index to

SCIENCE FICTION

anthologies and collections

A
Reference
Publication
in
Science Fiction

L. W. Currey
David G. Hartwell
Editors

index to

SCIENCE FICTION

anthologies and collections

WILLIAM CONTENTO

George Prior Publishers, London, England

G.K.HALL&CO.

70 LINCOLN STREET, BOSTON, MASS.

Available for sale in the British Commonwealth from
George Prior Publishers, 2 Rugby St., London, England
ISBN (U.K.)   0-86043-167-3

Library of Congress Cataloging in Publication Data

Contento, William.
    Index to science fiction.

    (A Reference publication in science fiction)
    Includes bibliographical references.
        1. Science fiction, American — Bibliography.
2. Science fiction, English — Bibliography.
3. Science fiction — Bibliography.   I. Title.   II. Series.
Z1231.F4C65   [PS374.S35]   016.813'0876   78-155
ISBN 0-8161-8092-X

This publication is printed on permanent/durable acid-free paper
MANUFACTURED IN THE UNITED STATES OF AMERICA

Contents

Introduction vii

How to Use the Index xi

Abbreviations 3

Checklist of Books Indexed 11

Author Index 27

Story Index 259

Book Contents 459

Introduction

This Index is intended to be a standard reference for locating stories that have appeared in science fiction anthologies and collections of stories by one author. For inclusion in the Index a book had to contain at least three stories. Anthologies had to contain mainly science fiction stories, while collections had to be written by authors associated with science fiction. Also covered, although not as thoroughly, are science fiction novels re-written from three or more stories.

In determining the selection criteria it was decided to include those science fiction stories which dealt with social and technical extrapolation and innovation while excluding stories that deal exclusively with horror, the weird, ghosts, mythology, sword and sorcery, the occult, and other fantasy. Of course there are always stories that fall into a gray area between fantasy and science fiction that should be included in a work of this type. For books containing such stories the following rule was used: where there was any doubt, the book was included. Also included are several books having only two stories or stories that are definitely not science fiction, which were added to maintain completeness with previous reference works.

This Index began, as many other specialty reference works have begun, as a catalog for a private collection of books. As I accumulated science fiction anthologies and collections I found more and more stories being duplicated, and also found it difficult to remember which book contained a specific story. As the collection approached 800 books I decided to index the stories, and having access to computers through my work, I used that medium. When the Index was complete I showed it to friends who knew of similar works and pointed out that the index contained more information than previous references (Cole covers 227 books and Siemon 237, Collins lists a like number of books, many fantasy). They encouraged me to expand the Index and

make it available to the public. I began adding new material and showing the Index at science fiction conventions until it developed into its present size and format. The Index now covers over 2,000 book titles with full contents listings of over 1,900 books containing 12,000 different stories by 2,500 authors. Of the books, I have personally examined about eighty-three percent, seen photocopies of the contents pages of five percent, and used other sources for twelve percent. Where it was necessary to use other sources an effort was made to find more than one source for each book.

An attempt has been made to include all English language science fiction anthologies and collections published through June 1977. While there are bound to be some omissions in the Index, I feel that it is complete for all commonly available books. Any information on omissions and corrections to the Index will be greatly appreciated.

The Index is divided into the following five sections:

I. *Abbreviations*

Lists abbreviations used for book type, publisher, story type, and original source of story.

II. *Checklist of Books Indexed*

Lists book titles followed by author or editor, type of book, publisher, date of publication, and notes about the book.

III. *Author Index*

Lists books and stories by author in the following basic format:

Author and notes on pseudonyms
(*indented one space*) Books by author
(*indented two spaces*) Stories by author
(*indented four spaces*) Books containing each
story

IV. *Story Index*

Lists all story titles. Basic format:
Story title, author
(*indented two spaces*) Books containing each
story

V. *Book Contents*

Lists books by title, followed by contents. Basic format:
Book title, author
(*indented two spaces*) Story title, author

With each story is also given an indicator of the story type (short story, novelette, etc.) and when available, the original source of the story and date of first publication. For a more detailed description of data formats see "How to Use the Index."

Special Considerations

Character set: Lower case letters were not available on the computer used to produce this Index.

Sorting rules: All data is sorted character by character in the following sequence:

1. blank or space
2. Special characters (except when they appear as the first character in a title, in which case special characters are ignored)
3. Letters
4. Numbers

Names: Prefixes to family names such as "DE," "DEL," "FITZ," "VAN," etc. are listed according to the sorting rules with the position of spaces determined by the common spelling of the name. Therefore "DE LA MARE" comes before "DEFORD." "MC" and "MAC" are treated as if spelled the same and appear before other M's.

Collaborations: Books that were joint authored are listed in the *Author Index* by the first author credited for the book, preceding individual works. Notes are made under the other author(s) to refer to the first author. In other sections joint authors' names are separated by '&' if two authors and by '/' if more than two. Story collaborations are indicated by the letter 'C' appearing after the story type code. If one book lists a story as a collaboration and another does not the story is listed twice.

Pseudonyms: Each story is listed under the author given for that story by the book containing the story. As a result some stories appear under the author's real name and under a pseudonym. Known pseudonyms that appear in the Index are cross-referenced with the author's real name in the *Author Index*. The title field of some stories also contains the name used by the author for the original publication of the story, indicated by '(AS name)' following the title, or the real name of the author when a pseudonym has been used by several authors.

Story titles: Each story title is the same as that given in the book containing the story. If the original story title is different or the story appears elsewhere in the Index under a different title that information is given in parentheses after the title. A cross-reference between the original title of a story and its reprint title is given in the author and title sections of the Index.

Abridged reprints of books: Abridged editions of books having the same title as the original edition are indicated by a comparison of the story counts in the title field. For example, "AWAY AND BEYOND (7 OF 9)" contains seven of the nine stories contained in the first edition. Abridged editions are not listed as sources of stories in the author and title sections of the Index, but the title of the first edition is prefixed by an asterisk indicating that an abridged edition is also listed in the *Book Contents* section.

Story types: Story types are the same as that given the story when it was first published. When this is not available or not given the type is determined from the book page length of the story, with a novel over 100 pages, novella or short novel over 50 pages, novelette over 20 pages and all else a short story.

General: When one book reprints the entire contents of another book along with other material the title of the reprinted book is listed in the contents instead of its individual stories.

The edition given of each book is the first American edition unless there was no American edition or I have personally examined the earlier edition.

This Index does not cover multi-volume reprints which together contain the complete contents of a single volume first edition and use the same title.

For books that have changed titles the contents are listed only under the original title except where the contents differ.

ACKNOWLEDGMENTS

I would like to thank the following people for their invaluable assistance and encouragement in preparing this Index:

Forrest J. Ackerman
Vicki Anders, Head, Separates Acquisitions, Texas A&M University Library

Neil Barron, Anatomy of Wonder, Bowker, N.Y. 1976.

Lloyd W. Currey, L. W. Currey Rare Books Incorporated, Dragon Press, Elizabethtown, N.Y.

Lou and Gini Donato, Bookstop III, San Diego, Cal.

Martin Harry Greenberg, Director of Graduate Studies, University of Wisconsin, Greenbay

Ronald G. Nelson

Fred Patton

De Wayne and Gwen White, The Amber Unicorn, San Diego, Cal.

REFERENCES

Cockcroft, Thomas G. L. *Index to the Weird Fiction Magazines*, Vols. 1 & 2. 1962, 1964. Reprinted by Arno Press, N.Y., 1975.

Collins, Len. *Science Fiction Collections Index and Cross Index.* South Porcupine, Ontario: Arthur Hayes, National Fantasy Fan Federation, 1970, 1971.

Cole, Walter R. *A Checklist of Science-Fiction Anthologies.* 1964. Reprinted by Arno Press, N.Y. 1974.

Crawford, William. *Index to Fantasy & Science Fiction in Munsey Publications.* 1976.

Day, Donald B. *Index to the Science Fiction Magazines 1926–1950.* Portland, Oregon: Perri Press, 1952.

Larson, Randall D. *The Robert Bloch Fanzine, September 1973 Edition.* Los Altos, California: Fandom Unlimited Enterprises.

The Magazine of Fantasy and Science Fiction.
for bibliographies from the following issues:
October 1960, Isaac Asimov;
September 1962, Theodore Sturgeon compiled by Sam Moskowitz;
May 1963, Ray Bradbury compiled by William F. Nolan;
June 1967, Charles Beaumont compiled by William F. Nolan;
July 1969, Fritz Leiber compiled by Al Lewis;
April 1971, Poul Anderson;
April 1972, James Blish compiled by Mike Owings;
September 1973, Frederik Pohl compiled by Mike Owings;
April 1974, Robert Silverberg compiled by Donald H. Tuck;
November 1976, Damon Knight compiled by Vincent Miranda;
July 1977, Harlan Ellison compiled by Leslie Kay Swigart.

McGhan, Barry. *Sciencefiction and Fantasy Pseudonyms.* Dearborn, Michigan: Misfit Press, 1976.

Metcalf, Norm. *The Index of Science Fiction Magazines 1951–1965.* El Cerrito, California: J. Ben Stark, 1968.

New England Science Fiction Association. *Index to the Science Fiction Magazines 1966–1970.* 1971.

New England Science Fiction Association Press. *The N.E.S.F.A. Index — Science Fiction Magazines and Original Anthologies, 1971–1972, 1973, 1974, 1975.*

Siemon, Frederick. *Science Fiction Story Index 1950–1968.* Chicago, Illinois: American Library Association.

Strauss, Erwin S. *The MIT Science Fiction Society's Index to the S-F Magazines 1951–1965.* 1966.

Swigart, Leslie Kay. *Harlan Ellison: A Bibliographical Checklist.* Dallas Texas: Williams Publishing Co. 1973.

Thiessen, J. Grant. *The Science-Fiction Collector.* Alberta, Canada: Calgary, 1976/1977.

Tuck, Donald H. *The Encyclopedia of Science Fiction and Fantasy,* Vol 1 & 2. Chicago, Illinois: Advent Publishers. Vol. 1, 1974; Vol. 2, to be published.

How to Use the Index

Format

The following is a detailed breakdown of the formats used in the five sections of the Index along with examples of the information contained therein.

I. *Abbreviations*

    ABR — ABBREVIATION

II. *Checklist of Books Indexed*

    BOOK TITLE   BOOK AUTHOR/EDITOR   BT S PUB PY PM
        BOOK NOTES

III. *Author Index*

    AUTHOR   AUTHOR NOTES   BT S PUB PY PM
       TITLE OF BOOK BY AUTHOR
         BOOK NOTES
       TITLE OF STORY BY AUTHOR   ST C SRC SY SM
         TITLE OF BOOK CONTAINING STORY   BOOK AUTHOR/EDITOR   BT

IV. *Story Index*

    STORY TITLE   AUTHOR OF STORY   ST C SRC SY SM
        TITLE OF BOOK CONTAINING STORY   BOOK AUTHOR/EDITOR   BT

V. *Book Contents*

    BOOK TITLE   BOOK AUTHOR/EDITOR   BT S PUB PY PM
        BOOK NOTES
       TITLE OF STORY IN BOOK   AUTHOR OF STORY   ST C SRC PY PM

In all cases if a book or story title is too long the title and subsequent information will be continued on the next line.

Explanation of codes and format

BOOK TITLE may include the number of stories contained in a reprint compared to the number of stories in the original edition.

   BT — Book Type. *Example:* AN, anthology

S — Book Size, Cover Type. *Examples:* H, hard cover; blank, paperback

PUB — Publisher. *Example:* DBL, Doubleday & Co., Inc.

PY — Year Published. *Example:* 65, 1965

PM — Month Published. *Example:* 05, May

Examples of book types and publishing information:

AC H GNM 57 One author collection in hard cover published by Gnome Press in 1957

AN   PKT 69 12 Anthology in paperback published by Pocket Books in December of 1969

BOOK NOTES may contain information on sub-titles, title changes or other appearances of the book.

AUTHOR NOTES may contain information on pseudonyms or other appearances of the author.

STORY TITLE may include original title of the story, alternate title of the story, pseudonym author used for first appearance of the story, real name of the author, author of the screenplay that the story is based on, notes about the story or alternate source for the story.

ST — Story Type. *Example:* SS, short story

C — Collaboration; more than one author participated in writing the story. If one book lists a story as a collaboration and another does not the story is listed twice.

SRC — Source of the story. *Examples:* GAL, *Galaxy Magazine;* ORB, Orbit original anthology (if SRC is an original anthology SM is the number of the anthology); NEW, the story first appeared in an anthology or collection (which is then given in SM)

SY — Year story first appeared or copyrighted. *Example:* 55, 1955

SM — 1) Month of publication. *Example:* 07, July
  2) Time of year: *Example:* WI, Winter
  3) Whole number of source (check abbreviations section for applicability). *Example:* 25, number twenty-five
  4) Type of book containing original story (where SRC is NEW); *Example:* AN, anthology

Examples of story type and source information:

NV   GAL 57 03   Novelette first appeared in the March 1957 issue of *Galaxy Magazine.*

SS   PLS 54 SU   Short story first appeared in the Summer 1954 issue of *Planet Stories.*

NV C INY 71 02   Novelette written as a collaboration first appeared in the original anthology *Infinity #2* in 1971.

SS   NEW 70 AC   Short story first appeared in a one author collection in 1970.

Sample entry from the Author Index:

(1) ANDERSON, POUL   ALSO AS   WINSTON P. SANDERS
(2)   MANY WORLDS OF POUL ANDERSON, THE   AC H CHL 74
(3)   EDITED BY ROGER ELWOOD,
            ALSO AS "THE BOOK OF POUL ANDERSON"
(4)   CHAPTER ENDS, THE   NV   DSF 54 01
(5)   ADVENTURES IN THE FAR FUTURE   WOLLHEIM, DONALD A. DA
(5)   NOVELETS OF SCIENCE FICTION   HOWARD, IVAN   AN

The above information is read:

(1) Poul Anderson also appears in the Index under the name Winston P. Sanders

(2) Anderson's collection *The Many Worlds of Poul Anderson* is covered in the Index and was published in hardcover by Chilton in 1974.

(3) The above collection was edited by Roger Elwood and also appears under the title *The*

Book of Poul Anderson.

(4) Anderson's novelette "The Chapter Ends" originally appeared in the January 1954 issue of *Dynamic Science Fiction.*

(5) The above story has been reprinted in the anthologies *Adventures in the Far Future* by Wollheim and *Novelets of Science Fiction* by Howard.

Abbreviations

* - LATER EDITIONS OF BOOK DO NOT CONTAIN ALL STORIES
    CHECK CONTENTS SECTION FOR REPRINT CONTENTS
C - COLLABORATION
D - DIGEST SIZE MAGAZINE
H - HARD COVER
L - LARGE PAPERBACK
AC - COLLECTION OF WORKS BY ONE AUTHOR
AI - AUTHOR'S INTRODUCTION TO STORY
AN - ANTHOLOGY
AR - ARTICLE
BR - BOOK REVIEW
CT - CARTOON
DA - ANTHOLOGY, ONE HALF OF A DOUBLE
DC - COLLECTION, ONE HALF OF A DOUBLE
DN - NOVEL, ONE HALF OF A DOUBLE
EC - EDITED COLLECTION, EDITOR IS NOT AUTHOR OF STORIES
ED - EDITORIAL
EX - EXCERPT
FA - FACETIOUS ARTICLE
FL - FALL
GR - GROUP OF RELATED STORIES
IL - ILLUSTRATION
IN - INTRODUCTION, PROLOG, FOREWARD, ETC.
MR - MOVIE REVIEW
MS - MISCELLANEOUS
NA - NOVELLA
NF - NON-FICTION COLLECTION
NO - NOVEL
NV - NOVELETTE
OA - ORIGINAL ANTHOLOGY- NEW STORIES
OC - ORIGINAL COLLECTION- NEW STORIES BY ONE AUTHOR
PB - PAPERBACK
PL - PLAY
PM - POEM
SA - STORY ADAPTATION OF SCREEN PLAY
SF - SPECIAL FEATURE
SG - SONG
SI - SECTION INTRODUCTION
SN - SHORT NOVEL
SP - SPRING
SS - SHORT STORY
SU - SUMMER
TC - STORY TITLE CROSS-REFERENCE
WI - WINTER
WS - WINTER-SPRING
AAM - ALL AROUND MAGAZINE
AAR - ANGUS AND ROBERTSON (PUBLISHERS) PTY LTD, SYDNEY
AAS - ARGOSY ALL-STORY WEEKLY
ABB - ABBOTTEMPO
ABC - AMERICAN BROADCASTING CORPORATION
ABE - ABELARD PRESS
ABR - ADAM BEDSIDE READER (NUMBERED)
ABS - ABELARD-SCHUMAN, LONDON
ABT - AMBIT
ACB - ACE, BRITISH
ACE - ACE BOOKS
ADM - ADAM
ADS - ARMADA SCI-FI (OA, NUMBERED)
ADT - AUDIT
ADV - ADVENTURE
ADW - ADDISON- WESLEY PUBLISHING CO., READING, MASS.
AFR - AVON FANTASY READER (NUMBERED)
AFT - AFTER HOURS
AHM - ALFRED HITCHCOCK MYSTERY MAGAZINE
ALB - ALLISON AND BUSBY, LONDON
ALC - ALIEN CONDITION (OA)
ALL - W. H. ALLEN, LONDON
ALM - AMERICAN LEGION MAGAZINE
ALN - G. ALLEN, LONDON
ALS - ALLISON & BUSBY, LONDON
ALT - ALTERNITIES (OC)
AMA - ASTOUNDING/JOHN W. CAMPBELL MEMORIAL ANTHOLOGY (OA)
AMB - THE AMERICAN BOY
AMD - AMAZING DETECTIVE TALES
AMM - AMERICAN MERCURY
AMQ - AMAZING STORIES QUARTERLY
AMR - AMERICA
AMS - AMATEUR SCIENCE STORIES
AMZ - AMAZING STORIES-AMAZING SCIENCE FICTION
ANA - ALCHEMY AND ACADEME (OA)
ANC - ANCHOR PRESS / DOUBLEDAY
ANL - EDWARD ARNOLD, NEW YORK
ANO - ARNO PUBLISHERS
ANT - AMERICAN ANTHROPOLOGIST
ARA - AMRA (NUMBERED FANZINE)
ARB - ARGOSY (BRITISH)
ARC - ARCO, LONDON
ARG - ARGOSY
ARK - ARKHAM HOUSE
ARM - ARMADA, LONDON
ARN - THE ARENA
ARS - ARKHAM SAMPLER
ARV - AMERICAN REVIEW
ARW - ARROW BOOKS, LONDON
ASA - AMAZING STORIES ANNUAL
ASC - ALL-STORY CAVALIER WEEKLY
ASF - ASTOUNDING/ANALOG SCIENCE FICTION
ASM - ALL-STORY MAGAZINE
ASR - AVON SCIENCE FICTION AND FANTASY READER
AST - ASTONISHING STORIES
ASW - ALL-STORY WEEKLY
ATH - ATHENEUM PUBS.
ATL - ATLANTIC MONTHLY
ATR - THE ANTIOCH REVIEW
ATS - ATLAS MAGAZINE
AUJ - AUSTRALIAN JOURNAL

AUR - AURORA PUBLISHERS, INC.
AUS - AUSTRALIAN SCIENCE FICTION REVIEW
AUT - AUTHENTIC SCIENCE FICTION (BRITISH)
AVL - AVALON
AVN - AVON BOOKS
AVS - AVON SCIENCE FICTION READER (NUMBERED)
AVT - ADVENT PUBLISHERS
AWD - AWARD BOOKS
AWR - AMERICAN WHIG REVIEW
BAC - BULLETIN OF ATOMIC SCIENTISTS
BAL - BALLANTINE BOOKS
BAN - BANTAM BOOKS
BAS - BASIC BOOKS
BAW - BLACK AND WHITE
BBC - BRITISH BROADCASTING CORPORATION (RADIO)
BBM - BLUE BOOK MAGAZINE
BCA - BOOK COMPANY OF AMERICA
BCH - THE BEECHHURST PRESS
BCN - BEACON BOOKS
BDL - BODLEY HEAD, LONDON
BDM - BOARDMAN, LONDON
BEA - BEAGLE BOOKS
BEL - BELMONT BOOKS
BEN - ERNEST BENN LIMITED, LONDON
BER - THE BERSERKERS (OA)
BET - BELMONT/TOWER BOOKS
BEY - BEYOND FANTASY FICTION
BFT - BOOKS FOR TODAY, LONDON
BGM - BURTON'S GENTLEMEN'S MAGAZINE
BGU - BOWLING GREEN UNIVERSITY POPULAR PRESS
BIZ - BIZARRE MYSTERY MAGAZINE
BKM - BERKLEY MEDALLION BOOKS
BKP - BERKLEY / PUTNAM
BLC - THE BLACK CAT
BLF - BOY'S LIFE
BLK - BLACKIE AND SON, LONDON
BLM - BLACK MASK
BML - THE BOBBS-MERRIL COMPANY, INC.
BMM - BESTSELLER MYSTERY MAGAZINE
BMR - BAD MOON RISING (OA)
BNA - BANANAS
BNC - BOND-CHARTERIS
BNY - BOYS OF NEW YORK (DIME NOVEL)
BNZ - BONANZA BOOKS
BOA - BOAC
BOK - THE BOOKMAN
BON - BOON
BPL - BEST ONE ACT PLAYS
BRD - BROADSIDE
BRK - BERKLEY BOOKS (CROWN)
BSJ - THE BAKER STREET JOURNAL
BSV - BALTIMORE SATURDAY VISITOR
BTH - BALTHUS
BTM - BELL TELEPHONE MAGAZINE
BUG - BOSTON UNIVERSITY GRADUATE JOURNAL
BUL - THE BULLETIN
BUR - BURROUGHS PUBLISHING
BUT - BUTTERFLY
BYI - BEYOND INFINITY
CAD - CAD MAGAZINE
CAM - CAMELOT BOOKS (AVON)
CAN - CANAVERAL
CAP - JONATHAN CAPE LTD., LONDON
CAS - CASSELL & COMPANY, LTD.
CAV - CAVALIER
CBS - COLUMBIA BROADCASTING SYSTEM (RADIO)
CCR - CALIFORNIA CHESS REVIEW
CEM - CHEMICAL ENGINEERING NEWS
CEO - CEOLFRITH PRESS
CFQ - CALIFORNIA QUARTERLY
CFU - CAPTAIN FUTURE
CHB - CHAMBERLAIN PRESS
CHJ - CONKEY'S HOME JOURNAL
CHL - CHILTON BOOK COMPANY
CHM - CHARM
CHN - CHAINS OF THE SEA (OA)
CHP - CHAPMAN
CHR - CONRAD H. RUPPERT
CHT - CHARTERHOUSE
CLB - COLLIER BOOKS
CLG - COLLAGE
CLM - CLIMAX
CLR - CLARION (OA)
CMC - COWARD-MCCANN
CMG - THE COURT MAGAZINE AND BELLE ASSEMBLEE
CMK - CORNMARKET REPRINTS LTD., LONDON
CMM - COMMENTARY
CMP - COSMOPOLITAN
CMT - COMET STORIES
CNC - CONCORDIA
CND - CORNUDO
CNL - CONSUL, LONDON
CNS - CONSULTANT
CNT - CORONET BOOKS (BRITISH)
CNY - THE CENTURY
COI - CHILDREN OF INFINITY (OA)
COL - COLLIERS
COM - COMMENT
CON - CONTACT
COQ - THE COLORADO QUARTERLY
COR - CORGI BOOKS
COS - COSMIC STORIES
COV - COVEN 13
CPR - CAPER
CPT - COMPACT PUB., LONDON
CPY - COPY

CRB - CROWN BONANZA
CRF - CRAWFORD PUBLICATIONS
CRN - CROWN PUBLISHERS, INC.
CRR - COURIER
CRS - CREST BOOKS
CRT - CORONET
CRV - CONTEMPORARY REVIEW
CRW - CRAWDADDY
CSB - THE CAVALIER AND THE SCRAP BOOK
CSL - CASSELL'S MAGAZINE
CSM - COSMOS SCIENCE FICTION AND FANTASY MAGAZINE
CTM - CONTINUUM (OA)
CUR - CURTIS BOOKS
CVL - THE CAVALIER
CYE - COLLINS YOUNG ELIZABETHAN
DAP - DAPPER
DAW - DAW BOOKS
DBL - DOUBLEDAY & CO., INC.
DBM - DETECTIVE BOOK MAGAZINE
DCH - THE DAILY CHRONICLE
DCM - DINERS CLUB MAGAZINE
DCT - DELACORTE PRESS
DDT - DIME DETECTIVE
DEL - DELL BOOKS
DEM - DEMON KIND (OA)
DIG - DIGIT, LONDON
DIP - DIPPLE CHRONICLE
DLM - DUBLIN LITERARY MAGAZINE
DMN - DIME MYSTERY NOVEL
DMR - DEMOCRATIC REVIEW
DMX - DIMENSION X, NBC RADIO SHOW
DOB - DOBSON
DOM - DODD MEAD
DOR - DORRANCE AND COMPANY, INC.
DOV - DOVER PUBLICATIONS, INC.
DPM - DATA PROCESSING MAGAZINE
DPS - THE DAILY POST
DRC - YE DRAGON RUNNERS' CHRONICLE (NUMBERED)
DSF - DYNAMIC SCIENCE FICTION
DSM - DETECTIVE STORY MAGAZINE
DSP - DESIGN PARTICIPATION - PROCEEDINGS OF THE
      DESIGN RESEARCH SOCIETY CONFRENCE
DTM - THE DAILY TELEGRAPH MAGAZINE
DUD - DUDE
DUT - E. P. DUTTON & CO., INC.
DVS - DANGEROUS VISIONS (1), AGAIN D.V. (2) (OA)
DYS - DYSTOPIAN VISIONS (OA)
EDG - EDGE (SF DIRECTIONS)
EIM - ENGLISH ILLUSTRATED MAGAZINE
EIO - EROS IN ORBIT (OA)
ELK - ELKS MAGAZINE
ELM - THE ELMFIELD PRESS
ELX - ELECTRICAL EXPERIMENTER
ENC - ENCOUNTER
EPC - EPOCH (OA)
EPM - THE (SAN FRANCISCO) EVENING POST MAGAZINE
EPO - EPOCH
EPS - THE EPISCOPALIAN
EQM - ELLERY QUEEN'S MYSTERY MAGAZINE
EQN - EQUINOX BOOKS (AVON)
ESC - ESCAPADE
ESQ - ESQUIRE
ESR - EAST SIDE REVIEW
ETN - ETERNITY
EVB - EVERYBODY'S MAGAZINE (BRITISH)
EVN - M. EVANS
EVW - EVERYWOMAN'S MAGAZINE
EXR - EXTRAPOLATION
EXT - EXTENSION
EYR - EYRE & SPOTTISWOODE
FAB - FABER AND FABER, LTD.
FAD - FANTASTIC ADVENTURES
FAL - FALCON BOOKS
FAN - FANTASTIC
FAW - FAWCETT CREST BOOKS
FBK - FANTASY BOOK (NUMBERED)
FCR - FUTURE CORRUPTION (OA)
FCT - FICTION (FRENCH VERSION OF "FANTASY & SCIENCE FICTION")
FDN - FOUNDATION: A REVIEW OF SCIENCE FICTION
FEL - FREDRICK FELL, INC.
FFM - FAMOUS FANTASTIC MYSTERIES
FFN - THE FANTASY FAN
FFS - FUTURE FANTASY AND SCIENCE FICTION
FFU - FOUR FUTURES (OA)
FGM - FAWCETT GOLD MEDAL BOOKS
FIF - FIFTEEN MYSTERY STORIES
FIN - THE FUTURE IS NOW (OA)
FKW - FUNK & WAGNALLS COMPANY
FLG - FLAGSHIP PUB.
FLK - FOLK REVIEW
FLM - FILM QUARTERLY
FLN - FLING
FLP - FOREIGN LANGUAGES PUBLISHING HOUSE, MOSCOW
FLS - FLASHING SWORDS (OA)
FMG - FANTASY MAGAZINE
FMS - FAMOUS MONSTERS
FND - FIENDETTA
FNF - FANTASY FICTION
FNK - W. FUNK
FNP - FANTASY PUBLICATIONS, EVERETT PA.
FOC - FOCUS BOOKS (LANCER)
FOL - FOLLETT
FON - FONTANA, LONDON
FOR - FORTUNE
FOS - FELLOWSHIP OF THE STARS (OA)
FPB - FANTASY PUBLISHING COMPANY, INC.

FPC - FLEET PRESS CORPORATION
FPL - FUTURA PUBLICATIONS LIMITED
FPR - FAWCETT PREMIER BOOKS
FPS - FANTASY PRESS
FRL - FRANK READE LIBRARY
FRM - THE FORUM
FRS - THE FARTHEST REACHES (OA)
FSB - FANTASY (BRITISH, FIRST 3 ISSUES NUMBERED, 1938-1939)
FSF - THE MAGAZINE OF FANTASY AND SCIENCE FICTION
FSM - FANTASTIC STORY MAGAZINE
FSP - FSB PUBLISHERS, LONDON
FSQ - FANTASTIC STORY QUARTERLY
FST - FINAL STAGE (OA)
FSY - FARRAR, STRAUS AND YOUNG
FTM - FORD TIMES MAGAZINE
FTP - FLAME TREE PLANET (OA)
FTS - FUTURES
FUC - FUTURE CITY (OA)
FUF - FUTURIA FANTASIA, FAN MAGAZINE PUBLISHED BY RAY BRADBURY
FUN - FANTASTIC UNIVERSE
FUP - THE FUTURE UNBOUND PROGRAM BOOK
FUQ - FUTURE QUEST (OA)
FUR - FURY
FUS - FUTURE COMBINED WITH SCIENCE FICTION STORIES
FUT - FUTURE SCIENCE FICTION
FVW - F. V. WHITE, LONDON
FWS - FANTASTIC WORLDS
GAL - GALAXY SCIENCE FICTION
GAM - GAMMA
GAN - GALAXY NOVELS (NUMBERED)
GBG - GREENBERG PUBLISHERS
GBK - GOLDEN BOOK
GCB - GARDEN CITY BOOKS
GDY - GODEY'S LADY'S BOOK
GEN - GENERATION (OA)
GFT - GIFT
GHK - GOOD HOUSEKEEPING
GLB - GLOBE BOOK CO.
GLG - GRAHAM'S LADY'S AND GENTILEMAN'S MAGAZINE
GLN - GLENCOE PRESS
GLR - GALLERY
GMB - GOLD MEDAL BOOKS
GMQ - GENTLEMAN'S QUARTERLY
GMS - G. M. SMITH
GND - GRAND MAGAZINE
GNM - GNOME PRESS
GNT - GENT
GOL - GOLLANCZ
GOM - GO: READING IN THE CONTENT AREAS
GOR - GOURMET
GPC - GALAXY PUBLISHING CORPORATION
GRG - GREGG PRESS
GRI - GRIFFIN PUBLISHING CO.
GRO - GROVE PRESS, INC.
GRP - THE GRAPHIC
GRS - GROSSET & DUNLAP
GRY - GRAYSON, LONDON
GYR - GOODYEAR PUBLISHING COMPANY, INC.
HAL - ROBERT HALE, LONDON
HAM - HAMPTON'S MAGAZINE
HAN - HANOVER HOUSE
HAS - THE HALL SYNDICATE
HAW - HAWTHORN BOOKS, INC.
HBJ - HARCOURT, BRACE & JOVANOVICH, INC.
HBK - HABAKKUK
HBW - HARCOURT, BRACE & WORLD, INC.
HBZ - HARPERS BAZAAR
HDL - HEIDELBERG PUBLISHERS, INC., AUSTIN TEXAS
HDS - HODDER STOUGHTON, LONDON
HDV - RUPERT HART-DAVIS, LONDON
HEI - HEINEMANN PUB. (LONDON)
HFI - HIGH FIDELITY MAGAZINE
HIL - HILLMAN
HIS - HISTORY TODAY
HLK - HORLICK'S MAGAZINE
HLP - HARVARD LAMPOON
HLT - HENRY HOLT
HMF - HOUGHTON MIFFLIN COMPANY
HML - HAMILTON AND CO., LONDON
HOH - THE HAUNT OF HORROR
HOR - HORIZON
HOS - HORROR STORIES
HPM - HARPER'S MONTHLY
HPR - HARPER & ROW
HRM - HARMSWORTH'S MAGAZINE
HRP - HARPERS
HRS - HEARST'S INTERNATIONAL
HRW - HOLT, RINEHART AND WINSTON
HSA - THE (OAKLAND) HIGH SCHOOL AEGIS
HUD - HUDSON REVIEW
HUM - HUMANIST
HUT - HUTCHINSON, LONDON
HWF - HARRIS-WOLFE
HWZ - HORWITZ, LONDON
HYP - HYPERION PRESS, INC.
IBM - IBM MAGAZINE
ICA - THE ICA EVENTSHEET
IDL - THE IDLER
IFS - IF, WORLDS OF SCIENCE FICTION
ILN - ILLUSTRATED LONDON NEWS
IMG - IMAGINATION
IMP - (SF) IMPULSE, FORMERLY SCIENCE FANTASY (BRITISH)
IMT - IMAGINATIVE TALES
INF - INFINITY SCIENCE FICTION
INS - INSIDE (FANZINE)
INT - INTERNATIONAL

INY - INFINITY (OA)
ISF - INTERNATIONAL SCIENCE FICTION
ISR - INTERNATIONAL SOCIALIST REVIEW
ITL - INTELLECTUAL DIGEST
ITM - INTERNATIONAL MAGAZINE
JAD - JADE
JAR - JARROLDS, LONDON
JBL - JUBILEE PUBLICATIONS PTY., LTD., SYDNEY
JCE - JOURNAL OF CHEMICAL ENGINEERING
JCW - JOHN C. WINSTON COMPANY
JKP - JOHN KNOX PRESS
JOS - MICHAEL JOSEPH, LONDON
KAK - KAKABEKA PUBLISHING CO., CANADA
KDK - KODAK NEWS
KEM - KEMSLEY NEWSPAPERS
KEN - KENNERLEY
KHM - KEYHOLE MYSTERY
KNK - KENNIKAT PRESS, PORT WASHINGTON, N.Y.
KNP - ALFRED A. KNOPF, INC.
KNT - KNIGHT
KNV - KNAVE
KPS - KEEPSAKE
KRP - KARL RAUCH PUBLISHERS, WEST GERMANY
LAF - LOS ANGELES FREE PRESS
LAN - LANCER BOOKS
LAS - LASL NEWS (LOS ALAMOS SCIENTIFIC LABORATORY)
LAT - LOS ANGELES TIMES
LAU - LAURIE, LONDON
LBR - LITTLE AND BROWN
LEI - LEISURE BOOKS
LER - LERNER SF LIBRARY
LES - LONDON EVENING STANDARD
LGH - LIGHTHOUSE
LHJ - LADIES HOME JOURNAL
LHT - LIBRAIRIE HACHETTE, PARIS
LIB - THE LIBERAL (NUMBERED)
LIF - LIFE
LIL - LILLIPUT
LIO - LION BOOKS, INC.
LIP - J. B. LIPPINCOTT COMPANY
LIS - THE LISTNER
LLL - LAUREL-LEAF LIBRARY (DELL PUBLISHING CO., INC.)
LMF - LITERARY MAGAZINE OF FANTASY AND TERROR
LMG - THE LITTLE MAGAZINE
LMR - LONDON MERCURY
LNE - LANE PUBLISHERS, LONDON
LNG - LONGMAN GROUP LIMITED, LONDON
LOB - THE LONDON OBSERVER
LOM - THE LONDON MAGAZINE
LOT - LOTHROP, LEE AND SHEPARD COMPANY
LPB - LANTERN PRESS BOOKS
LRV - THE LITERARY REVIEW
LST - LOS ANGELES STAFF
LSW - LUKE SHORT'S WESTERN MAGAZINE
LUD - THE LUDGATE MONTHLY
LVS - LEAVES, FANZINE PRODUCED BY R. H. BARLOW
MAC - THE MACMILLAN COMPANY
MAD - MADEMOISELLE
MAG - THE MATHEMATICAL GAZETTE
MAN - MANOR BOOKS
MAR - MARVEL SCIENCE FICTION
MAY - MAYFAIR
MBB - MACFADDEN-BARTELL BOOKS
MBR - MCBRIDE CO.
MCB - ED MCBAIN'S MYSTERY MAGAZINE
MCC - MCCALLS
MCD - MCDOUGAL, LITTELL & COMPANY
MCF - MACFADDEN BOOKS
MCG - MCCLURGE
MCK - DAVID MCKAY COMPANY, INC.
MCL - MACLEAN'S MAGAZINE
MCM - MACMILLAN, LONDON
MCS - MCCLURE'S MAGAZINE
MDL - THE MODERN LIBRARY
MDM - MYSTERY DIGEST MAGAZINE
MDN - MACDONALD, LONDON
MDT - MEREDITH PRESS
MEL - MODERN ELECTRONICS
MER - MERLIN PRESS, INC.
MES - JULIAN MESSNER
MFL - MAYFLOWER BOOKS, LONDON
MGC - THE MAGIC CARPET MAGAZINE
MGH - MCGRAW-HILL BOOK COMPANY
MHS - MAGAZINE OF HORROR AND THE STRANGE
MHT - MANHUNT
MIR - MIR PUBLISHERS, MOSCOW
MJR - MAJOR BOOKS
MLB - MCLOUGHLIN BROS.
MNS - MAN'S MAGAZINE
MNT - MENTOR BOOKS
MOB - MOEBIUS TRIP
MOH - MAGAZINE OF HORROR
MON - MONOCLE
MOP - THE MAGAZINE OF POETRY
MOR - WILLIAM MORROW & COMPANY, INC.
MOT - MOTIVE
MPM - METROPOLITAN MAGAZINE
MRG - THE MIRAGE PRESS, LTD., BALTIMORE
MRM - MR. MAGAZINE
MRV - MASSACHUSETTS REVIEW
MSM - MIKE SHANE MYSTERY MAGAZINE
MSP - MANUSCRIPT
MSS - MARVEL SCIENCE STORIES
MSW - MAN'S WORLD
MTH - METHUEN, LONDON
MTP - MANTRAP

MUR - J. MURRAY, LONDON
MUS - MUSEUM, LONDON
MVT - MARVEL TALES
MWS - THE MANY WORLDS OF SCIENCE FICTION (OA)
MYS - THE MYSTERIOUS PRESS, NEW YORK
NAL - THE NEW ATLANTIS (OA)
NAM - NEW AMERICAN LIBRARY
NAR - NEW AMERICAN REVIEW
NAT - THE NATION
NBC - NATIONAL BROADCASTING CORPORATION
NBG - NEW BUDGET
NBM - THE NEW BROADWAY MAGAZINE
NBS - NATION'S BUSINESS
NDB - NELSON DOUBLEDAY
NDM - NEW DIMENSIONS (OA)
NDR - NEW DIRECTIONS (NUMBERED)
NEA - NEA SERVICES, INC.
NEB - NEBULA SCIENCE FICTION (BRITISH)
NEL - THOMAS NELSON INC.
NEM - NEW ENGLAND MAGAZINE
NES - THE NESFA PRESS
NEW - STORY FIRST APPEARED IN AN ANTHOLOGY OR COLLECTION
NIE - NIEKAS (FANZINE PUBLISHED BY ED MESKYS)
NLB - NEW ENGLISH LIBRARY, LONDON
NLP - NATIONAL LAMPOON
NLS - NELSON, LONDON
NMD - THE NEW MIND (FRONTIERS 2, OA)
NMQ - NEW MEXICO QUARTERLY REVIEW
NOV - NOVA (OA)
NRV - NEW REVIEW
NSM - NEW STATESMAN
NSP - NEVILLE SPEARMAN, LTD., LONDON
NSR - NEW SCIENCE REVIEW
NST - NEW STORY MAGAZINE
NTC - NATIONAL TEXTBOOK COMPANY, SKOKIE, ILL.
NTL - NINE TALES OF SPACE AND TIME (OA)
NTR - NATURE
NTS - NEW TALES OF SPACE AND TIME (OA)
NUG - NUGGET
NWB - NEW WORLDS (QUARTERLY), (BRITISH OA, NUMBERED)
NWQ - NEW WORLDS (QUARTERLY), AMERICAN VERSION OF BRITISH OA,
      SAME CONTENTS BUT NUMBERED 1 LESS THAN BRITISH EDITION
NWR - NEW WRITINGS IN SCIENCE FICTION (OA)
NWS - NEW WORLDS (BRITISH, FIRST 5 NUMBERED, 1946-1949)
NYE - NEW YORK EVENING JOURNAL
NYH - NEW YORK HERALD TRIBUNE
NYM - NEW YORKER MAGAZINE
NYT - NEW YORK TIMES
NYU - NEW YORK UNIVERSITY PRESS
NYW - NEW YORK EVENING WORLD
OAW - ONCE A WEEK
OBS - THE OBSERVER
OFF - OFFBEAT
OMG - OMEGA (OA)
ORB - ORBIT (OA)
ORI - ORIENTAL STORIES
OSF - ORBIT SCIENCE FICTION (FIRST 2 NUMBERED, 1953-1954)
OTW - OUT OF THIS WORLD SCIENCE FICTION
OUT - OUTWORLDS (NUMBERED FANZINE)
OVL - THE OVERLAND MONTHLY
OWS - OTHER WORLDS
OXF - OXFORD BOOK COMPANY
PAA - PROCEEDINGS OF THE AMERICAN ACADEMY OF ARTS AND LETTERS
PAN - PAN BOOKS LTD.
PBK - PAPERBACK LIBRARY
PBP - PLAYBOY PRESS
PBW - PUBLISHERS WEEKLY
PBY - PLAYBOY
PDX - PARADOX PRESS, BERKELEY
PEL - PELLEGRINI CUDAHY
PEN - PENGUIN BOOKS
PER - PERENNIAL LIBRARY
PFL - PFLAUM PUBLISHING
PFP - POPULAR FICTION PUBLISHING CO.
PGM - PERGAMON
PGZ - PALL MALL GAZETTE
PHE - PHYSICS EDUCATION
PHI - S. G. PHILLIPS
PHS - PUBLISHERS-HALL SYNDICATE
PHT - PHANTAGRAPH
PHY - THE PHYSICS TEACHER
PIN - PINNACLE BOOKS
PIO - THE PIONEER
PKT - POCKET BOOKS
PLM - PLATT & MUNK CO., INC.
PLS - PLANET STORIES
PMA - PERMA BOOKS
PMB - PALL MALL BUDGET
PMG - PELICAN MAGAZINE, A.S.U.C.
PMP - PENGUIN MODERN POETS
PMY - PHIL MAY'S ANNUAL MAGAZINE
PND - PENDULUM, LONDON
PNM - PHANTOM
PNN - PENNANT BOOKS
PNT - PENTHOUSE
PNW - POETRY NORTHWEST
POM - THE POPULAR MAGAZINE
POP - POPULAR LIBRARY
POW - POWELL PUBLICATIONS
PPL - PAN PICCOLO, LONDON
PPR - THE PAPER: A CHICAGO WEEKLY
PRH - PRENTICE-HALL, INC.
PRI - PRIRODA (NATURE)
PRM - PRIME PRESS
PRP - PRIAPUS
PRS - PEARSON'S MAGAZINE

PRT - PROTOSTARS (OA)
PRV - PARIS REVIEW
PSD - PURSUED
PSM - P.S.
PSP - THE PACIFIC SPECTATOR
PSY - PSYCHOLOGY TODAY
PTH - PANTHER BOOKS LTD.
PTJ - PHOTOGRAPHIC JOURNAL
PTM - PUTNAM'S MONTHLY MAGAZINE
PTR - THE PARTISAN REVIEW
PUN - PUNCH
PUT - G. P. PUTNAM'S SONS
PYR - PYRAMID BOOKS
QBM - QUARBER MERKUR
QRK - QUARK (OA)
QRT - QUARTET BOOKS, LONDON
QUI - QUINN PUBLISHING CO., INC.
QUN - QUEEN
RAM - RAMPARTS
RAN - RAND MCNALLY
RAT - ROAD AND TRACK
RBM - THE RED BOOK MAGAZINE
RCH - RICH COWAN, LONDON
RDM - RANDOM HOUSE
RDN - RANDEN PUBLISHING CO., CULVER CITY, CALIFORNIA
RDT - REAL DETECTIVE TALES
REA - REASON
REG - HENRY REGNERY COMPANY
REL - REILLY AND LEE
REP - REPORTER
RET - RETORT
REV - FLEMING H. REVELL
RIN - RINEHART
RKS - ROCKET STORIES
RLS - THE REALIST
RNH - RINEHART AND COMPANY, INC.
ROG - ROGUE
ROT - THE ROTARIAN MAGAZINE
ROY - ROY PUBLISHERS
RPW - RAPP & WHITING, LONDON
RRV - THE RICHMOND REVIEW
RTR - RAINTREE PUBLISHERS LIMITED, MILWAUKEE
RUN - THE RUNNING MAN
RVP - REVUE PARISENNE
RVQ - RIVERSIDE QUARTERLY
SAD - STEIN AND DAY
SAG - SCIENCE AGAINST MAN (OA)
SAI - SCIENCE AND INVENTION
SAM - SCIENTIFIC AMERICAN
SAR - SAN FRANCISCO REVIEW
SAS - SIMON AND SCHUSTER
SAT - SATELLITE SCIENCE FICTION
SAW - SIGNS AND WONDERS (OA)
SBB - SCIENCE FICTION BOOK CLUB, BRITISH
SBS - SCHOLASTIC BOOK SERVICES
SCB - CHARLES SCRIBNER'S SONS
SCD - SCIENTIFIC DETECTIVE MONTHLY
SCF - SCIENCE FANTASY (BRITISH)
SCH - SCHOLASTIC
SCJ - WEST COAST SPORTS CAR JOURNAL
SCL - SIERRA CLUB BULLETIN
SCP - SCIENCE FICTION & FANTASY PUBLICATIONS
SCR - SCRIBNER'S MAGAZINE
SCS - SHOWCASE (OA)
SDG - SCIENCE DIGEST
SDM - SAINT DETECTIVE MAGAZINE (FRENCH & BRITISH)
SDT - SUNDAY TIMES, LONDON
SEA - THE SEABURY PRESS, INC.
SEE - SEELY & CO., LONDON
SEM - STANLEY ELLIN'S MYSTERY MAGAZINE
SEP - SATURDAY EVENING POST
SEV - SEVENTEEN
SEX - SEX AND CENSORSHIP
SFA - SCIENCE FICTION ADVENTURES
SFB - SCIENCE FICTION ADVENTURES, BRITISH
SFC - SCOTT, FORESMAN AND COMPANY
SFD - SCIENCE FICTION DIRECTIONS
SFE - SCIENCE FICTION EMPHASIS (OA)
SFF - SCIENCE FICTION FORUM
SFH - SCIENCE FICTION HORIZONS
SFM - SCIENCE FICTION MONTHLY (BRITISH)
SFP - SCIENCE FICTION PLUS
SFQ - SCIENCE FICTION QUARTERLY
SFR - SCIENCE FICTION REVIEW (NUMBERED FANZINE)
SFS - (THE ORIGINAL) SCIENCE FICTION STORIES
      (FIRST 2 NUMBERED, 1953-1954)
SFT - SCIENCE FICTION TALES (OA)
SGA - SAGA
SGN - SIGNATURE
SHB - SHERBOURNE PRESS, INC.
SHK - SHOCK
SHN - SHENANDOAH
SHR - SOUTHERN HUMANITIES REVIEW
SHS - SHASTA PUBLISHERS
SID - SIDGWICK & JACKSON
SIG - SIGNET BOOKS
SJG - ST. JAMES GAZETTE
SJR - SCIENCE JOURNAL
SKW - SECKER WARBURG, LONDON
SLG - STAR TREK LOG (NUMBERED)
SLM - SOUTHERN LITERARY MESSENGER
SLN - SLANT
SLP - THE SALOPIAN
SME - SMENA (CHANGE)
SMG - STAR SCIENCE FICTION (MAGAZINE)
SMM - SAINT MYSTERY MAGAZINE

SMP - ST. MARTIN'S PRESS, INC.
SMS - STARTLING MYSTERY STORIES
SMT - STREET AND SMITH
SMY - SMALL MAYNARD, PUB.
SND - THE STRAND MAGAZINE (LONDON)
SNG - SING
SNS - SWORD AND SORCERY
SOI - STORIES OF IMAGINATION
SOU - THE SOUTHERN REVIEW
SPC - SPACE (OA)
SPH - SPHERE BOOKS, LTD.
SPM - SPACE SCIENCE FICTION MAGAZINE
SPN - SPENCER PRESS
SPS - SPACE STORIES
SPT - SUSPECT
SPW - SPACE WORLD
SQU - SQUIRE
SRS - STRANGE STORIES
SRV - SATURDAY REVIEW
SRY - STORYTELLER MAGAZINE
SSF - SPACE SCIENCE FICTION
SSI - SHORT STORIES INTERNATIONAL
SSJ - THE SCIENCE SCHOOL JOURNAL
SSM - SHORT STORIES MAGAZINE
SSN - STAR SHORT NOVELS (OA)
SSR - SSR PUBLICATIONS
SSS - SUPER SCIENCE STORIES
SST - SCIENCE STORIES
STA - STATUS MAGAZINE
STD - SCIENCE-FICTION STUDIES
STE - STRANGE STORIES
STF - STEFANTASY
STG - STRANGE GODS (OA)
STI - STIRRING SCIENCE STORIES
STK - STAR TREK (OA)
STL - STELLAR (OA)
STM - SPACE TRAVEL MAGAZINE
STN - SATURN SCIENCE FICTION AND FANTASY
STO - STORY MAGAZINE
STP - STORY PARADE
STR - STAR SCIENCE FICTION (OA)
STS - STARTLING STORIES
STT - STRANGE TALES
STY - SANITY, THE JOURNAL OF THE CAMPAIGN FOR NUCLEAR DISARM.
SUN - THE SUN (NEWSPAPER)
SUP - SUPER SCIENCE FICTION
SUS - SUSPENSE
SVM - SCHOLASTIC VOICE MAGAZINE
SVN - SOUVENIER, LONDON
SVW - SAVING WORLDS (OA)
SWK - SWANK
SWL - SCIENCE WORLD
SWN - SWAN, LONDON
SWS - SCIENCE WONDER STORIES
SWY - SPACEWAY
SYR - SCIENCE YEAR
TAC - TOWN AND COUNTRY
TAL - TOMORROW'S ALTERNATIVES (FRONTIERS 1, OA)
TAP - TAPLINGER PUBLISHING COMPANY
TBT - TITBITS
TCH - TOUCHSTONE
TCS - TWO COMPLETE SCIENCE ADVENTURE BOOKS
TDM - TANDEM, LONDON
TDW - TODAY'S WOMAN
TDY - TODAY, THE PHILADELPHIA INQUIRER MAGAZINE
TEN - TECHNICAL ENGINEERING NEWS
TFT - THREE FOR TOMORROW (OA)
THN - THINK
TIC - TICKNOR, PUB.
TIG - TIGER
TIM - TIME, THE WEEKLY NEWSMAGAZINE
TIS - TOPS IN SCIENCE FICTION
TMM - TALES OF MAGIC AND MYSTERY
TMP - TEMPO BOOKS
TMS - THE TIMES
TMY - THRILLING MYSTERY STORIES
TOM - TOMORROW
TOP - TOPPER
TOR - TORQUIL PUB.
TOT - THREADS OF TIME (OA)
TOW - TALES OF WONDER (BRITISH, FIRST 2 NUMBERED, 1937-1938)
TPS - TEMPEST, LONDON
TRB - TRIBUNE
TRI - TRIDENT PRESS
TRU - TRUE
TRV - TRANSATLANTIC REVIEW
TRY - THE TRYOUT
TSB - THREE STAR BOOKS
TSF - TEN STORY FANTASY
TST - TEN STORY BOOK
TTB - THE THRILL BOOK
TTH - TRUTH
TTM - TEN TOMORROWS (OA)
TTP - TOWN TOPICS
TTT - THREE TRIPS IN TIME AND SPACE (OA)
TVW - TWO VIEWS OF WONDER (OA)
TWK - THIS WEEK
TWN - TWAYNE PUBLISHERS
TWR - TOWER BOOKS
TWS - THRILLING WONDER STORIES
TXQ - TEXAS QUARTERLY
UCL - UNIVERSITY OF CHICAGO LAW REVIEW
UCM - UNIVERSITY OF CHICAGO MAGAZINE
UCN - UNICORN
UKW - THE UNKNOWN WORLD
UNI - UNIVERSE (OA)

UNK - UNKNOWN, UNKNOWN WORLDS
UOL - UNIVERSITY OF LONDON (ENGLAND)
UPR - UNITY PRESS
USF - UNIVERSE SCIENCE FICTION
UTP - UTOPIAN PUBLISHERS, LONDON
VAN - VANGUARD SCIENCE FICTION
VAR - VARIETY
VCT - VECTOR
VIK - VIKING PRESS, INC.
VLG - THE VILLAGE VOICE
VNR - VAN NOSTRAND REINHOLD COMPANY
VNS - ARTIA VANOUS
VNT - VINTAGE BOOKS (RANDOM HOUSE)
VOB - VOGUE, BRITISH
VOG - VOGUE
VOR - VORTEX SCIENCE FICTION
VOT - VISIONS OF TOMORROW
VOX - VORTEX, GERMAN FANZINE
VPG - VORPAL GLASS (NUMBERED FANZINE)
VPR - THE VANGUARD PRESS, INC.
VQR - THE VIRGINIA QUARTERLY REVIEW
VSF - VENTURE SCIENCE FICTION
VTA - VENTURA
VTR - VENTURE- TRAVELER'S WORLD
VTX - VERTEX
WAB - WELCOME ABOARD
WAT - FRANKLIN WATTS, INC.
WBK - WARNER BOOKS
WBY - WORLDS BEYOND
WDG - WHAT'S DOING
WDM - WOMAN'S DAY MAGAZINE
WEI - WEIDENFELD NICOLSON, LONDON
WHC - WOMANS HOME COMPANION

WHL - WHITE LION, LONDON
WHP - WHITMAN PRESS, SYDNEY
WHS - WHISPERS (NUMBERED)
WHT - WHITMAN BOOKS
WHW - WHITING & WHEATON, LONDON
WKR - WALKER AND COMPANY
WKS - WORKSHOP NEW POETRY
WLK - AND WALK NOW GENTLY THROUGH THE FIRE (OA)
WMR - WESTMINSTER MAGAZINE
WMW - WILLIAM WILKINS, BALTIMORE
WND - C. WINDUS, PUB. (LONDON)
WOF - WORLDS OF FANTASY (FIRST 2 NUMBERED, 1968-1970)
WOR - WORLD PUBLISHING COMPANY
WOS - WONDER STORIES
WOT - WORLDS OF TOMORROW
WPB - WARNER PAPERBACK LIBRARY
WPC - WESTERN PUBLISHING COMPANY, INC.
WPS - THE WASHINGTON POST
WRN - WREN: SOUTH MELBOURNE, AUSTRALIA
WRP - WARD RITCHIE PRESS
WRT - WEIRD TALES
WRV - WORLD REVIEW
WSL - THE WEEKLY SUN LITERARY SUPPLEMENT
WSP - WASHINGTON SQUARE PRESS
WSQ - WONDER STORIES QUARTERLY
WTS - WITCHCRAFT & SORCERY (NUMBERED AFTER MAY, 1971)
WUM - WASHINGTON UNIVERSITY MAGAZINE
YBK - YELLOW BOOK
YNW - YOUNG WORLD MAGAZINE
YPB - YOUTH PUBLICATIONS/ THE SATURDAY EVENING POST CO.
YRT - THE YEAR 2000 (OA)
YRV - YALE REVIEW
ZEB - ZEBRA BOOKS
ZEN - ZENETH
ZGW - ZANE GREY'S WESTERN MAGAZINE

Checklist of Books Indexed

ABC OF SCIENCE FICTION, AN

ABC OF SCIENCE FICTION, AN	BOARDMAN, TOM JR.	AN	AVN	68	12
ABOMINABLE EARTHMAN, THE	POHL, FREDERIK	AC	BAL	63	
ABOVE THE HUMAN LANDSCAPE	MCNELLY & STOVER	AN H	GYR	72	

A SOCIAL SCIENCE FICTION ANTHOLOGY

ACE SCIENCE FICTION READER	WOLLHEIM, DONALD A.	AN	ACE	71	

IN ENGLAND AS "TRILOGY OF THE FUTURE"

ACROSS PARIS AND OTHER STORIES	AYME, MARCEL	AC H	BDL	57	

SEE "THE WALKER THROUGH WALLS"

ACROSS THE SEA OF STARS	CLARKE, ARTHUR C.	AC H	HBW	59	
AD 2500	WILSON, ANGUS	AN H	HEI	55	

THE OBSERVER PRIZE STORIES 1954

ADAM LINK- ROBOT	BINDER, EANDO	AC	PBK	65	09
ADRIFT IN SPACE AND OTHER STORIES	ELWOOD, ROGER	OA H	LER	74	
ADVENTURES IN DIMENSION	CONKLIN, GROFF	AN H	GRY	55	

SELECTIONS FROM "SCIENCE FICTION ADVENTURES IN DIMENSION"

ADVENTURES IN THE FAR FUTURE	WOLLHEIM, DONALD A.	DA	ACE	54	
ADVENTURES IN TIME AND SPACE	HEALY & MCCOMAS	AN H	RDM	46	08

SECOND EDITION, 1953, OMITS LAST FIVE STORIES,
ALSO AS "FAMOUS SCIENCE-FICTION STORIES"
DERIVATIVE ANTHOLOGY "MORE ADVENTURES IN TIME AND SPACE"
ADVENTURES IN TIME AND SPACE (BRITISH)

	HEALY & MCCOMAS	AN H	GRY	52	

ADVENTURES IN TIME AND SPACE (SELECTIONS FROM)

	HEALY & MCCOMAS	AN	BAN	54	
ADVENTURES IN TOMORROW	CROSSEN, KENDELL F.	AN H	GBG	51	
ADVENTURES ON OTHER PLANETS	WOLLHEIM, DONALD A.	AN	ACE	55	
ADVENTURES TO COME	ESENWEIN, J. BERG	OA H	MLB	37	
AFFAIR WITH GENIUS, AN	GREEN, JOSEPH	AC H	GOL	69	
AGAIN, DANGEROUS VISIONS	ELLISON, HARLAN	OA H	DBL	72	
AGENT OF THE TERRAN EMPIRE	ANDERSON, POUL	AC H	CHL	65	
AGENT OF VEGA	SCHMITZ, JAMES H.	AC H	GNM	60	
AHEAD OF TIME	KUTTNER, HENRY	AC	BAL	53	07
AIR FORCE!	HARVEY, FRANK	AC	BAL	59	
AIR OF MARS AND OTHER STORIES, THE					
	GINSBURG, MIRRA	AN H	MAC	76	
AIRS OF EARTH, THE	ALDISS, BRIAN W.	AC H	FAB	63	
ALCHEMY AND ACADEME	MCCAFFREY, ANNE	OA H	DBL	70	
ALFRED BESTER OMNIBUS, AN	BESTER, ALFRED	AC H	SID	67	
ALIEN CONDITION, THE	GOLDIN, STEPHEN	OA	BAL	73	04
ALIEN DUST	TUBB, E. C.	NO H	BDM	55	
ALIEN EARTH AND OTHER STORIES	ELWOOD & MOSKOWITZ	AN	MCF	69	
ALIEN HORIZONS	NOLAN, WILLIAM F.	AC	PKT	74	08
ALIEN LANDSCAPES	BURKE, JONATHAN F.	AC H	MUS	55	
ALIEN WORLDS	ELWOOD, ROGER	AN	PBK	64	09
ALIENS AMONG US, THE	WHITE, JAMES	AC	BAL	69	03
ALIENS FOR NEIGHBOURS	SIMAK, CLIFFORD D.	AC H	FAB	61	

9 STORIES FROM "THE WORLDS OF CLIFFORD SIMAK"

ALIENS 4	STURGEON, THEODORE	AC	AVN	59	
ALIENS, THE	LEINSTER, MURRAY	AC	BKM	60	03
ALIENS, THE	SILVERBERG, ROBERT	AN H	NEL	76	
ALL ABOUT THE FUTURE	GREENBERG, MARTIN	AN H	GNM	55	
ALL ABOUT VENUS	ALDISS, BRIAN W.	AN	DEL	68	12
ALL THE MYRIAD WAYS	NIVEN, LARRY	AC	BAL	71	06
ALL THE SOUNDS OF FEAR	ELLISON, HARLAN	AC	PTH	73	

FIRST 9 STORIES FROM "ALONE AGAINST TOMORROW"
ALL THE TRAPS OF EARTH AND OTHER STORIES

	SIMAK, CLIFFORD D.	AC H	DBL	62	

IN ENGLAND AS "THE NIGHT OF THE PUUDLY"
ALL THE TRAPS OF EARTH AND OTHER STORIES (BRITISH PB 2)

	SIMAK, CLIFFORD D.	AC	FSP	64	

ALL THE TRAPS OF EARTH AND OTHER STORIES (6 OF 9)

	SIMAK, CLIFFORD D.	AC	MCF	63	
ALLEY GOD, THE	FARMER, PHILIP JOSE	AC	BAL	62	
ALMOST HUMAN	NOLAN, WILLIAM F.	AN H	SVN	66	

SEE "THE PSEUDO-PEOPLE"

ALONE AGAINST TOMORROW	ELLISON, HARLAN	AC H	MAC	71	

IN ENGLAND AS "ALL THE SOUNDS OF FEAR" AND
"THE TIME OF THE EYE"

ALONE BY NIGHT	CONGDON, MICHAEL&DON	AN	BAL	62	01
ALPHA 1	SILVERBERG, ROBERT	AN	BAL	70	09
ALPHA 2	SILVERBERG, ROBERT	AN	BAL	71	11
ALPHA 3	SILVERBERG, ROBERT	AN	BAL	72	10
ALPHA 4	SILVERBERG, ROBERT	AN	BAL	73	10
ALPHA 5	SILVERBERG, ROBERT	AN	BAL	74	08
ALPHA 6	SILVERBERG, ROBERT	AN	BKM	76	04
ALPHA 7	SILVERBERG, ROBERT	AN	BKM	77	07
ALTERNATE ORBITS	CHANDLER, A. BERTRAM	DC	ACE	71	
ALTERNATIES	GERROLD, DAVID	OA	DEL	74	07
ALTERNATING CURRENTS	POHL, FREDERIK	AC	BAL	56	
ALYX	RUSS, JOANNA	AC H	GRG	76	06

AMERICAN GOVERNMENT THROUGH SCIENCE FICTION

	OLANDER/GREENBERG/&	AN L	RAN	74	
AMONG THE DEAD	BRYANT, EDWARD	AC H	MAC	73	
ANALOG ANNUAL	BOVA, BEN	OA	PYR	76	04
ANALOG ANTHOLOGY	CAMPBELL, JOHN W. JR	AN H	DOB	65	
ANALOG 1	CAMPBELL, JOHN W. JR	AN H	DBL	63	

IN "ANALOG ANTHOLOGY"

ANALOG 2	CAMPBELL, JOHN W. JR	AN H	DBL	64	

IN "ANALOG ANTHOLOGY"

ANALOG 3	CAMPBELL, JOHN W. JR	AN H	DBL	65	

ALSO AS "A WORLD BY THE TALE"

ANALOG 4	CAMPBELL, JOHN W. JR	AN H	DBL	66	

ALSO AS "THE PERMANENT IMPLOSION"

ANALOG 5	CAMPBELL, JOHN W. JR	AN H	DBL	67	

ALSO AS "COUNTERCOMMANDMENT"

ANALOG 6	CAMPBELL, JOHN W. JR	AN H	DBL	68	
ANALOG 7	CAMPBELL, JOHN W. JR	AN H	DBL	70	
ANALOG 8	CAMPBELL, JOHN W. JR	AN H	DBL	71	
ANALOG 9	BOVA, BEN	AN H	DBL	73	
ANCESTRAL VOICES	MENVILLE & REGINALD	AN H	ANO	74	
ANCIENT MYSTERIES READER, THE	HAINING, PETER	AN H	DBL	75	
ANCIENT, MY ENEMY	DICKSON, GORDON R.	AC H	DBL	74	
AND SOME WERE HUMAN	DEL REY, LESTER	AC H	PRM	48	
AND SOME WERE HUMAN (8 OF 12)	DEL REY, LESTER	AC	BAL	61	

BEST FROM FANTASY AND SCIENCE FICTION: 4

AND WALK NOW GENTLY THROUGH THE FIRE...					
	ELWOOD, ROGER	OA H	CHL	72	
ANDOVER AND THE ANDROID	WILHELM, KATE	AC H	DOB	66	

SEE "THE MILE-LONG SPACESHIP"
ANDROIDS, TIME MACHINES AND BLUE GIRAFFES

	ELWOOD & GHIDALIA	AN H	FOL	73	
ANDROMEDA I	WESTON, PETER	OA	FPL	76	
ANGELS AND SPACESHIPS	BROWN, FREDRIC	AC H	DUT	54	09

ALSO AS "STAR SHINE"

ANOTHER KIND	OLIVER, CHAD	AC H	BAL	55	
ANOTHER PART OF THE GALAXY	CONKLIN, GROFF	AN	FGM	66	
ANOTHER TOMORROW	HOLLISTER, BERNARD C	AN L	PFL	74	
ANOTHER WORLD	DOZOIS, GARDNER R.	AN H	FOL	77	

ANTHROPOLOGY THROUGH SCIENCE FICTION

	MASON, C/GREENBERG/&	AN H	SMP	74	
ANTIGRAV: COSMIC COMEDIES	STRICK, PHILIP	AN H	HUT	76	01
ANTON YORK, IMMORTAL	BINDER, EANDO	AC	BEL	65	
ANYTHING BOX, THE	HENDERSON, ZENNA	AC H	DBL	65	
ANYWHEN	BLISH, JAMES	AC H	DBL	70	

ANYWHEN (ENGLISH EDITION ADDS:)

	BLISH, JAMES	AC H	FAB	71	
ANYWHERE, ANYWHEN	ENGDAHL, SYLVIA	OA H	ATH	76	
APEMAN, SPACEMAN	STOVER & HARRISON	AN H	DBL	68	

ANTHROPOLOGICAL SCIENCE FICTION

APPROACHING OBLIVION	ELLISON, HARLAN	AC H	WKR	74	
ARENA: SPORTS SF	FERMAN & MALZBERG	AN H	DBL	76	
ARMADA SCI-FI ONE	DAVIS, RICHARD	OA	ARM	75	04
ARMADA SCI-FI TWO	DAVIS, RICHARD	OA	ARM	75	04
ARMCHAIR SCIENCE FICTION READER, THE	GORDON, I. & SORKIN	AN H	SAS	59	

ONLY SCIENCE FICTION LISTED

ARTHUR C. CLARKE OMNIBUS, AN	CLARKE, ARTHUR C.	AC H	SID	65	

ARTHUR C. CLARKE SECOND OMNIBUS, AN

	CLARKE, ARTHUR C.	AC H	SID	68	
AS TOMORROW BECOMES TODAY	SULLIVAN, CHARLES W.	AN L	PRH	74	
ASIMOV'S MYSTERIES	ASIMOV, ISAAC	AC H	DBL	68	
ASLEEP IN ARMAGEDDON	SISSONS, MICHAEL	AN	PTH	62	06
ASPECTS OF SCIENCE FICTION	DOHERTY, G. D.	AN H	MUR	59	
ASSIGNMENT IN ETERNITY	HEINLEIN, ROBERT A.	AC H	FPS	53	
ASSIGNMENT IN TOMORROW	POHL, FREDERIK	AN H	HAN	54	
ASTOUNDING	HARRISON, HARRY	OA H	RDM	73	

JOHN W. CAMPBELL MEMORIAL ANTHOLOGY
ASTOUNDING SCIENCE FICTION ANTHOLOGY, THE

	CAMPBELL, JOHN W. JR	AN H	SAS	52	

DERIVATIVE ANTHOLOGY "ASTOUNDING TALES OF SPACE AND TIME"
IN ENGLAND AS "THE FIRST AND SECOND ASTOUNDING SCIENCE
FICTION ANTHOLOGIES"
ASTOUNDING SCIENCE FICTION ANTHOLOGY, THE (8 OF 22)

	CAMPBELL, JOHN W. JR	AN	BRK	56	12

ASTOUNDING TALES OF SPACE AND TIME

	CAMPBELL, JOHN W. JR	AN	BRK	57	02

STORIES FROM "THE ASTOUNDING SCIENCE FICTION ANTHOLOGY"
ASTOUNDING-ANALOG READER, THE VOLUME ONE

	HARRISON & ALDISS	AN H	DBL	72	

ASTOUNDING-ANALOG READER, THE VOLUME TWO

	HARRISON & ALDISS	AN H	DBL	73	
ATOMS AND EVIL	BLOCH, ROBERT	AC	GMB	62	08
ATROCITY EXHIBITION	BALLARD, J. G.	AC H	CAP	70	

SEE "LOVE & NAPALM: EXPORT U.S.A."

AURORA: BEYOND EQUALITY	MCINTYRE & ANDERSON	OA	FGM	76	05
AUTHENTIC BOOK OF SPACE	CAMPBELL, H. J.	AN H	HML	54	
AUTUMN PEOPLE, THE	BRADBURY, RAY	AC	BAL	65	10

COMIC BOOK VERSIONS OF STORIES FROM E.C. COMICS

AVON FANTASY READER, THE	WOLLHEIM &ERNSBERGER	AN	AVN	68	
AWARD SCIENCE FICTION READER	NORTON, ALDEN H.	AN	AWD	66	
AWAY AND BEYOND	VAN VOGT, A. E.	AC H	PEL	52	
AWAY AND BEYOND (7 OF 9)	VAN VOGT, A. E.	AC	BKM	59	02
AWAY FROM THE HERE AND NOW	HARRIS, CLARE WINGER	AC H	DOR	47	
BACKDROP OF STARS	HARRISON, HARRY	AC H	DOB	68	

SEE "SF: AUTHORS' CHOICE"

BAD MOON RISING	DISCH, THOMAS M.	OA H	HPR	73	

BATTLE FOR THE PACIFIC AND OTHER ADVENTURES AT SEA, THE

	ANONYMOUS	AN H	HPR	08	

BATTLE OF THE MONSTERS AND OTHER STORIES, THE

	HARTWELL & CURREY	AN H	GRG	76	
BEACHHEADS IN SPACE	DERLETH, AUGUST	AN H	PEL	52	

ENGLISH DERIVATIVE ANTHOLOGY "FROM OTHER WORLDS"
BEACHHEADS IN SPACE (BRITISH PB)

	DERLETH, AUGUST	AN	FSP	64	
BEACHHEADS IN SPACE (BRITISH)	DERLETH, AUGUST	AN	WEI	54	
BEACHHEADS IN SPACE (7 OF 14)	DERLETH, AUGUST	AN	BRK	57	

BEAST THAT SHOUTED LOVE AT THE HEART OF THE WORLD, THE

	ELLISON, HARLAN	AC	AVN	69	07

ENGLISH EDITION (H. MILLINGTON, 1976) OMITS:
"ALONG THE SCENIC ROUTE", "THE PLACE WITH NO NAME"
AND "SHATTERED LIKE A GLASS GOBLIN"

BEAST, THE	VAN VOGT, A. E.	NO H	DBL	63	

ALSO IN "A VAN VOGT OMNIBUS"

BEFORE ARMAGEDDON	MOORCOCK, MICHAEL	AN H	ALL	75	

AN ANTHOLOGY OF VICTORIAN AND EDWARDIAN IMAGINATIVE FICTION
PUBLISHED BEFORE 1914

BEFORE THE GOLDEN AGE	ASIMOV, ISAAC	AN H	DBL	74	
BERSERKER	SABERHAGEN, FRED	AC	BAL	67	01
BERSERKERS, THE	ELWOOD, ROGER	OA H	TRI	74	
BEST FANTASY STORIES	ALDISS, BRIAN W.	AN H	FAB	62	
BEST FROM AMAZING, THE	WHITE, TED	AN	MAN	73	
BEST FROM FANTASTIC, THE	WHITE, TED	AN	MAN	73	

BEST FROM FANTASY AND SCIENCE FICTION

	BOUCHER & MCCOMAS	AN H	LBR	52	

BEST FROM FANTASY AND SCIENCE FICTION: 2

	BOUCHER & MCCOMAS	AN H	LBR	53	

BEST FROM FANTASY AND SCIENCE FICTION: 3

	BOUCHER & MCCOMAS	AN H	DBL	54	

ACE PB EDITION OMITS ALL POEMS
BEST FROM FANTASY AND SCIENCE FICTION: 4

	BOUCHER, ANTHONY	AN H	DBL	55	

ACE PB EDITION OMITS ALL POEMS EXCEPT ASIMOV'S

BEST FROM FANTASY AND SCIENCE FICTION: 5
                              BOUCHER, ANTHONY   AN H DBL 56
    ACE PB EDITION OMITS POEMS "1980 OVERTURES", "SILENT UPON TWO
    PEAKS" AND "THE GLASS OF THE FUTURE"
BEST FROM FANTASY AND SCIENCE FICTION: 6
                              BOUCHER, ANTHONY   AN H DBL 57
    ACE PB EDITION OMITS POEMS "FLYING CHAUCER" AND
    "I WANT MY NAME IN THE TITLE"
BEST FROM FANTASY AND SCIENCE FICTION: 7
                              BOUCHER, ANTHONY   AN H DBL 58
    ACE PB EDITION OMITS ALL POEMS EXCEPT BUCK'S
BEST FROM FANTASY AND SCIENCE FICTION: 8
                              BOUCHER, ANTHONY   AN H DBL 59
    ACE PB EDITION OMITS FEGHOOTS AND POEMS
BEST FROM FANTASY AND SCIENCE FICTION: 9
                              MILLS, ROBERT P.   AN H DBL 60
    ALSO AS "FLOWERS FOR ALGERNON AND OTHER STORIES"
    BRITISH EDITIONS OMIT FEGHOOTS,
    ACE PB EDITION OMITS FEGHOOTS AND POEMS
BEST FROM FANTASY AND SCIENCE FICTION: 10
                              MILLS, ROBERT P.   AN H DBL 61
BEST FROM FANTASY AND SCIENCE FICTION: 11
                              MILLS, ROBERT P.   AN H DBL 62
BEST FROM FANTASY AND SCIENCE FICTION: 11 (BRITISH)
                              MILLS, ROBERT P.   AN   PTH 66
BEST FROM FANTASY AND SCIENCE FICTION: 12
                              DAVIDSON, AVRAM   AN H DBL 63
BEST FROM FANTASY AND SCIENCE FICTION: 13
                              DAVIDSON, AVRAM   AN H DBL 64
BEST FROM FANTASY AND SCIENCE FICTION: 14
                              DAVIDSON, AVRAM   AN H DBL 65
BEST FROM FANTASY AND SCIENCE FICTION: 15
                              FERMAN, EDWARD L.   AN H DBL 66
BEST FROM FANTASY AND SCIENCE FICTION: 16
                              FERMAN, EDWARD L.   AN H DBL 67
BEST FROM FANTASY AND SCIENCE FICTION: 17
                              FERMAN, EDWARD L.   AN H DBL 68
BEST FROM FANTASY AND SCIENCE FICTION: 18
                              FERMAN, EDWARD L.   AN H DBL 69
BEST FROM FANTASY AND SCIENCE FICTION: 19
                              FERMAN, EDWARD L.   AN H DBL 71
BEST FROM FANTASY AND SCIENCE FICTION: 20
                              FERMAN, EDWARD L.   AN H DBL 73
BEST FROM FANTASY AND SCIENCE FICTION, 25TH ANNIV.
                              FERMAN, EDWARD L.   AN H DBL 74
BEST FROM GALAXY, THE   VOLUME I
                              GALAXY, EDITORS OF AN   AWD 72
BEST FROM GALAXY, THE   VOLUME II
                              GALAXY, EDITORS OF AN   AWD 74
BEST FROM GALAXY, THE   VOLUME III
                              BAEN, JAMES   AN   AWD 75
BEST FROM GALAXY, THE   VOLUME IV
                              BAEN, JAMES   AN   AWD 76
BEST FROM IF, THE   VOLUME I   IF, EDITORS OF   AN   AWD 73
BEST FROM IF, THE   VOLUME II   IF, EDITORS OF   AN   AWD 74
BEST FROM IF, THE   VOLUME III BAEN, JAMES   AN   AWD 76
BEST FROM NEW WORLDS SCIENCE FICTION, THE
                              CARNELL, JOHN   AN   BDM 55
BEST FROM NEW WRITINGS IN S-F FIRST SELECTION, THE
                              CARNELL, JOHN   AN H DOB 71
BEST FROM ORBIT, THE   KNIGHT, DAMON   AN H BRK 75
BEST FROM STARTLING STORIES, THE
                              MINES, SAMUEL   AN H HLT 53
    ALSO AS "STARTLING STORIES" AND "MOMENT WITHOUT TIME"
BEST FROM THE REST OF THE WORLD, THE
                              WOLLHEIM, DONALD A. AN H DBL 76
BEST LAID SCHEMES, THE   EISENBERG, LARRY   AC H MAC 71
BEST OF A. E. VAN VOGT, THE   VAN VOGT, A. E.   AC   PKT 76 07
BEST OF A. E. VAN VOGT, THE (BRITISH)
                              VAN VOGT, A. E.   AC H SID 74 05
    EDITED BY ANGUS WELLS
BEST OF AMAZING, THE   ROSS, JOSEPH   AN H DBL 67
BEST OF ARTHUR C. CLARKE: 1937-1971, THE
                              CLARKE, ARTHUR C.   AC H SID 73
BEST OF BARRY N. MALZBERG, THE MALZBERG, BARRY N. AC   PKT 76 01
BEST OF C. L. MOORE, THE   MOORE, C. L.   AC H NDB 75
    EDITED BY LESTER DEL REY
BEST OF C. M. KORNBLUTH, THE KORNBLUTH, C. M.   AC H NDB 76
    EDITED BY FREDERIK POHL
BEST OF CORDWAINER SMITH, THE SMITH, CORDWAINER   AC   BAL 75
    EDITED BY J. J. PIERCE
BEST OF DAMON KNIGHT, THE   KNIGHT, DAMON   AC H NDB 76
BEST OF E. E. 'DOC' SMITH, THE SMITH, EDWARD E. PHD AC H WEI 75
BEST OF EDMOND HAMILTON, THE HAMILTON, EDMOND   AC H NDB 77
    EDITED BY LEIGH BRACKETT
BEST OF FRANK HERBERT, THE   HERBERT, FRANK   AC H SID 75
    EDITED BY ANGUS WELLS
BEST OF FREDERIK POHL, THE   POHL, FREDERIK   AC H NDB 75
    EDITED BY LESTER DEL REY
BEST OF FREDRIC BROWN, THE   BROWN, FREDRIC   AC H NDB 76
    EDITED BY ROBERT BLOCH
BEST OF FRITZ LEIBER, THE   LEIBER, FRITZ   AC H NDB 74
BEST OF HARRY HARRISON, THE   HARRISON, HARRY   AC   PKT 76 06
BEST OF HARRY HARRISON, THE (BRITISH)
                              HARRISON, HARRY   AC H SID 76 09
BEST OF HENRY KUTTNER 1, THE KUTTNER, HENRY   AC   MFL 65
BEST OF HENRY KUTTNER 2, THE KUTTNER, HENRY   AC   MFL 66
BEST OF HENRY KUTTNER, THE   KUTTNER, HENRY   AC H NDB 75
BEST OF ISAAC ASIMOV, THE   ASIMOV, ISAAC   AC H SID 73
    EDITED BY ANGUS WELLS, U.S. EDITION OMITS
    BIBLIOGRAPHY AND PART OF INTRODUCTION
BEST OF J. G. BALLARD, THE   BALLARD, J. G.   AC   FPL 77
BEST OF JACK VANCE, THE   VANCE, JACK   AC   PKT 76 05
BEST OF JOHN JAKES, THE   JAKES, JOHN W.   AC   DAW 77 06
    EDITED BY MARTIN HARRY GREENBERG AND JOSEPH D. OLANDER
BEST OF JOHN W. CAMPBELL, THE CAMPBELL, JOHN W. JR AC BAL 76 05

    EDITED BY LESTER DEL REY
BEST OF JOHN W. CAMPBELL, THE (BRITISH)
                              CAMPBELL, JOHN W. JR AC H SID 73
    COMPILED BY GEORGE HAY
BEST OF JOHN WYNDHAM, THE   WYNDHAM, JOHN   AC   SPH 73
BEST OF JUDITH MERRIL, THE   MERRIL, JUDITH   AC   WBK 76 01
BEST OF KEITH LAUMER, THE   LAUMER, KEITH   AC   PKT 76 03
BEST OF LEIGH BRACKETT, THE   BRACKETT, LEIGH   AC H NDB 77
    EDITED BY EDMOND HAMILTON
BEST OF MACK REYNOLDS, THE   REYNOLDS, MACK   AC   PKT 76 04
BEST OF MURRAY LEINSTER, THE   LEINSTER, MURRAY   AC   COR 76
    EDITED BY BRIAN DAVIS
BEST OF NEW WORLDS, THE   MOORCOCK, MICHAEL   AN   CPT 65
BEST OF PHILIP K. DICK, THE   DICK, PHILIP K.   AC   BAL 77 03
    EDITED BY JOHN BRUNNER
BEST OF PLANET STORIES NO. 1, THE
                              BRACKETT, LEIGH   AN   BAL 75 01
BEST OF POUL ANDERSON, THE   ANDERSON, POUL   AC   PKT 76 08
BEST OF ROBERT HEINLEIN, THE   HEINLEIN, ROBERT A. AC H SID 73
BEST OF ROBERT SILVERBERG, THE SILVERBERG, ROBERT AC   PKT 76 02
BEST OF SCIENCE FICTION   CONKLIN, GROFF   AN H CRN 46
BEST OF SCIENCE FICTION (22 OF 40)
                              CONKLIN, GROFF   AN L CRB 63
BEST OF SCIENCE FICTION MONTHLY, THE
                              SACKS, JANET   AN H NLB 75
BEST OF SCIENCE FICTION 2, THE MERRIL, JUDITH   AN   MFL 64
    SEE "THE 7TH ANNUAL OF THE YEAR'S BEST S-F, THE"
BEST OF SCIENCE FICTION 4, THE MERRIL, JUDITH   AN   MFL 65
    SEE "THE 8TH ANNUAL OF THE YEAR'S BEST S-F, THE"
BEST OF SCIENCE FICTION 5, THE MERRIL, JUDITH   AN   MFL 66
    SEE "THE 5TH ANNUAL OF THE YEAR'S BEST S-F, THE"
BEST OF SCIENCE FICTION, THE   MERRIL, JUDITH   AN   MFL 63
    SEE "THE 6TH ANNUAL OF THE YEAR'S BEST S-F, THE"
BEST OF STANLEY G. WEINBAUM, THE
                              WEINBAUM, STANLEY G. AC   BAL 74
BEST SCIENCE FICTION FOR 1972 POHL, FREDERIK   AN   ACE 72 09
BEST SCIENCE FICTION FOR 1973 ACKERMAN, FORREST J. AN ACE 73
BEST SCIENCE FICTION FROM IF, THE
                              POHL, FREDERIK   AN D GPC 64
BEST SCIENCE FICTION FROM WORLDS OF TOMORROW, THE
                              POHL, FREDERIK   AN D GPC 64
BEST SCIENCE FICTION OF THE YEAR, THE
                              CARR, TERRY   AN   BAL 72 07
BEST SCIENCE FICTION OF THE YEAR, THE NO. 2
                              CARR, TERRY   AN   BAL 73 07
BEST SCIENCE FICTION OF THE YEAR, THE NO. 3
                              CARR, TERRY   AN   BAL 74 07
BEST SCIENCE FICTION OF THE YEAR, THE NO. 4
                              CARR, TERRY   AN   BAL 75 07
BEST SCIENCE FICTION OF THE YEAR, THE NO. 5
                              CARR, TERRY   AN   BAL 76 07
BEST SCIENCE FICTION OF THE YEAR, THE NO. 6
                              CARR, TERRY   AN   HRW 77 07
BEST SCIENCE FICTION STORIES AND NOVELS: 1955
                              DIKTY, T. E.   AN H FEL 55
    DERIVATIVE ANTHOLOGY "5 TALES FROM TOMORROW"
BEST SCIENCE FICTION STORIES AND NOVELS: 1956
                              DIKTY, T. E.   AN H FEL 56
    DERIVATIVE ANTHOLOGY "6 FROM WORLDS BEYOND"
BEST SCIENCE FICTION STORIES AND NOVELS: 9TH SERIES
                              DIKTY, T. E.   AN H AVT 58
BEST SCIENCE FICTION STORIES OF BRIAN W. ALDISS
                              ALDISS, BRIAN W.   AC H FAB 65
    ALSO AS "WHO CAN REPLACE A MAN?"
BEST SCIENCE FICTION STORIES OF BRIAN W. ALDISS (REVISED)
                              ALDISS, BRIAN W.   AC H FAB 71
BEST SCIENCE FICTION STORIES OF C. M. KORNBLUTH
                              KORNBLUTH, C. M.   AC H FAB 68
BEST SCIENCE FICTION STORIES OF CLIFFORD D. SIMAK
                              SIMAK, CLIFFORD D.   AC H FAB LM
BEST SCIENCE FICTION STORIES OF H. G. WELLS
                              WELLS, H. G.   AC L DOV 66
BEST SCIENCE FICTION STORIES OF JAMES BLISH
                              BLISH, JAMES   AC H FAB 65
BEST SCIENCE FICTION STORIES OF JAMES BLISH (REVISED)
                              BLISH, JAMES   AC H FAB 73
BEST SCIENCE FICTION STORIES OF THE YEAR (1971)
                              DEL REY, LESTER   AN H DUT 72
BEST SCIENCE FICTION STORIES OF THE YEAR (1972)
                              DEL REY, LESTER   AN H DUT 73
BEST SCIENCE FICTION STORIES OF THE YEAR (1973)
                              DEL REY, LESTER   AN H DUT 74
                              DEL REY, LESTER   AN H DUT 75
BEST SCIENCE FICTION STORIES OF THE YEAR (1974)
                              DEL REY, LESTER   AN H DUT 75
BEST SCIENCE FICTION STORIES OF THE YEAR (1975)
                              DEL REY, LESTER   AN H DUT 76
BEST SCIENCE FICTION STORIES OF THE YEAR (1976)
                              DOZOIS, GARDNER R.   AN H DUT 77 07
BEST SCIENCE FICTION STORIES 3, THE
                              SMITH, CORDELIA T.   AN   MFL 64
    SEE "GREAT SCIENCE FICTION STORIES"
BEST SCIENCE FICTION STORIES: FIFTH SERIES, THE
                              BLEILER & DIKTY   AN H GRY 56
    SEE "THE BEST SCIENCE-FICTION STORIES: 1954",
    OMITS STORIES BY LEIBER (2), MCINTOSH AND BESTER,
    "CRUCIFIXUS ETIAM" LISTED AS "THE SOWER DOES NOT REAP"
BEST SCIENCE FICTION STORIES: FOURTH SERIES, THE
                              BLEILER & DIKTY   AN H GRY 55
    SEE "THE BEST SCIENCE-FICTION STORIES: 1953", OMITS
    "THE FLY" AND "LOVER, WHEN YOU'RE NEAR ME"
BEST SCIENCE FICTION STORIES: SECOND SERIES, THE
                              BLEILER & DIKTY   AN H GRY 52
    SEE "THE BEST SCIENCE-FICTION STORIES: 1951", OMITS STORIES BY
    TEMPLE, BESTER, HARNESS AND LEIBER
BEST SCIENCE FICTION STORIES: THIRD SERIES, THE
                              BLEILER & DIKTY   AN H GRY 53

BEST SCIENCE FICTION STORIES: THIRD SERIES, THE

     SEE "THE BEST SCIENCE-FICTION STORIES: 1952", OMITS
    "DARK INTERLUDE" AND "THE PEDESTRIAN"
BEST SCIENCE FICTION STORIES, THE
                  BLEILER & DIKTY   AN H GRY 51
     SEE "THE BEST SCIENCE FICTION STORIES: 1950", OMITS STORIES BY
    STURGEON, KREPPS, BRADBURY (2) AND MACDONALD
BEST SCIENCE-FICTION STORIES: 1949, THE
                  BLEILER & DIKTY   AN H FEL 49 08
    ALSO IN "SCIENCE FICTION OMNIBUS"
BEST SCIENCE-FICTION STORIES: 1950, THE
                  BLEILER & DIKTY   AN H FEL 50 08
    ALSO IN "SCIENCE FICTION OMNIBUS"
    IN ENGLAND AS "THE BEST SCIENCE FICTION STORIES"
BEST SCIENCE-FICTION STORIES: 1951, THE
                  BLEILER & DIKTY   AN H FEL 51
    IN ENGLAND AS
    "THE BEST SCIENCE FICTION STORIES: SECOND SERIES"
BEST SCIENCE-FICTION STORIES: 1952, THE
                  BLEILER & DIKTY   AN H FEL 52
    IN ENGLAND AS "THE BEST SCIENCE FICTION STORIES: THIRD SERIES"
BEST SCIENCE-FICTION STORIES: 1953, THE
                  BLEILER & DIKTY   AN H FEL 53
    IN ENGLAND AS
    "THE BEST SCIENCE FICTION STORIES: FOURTH SERIES"
BEST SCIENCE-FICTION STORIES: 1954, THE
                  BLEILER & DIKTY   AN H FEL 54
    IN ENGLAND AS "THE BEST SCIENCE FICTION STORIES: FIFTH SERIES"
BEST SF   CRISPIN, EDMUND   AN H FAB 55
BEST SF 2   CRISPIN, EDMUND   AN H FAB 56
BEST SF 3   CRISPIN, EDMUND   AN H FAB 58
BEST SF 4   CRISPIN, EDMUND   AN H FAB 61
BEST SF 5   CRISPIN, EDMUND   AN H FAB 63
BEST SF 6   CRISPIN, EDMUND   AN H FAB 66
BEST SF 7   CRISPIN, EDMUND   AN H FAB 70
BEST SF STORIES FROM NEW WORLDS NO. 1, THE
             MOORCOCK, MICHAEL AN   BKM 67
BEST SF STORIES FROM NEW WORLDS NO. 2, THE
             MOORCOCK, MICHAEL AN   BKM 68
BEST SF STORIES FROM NEW WORLDS 3
             MOORCOCK, MICHAEL AN   BKM 68
BEST SF STORIES FROM NEW WORLDS 4
             MOORCOCK, MICHAEL AN   BKM 69
BEST SF STORIES FROM NEW WORLDS 5
             MOORCOCK, MICHAEL AN   BKM 69
BEST SF STORIES FROM NEW WORLDS 6
             MOORCOCK, MICHAEL AN   BKM 70
BEST SF STORIES FROM NEW WORLDS 7
             MOORCOCK, MICHAEL AN   PTH 71
BEST SF STORIES FROM NEW WORLDS 8
             MOORCOCK, MICHAEL AN   PTH 74
BEST SF: 1967   HARRISON & ALDISS AN   BKM 68 03
    IN ENGLAND AS "THE YEAR'S BEST SCIENCE FICTION NO. 1"
BEST SF: 1968   HARRISON & ALDISS AN H PUT 69
    IN ENGLAND AS "THE YEAR'S BEST SCIENCE FICTION NO. 2"
BEST SF: 1969   HARRISON & ALDISS AN H PUT 70
    IN ENGLAND AS "THE YEAR'S BEST SCIENCE FICTION NO. 3"
BEST SF: 1970   HARRISON & ALDISS AN H PUT 71
    IN ENGLAND AS "THE YEAR'S BEST SCIENCE FICTION NO. 4"
BEST SF: 1971   HARRISON & ALDISS AN H PUT 72
    IN ENGLAND AS "THE YEAR'S BEST SCIENCE FICTION NO. 5"
BEST SF: 1972   HARRISON & ALDISS AN H PUT 73
    IN ENGLAND AS "THE YEAR'S BEST SCIENCE FICTION NO. 6"
BEST SF: 1973   HARRISON & ALDISS AN H PUT 74
    IN ENGLAND AS "THE YEAR'S BEST SCIENCE FICTION NO. 7"
BEST SF: 1974   HARRISON & ALDISS AN H BML 75
    IN ENGLAND AS "THE YEAR'S BEST SCIENCE FICTION NO. 8"
BEST SF: 75, THE NINTH ANNUAL HARRISON & ALDISS AN H BML 76
    IN ENGLAND AS "THE YEAR'S BEST SCIENCE FICTION NO. 9"
BEST STORIES OF H. G. WELLS WELLS, H. G.   AC   BAL 60 08
BEWARE MORE BEASTS   GHIDALIA, V.& ELWOOD AN   MAN 75
BEWARE THE BEASTS   GHIDALIA, V.& ELWOOD AN   MBB 70
BEYOND   ANONYMOUS   AN   BKM 63 01
BEYOND   STURGEON, THEODORE AC   AVN 60
BEYOND BELIEF   HURLEY, RICHARD J. AN   SBS 64 04
BEYOND CONTROL   SILVERBERG, ROBERT AN H NEL 72
BEYOND HUMAN KEN   MERRIL, JUDITH   AN H RDM 52
BEYOND HUMAN KEN (BRITISH) MERRIL, JUDITH   AN H GRY 53
BEYOND HUMAN KEN (SELECTIONS FROM)
             MERRIL, JUDITH   AN   PNN 54 06
BEYOND INFINITY   CARR, ROBERT S.   AC H FPS 51
BEYOND INFINITY   NOURSE, ALAN E.   AC   COR 64
    SEE "TIGER BY THE TAIL"
BEYOND THE BARRIERS OF SPACE AND TIME
             MERRIL, JUDITH   AN H RDM 54
BEYOND THE BEYOND   ANDERSON, POUL   AN   SIG 69 08
    ENGLISH EDITION (GOL 70) OMITS STORY "DAY OF BURNING"
BEYOND THE END OF TIME   POHL, FREDERIK   AN H DBL 52
BEYOND THE GALACTIC RIM   CHANDLER, A. BERTRAM DC   ACE 63
BEYOND THE STARS AND OTHER STORIES
             ANONYMOUS   AN   JBL 58
BEYOND THIRTY & THE MAN-EATER BURROUGHS, EDGAR R. AC H SCP 57
BEYOND THIS HORIZON   CARRELL, CHRISTOPHER OA   CEO 73 10
BEYOND TIME   LEY, SANDRA   OA   PKT 76 10
BEYOND TIME AND SPACE   DERLETH, AUGUST   AN H PEL 50
BEYOND TIME AND SPACE (8 OF 32)
             DERLETH, AUGUST   AN   BRK 58
BEYOND TOMORROW   HARDING, LEE   AN H WRN 76
BEYOND TOMORROW   KNIGHT, DAMON   AN H HPR 65
BICENTENNIAL MAN AND OTHER STORIES, THE
             ASIMOV, ISAAC   AC H DBL 76
BIG BOOK OF SCIENCE FICTION CONKLIN, GROFF   AN H CRN 50
BIG BOOK OF SCIENCE FICTION (10 OF 32)
             CONKLIN, GROFF   AN   BRK 57
BIG SHOW, THE   LAUMER, KEITH   AC   ACE 72 10
BILLENIUM   BALLARD, J. G.   AC   BRK 62
BIO-FUTURES   SARGENT, PAMELA   AN   VNT 76 06

COLONIAL SURVEY

BIRD OF TIME, THE   WEST, WALLACE   NO H GNM 59
BLACK STAR PASSES, THE   CAMPBELL, JOHN W. JR AC H FPS 53
BLAL, THE   VAN VOGT, A. E.   AC   ZEB 76 08
    SEE "MONSTERS"
BLOCH AND BRADBURY   BRADBURY & BLOCH   AC   TWR 69
    IN ENGLAND AS "FEVER DREAM"
BLOOD RUNS COLD   BLOCH, ROBERT   AC H SAS 61
BLOOD RUNS COLD (BRITISH) BLOCH, ROBERT   AC   COR 64
BODYGUARD AND 4 OTHER SHORT SF NOVELS FROM GALAXY
             GOLD, H. L.   AN H DBL 60
BOGEY MEN   BLOCH, ROBERT   AC   PYR 63 03
BOLO   LAUMER, KEITH   AC H BKP 76
BOOK OF ANDRE NORTON, THE NORTON, ANDRE   AC   DAW 75 10
    SEE "THE MANY WORLDS OF ANDRE NORTON"
BOOK OF BRIAN ALDISS, THE ALDISS, BRIAN W.   AC   DAW 72
    IN ENGLAND AS "THE COMIC INFERNO"
BOOK OF FRANK HERBERT, THE HERBERT, FRANK   AC   DAW 73 01
BOOK OF FRITZ LEIBER, THE LEIBER, FRITZ   AC   DAW 74 01
BOOK OF GORDON DICKSON, THE DICKSON, GORDON R. AC   DAW 73 05
    SEE "DANGER- HUMAN"
BOOK OF JOHN BRUNNER, THE BRUNNER, JOHN   AC   DAW 76 01
BOOK OF PHILIP JOSE FARMER, THE
             FARMER, PHILIP JOSE AC   DAW 73 07
BOOK OF PHILIP K. DICK, THE DICK, PHILIP K.   AC   DAW 73 02
BOOK OF POUL ANDERSON, THE ANDERSON, POUL   AC   DAW 75 06
    SEE "THE MANY WORLDS OF POUL ANDERSON"
BOOK OF SABERHAGEN, THE   SABERHAGEN, FRED   AC   DAW 75 01
BOOK OF SKAITH, THE   BRACKETT, LEIGH   AC H NDB 76
    THE ADVENTURES OF ERIC JOHN STARK
BOOK OF VAN VOGT, THE   VAN VOGT, A. E.   AC   DAW 72
BORN OF MAN AND WOMAN   MATHESON, RICHARD AC H CHB 54 03
    DERIVATIVE COLLECTION "THIRD FROM THE SUN"
BORN WITH THE DEAD   SILVERBERG, ROBERT AC H RDM 74
BOYS' LIFE BOOK OF OUTER SPACE STORIES, THE
             BOY'S LIFE, ED. OF AN H RDM 64
BR-R-R-| CONKLIN, GROFF   AN   AVN 59
BREAKING POINT   GUNN, JAMES E.   AC H WKR 72
BRIAN ALDISS OMNIBUS 2   ALDISS, BRIAN W.   AC H SID 71
BRIAN ALDISS OMNIBUS, A   ALDISS, BRIAN W.   AC H SID 69
BROKE DOWN ENGINE AND OTHER TROUBLES WITH MACHINES
             GOULART, RON   AC H MAC 71
BUDRYS' INFERNO   BUDRYS, ALGIS   AC   BKM 63 07
    IN ENGLAND AS "THE FURIOUS FUTURE"
BUG-EYED MONSTERS   CHEETHAM, ANTHONY   AN   PTH 74
BULLARD OF THE SPACE PATROL JAMESON, MALCOLM   AC H WOR 51
    EDITED BY ANDRE NORTON, SECOND EDITION OMITS "THE BUREAUCRAT"
BURNING, THE   GUNN, JAMES E.   NO   DEL 72 02
BUY JUPITER AND OTHER STORIES ASIMOV, ISAAC   AC H DBL 75
BYPASS TO OTHERNESS   KUTTNER, HENRY   AC   BAL 61
CALLAHAN'S CROSSTIME SALOON ROBINSON, SPIDER   AC   ACE 77 06
CALLIBRATED ALLIGATOR AND OTHER SCIENCE FICTION STORIES, THE
             SILVERBERG, ROBERT AC H HRW 69
CALTRAPS OF TIME, THE   MASSON, DAVID I.   AC H FAB 68
CAN YOU FEEL ANYTHING WHEN I DO THIS?, AND OTHER STORIES
             SHECKLEY, ROBERT   AC H DBL 71
    IN ENGLAND AS "THE SAME TO YOU DOUBLED"
CANARY IN A CAT HOUSE   VONNEGUT, KURT JR. AC   FAW 61 09
CANOPY OF TIME, THE   ALDISS, BRIAN W.   AC H FAB 59
CANTICLE FOR LEIBOWITZ, A MILLER, WALTER M. JR NO H LIP 60
CAPRICORN GAMES   SILVERBERG, ROBERT AC H RDM 76
CASE AGAINST TOMORROW, THE POHL, FREDERIK   AC   BAL 57 05
CASE AND THE DREAMER   STURGEON, THEODORE AC H NDB 74
CASEY AGONISTES, AND OTHER S.F. & FANTASY STORIES
             MCKENNA, RICHARD M. AC H HPR 73
CATEGORY PHOENIX   BLEILER & DIKTY   AN H BDL 55
    SEE "YEAR'S BEST SCIENCE FICTION NOVELS: 1953"
    OMITS "THE GADGET HAD A GHOST" AND "CONDITIONALLY HUMAN"
CAUTION| INFLAMMABLE| SCORTIA, THOMAS N. AC H DBL 75 07
CAVE GIRL, THE   BURROUGHS, EDGAR R. AC H MCG 25
CAVIAR   STURGEON, THEODORE AC H BAL 55 11
    ALSO IN "SCIENCE FICTION SPECIAL 3"
CELESTIAL BLUEPRINT, THE FARMER, PHILIP JOSE DC   ACE 62
CENTURY OF GREAT SHORT SCIENCE FICTION NOVELS, A
             KNIGHT, DAMON   AN H DCT 64
CENTURY OF SCIENCE FICTION, A KNIGHT, DAMON   AN H SAS 62
CHAINS OF THE SEA   SILVERBERG, ROBERT OA H NDB 73
CHAMBER OF HORRORS   BLOCH, ROBERT   AC   AWD 66
CHAMELEON CORPS & OTHER SHAPE CHANGERS, THE
             GOULART, RON   AC H MAC 72
CHANGE THE SKY AND OTHER STORIES
             ST. CLAIR, MARGARET AC   ACE 74
CHILDREN OF INFINITY   ELWOOD, ROGER   OA H WAT 73
CHILDREN OF THE ATOM   SHIRAS, WILMAR H. AC H GNM 53
CHILDREN OF WONDER   TENN, WILLIAM   AN H SAS 53
    ALSO AS "OUTSIDERS: CHILDREN OF WONDER"
CHRONICLES OF A COMER AND OTHER RELIGIOUS SCIENCE FICTION
   STORIES   ELWOOD, ROGER   AN L JKP 74
CHRONOPOLIS AND OTHER STORIES BALLARD, J. G.   AC H PUT 71
CIRCUS OF DR. LAO AND OTHER IMPROBABLE STORIES
             BRADBURY, RAY   AN   BAN 56 10
CITIES IN FLIGHT   BLISH, JAMES   AC   AVN 70 02
CITIES OF WONDER   KNIGHT, DAMON   AN H DBL 66
CITIZEN IN SPACE   SHECKLEY, ROBERT   AC H BAL 55 12
CITY   SIMAK, CLIFFORD D. NO H GNM 52 05
CITY: 2000 A.D., THE   CLEM:GREENBERG:&   AN   FAW 76 07
CLARION   WILSON, ROBIN SCOTT OA   SIG 71 06
CLARION II   WILSON, ROBIN SCOTT OA   SIG 72 06
CLARION III   WILSON, ROBIN SCOTT OA   SIG 73 10
CLARION SF   WILHELM, KATE   OA   BKM 77 01
CLOAK OF AESIR   CAMPBELL, JOHN W. JR AC H SHS 52
CLOCK OF TIME, THE   FINNEY, JACK   AC H EYR 58
    SEE "THE THIRD LEVEL"
CLONED LIVES   SARGENT, PAMELA   NO   FGM 76 06
COLD CHILLS   BLOCH, ROBERT   AC H DBL 77
COLONIAL SURVEY   LEINSTER, MURRAY   NO H GNM 56
    ALSO AS "THE PLANET EXPLORER"

COMBAT SF	DICKSON, GORDON R.	AN	H	DBL	75
COMIC INFERNO, THE	ALDISS, BRIAN W.	AC		NLB	73 10
SEE "THE BOOK OF BRIAN ALDISS"					
COMING ATTRACTIONS	GREENBERG , MARTIN	NF	H	GNM	57
COMING OF CONAN, THE	HOWARD, ROBERT E.	AC	H	GNM	53
COMING OF THE ROBOTS, THE	MOSKOWITZ, SAM	AN		CLB	63
COMING OF THE TERRANS, THE	BRACKETT, LEIGH	NO		ACE	67
COMPLEAT WEREWOLF, THE	BOUCHER, ANTHONY	AC	H	SAS	69
COMPLETE FEGHOOT, THE	BRIARTON, GRENDEL	AC		MRG	75
COMPLETE VENUS EQUILATERAL, THE					
	SMITH, GEORGE O.	AC		BAL	76 11
IN ENGLAND (ORBIT, 1977) AS "VENUS EQUILATERAL"					
CONAN	HOWARD, R./DE CAMP/&	AC		LAN	67
CONAN THE ADVENTURER	HOWARD, R. & DE CAMP	AC		LAN	66
CONAN THE AVENGER	HOWARD, R./NYBERG/&	AC		LAN	68
CONAN THE BARBARIAN	HOWARD, ROBERT E.	AC	H	GNM	55
CONAN THE FREEBOOTER	HOWARD, R. & DE CAMP	AC		LAN	68
CONAN THE USURPER	HOWARD, R. & DE CAMP	AC		LAN	67
CONAN THE WANDERER	HOWARD, R./DE CAMP/&	AC		LAN	68
CONAN THE WARRIOR	HOWARD, R. & DE CAMP	AC		LAN	67
CONDITIONALLY HUMAN	MILLER, WALTER M. JR	AC		BAL	62
CONNOISSEUR'S S. F.	BOARDMAN, TOM JR.	AN		PEN	64
CONSCIENCE INTERPLANETARY	GREEN, JOSEPH	NO		DAW	74
CONSIDER HER WAYS AND OTHERS	WYNDHAM, JOHN	AC	H	JOS	61
CONTACT	KEYES, NOEL	AN		PBK	63 05
CONTINENT MAKERS AND OTHER TALES OF THE VIAGENS					
	DE CAMP, L. SPRAGUE	AC	H	TWN	53
CONTINUUM 1	ELWOOD, ROGER	OA	H	PUT	74
CONTINUUM 2	ELWOOD, ROGER	OA	H	BKP	74
CONTINUUM 3	ELWOOD, ROGER	OA	H	BKP	74
CONTINUUM 4	ELWOOD, ROGER	OA	H	BKP	75
COSMIC KALEIDOSCOPE	SHAW, BOB	AC	H	GOL	76
COSMIC LAUGHTER	HALDEMAN, JOE W.	AN	H	HRW	74
COSMICOMICS	CALVINO, ITALO	OC	H	HBW	68
COUNTERCOMMANDMENT	CAMPBELL, JOHN W. JR	AN		CUR	67
SEE "ANALOG 5"					
COUNTERFEIT MAN, THE	NOURSE, ALAN E.	AC	H	MCK	63
COUNTRY OF THE BLIND, THE	WELLS, H. G.	AC	H	NEL	13
CRASHING SUNS	HAMILTON, EDMOND	AC		ACE	65
CRAZY MIXED-UP PLANET	FRITCH, CHARLES E.	AC		POW	69 11
CREATURES FROM BEYOND	CARR, TERRY	AN	H	NEL	75
CRIME PREVENTION IN THE 30TH CENTURY					
	SANTESSON, HANS S.	AN	H	WLK	69
CRISIS	ELWOOD, ROGER	OA	H	NEL	74
CROSSROADS IN TIME	CONKLIN, GROFF	AN		PMA	53
CRUCIBLE OF POWER, THE	GREENBERG , MARTIN	AN	H	BDL	53
3 SELECTIONS FROM "FIVE SCIENCE FICTION NOVELS"					
CRYSTAL MAN, THE	MITCHELL, EDWARD P.	AC	H	DBL	73
CRYSTAL SHIP, THE	SILVERBERG, ROBERT	OA	H	NEL	76
CUBE ROOT OF UNCERTAINTY, THE	SILVERBERG, ROBERT	AC	H	MAC	70
CUPFUL OF SPACE, A	CLINGERMAN, MILDRED	AC		BAL	61
CURIOUS FRAGMENTS	LONDON, JACK	AC	H	KNK	75
EDITED BY DALE L. WALKER					
CUSTODIANS AND OTHER STORIES, THE					
	COWPER, RICHARD	AC	H	GOL	76
CYBERIAD, THE	LEM, STANISLAW	OC	H	SEA	74
DA VINCI MACHINE, THE	CONRAD, EARL	OC	H	FPC	68
DANDELION WINE	BRADBURY, RAY	NO	H	DBL	57
DANGER- HUMAN	DICKSON, GORDON R.	AC	H	DBL	70
ALSO AS "THE BOOK OF GORDON DICKSON"					
DANGEROUS VISIONS	ELLISON, HARLAN	OA	H	DBL	67 10
DARK BEASTS, THE	LONG, FRANK BELKNAP	AC		BEL	64 01
DARK CARNIVAL	BRADBURY, RAY	AC	H	ARK	47
DARK CARNIVAL (BRITISH)	BRADBURY, RAY	AC	H	HML	48
DARK INTRUDER & OTHER STORIES, THE					
	BRADLEY, MARION Z.	DC		ACE	64
DARK SIDE OF THE EARTH, THE	BESTER, ALFRED	AC		SIG	64 05
DARK SIDE, THE	KNIGHT, DAMON	AN	H	DBL	65
DARK STARS	SILVERBERG, ROBERT	AN		BAL	69 12
DARK TIDES	RUSSELL, ERIC FRANK	AC	H	DOB	62
DARK TOWER AND OTHER STORIES, THE					
	LEWIS, C. S.	AC	H	HBJ	77
EDITED BY WALTER HOOPER					
DARKNESS AND DAWN	ENGLAND, GEORGE A.	NO	H	SMY	14
DAUGHTERS OF EARTH	MERRIL, JUDITH	AC	H	DBL	68
DAW SCIENCE FICTION READER, THE					
	WOLLHEIM, DONALD A.	OA	H	DAW	76 07
DAWN OF FLAME	WEINBAUM, STANLEY G.	AC	H	CHR	36
THE WEINBAUM MEMORIAL VOLUME					
DAY BEFORE FOREVER AND THUNDER HEAD, THE					
	LAUMER, KEITH	AC	H	DBL	68
DAY IN THE LIFE, A	DOZOIS, GARDNER R.	AN	H	HPR	72
DAY IT RAINED FOREVER, THE	BRADBURY, RAY	AC	H	HDV	60
BRITISH VERSION OF "A MEDICINE FOR MELANCHOLY"					
DAY MILLION	POHL, FREDERIK	AC		BAL	70 06
DAY OF FOREVER, THE	BALLARD, J. G.	AC		PTH	67 09
DAY THE SUN STOOD STILL, THE	SILVERBERG, ROBERT	OA	H	NEL	72
DAYMARES	BROWN, FREDRIC	AC		LAN	68
DAYS AFTER TOMORROW, THE	SANTESSON, HANS S.	AN	H	LBR	71
DEAD ASTRONAUT, 10 STORIES OF SPACE FLIGHT, THE					
	PLAYBOY, EDITORS OF	AN		PBP	71
DEADLY LITTER	WHITE, JAMES	NO		BAL	64 10
DEALS WITH THE DEVIL	DAVENPORT, BASIL	AN	H	DOM	58
DEATHBIRD STORIES	ELLISON, HARLAN	AC	H	HPR	75
DEATHWORLD TRILOGY, THE	HARRISON, HARRY	AC	H	BKM	75
DECADE OF FANTASY AND SCIENCE FICTION, A					
	MILLS, ROBERT P.	AN	H	DBL	60
DECADE THE 1940S	ALDISS & HARRISON	AN	H	MCM	75
DECADE THE 1950S	ALDISS & HARRISON	AN	H	MCM	76
DECADE THE 1960S	ALDISS & HARRISON	AN	H	MCM	77
DEEP FIX, THE	COLVIN, JAMES	AC		CPT	66
DEEP SPACE	RUSSELL, ERIC FRANK	AC	H	FPS	54
BANTAM 1955 EDITION OMITS "FIRST PERSON SINGULAR"					
DEEP SPACE	SILVERBERG, ROBERT	AN	H	NDB	73
DEMON KIND	ELWOOD, ROGER	OA		AVN	73 03
DEPRESSION OR BUST	REYNOLDS, MACK	DN		ACE	74
DESTINATION: AMALTHEIA	DIXON, RICHARD	AN		FLP	63
DESTINATION: UNIVERSE¡	VAN VOGT, A. E.	AC	H	PEL	52
DEVIL HIS DUE, THE	HILL, DOUGLAS	AN		AVN	69 03
DEVIL'S GENERATION, THE	GHIDALIA, VIC	AN		LAN	73
DIGITS AND DASTARDS	POHL, FREDERIK	AC		BAL	66 06
DIMENSION THIRTEEN	SILVERBERG, ROBERT	AC		BAL	69 05
DIMENSION X	KNIGHT, DAMON	AN	H	SAS	70
DIMENSION 4	CONKLIN, GROFF	AN		PYR	64 02
DIPLOIDS AND OTHER FLIGHTS OF FANCY, THE					
	MACLEAN, KATHERINE	AC		AVN	62
DISASTER AREA, THE	BALLARD, J. G.	AC	H	CAP	67 10
DOCTOR TO THE STARS	LEINSTER, MURRAY	AC		PYR	64 03
DOES ANYONE ELSE HAVE SOMETHING FURTHER TO ADD?					
	LAFFERTY, R. A.	AC	H	SCB	74
DOOMSDAY ON AJIAT	JONES, NEIL R.	AC		ACE	68
DOOR IN THE WALL, THE	WELLS, H. G.	AC	H	KEN	11
DOOR TO ANYWHERE	POHL, FREDERIK	AN		CUR	67
SEE "THE TENTH GALAXY READER"					
DOORS OF HIS FACE, THE LAMPS OF HIS MOUTH, THE					
	ZELAZNY, ROGER	AC	H	DBL	71
DOORWAY INTO TIME	MOSKOWITZ, SAM	AN		MBB	66
AND OTHER STORIES FROM MODERN MASTERPIECES OF SCIENCE FICTION					
DOORWAYS TO SPACE	WELLS, BASIL	AC	H	FPB	51
DOUBLE IN SPACE	PRATT, FLETCHER	AC	H	DBL	51
DOUBLE JEOPARDY	PRATT, FLETCHER	AC	H	DBL	52
DOWN HERE IN THE DREAM QUARTER	MALZBERG, BARRY N.	AC	H	DBL	76
DOWN IN THE BLACK GANG AND OTHER STORIES					
	FARMER, PHILIP JOSE	AC	H	DBL	71
DOWNSTAIRS ROOM AND OTHER SPECULATIVE FICTION, THE					
	WILHELM, KATE	AC	H	DBL	68
DR. CYCLOPS	KUTTNER, HENRY	AN		POP	67
DRAGONFLIGHT	MCCAFFREY, ANNE	NO	H	WKR	69
DRAGONS AND NIGHTMARES	BLOCH, ROBERT	AC	H	BEL	69 11
DRIFTGLASS	DELANY, SAMUEL R.	AC		SIG	71 11
DROWNED WORLD AND THE WIND FROM NOWHERE, THE					
	BALLARD, J. G.	AC	H	DBL	65
DYING EARTH, THE	VANCE, JACK	OC		HIL	50
DYSTOPIAN VISIONS	ELWOOD, ROGER	OA	H	PRH	75
E PLURIBUS UNICORN	STURGEON, THEODORE	AC	H	ABE	53
EARLY ASIMOV, THE	ASIMOV, ISAAC	AC	H	DBL	72
EARLY DEL REY, THE	DEL REY, LESTER	AC	H	DBL	75
EARLY LONG, THE	LONG, FRANK BELKNAP	AC	H	DBL	75
EARLY POHL, THE	POHL, FREDERIK	AC	H	DBL	76
EARLY WILLIAMSON, THE	WILLIAMSON, JACK	AC	H	DBL	75
EARTH IN PERIL, THE	WOLLHEIM, DONALD A.	DA		ACE	57
EARTH IN TRANSIT	SCHWARTZ, SHEILA	AN		LLL	76 11
EARTH IS ROOM ENOUGH	ASIMOV, ISAAC	AC	H	DBL	57 10
EARTH IS THE STRANGEST PLANET	SILVERBERG, ROBERT	AN	H	NEL	77
EARTH'S OTHER SHADOW	SILVERBERG, ROBERT	AC		SIG	73 06
EARTHMAN'S BURDEN	ANDERSON, P.&DICKSON	AC	H	GNM	57
EARTHMAN, COME HOME	BLISH, JAMES	NO	H	PUT	55
EARTHMAN, GO HOME¡	ELLISON, HARLAN	AC		PBK	64 12
SEE "ELLISON WONDERLAND"					
EARTHMEN AND STRANGERS	SILVERBERG, ROBERT	AN	H	MDT	66
EARTHSEA	LE GUIN, URSULA K.	AC	H	GOL	77
ECO-FICTION	STADLER, JOHN	AN		WSP	71 04
EDGE OF FOREVER, THE	OLIVER, CHAD	AC	H	SHB	71
EDGE OF NEVER, THE	HOSKINS, ROBERT	AN		FPR	73 06
EDGE OF TOMORROW, THE	FAST, HOWARD	AC		BAN	61 06
ALSO IN "TIME AND THE RIDDLE"					
EDGE, THE	BEAUMONT, CHARLES	AC		PTH	66
EDITOR'S CHOICE IN SCIENCE FICTION					
	MOSKOWITZ, SAM	AN	H	MBR	54
EGG OF THE GLAK, AND OTHER STORIES, THE					
	JACOBS, HARVEY	AC	H	HPR	69
EIGHT FANTASMS AND MAGICS	VANCE, JACK	AC	H	MAC	69
EIGHTH GALAXY READER, THE	POHL, FREDERIK	AN	H	DBL	65
ALSO AS "FINAL ENCOUNTER"					
ELEMENT 79	HOYLE, FRED	AC	H	NAM	67
ELEVENTH GALAXY READER, THE	POHL, FREDERIK	AN	H	DBL	69
ELLISON WONDERLAND	ELLISON, HARLAN	AC		PBK	62 06
ALSO AS "EARTHMAN, GO HOME¡"					
ELSEWHERE AND ELSEWHEN	CONKLIN, GROFF	AN		BKM	68 05
ELSEWHERE, ELSEWHEN, ELSEHOW	DEFORD, MIRIAM ALLEN	AC	H	WLK	71
STORIES "MARTIE AND I" AND "THE CAGE" ARE LISTED IN THE					
ACKNOWLEDGEMENTS BUT ARE NOT IN THE BOOK					
EMPIRE OF THE ATOM	VAN VOGT, A. E.	NO	H	SHS	57
ENCOUNTERS WITH ALIENS	EARLEY, GEORGE W.	AN	H	SHB	68
END OF THE DREAMS, THE	GUNN, JAMES E.	AC	H	SCB	75
END OF THE WORLD, THE	WOLLHEIM, DONALD A.	AN		ACE	56
ENDS OF TIME, THE	SILVERBERG, ROBERT	AN	H	HAW	70
ENEMIES IN SPACE	CONKLIN, GROFF	AN		DIG	62
SELECTIONS FROM "INVADERS OF EARTH"					
ENGLAND SWINGS SF	MERRIL, JUDITH	AN	H	DBL	68
ENGLISH DERIVATIVE ANTHOLOGY "THE SPACE-TIME JOURNAL"					
ENQUIRIES OF DOCTOR ESZTERHAZY, THE					
	DAVIDSON, AVRAM	NO		WPB	75 12
ENTRY TO ELSEWHEN (STORIES REVISED)					
	BRUNNER, JOHN	AC		DAW	72 10
ENVOY TO NEW WORLDS	LAUMER, KEITH	AC		ACE	63
EPOCH	ELWOOD & SILVERBERG	OA	H	BRK	75
EROS IN ORBIT	ELDER, JOSEPH	OA	H	TRI	73
ESCALES DANS L'INFINI	GALLET, GEORGES H.	AN		LHT	54 04
SCALES OF THE INFINITE, STORIES IN FRENCH					
ESCAPE ON VENUS	BURROUGHS, EDGAR R.	NO	H	BUR	46
ESCAPE TO EARTH	HOWARD, IVAN	AC	H	BEL	63 09
ESKIMO INVASION	HOWARD, HAYDEN	NO		BAL	67
ETERNAL LOVER, THE	BURROUGHS, EDGAR R.	AC	H	MCG	25
EVERY BOY'S BOOK OF OUTER SPACE STORIES					
	DIKTY, T. E.	AN	H	FEL	60
EVERY BOY'S BOOK OF SCIENCE FICTION					
	WOLLHEIM, DONALD A.	AN	H	FEL	51
EVIL EARTHS	ALDISS, BRIAN W.	AN	H	WEI	75
AN ANTHOLOGY OF WAY-BACK-WHEN FUTURES					
EXALTATION OF STARS, AN	CARR, TERRY	OA	H	SAS	73

EXILE AND OTHER TALES OF FANTASY   GRAIN KINGS, THE

```
EXILE AND OTHER TALES OF FANTASY
                              CUMMINGS, M. A.      OC    FLG 68
EXODUS FROM ELYSIUM           BURKE, JONATHAN F.   AC    HWZ 65
EXPEDITION TO EARTH           CLARKE, ARTHUR C.    AC    BAL 53 12
    ALSO IN "AN ARTHUR C. CLARKE OMNIBUS"
EXPERT DREAMERS, THE          POHL, FREDERIK       AN H DBL 62
EXPLORERS OF SPACE            SILVERBERG, ROBERT   AN H NEL 75
EXPLORERS, THE                KORNBLUTH, C. M.           BAL 54 08
EXPLORING OTHER WORLDS        MOSKOWITZ, SAM       AN    CLB 63
EXTRAPOLASIS                  MALEC, ALEXANDER B.  AC H DBL 67
EYE AND THE FINGER            WANDREI, DONALD      AC H ARK 44
EYE OF THE LENS, THE          JONES, LANGDON       AC H MAC 72
FAHRENHEIT 451                BRADBURY, RAY        AC H BAL 53
FALLING TORCH, THE            BUDRYS, ALGIS        NO    PYR 59 06
FAMOUS SCIENCE-FICTION STORIES HEALY & MCCOMAS     AN H MDL 57
    SEE "ADVENTURES IN TIME AND SPACE"
FANTASIA MATHEMATICA          FADIMAN, CLIFTON     AN H SAS 58
FANTASTIC PULPS, THE          HAINING, PETER       AN H SMP 75
FANTASTIC UNIVERSE OMNIBUS, THE
                              SANTESSON, HANS S.   AN H PRH 60
FANTASY: THE LITERATURE OF THE MARVELOUS
                              KELLEY, LEO P.       AN L MGH 74
FAR AND AWAY                  BOUCHER, ANTHONY     AC    BAL 55
FAR BOUNDARIES                DERLETH, AUGUST      AN H PEL 52
FAR OUT                       KNIGHT, DAMON        AC H SAS 61
FAR SIDE OF TIME, THE         ELWOOD, ROGER        OA H DOM 74
FAR STARS                     RUSSELL, ERIC FRANK  AC H DOB 61
FAR-OUT PEOPLE, THE           HOSKINS, ROBERT      AN    SIG 71 07
FAR-OUT WORLDS OF A. E. VAN VOGT, THE
                              VAN VOGT, A. E.      AC    ACE 68
FAREWELL FANTASTIC VENUS      ALDISS & HARRISON    AN H MDN 68
FAREWELL TO YESTERDAY'S TOMORROW
                              PANSHIN, ALEXEI      AC H PUT 75
FARTHEST REACHES, THE         ELDER, JOSEPH        OA H TRI 68 08
FASTER THAN LIGHT             DANN & ZEBROWSKI     OA H HPR 76
FEAR TODAY, GONE TOMORROW     BLOCH, ROBERT        AC    AWD 71 09
FEAST OF ST. DIONYSUS, THE    SILVERBERG, ROBERT   AC H SCB 75 03
FELLOWSHIP OF THE STARS       CARR, TERRY          OA H SAS 74
FEVER DREAM                   BRADBURY & BLOCH     AC    SPH 70
    SEE "BLOCH AND BRADBURY"
FEW LAST WORDS, A             SALLIS, JAMES        AC H MAC 70
FIEND IN YOU, THE             BEAUMONT, CHARLES    AN    BAL 62
FIEND, THE                    PLAYBOY, EDITORS OF  AN    PBP 71
FIFTH GALAXY READER, THE      GOLD, H. L.          AN H DBL 61
FIFTH HEAD OF CERBERUS, THE   WOLFE, GENE          AC H SCB 72
FIFTY SHORT SCIENCE FICTION TALES
                              ASIMOV & CONKLIN     AN    CLB 63
FINAL ENCOUNTER               POHL, FREDERIK       AN    CUR 65
    SEE "THE EIGHTH GALAXY READER"
FINAL PROGRAMME, THE          MOORCOCK, MICHAEL    NO    AVN 68
FINAL STAGE                   FERMAN & MALZBERG    OA H CHT 74
FINAL WAR AND OTHER FANTASIES O'DONNELL, K. M.     DC    ACE 69
FIRST ASTOUNDING SCIENCE FICTION ANTHOLOGY, THE
                              CAMPBELL, JOHN W. JR AN H GRY 54
FIRST ASTOUNDING SCIENCE FICTION ANTHOLOGY, THE (PB)
                              CAMPBELL, JOHN W. JR AN    FSP 64
FIRST CONTACT                 KNIGHT, DAMON        AN    PIN 71 11
FIRST FLIGHT                  KNIGHT, DAMON        AN    LAN 63
    MAIDEN VOYAGES IN SPACE AND TIME,
    ALSO AS "NOW BEGINS TOMORROW"
FIRST FLIGHTS TO THE MOON     CLEMENT, HAL         AN H DBL 70
FIRST PERSON, PECULIAR        SHERRED, T. L.       AC    BAL 72 01
FIRST STEP OUTWARD            HOSKINS, ROBERT      AN    DEL 69 08
FIRST WORLD OF IF, THE        QUINN & WULFF        AN D QUI 57
FIVE FATES                    LAUMER, KEITH        AN H DBL 70
FIVE SCIENCE FICTION NOVELS   GREENBERG , MARTIN   AN H GNM 52
    ENGLISH DERIVATIVE ANTHOLOGY "CRUCIBLE OF POWER"
FIVE-ODD                      CONKLIN, GROFF       AN    PYR 64 08
    IN ENGLAND AS "POSSIBLE TOMORROWS"
FLAME TREE PLANET             ELWOOD, ROGER        OA    CNC 73
FLANDRY OF TERRA              ANDERSON, POUL       AC H CHL 65
FLIGHT INTO SPACE             WOLLHEIM, DONALD A.  AN H FEL 50
FLIGHT OF THE HORSE, THE      NIVEN, LARRY         AC    BAL 73 09
FLOWERS FOR ALGERNON AND OTHER STORIES
                              MILLS, ROBERT P.     AN    ACE 60
    SEE "BEST FROM FANTASY AND SCIENCE FICTION: 9"
FLYING SAUCERS IN FACT AND FICTION
                              SANTESSON, HANS S.   AN    LAN 68
FOLSOM FLINT AND OTHER CURIOUS TALES, THE
                              KELLER, DAVID H. MD. AC H ARK 69
FOREVER WAR, THE              HALDEMAN, JOE W.     NO H SMP 74
FORGETFUL ROBOT, THE          FAIRMAN, PAUL W.     OC H HRW 68
FORGOTTEN PLANET, THE         LEINSTER, MURRAY     AC H GNM 54
FORWARD IN TIME               BOVA, BEN            AC H WKR 73
FOUNDATION                    ASIMOV, ISAAC        NO H GNM 51
    ALSO IN "THE FOUNDATION TRILOGY" AND AS "THE 1,000 YEAR PLAN"
FOUNDATION AND EMPIRE         ASIMOV, ISAAC        NO H GNM 52
    ALSO IN "THE FOUNDATION TRILOGY" AND AS
    "THE MAN WHO UPSET THE UNIVERSE"
FOUNDATION TRILOGY, THE       ASIMOV, ISAAC        AC H DBL 64
    IN ENGLAND AS "AN ISAAC ASIMOV OMNIBUS"
FOUR FOR THE FUTURE           CONKLIN, GROFF       AN    PYR 59 08
FOUR FOR THE FUTURE           HARRISON, HARRY      AN H MAC 69
FOUR FOR TOMORROW             ZELAZNY, ROGER       AC    ACE 67 03
    IN ENGLAND AS "A ROSE FOR ECCLESIASTES"
FOUR FUTURES                  SILVERBERG, ROBERT   OA H HAW 71
FOUR-DIMENSIONAL NIGHTMARE, THE
                              BALLARD, J. G.       AC H GOL 63 05
FOUR-DIMENSIONAL NIGHTMARE, THE (REVISED)
                              BALLARD, J. G.       AC H GOL 74
FOURTH GALAXY READER, THE     GOLD, H. L.          AN H DBL 59
FOX WOMAN & OTHER STORIES, THE MERRITT, A.         AC    AVN 49
FREDERIK POHL OMNIBUS, THE    POHL, FREDERIK       AC H GOL 66
FROM DEATH TO THE STARS       HUBBARD, L. RON      AC H FPB 53
FROM FRANKENSTEIN TO ANDROMEDA BROWN, JAMES GOLDIE AN    MCM 66
FROM OFF THIS WORLD           MARGULIES & FRIEND   AN H MER 49

FROM OTHER WORLDS             DERLETH, AUGUST      AN    FSP 64
    STORIES FROM "BEACHHEADS IN SPACE"
FROM THE "S" FILE             PLAYBOY, EDITORS OF  AN    PBP 71
FROM THE LAND OF FEAR         ELLISON, HARLAN      AC    BEL 67 12
FROM THE OCEAN, FROM THE STARS CLARKE, ARTHUR C.   AC H HBW 61
FROM THE TWILIGHT ZONE        SERLING, ROD         AC H NDB 62
FROM THIS DAY FORWARD         BRUNNER, JOHN        AC H DBL 72
FROM UNKNOWN WORLDS           CAMPBELL, JOHN W. JR AN    SMT 53
FRONTIERS IN SPACE            BLEILER & DIKTY      AN    BAN 55 04
    SELECTIONS FROM "THE BEST SCIENCE FICTION STORIES 1951-1953"
FRONTIERS 1; TOMORROW'S ALTERNATIVES
                              ELWOOD, ROGER        OA H MAC 73
FRONTIERS 2; THE NEW MIND     ELWOOD, ROGER        OA H MAC 73
FROZEN PLANET AND 4 OTHER SF NOVELLAS, THE
                              ANONYMOUS            AN    MBB 66
FULLY AUTOMATED LOVE LIFE OF HENRY KEANRIDGE
                              PLAYBOY, EDITORS OF  AN    PBP 71
FUN WITH YOUR NEW HEAD        DISCH, THOMAS M.     AC H DBL 71
    IN ENGLAND AS "UNDER COMPULSION"
FURIOUS FUTURE, THE           BUDRYS, ALGIS        AC H GOL 64
    SEE "BUDRYS' INFERNO"
FUTURE CITY                   ELWOOD, ROGER        OA H TRI 73
FUTURE CORRUPTION             ELWOOD, ROGER        OA    WPB 75 01
FUTURE IMPERFECT              GUNN, JAMES E.       AC    BAN 64 01
FUTURE IS NOW, THE            NOLAN, WILLIAM F.    OA H SHB 70
FUTURE KIN                    ELWOOD, ROGER        OA H DBL 74
FUTURE MAKERS, THE            HAINING, PETER       AN    BEL 71 05
    ALSO IN "SCIENCE FICTION SPECIAL 5"
FUTURE NOW, THE               HOSKINS, ROBERT      AN    FCR 77 06
FUTURE PASTIMES               EDELSTEIN, SCOTT     OA H AUR 77
FUTURE PERFECT                FRANKLIN, H. BRUCE   AN H OXF 66
FUTURE POWER                  DANN & DOZOIS        OA H RDM 76
FUTURE QUEST                  ELWOOD, ROGER        OA    AVN 73 09
FUTURE TENSE                  CURTIS, RICHARD      AC    DEL 68 09
FUTURE TENSE                  VANCE, JACK          AC    BAL 64 06
FUTURE TENSE                  CROSSEN, KENDELL F.  AN H GBG 52 03
FUTURE TENSE (BRITISH)        CROSSEN, KENDELL F.  AN H BDL 54
FUTURE WITHOUT FUTURE         STERNBERG, JACQUES   OC H SEA 73
FUTURELOVE                    ELWOOD, ROGER        OA H BML 77
FUTURES TO INFINITY           MOSKOWITZ, SAM       AN    PYR 70 09
FUTURES UNLIMITED             NORTON, ALDEN H.     AN    PYR 69 06
GALACTIC CLUSTER              BLISH, JAMES         AC    SIG 59
GALACTIC CLUSTER (BRITISH PB) BLISH, JAMES         AC    FPS 63
GALACTIC CLUSTER (BRITISH)    BLISH, JAMES         AC H FAB 60
GALACTIC DIPLOMAT             LAUMER, KEITH        AC H DBL 65
GALACTIC EMPIRES VOLUME ONE   ALDISS, BRIAN W.     AN H WEI 76
    AN ANTHOLOGY OF WAY-BACK-WHEN FUTURES
GALACTIC EMPIRES VOLUME TWO   ALDISS, BRIAN W.     AN H WEI 76
    AN ANTHOLOGY OF WAY-BACK-WHEN FUTURES
GALAXIES LIKE GRAINS OF SAND  ALDISS, BRIAN W.     AC    SIG 60 07
GALAXY OF GHOULS              MERRIL, JUDITH       AN    LIO 55 05
    ALSO AS "OFF THE BEATEN ORBIT"
GALAXY OF STRANGERS, A        BIGGLE, LLOYD JR.    AC H DBL 76
GALAXY READER OF SCIENCE FICTION
                              GOLD, H. L.          AN H CRN 52
GALAXY READER OF SCIENCE FICTION (BRITISH)
                              GOLD, H. L.          AN H GRY 53
GALAXY SCIENCE FICTION OMNIBUS GOLD, H. L.         AN H GRY 55
    SELECTIONS FROM "SECOND GALAXY READER OF SCIENCE FICTION"
GAMBLES WITH DESTINY          GRIFFITH, GEORGE     AC H FVW 99
GARDEN OF FEAR AND OTHER STORIES, THE
                              CRAWFORD, WILLIAM L. AN    CRF 45
GATES TO TOMORROW             NORTON, AN.&DONALDY  AN H ATH 73
GATEWAY TO THE STARS          CARNELL, JOHN        AN    MUS 55
GATEWAY TO TOMORROW           CARNELL, JOHN        AN    MUS 54
GENERAL ZAPPED AN ANGEL, THE  FAST, HOWARD         OC H MOR 70
    ALSO IN "TIME AND THE RIDDLE"
GENERATION                    GERROLD, DAVID       OA    DEL 72 07
GENTLE INVADERS               SANTESSON, HANS S.   AN    BEL 69 05
GET OFF MY WORLD!             LEINSTER, MURRAY     AC    BEL 66 04
GET OFF THE UNICORN           MCCAFFREY, ANNE      AC    BAL 77 06
GET OUT OF MY SKY             MARGULIES, LEO       AN    CRS 60
GETTING INTO DEATH            DISCH, THOMAS M.     AC H HDV 73
    THE BEST SHORT STORIES OF THOMAS M. DISCH
GETTING INTO DEATH AND OTHER STORIES
                              DISCH, THOMAS M.     AC H KNP 76
GHOST BREAKER                 GOULART, RON         DC    ACE 71
GHOUL KEEPERS, THE            MARGULIES, LEO       AN    PYR 61
GHOULS, THE                   HAINING, PETER       AN H SAD 71 05
GIANT ANTHOLOGY OF SCIENCE FICTION
                              MARGULIES & FRIEND   AN H MER 54
    DERIVATIVE ANTHOLOGY "RACE TO THE STARS"
GIANTS UNLEASHED              CONKLIN, GROFF       AN H GRS 65
    ALSO AS "MINDS UNLEASHED"
GIFTS OF ASTI AND OTHER STORIES OF SCIENCE FICTION, THE
                              ELWOOD, ROGER        AN H FOL 75
GIRL WITH THE HUNGRY EYES, AND OTHER STORIES, THE
                              WOLLHEIM, DONALD A.  OA    AVN 49
GLASS OF STARS, A             YOUNG, ROBERT F.     AC H HWF 68
GNOME THERE WAS, A            PADGETT, LEWIS       AC H SAS 50
GODLING, GO HOME!             SILVERBERG, ROBERT   AC    BEL 64 06
GODS AND GOLEMS               DEL REY, LESTER      AC    BAL 73 02
GODS FOR TOMORROW             SANTESSON, HANS S.   AN    AWD 67
GOLD AT STARBOW'S END, THE    POHL, FREDERIK       AC    BAL 72 08
GOLDEN APPLES OF THE SUN      BRADBURY, RAY        AC H DBL 53 03
    ALSO IN "TWICE 22"
    ENGLISH EDITION (HDV 53) OMITS STORIES "THE BIG BLACK AND
    WHITE GAME" AND "THE GREAT FIRE"
GOLDEN ROAD, THE              KNIGHT, DAMON        AN H SAS 73
GOLLANCZ - SUNDAY TIMES BEST SF STORIES
                              ANONYMOUS            OA H GOL 75
GOOD NEIGHBORS AND OTHER STRANGERS
                              PANGBORN, EDGAR      AC H MAC 72
GRADUATED ROBOT AND OTHER STORIES, THE
                              ELWOOD, ROGER        OA H LER 74
GRAIN KINGS, THE              ROBERTS, KEITH       AC H HUT 76
```

GRAVEYARD READER, THE   CONKLIN, GROFF   AN   BAL 58
GREAT FOG AND OTHER WEIRD TALES, THE
                               HEARD, H. F.   OC H VPR 44
GREAT SCIENCE FICTION ABOUT DOCTORS
                               CONKLIN, G&FABRICANT AN   CLB 63
GREAT SCIENCE FICTION ADVENTURES
                               SHAW, LARRY T.   AN   LAN 63
GREAT SCIENCE FICTION BY SCIENTISTS
                               CONKLIN, GROFF   AN   CLB 62
GREAT SCIENCE FICTION STORIES SMITH, CORDELIA T. AN   DEL 64 02
    IN ENGLAND AS "THE BEST SCIENCE FICTION STORIES 3"
GREAT SCIENCE FICTION STORIES ABOUT MARS
                               DIKTY, T. E.   AN H FEL 66
GREAT SCIENCE FICTION STORIES ABOUT THE MOON
                               DIKTY, T. E.   AN H FEL 67
GREAT SCIENCE-FICTION   LICATA, TONY   AN   TSB 65
GREAT SHORT NOVELS OF SCIENCE FICTION
                               SILVERBERG, ROBERT AN   BAL 70 07
GREAT STORIES OF SCIENCE FICTION
                               LEINSTER, MURRAY   AN H RDM 51
GREAT STORIES OF SPACE TRAVEL CONKLIN, GROFF   AN H TMP 63 07
GREAT TALES OF FANTASY AND IMAGINATION
                               STERN, PHILIP VAN D. AN   PKT 54 11
    SEE "THE MOONLIGHT TRAVELER"
GREEN HILLS OF EARTH, THE   HEINLEIN, ROBERT A. AC H SHS 51
    ALSO IN "A ROBERT HEINLEIN OMNIBUS"
GREYLORN   LAUMER, KEITH   AC   BKM 68 02
GUARDIANS OF TIME   ANDERSON, POUL   AC   BAL 60 09
GUN FOR DINOSAUR AND OTHER IMAGINATIVE TALES
                               DE CAMP, L. SPRAGUE AC H DBL 63
HALFLING AND OTHER STORIES, THE
                               BRACKETT, LEIGH   AC   ACE 73 09
HANDFUL OF DARKNESS, A   DICK, PHILIP K.   AC H RCH 55
HANDFUL OF TIME, A   BROWN, ROSEL GEORGE AC   BAL 63
HARD WAY UP, THE   CHANDLER, A. BERTRAM DC   ACE 72
HARRIGAN'S FILE   DERLETH, AUGUST   AC H ARK 75
HARVEST OF HOODWINKS, A   LORY, ROBERT   DC   ACE 70
HAUNTER OF THE DARK, THE   LOVECRAFT, H. P.   AC H GOL 51
HAVE YOU SEEN THESE?   ASIMOV, ISAAC   AC H NES 74
    ALL STORIES ALSO IN "BUY JUPITER"
HAWK AMONG THE SPARROWS   MCLAUGHLIN, DEAN   AC H SCB 76
HEART OF THE SERPENT, THE   ANONYMOUS   AN H FLP 61
    SEE "MORE SOVIET SCIENCE FICTION"
HEINLEIN TRIAD, A   HEINLEIN, ROBERT A. AC H GOL 66
    SEE "THREE BY HEINLEIN"
HELL HATH FURY   HAY, GEORGE   AN H NSP 63 10
HIDDEN PLANET, THE   WOLLHEIM, DONALD A. AN   ACE 59
HIGH JUSTICE   POURNELLE, JERRY   AC   PKT 77 05
HISTORY OF THE SCIENCE FICTION MAGAZINE, THE   PART 1 1926-1935
                               ASHLEY, MICHAEL   AN H NLB 74
HISTORY OF THE SCIENCE FICTION MAGAZINE, THE   PART 2 1936-1945
                               ASHLEY, MICHAEL   AN H NLB 75
HISTORY OF THE SCIENCE FICTION MAGAZINE, THE   PART 3 1946-1955
                               ASHLEY, MICHAEL   AN H NLB 76
HOLDING WONDER   HENDERSON, ZENNA   AC H DBL 71
HOLDING YOUR EIGHT HANDS   LUCIE-SMITH, EDWARD AN H DBL 69
HOLE IN SPACE, A   NIVEN, LARRY   AC   BAL 74 06
HOMEBREW   ANDERSON, POUL   AC H NES 76
HOMEWARD AND BEYOND   ANDERSON, POUL   AC H DBL 75 06
HONEYMOON IN HELL   BROWN, FREDRIC   AC   BAN 58 08
HORN OF TIME, THE   ANDERSON, POUL   AC   SIG 68 01
HORROR FROM THE HILLS, THE   LONG, FRANK BELKNAP AC   DIG 65
    SEE "ODD SCIENCE FICTION"
HORROR ON THE ASTEROID AND OTHER TALES OF PLANETARY HORROR
                               HAMILTON, EDMOND   AC H GRG 75 06
    REPRINT OF 1936 EDITION PUBLISHED BY P. ALLEN, LONDON
HORROR TIMES TEN   NORTON, ALDEN H.   AN   BKM 67 06
HORROR-7   BLOCH, ROBERT   AC   BEL 63 02
HORSES' ASTEROID   FRITCH, CHARLES E. AC   POW 70
HOSPITAL STATION   WHITE, JAMES   AC   BAL 62
HOT & COLD RUNNING CITIES   MCHARGUE, GEORGESS AN H H&W 74
HOTHOUSE   ALDISS, BRIAN W.   NO H FAB 62
    SEE "THE LONG AFTERNOON OF EARTH"
HOUNDS OF TINDALOS, THE   LONG, FRANK BELKNAP AC H ARK 46
HOUNDS OF TINDALOS, THE (9 OF 21)
                               LONG, FRANK BELKNAP AC   BEL 63 08
HOUSE OF THE HATCHET AND OTHER TALES OF HORROR, THE
                               BLOCH, ROBERT   AC   TDM 65
    SEE "YOURS TRULY, JACK THE RIPPER"
HOUSE OF THE HATCHET, THE   BLOCH, ROBERT   AC   PTH 76
    11 STORIES FROM "THE OPENER OF THE WAY"
HUGO WINNERS, THE (VOLUME 1)   ASIMOV, ISAAC   AN H DBL 62
HUGO WINNERS, THE (VOLUME 2)   ASIMOV, ISAAC   AN H DBL 71
    DERIVATIVE ANTHOLOGIES "STORIES FROM THE HUGO WINNERS VOL. 2"
    AND "MORE STORIES FROM THE HUGO WINNERS VOL. 2"
HUMAN AND OTHER BEINGS   DEGRAEFF, ALLEN   AN   CLB 63
HUMAN ANGLE, THE   TENN, WILLIAM   AC   BAL 56 08
HUMAN EQUATION, THE   NOLAN, WILLIAM F.   AN H SHB 71
HUMAN ZERO, THE   MOSKOWITZ & ELWOOD AN   TWR 67
HUMAN?   MERRIL, JUDITH   AN   LIO 54 04
HUMAN-MACHINES   SCORTIA & ZEBROWSKI AN   VNT 75 11
HUNGER AND OTHER STORIES, THE BEAUMONT, CHARLES   AC H PUT 58 04
    IN ENGLAND AS "SHADOW PLAY", OMITS STORY "THE HUNGER"
I HAVE NO MOUTH, AND I MUST SCREAM
                               ELLISON, HARLAN   AC   PYR 67 04
I LOVE GALESBURG IN THE SPRINGTIME
                               FINNEY, JACK   AC H SAS 63
I SING THE BODY ELECTRIC   BRADBURY, RAY   AC H KNP 69
I, ROBOT   ASIMOV, ISAAC   AC H GNM 50
I, ROBOT (BRITISH PB)   ASIMOV, ISAAC   AC   DIG 58
    OMITS LAST TWO STORIES
IDES OF TOMORROW, THE   CARR, TERRY   OA H LBR 76
IF READER OF SCIENCE FICTION, THE
                               POHL, FREDERIK   AN H DBL 66
IF THIS GOES ON   NUETZEL, CHARLES   AN   BCA 65
    STORY "ALMOST THE END OF THE WORLD" BY RAY BRADBURY LISTED

    IN CONTENTS AND ON COVER BUT NOT IN BOOK
ILLUSTRATED MAN, THE   BRADBURY, RAY   AC H DBL 51 02
ILLUSTRATED MAN, THE (BRITISH) BRADBURY, RAY   AC H HDV 52
IMAGES OF TOMORROW   NUETZEL, CHARLES   AC   POW 69 03
IMAGINATION UNLIMITED   BLEILER & DIKTY   AN H FSY 52
    ALSO AS "MEN OF SPACE AND TIME"
IMAGINATION UNLIMITED (BRITISH)
                               BLEILER & DIKTY   AN H BDL 53
    FIRST 6 STORIES OF AMERICAN VERSION, REMAINDER IN
    "MEN OF SPACE AND TIME"
IMAGINATION UNLIMITED (7 OF 13)
                               BLEILER & DIKTY   AN   BRK 59 04
IMMORTALS, THE   GUNN, JAMES E.   NO   BAN 62 11
IMPACT-20   NOLAN, WILLIAM F.   AC   PBK 63 11
IMPOSSIBLE MAN, THE   BALLARD, J. G.   AC   BRK 66 04
IMPOSSIBLE?   JANIFER, LAURENCE M. AC   BEL 68 08
IN DEEP   KNIGHT, DAMON   AC   BKM 63
    BRITISH EDITIONS OMIT "THE HANDLER"
IN DREAMS AWAKE   FIEDLER, LESLIE A. AN   DEL 75 07
IN THE FOOTSTEPS OF THE ABOMINABLE SNOWMAN
                               NESVADBA, JOSEF   AC   70
    SEE "THE LOST FACE"
IN THE POCKET AND OTHER S-F STORIES
                               O'DONNELL, K. M.   DC   ACE 71
IN THE PROBLEM PIT   POHL, FREDERIK   AC   BAN 76 06
IN THE WAKE OF MAN   ELWOOD, ROGER   OA H BML 75
INCREDIBLE PLANET, THE   CAMPBELL, JOHN W. JR NO H FPS 49
INEXPERIENCED GHOST AND NINE OTHER STORIES, THE
                               WELLS, H. G.   AC   BAN 65 02
INFINITE ARENA, THE   CARR, TERRY   AN H NEL 77
INFINITE JESTS   SILVERBERG, ROBERT AN H CHL 74
INFINITE MOMENT, THE   WYNDHAM, JOHN   AC   BAL 61
INFINITY BOX, THE   WILHELM, KATE   AC H HPR 75
INFINITY 1   HOSKINS, ROBERT   OA   LAN 70
INFINITY 2   HOSKINS, ROBERT   OA   LAN 71
INFINITY 3   HOSKINS, ROBERT   OA   LAN 72
INFINITY 4   HOSKINS, ROBERT   OA   LAN 72
INFINITY 5   HOSKINS, ROBERT   OA   LAN 73
INNER LANDSCAPE, THE   MOORCOCK, MICHAEL   AN H ALS 69
INSIDE INFORMATION   MOWSHOWITZ, ABBE   AN L ADW 77
    COMPUTERS IN FICTION
INTANGIBLES INC. AND OTHER STORIES
                               ALDISS, BRIAN W.   AC H FAB 69
INTERPLANETARY HUNTER   BARNES, ARTHUR K.   AC H GNM 56
INTERSTELLAR EMPIRE   BRUNNER, JOHN   AC   DAW 76 09
INTO THE FOURTH DIMENSION   CUMMINGS, RAY   AN   SWN 41
INTO THE UNKNOWN   CARR, TERRY   AN H NEL 73
INTRODUCING SCIENCE FICTION   ALDISS, BRIAN W.   AN H FAB 64
INTRODUCTORY PSYCHOLOGY THROUGH SCIENCE FICTION
                               KATZ/WARRICK/&   AN L RAN 74
INVADERS FROM SPACE   SILVERBERG, ROBERT AN H HAW 72
INVADERS OF EARTH   CONKLIN, GROFF   AN H VPR 52
    ENGLISH DERIVATIVE ANTHOLOGY "ENEMIES IN SPACE"
INVADERS OF EARTH (BRITISH PB) CONKLIN, GROFF   AN   DIG 62
INVADERS OF EARTH (BRITISH)   CONKLIN, GROFF   AN H WEI 53
INVADERS OF EARTH (15 OF 22)   CONKLIN, GROFF   AN   PKT 55 09
INVADERS OF EARTH (17 OF 22)   CONKLIN, GROFF   AN   TMP 62 09
INVASION FROM MARS   WELLES, ORSON   AN   DEL 49
INVASION OF THE ROBOTS   ELWOOD, ROGER   AN   PBK 65 04
INVISIBLE MEN   DAVENPORT, BASIL   AN   BAL 60
IRRATIONAL NUMBERS   EFFINGER, GEO. ALEC AC H DBL 76
ISAAC ASIMOV OMNIBUS, AN   ASIMOV, ISAAC   AC H SID 65
    SEE "THE FOUNDATION TRILOGY"
ISAAC ASIMOV SECOND OMNIBUS, AN
                               ASIMOV, ISAAC   AC H SID 69
    SEE "TRIANGLE"
ISLAND OF FEAR AND OTHER SCIENCE FICTION
                               SAMBROT, WILLIAM   AC   PMA 63 03
IT'S A MAD, MAD, MAD GALAXY   LAUMER, KEITH   AC   BKM 68 12
JIREL OF JOIRY   MOORE, C. L.   AC   PBK 69 08
JIZZLE   WYNDHAM, JOHN   AC H DOB 54
JOHN CARSTAIRS: SPACE DETECTIVE
                               LONG, FRANK BELKNAP AC H FEL 49
JOHN CARTER OF MARS   BURROUGHS, EDGAR R. AC H CAN 64
JOHN W. CAMPBELL ANTHOLOGY: THREE NOVELS
                               CAMPBELL, JOHN W. JR AC H DBL 73
JOHN WYNDHAM OMNIBUS, THE   WYNDHAM, JOHN   AC H SAS 65
JOURNEY ACROSS THREE WORLDS   ANONYMOUS   AN H MIR 73
JOURNEY TO ANOTHER STAR AND OTHER STORIES
                               ELWOOD, ROGER   OA H LER 74
JOURNEY TO INFINITY   GREENBERG, MARTIN   AN H GNM 51
JOURNEYS IN SCIENCE FICTION   LOUGHLIN, RICHARD L. AN H GLB 61
JOY IN OUR CAUSE   EMSHWILLER, CAROL   AC H HPR 74
JOY MAKERS, THE   GUNN, JAMES E.   NO   BAN 61 03
JOYOUS INVASION, THE   STURGEON, THEODORE AC H GOL 65
JUDGEMENT NIGHT   MOORE, C. L.   AC H GNM 52
JULES VERNE- MASTER OF SCIENCE FICTION
                               VERNE, JULES   AC H SID 56
    EDITED BY I. O. EVANS
JUPITER   POHL, C. & F.   AN   BAL 73 12
KILLER PLANTS AND OTHER STORIES, THE
                               ELWOOD, ROGER   OA H LER 74
KING CONAN   HOWARD, ROBERT E.   AC H GNM 53
KING OF TERRORS, THE   BLOCH, ROBERT   AC H MYS 77
    TALES OF MADNESS AND DEATH
KINGSLAYER, THE   HUBBARD, L. RON   AC H FPB 49
    ALSO IN "FROM DEATH TO THE STARS"
    ALSO AS "SEVEN STEPS TO THE ARBITER"
LAMBDA I AND OTHER STORIES   CARNELL, JOHN   AN   BKM 64 04
LANCELOT BIGGS: SPACEMAN   BOND, NELSON S.   AC H DBL 50
LAND THAT TIME FORGOT AND THE MOON MAID, THE
                               BURROUGHS, EDGAR R. AC H DOV 63
LAND THAT TIME FORGOT, THE   BURROUGHS, EDGAR R. NO H MCG 24
LAST DOOR TO AIYA   GINSBURG, MIRRA   AN H PHI 68
LAST HURRAH OF THE GOLDEN HORDE, THE
                               SPINRAD, NORMAN   AC H DBL 70

```
LAST LEAP AND OTHER STORIES OF THE SUPER-MIND, THE
                         GALOUYE, DANIEL F.   AC   COR 64
LAST SPACESHIP, THE         LEINSTER, MURRAY    NO H FEL 49
LAST TRAIN TO LIMBO         PLAYBOY, EDITORS OF  AN   PBP 71
LATE GREAT FUTURE, THE      FITZ GERALD & DILLON AN   FCB 76
LAURIE'S SPACE ANNUAL       ANONYMOUS           AN H LAU 53
LEARNING MAZE AND OTHER STORIES, THE
                         ELWOOD, ROGER       OA H MES 74
LEGENDS FROM THE END OF TIME  MOORCOCK, MICHAEL  AC H HPR 76
LEST WE FORGET THEE, EARTH   KNOX, CALVIN M.     DN   ACE 58
LIBERATED FUTURE: VOYAGES INTO TOMORROW, THE
                         HOSKINS, ROBERT     AN   FAW 74 12
LIFE EVERLASTING AND OTHER TALES OF SCIENCE, FANTASY
  AND HORROR               KELLER, DAVID H. MD. AC H AVL 49
LIFE EVERLASTING AND OTHER TALES OF SCIENCE, FANTASY
  AND HORROR               KELLER, DAVID H. MD. AC H AVL 49
LIGHT AT THE END OF THE UNIVERSE, THE
                         CARR, TERRY         AC   PYR 76 10
LIGHT FANTASTIC, THE        BESTER, ALFRED      AC H BKP 76
  ALSO IN "STARLIGHT"
LIGHT FANTASTIC, THE        HARRISON, HARRY     AN H SCB 71
LIKE NOTHING ON EARTH       RUSSELL, ERIC FRANK AC H DOB 75
LINE TO TOMORROW AND OTHER STORIES OF FANTASY AND SCIENCE
  FICTION                  PADGETT, LEWIS      AC   BAN 54 08
LION OF COMARRE AND AGAINST THE FALL OF NIGHT
                         CLARKE, ARTHUR C.   AC H HBW 68
LISTENERS, THE              GUNN, JAMES E.      NO H SCB 72
LITTLE MONSTERS, THE        ELWOOD & GHIDALIA   AN   MBB 69
LIVES AND TIMES OF JERRY CORNELIUS, THE
                         MOORCOCK, MICHAEL   AC H ALB 76
LIVING DEMONS, THE          BLOCH, ROBERT       AC   BEL 67 09
LIVING WAY OUT              GUIN, WYMAN         AC   AVN 67 08
LLANA OF GATHOL             BURROUGHS, EDGAR R. NO H BUR 48
LONE STAR UNIVERSE          PROCTOR & UTLEY     OA H HDL 76
  SPECULATIVE FICTION & FANTASY FROM TEXAS
LONG AFTER MIDNIGHT         BRADBURY, RAY       AC H KNP 76
LONG AFTERNOON OF EARTH, THE ALDISS, BRIAN W.    NO   SIG 62 01
  IN ENGLAND AS "HOTHOUSE"
LONG ARM OF GIL HAMILTON, THE NIVEN, LARRY       AC   BAL 76 02
LONG EUREKA, THE            SELLINGS, ARTHUR    AC H DOB 68
LONG NIGHT OF WAITING AND OTHER STORIES
                         ELWOOD, ROGER       OA H AUR 74
LOOKING AHEAD               ALLEN, D. & L.      AN L HBL 75
  THE VISION OF SCIENCE FICTION
LOOKING FORWARD             LESSER, MILTON      AN H BCH 53
LOST CAVERN AND OTHER TALES OF THE FANTASTIC, THE
                         HEARD, H. F.        AC H VPR 48
LOST FACE, THE              NESVADBA, JOSEF     AC H TAP 71
  BEST SCIENCE FICTION FROM CZECHOSLOVAKIA
  IN ENGLAND AS "IN THE FOOTSTEPS OF THE ABOMINABLE SNOWMAN"
  ALL BUT FIRST AND THIRD STORIES ARE IN "VAMPIRES LTD."
LOVE & NAPALM: EXPORT U.S.A. BALLARD, J. G.      AC H GRV 72
  IN ENGLAND AS "ATROCITY EXHIBITION"
LOVE AIN'T NOTHING BUT SEX MISSPELLED
                         ELLISON, HARLAN     AC H TRI 68
LOVE AIN'T NOTHING BUT SEX MISSPELLED (REVISED)
                         ELLISON, HARLAN     AC   PYR 76 02
LOW-FLYING AIRCRAFT AND OTHER STORIES
                         BALLARD, J. G.      AC H CAP 76
M 33 IN ANDROMEDA           VAN VOGT, A. E.     AC   PBK 71 04
MACHINE IN SHAFT TEN AND OTHER STORIES, THE
                         HARRISON, M. JOHN   AC   PTH 75
MACHINE IN WARD ELEVEN, THE  WILLEFORD, CHARLES  NO   BEL 63 06
MACHINE-GOD LAUGHS, THE     ANONYMOUS           AN H GRI 49
MACHINERIES OF JOY, THE      BRADBURY, RAY       AC H SAS 64 02
  ENGLISH EDITION (HDV 64) OMITS "ALMOST THE END OF THE WORLD"
MACHINES AND MEN            ROBERTS, KEITH      AC H HUT 73
MAGIC MAN AND OTHER SCIENCE-FANTASY STORIES
                         BEAUMONT, CHARLES   AC   FAW 65
MAJOR OPERATION            WHITE, JAMES        NO   BAL 71 02
MAN AGAINST TOMORROW        NOLAN, WILLIAM F.   AN   AVN 65 12
MAN FROM BEYOND AND OTHER STORIES, THE
                         WYNDHAM, JOHN       AC H JOS 75
MAN WHO ATE THE WORLD, THE   POHL, FREDERIK      AC   BAL 60
MAN WHO SOLD THE MOON, THE   HEINLEIN, ROBERT A. AC H SHS 50
  ALSO IN "A ROBERT HEINLEIN OMNIBUS"
MAN WHO SOLD THE MOON, THE (4 OF 6)
                         HEINLEIN, ROBERT A. AC   SIG 51
MAN WHO UPSET THE UNIVERSE, THE
                         ASIMOV, ISAAC       DN   ACE 55
  SEE "FOUNDATION AND EMPIRE"
MANY WORLDS OF ANDRE NORTON, THE
                         NORTON, ANDRE       AC H CHL 74
  EDITED BY ROGER ELWOOD, ALSO AS "THE BOOK OF ANDRE NORTON"
MANY WORLDS OF BARRY MALZBERG, THE
                         MALZBERG, BARRY N.  AC   POP 75
MANY WORLDS OF MAGNUS RIDOLPH, THE
                         VANCE, JACK         DC   ACE 66
MANY WORLDS OF POUL ANDERSON, THE
                         ANDERSON, POUL      AC H CHL 74
  EDITED BY ROGER ELWOOD, ALSO AS "THE BOOK OF POUL ANDERSON"
MANY WORLDS OF SCIENCE FICTION, THE
                         BOVA, BEN           OA H DUT 71
MARACOT DEEP AND OTHER STORIES, THE
                         DOYLE, ARTHUR CONAN AC H DBL 29
MARCHING MORONS AND OTHER SCIENCE FICTION
                         KORNBLUTH, C. M.    AC   BAL 59 04
MARRIAGE AND THE FAMILY THROUGH SCIENCE FICTION
                         CLEAR/WARRICK/&     AN L SMP 76
MARS MOUNTAIN              KEY, EUGENE GEORGE  AC H FNP 34
MARS, WE LOVE YOU           HIPOLITO & MCNELLY  AN H DBL 71
MARTIAN CHRONICLES, THE      BRADBURY, RAY       AC H DBL 50 05
  IN ENGLAND AS "THE SILVER LOCUSTS"
MARTIAN CHRONICLES, THE (BRITISH SFBC, ADDS:)
                         BRADBURY, RAY       AC H SBB 53
  OMITS STORY "USHER II"

MARTIAN ENTERPRISE          REED, CLIFFORD C.   AC   DIG 62
MARTIAN ODYSSEY AND OTHER SCIENCE FICTION TALES, A
                         WEINBAUM, STANLEY G. AC H HYP 74
  EDITED BY SAM MOSKOWITZ
MARTIAN ODYSSEY AND OTHERS, A WEINBAUM, STANLEY G. AC H FPS 49
MARTIAN ODYSSEY, A          WEINBAUM, STANLEY G. AC   LAN 62
  AND OTHER CLASSICS OF SCIENCE FICTION, EDITED BY SAM MOSKOWITZ
MARTIAN SEXPOT             O'NEILL, SCOTT      AC   JAD 63
MARTIAN WAY AND OTHER STORIES, THE
                         ASIMOV, ISAAC       AC H DBL 55
MASKS                       PLAYBOY, EDITORS OF AN   PBP 71
MASTERPIECES OF SCIENCE FICTION
                         MOSKOWITZ, SAM      AN H WOR 66
MASTERS OF SCIENCE FICTION   HOWARD, IVAN        AN   BEL 64 10
MASTERS OF TIME             VAN VOGT, A. E.     AC H FPS 50
MASTERS' CHOICE            JANIFER, LAURENCE M. AN H SAS 66
  ALSO AS "18 GREAT SCIENCE FICTION STORIES"
MATHEMATICAL MAGPIE, THE     FADIMAN, CLIFTON    AN H SAS 62
MEDICINE FOR MELANCHOLY, A   BRADBURY, RAY       AC H DBL 58
  ALSO IN "TWICE 22"
  IN ENGLAND WITH SOME CONTENTS CHANGE AS
  "THE DAY IT RAINED FOREVER"
MEETING OVER TUSCARORA AND OTHER ADVENTURE TALES, A
                         YEFREMOV, IVAN      AC H HUT 46
MEN AGAINST THE STARS       GREENBERG, MARTIN   AN H GNM 50
MEN AGAINST THE STARS (BRITISH)
                         GREENBERG, MARTIN   AN H GRY 51
MEN AGAINST THE STARS (9 OF 12)
                         GREENBERG, MARTIN   AN   PYR 56 12
MEN AND MACHINES           SILVERBERG, ROBERT  AN H MDT 68
MEN AND THE MIRROR, THE      ROCKLYNNE, ROSS     AC   ACE 73 02
MEN OF SPACE AND TIME       BLEILER & DIKTY     AN H LNE 53
  LAST SEVEN STORIES FROM "IMAGINATION UNLIMITED"
MEN ON THE MOON            WOLLHEIM, DONALD A. DA   ACE 58
MEN WITHOUT BONES           KERSH, GERALD       AC   PKB 62 01
MEN, MARTIANS AND MACHINES   RUSSELL, ERIC FRANK AC H DOB 55
MENACE FROM EARTH, THE      HEINLEIN, ROBERT A. AC H GNM 59
MERCENARY, THE              POURNELLE, JERRY    NO   PKT 77 02
METAL SMILE, THE            KNIGHT, DAMON       AC   BEL 68
METALLIC MUSE, THE          BIGGLE, LLOYD JR.   AC H DBL 72
MICROCOSMIC GOD            MOSKOWITZ, SAM      AN   MBB 65
  AND OTHER STORIES FROM MODERN MASTERPIECES OF SCIENCE FICTION
MIDSUMMER CENTURY           BLISH, JAMES        AC   DAW 74 02
MILE BEYOND THE MOON, A      KORNBLUTH, C. M.    AC H DBL 58
MILE BEYOND THE MOON, A (11 OF 15)
                         KORNBLUTH, C. M.    AC   MCF 62
MILE-LONG SPACESHIP, THE     WILHELM, KATE       AC   BKM 63 12
  IN ENGLAND AS "ANDOVER AND THE ANDROID"
MIND ANGEL AND OTHER STORIES, THE
                         ELWOOD, ROGER       OA H LER 74
MIND PARTNER AND 8 OTHER NOVELETS FROM GALAXY
                         GOLD, H. L.         AN H DBL 61
MIND SPIDER AND OTHER STORIES, THE
                         LEIBER, FRITZ       DC   ACE 61
MIND SPIDER AND OTHER STORIES, THE (ACE 76)
                         LEIBER, FRITZ       AC   ACE 76
MIND TO MIND                SILVERBERG, ROBERT  AN H NEL 71
MINDS UNLEASHED             CONKLIN, GROFF      AN   TMP 70 10
  SEE "GIANTS UNLEASHED"
MINDWORM AND OTHER STORIES, THE
                         KORNBLUTH, C. M.    AC H JOS 55
MINDWORM, THE              ANONYMOUS           AN   TDM 67
MIRROR OF INFINITY, THE      SILVERBERG, ROBERT  AN H HPR 70
MISSING MAN, THE            MACLEAN, KATHERINE  NO   BKM 75
MISSING WORLD AND OTHER STORIES, THE
                         ELWOOD, ROGER       OA H LER 74
MISSION TO THE STARS        VAN VOGT, A. E.     NO   BKM 71 03
  SEE "THE MIXED MEN"
MISSION: INTERPLANETARY      VAN VOGT, A. E.     NO   NAM 52
  SEE "THE VOYAGE OF THE SPACE BEAGLE"
MISSION: MANSTOP           NEVILLE, KRIS       AC   LEI 71 10
MIXED FEELINGS              EFFINGER, GEO. ALEC AC   FPR 74
MIXED MEN, THE              VAN VOGT, A. E.     NO H GNM 52
  ALSO AS "MISSION TO THE STARS"
MODERAN                     BUNCH, DAVID R.     AC   AVN 71 05
MODERN MASTERPIECES OF SCIENCE FICTION
                         MOSKOWITZ, SAM      AN H WOR 65
  DERIVATIVE ANTHOLOGIES "DOORWAY INTO TIME", "MICROCOSMIC GOD"
  AND "THE VORTEX BLASTERS"
MODERN SCIENCE FICTION      SPINRAD, NORMAN     AN   ANC 74
MOLECULE MONSTERS, THE      ANONYMOUS           AN   WHP 50
MOMENT OF ECLIPSE, THE      ALDISS, BRIAN W.    AC H FAB 70
MOMENT WITHOUT TIME         MINES, SAMUEL       AN H SBB 52
  SEE "THE BEST FROM STARTLING STORIES"
MONADIC UNIVERSE, THE       ZEBROWSKI, GEORGE   AC   ACE 77 03
MONITOR FOUND IN ORBIT       CONEY, MICHAEL G.   AC   DAW 74 09
MONSTERS                    VAN VOGT, A. E.     AC   PKT 65
  EDITED BY FORREST J. ACKERMAN, ALSO AS "THE BLAL"
MONSTERS AND MEDICS         WHITE, JAMES        AC   BAL 77 03
MONSTERS AND SUCH          LEINSTER, MURRAY    AC   AVN 59
MOON CONQUERORS, THE        ANONYMOUS           AN   SWN 43
MOON ERA, THE               MOSKOWITZ, SAM      AN H DBL 67
  SEE "THREE STORIES"
MOON MAID, THE              BURROUGHS, EDGAR R. NO H MCG 26
MOON MOTH AND OTHER STORIES, THE
                         VANCE, JACK         AC H DOB 76
  SEE "THE WORLD BETWEEN AND OTHER STORIES"
MOON TERROR, THE            BIRCH, A. G.        AN H PFP 27
MOONFERNS & STARSONGS        SILVERBERG, ROBERT  AC   BAL 71 06
MOONLIGHT TRAVELER, THE      STERN, PHILIP VAN D. AN H DBL 43 05
  ALSO AS "GREAT TALES OF FANTASY AND IMAGINATION"
MOORCOCK'S BOOK OF MARTYRS   MOORCOCK, MICHAEL   AC   QRT 76
MORE ADVENTURES IN TIME AND SPACE
                         HEALY & MCCOMAS     AN   BAN 55 03
  STORIES FROM "ADVENTURES IN TIME AND SPACE"
```

MORE ADVENTURES ON OTHER PLANETS
                              WOLLHEIM, DONALD A.   AN   ACE 63
MORE LITTLE MONSTERS   ELWOOD & GHIDALIA   AN   MAN 73
MORE NIGHTMARES   BLOCH, ROBERT   AC   BEL 62 02
MORE PENGUIN SCIENCE FICTION ALDISS, BRIAN W.   AN   PEN 63
    ALSO IN "THE PENGUIN SCIENCE FICTION OMNIBUS"
MORE SCIENCE FICTION TALES   ELWOOD, ROGER   OA H RAN 74
MORE SOVIET SCIENCE FICTION   ANONYMOUS   AN   CLB 62
    ALSO AS "THE HEART OF THE SERPENT"
MORE STORIES FROM THE HUGO WINNERS VOLUME 2
                              ASIMOV, ISAAC   AN   FCR 73 12
    LAST 8 STORIES
MORE STORIES FROM THE TWILIGHT ZONE
                              SERLING, ROD   OC   BAN 61 04
MORE TERROR IN THE MODERN VEIN WOLLHEIM, DONALD A. AN   DIG 61
    7 STORIES FROM "TERROR IN THE MODERN VEIN"
MORE THAN HUMAN   STURGEON, THEODORE   NO H FSY 53
MORE THAN SUPERHUMAN   VAN VOGT, A. E.   AC   DEL 71 05
MORE WOMEN OF WONDER   SARGENT, PAMELA   AN   VNT 76 08
MORTAL ENGINES   LEM, STANISLAW   AC H SEA 77 05
MORTALS AND MONSTERS   DEL REY, LESTER   AC   BAL 65
MR. GEORGE AND OTHER ODD PERSONS
                              DERLETH, AUGUST   AC H ARK 63
MR. MERGENTHWIRKER'S LOBBIES AND OTHER FANTASTIC TALES
                              BOND, NELSON S.   AC H CMC 46
MURRAY LEINSTER OMNIBUS, A   LEINSTER, MURRAY   AC H SID 68
    ALSO IN "SCIENCE FICTION SPECIAL 7"
MUTANT   PADGETT, LEWIS   AC H GNM 53
MUTANTS   DICKSON, GORDON R.   AC H MAC 70
MUTANTS   SILVERBERG, ROBERT   AN H NDB 74
MY BEST SCIENCE FICTION STORY MARGULIES & FRIEND   AN H MER 49
MY BEST SCIENCE FICTION STORY (12 OF 25)
                              MARGULIES & FRIEND   AN   PKT 54 05
MY NAME IS LEGION   ZELAZNY, ROGER   AC   BAL 76 04
NATIVES OF SPACE   CLEMENT, HAL   AC   BAL 65 04
NEANDERTHAL PLANET   ALDISS, BRIAN W.   AC   AVN 70 01
NEBULA AWARD STORIES   KNIGHT, DAMON   AN H DBL 66
NEBULA AWARD STORIES   NO. 2 ALDISS & HARRISON   AN H DBL 67
NEBULA AWARD STORIES   NO. 3 ZELAZNY, ROGER   AN H DBL 68 12
NEBULA AWARD STORIES   NO. 4 ANDERSON, POUL   AN H DBL 69 12
NEBULA AWARD STORIES   NO. 5 BLISH, JAMES   AN H DBL 70 12
NEBULA AWARD STORIES   NO. 6 SIMAK, CLIFFORD D.   AN H DBL 71 12
NEBULA AWARD STORIES   NO. 7 BIGGLE, LLOYD JR.   AN H HPR 73
NEBULA AWARD STORIES   8   ASIMOV, ISAAC   AN H HPR 73
NEBULA AWARD STORIES   9   WILHELM, KATE   AN H HPR 74
NEBULA AWARD STORIES   10   GUNN, JAMES E.   AN H HPR 75
NEBULA AWARD STORIES   11   LE GUIN, URSULA K.   AN H HPR 77
NEEDLE IN A TIMESTACK   SILVERBERG, ROBERT   AC   BAL 66 11
NEUTRON STAR   NIVEN, LARRY   AC   BAL 68 04
NEVER IN THIS WORLD   STONE, IDELLA P.   AN   FGM 71 04
NEW ATLANTIS AND OTHER NOVELLAS OF S.F., THE
                              SILVERBERG, ROBERT   OA H HAW 75
NEW AWARENESS, THE   WARRICK & GREENBERG   AN H DCT 75
NEW CONSTELLATIONS   DISCH & NAYLOR   OA H HPR 76
NEW DIMENSIONS 1   SILVERBERG, ROBERT   OA H DBL 71
NEW DIMENSIONS 2   SILVERBERG, ROBERT   OA H DBL 72
NEW DIMENSIONS 3   SILVERBERG, ROBERT   OA   SIG 74 02
NEW DIMENSIONS 4   SILVERBERG, ROBERT   OA   SIG 74 10
NEW DIMENSIONS 5   SILVERBERG, ROBERT   OA H HPR 75
NEW DIMENSIONS 6   SILVERBERG, ROBERT   OA H HPR 76
NEW DIMENSIONS 7   SILVERBERG, ROBERT   OA H HPR 77
NEW DREAMS THIS MORNING   BLISH, JAMES   AN   BAL 66 10
NEW GODS LEAD, THE   WRIGHT, S. FOWLER   AC H JAR 32
    ALSO IN "THE THRONE OF SATURN"
NEW IMPROVED SUN, THE   DISCH, THOMAS M.   AN H HPR 75
NEW MIND, THE   ELWOOD, ROGER   OA H MAC 73
    SEE "FRONTIERS 2; THE NEW MIND"
NEW S.F., THE   JONES, LANGDON   OA H HUT 69
NEW STORIES FROM THE TWILIGHT ZONE
                              SERLING, ROD   OC   BAN 62 05
NEW TALES OF SPACE AND TIME   HEALY, RAYMOND J.   OA H HLT 51 11
NEW TOMORROWS, THE   SPINRAD, NORMAN   AN   BEL 71
NEW VOICES IN SCIENCE FICTION MARTIN, GEORGE R. R. AN H MAC 77
NEW WORLDS EIGHT   BAILEY, HILARY   OA   SPH 75 03
NEW WORLDS FOR OLD   DERLETH, AUGUST   AN   FSP 63
    9 STORIES FROM "WORLDS OF TOMORROW"
NEW WORLDS NINE   BAILEY, HILARY   OA   COR 75 11
NEW WORLDS NO. 5   MOORCOCK & PLATT   OA L EQN 73
NEW WORLDS NO. 6   PLATT & BAILEY   OA L EQN 74
NEW WORLDS OF FANTASY   CARR, TERRY   AN   ACE 67
    IN ENGLAND AS "STEP OUTSIDE YOUR MIND"
NEW WORLDS OF FANTASY NO. 2   CARR, TERRY   AN   ACE 70
NEW WORLDS OF FANTASY NO. 3   CARR, TERRY   AN   ACE 71
NEW WORLDS QUARTERLY NO. 1   MOORCOCK, MICHAEL   OA   BKM 71 09
NEW WORLDS QUARTERLY NO. 2   MOORCOCK, MICHAEL   OA   BKM 71 12
NEW WORLDS QUARTERLY NO. 3   MOORCOCK, MICHAEL   OA   BKM 72 03
NEW WORLDS QUARTERLY NO. 4   MOORCOCK, MICHAEL   OA   BKM 72 06
NEW WORLDS QUARTERLY NO. 5   MOORCOCK, MICHAEL   OA   SPH 73
NEW WRITINGS IN SF. 1   CARNELL, JOHN   OA   BAN 66 04
NEW WRITINGS IN SF. 2   CARNELL, JOHN   OA   BAN 66 10
NEW WRITINGS IN SF. 3   CARNELL, JOHN   OA   BAN 67 02
NEW WRITINGS IN SF. 4   CARNELL, JOHN   OA   BAN 68 03
NEW WRITINGS IN SF. 5   CARNELL, JOHN   OA   BAN 70 08
NEW WRITINGS IN SF. 6   CARNELL, JOHN   OA   BAN 71 03
NEW WRITINGS IN SF. 7   CARNELL, JOHN   AN   BAN 71 08
NEW WRITINGS IN SF. 7   CARNELL, JOHN   OA H DOB 66
NEW WRITINGS IN SF. 8   CARNELL, JOHN   AN   BAN 71 12
NEW WRITINGS IN SF. 8   CARNELL, JOHN   OA H DOB 66
NEW WRITINGS IN SF. 9   CARNELL, JOHN   AN   BAN 72 05
NEW WRITINGS IN SF. 9   CARNELL, JOHN   OA H DOB 66
NEW WRITINGS IN SF. 10   CARNELL, JOHN   OA H DOB 67
NEW WRITINGS IN SF. 11   CARNELL, JOHN   OA   COR 68
NEW WRITINGS IN SF. 12   CARNELL, JOHN   OA   COR 68
NEW WRITINGS IN SF. 13   CARNELL, JOHN   OA   COR 68
NEW WRITINGS IN SF. 14   CARNELL, JOHN   OA H DOB 69
NEW WRITINGS IN SF. 15   CARNELL, JOHN   OA H DOB 69

NEW WRITINGS IN SF. 16   CARNELL, JOHN   OA H DOB 69
NEW WRITINGS IN SF. 17   CARNELL, JOHN   OA H DOB 70
NEW WRITINGS IN SF. 18   CARNELL, JOHN   OA H DOB 71
NEW WRITINGS IN SF. 19   CARNELL, JOHN   OA H DOB 71
NEW WRITINGS IN SF. 20   CARNELL, JOHN   OA H DOB 72
NEW WRITINGS IN SF. 21   CARNELL, JOHN   OA H SID 73
NEW WRITINGS IN SF. 22   BULMER, KENNETH   OA H SID 73
NEW WRITINGS IN SF. 23   BULMER, KENNETH   OA H SID 74
NEW WRITINGS IN SF. 24   BULMER, KENNETH   OA H SID 74
NEW WRITINGS IN SF. 25   BULMER, KENNETH   OA H DOB 75
NEW WRITINGS IN SF. 26   BULMER, KENNETH   OA H DOB 75
NEW WRITINGS IN SF. 27   BULMER, KENNETH   OA H SID 75
NEW WRITINGS IN SF. 28   BULMER, KENNETH   OA H DOB 76
NEW WRITINGS IN SF. 29   BULMER, KENNETH   OA H SID 76
NEWS FROM ELSEWHERE   COOPER, EDMUND   AC   BKM 69 05
NEXT STOP THE STARS   SILVERBERG, ROBERT   DC   ACE 62
NICE DAY FOR SCREAMING, AND OTHER TALES OF THE HUB
                              SCHMITZ, JAMES H.   AC H CHL 65
NIGHT GALLERY   SERLING, ROD   OC   BAN 71 11
NIGHT GALLERY 2   SERLING, ROD   OC   BAN 72 12
NIGHT IN FUNLAND   BRONDFIELD, JEROME   AN   SBS 68
    AND OTHER STORIES FROM LITERARY CAVALCADE
NIGHT MONSTERS   LEIBER, FRITZ   DC   ACE 69
NIGHT OF THE PUUDLY, THE   SIMAK, CLIFFORD D.   AC   FSP 64
    5 STORIES FROM "ALL THE TRAPS OF EARTH"
NIGHT OF THE SPHINX AND OTHER STORIES
                              ELWOOD, ROGER   OA H LER 74
NIGHT OF THE WOLF, THE   LEIBER, FRITZ   AC   BAL 66 07
NIGHT RIDE AND OTHER JOURNEYS BEAUMONT, CHARLES   AC   BAN 60 03
NIGHT TIDE, A   INOUYE, JON   OC   RDN 76 12
NIGHT'S BLACK AGENTS   LEIBER, FRITZ   AC H ARK 47
    BALLANTINE 1961 EDITION OMITS "ADEPT'S GAMBIT"
NIGHTFALL AND OTHER STORIES   ASIMOV, ISAAC   AC H DBL 69
NIGHTMARE AGE   POHL, FREDERIK   AN   BAL 70 10
NIGHTMARE GARDEN   GHIDALIA, VIC   AN   MAN 76
NIGHTMARES   BLOCH, ROBERT   AC   BEL 61
    TEN WEIRD TALES FROM PLEASANT DREAMS
NIGHTMARES AND DAYDREAMS   BOND, NELSON S.   AC H ARK 68
NIGHTMARES AND GEEZENSTACKS   BROWN, FREDRIC   AC   BAN 61 07
NIGHTSHADE & DAMNATIONS   KERSH, GERALD   AC   FGM 68
NINE BILLION NAMES OF GOD, THE CLARKE, ARTHUR C.   AC H HBW 67
NINE BY LAUMER   LAUMER, KEITH   AC H DBL 67
NINE HUNDRED GRANDMOTHERS   LAFFERTY, R. A.   AC   ACE 70
NINE TOMORROWS   ASIMOV, ISAAC   AC H DBL 59
NINTH GALAXY READER, THE   POHL, FREDERIK   AN H DBL 66 02
NO BOUNDARIES   KUTTNER & MOORE   AC H BAL 55
NO DIRECTION HOME   SPINRAD, NORMAN   AC   PKT 75 05
    (STORIES REWRITTEN)
NO DOORS, NO WINDOWS   ELLISON, HARLAN   AC   PYR 75 11
NO FUTURE IN IT   BRUNNER, JOHN   AC H DBL 64
NO LIMITS   FERMAN, JOSEPH W.   AN   BAL 64 08
NO MIND OF MAN   SILVERBERG, ROBERT   OA H HAW 73
NO OTHER GODS BUT ME   BRUNNER, JOHN   AC   CPT 66
NO PLACE LIKE EARTH   CARNELL, JOHN   AN H BDM 52 10
NO PLACE LIKE EARTH (7 OF 10) CARNELL, JOHN   AN   BDM 54 02
NO TIME LIKE THE FUTURE   BOND, NELSON S.   AC   AVN 54
NO TIME LIKE TOMORROW   ALDISS, BRIAN W.   AC   SIG 59 07
NON-STATISTICAL MAN, THE   JONES, RAYMOND F.   AC   BEL 64
NORTHWEST OF EARTH   MOORE, C. L.   AC H GNM 54
NOT BEFORE TIME   BRUNNER, JOHN   AC   FSP 68
NOT LONG FOR THIS WORLD   DERLETH, AUGUST   AC H ARK 48
NOT WITHOUT SORCERY   STURGEON, THEODORE   AC   BAL 61 06
    8 STORIES FROM "WITHOUT SORCERY"
NOTES TO A SCIENCE FICTION WRITER
                              BOVA, BEN   AC H SCB 75
    ONLY STORIES USED TO ILLUSTRATE WRITING TECHNIQUES ARE LISTED
NOTIONS: UNLIMITED   SHECKLEY, ROBERT   AC   BAN 60 06
NOVA 1   HARRISON, HARRY   OA H DCT 70
NOVA 1 (BRITISH)   HARRISON, HARRY   OA H HAL 76
NOVA 2   HARRISON, HARRY   OA H WKR 72
NOVA 3   HARRISON, HARRY   OA H WKR 73
    ALSO AS "THE OUTDATED MAN"
NOVA 4   HARRISON, HARRY   OA H WKR 74
NOVELETS OF SCIENCE FICTION   HOWARD, IVAN   AN   BEL 63
NOVELS   VERNE, JULES   AC H GOL 29
    EDITED BY H. C. HARWOOD
NOW & BEYOND   HOWARD, IVAN   AN   BEL 65 09
NOW BEGINS TOMORROW   KNIGHT, DAMON   AN   LAN 69 11
    SEE "FIRST FLIGHT"
NOW THEN   BRUNNER, JOHN   AC   MFL 65 10
NUTZENBOLTS   GOULART, RON   AC H MAC 75
OCTOBER COUNTRY, THE   BRADBURY, RAY   AC H BAL 55
OCTOBER COUNTRY, THE (BRITISH) BRADBURY, RAY   AC H HDV 56
ODD JOB NO. 101   GOULART, RON   AC H SCB 75
ODD SCIENCE FICTION   LONG, FRANK BELKNAP   AC   BEL 64 08
    IN ENGLAND AS "THE HORROR FROM THE HILLS"
ODDBALLS, THE   GHIDALIA, VIC   AN   MAN 73
OF ALL POSSIBLE WORLDS   TENN, WILLIAM   AC   BAL 55
OF TIME AND STARS   CLARKE, ARTHUR C.   AC H GOL 72
OFF CENTER   KNIGHT, DAMON   DC   ACE 65
OFF CENTRE   KNIGHT, DAMON   AC H GOL 69
OFF THE BEATEN ORBIT   MERRIL, JUDITH   AN   PYR 59
    SEE "GALAXY OF GHOULS"
OLD DIE RICH AND OTHER SCIENCE FICTION, THE
                              GOLD, H. L.   AC H CRN 55
OLE DOC METHUSELAH   HUBBARD, L. RON   AC   DAW 70
OMEGA   ELWOOD, ROGER   OA H WKR 73
OMNIBUS OF SCIENCE FICTION   CONKLIN, GROFF   AN H CRN 52
    DERIVATIVE ANTHOLOGIES ARE "SCIENCE FICTION OMNIBUS",
    "STRANGE TRAVELS IN SCIENCE FICTION" AND
    "STRANGE ADVENTURES IN SCIENCE FICTION"
OMNIBUS OF TIME, THE   FARLEY, RALPH MILNE   AC H FPB 50
OMNIBUS, THE   VERNE, JULES   AC H LIP 31
ON AN ODD NOTE   KERSH, GERALD   AC   BAL 58
ON OUR WAY TO THE FUTURE   CARR, TERRY   AN   ACE 70

ONCE AND FUTURE TALES FROM THE MAGAZINE OF FANTASY AND
  SCIENCE FICTION   FERMAN, EDWARD L.   AN H HWF 68
ONCE THERE WAS A GIANT   LAUMER, KEITH   AC H DBL 71
ONE HUNDRED YEARS OF SCIENCE FICTION
                                  KNIGHT, DAMON   AN H SAS 68
ONE HUNDRED AND TWO H-BOMBS   DISCH, THOMAS M.   AC   CPT 66
ONE HUNDRED AND TWO H-BOMBS (U.S.)
                                  DISCH, THOMAS M.   AC   BKM 71 08
ONE IN THREE HUNDRED   MCINTOSH, J. T.   AC H DBL 54
ONE STEP FROM EARTH   HARRISON, HARRY   AC H MAC 70
OPENER OF THE WAY, THE   BLOCH, ROBERT   AC H ARK 45
  ENGLISH DERIVATIVE ANTHOLOGY "THE HOUSE OF THE HATCHET"
OPENER OF THE WAY, THE (BRITISH PB)
                                  BLOCH, ROBERT   AC   PTH 76
OPERATION CHAOS   ANDERSON, POUL   NO   LAN 71
OPERATION FUTURE   CONKLIN, GROFF   AN   PMA 55 05
OPUS 100   ASIMOV, ISAAC   AC H HMF 69
OR ALL THE SEAS WITH OYSTERS   DAVIDSON, AVRAM   AC   BKM 52
ORBIT   1   KNIGHT, DAMON   OA   BKM 66 10
ORBIT   2   KNIGHT, DAMON   OA   BKM 67 09
ORBIT   3   KNIGHT, DAMON   OA H PUT 68
ORBIT   4   KNIGHT, DAMON   OA H PUT 68
ORBIT   5   KNIGHT, DAMON   OA H PUT 69
ORBIT   6   KNIGHT, DAMON   OA H PUT 70
ORBIT   7   KNIGHT, DAMON   OA H PUT 70
ORBIT   8   KNIGHT, DAMON   OA H PUT 70
ORBIT   9   KNIGHT, DAMON   OA H PUT 71
ORBIT 10   KNIGHT, DAMON   OA H PUT 72
ORBIT 11   KNIGHT, DAMON   OA H PUT 73
ORBIT 12   KNIGHT, DAMON   OA H PUT 73
ORBIT 13   KNIGHT, DAMON   OA H PUT 74
ORBIT 14   KNIGHT, DAMON   OA H HPR 74
ORBIT 15   KNIGHT, DAMON   OA H HPR 74
ORBIT 16   KNIGHT, DAMON   OA H HPR 75
ORBIT 17   KNIGHT, DAMON   OA H HPR 75
ORBIT 18   KNIGHT, DAMON   OA H HPR 76
ORBIT UNLIMITED   ANDERSON, POUL   NO   PYR 61 05
ORPHANS OF THE SKY   HEINLEIN, ROBERT A.   NO H GOL 63
OTHER DAYS, OTHER EYES   SHAW, BOB   NO   ACE 72 07
OTHER DIMENSION, THE   ROSNER, SARA   AN   SBS 72 11
OTHER DIMENSIONS   SILVERBERG, ROBERT   AN H HAW 73
OTHER DIMENSIONS   SMITH, CLARK ASHTON   AC H ARK 70
OTHER PLACE, THE   PRIESTLEY, J. B.   AC H HPR 53
OTHER SIDE OF THE CLOCK, THE   STERN, PHILIP VAN D. AN H VNR 69
OTHER SIDE OF THE MOON, THE   DERLETH, AUGUST   AN H PEL 49
OTHER SIDE OF THE MOON, THE (BRITISH PB 1)
                                  DERLETH, AUGUST   AN   PTH 63
OTHER SIDE OF THE MOON, THE (BRITISH PB 2)
                                  DERLETH, AUGUST   AN   MFL 66
OTHER SIDE OF THE MOON, THE (BRITISH)
                                  DERLETH, AUGUST   AN H GRY 56
OTHER SIDE OF THE MOON, THE (10 OF 20)
                                  DERLETH, AUGUST   AN   BRK 59
OTHER SIDE OF THE SKY, THE   CLARKE, ARTHUR C.   AC H HBW 58
  ALSO IN "FROM THE OCEAN, FROM THE STARS"
OTHER SIDE OF TOMORROW, THE   ELWOOD, ROGER   OA H RDM 73
OTHER WORLDS OF CLIFFORD SIMAK   SIMAK, CLIFFORD D.   AC   AVN 62
  6 STORIES FROM "THE WORLDS OF CLIFFORD SIMAK"
OTHER WORLDS, OTHER GODS   MOHS, MAYO   AN H DBL 71
OTHER WORLDS, OTHER SEAS   SUVIN, DARKO   AN H RDM 70
OTHER WORLDS, OTHER TIMES   MOSKOWITZ & ELWOOD   AN   MBB 69
OTHER WORLDS, THE   STONG, PHILIP D.   AN H FNK 41
  ALSO AS "25 MODERN STORIES OF MYSTERY AND IMAGINATION"
OTHERS, THE   CARR, TERRY   AN   FGM 69
OUT FROM GANYMEDE   MALZBERG, BARRY N.   AC   WPB 74 12
OUT OF BOUNDS   MERRIL, JUDITH   AC   PYR 60 04
OUT OF MY MIND   BRUNNER, JOHN   AC   BAL 67 02
OUT OF MY MIND (BRITISH)   BRUNNER, JOHN   AC   FSP 68
OUT OF SPACE AND TIME   SMITH, CLARK ASHTON   AC H NSP 71
OUT OF THE SILENT SKY   BIGGLE, LLOYD JR.   AC   BET 77
  ON COVER AS "THE SILENT SKY", SEE "RULE OF THE DOOR"
OUT OF THE UNKNOWN   VAN VOGT & HULL   AC H FPB 48
  IN ENGLAND AS "THE SEA THING AND OTHER STORIES"
OUT OF THE UNKNOWN (ENGLISH EDITION ADDS:)
                                  VAN VOGT & HULL   AC H SID 70
OUT OF THIS WORLD   FAST, JULIUS   AN   PEN 44 06
OUT OF THIS WORLD   LEINSTER, MURRAY   NO H AVL 58
OUT OF THIS WORLD   1   WILLIAMS-ELLIS& OWEN AN H BLK 60
OUT OF THIS WORLD   2   WILLIAMS-ELLIS& OWEN AN H BLK 61
OUT OF THIS WORLD   3   WILLIAMS-ELLIS& OWEN AN H BLK 61
OUT OF THIS WORLD   4   WILLIAMS-ELLIS& OWEN AN H BLK 64
OUT OF THIS WORLD   5   WILLIAMS-ELLIS& OWEN AN H BLK 65
OUT OF THIS WORLD   6   WILLIAMS-ELLIS& OWEN AN H BLK 67
OUT OF THIS WORLD   7   WILLIAMS-ELLIS& OWEN AN H BLK 68
OUTDATED MAN, THE   HARRISON, HARRY   OA   DEL 75 04
  SEE "NOVA 3"
OUTER REACHES, THE   DERLETH, AUGUST   AN H PEL 51
  ENGLISH DERIVATIVE ANTHOLOGY "THE TIME OF INFINITY"
OUTER REACHES, THE (BRITISH)   DERLETH, AUGUST   AN   CNL 63
  FIRST 8 STORIES OF AMERICAN EDITION, LAST 9 IN
  "THE TIME OF INFINITY"
OUTER REACHES, THE (10 OF 17)   DERLETH, AUGUST   AN   BRK 58
OUTER SPACE STORIES   FURMAN, A. L.   AN   LPB 65 12
  SEE "TEEN-AGE OUTER SPACE STORIES"
OUTPOSTS IN SPACE   WEST, WALLACE   AC H AVL 62
OUTSIDERS: CHILDREN OF WONDER   TENN, WILLIAM   AN   PMA 54
  SEE "CHILDREN OF WONDER"
OUTWARD URGE, THE   WYNDHAM & PARKES   AC   BAL 59
  ONLY LATER EDITIONS CONTAIN "THE EMPTYNESS OF SPACE"
OVER THE EDGE   ELLISON, HARLAN   AC   BEL 70 05
OVERLOADED MAN, THE   BALLARD, J. G.   AC   PTH 67 11
PACIFIC BOOK OF AUSTRALIAN SCIENCE FICTION
                                  BAXTER, JOHN   AN   AAR 68
PAIL OF AIR, A   LEIBER, FRITZ   AC   BAL 64 07
PAINGOD AND OTHER DELUSIONS   ELLISON, HARLAN   AC   PYR 65 12

PAINGOD AND OTHER DELUSIONS (THIRD EDITION ADDS:)
                                  ELLISON, HARLAN   AC   PYR 75 03
PANDORA EFFECT, THE   WILLIAMSON, JACK   AC   ACE 69
PARADOX LOST, AND 12 OTHER GREAT S.F. STORIES
                                  BROWN, FREDRIC   AC H RDM 73
PARSECS AND PARABLES   SILVERBERG, ROBERT   AC H DBL 70
PARTNERS IN WONDER   ELLISON, HARLAN   AC H WKR 71
PASSING OF THE DRAGONS, THE   ROBERTS, KEITH   AC   BKM 77 04
PASSPORT TO ETERNITY   BALLARD, J. G.   AC   BKM 63 09
PAST THROUGH TOMORROW, THE   HEINLEIN, ROBERT A.   AC H PUT 67
PAST, PRESENT, AND FUTURE PERFECT
                                  WOLFE, J&FITZ GERALD AN   FPR 73 08
PATH INTO THE UNKNOWN   ANONYMOUS   AN H DCT 68
  THE BEST OF SOVIET SCIENCE FICTION
PAVANE   ROBERTS, KEITH   NO H DBL 68
PENGUIN SCIENCE FICTION   ALDISS, BRIAN W.   AN   PEN 61
  ALSO IN "THE PENGUIN SCIENCE FICTION OMNIBUS"
PENGUIN SCIENCE FICTION OMNIBUS, THE
                                  ALDISS, BRIAN W.   AN   PEN 73
PEOPLE MACHINES   WILLIAMSON, JACK   AC   ACE 71
PEOPLE TRAP AND OTHER PITFALLS, THE
                                  SHECKLEY, ROBERT   AC   DEL 68 12
PEOPLE: NO DIFFERENT FLESH, THE
                                  HENDERSON, ZENNA   AC H DBL 67
PERCHANCE TO DREAM   KNIGHT, DAMON   AC H DBL 72
PERMANENT IMPLOSION, THE   CAMPBELL, JOHN W. JR AN   CUR 66
  SEE "ANALOG 4"
PETRIFIED PLANET, THE   CLARK, JOHN D.   OA H TWN 52
PHILIP K. DICK OMNIBUS, A   DICK, PHILIP K.   AC H SID 70
PHILOSOPHICAL CORPS, THE   COLE, EVERETT B.   NO H GNM 62
PILGRIMAGE TO EARTH   SHECKLEY, ROBERT   AC   BAN 57 10
PILGRIMAGE: THE BOOK OF THE PEOPLE
                                  HENDERSON, ZENNA   AC H DBL 61
PILLAR OF FIRE AND OTHER PLAYS   BRADBURY, RAY   AC   BAN 57 11
PIRATES OF VENUS AND LOST ON VENUS, THE
                                  BURROUGHS, EDGAR R.   AC H DOV 63
PLANET EXPLORER, THE   LEINSTER, MURRAY   NO   AVN 57
  SEE "COLONIAL SURVEY"
PLANET OF DOOM AND OTHER STORIES
                                  ANONYMOUS   AN   JBL 58
PLANET OF THE DOUBLE SUN   JONES, NEIL R.   AC   ACE 67
PLANETEERS, THE   CAMPBELL, JOHN W. JR DC   ACE 66
PLANETS FOR SALE   HULL, E. MAYNE   AC H FEL 54
PLANETS OF ADVENTURE   WELLS, BASIL   AC H FPB 49
PLANETS OF WONDER   CARR, TERRY   AN H NEL 76
  A TREASURY OF SPACE OPERA
PLATTNER STORY AND OTHERS, THE   WELLS, H. G.   AC H MTH 97
PLATYPUS OF DOOM AND OTHER NIHILISTS, THE
                                  COVER, ARTHUR BYRON   OC   WPB 76 06
PLAYBOY BOOK OF HORROR AND THE SUPERNATURAL, THE
                                  PLAYBOY, EDITORS OF   AN H PBP 67
PLAYBOY BOOK OF SCIENCE FICTION AND FANTASY, THE
                                  PLAYBOY, EDITORS OF   AN H PBP 66
PLAYBOY'S STORIES OF THE SINISTER & STRANGE
                                  PLAYBOY, EDITORS OF   AN   PBP 69
PLEASANT DREAMS   BLOCH, ROBERT   AC H ARK 60
POCKET BOOK OF SCIENCE-FICTION, THE
                                  WOLLHEIM, DONALD A.   AN   PKT 43 03
POCKETFUL OF STARS, A   KNIGHT, DAMON   AN H DBL 71
POISON BELT, THE   DOYLE, ARTHUR CONAN   AC H MCM 64
POLITICAL SCIENCE FICTION   GREENBERG& WARRICK   AN L PRH 74
PORTABLE NOVELS OF SCIENCE   WOLLHEIM, DONALD A.   AN H VIK 45
PORTALS OF TOMORROW   DERLETH, AUGUST   AN H RNH 54
PORTRAITS IN MOONLIGHT   JACOBI, CARL   AC H ARK 64
POSITIVE CHARGE   RICHMOND, W. & L.   DC   ACE 70
POSSIBLE TOMORROWS   CONKLIN, GROFF   AN   71
  SEE "FIVE-ODD"
POSSIBLE WORLDS OF SCIENCE FICTION
                                  CONKLIN, GROFF   AN H VPR 51
POSSIBLE WORLDS OF SCIENCE FICTION (BRITISH)
                                  CONKLIN, GROFF   AN H GRY 51
POSSIBLE WORLDS OF SCIENCE FICTION (10 OF 22)
                                  CONKLIN, GROFF   AN   BRK 55 07
POST READER OF FANTASY AND SCIENCE FICTION
                                  SATURDAY EVE. POST   AN H DBL 64
PRELUDE TO MARS   CLARKE, ARTHUR C.   AC H HBW 65
PRESERVING MACHINE, THE   DICK, PHILIP K.   AC H ACE 69
  ENGLISH EDITION (GOL 71) OMITS STORY "WHAT THE DEAD MEN SAY"
PRIDE OF MONSTERS, A   SCHMITZ, JAMES H.   AC H MAC 70
PRIME NUMBER   HARRISON, HARRY   AC   BKM 70 07
PRINCESS OF MARS AND A FIGHTING MAN OF MARS, A
                                  BURROUGHS, EDGAR R.   AC H DOV 64
PRIZE SCIENCE FICTION   WOLLHEIM, DONALD A.   AN H MBR 53
  IN ENGLAND AS "PRIZE STORIES OF SPACE AND TIME"
PRIZE STORIES OF SPACE AND TIME
                                  WOLLHEIM, DONALD A.   AN H WEI 53
  SEE "PRIZE SCIENCE FICTION"
PROJECT BARRIER   GALOUYE, DANIEL F.   AC H GOL 68
PROLOGUE TO ANALOG   CAMPBELL, JOHN W. JR AN H DBL 62
  IN "ANALOG ANTHOLOGY"
PROTOSTARS   GERROLD & GOLDIN   OA   BAL 71 10
PROXY INTELLIGENCE AND OTHER MIND BENDERS
                                  VAN VOGT, A. E.   AC   PBK 71 01
PSEUDO PEOPLE, THE   NOLAN, WILLIAM F.   AN H SHB 65
  IN ENGLAND AS "ALMOST HUMAN"
PSI-HIGH AND OTHERS   NOURSE, ALAN E.   AC H MCK 67
QUADRATIC   CRAWFORD, WILLIAM L. AN H FPB 53
QUARK/1   DELANY & HACKER   OA   PBK 70 11
QUARK/2   DELANY & HACKER   OA   PBK 71 02
QUARK/3   DELANY & HACKER   OA   PBK 71 05
QUARK/4   DELANY & HACKER   OA   PBK 71 08
QUEEN OF AIR AND DARKNESS AND OTHER STORIES, THE
                                  ANDERSON, POUL   AC   SIG 73 12
QUEST   BISCHOFF, DAVID   OA H RTH 77
QUEST FOR THE FUTURE   VAN VOGT, A. E.   NO   ACE 70
QUEST OF THE THREE WORLDS   SMITH, CORDWAINER   NO   ACE 66

R IS FOR ROCKET   BRADBURY, RAY   AC H DBL 62 10
RACE TO THE STARS   MARGULIES & FRIEND   AN   CRS 58 10
    4 STORIES FROM "GIANT ANTHOLOGY OF SCIENCE FICTION"
RADIUM POOL, THE   REPP, ED EARL   AC H FPB 49
    ALSO IN "SCIENCE-FANTASY QUINTETTE"
RARE SCIENCE FICTION   HOWARD, IVAN   AN   BEL 63 01
REACH FOR TOMORROW   CLARKE, ARTHUR C.   AC   BAL 56 03
REAL-TIME WORLD   PRIEST, CHRISTOPHER   AC H NLB 74
REALITY TRIP, THE   SILVERBERG, ROBERT   AC   BAL 72 03
RED PERI, THE   WEINBAUM, STANLEY G.   AC H FPS 52
REST OF THE ROBOTS, THE   ASIMOV, ISAAC   AC H DBL 64
REST OF THE ROBOTS, THE (EIGHT STORIES FROM)
                                ASIMOV, ISAAC   AC   PYR 66 01
RETIEF OF THE CDT   LAUMER, KEITH   AC H DBL 71
RETIEF: AMBASSADOR TO SPACE   LAUMER, KEITH   AC H DBL 69
RETIEF: EMISSARY TO THE STARS   LAUMER, KEITH   AC   DEL 75 12
RETURN TO OTHERNESS   KUTTNER, HENRY   AC   BAL 62
REVOLT IN 2100   HEINLEIN, ROBERT A.   AC H SHS 53
RIM GODS, THE   CHANDLER, A. BERTRAM   DC   ACE 68
RIM OF MORNING, THE   SLOANE, WILLIAM   AC H DOM 64
RIM OF THE UNKNOWN   LONG, FRANK BELKNAP   AC H ARK 72
ROBERT HEINLEIN OMNIBUS, A   HEINLEIN, ROBERT A.   AC H SID 66
ROBERT SHECKLEY OMNIBUS, THE   SHECKLEY, ROBERT   AC H GOL 73
    EDITED BY ROBERT CONQUEST
ROBOT AND THE MAN, THE   GREENBERG , MARTIN   AN H GNM 53
ROBOTS AND CHANGELINGS   DEL REY, LESTER   AC   BAL 57
ROBOTS HAVE NO TAILS   PADGETT, LEWIS   AC H GNM 52
ROD SERLING'S THE TWILIGHT ZONE
                                SERLING, ROD   OC H GRS 63
ROD SERLING'S THE TWILIGHT ZONE (CHILLING STORIES FROM)
                                SERLING, ROD   OC   TMP 65 08
ROD SERLING'S TRIPLE W: WITCHES, WARLOCKS AND WEREWOLVES
                                SERLING, ROD   AN   BAN 63 05
ROD SERLING'S TWILIGHT ZONE REVISITED
                                SERLING, ROD   OC H GRS 64
ROGUE SHIP   VAN VOGT, A. E.   NO H DBL 65
ROLLERBALL   HARRISON, WILLIAM   AC   WPB 75 07
ROOTS OF EVIL, THE   PARRY, MICHEL   AN H TAP 76
ROSE FOR ECCLESIASTES, A   ZELAZNY, ROGER   AC H HDV 69
    SEE "FOUR FOR TOMORROW"
ROSE, THE   HARNESS, CHARLES L.   AC   CPT 66
RUINS OF EARTH, THE   DISCH, THOMAS M.   AN H PUT 71
RULE OF THE DOOR AND OTHER FANCIFUL REGULATIONS
                                BIGGLE, LLOYD JR.   AC H DBL 67
    ALSO AS "(OUT OF) THE SILENT SKY"
RULERS OF MEN   SANTESSON, HANS S.   AN   PYR 65
RUN TO STARLIGHT, SPORTS THROUGH SCIENCE FICTION
                                GREENBERG/OLANDER/&   AN H DCT 75
RUSSIAN SCIENCE FICTION   MAGIDOFF, ROBERT   AN H NYU 64
RUSSIAN SCIENCE FICTION, 1968   MAGIDOFF, ROBERT   AN H NYU 68
RUSSIAN SCIENCE FICTION, 1969   MAGIDOFF, ROBERT   AN H NYU 69
RX FOR TOMORROW   NOURSE, ALAN E.   AC H MCK 71
S IS FOR SPACE   BRADBURY, RAY   AC H DBL 66 08
S.O.S. FROM THREE WORLDS   LEINSTER, MURRAY   AC   ACE 66
SAGITTARIUS   RUSSELL, RAY   AC   PBP 71
SAINT'S CHOICE OF IMPOSSIBLE CRIME, THE
                                CHARTERIS, LESLIE   AN   BNC 45
SALIVA TREE AND OTHER STRANGE GROWTHS, THE
                                ALDISS, BRIAN W.   AC H FAB 66
SAME TO YOU DOUBLED AND OTHER STORIES, THE
                                SHECKLEY, ROBERT   AC   PAN 74
    SEE "CAN YOU FEEL ANYTHING WHEN I DO THIS?"
SANDS OF MARS AND OTHER STORIES, THE
                                ANONYMOUS   AN   JBL 58
SANTANA MORNING AND OTHER STORIES
                                DOLAN, MIKE   OC   POW 70
SARDONICUS AND OTHER STORIES   RUSSELL, RAY   AC   BAL 61
SATAN'S PETS   GHIDALIA, VIC   AN   MAN 72
SATURDAY EVENING POST FANTASY STORIES, THE
                                FLES, BARTHOLD   AN   AVN 51 10
SAVAGE PELLUCIDAR   BURROUGHS, EDGAR R.   NO H CAN 63
SAVING WORLDS   ELWOOD & KIDD   OA H DBL 73
    ALSO AS "THE WOUNDED PLANET"
SCATTER OF STARDUST, A   TUBB, E. C.   DC   ACE 72
SCHOOL AND SOCIETY THROUGH SCIENCE FICTION
                                OLANDER/GREENBERG/&   AN L RAN 74
SCIENCE AGAINST MAN   CHEETHAM, ANTHONY   OA   AVN 70 12
SCIENCE AND SORCERY   FORD, GARRET   AN H FPB 53
SCIENCE FACT/FICTION   FARRELL/GAGE/&   AN L SFC 74
SCIENCE FICTION   BRODKIN & PEARSON   AN L MCD 73
SCIENCE FICTION   BURTON, S. H.   AN   LNG 67
SCIENCE FICTION ADVENTURES FROM WAY OUT
                                ELWOOD, ROGER   OA L WHT 74
SCIENCE FICTION ADVENTURES IN DIMENSION
                                CONKLIN, GROFF   AN H VPR 53
    IN ENGLAND AS "ADVENTURES IN DIMENSION" (13 OF 23)
SCIENCE FICTION ADVENTURES IN DIMENSION (12 OF 23)
                                CONKLIN, GROFF   AN   BKM 65 03
SCIENCE FICTION ADVENTURES IN MUTATION
                                CONKLIN, GROFF   AN H VPR 55
SCIENCE FICTION ADVENTURES IN MUTATION (14 OF 20)
                                CONKLIN, GROFF   AN   BKM 65 06
SCIENCE FICTION AND READER'S GUIDE
                                BARROWS, MARJORIE   AN H SPN 54
    VOLUME 16 OF "THE CHILDREN'S HOUR" SET
SCIENCE FICTION ARGOSY, A   KNIGHT, DAMON   AN H SAS 72
SCIENCE FICTION BESTIARY, THE   SILVERBERG, ROBERT   AN H NEL 71
SCIENCE FICTION BY GASLIGHT   MOSKOWITZ, SAM   AN H WOR 68
    A HISTORY AND ANTHOLOGY OF SCIENCE FICTION
    IN THE POPULAR MAGAZINES 1891 TO 1911
SCIENCE FICTION DISCOVERIES   POHL, C. & F.   OA   BAN 76 08
SCIENCE FICTION EMPHASIS NO. 1 GERROLD, DAVID   OA   BAL 74 05
SCIENCE FICTION FOR PEOPLE WHO HATE SCIENCE FICTION
                                CARR, TERRY   AN H DBL 66
SCIENCE FICTION GALAXY, THE   CONKLIN, GROFF   AN   PMA 50

SCIENCE FICTION HALL OF FAME VOLUME 1
                                SILVERBERG, ROBERT   AN H DBL 70
SCIENCE FICTION HALL OF FAME VOLUME 2A
                                BOVA, BEN   AN H DBL 73
SCIENCE FICTION HALL OF FAME VOLUME 2B
                                BOVA, BEN   AN H DBL 73
SCIENCE FICTION HORIZONS NO. 1 BOARDMAN, TOM JR.   AN H DOB 68
SCIENCE FICTION INVENTIONS   KNIGHT, DAMON   AN   LAN 67
SCIENCE FICTION NOVELLAS   HARRISON & MCNELLY   AN L SCB 75
SCIENCE FICTION ODDITIES   CONKLIN, GROFF   AN   BKM 66 11
SCIENCE FICTION OF FRANK R. STOCKTON, THE
                                STOCKTON, FRANK R.   AC H GRG 76 06
SCIENCE FICTION OF JACK LONDON, THE
                                LONDON, JACK   AC H GRG 75
SCIENCE FICTION OF THE 30'S   KNIGHT, DAMON   AN H BML 75
SCIENCE FICTION OMNIBUS   BLEILER & DIKTY   AN H GCB 52 01
SCIENCE FICTION OMNIBUS   CONKLIN, GROFF   AN   BRK 56 08
    STORIES FROM "OMNIBUS OF SCIENCE FICTION"
SCIENCE FICTION OMNIBUS ON POLLUTION, A
                                ANONYMOUS   AN H SID 71
SCIENCE FICTION ROLL OF HONOR, THE
                                POHL, FREDERIK   AN H RDM 75
SCIENCE FICTION SHOWCASE   KORNBLUTH, MARY   AN H DBL 59
    CURTIS PB EDITION OMITS STORY "MED SERVICE"
SCIENCE FICTION SPECIAL   1   ANONYMOUS   AN H SID 70 08
SCIENCE FICTION SPECIAL   3   ANONYMOUS   AN H SID 71
SCIENCE FICTION SPECIAL   4   ANONYMOUS   AN H SID 71
SCIENCE FICTION SPECIAL   5   ANONYMOUS   AN H SID 71 07
SCIENCE FICTION SPECIAL   6   ANONYMOUS   AN H SID 73
SCIENCE FICTION SPECIAL   7   ANONYMOUS   AN H SID
SCIENCE FICTION SPECIAL   8   ANONYMOUS   AN H SID 73
SCIENCE FICTION STORIES   BRADLEY, JOHANNA   AN H YPB 75
SCIENCE FICTION STORIES   ELAM, RICHARD M. JR.   AC   LPB 64 12
    SEE "TEEN-AGE SCIENCE FICTION STORIES"
SCIENCE FICTION SUBTREASURY, THE
                                TUCKER, WILSON   AC H RIN 54 09
    ALSO AS "TIME: X"
SCIENCE FICTION TALES   ELWOOD, ROGER   OA H RAN 73
SCIENCE FICTION TERROR TALES   CONKLIN, GROFF   AN H GNM 55 01
SCIENCE FICTION THINKING MACHINES
                                CONKLIN, GROFF   AN H VPR 54
SCIENCE FICTION THINKING MACHINES (SELECTIONS FROM)
                                CONKLIN, GROFF   AN   BAN 55 08
SCIENCE FICTION THROUGH THE AGES 1
                                EVANS, I. O.   AN   PTH 66
SCIENCE FICTION THROUGH THE AGES 2
                                EVANS, I. O.   AN   PTH 66
SCIENCE FICTION WORLDS OF FORREST J. ACKERMAN & FRIENDS
                                ACKERMAN, FORREST J.   AC   POW 69 04
SCIENCE FICTION: THE FUTURE   ALLEN, DICK   AN H HBJ 71
SCIENCE FICTION: THE GREAT YEARS
                                POHL, C. & F.   AN   ACE 73 01
SCIENCE FICTION: THE GREAT YEARS, VOL. II
                                POHL, C. & F.   AN   ACE 76
SCIENCE IN FICTION   BAYLISS, A.E. & J.C. AN UOL 57
SCIENCE-FANTASY QUINTETTE   CRAWFORD, WILLIAM L. AN H FPB 53
SCIENCE-FICTION CARNIVAL   BROWN, F. & REYNOLDS AN H SHS 53 12
SCIENCE-FICTION CARNIVAL (11 OF 13)
                                BROWN, F. & REYNOLDS AN   BAN 57 06
SCIENCE-FICTIONAL SHERLOCK HOLMES, THE
                                COUNCIL OF FOUR   AN   60
SEA OF SPACE, A   NOLAN, WILLIAM F.   AN   BAN 70 05
SEAGULLS UNDER GLASS AND OTHER STORIES
                                TATE, PETER   AC H DBL 75
SECOND ASTOUNDING SCIENCE FICTION ANTHOLOGY, THE
                                CAMPBELL, JOHN W. JR AN H GRY 54
SECOND ASTOUNDING SCIENCE FICTION ANTHOLOGY, THE (PB)
                                CAMPBELL, JOHN W. JR AN   FSP 65
SECOND AVON FANTASY READER, THE
                                WOLLHEIM &ERNSBERGER AN   AVN 69
SECOND BOOK OF FRITZ LEIBER, THE
                                LEIBER, FRITZ   AC   DAW 75 09
SECOND FOUNDATION   ASIMOV, ISAAC   NO H GNM 53
    ALSO IN "THE FOUNDATION TRILOGY"
SECOND GALAXY READER OF SCIENCE FICTION
                                GOLD, H. L.   AN H CRN 54
    ENGLISH DERIVATIVE ANTHOLOGY "GALAXY SCIENCE FICTION OMNIBUS"
SECOND IF READER OF SCIENCE FICTION, THE
                                POHL, FREDERIK   AN H DBL 68
SECOND ORBIT   DOHERTY, G. D.   AN H MUR 65
SECOND PACIFIC BOOK OF SCIENCE FICTION, THE
                                BAXTER, JOHN   AN H AAR 71
SECOND WORLD OF IF, THE   QUINN & WULFF   AN D QUI 68
SECRET SONGS, THE   LEIBER, FRITZ   AC H HDV 68
SEEDLING STARS, THE   BLISH, JAMES   NO H GNM 56
SEEDS OF TIME, THE   WYNDHAM, JOHN   AC H JOS 56
SEETEE SHIP   STEWART, WILL   AC H GNM 51
SEETEE SHIP/SEETEE SHOCK   WILLIAMSON, JACK   AC   LAN
SENSE OF WONDER, A   MOSKOWITZ, SAM   AN H SID 67
    SEE "THREE STORIES"
SEVEN COME INFINITY   CONKLIN, GROFF   AN   FGM 66
SEVEN FAMOUS NOVELS BY H. G. WELLS
                                WELLS, H. G.   AC H KNP 34
    ALSO AS "SEVEN SCIENCE FICTION NOVELS"
SEVEN SCIENCE FICTION NOVELS   WELLS, H. G.   AC H DOV 50
    SEE "SEVEN FAMOUS NOVELS BY H. G. WELLS"
SEVEN SEXES, THE   TENN, WILLIAM   AC   BAL 68 06
SEVEN STEPS TO THE ARBITER   HUBBARD, L. RON   AC   MJR 75
    SEE "THE KINGSLAYER"
SEVEN TRIPS THROUGH TIME AND SPACE
                                CONKLIN, GROFF   AN   FGM 68
SEVENTH GALAXY READER, THE   POHL, FREDERIK   AN H DBL 64
SF: AUTHORS' CHOICE   HARRISON, HARRY   AN   BKM 68 06
    IN ENGLAND AS "BACKDROP OF STARS"
SF: AUTHORS' CHOICE 2   HARRISON, HARRY   AN   BKM 70 05
SF: AUTHORS' CHOICE 3   HARRISON, HARRY   AN H PUT 71

SF: AUTHORS' CHOICE 4   STRANGE DOINGS

SF: AUTHORS' CHOICE 4   HARRISON, HARRY   AN H PUT 74
SF: THE BEST OF THE BEST   MERRIL, JUDITH   AN H DCT 67
SF: THE YEAR'S GREATEST SCIENCE FICTION AND FANTASY
                               MERRIL, JUDITH   AN H GNM 56
SF: THE YEAR'S GREATEST SCIENCE-FICTION AND FANTASY, FOURTH
ANNUAL VOLUME   MERRIL, JUDITH   AN   DEL 59 06
    SEE "SF:59"
SF: THE YEAR'S GREATEST SCIENCE-FICTION AND FANTASY, SECOND
ANNUAL VOLUME   MERRIL, JUDITH   AN   DEL 57 06
    SEE "SF:57"
SF: THE YEAR'S GREATEST SCIENCE-FICTION AND FANTASY, THIRD
ANNUAL VOLUME   MERRIL, JUDITH   AN   DEL 58 07
    SEE "SF:58"
SF:57, THE YEAR'S GREATEST SCIENCE FICTION AND FANTASY
                               MERRIL, JUDITH   AN H GNM 57
SF:58, THE YEAR'S GREATEST SCIENCE FICTION AND FANTASY
                               MERRIL, JUDITH   AN H GNM 58
SF:59, THE YEAR'S GREATEST SCIENCE FICTION AND FANTASY
                               MERRIL, JUDITH   AN H GNM 59
SF12   MERRIL, JUDITH   AN H DCT 68
SHADOW OF TOMORROW   POHL, FREDERIK   AN H DBL 53
SHADOW PLAY   BEAUMONT, CHARLES   AC   PTH 64
    SEE "THE HUNGER AND OTHER STORIES"
SHADOWS WITH EYES   LEIBER, FRITZ   AC   BAL 62 03
SHAMBLEAU AND OTHERS   MOORE, C. L.   AC H GNM 53
    BRITISH CONSUL EDITION OMITS "JIREL MEETS MAGIC"
SHAMBLEAU AND OTHERS (3 OF 7) MOORE, C. L.   AC   GAN 58 31
SHANADU   BRINEY, ROBERT E.   OA   SSR 53 11
SHAPE OF SPACE, THE   NIVEN, LARRY   AC   BAL 69 09
SHAPE OF THINGS, THE   KNIGHT, DAMON   AN   POP 67
SHARDS OF SPACE   SHECKLEY, ROBERT   AC   BAN 62 07
SHIP WHO SANG, THE   MCCAFFREY, ANNE   AC H WKR 69
SHIPS TO THE STARS   LEIBER, FRITZ   DC   ACE 64
SHOCK II   MATHESON, RICHARD   AC   DEL 64 10
SHOCK III   MATHESON, RICHARD   AC   DEL 66 03
SHOCK WAVES   MATHESON, RICHARD   AC   DEL 70 10
SHOCK!   MATHESON, RICHARD   AC   DEL 61 06
SHOCKING THING, A   KNIGHT, DAMON   AN   PKT 74 11
SHORES BENEATH, THE   SALLIS, JAMES   AN   AVN 71 08
SHORES OF SPACE, THE   MATHESON, RICHARD   AC   BAN 57 02
SHORES OF TOMORROW, THE   SILVERBERG, ROBERT   AC H NEL 76
SHORT STORIES OF H. G. WELLS, THE
                               WELLS, H. G.   AC H BEN 27
SHOT IN THE DARK   MERRIL, JUDITH   AN   BAN 50
SHOWCASE   ELWOOD, ROGER   OA H HRP 73
SHROUDED PLANET, THE   RANDALL, ROBERT   AC H GNM 58
SIDEWISE IN TIME   LEINSTER, MURRAY   AC H SHS 50
SIGNS AND WONDERS   ELWOOD, ROGER   OA H REV 72
SILENT BULLET, THE   REEVE, ARTHUR B.   AC H DOM 12
SILKIE, THE   VAN VOGT, A. E.   NO   ACE 69
SILVER LOCUSTS, THE   BRADBURY, RAY   AC H HDV 51
    SEE "THE MARTIAN CHRONICLES", OMITS STORY "USHER II"
SINISTER RESEARCHES OF C. P. RANSOM, THE
                               NEARING, H. JR.   AC H DBL 54
SIX GREAT SHORT SCIENCE FICTION NOVELS
                               CONKLIN, GROFF   AN   DEL 60 11
SIX SCIENCE FICTION PLAYS   ELWOOD, ROGER   AN   WSP 76 01
SIX WORLDS YONDER   RUSSELL, ERIC FRANK   DC   ACE 58
SIXTH GALAXY READER, THE   GOLD, H. L.   AN H DBL 62
SKULL OF THE MARQUIS DE SADE, THE
                               BLOCH, ROBERT   AC   PYR 65 10
SMALL ASSASSIN, THE   BRADBURY, RAY   AC   ACB 62
SMALL CHANGES   CLEMENT, HAL   AC H DBL 69
    ALSO AS "SPACE LASH"
SO BRIGHT THE VISION   SIMAK, CLIFFORD D.   DC   ACE 68
SO CLOSE TO HOME   BLISH, JAMES   AC   BAL 61 02
SOCIAL PROBLEMS THROUGH SCIENCE FICTION
                               GREENBERG/MILSTEAD/& AN L SMP 75
SOCIOLOGY THROUGH SCIENCE FICTION
                               MILSTEAD/GREENBERG/& AN H SMP 74
SOFT COME THE DRAGONS   KOONTZ, DEAN R.   DC   ACE 70
SOME DREAMS ARE NIGHTMARES   GUNN, JAMES E.   AC H SCB 74
SOMETIME, NEVER   ANONYMOUS   OA   BAL 56
SOMEWHERE A VOICE   RUSSELL, ERIC FRANK   AC H DOB 65
SONG FOR LYA, A   MARTIN, GEORGE R. R. AC   AVN 76 02
SONGS OF STARS AND SHADOWS   MARTIN, GEORGE R. R. AC   PKT 77 07
SOULS IN METAL   ASHLEY, MICHAEL   AN H SMP 77
SOVIET SCIENCE FICTION   ANONYMOUS   AN   CLB 62
    ALSO AS "A VISITOR FROM OUTER SPACE"
SPACE   1   DAVIS, RICHARD   OA H ABS 73 06
SPACE   2   DAVIS, RICHARD   OA H ABS 74 01
SPACE ADVENTURES   FURMAN, A. L.   AN   LPB 75 01
    SEE "TEEN-AGE SPACE ADVENTURES"
SPACE BEYOND, THE   CAMPBELL, JOHN W. JR OC   PYR 76 06
SPACE BY THE TAIL   BIXBY, JEROME   AC   BAL 64
SPACE FRONTIERS, THE   VERNON, ROGER LEE   AC   SIG 55 08
SPACE HAWK   GILMORE, ANTHONY   AC H GBG 52
SPACE LASH   CLEMENT, HAL   AC   DEL 69 12
    SEE "SMALL CHANGES"
SPACE LORDS   SMITH, CORDWAINER   AC   PYR 65 05
SPACE MAGICIANS, THE   NORTON & MOSKOWITZ   AN   PYR 71 01
SPACE ODYSSEYS   ALDISS, BRIAN W.   AN H WEI 75
SPACE ON MY HANDS   BROWN, FREDRIC   AC H SHS 51 07
SPACE OPERA   ALDISS, BRIAN W.   AN H WEI 74
SPACE PIONEERS   NORTON, ANDRE   AN H WOR 54
SPACE POLICE   NORTON, ANDRE   AN H WOR 56
SPACE SCAVENGERS, THE   CARTMILL, CLEVE   NO   MAJ 75
SPACE SERVICE   NORTON, ANDRE   AN H WOR 53
SPACE STATION 42 AND OTHER STORIES
                               ANONYMOUS   AN   JBL 58
SPACE WAR   JONES, NEIL R.   AC   ACE 67
SPACE-TIME JOURNAL, THE   MERRIL, JUDITH   AN   PTH 72
    21 STORIES FROM "ENGLAND SWINGS SF"
SPACE, SPACE, SPACE   SLOANE, WILLIAM   AN H WAT 53
SPACE, TIME & CRIME   DEFORD, MIRIAM ALLEN AN   PBK 64 11
SPACE, TIME AND NATHANIEL   ALDISS, BRIAN W.   AC H FAB 57

    ALSO IN "BRIAN ALDISS OMNIBUS II"
SPECIAL WONDER   MCCOMAS, J. FRANCIS   AN H RDM 70
    THE ANTHONY BOUCHER MEMORIAL ANTHOLOGY OF FANTASY AND
    SCIENCE FICTION
SPECTRUM   AMIS & CONQUEST   AN H HBW 62
SPECTRUM   (7 OF 10)   AMIS & CONQUEST   AN   BKM 63 03
SPECTRUM 2   AMIS & CONQUEST   AN H HBW 63
SPECTRUM 3   AMIS & CONQUEST   AN H HBW 64
SPECTRUM 4   AMIS & CONQUEST   AN H HBW 65
SPECTRUM 5   AMIS & CONQUEST   AN H HBW 67
SPECTRUM OF WORLDS, A   CLARESON, THOMAS D.   AN H DBL 72
SPECULATIONS   SANDERS, THOMAS E.   AN L GLN 73
SPELL OF SEVEN, THE   DE CAMP, L. SPRAGUE   AN   PYR 65 06
SPRAGUE DE CAMP'S NEW ANTHOLOGY
                               DE CAMP, L. SPRAGUE   AC H HML 53
SQUARE ROOT OF MAN, THE   TENN, WILLIAM   AC   BAL 68 06
STAR FOURTEEN   POHL, FREDERIK   AN H WHW 66
    SEE "STAR OF STARS"
STAR FOX, THE   ANDERSON, POUL   AC H DBL 65
STAR LIGHT, STAR BRIGHT   BESTER, ALFRED   AC H BKP 76
    ALSO IN "STARLIGHT"
STAR OF STARS   POHL, FREDERIK   AN   BAL 60
    IN ENGLAND AS "STAR FOURTEEN"
STAR ROAD, THE   DICKSON, GORDON R.   AC H DBL 73
STAR SCIENCE FICTION STORIES   POHL, FREDERIK   OA H BAL 53
STAR SCIENCE FICTION STORIES NO. 2
                               POHL, FREDERIK   OA H BAL 53
STAR SCIENCE FICTION STORIES NO. 3
                               POHL, FREDERIK   OA H BAL 54
STAR SCIENCE FICTION STORIES NO. 4
                               POHL, FREDERIK   OA   BAL 58
STAR SCIENCE FICTION STORIES NO. 5
                               POHL, FREDERIK   OA   BAL 59
STAR SCIENCE FICTION STORIES NO. 6
                               POHL, FREDERIK   OA   BAL 59
STAR SHINE   BROWN, FREDRIC   AC   BAN 56 02
    SEE "ANGELS AND SPACESHIPS"
STAR SHORT NOVELS   POHL, FREDERIK   OA   BAL 54 10
STAR TREK   BLISH, JAMES   OC   BAN 67
    ALSO IN "THE STAR TREK READER II"
STAR TREK   2   BLISH, JAMES   OC   BAN 68
    ALSO IN "THE STAR TREK READER"
STAR TREK   3   BLISH, JAMES   OC   BAN 69 04
    ALSO IN "THE STAR TREK READER"
STAR TREK   4   BLISH, JAMES   OC   BAN 71 07
    ALSO IN "THE STAR TREK READER II"
STAR TREK   5   BLISH, JAMES   OC   BAN 72 02
STAR TREK   6   BLISH, JAMES   OC   BAN 72 04
STAR TREK   7   BLISH, JAMES   OC   BAN 72 07
STAR TREK   8   BLISH, JAMES   OC   BAN 72 11
    ALSO IN "THE STAR TREK READER"
STAR TREK   9   BLISH, JAMES   OC   BAN 73 08
    ALSO IN "THE STAR TREK READER II"
STAR TREK 10   BLISH, JAMES   OC   BAN 74 02
STAR TREK 11   BLISH, JAMES   OC   BAN 75 04
STAR TREK LOG FIVE   FOSTER, ALAN DEAN   OC   BAL 75 08
STAR TREK LOG FOUR   FOSTER, ALAN DEAN   OC   BAL 75 03
STAR TREK LOG ONE   FOSTER, ALAN DEAN   OC   BAL 74 06
STAR TREK LOG SIX   FOSTER, ALAN DEAN   OC   BAL 76 03
STAR TREK LOG THREE   FOSTER, ALAN DEAN   OC   BAL 75 01
STAR TREK LOG TWO   FOSTER, ALAN DEAN   OC   BAL 74 09
STAR TREK READER II, THE   BLISH, JAMES   AC H DUT 77
STAR TREK READER, THE   BLISH, JAMES   AC H DUT 76
STAR TREK: THE NEW VOYAGES   MARSHAK, S&CULBREATH OA   BAN 76 03
STARBURST   BESTER, ALFRED   AC   SIG 58
STARDREAMER   SMITH, CORDWAINER   AC   BEA 71 08
STARDRIFT AND OTHER FANTASTIC FLOTSAM
                               PETAJA, EMIL   AC H FPB 71
STARDUST VOYAGES, THE   TALL, STEPHEN   AC   BKM 75 10
STARLIGHT   BESTER, ALFRED   AC H NDB 76
STARLIT CORRIDOR, THE   MANSFIELD, ROGER   AN H PGM 67
STARS AND UNDER, THE   CRISPIN, EDMUND   AN H FAB 68
STARS AROUND US, THE   HOSKINS, ROBERT   AN   SIG 70 03
STARSHADOWS   SARGENT, PAMELA   AC   ACE 77 06
STARSHINE   STURGEON, THEODORE   AC   PYR 66 12
STARSWARM   ALDISS, BRIAN W.   AC   SIG 64 01
STARTLING STORIES   MINES, SAMUEL   AN H CAS 54
    SEE "THE BEST FROM STARTLING STORIES"
STATION IN SPACE   GUNN, JAMES E.   AC   BAN 58
STELLAR MISSILES, THE   REPP, ED EARL   AC H FPB 49
STELLAR SHORT NOVELS   DEL REY, JUDY-LYNN   OA   BAL 76 10
STELLAR 1   DEL REY, JUDY-LYNN   OA   BAL 74 09
STELLAR 2   DEL REY, JUDY-LYNN   OA   BAL 76 02
STEP OUTSIDE YOUR MIND   CARR, TERRY   AC H DOB 69
    SEE "NEW WORLDS OF FANTASY"
STOLEN BACILLUS AND OTHER INCIDENTS, THE
                               WELLS, H. G.   AC H MTH 95
STOPWATCH   HAY, GEORGE   OA H NEL 74 10
STORE OF INFINITY   SHECKLEY, ROBERT   AC   BAN 60 11
STORIES   YEFREMOV, IVAN   AC H FLP 54
STORIES FOR TOMORROW   SLOANE, WILLIAM   AN H FKW 54 06
STORIES FOR TOMORROW (BRITISH) SLOANE, WILLIAM   AN H EYR 55
STORIES FROM SCIENCE FICTION   DOHERTY, G. D.   AN H NLS 66
STORIES FROM THE HUGO WINNERS VOLUME 2
                               ASIMOV, ISAAC   AN   FCR 73 08
    FIRST 6 STORIES
STORIES FROM THE TWILIGHT ZONE SERLING, ROD   OC   BAN 60 04
STORIES OF SCIENTIFIC IMAGINATION
                               GALLANT, JOSEPH   AN   OXF 54
STRANGE ADVENTURES IN SCIENCE FICTION
                               CONKLIN, GROFF   AN H GRY 54
    STORIES FROM "OMNIBUS OF SCIENCE FICTION"
STRANGE BEASTS AND UNNATURAL MONSTERS
                               STERN, PHILIP VAN D. AN   FCR 68 08
STRANGE BED FELLOWS   SCORTIA, THOMAS N.   AN H RDM 72
STRANGE DOINGS   LAFFERTY, R. A.   AC H SCB 72

STRANGE ECSTASIES	PARRY, MICHEL	AN	PIN 74 10
STRANGE ENCOUNTERS	BISCHOFF, DAVID	OA H	RTR 77
STRANGE GIFTS	SILVERBERG, ROBERT	AN H	NEL 75
STRANGE GODS	ELWOOD, ROGER	OA	PKT 74 09
STRANGE HARVEST	WANDREI, DONALD	AC H	ARK 65
STRANGE LOVE STORIES	ANONYMOUS	AN	UTP 46
STRANGE PORTS OF CALL	DERLETH, AUGUST	AN H	PEL 48
STRANGE PORTS OF CALL (10 OF 20)			
	DERLETH, AUGUST	AN	BRK 58
STRANGE RELATIONS	FARMER, PHILIP JOSE	AC	BAL 60
STRANGE SEAS AND SHORES	DAVIDSON, AVRAM	AC H	DBL 71
STRANGE SIGNPOSTS	ELWOOD & MOSKOWITZ	AN H	HRW 66
STRANGE TOMORROWS	HOSKINS, ROBERT	AN	LAN 72
STRANGE TRAVELS IN SCIENCE FICTION			
	CONKLIN, GROFF	AN H	GRY 53
STORIES FROM "OMNIBUS OF SCIENCE FICTION"			
STRANGE WORLD OF SCIENCE FICTION			
	ANONYMOUS	OA	NLB 75 10
STRANGE WORLDS	FARLEY, RALPH MILNE	AC H	FPB 52
STRANGER THAN YOU THINK	EDMONDSON, G. C.	DC	ACE 65
STRANGERS FROM EARTH	ANDERSON, POUL	AC	BAL 61 05
STRANGERS IN THE UNIVERSE	SIMAK, CLIFFORD D.	AC H	SAS 56
STRANGERS IN THE UNIVERSE (BRITISH)			
	SIMAK, CLIFFORD D.	AC H	FAB 58
STRANGERS IN THE UNIVERSE (7 OF 11)			
	SIMAK, CLIFFORD D.	AC	BKM 57 09
STURGEON IN ORBIT	STURGEON, THEODORE	AC	PYR 64 02
STURGEON IS ALIVE AND WELL...	STURGEON, THEODORE	AC H	PUT 71
SUN DESTROYERS, THE	ROCKLYNNE, ROSS	DC	ACE 73 03
SUNDANCE AND OTHER SCIENCE FICTION STORIES			
	SILVERBERG, ROBERT	AC H	NEL 74
SUNLESS WORLD, THE	JONES, NEIL R.	AC	ACE 67
SUNRISE ON MERCURY AND OTHER SCIENCE FICTION STORIES			
	SILVERBERG, ROBERT	OA L	NDB 75
SUPER SCIENCE STORIES	ELAM, RICHARD M. JR.	AC	LPB 67 02
SEE "TEEN-AGE SUPER SCIENCE STORIES"			
SUPERNATURAL READER, THE	CONKLIN, G&L.	AN H	LIP 53
SURVIVAL FROM INFINITY	ELWOOD, ROGER	OA H	WAT 74
SURVIVAL PRINTOUT	TOTAL EFFECT	AN	VNT 73
SURVIVAL SHIP AND OTHER STORIES			
	MERRIL, JUDITH	AC	KAK 74
SURVIVOR AND OTHER STORIES, THE			
	LOVECRAFT & DERLETH	AC H	ARK 57
SWORD OF CONAN, THE	HOWARD, ROBERT E.	AC H	GNM 55
SWORDSMEN IN THE SKY	WOLLHEIM, DONALD A.	AN	ACE 64
TALES AND STORIES	SHELLEY, MARY W.	AC H	GRG 75
REPRINT OF 1891 EDITION PUBLISHED BY WM. PATERSON & CO, LONDON			
TALES BEYOND TIME	DE CAMP, L. S.&C.	AN H	LOT 73
TALES FROM GAVAGAN'S BAR	DE CAMP, L. S.&PRATT	AC H	TWN 53
TALES FROM THE GALAXIES	WILLIAMS-ELLIS& P.	AN	PPL 73
TALES FROM THE WHITE HART	CLARKE, ARTHUR C.	AC	BAL 57
TALES FROM UNDERWOOD	KELLER, DAVID H. MD.	AC H	PEL 52
TALES IN A JUGULAR VEIN	BLOCH, ROBERT	AC	PYR 65 02
TALES OF CONAN	HOWARD, R. & DE CAMP	AC H	GNM 55
TALES OF GOOSEFLESH AND LAUGHTER			
	WYNDHAM, JOHN	AC	BAL 56 12
TALES OF KNOWN SPACE: THE UNIVERSE OF LARRY NIVEN			
	NIVEN, LARRY	AC	BAL 75 08
TALES OF OUTER SPACE	WOLLHEIM, DONALD A.	DA	ACE 54
TALES OF SCIENCE AND SORCERY	SMITH, CLARK ASHTON	AC H	ARK 64
TALES OF SCIENCE FICTION	BALL, BRIAN N.	AN H	HML 64
TALES OF SPACE AND TIME	WELLS, H. G.	AC H	HPR 99
TALES OF TEN WORLDS	CLARKE, ARTHUR C.	AC H	HBW 62
TALES OF TERROR FROM OUTER SPACE			
	CHETWYND-HAYES, R.	AN	FON 75 05
TALES OF THE FLYING MOUNTAINS	ANDERSON, POUL	AC H	MAC 70
TALES OF THREE PLANETS	BURROUGHS, EDGAR R.	AC H	CAN 64
TALES OF TIME AND SPACE	OLNEY, ROSS R.	AN H	WPC 69
TEEN-AGE OUTER SPACE STORIES	FURMAN, A. L.	AN H	LPB 62
ALSO AS "OUTER SPACE STORIES"			
TEEN-AGE SCIENCE FICTION STORIES			
	ELAM, RICHARD M. JR.	AC H	LPB 52
ALSO AS "YOUNG READERS SCIENCE FICTION STORIES" AND			
"SCIENCE FICTION STORIES"			
TEEN-AGE SPACE ADVENTURES	FURMAN, A. L.	AN	LPB 72
ALSO AS "SPACE ADVENTURES"			
TEEN-AGE SUPER SCIENCE STORIES	ELAM, RICHARD M. JR.	AC H	LPB 58
ALSO AS "SUPER SCIENCE STORIES"			
TELZEY TOY, THE	SCHMITZ, JAMES H.	NO	DAW 73 12
TEN FROM TOMORROW	TUBB, E. C.	AC H	HDV 66
TEN THOUSAND LIGHT-YEARS FROM HOME			
	TIPTREE, JAMES JR.	AC	ACE 73 07
TEN TOMORROWS	ELWOOD, ROGER	OA	FGM 73 09
TENTH GALAXY READER, THE	POHL, FREDERIK	AN H	DBL 67
ALSO AS "DOOR TO ANYWHERE"			
TERMINAL BEACH (AMERICAN VERSION)			
	BALLARD, J. G.	AC	BKM 64 06
TERMINAL BEACH (BRITISH VERSION)			
	BALLARD, J. G.	AC H	GOL 64 06
TERROR IN THE MODERN VEIN	WOLLHEIM, DONALD A.	AN H	HAN 55 04
ENGLISH DERIVATIVE ANTHOLOGY "MORE TERROR IN THE MODERN VEIN"			
TERROR IN THE MODERN VEIN (BRITISH PB)			
	WOLLHEIM, DONALD A.	AN	DIG 61
THEMES IN SCIENCE FICTION	KELLEY, LEO P.	AN L	MGH 72
A JOURNEY INTO WONDER			
THING AND OTHER STORIES, THE	CAMPBELL, JOHN W. JR	AC	KEM 52
SEE "WHO GOES THERE?"			
THING FROM OUTER SPACE, THE	CAMPBELL, JOHN W. JR	AC	TDM 66
SEE "WHO GOES THERE?"			
THINGS	HOWARD, IVAN	AN	BEL 64 02
THIRD EYE, THE	COGSWELL, THEODORE R	AC	BEL 68 09
THIRD FROM THE SUN	MATHESON, RICHARD	AC	BAN 55 02
SELECTIONS FROM "BORN OF MAN AND WOMAN"			
THIRD GALAXY READER, THE	GOLD, H. L.	AN H	DBL 58
THIRD LEVEL, THE	FINNEY, JACK	AC H	RIN 57
IN ENGLAND AS "THE CLOCK OF TIME"			
THIRST QUENCHERS, THE	RAPHAEL, RICK	AC H	GOL 65
THIRTEEN O'CLOCK AND OTHER ZERO HOURS			
	KORNBLUTH, C. M.	AC	DEL 70
CECIL CORWIN STORIES, EDITED BY JAMES BLISH			
THIRTY STRANGE STORIES	WELLS, H. G.	AC H	ANL 97
THIS ISLAND EARTH	JONES, RAYMOND F.	NO H	SHS 52
THIS SIDE OF INFINITY	CARR, TERRY	AN	ACE 72 09
THOSE IDIOTS FROM EARTH	WILSON, RICHARD	AC	BAL 57
THOSE WHO CAN: A SCIENCE FICTION READER			
	WILSON, ROBIN SCOTT	AN	MNT 73 09
THREADS OF TIME	SILVERBERG, ROBERT	OA H	NDB 74
THREE BY HEINLEIN	HEINLEIN, ROBERT A.	AC H	DBL 51
IN ENGLAND AS "A HEINLEIN TRIAD"			
THREE FOR TOMORROW	SILVERBERG, ROBERT	OA H	MDT 69
THREE MARTIAN NOVELS	BURROUGHS, EDGAR R.	AC L	DOV 62
THREE NOVELS	KNIGHT, DAMON	AC H	DBL 67
THREE SCIENCE FICTION NOVELS	BURROUGHS, EDGAR R.	AC L	DOV 63
THREE SCIENCE FICTION NOVELS	TAINE, JOHN	AC L	DOV 64
THREE STORIES	MOSKOWITZ, SAM	AN H	DBL 67
ALSO AS "THE MOON ERA" AND "A SENSE OF WONDER"			
THREE TIMES INFINITY	MARGULIES, LEO	AN	GMB 58
THREE TO DORSAI!	DICKSON, GORDON R.	AC H	NDB 75
THREE TRIPS IN TIME AND SPACE	SILVERBERG, ROBERT	OA H	HAW 73
THREE WORLDS OF FUTURITY	ST. CLAIR, MARGARET	DC	ACE 64
THRONE OF SATURN, THE	WRIGHT, S. FOWLER	AC H	ARK 49
THROUGH A GLASS, CLEARLY	ASIMOV, ISAAC	AC	FSP 67
THROUGH TIME AND SPACE WITH FERDINAND FEGHOOT			
	BRIARTON, GRENDEL	AC H	PDX 62
IN "THE COMPLETE FEGHOOT"			
THUNDER AND ROSES	STURGEON, THEODORE	AC H	JOS 57
8 STORIES FROM "A WAY HOME"			
TIGER BY THE TAIL	NOURSE, ALAN E.	AC H	MCK 61
AND OTHER SCIENCE FICTION STORIES			
IN ENGLAND AS "BEYOND INFINITY"			
TIME AND STARS	ANDERSON, POUL	AC H	DBL 64
BRITISH EDITION OMITS "EVE TIMES FOUR"			
TIME AND THE RIDDLE	FAST, HOWARD	AC H	WRP 75
TIME CURVE, THE	MOSKOWITZ & ELWOOD	AN	TWR 68
TIME DWELLER, THE	MOORCOCK, MICHAEL	AC H	HDV 69
TIME IN ADVANCE	TENN, WILLIAM	AC	BAN 58 06
TIME MACHINE AND OTHER STORIES, THE			
	WELLS, H. G.	AC H	HLT 95
TIME MACHINE AND OTHER STORIES, THE (PB)			
	WELLS, H. G.	AC	SBS 63
TIME OF INFINITY, THE	DERLETH, AUGUST	AN	CNL 63
LAST 9 STORIES FROM "THE OUTER REACHES"			
TIME OF THE EYE, THE	ELLISON, HARLAN	AC	PTH 74
LAST 12 STORIES FROM "ALONE AGAINST TOMORROW"			
TIME OUT FOR TOMORROW	WILSON, RICHARD	AC	BAL 62
TIME OUT OF MIND	BOULLE, PIERRE	OC H	VAN 66
TIME PROBE: THE SCIENCES IN SF.			
	CLARKE, ARTHUR C.	AN H	DCT 66
TIME TO COME	DERLETH, AUGUST	OA H	FSY 54
TIME TO COME (10 OF 12, BRK 58)			
	DERLETH, AUGUST	OA	BRK 58 12
TIME TO COME (10 OF 12, TWR 65)			
	DERLETH, AUGUST	OA	TWR 65
TIME TRANSFER	SELLINGS, ARTHUR	AC H	JOS 56
TIME TRANSFER (11 OF 16)	SELLINGS, ARTHUR	AN	CPT 66
TIME UNTAMED	HOWARD, IVAN	AN	BEL 67
TIME WAITS FOR WINTHROP, AND FOUR OTHER SHORT NOVELS			
	POHL, FREDERIK	AN H	DBL 62
TIME: X	TUCKER, WILSON	AC	BAN 55 12
SEE "THE SCIENCE FICTION SUBTREASURY"			
TIME-JUMP	BRUNNER, JOHN	AC	DEL 73 12
TIMELESS STORIES FOR TODAY AND TOMORROW			
	BRADBURY, RAY	AN	BAN 52 09
TIMES WITHOUT NUMBER	BRUNNER, JOHN	NO	ACE 62
TIMES 4 (ABRIDGED STORIES)	ALLEN, VIRGINIA F.	AN	FAL
TIMETRACKS	LAUMER, KEITH	AC	BAL 72 04
TITAN, THE	MILLER, P. SCHUYLER	AC H	FPS 52
BRITISH EDITION OMITS "THE ARRHENIUS HORROR"			
TO HERE AND THE EASEL	STURGEON, THEODORE	AC H	GOL 73
TO OPEN THE SKY	SILVERBERG, ROBERT	NO	BAL 67 05
TO RIDE PEGASUS	MCCAFFREY, ANNE	AC	BAL 73 08
TO THE END OF TIME	STAPLEDON, OLAF	AC H	FKW 53
THE BEST OF OLAF STAPLEDON, EDITED BY BASIL DAVENPORT			
TO THE END OF TIME AND OTHER STORIES			
	WILLIAMS, ROBERT M.	DC	ACE 60
TO THE STARS	SILVERBERG, ROBERT	AN H	HAW 71
TO WORLDS BEYOND	SILVERBERG, ROBERT	AC H	CHL 65
TOMORROW AND TOMORROW	KNIGHT, DAMON	AN H	SAS 73
TOMORROW AND TOMORROW AND THE FAIRY CHESSMEN			
	PADGETT, LEWIS	AC H	GNM 51
TOMORROW CAME	COOPER, EDMUND	AC	PTH 63
TOMORROW LIES IN AMBUSH	SHAW, BOB	AC	ACE 73 02
ENGLISH EDITION (GOL 73) OMITS STORIES "STORMSEEKER"			
AND "ELEMENT OF CHANCE"			
TOMORROW MIDNIGHT	BRADBURY, RAY	AC	BAL 66
STORIES IN CARTOON FORM			
TOMORROW TIMES SEVEN	POHL, FREDERIK	AC	BAL 59 07
TOMORROW TODAY	ZEBROWSKI, GEORGE	OA L	UPR 75
TOMORROW X 4	KNIGHT, DAMON	AN	GMB 64
TOMORROW 1	HOSKINS, ROBERT	AN	SIG 71 06
TOMORROW: NEW WORLDS OF SCIENCE FICTION			
	ELWOOD, ROGER	OA H	EVN 76
TOMORROW'S ALTERNATIVES	ELWOOD, ROGER	OA H	MAC 73
SEE "FRONTIERS 1; TOMORROW'S ALTERNATIVES"			
TOMORROW'S CHILDREN	ASIMOV, ISAAC	AN H	DBL 66
TOMORROW'S GIFT	COOPER, EDMUND	AC	BAL 58
TOMORROW'S UNIVERSE	CAMPBELL, H. J.	AN H	HML 54 05
TOMORROW'S WORLDS	SILVERBERG, ROBERT	AN H	MDT 69
TOMORROW, AND TOMORROW, AND TOMORROW...			
	HEINTZ/HERBERT/JOOS/	AN L	HRW 74
TOMORROW, INC.	GREENBERG& OLANDER	AN L	TAP 76
TOMORROW, THE STARS	HEINLEIN, ROBERT A.	AN H	DBL 51

TORRENT OF FACES, A

TORRENT OF FACES, A   BLISH & KNIGHT, N.   NO H DBL 67
TOUCH OF INFINITY, A   ELLISON, HARLAN   DC   ACE 59
TOUCH OF INFINITY, A   FAST, HOWARD   OC H MOR 73
    ALSO IN "TIME AND THE RIDDLE"
TOUCH OF STRANGE, A   STURGEON, THEODORE   AC H DBL 58
TOUCH OF STRANGE, A (7 OF 9) STURGEON, THEODORE   AC   BRK 59
TOWARD INFINITY   KNIGHT, DAMON   AN H SAS 68
TOYMAKER, THE   JONES, RAYMOND F.   AC H FPB 51
TRADER TO THE STARS   ANDERSON, POUL   AC H DBL 64
TRANSFORMATIONS   ROSELLE, DANIEL   AN   FPR 73 12
    UNDERSTANDING WORLD HISTORY THROUGH SCIENCE FICTION
TRANSFORMATIONS II   ROSELLE, DANIEL   AN   FAW 74 11
    UNDERSTANDING AMERICAN HISTORY THROUGH SCIENCE FICTION
TRANSIT OF EARTH   PLAYBOY, EDITORS OF   AN   PBP 71
TRAPS OF TIME, THE   MOORCOCK, MICHAEL   AN H RPW 68
TRAVELER IN BLACK, THE   BRUNNER, JOHN   AC   ACE 71
TRAVELERS IN TIME   STERN, PHILIP VAN D.   AN H DBL 47 07
TRAVELLERS BY NIGHT   DERLETH, AUGUST   OA H ARK 67
TRAVELLERS OF SPACE   GREENBERG, MARTIN   AN H GNM 51
TREASURY OF GREAT SCIENCE FICTION, A VOL. 1
                            BOUCHER, ANTHONY   AN H DBL 59
TREASURY OF GREAT SCIENCE FICTION, A VOL. 2
                            BOUCHER, ANTHONY   AN H DBL 59
TREASURY OF SCIENCE FICTION CLASSICS, THE
                            KUEBLER, HAROLD W.   AN H HAN 54
TREASURY OF SCIENCE FICTION, A CONKLIN, GROFF   AN H CRN 48 11
TREASURY OF SCIENCE FICTION, A (8 OF 30)
                            CONKLIN, GROFF   AN   BRK 57 07
TRIAD   VAN VOGT, A. E.   AC H SAS 51
TRIAL OF TERRA, THE   WILLIAMSON, JACK   NO   ACE 62
TRIANGLE   ASIMOV, ISAAC   AC H DBL 61
    IN ENGLAND AS "AN ISAAC ASIMOV SECOND OMNIBUS"
TRILOGY OF THE FUTURE   WOLLHEIM, DONALD A.   AN H SID 62
    SEE "ACE SCIENCE FICTION READER"
TRITONIAN RING, THE   DE CAMP, L. SPRAGUE   AC H TWN 53
TROUBLE TWISTERS, THE   ANDERSON, POUL   AC H DBL 66
TUNNEL AND OTHER STORIES, THE ELWOOD, ROGER   OA H LER 74
TURN LEFT AT THURSDAY   POHL, FREDERIK   AC   BAL 61 03
TURNING ON   KNIGHT, DAMON   AC H DBL 66
    ACE 67 EDITION OMITS STORY "THE HANDLER"
TURNING PLACE, THE   KARL, JEAN E.   OC H DUT 76
    STORIES OF A FUTURE PAST
TWELVE STORIES AND A DREAM WELLS, H. G.   AC H MCM 03
TWENTY YEARS OF FANTASY & SCIENCE FICTION
                            FERMAN & MILLS   AN H PUT 70
TWENTY-EIGHT SCIENCE FICTION STORIES
                            WELLS, H. G.   AC H DOV 52
TWENTY-SECOND CENTURY, THE CHRISTOPHER, JOHN   AC H GRY 54
TWICE 22   BRADBURY, RAY   AC H DBL 66
TWILIGHT WORLD   ANDERSON, POUL   NO H TOR 61
TWIN WORLDS   JONES, NEIL R.   AC   ACE 67
TWISTED   CONKLIN, GROFF   AN   BEL 62
TWISTED (BRITISH)   CONKLIN, GROFF   AN   HWZ 63
TWISTED MEN, THE   VAN VOGT, A. E.   DC   ACE 64
TWISTS IN TIME   LEINSTER, MURRAY   AC   AVN 60
TWO DOZEN DRAGON EGGS   WOLLHEIM, DONALD A.   AC   POW 69 09
TWO TALES AND EIGHT TOMORROWS HARRISON, HARRY   AC   BAN 68 05
TWO VIEWS OF WONDER   SCORTIA & YARBRO   OA   BAL 73 12
TYRANT OF TIME, THE   ESHBACH, LLOYD A.   AC H FPS 55
UBERWINDUNG VON RAUM UND ZEIT GUNTHER, GOTTHARD   AN H KRP 52
    CONQUEST OF SPACE AND TIME, STORIES IN GERMAN
ULTIMATE INVADER, AND OTHER SCIENCE FICTION, THE
                            WOLLHEIM, DONALD A.   DA   ACE 54
ULTIMATE THRESHOLD, THE   GINSBURG, MIRRA   AN H HRW 70
UN-MAN AND OTHER NOVELLAS   ANDERSON, POUL   DC   ACE 62
UNBORN TOMORROW   COOPER, EDMUND   AC H HAL 71
UNDEFEATED, THE   LAUMER, KEITH   AC   DEL 74 06
UNDER COMPULSION   DISCH, THOMAS M.   AC H HDV 68
    SEE "FUN WITH YOUR NEW HEAD"
UNDER THE MOONS OF MARS   MOSKOWITZ, SAM   AN H HRW 70
UNEXPECTED DIMENSION, THE   BUDRYS, ALGIS   AC   BAL 60
UNEXPECTED, THE   MARGULIES, LEO   AN   PYR 61 02
UNFAMILIAR TERRITORY   SILVERBERG, ROBERT   AC H SCB 73
UNFRIENDLY FUTURE, THE   BOARDMAN, TOM JR.   AN   FSP 65
UNIVERSE AHEAD   ENGDAHL & ROBERSON   AN H ATH 76
UNIVERSE DAY   O'DONNELL, K. M.   NO   AVN 71 04
UNIVERSE 1   CARR, TERRY   OA   ACE 71
UNIVERSE 2   CARR, TERRY   OA   ACE 72
UNIVERSE 3   CARR, TERRY   OA H RDM 73
UNIVERSE 4   CARR, TERRY   OA H RDM 74
UNIVERSE 5   CARR, TERRY   OA H RDM 74
UNIVERSE 6   CARR, TERRY   OA H DBL 76
UNIVERSE 7   CARR, TERRY   OA H DBL 77 01
UNKNOWN 5, THE   BENSEN, D. R.   AN   PYR 64 01
UNKNOWN, THE   BENSEN, D. R.   AN   PYR 63 04
UNPLEASANT PROFESSION OF JONATHAN HOAG, THE
                            HEINLEIN, ROBERT A.   AC H GNM 59
    ALSO AS "6 X H"
UNTOUCHED BY HUMAN HANDS   SHECKLEY, ROBERT   AC H BAL 54 03
UNTOUCHED BY HUMAN HANDS (BRITISH)
                            SHECKLEY, ROBERT   AC   FSP 67
UNTRAVELLED WORLDS   BARTER & WILSON   AN   MCM 66
VALLEY BEYOND TIME   SILVERBERG, ROBERT   AC   DEL 73 01
VAMPIRES, LTD.   NESVADBA, JOSEF   AC   VNS 64
    SEE "THE LOST FACE"
VAN VOGT OMNIBUS, A   VAN VOGT, A. E.   AC H SID 67
VARIABLE MAN, THE   DICK, PHILIP K.   AC   ACE 57
VENUS EQUILATERAL   SMITH, GEORGE O.   AC H PRM 47
VENUS FACTOR, THE   GHIDALIA, V.& ELWOOD   AN   MBB 72
VERMILLION SANDS   BALLARD, J. G.   BKM 71 04
VERMILLION SANDS (BRITISH) BALLARD, J. G.   AC H CAP 73
VIEW FROM ANOTHER SHORE   ROTTENSTEINER, FRANZ AN H SEA 73
VIEW FROM THE STARS, THE   MILLER, WALTER M. JR AC   BAL 65 01
VINTAGE ANTHOLOGY OF SCIENCE FANTASY, THE
                            CERF, CHRISTOPHER   AN   VNT 66 02
VINTAGE BRADBURY, THE   BRADBURY, RAY   AC   VNT 65

WORLD'S BEST SCIENCE FICTION: 1967

VISIONS OF TOMORROW   ELWOOD, ROGER   AN   PKT 76 11
VISITOR FROM OUTER SPACE, A ANONYMOUS   AN H FLP 61
    SEE "SOVIET SCIENCE FICTION"
VOICE OF THE DOLPHINS, AND OTHER STORIES, THE
                            SZILARD, LEO   AC H SAS 61
VOICES IN THE DARK   COOPER, EDMUND   AC   DIG 60
VOICES OF TIME AND OTHER STORIES, THE
                            BALLARD, J. G.   AC   BKM 62 02
VOID BEYOND, AND OTHER STORIES, THE
                            WILLIAMS, ROBERT M.   DC   ACE 58
VORTEX BLASTERS, THE   MOSKOWITZ, SAM   AN   MBB 65
    AND OTHER STORIES FROM MODERN MASTERPIECES OF SCIENCE FICTION
VOYAGE OF THE SPACE BEAGLE, THE
                            VAN VOGT, A. E.   NO H SAS 50
    IN "TRIAD"
    ALSO AS "MISSION: INTERPLANETARY"
VOYAGERS IN TIME   SILVERBERG, ROBERT   AN H MDT 67
VOYAGES: SCENARIOS FOR A SHIP CALLED EARTH
                            SAUER, ROB   AN   BAL 71 04
WALKER THROUGH WALLS, THE   AYME, MARCEL   AC   BRK 62
    IN ENGLAND AS "ACROSS PARIS AND OTHER STORIES"
WALL AROUND THE WORLD, THE COGSWELL, THEODORE R AC   PYR 62 02
WANDERERS OF TIME   WYNDHAM, JOHN   AC   CNT 73
WANDERING STARS   DANN, JACK M.   AN H HPR 74
WAR AGAINST THE RULL, THE   VAN VOGT, A. E.   NO H SAS 59 09
WAR OF THE WORLDS, THE TIME MACHINE AND SELECTED SHORT STORIES
                            WELLS, H. G.   AC H PLM 63
WAR WITH THE ROBOTS   HARRISON, HARRY   AC   PYR 62 09
WARM WORLDS AND OTHERWISE   TIPTREE, JAMES JR.   AC   BAL 75 02
WAY HOME, A   STURGEON, THEODORE   AC H FKW 55
    EDITED BY GROFF CONKLIN
    ENGLISH DERIVATIVE COLLECTION "THUNDER AND ROSES"
WAY HOME, A (9 OF 11)   STURGEON, THEODORE   AC   PYR 56
    EDITED BY GROFF CONKLIN
WAY OUT   HOWARD, IVAN   AN   BEL 63 12
WEAPON SHOPS OF ISHER, THE VAN VOGT, A. E.   NO H GBG 51
    ALSO IN "A TREASURY OF GREAT SCIENCE FICTION VOL. 1"
WEIGHER OF SOULS AND THE EARTH DWELLERS, THE
                            MAUROIS, ANDRE   AC H MAC 63
WEIRD ONES, THE   HOWARD, IVAN   AN   BEL 62 07
WEIRD SHADOWS FROM BEYOND   CARNELL, JOHN   AN   AVN 69 04
WEIRD SHOW   PLAYBOY, EDITORS OF   AN   PBP 71
WEIRD TALES   MARGULIES, LEO   AN   PYR 64 05
WELCOME TO THE MONKEY HOUSE VONNEGUT, KURT JR.   AC H DCT 68
WHAT STRANGE STARS AND SKIES DAVIDSON, AVRAM   AC   ACE 65
WHAT'S BECOME OF SCREWLOOSE? AND OTHER INQUIRIES
                            GOULART, RON   AC H SCB 71
WHAT'S IT LIKE OUT THERE? AND OTHER STORIES
                            HAMILTON, EDMOND   AC   ACE 74
WHEELS OF IF, THE   DE CAMP, L. SPRAGUE   AC H SHS 48
WHEN HARLIE WAS ONE   GERROLD, DAVID   NO H NDB 72
WHEN TWO WORLDS MEET   WILLIAMS, ROBERT M.   AC   CUR 70
    STORIES OF MEN ON MARS
WHEN WOMEN RULE   MOSKOWITZ, SAM   AN H WKR 72
WHERE DO WE GO FROM HERE?   ASIMOV, ISAAC   AN H DBL 71
WHITE FANG GOES DINGO AND OTHER FUNNY S.F. STORIES
                            DISCH, THOMAS M.   AC   ARW 71
WHO CAN REPLACE A MAN?   ALDISS, BRIAN W.   AC H HBW 66
    SEE "BEST SCIENCE FICTION STORIES OF BRIAN W. ALDISS"
WHO FEARS THE DEVIL?   WELLMAN, MANLY WADE AC H ARK 63
WHO GOES THERE?   CAMPBELL, JOHN W. JR AC H SHS 48
    IN ENGLAND AS "THE THING AND OTHER STORIES" AND
    "THE THING FROM OUTER SPACE"
WHO GOES THERE? AND OTHER STORIES
                            CAMPBELL, JOHN W. JR AC   DEL 55
WHOLE MAN, THE   BRUNNER, JOHN   NO   BAL 64 08
WILDERNESS OF STARS, A   NOLAN, WILLIAM F.   AN H SHB 69
WIND FROM THE SUN, THE   CLARKE, ARTHUR C.   AC H HBJ 72
WINDOW ON THE FUTURE   HILL, DOUGLAS   AN H HDV 66
WINDOWS INTO TOMORROW   SILVERBERG, ROBERT   AN H HAW 74
WINDS TWELVE QUARTERS, THE LE GUIN, URSULA K.   AC H HPR 75
WINGS ACROSS TIME   ARNOLD, FRANK EDWARD AC   PND 46
WITCHES THREE   PRATT, FLETCHER   AN H TWN 52
WITCHFINDER, THE   WRIGHT, S. FOWLER   AC H BPT 46
WITCHING HOUR, THE   GUNN, JAMES E.   AC   DEL 70 06
WITH A FINGER IN MY I   GERROLD, DAVID   AC   BAL 72 06
WITHOUT SORCERY   STURGEON, THEODORE   AC H PRM 48
    DERIVATIVE COLLECTION "NOT WITHOUT SORCERY"
WIZARDS AND WARLOCKS   GHIDALIA, VIC   AN   MAN 72
WOLFSHEAD   HOWARD, ROBERT E.   AC   LAN 68
WOMEN OF WONDER   SARGENT, PAMELA   AN   VNT 75 01
WONDER EFFECT, THE   POHL, F. & KORNBLUTH AC   BAL 62
WONDERFUL ICE CREAM SUIT AND OTHER PLAYS, THE
                            BRADBURY, RAY   AC   BAN 72 04
WONDERMAKERS   HOSKINS, ROBERT   AN   FAW 72 05
WONDERMAKERS 2   HOSKINS, ROBERT   AN   FPR 74 02
WOODEN STAR, THE   TENN, WILLIAM   AC   BAL 68 06
WORLD BETWEEN AND OTHER STORIES, THE
                            VANCE, JACK   DC   ACE 65
    IN ENGLAND AS "THE MOON MOTH AND OTHER STORIES"
WORLD BY THE TALE, A   CAMPBELL, JOHN W. JR AN   CUR 65
    SEE "ANALOG 3"
WORLD INSIDE, THE   SILVERBERG, ROBERT   NO H DBL 71
WORLD NAMED CLEOPATRA, A   ANDERSON, POUL   OA   PYR 77 03
    PRODUCED BY ROGER ELWOOD
WORLD OF WONDER   PRATT, FLETCHER   AN H TWN 51
WORLD OUT OF TIME, A   NIVEN, LARRY   NO H HRW 76
WORLD THAT COULDN'T BE AND 8 OTHER SF NOVELETS
                            GOLD, H. L.   AN H DBL 59
WORLD'S BEST SCIENCE FICTION: 1965
                            WOLLHEIM & CARR   AN   ACE 65
WORLD'S BEST SCIENCE FICTION: 1966
                            WOLLHEIM & CARR   AN   ACE 66
WORLD'S BEST SCIENCE FICTION: 1967
                            WOLLHEIM & CARR   AN   ACE 67

WORLD'S BEST SCIENCE FICTION: 1968
                              WOLLHEIM & CARR   AN   ACE 68
WORLD'S BEST SCIENCE FICTION: 1969
                              WOLLHEIM & CARR   AN   ACE 69
WORLD'S BEST SCIENCE FICTION: 1970
                              WOLLHEIM & CARR   AN   ACE 70
WORLD'S BEST SCIENCE FICTION: 1971
                              WOLLHEIM & CARR   AN   ACE 71
WORLD'S BEST SF SHORT STORIES NO. 1, THE
                              WOLLHEIM, DONALD A. AN H ELM 75
     SEE "THE 1974 ANNUAL WORLD'S BEST SF"
WORLD'S BEST SF SHORT STORIES NO. 2, THE
                              WOLLHEIM, DONALD A. AN H ELM 76
     SEE "THE 1975 ANNUAL WORLD'S BEST SF"
WORLDS APART   LOCKE, GEORGE   AN H CMK
     AN ANTHOLOGY OF INTERPLANETARY FICTION
WORLDS APART   WILLIAMS-ELLIS& OWEN AN H BLK 66
WORLDS AT WAR   RAYER, FRANCIS G.   AN   TPS
WORLDS FAR AND NEAR   CARR, TERRY   AN H NEL 74
WORLDS OF A. E. VAN VOGT, THE VAN VOGT, A. E.   AC   ACE 74 01
WORLDS OF CLIFFORD SIMAK, THE SIMAK, CLIFFORD D.   AC H SAS 60
     DERIVATIVE COLLECTION "OTHER WORLDS OF CLIFFORD SIMAK"
     IN ENGLAND AS "ALIENS FOR NEIGHBOURS"
WORLDS OF CLIFFORD SIMAK, THE (BRITISH PB)
                              SIMAK, CLIFFORD D.   AC   FSP 63
WORLDS OF CLIFFORD SIMAK, THE (6 OF 12)
                              SIMAK, CLIFFORD D.   AC   AVN 61
WORLDS OF FRANK HERBERT, THE HERBERT, FRANK   AC   ACE 71
WORLDS OF FRITZ LEIBER, THE   LEIBER, FRITZ   AC   ACE 76 11
WORLDS OF JACK VANCE, THE   VANCE, JACK   AC   ACE 73 12
WORLDS OF MAYBE   SILVERBERG, ROBERT   AN H NEL 70
WORLDS OF POUL ANDERSON, THE ANDERSON, POUL   AC   ACE 74
WORLDS OF ROBERT A. HEINLEIN, THE
                              HEINLEIN, ROBERT A. AC   ACE 66
WORLDS OF ROBERT F. YOUNG, THE, THE YOUNG, ROBERT F. AC H SAS 65
WORLDS OF SCIENCE FICTION, THE MILLS, ROBERT P.   AN   PBK 63
WORLDS OF THEODORE STURGEON, THE
                              STURGEON, THEODORE   AC   ACE 72
WORLDS OF TOMORROW   DERLETH, AUGUST   AN H PEL 53
     ENGLISH DERIVATIVE ANTHOLOGY "NEW WORLDS FOR OLD"
WORLDS OF TOMORROW (BRITISH PB)
                              DERLETH, AUGUST   AN   FSP 63
     10 STORIES FROM AMERICAN EDITION,
     REMAINING 9 IN "NEW WORLDS FOR OLD"
WORLDS OF TOMORROW (BRITISH) DERLETH, AUGUST   AN H WEI 55
WORLDS OF TOMORROW (10 OF 19) DERLETH, AUGUST   AN   BRK 58 10
WORLDS OF WEIRD   MARGULIES, LEO   AN   PYR 65
WORLDS OF WHEN   CONKLIN, GROFF   AN   PYR 62 05
WORLDS OF WONDER   HARRISON, HARRY   AN H DBL 69
WORLDS OF WONDER   STAPLEDON, OLAF   AC H FPB 49
WORLDS TO COME   KNIGHT, DAMON   AN H HPR 67
WORLDS WITHOUT END   SIMAK, CLIFFORD D.   AC   BEL 64 04
WOUNDED PLANET, THE   ELWOOD, ROGER   AN   BAN 74 08
     SEE "SAVING WORLDS"
XENOGENESIS   DEFORD, MIRIAM ALLEN AC   BAL 69 03
YEAR AFTER TOMORROW, THE   DEL REY, L/MATSCHAT/ AN H JCW 51
YEAR 2000, THE   HARRISON, HARRY   OA H DBL 70
YEAR 2018!   BLISH, JAMES   NO   AVN 57
     IN ENGLAND AS "THEY SHALL HAVE STARS"
YEAR'S BEST HORROR STORIES: SERIES II, THE
                              DAVIS, RICHARD   AN   DAW 74 07
YEAR'S BEST HORROR STORIES: SERIES III, THE
                              DAVIS, RICHARD   AN   DAW 75 06
YEAR'S BEST HORROR STORIES: SERIES IV, THE
                              PAGE, GERALD W.   AN   DAW 76 11
YEAR'S BEST HORROR STORIES, THE
                              DAVIS, RICHARD   AN   DAW 71
YEAR'S BEST SCIENCE FICTION NO. 1, THE
                              HARRISON & ALDISS   AN   SPH 68
     SEE "BEST SF: 1967"
YEAR'S BEST SCIENCE FICTION NO. 2, THE
                              HARRISON & ALDISS   AN   SPH 69
     SEE "BEST SF: 1968"
YEAR'S BEST SCIENCE FICTION NO. 3, THE
                              HARRISON & ALDISS   AN   SPH 70
     SEE "BEST SF: 1969"
YEAR'S BEST SCIENCE FICTION NO. 4, THE
                              HARRISON & ALDISS   AN   SPH 71
     SEE "BEST SF: 1970"
YEAR'S BEST SCIENCE FICTION NO. 5, THE
                              HARRISON & ALDISS   AN   SPH 72
     SEE "BEST SF: 1971"
YEAR'S BEST SCIENCE FICTION NO. 6, THE
                              HARRISON & ALDISS   AN   SPH 73
     SEE "BEST SF: 1972"
YEAR'S BEST SCIENCE FICTION NO. 7, THE
                              HARRISON & ALDISS   AN   SPH 74
     SEE "BEST SF: 1973"
YEAR'S BEST SCIENCE FICTION NO. 8, THE
                              HARRISON & ALDISS   AN   SPH 75
     SEE "BEST SF: 1974"
YEAR'S BEST SCIENCE FICTION NO. 9, THE
                              HARRISON & ALDISS   AN H WEI 76
     SEE "BEST SF: 75, THE NINTH ANNUAL"
YEAR'S BEST SCIENCE FICTION NOVELS: SECOND SERIES, THE
                              BLEILER & DIKTY   AN H GRY 55
     SEE "YEAR'S BEST SCIENCE FICTION NOVELS: 1954"
     OMITS "SECOND VARIETY"
YEAR'S BEST SCIENCE FICTION NOVELS: 1952
                              BLEILER & DIKTY   AN H FEL 52
     IN ENGLAND AS "THE YEAR'S BEST SCIENCE FICTION NOVELS"
YEAR'S BEST SCIENCE FICTION NOVELS: 1953
                              BLEILER & DIKTY   AN H FEL 53 03
     IN ENGLAND AS "CATEGORY PHOENIX"
YEAR'S BEST SCIENCE FICTION NOVELS: 1954
                              BLEILER & DIKTY   AN H FEL 54 03
     IN ENGLAND AS
     "THE YEAR'S BEST SCIENCE FICTION NOVELS: SECOND SERIES
YEAR'S BEST SCIENCE FICTION NOVELS, THE
                              BLEILER & DIKTY   AN H GRY 54
     SEE "YEAR'S BEST SCIENCE FICTION NOVELS: 1952"
     OMITS "SEEKER OF THE SPHINX"
YESTERDAY AND TOMORROW   VERNE, JULES   AC H ARC 64
     EDITED BY I. O. EVANS
YET MORE PENGUIN SCIENCE FICTION
                              ALDISS, BRIAN W.   AN   PEN 64
     ALSO IN "THE PENGUIN SCIENCE FICTION OMNIBUS"
YONDER   BEAUMONT, CHARLES   AC   BAN 58 04
YOU AND SCIENCE FICTION   HOLLISTER, BERNARD C AN L NTC 76
     A HUMANISTIC APPROACH TO SCIENCE FICTION
YOU WILL NEVER BE THE SAME   SMITH, CORDWAINER   AC   BKM 63
YOU'RE ALL ALONE   LEIBER, FRITZ   AC   ACE 72
YOUNG DEMONS   ELWOOD & GHIDALIA   AN   AVN 72 04
YOUNG READERS SCIENCE FICTION STORIES
                              ELAM, RICHARD M. JR. AC H LPB 57
     SEE "TEEN-AGE SCIENCE FICTION STORIES"
YOURS TRULY, JACK THE RIPPER BLOCH, ROBERT   AC   BEL 62
     IN ENGLAND AS "THE HOUSE OF THE HATCHET AND OTHER TALES OF
     HORROR"
ZACHERLEY'S MIDNIGHT SNACKS   ZACHERLEY   AN   BAL 60
ZACHERLEY'S VULTURE STEW   ZACHERLEY   AN   BAL 60
ZOO 2000   YOLEN, JANE   AN H SEA 73
1,000 YEAR PLAN, THE   ASIMOV, ISAAC   DN   ACE 55
     ABRIDGED VERSION OF "FOUNDATION"
10TH ANNUAL OF THE YEAR'S BEST S-F, THE
                              MERRIL, JUDITH   AN H DCT 65
11TH ANNUAL OF THE YEAR'S BEST S-F, THE
                              MERRIL, JUDITH   AN H DCT 66
12 GREAT CLASSICS OF SCIENCE FICTION
                              CONKLIN, GROFF   AN   FGM 63
13 ABOVE THE NIGHT   CONKLIN, GROFF   AN   DEL 65
13 FRENCH SCIENCE-FICTION STORIES
                              KNIGHT, DAMON   AN   BAN 65
13 GREAT STORIES OF SCIENCE FICTION
                              CONKLIN, GROFF   AN   FGM 60
14 GREAT TALES OF ESP   STONE, IDELLA P.   AN   FGM 69 11
17 X INFINITY   CONKLIN, GROFF   AN   DEL 63 08
18 GREAT SCIENCE FICTION STORIES
                              JANIFER, LAURENCE M. AN   TMP 71 01
     SEE "MASTERS' CHOICE"
1972 ANNUAL WORLD'S BEST SF, THE
                              WOLLHEIM, DONALD A. AN H DAW 72
1973 ANNUAL WORLD'S BEST SF, THE
                              WOLLHEIM, DONALD A. AN H DAW 73
1974 ANNUAL WORLD'S BEST SF, THE
                              WOLLHEIM, DONALD A. AN H DAW 74
     IN ENGLAND AS "THE WORLD'S BEST SF SHORT STORIES NO. 1"
1975 ANNUAL WORLD'S BEST SF, THE
                              WOLLHEIM, DONALD A. AN   DAW 75
     IN ENGLAND AS "THE WORLD'S BEST SF SHORT STORIES NO. 2"
1976 ANNUAL WORLD'S BEST SF, THE
                              WOLLHEIM, DONALD A. AN   DAW 76 05
1977 ANNUAL WORLD'S BEST SF, THE
                              WOLLHEIM, DONALD A. AN   DAW 77 05
     WITH ARTHUR W. SAHA
2020 VISION   POURNELLE, JERRY   AN   AVN 74 02
2076: THE AMERICAN TRICENTENNIAL
                              BRYANT, EDWARD   OA   PYR 77
25 MODERN STORIES OF MYSTERY AND IMAGINATION
                              STONG, PHILIP D.   AN H GCB 42
     SEE "THE OTHER WORLDS"
3 FROM OUT THERE   MARGULIES, LEO   AN   CRS 59 03
3 IN 1   MARGULIES, LEO   AN   PYR 63 08
3 PROPHETIC SCIENCE FICTION NOVELS OF H. G. WELLS
                              WELLS, H. G.   AC L DOV 60
3 TO THE HIGHEST POWER   NOLAN, WILLIAM F.   AN   AVN 68 02
3000 YEARS OF FANTASY AND SCIENCE FICTION
                              DE CAMP, L. S.&C.   AN H LOT 72
31ST OF FEBRUARY, THE   BOND, NELSON S.   AC H GNM 49
334   DISCH, THOMAS M.   NO   AVN 74 02
5 GALAXY SHORT NOVELS   GOLD, H. L.   AN H DBL 58
5 TALES FROM TOMORROW   DIKTY, T. E.   AN   CRS 57 12
     5 STORIES FROM "BEST SCIENCE FICTION STORIES AND NOVELS: 1955"
5 UNEARTHLY VISIONS   CONKLIN, GROFF   AN   FGM 65
5TH ANNUAL OF THE YEAR'S BEST S-F, THE
                              MERRIL, JUDITH   AN H SAS 60
     IN ENGLAND AS "THE BEST OF SCIENCE FICTION 5"
6 AND THE SILENT SCREAM   HOWARD, IVAN   AN   BEL 63 05
6 FINGERS OF TIME AND 5 OTHER SCIENCE FICTION NOVELETS, THE
                              ANONYMOUS   AN   MBB 65
6 FROM WORLDS BEYOND   DIKTY, T. E.   AN   CRS 58 12
     6 STORIES FROM "BEST SCIENCE FICTION STORIES AND NOVELS: 1956"
6 GREAT SHORT NOVELS OF SCIENCE FICTION
                              CONKLIN, GROFF   AN   DEL 54
6 X H   HEINLEIN, ROBERT A. AC   PYR 61 08
     SEE "THE UNPLEASANT PROFESSION OF JONATHAN HOAG"
6TH ANNUAL OF THE YEAR'S BEST S-F, THE
                              MERRIL, JUDITH   AN H SAS 61
     IN ENGLAND AS "THE BEST OF SCIENCE FICTION"
7 CONQUESTS   ANDERSON, POUL   AC H MAC 69
7TH ANNUAL OF THE YEAR'S BEST S-F, THE
                              MERRIL, JUDITH   AN H SAS 62
     IN ENGLAND AS "THE BEST OF SCIENCE FICTION 2"
8TH ANNUAL OF THE YEAR'S BEST S-F, THE
                              MERRIL, JUDITH   AN H SAS 63
     IN ENGLAND AS "THE BEST OF SCIENCE FICTION 4"
9 TALES OF SPACE AND TIME   HEALY, RAYMOND J.   OA H HLT 54
9TH ANNUAL OF THE YEAR'S BEST S-F, THE
                              MERRIL, JUDITH   AN H SAS 64

Author Index

MISC. MATERIAL

MISC. MATERIAL
ABOUT H. G. WELLS: BIOGRAPHICAL NOTES   MS
   WAR OF THE WORLDS, THE TIME MACHINE AND SELECTED SHORT STORIES
                                              WELLS, H. G.   AC
ABOUT THE AUTHORS   MS
   AURORA: BEYOND EQUALITY   MCINTYRE & ANDERSON OA
   BEST SCIENCE-FICTION STORIES: 1950, THE
                                     BLEILER & DIKTY   AN
   BEST SCIENCE-FICTION STORIES: 1951, THE
                                     BLEILER & DIKTY   AN
   BEST SCIENCE-FICTION STORIES: 1952, THE
                                     BLEILER & DIKTY   AN
   BEST SCIENCE-FICTION STORIES: 1953, THE
                                     BLEILER & DIKTY   AN
   BEST SCIENCE-FICTION STORIES: 1954, THE
                                     BLEILER & DIKTY   AN
   BIO-FUTURES   SARGENT, PAMELA   AN
   MORE WOMEN OF WONDER   SARGENT, PAMELA   AN
   STAR SHORT NOVELS   POHL, FREDERIK   OA
   TOMORROW TODAY   ZEBROWSKI, GEORGE   OA
   WORLD NAMED CLEOPATRA, A   ANDERSON, POUL   OA
ABOUT THE EDITOR   MS
   CHILDREN OF WONDER   TENN, WILLIAM   AN
   MORE WOMEN OF WONDER   SARGENT, PAMELA   AN
   OTHER WORLDS, OTHER SEAS   SUVIN, DARKO   AN
ABOUT WILLIAM TENN   MS
   OF ALL POSSIBLE WORLDS   TENN, WILLIAM   AC
ADDITIONAL SIGNIFICANT WORKS OF SPECULATIVE FICTION
                                               MS
   MODERN SCIENCE FICTION   SPINRAD, NORMAN   AN
AFTERWORD: THE EPIC OF SPACE BY E. E. 'DOC' SMITH MS
   BEST OF E. E. 'DOC' SMITH, THE   SMITH, EDWARD E. PHD AC
ANDERSON BIBLIOGRAPHY   MS   FSF 71 04
   BEST FROM FANTASY AND SCIENCE FICTION, 25TH ANNIV.
                                     FERMAN, EDWARD L.   AN
APPENDICES   MS
   FANTASTIC PULPS, THE   HAINING, PETER   AN
   HISTORY OF THE SCIENCE FICTION MAGAZINE, THE   PART 1 1926-1935
                                     ASHLEY, MICHAEL   AN
   HISTORY OF THE SCIENCE FICTION MAGAZINE, THE   PART 2 1936-1945
                                     ASHLEY, MICHAEL   AN
   HISTORY OF THE SCIENCE FICTION MAGAZINE, THE   PART 3 1946-1955
                                     ASHLEY, MICHAEL   AN
APPENDIX   MS
   EARLY DEL REY   DEL REY, LESTER   AC
APPENDIX OF THEMES   MS
   TWO VIEWS OF WONDER   SCORTIA & YARBRO   OA
APPENDIX: THE HUGO AWARDS   MS
   HUGO WINNERS, THE (VOLUME 1)   ASIMOV, ISAAC   AN
ARCS & SECANTS
   ORBIT 12   KNIGHT, DAMON   OA
   ORBIT 13   KNIGHT, DAMON   OA
   ORBIT 14   KNIGHT, DAMON   OA
   ORBIT 15   KNIGHT, DAMON   OA
   ORBIT 16   KNIGHT, DAMON   OA
   ORBIT 17   KNIGHT, DAMON   OA
   ORBIT 18   KNIGHT, DAMON   OA
ARTICLES   AR
   AUTHENTIC BOOK OF SPACE   CAMPBELL, H. J.   AN
ASIMOV BIBLIOGRAPHY   MS   FSF 66 10
   BEST FROM FANTASY AND SCIENCE FICTION, 25TH ANNIV.
                                     FERMAN, EDWARD L.   AN
AUTHORS, THE   MS
   NEBULA AWARD STORIES 9   WILHELM, KATE   AN
   NEW WORLDS NO. 6   PLATT & BAILEY   OA
   NEW WORLDS QUARTERLY NO. 1   MOORCOCK, MICHAEL   OA
   NEW WORLDS QUARTERLY NO. 2   MOORCOCK, MICHAEL   OA
   NEW WORLDS QUARTERLY NO. 3   MOORCOCK, MICHAEL   OA
   NEW WORLDS QUARTERLY NO. 4   MOORCOCK, MICHAEL   OA
   NEW WORLDS QUARTERLY NO. 5   MOORCOCK, MICHAEL   OA
   SURVIVAL PRINTOUT   TOTAL EFFECT   AN
AWARD WINNING SCIENCE FICTION, 1965-1974   MS
   NEBULA AWARD STORIES 10   GUNN, JAMES E.   AN
BIBLIOGRAPHY   MS
   ANOTHER TOMORROW   HOLLISTER, BERNARD C AN
   AS TOMORROW BECOMES TODAY   SULLIVAN, CHARLES W. AN
   BEST OF A. E. VAN VOGT, THE (BRITISH) VAN VOGT, A. E. AC
   BEST OF ARTHUR C. CLARKE: 1937-1971, THE
                                     CLARKE, ARTHUR C.   AC
   BEST OF E. E. 'DOC' SMITH, THE   SMITH, EDWARD E. PHD AC
   BEST OF FRANK HERBERT, THE   HERBERT, FRANK   AC
   BEST OF JOHN W. CAMPBELL, THE (BRITISH)
                                     CAMPBELL, JOHN W. JR AC
   BEST OF ROBERT HEINLEIN, THE   HEINLEIN, ROBERT A. AC
  *BEYOND HUMAN KEN   MERRIL, JUDITH   AN
   FANTASTIC PULPS, THE   HAINING, PETER   AN
   HISTORY OF THE SCIENCE FICTION MAGAZINE, THE   PART 2 1936-1945
                                     ASHLEY, MICHAEL   AN
   HISTORY OF THE SCIENCE FICTION MAGAZINE, THE   PART 3 1946-1955
                                     ASHLEY, MICHAEL   AN
   INSIDE INFORMATION   MOWSHOWITZ, ABBE   AN
   INTRODUCTORY PSYCHOLOGY THROUGH SCIENCE FICTION
                                     KATZ/WARRICK/&   AN
   JULES VERNE- MASTER OF SCIENCE FICTION VERNE, JULES   AC
   SCIENCE FICTION OF THE 30'S   KNIGHT, DAMON   AN
   SCIENCE FICTION THROUGH THE AGES 1 EVANS, I. O.   AN
BIBLIOGRAPHY OF MUTATION STORIES   MS
  *SCIENCE FICTION ADVENTURES IN MUTATION CONKLIN, GROFF AN
BIBLIOGRAPHY OF PRINCIPAL NONFICTION WORKS CONSULTED
                                               MS
   ALL ABOUT VENUS   ALDISS, BRIAN W.   AN
BIBLIOGRAPHY OF ROBOT FICTION, A   MS
   PSEUDO PEOPLE, THE   NOLAN, WILLIAM F.   AN
BIBLIOGRAPHY: BOOKS BY ARTHUR C. CLARKE   MS
   OF TIME AND STARS   CLARKE, ARTHUR C.   AC

MISC. MATERIAL   (CONTINUED)
BIBLIOGRAPHY: THE CRITICAL LITERATURE OF S. F., A MS
   MIRROR OF INFINITY, THE   SILVERBERG, ROBERT AN
BIBLIOGRAPHY: THE WORLDS OF LARRY NIVEN   MS
   TALES OF KNOWN SPACE: THE UNIVERSE OF LARRY NIVEN
                                     NIVEN, LARRY   AC
BIOGRAPHICAL NOTES   MS
   HOLDING YOUR EIGHT HANDS   LUCIE-SMITH, EDWARD AN
BIOGRAPHIES OF AUTHORS   MS
   SCIENCE FACT/FICTION   FARRELL/GAGE/&   AN
BRITISH INTERPLANETARY SOCIETY, THE   MS
   LAURIE'S SPACE ANNUAL   ANONYMOUS   AN
CAST AND CREDITS   MS
   GHOULS, THE   HAINING, PETER   AN
CHAD OLIVER SF/FANTASY INDEX, A   MS
   3 TO THE HIGHEST POWER   NOLAN, WILLIAM F.   AN
CHECK YOUR UNDERSTANDING   MS
   JOURNEYS IN SCIENCE FICTION   LOUGHLIN, RICHARD L. AN
CHRONOLOGY OF SCIENCE FICTION, A   MS
   LOOKING AHEAD   ALLEN, D. & L.   AN
CLARK ASHTON SMITH: MASTER OF FANTASY   IN
   OUT OF SPACE AND TIME   SMITH, CLARK ASHTON AC
CONTRIBUTORS   MS
   CHRONICLES OF A COMER AND OTHER RELIGIOUS SCIENCE FICTION
   STORIES   ELWOOD, ROGER   AN
CONTRIBUTORS' NOTES   MS
   QUARK/1   DELANY & HACKER   OA
   QUARK/3   DELANY & HACKER   OA
CONTRIBUTORS, THE   MS
   FASTER THAN LIGHT   DANN & ZEBROWSKI   OA
CRITICAL WORKS ABOUT SCIENCE FICTION   MS
   SCIENCE FICTION NOVELLAS   HARRISON & MCNELLY AN
DISCUSSION QUESTIONS   MS
   SCIENCE FACT/FICTION   FARRELL/GAGE/&   AN
ED EMSHWILLER   MS
   AGAIN, DANGEROUS VISIONS   ELLISON, HARLAN   OA
EDITORS, THE   MS
   SURVIVAL PRINTOUT   TOTAL EFFECT   AN
FOR FURTHER READING   MS
   SCIENCE FICTION   BURTON, S. H.   AN
FROM SCIENCE FICTION TO SCIENCE FACT: THE UNIVERSE
                                               MS
   SF:59, THE YEAR'S GREATEST SCIENCE FICTION AND FANTASY
                                     MERRIL, JUDITH   AN
FURTHER READING   MS
   BIO-FUTURES   SARGENT, PAMELA   AN
   MORE WOMEN OF WONDER   SARGENT, PAMELA   AN
FURTHER READINGS   MS
   NEW AWARENESS, THE   WARRICK & GREENBERG AN
GALACTIC LOVEPOEM TWO   PM
   BEYOND THIS HORIZON   CARRELL, CHRISTOPHER OA
GENERALIZED NONFICTION BIBLIOGRAPHY   MS
   VOYAGES: SCENARIOS FOR A SHIP CALLED EARTH
                                     SAUER, ROB   AN
GLOSSARY   MS
   GREAT SCIENCE FICTION STORIES ABOUT THE MOON
                                     DIKTY, T. E.   AN
   INTRODUCING SCIENCE FICTION   ALDISS, BRIAN W.   AN
   SCIENCE FICTION   BURTON, S. H.   AN
HONOR ROLL, THE   MS
   MASTERS' CHOICE   JANIFER, LAURENCE M. AN
HONORABLE MENTIONS   MS
   BEST SCIENCE FICTION OF THE YEAR, THE NO. 2
                                     CARR, TERRY   AN
   BEST SCIENCE FICTION OF THE YEAR, THE NO. 3
                                     CARR, TERRY   AN
   10TH ANNUAL OF THE YEAR'S BEST S-F, THE
                                     MERRIL, JUDITH   AN
   6TH ANNUAL OF THE YEAR'S BEST S-F, THE MERRIL, JUDITH AN
   7TH ANNUAL OF THE YEAR'S BEST S-F, THE MERRIL, JUDITH AN
   8TH ANNUAL OF THE YEAR'S BEST S-F, THE MERRIL, JUDITH AN
   9TH ANNUAL OF THE YEAR'S BEST S-F, THE MERRIL, JUDITH AN
HUGO AWARDS   MS
   NEBULA AWARD STORIES 8   ASIMOV, ISAAC   AN
INDEX   MS
   INSIDE INFORMATION   MOWSHOWITZ, ABBE   AN
   NEW AWARENESS, THE   WARRICK & GREENBERG AN
INDEX OF AUTHORS   MS
   PLAYBOY BOOK OF HORROR AND THE SUPERNATURAL, THE
                                     PLAYBOY, EDITORS OF AN
   PLAYBOY BOOK OF SCIENCE FICTION AND FANTASY, THE
                                     PLAYBOY, EDITORS OF AN
INDEX OF AUTHORS AND TITLES   MS
   SCIENCE FACT/FICTION   FARRELL/GAGE/&   AN
INDEX TO VOLUMES 1-10   MS
   ORBIT 10   KNIGHT, DAMON   OA
INDEX, THE BEST SCIENCE-FICTION STORIES: 1949-1954
                                               MS
   BEST SCIENCE-FICTION STORIES: 1954, THE
                                     BLEILER & DIKTY   AN
JOHN JAKES BIBLIOGRAPHY, A   MS
   BEST OF JOHN JAKES, THE   JAKES, JOHN W.   AC
JOHN W. CAMPBELL, JR. AWARDS 1973 - 1975, THE MS
   NEW VOICES IN SCIENCE FICTION   MARTIN, GEORGE R. R. OA
LONGER STORIES TOO GOOD TO BE MISSED   MS
   TALES BEYOND TIME   DE CAMP, L. S.&C.   AN
MEMORY MACHINE, THE   MS
   ORBIT 14   KNIGHT, DAMON   OA
   ORBIT 15   KNIGHT, DAMON   OA
   ORBIT 16   KNIGHT, DAMON   OA
   ORBIT 17   KNIGHT, DAMON   OA
   ORBIT 18   KNIGHT, DAMON   OA
MILESTONES . NOVELS WORTH READING   MS
   3000 YEARS OF FANTASY AND SCIENCE FICTION
                                     DE CAMP, L. S.&C.   AN

MISC. MATERIAL   (CONTINUED)
MORE GOOD READING IN SCIENCE FICTION   MS
  BEYOND TOMORROW   KNIGHT, DAMON   AN
NEBULA AWARDS   MS
  NEBULA AWARD STORIES 8   ASIMOV, ISAAC   AN
NEBULA AWARDS, 1975: WIN, PLACE, AND SHOW   MS
  NEBULA AWARD STORIES 11   LE GUIN, URSULA K.   AN
NEBULA WINNERS, 1965-1973, THE   MS
  NEBULA AWARD STORIES 9   WILHELM, KATE   AN
NOTES FROM INFINITY   MS
  INFINITY 2   HOSKINS, ROBERT   OA
  INFINITY 3   HOSKINS, ROBERT   OA
  INFINITY 4   HOSKINS, ROBERT   OA
NOTES ON SOME OF THE AUTHORS   MS
  RUSSIAN SCIENCE FICTION, 1969   MAGIDOFF, ROBERT   AN
NOTES ON THE AUTHORS   MS
  AIR OF MARS AND OTHER STORIES, THE GINSBURG, MIRRA   AN
  VIEW FROM ANOTHER SHORE   ROTTENSTEINER, FRANZ AN
NOTES ON THE CONTRIBUTORS   MS
  NEW CONSTELLATIONS   DISCH & NAYLOR   OA
OBITUARIES: MAL DEAN, MAC KING   MS
  NEW WORLDS NO. 6   PLATT & BAILEY   OA
OTHER WORKS OF INTEREST   MS
  AURORA: BEYOND EQUALITY   MCINTYRE & ANDERSON   OA
PERUVIAN MUMMY MASK   IL
  SCIENCE FICTION   BRODKIN & PEARSON   AN
PREFACE   MS
  ABOVE THE HUMAN LANDSCAPE   MCNELLY & STOVER   AN
PRONUNCIATION KEY   MS
  SCIENCE FACT/FICTION   FARRELL/GAGE/&   AN
PULP ARTISTS, THE   IL
  FANTASTIC PULPS, THE   HAINING, PETER   AN
RAY BRADBURY SF/FANTASY INDEX, A   MS
  3 TO THE HIGHEST POWER   NOLAN, WILLIAM F.   AN
READER'S GUIDE TO SF   MS
  ANOTHER WORLD   DOZOIS, GARDNER R.   AN
RECOMMENDED OTHER STORIES   MS
  GREAT STORIES OF SCIENCE FICTION   LEINSTER, MURRAY   AN
RECOMMENDED READING   MS
  HUMAN-MACHINES   SCORTIA & ZEBROWSKI AN
  INTRODUCING SCIENCE FICTION   ALDISS, BRIAN W.   AN
SATURN FACTS   MS
  LAURIE'S SPACE ANNUAL   ANONYMOUS   AN
SCIENCE FICTION DICTIONARY   MS
  TRAVELLERS OF SPACE   GREENBERG , MARTIN   AN
SCIENCE-FICTION AWARDS   MS
  SCIENCE FACT/FICTION   FARRELL/GAGE/&   AN
SELECTED BIBLIOGRAPHY   MS
  AMERICAN GOVERNMENT THROUGH SCIENCE FICTION
                                     OLANDER/GREENBERG/&   AN
  SCHOOL AND SOCIETY THROUGH SCIENCE FICTION
                                     OLANDER/GREENBERG/&   AN
SELECTED BIBLIOGRAPHY: INTERSTELLAR TRAVEL, A   MS
  FASTER THAN LIGHT   DANN & ZEBROWSKI   OA
SIGNIFICANT EVENTS IN LUNAR EXPLORATION   MS
  GREAT SCIENCE FICTION STORIES ABOUT THE MOON
                                     DIKTY, T. E.   AN
SUGGESTED READING   MS
  CENTURY OF SCIENCE FICTION, A   KNIGHT, DAMON   AN
SUGGESTIONS FOR FURTHER READING   MS
  SCIENCE FICTION NOVELLAS   HARRISON & MCNELLY   AN
  SCIENCE FICTION THROUGH THE AGES 2 EVANS, I. O.   AN
  SCIENCE FICTION: THE FUTURE   ALLEN, DICK   AN
SUGGESTIONS FOR FURTHER READING AND VIEWING   MS
  LOOKING AHEAD   ALLEN, D. & L.   AN
TABLE OF COMPARISONS: EARTH AND MOON   MS
  GREAT SCIENCE FICTION STORIES ABOUT THE MOON
                                     DIKTY, T. E.   AN
THEMATIC CONTENTS   MS
  SPECULATIONS   SANDERS, THOMAS E.   AN
THEODORE STURGEON SF/FANTASY INDEX, A   MS
  3 TO THE HIGHEST POWER   NOLAN, WILLIAM F.   AN
TOPICS FOR SHORTER AND LONGER PAPERS   MS
  LOOKING AHEAD   ALLEN, D. & L.   AN
TOPICS OF WRITING AND RESEARCH   MS
  SCIENCE FICTION: THE FUTURE   ALLEN, DICK   AN
VILLAGE DANCE MASK FROM CEYLON   IL
  SCIENCE FICTION   BRODKIN & PEARSON   AN
ZERO POPULATION GROWTH: A STATEMENT   MS
  VOYAGES: SCENARIOS FOR A SHIP CALLED EARTH
                                     SAUER, ROB   AN

AANDAHL, VANCE
ADAM FROST   SS   PBY 62 04
  FIEND, THE   PLAYBOY, EDITORS OF AN
ADVENTURE IN THE YOLLA BOLLY MIDDLE EEL WILDERNESS, AN
                                         NV   FSF 69 08
  BEST FROM FANTASY AND SCIENCE FICTION: 19
                                     FERMAN, EDWARD L.   AN
BEYOND THE GAME   SS   FSF 68 05
  ARENA: SPORTS SF   FERMAN & MALZBERG   AN
  BEST FROM FANTASY AND SCIENCE FICTION: 18
                                     FERMAN, EDWARD L.   AN
  INTO THE UNKNOWN   CARR, TERRY   AN
  TRANSFORMATIONS II   ROSELLE, DANIEL   AN
IT'S A GREAT BIG WONDERFUL UNIVERSE   SS   FSF 60 11
  BEST FROM FANTASY AND SCIENCE FICTION: 10
                                     MILLS, ROBERT P.   AN
UNFORTUNATE MR. MORKY, THE   SS   FSF 62 10
  8TH ANNUAL OF THE YEAR'S BEST S-F, THE MERRIL, JUDITH   AN
WHEN LILACS LAST IN THE DOORYARD BLOOMED NV   FSF 62 05
  BEST FROM FANTASY AND SCIENCE FICTION: 12
                                     DAVIDSON, AVRAM   AN

ABBOTT, EDWIN A.
PLATLAND: TWO EXCERPTS   EX   SEE 84
  WONDERMAKERS   HOSKINS, ROBERT   AN

ABBOTT, GORDON
AURORA IN ZENITH   SS   NWQ 73 05
  NEW WORLDS NO. 5   MOORCOCK & PLATT   OA

ABERNATHY, ROBERT
AXOLOTL (ALSO AS DEEP SPACE)   SS   FSF 54 01
  BEST SCIENCE FICTION STORIES AND NOVELS: 1955
                                     DIKTY, T. E.   AN
CANAL BUILDERS, THE   SS   ASF 45 01
  EVERY BOY'S BOOK OF OUTER SPACE STORIES
                                     DIKTY, T. E.   AN
DEEP SPACE (AXOLOTL)   SS   FSF 54 01
  5 TALES FROM TOMORROW   DIKTY, T. E.   AN
GRANDMA'S LIE SOAP   SS   FUN 56 02
  SF:57, THE YEAR'S GREATEST SCIENCE FICTION AND FANTASY
                                     MERRIL, JUDITH   AN
HEIRS APPARENT   NV   FSF 54 06
  BEST FROM FANTASY AND SCIENCE FICTION: 4
                                     BOUCHER, ANTHONY   AN
  BEST SCIENCE FICTION STORIES AND NOVELS: 1955
                                     DIKTY, T. E.   AN
HERITAGE   NV   ASF 42 06
  OMNIBUS OF SCIENCE FICTION   CONKLIN, GROFF   AN
JUNIOR   SS   GAL 56 01
  SF: THE BEST OF THE BEST   MERRIL, JUDITH   AN
  SF: THE YEAR'S GREATEST SCIENCE FICTION AND FANTASY
                                     MERRIL, JUDITH   AN
PERIL OF THE BLUE WORLD   SS   PLS 42 WI
  FLIGHT INTO SPACE   WOLLHEIM, DONALD A.   AN
  STORIES OF SCIENTIFIC IMAGINATION GALLANT, JOSEPH   AN
PYRAMID   NV   ASF 54 07
  ANTHROPOLOGY THROUGH SCIENCE FICTION   MASON, C/GREENBERG/& AN
  ASTOUNDING-ANALOG READER, THE VOLUME TWO
                                     HARRISON & ALDISS   AN
  MORE PENGUIN SCIENCE FICTION   ALDISS, BRIAN W.   AN
ROTIFERS, THE   SS   IFS 53 03
  EARTH IS THE STRANGEST PLANET   SILVERBERG, ROBERT   AN
  FIRST WORLD OF IF, THE   QUINN & WULFF   AN
SINGLE COMBAT   SS   FSF 55 01
  CITIES OF WONDER   KNIGHT, DAMON   AN
  SOCIOLOGY THROUGH SCIENCE FICTION MILSTEAD/GREENBERG/& AN
STRANGE EXODUS   SS   PLS 50 FL
  SPACE ODYSSEYS   ALDISS, BRIAN W.   AN

ABLEMAN, PAUL
MAN'S ESTATE   SS   SAG 70
  SCIENCE AGAINST MAN   CHEETHAM, ANTHONY   OA

ABRAMOV, ALEXANDER
JOURNEY ACROSS THREE WORLDS   SS C
  JOURNEY ACROSS THREE WORLDS   ANONYMOUS   AN

ABRAMOV, SERGEI
JOURNEY ACROSS THREE WORLDS   SS C
  JOURNEY ACROSS THREE WORLDS   ANONYMOUS   AN

ACKERMAN, FORREST J.
BEST SCIENCE FICTION FOR 1973   AN   ACE 73
SCIENCE FICTION WORLDS OF FORREST J. ACKERMAN & FRIENDS
                                         AC   POW 69 04
  ABOUT THE AUTHOR   IN
    WORLDS OF A. E. VAN VOGT, THE   VAN VOGT, A. E.   AC
  AFTERWORD   MS
    BEST SCIENCE FICTION FOR 1973   ACKERMAN, FORREST J. AN
  AND THEN THE COVER WAS BARE   SS
    SCIENCE FICTION WORLDS OF FORREST J. ACKERMAN & FRIENDS
                                     ACKERMAN, FORREST J. AC
  ATOMIC MONUMENT, THE (MEMORIAL)   SS C ASF 46 04
    SCIENCE FICTION WORLDS OF FORREST J. ACKERMAN & FRIENDS
                                     ACKERMAN, FORREST J. AC
  BEHIND THE ATE BALL (SEE A MARTIAN ODDITY) TC
  BIG SLEEP, THE   SS   50
    SCIENCE FICTION WORLDS OF FORREST J. ACKERMAN & FRIENDS
                                     ACKERMAN, FORREST J. AC
  BURN WITCH, BURN   SS   SEX 58
    SCIENCE FICTION WORLDS OF FORREST J. ACKERMAN & FRIENDS
                                     ACKERMAN, FORREST J. AC
  CONFESSIONS OF A SCIENCE FICTION ADDICT AR AFT 57
    SCIENCE FICTION WORLDS OF FORREST J. ACKERMAN & FRIENDS
                                     ACKERMAN, FORREST J. AC
  COUNT DOWN TO DOOM   SS C FMS 66
    SCIENCE FICTION WORLDS OF FORREST J. ACKERMAN & FRIENDS
                                     ACKERMAN, FORREST J. AC
  DEATH RIDES THE SPACEWAYS   SS
    AUTHENTIC BOOK OF SPACE   CAMPBELL, H. J.   AN
  DHACTWHUJ- REMEMBER?   SS C SSS 49 04
    SCIENCE FICTION WORLDS OF FORREST J. ACKERMAN & FRIENDS
                                     ACKERMAN, FORREST J. AC
  DWELLERS IN THE DUST   SS   FBK 48 04
    SCIENCE FICTION WORLDS OF FORREST J. ACKERMAN & FRIENDS
                                     ACKERMAN, FORREST J. AC
  EGGS AND I, THE   IN
    TWO DOZEN DRAGON EGGS   WOLLHEIM, DONALD A.   AN
  FAR-OUT PHILOSOPHER OF SCIENCE FICTION, THE AR   49
    SCIENCE FICTION WORLDS OF FORREST J. ACKERMAN & FRIENDS
                                     ACKERMAN, FORREST J. AC
  GIRL WHO WASN'T THERE, THE   SS C GAM 63 01
    SCIENCE FICTION WORLDS OF FORREST J. ACKERMAN & FRIENDS
                                     ACKERMAN, FORREST J. AC
  HOUSE IN THE TWILIGHT ZONE, THE   AR
    SCIENCE FICTION WORLDS OF FORREST J. ACKERMAN & FRIENDS
                                     ACKERMAN, FORREST J. AC

ACKERMAN, FORREST J.   ALDISS, BRIAN W.

ACKERMAN, FORREST J. (CONTINUED)
  IN MEMORIAM- HARL VINCENT   MS
    NEBULA AWARD STORIES NO. 4   ANDERSON, POUL   AN
  INTRODUCTION   IN
    BEST SCIENCE FICTION FOR 1973   ACKERMAN, FORREST J. AN
    IF THIS GOES ON   NUETZEL, CHARLES   AN
    IMAGES OF TOMORROW   NUETZEL, CHARLES   AC
    SCIENCE FICTION WORLDS OF FORREST J. ACKERMAN & FRIENDS
                                    ACKERMAN, FORREST J. AC
    STARDRIFT AND OTHER FANTASTIC FLOTSAM PETAJA, EMIL   AC
  LADY TAKES A POWDER, THE   SS C INS 53
    SCIENCE FICTION WORLDS OF FORREST J. ACKERMAN & FRIENDS
                                    ACKERMAN, FORREST J. AC
  LAUGH, CLONE, LAUGH   SS C NEW 69 AC
    MORE THAN SUPERHUMAN   VAN VOGT, A. E.   AC
    SCIENCE FICTION WORLDS OF FORREST J. ACKERMAN & FRIENDS
                                    ACKERMAN, FORREST J. AC
  LETTER TO AN ANGEL   SS
    SCIENCE FICTION WORLDS OF FORREST J. ACKERMAN & FRIENDS
                                    ACKERMAN, FORREST J. AC
  LURE AND LORE OF "THE BLIND SPOT", THE   AR   51
    SCIENCE FICTION WORLDS OF FORREST J. ACKERMAN & FRIENDS
                                    ACKERMAN, FORREST J. AC
  MAN WHO WAS THIRSTY, THE   SS
    SCIENCE FICTION WORLDS OF FORREST J. ACKERMAN & FRIENDS
                                    ACKERMAN, FORREST J. AC
  MARTIAN ODDITY, A (BEHIND THE ATE BALL)   SS   MAR 50 11
    SCIENCE FICTION WORLDS OF FORREST J. ACKERMAN & FRIENDS
                                    ACKERMAN, FORREST J. AC
  METROPOLIS UEBER ALLES   AR   63
    SCIENCE FICTION WORLDS OF FORREST J. ACKERMAN & FRIENDS
                                    ACKERMAN, FORREST J. AC
  MICRO MAN   SS   NWS 46 02
    SCIENCE FICTION WORLDS OF FORREST J. ACKERMAN & FRIENDS
                                    ACKERMAN, FORREST J. AC
  MIRROR IMAGE (SEE TIME TO CHANGE)   TC C
  MONSTER MAN, SIRE OF SLAN, THE   IN
    MONSTERS   VAN VOGT, A. E.   AC
  MUTE QUESTION, THE   SS   OWS 50 09
    ADVENTURES IN TOMORROW   CROSSEN, KENDELL F. AN
    IF THIS GOES ON   NUETZEL, CHARLES   AN
    MUTANTS   SILVERBERG, ROBERT   AN
  RADCLYFFE EFFECT, THE   SS
    SCIENCE FICTION WORLDS OF FORREST J. ACKERMAN & FRIENDS
                                    ACKERMAN, FORREST J. AC
  RECORD, THE   SS C   40
    SCIENCE FICTION WORLDS OF FORREST J. ACKERMAN & FRIENDS
                                    ACKERMAN, FORREST J. AC
  SHORTEST SCIENCE FICTION STORY EVER TOLD, THE SS   VTX 73 06
    TOMORROW, AND TOMORROW, AND TOMORROW...
                                    HEINTZ/HERBERT/JOOS/ AN
  TARZAN AND THE GOLDEN LOIN   SS   48
    SCIENCE FICTION WORLDS OF FORREST J. ACKERMAN & FRIENDS
                                    ACKERMAN, FORREST J. AC
  TIME TO CHANGE (MIRROR IMAGE)   SS C   68
    SCIENCE FICTION WORLDS OF FORREST J. ACKERMAN & FRIENDS
                                    ACKERMAN, FORREST J. AC
  WHEN FRIGHTHOOD WAS IN FLOWER   SS
    SCIENCE FICTION WORLDS OF FORREST J. ACKERMAN & FRIENDS
                                    ACKERMAN, FORREST J. AC

ACKERSON, DUANE
  DNA   PM
    BEST SF: 1974   HARRISON & ALDISS   AN
  FUTURE SPORTSMAN'S MANUAL, THE   SS
    FUTURE PASTIMES   EDELSTEIN, SCOTT   OA
  SCIENCE FICTION STORY   PM   EDG 74
    BEST SF: 1974   HARRISON & ALDISS   AN
  SIGN AT THE END OF THE UNIVERSE   SS   ALT 74
    ALTERNATES   GERROLD, DAVID   OA

ADAM, HELEN
  DAUGHTER OF ROSES   PM   QRK 70 01
    QUARK/1   DELANY & HACKER   OA
  TRUE REASON FOR THE DREADFUL DEATH OF MR. REX ARUNDEL, THE
                                                 NV   QRK 71 04
    QUARK/4   DELANY & HACKER   OA

ADAMS, LOUIS J. A.
  DARK CONCEPTION   SS   FSF 64 11
    BEST FROM FANTASY AND SCIENCE FICTION: 14
                                    DAVIDSON, AVRAM   AN

ADAMS, PETE
  PLANTING TIME   SS C NEW 76 AN
    ANTIGRAV: COSMIC COMEDIES   STRICK, PHILIP   AN
    GALACTIC EMPIRES VOLUME ONE   ALDISS, BRIAN W.   AN

ADDOBATI, MICHAEL
  SIDE VIEW OF A CIRCLE   SS   NOV 74 04
    NOVA 4   HARRISON, HARRY   OA

ADLARD, MARK
  OTHER TRADITION, THE   AR
    BEYOND THIS HORIZON   CARRELL, CHRISTOPHER OA
  THEOPHILUS   SS
    BEYOND THIS HORIZON   CARRELL, CHRISTOPHER OA

AGEE, JAMES
  MOTHER'S TALE, A   NV   52
    ECO-FICTION   STADLER, JOHN   AN

AHERN, MICHAEL
  CAKE CHRONICLE, THE   SS   NWB 73 05
    NEW WORLDS QUARTERLY NO. 5   MOORCOCK, MICHAEL   OA

AICKMAN, ROBERT
  CICERONES, THE   SS
    TRAVELLERS BY NIGHT   DERLETH, AUGUST   OA

AIKEN, CONRAD
  MR. ARCULARIS   SS   22
    MOONLIGHT TRAVELER, THE   STERN, PHILIP VAN D. AN
    PERCHANCE TO DREAM   KNIGHT, DAMON   AN
  ONEIROMACHIA   PM   ATL 61 10
    7TH ANNUAL OF THE YEAR'S BEST S-F, THE MERRIL, JUDITH AN

AKERS, ALAN BURT
  WIZARD OF SCORPIO   NV
    DAW SCIENCE FICTION READER, THE WOLLHEIM, DONALD A. OA

ALBEE, GEORGE SUMNER
  TOP, THE   SS   FSF 62 08
    12 GREAT CLASSICS OF SCIENCE FICTION CONKLIN, GROFF AN

ALDANI, LINO
  GOOD NIGHT, SOPHIE   NV
    VIEW FROM ANOTHER SHORE   ROTTENSTEINER, FRANZ AN

ALDISS, BRIAN W. AND HARRY HARRISON
  DECADE THE 1940S   AN H MCM 75
  DECADE THE 1950S   AN H MCM 76
  DECADE THE 1960S   AN H MCM 77
  FAREWELL FANTASTIC VENUS   AN H MDN 68
  NEBULA AWARD STORIES NO. 2   AN H DBL 67

ALDISS, BRIAN W.   ALSO AS   C. C. SHACKLETON
                     SEE ALSO   CO-EDITOR HARRY HARRISON
  AIRS OF EARTH, THE   AC H FAB 63
  ALL ABOUT VENUS   AN   DEL 68 12
  BEST FANTASY STORIES   AN H FAB 62
  BEST SCIENCE FICTION STORIES OF BRIAN W. ALDISS AC H FAB 65
    ALSO AS "WHO CAN REPLACE A MAN?"
  BEST SCIENCE FICTION STORIES OF BRIAN W. ALDISS (REVISED)
                                                 AC H FAB 71
  BOOK OF BRIAN ALDISS, THE   AC   DAW 72
    IN ENGLAND AS "THE COMIC INFERNO"
  BRIAN ALDISS OMNIBUS 2   AC H SID 71
  BRIAN ALDISS OMNIBUS, A   AC H SID 69
  CANOPY OF TIME, THE   AC H FAB 59
  COMIC INFERNO, THE   AC   NLB 73 10
    SEE "THE BOOK OF BRIAN ALDISS"
  EVIL EARTHS   AN H WEI 75
    AN ANTHOLOGY OF WAY-BACK-WHEN FUTURES
  GALACTIC EMPIRES VOLUME ONE   AN H WEI 76
    AN ANTHOLOGY OF WAY-BACK-WHEN FUTURES
  GALACTIC EMPIRES VOLUME TWO   AN H WEI 76
    AN ANTHOLOGY OF WAY-BACK-WHEN FUTURES
  GALAXIES LIKE GRAINS OF SAND   AC   SIG 60 07
  HOTHOUSE   NO H FAB 62
    SEE "THE LONG AFTERNOON OF EARTH"
  INTANGIBLES INC. AND OTHER STORIES   AC H FAB 69
  INTRODUCING SCIENCE FICTION   AN H FAB 64
  LONG AFTERNOON OF EARTH, THE   NO   SIG 62 01
    IN ENGLAND AS "HOTHOUSE"
  MOMENT OF ECLIPSE, THE   AC H FAB 70
  MORE PENGUIN SCIENCE FICTION   AN   PEN 63
    ALSO IN "THE PENGUIN SCIENCE FICTION OMNIBUS"
  NEANDERTHAL PLANET   AC   AVN 70 01
  NO TIME LIKE TOMORROW   AC   SIG 59 07
  PENGUIN SCIENCE FICTION   AN   PEN 61
    ALSO IN "THE PENGUIN SCIENCE FICTION OMNIBUS"
  PENGUIN SCIENCE FICTION OMNIBUS, THE   AN   PEN 73
  SALIVA TREE AND OTHER STRANGE GROWTHS, THE   AC H FAB 66
  SPACE ODYSSEYS   AN H WEI 75
  SPACE OPERA   AN H WEI 74
  SPACE, TIME AND NATHANIEL   AC H FAB 57
    ALSO IN "BRIAN ALDISS OMNIBUS II"
  STARSWARM   AC   SIG 64 01
  WHO CAN REPLACE A MAN?   AC H HBW 66
    SEE "BEST SCIENCE FICTION STORIES OF BRIAN W. ALDISS"
  YET MORE PENGUIN SCIENCE FICTION   AN   PEN 64
    ALSO IN "THE PENGUIN SCIENCE FICTION OMNIBUS"
  AFTERWORD: A DAY IN THE LIFE-STYLE OF...   MS
    BEST SF: 1971   HARRISON & ALDISS   AN
  AFTERWORD: SCIENCE FICTION ON THE TITANIC   MS
    BEST SF: 75, THE NINTH ANNUAL   HARRISON & ALDISS   AN
  AFTERWORD: THE GALAXY BEGINS AT HOME   MS
    BEST SF: 1974   HARRISON & ALDISS   AN
  AFTERWORD: THE WIZARD AND THE PLUMBER   MS
    BEST SF: 1973   HARRISON & ALDISS   AN
  AFTERWORD: THE YEAR OF THE BIG SPRING CLEAN   MS
    BEST SF: 1972   HARRISON & ALDISS   AN
  AHEAD (THE FAILED MEN)   SS   SCF 56 05
    *BEST SCIENCE FICTION STORIES OF BRIAN W. ALDISS
                                    ALDISS, BRIAN W.   AC
  AIMEZ-VOUS HOLMAN HUNT?   SS   EPC 75
    EPOCH   ELWOOD & SILVERBERG OA
  ALL THE WORLD'S TEARS   SS   NEB 57 05
    BOOK OF BRIAN ALDISS, THE   ALDISS, BRIAN W.   AC
    CANOPY OF TIME, THE   ALDISS, BRIAN W.   AC
    GALAXIES LIKE GRAINS OF SAND   ALDISS, BRIAN W.   AC
  ALL THOSE ENDURING OLD CHARMS   SS   NWR 74 23
    NEW WRITINGS IN SF. 23   BULMER, KENNETH   OA
  ALWAYS SOMEBODY THERE   SS
    TOMORROW: NEW WORLDS OF SCIENCE FICTION
                                    ELWOOD, ROGER   OA
  AMEN AND OUT   SS   NWS 66 08
    BOOK OF BRIAN ALDISS, THE   ALDISS, BRIAN W.   AC
    WORLD'S BEST SCIENCE FICTION: 1967 WOLLHEIM & CARR   AN
  AND THE STAGNATION OF THE HEART   SS   NWS 68 12
    FOUR FOR THE FUTURE   HARRISON, HARRY   AN

ALDISS, BRIAN W.   (CONTINUED)
  MOMENT OF ECLIPSE, THE   ALDISS, BRIAN W.   AC
  THIS SIDE OF INFINITY   CARR, TERRY   AN
ANOTHER LITTLE BOY   SS   NWS 66 09
  BEST SCIENCE FICTION STORIES OF BRIAN W. ALDISS (REVISED)
                                          ALDISS, BRIAN W.   AC
  BEST SF STORIES FROM NEW WORLDS NO. 2, THE
                                          MOORCOCK, MICHAEL   AN
APERTURE MOMENT, THE   GR   EPC 75
  EPOCH   ELWOOD & SILVERBERG OA
APPEARANCE OF LIFE   SS   76
  ANDROMEDA I   WESTON, PETER   OA
  1977 ANNUAL WORLD'S BEST SF, THE   WOLLHEIM, DONALD A. AN
AS FOR OUR FATAL CONTINUITY...   SS   NWQ 72 03
  BEST SF: 1972   HARRISON & ALDISS   AN
  BOOK OF BRIAN ALDISS, THE   ALDISS, BRIAN W.   AC
  NEW WORLDS QUARTERLY NO. 3   MOORCOCK, MICHAEL   OA
AUTO-ANCESTRAL FRACTURE   NV   NWS 67 12
  SF: AUTHORS' CHOICE 2   HARRISON, HARRY   AN
AWFUL LOT OF COPY, AN   MS
  BEST SF: 1969   HARRISON & ALDISS   AN
BASIS FOR NEGOTIATION   NV   NWS 62 01
  AIRS OF EARTH, THE   ALDISS, BRIAN W.   AC
 *BEST SCIENCE FICTION STORIES OF BRIAN W. ALDISS
                                          ALDISS, BRIAN W.   AC
  BRIAN ALDISS OMNIBUS, A   ALDISS, BRIAN W.   AC
  LAMBDA I AND OTHER STORIES   CARNELL, JOHN   AN
BIG SISTER   SI
  ALL ABOUT VENUS   ALDISS, BRIAN W.   AN
BLIGHTED PROFILE   SS   SCF 58 06
  CANOPY OF TIME, THE   ALDISS, BRIAN W.   AC
  NO TIME LIKE TOMORROW   ALDISS, BRIAN W.   AC
BONES OF BERTRAND RUSSELL, THE   SS   NWR 76 28
  NEW WRITINGS IN SF. 28   BULMER, KENNETH   OA
BURNING QUESTION   SS   FSF 66 12
  POLITICAL SCIENCE FICTION   GREENBERG& WARRICK AN
BUT WHO CAN REPLACE A MAN?   SS   INF 58 06
  MEN AND MACHINES   SILVERBERG, ROBERT AN
  OUT OF THIS WORLD 2   WILLIAMS-ELLIS& OWEN AN
  TALES OF SCIENCE FICTION   BALL, BRIAN W.   AN
BUT WITHOUT ORIFICES   SS   EPC 75
  EPOCH   ELWOOD & SILVERBERG OA
CARDIAC ARREST   NV   FAN 70 12
  BOOK OF BRIAN ALDISS, THE   ALDISS, BRIAN W.   AC
CAREFULLY OBSERVED WOMEN   SS   NWR 75 26
  NEW WRITINGS IN SF. 26   BULMER, KENNETH   OA
CARRION COUNTRY   SS   NWS 58 11
  NO TIME LIKE TOMORROW   ALDISS, BRIAN W.   AC
CASTLE SCENE WITH PENITENTS   SS   ORB 73 12
  ORBIT 12   KNIGHT, DAMON   OA
CIRCULATION OF THE BLOOD, THE   NV   IMP 66 03
  FOUR FOR THE FUTURE   HARRISON, HARRY   AN
  MOMENT OF ECLIPSE, THE   ALDISS, BRIAN W.   AC
  WINDOW ON THE FUTURE   HILL, DOUGLAS   AN
CLOUDED JUDGEMENTS   SI
  ALL ABOUT VENUS   ALDISS, BRIAN W.   AN
COMIC INFERNO   NA   GAL 63 02
  BOOK OF BRIAN ALDISS, THE   ALDISS, BRIAN W.   AC
  EIGHTH GALAXY READER, THE   POHL, FREDERIK   AN
  SCIENCE FICTION HORIZONS NO. 1   BOARDMAN, TOM JR.   AN
CONFLUENCE   SS   PUN 67 08
  MOMENT OF ECLIPSE, THE   ALDISS, BRIAN W.   AC
  SF12   MERRIL, JUDITH   AN
CONVICTION   SS   NWS 56 09
  SPACE, TIME AND NATHANIEL   ALDISS, BRIAN W.   AC
CRIMINAL RECORD   SS   SCF 54 07
  SPACE, TIME AND NATHANIEL   ALDISS, BRIAN W.   AC
CROWDED CITIES OF PATAGONIA, THE   PL   NWB 75 09
  NEW WORLDS NINE   BAILEY, HILARY   OA
CULTURAL SIDE EFFECT, A   SS   FST 74
  FINAL STAGE   FERMAN & MALZBERG   OA
DAFFODIL RETURNS THE SMILE, THE   SS   NWR 75 26
  NEW WRITINGS IN SF. 26   BULMER, KENNETH   OA
DANGER: RELIGION| (MATRIX)   TC   SCF 62 10
  INNER LANDSCAPE, THE   MOORCOCK, MICHAEL   AN
  NEANDERTHAL PLANET   ALDISS, BRIAN W.   AC
  SALIVA TREE AND OTHER STRANGE GROWTHS, THE
                                          ALDISS, BRIAN W.   AC
  UNFRIENDLY FUTURE, THE   BOARDMAN, TOM JR.   AN
DARK SOUL OF THE NIGHT, THE   SS
  IDES OF TOMORROW, THE   CARR, TERRY   OA
DARK THEY WERE AND GOLEM-EYED   SI
  EVIL EARTHS   ALDISS, BRIAN W.   AN
DAY EQUALITY BROKE OUT, THE   MS
  BEST SF: 1970   HARRISON & ALDISS   AN
DAY OF THE DOOMED KING   SS   SCF 65 11
  SALIVA TREE AND OTHER STRANGE GROWTHS, THE
                                          ALDISS, BRIAN W.   AC
DAY WE EMBARKED FOR CYTHERA, THE   SS   NWQ 71 01
  MOMENT OF ECLIPSE, THE   ALDISS, BRIAN W.   AC
  NEW WORLDS QUARTERLY NO. 1   MOORCOCK, MICHAEL   OA
DELICIOUS CIRCLE, A   PL   NWB 75 09
  NEW WORLDS NINE   BAILEY, HILARY   OA
DIAGRAMS FOR THREE ENIGMATIC STORIES   GR   FST 74
  FINAL STAGE   FERMAN & MALZBERG   OA
DISHONESTIES OF A LONELY FILLING STATION   PL   NWB 75 09
  NEW WORLDS NINE   BAILEY, HILARY   OA
DOWN THE UP ESCALATION   SS   LOM 67
  MOMENT OF ECLIPSE, THE   ALDISS, BRIAN W.   AC
  NEW TOMORROWS, THE   SPINRAD, NORMAN   AN
DUMB SHOW   SS   NEB 56 12
  ASPECTS OF SCIENCE FICTION   DOHERTY, G. D.   AN
 *BEST SCIENCE FICTION STORIES OF BRIAN W. ALDISS
                                          ALDISS, BRIAN W.   AC
  SPACE, TIME AND NATHANIEL   ALDISS, BRIAN W.   AC

ALDISS, BRIAN W.   (CONTINUED)
E OF HER VOICE, THE   SS   NWR 73 22
  NEW WRITINGS IN SF. 22   BULMER, KENNETH   OA
ENVOI   MS
  SPACE OPERA   ALDISS, BRIAN W.   AN
EPILOGUE   MS
  GALACTIC EMPIRES VOLUME TWO   ALDISS, BRIAN W.   AN
EQUATOR   NA   NWS 58 09
  FUTURE MAKERS, THE   HAINING, PETER   AN
ERGOT SHOW, THE   SS   NOV 72 02
  ANTIGRAV: COSMIC COMEDIES   STRICK, PHILIP   AN
  NOVA 2   HARRISON, HARRY   AN
ETERNAL THEME OF EXILE, THE   SS   NWR 74 23
  NEW WRITINGS IN SF. 23   BULMER, KENNETH   OA
EVERGREEN   NV   FSF 61 12
  LONG AFTERNOON OF EARTH, THE   ALDISS, BRIAN W.   NO
EXILE IS OUR LOT   SI
  SPACE OPERA   ALDISS, BRIAN W.   AN
EXPENSIVE DELICATE SHIP, THE   SS   NOV 73 03
  NOVA 3   HARRISON, HARRY   AN
FAILED MEN, THE   SS   SCF 56 05
  NO TIME LIKE TOMORROW   ALDISS, BRIAN W.   AC
  SPACE, TIME AND NATHANIEL   ALDISS, BRIAN W.   AC
FLOWERS OF THE FOREST, THE   SS   SCF 57 08
  WEIRD SHADOWS FROM BEYOND   CARNELL, JOHN   AN
FOREWORD   IN
  ALL ABOUT VENUS   ALDISS, BRIAN W.   AN
FOREWORD TO "THE HEAT DEATH OF THE UNIVERSE" IN
  MIRROR OF INFINITY, THE   SILVERBERG, ROBERT AN
FULL SUN   SS   ORB 67 02
  CREATURES FROM BEYOND   CARR, TERRY   AN
  INSIDE INFORMATION   MOWSHOWITZ, ABBE   AN
  ORBIT   2   KNIGHT, DAMON   OA
  WORLD'S BEST SCIENCE FICTION: 1968   WOLLHEIM & CARR   OA
FUTURE ON A CHIPPED PLATE, THE   NV   NWB 73 05
  NEW WORLDS QUARTERLY NO. 5   MOORCOCK, MICHAEL   OA
GAME OF GOD, THE (SEGREGATION)   NV   NWS 58 07
  AIRS OF EARTH, THE   ALDISS, BRIAN W.   AC
  STARSWARM   ALDISS, BRIAN W.   AC
GENE-HIVE (JOURNEY TO THE INTERIOR)   NV   NEB 58 05
  CANOPY OF TIME, THE   ALDISS, BRIAN W.   AC
  GALAXIES LIKE GRAINS OF SAND   ALDISS, BRIAN W.   AC
GESTURE OF FAREWELL   SS   NWS 57 07
  INTRODUCING SCIENCE FICTION   ALDISS, BRIAN W.   AN
  NO TIME LIKE TOMORROW   ALDISS, BRIAN W.   AN
GIRL AND ROBOT WITH FLOWERS   SS   NWS 65 09
  BEST SCIENCE FICTION STORIES OF BRIAN W. ALDISS (REVISED)
                                          ALDISS, BRIAN W.   AC
  SALIVA TREE AND OTHER STRANGE GROWTHS, THE
                                          ALDISS, BRIAN W.   AC
GIRL IN THE TRU-DREAM, THE   SS   FST 74
  FINAL STAGE   FERMAN & MALZBERG   OA
GODLIKE MACHINES, THE   SI
  SPACE OPERA   ALDISS, BRIAN W.   AN
GREAT CHAIN OF BEING WHAT?, THE   SS   NWR 73 22
  NEW WRITINGS IN SF. 22   BULMER, KENNETH   OA
HAVE YOUR HATREDS READY (SEE SECRET OF A MIGHTY CITY)
                                            TC
HEARTS AND ENGINES (SOLDIERS RUNNING)   SS   NWS 60 06
  STARSWARM   ALDISS, BRIAN W.   AC
HERESIES OF THE HUGE GOD   FA   GAL 66 08
  BEST SF 7   CRISPIN, EDMUND   AN
  DARK STARS   SILVERBERG, ROBERT AN
  EVIL EARTHS   ALDISS, BRIAN W.   AN
  INFINITE JESTS   SILVERBERG, ROBERT AN
  INVADERS FROM SPACE   SILVERBERG, ROBERT AN
  MOMENT OF ECLIPSE, THE   ALDISS, BRIAN W.   AC
  TALES OF TERROR FROM OUTER SPACE   CHETWYND-HAYES, R. AN
  TENTH GALAXY READER, THE   POHL, FREDERIK   AN
HOTHOUSE   NV   FSF 61 02
  LONG AFTERNOON OF EARTH, THE   ALDISS, BRIAN W.   NO
  MUTANTS   SILVERBERG, ROBERT AN
  OUT OF THIS WORLD 4   WILLIAMS-ELLIS& OWEN AN
HOUSE THAT JULES BUILT, THE   MS
  BEST SF: 1968   HARRISON & ALDISS   AN
HOW TO BE A SOLDIER (SOLDIERS RUNNING)   SS   NWS 60 06
  AIRS OF EARTH, THE   ALDISS, BRIAN W.   AC
HUNTER AT HIS EASE, THE   SS   SAG 70
  BEST SF: 1971   HARRISON & ALDISS   AN
  SCIENCE AGAINST MAN   CHEETHAM, ANTHONY   AN
I CHING, WHO YOU?   SS   NWR 73 22
  NEW WRITINGS IN SF. 22   BULMER, KENNETH   OA
IMMOBILITY CREW, THE   SS   FST 74
  FINAL STAGE   FERMAN & MALZBERG   OA
IMPOSSIBLE STAR, THE   NV   WOT 63 08
  BEST SCIENCE FICTION FROM WORLDS OF TOMORROW, THE
                                          POHL, FREDERIK   AN
 *BEST SCIENCE FICTION STORIES OF BRIAN W. ALDISS
                                          ALDISS, BRIAN W.   AC
  BRIAN ALDISS OMNIBUS, A   ALDISS, BRIAN W.   AC
IN MEMORIAM- ANNA KAVAN   MS
  NEBULA AWARD STORIES NO. 4   ANDERSON, POUL   AN
IN THE ARENA   SS   IFS 63 07
  BEST SCIENCE FICTION FROM IF, THE   POHL, FREDERIK   AN
  BOOK OF BRIAN ALDISS, THE   ALDISS, BRIAN W.   AC
  SECOND IF READER OF SCIENCE FICTION, THE
                                          POHL, FREDERIK   AN
INCENTIVE   SS   NWS 58 12
  CANOPY OF TIME, THE   ALDISS, BRIAN W.   AC
  GALAXIES LIKE GRAINS OF SAND   ALDISS, BRIAN W.   AC
INTANGIBLES, INC.   NV   SCF 59 02
  BEST FANTASY STORIES   ALDISS, BRIAN W.   AN
  INTANGIBLES INC. AND OTHER STORIES   ALDISS, BRIAN W.   AC
  NEANDERTHAL PLANET   ALDISS, BRIAN W.   AC
INTERNATIONAL SMILE, THE   SS   NEW 63 07
  AIRS OF EARTH, THE   ALDISS, BRIAN W.   AC

ALDISS, BRIAN W.   ALDISS, BRIAN W.

```
ALDISS, BRIAN W.    (CONTINUED)
INTERPRETER, THE                                    SS
  BRIAN ALDISS OMNIBUS, A          ALDISS, BRIAN W.    AC
INTRODUCTION                                         IN
  AIRS OF EARTH, THE               ALDISS, BRIAN W.    AC
  BEST FANTASY STORIES             ALDISS, BRIAN W.    AN
  *BEST SCIENCE FICTION STORIES OF BRIAN W. ALDISS
                                   ALDISS, BRIAN W.    AC
  BOOK OF BRIAN ALDISS, THE        ALDISS, BRIAN W.    AC
  DECADE THE 1940S                 ALDISS & HARRISON   AN
  EVIL EARTHS                      ALDISS, BRIAN W.    AN
  GALACTIC EMPIRES VOLUME ONE      ALDISS, BRIAN W.    AN
  GALACTIC EMPIRES VOLUME TWO      ALDISS, BRIAN W.    AN
  GOLLANCZ - SUNDAY TIMES BEST SF STORIES
                                   ANONYMOUS           OA
  INTRODUCING SCIENCE FICTION      ALDISS, BRIAN W.    AN
  MORE PENGUIN SCIENCE FICTION     ALDISS, BRIAN W.    AN
  PENGUIN SCIENCE FICTION          ALDISS, BRIAN W.    AN
  PENGUIN SCIENCE FICTION OMNIBUS, THE  ALDISS, BRIAN W.  AN
  SPACE ODYSSEYS                   ALDISS, BRIAN W.    AN
  SPACE OPERA                      ALDISS, BRIAN W.    AN
  TWO TALES AND EIGHT TOMORROWS    HARRISON, HARRY     AC
  YET MORE PENGUIN SCIENCE FICTION ALDISS, BRIAN W.    AN
INTRODUCTION                                         IN C
  ASTOUNDING-ANALOG READER, THE VOLUME ONE
                                   HARRISON & ALDISS   AN
  ASTOUNDING-ANALOG READER, THE VOLUME TWO
                                   HARRISON & ALDISS   AN
  DECADE THE 1960S                 ALDISS & HARRISON   AN
  NEBULA AWARD STORIES   NO. 2     ALDISS & HARRISON   AN
IS EVERYTHING AN ILLUSION?                           SI
  SPACE OPERA                      ALDISS, BRIAN W.    AN
JOURNEY TO THE HEARTLAND                             NV  UNI 76 06
  UNIVERSE 6                       CARR, TERRY         OA
JOURNEY TO THE INTERIOR (SEE GENE-HIVE)              TC
JUDAS DANCED (JUDAS DANCING)                         SS  SMG 58 01
  ALPHA 4                          SILVERBERG, ROBERT  AN
  BEST SCIENCE FICTION STORIES OF BRIAN W. ALDISS (REVISED)
                                   ALDISS, BRIAN W.    AC
  CANOPY OF TIME, THE              ALDISS, BRIAN W.    AC
  NO TIME LIKE TOMORROW            ALDISS, BRIAN W.    AC
  SF: AUTHORS' CHOICE              HARRISON, HARRY     AN
JUDAS DANCING (SEE JUDAS DANCED)                     TC
JUNGLE SUBSTITUTE                                    NV  GAL 64 08
  NINTH GALAXY READER, THE         POHL, FREDERIK      AN
KIND OF ARTISTRY, A                                  SS  FSF 62 10
  AIRS OF EARTH, THE               ALDISS, BRIAN W.    AC
  BEST FROM FANTASY AND SCIENCE FICTION: 12
                                   DAVIDSON, AVRAM     AN
  *BEST SCIENCE FICTION STORIES OF BRIAN W. ALDISS
                                   ALDISS, BRIAN W.    AC
  STARSWARM                        ALDISS, BRIAN W.    AC
KNIGHTS OF THE PAPER SPACESHIP: A RETROSPECTIVE GLANCE AT
SCIENCE FICTION                                      MS
  BEST SF: 1967                    HARRISON & ALDISS   AN
LAMBETH BLOSSOM                                      SS  KNT 66 09
  STRANGE BED FELLOWS              SCORTIA, THOMAS N.  AN
LEGENDS OF SMITH'S BURST                             SS  NEB 59 06
  SALIVA TREE AND OTHER STRANGE GROWTHS, THE
                                   ALDISS, BRIAN W.    AC
  STARSWARM                        ALDISS, BRIAN W.    AC
LET'S BE FRANK                                       SS  SCF 57 06
  ABC OF SCIENCE FICTION, AN       BOARDMAN, TOM JR.   AN
  SF: THE BEST OF THE BEST         MERRIL, JUDITH      AN
  SF:58, THE YEAR'S GREATEST SCIENCE FICTION AND FANTASY
                                   MERRIL, JUDITH      AN
LISTEN WITH BIG BROTHER                              SS
  BEST SF: 1974                    HARRISON & ALDISS   AN
LIVE? OUR COMPUTERS WILL DO THAT FOR US              SS  ORB 74 15
  ORBIT 15                         KNIGHT, DAMON       OA
LONELY HABIT, THE                                    SS  EQM 66 06
  SALIVA TREE AND OTHER STRANGE GROWTHS, THE
                                   ALDISS, BRIAN W.    AC
LOOKING ON THE SUNNY SIDE OF AN ECLIPSE              SS  NWR 74 24
  NEW WRITINGS IN SF. 24           BULMER, KENNETH     OA
MALE RESPONSE, THE                                   NO  BCN 61
  BRIAN ALDISS OMNIBUS 2           ALDISS, BRIAN W.    AC
MAN IN HIS TIME                                      SS  SCF 65 04
  *BEST SCIENCE FICTION STORIES OF BRIAN W. ALDISS
                                   ALDISS, BRIAN W.    AC
  BRIAN ALDISS OMNIBUS, A          ALDISS, BRIAN W.    AC
  NEBULA AWARD STORIES   NO. 2     ALDISS & HARRISON   AN
  SCIENCE FICTION ARGOSY, A        KNIGHT, DAMON       AN
  TRAPS OF TIME, THE               MOORCOCK, MICHAEL   AN
MAN ON BRIDGE                                        SS  NWR 64 01
  BEST FROM NEW WRITINGS IN S-F FIRST SELECTION, THE
                                   CARNELL, JOHN       AN
  *BEST SCIENCE FICTION STORIES OF BRIAN W. ALDISS
                                   ALDISS, BRIAN W.    AC
  NEW WRITINGS IN SF.  1           CARNELL, JOHN       OA
MATRIX (SEE DANGER: RELIGION|)                       TC
MOMENT OF ECLIPSE, THE                               SS  NWS 69 05
  BEST SCIENCE FICTION STORIES OF BRIAN W. ALDISS (REVISED)
                                   ALDISS, BRIAN W.    AC
  MOMENT OF ECLIPSE, THE           ALDISS, BRIAN W.    AC
MONSTERS OF INGRATITUDE IV, THE                      SS  NOV 74 04
  NOVA 4                           HARRISON, HARRY     OA
MOON OF DELIGHT (SEE O MOON OF MY DELIGHT|)          TC
MORE PENGUIN SCIENCE FICTION                         AN  PEN 63
  PENGUIN SCIENCE FICTION OMNIBUS, THE  ALDISS, BRIAN W.  AN
MULTI-VALUE MOTORWAY                                 NV  NWS 67 08
  BEST SF STORIES FROM NEW WORLDS 3  MOORCOCK, MICHAEL  AN
MY LADY OF PSYCHIATRIC SORROWS                       SS  UNI 77 07
  UNIVERSE 7                       CARR, TERRY         OA
NEANDERTHAL PLANET (A TOUCH OF NEANDERTHAL)          NV  SFA 60 09
  INTANGIBLES INC. AND OTHER STORIES  ALDISS, BRIAN W.  AC

ALDISS, BRIAN W.       (CONTINUED)
NEANDERTHAL PLANET               ALDISS, BRIAN W.    AC
NEW FATHER CHRISTMAS, THE                            SS  FSF 58 01
  *BEST SCIENCE FICTION STORIES OF BRIAN W. ALDISS
                                   ALDISS, BRIAN W.    AC
  METAL SMILE, THE                 KNIGHT, DAMON       AN
  NO TIME LIKE TOMORROW            ALDISS, BRIAN W.    AC
NIGHT THAT ALL TIME BROKE OUT, THE                   SS  DVS 67 01
  DANGEROUS VISIONS                ELLISON, HARLAN     OA
  EARTH IS THE STRANGEST PLANET    SILVERBERG, ROBERT  AN
NOBODY SPOKE OR WAVED GOODBYE                        SS  NWR 74 23
  NEW WRITINGS IN SF. 23           BULMER, KENNETH     OA
NOMANSLAND                                           NV  FSF 61 04
  LONG AFTERNOON OF EARTH, THE     ALDISS, BRIAN W.    NO
NON-STOP                                             NO  FAB 58
  BRIAN ALDISS OMNIBUS 2           ALDISS, BRIAN W.    AC
NOT FOR AN AGE                                       SS  LOB 55 01
  AD 2500                          WILSON, ANGUS       AN
  *BEST SCIENCE FICTION STORIES OF BRIAN W. ALDISS
                                   ALDISS, BRIAN W.    AC
  NO TIME LIKE TOMORROW            ALDISS, BRIAN W.    AC
  SPACE, TIME AND NATHANIEL        ALDISS, BRIAN W.    AC
O ISHRAEL|                                           SS  NWS 57 04
  CANOPY OF TIME, THE              ALDISS, BRIAN W.    AC
  GALAXIES LIKE GRAINS OF SAND     ALDISS, BRIAN W.    AC
O MOON OF MY DELIGHT| (MOON OF DELIGHT)              NV  NWS 61 03
  AIRS OF EARTH, THE               ALDISS, BRIAN W.    AC
  STARSWARM                        ALDISS, BRIAN W.    AC
OH IN JOSE, THE                                      SS  IMP 66 07
  BEYOND TOMORROW                  HARDING, LEE        AN
OLD FLEEING AND FLEETING IMAGES, THE                 SS  NWR 74 24
  NEW WRITINGS IN SF. 24           BULMER, KENNETH     OA
OLD HUNDREDTH                                        SS  NWS 60 11
  AIRS OF EARTH, THE               ALDISS, BRIAN W.    AC
  ANOTHER WORLD                    DOZOIS, GARDNER R.  AN
  *BEST SCIENCE FICTION STORIES OF BRIAN W. ALDISS
                                   ALDISS, BRIAN W.    AC
  BEST SF  6                       CRISPIN, EDMUND     AN
  SF: AUTHORS' CHOICE 4            HARRISON, HARRY     AN
  STARSWARM                        ALDISS, BRIAN W.    AC
  6TH ANNUAL OF THE YEAR'S BEST S-F, THE  MERRIL, JUDITH  AN
ONE ROLE WITH RELISH                                 SS  NEW 66 AC
  SALIVA TREE AND OTHER STRANGE GROWTHS, THE
                                   ALDISS, BRIAN W.    AC
OPEN QUESTION, THE                                   SI
  ALL ABOUT VENUS                  ALDISS, BRIAN W.    AN
ORGY OF THE LIVING AND THE DYING                     NV  YRT 70
  MOMENT OF ECLIPSE, THE           ALDISS, BRIAN W.    AC
  YEAR 2000, THE                   HARRISON, HARRY     OA
OUR KIND OF KNOWLEDGE                                SS  NWS 55 06
  NO TIME LIKE TOMORROW            ALDISS, BRIAN W.    AC
  SPACE, TIME AND NATHANIEL        ALDISS, BRIAN W.    AC
OUT OF REACH                                         SS  AUT 57 08
  GALAXIES LIKE GRAINS OF SAND     ALDISS, BRIAN W.    AC
OUTSIDE                                              SS  NWS 55 01
  *BEST SCIENCE FICTION STORIES OF BRIAN W. ALDISS
                                   ALDISS, BRIAN W.    AC
  BEST SF  2                       CRISPIN, EDMUND     AN
  NO TIME LIKE TOMORROW            ALDISS, BRIAN W.    AC
  SECOND ORBIT                     DOHERTY, G. D.      AN
  SPACE, TIME AND NATHANIEL        ALDISS, BRIAN W.    AC
PANEL GAME                                           SS  NWS 55 12
  ASPECTS OF SCIENCE FICTION       DOHERTY, G. D.      AN
  SPACE, TIME AND NATHANIEL        ALDISS, BRIAN W.    AC
PATAGONIA'S DELICIOUS FILLING STATION                GR  NWB 75 09
  NEW WORLDS NINE                  BAILEY, HILARY      OA
PATERNAL CARE                                        SS  NEW 66 AC
  SALIVA TREE AND OTHER STRANGE GROWTHS, THE
                                   ALDISS, BRIAN W.    AC
PENGUIN SCIENCE FICTION                              AN  PEN 61
  PENGUIN SCIENCE FICTION OMNIBUS, THE  ALDISS, BRIAN W.  AN
PIT MY PARISH, THE                                   SS  NWS 58 01
  BEST OF NEW WORLDS, THE          MOORCOCK, MICHAEL   AN
PLEASURE SHARED, A                                   SS  SCF 65 06
  SALIVA TREE AND OTHER STRANGE GROWTHS, THE
                                   ALDISS, BRIAN W.    AC
POGSMITH                                             SS  AUT 55 05
  SPACE, TIME AND NATHANIEL        ALDISS, BRIAN W.    AC
POOR LITTLE WARRIOR|                                 SS  FSF 58 04
  ALPHA 1                          SILVERBERG, ROBERT  AN
  BEST FROM FANTASY AND SCIENCE FICTION: 8
                                   BOUCHER, ANTHONY    AN
  *BEST SCIENCE FICTION STORIES OF BRIAN W. ALDISS
                                   ALDISS, BRIAN W.    AC
  NO TIME LIKE TOMORROW            ALDISS, BRIAN W.    AC
  PENGUIN SCIENCE FICTION          ALDISS, BRIAN W.    AN
  RUN TO STARLIGHT, SPORTS THROUGH SCIENCE FICTION
                                   GREENBERG/OLANDER/& AN
  SHOCKING THING, A                KNIGHT, DAMON       AN
"PRECIPICES OF LIGHT THAT WENT FOREVER UP..."        SI
  SPACE OPERA                      ALDISS, BRIAN W.    AN
PRIMAL URGE, THE                                     SS
  BRIAN ALDISS OMNIBUS, A          ALDISS, BRIAN W.    AC
PROGRESSION OF THE SPECIES                           PM  PRP 67 SP
  BEST SF: 1969                    HARRISON & ALDISS   AN
  HOLDING YOUR EIGHT HANDS         LUCIE-SMITH, EDWARD AN
PSYCLOPS                                             SS  NWS 56 07
  *BEST SCIENCE FICTION STORIES OF BRIAN W. ALDISS
                                   ALDISS, BRIAN W.    AC
  BEST SF  4                       CRISPIN, EDMUND     AN
  MIND TO MIND                     SILVERBERG, ROBERT  AN
  NO TIME LIKE TOMORROW            ALDISS, BRIAN W.    AC
  SPACE, TIME AND NATHANIEL        ALDISS, BRIAN W.    AC
RANDY'S SYNDROME                                     NV  FSF 67 04
  BEST FROM FANTASY AND SCIENCE FICTION: 17
                                   FERMAN, EDWARD L.   AN
```

ALDISS, BRIAN W.   (CONTINUED)
  INTANGIBLES INC. AND OTHER STORIES   ALDISS, BRIAN W.   AC
SALIVA TREE, THE   SN   FSF 65 09
  BRIAN ALDISS OMNIBUS, A   ALDISS, BRIAN W.   AC
  DIMENSION X   KNIGHT, DAMON   AN
  NEBULA AWARD STORIES   KNIGHT, DAMON   AN
  SALIVA TREE AND OTHER STRANGE GROWTHS, THE   ALDISS, BRIAN W.   AC
SCARFE'S WORLD   NV   WOT 65 03
  11TH ANNUAL OF THE YEAR'S BEST S-F, THE   MERRIL, JUDITH   AN
SECRET OF A MIGHTY CITY (HAVE YOUR HATREDS READY) SS   FSF 58 05
  CANOPY OF TIME, THE   ALDISS, BRIAN W.   AC
  GALAXIES LIKE GRAINS OF SAND   ALDISS, BRIAN W.   AC
SECRET OF HOLMAN HUNT AND THE CRUDE DEATH RATE,THE   FA   NWS 70 01
  NEW WORLDS NO. 6   PLATT & BAILEY   OA
SEGREGATION (SEE THE GAME OF GOD)   TC
SEND HER VICTORIOUS   NV   AMZ 68 04
  BOOK OF BRIAN ALDISS, THE   ALDISS, BRIAN W.   AC
  INTANGIBLES INC. AND OTHER STORIES   ALDISS, BRIAN W.   AC
SERPENT BURNING ON AN ALTAR   SS   ORB 73 12
  BEST OF 1973   HARRISON & ALDISS   AN
  ORBIT 12   KNIGHT, DAMON   OA
SERPENT OF KUNDALINI, THE   SS   NWS 68 02
  BEST SF STORIES FROM NEW WORLDS 5   MOORCOCK, MICHAEL   AN
  BEST SF: 1968   HARRISON & ALDISS   AN
SHARDS   SS   FSF 62 04
  BEST SCIENCE FICTION STORIES OF BRIAN W. ALDISS (REVISED)   ALDISS, BRIAN W.   AC
  STARSWARM   ALDISS, BRIAN W.   AC
SHUBSHUB RACE, THE   SS   NEW 57 AC
  SPACE, TIME AND NATHANIEL   ALDISS, BRIAN W.   AC
SINCE THE ASSASSINATION   NV   NEW 69 AC
  INTANGIBLES INC. AND OTHER STORIES   ALDISS, BRIAN W.   AC
  NEANDERTHAL PLANET   ALDISS, BRIAN W.   AC
SMALL BETRAYING DETAIL, THE   SS   NWS 65 05
  BEST SF STORIES FROM NEW WORLDS NO. 1, THE   MOORCOCK, MICHAEL   AN
SO FAR FROM PRAGUE   SS
  NEW S.F., THE   JONES, LANGDON   OA
SOBER NOISES OF MORNING IN A MARGINAL LAND   NV   LOM 72 06
  BEST SCIENCE FICTION STORIES OF BRIAN W. ALDISS (REVISED)   ALDISS, BRIAN W.   AC
  SF: AUTHORS' CHOICE 3   HARRISON, HARRY   AN
SOFT PREDICAMENT, THE   NV   FSF 69 10
  BOOK OF BRIAN ALDISS, THE   ALDISS, BRIAN W.   AC
SOLDIERS RUNNING (SEE HEARTS AND ENGINES, HOW TO BE A SOLDIER)   TC
SOURCE, THE   SS   NWS 65 08
  BEST SF STORIES FROM NEW WORLDS 4   MOORCOCK, MICHAEL   AN
  SALIVA TREE AND OTHER STRANGE GROWTHS, THE   ALDISS, BRIAN W.   AC
SPACE BURIAL   PM   FSF 59 07
  BEST FROM FANTASY AND SCIENCE FICTION: 9   MILLS, ROBERT P.   AN
SPACE FOR REFLECTION, A   SS   NWR 76 29
  NEW WRITINGS IN SF. 29   BULMER, KENNETH   OA
SPACE, TIME AND NATHANIEL   AC   FAB 57
  BRIAN ALDISS OMNIBUS 2   ALDISS, BRIAN W.   AC
STILL TRAJECTORIES   SS   NWS 67 09
  BEST SCIENCE FICTION STORIES OF BRIAN W. ALDISS (REVISED)   ALDISS, BRIAN W.   AC
  ENGLAND SWINGS SF   MERRIL, JUDITH   AN
  SPACE-TIME JOURNAL, THE   MERRIL, JUDITH   AN
  SPECTRUM OF WORLDS, A   CLARESON, THOMAS D.   AN
STRANGE IN A FAMILIAR WAY   SS
  BEYOND THIS HORIZON   CARRELL, CHRISTOPHER OA
SUPER-TOYS LAST ALL SUMMER LONG   SS   HBZ 69 12
  MOMENT OF ECLIPSE, THE   ALDISS, BRIAN W.   AC
SUPERCITY   SS   NWS 65 07
  SPACE, TIME AND NATHANIEL   ALDISS, BRIAN W.   AC
SWASTIKA!   SS   NOV 70 01
  BEST SCIENCE FICTION STORIES OF BRIAN W. ALDISS (REVISED)   ALDISS, BRIAN W.   AC
  MOMENT OF ECLIPSE, THE   ALDISS, BRIAN W.   AC
  *NOVA 1   HARRISON, HARRY   OA
T   SS   NEB 56 11
  FIRST FLIGHT   KNIGHT, DAMON   AN
  NO TIME LIKE TOMORROW   ALDISS, BRIAN W.   AC
  SPACE, TIME AND NATHANIEL   ALDISS, BRIAN W.   AC
TASTE FOR DOSTOEVSKY, A   SS   NWR 67 10
  NEW WRITINGS IN SF. 10   CARNELL, JOHN   OA
  ON OUR WAY TO THE FUTURE   CARR, TERRY   AN
TEN-STORY JIGSAW   SS   NEB 58 01
  SF:59, THE YEAR'S GREATEST SCIENCE FICTION AND FANTASY   MERRIL, JUDITH   AN
THAT UNCOMFORTABLE PAUSE BETWEEN LIFE AND ART   SS   QUN 69 07
  MOMENT OF ECLIPSE, THE   ALDISS, BRIAN W.   AC
THERE IS A TIDE   SS   NWS 56 02
  SPACE, TIME AND NATHANIEL   ALDISS, BRIAN W.   AC
  SPECTRUM 2   AMIS & CONQUEST   AN
THEY SHALL INHERIT   SS   NEB 58 07
  CANOPY OF TIME, THE   ALDISS, BRIAN W.   AC
THING UNDER THE GLACIER, THE   SS   SPC 74 02
  SPACE 2   DAVIS, RICHARD   OA
THREE ENIGMAS: I   GR   NWR 73 22
  NEW WRITINGS IN SF. 22   BULMER, KENNETH   OA
THREE ENIGMAS: II   GR   NWR 74 23
  NEW WRITINGS IN SF. 23   BULMER, KENNETH   OA
THREE ENIGMAS: III   GR   NWR 74 24
  NEW WRITINGS IN SF. 24   BULMER, KENNETH   OA
THREE GREEN BLADES OF GRASS   SI
  EVIL EARTHS   ALDISS, BRIAN W.   AN
THREE'S A CLOUD (THE UNBEATEN TRACK)   SS   NWS 59 01
  CANOPY OF TIME, THE   ALDISS, BRIAN W.   AC

ALDISS, BRIAN W.   (CONTINUED)
  TIMBERLINE   NV   FSF 61 09
  LONG AFTERNOON OF EARTH, THE   ALDISS, BRIAN W.   NO
TOTAL ENVIRONMENT   NV   GAL 68 02
  ALPHA 3   SILVERBERG, ROBERT   AN
  CITY: 2000 A.D., THE   CLEM/GREENBERG/&   AN
  SOCIOLOGY THROUGH SCIENCE FICTION   MILSTEAD/GREENBERG/&   AN
  WORLD'S BEST SCIENCE FICTION: 1969   WOLLHEIM & CARR   AN
TOUCH OF NEANDERTHAL, A (SEE NEANDERTHAL PLANET)   TC
TOWARDS THE FALL OF NIGHT   SI
  EVIL EARTHS   ALDISS, BRIAN W.   AN
UNBEARABLENESS OF OTHER LIVES, THE   SS   NWR 74 24
  NEW WRITINGS IN SF. 24   BULMER, KENNETH   OA
UNBEATEN TRACK, THE (SEE THREE'S A CLOUD)   TC
UNDERGROWTH   NV   FSF 61 07
  LONG AFTERNOON OF EARTH, THE   ALDISS, BRIAN W.   NO
UNDERPRIVILEGED, THE   SS   NWS 63 05
  BOOK OF BRIAN ALDISS, THE   ALDISS, BRIAN W.   AC
  CITIES OF WONDER   KNIGHT, DAMON   AN
  STARSWARM   ALDISS, BRIAN W.   AC
UNREAL ESTATES   MS C SFH 64 01
  SPECTRUM 4   AMIS & CONQUEST   AN
"VENUS IS HELL!"   SI
  ALL ABOUT VENUS   ALDISS, BRIAN W.   AN
VILLAGE SWINDLER, THE   SS   INT 68 10
  DECADE THE 1960S   ALDISS & HARRISON   AN
  MOMENT OF ECLIPSE, THE   ALDISS, BRIAN W.   AC
VISITING AMOEBA (WHAT TRIUMPHS?)   NV   AUT 57 07
  CANOPY OF TIME, THE   ALDISS, BRIAN W.   AC
  GALAXIES LIKE GRAINS OF SAND   ALDISS, BRIAN W.   AC
WAITING FOR THE UNIVERSE TO BEGIN   SS   EPC 75
  EPOCH   ELWOOD & SILVERBERG   OA
"WHAT IS WRONG? WHAT IS RIGHT? ANYWAY, WE'RE HERE..."   SI
  EVIL EARTHS   ALDISS, BRIAN W.   AN
WHAT TRIUMPHS? (SEE VISITING AMOEBA)   TC
WHAT YOU GET FOR YOUR DOLLAR (FROM "THE SHAPE OF FURTHER THINGS")   EX   75
  NEW IMPROVED SUN, THE   DISCH, THOMAS M.   AN
WHEN I WAS VERY JUNG   SS   GAL 68 09
  ELEVENTH GALAXY READER, THE   POHL, FREDERIK   AN
WHO CAN REPLACE A MAN? (BUT WHO CAN REPLACE A MAN)   SS   INF 58 06
  ABOVE THE HUMAN LANDSCAPE   MCNELLY & STOVER   AN
  *BEST SCIENCE FICTION STORIES OF BRIAN W. ALDISS   ALDISS, BRIAN W.   AC
  BEST SF 5   CRISPIN, EDMUND   AN
  CANOPY OF TIME, THE   ALDISS, BRIAN W.   AC
  CENTURY OF SCIENCE FICTION, A   KNIGHT, DAMON   AN
  GALAXIES LIKE GRAINS OF SAND   ALDISS, BRIAN W.   AC
  SOULS IN METAL   ASHLEY, MICHAEL   AN
  STORIES FROM SCIENCE FICTION   DOHERTY, G. D.   AN
  WORLDS OF WONDER   HARRISON, HARRY   AN
WOMAN IN SUNLIGHT WITH MANDOLIN   SS   ORB 73 12
  ORBIT 12   KNIGHT, DAMON   OA
WORKING IN THE SPACESHIP YARDS   SS   PUN 69 04
  BEST SF: 1969   HARRISON & ALDISS   AN
  MOMENT OF ECLIPSE, THE   ALDISS, BRIAN W.   AC
WORM THAT FLIES, THE   SS   FRS 68
  FARTHEST REACHES, THE   ELDER, JOSEPH   OA
  MOMENT OF ECLIPSE, THE   ALDISS, BRIAN W.   AC
  WORLD'S BEST SCIENCE FICTION: 1969   WOLLHEIM & CARR   AN
YEAR BY YEAR THE EVIL GAINS   NV   NWR 75 27
  NEW WRITINGS IN SF. 27   BULMER, KENNETH   OA
YEAR OF THE QUIET COMPUTER, THE   SS   NWR 75 26
  NEW WRITINGS IN SF. 26   BULMER, KENNETH   OA
YESTERDAY, TOMORROW, AND THE DESERT   SI
  EVIL EARTHS   ALDISS, BRIAN W.   AN
YET MORE PENGUIN SCIENCE FICTION   AN   PEN 64
  PENGUIN SCIENCE FICTION OMNIBUS, THE   ALDISS, BRIAN W.   AN
YOUNG SOLDIER'S HOROSCOPE, THE   SS   ORB 73 12
  ORBIT 12   KNIGHT, DAMON   OA

ALEXANDER, DAVID
DISPOSAL UNIT MAN, THE   SS   NWS 63 08
  WINDOW ON THE FUTURE   HILL, DOUGLAS   AN

ALEXANDER, JAMES
HIBBIE, THE   SS
  GOLLANCZ - SUNDAY TIMES BEST SF STORIES   ANONYMOUS   OA

ALEXANDER, LLOYD
SACRED CITY OF CATS, THE (FROM TIME CAT)   EX   HRW 63
  TALES BEYOND TIME   DE CAMP, L. S.&C.   AN

ALEXANDER, W.
ONE LEG TOO MANY   SS   AMZ 29 10
  *BIG BOOK OF SCIENCE FICTION   CONKLIN, GROFF   AN

ALLEN, DICK AND LORI
LOOKING AHEAD   AN L HBL 75
  THE VISION OF SCIENCE FICTION

ALLEN, DICK
SCIENCE FICTION: THE FUTURE   AN H HBJ 71
ALTERNATIVE FUTURES: THE PRESENT AS FUTURE   SI
  SCIENCE FICTION: THE FUTURE   ALLEN, DICK   AN
BACKWARD, INTO BEASTS EVOLVING   PM
  BEST SF: 1974   HARRISON & ALDISS   AN
FIRST PERSPECTIVES   SI
  SCIENCE FICTION: THE FUTURE   ALLEN, DICK   AN
FUTURE, THE   SI
  SCIENCE FICTION: THE FUTURE   ALLEN, DICK   AN
HYPERSPACE   PM   EDG 73
  FASTER THAN LIGHT   DANN & ZEBROWSKI   OA

ALLEN, DICK

ANDERSON, POUL

ALLEN, DICK   (CONTINUED)
   INTRODUCTION   IN
      SCIENCE FICTION: THE FUTURE   ALLEN, DICK   AN
   NEW AGE, A   PM   SFD 72
      LOOKING AHEAD   ALLEN, D. & L.   AN
   PREFACE   IN
      SCIENCE FICTION: THE FUTURE   ALLEN, DICK   AN
   PREFACE   IN C
      LOOKING AHEAD   ALLEN, D. & L.   AN
   THEORIES   SI
      SCIENCE FICTION: THE FUTURE   ALLEN, DICK   AN
   WHEN I FIRST READ...   PM   ATR 66
      SF12   MERRIL, JUDITH   AN

ALLEN, EDWARD
   NOW IS FOREVER   SS
      STOPWATCH   HAY, GEORGE   OA

ALLEN, GRANT
   PAUSODYNE (1884)   SS   84
      *BEYOND TIME AND SPACE   DERLETH, AUGUST   AN
   THAMES VALLEY CATASTROPHY, THE   SS   SND 97 12
      SCIENCE FICTION BY GASLIGHT   MOSKOWITZ, SAM   AN

ALLEN, LORI   SEE ALSO   CO-EDITOR DICK ALLEN
   PREFACE   IN C
      LOOKING AHEAD   ALLEN, D. & L.   AN

ALLEN, MARIJANE
   NEANDERTHAL   PM   NYT 56
      APEMAN, SPACEMAN   STOVER & HARRISON AN

ALLEN, STEVE
   PUBLIC HATING, THE   SS   BBM 55 01
      SF: THE BEST OF THE BEST   MERRIL, JUDITH   AN
      SF: THE YEAR'S GREATEST SCIENCE FICTION AND FANTASY
                                      MERRIL, JUDITH   AN
      SOCIAL PROBLEMS THROUGH SCIENCE FICTION
                                      GREENBERG/MILSTEAD/& AN

ALLEN, VIRGINIA F.
   TIMES 4 (ABRIDGED STORIES)   AN   FAL

ALLINGHAM, MARGAREY
   SHE WAS ASKING FOR YOU   SS   46
      SHOT IN THE DARK   MERRIL, JUDITH   AN

ALLISON, RUTH   SEE PSEUD. ALLISON RICE (WITH JANE RICE)

ALLPORT, ARTHUR   PSEUD. FOR RAYMOND Z. GALLUN
   GENTLE BRAIN, THE   SS   SFQ 40 SU
   MOON CONQUERORS, THE   ANONYMOUS   AN

ALPER, GERALD ARTHUR
   MECHANICAL SWEETHEART, THE   SS   NEW 72 AN
      STRANGE BED FELLOWS   SCORTIA, THOMAS N. AN

ALPERT, HOLLIS
   SIMIAN PROBLEM, THE   SS   FSF 60 07
      17 X INFINITY   CONKLIN, GROFF   AN

ALTERMAN, PETER S.
   INTRODUCTION: FLASHFORWARD TO 2076   AR
      2076: THE AMERICAN TRICENTENNIAL BRYANT, EDWARD   OA

ALTOV, HENRIK
   ICARUS AND DAEDALUS   SS   68
      ULTIMATE THRESHOLD, THE   GINSBURG, MIRRA   AN
   MASTER BUILDER, THE   SS
      OTHER WORLDS, OTHER SEAS   SUVIN, DARKO   AN

ALTSHULER, HARRY
   WITCH IN THE FOG, THE   SS   WRT 38 09
      GHOUL KEEPERS, THE   MARGULIES, LEO   AN

AMIS, KINGSLEY AND ROBERT CONQUEST
SPECTRUM   AN H HBW 62
SPECTRUM (7 OF 10)   AN   BKM 63 03
SPECTRUM 2   AN H HBW 63
SPECTRUM 3   AN H HBW 64
SPECTRUM 4   AN H HBW 65
SPECTRUM 5   AN H HBW 67

AMIS, KINGSLEY
   FOREWORD TO "THE GAME OF RAT AND DRAGON"   IN
      MIRROR OF INFINITY, THE   SILVERBERG, ROBERT AN
   H. G. WELLS   IN
      WAR OF THE WORLDS, THE TIME MACHINE AND SELECTED SHORT STORIES
                                      WELLS, H. G.   AC
   HEMINGWAY IN SPACE   SS   PUN 60 12
      DECADE THE 1960S   ALDISS & HARRISON AN
      6TH ANNUAL OF THE YEAR'S BEST S-F, THE MERRIL, JUDITH AN
   INTRODUCTION   IN C
      *SPECTRUM   AMIS & CONQUEST   AN
      SPECTRUM 2   AMIS & CONQUEST   AN
      SPECTRUM 3   AMIS & CONQUEST   AN
      SPECTRUM 5   AMIS & CONQUEST   AN
   MASON'S LIFE   SS   SDT 72
      BEST SF: 1973   HARRISON & ALDISS AN
   PREFACE   IN C
      SPECTRUM 4   AMIS & CONQUEST   AN
   REPORT   PM   NSM 71
      BEST SF: 1971   HARRISON & ALDISS AN
   SCIENCE FICTION   PM   ENC 60 05
      SPECULATIONS   SANDERS, THOMAS E. AN
      STARLIT CORRIDOR, THE   MANSFIELD, ROGER   AN

AMIS, KINGSLEY   (CONTINUED)
   SOMETHING STRANGE   NV   FSF 61 07
      FIVE-ODD   CONKLIN, GROFF   AN
      LIGHT FANTASTIC, THE   HARRISON, HARRY   AN
   STARTING POINTS   AR   60
      SCIENCE FICTION: THE FUTURE   ALLEN, DICK   AN
   UNREAL ESTATES   MS C SFH 64 01
      SPECTRUM 4   AMIS & CONQUEST   AN

AMMONS, A. R.
   MISFIT, THE   PM   65
      SPECULATIONS   SANDERS, THOMAS E. AN

AMUNDSON, GRACE
   CHILD WHO BELIEVED, THE   SS   SEP 50 12
      SATURDAY EVENING POST FANTASY STORIES, THE
                                      FLES, BARTHOLD   AN

ANDERSON, JACK
   AESTHETICS OF THE MOON   PM
      SCIENCE FACT/FICTION   FARRELL/GAGE/&   AN

ANDERSON, JO   SEE PSEUD. STELLA BENSON

ANDERSON, KAREN
   IN MEMORIAM: HENRY KUTTNER   PM   FSF 58 05
      BEST FROM FANTASY AND SCIENCE FICTION: 8
                                      BOUCHER, ANTHONY   AN
   IN MEMORIAM- STUART PALMER   MS
      NEBULA AWARD STORIES NO. 4   ANDERSON, POUL   AN
   INNOCENT ARRIVAL, THE (INNOCENT AT LARGE) NV C GAL 58 07
      SPACE, TIME & CRIME   DEFORD, MIRIAM ALLEN AN
   INNOCENT AT LARGE (SEE THE INNOCENT ARRIVAL) TC C
   LANDSCAPE WITH SPHINXES   SS   FSF 62 11
      BEST FROM FANTASY AND SCIENCE FICTION: 12
                                      DAVIDSON, AVRAM   AN
   MURPHY'S HALL   NV C INY 71 02
      HOMEWARD AND BEYOND   ANDERSON, POUL   AC
      INFINITY 2   HOSKINS, ROBERT   OA
   ORIGIN OF THE SPECIES   PM   FSF 58 06
      BEST FROM FANTASY AND SCIENCE FICTION: 8
                                      BOUCHER, ANTHONY   AN
   PIEBALD HIPPOGRIFF, THE   SS   FAN 62 05
      8TH ANNUAL OF THE YEAR'S BEST S-F, THE MERRIL, JUDITH AN
   SIX HAIKU   PM   FSF 62 07
      FIFTY SHORT SCIENCE FICTION TALES ASIMOV & CONKLIN AN
      SPECULATIONS   SANDERS, THOMAS E. AN
   TREATY IN TARTESSOS   SS   FSF 63 05
      BEST FROM FANTASY AND SCIENCE FICTION: 13
                                      DAVIDSON, AVRAM   AN

ANDERSON, POUL AND GORDON R. DICKSON
   EARTHMAN'S BURDEN   AC H GNM 57

ANDERSON, POUL   ALSO AS   WINSTON P. SANDERS
   AGENT OF THE TERRAN EMPIRE   AC H CHL 65
   BEST OF POUL ANDERSON, THE   AC   PKT 76 08
   BEYOND THE BEYOND   AC   SIG 69 08
      ENGLISH EDITION (GOL 70) OMITS STORY "DAY OF BURNING"
   BOOK OF POUL ANDERSON, THE   AC   DAW 75 06
      SEE "THE MANY WORLDS OF POUL ANDERSON"
   FLANDRY OF TERRA   AC H CHL 65
   GUARDIANS OF TIME   AC   BAL 60 09
   HOMEBREW   AC H NES 76
   HOMEWARD AND BEYOND   AC H DBL 75 06
   HORN OF TIME, THE   AC   SIG 68 01
   MANY WORLDS OF POUL ANDERSON, THE   AC H CHL 74
      EDITED BY ROGER ELWOOD, ALSO AS "THE BOOK OF POUL ANDERSON"
   NEBULA AWARD STORIES NO. 4   AN H DBL 69 12
   OPERATION CHAOS   NO   LAN 71
   ORBIT UNLIMITED   NO   PYR 61 05
   QUEEN OF AIR AND DARKNESS AND OTHER STORIES, THE AC   SIG 73 12
   STAR FOX, THE   AC H DBL 65
   STRANGERS FROM EARTH   AC   BAL 61 05
   TALES OF THE FLYING MOUNTAINS   AC H MAC 70
   TIME AND STARS   AC H DBL 64
      BRITISH EDITION OMITS "EVE TIMES FOUR"
   TRADER TO THE STARS   AC H DBL 64
   TROUBLE TWISTERS, THE   AC H DBL 66
   TWILIGHT WORLD   NO H TOR 61
   UN-MAN AND OTHER NOVELLAS   DC   ACE 62
   WORLD NAMED CLEOPATRA, A   OA   PYR 77 03
      PRODUCED BY ROGER ELWOOD
   WORLDS OF POUL ANDERSON, THE   AC   ACE 74
   7 CONQUESTS   AC H MAC 69
   ADMIRALTY   SN   FSF 65 06
      STAR FOX, THE   ANDERSON, POUL   AC
   ADVENTURE OF THE MISPLACED HOUND, THE NV C USF 53 12
      EARTHMAN'S BURDEN   ANDERSON, P.&DICKSON AC
      SCIENCE-FICTIONAL SHERLOCK HOLMES, THE COUNCIL OF FOUR AN
   AFTERWORD: OUR MANY ROADS TO THE STARS AR   GAL 75 09
      FASTER THAN LIGHT   DANN & ZEBROWSKI   OA
   ALIEN ENEMY, THE (AS MICHAEL KARAGEORGE) SS   ASF 68 11
      QUEEN OF AIR AND DARKNESS AND OTHER STORIES, THE
                                      ANDERSON, POUL   AC
   AMBASSADORS OF FLESH, THE (SEE WARRIORS FROM NOWHERE)
                                      TC
   AMONG THIEVES   NV   ASF 57 06
      STRANGERS FROM EARTH   ANDERSON, POUL   AC
   ANCIENT GODS, THE (SEE WORLD WITHOUT STARS) TC
   AND YET SO FAR (CONDEMNED TO DEATH)   SS   FUN 59 10
      ORBIT UNLIMITED   ANDERSON, POUL   NO
   ARCHETYPICAL HOLMES, THE   AR   BSJ 68 09
      HOMEBREW   ANDERSON, POUL   AC
   ARSENAL PORT   SN   FSF 65 04
      STAR FOX, THE   ANDERSON, POUL   AC

ANDERSON, POUL   (CONTINUED)
BACKWARDNESS   SS   FSF 58 03
   BEST FROM FANTASY AND SCIENCE FICTION: 8
                                   BOUCHER, ANTHONY   AN
   SCHOOL AND SOCIETY THROUGH SCIENCE FICTION
                                   OLANDER/GREENBERG/&   AN
BALLADE OF AN ARTIFICIAL SATELLITE   PM   FSF 58 10
   FIFTY SHORT SCIENCE FICTION TALES   ASIMOV & CONKLIN   AN
   HOMEBREW   ANDERSON, POUL   AC
BARBARIAN, THE   SS   FSF 56 05
   BEST FROM FANTASY AND SCIENCE FICTION: 6
                                   BOUCHER, ANTHONY   AN
   BEST OF POUL ANDERSON, THE   ANDERSON, POUL   AC
   ODDBALLS, THE   GHIDALIA, VIC   AN
BIG RAIN, THE   SN   ASF 54 10
   ALL ABOUT VENUS   ALDISS, BRIAN W.   AN
   FAREWELL FANTASTIC VENUS   ALDISS & HARRISON   AN
BIRTHRIGHT   NV   ASF 70 02
   SOCIOLOGY THROUGH SCIENCE FICTION   MILSTEAD/GREENBERG/& AN
BITTER BREAD, THE   NV   ASF 75 12
   BEST SCIENCE FICTION STORIES OF THE YEAR (1975)
                                   DEL REY, LESTER   AN
BLESSEDNESS OF SAINTS, A   AR   VPG 62 04
   HOMEBREW   ANDERSON, POUL   AC
BRAIN WAVE   NO   BAL 54
   TREASURY OF GREAT SCIENCE FICTION, A VOL.2
                                   BOUCHER, ANTHONY   AN
BRAKE   NV   ASF 57 08
   BEYOND THE BEYOND   ANDERSON, POUL   AC
BRAVE TO BE A KING   NV   FSF 59 08
   GUARDIANS OF TIME   ANDERSON, POUL   AC
BURNING BRIDGE, THE   NV   ASF 60 01
   ORBIT UNLIMITED   ANDERSON, POUL   NO
BUTCH   NV   NWS 55 07
   *TIME TO COME   DERLETH, AUGUST   OA
CALL ME JOE   NV   ASF 57 04
   ALPHA 2   SILVERBERG, ROBERT   AN
   ASTOUNDING-ANALOG READER, THE VOLUME TWO
                                   HARRISON & ALDISS   AN
   BEST SCIENCE FICTION STORIES AND NOVELS: 9TH SERIES
                                   DIKTY, T. E.   AN
   BIO-FUTURES   SARGENT, PAMELA   AN
   CENTURY OF SCIENCE FICTION, A   KNIGHT, DAMON   AN
   JUPITER   POHL, C. & F.   AN
   SCIENCE FICTION HALL OF FAME VOLUME 2A BOVA, BEN   AN
   SCIENCE FICTION NOVELLAS   HARRISON & MCNELLY   AN
   SPECTRUM 3   AMIS & CONQUEST   AN
CHAIN OF LOGIC (LOGIC)   NV   ASF 47 07
   TWILIGHT WORLD   ANDERSON, POUL   NO
CHAPTER ENDS, THE   NV   DSF 54 01
   ADVENTURES IN THE FAR FUTURE   WOLLHEIM, DONALD A.   DA
   NOVELETS OF SCIENCE FICTION   HOWARD, IVAN   AN
CHAPTER OF REVELATION, A   NA
   DAY THE SUN STOOD STILL, THE   SILVERBERG, ROBERT   OA
CHILDREN OF FORTUNE   NV   NEW 61 NO
   TWILIGHT WORLD   ANDERSON, POUL   NO
COLD VICTORY   SS   FSF 57 05
   7 CONQUESTS   ANDERSON, POUL   AC
COMMUNICATORS, THE   SN   INY 70 01
   INFINITY 1   HOSKINS, ROBERT   OA
CONDEMNED TO DEATH (SEE AND YET SO FAR)   TC
COURIER OF CHAOS   NV   PUT 53 03
   THINGS   HOWARD, IVAN   AN
CRITIQUE OF IMPURE REASON, THE   NV   IFS 62 11
   NEVER IN THIS WORLD   STONE, IDELLA P.   AN
   TIME AND STARS   ANDERSON, POUL   AC
DAY OF BURNING (SUPERNOVA)   SN   ASF 67 01
   BEYOND THE BEYOND   ANDERSON, POUL   AC
   MANY WORLDS OF POUL ANDERSON, THE   ANDERSON, POUL   AC
DELENDA EST   NV   FSF 55 12
   GUARDIANS OF TIME   ANDERSON, POUL   AC
   WORLDS OF MAYBE   SILVERBERG, ROBERT   AN
DETAILS   SS   IFS 56 10
   7 CONQUESTS   ANDERSON, POUL   AC
DIALOGUE   NV   76
   FASTER THAN LIGHT   DANN & ZEBROWSKI   OA
DIPTEROID PHENOMENON, THE   SS
   FOUR FOR THE FUTURE   HARRISON, HARRY   AN
DISINHERITED, THE (ALSO AS HOME)   SS   ORB 66 01
   ORBIT 1   KNIGHT, DAMON   OA
DISINTEGRATING SKY, THE   NV   FUN 53 08
   STRANGERS FROM EARTH   ANDERSON, POUL   AC
DON JONES   NV C NEW 57 AC
   EARTHMAN'S BURDEN   ANDERSON, P.&DICKSON AC
DOOR TO ANYWHERE   NV   GAL 66 12
   TENTH GALAXY READER, THE   POHL, FREDERIK   AN
DOUBLE DYED VILLAINS, THE   NV   ASF 49 09
   TRAVELLERS OF SPACE   GREENBERG, MARTIN   AN
DUEL ON SYRTIS   SS   PLS 51 03
   BEST OF PLANET STORIES NO. 1, THE   BRACKETT, LEIGH   AN
   STRANGERS FROM EARTH   ANDERSON, POUL   AC
EARTHMAN, BEWARE!   NV   SSS 51 06
   HISTORY OF THE SCIENCE FICTION MAGAZINE, THE PART 3 1946-1955
                                   ASHLEY, MICHAEL   AN
   STRANGERS FROM EARTH   ANDERSON, POUL   AC
ENOUGH ROPE   NV   ASF 53 07
   FOUR FOR THE FUTURE   CONKLIN, GROFF   AN
EPILOGUE   MS
   TALES OF THE FLYING MOUNTAINS   ANDERSON, POUL   AC
EPILOGUE   SN   ASF 62 03
   ENDS OF TIME, THE   SILVERBERG, ROBERT   AN
   MANY WORLDS OF POUL ANDERSON, THE   ANDERSON, POUL   AC
   TIME AND STARS   ANDERSON, POUL   AC
ESCAPE FROM ORBIT   NV   AMZ 62 10
   TIME AND STARS   ANDERSON, POUL   AC

ANDERSON, POUL   (CONTINUED)
ESCAPE THE MORNING   SS   BLF 66 11
   WORLDS OF WONDER   HARRISON, HARRY   AN
EUTOPIA   SS   DVS 67 01
   DANGEROUS VISIONS   ELLISON, HARLAN   OA
   PAST, PRESENT, AND FUTURE PERFECT   WOLFE, J&FITZ GERALD AN
EVE TIMES FOUR   NV   FAN 60 04
   BEST FROM FANTASTIC, THE   WHITE, TED   AN
   TIME AND STARS   ANDERSON, POUL   AC
FAIR EXCHANGE, A   NV   CTM 74 03
   CONTINUUM 3   ELWOOD, ROGER   OA
FATAL FULFILLMENT, THE   SN   FSF 70 03
   BEST OF POUL ANDERSON, THE   ANDERSON, POUL   AC
   FIVE FATES   LAUMER, KEITH   AN
FAUN, THE   SS   BLF 68 09
   QUEEN OF AIR AND DARKNESS AND OTHER STORIES, THE
                                   ANDERSON, POUL   AC
FIRST LOVE, THE   PM   ABA 60 12
   HOMEBREW   ANDERSON, POUL   AC
FLIGHT TO FOREVER   NV   SSS 50 11
   YEAR'S BEST SCIENCE FICTION NOVELS: 1952
                                   BLEILER & DIKTY   AN
FOR THE DURATION   SS   VSF 57 09
   STRANGERS FROM EARTH   ANDERSON, POUL   AC
FOREWARD   IN
   HOMEBREW   ANDERSON, POUL   AC
FOREWORD   IN
   QUEEN OF AIR AND DARKNESS AND OTHER STORIES, THE
                                   ANDERSON, POUL   AC
   7 CONQUESTS   ANDERSON, POUL   AC
FORTUNE HUNTER   SS   INY 72 04
   BEST SCIENCE FICTION OF THE YEAR, THE NO. 2
                                   CARR, TERRY   AN
   INFINITY 4   HOSKINS, ROBERT   OA
GAME OF GLORY, THE   NV   VSF 58 03
   FLANDRY OF TERRA   ANDERSON, POUL   AC
GARDEN IN THE VOID   NV   GAL 52 05
   EXPLORING OTHER WORLDS   MOSKOWITZ, SAM   AN
GENIUS   NV   ASF 48 12
   BEST SCIENCE-FICTION STORIES: 1949, THE
                                   BLEILER & DIKTY   AN
   GIANTS UNLEASHED   CONKLIN, GROFF   AN
GHETTO   NV   FSF 54 05
   WILDERNESS OF STARS, A   NOLAN, WILLIAM F.   AN
GOAT SONG   NV   FSF 72 02
   HOMEWARD AND BEYOND   ANDERSON, POUL   AC
   NEBULA AWARD STORIES 8   ASIMOV, ISAAC   AN
   1973 ANNUAL WORLD'S BEST SF, THE   WOLLHEIM, DONALD A. AN
GREEN THUMB, THE   SS   SFQ 53 02
   MASTERS OF SCIENCE FICTION   HOWARD, IVAN   AN
GYPSY   SS   ASF 50 01
   EVERY BOY'S BOOK OF OUTER SPACE STORIES
                                   DIKTY, T. E.   AN
   STRANGERS FROM EARTH   ANDERSON, POUL   AC
   TO THE STARS   SILVERBERG, ROBERT   AN
HANDFUL OF STARS, A   NA   AMZ 59 06
   AGENT OF THE TERRAN EMPIRE   ANDERSON, POUL   AC
HELPING HAND, THE   NV   ASF 50 05
   GREAT STORIES OF SPACE TRAVEL   CONKLIN, GROFF   AN
   POLITICAL SCIENCE FICTION   GREENBERG& WARRICK   AN
   *POSSIBLE WORLDS OF SCIENCE FICTION   CONKLIN, GROFF   AN
   STARS AROUND US, THE   HOSKINS, ROBERT   AN
HEROES ARE MADE (SEE THE SHERIFF OF CANYON GULCH) TC C
HERRINGS   MS   59
   HOMEBREW   ANDERSON, POUL   AC
HIDING PLACE   NV   ASF 61 03
   BEST OF POUL ANDERSON, THE   ANDERSON, POUL   AC
   TRADER TO THE STARS   ANDERSON, POUL   AC
HIGH ONES, THE   NV   INF 58 06
   HORN OF TIME, THE   ANDERSON, POUL   AC
HIGH TREASON   SS   IMP 66 03
   FOUR FOR THE FUTURE   HARRISON, HARRY   AN
HOME (THE DISINHERITED)   SS   ORB 66 01
   FUTURE NOW, THE   HOSKINS, ROBERT   AN
   QUEEN OF AIR AND DARKNESS AND OTHER STORIES, THE
                                   ANDERSON, POUL   AC
HOMO AQUATICUS (SEE THE HORN OF TIME THE HUNTER) TC
HONORABLE ENEMIES   NV   FUT 51 05
   AGENT OF THE TERRAN EMPIRE   ANDERSON, POUL   AC
   WAY OUT   HOWARD, IVAN   AN
HORN OF TIME THE HUNTER, THE (HOMO AQUATICUS) SS AMZ 63 09
   BEST FROM AMAZING, THE   WHITE, TED   AN
   HORN OF TIME, THE   ANDERSON, POUL   AC
   WONDERMAKERS 2   HOSKINS, ROBERT   AN
HOUSE RULE   SS   NEW 76 01
   HOMEBREW   ANDERSON, POUL   AC
HOW TO BE ETHNIC IN ONE EASY LESSON   NV   FUQ 73
   FUTURE QUEST   ELWOOD, ROGER   OA
I TELL YOU, IT'S TRUE   NV   NOV 72 02
   EARTH IN TRANSIT   SCHWARTZ, SHEILA   AN
   NOVA 2   HARRISON, HARRY   AN
IMMORTAL GAME, THE   SS   FSF 54 02
   BEST FROM FANTASY AND SCIENCE FICTION: 4
                                   BOUCHER, ANTHONY   AN
   RUN TO STARLIGHT, SPORTS THROUGH SCIENCE FICTION
                                   GREENBERG/OLANDER/&   AN
IN HOKA SIGNO VINCES   NV C OWS 53 06
   EARTHMAN'S BURDEN   ANDERSON, P.&DICKSON AC
IN THE SHADOW (AS MICHAEL KARAGEORGE)   NV   ASF 67 03
   QUEEN OF AIR AND DARKNESS AND OTHER STORIES, THE
                                   ANDERSON, POUL   AC
INDUSTRIAL REVOLUTION (SEE THE ROGUE)   TC
INNOCENT ARRIVAL, THE (INNOCENT AT LARGE)   NV C GAL 58 07
   SPACE, TIME & CRIME   DEFORD, MIRIAM ALLEN AN
INNOCENT AT LARGE (SEE THE INNOCENT ARRIVAL)   TC C

ANDERSON, POUL

ANDERSON, POUL   (CONTINUED)
  INSIDE EARTH   NV   GAL 51 04
    *GALAXY READER OF SCIENCE FICTION   GOLD, H. L.   AN
  INSIDE STRAIGHT   SS   FSF 55 08
    7 CONQUESTS   ANDERSON, POUL   AC
  INTERLOPER   SS   FSF 51 04
    *OUTER REACHES, THE   DERLETH, AUGUST   AN
  INTRODUCTION   IN
    BEST OF POUL ANDERSON, THE   ANDERSON, POUL   AC
    COMPLETE PEGHOOT, THE   BRIARTON, GRENDEL   AC
    FIRST STEP OUTWARD   HOSKINS, ROBERT   AN
    HOMEWARD AND BEYOND   ANDERSON, POUL   AC
    NEBULA AWARD STORIES NO. 4   ANDERSON, POUL   AC
  JOURNEYS END   SS   FSF 57 02
    BEST FROM FANTASY AND SCIENCE FICTION: 7
                                        BOUCHER, ANTHONY   AN
    DARK STARS   SILVERBERG, ROBERT   AN
    EDGE OF NEVER, THE   HOSKINS, ROBERT   AN
    MANY WORLDS OF POUL ANDERSON, THE   ANDERSON, POUL   AC
    MIND TO MIND   SILVERBERG, ROBERT   AN
    SCIENCE FICTION ARGOSY, A   KNIGHT, DAMON   AN
    SPECIAL WONDER   MCCOMAS, J. FRANCIS AN
  JOY IN MUDVILLE   NV C FSF 55 11
    INFINITE ARENA, THE   CARR, TERRY   AN
  KINGS WHO DIE   NV   IFS 62 03
    SCIENCE FICTION ROLL OF HONOR, THE POHL, FREDERIK   AN
    7 CONQUESTS   ANDERSON, POUL   AC
    8TH ANNUAL OF THE YEAR'S BEST S-F, THE MERRIL, JUDITH   AN
  KYRIE   SS   FRS 68
    BEST OF POUL ANDERSON, THE   ANDERSON, POUL   AC
    EXPLORERS OF SPACE   SILVERBERG, ROBERT   AN
    FARTHEST REACHES, THE   ELDER, JOSEPH   OA
    UNIVERSE AHEAD   ENGDAHL & ROBERSON   AN
    WORLD'S BEST SCIENCE FICTION: 1969 WOLLHEIM & CARR   AN
  LAST MONSTER, THE (TERMINAL QUEST)   SS   SSS 51 08
    ALIEN WORLDS   ELWOOD, ROGER   AN
    LOOKING FORWARD   LESSER, MILTON   AN
  LAST OF THE DELIVERERS, THE   SS   FSF 58 02
    BEST OF POUL ANDERSON, THE   ANDERSON, POUL   AC
    POLITICAL SCIENCE FICTION   GREENBERG & WARRICK AN
    SF: AUTHORS' CHOICE   HARRISON, HARRY   AN
  LICENSE   NV   FSF 57 04
    7 CONQUESTS   ANDERSON, POUL   AC
  LIFE CYCLE   SS   FSF 57 07
    EARTHMEN AND STRANGERS   SILVERBERG, ROBERT   AN
  LIGHT, THE   NV   GAL 57 03
    SCIENCE FICTION THROUGH THE AGES 2 EVANS, I. O.   AN
    13 GREAT STORIES OF SCIENCE FICTION CONKLIN, GROFF   AN
  LIMERICKS   PM
    HOMEBREW   ANDERSON, POUL   AC
  LITTLE KNOWLEDGE, A   NV   ASF 71 08
    BEST SCIENCE FICTION STORIES OF THE YEAR (1971)
                                        DEL REY, LESTER   AN
    1972 ANNUAL WORLD'S BEST SF, THE   WOLLHEIM, DONALD A. AN
  LITTLE MONSTER, THE   NV
    SCIENCE FICTION ADVENTURES FROM WAY OUT
                                        ELWOOD, ROGER   OA
  LIVE COWARD, THE   SS   ASF 56 06
    ANOTHER PART OF THE GALAXY   CONKLIN, GROFF   AN
    UN-MAN AND OTHER NOVELLAS   ANDERSON, POUL   DC
  LODESTAR   NV   AMA 73
    ASTOUNDING   HARRISON, HARRY   OA
  LOGIC (SEE CHAIN OF LOGIC)   TC
  LONG REMEMBERING, THE   SS   FSF 57 11
    HOMEWARD AND BEYOND   ANDERSON, POUL   AC
    SCIENCE FICTION SHOWCASE   KORNBLUTH, MARY   AN
  LONGEST VOYAGE, THE   NV   ASF 60 12
    BEST OF POUL ANDERSON, THE   ANDERSON, POUL   AC
    HUGO WINNERS, THE (VOLUME 1)   ASIMOV, ISAAC   AN
    MANY WORLDS OF POUL ANDERSON, THE   ANDERSON, POUL   AC
  LORD OF A THOUSAND SUNS   NV   PLS 51 09
    GALACTIC EMPIRES VOLUME TWO   ALDISS, BRIAN W.   AN
    TALES OF OUTER SPACE   WOLLHEIM, DONALD A. DA
  LOST SECRETS REVEALED   AR   72
    HOMEBREW   ANDERSON, POUL   AC
  MAN TO MY WOUNDING, A (STATE OF ASSASSINATION) SS EQM 59 12
    HORN OF TIME, THE   ANDERSON, POUL   AC
  MAN WHO CAME EARLY, THE   NV   FSF 56 06
    ALPHA 1   SILVERBERG, ROBERT   AN
    BEST FROM FANTASY AND SCIENCE FICTION: 6
                                        BOUCHER, ANTHONY   AN
    BEYOND TOMORROW   HARDING, LEE   AN
    COMBAT SF   DICKSON, GORDON R.   AN
    HORN OF TIME, THE   ANDERSON, POUL   AC
    ONE HUNDRED YEARS OF SCIENCE FICTION KNIGHT, DAMON   AN
    THEMES IN SCIENCE FICTION   KELLEY, LEO P.   AN
  MARGIN OF PROFIT   SS   ASF 56 09
    UN-MAN AND OTHER NOVELLAS   ANDERSON, POUL   DC
  MARIUS   SS   ASF 57 03
    HORN OF TIME, THE   ANDERSON, POUL   AC
  MARQUE AND REPRISAL   SN   FSF 65 02
    STAR FOX, THE   ANDERSON, POUL   AC
  MARTIAN CROWN JEWELS, THE   SS   EQM 58 02
    GREAT SCIENCE FICTION STORIES   SMITH, CORDELIA T.   AN
    SCIENCE-FICTIONAL SHERLOCK HOLMES, THE COUNCIL OF FOUR   AN
    TALES OF TIME AND SPACE   OLNEY, ROSS R.   AN
    TREASURY OF GREAT SCIENCE FICTION, A VOL.1
                                        BOUCHER, ANTHONY   AN
  MARTYR, THE   NV   FSF 60 03
    BEST FROM FANTASY AND SCIENCE FICTION: 10
                                        MILLS, ROBERT P.   AN
    BEST SF 5   CRISPIN, EDMUND   AN
  MASTER KEY, THE   NV   ASF 64 07
    TRADER TO THE STARS   ANDERSON, POUL   AC
  MEMORY (A WORLD CALLED MAANEREK)   NV   GAL 57 07
    BEYOND THE BEYOND   ANDERSON, POUL   AC

ANDERSON, POUL   (CONTINUED)
  MESSAGE IN SECRET, A   NA   FAN 57 12
    FLANDRY OF TERRA   ANDERSON, POUL   AC
  MILL OF THE GODS, THE   NV   NEW 61 AC
    ORBIT UNLIMITED   ANDERSON, POUL   NO
  MOONRAKERS, THE   NV   IFS 66 01
    BEYOND THE BEYOND   ANDERSON, POUL   AC
  MURPHY'S HALL   NV C INY 71 02
    HOMEWARD AND BEYOND   ANDERSON, POUL   AC
    INFINITY 2   HOSKINS, ROBERT   OA
  MY OBJECT ALL SUBLIME   SS   GAL 61 06
    BEST OF POUL ANDERSON, THE   ANDERSON, POUL   AC
    12 GREAT CLASSICS OF SCIENCE FICTION CONKLIN, GROFF   AN
  MY OWN, MY NATIVE LAND   NV   CTM 74 01
    CONTINUUM 1   ELWOOD, ROGER   OA
  NEBULA AWARD S. F., 1965-1970, THE SCIENCE   MS
    NEBULA AWARD STORIES NO. 7   BIGGLE, LLOYD JR.   AN
  NIGHT PIECE   SS   FSF 61 07
    WORLDS OF SCIENCE FICTION, THE   MILLS, ROBERT P.   AN
  NO TRUCE WITH KINGS   NV   FSF 63 06
    HUGO WINNERS, THE (VOLUME 2)   ASIMOV, ISAAC   AN
    TIME AND STARS   ANDERSON, POUL   AC
  NOTES TOWARD A DEFINITION OF SCIENCE FICTION   AR   SFR 71 43
    HOMEBREW   ANDERSON, POUL   AC
  NOTHING SUCCEEDS LIKE FAILURE   SS   NEW 70 AC
    TALES OF THE FLYING MOUNTAINS   ANDERSON, POUL   AC
  ONLY GAME IN TOWN, THE   NV   FSF 60 01
    GUARDIANS OF TIME   ANDERSON, POUL   AC
  OPERATION AFREET   SS   FSF 56 09
    OPERATION CHAOS   ANDERSON, POUL   NO
  OPERATION CHANGELING   NA   FSF 69 05
    OPERATION CHAOS   ANDERSON, POUL   NO
  OPERATION INCUBUS   SS   FSF 59 10
    OPERATION CHAOS   ANDERSON, POUL   NO
  OPERATION SALAMANDER   NV   FSF 57 01
    OPERATION CHAOS   ANDERSON, POUL   NO
  PASSING THE LOVE OF WOMEN   NV   CTM 74 02
    CONTINUUM 2   ELWOOD, ROGER   OA
  PEAT BOG, THE   SS
    HOMEWARD AND BEYOND   ANDERSON, POUL   AC
  PEEK! I SEE YOU!   NV   ASF 68 02
    HOMEWARD AND BEYOND   ANDERSON, POUL   AC
  PHILOSOPHICAL DIALOGUE, A   AR   OUT 71 08
    HOMEBREW   ANDERSON, POUL   AC
  PIRATE, THE   NV   ASF 68 10
    HOMEWARD AND BEYOND   ANDERSON, POUL   AC
  PLAGUE OF MASTERS, A   NA   FAN 60 12
    FLANDRY OF TERRA   ANDERSON, POUL   AC
  PLANET OF NO RETURN (QUESTION AND ANSWER)   NO   ASF 54 06
    WORLDS OF POUL ANDERSON, THE   ANDERSON, POUL   AC
  PROBLEM OF PAIN, THE   NV   FSF 73 02
    BEST FROM FANTASY AND SCIENCE FICTION: 20
                                        FERMAN, EDWARD L.   AN
    BEST SCIENCE FICTION STORIES OF THE YEAR (1973)
                                        DEL REY, LESTER   AN
    CHRONICLES OF A COMET AND OTHER RELIGIOUS SCIENCE FICTION
    STORIES   ELWOOD, ROGER   AN
  PROGRESS   NV   FSF 62 01
    HORN OF TIME, THE   ANDERSON, POUL   AC
  PROLOGUE   IN
    TALES OF THE FLYING MOUNTAINS   ANDERSON, POUL   AC
  PUGILIST, THE   NV   FSF 73 11
    2020 VISION   POURNELLE, JERRY   AN
  QUE DONN'REZ VOUS? (WHAT'LL YOU GIVE?)   NV   ASF 63 04
    TALES OF THE FLYING MOUNTAINS   ANDERSON, POUL   AC
  QUEEN OF AIR AND DARKNESS, THE   SN   FSF 71 04
    BEST FROM FANTASY AND SCIENCE FICTION, 25TH ANNIV.
                                        FERMAN, EDWARD L.   AN
    BEST SCIENCE FICTION OF THE YEAR, THE CARR, TERRY   AN
    MANY WORLDS OF POUL ANDERSON, THE   ANDERSON, POUL   AC
    NEBULA AWARD STORIES NO. 7   BIGGLE, LLOYD JR.   AN
  QUEEN OF AIR AND DARKNESS AND OTHER STORIES, THE
                                        ANDERSON, POUL   AC
  QUESTION AND ANSWER (SEE PLANET OF NO RETURN)   TC
  QUIXOTE AND THE WINDMILL   SS   ASF 50 11
    METAL SMILE, THE   KNIGHT, DAMON   AN
    STRANGERS FROM EARTH   ANDERSON, POUL   AC
  RAMBLE WITH A GAMBLIN' MAN   NV   NEW 70 AC
    TALES OF THE FLYING MOUNTAINS   ANDERSON, POUL   AC
  RECRUITING NATION   NV   NEW 70 AC
    TALES OF THE FLYING MOUNTAINS   ANDERSON, POUL   AC
  ROBIN HOOD'S BARN   NV   ASF 59 01
    ORBIT UNLIMITED   ANDERSON, POUL   NO
  ROGUE, THE (INDUSTRIAL REVOLUTION)   SN   ASF 63 09
    TALES OF THE FLYING MOUNTAINS   ANDERSON, POUL   AC
  SAM HALL   NV   ASF 53 08
    BEST OF POUL ANDERSON, THE   ANDERSON, POUL   AC
    LIBERATED FUTURE: VOYAGES INTO TOMORROW, THE
                                        HOSKINS, ROBERT   AN
    *SCIENCE FICTION THINKING MACHINES CONKLIN, GROFF   AN
  SAY IT WITH FLOWERS   SS   ASF 65 09
    TALES OF THE FLYING MOUNTAINS   ANDERSON, POUL   AC
  SCIENCE FICTION AND FREEDOM   AR   SFR 69 30
    HOMEBREW   ANDERSON, POUL   AC
  SENSITIVE MAN, THE   NV   FUN 54 01
    BEYOND THE BEYOND   ANDERSON, POUL   AC
  SENTIMENT, INC.   NV   SFS 53 01
    WEIRD ONES, THE   HOWARD, IVAN   AN
  SERPENT IN EDEN, THE   NV   OMG 73
    OMEGA   ELWOOD, ROGER   OA
    VISIONS OF TOMORROW   ELWOOD, ROGER   AN
    WORLD NAMED CLEOPATRA, A   ANDERSON, POUL   OA
  SHARING OF FLESH, THE   NV   GAL 68 12
    ANTHROPOLOGY THROUGH SCIENCE FICTION MASON, C/GREENBERG/& AN
    ELEVENTH GALAXY READER, THE   POHL, FREDERIK   AN
    HUGO WINNERS, THE (VOLUME 2)   ASIMOV, ISAAC   AN

ANDERSON, POUL   (CONTINUED)
  SHERIFF OF CANYON GULCH, THE (HEROES ARE MADE)   NV C OWS 51 05
    EARTHMAN'S BURDEN   ANDERSON, P.&DICKSON AC
    GATES TO TOMORROW   NORTON, AN.&DONALDY AN
    MANY WORLDS OF POUL ANDERSON, THE   ANDERSON, POUL   AC
    SCIENCE FICTION BESTIARY, THE   SILVERBERG, ROBERT   AN
  SILENT VICTORY (SEE THE WAR OF TWO WORLDS) TC
  SISTER PLANET   SN SAT 59 05
    ALL ABOUT VENUS   ALDISS, BRIAN W.   AN
    FAREWELL FANTASTIC VENUS   ALDISS & HARRISON   AN
    GET OUT OF MY SKY   MARGULIES, LEO   AN
  SKY PEOPLE, THE   NV FSF 59 03
    BEST OF POUL ANDERSON, THE   ANDERSON, POUL   AC
    DECADE OF FANTASY AND SCIENCE FICTION, A
                                         MILLS, ROBERT P.   AN
  SOS   NV IFS 70 03
    BEST FROM IF, THE   VOLUME I   IF, EDITORS OF   AN
  STAR BEAST, THE   NV SSS 50 09
    AWARD SCIENCE FICTION READER   NORTON, ALDEN H.   AN
    STRANGERS FROM EARTH   ANDERSON, POUL   AN
  STAR PLUNDERER, THE   NV PLS 52 09
    GALACTIC EMPIRES VOLUME ONE   ALDISS, BRIAN W.   AN
  STAR SHIP   NV PLS 50 FL
    SPACE ODYSSEYS   ALDISS, BRIAN W.   AN
  STARFOG   SN ASF 67 08
    BEYOND THE BEYOND   ANDERSON, POUL   AC
  STATE OF ASSASSINATION (SEE A MAN TO MY WOUNDING) TC
  STRANGE BEDFELLOWS (TO BUILD A WORLD)   SN GAL 64 06
    7 CONQUESTS   ANDERSON, POUL   AC
  SUN INVISIBLE, A   NV ASF 66 04
    TROUBLE TWISTERS, THE   ANDERSON, POUL   AC
  SUNJAMMER   NV ASF 64 04
    ANALOG 4   CAMPBELL, JOHN W. JR AN
    TALES OF THE FLYING MOUNTAINS   ANDERSON, POUL   AN
  SUPERNOVA (SEE DAY OF BURNING)   TC
  SWORDSMAN OF LOST TERRA   NA PLS 51 11
    SWORDSMEN IN THE SKY   WOLLHEIM, DONALD A. AN
  TERMINAL QUEST (ALSO AS THE LAST MONSTER) SS SSS 51 08
    CHILDREN OF WONDER   TENN, WILLIAM   AN
  TERRITORY   SN ASF 63 06
    TOMORROW 1   HOSKINS, ROBERT   AN
    TRADER TO THE STARS   ANDERSON, POUL   AN
  THIRD STAGE   SS AMZ 62 02
    FIRST STEP OUTWARD   HOSKINS, ROBERT   AN
  THREE-CORNERED WHEEL, THE   NV ASF 63 10
    TROUBLE TWISTERS, THE   ANDERSON, POUL   AC
  TIDDLYWINK WARRIORS, THE   NV C FSF 55 08
    EARTHMAN'S BURDEN   ANDERSON, P.&DICKSON AC
  TIGER BY THE TAIL   NV PLS 51 01
    AGENT OF THE TERRAN EMPIRE   ANDERSON, POUL   AC
    MORE ADVENTURES ON OTHER PLANETS   WOLLHEIM, DONALD A. AN
  TIME HEALS   SS ASF 49 10
    VOYAGERS IN TIME   SILVERBERG, ROBERT   AN
  TIME LAG   NV FSF 61 01
    *BEST FROM FANTASY AND SCIENCE FICTION: 11
                                         MILLS, ROBERT P.   AN
    QUEEN OF AIR AND DARKNESS AND OTHER STORIES, THE
                                         ANDERSON, POUL   AC
  TIME PATROL   NV FSF 55 05
    GUARDIANS OF TIME   ANDERSON, POUL   AC
  TINKLER, THE   SS WBY 51 02
    *WORLDS OF TOMORROW   DERLETH, AUGUST   AN
  TO BUILD A WORLD (SEE STRANGE BEDFELLOWS) TC
  TO PROMOTE THE GENERAL WELFARE   NV CTM 75 04
    CONTINUUM 4   ELWOOD, ROGER   OA
  TOMORROW'S CHILDREN   NV ASF 47 03
    FIRST FLIGHT   KNIGHT, DAMON   AN
    MANY WORLDS OF POUL ANDERSON, THE   ANDERSON, POUL   AC
    TWILIGHT WORLD   ANDERSON, POUL   NO
  TOMORROW'S CHILDREN   NV C ASF 47 03
    MUTANTS   SILVERBERG, ROBERT   AN
    *TREASURY OF SCIENCE FICTION, A   CONKLIN, GROFF   AN
  TRADER TEAM (SEE THE TROUBLE TWISTERS)   TC
  TRESPASS!   SS C FSQ 50 SP
    BEST SCIENCE-FICTION STORIES: 1951, THE
                                         BLEILER & DIKTY   AN
    MINDWORM, THE   ANONYMOUS   AN
  TROUBLE TWISTERS, THE (TRADER TEAM)   NA ASF 65 07
    TROUBLE TWISTERS, THE   ANDERSON, POUL   AC
  TURNING POINT   NV IFS 63 05
    ELSEWHERE AND ELSEWHEN   CONKLIN, GROFF   AN
    TIME AND STARS   ANDERSON, POUL   AC
  TWO SONGS   SG
    HOMEBREW   ANDERSON, POUL   AC
  UN-MAN   SN ASF 53 01
    ALL ABOUT THE FUTURE   GREENBERG , MARTIN   AN
    UN-MAN AND OTHER NOVELLAS   ANDERSON, POUL   DC
  UNCLEAVISH TRUETHINKING   AR   60
    HOMEBREW   ANDERSON, POUL   AC
  UPON THE OCCASION OF BEING ASKED TO ARGUE THAT LOVE AND
  MARRIAGE ARE INCOMPATIBLE   PM DKC 73 01
    HOMEBREW   ANDERSON, POUL   AC
  VISITOR, THE   SS FSF 74 10
    HOMEWARD AND BEYOND   ANDERSON, POUL   AC
  VOORTREKKERS, THE   NV FST 74
    FINAL STAGE   FERMAN & MALZBERG   OA
  WAR OF TWO WORLDS, THE (SILENT VICTORY) NO TCS 53 WI
    WORLDS OF POUL ANDERSON, THE   ANDERSON, POUL   AC
  WARRIORS FROM NOWHERE (THE AMBASSADORS OF FLESH) SS PLS 54 SU
    AGENT OF THE TERRAN EMPIRE   ANDERSON, POUL   AC
  WHAT'LL YOU GIVE? (SEE QUE DONN'REZ VOUS?) TC
  WILDCAT   NV FSF 58 11
    7 CONQUESTS   ANDERSON, POUL   AC
  WINDMILL   NV SVW 73
    SAVING WORLDS   ELWOOD & KIDD   OA

ANDERSON, POUL   (CONTINUED)
                                         SS   COI 73
    CHILDREN OF INFINITY   ELWOOD, ROGER   OA
  WINGS OF VICTORY   SS ASF 72 04
    HOMEWARD AND BEYOND   ANDERSON, POUL   AC
  WIZARD OF NEHWON-, THE   IN
    BEST OF FRITZ LEIBER, THE   LEIBER, FRITZ   AC
  WOLFRAM   SS
    HOMEWARD AND BEYOND   ANDERSON, POUL   AC
  WORLD CALLED MAANEREK, A (SEE MEMORY)   TC
  WORLD NAMED CLEOPATRA, A   FA   NEW 74 AC
    MANY WORLDS OF POUL ANDERSON, THE   ANDERSON, POUL   AC
    WORLD NAMED CLEOPATRA, A   ANDERSON, POUL   OA
  WORLD WITHOUT STARS (THE ANCIENT GODS)   NO ASF 66 06
    WORLDS OF POUL ANDERSON, THE   ANDERSON, POUL   AC
  YO HO HOKA!   NV C FSF 55 03
    EARTHMAN'S BURDEN   ANDERSON, P.&DICKSON AC

ANDERSON, SUSAN J.   SEE ALSO   CO-EDITOR VONDA N. MCINTYRE
  FEMINISM AND SCIENCE FICTION: BEYOND BEMS AND BOOBS
                                         IN
    AURORA: BEYOND EQUALITY   MCINTYRE & ANDERSON OA

ANDERSSON, VIC
  WEREWOLF GIRL   SS
    MORE SCIENCE FICTION TALES   ELWOOD, ROGER   OA

ANDREVON, JEAN-PIERRE
  OBSERVATION OF QUADRAGNES   SS
    VIEW FROM ANOTHER SHORE   ROTTENSTEINER, FRANZ AN
  TIME OF THE BIG SLEEP, THE   NV   71
    SHOCKING THING, A   KNIGHT, DAMON   AN

ANDREW, WILLIAM
  RIGHT THING, THE   SS
    AD 2500   WILSON, ANGUS   AN

ANDREYEV, LEONID
  ABYSS, THE   SS   43
    SHOCKING THING, A   KNIGHT, DAMON   AN
  LAZARUS   SS WRT 27 03
    NEW WORLDS OF FANTASY NO. 2   CARR, TERRY   AN

ANFILOV, GLEB
  EREM   SS   63
    BEST SF: 1970   HARRISON & ALDISS   AN
    ULTIMATE THRESHOLD, THE   GINSBURG, MIRRA   AN

ANMAR, FRANK   PSEUD. FOR WILLIAM F. NOLAN
  FASTERFASTER AFFAIR, THE   SS NEW 65 AN
    PSEUDO PEOPLE, THE   NOLAN, WILLIAM F.   AN
  JENNY AMONG THE ZEEBS   SS PIN 70
    FUTURE IS NOW, THE   NOLAN, WILLIAM F.   OA

ANONYMOUS
  BATTLE FOR THE PACIFIC AND OTHER ADVENTURES AT SEA, THE
                                         AN H HPR 08
  BEYOND   AN BKM 63 01
  BEYOND THE STARS AND OTHER STORIES   AN JBL 58
  FROZEN PLANET AND 4 OTHER SF NOVELLAS, THE AN MBB 66
  GOLLANCZ - SUNDAY TIMES BEST SF STORIES OA H GOL 75
  HEART OF THE SERPENT, THE   AN H FLP 61
    SEE "MORE SOVIET SCIENCE FICTION"
  JOURNEY ACROSS THREE WORLDS   AN H MIR 73
  LAURIE'S SPACE ANNUAL   AN H LAU 53
  MACHINE-GOD LAUGHS, THE   AN H GRI 49
  MINDWORM, THE   AN TDM 67
  MOLECULE MONSTERS, THE   AN WHP 50
  MOON CONQUERORS, THE   AN SWN 43
  MORE SOVIET SCIENCE FICTION   AN CLB 62
    ALSO AS "THE HEART OF THE SERPENT"
  PATH INTO THE UNKNOWN   AN H DCT 68
    THE BEST OF SOVIET SCIENCE FICTION
  PLANET OF DOOM AND OTHER STORIES   AN JBL 58
  SANDS OF MARS AND OTHER STORIES, THE   AN JBL 58
  SCIENCE FICTION OMNIBUS ON POLLUTION, A AN H SID 71
  SCIENCE FICTION SPECIAL   1   AN H SID 71 08
  SCIENCE FICTION SPECIAL   3   AN H SID 71
  SCIENCE FICTION SPECIAL   4   AN H SID 71
  SCIENCE FICTION SPECIAL   5   AN H SID 71 07
  SCIENCE FICTION SPECIAL   6   AN H SID 73
  SCIENCE FICTION SPECIAL   7   AN H SID
  SCIENCE FICTION SPECIAL   8   AN H SID 73
  SOMETIME, NEVER   OA BAL 56
  SOVIET SCIENCE FICTION   AN CLB 62
    ALSO AS "A VISITOR FROM OUTER SPACE"
  SPACE STATION 42 AND OTHER STORIES   AN JBL 58
  STRANGE LOVE STORIES   AN UTP 46
  STRANGE WORLD OF SCIENCE FICTION   OA NLB 75 10
  VISITOR FROM OUTER SPACE, A   AN H FLP 61
    SEE "SOVIET SCIENCE FICTION"
  6 FINGERS OF TIME AND 5 OTHER SCIENCE FICTION NOVELETS, THE
                                         AN MBB 65
  APOTHEM   MS
    MATHEMATICAL MAGPIE, THE   FADIMAN, CLIFTON   AN
  COUNTESS KATHLEEN O'SHEA   SS
    DEALS WITH THE DEVIL   DAVENPORT, BASIL   AN
  CULVER CITY ARITHMATIC EXERCISE PAPER   MS NYM 61 02
    MATHEMATICAL MAGPIE, THE   FADIMAN, CLIFTON   AN
  DEATH OF A PLANET   CT
    LAURIE'S SPACE ANNUAL   ANONYMOUS   AN
  DOCTOR FAUSTUS   SS
    DEALS WITH THE DEVIL   DAVENPORT, BASIL   AN
  DREADED BLACK PLANET, THE   CT
    LAURIE'S SPACE ANNUAL   ANONYMOUS   AN

ANONYMOUS   ARRHENIUS, SVANTE

ANONYMOUS   (CONTINUED)   MS   67
  DREAM OF DISTANCE
    ALL ABOUT VENUS   ALDISS, BRIAN W.   AN
    FAREWELL FANTASTIC VENUS   ALDISS & HARRISON   AN
  ENGINEER'S YELL   PM
    MATHEMATICAL MAGPIE, THE   FADIMAN, CLIFTON   AN
  FABLE, A   PM   MAG 54 38
    FANTASIA MATHEMATICA   FADIMAN, CLIFTON   AN
  FOUR-DIMENSIONAL SPACE (1885)   AR   NTR 85
    FUTURE PERFECT   FRANKLIN, H. BRUCE   AN
  GRAVITY IS A THING   AR
    LAURIE'S SPACE ANNUAL   ANONYMOUS   AN
  HARRY AMONG THE ALIENS   SS
    STRANGE WORLD OF SCIENCE FICTION   ANONYMOUS   OA
  LETTER FROM TENNYSON, A   PM   MAG
    FANTASIA MATHEMATICA   FADIMAN, CLIFTON   AN
  MAN FROM OCCAM, THE   SS
    STRANGE WORLD OF SCIENCE FICTION   ANONYMOUS   OA
  MATHEMATICIAN CONFIDED, A   PM
    MATHEMATICAL MAGPIE, THE   FADIMAN, CLIFTON   AN
  MATHEMATICIAN NAMED KLEIN, A   PM
    MATHEMATICAL MAGPIE, THE   FADIMAN, CLIFTON   AN
  MATTER OF OVERTIME, A   AR   TIM 69 03
    SCIENCE FACT/FICTION   FARRELL/GAGE/&   AN
  MISSING ONE'S COACH: AN ANACHRONISM   SS   DLM 38
    FAR BOUNDARIES   DERLETH, AUGUST   AN
  MODERN HIAWATHA, THE   PM
    MATHEMATICAL MAGPIE, THE   FADIMAN, CLIFTON   AN
  MYSTERIOUS FOOTPRINTS, THE   SS
    STRANGE WORLD OF SCIENCE FICTION   ANONYMOUS   OA
  PROBLEM, A   PM   NYM 57 03
    FANTASIA MATHEMATICA   FADIMAN, CLIFTON   AN
  RELATIVITY   PM
    FANTASIA MATHEMATICA   FADIMAN, CLIFTON   AN
  RELATIVITY WINS AGAIN   AR   SDG 72 01
    SCIENCE FACT/FICTION   FARRELL/GAGE/&   AN
  RIDDLE   PM   51
    MATHEMATICAL MAGPIE, THE   FADIMAN, CLIFTON   AN
  SONG OF THE SCREW   PM
    MATHEMATICAL MAGPIE, THE   FADIMAN, CLIFTON   AN
  SPECIMEN, THE   SS
    STRANGE WORLD OF SCIENCE FICTION   ANONYMOUS   OA
  STORY OF SIDI NORMAN, THE   SS
    ROD SERLING'S TRIPLE W: WITCHES, WARLOCKS AND WEREWOLVES
                                        SERLING, ROD   AN
  TALE OF A CHEMIST (1843)   SS
    FAR BOUNDARIES   DERLETH, AUGUST   AN
  THERE WAS A YOUNG FELLOW NAMED FISK   PM
    FANTASIA MATHEMATICA   FADIMAN, CLIFTON   AN
  THERE WAS A YOUNG MAN FROM TRINITY   PM
    FANTASIA MATHEMATICA   FADIMAN, CLIFTON   AN
  THERE WAS AN OLD MAN WHO SAID, "DO"   PM
    FANTASIA MATHEMATICA   FADIMAN, CLIFTON   AN
    MATHEMATICAL MAGPIE, THE   FADIMAN, CLIFTON   AN
  VERSE   PM   51
    MATHEMATICAL MAGPIE, THE   FADIMAN, CLIFTON   AN
  WINDOWS OF HEAVEN, THE   SS
    UNTRAVELLED WORLDS   BARTER & WILSON   AN
  ZARGON MENACE, THE   SS
    STRANGE WORLD OF SCIENCE FICTION   ANONYMOUS   OA
  1,000,000 A.D.   PM   PUN 93
    APEMAN, SPACEMAN   STOVER & HARRISON   AN

ANTHONY, JOHN   PSEUD. FOR JOHN CIARDI
  HYPNOGLYPH, THE   SS   FSF 53 07
    DECADE OF FANTASY AND SCIENCE FICTION, A
                                        MILLS, ROBERT P.   AN
    PORTALS OF TOMORROW   DERLETH, AUGUST   AN

ANTHONY, PIERS   PSEUD. FOR PIERS ANTHONY DILLINGHAM JACOB
  IN THE BARN   NV   DVS 72 02
    AGAIN, DANGEROUS VISIONS   ELLISON, HARLAN   OA
  MESSAGE, THE   NV C ASF 66 07
    ANALOG 6   CAMPBELL, JOHN W. JR AN
  PHOG   SS   FAN 65 06
    SF: AUTHORS' CHOICE 3   HARRISON, HARRY   AN
  SMALL MOUTH, BAD TASTE   SS   SAG 70
    SCIENCE AGAINST MAN   CHEETHAM, ANTHONY   OA
  UP SCHIST CRICK   SS   GEN 72
    GENERATION   GERROLD, DAVID   OA
  WHOLE TRUTH, THE   SS   NOV 70 01
    *NOVA 1   HARRISON, HARRY   OA

ANTROBUS, ROSIE
  MONSTERS   IL
    BEYOND THIS HORIZON   CARRELL, CHRISTOPHER OA

ANVIL, CHRISTOPHER   PSEUD. FOR HARRY C. CROSBY
  BEHIND THE SANDRAT HOAX   NV   GAL 68 10
    ELEVENTH GALAXY READER, THE   POHL, FREDERIK   AN
  BILL FOR DELIVERY   SS   ASF 64 11
    WORLD'S BEST SCIENCE FICTION: 1965 WOLLHEIM & CARR   AN
  CAPTIVE DJINN, THE   SS   ASF 65 05
    WORLD'S BEST SCIENCE FICTION: 1966 WOLLHEIM & CARR   AN
  GADGET VS. TREND   SS   ASF 62 10
    ANOTHER TOMORROW   HOLLISTER, BERNARD C AN
    SOCIOLOGY THROUGH SCIENCE FICTION   MILSTEAD/GREENBERG/& AN
    SPECTRUM 4   AMIS & CONQUEST   AN
  GHOST FLEET   SS   ASF 61 02
    STARS AROUND US, THE   HOSKINS, ROBERT   AN
  GREAT INTELLECT BOOM, THE   SS   ASF 69 07
    SCHOOL AND SOCIETY THROUGH SCIENCE FICTION
                                        OLANDER/GREENBERG/& AN
    SOCIAL PROBLEMS THROUGH SCIENCE FICTION
                                        GREENBERG/MILSTEAD/& AN

ANVIL, CHRISTOPHER   (CONTINUED)   SS   ASF 61 07
  HUNCH, THE
    ANALOG 1   CAMPBELL, JOHN W. JR AN
  KNIFE AND THE SHEATH, THE   SS
    FUTURE KIN   ELWOOD, ROGER   OA
  MIND PARTNER   NV   GAL 60 08
    MIND PARTNER AND 8 OTHER NOVELETS FROM GALAXY
                                        GOLD, H. L.   AN
  NOT IN THE LITERATURE   SS   ASF 63 03
    ANALOG 3   CAMPBELL, JOHN W. JR AN
  PANDORA'S PLANET   NV   ASF 56 09
    PROLOGUE TO ANALOG   CAMPBELL, JOHN W. JR AN
  PHILOSOPHER'S STONE   SS   ASF 63 01
    ANALOG 2   CAMPBELL, JOHN W. JR AN
  POSITIVE FEEDBACK   SS   ASF 65 08
    ABOVE THE HUMAN LANDSCAPE   MCNELLY & STOVER   AN
    SOCIOLOGY THROUGH SCIENCE FICTION   MILSTEAD/GREENBERG/& AN
  PRISONER, THE   SS   ASF 56 02
    BEST SF 5   CRISPIN, EDMUND   AN
  ROSE BY OTHER NAME, A   SS   ASF 60 01
    6TH ANNUAL OF THE YEAR'S BEST S-F, THE MERRIL, JUDITH   AN
  STRANGLEHOLD   SS   ASF 66 06
    ANALOG 6   CAMPBELL, JOHN W. JR AN
  UNCALCULATED RISK   SS   ASF 62 03
    NIGHTMARE AGE   POHL, FREDERIK   AN
  UNINVITED GUEST, THE   SS   ASF 67 03
    ENCOUNTERS WITH ALIENS   EARLEY, GEORGE W.   AN

APOSTOLIDES, ALEX
  CIVILIZED (WE'RE CIVILIZED)   SS C GAL 53 08
    PORTALS OF TOMORROW   DERLETH, AUGUST   AN
  CRAZY JOEY   SS C ASF 53 08
    BEYOND THE BARRIERS OF SPACE AND TIME MERRIL, JUDITH   AN
  WE'RE CIVILIZED (ALSO AS CIVILIZED)   SS C GAL 53 08
    GALACTIC EMPIRES VOLUME ONE   ALDISS, BRIAN W.   AN
  WHAT THIN PARTITIONS   NV C ASF 53 09
    BEST SCIENCE-FICTION STORIES: 1954, THE
                                        BLEILER & DIKTY   AN
    EDITOR'S CHOICE IN SCIENCE FICTION MOSKOWITZ, SAM   AN
    14 GREAT TALES OF ESP   STONE, IDELLA P.   AN

ARATOVSKY, Y.
  INVISIBILITY COMPETITION   CT   PRI
    BEST SF: 1972   HARRISON & ALDISS   AN

ARISS, BRUCE
  ILLUSTRATIONS   IL
    THROUGH TIME AND SPACE WITH FERDINAND FEGHOOT
                                        BRIARTON, GRENDEL   AC

ARKIN, ALAN
  PEOPLE SOUP   SS   GAL 58 11
    SCIENCE FICTION ODDITIES   CONKLIN, GROFF   AN

ARNASON, ELEANOR
  ACE 167   SS   ORB 74 15
    ORBIT 15   KNIGHT, DAMON   OA
  CLEAR DAY IN THE MOTOR CITY, A   SS   NWQ 73 05
    NEW IMPROVED SUN, THE   DISCH, THOMAS M.   AN
    NEW WORLDS NO. 5   MOORCOCK & PLATT   OA
  FACE ON THE BARROOM FLOOR, THE   NV C
    STAR TREK: THE NEW VOYAGES   MARSHAK, S&CULBREATH OA
  HOUSE BY THE SEA, THE   SS   ORB 75 16
    ORBIT 16   KNIGHT, DAMON   OA
  WARLORD OF SATURN'S MOONS, THE   SS   NWQ 74 06
    NEW WORLDS NO. 6   PLATT & BAILEY   OA

ARNOLD, CHARLES
  MY EIGHT DAYS IN THE AUTOMOTIVE INDUSTRY   SS   NWQ 73 05
    NEW WORLDS NO. 5   MOORCOCK & PLATT   OA
  SPRING CAME TO BLUE RIDGE EARLY THIS YEAR   SS   ORB 74 13
    ORBIT 13   KNIGHT, DAMON   OA

ARNOLD, DOUGLAS
  LIKE NOTHING ON EARTH   AR   KDK 73 02
    BEYOND THIS HORIZON   CARRELL, CHRISTOPHER OA
  LIKENESS OF APOLLO, THE   AR   PTJ 73 03
    BEYOND THIS HORIZON   CARRELL, CHRISTOPHER OA

ARNOLD, FRANK EDWARD
  WINGS ACROSS TIME   AC   PND 46
  CITY OF MACHINES (SEE THE MAD MACHINES)   TC
    ENDLESS DIMENSIONS   NV
      WINGS ACROSS TIME   ARNOLD, FRANK EDWARD AC
  MAD MACHINES, THE (CITY OF MACHINES)   NV   TOW 39 SU
    WINGS ACROSS TIME   ARNOLD, FRANK EDWARD AC
  TWILIGHT PEOPLE, THE   NV   CMT 41 01
    WINGS ACROSS TIME   ARNOLD, FRANK EDWARD AC
  WINGS ACROSS TIME   NV   SFQ 42 WI
    WINGS ACROSS TIME   ARNOLD, FRANK EDWARD AC

ARNOLD, JACK
  LIFE BY TELEVISION, A   SS
    ADVENTURES TO COME   ESENWEIN, J. BERG   OA

AROUET, FRANCOIS M.   SEE PSEUD. VOLTAIRE

ARR, STEPHEN   PSEUD. FOR STEPHEN A. RYNAS
  CHAIN OF COMMAND   SS   GAL 54 05
    *SCIENCE FICTION ADVENTURES IN MUTATION CONKLIN, GROFF   AN

ARRHENIUS, SVANTE
  DESTINIES OF THE STARS   AR   18
    ALL ABOUT VENUS   ALDISS, BRIAN W.   AN
    FAREWELL FANTASTIC VENUS   ALDISS & HARRISON   AN

ARTHUR, ROBERT
EVOLUTION'S END SS TWS 41 04
ADVENTURES IN TOMORROW CROSSEN, KENDELL F. AN
NEW AWARENESS, THE WARRICK & GREENBERG AN
MR. JINX SS UNK 41 08
UNKNOWN, THE BENSEN, D. R. AN
POSTPAID TO PARADISE (POSTMARKED FOR PARADISE, IN FSF 50 WS)
SS ARG 40 06
BEST FROM FANTASY AND SCIENCE FICTION BOUCHER & MCCOMAS AN
GOLDEN ROAD, THE KNIGHT, DAMON AN
SATAN AND SAM SHAY SS ELK 42 08
DEALS WITH THE DEVIL DAVENPORT, BASIL AN
OUT OF THIS WORLD FAST, JULIUS AN
WHEEL OF TIME, THE SS SSS 50 03
*SCIENCE-FICTION CARNIVAL BROWN, F. & REYNOLDS AN

ASH, PAUL PSEUD. FOR PAULINE ASHWELL
BIG SWORD NV ASF 58 10
ANOTHER PART OF THE GALAXY CONKLIN, GROFF AN
SPECTRUM 5 AMIS & CONQUEST AN
WINGS OF A BAT, THE NV ASF 66 05
WORLD'S BEST SCIENCE FICTION: 1967 WOLLHEIM & CARR AN

ASHBY, RICHARD
COMMENCEMENT NIGHT SS ASF 53 08
GIANTS UNLEASHED CONKLIN, GROFF AN
SPECTRUM 5 AMIS & CONQUEST AN
MASTER RACE SS IMG 51 09
SPACE, SPACE, SPACE SLOANE, WILLIAM AN
TEEN-AGE SPACE ADVENTURES FURMAN, A. L. AN

ASHE, TAMSIN
QUALITY OF MERCY, THE SS TVW 73
TWO VIEWS OF WONDER SCORTIA & YARBRO OA

ASHLEY, MICHAEL
HISTORY OF THE SCIENCE FICTION MAGAZINE, THE PART 1 1926-1935
AN H NLB 74
HISTORY OF THE SCIENCE FICTION MAGAZINE, THE PART 2 1936-1945
AN H NLB 75
HISTORY OF THE SCIENCE FICTION MAGAZINE, THE PART 3 1946-1955
AN H NLB 76
SOULS IN METAL AN H SMP 77
AFTERWORD MS
SOULS IN METAL ASHLEY, MICHAEL AN
INTRODUCTION: AN AMAZING EXPERIMENT AR
HISTORY OF THE SCIENCE FICTION MAGAZINE, THE PART 1 1926-1935
ASHLEY, MICHAEL AN
INTRODUCTION: FROM BOMB TO BOOM IN
HISTORY OF THE SCIENCE FICTION MAGAZINE, THE PART 3 1946-1955
ASHLEY, MICHAEL AN
INTRODUCTION: SF BANDWAGON AR
HISTORY OF THE SCIENCE FICTION MAGAZINE, THE PART 2 1936-1945
ASHLEY, MICHAEL AN
PREFACE IN
HISTORY OF THE SCIENCE FICTION MAGAZINE, THE PART 1 1926-1935
ASHLEY, MICHAEL AN
HISTORY OF THE SCIENCE FICTION MAGAZINE, THE PART 2 1936-1945
ASHLEY, MICHAEL AN
HISTORY OF THE SCIENCE FICTION MAGAZINE, THE PART 3 1946-1955
ASHLEY, MICHAEL AN
SOULS IN METAL ASHLEY, MICHAEL AN

ASHWELL, PAULINE SEE PSEUD. PAUL ASH

ASIMOV, ISAAC AND GROFF CONKLIN
FIFTY SHORT SCIENCE FICTION TALES AN CLB 63

ASIMOV, ISAAC
ASIMOV'S MYSTERIES AC H DBL 68
BEFORE THE GOLDEN AGE AN H DBL 74
BEST OF ISAAC ASIMOV, THE AC H SID 73
EDITED BY ANGUS WELLS, U.S. EDITION OMITS
BIBLIOGRAPHY AND PART OF INTRODUCTION
BICENTENNIAL MAN AND OTHER STORIES, THE AC H DBL 76
BUY JUPITER AND OTHER STORIES AC H DBL 75
EARLY ASIMOV, THE AC H DBL 72
EARTH IS ROOM ENOUGH AC H DBL 57 10
FOUNDATION NO H GNM 51
ALSO IN "THE FOUNDATION TRILOGY" AND AS "THE 1,000 YEAR PLAN"
FOUNDATION AND EMPIRE NO H GNM 52
ALSO IN "THE FOUNDATION TRILOGY" AND AS
"THE MAN WHO UPSET THE UNIVERSE"
FOUNDATION TRILOGY, THE AC H DBL 64
IN ENGLAND AS "AN ISAAC ASIMOV OMNIBUS"
HAVE YOU SEEN THESE? AC H NES 74
ALL STORIES ALSO IN "BUY JUPITER"
HUGO WINNERS, THE (VOLUME 1) AN H DBL 62
HUGO WINNERS, THE (VOLUME 2) AN H DBL 71
DERIVATIVE ANTHOLOGIES "STORIES FROM THE HUGO WINNERS VOL. 2"
AND "MORE STORIES FROM THE HUGO WINNERS VOL. 2"
I, ROBOT AC H GNM 50
I, ROBOT (BRITISH PB) AC DIG 58
OMITS LAST TWO STORIES
ISAAC ASIMOV OMNIBUS, AN AC H SID 65
SEE "THE FOUNDATION TRILOGY"
ISAAC ASIMOV SECOND OMNIBUS, AN AC H SID 69
SEE "TRIANGLE"
MAN WHO UPSET THE UNIVERSE, THE DN ACE 55
SEE "FOUNDATION AND EMPIRE"
MARTIAN WAY AND OTHER STORIES, THE AC H DBL 55
MORE STORIES FROM THE HUGO WINNERS VOLUME 2 AN FCR 73 12
LAST 8 STORIES
NEBULA AWARD STORIES 8 AN H HPR 73
NIGHTFALL AND OTHER STORIES AC H DBL 69
NINE TOMORROWS AC H DBL 59

ASIMOV, ISAAC (CONTINUED)
OPUS 100 AC H HMF 69
REST OF THE ROBOTS, THE AC H DBL 64
REST OF THE ROBOTS, THE (EIGHT STORIES FROM) AC PYR 66 01
SECOND FOUNDATION NO H GNM 53
ALSO IN "THE FOUNDATION TRILOGY"
STORIES FROM THE HUGO WINNERS VOLUME 2 AN FCR 73 08
FIRST 6 STORIES
THROUGH A GLASS, CLEARLY AC FSP 67
TOMORROW'S CHILDREN AN H DBL 66
TRIANGLE AC H DBL 61
IN ENGLAND AS "AN ISAAC ASIMOV SECOND OMNIBUS"
WHERE DO WE GO FROM HERE? AN H DBL 71
1,000 YEAR PLAN, THE DN ACE 55
ABRIDGED VERSION OF "FOUNDATION"
ALL THE TROUBLES OF THE WORLD SS SUP 58 04
FUTURE NOW, THE HOSKINS, ROBERT AN
IF THIS GOES ON NUETZEL, CHARLES AN
NINE TOMORROWS ASIMOV, ISAAC AC
OUT OF THIS WORLD 6 WILLIAMS-ELLIS& OWEN AN
AND IT WILL SERVE US RIGHT AR PSY 69 04
SCIENCE FICTION BRODKIN & PEARSON AN
AND NOW YOU DON'T NO ASF 49 11
SECOND FOUNDATION ASIMOV, ISAAC NO
ANNIVERSARY SS AMZ 59 03
ASIMOV'S MYSTERIES ASIMOV, ISAAC AC
BEST OF AMAZING, THE ROSS, JOSEPH AN
BEST OF ISAAC ASIMOV, THE ASIMOV, ISAAC AC
APPENDIX: MY HUNDRED BOOKS MS
OPUS 100 ASIMOV, ISAAC AC
AUTHOR'S ORDEAL, THE PM SFQ 57 05
EARTH IS ROOM ENOUGH ASIMOV, ISAAC AC
AUTHOR! AUTHOR! NV NEW 64 AN
EARLY ASIMOV, THE ASIMOV, ISAAC AC
UNKNOWN 5, THE BENSEN, D. R. AN
BAD NEWS AND THE GOOD, THE IN
BEYOND TOMORROW HARDING, LEE AN
BELIEF NV ASF 53 10
BEYOND THE BARRIERS OF SPACE AND TIME MERRIL, JUDITH AN
PROLOGUE TO ANALOG CAMPBELL, JOHN W. JR AN
THROUGH A GLASS, CLEARLY ASIMOV, ISAAC AC
14 GREAT TALES OF ESP STONE, IDELLA P. AN
BICENTENNIAL MAN, THE NV STL 76 02
BEST SCIENCE FICTION OF THE YEAR, THE NO. 6
CARR, TERRY AN
BICENTENNIAL MAN AND OTHER STORIES, THE
ASIMOV, ISAAC AC
STELLAR 2 DEL REY, JUDY-LYNN OA
1977 ANNUAL WORLD'S BEST SF, THE WOLLHEIM, DONALD A. AN
BIG AND THE LITTLE, THE NV ASF 44 08
FOUNDATION ASIMOV, ISAAC NO
BIG GAME (WRITTEN 11/18/41) SS NEW 74 AN
BEFORE THE GOLDEN AGE ASIMOV, ISAAC AN
BIG, BIG, BIG IN
SPACE BEYOND, THE CAMPBELL, JOHN W. JR OC
BILLIARD BALL, THE NV IFS 67 03
ASIMOV'S MYSTERIES ASIMOV, ISAAC AC
BEST OF ISAAC ASIMOV, THE ASIMOV, ISAAC AC
SECOND IF READER OF SCIENCE FICTION, THE
POHL, FREDERIK AN
WORLD'S BEST SCIENCE FICTION: 1968 WOLLHEIM & CARR AN
BIRTH OF A NOTION SS AMZ 76 06
BICENTENNIAL MAN AND OTHER STORIES, THE
ASIMOV, ISAAC AC
BLACK FRIAR OF THE FLAME NV PLS 42 SP
EARLY ASIMOV, THE ASIMOV, ISAAC AC
BLANK! SS INF 57 06
BUY JUPITER AND OTHER STORIES ASIMOV, ISAAC AC
HAVE YOU SEEN THESE? ASIMOV, ISAAC AC
BLIND ALLEY SS ASF 45 03
*BEST OF SCIENCE FICTION CONKLIN, GROFF AN
EARLY ASIMOV, THE ASIMOV, ISAAC AC
GREAT STORIES OF SPACE TRAVEL CONKLIN, GROFF AN
BRAZEN LOCKED ROOM, THE (ALSO AS GIMMICKS THREE) SS FSF 56 11
DEALS WITH THE DEVIL DAVENPORT, BASIL AN
SPECIAL WONDER MCCOMAS, J. FRANCIS AN
BREEDS THERE A MAN...? NV ASF 51 06
*BEACHHEADS IN SPACE DERLETH, AUGUST AN
FROM OTHER WORLDS DERLETH, AUGUST AN
NIGHTFALL AND OTHER STORIES ASIMOV, ISAAC AC
THROUGH A GLASS, CLEARLY ASIMOV, ISAAC AC
BRIDLE AND SADDLE NV ASF 42 06
FOUNDATION ASIMOV, ISAAC NO
*MEN AGAINST THE STARS GREENBERG , MARTIN AN
BUTTON, BUTTON SS STS 53 01
BUY JUPITER AND OTHER STORIES ASIMOV, ISAAC AC
13 ABOVE THE NIGHT CONKLIN, GROFF AN
BUY JUPITER! SS VSF 58 05
BUY JUPITER AND OTHER STORIES ASIMOV, ISAAC AC
NO LIMITS FERMAN, JOSEPH W. AN
C-CHUTE, THE NV GAL 51 10
BEST OF ISAAC ASIMOV, THE ASIMOV, ISAAC AC
GALAXY SCIENCE FICTION OMNIBUS GOLD, H. L. AN
NIGHTFALL AND OTHER STORIES ASIMOV, ISAAC AC
SECOND GALAXY READER OF SCIENCE FICTION
GOLD, H. L. AN
SHADOW OF TOMORROW POHL, FREDERIK AN
THROUGH A GLASS, CLEARLY ASIMOV, ISAAC AC
CALLISTAN MENACE, THE SS AST 40 04
EARLY ASIMOV, THE ASIMOV, ISAAC AC
FUTURES UNLIMITED NORTON, ALDEN H. AN
CATCH THAT RABBIT SS ASF 44 02
I, ROBOT ASIMOV, ISAAC AC
CAVES OF STEEL, THE NO GAL 53 10
*REST OF THE ROBOTS, THE ASIMOV, ISAAC AC

ASIMOV, ISAAC   (CONTINUED)
  CHRISTMAS ON GANYMEDE   SS   STS 42 01
    ADVENTURES IN TOMORROW   CROSSEN, KENDELL F.   AN
    EARLY ASIMOV, THE   ASIMOV, ISAAC   AC
  CURRENTS OF SPACE, THE   NO   ASF 52 10
    TRIANGLE   ASIMOV, ISAAC   AC
  DARWINIAN POOL ROOM   SS   GAL 50 10
    BUY JUPITER AND OTHER STORIES ASIMOV, ISAAC   AC
  DAY OF THE HUNTERS   SS   FUT 50 11
    BUY JUPITER AND OTHER STORIES ASIMOV, ISAAC   AC
    HAVE YOU SEEN THESE?   ASIMOV, ISAAC   AC
  DEAD HAND   NV   ASF 45 04
    FOUNDATION AND EMPIRE   ASIMOV, ISAAC   NO
  DEAD PAST, THE   NV   ASF 56 04
    BEST OF ISAAC ASIMOV, THE   ASIMOV, ISAAC   AC
    BEYOND CONTROL   SILVERBERG, ROBERT   AN
    EARTH IS ROOM ENOUGH   ASIMOV, ISAAC   AC
    FIVE-ODD   CONKLIN, GROFF   AN
  DEATH SENTENCE   SS   ASF 43 11
    EARLY ASIMOV, THE   ASIMOV, ISAAC   AC
    *OUTER REACHES, THE   DERLETH, AUGUST   AN
  DEEP, THE   NV   GAL 52 12
    BEST OF ISAAC ASIMOV, THE   ASIMOV, ISAAC   AC
    MARTIAN WAY AND OTHER STORIES, THE ASIMOV, ISAAC   AC
  DOES A BEE CARE?   SS   IFS 57 06
    BUY JUPITER AND OTHER STORIES ASIMOV, ISAAC   AC
    OTHER WORLDS, OTHER TIMES   MOSKOWITZ & ELWOOD   AN
  DREAMING IS A PRIVATE THING   SS   FSF 55 12
    EARTH IS ROOM ENOUGH   ASIMOV, ISAAC   AC
    FANTASY: THE LITERATURE OF THE MARVELOUS
                                   KELLEY, LEO P.   AN
    NEW DREAMS THIS MORNING   BLISH, JAMES   AN
    SCIENCE FICTION INVENTIONS   KNIGHT, DAMON   AN
    SF: THE BEST OF THE BEST   MERRIL, JUDITH   AN
    SF: THE YEAR'S GREATEST SCIENCE FICTION AND FANTASY
                                   MERRIL, JUDITH   AN
    TOMORROW, INC.   GREENBERG& OLANDER   AN
  DREAMWORLD   SS   FSF 55 11
    BEST FROM FANTASY AND SCIENCE FICTION: 5
                                   BOUCHER, ANTHONY   AN
    NEVER IN THIS WORLD   STONE, IDELLA P.   AN
    OPUS 100   ASIMOV, ISAAC   AC
  DUST OF DEATH, THE   SS   VSF 57 01
    ASIMOV'S MYSTERIES   ASIMOV, ISAAC   AC
  DYING NIGHT, THE   SS   FSF 56 07
    ASIMOV'S MYSTERIES   ASIMOV, ISAAC   AC
    BEST OF ISAAC ASIMOV, THE   ASIMOV, ISAAC   AC
    NINE TOMORROWS   ASIMOV, ISAAC   AC
  EACH AN EXPLORER   SS   FUT 56 30
    BUY JUPITER AND OTHER STORIES ASIMOV, ISAAC   AC
    EXPLORERS OF SPACE   SILVERBERG, ROBERT   AN
    ODDBALLS   GHIDALIA, VIC   AN
    SF:57, THE YEAR'S GREATEST SCIENCE FICTION AND FANTASY
                                   MERRIL, JUDITH   AN
  ENDOCHRONIC PROPERTIES OF RESUBLIMATED THIOTIMOLINE, THE
                                                 FA   ASF 48 03
    EARLY ASIMOV, THE   ASIMOV, ISAAC   AC
  ESCAPE (PARADOXICAL ESCAPE)   SS   ASF 45 08
    I, ROBOT   ASIMOV, ISAAC   AC
  EVEREST   SS   USF 53 12
    BUY JUPITER AND OTHER STORIES ASIMOV, ISAAC   AC
    HAVE YOU SEEN THESE?   ASIMOV, ISAAC   AC
  EVIDENCE   SS   ASF 46 09
    I, ROBOT   ASIMOV, ISAAC   AC
    POLITICAL SCIENCE FICTION   GREENBERG& WARRICK   AN
    PSEUDO PEOPLE, THE   NOLAN, WILLIAM F.   AN
  EVITABLE CONFLICT, THE   NV   ASF 50 06
    I, ROBOT   ASIMOV, ISAAC   AC
  EXILE TO HELL   SS   ASF 68 05
    BUY JUPITER AND OTHER STORIES ASIMOV, ISAAC   AC
    FAR-OUT PEOPLE, THE   HOSKINS, ROBERT   AN
  EYES DO MORE THAN SEE   SS   FSF 65 04
    BEST FROM FANTASY AND SCIENCE FICTION: 15
                                   FERMAN, EDWARD L.   AN
    NIGHTFALL AND OTHER STORIES   ASIMOV, ISAAC   AC
    11TH ANNUAL OF THE YEAR'S BEST S-F, THE
                                   MERRIL, JUDITH   AN
  F & SF AND I   IN
    TWENTY YEARS OF FANTASY & SCIENCE FICTION
                                   FERMAN & MILLS   AN
  FATHER OF SCIENCE FICTION, THE   IN   AMA 73
    ASTOUNDING   HARRISON, HARRY   OA
  FEELING OF POWER, THE   SS   IFS 58 02
    INSIDE INFORMATION   MOWSHOWITZ, ABBE   AN
    MATHEMATICAL MAGPIE, THE   FADIMAN, CLIFTON   AN
    NINE TOMORROWS   ASIMOV, ISAAC   AC
    OPUS 100   ASIMOV, ISAAC   AC
    PAST, PRESENT, AND FUTURE PERFECT WOLFE, J&FITZ GERALD AN
    SCIENCE FICTION THROUGH THE AGES 2 EVANS, I. O.   AN
    SPECTRUM 2   AMIS & CONQUEST   AN
    STARS AROUND US, THE   HOSKINS, ROBERT   AN
  FEMININE INTUITION   NV   FSF 69 10
    BICENTENNIAL MAN AND OTHER STORIES, THE
                                   ASIMOV, ISAAC   AC
    TWENTY YEARS OF FANTASY & SCIENCE FICTION
                                   FERMAN & MILLS   AN
  FIRST LAW   SS   FUN 56 10
    FANTASTIC UNIVERSE OMNIBUS, THE SANTESSON, HANS S.   AN
    *REST OF THE ROBOTS, THE   ASIMOV, ISAAC   AC
  FLIES   SS   FSF 53 06
    NIGHTFALL AND OTHER STORIES   ASIMOV, ISAAC   AC
    SCIENCE FICTION TERROR TALES   CONKLIN, GROFF   AN
  FOREWORD   IN
    ADRIFT IN SPACE AND OTHER STORIES ELWOOD, ROGER   OA
    GRADUATED ROBOT AND OTHER STORIES, THE ELWOOD, ROGER   OA

ASIMOV, ISAAC   (CONTINUED)
  JOURNEY TO ANOTHER STAR AND OTHER STORIES
                                   ELWOOD, ROGER   OA
    KILLER PLANTS AND OTHER STORIES, THE ELWOOD, ROGER   OA
    MIND ANGEL AND OTHER STORIES, THE ELWOOD, ROGER   OA
    MISSING WORLD AND OTHER STORIES, THE ELWOOD, ROGER   OA
    NIGHT OF THE SPHINX AND OTHER STORIES ELWOOD, ROGER   OA
    TUNNEL AND OTHER STORIES, THE ELWOOD, ROGER   OA
    UNKNOWN, THE   BENSEN, D. R.   AN
  FOREWORD 1- THE SECOND REVOLUTION   IN   DVS 67 01
    DANGEROUS VISIONS   ELLISON, HARLAN   OA
  FOREWORD 2- HARLAN AND I   IN   DVS 67 01
    DANGEROUS VISIONS   ELLISON, HARLAN   OA
  FOREWORD: FOUR THEMES FOR FOUR FUTURES   IN   FFU 71
    FOUR FUTURES   SILVERBERG, ROBERT   OA
  FOREWORD- WHY READ SCIENCE FICTION?   IN
    3000 YEARS OF FANTASY AND SCIENCE FICTION
                                   DE CAMP, L. S.&C.   AN
  FOUNDATION   NO   GNM 51
    FOUNDATION TRILOGY, THE   ASIMOV, ISAAC   .AC
  FOUNDATION   NV   ASF 42 05
    FOUNDATION   ASIMOV, ISAAC   NO
    GALACTIC EMPIRES VOLUME ONE   ALDISS, BRIAN W.   AN
  FOUNDATION AND EMPIRE   NO   GNM 52
    FOUNDATION TRILOGY, THE   ASIMOV, ISAAC   AC
  FOUNDATION OF SCIENCE FICTION SUCCESS, THE   PM   FSF 54 10
    BEST FROM FANTASY AND SCIENCE FICTION: 4
                                   BOUCHER, ANTHONY   AN
    EARTH IS ROOM ENOUGH   ASIMOV, ISAAC   AC
  FOUNDING FATHER   SS   GAL 65 10
    BUY JUPITER AND OTHER STORIES ASIMOV, ISAAC   AC
    SCIENCE FACT/FICTION   FARRELL/GAGE/&   AN
    SF: AUTHORS' CHOICE   HARRISON, HARRY   AN
    THEMES IN SCIENCE FICTION   KELLEY, LEO P.   AN
  FRANCHISE   SS   IFS 55 08
    ALIEN EARTH AND OTHER STORIES ELWOOD & MOSKOWITZ   AN
    EARTH IS ROOM ENOUGH   ASIMOV, ISAAC   AC
    FIRST WORLD OF IF, THE   QUINN & WULFF   AN
    INSIDE INFORMATION   MOWSHOWITZ, ABBE   AN
    POLITICAL SCIENCE FICTION   GREENBERG& WARRICK   AN
  FROM "ASIMOV'S BIOGRAPHICAL ENCYCLOPEDIA OF SCIENCE"
                                                 AR   DBL 64
    OPUS 100   ASIMOV, ISAAC   AC
  FROM "ASIMOV'S GUIDE TO THE BIBLE"   AR   DBL 68
    OPUS 100   ASIMOV, ISAAC   AC
  FROM "BIOCHEMISTRY AND HUMAN METABOLISM"   AR   WMW 52
    OPUS 100   ASIMOV, ISAAC   AC
  FROM "GALAXIES"   AR   FOL 68
    OPUS 100   ASIMOV, ISAAC   AC
  FROM "I, ROBOT"   EX   GNM 50
    OPUS 100   ASIMOV, ISAAC   AC
  FROM "ISAAC ASIMOV EXPLAINS" (FORCE FIELDS)   AR   SDG 68
    OPUS 100   ASIMOV, ISAAC   AC
  FROM "ISAAC ASIMOV EXPLAINS" (IRRESISTABLE FORCE) AR   SDG 68
    OPUS 100   ASIMOV, ISAAC   AC
  FROM "LIAR!"   EX   ASF 41 05
    OPUS 100   ASIMOV, ISAAC   AC
  FROM "LUCKIE STARR AND THE MOONS OF JUPITER"   EX   DBL 57
    OPUS 100   ASIMOV, ISAAC   AC
  FROM "LUCKIE STARR AND THE OCEANS OF VENUS"   EX   DBL 54
    OPUS 100   ASIMOV, ISAAC   AC
  FROM "ONLY A TRILLION"   AR   ABE 57
    OPUS 100   ASIMOV, ISAAC   AC
  FROM "PHOTOSYNTHESIS"   AR   BAS 68
    OPUS 100   ASIMOV, ISAAC   AC
  FROM "QUICK AND EASY MATH"   AR   HMF 64
    OPUS 100   ASIMOV, ISAAC   AC
  FROM "RUNAROUND"   EX   ASF 42 03
    OPUS 100   ASIMOV, ISAAC   AC
  FROM "STRANGE PLAYFELLOW"   EX   SSS 40 09
    OPUS 100   ASIMOV, ISAAC   AC
  FROM "SUPERNUTRON"   EX   AST 41 09
    OPUS 100   ASIMOV, ISAAC   AC
  FROM "THE CALLISTAN MENACE"   EX   AST 40 04
    OPUS 100   ASIMOV, ISAAC   AC
  FROM "THE CHEMICALS OF LIFE"   AR   ABE 54
    OPUS 100   ASIMOV, ISAAC   AC
  FROM "THE DEAD HAND"   EX   ASF 45 04
    OPUS 100   ASIMOV, ISAAC   AC
  FROM "THE EGYPTIANS"   AR   HMF 67
    OPUS 100   ASIMOV, ISAAC   AC
  FROM "THE GREEKS"   AR   HMF 65
    OPUS 100   ASIMOV, ISAAC   AC
  FROM "THE INTELLIGENT MAN'S GUIDE TO SCIENCE" AR   BAS 60
    OPUS 100   ASIMOV, ISAAC   AC
  FROM "THE KINETICS OF THE REACTION INACTIVATION OF TYROSINASE
  DURING ITS CATALYSIS OF.."   AR   48
    OPUS 100   ASIMOV, ISAAC   AC
  FROM "THE MARTIAN WAY"   EX   GAL 52 11
    OPUS 100   ASIMOV, ISAAC   AC
  FROM "THE NEAR EAST"   AR   HMF 68
    OPUS 100   ASIMOV, ISAAC   AC
  FROM "THE NOBLE GASSES"   AR   BAS 66
    OPUS 100   ASIMOV, ISAAC   AC
  FROM "THE NUTRINO"   AR   DBL 66
    OPUS 100   ASIMOV, ISAAC   AC
  FROM "THE PERFECT MACHINE"   AR   SJR 68 10
    OPUS 100   ASIMOV, ISAAC   AC
  FROM "THE REALM OF NUMBERS"   AR   HMF 59
    OPUS 100   ASIMOV, ISAAC   AC
  FROM "THE ROMAN REPUBLIC"   AR   HMF 66
    OPUS 100   ASIMOV, ISAAC   AC
  FROM "THE SOUND OF PANTING"   AR   ASF 55 06
    OPUS 100   ASIMOV, ISAAC   AC
  FROM "THE UNIVERSE"   AR   WKR 66
    OPUS 100   ASIMOV, ISAAC   AC

ASIMOV, ISAAC   (CONTINUED)
FROM "THE WELLSPRINGS OF LIFE"   AR   ABE 60
   OPUS 100   ASIMOV, ISAAC   AC
FROM "THERE'S NOTHING LIKE A GOOD FOUNDATION"   AR   67
   OPUS 100   ASIMOV, ISAAC   AC
FROM "VIEW FROM AMALTHEA"   AR   FSF 68 12
   OPUS 100   ASIMOV, ISAAC   AC
FROM "WORDS FROM HISTORY"   AR   HMF 68
   OPUS 100   ASIMOV, ISAAC   AC
FROM "WORDS OF SCIENCE"   AR   HMF 59
   OPUS 100   ASIMOV, ISAAC   AC
FROM "WORDS ON THE MAP"   AR   HMF 62
   OPUS 100   ASIMOV, ISAAC   AC
FUN THEY HAD, THE (NEA 51 12)   SS   FSF 54 02
   AS TOMORROW BECOMES TODAY   SULLIVAN, CHARLES W. AN
   BEST OF ISAAC ASIMOV, THE   ASIMOV, ISAAC   AC
   CONNOISSEUR'S S. F.   BOARDMAN, TOM JR. AN
   EARTH IS ROOM ENOUGH   ASIMOV, ISAAC   AC
   FIFTY SHORT SCIENCE FICTION TALES   ASIMOV & CONKLIN AN
   JOURNEYS IN SCIENCE FICTION   LOUGHLIN, RICHARD L. AN
   OPERATION FUTURE   CONKLIN, GROFF   AN
   UNTRAVELLED WORLDS   BARTER & WILSON   AN
GALLEY SLAVE   NV   GAL 57 12
   *REST OF THE ROBOTS, THE   ASIMOV, ISAAC   AC
   SIX GREAT SHORT SCIENCE FICTION NOVELS CONKLIN, GROFF AN
   TIME WAITS FOR WINTHROP, AND FOUR OTHER SHORT NOVELS
                                        POHL, FREDERIK   AN
GENTLE VULTURES, THE   SS   SUP 57 12
   CONTACT   KEYES, NOEL   AN
   EARTHMEN AND STRANGERS   SILVERBERG, ROBERT AN
   NINE TOMORROWS   ASIMOV, ISAAC   AC
GIMMICKS THREE (THE BRAZEN LOCKED ROOM)   SS   FSF 56 11
   EARTH IS ROOM ENOUGH   ASIMOV, ISAAC   AC
GREATEST ASSET, THE   SS   ASF 72 01
   BEST SCIENCE FICTION STORIES OF THE YEAR (1972)
                                        DEL REY, LESTER   AN
   BUY JUPITER AND OTHER STORIES   ASIMOV, ISAAC   AC
GREEN PATCHES (MISBEGOTTEN MISSIONARY)   SS   GAL 50 11
   NIGHTFALL AND OTHER STORIES   ASIMOV, ISAAC   AC
   SCIENCE FICTION   BRODKIN & PEARSON AN
HALF-BAKED PUBLISHER'S DELIGHT   SS C IFS 74 08
   BEST FROM IF, THE VOLUME III   BAEN, JAMES   AN
HALF-BREED   SS   AST 40 02
   EARLY ASIMOV, THE   ASIMOV, ISAAC   AC
   SPACE MAGICIANS, THE   NORTON & MOSKOWITZ AN
   TOMORROW, AND TOMORROW, AND TOMORROW...
                                        HEINTZ/HERBERT/JOOS/ AN
HALF-BREEDS ON VENUS   SS   AST 40 12
   EARLY ASIMOV, THE   ASIMOV, ISAAC   AC
HAZING, THE   SS   TWS 42 10
   EARLY ASIMOV, THE   ASIMOV, ISAAC   AC
HELL-FIRE   SS   FUN 56 05
   EARTH IS ROOM ENOUGH   ASIMOV, ISAAC   AC
HERE I AM AGAIN   IN
   HUGO WINNERS, THE (VOLUME 2)   ASIMOV, ISAAC   AN
HEREDITY   SS   AST 41 04
   BEYOND THE END OF TIME   POHL, FREDERIK   AN
   EARLY ASIMOV, THE   ASIMOV, ISAAC   AC
HISTORY   SS   SSS 41 03
   EARLY ASIMOV, THE   ASIMOV, ISAAC   AC
HOLMES-GINSBOOK DEVICE, THE   SS   IFS 68 12
   OPUS 100   ASIMOV, ISAAC   AC
HOMO SOL   SS   ASF 40 09
   EARLY ASIMOV, THE   ASIMOV, ISAAC   AC
   OMNIBUS OF SCIENCE FICTION   CONKLIN, GROFF   AN
   SCIENCE FICTION OMNIBUS   CONKLIN, GROFF   AN
HOSTESS   NV   GAL 51 05
   *GALAXY READER OF SCIENCE FICTION   GOLD, H. L.   AN
   NIGHTFALL AND OTHER STORIES   ASIMOV, ISAAC   AC
I JUST MAKE THEM UP, SEE   PM   FSF 58 02
   NINE TOMORROWS   ASIMOV, ISAAC   AC
I'M IN MARSPORT WITHOUT HILDA   SS   VSF 57 11
   ASIMOV'S MYSTERIES   ASIMOV, ISAAC   AC
   NINE TOMORROWS   ASIMOV, ISAAC   AC
IDEAS DIE HARD   NV   GAL 57 10
   FIRST FLIGHTS TO THE MOON   CLEMENT, HAL   AN
   THIRD GALAXY READER, THE   GOLD, H. L.   AN
IMAGINARY, THE   SS   SSS 42 11
   EARLY ASIMOV, THE   ASIMOV, ISAAC   AC
   HUMAN ZERO, THE   MOSKOWITZ & ELWOOD AN
IMMORTAL BARD, THE   SS   USF 54 05
   EARTH IS ROOM ENOUGH   ASIMOV, ISAAC   AC
   INTRODUCING SCIENCE FICTION   ALDISS, BRIAN W. AN
IN A GOOD CAUSE-   NV   NTS 51
   NEW TALES OF SPACE AND TIME   HEALY, RAYMOND J. OA
   NIGHTFALL AND OTHER STORIES   ASIMOV, ISAAC   AC
IN MEMORIAM- GROFF CONKLIN   MS
   NEBULA AWARD STORIES NO. 4   ANDERSON, POUL   AN
IN RE SPRAGUE   MS
   CONTINENT MAKERS AND OTHER TALES OF THE VIAGENS
                                        DE CAMP, L. SPRAGUE AC
INSERT KNOB A IN HOLE B   SS   FSF 57 12
   NIGHTFALL AND OTHER STORIES   ASIMOV, ISAAC   AC
INTRODUCTION   IN
   ASIMOV'S MYSTERIES   ASIMOV, ISAAC   AC
   BEST OF ISAAC ASIMOV, THE   ASIMOV, ISAAC   AC
   FIRST FLIGHTS TO THE MOON   CLEMENT, HAL   AN
   HUGO WINNERS, THE (VOLUME 1)   ASIMOV, ISAAC   AN
   I, ROBOT   ASIMOV, ISAAC   AC
   MORE SOVIET SCIENCE FICTION   ANONYMOUS   AN
   OPUS 100   ASIMOV, ISAAC   AC
   *REST OF THE ROBOTS, THE   ASIMOV, ISAAC   AC
   SOVIET SCIENCE FICTION   ANONYMOUS   AN
   TOMORROW'S CHILDREN   ASIMOV, ISAAC   AN
   WHERE DO WE GO FROM HERE?   ASIMOV, ISAAC   AN

ASIMOV, ISAAC   (CONTINUED)
INTRODUCTION NO. 1   IN
   FIFTY SHORT SCIENCE FICTION TALES   ASIMOV & CONKLIN AN
INTRODUCTION PART 1: 1920 TO 1930   IN
   BEFORE THE GOLDEN AGE   ASIMOV, ISAAC   AC
INTRODUCTION: THE FUN IN FUTURE FUN   IN   67
   INFINITY 1   HOSKINS, ROBERT   OA
IS THERE HOPE FOR THE FUTURE?   AR   GAL 74 07
   BEST FROM GALAXY, THE VOLUME III   BAEN, JAMES   AN
IT'S ALL HOW YOU LOOK AT IT (SEE THE THUNDER-THIEVES)
                                                 TC
IT'S SUCH A BEAUTIFUL DAY   NV   STR 54 03
   BEYOND BELIEF   HURLEY, RICHARD J. AN
   ECO-FICTION   STADLER, JOHN   AN
   NIGHTFALL AND OTHER STORIES   ASIMOV, ISAAC   AC
   STAR SCIENCE FICTION STORIES NO. 3   POHL, FREDERIK   OA
   THROUGH A GLASS, CLEARLY   ASIMOV, ISAAC   AC
   TRANSFORMATIONS   ROSELLE, DANIEL   AN
   UNIVERSE AHEAD   ENGDAHL & ROBERSON AN
   YOU AND SCIENCE FICTION   HOLLISTER, BERNARD C AN
JOKSTER   SS   INF 56 12
   EARTH IS ROOM ENOUGH   ASIMOV, ISAAC   AC
   MORE PENGUIN SCIENCE FICTION   ALDISS, BRIAN W. AN
JUPITER THE GIANT   IN
   JUPITER   POHL, C. & F.   AN
KEY ITEM   SS   FSF 68 07
   BUY JUPITER AND OTHER STORIES   ASIMOV, ISAAC   AC
KEY, THE   NV   FSF 66 10
   ASIMOV'S MYSTERIES   ASIMOV, ISAAC   AC
   BEST FROM FANTASY AND SCIENCE FICTION: 16
                                        FERMAN, EDWARD L. AN
   BEST FROM FANTASY AND SCIENCE FICTION, 25TH ANNIV.
                                        FERMAN, EDWARD L. AN
KID STUFF   SS   BEY 53 09
   EARTH IS ROOM ENOUGH   ASIMOV, ISAAC   AC
LAST QUESTION, THE   SS   SFQ 56 11
   BEST OF ISAAC ASIMOV, THE   ASIMOV, ISAAC   AC
   NINE TOMORROWS   ASIMOV, ISAAC   AC
   OPUS 100   ASIMOV, ISAAC   AC
   SCIENCE FICTION ROLL OF HONOR, THE   POHL, FREDERIK   AN
   SPACE OPERA   ALDISS, BRIAN W. AN
   3000 YEARS OF FANTASY AND SCIENCE FICTION
                                        DE CAMP, L. S.&C. AN
LAST TRUMP, THE   SS   FUN 55 06
   EARTH IS ROOM ENOUGH   ASIMOV, ISAAC   AC
LASTBORN (SEE THE UGLY LITTLE BOY)   TC
LEGAL RITES   NV C WRT 50 09
   BR-R-R-| CONKLIN, GROFF   AN
   EARLY ASIMOV, THE   ASIMOV, ISAAC   AC
   EDGE OF NEVER, THE   HOSKINS, ROBERT   AN
   UNEXPECTED, THE   MARGULIES, LEO   AN
LENNY   SS   INF 58 01
   ANDROIDS, TIME MACHINES AND BLUE GIRAFFES
                                        ELWOOD & GHIDALIA AN
   EXPERT DREAMERS, THE   POHL, FREDERIK   AN
   *REST OF THE ROBOTS, THE   ASIMOV, ISAAC   AC
   VISIONS OF TOMORROW   ELWOOD, ROGER   AN
LET'S GET TOGETHER   SS   INF 57 02
   *REST OF THE ROBOTS, THE   ASIMOV, ISAAC   AC
   SF:58, THE YEAR'S GREATEST SCIENCE FICTION AND FANTASY
                                        MERRIL, JUDITH   AN
LET'S NOT   SS   BUG 54 12
   ALL ABOUT THE FUTURE   GREENBERG, MARTIN AN
   BUY JUPITER AND OTHER STORIES   ASIMOV, ISAAC   AC
LIAR| SS   ASF 41 05
   DOORWAY INTO TIME   MOSKOWITZ, SAM   AN
   HUMAN?   MERRIL, JUDITH   AN
   I, ROBOT   ASIMOV, ISAAC   AC
   IN DREAMS AWAKE   FIEDLER, LESLIE A. AN
   MIND TO MIND   SILVERBERG, ROBERT AN
   MODERN MASTERPIECES OF SCIENCE FICTION MOSKOWITZ, SAM AN
LIFE AND TIMES OF MULTIVAC, THE   SS   NYT 75 01
   BICENTENNIAL MAN AND OTHER STORIES, THE
                                        ASIMOV, ISAAC   AC
LIGHT VERSE   SS   SEP 73 09
   BUY JUPITER AND OTHER STORIES   ASIMOV, ISAAC   AC
LITTLE LOST ROBOT   SS   ASF 47 03
   BEST SF 2   CRISPIN, EDMUND   AN
   I, ROBOT   ASIMOV, ISAAC   AC
   STARS AND UNDER, THE   CRISPIN, EDMUND   AN
LITTLE MAN ON THE SUBWAY, THE   SS C FBK 50 06
   EARLY ASIMOV, THE   ASIMOV, ISAAC   AC
   SCIENCE AND SORCERY   FORD, GARRET   AN
LIVING SPACE   SS   SFS 56 05
   EARTH IS ROOM ENOUGH   ASIMOV, ISAAC   AC
   OUT OF THIS WORLD 3   WILLIAMS-ELLIS& OWEN AN
   WONDERMAKERS 2   HOSKINS, ROBERT   AN
   WORLDS OF MAYBE   SILVERBERG, ROBERT AN
LOINT OF PAW, A   SS   FSF 57 08
   ASIMOV'S MYSTERIES   ASIMOV, ISAAC   AC
   BEST FROM FANTASY AND SCIENCE FICTION: 7
                                        BOUCHER, ANTHONY AN
MACHINE THAT WON THE WAR, THE   SS   FSF 61 10
   *BEST FROM FANTASY AND SCIENCE FICTION: 11
                                        MILLS, ROBERT P. AN
   BEST SF 7   CRISPIN, EDMUND   AN
   NIGHTFALL AND OTHER STORIES   ASIMOV, ISAAC   AC
MAGNIFICENT POSESSION, THE   SS   FUT 40 07
   EARLY ASIMOV, THE   ASIMOV, ISAAC   AC
MALE STRIKEBREAKER (SEE STRIKEBREAKER)   TC
MARCHING IN   SS   HFI 76 04
   BICENTENNIAL MAN AND OTHER STORIES, THE
                                        ASIMOV, ISAAC   AC
MAROONED OFF VESTA   SS   AMZ 39 03
   ASIMOV'S MYSTERIES   ASIMOV, ISAAC   AC
   BEST OF AMAZING, THE   ROSS, JOSEPH   AN

```
ASIMOV, ISAAC    (CONTINUED)                          ASIMOV, ISAAC    (CONTINUED)
  BEST OF ISAAC ASIMOV, THE         ASIMOV, ISAAC  AC   I, ROBOT                         ASIMOV, ISAAC       AC
MARTIAN WAY, THE                    NA   GAL 52 11       SPACE ODYSSEYS                   ALDISS, BRIAN W.    AN
  BEST OF ISAAC ASIMOV, THE         ASIMOV, ISAAC  AC  RED QUEEN'S RACE, THE              NV   ASF 49 01
  MARTIAN WAY AND OTHER STORIES, THE ASIMOV, ISAAC AC    EARLY ASIMOV, THE                ASIMOV, ISAAC       AC
  SCIENCE FICTION HALL OF FAME VOLUME 2B BOVA, BEN  AN   SCIENCE FICTION ARGOSY, A        KNIGHT, DAMON       AN
  WORLDS TO COME                    KNIGHT, DAMON  AN     WORLD OF WONDER                  PRATT, FLETCHER     AN
MESSAGE, THE                        SS   FSF 56 02     REJECTION SLIPS                    PM   NEW 59 AC
  EARTH IS ROOM ENOUGH              ASIMOV, ISAAC  AC    NINE TOMORROWS                   ASIMOV, ISAAC       AC
MIRROR IMAGE                        SS   ASF 72 05     RING AROUND THE SUN                SS   FUT 40 03
  BEST OF ISAAC ASIMOV, THE         ASIMOV, ISAAC  AC    EARLY ASIMOV, THE                ASIMOV, ISAAC       AC
MISBEGOTTEN MISSIONARY (ALSO AS GREEN PATCHES) SS GAL 50 11  RISK                        NV   ASF 55 05
  FIRST STEP OUTWARD               HOSKINS, ROBERT AN    *REST OF THE ROBOTS, THE         ASIMOV, ISAAC       AC
  GIANTS UNLEASHED                  CONKLIN, GROFF AN  ROBBIE (STRANGE PLAYFELLOW)        SS   SSS 40 09
  SCIENCE FACT/FICTION              FARRELL/GAGE/&  AN    I, ROBOT                         ASIMOV, ISAAC       AC
  SPECULATIONS                      SANDERS, THOMAS E. AN  *SCIENCE FICTION THINKING MACHINES CONKLIN, GROFF  AN
  TOMORROW, THE STARS               HEINLEIN, ROBERT A. AN TALES BEYOND TIME               DE CAMP, L. S.&C.   AN
MONKEY'S FINGER, THE                SS   STS 53 02     ROBOT AL-76 GOES ASTRAY            SS   AMZ 42 02
  BUY JUPITER AND OTHER STORIES     ASIMOV, ISAAC  AC    *MY BEST SCIENCE FICTION STORY   MARGULIES & FRIEND  AN
  HAVE YOU SEEN THESE?              ASIMOV, ISAAC  AC    *REST OF THE ROBOTS, THE         ASIMOV, ISAAC       AC
MOTHER EARTH                        NV   ASF 49 05     ROMANCE OF MARS, THE               IN
  EARLY ASIMOV, THE                 ASIMOV, ISAAC  AC    MARS, WE LOVE YOU                HIPOLITO & MCNELLY  AN
  JOURNEY TO INFINITY               GREENBERG, MARTIN AN RUNAROUND                         SS   ASF 42 03
  3 FROM OUT THERE                  MARGULIES, LEO AN     AS TOMORROW BECOMES TODAY        SULLIVAN, CHARLES W. AN
MULE, THE                           SN   ASF 45 11       COMING OF THE ROBOTS, THE        MOSKOWITZ, SAM      AN
  FOUNDATION AND EMPIRE             ASIMOV, ISAAC  NO     I, ROBOT                         ASIMOV, ISAAC       AC
MY SON, THE PHYSICIST               SS   SAM 62 02     S AS IN ZEBATINSKY (SEE SPELL MY NAME WITH AN S)  TC
  NIGHTFALL AND OTHER STORIES       ASIMOV, ISAAC  AC  SALLY                              SS   FAN 53 05
  SCIENCE FICTION HORIZONS NO. 1    BOARDMAN, TOM JR. AN  BEST FROM FANTASTIC, THE        WHITE, TED          AN
NAKED SUN, THE                      NO   ASF 56 10       NIGHTFALL AND OTHER STORIES      ASIMOV, ISAAC       AC
  *REST OF THE ROBOTS, THE          ASIMOV, ISAAC  AC    TIME UNTAMED                     HOWARD, IVAN        AN
NIGHTFALL                           NV   ASF 41 09     SATISFACTION GUARANTEED            SS   AMZ 51 04
  *ADVENTURES IN TIME AND SPACE     HEALY & MCCOMAS AN    EARTH IS ROOM ENOUGH             ASIMOV, ISAAC       AC
  ANTHROPOLOGY THROUGH SCIENCE FICTION MASON, C/GREENBERG/& AN INVASION OF THE ROBOTS     ELWOOD, ROGER       AN
  *ASTOUNDING SCIENCE FICTION ANTHOLOGY, THE             *REST OF THE ROBOTS, THE         ASIMOV, ISAAC       AC
                                    CAMPBELL, JOHN W. JR AN SECOND FOUNDATION             NO   GNM 53
  ASTOUNDING-ANALOG READER, THE VOLUME ONE               FOUNDATION TRILOGY, THE          ASIMOV, ISAAC       AC
                                    HARRISON & ALDISS AN SECOND NOVA, THE                  IN
  BEST OF ISAAC ASIMOV, THE         ASIMOV, ISAAC  AC    BEST OF STANLEY G. WEINBAUM, THE WEINBAUM, STANLEY G. AC
  BEYOND TOMORROW                   KNIGHT, DAMON  AN  SECRET SENSE, THE                   SS   COS 41 03
  GREAT SCIENCE FICTION STORIES     SMITH, CORDELIA T. AN  EARLY ASIMOV, THE              ASIMOV, ISAAC       AC
  MIRROR OF INFINITY, THE           SILVERBERG, ROBERT AN  FUTURES TO INFINITY            MOSKOWITZ, SAM      AN
  MODERN SCIENCE FICTION            SPINRAD, NORMAN AN SEGREGATIONIST                     SS   ABB 67 04
  MORE ADVENTURES IN TIME AND SPACE HEALY & MCCOMAS AN    BEST SF: 1968                    HARRISON & ALDISS   AN
  NIGHTFALL AND OTHER STORIES       ASIMOV, ISAAC  AC    NIGHTFALL AND OTHER STORIES      ASIMOV, ISAAC       AC
  OTHER DIMENSION, THE              ROSNER, SARA   AN  SENSE OF WONDER, THE                IN
  PENGUIN SCIENCE FICTION           ALDISS, BRIAN W. AN   JOHN W. CAMPBELL ANTHOLOGY: THREE NOVELS
  SCIENCE FICTION                   BURTON, S. H.  AN                                     CAMPBELL, JOHN W. JR AC
  SCIENCE FICTION HALL OF FAME VOLUME 1 SILVERBERG, ROBERT AN SHAH GUIDO G.               SS   MAR 51 11
  SECOND ASTOUNDING SCIENCE FICTION ANTHOLOGY, THE (PB)   BUY JUPITER AND OTHER STORIES   ASIMOV, ISAAC       AC
                                    CAMPBELL, JOHN W. JR AN  HAVE YOU SEEN THESE?          ASIMOV, ISAAC       AC
  TOMORROW, AND TOMORROW, AND TOMORROW...               SILLY ASSES                       SS   FUT 58 02
                                    HEINTZ/HERBERT/JOOS/ AN  BUY JUPITER AND OTHER STORIES ASIMOV, ISAAC       AC
  UBERWINDUNG VON RAUM UND ZEIT     GUNTHER, GOTTHARD AN   HAVE YOU SEEN THESE?            ASIMOV, ISAAC       AC
NO CONNECTION                       SS   ASF 48 06     SINGING BELL, THE                  SS   FSF 55 01
  BEST SCIENCE-FICTION STORIES: 1949, THE                ASIMOV'S MYSTERIES               ASIMOV, ISAAC       AC
                                    BLEILER & DIKTY AN     BEST FROM FANTASY AND SCIENCE FICTION: 5
  EARLY ASIMOV, THE                 ASIMOV, ISAAC  AC                                     BOUCHER, ANTHONY    AN
NOBODY HERE BUT-                    SS   STR 53 01       TOMORROW, AND TOMORROW, AND TOMORROW...
  NIGHTFALL AND OTHER STORIES       ASIMOV, ISAAC  AC                                     HEINTZ/HERBERT/JOOS/ AN
  STAR SCIENCE FICTION STORIES      POHL, FREDERIK OA  SO WHY AREN'T WE RICH?              IN
NOT FINAL!                          SS   ASF 41 10       NEBULA AWARD STORIES  8          ASIMOV, ISAAC       AN
  ASLEEP IN ARMAGEDDON              SISSONS, MICHAEL AN SOCIAL SCIENCE FICTION             AR   NEW 53 NF
  EARLY ASIMOV, THE                 ASIMOV, ISAAC  AC    SCIENCE FICTION: THE FUTURE      ALLEN, DICK         AN
  FIRST CONTACT                     KNIGHT, DAMON  AN  SOMEDAY                             SS   INF 56 08
  *POSSIBLE WORLDS OF SCIENCE FICTION CONKLIN, GROFF AN   EARTH IS ROOM ENOUGH            ASIMOV, ISAAC       AC
  TIME PROBE: THE SCIENCES IN SF.   CLARKE, ARTHUR C. AN   METAL SMILE, THE               KNIGHT, DAMON       AN
  TOWARD INFINITY                   KNIGHT, DAMON  AN     WORLDS OF WONDER                 HARRISON, HARRY     AN
NOW YOU SEE IT...                   NV   ASF 48 01     SPELL MY NAME WITH AN S (S AS IN ZEBATINSKY) SS SMG 58 01
  SECOND FOUNDATION                 ASIMOV, ISAAC  NO     NINE TOMORROWS                   ASIMOV, ISAAC       AC
OBITUARY                            SS   FSF 59 08     STAR LIGHT                         SS   SAM 62 10
  ASIMOV'S MYSTERIES                ASIMOV, ISAAC  AC    ASIMOV'S MYSTERIES               ASIMOV, ISAAC       AC
OLD-FASHIONED                       SS   BTM 76 02       BEST FROM NEW WRITINGS IN S-F FIRST SELECTION, THE
  BICENTENNIAL MAN AND OTHER STORIES, THE                                                CARNELL, JOHN       AN
                                    ASIMOV, ISAAC  AC    NEW WRITINGS IN SF.  4           CARNELL, JOHN       OA
ON PREDICTION                       IN   68            STARS LIKE DUST, THE               NO   GAL 51 01
  FUTURE TENSE                      CURTIS, RICHARD AN    TRIANGLE                         ASIMOV, ISAAC       AC
OPUS 100                            ASIMOV, ISAAC  AC  STATUE FOR FATHER, A                SS   SAT 59 02
PATE DE FOIE GRAS                   SF   ASF 56 09       BUY JUPITER AND OTHER STORIES    ASIMOV, ISAAC       AC
  ASIMOV'S MYSTERIES                ASIMOV, ISAAC  AC  STRANGE PLAYFELLOW (ALSO AS ROBBIE) SS  SSS 40 09
  WHERE DO WE GO FROM HERE?         ASIMOV, ISAAC  AN    SHOT IN THE DARK                 MERRIL, JUDITH      AN
PAUSE, THE                          SS               STRANGER IN PARADISE                NV   IFS 74 06
  BUY JUPITER AND OTHER STORIES     ASIMOV, ISAAC  AC    BEST FROM IF, THE  VOLUME II     IF, EDITORS OF      AN
  HAVE YOU SEEN THESE?              ASIMOV, ISAAC  AC    BICENTENNIAL MAN AND OTHER STORIES, THE
  *TIME TO COME                     DERLETH, AUGUST OA                                    ASIMOV, ISAAC       AC
PEBBLE IN THE SKY                   NO   DBL 50          1975 ANNUAL WORLD'S BEST SF, THE WOLLHEIM, DONALD A. AN
  TRIANGLE                          ASIMOV, ISAAC  AC  STRIKEBREAKER (MALE STRIKEBREAKER)  SS   SFS 57 01
PLAYBOY AND THE SLIME GOD, THE (SEE WHAT IS THIS THING    ANTHROPOLOGY THROUGH SCIENCE FICTION MASON, C/GREENBERG/& AN
  CALLED LOVE?)                     TC                   NIGHTFALL AND OTHER STORIES      ASIMOV, ISAAC       AC
PRIME OF LIFE, THE                  PM   FSF 66 10       17 X INFINITY                    CONKLIN, GROFF      AN
  BICENTENNIAL MAN AND OTHER STORIES, THE              SUCKER BAIT                        SN   ASF 54 02
                                    ASIMOV, ISAAC  AC    MARTIAN WAY AND OTHER STORIES, THE ASIMOV, ISAAC     AC
PROFESSION                          SN   ASF 57 07     SUPER-NEUTRON                      SS   AST 41 09
  NINE TOMORROWS                    ASIMOV, ISAAC  AC    EARLY ASIMOV, THE                ASIMOV, ISAAC       AC
  SCHOOL AND SOCIETY THROUGH SCIENCE FICTION           TAKE A MATCH                       SS   NDM 72 02
                                    OLANDER/GREENBERG/& AN  BUY JUPITER AND OTHER STORIES ASIMOV, ISAAC       AC
PROFESSION (EDITED)                 SS   ASF 57 07       NEW DIMENSIONS 2                 SILVERBERG, ROBERT  OA
  YOU AND SCIENCE FICTION           HOLLISTER, BERNARD C AN TALKING STONE, THE            SS   FSF 55 10
PROPER STUDY, THE                   SS   BLF 68 09       ASIMOV'S MYSTERIES               ASIMOV, ISAAC       AC
  BUY JUPITER AND OTHER STORIES     ASIMOV, ISAAC  AC    SPACE, TIME & CRIME              DEFORD, MIRIAM ALLEN AN
RAIN, RAIN, GO AWAY                 SS   FUN 59 09     TERCENTENARY INCIDENT, THE         SS   EQM 76 08
  BUY JUPITER AND OTHER STORIES     ASIMOV, ISAAC  AC    BICENTENNIAL MAN AND OTHER STORIES, THE
  HAVE YOU SEEN THESE?              ASIMOV, ISAAC  AC                                     ASIMOV, ISAAC       AC
REASON                              SS   ASF 41 04     THAT THOU ART MINDFUL OF HIM!      NV   FSF 74 05
  CENTURY OF SCIENCE FICTION, A     KNIGHT, DAMON  AN    BICENTENNIAL MAN AND OTHER STORIES, THE
  DECADE THE 1940S                  ALDISS & HARRISON AN                                  ASIMOV, ISAAC       AC
```

ASIMOV, ISAAC   (CONTINUED)
 FINAL STAGE   FERMAN & MALZBERG OA
 SOULS IN METAL   ASHLEY, MICHAEL   AN
THINKING MACHINE, THE   AR SDG 67 12
 SCIENCE FACT/FICTION   FARRELL/GAGE/&   AN
THIOTIMOLINE AND THE SPACE AGE   SF ASF 60 10
 OPUS 100   ASIMOV, ISAAC   AC
 6TH ANNUAL OF THE YEAR'S BEST S-F, THE MERRIL, JUDITH AN
THIOTIMOLINE TO THE STARS   SS AMA 73
 ASTOUNDING   HARRISON, HARRY   OA
 BUY JUPITER AND OTHER STORIES ASIMOV, ISAAC   AC
THREE JOHNS, THE (ONLY IN REPRINT, LAN 72) AR
 CLOAK OF AESIR   CAMPBELL, JOHN W. JR AC
THUNDER-THIEVES, THE (IT'S ALL HOW YOU LOOK AT IT)
               PM FUT 58 10
SF:59, THE YEAR'S GREATEST SCIENCE FICTION AND FANTASY
              MERRIL, JUDITH   AN
TIME PUSSY   SS ASF 42 04
 EARLY ASIMOV, THE   ASIMOV, ISAAC   AC
TRENDS   SS ASF 39 07
 EARLY ASIMOV, THE   ASIMOV, ISAAC   AC
 FIRST FLIGHTS TO THE MOON   CLEMENT, HAL   AN
 GREAT SCIENCE FICTION STORIES ABOUT THE MOON
              DIKTY, T. E.   AN
 *MEN AGAINST THE STARS   GREENBERG, MARTIN AN
 SPECTRUM OF WORLDS, A   CLARESON, THOMAS D. AN
TWELVE POINT THREE SIX NINE   AR FSF 67 07
 OPUS 100   ASIMOV, ISAAC   AC
UGLY LITTLE BOY, THE (LASTBORN) NA GAL 58 09
 DIMENSION X   KNIGHT, DAMON   AN
 NINE TOMORROWS   ASIMOV, ISAAC   AC
 TOMORROW'S CHILDREN   ASIMOV, ISAAC   AN
 WORLDS OF SCIENCE FICTION, THE MILLS, ROBERT P.   AN
ULTIMATE SPEED LIMIT, THE   AR SRV 72
 FASTER THAN LIGHT   DANN & ZEBROWSKI OA
UNCOMPROMISING VIEW, AN   BR PHY 69 02
 OPUS 100   ASIMOV, ISAAC   AC
UNTO THE FOURTH GENERATION   SS FSF 59 04
 DECADE OF FANTASY AND SCIENCE FICTION, A
              MILLS, ROBERT P.   AN
 NIGHTFALL AND OTHER STORIES ASIMOV, ISAAC   AC
 WANDERING STARS   DANN, JACK M.   AN
UP-TO-DATE SORCERER, THE   SS FSF 58 07
 BEST FROM FANTASY AND SCIENCE FICTION: 8
              BOUCHER, ANTHONY AN
 NIGHTFALL AND OTHER STORIES ASIMOV, ISAAC   AC
VICTORY UNINTENTIONAL   SS SSS 42 08
 DAYS AFTER TOMORROW, THE   SANTESSON, HANS S. AN
 INVASION FROM MARS   WELLES, ORSON   AN
 JUPITER   POHL, C. & F.   AN
 LOOKING FORWARD   LESSER, MILTON   AN
 *REST OF THE ROBOTS, THE   ASIMOV, ISAAC   AC
WATERCLAP   NV IFS 70 04
 BEST FROM IF, THE VOLUME I IF, EDITORS OF   AN
 BICENTENNIAL MAN AND OTHER STORIES, THE
              ASIMOV, ISAAC   AC
 WORLD'S BEST SCIENCE FICTION: 1971 WOLLHEIM & CARR   AN
WATERY PLACE, THE   SS SAT 56 10
 EARTH IS ROOM ENOUGH   ASIMOV, ISAAC   AC
WEAPON TOO DREADFUL TO USE, THE SS AMZ 39 05
 EARLY ASIMOV, THE   ASIMOV, ISAAC   AC
 FUTURE MAKERS, THE   HAINING, PETER   AN
WEDGE, THE   SS ASF 44 10
 FOUNDATION   ASIMOV, ISAAC   NO
WHAT IF   SS FAN 52 SU
 ADVENTURES IN DIMENSION   CONKLIN, GROFF   AN
 GREAT SCIENCE FICTION BY SCIENTISTS CONKLIN, GROFF   AN
 NIGHTFALL AND OTHER STORIES ASIMOV, ISAAC   AC
 *SCIENCE FICTION ADVENTURES IN DIMENSION
              CONKLIN, GROFF   AN
WHAT IS THIS THING CALLED LOVE?(THE PLAYBOY AND THE SLIME GOD)
              SS AMZ 61 03
 NIGHTFALL AND OTHER STORIES ASIMOV, ISAAC   AC
 SCIENCE FICTION ODDITIES   CONKLIN, GROFF   AN
WHAT'S IN A NAME   SS SDM 56 05
 ASIMOV'S MYSTERIES   ASIMOV, ISAAC   AC
WHEN ARISTOTLE FAILS, TRY SCIENCE FICTION AR ITL 71
 SPECULATIONS   SANDERS, THOMAS E. AN
WHY I SELECTED ROBOT AL-76 GOES ASTRAY AI
 *MY BEST SCIENCE FICTION STORY MARGULIES & FRIEND AN
WHY ME?   IN
 WANDERING STARS   DANN, JACK M.   AN
WINNOWING, THE   SS ASF 76 02
 BICENTENNIAL MAN AND OTHER STORIES, THE
              ASIMOV, ISAAC   AC
YOUTH   NV SSF 52 05
 MARTIAN WAY AND OTHER STORIES, THE ASIMOV, ISAAC   AC
 SCIENCE FICTION   BURTON, S. H.   AN
2430 A.D.   SS IBM 70 10
 BUY JUPITER AND OTHER STORIES ASIMOV, ISAAC   AC

ASQUITH, CYNTHIA
GOD GRANTE THAT SHE LYE STILLE NV   31
 VENUS FACTOR, THE   GHIDALIA, V.& ELWOOD AN
PLAYFELLOW, THE   NV   47
 LITTLE MONSTERS, THE   ELWOOD & GHIDALIA AN

ATHERTON, GERTRUDE
FOGHORN, THE   SS
 VENUS FACTOR, THE   GHIDALIA, V.& ELWOOD AN

ATHERTON, JOHN
THREES (TO BE SUNG BY NIELS BOHR) PM NYM 57 03
 FANTASIA MATHEMATICA   FADIMAN, CLIFTON AN
WASTE NOT, WANT NOT   SS PBY 59 06

ATHERTON, JOHN   (CONTINUED)
 PLAYBOY BOOK OF SCIENCE FICTION AND FANTASY, THE
              PLAYBOY, EDITORS OF AN
 TRANSIT OF EARTH   PLAYBOY, EDITORS OF AN

ATKEY, BERTRAM
STRANGE CASE OF ALAN MORAINE, THE SS GND 12 09
 WORLDS APART   LOCKE, GEORGE   AN

ATTANASIO, A. A.
BLOOD'S HORIZON, THE   NV NDM 77 07
 NEW DIMENSIONS 7   SILVERBERG, ROBERT OA
INTERFACE   NA EPC 75
 EPOCH   ELWOOD & SILVERBERG OA
ONCE MORE, THE DREAM   SS NWQ 74 06
 NEW WORLDS NO. 6   PLATT & BAILEY   OA

AUDEN, W. H.
CURSE, A   PM DTM 72
 BEST SF: 1973   HARRISON & ALDISS AN
MOON LANDING   PM NYM 69
 SPECULATIONS   SANDERS, THOMAS E. AN
UNKNOWN CITIZEN, THE   PM   40
 SPECULATIONS   SANDERS, THOMAS E. AN

AUERBACH, ARNOLD M.
DAY REMBRANDT WENT PUBLIC, THE SS HRP 62 07
 FUTURE TENSE   CURTIS, RICHARD AN
 8TH ANNUAL OF THE YEAR'S BEST S-F, THE MERRIL, JUDITH AN
IF "HAIR" WERE REVIVED IN 2016 FA NYT 71
 BEST SF: 1971   HARRISON & ALDISS AN

AUMBRY, ALAN
MAN IN TRANSIT   SS NWQ 72 04
 NEW WORLDS QUARTERLY NO. 4 MOORCOCK, MICHAEL OA

AYCOCK, ROGER D. SEE PSEUD. ROGER DEE

AYME, MARCEL
ACROSS PARIS AND OTHER STORIES   AC H BDL 57
 SEE "THE WALKER THROUGH WALLS"
WALKER THROUGH WALLS, THE   AC BRK 62
 IN ENGLAND AS "ACROSS PARIS AND OTHER STORIES"
ACROSS PARIS   SS
 WALKER THROUGH WALLS, THE AYME, MARCEL   AC
DERMUCHE   SS
 WALKER THROUGH WALLS, THE AYME, MARCEL   AC
DWARF, THE   SS
 WALKER THROUGH WALLS, THE AYME, MARCEL   AC
LEGEND OF POLDEVIA   SS
 WALKER THROUGH WALLS, THE AYME, MARCEL   AC
MARTIN THE NOVELIST   SS
 WALKER THROUGH WALLS, THE AYME, MARCEL   AC
PICTURE-WELL, THE   SS
 WALKER THROUGH WALLS, THE AYME, MARCEL   AC
ROLL OF DAUGHTERS, A   SS
 WALKER THROUGH WALLS, THE AYME, MARCEL   AC
RUE D'EVANGILE   SS
 WALKER THROUGH WALLS, THE AYME, MARCEL   AC
SEVEN-LEAGUE BOOTS, THE   SS FSF 59 12
 WALKER THROUGH WALLS, THE AYME, MARCEL   AC
STATE OF GRACE, THE   SS FSF 59 08
 WALKER THROUGH WALLS, THE AYME, MARCEL   AC
WALKER-THROUGH-WALLS, THE   SS
 WALKER THROUGH WALLS, THE AYME, MARCEL   AC
WINE OF PARIS, THE   SS
 WALKER THROUGH WALLS, THE AYME, MARCEL   AC

B., E. D.
ESCAPIST, THE   PM FSF 53 02
 BEST FROM FANTASY AND SCIENCE FICTION: 3
              BOUCHER & MCCOMAS AN
SOLAR SYSTEMS...   PM FSF 53 02
 BEST FROM FANTASY AND SCIENCE FICTION: 3
              BOUCHER & MCCOMAS AN

BABER, ASA
LAST TRAIN TO LIMBO   SS PBY 70 07
 LAST TRAIN TO LIMBO   PLAYBOY, EDITORS OF AN

BACON, EDGAR MAYHEW
ITSELF   SS BLC 07 05
 SCIENCE FICTION BY GASLIGHT MOSKOWITZ, SAM   AN

BACON, FRANCIS
FROM "NEW ATLANTIS" (1624)   EX
 PAST, PRESENT, AND FUTURE PERFECT WOLFE, J&FITZ GERALD AN
NEW ATLANTIS, THE (1624)   EX
 *BEYOND TIME AND SPACE   DERLETH, AUGUST AN
UTOPIAN SCIENCE FICTION (FROM "THE NEW ATLANTIS") EX
 SCIENCE FICTION THROUGH THE AGES 1 EVANS, I. O.   AN

BACON, GERTRUDE
GORGON'S HEAD, THE   SS
 TRANSFORMATIONS   ROSELLE, DANIEL AN

BADE, WILLIAM L.
AMBITION   NV GAL 51 10
 *SCIENCE FICTION ADVENTURES IN DIMENSION
              CONKLIN, GROFF   AN

BAEN, JAMES
BEST FROM GALAXY, THE VOLUME III   AN AWD 75
BEST FROM GALAXY, THE VOLUME IV   AN AWD 76
BEST FROM IF, THE VOLUME III   AN AWD 76

BAGLEY, SIMON
    WELCOME, COMRADE   NV   FSF 64 04
        AMERICAN GOVERNMENT THROUGH SCIENCE FICTION
                                               OLANDER/GREENBERG/&   AN

BAILEY, HILARY   SEE ALSO   CO-EDITOR CHARLES PLATT
    NEW WORLDS EIGHT   OA   SPH 75 03
    NEW WORLDS NINE   OA   COR 75 11
    BELLA GOES TO THE DARK TOWER   SS   NWQ 73 05
        NEW WORLDS NO. 5   MOORCOCK & PLATT   OA
    CHRONICLE OF BLACKTON, A   SS   NWQ 72 03
        NEW WORLDS QUARTERLY NO. 3   MOORCOCK, MICHAEL   OA
    DEVIL OF A DRUMMER   SS   NEW 67 01
        DEVIL HIS DUE, THE   HILL, DOUGLAS   AN
    DOGMAN OF ISLINGTON   SS   QRK 70 01
        INTO THE UNKNOWN   CARR, TERRY   AN
        QUARK/1   DELANY & HACKER   OA
    DR. GELABIUS   SS   NWS 68 04
        BEST SF STORIES FROM NEW WORLDS 4   MOORCOCK, MICHAEL   AN
        ENGLAND SWINGS SF   MERRIL, JUDITH   AN
        SPACE-TIME JOURNAL, THE   MERRIL, JUDITH   AN
    FALL OF FRENCHY STEINER, THE   NV   NWS 64 08
        BEST OF NEW WORLDS, THE   MOORCOCK, MICHAEL   AN
        BEST SF STORIES FROM NEW WORLDS 8   MOORCOCK, MICHAEL   AN
        SF12   MERRIL, JUDITH   AN
    IN REASON'S EAR   SS   SCF 65 06
        BEST SF STORIES FROM NEW WORLDS 6   MOORCOCK, MICHAEL   AN
    INTRODUCTION   IN
        NEW WORLDS EIGHT   BAILEY, HILARY   OA
    RAMPARTS, THE   NV   UNI 74 05
        UNIVERSE 5   CARR, TERRY   AN
    TWENTY-FOUR LETTERS FROM UNDER THE EARTH   SS   QRK 71 03
        QUARK/3   DELANY & HACKER   OA

BAILEY, WILLIAM C.
    "X" FOR "EXPENDABLE"   NV   DSF 52 12
        WAY OUT   HOWARD, IVAN   AN

BAKER, DOROTHY
    GORGON'S HEAD, THE   SS   SND 99 12
        HORROR TIMES TEN   NORTON, ALDEN H.   AN

BAKER, JULES
    MONSTERS   IL
        BEYOND THIS HORIZON   CARRELL, CHRISTOPHER   OA

BAKER, RUSSELL
    MS. FOUND IN A BUS   SS   NYT 62
        8TH ANNUAL OF THE YEAR'S BEST S-F, THE MERRIL, JUDITH   AN
    SINISTER METAMORPHOSIS, A   SS   NYT 65
        10TH ANNUAL OF THE YEAR'S BEST S-F, THE
                                             MERRIL, JUDITH   AN

BAKER, W. R.
    MAGIC BOX, THE   SS   HRP 28 04
        MATHEMATICAL MAGPIE, THE   FADIMAN, CLIFTON   AN

BAKHNOV, VLADLEN
    MUTINY   SS
        RUSSIAN SCIENCE FICTION, 1968   MAGIDOFF, ROBERT   AN
    ROBOTNIKS, THE   SS
        RUSSIAN SCIENCE FICTION, 1968   MAGIDOFF, ROBERT   AN
    SPEAKING OF DEMONOLOGY   SS
        RUSSIAN SCIENCE FICTION, 1969   MAGIDOFF, ROBERT   AN
    TWELVE HOLIDAYS   SS   69
        AIR OF MARS AND OTHER STORIES, THE   GINSBURG, MIRRA   AN
    UNIQUE   SS
        RUSSIAN SCIENCE FICTION, 1969   MAGIDOFF, ROBERT   AN

BALCHIN, NIGEL
    CABINET DECISION (FROM "WHO IS MY NEIGHBOUR")   EX
        ARMCHAIR SCIENCE READER, THE   GORDON, I. & SORKIN   AN
    GOD AND THE MACHINE   SS   51
        FANTASIA MATHEMATICA   FADIMAN, CLIFTON   AN
    INTRODUCTION   IN
        AD 2500   WILSON, ANGUS   AN

BALKE, BETTY T.
    APOSTLE TO ALPHA   SS   EPS 66 01
        GODS FOR TOMORROW   SANTESSON, HANS S.   AN

BALL, BRIAN N.
    TALES OF SCIENCE FICTION   AN H HML 64
    ESCAPE VELOCITY   SS
        TALES OF SCIENCE FICTION   BALL, BRIAN N.   AN

BALL, SIR ROBERT
    STORY OF THE HEAVENS (1883)   AR   83
        FAREWELL FANTASTIC VENUS   ALDISS & HARRISON   AN

BALL, W. W. R.
    EXTINCTION BY SUBTRACTION   MS
        MATHEMATICAL MAGPIE, THE   FADIMAN, CLIFTON   AN
    PI AND THE ACTUARY   MS
        MATHEMATICAL MAGPIE, THE   FADIMAN, CLIFTON   AN

BALLARD, J. G.
    ATROCITY EXHIBITION   AC H CAP 70
        SEE "LOVE & NAPALM: EXPORT U.S.A."
    BEST OF J. G. BALLARD, THE   AC   FPL 77
    BILLENIUM   AC   BRK 62
    CHRONOPOLIS AND OTHER STORIES   AC H PUT 71
    DAY OF FOREVER, THE   AC   PTH 67 09
    DISASTER AREA, THE   AC H CAP 67 10
    DROWNED WORLD AND THE WIND FROM NOWHERE, THE   AC H DBL 65
    FOUR-DIMENSIONAL NIGHTMARE, THE   AC H GOL 63 05

BALLARD, J. G.   (CONTINUED)
    FOUR-DIMENSIONAL NIGHTMARE, THE (REVISED)   AC H GOL 74
    IMPOSSIBLE MAN, THE   AC   BRK 66 04
    LOVE & NAPALM: EXPORT U.S.A.   AC H GRV 72
        IN ENGLAND AS "ATROCITY EXHIBITION"
    LOW-FLYING AIRCRAFT AND OTHER STORIES   AC H CAP 76
    OVERLOADED MAN, THE   AC   PTH 67 11
    PASSPORT TO ETERNITY   AC   BKM 63 09
    TERMINAL BEACH (AMERICAN VERSION)   AC   BKM 64 06
    TERMINAL BEACH (BRITISH VERSION)   AC H GOL 64 06
    VERMILLION SANDS   AC   BKM 71 04
    VERMILLION SANDS (BRITISH)   AC H CAP 73
    VOICES OF TIME AND OTHER STORIES, THE   AC   BKM 62 02
    ASSASSINATION OF JOHN FITZGERALD KENNEDY CONSIDERED AS A
        DOWNHILL MOTOR RACE, THE   SS   NWS 67 02
        AMERICAN GOVERNMENT THROUGH SCIENCE FICTION
                                             OLANDER/GREENBERG/&   AN
        BEST SF: 1967   HARRISON & ALDISS   AN
        DAY OF FOREVER, THE   BALLARD, J. G.   AC
        DECADE THE 1960S   ALDISS & HARRISON   AN
        ENGLAND SWINGS SF   MERRIL, JUDITH   AN
        LOVE & NAPALM: EXPORT U.S.A.   BALLARD, J. G.   AC
    ASSASSINATION WEAPON, THE   SS   NWS 66 04
        BEST SF STORIES FROM NEW WORLDS NO. 1, THE
                                             MOORCOCK, MICHAEL   AN
        LOVE & NAPALM: EXPORT U.S.A.   BALLARD, J. G.   AC
    ATROCITY EXHIBITION, THE   SS   NWS 66 09
        LOVE & NAPALM: EXPORT U.S.A.   BALLARD, J. G.   AC
    BEACH MURDERS, THE (CONFETTI ROYALE, ROG 66 01)   SS   NWS 69 04
        BEST SF STORIES FROM NEW WORLDS 7   MOORCOCK, MICHAEL   AN
        LOW-FLYING AIRCRAFT AND OTHER STORIES BALLARD, J. G.   AC
    BILLENIUM   SS   NWS 61 11
        BEST OF J. G. BALLARD, THE   BALLARD, J. G.   AC
        BEST SF 6   CRISPIN, EDMUND   AN
        BILLENIUM   BALLARD, J. G.   AC
        CHRONOPOLIS AND OTHER STORIES   BALLARD, J. G.   AC
        CITIES OF WONDER   KNIGHT, DAMON   AN
        CITY: 2000 A.D., THE   CLEM/GREENBERG/&   AN
        EARTH IN TRANSIT   SCHWARTZ, SHEILA   AN
        FUTURE TENSE   CURTIS, RICHARD   AN
        OUT OF THIS WORLD 4   WILLIAMS-ELLIS& OWEN   AN
        SOCIAL PROBLEMS THROUGH SCIENCE FICTION
                                             GREENBERG/MILSTEAD/&   AN
        STARS AND UNDER, THE   CRISPIN, EDMUND   AN
        TERMINAL BEACH (BRITISH VERSION)   BALLARD, J. G.   AC
        VOYAGES: SCENARIOS FOR A SHIP CALLED EARTH
                                             SAUER, ROB   AN
        WINDOWS INTO TOMORROW   SILVERBERG, ROBERT   AN
        YOU AND SCIENCE FICTION   HOLLISTER, BERNARD C   AN
    BUILD-UP (ALSO AS THE CONCENTRATION CITY)   SS   NWS 57 01
        AS TOMORROW BECOMES TODAY   SULLIVAN, CHARLES W.   AN
        BILLENIUM   BALLARD, J. G.   AC
        CHRONOPOLIS AND OTHER STORIES   BALLARD, J. G.   AC
        CONNOISSEUR'S S. F.   BOARDMAN, TOM JR.   AN
    CAGE OF SAND, THE   SS   NWS 62 06
        BEST OF J. G. BALLARD, THE   BALLARD, J. G.   AC
        CHRONOPOLIS AND OTHER STORIES   BALLARD, J. G.   AC
        DARK STARS   SILVERBERG, ROBERT   AN
       *FOUR-DIMENSIONAL NIGHTMARE, THE   BALLARD, J. G.   AC
        PASSPORT TO ETERNITY   BALLARD, J. G.   AC
        RUINS OF EARTH, THE   DISCH, THOMAS M.   AN
    CHRONOPOLIS   NV   NWS 60 06
        BEST OF J. G. BALLARD, THE   BALLARD, J. G.   AC
        BILLENIUM   BALLARD, J. G.   AC
        CHRONOPOLIS AND OTHER STORIES   BALLARD, J. G.   AC
       *FOUR-DIMENSIONAL NIGHTMARE, THE   BALLARD, J. G.   AC
        VINTAGE ANTHOLOGY OF SCIENCE FANTASY, THE
                                             CERF, CHRISTOPHER   AN
    CLOUD-SCULPTORS OF CORAL D, THE   SS   FSF 67 12
        BEST FROM FANTASY AND SCIENCE FICTION: 18
                                             FERMAN, EDWARD L.   AN
        NEBULA AWARD STORIES   NO. 3   ZELAZNY, ROGER   AN
        SF12   MERRIL, JUDITH   AN
       *VERMILLION SANDS   BALLARD, J. G.   AC
    COMING OF THE UNCONSCIOUS, THE   BR   NWS 66 07
        OVERLOADED MAN, THE   BALLARD, J. G.   AC
    COMSAT ANGELS, THE   SS   IFS 68 12
        LOW-FLYING AIRCRAFT AND OTHER STORIES BALLARD, J. G.   AC
    CONCENTRATION CITY, THE (BUILD-UP)   SS   NWS 57 01
        BEST OF J. G. BALLARD, THE   BALLARD, J. G.   AC
        DISASTER AREA, THE   BALLARD, J. G.   AC
    CONFETTI ROYALE (SEE THE BEACH MURDERS)   TC   ROG 66 01
    CRASH¦   SS   ICA 69
        LOVE & NAPALM: EXPORT U.S.A.   BALLARD, J. G.   AC
    CRY HOPE, CRY FURY¦   SS   FSF 67 10
       *VERMILLION SANDS   BALLARD, J. G.   AC
    DAY OF FOREVER, THE   SS   NWS 67 01
        BEST OF J. G. BALLARD, THE   BALLARD, J. G.   AC
        DAY OF FOREVER, THE   BALLARD, J. G.   AC
        IMPOSSIBLE MAN, THE   BALLARD, J. G.   AC
    DEAD ASTRONAUT, THE   SS   PBY 68 05
        DEAD ASTRONAUT, 10 STORIES OF SPACE FLIGHT, THE
                                             PLAYBOY, EDITORS OF   AN
        LOW-FLYING AIRCRAFT AND OTHER STORIES BALLARD, J. G.   AC
    DEATH MODULE, THE (ALSO AS NOTES TOWARD A MENTAL BREAKDOWN)
                                                      SS   NWS 67 07
        BEST SF STORIES FROM NEW WORLDS 5   MOORCOCK, MICHAEL   AN
    DEEP END   SS   NWS 61 05
        CHRONOPOLIS AND OTHER STORIES   BALLARD, J. G.   AC
        TERMINAL BEACH (BRITISH VERSION)   BALLARD, J. G.   AC
        VOICES OF TIME AND OTHER STORIES, THE BALLARD, J. G.   AC
    DELTA AT SUNSET   SS   NEW 64 AC
        IMPOSSIBLE MAN, THE   BALLARD, J. G.   AC
        TERMINAL BEACH (BRITISH VERSION)   BALLARD, J. G.   AC
    DROWNED GIANT, THE (SOUVENIR)   SS   PBY 65 05
        CHRONOPOLIS AND OTHER STORIES   BALLARD, J. G.   AC

BALLARD, J. G.   (CONTINUED)
  IMPOSSIBLE MAN, THE   BALLARD, J. G.   AC
  INTO THE UNKNOWN   CARR, TERRY   AN
  NEBULA AWARD STORIES   KNIGHT, DAMON   AN
  TERMINAL BEACH (BRITISH VERSION)   BALLARD, J. G.   AC
  11TH ANNUAL OF THE YEAR'S BEST S-F, THE
                                      MERRIL, JUDITH   AN
DROWNED WORLD, THE (ENLARGED)   NO   SFB 62 01
DROWNED WORLD AND THE WIND FROM NOWHERE, THE
                                      BALLARD, J. G.   AC
ENCOUNTER, THE (SEE THE VENUS HUNTERS) TC
END-GAME   SS   NWS 63 06
  CHRONOPOLIS AND OTHER STORIES   BALLARD, J. G.   AC
  SF: AUTHORS' CHOICE   HARRISON, HARRY   AN
  TERMINAL BEACH (AMERICAN VERSION)   BALLARD, J. G.   AC
  TERMINAL BEACH (BRITISH VERSION)   BALLARD, J. G.   AC
ESCAPEMENT   SS   NWS 56 12
  OVERLOADED MAN, THE   BALLARD, J. G.   AC
  PASSPORT TO ETERNITY   BALLARD, J. G.   AC
GARDEN OF TIME, THE   SS   FSF 62 02
  BEST FROM FANTASY AND SCIENCE FICTION: 12
                                      DAVIDSON, AVRAM   AN
  BEST OF J. G. BALLARD, THE   BALLARD, J. G.   AC
  BEYOND TOMORROW   HARDING, LEE   AN
  BILLENIUM   BALLARD, J. G.   AC
  CHRONOPOLIS AND OTHER STORIES   BALLARD, J. G.   AC
  *FOUR-DIMENSIONAL NIGHTMARE, THE   BALLARD, J. G.   AC
  INTRODUCING SCIENCE FICTION   ALDISS, BRIAN W.   AN
  SPECULATIONS   SANDERS, THOMAS E. AN
GENERATIONS OF AMERICA, THE   SS   NWS 68 10
  LOVE & NAPALM: EXPORT U.S.A.   BALLARD, J. G.   AC
GENTLE ASSASSIN, THE   SS   NWS 61 12
  BILLENIUM   BALLARD, J. G.   AC
  DAY OF FOREVER, THE   BALLARD, J. G.   AC
GIOCONDA OF THE TWILIGHT NOON, THE   SS   NEW 64 AC
  IMPOSSIBLE MAN, THE   BALLARD, J. G.   AC
  TERMINAL BEACH (BRITISH VERSION)   BALLARD, J. G.   AC
GREAT AMERICAN NUDE, THE   SS   AMB 68 SU
  LOVE & NAPALM: EXPORT U.S.A.   BALLARD, J. G.   AC
GREATEST TELEVISION SHOW ON EARTH, THE SS ABT 72 WI
  LOW-FLYING AIRCRAFT AND OTHER STORIES BALLARD, J. G.   AC
ILLUMINATED MAN, THE   NV   FSF 64 05
  BEST FROM FANTASY AND SCIENCE FICTION: 14
                                      DAVIDSON, AVRAM   AN
  TERMINAL BEACH (BRITISH VERSION)   BALLARD, J. G.   AC
IMPOSSIBLE MAN, THE   SS   NEW 66 AC
  DISASTER AREA, THE   BALLARD, J. G.   AC
  IMPOSSIBLE MAN, THE   BALLARD, J. G.   AC
INSANE ONES, THE   SS   AMZ 62 01
  BEST OF J. G. BALLARD, THE   BALLARD, J. G.   AC
  BILLENIUM   BALLARD, J. G.   AC
  DAY OF FOREVER, THE   BALLARD, J. G.   AC
  8TH ANNUAL OF THE YEAR'S BEST S-F, THE MERRIL, JUDITH AN
INTRODUCTION   IN
  BEST OF J. G. BALLARD, THE   BALLARD, J. G.   AC
JOURNEY ACROSS A CRATER   SS   NWS 70 02
  NEW WORLDS QUARTERLY NO. 1   MOORCOCK, MICHAEL   OA
KILLING GROUND, THE   SS   NWS 69 03
  BEST SF STORIES FROM NEW WORLDS 6   MOORCOCK, MICHAEL   AN
  BEST SF: 1969   HARRISON & ALDISS   AN
LAST WORLD OF MR. GODDARD, THE   SS   SCF 60 10
  DAY OF FOREVER, THE   BALLARD, J. G.   AC
  TERMINAL BEACH (AMERICAN VERSION)   BALLARD, J. G.   AC
LIFE AND DEATH OF GOD, THE   SS
  LOW-FLYING AIRCRAFT AND OTHER STORIES BALLARD, J. G.   AC
LOST LEONARDO, THE   SS   FSF 64 03
  NEW WORLDS OF FANTASY   CARR, TERRY   AN
  TERMINAL BEACH (BRITISH VERSION)   BALLARD, J. G.   AC
LOVE AND NAPALM: EXPORT U.S.A.   SS   RUN 68 SU
  LOVE & NAPALM: EXPORT U.S.A.   BALLARD, J. G.   AC
LOW-FLYING AIRCRAFT   SS   BNA 75 SU
  LOW-FLYING AIRCRAFT AND OTHER STORIES BALLARD, J. G.   AC
MAN ON THE 99TH FLOOR, THE   SS   NWS 62 07
  DAY OF FOREVER, THE   BALLARD, J. G.   AC
  PASSPORT TO ETERNITY   BALLARD, J. G.   AC
MANHOLE 69   SS   NWS 57 11
  BEST OF J. G. BALLARD, THE   BALLARD, J. G.   AC
  CHRONOPOLIS AND OTHER STORIES   BALLARD, J. G.   AC
  DISASTER AREA, THE   BALLARD, J. G.   AC
  VOICES OF TIME AND OTHER STORIES, THE BALLARD, J. G.   AC
MINUS ONE   SS   SCF 63 06
  DISASTER AREA, THE   BALLARD, J. G.   AC
  TERMINAL BEACH (AMERICAN VERSION)   BALLARD, J. G.   AC
MOBILE (ALSO AS VENUS SMILES)   SS   SCF 57 06
  BILLENIUM   BALLARD, J. G.   AC
MR. F IS MR. F   SS   SCF 61 08
  DISASTER AREA, THE   BALLARD, J. G.   AC
  TRAPS OF TIME, THE   MOORCOCK, MICHAEL   AN
MY DREAM OF FLYING TO WAKE ISLAND   SS   ABT 74 WI
  LOW-FLYING AIRCRAFT AND OTHER STORIES BALLARD, J. G.   AC
NEW SCIENCE FICTION, THE   AR   C
  NEW S.F., THE   JONES, LANGDON   OA
NOTES TOWARD A MENTAL BREAKDOWN (THE DEATH MODULE)
                                     SS   NWS 67 07
  LOVE & NAPALM: EXPORT U.S.A.   BALLARD, J. G.   AC
NOW WAKES THE SEA   SS   FSF 63 05
  BEST FROM FANTASY AND SCIENCE FICTION: 13
                                      DAVIDSON, AVRAM   AN
  CHRONOPOLIS AND OTHER STORIES   BALLARD, J. G.   AC
  DISASTER AREA, THE   BALLARD, J. G.   AC
  TERMINAL BEACH (AMERICAN VERSION)   BALLARD, J. G.   AC
NOW: ZERO   SS   SCF 59 12
  BILLENIUM   BALLARD, J. G.   AC
  OVERLOADED MAN, THE   BALLARD, J. G.   AC
OVERLOADED MAN, THE   SS   NWS 61 07
  BEST OF J. G. BALLARD, THE   BALLARD, J. G.   AC

BALLARD, J. G.   (CONTINUED)
  FOUR-DIMENSIONAL NIGHTMARE, THE (REVISED)
                                      BALLARD, J. G.   AC
  OVERLOADED MAN, THE   BALLARD, J. G.   AC
  VOICES OF TIME AND OTHER STORIES, THE BALLARD, J. G.   AC
PASSPORT TO ETERNITY   SS   AMZ 62 06
  BEST OF J. G. BALLARD, THE   BALLARD, J. G.   AC
  OVERLOADED MAN, THE   BALLARD, J. G.   AC
  PASSPORT TO ETERNITY   BALLARD, J. G.   AC
PLACE AND TIME TO DIE, A   SS   NWS 69 10
  LOW-FLYING AIRCRAFT AND OTHER STORIES BALLARD, J. G.   AC
  NEW WORLDS QUARTERLY NO. 1   MOORCOCK, MICHAEL   OA
PLAN FOR THE ASSASSINATION OF JACQUELINE KENNEDY SS AMB 66 WI
  ENGLAND SWINGS SF   MERRIL, JUDITH   AN
  IN DREAMS AWAKE   FIEDLER, LESLIE A. AN
  LOVE & NAPALM: EXPORT U.S.A.   BALLARD, J. G.   AC
PRIMA BELLADONNA   SS   SCF 56 12
  BILLENIUM   BALLARD, J. G.   AC
  *FOUR-DIMENSIONAL NIGHTMARE, THE   BALLARD, J. G.   AC
  SF: THE BEST OF THE BEST   MERRIL, JUDITH   AN
  SF:57, THE YEAR'S GREATEST SCIENCE FICTION AND FANTASY
                                      MERRIL, JUDITH   AN
  *VERMILLION SANDS   BALLARD, J. G.   AC
PRISONER OF THE CORAL DEEP (ARG 64 03) SS NWS 65 05
  DAY OF FOREVER, THE   BALLARD, J. G.   AC
QUESTION OF RE-ENTRY, A   NV   FAN 63 03
  BEST OF J. G. BALLARD, THE   BALLARD, J. G.   AC
  PASSPORT TO ETERNITY   BALLARD, J. G.   AC
  TERMINAL BEACH (BRITISH VERSION)   BALLARD, J. G.   AC
RECOGNITION, THE   SS   DVS 67 01
  DANGEROUS VISIONS   ELLISON, HARLAN   OA
REPTILE ENCLOSURE, THE (THE SHERRINGTON THEORY) SS AMZ 63 03
  IMPOSSIBLE MAN, THE   BALLARD, J. G.   AC
  TERMINAL BEACH (BRITISH VERSION)   BALLARD, J. G.   AC
SALVADOR DALI   AR   NWS 69 02
  BEST SF STORIES FROM NEW WORLDS 8   MOORCOCK, MICHAEL   AN
SAY GOODBYE TO THE WIND   SS   FAN 70 08
  NEW WORLDS OF FANTASY NO. 3   CARR, TERRY   AN
  *VERMILLION SANDS   BALLARD, J. G.   AC
SCREEN GAME, THE   NV   FAN 63 10
  IMPOSSIBLE MAN, THE   BALLARD, J. G.   AC
  *VERMILLION SANDS   BALLARD, J. G.   AC
SHERRINGTON THEORY, THE (SEE THE REPTILE ENCLOSURE)
                                     TC
SINGING STATUES, THE   SS   FAN 62 07
SOUND-SWEEP, THE   NV   SCF 60 02
  BEST OF J. G. BALLARD, THE   BALLARD, J. G.   AC
  CHRONOPOLIS AND OTHER STORIES   BALLARD, J. G.   AC
  *FOUR-DIMENSIONAL NIGHTMARE, THE   BALLARD, J. G.   AC
  SF: THE BEST OF THE BEST   MERRIL, JUDITH   AN
  TOMORROW AND TOMORROW   KNIGHT, DAMON   AN
  VOICES OF TIME AND OTHER STORIES, THE BALLARD, J. G.   AC
  5TH ANNUAL OF THE YEAR'S BEST S-F, THE MERRIL, JUDITH AN
SOUVENIR (ALSO AS THE DROWNED GIANT) SS   PBY 65 05
  PLAYBOY BOOK OF SCIENCE FICTION AND FANTASY, THE
                                      PLAYBOY, EDITORS OF AN
  TRANSIT OF EARTH   PLAYBOY, EDITORS OF AN
STORM-BIRD, STORM-DREAMER   SS   NWS 66 11
  CHRONOPOLIS AND OTHER STORIES   BALLARD, J. G.   AC
  DISASTER AREA, THE   BALLARD, J. G.   AC
  IMPOSSIBLE MAN, THE   BALLARD, J. G.   AC
STORM-WIND (SEE THE WIND FROM NOWHERE) TC
STUDIO 5, THE STARS   NV   SCF 61 02
  BILLENIUM   BALLARD, J. G.   AC
  *FOUR-DIMENSIONAL NIGHTMARE, THE   BALLARD, J. G.   AC
  *VERMILLION SANDS   BALLARD, J. G.   AC
SUBLIMINAL MAN, THE   SS   NWS 63 01
  BEST OF J. G. BALLARD, THE   BALLARD, J. G.   AC
  DISASTER AREA, THE   BALLARD, J. G.   AC
  EARTH IN TRANSIT   SCHWARTZ, SHEILA   AN
  ECO-FICTION   STADLER, JOHN   AN
  INTRODUCTORY PSYCHOLOGY THROUGH SCIENCE FICTION
                                      KATZ/WARRICK/&   AN
  MIRROR OF INFINITY, THE   SILVERBERG, ROBERT AN
  STORIES FROM SCIENCE FICTION   DOHERTY, G. D.   AN
  TERMINAL BEACH (AMERICAN VERSION)   BALLARD, J. G.   AC
  TOMORROW, AND TOMORROW, AND TOMORROW...
                                      HEINTZ/HERBERT/JOOS/ AN
  TOMORROW, INC.   GREENBERG& OLANDER AN
  WINDOW ON THE FUTURE   HILL, DOUGLAS   AN
  YOU AND SCIENCE FICTION   HOLLISTER, BERNARD C AN
SUDDEN AFTERNOON, THE   SS   FAN 63 09
  DAY OF FOREVER, THE   BALLARD, J. G.   AC
  TERMINAL BEACH (AMERICAN VERSION)   BALLARD, J. G.   AC
SUMMER CANNIBALS, THE   SS   NWS 69 01
  LOVE & NAPALM: EXPORT U.S.A.   BALLARD, J. G.   AC
TERMINAL BEACH, THE   SS   NWS 64 03
  ALPHA 1   SILVERBERG, ROBERT AN
  BEST OF J. G. BALLARD, THE   BALLARD, J. G.   AC
  BEST OF NEW WORLDS, THE   MOORCOCK, MICHAEL   AN
  CHRONOPOLIS AND OTHER STORIES   BALLARD, J. G.   AC
  SURVIVAL PRINTOUT   TOTAL EFFECT   AN
  TERMINAL BEACH (AMERICAN VERSION)   BALLARD, J. G.   AC
  TERMINAL BEACH (BRITISH VERSION)   BALLARD, J. G.   AC
  10TH ANNUAL OF THE YEAR'S BEST S-F, THE
                                      MERRIL, JUDITH   AN
THIRTEEN TO CENTAURUS   NV   AMZ 62 04
  BEST OF J. G. BALLARD, THE   BALLARD, J. G.   AC
  FOUR-DIMENSIONAL NIGHTMARE, THE (REVISED)
                                      BALLARD, J. G.   AC
  LEARNING MAZE AND OTHER STORIES, THE ELWOOD, ROGER   OA
  OVERLOADED MAN, THE   BALLARD, J. G.   AC
  PASSPORT TO ETERNITY   BALLARD, J. G.   AC
  SPECTRUM OF WORLDS, A   CLARESON, THOMAS D. AN
THOUSAND DREAMS OF STELLAVISTA, THE SS   AMZ 62 03
  PASSPORT TO ETERNITY   BALLARD, J. G.   AC

BALLARD, J. G.   BARTER, ALAN FRANK   AN

BALLARD, J. G.   (CONTINUED)
  *VERMILLION SANDS   BALLARD, J. G.   AC
  TIME OF PASSAGE   SS   SCF 64 02
    IMPOSSIBLE MAN, THE   BALLARD, J. G.   AC
    OVERLOADED MAN, THE   BALLARD, J. G.   AC
  TIME-TOMBS, THE   NV   IFS 63 03
    OVERLOADED MAN, THE   BALLARD, J. G.   AC
    SECOND IF READER OF SCIENCE FICTION, THE
                                      POHL, FREDERIK   AN
    TERMINAL BEACH (AMERICAN VERSION) BALLARD, J. G.   AC
  TOLERANCES OF THE HUMAN FACE   SS   ENC 69 09
    LOVE & NAPALM: EXPORT U.S.A.   BALLARD, J. G.   AC
  TOMORROW IS A MILLION YEARS   SS   ARG 66 10
    DAY OF FOREVER, THE   BALLARD, J. G.   AC
    FARTHEST REACHES, THE   ELDER, JOSEPH   OA
  TRACK 12   SS   NWS 58 04
    OVERLOADED MAN, THE   BALLARD, J. G.   AC
    PASSPORT TO ETERNITY   BALLARD, J. G.   AC
    PENGUIN SCIENCE FICTION   ALDISS, BRIAN W.   AN
  ULTIMATE CITY, THE   NA
    LOW-FLYING AIRCRAFT AND OTHER STORIES BALLARD, J. G.   AC
  UNIVERSITY OF DEATH, THE   SS   TRV 68 SU
    LOVE & NAPALM: EXPORT U.S.A.   BALLARD, J. G.   AC
  VENUS HUNTERS, THE (THE ENCOUNTER)   NV   AMZ 63 06
    OVERLOADED MAN, THE   BALLARD, J. G.   AC
    TERMINAL BEACH (AMERICAN VERSION) BALLARD, J. G.   AC
  VENUS SMILES (MOBILE)   NV   IFS 67 09
    *VERMILLION SANDS   BALLARD, J. G.   AC
  VISIONS OF HELL   BR   NWS 66 03
    NEW WORLDS QUARTERLY NO. 2   MOORCOCK, MICHAEL   OA
  VOICES OF TIME, THE   SS   NWS 60 10
    ALPHA 2   SILVERBERG, ROBERT   AN
    BEST OF J. G. BALLARD, THE   BALLARD, J. G.   AC
    CHRONOPOLIS AND OTHER STORIES   BALLARD, J. G.   AC
    *FOUR-DIMENSIONAL NIGHTMARE, THE BALLARD, J. G.   AC
    INNER LANDSCAPE, THE   MOORCOCK, MICHAEL   AN
    MODERN SCIENCE FICTION   SPINRAD, NORMAN   AN
    ONE HUNDRED YEARS OF SCIENCE FICTION KNIGHT, DAMON   AN
    SPECTRUM 3   AMIS & CONQUEST   AN
    VOICES OF TIME AND OTHER STORIES, THE BALLARD, J. G.   AC
  VOLCANO DANCES, THE   SS   NEW 64 AC
    TERMINAL BEACH (BRITISH VERSION) BALLARD, J. G.   AC
    11TH ANNUAL OF THE YEAR'S BEST S-F, THE
                                      MERRIL, JUDITH   AN
  WAITING GROUNDS, THE   NV   NWS 59 11
    BEST OF J. G. BALLARD, THE   BALLARD, J. G.   AC
    DAY OF FOREVER, THE   BALLARD, J. G.   AC
    VOICES OF TIME AND OTHER STORIES, THE BALLARD, J. G.   AC
  WATCH-TOWERS, THE   NV   SCF 62 06
    CHRONOPOLIS AND OTHER STORIES   BALLARD, J. G.   AC
    *FOUR-DIMENSIONAL NIGHTMARE, THE BALLARD, J. G.   AC
    PASSPORT TO ETERNITY   BALLARD, J. G.   AC
  WHY I WANT TO FUCK RONALD REAGAN   SS   MOP 68 SU
    LOVE & NAPALM: EXPORT U.S.A.   BALLARD, J. G.   AC
  WIND FROM NOWHERE, THE (ENLARGED FROM STORM-WIND) NO   NWS 61 09
    DROWNED WORLD AND THE WIND FROM NOWHERE, THE
                                      BALLARD, J. G.   AC
  YOU AND ME AND THE CONTINUUM   SS   IMP 66 03
    ENGLAND SWINGS SF   MERRIL, JUDITH   AN
    LOVE & NAPALM: EXPORT U.S.A.   BALLARD, J. G.   AC
    SPACE-TIME JOURNAL, THE   MERRIL, JUDITH   AN
  YOU: COMA: MARILYN MONROE   SS   NWS 66 06
    BEST SF STORIES FROM NEW WORLDS NO. 2, THE
                                      MOORCOCK, MICHAEL   AN
    LOVE & NAPALM: EXPORT U.S.A.   BALLARD, J. G.   AC
    SF12   MERRIL, JUDITH   AN
  ZONE OF TERROR   SS   NWS 60 03
    CHRONOPOLIS AND OTHER STORIES   BALLARD, J. G.   AC
    DISASTER AREA, THE   BALLARD, J. G.   AC
    VOICES OF TIME AND OTHER STORIES, THE BALLARD, J. G.   AC

BALMER, EDWIN
  FROM "WHEN WORLDS COLLIDE"   EX C LIP 32
    TREASURY OF SCIENCE FICTION CLASSICS, THE
                                      KUEBLER, HAROLD W.   AN

BAMBER, GEORGE
  OTTMAR BALLEAU X 2   SS   ROG 61 03
    7TH ANNUAL OF THE YEAR'S BEST S-F, THE MERRIL, JUDITH   AN

BANGS, JOHN KENDRICK
  DISPUTED AUTHORSHIP, A (1895)   SS
    OUT OF THIS WORLD   FAST, JULIUS   AN
  GLANCE AHEAD: BEING A CHRISTMAS TALE OF A.D. 3568, A
                                                  SS   01
    ANCESTRAL VOICES   MENVILLE & REGINALD   AN

BANISTER, MANLY
  ESCAPE TO EARTH   NV   SFQ 57 11
    ESCAPE TO EARTH   HOWARD, IVAN   AN

BANKS, RAYMOND E.
  CHRISTMAS TROMBONE   SS   FSF 54 01
    BEST SCIENCE FICTION STORIES AND NOVELS: 1955
                                      DIKTY, T. E.   AN
  CITY THAT LOVES YOU, THE   SS   GAL 69 03
    HOT & COLD RUNNING CITIES   MCHARGUE, GEORGESS   AN
  DOUBLE DOME   SS   GAL 57 05
    HUMAN AND OTHER BEINGS   DEGRAEFF, ALLEN   AN
  EAR-FRIEND, THE   NV   SFS 55 03
    6 AND THE SILENT SCREAM   HOWARD, IVAN   AN
  LITTLEST PEOPLE, THE   NV   GAL 54 03
    BEST SCIENCE FICTION STORIES AND NOVELS: 1955
                                      DIKTY, T. E.   AN
  RABBITS TO THE MOON   SS   FSF 59 07

BANKS, RAYMOND E.   (CONTINUED)
    DECADE OF FANTASY AND SCIENCE FICTION, A
                                      MILLS, ROBERT P.   AN
  SHORT ONES, THE   NV   FSF 55 03
    BEST FROM FANTASY AND SCIENCE FICTION: 5
                                      BOUCHER, ANTHONY   AN
    POLITICAL SCIENCE FICTION   GREENBERG& WARRICK   AN
  THIS SIDE UP   SS   GAL 54 07
    FIFTH GALAXY READER, THE   GOLD, H. L.   AN
  WALTER PERKINS IS HERE| SS   FIN 70
    FUTURE IS NOW, THE   NOLAN, WILLIAM F.   OA
    INSIDE INFORMATION   MOWSHOWITZ, ABBE   AN

BARBET, PIERRE
  PROBLEM IN BIONICS, A   SS   74
    BEST FROM THE REST OF THE WORLD, THE WOLLHEIM, DONALD A. AN

BARCLAY, ALAN
  HARD WAY, THE   SS   NWS 53 06
    BEST FROM NEW WORLDS SCIENCE FICTION, THE
                                      CARNELL, JOHN   AN
  ONLY AN ECHO   SS   NWS 54 04
    GATEWAY TO THE STARS   CARNELL, JOHN   AN

BARCLAY, WILLIAM   PSEUD. FOR MICHAEL MOORCOCK

BARFOOT, JOHN
  CHRYSTALLIZATION OF THE MYTH   SS   ORB 72 11
    ORBIT 11   KNIGHT, DAMON   OA
  COILS   SS   ORB 74 13
    ORBIT 13   KNIGHT, DAMON   OA
  HOUSE   SS   ORB 75 17
    ORBIT 17   KNIGHT, DAMON   OA

BARING, MAURICE
  ALTERNATIVE, THE   SS   25
    TRAVELERS IN TIME   STERN, PHILIP VAN D.   AN

BARNES, ARTHUR K.
  INTERPLANETARY HUNTER   AC H GNM 56
  ALMUSSEN'S COMET (THE SEVEN SLEEPERS)   NV   TWS 40 05
    INTERPLANETARY HUNTER   BARNES, ARTHUR K.   AC
  GRIEF OF BAGDAD   SS   TWS 43 06
    *MY BEST SCIENCE FICTION STORY   MARGULIES & FRIEND   AN
  HOTHOUSE PLANET (SEE VENUS)   TC
  JUPITER (SATELLITE FIVE)   NV   TWS 38 10
    INTERPLANETARY HUNTER   BARNES, ARTHUR K.   AC
  NEPTUNE (SIREN SATELLITE)   NV   TWS 48 WI
    INTERPLANETARY HUNTER   BARNES, ARTHUR K.   AC
  SATELLITE FIVE (SEE JUPITER)   TC
  SATURN (TROUBLE ON TITAN)   NV   TWS 41 02
    INTERPLANETARY HUNTER   BARNES, ARTHUR K.   AC
  SEVEN SLEEPERS, THE (SEE ALMUSSEN'S COMET)   TC
  SIREN SATELLITE (SEE NEPTUNE)   TC
  TROUBLE ON TITAN (SEE SATURN)   TC
  VENUS (HOTHOUSE PLANET)   NV   TWS 37 10
    INTERPLANETARY HUNTER   BARNES, ARTHUR K.   AC
  WHY I SELECTED GRIEF OF BAGDAD   AI
    *MY BEST SCIENCE FICTION STORY   MARGULIES & FRIEND   AN

BARR, ROBERT
  DOOM OF LONDON, THE   SS   IDL 92 11
    SCIENCE FICTION BY GASLIGHT   MOSKOWITZ, SAM   AN
  REVOLT OF THE..., THE   SS   IDL 94 05
    MARRIAGE AND THE FAMILY THROUGH SCIENCE FICTION
                                      CLEAR/WARRICK/&   AN
    WHEN WOMEN RULE   MOSKOWITZ, SAM   AN

BARR, STEPHEN
  ABSOLUTE ULTIMATE INVENTION, THE   SS   INY 70 01
    INFINITY 1   HOSKINS, ROBERT   OA
  BACK OF OUR HEADS, THE   NV   GAL 58 07
    13 ABOVE THE NIGHT   CONKLIN, GROFF   AN
  CALLAHAN AND THE WHEELIES   NV   FSF 60 08
    SCIENCE FICTION ODDITIES   CONKLIN, GROFF   AN
  HOMING INSTINCT OF JOE VARGO, THE   SS   FSF 59 12
    *SPECTRUM   AMIS & CONQUEST   AN
  I AM A NUCLEUS   NV   GAL 57 02
    FOURTH GALAXY READER, THE   GOLD, H. L.   AN
  VERSE   PM C
    MATHEMATICAL MAGPIE, THE   FADIMAN, CLIFTON   AN

BARRETT, NEAL JR.
  GREYSPUN'S GIFT   SS   WOT 70 WI
    WORLD'S BEST SCIENCE FICTION: 1971 WOLLHEIM & CARR   AN
  NIGHTBEAT   SS   EPC 75
    EPOCH   ELWOOD & SILVERBERG   OA
  STENTORII LUGGAGE, THE   NV   GAL 60 10
    MIND PARTNER AND 8 OTHER NOVELETS FROM GALAXY
                                      GOLD, H. L.   AN
  TALKING, THE   SS
    LONE STAR UNIVERSE   PROCTOR & UTLEY   OA

BARROWS, MARJORIE
  SCIENCE FICTION AND READER'S GUIDE   AN H SPN 54
    VOLUME 16 OF "THE CHILDREN'S HOUR" SET

BARSHOFSKY, PHILIP
  ONE PREHISTORIC NIGHT   SS   WOS 34 11
    HISTORY OF THE SCIENCE FICTION MAGAZINE, THE PART 1 1926-1935
                                      ASHLEY, MICHAEL   AN

BARTER, ALAN FRANK AND R. WILSON
  UNTRAVELLED WORLDS   AN   MCM 66

BARTER, ALAN FRANK
    FOREWORD   IN C
        UNTRAVELLED WORLDS   BARTER & WILSON   AN

BARTH, JOHN
    FROM: GILES GOAT-BOY   EX   DBL 66
        INSIDE INFORMATION   MOWSHOWITZ, ABBE   AN

BARTHELME, DONALD
    BALLOON, THE   SS   NYM 66 04
        SCIENCE FICTION: THE FUTURE ALLEN, DICK   AN
        SF12   MERRIL, JUDITH   AN
    GAME   SS   NYM 65 07
        11TH ANNUAL OF THE YEAR'S BEST S-F, THE
                                     MERRIL, JUDITH   AN
    GENIUS, THE   SS   NYM 71 02
        BEST SF: 1971   HARRISON & ALDISS   AN
    REPORT   SS   NYM 66
        INSIDE INFORMATION   MOWSHOWITZ, ABBE   AN

BARTON, EUSTACE   SEE PSEUD. ROBERT EUSTACE

BARTON, RALPH
    TWINKLE, TWINKLE, LITTLE STAR   PM   24
        FANTASIA MATHEMATICA   FADIMAN, CLIFTON   AN

BASCH, JOAN PATRICIA
    MATOG   SS   FSF 66 08
        BEST FROM FANTASY AND SCIENCE FICTION: 16
                                     FERMAN, EDWARD L.   AN

BASS, T. J.
    RORQUAL MARU   NV   GAL 72 01
        1973 ANNUAL WORLD'S BEST SF, THE WOLLHEIM, DONALD A. AN

BATES, HARRY   ALSO AS
        ANTHONY GILMORE (WITH DESMOND W. HALL)
    ALAS, ALL THINKING!   SN   ASF 35 06
        *IMAGINATION UNLIMITED   BLEILER & DIKTY   AN
        OTHER WORLDS, THE   STONG, PHILIP D.   AN
        SCIENCE FICTION OF THE 30'S KNIGHT, DAMON   AN
    DEATH OF A SENSITIVE   NV   SFP 53 05
        EDITOR'S CHOICE IN SCIENCE FICTION MOSKOWITZ, SAM   AN
    FAREWELL TO THE MASTER   NV   ASF 40 10
        *ADVENTURES IN TIME AND SPACE   HEALY & MCCOMAS   AN
        ASTOUNDING-ANALOG READER, THE VOLUME ONE
                                     HARRISON & ALDISS   AN
    MATTER OF SIZE, A   NV   ASF 34 04
        *ADVENTURES IN TIME AND SPACE   HEALY & MCCOMAS   AN

BATES, RUSSELL L.
    HELLO, WALLS AND FENCES   SS   INY 73 05
        INFINITY 5   HOSKINS, ROBERT   OA
    LEGION   SS   INY 71 02
        INFINITY 2   HOSKINS, ROBERT   OA
    MODEST PROPOSAL, A   SS   CLR 72 02
        CLARION II   WILSON, ROBIN SCOTT   OA

BATTEAU, DWIGHT W.
    INTRODUCTION   IN
        COMING ATTRACTIONS   GREENBERG , MARTIN   NF

BAUER, GERALD M.
    FROM ALL OF US   SS   NMD 73
        FRONTIERS 2: THE NEW MIND   ELWOOD, ROGER   OA

BAUM, L. FRANK
    MARVELOUS POWDER OF LIFE, THE (FROM THE LAND OF OZ)
                                                EX   REL 04
        TALES BEYOND TIME   DE CAMP, L. S.&C.   AN

BAUM, THOMAS
    LOST AND FOUND   SS
        BEST SF: 1974   HARRISON & ALDISS   AN
    ON LOCATION   SS   PBY 70 07
        LAST TRAIN TO LIMBO   PLAYBOY, EDITORS OF   AN

BAXTER, CHARLES
    IDEAL POLICE STATE, THE   PM   LMG 71
        BEST SF: 1971   HARRISON & ALDISS   AN

BAXTER, JOHN
    PACIFIC BOOK OF AUSTRALIAN SCIENCE FICTION AN   AAR 68
    SECOND PACIFIC BOOK OF SCIENCE FICTION, THE AN H AAR 71
    APPLE   SS   NWR 67 10
        NEW WRITINGS IN SF. 8   CARNELL, JOHN   AN
        NEW WRITINGS IN SF. 10   CARNELL, JOHN   OA
        SECOND PACIFIC BOOK OF SCIENCE FICTION, THE
                                     BAXTER, JOHN   AN
        ZOO 2000   YOLEN, JANE   AN
    BEACH, THE   SS   NWR 68 13
        NEW WRITINGS IN SF. 13   CARNELL, JOHN   OA
        PACIFIC BOOK OF AUSTRALIAN SCIENCE FICTION
                                     BAXTER, JOHN   AN
    HANDS, THE   SS   NWR 65 06
        NEW WRITINGS IN SF. 6   CARNELL, JOHN   OA
    INTRODUCTION   IN
        PACIFIC BOOK OF AUSTRALIAN SCIENCE FICTION
                                     BAXTER, JOHN   AN
        SECOND PACIFIC BOOK OF SCIENCE FICTION, THE
                                     BAXTER, JOHN   AN
    TAKEOVER BID   NV   NWR 65 05
        BEYOND TOMORROW   HARDING, LEE   AN
        NEW WRITINGS IN SF. 5   CARNELL, JOHN   OA
    TESTAMENT   SS   NWR 65 03

BAXTER, JOHN   (CONTINUED)
    BEST FROM NEW WRITINGS IN S-F FIRST SELECTION, THE
                                     CARNELL, JOHN   AN
        NEW WRITINGS IN SF. 3   CARNELL, JOHN   OA
    TRAPS OF TIME, THE   SS   NWS 64 03
        BEST OF NEW WORLDS, THE   MOORCOCK, MICHAEL   AN
    TRYST   SS   NWR 66 08
        NEW WRITINGS IN SF. 8   CARNELL, JOHN   OA

BAYLEY, BARRINGTON J ALSO AS   P. F. WOODS
    ALL THE KING'S MEN   NV   NWS 65 03
        BEST OF NEW WORLDS, THE   MOORCOCK, MICHAEL   AN
        BEST SF STORIES FROM NEW WORLDS 7 MOORCOCK, MICHAEL AN
        ENGLAND SWINGS SF   MERRIL, JUDITH   AN
    BEES OF KNOWLEDGE, THE   NV   NWB 75 08
        NEW WORLDS EIGHT   BAILEY, HILARY   OA
        1976 ANNUAL WORLD'S BEST SF, THE WOLLHEIM, DONALD A. AN
    BIG SOUND, THE   SS   SFB 62 02
        BEST SF STORIES FROM NEW WORLDS 8 MOORCOCK, MICHAEL AN
    CABINET OF OLIVER NAYLOR, THE   SS   NWB 76 10
        1977 ANNUAL WORLD'S BEST SF, THE WOLLHEIM, DONALD A. AN
    DOUBLE TIME   SS   NWS 62 07
        BEST SF STORIES FROM NEW WORLDS 8 MOORCOCK, MICHAEL AN
    EXIT FROM CITY 5   NV   NWQ 71 01
        NEW WORLDS QUARTERLY NO. 1   MOORCOCK, MICHAEL   OA
    EXPLORATION OF SPACE, THE   SS   NWQ 72 04
        NEW WORLDS QUARTERLY NO. 4   MOORCOCK, MICHAEL   OA
    FOUR-COLOR PROBLEM   NV   NWQ 71 02
        NEW WORLDS QUARTERLY NO. 2   MOORCOCK, MICHAEL   OA
    MALADJUSTMENT   SS   NWQ 74 06
        NEW WORLDS NO. 6   PLATT & BAILEY   OA
    ME AND MY ANTRONOSCOPE   NV   NWB 73 05
        NEW WORLDS QUARTERLY NO. 5   MOORCOCK, MICHAEL   OA
    MUTATION PLANET   NV   TAL 73
        FRONTIERS 1: TOMORROW'S ALTERNATIVES ELWOOD, ROGER OA
    OVERLOAD, AN   SS   NWQ 73 05
        NEW WORLDS NO. 5   MOORCOCK & PLATT   AN
    RADIUS RIDERS, THE   SS   SFB 62 07
        BEST SF STORIES FROM NEW WORLDS 8 MOORCOCK, MICHAEL AN
    SEED OF EVIL, THE   NV   NWR 74 23
        NEW WRITINGS IN SF. 23   BULMER, KENNETH   OA
    SHIP OF DISASTER, THE   SS   NWS 65 06
        BEST SF STORIES FROM NEW WORLDS 4 MOORCOCK, MICHAEL AN
        NEW WORLDS OF FANTASY NO. 2 CARR, TERRY   AN
    SHIP THAT SAILED THE OCEAN OF SPACE, THE   SS   NWS
        BEST SF STORIES FROM NEW WORLDS 8 MOORCOCK, MICHAEL AN

BAYLISS, A.E. & J.C.
    SCIENCE IN FICTION   AN   UOL 57

BEAGLE, PETER S.
    COME LADY DEATH   SS   ATL 63 09
        NEW WORLDS OF FANTASY   CARR, TERRY   AN
    FARRELL AND LILA THE WEREWOLF   SS   GUA 69
        NEW WORLDS OF FANTASY NO. 3 CARR, TERRY   AN

BEAR, GREG
    PERIHESPERON   SS
        TOMORROW: NEW WORLDS OF SCIENCE FICTION
                                     ELWOOD, ROGER   OA
    WEBSTER   SS   ALT 74
        ALTERNATIES   GERROLD, DAVID   OA

BEARD, JAMES H.   ALSO AS   PHILIP JAMES (WITH LESTER DEL REY)
    CARILLON OF SKULLS   SS C UNK 41 02
        EARLY DEL REY   DEL REY, LESTER   AC
    DAWN OF REASON, THE   PM   UNK 39 10
        FROM UNKNOWN WORLDS   CAMPBELL, JOHN W. JR AN

BEAUMONT, CHARLES   PSEUD. FOR CHARLES NUTT
    EDGE, THE   AC   PTH 66
    FIEND IN YOU, THE   AN   BAL 62
    HUNGER AND OTHER STORIES, THE   AC H PUT 58 04
        IN ENGLAND AS "SHADOW PLAY", OMITS STORY "THE HUNGER"
    MAGIC MAN AND OTHER SCIENCE-FANTASY STORIES AC   FAW 65
    NIGHT RIDE AND OTHER JOURNEYS   AC   BAN 60 03
    SHADOW PLAY   AC   PTH 64
        SEE "THE HUNGER AND OTHER STORIES"
    YONDER   AC   BAN 58 04
    ANTHEM   SS   NEW 58 AC
        YONDER   BEAUMONT, CHARLES   AC
    BEAUTIFUL PEOPLE, THE (ALSO AS THE BEAUTIFUL WOMAN)
                                                SS   IFS 52 09
        YONDER   BEAUMONT, CHARLES   AC
    BEAUTIFUL WOMAN, THE (THE BEAUTIFUL PEOPLE) SS   IFS 52 09
        PRIZE SCIENCE FICTION   WOLLHEIM, DONALD A.   AN
    BLACK COUNTRY   SS   PBY 54 09
        HUNGER AND OTHER STORIES, THE BEAUMONT, CHARLES   AC
        MAGIC MAN AND OTHER SCIENCE-FANTASY STORIES
                                     BEAUMONT, CHARLES   AC
        PLAYBOY BOOK OF HORROR AND THE SUPERNATURAL, THE
                                     PLAYBOY, EDITORS OF   AN
    BLOOD BROTHER   SS   PBY 61 04
        PLAYBOY BOOK OF SCIENCE FICTION AND FANTASY, THE
                                     PLAYBOY, EDITORS OF   AN
    BUCK FEVER   SS   NEW 60 AC
        NIGHT RIDE AND OTHER JOURNEYS BEAUMONT, CHARLES   AC
    CLASSIC AFFAIR, A   SS   PBY 55
        MAGIC MAN AND OTHER SCIENCE-FANTASY STORIES
                                     BEAUMONT, CHARLES   AC
        NIGHT RIDE AND OTHER JOURNEYS BEAUMONT, CHARLES   AC
    CROOKED MAN, THE   SS   PBY 55 08
        FIEND, THE   PLAYBOY, EDITORS OF   AN
        HUNGER AND OTHER STORIES, THE BEAUMONT, CHARLES   AC
        MAGIC MAN AND OTHER SCIENCE-FANTASY STORIES
                                     BEAUMONT, CHARLES   AC

BEAUMONT, CHARLES   (CONTINUED)
    PLAYBOY BOOK OF SCIENCE FICTION AND FANTASY, THE
                                    PLAYBOY, EDITORS OF AN
CUSTOMERS, THE   SS   NEW 57 AC
    HUNGER AND OTHER STORIES, THE   BEAUMONT, CHARLES   AC
DARK MUSIC, THE   SS   PBY 56 12
    HUNGER AND OTHER STORIES, THE   BEAUMONT, CHARLES   AC
    MAGIC MAN AND OTHER SCIENCE-FANTASY STORIES
                                    BEAUMONT, CHARLES   AC
    PLAYBOY'S STORIES OF THE SINISTER & STRANGE
                                    PLAYBOY, EDITORS OF AN
DEADLY WILL TO WIN, THE (SEE A DEATH IN THE COUNTRY)
                                    TC
DEATH IN THE COUNTRY, A (THE DEADLY WILL TO WIN) SS PBY 57 11
    MAGIC MAN AND OTHER SCIENCE-FANTASY STORIES
                                    BEAUMONT, CHARLES   AC
    NIGHT RIDE AND OTHER JOURNEYS   BEAUMONT, CHARLES   AC
ELEGY   SS   IMG 53 02
    SCIENCE FACT/FICTION   FARRELL/GAGE/&   AN
    SEA OF SPACE, A   NOLAN, WILLIAM F.   AN
FAIR LADY   SS   NEW 57 AC
    HUNGER AND OTHER STORIES, THE   BEAUMONT, CHARLES   AC
    MAGIC MAN AND OTHER SCIENCE-FANTASY STORIES
                                    BEAUMONT, CHARLES   AC
FATHER, DEAR FATHER (OH FATHER OF MINE) SS VSF 57 01
    NIGHT RIDE AND OTHER JOURNEYS   BEAUMONT, CHARLES   AC
FREE DIRT   SS   FSF 55 05
    GRAVEYARD READER, THE   CONKLIN, GROFF   AN
    HUNGER AND OTHER STORIES, THE   BEAUMONT, CHARLES   AC
    TWENTY YEARS OF FANTASY & SCIENCE FICTION
                                    FERMAN & MILLS   AN
FRITZCHEN   SS   OSF 53 01
    *TERROR IN THE MODERN VEIN   WOLLHEIM, DONALD A. AN
    YONDER   BEAUMONT, CHARLES   AC
GUESTS OF CHANCE, THE   SS C INF 56 06
    NIGHT RIDE AND OTHER JOURNEYS   BEAUMONT, CHARLES   AC
HAIR OF THE DOG   SS   OSF 54 03
    YONDER   BEAUMONT, CHARLES   AC
HOWLING MAN, THE   SS   NEW 60 AC
    EDGE, THE   BEAUMONT, CHARLES   AC
    NIGHT RIDE AND OTHER JOURNEYS   BEAUMONT, CHARLES   AC
HUNGER, THE   SS   PBY 55 04
    HUNGER AND OTHER STORIES, THE   BEAUMONT, CHARLES   AC
    MAGIC MAN AND OTHER SCIENCE-FANTASY STORIES
                                    BEAUMONT, CHARLES   AC
I'LL DO ANYTHING (SEE A POINT OF HONOR) TC
IN HIS IMAGE (THE MAN WHO MADE HIMSELF) NV IMG 57 02
    YONDER   BEAUMONT, CHARLES   AC
INFERNAL BOUILLABAISSE, THE   SS   NEW 57 AC
    HUNGER AND OTHER STORIES, THE   BEAUMONT, CHARLES   AC
INTRODUCTION   IN
    FIEND IN YOU, THE   BEAUMONT, CHARLES   AN
JUNGLE, THE   NV   IFS 54 12
    SECOND WORLD OF IF, THE   QUINN & WULFF   AN
    YONDER   BEAUMONT, CHARLES   AC
KEEPER OF THE DREAM   SS   54
    *TIME TO COME   DERLETH, AUGUST   OA
LAST CAPER, THE   SS   FSF 54 03
    EDGE, THE   BEAUMONT, CHARLES   AC
    MAGIC MAN AND OTHER SCIENCE-FANTASY STORIES
                                    BEAUMONT, CHARLES   AC
    YONDER   BEAUMONT, CHARLES   AC
LAST NIGHT IN THE RAIN (SIN TOWER) SS   NUG 56
    HUNGER AND OTHER STORIES, THE   BEAUMONT, CHARLES   AC
LAST RITES   SS   IFS 55 10
    FIRST WORLD OF IF, THE   QUINN & WULFF   AN
    MAGIC MAN AND OTHER SCIENCE-FANTASY STORIES
                                    BEAUMONT, CHARLES   AC
    PSEUDO PEOPLE, THE   NOLAN, WILLIAM F.   AN
    YONDER   BEAUMONT, CHARLES   AC
LAST WORD, THE   SS C FSF 55 04
    BEST FROM FANTASY AND SCIENCE FICTION: 5
                                    BOUCHER, ANTHONY   AN
    EVIL EARTHS   ALDISS, BRIAN W.   AN
LOVE-MASTER, THE   SS   ROG 56
    EDGE, THE   BEAUMONT, CHARLES   AC
    MAGIC MAN AND OTHER SCIENCE-FANTASY STORIES
                                    BEAUMONT, CHARLES   AC
    NIGHT RIDE AND OTHER JOURNEYS   BEAUMONT, CHARLES   AC
MAGIC MAN, THE   SS   NEW 60 AC
    EDGE, THE   BEAUMONT, CHARLES   AC
    MAGIC MAN AND OTHER SCIENCE-FANTASY STORIES
                                    BEAUMONT, CHARLES   AC
    NIGHT RIDE AND OTHER JOURNEYS   BEAUMONT, CHARLES   AC
MAN WHO MADE HIMSELF, THE (SEE IN HIS IMAGE) TC
MASS FOR MIXED VOICES   SS   SFQ 54 05
    MAN AGAINST TOMORROW   NOLAN, WILLIAM F.   AN
MISS GENTILBELLE   SS   NEW 57 AC
    HUNGER AND OTHER STORIES, THE   BEAUMONT, CHARLES   AC
    MAGIC MAN AND OTHER SCIENCE-FANTASY STORIES
                                    BEAUMONT, CHARLES   AC
MONSTER SHOW, THE   SS   PBY 56 05
    LAST TRAIN TO LIMBO   PLAYBOY, EDITORS OF AN
    MAGIC MAN AND OTHER SCIENCE-FANTASY STORIES
                                    BEAUMONT, CHARLES   AC
    YONDER   BEAUMONT, CHARLES   AC
MOTHER'S DAY   SS   NEW 58 AC
    EDGE, THE   BEAUMONT, CHARLES   AC
    YONDER   BEAUMONT, CHARLES   AC
MOURNING SONG   SS   GAM 63 01
    9TH ANNUAL OF THE YEAR'S BEST S-F, THE MERRIL, JUDITH AN
MURDERERS, THE   SS   ESQ 55
    HUNGER AND OTHER STORIES, THE   BEAUMONT, CHARLES   AC
    MAGIC MAN AND OTHER SCIENCE-FANTASY STORIES
                                    BEAUMONT, CHARLES   AC

BEAUMONT, CHARLES   (CONTINUED)
    MUSIC OF THE YELLOW BRASS, THE   SS   PBY 59 01
    EDGE, THE   BEAUMONT, CHARLES   AC
    NIGHT RIDE AND OTHER JOURNEYS   BEAUMONT, CHARLES   AC
NEIGHBORS, THE   SS   NEW 60 AC
    EDGE, THE   BEAUMONT, CHARLES   AC
    NIGHT RIDE AND OTHER JOURNEYS   BEAUMONT, CHARLES   AC
NEW PEOPLE, THE   SS   ROG 58
    EDGE, THE   BEAUMONT, CHARLES   AC
    MAGIC MAN AND OTHER SCIENCE-FANTASY STORIES
                                    BEAUMONT, CHARLES   AC
    NIGHT RIDE AND OTHER JOURNEYS   BEAUMONT, CHARLES   AC
NEW SOUND, THE   SS   FSF 55 06
    ABOVE THE HUMAN LANDSCAPE   MCNELLY & STOVER   AN
    EDGE, THE   BEAUMONT, CHARLES   AC
    YONDER   BEAUMONT, CHARLES   AC
NIGHT RIDE   SS   PBY 57 03
    EDGE, THE   BEAUMONT, CHARLES   AC
    NIGHT RIDE AND OTHER JOURNEYS   BEAUMONT, CHARLES   AC
NURSERY RHYME   SS   NEW 57 AC
    BR-R-R-| CONKLIN, GROFF   AN
    HUNGER AND OTHER STORIES, THE   BEAUMONT, CHARLES   AC
OH FATHER OF MINE (SEE FATHER, DEAR FATHER) TC
OPEN HOUSE   SS   NEW 57 AC
    HUNGER AND OTHER STORIES, THE   BEAUMONT, CHARLES   AC
    MAGIC MAN AND OTHER SCIENCE-FANTASY STORIES
                                    BEAUMONT, CHARLES   AC
PERCHANCE TO DREAM   SS   PBY 58 10
    FIEND IN YOU, THE   BEAUMONT, CHARLES   AN
    MAGIC MAN AND OTHER SCIENCE-FANTASY STORIES
                                    BEAUMONT, CHARLES   AC
    MASKS   PLAYBOY, EDITORS OF AN
    NIGHT RIDE AND OTHER JOURNEYS   BEAUMONT, CHARLES   AC
PLACE OF MEETING   SS   OSF 54 02
    PLANET OF DOOM AND OTHER STORIES ANONYMOUS   AN
    YONDER   BEAUMONT, CHARLES   AC
POINT OF HONOR, A (I'LL DO ANYTHING) SS   MHT 55
    HUNGER AND OTHER STORIES, THE   BEAUMONT, CHARLES   AC
QUADRIOPTICON, THE   SS   FSF 54 08
    YONDER   BEAUMONT, CHARLES   AC
SIN TOWER (SEE LAST NIGHT IN THE RAIN) TC
SONG FOR A LADY   SS   NEW 60 AC
    EDGE, THE   BEAUMONT, CHARLES   AC
    NIGHT RIDE AND OTHER JOURNEYS   BEAUMONT, CHARLES   AC
SORCERER'S MOON   SS   PBY 59 07
    PLAYBOY BOOK OF HORROR AND THE SUPERNATURAL, THE
                                    PLAYBOY, EDITORS OF AN
TEARS OF THE MADONNA   SS   NEW 57 AC
    HUNGER AND OTHER STORIES, THE   BEAUMONT, CHARLES   AC
TRAIN, THE   SS   NEW 57 AC
    HUNGER AND OTHER STORIES, THE   BEAUMONT, CHARLES   AC
TRAUMEREI   SS   INF 56 02
    YONDER   BEAUMONT, CHARLES   AC
TRIGGER, THE   SS   MDM 58
    NIGHT RIDE AND OTHER JOURNEYS   BEAUMONT, CHARLES   AC
VANISHING AMERICAN, THE   SS   FSF 55 08
    BEST FROM FANTASY AND SCIENCE FICTION: 5
                                    BOUCHER, ANTHONY   AN
    CITY: 2000 A.D., THE   CLEM/GREENBERG/&   AN
    HUNGER AND OTHER STORIES, THE   BEAUMONT, CHARLES   AC
    INVISIBLE MEN   DAVENPORT, BASIL   AN
    MAGIC MAN AND OTHER SCIENCE-FANTASY STORIES
                                    BEAUMONT, CHARLES   AC
    SOCIAL PROBLEMS THROUGH SCIENCE FICTION
                                    GREENBERG/MILSTEAD/& AN
WORLD OF DIFFERENTS, A   SS   NEW 58 AC
    YONDER   BEAUMONT, CHARLES   AC
YOU CAN'T HAVE THEM ALL   SS   PBY 56 08
    BEST FANTASY STORIES   ALDISS, BRIAN W.   AN
    FIEND, THE   PLAYBOY, EDITORS OF AN
    YONDER   BEAUMONT, CHARLES   AC

BECKER, STEPHEN
    NEW ENCYCLOPAEDIST, THE   SS   FSF 64 05
    10TH ANNUAL OF THE YEAR'S BEST S-F, THE
                                    MERRIL, JUDITH   AN

BECKETT, SAMUEL
    SIXTEEN STORIES (TRANSLATED BY PATRICK BOWLES) SS 55
    MATHEMATICAL MAGPIE, THE   FADIMAN, CLIFTON   AN

BECKMAN, CHARLES JR.
    LAST MAN, THE (NOAH)   SS   OSF 54 11
    SPACE STATION 42 AND OTHER STORIES ANONYMOUS   AN
    NOAH (SEE THE LAST MAN)   TC

BEDFORD-JONES, HENRY
    WOLF WOMAN, THE   SS   BBM 34
    FANTASTIC PULPS, THE   HAINING, PETER   AN

BEER, LIONEL
    FLYING SAUCERS - PEOPLE AND REALITY   AR
    BEYOND THIS HORIZON   CARRELL, CHRISTOPHER OA

BEER, PATRICIA
    AFTER DEATH   PM   NSM 72
    BEST SF: 1972   HARRISON & ALDISS   AN

BEERBOHM, MAX
    ENOCH SOAMES   NV   CNY 16 05
    DEALS WITH THE DEVIL   DAVENPORT, BASIL   AN
    MOONLIGHT TRAVELER, THE   STERN, PHILIP VAN D. AN
    TRAVELERS IN TIME   STERN, PHILIP VAN D. AN
NOTE ON THE EINSTEIN THEORY, A   SS   46
    MATHEMATICAL MAGPIE, THE   FADIMAN, CLIFTON   AN

BEERBOHM, MAX   (CONTINUED)
  TEN YEARS AGO...   SS   72
    BEST SF: 1973   HARRISON & ALDISS   AN

BEETEM, DORIS
  HUNTING, THE   SS
    STAR TREK: THE NEW VOYAGES   MARSHAK, S&CULBREATH OA

BEHRENS, WILLIAM W.
  FROM "THE LIMITS TO GROWTH"   AR   C   72
    LOOKING AHEAD   ALLEN, D. & L.   AN

BELAVAL, EMILIO S.
  PURPLE CHILD, THE   SS   66
    VOYAGES: SCENARIOS FOR A SHIP CALLED EARTH
                                         SAUER, ROB   AN

BELAYEV, ALEXANDER
  HOITY-TOITY   NV
    SOVIET SCIENCE FICTION   ANONYMOUS   AN
  INVISIBLE LIGHT   SS
    RUSSIAN SCIENCE FICTION   MAGIDOFF, ROBERT   AN
  OVER THE ABYSS   SS
    DESTINATION: AMALTHEIA   DIXON, RICHARD   AN

BELCHER, C. DAVIS
  JUST DEAD ENOUGH (THE PRICE)   NV   ORB 69 05
    CLARION   WILSON, ROBIN SCOTT OA
  PRICE, THE (ALSO AS JUST DEAD ENOUGH)   NV   ORB 69 05
    ORBIT 5   KNIGHT, DAMON   OA

BELKIN, NORMAN
  VAMPIRE'S SAGA, A   PM   FSF 59 05
    BEST FROM FANTASY AND SCIENCE FICTION: 9
                                         MILLS, ROBERT P.   AN

BELL, ERIC TEMPLE   ALSO AS   JOHN TAINE
  ULTIMATE CATALYST, THE   NV   TWS 39 06
    GREAT SCIENCE FICTION BY SCIENTISTS CONKLIN, GROFF   AN

BELLAMY, EDWARD
  BLINDMAN'S WORLD, THE (1886)   SS   ATL 86
    *BEYOND TIME AND SPACE   DERLETH, AUGUST   AN
    FUTURE PERFECT   FRANKLIN, H. BRUCE AN
  FROM "LOOKING BACKWARD"   EX   TIC 88
    PAST, PRESENT, AND FUTURE PERFECT   WOLFE, J&FITZ GERALD AN
  MACHINES DO OUR WORK (FROM "LOOKING BACKWARD")   EX   TIC 88
    ARMCHAIR SCIENCE READER, THE   GORDON, I. & SORKIN AN
  TO WHOM THIS MAY COME (1888)   SS   HRP 88
    FUTURE PERFECT   FRANKLIN, H. BRUCE AN

BELLING, RUDOLPH
  HEAD   IL
    SCIENCE FICTION   BRODKIN & PEARSON   AN

BEMLEMANS, LUDWIG
  PUTZI   SS   39
    TIMELESS STORIES FOR TODAY AND TOMORROW
                                         BRADBURY, RAY   AN

BENEDICT, MYRLE
  SIT BY THE FIRE   SS   FUN 58 05
    FANTASTIC UNIVERSE OMNIBUS, THE   SANTESSON, HANS S. AN
    GENTLE INVADERS   SANTESSON, HANS S. AN

BENEDIKT, MICHAEL
  BELOVED HEAD, A   PM   69
    HOLDING YOUR EIGHT HANDS   LUCIE-SMITH, EDWARD AN

BENET, STEPHEN VINCENT
  ALL THAT MONEY CAN BUY (THE DEVIL AND DANIEL WEBSTER)
                                                      NV   SEP 36 10
    GHOULS, THE   HAINING, PETER   AN
  ANGEL WAS A YANKEE, THE   SS   MCL 40 10
    *BEYOND HUMAN KEN   MERRIL, JUDITH   AN
  BY THE WATERS OF BABYLON (THE PLACE OF THE GODS) SS SEP 37 07
    ARMCHAIR SCIENCE READER, THE   GORDON, I. & SORKIN AN
    CITIES OF WONDER   KNIGHT, DAMON   AN
    POCKET BOOK OF SCIENCE-FICTION, THE WOLLHEIM, DONALD A. AN
    SCIENCE FICTION   BRODKIN & PEARSON   AN
    SPECTRUM OF WORLDS, A   CLARESON, THOMAS D. AN
    SPECULATIONS   SANDERS, THOMAS E. AN
  CURFEW TOLLS, THE   SS   SEP 35 10
    MOONLIGHT TRAVELER, THE   STERN, PHILIP VAN D. AN
  DEVIL AND DANIEL WEBSTER, THE (ALSO AS ALL THAT MONEY CAN BUY)
                                                      NV   SEP 36 10
    DEALS WITH THE DEVIL   DAVENPORT, BASIL   AN
  KING OF THE CATS, THE   SS   HRP 29 02
    GOLDEN ROAD, THE   KNIGHT, DAMON   AN
    OUT OF THIS WORLD   FAST, JULIUS   AN
  METROPOLITAN NIGHTMARE   PM   27
    HOT & COLD RUNNING CITIES   MCHARGUE, GEORGESS AN
    WONDERMAKERS   HOSKINS, ROBERT   AN
  NIGHTMARE FOR FUTURE REFERENCE   PM   SCH 38 09
    CHILDREN OF WONDER   TENN, WILLIAM   AN
    VOICE OF THE DOLPHINS, AND OTHER STORIES, THE
                                         SZILARD, LEO   AC
  NIGHTMARE NUMBER THREE   PM   35
    METAL SMILE, THE   KNIGHT, DAMON   AN
    SHOT IN THE DARK   MERRIL, JUDITH   AN
    SPECULATIONS   SANDERS, THOMAS E. AN
    WONDERMAKERS   HOSKINS, ROBERT   AN
  PLACE OF THE GODS, THE   SS   SEP 37 07
    POST READER OF FANTASY AND SCIENCE FICTION
                                         SATURDAY EVE. POST AN
  TOMORROW'S CHILDREN   ASIMOV, ISAAC   AN

BENET, STEPHEN V.   (CONTINUED)
  TOO EARLY SPRING   SS   33
    NIGHT IN FUNLAND   BRONDFIELD, JEROME AN

BENFORD, GREGORY
  AND THE SEA LIKE MIRRORS   SS   DVS 72 02
    AGAIN, DANGEROUS VISIONS   ELLISON, HARLAN   OA
  CAMBRIDGE, 1:58 A.M.   SS   EPC 75
    EPOCH   ELWOOD & SILVERBERG OA
  DEEPER THAN THE DARKNESS   NV   FSF 69 04
    SOCIOLOGY THROUGH SCIENCE FICTION   MILSTEAD/GREENBERG/& AN
  DOING LENNON   SS   ASF 75 04
    BEST SCIENCE FICTION OF THE YEAR, THE NO. 5
                                         CARR, TERRY   AN
  IF THE STARS ARE GODS   NV   C UNI 74 04
    BEST SCIENCE FICTION OF THE YEAR, THE NO. 4
                                         CARR, TERRY   AN
    NEBULA AWARD STORIES 10   GUNN, JAMES E.   AN
    UNIVERSE 4   CARR, TERRY   AN
  INALIENABLE RITE   SS   QRK 70 01
    QUARK/1   DELANY & HACKER   OA
  JOHN OF THE APOCALYPSE   SS   C
    TOMORROW TODAY   ZEBROWSKI, GEORGE   OA
  KNOWING HER   SS   NDM 77 07
    NEW DIMENSIONS 7   SILVERBERG, ROBERT OA
  NOBODY LIVES ON BURTON STREET   SS   AMZ 70 05
    INSIDE INFORMATION   MOWSHOWITZ, ABBE   AN
    SOCIOLOGY THROUGH SCIENCE FICTION   MILSTEAD/GREENBERG/& AN
    WORLD'S BEST SCIENCE FICTION: 1971   WOLLHEIM & CARR   AN
  SEASCAPE   NV   76
    FASTER THAN LIGHT   DANN & ZEBROWSKI   OA
  THREADS OF TIME   NA   TOT 74
    THREADS OF TIME   SILVERBERG, ROBERT OA
  WEST WIND, FALLING   NV   C UNI 71 01
    UNIVERSE 1   CARR, TERRY   AN
  WHAT DID YOU DO LAST YEAR?   SS   C UNI 76 06
    UNIVERSE 6   CARR, TERRY   OA
  WHITE CREATURES   SS   NDM 75 05
    NEW DIMENSIONS 5   SILVERBERG, ROBERT OA

BENFORD, JAMES
  JOHN OF THE APOCALYPSE   SS   C
    TOMORROW TODAY   ZEBROWSKI, GEORGE   OA

BENNETT, G. J.
  TILTING ISLAND, THE   SS   C EVB 09 09
    SCIENCE FICTION BY GASLIGHT   MOSKOWITZ, SAM   AN

BENNETT, GERTRUDE   SEE PSEUD. FRANCIS STEVENS

BENNETT, KEITH
  ROCKETEERS HAVE SHAGGY EARS, THE   NV   PLS 50 SP
    BEST OF PLANET STORIES NO. 1, THE   BRACKETT, LEIGH   AN
    TRAVELLERS OF SPACE   GREENBERG , MARTIN AN

BENNETT, KEM
  DIFFERENT PURPOSE, A   SS   FSF 58 11
    BEST FROM FANTASY AND SCIENCE FICTION: 9
                                         MILLS, ROBERT P.   AN
  SOOTHSAYER, THE   SS   FSF 52 08
    BEST FROM FANTASY AND SCIENCE FICTION: 2
                                         BOUCHER & MCCOMAS   AN
  TRAP, THE   SS   SEP 56 01
    POST READER OF FANTASY AND SCIENCE FICTION
                                         SATURDAY EVE. POST AN

BENSEN, D. R.
  UNKNOWN 5, THE   AN   PYR 64 01
  UNKNOWN, THE   AN   PYR 63 04
    INTRODUCTION   IN
      UNKNOWN 5, THE   BENSEN, D. R.   AN
      UNKNOWN, THE   BENSEN, D. R.   AN

BENSON, E. F.
  CAT, THE   SS   12
    SATAN'S PETS   GHIDALIA, VIC   AN
  HOW FEAR DEPARTED FROM THE LONG GALLERY   SS   12
    LITTLE MONSTERS, THE   ELWOOD & GHIDALIA   AN
  MRS. AMWORTH (1922)   SS   FFM 50 06
    STRANGE BEASTS AND UNNATURAL MONSTERS STERN, PHILIP VAN D. AN

BENSON, STELLA   PSEUD. FOR JO ANDERSON
  MAN WHO MISSED THE BUS, THE   SS   36
    MOONLIGHT TRAVELER, THE   STERN, PHILIP VAN D. AN

BENVENISTE, ASA
  GARDENERS, THE   PM   68
    HOLDING YOUR EIGHT HANDS   LUCIE-SMITH, EDWARD AN

BERESFORD, JOHN D.
  APPEARANCE OF MAN, THE   PL   21
    *OTHER SIDE OF THE MOON, THE   DERLETH, AUGUST   AN

BERGER, MICHAEL
  FORBIDDEN FRUIT   SS   YNW
    SCIENCE FICTION STORIES   BRADLEY, JOHANNA   AN

BERGER, THOMAS
  PROFESSOR HYDE   SS   PBY 61 12
    FULLY AUTOMATED LOVE LIFE OF HENRY KEANRIDGE
                                         PLAYBOY, EDITORS OF AN

BERGSTRESSER, MARTA
  SMACK RUN   SS   NWB 73 05
    NEW WORLDS QUARTERLY NO. 5   MOORCOCK, MICHAEL   OA

BERMAN, RUTH

BESTER, ALFRED

BERMAN, RUTH
FACE ON THE BARROOM FLOOR, THE   NV C
  STAR TREK: THE NEW VOYAGES   MARSHAK, S&CULBREATH OA
LAKEWOOD CEMETERY   SS   NWQ 74 06
  NEW WORLDS NO. 6   PLATT & BAILEY   OA
TO CEREMARK   SS
  NEW VOICES IN SCIENCE FICTION   MARTIN, GEORGE R. R. OA
VISIT TO A WEIRD PLANET REVISITED   SS
  STAR TREK: THE NEW VOYAGES   MARSHAK, S&CULBREATH OA

BERMEL, ALBERT
END OF THE RACE, THE   SS   GAL 64 04
  EIGHTH GALAXY READER, THE   POHL, FREDERIK   AN

BERN, DONALD
MAN WHO KNEW ALL THE ANSWERS, THE   SS   AMZ 40 08
  OTHER WORLDS, THE   STONG, PHILIP D.   AN

BERNARD, KENNETH
SISTER FRANCETTA AND PIG BABY   SS   ARV 73 16
  BEST SF: 1973   HARRISON & ALDISS   AN

BERNOTT, JOAN
MY FATHER'S GUEST   SS   QRK 70 01
  QUARK/1   DELANY & HACKER   OA
TEST-TUBE CREATURE, AFTERWARD, THE   SS   DVS 72 02
  AGAIN, DANGEROUS VISIONS   ELLISON, HARLAN   OA
WAY HOME, THE   SS   QRK 71 02
  QUARK/2   DELANY & HACKER   OA

BERRY, JOHN
ONE WHO RETURNS, THE   SS   FSF 61 03
  *BEST FROM FANTASY AND SCIENCE FICTION: 11
                                     MILLS, ROBERT P.   AN

BERRYMAN, JOHN
BEROM   NV   ASF 51 01
  *IMAGINATION UNLIMITED   BLEILER & DIKTY   AN
BEYOND THE STARS (SPACE RATING)   SS   ASF 39 10
  BEYOND THE STARS AND OTHER STORIES ANONYMOUS   AN
SOMETHING TO SAY   NV   ASF 66 08
  ANALOG 6   CAMPBELL, JOHN W. JR AN
SPACE RATING (ALSO AS BEYOND THE STARS) SS   ASF 39 10
  *POSSIBLE WORLDS OF SCIENCE FICTION CONKLIN, GROFF   AN
SPECIAL FLIGHT   NV   ASF 39 05
  *SPECTRUM   AMIS & CONQUEST   AN
TROUBLE WITH TELSTAR, THE   NV   ASF 63 06
  ANALOG 3   CAMPBELL, JOHN W. JR AN

BERTIN, EDDY C.
CITY, DYING, THE   SS   NWR 68 13
  NEW WRITINGS IN SF. 9   CARNELL, JOHN   AN
  NEW WRITINGS IN SF. 13   CARNELL, JOHN   OA
I WONDER WHAT HE WANTED   SS   70
  YEAR'S BEST HORROR STORIES, THE DAVIS, RICHARD   AN
LIKE TWO WHITE SPIDERS   SS
  YEAR'S BEST HORROR STORIES: SERIES II, THE
                                     DAVIS, RICHARD   AN
MY EYES, THEY BURN¡   NV   75
  BEST FROM THE REST OF THE WORLD, THE WOLLHEIM, DONALD A. AN
TASTE OF YOUR LOVE, THE   SS   71
  YEAR'S BEST HORROR STORIES: SERIES III, THE
                                     DAVIS, RICHARD   AN
TIMESTORM   SS   71
  1972 ANNUAL WORLD'S BEST SF, THE WOLLHEIM, DONALD A. AN

ESTER, ALFRED
ALFRED BESTER OMNIBUS, AN   AC H SID 67
DARK SIDE OF THE EARTH, THE   AC   SIG 64 05
LIGHT FANTASTIC, THE   AC H BKP 76
  ALSO IN "STARLIGHT"
STAR LIGHT, STAR BRIGHT   AC H BKP 76
  ALSO IN "STARLIGHT"
STARBURST   AC   SIG 58
STARLIGHT   AC H NDB 76
  ADAM AND NO EVE   SS   ASF 41 09
  *ADVENTURES IN TIME AND SPACE HEALY & MCCOMAS   AN
  BEYOND CONTROL   SILVERBERG, ROBERT AN
  MORE ADVENTURES IN TIME AND SPACE HEALY & MCCOMAS AN
  STAR LIGHT, STAR BRIGHT   BESTER, ALFRED   AC
  STARBURST   BESTER, ALFRED   AC
ANIMAL FAIR, THE   NV   FSF 72 10
  BEST FROM FANTASY AND SCIENCE FICTION: 20
                                     FERMAN, EDWARD L.   AN
COMMENT ON FONDLY FAHRENHEIT   AR
  LIGHT FANTASTIC, THE   BESTER, ALFRED   AC
DARK SIDE OF THE EARTH, THE   AC   SIG 64 05
  ALFRED BESTER OMNIBUS, AN   BESTER, ALFRED   AC
DEMOLISHED MAN, THE   NO   GAL 52 01
  ALFRED BESTER OMNIBUS, AN   BESTER, ALFRED   AC
  SCIENCE FICTION ARGOSY, A   KNIGHT, DAMON   AN
DEVIL'S INVENTION, THE (SEE ODDY AND ID) TC
DIE-HARD, THE   SS   NEW 58 AC
  STARBURST   BESTER, ALFRED   AC
DISAPPEARING ACT   SS   STR 53 02
  CONNOISSEUR'S S. F.   BOARDMAN, TOM JR.   AN
  LIGHT FANTASTIC, THE   BESTER, ALFRED   AC
  OTHER DIMENSIONS   SILVERBERG, ROBERT AN
  POLITICAL SCIENCE FICTION   GREENBERG& WARRICK AN
  SCIENCE FACT/FICTION   FARRELL/GAGE/&   AN
  STAR OF STARS   POHL, FREDERIK   AN
  STAR SCIENCE FICTION STORIES NO. 2 POHL, FREDERIK OA
  STARBURST   BESTER, ALFRED   AC
  STARLIT CORRIDOR, THE   MANSFIELD, ROGER   AN
FLOWERED THUNDERMUG, THE   NV
  DARK SIDE OF THE EARTH, THE   BESTER, ALFRED   AC

BESTER, ALFRED (CONTINUED)
  HUMAN EQUATION, THE   NOLAN, WILLIAM F.   AN
FONDLY FAHRENHEIT   SS   FSF 54 08
  BEST FROM FANTASY AND SCIENCE FICTION: 4
                                     BOUCHER, ANTHONY   AN
  LIGHT FANTASTIC, THE   BESTER, ALFRED   AC
  SCIENCE FICTION HALL OF FAME VOLUME 1 SILVERBERG, ROBERT AN
  SF: AUTHORS' CHOICE 2   HARRISON, HARRY   AN
  SHOCKING THING, A   KNIGHT, DAMON   AN
  SPECTRUM 3   AMIS & CONQUEST   AN
  STARBURST   BESTER, ALFRED   AC
  STARS AROUND US, THE   HOSKINS, ROBERT   AN
  SURVIVAL PRINTOUT   TOTAL EFFECT   AN
FOUR-HOUR FUGUE, THE   SS   ASF 74 06
  BEST SF: 1974   HARRISON & ALDISS   AN
  LIGHT FANTASTIC, THE   BESTER, ALFRED   AC
  1975 ANNUAL WORLD'S BEST SF, THE WOLLHEIM, DONALD A. AN
HELL IS FOREVER   SN   UNK 42 08
  LIGHT FANTASTIC, THE   BESTER, ALFRED   AC
  UNKNOWN 5, THE   BENSEN, D. R.   AN
HOBSON'S CHOICE   SS   FSF 52 08
  BEST FROM FANTASY AND SCIENCE FICTION: 2
                                     BOUCHER & MCCOMAS   AN
  BEST SF 2   CRISPIN, EDMUND   AN
  INFINITE JESTS   SILVERBERG, ROBERT AN
  STAR LIGHT, STAR BRIGHT   BESTER, ALFRED   AC
  STARBURST   BESTER, ALFRED   AC
  TOMORROW AND TOMORROW   KNIGHT, DAMON   AN
ISAAC ASIMOV   AR   PBW 73
  STAR LIGHT, STAR BRIGHT   BESTER, ALFRED   AC
LIGHT FANTASTIC, THE   AC   BKP 76
  STARLIGHT   BESTER, ALFRED   AC
MEN WHO MURDERED MOHAMMED, THE   SS   FSF 58 10
  AS TOMORROW BECOMES TODAY   SULLIVAN, CHARLES W. AN
  BEST FROM FANTASY AND SCIENCE FICTION: 8
                                     BOUCHER, ANTHONY   AN
  COSMIC LAUGHTER   HALDEMAN, JOE W.   AN
  DARK SIDE OF THE EARTH, THE   BESTER, ALFRED   AC
  LIGHT FANTASTIC, THE   BESTER, ALFRED   AC
  VINTAGE ANTHOLOGY OF SCIENCE FANTASY, THE
                                     CERF, CHRISTOPHER   AN
  VOYAGERS IN TIME   SILVERBERG, ROBERT AN
MS. FOUND IN A CHAMPAGNE BOTTLE   SS   STA 68
  LIGHT FANTASTIC, THE   BESTER, ALFRED   AC
MY AFFAIR WITH SCIENCE FICTION   AR   NOV 74 04
  NOVA 4   HARRISON, HARRY   OA
  STAR LIGHT, STAR BRIGHT   BESTER, ALFRED   AC
MY PRIVATE WORLD OF SCIENCE FICTION   MS
  WORLDS OF SCIENCE FICTION   MILLS, ROBERT P.   AN
ODDY AND ID (THE DEVIL'S INVENTION)   SS   ASF 50 08
  BEST SCIENCE-FICTION STORIES: 1951, THE
                                     BLEILER & DIKTY   AN
  FRONTIERS IN SPACE   BLEILER & DIKTY   AN
  STAR LIGHT, STAR BRIGHT   BESTER, ALFRED   AC
  STARBURST   BESTER, ALFRED   AC
  STRANGE GIFTS   SILVERBERG, ROBERT AN
OF TIME AND THIRD AVENUE   SS   FSF 51 10
  BEST SCIENCE-FICTION STORIES: 1952, THE
                                     BLEILER & DIKTY   AN
  CENTURY OF SCIENCE FICTION, A KNIGHT, DAMON   AN
  STAR LIGHT, STAR BRIGHT   BESTER, ALFRED   AC
  STARBURST   BESTER, ALFRED   AC
OUT OF THIS WORLD   SS
  DARK SIDE OF THE EARTH, THE   BESTER, ALFRED   AC
PI MAN, THE   SS   FSF 59 10
  ALPHA 1   SILVERBERG, ROBERT AN
  BEST FROM FANTASY AND SCIENCE FICTION: 9
                                     MILLS, ROBERT P.   AN
  DARK SIDE OF THE EARTH, THE   BESTER, ALFRED   AC
  STAR LIGHT, STAR BRIGHT   BESTER, ALFRED   AC
PROBABLE MAN, THE   NV   ASF 41 07
  FUTURES TO INFINITY   MOSKOWITZ, SAM   AN
PUSH OF A FINGER, THE   NV   ASF 42 05
  ASTOUNDING-ANALOG READER, THE VOLUME ONE
                                     HARRISON & ALDISS   AN
ROLLER COASTER, THE   SS   FAN 53 06
  BEST FROM FANTASTIC, THE   WHITE, TED   AN
  STARBURST   BESTER, ALFRED   AC
SOMETHING UP THERE LIKES ME   NV   AMA 73
  ASTOUNDING   HARRISON, HARRY   OA
  BEST SCIENCE FICTION OF THE YEAR, THE NO. 3
                                     CARR, TERRY   AN
  BEST SCIENCE FICTION STORIES OF THE YEAR (1973)
                                     DEL REY, LESTER   AN
  STAR LIGHT, STAR BRIGHT   BESTER, ALFRED   AC
STAR LIGHT, STAR BRIGHT   AC   BKP 76
  STARLIGHT   BESTER, ALFRED   AC
STAR LIGHT, STAR BRIGHT   SS   FSF 53 07
  BEST FROM FANTASY AND SCIENCE FICTION: 3
                                     BOUCHER & MCCOMAS   AN
  STAR LIGHT, STAR BRIGHT   BESTER, ALFRED   AC
  STARBURST   BESTER, ALFRED   AC
STARCOMBER, THE (5,271,009)   NV   FSF 54 03
  STARBURST   BESTER, ALFRED   AC
STARS MY DESTINATION, THE (ALSO AS TIGER¡ TIGER¡) NO GAL 56 10
  TREASURY OF GREAT SCIENCE FICTION, A VOL.2
                                     BOUCHER, ANTHONY   AN
THEY DON'T MAKE LIFE LIKE THEY USED TO NV   FSF 63 10
  BEST FROM FANTASY AND SCIENCE FICTION: 13
                                     DAVIDSON, AVRAM   AN
  DARK SIDE OF THE EARTH, THE   BESTER, ALFRED   AC
  STAR LIGHT, STAR BRIGHT   BESTER, ALFRED   AC
  9TH ANNUAL OF THE YEAR'S BEST S-F, THE MERRIL, JUDITH AN
TIGER¡ TIGER¡ (THE STARS MY DESTINATION) NO GAL 56 10
  ALFRED BESTER OMNIBUS, AN   BESTER, ALFRED   AC

BESTER, ALFRED (CONTINUED)
TIME IS THE TRAITOR NV FSF 53 09
BEST SCIENCE-FICTION STORIES: 1954, THE
BLEILER & DIKTY AN
DARK SIDE OF THE EARTH, THE BESTER, ALFRED AC
SCIENCE FICTION: THE GREAT YEARS, VOL. II
POHL, C. & F. AN
SPACE ODYSSEYS ALDISS, BRIAN W. AN
STAR LIGHT, STAR BRIGHT BESTER, ALFRED AC
TRAVEL DIARY SS NEW 58 AC
STARBURST BESTER, ALFRED AC
TREMATODE, A CRITIQUE OF MODERN SCIENCE-FICTION BR
BEST SCIENCE-FICTION STORIES: 1953, THE
BLEILER & DIKTY AN
WILL YOU WAIT? SS FSF 59 03
DARK SIDE OF THE EARTH, THE BESTER, ALFRED AC
DECADE OF FANTASY AND SCIENCE FICTION, A
MILLS, ROBERT P. AN
GOLDEN ROAD, THE KNIGHT, DAMON AN
5,271,009 (ALSO AS THE STARCOMBER) NV FSF 54 03
ALPHA 4 SILVERBERG, ROBERT AN
ASSIGNMENT IN TOMORROW POHL, FREDERIK AN
LIGHT FANTASTIC, THE BESTER, ALFRED AC
MODERN SCIENCE FICTION SPINRAD, NORMAN AN
TWENTY YEARS OF FANTASY & SCIENCE FICTION
FERMAN & MILLS AN

BEVAN, ALISTAIR PSEUD. FOR KEITH ROBERTS
I LOSE MEDEA SS NWQ 72 03
NEW WORLDS QUARTERLY NO. 3 MOORCOCK, MICHAEL OA
SUSAN SS SCF 65 04
11TH ANNUAL OF THE YEAR'S BEST S-F, THE
MERRIL, JUDITH AN

BEYNON, JOHN PSEUD. FOR
JOHN BEYNON HARRIS (JOHN WYNDHAM PARKES LUCAS BEYNON HARRIS)
NO PLACE LIKE EARTH (SEE TIME TO REST) TC NWS 51 SP
TECHNICAL SLIP (ARS 49 WI) SS IMG 50 12
OPERATION FUTURE CONKLIN, GROFF AN
TIME TO REST (COMBINED WITH "NO PLACE LIKE EARTH", NWS 51 SP)
NV ARS 49 WI
*NO PLACE LIKE EARTH CARNELL, JOHN AN

BIANCHI, ED
HABITS OF THE RIGELIAN NIGHTFOX SS IFS 71 12
BEST FROM IF, THE VOLUME I IF, EDITORS OF AN

BIERCE, AMBROSE
BOTTOMLESS GRAVE, A SS
GRAVEYARD READER, THE CONKLIN, GROFF AN
DAMNED THING, THE (1893) SS WRT 23 09
SPECTRUM OF WORLDS, A CLARESON, THOMAS D. AN
TREASURY OF SCIENCE FICTION CLASSICS, THE
KUEBLER, HAROLD W. AN
HOLY TERROR, A SS 91
*TWISTED CONKLIN, GROFF AN
INCIDENT AT OWL CREEK (AN OCCURENCE AT OWL CREEK BRIDGE)
SS 91
GHOULS, THE HAINING, PETER AN
INGENIOUS PATRIOT, THE SS
ONE HUNDERED YEARS OF SCIENCE FICTION KNIGHT, DAMON AN
PAST, PRESENT, AND FUTURE PERFECT WOLFE, J&FITZ GERALD AN
INHABITANT OF CARCOSA, AN SS AFR 48 08
EDGE OF NEVER, THE HOSKINS, ROBERT AN
MOONLIT ROAD, THE SS 93
SUPERNATURAL READER, THE CONKLIN, G&L. AN
MOXON'S MASTER SS 93
ANDROIDS, TIME MACHINES AND BLUE GIRAFFES
ELWOOD & GHIDALIA AN
CENTURY OF SCIENCE FICTION, A KNIGHT, DAMON AN
FROM FRANKENSTEIN TO ANDROMEDA BROWN, JAMES GOLDIE AN
INSIDE INFORMATION MOWSHOWITZ, ABBE AN
JOURNEYS IN SCIENCE FICTION LOUGHLIN, RICHARD L. AN
POCKET BOOK OF SCIENCE-FICTION, THE WOLLHEIM, DONALD A. AN
*SCIENCE FICTION THINKING MACHINES CONKLIN, GROFF AN
WONDERMAKERS HOSKINS, ROBERT AN
MYSTERIOUS DISAPPEARANCES (1893) AR 93
FUTURE PERFECT FRANKLIN, H. BRUCE AN
OCCURANCE AT OWL CREEK BRIDGE, AN (ALSO AS INCIDENT AT
OWL CREEK) SS 91
PERCHANCE TO DREAM KNIGHT, DAMON AN
OIL OF DOG SS
SHOCKING THING, A KNIGHT, DAMON AN
PSYCHOLOGICAL SHIPWRECK, A (1893) SS 93
FUTURE PERFECT FRANKLIN, H. BRUCE AN

BIGGLE, LLOYD JR.
GALAXY OF STRANGERS, A AC H DBL 76
METALLIC MUSE, THE AC H DBL 72
NEBULA AWARD STORIES NO. 7 AN H HPR 73
OUT OF THE SILENT SKY AC BET 77
ON COVER AS "THE SILENT SKY", SEE "RULE OF THE DOOR"
RULE OF THE DOOR AND OTHER FANCIFUL REGULATIONS AC H DBL 67
ALSO AS "(OUT OF) THE SILENT SKY"
AND MADLY TEACH NV FSF 66 05
BEST FROM FANTASY AND SCIENCE FICTION: 16
FERMAN, EDWARD L. AN
GALAXY OF STRANGERS, A BIGGLE, LLOYD JR. AC
BEACHHEAD IN UTOPIA SS OMG 73
OMEGA ELWOOD, ROGER OA
BOTTICELLI HORROR, THE NV FAN 60 03
METALLIC MUSE, THE BIGGLE, LLOYD JR. AC
BRIDLE SHOWER (SEE SECRET WEAPON) TC
CHRONIUS OF THE D.F.C. (SEE D.F.C.) TC
D.F.C. (CHRONIUS OF THE D.F.C.) SS IFS 57 02

BIGGLE, LLOYD JR. (CONTINUED)
RULE OF THE DOOR AND OTHER FANCIFUL REGULATIONS
BIGGLE, LLOYD JR. AC
DOUBLE-EDGED ROPE, THE SS ASF 67 06
GALAXY OF STRANGERS, A BIGGLE, LLOYD JR. AC
ESIDARAP OT PIRT DNUOR (SEE ROUND TRIP TO ESIDARAP)
TC
EYE FOR AN EYE NV
FAR SIDE OF TIME, THE ELWOOD, ROGER OA
GALAXY OF STRANGERS, A BIGGLE, LLOYD JR. AC
FIRST LOVE SS AMZ 59 09
GALAXY OF STRANGERS, A BIGGLE, LLOYD JR. AC
FRAYED STRING ON THE STRETCHED FOREFINGER OF TIME, THE
SS FSF 71 05
BEST SCIENCE FICTION OF THE YEAR, THE CARR, TERRY AN
IN HIS OWN IMAGE SS FSF 68 01
BEST FROM FANTASY AND SCIENCE FICTION: 18
FERMAN, EDWARD L. AN
METALLIC MUSE, THE BIGGLE, LLOYD JR. AC
INTRODUCTION IN
GALAXY OF STRANGERS, A BIGGLE, LLOYD JR. AC
NEBULA AWARD STORIES NO. 7 BIGGLE, LLOYD JR. AN
RULE OF THE DOOR AND OTHER FANCIFUL REGULATIONS
BIGGLE, LLOYD JR. AC
JUDGEMENT DAY SS FUN 58 04
RULE OF THE DOOR AND OTHER FANCIFUL REGULATIONS
BIGGLE, LLOYD JR. AC
LEADING MAN SS GAL 57 06
METALLIC MUSE, THE BIGGLE, LLOYD JR. AC
MAN WHO WASN'T HOME, THE (SEE ORPHAN OF THE VOID) TC
MONUMENT NV ASF 61 06
ANALOG 1 CAMPBELL, JOHN W. JR AN
NO BIZ LIKE SHOW BIZ SS ASF 74 05
GALAXY OF STRANGERS, A BIGGLE, LLOYD JR. AC
ON THE DOTTED LINE NV IFS 57 06
RULE OF THE DOOR AND OTHER FANCIFUL REGULATIONS
BIGGLE, LLOYD JR. AC
ORPHAN OF THE VOID (THE MAN WHO WASN'T HOME) NV FAN 60 09
METALLIC MUSE, THE BIGGLE, LLOYD JR. AC
PARIAH PLANET (SEE THE PERFECT PUNISHMENT) TC
PERFECT PUNISHMENT, THE (PARIAH PLANET) NV WOT 65 03
RULE OF THE DOOR AND OTHER FANCIFUL REGULATIONS
BIGGLE, LLOYD JR. AC
PETTY LARCENY SS SAT 58 08
RULE OF THE DOOR AND OTHER FANCIFUL REGULATIONS
BIGGLE, LLOYD JR. AC
ROUND TRIP TO ESIDARAP (ESIDARAP OT PIRT DNUOR) SS IFS 60 11
GALAXY OF STRANGERS, A BIGGLE, LLOYD JR. AC
OUT OF THIS WORLD 3 WILLIAMS-ELLIS& OWEN AN
RULE OF THE DOOR, THE NV GAL 58 02
RULE OF THE DOOR AND OTHER FANCIFUL REGULATIONS
BIGGLE, LLOYD JR. AC
SECRET WEAPON (BRIDLE SHOWER) NV GAL 58 05
RULE OF THE DOOR AND OTHER FANCIFUL REGULATIONS
BIGGLE, LLOYD JR. AC
SLIGHT CASE OF LIMBO, A SS ASF 63 04
RULE OF THE DOOR AND OTHER FANCIFUL REGULATIONS
BIGGLE, LLOYD JR. AC
9TH ANNUAL OF THE YEAR'S BEST S-F, THE MERRIL, JUDITH AN
SPARE THE ROD NV GAL 58 03
METALLIC MUSE, THE BIGGLE, LLOYD JR. AC
TUNESMITH, THE NV IFS 57 08
BEST SCIENCE FICTION STORIES AND NOVELS: 9TH SERIES
DIKTY, T. E. AN
METALLIC MUSE, THE BIGGLE, LLOYD JR. AC
WELL OF THE DEEP WISH NV IFS 61 03
METALLIC MUSE, THE BIGGLE, LLOYD JR. AC
WHAT HATH GOD WROUGHT| NV STG 74
GALAXY OF STRANGERS, A BIGGLE, LLOYD JR. AC
STRANGE GODS ELWOOD, ROGER OA
WHO'S ON FIRST? NV IFS 58 08
GALAXY OF STRANGERS, A BIGGLE, LLOYD JR. AC
WINGS OF SONG SS FSF 63 11
RULE OF THE DOOR AND OTHER FANCIFUL REGULATIONS
BIGGLE, LLOYD JR. AC

BILENKIN, DMITRY
AIR OF MARS, THE SS 69
AIR OF MARS AND OTHER STORIES, THE GINSBURG, MIRRA AN

BILKER, AUDREY L.
ALL YOU CAN EAT NV C COI 73
CHILDREN OF INFINITY ELWOOD, ROGER OA
APARTMENT HUNTING SS C FUC 73
FUTURE CITY ELWOOD, ROGER OA
EPILOGUE: THE FUTURE OF SCIENCE FICTION MS C
LONG NIGHT OF WAITING AND OTHER STORIES
ELWOOD, ROGER OA
THEN YOU CAN DO WHAT YOU WANT SS C
LEARNING MAZE AND OTHER STORIES, THE ELWOOD, ROGER OA

BILKER, HARVEY L.
ALL YOU CAN EAT NV C COI 73
CHILDREN OF INFINITY ELWOOD, ROGER OA
APARTMENT HUNTING SS C FUC 73
FUTURE CITY ELWOOD, ROGER OA
EPILOGUE: THE FUTURE OF SCIENCE FICTION MS C
LONG NIGHT OF WAITING AND OTHER STORIES
ELWOOD, ROGER OA
GENETIC FAUX PAS SS RLS 65 03
STRANGE BED FELLOWS SCORTIA, THOMAS N. AN
THEN YOU CAN DO WHAT YOU WANT SS C
LEARNING MAZE AND OTHER STORIES, THE ELWOOD, ROGER OA

BINDER, EANDO   BLACK, D. M.

BINDER, EANDO   PSEUD. FOR
    EARL AND OTTO BINDER (MOST STORIES AFTER 1940 BY OTTO ONLY)
ADAM LINK- ROBOT   AC PBK 65 09
ANTON YORK, IMMORTAL   AC BEL 65
  ADAM LINK IN BUSINESS   SS AMZ 40 01
    ADAM LINK- ROBOT   BINDER, EANDO   AC
  ADAM LINK SAVES THE WORLD   SS AMZ 42 04
    ADAM LINK- ROBOT   BINDER, EANDO   AC
  ADAM LINK'S VENGEANCE   NV AMZ 40 02
    ADAM LINK- ROBOT   BINDER, EANDO   AC
    OTHER WORLDS, THE   STONG, PHILIP D.   AN
  ADAM LINK, CHAMPION ATHLETE   SS AMZ 40 07
    ADAM LINK- ROBOT   BINDER, EANDO   AC
  ADAM LINK, ROBOT DETECTIVE   SS AMZ 40 05
    ADAM LINK- ROBOT   BINDER, EANDO   AC
ALL IN GOOD TIME   SS SAW 72
    SIGNS AND WONDERS   ELWOOD, ROGER   OA
ANY RESEMBLANCE TO MAGIC   SS
    LONG NIGHT OF WAITING AND OTHER STORIES
                                 ELWOOD, ROGER   OA
BETTER DUMB THAN DEAD   SS
    JOURNEY TO ANOTHER STAR AND OTHER STORIES
                                 ELWOOD, ROGER   OA
CONQUEST OF LIFE   SS TWS 37 08
    ANTON YORK, IMMORTAL   BINDER, EANDO   AC
    FROM OFF THIS WORLD   MARGULIES & FRIEND   AN
I, ROBOT   SS AMZ 39 01
    ADAM LINK- ROBOT   BINDER, EANDO   AC
    COMING OF THE ROBOTS, THE   MOSKOWITZ, SAM   AN
    EDITOR'S CHOICE IN SCIENCE FICTION MOSKOWITZ, SAM AN
IRON MAN   SS FUT 55 28
    WEIRD ONES, THE   HOWARD, IVAN   AN
LIFE ETERNAL   NV TWS 38 02
    ANTON YORK, IMMORTAL   BINDER, EANDO   AC
MISSING WORLD, THE   SS
    MISSING WORLD AND OTHER STORIES, THE ELWOOD, ROGER OA
SECRET OF ANTON YORK, THE   NV TWS 40 08
    ANTON YORK, IMMORTAL   BINDER, EANDO   AC
SON OF THE STARS   SS FFM 40 02
    ANDROIDS, TIME MACHINES AND BLUE GIRAFFES
                                 ELWOOD & GHIDALIA   AN
TEACHER FROM MARS, THE   SS TWS 41 02
    *MY BEST SCIENCE FICTION STORY MARGULIES & FRIEND AN
THREE ETERNALS, THE   NV TWS 39 12
    ANTON YORK, IMMORTAL   BINDER, EANDO   AC
TRIAL OF ADAM LINK, THE   SS AMZ 39 07
    ADAM LINK- ROBOT   BINDER, EANDO   AC
VIA ASTEROID   SS TWS 38 02
    EXPLORING OTHER WORLDS   MOSKOWITZ, SAM   AN
VIA DEATH   SS TWS 38 08
    GREAT SCIENCE FICTION STORIES ABOUT THE MOON
                                 DIKTY, T. E.   AN
VIA ETHERLINE   SS TWS 37 10
    GREAT SCIENCE FICTION STORIES ABOUT MARS
                                 DIKTY, T. E.   AN
WHY I SELECTED THE TEACHER FROM MARS   AI
    *MY BEST SCIENCE FICTION STORY MARGULIES & FRIEND AN

BINDER, EARL   SEE PSEUD.
    EANDO BINDER AND JOHN COLERIDGE (BOTH WITH OTTO BINDER)

BINDER, OTTO   SEE PSEUD.
    EANDO BINDER AND JOHN COLERIDGE (BOTH WITH EARL BINDER)

BING, JON
    WHITER SHADE OF PALE, A   SS   74
    BEST FROM THE REST OF THE WORLD, THE WOLLHEIM, DONALD A. AN

BIRCH, A. G.
    MOON TERROR, THE   AN H PFP 27
    MOON TERROR, THE   NA WRT 23 05
    MOON TERROR, THE   BIRCH, A. G.   AN

BIRD, CHRISTOPHER
    LOVE AMONG THE CABBAGES   AR C HRP 72 11
    SCIENCE FACT/FICTION   FARRELL/GAGE/&   AN

BIRD, CORDWAINER PSEUD. FOR HARLAN ELLISON

BIRELEY, RICHARD
    BINARY JUSTICE   SS ORB 75 16
    ORBIT 16   KNIGHT, DAMON   OA
    NOT A PETAL FALLS   SS NOV 74 04
    NOVA 4   HARRISON, HARRY   OA

BIRKIN, CHARLES
    NO MORE FOR MARY   SS   66
    TALES OF TERROR FROM OUTER SPACE CHETWYND-HAYES, R. AN

BIRLEY, JULIA
    RAINS OF ALPHA ALEPH, THE   SS ADS 75 01
    ARMADA SCI-FI ONE   DAVIS, RICHARD   OA

BISCHOFF, DAVE
    HEAVY METAL   SS
    FUTURE PASTIMES   EDELSTEIN, SCOTT   OA

BISCHOFF, DAVID
    QUEST   OA H RTR 77
    STRANGE ENCOUNTERS   OA H RTR 77

BISHOP, GERALD
    BIBLIOGRAPHY   MS
    BEST OF ISAAC ASIMOV, THE   ASIMOV, ISAAC   AC
    BEST OF JOHN WYNDHAM, THE   WYNDHAM, JOHN   AC

BISHOP, H. G.
    CONGEALING THE ICE TRUST   SS NBM 07 12
    SCIENCE FICTION BY GASLIGHT MOSKOWITZ, SAM   AN

BISHOP, MICHAEL
    ALLEGIANCES   NA GAL 75 02
    BEST FROM GALAXY, THE VOLUME IV BAEN, JAMES   AN
    1976 ANNUAL WORLD'S BEST SF, THE WOLLHEIM, DONALD A. AN
    BLOODED ON ARACHNE   NV EPC 75
    EPOCH   ELWOOD & SILVERBERG   OA
    CATHADONIAN ODYSSEY   SS FSF 74 09
    1975 ANNUAL WORLD'S BEST SF, THE WOLLHEIM, DONALD A. AN
    CONTRIBUTORS TO PLENUM FOUR, THE   SS NDM 75 05
    NEW DIMENSIONS 5   SILVERBERG, ROBERT   OA
    DEATH AND DESIGNATION AMONG THE ASADI   NA IFS 73 02
    BEST FROM IF, THE VOLUME II IF, EDITORS OF   AN
    1974 ANNUAL WORLD'S BEST SF, THE WOLLHEIM, DONALD A. AN
    IN CHINISTREX FORTRONZA THE PEOPLE ARE MACHINES SS
    NEW CONSTELLATIONS   DISCH & NAYLOR   OA
    IN THE LILLIPUTIAN ASYLUM: A STORY IN 8 POEMS AND AN
    INTRODUCTION   PM ORB 74 15
    ORBIT 15   KNIGHT, DAMON   OA
    ON THE STREET OF SERPENTS,OR THE ASSASSINATION OF CHAIRMAN MAO
    AS EFFECTED BY THE AUTHOR   NV SFE 74 01
    SCIENCE FICTION EMPHASIS NO. 1 GERROLD, DAVID   OA
    ROGUE TOMATO   SS NDM 75 05
    NEW DIMENSIONS 5   SILVERBERG, ROBERT   OA
    SAMURAI AND THE WILLOWS, THE   NV FSF 76 02
    BEST SCIENCE FICTION STORIES OF THE YEAR (1976)
                                 DOZOIS, GARDNER R.   AN
    WINDOWS IN DANTE'S HELL, THE   SS ORB 73 12
    BEST SF: 1973   HARRISON & ALDISS   AN
    ORBIT 12   KNIGHT, DAMON   OA

BISHOP, MORRIS
    E=MC2   PM NYM 46
    MATHEMATICAL MAGPIE, THE   FADIMAN, CLIFTON   AN
    SPECULATIONS   SANDERS, THOMAS E.   AN

BISHOP, ZEALIA BROWN
    CURSE OF YIG, THE   SS WRT 29 11
    SECOND AVON FANTASY READER, THE WOLLHEIM &ERNSBERGER AN

BIXBY, DREXEL J.   SEE PSEUD. JEROME BIXBY

BIXBY, JEROME   PSEUD. FOR DREXEL J. BIXBY
    SPACE BY THE TAIL   AC BAL 64
    ANGELS IN THE JETS   SS FAN 52 FL
    ASSIGNMENT IN TOMORROW   POHL, FREDERIK   AN
    BEST FROM FANTASTIC, THE   WHITE, TED   AN
    SPACE BY THE TAIL   BIXBY, JEROME   AC
    BAD LIFE, THE   NA GAL 63 02
    SPACE BY THE TAIL   BIXBY, JEROME   AC
    BATTLE OF THE BELLS, THE   SS IMG 54 09
    SPACE BY THE TAIL   BIXBY, JEROME   AC
    CAN SUCH BEAUTY BE?   SS BEY 53 09
    BEYOND   ANONYMOUS   AN
    DRAW, THE   SS AMZ 54 03
    SPACE BY THE TAIL   BIXBY, JEROME   AC
    GOOD DOG, THE   SS FAN 54 02
    SPACE BY THE TAIL   BIXBY, JEROME   AC
    HOLES AROUND MARS, THE   SS GAL 54 01
    DECADE THE 1950S   ALDISS & HARRISON   AN
    GREAT STORIES OF SPACE TRAVEL CONKLIN, GROFF   AN
    OPERATION FUTURE   CONKLIN, GROFF   AN
    WHERE DO WE GO FROM HERE?   ASIMOV, ISAAC   AN
    IT'S A GOOD LIFE   SS STR 53 02
    BEST SF 4   CRISPIN, EDMUND   AN
    IN DREAMS AWAKE   FIEDLER, LESLIE A.   AN
    INTRODUCING SCIENCE FICTION ALDISS, BRIAN W.   AN
    MASTERS' CHOICE   JANIFER, LAURENCE M. AN
    MUTANTS   SILVERBERG, ROBERT   AN
    SCIENCE FICTION HALL OF FAME VOLUME 1 SILVERBERG, ROBERT AN
    SPECULATIONS   SANDERS, THOMAS E.   AN
    STAR OF STARS   POHL, FREDERIK   AN
    STAR SCIENCE FICTION STORIES NO. 2 POHL, FREDERIK OA
    TOMORROW'S CHILDREN   ASIMOV, ISAAC   AN
    LABORATORY   NV IFS 55 12
    FIRST WORLD OF IF, THE   QUINN & WULFF   AN
    SPACE BY THE TAIL   BIXBY, JEROME   AC
    MAGIC TYPEWRITER, THE   SS   63
    SPACE BY THE TAIL   BIXBY, JEROME   AC
    OLD TESTAMENT   SS IFS 64 07
    IF READER OF SCIENCE FICTION, THE POHL, FREDERIK AN
    ONE WAY STREET   SS AMZ 54 01
    BEST SCIENCE FICTION STORIES AND NOVELS: 1955
                                 DIKTY, T. E.   AN
    SPACE BY THE TAIL   BIXBY, JEROME   AC
    PAGE AND PLAYER   NV STS 52 08
    SPACE PIONEERS   NORTON, ANDRE   AN
    SHARE ALIKE   SS C BEY 53 07
    GALAXY OF GHOULS   MERRIL, JUDITH   AN
    ZACHERLEY'S MIDNIGHT SNACKS ZACHERLEY   AN
    SMALL WAR   SS SFQ 54 05
    SPACE BY THE TAIL   BIXBY, JEROME   AC
    TRACE   SS   61
    SPACE BY THE TAIL   BIXBY, JEROME   AC
    YOUNG ONE, THE   NV FAN 54 05
    SPACE BY THE TAIL   BIXBY, JEROME   AC
    ZEN   SS GAL 52 10
    CROSSROADS IN TIME   CONKLIN, GROFF   AN

BLACK, D. M.
    BASILISK, THE   PM   69
    HOLDING YOUR EIGHT HANDS   LUCIE-SMITH, EDWARD   AN

BLACK, D. M.   (CONTINUED)
  MY SPECIES   PM   67
    HOLDING YOUR EIGHT HANDS   LUCIE-SMITH, EDWARD AN

BLACKIE, J.
  SPACE PILOT, THE   PM
    STARLIT CORRIDOR, THE   MANSFIELD, ROGER   AN

BLACKWOOD, ALGERNON
  EGYPTIAN HORNET, AN   SS   17
    BR-R-R-| CONKLIN, GROFF   AN
  ELSEWHERE AND OTHERWISE   SS   36
    TRAVELERS IN TIME   STERN, PHILIP VAN D. AN
  OLD CLOTHES   NV   17
    LITTLE MONSTERS, THE   ELWOOD & GHIDALIA   AN
  OTHER WING, THE   SS APR 48 08
    DEVIL'S GENERATION, THE   GHIDALIA, VIC   AN
  TRANSFER, THE   SS   12
    MORE LITTLE MONSTERS   ELWOOD & GHIDALIA   AN
  VICTIM OF HIGHER SPACE, A (1917)   NV APR 52 18
    AVON FANTASY READER, THE   WOLLHEIM &ERNSBERGER AN
  WENDIGO, THE (1910)   NV FFM 44 06
    BEWARE THE BEASTS   GHIDALIA, V.& ELWOOD AN

BLAIR, ERIC   SEE PSEUD. GEORGE ORWELL

BLAKE, E. MICHAEL
  FOREIGNER, THE   SS INY 72 04
    INFINITY 4   HOSKINS, ROBERT   OA
  GOAL TENDING   NV   75
    RUN TO STARLIGHT, SPORTS THROUGH SCIENCE FICTION
                                   GREENBERG/OLANDER/& AN
  LEGEND OF LONNIE AND THE SEVEN TEN SPLIT, THE NV ALT 74
    ALTERNATES   GERROLD, DAVID   OA
  TRANSLATOR, THE   SS
    MIND ANGEL AND OTHER STORIES, THE ELWOOD, ROGER   OA

BLAND, FREDERICK
  FIFTEENTH WIND OF MARCH, THE   NV FSF 62 06
    ONCE AND FUTURE TALES FROM THE MAGAZINE OF FANTASY AND
    SCIENCE FICTION   FERMAN, EDWARD L.   AN

BLAUSTEIN, ALBERT P. SEE PSEUD. ALLEN DEGRAEFF

BLEILER, EVERETT F. AND T. E. DIKTY
  BEST SCIENCE FICTION STORIES: FIFTH SERIES, THE AN H GRY 56
    SEE "THE BEST SCIENCE-FICTION STORIES: 1954",
    OMITS STORIES BY LEIBER (2), MCINTOSH AND BESTER,
    "CRUCIFIXUS ETIAM" LISTED AS "THE SOWER DOES NOT REAP"
  BEST SCIENCE FICTION STORIES: FOURTH SERIES, THE AN H GRY 55
    SEE "THE BEST SCIENCE-FICTION STORIES: 1953", OMITS
    "THE FLY" AND "LOVER, WHEN YOU'RE NEAR ME"
  BEST SCIENCE FICTION STORIES: SECOND SERIES, THE AN H GRY 52
    SEE "THE BEST SCIENCE-FICTION STORIES: 1951", OMITS STORIES BY
    TEMPLE, BESTER, HARNESS AND LEIBER
  BEST SCIENCE FICTION STORIES: THIRD SERIES, THE AN H GRY 53
    SEE "THE BEST SCIENCE-FICTION STORIES: 1952", OMITS
    "DARK INTERLUDE" AND "THE PEDESTRIAN"
  BEST SCIENCE FICTION STORIES, THE   AN H GRY 51
    SEE "THE BEST SCIENCE-FICTION STORIES: 1950", OMITS STORIES BY
    STURGEON, KREPPS, BRADBURY (2) AND MACDONALD
  BEST SCIENCE-FICTION STORIES: 1949, THE   AN H FEL 49 08
    ALSO IN "SCIENCE FICTION OMNIBUS"
  BEST SCIENCE-FICTION STORIES: 1950, THE   AN H FEL 50 08
    ALSO IN "SCIENCE FICTION OMNIBUS"
    IN ENGLAND AS "THE BEST SCIENCE FICTION STORIES"
  BEST SCIENCE-FICTION STORIES: 1951, THE   AN H FEL 51
    IN ENGLAND AS
    "THE BEST SCIENCE FICTION STORIES: SECOND SERIES"
  BEST SCIENCE-FICTION STORIES: 1952, THE   AN H FEL 52
    IN ENGLAND AS "THE BEST SCIENCE FICTION STORIES: THIRD SERIES"
  BEST SCIENCE-FICTION STORIES: 1953, THE   AN H FEL 53
    IN ENGLAND AS
    "THE BEST SCIENCE FICTION STORIES: FOURTH SERIES"
  BEST SCIENCE-FICTION STORIES: 1954, THE   AN H FEL 54
    IN ENGLAND AS "THE BEST SCIENCE FICTION STORIES: FIFTH SERIES"
  CATEGORY PHOENIX   AN H BDL 55
    SEE "YEAR'S BEST SCIENCE FICTION NOVELS: 1953"
    OMITS "THE GADGET HAD A GHOST" AND "CONDITIONALLY HUMAN"
  FRONTIERS IN SPACE   AN BAN 55 04
    SELECTIONS FROM "THE BEST SCIENCE FICTION STORIES 1951-1953"
  IMAGINATION UNLIMITED   AN H FSY 52
    ALSO AS "MEN OF SPACE AND TIME"
  IMAGINATION UNLIMITED (BRITISH)   AN H BDL 53
    FIRST 6 STORIES OF AMERICAN VERSION, REMAINDER IN
    "MEN OF SPACE AND TIME"
  IMAGINATION UNLIMITED (7 OF 13)   AN BRK 59 04
  MEN OF SPACE AND TIME   AN H LNE 53
    LAST SEVEN STORIES FROM "IMAGINATION UNLIMITED"
  SCIENCE FICTION OMNIBUS   AN H GCB 52 01
  YEAR'S BEST SCIENCE FICTION NOVELS: SECOND SERIES, THE
                                               AN H GRY 55
    SEE "YEAR'S BEST SCIENCE FICTION NOVELS: 1954"
    OMITS "SECOND VARIETY"
  YEAR'S BEST SCIENCE FICTION NOVELS: 1952   AN H FEL 52
    IN ENGLAND AS "THE YEAR'S BEST SCIENCE FICTION NOVELS"
  YEAR'S BEST SCIENCE FICTION NOVELS: 1953   AN H FEL 53 03
    IN ENGLAND AS "CATEGORY PHOENIX"
  YEAR'S BEST SCIENCE FICTION NOVELS: 1954   AN H FEL 54 03
    IN ENGLAND AS
    "THE YEAR'S BEST SCIENCE FICTION NOVELS: SECOND SERIES
  YEAR'S BEST SCIENCE FICTION NOVELS, THE   AN H GRY 54
    SEE "YEAR'S BEST SCIENCE FICTION NOVELS: 1952"
    OMITS "SEEKER OF THE SPHINX"
  BEST SCIENCE-FICTION STORIES: 1949, THE   AN FEL 49 08
    SCIENCE FICTION OMNIBUS   BLEILER & DIKTY   AN

BLEILER & DIKTY   (CONTINUED)
  BEST SCIENCE-FICTION STORIES: 1950, THE   AN FEL 50 08
    SCIENCE FICTION OMNIBUS   BLEILER & DIKTY   AN

BLEILER, EVERETT F.
  EDITORS' PREFACE   IN C
    BEST SCIENCE-FICTION STORIES: 1954, THE
                                     BLEILER & DIKTY   AN
  INTRODUCTION   IN C
    *IMAGINATION UNLIMITED   BLEILER & DIKTY   AN
    YEAR'S BEST SCIENCE FICTION NOVELS: 1953
                                     BLEILER & DIKTY   AN
    YEAR'S BEST SCIENCE FICTION NOVELS: 1954
                                     BLEILER & DIKTY   AN
  INTRODUCTION TO THE DOVER EDITION   IN
    3 PROPHETIC SCIENCE FICTION NOVELS OF H. G. WELLS
                                     WELLS, H. G.   AC

BLISH, JAMES AND NORMAN L. KNIGHT
  TORRENT OF FACES, A   NO H DBL 67

BLISH, JAMES
  ANYWHEN   AC H DBL 70
  ANYWHEN (ENGLISH EDITION ADDS:)   AC H FAB 71
  BEST SCIENCE FICTION STORIES OF JAMES BLISH AC H FAB 65
  BEST SCIENCE FICTION STORIES OF JAMES BLISH (REVISED)
                                               AC H FAB 73
  CITIES IN FLIGHT   AC AVN 70 02
  EARTHMAN, COME HOME   NO H PUT 55
  GALACTIC CLUSTER   AC SIG 59
  GALACTIC CLUSTER (BRITISH PB)   AC FPS 63
  GALACTIC CLUSTER (BRITISH)   AC H FAB 60
  MIDSUMMER CENTURY   AC DAW 74 02
  NEBULA AWARD STORIES NO. 5   AN H DBL 70 12
  NEW DREAMS THIS MORNING   AN BAL 66 10
  SEEDLING STARS, THE   NO H GNM 56
  SO CLOSE TO HOME   AC BAL 61 02
  STAR TREK   OC BAN 67
    ALSO IN "THE STAR TREK READER II"
  STAR TREK   2   OC BAN 68
    ALSO IN "THE STAR TREK READER"
  STAR TREK   3   OC BAN 69 04
    ALSO IN "THE STAR TREK READER"
  STAR TREK   4   OC BAN 71 07
    ALSO IN "THE STAR TREK READER II"
  STAR TREK   5   OC BAN 72 02
  STAR TREK   6   OC BAN 72 04
  STAR TREK   7   OC BAN 72 07
  STAR TREK   8   OC BAN 72 11
    ALSO IN "THE STAR TREK READER"
  STAR TREK   9   OC BAN 73 08
    ALSO IN "THE STAR TREK READER II"
  STAR TREK 10   OC BAN 74 02
  STAR TREK 11   OC BAN 75 04
  STAR TREK READER II, THE   AC H DUT 77
  STAR TREK READER, THE   AC H DUT 76
  THIRTEEN O'CLOCK AND OTHER ZERO HOURS (LISTED UNDER
    C. M. KORNBLUTH)   EC DEL 70
  YEAR 2018| NO AVN 57
    IN ENGLAND AS "THEY SHALL HAVE STARS"
  ABATTOIR EFFECT, THE   SS NEW 61 AC
    SO CLOSE TO HOME   BLISH, JAMES   AC
  ALL OUR YESTERDAYS (JEAN LISETTE AROESTE)   SA STK 71 04
    STAR TREK   4   BLISH, JAMES   OC
  ALTERNATIVE FACTOR, THE (DON INGALLS)   SA STK 74 10
    STAR TREK 10   BLISH, JAMES   OC
  AMOK TIME (THEODORE STURGEON)   SA STK 69 03
    STAR TREK   3   BLISH, JAMES   OC
  AND SOME WERE SAVAGES   NV AMZ 60 11
    ANYWHEN   BLISH, JAMES   AC
  APPLE, THE (MAX EHRLICH & GENE L. COON)   SA STK 72 06
    STAR TREK   6   BLISH, JAMES   OC
  ARENA (GENE L. COON)   SA STK 68 02
    STAR TREK   2   BLISH, JAMES   OC
  ART-WORK (SEE A WORK OF ART)   TC
  ASSIGNMENT: EARTH (GENE RODDENBERRY & ART WALLACE)
                                               SA STK 69 03
    STAR TREK   3   BLISH, JAMES   OC
  AT DEATH'S END   NV ASF 54 05
    YEAR 2018| BLISH, JAMES   NO
  BALANCE OF TERROR (PAUL SCHNEIDER)   SA STK 67 01
    STAR TREK   BLISH, JAMES   OC
  BATTLE OF THE UNBORN (ALSO AS STRUGGLE IN THE WOMB)
                                               SS FUT 50 05
    *SCIENCE FICTION ADVENTURES IN MUTATION CONKLIN, GROFF AN
  BEANSTALK   NA NEW 52 AN
    *FUTURE TENSE   CROSSEN, KENDELL F. AN
  BEEP   NV GAL 54 02
    *GALACTIC CLUSTER   BLISH, JAMES   AC
    GALACTIC EMPIRES VOLUME TWO   ALDISS, BRIAN W.   AN
    SPACE POLICE   NORTON, ANDRE   AN
    *STORIES FOR TOMORROW   SLOANE, WILLIAM   AN
  BINDLESTIFF   NV ASF 50 12
    EARTHMAN, COME HOME   BLISH, JAMES   NO
  BOX, THE   SS TWS 49 04
    BEYOND CONTROL   SILVERBERG, ROBERT AN
    OMNIBUS OF SCIENCE FICTION   CONKLIN, GROFF   AN
    SHAPE OF THINGS, THE   KNIGHT, DAMON   AN
    SO CLOSE TO HOME   BLISH, JAMES   AC
    STRANGE ADVENTURES IN SCIENCE FICTION CONKLIN, GROFF AN
  BREAD AND CIRCUSES (GENE RODDENBERRY & G. L. COON)
                                               SA STK 75 11
    STAR TREK 11   BLISH, JAMES   OC
  BRIDGE   NV ASF 52 02
    ASTOUNDING-ANALOG READER, THE VOLUME TWO
                                   HARRISON & ALDISS   AN

BLISH, JAMES   BLISH, JAMES

BLISH, JAMES   (CONTINUED)
  JUPITER   POHL, C. & F.   AN
  SPECTRUM 2   AMIS & CONQUEST   AN
  YEAR 2018!   BLISH, JAMES   NO
BY ANY OTHER NAME (D. C. FONTANA & JEROME BIXBY) SA   STK 72 06
  STAR TREK 6   BLISH, JAMES   OC
CASE OF CONSCIENCE, A   SN   IFS 53 09
  BEST SF   CRISPIN, EDMUND   AN
CATSPAW (ROBERT BLOCH)   SA   STK 72 08
  STAR TREK 8   BLISH, JAMES   OC
CHANGELING, THE (JOHN MEREDYTH LUCAS)   SA   STK 72 07
  STAR TREK 7   BLISH, JAMES   OC
CHARLIE X (SEE CHARLIE'S LAW)   TC
CHARLIE'S LAW (CHARLIE X, FONTANA & RODDENBERRY) SA   STK 67 01
  STAR TREK   BLISH, JAMES   OC
CHRONOLOGY OF CITIES IN FLIGHT   MS
  YEAR 2018!   BLISH, JAMES   NO
CITY ON THE EDGE OF FOREVER, THE (HARLAN ELLISON) SA   STK 68 02
  STAR TREK 2   BLISH, JAMES   OC
CLASH OF CYMBALS, A (SEE THE TRIUMPH OF TIME)   TC
CLOUD MINERS, THE (ARMEN, GERROLD & CRAWFORD)   SA   STK 72 06
  STAR TREK 6   BLISH, JAMES   OC
COMMON TIME   SS   SFQ 53 08
  *BEST SCIENCE FICTION STORIES OF JAMES BLISH
                                          BLISH, JAMES   AC
  *GALACTIC CLUSTER   BLISH, JAMES   AC
  MIRROR OF INFINITY, THE   SILVERBERG, ROBERT   AN
  SECOND ORBIT   DOHERTY, G. D.   AN
  SHADOW OF TOMORROW   POHL, FREDERICK   AN
  SURVIVAL PRINTOUT   TOTAL EFFECT   AN
  TO THE STARS   SILVERBERG, ROBERT   AN
  YET MORE PENGUIN SCIENCE FICTION   ALDISS, BRIAN W.   AN
CONSCIENCE OF THE KING, THE (BARRY TRIVERS)   SA   STK 67 01
  STAR TREK   BLISH, JAMES   OC
COURT MARTIAL (D. M. MANKIEWICZ & S. CARABATSOS) SA   STK 68 02
  STAR TREK 2   BLISH, JAMES   OC
CREDO   IN
  BEST SF: 1967   HARRISON & ALDISS   AN
DAGGER OF THE MIND (S. BAR-DAVID)   SA   STK 67 01
  STAR TREK   BLISH, JAMES   OC
DARK NIGHT OF THE SOUL, THE (GENIUS HEAP)   SS   GAL 56 08
  NEW DREAMS THIS MORNING   BLISH, JAMES   AN
DARKSIDE CROSSING   NV   GAL 70 12
  BEST FROM GALAXY, THE VOLUME I   GALAXY, EDITORS OF   AN
DAY OF THE DOVE (JEROME BIXBY)   SA   STK 75 11
  STAR TREK 11   BLISH, JAMES   OC
DEADLY YEARS, THE (DAVID P. HARMON)   SA   STK 72 07
  STAR TREK 7   BLISH, JAMES   OC
DEVIL IN THE DARK, THE (GENE L. COON)   SA   STK 71 04
  STAR TREK 4   BLISH, JAMES   OC
DOOMSDAY MACHINE, THE (NORMAN SPINRAD)   SA   STK 69 03
  STAR TREK 3   BLISH, JAMES   OC
DUSK OF IDOLS, A   NV   AMZ 61 03
  ANYWHEN   BLISH, JAMES   AC
EARTHMAN, COME HOME   NO   PUT 55
  CITIES IN FLIGHT   BLISH, JAMES   AC
EARTHMAN, COME HOME   NV   ASF 53 11
  EARTHMAN, COME HOME   BLISH, JAMES   NO
  SCIENCE FICTION HALL OF FAME VOLUME 2B BOVA, BEN   AN
ELAAN OF TROYIUS (JOHN MEREDYTH LUCAS)   SA   STK 72 07
  STAR TREK 7   BLISH, JAMES   OC
EMPATH, THE (JOYCE MUSKAT)   SA   STK 74 10
  STAR TREK 10   BLISH, JAMES   OC
ENEMY WITHIN, THE (RICHARD MATHESON)   SA   STK 72 08
  STAR TREK 8   BLISH, JAMES   OC
ENTERPRISE INCIDENT, THE (D. C. FONTANA)   SA   STK 71 04
  STAR TREK 4   BLISH, JAMES   OC
EPIGRAPH (FROM "THE SCIENCE IN SCIENCE FICTION")   EX   VCT 75 SU
  FASTER THAN LIGHT   DANN & ZEBROWSKI   OA
ERRAND OF MERCY (GENE L. COON)   SA   STK 68 02
  STAR TREK 2   BLISH, JAMES   OC
F Y I   SS   STR 53 02
  BEYOND THIS HORIZON   CARRELL, CHRISTOPHER   OA
  MATHEMATICAL MAGPIE, THE   FADIMAN, CLIFTON   AN
  SO CLOSE TO HOME   BLISH, JAMES   AC
  STAR SCIENCE FICTION STORIES NO. 2   POHL, FREDERIK   OA
FIRST STRIKE   SS   FSF 53 06
  SO CLOSE TO HOME   BLISH, JAMES   AC
FOR THE WORLD IS HOLLOW AND I HAVE TOUCHED THE SKY
  (RIK VOLLAERTS)   SA   STK 72 08
  STAR TREK 8   BLISH, JAMES   OC
FOREWORD TO "PRIVATE EYE"   IN
  MIRROR OF INFINITY, THE   SILVERBERG, ROBERT   AN
FRIDAY'S CHILD (D. C. FONTANA)   SA   STK 69 03
  STAR TREK 3   BLISH, JAMES   OC
GALILEO SEVEN, THE (S. WINCELBERG & O. CRAWFORD) SA   STK 74 10
  STAR TREK 10   BLISH, JAMES   OC
GENIUS HEAP, THE (ALSO AS THE DARK NIGHT OF THE SOUL)
                                                   SS   GAL 56 08
  SIXTH GALAXY READER, THE   GOLD, H. L.   AN
GET OUT OF MY SKY   SN   ASF 57 01
  GET OUT OF MY SKY   MARGULIES, LEO   AN
GETTING ALONG   NV C   DVS 72 02
  AGAIN, DANGEROUS VISIONS   ELLISON, HARLAN   OA
GLITCH, THE   NV C   GAL 74 06
  ANTIGRAV: COSMIC COMEDIES   STRICK, PHILIP   AN
  BEST FROM GALAXY, THE VOLUME III   BAEN, JAMES   AN
HERO'S LIFE, A (ALSO AS A STYLE IN TREASON)   NV   IMP 66 03
  FOUR FOR THE FUTURE   HARRISON, HARRY   AN
HOW BEAUTIFUL WITH BANNERS   SS   ORB 66 01
  ANYWHEN   BLISH, JAMES   AC
  BEST SCIENCE FICTION STORIES OF JAMES BLISH (REVISED)
                                          BLISH, JAMES   AC
  LATE GREAT FUTURE, THE   FITZ GERALD & DILLON   AN
  ORBIT 1   KNIGHT, DAMON   OA
  SCIENCE FICTION ROLL OF HONOR, THE   POHL, FREDERICK   AN

BLISH, JAMES   (CONTINUED)
IMMUNITY SYNDROME, THE (ROBERT SABAROFF)   SA   STK 73 09
  STAR TREK 9   BLISH, JAMES   OC
IN MEMORIAM: FLETCHER PRATT   PM   FSF 57 01
  BEST FROM FANTASY AND SCIENCE FICTION: 7
                                          BOUCHER, ANTHONY   AN
IN TOMORROW'S LITTLE BLACK BAG   AR
  7TH ANNUAL OF THE YEAR'S BEST S-F, THE MERRIL, JUDITH   AN
INTRODUCTION   IN
  BEST OF JOHN W. CAMPBELL, THE (BRITISH)
                                          CAMPBELL, JOHN W. JR   AC
  NEBULA AWARD STORIES NO. 5   BLISH, JAMES   AN
INTRODUCTION- THE FUNCTION OF SCIENCE FICTION   IN
  LIGHT FANTASTIC, THE   HARRISON, HARRY   AN
IS THERE NO TRUTH IN BEAUTY? (JEAN LISETTE AROESTE)
                                                   SA   STK 74 10
  STAR TREK 10   BLISH, JAMES   OC
JOURNEY TO BABEL (D. C. FONTANA)   SA   STK 71 04
  STAR TREK 4   BLISH, JAMES   OC
KING OF THE HILL   SS   INF 55 11
  *GALACTIC CLUSTER   BLISH, JAMES   AC
LAST GUNFIGHT, THE (LEE CRONIN)   SA   STK 69 03
  STAR TREK 3   BLISH, JAMES   OC
LET THAT BE YOUR LAST BATTLEFIELD (CRAWFORD & CRONIN)
                                                   SA   STK 72 05
  STAR TREK 5   BLISH, JAMES   OC
LIFE FOR THE STARS, A   NO   ASF 62 09
  CITIES IN FLIGHT   BLISH, JAMES   AC
LIGHTS OF ZETAR, THE (JEREMY TARCHER & SHARI LEWIS)
                                                   SA   STK 72 06
  STAR TREK 6   BLISH, JAMES   OC
MAN TRAP, THE (SEE THE UNREAL MCCOY)   TC
MARK OF GIDEON, THE (G. F. SLAVIN & S. ADAMS)   SA   STK 72 06
  STAR TREK 6   BLISH, JAMES   OC
MASKS, THE   SS   FSF 59 11
  SO CLOSE TO HOME   BLISH, JAMES   AC
MATTER OF ENERGY, A (WITH MALICE TO COME)   SS   FSF 55 05
  BEST FROM FANTASY AND SCIENCE FICTION: 5
                                          BOUCHER, ANTHONY   AN
MENAGERIE (GENE RODDENBERRY)   SA   STK 71 04
  STAR TREK 4   BLISH, JAMES   OC
METAMORPHOSIS (GENE L. COON)   SA   STK 72 07
  STAR TREK 7   BLISH, JAMES   OC
MIDSUMMER CENTURY   NO   DBL 72
  MIDSUMMER CENTURY   BLISH, JAMES   AC
MIDSUMMER CENTURY   SN   FSF 72 04
  BEST FROM FANTASY AND SCIENCE FICTION, 25TH ANNIV.
                                          FERMAN, EDWARD L.   AN
MIRI (ADRIAN SPIES)   SA   STK 67 01
  STAR TREK   BLISH, JAMES   OC
MIRROR, MIRROR (JEROME BIXBY)   SA   STK 69 03
  STAR TREK 3   BLISH, JAMES   OC
MISTAKE INSIDE   NV   STS 48 03
  DARK SIDE, THE   KNIGHT, DAMON   AN
  WORLD OF WONDER   PRATT, FLETCHER   AN
MORE LIGHT   SS   ANA 70
  ALCHEMY AND ACADEME   MCCAFFREY, ANNE   OA
NAKED TIME, THE (JOHN D. F. BLACK)   SA   STK 67 01
  STAR TREK   BLISH, JAMES   OC
NO JOKES ON MARS   SS   FSF 65 10
  ANYWHEN   BLISH, JAMES   AC
  SPACE 1   DAVIS, RICHARD   OA
NONE SO BLIND (WHO'S IN CHARGE HERE?)   SS   FSF 62 05
  ANYWHEN   BLISH, JAMES   AC
NOR IRON BARS (INCLUDES "DETOUR TO THE STARS" INF 56 12)
                                                   SS   INF 57 11
  *GALACTIC CLUSTER   BLISH, JAMES   AC
OATH, THE   SS   FSF 60 10
  *BEST SCIENCE FICTION STORIES OF JAMES BLISH
                                          BLISH, JAMES   AC
  BEYOND TOMORROW   HARDING, LEE   AN
  SO CLOSE TO HOME   BLISH, JAMES   AC
OBSESSION (ART WALLACE)   SA   STK 73 09
  STAR TREK 9   BLISH, JAMES   OC
OKIE   NV   ASF 50 04
  CITIES OF WONDER   KNIGHT, DAMON   AN
  EARTHMAN, COME HOME   BLISH, JAMES   NO
  *STORIES FOR TOMORROW   SLOANE, WILLIAM   AN
OMEGA GLORY, THE (GENE RODDENBERRY)   SA   STK 74 10
  STAR TREK 10   BLISH, JAMES   OC
ON THE WALL OF THE LODGE   NV C   GAL 62 04
  DARK STARS   SILVERBERG, ROBERT   AN
ONE-SHOT   SS   ASF 55 08
  SO CLOSE TO HOME   BLISH, JAMES   AC
OPERATION- ANNIHILATE! (S. W. CARABATSOS)   SA   STK 68 02
  STAR TREK 2   BLISH, JAMES   OC
PARADISE SYNDROME, THE (MARGARET ARMEN)   SA   STK 72 07
  STAR TREK 7   BLISH, JAMES   OC
PIECE OF THE ACTION, A (D. P. HARMON & G. L. COON)
                                                   SA   STK 71 04
  STAR TREK 4   BLISH, JAMES   OC
PIPER OF DIS, THE   NV C   GAL 66 08
  TORRENT OF FACES, A   BLISH & KNIGHT, N.   NO
PLATO'S STEPCHILDREN (MEYER DOLINSKY)   SA   STK 75 11
  STAR TREK 11   BLISH, JAMES   OC
PREFACE   IN
  ANYWHEN   BLISH, JAMES   AC
  BEST SCIENCE FICTION STORIES OF JAMES BLISH (REVISED)
                                          BLISH, JAMES   AC
  NEW DREAMS THIS MORNING   BLISH, JAMES   AN
  STAR TREK 4   BLISH, JAMES   OC
  STAR TREK 5   BLISH, JAMES   OC
  STAR TREK 6   BLISH, JAMES   OC
  STAR TREK 9   BLISH, JAMES   OC
  STAR TREK 10   BLISH, JAMES   OC
  STAR TREK 11   BLISH, JAMES   OC

BLISH, JAMES   (CONTINUED)
    THIRTEEN O'CLOCK AND OTHER ZERO HOURS KORNBLUTH, C. M.   AC
PREFACE: SOME AWARDS FOR STAR TREK- AND AN OPEN LETTER
                                                          IN
    STAR TREK 3   BLISH, JAMES   OC
PRICE OF A DRINK, A   SS   BER 74
    BERSERKERS, THE   ELWOOD, ROGER   OA
PRIVATE LITTLE WAR, A (D. INGALLS & G. RODDENBERRY)
                                          SA   STK 74 10
    STAR TREK 10   BLISH, JAMES   OC
REQUIEM FOR METHUSELAH (JEROME BIXBY)   SA   STK 72 05
    STAR TREK 5   BLISH, JAMES   OC
RETURN OF THE ARCHONS, THE (BORIS SOBELMAN) SA STK 73 09
    STAR TREK 9   BLISH, JAMES   OC
RETURN TO TOMORROW (G. RODDENBERRY & J. T. DOUGAN)
                                          SA   STK 73 09
    STAR TREK 9   BLISH, JAMES   OC
SARGASSO OF LOST CITIES   SN   TCS 53 SP
    EARTHMAN, COME HOME   BLISH, JAMES   NO
SAVAGE CURTAIN, THE (G. RODDENBERRY & A. HEINEMANN)
                                          SA   STK 72 06
    STAR TREK 6   BLISH, JAMES   OC
SEEDING PROGRAMME (A TIME TO SURVIVE)   SS   FSF 56 02
    SEEDLING STARS, THE   BLISH, JAMES   NO
SHIPWRECKED HOTEL, THE   NV C GAL 65 08
    SCIENCE FICTION HORIZONS NO. 1   BOARDMAN, TOM JR.   AN
    TORRENT OF FACES, A   BLISH & KNIGHT, N.   NO
SKYSIGN   NV   ASF 68 05
    ANYWHEN (ENGLISH EDITION ADDS:)   BLISH, JAMES   AC
    FOUR FOR THE FUTURE   HARRISON, HARRY   AN
    MIDSUMMER CENTURY   BLISH, JAMES   AC
SOLAR PLEXUS   SS   AST 41 09
    *BEYOND HUMAN KEN   MERRIL, JUDITH   AN
    HUMAN-MACHINES   SCORTIA & ZEBROWSKI   AN
    MEN AND MACHINES   SILVERBERG, ROBERT   AN
SPACE SEED (C. WILBER & GENE L. COON)   SA   STK 68 02
    STAR TREK 2   BLISH, JAMES   OC
SPOCK'S BRAIN (LEE CRONIN)   SA   STK 72 08
    STAR TREK 8   BLISH, JAMES   OC
SPONGE DIVE   SS   INF 56 06
    SO CLOSE TO HOME   BLISH, JAMES   AC
SQUIRE OF GOTHOS, THE (PAUL SCHNEIDER)   SA   STK 75 11
    STAR TREK 11   BLISH, JAMES   OC
STAR TREK   OC   BAN 67
    STAR TREK READER II, THE   BLISH, JAMES   AC
STAR TREK 2   OC   BAN 68
    STAR TREK READER, THE   BLISH, JAMES   AC
STAR TREK 3   OC   BAN 69 04
    STAR TREK READER, THE   BLISH, JAMES   AC
STAR TREK 4   OC   BAN 71 07
    STAR TREK READER II, THE   BLISH, JAMES   AC
STAR TREK 8   OC   BAN 72 11
    STAR TREK READER, THE   BLISH, JAMES   AC
STAR TREK 9   OC   BAN 73 08
    STAR TREK READER II, THE   BLISH, JAMES   AC
STATISTICIAN'S DAY   SS   SAG 70
    BEST SF: 1971   HARRISON & ALDISS   AN
    SCIENCE AGAINST MAN   CHEETHAM, ANTHONY   OA
STRUGGLE IN THE WOMB (BATTLE OF THE UNBORN) SS   FUT 50 05
    SO CLOSE TO HOME   BLISH, JAMES   AC
STYLE IN TREASON, A (A HERO'S LIFE)   NV   IMP 66 03
    ANYWHEN   BLISH, JAMES   AC
    MIDSUMMER CENTURY   BLISH, JAMES   AC
SUNKEN UNIVERSE (AS ARTHUR MERLYN, SEE ALSO SURFACE TENSION)
                                              NV   SSS 42 05
    WORLDS TO COME   KNIGHT, DAMON   AN
SURFACE TENSION   NA   GAL 52 08
    *BEST SCIENCE FICTION STORIES OF JAMES BLISH
                                          BLISH, JAMES   AC
    BUG-EYED MONSTERS   CHEETHAM, ANTHONY   AN
    SCIENCE FICTION HALL OF FAME VOLUME 1 SILVERBERG, ROBERT   AN
    SECOND GALAXY READER OF SCIENCE FICTION
                                          GOLD, H. L.   AN
    WHERE DO WE GO FROM HERE?   ASIMOV, ISAAC   AN
    WONDERMAKERS   HOSKINS, ROBERT   AN
    YEAR'S BEST SCIENCE FICTION NOVELS: 1953
                                          BLEILER & DIKTY   AN
    6 GREAT SHORT NOVELS OF SCIENCE FICTION
                                          CONKLIN, GROFF   AN
SURFACE TENSION (COMBINED WITH "SUNKEN UNIVERSE", SSS 42 05)
                                              NA   GAL 52 08
    SEEDLING STARS, THE   BLISH, JAMES   NO
TASTE OF ARMAGEDDON, A (R. HAMNER & G. L. COON) SA STK 68 02
    STAR TREK 2   BLISH, JAMES   OC
TESTAMENT OF ANDROS   NV   FUT 53 01
    ALPHA 1   SILVERBERG, ROBERT   AN
    *BEST SCIENCE FICTION STORIES OF JAMES BLISH
                                          BLISH, JAMES   AC
    NOVELETS OF SCIENCE FICTION   HOWARD, IVAN   AN
    PORTALS OF TOMORROW   DERLETH, AUGUST   AN
    SO CLOSE TO HOME   BLISH, JAMES   AC
THAT WHICH SURVIVES (J. M. LUCAS & D. C. FONTANA) SA STK 73 09
    STAR TREK 9   BLISH, JAMES   OC
THERE SHALL BE NO DARKNESS   SS   TWS 50 04
    *BEST SCIENCE FICTION STORIES OF JAMES BLISH
                                          BLISH, JAMES   AC
    WITCHES THREE   PRATT, FLETCHER   AN
    ZACHERLEY'S VULTURE STEW   ZACHERLEY   AN
THEY SHALL HAVE STARS (IN U.S. AS "YEAR 2018!") NO FAB 56
    CITIES IN FLIGHT   BLISH, JAMES   AC
THING IN THE ATTIC, THE   SS   IFS 54 07
    SECOND WORLD OF IF, THE   QUINN & WULFF   AN
    SEEDLING STARS, THE   BLISH, JAMES   NO
THIS EARTH OF HOURS   SS   FSF 59 06
    *GALACTIC CLUSTER   BLISH, JAMES   AC

BLISH, JAMES   (CONTINUED)
THIS SIDE OF PARADISE (N. BUTLER & D. C. FONTANA) SA STK 72 05
    STAR TREK 5   BLISH, JAMES   OC
THOLIAN WEB, THE (JUDY BURNS & CHET RICHARDS) SA STK 72 05
    STAR TREK 5   BLISH, JAMES   OC
TIGER RIDE   SS C ASF 48 10
    SF: AUTHORS' CHOICE   HARRISON, HARRY   AN
TIME TO SURVIVE, A (SEE SEEDING PROGRAMME)   TC
TO LOVE ANOTHER   NV C ASF 67 04
    TORRENT OF FACES, A   BLISH & KNIGHT, N.   NO
TO PAY THE PIPER   SS   IFS 56 02
    *GALACTIC CLUSTER   BLISH, JAMES   AC
TOMB TAPPER   SS   ASF 56 07
    *BEST SCIENCE FICTION STORIES OF JAMES BLISH
                                          BLISH, JAMES   AC
    *GALACTIC CLUSTER   BLISH, JAMES   AC
TOMORROW IS YESTERDAY (D. C. FONTANA)   SA   STK 68 02
    STAR TREK 2   BLISH, JAMES   OC
TRIUMPH OF TIME, THE (IN ENGLAND AS "A CLASH OF CYMBOLS")
                                              NO   AVN 58
    CITIES IN FLIGHT   BLISH, JAMES   AC
TROUBLE WITH TRIBBLES, THE (DAVID GERROLD) SA STK 69 03
    STAR TREK 3   BLISH, JAMES   OC
TRUE BILL, A   NV   TTM 73
    TEN TOMORROWS   ELWOOD, ROGER   OA
TURN OF A CENTURY   SS   DSF 53 03
    THINGS   HOWARD, IVAN   AN
TURNABOUT INTRUDER (G. RODDENBERRY & A. H. SINGER)
                                          SA   STK 72 05
    STAR TREK 5   BLISH, JAMES   OC
ULTIMATE COMPUTER, THE (D. C. FONTANA & L. WOLFE) SA STK 73 09
    STAR TREK 9   BLISH, JAMES   OC
UNREAL MCCOY, THE (THE MAN TRAP, GEORGE C. JOHNSON)
                                          SA   STK 67 01
    STAR TREK   BLISH, JAMES   OC
WATERSHED   SS   IFS 55 05
    BIO-FUTURES   SARGENT, PAMELA   AN
    FIRST WORLD OF IF, THE   QUINN & WULFF   AN
    MUTANTS   SILVERBERG, ROBERT   AN
    SEEDLING STARS, THE   BLISH, JAMES   NO
WAY TO EDEN, THE (A. HEINEMANN & M. RICHARDS) SA STK 72 05
    STAR TREK 5   BLISH, JAMES   OC
WE ALL DIE NAKED   NA   TFT 69
    ALPHA 4   SILVERBERG, ROBERT   AN
    BEST SCIENCE FICTION STORIES OF JAMES BLISH (REVISED)
                                          BLISH, JAMES   AC
    THREE FOR TOMORROW   SILVERBERG, ROBERT   OA
WHAT ARE LITTLE GIRLS MADE OF? (ROBERT BLOCH) SA STK 75 11
    STAR TREK 11   BLISH, JAMES   OC
WHERE NO MAN HAS GONE BEFORE (SAMUEL A. PEEPLES) SA STK 72 08
    STAR TREK 8   BLISH, JAMES   OC
WHO MOURNS FOR ADONAIS? (G. RALSTON & G. COON) SA STK 72 07
    STAR TREK 7   BLISH, JAMES   OC
WHO'S IN CHARGE HERE? (ALSO AS NONE SO BLIND) SS FSF 62 05
    BEST FROM FANTASY AND SCIENCE FICTION: 12
                                          DAVIDSON, AVRAM   AN
WHOM GODS DESTROY (LEE ERWIN & JERRY SOHL) SA STK 72 05
    STAR TREK 5   BLISH, JAMES   OC
WINK OF AN EYE (ARTHUR HEINEMANN & LEE CRONIN) SA STK 75 11
    STAR TREK 11   BLISH, JAMES   OC
WITH MALACE TO COME (SEE A MATTER OF ENERGY) TC
WOLF IN THE FOLD (ROBERT BLOCH)   SA   STK 72 08
    STAR TREK 8   BLISH, JAMES   OC
WORK OF ART, A (ART-WORK)   SS   SFS 56 07
    *BEST SCIENCE FICTION STORIES OF JAMES BLISH
                                          BLISH, JAMES   AC
    BEST SF 6   CRISPIN, EDMUND   AN
    *GALACTIC CLUSTER   BLISH, JAMES   AC
    NEW DREAMS THIS MORNING   BLISH, JAMES   AN
    SCIENCE FICTION SHOWCASE   KORNBLUTH, MARY   AN
    STARS AROUND US, THE   HOSKINS, ROBERT   AN
    WORLDS OF SCIENCE FICTION, THE   MILLS, ROBERT P.   AN
WRITING OF THE RAT, THE   SS   GAL 56 06
    ANYWHEN   BLISH, JAMES   AC
YEAR 2018! (SEE THEY SHALL HAVE STARS)   TC

BLOCH, ALAN
MEN ARE DIFFERENT   SS   NEW 54 AN
    FIFTY SHORT SCIENCE FICTION TALES   ASIMOV & CONKLIN   AN
    *SCIENCE FICTION THINKING MACHINES   CONKLIN, GROFF   AN

BLOCH, ROBERT   SEE ALSO   CO-AUTHOR RAY BRADBURY
ATOMS AND EVIL   AC   GMB 62 08
BEST OF FREDRIC BROWN, THE (LISTED UNDER FREDRIC BROWN)
                                              EC H NDB 76
BLOOD RUNS COLD   AC H SAS 61
BLOOD RUNS COLD (BRITISH)   AC   COR 64
BOGEY MEN   AC   PYR 63 03
CHAMBER OF HORRORS   AC   AWD 66
COLD CHILLS   AC H DBL 77
DRAGONS AND NIGHTMARES   AC   BEL 69 11
FEAR TODAY, GONE TOMORROW   AC   AWD 71 09
HORROR-7   AC   BEL 63 02
HOUSE OF THE HATCHET AND OTHER TALES OF HORROR, THE
                                              AC   TDM 65
    SEE "YOURS TRULY, JACK THE RIPPER"
HOUSE OF THE HATCHET, THE   AC   PTH 76
    11 STORIES FROM "THE OPENER OF THE WAY"
KING OF TERRORS, THE   AC H MYS 77
    TALES OF MADNESS AND DEATH
LIVING DEMONS, THE   AC   BEL 67 09
MORE NIGHTMARES   AC   BEL 62 02
NIGHTMARES   AC   BEL 61
    TEN WEIRD TALES FROM PLEASANT DREAMS
OPENER OF THE WAY, THE   AC H ARK 45
    ENGLISH DERIVATIVE ANTHOLOGY "THE HOUSE OF THE HATCHET"

BLOCH, ROBERT   BLOCH, ROBERT

BLOCH, ROBERT   (CONTINUED)   BLOCH, ROBERT   (CONTINUED)
OPENER OF THE WAY, THE (BRITISH PB)   AC   PTH 76   YOURS TRULY, JACK THE RIPPER   BLOCH, ROBERT   AC
PLEASANT DREAMS   AC H ARK 60   DRUIDIC DOOM, THE   SS   WRT 36 04
SKULL OF THE MARQUIS DE SADE, THE   AC   PYR 65 10   BLOCH AND BRADBURY   BRADBURY & BLOCH   AC
TALES IN A JUGULAR VEIN   AC   PYR 65 02   EAGER DRAGON, THE   NV   WRT 43 01
YOURS TRULY, JACK THE RIPPER   AC   BEL 62   DRAGONS AND NIGHTMARES   BLOCH, ROBERT   AC
  IN ENGLAND AS "THE HOUSE OF THE HATCHET AND OTHER TALES OF   EDIFICE COMPLEX   SS   ESC 58 02
  HORROR"   ATOMS AND EVIL   BLOCH, ROBERT   AC
ALL ON A GOLDEN AFTERNOON   NV   FSF 56 06   EGGHEAD   SS   FUN 58 07
*BLOOD RUNS COLD   BLOCH, ROBERT   AC   ATOMS AND EVIL   BLOCH, ROBERT   AC
ALMOST HUMAN (AS TARLETON FISKE)   SS   FAD 43 06   EGO TRIP   SS   PNT 72 03
HISTORY OF THE SCIENCE FICTION MAGAZINE, THE   PART 2 1936-1945   COLD CHILLS   BLOCH, ROBERT   AC
                                      ASHLEY, MICHAEL   AN   ENOCH   SS   WRT 46 09
  INVASION OF THE ROBOTS   ELWOOD, ROGER   AN   ALONE BY NIGHT   CONGDON, MICHAEL&DON   AN
  *MY BEST SCIENCE FICTION STORY   MARGULIES & FRIEND   AN   HORROR-7   BLOCH, ROBERT   AC
ANIMAL FAIR, THE   SS   PBY 71 05   PLEASANT DREAMS   BLOCH, ROBERT   AC
  COLD CHILLS   BLOCH, ROBERT   AC   EYES OF THE MUMMY, THE   SS   WRT 38 04
  YEAR'S BEST HORROR STORIES: SERIES II, THE   HOUSE OF THE HATCHET, THE   BLOCH, ROBERT   AC
                                      DAVIS, RICHARD   AN   *OPENER OF THE WAY, THE   BLOCH, ROBERT   AC
BACK WORD   MS   YOURS TRULY, JACK THE RIPPER   BLOCH, ROBERT   AC
  DRAGONS AND NIGHTMARES   BLOCH, ROBERT   AC   F.O.B. VENUS   SS   FAN 58 11
BALD-HEADED MIRAGE, THE   SS   AMZ 60 06   FEAR TODAY, GONE TOMORROW   BLOCH, ROBERT   AC
  ANCIENT MYSTERIES READER, THE   HAINING, PETER   AN   FACELESS GOD, THE   SS   WRT 36 05
  FEAR TODAY, GONE TOMORROW   BLOCH, ROBERT   AC   *OPENER OF THE WAY, THE   BLOCH, ROBERT   AC
BEASTS OF BARSAC, THE   SS   WRT 44 07   YOURS TRULY, JACK THE RIPPER   BLOCH, ROBERT   AC
  LIVING DEMONS, THE   BLOCH, ROBERT   AC   FAT CHANCE   SS   KHM 60 08
BEAUTY'S BEAST   SS   WRT 41 05   CHAMBER OF HORRORS   BLOCH, ROBERT   AC
  LIVING DEMONS, THE   BLOCH, ROBERT   AC   KING OF TERRORS, THE   BLOCH, ROBERT   AC
BEELZEBUB   SS   PBY 63 12   FEAR PLANET, THE   SS   SSS 43 02
  CHAMBER OF HORRORS   BLOCH, ROBERT   AC   ALIEN WORLDS   ELWOOD, ROGER   AN
  PLAYBOY BOOK OF HORROR AND THE SUPERNATURAL, THE   FAR BOUNDARIES   DERLETH, AUGUST   AN
                                      PLAYBOY, EDITORS OF   AN   FEAST IN THE ABBEY, THE   SS   WRT 35 01
BEETLES   SS   WRT 38 12   HOUSE OF THE HATCHET, THE   BLOCH, ROBERT   AC
  *OPENER OF THE WAY, THE   BLOCH, ROBERT   AC   MORE NIGHTMARES   BLOCH, ROBERT   AC
  YOURS TRULY, JACK THE RIPPER   BLOCH, ROBERT   AC   *OPENER OF THE WAY, THE   BLOCH, ROBERT   AC
BETSY BLAKE WILL LIVE FOREVER (SEE IS BETSY BLAKE STILL ALIVE)   FIDDLER'S FEE, THE   SS   WRT 40 07
                                           TC   MORE NIGHTMARES   BLOCH, ROBERT   AC
BIG KICK, THE   SS   ROG 59 07   *OPENER OF THE WAY, THE   BLOCH, ROBERT   AC
  *BLOOD RUNS COLD   BLOCH, ROBERT   AC   FINAL PERFORMANCE   NV   SHK 60 09
BLACK BARGAIN   SS   WRT 42 05   *BLOOD RUNS COLD   BLOCH, ROBERT   AC
  LIVING DEMONS, THE   BLOCH, ROBERT   AC   FLORAL TRIBUTE   SS   WRT 49 07
BLACK KISS, THE   SS   WRT 37 06   DEVIL'S GENERATION, THE   GHIDALIA, VIC   AN
  SECOND AVON FANTASY READER, THE   WOLLHEIM &ERNSBERGER   AN   FOREVER AND AMEN   SS   WLK 73
BLOCK THAT METAPHOR   SS   GAL 58 10   AND WALK NOW GENTLY THROUGH THE FIRE...
  ATOMS AND EVIL   BLOCH, ROBERT   AC   ELWOOD, ROGER   OA
BOGEY MAN WILL GET YOU, THE   SS   WRT 46 03   BEST SCIENCE FICTION FOR 1973   ACKERMAN, FORREST J.   AN
  SKULL OF THE MARQUIS DE SADE, THE BLOCH, ROBERT   AC   COLD CHILLS   BLOCH, ROBERT   AC
BROOMSTICK RIDE   SS   SUP 57 12   GIFTS OF ASTI AND OTHER STORIES OF SCIENCE FICTION, THE
  BOGEY MEN   BLOCH, ROBERT   AC   ELWOOD, ROGER   AN
BY WAY OF INTRODUCTION   IN   FOUNDING FATHERS   SS   FUN 56 07
  OPENER OF THE WAY, THE (BRITISH PB) BLOCH, ROBERT   AC   TALES IN A JUGULAR VEIN   BLOCH, ROBERT   AC
CATNIP   SS   WRT 48 03   FROZEN FEAR   SS   WRT 46 05
  NIGHTMARES   BLOCH, ROBERT   AC   CHAMBER OF HORRORS   BLOCH, ROBERT   AC
  PLEASANT DREAMS   BLOCH, ROBERT   AC   FUNNEL OF GOD, THE   NV   FAN 60 01
CHANGE OF HEART   SS   ARS 48 FL   FEAR TODAY, GONE TOMORROW   BLOCH, ROBERT   AC
  ATOMS AND EVIL   BLOCH, ROBERT   AC   GHOST WRITER, THE   SS   WRT 40 05
CHEATERS, THE   NV   WRT 47 11   BOGEY MEN   BLOCH, ROBERT   AC
  EDGE OF NEVER, THE   HOSKINS, ROBERT   AN   GIRL FROM MARS, THE   SS   FAD 50 03
  FANTASY: THE LITERATURE OF THE MARVELOUS   LIVING DEMONS, THE   BLOCH, ROBERT   AC
                                      KELLEY, LEO P.   AN   TALES OF TERROR FROM OUTER SPACE CHETWYND-HAYES, R.   AN
  MORE NIGHTMARES   BLOCH, ROBERT   AC   GLOATING PLACE, THE   SS   ROG 59 06
  PLEASANT DREAMS   BLOCH, ROBERT   AC   *BLOOD RUNS COLD   BLOCH, ROBERT   AC
CLOAK, THE   SS   UNK 39 05   GODDESS OF WISDOM, THE   SS   FUN 54 05
  FROM UNKNOWN WORLDS   CAMPBELL, JOHN W. JR AN   FEAR TODAY, GONE TOMORROW   BLOCH, ROBERT   AC
  HELL HATH FURY   HAY, GEORGE   AN   GODS ARE NOT MOCKED, THE   SS   EQM 68 08
  *OPENER OF THE WAY, THE   BLOCH, ROBERT   AC   COLD CHILLS   BLOCH, ROBERT   AC
  YOURS TRULY, JACK THE RIPPER   BLOCH, ROBERT   AC   FEAR TODAY, GONE TOMORROW   BLOCH, ROBERT   AC
COMFORT ME, MY ROBOT   SS   IMG 55 01   GOOD IMAGINATION, A   SS   SUS 56 01
  ATOMS AND EVIL   BLOCH, ROBERT   AC   KING OF TERRORS, THE   BLOCH, ROBERT   AC
CONSTANT READER   SS   USF 53 06   GOOD KNIGHT'S WORK, A   NV   UNK 41 10
  ATOMS AND EVIL   BLOCH, ROBERT   AC   DRAGONS AND NIGHTMARES   BLOCH, ROBERT   AC
  SCIENCE FACT/FICTION   FARRELL/GAGE/&   AN   GRINNING GHOUL, THE   SS   WRT 36 06
  SPACE MAGICIANS, THE   NORTON & MOSKOWITZ   AN   BLOCH AND BRADBURY   BRADBURY & BLOCH   AC
CRIME IN RHYME (SEE RHYME NEVER PAYS)   TC   HEAD HUNTER, THE (THE HEAD MAN)   SS   FIF 50 06
CRIME MACHINE   SS   GAL 61 10   CHAMBER OF HORRORS   BLOCH, ROBERT   AC
  FEAR TODAY, GONE TOMORROW   BLOCH, ROBERT   AC   HEAD MAN, THE (SEE THE HEAD HUNTER)   TC
  SEVENTH GALAXY READER, THE   POHL, FREDERIK   AN   HEAD, THE   SS
CURE, THE   SS   PBY 57 10   IDES OF TOMORROW, THE   CARR, TERRY   OA
  *BLOOD RUNS COLD   BLOCH, ROBERT   AC   HOME AWAY FROM HOME, A   SS   AHM 61 06
DARK DEMON, THE   SS   WRT 36 11   KING OF TERRORS, THE   BLOCH, ROBERT   AC
  MORE NIGHTMARES   BLOCH, ROBERT   AC   TALES IN A JUGULAR VEIN   BLOCH, ROBERT   AC
  *OPENER OF THE WAY, THE   BLOCH, ROBERT   AC   HOUSE OF THE HATCHET, THE   SS   WRT 41 01
DAYBROKE   SS   SMG 58 01   HOUSE OF THE HATCHET, THE   BLOCH, ROBERT   AC
  *BLOOD RUNS COLD   BLOCH, ROBERT   AC   *OPENER OF THE WAY, THE   BLOCH, ROBERT   AC
  SCIENCE FICTION ROLL OF HONOR, THE POHL, FREDERIK   AN   YOURS TRULY, JACK THE RIPPER   BLOCH, ROBERT   AC
  STAR OF STARS   POHL, FREDERIK   AN   HOW LIKE A GOD   SS   GAL 69 04
DEAD-END DOCTOR   SS   GAL 56 02   COLD CHILLS   BLOCH, ROBERT   AC
  ATOMS AND EVIL   BLOCH, ROBERT   AC   HUNGARIAN RHAPSODY (AS WILSON KANE)   SS   FAN 58 06
DEADLIEST ART, THE   SS   BMM 58 11   NIGHTMARES   BLOCH, ROBERT   AC
  KING OF TERRORS, THE   BLOCH, ROBERT   AC   PLEASANT DREAMS   BLOCH, ROBERT   AC
  TALES IN A JUGULAR VEIN   BLOCH, ROBERT   AC   HUNGRY EYE, THE   NV   FAN 59 05
DEADLY JOKER, THE (SEE IMPRACTICAL JOKER) TC   FEAR TODAY, GONE TOMORROW   BLOCH, ROBERT   AC
DEVIL'S TICKET, THE   SS   WRT 44 09   TIME UNTAMED   HOWARD, IVAN   AN
  SKULL OF THE MARQUIS DE SADE, THE BLOCH, ROBERT   AC   HUNGRY HOUSE, THE   NV   IMG 51 04
DIG THAT CRAZY GRAVE| SS   EQM 57 06   NIGHTMARES   BLOCH, ROBERT   AC
  *BLOOD RUNS COLD   BLOCH, ROBERT   AC   PLEASANT DREAMS   BLOCH, ROBERT   AC
DOUBLE TRAGEDY (SEE DOUBLE-CROSS)   TC   I DO NOT LOVE THEE, DOCTOR FELL   SS   FSF 55 03
DOUBLE WHAMMY   SS   FAN 70 02   BEST SCIENCE FICTION STORIES AND NOVELS: 1956
  COLD CHILLS   BLOCH, ROBERT   AC   DIKTY, T. E.   AN
  YEAR'S BEST HORROR STORIES, THE   DAVIS, RICHARD   AN   *BLOOD RUNS COLD   BLOCH, ROBERT   AC
DOUBLE-CROSS (DOUBLE TRAGEDY)   SS   MSM 59 10   6 FROM WORLDS BEYOND   DIKTY, T. E.   AN
  TALES IN A JUGULAR VEIN   BLOCH, ROBERT   AC   I KISS YOUR SHADOW   SS   FSF 56 04
DREAM MAKERS, THE   NV   BEY 53 09   NIGHTMARES   BLOCH, ROBERT   AC
  MORE TERROR IN THE MODERN VEIN   WOLLHEIM, DONALD A.   AN   PLEASANT DREAMS   BLOCH, ROBERT   AC
  PLEASANT DREAMS   BLOCH, ROBERT   AC   I LIKE BLONDES   SS   PBY 56 01
  *TERROR IN THE MODERN VEIN   WOLLHEIM, DONALD A.   AN   *BLOOD RUNS COLD   BLOCH, ROBERT   AC

BLOCH, ROBERT (CONTINUED)
FIEND, THE PLAYBOY, EDITORS OF AN
IMPRACTICAL JOKER (THE DEADLY JOKER) SS SMM 65 08
CHAMBER OF HORRORS BLOCH, ROBERT AC
IN THE CARDS SS WOF 70 WI
COLD CHILLS BLOCH, ROBERT AC
INDIAN SPIRIT GUIDE, THE SS WRT 48 11
LIVING DEMONS, THE BLOCH, ROBERT AC
INTRODUCTION IN
BEST OF FREDRIC BROWN, THE BROWN, FREDRIC AC
COLD CHILLS BLOCH, ROBERT AC
HOUSE OF THE HATCHET, THE BLOCH, ROBERT AC
KING OF TERRORS, THE BLOCH, ROBERT AC
LIVING DEMONS, THE BLOCH, ROBERT AC
*OPENER OF THE WAY, THE BLOCH, ROBERT AC
YOURS TRULY, JACK THE RIPPER BLOCH, ROBERT AC
INTRODUCTION TO NIGHTMARES, AN IN
NIGHTMARES BLOCH, ROBERT AC
IRON MASK NV WRT 44 05
FANTASTIC PULPS, THE HAINING, PETER AN
IS BETSY BLAKE STILL ALIVE? (BETSY BLAKE WILL LIVE FOREVER)
SS EQM 58 04
*BLOOD RUNS COLD BLOCH, ROBERT AC
IT HAPPENED TOMORROW NV SSS 51 06
FUTURES UNLIMITED NORTON, ALDEN H. AN
LEARNING MAZE, THE SS
COLD CHILLS BLOCH, ROBERT AC
LEARNING MAZE AND OTHER STORIES, THE ELWOOD, ROGER OA
LEFTY FEEP GETS HENPECKED NV FAD 45 04
SATAN'S PETS GHIDALIA, VIC AN
LIFE IN OUR TIME SS EQM 66 10
LIVING DEMONS, THE BLOCH, ROBERT AC
LIGHT-HOUSE, THE SS FAN 53 02
NIGHTMARES BLOCH, ROBERT AC
PLEASANT DREAMS BLOCH, ROBERT AC
LIVING DEAD, THE SS EQM 67 04
KING OF TERRORS, THE BLOCH, ROBERT AC
LIVING END, THE SS SMM 63 05
CHAMBER OF HORRORS BLOCH, ROBERT AC
"LIZZIE BORDEN TOOK AN AXE..." SS WRT 46 11
SKULL OF THE MARQUIS DE SADE, THE BLOCH, ROBERT AC
LUCY COMES TO STAY SS WRT 52 01
FIEND IN YOU, THE BEAUMONT, CHARLES AN
LIVING DEMONS, THE BLOCH, ROBERT AC
MAN WHO COLLECTED POE, THE SS FFM 51 10
BOGEY MEN BLOCH, ROBERT AC
MAN WHO CRIED WOLF!, THE SS WRT 45 05
BLOCH AND BRADBURY BRADBURY & BLOCH AC
MAN WHO KNEW WOMEN, THE SS SMM 59 07
KING OF TERRORS, THE BLOCH, ROBERT AC
SKULL OF THE MARQUIS DE SADE, THE BLOCH, ROBERT AC
MAN WHO MURDERED TOMORROW, THE SS AMZ 60 03
BOGEY MEN BLOCH, ROBERT AC
MANDARIN'S CANARIES, THE SS WRT 38 09
HORROR-7 BLOCH, ROBERT AC
HOUSE OF THE HATCHET, THE BLOCH, ROBERT AC
*OPENER OF THE WAY, THE BLOCH, ROBERT AC
MANNIKIN, THE (ALSO AS MANNIKINS OF HORROR) SS WRT 37 04
*OPENER OF THE WAY, THE BLOCH, ROBERT AC
YOURS TRULY, JACK THE RIPPER BLOCH, ROBERT AC
MANNIKINS OF HORROR (THE MANNIKIN) SS WRT 37 04
BLOCH AND BRADBURY BRADBURY & BLOCH AC
MASTERPIECE, THE SS ROG 60 06
*BLOOD RUNS COLD BLOCH, ROBERT AC
MATTER OF LIFE, A SS KHM 60 06
BOGEY MEN BLOCH, ROBERT AC
MEMO TO A MOVIE-MAKER SS DUD 61 01
BOGEY MEN BLOCH, ROBERT AC
METHOD FOR MURDER SS FUR 62 07
CHAMBER OF HORRORS BLOCH, ROBERT AC
KING OF TERRORS, THE BLOCH, ROBERT AC
MODEL WIFE, THE SS SWK 61 11
BOGEY MEN BLOCH, ROBERT AC
MODEL, THE SS GLR 75 11
COLD CHILLS BLOCH, ROBERT AC
MOTHER OF SERPENTS SS WRT 36 12
HOUSE OF THE HATCHET, THE BLOCH, ROBERT AC
MORE NIGHTMARES BLOCH, ROBERT AC
*OPENER OF THE WAY, THE BLOCH, ROBERT AC
MOVIE PEOPLE, THE SS FSF 69 10
COLD CHILLS BLOCH, ROBERT AC
NEW WORLDS OF FANTASY NO. 2 CARR, TERRY AN
MR. STEINWAY SS FAN 54 04
NIGHTMARES BLOCH, ROBERT AC
PLEASANT DREAMS BLOCH, ROBERT AC
NIGHT SCHOOL SS ROG 59 08
TALES IN A JUGULAR VEIN BLOCH, ROBERT AC
NIGHTMARE NUMBER FOUR PM NEW 59 AN
SCIENCE FICTION SHOWCASE KORNBLUTH, MARY AN
NURSEMAID TO NIGHTMARES NV WRT 42 11
DRAGONS AND NIGHTMARES BLOCH, ROBERT AC
OLD COLLEGE TRY, THE SS GAM 63 02
FEAR TODAY, GONE TOMORROW BLOCH, ROBERT AC
SEA OF SPACE, A NOLAN, WILLIAM F. AN
ONE WAY TO MARS SS WRT 45 07
HOUSE OF THE HATCHET, THE BLOCH, ROBERT AC
MORE NIGHTMARES BLOCH, ROBERT AC
*OPENER OF THE WAY, THE BLOCH, ROBERT AC
STRANGE SIGNPOSTS ELWOOD & MOSKOWITZ AN
OPENER OF THE WAY, THE SS WRT 36 10
HORROR-7 BLOCH, ROBERT AC
*OPENER OF THE WAY, THE BLOCH, ROBERT AC
ORACLE, THE SS PNT 71 05
COLD CHILLS BLOCH, ROBERT AC
PAST MASTER, THE NV BBM 55 01
ALIEN EARTH AND OTHER STORIES ELWOOD & MOSKOWITZ AN

BLOCH, ROBERT (CONTINUED)
TALES IN A JUGULAR VEIN BLOCH, ROBERT AC
PHILTRE TIP SS ROG 61 03
LIVING DEMONS, THE BLOCH, ROBERT AC
PIN-UP GIRL SS SHK 60 07
TALES IN A JUGULAR VEIN BLOCH, ROBERT AC
PIN, THE SS AMZ 54 01
*BLOOD RUNS COLD BLOCH, ROBERT AC
PLAY'S THE THING, THE SS AHM 71 05
COLD CHILLS BLOCH, ROBERT AC
PLOT IS THE THING, THE SS FSF 66 07
LIVING DEMONS, THE BLOCH, ROBERT AC
NEW WORLDS OF FANTASY NO. 3 CARR, TERRY AN
PRIDE GOES- SS SMM 66 08
CHAMBER OF HORRORS BLOCH, ROBERT AC
PROFESSOR PLAYS IT SQUARE, THE SS ARG 57 09
ATOMS AND EVIL BLOCH, ROBERT AC
PROPER SPIRIT, THE SS FSF 57 03
NIGHTMARES BLOCH, ROBERT AC
PLEASANT DREAMS BLOCH, ROBERT AC
PROXY HEAD, THE SS SFP 53 05
HUMAN ZERO, THE MOSKOWITZ & ELWOOD AN
QUESTION OF ETIQUETTE, A SS WRT 42 09
BLOCH AND BRADBURY BRADBURY & BLOCH AC
WEIRD TALES MARGULIES, LEO AN
QUIET FUNERAL, A SS
SKULL OF THE MARQUIS DE SADE, THE BLOCH, ROBERT AC
REAL BAD FRIEND, THE NV MSM 57 02
KING OF TERRORS, THE BLOCH, ROBERT AC
REPORT ON SOL III SS AMZ 58 07
FEAR TODAY, GONE TOMORROW BLOCH, ROBERT AC
RETURN TO THE SABBATH SS WRT 38 07
HORROR-7 BLOCH, ROBERT AC
HOUSE OF THE HATCHET, THE BLOCH, ROBERT AC
*OPENER OF THE WAY, THE BLOCH, ROBERT AC
RHYME NEVER PAYS (CRIME IN RHYME) SS EQM 57 09
TALES IN A JUGULAR VEIN BLOCH, ROBERT AC
SABBATICAL SS GAL 59 12
TALES IN A JUGULAR VEIN BLOCH, ROBERT AC
SALES OF A DEATHMAN SS GAL 68 02
FEAR TODAY, GONE TOMORROW BLOCH, ROBERT AC
SCREAMING PEOPLE, THE NV FAN 59 01
CHAMBER OF HORRORS BLOCH, ROBERT AC
SEAL OF THE SATYR, THE SS SRS 39 06
MORE NIGHTMARES BLOCH, ROBERT AC
*OPENER OF THE WAY, THE BLOCH, ROBERT AC
SECRET OF SEBEK, THE SS WRT 37 11
HORROR-7 BLOCH, ROBERT AC
HOUSE OF THE HATCHET, THE BLOCH, ROBERT AC
*OPENER OF THE WAY, THE BLOCH, ROBERT AC
WIZARDS AND WARLOCKS GHIDALIA, VIC AN
SEE HOW THEY RUN SS EQM 73 04
COLD CHILLS BLOCH, ROBERT AC
SHADOW FROM THE STEEPLE, THE NV WRT 50 08
BLOCH AND BRADBURY BRADBURY & BLOCH AC
SHAMBLER FROM THE STARS, THE SS WRT 35 09
HORROR-7 BLOCH, ROBERT AC
HOUSE OF THE HATCHET, THE BLOCH, ROBERT AC
*OPENER OF THE WAY, THE BLOCH, ROBERT AC
SHOES, THE SS UNK 42 02
BOGEY MEN BLOCH, ROBERT AC
SHOW BIZ SS EQM 59 05
*BLOOD RUNS COLD BLOCH, ROBERT AC
SHOW MUST GO ON, THE SS MSM 60 01
*BLOOD RUNS COLD BLOCH, ROBERT AC
SKELETON IN THE CLOSET, THE SS FAD 43 06
HORROR TIMES TEN NORTON, ALDEN H. AN
SKULL OF THE MARQUIS DE SADE, THE SS WRT 45 09
BOGEY MEN BLOCH, ROBERT AC
SKULL OF THE MARQUIS DE SADE, THE BLOCH, ROBERT AC
SKULL, THE (THE SKULL OF THE MARQUIS DE SADE) SS WRT 45 09
GHOULS, THE HAINING, PETER AN
SLAVE OF THE FLAMES SS WRT 38 06
HOUSE OF THE HATCHET, THE BLOCH, ROBERT AC
MORE NIGHTMARES BLOCH, ROBERT AC
*OPENER OF THE WAY, THE BLOCH, ROBERT AC
SLEEPING BEAUTY, THE (THE SLEEPING REDHEADS) SS SWK 58 03
NIGHTMARES BLOCH, ROBERT AC
PLEASANT DREAMS BLOCH, ROBERT AC
SLEEPING REDHEADS, THE (SEE THE SLEEPING BEAUTY) TC
SOCK FINISH SS EQM 57 10
*BLOOD RUNS COLD BLOCH, ROBERT AC
SORCERER'S APPRENTICE, THE SS WRT 49 01
GHOUL KEEPERS, THE MARGULIES, LEO AN
NIGHTMARES BLOCH, ROBERT AC
PLEASANT DREAMS BLOCH, ROBERT AC
SPACE-BORN NV COI 73
CHILDREN OF INFINITY ELWOOD, ROGER OA
COLD CHILLS BLOCH, ROBERT AC
STANLEY G. WEINBAUM: A PERSONAL RECOLLECTION AR
BEST OF STANLEY G. WEINBAUM, THE WEINBAUM, STANLEY G. AC
STRANGE FLIGHT OF RICHARD CLAYTON, THE SS AMZ 39 03
HORROR-7 BLOCH, ROBERT AC
MODERN MASTERPIECES OF SCIENCE FICTION MOSKOWITZ, SAM AN
*OPENER OF THE WAY, THE BLOCH, ROBERT AC
STRANGE ISLAND OF DR. NORK, THE SS WRT 49 03
UNEXPECTED, THE MARGULIES, LEO AN
STRING OF PEARLS SS SMM 56 08
KING OF TERRORS, THE BLOCH, ROBERT AC
SWEET SIXTEEN SS
NIGHTMARES BLOCH, ROBERT AC
PLEASANT DREAMS BLOCH, ROBERT AC
SWEETS TO THE SWEET SS WRT 47 03
ALONE BY NIGHT CONGDON, MICHAEL& DON AN
MORE LITTLE MONSTERS ELWOOD & GHIDALIA AN
PLEASANT DREAMS BLOCH, ROBERT AC

BLOCH, ROBERT   (CONTINUED)
  YOURS TRULY, JACK THE RIPPER   BLOCH, ROBERT   AC
TALENT   SS   IFS 60 07
  ATOMS AND EVIL   BLOCH, ROBERT   AC
  BEST SCIENCE FICTION FROM IF, THE   POHL, FREDERIK   AN
  ODDBALLS, THE   GHIDALIA, VIC   AN
TELL YOUR FORTUNE   SS   WRT 50 05
  LIVING DEMONS, THE   BLOCH, ROBERT   AC
TERROR IN THE NIGHT   SS   MHT 56 02
  KING OF TERRORS, THE   BLOCH, ROBERT   AC
TERROR OVER HOLLYWOOD   SS   FUN 57 06
  TALES IN A JUGULAR VEIN   BLOCH, ROBERT   AC
THAT HELL-BOUND TRAIN   SS   FSF 58 09
  HUGO WINNERS, THE (VOLUME 1)   ASIMOV, ISAAC   AN
  MORE NIGHTMARES   BLOCH, ROBERT   AC
  PLEASANT DREAMS   BLOCH, ROBERT   AC
  TWENTY YEARS OF FANTASY & SCIENCE FICTION
                                        FERMAN & MILLS   AN
THINKING CAP, THE   NV   OWS 53 06
  BOGEY MEN   BLOCH, ROBERT   AC
TIME WOUNDS ALL HEELS   SS   FAD 42 04
  TIME CURVE, THE   MOSKOWITZ & ELWOOD   AN
TIN YOU LOVE TO TOUCH, THE   SS   OWS 51 07
  OTHER WORLDS, OTHER TIMES   MOSKOWITZ & ELWOOD   AN
TOY FOR JULIETTE, A   SS   DVS 67 07
  DANGEROUS VISIONS   ELLISON, HARLAN   OA
  FEAR TODAY, GONE TOMORROW   BLOCH, ROBERT   AC
  PARTNERS IN WONDER   ELLISON, HARLAN   AC
TRAVELING SALESMAN, THE   SS   PBY 57 02
  PLAYBOY BOOK OF HORROR AND THE SUPERNATURAL, THE
                                        PLAYBOY, EDITORS OF   AN
TRY THIS FOR PSIS   SS   FSF 56 10
  ATOMS AND EVIL   BLOCH, ROBERT   AC
TWO OF A KIND   SS   61
  CHAMBER OF HORRORS   BLOCH, ROBERT   AC
UNDER THE HORNS   SS   62
  KING OF TERRORS, THE   BLOCH, ROBERT   AC
UNDERGROUND   SS   67
  LIVING DEMONS, THE   BLOCH, ROBERT   AC
UNPARDONABLE CRIME, THE   SS   SWK 61 09
  CHAMBER OF HORRORS   BLOCH, ROBERT   AC
  KING OF TERRORS, THE   BLOCH, ROBERT   AC
UNSPEAKABLE BETROTHAL, THE   SS   AFR 49 09
  LIVING DEMONS, THE   BLOCH, ROBERT   AC
UNTOUCHABLE   SS   SMM 62 03
  CHAMBER OF HORRORS   BLOCH, ROBERT   AC
  KING OF TERRORS, THE   BLOCH, ROBERT   AC
WATER'S EDGE   SS   MSM 56 09
  KING OF TERRORS, THE   BLOCH, ROBERT   AC
WAXWORKS   SS   WRT 39 01
  HOUSE OF THE HATCHET, THE   BLOCH, ROBERT   AC
  MORE NIGHTMARES   BLOCH, ROBERT   AC
  *OPENER OF THE WAY, THE   BLOCH, ROBERT   AC
WAY OF LIFE, A   SS   FUN 56 10
  FANTASTIC UNIVERSE OMNIBUS, THE   SANTESSON, HANS S.   AN
  RULERS OF MEN   SANTESSON, HANS S.   AN
WEIRD TAILOR, THE   SS   WRT 50 07
  SKULL OF THE MARQUIS DE SADE, THE   BLOCH, ROBERT   AC
WELCOME, STRANGER   SS   SAT 57 04
  FLYING SAUCERS IN FACT AND FICTION   SANTESSON, HANS S.   AN
WHEEL AND DEAL   SS   NEW 62 AC
  ATOMS AND EVIL   BLOCH, ROBERT   AC
WHERE THE BUFFALO ROAM   SS   OWS 55 05
  *BLOOD RUNS COLD   BLOCH, ROBERT   AC
WHY I SELECTED ALMOST HUMAN   AI
  *MY BEST SCIENCE FICTION STORY   MARGULIES & FRIEND   AN
WORD OF HONOR   SS   PBY 58 08
  *BLOOD RUNS COLD   BLOCH, ROBERT   AC
  LAST TRAIN TO LIMBO   PLAYBOY, EDITORS OF   AN
  PLAYBOY BOOK OF SCIENCE FICTION AND FANTASY, THE
                                        PLAYBOY, EDITORS OF   AN
WORLD-TIMER, THE   SS   FAN 60 08
  FEAR TODAY, GONE TOMORROW   BLOCH, ROBERT   AC
YOU COULD BE WRONG   SS   AMZ 55 03
  ATOMS AND EVIL   BLOCH, ROBERT   AC
YOU GOT TO HAVE BRAINS   SS   FUN 56 01
  ATOMS AND EVIL   BLOCH, ROBERT   AC
YOURS TRULY, JACK THE RIPPER   SS   WRT 43 07
  *OPENER OF THE WAY, THE   BLOCH, ROBERT   AC
  YOURS TRULY, JACK THE RIPPER   BLOCH, ROBERT   AC

BLOCK, LAWRENCE
  MAKE A PRISON   SS   SFS 59 01
  5TH ANNUAL OF THE YEAR'S BEST S-F, THE MERRIL, JUDITH   AN

BOARDMAN, TOM JR.
  ABC OF SCIENCE FICTION, AN   AN   AVN 68 12
  CONNOISSEUR'S S. F.   AN   PEN 64
  SCIENCE FICTION HORIZONS NO. 1   AN H DOB 68
  UNFRIENDLY FUTURE, THE   AN   FSP 65
  FOREWORD   IN
    SCIENCE FICTION HORIZONS NO. 1   BOARDMAN, TOM JR.   AN
  INTRODUCTION   IN
    ABC OF SCIENCE FICTION, AN   BOARDMAN, TOM JR.   AN
    CONNOISSEUR'S S. F.   BOARDMAN, TOM JR.   AN
    UNFRIENDLY FUTURE, THE   BOARDMAN, TOM JR.   AN

BOLES, NICK
  TWO YEARS TO GAEA   SS   SFT 73
    SCIENCE FICTION TALES   ELWOOD, ROGER   OA

BOLSOVER, JOHN
  JACKSON'S WRONG STORY   SS
    AD 2500   WILSON, ANGUS   AN

BOLTON, RICHARD
  SHOCK TROOP   SS   IFS 56 10
    FIRST WORLD OF IF, THE   QUINN & WULFF   AN

BOND, NELSON S.
  LANCELOT BIGGS: SPACEMAN   AC H DBL 50
  MR. MERGENTHWIRKER'S LOBBIES AND OTHER FANTASTIC TALES
                                        AC H CMC 46
  NIGHTMARES AND DAYDREAMS   AC H ARK 68
  NO TIME LIKE THE FUTURE   AC   AVN 54
  31ST OF FEBRUARY, THE   AC H GNM 49
  ABDUCTION OF ABNER GREER, THE   SS   BBM 41 06
    NIGHTMARES AND DAYDREAMS   BOND, NELSON S.   AC
    *SCIENCE-FICTION CARNIVAL   BROWN, F. & REYNOLDS   AN
  AL HADDON'S LAMP   NV   UNK 42 06
    NIGHTMARES AND DAYDREAMS   BOND, NELSON S.   AC
  AND LO| THE BIRD   SS   BBM 50 09
    EARTH IS THE STRANGEST PLANET   SILVERBERG, ROBERT   AN
    FAR BOUNDARIES   DERLETH, AUGUST   AN
    NO TIME LIKE THE FUTURE   BOND, NELSON S.   AC
  ANOTHER WORLD BEGINS (SEE THE CUNNING OF THE BEAST)
                                        TC
  BACULAR CLOCK, THE   SS   BBM 42 07
    MR. MERGENTHWIRKER'S LOBBIES AND OTHER FANTASTIC TALES
                                        BOND, NELSON S.   AC
  BIRD OF PREY   SS   BBM 49 08
    NIGHTMARES AND DAYDREAMS   BOND, NELSON S.   AC
  BOOKSHOP, THE   SS
    MR. MERGENTHWIRKER'S LOBBIES AND OTHER FANTASTIC TALES
                                        BOND, NELSON S.   AC
  BUTTON, BUTTON   SS
    NO TIME LIKE THE FUTURE   BOND, NELSON S.   AC
  CARTWRIGHT'S CAMERA (SEE JOHNNY CARTWRIGHT'S CAMERA)
                                        TC
  CASTAWAY, THE   SS   PLS 40 WI
    INVASION FROM MARS   WELLES, ORSON   AN
  CONQUEROR'S ISLE   SS   BBM 46 06
    MR. MERGENTHWIRKER'S LOBBIES AND OTHER FANTASTIC TALES
                                        BOND, NELSON S.   AC
    NO TIME LIKE THE FUTURE   BOND, NELSON S.   AC
    *OTHER SIDE OF THE MOON, THE   DERLETH, AUGUST   AN
    STORIES OF SCIENTIFIC IMAGINATION   GALLANT, JOSEPH   AN
    WORLD OF WONDER   PRATT, FLETCHER   AN
  CUNNING OF THE BEAST, THE (ANOTHER WORLD BEGINS) SS BBM 42 11
    NO TIME LIKE THE FUTURE   BOND, NELSON S.   AC
    OTHER WORLDS, OTHER GODS   MOHS, MAYO   AN
    *STRANGE PORTS OF CALL   DERLETH, AUGUST   AN
    31ST OF FEBRUARY, THE   BOND, NELSON S.   AC
  DARK DOOR, THE   SS   BBM 52 05
    NIGHTMARES AND DAYDREAMS   BOND, NELSON S.   AC
  DAY WE CELEBRATE, THE   SS   ASF 41 01
    *POSSIBLE WORLDS OF SCIENCE FICTION CONKLIN, GROFF   AN
  DEVIL TO PAY, THE   SS   BBM 51 02
    NIGHTMARES AND DAYDREAMS   BOND, NELSON S.   AC
  DOWN WILL COME THE SKY   SS   USF 53 06
    NIGHTMARES AND DAYDREAMS   BOND, NELSON S.   AC
  DR. PUDDLE'S FINGERS   SS
    MR. MERGENTHWIRKER'S LOBBIES AND OTHER FANTASTIC TALES
                                        BOND, NELSON S.   AC
  EINSTEIN INSHOOT, THE   SS   ASF 38 11
    MR. MERGENTHWIRKER'S LOBBIES AND OTHER FANTASTIC TALES
                                        BOND, NELSON S.   AC
  ENCHANTED PENCIL, THE   SS
    31ST OF FEBRUARY, THE   BOND, NELSON S.   AC
  F.O.B. VENUS   SS   FAD 39 11
    LANCELOT BIGGS: SPACEMAN   BOND, NELSON S.   AC
  FINAL REPORT   PM   FUN 58 01
    NIGHTMARES AND DAYDREAMS   BOND, NELSON S.   AC
  FIVE LIVES OF ROBERT JORDAN, THE   SS
    31ST OF FEBRUARY, THE   BOND, NELSON S.   AC
  FOUNTAIN, THE   SN   UNK 41 06
    MR. MERGENTHWIRKER'S LOBBIES AND OTHER FANTASTIC TALES
                                        BOND, NELSON S.   AC
  GENIUS OF LANCELOT BIGGS, THE   SS   FAD 40 06
    LANCELOT BIGGS: SPACEMAN   BOND, NELSON S.   AC
  GHOST OF LANCELOT BIGGS, THE   SS   WRT 42 01
    LANCELOT BIGGS: SPACEMAN   BOND, NELSON S.   AC
  GRIPES OF WRAITH, THE   SS
    31ST OF FEBRUARY, THE   BOND, NELSON S.   AC
  HONEYMOON IN BEDLAM   SS   WRT 41 01
    LANCELOT BIGGS: SPACEMAN   BOND, NELSON S.   AC
  JOHNNY CARTWRIGHT'S CAMERA (CARTWRIGHT'S CAMERA) SS UNK 40 11
    MR. MERGENTHWIRKER'S LOBBIES AND OTHER FANTASTIC TALES
                                        BOND, NELSON S.   AC
  LANCELOT BIGGS COOKS A PIRATE   SS   FAD 40 02
    LANCELOT BIGGS: SPACEMAN   BOND, NELSON S.   AC
  LANCELOT BIGGS ON THE SATURN (FROM L.B.: SPACEMAN)
                                        EX   DBL 50
    SCIENCE FICTION AND READER'S GUIDE BARROWS, MARJORIE   AN
  LANCELOT BIGGS, MASTER NAVIGATOR   SS   FAD 40 05
    LANCELOT BIGGS: SPACEMAN   BOND, NELSON S.   AC
  LAST INNING   SS   BBM 48 05
    NIGHTMARES AND DAYDREAMS   BOND, NELSON S.   AC
  LAST OUTPOST, THE   NV
    NO TIME LIKE THE FUTURE   BOND, NELSON S.   AC
  LIFE GOES ON   SS
    NO TIME LIKE THE FUTURE   BOND, NELSON S.   AC
  LOVE SONG OF LANCELOT BIGGS, THE   SS   AMZ 42 09
    LANCELOT BIGGS: SPACEMAN   BOND, NELSON S.   AC
  MADNESS OF LANCELOT BIGGS, THE   SS   FAD 40 04
    LANCELOT BIGGS: SPACEMAN   BOND, NELSON S.   AC
  MAGIC CITY   NV   ASF 41 02
    TREASURY OF GREAT SCIENCE FICTION, A VOL.2
                                        BOUCHER, ANTHONY   AN
  MAGIC STAIR-CASE, THE   SS

BOND, NELSON S.   (CONTINUED)
    MR. MERGENTHWIRKER'S LOBBIES AND OTHER FANTASTIC TALES
                                BOND, NELSON S.   AC
MAN WHO WALKED THROUGH GLASS, THE   SS   ESQ 38 11
    ODDBALLS, THE   GHIDALIA, VIC   AN
    31ST OF FEBRUARY, THE   BOND, NELSON S.   AC
MASK OF MEDUSA, THE   SS
    31ST OF FEBRUARY, THE   BOND, NELSON S.   AC
MASTER OF COTSWOLD, THE   SS   WRT 44 01
    MR. MERGENTHWIRKER'S LOBBIES AND OTHER FANTASTIC TALES
                                BOND, NELSON S.   AC
MONSTER FROM NOWHERE, THE   SS   FAD 39 07
    AS TOMORROW BECOMES TODAY   SULLIVAN, CHARLES W.   AN
    *BEST OF SCIENCE FICTION   CONKLIN, GROFF   AN
    31ST OF FEBRUARY, THE   BOND, NELSON S.   AC
MR. BIGGS GOES TO TOWN   SS   AMZ 42 10
    LANCELOT BIGGS: SPACEMAN   BOND, NELSON S.   AC
MR. MERGENTHWIRKER'S LOBBIES   SS   SCR 37 11
    MR. MERGENTHWIRKER'S LOBBIES AND OTHER FANTASTIC TALES
                                BOND, NELSON S.   AC
    OUT OF THIS WORLD   FAST, JULIUS   AN
MUCH ADO ABOUT PENDING   SS   BBM 47 04
    NIGHTMARES AND DAYDREAMS   BOND, NELSON S.   AC
MY NEPHEW NORVELL   SS
    31ST OF FEBRUARY, THE   BOND, NELSON S.   AC
ORDEAL OF LANCELOT BIGGS, THE   SS   AMZ 43 05
    LANCELOT BIGGS: SPACEMAN   BOND, NELSON S.   AC
PET SHOP, THE   SS   BBM 50 03
    NIGHTMARES AND DAYDREAMS   BOND, NELSON S.   AC
PETERSEN'S EYE   SS   BBM 49 03
    NIGHTMARES AND DAYDREAMS   BOND, NELSON S.   AC
PILGRIMAGE (THE PRIESTESS WHO REBELLED)   SS AMZ 39 10
    BEST OF AMAZING, THE   ROSS, JOSEPH   AN
    MARRIAGE AND THE FAMILY THROUGH SCIENCE FICTION
                                CLEAR/WARRICK/&   AN
    31ST OF FEBRUARY, THE   BOND, NELSON S.   AC
PRESCIENCE   SS   UNK 41 10
    UNKNOWN, THE   BENSEN, D. R.   AN
PRIESTESS WHO REBELLED, THE (ALSO AS PILGRIMAGE) SS AMZ 39 10
    WHEN WOMEN RULE   MOSKOWITZ, SAM   AN
REMARKABLE TALENT OF EGBERT HAW, THE SS   41
    MR. MERGENTHWIRKER'S LOBBIES AND OTHER FANTASTIC TALES
                                BOND, NELSON S.   AC
    SATAN'S PETS   GHIDALIA, VIC   AN
RETURN OF LANCELOT BIGGS, THE   SS   AMZ 42 05
    LANCELOT BIGGS: SPACEMAN   BOND, NELSON S.   AC
RING, THE   SS
    31ST OF FEBRUARY, THE   BOND, NELSON S.   AC
ROSY FUTURE FOR RODERICK, A   SS   BBM 52 08
    MORE LITTLE MONSTERS   ELWOOD & GHIDALIA   AN
    NIGHTMARES AND DAYDREAMS   BOND, NELSON S.   AC
SAINT MULLIGAN   SS   FAD 43 05
    31ST OF FEBRUARY, THE   BOND, NELSON S.   AC
SCIENTIFIC PIONEER RETURNS, THE   SS   AMZ 40 11
    LANCELOT BIGGS: SPACEMAN   BOND, NELSON S.   AC
SILENT PLANET, THE   SS
    NO TIME LIKE THE FUTURE   BOND, NELSON S.   AC
SOCRATES OF THE SOUTH FORTY   SS
    MR. MERGENTHWIRKER'S LOBBIES AND OTHER FANTASTIC TALES
                                BOND, NELSON S.   AC
SONG, THE   SS   BBM 49 04
    NIGHTMARES AND DAYDREAMS   BOND, NELSON S.   AC
SPINSTERS, THE   SS   BBM 50 01
    NIGHTMARES AND DAYDREAMS   BOND, NELSON S.   AC
SPORTSMAN, THE   SS
    31ST OF FEBRUARY, THE   BOND, NELSON S.   AC
TAKE MY DRUM TO ENGLAND-   SS   UNK 41 08
    31ST OF FEBRUARY, THE   BOND, NELSON S.   AC
THIS IS THE LAND   SS   BBM 51 04
    NO TIME LIKE THE FUTURE   BOND, NELSON S.   AC
    *OUTER REACHES, THE   DERLETH, AUGUST   AN
TO PEOPLE A NEW WORLD   SS   BBM 50 11
    *BEACHHEADS IN SPACE   DERLETH, AUGUST   AN
    NIGHTMARES AND DAYDREAMS   BOND, NELSON S.   AC
UNCOMMON CASTAWAY   SS   AFR 49 11
    NO TIME LIKE THE FUTURE   BOND, NELSON S.   AC
UNION IN GEHENNA   NV   FAD 42 11
    MR. MERGENTHWIRKER'S LOBBIES AND OTHER FANTASTIC TALES
                                BOND, NELSON S.   AC
VITAL FACTOR   SS   51
    GREAT SCIENCE FICTION STORIES SMITH, CORDELIA T.   AN
    NO TIME LIKE THE FUTURE   BOND, NELSON S.   AC
VOICE FROM THE CURIOUS CUBE, THE   SS
    NO TIME LIKE THE FUTURE   BOND, NELSON S.   AC
WHERE ARE YOU, MR. BIGGS?   SS   WRT 41 09
    LANCELOT BIGGS: SPACEMAN   BOND, NELSON S.   AC
WORLD OF WILLIAM GRESHAM, THE   NV
    NO TIME LIKE THE FUTURE   BOND, NELSON S.   AC

BONE, J. F.
FOUNDING FATHER   NA   GAL 62 04
    13 ABOVE THE NIGHT   CONKLIN, GROFF   AN
GAMESMAN   NV
    CRISIS   ELWOOD, ROGER   OA
HIGH PRIEST   SS   STG 74
    STRANGE GODS   ELWOOD, ROGER   OA
    VISIONS OF TOMORROW   ELWOOD, ROGER   AN
INSIDEKICK   NV   GAL 59 02
    ANOTHER PART OF THE GALAXY   CONKLIN, GROFF   AN
    SIXTH GALAXY READER, THE   GOLD, H. L.   AN
ON THE FOURTH PLANET   SS   GAL 63 04
    12 GREAT CLASSICS OF SCIENCE FICTION CONKLIN, GROFF AN
    9TH ANNUAL OF THE YEAR'S BEST S-F, THE MERRIL, JUDITH AN
PRIZE FOR EDIE, A   SS   ASF 61 04
    NEVER IN THIS WORLD   STONE, IDELLA P.   AN
    7TH ANNUAL OF THE YEAR'S BEST S-F, THE MERRIL, JUDITH AN

BONE, J. F.   (CONTINUED)
    SCENTS OF IT, THE   NV   INY 71 02
    INFINITY 2   HOSKINS, ROBERT   OA
TRIGGERMAN   SS   ASF 58 12
    JOURNEYS IN SCIENCE FICTION   LOUGHLIN, RICHARD L.   AN
    POLITICAL SCIENCE FICTION   GREENBERG& WARRICK   AN
    PROLOGUE TO ANALOG   CAMPBELL, JOHN W. JR   AN
    SF:59, THE YEAR'S GREATEST SCIENCE FICTION AND FANTASY
                                MERRIL, JUDITH   AN

BONFIGLIOLI, KYRIL
BLASTOFF   SS   64
    ENGLAND SWINGS SF   MERRIL, JUDITH   AN
    SPACE-TIME JOURNAL, THE   MERRIL, JUDITH   AN

BOOTH, PHILIP
LET THE TREES   PM   PNW 69 FL
    SPECULATIONS   SANDERS, THOMAS E.   AN

BORGES, JORGE LUIS
CIRCULAR RUINS, THE (TRANSLATED BY JAMES E. IRBY) SS 62
    LIGHT FANTASTIC, THE   HARRISON, HARRY   AN
    PERCHANCE TO DREAM   KNIGHT, DAMON   AN
    11TH ANNUAL OF THE YEAR'S BEST S-F, THE
                                MERRIL, JUDITH   AN
    FUNES THE MEMORIOUS   SS   62
    NEW WORLDS OF FANTASY NO. 3   CARR, TERRY   AN
GARDEN OF FORKING PATHS, THE   SS   62
    TRAPS OF TIME, THE   MOORCOCK, MICHAEL   AN
IMMORTAL, THE   SS   62
    NEW WORLDS OF FANTASY   CARR, TERRY   AN
LIBRARY OF BABEL, THE   SS   62
    MIRROR OF INFINITY, THE   SILVERBERG, ROBERT   AN
    NEW WORLDS OF FANTASY NO. 2   CARR, TERRY   AN
LOTTERY IN BABYLON, THE   SS   62
    INTO THE UNKNOWN   CARR, TERRY   AN

BORGESE, ELISABETH M
IMMORTAL FISH, THE   SS   57
    PAST, PRESENT, AND FUTURE PERFECT WOLFE, J&FITZ GERALD AN
TRUE SELF   SS   GAL 59 10
    SIXTH GALAXY READER, THE   GOLD, H. L.   AN
TWIN'S WAIL   NV   STR 59 06
    STAR OF STARS   POHL, FREDERIK   AN
    STAR SCIENCE FICTION STORIES NO. 6 POHL, FREDERIK   OA

BORSKI, ROBERT
IN THE CROWDED PART OF HEAVEN   SS   SFE 74 01
    SCIENCE FICTION EMPHASIS NO. 1 GERROLD, DAVID   OA
IN THE HOUR OF NOT QUITE RAIN   SS   SFM 74 07
    BEST OF SCIENCE FICTION MONTHLY, THE SACKS, JANET   AN
TROLLS   SS   FSF 74 05
    ANTIGRAV: COSMIC COMEDIES   STRICK, PHILIP   AN

BOSTON, BRUCE
BREAK   SS   NWQ 74 06
    NEW WORLDS NO. 6   PLATT & BAILEY   OA
TARFU'S LAST SHOW   SS
    FUTURE PASTIMES   EDELSTEIN, SCOTT   OA

BOSTWICK, ARTHUR E.
FROM "FOUR-DIMENSIONAL SPACE" (1896) AR   NSR 96
    FUTURE PERFECT   FRANKLIN, H. BRUCE   AN

BOSWORTH, ALAN R.
JESUS SHOES   SS   UNK 42 04
    FROM UNKNOWN WORLDS   CAMPBELL, JOHN W. JR   AN

BOUCHER, ANTHONY AND J. FRANCIS MCCOMAS
BEST FROM FANTASY AND SCIENCE FICTION   AN H LBR 52
BEST FROM FANTASY AND SCIENCE FICTION: 2   AN H LBR 53
BEST FROM FANTASY AND SCIENCE FICTION: 3   AN H DBL 54
    ACE PB EDITION OMITS ALL POEMS

BOUCHER, ANTHONY   PSEUD. FOR WILLIAM ANTHONY PARKER WHITE
BEST FROM FANTASY AND SCIENCE FICTION: 4   AN H DBL 55
    ACE PB EDITION OMITS ALL POEMS EXCEPT ASIMOV'S
BEST FROM FANTASY AND SCIENCE FICTION: 5   AN H DBL 56
    ACE PB EDITION OMITS POEMS "1980 OVERTURES", "SILENT UPON TWO
    PEAKS" AND "THE GLASS OF THE FUTURE"
BEST FROM FANTASY AND SCIENCE FICTION: 6   AN H DBL 57
    ACE PB EDITION OMITS POEMS "FLYING CHAUCER" AND
    "I WANT MY NAME IN THE TITLE"
BEST FROM FANTASY AND SCIENCE FICTION: 7   AN H DBL 58
    ACE PB EDITION OMITS ALL POEMS EXCEPT BUCK'S
BEST FROM FANTASY AND SCIENCE FICTION: 8   AN H DBL 59
    ACE PB EDITION OMITS FEGHOOTS AND POEMS
COMPLEAT WEREWOLF, THE   AC H SAS 69
FAR AND AWAY   AC   BAL 55
TREASURY OF GREAT SCIENCE FICTION, A VOL.1   AN H DBL 59
TREASURY OF GREAT SCIENCE FICTION, A VOL.2   AN H DBL 59
    AMBASSADORS, THE   SS   STS 52 06
    FIFTY SHORT SCIENCE FICTION TALES ASIMOV & CONKLIN   AN
    *FUTURE TENSE   CROSSEN, KENDELL F.   AN
    GALAXY OF GHOULS   MERRIL, JUDITH   AN
    SHAPE OF THINGS, THE   KNIGHT, DAMON   AN
ANOMALY OF THE EMPTY MAN, THE   SS   FSF 52 04
    FAR AND AWAY   BOUCHER, ANTHONY   AC
    SCIENCE-FICTIONAL SHERLOCK HOLMES, THE COUNCIL OF FOUR AN
BALAAM   SS   NTL 54
    BEST SF 4   CRISPIN, EDMUND   AN
    FAR AND AWAY   BOUCHER, ANTHONY   AC
    GODS FOR TOMORROW   SANTESSON, HANS S.   AN
    OTHER WORLDS, OTHER GODS   MOHS, MAYO   AN
    9 TALES OF SPACE AND TIME   HEALY, RAYMOND J.   OA

BOUCHER, ANTHONY

BOVA, BEN

BOUCHER, ANTHONY   (CONTINUED)
BARRIER   NV ASF 42 09
    SPECTRUM 4   AMIS & CONQUEST   AN
    6 GREAT SHORT NOVELS OF SCIENCE FICTION
                                        CONKLIN, GROFF   AN
BEFORE THE CURTAIN...   IN
    TREASURY OF GREAT SCIENCE FICTION, A VOL.1
                                        BOUCHER, ANTHONY   AN
BOOKS   MS
    7TH ANNUAL OF THE YEAR'S BEST S-F, THE MERRIL, JUDITH   AN
    8TH ANNUAL OF THE YEAR'S BEST S-F, THE MERRIL, JUDITH   AN
    9TH ANNUAL OF THE YEAR'S BEST S-F, THE MERRIL, JUDITH   AN
    C. M. KORNBLUTH: A MEMORIAL BIBLIOGRAPHY MS FSF 58 07
    BEST FROM FANTASY AND SCIENCE FICTION: 8
                                        BOUCHER, ANTHONY   AN
CHRONOKINESIS OF JONATHAN HULL, THE   SS ASF 46 06
    GREAT STORIES OF SCIENCE FICTION   LEINSTER, MURRAY   AN
COMPLEAT WEREWOLF, THE   NV UNK 42 04
    *BEYOND HUMAN KEN   MERRIL, JUDITH   AN
    COMPLEAT WEREWOLF, THE   BOUCHER, ANTHONY   AC
    FROM UNKNOWN WORLDS   CAMPBELL, JOHN W. JR AN
CONQUEST   SS STR 53 02
    STAR SCIENCE FICTION STORIES NO. 2 POHL, FREDERIK   OA
ELSEWHEN   NV ASF 43 01
    FAR AND AWAY   BOUCHER, ANTHONY   AC
EXPEDITION   SS TWS 43 08
    *BEST OF SCIENCE FICTION   CONKLIN, GROFF   AN
    COMPLEAT WEREWOLF, THE   BOUCHER, ANTHONY   AC
    INVASION FROM MARS   WELLES, ORSON   AN
    MARS, WE LOVE YOU   HIPOLITO & MCNELLY   AN
FANTASY AND/OR SCIENCE FICTION   IN
    WALL AROUND THE WORLD, THE   COGSWELL, THEODORE R AC
FIRST, THE   SS FSF 52 10
    FAR AND AWAY   BOUCHER, ANTHONY   AC
GANDOLPHUS   SS FSF 56 12
    DECADE OF FANTASY AND SCIENCE FICTION, A
                                        MILLS, ROBERT P.   AN
GHOST OF ME, THE   SS UNK 42 06
    BEYOND THE BARRIERS OF SPACE AND TIME MERRIL, JUDITH   AN
    COMPLEAT WEREWOLF, THE   BOUCHER, ANTHONY   AC
GREATEST TERTIAN, THE   SS NEW 52 AN
    ENEMIES IN SPACE   CONKLIN, GROFF   AN
    *INVADERS OF EARTH   CONKLIN, GROFF   AN
    SCIENCE-FICTIONAL SHERLOCK HOLMES, THE COUNCIL OF FOUR   AN
INTRODUCTION   IN
    BEST FROM FANTASY AND SCIENCE FICTION: 4
                                        BOUCHER, ANTHONY   AN
    BEST FROM FANTASY AND SCIENCE FICTION: 6
                                        BOUCHER, ANTHONY   AN
    BEST FROM FANTASY AND SCIENCE FICTION: 7
                                        BOUCHER, ANTHONY   AN
    BEST FROM FANTASY AND SCIENCE FICTION: 8
                                        BOUCHER, ANTHONY   AN
    FAR OUT   KNIGHT, DAMON   AC
INTRODUCTION   IN C
    BEST FROM FANTASY AND SCIENCE FICTION BOUCHER & MCCOMAS AN
    BEST FROM FANTASY AND SCIENCE FICTION: 2
                                        BOUCHER & MCCOMAS   AN
    BEST FROM FANTASY AND SCIENCE FICTION: 3
                                        BOUCHER & MCCOMAS   AN
KHARTOUM: A PROSE LIMERICK   SS STF 55 08
    STRANGE BED FELLOWS   SCORTIA, THOMAS N.   AN
MR. LUPESCU   SS WRT 45 09
    COMPLEAT WEREWOLF, THE   BOUCHER, ANTHONY   AC
    DEVIL'S GENERATION, THE   GHIDALIA, VIC   AN
    SHOT IN THE DARK   MERRIL, JUDITH   AN
NELLTHU   SS FSF 55 08
    BEST FROM FANTASY AND SCIENCE FICTION: 5
                                        BOUCHER, ANTHONY   AN
    DARK SIDE, THE   KNIGHT, DAMON   AN
    DEALS WITH THE DEVIL   DAVENPORT, BASIL   AN
NINE-FINGER JACK   SS ESQ 51 05
    BEST SCIENCE-FICTION STORIES: 1952, THE
                                        BLEILER & DIKTY   AN
    FRONTIERS IN SPACE   BLEILER & DIKTY   AN
OTHER INAUGURATION, THE   SS FSF 53 03
    FAR AND AWAY   BOUCHER, ANTHONY   AC
    SCIENCE FICTION TERROR TALES   CONKLIN, GROFF   AN
PINK CATERPILLAR, THE   SS ADV 45 02
    COMPLEAT WEREWOLF, THE   BOUCHER, ANTHONY   AC
PUBLIC EYE   SS TWS 52 04
    SPACE, TIME & CRIME   DEFORD, MIRIAM ALLEN AN
Q.U.R.   SS ASF 43 03
    *ADVENTURES IN TIME AND SPACE   HEALY & MCCOMAS   AN
    COMPLEAT WEREWOLF, THE   BOUCHER, ANTHONY   AC
QUEST FOR SAINT AQUIN, THE   SS NTS 51
    BEST SF 5   CRISPIN, EDMUND   AN
    NEW TALES OF SPACE AND TIME   HEALY, RAYMOND J.   OA
    ONE HUNDRED YEARS OF SCIENCE FICTION KNIGHT, DAMON   AN
    OTHER WORLDS, OTHER GODS   MOHS, MAYO   AN
    SCIENCE FICTION HALL OF FAME VOLUME 1 SILVERBERG, ROBERT AN
    WORLDS OF SCIENCE FICTION, THE   MILLS, ROBERT P.   AN
REVIEW COPY   SS FSF 49 FL
    FAR AND AWAY   BOUCHER, ANTHONY   AC
ROBINC   SS ASF 43 09
    COMPLEAT WEREWOLF, THE   BOUCHER, ANTHONY   AC
S-F BOOKS- 1960   MS
    6TH ANNUAL OF THE YEAR'S BEST S-F, THE MERRIL, JUDITH   AN
SCIENCE FICTION STILL LEADS SCIENCE FACT AR NYT 57 12
    SF:58, THE YEAR'S GREATEST SCIENCE FICTION AND FANTASY
                                        MERRIL, JUDITH   AN
SCRAWNY ONE, THE   SS WRT 49 05
    UNEXPECTED, THE   MARGULIES, LEO   AN
SECRET OF THE HOUSE   SS GAL 53 03
    FAR AND AWAY   BOUCHER, ANTHONY   AC

BOUCHER, ANTHONY   (CONTINUED)
SHAPE IN TIME, A   SS FIN 70
    FUTURE IS NOW, THE   NOLAN, WILLIAM F.   OA
SHERLOCK HOLMES AND SCIENCE FICTION   IN
    SCIENCE-FICTIONAL SHERLOCK HOLMES, THE COUNCIL OF FOUR   AN
SNULBUG (FIRST IN UNKNOWN, DEC. 1941)   SS FSF 53 05
    BEST FROM FANTASY AND SCIENCE FICTION: 3
                                        BOUCHER & MCCOMAS   AN
    COMPLEAT WEREWOLF, THE   BOUCHER, ANTHONY   AC
    FAR AND AWAY   BOUCHER, ANTHONY   AC
    UNKNOWN, THE   BENSEN, D. R.   AN
SRIBERDEGIBIT   NV UNK 43 06
    FAR AND AWAY   BOUCHER, ANTHONY   AC
STAR BRIDE   SS TWS 51 12
    FAR AND AWAY   BOUCHER, ANTHONY   AC
    *STORIES FOR TOMORROW   SLOANE, WILLIAM   AN
STAR DUMMY, THE   SS FAN 52 FL
    OMNIBUS OF SCIENCE FICTION   CONKLIN, GROFF   AN
    SCIENCE FICTION OMNIBUS   CONKLIN, GROFF   AN
    STRANGE TRAVELS IN SCIENCE FICTION CONKLIN, GROFF   AN
THEY BITE   SS UNK 43 08
    COMPLEAT WEREWOLF, THE   BOUCHER, ANTHONY   AC
    FAR AND AWAY   BOUCHER, ANTHONY   AC
    ZACHERLEY'S VULTURE STEW   ZACHERLEY   AN
TRANSFER POINT   SS GAL 50 11
    ADVENTURES IN TOMORROW   CROSSEN, KENDELL F. AN
    ALPHA 7   SILVERBERG, ROBERT   AN
    SHADOW OF TOMORROW   POHL, FREDERIK   AN
WE PRINT THE TRUTH   NV ASF 43 12
    COMPLEAT WEREWOLF, THE   BOUCHER, ANTHONY   AC

BOUCHER, SANDY
SHADES   SS QRK 70 01
    QUARK/1   DELANY & HACKER   OA

BOULLE, PIERRE
TIME OUT OF MIND   OC H VAN 66
    AGE OF WISDOM, THE   SS
        TIME OUT OF MIND   BOULLE, PIERRE   OC
    DIABOLICAL WEAPON, THE   SS
        TIME OUT OF MIND   BOULLE, PIERRE   OC
    E=MC2   NV
        TIME OUT OF MIND   BOULLE, PIERRE   OC
    ENIGMATIC SAINT, THE   NV
        TIME OUT OF MIND   BOULLE, PIERRE   OC
    HALLUCINATION, THE   SS
        TIME OUT OF MIND   BOULLE, PIERRE   OC
    LOVE AND GRAVITY   NV
        TIME OUT OF MIND   BOULLE, PIERRE   OC
    LUNIANS, THE   NV
        TIME OUT OF MIND   BOULLE, PIERRE   OC
    MAN WHO HATED MACHINES, THE   SS
        TIME OUT OF MIND   BOULLE, PIERRE   OC
    MAN WHO PICKED UP PINS, THE   SS
        TIME OUT OF MIND   BOULLE, PIERRE   OC
    MIRACLE, THE   SS
        TIME OUT OF MIND   BOULLE, PIERRE   OC
    PERFECT ROBOT, THE   NV
        TIME OUT OF MIND   BOULLE, PIERRE   OC
    TIME OUT OF MIND   NV
        TIME OUT OF MIND   BOULLE, PIERRE   OC

BOULT, S. KYE
SAFETY ENGINEER, THE   NV ALC 73
    ALIEN CONDITION, THE   GOLDIN, STEPHEN   OA

BOUNDS, SYDNEY J.
ANIMATORS, THE   SS NEW 75 AN
    TALES OF TERROR FROM OUTER SPACE   CHETWYND-HAYES, R.   AN
BALLAD OF LUNA LIL, THE   SS NWR 69 14
    NEW WRITINGS IN SF. 14   CARNELL, JOHN   OA
LIAISON SERVICE   NV NWS 51 WI
    LAURIE'S SPACE ANNUAL   ANONYMOUS   AN
MATTER OF SALVAGE, A   SS NWS 52 01
    LAURIE'S SPACE ANNUAL   ANONYMOUS   AN
MONITOR   SS NWR 73 22
    NEW WRITINGS IN SF. 22   BULMER, KENNETH   OA
POSSESSED, THE   SS NWR 73 21
    NEW WRITINGS IN SF. 21   CARNELL, JOHN   OA
PUBLIC SERVICE   SS NWR 68 13
    NEW WRITINGS IN SF. 13   CARNELL, JOHN   OA
STARPORT   SS SFM 74 03
    BEST OF SCIENCE FICTION MONTHLY, THE SACKS, JANET   AN
TALENT SPOTTER   SS NWR 75 25
    NEW WRITINGS IN SF. 25   BULMER, KENNETH   OA
THROWBACK   SS NWR 69 16
    NEW WRITINGS IN SF. 16   CARNELL, JOHN   OA

BOVA, BEN
ANALOG ANNUAL   OA PYR 76 04
ANALOG 9   AN H DBL 73
FORWARD IN TIME   AC H WKR 73
MANY WORLDS OF SCIENCE FICTION, THE   OA H DUT 71
NOTES TO A SCIENCE FICTION WRITER   AC H SCB 75
    ONLY STORIES USED TO ILLUSTRATE WRITING TECHNIQUES ARE LISTED
SCIENCE FICTION HALL OF FAME VOLUME 2A   AN H DBL 73
SCIENCE FICTION HALL OF FAME VOLUME 2B   AN H DBL 73
BLOOD OF TYRANTS   NV AMZ 70 05
    FORWARD IN TIME   BOVA, BEN   AC
BRILLO   NV C ASF 70 08
    PARTNERS IN WONDER   ELLISON, HARLAN   AC
BUILD ME A MOUNTAIN   SS NEW 74 AN
    2020 VISION   POURNELLE, JERRY   AN
BUT WHAT IF WE TRIED IT?   AR 76
    FASTER THAN LIGHT   DANN & ZEBROWSKI   OA

BOVA, BEN   (CONTINUED)
DUELING MACHINE, THE (SEE THE PERFECT WARRIOR)   TC C
FIFTEEN MILES   SS   FSF 67 05
  BEST SF: 1967   HARRISON & ALDISS   AN
  FORWARD IN TIME   BOVA, BEN   AC
  NOTES TO A SCIENCE FICTION WRITER BOVA, BEN   AC
  POCKETFUL OF STARS, A   KNIGHT, DAMON   AN
FUTURE OF SCIENCE: PROMETHEUS, APOLLO, ATHENA, THE   AR
  NEBULA AWARD STORIES 9   WILHELM, KATE   AN
GREAT SUPERSONIC ZEPPELIN RACE, THE   NV
  FAR SIDE OF TIME, THE   ELWOOD, ROGER   OA
INTRODUCTION   IN
  ANALOG 9   BOVA, BEN   AN
  FORWARD IN TIME   BOVA, BEN   AC
  MANY WORLDS OF SCIENCE FICTION, THE BOVA, BEN   OA
  NEW VOICES IN SCIENCE FICTION   MARTIN, GEORGE R. R.   OA
  SCIENCE FICTION HALL OF FAME VOLUME 2A BOVA, BEN   AN
  SCIENCE FICTION HALL OF FAME VOLUME 2B BOVA, BEN   AN
INTRODUCTION: HUGO, JOHN AND THE MAGAZINES   IN
  ANALOG ANNUAL   BOVA, BEN   OA
INTRODUCTION: SPIDER ROBINSON: THE SF WRITER AS EMPATH   IN
  CALLAHAN'S CROSSTIME SALOON   ROBINSON, SPIDER   AC
MAN WHO SAW GUNGA DIN THIRTY TIMES, THE   SS   SCS 73
  SHOWCASE   ELWOOD, ROGER   OA
MEN OF GOOD WILL   SS C GAL 64 06
  COMBAT SF   DICKSON, GORDON R.   AN
  FORWARD IN TIME   BOVA, BEN   AC
  NOTES TO A SCIENCE FICTION WRITER BOVA, BEN   AC
  WORLD'S BEST SCIENCE FICTION: 1965 WOLLHEIM & CARR   AN
NEXT LOGICAL STEP, THE   SS   ASF 62 05
  FORWARD IN TIME   BOVA, BEN   AC
PERFECT WARRIOR, THE (THE DUELING MACHINE)   SN C ASF 63 05
  FORWARD IN TIME   BOVA, BEN   AC
SHINING ONES, THE (FULL VERSION)   NV   BLF 74 02
  NOTES TO A SCIENCE FICTION WRITER BOVA, BEN   AC
SIGHTSEERS, THE   SS   FUC 73
  FUTURE CITY   ELWOOD, ROGER   OA
SLIGHT MISCALCULATION, A   SS   FSF 71 08
  COSMIC LAUGHTER   HALDEMAN, JOE W.   AN
  FORWARD IN TIME   BOVA, BEN   AC
STARS, WON'T YOU HIDE ME?   SS   WOT 66 01
  FORWARD IN TIME   BOVA, BEN   AC
  NOTES TO A SCIENCE FICTION WRITER BOVA, BEN   AC
TEST IN ORBIT   SS   ASF 65 09
  FORWARD IN TIME   BOVA, BEN   AC
WEATHERMAKERS, THE   NV   ASF 66 12
  FORWARD IN TIME   BOVA, BEN   AC
WHERE IS EVERYBODY?   AR   AMZ 63 05
  9TH ANNUAL OF THE YEAR'S BEST S-F, THE MERRIL, JUDITH   AN
ZERO GEE   NV   DVS 72 02
  AGAIN, DANGEROUS VISIONS   ELLISON, HARLAN   OA
  BEST SCIENCE FICTION OF THE YEAR, THE NO. 2
                                   CARR, TERRY   AN
  FORWARD IN TIME   BOVA, BEN   AC

BOWEN, ELIZABETH
CHEERY SOUL, THE (1945)   SS   FSF 52 04
  BEST FROM FANTASY AND SCIENCE FICTION: 2
                                   BOUCHER & MCCOMAS   AN

BOY'S LIFE, ED. OF
BOYS' LIFE BOOK OF OUTER SPACE STORIES, THE   AN H RDM 64

BOYD, FELIX   PSEUD. FOR HARRY HARRISON
ROBOT WHO WANTED TO KNOW, THE   SS   FUN 58 03
  FANTASTIC UNIVERSE OMNIBUS, THE SANTESSON, HANS S.   AN

BOYD, LYLE   SEE PSEUD.
  BOYD ELLANBY (WITH WILLIAM C. BOYD)

BOYD, WILLIAM C.   SEE PSEUD. BOYD ELLANBY (WITH LYLE BOYD)

BRACKETT, LEIGH   (MRS. EDMOND HAMILTON)
BEST OF EDMOND HAMILTON, THE (LISTED UNDER EDMOND HAMILTON)
                                                  EC H NDB 77
BEST OF LEIGH BRACKETT, THE   AC H NDB 77
  EDITED BY EDMOND HAMILTON
BEST OF PLANET STORIES NO. 1, THE   AN   BAL 75 01
BOOK OF SKAITH, THE   AC H NDB 76
  THE ADVENTURES OF ERIC JOHN STARK
COMING OF THE TERRANS, THE   NO   ACE 67
HALFLING AND OTHER STORIES, THE   AC   ACE 73 09
  AFTERWORD   MS
    BEST OF LEIGH BRACKETT, THE   BRACKETT, LEIGH   AC
ALL THE COLORS OF THE RAINBOW   SS   VSF 57 11
  HALFLING AND OTHER STORIES, THE BRACKETT, LEIGH   AC
  HUMAN AND OTHER BEINGS   DEGRAEFF, ALLEN   AN
  NO LIMITS   FERMAN, JOSEPH W.   AN
BEAST-JEWEL OF MARS, THE   SS   PLS 55 SP
  COMING OF THE TERRANS, THE   BRACKETT, LEIGH   NO
BEYOND OUR NARROW SKIES   IN
  BEST OF PLANET STORIES NO. 1, THE BRACKETT, LEIGH   AN
CHILD OF THE SUN   SS   PLS 42 SP
  MORE ADVENTURES ON OTHER PLANETS WOLLHEIM, DONALD A.   AN
CITADEL OF LOST AGES, THE   NV   TWS 50 12
  HALFLING AND OTHER STORIES, THE BRACKETT, LEIGH   AC
CITY OF THE LOST ONES (ENCHANTRESS OF VENUS)   NV   PLS 49 FL
  RACE TO THE STARS   MARGULIES & FRIEND   AN
COME SING THE MOONS OF MORAVENN   NV
  OTHER SIDE OF TOMORROW, THE   ELWOOD, ROGER   OA
DANCING GIRL OF GANYMEDE, THE   SS   TWS 50 02
  AWARD SCIENCE FICTION READER   NORTON, ALDEN H.   AN
  HALFLING AND OTHER STORIES, THE BRACKETT, LEIGH   AC

BRACKETT, LEIGH   (CONTINUED)
ENCHANTRESS OF VENUS (ALSO AS CITY OF THE LOST ONES)
                                                  NV   PLS 49 FL
  BEST OF LEIGH BRACKETT, THE   BRACKETT, LEIGH   AC
  GIANT ANTHOLOGY OF SCIENCE FICTION MARGULIES & FRIEND   AN
  HALFLING AND OTHER STORIES, THE BRACKETT, LEIGH   AC
FIFTY YEARS OF WONDER   IN
  BEST OF EDMOND HAMILTON, THE   HAMILTON, EDMOND   AC
GINGER STAR, THE   NO   IFS 74 02
  BOOK OF SKAITH, THE   BRACKETT, LEIGH   AC
HALFLING, THE   SS   AST 43 02
  HALFLING AND OTHER STORIES, THE BRACKETT, LEIGH   AC
  SHOT IN THE DARK   MERRIL, JUDITH   AN
HOUNDS OF SKAITH, THE   NO   BAL 74 10
  BOOK OF SKAITH, THE   BRACKETT, LEIGH   AC
HOW BRIGHT THE STARS   SS   FTP 73
  FLAME TREE PLANET   ELWOOD, ROGER   OA
JEWEL OF BAS, THE   NV   PLS 44 SP
  BEST OF LEIGH BRACKETT, THE   BRACKETT, LEIGH   AC
LAKE OF THE GONE FOREVER, THE   NV   TWS 49 10
  HALFLING AND OTHER STORIES, THE BRACKETT, LEIGH   AC
  MORE WOMEN OF WONDER   SARGENT, PAMELA   AN
  SPACE ODYSSEYS   ALDISS, BRIAN W.   AN
LAST DAYS OF SHANDAKOR, THE   NV   STS 52 04
  BEST OF LEIGH BRACKETT, THE   BRACKETT, LEIGH   AC
  COMING OF THE TERRANS, THE   BRACKETT, LEIGH   NO
  PRIZE SCIENCE FICTION   WOLLHEIM, DONALD A.   AN
LORELEI OF THE RED MIST   NV C PLS 46 SU
  BEST OF PLANET STORIES NO. 1, THE BRACKETT, LEIGH   AN
  HUMAN EQUATION, THE   NOLAN, WILLIAM F.   AN
  THREE TIMES INFINITY   MARGULIES, LEO   AN
MARS MINUS BISHA   SS   PLS 54 01
  COMING OF THE TERRANS, THE   BRACKETT, LEIGH   NO
MOMMIES AND DADDIES   SS
  CRISIS   ELWOOD, ROGER   OA
MOON THAT VANISHED, THE   NV   TWS 48 10
  BEST OF LEIGH BRACKETT, THE   BRACKETT, LEIGH   AC
  SWORDSMEN IN THE SKY   WOLLHEIM, DONALD A.   AN
OTHER PEOPLE, THE (THE QUEER ONES)   NV   VSF 57 03
  BEST SCIENCE FICTION STORIES AND NOVELS: 9TH SERIES
                                   DIKTY, T. E.   AN
PURPLE PRIESTESS OF THE MAD MOON   SS   FSF 64 10
  COMING OF THE TERRANS, THE   BRACKETT, LEIGH   NO
QUEER ONES, THE (ALSO AS THE OTHER PEOPLE)   NV   VSF 57 03
  BEST OF LEIGH BRACKETT, THE   BRACKETT, LEIGH   AC
  GENTLE INVADERS   SANTESSON, HANS S.   AN
REAVERS OF SKAITH, THE   NO   BAL 76 08
  BOOK OF SKAITH, THE   BRACKETT, LEIGH   AC
RETREAT TO THE STARS   SS   AST 41 11
  ADVENTURES IN TOMORROW   CROSSEN, KENDELL F.   AN
ROAD TO SINHARAT, THE   NV   AMZ 63 05
  COMING OF THE TERRANS, THE   BRACKETT, LEIGH   NO
SEA-KINGS OF MARS (SEE THE SWORD OF RHIANNON)   TC
SHADOWS, THE   SS   STS 52 02
  HALFLING AND OTHER STORIES, THE BRACKETT, LEIGH   AC
SHANNACH- THE LAST   NO   PLS 52 11
  BEST OF LEIGH BRACKETT, THE   BRACKETT, LEIGH   AC
SWORD OF RHIANNON, THE (SEA-KINGS OF MARS)   EX   TWS 49 06
  SPACE OPERA   ALDISS, BRIAN W.   AN
TERROR OUT OF SPACE   SS   PLS 44 SU
  HIDDEN PLANET, THE   WOLLHEIM, DONALD A.   AN
TRUANTS, THE   SS   STS 50 07
  HALFLING AND OTHER STORIES, THE BRACKETT, LEIGH   AC
TWEENER, THE   SS   FSF 55 02
  BEST OF LEIGH BRACKETT, THE   BRACKETT, LEIGH   AC
VANISHING VENUSIANS, THE   SS   PLS 45 SP
  BEST OF LEIGH BRACKETT, THE   BRACKETT, LEIGH   AC
VEIL OF ASTELLAR, THE   SS   TWS 44 SP
  BEST OF LEIGH BRACKETT, THE   BRACKETT, LEIGH   AC
  PLANETS OF WONDER   CARR, TERRY   AN
WOMAN FROM ALTAIR, THE   NV   STS 51 07
  BEST OF LEIGH BRACKETT, THE   BRACKETT, LEIGH   AC

BRADBURY, RAY AND ROBERT BLOCH
BLOCH AND BRADBURY   AC   TWR 69
  IN ENGLAND AS "FEVER DREAM"
FEVER DREAM   AC   SPH 70
  SEE "BLOCH AND BRADBURY"

BRADBURY, RAY
AUTUMN PEOPLE, THE   AC   BAL 65 10
  COMIC BOOK VERSIONS OF STORIES FROM E.C. COMICS
CIRCUS OF DR. LAO AND OTHER IMPROBABLE STORIES   AN   BAN 56 10
DANDELION WINE   NO H DBL 57
DARK CARNIVAL   AC H ARK 47
DARK CARNIVAL (BRITISH)   AC H HML 48
DAY IT RAINED FOREVER, THE   AC H HDV 60
  BRITISH VERSION OF "A MEDICINE FOR MELANCHOLY"
FAHRENHEIT 451   AC H BAL 53
GOLDEN APPLES OF THE SUN   AC H DBL 53 03
  ALSO IN "TWICE 22"
  ENGLISH EDITION (HDV 53) OMITS STORIES "THE BIG BLACK AND
  WHITE GAME" AND "THE GREAT FIRE"
I SING THE BODY ELECTRIC   AC H KNP 69
ILLUSTRATED MAN, THE   AC H DBL 51 02
ILLUSTRATED MAN, THE (BRITISH)   AC H HDV 52
LONG AFTER MIDNIGHT   AC H KNP 76
MACHINERIES OF JOY, THE   AC H SAS 64 02
  ENGLISH EDITION (HDV 64) OMITS "ALMOST THE END OF THE WORLD"
MARTIAN CHRONICLES, THE   AC H DBL 50 05
  IN ENGLAND AS "THE SILVER LOCUSTS"
MARTIAN CHRONICLES, THE (BRITISH SFBC, ADDS:)   AC H SBB 53
  OMITS STORY "USHER II"
MEDICINE FOR MELANCHOLY, A   AC H DBL 58
  ALSO IN "TWICE 22"
  IN ENGLAND WITH SOME CONTENTS CHANGE AS

BRADBURY, RAY

    "THE DAY IT RAINED FOREVER"
OCTOBER COUNTRY, THE   AC H BAL 55
OCTOBER COUNTRY, THE (BRITISH)   AC H HDV 56
PILLAR OF FIRE AND OTHER PLAYS   AC   BAN 57 11
R IS FOR ROCKET   AC H DBL 62 10
S IS FOR SPACE   AC H DBL 66 08
SILVER LOCUSTS, THE   AC H HDV 51
    SEE "THE MARTIAN CHRONICLES", OMITS STORY "USHER II"
SMALL ASSASSIN, THE   AC   ACB 62
TIMELESS STORIES FOR TODAY AND TOMORROW   AN   BAN 52 09
TOMORROW MIDNIGHT   AC   BAL 66
    STORIES IN CARTOON FORM
TWICE 22   AC H DBL 66
VINTAGE BRADBURY, THE   AC   VNT 65
WONDERFUL ICE CREAM SUIT AND OTHER PLAYS, THE   AC   BAN 72 04
    ABOUT BILL NOLAN   IN
       IMPACT-20   NOLAN, WILLIAM F.   AC
ALL SUMMER IN A DAY   SS   FSF 54 03
    BEST FROM FANTASY AND SCIENCE FICTION: 4
                                     BOUCHER, ANTHONY   AN
    MEDICINE FOR MELANCHOLY, A   BRADBURY, RAY   AC
    SPACE OPERA   ALDISS, BRIAN W.   AN
    TOMORROW'S CHILDREN   ASIMOV, ISAAC   AN
    VOYAGES: SCENARIOS FOR A SHIP CALLED EARTH
                                     SAUER, ROB   AN
    YOU AND SCIENCE FICTION   HOLLISTER, BERNARD C AN
ALMOST THE END OF THE WORLD   SS   REP 57 12
    DAY IT RAINED FOREVER, THE   BRADBURY, RAY   AC
    MACHINERIES OF JOY, THE   BRADBURY, RAY   AC
AND SO DIED RIABOUCHINSKA   SS   SDM 53 06
    MACHINERIES OF JOY, THE   BRADBURY, RAY   AC
AND THE MOON BE STILL AS BRIGHT   SS   TWS 48 06
    BEST SCIENCE-FICTION STORIES: 1949, THE
                                     BLEILER & DIKTY   AN
    MARTIAN CHRONICLES, THE   BRADBURY, RAY   AC
AND THE ROCK CRIED OUT (THE MILLIONTH MURDER)   SS   MHT 53 09
    DAY IT RAINED FOREVER, THE   BRADBURY, RAY   AC
    FAHRENHEIT 451   BRADBURY, RAY   AC
    VINTAGE BRADBURY, THE   BRADBURY, RAY   AC
AND THE SAILOR, HOME FROM THE SEA (FOREVER VOYAGE)
                                         SS   SEP 60 01
    MACHINERIES OF JOY, THE   BRADBURY, RAY   AC
AND THIS DID DANTE DO   SS   NOV 70 01
    *NOVA 1   HARRISON, HARRY   OA
ANTHEM SPRINTERS, THE (THE QUEEN'S OWN EVADERS) SS   PBY 63 06
    MACHINERIES OF JOY, THE   BRADBURY, RAY   AC
    VINTAGE BRADBURY, THE   BRADBURY, RAY   AC
ANY FRIEND OF NICHOLAS NICKLEBY'S IS A FRIEND OF MINE
    (THE BEST OF TIMES)   NV   MCC 66 01
    I SING THE BODY ELECTRIC   BRADBURY, RAY   AC
APRIL WITCH, THE   SS   SEP 52 04
    *GOLDEN APPLES OF THE SUN   BRADBURY, RAY   AC
ASLEEP IN ARMAGEDDON (ALSO AS PERCHANCE TO DREAM) SS   PLS 48 WI
    ASLEEP IN ARMAGEDDON   SISSONS, MICHAEL   AN
    BEYOND THE STARS AND OTHER STORIES   ANONYMOUS   AN
    *POSSIBLE WORLDS OF SCIENCE FICTION   CONKLIN, GROFF   AN
AUGUST 2026: THERE WILL COME SOFT RAINS   SS   COL 50 05
    IN DREAMS AWAKE   FIEDLER, LESLIE A.   AN
BEAST FROM 20,000 FATHOMS, THE (ALSO AS THE FOGHORN)
                                         SS   SEP 51 06
    GHOULS, THE   HAINING, PETER   AN
BEAUTIFUL ONE IS HERE, THE (SEE I SING THE BODY ELECTRIC)
                                         TC
BEGGAR ON DUBLIN BRIDGE, THE (SEE THE BEGGAR ON O'CONNELL
BRIDGE)   TC
BEGGAR ON O'CONNELL BRIDGE, THE (THE BEGGAR ON DUBLIN BRIDGE)
                                         SS   SEP 61 01
    MACHINERIES OF JOY, THE   BRADBURY, RAY   AC
BEST OF ALL POSSIBLE WORLDS   SS   PBY 60 08
    MACHINERIES OF JOY, THE   BRADBURY, RAY   AC
BEST OF TIMES, THE (SEE ANY FRIEND OF NICHOLAS NICKLEBY'S IS A
FRIEND OF MINE)   TC
BETTER PART OF WISDOM, THE   SS
    LONG AFTER MIDNIGHT   BRADBURY, RAY   AC
BIG BLACK AND WHITE GAME, THE   SS   AMM 45 08
    *GOLDEN APPLES OF THE SUN   BRADBURY, RAY   AC
BLACK FERRIS, THE   SS   WRT 48 05
    DARK SIDE, THE   KNIGHT, DAMON   AN
    DEVIL'S GENERATION, THE   GHIDALIA, VIC   AN
BLUE BOTTLE, THE (DEATH WISH)   SS   PLS 50 FL
    LONG AFTER MIDNIGHT   BRADBURY, RAY   AC
    SEA OF SPACE, A   NOLAN, WILLIAM F.   AN
BOYS, RAISE GIANT MUSHROOMS IN YOUR CELLAR (COME INTO MY
CELLAR)   SS   GAL 62 10
    MACHINERIES OF JOY, THE   BRADBURY, RAY   AC
BURNING MAN, THE   SS
    LONG AFTER MIDNIGHT   BRADBURY, RAY   AC
CARNIVAL OF MADNESS (SEE USHER II)   TC
CHANGELING   SS   SSS 49 07
    PSEUDO PEOPLE, THE   NOLAN, WILLIAM F.   AN
CHRIST, OLD STUDENT IN A NEW SCHOOL   PM   DVS 72 02
    AGAIN, DANGEROUS VISIONS   ELLISON, HARLAN   OA
CHRISTUS APOLLO   PM   NEW 69 AC
    I SING THE BODY ELECTRIC   BRADBURY, RAY   AC
CHRISTUS APOLLO (SELECTION)   PM   NEW 69 AC
    OTHER WORLDS, OTHER GODS   MOHS, MAYO   AN
CHRYSALIS   SS   AMZ 46 07
    S IS FOR SPACE   BRADBURY, RAY   AC
CISTERN, THE   SS   MAD 47 05
    *DARK CARNIVAL   BRADBURY, RAY   AC
    *OCTOBER COUNTRY, THE   BRADBURY, RAY   AC
    SMALL ASSASSIN, THE   BRADBURY, RAY   AC
CITY, THE (PURPOSE)   SS   STS 50 07
    *ILLUSTRATED MAN, THE   BRADBURY, RAY   AC
COFFIN, THE (WAKE FOR THE LIVING)   SS   DMN 47 09
    AUTUMN PEOPLE, THE   BRADBURY, RAY   AC

BRADBURY, RAY   (CONTINUED)
    *DARK CARNIVAL   BRADBURY, RAY   AC
COLD WIND AND THE WARM, THE   SS   HRP 64 07
    I SING THE BODY ELECTRIC   BRADBURY, RAY   AC
COME INTO MY CELLAR (ALSO AS BOYS, RAISE GIANT MUSHROOMS
    IN YOUR CELLAR)   SS   GAL 62 10
    NIGHTMARE GARDEN   GHIDALIA, VIC   AN
    S IS FOR SPACE   BRADBURY, RAY   AC
    SEVENTH GALAXY READER, THE   POHL, FREDERIK   AN
    17 X INFINITY   CONKLIN, GROFF   AN
CONCRETE MIXER, THE   SS   TWS 49 04
    *ILLUSTRATED MAN, THE   BRADBURY, RAY   AC
CORA AND THE GREAT WIDE WORLD OVER THERE (SEE THE GREAT WIDE
WORLD OVER THERE)   TC
CREATURES THAT TIME FORGOT, THE (SEE FROST AND FIRE)
                                        TC
CROWD, THE   SS   WRT 43 05
    *DARK CARNIVAL   BRADBURY, RAY   AC
    *OCTOBER COUNTRY, THE   BRADBURY, RAY   AC
    SMALL ASSASSIN, THE   BRADBURY, RAY   AC
    *TERROR IN THE MODERN VEIN   WOLLHEIM, DONALD A. AN
DANDELION WINE   SS   GOR 53 06
    DANDELION WINE   BRADBURY, RAY   NO
    VINTAGE BRADBURY, THE   BRADBURY, RAY   AC
DARK THEY WERE, AND GOLDEN-EYED (THE NAMING OF NAMES)
                                       SS   TWS 49 08
    DAY IT RAINED FOREVER, THE   BRADBURY, RAY   AC
    MEDICINE FOR MELANCHOLY, A   BRADBURY, RAY   AC
    OTHER DIMENSION, THE   ROSNER, SARA   AN
    S IS FOR SPACE   BRADBURY, RAY   AC
    SCIENCE FICTION   BURTON, S. H.   AN
DARLING ADOLPH   SS
    LONG AFTER MIDNIGHT   BRADBURY, RAY   AC
DAY IT RAINED FOREVER, THE   SS   HRP 57 07
    DAY IT RAINED FOREVER, THE   BRADBURY, RAY   AC
    MEDICINE FOR MELANCHOLY, A   BRADBURY, RAY   AC
DAY OF DEATH, THE (SEE EL DIA DE MUERTE)   TC
DEAD MAN, THE   SS   WRT 45 07
    BLOCH AND BRADBURY   BRADBURY & BLOCH   AC
    *DARK CARNIVAL   BRADBURY, RAY   AC
    SMALL ASSASSIN, THE   BRADBURY, RAY   AC
DEATH AND THE MAIDEN   SS   FSF 60 03
    MACHINERIES OF JOY, THE   BRADBURY, RAY   AC
DEATH WISH (SEE THE BLUE BOTTLE)   TC
DEATH-BY-RAIN (SEE THE LONG RAIN)   TC
DINNER AT DAWN   SS   EVW 54 02
    DANDELION WINE   BRADBURY, RAY   NO
DOODAD   SS   ASF 43 09
    ALIEN EARTH AND OTHER STORIES   ELWOOD & MOSKOWITZ AN
    STRANGE SIGNPOSTS   ELWOOD & MOSKOWITZ AN
DOWNWIND FROM GETTYSBURG   SS   PBY 69 06
    I SING THE BODY ELECTRIC   BRADBURY, RAY   AC
DRAGON, THE   SS   FSF 56 03
    DAY IT RAINED FOREVER, THE   BRADBURY, RAY   AC
    MEDICINE FOR MELANCHOLY, A   BRADBURY, RAY   AC
    R IS FOR ROCKET   BRADBURY, RAY   AC
DRINK ENTIRE: AGAINST THE MADNESS OF CROWDS   SS   GLR
    LONG AFTER MIDNIGHT   BRADBURY, RAY   AC
DRUMMER BOY OF SHILOH, THE   SS   SEP 60 04
    MACHINERIES OF JOY, THE   BRADBURY, RAY   AC
    TRANSFORMATIONS II   ROSELLE, DANIEL   AN
DWARF, THE   SS   FAN 54 01
    *OCTOBER COUNTRY, THE   BRADBURY, RAY   AC
    VINTAGE BRADBURY, THE   BRADBURY, RAY   AC
DWELLERS IN SILENCE (THE LONG YEARS)   SS   MCL 48 09
    BEST SCIENCE-FICTION STORIES: 1950, THE
                                     BLEILER & DIKTY   AN
EARTH MEN, THE   SS   TWS 48 08
    MARTIAN CHRONICLES, THE   BRADBURY, RAY   AC
    *OTHER SIDE OF THE MOON, THE   DERLETH, AUGUST   AN
    TOWARD INFINITY   KNIGHT, DAMON   AN
EL DIA DE MUERTE (THE DAY OF DEATH)   SS   TCH 47 FL
    MACHINERIES OF JOY, THE   BRADBURY, RAY   AC
EMBROIDERY   SS   MAR 51 11
    *GOLDEN APPLES OF THE SUN   BRADBURY, RAY   AC
EMISSARY, THE   SS   NEW 47 AC
    *DARK CARNIVAL   BRADBURY, RAY   AC
    *OCTOBER COUNTRY, THE   BRADBURY, RAY   AC
EN LA NOCHE (TORRID SACRIFICE)   SS   CAV 52 11
    *GOLDEN APPLES OF THE SUN   BRADBURY, RAY   AC
END OF THE BEGINNING, THE (NEXT STOP: THE STARS) SS   MCL 56 10
    DAY IT RAINED FOREVER, THE   BRADBURY, RAY   AC
    MEDICINE FOR MELANCHOLY, A   BRADBURY, RAY   AC
    R IS FOR ROCKET   BRADBURY, RAY   AC
    SCIENCE FICTION SHOWCASE   KORNBLUTH, MARY   AN
EPILOGUE   MS   51
    *ILLUSTRATED MAN, THE   BRADBURY, RAY   AC
EXILES, THE (THE MAD WIZARDS OF MARS, MCL 49 09) SS   FSF 50 WS
    *BEYOND TIME AND SPACE   DERLETH, AUGUST   AN
    *ILLUSTRATED MAN, THE   BRADBURY, RAY   AC
    R IS FOR ROCKET   BRADBURY, RAY   AC
FAHRENHEIT 451 (EXPANSION OF "THE FIREMAN")   NO   GAL 51 02
    FAHRENHEIT 451   BRADBURY, RAY   AC
FEVER DREAM   SS   WRT 48 09
    BLOCH AND BRADBURY   BRADBURY & BLOCH   AC
    DAY IT RAINED FOREVER, THE   BRADBURY, RAY   AC
    MEDICINE FOR MELANCHOLY, A   BRADBURY, RAY   AC
    VINTAGE BRADBURY, THE   BRADBURY, RAY   AC
FINAL SCEPTRE, A LASTING CROWN, A (ALSO AS HENRY THE NINTH)
                                      SS   FSF 69 10
    TWENTY YEARS OF FANTASY & SCIENCE FICTION
                                     FERMAN & MILLS   AN
FIRE BALLOONS, THE (IN THIS SIGN)   SS   IMG 51 04
    BEST SF   CRISPIN, EDMUND   AN
    CONTACT   KEYES, NOEL   AN
    *ILLUSTRATED MAN, THE   BRADBURY, RAY   AC

BRADBURY, RAY

BRADBURY, RAY

BRADBURY, RAY   (CONTINUED)
  MARTIAN CHRONICLES, THE (BRITISH SFBC, ADDS:)
                           BRADBURY, RAY   AC
    NEW AWARENESS, THE   WARRICK & GREENBERG   AN
    SILVER LOCUSTS, THE   BRADBURY, RAY   AC
    SPECIAL WONDER   MCCOMAS, J. FRANCIS   AN
  FIREMAN, THE (SEE FAHRENHEIT 451)   TC
  FIRST NIGHT OF LENT, THE   SS   PBY 56 03
    MEDICINE FOR MELANCHOLY, A   BRADBURY, RAY   AC
  FLIGHT OF RAVENS, A   SS   CFQ 52 WI
    MACHINERIES OF JOY, THE   BRADBURY, RAY   AC
  FLYING MACHINE, THE   SS   NEW 53 AC
    *GOLDEN APPLES OF THE SUN   BRADBURY, RAY   AC
    S IS FOR SPACE   BRADBURY, RAY   AC
  FOG HORN, THE (THE BEAST FROM 20,000 FATHOMS) SS   SEP 51 06
    *GOLDEN APPLES OF THE SUN   BRADBURY, RAY   AC
    R IS FOR ROCKET   BRADBURY, RAY   AC
    SPECULATIONS   SANDERS, THOMAS E.   AN
    VINTAGE BRADBURY, THE   BRADBURY, RAY   AC
  FOGHORN, THE   PL   SEP 51 06
    PILLAR OF FIRE AND OTHER PLAYS   BRADBURY, RAY   AC
  FOREVER AND THE EARTH   SS   PLS 50 SP
    *BIG BOOK OF SCIENCE FICTION   CONKLIN, GROFF   AN
    LONG AFTER MIDNIGHT   BRADBURY, RAY   AC
  FOREVER VOYAGE (SEE AND THE SAILOR, HOME FROM THE SEA)

  FOREWORD   IN
    AUTUMN PEOPLE, THE   BRADBURY, RAY   AC
    MAGIC MAN AND OTHER SCIENCE-FANTASY STORIES
                           BEAUMONT, CHARLES   AC
    TOMORROW MIDNIGHT   BRADBURY, RAY   AC
  FOX AND THE FOREST, THE (TO THE FUTURE) SS   COL 50 05
    BEST SCIENCE-FICTION STORIES: 1951, THE
                          BLEILER & DIKTY   AN
    FRONTIERS IN SPACE   BLEILER & DIKTY   AN
    *ILLUSTRATED MAN, THE   BRADBURY, RAY   AC
    MINDWORM, THE   ANONYMOUS   AN
    VINTAGE BRADBURY, THE   BRADBURY, RAY   AC
  FROST AND FIRE (THE CREATURES THAT TIME FORGOT) NV   PLS 46 FL
    R IS FOR ROCKET   BRADBURY, RAY   AC
  FRUIT AT THE BOTTOM OF THE BOWL, THE (TOUCH AND GO)
                          SS   DBM 48 11
    *GOLDEN APPLES OF THE SUN   BRADBURY, RAY   AC
    VINTAGE BRADBURY, THE   BRADBURY, RAY   AC
  G.B.S.-MARK V   SS
    LONG AFTER MIDNIGHT   BRADBURY, RAY   AC
  GARBAGE COLLECTOR, THE   SS   NAT 53 10
    *GOLDEN APPLES OF THE SUN   BRADBURY, RAY   AC
  GETTING THROUGH SUNDAY SOMEHOW   SS
    LONG AFTER MIDNIGHT   BRADBURY, RAY   AC
  GIFT, THE   SS   FAN 59 07
    DAY IT RAINED FOREVER, THE   BRADBURY, RAY   AC
    MEDICINE FOR MELANCHOLY, A   BRADBURY, RAY   AC
    R IS FOR ROCKET   BRADBURY, RAY   AC
  GOLDEN APPLES OF THE SUN   AC   DBL 53
    TWICE 22   BRADBURY, RAY   AC
  GOLDEN APPLES OF THE SUN, THE   SS   PLS 53 11
    *GOLDEN APPLES OF THE SUN   BRADBURY, RAY   AC
    R IS FOR ROCKET   BRADBURY, RAY   AC
    STORIES FROM SCIENCE FICTION   DOHERTY, G. D.   AN
  GOLDEN KITE, THE SILVER WIND, THE   SS   EPO 53 WI
    *GOLDEN APPLES OF THE SUN   BRADBURY, RAY   AC
  GOOD-BY, GRANDMA   SS   SEP 57 05
    DANDELION WINE   BRADBURY, RAY   NO
  GREAT COLLISION OF MONDAY LAST, THE SS   CON 58 01
    MEDICINE FOR MELANCHOLY, A   BRADBURY, RAY   AC
  GREAT FIRE, THE   SS   SEV 49 03
    *GOLDEN APPLES OF THE SUN   BRADBURY, RAY   AC
  GREAT WIDE WORLD OVER THERE, THE (CORA AND THE GREAT WIDE
    WORLD OVER THERE)   SS   MCL 52 08
    *GOLDEN APPLES OF THE SUN   BRADBURY, RAY   AC
  GREEN MACHINE, THE   SS   ARG 51 03
    DANDELION WINE   BRADBURY, RAY   NO
  GREEN MORNING, THE   SS   NEW 51 AC
    MARTIAN CHRONICLES, THE   BRADBURY, RAY   AC
  GREEN WINE FOR DREAMING   SS   NEW 57 NO
    VINTAGE BRADBURY, THE   BRADBURY, RAY   AC
  HAIL AND FAREWELL   SS   TDY 53 03
    *GOLDEN APPLES OF THE SUN   BRADBURY, RAY   AC
    S IS FOR SPACE   BRADBURY, RAY   AC
    VINTAGE BRADBURY, THE   BRADBURY, RAY   AC
  HANDLER, THE   SS   WRT 47 01
    AUTUMN PEOPLE, THE   BRADBURY, RAY   AC
    BLOCH AND BRADBURY   BRADBURY & BLOCH   AC
    BR-R-R-| CONKLIN, GROFF   AN
    *DARK CARNIVAL   BRADBURY, RAY   AC
    SMALL ASSASSIN, THE   BRADBURY, RAY   AC
    UNEXPECTED, THE   MARGULIES, LEO   AN
  HAPPINESS MACHINE, THE (ALSO AS THE TIME MACHINE) SS   SEP 57 09
    DANDELION WINE   BRADBURY, RAY   NO
  HAUNTING OF THE NEW, THE   SS   VOB 69 10
    I SING THE BODY ELECTRIC   BRADBURY, RAY   AC
  HAVE I GOT A CHOCOLATE BAR FOR YOU| SS   PNT 73 10
    LONG AFTER MIDNIGHT   BRADBURY, RAY   AC
  HEADPIECE, THE   SS   LIL 58 05
    DAY IT RAINED FOREVER, THE   BRADBURY, RAY   AC
    MEDICINE FOR MELANCHOLY, A   BRADBURY, RAY   AC
  HEAVY-SET   SS   PBY 64 10
    I SING THE BODY ELECTRIC   BRADBURY, RAY   AC
    PLAYBOY BOOK OF HORROR AND THE SUPERNATURAL, THE
                          PLAYBOY, EDITORS OF   AN
  HENRY KUTTNER: A NEGLECTED MASTER   IN   75
    BEST OF HENRY KUTTNER, THE   KUTTNER, HENRY   AC
  HENRY THE NINTH (FINAL SCEPTRE, A LASTING CROWN) SS   FSF 69 10
    I SING THE BODY ELECTRIC   BRADBURY, RAY   AC

BRADBURY, RAY   (CONTINUED)
  HERE THERE BE TYGERS   SS   NTS 51
    DAY IT RAINED FOREVER, THE   BRADBURY, RAY   AC
    NEW TALES OF SPACE AND TIME   HEALY, RAYMOND J.   OA
    R IS FOR ROCKET   BRADBURY, RAY   AC
    TOMORROW, AND TOMORROW, AND TOMORROW...
                          HEINTZ/HERBERT/JOOS/   AN
  HIGHWAY, THE (AS LEONARD SPALDING)   SS   CPY 50 SP
    ABOVE THE HUMAN LANDSCAPE   MCNELLY & STOVER   AN
    *ILLUSTRATED MAN, THE   BRADBURY, RAY   AC
  HOLIDAY   SS   ARS 49 FL
    FAR BOUNDARIES   DERLETH, AUGUST   AN
  HOMECOMING, THE   SS   MAD 46 10
    *DARK CARNIVAL   BRADBURY, RAY   AC
    GALAXY OF GHOULS   MERRIL, JUDITH   AN
    *OCTOBER COUNTRY, THE   BRADBURY, RAY   AC
  I SEE YOU NEVER   SS   NYM 47 11
    *GOLDEN APPLES OF THE SUN   BRADBURY, RAY   AC
  I SING THE BODY ELECTRIC (BEAUTIFUL ONE IS HERE) NV   MCC 69 08
    I SING THE BODY ELECTRIC   BRADBURY, RAY   AC
  I'LL NOT LOOK FOR WINE (SEE YLLA)   TC
  I, MARS   SS   SSS 49 04
    TALES OF TERROR FROM OUTER SPACE   CHETWYND-HAYES, R.   AN
    WILDERNESS OF STARS, A   NOLAN, WILLIAM F.   AN
  I, ROCKET   SS   AMZ 44 05
    HUMAN ZERO, THE   MOSKOWITZ & ELWOOD   AN
    TOMORROW MIDNIGHT   BRADBURY, RAY   AC
  ICARUS MONTGOLFIER WRIGHT   SS   FSF 56 05
    BEST FROM FANTASY AND SCIENCE FICTION: 6
                          BOUCHER, ANTHONY   AN
    DAY IT RAINED FOREVER, THE   BRADBURY, RAY   AC
    MEDICINE FOR MELANCHOLY, A   BRADBURY, RAY   AC
    S IS FOR SPACE   BRADBURY, RAY   AC
  ILLUMINATION   SS   REP 57 05
    DANDELION WINE   BRADBURY, RAY   NO
    VINTAGE BRADBURY, THE   BRADBURY, RAY   AC
  ILLUSTRATED MAN, THE   SS   NEW 51 AC
    VINTAGE BRADBURY, THE   BRADBURY, RAY   AC
  ILLUSTRATED WOMAN, THE   SS   PBY 61 03
    LAST TRAIN TO LIMBO   PLAYBOY, EDITORS OF   AN
    MACHINERIES OF JOY, THE   BRADBURY, RAY   AC
  IMPOSSIBLE (SEE THE MARTIAN)   TC
  IN A SEASON OF CALM WEATHER   SS   PBY 57 01
    BEST FANTASY STORIES   ALDISS, BRIAN W.   AN
    DAY IT RAINED FOREVER, THE   BRADBURY, RAY   AC
    MEDICINE FOR MELANCHOLY, A   BRADBURY, RAY   AC
  IN THIS SIGN (ALSO AS THE FIRE BALLOONS) SS   IMG 51 04
    CHRONICLES OF A COMER AND OTHER RELIGIOUS SCIENCE FICTION
      STORIES   ELWOOD, ROGER   AN
    LOOKING FORWARD   LESSER, MILTON   AN
  INSPIRED CHICKEN MOTEL, THE   SS   LAT 69 11
    I SING THE BODY ELECTRIC   BRADBURY, RAY   AC
  INTERIM   SS   WRT 47 07
    *DARK CARNIVAL   BRADBURY, RAY   AC
    MARTIAN CHRONICLES, THE   BRADBURY, RAY   AC
  INTERVAL IN SUNLIGHT   NV   ESQ 54 03
    LONG AFTER MIDNIGHT   BRADBURY, RAY   AC
  INTRODUCTION   IN
    CIRCUS OF DR. LAO AND OTHER IMPROBABLE STORIES
                          BRADBURY, RAY   AN
    PILLAR OF FIRE AND OTHER PLAYS   BRADBURY, RAY   AC
    R IS FOR ROCKET   BRADBURY, RAY   AC
    S IS FOR SPACE   BRADBURY, RAY   AC
    TIMELESS STORIES FOR TODAY AND TOMORROW
                          BRADBURY, RAY   AN
    WITHOUT SORCERY   STURGEON, THEODORE   AC
  INTRODUCTION, WITH NOTES ON STAGING IN
    WONDERFUL ICE CREAM SUIT AND OTHER PLAYS, THE
                          BRADBURY, RAY   AC
  INVISIBLE BOY   SS   MAD 45 11
    *GOLDEN APPLES OF THE SUN   BRADBURY, RAY   AC
    INVISIBLE MEN   DAVENPORT, BASIL   AN
    S IS FOR SPACE   BRADBURY, RAY   AC
    VINTAGE BRADBURY, THE   BRADBURY, RAY   AC
  JACK-IN-THE-BOX   SS   NEW 47 AC
    *DARK CARNIVAL   BRADBURY, RAY   AC
    *OCTOBER COUNTRY, THE   BRADBURY, RAY   AC
    SMALL ASSASSIN, THE   BRADBURY, RAY   AC
  JAR, THE   SS   WRT 44 11
    *DARK CARNIVAL   BRADBURY, RAY   AC
    *OCTOBER COUNTRY, THE   BRADBURY, RAY   AC
  KALEIDOSCOPE   PL   DMX 51 09
    PILLAR OF FIRE AND OTHER PLAYS   BRADBURY, RAY   AC
  KALEIDOSCOPE   SS   TWS 49 10
    BEST SF 6   CRISPIN, EDMUND   AN
    GREAT STORIES OF SPACE TRAVEL   CONKLIN, GROFF   AN
    HISTORY OF THE SCIENCE FICTION MAGAZINE, THE   PART 3 1946-1955
                          ASHLEY, MICHAEL   AN
    *ILLUSTRATED MAN, THE   BRADBURY, RAY   AC
    OMNIBUS OF SCIENCE FICTION   CONKLIN, GROFF   AN
    SCIENCE FICTION OMNIBUS   CONKLIN, GROFF   AN
    STRANGE TRAVELS IN SCIENCE FICTION   CONKLIN, GROFF   AN
    VINTAGE BRADBURY, THE   BRADBURY, RAY   AC
  KILEMANJARO DEVICE, THE (THE KILIMANJARO MACHINE) SS   LIF 65 01
    I SING THE BODY ELECTRIC   BRADBURY, RAY   AC
  KILIMANJARO MACHINE, THE (SEE THE KILIMANJARO DEVICE)
                          TC
  KING OF THE GRAY SPACES (ALSO AS R IS FOR ROCKET) SS   FFM 43 12
    EVERY BOY'S BOOK OF SCIENCE FICTION WOLLHEIM, DONALD A.   AN
    SCIENCE FICTION GALAXY, THE   CONKLIN, GROFF   AN
    TOMORROW MIDNIGHT   BRADBURY, RAY   AC
  LAKE, THE   SS   WRT 44 05
    AUTUMN PEOPLE, THE   BRADBURY, RAY   AC
    *DARK CARNIVAL   BRADBURY, RAY   AC
    GHOUL KEEPERS, THE   MARGULIES, LEO   AN
    *OCTOBER COUNTRY, THE   BRADBURY, RAY   AC

BRADBURY, RAY   BRADBURY, RAY

BRADBURY, RAY   (CONTINUED)
    SMALL ASSASSIN, THE   BRADBURY, RAY   AC
LAST NIGHT OF THE WORLD, THE   SS   ESQ 51 02
    *ILLUSTRATED MAN, THE   BRADBURY, RAY   AC
LAST, THE VERY LAST, THE   SS   REP 55 06
    DANDELION WINE   BRADBURY, RAY   NO
LAWNS OF SUMMER, THE   SS   NBS 52 02
    DANDELION WINE   BRADBURY, RAY   NO
LET'S PLAY POISON   SS   WRT 46 11
    AUTUMN PEOPLE, THE   BRADBURY, RAY   AC
    *DARK CARNIVAL   BRADBURY, RAY   AC
    LITTLE MONSTERS, THE   ELWOOD & GHIDALIA   AN
    SMALL ASSASSIN, THE   BRADBURY, RAY   AC
LIFE WORK OF JUAN DIAZ, THE   SS   PBY 63 09
    MACHINERIES OF JOY, THE   BRADBURY, RAY   AC
    PLAYBOY BOOK OF HORROR AND THE SUPERNATURAL, THE
                                         PLAYBOY, EDITORS OF AN
LITTLE JOURNEY, A   SS   GAL 51 08
    *GALAXY READER OF SCIENCE FICTION   GOLD, H. L.   AN
LITTLE MICE, THE (THE MICE)   SS   ESC 55 10
    DAY IT RAINED FOREVER, THE   BRADBURY, RAY   AC
    MEDICINE FOR MELANCHOLY, A   BRADBURY, RAY   AC
    VINTAGE BRADBURY, THE   BRADBURY, RAY   AC
LOCUSTS, THE   SS   NEW 51 AC
    MARTIAN CHRONICLES, THE   BRADBURY, RAY   AC
LONG AFTER MIDNIGHT   SS
    LONG AFTER MIDNIGHT   BRADBURY, RAY   AC
LONG RAIN, THE (DEATH-BY-RAIN)   SS   PLS 50 SU
    *ILLUSTRATED MAN, THE   BRADBURY, RAY   AC
    R IS FOR ROCKET   BRADBURY, RAY   AC
LONG YEARS, THE (ALSO AS DWELLERS IN SILENCE)   SS   MCL 48 09
    MARTIAN CHRONICLES, THE   BRADBURY, RAY   AC
    TOMORROW MIDNIGHT   BRADBURY, RAY   AC
LORELEI OF THE RED MIST   NV C PLS 46 SU
    BEST OF PLANET STORIES NO. 1, THE   BRACKETT, LEIGH   AN
    HUMAN EQUATION, THE   NOLAN, WILLIAM F.   AN
    THREE TIMES INFINITY   MARGULIES, LEO   AN
LOST CITY OF MARS, THE   NV   PBY 67 01
    I SING THE BODY ELECTRIC   BRADBURY, RAY   AC
    LAST TRAIN TO LIMBO   PLAYBOY, EDITORS OF AN
    MARS, WE LOVE YOU   HIPOLITO & MCNELLY AN
    3 TO THE HIGHEST POWER   NOLAN, WILLIAM F.   AN
LUGGAGE STORE, THE   SS   NEW 51 AC
    MARTIAN CHRONICLES, THE   BRADBURY, RAY   AC
MACHINERIES OF JOY, THE   SS   PBY 62 12
    MACHINERIES OF JOY, THE   BRADBURY, RAY   AC
    TRANSIT OF EARTH   PLAYBOY, EDITORS OF AN
MAD WIZARDS OF MARS, THE (SEE THE EXILES)   TC
MADEN, THE   SS   NEW 47 AC
    *DARK CARNIVAL   BRADBURY, RAY   AC
MAGIC WHITE SUIT, THE (SEE THE WONDERFUL ICE CREAM SUIT)
                                                  TC
MAN IN THE RORSCHACH SHIRT, THE   SS   PBY 66 10
    I SING THE BODY ELECTRIC   BRADBURY, RAY   AC
    INTRODUCTORY PSYCHOLOGY THROUGH SCIENCE FICTION
                                         KATZ/WARRICK/&   AN
    TRANSIT OF EARTH   PLAYBOY, EDITORS OF AN
MAN UPSTAIRS, THE   SS   HRP 47 03
    *DARK CARNIVAL   BRADBURY, RAY   AC
    *OCTOBER COUNTRY, THE   BRADBURY, RAY   AC
    SMALL ASSASSIN, THE   BRADBURY, RAY   AC
MAN, THE   SS   TWS 49 02
    BEST SCIENCE-FICTION STORIES: 1950, THE
                                         BLEILER & DIKTY   AN
    BOYS' LIFE BOOK OF OUTER SPACE STORIES, THE
                                         BOY'S LIFE, ED. OF AN
    *ILLUSTRATED MAN, THE   BRADBURY, RAY   AC
    S IS FOR SPACE   BRADBURY, RAY   AC
MARIONETTES, INC.   SS   STS 49 03
    *ILLUSTRATED MAN, THE   BRADBURY, RAY   AC
MARRIAGE MENDER, THE   SS   COL 54 01
    DAY IT RAINED FOREVER, THE   BRADBURY, RAY   AC
    MEDICINE FOR MELANCHOLY, A   BRADBURY, RAY   AC
MARS IS HEAVEN¡   SS   PLS 48 FL
    BEST SCIENCE-FICTION STORIES: 1949, THE
                                         BLEILER & DIKTY   AN
    SCIENCE FICTION HALL OF FAME VOLUME 1 SILVERBERG, ROBERT AN
    SHOT IN THE DARK   MERRIL, JUDITH   AN
    TOMORROW MIDNIGHT   BRADBURY, RAY   AC
    WORLDS TO COME   KNIGHT, DAMON   AN
MARTIAN, THE (IMPOSSIBLE)   SS   SSS 49 11
    MARTIAN CHRONICLES, THE   BRADBURY, RAY   AC
MCGILLAHEE'S BRAT (WAB 70 FL)   SS   FSF 72 01
    INTO THE UNKNOWN   CARR, TERRY   AN
MEADOW, THE   PL   BPL 48
    *GOLDEN APPLES OF THE SUN   BRADBURY, RAY   AC
MEDICINE FOR MELANCHOLY, A   AC   DBL 58
    TWICE 22   BRADBURY, RAY   AC
MEDICINE FOR MELANCHOLY, A   SS   NEW 59 AC
    MEDICINE FOR MELANCHOLY, A   BRADBURY, RAY   AC
    VINTAGE BRADBURY, THE   BRADBURY, RAY   AC
MESSIAH, THE   SS   WAB 71 SP
    LONG AFTER MIDNIGHT   BRADBURY, RAY   AC
MICE, THE (SEE THE LITTLE MICE)   TC
MILLION-YEAR PICNIC, THE   SS   PLS 46 SU
    BEYOND TOMORROW   KNIGHT, DAMON   AN
    INVASION FROM MARS   WELLES, ORSON   AN
    MARTIAN CHRONICLES, THE   BRADBURY, RAY   AC
    S IS FOR SPACE   BRADBURY, RAY   AC
    *STRANGE PORTS OF CALL   DERLETH, AUGUST   AN
    WORLD OF WONDER   PRATT, FLETCHER   AN
MILLIONTH MURDER, THE (SEE AND THE ROCK CRIED OUT)
                                                  TC
MIRACLE OF RARE DEVICE, A   SS   PBY 62 01
    FANTASY: THE LITERATURE OF THE MARVELOUS
                                         KELLEY, LEO P.   AN

BRADBURY, RAY   (CONTINUED)
    FULLY AUTOMATED LOVE LIFE OF HENRY KEANRIDGE
                                         PLAYBOY, EDITORS OF AN
    MACHINERIES OF JOY, THE   BRADBURY, RAY   AC
    WORLDS OF SCIENCE FICTION, THE   MILLS, ROBERT P.   AN
    8TH ANNUAL OF THE YEAR'S BEST S-F, THE MERRIL, JUDITH   AN
MIRACLES OF JAMIE, THE   SS   CHM 46 04
    LONG AFTER MIDNIGHT   BRADBURY, RAY   AC
MURDERER, THE   SS   ARG 53 06
    *GOLDEN APPLES OF THE SUN   BRADBURY, RAY   AC
MUSICIANS, THE   SS   NEW 51 AC
    MARTIAN CHRONICLES, THE   BRADBURY, RAY   AC
MY PERFECT MURDER (SEE THE UTTERLY PERFECT MURDER)
                                                  TC
NAMING OF NAMES, THE (ALSO AS DARK THEY WERE, AND GOLDEN-EYED)
                                                  SS   TWS 49 08
    BEST FROM STARTLING STORIES, THE   MINES, SAMUEL   AN
    GATES TO TOMORROW   NORTON, AN.&DONALDY AN
    MARTIAN CHRONICLES, THE   BRADBURY, RAY   AC
    SCIENCE AND SORCERY   FORD, GARRET   AN
NEXT IN LINE, THE   NV   NEW 47 AC
    *DARK CARNIVAL   BRADBURY, RAY   AC
    *OCTOBER COUNTRY, THE   BRADBURY, RAY   AC
    SMALL ASSASSIN, THE   BRADBURY, RAY   AC
NEXT STOP: THE STARS (SEE THE END OF THE BEGINNING)
                                                  TC
NIGHT CALL, COLLECT   SS   NEW 69 AC
    I SING THE BODY ELECTRIC   BRADBURY, RAY   AC
NIGHT MEETING   SS   NEW 51 AC
    ADVENTURES IN DIMENSION   CONKLIN, GROFF   AN
    MARTIAN CHRONICLES, THE   BRADBURY, RAY   AC
    *SCIENCE FICTION ADVENTURES IN DIMENSION
                                         CONKLIN, GROFF   AN
    VINTAGE BRADBURY, THE   BRADBURY, RAY   AC
NIGHT SETS, THE   SS   NEW 47 AC
    *DARK CARNIVAL   BRADBURY, RAY   AC
NIGHT, THE   SS   WRT 46 07
    DANDELION WINE   BRADBURY, RAY   NO
    *DARK CARNIVAL   BRADBURY, RAY   AC
    SMALL ASSASSIN, THE   BRADBURY, RAY   AC
NO PARTICULAR NIGHT OR MORNING   SS   NEW 51 AC
    *ILLUSTRATED MAN, THE   BRADBURY, RAY   AC
OCTOBER GAME, THE   SS   WRT 48 03
    LONG AFTER MIDNIGHT   BRADBURY, RAY   AC
OFF SEASON, THE   SS   TWS 48 12
    MARTIAN CHRONICLES, THE   BRADBURY, RAY   AC
OLD ONES, THE   SS   NEW 51 AC
    MARTIAN CHRONICLES, THE   BRADBURY, RAY   AC
ONE TIMELESS SPRING   SS   COL 46 04
    LONG AFTER MIDNIGHT   BRADBURY, RAY   AC
ONE WHO WAITS, THE   SS   FSF 51 02
    FAR BOUNDARIES   DERLETH, AUGUST   AN
    MACHINERIES OF JOY, THE   BRADBURY, RAY   AC
    TOMORROW MIDNIGHT   BRADBURY, RAY   AC
OTHER FOOT, THE   SS   NST 51 03
    HUMAN AND OTHER BEINGS   DEGRAEFF, ALLEN   AN
    *ILLUSTRATED MAN, THE   BRADBURY, RAY   AC
    SOCIAL PROBLEMS THROUGH SCIENCE FICTION
                                         GREENBERG/MILSTEAD/& AN
    TOMORROW, AND TOMORROW, AND TOMORROW...
                                         HEINTZ/HERBERT/JOOS/ AN
OUTCASTS OF THE STARS (ALSO AS THE ROCKET)   SS   SSS 50 03
    TOMORROW MIDNIGHT   BRADBURY, RAY   AC
PARROT WHO MET PAPA, THE   SS   PBY 72 01
    LONG AFTER MIDNIGHT   BRADBURY, RAY   AC
PAYMENT IN FULL   SS   TWS 50 02
    MAN AGAINST TOMORROW   NOLAN, WILLIAM F.   AN
PEDESTRIAN, THE (REP 51 08)   SS   FSF 52 02
    BEST SCIENCE-FICTION STORIES: 1952, THE
                                         BLEILER & DIKTY   AN
    DECADE THE 1950S   ALDISS & HARRISON   AN
    *GOLDEN APPLES OF THE SUN   BRADBURY, RAY   AC
    LATE GREAT FUTURE, THE   FITZ GERALD & DILLON AN
    S IS FOR SPACE   BRADBURY, RAY   AC
    SOCIOLOGY THROUGH SCIENCE FICTION   MILSTEAD/GREENBERG/& AN
    TIMELESS STORIES FOR TODAY AND TOMORROW
                                         BRADBURY, RAY   AN
PERCHANCE TO DREAM (ASLEEP IN ARMAGEDDON)   SS   PLS 48 WI
    DAY IT RAINED FOREVER, THE   BRADBURY, RAY   AC
PERHAPS WE ARE GOING AWAY   SS   TOP 62 01
    MACHINERIES OF JOY, THE   BRADBURY, RAY   AC
PIECE OF WOOD, A   SS   ESQ 52 06
    LONG AFTER MIDNIGHT   BRADBURY, RAY   AC
PILLAR OF FIRE   NV   PLS 48 SU
    *OTHER SIDE OF THE MOON, THE   DERLETH, AUGUST   AN
    S IS FOR SPACE   BRADBURY, RAY   AC
    TREASURY OF GREAT SCIENCE FICTION, A VOL.1
                                         BOUCHER, ANTHONY   AN
PILLAR OF FIRE   PL   PLS 48 SU
    PILLAR OF FIRE AND OTHER PLAYS   BRADBURY, RAY   AC
PIPER, THE   SS   TWS 43 02
    FUTURE MAKERS, THE   HAINING, PETER   AN
    FUTURES TO INFINITY   MOSKOWITZ, SAM   AN
PLAYGROUND, THE   SS   ESQ 53 10
    FAHRENHEIT 451   BRADBURY, RAY   AC
    ILLUSTRATED MAN, THE (BRITISH)   BRADBURY, RAY   AC
    INTRODUCTORY PSYCHOLOGY THROUGH SCIENCE FICTION
                                         KATZ/WARRICK/&   AN
    PORTALS OF TOMORROW   DERLETH, AUGUST   AN
    *TWISTED   CONKLIN, GROFF   AN
POWERHOUSE   SS   CHM 48 03
    *GOLDEN APPLES OF THE SUN   BRADBURY, RAY   AC
PREHISTORIC PRODUCER, THE (SEE TYRANNOSAURUS REX) TC
PROLOGUE: THE ILLUSTRATED MAN   SS   NEW 51 AC
    *ILLUSTRATED MAN, THE   BRADBURY, RAY   AC

BRADBURY, RAY   (CONTINUED)
PUMPERNICKEL, THE   SS   COL 51 05
  LONG AFTER MIDNIGHT   BRADBURY, RAY   AC
PUNISHMENT WITHOUT CRIME   SS   OWS 50 03
  LONG AFTER MIDNIGHT   BRADBURY, RAY   AC
  SCIENCE FICTION TERROR TALES   CONKLIN, GROFF   AN
  TOMORROW MIDNIGHT   BRADBURY, RAY   AC
PURPOSE (SEE THE CITY)   TC
QUEEN'S OWN EVADERS, THE (SEE THE ANTHEM SPRINTERS)
                                                TC
R IS FOR ROCKET (KING OF THE GRAY SPACES)   SS   FFM 43 12
  R IS FOR ROCKET   BRADBURY, RAY   AC
RECORD, THE   SS C   40
  SCIENCE FICTION WORLDS OF FORREST J. ACKERMAN & FRIENDS
                                   ACKERMAN, FORREST J. AC
REFERENT (AS BRETT STERLING)   SS   TWS 48 10
  DAY IT RAINED FOREVER, THE   BRADBURY, RAY   AC
  *IMAGINATION UNLIMITED   BLEILER & DIKTY   AN
REUNION   SS   WRT 44 03
  *DARK CARNIVAL   BRADBURY, RAY   AC
ROCKET MAN, THE   SS   MCL 51 05
  *ILLUSTRATED MAN, THE   BRADBURY, RAY   AC
  R IS FOR ROCKET   BRADBURY, RAY   AC
ROCKET SUMMER   SS   PLS 47 SP
  MARTIAN CHRONICLES, THE   BRADBURY, RAY   AC
ROCKET, THE (OUTCAST OF THE STARS)   SS   SSS 50 03
  *ILLUSTRATED MAN, THE   BRADBURY, RAY   AC
  R IS FOR ROCKET   BRADBURY, RAY   AC
SCENT OF SARSAPARILLA, A   SS   STR 53 01
  DAY IT RAINED FOREVER, THE   BRADBURY, RAY   AC
  MEDICINE FOR MELANCHOLY, A   BRADBURY, RAY   AC
  STAR SCIENCE FICTION STORIES   POHL, FREDERIK   OA
  *STORIES FOR TOMORROW   SLOANE, WILLIAM   AN
  TRANSFORMATIONS II   ROSELLE, DANIEL   AN
SCIENCE FICTION: BEFORE CHRIST AND AFTER 2001   IN
  SCIENCE FACT/FICTION   FARRELL/GAGE/&   AN
SCREAMING WOMAN, THE   SS   TDY 51 05
  AUTUMN PEOPLE, THE   BRADBURY, RAY   AC
  GRAVEYARD READER, THE   CONKLIN, GROFF   AN
  S IS FOR SPACE   BRADBURY, RAY   AC
SCYTHE, THE   SS   WRT 43 07
  *DARK CARNIVAL   BRADBURY, RAY   AC
  *OCTOBER COUNTRY, THE   BRADBURY, RAY   AC
SEA SHELLS, THE   SS   WRT 44 01
  FANTASTIC PULPS, THE   HAINING, PETER   AN
SEASON OF DISBELIEF   SS   COL 50 11
  DANDELION WINE   BRADBURY, RAY   NO
SEASON OF SITTING, THE   AR   CHM 51 08
  DANDELION WINE   BRADBURY, RAY   NO
SERIOUS SEARCH FOR WEIRD WORLDS, A   AR   LIF 60 10
  6TH ANNUAL OF THE YEAR'S BEST S-F, THE MERRIL, JUDITH AN
SETTLERS, THE   SS   NEW 51 AC
  MARTIAN CHRONICLES, THE   BRADBURY, RAY   AC
SHAPE OF THINGS, THE   SS   TWS 48 02
  SHAPE OF THINGS, THE   KNIGHT, DAMON   AN
  TRAVELLERS OF SPACE   GREENBERG, MARTIN   AN
SHOPPING FOR DEATH (SEE TOUCHED WITH FIRE)   TC
SHORE, THE   SS   NEW 51 AC
  MARTIAN CHRONICLES, THE   BRADBURY, RAY   AC
SHORELINE AT SUNSET, THE (ALSO AS THE SUNSET HARP)
                                                SS   FSF 59 03
  MEDICINE FOR MELANCHOLY, A   BRADBURY, RAY   AC
  5TH ANNUAL OF THE YEAR'S BEST S-F, THE MERRIL, JUDITH AN
SILENT TOWNS, THE   SS   CHM 49 03
  MARTIAN CHRONICLES, THE   BRADBURY, RAY   AC
SKELETON   SS   WRT 45 09
  *DARK CARNIVAL   BRADBURY, RAY   AC
  *OCTOBER COUNTRY, THE   BRADBURY, RAY   AC
  STRANGE BEASTS AND UNNATURAL MONSTERS STERN, PHILIP VAN D. AN
  VINTAGE BRADBURY, THE   BRADBURY, RAY   AC
SMALL ASSASSIN, THE   SS   DMN 46 11
  AUTUMN PEOPLE, THE   BRADBURY, RAY   AC
  CHILDREN OF WONDER   TENN, WILLIAM   AN
  *DARK CARNIVAL   BRADBURY, RAY   AC
  *OCTOBER COUNTRY, THE   BRADBURY, RAY   AC
  SMALL ASSASSIN, THE   BRADBURY, RAY   AC
  VINTAGE BRADBURY, THE   BRADBURY, RAY   AC
  YOUNG DEMONS   ELWOOD & GHIDALIA   AN
SMILE, THE   SS   FAN 52 SU
  DAY IT RAINED FOREVER, THE   BRADBURY, RAY   AC
  MEDICINE FOR MELANCHOLY, A   BRADBURY, RAY   AC
  NEW WORLDS FOR OLD   DERLETH, AUGUST   AN
  S IS FOR SPACE   BRADBURY, RAY   AC
  TRANSFORMATIONS   ROSELLE, DANIEL   AN
  *WORLDS OF TOMORROW   DERLETH, AUGUST   AN
  YOU AND SCIENCE FICTION   HOLLISTER, BERNARD C   AN
SMILING PEOPLE, THE   SS   WRT 46 05
  *DARK CARNIVAL   BRADBURY, RAY   AC
  SMALL ASSASSIN, THE   BRADBURY, RAY   AC
SOME LIVE LIKE LAZARUS (VERY LATE IN THE EVENING) SS PBY 60 12
  MACHINERIES OF JOY, THE   BRADBURY, RAY   AC
SOUND OF SUMMER RUNNING, THE (SUMMER IN THE AIR) SS   SEP 56 02
  R IS FOR ROCKET   BRADBURY, RAY   AC
SOUND OF THUNDER, A   SS   COL 52 06
  ASPECTS OF SCIENCE FICTION   DOHERTY, G. D.   AN
  ECO-FICTION   STADLER, JOHN   AN
  *GOLDEN APPLES OF THE SUN   BRADBURY, RAY   AC
  R IS FOR ROCKET   BRADBURY, RAY   AC
  SCIENCE FACT/FICTION   FARRELL/GAGE/&   AN
  SCIENCE FICTION   BRODKIN & PEARSON   AN
  SCIENCE FICTION FOR PEOPLE WHO HATE SCIENCE FICTION
                                   CARR, TERRY   AN
  SCIENCE FICTION THROUGH THE AGES 2 EVANS, I. O.   AN
  STARS AND UNDER, THE   CRISPIN, EDMUND   AN
  TRANSFORMATIONS   ROSELLE, DANIEL   AN

BRADBURY, RAY   (CONTINUED)
SPRING NIGHT, THE (SEE THE SUMMER NIGHT)   TC
STATUES   SS   NEW 57 NO
  DANDELION WINE   BRADBURY, RAY   NO
  VINTAGE BRADBURY, THE   BRADBURY, RAY   AC
STORY OF LOVE, A   SS
  LONG AFTER MIDNIGHT   BRADBURY, RAY   AC
STRAWBERRY WINDOW, THE   SS   STR 54 03
  DAY IT RAINED FOREVER, THE   BRADBURY, RAY   AC
  MEDICINE FOR MELANCHOLY, A   BRADBURY, RAY   AC
  R IS FOR ROCKET   BRADBURY, RAY   AC
  STAR SCIENCE FICTION STORIES NO. 3 POHL, FREDERIK   OA
SUBTERFUGE   SS   AST 43 04
  ASSIGNMENT IN TOMORROW   POHL, FREDERIK   AN
SUMMER IN THE AIR (ALSO AS THE SOUND OF SUMMER RUNNING)
                                                SS   SEP 56 02
  DANDELION WINE   BRADBURY, RAY   NO
SUMMER NIGHT, THE (THE SPRING NIGHT)   SS   ARS 48 WI
  MARTIAN CHRONICLES, THE   BRADBURY, RAY   AC
SUN AND SHADOW   SS   REP 53 03
  *GOLDEN APPLES OF THE SUN   BRADBURY, RAY   AC
  VINTAGE BRADBURY, THE   BRADBURY, RAY   AC
SUNSET HARP, THE (THE SHORELINE AT SUNSET)   SS   FSF 59 03
  DAY IT RAINED FOREVER, THE   BRADBURY, RAY   AC
SWAN, THE   SS   CMP 54 09
  DANDELION WINE   BRADBURY, RAY   NO
TAXPAYER, THE   SS   NEW 51 AC
  MARTIAN CHRONICLES, THE   BRADBURY, RAY   AC
TERRIBLE CONFLAGRATION UP AT THE PLACE   SS   NEW 69 AC
  I SING THE BODY ELECTRIC   BRADBURY, RAY   AC
THERE WAS AN OLD WOMAN   SS   WRT 44 07
  AUTUMN PEOPLE, THE   BRADBURY, RAY   AC
  *DARK CARNIVAL   BRADBURY, RAY   AC
  *OCTOBER COUNTRY, THE   BRADBURY, RAY   AC
THERE WILL COME SOFT RAINS   SS   COL 50 05
  ADVENTURES IN TOMORROW   CROSSEN, KENDELL F.   AN
  BEYOND THE END OF TIME   POHL, FREDERIK   AN
  FROM FRANKENSTEIN TO ANDROMEDA   BROWN, JAMES GOLDIE   AN
  MARTIAN CHRONICLES, THE   BRADBURY, RAY   AC
  SCIENCE FACT/FICTION   FARRELL/GAGE/&   AN
  TOMORROW MIDNIGHT   BRADBURY, RAY   AC
  VINTAGE ANTHOLOGY OF SCIENCE FANTASY, THE
                                   CERF, CHRISTOPHER   AN
  VINTAGE BRADBURY, THE   BRADBURY, RAY   AC
THIRD EXPEDITION, THE   SS   PLS 48 FL
  MARTIAN CHRONICLES, THE   BRADBURY, RAY   AC
TIME IN THY FLIGHT   SS   FUN 53 06
  S IS FOR SPACE   BRADBURY, RAY   AC
TIME MACHINE, THE (THE HAPPINESS MACHINE)   SS   SEP 57 09
  R IS FOR ROCKET   BRADBURY, RAY   AC
TIME OF GOING AWAY, THE   SS   REP 56 11
  DAY IT RAINED FOREVER, THE   BRADBURY, RAY   AC
  MEDICINE FOR MELANCHOLY, A   BRADBURY, RAY   AC
TO THE CHICAGO ABYSS   PL   FSF 63 05
  WONDERFUL ICE CREAM SUIT AND OTHER PLAYS, THE
                                   BRADBURY, RAY   AC
TO THE CHICAGO ABYSS   SS   FSF 63 05
  BEST FROM FANTASY AND SCIENCE FICTION, 25TH ANNIV.
                                   FERMAN, EDWARD L.   AN
  MACHINERIES OF JOY, THE   BRADBURY, RAY   AC
  SCIENCE FICTION: THE FUTURE   ALLEN, DICK   AN
TO THE FUTURE (SEE THE FOX AND THE FOREST)   TC
TOMBLING DAY, THE   SS   SHN 52 FL
  I SING THE BODY ELECTRIC   BRADBURY, RAY   AC
  SUPERNATURAL READER, THE   CONKLIN, G&L.   AN
TOMBSTONE, THE   SS   WRT 45 03
  *DARK CARNIVAL   BRADBURY, RAY   AC
  SMALL ASSASSIN, THE   BRADBURY, RAY   AC
TOMORROW AND TOMORROW   SS   FAN 65 11
  TIME UNTAMED   HOWARD, IVAN   AN
TOMORROW'S CHILD   SS   NEW 69 AC
  I SING THE BODY ELECTRIC   BRADBURY, RAY   AC
  SPACE   2   DAVIS, RICHARD   OA
TORRID SACRIFICE (SEE EN LA NOCHE)   TC
TOUCH AND GO (ALSO AS THE FRUIT AT THE BOTTOM OF THE BOWL)
                                                SS   DBM 48 11
  AUTUMN PEOPLE, THE   BRADBURY, RAY   AC
TOUCHED WITH FIRE (SHOPPING FOR DEATH)   SS   MCL 54 06
  *OCTOBER COUNTRY, THE   BRADBURY, RAY   AC
TOWN WHERE NO ONE GOT OFF, THE   SS   EQM 58 10
  DAY IT RAINED FOREVER, THE   BRADBURY, RAY   AC
  MEDICINE FOR MELANCHOLY, A   BRADBURY, RAY   AC
TRAVELLER, THE   SS   WRT 46 03
  *DARK CARNIVAL   BRADBURY, RAY   AC
TROLLEY, THE   SS   GHK 55 07
  DANDELION WINE   BRADBURY, RAY   NO
  S IS FOR SPACE   BRADBURY, RAY   AC
TRUNK LADY, THE   SS   DMM 48 01
  HORROR TIMES TEN   NORTON, ALDEN H.   AN
TYRANNOSAURUS REX (THE PREHISTORIC PRODUCER)   SS   SEP 62 06
  MACHINERIES OF JOY, THE   BRADBURY, RAY   AC
UNCLE EINAR   SS   NEW 47 AC
  *DARK CARNIVAL   BRADBURY, RAY   AC
  *OCTOBER COUNTRY, THE   BRADBURY, RAY   AC
  R IS FOR ROCKET   BRADBURY, RAY   AC
USHER II (CARNIVAL OF MADNESS)   SS   TWS 50 04
  ILLUSTRATED MAN, THE (BRITISH)   BRADBURY, RAY   AC
  MARTIAN CHRONICLES, THE   BRADBURY, RAY   AC
UTTERLY PERFECT MURDER, THE (MY PERFECT MURDER) SS   PBY 71 08
  LONG AFTER MIDNIGHT   BRADBURY, RAY   AC
VACATION, THE   SS   PBY 63 12
  MACHINERIES OF JOY, THE   BRADBURY, RAY   AC
  PLAYBOY BOOK OF SCIENCE FICTION AND FANTASY, THE
                                   PLAYBOY, EDITORS OF   AN
VELDT, THE   PL   SEP 50 09

BRADBURY, RAY   (CONTINUED)
     WONDERFUL ICE CREAM SUIT AND OTHER PLAYS, THE
                                           BRADBURY, RAY   AC
VELDT, THE (THE WORLD THE CHILDREN MADE)   SS   SEP 50 09
     BEYOND THE BARRIERS OF SPACE AND TIME MERRIL, JUDITH   AN
     *ILLUSTRATED MAN, THE   BRADBURY, RAY   AC
     MASTERS' CHOICE   JANIFER, LAURENCE M.   AN
     PAST, PRESENT, AND FUTURE PERFECT   WOLFE, J&FITZ GERALD   AN
     SECOND ORBIT   DOHERTY, G. D.   AN
     TOMORROW, AND TOMORROW, AND TOMORROW...
                                           HEINTZ/HERBERT/JOOS/   AN
     UNTRAVELLED WORLDS   BARTER & WILSON   AN
     VINTAGE BRADBURY, THE   BRADBURY, RAY   AC
VERY LATE IN THE EVENING (SEE SOME LIVE LIKE LAZARUS)
                                           TC
VISITOR, THE   SS   STS 48 11
     *ILLUSTRATED MAN, THE   BRADBURY, RAY   AC
WAKE FOR THE LIVING (ALSO AS THE COFFIN)   SS   DMN 47 09
     MICROCOSMIC GOD   MOSKOWITZ, SAM   AN
     MODERN MASTERPIECES OF SCIENCE FICTION MOSKOWITZ, SAM   AN
WATCHERS, THE   SS   WRT 45 05
     BLOCH AND BRADBURY   BRADBURY & BLOCH   AC
     MARTIAN CHRONICLES, THE   BRADBURY, RAY   AC
WATCHFUL POKER CHIP OF H. MATISSE, THE   SS   BEY 54 03
     BEYOND   ANONYMOUS   AN
     *OCTOBER COUNTRY, THE   BRADBURY, RAY   AC
     VINTAGE BRADBURY, THE   BRADBURY, RAY   AC
WAY IN THE MIDDLE OF THE AIR   SS   OWS 50 07
     HUMAN AND OTHER BEINGS   DEGRAEFF, ALLEN   AN
     MARTIAN CHRONICLES, THE   BRADBURY, RAY   AC
WHOLE TOWN'S SLEEPING, THE   SS   MCC 50 09
     DANDELION WINE   BRADBURY, RAY   NO
WHY I SELECTED ZERO HOUR   AI
     *MY BEST SCIENCE FICTION STORY   MARGULIES & FRIEND   AN
WILDERNESS, THE   SS   FSF 52 11
     *GOLDEN APPLES OF THE SUN   BRADBURY, RAY   AC
     MARTIAN CHRONICLES, THE (BRITISH SFBC, ADDS:)
                                           BRADBURY, RAY   AC
     *STORIES FOR TOMORROW   SLOANE, WILLIAM   AN
     UNIVERSE AHEAD   ENGDAHL & ROBERSON   AN
WIND, THE   SS   WRT 43 03
     *DARK CARNIVAL   BRADBURY, RAY   AC
     GREAT SCIENCE-FICTION   LICATA, TONY   AN
     *OCTOBER COUNTRY, THE   BRADBURY, RAY   AC
WINDOW, THE   SS   COL 50 08
     DANDELION WINE   BRADBURY, RAY   NO
WISH, THE   SS   WDM 73 12
     LONG AFTER MIDNIGHT   BRADBURY, RAY   AC
WOMEN, THE   SS   FFM 48 10
     FIEND IN YOU, THE   BEAUMONT, CHARLES   AN
     I SING THE BODY ELECTRIC   BRADBURY, RAY   AC
WONDERFUL DEATH OF DUDLEY STONE, THE   SS   CHM 54 07
     *OCTOBER COUNTRY, THE   BRADBURY, RAY   AC
WONDERFUL ICE CREAM SUIT, THE   PL   SEP 58 10
     WONDERFUL ICE CREAM SUIT AND OTHER PLAYS, THE
                                           BRADBURY, RAY   AC
WONDERFUL ICE CREAM SUIT, THE (THE MAGIC WHITE SUIT)
                                           SS   SEP 58 10
     DAY IT RAINED FOREVER, THE   BRADBURY, RAY   AC
     MEDICINE FOR MELANCHOLY, A   BRADBURY, RAY   AC
     VINTAGE BRADBURY, THE   BRADBURY, RAY   AC
WORLD THE CHILDREN MADE, THE (SEE THE VELDT) TC
YES, WE'LL GATHER AT THE RIVER   SS   NEW 69 AC
     I SING THE BODY ELECTRIC   BRADBURY, RAY   AC
YLLA (I'LL NOT LOOK FOR WINE)   SS   MCL 50 01
     MARTIAN CHRONICLES, THE   BRADBURY, RAY   AC
     *OUTER REACHES, THE   DERLETH, AUGUST   AN
     VINTAGE BRADBURY, THE   BRADBURY, RAY   AC
ZERO HOUR   SS   PLS 47 PL
     ASPECTS OF SCIENCE FICTION   DOHERTY, G. D.   AN
     BEST SF 2   CRISPIN, EDMUND   AN
     *ILLUSTRATED MAN, THE   BRADBURY, RAY   AC
     INVASION FROM MARS   WELLES, ORSON   AN
     *MY BEST SCIENCE FICTION STORY   MARGULIES & FRIEND   AN
     S IS FOR SPACE   BRADBURY, RAY   AC
     SCIENCE FICTION   BRODKIN & PEARSON   AN

BRADFIELD, SCOTT
HALCYON IN A MIRROR AT MIDNIGHT   SS
     FUTURE PASTIMES   EDELSTEIN, SCOTT   OA
WHAT MAKES A CAGE, JAMIE KNOWS   SS   PRT 71
     PROTOSTARS   GERROLD & GOLDIN   OA

BRADFORD, JAMES S.
PIRATE OF THE AIR   SS
     ADVENTURES TO COME   ESENWEIN, J. BERG   OA

BRADFORD, RONALD
SURPRISE!   SS   62
     FIEND IN YOU, THE   BEAUMONT, CHARLES   AN

BRADLEY, JOHANNA
SCIENCE FICTION STORIES   AN H YPB 75

BRADLEY, MARION ZIMMER
DARK INTRUDER & OTHER STORIES, THE   DC   ACE 64
BLACK AND WHITE   SS   AMZ 62 11
     DARK INTRUDER & OTHER STORIES, THE   BRADLEY, MARION Z.   DC
CLIMBING WAVE, THE   SS   FSF 55 02
     IF THIS GOES ON   NUETZEL, CHARLES   AN
CRIME THERAPIST, THE   SS   FUT 54 10
     DARK INTRUDER & OTHER STORIES, THE   BRADLEY, MARION Z.   DC
DARK INTRUDER, THE (MEASURELESS TO MAN)   NV   AMZ 62 12
     DARK INTRUDER & OTHER STORIES, THE   BRADLEY, MARION Z.   DC
DAY OF THE BUTTERFLIES, THE   SS
     DAW SCIENCE FICTION READER, THE   WOLLHEIM, DONALD A. OA

BRADLEY, MARION Z.   (CONTINUED)
DEATH BETWEEN THE STARS   SS   FUN 56 03
     DARK INTRUDER & OTHER STORIES, THE   BRADLEY, MARION Z.   DC
EXILES OF TOMORROW   SS   FUN 55 03
     DARK INTRUDER & OTHER STORIES, THE   BRADLEY, MARION Z.   DC
INTRODUCTION   IN
     DARK INTRUDER & OTHER STORIES, THE   BRADLEY, MARION Z.   DC
JACKIE SEES A STAR   SS   FUN 54 09
     DARK INTRUDER & OTHER STORIES, THE   BRADLEY, MARION Z.   DC
MEASURELESS TO MAN (SEE THE DARK INTRUDER) TC
PHOENIX   SS C AMZ 63 02
     BEST FROM AMAZING, THE   WHITE, TED   AN
STARS ARE WAITING, THE   SS   STN 58 03
     DARK INTRUDER & OTHER STORIES, THE   BRADLEY, MARION Z.   DC
WIND PEOPLE, THE   SS   IFS 59 02
     CENTURY OF SCIENCE FICTION, A   KNIGHT, DAMON   AN
     WOMEN OF WONDER   SARGENT, PAMELA   AN

BRALY, MALCOLM
OUTLINE OF HISTORY, AN   SS   BMR 73
     BAD MOON RISING   DISCH, THOMAS M.   OA

BRAND, JONATHAN
ENCOUNTER WITH A HICK   SS   DVS 67 01
     DANGEROUS VISIONS   ELLISON, HARLAN   OA
LONG DAY IN COURT   SS   IFS 63 11
     IF READER OF SCIENCE FICTION, THE   POHL, FREDERICK   AN
VANISHING POINT   NV   IFS 65 01
     WORLD'S BEST SCIENCE FICTION: 1966   WOLLHEIM & CARR   AN

BRAND, MAX   PSEUD. FOR FREDERICK FAUST
JOHN OVINGTON RETURNS   SS   ASW 18 06
     FANTASTIC PULPS, THE   HAINING, PETER   AN
RECEDING BROW, THAT   NV   ASW 19 02
     HORROR TIMES TEN   NORTON, ALDEN H.   AN

BRAND, THOMAS
DON SLOW AND HIS ELECTRIC GIRL GETTER   SS   EIO 73
     EROS IN ORBIT   ELDER, JOSEPH   OA

BRANDIS, YEVGENY
IN THE LAND OF SCIENCE FICTION   SS C
     RUSSIAN SCIENCE FICTION, 1969   MAGIDOFF, ROBERT   AN

BRANDNER, GARY
PRICE OF A DEMON, THE   SS   WTS 72 07
     YEAR'S BEST HORROR STORIES: SERIES II, THE
                                           DAVIS, RICHARD   AN

BRANDON, CARL   PSEUD. FOR TERRY CARR

BRAUTIGAN, RICHARD
ALL WATCHED OVER BY MACHINES OF LOVING GRACE PM   68
     INSIDE INFORMATION   MOWSHOWITZ, ABBE   AN
     SCIENCE FACT/FICTION   FARRELL/GAGE/&   AN

BREADY, RICHARD S.
ENEMY YOU KILLED, MY FRIEND, THE   SS
     CLARION SF   WILHELM, KATE   OA

BRENNAN, JOSEPH P.
EPISODE ON CAIN STREET   SS
     TRAVELLERS BY NIGHT   DERLETH, AUGUST   OA
HOUSE ON STILLCROFT STREET, THE   SS   AHM 75 06
     YEAR'S BEST HORROR STORIES: SERIES IV, THE
                                           PAGE, GERALD W.   AN
SLIME   NV   WRT 53 03
     STRANGE BEASTS AND UNNATURAL MONSTERS STERN, PHILIP VAN D. AN

BRENNAN, KATHLEEN
ARE YOUR HOME GROWN VEGETABLES RADIOACTIVE? SS
     STOPWATCH   HAY, GEORGE   OA

BRENNERT, ALAN
BRIAN IN THE DREAMING SEAT   SS
     CLARION SF   WILHELM, KATE   OA
IN THIS IMAGE   NV   FOS 74
     FELLOWSHIP OF THE STARS   CARR, TERRY   OA
JAMIE'S SMILE   SS
     IDES OF TOMORROW, THE   CARR, TERRY   OA
NOSTALGIA TRIPPING   SS   INY 73 05
     INFINITY 5   HOSKINS, ROBERT   OA
SKYGHOSTS AND DUSK-DEVILS   SS
     FUTURE PASTIMES   EDELSTEIN, SCOTT   OA

BRETNOR, REGINALD   ALSO AS   GRENDEL BRIARTON
ALL THE TEA IN CHINA   SS   FSF 61 05
     7TH ANNUAL OF THE YEAR'S BEST S-F, THE MERRIL, JUDITH   AN
DOORSTOP, THE   SS   ASF 56 11
     SF:57, THE YEAR'S GREATEST SCIENCE FICTION AND FANTASY
                                           MERRIL, JUDITH   AN
DR. BIRDMOUSE   SS   FAN 62 04
     STRANGE BED FELLOWS   SCORTIA, THOMAS N.   AN
EARTHWOMAN   SS   FSF 67 08
     MARRIAGE AND THE FAMILY THROUGH SCIENCE FICTION
                                           CLEAR/WARRICK/&   AN
GENIUS OF THE SPECIES   SS   FSF 56 06
     9 TALES OF SPACE AND TIME   HEALY, RAYMOND J.   OA
GNURRS COME FROM THE VOODVORK OUT, THE   SS   FSF 50 WS
     BEST SCIENCE-FICTION STORIES: 1951, THE
                                           BLEILER & DIKTY   AN
     SCIENCE FICTION BESTIARY, THE   SILVERBERG, ROBERT   AN
     SPECIAL WONDER   MCCOMAS, J. FRANCIS   AN
GRATITUDE GUARANTEED   SS C FSF 53 08
     PORTALS OF TOMORROW   DERLETH, AUGUST   AN

BRETNOR, REGINALD   (CONTINUED)
    TWENTY YEARS OF FANTASY & SCIENCE FICTION
                                            FERMAN & MILLS   AN
    LITTLE ANTON   NV   NTS 51
      NEVER IN THIS WORLD   STONE, IDELLA P.   AN
      NEW TALES OF SPACE AND TIME   HEALY, RAYMOND J.   OA
    MAN ON TOP, THE (SCH 51 10)   SS   FSF 60 09
      TRANSFORMATIONS   ROSELLE, DANIEL   AN
      14 GREAT TALES OF ESP   STONE, IDELLA P.   AN
      6TH ANNUAL OF THE YEAR'S BEST S-F, THE MERRIL, JUDITH   AN
    MAYBE JUST A LITTLE ONE (HRP 47 08)   SS   FSF 53 02
      BEST FROM FANTASY AND SCIENCE FICTION: 3
                                            BOUCHER & MCCOMAS   AN
    MRS. PIGAFETTA SWIMS WELL   SS   FSF 63 05
      9TH ANNUAL OF THE YEAR'S BEST S-F, THE MERRIL, JUDITH   AN
    MRS. POPPLEDORE'S ID   SS   FSF 52 02
      SCIENCE FICTION ODDITIES   CONKLIN, GROFF   AN
    PAPA SCHIMMELHORN AND THE S.O.D.O.M. SERUM NV   TVW 73
      TWO VIEWS OF WONDER   SCORTIA & YARBRO   OA
    PAST AND IT'S DEAD PEOPLE, THE   SS   FSF 56 09
      SPACE, TIME & CRIME   DEFORD, MIRIAM ALLEN AN

BREUER, MILES J. MD.
    APPENDIX AND THE SPECTACLES, THE   SS   AMZ 28 12
      MATHEMATICAL MAGPIE, THE   FADIMAN, CLIFTON   AN
      SCIENCE FICTION GALAXY, THE   CONKLIN, GROFF   AN
    BABY ON NEPTUNE, A   SS C   AMZ 29 12
      AWAY FROM THE HERE AND NOW   HARRIS, CLARE WINGER AC
      FLIGHT INTO SPACE   WOLLHEIM, DONALD A. AN
    CAPTURED CROSS-SECTION, THE   SS   AMZ 29 02
      FANTASIA MATHEMATICA   FADIMAN, CLIFTON   AN
      OTHER DIMENSIONS   SILVERBERG, ROBERT   AN
    GOSTAK AND THE DOSHES, THE   SS   AMZ 30 03
      ADVENTURES IN DIMENSION   CONKLIN, GROFF   AN
      GREAT SCIENCE FICTION BY SCIENTISTS   CONKLIN, GROFF   AN
      *SCIENCE FICTION ADVENTURES IN DIMENSION
                                            CONKLIN, GROFF   AN
    HUNGRY GUINEA PIG, THE   SS   AMZ 30 01
      *SCIENCE FICTION ADVENTURES IN MUTATION CONKLIN, GROFF   AN
    MAN WITH THE STRANGE HEAD, THE   SS   AMZ 27 01
      *BIG BOOK OF SCIENCE FICTION   CONKLIN, GROFF   AN
    MAN WITHOUT AN APPETITE   SS   16
      GREAT SCIENCE FICTION ABOUT DOCTORS   CONKLIN, G&FABRICANT AN
    MARS COLONIZERS   SS   MVT 35 SU
      GARDEN OF FEAR AND OTHER STORIES, THE CRAWFORD, WILLIAM L. AN

BRIARTON, GRENDEL   PSEUD. FOR REGINALD BRETNOR
    COMPLETE FEGHOOT, THE   AC   MRG 75
    THROUGH TIME AND SPACE WITH FERDINAND FEGHOOT AC H PDX 62
      IN "THE COMPLETE FEGHOOT"
    ADDITIONAL FEGHOOT PUNS (LAST IN BSJ)   MS
      COMPLETE FEGHOOT, THE   BRIARTON, GRENDEL   AC
    THROUGH TIME AND SPACE WITH FERDINAND FEGHOOT AC   PDX 62
      COMPLETE FEGHOOT, THE   BRIARTON, GRENDEL   AC
    THROUGH TIME AND SPACE WITH FERDINAND FEGHOOT SS   BSJ 67
      SPECIAL WONDER   MCCOMAS, J. FRANCIS AN
    THROUGH TIME AND SPACE WITH FERDINAND FEGHOOT: VII
                                            SS   FSF 58 03
      BEST FROM FANTASY AND SCIENCE FICTION: 8
                                            BOUCHER, ANTHONY   AN
    THROUGH TIME AND SPACE WITH FERDINAND FEGHOOT: VIII
                                            SS   FSF 58 08
      BEST FROM FANTASY AND SCIENCE FICTION: 8
                                            BOUCHER, ANTHONY   AN
    THROUGH TIME AND SPACE WITH FERDINAND FEGHOOT: X SS FSF 59 01
      BEST FROM FANTASY AND SCIENCE FICTION: 9
                                            MILLS, ROBERT P.   AN
    THROUGH TIME AND SPACE WITH FERDINAND FEGHOOT: XI SS FSF 59 02
      BEST FROM FANTASY AND SCIENCE FICTION: 9
                                            MILLS, ROBERT P.   AN
    THROUGH TIME AND SPACE WITH FERDINAND FEGHOOT: XII
                                            SS   FSF 59 03
      BEST FROM FANTASY AND SCIENCE FICTION: 9
                                            MILLS, ROBERT P.   AN
      NEVER IN THIS WORLD   STONE, IDELLA P.   AN
    THROUGH TIME AND SPACE WITH FERDINAND FEGHOOT: XIII
                                            SS   FSF 59 04
      BEST FROM FANTASY AND SCIENCE FICTION: 9
                                            MILLS, ROBERT P.   AN
    THROUGH TIME AND SPACE WITH FERDINAND FEGHOOT: XIV
                                            SS   FSF 59 05
      BEST FROM FANTASY AND SCIENCE FICTION: 9
                                            MILLS, ROBERT P.   AN
    THROUGH TIME AND SPACE WITH FERDINAND FEGHOOT: XV SS FSF 59 06
      BEST FROM FANTASY AND SCIENCE FICTION: 9
                                            MILLS, ROBERT P.   AN
    50 FEGHOOT PUNS, 45 FROM F&SF AND 5 ORIGINAL   MS
      THROUGH TIME AND SPACE WITH FERDINAND FEGHOOT
                                            BRIARTON, GRENDEL   AC

BRINEY, ROBERT E.   ALSO AS   ANDREW DUANE
    SHANADU   OA   SSR 53 11

BRINGSVAERD, TOR AGE
    CODEMUS   SS   68
      BEST FROM THE REST OF THE WORLD, THE WOLLHEIM, DONALD A. AN
    MAN WHO COLLECTED THE FIRST OF SEPTEMBER 1973, THE
                                            SS   73
      BEST SF: 1973   HARRISON & ALDISS   AN

BRODE, ANTHONY
    BETTER BET, THE   PM   FSF 58 02
      BEST FROM FANTASY AND SCIENCE FICTION: 8
                                            BOUCHER, ANTHONY   AN
    CALL ME MISTER   PM   FSF 59 02

BRODE, ANTHONY   (CONTINUED)
      BEST FROM FANTASY AND SCIENCE FICTION: 9
                                            MILLS, ROBERT P.   AN
    FLYING CHAUCER   PM   FSF 56 03
      BEST FROM FANTASY AND SCIENCE FICTION: 6
                                            BOUCHER, ANTHONY   AN
    WATCHERS, THE   PM   FSF 58 04
      BEST FROM FANTASY AND SCIENCE FICTION: 8
                                            BOUCHER, ANTHONY   AN
    YES, BUT...   PM   FSF 57 09
      BEST FROM FANTASY AND SCIENCE FICTION: 7
                                            BOUCHER, ANTHONY   AN

BRODERICK, DAMIEN
    ALL MY YESTERDAYS   SS   65
      PACIFIC BOOK OF AUSTRALIAN SCIENCE FICTION
                                            BAXTER, JOHN   AN
    SEA'S FURTHEST END, THE   NV   NWR 64 01
      NEW WRITINGS IN SF. 1   CARNELL, JOHN   OA

BRODKIN, SYLVIA Z. AND ELIZABETH J. PEARSON
    SCIENCE FICTION   AN L MCD 73

BRONDFIELD, JEROME
    NIGHT IN FUNLAND   AN   SBS 68
      AND OTHER STORIES FROM LITERARY CAVALCADE
      FOREWORD   IN
        NIGHT IN FUNLAND   BRONDFIELD, JEROME   AN

BRONK, WILLIAM
    OUTER BECOMING INNER, THE   PM   SAR 49
      SPECULATIONS   SANDERS, THOMAS E.   AN

BRONSON, DONNA
    CANIS FAMILIARIS   SS C
      FUTURE PASTIMES   EDELSTEIN, SCOTT   OA

BROOKS, RICK
    ANDRE NORTON: LOSS OF FAITH   AR   DIP 71 11
      MANY WORLDS OF ANDRE NORTON, THE   NORTON, ANDRE   AC

BROSNAN, JOHN
    CONVERSATION ON A STARSHIP IN WARPDRIVE SS   NEW 76 AN
      ANTIGRAV: COSMIC COMEDIES   STRICK, PHILIP   AN

BROUGHTON, RHODA
    BEHOLD IT WAS A DREAM (1873)   SS
      BEYOND THE BARRIERS OF SPACE AND TIME MERRIL, JUDITH   AN

BROUN, HEYWOOD
    ARTIST UNKNOWN   SS   41
      GOLDEN ROAD, THE   KNIGHT, DAMON   AN

BROWN, BILL
    MEDICINE DANCER   SS   FNF 53 11
      BEYOND THE BARRIERS OF SPACE AND TIME MERRIL, JUDITH   AN
    STAR DUCKS, THE   SS   FSF 50 PL
      BEST SCIENCE-FICTION STORIES: 1951, THE
                                            BLEILER & DIKTY   AN
      BEST SF 6   CRISPIN, EDMUND   AN
      FRONTIERS IN SPACE   BLEILER & DIKTY   AN
      SCIENCE FICTION AND READER'S GUIDE   BARROWS, MARJORIE   AN
      STARS AND UNDER, THE   CRISPIN, EDMUND   AN

BROWN, CHARLES N.
    SCIENCE FICTION YEAR, THE   MS
      BEST SCIENCE FICTION OF THE YEAR, THE NO. 4
                                            CARR, TERRY   AN
      BEST SCIENCE FICTION OF THE YEAR, THE NO. 5
                                            CARR, TERRY   AN

BROWN, ELIZABETH
    INTRODUCTION   IN
      PARADOX LOST, AND 12 OTHER GREAT S.F. STORIES
                                            BROWN, FREDRIC   AC

BROWN, FREDRIC AND MACK REYNOLDS
    SCIENCE-FICTION CARNIVAL   AN H SHS 53 12
    SCIENCE-FICTION CARNIVAL (11 OF 13)   AN   BAN 57 06

BROWN, FREDRIC
    ANGELS AND SPACESHIPS   AC H DUT 54 09
      ALSO AS "STAR SHINE"
    BEST OF FREDRIC BROWN, THE   AC H NDB 76
      EDITED BY ROBERT BLOCH
    DAYMARES   AC   LAN 68
    HONEYMOON IN HELL   AC   BAN 58 08
    NIGHTMARES AND GEEZENSTACKS   AC   BAN 61 07
    PARADOX LOST, AND 12 OTHER GREAT S.F. STORIES AC H RDM 73
    SPACE ON MY HANDS   AC H SHS 51 07
    STAR SHINE   AC   BAN 56 02
      SEE "ANGELS AND SPACESHIPS"
    ABOMINABLE   SS   DUD 60 03
      BEST OF FREDRIC BROWN, THE   BROWN, FREDRIC   AC
      NIGHTMARES AND GEEZENSTACKS   BROWN, FREDRIC   AC
      6TH ANNUAL OF THE YEAR'S BEST S-F, THE MERRIL, JUDITH   AN
    AELUROPHOBE   SS   DUD 62
      PARADOX LOST, AND 12 OTHER GREAT S.F. STORIES
                                            BROWN, FREDRIC   AC
    ALL GOOD BEMS   SS   TWS 49 04
      SPACE ON MY HANDS   BROWN, FREDRIC   AC
    AND THE GODS LAUGHED   SS   TIS 53 PL
      HONEYMOON IN HELL   BROWN, FREDRIC   AC
    ANGELIC ANGLEWORM, THE   NV   UNK 43 02
      ANGELS AND SPACESHIPS   BROWN, FREDRIC   AC
      DAYMARES   BROWN, FREDRIC   AC

BROWN, FREDRIC   BROWN, FREDRIC

BROWN, FREDRIC   (CONTINUED)   BROWN, FREDRIC   (CONTINUED)
  ANSWER   SS   NEW 54 AC   FIRST TIME MACHINE   SS   EQM 55 09
    ANGELS AND SPACESHIPS   BROWN, FREDRIC   AC   HONEYMOON IN HELL   BROWN, FREDRIC   AC
    BEST OF FREDRIC BROWN, THE   BROWN, FREDRIC   AC   FISH STORY   SS
    BEST SF 3   CRISPIN, EDMUND   AN   NIGHTMARES AND GEEZENSTACKS BROWN, FREDRIC   AC
    INSIDE INFORMATION   MOWSHOWITZ, ABBE   AN   GATEWAY TO DARKNESS   NV   SSS 49 11
    METAL SMILE, THE   KNIGHT, DAMON   AN   DAYMARES   BROWN, FREDRIC   AC
    STARS AND UNDER, THE   CRISPIN, EDMUND   AN   GIANT ANTHOLOGY OF SCIENCE FICTION MARGULIES & FRIEND AN
  ARENA   NV   ASF 44 06   GEEZENSTACKS, THE   SS   WRT 43 09
    ALIENS, THE   SILVERBERG, ROBERT AN   BEST OF FREDRIC BROWN, THE BROWN, FREDRIC   AC
    ANTHROPOLOGY THROUGH SCIENCE FICTION MASON, C/GREENBERG/& AN   NIGHTMARES AND GEEZENSTACKS BROWN, FREDRIC   AC
    ARENA: SPORTS SF   FERMAN & MALZBERG   AN   GRANNY'S BIRTHDAY   SS
    BEST OF FREDRIC BROWN, THE   BROWN, FREDRIC   AC   NIGHTMARES AND GEEZENSTACKS BROWN, FREDRIC   AC
    *BIG BOOK OF SCIENCE FICTION CONKLIN, GROFF   AN   GREAT LOST DISCOVERIES I - INVISIBILITY SS
    BUG-EYED MONSTERS   CHEETHAM, ANTHONY   AN   NIGHTMARES AND GEEZENSTACKS BROWN, FREDRIC   AC
    DECADE THE 1940S   ALDISS & HARRISON   AN   GREAT LOST DISCOVERIES II - INVULNERABILITY SS
    HONEYMOON IN HELL   BROWN, FREDRIC   AC   NIGHTMARES AND GEEZENSTACKS BROWN, FREDRIC   AC
    INTRODUCING SCIENCE FICTION ALDISS, BRIAN W.   AN   GREAT LOST DISCOVERIES III - IMMORTALITY SS NEW 61 AC
    SCIENCE FICTION HALL OF FAME VOLUME 1 SILVERBERG, ROBERT AN   NIGHTMARES AND GEEZENSTACKS BROWN, FREDRIC   AC
    SCIENCE FICTION TERROR TALES CONKLIN, GROFF   AN   HALL OF MIRRORS   SS   GAL 53 12
    TOMORROW, AND TOMORROW, AND TOMORROW...   ASSIGNMENT IN TOMORROW   POHL, FREDERIK   AN
                                 HEINTZ/HERBERT/JOOS/ AN   BEST OF FREDRIC BROWN, THE BROWN, FREDRIC   AC
  ARMAGEDDON   SS   UNK 41 08   HONEYMOON IN HELL   BROWN, FREDRIC   AC
    ANGELS AND SPACESHIPS   BROWN, FREDRIC   AC   HAT TRICK, THE   SS   UNK 43 02
    BEST OF FREDRIC BROWN, THE   BROWN, FREDRIC   AC   ANGELS AND SPACESHIPS   BROWN, FREDRIC   AC
    EDGE OF NEVER, THE   HOSKINS, ROBERT   AN   HOBBYIST   SS   PBY 61 05
    UNKNOWN, THE   BENSEN, D. R.   AN   NIGHTMARES AND GEEZENSTACKS BROWN, FREDRIC   AC
  BEAR POSSIBILITY   SS   HONEYMOON IN HELL   NV   GAL 50 11
    NIGHTMARES AND GEEZENSTACKS BROWN, FREDRIC   AC   DAYMARES   BROWN, FREDRIC   AC
  BLOOD   SS   FSF 55 02   *GALAXY READER OF SCIENCE FICTION GOLD, H. L.   AN
    GALAXY OF GHOULS   MERRIL, JUDITH   AN   GREAT SCIENCE FICTION STORIES ABOUT THE MOON
    HONEYMOON IN HELL   BROWN, FREDRIC   AC   DIKTY, T. E.   AN
  BRIGHT BEARD   SS   HONEYMOON IN HELL   BROWN, FREDRIC   AC
    NIGHTMARES AND GEEZENSTACKS BROWN, FREDRIC   AC   HORSE RACE   SS
  CARTOONIST   SS C   NIGHTMARES AND GEEZENSTACKS BROWN, FREDRIC   AC
    NIGHTMARES AND GEEZENSTACKS BROWN, FREDRIC   AC   HOUSE, THE   SS   PAN 60 08
  CAT BURGLAR   SS   NIGHTMARES AND GEEZENSTACKS BROWN, FREDRIC   AC
    NIGHTMARES AND GEEZENSTACKS BROWN, FREDRIC   AC   IMAGINE, A PROEM   PM   FSF 55 05
  COME AND GO MAD   NV   WRT 49 07   BEST FROM FANTASY AND SCIENCE FICTION: 5
    BEST OF FREDRIC BROWN, THE   BROWN, FREDRIC   AC   BOUCHER, ANTHONY   AN
    DAYMARES   BROWN, FREDRIC   AC   BEST OF FREDRIC BROWN, THE BROWN, FREDRIC   AC
    SPACE ON MY HANDS   BROWN, FREDRIC   AC   HONEYMOON IN HELL   BROWN, FREDRIC   AC
    UNEXPECTED, THE   MARGULIES, LEO   AN   IMMORTALITY (GREAT LOST DISCOVERIES III) SS NEW 61 AC
  CONTACT   SS   VINTAGE ANTHOLOGY OF SCIENCE FANTASY, THE
    NIGHTMARES AND GEEZENSTACKS BROWN, FREDRIC   AC   CERF, CHRISTOPHER   AN
  CRISIS, 1999   SS   EQM 49 08   INTRODUCTION   IN
    SPACE ON MY HANDS   BROWN, FREDRIC   AC   ANGELS AND SPACESHIPS   BROWN, FREDRIC   AC
    SPACE, TIME & CRIME   DEFORD, MIRIAM ALLEN AN   HUMAN?   MERRIL, JUDITH   AN
  DAISIES (TRIPLICATE TWISTEROO)   SS   PBY 57 03   *SCIENCE-FICTION CARNIVAL   BROWN, F. & REYNOLDS AN
    ANGELS AND SPACESHIPS   BROWN, FREDRIC   AC   SPACE ON MY HANDS   BROWN, FREDRIC   AC
  DARK INTERLUDE   SS C GAL 51 01   IT DIDN'T HAPPEN   SS   PBY 63 10
    BEST SCIENCE-FICTION STORIES: 1952, THE   BEST OF FREDRIC BROWN, THE BROWN, FREDRIC   AC
                                 BLEILER & DIKTY   AN   PARADOX LOST, AND 12 OTHER GREAT S.F. STORIES
    FRONTIERS IN SPACE   BLEILER & DIKTY   AN   BROWN, FREDRIC   AC
    *GALAXY READER OF SCIENCE FICTION GOLD, H. L.   AN   TRANSIT OF EARTH   PLAYBOY, EDITORS OF AN
    HUMAN AND OTHER BEINGS   DEGRAEFF, ALLEN   AN   JAYCEE   SS   FSF 55
    NIGHTMARES AND GEEZENSTACKS BROWN, FREDRIC   AC   BEST OF FREDRIC BROWN, THE BROWN, FREDRIC   AC
  DASIES (TRIPLICATE TWISTEROO)   SS   PBY 57 03   NIGHTMARES AND GEEZENSTACKS BROWN, FREDRIC   AC
    ROOTS OF EVIL, THE   PARRY, MICHEL   AN   JOKE, THE   SS
  DAYMARE   NV   TWS 43 FL   NIGHTMARES AND GEEZENSTACKS BROWN, FREDRIC   AC
    DAYMARES   BROWN, FREDRIC   AC   KEEP OUT   SS   AMZ 54 03
    SAINT'S CHOICE OF IMPOSSIBLE CRIME, THE   HONEYMOON IN HELL   BROWN, FREDRIC   AC
                                 CHARTERIS, LESLIE   AN   *SCIENCE FICTION ADVENTURES IN MUTATION CONKLIN, GROFF AN
    SPACE ON MY HANDS   BROWN, FREDRIC   AC   KNOCK   SS   TWS 48 12
  DEAD LETTER   SS   BEST OF FREDRIC BROWN, THE   BROWN, FREDRIC   AC
    NIGHTMARES AND GEEZENSTACKS BROWN, FREDRIC   AC   BEST SCIENCE-FICTION STORIES: 1949, THE
  DEATH ON THE MOUNTAIN   SS   BLEILER & DIKTY   AN
    NIGHTMARES AND GEEZENSTACKS BROWN, FREDRIC   AC   CONTACT   KEYES, NOEL   AN
  DOME, THE   SS   TWS 51 08   PARADOX LOST, AND 12 OTHER GREAT S.F. STORIES
    HONEYMOON IN HELL   BROWN, FREDRIC   AC   BROWN, FREDRIC   AC
  DOUBLE STANDARD   SS   PBY 63   SHOT IN THE DARK   MERRIL, JUDITH   AN
    FIEND, THE   PLAYBOY, EDITORS OF AN   SPACE IN HAND   BROWN, FREDRIC   AC
    PARADOX LOST, AND 12 OTHER GREAT S.F. STORIES   LAST MARTIAN, THE   SS   GAL 50 10
                                 BROWN, FREDRIC   AC   BEST SCIENCE-FICTION STORIES: 1951, THE
    9TH ANNUAL OF THE YEAR'S BEST S-F, THE MERRIL, JUDITH AN   BLEILER & DIKTY   AN
  DOUBLE WHAMMY (SEE NATURALLY AND VOODOO) TC   *GALAXY READER OF SCIENCE FICTION GOLD, H. L.   AN
  EARTHMEN BEARING GIFTS   SS   GAL 60 06   HONEYMOON IN HELL   BROWN, FREDRIC   AC
    BEST OF FREDRIC BROWN, THE   BROWN, FREDRIC   AC   MINDWORM, THE   ANONYMOUS   AN
    SCIENCE FACT/FICTION   FARRELL/GAGE/&   AN   LAST TRAIN, THE   SS   WRT 50 01
    SEVENTH GALAXY READER, THE   POHL, FREDERIK   AN   PARADOX LOST, AND 12 OTHER GREAT S.F. STORIES
    12 GREAT CLASSICS OF SCIENCE FICTION CONKLIN, GROFF AN   BROWN, FREDRIC   AC
  EINE KLEINE NACHTMUSIK   SS C FSF 65 06   LETTER TO A PHOENIX   SS   ASF 49 08
    BEST OF FREDRIC BROWN, THE   BROWN, FREDRIC   AC   ANGELS AND SPACESHIPS   BROWN, FREDRIC   AC
    PARADOX LOST, AND 12 OTHER GREAT S.F. STORIES   BEST OF FREDRIC BROWN, THE BROWN, FREDRIC   AC
                                 BROWN, FREDRIC   AC   BEST SF 6   CRISPIN, EDMUND   AN
  END, THE   SS   NEW 61 AC   JOURNEY TO INFINITY   GREENBERG, MARTIN   AN
    BEST OF FREDRIC BROWN, THE   BROWN, FREDRIC   AC   LITTLE LAMB, THE   SS
    NIGHTMARES AND GEEZENSTACKS BROWN, FREDRIC   AC   NIGHTMARES AND GEEZENSTACKS BROWN, FREDRIC   AC
  ENTITY TRAP   SS   MAN OF DISTINCTION   SS   TWS 51 02
    NIGHTMARES AND GEEZENSTACKS BROWN, FREDRIC   AC   HONEYMOON IN HELL   BROWN, FREDRIC   AC
  ETAOIN SHRDLU   SS   UNK 42 02   ME AND FLAPJACK AND THE MARTIANS SS C ASF 52 12
    ANGELS AND SPACESHIPS   BROWN, FREDRIC   AC   NIGHTMARES AND GEEZENSTACKS BROWN, FREDRIC   AC
    BEST OF FREDRIC BROWN, THE   BROWN, FREDRIC   AC   MILLENNIUM   SS   FSF 55 03
    STORIES FROM SCIENCE FICTION DOHERTY, G. D.   AN   HONEYMOON IN HELL   BROWN, FREDRIC   AC
    WORLD OF WONDER   PRATT, FLETCHER   AN   MOUSE   SS   TWS 49 06
  EXPEDITION   SS   FSF 57 02   BEST SCIENCE-FICTION STORIES: 1950, THE
    BEST FROM FANTASY AND SCIENCE FICTION: 7   BLEILER & DIKTY   AN
                                 BOUCHER, ANTHONY   AN   GREAT SCIENCE-FICTION   LICATA, TONY   AN
    FANTASIA MATHEMATICA   FADIMAN, CLIFTON   AN   HONEYMOON IN HELL   BROWN, FREDRIC   AC
    NIGHTMARES AND GEEZENSTACKS BROWN, FREDRIC   AC   MURDER IN TEN EASY LESSONS   SS
  EXPERIMENT (TWO TIMER)   SS   GAL 54 02   NIGHTMARES AND GEEZENSTACKS BROWN, FREDRIC   AC
    BEST OF FREDRIC BROWN, THE   BROWN, FREDRIC   AC   NASTY   SS   PBY 59 04
    HONEYMOON IN HELL   BROWN, FREDRIC   AC   NIGHTMARES AND GEEZENSTACKS BROWN, FREDRIC   AC
  FATAL ERROR   SS   PLAYBOY BOOK OF HORROR AND THE SUPERNATURAL, THE
    NIGHTMARES AND GEEZENSTACKS BROWN, FREDRIC   AC   PLAYBOY, EDITORS OF AN
                                                             WEIRD SHOW   PLAYBOY, EDITORS OF AN

BROWN, FREDRIC   (CONTINUED)
  NATURALLY (DOUBLE WHAMMY)   SS   BEY 54 09
    BEYOND   ANONYMOUS   AN
    HONEYMOON IN HELL   BROWN, FREDRIC   AC
  NEW ONE, THE   SS   UNK 42 10
    PARADOX LOST, AND 12 OTHER GREAT S.F. STORIES
                                       BROWN, FREDRIC   AC
  NIGHTMARE IN BLUE   SS
    NIGHTMARES AND GEEZENSTACKS   BROWN, FREDRIC   AC
  NIGHTMARE IN GRAY   SS
    NIGHTMARES AND GEEZENSTACKS   BROWN, FREDRIC   AC
  NIGHTMARE IN GREEN   SS
    NIGHTMARES AND GEEZENSTACKS   BROWN, FREDRIC   AC
  NIGHTMARE IN RED   SS
    NIGHTMARES AND GEEZENSTACKS   BROWN, FREDRIC   AC
  NIGHTMARE IN TIME   SS   DUD 61
    7TH ANNUAL OF THE YEAR'S BEST S-F, THE MERRIL, JUDITH   AN
  NIGHTMARE IN WHITE   SS
    NIGHTMARES AND GEEZENSTACKS   BROWN, FREDRIC   AC
  NIGHTMARE IN YELLOW   SS   DUD 61 05
    BEST OF FREDRIC BROWN, THE   BROWN, FREDRIC   AC
    NIGHTMARES AND GEEZENSTACKS   BROWN, FREDRIC   AC
  NOT YET THE END   SS   CFU 41 WI
    BEST OF FREDRIC BROWN, THE   BROWN, FREDRIC   AC
    GALACTIC EMPIRES VOLUME TWO   ALDISS, BRIAN W.   AN
    NIGHTMARES AND GEEZENSTACKS   BROWN, FREDRIC   AC
  NOTHING SIRIUS   SS   CFU 44 SP
    BEST OF FREDRIC BROWN, THE   BROWN, FREDRIC   AC
    *MY BEST SCIENCE FICTION STORY   MARGULIES & FRIEND AN
    PARADOX LOST, AND 12 OTHER GREAT S.F. STORIES
                                       BROWN, FREDRIC   AC
    SPACE ON MY HANDS   BROWN, FREDRIC   AC
  OBEDIENCE (THE UNDYING ONES)   SS   SSS 50 09
    PARADOX LOST, AND 12 OTHER GREAT S.F. STORIES
                                       BROWN, FREDRIC   AC
  PARADOX LOST   SS   ASF 43 10
    PARADOX LOST, AND 12 OTHER GREAT S.F. STORIES
                                       BROWN, FREDRIC   AC
    *SCIENCE-FICTION CARNIVAL   BROWN, F. & REYNOLDS AN
  PATTERN   SS   NEW 54 AC
    ABC OF SCIENCE FICTION, AN   BOARDMAN, TOM JR.   AN
    ANGELS AND SPACESHIPS   BROWN, FREDRIC   AC
    BEST OF FREDRIC BROWN, THE   BROWN, FREDRIC   AC
    VOYAGES: SCENARIOS FOR A SHIP CALLED EARTH
                                       SAUER, ROB   AN
  PI IN THE SKY   SS   TWS 45 WI
    BEST OF FREDRIC BROWN, THE   BROWN, FREDRIC   AC
    DAYMARES   BROWN, FREDRIC   AC
    SPACE ON MY HANDS   BROWN, FREDRIC   AC
  PLACET IS A CRAZY PLACE   SS   ASF 46 05
    ANGELS AND SPACESHIPS   BROWN, FREDRIC   AC
    ASTOUNDING-ANALOG READER, THE VOLUME ONE
                                       HARRISON & ALDISS   AN
    BEST SF 2   CRISPIN, EDMUND   AN
    OUT OF THIS WORLD 1   WILLIAMS-ELLIS& OWEN AN
    SCIENCE FICTION: THE GREAT YEARS   POHL, C. & F.   AN
    TRAVELLERS OF SPACE   GREENBERG , MARTIN AN
  POLITENESS (TRIPLICATE TWISTEROO)   SS   PBY 57 03
    ANGELS AND SPACESHIPS   BROWN, FREDRIC   AC
  PREPOSTEROUS   SS   NEW 54 AC
    ANGELS AND SPACESHIPS   BROWN, FREDRIC   AC
    IF THIS GOES ON   NUETZEL, CHARLES   AN
    14 GREAT TALES OF ESP   STONE, IDELLA P.   AN
  PUPPET SHOW   SS   PBY 62 11
    BEST OF FREDRIC BROWN, THE   BROWN, FREDRIC   AC
    LAST TRAIN TO LIMBO   PLAYBOY, EDITORS OF AN
    PARADOX LOST, AND 12 OTHER GREAT S.F. STORIES
                                       BROWN, FREDRIC   AC
    PLAYBOY BOOK OF SCIENCE FICTION AND FANTASY, THE
                                       PLAYBOY, EDITORS OF AN
    SCIENCE FACT/FICTION   FARRELL/GAGE/&   AN
    SPECIAL WONDER   MCCOMAS, J. FRANCIS AN
    TALES OF TIME AND SPACE   OLNEY, ROSS R.   AN
    THEMES IN SCIENCE FICTION   KELLEY, LEO P.   AN
    8TH ANNUAL OF THE YEAR'S BEST S-F, THE MERRIL, JUDITH   AN
  REBOUND   SS   NEW 61 AC
    BEST OF FREDRIC BROWN, THE   BROWN, FREDRIC   AC
    NIGHTMARES AND GEEZENSTACKS   BROWN, FREDRIC   AC
  RECESSIONAL   SS   DUD 60 03
    BEST OF FREDRIC BROWN, THE   BROWN, FREDRIC   AC
    NIGHTMARES AND GEEZENSTACKS   BROWN, FREDRIC   AC
  RECONCILIATION   SS   NEW 54 AC
    ANGELS AND SPACESHIPS   BROWN, FREDRIC   AC
    BEST OF FREDRIC BROWN, THE   BROWN, FREDRIC   AC
  RING OF HANS CARVEL, THE   SS
    NIGHTMARES AND GEEZENSTACKS   BROWN, FREDRIC   AC
  ROPE TRICK   SS
    NIGHTMARES AND GEEZENSTACKS   BROWN, FREDRIC   AC
  RUNAROUND   SS
    NIGHTMARES AND GEEZENSTACKS   BROWN, FREDRIC   AC
  RUSTLE OF WINGS   SS   FSF 53 08
    HONEYMOON IN HELL   BROWN, FREDRIC   AC
    PORTALS OF TOMORROW   DERLETH, AUGUST   AN
  SEARCH   SS
    ANGELS AND SPACESHIPS   BROWN, FREDRIC   AC
  SECOND CHANCE   SS
    NIGHTMARES AND GEEZENSTACKS   BROWN, FREDRIC   AC
  SENTENCE (TRIPLICATE TWISTEROO)   SS   PBY 57 03
    ANGELS AND SPACESHIPS   BROWN, FREDRIC   AC
  SENTRY (TWO TIMER)   SS   GAL 54 02
    HONEYMOON IN HELL   BROWN, FREDRIC   AC
  SHORT HAPPY LIVES OF EUSTACE WEAVER I, THE   SS   EQM 61 06
    BEST OF FREDRIC BROWN, THE   BROWN, FREDRIC   AC
    NIGHTMARES AND GEEZENSTACKS   BROWN, FREDRIC   AC
  SHORT HAPPY LIVES OF EUSTACE WEAVER II, THE   SS   EQM 61 06
    BEST OF FREDRIC BROWN, THE   BROWN, FREDRIC   AC

BROWN, FREDRIC   (CONTINUED)
  NIGHTMARES AND GEEZENSTACKS   BROWN, FREDRIC   AC
  SHORT HAPPY LIVES OF EUSTACE WEAVER III, THE   SS   EQM 61 06
    BEST OF FREDRIC BROWN, THE   BROWN, FREDRIC   AC
    NIGHTMARES AND GEEZENSTACKS   BROWN, FREDRIC   AC
  SOLIPSIST   SS
    ANGELS AND SPACESHIPS   BROWN, FREDRIC   AC
  SOMETHING GREEN   SS   NEW 51 AC
    EXPLORING OTHER WORLDS   MOSKOWITZ, SAM   AN
    PARADOX LOST, AND 12 OTHER GREAT S.F. STORIES
                                       BROWN, FREDRIC   AC
    SPACE ON MY HANDS   BROWN, FREDRIC   AC
  STAR MOUSE, THE   SS   PLS 42 02
    *ADVENTURES IN TIME AND SPACE   HEALY & MCCOMAS   AN
    BEST OF FREDRIC BROWN, THE   BROWN, FREDRIC   AC
    BEST OF PLANET STORIES NO. 1, THE BRACKETT, LEIGH   AN
    DAYMARES   BROWN, FREDRIC   AC
    INVASION FROM MARS   WELLES, ORSON   AN
    SPACE ON MY HANDS   BROWN, FREDRIC   AC
  TEN PERCENTER   SS
    PARADOX LOST, AND 12 OTHER GREAT S.F. STORIES
                                       BROWN, FREDRIC   AC
  THREE LITTLE OWLS   SS
    NIGHTMARES AND GEEZENSTACKS   BROWN, FREDRIC   AC
  TOO FAR   SS   FSF 55 09
    BEST FROM FANTASY AND SCIENCE FICTION: 5
                                       BOUCHER, ANTHONY   AN
    HONEYMOON IN HELL   BROWN, FREDRIC   AC
  TRIPLICATE TWISTEROO (SEE DASIES, POLITENESS AND SENTENCE)
                                                    TC
  TWO TIMER (SEE EXPERIMENT AND SENTRY)   TC
  UNDYING ONES, THE (SEE OBEDIENCE)   TC
  UNFORTUNATELY   SS   FSF 58 10
    NIGHTMARES AND GEEZENSTACKS   BROWN, FREDRIC   AC
  VENGEANCE FLEET (VENGEANCE, UNLIMITED)   SS   SSS 50 07
    NIGHTMARES AND GEEZENSTACKS   BROWN, FREDRIC   AC
  VENGEANCE, UNLIMITED (SEE VENGEANCE FLEET)   TC
  VOODOO (DOUBLE WHAMMY)   SS   BEY 54 09
    BEYOND   ANONYMOUS   AN
    HONEYMOON IN HELL   BROWN, FREDRIC   AC
  WAVERIES, THE   SS   ASF 45 01
    ABOVE THE HUMAN LANDSCAPE   MCNELLY & STOVER   AN
    ANGELS AND SPACESHIPS   BROWN, FREDRIC   AC
    CONNOISSEUR'S S. F.   BOARDMAN, TOM JR.   AN
    ENEMIES IN SPACE   CONKLIN, GROFF   AN
    FIRST CONTACT   KNIGHT, DAMON   AN
    *INVADERS OF EARTH   CONKLIN, GROFF   AN
    SPECULATIONS   SANDERS, THOMAS E. AN
    TOMORROW, AND TOMORROW, AND TOMORROW...
                                       HEINTZ/HERBERT/JOOS/ AN
  WEAPON, THE   SS   ASF 51 04
    ASLEEP IN ARMAGEDDON   SISSONS, MICHAEL   AN
    FIFTY SHORT SCIENCE FICTION TALES ASIMOV & CONKLIN   AN
    HONEYMOON IN HELL   BROWN, FREDRIC   AC
    OMNIBUS OF SCIENCE FICTION   CONKLIN, GROFF   AN
    SCIENCE FICTION FOR PEOPLE WHO HATE SCIENCE FICTION
                                       CARR, TERRY   AN
    SCIENCE FICTION OMNIBUS   CONKLIN, GROFF   AN
    STRANGE TRAVELS IN SCIENCE FICTION CONKLIN, GROFF   AN
  WHY I SELECTED NOTHING SIRIUS   AI
    *MY BEST SCIENCE FICTION STORY   MARGULIES & FRIEND AN
  WORD FROM OUR SPONSOR, A   SS   OWS 51 09
    HONEYMOON IN HELL   BROWN, FREDRIC   AC
  YEHUDI PRINCIPLE, THE   SS   ASF 44 05
    ANGELS AND SPACESHIPS   BROWN, FREDRIC   AC
    BEST OF FREDRIC BROWN, THE   BROWN, FREDRIC   AC

BROWN, JAMES GOLDIE
  FROM FRANKENSTEIN TO ANDROMEDA   AN   MCM 66

BROWN, ROSEL GEORGE
  HANDFUL OF TIME, A   AC   BAL 63
  CAR POOL   NV   IFS 59 07
    HANDFUL OF TIME, A   BROWN, ROSEL GEORGE AC
  DAVID'S DADDY   SS   FAN 60 06
    6TH ANNUAL OF THE YEAR'S BEST S-F, THE MERRIL, JUDITH   AN
  DEVALUATION OF THE SYMBOL, THE   SS   NEW 63 AC
    HANDFUL OF TIME, A   BROWN, ROSEL GEORGE AC
  FLOWER ARRANGEMENT   SS   GAL 59 12
    SIXTH GALAXY READER, THE   GOLD, H. L.   AN
  FRUITING BODY   NV   FSF 62 08
    HANDFUL OF TIME, A   BROWN, ROSEL GEORGE AC
    ONCE AND FUTURE TALES FROM THE MAGAZINE OF FANTASY AND
      SCIENCE FICTION   FERMAN, EDWARD L.   AN
  HAIR-RAISING ADVENTURE   SS   STR 59 05
    STAR SCIENCE FICTION STORIES NO. 5 POHL, FREDERIK   OA
  JUST A SUGGESTION   SS   FSF 60 08
    HANDFUL OF TIME, A   BROWN, ROSEL GEORGE AC
  LITTLE HUMAN CONTACT, A   SS   FSF 60 04
    HANDFUL OF TIME, A   BROWN, ROSEL GEORGE AC
  LOST IN TRANSLATION   SS   FSF 59 05
    HANDFUL OF TIME, A   BROWN, ROSEL GEORGE AC
  OF ALL POSSIBLE WORLDS   SS   FSF 61 02
    HANDFUL OF TIME, A   BROWN, ROSEL GEORGE AC
  SAVE YOUR CONFEDERATE MONEY, BOYS   SS   FUN 59 11
    HANDFUL OF TIME, A   BROWN, ROSEL GEORGE AC
  SIGNS OF THE TIMES   SS   AMZ 59 12
    HANDFUL OF TIME, A   BROWN, ROSEL GEORGE AC
  SMITH'S REVENGE   SS   NEW 63 AC
    HANDFUL OF TIME, A   BROWN, ROSEL GEORGE AC
  STEP IV   SS   AMZ 60 06
    HANDFUL OF TIME, A   BROWN, ROSEL GEORGE AC
  VISITING PROFESSOR   SS   FAN 61 02
    HANDFUL OF TIME, A   BROWN, ROSEL GEORGE AC

BROWN, T. K. III
  HAUNTS OF THE VERY RICH   NV   PBY 71 05
    YEAR'S BEST HORROR STORIES: SERIES II, THE
                                                   DAVIS, RICHARD   AN
  MAN WITH A PAST   SS   PBY 63 05
    LAST TRAIN TO LIMBO   PLAYBOY, EDITORS OF AN
  WHEN THE STARS ANSWER   SS   WOT 64 02
    BEST SCIENCE FICTION FROM WORLDS OF TOMORROW, THE
                                                   POHL, FREDERIK   AN

BROWN, WENZELL
  MURDERER'S CHAIN   SS   FUN 60 03
    RULERS OF MEN   SANTESSON, HANS S. AN

BROWNING, JOHN S.   PSEUD. FOR ROBERT MOORE WILLIAMS
  BURNING BRIGHT   SS   ASF 48 07
    ROBOT AND THE MAN, THE   GREENBERG , MARTIN AN

BROWNJOHN, ALAN
  TO SEE THE RABBIT   PM
    STARLIT CORRIDOR, THE   MANSFIELD, ROGER   AN

BROWNLOW, CATHERINE
  VOICE FROM THE GALLERY   SS
    AD 2500   WILSON, ANGUS   AN

BROWNSTEIN, MICHAEL
  PLOT TO SAVE THE WORLD, THE   SS   PRV 70 48
    RUINS OF EARTH, THE   DISCH, THOMAS M.   AN

BROXON, MILDRED D.
  ANTRIM HILLS, THE   NV
    AURORA: BEYOND EQUALITY   MCINTYRE & ANDERSON OA
  ASCLEPIUS HAS PAWS   SS   CLR 73 03
    CLARION III   WILSON, ROBIN SCOTT OA
  NIGHT IS COLD, THE STARS ARE FAR AWAY, THE   SS   UNI 74 05
    BEST SCIENCE FICTION STORIES OF THE YEAR (1974)
                                                   DEL REY, LESTER   AN
    UNIVERSE 5   CARR, TERRY   OA
  STONES HAVE NAMES, THE   SS   FOS 74
    FELLOWSHIP OF THE STARS   CARR, TERRY   OA

BRUNNER, JOHN   ALSO AS   K. HOUSTON BRUNNER
  BEST OF PHILIP K. DICK, THE (LISTED UNDER PHILIP K. DICK)
                                                   EC   BAL 77 03
  BOOK OF JOHN BRUNNER, THE   AC   DAW 76 01
  ENTRY TO ELSEWHEN (STORIES REVISED)   AC   DAW 72 10
  FROM THIS DAY FORWARD   AC H DBL 72
  INTERSTELLAR EMPIRE   AC   DAW 76 09
  NO FUTURE IN IT   AC H DBL 64
  NO OTHER GODS BUT ME   AC   CPT 66
  NOT BEFORE TIME   AC   FSP 68
  NOW THEN   AC   MFL 65 10
  OUT OF MY MIND   AC   BAL 67 02
  OUT OF MY MIND (BRITISH)   AC   FSP 68
  TIME-JUMP   AC   DEL 73 12
  TIMES WITHOUT NUMBER   NO   ACE 62
  TRAVELER IN BLACK, THE   AC   ACE 71
  WHOLE MAN, THE   NO   BAL 64 08
  AGAINST THE ODDS (SEE THE ODDS AGAINST YOU)   TC
  ALTAR OF ASCONEL   NO   IFS 65 04
    INTERSTELLIAR EMPIRE   BRUNNER, JOHN   AC
  ATOM BOMB IS TWENTY-FIVE THIS YEAR, THE   PM   STY 70
    BOOK OF JOHN BRUNNER, THE   BRUNNER, JOHN   AC
  BADMAN   SS   NWS 60 03
    NO FUTURE IN IT   BRUNNER, JOHN   AC
    OUT OF THIS WORLD 5   WILLIAMS-ELLIS& OWEN AN
  "BALLAD OF TEDDY HART, THE"   SG   NEW 76 AC
    BOOK OF JOHN BRUNNER, THE   BRUNNER, JOHN   AC
  BETTER MOUSETRAP, A   NV   IFS 63 11
    IF READER OF SCIENCE FICTION, THE   POHL, FREDERIK   AN
    NOT BEFORE TIME   BRUNNER, JOHN   AC
    *OUT OF MY MIND   BRUNNER, JOHN   AC
  BIGGEST GAME, THE (AS KEITH WOODCOTT)   SS   SCF 56 02
    FROM THIS DAY FORWARD   BRUNNER, JOHN   AC
  BLOODSTREAM   SS   VTX 74 06
    BOOK OF JOHN BRUNNER, THE   BRUNNER, JOHN   AC
  BREAK THE DOOR OF HELL   NV   IMP 66 04
    NEW WORLDS OF FANTASY   CARR, TERRY   AN
    TRAVELER IN BLACK, THE   BRUNNER, JOHN   AC
  BY THE NAME OF MAN (SUBSTITUTE GOD, FUN 58 08)   NV   NEB 56 01
    MORE ADVENTURES ON OTHER PLANETS   WOLLHEIM, DONALD A. AN
  CHILDREN IN HIDING (SEE SIEZURE)   TC
  CITIZEN BACILLUS   PM   69
    HOLDING YOUR EIGHT HANDS   LUCIE-SMITH, EDWARD AN
  CITY OF THE TIGER   SN   SCF 58 12
    WHOLE MAN, THE   BRUNNER, JOHN   NO
  COINCIDENCE DAY   SS   ASF 65 02
    ANALOG 5   CAMPBELL, JOHN W. JR AN
    NOT BEFORE TIME   BRUNNER, JOHN   AC
    TIME-JUMP   BRUNNER, JOHN   AC
  CORRIDA (BY RAINER MARIA RILKE, TRANSLATION)   PM   CHP 73
    BOOK OF JOHN BRUNNER, THE   BRUNNER, JOHN   AC
  CROSSWORD   MS
    BOOK OF JOHN BRUNNER, THE   BRUNNER, JOHN   AC
  CURATIVE TELEPATH   NV   FUN 59 12
    WHOLE MAN, THE   BRUNNER, JOHN   NO
  DEATH DO US PART   SS   SCF 55 11
    TIME-JUMP   BRUNNER, JOHN   AC
  DIE SPANGE (BY STEFAN GEORGE, TRANSLATION)   PM   NEW 76 AC
    BOOK OF JOHN BRUNNER, THE   BRUNNER, JOHN   AC
  DIFFERENT KICK, OR HOW TO GET HIGH WITHOUT ACTUALLY GOING
    INTO ORBIT, A   AR   NIE 65
    BOOK OF JOHN BRUNNER, THE   BRUNNER, JOHN   AC
  DOMESTIC CRISIS 2017   PM   TRB 74 03
    BOOK OF JOHN BRUNNER, THE   BRUNNER, JOHN   AC

BRUNNER, JOHN   (CONTINUED)
  DREAD EMPIRE   SN   FAN 71 04
    TRAVELER IN BLACK, THE   BRUNNER, JOHN   AC
  EASY WAY OUT, THE   NV   IFS 71 06
    BEST SCIENCE FICTION FOR 1972   POHL, FREDERIK   AN
  EDUCATIONAL RELEVANCE OF SCIENCE FICTION, THE   AR   PHE 71 06
    BOOK OF JOHN BRUNNER, THE   BRUNNER, JOHN   AC
  ELECTED SILENCE (SILENCE)   NV   GAL 59 10
    NO FUTURE IN IT   BRUNNER, JOHN   AC
  ELIXER FOR THE EMPEROR, THE   SS   FAN 64 11
    FROM THIS DAY FORWARD   BRUNNER, JOHN   AC
  EPIGRAMMATA LXV (BY DECIMUS MAGNUS AUSONIUS, TRANS)
                                                   PM   NEW 76 AC
    BOOK OF JOHN BRUNNER, THE   BRUNNER, JOHN   AC
  EVEN CHANCE   SS   ASF 65 11
    FROM THIS DAY FORWARD   BRUNNER, JOHN   AC
  EVOLUTION OF A SCIENCE FICTION WRITER, THE   AR   FDN 72 01
    BOOK OF JOHN BRUNNER, THE   BRUNNER, JOHN   AC
  EXCERPT FROM A SOCIAL HISTORY OF THE 20TH CENTURY SS   70
    BOOK OF JOHN BRUNNER, THE   BRUNNER, JOHN   AC
  EYE OF THE BEHOLDER, THE   SS   FUN 57 01
    NOT BEFORE TIME   BRUNNER, JOHN   AC
    *OUT OF MY MIND   BRUNNER, JOHN   AC
  FACTSHEET SIX   NV   GAL 68 07
    FROM THIS DAY FORWARD   BRUNNER, JOHN   AC
  FAIR (AS KEITH WOODCOTT)   SS   NWS 56 03
    NO FUTURE IN IT   BRUNNER, JOHN   AC
    SF: AUTHORS' CHOICE 4   HARRISON, HARRY   AN
  FAIR WARNING   SS   ASF 64 05
    NOT BEFORE TIME   BRUNNER, JOHN   AC
    *OUT OF MY MIND   BRUNNER, JOHN   AC
  FAIRY TALE   SS   VOT 70 07
    FROM THIS DAY FORWARD   BRUNNER, JOHN   AC
  "FAITHLESS JACK THE SPACEMAN"   SG   NEW 76 AC
    BOOK OF JOHN BRUNNER, THE   BRUNNER, JOHN   AC
  FEGHOOT I   SS   FSF 62 06
    BOOK OF JOHN BRUNNER, THE   BRUNNER, JOHN   AC
  FEGHOOT II   SS   NEW 76 AC
    BOOK OF JOHN BRUNNER, THE   BRUNNER, JOHN   AC
  FEGHOOT III   SS   NEW 76 AC
    BOOK OF JOHN BRUNNER, THE   BRUNNER, JOHN   AC
  FIFTH COMMANDMENT   SS   VOT 70 03
    FROM THIS DAY FORWARD   BRUNNER, JOHN   AC
  FOURTH POWER, THE   NV   NWS 60 04
    *OUT OF MY MIND   BRUNNER, JOHN   AC
  "FROM THIS DAY FOREWORD", AS IT WERE, A   IN
    FROM THIS DAY FORWARD   BRUNNER, JOHN   AC
  FROM:THE JAGGED ORBIT   EX   ACE 69
    INSIDE INFORMATION   MOWSHOWITZ, ABBE   AN
  FULLNESS OF TIME, THE   NV   SPA 62 07
    TIMES WITHOUT NUMBER   BRUNNER, JOHN   NO
  GALACTIC CONSUMER REPORT NO. 1: INEXPENSIVE TIME MACHINES
                                                   FA   GAL 65 12
    TIME-JUMP   BRUNNER, JOHN   AC
  GALACTIC CONSUMER REPORT NO. 2: AUTOMATIC TWIN-TUBE WISHING
    MACHINES   FA   GAL 66 06
    TIME-JUMP   BRUNNER, JOHN   AC
  GALACTIC CONSUMER REPORT NO. 3: A SURVEY OF THE MEMBERSHIP
                                                   FA   GAL 67 12
    TIME-JUMP   BRUNNER, JOHN   AC
  "H-BOMBS' THUNDER, THE"   SG   SNG 58 10
    BOOK OF JOHN BRUNNER, THE   BRUNNER, JOHN   AC
  HIDE AND SEEK (CACHE-CACHE BY GERARD KLEIN, TRANS)
                                                   SS   73
    BOOK OF JOHN BRUNNER, THE   BRUNNER, JOHN   AC
  HOST AGE   NV   NWS 56 01
    ENTRY TO ELSEWHEN (STORIES REVISED)   BRUNNER, JOHN   AC
  IMPRINT OF CHAOS   NV   SCF 60 08
    NOW THEN   BRUNNER, JOHN   AC
    TRAVELER IN BLACK, THE   BRUNNER, JOHN   AC
  INCEPTION OF THE EPOCH OF MRS. BEDONEBYASYOUDID, THE
                                                   SS   QRK 71 02
    BEYOND THIS HORIZON   CARRELL, CHRISTOPHER OA
    FROM THIS DAY FORWARD   BRUNNER, JOHN   AC
    QUARK/2   DELANY & HACKER   OA
  INTRODUCTION   IN
    TIME-JUMP   BRUNNER, JOHN   AC
  INTRODUCTION: THE REALITY OF PHILIP K. DICK   IN
    BEST OF PHILIP K. DICK, THE   DICK, PHILIP K.   AC
  INVISIBLE IDIOT, THE   SS   SAG 70
    SCIENCE AGAINST MAN   CHEETHAM, ANTHONY   OA
  IRON JACKASS, THE   SS   ASF 62 03
    NO FUTURE IN IT   BRUNNER, JOHN   AC
  JACK FELL DOWN   NV   SFA 63 03
    CRIME PREVENTION IN THE 30TH CENTURY   SANTESSON, HANS S. AN
  JUDAS   SS   DVS 67 01
    DANGEROUS VISIONS   ELLISON, HARLAN   OA
    FROM THIS DAY FORWARD   BRUNNER, JOHN   AC
    OTHER WORLDS, OTHER GODS   MOHS, MAYO   AN
    PAST, PRESENT, AND FUTURE PERFECT   WOLFE, J&FITZ GERALD AN
  LAST LONELY MAN, THE   SS   NWS 64 06
    BEST OF NEW WORLDS, THE   MOORCOCK, MICHAEL   AN
    BEST SF STORIES FROM NEW WORLDS 8   MOORCOCK, MICHAEL   AN
    MARRIAGE AND THE FAMILY THROUGH SCIENCE FICTION
                                                   CLEAR/WARRICK/&   AN
    *OUT OF MY MIND   BRUNNER, JOHN   AC
    WORLD'S BEST SCIENCE FICTION: 1965   WOLLHEIM & CARR   AN
    10TH ANNUAL OF THE YEAR'S BEST S-F, THE
                                                   MERRIL, JUDITH   AN
  LIMERICK NO. 1   PM   ARA
    BOOK OF JOHN BRUNNER, THE   BRUNNER, JOHN   AC
  LIMERICK NO. 2   PM   ARA
    BOOK OF JOHN BRUNNER, THE   BRUNNER, JOHN   AC
  LIMERICK NO. 3   PM   VCT
    BOOK OF JOHN BRUNNER, THE   BRUNNER, JOHN   AC

BRUNNER, JOHN   (CONTINUED)
  LIMERICK NO. 4   PM   NEW 76 AC
    BOOK OF JOHN BRUNNER, THE   BRUNNER, JOHN   AC
  LIMERICK NO. 5   PM   NEW 76 AC
    BOOK OF JOHN BRUNNER, THE   BRUNNER, JOHN   AC
  LOSTLING   SS
    FAR SIDE OF TIME, THE   ELWOOD, ROGER   OA
  "LULLABY FOR THE MAD SCIENTIST'S DAUGHTER" SG   NEW 76 AC
    BOOK OF JOHN BRUNNER, THE   BRUNNER, JOHN   AC
  LUNGFISH (RENDEZVOUS WITH DESTINY, FUN 58 03) NV SCF 57 12
    ENTRY TO ELSEWHEN (STORIES REVISED) BRUNNER, JOHN   AC
  MAN FROM THE BIG DARK, THE   SN   SFA 58 06
    GREAT SCIENCE FICTION ADVENTURES SHAW, LARRY T.   AN
    INTERSTELLIAR EMPIRE   BRUNNER, JOHN   AC
    NO OTHER GODS BUT ME   BRUNNER, JOHN   AC
  MAN WHO PLAYED THE BLUES   SS   SCF 56 02
    OUT OF MY MIND (BRITISH)   BRUNNER, JOHN   AC
  MANALIVE   EX   REA 64 04
    BOOK OF JOHN BRUNNER, THE   BRUNNER, JOHN   AC
  MATTHEW XVIII, 6   PM   WKS 71 15
    BOOK OF JOHN BRUNNER, THE   BRUNNER, JOHN   AC
  NAIL IN THE MIDDLE OF THE HAND, THE   SS   SMM 65 07
    *OUT OF MY MIND   BRUNNER, JOHN   AC
  NEW THING, THE   SS   IFS 69 12
    BOOK OF JOHN BRUNNER, THE   BRUNNER, JOHN   AC
  NO FUTURE IN IT   SS   SCF 55 09
    NO FUTURE IN IT   BRUNNER, JOHN   AC
  NO OTHER GODS BUT ME (BASED ON A TIME TO REND) NV SCF 56 12
    ENTRY TO ELSEWHEN (STORIES REVISED) BRUNNER, JOHN   AC
    NO OTHER GODS BUT ME   BRUNNER, JOHN   AC
  NOBODY AXED YOU   NV   NWS 65 05
    BEST SF STORIES FROM NEW WORLDS NO. 1, THE
                                     MOORCOCK, MICHAEL   AN
    TIME-JUMP   BRUNNER, JOHN   AC
  ODDS AGAINST YOU, THE (AGAINST THE ODDS)   SS   IFS 65 08
    NO OTHER GODS BUT ME   BRUNNER, JOHN   AC
  OLDEST GLASS, THE   PM   72
    FROM THIS DAY FORWARD   BRUNNER, JOHN   AC
  ORPHEUS'S BROTHER   SS   MHS 65 04
    *OUT OF MY MIND   BRUNNER, JOHN   AC
  OUT OF MINDSHOT   SS   GAL 70 06
    BEST FROM GALAXY, THE   VOLUME I GALAXY, EDITORS OF AN
  OUT OF ORDER   SS   NWS 57 04
    NO FUTURE IN IT   BRUNNER, JOHN   AC
  PLANETFALL   SS   ASF 65 05
    FROM THIS DAY FORWARD   BRUNNER, JOHN   AC
  POND WATER   SS   FRS 68
    FARTHEST REACHES, THE   ELDER, JOSEPH   OA
  PREFACE   IN
    NOW THEN   BRUNNER, JOHN   AC
  PREMUMBLE   MS
    BOOK OF JOHN BRUNNER, THE   BRUNNER, JOHN   AC
  PREROGATIVE   SS   NWS 60 11
    NOT BEFORE TIME   BRUNNER, JOHN   AC
    *OUT OF MY MIND   BRUNNER, JOHN   AC
  PRODUCT OF THE MASSES, THE   NV   IFS 68 04
    TIME-JUMP   BRUNNER, JOHN   AC
  PROTECT ME FROM MY FRIENDS   SS   FSF 62 11
    BEST SF 7   CRISPIN, EDMUND   AN
    NO FUTURE IN IT   BRUNNER, JOHN   AC
  PROTOCOLS OF THE ELDERS OF BRITAIN, THE   SS
    STOPWATCH   HAY, GEORGE   OA
    1976 ANNUAL WORLD'S BEST SF, THE WOLLHEIM, DONALD A. AN
  PUZZLE FOR SPACEMEN   SS   NWS 55 12
    NO FUTURE IN IT   BRUNNER, JOHN   AC
    SPECIAL WONDER   MCCOMAS, J. FRANCIS AN
  RENDEZVOUS WITH DESTINY (SEE LUNGFISH)   TC   FUN 58 03
  REPORT ON THE NATURE OF THE LUNAR SURFACE   SS   ASF 60 08
    FIRST FLIGHTS TO THE MOON   CLEMENT, HAL   AN
    FROM FRANKENSTEIN TO ANDROMEDA   BROWN, JAMES GOLDIE AN
    NO FUTURE IN IT   BRUNNER, JOHN   AC
    WONDERMAKERS 2   HOSKINS, ROBERT   AN
  6TH ANNUAL OF THE YEAR'S BEST S-F, THE MERRIL, JUDITH AN
  ROUND TRIP   SS   FUN 59 09
    NOT BEFORE TIME   BRUNNER, JOHN   AC
    *OUT OF MY MIND   BRUNNER, JOHN   AC
  SEE WHAT I MEAN¡   SS   ASF 64 01
    *OUT OF MY MIND   BRUNNER, JOHN   AC
  SIEZURE (CHILDREN IN HIDING)   SS   GAL 66 12
    NOT BEFORE TIME   BRUNNER, JOHN   AC
  SILENCE (SEE ELECTED SILENCE)   TC
  SINGLEMINDED   NV   IFS 63 05
    ALIEN WORLDS   ELWOOD, ROGER   AN
    NOT BEFORE TIME   BRUNNER, JOHN   AC
    *OUT OF MY MIND   BRUNNER, JOHN   AC
  SOLUTION TO CROSSWORD   MS
    BOOK OF JOHN BRUNNER, THE   BRUNNER, JOHN   AC
  SOME LAPSE OF TIME   NV   SCF 63 02
    NOW THEN   BRUNNER, JOHN   AC
  "SPACEWRECK OF THE OLD 97, THE"   SG   NEW 76 AC
    BOOK OF JOHN BRUNNER, THE   BRUNNER, JOHN   AC
  SPARTANS' EPITAPH AT THERMOPYLAE (FROM GREEK ANTH)
                                              MS   NEW 76 AC
    BOOK OF JOHN BRUNNER, THE   BRUNNER, JOHN   AC
  SPEECH IS SILVER   SS   AMZ 65 04
    TIME-JUMP   BRUNNER, JOHN   AC
  SPOIL OF YESTERDAY   NV   SFA 62 03
    TIMES WITHOUT NUMBER   BRUNNER, JOHN   NO
  STIMULUS   SS   NWS 62 03
    NO FUTURE IN IT   BRUNNER, JOHN   AC
    OUT OF THIS WORLD 6   WILLIAMS-ELLIS& OWEN AN
  SUBSTITUTE GOD (SEE BY THE NAME OF MAN)   TC   FUN 58 08
  SUCH STUFF   SS   FSF 62 06
    INTRODUCTORY PSYCHOLOGY THROUGH SCIENCE FICTION
                                     KATZ/WARRICK/&   AN
    *OUT OF MY MIND   BRUNNER, JOHN   AC

BRUNNER, JOHN   (CONTINUED)
  SPECTRUM 4   AMIS & CONQUEST   AN
  8TH ANNUAL OF THE YEAR'S BEST S-F, THE MERRIL, JUDITH   AN
  TECHNOLOGICAL FOLK HERO: HAS HE A FUTURE?, THE AR FLK 72 05
    BOOK OF JOHN BRUNNER, THE   BRUNNER, JOHN   AC
  THEM AS CAN, DOES   AR   NWS 66 01
    BOOK OF JOHN BRUNNER, THE   BRUNNER, JOHN   AC
  THOU GOOD AND FAITHFUL (AS JOHN LOXMITH)   NV   ASF 53 03
    NOW THEN   BRUNNER, JOHN   AC
  TIME TO REND, A (SEE NO OTHER GODS BUT ME) TC
  TIMESCOOP   NO   69
    SCIENCE FICTION SPECIAL 8   ANONYMOUS   AN
  TO MYSELF ON THE OCCASION OF MY TWENTY-FIRST CENTURY
                                              PM   69
    HOLDING YOUR EIGHT HANDS   LUCIE-SMITH, EDWARD AN
  TOTALLY RICH, THE   NV   WOT 63 06
    DARK STARS   SILVERBERG, ROBERT   AN
    LATE GREAT FUTURE, THE   FITZ GERALD & DILLON AN
    *OUT OF MY MIND   BRUNNER, JOHN   AC
  TREASON IS A TWO-EDGED SWORD (TREASON)   NV   NEB 57 05
    NOT BEFORE TIME   BRUNNER, JOHN   AC
  TROUBLE I SEE, THE   SS   NWS 59 03
    FROM THIS DAY FORWARD   BRUNNER, JOHN   AC
  TWO BY TWO (SEE THE WINDOWS OF HEAVEN)   TC
  VITANULS, THE   SS   FSF 67 07
    FROM THIS DAY FORWARD   BRUNNER, JOHN   AC
    OTHER WORLDS, OTHER GODS   MOHS, MAYO   AN
  WAGER LOST BY WINNING, THE   NV   FAN 70 04
    TRAVELER IN BLACK, THE   BRUNNER, JOHN   AC
  WANTON OF ARGUS   NO   TCS 53 SU
    INTERSTELLIAR EMPIRE   BRUNNER, JOHN   AC
  WARP AND THE WOOF-WOOF, THE   SS   SCF 66 02
    NOT BEFORE TIME   BRUNNER, JOHN   AC
    TIME-JUMP   BRUNNER, JOHN   AC
  WASTED ON THE YOUNG   SS   GAL 65 04
    FROM THIS DAY FORWARD   BRUNNER, JOHN   AC
    NINTH GALAXY READER, THE   POHL, FREDERIK   AN
    WINDOW ON THE FUTURE   HILL, DOUGLAS   AN
  WHAT FRIENDS ARE FOR   SS   FOS 74
    BEST SCIENCE FICTION STORIES OF THE YEAR (1974)
                                     DEL REY, LESTER   AN
    FELLOWSHIP OF THE STARS   CARR, TERRY   OA
  WHAT WE HAVE HERE   PM   70
    BOOK OF JOHN BRUNNER, THE   BRUNNER, JOHN   AC
  WHEN GABRIEL...   SS   SCF 56 08
    BOOK OF JOHN BRUNNER, THE   BRUNNER, JOHN   AC
    OUT OF MY MIND (BRITISH)   BRUNNER, JOHN   AC
  WHIRLIGIG¡   SS   BYI 67 11
    OUT OF MY MIND (BRITISH)   BRUNNER, JOHN   AC
    TIME-JUMP   BRUNNER, JOHN   AC
  WHO STEALS MY PURSE   NV   ASF 73 03
    BOOK OF JOHN BRUNNER, THE   BRUNNER, JOHN   AC
  WHOLE MAN, THE   SN   SCF 59 04
    WHOLE MAN, THE   BRUNNER, JOHN   NO
  WINDOWS OF HEAVEN, THE (TWO BY TWO)   SS   NWS 56 05
    NO FUTURE IN IT   BRUNNER, JOHN   AC
    SCIENCE FICTION   BURTON, S. H.   AN
    YET MORE PENGUIN SCIENCE FICTION ALDISS, BRIAN W.   AN
  WORD NOT WRITTEN, THE   NV   SFA 62 06
    TIMES WITHOUT NUMBER   BRUNNER, JOHN   NO
  YOU'LL TAKE THE HIGH ROAD   NA   TTT 73
    THREE TRIPS IN TIME AND SPACE   SILVERBERG, ROBERT   OA

BRUNNER, K. HOUSTON PSEUD. FOR JOHN BRUNNER
  THOU GOOD AND FAITHFUL   NV   ASF 53 03
    SPACE PIONEERS   NORTON, ANDRE   AN

BRUSSOV, VALERY
  REPUBLIC OF THE SOUTHERN CROSS, THE   SS   19
    MORE TERROR IN THE MODERN VEIN   WOLLHEIM, DONALD A. AN
    *TERROR IN THE MODERN VEIN   WOLLHEIM, DONALD A. AN

BRUST, JOHN C. M.
  RED WHITE AND BLUE RUM COLLINS, THE   SS   HLP
    VINTAGE ANTHOLOGY OF SCIENCE FANTASY, THE
                                     CERF, CHRISTOPHER   AN

BRYANT, EDWARD
  AMONG THE DEAD   AC H MAC 73
  2076: THE AMERICAN TRICENTENNIAL   OA   PYR 77
  ADRIFT ON THE FREEWAY   SS   QRK 70 01
    AMONG THE DEAD   BRYANT, EDWARD   AC
    QUARK/1   DELANY & HACKER   OA
  AMONG THE DEAD   SS   QRK 71 02
    AMONG THE DEAD   BRYANT, EDWARD   AC
    QUARK/2   DELANY & HACKER   OA
  AUDITION: SOON TO BE A MAJOR PRODUCTION   SS   INY 72 04
    INFINITY 4   HOSKINS, ROBERT   OA
  BESIDE STILL WATERS   SS C GEN 72
    GENERATION   GERROLD, DAVID   OA
  BEYOND THE SAND RIVER RANGE   SS   INY 72 03
    INFINITY 3   HOSKINS, ROBERT   OA
  COWBOYS, INDIANS   SS   ALT 74
    ALTERNATIES   GERROLD, DAVID   OA
  DUNE'S EDGE   SS   ORB 72 11
    AMONG THE DEAD   BRYANT, EDWARD   AC
    ORBIT 11   KNIGHT, DAMON   OA
  EYES OF ONYX   SS   PRT 71
    NEW AWARENESS, THE   WARRICK & GREENBERG AN
    PROTOSTARS   GERROLD & GOLDIN   OA
  FILE ON THE PLAGUE   SS   NLP 71 04
    AMONG THE DEAD   BRYANT, EDWARD   AC
  GOING WEST   SS   ORB 74 13
    ORBIT 13   KNIGHT, DAMON   OA
  HANGED MAN, THE   SS   CLR 72 02
    AMONG THE DEAD   BRYANT, EDWARD   AC

BRYANT, EDWARD   BUDRYS, ALGIS

BRYANT, EDWARD   (CONTINUED)
  CLARION II   WILSON, ROBIN SCOTT OA
  HUMAN SIDE OF THE VILLAGE MONSTER, THE   SS   UNI 71 01
    AMONG THE DEAD   BRYANT, EDWARD   AC
    UNIVERSE 1   CARR, TERRY   OA
  INTRODUCTION: LOCI   IN
    AMONG THE DEAD   BRYANT, EDWARD   AC
  JADE BLUE   SS   UNI 71 01
    UNIVERSE 1   CARR, TERRY   OA
  JODY AFTER THE WAR   SS   ORB 72 10
    AMONG THE DEAD   BRYANT, EDWARD   AC
    ORBIT 10   KNIGHT, DAMON   OA
  LEGEND OF COUGAR LOU LANDIS, THE   SS   UNI 73 03
    UNIVERSE 3   CARR, TERRY   OA
  LOVE SONG OF HERSELF   SS   NDM 71 01
    AMONG THE DEAD   BRYANT, EDWARD   AC
    NEW DIMENSIONS 1   SILVERBERG, ROBERT   OA
  NO. 2 PLAIN TANK AUXILIARY FILL STRUCTURAL LIMIT 17,605 LBS.
    FUEL-PWA SPEC. 522 REVISED   SS   NDM 72 02
    AMONG THE DEAD   BRYANT, EDWARD   AC
    NEW DIMENSIONS 2   SILVERBERG, ROBERT   OA
  NOVA MORNING   SS C GEN 72
    GENERATION   GERROLD, DAVID   OA
  PINUP   SS   ORB 73 12
    AMONG THE DEAD   BRYANT, EDWARD   AC
    ORBIT 12   KNIGHT, DAMON   OA
  POET IN THE HOLOGRAM IN THE MIDDLE OF PRIME TIME, THE
                                              SS   NOV 72 02
    AMONG THE DEAD   BRYANT, EDWARD   AC
    FUTURE PASTIMES   EDELSTEIN, SCOTT   OA
    NOVA 2   HARRISON, HARRY   AN
  ROAD TO CINNABAR, THE   SS   INY 71 02
    INFINITY 2   HOSKINS, ROBERT   OA
  SENDING THE VERY BEST   SS   NWS 70 01
    AMONG THE DEAD   BRYANT, EDWARD   AC
    CLARION   WILSON, ROBIN SCOTT OA
    NEW TOMORROWS, THE   SPINRAD, NORMAN   AN
  SHARK   NV   ORB 73 12
    AMONG THE DEAD   BRYANT, EDWARD   AC
    FUTURE NOW, THE   HOSKINS, ROBERT   AN
    NEBULA AWARD STORIES 9   WILHELM, KATE   AN
    ORBIT 12   KNIGHT, DAMON   OA
  SOFT BLUE BUNNY RABBIT STORY, THE   SS   CLR 71 01
    AMONG THE DEAD   BRYANT, EDWARD   AC
    CLARION   WILSON, ROBIN SCOTT OA
  TACTICS   SS   NEW 73 AC
    AMONG THE DEAD   BRYANT, EDWARD   AC
  TELEIDOSCOPE   SS   NEW 73 AC
    AMONG THE DEAD   BRYANT, EDWARD   AC
  THEIR THOUSANDTH SEASON   SS   CLR 72 02
    AMONG THE DEAD   BRYANT, EDWARD   AC
    BEST SCIENCE FICTION OF THE YEAR, THE NO. 2
                                              CARR, TERRY   AN
    CLARION II   WILSON, ROBIN SCOTT OA
  XENOFREAK/XENOPHOBE   SS   DYS 75
    DYSTOPIAN VISIONS   ELWOOD, ROGER   OA
  10:00 REPORT IS BROUGHT TO YOU BY..., THE   SS   DVS 72 02
    AGAIN, DANGEROUS VISIONS   ELLISON, HARLAN   OA
  2.46593   SS   EIO 73
    EROS IN ORBIT   ELDER, JOSEPH   OA

BRYNING, FRANK B.
  FOR MEN MUST WORK (AUJ 55 08)   SS   FUN 56 02
    PACIFIC BOOK OF AUSTRALIAN SCIENCE FICTION
                                              BAXTER, JOHN   AN

BUCHAN, JOHN
  SPACE   SS   LVA 11 06
    *BEYOND TIME AND SPACE   DERLETH, AUGUST   AN

BUCHWALD, ART
  MARS IS OURS¡   SS   65
    POLITICAL SCIENCE FICTION   GREENBERG& WARRICK   AN
    11TH ANNUAL OF THE YEAR'S BEST S-F, THE
                                              MERRIL, JUDITH   AN

BUCK, DORIS PITKIN
  AUNT AGATHA   SS   FSF 52 10
    SPECIAL WONDER   MCCOMAS, J. FRANCIS AN
  CLASSICAL QUERY COMPOSED WHILE SHAMPOOING   PM   FSF 59 07
    BEST FROM FANTASY AND SCIENCE FICTION: 9
                                              MILLS, ROBERT P.   AN
  EPITHALAMIUM   PM   FSF 58 01
    BEST FROM FANTASY AND SCIENCE FICTION: 8
                                              BOUCHER, ANTHONY   AN
  FROM TWO UNIVERSES   PM   FSF 64 12
    BEST FROM FANTASY AND SCIENCE FICTION: 15
                                              FERMAN, EDWARD L.   AN
  GIBEREL, THE   SS   NDM 71 01
    NEBULA AWARD STORIES NO. 7   BIGGLE, LLOYD JR.   AN
    NEW DIMENSIONS 1   SILVERBERG, ROBERT   OA
  LYRIC FOR ATOM SPLITTERS   PM   FSF 57 05
    BEST FROM FANTASY AND SCIENCE FICTION: 7
                                              BOUCHER, ANTHONY   AN
  MICKEY FINN   PM   FSF 66 03
    BEST FROM FANTASY AND SCIENCE FICTION: 16
                                              FERMAN, EDWARD L.   AN
  SPORTSMAN'S DIFFICULTY   PM   FSF 59 03
    BEST FROM FANTASY AND SCIENCE FICTION: 9
                                              MILLS, ROBERT P.   AN
  WHY THEY MOBBED THE WHITE HOUSE   SS   ORB 68 03
    ORBIT 3   KNIGHT, DAMON   OA

BUDRYS, ALGIS   ALSO AS   IVAN JANVIER
  BUDRYS' INFERNO   AC   BKM 63 07
    IN ENGLAND AS "THE FURIOUS FUTURE"

BUDRYS, ALGIS   (CONTINUED)
  FALLING TORCH, THE   NO   PYR 59 06
  FURIOUS FUTURE, THE   AC H GOL 64
    SEE "BUDRYS' INFERNO"
  UNEXPECTED DIMENSION, THE   AC   BAL 60
  AND THEN SHE FOUND HIM...   SS   VSF 57 07
    BUDRYS' INFERNO   BUDRYS, ALGIS   AC
    NO LIMITS   FERMAN, JOSEPH W.   AN
  ATTIC VOICE, THE (SEE NIGHTSOUND)   TC
  BE MERRY   NV   IFS 66 12
    ON OUR WAY TO THE FUTURE   CARR, TERRY   AN
  BETWEEN THE DARK AND THE DAYLIGHT   SS   INF 58 10
    BUDRYS' INFERNO   BUDRYS, ALGIS   AC
  BURNING WORLD, THE   NV   INF 57 07
    UNEXPECTED DIMENSION, THE   BUDRYS, ALGIS   AC
  CHAIN REACTION (AS JOHN A. SENTRY)   NV   ASF 57 04
    SIX GREAT SHORT SCIENCE FICTION NOVELS   CONKLIN, GROFF   AN
  CONGRUENT PEOPLE, THE   SS   STR 53 02
    STAR SCIENCE FICTION STORIES NO. 2   POHL, FREDERIK   OA
  CONTACT BETWEEN EQUALS   SS   VSF 58 07
    BUDRYS' INFERNO   BUDRYS, ALGIS   AC
    SF: AUTHORS' CHOICE 2   HARRISON, HARRY   AN
  DEATH MARCH   NV   ASF 56 10
    BEST SF 6   CRISPIN, EDMUND   AN
  DIE, SHADOW¡   NV   IFS 63 05
    BEST SCIENCE FICTION FROM IF, THE   POHL, FREDERIK   AN
    SECOND IF READER OF SCIENCE FICTION, THE
                                              POHL, FREDERIK   AN
  DISTANT SOUND OF ENGINES, THE   SS   FSF 59 03
    UNEXPECTED DIMENSION, THE   BUDRYS, ALGIS   AC
  DREAM OF VICTORY   NV   AMZ 53 09
    BUDRYS' INFERNO   BUDRYS, ALGIS   AC
  DUE PROCESS   SS   ASF 60 02
    12 GREAT CLASSICS OF SCIENCE FICTION   CONKLIN, GROFF   AN
  EDGE OF THE SEA, THE   SS   VSF 58 03
    DECADE THE 1950S   ALDISS & HARRISON   AN
    INTRODUCING SCIENCE FICTION   ALDISS, BRIAN W.   AN
    SF:58, THE YEAR'S GREATEST SCIENCE FICTION AND FANTASY
                                              MERRIL, JUDITH   AN
    WORLDS TO COME   KNIGHT, DAMON   AN
  END OF SUMMER, THE   NV   ASF 54 11
    PENGUIN SCIENCE FICTION   ALDISS, BRIAN W.   AN
    UNEXPECTED DIMENSION, THE   BUDRYS, ALGIS   AC
  END OF WINTER, THE (SEE GO AND BEHOLD THEM)   TC
  EXECUTIONER, THE   NV   ASF 56 01
    *SPECTRUM   AMIS & CONQUEST   AN
    UNEXPECTED DIMENSION, THE   BUDRYS, ALGIS   AC
  FALLING TORCH   NV   VSF 58 01
    FALLING TORCH, THE   BUDRYS, ALGIS   NO
  FIRST TO SERVE   SS   ASF 54 05
    METAL SMILE, THE   KNIGHT, DAMON   AN
    UNEXPECTED DIMENSION, THE   BUDRYS, ALGIS   AC
  FOR LOVE   NV   GAL 62 06
    ALPHA 7   SILVERBERG, ROBERT   AN
    SEVENTH GALAXY READER, THE   POHL, FREDERIK   AN
  FOREWORD TO "TWILIGHT"   IN
    MIRROR OF INFINITY, THE   SILVERBERG, ROBERT   AN
  FRIGHTENED TREE, THE (PROTECTIVE MIMICRY)   SS   GAL 53 02
    ASSIGNMENT IN TOMORROW   POHL, FREDERIK   AN
  GO AND BEHOLD THEM (THE END OF WINTER, AS WILLIAM SCARFF)
                                              SS   VSF 58 01
    UNEXPECTED DIMENSION, THE   BUDRYS, ALGIS   AC
  HOT POTATO   SS   ASF 57 07
    FALLING TORCH, THE   BUDRYS, ALGIS   NO
  IN HUMAN HANDS   NV   SFS 54 02
    RARE SCIENCE FICTION   HOWARD, IVAN   AN
  INTRODUCTION   IN
    BUDRYS' INFERNO   BUDRYS, ALGIS   AC
  LOWER THAN ANGELS   SN   INF 56 10
    BUDRYS' INFERNO   BUDRYS, ALGIS   AC
    EARTHMEN AND STRANGERS   SILVERBERG, ROBERT   AN
    UNIVERSE AHEAD   ENGDAHL & ROBERSON   AN
  MAN IN THE SKY   SS   ASF 56 03
    EVERY BOY'S BOOK OF OUTER SPACE STORIES
                                              DIKTY, T. E.   AN
  MAN WHO ALWAYS KNEW, THE   SS   ASF 56 04
    BEST SCIENCE FICTION STORIES AND NOVELS: 1956
                                              DIKTY, T. E.   AN
    TOMORROW AND TOMORROW   KNIGHT, DAMON   AN
  MAN WHO DID NOT FIT, THE   SS   ASF 59 03
    FALLING TORCH, THE   BUDRYS, ALGIS   NO
  MAN WHO TASTED ASHES, THE   SS   IFS 59 02
    BUDRYS' INFERNO   BUDRYS, ALGIS   AC
    STORIES FROM SCIENCE FICTION   DOHERTY, G. D.   AN
  NEVER MEET AGAIN   SS   INF 58 03
    UNEXPECTED DIMENSION, THE   BUDRYS, ALGIS   AC
  NIGHTSOUND (THE ATTIC VOICE)   SS   SAT 57 02
    BEST SCIENCE FICTION STORIES AND NOVELS: 9TH SERIES
                                              DIKTY, T. E.   AN
  NOBODY BOTHERS GUS (AS PAUL JANVIER)   SS   ASF 55 11
    ARENA: SPORTS SF   FERMAN & MALZBERG   AN
    ODDBALLS, THE   GHIDALIA, VIC   AN
    ONE HUNDRED YEARS OF SCIENCE FICTION   KNIGHT, DAMON   AN
    SF: THE BEST OF THE BEST   MERRIL, JUDITH   AN
    SF: THE YEAR'S GREATEST SCIENCE FICTION AND FANTASY
                                              MERRIL, JUDITH   AN
  NOW HEAR THE WORD OF THE LORD   SS   GAL 69 02
    BEST SF: 1969   HARRISON & ALDISS   AN
  PEASANT GIRL, THE   SS   ASF 56 06
    BUDRYS' INFERNO   BUDRYS, ALGIS   AC
  PROTECTIVE MIMICRY (SEE THE FRIGHTENED TREE)   TC
  REAL PEOPLE, THE   NA   BEY 53 11
    BEYOND   ANONYMOUS   AN
  RIYA'S FOUNDLING   SS   SFS 53 01
    HUMAN?   MERRIL, JUDITH   AN
    MIND TO MIND   SILVERBERG, ROBERT   AN

BUDRYS, ALGIS   BUNCH, DAVID R.

BUDRYS, ALGIS   (CONTINUED)   BUNCH, DAVID R.   (CONTINUED)
ROGUE MOON   SN FSF 60 12   COMPLETE FATHER, A   SS FAN 60 01
  SCIENCE FICTION HALL OF FAME VOLUME 2B BOVA, BEN AN   MODERAN   BUNCH, DAVID R.   AC
SCRAPING AT THE BONES, A   SS ASF 75 05   DIRTY WAR, THE   SS FAN 60 01
  BEST SF: 75, THE NINTH ANNUAL HARRISON & ALDISS AN   FUTURE PASTIMES   EDELSTEIN, SCOTT   OA
SILENT BROTHER   SS ASF 56 02   EDUCATIONAL   SS
  BUDRYS' INFERNO   BUDRYS, ALGIS   AC   MODERAN   BUNCH, DAVID R.   AC
  SF:57, THE YEAR'S GREATEST SCIENCE FICTION AND FANTASY ESCAPING, THE   SS DVS 67 01
                        MERRIL, JUDITH   AN   DANGEROUS VISIONS   ELLISON, HARLAN   OA
SILENT EYES OF TIME, THE   NA FSF 75 11   FINAL DECISION, THE   SS AMZ 61 02
  BEST SCIENCE FICTION OF THE YEAR, THE NO. 5   MODERAN   BUNCH, DAVID R.   AC
                        CARR, TERRY   AN   FLESH-MAN FROM FAR WIDE, THE   SS AMZ 59 11
SKIRMISHER, THE   SS INF 57 11   MODERAN   BUNCH, DAVID R.   AC
  BUDRYS' INFERNO   BUDRYS, ALGIS   AC   GETTING REGULAR   SS AMZ 60 08
SNAIL'S PACE   SS DSF 53 10   MODERAN   BUNCH, DAVID R.   AC
  WAY OUT   HOWARD, IVAN   AN   GLANCE AT THE PAST, A   SS FAN 70 10
STAR DESCENDING   SS STR 59 05   MODERAN   BUNCH, DAVID R.   AC
  STAR SCIENCE FICTION STORIES NO. 5 POHL, FREDERIK OA HAS ANYONE SEEN THIS HORSEMAN?   SS
TO CIVILIZE   SS FUT 54 01   MODERAN   BUNCH, DAVID R.   AC
  GALACTIC EMPIRES VOLUME TWO ALDISS, BRIAN W. AN   HEAD THUMPING THE TROOPS   SS
ULTIMATE BRUNETTE, THE   SS PBY 65 09   MODERAN   BUNCH, DAVID R.   AC
  FIEND, THE   PLAYBOY, EDITORS OF   AN   HOLDHOLTZER'S BOX   SS PRT 71
WALK TO THE WORLD   SS SSF 52 11   PROTOSTARS   GERROLD & GOLDIN   OA
  FIRST FLIGHT   KNIGHT, DAMON   AN   HOW IT ENDED   SS AMZ 69 01
WALL OF CRYSTAL, EYE OF NIGHT   NV GAL 61 12   MODERAN   BUNCH, DAVID R.   AC
  ALPHA 2   SILVERBERG, ROBERT   AN   HOW THEY TOOK CARE OF SOUL IN A LAST DAY FOR A NON-BEGINNING
  TENTH GALAXY READER, THE POHL, FREDERIK   AN   SS
WAR IS OVER, THE   SS ASF 57 02   MODERAN   BUNCH, DAVID R.   AC
  13 GREAT STORIES OF SCIENCE FICTION CONKLIN, GROFF AN HOW XMAS GHOSTS ARE MADE   SS ALT 74
WEEBLIES, THE   SS FNF 53 06   ALTERNATES   GERROLD, DAVID   OA
  GOLDEN ROAD, THE   KNIGHT, DAMON   AN   HUSBAND'S SHARE, A   SS FAN 60 10
WONDERBIRD   SS C INF 57 09   MODERAN   BUNCH, DAVID R.   AC
  PARTNERS IN WONDER   ELLISON, HARLAN   AC   IN THE INNERMOST ROOM OF AUTHORITY SS
                                                        MODERAN   BUNCH, DAVID R.   AC
BULFINCH, THOMAS   INCIDENT IN MODERAN   SS DVS 67 01
DAEDALUS (1855)   SS   DANGEROUS VISIONS   ELLISON, HARLAN   OA
  JOURNEYS IN SCIENCE FICTION LOUGHLIN, RICHARD L. AN   MODERAN   BUNCH, DAVID R.   AC
                                                      INTERRUPTION IN CARNAGE   SS
BULLER, E. REGINALD   MODERAN   BUNCH, DAVID R.   AC
THERE WAS A YOUNG LADY NAMED BRIGHT PM   INTRODUCTION   IN
  FASTER THAN LIGHT   DANN & ZEBROWSKI   OA   MODERAN   BUNCH, DAVID R.   AC
  MATHEMATICAL MAGPIE, THE FADIMAN, CLIFTON   AN   INVESTIGATING THE BIDWELL ENDEAVORS SS 65
                                                        11TH ANNUAL OF THE YEAR'S BEST S-F, THE
BULLOCK, ALICE   MERRIL, JUDITH   AN
ASYLUM   SS FUT 54 08   IT WAS BLACK CAT WEATHER   SS FAN 63 02
  RARE SCIENCE FICTION   HOWARD, IVAN   AN   MODERAN   BUNCH, DAVID R.   AC
                                                      LADY WAS FOR KROINKING, THE   SS GEN 72
BULMER, KENNETH   FUTURE PASTIMES   EDELSTEIN, SCOTT   OA
NEW WRITINGS IN SF. 22   OA H SID 73   GENERATION   GERROLD, DAVID   OA
NEW WRITINGS IN SF. 23   OA H SID 74   LITTLE GIRL'S XMAS IN MODERAN, A   SS FSF 60 01
NEW WRITINGS IN SF. 24   OA H SID 74   MODERAN   BUNCH, DAVID R.   AC
NEW WRITINGS IN SF. 25   OA H DOB 75   MIRACLE OF THE FLOWERS, THE   SS
NEW WRITINGS IN SF. 26   OA H SID 75   MODERAN   BUNCH, DAVID R.   AC
NEW WRITINGS IN SF. 27   OA H SID 75   NEW KINGS ARE NOT FOR LAUGHING   SS
NEW WRITINGS IN SF. 28   OA H DOB 76   MODERAN   BUNCH, DAVID R.   AC
NEW WRITINGS IN SF. 29   OA H SID 76   NEW-METAL   SS
ADJUSTED, THE   SS FSF 66 06   MODERAN   BUNCH, DAVID R.   AC
  BEST FROM FANTASY AND SCIENCE FICTION: 16   NEW-METAL MISTRESS TIME   SS
                        FERMAN, EDWARD L.   AN   MODERAN   BUNCH, DAVID R.   AC
  MARRIAGE AND THE FAMILY THROUGH SCIENCE FICTION   NO CRACKS OR SAGGINGS   SS
                        CLEAR/WARRICK/&   AN   MODERAN   BUNCH, DAVID R.   AC
AQUAMAN   SS SPC 74 02   OF HAMMERS AND MEN   SS
  SPACE   2   DAVIS, RICHARD   OA   MODERAN   BUNCH, DAVID R.   AC
FOREWORD   IN   ONE FALSE STEP   SS
  NEW WRITINGS IN SF. 22   BULMER, KENNETH   OA   MODERAN   BUNCH, DAVID R.   AC
  NEW WRITINGS IN SF. 23   BULMER, KENNETH   OA   ONE FROM CAMELOT MODERAN, THE   SS
  NEW WRITINGS IN SF. 24   BULMER, KENNETH   OA   MODERAN   BUNCH, DAVID R.   AC
  NEW WRITINGS IN SF. 25   BULMER, KENNETH   OA   ONE TIME, A RED CARPET...   SS
  NEW WRITINGS IN SF. 26   BULMER, KENNETH   OA   MODERAN   BUNCH, DAVID R.   AC
  NEW WRITINGS IN SF. 27   BULMER, KENNETH   OA   PENANCE DAY IN MODERAN   SS AMZ 60 07
  NEW WRITINGS IN SF. 28   BULMER, KENNETH   OA   MODERAN   BUNCH, DAVID R.   AC
  NEW WRITINGS IN SF. 29   BULMER, KENNETH   OA   PLAYMATE   SS FAN 65 05
FOWLING, THE   EX   MODERAN   BUNCH, DAVID R.   AC
  BEYOND THIS HORIZON   CARRELL, CHRISTOPHER OA   PROBLEM, THE   SS
MEMORY OF GOLDEN SUNSHINE, A   SS NWR 71 19   MODERAN   BUNCH, DAVID R.   AC
  NEW WRITINGS IN SF. 19   CARNELL, JOHN   OA   REMEMBERING   SS AMZ 60 04
OUR FRIENDS THE ALIENS   SS   MODERAN   BUNCH, DAVID R.   AC
  AUTHENTIC BOOK OF SPACE CAMPBELL, H. J.   AN   REUNION   SS AMZ 65 02
STATION HR972   SS WOT 67 02   MODERAN   BUNCH, DAVID R.   AC
  NIGHTMARE AGE   POHL, FREDERIK   AN   SMALL MIRACLE OF FISHHOOKS AND STRAIGHT PINS, A NV FAN 61 06
                                                        7TH ANNUAL OF THE YEAR'S BEST S-F, THE MERRIL, JUDITH AN
BULYCHEV, KIRILL   SOMETIMES I GET SO HAPPY   SS FAN 63 08
GIRL NOTHING HAPPENS TO, THE   SS   MODERAN   BUNCH, DAVID R.   AC
  JOURNEY ACROSS THREE WORLDS ANONYMOUS   AN   STRANGE SHAPE IN THE STRONGHOLD   SS FAN 60 03
LIFE IS SO DULL FOR LITTLE GIRLS   SS   MODERAN   BUNCH, DAVID R.   AC
  RUSSIAN SCIENCE FICTION, 1968 MAGIDOFF, ROBERT   AN   STRONGHOLD, THE   SS
TACAN FOR THE CHILDREN OF EARTH, A SS 72   MODERAN   BUNCH, DAVID R.   AC
  AIR OF MARS AND OTHER STORIES, THE GINSBURG, MIRRA AN SURVIVAL PACKAGES   SS FAN 63 04
                                                        MODERAN   BUNCH, DAVID R.   AC
BUNCH, DAVID R.   THAT HIGH-UP BLUE DAY THAT SAW THE BLACK SKY-TRAIN COME
MODERAN   AC AVN 71 05   SPINNING   SS FSF 68 03
AMONG THE METAL-AND-PEOPLE PEOPLE   SS NDM 74 04   BEST FROM FANTASY AND SCIENCE FICTION: 18
  NEW DIMENSIONS 4   SILVERBERG, ROBERT   OA   FERMAN, EDWARD L. AN
AND SO WHITE WITCH VALLEY   SS   THINKING BACK (OUR GOD IS A HELPFUL GOD!) SS
  MODERAN   BUNCH, DAVID R.   AC   MODERAN   BUNCH, DAVID R.   AC
BATTLE WON   SS   TO FACE ETERNITY   SS
  MODERAN   BUNCH, DAVID R.   AC   MODERAN   BUNCH, DAVID R.   AC
BIRD MAN OF MODERAN, THE   SS   TRAINING TALK   SS FAN 64 03
  MODERAN   BUNCH, DAVID R.   AC   10TH ANNUAL OF THE YEAR'S BEST S-F, THE
BREAKOUT IN ECOL 2   SS NOV 73 03   MERRIL, JUDITH   AN
  NOVA 3   HARRISON, HARRY   OA   WALKING, TALKING I-DON'T-CARE MAN, THE SS AMZ 65 06
BUBBLE-DOME HOMES   SS   MODERAN   BUNCH, DAVID R.   AC
  MODERAN   BUNCH, DAVID R.   AC   WARNING, THE   SS AMZ 60 11
BUTTERFLIES WERE EAGLE-BIG THAT DAY, THE SS   MODERAN   BUNCH, DAVID R.   AC
  MODERAN   BUNCH, DAVID R.   AC   WAS SHE HORRID?   SS FAN 59 12
                                                        MODERAN   BUNCH, DAVID R.   AC

BUNCH, DAVID R.   (CONTINUED)
  WILL-HUNG AND WAITING   SS
    MODERAN   BUNCH, DAVID R.   AC
  2064, OR THEREABOUTS   SS   FAN 64 09
    MODERAN   BUNCH, DAVID R.   AC

BUNCH, MIRIAM
  SINGING CLIFFS OF FAUNUS, THE   SS
    LONG NIGHT OF WAITING AND OTHER STORIES
                                       ELWOOD, ROGER   OA

BUPP, WALTER   PSEUD. FOR RANDALL GARRETT
  MODUS VIVENDI   NV   ASF 61 09
    EARTH IN TRANSIT   SCHWARTZ, SHEILA   AN
    14 GREAT TALES OF ESP   STONE, IDELLA P.   AN

BURDICK, EUGENE
  FROM: THE 480   EX   MGH 64
    INSIDE INFORMATION   MOWSHOWITZ, ABBE   AN

BURGESS, ANTHONY   PSEUD. FOR JOHN ANTHONY BURGESS WILSON
  MUSE, THE   SS   HUD 68
    BEST SF: 1969   HARRISON & ALDISS   AN
    IN DREAMS AWAKE   FIEDLER, LESLIE A.   AN
    LIGHT FANTASTIC, THE   HARRISON, HARRY   AN

BURHOE, B. ALAN
  ORNITHANTHROPUS   SS   IFS 71 12
    BEST SCIENCE FICTION STORIES OF THE YEAR (1971)
                                       DEL REY, LESTER   AN
    BEST SF: 1971   HARRISON & ALDISS   AN

BURKE, JONATHAN F.
  ALIEN LANDSCAPES   AC H MUS 55
  EXODUS FROM ELYSIUM   AC H HWZ 65
    ALL MAD, EXCEPT ME   SS
      EXODUS FROM ELYSIUM   BURKE, JONATHAN F.   AC
    APPLE FOR THE TEACHER, AN   SS   NEB 55 04
      ALIEN LANDSCAPES   BURKE, JONATHAN F.   AC
    CENSORS, THE   SS   AUT 54 01
      ALIEN LANDSCAPES   BURKE, JONATHAN F.   AC
    ENTITY STRIKES TWICE, THE   SS
      EXODUS FROM ELYSIUM   BURKE, JONATHAN F.   AC
    EXODUS FROM ELYSIUM   SN
      EXODUS FROM ELYSIUM   BURKE, JONATHAN F.   AC
    FOR YOU, THE POSSESSED   SS   AUT 53 12
      ALIEN LANDSCAPES   BURKE, JONATHAN F.   AC
    OLD MAN OF THE STARS, THE   SN   AUT 53 10
      ALIEN LANDSCAPES   BURKE, JONATHAN F.   AC
    ONCE UPON A TIME   SS   SCF 54 05
      ALIEN LANDSCAPES   BURKE, JONATHAN F.   AC
    ROBOT WIFE, THE   SS
      EXODUS FROM ELYSIUM   BURKE, JONATHAN F.   AC
    STAND-IN   SS   AUT 54 03
      ALIEN LANDSCAPES   BURKE, JONATHAN F.   AC

BURKS, ARTHUR J.
  ESCAPE TO YESTERDAY   SS   NEW 53 AN
    SCIENCE AND SORCERY   FORD, GARRET   AN

BURNETT, WHIT
  NIGHT OF THE GRAN BAILE MASCARA, THE (1935)   SS   EQM 65 07
    FIEND IN YOU, THE   BEAUMONT, CHARLES   AN

BURRAGE, A. M.
  BETWEEN THE MINUTE AND THE HOUR   SS   27
    TRAVELERS IN TIME   STERN, PHILIP VAN D. AN

BURROUGHS, EDGAR RICE
  BEYOND THIRTY & THE MAN-EATER   AC H SCP 57
  CAVE GIRL, THE   AC H MCG 25
  ESCAPE ON VENUS   NO H BUR 46
  ETERNAL LOVER, THE   AC H MCG 25
  JOHN CARTER OF MARS   AC H CAN 64
  LAND THAT TIME FORGOT AND THE MOON MAID, THE   AC H DOV 63
  LAND THAT TIME FORGOT, THE   NO H MCG 24
  LLANA OF GATHOL   NO H BUR 48
  MOON MAID, THE   NO H MCG 26
  PIRATES OF VENUS AND LOST ON VENUS, THE   AC H DOV 63
  PRINCESS OF MARS AND A FIGHTING MAN OF MARS, A AC H DOV 64
  SAVAGE PELLUCIDAR   NO H CAN 63
  TALES OF THREE PLANETS   AC H CAN 64
  THREE MARTIAN NOVELS   AC L DOV 62
  THREE SCIENCE FICTION NOVELS   AC L DOV 63
    AT THE EARTH'S CORE   NO   ASW 14 04
      THREE SCIENCE FICTION NOVELS   BURROUGHS, EDGAR R.   AC
    BEYOND THE FARTHEST STAR (INCLUDES UNPUBLISHED SEQUEL,
      TANGOR RETURNS)   NV   BBM 42 01
      TALES OF THREE PLANETS   BURROUGHS, EDGAR R.   AC
    BEYOND THIRTY   NV   AAM 16 02
      BEYOND THIRTY & THE MAN-EATER   BURROUGHS, EDGAR R.   AC
    BLACK PIRATES OF BARSOOM   NV   AMZ 41 06
      LLANA OF GATHOL   BURROUGHS, EDGAR R.   NO
    CAVE GIRL, THE   NO   ASM 13 07
      CAVE GIRL, THE   BURROUGHS, EDGAR R.   AC
    CAVE MAN, THE   NO   ASW 17 03
      CAVE GIRL, THE   BURROUGHS, EDGAR R.   AC
    CHESSMEN OF MARS, THE   NO   AAS 22 02
      THREE MARTIAN NOVELS   BURROUGHS, EDGAR R.   AC
    CITY OF THE MUMMIES, THE   NV   AMZ 41 03
      LLANA OF GATHOL   BURROUGHS, EDGAR R.   NO
    ETERNAL LOVER, THE   NV   ASW 14 03
      ETERNAL LOVER, THE   BURROUGHS, EDGAR R.   AC
    FIGHTING MAN OF MARS, A   NO   BBM 30 04
      PRINCESS OF MARS AND A FIGHTING MAN OF MARS, A
                                       BURROUGHS, EDGAR R. AC

BURROUGHS, EDGAR R.   (CONTINUED)
  GODDESS OF FIRE   NV   FAD 41 07
    ESCAPE ON VENUS   BURROUGHS, EDGAR R.   NO
  INVISIBLE MEN OF MARS   NV   AMZ 41 10
    LLANA OF GATHOL   BURROUGHS, EDGAR R.   NO
  JOHN CARTER AND THE GIANTS OF MARS   NV   AMZ 41 01
    JOHN CARTER OF MARS   BURROUGHS, EDGAR R.   AC
  LAND THAT TIME FORGOT, THE   NO   BBM 18 08
    LAND THAT TIME FORGOT AND THE MOON MAID, THE
                                       BURROUGHS, EDGAR R. AC
    LAND THAT TIME FORGOT, THE   BURROUGHS, EDGAR R.   AC
  LIVING DEAD, THE   NV   FAD 41 11
    ESCAPE ON VENUS   BURROUGHS, EDGAR R.   NO
  LOST ON VENUS   NO   ARG 33 03
    PIRATES OF VENUS AND LOST ON VENUS, THE
                                       BURROUGHS, EDGAR R. AC
  MAN-EATER, THE   NO   NYW 15 11
    BEYOND THIRTY & THE MAN-EATER   BURROUGHS, EDGAR R.   NO
  MASTER MINDS OF MARS, THE   NO   ASA 27
    THREE MARTIAN NOVELS   BURROUGHS, EDGAR R.   AC
  MEN OF THE BRONZE AGE   NV   AMZ 42 03
    SAVAGE PELLUCIDAR   BURROUGHS, EDGAR R.   NO
  MOON MAID, THE   NO   AAS 23 05
    LAND THAT TIME FORGOT AND THE MOON MAID, THE
                                       BURROUGHS, EDGAR R. AC
    MOON MAID, THE   BURROUGHS, EDGAR R.   NO
  MOON MEN, THE   NV   AAS 25 02
    MOON MAID, THE   BURROUGHS, EDGAR R.   NO
  OUT OF TIME'S ABYSS   NV   BBM 18 12
    LAND THAT TIME FORGOT, THE   BURROUGHS, EDGAR R.   NO
  PELLUCIDAR   NO   ASC 15 05
    THREE SCIENCE FICTION NOVELS   BURROUGHS, EDGAR R.   AC
  PEOPLE THAT TIME FORGOT, THE   NV   BBM 18 10
    LAND THAT TIME FORGOT, THE   BURROUGHS, EDGAR R.   NO
  PIRATES OF VENUS (SELECTION)   EX   ARG 32 09
    ALL ABOUT VENUS   ALDISS, BRIAN W.   AN
    FAREWELL FANTASTIC VENUS   ALDISS & HARRISON   AN
  PIRATES OF VENUS, THE   NO   ARG 32 09
    PIRATES OF VENUS AND LOST ON VENUS, THE
                                       BURROUGHS, EDGAR R. AC
  PRINCESS OF MARS, A (EXCERPT FROM "UNDER THE MOONS OF MARS")
                                                 EX   ASM 12 02
    MARS, WE LOVE YOU   HIPOLITO & MCNELLY   AN
  PRINCESS OF MARS, A (UNDER THE MOONS OF MARS) NO   ASM 12 02
    PRINCESS OF MARS AND A FIGHTING MAN OF MARS, A
                                       BURROUGHS, EDGAR R. AC
  RED HAWK, THE   NV   AAS 25 09
    MOON MAID, THE   BURROUGHS, EDGAR R.   NO
  RESURRECTION OF JIMBER-JAW, THE   NV   ARG 37 02
    FANTASTIC PULPS, THE   HAINING, PETER   AN
    MASTERPIECES OF SCIENCE FICTION   MOSKOWITZ, SAM   AN
    TALES OF THREE PLANETS   BURROUGHS, EDGAR R.   AC
  RETURN TO PELLUCIDAR, THE   NV   AMZ 42 02
    SAVAGE PELLUCIDAR   BURROUGHS, EDGAR R.   NO
  SAVAGE PELLUCIDAR   NV   AMZ 63 11
    SAVAGE PELLUCIDAR   BURROUGHS, EDGAR R.   NO
  SKELETON MEN OF JUPITER   NV   AMZ 43 02
    JOHN CARTER OF MARS   BURROUGHS, EDGAR R.   AC
    STRANGE SIGNPOSTS   ELWOOD & MOSKOWITZ   AN
  SLAVES OF THE FISH MEN   NV   FAD 41 03
    ESCAPE ON VENUS   BURROUGHS, EDGAR R.   NO
  SWEETHEART PRIMEVAL   NO   ASC 15 01
    ETERNAL LOVER, THE   BURROUGHS, EDGAR R.   AC
  TANAR OF PELLUCIDAR   NO   BBM 29 03
    THREE SCIENCE FICTION NOVELS   BURROUGHS, EDGAR R.   AC
  THUVIA, MAID OF MARS   NO   ASW 16 04
    THREE MARTIAN NOVELS   BURROUGHS, EDGAR R.   AC
  TIGER GIRL   NV   AMZ 42 04
    SAVAGE PELLUCIDAR   BURROUGHS, EDGAR R.   NO
  UNDER THE MOONS OF MARS (ALSO AS A PRINCESS OF MARS)
                                                 NV   ASM 12 02
    UNDER THE MOONS OF MARS   MOSKOWITZ, SAM   AN
  WAR ON VENUS   NV   FAD 42 03
    ESCAPE ON VENUS   BURROUGHS, EDGAR R.   NO
  WIZARD OF VENUS, THE   NV   NEW 64 AC
    TALES OF THREE PLANETS   BURROUGHS, EDGAR R.   AC
  YELLOW MEN OF MARS   NV   AMZ 41 08
    LLANA OF GATHOL   BURROUGHS, EDGAR R.   NO

BURROUGHS, JOHN C.
  ILLUSTRATIONS   IL
    ESCAPE ON VENUS   BURROUGHS, EDGAR R.   NO
    LLANA OF GATHOL   BURROUGHS, EDGAR R.   NO

BURROUGHS, WILLIAM
  PREFACE   IN
    LOVE & NAPALM: EXPORT U.S.A.   BALLARD, J. G.   AC
  THEY DO NOT ALWAYS REMEMBER   SS   ESQ 66 05
    SF12   MERRIL, JUDITH   AN

BURTON, S. H.
  SCIENCE FICTION   AN   LNG 67
  INTRODUCTION   IN
    SCIENCE FICTION   BURTON, S. H.   AN

BUSBY, F. M.
  HERE, THERE, AND EVERYWHERE   SS   CLR 72 02
    CLARION II   WILSON, ROBIN SCOTT   OA
  I'M GOING TO GET YOU   SS   FAN 74 03
    SPACE ODYSSEYS   ALDISS, BRIAN W.   AN
  IF THIS IS WINNETKA, YOU MUST BE JUDY   NV   UNI 74 05
    BEST SCIENCE FICTION STORIES OF THE YEAR (1974)
                                       DEL REY, LESTER   AN
    UNIVERSE 5   CARR, TERRY   OA
  PLAY IT AGAIN, SAM   SS   CLR 73 03
    CLARION III   WILSON, ROBIN SCOTT   OA

BUSBY, F. M.   CAMPBELL, JOHN W. JR

BUSBY, F. M.   (CONTINUED)
  ROAD MAP   SS   CLR 73 03
    CLARION III   WILSON, ROBIN SCOTT OA
  TELL ME ALL ABOUT YOURSELF   SS   NDM 73 03
    BEST SCIENCE FICTION OF THE YEAR, THE NO. 3
                                     CARR, TERRY   AN
    NEW DIMENSIONS 3   SILVERBERG, ROBERT   OA

BUTLER, BILL
  FIRST GORILLA ON THE MOON, THE   PM   NEW 68 AN
    ENGLAND SWINGS SF   MERRIL, JUDITH   AN
    SPACE-TIME JOURNAL, THE   MERRIL, JUDITH   AN
  LETTER TO A TYRANT KING   PM   FSF 66 08
    BEST FROM FANTASY AND SCIENCE FICTION: 16
                                     FERMAN, EDWARD L.   AN

BUTLER, ELLIS PARKER
  EXPERIMENT IN GYRO-HATS, AN   SS   HAM 10 06
    SCIENCE FICTION BY GASLIGHT   MOSKOWITZ, SAM   AN

BUTLER, MILDRED
  TIMESCAPE   NV C
    ANYWHERE, ANYWHEN   ENGDAHL, SYLVIA   OA

BUTLER, OCTAVIA E.
  CROSSOVER   SS   CLR 71 01
    CLARION   WILSON, ROBIN SCOTT OA

BUTLER, SAMUEL
  FROM "EREWHON, OR OVER THE RANGE" (1872)   EX
    PAST, PRESENT, AND FUTURE PERFECT WOLFE, J&FITZ GERALD AN
  MENACE OF THE MACHINE, THE (FROM "EREWHON") EX
    SCIENCE FICTION THROUGH THE AGES 1 EVANS, I. O.   AN
  USES OF MATHEMATICS, THE (1863)   PM
    FANTASIA MATHEMATICA   FADIMAN, CLIFTON   AN

BUTTERWORTH, MICHAEL
  BAKED BEAN FACTORY, THE   SS   NWS 67 10
    ENGLAND SWINGS SF   MERRIL, JUDITH   AN
    SPACE-TIME JOURNAL, THE   MERRIL, JUDITH   AN
  CIRCULARIZATION OF CONDENSED CONVENTIONAL STRAIGHT-LINE
    WORD-IMAGE STRUCTURES   SS   NWS 69 07
    NEW TOMORROWS, THE   SPINRAD, NORMAN   AN
  DISINTEGRATION   SS   NWQ 73 05
    NEW WORLDS NO. 5   MOORCOCK & PLATT   OA
  POSTATOMIC   SS
    NEW S.F., THE   JONES, LANGDON   OA

BYRAM, GEORGE
  WONDER HORSE, THE   SS   ATL 57 08
    SF: THE BEST OF THE BEST   MERRIL, JUDITH   AN
  SF:58, THE YEAR'S GREATEST SCIENCE FICTION AND FANTASY
                                     MERRIL, JUDITH   AN

BYRNE, JOHNNY
  YESTERDAYS' GARDENS   SS   SCF 65 11
    11TH ANNUAL OF THE YEAR'S BEST S-F, THE
                                     MERRIL, JUDITH   AN

CABELL, JAMES BRANCH
  JURGEN PROVES IT BY MATHEMATICS   EX   MBR 19
    FANTASIA MATHEMATICA   FADIMAN, CLIFTON   AN

CABRAL, OLGA
  ELECTRONIC TAPE FOUND IN A BOTTLE   PM
    SCIENCE FACT/FICTION   FARRELL/GAGE/&   AN

CACCHIONI, MARCO
  SONG OF PASSING, THE   PM   QRK 71 04
    QUARK/4   DELANY & HACKER   OA

CAHN, LEE
  SECRET   SS   ASF 53 01
    CROSSROADS IN TIME   CONKLIN, GROFF   AN

CAIN, RONALD
  TELEPATHOS   NV   SFE 74 01
    SCIENCE FICTION EMPHASIS NO. 1   GERROLD, DAVID   OA

CALDER, JOHN
  SIGNALS   SS   NWS 66 09
    ENGLAND SWINGS SF   MERRIL, JUDITH   AN
    SPACE-TIME JOURNAL, THE   MERRIL, JUDITH   AN

CALDER, NIGEL
  EXPLODING STARS   AR   69
    SURVIVAL PRINTOUT   TOTAL EFFECT   AN

CALISHER, HORTENSE
  HEARTBURN   SS   AMM 51 01
    TIMELESS STORIES FOR TODAY AND TOMORROW
                                     BRADBURY, RAY   AN
  JOURNAL FROM ELLIPSIA (EXCERPT)   EX   LBR 65
    SF12   MERRIL, JUDITH   AN

CALKINS, ERNEST ELMO
  SUPERLATIVE DEGREE, THE   PM   SRV 59 05
    MATHEMATICAL MAGPIE, THE   FADIMAN, CLIFTON   AN

CALVERT, ROBERT
  ODE TO A TIME FLOWER   PM   NWB 73 05
    NEW WORLDS QUARTERLY NO. 5   MOORCOCK, MICHAEL   OA

CALVINO, ITALO
  COSMICOMICS   OC H HBW 68

CALVINO, ITALO   (CONTINUED)
  ALL AT ONE POINT   SS
    COSMICOMICS   CALVINO, ITALO   OC
  AQUATIC UNCLE, THE   SS
    COSMICOMICS   CALVINO, ITALO   OC
  AT DAYBREAK   SS
    COSMICOMICS   CALVINO, ITALO   OC
  DINOSAURS, THE   SS
    COSMICOMICS   CALVINO, ITALO   OC
  DISTANCE OF THE MOON, THE   SS
    COSMICOMICS   CALVINO, ITALO   OC
  FORM OF SPACE, THE   SS
    COSMICOMICS   CALVINO, ITALO   OC
  GAMES WITHOUT END   SS
    COSMICOMICS   CALVINO, ITALO   OC
  HOW MUCH SHALL WE BET?   SS
    COSMICOMICS   CALVINO, ITALO   OC
  LIGHT YEARS, THE   SS
    COSMICOMICS   CALVINO, ITALO   OC
  ORIGIN OF EVERYTHING, THE   SS   PBY 68 03
    LAST TRAIN TO LIMBO   PLAYBOY, EDITORS OF AN
  SIGN IN SPACE, A   SS   68
    COSMICOMICS   CALVINO, ITALO   OC
  TOMORROW AND TOMORROW   KNIGHT, DAMON   AN
  SPIRAL, THE   SS
    COSMICOMICS   CALVINO, ITALO   OC
  WITHOUT COLORS   SS
    COSMICOMICS   CALVINO, ITALO   OC

CAMPANELLA, G. D.
  CITY OF THE SUN, THE (1623)   EX
    *BEYOND TIME AND SPACE   DERLETH, AUGUST   AN
  FROM "THE CITY OF THE SUN" (1623)   EX
    PAST, PRESENT, AND FUTURE PERFECT WOLFE, J&FITZ GERALD AN

CAMPBELL, H. J.
  AUTHENTIC BOOK OF SPACE   AN H HML 54
  TOMORROW'S UNIVERSE   AN H HML 54 05

CAMPBELL, J. RAMSEY
  CELLARS, THE   SS
    TRAVELLERS BY NIGHT   DERLETH, AUGUST   OA
  CHRISTMAS PRESENT   SS   BBC 69 12
    YEAR'S BEST HORROR STORIES: SERIES IV, THE
                                     PAGE, GERALD W.   AN
  HEIGHT OF THE SCREAM, THE   EX
    BEYOND THIS HORIZON   CARRELL, CHRISTOPHER OA
  MAN IN THE UNDERPASS, THE   SS   NEW 75 AN
    YEAR'S BEST HORROR STORIES: SERIES III, THE
                                     DAVIS, RICHARD   AN
  MURDERS   SS   NWR 75 26
    NEW WRITINGS IN SF. 26   BULMER, KENNETH   OA
  NAPIER COURT   SS
    YEAR'S BEST HORROR STORIES: SERIES II, THE
                                     DAVIS, RICHARD   AN
  OLD HORNS, THE   SS
    YEAR'S BEST HORROR STORIES: SERIES II, THE
                                     DAVIS, RICHARD   AN
  SCAR, THE   SS   SMS 69 SU
    YEAR'S BEST HORROR STORIES, THE DAVIS, RICHARD   AN

CAMPBELL, J. SCOTT
  FILM OF DEATH   SS   ASF 48 03
    EVIL EARTHS   ALDISS, BRIAN W.   AN

CAMPBELL, JOHN W. JR ALSO AS   DON A. STUART
  ANALOG ANTHOLOGY   AN H DOB 65
  ANALOG 1   AN H DBL 63
    IN "ANALOG ANTHOLOGY"
  ANALOG 2   AN H DBL 64
    IN "ANALOG ANTHOLOGY"
  ANALOG 3   AN H DBL 65
    ALSO AS "A WORLD BY THE TALE"
  ANALOG 4   AN H DBL 66
    ALSO AS "THE PERMANENT IMPLOSION"
  ANALOG 5   AN H DBL 67
    ALSO AS "COUNTERCOMMANDMENT"
  ANALOG 6   AN H DBL 68
  ANALOG 7   AN H DBL 70
  ANALOG 8   AN H DBL 71
  ASTOUNDING SCIENCE FICTION ANTHOLOGY, THE   AN H SAS 52
    DERIVATIVE ANTHOLOGY "ASTOUNDING TALES OF SPACE AND TIME"
    IN ENGLAND AS "THE FIRST AND SECOND ASTOUNDING SCIENCE
    FICTION ANTHOLOGIES"
  ASTOUNDING SCIENCE FICTION ANTHOLOGY, THE (8 OF 22)
                                               AN   BRK 56 12
  ASTOUNDING TALES OF SPACE AND TIME   AN   BRK 57 02
    STORIES FROM "THE ASTOUNDING SCIENCE FICTION ANTHOLOGY"
  BEST OF JOHN W. CAMPBELL, THE   AC   BAL 76 05
    EDITED BY LESTER DEL REY
  BEST OF JOHN W. CAMPBELL, THE (BRITISH)   AC H SID 73
    COMPILED BY GEORGE HAY
  BLACK STAR PASSES, THE   AC H FPS 53
  CLOAK OF AESIR   AC H SHS 52
  COUNTERCOMMANDMENT   AN   CUR 67
    SEE "ANALOG 5"
  FIRST ASTOUNDING SCIENCE FICTION ANTHOLOGY, THE AN H GRY 54
  FIRST ASTOUNDING SCIENCE FICTION ANTHOLOGY, THE (PB)
                                               AN   FSP 64
  FROM UNKNOWN WORLDS   AN   SMT 53
  INCREDIBLE PLANET, THE   NO H FPS 49
  JOHN W. CAMPBELL ANTHOLOGY: THREE NOVELS   AC H DBL 73
  PERMANENT IMPLOSION, THE   AN   CUR 66
    SEE "ANALOG 4"
  PLANETEERS, THE   DC   ACE 66
  PROLOGUE TO ANALOG   AN H DBL 62

CAMPBELL, JOHN W. JR   CARAVAN, T. P.

    IN "ANALOG ANTHOLOGY"
  SECOND ASTOUNDING SCIENCE FICTION ANTHOLOGY, THE   AN H GRY 54
  SECOND ASTOUNDING SCIENCE FICTION ANTHOLOGY, THE (PB)
                                                      AN   FSP 65
  SPACE BEYOND, THE   OC   PYR 76 06
  THING AND OTHER STORIES, THE   AC   KEM 52
    SEE "WHO GOES THERE?"
  THING FROM OUTER SPACE, THE   AC   TDM 66
    SEE "WHO GOES THERE?"
  WHO GOES THERE?   AC H SHS 48
    IN ENGLAND AS "THE THING AND OTHER STORIES" AND
    "THE THING FROM OUTER SPACE"
  WHO GOES THERE? AND OTHER STORIES   AC   DEL 55
  WORLD BY THE TALE, A   AN   CUR 65
    SEE "ANALOG 3"
  ALL   SN
    SPACE BEYOND, THE   CAMPBELL, JOHN W. JR OC
  ANALOG 1   AN   DBL 63
    ANALOG ANTHOLOGY   CAMPBELL, JOHN W. JR AN
  ANALOG 2   AN   DBL 64
    ANALOG ANTHOLOGY   CAMPBELL, JOHN W. JR AN
  BATTERY OF HATE, THE   SS   AMZ 33 11
    SCIENCE FICTION OF THE 30'S   KNIGHT, DAMON   AN
  BLACK STAR PASSES, THE   NA   AMQ 30 FL
    BLACK STAR PASSES, THE   CAMPBELL, JOHN W. JR AC
    JOHN W. CAMPBELL ANTHOLOGY: THREE NOVELS
                                    CAMPBELL, JOHN W. JR AC
  BLINDNESS   SS   ASF 35 03
    *BEST OF JOHN W. CAMPBELL, THE CAMPBELL, JOHN W. JR AC
    *MY BEST SCIENCE FICTION STORY MARGULIES & FRIEND   AN
    WHO GOES THERE?   CAMPBELL, JOHN W. JR AC
    WHO GOES THERE? AND OTHER STORIES CAMPBELL, JOHN W. JR AC
  BRAIN PIRATES, THE   SS   TWS 38 10
    PLANETEERS, THE   CAMPBELL, JOHN W. JR DC
  BRAIN STEALERS OF MARS, THE   SS   TWS 36 12
    ALIEN WORLDS   ELWOOD, ROGER   AN
    BEFORE THE GOLDEN AGE   ASIMOV, ISAAC   AN
    PLANETEERS, THE   CAMPBELL, JOHN W. JR DC
  CLOAK OF AESIR   NV   ASF 39 03
    *BEST OF JOHN W. CAMPBELL, THE CAMPBELL, JOHN W. JR AC
    CLOAK OF AESIR   CAMPBELL, JOHN W. JR AC
    WHO GOES THERE? AND OTHER STORIES CAMPBELL, JOHN W. JR AC
  CONCERNING SCIENCE FICTION   IN
    *BEST OF SCIENCE FICTION   CONKLIN, GROFF   AN
  DEAD KNOWLEDGE   NV   ASF 38 01
    WHO GOES THERE?   CAMPBELL, JOHN W. JR AC
  DOUBLE MINDS, THE   NV   TWS 37 08
    BEST OF JOHN W. CAMPBELL, THE (BRITISH)
                                    CAMPBELL, JOHN W. JR AC
    PLANETEERS, THE   CAMPBELL, JOHN W. JR DC
  ELIMINATION   SS   ASF 36 05
    *BEST OF JOHN W. CAMPBELL, THE CAMPBELL, JOHN W. JR AC
    WHO GOES THERE?   CAMPBELL, JOHN W. JR AC
  ESCAPE, THE   NV   ASF 35 05
    CLOAK OF AESIR   CAMPBELL, JOHN W. JR AC
  FOREWORD   IN
    FROM UNKNOWN WORLDS   CAMPBELL, JOHN W. JR AN
  FORGETFULNESS   SN   ASF 37 06
    *BEST OF JOHN W. CAMPBELL, THE CAMPBELL, JOHN W. JR AC
    CLOAK OF AESIR   CAMPBELL, JOHN W. JR AC
  FRICTIONAL LOSSES   NV   ASF 36 07
    WHO GOES THERE?   CAMPBELL, JOHN W. JR AC
  IDEALIST, THE   NV   NTL 54
    9 TALES OF SPACE AND TIME   HEALY, RAYMOND J.   OA
  IMMORTALITY SEEKERS, THE   NV   TWS 37 10
    PLANETEERS, THE   CAMPBELL, JOHN W. JR DC
  IN MEMORIAM- BERNARD I. KAHN   MS
    NEBULA AWARD STORIES NO. 4   ANDERSON, POUL   AN
  INCREDIBLE PLANET, THE   NV
    INCREDIBLE PLANET, THE   CAMPBELL, JOHN W. JR NO
  INFINITE ATOM, THE   NV
    INCREDIBLE PLANET, THE   CAMPBELL, JOHN W. JR NO
  INTERSTELLAR SEARCH, THE   NV
    INCREDIBLE PLANET, THE   CAMPBELL, JOHN W. JR NO
  INTRODUCTION   IN
    ANALOG 1   CAMPBELL, JOHN W. JR AN
    ANALOG 3   CAMPBELL, JOHN W. JR AN
    ANALOG 6   CAMPBELL, JOHN W. JR AN
    *ASTOUNDING SCIENCE FICTION ANTHOLOGY, THE
                                    CAMPBELL, JOHN W. JR AN
    BLACK STAR PASSES, THE   CAMPBELL, JOHN W. JR AC
    CLOAK OF AESIR   CAMPBELL, JOHN W. JR AC
    *MAN WHO SOLD THE MOON, THE   HEINLEIN, ROBERT A. AC
    PROLOGUE TO ANALOG   CAMPBELL, JOHN W. JR AN
    VENUS EQUILATERAL   SMITH, GEORGE O.   AC
    14 GREAT TALES OF ESP   STONE, IDELLA P.   AN
  INVADERS FROM THE INFINITE   NO   FPS 61
    JOHN W. CAMPBELL ANTHOLOGY: THREE NOVELS
                                    CAMPBELL, JOHN W. JR AC
  INVADERS, THE   NV   ASF 35 06
    *BEST OF JOHN W. CAMPBELL, THE CAMPBELL, JOHN W. JR AC
    CLOAK OF AESIR   CAMPBELL, JOHN W. JR AC
  ISLANDS OF SPACE   NO   FPS 56
    JOHN W. CAMPBELL ANTHOLOGY: THREE NOVELS
                                    CAMPBELL, JOHN W. JR AC
  LAST EVOLUTION, THE   SS   AMZ 32 08
    AWARD SCIENCE FICTION READER   NORTON, ALDEN H.   AN
    *BEST OF JOHN W. CAMPBELL, THE CAMPBELL, JOHN W. JR AC
  MACHINE, THE   SS   ASF 35 02
    ANDROIDS, TIME MACHINES AND BLUE GIRAFFES
                                    ELWOOD & GHIDALIA   AN
    *BEST OF JOHN W. CAMPBELL, THE CAMPBELL, JOHN W. JR AC
    *BEST OF SCIENCE FICTION   CONKLIN, GROFF   AN
    CLOAK OF AESIR   CAMPBELL, JOHN W. JR AC
  MAROONED   SN
    SPACE BEYOND, THE   CAMPBELL, JOHN W. JR OC

CAMPBELL, JOHN W. JR (CONTINUED)
  NIGHT   NV   ASF 35 10
    EVIL EARTHS   ALDISS, BRIAN W.   AN
    MICROCOSMIC GOD   MOSKOWITZ, SAM   AN
    MODERN MASTERPIECES OF SCIENCE FICTION MOSKOWITZ, SAM AN
    WHERE DO WE GO FROM HERE?   ASIMOV, ISAAC   AN
    WHO GOES THERE?   CAMPBELL, JOHN W. JR AC
    WHO GOES THERE? AND OTHER STORIES CAMPBELL, JOHN W. JR AC
  OTHER EYES WATCHING   AR   ASF 37 02
    BEFORE THE GOLDEN AGE   ASIMOV, ISAAC   AN
  OUT OF NIGHT   NV   ASF 37 10
    *BEST OF JOHN W. CAMPBELL, THE CAMPBELL, JOHN W. JR AC
    CLOAK OF AESIR   CAMPBELL, JOHN W. JR AC
    WHO GOES THERE? AND OTHER STORIES CAMPBELL, JOHN W. JR AC
  PIRACY PREFERRED   NV   AMZ 30 06
    BLACK STAR PASSES, THE   CAMPBELL, JOHN W. JR AC
  PREFACE   IN
    ANALOG 2   CAMPBELL, JOHN W. JR AN
  PROLOGUE TO ANALOG   AN   DBL 62
    ANALOG ANTHOLOGY   CAMPBELL, JOHN W. JR AN
  REBELLION   NV   ASF 35 08
    *BEST OF JOHN W. CAMPBELL, THE CAMPBELL, JOHN W. JR AC
    CLOAK OF AESIR   CAMPBELL, JOHN W. JR AC
    FUTURES UNLIMITED   NORTON, ALDEN H.   AN
  "SCIENTISTS ARE STUPID!"   IN
    ANALOG 5   CAMPBELL, JOHN W. JR AN
  SOLARITE   NV   AMZ 30 11
    BLACK STAR PASSES, THE   CAMPBELL, JOHN W. JR AC
  SPACE BEYOND, THE   SN
    SPACE BEYOND, THE   CAMPBELL, JOHN W. JR OC
  SPACE FOR INDUSTRY   AR   ASF 60 04
    *BEST OF JOHN W. CAMPBELL, THE CAMPBELL, JOHN W. JR AC
  TENTH WORLD, THE   SS   TWS 37 12
    PLANETEERS, THE   CAMPBELL, JOHN W. JR DC
  THESE STORIES MAY UPSET YOU   IN
    ANALOG 4   CAMPBELL, JOHN W. JR AN
  TWILIGHT   SS   ASF 34 11
    *BEST OF JOHN W. CAMPBELL, THE CAMPBELL, JOHN W. JR AC
    ENDS OF TIME, THE   SILVERBERG, ROBERT   AN
    MIRROR OF INFINITY, THE   SILVERBERG, ROBERT   AN
    MODERN SCIENCE FICTION   SPINRAD, NORMAN   AN
    SCIENCE FICTION HALL OF FAME VOLUME 1 SILVERBERG, ROBERT AN
    WHO GOES THERE?   CAMPBELL, JOHN W. JR AC
    WHO GOES THERE? AND OTHER STORIES CAMPBELL, JOHN W. JR AC
  "WHAT DO YOU MEAN...HUMAN?"   ED   ASF 59 09
    5TH ANNUAL OF THE YEAR'S BEST S-F, THE MERRIL, JUDITH AN
  WHO GOES THERE   NV   ASF 38 08
    *BEST OF JOHN W. CAMPBELL, THE CAMPBELL, JOHN W. JR AC
    SCIENCE FICTION HALL OF FAME VOLUME 2A BOVA, BEN   AN
    SCIENCE FICTION ROLL OF HONOR, THE POHL, FREDERIK   AN
    UBERWINDUNG VON RAUM UND ZEIT   GUNTHER, GOTTHARD   AN
    WHO GOES THERE?   CAMPBELL, JOHN W. JR AC
    WHO GOES THERE? AND OTHER STORIES CAMPBELL, JOHN W. JR AC
  WHY I SELECTED BLINDNESS   AI
    *MY BEST SCIENCE FICTION STORY MARGULIES & FRIEND   AN

CAMPBELL, MRS. JOHN
  AFTERWORD: POSTSCRIPTUM   MS
    *BEST OF JOHN W. CAMPBELL, THE CAMPBELL, JOHN W. JR AC

CAMPTON, DAVID
  AT THE BOTTOM OF THE GARDEN   NV   ADS 75 01
    ARMADA SCI-FI ONE   DAVIS, RICHARD   OA
  DESMOND'S DINOSAUR   SS   ADS 75 02
    ARMADA SCI-FI TWO   DAVIS, RICHARD   OA
  LAPIDA MENACE, THE   NV   ADS 75 02
    ARMADA SCI-FI TWO   DAVIS, RICHARD   OA

CANNING, GEORGE
  LOVES OF THE TRIANGLES, THE   PM C
    MATHEMATICAL MAGPIE, THE   FADIMAN, CLIFTON   AN

CANTINE, HOLLEY
  DOUBLE, DOUBLE, TOIL AND TROUBLE   SS   FSF 60 01
    BEST FROM FANTASY AND SCIENCE FICTION: 10
                                    MILLS, ROBERT P.   AN
    6TH ANNUAL OF THE YEAR'S BEST S-F, THE MERRIL, JUDITH AN

CAPEK, JOSEF
  SYSTEM   SS C 08
    MASTERPIECES OF SCIENCE FICTION MOSKOWITZ, SAM   AN

CAPEK, KAREL
  ABSOLUTE AT LARGE, THE   SN   MAC 27
    CENTURY OF GREAT SHORT SCIENCE FICTION NOVELS, A
                                    KNIGHT, DAMON   AN
  DEATH OF ARCHIMEDES, THE   SS   49
    FANTASIA MATHEMATICA   FADIMAN, CLIFTON   AN
  R.U.R.   PL   21
    SCIENCE FACT/FICTION   FARRELL/GAGE/&   AN
    *SCIENCE FICTION THINKING MACHINES CONKLIN, GROFF   AN
    TREASURY OF SCIENCE FICTION CLASSICS, THE
                                    KUEBLER, HAROLD W.   AN
  SYSTEM   SS C 08
    MASTERPIECES OF SCIENCE FICTION MOSKOWITZ, SAM   AN

CAPOTE, TRUMAN
  MIRIAM   SS   45
    CHILDREN OF WONDER   TENN, WILLIAM   AN

CAPPS, CARROLL M.   SEE PSEUD. C. C. MACAPP

CARAVAN, T. P.
  COURT OF TARTARY, THE   SS   FSF 63 12
    BEST FROM FANTASY AND SCIENCE FICTION: 14
                                    DAVIDSON, AVRAM   AN

CARAVAN, T. P.   (CONTINUED)
    RANDOM SAMPLE   SS   FSF 53 04
        FIFTY SHORT SCIENCE FICTION TALES   ASIMOV & CONKLIN   AN
        SCIENCE FACT/FICTION   FARRELL/GAGE/&   AN

CARLETON, WILLIAM
    LEGEND OF FIN M'COUL, THE   SS
        FANTASY: THE LITERATURE OF THE MARVELOUS
                                             KELLEY, LEO P.   AN

CARLFI, CHESTER H.
    INTRODUCTION   IN
        CRAZY MIXED-UP PLANET   FRITCH, CHARLES E.   AC

CARLSON, ESTHER
    MUSEUM PIECE   SS   47
        WORLD OF WONDER   PRATT, FLETCHER   AN
    ROOM WITH A VIEW   SS   FAN 53 05
        FIEND IN YOU, THE   BEAUMONT, CHARLES   AN

CARLSON, WILLIAM
    CALL FROM KERLYANA   SS C ALC 73
        ALIEN CONDITION, THE   GOLDIN, STEPHEN   OA
    DINNER AT HELEN'S   SS   NEW 72 AN
        STRANGE BED FELLOWS   SCORTIA, THOMAS N.   AN
    FIRST MISSION   NV
        LONG NIGHT OF WAITING AND OTHER STORIES
                                             ELWOOD, ROGER   OA

CARLSSON, PEDER
    GORGIAS   SS   NWQ 73 05
        NEW WORLDS NO. 5   MOORCOCK & PLATT   OA

CARMER, CARL   SEE ALSO   CO-EDITOR LESTER DEL REY

CARNEIRO, ANDRE
    DARKNESS (TRANSLATED BY LEO L. BARROW)   SS   NOV 72 02
        BEST SF: 1972   HARRISON & ALDISS   AN
        NOVA 2   HARRISON, HARRY   OA

CARNELL, JOHN
    BEST FROM NEW WORLDS SCIENCE FICTION, THE   AN   BDM 55
    BEST FROM NEW WRITINGS IN S-F FIRST SELECTION, THE AN H DOB 71
    GATEWAY TO THE STARS   AN   MUS 55
    GATEWAY TO TOMORROW   AN   MUS 54
    LAMBDA I AND OTHER STORIES   AN   BKM 64 02
    NEW WRITINGS IN SF. 1   OA   BAN 66 04
    NEW WRITINGS IN SF. 2   OA   BAN 66 10
    NEW WRITINGS IN SF. 3   OA   BAN 67 02
    NEW WRITINGS IN SF. 4   OA   BAN 68 03
    NEW WRITINGS IN SF. 5   OA   BAN 70 08
    NEW WRITINGS IN SF. 6   OA   BAN 71 03
    NEW WRITINGS IN SF. 7   AN   BAN 71 08
    NEW WRITINGS IN SF. 7   OA H DOB 66
    NEW WRITINGS IN SF. 8   AN   BAN 71 12
    NEW WRITINGS IN SF. 8   OA H DOB 66
    NEW WRITINGS IN SF. 9   AN   BAN 72 05
    NEW WRITINGS IN SF. 9   OA H DOB 66
    NEW WRITINGS IN SF. 10   OA H DOB 67
    NEW WRITINGS IN SF. 11   OA   COR 68
    NEW WRITINGS IN SF. 12   OA   COR 68
    NEW WRITINGS IN SF. 13   OA   COR 68
    NEW WRITINGS IN SF. 14   OA H DOB 69
    NEW WRITINGS IN SF. 15   OA H DOB 69
    NEW WRITINGS IN SF. 16   OA H DOB 69
    NEW WRITINGS IN SF. 17   OA H DOB 70
    NEW WRITINGS IN SF. 18   OA H DOB 71
    NEW WRITINGS IN SF. 19   OA H DOB 71
    NEW WRITINGS IN SF. 20   OA H DOB 72
    NEW WRITINGS IN SF. 21   OA H SID 73
    NO PLACE LIKE EARTH   AN H BDM 52 10
    NO PLACE LIKE EARTH (7 OF 10)   AN   BDM 54 02
    WEIRD SHADOWS FROM BEYOND   AN   AVN 69 04
        FOREWORD   IN
            BEST FROM NEW WORLDS SCIENCE FICTION, THE
                                             CARNELL, JOHN   AN
            BEST FROM NEW WRITINGS IN S-F FIRST SELECTION, THE
                                             CARNELL, JOHN   AN
            LAMBDA I AND OTHER STORIES   CARNELL, JOHN   AN
            NEW WRITINGS IN SF. 1   CARNELL, JOHN   OA
            NEW WRITINGS IN SF. 2   CARNELL, JOHN   OA
            NEW WRITINGS IN SF. 3   CARNELL, JOHN   OA
            NEW WRITINGS IN SF. 4   CARNELL, JOHN   OA
            NEW WRITINGS IN SF. 5   CARNELL, JOHN   OA
            NEW WRITINGS IN SF. 6   CARNELL, JOHN   OA
            NEW WRITINGS IN SF. 7   CARNELL, JOHN   AN
            NEW WRITINGS IN SF. 7   CARNELL, JOHN   OA
            NEW WRITINGS IN SF. 8   CARNELL, JOHN   AN
            NEW WRITINGS IN SF. 8   CARNELL, JOHN   OA
            NEW WRITINGS IN SF. 9   CARNELL, JOHN   AN
            NEW WRITINGS IN SF. 9   CARNELL, JOHN   OA
            NEW WRITINGS IN SF. 10   CARNELL, JOHN   OA
            NEW WRITINGS IN SF. 11   CARNELL, JOHN   OA
            NEW WRITINGS IN SF. 12   CARNELL, JOHN   OA
            NEW WRITINGS IN SF. 13   CARNELL, JOHN   OA
            NEW WRITINGS IN SF. 14   CARNELL, JOHN   OA
            NEW WRITINGS IN SF. 15   CARNELL, JOHN   OA
            NEW WRITINGS IN SF. 16   CARNELL, JOHN   OA
            NEW WRITINGS IN SF. 17   CARNELL, JOHN   OA
            NEW WRITINGS IN SF. 18   CARNELL, JOHN   OA
            NEW WRITINGS IN SF. 19   CARNELL, JOHN   OA
            NEW WRITINGS IN SF. 20   CARNELL, JOHN   OA
    INTRODUCTION   IN
        WEIRD SHADOWS FROM BEYOND   CARNELL, JOHN   AN

CARNELL, TED
    IN MEMORIAM- ARTHUR SELLINGS   MS
        NEBULA AWARD STORIES NO. 4   ANDERSON, POUL   AN

CARO, DENNIS R.
    CANTALOUPES AND KANGAROOS   SS   CLR 73 03
        CLARION III   WILSON, ROBIN SCOTT   OA

CARR, CAROL
    INSIDE   SS   ORB 70 08
        INTO THE UNKNOWN   CARR, TERRY   AN
        ORBIT 8   KNIGHT, DAMON   OA
        OTHER DIMENSIONS   SILVERBERG, ROBERT   AN
    LOOK, YOU THINK YOU'VE GOT TROUBLES   SS   ORB 69 05
        ALIENS, THE   SILVERBERG, ROBERT   AN
        ANTIGRAV: COSMIC COMEDIES   STRICK, PHILIP   AN
        BEST FROM ORBIT, THE   KNIGHT, DAMON   AN
        MARRIAGE AND THE FAMILY THROUGH SCIENCE FICTION
                                             CLEAR/WARRICK/&   AN
        ORBIT 5   KNIGHT, DAMON   OA
        POCKETFUL OF STARS, A   KNIGHT, DAMON   AN
        THEMES IN SCIENCE FICTION   KELLEY, LEO P.   AN
        WANDERING STARS   DANN, JACK M.   AN
    SOME ARE BORN CATS   SS C SFT 73
        CREATURES FROM BEYOND   CARR, TERRY   AN
        SCIENCE FICTION TALES   ELWOOD, ROGER   OA

CARR, JOHN D.
    MANY-SIDED CONAN DOYLE, THE   IN
        POISON BELT, THE   DOYLE, ARTHUR CONAN AC

CARR, ROBERT S.
    BEYOND INFINITY   AC H FPS 51
    BEYOND INFINITY   NV   NEW 51 AC
        BEYOND INFINITY   CARR, ROBERT S.   AC
    EASTER EGGS (ALSO AS THOSE MEN FROM MARS) NV   SEP 49 09
        BEST SCIENCE-FICTION STORIES: 1950, THE
                                             BLEILER & DIKTY   AN
    MORNING STAR   NV   SEP 47 12
        BEYOND INFINITY   CARR, ROBERT S.   AC
    MUTATION   NV   NEW 51 AC
        BEYOND INFINITY   CARR, ROBERT S.   AC
    THOSE MEN FROM MARS (EASTER EGGS)   NV   SEP 49 09
        BEYOND INFINITY   CARR, ROBERT S.   AC

CARR, TERRY   SEE ALSO   CO-EDITOR DONALD A. WOLLHEIM
    BEST SCIENCE FICTION OF THE YEAR, THE   AN   BAL 72 07
    BEST SCIENCE FICTION OF THE YEAR, THE NO. 2 AN   BAL 73 07
    BEST SCIENCE FICTION OF THE YEAR, THE NO. 3 AN   BAL 74 07
    BEST SCIENCE FICTION OF THE YEAR, THE NO. 4 AN   BAL 75 07
    BEST SCIENCE FICTION OF THE YEAR, THE NO. 5 AN   BAL 76 07
    BEST SCIENCE FICTION OF THE YEAR, THE NO. 6 AN   HRW 77 07
    CREATURES FROM BEYOND   AN H NEL 75
    EXALTATION OF STARS, AN   OA H SAS 73
    FELLOWSHIP OF THE STARS   OA H SAS 74
    IDES OF TOMORROW, THE   OA H LBR 76
    INFINITE ARENA, THE   AN H NEL 77
    INTO THE UNKNOWN   AN H NEL 73
    LIGHT AT THE END OF THE UNIVERSE, THE   AC   PYR 76 10
    NEW WORLDS OF FANTASY   AN   ACE 67
        IN ENGLAND AS "STEP OUTSIDE YOUR MIND"
    NEW WORLDS OF FANTASY NO. 2   AN   ACE 70
    NEW WORLDS OF FANTASY NO. 3   AN   ACE 71
    ON OUR WAY TO THE FUTURE   AN   ACE 70
    OTHERS, THE   AN   FGM 69
    PLANETS OF WONDER   AN H NEL 76
        A TREASURY OF SPACE OPERA
    SCIENCE FICTION FOR PEOPLE WHO HATE SCIENCE FICTION
                                               AN H DBL 66
    STEP OUTSIDE YOUR MIND   AC H DOB 69
        SEE "NEW WORLDS OF FANTASY"
    THIS SIDE OF INFINITY   AN   ACE 72 09
    UNIVERSE 1   OA   ACE 71
    UNIVERSE 2   OA   ACE 72
    UNIVERSE 3   OA H RDM 73
    UNIVERSE 4   OA H RDM 74
    UNIVERSE 5   OA H RDM 74
    UNIVERSE 6   OA H DBL 76
    UNIVERSE 7   OA H DBL 77 01
    WORLDS FAR AND NEAR   AN H NEL 74
        ANSWER, THE   SS   TAL 73
            FRONTIERS 1; TOMORROW'S ALTERNATIVES ELWOOD, ROGER   OA
        BROWN ROBERT   SS   FSF 62 07
            ALPHA 6   SILVERBERG, ROBERT   AN
            LIGHT AT THE END OF THE UNIVERSE, THE CARR, TERRY   AC
        CASTLE IN THE STARS   SS
            TOMORROW: NEW WORLDS OF SCIENCE FICTION
                                             ELWOOD, ROGER   OA
        CHANGING OF THE GODS   NV   INY 73 05
            INFINITY 5   HOSKINS, ROBERT   OA
            LIGHT AT THE END OF THE UNIVERSE, THE CARR, TERRY   AC
        CITY OF YESTERDAY   SS   IFS 67 12
            BEYOND CONTROL   SILVERBERG, ROBERT   AN
            EARTH IN TRANSIT   SCHWARTZ, SHEILA   AN
        COLORS OF FEAR, THE   SS   NDM 74 04
            LIGHT AT THE END OF THE UNIVERSE, THE CARR, TERRY   AC
            NEW DIMENSIONS 4   SILVERBERG, ROBERT   AN
        DANCE OF THE CHANGER AND THE THREE, THE SS   FRS 68
            BUG-EYED MONSTERS   CHEETHAM, ANTHONY   AN
            DEEP SPACE   SILVERBERG, ROBERT   AN
            FARTHEST REACHES, THE   ELDER, JOSEPH   OA
            LIGHT AT THE END OF THE UNIVERSE, THE CARR, TERRY   AC
            NEBULA AWARD STORIES NO. 4   ANDERSON, POUL   AN
            WORLD'S BEST SCIENCE FICTION: 1969 WOLLHEIM & CARR   AN
        FROM DARKNESS TO DARKNESS   SS   DEM 73
            DEMON KIND   ELWOOD, ROGER   OA

```
CARR, TERRY   (CONTINUED)
  HONORABLE MENTIONS- 1974                    MS
    BEST SCIENCE FICTION OF THE YEAR, THE NO. 4
                                      CARR, TERRY          AN
  HOP-FRIEND                                  SS   FSF 62 11
    ALIENS, THE                     SILVERBERG, ROBERT     AN
    BEST FROM FANTASY AND SCIENCE FICTION: 12
                                    DAVIDSON, AVRAM        AN
    FIRST STEP OUTWARD              HOSKINS, ROBERT        AN
    LIGHT AT THE END OF THE UNIVERSE, THE  CARR, TERRY     AC
    POCKETFUL OF STARS, A          KNIGHT, DAMON          AN
  IN HIS IMAGE (IN MAN'S IMAGE)               SS   AMZ 71 11
    ALPHA 4                         SILVERBERG, ROBERT     AN
    LIGHT AT THE END OF THE UNIVERSE, THE  CARR, TERRY     AC
  IN MAN'S IMAGE (SEE IN HIS IMAGE)           TC
  INTRODUCTION                                IN
    BEST SCIENCE FICTION OF THE YEAR, THE  CARR, TERRY     AN
    BEST SCIENCE FICTION OF THE YEAR, THE NO. 2
                                    CARR, TERRY            AN
    BEST SCIENCE FICTION OF THE YEAR, THE NO. 3
                                    CARR, TERRY            AN
    BEST SCIENCE FICTION OF THE YEAR, THE NO. 4
                                    CARR, TERRY            AN
    BEST SCIENCE FICTION OF THE YEAR, THE NO. 5
                                    CARR, TERRY            AN
    CREATURES FROM BEYOND          CARR, TERRY            AN
    EXALTATION OF STARS, AN        CARR, TERRY            OA
    FELLOWSHIP OF THE STARS        CARR, TERRY            OA
    INFINITE ARENA, THE            CARR, TERRY            AN
    INTO THE UNKNOWN               CARR, TERRY            AN
    NEW WORLDS OF FANTASY          CARR, TERRY            AN
    NEW WORLDS OF FANTASY NO. 2    CARR, TERRY            AN
    NEW WORLDS OF FANTASY NO. 3    CARR, TERRY            AN
    ON OUR WAY TO THE FUTURE       CARR, TERRY            AN
    SCIENCE FICTION FOR PEOPLE WHO HATE SCIENCE FICTION
                                    CARR, TERRY            AN
    STARSHADOWS                    SARGENT, PAMELA        AC
    THIS SIDE OF INFINITY          CARR, TERRY            AN
    UNIVERSE 1                     CARR, TERRY            OA
    UNIVERSE 3                     CARR, TERRY            OA
    WORLDS FAR AND NEAR            CARR, TERRY            AN
  INTRODUCTION                                IN C
    WORLD'S BEST SCIENCE FICTION: 1965  WOLLHEIM & CARR    AN
    WORLD'S BEST SCIENCE FICTION: 1966  WOLLHEIM & CARR    AN
    WORLD'S BEST SCIENCE FICTION: 1967  WOLLHEIM & CARR    AN
    WORLD'S BEST SCIENCE FICTION: 1968  WOLLHEIM & CARR    AN
    WORLD'S BEST SCIENCE FICTION: 1969  WOLLHEIM & CARR    AN
    WORLD'S BEST SCIENCE FICTION: 1970  WOLLHEIM & CARR    AN
    WORLD'S BEST SCIENCE FICTION: 1971  WOLLHEIM & CARR    AN
  OLD MAN OF THE MOUNTAINS, THE               SS   FSF 63 04
    LIGHT AT THE END OF THE UNIVERSE, THE  CARR, TERRY     AC
    NEW WORLDS OF FANTASY NO. 2    CARR, TERRY            AN
  OZYMANDIAS                                  SS   DVS 72 02
    AGAIN, DANGEROUS VISIONS       ELLISON, HARLAN        OA
    LIGHT AT THE END OF THE UNIVERSE, THE  CARR, TERRY     AC
    MUTANTS                        SILVERBERG, ROBERT     AN
  RECOMMENDED READING- 1975                   MS
    BEST SCIENCE FICTION OF THE YEAR, THE NO. 5
                                    CARR, TERRY            AN
  REJOICE, REJOICE, WE HAVE NO CHOICE         SS
    ALPHA 7                        SILVERBERG, ROBERT     AN
    FUTURE KIN                     ELWOOD, ROGER          OA
    LIGHT AT THE END OF THE UNIVERSE, THE  CARR, TERRY     AC
  ROBOTS ARE HERE, THE                        NV   IFS 67 05
    COSMIC LAUGHTER                HALDEMAN, JOE W.       AN
    LIGHT AT THE END OF THE UNIVERSE, THE  CARR, TERRY     AC
  SAVING THE WORLD                            SS   SVW 73
    SAVING WORLDS                  ELWOOD & KIDD          OA
  SLEEPING BEAUTY                             SS   FSF 67 05
    LIGHT AT THE END OF THE UNIVERSE, THE  CARR, TERRY     AC
    NEW WORLDS OF FANTASY NO. 3    CARR, TERRY            AN
  SOME ARE BORN CATS                          SS C SFT 73
    CREATURES FROM BEYOND          CARR, TERRY            AN
    SCIENCE FICTION TALES          ELWOOD, ROGER          OA
  STANLEY TOOTHBRUSH (AS CARL BRANDON)        SS   FSF 62 07
    LIGHT AT THE END OF THE UNIVERSE, THE  CARR, TERRY     AC
    NEW WORLDS OF FANTASY          CARR, TERRY            AN
    OTHER DIMENSIONS               SILVERBERG, ROBERT     AN
  THEY LIVE ON LEVELS                         SS   NDM 73 03
    LIGHT AT THE END OF THE UNIVERSE, THE  CARR, TERRY     AC
    NEW DIMENSIONS 3               SILVERBERG, ROBERT     OA
    WORLDS FAR AND NEAR            CARR, TERRY            AN
  TOUCHSTONE                                  SS   FSF 64 05
    BEST FROM FANTASY AND SCIENCE FICTION: 14
                                    DAVIDSON, AVRAM        AN
    INTO THE UNKNOWN               CARR, TERRY            AN
    LIGHT AT THE END OF THE UNIVERSE, THE  CARR, TERRY     AC
  WINDS AT STARMONT, THE                      NA
    LIGHT AT THE END OF THE UNIVERSE, THE  CARR, TERRY     AC
    NO MIND OF MAN                 SILVERBERG, ROBERT     OA

CARRELL, CHRISTOPHER
  BEYOND THIS HORIZON                      OA   CEO 73 10

CARRINGTON, GRANT
  FOUNTAIN OF FORCE                        SS C INY 72 04
    INFINITY 4                     HOSKINS, ROBERT        OA

CARROLL, LEWIS    PSEUD. FOR CHARLES LUTWIDGE DODGSON
  APOTHEM                                     MS   96
    MATHEMATICAL MAGPIE, THE       FADIMAN, CLIFTON       AN
  ETERNITY: A NIGHTMARE                       PM   93
    FANTASIA MATHEMATICA           FADIMAN, CLIFTON       AN
  PURSE OF FORTUNATUS, THE                    SS   89
    MATHEMATICAL MAGPIE, THE       FADIMAN, CLIFTON       AN

CARROLL, LEWIS    (CONTINUED)
  YET WHAT ARE ALL...                         PM
    FANTASIA MATHEMATICA           FADIMAN, CLIFTON       AN

CARROLL, SIDNEY
  NONE BEFORE ME                              SS   CMP 49 07
    TIMELESS STORIES FOR TODAY AND TOMORROW
                                    BRADBURY, RAY          AN
  NOTE FOR THE MILKMAN, A                     SS   TDW 50 04
    TIMELESS STORIES FOR TODAY AND TOMORROW
                                    BRADBURY, RAY          AN

CARTER, ANGELA
  EXECUTIONER'S BEAUTIFUL DAUGHTER, THE       SS
    BEST SF: 1974                  HARRISON & ALDISS      AN

CARTER, LIN        SEE ALSO    CO-AUTHOR ROBERT E. HOWARD
  BLACK TEARS                                 SS C
    CONAN THE WANDERER             HOWARD, R./DE CAMP/& AC
  CHAINS OF SHAMBALLAH                        SS C
    CONAN                          HOWARD, R./DE CAMP/& AC
  HAND OF NERGAL, THE                         SS C
    CONAN                          HOWARD, R./DE CAMP/& AC
  MARTIAN EL DORADO OF PARKER WINTLEY, THE    SS
    DAW SCIENCE FICTION READER, THE  WOLLHEIM, DONALD A.  OA
  UNCOLLECTED WORKS                           SS   FSF 65 03
    WORLD'S BEST SCIENCE FICTION: 1966  WOLLHEIM & CARR    AN

CARTER, PAUL A.
  CONSTITUTION IN E FLAT                      SS   GEN 72
    GENERATION                     GERROLD, DAVID         OA
  LAST OBJECTIVE, THE                         NV   ASF 46 08
    DECADE THE 1940S               ALDISS & HARRISON      AN
    *TREASURY OF SCIENCE FICTION, A  CONKLIN, GROFF       AN
  MAN WHO RODE THE TRAINS, THE                SS
    TRAVELLERS BY NIGHT            DERLETH, AUGUST        OA
  OUNCE OF PREVENTION, AN                     SS   FSF 50 SU
    FAR BOUNDARIES                 DERLETH, AUGUST        AN

CARTIER, EDD
  LIFE ON OTHER WORLDS                        IL
    TRAVELLERS OF SPACE            GREENBERG , MARTIN     AN

CARTMILL, CLEVE
  SPACE SCAVENGERS, THE                       NO   MAJ 75
  BARGAIN, THE                                SS   UNK 42 08
    UNKNOWN 5, THE                 BENSEN, D. R.          AN
  DEAD RUN                                    NV   TWS 50 02
    SPACE SCAVENGERS, THE          CARTMILL, CLEVE        NO
  DEADLINE                                    NV   ASF 44 03
    *BEST OF SCIENCE FICTION       CONKLIN, GROFF         AN
  GREEN CAT, THE                              SS   WBY 51 01
    *OUTER REACHES, THE            DERLETH, AUGUST        AN
  HELL HATH FURY                              SN   UNK 43 08
    HELL HATH FURY                 HAY, GEORGE            AN
  HIGH JACK AND DAME                          NV   TWS 49 10
    SPACE SCAVENGERS, THE          CARTMILL, CLEVE        NO
  HUGE BEAST                                  SS   FSF 50 SU
    BEST FROM FANTASY AND SCIENCE FICTION  BOUCHER & MCCOMAS  AN
  LINK, THE                                   SS   ASF 42 08
    *ADVENTURES IN TIME AND SPACE  HEALY & MCCOMAS        AN
    MORE ADVENTURES IN TIME AND SPACE  HEALY & MCCOMAS    AN
    POLITICAL SCIENCE FICTION      GREENBERG& WARRICK     AN
  LITTLE JOE                                  NV   TWS 50 04
    SPACE SCAVENGERS, THE          CARTMILL, CLEVE        NO
  NO HIDING PLACE                             NA   TWS 50 06
    SPACE SCAVENGERS, THE          CARTMILL, CLEVE        NO
  NUMBER NINE                                 SS   ASF 50 02
    GREAT STORIES OF SCIENCE FICTION  LEINSTER, MURRAY    AN
  OSCAR                                       SS   UNK 41 02
    FIFTY SHORT SCIENCE FICTION TALES  ASIMOV & CONKLIN   AN
  OVERTHROW                                   SN   ASF 42 11
    JOURNEY TO INFINITY            GREENBERG , MARTIN     AN
  SALVAGE                                     NV   TWS 49 08
    SPACE SCAVENGERS, THE          CARTMILL, CLEVE        NO
  SOME DAY WE'LL FIND YOU                     NV   ASF 42 12
    DIMENSION 4                    CONKLIN, GROFF         AN
  THICKER THAN WATER                          NV   TWS 49 12
    SPACE SCAVENGERS, THE          CARTMILL, CLEVE        NO
  VISITING YOKEL                              SS   TWS 43 08
    *MY BEST SCIENCE FICTION STORY  MARGULIES & FRIEND    AN
    WHY I SELECTED VISITING YOKEL  AI
    *MY BEST SCIENCE FICTION STORY  MARGULIES & FRIEND    AN
  WITH FLAMING SWORDS                         NV   ASF 42 09
    *TREASURY OF SCIENCE FICTION, A  CONKLIN, GROFF       AN
  YOU CAN'T SAY THAT                          NV   NTS 51
    NEW TALES OF SPACE AND TIME    HEALY, RAYMOND J.      OA

CARTUR, PETER
  MIST, THE                                   SS   FSF 52 09
    ADVENTURES IN DIMENSION        CONKLIN, GROFF         AN
    FIFTY SHORT SCIENCE FICTION TALES  ASIMOV & CONKLIN   AN
    *SCIENCE FICTION ADVENTURES IN DIMENSION
                                    CONKLIN, GROFF         AN

CARVER, JEFFREY A.
  LOVE ROGO                                   NA
    FUTURELOVE                     ELWOOD, ROGER          OA

CASSILL, R. V.
  WAR IN THE AIR, THE                         SS   FSF 56 09
    WORLDS OF SCIENCE FICTION, THE  MILLS, ROBERT P.      AN

CASTELL, DAPHNE
  COLD STORAGE                                SS
```

CASTELL, DAPHNE   (CONTINUED)
  GOLLANCZ - SUNDAY TIMES BEST SF STORIES
                                           ANONYMOUS   OA
    COME UP AND SEE ME   SS   ANA 70
      ALCHEMY AND ACADEME   MCCAFFREY, ANNE   OA
    ESMERALDA   SS
      GOLLANCZ - SUNDAY TIMES BEST SF STORIES
                                           ANONYMOUS   OA
    PATENT MEDICINE MAN, THE   SS   BER 74
      BERSERKERS, THE   ELWOOD, ROGER   OA
    WHO'S IN THERE WITH ME?   SS   NEW 68 AN
      ENGLAND SWINGS SF   MERRIL, JUDITH   AN
      SPACE-TIME JOURNAL, THE   MERRIL, JUDITH   AN

CAUSEY, JAMES
    EXPLOITERS' END   SS   OSF 54 02
      BEYOND THE STARS AND OTHER STORIES   ANONYMOUS   AN
    FELONY   SS   GAL 54 07
      BEST SCIENCE FICTION STORIES AND NOVELS: 1955
                                           DIKTY, T. E.   AN
    SHOW MUST GO ON, THE (SO LOVELY, SO LOST)   SS   OSF 54 11
      PSEUDO PEOPLE, THE   NOLAN, WILLIAM F.   AN
    SO LOVELY, SO LOST (SEE THE SHOW MUST GO ON)   TC
    TEETHING RING   SS   GAL 53 01
      FIFTY SHORT SCIENCE FICTION TALES   ASIMOV & CONKLIN   AN
      SECOND GALAXY READER OF SCIENCE FICTION
                                           GOLD, H. L.   AN

CAWOOD, HAP
    SYNCHROMOCRACY   SS   MOT 64
      10TH ANNUAL OF THE YEAR'S BEST S-F, THE
                                           MERRIL, JUDITH   AN

CERF, CHRISTOPHER
    VINTAGE ANTHOLOGY OF SCIENCE FANTASY, THE   AN   VNT 66 02
    INTRODUCTION   IN
      VINTAGE ANTHOLOGY OF SCIENCE FANTASY, THE
                                           CERF, CHRISTOPHER   AN

CHAIN, JULIAN   PSEUD. FOR JULIAN CHAIN MAY DIKTY
    CAPTIVES, THE   NV   ASP 53 01
      APEMAN, SPACEMAN   STOVER & HARRISON   AN

CHAMBERS, ROBERT W.
    DEMOISELLE D'YS, THE   SS   WRT 28 08
      EDITOR'S CHOICE IN SCIENCE FICTION   MOSKOWITZ, SAM   AN
    IN SEARCH OF THE UNKNOWN (EXCERPT)   EX   04
      SPACE MAGICIANS, THE   NORTON & MOSKOWITZ   AN
    REPAIRER OF REPUTATIONS, THE (1895)   NV   95
      BATTLE OF THE MONSTERS AND OTHER STORIES, THE
                                           HARTWELL & CURREY   AN
    THIRD EYE, THE   SS   15
      ANCESTRAL VOICES   MENVILLE & REGINALD   AN
    YELLOW SIGN, THE (1895)   NV   FFM 43 09
      EDGE OF NEVER, THE   HOSKINS, ROBERT   AN

CHAMPAGNE, TERRY
    SURFACE IF YOU CAN   SS   NWS 69 07
      NEW TOMORROWS, THE   SPINRAD, NORMAN   AN

CHANDLER, A. BERTRAM ALSO AS   GEORGE WHITLEY
    ALTERNATE ORBITS   DC   ACE 71
    BEYOND THE GALACTIC RIM   DC   ACE 63
    HARD WAY UP, THE   DC   ACE 72
    RIM GODS, THE   DC   ACE 68
    ALL LACED UP   SS   NWS 61 11
      PACIFIC BOOK OF AUSTRALIAN SCIENCE FICTION
                                           BAXTER, JOHN   AN
    BIRD-BRAINED NAVIGATOR, THE   NV   IFS 68 06
      RIM GODS, THE   CHANDLER, A. BERTRAM DC
    CAGE, THE   SS   FSF 57 06
      ANTHROPOLOGY THROUGH SCIENCE FICTION MASON, C/GREENBERG/& AN
      BEST FROM FANTASY AND SCIENCE FICTION: 7
                                           BOUCHER, ANTHONY   AN
      YET MORE PENGUIN SCIENCE FICTION   ALDISS, BRIAN W.   AN
      12 GREAT CLASSICS OF SCIENCE FICTION CONKLIN, GROFF   AN
    CASTAWAY   SS   WRT 47 11
      *SCIENCE FICTION ADVENTURES IN DIMENSION
                                           CONKLIN, GROFF   AN
    CRITICAL ANGLE   SS   FSF 58 11
      FIRST FLIGHTS TO THE MOON   CLEMENT, HAL   AN
    FALL OF KNIGHT   SS   FUN 58 06
      FANTASTIC UNIVERSE OMNIBUS, THE   SANTESSON, HANS S.   AN
      RULERS OF MEN   SANTESSON, HANS S.   AN
    FALSE DAWN   NV   ASF 46 10
      JOURNEY TO INFINITY   GREENBERG, MARTIN   AN
    FINISHING TOUCH   SS   NWS 52 07
      GATEWAY TO TOMORROW   CARNELL, JOHN   AN
    FORBIDDEN PLANET   SS   FUN 59 07
      BEYOND THE GALACTIC RIM   CHANDLER, A. BERTRAM DC
    GIANT KILLER   NV   ASF 45 10
      ASTOUNDING-ANALOG READER, THE VOLUME ONE
                                           HARRISON & ALDISS   AN
      GREAT SHORT NOVELS OF SCIENCE FICTION SILVERBERG, ROBERT   AN
      WORLD OF WONDER   PRATT, FLETCHER   AN
    HALF PAIR, THE   SS   NWS 57 11
      PENGUIN SCIENCE FICTION   ALDISS, BRIAN W.   AN
    HALL OF FAME (KINGSOLVING'S PLANET IRREGULARS)   NV   GAL 69 07
      ALTERNATE ORBITS   CHANDLER, A. BERTRAM DC
    JETSAM   SS   NWS 53 03
      BEST FROM NEW WORLDS SCIENCE FICTION, THE
                                           CARNELL, JOHN   AN
      FIRST FLIGHTS TO THE MOON   CLEMENT, HAL   AN
      FIRST STEP OUTWARD   HOSKINS, ROBERT   AN
      MEN ON THE MOON   WOLLHEIM, DONALD A.   DA

CHANDLER, A. BERTRAM (CONTINUED)
      KEY, THE   NV   FAN 59 07
      BEYOND THE GALACTIC RIM   CHANDLER, A. BERTRAM DC
    KINGSOLVING'S PLANET IRREGULARS (SEE HALL OF FAME)
                                           TC
    LAST DREAMER   NV   IFS 68 08
      RIM GODS, THE   CHANDLER, A. BERTRAM DC
    LATE   SS   SCF 55 04
      BEYOND TOMORROW   HARDING, LEE   AN
      SF: AUTHORS' CHOICE 2   HARRISON, HARRY   AN
    LEFT-HAND WAY, THE   SS   AUS 67
      BEST SF: 1967   HARRISON & ALDISS   AN
    MAN WHO COULD NOT STOP, THE   NV   FSF 59 05
      BEYOND THE GALACTIC RIM   CHANDLER, A. BERTRAM DC
    MAN WHO SAILED THE SKY, THE   NV
      ALTERNATE ORBITS   CHANDLER, A. BERTRAM DC
    MOUNTAIN MOVERS, THE   NV   GAL 71 03
      HARD WAY UP, THE   CHANDLER, A. BERTRAM DC
    RIM GODS, THE   NV   IFS 68 04
      RIM GODS, THE   CHANDLER, A. BERTRAM DC
    RUB, THE   NV   GAL 70 04
      ALTERNATE ORBITS   CHANDLER, A. BERTRAM DC
    SEA CHANGE   NV   YRT 70
      YEAR 2000, THE   HARRISON, HARRY   OA
    SENSE OF WONDER   SS   FUN 58 02
      FLYING SAUCERS IN FACT AND FICTION   SANTESSON, HANS S.   AN
    SISTER SHIPS, THE   NV   GAL 71 09
      ALTERNATE ORBITS   CHANDLER, A. BERTRAM DC
    SLEEPING BEAUTY, THE   NV   GAL 70 02
      HARD WAY UP, THE   CHANDLER, A. BERTRAM DC
    SOUL MACHINE, THE   SS   GAL 69 10
      BEST FROM GALAXY, THE   VOLUME I   GALAXY, EDITORS OF   AN
    SUBTRACTER, THE   SS
      HARD WAY UP, THE   CHANDLER, A. BERTRAM DC
    TIN FISHES, THE   NV   IFS 68 12
      RIM GODS, THE   CHANDLER, A. BERTRAM DC
    TIN MESSIAH, THE   SS
      HARD WAY UP, THE   CHANDLER, A. BERTRAM DC
    WANDERING BOUY, THE   SS   ASF 70 09
      HARD WAY UP, THE   CHANDLER, A. BERTRAM DC
    WET PAINT   NV   AMZ 59 05
      BEYOND THE GALACTIC RIM   CHANDLER, A. BERTRAM DC
    WHAT YOU KNOW   NV   GAL 71 01
      HARD WAY UP, THE   CHANDLER, A. BERTRAM DC
    WITH GOOD INTENTIONS   SS
      HARD WAY UP, THE   CHANDLER, A. BERTRAM DC

CHANG, GLENN
    STARS AND DARKNESS   NV   UNI 76 06
      UNIVERSE 6   CARR, TERRY   OA

CHAPDELAINE, PERRY A
    CHARLEY   SS
      STOPWATCH   HAY, GEORGE   OA

CHAPLIN, SAUL
    SQUARE OF THE HYPOTENUSE, THE (MUSIC) SG C   58
      MATHEMATICAL MAGPIE, THE   FADIMAN, CLIFTON   AN

CHAPMAN, STEVE
    AUTOPSY IN TRANSIT   SS   ORB 75 17
      ORBIT 17   KNIGHT, DAMON   OA
    BURGER CREATURE   SS   ORB 73 12
      ORBIT 12   KNIGHT, DAMON   OA
      YEAR'S BEST HORROR STORIES: SERIES III, THE
                                           DAVIS, RICHARD   AN
    TESTING...ONE, TWO, THREE, FOUR   SS   ASF 69 12
      ANALOG 8   CAMPBELL, JOHN W. JR AN
      BEST OF SCIENCE FICTION MONTHLY, THE SACKS, JANET   AN
    TROIKA   SS   ORB 74 13
      ORBIT 13   KNIGHT, DAMON   OA

CHARLOTTE, JEAN
    RED SKY AT NIGHT   SS   NWQ 74 06
      NEW WORLDS NO. 6   PLATT & BAILEY   OA

CHARNEY, DAVID H.
    MOMMY LOVES YA   SS   TAL 73
      FRONTIERS 1: TOMORROW'S ALTERNATIVES ELWOOD, ROGER   OA
    TRIPLE MOONS OF DENEB II, THE   SS   SFT 73
      SCIENCE FICTION TALES   ELWOOD, ROGER   OA

CHARNOCK, GRAHAM
    CHINESE BOXES, THE   SS   ORB 70 08
      ORBIT 8   KNIGHT, DAMON   OA
    EROGENOUS ZONE, THE   SS   NWS 69 07
      BEST SF STORIES FROM NEW WORLDS 8   MOORCOCK, MICHAEL   AN
    OBSERVER, THE   SS   NWR 75 27
      NEW WRITINGS IN SF. 27   BULMER, KENNETH   OA

CHARTERIS, LESLIE   PSEUD. FOR LESLIE CHARLES BOWYER YIN
    SAINT'S CHOICE OF IMPOSSIBLE CRIME, THE   AN   BNC 45
    CONVENIENT MONSTER, THE   SS
      ANCIENT MYSTERIES READER, THE   HAINING, PETER   AN
    FISH STORY   SS   BBM 53 11
      GALAXY OF GHOULS   MERRIL, JUDITH   AN
    GOLD STANDARD, THE   SS   33
      SAINT'S CHOICE OF IMPOSSIBLE CRIME, THE
                                           CHARTERIS, LESLIE   AN

CHEETHAM, ANTHONY
    BUG-EYED MONSTERS   AN   PTH 74
    SCIENCE AGAINST MAN   OA   AVN 70 12
    INTRODUCTION   IN
      BUG-EYED MONSTERS   CHEETHAM, ANTHONY   AN
      SCIENCE AGAINST MAN   CHEETHAM, ANTHONY   OA

CHEEVER, JOHN
  ENORMOUS RADIO, THE   SS   NYM 47 05
    LIGHT FANTASTIC, THE   HARRISON, HARRY   AN
    TIMELESS STORIES FOR TODAY AND TOMORROW
                                BRADBURY, RAY   AN
  YELLOW ROOM, THE   NV   PBY 68 01
    MASKS   PLAYBOY, EDITORS OF   AN

CHEINISSE, CLAUDE F.
  JULIETTE   SS   59
    13 FRENCH SCIENCE-FICTION STORIES   KNIGHT, DAMON   AN

CHESNEY, G. T.
  BATTLE OF DORKING, THE   NA
    BEFORE ARMAGEDDON   MOORCOCK, MICHAEL   AN

CHETWYND-HAYES, R.
  TALES OF TERROR FROM OUTER SPACE   AN   FON 75 05
    INTRODUCTION   IN
    TALES OF TERROR FROM OUTER SPACE   CHETWYND-HAYES, R.   AN
  SHIPWRECK   SS   NEW 75 AN
    TALES OF TERROR FROM OUTER SPACE   CHETWYND-HAYES, R.   AN

CHILDS, BERNARD
  EYEBALL OF THE SUN   IL
    SCIENCE FICTION   BRODKIN & PEARSON   AN

CHILSON, ROBERT
  DEVIL AND THE DEEP BLUE SEA, THE   SS
    BEYOND TIME   LEY, SANDRA   OA
  IN HIS IMAGE   NV   ASF 69 09
    ANALOG 8   CAMPBELL, JOHN W. JR   AN
  PEOPLE REVIEWS   SS   UNI 77 07
    UNIVERSE 7   CARR, TERRY   OA

CHORON, JACQUES
  EPILOGUE   MS
    WEIGHER OF SOULS AND THE EARTH DWELLERS, THE
                                MAUROIS, ANDRE   AC

CHRISTIE, AGATHA
  LAST SEANCE, THE (1926)   SS   EQM 71 11
    BEYOND THE BARRIERS OF SPACE AND TIME MERRIL, JUDITH   AN
    VENUS FACTOR, THE   GHIDALIA, V.& ELWOOD   AN

CHRISTIE, WILLIAM H. SEE PSEUD. CECIL B. WHITE

CHRISTOPHER, JOHN   PSEUD. FOR CHRISTOPHER YOUD
  TWENTY-SECOND CENTURY, THE   AC H GRY 54
    BALANCE   SS   NWS 51 SP
      BEST SCIENCE-FICTION STORIES: 1952, THE
                                BLEILER & DIKTY   AN
     *NO PLACE LIKE EARTH   CARNELL, JOHN   AN
    BEGIN AGAIN   SS   ESQ
      TWENTY-SECOND CENTURY, THE   CHRISTOPHER, JOHN   AC
    BLEMISH   SS   AUT 53 11
      TWENTY-SECOND CENTURY, THE   CHRISTOPHER, JOHN   AC
    BREAKING POINT   SS   NWS 52 05
      TWENTY-SECOND CENTURY, THE   CHRISTOPHER, JOHN   AC
    CHRISTMAS ROSES (CHRISTMAS TREE)   SS   ASF 49 02
      TWENTY-SECOND CENTURY, THE   CHRISTOPHER, JOHN   AC
    COLONIAL   NV   ASF 49 04
      OUT OF THIS WORLD 5   WILLIAMS-ELLIS& OWEN AN
      TWENTY-SECOND CENTURY, THE   CHRISTOPHER, JOHN   AC
    CONSPIRACY   SS   AUT 55 01
      GATEWAY TO THE STARS   CARNELL, JOHN   AN
    DEATH SENTENCE (SEE SENTENCE OF DEATH)   TC
    DECOY   SS   SFS 55 07
      TWENTY-SECOND CENTURY, THE   CHRISTOPHER, JOHN   AC
    DROP, THE   SS   GAL 53 03
      GATEWAY TO TOMORROW   CARNELL, JOHN   AN
    FEW KINDRED SPIRITS, A   SS   FSF 65 11
      BEST FROM FANTASY AND SCIENCE FICTION: 16
                                FERMAN, EDWARD L.   AN
    MAN OF DESTINY   SS   GAL 51 05
     *GALAXY READER OF SCIENCE FICTION   GOLD, H. L.   AN
      LOOKING FORWARD   LESSER, MILTON   AN
    MONSTER   SS   SCF 50 SU
      TWENTY-SECOND CENTURY, THE   CHRISTOPHER, JOHN   AC
    MR. KOWTSHOOK   SS   ASF 53 01
      TALES OF SCIENCE FICTION   BALL, BRIAN N.   AN
      TWENTY-SECOND CENTURY, THE   CHRISTOPHER, JOHN   AC
    MUSEUM PIECE   SS   NWS 54 04
      TWENTY-SECOND CENTURY, THE   CHRISTOPHER, JOHN   AC
    NEW WINE, THE   SS   FSM 54 SU
      BEST SF   CRISPIN, EDMUND   AN
      SCIENCE FICTION   BURTON, S. H.   AN
      TWENTY-SECOND CENTURY, THE   CHRISTOPHER, JOHN   AC
    OCCUPATIONAL RISK   SS   SFS 57 01
      TWENTY-SECOND CENTURY, THE   CHRISTOPHER, JOHN   AC
    PROPHET, THE   SS   NWS 53 03
      TWENTY-SECOND CENTURY, THE   CHRISTOPHER, JOHN   AC
    RATHER IMPROBABLE HISTORY OF HILIARY KIFFER, THE SS AVS 53 04
      TWENTY-SECOND CENTURY, THE   CHRISTOPHER, JOHN   AC
    RENDEZVOUS   SS   PBY 66 09
      PLAYBOY BOOK OF HORROR AND THE SUPERNATURAL, THE
                                PLAYBOY, EDITORS OF   AN
    RICH AND STRANGE   SS
      TWENTY-SECOND CENTURY, THE   CHRISTOPHER, JOHN   AC
    ROCK-A-BYE   SS
      TWENTY-SECOND CENTURY, THE   CHRISTOPHER, JOHN   AC
    SENTENCE OF DEATH (DEATH SENTENCE)   SS   IMG 53 06
      TWENTY-SECOND CENTURY, THE   CHRISTOPHER, JOHN   AC
    SOCRATES   SS   GAL 51 03
     *BEYOND HUMAN KEN   MERRIL, JUDITH   AN

CHRISTOPHER, JOHN   (CONTINUED)
    INTRODUCTORY PSYCHOLOGY THROUGH SCIENCE FICTION
                                KATZ/WARRICK/&   AN
     *STORIES FOR TOMORROW   SLOANE, WILLIAM   AN
    TIME OF PEACE, A   SS   STN 57 10
      TWENTY-SECOND CENTURY, THE   CHRISTOPHER, JOHN   AC
    TREE, THE   SS   NWS 51 FL
      TWENTY-SECOND CENTURY, THE   CHRISTOPHER, JOHN   AC
    WEAPON   SS   NEW 54 AC
      BEST SF 6   CRISPIN, EDMUND   AN
      TWENTY-SECOND CENTURY, THE   CHRISTOPHER, JOHN   AC
    $64 QUESTION, THE   SS   NEW 54 AC
      TWENTY-SECOND CENTURY, THE   CHRISTOPHER, JOHN   AC

CHURCHILL, JOYCE   PSEUD. FOR M. JOHN HARRISON
    MACHINE IN SHAFT TEN, THE   SS   NWQ 72 03
      NEW WORLDS QUARTERLY NO. 3   MOORCOCK, MICHAEL   OA

CHURCHILL, WINSTON
    APOTHEM   MS
      MATHEMATICAL MAGPIE, THE   FADIMAN, CLIFTON   AN

CIARDI, JOHN   ALSO AS   JOHN ANTHONY
    LOVE LETTERS FROM MARS   PM   FSF 65 01
      BEST FROM FANTASY AND SCIENCE FICTION: 15
                                FERMAN, EDWARD L.   AN
    MAGUS, A   PM   SRV 65 12
      HOLDING YOUR EIGHT HANDS   LUCIE-SMITH, EDWARD   AN
      11TH ANNUAL OF THE YEAR'S BEST S-F, THE
                                MERRIL, JUDITH   AN

CLARESON, THOMAS D.
    SPECTRUM OF WORLDS, A   AN H DBL 72
      FOREWORD TO "THE SENTINEL"   IN
      MIRROR OF INFINITY, THE   SILVERBERG, ROBERT   AN
    INTRODUCTION: A SPECTRUM OF WORLDS   IN
      SPECTRUM OF WORLDS, A   CLARESON, THOMAS D.   AN
    SCIENCE FICTION AND LITERARY TRADITION   MS
      NEBULA AWARD STORIES   NO. 6   SIMAK, CLIFFORD D.   AN

CLARK, CURT
    NACKLES   SS   FSF 64 01
      NEW WORLDS OF FANTASY   CARR, TERRY   AN

CLARK, EVERT
    SCIENTIST SAYS ICECAP ON VENUS WOULD MAKE LIFE POSSIBLE
                                             AR   NYT 68 03
      FAREWELL FANTASTIC VENUS   ALDISS & HARRISON   AN

CLARK, JOHN D.
    PETRIFIED PLANET, THE   OA H TWN 52
      INFORMAL BIOGRAPHY OF CONAN THE CIMMERIAN, AN   AR C
      COMING OF CONAN, THE   HOWARD, ROBERT E.   AC
    INTRODUCTION   IN
      PETRIFIED PLANET, THE   CLARK, JOHN D.   OA
    MINUS PLANET   NV   ASF 37 04
      BEFORE THE GOLDEN AGE   ASIMOV, ISAAC   AN

CLARK, WALTER VAN TILBERG
    GHOST OF AN APPREHENSION, THE   AR   PSP 49 SU
      SPECULATIONS   SANDERS, THOMAS E.   AN
    PORTABLE PHONOGRAPH, THE   SS   41
      ADVENTURES IN TOMORROW   CROSSEN, KENDELL F.   AN
      ANOTHER TOMORROW   HOLLISTER, BERNARD C   AN
      ARMCHAIR SCIENCE READER, THE   GORDON, I. & SORKIN AN
      SPECULATIONS   SANDERS, THOMAS E.   AN
      TIMELESS STORIES FOR TODAY AND TOMORROW
                                BRADBURY, RAY   AN
      TOMORROW AND TOMORROW   KNIGHT, DAMON   AN
      TRANSFORMATIONS II   ROSELLE, DANIEL   AN

CLARKE, ARTHUR C.
    ACROSS THE SEA OF STARS   AC H HBW 59
    ARTHUR C. CLARKE OMNIBUS, AN   AC H SID 65
    ARTHUR C. CLARKE SECOND OMNIBUS, AN   AC H SID 68
    BEST OF ARTHUR C. CLARKE: 1937-1971, THE AC H SID 73
    EXPEDITION TO EARTH   AC   BAL 53 12
      ALSO IN "AN ARTHUR C. CLARKE OMNIBUS"
    FROM THE OCEAN, FROM THE STARS   AC H HBW 61
    LION OF COMARRE AND AGAINST THE FALL OF NIGHT AC H HBW 68
    NINE BILLION NAMES OF GOD, THE   AC H HBW 67
    OF TIME AND STARS   AC H GOL 72
    OTHER SIDE OF THE SKY, THE   AC H HBW 58
      ALSO IN "FROM THE OCEAN, FROM THE STARS"
    PRELUDE TO MARS   AC H HBW 65
    REACH FOR TOMORROW   AC   BAL 56 03
    TALES FROM THE WHITE HART   AC   BAL 57
    TALES OF TEN WORLDS   AC H HBW 62
    TIME PROBE: THE SCIENCES IN SF.   AN H DCT 66
    WIND FROM THE SUN, THE   AC H HBJ 72
    AGAINST THE FALL OF NIGHT   NO   STS 48 11
      LION OF COMARRE AND AGAINST THE FALL OF NIGHT
                                CLARKE, ARTHUR C.   AC
    ALL THAT GLITTERS (VENTURE TO THE MOON)   SS   FSF 57 01
      OTHER SIDE OF THE SKY, THE   CLARKE, ARTHUR C.   AC
    ALL THE TIME IN THE WORLD   SS   STS 52 07
      OF TIME AND STARS   CLARKE, ARTHUR C.   AC
      OTHER SIDE OF THE SKY, THE   CLARKE, ARTHUR C.   AC
      PRIZE SCIENCE FICTION   WOLLHEIM, DONALD A.   AN
      TALES OF TIME AND SPACE   OLNEY, ROSS R.   AN
    APE ABOUT THE HOUSE, AN   SS   DUD 62
      OF TIME AND STARS   CLARKE, ARTHUR C.   AC
      TALES OF TEN WORLDS   CLARKE, ARTHUR C.   AC
    ARMAMENTS RACE   SS   ADV 54 04
      ACROSS THE SEA OF STARS   CLARKE, ARTHUR C.   AC
      TALES FROM THE WHITE HART CLARKE, ARTHUR C.   AC

CLARKE, ARTHUR C.   (CONTINUED)
  AT THE END OF THE ORBIT   NV   IFS 61 11
    EXPERT DREAMERS, THE   POHL, FREDERIK   AN
  AWAKENING, THE   SS   ZEN 42 02
    ABC OF SCIENCE FICTION, AN   BOARDMAN, TOM JR.   AN
    BEST OF ARTHUR C. CLARKE: 1937-1971, THE
                                      CLARKE, ARTHUR C.   AC
    ENDS OF TIME, THE   SILVERBERG, ROBERT   AN
    PRELUDE TO MARS   CLARKE, ARTHUR C.   AC
    REACH FOR TOMORROW   CLARKE, ARTHUR C.   AC
  BEFORE EDEN   SS   AMZ 61 06
    ALL ABOUT VENUS   ALDISS, BRIAN W.   AN
    DOORWAY INTO TIME   MOSKOWITZ, SAM   AN
    FAREWELL FANTASTIC VENUS   ALDISS & HARRISON   AN
    MODERN MASTERPIECES OF SCIENCE FICTION MOSKOWITZ, SAM   AN
    NINE BILLION NAMES OF GOD, THE   CLARKE, ARTHUR C.   AC
    STARLIT CORRIDOR, THE   MANSFIELD, ROGER   AN
    TALES OF TEN WORLDS   CLARKE, ARTHUR C.   AC
    TOMORROW'S WORLDS   SILVERBERG, ROBERT   AN
    YET MORE PENGUIN SCIENCE FICTION ALDISS, BRIAN W.   AN
    3000 YEARS OF FANTASY AND SCIENCE FICTION
                                      DE CAMP, L. S.&C.   AN
  BIBLIOGRAPHICAL NOTE   IN
    OTHER SIDE OF THE SKY, THE   CLARKE, ARTHUR C.   AC
  BIG GAME HUNT   SS   54
    PRELUDE TO MARS   CLARKE, ARTHUR C.   AC
    TALES FROM THE WHITE HART   CLARKE, ARTHUR C.   AC
  BREAKING STRAIN (THIRTY SECONDS - THIRTY DAYS) NV   TWS 49 12
    ACROSS THE SEA OF STARS   CLARKE, ARTHUR C.   AC
    EXPEDITION TO EARTH   CLARKE, ARTHUR C.   AC
   *NO PLACE LIKE EARTH   CARNELL, JOHN   AN
    OUT OF THIS WORLD 1   WILLIAMS-ELLIS& OWEN AN
  CALL OF THE STARS, THE (THE OTHER SIDE OF THE SKY)
                                                  SS   INF 57 10
    NINE BILLION NAMES OF GOD, THE   CLARKE, ARTHUR C.   AC
    OTHER SIDE OF THE SKY, THE   CLARKE, ARTHUR C.   AC
  CAPTAIN WYXTPTHLL'S FLYING SAUCER (SEE TROUBLE WITH
    THE NATIVES)   TC
  CASE OF THE SNORING HEIR, THE (SEE SLEEPING BEAUTY)
                                                  TC
  CASTAWAY   SS   FSB 47 04
    BEST OF ARTHUR C. CLARKE: 1937-1971, THE
                                      CLARKE, ARTHUR C.   AC
    FUTURE MAKERS, THE   HAINING, PETER   AN
    STRANGE SIGNPOSTS   ELWOOD & MOSKOWITZ   AN
  CHILDHOOD'S END (EXPANDED FROM "GUARDIAN ANGEL") NO NWS 50 WI
    ACROSS THE SEA OF STARS   CLARKE, ARTHUR C.   AC
    ARTHUR C. CLARKE OMNIBUS, AN   CLARKE, ARTHUR C.   AC
  CITY AND THE STARS, THE   NO   HBW 56
    FROM THE OCEAN, FROM THE STARS   CLARKE, ARTHUR C.   AC
  COLD WAR   SS   SAT 57 04
    PRELUDE TO MARS   CLARKE, ARTHUR C.   AC
    TALES FROM THE WHITE HART   CLARKE, ARTHUR C.   AC
  COSMIC CASANOVA   SS   VSF 58 05
    OTHER SIDE OF THE SKY, THE   CLARKE, ARTHUR C.   AC
  CRIME ON MARS (SEE TROUBLE WITH TIME)   TC
  CRITICAL MASS (ORIGINAL VERSION IN LILLIPUT MARCH 1949)
                                                  SS   SPM 57 08
    PRELUDE TO MARS   CLARKE, ARTHUR C.   AC
    TALES FROM THE WHITE HART   CLARKE, ARTHUR C.   AC
  CRUEL SKY, THE   SS
    WIND FROM THE SUN, THE   CLARKE, ARTHUR C.   AC
  CRUSADE   SS   FRS 68
    FARTHEST REACHES, THE   ELDER, JOSEPH   OA
    WIND FROM THE SUN, THE   CLARKE, ARTHUR C.   AC
  CURSE, THE   SS   CSM 53 09
    FROM FRANKENSTEIN TO ANDROMEDA   BROWN, JAMES GOLDIE   AN
    NINE BILLION NAMES OF GOD, THE   CLARKE, ARTHUR C.   AC
    PRELUDE TO MARS   CLARKE, ARTHUR C.   AC
    REACH FOR TOMORROW   CLARKE, ARTHUR C.   AC
  DEATH AND THE SENATOR   NV   ASF 61 05
    BEST OF ARTHUR C. CLARKE: 1937-1971, THE
                                      CLARKE, ARTHUR C.   AC
    NINE BILLION·NAMES OF GOD, THE   CLARKE, ARTHUR C.   AC
    POLITICAL SCIENCE FICTION   GREENBERG& WARRICK   AN
    TALES OF TEN WORLDS   CLARKE, ARTHUR C.   AC
    WORLDS OF WHEN   CONKLIN, GROFF   AN
  DEEP RANGE, THE (ARB 54 04)   NO   STR 54 03
    FROM THE OCEAN, FROM THE STARS   CLARKE, ARTHUR C.   AC
  DEEP RANGE, THE (ARB 54 04)   NV   STR 54 03
    BEYOND TOMORROW   KNIGHT, DAMON   AN
    FROM FRANKENSTEIN TO ANDROMEDA   BROWN, JAMES GOLDIE   AN
    GIANTS UNLEASHED   CONKLIN, GROFF   AN
    STAR OF STARS   POHL, FREDERIK   AN
    STAR SCIENCE FICTION STORIES NO. 3 POHL, FREDERIK   OA
    WHERE DO WE GO FROM HERE?   ASIMOV, ISAAC   AN
    ZOO 2000   YOLEN, JANE   AN
  DEFENESTRATION OF ERMINTRUDE INCH, THE   SS
    TALES FROM THE WHITE HART   CLARKE, ARTHUR C.   AC
  DIAL "F" FOR FRANKENSTEIN   SS   PBY 65 01
    LAST TRAIN TO LIMBO   PLAYBOY, EDITORS OF AN
    PLAYBOY BOOK OF SCIENCE FICTION AND FANTASY, THE
                                      PLAYBOY, EDITORS OF AN
    WIND FROM THE SUN, THE   CLARKE, ARTHUR C.   AC
  DOG STAR (MOONDOG)   SS   GAL 62 04
    NINE BILLION NAMES OF GOD, THE   CLARKE, ARTHUR C.   AC
    SCIENCE FICTION ROLL OF HONOR, THE POHL, FREDERIK   AN
    TALES OF TEN WORLDS   CLARKE, ARTHUR C.   AC
  EARTHLIGHT   NO   TWS 51 08
    ACROSS THE SEA OF STARS   CLARKE, ARTHUR C.   AC
    ARTHUR C. CLARKE SECOND OMNIBUS, AN CLARKE, ARTHUR C. AC
  ENCOUNTER AT DAWN (ENCOUNTER IN THE DAWN)   SS   AMZ 53 07
    ACROSS THE SEA OF STARS   CLARKE, ARTHUR C.   AC
    NINE BILLION NAMES OF GOD, THE   CLARKE, ARTHUR C.   AC
    OF TIME AND STARS   CLARKE, ARTHUR C.   AC

CLARKE, ARTHUR C.   (CONTINUED)
  ENCOUNTER IN THE DAWN (SEE ENCOUNTER AT DAWN AND EXPEDITION
    TO EARTH)   TC
  EXILE OF THE EONS   SS   SSS 50 03
    AWARD SCIENCE FICTION READER   NORTON, ALDEN H.   AN
    EXPEDITION TO EARTH   CLARKE, ARTHUR C.   AC
    FUTURES UNLIMITED   NORTON, ALDEN H.   AN
    PRELUDE TO MARS   CLARKE, ARTHUR C.   AC
  EXPEDITION TO EARTH   AC   BAL 53 12
    ARTHUR C. CLARKE OMNIBUS, AN   CLARKE, ARTHUR C.   AC
  EXPEDITION TO EARTH (ENCOUNTER IN THE DAWN)   SS   AMZ 53 07
    EXPEDITION TO EARTH   CLARKE, ARTHUR C.   AC
  FALL OF MOONDUST, A   NO   GOL 61
    ARTHUR C. CLARKE SECOND OMNIBUS, AN CLARKE, ARTHUR C. AC
  FEATHERED FRIEND (THE OTHER SIDE OF THE SKY)   SS   INF 57 09
    OF TIME AND STARS   CLARKE, ARTHUR C.   AC
    OTHER SIDE OF THE SKY, THE   CLARKE, ARTHUR C.   AC
  FIRES WITHIN, THE   SS   FSB 47 08
    ACROSS THE SEA OF STARS   CLARKE, ARTHUR C.   AC
    HISTORY OF THE SCIENCE FICTION MAGAZINE, THE PART 3 1946-1955
                                      ASHLEY, MICHAEL   AN
    NEW WORLDS FOR OLD   DERLETH, AUGUST   AN
    OF TIME AND STARS   CLARKE, ARTHUR C.   AC
    REACH FOR TOMORROW   CLARKE, ARTHUR C.   AC
    SCIENCE FICTION GALAXY, THE   CONKLIN, GROFF   AN
   *WORLDS OF TOMORROW   DERLETH, AUGUST   AN
  FOOD OF THE GODS, THE   SS   PBY 64 05
    LAST TRAIN TO LIMBO   PLAYBOY, EDITORS OF AN
    WIND FROM THE SUN, THE   CLARKE, ARTHUR C.   AC
  FOREWORD   IN
    AUTHENTIC BOOK OF SPACE   CAMPBELL, H. J.   AN
    OF TIME AND STARS   CLARKE, ARTHUR C.   AC
    PRELUDE TO MARS   CLARKE, ARTHUR C.   AC
    THREE FOR TOMORROW   SILVERBERG, ROBERT   OA
  FORGOTTEN ENEMY, THE   SS   NWS 49 05
    MORE PENGUIN SCIENCE FICTION   ALDISS, BRIAN W.   AN
    OF TIME AND STARS   CLARKE, ARTHUR C.   AC
    PRELUDE TO MARS   CLARKE, ARTHUR C.   AC
    REACH FOR TOMORROW   CLARKE, ARTHUR C.   AC
    SCIENCE FACT/FICTION   FARRELL/GAGE/&   AN
    SF: AUTHORS' CHOICE 4   HARRISON, HARRY   AN
    STARS AND UNDER, THE   CRISPIN, EDMUND   AN
   *STORIES FOR TOMORROW   SLOANE, WILLIAM   AN
  FREEDOM OF SPACE (THE OTHER SIDE OF THE SKY)   SS   INF 57 10
    OTHER SIDE OF THE SKY, THE   CLARKE, ARTHUR C.   AC
  FROM: THE CITY AND THE STARS   EX   HBW 56
    INSIDE INFORMATION   MOWSHOWITZ, ABBE   AN
  GREEN FINGERS (VENTURE TO THE MOON)   SS   FSF 57 01
    DAYS AFTER TOMORROW, THE   SANTESSON, HANS S.   AN
    OF TIME AND STARS   CLARKE, ARTHUR C.   AC
    OTHER SIDE OF THE SKY, THE   CLARKE, ARTHUR C.   AC
  GUARDIAN ANGEL (SEE CHILDHOOD'S END, REWRITTEN BY JAMES BLISH)
                                      TC   FFM 50 04
  HATE (AT THE END OF THE ORBIT)   NV   IFS 61 11
    BEST OF ARTHUR C. CLARKE: 1937-1971, THE
                                      CLARKE, ARTHUR C.   AC
    TALES OF TEN WORLDS   CLARKE, ARTHUR C.   AC
  HAUNTED SPACESUIT, THE (WHO'S THERE?)   SS   NWS 58 11
    FIFTY SHORT SCIENCE FICTION TALES ASIMOV & CONKLIN   AN
  HERBERT GEORGE MORLEY ROBERTS WELLS, ESQ.   ED   IFS 67 12
    WIND FROM THE SUN, THE   CLARKE, ARTHUR C.   AC
  HIDE AND SEEK   SS   ASF 49 09
    ACROSS THE SEA OF STARS   CLARKE, ARTHUR C.   AC
    ASTOUNDING-ANALOG READER, THE VOLUME TWO
                                      HARRISON & ALDISS   AN
    BEST OF ARTHUR C. CLARKE: 1937-1971, THE
                                      CLARKE, ARTHUR C.   AC
    EXPEDITION TO EARTH   CLARKE, ARTHUR C.   AC
    GATEWAY TO TOMORROW   CARNELL, JOHN   AN
    NINE BILLION NAMES OF GOD, THE   CLARKE, ARTHUR C.   AC
    OF TIME AND STARS   CLARKE, ARTHUR C.   AC
    SPACE, SPACE, SPACE   SLOANE, WILLIAM   AN
    TALES OF SCIENCE FICTION   BALL, BRIAN N.   AN
  HISTORY LESSON   SS   STS 49 05
    ACROSS THE SEA OF STARS   CLARKE, ARTHUR C.   AC
    ANOTHER TOMORROW   HOLLISTER, BERNARD C AN
    BEST OF ARTHUR C. CLARKE: 1937-1971, THE
                                      CLARKE, ARTHUR C.   AC
    BEYOND BELIEF   HURLEY, RICHARD J.   AN
    EARTH IN TRANSIT   SCHWARTZ, SHEILA   AN
    EXPEDITION TO EARTH   CLARKE, ARTHUR C.   AC
    GREAT SCIENCE FICTION STORIES   SMITH, CORDELIA T.   AN
    GREAT SCIENCE-FICTION   LICATA, TONY   AN
    OMNIBUS OF SCIENCE FICTION   CONKLIN, GROFF   AN
    SCIENCE FICTION OMNIBUS   CONKLIN, GROFF   AN
    SCIENCE FICTION: THE FUTURE   ALLEN, DICK   AN
    TRANSFORMATIONS II   ROSELLE, DANIEL   AN
  HOTTEST PIECE OF REAL ESTATE IN THE SOLAR SYSTEM, THE
    (SEE SUMMERTIME ON ICARUS)   TC
  I REMEMBER BABYLON   SS   PBY 60 05
    FIEND, THE   PLAYBOY, EDITORS OF AN
    NINE BILLION NAMES OF GOD, THE   CLARKE, ARTHUR C.   AC
    PLAYBOY BOOK OF SCIENCE FICTION AND FANTASY, THE
                                      PLAYBOY, EDITORS OF AN
    TALES OF TEN WORLDS   CLARKE, ARTHUR C.   AC
    6TH ANNUAL OF THE YEAR'S BEST S-F, THE MERRIL, JUDITH   AN
  IF I FORGET THEE, OH EARTH...   SS   FUT 51 09
    ACROSS THE SEA OF STARS   CLARKE, ARTHUR C.   AC
    EVIL EARTHS   ALDISS, BRIAN W.   AN
    EXPEDITION TO EARTH   CLARKE, ARTHUR C.   AC
    NINE BILLION NAMES OF GOD, THE   CLARKE, ARTHUR C.   AC
    OF TIME AND STARS   CLARKE, ARTHUR C.   AC
    SPECTRUM OF WORLDS, A   CLARESON, THOMAS D.   AN
  INHERITANCE (NWS 47 03)   SS   ASF 48 09
    ACROSS THE SEA OF STARS   CLARKE, ARTHUR C.   AC
    EXPEDITION TO EARTH   CLARKE, ARTHUR C.   AC

CLARKE, ARTHUR C.

CLARKE, ARTHUR C.   (CONTINUED)
INSIDE THE COMET (ALSO AS INTO THE COMET)   SS   FSF 60 10
  OUT OF THIS WORLD 4   WILLIAMS-ELLIS& OWEN AN
INTO THE COMET (INSIDE THE COMET)   SS   FSF 60 10
  BEST OF ARTHUR C. CLARKE: 1937-1971, THE
                                 CLARKE, ARTHUR C.   AC
  OF TIME AND STARS   CLARKE, ARTHUR C.   AC
  TALES OF TEN WORLDS   CLARKE, ARTHUR C.   AC
INTRODUCTION   IN
  COMPLETE VENUS EQUILATERAL, THE SMITH, GEORGE O.   AC
  FROM THE OCEAN, FROM THE STARS CLARKE, ARTHUR C.   AC
  NINE BILLION NAMES OF GOD, THE CLARKE, ARTHUR C.   AC
JUPITER FIVE   NV   IFS 53 05
  ACROSS THE SEA OF STARS   CLARKE, ARTHUR C.   AC
  EXPLORERS OF SPACE   SILVERBERG, ROBERT   AN
  REACH FOR TOMORROW   CLARKE, ARTHUR C.   AC
LAST COMMAND, THE   SS   BIZ 65 11
  WIND FROM THE SUN, THE   CLARKE, ARTHUR C.   AC
LET THERE BE LIGHT   SS   PBY 58 02
  TALES OF TEN WORLDS   CLARKE, ARTHUR C.   AC
  TRANSIT OF EARTH   PLAYBOY, EDITORS OF AN
LIGHT OF DARKNESS, THE   SS
  WIND FROM THE SUN, THE   CLARKE, ARTHUR C.   AC
LION OF COMARRE   NV   TWS 49 08
  LION OF COMARRE AND AGAINST THE FALL OF NIGHT
                                 CLARKE, ARTHUR C.   AC
LONGEST SCIENCE-FICTION STORY EVER TOLD, THE   SS
  WIND FROM THE SUN, THE   CLARKE, ARTHUR C.   AC
LOOPHOLE   SS   ASF 46 04
  EXPEDITION TO EARTH   CLARKE, ARTHUR C.   AC
  FIRST FLIGHT   KNIGHT, DAMON   AN
  MARS, WE LOVE YOU   HIPOLITO & MCNELLY   AN
  *TREASURY OF SCIENCE FICTION, A CONKLIN, GROFF   AN
LOVE THAT UNIVERSE   SS
  WIND FROM THE SUN, THE   CLARKE, ARTHUR C.   AC
MAELSTROM II   SS   PBY 65 04
  DEAD ASTRONAUT, 10 STORIES OF SPACE FLIGHT, THE
                                 PLAYBOY, EDITORS OF AN
  THEMES IN SCIENCE FICTION   KELLEY, LEO P.   AN
  WIND FROM THE SUN, THE   CLARKE, ARTHUR C.   AC
  11TH ANNUAL OF THE YEAR'S BEST S-F, THE
                                 MERRIL, JUDITH   AN
MAN WHO PLOUGHED THE SEA, THE   SS   SAT 57 06
  HUMAN ZERO, THE   MOSKOWITZ & ELWOOD   AN
  PRELUDE TO MARS   CLARKE, ARTHUR C.   AC
  TALES FROM THE WHITE HART   CLARKE, ARTHUR C.   AC
MEETING WITH MEDUSA, A   NA   PBY 71 12
  BEST OF ARTHUR C. CLARKE: 1937-1971, THE
                                 CLARKE, ARTHUR C.   AC
  BEST SCIENCE FICTION OF THE YEAR, THE CARR, TERRY   AN
  BEST SF: 1971   HARRISON & ALDISS   AN
  JUPITER   POHL, C. & F.   AN
  NEBULA AWARD STORIES 8   ASIMOV, ISAAC   AN
  WIND FROM THE SUN, THE   CLARKE, ARTHUR C.   AC
MOONDOG (SEE DOG STAR)   TC
MOVING SPIRIT   SS
  PRELUDE TO MARS   CLARKE, ARTHUR C.   AC
  TALES FROM THE WHITE HART   CLARKE, ARTHUR C.   AC
NEUTRON TIDE, THE   SS   GAL 70 05
  WIND FROM THE SUN, THE   CLARKE, ARTHUR C.   AC
NEXT TENANTS, THE   SS   SAT 57 02
  ACROSS THE SEA OF STARS   CLARKE, ARTHUR C.   AC
  TALES FROM THE WHITE HART   CLARKE, ARTHUR C.   AC
NINE BILLION NAMES OF GOD, THE   SS   STR 53 01
  APEMAN, SPACEMAN   STOVER & HARRISON   AN
  ASPECTS OF SCIENCE FICTION   DOHERTY, G. D.   AN
  BEST SF   CRISPIN, EDMUND   AN
  IN DREAMS AWAKE   FIEDLER, LESLIE A.   AN
  INSIDE INFORMATION   MOWSHOWITZ, ABBE   AN
  MATHEMATICAL MAGPIE, THE   FADIMAN, CLIFTON   AN
  NEW AWARENESS, THE   WARRICK & GREENBERG AN
  NINE BILLION NAMES OF GOD, THE CLARKE, ARTHUR C.   AC
  OF TIME AND STARS   CLARKE, ARTHUR C.   AC
  ONE HUNDRED YEARS OF SCIENCE FICTION KNIGHT, DAMON AN
  OTHER SIDE OF THE SKY, THE   CLARKE, ARTHUR C.   AC
  OTHER WORLDS, OTHER GODS   MOHS, MAYO   AN
  OUT OF THIS WORLD 6   WILLIAMS-ELLIS& OWEN AN
  SCIENCE FICTION HALL OF FAME VOLUME 1 SILVERBERG, ROBERT AN
  STAR SCIENCE FICTION STORIES   POHL, FREDERIK   OA
  *STORIES FOR TOMORROW   SLOANE, WILLIAM   AN
NO MORNING AFTER   SS   FSF 56 07
  NINE BILLION NAMES OF GOD, THE CLARKE, ARTHUR C.   AC
  OF TIME AND STARS   CLARKE, ARTHUR C.   AC
  OTHER SIDE OF THE SKY, THE   CLARKE, ARTHUR C.   AC
  TALES OF TERROR FROM OUTER SPACE CHETWYND-HAYES, R. AN
  *TIME TO COME   DERLETH, AUGUST   OA
OBSOLESCENCE OF MAN, THE   AR   PBY 61
  LOOKING AHEAD   ALLEN, D. & L.   AN
OTHER SIDE OF THE SKY, THE   GR   INF 57 09
  FROM THE OCEAN, FROM THE STARS CLARKE, ARTHUR C.   AC
  TREASURY OF GREAT SCIENCE FICTION, A VOL.2
                                 BOUCHER, ANTHONY   AN
OTHER TIGER, THE   SS   FUN 53 06
  PORTALS OF TOMORROW   DERLETH, AUGUST   AN
OUT OF THE CRADLE, ENDLESSLY ORBITING   SS   DUD 59 03
  GREAT SCIENCE FICTION ABOUT DOCTORS CONKLIN, G&FABRICANT AN
  TALES OF TEN WORLDS   CLARKE, ARTHUR C.   AC
OUT OF THE SUN   SS   IFS 58 02
  EARTHMEN AND STRANGERS   SILVERBERG, ROBERT   AN
  NINE BILLION NAMES OF GOD, THE CLARKE, ARTHUR C.   AC
  OTHER SIDE OF THE SKY, THE   CLARKE, ARTHUR C.   AC
PACIFIST, THE   SS   FUN 56 10
  ACROSS THE SEA OF STARS   CLARKE, ARTHUR C.   AC
  FANTASTIC UNIVERSE OMNIBUS, THE SANTESSON, HANS S. AN
  MATHEMATICAL MAGPIE, THE   FADIMAN, CLIFTON   AN
  TALES FROM THE WHITE HART   CLARKE, ARTHUR C.   AC

CLARKE, ARTHUR C.

CLARKE, ARTHUR C.   (CONTINUED)
PARASITE, THE   SS   AVS 53 04
  PRELUDE TO MARS   CLARKE, ARTHUR C.   AC
  REACH FOR TOMORROW   CLARKE, ARTHUR C.   AC
PASSER-BY (THE OTHER SIDE OF THE SKY)   SS   INF 57 10
  OTHER SIDE OF THE SKY, THE   CLARKE, ARTHUR C.   AC
PATENT PENDING   SS   54
  NINE BILLION NAMES OF GOD, THE CLARKE, ARTHUR C.   AC
  TALES FROM THE WHITE HART   CLARKE, ARTHUR C.   AC
  TOMORROW, INC.   GREENBERG& OLANDER   AN
  VINTAGE ANTHOLOGY OF SCIENCE FANTASY, THE
                                 CERF, CHRISTOPHER   AN
PLAYBACK   SS   PBY 66 12
  WIND FROM THE SUN, THE   CLARKE, ARTHUR C.   AC
POSSESSED, THE   SS   DSF 53 03
  GALACTIC EMPIRES VOLUME ONE   ALDISS, BRIAN W.   AN
  NINE BILLION NAMES OF GOD, THE CLARKE, ARTHUR C.   AC
  NOVELETS OF SCIENCE FICTION   HOWARD, IVAN   AN
  PRELUDE TO MARS   CLARKE, ARTHUR C.   AC
  REACH FOR TOMORROW   CLARKE, ARTHUR C.   AC
POSSIBLE, THAT'S ALL!   AR   FSF 68 10
  FASTER THAN LIGHT   DANN & ZEBROWSKI   OA
PREFACE   IN
  REACH FOR TOMORROW   CLARKE, ARTHUR C.   AC
  TALES FROM THE WHITE HART   CLARKE, ARTHUR C.   AC
  WIND FROM THE SUN, THE   CLARKE, ARTHUR C.   AC
PRELUDE TO SPACE   EX   GAN 51 03
  SCIENCE IN FICTION   BAYLISS, A. E. & J.C. AN
PRELUDE TO SPACE   NO   GAN 51 03
  ARTHUR C. CLARKE OMNIBUS, AN   CLARKE, ARTHUR C.   AC
  PRELUDE TO MARS   CLARKE, ARTHUR C.   AC
PUBLICITY CAMPAIGN   SS   SAT 56 10
  OTHER SIDE OF THE SKY, THE   CLARKE, ARTHUR C.   AC
QUESTION OF RESIDENCE, A (VENTURE TO THE MOON)   SS   FSF 57 02
  OTHER SIDE OF THE SKY, THE   CLARKE, ARTHUR C.   AC
REFUGEE (CONTEST STORY, ORIGINAL TITLE THIS EARTH OF MAJESTY)
                                                 SS   FSF 55 07
  BEST OF ARTHUR C. CLARKE: 1937-1971, THE
                                 CLARKE, ARTHUR C.   AC
  OTHER SIDE OF THE SKY, THE   CLARKE, ARTHUR C.   AC
  SCIENCE FICTION THROUGH THE AGES 2 EVANS, I. O.   AN
RELUCTANT ORCHID, THE   SS   SAT 56 12
  ACROSS THE SEA OF STARS   CLARKE, ARTHUR C.   AC
  NINE BILLION NAMES OF GOD, THE CLARKE, ARTHUR C.   AC
  OF TIME AND STARS   CLARKE, ARTHUR C.   AC
  SCIENCE FACT/FICTION   FARRELL/GAGE/&   AN
  TALES FROM THE WHITE HART   CLARKE, ARTHUR C.   AC
RENDEZVOUS WITH RAMA (CHAPTER 1)   EX   NWR 73 22
  NEW WRITINGS IN SF. 22   BULMER, KENNETH   OA
RESCUE PARTY   NV   ASF 46 05
  ACROSS THE SEA OF STARS   CLARKE, ARTHUR C.   AC
  ALPHA 3   SILVERBERG, ROBERT   AN
  BEYOND THE END OF TIME   POHL, FREDERIK   AN
  END OF THE WORLD, THE   WOLLHEIM, DONALD A. AN
  NINE BILLION NAMES OF GOD, THE CLARKE, ARTHUR C.   AC
  REACH FOR TOMORROW   CLARKE, ARTHUR C.   AC
  TOMORROW, AND TOMORROW, AND TOMORROW...
                                 HEINTZ/HERBERT/JOOS/ AN
  *TREASURY OF SCIENCE FICTION, A CONKLIN, GROFF   AN
RETREAT FROM EARTH   SS   AMS 38 03
  BEST OF ARTHUR C. CLARKE: 1937-1971, THE
                                 CLARKE, ARTHUR C.   AC
REUNION   SS   INY 71 02
  INFINITY 2   HOSKINS, ROBERT   OA
  WIND FROM THE SUN, THE   CLARKE, ARTHUR C.   AC
REVERSED MAN, THE (SEE TECHNICAL ERROR)   TC   TWS 50 06
ROAD TO THE SEA, THE (SEEKER OF THE SPHINX)   NV   TCS 51 SP
  TALES OF TEN WORLDS   CLARKE, ARTHUR C.   AC
ROBIN HOOD, F.R.S. (VENTURE TO THE MOON)   SS   FSF 56 12
  OF TIME AND STARS   CLARKE, ARTHUR C.   AC
  OTHER SIDE OF THE SKY, THE   CLARKE, ARTHUR C.   AC
SANDS OF MARS, THE   NO   SID 51
  ARTHUR C. CLARKE SECOND OMNIBUS, AN CLARKE, ARTHUR C. AC
  PRELUDE TO MARS   CLARKE, ARTHUR C.   AC
SATURN RISING   SS   FSF 61 03
  TALES OF TEN WORLDS   CLARKE, ARTHUR C.   AC
SCIENCE AND SCIENCE FICTION   IN
  TIME PROBE: THE SCIENCES IN SF. CLARKE, ARTHUR C.   AN
SECOND DAWN   NV   SFQ 51 08
  BEST OF ARTHUR C. CLARKE: 1937-1971, THE
                                 CLARKE, ARTHUR C.   AC
  EXPEDITION TO EARTH   CLARKE, ARTHUR C.   AC
  PRELUDE TO MARS   CLARKE, ARTHUR C.   AC
SECRET, THE   SS
  WIND FROM THE SUN, THE   CLARKE, ARTHUR C.   AC
SECURITY CHECK   SS   FSF 57 06
  FUTURE TENSE   CURTIS, RICHARD   AN
  OF TIME AND STARS   CLARKE, ARTHUR C.   AC
  OTHER SIDE OF THE SKY, THE   CLARKE, ARTHUR C.   AC
SEEKER OF THE SPHINX (ALSO AS THE ROAD TO THE SEA)
                                                 NV   TCS 51 SP
YEAR'S BEST SCIENCE FICTION NOVELS: 1952
                                 BLEILER & DITKY   AN
SENTINEL OF ETERNITY (SEE THE SENTINEL)   TC
SENTINEL, THE (SENTINEL OF ETERNITY)   SS   TSF 51 SP
  ACROSS THE SEA OF STARS   CLARKE, ARTHUR C.   AC
  AS TOMORROW BECOMES TODAY   SULLIVAN, CHARLES W. AN
  BEST OF ARTHUR C. CLARKE: 1937-1971, THE
                                 CLARKE, ARTHUR C.   AC
  EXPEDITION TO EARTH   CLARKE, ARTHUR C.   AC
  MIRROR OF INFINITY, THE   SILVERBERG, ROBERT   AN
  NINE BILLION NAMES OF GOD, THE CLARKE, ARTHUR C.   AC
  OF TIME AND STARS   CLARKE, ARTHUR C.   AC
  PAST, PRESENT, AND FUTURE PERFECT WOLFE, J&FITZ GERALD AN
  SCIENCE FICTION   BRODKIN & PEARSON   AN
  SPACE ODYSSEYS   ALDISS, BRIAN W.   AN

CLARKE, ARTHUR C.   (CONTINUED)
  SPECTRUM 3   AMIS & CONQUEST   AN
  TOMORROW, AND TOMORROW, AND TOMORROW...
                                       HEINTZ/HERBERT/JOOS/ AN
  WORLDS TO COME   KNIGHT, DAMON   AN
SHINING ONES, THE   SS   PBY 64 08
  WIND FROM THE SUN, THE   CLARKE, ARTHUR C.   AC
  10TH ANNUAL OF THE YEAR'S BEST S-F, THE
                                       MERRIL, JUDITH   AN
SILENCE, PLEASE   SS   SCF 50 WI
  ACROSS THE SEA OF STARS   CLARKE, ARTHUR C.   AC
  TALES FROM THE WHITE HART   CLARKE, ARTHUR C.   AC
  13 GREAT STORIES OF SCIENCE FICTION CONKLIN, GROFF   AN
SLEEPING BEAUTY (THE CASE OF THE SNORING HEIR) SS INF 57 04
  TALES FROM THE WHITE HART   CLARKE, ARTHUR C.   AC
SLIGHT CASE OF SUNSTROKE, A (STROKE OF THE SUN) SS GAL 58 09
  TALES OF TEN WORLDS   CLARKE, ARTHUR C.   AC
SOCIAL CONSEQUENCES OF COMMUNICATIONS SATELLITES, THE
                                       AR   65
  SURVIVAL PRINTOUT   TOTAL EFFECT   AN
SONGS OF DISTANT EARTH, THE   NV   IFS 58 06
  OTHER SIDE OF THE SKY, THE   CLARKE, ARTHUR C.   AC
SPECIAL DELIVERY (THE OTHER SIDE OF THE SKY)   SS   INF 57 09
  OTHER SIDE OF THE SKY, THE   CLARKE, ARTHUR C.   AC
STAR, THE   SS   INF 55 11
  BEST OF ARTHUR C. CLARKE: 1937-1971, THE
                                       CLARKE, ARTHUR C.   AC
  BEST SF 5   CRISPIN, EDMUND   AN
  CENTURY OF SCIENCE FICTION, A   KNIGHT, DAMON   AN
  DECADE THE 1950S   ALDISS & HARRISON   AN
  HUGO WINNERS, THE (VOLUME 1)   ASIMOV, ISAAC   AN
  INFINITY 1   HOSKINS, ROBERT   OA
  MODERN SCIENCE FICTION   SPINRAD, NORMAN   AN
  NINE BILLION NAMES OF GOD, THE   CLARKE, ARTHUR C.   AC
  OTHER SIDE OF THE SKY, THE   CLARKE, ARTHUR C.   AC
  SCIENCE FICTION   BURTON, S. H.   AN
  SCIENCE FICTION FOR PEOPLE WHO HATE SCIENCE FICTION
                                       CARR, TERRY   AN
  SECOND ORBIT   DOHERTY, G. D.   AN
  SPECULATIONS   SANDERS, THOMAS E.   AN
STARTING LINE, THE (VENTURE TO THE MOON) SS   FSF 56 12
  OTHER SIDE OF THE SKY, THE   CLARKE, ARTHUR C.   AC
STROKE OF THE SUN (SEE A SLIGHT CASE OF SUNSTROKE)
                                       TC
SUMMERTIME ON ICARUS (THE HOTTEST PIECE OF REAL ESTATE IN THE
  SOLAR SYSTEM)   SS   VOG 60 06
  BEST OF ARTHUR C. CLARKE: 1937-1971, THE
                                       CLARKE, ARTHUR C.   AC
  GREAT SCIENCE FICTION BY SCIENTISTS CONKLIN, GROFF   AN
  NINE BILLION NAMES OF GOD, THE   CLARKE, ARTHUR C.   AC
  SCIENCE FICTION   BRODKIN & PEARSON   AN
  TALES OF TEN WORLDS   CLARKE, ARTHUR C.   AC
  UNTRAVELLED WORLDS   BARTER & WILSON   AN
SUNJAMMER (ALSO AS THE WIND FROM THE SUN) SS   BLF 64
  ANDROIDS, TIME MACHINES AND BLUE GIRAFFES
                                       ELWOOD & GHIDALIA   AN
  BEST OF ARTHUR C. CLARKE: 1937-1971, THE
                                       CLARKE, ARTHUR C.   AC
  INFINITE ARENA, THE   CARR, TERRY   AN
  STORIES FROM SCIENCE FICTION   DOHERTY, G. D.   AN
  VISIONS OF TOMORROW   ELWOOD, ROGER   AN
  WILDERNESS OF STARS, A   NOLAN, WILLIAM F.   AN
  WORLD'S BEST SCIENCE FICTION: 1966   WOLLHEIM & CARR   AN
  WORLDS OF WONDER   HARRISON, HARRY   AN
SUPERIORITY   SS   FSF 51 08
  ACROSS THE SEA OF STARS   CLARKE, ARTHUR C.   AC
  EXPEDITION TO EARTH   CLARKE, ARTHUR C.   AC
  FANTASIA MATHEMATICA   FADIMAN, CLIFTON   AN
  NINE BILLION NAMES OF GOD, THE   CLARKE, ARTHUR C.   AC
  POLITICAL SCIENCE FICTION   GREENBERG& WARRICK   AN
  *WORLDS OF TOMORROW   DERLETH, AUGUST   AN
TAKE A DEEP BREATH (THE OTHER SIDE OF THE SKY) SS INF 57 09
  OTHER SIDE OF THE SKY, THE   CLARKE, ARTHUR C.   AC
  TIME PROBE: THE SCIENCES IN SF.   CLARKE, ARTHUR C.   AC
TECHNICAL ERROR (THE REVERSED MAN)   SS   FSB 46 12
  ACROSS THE SEA OF STARS   CLARKE, ARTHUR C.   AC
  REACH FOR TOMORROW   CLARKE, ARTHUR C.   AC
THIRTY SECONDS- THIRTY DAYS (ALSO AS BREAKING STRAIN)
                                       NV   TWS 49 12
  BEST FROM STARTLING STORIES, THE   MINES, SAMUEL   AN
THIS EARTH OF MAJESTY (CONTEST STORY WINNING TITLE REFUGEE)
                                       SS   FSF 55 07
  BEST FROM FANTASY AND SCIENCE FICTION: 5
                                       BOUCHER, ANTHONY   AN
  RULERS OF MEN   SANTESSON, HANS S.   AN
TIME'S ARROW   SS   SCF 50 SU
  ACROSS THE SEA OF STARS   CLARKE, ARTHUR C.   AC
  REACH FOR TOMORROW   CLARKE, ARTHUR C.   AC
TRANSCIENCE   SS   STS 49 07
  LOOKING FORWARD   LESSER, MILTON   AN
  NINE BILLION NAMES OF GOD, THE   CLARKE, ARTHUR C.   AC
  OTHER SIDE OF THE SKY, THE   CLARKE, ARTHUR C.   AC
TRANSIT OF EARTH   SS   PBY 71 01
  TRANSIT OF EARTH   PLAYBOY, EDITORS OF   AN
  WIND FROM THE SUN, THE   CLARKE, ARTHUR C.   AC
  1972 ANNUAL WORLD'S BEST SF, THE   WOLLHEIM, DONALD A.   AN
TRANSITION- FROM FANTASY TO SCIENCE   AR   57
  SF:58, THE YEAR'S GREATEST SCIENCE FICTION AND FANTASY
                                       MERRIL, JUDITH   AN
TRAVEL BY WIRE   SS   AMS 37 12
  BEST OF ARTHUR C. CLARKE: 1937-1971, THE
                                       CLARKE, ARTHUR C.   AC
TROUBLE WITH THE NATIVES (CAPTAIN WYXTPTHLL'S FLYING SAUCER)
                                       SS   MAR 51 05
  OF TIME AND STARS   CLARKE, ARTHUR C.   AC
  PRELUDE TO MARS   CLARKE, ARTHUR C.   AC

CLARKE, ARTHUR C.   (CONTINUED)
  REACH FOR TOMORROW   CLARKE, ARTHUR C.   AC
TROUBLE WITH TIME (CRIME ON MARS, EQM 60 07)   SS   FSF 61 06
  INTRODUCING SCIENCE FICTION   ALDISS, BRIAN W.   AN
  NINE BILLION NAMES OF GOD, THE   CLARKE, ARTHUR C.   AC
  TALES OF TEN WORLDS   CLARKE, ARTHUR C.   AC
ULTIMATE MELODY, THE   SS   IFS 57 02
  ALIEN EARTH AND OTHER STORIES   ELWOOD & MOSKOWITZ   AN
  PRELUDE TO MARS   CLARKE, ARTHUR C.   AC
  TALES FROM THE WHITE HART   CLARKE, ARTHUR C.   AC
VENTURE TO THE MOON   GR   FSF 56 12
  BEST FROM FANTASY AND SCIENCE FICTION: 7
                                       BOUCHER, ANTHONY   AN
  BEST OF ARTHUR C. CLARKE: 1937-1971, THE
                                       CLARKE, ARTHUR C.   AC
  FIRST FLIGHTS TO THE MOON   CLEMENT, HAL   AN
WALK IN THE DARK, A   SS   TWS 50 08
  GREAT STORIES OF SPACE TRAVEL   CONKLIN, GROFF   AN
  NINE BILLION NAMES OF GOD, THE   CLARKE, ARTHUR C.   AC
  *POSSIBLE WORLDS OF SCIENCE FICTION CONKLIN, GROFF   AN
  PRELUDE TO MARS   CLARKE, ARTHUR C.   AC
  REACH FOR TOMORROW   CLARKE, ARTHUR C.   AC
  TO THE STARS   SILVERBERG, ROBERT   AN
WALL OF DARKNESS, THE   SS   SSS 49 07
  EDITOR'S CHOICE IN SCIENCE FICTION   MOSKOWITZ, SAM   AN
  NINE BILLION NAMES OF GOD, THE   CLARKE, ARTHUR C.   AC
  OTHER DIMENSIONS   SILVERBERG, ROBERT   AN
  OTHER SIDE OF THE SKY, THE   CLARKE, ARTHUR C.   AC
WATCH THIS SPACE (VENTURE TO THE MOON) SS   FSF 57 02
  OTHER SIDE OF THE SKY, THE   CLARKE, ARTHUR C.   AC
WE'LL NEVER CONQUER SPACE   AR   SDG 60 06
  SCIENCE FACT/FICTION   FARRELL/GAGE/&   AN
WHACKY   SS   FNT 42 07
  BEST OF ARTHUR C. CLARKE: 1937-1971, THE
                                       CLARKE, ARTHUR C.   AC
WHAT GOES UP   SS   FSF 56 01
  PRELUDE TO MARS   CLARKE, ARTHUR C.   AC
  TALES FROM THE WHITE HART   CLARKE, ARTHUR C.   AC
WHO'S THERE? (ALSO AS THE HAUNTED SPACESUIT)   SS   NWS 58 11
  NINE BILLION NAMES OF GOD, THE   CLARKE, ARTHUR C.   AC
  OF TIME AND STARS   CLARKE, ARTHUR C.   AC
  OUT OF THIS WORLD 3   WILLIAMS-ELLIS& OWEN AN
  SCIENCE FACT/FICTION   FARRELL/GAGE/&   AN
  TALES OF TEN WORLDS   CLARKE, ARTHUR C.   AC
WIND FROM THE SUN, THE (SUNJAMMER)   SS   BLF 64
  WIND FROM THE SUN, THE   CLARKE, ARTHUR C.   AC
1933: A SCIENCE FICTION ODYSSEY   IN
  BEST OF ARTHUR C. CLARKE: 1937-1971, THE
                                       CLARKE, ARTHUR C.   AC

CLARKE, I. F.
  H. G. WELLS: EXPONENT OF EXTRAPOLATION   AR   FTS 70 06
  BEYOND THIS HORIZON   CARRELL, CHRISTOPHER OA
  TRIBULATIONS OF TECHNOLOGY, THE   AR   FTS 71 06
  BEYOND THIS HORIZON   CARRELL, CHRISTOPHER OA

CLARKE, JOHN
  SAINT 505   SS   NWS 67 01
  ENGLAND SWINGS SF   MERRIL, JUDITH   AN
  SPACE-TIME JOURNAL, THE   MERRIL, JUDITH   AN

CLAUDY, CARL H.
  LAND OF NO SHADOW, THE   NV   AMB 31 02
  YEAR AFTER TOMORROW, THE   DEL REY, L/MATSCHAT/ AN
  MIND MASTERS OF MARS, THE   NV   AMB 31 09
  YEAR AFTER TOMORROW, THE   DEL REY, L/MATSCHAT/ AN
  TONGUE OF BEAST   SS   AMB 39 05
  YEAR AFTER TOMORROW, THE   DEL REY, L/MATSCHAT/ AN

CLEAR, VAL, PATRICIA S. WARRICK, MARTIN HARRY GREENBERG
  AND JOSEPH D. OLANDER
MARRIAGE AND THE FAMILY THROUGH SCIENCE FICTION   AN L SMP 76

CLEAR, VAL
  INTRODUCTION   IN C
  MARRIAGE AND THE FAMILY THROUGH SCIENCE FICTION
                                       CLEAR/WARRICK/&   AN

CLEAVER, PAMELA
  ALL IN THE MIND   SS   ADS 75 02
  ARMADA SCI-FI TWO   DAVIS, RICHARD   OA
  HARMONY AGGRO, THE   SS   SPC 74 02
  SPACE 2   DAVIS, RICHARD   OA

CLEEVE, BRIAN
  ANGELA'S SATYR   SS   SEP 62 11
  8TH ANNUAL OF THE YEAR'S BEST S-F, THE MERRIL, JUDITH   AN
  DEVIL AND DEMOCRACY, THE   SS   FSF 66 11
  BEST FROM FANTASY AND SCIENCE FICTION: 17
                                       FERMAN, EDWARD L.   AN

CLEM, RALPH, MARTIN HARRY GREENBERG AND JOSEPH D. OLANDER

CLEM:GREENBERG:&
  CITY: 2000 A.D., THE   AN   FAW 76 07

CLEM, RALPH
  INTRODUCTION: WHY THE CITY   IN C
  CITY: 2000 A.D., THE   CLEM/GREENBERG/&   AN

CLEMENS, SAMUEL L.   SEE PSEUD. MARK TWAIN

CLEMENT, HAL   PSEUD. FOR HARRY CLEMENT STUBBS
  FIRST FLIGHTS TO THE MOON   AN H DBL 70
  NATIVES OF SPACE   AC H BAL 65 04
  SMALL CHANGES   AC H DBL 69

CLEMENT, HAL

```
    ALSO AS "SPACE LASH"
SPACE LASH                                  AC    DEL 69 12
    SEE "SMALL CHANGES"
ANSWER                                      SS    ASF 47 04
    *SCIENCE FICTION THINKING MACHINES  CONKLIN, GROFF     AN
ASSUMPTION UNJUSTIFIED                      NV    ASF 46 10
    CROSSROADS IN TIME                  CONKLIN, GROFF     AN
    NATIVES OF SPACE                    CLEMENT, HAL       AC
ATTITUDE                                    NV    ASF 43 09
    TRAVELLERS OF SPACE                 GREENBERG , MARTIN AN
COLD FRONT                                  NV    ASF 46 07
    *MEN AGAINST THE STARS              GREENBERG, MARTIN  AN
CRITICAL FACTOR                             SS    STR 53 02
    STAR SCIENCE FICTION STORIES NO. 2  POHL, FREDERIK     OA
DUST RAG                                    SS    ASF 56 09
    SMALL CHANGES                       CLEMENT, HAL       AC
    WHERE DO WE GO FROM HERE?           ASIMOV, ISAAC      AN
FIREPROOF                                   SS    ASF 49 03
    DECADE THE 1940S                    ALDISS & HARRISON  AN
    SMALL CHANGES                       CLEMENT, HAL       AC
FOUNDLING STARS, THE                        SS    IFS 66 08
    SECOND IF READER OF SCIENCE FICTION, THE
                                        POHL, FREDERIK     AN
    SMALL CHANGES                       CLEMENT, HAL       AC
HALO                                        NV    GAL 52 10
    SHADOW OF TOMORROW                  POHL, FREDERIK     AN
    SMALL CHANGES                       CLEMENT, HAL       AC
HOT PLANET                                  NV    GAL 63 08
    EIGHTH GALAXY READER, THE           POHL, FREDERIK     AN
    SPECTRUM 4                          AMIS & CONQUEST    AN
    9TH ANNUAL OF THE YEAR'S BEST S-F, THE MERRIL, JUDITH  AN
IMPEDIMENT                                  NV    ASF 42 08
    NATIVES OF SPACE                    CLEMENT, HAL       AC
LECTURE DEMONSTRATION                       SS    AMA 73
    ASTOUNDING                          HARRISON, HARRY    OA
LOGICAL LIFE, THE                           SS    STL 74 01
    STELLAR 1                           DEL REY, JUDY-LYNN OA
LONGLINE                                    NV    76
    FASTER THAN LIGHT                   DANN & ZEBROWSKI   OA
MECHANIC, THE                               NV    ASF 66 09
    SMALL CHANGES                       CLEMENT, HAL       AC
PLANET FOR PLUNDER (SEE PLANETFALL)         TC
PLANETFALL (PLANET FOR PLUNDER)             SN    SAT 57 02
    STRANGE TOMORROWS                   HOSKINS, ROBERT    AN
PROOF                                       SS    ASF 42 06
    *POSSIBLE WORLDS OF SCIENCE FICTION CONKLIN, GROFF     AN
    SF: AUTHORS' CHOICE 2               HARRISON, HARRY    AN
    WHERE DO WE GO FROM HERE?           ASIMOV, ISAAC      AN
QUESTION OF GUILT, A                        NV    NEW 76 AN
    YEAR'S BEST HORROR STORIES: SERIES IV, THE
                                        PAGE, GERALD W.    AN
RAINDROP                                    NV    IFS 65 05
    SMALL CHANGES                       CLEMENT, HAL       AC
STUCK WITH IT                               NV    STL 76 02
    STELLAR 2                           DEL REY, JUDY-LYNN OA
SUN SPOT                                    SS    ASF 60 11
    SMALL CHANGES                       CLEMENT, HAL       AC
TECHNICAL ERROR                             NV    ASF 44 01
    NATIVES OF SPACE                    CLEMENT, HAL       AC
TROJAN FALL                                 SS    ASF 44 06
    SMALL CHANGES                       CLEMENT, HAL       AC
UNCOMMON SENSE                              SS    ASF 45 09
    SMALL CHANGES                       CLEMENT, HAL       AC

CLIFF, CATHERINE
CHAIN OF LOVE, THE                          SS    55
    13 FRENCH SCIENCE-FICTION STORIES   KNIGHT, DAMON      AN

CLIFTON, MARK
CIVILIZED (WE'RE CIVILIZED)                 SS  C GAL 53 08
    PORTALS OF TOMORROW                 DERLETH, AUGUST    AN
CLERICAL ERROR                              NV    ASF 56 02
    BEST SCIENCE FICTION STORIES AND NOVELS: 1956
                                        DIKTY, T. E.       AN
CONQUEROR, THE                              SS    ASF 52 08
    BEST SCIENCE-FICTION STORIES: 1953, THE
                                        BLEILER & DIKTY    AN
    MUTANTS                             SILVERBERG, ROBERT AN
    OMNIBUS OF SCIENCE FICTION          CONKLIN, GROFF     AN
CRAZY JOEY                                  SS  C ASF 53 08
    BEYOND THE BARRIERS OF SPACE AND TIME MERRIL, JUDITH   AN
HANG HEAD, VANDAL|                          SS    AMZ 62 04
    8TH ANNUAL OF THE YEAR'S BEST S-F, THE MERRIL, JUDITH  AN
HOW ALLIED                                  NV    ASF 57 03
    ELSEWHERE AND ELSEWHEN              CONKLIN, GROFF     AN
SENSE FROM THOUGHT DIVIDE                   NV    ASF 55 03
    SF: THE BEST OF THE BEST            MERRIL, JUDITH     AN
    SF: THE YEAR'S GREATEST SCIENCE FICTION AND FANTASY
                                        MERRIL, JUDITH     AN
    SPECTRUM 2                          AMIS & CONQUEST    AN
STAR, BRIGHT                                NV    GAL 52 07
    GALAXY SCIENCE FICTION OMNIBUS      GOLD, H. L.        AN
    MATHEMATICAL MAGPIE, THE            FADIMAN, CLIFTON   AN
    PRIZE SCIENCE FICTION               WOLLHEIM, DONALD A. AN
    SECOND GALAXY READER OF SCIENCE FICTION
                                        GOLD, H. L.        AN
    SPECULATIONS                        SANDERS, THOMAS E. AN
    TOMORROW'S CHILDREN                 ASIMOV, ISAAC      AN
WE'RE CIVILIZED (ALSO AS CIVILIZED)         SS  C GAL 53 08
    GALACTIC EMPIRES VOLUME ONE         ALDISS, BRIAN W.   AN
WHAT HAVE I DONE?                           SS    ASF 52 05
    ASTOUNDING-ANALOG READER, THE VOLUME TWO
                                        HARRISON & ALDISS  AN
    *BEYOND HUMAN KEN                   MERRIL, JUDITH     AN
WHAT NOW, LITTLE MAN?                       NV    FSF 59 12
    5TH ANNUAL OF THE YEAR'S BEST S-F, THE MERRIL, JUDITH  AN
```

CLIFTON, MARK   (CONTINUED)

```
    WHAT THIN PARTITIONS                    NV  C ASF 53 09
    BEST SCIENCE-FICTION STORIES: 1954, THE
                                        BLEILER & DIKTY    AN
    EDITOR'S CHOICE IN SCIENCE FICTION  MOSKOWITZ, SAM     AN
    14 GREAT TALES OF ESP               STONE, IDELLA P.   AN
WOMAN'S PLACE, A                            NV    GAL 55 05
    WORLD THAT COULDN'T BE AND 8 OTHER SF NOVELETS
                                        GOLD, H. L.        AN

CLINE, STEVE
THERE IS NO MORE AWAY                       SS    NWQ 73 05
    NEW WORLDS NO. 5                    MOORCOCK & PLATT   OA

CLINGAN, C. C.
HIGH BANK                                   SS
    FUTURE PASTIMES                     EDELSTEIN, SCOTT   OA

CLINGERMAN, MILDRED
CUPFUL OF SPACE, A                          AC    BAL 61
BIRDS CAN'T COUNT                           SS    FSF 55 02
    BEST FROM FANTASY AND SCIENCE FICTION: 5
                                        BOUCHER, ANTHONY   AN
    CUPFUL OF SPACE, A                  CLINGERMAN, MILDRED AC
    SF: THE YEAR'S GREATEST SCIENCE FICTION AND FANTASY
                                        MERRIL, JUDITH     AN
DAY FOR WAVING, A                           SS    FSF 57 08
    CUPFUL OF SPACE, A                  CLINGERMAN, MILDRED AC
DAY OF THE GREEN VELVET CLOAK, THE          SS    FSF 58 07
    CUPFUL OF SPACE, A                  CLINGERMAN, MILDRED AC
FIRST LESSON                                SS    FSF 56 12
    CUPFUL OF SPACE, A                  CLINGERMAN, MILDRED AC
    DECADE OF FANTASY AND SCIENCE FICTION, A
                                        MILLS, ROBERT P.   AN
GAY DECEIVER, THE                           SS    NEW 61 AC
    CUPFUL OF SPACE, A                  CLINGERMAN, MILDRED AC
LAST PROPHET, THE                           SS    FSF 55 08
    BEST FROM FANTASY AND SCIENCE FICTION: 5
                                        BOUCHER, ANTHONY   AN
    CUPFUL OF SPACE, A                  CLINGERMAN, MILDRED AC
LETTERS FROM LAURA                          SS    FSF 54 10
    CUPFUL OF SPACE, A                  CLINGERMAN, MILDRED AC
    TREASURY OF GREAT SCIENCE FICTION, A VOL.2
                                        BOUCHER, ANTHONY   AN
LITTLE WITCH OF ELM STREET, THE             SS    WHC 56
    CUPFUL OF SPACE, A                  CLINGERMAN, MILDRED AC
    MORE LITTLE MONSTERS                ELWOOD & GHIDALIA  AN
MINISTER WITHOUT PORTFOLIO                  SS    FSF 52 02
    CUPFUL OF SPACE, A                  CLINGERMAN, MILDRED AC
    ENCOUNTERS WITH ALIENS              EARLEY, GEORGE W.  AN
    *INVADERS OF EARTH                  CONKLIN, GROFF     AN
    *STORIES FOR TOMORROW               SLOANE, WILLIAM    AN
MR. SAKRIS'S HALT                           SS    FSF 56 01
    BEST FROM FANTASY AND SCIENCE FICTION: 6
                                        BOUCHER, ANTHONY   AN
    CUPFUL OF SPACE, A                  CLINGERMAN, MILDRED AC
RED HEART AND BLUE ROSES, A                 SS    NEW 61 AC
    CUPFUL OF SPACE, A                  CLINGERMAN, MILDRED AC
    NEW WORLDS OF FANTASY               CARR, TERRY        AN
STAIR TRICK                                 SS    FSF 52 08
    BEST FROM FANTASY AND SCIENCE FICTION: 2
                                        BOUCHER & MCCOMAS  AN
    CUPFUL OF SPACE, A                  CLINGERMAN, MILDRED AC
    FIFTY SHORT SCIENCE FICTION TALES   ASIMOV & CONKLIN   AN
STICKENEY AND THE CRITIC                    SS    FSF 53 02
    CUPFUL OF SPACE, A                  CLINGERMAN, MILDRED AC
    PORTALS OF TOMORROW                 DERLETH, AUGUST    AN
WILD WOOD, THE                              SS    FSF 57 01
    BEST FROM FANTASY AND SCIENCE FICTION: 7
                                        BOUCHER, ANTHONY   AN
    CUPFUL OF SPACE, A                  CLINGERMAN, MILDRED AC
    SPECIAL WONDER                      MCCOMAS, J. FRANCIS AN
WINNING RECIPE                              SS    FSF 52 11
    CUPFUL OF SPACE, A                  CLINGERMAN, MILDRED AC
WORD, THE                                   SS    FSF 53 11
    CUPFUL OF SPACE, A                  CLINGERMAN, MILDRED AC
    PORTALS OF TOMORROW                 DERLETH, AUGUST    AN

CLINTON, ED M. JR.
SMALL WORLD OF M-75, THE                    SS    IFS 54 07
    FIRST WORLD OF IF, THE              QUINN & WULFF      AN
    *SCIENCE FICTION ADVENTURES IN MUTATION CONKLIN, GROFF AN

CLOETE, STUART
BLAST, THE                                  NV    COL 47 04
    6 GREAT SHORT NOVELS OF SCIENCE FICTION
                                        CONKLIN, GROFF     AN

CLOUGH, ROY L.
BAIT                                        SS    ASF 51 06
    SPACE POLICE                        NORTON, ANDRE      AN

CLUTE, JOHN
BIRDSEED FOR OUR FEATHERED FANS             BR    NWQ 74 06
    NEW WORLDS NO. 6                    PLATT & BAILEY     OA
DISINHERITING PARTY, THE                    NV    NWB 73 05
    NEW WORLDS QUARTERLY NO. 5          MOORCOCK, MICHAEL  OA
I SAY BEGONE| APOTROPAIC NARCOSIS, I'M GOING TO READ THE
    DAMNED THING, HA HA                     BR    NWB 75 08
    NEW WORLDS EIGHT                    BAILEY, HILARY     OA
MAN MUST DIE, A                             SS    NWS 66 11
    ALPHA 5                             SILVERBERG, ROBERT AN
    BEST SF STORIES FROM NEW WORLDS 6   MOORCOCK, MICHAEL  AN
SCHOLIA, SEASONED WITH CRABS, BLISH IS      AR    NWQ 73 05
    NEW WORLDS NO. 5                    MOORCOCK & PLATT   OA
```

CLUTE, JOHN

CLUTE, JOHN   (CONTINUED)
  SHUCKSMA   SS   NWB 73 05
    NEW WORLDS QUARTERLY NO. 5   MOORCOCK, MICHAEL   OA

COATES, ROBERT M.
  HOUR AFTER WESTERLY, THE   SS   NYM 47 11
    TIMELESS STORIES FOR TODAY AND TOMORROW
                                  BRADBURY, RAY   AN
  LAW, THE   SS   NYM 47 11
    ECO-FICTION   STADLER, JOHN   AN
    MATHEMATICAL MAGPIE, THE   FADIMAN, CLIFTON   AN
  MAN WHO VANISHED, THE   SS   NYM 55 10
    CIRCUS OF DR. LAO AND OTHER IMPROBABLE STORIES
                                  BRADBURY, RAY   AN

COBLENTZ, STANTON A.
  SCARLET LUNES, THE   SS   FBK 50 06
    SCIENCE AND SORCERY   FORD, GARRET   AN
  SUNWARD   SS   TWS 40 04
    FLIGHT INTO SPACE   WOLLHEIM, DONALD A. AN

COE, NANCY FORSYTHE
  NIGHT BEFORE CHRISTMAS, THE   PM   59
    FLYING SAUCERS IN FACT AND FICTION SANTESSON, HANS S. AN

COFFIN, CARLYN
  SURVIVAL   PM   FSF 55 06
    BEST FROM FANTASY AND SCIENCE FICTION: 5
                                  BOUCHER, ANTHONY   AN

COGSWELL, GEORGE RAE
  CONTACT POINT   PL C   75
    SIX SCIENCE FICTION PLAYS   ELWOOD, ROGER   AN

COGSWELL, THEODORE R
  THIRD EYE, THE   AC   BEL 68 09
  WALL AROUND THE WORLD, THE   AC   PYR 62 02
  BIG STINK, THE   SS   IFS 54 07
    HUMAN AND OTHER BEINGS   DEGRAEFF, ALLEN   AN
  BLOWUP BLUES   SG   60
    6TH ANNUAL OF THE YEAR'S BEST S-F, THE MERRIL, JUDITH AN
  BURNING, THE   SS   FSF 60 07
    POCKETFUL OF STARS, A   KNIGHT, DAMON   AN
    WALL AROUND THE WORLD, THE   COGSWELL, THEODORE R AC
  CABBAGE PATCH, THE   SS   FSF 57 12
    SHOCKING THING, A   KNIGHT, DAMON   AN
    THIRD EYE, THE   COGSWELL, THEODORE R AC
  CONSUMER'S REPORT (NO GUN TO THE VICTOR)   SS   IMG 55 10
    SF: AUTHORS' CHOICE   HARRISON, HARRY   AN
    VOYAGES: SCENARIOS FOR A SHIP CALLED EARTH
                                  SAUER, ROB   AN
    YOU AND SCIENCE FICTION   HOLLISTER, BERNARD C AN
  CONTACT POINT   PL C   75
    SIX SCIENCE FICTION PLAYS   ELWOOD, ROGER   AN
  CONVENTIONAL ENDING   SS   FUT 54 10
    THIRD EYE, THE   COGSWELL, THEODORE R AC
  DISASSEMBLY LINE   SS   BEY 54 07
    THIRD EYE, THE   COGSWELL, THEODORE R AC
  EARLY BIRD   SS C AMA 73
    ASTOUNDING   HARRISON, HARRY   OA
    BEST SF: 1973   HARRISON & ALDISS   AN
  EMERGENCY RATIONS   SS   IMG 53 09
    WALL AROUND THE WORLD, THE   COGSWELL, THEODORE R AC
  FAEX DELENDA EST   PM   CND 72
    BEST SF: 1972   HARRISON & ALDISS   AN
  IMPACT WITH THE DEVIL   SS   FSF 56 11
    DEALS WITH THE DEVIL   DAVENPORT, BASIL   AN
    THIRD EYE, THE   COGSWELL, THEODORE R AC
  INVASION REPORT   SS   GAL 54 08
    WALL AROUND THE WORLD, THE   COGSWELL, THEODORE R AC
  LIMITING FACTOR   SS   GAL 54 04
    *SCIENCE FICTION ADVENTURES IN MUTATION CONKLIN, GROFF AN
    THIRD EYE, THE   COGSWELL, THEODORE R AC
    THIRD GALAXY READER, THE   GOLD, H. L.   AN
  LOVER BOY   SS   BEY 54 03
    THIRD EYE, THE   COGSWELL, THEODORE R AC
  MACHINE RECORD   SS   SFA 61 05
    THIRD EYE, THE   COGSWELL, THEODORE R AC
  MAN WHO KNEW GRODNIK, THE   SS   SCF 62 06
    THIRD EYE, THE   COGSWELL, THEODORE R AC
  MASTERS, THE   SS   TWS 54 SU
    WALL AROUND THE WORLD, THE   COGSWELL, THEODORE R AC
  MINIMUM SENTENCE   SS   GAL 53 08
    GALAXY SCIENCE FICTION OMNIBUS GOLD, H. L.   AN
    SECOND GALAXY READER OF SCIENCE FICTION
                                  GOLD, H. L.   AN
    THIRD EYE, THE   COGSWELL, THEODORE R AC
  MR. HOSKIN'S HEEL   SS   FUN 54 11
    THIRD EYE, THE   COGSWELL, THEODORE R AC
  NO GUN TO THE VICTOR (ALSO AS CONSUMER'S REPORT) SS IMG 55 10
    THIRD EYE, THE   COGSWELL, THEODORE R AC
  ONE TO A CUSTOMER   SS   SUP 58 06
    THIRD EYE, THE   COGSWELL, THEODORE R AC
  OTHER CHEEK, THE   NA   SFA 53 05
    THIRD EYE, THE   COGSWELL, THEODORE R AC
  POPULATION IMPLOSION, THE (PROBABILITY ZERO)   SS AMA 73
    BEST SCIENCE FICTION STORIES OF THE YEAR (1973)
                                  DEL REY, LESTER   AN
  PRISONER OF LOVE   SS   NEW 62 AC
    WALL AROUND THE WORLD, THE   COGSWELL, THEODORE R AC
  PROBABILITY ZERO| THE POPULATION IMPLOSION   SS   AMA 73
    ASTOUNDING   HARRISON, HARRY   OA
  RADIATION BLUES   SG   60
    6TH ANNUAL OF THE YEAR'S BEST S-F, THE MERRIL, JUDITH AN
  SHORT COUNT, THE   SS   AVS 53 01
    THIRD EYE, THE   COGSWELL, THEODORE R AC

COGSWELL, THEODORE R (CONTINUED)
  SPECTER GENERAL, THE   NV   ASF 52 06
    SCIENCE FICTION HALL OF FAME VOLUME 2B BOVA, BEN   AN
    SPACE SERVICE   NORTON, ANDRE   AN
    WALL AROUND THE WORLD, THE   COGSWELL, THEODORE R AC
  SPUDGET FOR THWILBERT, A   SS   FUN 58 04
    THIRD EYE, THE   COGSWELL, THEODORE R AC
  TEST AREA   SS   FUN 55 02
    WALL AROUND THE WORLD, THE   COGSWELL, THEODORE R AC
  THINGS   SS   FSF 58 05
    WALL AROUND THE WORLD, THE   COGSWELL, THEODORE R AC
  THREESIE   SS   FSF 56 01
    DEALS WITH THE DEVIL   DAVENPORT, BASIL   AN
  TRAINING DEVICE   SS   IMG 55 03
    THIRD EYE, THE   COGSWELL, THEODORE R AC
  WALL AROUND THE WORLD, THE   NV   BEY 53 09
    BEYOND THE BARRIERS OF SPACE AND TIME MERRIL, JUDITH AN
    WALL AROUND THE WORLD, THE   COGSWELL, THEODORE R AC
    WORLDS OF WONDER   HARRISON, HARRY   AN
    YET MORE PENGUIN SCIENCE FICTION ALDISS, BRIAN W. AN
  WOLFIE   SS   BEY 54 01
    WALL AROUND THE WORLD, THE   COGSWELL, THEODORE R AC
  YOU KNOW WILLIE   SS   FSF 57 05
    SF: THE BEST OF THE BEST   MERRIL, JUDITH   AN
    SF:58, THE YEAR'S GREATEST SCIENCE FICTION AND FANTASY
                                  MERRIL, JUDITH   AN

COGSWELL, THOMAS
  PARADISE REGAINED   SS   SVW 73
    BEST SCIENCE FICTION STORIES OF THE YEAR (1973)
                                  DEL REY, LESTER   AN
    SAVING WORLDS   ELWOOD & KIDD   OA

COHN, GARY
  RULES OF MOOPSBALL   AR   ORB 76 18
    ORBIT 18   KNIGHT, DAMON   OA

COLE, ADRIAN
  GENUINE ARTICLE, THE   SS   BER 74
    BERSERKERS, THE   ELWOOD, ROGER   OA

COLE, BARRY
  END TO COMPLACENCY, AN   PM   69
    HOLDING YOUR EIGHT HANDS   LUCIE-SMITH, EDWARD AN
  MEN ARE COMING BACK|, THE   PM   NWS 67 10
    HOLDING YOUR EIGHT HANDS   LUCIE-SMITH, EDWARD AN

COLE, EVERETT B.
  PHILOSOPHICAL CORPS, THE   NO H GNM 62
  EXILE   SN   ASF 54 01
    BEST SCIENCE FICTION STORIES AND NOVELS: 1955
                                  DIKTY, T. E.   AN
    5 TALES FROM TOMORROW   DIKTY, T. E.   AN
  FIGHTING PHILOSOPHER   NV   ASF 54 04
    PHILOSOPHICAL CORPS, THE   COLE, EVERETT B.   NO
  PHILOSOPHICAL CORPS   NV   ASF 51 03
    PHILOSOPHICAL CORPS, THE   COLE, EVERETT B.   NO
  PLAYERS, THE   NV   ASF 55 04
    PHILOSOPHICAL CORPS, THE   COLE, EVERETT B.   NO

COLERIDGE, JOHN   PSEUD. FOR EARL AND OTTO BINDER
  POLAR DOOM   SS   SFQ 40 SU
    MOON CONQUERORS, THE   ANONYMOUS   AN

COLES, DAVID
  CRITICAL PATH   SS   NWR 71 19
    NEW WRITINGS IN SF. 19   CARNELL, JOHN   OA

COLIN, VLADIMIR
  CONTACT, THE   SS
    OTHER WORLDS, OTHER SEAS   SUVIN, DARKO   AN

COLLADAY, MORRISON
  GIANT IN THE EARTH   SS   WOS 33 04
    *BEST OF SCIENCE FICTION   CONKLIN, GROFF   AN
  PLANETOID OF DOOM, THE   SS   WOS 32 12
    *BIG BOOK OF SCIENCE FICTION CONKLIN, GROFF   AN

COLLIER, JOHN
  ARE YOU TOO LATE OR WAS I TOO EARLY   SS   NYM 51 04
    GOLDEN ROAD, THE   KNIGHT, DAMON   AN
  BIRD OF PREY   SS   41
    SUPERNATURAL READER, THE   CONKLIN, G&L.   AN
  DEVIL, GEORGE, AND ROSIE, THE   SS   34
    DEALS WITH THE DEVIL   DAVENPORT, BASIL   AN
  EVENING PRIMROSE (1941)   SS   AFR 47 03
    FANTASY: THE LITERATURE OF THE MARVELOUS
                                  KELLEY, LEO P.   AN
    OUT OF THIS WORLD   FAST, JULIUS   AN
    WORLDS OF SCIENCE FICTION, THE MILLS, ROBERT P.   AN
  GREEN THOUGHTS   SS   31
    POCKET BOOK OF SCIENCE-FICTION, THE WOLLHEIM, DONALD A. AN
    ROOTS OF EVIL, THE   PARRY, MICHEL   AN
    SCIENCE FICTION ARGOSY, A   KNIGHT, DAMON   AN
  INCIDENT ON A LAKE   SS
    BEST FANTASY STORIES   ALDISS, BRIAN W.   AN
  INTERPRETATION OF A DREAM   SS   NYM 51 05
    BEYOND THE BARRIERS OF SPACE AND TIME MERRIL, JUDITH AN
    PERCHANCE TO DREAM   KNIGHT, DAMON   AN
  INVISIBLE DOVE DANCER OF STRATHPEEN ISLAND, THE SS 41
    INVISIBLE MEN   DAVENPORT, BASIL   AN
  MAN OVERBOARD   NV   FSF 60 03
    BEST FROM FANTASY AND SCIENCE FICTION: 10
                                  MILLS, ROBERT P.   AN
  MEETING OF RELATIONS (YRV 41 12)   SS   FSF 59 01

COLLIER, JOHN

CONKLIN, GROFF

COLLIER, JOHN   (CONTINUED)
  DECADE OF FANTASY AND SCIENCE FICTION, A
                                     MILLS, ROBERT P.   AN
  ROPE ENOUGH   SS   NYM 39 11
  HUMAN?   MERRIL, JUDITH   AN
  SOFTLY WALKS THE BEETLE   SS   PBY 60 01
  PLAYBOY BOOK OF HORROR AND THE SUPERNATURAL, THE
                                     PLAYBOY, EDITORS OF   AN
  WEIRD SHOW   PLAYBOY, EDITORS OF   AN
  SPECIAL DELIVERY   NV   41
  GRAVEYARD READER, THE   CONKLIN, GROFF   AN
  THUS I REFUTE BEELZY   SS   43
  OUT OF THIS WORLD   FAST, JULIUS   AN
  TOUCH OF NUTMEG MAKES IT, THE   SS   43
  SHOCKING THING, A   KNIGHT, DAMON   AN

COLLIGAN, DOUGLAS
  BRACE YOURSELF FOR ANOTHER ICE AGE AR   SDG 73 02
  SCIENCE FACT/FICTION   FARRELL/GAGE/&   AN

COLLYN, GEORGE
  IN PASSAGE OF THE SUN   SS   NWS 66 07
  BEST SF STORIES FROM NEW WORLDS 3 MOORCOCK, MICHAEL   AN
  MIX-UP   SS   NWS 64 12
  BEST SF STORIES FROM NEW WORLDS 7 MOORCOCK, MICHAEL   AN
  OUT OF TIME, OUT OF PLACE   SS   FSF 67 09
  BEST FROM FANTASY AND SCIENCE FICTION: 17
                                     FERMAN, EDWARD L.   AN
  SINGULAR QUEST OF MARTIN BORG, THE SS   NWS 65 02
  BEST SF STORIES FROM NEW WORLDS NO. 2, THE
                                     MOORCOCK, MICHAEL   AN
  ENGLAND SWINGS SF   MERRIL, JUDITH   AN
  SPACE-TIME JOURNAL, THE   MERRIL, JUDITH   AN
  UNIFICATION DAY   SS   NWS 66 05
  TRAPS OF TIME, THE   MOORCOCK, MICHAEL   AN

COLOMBO, JOHN ROBERT
  FRANKENSTEIN   PM   69
  HOLDING YOUR EIGHT HANDS   LUCIE-SMITH, EDWARD   AN

COLVIN, JAMES   PSEUD. FOR MICHAEL MOORCOCK
  DEEP FIX, THE   AC   CPT 66
  DEEP FIX, THE   NV   SCF 64 04
  DEEP FIX, THE   COLVIN, JAMES   AC
  LOVEBEAST, THE   SS
  DEEP FIX, THE   COLVIN, JAMES   AC
  MOUNTAIN, THE   SS   NWS 65 02
  BEST OF NEW WORLDS, THE   MOORCOCK, MICHAEL   AN
  BEST SF STORIES FROM NEW WORLDS 3 MOORCOCK, MICHAEL   AN
  PEACE ON EARTH   SS   NWS 59 12
  DEEP FIX, THE   COLVIN, JAMES   AC
  PLEASURE GARDEN OF FELIPE SAGITTARIUS, THE SS NWS 65 09
  BEST SF STORIES FROM NEW WORLDS NO. 2, THE
                                     MOORCOCK, MICHAEL   AN
  DEEP FIX, THE   COLVIN, JAMES   AC
  REAL LIFE OF MR. NEWMAN, THE   SS
  DEEP FIX, THE   COLVIN, JAMES   AC

COMPTON, D. G.
  FROM: THE STEEL CROCODILE   EX   ACE 70
  INSIDE INFORMATION   MOWSHOWITZ, ABBE   AN
  IT'S SMART TO HAVE AN ENGLISH ADDRESS SS IMP 67 02
  WORLD'S BEST SCIENCE FICTION: 1968 WOLLHEIM & CARR   AN

CONDIT, TOM
  TROUBLE WITH TREATIES   NV C STR 59 05
  STAR SCIENCE FICTION STORIES NO. 5 POHL, FREDERIK   OA

CONESA, LISA
  EYES OF A WOMAN- FROM A PORTRAIT BY PICASSO PM
  BEST SF: 1974   HARRISON & ALDISS   AN

CONEY, MICHAEL G.
  MONITOR FOUND IN ORBIT   AC   DAW 74 09
  BARTHOLOMEW & SON (AND THE FISH-GIRL) NV NWR 75 27
  NEW WRITINGS IN SF. 27   BULMER, KENNETH   OA
  BENEATH STILL WATERS   SS   IFS 71 01
  MONITOR FOUND IN ORBIT   CONEY, MICHAEL G.   AC
  ESMERALDA   SS   GAL 72 01
  MONITOR FOUND IN ORBIT   CONEY, MICHAEL G.   AC
  HOLD MY HAND, MY LOVE   SS   WOT 71 SP
  MONITOR FOUND IN ORBIT   CONEY, MICHAEL G.   AC
  INTRODUCTION   IN
  MONITOR FOUND IN ORBIT   CONEY, MICHAEL G.   AC
  MANYA, THE   SS   FSF 73 03
  MONITOR FOUND IN ORBIT   CONEY, MICHAEL G.   AC
  MIND PRISON, THE   SS   NWR 71 19
  MONITOR FOUND IN ORBIT   CONEY, MICHAEL G.   AC
  NEW WRITINGS IN SF. 19   CARNELL, JOHN   OA
  MONITOR FOUND IN ORBIT   SS   NWQ 71 02
  MONITOR FOUND IN ORBIT   CONEY, MICHAEL G.   AC
  NEW WORLDS QUARTERLY NO. 2   MOORCOCK, MICHAEL   AN
  OH, VALINDA!   NV   NWR 72 20
  NEW WRITINGS IN SF. 20   CARNELL, JOHN   OA
  1973 ANNUAL WORLD'S BEST SF, THE   WOLLHEIM, DONALD A.   AN
  R26/5/PSY AND I   NV   NWR 69 16
  MONITOR FOUND IN ORBIT   CONEY, MICHAEL G.   AC
  NEW WRITINGS IN SF. 16   CARNELL, JOHN   OA
  SHARKS OF PENTREATH, THE   SS   GAL 71 02
  BEST FROM GALAXY, THE VOLUME I   GALAXY, EDITORS OF   AN
  1972 ANNUAL WORLD'S BEST SF, THE   WOLLHEIM, DONALD A.   AN
  SIXTH SENSE   SS   VOT 69 08
  WORLD'S BEST SCIENCE FICTION: 1970 WOLLHEIM & CARR   AN
  STARTHINKER 9   SS
  ANDROMEDA I   WESTON, PETER   OA

CONEY, MICHAEL G.   (CONTINUED)
  SYMBIOTE   NV   NWR 69 15
  NEW WRITINGS IN SF. 9   CARNELL, JOHN   AN
  NEW WRITINGS IN SF. 15   CARNELL, JOHN   OA
  TERTIARY JUSTIFICATION, THE   NV   NWR 73 21
  NEW WRITINGS IN SF. 21   CARNELL, JOHN   OA
  THOSE GOOD OLD DAYS OF LIQUID FUEL SS   FSF 76 01
  1977 ANNUAL WORLD'S BEST SF, THE   WOLLHEIM, DONALD A.   AN
  TROUBLESHOOTER   SS   IFS 70 05
  BEST FROM IF, THE VOLUME I   IF, EDITORS OF   AN
  TRUE WORTH OF RUTH VILLIERS, THE   SS   NWR 70 17
  MONITOR FOUND IN ORBIT   CONEY, MICHAEL G.   AC
  NEW WRITINGS IN SF. 17   CARNELL, JOHN   OA
  UNSAVORY EPISODE OF MRS. HECTOR POWELL-CHALLENGER, THE
                                     SS
  MONITOR FOUND IN ORBIT   CONEY, MICHAEL G.   AC
  WHATEVER BECAME OF THE MCGOWANS?   NV   GAL 70 05
  WORLD'S BEST SCIENCE FICTION: 1971 WOLLHEIM & CARR   AN

CONGDON, MICHAEL&DON
  ALONE BY NIGHT   AN   BAL 62 01

CONKLIN, GROFF AND NOAH D. FABRICANT
  GREAT SCIENCE FICTION ABOUT DOCTORS AN CLB 63

CONKLIN, GROFF AND LUCY
  SUPERNATURAL READER, THE   AN H LIP 53

CONKLIN, GROFF   SEE ALSO   CO-EDITOR ISAAC ASIMOV
  ADVENTURES IN DIMENSION   AN H GRY 55
    SELECTIONS FROM "SCIENCE FICTION ADVENTURES IN DIMENSION"
  ANOTHER PART OF THE GALAXY   AN   FGM 66
  BEST OF SCIENCE FICTION   AN H CRN 46
  BEST OF SCIENCE FICTION (22 OF 40) AN L CRB 63
  BIG BOOK OF SCIENCE FICTION   AN H CRN 50
  BIG BOOK OF SCIENCE FICTION (10 OF 32) AN BRK 57
  BR-R-R-!   AN   AVN 59
  CROSSROADS IN TIME   AN   PMA 53
  DIMENSION 4   AN   PYR 64 02
  ELSEWHERE AND ELSEWHEN   AN   BKM 68 05
  ENEMIES IN SPACE   AN   DIG 62
    SELECTIONS FROM "INVADERS OF EARTH"
  FIVE-ODD   AN   PYR 64 08
    IN ENGLAND AS "POSSIBLE TOMORROWS"
  FOUR FOR THE FUTURE   AN   PYR 59 08
  GIANTS UNLEASHED   AN H GRS 65
    ALSO AS "MINDS UNLEASHED"
  GRAVEYARD READER, THE   AN   BAL 58
  GREAT SCIENCE FICTION BY SCIENTISTS AN   CLB 62
  GREAT STORIES OF SPACE TRAVEL   AN   TMP 63 07
  INVADERS OF EARTH   AN H VPR 52
    ENGLISH DERIVATIVE ANTHOLOGY "ENEMIES IN SPACE"
  INVADERS OF EARTH (BRITISH PB)   AN   DIG 62
  INVADERS OF EARTH (BRITISH)   AN H WEI 53
  INVADERS OF EARTH (15 OF 22)   AN   PKT 55 09
  INVADERS OF EARTH (17 OF 22)   AN   TMP 62 09
  MINDS UNLEASHED   AN   TMP 70 10
    SEE "GIANTS UNLEASHED"
  OMNIBUS OF SCIENCE FICTION   AN H CRN 52
    DERIVATIVE ANTHOLOGIES ARE "SCIENCE FICTION OMNIBUS",
    "STRANGE TRAVELS IN SCIENCE FICTION" AND
    "STRANGE ADVENTURES IN SCIENCE FICTION"
  OPERATION FUTURE   AN   PMA 55 05
  POSSIBLE TOMORROWS   AN   71
    SEE "FIVE-ODD"
  POSSIBLE WORLDS OF SCIENCE FICTION AN H VPR 51
  POSSIBLE WORLDS OF SCIENCE FICTION (BRITISH) AN H GRY 51
  POSSIBLE WORLDS OF SCIENCE FICTION (10 OF 22) AN BRK 55 07
  SCIENCE FICTION ADVENTURES IN DIMENSION AN H VPR 53
    IN ENGLAND AS "ADVENTURES IN DIMENSION" (13 OF 23)
  SCIENCE FICTION ADVENTURES IN DIMENSION (12 OF 23) AN BKM 65 03
  SCIENCE FICTION ADVENTURES IN MUTATION AN H VPR 55
  SCIENCE FICTION ADVENTURES IN MUTATION (14 OF 20) AN BKM 65 06
  SCIENCE FICTION GALAXY, THE   AN   PMA 50
  SCIENCE FICTION ODDITIES   AN   BKM 66 11
  SCIENCE FICTION OMNIBUS   AN   BRK 56 08
    STORIES FROM "OMNIBUS OF SCIENCE FICTION"
  SCIENCE FICTION TERROR TALES   AN H GNM 55 01
  SCIENCE FICTION THINKING MACHINES AN H VPR 54
  SCIENCE FICTION THINKING MACHINES (SELECTIONS FROM)
                                     AN   BAN 55 08
  SEVEN COME INFINITY   AN   FGM 66
  SEVEN TRIPS THROUGH TIME AND SPACE AN   FGM 68
  SIX GREAT SHORT SCIENCE FICTION NOVELS AN DEL 60 11
  STRANGE ADVENTURES IN SCIENCE FICTION   AN H GRY 54
    STORIES FROM "OMNIBUS OF SCIENCE FICTION"
  STRANGE TRAVELS IN SCIENCE FICTION AN H GRY 53
    STORIES FROM "OMNIBUS OF SCIENCE FICTION"
  TREASURY OF SCIENCE FICTION, A   AN H CRN 48 11
  TREASURY OF SCIENCE FICTION, A (8 OF 30) AN BRK 57 07
  TWISTED   AN   BEL 62
  TWISTED (BRITISH)   AN   HWZ 63
  WAY HOME, A (LISTED UNDER THEODORE STURGEON) EC H FKW 55
  WORLDS OF WHEN   AN   PYR 62 05
  12 GREAT CLASSICS OF SCIENCE FICTION AN FGM 63
  13 ABOVE THE NIGHT   AN   DEL 65
  13 GREAT STORIES OF SCIENCE FICTION AN   FGM 60
  17 X INFINITY   AN   DEL 63 08
  5 UNEARTHLY VISIONS   AN   FGM 65
  6 GREAT SHORT NOVELS OF SCIENCE FICTION AN DEL 54
  "ACT III. SCENE V. ANOTHER PART OF THE FOREST" IN
    ANOTHER PART OF THE GALAXY   CONKLIN, GROFF   AN
  ESSAY ON STURGEON   IN
  E PLURIBUS UNICORN   STURGEON, THEODORE   AC
  INTRODUCTION   IN
  ADVENTURES IN DIMENSION   CONKLIN, GROFF   AN

CONKLIN, GROFF

COOPER, EDMUND

CONKLIN, GROFF   (CONTINUED)
*BEST OF SCIENCE FICTION   CONKLIN, GROFF   AN
*BIG BOOK OF SCIENCE FICTION   CONKLIN, GROFF   AN
 BR-R-R-!   CONKLIN, GROFF   AN
 ELSEWHERE AND ELSEWHEN   CONKLIN, GROFF   AN
 FIVE-ODD   CONKLIN, GROFF   AN
 GRAVEYARD READER, THE   CONKLIN, GROFF   AN
 GREAT STORIES OF SPACE TRAVEL   CONKLIN, GROFF   AN
*INVADERS OF EARTH   CONKLIN, GROFF   AN
 OMNIBUS OF SCIENCE FICTION   CONKLIN, GROFF   AN
 OPERATION FUTURE   CONKLIN, GROFF   AN
*POSSIBLE WORLDS OF SCIENCE FICTION   CONKLIN, GROFF   AN
*SCIENCE FICTION ADVENTURES IN DIMENSION
                                                  CONKLIN, GROFF   AN
*SCIENCE FICTION ADVENTURES IN MUTATION CONKLIN, GROFF   AN
 SCIENCE FICTION GALAXY, THE   CONKLIN, GROFF   AN
 SCIENCE FICTION ODDITIES   CONKLIN, GROFF   AN
 SCIENCE FICTION TERROR TALES   CONKLIN, GROFF   AN
*SCIENCE FICTION THINKING MACHINES   CONKLIN, GROFF   AN
 SEVEN TRIPS THROUGH TIME AND SPACE   CONKLIN, GROFF   AN
 SIX GREAT SHORT SCIENCE FICTION NOVELS CONKLIN, GROFF   AN
 STRANGE ADVENTURES IN SCIENCE FICTION   CONKLIN, GROFF   AN
 STRANGE TRAVELS IN SCIENCE FICTION   CONKLIN, GROFF   AN
 SUPERNATURAL READER, THE   CONKLIN, G&L.   AN
 THUNDER AND ROSES   STURGEON, THEODORE AC
*TREASURY OF SCIENCE FICTION, A   CONKLIN, GROFF   AN
*TWISTED   CONKLIN, GROFF   AN
*WAY HOME, A   STURGEON, THEODORE AC
 12 GREAT CLASSICS OF SCIENCE FICTION   CONKLIN, GROFF   AN
 13 ABOVE THE NIGHT   CONKLIN, GROFF   AN
 13 GREAT STORIES OF SCIENCE FICTION   CONKLIN, GROFF   AN
 17 X INFINITY   CONKLIN, GROFF   AN
 6 GREAT SHORT NOVELS OF SCIENCE FICTION
                                                  CONKLIN, GROFF   AN
 INTRODUCTION   IN C
   GREAT SCIENCE FICTION ABOUT DOCTORS   CONKLIN, G&FABRICANT AN
 INTRODUCTION NO. 2   IN
   FIFTY SHORT SCIENCE FICTION TALES   ASIMOV & CONKLIN   AN
 INTRODUCTORY NOTE   IN
   WORLDS OF WHEN   CONKLIN, GROFF   AN
 NON-LIMITATION OF INTELLIGENCE, THE   IN
   GIANTS UNLEASHED   CONKLIN, GROFF   AN
 ON SCIENCE FICTION BY SCIENTISTS   IN
   GREAT SCIENCE FICTION BY SCIENTISTS   CONKLIN, GROFF   AN
 PREFACE   IN
   SEVEN COME INFINITY   CONKLIN, GROFF   AN
 SCIENCE FICTION AND IDEAS   IN
   HUMAN AND OTHER BEINGS   DEGRAEFF, ALLEN   AN

CONKLIN, LUCY   SEE ALSO   CO-EDITOR GROFF CONKLIN

CONNELL, RICHARD
 MOST DANGEROUS GAME, THE   NV   24
   GHOULS, THE   HAINING, PETER   AN
   NIGHT IN FUNLAND   BRONDFIELD, JEROME AN

CONNER, MICHAEL
 EXTINCTION OF CONFIDENCE, THE EXERCISE OF HONESTY SS
   NEW CONSTELLATIONS   DISCH & NAYLOR   OA

CONNER, PATRICK G.
 TINDAR-B   NV   STL 76 02
   STELLAR 2   DEL REY, JUDY-LYNN OA

CONNOLLY, CYRIL
 YEAR NINE   SS   46
   PAST, PRESENT, AND FUTURE PERFECT   WOLFE, J&FITZ GERALD AN

CONQUEST, ROBERT   SEE ALSO   CO-EDITOR KINGSLEY AMIS
ROBERT SHECKLEY OMNIBUS, THE (LISTED UNDER ROBERT SHECKLEY)
                                                  EC H GOL 73
                                                  PM   69
 FAR OUT
   HOLDING YOUR EIGHT HANDS   LUCIE-SMITH, EDWARD AN
 FOREWORD TO "SPECIALIST"   IN
   MIRROR OF INFINITY, THE   SILVERBERG, ROBERT AN
 GOLDEN AGE, THE   PM   69
   HOLDING YOUR EIGHT HANDS   LUCIE-SMITH, EDWARD AN
 INTRODUCTION   IN
   ROBERT SHECKLEY OMNIBUS, THE   SHECKLEY, ROBERT   AC
 INTRODUCTION   IN C
*SPECTRUM   AMIS & CONQUEST   AN
 SPECTRUM   2   AMIS & CONQUEST   AN
 SPECTRUM   3   AMIS & CONQUEST   AN
 SPECTRUM   5   AMIS & CONQUEST   AN
 PREFACE   IN C
 SPECTRUM   4   AMIS & CONQUEST   AN

CONRAD, EARL
 DA VINCI MACHINE, THE   OC H FPC 68
 COSMIC MEGILLAH, THE   SS
   DA VINCI MACHINE, THE   CONRAD, EARL   OC
 DA VINCI MACHINE, THE   SS
   DA VINCI MACHINE, THE   CONRAD, EARL   OC
 ECSTASY MACHINE OR PROFESSOR A'GLEY IN ANTIMATTERLAND, THE
                                                  NA
   DA VINCI MACHINE, THE   CONRAD, EARL   OC
 FEASIBILITY PLAN, THE   SS
   DA VINCI MACHINE, THE   CONRAD, EARL   OC
 HODSON'S CAPER   SS
   DA VINCI MACHINE, THE   CONRAD, EARL   OC
 JACOB WRESTLES WITH THE ANGEL   SS
   DA VINCI MACHINE, THE   CONRAD, EARL   OC
 MADE HE A RIB   SS
   DA VINCI MACHINE, THE   CONRAD, EARL   OC
 MATURATION OF THE ABORIGINES   SS
   DA VINCI MACHINE, THE   CONRAD, EARL   OC

CONRAD, EARL   (CONTINUED)
 MEDICAL CHART OF STEPHEN PAYNE   SS
   DA VINCI MACHINE, THE   CONRAD, EARL   OC
 OOK OOK OOK   SS
   DA VINCI MACHINE, THE   CONRAD, EARL   OC
 ORIGINS OF PILL AND HAMMER   SS
   DA VINCI MACHINE, THE   CONRAD, EARL   OC
 PROOF WAS IN DRINKWATER'S PUDDING, THE   SS
   DA VINCI MACHINE, THE   CONRAD, EARL   OC
 REPORT ON THE CONDITION OF POETRY CIRCA A.D. 2022 SS
   DA VINCI MACHINE, THE   CONRAD, EARL   OC
 THERMIDOR   SS
   DA VINCI MACHINE, THE   CONRAD, EARL   OC
 TWO BY FOURS, THE   SS
   DA VINCI MACHINE, THE   CONRAD, EARL   OC
 UPSHAW'S UPSET   SS
   DA VINCI MACHINE, THE   CONRAD, EARL   OC

CONRAD, JOSEPH   PSEUD. FOR TEODOR JOSEF KONRAD KORZENIOWSKI
 NIGGER OF THE NARCISSUS   EX
 VOYAGES: SCENARIOS FOR A SHIP CALLED EARTH
                                                  SAUER, ROB   AN

CONTOSKI, VICTOR
 VON GOOM'S GAMBIT   SS   FSF 66 12
   BEST FROM FANTASY AND SCIENCE FICTION: 17
                                        FERMAN, EDWARD L. AN
   NEW WORLDS OF FANTASY NO. 3   CARR, TERRY   AN

CONWAY, GERARD F.
 BABY MAKES TWO   SS   CLR 73 03
   CLARION III   WILSON, ROBIN SCOTT OA
 FUNERAL SERVICE   SS   UNI 72 02
   UNIVERSE 2   CARR, TERRY   OA
 MINDSHIP   SS   UNI 71 01
   UNIVERSE 1   CARR, TERRY   OA
 SILENT HANDS   SS   CLR 71 01
   CLARION   WILSON, ROBIN SCOTT OA

COOK, GLEN
 AND DRAGONS IN THE SKY   NV   CLR 72 02
   CLARION II   WILSON, ROBIN SCOTT OA
 IN THE WIND   NV
   TOMORROW TODAY   ZEBROWSKI, GEORGE OA
 SONG FROM A FORGOTTEN HILL   SS   WOT 71
   CLARION   WILSON, ROBIN SCOTT OA

COOK, STEPHEN
 FINAL FLOWER   SS   NEW 68 AN
   PACIFIC BOOK OF AUSTRALIAN SCIENCE FICTION
                                        BAXTER, JOHN   AN

COOKE, DAVID C.
 PACKAGE OF POWER   SS   SFQ 40 SU
   MOON CONQUERORS, THE   ANONYMOUS   AN

COOMBS, CHARLES
 ROCKET RIDER   SS   BLF 59
   TEEN-AGE OUTER SPACE STORIES   FURMAN, A. L.   AN

COON, CARLETON S.
 FOREWORD   IN
   APEMAN, SPACEMAN   STOVER & HARRISON AN
 FUTURE OF THE RACES OF MAN, THE   AR   65
   APEMAN, SPACEMAN   STOVER & HARRISON AN

COOPER, EDMUND
 NEWS FROM ELSEWHERE   AC   BKM 69 05
 TOMORROW CAME   AC   PTH 63
 TOMORROW'S GIFT   AC   BAL 58
 UNBORN TOMORROW   AC H HAL 71
 VOICES IN THE DARK   AC   DIG 60
 BOY DAVID, THE   SS
   VOICES IN THE DARK   COOPER, EDMUND   AC
 BRAIN CHILD (INVISIBLE BOY)   SS   SEP 56 06
   TOMORROW'S GIFT   COOPER, EDMUND   AC
 BURNT UMBER   SS
   VOICES IN THE DARK   COOPER, EDMUND   AC
 BUTTERFLIES, THE   SS
   NEWS FROM ELSEWHERE   COOPER, EDMUND   AC
   TOMORROW'S GIFT   COOPER, EDMUND   AC
   UNBORN TOMORROW   COOPER, EDMUND   AC
 DEATH WATCH   SS
   TOMORROW CAME   COOPER, EDMUND   AC
 DOOMSDAY STORY, THE   SS
   TOMORROW CAME   COOPER, EDMUND   AC
 DUET FOR ONE FINGER   SS
   VOICES IN THE DARK   COOPER, EDMUND   AC
 END OF THE JOURNEY, THE (SEE M81: URSA MAJOR)   TC
 ENLIGHTENED ONES, THE   NV   FUN 59 01
   NEWS FROM ELSEWHERE   COOPER, EDMUND   AC
   TOMORROW'S GIFT   COOPER, EDMUND   AC
   UNBORN TOMORROW   COOPER, EDMUND   AC
 FALCON CHASE   SS
   TOMORROW'S GIFT   COOPER, EDMUND   AC
 FIRST MARTIAN, THE   SS
   TOMORROW CAME   COOPER, EDMUND   AC
   VOICES IN THE DARK   COOPER, EDMUND   AC
 I AM A GHOST   SS
   VOICES IN THE DARK   COOPER, EDMUND   AC
 INTRODUCTION   IN
   UNBORN TOMORROW   COOPER, EDMUND   AC
 INTRUDERS (INTRUDERS ON THE MOON)   NV   FUN 57 04
   FIRST FLIGHTS TO THE MOON   CLEMENT, HAL   AN
   NEWS FROM ELSEWHERE   COOPER, EDMUND   AC
   TOMORROW'S GIFT   COOPER, EDMUND   AC

```
COOPER, EDMUND       (CONTINUED)
    UNBORN TOMORROW                        COOPER, EDMUND       AC
    INVISIBLE BOY (SEE BRAIN CHILD)                             TC
                                           SS    AUT 54 09
JAR OF LATAKIA, THE
    TOMORROW'S GIFT                        COOPER, EDMUND       AC
                                           SS
JUDGEMENT DAY
    NEWS FROM ELSEWHERE                    COOPER, EDMUND       AC
    TOMORROW CAME                          COOPER, EDMUND       AC
JUPITER LAUGHS
    BEYOND TIME                            LEY, SANDRA          OA
                                           SS
LAST ACT, THE
    VOICES IN THE DARK                     COOPER, EDMUND       AC
LIFE AND DEATH OF PLUNKY GOO, THE          SS
    TOMORROW CAME                          COOPER, EDMUND       AC
    UNBORN TOMORROW                        COOPER, EDMUND       AC
LIONS AND THE HARP, THE                    SS
    VOICES IN THE DARK                     COOPER, EDMUND       AC
                                           SS    FUN 58 08
LIZARD OF WOZ, THE
    NEWS FROM ELSEWHERE                    COOPER, EDMUND       AC
    TOMORROW CAME                          COOPER, EDMUND       AC
    UNBORN TOMORROW                        COOPER, EDMUND       AC
                                           SS
MENHIR, THE
    NEWS FROM ELSEWHERE                    COOPER, EDMUND       AC
                                           SS
MILLER'S DAUGHTER
    VOICES IN THE DARK                     COOPER, EDMUND       AC
                                           SS
MOUSE THAT ROARED, THE
    TOMORROW CAME                          COOPER, EDMUND       AC
    VOICES IN THE DARK                     COOPER, EDMUND       AC
M81: URSA MAJOR (THE END OF THE JOURNEY)   SS    FUN 56 02
    NEWS FROM ELSEWHERE                    COOPER, EDMUND       AC
    TOMORROW'S GIFT                        COOPER, EDMUND       AC
    UNBORN TOMORROW                        COOPER, EDMUND       AC
                                           SS
NINETEEN NINETY-FOUR
    TOMORROW CAME                          COOPER, EDMUND       AC
    VOICES IN THE DARK                     COOPER, EDMUND       AC
                                           SS
PICCADILLY INTERVAL
    TOMORROW CAME                          COOPER, EDMUND       AC
                                           NV    FUN 56 05
QUESTION OF TIME, A
    TOMORROW'S GIFT                        COOPER, EDMUND       AC
REPEAT PERFORMANCE                         SS
    TOMORROW'S GIFT                        COOPER, EDMUND       AC
SECOND CHANCE                              SS
    UNBORN TOMORROW                        COOPER, EDMUND       AC
SENTIMENTAL JOURNEY                        SS
    VOICES IN THE DARK                     COOPER, EDMUND       AC
SIX EGGS FOR MAFEKING                      SS
    VOICES IN THE DARK                     COOPER, EDMUND       AC
SO I NEVER LEFT HOME                       SS
    VOICES IN THE DARK                     COOPER, EDMUND       AC
TOMORROW'S GIFT                            SS    STR 58 04
    STAR SCIENCE FICTION STORIES NO. 4     POHL, FREDERIK       OA
    TOMORROW'S GIFT                        COOPER, EDMUND       AC
UNICORN, THE                               SS
    VOICES IN THE DARK                     COOPER, EDMUND       AC
VERTICAL HOLD                              SS
    TOMORROW CAME                          COOPER, EDMUND       AC
WELCOME HOME                               SS
    NEWS FROM ELSEWHERE                    COOPER, EDMUND       AC
    TOMORROW CAME                          COOPER, EDMUND       AC
WHEN THE SAUCERS CAME
    TOMORROW CAME                          COOPER, EDMUND       AC
    UNBORN TOMORROW                        COOPER, EDMUND       AC
    VOICES IN THE DARK                     COOPER, EDMUND       AC

COOPER, RALPH S.
    NEUTRINO BOMB, THE                     SS    LAS 61 07
    GREAT SCIENCE FICTION BY SCIENTISTS    CONKLIN, GROFF       AN

COOVER, ROBERT
    HAT ACT, THE                           SS    PBY 68 02
    MASKS                                  PLAYBOY, EDITORS OF  AN
    INCIDENT IN THE STREETS OF THE CITY (SEE A PEDESTRIAN ACCIDENT)
                                           TC
    PEDESTRIAN ACCIDENT, A (INCIDENT IN THE STREETS OF THE CITY)
                                           SS    PBY 69 01
    BEST SF: 1970                          HARRISON & ALDISS    AN

COPEMAN, BERGER
    DAWN ATTACK                            SS
    ADVENTURES TO COME                     ESENWEIN, J. BERG    OA
    MAN IN THE MOON COMES DOWN, A          SS
    ADVENTURES TO COME                     ESENWEIN, J. BERG    OA

COPPARD, A. E.
    ADAM AND EVE AND PINCH ME              SS    21
    CHILDREN OF WONDER                     TENN, WILLIAM        AN
    MOONLIGHT TRAVELER, THE                STERN, PHILIP VAN D. AN
    FAIR YOUNG WILLOWY TREE, THE           SS
    ECO-FICTION                            STADLER, JOHN        AN
    GONE AWAY                              SS    46
    MORE TERROR IN THE MODERN VEIN         WOLLHEIM, DONALD A.  AN
    *TERROR IN THE MODERN VEIN             WOLLHEIM, DONALD A.  AN
    HOMELESS ONE, THE                      SS    46
    TRAVELERS IN TIME                      STERN, PHILIP VAN D. AN
    PIFFINGCAP                             SS    21
    SUPERNATURAL READER, THE               CONKLIN, G&L.        AN

COPPEL, ALFRED
    BLOOD LANDS                            SS    DSF 52 12
    WAY OUT                                HOWARD, IVAN         AN
                                           SS    FSF 52 04
    DREAMER, THE
    BEST SCIENCE-FICTION STORIES: 1953, THE
                                           BLEILER & DIKTY      AN
                                           SS    ASF 52 10
    EXILE, THE
    *STORIES FOR TOMORROW                  SLOANE, WILLIAM      AN

COPPEL, ALFRED       (CONTINUED)
    LAST NIGHT OF SUMMER, THE              SS    OSF 54 09
    END OF THE WORLD, THE                  WOLLHEIM, DONALD A.  AN
    PLANET OF DOOM AND OTHER STORIES       ANONYMOUS            AN
    PEACEMAKER, THE                        SS    IFS 53 01
    PRIZE SCIENCE FICTION                  WOLLHEIM, DONALD A.  AN
    REBEL OF VALKYR, THE                   NV    PLS 50 FL
    GALACTIC EMPIRES VOLUME ONE            ALDISS, BRIAN W.     AN
    WHAT GOES UP                           SS    FBK 50 06
    SCIENCE AND SORCERY                    FORD, GARRET         AN

COPPER, BASIL
    KNOCKER AT THE PORTICO, THE            SS
    YEAR'S BEST HORROR STORIES: SERIES II, THE
                                           DAVIS, RICHARD       AN
    MESSAGE FROM THE STARS                 SS    SPC 74 02
    SPACE   2                              DAVIS, RICHARD       OA
    TRODES, THE                            SS    ADS 75 01
    ARMADA SCI-FI ONE                      DAVIS, RICHARD       OA

COREN, ALAN
    OWING TO CIRCUMSTANCES BEYOND OUR CONTROL 1984 HAS BEEN
    UNAVOIDABLY DETAINED                   SS    PUN
    BEST SF: 1974                          HARRISON & ALDISS    AN

CORES, LUCY
    HAIL TO THE CHIEF                      NV
    BEYOND TIME                            LEY, SANDRA          OA

COREY, PAUL
    IF YOU'RE SO SMART                     SS    NWR 69 14
    NEW WRITINGS IN SF.  9                 CARNELL, JOHN        AN
    NEW WRITINGS IN SF. 14                 CARNELL, JOHN        OA

CORMAN, CID
    COMPASS, THE                           PM    67
    SPECULATIONS                           SANDERS, THOMAS E.   AN

CORREA, HUGO
    ALTER EGO                              SS    FSF 67 07
    INTRODUCTORY PSYCHOLOGY THROUGH SCIENCE FICTION
                                           KATZ/WARRICK/&       AN

CORREY, LEE          PSEUD. FOR G. HARRY STINE
    AND A STAR TO STEER HER BY             NV    ASF 53 06
    EVERY BOY'S BOOK OF OUTER SPACE STORIES
                                           DIKTY, T. E.         AN
    EASY WAY OUT, THE                      SS    ASF 66 04
    ANALOG 6                               CAMPBELL, JOHN W. JR AN
    SOMETHING IN THE SKY                   SS    ASF 57 05
    ENCOUNTERS WITH ALIENS                 EARLEY, GEORGE W.    AN
    TEST STAND, THE                        SS    ASF 55 03
    EXPERT DREAMERS, THE                   POHL, FREDERIK       AN

CORWIN, CECIL        PSEUD. FOR C. M. KORNBLUTH
    MASK OF DEMETER                        SS C  FSF 53 01
    PRIZE SCIENCE FICTION                  WOLLHEIM, DONALD A.  AN

CORWIN, NORMAN
    BELLES LETTRES, 2272                   SS    FIN 70
    FUTURE IS NOW, THE                     NOLAN, WILLIAM F.    OA
    IN SPACE WITH RUNYON JONES             SS    52
    SEA OF SPACE, A                        NOLAN, WILLIAM F.    AN

COTTON, JOHN
    COLUMBUS ON ST. DOMENICA               PM    72
    BEST SF: 1972                          HARRISON & ALDISS    AN
    REPORT BACK                            PM    69
    BEST SF: 1969                          HARRISON & ALDISS    AN
    HOLDING YOUR EIGHT HANDS               LUCIE-SMITH, EDWARD  AN

COTTRELL, C. L.
    DANGER! CHILD AT LARGE                 NV    STR 59 06
    STAR SCIENCE FICTION STORIES NO. 6     POHL, FREDERIK       OA

COULSON, JUANITA
    INTERSECTION POINT                     NV
    STAR TREK: THE NEW VOYAGES             MARSHAK, S&CULBREATH OA
    UNSCHEDULED FLIGHT                     SS
    BEYOND TIME                            LEY, SANDRA          OA

CCULSON, ROBERT
    SOY LA LIBERTAD                        SS
    BEYOND TIME                            LEY, SANDRA          OA

COUNCIL OF FOUR
    SCIENCE-FICTIONAL SHERLOCK HOLMES, THE           AN    60

COUNSELMAN, MARY ELIZABETH
    HANDFUL OF SILVER, A                   SS
    TRAVELLERS BY NIGHT                    DERLETH, AUGUST      OA
    NIGHT COURT                            NV    WRT 53 03
    GRAVEYARD READER, THE                  CONKLIN, GROFF       AN
    TREE'S WIFE, THE                       SS    WRT 50 03
    ROOTS OF EVIL, THE                     PARRY, MICHEL        AN
    SUPERNATURAL READER, THE               CONKLIN, G&L.        AN
    UNWANTED, THE                          SS    WRT 51 01
    UNEXPECTED, THE                        MARGULIES, LEO       AN

COUPLING, J. J.      PSEUD. FOR JOHN R. PIERCE
    MR. KINKAID'S PASTS                    SS    FSF 53 08
    BEYOND THE BARRIERS OF SPACE AND TIME  MERRIL, JUDITH       AN
    PERIOD PIECE                           SS    ASF 48 11
    BEST SCIENCE-FICTION STORIES: 1949, THE
                                           BLEILER & DIKTY      AN
    HUMAN-MACHINES                         SCORTIA & ZEBROWSKI  AN
```

COUPLING, J. J.   (CONTINUED)
  TO BE A MAN   SS   YRT 70
    YEAR 2000, THE   HARRISON, HARRY   OA

COURTNEY, ROBERT
  ROVER I WILL BE, A   SS C
    EVERY BOY'S BOOK OF OUTER SPACE STORIES
                          DIKTY, T. E.   AN

COUZYN, JENI
  DAY WE EMBARKED FOR CYTHERA, THE   PM
    BEYOND THIS HORIZON   CARRELL, CHRISTOPHER OA
  HERESIES OF THE HUGE GOD   PM
    BEYOND THIS HORIZON   CARRELL, CHRISTOPHER OA
  TWO POEMS AFTER STORIES BY BRIAN ALDISS GR
    BEYOND THIS HORIZON   CARRELL, CHRISTOPHER OA

COVER, ARTHUR BYRON
  PLATYPUS OF DOOM AND OTHER NIHILISTS, THE   OC   WPB 76 06
  AARDVARK OF DESPAIR, THE   NV
    PLATYPUS OF DOOM AND OTHER NIHILISTS, THE
                          COVER, ARTHUR BYRON OC
  ARMADILLO OF DESTRUCTION, THE   NV
    PLATYPUS OF DOOM AND OTHER NIHILISTS, THE
                          COVER, ARTHUR BYRON OC
  CLAM OF CATASTROPHE, THE   NV
    PLATYPUS OF DOOM AND OTHER NIHILISTS, THE
                          COVER, ARTHUR BYRON OC
  GEE, ISN'T HE THE CUTEST LITTLE THING? SS   ALC 73
    ALIEN CONDITION, THE GOLDIN, STEPHEN   OA
  GROSS LOVE STORY, A   SS   ALT 74
    ALTERNATIVES   GERROLD, DAVID   OA
  IN BETWEEN THEN AND NOW   SS   INY 73 05
    INFINITY 5   HOSKINS, ROBERT   OA
  LIFEGUARD   SS   75
    YEAR'S BEST HORROR STORIES: SERIES IV, THE
                          PAGE, GERALD W.   AN
  MESSAGE OF JOY   SS   ALT 74
    ALTERNATIVES   GERROLD, DAVID   OA
  PLATYPUS OF DOOM, THE   NV
    PLATYPUS OF DOOM AND OTHER NIHILISTS, THE
                          COVER, ARTHUR BYRON OC

COWIE, GEORGE R.
  DEMOBILIZATION   SS   VOX 47
    SCIENCE AND SORCERY   FORD, GARRET   AN

COWPER, RICHARD   PSEUD. FOR JOHN MIDDLETON MURRY
  CUSTODIANS AND OTHER STORIES, THE   AC H GOL 76
  CUSTODIANS, THE   NV   FSF 75 10
    BEST SF: 75, THE NINTH ANNUAL   HARRISON & ALDISS AN
    CUSTODIANS AND OTHER STORIES, THE   COWPER, RICHARD AC
    1976 ANNUAL WORLD'S BEST SF, THE   WOLLHEIM, DONALD A. AN
  HERTFORD MANUSCRIPT, THE   NV   FSF 76 10
    CUSTODIANS AND OTHER STORIES, THE   COWPER, RICHARD AC
    1977 ANNUAL WORLD'S BEST SF, THE   WOLLHEIM, DONALD A. AN
  PARADISE BEACH   NV
    CUSTODIANS AND OTHER STORIES, THE   COWPER, RICHARD AC
  PIPER AT THE GATES OF DAWN   NA
    CUSTODIANS AND OTHER STORIES, THE   COWPER, RICHARD AC

COX, ARTHUR JEAN
  BLIGHT, THE   NV
    *TIME TO COME   DERLETH, AUGUST   OA
  FAME   SS   ORB 70 06
    ORBIT 6   KNIGHT, DAMON   OA
  OCCURRENCE AT THE OWL CREEK REST HOME, AN   NV
    SCIENCE FICTION DISCOVERIES   POHL, C. & F. OA
  SEA CHANGE, THE   SS   FSF 67 03
    BEST FROM FANTASY AND SCIENCE FICTION: 17
                          FERMAN, EDWARD L. AN

COX, IRVING E. JR.
  HOLE IN THE SKY   NV
    *TIME TO COME   DERLETH, AUGUST   OA
  LIKE GODS THEY CAME   SS   AUS 53 01
    SPACE, SPACE, SPACE   SLOANE, WILLIAM   AN
  NO MORE THE STARS   SS   OSF 54 09
    SANDS OF MARS AND OTHER STORIES, THE   ANONYMOUS   AN
  PEACE ON EARTH   NV   FUT 54 06
    6 AND THE SILENT SCREAM   HOWARD, IVAN   AN

COZZI, LUIGI
  RAINY DAY REVOLUTION NO. 39   SS   ISF 67 11
    BEST FROM THE REST OF THE WORLD, THE   WOLLHEIM, DONALD A. AN

CRAIG, WILLIAM
  FROM "THE FALL OF JAPAN"   AR   67
    LOOKING AHEAD   ALLEN, D. & L.   AN

CRAIS, ROBERT
  DUST OF EVENING, THE   SS
    2076: THE AMERICAN TRICENTENNIAL   BRYANT, EDWARD   OA
  WITH CROOKED HANDS   SS
    CLARION SF   WILHELM, KATE   OA

CRAM, RALPH ADAMS
  DEAD VALLEY, THE   SS   95
    HORROR TIMES TEN   NORTON, ALDEN H. AN

CRANE, ROBERT   PSEUD. FOR BERNARD GLEMSER
  PURPLE FIELDS, THE   SS   STR 53 02
    STAR SCIENCE FICTION STORIES NO. 2   POHL, FREDERIK OA

CRANE, STEPHEN
  MAN SAID TO THE UNIVERSE, A   PM
    SPECULATIONS   SANDERS, THOMAS E. AN
  MANACLED   SS   ARG 00 08
    FANTASTIC PULPS, THE HAINING, PETER   AN
  UPTURNED FACE, THE   SS
    *TWISTED   CONKLIN, GROFF   AN

CRAVENS, GWYNETH
  MISS SUBWAYS   SS   NWQ 74 06
    NEW WORLDS NO. 6   PLATT & BAILEY   AN
  ORIGINS OF THE UNIVERSE   SS   NWQ 73 05
    NEW WORLDS NO. 5   MOORCOCK & PLATT OA

CRAWFORD, F. MARION
  FOR THE BLOOD IS THE LIFE   SS   11
    ALONE BY NIGHT   CONGDON, MICHAEL&DON AN
    SUPERNATURAL READER, THE   CONKLIN, G&L. AN

CRAWFORD, MARGARET   SEE PSEUD.
    GARRET FORD (WITH WILLIAM CRAWFORD)

CRAWFORD, WILLIAM L. ALSO AS
    GARRET FORD (WITH MARGARET CRAWFORD)
  GARDEN OF FEAR AND OTHER STORIES, THE   AN   CRF 45
  QUADRATIC   AN H FPB 53
  SCIENCE-FANTASY QUINTETTE   AN H FPB 53

CRICHTON, MICHAEL
  APPROACHING ELLISON   MS
    APPROACHING OBLIVION ELLISON, HARLAN AC

CRISPIN, EDMUND   PSEUD. FOR R. BRUCE MONTGOMERY
  BEST SF   AN H FAB 55
  BEST SF 2   AN H FAB 56
  BEST SF 3   AN H FAB 58
  BEST SF 4   AN H FAB 61
  BEST SF 5   AN H FAB 63
  BEST SF 6   AN H FAB 66
  BEST SF 7   AN H FAB 70
  STARS AND UNDER, THE   AN H FAB 68
  FOREWORD   IN
    BEST SF 6   CRISPIN, EDMUND AN
    BEST SF 7   CRISPIN, EDMUND AN
  INTRODUCTION   IN
    BEST SCIENCE FICTION STORIES OF C. M. KORNBLUTH
                          KORNBLUTH, C. M. AC
    BEST SF   CRISPIN, EDMUND AN
    BEST SF 2   CRISPIN, EDMUND AN
    BEST SF 3   CRISPIN, EDMUND AN
    BEST SF 4   CRISPIN, EDMUND AN
    BEST SF 5   CRISPIN, EDMUND AN
  WHAT SCIENCE FICTION IS   IN
    STARS AND UNDER, THE CRISPIN, EDMUND AN

CROKER, T. CROFTON
  SOUL CAGES, THE   SS
    FANTASY: THE LITERATURE OF THE MARVELOUS
                          KELLEY, LEO P.   AN

CROOK, COMPTON N.   SEE PSEUD. STEPHEN TALL

CROSBY, HARRY C.   SEE PSEUD. CHRISTOPHER ANVIL

CROSS, JAMES
  DOLL-HOUSE, THE   SS   DVS 67 01
    DANGEROUS VISIONS   ELLISON, HARLAN OA
    FANTASY: THE LITERATURE OF THE MARVELOUS
                          KELLEY, LEO P.   AN

CROSS, JOHN KEIR
  BEST HOLIDAY I EVER HAD, THE   SS
    LAURIE'S SPACE ANNUAL ANONYMOUS   AN
  GLASS EYE, THE   SS   46
    TIMELESS STORIES FOR TODAY AND TOMORROW
                          BRADBURY, RAY   AN

CROSS, POLTON   PSEUD. FOR JOHN RUSSELL FEARN
  WINGS ACROSS THE COSMOS   SS   TWS 38 06
    *TREASURY OF SCIENCE FICTION, A   CONKLIN, GROFF   AN

CROSS, RONALD A.
  GETTING OFF   SS
    FUTURE PASTIMES   EDELSTEIN, SCOTT OA
  JEWEL THIEF, THE   SS   NWQ 74 06
    NEW WORLDS NO. 6   PLATT & BAILEY   OA
  STORY OF THREE CITIES, THE   SS   NWQ 73 05
    NEW WORLDS NO. 5   MOORCOCK & PLATT OA

CROSSEN, KENDELL F. ALSO AS   CHRISTOPHER MONIG
  ADVENTURES IN TOMORROW   AN H GBG 51
  FUTURE TENSE   AN H GBG 52 03
  FUTURE TENSE (BRITISH)   AN H BDL 54
  AMBASSADORS FROM VENUS, THE   NV   PLS 52 03
    *BEACHHEADS IN SPACE DERLETH, AUGUST AN
    FROM OTHER WORLDS   DERLETH, AUGUST AN
  ASSIGNMENT IN ALDEBARAN   NV   TWS 53 02
    YEAR'S BEST SCIENCE FICTION NOVELS: 1954
                          BLEILER & DIKTY   AN
  CLOSED DOOR, THE   SS   AMZ 53 09
    SPACE POLICE   NORTON, ANDRE   AN
  EDITOR'S NOTE   IN
    ADVENTURES IN TOMORROW   CROSSEN, KENDELL F. AN
  RESTRICTED CLIENTELE   SS   TWS 51 02
    ADVENTURES IN TOMORROW   CROSSEN, KENDELL F. AN

CROSSEN, KENDELL F. (CONTINUED)
    AMERICAN GOVERNMENT THROUGH SCIENCE FICTION
                                        OLANDER/GREENBERG/& AN
                                        NV STS 52 03
    THINGS OF DISTINCTION
    *FUTURE TENSE   CROSSEN, KENDELL F. AN
    TOMORROW IS HERE TO STAY   IN
    *FUTURE TENSE   CROSSEN, KENDELL F. AN

CROUTCH, LESLIE A.
    PLAYMATE   SS IMG 51 11
    AUTHENTIC BOOK OF SPACE   CAMPBELL, H. J.   AN
    TALES BEYOND TIME   DE CAMP, L. S.&C.   AN

CULBREATH, MYRNA   SEE ALSO CO-EDITOR SONDRA MARSHAK
    INTRODUCTION TO THE HUNTING   IN C
    STAR TREK: THE NEW VOYAGES   MARSHAK, S&CULBREATH OA
    INTRODUCTION: THE ONCE AND FUTURE VOYAGES IN C
    STAR TREK: THE NEW VOYAGES   MARSHAK, S&CULBREATH OA

CUMMINGS, E. E.
    PITY THIS BUSY MONSTER, MANUNKIND   PM   44
    SPECULATIONS   SANDERS, THOMAS E.   AN

CUMMINGS, M. A.
    EXILE AND OTHER TALES OF FANTASY   OC FLG 68
    ALIENS AREN'T WANTED   SS
    EXILE AND OTHER TALES OF FANTASY   CUMMINGS, M. A.   OC
    BUY ME A WOOFL   SS
    EXILE AND OTHER TALES OF FANTASY   CUMMINGS, M. A.   OC
    CAT WHO LIKED THRILLERS, THE   SS
    EXILE AND OTHER TALES OF FANTASY   CUMMINGS, M. A.   OC
    DON'T YOU REMEMBER?   SS
    EXILE AND OTHER TALES OF FANTASY   CUMMINGS, M. A.   OC
    EXILE   SN
    EXILE AND OTHER TALES OF FANTASY   CUMMINGS, M. A.   OC
    FULL MOON   SS
    EXILE AND OTHER TALES OF FANTASY   CUMMINGS, M. A.   OC
    GET RICH QUICK   SS
    EXILE AND OTHER TALES OF FANTASY   CUMMINGS, M. A.   OC
    GIRL WITH THE GREEN GLASS EYES, THE SS
    EXILE AND OTHER TALES OF FANTASY   CUMMINGS, M. A.   OC
    LITTLE OLD LADY   SS
    EXILE AND OTHER TALES OF FANTASY   CUMMINGS, M. A.   OC
    MOON DOWN   SS
    EXILE AND OTHER TALES OF FANTASY   CUMMINGS, M. A.   OC
    SPECIMEN   SS
    EXILE AND OTHER TALES OF FANTASY   CUMMINGS, M. A.   OC
    THOSE WERE GIANTS   SS
    EXILE AND OTHER TALES OF FANTASY   CUMMINGS, M. A.   OC
    TO CHANGE THE PAST   SS
    EXILE AND OTHER TALES OF FANTASY   CUMMINGS, M. A.   OC
    WHAT HAPPENED TO TUESDAY?   SS
    EXILE AND OTHER TALES OF FANTASY   CUMMINGS, M. A.   OC

CUMMINGS, PARKE
    NEEDED: FEMININE MATH   AR   61
    MATHEMATICAL MAGPIE, THE   FADIMAN, CLIFTON   AN

CUMMINGS, RAY
    INTO THE FOURTH DIMENSION   AN SWN 41
    GIRL IN THE GOLDEN ATOM, THE   NA ASW 19 03
    GIANT ANTHOLOGY OF SCIENCE FICTION MARGULIES & FRIEND   AN
    UNDER THE MOONS OF MARS   MOSKOWITZ, SAM   AN
    GRAVITY PROFESSOR   SS AAS 21 05
    EVERY BOY'S BOOK OF SCIENCE FICTION WOLLHEIM, DONALD A. AN
    INTO THE FOURTH DIMENSION   NO SAI 26 09
    INTO THE FOURTH DIMENSION   CUMMINGS, RAY   AN
    MADMAN'S MURDER MELODY   SS HOS 40 12
    FANTASTIC PULPS, THE   HAINING, PETER   AN

CUMMINS, HARLE OREN
    SPACE ANNIHILATOR, THE   SS   02
    ANCESTRAL VOICES   MENVILLE & REGINALD AN

CUNNINGHAM, BEN
    EQUIVOCATION   IL
    SCIENCE FICTION   BRODKIN & PEARSON   AN

CURLOVICH, JOHN M.
    QUITE LATE ONE SPRING NIGHT   SS ORB 75 17
    ORBIT 17   KNIGHT, DAMON   OA

CURREY, L. W.   SEE ALSO CO-EDITOR DAVID G. HARTWELL
    INTRODUCTION   IN C
    BATTLE OF THE MONSTERS AND OTHER STORIES, THE
                                        HARTWELL & CURREY   AN

CURTIS, BETSY
    KEY TO OUT, THE   SS ANA 70
    ALCHEMY AND ACADEME   MCCAFFREY, ANNE   OA
    PECULIAR PEOPLE, A   SS FSF 51 08
    BEST SCIENCE-FICTION STORIES: 1952, THE
                                        BLEILER & DIKTY   AN

CURTIS, RICHARD
    FUTURE TENSE   AN DEL 68 09
    ZOO 2000   SS NEW 72 AN
    ZOO 2000   YOLEN, JANE   AN

CURTIS, WARDON ALLEN
    MONSTER OF LAKE LAMETRIE, THE   SS PRS 99 09
    SCIENCE FICTION BY GASLIGHT   MOSKOWITZ, SAM   AN

CUTHBERT, CHESTER D.
    SUBLIME VIGIL, THE   SS WOS 34 02
    EDITOR'S CHOICE IN SCIENCE FICTION MOSKOWITZ, SAM   AN

DAHL, ROALD
    GREAT AUTOMATIC GRAMMATISATOR, THE SS   53
    VINTAGE ANTHOLOGY OF SCIENCE FANTASY, THE
                                        CERF, CHRISTOPHER   AN
    IN THE RUINS   SS   64
    11TH ANNUAL OF THE YEAR'S BEST S-F, THE
                                        MERRIL, JUDITH   AN
    MAN FROM THE SOUTH   SS   53
    SHOCKING THING, A   KNIGHT, DAMON   AN
    SKIN   SS NYM 52 05
    GRAVEYARD READER, THE   CONKLIN, GROFF   AN
    SOUND MACHINE, THE   SS NYM 49 09
    BR-R-R-| CONKLIN, GROFF   AN
    SCIENCE FACT/FICTION   FARRELL/GAGE/&   AN
    TIMELESS STORIES FOR TODAY AND TOMORROW
                                        BRADBURY, RAY   AN
    WILLIAM AND MARY   NV   59
    LATE GREAT FUTURE, THE   FITZ GERALD & DILLON AN
    WISH, THE   SS   53
    CIRCUS OF DR. LAO AND OTHER IMPROBABLE STORIES
                                        BRADBURY, RAY   AN

DALEY, JOHN BERNARD
    MAN WHO LIKED LIONS, THE   SS INF 56 10
    SF:57, THE YEAR'S GREATEST SCIENCE FICTION AND FANTASY
                                        MERRIL, JUDITH   AN

DALY, MARSHA
    INTRODUCTION   IN
    AND WALK NOW GENTLY THROUGH THE FIRE...
                                        ELWOOD, ROGER   OA

DAMONTI, HENRI
    NOTARY AND THE CONSPIRACY, THE   SS   62
    13 FRENCH SCIENCE-FICTION STORIES   KNIGHT, DAMON   AN
    OLIVIA   SS   60
    13 FRENCH SCIENCE-FICTION STORIES   KNIGHT, DAMON   AN

DANCE, CLIFTON JR.
    BROTHERS, THE   SS FSF 52 06
    GREAT SCIENCE FICTION ABOUT DOCTORS CONKLIN, G&FABRICANT AN

DANCEY, MAX
    COLLECTORS, THE   SS C AMZ 53 07
    BEST SCIENCE-FICTION STORIES: 1954, THE
                                        BLEILER & DIKTY   AN

DANIEL, MOLLY
    WINTER HOUSECLEANING   SS CLR 72 02
    CLARION II   WILSON, ROBIN SCOTT OA

DANN, JACK M. AND GARDNER R. DOZOIS
    FUTURE POWER   OA H RDM 76

DANN, JACK M. AND GEORGE ZEBROWSKI
    FASTER THAN LIGHT   OA H HPR 76

DANN, JACK M.
    WANDERING STARS   AN H HPR 74
    AMONG THE MOUNTAINS   NV
    WORLD NAMED CLEOPATRA, A   ANDERSON, POUL   OA
    DRUM LOLLIPOP, THE   SS ORB 72 11
    ORBIT 11   KNIGHT, DAMON   OA
    DYBBUK DOLLS, THE   SS NDM 75 05
    NEW DIMENSIONS 5   SILVERBERG, ROBERT   OA
    FACES FORWARD   SS C DYS 75
    DYSTOPIAN VISIONS   ELWOOD, ROGER   OA
    FLOWER THAT MISSED THE MORNING, THE SS C
    KILLER PLANTS AND OTHER STORIES, THE ELWOOD, ROGER   OA
    FRAGMENTARY BLUE   NV FAN 75 04
    FUTURE PASTIMES   EDELSTEIN, SCOTT   OA
    GOOD OLD DAYS, THE   SS
    JOURNEY TO ANOTHER STAR AND OTHER STORIES
                                        ELWOOD, ROGER   OA
    I'M WITH YOU IN ROCKLAND   SS NEW 72 AN
    HUMAN-MACHINES   SCORTIA & ZEBROWSKI AN
    STRANGE BED FELLOWS   SCORTIA, THOMAS N.   AN
    INTRODUCTION   IN SCS 73
    SHOWCASE   ELWOOD, ROGER   OA
    INTRODUCTION   IN C
    FUTURE POWER   DANN & DOZOIS   OA
    INTRODUCTION: DREAMING AGAIN   IN C
    FASTER THAN LIGHT   DANN & ZEBROWSKI   OA
    LISTEN, LOVE   SS C NWQ 71 02
    NEW WORLDS QUARTERLY NO. 2   MOORCOCK, MICHAEL   OA
    MARKS OF PAINTED TEETH, THE   SS DEM 73
    DEMON KIND   ELWOOD, ROGER   OA
    OD   SS C OMG 73
    OMEGA   ELWOOD, ROGER   OA
    THERE ARE NO BANISTERS   SS NWB 73 05
    NEW WORLDS QUARTERLY NO. 5   MOORCOCK, MICHAEL   OA
    THIRTY-THREE AND ONE-THIRD   SS C
    LONG NIGHT OF WAITING AND OTHER STORIES
                                        ELWOOD, ROGER   OA
    TIMETIPPING   SS EPC 75
    EPOCH   ELWOOD & SILVERBERG OA
    TULPA   SS NWQ 73 05
    NEW WORLDS NO. 5   MOORCOCK & PLATT   OA
    WHIRL CAGE   SS ORB 72 10
    ORBIT 10   KNIGHT, DAMON   OA
    WINDOWS   SS NWQ 72 03
    NEW WORLDS QUARTERLY NO. 3   MOORCOCK, MICHAEL   OA
    YELLOWHEAD   SS C
    NEW CONSTELLATIONS   DISCH & NAYLOR   OA

```
DANTON, WILLIAM
  BEND OF TIME, THE                                   SS
    MORE SCIENCE FICTION TALES        ELWOOD, ROGER        OA

DANZIG, ALLAN
  GREAT NEBRASKA SEA, THE                    FA   GAL 63 08
    SPECTRUM 4                        AMIS & CONQUEST      AN
    9TH ANNUAL OF THE YEAR'S BEST S-F, THE MERRIL, JUDITH  AN

DARLINGTON, ANDREW
  WHEN THE MUSIC'S OVER                      SS
    STOPWATCH                         HAY, GEORGE          OA

DARNAY, ARSEN
  GUT IN PERIL                               SS   IFS 74 12
    BEST FROM IF, THE   VOLUME III    BAEN, JAMES          AN
  SPLENDID FREEDOM, THE                      NV   GAL 74 09
    BEST FROM GALAXY, THE   VOLUME III BAEN, JAMES         AN

DAULTON, GEORGE
  DEATH-TRAP, THE                            SS   PRS 08 03
    SCIENCE FICTION BY GASLIGHT       MOSKOWITZ, SAM       AN

DAVENPORT, BASIL
  DEALS WITH THE DEVIL                       AN H DOM 58
  INVISIBLE MEN                              AN   BAL 60
  TO THE END OF TIME (LISTED UNDER OLAF STAPLEDON) EC H FKW 53
    INTRODUCTION                             IN
      DEALS WITH THE DEVIL            DAVENPORT, BASIL     AN
    VISION OF OLAF STAPLEDON, THE            AR
      TO THE END OF TIME             STAPLEDON, OLAF      AC

DAVIDSON, AVRAM
  BEST FROM FANTASY AND SCIENCE FICTION: 12   AN H DBL 63
  BEST FROM FANTASY AND SCIENCE FICTION: 13   AN H DBL 64
  BEST FROM FANTASY AND SCIENCE FICTION: 14   AN H DBL 65
  ENQUIRIES OF DOCTOR ESZTERHAZY, THE        NO   WPB 75 12
  OR ALL THE SEAS WITH OYSTERS               AC   BKM 52
  STRANGE SEAS AND SHORES                    AC H DBL 71
  WHAT STRANGE STARS AND SKIES               AC   ACE 65
  AND DON'T FORGET THE ONE RED ROSE          SS   PBY 75 09
    YEAR'S BEST HORROR STORIES: SERIES IV, THE
                                      PAGE, GERALD W.      AN
  APRES NOUS                                 SS   FSF 60 03
    BEST FROM FANTASY AND SCIENCE FICTION: 10
                                      MILLS, ROBERT P.     AN
    STRANGE SEAS AND SHORES           DAVIDSON, AVRAM      AC
  AUTHOR, AUTHOR                             SS   FSF 59 07
    OR ALL THE SEAS WITH OYSTERS      DAVIDSON, AVRAM      AC
  BASILEIKON: SUMMER                         SS   QRK 71 04
    QUARK/4                           DELANY & HACKER      OA
  BASILISK                                   NV   NEW 67 AN
    NEW WORLDS OF FANTASY             CARR, TERRY          AN
  BIG SAM                                    SS   ANA 70
    ALCHEMY AND ACADEME               MCCAFFREY, ANNE      OA
    NEW WORLDS OF FANTASY NO. 3       CARR, TERRY          AN
  BOTTLE FULL OF KISMET, A                   SS
    STRANGE SEAS AND SHORES           DAVIDSON, AVRAM      AC
  BOUNTY HUNTER, THE                         SS   FUN 58 03
    FANTASTIC UNIVERSE OMNIBUS, THE   SANTESSON, HANS S.   AN
    GALACTIC EMPIRES VOLUME TWO       ALDISS, BRIAN W.     AN
    WHAT STRANGE STARS AND SKIES      DAVIDSON, AVRAM      AC
  BUMBERBOOM                                 NV   FSF 66 12
    BEST FROM FANTASY AND SCIENCE FICTION: 17
                                      FERMAN, EDWARD L.    AN
    WORLD'S BEST SCIENCE FICTION: 1967 WOLLHEIM & CARR     AN
  CASE OF THE MOTHER-IN-LAW OF PEARL, THE    NV   FAN 75 10
    ENQUIRIES OF DOCTOR ESZTERHAZY, THE DAVIDSON, AVRAM    NO
  CEASELESS STONES, THE                      NV
    ENQUIRIES OF DOCTOR ESZTERHAZY, THE DAVIDSON, AVRAM    NO
  CERTIFICATE, THE                           SS   FSF 59 03
    DECADE OF FANTASY AND SCIENCE FICTION, A
                                      MILLS, ROBERT P.     AN
    STRANGE SEAS AND SHORES           DAVIDSON, AVRAM      AC
  CHURCH OF SAINT SATAN AND PANDAEMONS, THE  NV   FAN 75 12
    ENQUIRIES OF DOCTOR ESZTERHAZY, THE DAVIDSON, AVRAM    NO
  CLIMACTERIC                                SS   FSF 60 08
    STRANGE SEAS AND SHORES           DAVIDSON, AVRAM      AC
  CROWN JEWELS OF JERUSALEM, OR, THE TELL-TALE HEAD, THE
                                             NV   FSF 75 08
    ENQUIRIES OF DOCTOR ESZTERHAZY, THE DAVIDSON, AVRAM    NO
  DAGON                                      SS   FSF 59 10
    BEST FROM FANTASY AND SCIENCE FICTION: 9
                                      MILLS, ROBERT P.     AN
    OR ALL THE SEAS WITH OYSTERS      DAVIDSON, AVRAM      AC
  DR. MORRIS GOLDPEPPER RETURNS              SS   GAL 62 12
    STRANGE SEAS AND SHORES           DAVIDSON, AVRAM      AC
  FAED-OUT                                   SS   FSF 63 10
    WHAT STRANGE STARS AND SKIES      DAVIDSON, AVRAM      AC
  FAIR TRADE                                 SS   FSF 60 07
    WHAT STRANGE STARS AND SKIES      DAVIDSON, AVRAM      AC
  GOLEM, THE                                 SS   FSF 55 03
    BEST FROM FANTASY AND SCIENCE FICTION: 5
                                      BOUCHER, ANTHONY     AN
    DARK SIDE, THE                    KNIGHT, DAMON        AN
    GREAT SCIENCE-FICTION             LICATA, TONY         AN
    MASTERS' CHOICE                   JANIFER, LAURENCE M. AN
    OR ALL THE SEAS WITH OYSTERS      DAVIDSON, AVRAM      AC
    SF: THE BEST OF THE BEST          MERRIL, JUDITH       AN
    SF: THE YEAR'S GREATEST SCIENCE FICTION AND FANTASY
                                      MERRIL, JUDITH       AN
    WANDERING STARS                   DANN, JACK M.        AN
  GOOBERS, THE                               SS   SWK 65 11
    STRANGE SEAS AND SHORES           DAVIDSON, AVRAM      AC
  GOSLIN DAY                                 SS   ORB 70 06
    ORBIT  6                          KNIGHT, DAMON        OA

DAVIDSON, AVRAM    (CONTINUED)
    WANDERING STARS                   DANN, JACK M.        AN
  GRANTHA SIGHTING, THE                      SS   FSF 58 04
    BEST FROM FANTASY AND SCIENCE FICTION: 8
                                      BOUCHER, ANTHONY     AN
    ENCOUNTERS WITH ALIENS            EARLEY, GEORGE W.    AN
    OR ALL THE SEAS WITH OYSTERS      DAVIDSON, AVRAM      AC
  GREAT IS DIANA                             SS   FSF 58 08
    OR ALL THE SEAS WITH OYSTERS      DAVIDSON, AVRAM      AC
  HELP! I AM DR. MORRIS GOLDPEPPER           NV   GAL 57 07
    INFINITE JESTS                    SILVERBERG, ROBERT   AN
    OR ALL THE SEAS WITH OYSTERS      DAVIDSON, AVRAM      AC
    THIRD GALAXY READER, THE          GOLD, H. L.          AN
  HOUSE THE BLAKENEYS BUILT, THE             SS   FSF 65 01
    ANTHROPOLOGY THROUGH SCIENCE FICTION MASON, C/GREENBERG/& AN
    BEST FROM FANTASY AND SCIENCE FICTION: 15
                                      FERMAN, EDWARD L.    AN
    STRANGE SEAS AND SHORES           DAVIDSON, AVRAM      AC
  I DO NOT HEAR YOU, SIR                     SS   FSF 58 02
    ABC OF SCIENCE FICTION, AN        BOARDMAN, TOM JR.    AN
    OR ALL THE SEAS WITH OYSTERS      DAVIDSON, AVRAM      AC
    TRANSFORMATIONS II                ROSELLE, DANIEL      AN
  INTRODUCTION                               IN
    BEST FROM FANTASY AND SCIENCE FICTION: 12
                                      DAVIDSON, AVRAM      AN
    BEST FROM FANTASY AND SCIENCE FICTION: 13
                                      DAVIDSON, AVRAM      AN
    BEST FROM FANTASY AND SCIENCE FICTION: 14
                                      DAVIDSON, AVRAM      AN
    STRANGE SEAS AND SHORES           DAVIDSON, AVRAM      AC
    WHAT STRANGE STARS AND SKIES      DAVIDSON, AVRAM      AC
    WORLDS OF ROBERT F. YOUNG, THE    YOUNG, ROBERT F.     AC
  INVASION, THE                              SS   PBY 65 07
    TRANSIT OF EARTH                  PLAYBOY, EDITORS OF  AN
  JURY-RIG                                   SS   VSF 57 11
    WHAT STRANGE STARS AND SKIES      DAVIDSON, AVRAM      AC
  KAPPA NU NEXUS, THE                        SS C FSF 61 08
    13 ABOVE THE NIGHT                CONKLIN, GROFF       AN
  KING'S EVIL                                SS   FSF 56 10
    BEST FROM FANTASY AND SCIENCE FICTION: 6
                                      BOUCHER, ANTHONY     AN
    OR ALL THE SEAS WITH OYSTERS      DAVIDSON, AVRAM      AC
    SPECIAL WONDER                    MCCOMAS, J. FRANCIS  AN
  KING'S SHADOW HAS NO LIMITS, THE           SS   WHS 75 04
    ENQUIRIES OF DOCTOR ESZTERHAZY, THE
  LINEAMENTS OF GRATIFIED DESIRE, THE        SS
    WHAT STRANGE STARS AND SKIES      DAVIDSON, AVRAM      AC
  LOVE CALLED THIS THING                     SS C GAL 59 04
    SCIENCE FICTION FOR PEOPLE WHO HATE SCIENCE FICTION
                                      CARR, TERRY          AN
    SIXTH GALAXY READER, THE          GOLD, H. L.          AN
    WHAT STRANGE STARS AND SKIES      DAVIDSON, AVRAM      AC
  MILORD SIR SMIHT, THE ENGLISH WIZARD       NV
    ENQUIRIES OF DOCTOR ESZTERHAZY, THE DAVIDSON, AVRAM    NO
  MISS BUTTERMOUTH                           SS   FSF 62 05
    WHAT STRANGE STARS AND SKIES      DAVIDSON, AVRAM      AC
  MONTAVARDE CAMERA, THE                     SS   FSF 59 05
    OR ALL THE SEAS WITH OYSTERS      DAVIDSON, AVRAM      AC
  MR. STILWELL'S STAGE                       SS   FSF 57 09
    BEST FROM FANTASY AND SCIENCE FICTION: 7
                                      BOUCHER, ANTHONY     AN
    WHAT STRANGE STARS AND SKIES      DAVIDSON, AVRAM      AC
  MY BOYFRIEND'S NAME IS JELLO               SS   FSF 54 07
    BEST FROM FANTASY AND SCIENCE FICTION: 4
                                      BOUCHER, ANTHONY     AN
    OR ALL THE SEAS WITH OYSTERS      DAVIDSON, AVRAM      AC
  NEGRA SUM                                  SS   FSF 57 11
    OR ALL THE SEAS WITH OYSTERS      DAVIDSON, AVRAM      AC
  NO FIRE BURNS                              SS   PBY 59 07
    5TH ANNUAL OF THE YEAR'S BEST S-F, THE MERRIL, JUDITH  AN
  NOW LET US SLEEP                           SS   VSF 57 09
    NO LIMITS                         FERMAN, JOSEPH W.    AC
    OR ALL THE SEAS WITH OYSTERS      DAVIDSON, AVRAM      AC
    SF:58, THE YEAR'S GREATEST SCIENCE FICTION AND FANTASY
                                      MERRIL, JUDITH       AN
    WORLDS OF SCIENCE FICTION, THE    MILLS, ROBERT P.     AN
    YOU AND SCIENCE FICTION           HOLLISTER, BERNARD C AN
  O BRAVE OLD WORLD!                         NV
    BEYOND TIME                       LEY, SANDRA          OA
  OGRE IN THE VLY                            SS   IFS 59 07
    STRANGE SEAS AND SHORES           DAVIDSON, AVRAM      AC
  OGRE, THE                                  SS   IFS 59 07
    WHAT STRANGE STARS AND SKIES      DAVIDSON, AVRAM      AC
  OLD WOMAN WHO LIVED WITH A BEAR, THE       NV
    ENQUIRIES OF DOCTOR ESZTERHAZY, THE DAVIDSON, AVRAM    NO
  OR ALL THE SEAS WITH OYSTERS               SS   GAL 58 05
    EARTH IS THE STRANGEST PLANET     SILVERBERG, ROBERT   AN
    FANTASY: THE LITERATURE OF THE MARVELOUS
                                      KELLEY, LEO P.       AN
    FOURTH GALAXY READER, THE         GOLD, H. L.          AN
    HUGO WINNERS, THE (VOLUME 1)      ASIMOV, ISAAC        AN
    OR ALL THE SEAS WITH OYSTERS      DAVIDSON, AVRAM      AC
    SF:59, THE YEAR'S GREATEST SCIENCE FICTION AND FANTASY
                                      MERRIL, JUDITH       AN
    VINTAGE ANTHOLOGY OF SCIENCE FANTASY, THE
                                      CERF, CHRISTOPHER    AN
  OR THE GRASSES GROW                        SS   FSF 58 11
    OR ALL THE SEAS WITH OYSTERS      DAVIDSON, AVRAM      AC
    SCIENCE FICTION SHOWCASE          KORNBLUTH, MARY      AN
  PARAMOUNT ULJ                              SS   GAL 58 10
    STRANGE SEAS AND SHORES           DAVIDSON, AVRAM      AC
  POLLY CHARMS, THE SLEEPING WOMAN           NV   FSF 75 02
    ENQUIRIES OF DOCTOR ESZTERHAZY, THE DAVIDSON, AVRAM    NO
  POWER OF EVERY ROOT, THE                   NV   FSF 67 10
    SF: AUTHORS' CHOICE 3             HARRISON, HARRY      AN
    STRANGE SEAS AND SHORES           DAVIDSON, AVRAM      AC
```

DAVIDSON, AVRAM   DE CAMP, L. SPRAGUE

DAVIDSON, AVRAM   (CONTINUED)   DAVIS, HANK
  PREFACE   IN   TO PLANT A SEED   SS   ORB 72 11
    STRANGE SEAS AND SHORES   DAVIDSON, AVRAM   AC   ORBIT 11   KNIGHT, DAMON   OA
  RITE OF SPRING   SS   ORB 70 08
    BEST FROM ORBIT, THE   KNIGHT, DAMON   AN   DAVIS, RICHARD
    ORBIT   8   KNIGHT, DAMON   OA   ARMADA SCI-FI ONE   OA   ARM 75 04
  ROADS, THE ROADS, THE BEAUTIFUL ROADS, THE   SS   ORB 69 05   ARMADA SCI-FI TWO   OA   ARM 75 04
    ORBIT   5   KNIGHT, DAMON   OA   SPACE   1   OA H ABS 73 06
  SACHEVERELL   SS   FSF 64 03   SPACE   2   OA H ABS 74 01
    BEST FROM FANTASY AND SCIENCE FICTION: 14   YEAR'S BEST HORROR STORIES: SERIES II, THE   AN   DAW 74 07
                                   DAVIDSON, AVRAM   AN   YEAR'S BEST HORROR STORIES: SERIES III, THE AN   DAW 75 06
    STRANGE SEAS AND SHORES   DAVIDSON, AVRAM   AC   YEAR'S BEST HORROR STORIES, THE   AN   DAW 71
  SELECTRA SIX-TEN   SS   FSF 70 10   INTRODUCTION   IN
    BEST FROM FANTASY AND SCIENCE FICTION: 19   YEAR'S BEST HORROR STORIES: SERIES III, THE
                                   FERMAN, EDWARD L. AN   DAVIS, RICHARD   AN
  SENSIBLE MAN, THE   SS   PBY 59 02
    DEAD ASTRONAUT, 10 STORIES OF SPACE FLIGHT, THE   DAVIS, ROBERT L.
                               PLAYBOY, EDITORS OF AN   TERATOHIPPUS   NV   IFS 72 12
    PLAYBOY BOOK OF SCIENCE FICTION AND FANTASY, THE   BEST SCIENCE FICTION STORIES OF THE YEAR (1972)
                               PLAYBOY, EDITORS OF AN   DEL REY, LESTER   AN
  SINGULAR EVENTS WHICH OCCURRED IN THE HOVEL ON THE ALLEY OFF
    OF EYE STREET, THE   SS   FSF 62 02   DAVIS, WESLEY FORD
    BEST FROM FANTASY AND SCIENCE FICTION: 12   ASK AND IT MAY BE GIVEN   SS   FSF 71 10
                                   DAVIDSON, AVRAM   AN   NEW AWARENESS, THE   WARRICK & GREENBERG AN
    WHAT STRANGE STARS AND SKIES   DAVIDSON, AVRAM   AC
  SIXTH SEASON, THE   SS   FSF 60 06   DAVISON, L.
    OR ALL THE SEAS WITH OYSTERS   DAVIDSON, AVRAM   AC   ASPECT OF ENVIRONMENT   SS   NWR 70 17
  SIXTY-THIRD STREET STATION, THE   SS   FSF 62 03   NEW WRITINGS IN SF. 17   CARNELL, JOHN   OA
    STRANGE SEAS AND SHORES   DAVIDSON, AVRAM   AC
  SOURCES OF THE NILE, THE   NV   FSF 61 01   DAVY, JOHN
  *BEST FROM FANTASY AND SCIENCE FICTION: 11   VENUS MYSTERY FOR SCIENTISTS   AR   OBS 67 10
                                   MILLS, ROBERT P. AN   ALL ABOUT VENUS   ALDISS, BRIAN W.   AN
    POCKETFUL OF STARS, A   KNIGHT, DAMON   AN   FAREWELL FANTASTIC VENUS   ALDISS & HARRISON   AN
    STRANGE SEAS AND SHORES   DAVIDSON, AVRAM   AC
    TOMORROW X 4   KNIGHT, DAMON   AN   DAY, PRICE
  SUMMERLAND   SS   FSF 57 07   4 O'CLOCK   SS   58
    OR ALL THE SEAS WITH OYSTERS   DAVIDSON, AVRAM   AC   NIGHT IN FUNLAND   BRONDFIELD, JEROME   AN
  TAIL-TIED KINGS, THE   SS   GAL 62 04
    SEVENTH GALAXY READER, THE   POHL, FREDERIK   AN   DE BERGERAC, CYRANO
    STRANGE SEAS AND SHORES   DAVIDSON, AVRAM   AC   FROM "A VOYAGE TO THE MOON" (1650)   EX
  TAKE WOODEN INDIANS   NV   GAL 59 06   PAST, PRESENT, AND FUTURE PERFECT WOLFE, J&FITZ GERALD AN
    FIFTH GALAXY READER, THE   GOLD, H. L.   AN   JOURNEY TO THE MOON, A (ABRIDGED)   NV
    STRANGE SEAS AND SHORES   DAVIDSON, AVRAM   AC   3000 YEARS OF FANTASY AND SCIENCE FICTION
  TEETH OF DESPAIR, THE   SS C FSF 61 05   DE CAMP, L. S.&C. AN
    SCIENCE FICTION ODDITIES   CONKLIN, GROFF   AN   VOYAGE TO THE MOON (CONDENSED)   SS
    WHAT STRANGE STARS AND SKIES   DAVIDSON, AVRAM   AC   MASTERPIECES OF SCIENCE FICTION MOSKOWITZ, SAM   AN
  THEY LOVED ME IN UTICA   SS   NEW 70 AN
    NEW WORLDS OF FANTASY NO. 2   CARR, TERRY   AN   DE CAMP, CATHERINE CROOK
  UNKNOWN LAW, THE   NV   FSF 64 06   SEE ALSO   CO-EDITOR L. SPRAGUE DE CAMP
    WHAT STRANGE STARS AND SKIES   DAVIDSON, AVRAM   AC   ICARUS   SS   NEW 73 AN
  UP CHRISTOPHER TO MADNESS   SS C KNT 65 11   TALES BEYOND TIME   DE CAMP, L. S.&C. AN
    PARTNERS IN WONDER   ELLISON, HARLAN AC   INTRODUCTION: YESTERDAY, TOMORROW, AND MAYBY IN C
  UP THE CLOSE AND DOWN THE STAIR   SS   FSF 58 05   TALES BEYOND TIME   DE CAMP, L. S.&C. AN
    OR ALL THE SEAS WITH OYSTERS   DAVIDSON, AVRAM   AC   INTRODUCTION- BEYOND THE WORLD WE KNOW   IN C
  VAT, THE   SS   FSF 61 10   3000 YEARS OF FANTASY AND SCIENCE FICTION
    STRANGE SEAS AND SHORES   DAVIDSON, AVRAM   AC   DE CAMP, L. S.&C. AN
  WHAT STRANGE STARS AND SKIES   SS   FSF 63 12
    BEST FROM FANTASY AND SCIENCE FICTION: 13   DE CAMP, L. SPRAGUE AND CATHERINE CROOK DE CAMP
                                   DAVIDSON, AVRAM   AN   TALES BEYOND TIME   AN H LOT 73
    WHAT STRANGE STARS AND SKIES   DAVIDSON, AVRAM   AC   3000 YEARS OF FANTASY AND SCIENCE FICTION   AN H LOT 72
  WHERE DO YOU LIVE, QUEEN ESTHER?   SS   FSF 64 11
    WHAT STRANGE STARS AND SKIES   DAVIDSON, AVRAM   AC   DE CAMP, L. SPRAGUE AND PLETCHER PRATT
  WOMAN WHO THOUGHT SHE COULD READ, THE SS FSF 59 01   TALES FROM GAVAGAN'S BAR   AC H TWN 53
    OR ALL THE SEAS WITH OYSTERS   DAVIDSON, AVRAM   AC
  YO-HO, AND UP   SS   FSF 60 12   DE CAMP, L. SPRAGUE SEE ALSO   CO-AUTHOR ROBERT E. HOWARD
    STRANGE SEAS AND SHORES   DAVIDSON, AVRAM   AC   CONTINENT MAKERS AND OTHER TALES OF THE VIAGENS AC H TWN 53
                                                                     GUN FOR DINOSAUR AND OTHER IMAGINATIVE TALES   AC H DBL 63
DAVIES, HOWELL   SEE PSEUD. ANDREW MARVELL   SPELL OF SEVEN, THE   AN   PYR 65 06
                                                                     SPRAGUE DE CAMP'S NEW ANTHOLOGY   AC H HML 53
DAVIS, BRIAN   TRITONIAN RING, THE   AC H TWN 53
  BEST OF MURRAY LEINSTER, THE (LISTED UNDER MURRAY LEINSTER)   WHEELS OF IF, THE   AC H SHS 48
                                   EC   COR 76   ALL THAT GLITTERS   SS C NEW 53 AC
  INTRODUCTION   IN   TALES FROM GAVAGAN'S BAR   DE CAMP, L. S.&PRATT AC
    BEST OF MURRAY LEINSTER, THE   LEINSTER, MURRAY AC   ANCESTRAL AMETHYST, THE   SS C FSF 52 08
                                                                       TALES FROM GAVAGAN'S BAR   DE CAMP, L. S.&PRATT AC
DAVIS, CHAN   ANIMAL-CRACKER PLOT, THE   SS C FSF 49 07
  ADRIFT ON THE POLICY LEVEL   SS   STR 59 05   CONTINENT MAKERS AND OTHER TALES OF THE VIAGENS
    ABOVE THE HUMAN LANDSCAPE   MCNELLY & STOVER AN   DE CAMP, L. SPRAGUE AC
    EXPERT DREAMERS, THE   POHL, FREDERIK   AN   ARISTOTLE AND THE GUN   NV   ASF 58 02
    POLITICAL SCIENCE FICTION   GREENBERG& WARRICK AN   ALPHA 3   SILVERBERG, ROBERT AN
    STAR SCIENCE FICTION STORIES NO. 5 POHL, FREDERIK OA   GUN FOR DINOSAUR AND OTHER IMAGINATIVE TALES
  HEXAMINATION   SS   NOV 70 01   DE CAMP, L. SPRAGUE AC
    *NOVA 1   HARRISON, HARRY OA   AUTHOR'S NOTE   IN
  LAST YEAR'S GRAVE UNDUG   SS C NEW 62 AN   CONTINENT MAKERS AND OTHER TALES OF THE VIAGENS
    GREAT SCIENCE FICTION BY SCIENTISTS CONKLIN, GROFF AN   DE CAMP, L. SPRAGUE AC
  LETTER TO ELLEN   SS   ASF 47 06   BEASTS OF BOURBON   SS C FSF 51 10
    *SCIENCE FICTION THINKING MACHINES CONKLIN, GROFF AN   TALES FROM GAVAGAN'S BAR   DE CAMP, L. S.&PRATT AC
  NIGHTMARE, THE   NV   ASF 46 05   BEST-LAID SCHEME, THE   SS   ASF 41 02
    *TREASURY OF SCIENCE FICTION, A CONKLIN, GROFF   AN   WHEELS OF IF, THE   DE CAMP, L. SPRAGUE AC
                                                                     BETTER MOUSETRAP, THE   SS C FSF 50 12
DAVIS, DOROTHY S.   TALES FROM GAVAGAN'S BAR   DE CAMP, L. S.&PRATT AC
  MUTED HORN, THE   SS   FUN 57 05   BLACK BALL, THE   SS C FSF 52 10
    FANTASTIC UNIVERSE OMNIBUS, THE SANTESSON, HANS S. AN   BEST FROM FANTASY AND SCIENCE FICTION: 2
                                                                                                     BOUCHER & MCCOMAS AN
DAVIS, F. H.   TALES FROM GAVAGAN'S BAR   DE CAMP, L. S.&PRATT AC
  DREAM PILLS, THE   SS   20   BLACK STRANGER, THE (SEE THE TREASURE OF TRANICOS)
    STRANGE ECSTASIES   PARRY, MICHEL   AN   TC C
                                                                     BLACK TEARS   SS C
DAVIS, GRANIA   CONAN THE WANDERER   HOWARD, R./DE CAMP/& AC
  MY HEAD'S IN A DIFFERENT PLACE, NOW NV   UNI 72 02   BLUE GIRAFFE, THE   NV   ASF 39 08
    UNIVERSE 2   CARR, TERRY   OA   *ADVENTURES IN TIME AND SPACE   HEALY & MCCOMAS   AN
  YOUNG LOVE   NV   ORB 74 13   ANDROIDS, TIME MACHINES AND BLUE GIRAFFES
    ORBIT 13   KNIGHT, DAMON   OA   ELWOOD & GHIDALIA AN
                                                                     ESCALES DANS L'INFINI   GALLET, GEORGES H. AN
                                                                     SCIENCE FICTION BESTIARY, THE SILVERBERG, ROBERT AN
                                                                     WORLD OF WONDER   PRATT, FLETCHER   AN

DE CAMP, L. SPRAGUE   DE CAMP, L. SPRAGUE

DE CAMP, L. SPRAGUE (CONTINUED)
  CALORIES   SS   TST 51 SP
    SPRAGUE DE CAMP'S NEW ANTHOLOGY   DE CAMP, L. SPRAGUE AC
  CAVEAT EMPTOR   SS C WRT 53 03
    DEALS WITH THE DEVIL   DAVENPORT, BASIL   AN
    TALES FROM GAVAGAN'S BAR   DE CAMP, L. S.&PRATT AC
  CHAINS OF SHAMBALLAH   SS C
    CONAN   HOWARD, R./DE CAMP/& AC
  COLORFUL CHARACTER, THE   SS   TWS 49 12
    SPRAGUE DE CAMP'S NEW ANTHOLOGY   DE CAMP, L. SPRAGUE AC
  COMMAND, THE   SS   ASF 38 10
    DOORWAY INTO TIME   MOSKOWITZ, SAM   AN
    MODERN MASTERPIECES OF SCIENCE FICTION MOSKOWITZ, SAM AN
  CONAN THE VICTORIOUS (SEE THE RETURN OF CONAN) TC C
  CONAN, MAN OF DESTINY (SEE THE ROAD OF THE EAGLES)
                                             TC C
  CONTINENT MAKERS, THE   NA   TWS 51 04
    CONTINENT MAKERS AND OTHER TALES OF THE VIAGENS
                                      DE CAMP, L. SPRAGUE AC
  CONTRABAND COW, THE   SS   ASF 42 07
    WHEELS OF IF, THE   DE CAMP, L. SPRAGUE AC
  CORNZAN THE MIGHTY   SS   FUT 55 28
    GUN FOR DINOSAUR AND OTHER IMAGINATIVE TALES
                                      DE CAMP, L. SPRAGUE AC
  CORPUS DELECTABLE   SS C NEW 53 AC
    TALES FROM GAVAGAN'S BAR   DE CAMP, L. S.&PRATT AC
  DIME BRINGS YOU SUCCESS, A   SS C NEW 53 AC
    TALES FROM GAVAGAN'S BAR   DE CAMP, L. S.&PRATT AC
  DRUMS OF TOMBALKU   SS C
    CONAN THE ADVENTURER   HOWARD, R. & DE CAMP AC
  EGG, THE   SS   SAT 56 10
    GUN FOR DINOSAUR AND OTHER IMAGINATIVE TALES
                                      DE CAMP, L. SPRAGUE AC
  ELEPHAS FRUMENTI   SS C FSP 50 WS
    BEST FROM FANTASY AND SCIENCE FICTION BOUCHER & MCCOMAS AN
    TALES FROM GAVAGAN'S BAR   DE CAMP, L. S.&PRATT AC
  EMPEROR'S FAN, THE   NV   AMA 73
    ASTOUNDING   HARRISON, HARRY   OA
  EMPLOYMENT (AS LYMAN R. LYON)   SS   ASF 39 05
    *IMAGINATION UNLIMITED   BLEILER & DIKTY   AN
    SCIENCE FICTION INVENTIONS   KNIGHT, DAMON   AN
  EVE OF ST. JOHN, THE   SS C NEW 53 AC
    TALES FROM GAVAGAN'S BAR   DE CAMP, L. S.&PRATT AC
  EXALTED, THE   NV   ASF 40 11
    *ASTOUNDING SCIENCE FICTION ANTHOLOGY, THE
                                      CAMPBELL, JOHN W. JR AN
  EYE OF TANDYLA, THE   NV   FAD 51 05
    TIME UNTAMED   HOWARD, IVAN   AN
    TRITONIAN RING, THE   DE CAMP, L. SPRAGUE AC
  FINISHED   SS   ASF 49 11
    CONTINENT MAKERS AND OTHER TALES OF THE VIAGENS
                                      DE CAMP, L. SPRAGUE AC
  FOREWORD   IN
    WHEELS OF IF, THE   DE CAMP, L. SPRAGUE AC
  FROST-GIANT'S DAUGHTER, THE   SS C FMG 53 08
    COMING OF CONAN, THE   HOWARD, ROBERT E.   AC
  GALTON WHISTLE, THE (ULTRASONIC GOD)   NV   FUT 51 07
    CONTINENT MAKERS AND OTHER TALES OF THE VIAGENS
                                      DE CAMP, L. SPRAGUE AC
  GIFT OF GOD, THE   SS C FSP 50 WS
    BEST FROM FANTASY AND SCIENCE FICTION BOUCHER & MCCOMAS AN
    TALES FROM GAVAGAN'S BAR   DE CAMP, L. S.&PRATT AC
  GIN COMES IN BOTTLES   SS C NEW 53 AC
    TALES FROM GAVAGAN'S BAR   DE CAMP, L. S.&PRATT AC
  GIT ALONG!   SS   ASF 50 08
    CONTINENT MAKERS AND OTHER TALES OF THE VIAGENS
                                      DE CAMP, L. SPRAGUE AC
  *OUTER REACHES, THE   DERLETH, AUGUST   AN
  GNARLY MAN, THE   NV   UNK 39 06
    HUMAN?   MERRIL, JUDITH   AN
    UNKNOWN, THE   BENSEN, D. R.   AN
    WHEELS OF IF, THE   DE CAMP, L. SPRAGUE AC
  GRATITUDE (PROPERTY OF VENUS)   NV   GAL 55 07
    GUN FOR DINOSAUR AND OTHER IMAGINATIVE TALES
                                      DE CAMP, L. SPRAGUE AC
  GREEN THUMB, THE   SS C FSP 53 02
    TALES FROM GAVAGAN'S BAR   DE CAMP, L. S.&PRATT AC
  GUIDED MAN, THE   NV   STS 52 10
    GUN FOR DINOSAUR AND OTHER IMAGINATIVE TALES
                                      DE CAMP, L. SPRAGUE AC
  GUN FOR DINOSAUR, A   NV   GAL 56 03
    GUN FOR DINOSAUR AND OTHER IMAGINATIVE TALES
                                      DE CAMP, L. SPRAGUE AC
    TIME CURVE, THE   MOSKOWITZ & ELWOOD   AN
    WORLD THAT COULDN'T BE AND 8 OTHER SF NOVELETS
                                      GOLD, H. L.   AN
    3000 YEARS OF FANTASY AND SCIENCE FICTION
                                      DE CAMP, L. S.&C.   AN
  HALL OF THE DEAD, THE   NV C FSP 67 02
    CONAN   HOWARD, R./DE CAMP/& AC
  HAWKS OVER SHEM (FROM "HAWKS OVER EGYPT" BY REH.) NV C FUN 55 10
    CONAN THE FREEBOOTER   HOWARD, R. & DE CAMP AC
    TALES OF CONAN   HOWARD, R. & DE CAMP AC
  HERE, PUTZI!   SS C NEW 53 AC
    TALES FROM GAVAGAN'S BAR   DE CAMP, L. S.&PRATT AC
  HIBITED MAN, THE   SS   TWS 49 10
    *MY BEST SCIENCE FICTION STORY   MARGULIES & FRIEND   AN
    SHAPE OF THINGS, THE   KNIGHT, DAMON   AN
  HUNGRY HERCYNIAN, THE   NV   USF 53 12
    SPELL OF SEVEN, THE   DE CAMP, L. SPRAGUE AN
  HYPERPELOSITY   SS   ASF 38 04
    OMNIBUS OF SCIENCE FICTION   CONKLIN, GROFF   AN
    SCIENCE FICTION OF THE 30'S   KNIGHT, DAMON   AN
    WHEELS OF IF, THE   DE CAMP, L. SPRAGUE AC
  IMPRACTICAL JOKE   SS   FUT 56 29

DE CAMP, L. SPRAGUE (CONTINUED)
  GUN FOR DINOSAUR AND OTHER IMAGINATIVE TALES
                                      DE CAMP, L. SPRAGUE AC
    WEIRD ONES, THE   HOWARD, IVAN   AC
  IN-GROUP   SS   MAR 52 05
    GUN FOR DINOSAUR AND OTHER IMAGINATIVE TALES
                                      DE CAMP, L. SPRAGUE AC
  INCORRIGIBLE, THE   SS   ASF 39 01
    FUTURES TO INFINITY   MOSKOWITZ, SAM   AN
  INSPECTOR'S TEETH, THE   SS   ASF 50 04
    CONTINENT MAKERS AND OTHER TALES OF THE VIAGENS
                                      DE CAMP, L. SPRAGUE AC
  INTERNAL COMBUSTION   SS   INF 56 02
    GUN FOR DINOSAUR AND OTHER IMAGINATIVE TALES
                                      DE CAMP, L. SPRAGUE AC
    SOULS IN METAL   ASHLEY, MICHAEL   AN
  INTRODUCTION   IN
    COMING OF CONAN, THE   HOWARD, ROBERT E.   AC
    CONAN   HOWARD, R./DE CAMP/& AC
    CONAN THE ADVENTURER   HOWARD, R. & DE CAMP AC
    CONAN THE AVENGER   HOWARD, R./NYBERG/& AC
    CONAN THE FREEBOOTER   HOWARD, R. & DE CAMP AC
    CONAN THE USURPER   HOWARD, R. & DE CAMP AC
    CONAN THE WANDERER   HOWARD, R./DE CAMP/& AC
    CONAN THE WARRIOR   HOWARD, R. & DE CAMP AC
    KING CONAN   HOWARD, ROBERT E.   AC
  INTRODUCTION: YESTERDAY, TOMORROW, AND MAYBY   IN C
    TALES BEYOND TIME   DE CAMP, L. S.&C.   AN
  INTRODUCTION- BEYOND THE WORLD WE KNOW   IN C
    3000 YEARS OF FANTASY AND SCIENCE FICTION
                                      DE CAMP, L. S.&C.   AN
  ISAAC ASIMOV (YOU CAN'T BEAT BRAINS)   AR   FSP 66 10
    BEST FROM FANTASY AND SCIENCE FICTION, 25TH ANNIV.
                                      FERMAN, EDWARD L.   AN
  ISOLINGUALS, THE   SS   ASF 37 09
    FIRST FLIGHT   KNIGHT, DAMON   AN
  JUDGMENT DAY   SS   ASF 55 08
    BEST SCIENCE FICTION STORIES AND NOVELS: 1956
                                      DIKTY, T. E.   AN
    GREAT SCIENCE-FICTION   LICATA, TONY   AN
    GUN FOR DINOSAUR AND OTHER IMAGINATIVE TALES
                                      DE CAMP, L. SPRAGUE AC
    SCIENCE FICTION ARGOSY, A   KNIGHT, DAMON   AN
  JUICE   SS   SSS 40 05
    SPRAGUE DE CAMP'S NEW ANTHOLOGY   DE CAMP, L. SPRAGUE AC
  LAMENT BY A MAKER   PM   FSP 55 01
    BEST FROM FANTASY AND SCIENCE FICTION: 5
                                      BOUCHER, ANTHONY   AN
  LANGUAGE FOR TIME TRAVELERS   AR   ASF 38 07
    COMING ATTRACTIONS   GREENBERG , MARTIN   NF
  LET'S HAVE FUN   SS   SFQ 57 05
    GUN FOR DINOSAUR AND OTHER IMAGINATIVE TALES
                                      DE CAMP, L. SPRAGUE AC
    RARE SCIENCE FICTION   HOWARD, IVAN   AN
  LIVING FOSSIL   SS   ASF 39 02
    GATES TO TOMORROW   NORTON, AN.&DONALDY AN
    *TREASURY OF SCIENCE FICTION, A   CONKLIN, GROFF   AN
  LOVE-NEST, THE   SS C NEW 53 AC
    TALES FROM GAVAGAN'S BAR   DE CAMP, L. S.&PRATT AC
  MERMAN, THE   SS   ASF 38 12
    SCIENCE FICTION OF THE 30'S   KNIGHT, DAMON   AN
    WHEELS OF IF, THE   DE CAMP, L. SPRAGUE AC
  MORE THAN SKIN DEEP   SS C FSP 51 04
    TALES FROM GAVAGAN'S BAR   DE CAMP, L. S.&PRATT AC
  MY BROTHER'S KEEPER   SS C NEW 53 AC
    TALES FROM GAVAGAN'S BAR   DE CAMP, L. S.&PRATT AC
  NEW ARCADIA   NV   FUT 56 30
    GUN FOR DINOSAUR AND OTHER IMAGINATIVE TALES
                                      DE CAMP, L. SPRAGUE AC
  NO FORWARDING ADDRESS   SS C NEW 53 AC
    TALES FROM GAVAGAN'S BAR   DE CAMP, L. S.&PRATT AC
  NOTHING IN THE RULES   NV   UNK 39 07
    FROM UNKNOWN WORLDS   CAMPBELL, JOHN W. JR AN
  ORDEAL OF PROFESSOR KLEIN, THE   SS   SFA 52 11
    *BEACHHEADS IN SPACE   DERLETH, AUGUST   AN
  OWL AND THE APE, THE   SS   IMG 51 11
    TRITONIAN RING, THE   DE CAMP, L. SPRAGUE AC
  PALIMPSEST OF ST. AUGUSTINE, THE   SS C NEW 53 AC
    TALES FROM GAVAGAN'S BAR   DE CAMP, L. S.&PRATT AC
  PERPETUAL MOTION (WIDE-OPEN PLANET)   NV   FUT 50 09
    CONTINENT MAKERS AND OTHER TALES OF THE VIAGENS
                                      DE CAMP, L. SPRAGUE AC
  PROPERTY OF VENUS (SEE GRATITUDE)   TC
  PROPOSAL   SS   STS 52 11
    SF: AUTHORS' CHOICE   HARRISON, HARRY   AN
    SPRAGUE DE CAMP'S NEW ANTHOLOGY   DE CAMP, L. SPRAGUE AC
  RAPE OF THE LOCK, THE   SS C FSP 52 02
    TALES FROM GAVAGAN'S BAR   DE CAMP, L. S.&PRATT AC
  RETURN OF CONAN, THE (EXPANDED FROM "CONAN THE VICTORIOUS",
    PUBLISHED BY GNOME, 1957)   NO C FUN 57 09
    CONAN THE AVENGER   HOWARD, R./NYBERG/& AC
  ROAD OF THE EAGLES, THE (CONAN, MAN OF DESTINY) NV C FUN 55 12
    CONAN THE FREEBOOTER   HOWARD, R. & DE CAMP AC
    TALES OF CONAN   HOWARD, R. & DE CAMP AC
  SAXON PRETENDER, THE   SS
    SPRAGUE DE CAMP'S NEW ANTHOLOGY   DE CAMP, L. SPRAGUE AC
  SOARING STATUE, THE   SS   NEW 54 09
    TOMORROW'S UNIVERSE   CAMPBELL, H. J.   AN
  SORCERERS, THE   PM   ANA 70
    ALCHEMY AND ACADEME   MCCAFFREY, ANNE   OA
  SPACE CLAUSE, THE   SS   IFS 52 09
    SPRAGUE DE CAMP'S NEW ANTHOLOGY   DE CAMP, L. SPRAGUE AC
  STONE OF THE SAGES, THE   SS C NEW 53 AC
    TALES FROM GAVAGAN'S BAR   DE CAMP, L. S.&PRATT AC
  STRONGER SPELL, THE   SS   FNF 53 11
    TRITONIAN RING, THE   DE CAMP, L. SPRAGUE AC

DE CAMP, L. SPRAGUE

DE CAMP, L. SPRAGUE (CONTINUED)
   SUMMER WEAR   SS   STS 50 05
      BEST SCIENCE-FICTION STORIES: 1951, THE
                                          BLEILER & DIKTY   AN
   CONTINENT MAKERS AND OTHER TALES OF THE VIAGENS
                                          DE CAMP, L. SPRAGUE AC
   THING OF CUSTOM, A   SS   FUN 57 01
      FANTASTIC UNIVERSE OMNIBUS, THE   SANTESSON, HANS S.   AN
   GUN FOR DINOSAUR AND OTHER IMAGINATIVE TALES
                                          DE CAMP, L. SPRAGUE AC
   LATE GREAT FUTURE, THE   FITZ GERALD & DILLON AN
   RULERS OF MEN   SANTESSON, HANS S.   AN
   THROWBACK   NV   ASF 49 03
      APEMAN, SPACEMAN   STOVER & HARRISON   AN
   GUN FOR DINOSAUR AND OTHER IMAGINATIVE TALES
                                          DE CAMP, L. SPRAGUE AC
   TREASURE OF TRANICOS, THE (THE BLACK STRANGER) NA C FMG 53 03
      CONAN THE USURPER   HOWARD, R. & DE CAMP AC
      KING CONAN   HOWARD, ROBERT E.   AC
   TRITONIAN RING, THE   NO   TCS 51 WI
      TRITONIAN RING, THE   DE CAMP, L. SPRAGUE AC
   ULTRASONIC GOD (ALSO AS THE GALTON WHISTLE)   NV   FUT 51 07
      NOVELETS OF SCIENCE FICTION   HOWARD, IVAN   AN
   UNTIMELY TOPPER, THE   SS C FSF 53 07
      BEST FROM FANTASY AND SCIENCE FICTION: 3
                                          BOUCHER & MCCOMAS   AN
   WARRIOR RACE, THE   SS   ASF 40 10
      WHEELS OF IF, THE   DE CAMP, L. SPRAGUE AC
   WEISSENBROCH SPECTACLES, THE   SS C FSF 54 11
      INVISIBLE MEN   DAVENPORT, BASIL   AN
   WHEELS OF IF, THE   SN   UNK 40 10
      WHEELS OF IF, THE   DE CAMP, L. SPRAGUE AC
   WHEN THE NIGHT WIND HOWLS   SS C WRT 51 11
      GHOUL KEEPERS, THE   MARGULIES, LEO   AN
      TALES FROM GAVAGAN'S BAR   DE CAMP, L. S.&PRATT AC
   WHERE TO, PLEASE?   SS C WRT 52 09
      TALES FROM GAVAGAN'S BAR   DE CAMP, L. S.&PRATT AC
   WHY I SELECTED THE HIBITED MAN   AI
      *MY BEST SCIENCE FICTION STORY   MARGULIES & FRIEND   AN
   WIDE-OPEN PLANET (SEE PERPETUAL MOTION)   TC
   WIZARDS AND WARRIORS   IN
      SPELL OF SEVEN, THE   DE CAMP, L. SPRAGUE AN
   WOLVES BEYOND THE BORDER   SS C
      CONAN THE USURPER   HOWARD, R. & DE CAMP AC
   YOU CAN'T BEAT BRAINS (SEE ISAAC ASIMOV)   TC

DE CHIRICO, GIORGIO
   MELANCHOLY AND MYSTERY OF A STREET, THE   IL
      SCIENCE FICTION   BRODKIN & PEARSON   AN

DE CLES, JON
   CRUELTY   SS   NEW 71 AN
      SPECIAL WONDER   MCCOMAS, J. FRANCIS AN

DE CONDILLAC, E. B.
   APOTHEM   MS
      MATHEMATICAL MAGPIE, THE   FADIMAN, CLIFTON   AN

DE COURCY, DOROTHY
   ALCHEMY   SS C OTW 50 12
      FAREWELL FANTASTIC VENUS   ALDISS & HARRISON   AN
   RAT RACE   SS C STS 48 09
      *BIG BOOK OF SCIENCE FICTION   CONKLIN, GROFF   AN

DE COURCY, JOHN
   ALCHEMY   SS C OTW 50 12
      FAREWELL FANTASTIC VENUS   ALDISS & HARRISON   AN
   RAT RACE   SS C STS 48 09
      *BIG BOOK OF SCIENCE FICTION   CONKLIN, GROFF   AN

DE LA MARE, WALTER
   ALL HALLOWS   SS   26
      MOONLIGHT TRAVELER, THE   STERN, PHILIP VAN D. AN
   LISTENERS, THE   PM
      LOOKING AHEAD   ALLEN, D. & L.   AN

DE LA REE, GERRY
   INTRODUCTION   IN
      HORROR ON THE ASTEROID AND OTHER TALES OF PLANETARY HORROR
                                          HAMILTON, EDMOND   AC

DE MAUPASSANT, GUY
   DIARY OF A MADMAN, THE   SS
      *TWISTED   CONKLIN, GROFF   AN
   HORLA, THE (1886)   SS   WRT 26 08
      ANDROIDS, TIME MACHINES AND BLUE GIRAFFES
                                          ELWOOD & GHIDALIA   AN
   LEGEND OF MONT ST. MICHEL, THE   SS
      DEALS WITH THE DEVIL   DAVENPORT, BASIL   AN

DE WEESE, GENE
   SPACESHIP, THE   SS
      STRANGE ENCOUNTERS   BISCHOFF, DAVID   OA

DEAL, BORDEN
   ANTAEUS   SS   61
      NIGHT IN FUNLAND   BRONDFIELD, JEROME   AN

DEAN, ABNER
   CARTOON   CT   47
      MATHEMATICAL MAGPIE, THE   FADIMAN, CLIFTON   AN

DEAN, JOE E.
   SHARE ALIKE   SS C BEY 53 07
      GALAXY OF GHOULS   MERRIL, JUDITH   AN
      ZACHERLEY'S MIDNIGHT SNACKS   ZACHERLEY   AN

DEFORD, MIRIAM ALLEN

DEAN, MAL
   SLOW DRAG   SS   NWB 75 08
      NEW WORLDS EIGHT   BAILEY, HILARY   OA

DEE, ROGER   PSEUD. FOR ROGER D. AYCOCK
   INTERLOPERS, THE   SS   ASF 54 09
      GALACTIC EMPIRES VOLUME TWO   ALDISS, BRIAN W.   AN
   OBLIGATION, THE   NV   STS 52 09
      ADVENTURES ON OTHER PLANETS   WOLLHEIM, DONALD A. AN
   PROBLEM ON BALAK   SS   GAL 53 09
      GALAXY SCIENCE FICTION OMNIBUS   GOLD, H. L.   AN
      SECOND GALAXY READER OF SCIENCE FICTION
                                          GOLD, H. L.   AN
   UNWELCOME TENANT   SS   PLS 50 SU
      *BEYOND HUMAN KEN   MERRIL, JUDITH   AN
      FIFTY SHORT SCIENCE FICTION TALES   ASIMOV & CONKLIN   AN

DEEGAN, JON J.
   OLD GROWLER SPACE SHIP NO. 2213   CT   AUT 51 04
      AUTHENTIC BOOK OF SPACE   CAMPBELL, H. J.   AN

DEELEY, ROGER
   FIVE-DIMENSIONAL SUGAR CUBE, THE   SS   PRT 71
      PROTOSTARS   GERROLD & GOLDIN   OA
   HERE'S A HEALTH UNTO HIS MAJESTY   SS   GEN 72
      GENERATION   GERROLD, DAVID   OA
   SHORTEST SCIENCE-FICTION STORY EVER TOLD, THE SS   GEN 72
      GENERATION   GERROLD, DAVID   OA

DEFOE, DANIEL
   FRIENDLY DEMON, THE (1726)   SS   FSF 51 02
      BEST FROM FANTASY AND SCIENCE FICTION BOUCHER & MCCOMAS AN

DEFORD, MIRIAM ALLEN
   ELSEWHERE, ELSEWHEN, ELSEHOW   AC H WLK 71
      STORIES "MARTIE AND I" AND "THE CAGE" ARE LISTED IN THE
      ACKNOWLEDGEMENTS BUT ARE NOT IN THE BOOK
   SPACE, TIME & CRIME   AN   PBK 64 11
   XENOGENESIS   AC   BAL 69 03
   ABSOLUTELY PERFECT MURDER, THE   SS   FSF 65 02
      XENOGENESIS   DEFORD, MIRIAM ALLEN AC
   AGAINST AUTHORITY   NV   FSF 66 02
      VENUS FACTOR, THE   GHIDALIA, V.& ELWOOD AN
   AJERI DIARY, THE   SS   FSF 68 03
      XENOGENESIS   DEFORD, MIRIAM ALLEN AC
   ALL IN GOOD TIME   SS   FSF 60 07
      XENOGENESIS   DEFORD, MIRIAM ALLEN AC
   APOTHEOSIS OF KI, THE   SS   FSF 56 12
      ELSEWHERE, ELSEWHEN, ELSEHOW   DEFORD, MIRIAM ALLEN AC
      SPECIAL WONDER   MCCOMAS, J. FRANCIS AN
   APPRENTICE GOD, THE   PM   WOT 64 04
      BEST SCIENCE FICTION FROM WORLDS OF TOMORROW, THE
                                          POHL, FREDERIK   AN
   BEAST IN VIEW   SS   OMG 73
      OMEGA   ELWOOD, ROGER   OA
   CHILDREN, THE   NV   STS 52 12
      XENOGENESIS   DEFORD, MIRIAM ALLEN AC
   COLONY, THE   SS   FSF 66 05
      ELSEWHERE, ELSEWHEN, ELSEHOW   DEFORD, MIRIAM ALLEN AC
   CRIB CIRCUIT, THE   SS   FSF 69 11
      ELSEWHERE, ELSEWHEN, ELSEHOW   DEFORD, MIRIAM ALLEN AC
   DAUGHTER OF THE TREE, THE   SS   FSF 51 08
      STRANGE BED FELLOWS   SCORTIA, THOMAS N.   AN
      XENOGENESIS   DEFORD, MIRIAM ALLEN AC
   EEL, THE   SS   GAL 58 04
      CRIME PREVENTION IN THE 30TH CENTURY SANTESSON, HANS S. AN
      ELSEWHERE, ELSEWHEN, ELSEHOW   DEFORD, MIRIAM ALLEN AC
      FIFTH GALAXY READER, THE   GOLD, H. L.   AN
   FEATHERBED ON CHLYNTHA   SS   VSF 57 11
      XENOGENESIS   DEFORD, MIRIAM ALLEN AC
   FIRST DIG   SS   FSF 59 05
      ELSEWHERE, ELSEWHEN, ELSEHOW   DEFORD, MIRIAM ALLEN AC
   FREAK SHOW   SS   FUN 58 02
      ELSEWHERE, ELSEWHEN, ELSEHOW   DEFORD, MIRIAM ALLEN AC
   GENTLE INVADERS   SANTESSON, HANS S.   AN
   GATHI   SS   FSF 58 06
      XENOGENESIS   DEFORD, MIRIAM ALLEN AC
   GONE TO THE DOGS (HENRY MARTINDALE, GREAT DANE) SS   BEY 54 03
      ELSEWHERE, ELSEWHEN, ELSEHOW   DEFORD, MIRIAM ALLEN AC
   HENRY MARTINDALE, GREAT DANE (SEE GONE TO THE DOGS)
                                                  TC
   INTRODUCTION   IN
      SPACE, TIME & CRIME   DEFORD, MIRIAM ALLEN AN
   LAST GENERATION, THE   SS   FSF 50 12
      XENOGENESIS   DEFORD, MIRIAM ALLEN AC
   LAZARUS II   SS   NDM 72 02
      NEW DIMENSIONS 2   SILVERBERG, ROBERT   OA
   LONE WARRIOR   SS   TVW 73
      TWO VIEWS OF WONDER   SCORTIA & YARBRO   OA
   LONG ECHO, THE   SS   STR 58 04
      STAR SCIENCE FICTION STORIES NO. 4 POHL, FREDERIK   OA
   MALLEY SYSTEM, THE   SS   DVS 67 01
      DANGEROUS VISIONS   ELLISON, HARLAN   OA
   MARGENES, THE   SS   IFS 56 02
      ELSEWHERE, ELSEWHEN, ELSEHOW   DEFORD, MIRIAM ALLEN AC
      FIRST WORLD OF IF, THE   QUINN & WULFF   AN
   MONSTER, THE   SS   FSF 60 03
      ELSEWHERE, ELSEWHEN, ELSEHOW   DEFORD, MIRIAM ALLEN AC
   MRS. HINCK   SS   FSF 54 03
      ELSEWHERE, ELSEWHEN, ELSEHOW   DEFORD, MIRIAM ALLEN AC
   NEITHER SNOW NOR RAIN (NOT SNOW NOR RAIN)   SS   IFS 59 11
      FLYING SAUCERS IN FACT AND FICTION SANTESSON, HANS S.   AN
   NOT SNOW NOR RAIN (ALSO AS NEITHER SNOW NOR RAIN) SS IFS 59 11
      ELSEWHERE, ELSEWHEN, ELSEHOW   DEFORD, MIRIAM ALLEN AC
   OLD BUNCH AND DUSTY STIGGINS, THE   SS   FSF 70 10
      ELSEWHERE, ELSEWHEN, ELSEHOW   DEFORD, MIRIAM ALLEN AC

DEFORD, MIRIAM ALLEN   DEL REY, LESTER

DEFORD, MIRIAM ALLEN (CONTINUED)
  OLD MAN MORGAN'S GRAVE   SS   FSF 52 10
    ELSEWHERE, ELSEWHEN, ELSEHOW   DEFORD, MIRIAM ALLEN AC
  OLD WOMAN, THE   SS   FUN 57 10
    ELSEWHERE, ELSEWHEN, ELSEHOW   DEFORD, MIRIAM ALLEN AC
  ONE-WAY JOURNEY (ONE WAY)   SS   GAL 55 03
    XENOGENESIS   DEFORD, MIRIAM ALLEN AC
  OPERATION CASSANDRA   NV   FUN 58 11
    XENOGENESIS   DEFORD, MIRIAM ALLEN AC
  PEAK LORDS, THE   SS   IFS 66 02
    ELSEWHERE, ELSEWHEN, ELSEHOW   DEFORD, MIRIAM ALLEN AC
  PRESS CONFERENCE   SS   STR 59 06
    STAR SCIENCE FICTION STORIES NO. 6 POHL, FREDERIK   OA
  PRISON BREAK   SS   FUN 59 07
    ELSEWHERE, ELSEWHEN, ELSEHOW   DEFORD, MIRIAM ALLEN AC
    RULERS OF MEN   SANTESSON, HANS S.   AN
  QUICK TO HASTE   SS   NEW 69 AC
    XENOGENESIS   DEFORD, MIRIAM ALLEN AC
  SEASON OF THE BABIES, THE   SS   FUN 59 12
    XENOGENESIS   DEFORD, MIRIAM ALLEN AC
  SLIPS TAKE OVER   SS   FSF 64 09
    WORLDS OF MAYBE   SILVERBERG, ROBERT   AN
  SMILING FUTURE, THE   SS   IFS 65 10
    XENOGENESIS   DEFORD, MIRIAM ALLEN AC
  SUPERIOR SEX, THE   SS   FSF 68 04
    XENOGENESIS   DEFORD, MIRIAM ALLEN AC
  THROWBACK   SS   STS 52 10
    *FUTURE TENSE   CROSSEN, KENDELL F. AN
    XENOGENESIS   DEFORD, MIRIAM ALLEN AC
  TIGER, THE   SS   INY 70 01
    INFINITY 1   HOSKINS, ROBERT   OA
  TRAMMEL, THE   SS
    DEALS WITH THE DEVIL   DAVENPORT, BASIL   AN
  TRANSIT OF VENUS, THE   SS   FSF 62 06
    XENOGENESIS   DEFORD, MIRIAM ALLEN AC
  VOOREMP: SPY   SS   INY 72 03
    INFINITY 3   HOSKINS, ROBERT   OA
  VOYAGE OF THE "DEBORAH PRATT", THE   SS   FSF 63 04
    ELSEWHERE, ELSEWHEN, ELSEHOW   DEFORD, MIRIAM ALLEN AC
  WAY OUT, A   SS   ALC 73
    ALIEN CONDITION, THE   GOLDIN, STEPHEN   OA
  WORD IN ADVANCE, A   IN
    ELSEWHERE, ELSEWHEN, ELSEHOW   DEFORD, MIRIAM ALLEN AC
  1980 PRESIDENT, THE   SS   GAL 64 10
    AMERICAN GOVERNMENT THROUGH SCIENCE FICTION
                                      OLANDER/GREENBERG/& AN
    ELSEWHERE, ELSEWHEN, ELSEHOW   DEFORD, MIRIAM ALLEN AC
  5,000,000 A.D.   SS   FUC 73
    FUTURE CITY   ELWOOD, ROGER   OA

DEGRAEFF, ALLEN   PSEUD. FOR ALBERT PAUL BLAUSTEIN
  HUMAN AND OTHER BEINGS   AN   CLB 63
  PREFACE   IN
    HUMAN AND OTHER BEINGS   DEGRAEFF, ALLEN   AN

DEGRAW, PAT
  INSIDE MOTHER   SS   INY 70 01
    INFINITY 1   HOSKINS, ROBERT   OA
  MEMO TO SECRETARY   PM   FSF 66 06
    BEST FROM FANTASY AND SCIENCE FICTION: 16
                                      FERMAN, EDWARD L.   AN

DEHN, PAUL
  QUAKE, QUAKE, QUAKE (EXCERPT)   PM   61
    7TH ANNUAL OF THE YEAR'S BEST S-F, THE MERRILL, JUDITH AN
  RHYMES FOR A MODERN NURSERY (FROM "QUAKE, QUAKE, QUAKE")
                                                  PM   61
    SPECULATIONS   SANDERS, THOMAS E.   AN

DEKKER, THOMAS
  CIRCLE AND THE SQUARE, THE   PM
    FANTASIA MATHEMATICA   FADIMAN, CLIFTON   AN

DEL REY, JUDY-LYNN
  STELLAR SHORT NOVELS   OA   BAL 76 10
  STELLAR 1   OA   BAL 74 09
  STELLAR 2   OA   BAL 76 02
  INTRODUCTION: AN ENDANGERED SPECIES   IN
    STELLAR SHORT NOVELS   DEL REY, JUDY-LYNN   OA
  WHY ANTHOLOGIZE?   IN
    STELLAR 1   DEL REY, JUDY-LYNN   OA

DEL REY, LESTER, CECILE MATSCHAT AND CARL CARMER
  YEAR AFTER TOMORROW, THE   AN H JCW 51

DEL REY, LESTER   PSEUD. FOR
    RAMON FELIPE SAN JUAN MARIO SILVIO ENRICO ALVAREZ DEL REY
      ALSO AS
    PHILIP JAMES (WITH JAMES H. BEARD), PHILIP ST. JOHN
  AND SOME WERE HUMAN   AC H PRM 48
  AND SOME WERE HUMAN (8 OF 12)   AC   BAL 61
  BEST OF C. L. MOORE, THE (LISTED UNDER C. L. MOORE)
                                                  EC H NDB 75
  BEST OF FREDERIK POHL, THE (LISTED UNDER FREDERIK POHL)
                                                  EC H NDB 75
  BEST OF JOHN W. CAMPBELL, THE (LISTED UNDER JOHN W. CAMPBELL)
                                                  EC H BAL 76 05
  BEST SCIENCE FICTION STORIES OF THE YEAR (1971) AN H DUT 72
  BEST SCIENCE FICTION STORIES OF THE YEAR (1972) AN H DUT 73
  BEST SCIENCE FICTION STORIES OF THE YEAR (1973) AN H DUT 74
  BEST SCIENCE FICTION STORIES OF THE YEAR (1974) AN H DUT 75
  BEST SCIENCE FICTION STORIES OF THE YEAR (1975) AN H DUT 76
  EARLY DEL REY   AC H DBL 75
  GODS AND GOLEMS   AC   BAL 73 02
  MORTALS AND MONSTERS   AC   BAL 65
  ROBOTS AND CHANGELINGS   AC   BAL 57

DEL REY, LESTER   (CONTINUED)
  ALIEN   SS   STR 54 03
    STAR SCIENCE FICTION STORIES NO. 3 POHL, FREDERIK   OA
  AND IT COMES OUT HERE   SS   GAL 51 02
    MORTALS AND MONSTERS   DEL REY, LESTER   AC
    OTHER SIDE OF THE CLOCK, THE   STERN, PHILIP VAN D. AN
    *SCIENCE FICTION ADVENTURES IN DIMENSION
                                      CONKLIN, GROFF   AN
    VOYAGERS IN TIME   SILVERBERG, ROBERT   AN
  AND THE DARKNESS (OMEGA AND THE WOLF GIRL)   SS   OTW 50 07
    EARLY DEL REY   DEL REY, LESTER   AC
  AND THE TRUTH (DEAD RINGER)   SS   GAL 56 11
    MORTALS AND MONSTERS   DEL REY, LESTER   AC
  ANYTHING   SS   UNK 39 10
    EARLY DEL REY   DEL REY, LESTER   AC
  CARILLON OF SKULLS   SS C UNK 41 02
    EARLY DEL REY   DEL REY, LESTER   AC
  CONDITIONED REFLEX (MIND OF TOMORROW)   SS   FUT 51 05
    EARLY DEL REY   DEL REY, LESTER   AC
  COPPERSMITH, THE   SS   UNK 39 09
    *AND SOME WERE HUMAN   DEL REY, LESTER   AC
    ROBOTS AND CHANGELINGS   DEL REY, LESTER   AC
  COURSE OF LOGIC, THE   SS   IFS 63 09
    MORTALS AND MONSTERS   DEL REY, LESTER   AC
  CROSS OF FIRE   SS   WRT 39 05
    EARLY DEL REY   DEL REY, LESTER   AC
  DARK MISSION   SS   ASF 40 07
    *AND SOME WERE HUMAN   DEL REY, LESTER   AC
    GREAT SCIENCE-FICTION   LICATA, TONY   AN
    MARS, WE LOVE YOU   HIPOLITO & MCNELLY   AN
    *TREASURY OF SCIENCE FICTION, A   CONKLIN, GROFF   AN
  DAY IS DONE, THE   SS   ASF 39 05
    *AND SOME WERE HUMAN   DEL REY, LESTER   AC
    OPERATION FUTURE   CONKLIN, GROFF   AN
    SCIENCE FICTION OF THE 30'S   KNIGHT, DAMON   AN
    WHERE DO WE GO FROM HERE?   ASIMOV, ISAAC   AN
  DEAD RINGER (ALSO AS AND THE TRUTH)   SS   GAL 56 11
    THIRD GALAXY READER, THE   GOLD, H. L.   AN
  DONE WITHOUT EAGLES   SS   ASF 40 08
    EARLY DEL REY   DEL REY, LESTER   AC
  DOUBLED IN BRASS   SS   UNK 40 01
    EARLY DEL REY   DEL REY, LESTER   AC
  DWINDLING YEARS, THE   SS   GAL 56 01
    MORTALS AND MONSTERS   DEL REY, LESTER   AC
  EVENSONG   SS   DVS 67 01
    DANGEROUS VISIONS   ELLISON, HARLAN   OA
    OTHER WORLDS, OTHER GODS   MOHS, MAYO   AN
  FAITHFUL, THE   SS   ASF 38 04
    *AND SOME WERE HUMAN   DEL REY, LESTER   AC
    EARLY DEL REY   DEL REY, LESTER   AC
    FIRST FLIGHT   KNIGHT, DAMON   AN
  FIFTH FREEDOM   SS   ASF 43 05
    EARLY DEL REY   DEL REY, LESTER   AC
  FLYING SAUCER MYTH, THE   AR   FUN 57 08
    FLYING SAUCERS IN FACT AND FICTION SANTESSON, HANS S. AN
  FOOL'S ERRAND   SS   SFQ 51 11
    EARLY DEL REY   DEL REY, LESTER   AC
  FOR I AM A JEALOUS PEOPLE!   SN   SSN 54
    GODS AND GOLEMS   DEL REY, LESTER   AC
    STAR SHORT NOVELS   POHL, FREDERIK   OA
  FOREWORD   IN
    *AND SOME WERE HUMAN   DEL REY, LESTER   AC
    DAY THE SUN STOOD STILL, THE   SILVERBERG, ROBERT   OA
    YEAR AFTER TOMORROW, THE   DEL REY, L/MATSCHAT/ AN
  FOREWORD: A SPATE OF CHANGES   IN
    BEST SCIENCE FICTION STORIES OF THE YEAR (1973)
                                      DEL REY, LESTER   AN
  FOREWORD: ALTERNATE POSSIBILITIES   IN
    BEST SCIENCE FICTION STORIES OF THE YEAR (1971)
                                      DEL REY, LESTER   AN
  FOREWORD: FIFTY YEARS OF SCIENCE FICTION   IN
    BEST SCIENCE FICTION STORIES OF THE YEAR (1975)
                                      DEL REY, LESTER   AN
  FOREWORD: THE SENSE OF WONDER   IN
    BEST SCIENCE FICTION STORIES OF THE YEAR (1974)
                                      DEL REY, LESTER   AN
  FOREWORD: THE SPICE OF VARIETY   IN
    BEST SCIENCE FICTION STORIES OF THE YEAR (1972)
                                      DEL REY, LESTER   AN
  FORGIVE US OUR DEBTS (ALSO AS RECESSIONAL)   SS   FUT 52 05
    MASTERS OF SCIENCE FICTION   HOWARD, IVAN   AN
  FORSAKING ALL OTHERS   SS   UNK 39 08
    *AND SOME WERE HUMAN   DEL REY, LESTER   AC
  FORTY YEARS OF C. L. MOORE   IN
    BEST OF C. L. MOORE, THE   MOORE, C. L.   AC
  GAME OF FUTURES- AN INTRODUCTION, A   IN
    CHILDREN OF INFINITY   ELWOOD, ROGER   OA
  HABIT   SS   ASF 39 11
    EARLY DEL REY   DEL REY, LESTER   AC
    JUPITER   POHL, C. & F.   AN
  HELEN O'LOY   SS   ASF 38 12
    *AND SOME WERE HUMAN   DEL REY, LESTER   AC
    ASSIGNMENT IN TOMORROW   POHL, FREDERIK   AN
    *BEYOND HUMAN KEN   MERRIL, JUDITH   AN
    COMING OF THE ROBOTS, THE   MOSKOWITZ, SAM   AN
    IN DREAMS AWAKE   FIEDLER, LESLIE A.   AN
    MASTERS' CHOICE   JANIFER, LAURENCE M. AN
    MODERN SCIENCE FICTION   SPINRAD, NORMAN   AN
    SCIENCE FICTION HALL OF FAME VOLUME 1 SILVERBERG, ROBERT AN
    SOULS IN METAL   ASHLEY, MICHAEL   AN
    3000 YEARS OF FANTASY AND SCIENCE FICTION
                                      DE CAMP, L. S.&C.   AN
  HELPING HAND   NV   STR 58 04
    STAR SCIENCE FICTION STORIES NO. 4 POHL, FREDERIK   OA
  HEREAFTER, INC.   SS   UNK 41 12
    *AND SOME WERE HUMAN   DEL REY, LESTER   AC

DEL REY, LESTER   DELANY, SAMUEL R.

DEL REY, LESTER   (CONTINUED)
I AM TOMORROW   NV   DSF 52 12
   NOVELETS OF SCIENCE FICTION   HOWARD, IVAN   AN
IDEALIST   SS   STR 53 01
   STAR SCIENCE FICTION STORIES   POHL, FREDERIK   AN
INSTINCT   SS   ASF 52 01
   INSIDE INFORMATION   MOWSHOWITZ, ABBE   AN
   INTRODUCTORY PSYCHOLOGY THROUGH SCIENCE FICTION
                                       KATZ/WARRICK/&   AN
   MEN AND MACHINES   SILVERBERG, ROBERT   AN
   MORTALS AND MONSTERS   DEL REY, LESTER   AC
   OMNIBUS OF SCIENCE FICTION   CONKLIN, GROFF   AN
   SCIENCE FICTION OMNIBUS   CONKLIN, GROFF   AN
INTO THY HANDS   SS   ASF 45 08
   INVASION OF THE ROBOTS   ELWOOD, ROGER   AN
   LOOKING FORWARD   LESSER, MILTON   AN
   ROBOT AND THE MAN, THE   GREENBERG, MARTIN   AN
   ROBOTS AND CHANGELINGS   DEL REY, LESTER   AC
INTRODUCTION   IN
   FANTASTIC UNIVERSE OMNIBUS, THE   SANTESSON, HANS S.   AN
INTRODUCTION: THE THREE CAREERS OF JOHN W. CAMPBELL
                                                   IN
   *BEST OF JOHN W. CAMPBELL, THE   CAMPBELL, JOHN W. JR AC
KEEPERS OF THE HOUSE   SS   FUN 56 01
   DARK STARS   SILVERBERG, ROBERT   AN
   ROBOTS AND CHANGELINGS   DEL REY, LESTER   AC
KINDNESS   SS   ASF 44 10
   MODERN MASTERPIECES OF SCIENCE FICTION MOSKOWITZ, SAM   AN
   ROBOTS AND CHANGELINGS   DEL REY, LESTER   AC
   VORTEX BLASTERS, THE   MOSKOWITZ, SAM   AN
   YEAR AFTER TOMORROW, THE   DEL REY, L/MATSCHAT/   AN
LADY OF SPACE   SS   VSF 58 07
   MORTALS AND MONSTERS   DEL REY, LESTER   AC
LAST TRUE GOD, THE   SS   IFS 69 09
   BEST FROM IF, THE VOLUME I   IF, EDITORS OF   AN
   LOOKING AHEAD   ALLEN, D. & L.   AN
LIFE WATCH   NV   FUN 54 09
   GODS AND GOLEMS   DEL REY, LESTER   AC
LITTLE JIMMY   SS   FSF 57 04
   MORE LITTLE MONSTERS   ELWOOD & GHIDALIA   AN
   ROBOTS AND CHANGELINGS   DEL REY, LESTER   AC
LUCK OF IGNATZ, THE   NV   ASF 39 08
   *AND SOME WERE HUMAN   DEL REY, LESTER   AN
   HIDDEN PLANET, THE   WOLLHEIM, DONALD A.   AN
   YEAR AFTER TOMORROW, THE   DEL REY, L/MATSCHAT/   AN
LUNAR LANDING   NV   ASF 42 10
   EARLY DEL REY   DEL REY, LESTER   AC
MIND OF TOMORROW (ALSO AS CONDITIONED REFLEX) SS FUT 51 05
   THINGS   HOWARD, IVAN   AN
MONSTER, THE   SS   ARG 51 06
   ROBOTS AND CHANGELINGS   DEL REY, LESTER   AC
   SCIENCE FICTION ROLL OF HONOR, THE POHL, FREDERIK   AN
   TOMORROW, THE STARS   HEINLEIN, ROBERT A.   AN
MY NAME IS LEGION   NV   ASF 42 06
   EARLY DEL REY   DEL REY, LESTER   AC
NATURAL ADVANTAGE   SS   AMZ 76 06
   1977 ANNUAL WORLD'S BEST SF, THE   WOLLHEIM, DONALD A.   AN
NERVES   NV   ASF 42 09
   *ADVENTURES IN TIME AND SPACE   HEALY & MCCOMAS   AN
   *AND SOME WERE HUMAN   DEL REY, LESTER   AC
   SCIENCE FICTION HALL OF FAME VOLUME 2A BOVA, BEN   AN
NEW GODS LEAD, THE (SEE THE OLD ORDER)   TC
NO PLACE LIKE HOME   SS   ASF 52 08
   MORTALS AND MONSTERS   DEL REY, LESTER   AC
NO STRINGS ATTACHED   SS   IFS 54 06
   ROBOTS AND CHANGELINGS   DEL REY, LESTER   AC
OF DESTINY AND WONDER   IN
   JOHN W. CAMPBELL ANTHOLOGY: THREE NOVELS
                                       CAMPBELL, JOHN W. JR AC
OLD ORDER, THE (THE NEW GODS LEAD)   SS   MSS 51 02
   SHADOW OF TOMORROW   POHL, FREDERIK   AN
ONE-EYED MAN, THE   SS   ASF 45 05
   EARLY DEL REY   DEL REY, LESTER   AC
OVER THE TOP   SS   ASF 49 11
   *ASTOUNDING SCIENCE FICTION ANTHOLOGY, THE
                                       CAMPBELL, JOHN W. JR AN
   EARLY DEL REY   DEL REY, LESTER   AC
   SECOND ASTOUNDING SCIENCE FICTION ANTHOLOGY, THE (PB)
                                       CAMPBELL, JOHN W. JR AN
PIPES OF PAN, THE   SS   UNK 40 05
   OTHER WORLDS, THE   STONG, PHILIP D.   AN
   ROBOTS AND CHANGELINGS   DEL REY, LESTER   AC
POUND OF CURE, A   SS   STR 53 02
   STAR SCIENCE FICTION STORIES NO. 2 POHL, FREDERIK   OA
PSALM   PM   FUN 60 02
   6TH ANNUAL OF THE YEAR'S BEST S-F, THE MERRIL, JUDITH   AN
PURSUIT   NA   SSF 52 05
   GODS AND GOLEMS   DEL REY, LESTER   AC
READING ROOM   BR   IFS 74 12
   BEST FROM IF, THE VOLUME III   BAEN, JAMES   AN
RECESSIONAL (FORGIVE US OUR DEBTS)   SS   FUT 52 05
   MORTALS AND MONSTERS   DEL REY, LESTER   AC
REINCARNATE   NV   ASF 40 04
   EARLY DEL REY   DEL REY, LESTER   AC
RENEGADE, THE   SS   ASF 43 07
   *AND SOME WERE HUMAN   DEL REY, LESTER   AC
   APEMAN, SPACEMAN   STOVER & HARRISON   AN
RETURN ENGAGEMENT   SS   GAL 61 08
   MORTALS AND MONSTERS   DEL REY, LESTER   AC
   SEVENTH GALAXY READER, THE   POHL, FREDERIK   AN
SCIENCE FICTION YEARBOOK, THE   MS
   BEST SCIENCE FICTION STORIES OF THE YEAR (1971)
                                       DEL REY, LESTER   AN
   BEST SCIENCE FICTION STORIES OF THE YEAR (1972)
                                       DEL REY, LESTER   AN

DEL REY, LESTER   (CONTINUED)
   BEST SCIENCE FICTION STORIES OF THE YEAR (1973)
                                       DEL REY, LESTER   AN
   BEST SCIENCE FICTION STORIES OF THE YEAR (1974)
                                       DEL REY, LESTER   AN
   BEST SCIENCE FICTION STORIES OF THE YEAR (1975)
                                       DEL REY, LESTER   AN
SEAT OF JUDGMENT, THE   SS   VSP 57 07
   MORTALS AND MONSTERS   DEL REY, LESTER   AC
   NO LIMITS   FERMAN, JOSEPH W.   AN
SHADOWS OF EMPIRE   SS   FUT 50 07
   EARLY DEL REY   DEL REY, LESTER   AC
SMALLEST GOD, THE   NV   ASF 40 01
   EARLY DEL REY   DEL REY, LESTER   AC
SPAWNING GROUND   SS   IFS 61 09
   BEST SCIENCE FICTION FROM IF, THE   POHL, FREDERIK   AN
   MORTALS AND MONSTERS   DEL REY, LESTER   AC
STABILITY   SS   VOR 53 01
   ROBOTS AND CHANGELINGS   DEL REY, LESTER   AC
STARS LOOK DOWN, THE   NV   ASF 40 08
   *AND SOME WERE HUMAN   DEL REY, LESTER   AC
   EARLY DEL REY   DEL REY, LESTER   AC
STILL WATERS, THE   SS   FAN 55 04
   OUT OF THIS WORLD 2   WILLIAMS-ELLIS& OWEN   AN
   ROBOTS AND CHANGELINGS   DEL REY, LESTER   AC
SUPERSTITION   NV   ASF 54 08
   GODS AND GOLEMS   DEL REY, LESTER   AC
THOUGH DREAMERS DIE   SS   ASF 44 02
   EARLY DEL REY   DEL REY, LESTER   AC
   ROBOT AND THE MAN, THE   GREENBERG, MARTIN   AN
THOUGH POPPIES GROW   NV   UNK 42 08
   EARLY DEL REY   DEL REY, LESTER   AC
TO AVENGE MAN (ALSO AS VENGEANCE IS MINE)   NV   GAL 64 12
   NINTH GALAXY READER, THE   POHL, FREDERIK   AN
UNEASY LIES THE HEAD   SS   TSF 51 SP
   ROBOTS AND CHANGELINGS   DEL REY, LESTER   AC
UNREASONABLE FACSIMILE   SS   FUT 52 07
   EARLY DEL REY   DEL REY, LESTER   AC
   NOW & BEYOND   HOWARD, IVAN   AN
UNTO HIM THAT HATH   NV   SSF 52 11
   TIME CURVE, THE   MOSKOWITZ & ELWOOD   AN
VARIETY OF EXCELLENCE, A   IN
   BEST OF FREDERIK POHL, THE   POHL, FREDERIK   AC
VENGEANCE IS MINE (TO AVENGE MAN)   NV   GAL 64 12
   GODS AND GOLEMS   DEL REY, LESTER   AC
WHOM THE GODS LOVE   SS   ASF 43 06
   EARLY DEL REY   DEL REY, LESTER   AC
WIND BETWEEN THE WORLDS, THE   NV   GAL 51 03
   ADVENTURES IN THE FAR FUTURE   WOLLHEIM, DONALD A.   DA
   EARLY DEL REY   DEL REY, LESTER   AC
WINGS OF NIGHT, THE   SS   ASF 42 03
   *AND SOME WERE HUMAN   DEL REY, LESTER   AC
   *BIG BOOK OF SCIENCE FICTION   CONKLIN, GROFF   AN
   GREAT STORIES OF SPACE TRAVEL   CONKLIN, GROFF   AN
"YEARS DRAW NIGH, THE"   SS   ASF 51 10
   *BEACHHEADS IN SPACE   DERLETH, AUGUST   AN
   MORTALS AND MONSTERS   DEL REY, LESTER   AC
2001: A SPACE ODYSSEY- REVIEW 1   MR   GAL 68 07
   BEST SF: 1968   HARRISON & ALDISS   AN

DEL REY, RAMON F. A. SEE PSEUD. LESTER DEL REY

DELANY, SAMUEL R. AND MARILYN HACKER
QUARK/1   OA   PBK 70 11
QUARK/2   OA   PBK 71 02
QUARK/3   OA   PBK 71 05
QUARK/4   OA   PBK 71 08

DELANY, SAMUEL R.
DRIFTGLASS   AC   SIG 71 11
AYE, AND GOMORRAH...   SS   DVS 67 01
   DANGEROUS VISIONS   ELLISON, HARLAN   OA
   DRIFTGLASS   DELANY, SAMUEL R.   AC
   MODERN SCIENCE FICTION   SPINRAD, NORMAN   AN
   NEBULA AWARD STORIES NO. 3   ZELAZNY, ROGER   AN
CAGE OF BRASS   SS   IFS 68 06
   DRIFTGLASS   DELANY, SAMUEL R.   AC
CORONA   SS   FSF 67 10
   BEST FROM FANTASY AND SCIENCE FICTION: 17
                                       FERMAN, EDWARD L.   AN
   DRIFTGLASS   DELANY, SAMUEL R.   AC
   LOOKING AHEAD   ALLEN, D. & L.   AN
CRITICAL METHODS: SPECULATIVE FICTION   AR   QRK 70 01
   QUARK/1   DELANY & HACKER   OA
DOG IN A FISHERMAN'S NET   SS   QRK 71 03
   DRIFTGLASS   DELANY, SAMUEL R.   AC
   QUARK/3   DELANY & HACKER   OA
DRIFTGLASS   NV   IFS 67 06
   DAY IN THE LIFE, A   DOZOIS, GARDNER R.   AN
   DRIFTGLASS   DELANY, SAMUEL R.   AC
   NEW TOMORROWS, THE   SPINRAD, NORMAN   AN
   SPECTRUM OF WORLDS, A   CLARESON, THOMAS D.   AN
   SURVIVAL PRINTOUT   TOTAL EFFECT   AN
   WORLD'S BEST SCIENCE FICTION: 1968 WOLLHEIM & CARR   AN
EDITORIAL   ED C QRK 70 01
   QUARK/1   DELANY & HACKER   OA
EMPIRE STAR   NO   ACE 66
   ACE SCIENCE FICTION READER   WOLLHEIM, DONALD A.   AN
FOREWORD   IN C
   QUARK/3   DELANY & HACKER   OA
FROM: NOVA   EX   DBL 68
   INSIDE INFORMATION   MOWSHOWITZ, ABBE   AN
HIGH WEIR   NV   IFS 68 10
   DRIFTGLASS   DELANY, SAMUEL R.   AC
   WONDERMAKERS 2   HOSKINS, ROBERT   AN

```
DELANY, SAMUEL R.

DELANY, SAMUEL R.    (CONTINUED)
  INTRODUCTION                                    IN
    ALYX                            RUSS, JOANNA          AC
  INTRODUCTION                                    IN C
    QUARK/2                         DELANY & HACKER       OA
  NIGHT AND THE LOVES OF JOE DICOSTANZO           SS   ANA 70
    ALCHEMY AND ACADEME             MCCAFFREY, ANNE       OA
  DRIFTGLASS                        DELANY, SAMUEL R.     AC
  ON SPECULATIVE FICTION                          IN C
    QUARK/4                         DELANY & HACKER       OA
  POWER OF THE NAIL, THE                          SS C AMZ 68 11
    PARTNERS IN WONDER              ELLISON, HARLAN       AC
  READING BETWEEN THE WORDS                       AR   CLR 71 01
    CLARION                         WILSON, ROBIN SCOTT   OA
  STAR PIT, THE                                   NV   WOT 67 02
    ALPHA 5                         SILVERBERG, ROBERT    AN
    DRIFTGLASS                      DELANY, SAMUEL R.     AC
    SF12                            MERRIL, JUDITH        AN
  STARS IN MY POCKET LIKE GRAINS OF SAND          EX
    BEYOND THIS HORIZON             CARRELL, CHRISTOPHER  OA
  THICKENING THE PLOT                             AR
    THOSE WHO CAN: A SCIENCE FICTION READER
                                    WILSON, ROBIN SCOTT   AN
  TIME CONSIDERED AS A HELIX OF SEMI-PRECIOUS STONES
                                                  SS   NWS 68 12
    BEST SF STORIES FROM NEW WORLDS 7  MOORCOCK, MICHAEL  AN
    DRIFTGLASS                      DELANY, SAMUEL R.     AC
    HUGO WINNERS, THE (VOLUME 2)    ASIMOV, ISAAC         AN
    IN DREAMS AWAKE                 FIEDLER, LESLIE A.    AN
    NEBULA AWARD STORIES  NO. 5     BLISH, JAMES          AN
    SHORES BENEATH, THE             SALLIS, JAMES         AN
    WORLD'S BEST SCIENCE FICTION: 1969  WOLLHEIM & CARR   AN
  WE, IN SOME STRANGE POWER'S EMPLOY, MOVE ON A RIGOROUS LINE
                                                  NV   FSF 68 05
    DRIFTGLASS                      DELANY, SAMUEL R.     AC
    THOSE WHO CAN: A SCIENCE FICTION READER
                                    WILSON, ROBIN SCOTT   AN
  2001: A SPACE ODYSSEY- REVIEW 2                 MR   FSF 68 08
    BEST SF: 1968                   HARRISON & ALDISS     AN

DELL, DUDLEY       PSEUD. FOR HORACE L. GOLD
  BIOGRAPHY PROJECT, THE                          SS   GAL 51 09
    *GALAXY READER OF SCIENCE FICTION  GOLD, H. L.        AN

DEMARE, LEO
  CARTOON                                         CT   MNS 58
    MATHEMATICAL MAGPIE, THE        FADIMAN, CLIFTON      AN

DEMING, RICHARD
  SHAPE OF THINGS THAT CAME, THE                  SS   FSF 51 10
    SPECIAL WONDER                  MCCOMAS, J. FRANCIS   AN
    TREASURY OF GREAT SCIENCE FICTION, A VOL.1
                                    BOUCHER, ANTHONY      AN

DEMMON, CALVIN
  SERVO                                           SS
    FUTURE PASTIMES                 EDELSTEIN, SCOTT      OA

DEMORGAN, AUGUSTUS
  APOTHEM (1872)                                  MS
    MATHEMATICAL MAGPIE, THE        FADIMAN, CLIFTON      AN
  EULER, DIDEROT, ALGEBRA AND GOD (1872)          MS
    MATHEMATICAL MAGPIE, THE        FADIMAN, CLIFTON      AN

DEMPSEY, HANK      PSEUD. FOR HARRY HARRISON
  CWACC STRIKES AGAIN                             NV   ASF 66 06
    ANALOG 6                        CAMPBELL, JOHN W. JR  AN
  DEFENSIVE BOMBER, THE                           SS   NOV 73 03
    NOVA 3                          HARRISON, HARRY       OA

DENTINGER, STEPHEN
  FUTURE IS OURS, THE                             SS   NEW 69 AN
    CRIME PREVENTION IN THE 30TH CENTURY  SANTESSON, HANS S.  AN
  GOD OF THE PLAYBACK                             SS   NEW 67 AN
    GODS FOR TOMORROW               SANTESSON, HANS S.    AN

DENTON, KIT
  BURNING SPEAR                                   SS   FSF 64 02
    PACIFIC BOOK OF AUSTRALIAN SCIENCE FICTION
                                    BAXTER, JOHN          AN

DERBY, PAT
  WE ARE WAITING                                  SS   YNW
    SCIENCE FICTION STORIES         BRADLEY, JOHANNA      AN

DERLETH, AUGUST    SEE ALSO    CO-AUTHOR H. P. LOVECRAFT
                   ALSO AS     STEPHEN GRENDON AND KENYON HOLMES
  BEACHHEADS IN SPACE                             AN H PEL 52
    ENGLISH DERIVATIVE ANTHOLOGY "FROM OTHER WORLDS"
  BEACHHEADS IN SPACE (BRITISH PB)                AN   FSP 64
  BEACHHEADS IN SPACE (BRITISH)                   AN H WEI 54
  BEACHHEADS IN SPACE (7 OF 14)                   AN   BRK 57
  BEYOND TIME AND SPACE                           AN H PEL 50
  BEYOND TIME AND SPACE (8 OF 32)                 AN   BRK 58
  FAR BOUNDARIES                                  AN H PEL 52
  FROM OTHER WORLDS                               AN   FSP 64
    STORIES FROM "BEACHHEADS IN SPACE"
  HARRIGAN'S FILE                                 AC H ARK 75
  MR. GEORGE AND OTHER ODD PERSONS                AC H ARK 63
  NEW WORLDS FOR OLD                              AN   FSP 63
    9 STORIES FROM "WORLDS OF TOMORROW"
  NOT LONG FOR THIS WORLD                         AC H ARK 48
  OTHER SIDE OF THE MOON, THE                     AN H PEL 49
  OTHER SIDE OF THE MOON, THE (BRITISH PB 1)      AN   PTH 63
  OTHER SIDE OF THE MOON, THE (BRITISH PB 2)      AN   MFL 66
  OTHER SIDE OF THE MOON, THE (BRITISH)           AN H GRY 56

DERLETH, AUGUST    (CONTINUED)
  OTHER SIDE OF THE MOON, THE (10 OF 20)          AN   BRK 59
  OUTER REACHES, THE                              AN H PEL 51
    ENGLISH DERIVATIVE ANTHOLOGY "THE TIME OF INFINITY"
  OUTER REACHES, THE (BRITISH)                    AN   CNL 63
    FIRST 8 STORIES OF AMERICAN EDITION, LAST 9 IN
    "THE TIME OF INFINITY"
  OUTER REACHES, THE (10 OF 17)                   AN   BRK 58
  PORTALS OF TOMORROW                             AN H RNH 54
  STRANGE PORTS OF CALL                           AN H PEL 48
  STRANGE PORTS OF CALL (10 OF 20)                AN   BRK 58
  TIME OF INFINITY, THE                           AN   CNL 63
    LAST 9 STORIES FROM "THE OUTER REACHES"
  TIME TO COME                                    OA H FSY 54
  TIME TO COME (10 OF 12, BRK 58)                 OA   BRK 58 12
  TIME TO COME (10 OF 12, TWR 65)                 OA   TWR 65
  TRAVELLERS BY NIGHT                             OA H ARK 67
  WORLDS OF TOMORROW                              AN H PEL 53
    ENGLISH DERIVATIVE ANTHOLOGY "NEW WORLDS FOR OLD"
  WORLDS OF TOMORROW (BRITISH PB)                 AN   FSP 63
    10 STORIES FROM AMERICAN EDITION,
    REMAINING 9 IN "NEW WORLDS FOR OLD"
  WORLDS OF TOMORROW (BRITISH)                    AN H WEI 55
  WORLDS OF TOMORROW (10 OF 19)                   AN   BRK 58 10
  ADVENTURE OF THE BALL OF NOSTRADAMUS, THE       SS C FSF 55 06
    SCIENCE-FICTIONAL SHERLOCK HOLMES, THE COUNCIL OF FOUR  AN
  ADVENTURE OF THE SNITCH IN TIME, THE            SS C FSF 53 07
    SCIENCE-FICTIONAL SHERLOCK HOLMES, THE COUNCIL OF FOUR  AN
    SPACE, TIME & CRIME             DEFORD, MIRIAM ALLEN  AN
  AFTER YOU, MR. HENDERSON                        SS   SRS 40 06
    NOT LONG FOR THIS WORLD         DERLETH, AUGUST       AC
  ALANNAH                                         SS   WRT 45 03
    MR. GEORGE AND OTHER ODD PERSONS  DERLETH, AUGUST     AC
  ANCESTOR, THE                                   SS C
    FANTASY: THE LITERATURE OF THE MARVELOUS
                                    KELLEY, LEO P.        AN
    SURVIVOR AND OTHER STORIES, THE  LOVECRAFT & DERLETH  AC
  BALU                                            SS   WRT 49 01
    MR. GEORGE AND OTHER ODD PERSONS  DERLETH, AUGUST     AC
  BAYNTER'S IMP                                   SS   WRT 43 09
    ALONE BY NIGHT                  CONGDON, MICHAEL&DON  AN
    NOT LONG FOR THIS WORLD         DERLETH, AUGUST       AC
  BEYOND THE THRESHOLD                            NV   WRT 41 09
    BEWARE MORE BEASTS              GHIDALIA, V.& ELWOOD  AN
  BIRKETT'S TWELFTH CORPSE                        SS   SRS 40 08
    NOT LONG FOR THIS WORLD         DERLETH, AUGUST       AC
  BISHOP'S GAMBIT                                 SS   AFR 47 03
    MR. GEORGE AND OTHER ODD PERSONS  DERLETH, AUGUST     AC
  BLESSED ARE THE MEEK                            SS   WRT 48 11
    MR. GEORGE AND OTHER ODD PERSONS  DERLETH, AUGUST     AC
  BLUE SPECTACLES, THE                            SS   WRT 49 07
    MR. GEORGE AND OTHER ODD PERSONS  DERLETH, AUGUST     AC
  BRIDGE OF SIGHS, THE                            SS   WRT 31 09
    NOT LONG FOR THIS WORLD         DERLETH, AUGUST       AC
  BY ROCKET TO THE MOON                           SS   VTA 65
    HARRIGAN'S FILE                 DERLETH, AUGUST       AC
  CENTURY JUMPER (A TRAVELLER IN TIME)            SS   OSF 54 02
    BEYOND THE STARS AND OTHER STORIES  ANONYMOUS         AN
  CLOAK FROM MESSER LANDO, A                      SS   WRT 34 09
    NOT LONG FOR THIS WORLD         DERLETH, AUGUST       AC
  COLLECTOR OF STONES, A                          SS   WRT 46 11
    NOT LONG FOR THIS WORLD         DERLETH, AUGUST       AC
  CORNER FOR LUCIA, A                             SS   WRT 53 05
    HARRIGAN'S FILE                 DERLETH, AUGUST       AC
  DEAD MAN'S SHOES                                SS   WRT 46 03
    MR. GEORGE AND OTHER ODD PERSONS  DERLETH, AUGUST     AC
  DETECTIVE AND THE SENATOR, THE                  SS   SDM 53 08
    HARRIGAN'S FILE                 DERLETH, AUGUST       AC
  DINNER AT IMOLA, A                              SS   WRT 29 04
    NOT LONG FOR THIS WORLD         DERLETH, AUGUST       AC
  DRIFTING SNOW, THE                              SS   WRT 39 02
    NOT LONG FOR THIS WORLD         DERLETH, AUGUST       AC
    WEIRD TALES                     MARGULIES, LEO        AN
  EXTRA PASSENGER, THE                            SS   WRT 47 01
    MR. GEORGE AND OTHER ODD PERSONS  DERLETH, AUGUST     AC
  EYE FOR HISTORY, AN                             SS
    HARRIGAN'S FILE                 DERLETH, AUGUST       AC
  FEIGMAN'S BEARD                                 SS   WRT 34 11
    NOT LONG FOR THIS WORLD         DERLETH, AUGUST       AC
  FERGUSON'S CAPSULES                             SS
    HARRIGAN'S FILE                 DERLETH, AUGUST       AC
  FOREWORD                                        IN
    NOT LONG FOR THIS WORLD         DERLETH, AUGUST       AC
    *OUTER REACHES, THE             DERLETH, AUGUST       AN
    *TIME TO COME                   DERLETH, AUGUST       OA
  GABEL WINDOW, THE (THE MURKY GLASS)             SS C STN 57 05
    SURVIVOR AND OTHER STORIES, THE  LOVECRAFT & DERLETH  AC
  GENTLEMAN FROM PRAGUE, A                        SS   WRT 44 11
    MR. GEORGE AND OTHER ODD PERSONS  DERLETH, AUGUST     AC
  GOD-BOX, THE                                    SS   WRT 45 09
    NOT LONG FOR THIS WORLD         DERLETH, AUGUST       AC
  HE SHALL COME                                   SS   MSP 29 12
    NOT LONG FOR THIS WORLD         DERLETH, AUGUST       AC
  HERE, DAEMOS!                                   SS   WRT 42 03
    BEWARE THE BEASTS               GHIDALIA, V.& ELWOOD  AN
  HOUSE IN THE VALLEY, THE                        NV   WRT 53 07
    ANDROIDS, TIME MACHINES AND BLUE GIRAFFES
                                    ELWOOD & GHIDALIA     AN
  IN THE LEFT WING                                SS C WRT 32 06
    WIZARDS AND WARLOCKS            GHIDALIA, VIC         AN
  INTRODUCTION                                    IN
    *BEACHHEADS IN SPACE            DERLETH, AUGUST       AN
    *BEYOND TIME AND SPACE          DERLETH, AUGUST       AN
    FROM OTHER WORLDS               DERLETH, AUGUST       AN
    HAUNTER OF THE DARK, THE        LOVECRAFT, H. P.      AC
    MR. GEORGE AND OTHER ODD PERSONS  DERLETH, AUGUST     AC
```

DERLETH, AUGUST   (CONTINUED)
  PORTALS OF TOMORROW   DERLETH, AUGUST   AN
  *STRANGE PORTS OF CALL   DERLETH, AUGUST   AN
  *WORLDS OF TOMORROW   DERLETH, AUGUST   AN
INVADERS FROM THE MICROCOSM (INVASION FROM THE MICROCOSM)
                                        SS   OSF 53 01
  HARRIGAN'S FILE   DERLETH, AUGUST   AC
INVASION FROM THE MICROCOSM (SEE INVADERS FROM THE MICROCOSM)
                                        TC
"JUST A SONG AT TWILIGHT"   SS   WRT 30 08
  NOT LONG FOR THIS WORLD   DERLETH, AUGUST   AC
LAMP OF ALHAZRED, THE   SS C
  SURVIVOR AND OTHER STORIES, THE   LOVECRAFT & DERLETH   AC
LESANDRO'S FAMILIAR   SS   WRT 36 05
  NOT LONG FOR THIS WORLD   DERLETH, AUGUST   AC
LILAC BUSH, THE   SS   WRT 30 02
  NOT LONG FOR THIS WORLD   DERLETH, AUGUST   AC
LITTLE KNOWLEDGE, A   SS
  NOT LONG FOR THIS WORLD   DERLETH, AUGUST   AC
LOGODA'S HEADS   SS   SRS 39 04
  NOT LONG FOR THIS WORLD   DERLETH, AUGUST   AC
LONESOME PLACE, THE   SS   FFM 48 02
  HORROR TIMES TEN   NORTON, ALDEN H.   AN
LORD OF EVIL (SEE THE SECOND PRINT)   TC
LOST DAY, THE   SS   WRT 45 05
  NOT LONG FOR THIS WORLD   DERLETH, AUGUST   AC
MAN ON B-17, THE   SS   WRT 50 05
  MR. GEORGE AND OTHER ODD PERSONS   DERLETH, AUGUST   AC
MAN WHO RODE THE SAUCER, THE   SS   NEW 52 AN
  HARRIGAN'S FILE   DERLETH, AUGUST   AC
MARA   SS   ARS 48 WI
  MR. GEORGE AND OTHER ODD PERSONS   DERLETH, AUGUST   AC
MARK VII (THE THINKER AND THE THOUGHT) SS   OSF 54 09
  HARRIGAN'S FILE   DERLETH, AUGUST   AC
MARTIAN ARTIFACT, THE   SS   STN 57 07
  HARRIGAN'S FILE   DERLETH, AUGUST   AC
MATTER OF SIGHT, A   SS   WRT 30 01
  NOT LONG FOR THIS WORLD   DERLETH, AUGUST   AC
MAUGHAM OBSESSION, THE   SS   FUN 53 06
  HARRIGAN'S FILE   DERLETH, AUGUST   AC
MCILVAINE'S STAR   SS   IFS 52 07
  HARRIGAN'S FILE   DERLETH, AUGUST   AC
  PRIZE SCIENCE FICTION   WOLLHEIM, DONALD A.   AN
  *WORLDS OF TOMORROW   DERLETH, AUGUST   AN
MECHANICAL HOUSE, THE (THE UNGRATEFUL HOUSE) SS   OSF 54 03
  HARRIGAN'S FILE   DERLETH, AUGUST   AC
METRONOME, THE   SS   WRT 35 02
  LITTLE MONSTERS, THE   ELWOOD & GHIDALIA   AN
MISS ESPERSON   SS   62
  MR. GEORGE AND OTHER ODD PERSONS   DERLETH, AUGUST   AC
MR. BERBECK HAD A DREAM   SS   WRT 35 11
  NOT LONG FOR THIS WORLD   DERLETH, AUGUST   AC
MR. GEORGE   NV   WRT 47 03
  MR. GEORGE AND OTHER ODD PERSONS   DERLETH, AUGUST   AC
MRS. BENTLEY'S DAUGHTER   SS   WRT 30 10
  NOT LONG FOR THIS WORLD   DERLETH, AUGUST   AC
MRS. ELTING DOES HER PART   SS   SRS 39 08
  NOT LONG FOR THIS WORLD   DERLETH, AUGUST   AC
MRS. LANNISFREE   SS   WRT 45 11
  NOT LONG FOR THIS WORLD   DERLETH, AUGUST   AC
MRS. MANIFOLD   SS   49
  MR. GEORGE AND OTHER ODD PERSONS   DERLETH, AUGUST   AC
MURKY GLASS, THE (SEE THE GABEL WINDOW) TC C
NELLIE FOSTER   SS   WRT 33 06
  NOT LONG FOR THIS WORLD   DERLETH, AUGUST   AC
NIGHT TRAIN TO LOST VALLEY, THE   SS   WRT 48 01
  MR. GEORGE AND OTHER ODD PERSONS   DERLETH, AUGUST   AC
OTHER SIDE OF THE WALL, THE   SS   TSF 51 SP
  HARRIGAN'S FILE   DERLETH, AUGUST   AC
PANELLED ROOM, THE   SS   WMR 33 09
  OTHER WORLDS, THE   STONG, PHILIP D.   AN
PARRINGTON'S POOL   SS   WRT 47 07
  MR. GEORGE AND OTHER ODD PERSONS   DERLETH, AUGUST   AC
PEABODY HERITAGE, THE   NV C
  SURVIVOR AND OTHER STORIES, THE   LOVECRAFT & DERLETH   AC
PENFIELD MISADVENTURE, THE   SS   OSF 54 11
  HARRIGAN'S FILE   DERLETH, AUGUST   AC
PLACE IN THE WOODS, THE   SS   WRT 54 05
  DEVIL'S GENERATION, THE   GHIDALIA, VIC   AN
PRINCE BORGIA'S MASS   SS   WRT 31 08
  NOT LONG FOR THIS WORLD   DERLETH, AUGUST   AC
PROTOPLASMA   SS
  HARRIGAN'S FILE   DERLETH, AUGUST   AC
REMARKABLE DINGDONG, THE   SS   SWY 54 04
  HARRIGAN'S FILE   DERLETH, AUGUST   AC
RETURN OF ANDREW BENTLEY, THE   SS C WRT 33 09
  OTHER WORLDS, THE   STONG, PHILIP D.   AN
RETURN OF SARAH PURCELL, THE   SS   WRT 36 07
  NOT LONG FOR THIS WORLD   DERLETH, AUGUST   AC
SAUNDER'S LITTLE FRIEND   SS   WRT 48 05
  NOT LONG FOR THIS WORLD   DERLETH, AUGUST   AC
SECOND PRINT, THE (LORD OF EVIL)   SS   SRS 39 04
  NOT LONG FOR THIS WORLD   DERLETH, AUGUST   AC
SHADOW ON THE SKY, THE   SS   STT 32 01
  NOT LONG FOR THIS WORLD   DERLETH, AUGUST   AC
SHADOW OUT OF SPACE, THE   NV C
  SURVIVOR AND OTHER STORIES, THE   LOVECRAFT & DERLETH   AC
SOMETHING IN WOOD   SS   WRT 48 03
  FANTASY: THE LITERATURE OF THE MARVELOUS
                                        KELLEY, LEO P.   AN
SURVIVOR, THE   NV C WRT 54 07
  SURVIVOR AND OTHER STORIES, THE   LOVECRAFT & DERLETH   AC
TENANT, THE   SS   WRT 28 03
  NOT LONG FOR THIS WORLD   DERLETH, AUGUST   AC
THINKER AND THE THOUGHT, THE (SEE MARK VII AND THINKER)
                                        TC

DERLETH, AUGUST   (CONTINUED)
  THINKER, MARK VII (THE THINKER AND THE THOUGHT) SS   OSF 54 09
  SANDS OF MARS AND OTHER STORIES, THE ANONYMOUS   AN
THOSE WHO SEEK   SS   WRT 32 01
  NOT LONG FOR THIS WORLD   DERLETH, AUGUST   AC
TRAVELLER IN TIME, A (ALSO AS CENTURY JUMPER) SS   OSF 54 02
  HARRIGAN'S FILE   DERLETH, AUGUST   AC
TSANTSA IN THE PARLOR, THE   SS   WRT 48 07
  MR. GEORGE AND OTHER ODD PERSONS   DERLETH, AUGUST   AC
TWILIGHT PLAY   SS   WRT 49 11
  MORE LITTLE MONSTERS   ELWOOD & GHIDALIA   AN
UNGRATEFUL HOUSE, THE (SEE THE MECHANICAL HOUSE) TC
WENTWORTH'S DAY   SS C
  SURVIVOR AND OTHER STORIES, THE   LOVECRAFT & DERLETH   AC
WHITE MOTH, THE   SS   WRT 33 04
  NOT LONG FOR THIS WORLD   DERLETH, AUGUST   AC
"WHO SHALL I SAY IS CALLING?"   SS   FSF 52 08
  HUMAN?   MERRIL, JUDITH   AN
WILD GRAPES   SS   WRT 34 07
  NOT LONG FOR THIS WORLD   DERLETH, AUGUST   AC
WIND IN THE LILACS, THE   SS   ARS 48 SP
  MR. GEORGE AND OTHER ODD PERSONS   DERLETH, AUGUST   AC

DEUTSCH, A. J.
SUBWAY NAMED MOBIUS, A   SS   ASF 50 12
  BEST SF 4   CRISPIN, EDMUND   AN
  FANTASIA MATHEMATICA   FADIMAN, CLIFTON   AN
  OMNIBUS OF SCIENCE FICTION   CONKLIN, GROFF   AN
  ONE HUNDRED YEARS OF SCIENCE FICTION KNIGHT, DAMON   AN
  SCIENCE FICTION OMNIBUS   CONKLIN, GROFF   AN
  STRANGE TRAVELS IN SCIENCE FICTION   CONKLIN, GROFF   AN
  WHERE DO WE GO FROM HERE?   ASIMOV, ISAAC   AN

DEUTSCH, BABETTE
ELECTRONIC CONCERT   PM   63
  SCIENCE FICTION   BRODKIN & PEARSON   AN
SPACE MAN   PM   69
  SCIENCE FICTION   BRODKIN & PEARSON   AN
TO THE MOON, 1969   PM
  SPECULATIONS   SANDERS, THOMAS E.   AN

DEUTSCH, R. H.
WATCHERS, THE   SS   NEW 53 AN
  SCIENCE AND SORCERY   FORD, GARRET   AN

DEVET, CHARLES V.
PROTECTIVE CAMOUFLAGE   NV   SFS 55 05
  RARE SCIENCE FICTION   HOWARD, IVAN   AN
SECOND GAME   NV C ASF 58 03
  GREAT SHORT NOVELS OF SCIENCE FICTION SILVERBERG, ROBERT   AN
SPECIAL FEATURE   NV   ASF 58 05
  SEVEN COME INFINITY   CONKLIN, GROFF   AN

DEWEESE, EUGENE
QUEST OF THE VEIL   NV
  SHANADU   BRINEY, ROBERT E.   OA

DEWEY, G. GORDON
COLLECTORS, THE   SS C AMZ 53 07
  BEST SCIENCE-FICTION STORIES: 1954, THE
                                        BLEILER & DIKTY   AN
TOOTH, THE   SS   FSF 52 08
  BEST FROM FANTASY AND SCIENCE FICTION: 2
                                        BOUCHER & MCCOMAS   AN

DEXTER, RALPH W.
ELTONIAN PYRAMID   MS   SCM 52 10
  APEMAN, SPACEMAN   STOVER & HARRISON   AN

DICK, PHILIP K.
BEST OF PHILIP K. DICK, THE   AC   BAL 77 03
  EDITED BY JOHN BRUNNER
BOOK OF PHILIP K. DICK, THE   AC   DAW 73 02
HANDFUL OF DARKNESS, A   AC H RCH 55
PHILIP K. DICK OMNIBUS, A   AC H SID 70
PRESERVING MACHINE, THE   AC H ACE 69
  ENGLISH EDITION (GOL 71) OMITS STORY "WHAT THE DEAD MEN SAY"
VARIABLE MAN, THE   AC   ACE 57
ADJUSTMENT TEAM   NV   OSF 54 09
  BOOK OF PHILIP K. DICK, THE   DICK, PHILIP K.   AC
  SANDS OF MARS AND OTHER STORIES, THE ANONYMOUS   AN
  AFTERTHOUGHTS BY THE AUTHOR   MS
  BEST OF PHILIP K. DICK, THE   DICK, PHILIP K.   AC
AUTOFAC   NV   GAL 55 11
  BEST OF PHILIP K. DICK, THE   DICK, PHILIP K.   AC
  BEYOND CONTROL   SILVERBERG, ROBERT   AN
  RUINS OF EARTH, THE   DISCH, THOMAS M.   AN
  SCIENCE FACT/FICTION   FARRELL/GAGE/&   AN
  VARIABLE MAN, THE   DICK, PHILIP K.   AC
BEYOND LIES THE WUB   SS   PLS 52 07
  ALPHA 3   SILVERBERG, ROBERT   AN
  BEST OF PHILIP K. DICK, THE   DICK, PHILIP K.   AC
  PRESERVING MACHINE, THE   DICK, PHILIP K.   AC
BREAKFAST AT TWILIGHT   SS   AMZ 54 07
  BEST OF PHILIP K. DICK, THE   DICK, PHILIP K.   AC
  BOOK OF PHILIP K. DICK, THE   DICK, PHILIP K.   AC
BUILDER, THE   SS   AMZ 54 01
  HANDFUL OF DARKNESS, A   DICK, PHILIP K.   AC
CANTATA 140 (SEE THE CRACK IN SPACE)   TC   FSF 64 07
CAPTIVE MARKET   SS   IFS 55 04
  FIRST WORLD OF IF, THE   QUINN & WULFF   AN
  PRESERVING MACHINE, THE   DICK, PHILIP K.   AC
  TOMORROW, INC.   GREENBERG& OLANDER   AN
COLONY   NV   GAL 53 06
  BEST OF PHILIP K. DICK, THE   DICK, PHILIP K.   AC
  HANDFUL OF DARKNESS, A   DICK, PHILIP K.   AC

DICK, PHILIP K.   (CONTINUED)
    SPACE OPERA   ALDISS, BRIAN W.   AN
                                          SS   AMZ 53 09
      BEYOND TOMORROW   HARDING, LEE   AN
    BOOK OF PHILIP K. DICK, THE   DICK, PHILIP K.   AC
COOKIE LADY, THE   SS   FNF 53 06
    HANDFUL OF DARKNESS, A   DICK, PHILIP K.   AC
COSMIC POACHERS, THE   SS   IMG 53 07
    ALIEN WORLDS   ELWOOD, ROGER   AN
CRACK IN SPACE, THE (CANTATA 140, FSF 64 07)   NO   ACE 66
    PHILIP K. DICK OMNIBUS, A   DICK, PHILIP K.   AC
CRAWLERS, THE   SS   IMG 54 07
    PRESERVING MACHINE, THE   DICK, PHILIP K.   AC
    YOU AND SCIENCE FICTION   HOLLISTER, BERNARD C   AN
DAYS OF PERKY PAT, THE   NV   AMZ 63 12
    BEST OF PHILIP K. DICK, THE   DICK, PHILIP K.   AC
DEFENDERS, THE   NV   GAL 53 01
    BOOK OF PHILIP K. DICK, THE   DICK, PHILIP K.   AC
    INVASION OF THE ROBOTS   ELWOOD, ROGER   AN
DR. FUTURITY (TIME PAWN, TWS 54 SU)   DN   ACE 60
    PHILIP K. DICK OMNIBUS, A   DICK, PHILIP K.   AC
ELECTRIC ANT, THE   NV   FSF 69 10
    BEST OF PHILIP K. DICK, THE   DICK, PHILIP K.   AC
    BEST SF: 1969   HARRISON & ALDISS   AN
    DECADE THE 1960S   ALDISS & HARRISON   AN
    WINDOWS INTO TOMORROW   SILVERBERG, ROBERT   AN
EXHIBIT PIECE   SS   IFS 54 08
    HANDFUL OF DARKNESS, A   DICK, PHILIP K.   AC
EXPENDABLE   SS   FSF 53 07
    BEST OF PHILIP K. DICK, THE   DICK, PHILIP K.   AC
    HANDFUL OF DARKNESS, A   DICK, PHILIP K.   AC
    SCIENCE FICTION SHOWCASE   KORNBLUTH, MARY   AN
FAITH OF OUR FATHERS   NV   DVS 67 01
    ALPHA 2   SILVERBERG, ROBERT   AN
    BEST OF PHILIP K. DICK, THE   DICK, PHILIP K.   AC
    DANGEROUS VISIONS   ELLISON, HARLAN   OA
    MODERN SCIENCE FICTION   SPINRAD, NORMAN   AN
FATHER-THING, THE   SS   FSF 54 12
    BEST OF PHILIP K. DICK, THE   DICK, PHILIP K.   AC
    SOCIAL PROBLEMS THROUGH SCIENCE FICTION
                                      GREENBERG/MILSTEAD/&   AN
    THEMES IN SCIENCE FICTION   KELLEY, LEO P.   AN
    TOMORROW'S CHILDREN   ASIMOV, ISAAC   AN
    TREASURY OF GREAT SCIENCE FICTION, A VOL.1
                                      BOUCHER, ANTHONY   AN
FOSTER, YOU'RE DEAD   NV   STR 54 03
    BEST OF PHILIP K. DICK, THE   DICK, PHILIP K.   AC
    STAR SCIENCE FICTION STORIES NO. 3   POHL, FREDERIK   OA
GOLDEN MAN, THE   NV   IFS 54 04
    BEYOND THE BARRIERS OF SPACE AND TIME   MERRIL, JUDITH   AN
    EVIL EARTHS   ALDISS, BRIAN W.   AN
    STRANGE GIFTS   SILVERBERG, ROBERT   AN
HUMAN IS   SS   STS 55 WI
    BEST OF PHILIP K. DICK, THE   DICK, PHILIP K.   AC
IF THERE WERE NO BENNY CEMOLI   SS   GAL 63 12
    BEST OF PHILIP K. DICK, THE   DICK, PHILIP K.   AC
    EIGHTH GALAXY READER, THE   POHL, FREDERIK   AN
    PRESERVING MACHINE, THE   DICK, PHILIP K.   AC
IMPOSSIBLE PLANET, THE   SS   IFS 53 10
    HANDFUL OF DARKNESS, A   DICK, PHILIP K.   AC
    SPACE ODYSSEYS   ALDISS, BRIAN W.   AN
IMPOSTOR   SS   ASF 53 06
    ASTOUNDING-ANALOG READER, THE VOLUME TWO
                                      HARRISON & ALDISS   AN
    BEST OF PHILIP K. DICK, THE   DICK, PHILIP K.   AC
    BEST SF 2   CRISPIN, EDMUND   AN
    DARK STARS   SILVERBERG, ROBERT   AN
    END OF THE WORLD, THE   WOLLHEIM, DONALD A.   AN
    HANDFUL OF DARKNESS, A   DICK, PHILIP K.   AC
    METAL SMILE, THE   KNIGHT, DAMON   AN
    SCIENCE FICTION TERROR TALES   CONKLIN, GROFF   AN
    SOULS IN METAL   ASHLEY, MICHAEL   AN
    UNTRAVELLED WORLDS   BARTER & WILSON   AN
INDEFATIGABLE FROG, THE   SS   FSM 53 07
    HANDFUL OF DARKNESS, A   DICK, PHILIP K.   AC
JON'S WORLD   NV
    *TIME TO COME   DERLETH, AUGUST   OA
LAST OF THE MASTERS, THE   SS   OSF 54 11
    SPACE STATION 42 AND OTHER STORIES   ANONYMOUS   AN
LITTLE MOVEMENT, THE   SS   FSF 52 11
    HANDFUL OF DARKNESS, A   DICK, PHILIP K.   AC
LITTLE SOMETHING FOR US TEMPUNAUTS, A   NV   FST 74
    BEST OF PHILIP K. DICK, THE   DICK, PHILIP K.   AC
    BEST SCIENCE FICTION OF THE YEAR, THE NO. 4
                                      CARR, TERRY   AN
    FINAL STAGE   FERMAN & MALZBERG   OA
MINORITY REPORT, THE   SS   FUN 56 01
    VARIABLE MAN, THE   DICK, PHILIP K.   AC
MOLD OF YANCY, THE   NV   IFS 55 08
    SECOND WORLD OF IF, THE   QUINN & WULFF   AN
NANNY   SS   STS 55 SP
    BOOK OF PHILIP K. DICK, THE   DICK, PHILIP K.   AC
NOVELTY ACT   NV   FAN 64 02
    HUMAN EQUATION, THE   NOLAN, WILLIAM F.   AN
OH, TO BE A BLOBEL| SS   GAL 64 02
    BEST OF PHILIP K. DICK, THE   DICK, PHILIP K.   AC
    INFINITE JESTS   SILVERBERG, ROBERT   AN
    PRESERVING MACHINE, THE   DICK, PHILIP K.   AC
    WORLD'S BEST SCIENCE FICTION: 1965   WOLLHEIM & CARR   AN
OUT IN THE GARDEN   SS   FNF 53 08
    SATAN'S PETS   GHIDALIA, VIC   AN
PAY FOR THE PRINTER   SS   SAT 56 10
    PRESERVING MACHINE, THE   DICK, PHILIP K.   AC
PAYCHECK   NV   IMG 53 06
    BEST OF PHILIP K. DICK, THE   DICK, PHILIP K.   AC

DICK, PHILIP K.   (CONTINUED)
    PHILIP K. DICK OMNIBUS, A   DICK, PHILIP K.   AC   SID 70
    SCIENCE FICTION SPECIAL 7   ANONYMOUS   AN
PIPER IN THE WOODS   SS   IMG 53 02
    OTHER WORLDS, OTHER TIMES   MOSKOWITZ & ELWOOD   AN
PLANET FOR TRANSIENTS   SS   FUN 53 10
    HANDFUL OF DARKNESS, A   DICK, PHILIP K.   AC
PRESENT FOR PAT, A   SS   STS 54 01
    BOOK OF PHILIP K. DICK, THE   DICK, PHILIP K.   AC
PRESERVING MACHINE, THE   SS   FSF 53 06
    HANDFUL OF DARKNESS, A   DICK, PHILIP K.   AC
    PRESERVING MACHINE, THE   DICK, PHILIP K.   AC
    SCIENCE FICTION BESTIARY, THE   SILVERBERG, ROBERT   AN
PROGENY   SS   IFS 54 11
    HANDFUL OF DARKNESS, A   DICK, PHILIP K.   AC
    MARRIAGE AND THE FAMILY THROUGH SCIENCE FICTION
                                      CLEAR/WARRICK/&   AN
    SCHOOL AND SOCIETY THROUGH SCIENCE FICTION
                                      OLANDER/GREENBERG/&   AN
PROMINANT AUTHOR   SS   IFS 54 05
    HANDFUL OF DARKNESS, A   DICK, PHILIP K.   AC
PSI-MAN (PSI-MAN HEAL MY CHILD)   NV   IMT 55 11
    BOOK OF PHILIP K. DICK, THE   DICK, PHILIP K.   AC
RETREAT FROM RIGEL (TONY AND THE BEETLES)   SS   OSF 54 02
    PLANET OF DOOM AND OTHER STORIES ANONYMOUS   AN
RETREAT SYNDROME   SS   WOT 65 01
    PRESERVING MACHINE, THE   DICK, PHILIP K.   AC
ROOG   SS   FSF 53 02
    BEST OF PHILIP K. DICK, THE   DICK, PHILIP K.   AC
    INVADERS FROM SPACE   SILVERBERG, ROBERT   AN
    OTHERS, THE   CARR, TERRY   AN
    PRESERVING MACHINE, THE   DICK, PHILIP K.   AC
SECOND VARIETY   NV   SSF 53 05
    BEST OF PHILIP K. DICK, THE   DICK, PHILIP K.   AC
    SPECTRUM 2   AMIS & CONQUEST   AN
    VARIABLE MAN, THE   DICK, PHILIP K.   AC
    YEAR'S BEST SCIENCE FICTION NOVELS: 1954
                                      BLEILER & DIKTY   AN
SERVICE CALL   SS   SFS 55 07
    BEST OF PHILIP K. DICK, THE   DICK, PHILIP K.   AC
    MASTERS OF SCIENCE FICTION   HOWARD, IVAN   AN
SHELL GAME   SS   GAL 54 09
    BOOK OF PHILIP K. DICK, THE   DICK, PHILIP K.   AC
STAND-BY (SEE TOP STAND-BY JOB)   TC
TIME PAWN (SEE DR. FUTURITY)   TC   TWS 54 SU
TONY AND THE BEETLES (SEE RETREAT FROM RIGEL)   TC
TOP STAND-BY JOB (STAND-BY)   SS   AMZ 63 10
    INSIDE INFORMATION   MOWSHOWITZ, ABBE   AN
    PRESERVING MACHINE, THE   DICK, PHILIP K.   AC
TURNING WHEEL, THE   SS   SFS 54 02
    BOOK OF PHILIP K. DICK, THE   DICK, PHILIP K.   AC
    HANDFUL OF DARKNESS, A   DICK, PHILIP K.   AC
    NOW & BEYOND   HOWARD, IVAN   AN
UNTELEPORTED MAN, THE   SN   FAN 64 12
    PHILIP K. DICK OMNIBUS, A   DICK, PHILIP K.   AC
UPON THE DULL EARTH   NV   BEY 54 09
    HANDFUL OF DARKNESS, A   DICK, PHILIP K.   AC
    PRESERVING MACHINE, THE   DICK, PHILIP K.   AC
VARIABLE MAN, THE   NA   SSF 53 09
    VARIABLE MAN, THE   DICK, PHILIP K.   AC
VULCAN'S HAMMER   NV   FUT 56 29
    6 AND THE SILENT SCREAM   HOWARD, IVAN   AN
WAR GAME   SS   GAL 59 12
    PRESERVING MACHINE, THE   DICK, PHILIP K.   AC
WAR VETERAN   NV   IFS 55 03
    PRESERVING MACHINE, THE   DICK, PHILIP K.   AC
WE CAN REMEMBER IT FOR YOU WHOLESALE   NV   FSF 66 04
    ALPHA 5   SILVERBERG, ROBERT   AN
    BEST FROM FANTASY AND SCIENCE FICTION: 16
                                      FERMAN, EDWARD L.   AN
    EARTH IN TRANSIT   SCHWARTZ, SHEILA   AN
    NEBULA AWARD STORIES NO. 2   ALDISS & HARRISON   AN
    PRESERVING MACHINE, THE   DICK, PHILIP K.   AC
    TWENTY YEARS OF FANTASY & SCIENCE FICTION
                                      FERMAN & MILLS   AN
    WORLD'S BEST SCIENCE FICTION: 1967   WOLLHEIM & CARR   AN
WHAT THE DEAD MEN SAY   SN   WOT 64 06
    PRESERVING MACHINE, THE   DICK, PHILIP K.   AC
WORLD OF TALENT, A   NV   GAL 54 10
    VARIABLE MAN, THE   DICK, PHILIP K.   AC
WORLD THAT JONES MADE, THE   NO   ACE 56
    SCIENCE FICTION SPECIAL 1   ANONYMOUS   AN

DICKENS, CHARLES
    DEVIL AND MR. CHIPS, THE (THE RAT THAT COULD SPEAK)
                                          SS   FSF 51 08
    DEALS WITH THE DEVIL   DAVENPORT, BASIL   AN
    RAT THAT COULD SPEAK, THE (ALSO AS THE DEVIL AND MR. CHIPS)
                                          SS   FSF 51 08
    BEST FROM FANTASY AND SCIENCE FICTION   BOUCHER & MCCOMAS   AN
    EDGE OF NEVER, THE   HOSKINS, ROBERT   AN

DICKEY, JAMES
    APOLLO   PM   LIF 69
    SPECULATIONS   SANDERS, THOMAS E.   AN

DICKEY, WILLIAM
    VOYAGE TO THE MOON   PM   TXQ 64 03
    SCIENCE FICTION   BRODKIN & PEARSON   AN

DICKINSON, JOSEPH
    THREE FOR THE STARS   SS   FSF 62 04
    BEST FROM FANTASY AND SCIENCE FICTION: 12
                                      DAVIDSON, AVRAM   AN

DICKSON, GORDON R.   DICKSON, GORDON R.

```
DICKSON, GORDON R.   SEE ALSO   CO-AUTHOR POUL ANDERSON
ANCIENT, MY ENEMY                                   AC H DBL 74
BOOK OF GORDON DICKSON, THE                         AC   DAW 73 05
    SEE "DANGER- HUMAN"
COMBAT SF                                           AN H DBL 75
DANGER- HUMAN                                       AC H DBL 70
    ALSO AS "THE BOOK OF GORDON DICKSON"
MUTANTS                                             AC H MAC 70
STAR ROAD, THE                                      AC H DBL 73
THREE TO DORSAI|                                    AC H NDB 75
  ADVENTURE OF THE MISPLACED HOUND, THE             NV C USF 53 12
    EARTHMAN'S BURDEN              ANDERSON, P.&DICKSON AC
    SCIENCE-FICTIONAL SHERLOCK HOLMES, THE COUNCIL OF FOUR  AN
  AMULET, THE                                       SS   FSF 59 04
    ROD SERLING'S TRIPLE W: WITCHES, WARLOCKS AND WEREWOLVES
                                    SERLING, ROD        AN
  ANCIENT, MY ENEMY                                 NV   IFS 69 12
    ANCIENT, MY ENEMY             DICKSON, GORDON R.    AC
  AND THEN THERE WAS PEACE                          SS   IFS 62 09
    DANGER- HUMAN                 DICKSON, GORDON R.    AC
  BALLAD OF THE SHOSHONU                            SG   NEW 61 AN
    6TH ANNUAL OF THE YEAR'S BEST S-F, THE MERRIL, JUDITH   AN
  BLACK CHARLIE                                     SS   GAL 54 04
    DANGER- HUMAN                 DICKSON, GORDON R.    AC
    FIFTH GALAXY READER, THE      GOLD, H. L.          AN
    ONE HUNDERED YEARS OF SCIENCE FICTION KNIGHT, DAMON    AN
  BLEAK AND BARREN LAND, THE                        NV   SPS 53 02
    ANCIENT, MY ENEMY             DICKSON, GORDON R.    AC
  BROTHERS                                          NV   AMA 73
    ASTOUNDING                    HARRISON, HARRY      OA
  BUILDING ON THE LINE                              NV   GAL 68 11
    STAR ROAD, THE                DICKSON, GORDON R.    AC
  BY NEW HEARTH FIRES                               SS   ASF 59 01
    MUTANTS                       DICKSON, GORDON R.    AC
  CALL HIM LORD                                     SS   ASF 66 05
    ANALOG 6                      CAMPBELL, JOHN W. JR AN
    BEYOND TOMORROW               HARDING, LEE         AN
    DANGER- HUMAN                 DICKSON, GORDON R.    AC
    NEBULA AWARD STORIES  NO. 2   ALDISS & HARRISON    AN
    POLITICAL SCIENCE FICTION     GREENBERG& WARRICK   AN
  CATCH, THE                                        SS   ASF 59 04
    STAR ROAD, THE                DICKSON, GORDON R.    AC
  CHRISTMAS PRESENT, THE                            SS   FSF 58 01
    STAR ROAD, THE                DICKSON, GORDON R.    AC
    UNIVERSE AHEAD                ENGDAHL & ROBERSON   AN
  COMBAT SF: INTRODUCTION                           IN
    COMBAT SF                     DICKSON, GORDON R.   AN
  COMPUTERS DON'T ARGUE                             SS   ASF 65 09
    ANALOG 5                      CAMPBELL, JOHN W. JR AN
    ASTOUNDING-ANALOG READER, THE VOLUME TWO
                                  HARRISON & ALDISS    AN
    DECADE THE 1960S              ALDISS & HARRISON    AN
    NEBULA AWARD STORIES          KNIGHT, DAMON        AN
    TRANSFORMATIONS II            ROSELLE, DANIEL      AN
    WONDERMAKERS 2                HOSKINS, ROBERT      AN
    YOU AND SCIENCE FICTION       HOLLISTER, BERNARD C AN
  DANGER- HUMAN|                                    SS   ASF 57 12
    DANGER- HUMAN                 DICKSON, GORDON R.    AC
    MUTANTS                       DICKSON, GORDON R.    AC
    STRANGE GIFTS                 SILVERBERG, ROBERT   AN
  DOLPHIN'S WAY                                     SS   ASF 64 06
    DANGER- HUMAN                 DICKSON, GORDON R.    AC
  DON JONES                                         NV C NEW 57 04
    EARTHMAN'S BURDEN             ANDERSON, P.&DICKSON AC
  DORSAI|                                           NO   ASF 59 05
    THREE TO DORSAI|              DICKSON, GORDON R.    AC
  DREAMSMAN, THE                                    SS   STR 59 06
    STAR SCIENCE FICTION STORIES NO. 6  POHL, FREDERIK   OA
    5TH ANNUAL OF THE YEAR'S BEST S-F, THE MERRIL, JUDITH AN
  ENTER A PILGRIM                                   SS   ASF 74 08
    BEST SCIENCE FICTION STORIES OF THE YEAR (1974)
                                  DEL REY, LESTER      AN
  EPILIGUE                                          MS
    THREE TO DORSAI|              DICKSON, GORDON R.    AC
  FLAT TIGER                                        SS   GAL 56 03
    DANGER- HUMAN                 DICKSON, GORDON R.    AC
  FRIENDLY MAN, THE                                 SS   ASF 51 02
    ANCIENT, MY ENEMY             DICKSON, GORDON R.    AC
  HALF A HOKA- POUL ANDERSON                        AR   59
    SCIENCE-FICTIONAL SHERLOCK HOLMES, THE COUNCIL OF FOUR AN
  HAUNTED VILLAGE, THE                              NV   FSF 61 08
    *BEST FROM FANTASY AND SCIENCE FICTION: 11
                                  MILLS, ROBERT P.     AN
  HEROES ARE MADE (SEE THE SHERIFF OF CANYON GULCH) TC C
  HILIFTER                                          SS   ASF 63 02
    ANALOG 3                      CAMPBELL, JOHN W. JR AN
    SPECULATIONS                  SANDERS, THOMAS E.   AN
    STAR ROAD, THE                DICKSON, GORDON R.    AC
  HOME FROM THE SHORE                               NA   GAL 63 02
    MUTANTS                       DICKSON, GORDON R.    AC
    8TH ANNUAL OF THE YEAR'S BEST S-F, THE MERRIL, JUDITH AN
  HONORABLE DEATH, AN                               NV   GAL 61 02
    ALPHA 6                       SILVERBERG, ROBERT   AN
    DANGER- HUMAN                 DICKSON, GORDON R.    AC
    POCKETFUL OF STARS, A         KNIGHT, DAMON        AN
  IDIOT SOLVANT                                     SS   ASF 62 01
    MUTANTS                       DICKSON, GORDON R.    AC
    13 ABOVE THE NIGHT            CONKLIN, GROFF       AN
  IMMORTAL, THE                                     NV   FSF 65 08
    MUTANTS                       DICKSON, GORDON R.    AC
  IN HOKA SIGNO VINCES                              NV C OWS 53 06
    EARTHMAN'S BURDEN             ANDERSON, P.&DICKSON AC
  IN THE BONE                                       NV   IFS 66 10
    ANCIENT, MY ENEMY             DICKSON, GORDON R.    AC
  INTERLUDE                                         MS
    THREE TO DORSAI|              DICKSON, GORDON R.    AC

DICKSON, GORDON R.   (CONTINUED)
    THREE TO DORSAI|              DICKSON, GORDON R.    AC
  INTRODUCTION                                      IN
    FUTURELOVE                    ELWOOD, ROGER        OA
    MUTANTS                       DICKSON, GORDON R.    AC
    THREE TO DORSAI|              DICKSON, GORDON R.    AC
  JACKAL'S MEAL                                     SS   ASF 69 06
    STAR ROAD, THE                DICKSON, GORDON R.    AC
  JAMES                                             SS   FSF 55 05
    DANGER- HUMAN                 DICKSON, GORDON R.    AC
  JEAN DUPRES                                       NV   NOV 70 01
    *NOVA 1                       HARRISON, HARRY      OA
  JOY IN MUDVILLE                                   NV C FSF 55 11
    INFINITE ARENA, THE           CARR, TERRY          AN
  LAW-TWISTER SHORTY, THE                           NV   MWS 71
    MANY WORLDS OF SCIENCE FICTION, THE  BOVA, BEN     OA
  LISTEN                                            SS   FSF 52 08
    MUTANTS                       DICKSON, GORDON R.    AC
    PRIZE SCIENCE FICTION         WOLLHEIM, DONALD A.  AN
  LOVE ME TRUE                                      SS   ASF 61 10
    ANCIENT, MY ENEMY             DICKSON, GORDON R.    AC
  LULUNGOMEENA                                      NV   GAL 54 01
    DANGER- HUMAN                 DICKSON, GORDON R.    AC
    DEEP SPACE                    SILVERBERG, ROBERT   AN
    LOOKING FORWARD               LESSER, MILTON       AN
  MAN FROM EARTH, THE                               SS   GAL 64 06
    DANGER- HUMAN                 DICKSON, GORDON R.    AC
  MAVERICK (WALKER BETWEEN THE PLANES)              NV   WOF 70 02
    FIVE FATES                    LAUMER, KEITH        AN
  MISS PRINKS                                       SS   FSF 54 06
    MUTANTS                       DICKSON, GORDON R.    AC
  MONKEY WRENCH, THE                                SS   ASF 51 08
    ANCIENT, MY ENEMY             DICKSON, GORDON R.    AC
    METAL SMILE, THE              KNIGHT, DAMON        AN
    MORE PENGUIN SCIENCE FICTION  ALDISS, BRIAN W.     AN
  MORTAL AND THE MONSTER, THE                       NA
    STELLAR SHORT NOVELS          DEL REY, JUDY-LYNN   OA
  MOUSETRAP, THE                                    SS   GAL 52 09
    STAR ROAD, THE                DICKSON, GORDON R.    AC
  NECROMANCER                                       NO   DBL 62
    THREE TO DORSAI|              DICKSON, GORDON R.    AC
  ODD ONES, THE                                     NV   IFS 55 02
    ANCIENT, MY ENEMY             DICKSON, GORDON R.    AC
    SECOND WORLD OF IF, THE       QUINN & WULFF        AN
  OF THE PEOPLE                                     SS   FSF 55 12
    MUTANTS                       DICKSON, GORDON R.    AC
  ON MESSENGER MOUNTAIN                             NV   WOT 64 06
    STAR ROAD, THE                DICKSON, GORDON R.    AC
  OPERATION P-BUTTON                                SS   INY 70 01
    INFINITY 1                    HOSKINS, ROBERT      OA
  OUR FIRST DEATH                                   SS   FSF 55 08
    ANCIENT, MY ENEMY             DICKSON, GORDON R.    AC
  POUL ANDERSON                                     AR   FSF 71 04
    BEST FROM FANTASY AND SCIENCE FICTION, 25TH ANNIV.
                                  FERMAN, EDWARD L.    AN
  PROLOGUE                                          MS
    THREE TO DORSAI|              DICKSON, GORDON R.    AC
  QUARRY, THE                                       SS   ASF 58 09
    DANGER- HUMAN                 DICKSON, GORDON R.    AC
  REHABILITATED                                     SS   FSF 61 01
    MUTANTS                       DICKSON, GORDON R.    AC
  RICOCHET ON MIZA                                  SS   PLS 52 03
    COMBAT SF.                    DICKSON, GORDON R.   AN
  ROOFS OF SILVER                                   NV   FSF 62 12
    MUTANTS                       DICKSON, GORDON R.    AC
  SHERIFF OF CANYON GULCH, THE (HEROES ARE MADE)    NV C OWS 51 05
    EARTHMAN'S BURDEN             ANDERSON, P.&DICKSON AC
    GATES TO TOMORROW             NORTON, AN.&DONALDY  AN
    MANY WORLDS OF POUL ANDERSON, THE  ANDERSON, POUL  AC
    SCIENCE FICTION BESTIARY, THE SILVERBERG, ROBERT  AN
  SLIGHT OF WIT                                     SS   ASF 61 12
    ANALOG 1                      CAMPBELL, JOHN W. JR AN
  SOLDIER, ASK NOT                                  SN   GAL 64 10
    HUGO WINNERS, THE (VOLUME 2)  ASIMOV, ISAAC        AN
  SPACE SWIMMERS                                    NO   BKM 67
    SCIENCE FICTION SPECIAL  1    ANONYMOUS          AN
  STEEL BROTHER                                     NV   ASF 52 02
    DANGER- HUMAN                 DICKSON, GORDON R.    AC
    SPACE SERVICE                 NORTON, ANDRE        AN
  TACTICS OF MISTAKE                                NO   ASF 70 10
    THREE TO DORSAI|              DICKSON, GORDON R.    AC
  TEN YEARS OF NEBULA AWARDS                        AR   NEW 75 AN
    NEBULA AWARD STORIES 10       GUNN, JAMES E.       AN
  THINGS WHICH ARE CAESAR'S                         NA
    DAY THE SUN STOOD STILL, THE  SILVERBERG, ROBERT  OA
  THREE-PART PUZZLE                                 SS   ASF 62 06
    STAR ROAD, THE                DICKSON, GORDON R.    AC
  THREE, THE                                        SS   STS 53 05
    SPECIAL WONDER                MCCOMAS, J. FRANCIS  AN
  TIDDLYWINK WARRIORS, THE                          NV C FSF 55 08
    EARTHMAN'S BURDEN             ANDERSON, P.&DICKSON AC
  TIGER GREEN                                       NV   IFS 65 11
    ANCIENT, MY ENEMY             DICKSON, GORDON R.    AC
  TRESPASS|                                         SS C FSQ 50 SP
    BEST SCIENCE-FICTION STORIES: 1951, THE
                                  BLEILER & DIKTY      AN
    MINDWORM, THE                 ANONYMOUS            AN
  TWIG                                              NV   STL 74 01
    STELLAR 1                     DEL REY, JUDY-LYNN   OA
    1975 ANNUAL WORLD'S BEST SF, THE  WOLLHEIM, DONALD A. AN
  WALKER BETWEEN THE PLANES (SEE MAVERICK)          TC
  WARRIOR                                           SS   ASF 65 12
    DAW SCIENCE FICTION READER, THE  WOLLHEIM, DONALD A. OA
    MUTANTS                       DICKSON, GORDON R.    AC
    SF: AUTHORS' CHOICE 4         HARRISON, HARRY      AN
```

DICKSON, GORDON R.   DISCH, THOMAS M.

DICKSON, GORDON R.   (CONTINUED)   DISCH, THOMAS M.   (CONTINUED)
  11TH ANNUAL OF THE YEAR'S BEST S-F, THE   ALTERNATE UNIVERSE I   PM
                              MERRIL, JUDITH   AN   BEYOND TIME   LEY, SANDRA   OA
    WHATEVER GODS THERE BE   SS   AMZ 61 07   ALTERNATE UNIVERSE II   PM
    STAR ROAD, THE   DICKSON, GORDON R.   AC   BEYOND TIME   LEY, SANDRA   OA
    YO HO HOKA| NV C FSF 55 03   ALTERNATE UNIVERSE III   PM
    EARTHMAN'S BURDEN   ANDERSON, P.&DICKSON AC   BEYOND TIME   LEY, SANDRA   OA
    ZEEPSDAY   SS   FSF 56 11   ANGOULEME   SS   NWQ 71 01
    DANGER- HUMAN   DICKSON, GORDON R.   AC   BEST SF: 1971   HARRISON & ALDISS   AN
                                                         NEW WORLDS QUARTERLY NO. 1
DIEFENDORF, DAVID   MOORCOCK, MICHAEL   OA
  FABLES (THE FROG PRINCE & MICKEY MOUSE) SS NYT 75 12   334   DISCH, THOMAS M.   NO
  NEW CONSTELLATIONS   DISCH & NAYLOR   OA   APOLLO   SS
                                                         GETTING INTO DEATH AND OTHER STORIES DISCH, THOMAS M. AC
DIFFIN, CHARLES W.   ASIAN SHORE, THE   NV   ORB 70 06
  POWER AND THE GLORY, THE   SS   ASF 30 07   BEST SF: 1970   HARRISON & ALDISS   AN
    HISTORY OF THE SCIENCE FICTION MAGAZINE, THE PART 1 1926-1935 *GETTING INTO DEATH DISCH, THOMAS M. AC
                              ASHLEY, MICHAEL AN   ORBIT 6   KNIGHT, DAMON   OA
  SPAWN OF THE STARS   NV   ASF 30 02   SCIENCE FICTION NOVELLAS HARRISON & MCNELLY AN
    *BEST OF SCIENCE FICTION   CONKLIN, GROFF   AN   SHORES BENEATH, THE   SALLIS, JAMES   AN
                                                       ASSASSINATION OF THE MAYOR, THE SS   NWB 73 05
DIGHTON, RALPH   NEW WORLDS QUARTERLY NO. 5
  SIERRA SAM   AR   NYT 60 01   MOORCOCK, MICHAEL   OA
    5TH ANNUAL OF THE YEAR'S BEST S-F, THE MERRIL, JUDITH AN ATHEIST'S BARGAIN, THE   SS C NEW 67 AN
                                                         DEVIL HIS DUE, THE   HILL, DOUGLAS   AN
DIKTY, JULIAN CHAIN   SEE PSEUD. JULIAN CHAIN AND JULIAN C. MAY BEGINNING OF APRIL OR THE END OF MARCH, THE SS FSF 71 02
                                                         *GETTING INTO DEATH   DISCH, THOMAS M.   AC
DIKTY, T. E.   SEE ALSO   CO-EDITOR EVERETT F. BLEILER BIRDS, THE   SS   73
  BEST SCIENCE FICTION STORIES AND NOVELS: 1955 AN H FEL 55 BEST SF: 1973   HARRISON & ALDISS   AN
    DERIVATIVE ANTHOLOGY "5 TALES FROM TOMORROW"   GETTING INTO DEATH AND OTHER STORIES DISCH, THOMAS M. AC
  BEST SCIENCE FICTION STORIES AND NOVELS: 1956 AN H FEL 56 BODIES   NV   QRK 71 04
    DERIVATIVE ANTHOLOGY "6 FROM WORLDS BEYOND"   QUARK/4   DELANY & HACKER   OA
  BEST SCIENCE FICTION STORIES AND NOVELS: 9TH SERIES   334   DISCH, THOMAS M.   NO
                                    AN H AVT 58   BONE OF CONTENTION   SS   AHM 66
  EVERY BOY'S BOOK OF OUTER SPACE STORIES AN H FEL 60   *ONE HUNDRED AND TWO H-BOMBS DISCH, THOMAS M. AC
  GREAT SCIENCE FICTION STORIES ABOUT MARS AN H FEL 66   WHITE FANG GOES DINGO AND OTHER FUNNY S.F. STORIES
  GREAT SCIENCE FICTION STORIES ABOUT THE MOON AN H FEL 67   DISCH, THOMAS M.   AC
  5 TALES FROM TOMORROW   AN   CRS 57 12   CASABLANCA   NV   67
    5 STORIES FROM "BEST SCIENCE FICTION STORIES AND NOVELS: 1955" ALPHA 4   SILVERBERG, ROBERT AN
  6 FROM WORLDS BEYOND   AN   CRS 58 12   FUN WITH YOUR NEW HEAD DISCH, THOMAS M. AC
    6 STORIES FROM "BEST SCIENCE FICTION STORIES AND NOVELS: 1956" CEPHALOTRON (ALSO AS FUN WITH YOUR NEW HEAD) SS PBY 66 12
  EARTH'S NATURAL SATELLITE   IN   TRANSIT OF EARTH   PLAYBOY, EDITORS OF AN
    GREAT SCIENCE FICTION STORIES ABOUT THE MOON   CHOCOLATE EGG, THE   SS
                              DIKTY, T. E.   AN   *GETTING INTO DEATH   DISCH, THOMAS M.   AC
  EDITORS' PREFACE   IN C   CITY OF PENETRATING LIGHT, THE   SS
    BEST SCIENCE-FICTION STORIES: 1954, THE   FUN WITH YOUR NEW HEAD DISCH, THOMAS M. AC
                              BLEILER & DIKTY   AN   COLORS, THE   SS   NWS 68 12
  INTRODUCTION   IN C   *GETTING INTO DEATH   DISCH, THOMAS M.   AC
    *IMAGINATION UNLIMITED   BLEILER & DIKTY   AN   COME TO VENUS MELANCHOLY   SS   FSF 65 11
  YEAR'S BEST SCIENCE FICTION NOVELS: 1953   ALPHA 3   SILVERBERG, ROBERT   AN
                              BLEILER & DIKTY   AN   BEST SF 7   CRISPIN, EDMUND   AN
  YEAR'S BEST SCIENCE FICTION NOVELS: 1954   FUN WITH YOUR NEW HEAD DISCH, THOMAS M. AN
                              BLEILER & DIKTY   AN   LATE GREAT FUTURE, THE FITZ GERALD & DILLON AN
  RED PLANET, THE   IN   COMPLETE SHORT STORIES, THE   GR
    GREAT SCIENCE FICTION STORIES ABOUT MARS   *GETTING INTO DEATH   DISCH, THOMAS M.   AC
                              DIKTY, T. E.   AN   CONTEST, THE   SS   NWS 67 03
  SCIENCE-FICTION YEAR, THE   MS   BEST SF STORIES FROM NEW WORLDS NO. 2, THE
    BEST SCIENCE FICTION STORIES AND NOVELS: 1955   MOORCOCK, MICHAEL   AN
                              DIKTY, T. E.   AN   FUN WITH YOUR NEW HEAD DISCH, THOMAS M. AC
    BEST SCIENCE FICTION STORIES AND NOVELS: 1956   COTTONWOOD TREE, THE   SS
                              DIKTY, T. E.   AN   *GETTING INTO DEATH   DISCH, THOMAS M.   AC
    BEST SCIENCE FICTION STORIES AND NOVELS: 9TH SERIES DANGEROUS FLAGS   SS   FAN 64 08
                              DIKTY, T. E.   AN   *ONE HUNDRED AND TWO H-BOMBS DISCH, THOMAS M. AC
                                                         WHITE FANG GOES DINGO AND OTHER FUNNY S.F. STORIES
DILLINGHAM, PETER   DISCH, THOMAS M.   AC
  X-2076   PM   DANNY'S NEW FRIENDS FROM DENEB
    2076: THE AMERICAN TRICENTENNIAL BRYANT, EDWARD OA WHITE FANG GOES DINGO AND OTHER FUNNY S.F. STORIES
                                                                             DISCH, THOMAS M.   AC
DILLON, JOHN   SEE ALSO   CO-EDITOR GREGORY FITZ GERALD DAWN BREAKS OVER CRAKOW   SS
  INTRODUCTION   IN C   *GETTING INTO DEATH   DISCH, THOMAS M.   AC
    LATE GREAT FUTURE, THE   FITZ GERALD & DILLON AN DAY EUTERPE DIED, THE   PM   69
                                                         HOLDING YOUR EIGHT HANDS LUCIE-SMITH, EDWARD AN
DINGLE, HERBERT   DAY IN THE LIFE OF THE ARTIST, A   SS
  HE THOUGHT HE SAW ELECTRONS SWIFT PM   *GETTING INTO DEATH   DISCH, THOMAS M.   AC
    FANTASIA MATHEMATICA   FADIMAN, CLIFTON   AN   DEATH AND THE SINGLE GIRL   SS
                                                       DEATH OF SOCRATES, THE   NV
DIONNE, ROGER   334   DISCH, THOMAS M.   NO
  ACCIDENTS OF A COUNTRY ROAD   SS   PBY 70 11   DEMI-URGE, THE   SS   AMZ 63 06
    WEIRD SHOW   PLAYBOY, EDITORS OF AN   *ONE HUNDRED AND TWO H-BOMBS DISCH, THOMAS M. AC
                                                         WHITE FANG GOES DINGO AND OTHER FUNNY S.F. STORIES
DIRAC, HUGH   DISCH, THOMAS M.   AC
  PROFIT OF DOOM, THE   NO   70   DESCENDING   SS   FAN 64 07
    SCIENCE FICTION SPECIAL 8 ANONYMOUS   AN   DECADE THE 1960S   ALDISS & HARRISON   AN
                                                         FUN WITH YOUR NEW HEAD DISCH, THOMAS M. AC
DISCH, THOMAS M. AND CHARLES NAYLOR   MODERN SCIENCE FICTION SPINRAD, NORMAN   AN
  NEW CONSTELLATIONS   OA H HPR 76   10TH ANNUAL OF THE YEAR'S BEST S-F, THE
                                                                             MERRIL, JUDITH   AN
DISCH, THOMAS M.   DESCENT OF THE WEST END, THE   SS   NWS 67 03
  BAD MOON RISING   OA H HPR 73   BEST SF STORIES FROM NEW WORLDS NO. 2, THE
  FUN WITH YOUR NEW HEAD   AC H DBL 71   MOORCOCK, MICHAEL   AN
    IN ENGLAND AS "UNDER COMPULSION"   WHITE FANG GOES DINGO AND OTHER FUNNY S.F. STORIES
  GETTING INTO DEATH   AC H HDV 73   DISCH, THOMAS M.   AC
    THE BEST SHORT STORIES OF THOMAS M. DISCH   DISCOVERY OF THE NULLITRON, THE FA C GAL 67 02
  GETTING INTO DEATH AND OTHER STORIES AC H KNP 76   WHITE FANG GOES DINGO AND OTHER FUNNY S.F. STORIES
  NEW IMPROVED SUN   AN H HPR 75   DISCH, THOMAS M.   AC
  ONE HUNDRED AND TWO H-BOMBS   AC   CPT 66   DISPLAYING THE FLAG   SS
  ONE HUNDRED AND TWO H-BOMBS (U.S.) AC   BKM 71 08   *GETTING INTO DEATH   DISCH, THOMAS M.   AC
  RUINS OF EARTH, THE   AN H PUT 71   EMANCIPATION: A ROMANCE OF THE TIMES TO COME NV NDM 71 01
  UNDER COMPULSION   AC H HDV 68   BIO-FUTURES   SARGENT, PAMELA   AN
    SEE "FUN WITH YOUR NEW HEAD"   NEW DIMENSIONS 1   SILVERBERG, ROBERT   OA
  WHITE FANG GOES DINGO AND OTHER FUNNY S.F. STORIES AC ARW 71 334   DISCH, THOMAS M.   NO
  334   NO   AVN 74 02   EMPTY ROOM, THE   SS   NWS 67 03
    AFFLUENCE OF EDWIN LOLLARD, THE SS   NWR 67 10   BEST SF STORIES FROM NEW WORLDS NO. 2, THE
      NEW WRITINGS IN SF. 10   CARNELL, JOHN   OA   MOORCOCK, MICHAEL   AN
    WHITE FANG GOES DINGO AND OTHER FUNNY S.F. STORIES   FUN WITH YOUR NEW HEAD DISCH, THOMAS M. AC
                              DISCH, THOMAS M.   AC ENCHANTED PRINCE, THE (SEE THE PRINCESS' CARILLON)
                                                                                  TC

DISCH, THOMAS M.   (CONTINUED)
ET IN ARCADIA EGO (ALSO AS THE PLANET ARCADIA)   SS   QRK 71 02
   QUARK/2   DELANY & HACKER   OA
   SF: AUTHORS' CHOICE 4   HARRISON, HARRY   AN
EVERYDAY LIFE IN THE LATER ROMAN EMPIRE   NV   BMR 73
   BAD MOON RISING   DISCH, THOMAS M.   OA
   334   DISCH, THOMAS M.   NO
EXTENSION CORD, THE   SS
   *GETTING INTO DEATH   DISCH, THOMAS M.   AC
FAREWELL TO THE RIVIERA   SS
   *GETTING INTO DEATH   DISCH, THOMAS M.   AC
FEATHERS FROM THE WINGS OF AN ANGEL   SS   NWS 71 03
   *GETTING INTO DEATH   DISCH, THOMAS M.   AC
   NEW WORLDS QUARTERLY NO. 2   MOORCOCK, MICHAEL   OA
FINAL AUDIT   SS   FAN 63 07
   *ONE HUNDRED AND TWO H-BOMBS   DISCH, THOMAS M.   AC
   WHITE FANG GOES DINGO AND OTHER FUNNY S.F. STORIES
                                                    DISCH, THOMAS M.   AC
FLIGHT USELESS, INEXORABLE THE PURSUIT   SS
   FUN WITH YOUR NEW HEAD   DISCH, THOMAS M.   AC
   NEW TOMORROWS, THE   SPINRAD, NORMAN   AN
FUN WITH YOUR NEW HEAD (CEPHALOTRON)   SS   PBY 66 12
   FUN WITH YOUR NEW HEAD   DISCH, THOMAS M.   AC
GENETIC CODA   SS   FAN 64 06
   *ONE HUNDRED AND TWO H-BOMBS   DISCH, THOMAS M.   AC
   WHITE FANG GOES DINGO AND OTHER FUNNY S.F. STORIES
                                                    DISCH, THOMAS M.   AC
GETTING INTO DEATH   NV
   *GETTING INTO DEATH   DISCH, THOMAS M.   AC
GOLDEN LEMONS, THE   SS
   *GETTING INTO DEATH   DISCH, THOMAS M.   AC
GRATITUDE, OR, THE SERPENT'S TOOTH   SS
   *GETTING INTO DEATH   DISCH, THOMAS M.   AC
HAPPY FAMILIES ALL LIKE SCRABBLE   SS
   *GETTING INTO DEATH   DISCH, THOMAS M.   AC
HAPPY STORY, THE   SS
   *GETTING INTO DEATH   DISCH, THOMAS M.   AC
   WHITE FANG GOES DINGO AND OTHER FUNNY S.F. STORIES
                                                    DISCH, THOMAS M.   AC
HIS OWN KIND   SS   NEW 70 AN
   NEW WORLDS OF FANTASY NO. 2   CARR, TERRY   AN
IN PRAISE OF NEW YORK   PM   FUC 73
   FUTURE CITY   ELWOOD, ROGER   OA
INTRODUCTION   IN
   *ONE HUNDRED AND TWO H-BOMBS   DISCH, THOMAS M.   AC
INTRODUCTION: BUCK ROGERS IN THE NEW JERUSALEM   IN
   NEW IMPROVED SUN, THE   DISCH, THOMAS M.   AN
INTRODUCTION: MYTHOLOGY AND SCIENCE FICTION   IN
   NEW CONSTELLATIONS   DISCH & NAYLOR   OA
INTRODUCTION: ON THE ROAD TO 1984   IN
   BAD MOON RISING   DISCH, THOMAS M.   OA
INVADED BY LOVE   SS   NWS 66 09
   *ONE HUNDRED AND TWO H-BOMBS   DISCH, THOMAS M.   AC
   WHITE FANG GOES DINGO AND OTHER FUNNY S.F. STORIES
                                                    DISCH, THOMAS M.   AC
INVASION OF THE GIANT STUPID DINOSAURS, THE   SS   AMZ 69 03
   *GETTING INTO DEATH   DISCH, THOMAS M.   AC
   WHITE FANG GOES DINGO AND OTHER FUNNY S.F. STORIES
                                                    DISCH, THOMAS M.   AC
JESSICA, RAYMOND, AND JACK   SS
   *GETTING INTO DEATH   DISCH, THOMAS M.   AC
JOYCELIN SHRAGER STORY, THE   NV
   *GETTING INTO DEATH   SS
KISS GOODBYE, A   SS
   *GETTING INTO DEATH   DISCH, THOMAS M.   AC
L'HOMME   SS
   *GETTING INTO DEATH   DISCH, THOMAS M.   AC
LEADER OF THE REVOLUTION   SS   BIZ 65 10
   *ONE HUNDRED AND TWO H-BOMBS   DISCH, THOMAS M.   AC
LET US QUICKLY HASTEN TO THE GATE OF IVORY   SS   QRK 70 01
   *GETTING INTO DEATH   DISCH, THOMAS M.   AC
   QUARK/1   DELANY & HACKER   OA
LINDA AND DANIEL AND SPIKE   SS   NWS 67 12
   BEST SF STORIES FROM NEW WORLDS 4   MOORCOCK, MICHAEL   AN
   FUN WITH YOUR NEW HEAD   DISCH, THOMAS M.   AC
MAN WHO DIDN'T DOUBT IT, THE   SS
   *GETTING INTO DEATH   DISCH, THOMAS M.   AC
MAN WHO UNDERSTOOD THE DIFFERENCE BETWEEN SALMON AND
ORANGE CHIFFON, THE   SS
   *GETTING INTO DEATH   DISCH, THOMAS M.   AC
MASTER OF THE MILFORD ALTARPIECE, THE   SS   PRV 68
   *GETTING INTO DEATH   DISCH, THOMAS M.   AC
MIMI SMITH   SS
   *GETTING INTO DEATH   DISCH, THOMAS M.   AC
MOONDUST, THE SMELL OF HAY, AND DIALECTICAL MATERIALISM
                                                    SS   FSF 67 08
   FIRST FLIGHTS TO THE MOON   CLEMENT, HAL   AN
   FUN WITH YOUR NEW HEAD   DISCH, THOMAS M.   AC
MRS. GALLAGHER'S PSYCHOANALYSIS   SS
   *GETTING INTO DEATH   DISCH, THOMAS M.   AC
MYSTERY DIET OF THE GODS: A REVELATION   SS C SWK 76 10
   NEW CONSTELLATIONS   DISCH & NAYLOR   OA
NADA   SS   FSF 64 08
   BEST FROM FANTASY AND SCIENCE FICTION: 14
                                                    DAVIDSON, AVRAM   AN
   FUN WITH YOUR NEW HEAD   DISCH, THOMAS M.   AC
   SCHOOL AND SOCIETY THROUGH SCIENCE FICTION
                                                    OLANDER/GREENBERG/& AN
NARCISSUS   PM   69
   HOLDING YOUR EIGHT HANDS   LUCIE-SMITH, EDWARD AN
NOVELIST WITH WOODEN CHARACTER, THE   SS
   *GETTING INTO DEATH   DISCH, THOMAS M.   AC
NOW IS FOREVER   SS   AMZ 64 03
   FUN WITH YOUR NEW HEAD   DISCH, THOMAS M.   AC
   TRAPS OF TIME, THE   MOORCOCK, MICHAEL   AN
   WORLD'S BEST SCIENCE FICTION: 1965   WOLLHEIM & CARR   AN

DISCH, THOMAS M.   (CONTINUED)
NUMBER YOU HAVE REACHED, THE   SS   IMP 67 02
   FUN WITH YOUR NEW HEAD   DISCH, THOMAS M.   AC
   SOCIAL PROBLEMS THROUGH SCIENCE FICTION
                                                    GREENBERG/MILSTEAD/& AN
   WORLD'S BEST SCIENCE FICTION: 1968   WOLLHEIM & CARR   AN
ODE ON THE SOURCE OF THE CLITUMNUS   PM   SVW 73
   SAVING WORLDS   ELWOOD & KIDD   OA
ON SAVING THE WORLD   IN
   RUINS OF EARTH, THE   DISCH, THOMAS M.   AN
PAGE FOR OCTOBER HAS BEEN TORN OFF, THE   SS
   *GETTING INTO DEATH   DISCH, THOMAS M.   AC
PEARL NECKLACE, THE   SS
   *GETTING INTO DEATH   DISCH, THOMAS M.   AC
PERSISTENCE OF DESIRE, THE   SS
   *GETTING INTO DEATH   DISCH, THOMAS M.   AC
PLANET ARCADIA, THE (ET IN ARCADIA EGO)   SS   QRK 71 02
   *GETTING INTO DEATH   DISCH, THOMAS M.   AC
POCKET FROM BROOKS BROTHERS, THE   SS
   *GETTING INTO DEATH   DISCH, THOMAS M.   AC
POLITICS OF DARKNESS, THE   PM   SVW 73
   SAVING WORLDS   ELWOOD & KIDD   OA
PRESSURE OF TIME, THE   NV   ORB 70 07
   ORBIT 7   KNIGHT, DAMON   OA
PRINCESS' CARILLON, THE (THE ENCHANTED PRINCE)   SS   FAN 63 08
   *ONE HUNDRED AND TWO H-BOMBS   DISCH, THOMAS M.   AC
   WHITE FANG GOES DINGO AND OTHER FUNNY S.F. STORIES
                                                    DISCH, THOMAS M.   AC
PROBLEMS OF CREATIVENESS   SS   FSF 67 04
   BEST FROM FANTASY AND SCIENCE FICTION: 17
                                                    FERMAN, EDWARD L.   AN
PYRAMIDS FOR MINNESOTA: A SERIOUS PROPOSAL   FA   HRP 74 01
   NEW IMPROVED SUN, THE   DISCH, THOMAS M.   AN
QUINCUNX   SS
   *GETTING INTO DEATH   DISCH, THOMAS M.   AC
   NEW S.F., THE   JONES, LANGDON   OA
RETURN OF THE MEDUSAE, THE   SS   FAN 63 08
   *ONE HUNDRED AND TWO H-BOMBS   DISCH, THOMAS M.   AC
   WHITE FANG GOES DINGO AND OTHER FUNNY S.F. STORIES
                                                    DISCH, THOMAS M.   AC
ROACHES, THE   SS   ESC 65 10
   FUN WITH YOUR NEW HEAD   DISCH, THOMAS M.   AC
   11TH ANNUAL OF THE YEAR'S BEST S-F, THE
                                                    MERRIL, JUDITH   AN
ROMANCE OF THE BOY AND THE GIRL, THE   SS
   *GETTING INTO DEATH   DISCH, THOMAS M.   AC
SANTA CLAUS COMPROMISE, THE   SS   CRW 74 12
   BEST SF: 75, THE NINTH ANNUAL   HARRISON & ALDISS   AN
SIGHTSEERS, THE   SS   WOT 65 11
   *ONE HUNDRED AND TWO H-BOMBS   DISCH, THOMAS M.   AC
SLAVES   SS   TRV 67
   *GETTING INTO DEATH   DISCH, THOMAS M.   AC
SOLILOQUY IN THE LAST ACT, THE   SS
   *GETTING INTO DEATH   DISCH, THOMAS M.   AC
SQUIRREL CAGE, THE   SS   NWS 66 10
   BEST SF STORIES FROM NEW WORLDS NO. 1, THE
                                                    MOORCOCK, MICHAEL   AN
   ENGLAND SWINGS SF   MERRIL, JUDITH   AN
   FUN WITH YOUR NEW HEAD   DISCH, THOMAS M.   AC
   NEW WORLDS OF FANTASY   CARR, TERRY   AN
THESIS ON SOCIAL FORMS AND SOCIAL CONTROLS IN THE U.S.A.
                                                    SS   FAN 64 01
   FUN WITH YOUR NEW HEAD   DISCH, THOMAS M.   AC
THINGS LOST   NV   DVS 72 02
   AGAIN, DANGEROUS VISIONS   ELLISON, HARLAN   OA
THREE POINTS ON THE DEMOGRAPHIC CURVE   SS   IMP 66 12
   ONE HUNDRED AND TWO H-BOMBS (U.S.)   DISCH, THOMAS M.   AC
TIC, THE   SS
   *GETTING INTO DEATH   DISCH, THOMAS M.   AC
UNSPOKEN WISH, THE   SS
   *GETTING INTO DEATH   DISCH, THOMAS M.   AC
UTOPIA? NEVER!   SS   AMZ 63 08
   *ONE HUNDRED AND TWO H-BOMBS   DISCH, THOMAS M.   AC
   WHITE FANG GOES DINGO AND OTHER FUNNY S.F. STORIES
                                                    DISCH, THOMAS M.   AC
VACATION ON EARTH, A   PM   66
   HOLDING YOUR EIGHT HANDS   LUCIE-SMITH, EDWARD AN
   SF12   MERRIL, JUDITH   AN
VAMP, THE   SS   FAN 65 02
   *ONE HUNDRED AND TWO H-BOMBS   DISCH, THOMAS M.   AC
   WHITE FANG GOES DINGO AND OTHER FUNNY S.F. STORIES
                                                    DISCH, THOMAS M.   AC
VAPORS   SS
   *GETTING INTO DEATH   DISCH, THOMAS M.   AC
WHAT THEY DO WITH MOTHERS-IN-LAW IN TIERRA DEL FUEGO
                                                    SS
   *GETTING INTO DEATH   DISCH, THOMAS M.   AC
WHITE FANG GOES DINGO   NV   IFS 65 04
   *ONE HUNDRED AND TWO H-BOMBS   DISCH, THOMAS M.   AC
   WHITE FANG GOES DINGO AND OTHER FUNNY S.F. STORIES
                                                    DISCH, THOMAS M.   AC
WONDERFUL WORLD OF GRISWALD TRACTORS, THE   SS   NWQ 72 03
   NEW WORLDS QUARTERLY NO. 3   MOORCOCK, MICHAEL   OA
   WHITE FANG GOES DINGO AND OTHER FUNNY S.F. STORIES
                                                    DISCH, THOMAS M.   AC
                                                    SS   FAN 69 12
[X] YES
   *GETTING INTO DEATH   DISCH, THOMAS M.   AC
1-A   SS   NWS 68 04
   FUN WITH YOUR NEW HEAD   DISCH, THOMAS M.   AC
102 H-BOMBS   NV   FAN 65 03
   *ONE HUNDRED AND TWO H-BOMBS   DISCH, THOMAS M.   AC
   WHITE FANG GOES DINGO AND OTHER FUNNY S.F. STORIES
                                                    DISCH, THOMAS M.   AC
                                                    NA   NWQ 72 04
334
   NEW WORLDS QUARTERLY NO. 4   MOORCOCK, MICHAEL   OA
   334   DISCH, THOMAS M.   NO

DISCH, THOMAS M.   (CONTINUED)
  5 EGGS   SS   ORB 66 01
    ONE HUNDRED AND TWO H-BOMBS (U.S.)   DISCH, THOMAS M.   AC
    ORBIT 1   KNIGHT, DAMON   OA

DIXON, RICHARD
  DESTINATION: AMALTHEIA   AN   FLP 63

DIXON, TERRY
  BARD'S TALE, THE   SS   INY 72 03
    INFINITY 3   HOSKINS, ROBERT   OA
  HATE IS A SANDPAPER ICE CUBE WITH POLKA DOTS OF LOVE ON IT
                                                 SS   FIN 70
    FUTURE IS NOW, THE   NOLAN, WILLIAM F.   OA
  PROPHET OF ZORAYNE, THE   SS   STG 74
    STRANGE GODS   ELWOOD, ROGER   OA

DMITRVSKY, VLADIMIR
  IN THE LAND OF SCIENCE FICTION   SS C
    RUSSIAN SCIENCE FICTION, 1969   MAGIDOFF, ROBERT   AN

DNIEPROV, ANATOLY   PSEUD. FOR A. P. MITSKEVICH
  CRABS TAKE OVER THE ISLAND   SS   ISF 68 06
    RUSSIAN SCIENCE FICTION, 1969   MAGIDOFF, ROBERT   AN
    SCIENCE FACT/FICTION   FARRELL/GAGE/&   AN
  FORMULA FOR IMMORTALITY   NV   63
    ULTIMATE THRESHOLD, THE   GINSBURG, MIRRA   AN
  HEROIC FEAT, THE   SS
    RUSSIAN SCIENCE FICTION, 1968   MAGIDOFF, ROBERT   AN
  INTERVIEW WITH A TRAFFIC POLICEMAN
    OTHER WORLDS, OTHER SEAS   SUVIN, DARKO   AN
  ISLAND OF THE CRABS, THE   SS   ISF 68 06
    OTHER WORLDS, OTHER SEAS   SUVIN, DARKO   AN
  MAXWELL EQUATIONS, THE   SS
    DESTINATION: AMALTHEIA   DIXON, RICHARD   AN
    RUSSIAN SCIENCE FICTION   MAGIDOFF, ROBERT   AN
  PURPLE MUMMY, THE   SS
    PATH INTO THE UNKNOWN   ANONYMOUS   AN
  S*T*A*P*L*E FARM, THE   SS
    OTHER WORLDS, OTHER SEAS   SUVIN, DARKO   AN
  SIEMA   NV
    MORE SOVIET SCIENCE FICTION   ANONYMOUS   AN
  WHEN QUESTIONS ARE ASKED   SS   63
    ULTIMATE THRESHOLD, THE   GINSBURG, MIRRA   AN
  WORLD IN WHICH I DISAPPEARED, THE   SS   ISF 68 06
    LAST DOOR TO AIYA   GINSBURG, MIRRA   AN

DOAR, GRAHAM
  OUTER LIMIT, THE   SS   SEP 49 12
    *BIG BOOK OF SCIENCE FICTION   CONKLIN, GROFF   AN
  WHO KNOWS HIS BROTHER   SS   STS 52 02
    HUMAN?   MERRIL, JUDITH   AN

DOBINSON, FRANK
  MASTER COPY, THE   SS   PBY 66 05
    FIEND, THE   PLAYBOY, EDITORS OF AN

DODGSON, CHARLES L.   SEE PSEUD. LEWIS CARROLL

DOGGE, MARY
  BLUE CLOUD, THE   SS
    AUTHENTIC BOOK OF SPACE   CAMPBELL, H. J.   AN

DOHERTY, G. D.
  ASPECTS OF SCIENCE FICTION   AN H MUR 59
  SECOND ORBIT   AN H MUR 65
  STORIES FROM SCIENCE FICTION   AN H NLS 66
  INTRODUCTION   IN
    SECOND ORBIT   DOHERTY, G. D.   AN
    STORIES FROM SCIENCE FICTION   DOHERTY, G. D.   AN

DOLAN, MIKE
  SANTANA MORNING AND OTHER STORIES   OC   POW 70
  CITY, THE   SS
    SANTANA MORNING AND OTHER STORIES   DOLAN, MIKE   OC
  DYNAMO   SS
    SANTANA MORNING AND OTHER STORIES   DOLAN, MIKE   OC
  FOG, THE   SS
    SANTANA MORNING AND OTHER STORIES   DOLAN, MIKE   OC
  FOREWORD   IN
    SANTANA MORNING AND OTHER STORIES   DOLAN, MIKE   OC
  GOLDEN EFFECT, THE   SS
    SANTANA MORNING AND OTHER STORIES   DOLAN, MIKE   OC
  GRASS, THE   SS
    SANTANA MORNING AND OTHER STORIES   DOLAN, MIKE   OC
  HANDS, THE   SS
    SANTANA MORNING AND OTHER STORIES   DOLAN, MIKE   OC
  HOLE, THE   SS
    SANTANA MORNING AND OTHER STORIES   DOLAN, MIKE   OC
  INTRUDER   SS
    SANTANA MORNING AND OTHER STORIES   DOLAN, MIKE   OC
  JOURNEY BY HELIODROME   SS
    SANTANA MORNING AND OTHER STORIES   DOLAN, MIKE   OC
  MEMORY   SS
    SANTANA MORNING AND OTHER STORIES   DOLAN, MIKE   OC
  MIRROR, THE   SS
    SANTANA MORNING AND OTHER STORIES   DOLAN, MIKE   OC
  NIGHTMARE   SS
    SANTANA MORNING AND OTHER STORIES   DOLAN, MIKE   OC
  NUCLEAR GENESIS   SS
    SANTANA MORNING AND OTHER STORIES   DOLAN, MIKE   OC
  OF A YELLOW SUMMER   SS
    SANTANA MORNING AND OTHER STORIES   DOLAN, MIKE   OC
  ROAD, THE   SS
    SANTANA MORNING AND OTHER STORIES   DOLAN, MIKE   OC

DOLAN, MIKE   (CONTINUED)
  SANTANA MORNING   SS
    SANTANA MORNING AND OTHER STORIES   DOLAN, MIKE   OC

DOMINGO, PEDRO   SEE PSEUD. DOMINGO SANTOS

DONALDY, ERNESTINE   SEE ALSO   CO-EDITOR ANDRE NORTON
  INTRODUCTION   IN C
    GATES TO TOMORROW   NORTON, AN.&DONALDY AN

DONEV, ANTON
  WHY ATLANTIS SANK   SS
    OTHER WORLDS, OTHER SEAS   SUVIN, DARKO   AN

DONOVAN, FRANCIS
  SHORT LIFE, THE   SN   ASF 55 10
    BEST SF 4   CRISPIN, EDMUND   AN

DOOHAN, JAMES
  INTRODUCTION TO INTERSECTION POINT   IN
    STAR TREK: THE NEW VOYAGES   MARSHAK, S&CULBREATH OA

DOREMIEUX, ALAIN
  VANA, THE   SS   59
    13 FRENCH SCIENCE-FICTION STORIES   KNIGHT, DAMON   AN

DORMAN, SONYA
  BITCHING IT   SS   QRK 71 02
    QUARK/2   DELANY & HACKER   OA
  CHILD DREAMS, THE   PM
    WOMEN OF WONDER   SARGENT, PAMELA   AN
  CORRUPTION OF METALS   PM
    2076: THE AMERICAN TRICENTENNIAL   BRYANT, EDWARD   OA
  DEATH OR CONSEQUENCES   SS
    TOMORROW: NEW WORLDS OF SCIENCE FICTION
                                         ELWOOD, ROGER   OA
  DEEPEST BLUE IN THE WORLD, THE   SS   FSF 64 09
    SF: AUTHORS' CHOICE 3   HARRISON, HARRY   AN
  GO, GO, GO, SAID THE BIRD   SS   DVS 67 01
    DANGEROUS VISIONS   ELLISON, HARLAN   AN
  HARRY THE TAILOR   SS   CMP 61
    POCKETFUL OF STARS, A   KNIGHT, DAMON   AN
  LIVING END, THE   SS   ORB 70 07
    ORBIT 7   KNIGHT, DAMON   OA
  LUNATIC ASSIGNMENT   SS   FSF 68 01
    BEST FROM FANTASY AND SCIENCE FICTION: 18
                                         FERMAN, EDWARD L.   AN
  MESS OF PORRIDGE, A   SS   ANA 70
    ALCHEMY AND ACADEME   MCCAFFREY, ANNE   OA
  SPLICE OF LIFE   SS   ORB 66 01
    ONE HUNDRED YEARS OF SCIENCE FICTION KNIGHT, DAMON   AN
    ORBIT 1   KNIGHT, DAMON   OA
  TIME BEND   SS   ORB 74 13
    ORBIT 13   KNIGHT, DAMON   OA
  VANISHING POINTS   PM   QRK 71 03
    QUARK/3   DELANY & HACKER   OA
  WHEN I WAS MISS DOW   SS   GAL 66 06
    NEBULA AWARD STORIES NO. 2   ALDISS & HARRISON   AN
    SF12   MERRIL, JUDITH   AN
    WOMEN OF WONDER   SARGENT, PAMELA   AN

DOS PASSOS, JOHN
  THREE PROLOGUES AND AN EPILOGUE   PM   ADT 61 SP
    7TH ANNUAL OF THE YEAR'S BEST S-F, THE MERRIL, JUDITH   AN

DOSTOEVSKY, FYODOR
  DREAM OF A RIDICULOUS MAN, THE   SS
    PERCHANCE TO DREAM   KNIGHT, DAMON   AN

DOUGLASS, ELLSWORTH
  WHEELS OF DR. GINOCHIO GYVES, THE   SS C CSL 99 09
    WORLDS APART   LOCKE, GEORGE   AN

DOYLE, ARTHUR CONAN
  MARACOT DEEP AND OTHER STORIES, THE   AC H DBL 29
  POISON BELT, THE   AC H MCM 64
  CAPTAIN OF THE "POLE STAR", THE   NV   94
    HORROR TIMES TEN   NORTON, ALDEN H.   AN
  DISINTEGRATION MACHINE, THE   SS   CMP 28
    JOURNEYS IN SCIENCE FICTION   LOUGHLIN, RICHARD L. AN
    MARACOT DEEP AND OTHER STORIES, THE DOYLE, ARTHUR CONAN AC
    POISON BELT, THE   DOYLE, ARTHUR CONAN AC
    WONDERMAKERS   HOSKINS, ROBERT   AN
  FROM "THE POISON BELT"   EX   SND 13 03
    PAST, PRESENT, AND FUTURE PERFECT   WOLFE, J&FITZ GERALD AN
  GREAT KEINPLATZ EXPERIMENT, THE   SS   WRT 36 10
    *BEST OF SCIENCE FICTION   CONKLIN, GROFF   AN
    GREAT SCIENCE FICTION ABOUT DOCTORS CONKLIN, G&FABRICANT AN
  HORROR OF THE HEIGHTS, THE   SS   EVB 13 11
    FUTURES UNLIMITED   NORTON, ALDEN H.   AN
  LOS AMIGOS FIASCO, THE   SS   IDL 92 12
    MASTERPIECES OF SCIENCE FICTION   MOSKOWITZ, SAM   AN
  LOST WORLD, THE   EX   HDS 12
    FROM FRANKENSTEIN TO ANDROMEDA   BROWN, JAMES GOLDIE AN
  MARACOT DEEP, THE   NO   SEP 27 10
    MARACOT DEEP AND OTHER STORIES, THE DOYLE, ARTHUR CONAN AC
    TREASURY OF SCIENCE FICTION CLASSICS, THE
                                         KUEBLER, HAROLD W.   AN
  POISON BELT, THE   NO   HDS 13
    POISON BELT, THE   DOYLE, ARTHUR CONAN AC
  RACE WITH A DINOSAUR, A (FROM "THE LOST WORLD") EX HDS 12
    SCIENCE IN FICTION   BAYLISS, A.E. & J.C. AN
  SILVER MIRROR, THE   SS   25
    TRAVELERS IN TIME   STERN, PHILIP VAN D. AN
  SPODEGUE'S DROOPER   SS
    MARACOT DEEP AND OTHER STORIES, THE DOYLE, ARTHUR CONAN AC

DOYLE, ARTHUR CONAN

EARL, STEPHEN

DOYLE, ARTHUR CONAN (CONTINUED)
    TERROR OF BLUE JOHN GAP, THE   SS   10
        ANCIENT MYSTERIES READER, THE   HAINING, PETER   AN
        STRANGE BEASTS AND UNNATURAL MONSTERS STERN, PHILIP VAN D. AN
    WHEN THE WORLD SCREAMED   SS   29
        MARACOT DEEP AND OTHER STORIES, THE DOYLE, ARTHUR CONAN AC
        POISON BELT, THE   DOYLE, ARTHUR CONAN AC

DOZOIS, GARDNER R.   SEE ALSO   CO-EDITOR JACK M. DANN
    ANOTHER WORLD   AN H POL 77
    BEST SCIENCE FICTION STORIES OF THE YEAR (1976) AN H DUT 77 07
                                                  AN H HPR 72
    DAY IN THE LIFE, A   NA   CHN 73
    CHAINS OF THE SEA
        CHAINS OF THE SEA   SILVERBERG, ROBERT   OA
    CONDITIONED REFLEX   SS   GEN 72
        GENERATION   GERROLD, DAVID   OA
    DREAM AT NOONDAY, A   SS   ORB 70 07
        ORBIT   7   KNIGHT, DAMON   OA
    FLASH POINT   NV   ORB 74 13
        ORBIT 13   KNIGHT, DAMON   OA
    HORSE OF AIR   SS   ORB 70 08
        BEST FROM ORBIT, THE   KNIGHT, DAMON   AN
        NEBULA AWARD STORIES NO. 7   BIGGLE, LLOYD JR.   AN
        ORBIT   8   KNIGHT, DAMON   OA
    IN A CROOKED YEAR   NV   TTM 73
        TEN TOMORROWS   ELWOOD, ROGER   OA
    INTRODUCTION   IN
        ANOTHER WORLD   DOZOIS, GARDNER R.   AN
        DAY IN THE LIFE, A   DOZOIS, GARDNER R.   AN
    INTRODUCTION   IN C
        FUTURE POWER   DANN & DOZOIS   OA
    KING HARVEST   NV   NDM 72 02
        NEW DIMENSIONS 2   SILVERBERG, ROBERT   OA
    KINGDOM BY THE SEA, A   NV   ORB 72 10
        ORBIT 10   KNIGHT, DAMON   OA
    LAST DAY OF JULY, THE   NV   NDM 73 03
        NEW DIMENSIONS 3   SILVERBERG, ROBERT   OA
    MACHINES OF LOVING GRACE   SS   ORB 72 11
        INSIDE INFORMATION   MOWSHOWITZ, ABBE   AN
        ORBIT 11   KNIGHT, DAMON   OA
    MAN WHO WAVED HELLO, THE   SS   UNI 72 02
        UNIVERSE 2   CARR, TERRY   OA
    SOUND OF MUZAK, THE   NV   QRK 70 01
        QUARK/1   DELANY & HACKER   AN
    SPECIAL KIND OF MORNING, A   NV   NDM 71 01
        ALPHA 5   SILVERBERG, ROBERT   AN
        NEW DIMENSIONS 1   SILVERBERG, ROBERT   OA
    STORM, THE   NV   FCR 75
        FUTURE CORRUPTION   ELWOOD, ROGER   OA
        VISIONS OF TOMORROW   ELWOOD, ROGER   AN
    STRANGERS   NA   NDM 74 04
        NEW DIMENSIONS 4   SILVERBERG, ROBERT   OA
    WHERE NO SUN SHINES   SS   ORB 70 06
        ORBIT   6   KNIGHT, DAMON   OA

DRACO, S.
    MASQUE   SS
        WORLDS AT WAR   RAYER, FRANCIS G.   AN

DRAKE, DAVID
    BUTCHER'S BILL, THE   NV   GAL 74 11
        COMBAT SF   DICKSON, GORDON R.   AN
    DENKIRK   SS
        TRAVELLERS BY NIGHT   DERLETH, AUGUST   OA
    SOMETHING HAD TO BE DONE   SS   FSF 75 02
        YEAR'S BEST HORROR STORIES: SERIES IV, THE
                                            PAGE, GERALD W.   AN

DRAKE, LEAH BODINE
    WOODS GROW DARKER, THE   PM   FSF 55 11
        BEST FROM FANTASY AND SCIENCE FICTION: 6
                                            BOUCHER, ANTHONY   AN

DRAKE, W. RAYMOND
    SPACEMEN THROUGHOUT HISTORY   AR
        BEYOND THIS HORIZON   CARRELL, CHRISTOPHER OA

DRAPER, HAL
    MS FND IN A LBRY   SS   FSF 61 12
        INSIDE INFORMATION   MOWSHOWITZ, ABBE   AN
        17 X INFINITY   CONKLIN, GROFF   AN

DRESSLER, DR. DANIEL
    WHITE ARMY, THE   SS   AMZ 29 09
        EVERY BOY'S BOOK OF SCIENCE FICTION WOLLHEIM, DONALD A. AN
        STORIES OF SCIENTIFIC IMAGINATION   GALLANT, JOSEPH   AN

DRISCOLL, DENNIS
    GOING UP! (FROM THE ARTICLE "SPACE TRAVEL") AR   BLF 57 05
        SF:58, THE YEAR'S GREATEST SCIENCE FICTION AND FANTASY
                                            MERRIL, JUDITH   AN

DRURY, ALLEN
    SOMETHING   SS   FSF 60 10
        BEST FROM FANTASY AND SCIENCE FICTION: 10
                                            MILLS, ROBERT P.   AN

DRUSSAI, GAREN
    TWILIGHT YEARS, THE   NV C IFS 55 06
        FIRST WORLD OF IF, THE   QUINN & WULFF   AN

DRUSSAI, KIRK
    TWILIGHT YEARS, THE   NV C IFS 55 06
        FIRST WORLD OF IF, THE   QUINN & WULFF   AN

DRYER, STAN
    FULLY AUTOMATED LOVE LIFE OF HENRY KEANRIDGE, THE NV PBY 68 07
    FULLY AUTOMATED LOVE LIFE OF HENRY KEANRIDGE
                                            PLAYBOY, EDITORS OF AN

DRYFOOS, DAVE
    BLUNDER ENLIGHTENING   NV   DSF 52 12
        WAY OUT   HOWARD, IVAN   AN
    BRIDGE CROSSING   SS   GAL 51 05
        BEYOND THE END OF TIME   POHL, FREDERIK   AN
    JOURNEY WORK   SS   IFS 55 01
        FIRST WORLD OF IF, THE   QUINN & WULFF   AN

DU BOIS, WILLIAM P.
    ILLUSTRATIONS   IL
        POISON BELT, THE   DOYLE, ARTHUR CONAN AC

DU MAURIER, DAPHNE
    BIRDS, THE   NV   GHK 52 10
        ECO-FICTION   STADLER, JOHN   AN
        RUINS OF EARTH, THE   DISCH, THOMAS M.   AN
        STRANGE BEASTS AND UNNATURAL MONSTERS STERN, PHILIP VAN D. AN
        YOU AND SCIENCE FICTION   HOLLISTER, BERNARD C AN
    BLUE LENSES, THE   NV   59
        OTHERS, THE   CARR, TERRY   AN

DUANE, ANDREW   PSEUD. FOR ROBERT E. BRINEY
    BLACK TOWER, THE   NV   C
        SHANADU   BRINEY, ROBERT E.   OA

DUANE, TOBY   PSEUD. FOR W. PAUL GANLEY
    FIRE BORN, THE   NV
        SHANADU   BRINEY, ROBERT E.   OA

DUDINTSEV, VLADIMIR
    NEW YEAR'S FAIRY TALE, A   SS
        RUSSIAN SCIENCE FICTION   MAGIDOFF, ROBERT   AN

DUNCAN, DAVID
    REQUIEM ON THE MOON   SS   PBY 64 10
        DEAD ASTRONAUT, 10 STORIES OF SPACE FLIGHT, THE
                                            PLAYBOY, EDITORS OF AN

DUNN, ALAN
    CARTOON   CT   SRV 55 03
        MATHEMATICAL MAGPIE, THE   FADIMAN, CLIFTON   AN

DUNSANY, LORD   PSEUD. FOR EDWARD JOHN MORTON DRAX PLUNKETT
    CLUB SECRETARY   SS   34
        OUT OF THIS WORLD   FAST, JULIUS   AN
    DEAL WITH THE DEVIL, A   SS   48
        DEALS WITH THE DEVIL   DAVENPORT, BASIL   AN
    HASHISH MAN, THE   SS   FFM 45 12
        FUTURES UNLIMITED   NORTON, ALDEN H.   AN
    HOARD OF THE GIBBELINS, THE   SS   AFR 47 04
        SPELL OF SEVEN, THE   DE CAMP, L. SPRAGUE AN
    MARS ON THE ETHER   SS   CRT 37 09
        *STRANGE PORTS OF CALL   DERLETH, AUGUST   AN
    MISADVENTURE   SS   FSF 54 10
        BEST FROM FANTASY AND SCIENCE FICTION: 4
                                            BOUCHER, ANTHONY   AN
    OUR DISTANT COUSINS   SS   31
        ARMCHAIR SCIENCE READER, THE   GORDON, I. & SORKIN AN
    MOONLIGHT TRAVELER, THE   STERN, PHILIP VAN D. AN
    STRANGE DRUG OF DR. CABER, THE   SS   48
        *OTHER SIDE OF THE MOON, THE   DERLETH, AUGUST   AN
    THIRTEEN AT TABLE   SS   16
        SUPERNATURAL READER, THE   CONKLIN, G&L.   AN

DUNTEMANN, JEFF
    OUR LADY OF THE ENDLESS SKY   NV   NOV 74 04
        NOVA 4   HARRISON, HARRY   OA
    STEEL SONNETS, THE   SS   ORB 75 17
        ORBIT 17   KNIGHT, DAMON   OA

DURRELL, LAWRENCE
    HIGH BARBARY   SS   MAD 61 09
        7TH ANNUAL OF THE YEAR'S BEST S-F, THE MERRIL, JUDITH   AN

DUTTA, REX
    MAJORITY OF PEOPLE NOW BELIEVE IN FLYING SAUCERS, THE
                                                     AR
        BEYOND THIS HORIZON   CARRELL, CHRISTOPHER OA

DYALHIS, NICTZIN
    SAPPHIRE GODDESS, THE   NV   WRT 34 02
        WORLDS OF WEIRD   MARGULIES, LEO   AN
    SAPPHIRE SIREN, THE   NV   WRT 34 02
        AVON FANTASY READER, THE   WOLLHEIM &ERNSBERGER AN
    SEA WITCH, THE   NV   WRT 37 12
        WEIRD TALES   MARGULIES, LEO   AN
    WHEN THE GREEN STAR WANED   SS   WRT 25 04
        *BEYOND TIME AND SPACE   DERLETH, AUGUST   AN

DYBEK, STUART
    MAZE, THE   SS   ORB 75 17
        ORBIT 17   KNIGHT, DAMON   OA

DYE, CHARLES   PSEUD. FOR KATHERINE MACLEAN
    SYNDROME JOHNNY   SS   GAL 51 07
        *GALAXY READER OF SCIENCE FICTION   GOLD, H. L.   AN

EARL, STEPHEN
    WALKABOUT   SS
        AD 2500   WILSON, ANGUS   AN

EARLE, WARREN
   IN RE STATE VS. FORBES   SS   BLC 07 06
      SCIENCE FICTION BY GASLIGHT   MOSKOWITZ, SAM   AN

EARLEY, GEORGE W.
   ENCOUNTERS WITH ALIENS   AN H SHB 68
      EDITOR'S PREFACE   IN
      ENCOUNTERS WITH ALIENS   EARLEY, GEORGE W.   AN

EARLS, WILLIAM
   BUS STATION   SS   CLR 73 03
      CLARION III   WILSON, ROBIN SCOTT OA
   JUMP   SS   ASF 69 10
      ANALOG 8   CAMPBELL, JOHN W. JR AN
   TRAFFIC PROBLEM   SS   GAL 70 10
      BEST FROM GALAXY, THE VOLUME I GALAXY, EDITORS OF   AN
      BEST SF: 1970   HARRISON & ALDISS   AN
      CITY: 2000 A.D., THE   CLEM/GREENBERG/&   AN

EARLY, DAVID
   ASTRONOMY AND ART: PAINTINGS   IL
      BEYOND THIS HORIZON   CARRELL, CHRISTOPHER OA

EBERHART, RICHARD
   ON SHOOTING PARTICLES BEYOND THE WORLD   PM   60
      LOOKING AHEAD   ALLEN, D. & L.   AN

EBERHART, SHERI
   EXTRATERRESTRIAL TRILOGUE ON TERRAN SELF-DESTRUCTION
                                                PM   GAL 61 08
      7TH ANNUAL OF THE YEAR'S BEST S-F, THE MERRIL, JUDITH AN

ECHAURREN, ROBERTO
   EARTH IS A MAN, THE   IL
      SCIENCE FICTION   BRODKIN & PEARSON   AN

EDDINGTON, ARTHUR
   INFINITY   PM   35
      FANTASIA MATHEMATICA   FADIMAN, CLIFTON   AN
   THERE ONCE WAS A BREATHY BABOON   PM
      FANTASIA MATHEMATICA   FADIMAN, CLIFTON   AN

EDELSON, EDWARD
   OUTER LIMITS OF SPACE, THE   AR   SRV 73 10
      LOOKING AHEAD   ALLEN, D. & L.   AN

EDELSTEIN, SCOTT
   FUTURE PASTIMES   OA H AUR 77
      AGE OF LIBRA, THE   SS
         SCIENCE FICTION DISCOVERIES   POHL, C. & F.   OA
      EXHIBITION, THE   SS   NOV 73 03
         BEST OF SCIENCE FICTION MONTHLY, THE SACKS, JANET AN
         NOVA 3   HARRISON, HARRY   OA
      ISAAC UNDER PRESSURE   SS   INY 73 05
         INFINITY 5   HOSKINS, ROBERT   OA
      SLIME DWELLERS, THE   SS   VTX 75 06
         CITY: 2000 A.D., THE   CLEM/GREENBERG/&   AN
      TIME ON OUR HANDS: AN INTRODUCTION   IN
         FUTURE PASTIMES   EDELSTEIN, SCOTT   OA
      UNPLEASANT END, AN   SS   NWQ 73 05
         NEW WORLDS NO. 5   MOORCOCK & PLATT   OA

EDMONDSON, G. C.
   STRANGER THAN YOU THINK   DC   ACE 65
      COUNTRY BOY, THE   SS   FSF 61 05
         STRANGER THAN YOU THINK   EDMONDSON, G. C.   DC
      "FROM CARIBOU TO CARRY NATION"   SS   FSF 59 11
         STRANGER THAN YOU THINK   EDMONDSON, G. C.   DC
      GALACTIC CALABASH, THE   SS   FSF 60 01
         SCIENCE FICTION ODDITIES   CONKLIN, GROFF   AN
         STRANGER THAN YOU THINK   EDMONDSON, G. C.   DC
      MISFIT, THE   SS   FSF 59 02
         STRANGER THAN YOU THINK   EDMONDSON, G. C.   DC
      RESCUE   SS   FSF 57 06
         BEST FROM FANTASY AND SCIENCE FICTION: 7
                                       BOUCHER, ANTHONY   AN
      RINGER   SS   FSF 60 04
         ENCOUNTERS WITH ALIENS   EARLEY, GEORGE W.   AN
      SIGN OF THE GOOSE, THE   SS   FSF 60 08
         STRANGER THAN YOU THINK   EDMONDSON, G. C.   DC
      TECHNOLOGICAL RETREAT   SS   FSF 56 05
         13 GREAT STORIES OF SCIENCE FICTION CONKLIN, GROFF AN
      TEMPOLLUTERS, THE   SS   INY 72 04
         INFINITY 4   HOSKINS, ROBERT   OA
      THIRD BUBBLE, THE   SS   FSF 64 06
         STRANGER THAN YOU THINK   EDMONDSON, G. C.   DC
      WORLD MUST NEVER KNOW, THE   SS   FSF 63 04
         STRANGER THAN YOU THINK   EDMONDSON, G. C.   DC

EDMONDSON, WALLACE   PSEUD. FOR HARLAN ELLISON

EDWARDS, DOLTON   PSEUD. FOR W. K. LAISSING
   MEIHEM IN CE KLASRUM   AR   ASF 46 09
      *ASTOUNDING SCIENCE FICTION ANTHOLOGY, THE
                                       CAMPBELL, JOHN W. JR AN
      *SECOND ASTOUNDING SCIENCE FICTION ANTHOLOGY, THE
                                       CAMPBELL, JOHN W. JR AN

EDWARDS, KELLEY
   COUNTERSPY   SS   ASF 53 12
      BEST SF 3   CRISPIN, EDMUND   AN

EFFINGER, GEO. ALEC
   IRRATIONAL NUMBERS   AC H DBL 76
   MIXED FEELINGS   AC H HPR 74

EFFINGER, GEO. ALEC   (CONTINUED)
   ALL THE LAST WARS AT ONCE   SS   UNI 71 01
      BEST SCIENCE FICTION OF THE YEAR, THE CARR, TERRY   AN
      INTRODUCTORY PSYCHOLOGY THROUGH SCIENCE FICTION
                                       KATZ/WARRICK/&   AN
         MIXED FEELINGS   EFFINGER, GEO. ALEC AC
         UNIVERSE 1   CARR, TERRY   OA
         WINDOWS INTO TOMORROW   SILVERBERG, ROBERT   AN
   AND US, TOO, I GUESS   NA   CHN 73
      CHAINS OF THE SEA   SILVERBERG, ROBERT   OA
      IRRATIONAL NUMBERS   EFFINGER, GEO. ALEC AC
   ASHES ALL MY LUST   NV   FOS 74
      FELLOWSHIP OF THE STARS   CARR, TERRY   OA
   AT THE BRAN FOUNDRY   SS   NDM 73 03
      IRRATIONAL NUMBERS   EFFINGER, GEO. ALEC AC
      NEW DIMENSIONS 3   SILVERBERG, ROBERT   OA
   BITING DOWN HARD ON TRUTH   NV   ORB 74 15
      IRRATIONAL NUMBERS   EFFINGER, GEO. ALEC AC
      ORBIT 15   KNIGHT, DAMON   OA
   CHASE OUR BLUES AWAY   SS   NDM 76 06
      NEW DIMENSIONS 6   SILVERBERG, ROBERT   OA
   CONTENTMENT, SATISFACTION, CHEER, WELL-BEING, GLADNESS, JOY,
      COMFORT, AND NOT HAVING...   NV   76
      FUTURE POWER   DANN & DOZOIS   OA
   CURTAINS   SS   FSF 74 08
      IRRATIONAL NUMBERS   EFFINGER, GEO. ALEC AC
   EARLY TO BED   SS   CLR 72 02
      CLARION II   WILSON, ROBIN SCOTT OA
   F (X) = (11/15/67) X=HER, F(X)≠0   SS   NDM 72 02
      MIXED FEELINGS   EFFINGER, GEO. ALEC AC
      NEW DIMENSIONS 2   SILVERBERG, ROBERT   OA
   FREE PASS TO THE CARNIVAL, A   SS   FSF 71 05
      CLARION   WILSON, ROBIN SCOTT OA
   GHOST WRITER, THE   SS   UNI 73 03
      MIXED FEELINGS   EFFINGER, GEO. ALEC AC
      UNIVERSE 3   CARR, TERRY   OA
   HARD TIMES   SS   AMZ 73 03
      IRRATIONAL NUMBERS   EFFINGER, GEO. ALEC AC
   HORSE WITH ONE LEG, THE   SS   NEW 74 AN
      WORLDS FAR AND NEAR   CARR, TERRY   AN
   HOW IT FELT   SS   UNI 74 05
      IRRATIONAL NUMBERS   EFFINGER, GEO. ALEC AC
      UNIVERSE 5   CARR, TERRY   OA
   IBID   SS   UNI 77 07
      UNIVERSE 7   CARR, TERRY   OA
   LIGHTS OUT   NV   FSF 73 10
      MIXED FEELINGS   EFFINGER, GEO. ALEC AC
   LIVE, FROM BERCHTESGADEN   SS   ORB 72 10
      ALPHA 5   SILVERBERG, ROBERT   AN
      BEST FROM ORBIT, THE   KNIGHT, DAMON   AN
      ORBIT 10   KNIGHT, DAMON   OA
   LYDECTES: ON THE NATURE OF SPORT   NV   FAN 75 12
      IRRATIONAL NUMBERS   EFFINGER, GEO. ALEC AC
   MOM'S DIFFERENTIALS   SS
      NEW VOICES IN SCIENCE FICTION   MARTIN, GEORGE R. R. OA
   MOTHERS' MARCH ON ECSTACY, THE   SS   NDM 75 05
      NEW DIMENSIONS 5   SILVERBERG, ROBERT   OA
   NAKED TO THE INVISIBLE EYE   NV   ASF 73 05
      MIXED FEELINGS   EFFINGER, GEO. ALEC AC
   RUN TO STARLIGHT, SPORTS THROUGH SCIENCE FICTION
                                       GREENBERG/OLANDER/& AN
   NEW NEW YORK NEW ORLEANS   SS   NMD 73
      FRONTIERS 2; THE NEW MIND   ELWOOD, ROGER   OA
   PARADISE LAST   NV   NEW 74 AN
      WANDERING STARS   DANN, JACK M.   AN
   RELATIVES   SS   BMR 73
      BAD MOON RISING   DISCH, THOMAS M.   OA
   SAND AND STONES   SS   CLR 72 02
      CLARION II   WILSON, ROBIN SCOTT OA
   STEVE WEINRAUB AND THE SECRET EMPIRE   SS
      MIXED FEELINGS   EFFINGER, GEO. ALEC AC
   TARGET: BERLIN| NV   NDM 76 06
      NEW DIMENSIONS 6   SILVERBERG, ROBERT   OA
   THINGS GO BETTER   SS   ORB 72 11
      MIXED FEELINGS   EFFINGER, GEO. ALEC AC
      ORBIT 11   KNIGHT, DAMON   OA
   THIS WRITING "GAME"   SS
      MIXED FEELINGS   EFFINGER, GEO. ALEC AC
   TROUBLE FOLLOWS   SS   CLR 71 01
      CLARION   WILSON, ROBIN SCOTT OA
   TWO SADNESSES   SS   BMR 73
      BAD MOON RISING   DISCH, THOMAS M.   OA
      MIXED FEELINGS   EFFINGER, GEO. ALEC AC
   WEDNESDAY, NOVEMBER 15, 1967   SS   NEW 71 AN
      MIXED FEELINGS   EFFINGER, GEO. ALEC AC
      RUINS OF EARTH, THE   DISCH, THOMAS M.   AN
   WESTFIELD HEIGHTS MALL MONSTER, THE   SS   CLR 71 01
      CLARION   WILSON, ROBIN SCOTT OA
   WORLD WAR TWO   SS   VTX 73 10
      ALPHA 7   SILVERBERG, ROBERT   AN
      MIXED FEELINGS   EFFINGER, GEO. ALEC AC
   25 CRUNCH SPLIT RIGHT ON TWO   NV   FSF 75 04
      IRRATIONAL NUMBERS   EFFINGER, GEO. ALEC AC

EHRLICH, ANNE H.
   FOREWORD   IN C
      VOYAGES: SCENARIOS FOR A SHIP CALLED EARTH
                                       SAUER, ROB   AN

EHRLICH, DR. PAUL R.
   ECO-CATASTROPHE| SS   RAM 69 09
      BEST SF: 1969   HARRISON & ALDISS   AN
      NIGHTMARE AGE   POHL, FREDERIK   AN
   FOREWORD   IN C
      VOYAGES: SCENARIOS FOR A SHIP CALLED EARTH
                                       SAUER, ROB   AN

EIDE, EDYTHE   SEE PSEUD. TIGRINA

EISELEY, LOREN
  BUSBY'S PETRIFIED WOMAN   SS   HRP 48 11
    CIRCUS OF DR. LAO AND OTHER IMPROBABLE STORIES
                                   BRADBURY, RAY   AN

EISELEY, SIMON
  STAR THROWER, THE   AR   69
    SURVIVAL PRINTOUT   TOTAL EFFECT   AN

EISENBERG, LARRY
  BEST LAID SCHEMES, THE   AC H MAC 71
  CHAMELEON, THE   SS   FSF 70 03
    AMERICAN GOVERNMENT THROUGH SCIENCE FICTION
                                   OLANDER/GREENBERG/&   AN
    BEST LAID SCHEMES, THE   EISENBERG, LARRY   AC
  CHILD'S PLAY (SEE UNCLE SAM'S CHILDREN)   TC
  CONQUEROR   SS   IFS 67 10
    BEST LAID SCHEMES, THE   EISENBERG, LARRY   AC
  DUCKWORTH'S FOREVER   SS   NEW 71 AC
    BEST LAID SCHEMES, THE   EISENBERG, LARRY   AC
  DUCKWORTH'S IQ SOUP (IQ SOUP)   SS   VSF 69 11
    BEST LAID SCHEMES, THE   EISENBERG, LARRY   AC
  FASTEST DRAW, THE (SEE THE MARVELOUS MARSHAL) TC
  HOLD YOUR FIRE   SS   NEW 71 AC
    BEST LAID SCHEMES, THE   EISENBERG, LARRY   AC
  INTRODUCTION   IN
    BEST LAID SCHEMES, THE   EISENBERG, LARRY   AC
  IQ SOUP (SEE DUCKWORTH'S IQ SOUP)   TC
  IRRESISTIBLE PARTY CHAIRMAN, THE   SS   NEW 71 AC
    BEST LAID SCHEMES, THE   EISENBERG, LARRY   AC
  IS THERE LIFE IN INNER SPACE?   SS   NEW 71 AC
    BEST LAID SCHEMES, THE   EISENBERG, LARRY   AC
  MARVELOUS MARSHAL, THE (THE FASTEST DRAW)   SS   AMZ 63 10
    BEST LAID SCHEMES, THE   EISENBERG, LARRY   AC
  MATTER OF RECORDINGS, A   SS   IFS 70 02
    BEST LAID SCHEMES, THE   EISENBERG, LARRY   AC
  MATTER OF TIME AND PLACE, A   SS   FSF 70 01
    BEST LAID SCHEMES, THE   EISENBERG, LARRY   AC
  MIGHTY MATTERHORN, THE   SS   NEW 71 AC
    BEST LAID SCHEMES, THE   EISENBERG, LARRY   AC
  OPEN SECRETS, THE   SS   GAL 69 05
    BEST LAID SCHEMES, THE   EISENBERG, LARRY   AC
  PIROKIN EFFECT, THE   SS   AMZ 64 06
    BEST LAID SCHEMES, THE   EISENBERG, LARRY   AC
    10TH ANNUAL OF THE YEAR'S BEST S-F, THE
                                   MERRIL, JUDITH   AN
  PROJECT AMNION   SS   VSF 69 08
    BEST LAID SCHEMES, THE   EISENBERG, LARRY   AC
  SAGA OF DMM, THE   SS   FSF 67 12
    BEST LAID SCHEMES, THE   EISENBERG, LARRY   AC
  TIME OF HIS LIFE, THE   SS   FSF 68 04
    ALPHA 1   SILVERBERG, ROBERT   AN
    BEST LAID SCHEMES, THE   EISENBERG, LARRY   AC
  TOO MANY COOKS   SS   NEW 71 AC
    BEST LAID SCHEMES, THE   EISENBERG, LARRY   AC
  TWO LIVES OF BEN COULTER, THE   SS   FSF 67 04
    BEST LAID SCHEMES, THE   EISENBERG, LARRY   AC
  UNCLE SAM'S CHILDREN (CHILD'S PLAY)   SS   IFS 70 01
    BEST LAID SCHEMES, THE   EISENBERG, LARRY   AC
  VANISHING BOROUGH, THE   SS   NEW 71 AC
    BEST LAID SCHEMES, THE   EISENBERG, LARRY   AC
  WHAT HAPPENED TO AUGUSTE CLAROT?   SS   DVS 67 01
    BEST LAID SCHEMES, THE   EISENBERG, LARRY   AC
    DANGEROUS VISIONS   ELLISON, HARLAN   OA

EISENSTEIN, ALEX
  TROUBLE WITH THE PAST, THE   SS C NDM 71 01
    NEW DIMENSIONS 1   SILVERBERG, ROBERT   OA
  YOU ARE HERE   NV C NDM 77 07
    NEW DIMENSIONS 7   SILVERBERG, ROBERT   OA

EISENSTEIN, PHYLLIS
  BORN TO EXILE   NV   FSF 71 08
    BEST FROM FANTASY AND SCIENCE FICTION: 20
                                   FERMAN, EDWARD L.   AN
  TELEPROBE   SS
    LONG NIGHT OF WAITING AND OTHER STORIES
                                   ELWOOD, ROGER   OA
  TREE OF LIFE   SS   GAL 75 03
    BEST SCIENCE FICTION STORIES OF THE YEAR (1975)
                                   DEL REY, LESTER   AN
  TROUBLE WITH THE PAST, THE   SS C NDM 71 01
    NEW DIMENSIONS 1   SILVERBERG, ROBERT   OA
  YOU ARE HERE   NV C NDM 77 07
    NEW DIMENSIONS 7   SILVERBERG, ROBERT   OA

EISNER, SIMON   PSEUD. FOR C. M. KORNBLUTH
  LUCKIEST MAN IN DENV, THE   SS   GAL 52 06
    SHADOW OF TOMORROW   POHL, FREDERIK   AN

EKLUND, GORDON
  AMBIGUITIES OF YESTERDAY, THE   SS
    FAR SIDE OF TIME, THE   ELWOOD, ROGER   OA
  ANGEL OF TRUTH   NV   EPC 75
    EPOCH   ELWOOD & SILVERBERG   OA
  DEAR AUNT ANNIE   NV   FAN 70 04
    WORLD'S BEST SCIENCE FICTION: 1971 WOLLHEIM & CARR   AN
  EXAMINATION DAY   NV
    OTHER SIDE OF TOMORROW, THE   ELWOOD, ROGER   OA
  FREE CITY BLUES   NV   UNI 73 03
    UNIVERSE 3   CARR, TERRY   OA
  GRASSHOPPER TIME   SS   FSF 72 03
    BEST SCIENCE FICTION OF THE YEAR, THE NO. 2
                                   CARR, TERRY   AN

EKLUND, GORDON   (CONTINUED)
  HOME AGAIN, HOME AGAIN   SS   QRK 71 03
    QUARK/3   DELANY & HACKER   OA
  IF THE STARS ARE GODS   NV C UNI 74 04
    BEST SCIENCE FICTION OF THE YEAR, THE NO. 4
                                   CARR, TERRY   AN
    NEBULA AWARD STORIES 10   GUNN, JAMES E.   AN
    UNIVERSE 4   CARR, TERRY   OA
  LOVEMAKER   SS   EIO 73
    EROS IN ORBIT   ELDER, JOSEPH   OA
  MOBY, TOO   SS   AMZ 73 12
    1974 ANNUAL WORLD'S BEST SF, THE WOLLHEIM, DONALD A. AN
  PSYCHOSOMATICA   NV
    CRISIS   ELWOOD, ROGER   OA
  RAMONA, COME SOFTLY   NV   QRK 70 01
    QUARK/1   DELANY & HACKER   OA
  RETRO MAN, THE   NV   NDM 77 07
    NEW DIMENSIONS 7   SILVERBERG, ROBERT   OA
  RISING OF THE SUN, THE   SS
    BEYOND TIME   LEY, SANDRA   OA
  SHRINE OF SEBASTIAN, THE   NA   CHN 73
    CHAINS OF THE SEA   SILVERBERG, ROBERT   OA
  STALKING THE SUN   NV   UNI 72 02
    UNIVERSE 2   CARR, TERRY   OA
  THREE COMEDIANS   NV   NDM 73 03
    NEW DIMENSIONS 3   SILVERBERG, ROBERT   OA
  UNDERBELLY   SS   IFS 72 10
    BEST SCIENCE FICTION STORIES OF THE YEAR (1972)
                                   DEL REY, LESTER   AN
  WEST WIND, FALLING   NV C UNI 71 01
    UNIVERSE 1   CARR, TERRY   OA
  WHAT DID YOU DO LAST YEAR?   SS C UNI 76 06
    UNIVERSE 6   CARR, TERRY   OA
  WHITE SUMMER IN MEMPHIS   NV   NDM 72 02
    NEW DIMENSIONS 2   SILVERBERG, ROBERT   OA

ELA, JONATHAN
  FROM SEA TO SHINING SEA   PA   SCL 72
    BEST SF: 1972   HARRISON & ALDISS   AN

ELAM, RICHARD M. JR.
  SCIENCE FICTION STORIES   AC   LPB 64 12
    SEE "TEEN-AGE SCIENCE FICTION STORIES"
  SUPER SCIENCE STORIES   AC   LPB 67 02
    SEE "TEEN-AGE SUPER SCIENCE STORIES"
  TEEN-AGE SCIENCE FICTION STORIES   AC H LPB 52
    ALSO AS "YOUNG READERS SCIENCE FICTION STORIES" AND
    "SCIENCE FICTION STORIES"
  TEEN-AGE SUPER SCIENCE STORIES   AC H LPB 58
    ALSO AS "SUPER SCIENCE STORIES"
  YOUNG READERS SCIENCE FICTION STORIES   AC H LPB 57
    SEE "TEEN-AGE SCIENCE FICTION STORIES"
  ADVENTURES ON MARS   SS   STP 52 12
    SCIENCE FICTION AND READER'S GUIDE BARROWS, MARJORIE AN
  BY JUPITER   SS   BLF 51
    TEEN-AGE SCIENCE FICTION STORIES ELAM, RICHARD M. JR. AC
  DAY THE FLAG FELL, THE   SS
    TEEN-AGE SCIENCE FICTION STORIES ELAM, RICHARD M. JR. AC
  EXPEDITION PLUTO   NV
    TEEN-AGE SUPER SCIENCE STORIES ELAM, RICHARD M. JR. AC
  FIRST MAN INTO SPACE, THE   NV
    TEEN-AGE SUPER SCIENCE STORIES ELAM, RICHARD M. JR. AC
  FLIGHT OF THE CENTAURUS   SS
    TEEN-AGE SUPER SCIENCE STORIES ELAM, RICHARD M. JR. AC
  GHOST SHIP OF SPACE, THE   NV
    TEEN-AGE SUPER SCIENCE STORIES ELAM, RICHARD M. JR. AC
  HANDS ACROSS THE DEEP   SS
    TEEN-AGE SCIENCE FICTION STORIES ELAM, RICHARD M. JR. AC
  IRON MOON, THE   NV   BLF 51
    TEEN-AGE SCIENCE FICTION STORIES ELAM, RICHARD M. JR. AC
  LUNAR TRAP   NV   BLF 49
    TEEN-AGE SCIENCE FICTION STORIES ELAM, RICHARD M. JR. AC
  MERCY FLIGHT TO LUNA   SS
    TEEN-AGE SUPER SCIENCE STORIES ELAM, RICHARD M. JR. AC
  MYSTERY EYES OVER EARTH   SS
    TEEN-AGE SUPER SCIENCE STORIES ELAM, RICHARD M. JR. AC
  PERIL FROM OUTER SPACE, THE   NV
    TEEN-AGE SUPER SCIENCE STORIES ELAM, RICHARD M. JR. AC
  PROJECT OCEAN FLOOR   SS
    TEEN-AGE SCIENCE FICTION STORIES ELAM, RICHARD M. JR. AC
  RACE AROUND THE SUN   SS
    TEEN-AGE SUPER SCIENCE STORIES ELAM, RICHARD M. JR. AC
  RED SANDS   SS
    TEEN-AGE SCIENCE FICTION STORIES ELAM, RICHARD M. JR. AC
  SOL'S LITTLE BROTHER   SS
    TEEN-AGE SCIENCE FICTION STORIES ELAM, RICHARD M. JR. AC
  SPACE STEWARD   NV
    TEEN-AGE SUPER SCIENCE STORIES ELAM, RICHARD M. JR. AC
  STRANGE MEN, THE   SS
    TEEN-AGE SCIENCE FICTION STORIES ELAM, RICHARD M. JR. AC
  VENUSWAY   SS   BLF 51
    TEEN-AGE SCIENCE FICTION STORIES ELAM, RICHARD M. JR. AC
  WHAT TIME IS IT?   NV
    SCIENCE FICTION AND READER'S GUIDE BARROWS, MARJORIE AN
    TEEN-AGE SCIENCE FICTION STORIES ELAM, RICHARD M. JR. AC

ELDER, JOSEPH
  EROS IN ORBIT   OA H TRI 73
  FARTHEST REACHES, THE   OA H TRI 68 08
  FOREWORD   IN
    FARTHEST REACHES, THE   ELDER, JOSEPH   OA
  PREFACE   IN
    EROS IN ORBIT   ELDER, JOSEPH   OA

ELGIN, SUZETTE HADEN
  FOR THE SAKE OF GRACE   NV   FSF 69 05
  TOMORROW, AND TOMORROW, AND TOMORROW...
                                                   HEINTZ/HERBERT/JOOS/ AN
    WORLD'S BEST SCIENCE FICTION: 1970   WOLLHEIM & CARR   AN

ELLANBY, BOYD   PSEUD. FOR WILLIAM C. AND LYLE BOYD
  CATEGORY PHOENIX   NA   GAL 52 05
    YEAR'S BEST SCIENCE FICTION NOVELS: 1953
                                                   BLEILER & DIKTY   AN
  CHAIN REACTION   NV   GAL 56 09
    EXPERT DREAMERS, THE   POHL, FREDERIK   AN

ELLERMAN, GENE   PSEUD. FOR BASIL WELLS

ELLERN, WILLIAM B.
  MOON PROSPECTOR   NV   ASF 66 04
    GREAT SCIENCE FICTION STORIES ABOUT THE MOON
                                                   DIKTY, T. E.   AN

ELLIN, STANLEY
  FOOL'S MATE   SS   SEM 48
    FIEND IN YOU, THE   BEAUMONT, CHARLES   AN

ELLIOT, JOHN
  A FOR ANDROMEDA   EX C SVN 62
    FROM FRANKENSTEIN TO ANDROMEDA   BROWN, JAMES GOLDIE   AN

ELLIOTT, BRUCE
  BATTLE OF THE S...S, THE   SS   NEW 52 AN
   *FUTURE TENSE   CROSSEN, KENDELL F.   AN
  DEVIL WAS SICK, THE   SS   FSF 51 04
    ADVENTURES IN TOMORROW   CROSSEN, KENDELL F.   AN
    DEALS WITH THE DEVIL   DAVENPORT, BASIL   AN
  FEARSOME FABLE   SS   FSF 51 02
    BEST FROM FANTASY AND SCIENCE FICTION   BOUCHER & MCCOMAS   AN
    FANTASIA MATHEMATICA   FADIMAN, CLIFTON   AN
  LAST MAGICIAN, THE   SS   FSF 53 01
    FANTASIA MATHEMATICA   FADIMAN, CLIFTON   AN
  SO SWEET AS MAGIC...   NV   FNF 53 08
    WIZARDS AND WARLOCKS   GHIDALIA, VIC   AN
  WOLVES DON'T CRY   SS   FSF 54 04
    GALAXY OF GHOULS   MERRIL, JUDITH   AN
    ROD SERLING'S TRIPLE W: WITCHES, WARLOCKS AND WEREWOLVES
                                                   SERLING, ROD   AN

ELLIOTT, GEORGE P.
  AMONG THE DANGS (EXCERPT)   EX   ESQ 58 06
    7TH ANNUAL OF THE YEAR'S BEST S-F, THE MERRIL, JUDITH   AN
  FAQ!   SS   FSF 61 11
    WORLDS OF SCIENCE FICTION, THE   MILLS, ROBERT P.   AN
  INVASION OF THE PLANET OF LOVE   SS   FSF 59 01
    BEST FROM FANTASY AND SCIENCE FICTION: 9
                                                   MILLS, ROBERT P.   AN
  NRACP, THE   NV   HUD 49 FL
    HUMAN AND OTHER BEINGS   DEGRAEFF, ALLEN   AN
    SOCIAL PROBLEMS THROUGH SCIENCE FICTION
                                                   GREENBERG/MILSTEAD/& AN
  SANDRA   SS   FSF 57 10
    TREASURY OF GREAT SCIENCE FICTION, A VOL.1
                                                   BOUCHER, ANTHONY   AN

ELLIOTT, H. CHANDLER
  DAY ON DEATH HIGHWAY, A   NV   GAL 63 10
    EIGHTH GALAXY READER, THE   POHL, FREDERIK   AN
  INANIMATE OBJECTION   NV   GAL 54 02
   *SPECTRUM   AMIS & CONQUEST   AN

ELLIOTT, ROSE B.
  BABY KILLERS   SS   NEW 52 AN
   *FUTURE TENSE   CROSSEN, KENDELL F.   AN

ELLIS, H. F.
  SPACE-CRIME CONTINUUM   SS   FSF 54 09
    SCIENCE FICTION ODDITIES   CONKLIN, GROFF   AN

ELLISON, HARLAN
  AGAIN, DANGEROUS VISIONS   OA H DBL 72
  ALL THE SOUNDS OF FEAR   AC   PTH 73
    FIRST 9 STORIES FROM "ALONE AGAINST TOMORROW"
  ALONE AGAINST TOMORROW   AC H MAC 71
    IN ENGLAND AS "ALL THE SOUNDS OF FEAR" AND
    "THE TIME OF THE EYE"
  APPROACHING OBLIVION   AC H WKR 74
  BEAST THAT SHOUTED LOVE AT THE HEART OF THE WORLD, THE
                                                   AC   AVN 69 07
    ENGLISH EDITION (H. MILLINGTON, 1976) OMITS:
    "ALONG THE SCENIC ROUTE", "THE PLACE WITH NO NAME"
    AND "SHATTERED LIKE A GLASS GOBLIN"
  DANGEROUS VISIONS   OA H DBL 67 10
  DEATHBIRD STORIES   AC H HPR 75
  EARTHMAN, GO HOME!   AC   PBK 64 12
    SEE "ELLISON WONDERLAND"
  ELLISON WONDERLAND   AC   PBK 62 06
    ALSO AS "EARTHMAN, GO HOME!"
  FROM THE LAND OF FEAR   AC   BEL 67 12
  I HAVE NO MOUTH, AND I MUST SCREAM   AC   PYR 67 04
  LOVE AIN'T NOTHING BUT SEX MISSPELLED   AC H TRI 68
  LOVE AIN'T NOTHING BUT SEX MISSPELLED (REVISED) AC   PYR 76 02
  NO DOORS, NO WINDOWS (STORIES REWRITTEN)   AC   PYR 75 11
  OVER THE EDGE   AC   BEL 70 05
  PAINGOD AND OTHER DELUSIONS   AC   PYR 65 12
  PAINGOD AND OTHER DELUSIONS (THIRD EDITION ADDS:) AC   PYR 75 03
  PARTNERS IN WONDER   AC H WKR 71
  TIME OF THE EYE, THE   AC   PTH 74
    LAST 12 STORIES FROM "ALONE AGAINST TOMORROW"

ELLISON, HARLAN   (CONTINUED)
  TOUCH OF INFINITY, A   DC   ACE 59
  ABNORMALS, THE (SEE THE DISCARDED)   TC
  ADRIFT JUST OFF THE ISLETS OF LANGERHANS: LATITUDE 38° 54' N,
    LONGITUDE 77° 00' 13" W   NV   FSF 74 10
    DEATHBIRD STORIES   ELLISON, HARLAN   AC
  ALL THE SOUNDS OF FEAR   SS   SDM 62 07
    ALONE AGAINST TOMORROW   ELLISON, HARLAN   AC
    ELLISON WONDERLAND   ELLISON, HARLAN   AC
   *LOVE AIN'T NOTHING BUT SEX MISSPELLED   ELLISON, HARLAN   AC
    8TH ANNUAL OF THE YEAR'S BEST S-F, THE MERRIL, JUDITH   AN
  ALONG THE SCENIC ROUTE (DOGFIGHT ON 101)   SS   AMZ 69 09
    BEAST THAT SHOUTED LOVE AT THE HEART OF THE WORLD, THE
                                                   ELLISON, HARLAN   AC
    DEATHBIRD STORIES   ELLISON, HARLAN   AC
  ARE YOU LISTENING?   SS   AMZ 58 12
    ALONE AGAINST TOMORROW   ELLISON, HARLAN   AC
    BEAST THAT SHOUTED LOVE AT THE HEART OF THE WORLD, THE
                                                   ELLISON, HARLAN   AC
    INTO THE UNKNOWN   CARR, TERRY   AN
  ASLEEP: WITH STILL HANDS (THE SLEEPER WITH STILL HANDS)
                                                   NV   IFS 68 07
    BEAST THAT SHOUTED LOVE AT THE HEART OF THE WORLD, THE
                                                   ELLISON, HARLAN   AC
  ASSAULT ON NEW DREAMERS, AN   IN   DVS 72 02
    AGAIN, DANGEROUS VISIONS   ELLISON, HARLAN   OA
  AT THE MOUSE CIRCUS   SS   NDM 71 01
    BEST SCIENCE FICTION FOR 1972   POHL, FREDERIK   AN
    DEATHBIRD STORIES   ELLISON, HARLAN   AC
    MODERN SCIENCE FICTION   SPINRAD, NORMAN   AN
    NEW DIMENSIONS 1   SILVERBERG, ROBERT   OA
  BACK TO THE DRAWING BOARDS   SS   FUN 58 08
    ELLISON WONDERLAND   ELLISON, HARLAN   AC
    FROM THE LAND OF FEAR   ELLISON, HARLAN   AC
    TOUCH OF INFINITY, A   ELLISON, HARLAN   DC
  BASILISK   SS   FSF 72 08
    DEATHBIRD STORIES   ELLISON, HARLAN   AC
  BATTLE WITHOUT BANNERS   SS   NEW 64 OC
    FROM THE LAND OF FEAR   ELLISON, HARLAN   AC
   *LOVE AIN'T NOTHING BUT SEX MISSPELLED   ELLISON, HARLAN   AC
  BATTLEFIELD (HIS FIRST DAY AT WAR)   SS   STM 58 11
    ELLISON WONDERLAND   ELLISON, HARLAN   AC
    WINDOWS INTO TOMORROW   SILVERBERG, ROBERT   AN
  BEAST THAT SHOUTED LOVE AT THE HEART OF THE WORLD, THE
                                                   NV   GAL 68 06
    BEAST THAT SHOUTED LOVE AT THE HEART OF THE WORLD, THE
                                                   ELLISON, HARLAN   AC
    DARK STARS   SILVERBERG, ROBERT   AN
    HUGO WINNERS, THE (VOLUME 2)   ASIMOV, ISAAC   AN
  BIG SAM WAS MY FRIEND   SS   SFA 58 03
    I HAVE NO MOUTH, AND I MUST SCREAM   ELLISON, HARLAN   AC
  BLANK   SS   INF 57 06
    OVER THE EDGE   ELLISON, HARLAN   AC
  BLEEDING STONES   SS   VTX 73 04
    DEATHBIRD STORIES   ELLISON, HARLAN   AC
  BLIND BIRD, BLIND BIRD, GO AWAY FROM ME!   SS   KNT 63 07
   *LOVE AIN'T NOTHING BUT SEX MISSPELLED   ELLISON, HARLAN   AC
  BLIND LIGHTNING   SS   FUN 56 06
    ALONE AGAINST TOMORROW   ELLISON, HARLAN   AC
    EARTHMEN AND STRANGERS   SILVERBERG, ROBERT   AN
    OVER THE EDGE   ELLISON, HARLAN   AC
    TOUCH OF INFINITY, A   ELLISON, HARLAN   DC
  BLOOD/THOUGHTS   IN
    NO DOORS, NO WINDOWS (STORIES REWRITTEN)
                                                   ELLISON, HARLAN   AC
  BOY AND HIS DOG, A   NV   NWS 69 04
    AS TOMORROW BECOMES TODAY   SULLIVAN, CHARLES W. AN
    BEAST THAT SHOUTED LOVE AT THE HEART OF THE WORLD, THE
                                                   ELLISON, HARLAN   AC
    BEST SF STORIES FROM NEW WORLDS 8   MOORCOCK, MICHAEL   AN
    NEBULA AWARD STORIES   NO. 5   BLISH, JAMES   AN
    WORLD'S BEST SCIENCE FICTION: 1970   WOLLHEIM & CARR   AN
  BRIGHT EYES   SS   FAN 65 04
    ALONE AGAINST TOMORROW   ELLISON, HARLAN   AC
   *PAINGOD AND OTHER DELUSIONS   ELLISON, HARLAN   AC
  BRILLO   NV C ASF 70 08
    PARTNERS IN WONDER   ELLISON, HARLAN   AC
  BRINKMANSHIP   IN
    OVER THE EDGE   ELLISON, HARLAN   AC
  CASE OF PTOMAINE, A (SEE MEALTIME)   TC
  CATMAN   NV   FST 74
    APPROACHING OBLIVION   ELLISON, HARLAN   AC
    FINAL STAGE   FERMAN & MALZBERG   OA
  CHILDREN'S HOUR, THE (AS WALLACE EDMONDSON)   SS   FUN 58 07
    NO DOORS, NO WINDOWS (STORIES REWRITTEN)
                                                   ELLISON, HARLAN   AC
  CITY ON THE EDGE OF FOREVER, THE   PL   NBC 67 04
    SIX SCIENCE FICTION PLAYS   ELWOOD, ROGER   AN
  COLD FRIEND   SS   GAL 73 10
    APPROACHING OBLIVION   ELLISON, HARLAN   AC
    BEST FROM GALAXY, THE VOLUME II   GALAXY, EDITORS OF   AN
  COME TO ME NOT IN WINTER'S WHITE   SS C FSF 69 10
    PARTNERS IN WONDER   ELLISON, HARLAN   AC
  COMMUTER'S PROBLEM   SS   FUN 57 06
    ELLISON WONDERLAND   ELLISON, HARLAN   AC
  CORPSE   SS   FSF 72 01
    DEATHBIRD STORIES   ELLISON, HARLAN   AC
  CRACKPOTS, THE   NV   IFS 56 06
   *PAINGOD AND OTHER DELUSIONS   ELLISON, HARLAN   AC
  CROATOAN   SS   FSF 75 05
    BEST SCIENCE FICTION OF THE YEAR, THE NO. 5
                                                   CARR, TERRY   AN
  DANIEL WHITE FOR THE GREATER GOOD   SS   ROG 61 03
   *LOVE AIN'T NOTHING BUT SEX MISSPELLED   ELLISON, HARLAN   AC
  DEAL FROM THE BOTTOM   SS   ROG 60 01
    ELLISON WONDERLAND   ELLISON, HARLAN   AC

ELLISON, HARLAN

ELLISON, HARLAN   (CONTINUED)
DEATHBIRD, THE   NV   FSF 73 03
    BEST FROM FANTASY AND SCIENCE FICTION: 20
                                            FERMAN, EDWARD L.   AN
    BEST SCIENCE FICTION OF THE YEAR, THE NO. 3
                                            CARR, TERRY   AN
    DEATHBIRD STORIES   ELLISON, HARLAN   AC
    NEBULA AWARD STORIES 9   WILHELM, KATE   AN
    1974 ANNUAL WORLD'S BEST SF, THE   WOLLHEIM, DONALD A. AN
DEEPER THAN DARKNESS   NV   INF 57 04
    ALONE AGAINST TOMORROW   ELLISON, HARLAN   AC
    *PAINGOD AND OTHER DELUSIONS   ELLISON, HARLAN   AC
DELUSION FOR A DRAGON SLAYER   SS   KNT 66 09
    DEATHBIRD STORIES   ELLISON, HARLAN   AC
    I HAVE NO MOUTH, AND I MUST SCREAM   ELLISON, HARLAN   AC
    *LOVE AIN'T NOTHING BUT SEX MISSPELLED ELLISON, HARLAN   AC
DISCARDED, THE (THE ABNORMALS)   SS   FAN 59 04
    ALONE AGAINST TOMORROW   ELLISON, HARLAN   AC
    *PAINGOD AND OTHER DELUSIONS   ELLISON, HARLAN   AC
DO-IT-YOURSELF   SS C ROG 61 02
    ELLISON WONDERLAND   ELLISON, HARLAN   AC
DOGFIGHT ON 101 (SEE ALONG THE SCENIC ROUTE)   TC
DOWN IN THE DARK (AS ELLIS HART)   SS   ABR 67 30
    NO DOORS, NO WINDOWS (STORIES REWRITTEN)
                                            ELLISON, HARLAN   AC
DREAMERS ON THE BARRICADES   AR   CLR 71 01
    CLARION   WILSON, ROBIN SCOTT OA
DUNDERBIRD (SEE STREET SCENE)   TC C
ECOWARENESS   SS   NEW 74 AC
    APPROACHING OBLIVION   ELLISON, HARLAN   AC
EDDIE, YOU'RE MY FRIEND   SS   KNT 75
    NO DOORS, NO WINDOWS (STORIES REWRITTEN)
                                            ELLISON, HARLAN   AC
ELLISON'S GRAMMATICAL GUIDE AND GLOSSARY FOR GOYIM
                                                         MS
    WANDERING STARS   DANN, JACK M.   AN
EMISSARY FROM HAMELIN   SS
    2076: THE AMERICAN TRICENTENNIAL   BRYANT, EDWARD   OA
ENTER THE FANATIC, STAGE CENTER   SS   ADM 66 07
    OVER THE EDGE   ELLISON, HARLAN   AC
ERNEST AND THE MACHINE GOD   NV   KNT 68 01
    DEATHBIRD STORIES   ELLISON, HARLAN   AC
    *LOVE AIN'T NOTHING BUT SEX MISSPELLED ELLISON, HARLAN   AC
    OVER THE EDGE   ELLISON, HARLAN   AC
EROTOPHOBIA   SS   PNT 71 08
    APPROACHING OBLIVION   ELLISON, HARLAN   AC
EYES OF DUST   SS   ROG 59 12
    ALONE AGAINST TOMORROW   ELLISON, HARLAN   AC
    I HAVE NO MOUTH, AND I MUST SCREAM   ELLISON, HARLAN   AC
FACE OF HELENE BOURNOUW, THE   SS   CLG 60 10
    DEATHBIRD STORIES   ELLISON, HARLAN   AC
    *LOVE AIN'T NOTHING BUT SEX MISSPELLED ELLISON, HARLAN   AC
FINAL SHTICK   SS   ROG 60 08
    *LOVE AIN'T NOTHING BUT SEX MISSPELLED ELLISON, HARLAN   AC
FINAL TROPHY   NV   SUP 57 06
    OVER THE EDGE   ELLISON, HARLAN   AC
    TOUCH OF INFINITY, A   ELLISON, HARLAN   DC
FRIEND TO MAN, A   SS   FUN 59 10
    FROM THE LAND OF FEAR   ELLISON, HARLAN   AC
G.B.K. - A MANY FLAVORED BIRD   SS   ROG 62 06
    *LOVE AIN'T NOTHING BUT SEX MISSPELLED ELLISON, HARLAN   AC
GNOMEBODY   SS   AMZ 56 10
    ELLISON WONDERLAND   ELLISON, HARLAN   AC
HADJ   SS   SFA 56 12
    ELLISON WONDERLAND   ELLISON, HARLAN   AC
HINDSIGHT: 480 SECONDS   SS   FUC 73
    APPROACHING OBLIVION   ELLISON, HARLAN   AC
    FUTURE CITY   ELWOOD, ROGER   OA
HIS FIRST DAY AT WAR (SEE BATTLEFIELD)   TC
HOW SCIENCE FICTION SAVED ME FROM A LIFE OF CRIME IN
    I HAVE NO MOUTH, AND I MUST SCREAM   ELLISON, HARLAN   AC
HUMAN OPERATORS, THE   NV C FSF 71 01
    BEST SCIENCE FICTION STORIES OF THE YEAR (1971)
                                            DEL REY, LESTER   AN
    PARTNERS IN WONDER   ELLISON, HARLAN   AC
I CURSE THE LESSON AND BLESS THE KNOWLEDGE   SS   75
    LOVE AIN'T NOTHING BUT SEX MISSPELLED (REVISED)
                                            ELLISON, HARLAN   AC
I HAVE NO MOUTH, AND I MUST SCREAM   SS   IFS 67 03
    ALONE AGAINST TOMORROW   ELLISON, HARLAN   AC
    HUGO WINNERS, THE (VOLUME 2)   ASIMOV, ISAAC   AN
    I HAVE NO MOUTH, AND I MUST SCREAM   ELLISON, HARLAN   AC
    MIRROR OF INFINITY, THE   SILVERBERG, ROBERT   AN
    POCKETFUL OF STARS, A   KNIGHT, DAMON   AN
    SURVIVAL PRINTOUT   TOTAL EFFECT   AN
    WORLD'S BEST SCIENCE FICTION: 1968   WOLLHEIM & CARR   AN
I SEE A MAN SITTING IN A CHAIR,AND THE CHAIR IS BITING HIS LEG
                                                         NV C FSF 68 01
    PARTNERS IN WONDER   ELLISON, HARLAN   AC
I'M LOOKING FOR KADAK   NV   NEW 74 AN
    APPROACHING OBLIVION   ELLISON, HARLAN   AC
    WANDERING STARS   DANN, JACK M.   AN
IN EXORCISING TEXAS: AN INTRODUCTION   IN
    LONE STAR UNIVERSE   PROCTOR & UTLEY   OA
IN LONELY LANDS   SS   FUN 59 01
    ALONE AGAINST TOMORROW   ELLISON, HARLAN   AC
    ELLISON WONDERLAND   ELLISON, HARLAN   AC
    FANTASTIC UNIVERSE OMNIBUS, THE   SANTESSON, HANS S.   AN
    MARS, WE LOVE YOU   HIPOLITO & MCNELLY   AN
IN MEMORIAM- GERALD KERSH   MS
    NEBULA AWARD STORIES NO. 4   ANDERSON, POUL   AN
INTRODUCTION   IN
    TOUCH OF INFINITY, A   ELLISON, HARLAN   DC
INTRODUCTION TO THE CITY ON THE EDGE OF FOREVER   AI
    SIX SCIENCE FICTION PLAYS   ELWOOD, ROGER   AN

ELLISON, HARLAN

ELLISON, HARLAN   (CONTINUED)
INTRODUCTION TO THE FIRST EDITION   IN
    LOVE AIN'T NOTHING BUT SEX MISSPELLED (REVISED)
                                            ELLISON, HARLAN   AC
INTRODUCTION: OBLATIONS AT ALIEN ALTARS   IN
    DEATHBIRD STORIES   ELLISON, HARLAN   AC
KERSH, THE DEMON PRINCE   IN
    NIGHTSHADE & DAMNATIONS   KERSH, GERALD   AC
KISS OF FIRE   SS   TVW 73
    APPROACHING OBLIVION   ELLISON, HARLAN   AC
    TWO VIEWS OF WONDER   SCORTIA & YARBRO   OA
KNOX   SS   CRW 74 03
    APPROACHING OBLIVION   ELLISON, HARLAN   AC
KONG PAPERS, THE   SS C KNT 73 04
    PARTNERS IN WONDER   ELLISON, HARLAN   AC
LAST DAY, THE (SEE THE VERY LAST DAY OF A GOOD WOMAN)
                                                         TC
LIFE HUTCH   SS   IFS 56 04
    ALONE AGAINST TOMORROW   ELLISON, HARLAN   AC
    DEEP SPACE   SILVERBERG, ROBERT   AN
    FROM THE LAND OF FEAR   ELLISON, HARLAN   AC
    TOUCH OF INFINITY, A   ELLISON, HARLAN   DC
LONELYACHE   SS   KNT 64 07
    ALONE AGAINST TOMORROW   ELLISON, HARLAN   AC
    I HAVE NO MOUTH, AND I MUST SCREAM   ELLISON, HARLAN   AC
    *LOVE AIN'T NOTHING BUT SEX MISSPELLED ELLISON, HARLAN   AC
MAN ON THE JUICE WAGON, THE (AS CORDWAINER BIRD)   SS   ABR 63 14
    NO DOORS, NO WINDOWS (STORIES REWRITTEN)
                                            ELLISON, HARLAN   AC
MAN WITH THE GREEN NOSE, THE (SEE SURVIVOR NO. 1) TC C
MEALTIME (A CASE OF PTOMAINE)   SS   STM 58 09
    ELLISON WONDERLAND   ELLISON, HARLAN   AC
MONA AT HER WINDOWS   SS   ROG 62 06
    *LOVE AIN'T NOTHING BUT SEX MISSPELLED ELLISON, HARLAN   AC
MOTHERHOOD, APPLE PIE AND THE AMERICAN WAY   IN
    *LOVE AIN'T NOTHING BUT SEX MISSPELLED ELLISON, HARLAN   AC
MOURNERS FOR HIRE (SEE WE MOURN FOR ANYONE...)   TC
MY BROTHER PAULIE   SS   SAT 58 12
    FROM THE LAND OF FEAR   ELLISON, HARLAN   AC
NEDRA AT F:5.6 (THE HUNGRY ONE)   SS   GNT 57 03
    NO DOORS, NO WINDOWS (STORIES REWRITTEN)
                                            ELLISON, HARLAN   AC
NEITHER YOUR JENNY NOR MINE   SS   KNT 64 04
    *LOVE AIN'T NOTHING BUT SEX MISSPELLED ELLISON, HARLAN   AC
NEON   SS   HOH 73 08
    DEATHBIRD STORIES   ELLISON, HARLAN   AC
NEW INTRODUCTION: HAVING AN AFFAIR WITH A TROLL IN
    LOVE AIN'T NOTHING BUT SEX MISSPELLED (REVISED)
                                            ELLISON, HARLAN   AC
NEW INTRODUCTION: YOUR BASIC CROWN OF THORNS   IN
    PAINGOD AND OTHER DELUSIONS (THIRD EDITION ADDS:)
                                            ELLISON, HARLAN   AC
NICE GUYS FINISH SOMEWHERE IN THE MIDDLE   IN
    LIGHT AT THE END OF THE UNIVERSE, THE CARR, TERRY   AC
NIGHT OF DELICATE TERRORS, THE   SS   PPR 61 04
    *LOVE AIN'T NOTHING BUT SEX MISSPELLED ELLISON, HARLAN   AC
NIGHT VIGIL (YELLOW STREAK HERO)   SS   AMZ 57 05
    ALONE AGAINST TOMORROW   ELLISON, HARLAN   AC
    OVER THE EDGE   ELLISON, HARLAN   AC
NOTHING FOR MY NOON MEAL   SS   NEB 58 05
    ALONE AGAINST TOMORROW   ELLISON, HARLAN   AC
    ELLISON WONDERLAND   ELLISON, HARLAN   AC
O YE OF LITTLE FAITH   SS   KNT 68 09
    ALONE AGAINST TOMORROW   ELLISON, HARLAN   AC
    DEATHBIRD STORIES   ELLISON, HARLAN   AC
    *LOVE AIN'T NOTHING BUT SEX MISSPELLED ELLISON, HARLAN   AC
    SF: AUTHORS' CHOICE 3   HARRISON, HARRY   AN
ON THE DOWNHILL SIDE   SS   UNI 72 02
    DEATHBIRD STORIES   ELLISON, HARLAN   AC
    NEBULA AWARD STORIES 8   ASIMOV, ISAAC   AN
    UNIVERSE 2   CARR, TERRY   OA
ONE LIFE, FURNISHED IN EARLY POVERTY   SS   ORB 70 08
    APPROACHING OBLIVION   ELLISON, HARLAN   AC
    BEST FROM ORBIT, THE   KNIGHT, DAMON   AN
    ORBIT 8   KNIGHT, DAMON   OA
    1972 ANNUAL WORLD'S BEST SF, THE   WOLLHEIM, DONALD A. AN
OPPOSITES ATTRACT (MAD BOMBER)   SS   CPR 57 11
    NO DOORS, NO WINDOWS (STORIES REWRITTEN)
                                            ELLISON, HARLAN   AC
ORMOND ALWAYS PAYS HIS BILLS   SS   PSD 57 07
    NO DOORS, NO WINDOWS (STORIES REWRITTEN)
                                            ELLISON, HARLAN   AC
PAINGOD   SS   FAN 64 06
    BEST FROM FANTASTIC, THE   WHITE, TED   AN
    DEATHBIRD STORIES   ELLISON, HARLAN   AC
    *PAINGOD AND OTHER DELUSIONS   ELLISON, HARLAN   AC
PATH THROUGH THE DARKNESS, A   NV   FLN 63 01
    *LOVE AIN'T NOTHING BUT SEX MISSPELLED ELLISON, HARLAN   AC
PAULIE CHARMED THE SLEEPING WOMAN   SS   FSF 62 08
    APPROACHING OBLIVION   ELLISON, HARLAN   AC
PAWOB DIVISION, THE (SEE THE PITLL PAWOB DIVISION)
                                                         TC
PENNIES, OFF A DEAD MAN'S EYES   SS   GAL 69 11
    ALONE AGAINST TOMORROW   ELLISON, HARLAN   AC
    BEST FROM GALAXY, THE   VOLUME I   GALAXY, EDITORS OF   AN
    NEW TOMORROWS, THE   SPINRAD, NORMAN   AN
    OVER THE EDGE   ELLISON, HARLAN   AC
PHOENIX (PHOENIX LAND)   SS   IFS 69 03
    BEAST THAT SHOUTED LOVE AT THE HEART OF THE WORLD, THE
                                            ELLISON, HARLAN   AC
PHOENIX WITHOUT ASHES   PL   76
    FASTER THAN LIGHT   DANN & ZEBROWSKI   OA
PITLL PAWOB DIVISION, THE (THE PAWOB DIVISION)   SS   IFS 68 12
    BEAST THAT SHOUTED LOVE AT THE HEART OF THE WORLD, THE
                                            ELLISON, HARLAN   AC

ELLISON, HARLAN   (CONTINUED)
PLACE WITH NO NAME, THE   SS   FSF 69 07
   BEAST THAT SHOUTED LOVE AT THE HEART OF THE WORLD, THE
                                          ELLISON, HARLAN   AC
   DEATHBIRD STORIES   ELLISON, HARLAN   AC
POWER OF THE NAIL, THE   SS C AMZ 68 11
   PARTNERS IN WONDER   ELLISON, HARLAN   AC
PRAYER FOR ONE'S ENEMY, A   NV   CAD 66 03
   *LOVE AIN'T NOTHING BUT SEX MISSPELLED ELLISON, HARLAN   AC
PRETTY MAGGIE MONEYEYES   NV   KNT 67 05
   BEST SF: 1967   HARRISON & ALDISS   AN
   DEATHBIRD STORIES   ELLISON, HARLAN   AC
   I HAVE NO MOUTH, AND I MUST SCREAM   ELLISON, HARLAN   AC
   *LOVE AIN'T NOTHING BUT SEX MISSPELLED ELLISON, HARLAN   AC
   NEBULA AWARD STORIES   NO. 3   ZELAZNY, ROGER   AN
   SPECIAL WONDER   MCCOMAS, J. FRANCIS AN
   THOSE WHO CAN: A SCIENCE FICTION READER
                                          WILSON, ROBIN SCOTT AN
PRIDE IN THE PROFESSION   SS   ADM 66 08
   NO DOORS, NO WINDOWS (STORIES REWRITTEN)
                                          ELLISON, HARLAN   AC
PROMISES OF LAUGHTER   SS   ADM 69 11
   NO DOORS, NO WINDOWS (STORIES REWRITTEN)
                                          ELLISON, HARLAN   AC
PROWLER IN THE CITY AT THE EDGE OF THE WORLD, THE NV DVS 67 01
   DANGEROUS VISIONS   ELLISON, HARLAN   OA
   OVER THE EDGE   ELLISON, HARLAN   AC
   PARTNERS IN WONDER   ELLISON, HARLAN   AC
PUNKY AND THE YALE MAN   NV   KNT 66 01
   *LOVE AIN'T NOTHING BUT SEX MISSPELLED ELLISON, HARLAN   AC
RAIN, RAIN, GO AWAY   SS   SCF 56 12
   ELLISON WONDERLAND   ELLISON, HARLAN   AC
REAPING THE WHIRLWIND
   APPROACHING OBLIVION   IN
                                          ELLISON, HARLAN   AC
REGION BETWEEN, THE   NA   GAL 70 03
   FIVE FATES   LAUMER, KEITH   AN
"REPENT, HARLEQUIN!" SAID THE TICKTOCKMAN   SS   GAL 65 12
   ABOVE THE HUMAN LANDSCAPE   MCNELLY & STOVER   AN
   ALONE AGAINST TOMORROW   ELLISON, HARLAN   AC
   ANOTHER TOMORROW   HOLLISTER, BERNARD C AN
   AS TOMORROW BECOMES TODAY   SULLIVAN, CHARLES W. AN
   FANTASY: THE LITERATURE OF THE MARVELOUS
                                          KELLEY, LEO P.   AN
   HUGO WINNERS, THE (VOLUME 2)   ASIMOV, ISAAC   AN
   IN DREAMS AWAKE   FIEDLER, LESLIE A.   AN
   NEBULA AWARD STORIES   KNIGHT, DAMON   AN
   *PAINGOD AND OTHER DELUSIONS   ELLISON, HARLAN   AC
   POLITICAL SCIENCE FICTION   GREENBERG& WARRICK   AN
   SCIENCE FICTION: THE FUTURE   ALLEN, DICK   AN
   SPECULATIONS   SANDERS, THOMAS E.   AN
   TENTH GALAXY READER, THE   POHL, FREDERIK   AN
   TOMORROW, AND TOMORROW, AND TOMORROW...
                                          HEINTZ/HERBERT/JOOS/ AN
   TRANSFORMATIONS   ROSELLE, DANIEL   AN
   WORLD'S BEST SCIENCE FICTION: 1966   WOLLHEIM & CARR   AN
RESURGENCE OF MISS ANKLE-STRAP WEDGIE, THE   SS   NEW 68 AC
   *LOVE AIN'T NOTHING BUT SEX MISSPELLED ELLISON, HARLAN   AC
RIDING THE DARK TRAIN OUT   SS   ROG 61 05
   *LOVE AIN'T NOTHING BUT SEX MISSPELLED ELLISON, HARLAN   AC
ROBERT BLAKE'S UNIVERSE (SEE THE UNIVERSE OF ROBERT BLAKE)
                                          TC
ROCK GOD   SS   COV 69 11
   DEATHBIRD STORIES   ELLISON, HARLAN   AC
   OVER THE EDGE   ELLISON, HARLAN   AC
RODNEY PARISH FOR HIRE   SS C SWK 62 05
   PARTNERS IN WONDER   ELLISON, HARLAN   AC
RUN FOR THE STARS   NV   SFA 57 06
   BEAST THAT SHOUTED LOVE AT THE HEART OF THE WORLD, THE
                                          ELLISON, HARLAN   AC
   TOUCH OF INFINITY, A   ELLISON, HARLAN   DC
RUNESMITH   SS C FSF 70 05
   PARTNERS IN WONDER   ELLISON, HARLAN   AC
SANTA CLAUS VS. S.P.I.D.E.R.   NV   FSF 69 01
   BEAST THAT SHOUTED LOVE AT THE HEART OF THE WORLD, THE
                                          ELLISON, HARLAN   AC
SAVAGE WIND (SEE THE WIND FROM BEYOND THE MOUNTAINS)
                                          TC
SCHERZO FOR SCHIZOIDS: NOTES ON A COLLABORATION MS KNT 65 11
   PARTNERS IN WONDER   ELLISON, HARLAN   AC
SEEING   SS
   ANDROMEDA I   WESTON, PETER   OA
   BEST SCIENCE FICTION OF THE YEAR, THE NO. 6
                                          CARR, TERRY   AN
   IDES OF TOMORROW, THE   CARR, TERRY   OA
SHATTERDAY   SS   GLR 75 09
   NEBULA AWARD STORIES 11   LE GUIN, URSULA K.   AN
SHATTERED LIKE A GLASS GOBLIN   SS   ORB 68 04
   ABOVE THE HUMAN LANDSCAPE   MCNELLY & STOVER   AN
   BEAST THAT SHOUTED LOVE AT THE HEART OF THE WORLD, THE
                                          ELLISON, HARLAN   AC
   BEST FROM ORBIT, THE   KNIGHT, DAMON   AN
   DEATHBIRD STORIES   ELLISON, HARLAN   AC
   ORBIT 4   KNIGHT, DAMON   OA
SILENT IN GEHENNA   SS   MWS 71
   APPROACHING OBLIVION   ELLISON, HARLAN   AC
   BEST SCIENCE FICTION FOR 1972   POHL, FREDERIK   AN
   FUTURE NOW, THE   HOSKINS, ROBERT   AN
   MANY WORLDS OF SCIENCE FICTION, THE   BOVA, BEN   OA
   2020 VISION   POURNELLE, JERRY   AN
SILVER CORRIDOR, THE   NV   INF 56 10
   ALONE AGAINST TOMORROW   ELLISON, HARLAN   AC
   ELLISON WONDERLAND   ELLISON, HARLAN   AC
SKY IS BURNING, THE   SS   IFS 58 08
   ELLISON WONDERLAND   ELLISON, HARLAN   AC
   FROM THE LAND OF FEAR   ELLISON, HARLAN   AC
   TOUCH OF INFINITY, A   ELLISON, HARLAN   DC

ELLISON, HARLAN   (CONTINUED)
SLEEPER WITH STILL HANDS, THE (SEE ASLEEP: WITH STILL HANDS)
                                          TC
SLEEPING DOGS   SS   ASF 74 10
   BEST SCIENCE FICTION STORIES OF THE YEAR (1974)
                                          DEL REY, LESTER   AN
   PAINGOD AND OTHER DELUSIONS (THIRD EDITION ADDS:)
                                          ELLISON, HARLAN   AC
SOLDIER (SOLDIER FROM TOMORROW)   SS   FUN 57 10
   FROM THE LAND OF FEAR   ELLISON, HARLAN   AC
   THEMES IN SCIENCE FICTION   KELLEY, LEO P.   AN
SOLDIER (TELEVISION SCRIPT VERSION)   PL   ABC 64 09
   FROM THE LAND OF FEAR   ELLISON, HARLAN   AC
SONG OF THE SOUL, THE   IN
   ALONE AGAINST TOMORROW   ELLISON, HARLAN   AC
SONG THE ZOMBIE SANG, THE   SS C CMP 70 12
   EARTH'S OTHER SHADOW   SILVERBERG, ROBERT   AC
   PARTNERS IN WONDER   ELLISON, HARLAN   AC
SONS OF JANUS   IN
   PARTNERS IN WONDER   ELLISON, HARLAN   AC
SPERO MELIORA   IN
   *PAINGOD AND OTHER DELUSIONS   ELLISON, HARLAN   AC
STATUS QUO AT TROYDEN'S   SS   SMM 58 11
   NO DOORS, NO WINDOWS (STORIES REWRITTEN)
                                          ELLISON, HARLAN   AC
STREET SCENE (DUNDERBIRD)   NV C GAL 69 01
   PARTNERS IN WONDER   ELLISON, HARLAN   AC
SURVIVOR NO. 1 (THE MAN WITH THE GREEN NOSE) SS C KNV 59 09
   PARTNERS IN WONDER   ELLISON, HARLAN   AC
TEDDY|CRAZY||SHOW|||, |||THE|| NV   ADM 68 10
   OVER THE EDGE   ELLISON, HARLAN   AC
THICKER THAN BLOOD   SS   MSM 58 02
   NO DOORS, NO WINDOWS (STORIES REWRITTEN)
                                          ELLISON, HARLAN   AC
THIRTY-TWO SOOTHSAYERS   IN   DVS 67 01
   DANGEROUS VISIONS   ELLISON, HARLAN   OA
TIME OF THE EYE, THE   SS   SMM 59 05
   ALONE AGAINST TOMORROW   ELLISON, HARLAN   AC
   FROM THE LAND OF FEAR   ELLISON, HARLAN   AC
TINY ALLY   SS   STN 57 10
   OVER THE EDGE   ELLISON, HARLAN   AC
TIRED OLD MAN   SS   MSM 76 01
   NO DOORS, NO WINDOWS (STORIES REWRITTEN)
                                          ELLISON, HARLAN   AC
TOE THE LINE   SS   SMM 57 06
   NO DOORS, NO WINDOWS (STORIES REWRITTEN)
                                          ELLISON, HARLAN   AC
TRY A DULL KNIFE   SS   FSF 68 10
   ALONE AGAINST TOMORROW   ELLISON, HARLAN   AC
   BEAST THAT SHOUTED LOVE AT THE HEART OF THE WORLD, THE
                                          ELLISON, HARLAN   AC
TWO INCHES IN TOMORROW'S COLUMN (AS ELLIS HART) SS ABR 65 21
   NO DOORS, NO WINDOWS (STORIES REWRITTEN)
                                          ELLISON, HARLAN   AC
UNIVERSE ACCORDING TO LAUMER, THE   IN
   NINE BY LAUMER   LAUMER, KEITH   AC
UNIVERSE OF ROBERT BLAKE, THE (ROBERT BLAKE'S UNIVERSE)
                                             SS   ROG 62 06
   *LOVE AIN'T NOTHING BUT SEX MISSPELLED ELLISON, HARLAN   AC
UP CHRISTOPHER TO MADNESS   SS C KNT 65 11
   PARTNERS IN WONDER   ELLISON, HARLAN   AC
VALERIE   SS   LAF 72 11
   LOVE AIN'T NOTHING BUT SEX MISSPELLED (REVISED)
                                          ELLISON, HARLAN   AC
VERY LAST DAY OF A GOOD WOMAN, THE (THE LAST DAY) SS ROG 58 11
   ALONE AGAINST TOMORROW   ELLISON, HARLAN   AC
   ELLISON WONDERLAND   ELLISON, HARLAN   AC
VOICE IN THE GARDEN, THE   SS   LGH 67 06
   FROM THE LAND OF FEAR   ELLISON, HARLAN   AC
WANTED IN SURGERY   NV   IFS 57 08
   *PAINGOD AND OTHER DELUSIONS   ELLISON, HARLAN   AC
WAVES IN RIO, THE   IN
   BEAST THAT SHOUTED LOVE AT THE HEART OF THE WORLD, THE
                                          ELLISON, HARLAN   AC
WE MOURN FOR ANYONE... (MOURNERS FOR HIRE)   SS   FAN 57 05
   FROM THE LAND OF FEAR   ELLISON, HARLAN   AC
WHAT I DID ON MY VACATION THIS SUMMER BY LITTLE BOBBY
HIRSCHHORN, AGE 27   SS   KNT 64 11
   *LOVE AIN'T NOTHING BUT SEX MISSPELLED ELLISON, HARLAN   AC
WHEN DREAMS BECOME NIGHTMARES: SOME CAUTIONARY NOTES ON THE
CLARION EXPERIENCE   AR   CLR 73 03
   CLARION III   WILSON, ROBIN SCOTT OA
WHEN I WAS A HIRED GUN   SS   LAF 73 06
   LOVE AIN'T NOTHING BUT SEX MISSPELLED (REVISED)
                                          ELLISON, HARLAN   AC
WHERE THE STRAY DREAMS GO   IN
   FROM THE LAND OF FEAR   ELLISON, HARLAN   AC
WHIMPER OF WHIPPED DOGS, THE   NV   BMR 73
   BAD MOON RISING   DISCH, THOMAS M.   OA
   DEATHBIRD STORIES   ELLISON, HARLAN   AC
   NO DOORS, NO WINDOWS (STORIES REWRITTEN)
                                          ELLISON, HARLAN   AC
   YEAR'S BEST HORROR STORIES: SERIES III, THE
                                          DAVIS, RICHARD   AN
WHITE ON WHITE   SS   KNT 68 11
   BEAST THAT SHOUTED LOVE AT THE HEART OF THE WORLD, THE
                                          ELLISON, HARLAN   AC
WHITE TRASH DON'T EXIST (MURDER BAIT)   SS   MTP 56 10
   NO DOORS, NO WINDOWS (STORIES REWRITTEN)
                                          ELLISON, HARLAN   AC
WHORE WITH A HEART OF IRON PYRITES: OR, WHERE DOES A WRITER GO
TO FIND A MAGGIE?   AR
   THOSE WHO CAN: A SCIENCE FICTION READER
                                          WILSON, ROBIN SCOTT AN
WIND FROM BEYOND THE MOUNTAINS, THE (SAVAGE WIND) SS AMZ 57 01
   ELLISON WONDERLAND   ELLISON, HARLAN   AC

ELLISON, HARLAN   EMSHWILLER, CAROL

ELLISON, HARLAN   (CONTINUED)
  WINE HAS BEEN LEFT OPEN TOO LONG AND THE MEMORY HAS
    GONE FLAT, THE   SS   UNI 76 06
    UNIVERSE 6   CARR, TERRY   OA
  WONDERBIRD   SS C INF 57 09
    PARTNERS IN WONDER   ELLISON, HARLAN   AC
  WORLD OF THE MYTH   NV   KNT 64 08
    I HAVE NO MOUTH, AND I MUST SCREAM   ELLISON, HARLAN   AC
  WORLDS TO KILL   NV   IFS 68 03
    BEAST THAT SHOUTED LOVE AT THE HEART OF THE WORLD, THE
                                     ELLISON, HARLAN   AC
  YELLOW STREAK HERO (SEE NIGHT VIGIL)   TC
  YOU ARE WHAT YOU WRITE   AR   CLR 72 02
    CLARION II   WILSON, ROBIN SCOTT   OA
  3 FACES OF FEAR: AN ESSAY   MS
    OVER THE EDGE   ELLISON, HARLAN   AC

ELMSLIE, KENWARD
  ACCIDENT VERTIGO   SS   PRV 71 50
    RUINS OF EARTH, THE   DISCH, THOMAS M.   AN

ELWOOD, ROGER AND VIC GHIDALIA
  ANDROIDS, TIME MACHINES AND BLUE GIRAFFES   AN H FOL 73
  LITTLE MONSTERS, THE   AN   MBB 69
  MORE LITTLE MONSTERS   AN   MAN 73
  YOUNG DEMONS   AN   AVN 72 04

ELWOOD, ROGER AND VIRGINIA KIDD
  SAVING WORLDS   OA H DBL 73
    ALSO AS "THE WOUNDED PLANET"

ELWOOD, ROGER AND SAM MOSKOWITZ
  ALIEN EARTH AND OTHER STORIES   AN   MCF 69
  STRANGE SIGNPOSTS   AN H HRW 66

ELWOOD, ROGER AND ROBERT SILVERBERG
  EPOCH   OA H BRK 75

ELWOOD, ROGER   SEE ALSO
    CO-EDITORS VIC GHIDALIA AND SAM MOSKOWITZ
  ADRIFT IN SPACE AND OTHER STORIES   OA H LER 74
  ALIEN WORLDS   AN   PBK 64 09
  AND WALK NOW GENTLY THROUGH THE FIRE...   OA H CHL 72
  BERSERKERS, THE   OA H TRI 74
  CHILDREN OF INFINITY   OA H WAT 73
  CHRONICLES OF A COMER AND OTHER RELIGIOUS SCIENCE FICTION
    STORIES   AN L JKP 74
  CONTINUUM 1   OA H PUT 74
  CONTINUUM 2   OA H BKP 74
  CONTINUUM 3   OA H BKP 74
  CONTINUUM 4   OA H BKP 75
  CRISIS   OA H NEL 74
  DEMON KIND   OA   AVN 73 03
  DYSTOPIAN VISIONS   OA H PRH 75
  FAR SIDE OF TIME, THE   OA H DOM 74
  FLAME TREE PLANET   OA   CNC 73
  FRONTIERS 1: TOMORROW'S ALTERNATIVES   OA H MAC 73
  FRONTIERS 2: THE NEW MIND   OA H MAC 73
  FUTURE CITY   OA H TRI 73
  FUTURE CORRUPTION   OA   WPB 75 01
  FUTURE KIN   OA H DBL 74
  FUTURE QUEST   OA   AVN 73 09
  FUTURELOVE   OA H BML 77
  GIFTS OF ASTI AND OTHER STORIES OF SCIENCE FICTION, THE
                                                AN H FOL 75
  GRADUATED ROBOT AND OTHER STORIES, THE   OA H LER 74
  IN THE WAKE OF MAN   OA H BML 75
  INVASION OF THE ROBOTS   AN   PBK 65 04
  JOURNEY TO ANOTHER STAR AND OTHER STORIES   OA H LER 74
  KILLER PLANTS AND OTHER STORIES, THE   OA H LER 74
  LEARNING MAZE AND OTHER STORIES, THE   OA H MES 74
  LONG NIGHT OF WAITING AND OTHER STORIES   OA H AUR 74
  MANY WORLDS OF ANDRE NORTON, THE (LISTED UNDER ANDRE NORTON)
                                                EC H CHL 74
  MANY WORLDS OF POUL ANDERSON, THE (LISTED UNDER POUL ANDERSON)
                                                EC H CHL 74
  MIND ANGEL AND OTHER STORIES, THE   OA H LER 74
  MISSING WORLD AND OTHER STORIES, THE   OA H LER 74
  MORE SCIENCE FICTION TALES   OA H RAN 74
  NEW MIND, THE   OA H MAC 73
    SEE "FRONTIERS 2: THE NEW MIND"
  NIGHT OF THE SPHINX AND OTHER STORIES   OA H LER 74
  OMEGA   OA H WKR 73
  OTHER SIDE OF TOMORROW, THE   OA H RDM 73
  SCIENCE FICTION ADVENTURES FROM WAY OUT   OA L WHT 74
  SCIENCE FICTION TALES   OA H RAN 74
  SHOWCASE   OA H HRP 73
  SIGNS AND WONDERS   OA H REV 72
  SIX SCIENCE FICTION PLAYS   AN   WSP 76 01
  STRANGE GODS   OA   PKT 74 09
  SURVIVAL FROM INFINITY   OA H WAT 74
  TEN TOMORROWS   OA   FGM 73 09
  TOMORROW: NEW WORLDS OF SCIENCE FICTION   OA H EVN 76
  TOMORROW'S ALTERNATIVES   OA H MAC 73
    SEE "FRONTIERS 1: TOMORROW'S ALTERNATIVES"
  TUNNEL AND OTHER STORIES, THE   OA H LER 74
  VISIONS OF TOMORROW   AN   PKT 76 11
  WOUNDED PLANET, THE   AN   BAN 74 08
    SEE "SAVING WORLDS"
  ARIEL   SS   NDM 74 04
    NEW DIMENSIONS 4   SILVERBERG, ROBERT   OA
    VISIONS OF TOMORROW   ELWOOD, ROGER   AN
  EDITOR'S INTRODUCTION   IN
    ALIEN WORLDS   ELWOOD, ROGER   AN
  EDITOR'S NOTE   IN
    SURVIVAL FROM INFINITY   ELWOOD, ROGER   OA

ELWOOD, ROGER   (CONTINUED)
  EDITOR'S PREFACE   IN
    FUTURE CORRUPTION   ELWOOD, ROGER   OA
  FEAST   SS   FCR 75
    FUTURE CORRUPTION   ELWOOD, ROGER   OA
  FOREWORD   IN
    CHILDREN OF INFINITY   ELWOOD, ROGER   OA
  CHRONICLES OF A COMER AND OTHER RELIGIOUS SCIENCE FICTION
    STORIES   ELWOOD, ROGER   AN
  FAR SIDE OF TIME, THE   ELWOOD, ROGER   OA
  INTRODUCTION   IN
    BERSERKERS, THE   ELWOOD, ROGER   OA
    CONTINUUM 1   ELWOOD, ROGER   OA
    CONTINUUM 2   ELWOOD, ROGER   OA
    CONTINUUM 3   ELWOOD, ROGER   OA
    CRISIS   ELWOOD, ROGER   OA
    DEMON KIND   ELWOOD, ROGER   OA
    DYSTOPIAN VISIONS   ELWOOD, ROGER   OA
    FUTURE KIN   ELWOOD, ROGER   OA
    INVASION OF THE ROBOTS   ELWOOD, ROGER   AN
    LEARNING MAZE AND OTHER STORIES, THE ELWOOD, ROGER   OA
    OTHER SIDE OF TOMORROW, THE   ELWOOD, ROGER   OA
    SCIENCE FICTION ADVENTURES FROM WAY OUT
                                    ELWOOD, ROGER   OA
    SIGNS AND WONDERS   ELWOOD, ROGER   OA
    SIX SCIENCE FICTION PLAYS   ELWOOD, ROGER   AN
  INTRODUCTION   IN C
    EPOCH   ELWOOD & SILVERBERG   OA
  OTHER SIDE OF THE CURTAIN- A REFLECTION OF THE FUTURE, THE
                                                IN C
    STRANGE SIGNPOSTS   ELWOOD & MOSKOWITZ   AN
  PREFACE   IN
    ANDROIDS, TIME MACHINES AND BLUE GIRAFFES
                                    ELWOOD & GHIDALIA   AN
    FRONTIERS 1: TOMORROW'S ALTERNATIVES ELWOOD, ROGER   OA
    FRONTIERS 2: THE NEW MIND   ELWOOD, ROGER   OA
    FUTURE CITY   ELWOOD, ROGER   OA
    MANY WORLDS OF BARRY MALZBERG, THE MALZBERG, BARRY N. AC
  TOMORROW: NEW WORLDS OF SCIENCE FICTION
                                    ELWOOD, ROGER   OA
  THROWBACK   SS   STG 74
    STRANGE GODS   ELWOOD, ROGER   OA

ELY, DAVID
  ACADEMY, THE   SS   PBY 65 06
    FANTASY: THE LITERATURE OF THE MARVELOUS
                                    KELLEY, LEO P.   AN
    PLAYBOY BOOK OF HORROR AND THE SUPERNATURAL, THE
                                    PLAYBOY, EDITORS OF   AN
    WEIRD SHOW   PLAYBOY, EDITORS OF   AN
  HUMAN FACTOR, THE   SS   SEP 63 11
    SCIENCE FACT/FICTION   FARRELL/GAGE/&   AN

EMANUEL, VICTOR R.   SEE PSEUD. VICTOR ROUSSEAU

EMMETT, ELIZABETH
  ENCHANTMENT   SS   SEP 60 10
    6TH ANNUAL OF THE YEAR'S BEST S-F, THE MERRIL, JUDITH AN

EMSHWILLER, CAROL
  JOY IN OUR CAUSE   AC H HPR 74
  AL   SS   ORB 72 10
    BEST FROM ORBIT, THE   KNIGHT, DAMON   AN
    JOY IN OUR CAUSE   EMSHWILLER, CAROL   AC
    ORBIT 10   KNIGHT, DAMON   OA
  ANIMAL   SS   ORB 68 04
    JOY IN OUR CAUSE   EMSHWILLER, CAROL   AC
    ORBIT   4   KNIGHT, DAMON   OA
  AUTOBIOGRAPHY   SS
    JOY IN OUR CAUSE   EMSHWILLER, CAROL   AC
  BIOGRAPHY OF AN UNCIRCUMCISED MAN (INCLUDING INTERVIEW)
                                                SS
    JOY IN OUR CAUSE   EMSHWILLER, CAROL   AC
  BUT SOFT, WHAT LIGHT...   SS   FSF 66 04
    SF: AUTHORS' CHOICE 4   HARRISON, HARRY   AN
  CHICKEN ICARUS (A DREAM OF FLYING)   SS   CAV 66
    JOY IN OUR CAUSE   EMSHWILLER, CAROL   AC
    SF12   MERRIL, JUDITH   AN
  CHILDHOOD OF THE HUMAN HERO, THE   SS   SCS 73
    JOY IN OUR CAUSE   EMSHWILLER, CAROL   AC
    NEBULA AWARD STORIES 9   WILHELM, KATE   AN
    SHOWCASE   ELWOOD, ROGER   OA
  DAY AT THE BEACH   SS   FSF 59 08
    ABC OF SCIENCE FICTION, AN   BOARDMAN, TOM JR.   AN
    FANTASY: THE LITERATURE OF THE MARVELOUS
                                    KELLEY, LEO P.   AN
    SF: THE BEST OF THE BEST   MERRIL, JUDITH   AN
    5TH ANNUAL OF THE YEAR'S BEST S-F, THE MERRIL, JUDITH AN
  DEBUT   SS   ORB 70 06
    ORBIT   6   KNIGHT, DAMON   OA
  DESTINATIONS, PREMONITIONS AND THE NATURE OF ANXIETY
                                                SS
    JOY IN OUR CAUSE   EMSHWILLER, CAROL   AC
  DOG IS DEAD   SS
    JOY IN OUR CAUSE   EMSHWILLER, CAROL   AC
  DREAM OF FLYING, A (SEE CHICKEN ICARUS)   TC
  EOHIPPUS   SS   TRV
    JOY IN OUR CAUSE   EMSHWILLER, CAROL   AC
  ESCAPE IS NO ACCIDENT   SS
    2076: THE AMERICAN TRICENTENNIAL BRYANT, EDWARD   OA
  HUNTING MACHINE, THE   SS   SFS 57 05
    BEST SCIENCE FICTION STORIES AND NOVELS: 9TH SERIES
                                    DIKTY, T. E.   AN
    SCIENCE FICTION INVENTIONS   KNIGHT, DAMON   AN
  I LOVE YOU   SS   EPO
    JOY IN OUR CAUSE   EMSHWILLER, CAROL   AC

EMSHWILLER, CAROL   (CONTINUED)
  INSTITUTE, THE   SS   ANA 70
    ALCHEMY AND ACADEME   MCCAFFREY, ANNE   OA
  JOY IN OUR CAUSE   SS
    JOY IN OUR CAUSE   EMSHWILLER, CAROL   AC
  LIB   SS   NWS 68 03
    BEST SF STORIES FROM NEW WORLDS 6   MOORCOCK, MICHAEL AN
    JOY IN OUR CAUSE   EMSHWILLER, CAROL   AC
  MAYBE ANOTHER LONG MARCH ACROSS CHINA 80,000 STRONG
                                                    SS
    JOY IN OUR CAUSE   EMSHWILLER, CAROL   AC
  METHAPYRILENE HYDROCHLORIDE SOMETIMES HELPS   SS   NWS 68 07
    JOY IN OUR CAUSE   EMSHWILLER, CAROL   AC
  PELT   SS   FSF 58 11
    POCKETFUL OF STARS, A   KNIGHT, DAMON   AN
    SF: THE BEST OF THE BEST   MERRIL, JUDITH   AN
    SF:59, THE YEAR'S GREATEST SCIENCE FICTION AND FANTASY
                                  MERRIL, JUDITH   AN
  PENINSULA   SS   RRV
    JOY IN OUR CAUSE   EMSHWILLER, CAROL   AC
  POSSIBLE EPISODE IN THE PICARESQUE ADVENTURES OF MR. J.H.B.
    MONSTROSEE, A   SS   QRK 71 02
    QUARK/2   DELANY & HACKER   OA
  QUEEN OF SLEEP, THE   SS   NDR
    JOY IN OUR CAUSE   EMSHWILLER, CAROL   AC
  SEX AND/OR MR. MORRISON   SS   DVS 67 01
    DANGEROUS VISIONS   ELLISON, HARLAN   OA
    JOY IN OUR CAUSE   EMSHWILLER, CAROL   AC
    WOMEN OF WONDER   SARGENT, PAMELA   AN
  STRANGERS   SS   BMR 73
    BAD MOON RISING   DISCH, THOMAS M.   OA
    JOY IN OUR CAUSE   EMSHWILLER, CAROL   AC
  TO THE ASSOCIATION   SS
    JOY IN OUR CAUSE   EMSHWILLER, CAROL   AC
  WOMAN WAITING   SS   ORB 70 07
    ORBIT   7   KNIGHT, DAMON   OA
  YES, VIRGINIA   SS   TRV
    JOY IN OUR CAUSE   EMSHWILLER, CAROL   AC

EMSHWILLER, ED
  2001: A SPACE ODYSSEY- REVIEW 3   MR   FSF 68 08
    BEST SF: 1968   HARRISON & ALDISS   AN

ENDORE, GUY
  DAY OF THE DRAGON, THE   NV   AFR 47 02
    ZOO 2000   YOLEN, JANE   AN
  MEN OF IRON (1940)   SS   FSF 49 FL
    DECADE OF FANTASY AND SCIENCE FICTION, A
                                  MILLS, ROBERT P.   AN
    HUMAN-MACHINES   SCORTIA & ZEBROWSKI AN

ENEVER, J. E.
  GIANT METEOR IMPACT   AR   ASF 66 03
    ANALOG 6   CAMPBELL, JOHN W. JR AN

ENGDAHL, SYLVIA AND RICK ROBERSON
  UNIVERSE AHEAD   AN H ATH 76

ENGDAHL, SYLVIA
  ANYWHERE, ANYWHEN   OA H ATH 76
  BECKONING TRAIL, THE   NV C NEW 76 AN
    UNIVERSE AHEAD   ENGDAHL & ROBERSON AN
  FOREWORD   IN
    ANYWHERE, ANYWHEN   ENGDAHL, SYLVIA   OA
  PREFACE   IN
    UNIVERSE AHEAD   ENGDAHL & ROBERSON AN
  TIMESCAPE   NV C
    ANYWHERE, ANYWHEN   ENGDAHL, SYLVIA   OA

ENGLAND, GEORGE A.
  DARKNESS AND DAWN   NO H SMY 14
    AFTERGLOW, THE   NO   CSB 13 06
    DARKNESS AND DAWN   ENGLAND, GEORGE A.   NO
    BEYOND THE GREAT OBLIVION   NO   CSB 13 01
    DARKNESS AND DAWN   ENGLAND, GEORGE A.   NO
    DARKNESS AND DAWN   NO   CSB 12 01
    DARKNESS AND DAWN   ENGLAND, GEORGE A.   NO
    UNDER THE MOONS OF MARS   MOSKOWITZ, SAM   AN
  JUNE 6, 2016   NV   COL 16 04
    WHEN WOMEN RULE   MOSKOWITZ, SAM   AN
  MAN WITH THE GLASS HEART, THE   SS   CVL 11 05
    FANTASTIC PULPS, THE   HAINING, PETER   AN
  MESSAGE FROM THE MOON, A   SS   PRS 07 04
    WORLDS APART   LOCKE, GEORGE   AN
  THING FROM OUTSIDE, THE (AMZ 26 04)   SS   SAI 23 04
    *STRANGE PORTS OF CALL   DERLETH, AUGUST   AN

ERCKMANN-CHATRIAN
  HANS SCHNAP'S SPY-GLASS   SS
    STRANGE SIGNPOSTS   ELWOOD & MOSKOWITZ AN

ERICSON, MARCIA
  ENCHANTED POOL, THE   NV
    STAR TREK: THE NEW VOYAGES   MARSHAK, S&CULBREATH OA

ERNSBERGER, GEORGE   SEE ALSO   CO-EDITOR DONALD A. WOLLHEIM
  FOREWORD   IN
    AVON FANTASY READER, THE   WOLLHEIM &ERNSBERGER AN
    SECOND AVON FANTASY READER, THE   WOLLHEIM &ERNSBERGER AN

ERNST, MAX
  EUROPE AFTER THE RAIN   IL
    SCIENCE FICTION   BRODKIN & PEARSON   AN
  PHASES OF THE NIGHT, THE   IL
    SCIENCE FICTION   BRODKIN & PEARSON   AN

ERNST, MAX   (CONTINUED)
  SEA, THE   IL
    SCIENCE FICTION   BRODKIN & PEARSON   AN
  SUN AND FOREST   IL
    SCIENCE FICTION   BRODKIN & PEARSON   AN
  WHOLE CITY, THE   IL
    SCIENCE FICTION   BRODKIN & PEARSON   AN

ERNST, PAUL
  ESCAPE   SS   WRT 38 07
    OTHER WORLDS, THE   STONG, PHILIP D.   AN
  MICROSCOPIC GIANTS, THE   SS   TWS 36 10
    FROM OFF THIS WORLD   MARGULIES & FRIEND AN
    SCIENCE FICTION TERROR TALES CONKLIN, GROFF   AN
  NOTHING HAPPENS ON THE MOON   SS   ASF 39 02
    OMNIBUS OF SCIENCE FICTION   CONKLIN, GROFF   AN
    STRANGE TRAVELS IN SCIENCE FICTION   CONKLIN, GROFF AN
    TALES OF SCIENCE FICTION   BALL, BRIAN N.   AN
  THING IN THE POND, THE   SS   ASF 34 06
    *MY BEST SCIENCE FICTION STORY   MARGULIES & FRIEND AN
  WHY I SELECTED THE THING IN THE POND   AI
    *MY BEST SCIENCE FICTION STORY   MARGULIES & FRIEND AN
  32ND OF MAY, THE   SS   ASF 35 04
    *BEST OF SCIENCE FICTION   CONKLIN, GROFF   AN

ESCHER, M. C.
  BUTTERFLIES   IL
    SCIENCE FICTION   BRODKIN & PEARSON   AN
  PUDDLE   IL
    SCIENCE FICTION   BRODKIN & PEARSON   AN
  UP AND DOWN   IL
    SCIENCE FICTION   BRODKIN & PEARSON   AN

ESENWEIN, J. BERG
  ADVENTURES TO COME   OA H MLB 37

ESHBACH, LLOYD A.
  TYRANT OF TIME, THE   AC H FPS 55
    CAULDRON OF LIFE, THE (THE CAULDRON) SS   SRS 40 04
    TYRANT OF TIME, THE   ESHBACH, LLOYD A.   AC
    CITY OF DREAD, THE   SS
    TYRANT OF TIME, THE   ESHBACH, LLOYD A.   AC
    DUST   SS   MSS 39 08
    SCIENCE FICTION ROLL OF HONOR, THE   POHL, FREDERIK AN
    GOD OF LIGHT (SEE THE LIGHT FROM BEYOND)   TC
    GOD THAT SCIENCE MADE, THE (SEE THE PLACE OF ORCHIDS)
                                                    TC
    LIGHT FROM BEYOND, THE (GOD OF LIGHT) SS   TWS 44 SU
    TYRANT OF TIME, THE   ESHBACH, LLOYD A.   AC
    MAN WITH THE HOUR GLASS, THE   SS   MVT 34 05
    GARDEN OF FEAR AND OTHER STORIES, THE CRAWFORD, WILLIAM L. AN
    METEOR MINERS, THE   SS   AMZ 35 12
    TYRANT OF TIME, THE   ESHBACH, LLOYD A.   AC
    PLACE OF ORCHIDS, THE (THE GOD THAT SCIENCE MADE) SS SFS 39 08
    TYRANT OF TIME, THE   ESHBACH, LLOYD A.   AC
    SINGING BLADES   SS   SRS 40 02
    TYRANT OF TIME, THE   ESHBACH, LLOYD A.   AC
    SPACEWAYS INCIDENT   SS
    TYRANT OF TIME, THE   ESHBACH, LLOYD A.   AC
    TIME CONQUEROR, THE (SEE THE TYRANT OF TIME)   TC
    TYRANT OF TIME, THE (THE TIME CONQUEROR) SS   WOS 32 07
    TYRANT OF TIME, THE   ESHBACH, LLOYD A.   AC
    VOICE FROM THE ETHER, THE   NV   AMZ 31 05
    HISTORY OF THE SCIENCE FICTION MAGAZINE, THE   PART 1 1926-1935
                                  ASHLEY, MICHAEL   AN

ETCHISON, DENNIS
  BLACK SUN   SS   ORB 74 13
    ORBIT   13   KNIGHT, DAMON   OA
  BRIGHT ARE THE STARS THAT SHINE, DARK IS THE SKY SS   NWR 68 11
    NEW WRITINGS IN SF. 11   CARNELL, JOHN   OA
  COUNTRY OF THE STRONG, THE   SS   SEV 62
    NEW WRITINGS IN SF. 4   CARNELL, JOHN   OA
  DAMECHILD   SS   FIN 70
    FUTURE IS NOW, THE   NOLAN, WILLIAM F.   OA
  FIRES OF NIGHT, THE   SS   NEW 65 AN
    PSEUDO PEOPLE, THE   NOLAN, WILLIAM F.   AN
  ODD BOY OUT   SS   ESC 61
    NEW WRITINGS IN SF. 2   CARNELL, JOHN   OA

EUSTACE, ROBERT   PSEUD. FOR EUSTACE BARTON
  WHERE THE AIR QUIVERED   SS C SND 98 12
    SCIENCE FICTION BY GASLIGHT   MOSKOWITZ, SAM   AN

EUSTIS, HELEN
  MR. DEATH AND THE REDHEADED WOMAN   SS   SEP 50 02
    TIMELESS STORIES FOR TODAY AND TOMORROW
                                  BRADBURY, RAY   AN

EVANS, CHRISTOPHER
  CHATTING WITH COMPUTERS (REVISED)   AR   DSP 73 10
    BEYOND THIS HORIZON   CARRELL, CHRISTOPHER OA

EVANS, DEAN
  NOT A CREATURE WAS STIRRING   SS   GAL 51 12
    SHADOW OF TOMORROW   POHL, FREDERIK   AN

EVANS, DON
  SUMMONS, THE   SS   UNK 39 06
    FROM UNKNOWN WORLDS   CAMPBELL, JOHN W. JR   AN

EVANS, E. EVERETT
  SHED, THE   SS   ASR 53 01
    *STORIES FOR TOMORROW   SLOANE, WILLIAM   AN
    TALES BEYOND TIME   DE CAMP, L. S.&C.   AN
    ZACHERLEY'S VULTURE STEW   ZACHERLEY   AN

EVANS, GLADYS   FARMER, PHILIP JOSE

EVANS, GLADYS
  TRANSLATION   MS
    JOURNEY ACROSS THREE WORLDS   ANONYMOUS   AN

EVANS, I. O.
  JULES VERNE- MASTER OF SCIENCE FICTION (LISTED UNDER
    JULES VERNE)   EC H SID 56
  SCIENCE FICTION THROUGH THE AGES 1   AN   PTH 66
  SCIENCE FICTION THROUGH THE AGES 2   AN   PTH 66
  YESTERDAY AND TOMORROW (LISTED UNDER JULES VERNE) EC H ARC 64
  FLINTIES, THE   SS
    SCIENCE FICTION THROUGH THE AGES 2 EVANS, I. O.   AN
  INTRODUCTION   IN
    JULES VERNE- MASTER OF SCIENCE FICTION VERNE, JULES   AC
    SCIENCE FICTION THROUGH THE AGES 1 EVANS, I. O.   AN
    SCIENCE FICTION THROUGH THE AGES 2 EVANS, I. O.   AN
    YESTERDAY AND TOMORROW   VERNE, JULES   AC

EVANS, MIKE
  MUSHROOMS   PM   69
    HOLDING YOUR EIGHT HANDS   LUCIE-SMITH, EDWARD   AN
    SCIENCE FICTION   BRODKIN & PEARSON   AN
  WE'LL ALL BE SPACEMEN BEFORE WE DIE   PM   NWS 68 10
    HOLDING YOUR EIGHT HANDS   LUCIE-SMITH, EDWARD   AN
    SCIENCE FICTION   BRODKIN & PEARSON   AN

EVERETT, WALKER G.
  WOMAN IN GRAY, THE   SS   WRT 35 06
    OTHER WORLDS, THE   STONG, PHILIP D.   AN

EXTER, MAUREEN
  NIGHT OF THE SPHINX   SS
    NIGHT OF THE SPHINX AND OTHER STORIES ELWOOD, ROGER   OA
  SPACERS' DANCE, THE   NV
    CRISIS   ELWOOD, ROGER   OA

FABRICANT, NOAH D.   SEE ALSO   CO-EDITOR GROFF CONKLIN
  INTRODUCTION   IN C
    GREAT SCIENCE FICTION ABOUT DOCTORS CONKLIN, G&FABRICANT AN

FADIMAN, CLIFTON
  FANTASIA MATHEMATICA   AN H SAS 58
  MATHEMATICAL MAGPIE, THE   AN H SAS 62
  INTRODUCTION   IN
    ACROSS THE SEA OF STARS   CLARKE, ARTHUR C.   AC
    FANTASIA MATHEMATICA   FADIMAN, CLIFTON   AN
    GREAT STORIES OF SCIENCE FICTION LEINSTER, MURRAY   AN
    MATHEMATICAL MAGPIE, THE   FADIMAN, CLIFTON   AN

FAINLIGHT, RUTH
  REPORT, A   PM   69
    HOLDING YOUR EIGHT HANDS   LUCIE-SMITH, EDWARD AN

FAIRFAX, JOHN
  ALL ADAM AGAIN   PM
    BEYOND THIS HORIZON   CARRELL, CHRISTOPHER OA
  BEYOND ASTRONAUT   PM   69
    HOLDING YOUR EIGHT HANDS   LUCIE-SMITH, EDWARD AN
  TWELVE STATIONS FROM GEMINI   PM
    BEYOND THIS HORIZON   CARRELL, CHRISTOPHER OA

FAIRMAN, PAUL W.
  FORGETFUL ROBOT, THE   OC H HRW 68
  BROTHERS BEYOND THE VOID   SS   FAD 52 03
    *WORLDS OF TOMORROW   DERLETH, AUGUST   AN
  BROWN PACKAGE, THE   SS
    FORGETFUL ROBOT, THE   FAIRMAN, PAUL W.   OC
  CULTURE FOR THE PLANETS   SS
    FORGETFUL ROBOT, THE   FAIRMAN, PAUL W.   OC
  DELENDA EST CARTHAGO   SS
    FORGETFUL ROBOT, THE   FAIRMAN, PAUL W.   OC
  GALLANT LADY, THE   SS
    FORGETFUL ROBOT, THE   FAIRMAN, PAUL W.   OC
  INTERLUDE IN THE DESERT   SS
    FORGETFUL ROBOT, THE   FAIRMAN, PAUL W.   OC
  LONG HOP   SS
    FORGETFUL ROBOT, THE   FAIRMAN, PAUL W.   OC
  LOST IN A JUNKYARD   SS
    FORGETFUL ROBOT, THE   FAIRMAN, PAUL W.   OC
  MASTERMIND OF ZARK   SS
    FORGETFUL ROBOT, THE   FAIRMAN, PAUL W.   OC
  MINEFIELD, THE   SS
    FORGETFUL ROBOT, THE   FAIRMAN, PAUL W.   OC
  MISSING SYMBOL, THE   SS   FAN 52 12
    FIRST FLIGHTS TO THE MOON   CLEMENT, HAL   AN
  NOT BORN TO GREATNESS   SS
    FORGETFUL ROBOT, THE   FAIRMAN, PAUL W.   OC
  PHANTOMS OF ZARK   SS
    FORGETFUL ROBOT, THE   FAIRMAN, PAUL W.   OC
  PIT, THE   SS
    FORGETFUL ROBOT, THE   FAIRMAN, PAUL W.   OC
  ROBOTS SHOULD STICK TOGETHER   SS
    FORGETFUL ROBOT, THE   FAIRMAN, PAUL W.   OC
  SPACE MUSEUM, THE   SS
    FORGETFUL ROBOT, THE   FAIRMAN, PAUL W.   OC
  THOSE REMARKABLE RAVENCRAFTS   SS
    FORGETFUL ROBOT, THE   FAIRMAN, PAUL W.   OC

FANCETT, ELIZABETH
  MUSEUM PIECE   SS   SPC 73 01
    SPACE 1   DAVIS, RICHARD   OA
  REFUGEES, THE   NV   SPC 74 02
    SPACE 2   DAVIS, RICHARD   OA
  STAR-BOY   NV   ADS 75 02
    ARMADA SCI-FI TWO   DAVIS, RICHARD   OA

FANCETT, ELIZABETH   (CONTINUED)
  WHEN MORNING COMES   SS   69
    YEAR'S BEST HORROR STORIES, THE DAVIS, RICHARD   AN
  WHO IS CINDY?   SS   ADS 75 01
    ARMADA SCI-FI ONE   DAVIS, RICHARD   OA

FARBER, JERRY
  GORMAN   SS   69
    BEST SF: 1970   HARRISON & ALDISS   AN
    SCHOOL AND SOCIETY THROUGH SCIENCE FICTION
                                OLANDER/GREENBERG/& AN

FARLEY, CAROL
  DILOPS ARE COMING, THE   NV
    ANYWHERE, ANYWHEN   ENGDAHL, SYLVIA   OA

FARLEY, RALPH MILNE PSEUD. FOR ROGER SHERMAN HOAR
  OMNIBUS OF TIME, THE   AC H FPB 50
  STRANGE WORLDS   AC H FPB 52
  AFTER MATH   AR
    OMNIBUS OF TIME, THE   FARLEY, RALPH MILNE AC
  END OF THE WORLD, THE   SS
    OMNIBUS OF TIME, THE   FARLEY, RALPH MILNE AC
  GOLDEN CITY, THE   EX   ARG 33 05
    OMNIBUS OF TIME, THE   FARLEY, RALPH MILNE AC
  HIDDEN UNIVERSE, THE   EX   AMZ 39 11
    OMNIBUS OF TIME, THE   FARLEY, RALPH MILNE AC
  HIDDEN UNIVERSE, THE   NO   AMZ 39 11
    STRANGE WORLDS   FARLEY, RALPH MILNE AC
  HOUSE OF ECSTASY, THE   SS   WRT 38 04
    OTHER WORLDS, THE   STONG, PHILIP D.   AN
  I KILLER HITLER   SS   WRT 41 07
    OMNIBUS OF TIME, THE   FARLEY, RALPH MILNE AC
  IMMORTALITY OF ALAN WHIDDEN, THE   SS   AMZ 42 02
    OMNIBUS OF TIME, THE   FARLEY, RALPH MILNE AC
  INVISIBLE BOMBER, THE   SS   AMZ 38 06
    OMNIBUS OF TIME, THE   FARLEY, RALPH MILNE AC
  LIQUID LIFE   NV   TWS 36 10
    *BEST OF SCIENCE FICTION   CONKLIN, GROFF   AN
    GREAT STORIES OF SCIENCE FICTION LEINSTER, MURRAY   AN
    MUTANTS   SILVERBERG, ROBERT   AN
  LIVING MIST, THE (SEE WE, THE MIST)   TC
  MAN WHO COULD TURN BACK THE CLOCK, THE   SS
    OMNIBUS OF TIME, THE   FARLEY, RALPH MILNE AC
  MAN WHO LIVED BACKWARDS, THE   SS
    OMNIBUS OF TIME, THE   FARLEY, RALPH MILNE AC
  MAN WHO MET HIMSELF, THE   SS
    OMNIBUS OF TIME, THE   FARLEY, RALPH MILNE AC
  MONTH A MINUTE, A   SS   TWS 37 12
    OMNIBUS OF TIME, THE   FARLEY, RALPH MILNE AC
  RADIO MAN, THE   NO   AAS 24 06
    STRANGE WORLDS   FARLEY, RALPH MILNE AC
  RADIO WAR, THE (MISSING FIRST CHAPTER OF)   EX   ARG 32 07
    OMNIBUS OF TIME, THE   FARLEY, RALPH MILNE AC
  RESCUE INTO THE PAST   SS   AMZ 40 10
    OMNIBUS OF TIME, THE   FARLEY, RALPH MILNE AC
  REVENGE OF THE GREAT WHITE LODGE, THE   SS
    OMNIBUS OF TIME, THE   FARLEY, RALPH MILNE AC
  STRANDED IN TIME   SS
    OMNIBUS OF TIME, THE   FARLEY, RALPH MILNE AC
  TIME FOR SALE   SS   AMZ 38 08
    ANDROIDS, TIME MACHINES AND BLUE GIRAFFES
                                ELWOOD & GHIDALIA   AN
    OMNIBUS OF TIME, THE   FARLEY, RALPH MILNE AC
  TIME TRAVELLER, THE   SS   WRT 31 08
    OMNIBUS OF TIME, THE   FARLEY, RALPH MILNE AC
  TIME-WISE GUY, THE   SS   AMZ 40 05
    OMNIBUS OF TIME, THE   FARLEY, RALPH MILNE AC
  WE, THE MIST (THE LIVING MIST)   NV   AMZ 40 08
    STRANGE WORLDS   FARLEY, RALPH MILNE AC

FARMER, PHILIP JOSE
  ALLEY GOD, THE   AC   BAL 62
  BOOK OF PHILIP JOSE FARMER, THE   AC   DAW 73 07
  CELESTIAL BLUEPRINT, THE   DC   ACE 62
  DOWN IN THE BLACK GANG AND OTHER STORIES   AC H DBL 71
  STRANGE RELATIONS   AC   BAL 60
  AFTER KING KONG FELL   SS   OMG 73
    BEST SF: 1974   HARRISON & ALDISS   AN
    NEBULA AWARD STORIES 10   GUNN, JAMES E.   AN
    OMEGA   ELWOOD, ROGER   OA
  ALLEY MAN, THE   NV   FSF 59 06
    ALLEY GOD, THE   FARMER, PHILIP JOSE AC
    BOOK OF PHILIP JOSE FARMER, THE FARMER, PHILIP JOSE AC
  ATTITUDES   NV   FSF 53 10
    BEST FROM FANTASY AND SCIENCE FICTION: 3
                                BOUCHER & MCCOMAS   AN
  BLASPHEMERS, THE   NV   GAL 64 04
    DOWN IN THE BLACK GANG AND OTHER STORIES
                                FARMER, PHILIP JOSE AC
  BOWL BIGGER THAN EARTH, A   NV   IFS 67 09
    DOWN IN THE BLACK GANG AND OTHER STORIES
                                FARMER, PHILIP JOSE AC
  BRASS AND GOLD, OR HORSE AND ZEPPELIN IN BEVERLY HILLS
                                                 SS   QRK 71 04
    BOOK OF PHILIP JOSE FARMER, THE FARMER, PHILIP JOSE AC
    QUARK/4   DELANY & HACKER   OA
  CAPTAIN'S DAUGHTER, THE (STRANGE COMPULSION)   SN   SFP 53 10
    ALLEY GOD, THE   FARMER, PHILIP JOSE AC
  CELESTIAL BLUEPRINT, THE   SS   FUN 54 07
    CELESTIAL BLUEPRINT, THE   FARMER, PHILIP JOSE DC
  DAUGHTER   SS   TWS 54 WI
    STRANGE RELATIONS   FARMER, PHILIP JOSE AC
  DON'T WASH THE CARATS   SS   ORB 68 03
    BEST FROM ORBIT, THE   KNIGHT, DAMON   AN
    BOOK OF PHILIP JOSE FARMER, THE FARMER, PHILIP JOSE AC

FARMER, PHILIP JOSE (CONTINUED)
  MODERN SCIENCE FICTION   SPINRAD, NORMAN   AN
  ORBIT   3   KNIGHT, DAMON   OA
DOWN IN THE BLACK GANG   NV   IFS 69 03
  DOWN IN THE BLACK GANG AND OTHER STORIES
                                  FARMER, PHILIP JOSE AC
EXCLUSIVE INTERVIEW WITH LORD GREYSTOKE, AN (TARZAN LIVES)
                                        SS   ESQ 72 04
  BOOK OF PHILIP JOSE FARMER, THE   FARMER, PHILIP JOSE AC
FATHER   NV   FSF 55 07
  STRANGE RELATIONS   FARMER, PHILIP JOSE AC
FATHER'S IN THE BASEMENT   SS   ORB 72 11
  BOOK OF PHILIP JOSE FARMER, THE   FARMER, PHILIP JOSE AC
  ORBIT 11   KNIGHT, DAMON   OA
FEW MILES, A   NV   FSF 60 10
  DOWN IN THE BLACK GANG AND OTHER STORIES
                                  FARMER, PHILIP JOSE AC
FOREWORD   IN
  BOOK OF PHILIP JOSE FARMER, THE   FARMER, PHILIP JOSE AC
GOD BUSINESS, THE   NA   BEY 54 03
  ALLEY GOD, THE   FARMER, PHILIP JOSE AC
HOW DEEP THE GROOVES   SS   AMZ 63 02
  DOWN IN THE BLACK GANG AND OTHER STORIES
                                  FARMER, PHILIP JOSE AC
JUNGLE ROT KID ON THE NOD, THE   SS   NWS 70 04
  NEW TOMORROWS, THE   SPINRAD, NORMAN   AN
KING OF THE BEASTS, THE   SS   GAL 64 06
  ABC OF SCIENCE FICTION, AN   BOARDMAN, TOM JR.   AN
  NINTH GALAXY READER, THE   POHL, FREDERIK   AN
  SCIENCE FACT/FICTION   FARRELL/GAGE/&   AN
  ZOO 2000   YOLEN, JANE   AN
MONOLOGUE   SS   DEM 73
  DEMON KIND   ELWOOD, ROGER   OA
MOTHER   NV   TWS 53 04
  ALPHA 4   SILVERBERG, ROBERT   AN
  ASSIGNMENT IN TOMORROW   POHL, FREDERIK   AN
  BUG-EYED MONSTERS   CHEETHAM, ANTHONY   AN
  IN DREAMS AWAKE   FIEDLER, LESLIE A.   AN
  INTRODUCTORY PSYCHOLOGY THROUGH SCIENCE FICTION
                                  KATZ/WARRICK/&   AN
  MICROCOSMIC GOD   MOSKOWITZ, SAM   AN
  MODERN MASTERPIECES OF SCIENCE FICTION MOSKOWITZ, SAM AN
  STRANGE BED FELLOWS   SCORTIA, THOMAS N.   AN
  STRANGE RELATIONS   FARMER, PHILIP JOSE AC
MOTHER EARTH WANTS YOU   SS   WLK 73
  AND WALK NOW GENTLY THROUGH THE FIRE...
                                  ELWOOD, ROGER   OA
MY SISTER'S BROTHER (OPEN TO ME, MY SISTER)   NV   FSF 60 05
  BOOK OF PHILIP JOSE FARMER, THE   FARMER, PHILIP JOSE AC
  STRANGE RELATIONS   FARMER, PHILIP JOSE AC
OBSCURE LIFE AND HARD TIMES OF KILGORE TROUT, THE SS MOB 71 12
  BOOK OF PHILIP JOSE FARMER, THE   FARMER, PHILIP JOSE AC
ONLY WHO CAN MAKE A TREE?   SS   FSF 71 11
  BOOK OF PHILIP JOSE FARMER, THE   FARMER, PHILIP JOSE AC
OOGENESIS OF BIRD CITY, THE   SS   AMZ 70 09
  AMERICAN GOVERNMENT THROUGH SCIENCE FICTION
                                  OLANDER/GREENBERG/& AN
OPEN TO ME, MY SISTER (ALSO AS MY SISTER'S BROTHER)
                                        NV   FSF 60 05
  ONCE AND FUTURE TALES FROM THE MAGAZINE OF FANTASY AND
  SCIENCE FICTION   FERMAN, EDWARD L.   AN
OPENING THE DOOR   SS   COI 73
  CHILDREN OF INFINITY   ELWOOD, ROGER   OA
OSIRIS ON CRUTCHES   SS C NDM 76 06
  NEW DIMENSIONS 6   SILVERBERG, ROBERT   OA
POLYTROPICAL PARAMYTHS   AI
  BOOK OF PHILIP JOSE FARMER, THE   FARMER, PHILIP JOSE AC
PREFACE   IN
  CURIOUS FRAGMENTS   LONDON, JACK   AC
PROMETHEUS   NV   FSF 61 03
  DOWN IN THE BLACK GANG AND OTHER STORIES
                                  FARMER, PHILIP JOSE AC
  OTHER WORLDS, OTHER GODS   MOHS, MAYO   AN
  SPECIAL WONDER   MCCOMAS, J. FRANCIS AN
RASTIGNAC THE DEVIL   SS   FUN 54 05
  CELESTIAL BLUEPRINT, THE   FARMER, PHILIP JOSE DC
RIDERS OF THE PURPLE WAGE   NA   DVS 67 01
  DANGEROUS VISIONS   ELLISON, HARLAN   OA
  HUGO WINNERS, THE (VOLUME 2)   ASIMOV, ISAAC   AN
RIVERWORLD   NV   WOT 66 01
  DOWN IN THE BLACK GANG AND OTHER STORIES
                                  FARMER, PHILIP JOSE AC
SAIL ON! SAIL ON!   SS   STS 52 12
  CENTURY OF SCIENCE FICTION, A   KNIGHT, DAMON   AN
  DECADE THE 1950S   ALDISS & HARRISON   AN
  SF: AUTHORS' CHOICE   HARRISON, HARRY   AN
  WORLDS OF MAYBE   SILVERBERG, ROBERT   AN
SEVENTY YEARS OF DECPOP   NA   GAL 72 07
  BEST SCIENCE FICTION FOR 1973   ACKERMAN, FORREST J. AN
SEXUAL IMPLICATIONS OF THE CHARGE OF THE LIGHT BRIGADE
                                        SS   DVS 67 01
  BOOK OF PHILIP JOSE FARMER, THE   FARMER, PHILIP JOSE AC
SHADOW OF SPACE, THE   NV   IFS 67 11
  ALPHA 3   SILVERBERG, ROBERT   AN
  DOWN IN THE BLACK GANG AND OTHER STORIES
                                  FARMER, PHILIP JOSE AC
SKETCHES AMONG THE RUINS OF MY MIND   NV   NOV 73 03
  BEST SCIENCE FICTION OF THE YEAR, THE NO. 3
                                  CARR, TERRY   AN
  NOVA 3   HARRISON, HARRY   OA
SKINBURN   SS   FSF 72 10
  BOOK OF PHILIP JOSE FARMER, THE   FARMER, PHILIP JOSE AC
SLICED-CROSSWISE ONLY-ON-TUESDAY WORLD, THE   SS   NDM 71 01
  BEST SCIENCE FICTION OF THE YEAR, THE CARR, TERRY   AN
  BEST SCIENCE FICTION STORIES OF THE YEAR (1971)
                                  DEL REY, LESTER   AN

FARMER, PHILIP JOSE (CONTINUED)
  NEW DIMENSIONS 1   SILVERBERG, ROBERT   OA
  SOCIAL PROBLEMS THROUGH SCIENCE FICTION
                                  GREENBERG/MILSTEAD/& AN
SON (QUEEN OF THE DEEP)   SS   ARG 54 03
  STRANGE RELATIONS   FARMER, PHILIP JOSE AC
STATIONS OF THE NIGHTMARE- PART 1   NV   CTM 74 01
  CONTINUUM 1   ELWOOD, ROGER   OA
STATIONS OF THE NIGHTMARE- PART 2: THE STARTOUCHED
                                        NV   CTM 74 02
  CONTINUUM 2   ELWOOD, ROGER   OA
STATIONS OF THE NIGHTMARE- PART 3: THE EVOLUTION OF PAUL EYRE
                                        NV   CTM 74 03
  CONTINUUM 3   ELWOOD, ROGER   OA
STATIONS OF THE NIGHTMARE- PART 4: PASSING ON   NV   CTM 75 04
  CONTINUUM 4   ELWOOD, ROGER   OA
STRANGE COMPULSION (SEE THE CAPTAIN'S DAUGHTER) TC
SUMERIAN OATH, THE   SS   NOV 72 02
  BOOK OF PHILIP JOSE FARMER, THE   FARMER, PHILIP JOSE AC
  NOVA 2   HARRISON, HARRY   OA
TARZAN LIVES (SEE AN EXCLUSIVE INTERVIEW WITH LORD GREYSTOKE)
                                        TC
THEY TWINKLED LIKE JEWELS   SS   FUN 54 01
  CELESTIAL BLUEPRINT, THE   FARMER, PHILIP JOSE DC
TOTEM AND TABOO   SS   FSF 54 12
  BOOK OF PHILIP JOSE FARMER, THE   FARMER, PHILIP JOSE AC
  CELESTIAL BLUEPRINT, THE   FARMER, PHILIP JOSE DC
TOWARDS THE BELOVED CITY   NV   SAW 72
  BOOK OF PHILIP JOSE FARMER, THE   FARMER, PHILIP JOSE AC
  CHRONICLES OF A COMER AND OTHER RELIGIOUS SCIENCE FICTION
  STORIES   ELWOOD, ROGER   AN
  SIGNS AND WONDERS   ELWOOD, ROGER   OA
  VISIONS OF TOMORROW   ELWOOD, ROGER   AN
VOICE OF THE SONAR IN MY VERMIFORM APPENDIX, THE SS QRK 71 02
  BOOK OF PHILIP JOSE FARMER, THE   FARMER, PHILIP JOSE AC
  QUARK/2   DELANY & HACKER   OA

FARNSWORTH, MONA
ALL ROADS   SS   UNK 40 08
  EDITOR'S CHOICE IN SCIENCE FICTION MOSKOWITZ, SAM   AN

FARRELL/GAGE/&
SCIENCE FACT/FICTION   AN L SPC 74

FARRELL, JAMES T.
BENEFACTOR OF HUMANITY, A   SS   SSI 58
  10TH ANNUAL OF THE YEAR'S BEST S-F, THE
                                  MERRIL, JUDITH   AN

FAST, HOWARD
EDGE OF TOMORROW, THE   AC   BAN 61 06
  ALSO IN "TIME AND THE RIDDLE"
GENERAL ZAPPED AN ANGEL, THE   OC H MOR 70
  ALSO IN "TIME AND THE RIDDLE"
TIME AND THE RIDDLE   AC H WRP 75
TOUCH OF INFINITY, A   OC H MOR 73
  ALSO IN "TIME AND THE RIDDLE"
AFTERWORD   MS
  TIME AND THE RIDDLE   FAST, HOWARD   AC
BIG ANT, THE (SEE THE LARGE ANT)   TC
CATO THE MARTIAN   SS   FSF 60 06
  EDGE OF TOMORROW, THE   FAST, HOWARD   AC
  SPECULATIONS   SANDERS, THOMAS E.   AN
  17 X INFINITY   CONKLIN, GROFF   AN
CEPHES 5   SS
  TOUCH OF INFINITY, A   FAST, HOWARD   OC
COLD, COLD BOX, THE   SS   FSF 59 07
  EDGE OF TOMORROW, THE   FAST, HOWARD   AC
  OUT OF THIS WORLD 7   WILLIAMS-ELLIS& OWEN AN
ECHINOMASTUS CONTENTII   SS
  TIME AND THE RIDDLE   FAST, HOWARD   AC
EDGE OF TOMORROW, THE (OMITS STORY "THE FIRST MEN")
                                        AC   BAN 61 06
  TIME AND THE RIDDLE   FAST, HOWARD   AC
EGG, THE   SS
  TOUCH OF INFINITY, A   FAST, HOWARD   OC
FIRST MEN, THE   NV   FSF 60 02
  EDGE OF TOMORROW, THE   FAST, HOWARD   AC
  INTRODUCTORY PSYCHOLOGY THROUGH SCIENCE FICTION
                                  KATZ/WARRICK/&   AN
  MORE PENGUIN SCIENCE FICTION   ALDISS, BRIAN W.   AN
  SCHOOL AND SOCIETY THROUGH SCIENCE FICTION
                                  OLANDER/GREENBERG/& AN
  WORLDS OF SCIENCE FICTION, THE MILLS, ROBERT P.   AN
FOREWORD   IN
  TIME AND THE RIDDLE   FAST, HOWARD   AC
GENERAL HARDY'S PROFESSION   SS
  TOUCH OF INFINITY, A   FAST, HOWARD   OC
GENERAL ZAPPED AN ANGEL, THE   OC   MOR 70
  TIME AND THE RIDDLE   FAST, HOWARD   AC
GENERAL ZAPPED AN ANGEL, THE   SS
  GENERAL ZAPPED AN ANGEL, THE   FAST, HOWARD   OC
  POLITICAL SCIENCE FICTION   GREENBERG& WARRICK   AN
HOLE IN THE FLOOR, THE   SS
  TOUCH OF INFINITY, A   FAST, HOWARD   OC
HOOP, THE   SS   FSF 72 10
  TOUCH OF INFINITY, A   FAST, HOWARD   OC
HUNTER, THE   NV
  TIME AND THE RIDDLE   FAST, HOWARD   AC
INSECTS, THE   SS
  GENERAL ZAPPED AN ANGEL, THE   FAST, HOWARD   OC
INTERVAL, THE   SS
  GENERAL ZAPPED AN ANGEL, THE   FAST, HOWARD   OC
INTRODUCTION   IN
  TIME AND THE RIDDLE   FAST, HOWARD   AC

FAST, HOWARD

FINCH, CHRISTOPHER

FAST, HOWARD   (CONTINUED)
  LARGE ANT, THE (THE BIG ANT)   SS   FUN 60 02
    CONTACT   KEYES, NOEL   AN
    DECADE THE 1950S   ALDISS & HARRISON   AN
    EDGE OF TOMORROW, THE   FAST, HOWARD   AC
    SPECTRUM 4   AMIS & CONQUEST   AN
    6TH ANNUAL OF THE YEAR'S BEST S-F, THE MERRIL, JUDITH AN
  MARTIAN SHOP, THE   SS   FSF 59 11
    DECADE OF FANTASY AND SCIENCE FICTION, A
                                     MILLS, ROBERT P.   AN
    EDGE OF TOMORROW, THE   FAST, HOWARD   AC
  MATTER OF SIZE, A   SS
    TOUCH OF INFINITY, A   FAST, HOWARD   OC
  MIND OF GOD, THE   SS
    TOUCH OF INFINITY, A   FAST, HOWARD   OC
  MOHAWK, THE
    GENERAL ZAPPED AN ANGEL, THE   FAST, HOWARD   OC
  MOUSE, THE   SS   FSF 69 11
    GENERAL ZAPPED AN ANGEL, THE   FAST, HOWARD   OC
    ZOO 2000   YOLEN, JANE   AN
  MOVIE HOUSE, THE   NV
    GENERAL ZAPPED AN ANGEL, THE   FAST, HOWARD   OC
  NOT WITH A BANG   SS
    TOUCH OF INFINITY, A   FAST, HOWARD   OC
  OF TIME AND CATS   SS   FSF 59 03
    EDGE OF TOMORROW, THE   FAST, HOWARD   AC
  PRAGMATIC SEED, THE   SS
    TOUCH OF INFINITY, A   FAST, HOWARD   OC
  PRICE, THE   SS
    TOUCH OF INFINITY, A   FAST, HOWARD   OC
  SHOW CAUSE   SS
    TOUCH OF INFINITY, A   FAST, HOWARD   OC
  SIGHT OF EDEN, THE   SS   FSF 60 10
    EDGE OF TOMORROW, THE   FAST, HOWARD   AC
  TALENT OF HARVEY, THE   NV
    TOUCH OF INFINITY, A   FAST, HOWARD   OC
  TOMORROW'S WALL STREET JOURNAL   SS
    GENERAL ZAPPED AN ANGEL, THE   FAST, HOWARD   OC
  TOUCH OF INFINITY, A   OC   MOR 73
  TIME AND THE RIDDLE   NA
    TRAP, THE   FAST, HOWARD   AC
  TIME AND THE RIDDLE   SS
    UFO   FAST, HOWARD   AC
  TOUCH OF INFINITY, A   SS
    VISION OF MILTY BOIL, THE   FAST, HOWARD   OC
  GENERAL ZAPPED AN ANGEL, THE   SS   70
  WOUND, THE
    EVIL EARTHS   ALDISS, BRIAN W.   AN
    GENERAL ZAPPED AN ANGEL, THE   FAST, HOWARD   OC
    SCIENCE FACT/FICTION   FARRELL/GAGE/&   AN

FAST, JON
  EARTHBLOSSOM   SS
    NEW CONSTELLATIONS   DISCH & NAYLOR   OA

FAST, JULIUS
  OUT OF THIS WORLD   AN   PEN 44 06
    MY FRIEND MERTON   SS   NEW 44 AN
    OUT OF THIS WORLD   FAST, JULIUS   AN
  WORD FROM THE EDITOR, A   IN
    OUT OF THIS WORLD   FAST, JULIUS   AN

FAUST, FREDERICK   SEE PSEUD. MAX BRAND

FAWCETT, DOUGLAS
  ANARCHIST; OR, THE DOOM OF THE GREAT CITY, THE   SS
    WORLDS APART   WILLIAMS-ELLIS& OWEN AN

FAYETTE, MICHAEL
  MAN ON THE HILL, THE   SS   INY 70 01
    INFINITY 1   HOSKINS, ROBERT   OA
  MONSTER IN THE CLEARING, THE   SS   INY 71 02
    INFINITY 2   HOSKINS, ROBERT   OA
  SAVIOR SOLE   SS   71
    FAR-OUT PEOPLE, THE   HOSKINS, ROBERT   AN

FEARN, JOHN RUSSELL ALSO AS POLTON CROSS
  WANDERER OF TIME   SS   STS 44 SU
    HISTORY OF THE SCIENCE FICTION MAGAZINE, THE PART 2 1936-1945
                                     ASHLEY, MICHAEL   AN
    *MY BEST SCIENCE FICTION STORY   MARGULIES & FRIEND   AN
  WHY I SELECTED WANDERER OF TIME   AI
    *MY BEST SCIENCE FICTION STORY   MARGULIES & FRIEND   AN

FEDER, MOSHE
  SANDIAL   SS   ORB 75 16
    ORBIT 16   KNIGHT, DAMON   OA

FEHRENBACH, T. R.
  FROM THE TOWER OF ERIDU   SS
    LONE STAR UNIVERSE   PROCTOR & UTLEY   OA
  REMEMBER THE ALAMO!   SS   ASF 61 12
    ANALOG 1   CAMPBELL, JOHN W. JR AN
    POLITICAL SCIENCE FICTION   GREENBERG& WARRICK   AN
    TRANSFORMATIONS II   ROSELLE, DANIEL   AN

PEIFFER, JULES
  DOG EAT DOG   CT   63
    9TH ANNUAL OF THE YEAR'S BEST S-F, THE MERRIL, JUDITH AN
  LOOKING BACKWARD   CT   HAS 61 12
    7TH ANNUAL OF THE YEAR'S BEST S-F, THE MERRIL, JUDITH AN

*FELDMAN, ARTHUR
  MATHEMATICIANS, THE   SS   AMZ 53 11
    FIFTY SHORT SCIENCE FICTION TALES ASIMOV & CONKLIN   AN

FELDSTEIN, ALBERT B.
  ADAPTATION   MS
    AUTUMN PEOPLE, THE   BRADBURY, RAY   AC
    TOMORROW MIDNIGHT   BRADBURY, RAY   AC

FELSEN, HENRY GREGOR
  SPACEMAN COMETH, THE   SS   FSF 56 04
    17 X INFINITY   CONKLIN, GROFF   AN

FENNEL, ERIC
  DOUGHNUT JOCKEY   SS   BBM 48 05
    BEST SCIENCE-FICTION STORIES: 1949, THE
                                     BLEILER & DIKTY   AN

FENTON, FRANK
  CHICKEN OR THE EGG-HEAD, THE   SS   NTL 54
    9 TALES OF SPACE AND TIME   HEALY, RAYMOND J.   OA
  TOLLIVER'S TRAVELS   NV C NTS 51
    NEW TALES OF SPACE AND TIME   HEALY, RAYMOND J.   OA

FERGUSON, BIRD
  INTERVIEW   PM   FSF 55 12
    BEST FROM FANTASY AND SCIENCE FICTION: 6
                                     BOUCHER, ANTHONY   AN

FERGUSON, DALE
  ISLAND OF THE ENDANGERED, THE   SS   NEW 72 AN
    ZOO 2000   YOLEN, JANE   AN

FERMAN, EDWARD L. AND BARRY N. MALZBERG
  ARENA: SPORTS SF   AN H DBL 76
  FINAL STAGE   OA H CHT 74

FERMAN, EDWARD L. AND ROBERT P. MILLS
  TWENTY YEARS OF FANTASY & SCIENCE FICTION   AN H PUT 70

FERMAN, EDWARD L.
  BEST FROM FANTASY AND SCIENCE FICTION: 15   AN H DBL 66
  BEST FROM FANTASY AND SCIENCE FICTION: 16   AN H DBL 67
  BEST FROM FANTASY AND SCIENCE FICTION: 17   AN H DBL 68
  BEST FROM FANTASY AND SCIENCE FICTION: 18   AN H DBL 69
  BEST FROM FANTASY AND SCIENCE FICTION: 19   AN H DBL 71
  BEST FROM FANTASY AND SCIENCE FICTION: 20   AN H DBL 73
  BEST FROM FANTASY AND SCIENCE FICTION, 25TH ANNIV. AN H DBL 74
  ONCE AND FUTURE TALES FROM THE MAGAZINE OF FANTASY AND
    SCIENCE FICTION   AN H HWF 68
  INTRODUCTION   IN
    BEST FROM FANTASY AND SCIENCE FICTION: 15
                                     FERMAN, EDWARD L.   AN
    BEST FROM FANTASY AND SCIENCE FICTION: 16
                                     FERMAN, EDWARD L.   AN
    BEST FROM FANTASY AND SCIENCE FICTION: 17
                                     FERMAN, EDWARD L.   AN
    BEST FROM FANTASY AND SCIENCE FICTION, 25TH ANNIV.
                                     FERMAN, EDWARD L.   AN
  INTRODUCTION   IN C
    FINAL STAGE   FERMAN & MALZBERG   OA

FERMAN, JOSEPH W.
  NO LIMITS   AN   BAL 64 08

FESSIER, MICHAEL
  FASCINATING STRANGER, THE   NV   SEP 48 05
    GREAT STORIES OF SCIENCE FICTION LEINSTER, MURRAY   AN
  MAN IN THE BLACK HAT, THE   SS   ESQ 34 02
    OTHER WORLDS, THE   STONG, PHILIP D.   AN

FFOLKES, MICHAEL
  OBVIOUS!   CT   FUN 56 10
    6TH ANNUAL OF THE YEAR'S BEST S-F, THE MERRIL, JUDITH AN

FIEDLER, LESLIE A.
  IN DREAMS AWAKE   AN   DEL 75 07
    BEGINNINGS, THE   SI
      IN DREAMS AWAKE   FIEDLER, LESLIE A.   AN
    CROSS THE BORDER, CLOSE THE GAP   AR
      LOOKING AHEAD   ALLEN, D. & L.   AN
    GOLDEN AGE, THE   SI
      IN DREAMS AWAKE   FIEDLER, LESLIE A.   AN
    INTRODUCTION   IN
      IN DREAMS AWAKE   FIEDLER, LESLIE A.   AN
    NEW DIRECTIONS   SI
      IN DREAMS AWAKE   FIEDLER, LESLIE A.   AN
  THANKS FOR THE FEAST, NOTES ON PHILIP JOSE FARMER MS
    BOOK OF PHILIP JOSE FARMER, THE FARMER, PHILIP JOSE AC

FILER, BURT K.
  BACKTRACKED   SS   FSF 68 06
    AS TOMORROW BECOMES TODAY   SULLIVAN, CHARLES W. AN
    WORLD'S BEST SCIENCE FICTION: 1969 WOLLHEIM & CARR   AN
  EYE OF THE BEHOLDER   SS   DVS 72 02
    AGAIN, DANGEROUS VISIONS   ELLISON, HARLAN   OA
  HOT POTATO   SS   MWS 71
    BEST SCIENCE FICTION STORIES OF THE YEAR (1971)
                                     DEL REY, LESTER   AN
    MANY WORLDS OF SCIENCE FICTION, THE BOVA, BEN   OA
  SUN   SS   NEW 71 AN
    POCKETFUL OF STARS, A   KNIGHT, DAMON   AN
  TIME TRAWLERS, THE   SS   GAL 68 08
    ELEVENTH GALAXY READER, THE   POHL, FREDERICK   AN

FINCH, CHRISTOPHER
  LANDSCAPE OF SHALLOWS, A   SS   NWS 68 07
    BEST SF STORIES FROM NEW WORLDS 5 MOORCOCK, MICHAEL AN

FINK, DAVID H. MD.
    COMPOUND B   NV   NTL 54
        GREAT SCIENCE FICTION ABOUT DOCTORS   CONKLIN, G&FABRICANT AN
        9 TALES OF SPACE AND TIME   HEALY, RAYMOND J.   OA

FINNEY, CHARLES G.
    BLACK RETRIEVER, THE   SS   FSF 58 10
        ROD SERLING'S TRIPLE W: WITCHES, WARLOCKS AND WEREWOLVES
                                              SERLING, ROD   AN
    CAPTIVITY, THE   SS   FSF 61 10
        *BEST FROM FANTASY AND SCIENCE FICTION: 11
                                              MILLS, ROBERT P.   AN
    CIRCUS OF DR. LAO, THE   NA   35
        CIRCUS OF DR. LAO AND OTHER IMPROBABLE STORIES
                                              BRADBURY, RAY   AN

FINNEY, JACK   PSEUD. FOR WALTER B. FINNEY
    CLOCK OF TIME, THE   AC H EYR 58
        SEE "THE THIRD LEVEL"
    I LOVE GALESBURG IN THE SPRINGTIME   AC H SAS 63
    THIRD LEVEL, THE   AC H RIN 57
        IN ENGLAND AS "THE CLOCK OF TIME"
    COIN COLLECTOR, THE (THE OTHER WIFE)   SS   SEP 60 01
        I LOVE GALESBURG IN THE SPRINGTIME   FINNEY, JACK   AC
    CONTENTS OF THE DEAD MAN'S POCKETS   NV   NEW 57 AC
        NIGHT IN FUNLAND   BRONDFIELD, JEROME   AN
        THIRD LEVEL, THE   FINNEY, JACK   AC
    COUSIN LEN'S WONDERFUL ADJECTIVE CELLAR   SS
        BEST FANTASY STORIES   ALDISS, BRIAN W.   AN
        THIRD LEVEL, THE   FINNEY, JACK   AC
    DASH OF SPRING, A   SS
        THIRD LEVEL, THE   FINNEY, JACK   AC
    DOUBLE TAKE   SS   PBY 65 04
        PLAYBOY BOOK OF SCIENCE FICTION AND FANTASY, THE
                                              PLAYBOY, EDITORS OF AN
    FACE IN THE PHOTO, THE (TIME HAS NO BOUNDARIES)   SS   SEP 62 10
        I LOVE GALESBURG IN THE SPRINGTIME   FINNEY, JACK   AC
        TIMES 4 (ABRIDGED STORIES)   ALLEN, VIRGINIA F.   AN
        8TH ANNUAL OF THE YEAR'S BEST S-F, THE MERRIL, JUDITH   AN
    HEY! LOOK AT ME!   SS   PBY 62 09
        I LOVE GALESBURG IN THE SPRINGTIME   FINNEY, JACK   AC
        PLAYBOY BOOK OF HORROR AND THE SUPERNATURAL, THE
                                              PLAYBOY, EDITORS OF AN
    "I LOVE GALESBURG IN THE SPRINGTIME"   NV   MCC 60 04
        I LOVE GALESBURG IN THE SPRINGTIME   FINNEY, JACK   AC
    I'M SCARED   SS   COL 51 09
        THIRD LEVEL, THE   FINNEY, JACK   AC
        TOMORROW, THE STARS   HEINLEIN, ROBERT A.   AN
    INTREPID AERONAUT, THE (AN OLD TUNE)   NV   MCC 61 10
        I LOVE GALESBURG IN THE SPRINGTIME   FINNEY, JACK   AC
    LOVE LETTER, THE   SS   SEP 59 08
        I LOVE GALESBURG IN THE SPRINGTIME   FINNEY, JACK   AC
    LOVE, YOUR MAGIC SPELL IS EVERYWHERE (THE MAN WITH THE MAGIC
        GLASSES)   NV   MCC 62 03
        I LOVE GALESBURG IN THE SPRINGTIME   FINNEY, JACK   AC
    MAN WITH THE MAGIC GLASSES, THE (SEE LOVE, YOUR MAGIC
        SPELL IS EVERYWHERE)   TC
    OF MISSING PERSONS   SS   GHK 55 03
        FANTASY: THE LITERATURE OF THE MARVELOUS
                                              KELLEY, LEO P.   AN
        SCIENCE FICTION   BRODKIN & PEARSON   AN
        SF: THE YEAR'S GREATEST SCIENCE FICTION AND FANTASY
                                              MERRIL, JUDITH   AN
        TALES OF TIME AND SPACE   OLNEY, ROSS R.   AN
        THIRD LEVEL, THE   FINNEY, JACK   AC
    OLD TUNE, AN (SEE THE INTREPID AERONAUT)   TC
    OTHER WIFE, THE (ALSO AS THE COIN COLLECTOR)   SS   SEP 60 01
        5TH ANNUAL OF THE YEAR'S BEST S-F, THE MERRIL, JUDITH   AN
    POSSIBLE CANDIDATE FOR THE PRESIDENCY, A (TIGER TAMER)
                                                      SS   COL 52 05
        I LOVE GALESBURG IN THE SPRINGTIME   FINNEY, JACK   AC
    PRISON LEGEND (SEVEN DAYS TO LIVE)   NV   SEP 59 10
        I LOVE GALESBURG IN THE SPRINGTIME   FINNEY, JACK   AC
    QUIT ZOOMIN' THOSE HANDS THROUGH THE AIR   SS   FSF 52 12
        CONNOISSEUR'S S. F.   BOARDMAN, TOM JR.   AN
        JOURNEYS IN SCIENCE FICTION   LOUGHLIN, RICHARD L. AN
        OPERATION FUTURE   CONKLIN, GROFF   AN
        THIRD LEVEL, THE   FINNEY, JACK   AC
    SECOND CHANCE   SS
        THIRD LEVEL, THE   FINNEY, JACK   AC
    SEVEN DAYS TO LIVE (SEE PRISON LEGEND)   TC
    SOMETHING IN A CLOUD   SS
        THIRD LEVEL, THE   FINNEY, JACK   AC
    SUCH INTERESTING NEIGHBORS   SS   COL 51 01
        BEYOND THE END OF TIME   POHL, FREDERIK   AN
        OTHER SIDE OF THE CLOCK, THE   STERN, PHILIP VAN D. AN
        THIRD LEVEL, THE   FINNEY, JACK   AC
    THERE IS A TIDE   SS   FSF 54 09
        THIRD LEVEL, THE   FINNEY, JACK   AC
    THIRD LEVEL, THE (COL 50 10)   SS   FSF 52 10
        BEST FROM FANTASY AND SCIENCE FICTION: 2
                                              BOUCHER & MCCOMAS   AN
        FIFTY SHORT SCIENCE FICTION TALES   ASIMOV & CONKLIN   AN
        SCIENCE FACT/FICTION   FARRELL/GAGE/&   AN
        SCIENCE FICTION ARGOSY, A   KNIGHT, DAMON   AN
        THIRD LEVEL, THE   FINNEY, JACK   AC
    TIGER TAMER (SEE A POSSIBLE CANDIDATE FOR THE PRESIDENCY)
                                                      TC
    TIME HAS NO BOUNDARIES (SEE THE FACE IN THE PHOTO)
                                                      TC
    WHERE THE CLUETTS ARE   NV   MCC 62 01
        I LOVE GALESBURG IN THE SPRINGTIME   FINNEY, JACK   AC

FINNEY, WALTER B.   SEE PSEUD. JACK FINNEY

FIRSOFF, V. A.
    EXPLORING THE PLANETS   AR   SID 64
        ALL ABOUT VENUS   ALDISS, BRIAN W.   AN
        FAREWELL FANTASTIC VENUS   ALDISS & HARRISON   AN

FISCHER, JOHN
    SURVIVAL U: PROSPECTUS FOR A REALLY RELEVANT UNIVERSITY
                                                      AR   HRP 69 09
        LOOKING AHEAD   ALLEN, D. & L.   AN

FISCHER, MICHAEL
    MISFIT   SS   SFP 53 12
        COMING OF THE ROBOTS, THE   MOSKOWITZ, SAM   AN

FISH, ROBERT L.
    TO HELL WITH THE ODDS   SS   FSF 58 02
        RUN TO STARLIGHT, SPORTS THROUGH SCIENCE FICTION
                                              GREENBERG/OLANDER/& AN

FISHER, GENE
    STIMULUS-REWARD SITUATION   SS   ASF 73 08
        SCHOOL AND SOCIETY THROUGH SCIENCE FICTION
                                              OLANDER/GREENBERG/& AN

FISHER, LEONARD E.
    ILLUSTRATIONS   IL
        WEIGHER OF SOULS AND THE EARTH DWELLERS, THE
                                              MAUROIS, ANDRE   AC

FISHER, LOU
    BLOODSTREAM   SS   EPC 75
        EPOCH   ELWOOD & SILVERBERG   OA
    TRIGGERMAN   SS   GAL 73 09
        BEST FROM GALAXY, THE   VOLUME II   GALAXY, EDITORS OF   AN

FISHER, PHILIP M. JR
    LIGHTS   SS   AAS 22 07
        SUPERNATURAL READER, THE   CONKLIN, G&L.   AN
    STRANGE CASE OF LEMUEL JENKINS, THE   SS   ASW 19 07
        *TERROR IN THE MODERN VEIN   WOLLHEIM, DONALD A.   AN

FISK, NICHOLAS
    FIND THE LADY   SS   NDM 75 05
        NEW DIMENSIONS 5   SILVERBERG, ROBERT   OA

FISKE, TARLETON   PSEUD. FOR ROBERT BLOCH

FITZ GEROLD, GREGORY AND JOHN DILLON
    LATE GREAT FUTURE, THE   AN   FCR 76

FITZ GERALD, GREGORY SEE ALSO   CO-EDITOR JACK C. WOLFE
    HALLOWEEN STORY   SS   BTH 73
        YEAR'S BEST HORROR STORIES: SERIES III, THE
                                              DAVIS, RICHARD   AN
    INTRODUCTION   IN C
        LATE GREAT FUTURE, THE   FITZ GERALD & DILLON AN
    PAST, PRESENT, AND FUTURE PERFECT   WOLFE, J&FITZ GERALD AN
    PREFACE   IN C
        PAST, PRESENT, AND FUTURE PERFECT   WOLFE, J&FITZ GERALD AN

FITZGERALD, F. SCOTT
    CURIOUS CASE OF BENJAMIN BUTTON, THE   SS   COL 22 05
        TRAVELERS IN TIME   STERN, PHILIP VAN D. AN
        TREASURY OF SCIENCE FICTION CLASSICS, THE
                                              KUEBLER, HAROLD W.   AN
    DIAMOND AS BIG AS THE RITZ, THE   SS   22
        MOONLIGHT TRAVELER, THE   STERN, PHILIP VAN D. AN

FITZGERALD, RUSSELL
    LAST SUPPER, THE   SS   QRK 71 02
        QUARK/2   DELANY & HACKER   OA
    TWELVE ANCILLARY APPROXIMATIONS FOR THE QUARK/ COVER CALLED
        APPOMATTOX   IL   QRK 70 01
        QUARK/1   DELANY & HACKER   OA

FITZGIBBON, C.
    SPACE PROBE TO VENUS   PM
        STARLIT CORRIDOR, THE   MANSFIELD, ROGER   AN

FITZPATRICK, E. D.
    SHADOW PLAY   SS
        AD 2500   WILSON, ANGUS   AN

FITZPATRICK, E. M.
    VENUS AND THE RABBIT   SS
        AD 2500   WILSON, ANGUS   AN

FITZPATRICK, R. C.
    CIRCUIT RIDERS, THE   SS   ASF 62 04
        ANALOG 2   CAMPBELL, JOHN W. JR AN
        8TH ANNUAL OF THE YEAR'S BEST S-F, THE MERRIL, JUDITH   AN
    WINKIN, BLINKIN AND PI R SQUARE   SS   ASF 68 07
        ANALOG 8   CAMPBELL, JOHN W. JR AN

FLAGG, FRANCIS   PSEUD. FOR GEORGE HENRY WEISS
    MACHINE MAN OF ARDATHIA, THE   SS   AMZ 27 11
        ESCALES DANS L'INFINI   GALLET, GEORGES H.   AN
        HISTORY OF THE SCIENCE FICTION MAGAZINE, THE PART 1 1926-1935
                                              ASHLEY, MICHAEL   AN

FLANDERS, JOHN   PSEUD. FOR JEAN RAY
    MYSTERY OF THE LAST GUEST, THE   SS   WRT 35 10
        OTHER WORLDS, THE   STONG, PHILIP D.   AN

LEHR, PAUL   FRIEDBERG, GERTRUDE

LEHR, PAUL   PSEUD. FOR FREDERIK POHL
  HATED, THE   SS   GAL 58 01
    FOURTH GALAXY READER, THE   GOLD, H. L.   AN
  WE NEVER MENTION AUNT NORA   SS   GAL 58 07
    FIFTH GALAXY READER, THE   GOLD, H. L.   AN

LEMING, PETER
  KILL, THE   SS   42
    STRANGE BEASTS AND UNNATURAL MONSTERS STERN, PHILIP VAN D. AN

LES, BARTHOLD
  SATURDAY EVENING POST FANTASY STORIES, THE   AN AVN 51 10

LINT, HOMER EON
  BLIND SPOT, THE   NV C AAS 21 05
    UNDER THE MOONS OF MARS   MOSKOWITZ, SAM   AN

LOOD, LESLIE
  INTRODUCTION   IN
    BEST OF JOHN WYNDHAM, THE   WYNDHAM, JOHN   AC

ONTENAY, CHARLES L.
  DISQUALIFIED   SS   IFS 54 09
    FIRST WORLD OF IF, THE   QUINN & WULFF   AN
  SILK AND THE SONG, THE   NV   FSF 56 07
    BEST FROM FANTASY AND SCIENCE FICTION: 6
                                   BOUCHER, ANTHONY   AN
    THEMES IN SCIENCE FICTION   KELLEY, LEO P.   AN
  Z   NV   IFS 56 06
    SECOND WORLD OF IF, THE   QUINN & WULFF   AN

ORD, COREY
  WONDERFUL WORLD OF FIGURES, THE   AR   61
    MATHEMATICAL MAGPIE, THE   FADIMAN, CLIFTON   AN

ORD, GARRET   PSEUD. FOR MARGARET AND WILLIAM CRAWFORD
  SCIENCE AND SORCERY   AN H FPB 53

ORSTER, E. M.
  CELESTIAL OMNIBUS, THE   SS   23
    MOONLIGHT TRAVELER, THE   STERN, PHILIP VAN D. AN
  CURATE'S FRIEND, THE   SS   47
    SUPERNATURAL READER, THE   CONKLIN, G&L.   AN
  MACHINE STOPS, THE   NV   28
    ARMCHAIR SCIENCE READER, THE   GORDON, I. & SORKIN AN
    CITIES OF WONDER   KNIGHT, DAMON   AN
    LIGHT FANTASTIC, THE   HARRISON, HARRY   AN
    SCIENCE FICTION GALAXY, THE   CONKLIN, GROFF   AN
    SCIENCE FICTION HALL OF FAME VOLUME 2B BOVA, BEN   AN
    SCIENCE FICTION: THE FUTURE   ALLEN, DICK   AN
    TREASURY OF SCIENCE FICTION CLASSICS, THE
                                   KUEBLER, HAROLD W.   AN
    WONDERMAKERS   HOSKINS, ROBERT   AN
    17 X INFINITY   CONKLIN, GROFF   AN
  STORY OF A PANIC, THE   SS   47
    CHILDREN OF WONDER   TENN, WILLIAM   AN

ORTEY, BRYN
  WORDSMITH   SS   NWR 76 28
    NEW WRITINGS IN SF. 28   BULMER, KENNETH   OA

FOSTER, ALAN DEAN
  STAR TREK LOG FIVE   OC   BAL 75 08
  STAR TREK LOG FOUR   OC   BAL 75 03
  STAR TREK LOG ONE   OC   BAL 74 06
  STAR TREK LOG SIX   OC   BAL 75 03
  STAR TREK LOG THREE   OC   BAL 75 01
  STAR TREK LOG TWO   OC   BAL 74 09
  ALBATROSS (DARIO FINELLI)   SA   SLG 76 06
    STAR TREK LOG SIX   FOSTER, ALAN DEAN   OC
  AMBERGRIS ELEMENT, THE (MARGARET ARMEN) SA   SLG 75 05
    STAR TREK LOG FIVE   FOSTER, ALAN DEAN   OC
  BEYOND THE FARTHEST STAR (SAMUEL A. PEEPLES) SA SLG 74 01
    STAR TREK LOG ONE   FOSTER, ALAN DEAN   OC
  DREAM DONE GREEN   SS   FOS 74
    BEST SCIENCE FICTION STORIES OF THE YEAR (1974)
                                   DEL REY, LESTER   AN
    FELLOWSHIP OF THE STARS   CARR, TERRY   OA
  EMPIRE OF T'ANG LANG, THE   SS   ALC 73
    ALIEN CONDITION, THE   GOLDIN, STEPHEN   OA
  HOW SHARPER THAN A SERPENT'S TOOTH (RUSSELL BATES &DAVID WISE)
                                         SA   SLG 76 06
    STAR TREK LOG SIX   FOSTER, ALAN DEAN   OC
  INFINITE VULCAN, THE (WALTER KOENIG)   SA   SLG 74 02
    STAR TREK LOG TWO   FOSTER, ALAN DEAN   OC
  JIHAD (STEPHEN KANDEL)   SA   SLG 75 05
    STAR TREK LOG FIVE   FOSTER, ALAN DEAN   OC
  LORELEI SIGNAL, THE (MARGARET ARMEN)   SA   SLG 74 02
    STAR TREK LOG TWO   FOSTER, ALAN DEAN   OC
  MAGICKS OF MEGAS-TU, THE (LARRY BRODY) SA   SLG 75 03
    STAR TREK LOG THREE   FOSTER, ALAN DEAN   OC
  MIRACLE OF SMALL FISHES, A   NV   STL 74 01
    STELLAR 1   DEL REY, JUDY-LYNN   OA
  MORE TRIBBLES, MORE TROUBLES (DAVID GERROLD) SA SLG 75 04
    STAR TREK LOG FOUR   FOSTER, ALAN DEAN   OC
  MUDD'S PASSION (STEPHEN KANDEL)   SA   SLG 75 03
    STAR TREK LOG THREE   FOSTER, ALAN DEAN   OC
  ONCE UPON A PLANET (LEN JANSON & CHUCK MENVILLE) SA SLG 75 03
    STAR TREK LOG THREE   FOSTER, ALAN DEAN   OC
  ONE OF OUR PLANETS IS MISSING (MARC DANIELS) SA SLG 74 01
    STAR TREK LOG ONE   FOSTER, ALAN DEAN   OC
  PIRATES OF ORION, THE (HOWARD WEINSTEIN) SA SLG 75 05
    STAR TREK LOG FIVE   FOSTER, ALAN DEAN   OC
  POLONAISE   SS
    BEYOND TIME   LEY, SANDRA   OA

FOSTER, ALAN DEAN   (CONTINUED)
  PRACTICAL JOKER, THE (CHUCK MENVILLE) SA   SLG 76 06
    STAR TREK LOG SIX   FOSTER, ALAN DEAN   OC
  SURVIVOR, THE (JAMES SCHERMER)   SA   SLG 74 02
    STAR TREK LOG TWO   FOSTER, ALAN DEAN   OC
  TERRATIN INCIDENT, THE (PAUL SCHNEIDER) SA   SLG 75 04
    STAR TREK LOG FOUR   FOSTER, ALAN DEAN   OC
  TIME TRAP (JOYCE PERRY)   SA   SLG 75 04
    STAR TREK LOG FOUR   FOSTER, ALAN DEAN   OC
  WITH FRIENDS LIKE THESE...   SS   ASF 71 06
    1972 ANNUAL WORLD'S BEST SF, THE WOLLHEIM, DONALD A. AN
  YESTERYEAR (D. C. FONTANA)   SA   SLG 74 01
    STAR TREK LOG ONE   FOSTER, ALAN DEAN   OC

FOSTER, HUGH G.
  TASTE OF FEAR, THE   SS   PBY 59 09
    PLAYBOY BOOK OF HORROR AND THE SUPERNATURAL, THE
                                   PLAYBOY, EDITORS OF AN
    WEIRD SHOW   PLAYBOY, EDITORS OF AN

FOWLER, ALASTAIR
  NOTES TO AFTER TEN YEARS   MS
    DARK TOWER AND OTHER STORIES, THE LEWIS, C. S.   AC

FOX, GARDNER F.
  TONIGHT THE STARS REVOLT| NA   PLS 52 03
    GALACTIC EMPIRES VOLUME TWO   ALDISS, BRIAN W.   AN

FOX, WILLIAM
  SOFT LANDING   PM
    MARS, WE LOVE YOU   HIPOLITO & MCNELLY   AN

FRANCIS, NIGEL
  BLACK HOLE   SS   NWB 75 08
    NEW WORLDS EIGHT   BAILEY, HILARY   OA
  BROKEN FIELD, THE   SS   NWB 75 08
    NEW WORLDS EIGHT   BAILEY, HILARY   OA

FRANKE, HERBERT W.
  PARADISE 3000   SS   75
    BEST FROM THE REST OF THE WORLD, THE WOLLHEIM, DONALD A. AN
  SLUM   SS
    VIEW FROM ANOTHER SHORE   ROTTENSTEINER, FRANZ AN

FRANKFORT, JAMES
  CARTOON   CT   VLG 61 10
    MATHEMATICAL MAGPIE, THE   FADIMAN, CLIFTON   AN

FRANKLIN, DONALD
  NIGHT SEARCH   SS
    STRANGE ENCOUNTERS   BISCHOFF, DAVID   OA

FRANKLIN, H. BRUCE
  FUTURE PERFECT   AN H OXF 66
  FOREWORD TO "THE SUBLIMINAL MAN"   AR   70
    MIRROR OF INFINITY, THE   SILVERBERG, ROBERT   AN
  INTRODUCTION   IN
    FUTURE PERFECT   FRANKLIN, H. BRUCE   AN

FRANTHWAY, BURKE
  IT'S GOING TO BE TRUE| SS
    ADVENTURES TO COME   ESENWEIN, J. BERG   OA

FREDERIC, GEORGE   PSEUD. FOR CHARLES NUETZEL
  VERY CULTURED TASTE, A   SS   60
    IF THIS GOES ON   NUETZEL, CHARLES   AN

FREE, COLIN
  WEATHER IN THE UNDERWORLD, THE   SS   SQU 65 06
    PACIFIC BOOK OF AUSTRALIAN SCIENCE FICTION
                                   BAXTER, JOHN   AN
    WORLD'S BEST SCIENCE FICTION: 1965 WOLLHEIM & CARR AN

FREEMAN, AUSTIN
  BRONZE PARROT, THE   SS   24
    SHOT IN THE DARK   MERRIL, JUDITH   AN

FREMAN, EDWARD L.
  INTRODUCTION   IN
    ARENA: SPORTS SF   FERMAN & MALZBERG   AN

FREMLIN, CELIA
  QUIET GAME, A   SS   ..RG 70
    YEAR'S BEST HORROR STORIES, THE DAVIS, RICHARD   AN

FRENKEL, JAMES
  HEADNOTES   MS
    BEST FROM IF, THE VOLUME I   IF, EDITORS OF   AN

FRERE, JOHN H.
  LOVES OF THE TRIANGLES, THE   PM C
    MATHEMATICAL MAGPIE, THE   FADIMAN, CLIFTON   AN

FRIBORG, ALBERT C.
  CARELESS LOVE (ALSO AS PUSH-BUTTON PASSION) SS FSF 54 07
    BEST FROM FANTASY AND SCIENCE FICTION: 4
                                   BOUCHER, ANTHONY   AN
    BEST SCIENCE FICTION STORIES AND NOVELS: 1955
                                   DIKTY, T. E.   AN
  PUSH-BUTTON PASSION (CARELESS LOVE)   SS   FSF 54 07
    5 TALES FROM TOMORROW   DIKTY, T. E.   AN

FRIEDBERG, GERTRUDE
  WAYWARD CRAVAT, THE   SS   58
    TOMORROW'S CHILDREN   ASIMOV, ISAAC   AN

FRIEDMAN, BRUCE JAY
  FOOT IN THE DOOR, A   SS   PBY 60 10
    FULLY AUTOMATED LOVE LIFE OF HENRY KEANRIDGE
                                      PLAYBOY, EDITORS OF AN
    PLAYBOY BOOK OF SCIENCE FICTION AND FANTASY, THE
                                      PLAYBOY, EDITORS OF AN
  INVESTOR, THE   SS   PBY 62 02
    PLAYBOY'S STORIES OF THE SINISTER & STRANGE
                                      PLAYBOY, EDITORS OF AN
  KILLER IN THE TV SET, THE   SS   PBY 61 08
    FULLY AUTOMATED LOVE LIFE OF HENRY KEANRIDGE
                                      PLAYBOY, EDITORS OF AN
    PLAYBOY BOOK OF SCIENCE FICTION AND FANTASY, THE
                                      PLAYBOY, EDITORS OF AN
  NIGHT BOXING ENDED, THE   SS   GMQ 66
    ARENA: SPORTS SF   FERMAN & MALZBERG   AN
  YES, WE HAVE NO RITCHARD   SS   FSF 60 11
    TWENTY YEARS OF FANTASY & SCIENCE FICTION
                                   FERMAN & MILLS   AN

FRIEDMAN, STUART
  BEAUTIFUL, BEAUTIFUL, BEAUTIFUL   SS   FUT 52 03
    FIFTY SHORT SCIENCE FICTION TALES ASIMOV & CONKLIN AN
    *WORLDS OF TOMORROW   DERLETH, AUGUST   AN

FRIEND, OSCAR J.   SEE ALSO   CO-EDITOR LEO MARGULIES
  IMPOSSIBLE HIGHWAY, THE   SS   TWS 40 08
    GREAT STORIES OF SCIENCE FICTION LEINSTER, MURRAY   AN
    MOLECULE MONSTERS, THE   ANONYMOUS   AN
    SAINT'S CHOICE OF IMPOSSIBLE CRIME, THE
                                    CHARTERIS, LESLIE   AN
  INTRODUCTION   IN C
    *MY BEST SCIENCE FICTION STORY MARGULIES & FRIEND   AN
  INTRODUCTION TO THE POCKET BOOK EDITION   IN C
  MOLECULE MONSTERS, THE   SS
    MOLECULE MONSTERS, THE   ANONYMOUS   AN
  OF JOVIAN BUILD   SS   TWS 38 10
    *TREASURY OF SCIENCE FICTION, A CONKLIN, GROFF   AN

FRISCH, O. R.
  ON THE FEASIBILITY OF COAL-DRIVEN POWER STATIONS SS SAM 56 03
    EXPERT DREAMERS, THE   POHL, FREDERIK   AN

FRITCH, CHARLES E.
  CRAZY MIXED-UP PLANET   AC   POW 69 11
  HORSES' ASTEROID   AC   POW 70
  ATAVIST, THE   SS
    HORSES' ASTEROID   FRITCH, CHARLES E.   AC
  BIG LEAP, THE   SS   IFS 55 02
    HORSES' ASTEROID   FRITCH, CHARLES E.   AC
  BIG, WIDE, WONDERFUL WORLD   SS   FSF 58 03
    CRAZY MIXED-UP PLANET   FRITCH, CHARLES E.   AC
    FIEND IN YOU, THE   BEAUMONT, CHARLES   AN
    YEAR'S BEST HORROR STORIES: SERIES III, THE
                                    DAVIS, RICHARD   AN
  BIRTHDAY PRESENT   SS   SCF 55 09
    CRAZY MIXED-UP PLANET   FRITCH, CHARLES E.   AC
    MAN AGAINST TOMORROW   NOLAN, WILLIAM F.   AN
  BLOODMOBILE   SS
    HORSES' ASTEROID   FRITCH, CHARLES E.   AC
  BREATHES THERE A MAN   SS   RKS 53 07
    HORSES' ASTEROID   FRITCH, CHARLES E.   AC
  CASTAWAY, THE   SS   GAM 63 02
    WILDERNESS OF STARS, A   NOLAN, WILLIAM F.   AN
  COG, THE   SS   ASF 53 02
    CRAZY MIXED-UP PLANET   FRITCH, CHARLES E.   AC
  COME INTO MY PARLOR   SS   SFA 53 02
    CRAZY MIXED-UP PLANET   FRITCH, CHARLES E.   AC
  CRAZY, MIXED-UP PLANET   NV   FUN 55 08
    CRAZY MIXED-UP PLANET   FRITCH, CHARLES E.   AC
  DANGER IN THE VOID   SS   INF 54 08
    HORSES' ASTEROID   FRITCH, CHARLES E.   AC
  EMISSARY   SS   FNF 53 06
    CRAZY MIXED-UP PLANET   FRITCH, CHARLES E.   AC
  ESCAPE MECHANISM   SS   IFS 55 04
    HORSES' ASTEROID   FRITCH, CHARLES E.   AC
  GEEVER'S FLIGHT   SS   NEW 65 AN
    PSEUDO PEOPLE, THE   NOLAN, WILLIAM F.   AN
  GIRL WHO WASN'T THERE, THE   SS C GAM 63 01
    SCIENCE FICTION WORLDS OF FORREST J. ACKERMAN & FRIENDS
                                    ACKERMAN, FORREST J. AC
  HONEYMOON   SS   VOR 53 05
    HORSES' ASTEROID   FRITCH, CHARLES E.   AC
  HORSES' ASTEROID   SS   58
    HORSES' ASTEROID   FRITCH, CHARLES E.   AC
  I LIKE MARTIAN MUSIC   SS   FUN 57 09
    CRAZY MIXED-UP PLANET   FRITCH, CHARLES E.   AC
  IF AT FIRST-   SS
    CRAZY MIXED-UP PLANET   FRITCH, CHARLES E.   AC
  MANY DREAMS OF EARTH (SEE SPACE STATION 42) TC
  NIGHT TALK   SS   STS 52 09
    CRAZY MIXED-UP PLANET   FRITCH, CHARLES E.   AC
  NO WORLD FOR THE TIMID   SS   AMZ 57 05
    CRAZY MIXED-UP PLANET   FRITCH, CHARLES E.   AC
  OFFICE CALL   SS   FUN 54 10
    CRAZY MIXED-UP PLANET   FRITCH, CHARLES E.   AC
  PACIFISTS, THE   SS   IFS 55 05
    HORSES' ASTEROID   FRITCH, CHARLES E.   AC
  SHAGGY DOG   SS   STN 58 03
    HORSES' ASTEROID   FRITCH, CHARLES E.   AC
  SHOCK TREATMENT   SS   FUN 55 02
    HORSES' ASTEROID   FRITCH, CHARLES E.   AC
  SKIN GAME   SS   IFS 54 05
    CRAZY MIXED-UP PLANET   FRITCH, CHARLES E.   AC
  SPACE STATION 42 (MANY DREAMS OF EARTH)   SS   OSF 54 11
    SPACE STATION 42 AND OTHER STORIES ANONYMOUS   AN

FRITCH, CHARLES E.   (CONTINUED)
  TRICK OR TREAT   SS   AMZ 57 07
    HORSES' ASTEROID   FRITCH, CHARLES E.   AC
  VENUS PLUS THREE   NV   GAM 63 01
    HORSES' ASTEROID   FRITCH, CHARLES E.   AC
  WATCHER, THE   SS   STS 52 06
    CRAZY MIXED-UP PLANET   FRITCH, CHARLES E.   AC
  WELCOME TO PROCYON IV   SS   65
    CRAZY MIXED-UP PLANET   FRITCH, CHARLES E.   AC

FRITH, UTA
  EMERGENCY SOCIETY   SS   NEW 76 AN
    ANTIGRAV: COSMIC COMEDIES   STRICK, PHILIP   AN

FROST, NEMI
  FIVE DRAWINGS   IL   QRK 71 02
    QUARK/2   DELANY & HACKER   OA

FROST, ROBERT
  STAR-SPLITTER, THE   PM   23
    LOOKING AHEAD   ALLEN, D. & L.   AN

FRUCH, A.
  CARTOON   CT   NYM 58 04
    MATHEMATICAL MAGPIE, THE   FADIMAN, CLIFTON   AN

FULLER, BUCKMINSTER
  SPACESHIP EARTH   AR   69
    SCIENCE FACT/FICTION   FARRELL/GAGE/&   AN

FULTHORPE, DOUGLAS
  DEATH OF MAN, THE   SS   SFM 74 05
    BEST OF SCIENCE FICTION MONTHLY, THE SACKS, JANET   AN

FURMAN, A. L.
  OUTER SPACE STORIES   AN   LPB 65 12
    SEE "TEEN-AGE OUTER SPACE STORIES"
  SPACE ADVENTURES   AN   LPB 75 01
    SEE "TEEN-AGE SPACE ADVENTURES"
  TEEN-AGE OUTER SPACE STORIES   AN H LPB 62
    ALSO AS "OUTER SPACE STORIES"
  TEEN-AGE SPACE ADVENTURES   AN   LPB 72
    ALSO AS "SPACE ADVENTURES"

FURNAS, J. C.
  LAOCOON COMPLEX, THE   SS   ESQ 37 04
    BEYOND THE BARRIERS OF SPACE AND TIME MERRIL, JUDITH AN
    TIMELESS STORIES FOR TODAY AND TOMORROW
                                    BRADBURY, RAY   AN

FYFE, H. B.
  AFTERTHOUGHT   SS   FUS 51 01
    *BEYOND HUMAN KEN   MERRIL, JUDITH   AN
  BUREAU OF SLICK TRICKS   SS   ASF 48 12
    TRAVELLERS OF SPACE   GREENBERG, MARTIN   AN
  IMPLODE AND PEDDLE   NV   ASF 51 11
    SPACE SERVICE   NORTON, ANDRE   AN
  IN VALUE DECEIVED   SS   ASF 50 11
    FIRST CONTACT   KNIGHT, DAMON   AN
    *POSSIBLE WORLDS OF SCIENCE FICTION CONKLIN, GROFF AN
    *STORIES FOR TOMORROW   SLOANE, WILLIAM   AN
    STORIES OF SCIENTIFIC IMAGINATION GALLANT, JOSEPH   AN
  KNOWLEDGE IS POWER   NV   DSF 52 12
    WAY OUT   HOWARD, IVAN   AN
  LET THERE BE LIGHT   SS   IFS 52 11
    CROSSROADS IN TIME   CONKLIN, GROFF   AN
    FIRST WORLD OF IF, THE   QUINN & WULFF   AN
  LOCKED OUT   SS   ASF 40 02
    *MEN AGAINST THE STARS   GREENBERG, MARTIN   AN
  LUNAR ESCAPADE   SS   OSF 54 02
    PLANET OF DOOM AND OTHER STORIES ANONYMOUS   AN
  MANNERS OF THE AGE   SS   GAL 52 03
    OMNIBUS OF SCIENCE FICTION   CONKLIN, GROFF   AN
    STRANGE TRAVELS IN SCIENCE FICTION CONKLIN, GROFF   AN
  MOONWALK   NA   SSF 52 11
    MEN ON THE MOON   WOLLHEIM, DONALD A.   DA
    SPACE PIONEERS   NORTON, ANDRE   AN
    WORLDS TO COME   KNIGHT, DAMON   AN
  PROTECTED SPECIES   SS   ASF 51 03
    *ASTOUNDING SCIENCE FICTION ANTHOLOGY, THE
                                 CAMPBELL, JOHN W. JR AN
    ASTOUNDING TALES OF SPACE AND TIME CAMPBELL, JOHN W. JR AN
    GALACTIC EMPIRES VOLUME ONE   ALDISS, BRIAN W.   AN
    SCIENCE FICTION   BURTON, S. H.   AN
    *SECOND ASTOUNDING SCIENCE FICTION ANTHOLOGY, THE
                                 CAMPBELL, JOHN W. JR AN
    YET MORE PENGUIN SCIENCE FICTION ALDISS, BRIAN W. AN
  RANSOM   SS   FSF 52 02
    BEST FROM FANTASY AND SCIENCE FICTION: 2
                                 BOUCHER & MCCOMAS   AN
    SPECIAL WONDER   MCCOMAS, J. FRANCIS   AN
  STAR-LINKED   SS   ASF 52 02
    SPACE SERVICE   NORTON, ANDRE   AN
    WELL-OILED MACHINE, THE   NV   FSF 50 12
    *SCIENCE-FICTION CARNIVAL   BROWN, F. & REYNOLDS AN

GABBARD, G. N.
  RECRUDESCENCE OF GEOFFREY MARVELL, THE   SS   NEW 76 AN
    YEAR'S BEST HORROR STORIES: SERIES IV, THE
                                 PAGE, GERALD W.   AN

GABRIEL, CLAIRE
  NI VAR   NV
    STAR TREK: THE NEW VOYAGES   MARSHAK, S&CULBREATH OA

GADE, HENRY
   CITY ON VENUS, A   SS
      FAREWELL FANTASTIC VENUS   ALDISS & HARRISON   AN

GALAXY, EDITORS OF
   BEST FROM GALAXY, THE VOLUME I   AN   AWD 72
   BEST FROM GALAXY, THE VOLUME II   AN   AWD 74

GALLAGHER, JOHN
   TREE TRUNKS   CT   SEP 63
     9TH ANNUAL OF THE YEAR'S BEST S-F, THE MERRIL, JUDITH   AN

GALLANT, JOSEPH
   STORIES OF SCIENTIFIC IMAGINATION   AN   OXF 54
   PREFACE   IN
     STORIES OF SCIENTIFIC IMAGINATION GALLANT, JOSEPH   AN

GALLERY, D. V.
   ENEMY PLANET, THE   SS   SEP 50 09
     SATURDAY EVENING POST FANTASY STORIES, THE
                      FLES, BARTHOLD   AN

GALLET, GEORGES H.
   ESCALES DANS L'INFINI   AN   LHT 54 04
     SCALES OF THE INFINITE, STORIES IN FRENCH

GALLICO, PAUL
   TERRIBLE ANSWER, THE   SS   SEP 50 01
     SATURDAY EVENING POST FANTASY STORIES, THE
                      FLES, BARTHOLD   AN

GALLUN, RAYMOND Z.   ALSO AS   ARTHUR ALLPORT
   ASTEROID OF FEAR   NV   PLS 51 03
     SPACE PIONEERS   NORTON, ANDRE   AN
   BEAST OF THE VOID, A   SS   ASF 36 09
     ESCALES DANS L'INFINI   GALLET, GEORGES H.   AN
   DAVEY JONES' AMBASSADOR   NV   ASF 35 12
     *BEST OF SCIENCE FICTION   CONKLIN, GROFF   AN
     HISTORY OF THE SCIENCE FICTION MAGAZINE, THE PART 1 1926-1935
                      ASHLEY, MICHAEL   AN
     SCIENCE FICTION OF THE 30'S   KNIGHT, DAMON   AN
   DAVY JONES' AMBASSADOR   NV   ASF 35 12
     EARTH IS THE STRANGEST PLANET   SILVERBERG, ROBERT   AN
   DERELICT   SS   ASF 35 10
     COMING OF THE ROBOTS, THE   MOSKOWITZ, SAM   AN
   LOTUS-ENGINE, THE   SS   SSS 40 03
     JUPITER   POHL, C. & F.   AN
   OLD FAITHFUL   NV   ASF 34 12
     BEFORE THE GOLDEN AGE   ASIMOV, ISAAC   AN
     *IMAGINATION UNLIMITED   BLEILER & DIKTY   AN
     SCIENCE FICTION: THE GREAT YEARS POHL, C. & F.   AN
   OPERATION PUMICE   SS   TWS 49 04
     MEN ON THE MOON   WOLLHEIM, DONALD A.   DA
     *POSSIBLE WORLDS OF SCIENCE FICTION CONKLIN, GROFF   AN
   RETURN OF A LEGEND   SS   PLS 52 03
     BEST OF PLANET STORIES NO. 1, THE BRACKETT, LEIGH   AN
     SPACE SERVICE   NORTON, ANDRE   AN
   SCARAB, THE   SS   ASF 36 08
     *SCIENCE FICTION THINKING MACHINES CONKLIN, GROFF   AN
   SEEDS OF THE DUSK   NV   ASF 38 06
     *ADVENTURES IN TIME AND SPACE   HEALY & MCCOMAS   AN
     ASTOUNDING-ANALOG READER, THE VOLUME ONE
                      HARRISON & ALDISS   AN
     TOMORROW'S WORLDS   SILVERBERG, ROBERT   AN
     TOMORROW, AND TOMORROW, AND TOMORROW...
                      HEINTZ/HERBERT/JOOS/ AN
   STAMPED CAUTION   NV   GAL 53 08
     5 UNEARTHLY VISIONS   CONKLIN, GROFF   AN
   STEPSON OF SPACE   SS   AST 40 10
     BEYOND THE END OF TIME   POHL, FREDERIK   AN
   TRAIL BLAZER   SS   FSM 51 FL
     SPACE PIONEERS   NORTON, ANDRE   AN

GALLUP, DICK
   COLD TURKEY   SS C BMR 73
     BAD MOON RISING   DISCH, THOMAS M.   OA

GALOUYE, DANIEL F.
  LAST LEAP AND OTHER STORIES OF THE SUPER-MIND, THE AC COR 64
  PROJECT BARRIER   AC H GOL 68
  CITY OF FORCE, THE   NA   GAL 59 04
    BODYGUARD AND 4 OTHER SHORT SF NOVELS FROM GALAXY
                      GOLD, H. L.   AN
  DEADLINE SUNDAY   NV   IMG 55 10
    LAST LEAP AND OTHER STORIES OF THE SUPER-MIND, THE
                      GALOUYE, DANIEL F.   AC
  DIPLOMATIC COOP   SS   STR 59 05
    SF: AUTHORS' CHOICE 2   HARRISON, HARRY   AN
    STAR SCIENCE FICTION STORIES NO. 5 POHL, FREDERIK   OA
  FIGHTING SPIRIT   NV   GAL 60 12
    LAST LEAP AND OTHER STORIES OF THE SUPER-MIND, THE
                      GALOUYE, DANIEL F.   AC
  HOMEY ATMOSPHERE   SS   GAL 61 04
    ABC OF SCIENCE FICTION, AN   BOARDMAN, TOM JR.   AN
  IN MEMORIAM- ROSEL GEORGE BROWN   MS
    NEBULA AWARD STORIES NO. 4   ANDERSON, POUL   AN
  JEBABURBA   SS   GAL 54 10
    LAST LEAP AND OTHER STORIES OF THE SUPER-MIND, THE
                      GALOUYE, DANIEL F.   AC
  KANGAROO COURT   SN   IFS 60 09
    LAST LEAP AND OTHER STORIES OF THE SUPER-MIND, THE
                      GALOUYE, DANIEL F.   AC
  LAST LEAP, THE   NV   IFS 60 01
    LAST LEAP AND OTHER STORIES OF THE SUPER-MIND, THE
                      GALOUYE, DANIEL F.   AC

GALOUYE, DANIEL F.   (CONTINUED)
  PROJECT BARRIER   SS FUN 58 01
    PROJECT BARRIER   GALOUYE, DANIEL F.   AC
  PROMETHEUS REBOUND   NV YRT 70
    YEAR 2000, THE   HARRISON, HARRY   OA
  RECOVERY AREA   NA AMZ 63 02
    PROJECT BARRIER   GALOUYE, DANIEL F.   AC
  REIGN OF THE TELEPUPPETS   NA AMZ 63 08
    PROJECT BARRIER   GALOUYE, DANIEL F.   AC
  RUB-A-DUB   SS
    PROJECT BARRIER   GALOUYE, DANIEL F.   AC
  SANCTUARY   NV FSF 54 02
    BEST FROM FANTASY AND SCIENCE FICTION: 4
                      BOUCHER, ANTHONY   AN
    LAST LEAP AND OTHER STORIES OF THE SUPER-MIND, THE
                      GALOUYE, DANIEL F.   AC
  SEEING-EYE DOG   SS GAL 56 09
    LAST LEAP AND OTHER STORIES OF THE SUPER-MIND, THE
                      GALOUYE, DANIEL F.   AC
  SHUFFLE BOARD   SS IFS 57 06
    PROJECT BARRIER   GALOUYE, DANIEL F.   AC
  SITTING DUCK   SS IFS 59 07
    6 FINGERS OF TIME AND 5 OTHER SCIENCE FICTION NOVELETS, THE
                      ANONYMOUS   AN
  TONIGHT THE SKY WILL FALL| SN IMG 52 05
    SPACE OPERA   ALDISS, BRIAN W.   AN

GAMOW, GEORGE
  HEART ON THE OTHER SIDE, THE   SS
    EXPERT DREAMERS, THE   POHL, FREDERIK   AN
  INFINITY OF GUESTS, A   PM   47
    FANTASIA MATHEMATICA   FADIMAN, CLIFTON   AN
  WITH APOLOGIES TO ROYAL   MS   47
    MATHEMATICAL MAGPIE, THE   FADIMAN, CLIFTON   AN

GANLEY, W. PAUL   SEE PSEUD. TOBY DUANE

GANSOVSKY, SEVER
  DAY OF WRATH, A   SS
    PATH INTO THE UNKNOWN   ANONYMOUS   AN
  NEW SIGNAL STATION, THE   SS
    LAST DOOR TO AIYA   GINSBURG, MIRRA   AN
  PROVING GROUND, THE   SS
    VIEW FROM ANOTHER SHORE   ROTTENSTEINER, FRANZ AN
  TWO, THE   NV
    JOURNEY ACROSS THREE WORLDS ANONYMOUS   AN
  WE ARE NOT ALONE   SS   64
    AIR OF MARS AND OTHER STORIES, THE GINSBURG, MIRRA   AN

GARDNER, EARL STANLEY
  HUMAN ZERO, THE   NV ARG 31 12
    HUMAN ZERO, THE   MOSKOWITZ & ELWOOD   AN
  NEW WORLDS   NV ARG 32 12
    OTHER WORLDS, OTHER TIMES MOSKOWITZ & ELWOOD   AN
  RAIN MAGIC   NV AAS 28 10
    ALIEN EARTH AND OTHER STORIES ELWOOD & MOSKOWITZ   AN

GARDNER, MARTIN
  ISLAND OF THE FIVE COLORS, THE   SS NEW 52 AN
    FANTASIA MATHEMATICA   FADIMAN, CLIFTON   AN
    *FUTURE TENSE   CROSSEN, KENDELL F.   AN
  NO-SIDED PROFESSOR (ESQ 47 01)   SS FSF 51 02
    AS TOMORROW BECOMES TODAY SULLIVAN, CHARLES W.   AN
    BEST FROM FANTASY AND SCIENCE FICTION BOUCHER & MCCOMAS   AN
    FANTASIA MATHEMATICA   FADIMAN, CLIFTON   AN
    VINTAGE ANTHOLOGY OF SCIENCE FANTASY, THE
                      CERF, CHRISTOPHER   AN
  THANG   SS COM 48 FL
    BEST SCIENCE-FICTION STORIES: 1949, THE
                      BLEILER & DIKTY   AN

GARDNER, THOMAS S.
  LAST WOMAN, THE   SS WOS 32 04
    FROM OFF THIS WORLD   MARGULIES & FRIEND   AN
    WHEN WOMEN RULE   MOSKOWITZ, SAM   AN

GARIS, HOWARD R.
  PROFESSOR JONKIN'S CANNIBAL PLANT SS ARG 05 08
    SCIENCE FICTION BY GASLIGHT MOSKOWITZ, SAM   AN

GARNETT, BILL
  SINGULAR   SS NOV 74 C4
    NOVA 4   HARRISON, HARRY   OA

GARNETT, DAVID S.
  MAN WHO, THE   SS NWR 75 26
    NEW WRITINGS IN SF. 26   BULMER, KENNETH   OA
  NOW HEAR THE WORD   NV NWR 74 24
    NEW WRITINGS IN SF. 24   BULMER, KENNETH   OA
  RAINBOW   SS NWR 74 23
    NEW WRITINGS IN SF. 23   BULMER, KENNETH   OA

GARNETT, RICHARD,LLD
  INTRODUCTION   IN
    TALES AND STORIES   SHELLEY, MARY W.   AC

GARRETT, RANDALL   ALSO AS
  WALTER BUPP, DARREL T. LANGART, SEATON MCKETTRIG AND ROBERT
  RANDALL (WITH R.SILVERBERG)
  AFTER A FEW WORDS   SS ASF 62 10
    ASTOUNDING-ANALOG READER, THE VOLUME TWO
                      HARRISON & ALDISS   AN
  ALL ABOUT "THE THING" (PARODIES TOSSED) PM SFS 56 05
    SF:57, THE YEAR'S GREATEST SCIENCE FICTION AND FANTASY
                      MERRIL, JUDITH   AN

GARRETT, RANDALL   (CONTINUED)
  BEST POLICY, THE   SS   ASF 57 07
    EARTHMEN AND STRANGERS   SILVERBERG, ROBERT   AN
  BLAZE OF GLORY   PM   FSF 55 12
    BEST FROM FANTASY AND SCIENCE FICTION: 6
                                BOUCHER, ANTHONY   AN
  CASE OF IDENTITY, A   NV   ASF 64 09
    ANALOG 4   CAMPBELL, JOHN W. JR AN
  EYES HAVE IT, THE   NV   ASF 64 01
    RULERS OF MEN   SANTESSON, HANS S.   AN
  FIGHTING DIVISION   SS   ASF 65 08
    ANALOG 5   CAMPBELL, JOHN W. JR AN
  FOREIGN HAND TIE, THE   NV   ASF 61 12
    14 GREAT TALES OF ESP   STONE, IDELLA P.   AN
  GREAT KLADNAR RACE, THE (AS RICHARD GREER)   SS C AMZ 56 12
    INFINITE ARENA, THE   CARR, TERRY   AN
  HAIL TO THE CHIEF   SS   ASF 62
    AMERICAN GOVERNMENT THROUGH SCIENCE FICTION
                                OLANDER/GREENBERG/& AN
  HOT ARGUMENT   PM   FSF 60 02
    5TH ANNUAL OF THE YEAR'S BEST S-F, THE MERRIL, JUDITH AN
  HUNTING LODGE, THE   NV   ASF 54 07
    MEN AND MACHINES   SILVERBERG, ROBERT   AN
  LOOK OUT! DUCK!   NV   ASF 57 09
    NEVER IN THIS WORLD   STONE, IDELLA P.   AN
  MUDDLE OF THE WOAD, THE   NV   ASF 65 06
    SPECIAL WONDER   MCCOMAS, J. FRANCIS AN
  SOUND DECISION   NV C ASF 56 10
    DAYS AFTER TOMORROW, THE   SANTESSON, HANS S.   AN
    PROLOGUE TO ANALOG   CAMPBELL, JOHN W. JR AN
    SHORES OF TOMORROW, THE   SILVERBERG, ROBERT   AC
  TIME FUZE   SS   IFS 54 03
    SPACE OPERA   ALDISS, BRIAN W.   AN
  TIN LIZZIE   NV   AMZ 64 06
    GREAT SCIENCE FICTION STORIES ABOUT MARS
                                DIKTY, T. E.   AN

GARY, ROMAIN
  DECADENCE (TRANSLATED BY RICHARD HOWARD)   SS   SGA 64
    10TH ANNUAL OF THE YEAR'S BEST S-F, THE
                                MERRIL, JUDITH   AN

GAT, DIMITRI V.
  U-GENIE SX-1--HUMAN ENTREPRENEUR: NATURALLY RAPACIOUS YANKEE
                                                SS
    BEYOND TIME   LEY, SANDRA   OA

GAULT, WILLIAM C.
  FOG   SS   TWS 51 06
    TALES OF TIME AND SPACE   OLNEY, ROSS R.   AN
  MADE TO MEASURE   SS   GAL 51 01
    *GALAXY READER OF SCIENCE FICTION GOLD, H. L.   AN
  TITLE FIGHT   SS   FUN 56 12
    FANTASTIC UNIVERSE OMNIBUS, THE SANTESSON, HANS S. AN
    RUN TO STARLIGHT, SPORTS THROUGH SCIENCE FICTION
                                GREENBERG/OLANDER/& AN

GEHMAN, RICHARD
  HICKORY, DICKORY, KEROUAC (AS MARTIN SCOTT)   SS   PBY 58 03
    FANTASY: THE LITERATURE OF THE MARVELOUS
                                KELLEY, LEO P.   AN
    SF: THE BEST OF THE BEST   MERRIL, JUDITH   AN
    SF:59, THE YEAR'S GREATEST SCIENCE FICTION AND FANTASY
                                MERRIL, JUDITH   AN
  MACHINE, THE   SS   COL 46 12
    13 GREAT STORIES OF SCIENCE FICTION CONKLIN, GROFF AN

GEIER, CHESTER S.
  ENVIRONMENT   SS   ASF 44 05
    OMNIBUS OF SCIENCE FICTION CONKLIN, GROFF   AN
    STRANGE ADVENTURES IN SCIENCE FICTION CONKLIN, GROFF AN

GEIS, RICHARD E.
  ALIEN VIEWPOINT, THE   AR   IFS 74 10
    BEST FROM IF, THE VOLUME III BAEN, JAMES   AN

GELLMAN, RICK
  RETURN OF THE MANDARIN, THE   SS   NWQ 74 06
    NEW WORLDS NO. 6   PLATT & BAILEY   OA

GENOVES, JUAN
  MAN FALLING FORWARD   IL
    SCIENCE FICTION   BRODKIN & PEARSON   AN
  PHOTOGRAPHIC EVIDENCE   IL
    SCIENCE FICTION   BRODKIN & PEARSON   AN

GERAHTY, DIGBY G.   SEE PSEUD. ROBERT STANDISH

GERNBERG, MORT
  IBM   CT   DUD 63
    9TH ANNUAL OF THE YEAR'S BEST S-F, THE MERRIL, JUDITH AN

GERNSBACK, HUGO
  ACTION FROM A DISTANCE (FROM "RALPH 124C 41+")   EX MEL 11 04
    SCIENCE FICTION THROUGH THE AGES 2 EVANS, I. O. AN
  BARON MUNCHAUSEN'S SCIENTIFIC ADVENTURES (HOW THE MARTIAN
    CANALS ARE BUILT)   SS   ELX 16 11
    FANTASTIC PULPS, THE   HAINING, PETER   AN
  EXTRA SENSORY PERFECTION   SS
    MASTERPIECES OF SCIENCE FICTION MOSKOWITZ, SAM AN
  NEW YORK A.D. 2660 (RALPH 124C 41+)   EX   MEL 11 04
    CITY: 2000 A.D., THE   CLEM/GREENBERG/&   AN
    FUTURE TENSE   CURTIS, RICHARD   AN
  PROPHETS OF DOOM, THE   AR
    SCIENCE FICTION ROLL OF HONOR, THE POHL, FREDERIK AN

GEROULD, KATHERINE F
  ON THE STAIRCASE   SS   SCR 13 12
    TRAVELERS IN TIME   STERN, PHILIP VAN D. AN

GERROLD, DAVID AND STEPHEN GOLDIN
  PROTOSTARS   OA   BAL 71 10

GERROLD, DAVID
  ALTERNATES   OA   DEL 74 07
  GENERATION   OA   DEL 72 07
  SCIENCE FICTION EMPHASIS NO. 1   OA   BAL 74 05
  WHEN HARLIE WAS ONE   NO H NDB 72
  WITH A FINGER IN MY I   AC   BAL 72 06
  AFTERNOON WITH A DEAD BUS   SS   PRT 71
    FANTASY: THE LITERATURE OF THE MARVELOUS
                                KELLEY, LEO P.   AN
    PROTOSTARS   GERROLD & GOLDIN   OA
  ALL OF THEM WERE EMPTY   SS   NEW 72 AC
    GENERATION   GERROLD, DAVID   OA
    WITH A FINGER IN MY I   GERROLD, DAVID   OA
  BATTLE HUM AND THE BOJE   NV   NEW 72 AC
    WITH A FINGER IN MY I   GERROLD, DAVID   AC
  CRYSTAL CASTLE, THE   SS   NEW 72 AC
    WITH A FINGER IN MY I   GERROLD, DAVID   AC
  FOR G.O.D.'S SAKE   NV   GAL 72 07
    WHEN HARLIE WAS ONE   GERROLD, DAVID   NO
  GOD MACHINE, THE   NV   GAL 70 05
    WHEN HARLIE WAS ONE   GERROLD, DAVID   NO
  HOW WE SAVED THE HUMAN RACE   NV   NEW 72 AC
    WITH A FINGER IN MY I   GERROLD, DAVID   AC
  IN THE DEADLANDS   NV   NEW 72 AC
    WITH A FINGER IN MY I   GERROLD, DAVID   AC
  INFINITY OF LOVING, AN   SS   TTM 73
    TEN TOMORROWS   ELWOOD, ROGER   OA
  INTRODUCTION   IN
    ALTERNATES   GERROLD, DAVID   OA
    GENERATION   GERROLD, DAVID   OA
    SCIENCE FICTION EMPHASIS NO. 1 GERROLD, DAVID   OA
  LOVE STORY IN THREE ACTS   SS   NOV 70 01
    *NOVA 1   HARRISON, HARRY   OA
    WITH A FINGER IN MY I   GERROLD, DAVID   OA
  ORACLE FOR A WHITE RABBIT   NV   GAL 69 12
    WHEN HARLIE WAS ONE   GERROLD, DAVID   NO
    WITH A FINGER IN MY I   GERROLD, DAVID   NO
  SKINFLOWERS   SS   BER 74
    BERSERKERS, THE   ELWOOD, ROGER   OA
  SORT OF INTRODUCTION, A   IN
    PROTOSTARS   GERROLD & GOLDIN   OA
  TROUBLE WITH G.O.D., THE   NV   GAL 72 05
    WHEN HARLIE WAS ONE   GERROLD, DAVID   NO
  WITH A FINGER IN MY I   SS   DVS 72 02
    AGAIN, DANGEROUS VISIONS   ELLISON, HARLAN   OA
    WITH A FINGER IN MY I   GERROLD, DAVID   AC
  YARST!   SS   NEW 72 AC
    WITH A FINGER IN MY I   GERROLD, DAVID   AC

GHIDALIA, ROBERTA
  FRIENDS?   SS   NEW 73 AN
    MORE LITTLE MONSTERS   ELWOOD & GHIDALIA   AN

GHIDALIA, VIC AND ROGER ELWOOD
  BEWARE MORE BEASTS   AN   MAN 75
  BEWARE THE BEASTS   AN   MBB 70
  VENUS FACTOR, THE   AN   MBB 72

GHIDALIA, VIC   SEE ALSO   CO-EDITOR ROGER ELWOOD
  DEVIL'S GENERATION, THE   AN   LAN 73
  NIGHTMARE GARDEN   AN   MAN 76
  ODDBALLS, THE   AN   MAN 73
  SATAN'S PETS   AN   MAN 72
  WIZARDS AND WARLOCKS   AN   MAN 72
    INTRODUCTION   IN
    DEVIL'S GENERATION, THE   GHIDALIA, VIC   AN

GIANNATTASIO, GERARD
  G. I. SPARROW   SS   NWQ 74 06
    NEW WORLDS NO. 6   PLATT & BAILEY   OA
  PROTECTIVE TEMPORAL STRIKE   SS   NOV 74 04
    NOVA 4   HARRISON, HARRY   OA

GIBSON, WALTER B.
  ADAPTATION   MS
    *ROD SERLING'S THE TWILIGHT ZONE SERLING, ROD   OC
    ROD SERLING'S TWILIGHT ZONE REVISITED SERLING, ROD OC

GIESY, J. U.
  BLIND MAN'S BUFF   SS   ASW 20 01
    ESCALES DANS L'INFINI   GALLET, GEORGES H.   AN
  PALOS OF THE DOG STAR PACK   NV   ASW 18 07
    UNDER THE MOONS OF MARS   MOSKOWITZ, SAM   AN

GILBERT, DOROTHY
  SOLFY DRINK, A SAFFEL FRAGRANCE, A   SS   NDM 75 05
    NEW DIMENSIONS 5   SILVERBERG, ROBERT   AN

GILBERT, ROBERT E.
  FOOTPRINTS   SS   FBK 51 08
    SCIENCE AND SORCERY   FORD, GARRET   AN

GILCHRIST, JEREMY
  THALIDOMIDE KID, THE   SS   NWQ 74 06
    NEW WORLDS NO. 6   PLATT & BAILEY   OA

GILDEN, MEL
  EVERYBODY LOVES: IN A CIRCULAR MOTION   SS   CLR 73 03
    CLARION III   WILSON, ROBIN SCOTT OA

GILDEN, MEL   GOLD, H. L.

GILDEN, MEL   (CONTINUED)
  WHAT ABOUT US GRILS?   SS   CLR 71 01
    CLARION   WILSON, ROBIN SCOTT   OA
    STRANGE BED FELLOWS   SCORTIA, THOMAS N.   AN
  WHAT'S THE MATTER WITH HERBIE?   NV   ORB 73 12
    ORBIT 12   KNIGHT, DAMON   OA

GILDEN, STEPHEN
  FRONTISPIECE   MS   QRK 70 01
    QUARK/1   DELANY & HACKER   OA
  SIX DRAWINGS   IL   QRK 70 01
    QUARK/1   DELANY & HACKER   OA

GILES, GORDON A.
  KILLER PLANTS, THE   SS
    KILLER PLANTS AND OTHER STORIES, THE ELWOOD, ROGER   OA

GILIEN, SASHA
  TWO'S A CROWD   SS   FSF 62 07
    BEST FROM FANTASY AND SCIENCE FICTION: 12
                                        DAVIDSON, AVRAM   AN

GILLESPIE, ALFRED
  EVIL EYE, THE   NV   SEP 66 01
    NEW WORLDS OF FANTASY   CARR, TERRY   AN

GILLETTE, GLEN L.
  FIDDLE ESS   NV
    LONE STAR UNIVERSE   PROCTOR & UTLEY   OA

GILLINGS, WALTER
  BEFORE THE TRIFFIDS...   IN
    WANDERERS OF TIME   WYNDHAM, JOHN   AC
  FOREWORD   IN
    BEST OF E. E. 'DOC' SMITH, THE   SMITH, EDWARD E. PHD   AC

GILMORE, ANTHONY   PSEUD. FOR HARRY BATES AND DESMOND W. HALL
  SPACE HAWK   AC H GBG 52
  AFFAIR OF THE BRAINS, THE   NV   ASF 32 03
    SPACE HAWK   GILMORE, ANTHONY   AC
  BLUFF OF THE HAWK, THE   SS   ASF 32 05
    SPACE HAWK   GILMORE, ANTHONY   AC
  HAWK CARSE   NV   ASF 31 11
    SPACE HAWK   GILMORE, ANTHONY   AC
  PASSING OF KU SUI, THE   NV   ASF 32 11
    SPACE HAWK   GILMORE, ANTHONY   AC
  RETURN OF HAWK CARSE, THE (HARRY BATES)   NA   AMZ 42 07
    SPACE HAWK   GILMORE, ANTHONY   AC

GINSBERG, ALLEN
  POEM ROCKET   PM   61
    SCIENCE FICTION: THE FUTURE   ALLEN, DICK   AN
    SPECULATIONS   SANDERS, THOMAS E.   AN

GINSBURG, MIRRA
  AIR OF MARS AND OTHER STORIES, THE   AN H MAC 76
  LAST DOOR TO AIYA   AN H PHI 68
  ULTIMATE THRESHOLD, THE   AN H HRW 70
  EDITOR'S NOTE   IN
    AIR OF MARS AND OTHER STORIES, THE GINSBURG, MIRRA   AN
  INTRODUCTION   IN
    LAST DOOR TO AIYA   GINSBURG, MIRRA   AN
  PREFACE   IN
    ULTIMATE THRESHOLD, THE   GINSBURG, MIRRA   AN

GIRAD, DIAN
  EAT, DRINK, AND BE MERRY   SS   NEW 74 AN
    2020 VISION   POURNELLE, JERRY   AN

GIRARD, JAMES P.
  ALTERNATES, THE   NV   NDM 76 06
    NEW DIMENSIONS 6   SILVERBERG, ROBERT   OA

GIRONELLA,JOSE MARIA
  DEATH OF THE SEA, THE   SS   64
    VINTAGE ANTHOLOGY OF SCIENCE FANTASY, THE
                                        CERF, CHRISTOPHER   AN
  RED EGG, A (TRANSLATED BY TERRY BROCH FONTSERE) SS   64
    10TH ANNUAL OF THE YEAR'S BEST S-F, THE
                                        MERRIL, JUDITH   AN

GLASER, ALICE
  TUNNEL AHEAD, THE   SS   FSF 61 11
    AS TOMORROW BECOMES TODAY   SULLIVAN, CHARLES W. AN
    VOYAGES: SCENARIOS FOR A SHIP CALLED EARTH
                                        SAUER, ROB   AN
    7TH ANNUAL OF THE YEAR'S BEST S-F, THE MERRIL, JUDITH   AN

GLASGOW, ELLEN
  SHADOWY THIRD, THE   NV
    MORE LITTLE MONSTERS   ELWOOD & GHIDALIA   AN

GLASS, DICK
  ULTIMATE END, THE   SS   NOV 73 03
    NOVA 3   HARRISON, HARRY   OA

GLEMSER, BERNARD   SEE PSEUD. ROBERT CRANE

GLOECKNER, CAROLYN
  ANDREW   SS   FCR 75
    FUTURE CORRUPTION   ELWOOD, ROGER   OA
  EARTH MOTHER   SS   74
    BEST SCIENCE FICTION STORIES OF THE YEAR (1974)
                                        DEL REY, LESTER   AN
    LONG NIGHT OF WAITING AND OTHER STORIES
                                        ELWOOD, ROGER   OA

GLOECKNER, CAROLYN   (CONTINUED)
  MISCOUNT   SS   ASF 72 11
    BEST SCIENCE FICTION STORIES OF THE YEAR (1972)
                                        DEL REY, LESTER   AN
  SKYHOOK   SS
    NIGHT OF THE SPHINX AND OTHER STORIES ELWOOD, ROGER   OA

GODWIN, FRANCIS
  MAN ON THE MOONE, THE (1638)   EX
    *BEYOND TIME AND SPACE   DERLETH, AUGUST   AN

GODWIN, TOM
  COLD EQUATIONS, THE   NV   ASF 54 08
    ASPECTS OF SCIENCE FICTION   DOHERTY, G. D.   AN
    ASTOUNDING-ANALOG READER, THE VOLUME TWO
                                        HARRISON & ALDISS   AN
    BEST SCIENCE FICTION STORIES AND NOVELS: 1955
                                        DIKTY, T. E.   AN
    BEST SF 3   CRISPIN, EDMUND   AN
    BEYOND THE STARS AND OTHER STORIES ANONYMOUS   AN
    IN DREAMS AWAKE   FIEDLER, LESLIE A.   AN
    MASTERS' CHOICE   JANIFER, LAURENCE M.   AN
    MODERN SCIENCE FICTION   SPINRAD, NORMAN   AN
    NEW AWARENESS, THE   WARRICK & GREENBERG   AN
    SCIENCE FICTION HALL OF FAME VOLUME 1 SILVERBERG, ROBERT AN
    SCIENCE FICTION THROUGH THE AGES 2 EVANS, I. O.   AN
    THEMES IN SCIENCE FICTION   KELLEY, LEO P.   AN
    3000 YEARS OF FANTASY AND SCIENCE FICTION
                                        DE CAMP, L. S.&C.   AN
    5 TALES FROM TOMORROW   DIKTY, T. E.   AN
  GENTLE CAPTIVE, THE   SS   SAW 72
    SIGNS AND WONDERS   ELWOOD, ROGER   OA
    VISIONS OF TOMORROW   ELWOOD, ROGER   OA
  GREATER THING, THE   NV   ASF 54 02
    MORE PENGUIN SCIENCE FICTION   ALDISS, BRIAN W.   AN
  LAST VICTORY, THE   SS   IFS 57 08
    BEST SCIENCE FICTION STORIES AND NOVELS: 9TH SERIES
                                        DIKTY, T. E.   AN
  MOTHER OF INVENTION   SN   ASF 53 12
    SPECTRUM 5   AMIS & CONQUEST   AN
  WE'LL WALK AGAIN IN THE MOONLIGHT   SS
    CRISIS   ELWOOD, ROGER   OA
  YOU CREATED US   SS   FUN 55 10
    BEST SCIENCE FICTION STORIES AND NOVELS: 1956
                                        DIKTY, T. E.   AN
    6 FROM WORLDS BEYOND   DIKTY, T. E.   AN

GOETHE, J. V.
  APOTHEM   MS
    MATHEMATICAL MAGPIE, THE   FADIMAN, CLIFTON   AN

GOFORTH, LAURA
  LOVE CALLED THIS THING   SS C GAL 59 04
    SCIENCE FICTION FOR PEOPLE WHO HATE SCIENCE FICTION
                                        CARR, TERRY   AN
    SIXTH GALAXY READER, THE   GOLD, H. L.   AN
    WHAT STRANGE STARS AND SKIES   DAVIDSON, AVRAM   AC

GOGGIN, RICHARD
  FRANCES HARKINS   SS   FSF 52 12
    SPECULATIONS   SANDERS, THOMAS E.   AN
    17 X INFINITY   CONKLIN, GROFF   AN

GOGOL, NIKOLAI
  BLACK SUNDAY (THE VIY)   NV
    GHOULS, THE   HAINING, PETER   AN

GOHMAN, FRED
  FLYING TEACUP   SS   53
    TEEN-AGE OUTER SPACE STORIES   FURMAN, A. L.   AN

GOLD, H. L.   ALSO AS   DUDLEY DELL
  BODYGUARD AND 4 OTHER SHORT SF NOVELS FROM GALAXY AN H DBL 60
  FIFTH GALAXY READER, THE   AN H DBL 61
  FOURTH GALAXY READER, THE   AN H DBL 59
  GALAXY READER OF SCIENCE FICTION   AN H CRN 52
  GALAXY READER OF SCIENCE FICTION (BRITISH)   AN H GRY 53
  GALAXY SCIENCE FICTION OMNIBUS   AN H GRY 55
    SELECTIONS FROM "SECOND GALAXY READER OF SCIENCE FICTION"
  MIND PARTNER AND 8 OTHER NOVELETS FROM GALAXY AN H DBL 61
  OLD DIE RICH AND OTHER SCIENCE FICTION, THE AC H CRN 55
  SECOND GALAXY READER OF SCIENCE FICTION   AN H CRN 54
    ENGLISH DERIVATIVE ANTHOLOGY "GALAXY SCIENCE FICTION OMNIBUS"
  SIXTH GALAXY READER, THE   AN H DBL 62
  THIRD GALAXY READER, THE   AN H DBL 58
  WORLD THAT COULDN'T BE AND 8 OTHER SF NOVELETS AN H DBL 59
  5 GALAXY SHORT NOVELS   AN H DBL 58
  AND THREE TO GET READY   SS   FAN 52 SU
    OLD DIE RICH AND OTHER SCIENCE FICTION, THE
                                        GOLD, H. L.   AC
  AT THE POST   NV   GAL 53 10
    OLD DIE RICH AND OTHER SCIENCE FICTION, THE
                                        GOLD, H. L.   AC
  BIOGRAPHY PROJECT, THE   SS   GAL 51 09
    OLD DIE RICH AND OTHER SCIENCE FICTION, THE
                                        GOLD, H. L.   AC
  DON'T TAKE IT TO HEART   SS   FAN 53 08
    OLD DIE RICH AND OTHER SCIENCE FICTION, THE
                                        GOLD, H. L.   AC
  ENORMOUS ROOM, THE   SN C AMZ 53 11
    WORLDS APART   WILLIAMS-ELLIS& OWEN AN
    YEAR'S BEST SCIENCE FICTION NOVELS: 1954
                                        BLEILER & DIKTY   AN
  HERO   SS   TWS 39 10
    OLD DIE RICH AND OTHER SCIENCE FICTION, THE
                                        GOLD, H. L.   AC

```
GOLD, H. L.          (CONTINUED)
  HOW DO YOU KNOW YOU CAN'T WRITE SCIENCE FICTION?  IN
    WORLD THAT COULDN'T BE AND 8 OTHER SF NOVELETS
                                GOLD, H. L.           AN
  IN THIS CORNER                                      IN
    FOURTH GALAXY READER, THE   GOLD, H. L.           AN
  LOVE ETHEREAL (SEE LOVE IN THE DARK)                TC
  LOVE IN THE DARK (LOVE ETHEREAL)   SS   SUS 51 FL
    BEYOND THE END OF TIME      POHL, FREDERIK        AN
    INVISIBLE MEN               DAVENPORT, BASIL      AN
    OLD DIE RICH AND OTHER SCIENCE FICTION, THE
                                GOLD, H. L.           AC
    SF: AUTHORS' CHOICE 2       HARRISON, HARRY       AN
  MAN OF PARTS                     SS   NTL 54
    ALPHA 6                     SILVERBERG, ROBERT    AN
    OLD DIE RICH AND OTHER SCIENCE FICTION, THE
                                GOLD, H. L.           AC
  9 TALES OF SPACE AND TIME     HEALY, RAYMOND J.     OA
  MAN WITH ENGLISH, THE            SS   STR 53 01
    OLD DIE RICH AND OTHER SCIENCE FICTION, THE
                                GOLD, H. L.           AC
  SCIENCE FICTION FOR PEOPLE WHO HATE SCIENCE FICTION
                                CARR, TERRY           AN
    STAR OF STARS               POHL, FREDERIK        AN
    STAR SCIENCE FICTION STORIES POHL, FREDERIK       OA
    STRANGE GIFTS               SILVERBERG, ROBERT    AN
  MATTER OF FORM, A                SN   ASF 38 12
    ASSIGNMENT IN TOMORROW      POHL, FREDERIK        AN
    *BIG BOOK OF SCIENCE FICTION CONKLIN, GROFF       AN
    SCIENCE FICTION: THE GREAT YEARS POHL, C. & F.    AN
  MY WORD                                             IN
    WEIRD ONES, THE             HOWARD, IVAN          AN
  NO CHARGE FOR ALTERATIONS        NV   AMZ 53 05
    BEST FROM AMAZING, THE      WHITE, TED            AN
    OLD DIE RICH AND OTHER SCIENCE FICTION, THE
                                GOLD, H. L.           AC
  OLD DIE RICH, THE                NA   GAL 53 03
    OLD DIE RICH AND OTHER SCIENCE FICTION, THE
                                GOLD, H. L.           AC
  PERFECT MURDER                   SS   TWS 40 03
    *SCIENCE FICTION ADVENTURES IN DIMENSION
                                CONKLIN, GROFF        AN
  PERSONNEL PROBLEM                SS   GAL 58 09
    SIXTH GALAXY READER, THE    GOLD, H. L.           AN
  PROBLEM IN MURDER                NV   ASF 39 03
    OLD DIE RICH AND OTHER SCIENCE FICTION, THE
                                GOLD, H. L.           AC
  PROGRAM NOTES                                       IN
    THIRD GALAXY READER, THE    GOLD, H. L.           AN
  TO THE HILLS|                    ED   GAL 53 10
    SECOND GALAXY READER OF SCIENCE FICTION
                                GOLD, H. L.           AN
  TODAY'S TOMORROWS                                   IN
    5 GALAXY SHORT NOVELS       GOLD, H. L.           AN
  TROUBLE WITH WATER               SS   UNK 39 03
    DARK SIDE, THE              KNIGHT, DAMON         AN
    FROM UNKNOWN WORLDS         CAMPBELL, JOHN W. JR  AN
    OLD DIE RICH AND OTHER SCIENCE FICTION, THE
                                GOLD, H. L.           AC
    UNKNOWN, THE                BENSEN, D. R.         AN
    WANDERING STARS             DANN, JACK M.         AN
  WARM, DARK PLACES                SS   UNK 40 10
    BR-R-R-|                    CONKLIN, GROFF        AN

GOLD, HERBERT
  DAY THEY GOT BOSTON, THE         SS   FSF 61 09
    POLITICAL SCIENCE FICTION   GREENBERG& WARRICK    AN
    17 X INFINITY               CONKLIN, GROFF        AN
  WEIRD SHOW                       SS   PBY 58 04
    PLAYBOY BOOK OF HORROR AND THE SUPERNATURAL, THE
                                PLAYBOY, EDITORS OF   AN
    WEIRD SHOW                  PLAYBOY, EDITORS OF   AN

GOLDBARTH, ALBERT
  STARBIRTH (ENVOI: STARBIRTH)     SS   LMG 75
    NEW CONSTELLATIONS          DISCH & NAYLOR        OA

GOLDIN, STEPHEN          CO-EDITOR DAVID GERROLD
  ALIEN CONDITION, THE             OA   BAL 73 04
  BUT AS A SOLDIER, FOR HIS COUNTRY SS  UNI 74 05
    UNIVERSE 5                  CARR, TERRY           OA
  HARRIET                          SS C TAL 73
    FRONTIERS 1; TOMORROW'S ALTERNATIVES ELWOOD, ROGER OA
  INTRODUCTION                                        IN
    ALIEN CONDITION, THE        GOLDIN, STEPHEN       OA
  LAST GHOST, THE                  SS   PRT 71
    NEBULA AWARD STORIES  NO. 7 BIGGLE, LLOYD JR.     AN
    PROTOSTARS                  GERROLD & GOLDIN      OA
  NOR IRON BARS A CAGE             SS C ALC 73
    ALIEN CONDITION, THE        GOLDIN, STEPHEN       OA
  PRELUDE TO A SYMPHONY OF UNBORN SHOUTS SS FCR 75
    FUTURE CORRUPTION           ELWOOD, ROGER         OA
  STUBBORN                         SS   GEN 72
    GENERATION                  GERROLD, DAVID        OA
  SWEET DREAMS, MELISSA            SS   GAL 68 12
    BEST SF: 1968               HARRISON & ALDISS     AN
    ELEVENTH GALAXY READER, THE POHL, FREDERIK        AN
  WORLD WHERE WISHES WORKED, THE   SS   PRT 71
    PROTOSTARS                  GERROLD & GOLDIN      OA

GOLDING, WILLIAM
  ENVOY EXTRAORDINARY              NV   56
    SOMETIME, NEVER             ANONYMOUS             OA

GOLDSMITH, HOWARD
  LAST CONGREGATION, THE           SS   FCR 75
    FUTURE CORRUPTION           ELWOOD, ROGER         OA
    VISIONS OF TOMORROW         ELWOOD, ROGER         OA
  MUSIC OF MINOX, THE              SS
    MORE SCIENCE FICTION TALES  ELWOOD, ROGER         OA
  PLASTIC AGE, THE                 SS
    ADRIFT IN SPACE AND OTHER STORIES ELWOOD, ROGER   OA
  PROUST SYNDROME, THE             SS
    CRISIS                      ELWOOD, ROGER         OA

GOLDSMITH, RUTH M.
  YANKEE EXODUS                    SS   FSF 53 07
    BEST SCIENCE-FICTION STORIES: 1954, THE
                                BLEILER & DIKTY       AN

GOLDSTONE, HERBERT
  VIRTUOSO                         SS   FSF 53 02
    *SCIENCE FICTION THINKING MACHINES CONKLIN, GROFF AN

GOODALE, EARL
  SUCCESS STORY                    NV   GAL 60 04
    SIXTH GALAXY READER, THE    GOLD, H. L.           AN

GOODWIN, JOHN B. L.
  COCOON, THE                      SS   STO 46 10
    STRANGE BEASTS AND UNNATURAL MONSTERS STERN, PHILIP VAN D. AN
    TIMELESS STORIES FOR TODAY AND TOMORROW
                                BRADBURY, RAY         AN

GOR, GENNADY
  BOY, THE                         SS
    PATH INTO THE UNKNOWN       ANONYMOUS             AN
  DWELLER IN TWO WORLDS, A         SS
    RUSSIAN SCIENCE FICTION, 1968 MAGIDOFF, ROBERT    AN
  GARDEN, THE                      SS   68
    AIR OF MARS AND OTHER STORIES, THE GINSBURG, MIRRA AN
    RUSSIAN SCIENCE FICTION, 1969 MAGIDOFF, ROBERT    AN
  MINOTAUR, THE                    SS
    RUSSIAN SCIENCE FICTION, 1969 MAGIDOFF, ROBERT    AN

GORDON, GILES
  FOURTEEN STATIONS ON THE NORTHERN LINE  SS
    NEW S.F., THE               JONES, LANGDON        OA
  ILLUSIONIST, THE                 SS   NWB 75 09
    NEW WORLDS NINE             BAILEY, HILARY        OA
  MAESTRO                          SS   NWB 75 09
    NEW WORLDS NINE             BAILEY, HILARY        OA
  OFFICE MEETING, AN               SS   NWQ 73 05
    NEW WORLDS NO. 5            MOORCOCK & PLATT      OA
  SCREAM                           SS   NWS 68 07
    BEST SF STORIES FROM NEW WORLDS 5 MOORCOCK, MICHAEL AN

GORDON, ISABEL S. AND SOPHIE SORKIN
  ARMCHAIR SCIENCE READER, THE     AN H SAS 59
    ONLY SCIENCE FICTION LISTED

GORDON, RICHARD M.
  PUNISHMENT TO FIT THE CRIMES, A  SS   62
    FIEND IN YOU, THE           BEAUMONT, CHARLES     AN

GORDON, W. J. J.
  NOBEL PRIZE WINNERS              SS   ATL 63 11
    9TH ANNUAL OF THE YEAR'S BEST S-F, THE MERRIL, JUDITH AN

GORES, JOE
  CRIMINAL, THE                    SS   ADM 70 12
    STRANGE BED FELLOWS         SCORTIA, THOMAS N.    AN
  FAULTY REGISTER                  SS   TVW 73
    TWO VIEWS OF WONDER         SCORTIA & YARBRO      OA

GOREY, EDWARD
  QUAKE, QUAKE, QUAKE (EXCERPT)    IL   61
    7TH ANNUAL OF THE YEAR'S BEST S-F, THE MERRIL, JUDITH AN

GOSSETT, THOROLD
  KISS PRECISE (GENERALIZED), THE  PM   NTR 37 01
    MATHEMATICAL MAGPIE, THE    FADIMAN, CLIFTON      AN

GOTLEIB, PHYLLIS
  PLANETOID IDIOT                  NV   FSF 67 05
    TO THE STARS                SILVERBERG, ROBERT    AN

GOTSCHALK, FELIX C.
  BONUS BABY                       SS   SFE 74 01
    SCIENCE FICTION EMPHASIS NO. 1 GERROLD, DAVID     OA
  CHARISMA LEAK                    NV   NDM 76 06
    NEW DIMENSIONS 6            SILVERBERG, ROBERT    OA
  DAY IN THE SOUTH QUAD, A         SS   NDM 75 05
    NEW DIMENSIONS 5            SILVERBERG, ROBERT    OA
  DAY OF THE BIG TEST, THE         NV   76
    FUTURE POWER                DANN & DOZOIS         OA
  EXAMINATION, THE                 SS   NDM 74 04
    NEW DIMENSIONS 4            SILVERBERG, ROBERT    OA
  FAMILY WINTER OF 1986, THE       SS   ORB 76 18
    ORBIT 18                    KNIGHT, DAMON         OA
  HOME SWEET GERIATRIC DOME        SS   NDM 77 07
    NEW DIMENSIONS 7            SILVERBERG, ROBERT    OA
  MAN WITH THE GOLDEN RETICULATES, THE SS ORB 75 17
    ORBIT 17                    KNIGHT, DAMON         OA
  NAPOLEONIC WARS, THE             SS
    BEYOND TIME                 LEY, SANDRA           OA
  OUTER CONCENTRIC                 SS   NDM 74 04
    NEW DIMENSIONS 4            SILVERBERG, ROBERT    OA
```

GOTTESMAN, S. D.

GOULART, RON

GOTTESMAN, S. D.
  SIR MALLORY'S MAGNITUDE   SS   SFQ 41 WI
    INTO THE FOURTH DIMENSION   CUMMINGS, RAY   AN

GOULART, RON
  BROKE DOWN ENGINE AND OTHER TROUBLES WITH MACHINES AC H MAC 71
  CHAMELEON CORPS & OTHER SHAPE CHANGERS, THE   AC H MAC 72
  GHOST BREAKER   DC   ACE 71
  NUTZENBOLTS   AC H MAC 75
  ODD JOB NO. 101   AC H SCB 75
  WHAT'S BECOME OF SCREWLOOSE? AND OTHER INQUIRIES AC H SCB 71
  ALL FOR LOVE (BY WAY OF MARS)   SS   WOT 65 03
    BROKE DOWN ENGINE AND OTHER TROUBLES WITH MACHINES
                                    GOULART, RON   AC
  ANYTHING FOR LAUGHS (SEE JOKER FOR HIRE)   TC
  BADINAGE   SS   NEW 65 AN
    NUTZENBOLTS   GOULART, RON   AC
    PSEUDO PEOPLE, THE   NOLAN, WILLIAM F.   AN
  BREAKAWAY HOUSE   SS   FSF 66 05
    GHOST BREAKER   GOULART, RON   DC
  BROKE AND HUNGRY, NO PLACE TO GO (SEE BROKE DOWN ENGINE)
                                                   TC
  BROKE DOWN ENGINE (BROKE AND HUNGRY, NO PLACE TO GO)
                                                   SS   GAL 69 11
    BROKE DOWN ENGINE AND OTHER TROUBLES WITH MACHINES
                                    GOULART, RON   AC
  BY WAY OF MARS (SEE ALL FOR LOVE)   TC
  CALLING DR. CLOCKWORK   SS   AMZ 65 03
    ANDROIDS, TIME MACHINES AND BLUE GIRAFFES
                                    ELWOOD & GHIDALIA   AN
    AS TOMORROW BECOMES TODAY   SULLIVAN, CHARLES W. AN
    BROKE DOWN ENGINE AND OTHER TROUBLES WITH MACHINES
                                    GOULART, RON   AC
    WORLD'S BEST SCIENCE FICTION: 1966 WOLLHEIM & CARR AN
  CHAMELEON   SS   FSF 64 09
    CHAMELEON CORPS & OTHER SHAPE CHANGERS, THE
                                    GOULART, RON   AC
  CHANGE OVER   SS   NEW 72 AC
    CHAMELEON CORPS & OTHER SHAPE CHANGERS, THE
                                    GOULART, RON   AC
  CONFESSIONS   NV   FSF 70 08
    BEST FROM FANTASY AND SCIENCE FICTION: 19
                                    FERMAN, EDWARD L.   AN
    WHAT'S BECOME OF SCREWLOOSE? AND OTHER INQUIRIES
                                    GOULART, RON   AC
    WORLD'S BEST SCIENCE FICTION: 1971 WOLLHEIM & CARR AN
  COPSTATE   SS   FSF 69 05
    CHAMELEON CORPS & OTHER SHAPE CHANGERS, THE
                                    GOULART, RON   AC
  CYBERNETIC TABERNACLE JOB, THE   NV   INY 72 03
    INFINITY 3   HOSKINS, ROBERT   OA
    ODD JOB NO. 101   GOULART, RON   AC
  DINGBAT   NV   IFS 73 12
    NUTZENBOLTS   GOULART, RON   AC
  DISPOSAL   SS   VSF 70 02
    BROKE DOWN ENGINE AND OTHER TROUBLES WITH MACHINES
                                    GOULART, RON   AC
    CITY: 2000 A.D., THE   CLEM/GREENBERG/&   AN
  DOWN AND OUT   SS   FSF 73 08
    NUTZENBOLTS   GOULART, RON   AC
  EXPERIMENT IN AUTOBIOGRAPHY   SS   FSF 66 07
    BEST FROM FANTASY AND SCIENCE FICTION: 16
                                    FERMAN, EDWARD L.   AN
  FILL IN THE BLANK   SS   FSF 67 05
    BEST FROM FANTASY AND SCIENCE FICTION: 17
                                    FERMAN, EDWARD L.   AN
    GHOST BREAKER   GOULART, RON   DC
  FOREWORD: MAN OF A THOUSAND FACES   IN
    CHAMELEON CORPS & OTHER SHAPE CHANGERS, THE
                                    GOULART, RON   AC
  FOREWORD: POPULAR MECHANICS   IN
    NUTZENBOLTS   GOULART, RON   AC
  FREE AT LAST   SS   INY 73 05
    INFINITY 5   HOSKINS, ROBERT   OA
    NUTZENBOLTS   GOULART, RON   AC
  GHOST PATROL, THE   SS   FSF 68 10
    GHOST BREAKER   GOULART, RON   DC
  GIGOLO   SS   FSF 72 08
    MARRIAGE AND THE FAMILY THROUGH SCIENCE FICTION
                                    CLEAR/WARRICK/&   AN
    NUTZENBOLTS   GOULART, RON   AC
  HARDCASTLE   SS   NEW 71 AC
    ANTIGRAV: COSMIC COMEDIES   STRICK, PHILIP   AN
    INSIDE INFORMATION   MOWSHOWITZ, ABBE   AN
    WHAT'S BECOME OF SCREWLOOSE? AND OTHER INQUIRIES
                                    GOULART, RON   AC
  HELP STAMP OUT CHESNEY   SS   NEW 71 DC
    GHOST BREAKER   GOULART, RON   DC
  HOBO JUNGLE   NV   FSF 70 06
    WHAT'S BECOME OF SCREWLOOSE? AND OTHER INQUIRIES
                                    GOULART, RON   AC
  IGNATZ   SS   IFS 60 03
    CHAMELEON CORPS & OTHER SHAPE CHANGERS, THE
                                    GOULART, RON   AC
  INNOCENCE OF FATHER BANGS, THE   SS   PNT 72
    NUTZENBOLTS   GOULART, RON   AC
  INTO THE SHOP   SS   FSF 64 04
    BEST FROM FANTASY AND SCIENCE FICTION: 14
                                    DAVIDSON, AVRAM   AN
    SPECTRUM 4   AMIS & CONQUEST   AN
    WHAT'S BECOME OF SCREWLOOSE? AND OTHER INQUIRIES
                                    GOULART, RON   AC
    YOU AND SCIENCE FICTION   HOLLISTER, BERNARD C AN
  JOKER FOR HIRE (ANYTHING FOR LAUGHS)   NV   FAN 63 05
    BROKE DOWN ENGINE AND OTHER TROUBLES WITH MACHINES
                                    GOULART, RON   AC

GOULART, RON   (CONTINUED)
  JUNIOR PARTNER   SS   FAN 62 09
    WHAT'S BECOME OF SCREWLOOSE? AND OTHER INQUIRIES
                                    GOULART, RON   AC
  KATY DIALOGUES, THE   SS   FSF 58 07
    BROKE DOWN ENGINE AND OTHER TROUBLES WITH MACHINES
                                    GOULART, RON   AC
  KEARNY'S LAST CASE   SS   FSF 65 09
    GHOST BREAKER   GOULART, RON   DC
  KEEPING AN EYE ON JANEY   SS   INY 70 01
    INFINITY 1   HOSKINS, ROBERT   OA
    WHAT'S BECOME OF SCREWLOOSE? AND OTHER INQUIRIES
                                    GOULART, RON   AC
  LETTERS TO THE EDITOR (PMG 50 10)   SS   FSF 52 04
    BEST FROM FANTASY AND SCIENCE FICTION: 2
                                    BOUCHER & MCCOMAS   AN
  LOFTHOUSE (A MAN'S HOME IS HIS CASTLE)   SS   PBY 69 03
    BROKE DOWN ENGINE AND OTHER TROUBLES WITH MACHINES
                                    GOULART, RON   AC
  LOOKING INTO IT   SS   NEW 72 AC
    CHAMELEON CORPS & OTHER SHAPE CHANGERS, THE
                                    GOULART, RON   AC
  MAN'S HOME IS HIS CASTLE, A (ALSO AS LOFTHOUSE) SS   PBY 69 03
    FULLY AUTOMATED LOVE LIFE OF HENRY KEANRIDGE
                                    PLAYBOY, EDITORS OF AN
  MASTERPIECE   SS   FSF 72 05
    CHAMELEON CORPS & OTHER SHAPE CHANGERS, THE
                                    GOULART, RON   AC
  MCNAMARA'S FISH   SS   FSF 63 07
    BEST FROM FANTASY AND SCIENCE FICTION: 13
                                    DAVIDSON, AVRAM   AN
    GHOST BREAKER   GOULART, RON   DC
  MONTE CRISTO COMPLEX   SS
    WHAT'S BECOME OF SCREWLOOSE? AND OTHER INQUIRIES
                                    GOULART, RON   AC
  MUSCADINE   SS   FSF 68 04
    BEST FROM FANTASY AND SCIENCE FICTION: 18
                                    FERMAN, EDWARD L.   AN
    BROKE DOWN ENGINE AND OTHER TROUBLES WITH MACHINES
                                    GOULART, RON   AC
  NEW LO|, A   SS   FSF 58 01
    BEST FROM FANTASY AND SCIENCE FICTION: 8
                                    BOUCHER, ANTHONY   AN
  NOBODY STARVES   SS   FSF 64 02
    BROKE DOWN ENGINE AND OTHER TROUBLES WITH MACHINES
                                    GOULART, RON   AC
    MAN AGAINST TOMORROW   NOLAN, WILLIAM F.   AN
  NOT THAT SHAGGY   SS   INY 72 04
    INFINITY 4   HOSKINS, ROBERT   OA
    NUTZENBOLTS   GOULART, RON   AC
  ODD JOB NO. 101   SS   FSF 74
    ODD JOB NO. 101   GOULART, RON   AC
  PASSAGE TO MURDSTONE   SS   FSF 71 10
    ODD JOB NO. 101   GOULART, RON   AC
  PLEASE STAND BY   NV   FSF 62 01
    BEST FROM FANTASY AND SCIENCE FICTION: 12
                                    DAVIDSON, AVRAM   AN
    CHAMELEON CORPS & OTHER SHAPE CHANGERS, THE
                                    GOULART, RON   AC
    GHOST BREAKER   GOULART, RON   DC
  PLUMROSE   SS   FAN 63 06
    ODD JOB NO. 101   GOULART, RON   AC
  PREZ   SS   IFS 70 02
    BEST FROM IF, THE VOLUME I   IF, EDITORS OF   AN
    WHAT'S BECOME OF SCREWLOOSE? AND OTHER INQUIRIES
                                    GOULART, RON   AC
  PRINCESS NO. 22   SS   FSF 62 05
    BROKE DOWN ENGINE AND OTHER TROUBLES WITH MACHINES
                                    GOULART, RON   AC
  RAKE   SS   FSF 65 06
    BEST FROM FANTASY AND SCIENCE FICTION: 15
                                    FERMAN, EDWARD L.   AN
    CHAMELEON CORPS & OTHER SHAPE CHANGERS, THE
                                    GOULART, RON   AC
  RALPH WOLLSTONECRAFT HEDGE: A MEMOIR   SS   FSF 59 05
    BEST FROM FANTASY AND SCIENCE FICTION: 9
                                    MILLS, ROBERT P.   AN
  REGARDING PATIENT 724   SS   ASF 73 11
    ODD JOB NO. 101   GOULART, RON   AC
  ROMANCE OF DR. TANNER, THE   SS   UNI 71 01
    UNIVERSE 1   CARR, TERRY   OA
  SHANDY   SS   IFS 58 10
    CHAMELEON CORPS & OTHER SHAPE CHANGERS, THE
                                    GOULART, RON   AC
  SOCIETY FOR THE PREVENTION   SS   GAM 64 03
    SEA OF SPACE, A   NOLAN, WILLIAM F.   AN
  STOCKYARD BLUES   SS   COV 70 01
    NUTZENBOLTS   GOULART, RON   AC
  STRAWHOUSE PAVILION, THE   SS   UNI 74 04
    GHOST BREAKER   GOULART, RON   DC
  STUNGUN SLIM   SS   GAL 60 12
    UNIVERSE 4   CARR, TERRY   OA
  SUBJECT TO CHANGE   NV   FSF 70 08
    CHAMELEON CORPS & OTHER SHAPE CHANGERS, THE
                                    GOULART, RON   AC
  SUNFLOWER   SS   IFS 70 04
    CHAMELEON CORPS & OTHER SHAPE CHANGERS, THE
                                    GOULART, RON   AC
  SWAP   NV   FSF 67 11
    NUTZENBOLTS   GOULART, RON   AC
  SWORD SWALLOWER, THE   SS   FAN 65 05
    WORLD'S BEST SCIENCE FICTION: 1968 WOLLHEIM & CARR AN
  TERMINAL
    BROKE DOWN ENGINE AND OTHER TROUBLES WITH MACHINES
                                    GOULART, RON   AC

GOULART, RON   (CONTINUED)
  11TH ANNUAL OF THE YEAR'S BEST S-F, THE
                                 MERRIL, JUDITH   AN
  TO THE RESCUE   SS   FSF 66 01
    BROKE DOWN ENGINE AND OTHER TROUBLES WITH MACHINES
                                 GOULART, RON   AC
  TROUBLE WITH MACHINES, THE   SS   PBY 68 08
    BROKE DOWN ENGINE AND OTHER TROUBLES WITH MACHINES
                                 GOULART, RON   AC
  FULLY AUTOMATED LOVE LIFE OF HENRY KEANRIDGE
                                 PLAYBOY, EDITORS OF AN
  TWO DAYS RUNNING AND THEN SKIP A DAY SS AMZ 67 02
    NUTZENBOLTS   GOULART, RON   AC
  UNCLE ARLY   SS   FSF 62 07
    GHOST BREAKER   GOULART, RON   DC
  VARIETIES OF RELIGIOUS EXPERIENCE SS FSF 73 06
    ODD JOB NO. 101   GOULART, RON   AC
  WAY THINGS DON'T WORK, THE   IN
    BROKE DOWN ENGINE AND OTHER TROUBLES WITH MACHINES
                                 GOULART, RON   AC
  WAY THINGS WORK, THE   SS   FSF 71 03
    ODD JOB NO. 101   GOULART, RON   AC
  WHAT'S BECOME OF SCREWLOOSE?   SS   IFS 70 07
    WHAT'S BECOME OF SCREWLOOSE? AND OTHER INQUIRIES
                                 GOULART, RON   AC
  WHISTLER   SS   EIO 73
    EROS IN ORBIT   ELDER, JOSEPH   OA
    NUTZENBOLTS   GOULART, RON   AC
  WHOLE ROUND WORLD, THE   NV   FIN 70
    FUTURE IS NOW, THE   NOLAN, WILLIAM F.   OA
  YES-MEN OF VENUS, THE   SS   AMZ 63 07
    WHAT'S BECOME OF SCREWLOOSE? AND OTHER INQUIRIES
                                 GOULART, RON   AC

GOVAN, CHRISTINE N.
  MISS WINTERS AND THE WIND   SS   TOM 46 05
    TIMELESS STORIES FOR TODAY AND TOMORROW
                                 BRADBURY, RAY   AN

GRAHAM, HOWARD W.   PSEUD. FOR HOWARD E. WANDREI
  OTHER, THE   SS   ASF 34 12
    SCIENCE FICTION OF THE 30'S KNIGHT, DAMON   AN
  WALL, THE   SS   ASF 34 05
    SCIENCE FICTION OF THE 30'S KNIGHT, DAMON   AN

GRAHAM, JOYCE M.   SEE PSEUD. JAN STRUTHER

GRAHAM, L. A.
  MINIVER PROBLEM, THE (SOLUTION) AR 59
    MATHEMATICAL MAGPIE, THE   FADIMAN, CLIFTON   AN
  THREE VERSES   PM   59
    MATHEMATICAL MAGPIE, THE   FADIMAN, CLIFTON   AN

GRAHAM, ROGER P.   SEE PSEUD. ROG PHILLIPS

GRANIN, DANIIL
  JOURNEY INTO THE FUTURE   SS
    RUSSIAN SCIENCE FICTION, 1969 MAGIDOFF, ROBERT AN

GRANOSKI, CLARENCE
  EPHONY'S SPECTACLES   SS   SFQ 41 WI
    INTO THE FOURTH DIMENSION   CUMMINGS, RAY   AN

GRANT, ALLAN
  FICTION   PM   UNK 41 02
    FROM UNKNOWN WORLDS   CAMPBELL, JOHN W. JR AN

GRANT, C. L.
  EVERYBODY A WINNER, THE BARKER CRIED SS ORB 74 13
    ORBIT 13   KNIGHT, DAMON   OA
  IN DONOVAN'S TIME   SS   ORB 75 16
    ORBIT 16   KNIGHT, DAMON   OA
  MAGIC CHILD, THE   SS   NMD 73
    FRONTIERS 2: THE NEW MIND   ELWOOD, ROGER   OA
  REST IS SILENCE, THE   SS   FSF 74 09
    NEBULA AWARD STORIES 10   GUNN, JAMES E.   AN
  SUMMER OF THE IRISH SEA, THE   SS   ORB 72 11
    FUTURE PASTIMES   EDELSTEIN, SCOTT   OA
    ORBIT 11   KNIGHT, DAMON   OA
  WEEP NO MORE, OLD LADY   SS   FUQ 73
    FUTURE QUEST   ELWOOD, ROGER   OA
  WHITE WOLF CALLING   SS   FSF 75 04
    YEAR'S BEST HORROR STORIES: SERIES IV, THE
                                 PAGE, GERALD W.   AN

GRANT, GORDON
  ILLUSTRATIONS TO "THE SCARLET PLAGUE" IL
    SCIENCE FICTION OF JACK LONDON, THE LONDON, JACK AC

GRASS, GUNTER
  IN THE EGG (TRANSLATED BY MICHAEL HAMBURGER) PM 66
    SF12   MERRIL, JUDITH   AN

GRASTY, WILLIAM K.
  ONE AFTERNOON IN BUSTERVILLE   SS   STG 74
    STRANGE GODS   ELWOOD, ROGER   OA

GRAVES, JOCELYN
  PIE IN THE SKY   SS   ADS 75 02
    ARMADA SCI-FI TWO   DAVIS, RICHARD   OA

GRAVES, ROBERT
  ABOMINABLE MR. GUNN, THE   SS
    MATHEMATICAL MAGPIE, THE   FADIMAN, CLIFTON   AN
  SHOUT, THE (1929)   SS   FSF 52 04

GRAVES, ROBERT   (CONTINUED)
  BEST FROM FANTASY AND SCIENCE FICTION: 2
                                 BOUCHER & MCCOMAS   AN
  LIGHT FANTASTIC, THE   HARRISON, HARRY   AN

GRAY, WILL H.
  BEES FROM BORNEO, THE   SS   AMZ 31 02
    OMNIBUS OF SCIENCE FICTION   CONKLIN, GROFF   AN

GREEN, GERALD
  DISPATCHER, THE   NV   PBY 67 08
    PLAYBOY'S STORIES OF THE SINISTER & STRANGE
                                 PLAYBOY, EDITORS OF AN

GREEN, JOSEPH
  AFFAIR WITH GENIUS, AN   AC H GOL 69
  CONSCIENCE INTERPLANETARY   NO   DAW 74
  AFFAIR WITH GENIUS, AN   SS   FSF 69 03
    AFFAIR WITH GENIUS, AN   GREEN, JOSEPH   AC
  BIRD LOVER, THE   NV   SCS 73
    SHOWCASE   ELWOOD, ROGER   OA
  BIRTH OF A BUTTERFLY   SS   NWR 67 10
    NEW WRITINGS IN SF. 8   CARNELL, JOHN   AN
    NEW WRITINGS IN SF. 10   CARNELL, JOHN   OA
  BUTTERFLYS OF BEAUTY, THE   NV   FSF 71 06
    CONSCIENCE INTERPLANETARY   GREEN, JOSEPH   NO
  CREATORS, THE   SS   NWR 64 02
    BEST FROM NEW WRITINGS IN S-F FIRST SELECTION, THE
                                 CARNELL, JOHN   AN
    NEW WRITINGS IN SF. 2   CARNELL, JOHN   OA
  CRYER OF CRYSTAL, THE   SS   ASF 71 10
    CONSCIENCE INTERPLANETARY   GREEN, JOSEPH   NO
  DANCE OF THE CATS   SS   NWS 65 12
    AFFAIR WITH GENIUS, AN   GREEN, JOSEPH   AC
  DEATH AND THE SENSPERIENCE POET SS NWR 70 17
    NEW WRITINGS IN SF. 17   CARNELL, JOHN   OA
  DEATH IN COVENTRY, A   SS   DYS 75
    DYSTOPIAN VISIONS   ELWOOD, ROGER   OA
  DECISION MAKERS, THE   NV   GAL 65 04
    AFFAIR WITH GENIUS, AN   GREEN, JOSEPH   AC
    AS TOMORROW BECOMES TODAY   SULLIVAN, CHARLES W. AN
    CONSCIENCE INTERPLANETARY   GREEN, JOSEPH   NO
    WORLD'S BEST SCIENCE FICTION: 1966 WOLLHEIM & CARR AN
  ENCOUNTER WITH A CARNIVORE   SS   EPC 75
    EPOCH   ELWOOD & SILVERBERG OA
  ENGINEER, THE   SS   NWS 62 02
    AFFAIR WITH GENIUS, AN   GREEN, JOSEPH   AC
  FIRST LIGHT ON A DARKLING PLAIN SS NWR 71 19
    NEW WRITINGS IN SF. 19   CARNELL, JOHN   OA
  HAGGARD HONEYMOON   NV C NWR 64 01
    NEW WRITINGS IN SF. 1   CARNELL, JOHN   OA
  JINN   SS   GAL 68 12
    AFFAIR WITH GENIUS, AN   GREEN, JOSEPH   AC
    ELEVENTH GALAXY READER, THE POHL, FREDERIK   AN
  LET MY PEOPLE GO!   SS
    OTHER SIDE OF TOMORROW, THE ELWOOD, ROGER   OA
  LIFE-FORCE   SS   NWS 62 11
    AFFAIR WITH GENIUS, AN   GREEN, JOSEPH   AC
  ONCE AROUND ARCTURUS   NV   IFS 62 09
    AFFAIR WITH GENIUS, AN   GREEN, JOSEPH   AC
  SHAMBLERS OF MISERY, THE   NV   FSF 69 08
    CONSCIENCE INTERPLANETARY   GREEN, JOSEPH   NO
  SINGLE COMBAT   SS   NWS 64 08
    AFFAIR WITH GENIUS, AN   GREEN, JOSEPH   AC
    COMBAT SF   DICKSON, GORDON R. AN
  SPACE TO MOVE   SS   NMD 73
    FRONTIERS 2: THE NEW MIND   ELWOOD, ROGER   OA
  TREASURE HUNT   SS   NWR 65 05
    NEW WRITINGS IN SF. 5   CARNELL, JOHN   OA
  TUNNEL OF LOVE   SS   NWS 65 01
    AFFAIR WITH GENIUS, AN   GREEN, JOSEPH   AC
  WAITING WORLD, THE   SS
    FUTURE KIN   ELWOOD, ROGER   OA
  WHEN I HAVE PASSED AWAY   NV   NWR 69 15
    NEW WRITINGS IN SF. 9   CARNELL, JOHN   AN
    NEW WRITINGS IN SF. 15   CARNELL, JOHN   OA

GREEN, ROBERT M. JR.
  APOLOGY TO INKY   NV   FSF 66 01
    BEST FROM FANTASY AND SCIENCE FICTION: 16
                                 FERMAN, EDWARD L.   AN
    SCIENCE FICTION ARGOSY, A   KNIGHT, DAMON   AN

GREEN, ROGER L.
  NOTES TO AFTER TEN YEARS   MS
    DARK TOWER AND OTHER STORIES, THE LEWIS, C. S.   AC

GREENBERG, ALVIN
  "FRANZ KAFKA" BY JORGE LUIS BORGES SS NAR 70 08
    BEST SF: 1970   HARRISON & ALDISS   AN

GREENBERG, MARTIN
  ALL ABOUT THE FUTURE   AN H GNM 55
  COMING ATTRACTIONS   NF H GNM 57
  CRUCIBLE OF POWER, THE   AN H BDL 53
    3 SELECTIONS FROM "FIVE SCIENCE FICTION NOVELS"
  FIVE SCIENCE FICTION NOVELS   AN H GNM 52
    ENGLISH DERIVATIVE ANTHOLOGY "CRUCIBLE OF POWER"
  JOURNEY TO INFINITY   AN H GNM 51
  MEN AGAINST THE STARS   AN H GNM 50
  MEN AGAINST THE STARS (BRITISH) AN H GRY 51
  MEN AGAINST THE STARS (9 OF 12) AN PYR 56 12
  ROBOT AND THE MAN, THE   AN H GNM 53
  TRAVELLERS OF SPACE   IN
    FOREWORD   AN H GNM 53
    ALL ABOUT THE FUTURE   GREENBERG, MARTIN   AN

GREENBERG , MARTIN

GREENBERG , MARTIN   GRINNELL, DAVID

GREENBERG , MARTIN   (CONTINUED)
  JOURNEY TO INFINITY   GREENBERG , MARTIN   AN
  *MEN AGAINST THE STARS   GREENBERG , MARTIN   AN
  ROBOT AND THE MAN, THE   GREENBERG , MARTIN   AN
  TRAVELLERS OF SPACE   GREENBERG , MARTIN   AN
  PREFACE   IN
  COMING ATTRACTIONS   GREENBERG , MARTIN   NF

GREENBERG, MARTIN HARRY, JOHN W. MILSTEAD, JOSEPH D. OLANDER
  AND PATRICIA S. WARRICK
  SOCIAL PROBLEMS THROUGH SCIENCE FICTION   AN L SMP 75

GREENBERG, MARTIN HARRY, JOSEPH D. OLANDER AND
  PATRICIA S. WARRICK
  RUN TO STARLIGHT, SPORTS THROUGH SCIENCE FICTION   AN H DCT 75

GREENBERG, MARTIN HARRY AND JOSEPH D. OLANDER
  BEST OF JOHN JAKES, THE (LISTED UNDER JOHN JAKES)   EC   DAW 77 06
  TOMORROW, INC.   AN L TAP 76

GREENBERG, MARTIN HARRY AND PATRICIA S. WARRICK
  POLITICAL SCIENCE FICTION   AN L PRH 74

GREENBERG, MARTIN HARRY
              SEE ALSO
  CO-EDITORS V. CLEAR, R. CLEM, H. KATZ, C. MASON, J. MILSTEAD,
     J. OLANDER AND P. WARRICK
  INTRODUCTION   IN C
  BEST OF JOHN JAKES, THE   JAKES, JOHN W.   AC
  MARRIAGE AND THE FAMILY THROUGH SCIENCE FICTION
                                  CLEAR/WARRICK/&   AN
  NEW AWARENESS, THE   WARRICK & GREENBERG AN
  POLITICAL SCIENCE FICTION   GREENBERG& WARRICK   AN
  RUN TO STARLIGHT, SPORTS THROUGH SCIENCE FICTION
                                  GREENBERG/OLANDER/& AN
  SCHOOL AND SOCIETY THROUGH SCIENCE FICTION
                                  OLANDER/GREENBERG/& AN
  SOCIAL PROBLEMS THROUGH SCIENCE FICTION
                                  GREENBERG/MILSTEAD/& AN
  SOCIOLOGY THROUGH SCIENCE FICTION   MILSTEAD/GREENBERG/& AN
  TOMORROW, INC.   GREENBERG& OLANDER   AN
  INTRODUCTION: WHY THE CITY   IN C
  CITY: 2000 A.D., THE   CLEM/GREENBERG/&   AN
  PREFACE   IN C
  AMERICAN GOVERNMENT THROUGH SCIENCE FICTION
                                  OLANDER/GREENBERG/& AN
  ANTHROPOLOGY THROUGH SCIENCE FICTION   MASON, C/GREENBERG/& AN
  INTRODUCTORY PSYCHOLOGY THROUGH SCIENCE FICTION
                                  KATZ/WARRICK/&   AN
  NEW AWARENESS, THE   WARRICK & GREENBERG AN
  POLITICAL SCIENCE FICTION   GREENBERG& WARRICK   AN

GREENBLATT, JONATHAN
  ZEN ARCHER, THE   SS   NEW 75 AN
  NEW IMPROVED SUN, THE   DISCH, THOMAS M.   AN

GREENE, GRAHAM
  DISCOVERY IN THE WOODS, A   NV   63
  PAST, PRESENT, AND FUTURE PERFECT   WOLFE, J&FITZ GERALD AN
  SPECULATIONS   SANDERS, THOMAS E.   AN
  END OF THE PARTY, THE (1947)   SS   WBY 50 12
  CHILDREN OF WONDER   TENN, WILLIAM   AN
  LIGHT FANTASTIC, THE   HARRISON, HARRY   AN
  PERCHANCE TO DREAM   KNIGHT, DAMON   AN
  PROOF POSITIVE (HRP 47 10)   SS   FSF 52 08
  DECADE OF FANTASY AND SCIENCE FICTION, A
                                  MILLS, ROBERT P.   AN

GREENFIELD, IRVING A
  WATERS OF DEATH   NO   LAN 67
  SCIENCE FICTION SPECIAL 1   ANONYMOUS   AN

GREENHOUGH, TERRY
  DOLL   SS
  ANDROMEDA I   WESTON, PETER   OA
  TREE IN THE FOREST, THE   SS   SFM 74 02
  BEST OF SCIENCE FICTION MONTHLY, THE   SACKS, JANET
  WILBUR   SS   SFM 74 04
  BEST OF SCIENCE FICTION MONTHLY, THE   SACKS, JANET AN

GREER, WILLIAM W.
  QUADS FROM MARS   SS   BLF
  BOYS' LIFE BOOK OF OUTER SPACE STORIES, THE
                                  BOY'S LIFE, ED. OF   AN

GREGOR, LEE   PSEUD. FOR MILTON A. ROTHMAN
  HEAVY PLANET   SS   ASF 39 08
  *ADVENTURES IN TIME AND SPACE   HEALY & MCCOMAS   AN
  EXPERT DREAMERS, THE   POHL, FREDERIK   AN
  MORE ADVENTURES IN TIME AND SPACE   HEALY & MCCOMAS AN
  POWER PLANT   SS   SFQ 41 WI
  INTO THE FOURTH DIMENSION   CUMMINGS, RAY   AN

GRENDON, EDWARD
  CRISIS   SS   ASF 51 06
  *INVADERS OF EARTH   CONKLIN, GROFF   AN
  FIGURE, THE   SS   ASF 47 07
  FIFTY SHORT SCIENCE FICTION TALES   ASIMOV & CONKLIN AN
  *TREASURY OF SCIENCE FICTION, A CONKLIN, GROFF   AN
  TRIP ONE   SS   ASF 49 07
  GIANTS UNLEASHED   CONKLIN, GROFF   AN
  SPACE, SPACE, SPACE   SLOANE, WILLIAM   AN

GRENDON, STEPHEN   PSEUD. FOR AUGUST DERLETH
  MR. GEORGE   NV   WRT 47 03
  MORE LITTLE MONSTERS   ELWOOD & GHIDALIA   AN

GRENDON, STEPHEN   (CONTINUED)
  MRS. MANIFOLD   SS   49
  GIRL WITH THE HUNGRY EYES, AND OTHER STORIES, THE
                                  WOLLHEIM, DONALD A. OA
  SUPERNATURAL READER, THE   CONKLIN, G&L.   AN
  *TWISTED   CONKLIN, GROFF   AN
  OPEN, SESAME¡   SS   ARS 49 WI
  FAR BOUNDARIES   DERLETH, AUGUST   AN
  SONG OF THE PEWEE, THE   SS   ARS 49 FL
  FAR BOUNDARIES   DERLETH, AUGUST   AN

GRESHAM, WILLIAM L.
  STAR GYPSIES, THE   SS   FSF 53 07
  BEST FROM FANTASY AND SCIENCE FICTION: 3
                                  BOUCHER & MCCOMAS   AN

GRESHNOV, M.
  GOLDEN LOTUS, A LEGEND, THE   SS
  LAST DOOR TO AIYA   GINSBURG, MIRRA   AN

GREY, CHARLES   PSEUD. FOR E. C. TUBB
  ACCOLADE   SS   NWR 74 23
  NEW WRITINGS IN SF. 23   BULMER, KENNETH   OA

GRIBBIN, DR. JOHN
  CLIMATIC THREAT, THE   AR
  ANALOG ANNUAL   BOVA, BEN   OA

GRIFFITH, ANN WARREN
  CAPTIVE AUDIENCE   SS   FSF 53 08
  BEST FROM FANTASY AND SCIENCE FICTION: 3
                                  BOUCHER & MCCOMAS   AN
  TOMORROW, INC.   GREENBERG& OLANDER   AN
  ZERITSKY'S LAW   SS   GAL 51 11
  OMNIBUS OF SCIENCE FICTION   CONKLIN, GROFF   AN

GRIFFITH, GEORGE
  GAMBLES WITH DESTINY   AC H FVW 99
  CORNER IN LIGHTNING, A   SS   PRS 98 03
  ANCESTRAL VOICES   MENVILLE & REGINALD AN
  GAMBLES WITH DESTINY   GRIFFITH, GEORGE   AC
  SCIENCE FICTION BY GASLIGHT   MOSKOWITZ, SAM   AN
  GENIUS FOR A YEAR, A   SS
  GAMBLES WITH DESTINY   GRIFFITH, GEORGE   AC
  GLIMPSE OF THE SINLESS STAR, A   SS   PRS 00 03
  WORLDS APART   LOCKE, GEORGE   AN
  GREAT CRELLIN COMET, THE   SS
  GAMBLES WITH DESTINY   GRIFFITH, GEORGE   AC
  HELLVILLE U.S.A.   SS
  GAMBLES WITH DESTINY   GRIFFITH, GEORGE   AC
  HOMEWARD BOUND   SS   PRS 00 06
  WORLDS APART   LOCKE, GEORGE   AN
  HONEYMOON IN SPACE, A   EX   PRS 00 01
  FAREWELL FANTASTIC VENUS   ALDISS & HARRISON   AN
  SPACE OPERA   ALDISS, BRIAN W.   AN
  IN SATURN'S REALM   SS   PRS 00 05
  WORLDS APART   LOCKE, GEORGE   AN
  PLAGUE-SHIP "TUPISA", THE   SS
  GAMBLES WITH DESTINY   GRIFFITH, GEORGE   AC
  RAID OF LE VENGEUR, THE   SS   PRS 01 02
  BEFORE ARMAGEDDON   MOORCOCK, MICHAEL   AN
  STORIES OF OTHER WORLDS   GR
  WORLDS APART   LOCKE, GEORGE   AN
  VISIT TO THE MOON, A   SS   PRS 00 01
  WORLDS APART   LOCKE, GEORGE   AN
  WORLD OF CRYSTAL CITIES, THE   SS   PRS 00 04
  WORLDS APART   LOCKE, GEORGE   AN
  WORLD OF THE WAR GOD, THE   SS   PRS 00 02
  WORLDS APART   LOCKE, GEORGE   AN

GRIGG, DAVID
  SONG BEFORE SUNSET, A   SS
  BEYOND TOMORROW   HARDING, LEE   AN

GRIGORIEV, VLADIMIR
  HORN OF PLENTY, THE   SS   GAL 69 12
  ULTIMATE THRESHOLD, THE   GINSBURG, MIRRA   AN
  MY COLLEAGUE   SS
  LAST DOOR TO AIYA   GINSBURG, MIRRA   AN
  VANYA   SS
  LAST DOOR TO AIYA   GINSBURG, MIRRA   AN

GRIMM, CHRISTOPHER
  BODYGUARD   NA   GAL 56 02
  BODYGUARD AND 4 OTHER SHORT SF NOVELS FROM GALAXY
                                  GOLD, H. L.   AN

GRINNELL, DAVID   PSEUD. FOR DONALD A. WOLLHEIM
  EXTENDING THE HOLDINGS   SS   FSF 51 04
  BEST SCIENCE-FICTION STORIES: 1952, THE
                                  BLEILER & DIKTY   AN
  FIRST FLIGHTS TO THE MOON   CLEMENT, HAL   AN
  LYSENKO MAZE, THE   SS   FSF 54 07
  FUTURE TENSE   CURTIS, RICHARD   AN
  *SCIENCE FICTION ADVENTURES IN MUTATION CONKLIN, GROFF AN
  MALICE AFORETHOUGHT   SS   FSF 52 11
  BEYOND THE BARRIERS OF SPACE AND TIME MERRIL, JUDITH AN
  RAG THING, THE   SS   FSF 51 10
  FIFTY SHORT SCIENCE FICTION TALES   ASIMOV & CONKLIN AN
  OMNIBUS OF SCIENCE FICTION   CONKLIN, GROFF   AN
  *TERROR IN THE MODERN VEIN   WOLLHEIM, DONALD A. AN
  TOP SECRET   SS   FSF 50 FL
  *INVADERS OF EARTH   CONKLIN, GROFF   AN

GROSS, MARION
    GOOD PROVIDER, THE   SS   FSF 52 09
        FIFTY SHORT SCIENCE FICTION TALES   ASIMOV & CONKLIN   AN
        SCIENCE FACT/FICTION   FARRELL/GAGE/&   AN
        *SCIENCE FICTION ADVENTURES IN DIMENSION
                                               CONKLIN, GROFF   AN
        THEMES IN SCIENCE FICTION   KELLEY, LEO P.   AN

GROSSER, E. A.
    PSYCHOMORPH   SS   UNK 40 02
        FROM UNKNOWN WORLDS   CAMPBELL, JOHN W. JR AN

GROSSMAN, NANCY
    MALE FIGURE   IL
        SCIENCE FICTION   BRODKIN & PEARSON   AN

GROVE, WALT
    JOHN GRANT'S LITTLE ANGEL   SS   PBY 64 07
        PLAYBOY BOOK OF SCIENCE FICTION AND FANTASY, THE
                                               PLAYBOY, EDITORS OF AN

GROVES, J. W.
    ROBOTS DON'T BLEED   SS   NWS 50 WI
        BEST FROM NEW WORLDS SCIENCE FICTION, THE
                                               CARNELL, JOHN   AN
        *NO PLACE LIKE EARTH   CARNELL, JOHN   AN

GROW, JULIAN F.
    FASTEST GUN DEAD, THE   SS   IFS 61 03
        7TH ANNUAL OF THE YEAR'S BEST S-F, THE MERRIL, JUDITH   AN
    TROUBLE WITH TRUTH, THE   NV   WOT 63 12
        BEST SCIENCE FICTION FROM WORLDS OF TOMORROW, THE
                                               POHL, FREDERIK   AN

GRUNERT, KARL
    ENEMIES IN SPACE (TRANSLATED BY WILLY LEY)   SS   07
        *INVADERS OF EARTH   CONKLIN, GROFF   AN

GUERNSEY, H. W.   PSEUD. FOR HOWARD E. WANDREI
    HEXER, THE   SS   UNK 39 06
        FROM UNKNOWN WORLDS   CAMPBELL, JOHN W. JR AN

GUIN, WYMAN
    LIVING WAY OUT   AC   AVN 67 08
    BEYOND BEDLAM   NA   GAL 51 08
        *GALAXY READER OF SCIENCE FICTION   GOLD, H. L.   AN
        GREAT SHORT NOVELS OF SCIENCE FICTION SILVERBERG, ROBERT AN
        LIVING WAY OUT   GUIN, WYMAN   AC
        SPECTRUM 2   AMIS & CONQUEST   AN
    DELEGATE FROM GUAPANGA, THE   NV   GAL 64 08
        AMERICAN GOVERNMENT THROUGH SCIENCE FICTION
                                               OLANDER/GREENBERG/& AN
        LIVING WAY OUT   GUIN, WYMAN   AC
    MAN OF THE RENAISSANCE, A   SS   GAL 64 12
        ALPHA 2   SILVERBERG, ROBERT AN
        LIVING WAY OUT   GUIN, WYMAN   AC
    MY DARLING HECATE   NV   BEY 53 11
        LIVING WAY OUT   GUIN, WYMAN   AC
    ROOT AND THE RING, THE   NV   BEY 54 09
        BEYOND   ANONYMOUS   AN
        LIVING WAY OUT   GUIN, WYMAN   AC
    TRIGGER TIDE   SS   ASF 50 10
        LIVING WAY OUT   GUIN, WYMAN   AC
        OMNIBUS OF SCIENCE FICTION   CONKLIN, GROFF   AN
    VOLPLA   NV   GAL 56 05
        LIVING WAY OUT   GUIN, WYMAN   AC
        THIRD GALAXY READER, THE   GOLD, H. L.   AN
        13 GREAT STORIES OF SCIENCE FICTION   CONKLIN, GROFF   AN

GUNN, JAMES E.
    BREAKING POINT   AC H WKR 72
    BURNING, THE   NO   DEL 72 02
    END OF THE DREAMS, THE   AC H SCB 75
    FUTURE IMPERFECT   AC   BAN 64 01
    IMMORTALS, THE   NO   BAN 62 11
    JOY MAKERS, THE   NO   BAN 61 03
    LISTENERS, THE   NO H SCB 72
    NEBULA AWARD STORIES 10   AN H HPR 75
    SOME DREAMS ARE NIGHTMARES   AC H SCB 74
    STATION IN SPACE   AC   BAN 58
    WITCHING HOUR, THE   AC   DEL 70 06
    ANDREW WHITE- 2028 (THE ANSWER)   NV   GAL 72 01
        LISTENERS, THE   GUNN, JAMES E.   NO
    ANSWER, THE (SEE ANDREW WHITE- 2028)   TC
    BEAUTIFUL BREW, THE   NV   BEY 54 09
        BEYOND   ANONYMOUS   AN
        WITCHING HOUR, THE   GUNN, JAMES E.   AC
    BIG WHEEL, THE   SS   FUN 56 09
        STATION IN SPACE   GUNN, JAMES E.   AC
    BREAKING POINT   NV   SSF 53 03
        BREAKING POINT   GUNN, JAMES E.   AC
    CAVE OF NIGHT, THE   SS   GAL 55 02
        SF: THE YEAR'S GREATEST SCIENCE FICTION AND FANTASY
                                               MERRIL, JUDITH   AN
        SOME DREAMS ARE NIGHTMARES   GUNN, JAMES E.   AC
        STATION IN SPACE   GUNN, JAMES E.   AC
        WHERE DO WE GO FROM HERE?   ASIMOV, ISAAC   AN
    CINDERELLA STORY (WHEN THE SHOE FITS)   SS   VAN 58 06
        BREAKING POINT   GUNN, JAMES E.   AC
    COMPUTER- 2118, THE (THE REPLY)   NV   GAL 72 05
        LISTENERS, THE   GUNN, JAMES E.   NO
    DONOR   NV   FAN 60 11
        IMMORTALS, THE   GUNN, JAMES E.   NO
    EVERY DAY IS CHRISTMAS   NV   SUP 57 02
        FUTURE IMPERFECT   GUNN, JAMES E.   AC

GUNN, JAMES E.   (CONTINUED)
    FEEDING TIME   SS   ASF 55 08
        FUTURE IMPERFECT   GUNN, JAMES E.   AC
    GEORGE THOMAS- 2027 (THE VOICES)   NV   FSF 72 09
        LISTENERS, THE   GUNN, JAMES E.   NO
    GIRLS WHO WERE REALLY BUILT, THE (NEOSHO'S CHOICEST)
                                                    SS   FAN 58 06
        FUTURE IMPERFECT   GUNN, JAMES E.   AC
    GREEN THUMB   NV   IFS 57 04
        BREAKING POINT   GUNN, JAMES E.   AC
    HEDONIST, THE (NAME YOUR PLEASURE)   NA   TWS 55 WI
        SOME DREAMS ARE NIGHTMARES   GUNN, JAMES E.   AC
    HOAX   NV   IFS 55 12
        STATION IN SPACE   GUNN, JAMES E.   AC
    IMMORTAL (THE IMMORTALS)   NV   STR 58 04
        IMMORTALS, THE   GUNN, JAMES E.   NO
    IMMORTAL, THE   NV   STR 58 04
        END OF THE DREAMS, THE   GUNN, JAMES E.   AC
    IMMORTALS, THE (ALSO AS IMMORTAL)   NV   STR 58 04
        BIO-FUTURES   SARGENT, PAMELA   AN
        STAR SCIENCE FICTION STORIES NO. 4   POHL, FREDERIK   OA
    INTRODUCTION   IN
        BREAKING POINT   GUNN, JAMES E.   AC
        END OF THE DREAMS, THE   GUNN, JAMES E.   AC
        NEBULA AWARD STORIES 10   GUNN, JAMES E.   AN
        SOME DREAMS ARE NIGHTMARES   GUNN, JAMES E.   AC
    JOY RIDE, THE (THE NAKED SKY)   NA   STS 55 FL
        END OF THE DREAMS, THE   GUNN, JAMES E.   AC
    LAST WORD, THE   SS   NEW 64 AC
        FUTURE IMPERFECT   GUNN, JAMES E.   AC
    LISTENERS, THE (ALSO AS ROBERT MACDONALD- 2025) NV   GAL 68 09
        BREAKING POINT   GUNN, JAMES E.   AC
        NEBULA AWARD STORIES NO. 4   ANDERSON, POUL   AN
        STARS AROUND US, THE   HOSKINS, ROBERT   AN
        THOSE WHO CAN: A SCIENCE FICTION READER
                                               WILSON, ROBIN SCOTT AN
    LITTLE ORPHAN ANDROID   NV   GAL 55 09
        FUTURE IMPERFECT   GUNN, JAMES E.   AC
    MAGICIANS, THE (SINE OF THE MAGUS)   NA   BEY 54 05
        WITCHING HOUR, THE   GUNN, JAMES E.   AC
    MAN WHO OWNED TOMORROW, THE   SS   ARG 53 10
        BREAKING POINT   GUNN, JAMES E.   AC
    MAN WHO WOULD NOT BE, THE (SEE THE POWER AND THE GLORY)
                                                    TC
    MEDIC (NOT SO GREAT AN ENEMY)   NV   VSF 57 07
        IMMORTALS, THE   GUNN, JAMES E.   NO
        SOME DREAMS ARE NIGHTMARES   GUNN, JAMES E.   AC
    MESSAGE, THE (SEE WILLIAM MITCHELL- 2028)   TC
    MISOGYNIST, THE   SS   GAL 52 11
        FUTURE IMPERFECT   GUNN, JAMES E.   AC
        GALAXY SCIENCE FICTION OMNIBUS   GOLD, H. L.   AN
        SECOND GALAXY READER OF SCIENCE FICTION
                                               GOLD, H. L.   AN
        SF: AUTHORS' CHOICE 4   HARRISON, HARRY   AN
        SHADOW OF TOMORROW   POHL, FREDERIK   AN
    MONSTER NAMED SMITH, A   NV   IFS 54 07
        BREAKING POINT   GUNN, JAMES E.   AC
        SECOND WORLD OF IF, THE   QUINN & WULFF   AN
    NAKED SKY, THE (ALSO AS THE JOY RIDE)   NA   STS 55 FL
        JOY MAKERS, THE   GUNN, JAMES E.   NO
    NAME YOUR PLEASURE (ALSO AS THE HEDONIST)   NA   TWS 55 WI
        JOY MAKERS, THE   GUNN, JAMES E.   NO
    NEOSHO'S CHOICEST (SEE THE GIRLS WHO WERE REALLY BUILT)
                                                    TC
    NEW BLOOD   NV   ASF 55 10
        IMMORTALS, THE   GUNN, JAMES E.   NO
        SOME DREAMS ARE NIGHTMARES   GUNN, JAMES E.   AC
    NOT SO GREAT AN ENEMY (SEE MEDIC)   TC
    OLD FOLKS, THE   SS   NOV 72 02
        BEST SF: 1972   HARRISON & ALDISS   AN
        INTO THE UNKNOWN   CARR, TERRY   AN
        NOVA 2   HARRISON, HARRY   OA
    ON STYLE   AR
        THOSE WHO CAN: A SCIENCE FICTION READER
                                               WILSON, ROBIN SCOTT AN
    OPEN WARFARE   NV   GAL 54 05
        ARENA: SPORTS SF   FERMAN & MALZBERG   AN
    POWDER KEG   NV   IFS 58 04
        STATION IN SPACE   GUNN, JAMES E.   AC
    POWER AND THE GLORY, THE (THE MAN WHO WOULD NOT) SS   IFS 69 12
        BREAKING POINT   GUNN, JAMES E.   AC
    RELUCTANT WITCH, THE (WHEREVER YOU MAY BE)   NA   GAL 53 05
        WITCHING HOUR, THE   GUNN, JAMES E.   AC
    REPLY, THE (SEE THE COMPUTER- 2118)   TC
    ROBERT MACDONALD- 2025 (THE LISTENERS)   NV   GAL 68 09
        LISTENERS, THE   GUNN, JAMES E.   NO
    ROBERT MACDONALD- 2058   NV
        LISTENERS, THE   GUNN, JAMES E.   NO
    SINE OF THE MAGUS (SEE THE MAGICIANS)   TC
    SKIN GAME   SS   VSF 58 01
        FUTURE IMPERFECT   GUNN, JAMES E.   AC
    SPACE IS A LONELY PLACE   NV   VSF 57 05
        END OF THE DREAMS, THE   GUNN, JAMES E.   AC
        STATION IN SPACE   GUNN, JAMES E.   AC
    STILLED PATTER, THE   SS   INF 56 06
        FUTURE IMPERFECT   GUNN, JAMES E.   AC
    SURVIVAL POLICY (AS EDWIN JAMES)   NV   ASF 52 10
        FUTURE IMPERFECT   GUNN, JAMES E.   AC
    TECHNOLOGICAL REVOLUTION, THE   SS   INY 71 02
        INFINITY 2   HOSKINS, ROBERT   OA
    TEDDY BEAR   SS   WOF 70 02
        BREAKING POINT   GUNN, JAMES E.   AC
    TRANSLATIONS   MS
        BREAKING POINT   GUNN, JAMES E.   AC
    TRIAL BY FIRE   SN   IFS 69 02
        BURNING, THE   GUNN, JAMES E.   NO

GUNN, JAMES E.   HAMBURGER, MICHAEL

GUNN, JAMES E.   (CONTINUED)
  TSYLANA   NV   GAL 56 03
    FUTURE IMPERFECT   GUNN, JAMES E.   AC
  UNHAPPY MAN, THE   NV   FUN 55 02
    JOY MAKERS, THE   GUNN, JAMES E.   NO
  VOICES, THE (SEE GEORGE THOMAS- 2027)   TC
  WHEN THE SHOE FITS (SEE CINDERELLA STORY)   TC
  WHEREVER YOU MAY BE (ALSO AS THE RELUCTANT WITCH) NA   GAL 53 05
    5 GALAXY SHORT NOVELS   GOLD, H. L.   AN
  WILLIAM MITCHELL- 2028 (THE MESSAGE)   NV   GAL 71 05
    LISTENERS, THE   GUNN, JAMES E.   NO
  WITCH HUNT   NV   GAL 69 04
    BURNING, THE   GUNN, JAMES E.   NO
  WITCHES MUST BURN   NV   ASF 56 08
    BURNING, THE   GUNN, JAMES E.   NO

GUNTHER, GOTTHARD
  UBERWINDUNG VON RAUM UND ZEIT   AN H KRP 52
    CONQUEST OF SPACE AND TIME, STORIES IN GERMAN

GUPPY, PAULINE D.
  VISITOR FROM SPACE   SS   YNW
    SCIENCE FICTION STORIES   BRADLEY, JOHANNA   AN

GUREVICH, G.
  FOREWORD   IN
    JOURNEY ACROSS THREE WORLDS ANONYMOUS   AN
  INFRA DRACONIS   NV
    SOVIET SCIENCE FICTION   ANONYMOUS   AN
    WORLDS APART   WILLIAMS-ELLIS& OWEN AN

GUTHRIE, ALAN   PSEUD. FOR E. C. TUBB

GUTTRIDGE, JENNIFER
  WINGED DREAMERS, THE   NV
    STAR TREK: THE NEW VOYAGES MARSHAK, S&CULBREATH OA

GUTTRIDGE, LEN
  AUNT MILLICENT AT THE RACES   SS   FSF 65 04
    BEST FROM FANTASY AND SCIENCE FICTION: 15
                                FERMAN, EDWARD L.   AN

GYLES, GORDON A.
  GLIMPSE OF MARY, A   SS   SAW 72
    SIGNS AND WONDERS   ELWOOD, ROGER   OA

HAAS, CHARLIE
  SHIFTING PARAMETERS IN DISAPPEARANCE AND MEMORY NV   UNI 76 06
    UNIVERSE 6   CARR, TERRY   OA

HAASE, JOHN
  COUNTDOWN, THE   SS   NYM 61 10
    7TH ANNUAL OF THE YEAR'S BEST S-F, THE MERRIL, JUDITH   AN

HACKER, MARILYN   SEE ALSO   CO-EDITOR SAMUEL R. DELANY
  EDITORIAL   ED C QRK 70 01
    QUARK/1   DELANY & HACKER   OA
  ELEGY FOR JANIS JOPLIN   PM   BMR 73
    BAD MOON RISING   DISCH, THOMAS M.   OA
  FOREWORD   IN C
    QUARK/3   DELANY & HACKER   OA
  INTRODUCTION   IN C
    QUARK/2   DELANY & HACKER   OA
  LANDSCAPE FOR INSURRECTION   PM   QRK 71 02
    QUARK/2   DELANY & HACKER   OA
  NIGHTSONG   PM   QRK 71 04
    QUARK/4   DELANY & HACKER   OA
  ON SPECULATIVE FICTION   IN C
    QUARK/4   DELANY & HACKER   OA
  UNTOWARD OCCURENCE AT EMBASSY POETRY READING   PM   BMR 73
    BAD MOON RISING   DISCH, THOMAS M.   OA

HADEN-GUEST, ANTHONY
  AUTO-APOTHEOSIS   PM   DTM 72
    BEST SF: 1973   HARRISON & ALDISS   AN
  HOW THE CONSOLATIONS OF PHILOSOPHY WORKED OUT IN ACTUAL
    PRACTICE   PM   69
    HOLDING YOUR EIGHT HANDS   LUCIE-SMITH, EDWARD AN

HAGGERT, W. T.
  LEX   NV   GAL 59 08
    SIXTH GALAXY READER, THE   GOLD, H. L.   AN

HAIL, STEVE
  CABLES PARTING| (NOT SF)   SS
    MOLECULE MONSTERS, THE   ANONYMOUS   AN

HAINING, PETER
  ANCIENT MYSTERIES READER, THE   AN H DBL 75
  FANTASTIC PULPS, THE   AN H SMP 75
  FUTURE MAKERS, THE   AN   BEL 71 05
    ALSO IN "SCIENCE FICTION SPECIAL 5"
  GHOULS, THE   AN H SAD 71 05
    EDITOR'S FOREWORD   IN
      GHOULS, THE   HAINING, PETER   AN
  FUTURE MAKERS, THE   AN   BEL 71 05
    SCIENCE FICTION SPECIAL 5 ANONYMOUS   AN
  INTRODUCTION   IN
    FANTASTIC PULPS, THE   HAINING, PETER   AN
    FUTURE MAKERS, THE   HAINING, PETER   AN

HALDANE, J. B. S.
  GOLD-MAKERS, THE (1932)   SS   EQM 52 10
    GREAT SCIENCE FICTION BY SCIENTISTS CONKLIN, GROFF AN

HALDEMAN, JACK C. II
  SAND CASTLES   SS   ALT 74
    ALTERNATIVES   GERROLD, DAVID   OA
  SLUGGING IT OUT   SS
    FAR SIDE OF TIME, THE   ELWOOD, ROGER   OA
  SONGS OF DYING SWANS   SS   STL 76 02
    STELLAR 2   DEL REY, JUDY-LYNN   OA
  WATCHDOG   SS   AMZ 72 05
    BEST SCIENCE FICTION STORIES OF THE YEAR (1972)
                                DEL REY, LESTER   AN

HALDEMAN, JOE W.
  COSMIC LAUGHTER   AN H HRW 74
  FOREVER WAR, THE   NO H SMP 74
  ARMAJA DAS   SS   76
    BEST SCIENCE FICTION STORIES OF THE YEAR (1976)
                                DOZOIS, GARDNER R.   AN
  COUNTERPOINT   SS   ORB 72 11
    ORBIT 11   KNIGHT, DAMON   OA
  END GAME   NV   ASF 75 01
    BEST SF: 75, THE NINTH ANNUAL   HARRISON & ALDISS   AN
    FOREVER WAR, THE   HALDEMAN, JOE W.   NO
    NEBULA AWARD STORIES 11   LE GUIN, URSULA K.   AN
  HERO   NV   ASF 72 06
    ANALOG 9   BOVA, BEN   AN
    BEST SCIENCE FICTION OF THE YEAR, THE NO. 2
                                CARR, TERRY   AN
    BEST SF: 1972   HARRISON & ALDISS   AN
    FOREVER WAR, THE   HALDEMAN, JOE W.   NO
  I OF NEWTON   SS
    COSMIC LAUGHTER   HALDEMAN, JOE W.   AN
  INTRODUCTION   IN
    COSMIC LAUGHTER   HALDEMAN, JOE W.   AN
  JOHN'S OTHER LIFE   SS   SCS 73
    SHOWCASE   ELWOOD, ROGER   OA
  OUT OF PHASE   SS   GAL 69 09
    BEST FROM GALAXY, THE VOLUME I   GALAXY, EDITORS OF AN
  PRIVATE WAR OF PVT. JACOB, THE   SS   GAL 74 06
    BEST FROM GALAXY, THE VOLUME III BAEN, JAMES   AN
  THIS BEST OF ALL POSSIBLE WORLDS   SS   ASF 74 11
    FOREVER WAR, THE   HALDEMAN, JOE W.   NO
  TIME PIECE   SS   IFS 70 07
    COMBAT SF   DICKSON, GORDON R.   AN
  WE ARE VERY HAPPY HERE   NV   ASF 73 11
    BEST SF: 1973   HARRISON & ALDISS   AN
    FOREVER WAR, THE   HALDEMAN, JOE W.   NO

HALE, EDWARD EVERETT
  BRICK MOON, THE (1869, INCLUDES SEQUEL "LIFE IN THE
    BRICK MOON" ATL 70 02)   NA   ATL 69 10
    MASTERPIECES OF SCIENCE FICTION MOSKOWITZ, SAM   AN

HALE, ROBERT BEVERLY
  IMMEDIATELY YOURS   SS   MAD 61 11
    7TH ANNUAL OF THE YEAR'S BEST S-F, THE MERRIL, JUDITH   AN

HALL, AUSTIN
  BLIND SPOT, THE   NV C AAS 21 05
    UNDER THE MOONS OF MARS   MOSKOWITZ, SAM   AN
  MAN WHO SAVED THE EARTH, THE   SS   ASW 19 12
    *BEST OF SCIENCE FICTION   CONKLIN, GROFF   AN

HALL, DESMOND W.   SEE PSEUD. ANTHONY GILMORE (WITH HARRY BATES)

HALL, DONALD
  WONDERFUL DOG SUIT, THE   SS
    10TH ANNUAL OF THE YEAR'S BEST S-F, THE
                                MERRIL, JUDITH   AN

HALL, FRANCES
  MESSAGE, THE   NV C ASF 66 07
    ANALOG 6   CAMPBELL, JOHN W. JR AN

HALL, GRAHAM M.
  SUN PUSH   SS   NWS 67 01
    ENGLAND SWINGS SF   MERRIL, JUDITH   AN
    SPACE-TIME JOURNAL, THE   MERRIL, JUDITH   AN
  TENNYSON EFFECT, THE   SS   NWS 66 11
    BEST SF STORIES FROM NEW WORLDS 5 MOORCOCK, MICHAEL AN

HALL, OWEN
  WARM CORNER IN SOOLOO, A   SS
    BATTLE FOR THE PACIFIC AND OTHER ADVENTURES AT SEA, THE
                                ANONYMOUS   AN

HALL, STEVE
  ROUND BILLIARD TABLE, A   SS   NWR 64 02
    NEW WRITINGS IN SF. 2   CARNELL, JOHN   OA

HALL, WILLIAM C.
  MEDAL FOR HORATIUS, A   SS   ARM 55 01
    APEMAN, SPACEMAN   STOVER & HARRISON   AN

HALLUS, TAK   PSEUD. FOR STEPHEN ROBINETT

HALSTEAD, WILLIAM F.
  SPACE LANE CADET   SS   BLF
    BOYS' LIFE BOOK OF OUTER SPACE STORIES, THE
                                BOY'S LIFE, ED. OF   AN

HAMBURGER, MICHAEL
  REPORT ON A SUPERMARKET   PM
    ENGLAND SWINGS SF   MERRIL, JUDITH   AN
    SPACE-TIME JOURNAL, THE   MERRIL, JUDITH   AN

HAMILTON-PATTERSON,J
  TEDDYSAURS, THE   SS   SPC 73 01
    SPACE 1   DAVIS, RICHARD   OA

HAMILTON, ALEX
  WORDS OF WARNING   SS   72
    BEST SF: 1972   HARRISON & ALDISS   AN

HAMILTON, EDMOND
  BEST OF EDMOND HAMILTON, THE   AC H NDB 77
    EDITED BY LEIGH BRACKETT
  BEST OF LEIGH BRACKETT, THE (LISTED UNDER LEIGH BRACKETT)
                                               EC H NDB 77
  CRASHING SUNS   AC   ACE 65
  HORROR ON THE ASTEROID AND OTHER TALES OF PLANETARY HORROR
                                               AC H GRG 75 06
    REPRINT OF 1936 EDITION PUBLISHED BY P. ALLEN, LONDON
  WHAT'S IT LIKE OUT THERE? AND OTHER STORIES AC   ACE 74
  ACCURSED GALAXY, THE   SS   ASF 35 07
    BEFORE THE GOLDEN AGE   ASIMOV, ISAAC   AN
    BEST OF EDMOND HAMILTON, THE   HAMILTON, EDMOND   AC
    HORROR ON THE ASTEROID AND OTHER TALES OF PLANETARY HORROR
                                   HAMILTON, EDMOND   AC
  AFTER A JUDGMENT DAY   SS   FSF 63 12
    BEST OF EDMOND HAMILTON, THE   HAMILTON, EDMOND   AC
  AFTERWORD   MS
    BEST OF EDMOND HAMILTON, THE   HAMILTON, EDMOND   AC
  ALIEN EARTH   SS   TWS 49 04
    ALIEN EARTH AND OTHER STORIES ELWOOD & MOSKOWITZ   AN
    BEST OF EDMOND HAMILTON, THE   HAMILTON, EDMOND   AC
  CASTAWAY   SS   68
    BEST OF EDMOND HAMILTON, THE   HAMILTON, EDMOND   AC
    WHAT'S IT LIKE OUT THERE? AND OTHER STORIES
                                   HAMILTON, EDMOND   AC
  CHILD OF THE WINDS   SS   WRT 36 05
    BEST OF EDMOND HAMILTON, THE   HAMILTON, EDMOND   AC
  COMET DRIVERS, THE   NV   WRT 30 02
    CRASHING SUNS   HAMILTON, EDMOND   AC
  CONQUEST OF TWO WORLDS, A   NV   WOS 32 02
    BEST OF EDMOND HAMILTON, THE   HAMILTON, EDMOND   AC
    EVERY BOY'S BOOK OF SCIENCE FICTION WOLLHEIM, DONALD A. AN
  COSMIC CLOUD, THE   NV   WRT 30 11
    CRASHING SUNS   HAMILTON, EDMOND   AC
  CRASHING SUNS   NV   WRT 28 08
    CRASHING SUNS   HAMILTON, EDMOND   AC
  DAY OF JUDGMENT   SS   WRT 46 09
    BEST OF EDMOND HAMILTON, THE   HAMILTON, EDMOND   AC
  DEAD PLANET, THE   SS   STS 46 SP
    EXPLORING OTHER WORLDS   MOSKOWITZ, SAM   AN
    *WORLDS OF TOMORROW   DERLETH, AUGUST   AN
  DEVOLUTION   SS   AMZ 36 12
    BEFORE THE GOLDEN AGE   ASIMOV, ISAAC   AN
  DOGS OF DOCTOR DWANN, THE   NV   WRT 32 10
    SATAN'S PETS   GHIDALIA, VIC   AN
  DREAMER'S WORLD   NV   WRT 41 11
    WHAT'S IT LIKE OUT THERE? AND OTHER STORIES
                                   HAMILTON, EDMOND   AC
  EARTH-BRAIN, THE   SS   WRT 32 04
    HORROR ON THE ASTEROID AND OTHER TALES OF PLANETARY HORROR
                                   HAMILTON, EDMOND   AC
  EASY MONEY   SS   TWS 38 04
    BEST OF EDMOND HAMILTON, THE   HAMILTON, EDMOND   AC
  EXILE   SS   SSS 43 05
    BEST OF EDMOND HAMILTON, THE   HAMILTON, EDMOND   AC
    LOOKING FORWARD   LESSER, MILTON   AN
  FESSENDEN'S WORLDS   SS   WRT 37 04
    BEST OF EDMOND HAMILTON, THE   HAMILTON, EDMOND   AC
    *BEYOND TIME AND SPACE   DERLETH, AUGUST   AN
  FORGOTTEN WORLD   NV   TWS 46 WI
    GIANT ANTHOLOGY OF SCIENCE FICTION MARGULIES & FRIEND   AN
    RACE TO THE STARS   MARGULIES & FRIEND   AN
  HARPERS OF TITAN, THE   SS   STS 50 09
    DR. CYCLOPS   KUTTNER, HENRY   AN
  HE THAT HATH WINGS   SS   WRT 38 07
    BEST OF EDMOND HAMILTON, THE   HAMILTON, EDMOND   AC
    WORLDS OF WEIRD   MARGULIES, LEO   AN
  HORROR ON THE ASTEROID   SS   WRT 33 09
    HORROR ON THE ASTEROID AND OTHER TALES OF PLANETARY HORROR
                                   HAMILTON, EDMOND   AC
  IN THE WORLD'S DUSK   SS   WRT 36 03
    BEST OF EDMOND HAMILTON, THE   HAMILTON, EDMOND   AC
    END OF THE WORLD, THE   WOLLHEIM, DONALD A.   AN
  INN OUTSIDE THE WORLD, THE   SS   WRT 45 07
    *MY BEST SCIENCE FICTION STORY MARGULIES & FRIEND   AN
    SCIENCE FACT/FICTION   FARRELL/GAGE/&   AN
    WHAT'S IT LIKE OUT THERE? AND OTHER STORIES
                                   HAMILTON, EDMOND   AC
  IRON ONE, THE   SS   SAW 72
    SIGNS AND WONDERS   ELWOOD, ROGER   OA
  ISLAND OF UNREASON, THE   SS   WOS 33 05
    BEST OF EDMOND HAMILTON, THE   HAMILTON, EDMOND   AC
    HISTORY OF THE SCIENCE FICTION MAGAZINE, THE PART 1 1926-1935
                                   ASHLEY, MICHAEL   AN
  ISLE OF THE SLEEPER, THE   SS   WRT 51 05
    GHOUL KEEPERS, THE   MARGULIES, LEO   AN
    WHAT'S IT LIKE OUT THERE? AND OTHER STORIES
                                   HAMILTON, EDMOND   AC
  KALDAR, WORLD OF ANTARES   NV   MGC 33 04
    SWORDSMEN IN THE SKY   WOLLHEIM, DONALD A.   AN
  KING OF SHADOWS, THE   NV   WRT 47 01
    WHAT'S IT LIKE OUT THERE? AND OTHER STORIES
                                   HAMILTON, EDMOND   AC
  KINGDOMS OF THE STARS   NV   AMZ 64 09
    PLANETS OF WONDER   CARR, TERRY   AN
  MAN WHO EVOLVED, THE   SS   WOS 31 04
    BEFORE THE GOLDEN AGE   ASIMOV, ISAAC   AN

HAMILTON, EDMOND   (CONTINUED)
    BEST OF EDMOND HAMILTON, THE   HAMILTON, EDMOND   AC
    FROM OFF THIS WORLD   MARGULIES & FRIEND AN
    HORROR ON THE ASTEROID AND OTHER TALES OF PLANETARY HORROR
                                   HAMILTON, EDMOND   AC
  MAN WHO RETURNED, THE   SS   WRT 34 02
    BEST OF EDMOND HAMILTON, THE   HAMILTON, EDMOND   AC
    WEIRD TALES   MARGULIES, LEO   AN
  MAN WHO SAW EVERYTHING, THE   SS   AMZ 30 10
    HORROR ON THE ASTEROID AND OTHER TALES OF PLANETARY HORROR
                                   HAMILTON, EDMOND   AC
  MAN WHO SAW THE FUTURE, THE   SS   AMZ 30 10
    FANTASTIC PULPS, THE   HAINING, PETER   AN
    OTHER WORLDS, OTHER TIMES   MOSKOWITZ & ELWOOD   AN
    STRANGE SIGNPOSTS   ELWOOD & MOSKOWITZ   AN
  MONSTER-GOD OF MAMURTH, THE   SS   WRT 26 08
    BEST OF EDMOND HAMILTON, THE   HAMILTON, EDMOND   AC
    HORROR ON THE ASTEROID AND OTHER TALES OF PLANETARY HORROR
                                   HAMILTON, EDMOND   AC
  PLANT REVOLT, THE   SS   WRT 30 04
    EARTH IN PERIL, THE   WOLLHEIM, DONALD A.   DA
  PRO, THE   SS   FSF 64 10
    BEST OF EDMOND HAMILTON, THE   HAMILTON, EDMOND   AC
    GREAT SCIENCE FICTION STORIES ABOUT THE MOON
                                   DIKTY, T. E.   AN
  REIGN OF THE ROBOTS, THE   SS   WOS 31 12
    STRANGE LOVE STORIES   ANONYMOUS   AN
  REQUIEM   SS   AMZ 62 04
    BEST OF EDMOND HAMILTON, THE   HAMILTON, EDMOND   AC
    LEARNING MAZE AND OTHER STORIES, THE ELWOOD, ROGER   OA
    MODERN MASTERPIECES OF SCIENCE FICTION MOSKOWITZ, SAM   AN
    VORTEX BLASTERS   MOSKOWITZ, SAM   AN
  SEEDS FROM OUTSIDE, THE   SS   WRT 37 03
    BEST OF EDMOND HAMILTON, THE   HAMILTON, EDMOND   AC
  SERPENT PRINCESS   NV   WRT 48 01
    WHAT'S IT LIKE OUT THERE? AND OTHER STORIES
                                   HAMILTON, EDMOND   AC
  SON OF TWO WORLDS   NA   TWS 41 08
    3 FROM OUT THERE   MARGULIES, LEO   AN
  STAR OF LIFE, THE   EX   STS 47 01
    SPACE OPERA   ALDISS, BRIAN W.   AN
  STAR STEALERS, THE   NV   WRT 29 02
    CRASHING SUNS   HAMILTON, EDMOND   AC
  STARCOMBERS, THE   SN   SPA 56 12
    GREAT SCIENCE FICTION ADVENTURES SHAW, LARRY T.   AN
  STARS, MY BROTHERS, THE   NV   AMZ 62 05
    ALIEN WORLDS   ELWOOD, ROGER   AN
    WHAT'S IT LIKE OUT THERE? AND OTHER STORIES
                                   HAMILTON, EDMOND   AC
  STORY-TELLER OF MANY WORLDS   IN
    BEST OF LEIGH BRACKETT, THE   BRACKETT, LEIGH   AC
  SUNFIRE!   SS   AMZ 62 09
    BEST OF AMAZING, THE   ROSS, JOSEPH   AN
    WHAT'S IT LIKE OUT THERE? AND OTHER STORIES
                                   HAMILTON, EDMOND   AC
  THUNDERING WORLDS   NV   WRT 34 03
    BEST OF EDMOND HAMILTON, THE   HAMILTON, EDMOND   AC
  TRANSURANIC   SS   TWS 48 02
    WHAT'S IT LIKE OUT THERE? AND OTHER STORIES
                                   HAMILTON, EDMOND   AC
  TWILIGHT OF THE GODS   NV   WRT 48 07
    WHAT'S IT LIKE OUT THERE? AND OTHER STORIES
                                   HAMILTON, EDMOND   AC
  WATCHER OF THE AGES, THE   SS   WRT 48 09
    WHAT'S IT LIKE OUT THERE? AND OTHER STORIES
                                   HAMILTON, EDMOND   AC
  WHAT'S IT LIKE OUT THERE?   NV   TWS 52 12
    BEST FROM STARTLING STORIES, THE MINES, SAMUEL   AN
    BEST OF EDMOND HAMILTON, THE   HAMILTON, EDMOND   AC
    CENTURY OF SCIENCE FICTION, A KNIGHT, DAMON   AN
    EXPLORERS OF SPACE   SILVERBERG, ROBERT   AN
    SCIENCE FICTION FOR PEOPLE WHO HATE SCIENCE FICTION
                                   CARR, TERRY   AN
    WHAT'S IT LIKE OUT THERE? AND OTHER STORIES
                                   HAMILTON, EDMOND   AC
  WHY I SELECTED THE INN OUTSIDE THE WORLD   AI
    *MY BEST SCIENCE FICTION STORY MARGULIES & FRIEND   AN
  WITHIN THE NEBULA   NV   WRT 28 05
    CRASHING SUNS   HAMILTON, EDMOND   AC

HAMM, THELMA D.
  NATIVE SON   SS   IMG 53 07
    TALES BEYOND TIME   DE CAMP, L. S.&C.   AN
  TICKING HIS LIFE AWAY   SS   NEW 54 AN
    TOMORROW'S UNIVERSE   CAMPBELL, H. J.   AN

HAMMETT, DASHIELL
  SARDONIC STAR OF TOM DOODY, THE   SS   BLM 24
    FANTASTIC PULPS, THE   HAINING, PETER   AN

HANEY, LAURA
  TO THE MOUNTAINS   SS   CLR 72 02
    CLARION II   WILSON, ROBIN SCOTT   OA

HANIWA
  TWO DANCERS   IL
    SCIENCE FICTION   BRODKIN & PEARSON   AN

HANNAH, E.
  SCAPEGOAT   SS
    WORLDS AT WAR   RAYER, FRANCIS G.   AN

HANNIGAN, D. F.
  OLD DOCTOR RUTHERFORD   SS   LUD 91 09
    SCIENCE FICTION BY GASLIGHT   MOSKOWITZ, SAM   AN

```
HANSEN, KARL
  RED, WHITE AND BLUE FOURTH OF JULY, A        NV
    2076: THE AMERICAN TRICENTENNIAL   BRYANT, EDWARD       OA

HARBEN, WILLIAM
  IN THE YEAR TEN THOUSAND (1892)              SS   ARN 92
    FUTURE PERFECT                     FRANKLIN, H. BRUCE   AN

HARBOTTLE, PHILIP
  HISTORY OF BRITISH SCIENCE FICTION MAGAZINES, A  AR
    BEYOND THIS HORIZON                CARRELL, CHRISTOPHER OA
  PREFACE                                      IN
    BEST OF E. E. 'DOC' SMITH, THE     SMITH, EDWARD E. PHD AC

HARDING, LEE       PSEUD. FOR LEO HARDING
  BEYOND TOMORROW                              AN H WRN 76
  DANCING GERONTIUS                            SS   VOT 69 12
    SECOND PACIFIC BOOK OF SCIENCE FICTION, THE
                                       BAXTER, JOHN         AN
  EVIDENCE, THE                                SS   NWS 64 08
    PACIFIC BOOK OF AUSTRALIAN SCIENCE FICTION
                                       BAXTER, JOHN         AN
  LIBERATORS, THE                              SS   NWR 65 05
    NEW WRITINGS IN SF.  5             CARNELL, JOHN        OA
  MISTRESS OF THE MIND                         NV   NWR 71 18
    NEW WRITINGS IN SF. 18             CARNELL, JOHN        OA
  QUEST                                        SS   NWS 63 04
    LAMBDA I AND OTHER STORIES         CARNELL, JOHN        AN
  SHOCK TREATMENT                              SS   NWR 68 11
    NEW WRITINGS IN SF.  8             CARNELL, JOHN        AN
    NEW WRITINGS IN SF. 11             CARNELL, JOHN        OA
  SOUL SURVIVORS                               NV   NWR 70 17
    NEW WRITINGS IN SF. 17             CARNELL, JOHN        OA

HARDING, LEO        SEE PSEUD. LEE HARDING

HARDY, DAVID A.
  LANDSCAPES IN SPACE                          AR
    BEYOND THIS HORIZON                CARRELL, CHRISTOPHER OA

HARDY, G. H.
  BERTRAND RUSSELL'S DREAM                     PM        48
    FANTASIA MATHEMATICA               FADIMAN, CLIFTON     AN

HARDY, THOMAS
  POEM AT A LUNAR ECLIPSE                      PM
    MOMENT OF ECLIPSE, THE             ALDISS, BRIAN W.     AC

HARGREAVES, H. A.
  CAIN N                                       NV   NWR 72 20
    NEW WRITINGS IN SF. 20             CARNELL, JOHN        OA
  DEAD TO THE WORLD                            SS   NWR 68 11
    NEW WRITINGS IN SF.  8             CARNELL, JOHN        AN
    NEW WRITINGS IN SF. 11             CARNELL, JOHN        OA
  MORE THINGS IN HEAVEN AND EARTH              NV   NWR 70 17
    NEW WRITINGS IN SF. 17             CARNELL, JOHN        OA
  TANGLED WEB                                  NV   NWR 73 21
    NEW WRITINGS IN SF. 21             CARNELL, JOHN        OA

HARLEY, ALAN
  VICIOUS CIRCLE                               SS   SFM 74 02
    BEST OF SCIENCE FICTION MONTHLY, THE   SACKS, JANET     AN

HARMON, JIM
  LUCK, INC.                                   SS   SFS 59 11
    RARE SCIENCE FICTION               HOWARD, IVAN         AN
  NAME YOUR SYMPTOM                            SS   GAL 56 05
    FOURTH GALAXY READER, THE          GOLD, H. L.          AN
  PLACE WHERE CHICAGO WAS, THE                 NV   GAL 62 02
    HOT & COLD RUNNING CITIES          MCHARGUE, GEORGESS   AN
    TENTH GALAXY READER, THE           POHL, FREDERIK       AN

HARMON, SETH
  MOON GOLD                                    SS        58
    TEEN-AGE OUTER SPACE STORIES       FURMAN, A. L.        AN

HARNESS, CHARLES L.
  ROSE, THE                                    AC   CPT 66
  BOOKMOBILE                                   SS   IFS 68 11
    SCHOOL AND SOCIETY THROUGH SCIENCE FICTION
                                       OLANDER/GREENBERG/&  AN
  CHESSPLAYERS, THE                            SS   FSF 53 10
    ROSE, THE                          HARNESS, CHARLES L.  AC
    SCIENCE FICTION ODDITIES           CONKLIN, GROFF       AN
  CHILD BY CHRONOS                             SS   FSF 53 06
    BEST FROM FANTASY AND SCIENCE FICTION:  3
                                       BOUCHER & MCCOMAS    AN
  HERITAGE                                     SS   FSF 50 FL
    TOMORROW'S UNIVERSE                CAMPBELL, H. J.      AN
  NEW REALITY, THE                             NV   TWS 50 12
    AS TOMORROW BECOMES TODAY          SULLIVAN, CHARLES W. AN
    BEST SCIENCE-FICTION STORIES: 1951, THE
                                       BLEILER & DIKTY      AN
    ROSE, THE                          HARNESS, CHARLES L.  AC
    SHAPE OF THINGS, THE               KNIGHT, DAMON        AN
  ORNAMENT TO HIS PROFESSION, AN               NV   ASF 66 02
    SCIENCE FICTION ARGOSY, A          KNIGHT, DAMON        AN
    SF12                               MERRIL, JUDITH       AN
  PARADOX MEN, THE                             NV        49
    SPACE OPERA                        ALDISS, BRIAN W.     AN
  PROBABLE CAUSE                               NA   ORB 68 04
    ORBIT  4                           KNIGHT, DAMON        AN
  ROSE, THE                                    NO   AUT 53 03
    ROSE, THE                          HARNESS, CHARLES L.  AC
    SCIENCE FICTION SPECIAL  4         ANONYMOUS            AN

HARNESS, CHARLES L.   (CONTINUED)
  TIME TRAP                                    NV   ASF 48 08
    ALPHA 1                            SILVERBERG, ROBERT   AN
    TRAPS OF TIME, THE                 MOORCOCK, MICHAEL    AN

HARPER, JO ANN
  FEMININE DEMYSTIFICATION                     PM
    2076: THE AMERICAN TRICENTENNIAL   BRYANT, EDWARD       OA

HARPER, JODY
  NOVA MORNING                                 SS C GEN 72
    GENERATION                         GERROLD, DAVID       OA

HARPER, RICHARD
  SAMARITAN, THE                               SS   BLF
    BOYS' LIFE BOOK OF OUTER SPACE STORIES, THE
                                       BOY'S LIFE, ED. OF   AN
    UNIVERSE AHEAD                     ENGDAHL & ROBERSON   AN

HARRIS-BURLAND, J.B.
  LORD BEDEN'S MOTOR                           SS   SND 01 12
    SCIENCE FICTION BY GASLIGHT        MOSKOWITZ, SAM       AN

HARRIS, CLARE WINGER
  AWAY FROM THE HERE AND NOW                   AC H DOR 47
  APE CYCLE, THE                               SS   WSQ 30 SP
    AWAY FROM THE HERE AND NOW         HARRIS, CLARE WINGER AC
  ARTIFICIAL MAN, THE                          SS   WSQ 29 FL
    AWAY FROM THE HERE AND NOW         HARRIS, CLARE WINGER AC
  BABY ON NEPTUNE, A                           SS C AMZ 29 12
    AWAY FROM THE HERE AND NOW         HARRIS, CLARE WINGER AC
    FLIGHT INTO SPACE                  WOLLHEIM, DONALD A.  AN
  CERTAIN SOLDIER, A                           SS   WRT 27 11
    AWAY FROM THE HERE AND NOW         HARRIS, CLARE WINGER AC
  DIABOLICAL DRUG, THE                         SS   AMZ 29 05
    AWAY FROM THE HERE AND NOW         HARRIS, CLARE WINGER AC
  EVOLUTIONARY MONSTROSITY, THE                SS   AMQ 29 WI
    AWAY FROM THE HERE AND NOW         HARRIS, CLARE WINGER AC
  FATE OF THE POSEIDONIA, THE                  SS   AMZ 27 06
    AWAY FROM THE HERE AND NOW         HARRIS, CLARE WINGER AC
  FIFTH DIMENSION, THE                         SS   AMZ 28 12
    AWAY FROM THE HERE AND NOW         HARRIS, CLARE WINGER AC
  MENACE OF MARS, THE                          SS   AMZ 28 10
    AWAY FROM THE HERE AND NOW         HARRIS, CLARE WINGER AC
  MIRACLE OF THE LILY, THE                     SS   AMZ 28 04
    AWAY FROM THE HERE AND NOW         HARRIS, CLARE WINGER AC
  RUNAWAY WORLD, A                             SS   WRT 26 07
    AWAY FROM THE HERE AND NOW         HARRIS, CLARE WINGER AC

HARRIS, JOHN BEYNON   ALSO AS
  JOHN BEYNON, LUCAS PARKES AND JOHN WYNDHAM
  LOST MACHINE, THE                            SS   AMZ 32 04
    BEST OF AMAZING, THE               ROSS, JOSEPH         AN
  METEOR (PHONEY METEOR)                       SS   AMZ 41 03
    *BEACHHEADS IN SPACE               DERLETH, AUGUST      AN
    FROM OTHER WORLDS                  DERLETH, AUGUST      AN
  TIME TO REST                                 SS   ARS 49 WI
    FAR BOUNDARIES                     DERLETH, AUGUST      AN

HARRIS, LARRY M.     ALSO AS   LAURENCE M. JANIFER
  MEX                                          SS   FUN 57 01
    FANTASTIC UNIVERSE OMNIBUS, THE    SANTESSON, HANS S.   AN

HARRISON, HARRY AND BRIAN W. ALDISS
  ASTOUNDING-ANALOG READER, THE VOLUME ONE     AN H DBL 72
  ASTOUNDING-ANALOG READER, THE VOLUME TWO     AN H DBL 73
  BEST SF: 1967                                AN   BKM 68 03
    IN ENGLAND AS "THE YEAR'S BEST SCIENCE FICTION NO. 1"
  BEST SF: 1968                                AN H PUT 69
    IN ENGLAND AS "THE YEAR'S BEST SCIENCE FICTION NO. 2"
  BEST SF: 1969                                AN H PUT 70
    IN ENGLAND AS "THE YEAR'S BEST SCIENCE FICTION NO. 3"
  BEST SF: 1970                                AN H PUT 71
    IN ENGLAND AS "THE YEAR'S BEST SCIENCE FICTION NO. 4"
  BEST SF: 1971                                AN H PUT 72
    IN ENGLAND AS "THE YEAR'S BEST SCIENCE FICTION NO. 5"
  BEST SF: 1972                                AN H PUT 73
    IN ENGLAND AS "THE YEAR'S BEST SCIENCE FICTION NO. 6"
  BEST SF: 1973                                AN H PUT 74
    IN ENGLAND AS "THE YEAR'S BEST SCIENCE FICTION NO. 7"
  BEST SF: 1974                                AN H BML 75
    IN ENGLAND AS "THE YEAR'S BEST SCIENCE FICTION NO. 8"
  BEST SF: 75, THE NINTH ANNUAL                AN H BML 76
    IN ENGLAND AS "THE YEAR'S BEST SCIENCE FICTION NO. 9"
  YEAR'S BEST SCIENCE FICTION NO. 1, THE       AN   SPH 68
    SEE "BEST SF: 1967"
  YEAR'S BEST SCIENCE FICTION NO. 2, THE       AN   SPH 69
    SEE "BEST SF: 1968"
  YEAR'S BEST SCIENCE FICTION NO. 3, THE       AN   SPH 70
    SEE "BEST SF: 1969"
  YEAR'S BEST SCIENCE FICTION NO. 4, THE       AN   SPH 71
    SEE "BEST SF: 1970"
  YEAR'S BEST SCIENCE FICTION NO. 5, THE       AN   SPH 72
    SEE "BEST SF: 1971"
  YEAR'S BEST SCIENCE FICTION NO. 6, THE       AN   SPH 73
    SEE "BEST SF: 1972"
  YEAR'S BEST SCIENCE FICTION NO. 7, THE       AN   SPH 74
    SEE "BEST SF: 1973"
  YEAR'S BEST SCIENCE FICTION NO. 8, THE       AN   SPH 75
    SEE "BEST SF: 1974"
  YEAR'S BEST SCIENCE FICTION NO. 9, THE       AN H WEI 76
    SEE "BEST SF: 75, THE NINTH ANNUAL"

HARRISON, HARRY AND WILLIS E. MCNELLY
  SCIENCE FICTION NOVELLAS                     AN L SCB 75
```

HARRISON, HARRY   SEE ALSO
   CO-EDITORS BRIAN W. ALDISS AND LEON E. STOVER
         ALSO AS   FELIX BOYD AND HANK DEMPSEY
ASTOUNDING   OA H RDM 73
   JOHN W. CAMPBELL MEMORIAL ANTHOLOGY
BACKDROP OF STARS   AC H DOB 68
   SEE "SF: AUTHORS' CHOICE"
BEST OF HARRY HARRISON, THE   AC PKT 76 06
BEST OF HARRY HARRISON, THE (BRITISH)   AC H SID 76 09
DEATHWORLD TRILOGY, THE   AC H BKM 75
FOUR FOR THE FUTURE   AN H MAC 69
LIGHT FANTASTIC, THE   AN H SCB 71
NOVA 1   OA H DCT 70
NOVA 1 (BRITISH)   OA H HAL 76
NOVA 2   OA H WKR 72
NOVA 3   OA H WKR 73
   ALSO AS "THE OUTDATED MAN"
NOVA 4   OA H WKR 74
ONE STEP FROM EARTH   AC H MAC 70
OUTDATED MAN, THE   OA DEL 75 04
   SEE "NOVA 3"
PRIME NUMBER   AC BKM 70 07
SF: AUTHORS' CHOICE   AN BKM 68 06
   IN ENGLAND AS "BACKDROP OF STARS"
SF: AUTHORS' CHOICE 2   AN BKM 70 05
SF: AUTHORS' CHOICE 3   AN H PUT 71
SF: AUTHORS' CHOICE 4   AN H PUT 74
TWO TALES AND EIGHT TOMORROWS   AC BAN 68 05
WAR WITH THE ROBOTS   AC PYR 62 09
WORLDS OF WONDER   AN H DBL 69
YEAR 2000, THE   OA H DBL 70
ACCORDING TO HIS ABILITIES   SS AMZ 64 05
   TWO TALES AND EIGHT TOMORROWS   HARRISON, HARRY   AC
AD ASTRA   SS VTX 74 08
   BEST SCIENCE FICTION STORIES OF THE YEAR (1974)
                                    DEL REY, LESTER   AN
AFTERWORD   MS
   LIGHT FANTASTIC, THE   HARRISON, HARRY   AN
   NOVA 4   HARRISON, HARRY   OA
ALIEN AGONY, AN (THE STREETS OF ASHKELON) SS NWS 62 09
   MORE PENGUIN SCIENCE FICTION   ALDISS, BRIAN W.   AN
AMERICAN DEAD   SS YRT 70
   YEAR 2000, THE   HARRISON, HARRY   OA
ARM OF THE LAW   SS FUN 58 08
   WAR WITH THE ROBOTS   HARRISON, HARRY   AC
AT LAST, THE TRUE STORY OF FRANKENSTEIN   SS FSF 63
   *BEST OF HARRY HARRISON, THE   HARRISON, HARRY   AC
BRAVE NEWER WORLD   NV FFU 71
   *BEST OF HARRY HARRISON, THE   HARRISON, HARRY   AC
   FOUR FUTURES   SILVERBERG, ROBERT   OA
BY THE FALLS   SS IFS 70 01
   BEST FROM IF, THE VOLUME I   IF, EDITORS OF   AN
   *BEST OF HARRY HARRISON, THE   HARRISON, HARRY   AC
   NEBULA AWARD STORIES NO. 6   SIMAK, CLIFFORD D.   AN
   NEW WORLDS OF FANTASY NO. 2   CARR, TERRY   AN
   SF: AUTHORS' CHOICE 3   HARRISON, HARRY   AN
CAPTAIN BEDLAM   SS SFA 57 12
   TWO TALES AND EIGHT TOMORROWS   HARRISON, HARRY   AC
CAPTAIN HONARIO HARPPLAYER, R.N.   SS FSF 63 03
   BEST FROM FANTASY AND SCIENCE FICTION: 13
                                    DAVIDSON, AVRAM   AN
   *BEST OF HARRY HARRISON, THE   HARRISON, HARRY   AC
   SPECTRUM OF WORLDS, A   CLARESON, THOMAS D.   AN
   TWO TALES AND EIGHT TOMORROWS   HARRISON, HARRY   AC
CIVIL SERVICE SERVANT, A (THE FAIRLY CIVIL SERVANT)
                                           SS GAL 67 12
   PRIME NUMBER   HARRISON, HARRY   AC
COMMANDO RAID   SS NEW 70 AC
   PRIME NUMBER   HARRISON, HARRY   AC
CONTACT MAN   SS   66
   PRIME NUMBER   HARRISON, HARRY   AC
CRIMINAL ACT, A   SS ASF 67 01
   *BEST OF HARRY HARRISON, THE   HARRISON, HARRY   AC
   PRIME NUMBER   HARRISON, HARRY   AC
DEATHWORLD   NO ASF 60 01
   DEATHWORLD TRILOGY, THE   HARRISON, HARRY   AC
DEATHWORLD 2 (THE ETHICAL ENGINEER)   NO ASF 63 07
   DEATHWORLD TRILOGY, THE   HARRISON, HARRY   AC
DEATHWORLD 3 (THE HORSE BARBARIANS)   NO ASF 68 02
   DEATHWORLD TRILOGY, THE   HARRISON, HARRY   AC
DOWN TO EARTH   SS AMZ 63 11
   PRIME NUMBER   HARRISON, HARRY   AC
EDITORIAL   ED
   BEST SF: 1974   HARRISON & ALDISS   AN
ETHICAL ENGINEER, THE (SEE DEATHWORLD 2)   TC
EVER-BRANCHING TREE, THE   SS SAG 70
   *BEST OF HARRY HARRISON, THE   HARRISON, HARRY   AC
   SCHOOL AND SOCIETY THROUGH SCIENCE FICTION
                                    OLANDER/GREENBERG/&   AN
   SCIENCE AGAINST MAN   CHEETHAM, ANTHONY   OA
FAIRLY CIVIL SERVANT, THE (SEE A CIVIL SERVICE SERVANT)
                                           TC
FAMOUS FIRST WORDS   SS FSF 65 01
   PRIME NUMBER   HARRISON, HARRY   AC
FINAL BATTLE   SS NEW 70 AC
   PRIME NUMBER   HARRISON, HARRY   AC
FINAL ENCOUNTER   NV GAL 64 04
   EIGHTH GALAXY READER, THE   POHL, FREDERIK   AN
   GALACTIC EMPIRES VOLUME TWO   ALDISS, BRIAN W.   AN
   TWO TALES AND EIGHT TOMORROWS   HARRISON, HARRY   AC
FINEST HUNTER IN THE WORLD, THE   SS NEW 70 AC
   PRIME NUMBER   HARRISON, HARRY   AC
FOREWORD TO "NIGHTFALL"   IN
   MIRROR OF INFINITY, THE   SILVERBERG, ROBERT   AN
FROM FANATICISM, OR FOR REWARD   SS ASF 69 03
   *BEST OF HARRY HARRISON, THE   HARRISON, HARRY   AC

HARRISON, HARRY   (CONTINUED)
   ONE STEP FROM EARTH   HARRISON, HARRY   AC
GHOUL SQUAD, THE   SS ASF 69 06
   PRIME NUMBER   HARRISON, HARRY   AC
GHOUL, THE   SS
   FOUR FOR THE FUTURE   HARRISON, HARRY   AN
GODS THEMSELVES THROW INCENSE, THE   SS IMP 66 03
   FOUR FOR THE FUTURE   HARRISON, HARRY   AN
GREATEST CAR IN THE WORLD, THE   SS NWS 66 10
   PRIME NUMBER   HARRISON, HARRY   AC
HEAVY DUTY (AS HANK DEMPSEY)   SS ASF 70 05
   ONE STEP FROM EARTH   HARRISON, HARRY   AC
HONEST DAY'S WORK, AN   NV NWR 73 22
   *BEST OF HARRY HARRISON, THE   HARRISON, HARRY   AC
   NEW WRITINGS IN SF. 22   BULMER, KENNETH   OA
HORSE BARBARIANS, THE (SEE DEATHWORLD 3)   TC
HOW THE OLD WORLD DIED   SS GAL 64 10
   NINTH GALAXY READER, THE   POHL, FREDERIK   AN
I ALWAYS DO WHAT TEDDY SAYS   SS EQM 65 06
   *BEST OF HARRY HARRISON, THE   HARRISON, HARRY   AC
   DAYS AFTER TOMORROW, THE   SANTESSON, HANS S.   AN
   NEW IMPROVED SUN, THE   DISCH, THOMAS M.   AN
   SCIENCE FACT/FICTION   FARRELL/GAGE/&   AN
   TWO TALES AND EIGHT TOMORROWS   HARRISON, HARRY   AC
I HAVE MY VIGIL   SS FSF 68 02
   BEST FROM FANTASY AND SCIENCE FICTION: 18
                                    FERMAN, EDWARD L.   AN
   *BEST OF HARRY HARRISON, THE   HARRISON, HARRY   AC
   WONDERMAKERS 2   HOSKINS, ROBERT   AN
I SEE YOU (ROBOT JUSTICE, FUN 59 07)   SS NWS 59 05
   BEST OF NEW WORLDS, THE   MOORCOCK, MICHAEL   AN
   WAR WITH THE ROBOTS   HARRISON, HARRY   AC
IF (PRAISEWORTHY SAUR)   SS IFS 69 02
   *BEST OF HARRY HARRISON, THE   HARRISON, HARRY   AC
   PRIME NUMBER   HARRISON, HARRY   AC
   WORLDS OF WONDER   HARRISON, HARRY   AN
INCIDENT IN THE IND   SS FSF 64 03
   PRIME NUMBER   HARRISON, HARRY   AC
INTRODUCTION   IN
   BEST SF: 1967   HARRISON & ALDISS   AN
   BEST SF: 1968   HARRISON & ALDISS   AN
   BEST SF: 1969   HARRISON & ALDISS   AN
   BEST SF: 1971   HARRISON & ALDISS   AN
   BEST SF: 1972   HARRISON & ALDISS   AN
   BEST SF: 1973   HARRISON & ALDISS   AN
   BEST SF: 75, THE NINTH ANNUAL   HARRISON & ALDISS   AN
   DECADE THE 1950S   ALDISS & HARRISON   AN
   FOUR FOR THE FUTURE   HARRISON, HARRY   AN
   *NOVA 1   HARRISON, HARRY   AN
   NOVA 2   HARRISON, HARRY   OA
   SF: AUTHORS' CHOICE   HARRISON, HARRY   AN
   SF: AUTHORS' CHOICE 2   HARRISON, HARRY   AN
   SF: AUTHORS' CHOICE 3   HARRISON, HARRY   AN
   TEN THOUSAND LIGHT-YEARS FROM HOME TIPTREE, JAMES JR. AC
   WORLDS OF WONDER   HARRISON, HARRY   AN
INTRODUCTION   IN C
   APEMAN, SPACEMAN   STOVER & HARRISON   AN
   ASTOUNDING-ANALOG READER, THE VOLUME ONE
                                    HARRISON & ALDISS   AN
   ASTOUNDING-ANALOG READER, THE VOLUME TWO
                                    HARRISON & ALDISS   AN
   DECADE THE 1960S   ALDISS & HARRISON   AN
   NEBULA AWARD STORIES NO. 2   ALDISS & HARRISON   AN
K-FACTOR, THE   NV ASF 60 12
   RULERS OF MEN   SANTESSON, HANS S.   AN
LIFE PRESERVERS, THE (AS HANK DEMPSEY)   NV ASF 70 04
   ONE STEP FROM EARTH   HARRISON, HARRY   AC
MAKE ROOM! MAKE ROOM!   NO IMP 66 08
   SCIENCE FICTION OMNIBUS ON POLLUTION, A
                                    ANONYMOUS   AN
MANY DOOMS, THE (SEE UNTO MY MANIFOLD DOOMS) TC
MATTER TRANSMITTER, THE   IN
   ONE STEP FROM EARTH   HARRISON, HARRY   AC
MOTHBALLED SPACESHIP, THE   SS AMA 73
   ASTOUNDING   HARRISON, HARRY   OA
   *BEST OF HARRY HARRISON, THE   HARRISON, HARRY   AC
MUTE MILTON   SS AMZ 66 02
   ABC OF SCIENCE FICTION, AN   BOARDMAN, TOM JR.   AN
   *BEST OF HARRY HARRISON, THE   HARRISON, HARRY   AC
   PRIME NUMBER   HARRISON, HARRY   AC
NO WAR, OR BATTLE'S SOUND   NV   68
   COMBAT SF   DICKSON, GORDON R.   AN
   ONE STEP FROM EARTH   HARRISON, HARRY   AC
NOT ME, NOT AMOS CABOT!   SS SCF 65 01
   *BEST OF HARRY HARRISON, THE   HARRISON, HARRY   AC
   PRIME NUMBER   HARRISON, HARRY   AC
   SCIENCE FICTION HORIZONS NO. 1   BOARDMAN, TOM JR.   AN
ONE STEP FROM EARTH (AS HANK DEMPSEY)   SS ASF 70 03
   MARS, WE LOVE YOU   HIPOLITO & MCNELLY   AN
   ONE STEP FROM EARTH   HARRISON, HARRY   AC
PAD, THE   SS NEW 70 AC
   PRIME NUMBER   HARRISON, HARRY   AC
PLIABLE ANIMAL, THE   NV SDM 62 09
   TWO TALES AND EIGHT TOMORROWS   HARRISON, HARRY   AC
PORTRAIT OF THE ARTIST   SS FSF 64 11
   *BEST OF HARRY HARRISON, THE   HARRISON, HARRY   AC
   NEW DREAMS THIS MORNING   BLISH, JAMES   AN
   TWO TALES AND EIGHT TOMORROWS   HARRISON, HARRY   AC
POWERS OF OBSERVATION, THE   SS ASF 68 09
   ANALOG 8   CAMPBELL, JOHN W. JR AN
   PRIME NUMBER   HARRISON, HARRY   AC
PRAISEWORTHY SAUR (SEE IF)   TC
PRESSURE   SS ASF 69 08
   ONE STEP FROM EARTH   HARRISON, HARRY   AC
   TOMORROW'S WORLDS   SILVERBERG, ROBERT   AN

HARRISON, HARRY   (CONTINUED)
REPAIRMAN, THE   SS   GAL 58 02
  WAR WITH THE ROBOTS   HARRISON, HARRY   AC
RESCUE OPERATION   SS   ASF 64 12
  ABOVE THE HUMAN LANDSCAPE   MCNELLY & STOVER   AN
  ASTOUNDING-ANALOG READER, THE VOLUME TWO
                               HARRISON & ALDISS   AN
 *BEST OF HARRY HARRISON, THE   HARRISON, HARRY   AC
  STORIES FROM SCIENCE FICTION DOHERTY, G. D.   AN
  TWO TALES AND EIGHT TOMORROWS HARRISON, HARRY   AC
  UNFRIENDLY FUTURE, THE   BOARDMAN, TOM JR.   AN
ROBOT JUSTICE (SEE I SEE YOU)   TC
ROBOT WHO WANTED TO KNOW, THE   SS   FUN 58 03
  WAR WITH THE ROBOTS   HARRISON, HARRY   AC
ROCK DIVER   SS   WBY 51 02
  BEYOND THE END OF TIME   POHL, FREDERIK   AN
  EARTH IS THE STRANGEST PLANET SILVERBERG, ROBERT   AN
  SCIENCE FICTION INVENTIONS   KNIGHT, DAMON   AN
ROOMMATES (BASIS FOR NOVEL "MAKE ROOM! MAKE ROOM!")
                                        NV   NEW 71 AN
  ABOVE THE HUMAN LANDSCAPE   MCNELLY & STOVER   AN
 *BEST OF HARRY HARRISON, THE   HARRISON, HARRY   AC
  EARTH IN TRANSIT   SCHWARTZ, SHEILA   AN
  RUINS OF EARTH, THE   DISCH, THOMAS M.   AN
RUN FROM THE FIRE   NV   EPC 75
  EPOCH   ELWOOD & SILVERBERG   OA
SECRET OF STONEHENGE, THE   SS   FSF 68 06
  ANCIENT MYSTERIES READER, THE HAINING, PETER   AN
  PRIME NUMBER   HARRISON, HARRY   AC
SIMULATED TRAINER (TRAINEE FOR MARS)   SS   FUN 58 06
  WAR WITH THE ROBOTS   HARRISON, HARRY   AC
SPACE RATS OF THE C.C.C.   NV   FST 74
  ANTIGRAV: COSMIC COMEDIES   STRICK, PHILIP   AN
 *BEST OF HARRY HARRISON, THE   HARRISON, HARRY   AC
  FINAL STAGE   FERMAN & MALZBERG   OA
STREETS OF ASHKELON, THE (ALSO AS AN ALIEN AGONY) SS NWS 62 09
 *BEST OF HARRY HARRISON, THE   HARRISON, HARRY   AC
  DARK STARS   SILVERBERG, ROBERT   AN
  GODS FOR TOMORROW   SANTESSON, HANS S.   AN
  NEW AWARENESS, THE   WARRICK & GREENBERG   AN
  SCIENCE FICTION NOVELLAS   HARRISON & MCNELLY   AN
  TWO TALES AND EIGHT TOMORROWS HARRISON, HARRY   AC
SURVIVAL PLANET   SS   FSF 61 08
  WAR WITH THE ROBOTS   HARRISON, HARRY   AC
TALE OF THE ENDING, A (AS HANK DEMPSEY) SS   ASF 70 06
  ONE STEP FROM EARTH   HARRISON, HARRY   AC
THINGS TO COME   IN C
  SCIENCE FICTION NOVELLAS   HARRISON & MCNELLY   AN
TOY SHOP   SS   ASF 62 04
  PRIME NUMBER   HARRISON, HARRY   AC
  8TH ANNUAL OF THE YEAR'S BEST S-F, THE MERRIL, JUDITH AN
TRAINEE FOR MARS (ALSO AS SIMULATED TRAINER) SS FUN 58 06
  SECOND ORBIT   DOHERTY, G. D.   AN
UNTO MY MANIFOLD DOOMS (THE MANY DOOMS) SS   GAL 64 06
  TWO TALES AND EIGHT TOMORROWS HARRISON, HARRY   AC
VELVET GLOVE, THE   NV   FUN 56 11
  CRIME PREVENTION IN THE 30TH CENTURY SANTESSON, HANS S. AN
  FANTASTIC UNIVERSE OMNIBUS, THE SANTESSON, HANS S. AN
  SOULS IN METAL   ASHLEY, MICHAEL   AN
  WAR WITH THE ROBOTS   HARRISON, HARRY   AC
WAITING PLACE   SS   GAL 68 06
 *BEST OF HARRY HARRISON, THE   HARRISON, HARRY   AC
  ONE STEP FROM EARTH   HARRISON, HARRY   AC
WAR WITH THE ROBOTS   SS   SFE 62 07
  WAR WITH THE ROBOTS   HARRISON, HARRY   AC
WE ATE THE WHOLE THING   SS   VTX 73 04
  BEST OF HARRY HARRISON, THE (BRITISH) HARRISON, HARRY AC
WICKED FLEE, THE   SS   NDM 71 01
  BEST OF HARRY HARRISON, THE (BRITISH) HARRISON, HARRY AC
  BEST SCIENCE FICTION STORIES OF THE YEAR (1971)
                               DEL REY, LESTER   AN
  NEW DIMENSIONS 1   SILVERBERG, ROBERT   OA
WIFE TO THE LORD   SS   FSF 70 06
  ONE STEP FROM EARTH   HARRISON, HARRY   AC
WORD FROM THE (HUMAN) EDITOR..., A   IN
  WAR WITH THE ROBOTS   HARRISON, HARRY   AC
WORLD OTALMI MADE, THE   SN   SFA 58 06
  GREAT SCIENCE FICTION ADVENTURES SHAW, LARRY T.   AN
YOU MEN OF VIOLENCE   SS   GAL 67 04
  PRIME NUMBER   HARRISON, HARRY   AC

HARRISON, LIZ
METAMORPHOSIS   IL C
  BEYOND THIS HORIZON   CARRELL, CHRISTOPHER OA

HARRISON, M. JOHN
MACHINE IN SHAFT TEN AND OTHER STORIES, THE AC PTH 75
ABSORBING THE MIRACULOUS   BR   NWQ 74 06
  NEW WORLDS NO. 6   PLATT & BAILEY   OA
ASH CIRCUS, THE   SS   NWS 69 04
  BEST SF STORIES FROM NEW WORLDS 7 MOORCOCK, MICHAEL AN
BAA BAA BLOCKSHEEP   SS   NWS 68 11
  BEST SF STORIES FROM NEW WORLDS 6 MOORCOCK, MICHAEL AN
BAIT PRINCIPLE, THE   SS   NWS 70 02
  BEST SF STORIES FROM NEW WORLDS 8 MOORCOCK, MICHAEL AN
  MACHINE IN SHAFT TEN AND OTHER STORIES, THE
                               HARRISON, M. JOHN   AC
BLACK GLAK, THE   AR   NWQ 72 03
  NEW WORLDS QUARTERLY NO. 3   MOORCOCK, MICHAEL   OA
BRINGER WITH THE WINDOW, THE (LAMIA MUTABLE) SS DVS 72 02
  MACHINE IN SHAFT TEN AND OTHER STORIES, THE
                               HARRISON, M. JOHN   AC
BY TENNYSON OUT OF DISNEY   SS   NWQ 71 02
  NEW WORLDS QUARTERLY NO. 2   MOORCOCK, MICHAEL   OA
CAUSEWAY, THE   SS   NWQ 71 02

HARRISON, M. JOHN   (CONTINUED)
  MACHINE IN SHAFT TEN AND OTHER STORIES, THE
                               HARRISON, M. JOHN   AC
  NEW WORLDS QUARTERLY NO. 2   MOORCOCK, MICHAEL   OA
COMING FROM BEHIND   SS   NWQ 73 05
  MACHINE IN SHAFT TEN AND OTHER STORIES, THE
                               HARRISON, M. JOHN   AC
  NEW WORLDS NO. 5   MOORCOCK & PLATT   OA
COMING TO LIFE   MS   NWB 75 08
  NEW WORLDS EIGHT   BAILEY, HILARY   OA
ESSAY: A LITERATURE OF COMFORT   BR   NWQ 71 01
  NEW WORLDS QUARTERLY NO. 1   MOORCOCK, MICHAEL   OA
EVENTS WITNESSED FROM A CITY   SS
  MACHINE IN SHAFT TEN AND OTHER STORIES, THE
                               HARRISON, M. JOHN   AC
FILLING US UP   SS   NWQ 73 05
  NEW WORLDS NO. 5   MOORCOCK & PLATT   OA
GREEN FIVE RENEGADE   NV   NWR 69 14
  NEW WRITINGS IN SF. 14   CARNELL, JOHN   OA
LAMIA AND LORD CROMIS, THE   NV   NWQ 71 01
  MACHINE IN SHAFT TEN AND OTHER STORIES, THE
                               HARRISON, M. JOHN   AC
  NEW WORLDS QUARTERLY NO. 1   MOORCOCK, MICHAEL   OA
LAMIA MUTABLE (ALSO AS THE BRINGER WITH THE WINDOW)
                                        SS   DVS 72 02
  AGAIN, DANGEROUS VISIONS   ELLISON, HARLAN   OA
LONDON MELANCHOLY   SS   FSF 69 05
  MACHINE IN SHAFT TEN AND OTHER STORIES, THE
                               HARRISON, M. JOHN   AC
MACBETH EXPIATION, THE   SS   NWR 68 13
  NEW WRITINGS IN SF. 9   CARNELL, JOHN   AN
  NEW WRITINGS IN SF. 13   CARNELL, JOHN   OA
MACHINE IN SHAFT TEN, THE (AS JOYCE CHURCHILL) SS NWQ 72 03
  MACHINE IN SHAFT TEN AND OTHER STORIES, THE
                               HARRISON, M. JOHN   AC
ORGASM BAND, THE   SS   TRV
  MACHINE IN SHAFT TEN AND OTHER STORIES, THE
                               HARRISON, M. JOHN   AC
PROBLEM OF SYMPATHY, THE   BR   NWQ 72 04
  NEW WORLDS QUARTERLY NO. 4   MOORCOCK, MICHAEL   OA
RING OF PAIN   SS   QRK 71 03
  MACHINE IN SHAFT TEN AND OTHER STORIES, THE
                               HARRISON, M. JOHN   AC
  QUARK/3   DELANY & HACKER   OA
RUNNING DOWN   NV   NWB 75 08
  MACHINE IN SHAFT TEN AND OTHER STORIES, THE
                               HARRISON, M. JOHN   AC
  NEW WORLDS EIGHT   BAILEY, HILARY   OA
SETTLING THE WORLD   NV   NEW 75 AN
  BEST SF: 75, THE NINTH ANNUAL HARRISON & ALDISS   AN
  NEW IMPROVED SUN, THE   DISCH, THOMAS M.   AN
TO THE STARS AND BEYOND ON THE FABULOUS ANTI-SYNTAX DRIVE
                                        SS   NWB 73 05
  NEW WORLDS QUARTERLY NO. 5   MOORCOCK, MICHAEL   OA
VISIONS OF MONAD   SS   NWR 68 12
  MACHINE IN SHAFT TEN AND OTHER STORIES, THE
                               HARRISON, M. JOHN   AC
  NEW WRITINGS IN SF. 8   CARNELL, JOHN   AN
  NEW WRITINGS IN SF. 12   CARNELL, JOHN   OA
WOLF THAT FOLLOWS, THE   NV   NWQ 74 06
  NEW WORLDS NO. 6   PLATT & BAILEY   OA

HARRISON, WILLIAM
ROLLERBALL   AC   WPB 75 07
ARSONS OF DESIRE, THE   SS   72
  ROLLERBALL   HARRISON, WILLIAM   AC
BLURB KING, THE   SS   71
  ROLLERBALL   HARRISON, WILLIAM   AC
COOK'S TALE, A   NV   66
  ROLLERBALL   HARRISON, WILLIAM   AC
DOWN THE BLUE HOLE   SS   73
  ROLLERBALL   HARRISON, WILLIAM   AC
EATING IT   SS   70
  ROLLERBALL   HARRISON, WILLIAM   AC
GOOD SHIP ERASMUS, THE   SS   71
  ROLLERBALL   HARRISON, WILLIAM   AC
HERMIT, THE   SS   68
  ROLLERBALL   HARRISON, WILLIAM   AC
NIRVANA, GOTTERDAMMERUNG, AND THE SHOT PUT SS   72
  ROLLERBALL   HARRISON, WILLIAM   AC
PINBALL MACHINES, THE   SS   SEP 67 04
  ROLLERBALL   HARRISON, WILLIAM   AC
PREFACE   IN
  ROLLERBALL   HARRISON, WILLIAM   AC
ROLLER BALL MURDERS   SS   ESQ 73 09
  BEST SF: 1973   HARRISON & ALDISS   AN
  ROLLERBALL   HARRISON, WILLIAM   AC
UNDER THE HOUSE   SS   72
  ROLLERBALL   HARRISON, WILLIAM   AC
WARRIOR, THE   SS   ESQ 71 11
  ROLLERBALL   HARRISON, WILLIAM   AC
WEATHERMAN: A THEOLOGICAL NARRATIVE   SS   73
  ROLLERBALL   HARRISON, WILLIAM   AC

HART, ELLIS   PSEUD. FOR HARLAN ELLISON

HART, JAMES S.
TRAITOR, THE   SS   FSF 50 FL
  SUPERNATURAL READER, THE   CONKLIN, G&L.   AN

HART, JOHNNY
B.C.   CT   NYH 61 08
  MATHEMATICAL MAGPIE, THE   FADIMAN, CLIFTON   AN

HARTRIDGE, JON
  LIKE FATHER   SS   NWS 69 08
    BEST SF: 1969   HARRISON & ALDISS   AN

HARTWELL, DAVID G. AND L. W. CURREY
  BATTLE OF THE MONSTERS AND OTHER STORIES, THE   AN H GRG 76

HARTWELL, DAVID G.
  INTRODUCTION   IN C
    BATTLE OF THE MONSTERS AND OTHER STORIES, THE
                                           HARTWELL & CURREY   AN

HARVEY, FRANK
  AIR FORCE¡   AC   BAL 59
  DEATH DUST, THE   SS   SEP 59 08
    POST READER OF FANTASY AND SCIENCE FICTION
                                           SATURDAY EVE. POST   AN
  DESTRUCT BUTTON   SS   AUG 59
    AIR FORCE¡   HARVEY, FRANK   AC
  JINX JET   SS   CAV 57
    AIR FORCE¡   HARVEY, FRANK   AC
  MOON SHOT   SS   SEP 58 05
    AIR FORCE¡   HARVEY, FRANK   AC
  ORBIT FLIGHT   SS   SEP 58 10
    AIR FORCE¡   HARVEY, FRANK   AC
  PANIC ON RUNWAY 6   SS   SEP 56 07
    AIR FORCE¡   HARVEY, FRANK   AC
  RUNAWAY PROP   SS   SEP 59 05
    AIR FORCE¡   HARVEY, FRANK   AC
  TEST JUMP   SS   SEP 56 06
    AIR FORCE¡   HARVEY, FRANK   AC
  100 MILES UP   SS   AUG 58
    AIR FORCE¡   HARVEY, FRANK   AC

HARVEY, WILLIAM F.
  AUGUST HEAT   SS   28
    NIGHT IN FUNLAND   BRONDFIELD, JEROME   AN
    OTHER SIDE OF THE CLOCK, THE   STERN, PHILIP VAN D. AN
    TRAVELERS IN TIME   STERN, PHILIP VAN D. AN
  BEAST WITH FIVE FINGERS, THE   NV
    GHOULS, THE   HAINING, PETER   AN

HARWOOD, H. C.
  NOVELS (LISTED UNDER JULES VERNE)   EC H GOL 29

HASFORD, GUSTAV
  HEARTLAND   SS   ORB 75 16
    ORBIT 16   KNIGHT, DAMON   OA

HASSE, HENRY
  EYES, THE   SS   FBK 51 08
    SCIENCE AND SORCERY   FORD, GARRET   AN
  HE WHO SHRANK   NV   AMZ 36 08
    *ADVENTURES IN TIME AND SPACE   HEALY & MCCOMAS   AN
    BEFORE THE GOLDEN AGE   ASIMOV, ISAAC   AN

HASTINGS, CHRISTEL
  BLACK CATS   PM   UNK 40 12
    FROM UNKNOWN WORLDS   CAMPBELL, JOHN W. JR AN

HASTINGS, HUDSON   PSEUD. FOR HENRY KUTTNER

HATCHER, JACK
  FUEL FOR THE FUTURE   AR   ASF 40 03
    COMING ATTRACTIONS   GREENBERG , MARTIN   NF

HAUSMANN, RAOUL
  MECHANICAL HEAD   IL
    SCIENCE FICTION   BRODKIN & PEARSON   AN

HAWKINS, PETER
  CIRCUS   SS   SCF 52 FL
    GATEWAY TO THE STARS   CARNELL, JOHN   AN
  LIFE CYCLE   SS   NWS 51 SP
    GATEWAY TO TOMORROW   CARNELL, JOHN   AN
  SHIP FROM THE STARS   SS   NWS 54 07
    BEST FROM NEW WORLDS SCIENCE FICTION, THE
                                           CARNELL, JOHN   AN

HAWKINS, WILLIAM
  DWINDLING SPHERE, THE   SS   ASF 40 03
    MASTERS' CHOICE   JANIFER, LAURENCE M. AN

HAWTHORNE, NATHANIEL
  ARTIST OF THE BEAUTIFUL, THE (1844)   NV   DMR 44 06
    FUTURE PERFECT   FRANKLIN, H. BRUCE   AN
    LOOKING AHEAD   ALLEN, D. & L.   AN
  BIRTHMARK, THE (1843)   SS   PIO 43 03
    FUTURE PERFECT   FRANKLIN, H. BRUCE   AN
    JOURNEYS IN SCIENCE FICTION   LOUGHLIN, RICHARD L. AN
    PAST, PRESENT, AND FUTURE PERFECT   WOLFE, J&FITZ GERALD AN
  EARTH'S HOLOCAUST   SS   GLG 44 05
    CIRCUS OF DR. LAO AND OTHER IMPROBABLE STORIES
                                           BRADBURY, RAY   AN
    SCIENCE FICTION: THE FUTURE   ALLEN, DICK   AN
    SPECULATIONS   SANDERS, THOMAS E.   AN
  FEATHERTOP (SEE PURITAN PASSIONS)   TC
  PURITAN PASSIONS (FEATHERTOP)   SS   ITM 52 02
    GHOULS, THE   HAINING, PETER   AN
  RAPPACCINI'S DAUGHTER (1844)   NV   DMR 44 12
    FUTURE PERFECT   FRANKLIN, H. BRUCE   AN
    GREAT SCIENCE FICTION ABOUT DOCTORS   CONKLIN, G&FABRICANT AN
    NIGHTMARE GARDEN   GHIDALIA, VIC   AN
    OTHER DIMENSION, THE   ROSNER, SARA   AN
    ROOTS OF EVIL, THE   PARRY, MICHEL   AN
    STRANGE SIGNPOSTS   ELWOOD & MOSKOWITZ   AN

HAWTHORNE, NATHANIEL (CONTINUED)
  YOUNG GOODMAN BROWN (1835)   SS   NEM 35 04
    ROD SERLING'S TRIPLE W: WITCHES, WARLOCKS AND WEREWOLVES
                                           SERLING, ROD   AN
    WIZARDS AND WARLOCKS   GHIDALIA, VIC   AN

HAY, GEORGE
  BEST OF JOHN W. CAMPBELL, THE (LISTED UNDER JOHN W. CAMPBELL)
                                                      EC H SID 73
  HELL HATH FURY   AN H NSP 63 10
  STOPWATCH   OA H NEL 74 10
    INTRODUCTION   IN
      STOPWATCH   HAY, GEORGE   OA
  INTRODUCTION: SCIENCE FICTION - SCIENCE FACT   IN
    BEYOND THIS HORIZON   CARRELL, CHRISTOPHER OA

HAYCOCK, CHRISTINE
  PHOTOGRAPHY   IL
    SCIENCE FICTION BY GASLIGHT   MOSKOWITZ, SAM   AN

HEALY, RAYMOND J. AND J. FRANCIS MCCOMAS
  ADVENTURES IN TIME AND SPACE   AN H RDM 46 08
    SECOND EDITION, 1953, OMITS LAST FIVE STORIES,
    ALSO AS "FAMOUS SCIENCE-FICTION STORIES"
    DERIVATIVE ANTHOLOGY "MORE ADVENTURES IN TIME AND SPACE"
  ADVENTURES IN TIME AND SPACE (BRITISH)   AN H GRY 52
  ADVENTURES IN TIME AND SPACE (SELECTIONS FROM)   AN   BAN 54
  FAMOUS SCIENCE-FICTION STORIES   AN H MDL 57
    SEE "ADVENTURES IN TIME AND SPACE"
  MORE ADVENTURES IN TIME AND SPACE   AN   BAN 55 0
    STORIES FROM "ADVENTURES IN TIME AND SPACE"

HEALY, RAYMOND J.
  NEW TALES OF SPACE AND TIME   OA H HLT 51 11
  9 TALES OF SPACE AND TIME   OA H HLT 54
  GREAT DEVON MYSTERY, THE   SS   NTL 54
    9 TALES OF SPACE AND TIME   HEALY, RAYMOND J.   OA
  INTRODUCTION   IN
    NEW TALES OF SPACE AND TIME   HEALY, RAYMOND J.   OA

HEARD, GERALD   PSEUD. FOR H. F. HEARD
  B + M - PLANET 4   NV   NTS 51
    NEW TALES OF SPACE AND TIME   HEALY, RAYMOND J.   OA
  SCIENCE FICTION, MORALS, AND RELIGION   AR   NEW 53 NF
  SCIENCE FICTION: THE FUTURE   ALLEN, DICK   AN

HEARD, H. F.   ALSO AS   GERALD HEARD
  GREAT FOG AND OTHER WEIRD TALES, THE   OC H VPR 44
  LOST CAVERN AND OTHER TALES OF THE FANTASTIC, THE AC H VPR 48
  CAT "I AM"   SS
    GREAT FOG AND OTHER WEIRD TALES, THE   HEARD, H. F.   OC
  CHAPEL OF EASE, THE   NV
    LOST CAVERN AND OTHER TALES OF THE FANTASTIC, THE
                                           HEARD, H. F.   AC
  COLLECTOR, THE   SS   FSF 51 08
    BEST FROM FANTASY AND SCIENCE FICTION BOUCHER & MCCOMAS   AN
  CRAYFISH, THE   SS
    GREAT FOG AND OTHER WEIRD TALES, THE   HEARD, H. F.   OC
  CUP, THE   NV
    LOST CAVERN AND OTHER TALES OF THE FANTASTIC, THE
                                           HEARD, H. F.   AC
  CYCLOPS   SS   NEW 52 AN
    *FUTURE TENSE   CROSSEN, KENDELL F.   AN
  DROMENON   SS
    GREAT FOG AND OTHER WEIRD TALES, THE   HEARD, H. F.   OC
  ECLIPSE   SS
    GREAT FOG AND OTHER WEIRD TALES, THE   HEARD, H. F.   OC
  GREAT FOG, THE   SS   44
    GREAT FOG AND OTHER WEIRD TALES, THE   HEARD, H. F.   OC
    *TREASURY OF SCIENCE FICTION, A   CONKLIN, GROFF   AN
  LOST CAVERN, THE   NV
    LOST CAVERN AND OTHER TALES OF THE FANTASTIC, THE
                                           HEARD, H. F.   AC
  ROUSING OF MR. BRADEGAR, THE   SS   44
    GREAT FOG AND OTHER WEIRD TALES, THE   HEARD, H. F.   OC
    TRAVELERS IN TIME   STERN, PHILIP VAN D. AN
  SWAP, THE   SS   44
    GREAT FOG AND OTHER WEIRD TALES, THE   HEARD, H. F.   OC
    SUPERNATURAL READER, THE   CONKLIN, G&L.   AN
  THAW PLAN, THE   NV
    LOST CAVERN AND OTHER TALES OF THE FANTASTIC, THE
                                           HEARD, H. F.   AC
  VINDICAE FLAMMAE   SS
    GREAT FOG AND OTHER WEIRD TALES, THE   HEARD, H. F.   OC
  WINGLESS VICTORY   SS   44
    *BEYOND TIME AND SPACE   DERLETH, AUGUST   AN
    GREAT FOG AND OTHER WEIRD TALES, THE   HEARD, H. F.   OC

HEARN, LAFCADIO
  MOUND BUILDERS, THE   AR
    ANCIENT MYSTERIES READER, THE   HAINING, PETER   AN

HEATH-STUBBS, JOHN
  FROM AN ECCLESIASTICAL CHRONICLE   PM
    HOLDING YOUR EIGHT HANDS   LUCIE-SMITH, EDWARD   AN

HECHT, BEN
  IN THE MIDST OF DEATH   SS   45
    ALONE BY NIGHT   CONGDON, MICHAEL&DON AN

HEIDENRY, JOHN
  COUNTERPOINT OF VIEW, THE   MS   DVS 72 02
    AGAIN, DANGEROUS VISIONS   ELLISON, HARLAN   OA

HEINLEIN, ROBERT A.

HEINLEIN, ROBERT A.   ALSO AS   ANSON MACDONALD AND LYLE MONROE
ASSIGNMENT IN ETERNITY   AC H FPS 53
BEST OF ROBERT HEINLEIN, THE   AC H SID 73
GREEN HILLS OF EARTH, THE   AC H SHS 51
    ALSO IN "A ROBERT HEINLEIN OMNIBUS"
HEINLEIN TRIAD, A   AC H GOL 66
    SEE "THREE BY HEINLEIN"
MAN WHO SOLD THE MOON, THE   AC H SHS 50
    ALSO IN "A ROBERT HEINLEIN OMNIBUS"
MAN WHO SOLD THE MOON, THE (4 OF 6)   AC SIG 51
MENACE FROM EARTH, THE   AC H GNM 59
ORPHANS OF THE SKY   NO H GOL 63
PAST THROUGH TOMORROW, THE   AC H PUT 67
REVOLT IN 2100   AC H SHS 53
ROBERT HEINLEIN OMNIBUS, A   AC H GOL 66
THREE BY HEINLEIN   AC H DBL 51
    IN ENGLAND AS "A HEINLEIN TRIAD"
TOMORROW, THE STARS   AN H DBL 51
UNPLEASANT PROFESSION OF JONATHAN HOAG, THE   AC H GNM 59
    ALSO AS "6 X H"
WORLDS OF ROBERT A. HEINLEIN, THE   AC ACE 66
6 X H   AC PYR 61 08
    SEE "THE UNPLEASANT PROFESSION OF JONATHAN HOAG"
ALL YOU ZOMBIES-   SS FSF 59 03
    AS TOMORROW BECOMES TODAY   SULLIVAN, CHARLES W. AN
    BEST FROM FANTASY AND SCIENCE FICTION: 9
                                     MILLS, ROBERT P.   AN
    BEST OF ROBERT HEINLEIN, THE   HEINLEIN, ROBERT A. AC
    MIRROR OF INFINITY, THE   SILVERBERG, ROBERT AN
    SURVIVAL PRINTOUT   TOTAL EFFECT   AN
    UNPLEASANT PROFESSION OF JONATHAN HOAG, THE
                                     HEINLEIN, ROBERT A. AC
    WORLDS OF SCIENCE FICTION, THE   MILLS, ROBERT P.   AN
AND HE BUILT A CROOKED HOUSE   SS ASF 41 02
    AS TOMORROW BECOMES TODAY   SULLIVAN, CHARLES W. AN
    BEST OF ROBERT HEINLEIN, THE   HEINLEIN, ROBERT A. AC
    FANTASIA MATHEMATICA   FADIMAN, CLIFTON   AN
    INTRODUCTORY PSYCHOLOGY THROUGH SCIENCE FICTION
                                     KATZ/WARRICK/&   AN
    OTHER DIMENSIONS   SILVERBERG, ROBERT AN
    OTHER SIDE OF THE CLOCK, THE   STERN, PHILIP VAN D. AN
    POCKET BOOK OF SCIENCE-FICTION, THE WOLLHEIM, DONALD A. AN
    SCIENCE FICTION   BRODKIN & PEARSON   AN
    TIME PROBE: THE SCIENCES IN SF. CLARKE, ARTHUR C.   AN
    UNPLEASANT PROFESSION OF JONATHAN HOAG, THE
                                     HEINLEIN, ROBERT A. AC
    WHERE DO WE GO FROM HERE?   ASIMOV, ISAAC   AN
BEYOND DOUBT   SS C AST 41 04
    BEYOND THE END OF TIME   POHL, FREDERIK   AN
BEYOND THIS HORIZON   NO ASF 42 04
    ROBERT HEINLEIN OMNIBUS, A   HEINLEIN, ROBERT A. AC
BLACK PITS OF LUNA, THE   SS SEP 48 01
    GREEN HILLS OF EARTH, THE   HEINLEIN, ROBERT A. AC
    PAST THROUGH TOMORROW, THE   HEINLEIN, ROBERT A. AC
    *POSSIBLE WORLDS OF SCIENCE FICTION CONKLIN, GROFF AN
    SCIENCE FICTION AND READER'S GUIDE BARROWS, MARJORIE AN
    STORIES OF SCIENTIFIC IMAGINATION GALLANT, JOSEPH   AN
    TOMORROW'S WORLDS   SILVERBERG, ROBERT AN
BLOWUPS HAPPEN   NV ASF 40 09
    *ASTOUNDING SCIENCE FICTION ANTHOLOGY, THE
                                     CAMPBELL, JOHN W. JR AN
    *BEST OF SCIENCE FICTION   CONKLIN, GROFF   AN
    BEST SF 2   CRISPIN, EDMUND   AN
    *FIRST ASTOUNDING SCIENCE FICTION ANTHOLOGY, THE
                                     CAMPBELL, JOHN W. JR AN
    *MAN WHO SOLD THE MOON, THE   HEINLEIN, ROBERT A. AC
    PAST THROUGH TOMORROW, THE   HEINLEIN, ROBERT A. AC
    WORLDS OF ROBERT A. HEINLEIN, THE HEINLEIN, ROBERT A. AC
BY HIS BOOTSTRAPS (ALSO AS THE TIME GATE)   NV ASF 41 10
    GIANT ANTHOLOGY OF SCIENCE FICTION MARGULIES & FRIEND AN
    MENACE FROM EARTH, THE   HEINLEIN, ROBERT A. AC
    *SPECTRUM   AMIS & CONQUEST   AN
COLUMBUS WAS A DOPE   SS STS 47 05
    FIFTY SHORT SCIENCE FICTION TALES ASIMOV & CONKLIN AN
    FUTURE MAKERS, THE   HAINING, PETER   AN
    MENACE FROM EARTH, THE   HEINLEIN, ROBERT A. AC
    SCIENCE FICTION: THE GREAT YEARS, VOL. II
                                     POHL, C. & F.   AN
COMMON SENSE   NV ASF 41 10
    ORPHANS OF THE SKY   HEINLEIN, ROBERT A. NO
CONCERNING STORIES NEVER WRITTEN: POSTSCRIPT   MS
    REVOLT IN 2100   HEINLEIN, ROBERT A. AC
COVENTRY   NV ASF 40 07
    BEYOND TOMORROW   KNIGHT, DAMON   AN
    PAST THROUGH TOMORROW, THE   HEINLEIN, ROBERT A. AC
    REVOLT IN 2100   HEINLEIN, ROBERT A. AC
    6 GREAT SHORT NOVELS OF SCIENCE FICTION
                                     CONKLIN, GROFF   AN
DELILAH AND THE SPACE-RIGGER   SS BBM 49 12
    GREEN HILLS OF EARTH, THE   HEINLEIN, ROBERT A. AC
    PAST THROUGH TOMORROW, THE   HEINLEIN, ROBERT A. AC
DESTINATION MOON   NV SSM 50 09
    THREE TIMES INFINITY   MARGULIES, LEO   AN
DEVIL MAKES THE LAW, THE (SEE MAGIC, INC.)   TC
DOUBLE STAR (EXCERPT)   EX ASF 56 02
    MARS, WE LOVE YOU   HIPOLITO & MCNELLY AN
ELEPHANT CIRCUIT, THE (SEE THE MAN WHO TRAVELED IN ELEPHANTS)
                                                 TC
ELSEWHEN (ELSEWHERE)   NV ASF 41 09
    ASSIGNMENT IN ETERNITY   HEINLEIN, ROBERT A. AC
ELSEWHERE (SEE ELSEWHEN)   TC
FREE MEN   NV NEW 66 AC
    WORLDS OF ROBERT A. HEINLEIN, THE HEINLEIN, ROBERT A. AC
FROM: THE MOON IS A HARSH MISTRESS   EX IFS 65 12
    INSIDE INFORMATION   MOWSHOWITZ, ABBE   AN

HEINLEIN, ROBERT A.

HEINLEIN, ROBERT A.   (CONTINUED)
GENTLEMEN, BE SEATED¦   SS ARG 48 05
    FIRST STEP OUTWARD   HOSKINS, ROBERT   AN
    GREEN HILLS OF EARTH, THE   HEINLEIN, ROBERT A. AC
    PAST THROUGH TOMORROW, THE   HEINLEIN, ROBERT A. AC
    SHOT IN THE DARK   MERRIL, JUDITH   AN
GOLDFISH BOWL   NV ASF 42 03
    APEMAN, SPACEMAN   STOVER & HARRISON   AN
    *BEST OF SCIENCE FICTION   CONKLIN, GROFF   AN
    FIRST CONTACT   KNIGHT, DAMON   AN
    MENACE FROM EARTH, THE   HEINLEIN, ROBERT A. AC
    TOMORROW, AND TOMORROW, AND TOMORROW...
                                     HEINTZ/HERBERT/JOOS/ AN
GREEN HILLS OF EARTH, THE   AC SHS 51
    ROBERT HEINLEIN OMNIBUS, A   HEINLEIN, ROBERT A. AC
GREEN HILLS OF EARTH, THE   SS SEP 47 02
    BEST OF ROBERT HEINLEIN, THE   HEINLEIN, ROBERT A. AC
    GREEN HILLS OF EARTH, THE   HEINLEIN, ROBERT A. AC
    IN DREAMS AWAKE   FIEDLER, LESLIE A. AN
    INVASION FROM MARS   WELLES, ORSON   AN
    *MY BEST SCIENCE FICTION STORY   MARGULIES & FRIEND AN
    PAST THROUGH TOMORROW, THE   HEINLEIN, ROBERT A. AC
    POST READER OF FANTASY AND SCIENCE FICTION
                                     SATURDAY EVE. POST AN
    SCIENCE FICTION: THE FUTURE   ALLEN, DICK   AN
    SPECULATIONS   SANDERS, THOMAS E. AN
    *STRANGE PORTS OF CALL   DERLETH, AUGUST   AN
GULF   SN ASF 49 11
    ASSIGNMENT IN ETERNITY   HEINLEIN, ROBERT A. AC
    CENTURY OF GREAT SHORT SCIENCE FICTION NOVELS, A
                                     KNIGHT, DAMON   AN
HEIL¦   SS FUF 40 04
    FUTURES TO INFINITY   MOSKOWITZ, SAM   AN
IF THIS GOES ON-   SN ASF 40 02
    PAST THROUGH TOMORROW, THE   HEINLEIN, ROBERT A. AC
    REVOLT IN 2100   HEINLEIN, ROBERT A. AC
INTRODUCTION   IN
    BEST FROM STARTLING STORIES, THE MINES, SAMUEL   AN
    BEST OF ROBERT HEINLEIN, THE   HEINLEIN, ROBERT A. AC
    TOMORROW, THE STARS   HEINLEIN, ROBERT A. AC
"IT DOES NOT PAY A PROPHET TO BE TOO SPECIFIC"   IN
    *MAN WHO SOLD THE MOON, THE   HEINLEIN, ROBERT A. AC
IT'S GREAT TO BE BACK¦   SS SEP 47 07
    CITIES OF WONDER   KNIGHT, DAMON   AN
    GREEN HILLS OF EARTH, THE   HEINLEIN, ROBERT A. AC
    PAST THROUGH TOMORROW, THE   HEINLEIN, ROBERT A. AC
    *TREASURY OF SCIENCE FICTION, A CONKLIN, GROFF   AN
JERRY WAS A MAN (JERRY IS A MAN)   SS TWS 47 10
    ASSIGNMENT IN ETERNITY   HEINLEIN, ROBERT A. AC
LET THERE BE LIGHT   SS SSS 40 05
    *MAN WHO SOLD THE MOON, THE   HEINLEIN, ROBERT A. AC
LIFE-LINE   SS ASF 39 08
    BEST OF ROBERT HEINLEIN, THE   HEINLEIN, ROBERT A. AC
    FIRST FLIGHT   KNIGHT, DAMON   AN
    *MAN WHO SOLD THE MOON, THE   HEINLEIN, ROBERT A. AC
    PAST THROUGH TOMORROW, THE   HEINLEIN, ROBERT A. AC
    TALES OF SCIENCE FICTION   BALL, BRIAN N.   AN
    WORLDS OF ROBERT A. HEINLEIN, THE HEINLEIN, ROBERT A. AC
LOGIC OF EMPIRE   NV ASF 41 03
    GREEN HILLS OF EARTH, THE   HEINLEIN, ROBERT A. AC
    PAST THROUGH TOMORROW, THE   HEINLEIN, ROBERT A. AC
LONG WATCH, THE   SS ALM 49 12
    BEST OF ROBERT HEINLEIN, THE   HEINLEIN, ROBERT A. AC
    *BEYOND TIME AND SPACE   DERLETH, AUGUST   AN
    GREEN HILLS OF EARTH, THE   HEINLEIN, ROBERT A. AC
    PAST THROUGH TOMORROW, THE   HEINLEIN, ROBERT A. AC
    SCIENCE FICTION ROLL OF HONOR, THE POHL, FREDERIK   AN
LOST LEGACY (LOST LEGION)   NV SSS 41 11
    ASSIGNMENT IN ETERNITY   HEINLEIN, ROBERT A. AC
LOST LEGION (SEE LOST LEGACY)   TC
MAGIC, INC. (THE DEVIL MAKES THE LAW)   SN UNK 40 09
    GOLDEN ROAD, THE   KNIGHT, DAMON   AN
    THREE BY HEINLEIN   HEINLEIN, ROBERT A. AC
MAN WHO SOLD THE MOON, THE   AC SHS 50
    ROBERT HEINLEIN OMNIBUS, A   HEINLEIN, ROBERT A. AC
MAN WHO SOLD THE MOON, THE   NV NEW 50 AC
    BEST OF ROBERT HEINLEIN, THE   HEINLEIN, ROBERT A. AC
    DIMENSION X   KNIGHT, DAMON   AN
    *MAN WHO SOLD THE MOON, THE   HEINLEIN, ROBERT A. AC
    PAST THROUGH TOMORROW, THE   HEINLEIN, ROBERT A. AC
    TREASURY OF GREAT SCIENCE FICTION, A VOL.2
                                     BOUCHER, ANTHONY   AN
MAN WHO TRAVELED IN ELEPHANTS, THE (THE ELEPHANT CIRCUIT)
                                                 SS STN 57 10
    UNPLEASANT PROFESSION OF JONATHAN HOAG, THE
                                     HEINLEIN, ROBERT A. AC
MENACE FROM EARTH, THE   SS FSF 57 08
    HOT & COLD RUNNING CITIES   MCHARGUE, GEORGESS AN
    MENACE FROM EARTH, THE   HEINLEIN, ROBERT A. AC
    PAST THROUGH TOMORROW, THE   HEINLEIN, ROBERT A. AC
    TOMORROW'S CHILDREN   ASIMOV, ISAAC   AN
METHUSELAH'S CHILDREN   NO ASF 41 07
    PAST THROUGH TOMORROW, THE   HEINLEIN, ROBERT A. AC
MISFIT   SS ASF 39 11
    GIANTS UNLEASHED   CONKLIN, GROFF   AN
    PAST THROUGH TOMORROW, THE   HEINLEIN, ROBERT A. AC
    REVOLT IN 2100   HEINLEIN, ROBERT A. AC
ORDEAL IN SPACE   SS TAC 48 05
    GREEN HILLS OF EARTH, THE   HEINLEIN, ROBERT A. AC
    OUT OF THIS WORLD 7   WILLIAMS-ELLIS& OWEN AN
    PAST THROUGH TOMORROW, THE   HEINLEIN, ROBERT A. AC
    WORLDS TO COME   KNIGHT, DAMON   AN
OUR FAIR CITY   SS WRT 49 01
    *BEYOND HUMAN KEN   MERRIL, JUDITH   AN
    UNPLEASANT PROFESSION OF JONATHAN HOAG, THE
                                     HEINLEIN, ROBERT A. AC

```
HEINLEIN, ROBERT A.

HEINLEIN, ROBERT A.  (CONTINUED)
  PANDORA'S BOX (WHERE TO?)                      IN   GAL 52 02
    WORLDS OF ROBERT A. HEINLEIN, THE    HEINLEIN, ROBERT A.  AC
  PROJECT NIGHTMARE                              NV   AMZ 53 05
    MENACE FROM EARTH, THE               HEINLEIN, ROBERT A.  AC
    14 GREAT TALES OF ESP                STONE, IDELLA P.     AN
  PUPPET MASTERS, THE                            NO   GAL 51 09
    THREE BY HEINLEIN                    HEINLEIN, ROBERT A.  AC
  REQUIEM                                        SS   ASF 40 01
    *ADVENTURES IN TIME AND SPACE        HEALY & MCCOMAS      AN
    *MAN WHO SOLD THE MOON, THE          HEINLEIN, ROBERT A.  AC
    MASTERS' CHOICE                      JANIFER, LAURENCE M. AN
    PAST THROUGH TOMORROW, THE           HEINLEIN, ROBERT A.  AC
    SCIENCE FICTION                      BURTON, S. H.        AN
  ROADS MUST ROLL, THE                           NV   ASF 40 06
    *ADVENTURES IN TIME AND SPACE        HEALY & MCCOMAS      AN
    BEST OF ROBERT HEINLEIN, THE         HEINLEIN, ROBERT A.  AC
    GREAT SCIENCE FICTION STORIES        SMITH, CORDELIA T.   AN
    JOURNEYS IN SCIENCE FICTION          LOUGHLIN, RICHARD L. AN
    *MAN WHO SOLD THE MOON, THE          HEINLEIN, ROBERT A.  AC
    MORE ADVENTURES IN TIME AND SPACE    HEALY & MCCOMAS      AN
    PAST THROUGH TOMORROW, THE           HEINLEIN, ROBERT A.  AC
    SCIENCE FICTION HALL OF FAME VOLUME 1 SILVERBERG, ROBERT  AN
    TOMORROW X 4                         KNIGHT, DAMON        AN
  SEARCHLIGHT                                    SS   SAM 62 08
    PAST THROUGH TOMORROW, THE           HEINLEIN, ROBERT A.  AC
    WORLDS OF ROBERT A. HEINLEIN, THE    HEINLEIN, ROBERT A.  AC
  SKY LIFT                                       SS   IMG 53 11
    CENTURY OF SCIENCE FICTION, A        KNIGHT, DAMON        AN
    MENACE FROM EARTH, THE               HEINLEIN, ROBERT A.  AC
  SOLUTION UNSATISFACTORY                        NV   ASF 41 05
    FUTURE TENSE                         CURTIS, RICHARD      AN
    WORLDS OF ROBERT A. HEINLEIN, THE    HEINLEIN, ROBERT A.  AC
  SPACE JOCKEY                                   SS   SEP 47 04
    GREEN HILLS OF EARTH, THE            HEINLEIN, ROBERT A.  AC
    PAST THROUGH TOMORROW, THE           HEINLEIN, ROBERT A.  AC
  THEY                                           SS   UNK 41 04
    ABOVE THE HUMAN LANDSCAPE            MCNELLY & STOVER     AN
    DARK SIDE, THE                       KNIGHT, DAMON        AN
    OTHERS, THE                          CARR, TERRY          AN
    SCIENCE FICTION TERROR TALES         CONKLIN, GROFF       AN
    SCIENCE FICTION: THE FUTURE          ALLEN, DICK          AN
    *TERROR IN THE MODERN VEIN           WOLLHEIM, DONALD A.  AN
    UNPLEASANT PROFESSION OF JONATHAN HOAG, THE
                                         HEINLEIN, ROBERT A.  AC
    WORLD OF WONDER                      PRATT, FLETCHER      AN
  TIME GATE, THE (BY HIS BOOTSTRAPS)             NV   ASF 41 10
    RACE TO THE STARS                    MARGULIES & FRIEND   AN
  UNIVERSE                                       NV   ASF 41 05
    *BEST OF SCIENCE FICTION             CONKLIN, GROFF       AN
    ORPHANS OF THE SKY                   HEINLEIN, ROBERT A.  NO
    SCIENCE FICTION HALL OF FAME VOLUME 2A BOVA, BEN          AN
  UNPLEASANT PROFESSION OF JONATHAN HOAG, THE    SN   UNK 42 10
    BEST OF ROBERT HEINLEIN, THE         HEINLEIN, ROBERT A.  AC
    UNPLEASANT PROFESSION OF JONATHAN HOAG, THE
                                         HEINLEIN, ROBERT A.  AC
  WALDO                                          SN   ASF 42 08
    THREE BY HEINLEIN                    HEINLEIN, ROBERT A.  AC
    TREASURY OF GREAT SCIENCE FICTION, A VOL.1
                                         BOUCHER, ANTHONY     AN
  WATER IS FOR WASHING                           SS   ARG 47 11
    MENACE FROM EARTH, THE               HEINLEIN, ROBERT A.  AC
  WE ALSO WALK DOGS                              SS   ASF 41 07
    GREEN HILLS OF EARTH, THE            HEINLEIN, ROBERT A.  AC
    MODERN MASTERPIECES OF SCIENCE FICTION MOSKOWITZ, SAM     AN
    PAST THROUGH TOMORROW, THE           HEINLEIN, ROBERT A.  AC
    VORTEX BLASTERS, THE                 MOSKOWITZ, SAM       AN
  WHERE TO? (ALSO AS PANDORA'S BOX)              IN   GAL 52 02
    ALL ABOUT THE FUTURE                 GREENBERG , MARTIN   AN
  WHY I SELECTED THE GREEN HILLS OF EARTH        AI
    *MY BEST SCIENCE FICTION STORY       MARGULIES & FRIEND   AN
  YEAR OF THE JACKPOT, THE                       NV   GAL 52 03
    END OF THE WORLD, THE                WOLLHEIM, DONALD A.  AN
    LOOKING AHEAD                        ALLEN, D. & L.       AN
    MENACE FROM EARTH, THE               HEINLEIN, ROBERT A.  AC
    NIGHTMARE AGE                        POHL, FREDERIK       AN
    SCIENCE FICTION FOR PEOPLE WHO HATE SCIENCE FICTION
                                         CARR, TERRY          AN
    SECOND GALAXY READER OF SCIENCE FICTION
                                         GOLD, H. L.          AN
    SHADOW OF TOMORROW                   POHL, FREDERIK       AN
    SHOCKING THING, A                    KNIGHT, DAMON        AN
    WINDOWS INTO TOMORROW                SILVERBERG, ROBERT   AN

HEINTZ, BONNIE L., FRANK HERBERT, DONALD A. JOOS AND
  JANE AGORN MCGEE
  TOMORROW, AND TOMORROW, AND TOMORROW...        AN L HRW 74

HEINTZ, BONNIE L.
  PREFACE                                        IN C
  TOMORROW, AND TOMORROW, AND TOMORROW...
                                         HEINTZ/HERBERT/JOOS/ AN

HEMESATH, JAMES B.
  HARRY THE HARE                                 SS   DVS 72 02
    AGAIN, DANGEROUS VISIONS             ELLISON, HARLAN      OA

HENDERSON, GENE L.
  TIGER BY THE TAIL                              SS   BLF
    BOYS' LIFE BOOK OF OUTER SPACE STORIES, THE
                                         BOY'S LIFE, ED. OF   AN

HENDERSON, WILLIAM J
  HARRY BORDEN'S NAVAL MONSTER                   SS
    BATTLE FOR THE PACIFIC AND OTHER ADVENTURES AT SEA, THE
                                         ANONYMOUS            AN

HENDERSON, WILLIAM J (CONTINUED)
  BATTLE OF THE MONSTERS AND OTHER STORIES, THE
                                         HARTWELL & CURREY    AN
  JOE GRIFFIN'S GREAT JUMP                       SS
    BATTLE FOR THE PACIFIC AND OTHER ADVENTURES AT SEA, THE
                                         ANONYMOUS            AN
  MUTINY ON THE SWALLOW, THE                     SS
    BATTLE FOR THE PACIFIC AND OTHER ADVENTURES AT SEA, THE
                                         ANONYMOUS            AN

HENDERSON, ZENNA
  ANYTHING BOX, THE                              AC H DBL 65
  HOLDING WONDER                                 AC H DBL 71
  PEOPLE: NO DIFFERENT FLESH, THE                AC H DBL 67
  PILGRIMAGE: THE BOOK OF THE PEOPLE             AC H DBL 61
  AD ASTRA                                       SS   NEW 71 AC
    HOLDING WONDER                       HENDERSON, ZENNA     AC
  AND A LITTLE CHILD-                            SS   FSF 59 10
    ANYTHING BOX, THE                    HENDERSON, ZENNA     AC
  ANGELS UNAWARES                                NV   FSF 66 03
    PEOPLE: NO DIFFERENT FLESH, THE      HENDERSON, ZENNA     AC
  ANYTHING BOX                                   SS   FSF 56 10
    ANYTHING BOX, THE                    HENDERSON, ZENNA     AC
    GOLDEN ROAD, THE                     KNIGHT, DAMON        AN
    SF: THE BEST OF THE BEST             MERRIL, JUDITH       AN
    SF:57, THE YEAR'S GREATEST SCIENCE FICTION AND FANTASY
                                         MERRIL, JUDITH       AN
  ARARAT                                         SS   FSF 52 10
    BEST SCIENCE-FICTION STORIES: 1953, THE
                                         BLEILER & DIKTY      AN
    FRONTIERS IN SPACE                   BLEILER & DIKTY      AN
    OUT OF THIS WORLD 3                  WILLIAMS-ELLIS& OWEN AN
    PILGRIMAGE: THE BOOK OF THE PEOPLE   HENDERSON, ZENNA     AC
    UNIVERSE AHEAD                       ENGDAHL & ROBERSON   AN
    14 GREAT TALES OF ESP                STONE, IDELLA P.     AN
  AS SIMPLE AS THAT                              SS   NEW 71 AC
    HOLDING WONDER                       HENDERSON, ZENNA     AC
  BELIEVING CHILD, THE                           SS   FSF 70 06
    HOLDING WONDER                       HENDERSON, ZENNA     AC
  BOONA ON SCANCIA                               SS   NEW 71 AC
    HOLDING WONDER                       HENDERSON, ZENNA     AC
  CAPTIVITY                                      SS   FSF 58 06
    BEST FROM FANTASY AND SCIENCE FICTION:  8
                                         BOUCHER, ANTHONY     AN
    PILGRIMAGE: THE BOOK OF THE PEOPLE   HENDERSON, ZENNA     AC
    WORLDS APART                         WILLIAMS-ELLIS& OWEN AN
  CLOSEST SCHOOL, THE                            SS   FAN 60 04
    HOLDING WONDER                       HENDERSON, ZENNA     AC
  COME ON, WAGON!                                SS   FSF 51 12
    ANYTHING BOX, THE                    HENDERSON, ZENNA     AC
    BEST FROM FANTASY AND SCIENCE FICTION:  2
                                         BOUCHER & MCCOMAS    AN
  CROWNING GLORY                                 SS   NEW 71 AC
    HOLDING WONDER                       HENDERSON, ZENNA     AC
  DARK CAME OUT TO PLAY, THE (SEE STEVIE AND THE DARK)
                                         TC
  DELUGE                                         NV   FSF 63 10
    BEST FROM FANTASY AND SCIENCE FICTION: 13
                                         DAVIDSON, AVRAM      AN
    PEOPLE: NO DIFFERENT FLESH, THE      HENDERSON, ZENNA     AC
  EFFECTIVES, THE                                SS   WOT 65 05
    HOLDING WONDER                       HENDERSON, ZENNA     AC
  FOOD TO ALL FLESH                              SS   FSF 53 12
    ANYTHING BOX, THE                    HENDERSON, ZENNA     AC
    BEST SF  3                           CRISPIN, EDMUND      AN
    STARS AND UNDER, THE                 CRISPIN, EDMUND      AN
  GILEAD                                         SS   FSF 54 08
    PILGRIMAGE: THE BOOK OF THE PEOPLE   HENDERSON, ZENNA     AC
    TOMORROW'S CHILDREN                  ASIMOV, ISAAC        AN
    YOU AND SCIENCE FICTION              HOLLISTER, BERNARD C AN
  GRUNDER, THE                                   SS   IMG 53 06
    ANYTHING BOX, THE                    HENDERSON, ZENNA     AC
  HUSH!                                          SS   BEY 53 11
    ANYTHING BOX, THE                    HENDERSON, ZENNA     AC
  INCIDENT AFTER                                 SS   NEW 71 AC
    HOLDING WONDER                       HENDERSON, ZENNA     AC
  INDELIBLE KIND, THE                            NV   FSF 68 12
    HOLDING WONDER                       HENDERSON, ZENNA     AC
  J-LINE TO NOWHERE                              NV   FSF 69 09
    HOLDING WONDER                       HENDERSON, ZENNA     AC
    VENUS FACTOR, THE                    GHIDALIA, V.& ELWOOD AN
  JORDAN                                         SS   FSF 59 03
    DECADE OF FANTASY AND SCIENCE FICTION, A
                                         MILLS, ROBERT P.     AN
    PILGRIMAGE: THE BOOK OF THE PEOPLE   HENDERSON, ZENNA     AC
  LAST STEP, THE                                 SS   FSF 58 02
    ANYTHING BOX, THE                    HENDERSON, ZENNA     AC
  LOO REE                                        SS   FSF 53 02
    HOLDING WONDER                       HENDERSON, ZENNA     AC
  LOVE EVERY THIRD STIR                          SS   NEW 71 AC
    HOLDING WONDER                       HENDERSON, ZENNA     AC
  NO DIFFERENT FLESH                             NV   FSF 65 05
    BEST FROM FANTASY AND SCIENCE FICTION: 15
                                         FERMAN, EDWARD L.    AN
    PEOPLE: NO DIFFERENT FLESH, THE      HENDERSON, ZENNA     AC
  ONE OF THEM                                    SS   NEW 71 AC
    HOLDING WONDER                       HENDERSON, ZENNA     AC
  POTTAGE                                        NV   FSF 55 09
    BEST FROM FANTASY AND SCIENCE FICTION:  5
                                         BOUCHER, ANTHONY     AN
    GREAT SCIENCE FICTION STORIES        SMITH, CORDELIA T.   AN
    PILGRIMAGE: THE BOOK OF THE PEOPLE   HENDERSON, ZENNA     AC
    SCHOOL AND SOCIETY THROUGH SCIENCE FICTION
                                         OLANDER/GREENBERG/&  AN
    SF: THE YEAR'S GREATEST SCIENCE FICTION AND FANTASY
                                         MERRIL, JUDITH       AN
```

HENDERSON, ZENNA

HERBERT, FRANK

HENDERSON, ZENNA   (CONTINUED)
RETURN   NV   FSP 61 03
    PEOPLE: NO DIFFERENT FLESH, THE   HENDERSON, ZENNA   AC
SHADOW ON THE MOON   SS   FSP 62 03
    PEOPLE: NO DIFFERENT FLESH, THE   HENDERSON, ZENNA   AC
SHARING TIME   SS   NEW 71 AC
    HOLDING WONDER   HENDERSON, ZENNA   AC
SOMETHING BRIGHT   SS   GAL 60 02
    ANYTHING BOX, THE   HENDERSON, ZENNA   AC
    SEVENTH GALAXY READER, THE   POHL, FREDERIK   AN
    TALES BEYOND TIME   DE CAMP, L. S.&C.   AN
STEVIE AND THE DARK (THE DARK CAME OUT TO PLAY) SS   IMG 52 05
    ANYTHING BOX, THE   HENDERSON, ZENNA   AC
    6TH ANNUAL OF THE YEAR'S BEST S-F, THE MERRIL, JUDITH   AN
SUBCOMMITTEE   NV   FSF 62 07
    ANYTHING BOX, THE   HENDERSON, ZENNA   AC
    GENTLE INVADERS   SANTESSON, HANS S.   AN
    8TH ANNUAL OF THE YEAR'S BEST S-F, THE MERRIL, JUDITH   AN
SUBSTITUTE, THE   SS   IMG 53 08
    ANYTHING BOX, THE   HENDERSON, ZENNA   AC
SWEPT AND GARNISHED   SS   NEW 71 AC
    HOLDING WONDER   HENDERSON, ZENNA   AC
TASTE OF AUNT SOPHRONIA, THE   SS   NEW 71 AC
    HOLDING WONDER   HENDERSON, ZENNA   AC
THINGS   SS   FSP 60 07
    ANYTHING BOX, THE   HENDERSON, ZENNA   AC
    12 GREAT CLASSICS OF SCIENCE FICTION CONKLIN, GROFF   AN
THREE-CORNERED AND SECURE   SS   NEW 71 AC
    HOLDING WONDER   HENDERSON, ZENNA   AC
THROUGH A GLASS- DARKLY   NV   FSP 70 10
    HOLDING WONDER   HENDERSON, ZENNA   AC
    NEW WORLDS OF FANTASY NO. 3   CARR, TERRY   AN
TROUBLING OF THE WATER   NV   FSP 66 09
    PEOPLE: NO DIFFERENT FLESH, THE   HENDERSON, ZENNA   AC
TURN THE PAGE   SS   FSP 57 05
    ANYTHING BOX, THE   HENDERSON, ZENNA   AC
WALKING AUNT DAID   SS   FSP 55 07
    ANYTHING BOX, THE   HENDERSON, ZENNA   AC
WALLS, THE   SS   NEW 71 AC
    HOLDING WONDER   HENDERSON, ZENNA   AC
WILDERNESS   SS   FSP 57 01
    PILGRIMAGE: THE BOOK OF THE PEOPLE HENDERSON, ZENNA   AC
    SF:58, THE YEAR'S GREATEST SCIENCE FICTION AND FANTASY
                                        MERRIL, JUDITH   AN
YOU KNOW WHAT, TEACHER?   SS   EQM 54 09
    HOLDING WONDER   HENDERSON, ZENNA   AC

HENNEBERG, CHARLES
BLIND PILOT, THE (TRANSLATED BY DAMON KNIGHT)   SS   FSF 60 01
    BEST FROM FANTASY AND SCIENCE FICTION: 10
                                        MILLS, ROBERT P.   AN
    FIRST CONTACT   KNIGHT, DAMON   AN
    13 FRENCH SCIENCE-FICTION STORIES   KNIGHT, DAMON   AN
MOON-FISHERS   NV   59
    13 FRENCH SCIENCE-FICTION STORIES   KNIGHT, DAMON   AN
NON-HUMANS, THE   SS   58
    13 FRENCH SCIENCE-FICTION STORIES   KNIGHT, DAMON   AN
YSOLDE   SS   ISF 68 06
    BEST FROM THE REST OF THE WORLD, THE WOLLHEIM, DONALD A. AN

HENRI, ADRIAN
GALACTIC LOVEPOEM   PM   68
    HOLDING YOUR EIGHT HANDS   LUCIE-SMITH, EDWARD   AN
UNIVERSES   PM   68
    HOLDING YOUR EIGHT HANDS   LUCIE-SMITH, EDWARD   AN

HENRY, O.   PSEUD. FOR WILLIAM SIDNEY PORTER
ROADS OF DESTINY   NV   09
    FANTASY: THE LITERATURE OF THE MARVELOUS
                                        KELLEY, LEO P.   AN
    MOONLIGHT TRAVELER, THE   STERN, PHILIP VAN D. AN
    WORLD OF WONDER   PRATT, FLETCHER   AN

HENSEL, C. F.
HARRIET   SS C TAL 73
    FRONTIERS 1: TOMORROW'S ALTERNATIVES ELWOOD, ROGER   OA
NOR IRON BARS A CAGE   SS C ALC 73
    ALIEN CONDITION, THE   GOLDIN, STEPHEN   OA
SENSE OF THYME, A   SS   GEN 72
    GENERATION   GERROLD, DAVID   OA

HENSLEY, JOE L.
AND NOT QUITE HUMAN   SS   BEY 53 09
    ROD SERLING'S TRIPLE W: WITCHES, WARLOCKS AND WEREWOLVES
                                        SERLING, ROD   AN
DO-IT-YOURSELF   SS C ROG 61 02
    ELLISON WONDERLAND   ELLISON, HARLAN   AC
IN DARK PLACES   SS   FUC 73
    CITY: 2000 A.D., THE   CLEM/GREENBERG/&   AN
    FUTURE CITY   ELWOOD, ROGER   OA
LORD RANDY, MY SON   SS   DVS 67 01
    DANGEROUS VISIONS   ELLISON, HARLAN   OA
    FANTASY: THE LITERATURE OF THE MARVELOUS
                                        KELLEY, LEO P.   AN
PAIR, THE   SS   FUN 58 07
    COMBAT SF   DICKSON, GORDON R.   AN
RODNEY PARISH FOR HIRE   SS C SWK 62 05
    PARTNERS IN WONDER   ELLISON, HARLAN   AC
RUN FROM HOME, THE   SS   FSF 70 12
    LIBERATED FUTURE: VOYAGES INTO TOMORROW, THE
                                        HOSKINS, ROBERT   AN
SHUT THE LAST DOOR   SS   ANA 70
    ALCHEMY AND ACADEME   MCCAFFREY, ANNE   OA
    YOUNG DEMONS   ELWOOD & GHIDALIA   AN

HERBERT, BENSON
WORLD WITHOUT, THE   SS   WOS 31 02
    FROM OFF THIS WORLD   MARGULIES & FRIEND   AN

HERBERT, FRANK   SEE ALSO   CO-EDITOR BONNIE L. HEINTZ
BEST OF FRANK HERBERT, THE   AC H SID 75
    EDITED BY ANGUS WELLS
BOOK OF FRANK HERBERT, THE   AC   DAW 73 01
WORLDS OF FRANK HERBERT, THE   AC   ACE 71
A-W-F, UNLIMITED   NV   GAL 61 06
    WORLDS OF FRANK HERBERT, THE   HERBERT, FRANK   AC
    17 X INFINITY   CONKLIN, GROFF   AN
BEING MACHINE, THE (THE MIND BOMB)   NV   IFS 69 10
    BEST OF FRANK HERBERT, THE   HERBERT, FRANK   AC
BY THE BOOK   NV   ASF 66 08
    BEST OF FRANK HERBERT, THE   HERBERT, FRANK   AC
    WORLDS OF FRANK HERBERT, THE   HERBERT, FRANK   AC
CARTHAGE: REFLECTIONS OF A MARTIAN   PM   NEW 71 AN
    MARS, WE LOVE YOU   HIPOLITO & MCNELLY   AN
CEASE FIRE   SS   ASF 58 01
    CENTURY OF SCIENCE FICTION, A   KNIGHT, DAMON   AN
COMMITTEE OF THE WHOLE   NV   GAL 65 04
    BEST OF FRANK HERBERT, THE   HERBERT, FRANK   AC
    SCIENCE FICTION INVENTIONS   KNIGHT, DAMON   AN
    WORLDS OF FRANK HERBERT, THE   HERBERT, FRANK   AC
DEATH OF A CITY   SS   FUC 73
    FUTURE CITY   ELWOOD, ROGER   OA
DRAGON IN THE SEA (UNDER PRESSURE)   EX   ASF 55 11
    BEST OF FRANK HERBERT, THE   HERBERT, FRANK   AC
DUNE   EX   CHL 65
    BEST OF FRANK HERBERT, THE   HERBERT, FRANK   AC
EGG AND ASHES   SS   IFS 60 11
    BEST OF FRANK HERBERT, THE   HERBERT, FRANK   AC
    BEST SCIENCE FICTION FROM IF, THE   POHL, FREDERIK   AN
ENCOUNTER IN A LONELY PLACE   SS   NEW 73 AC
    BOOK OF FRANK HERBERT, THE   HERBERT, FRANK   AC
ESCAPE FELICITY   SS   ASF 66 06
    WORLDS OF FRANK HERBERT, THE   HERBERT, FRANK   AC
FEATHERBEDDERS, THE   NV   ASF 67 08
    ANALOG 7   CAMPBELL, JOHN W. JR AN
    WORLDS OF FRANK HERBERT, THE   HERBERT, FRANK   AC
GAMBLING DEVICE   SS   NEW 73 AC
    BOOK OF FRANK HERBERT, THE   HERBERT, FRANK   AC
GM EFFECT, THE   SS   ASF 65 06
    WORLDS OF FRANK HERBERT, THE   HERBERT, FRANK   AC
GONE DOGS, THE   SS   AMZ 54 11
    BOOK OF FRANK HERBERT, THE   HERBERT, FRANK   AC
GREENSLAVES   NV   AMZ 65 03
    BUG-EYED MONSTERS   CHEETHAM, ANTHONY   AN
    ON OUR WAY TO THE FUTURE   CARR, TERRY   AN
HEAVEN MAKERS, THE   EX   AMZ 67 04
    BEST OF FRANK HERBERT, THE   HERBERT, FRANK   AC
INTRODUCTION   IN
    BEST OF FRANK HERBERT, THE   HERBERT, FRANK   AC
    SAVING WORLDS   ELWOOD & KIDD   OA
LOOKING FOR SOMETHING?   SS   STS 52 04
    BEST OF FRANK HERBERT, THE   HERBERT, FRANK   AC
    BOOK OF FRANK HERBERT, THE   HERBERT, FRANK   AC
MARY CELESTE MOVE, THE   SS   ASF 64 10
    ANALOG 4   CAMPBELL, JOHN W. JR AN
    BEST OF FRANK HERBERT, THE   HERBERT, FRANK   AC
    ECO-FICTION   STADLER, JOHN   AN
MATING CALL   SS   GAL 61 10
    WORLDS OF FRANK HERBERT, THE   HERBERT, FRANK   AC
    13 ABOVE THE NIGHT   CONKLIN, GROFF   AN
MIND BOMB, THE (ALSO AS THE BEING MACHINE)   NV   IFS 69 10
    BEST FROM IF, THE   VOLUME I   IF, EDITORS OF   AN
MISSING LINK   SS   ASF 59 02
    SF: AUTHORS' CHOICE   HARRISON, HARRY   AN
MURDER WILL IN   NV   FSF 70 05
    FIVE FATES   LAUMER, KEITH   AN
NIGHTMARE BLUES (OPERATION SYNDROME)   NV   ASF 54 06
    BEST OF FRANK HERBERT, THE   HERBERT, FRANK   AC
    BEST SCIENCE FICTION STORIES AND NOVELS: 1955
                                        DIKTY, T. E.   AN
NOTHING, THE   SS   FUN 56 01
    BOOK OF FRANK HERBERT, THE   HERBERT, FRANK   AC
    TOMORROW, AND TOMORROW, AND TOMORROW...
                                        HEINTZ/HERBERT/JOOS/ AN
OCCUPATION FORCE   SS   FAN 55 08
    BOOK OF FRANK HERBERT, THE   HERBERT, FRANK   AC
OLD RAMBLING HOUSE   SS   GAL 58 04
    WORLDS OF FRANK HERBERT, THE   HERBERT, FRANK   AC
OPERATION SYNDROME (ALSO AS NIGHTMARE BLUES)   NV   ASF 54 06
    BOOK OF FRANK HERBERT, THE   HERBERT, FRANK   AC
PASSAGE FOR PIANO   NV   NEW 73 AC
    BOOK OF FRANK HERBERT, THE   HERBERT, FRANK   AC
PREFACE   IN C
    TOMORROW, AND TOMORROW, AND TOMORROW...
                                        HEINTZ/HERBERT/JOOS/ AN
PRIMATIVES, THE   NV   GAL 66 04
    BEST OF FRANK HERBERT, THE   HERBERT, FRANK   AC
    TENTH GALAXY READER, THE   POHL, FREDERIK   AN
RAT RACE   NV   ASF 55 07
    BOOK OF FRANK HERBERT, THE   HERBERT, FRANK   AC
SCIENCE FICTION AND YOU   IN
    TOMORROW, AND TOMORROW, AND TOMORROW...
                                        HEINTZ/HERBERT/JOOS/ AN
SEASE FIRE   SS   ASF 58 01
    BEST OF FRANK HERBERT, THE   HERBERT, FRANK   AC
SEED STOCK   SS   ASF 70 04
    BEST OF FRANK HERBERT, THE   HERBERT, FRANK   AC
    BOOK OF FRANK HERBERT, THE   HERBERT, FRANK   AC
    NIGHTMARE GARDEN   GHIDALIA, VIC   AN
TACTFUL SABOTEUR, THE   NV   GAL 64 10
    SEVEN TRIPS THROUGH TIME AND SPACE CONKLIN, GROFF   AN

HERBERT, FRANK   (CONTINUED)
    WORLDS OF FRANK HERBERT, THE   HERBERT, FRANK   AC
    TOMORROW'S ALTERNATIVES?   IN TAL 73
        FRONTIERS 1; TOMORROW'S ALTERNATIVES   ELWOOD, ROGER   OA
    TRY TO REMEMBER!   NV AMZ 61 10
        BEST OF AMAZING, THE   ROSS, JOSEPH   AN
    UNDER PRESSURE (SEE DRAGON IN THE SEA)   TC

HERBST, STEVE
    CREATION OF A FUTURE WORLD IN THE TRACER   SS ORB 74 13
        ORBIT 13   KNIGHT, DAMON   OA
    MAGIC PASSES   SS CLR 72 02
        CLARION II   WILSON, ROBIN SCOTT   OA
    OLD SOUL   SS ORB 72 11
        ORBIT 11   KNIGHT, DAMON   OA
    UNEVEN EVENING, AN   SS CLR 71 01
        BEST SF: 1971   HARRISON & ALDISS   AN
        CLARION   WILSON, ROBIN SCOTT   OA
        FUTURE PASTIMES   EDELSTEIN, SCOTT   OA

HERNHUNTER, ALBERT
    TEXAS WEEK   SS FUN 54 01
        FIFTY SHORT SCIENCE FICTION TALES   ASIMOV & CONKLIN   AN
    TOMORROW, AND TOMORROW, AND TOMORROW...
                                               HEINTZ/HERBERT/JOOS/

HERODOTUS
    AMAZONS, THE (500 B.C.)   AR
        WHEN WOMEN RULE   MOSKOWITZ, SAM   AN

HERSHMAN, MORRIS
    LET THERE BE NIGHT!   NV FAN 63 10
        CRIME PREVENTION IN THE 30TH CENTURY   SANTESSON, HANS S.   AN

HERZOG, EMILE   SEE PSEUD. ANDRE MAUROIS

HERZOG, TOM
    INVESTIGATING THE CURIOSITY DRIVE   SS FSF 68 11
        SCHOOL AND SOCIETY THROUGH SCIENCE FICTION
                                               OLANDER/GREENBERG/&   AN
    PLOT, THE   SS ROG 65
        INTRODUCTORY PSYCHOLOGY THROUGH SCIENCE FICTION
                                               KATZ/WARRICK/&   AN
        11TH ANNUAL OF THE YEAR'S BEST S-F, THE
                                               MERRIL, JUDITH   AN

HETSCHEL, DICK
    FIRST STAGE: MOON   SS IFS 54 12
        FIRST WORLD OF IF, THE   QUINN & WULFF   AN

HICKEY, H. B.   PSEUD. FOR HERB AND BERKELEY LIVINGSTON
    GONE ARE THE LUPO   SS QRK 70 01
        QUARK/1   DELANY & HACKER   OA
        WORLD'S BEST SCIENCE FICTION: 1971   WOLLHEIM & CARR   AN
    HILDA   SS FSF 52 09
        FIFTY SHORT SCIENCE FICTION TALES   ASIMOV & CONKLIN   AN
        OPERATION FUTURE   CONKLIN, GROFF   AN
    LIKE A BIRD, LIKE A FISH   SS WBY 51 02
        *WORLDS OF TOMORROW   DERLETH, AUGUST   AN

HIGGINSON, THOMAS W.
    MONARCH OF DREAMS, THE (1886)   SS 86
        FUTURE PERFECT   FRANKLIN, H. BRUCE   AN

HIGH, PHILIP E.
    BOTTOMLESS PIT   SS NWS 63 03
        OUT OF THIS WORLD 5   WILLIAMS-ELLIS& OWEN   AN
    ROUTINE EXERCISE   SS NWS 61 02
        LAMBDA I AND OTHER STORIES   CARNELL, JOHN   AN

HIGHET, GILBERT
    INTRODUCTION   IN
        VINTAGE BRADBURY, THE   BRADBURY, RAY   AC

HIGHSMITH, PATRICIA
    SNAIL-WATCHER, THE   SS GAM 64 03
        SHOCKING THING, A   KNIGHT, DAMON   AN

HIGHSTONE, H. A.
    FRANKENSTEIN UNLIMITED   SS ASF 36 12
        FAR BOUNDARIES   DERLETH, AUGUST   AN

HILL, DOUGLAS
    DEVIL HIS DUE, THE   AN AVN 69 03
    WINDOW ON THE FUTURE   AN H HDV 66
    INTRODUCTION   IN
        DEVIL HIS DUE, THE   HILL, DOUGLAS   AN

HILL, ERNEST
    ATROPHY   SS NWR 65 06
        NEW WRITINGS IN SF. 6   CARNELL, JOHN   OA
    HERO, THE   SS NWR 70 17
        NEW WRITINGS IN SF. 17   CARNELL, JOHN   OA
    Z FACTOR, THE   NV NWR 76 29
        NEW WRITINGS IN SF. 29   BULMER, KENNETH   OA

HILL, RICHARD
    AGENT, THE   SS
        FUTURE PASTIMES   EDELSTEIN, SCOTT   OA
    BRAVE SALT   SS QRK 71 03
        QUARK/3   DELANY & HACKER   OA
    MOTH RACE   SS DVS 72 02
        AGAIN, DANGEROUS VISIONS   ELLISON, HARLAN   OA
    TO SPORT WITH AMARYLLIS   SS ORB 70 07
        ORBIT 7   KNIGHT, DAMON   OA

HILLIARD, A. ROWLEY
    DEATH FROM THE STARS   NV WOS 31 10
        SCIENCE FICTION GALAXY, THE   CONKLIN, GROFF   AN
    GREEN TORTURE, THE   SS WOS 31 03
        FROM OFF THIS WORLD   MARGULIES & FRIEND   AN

HILLMAN, MARTIN
    FACTS OF LIFE, THE   SS
        WINDOW ON THE FUTURE   HILL, DOUGLAS   AN

HILTON-YOUNG, WAYLAND
    CHOICE, THE   SS PUN 52 03
        FIFTY SHORT SCIENCE FICTION TALES   ASIMOV & CONKLIN   AN
        OMNIBUS OF SCIENCE FICTION   CONKLIN, GROFF   AN
        SPECTRUM 4   AMIS & CONQUEST   AN
        STRANGE ADVENTURES IN SCIENCE FICTION CONKLIN, GROFF   AN
        VOYAGES: SCENARIOS FOR A SHIP CALLED EARTH
                                               SAUER, ROB   AN

HILTON, A. C.
    YOUNG MAN OF SID SUSSEX, THE   PM 45
        MATHEMATICAL MAGPIE, THE   FADIMAN, CLIFTON   AN

HILTS, PHILIP J.
    UFO DETECTIVE SOLVES 'EM ALL- WELL ALMOST   AR WPS 73
        SCIENCE FACT/FICTION   FARRELL/GAGE/&   AN

HINRICHS, JAMES V.
    TERRIBLE INTRUDERS, THE   SS BLF
        BOYS' LIFE BOOK OF OUTER SPACE STORIES, THE
                                               BOY'S LIFE, ED. OF   AN

HIPOLITO, JANE AND WILLIS E. MCNELLY
    MARS, WE LOVE YOU   AN H DBL 71

HIPOLITO, JANE
    FOREWORD   IN C
        MARS, WE LOVE YOU   HIPOLITO & MCNELLY   AN

HIRSHFIELD, HENRY I.
    ON HANDLING THE DATA   SS C ASF 59 09
        BEST SF 5   CRISPIN, EDMUND   AN

HOAGLAND, RICHARD C.
    FOLLOWING YONDER STAR   AR IFS 74 12
        BEST FROM IF, THE VOLUME III   BAEN, JAMES   AN

HOAR, ROGER SHERMAN   SEE PSEUD. RALPH MILNE FARLEY

HOCH, EDWARD D.
    BOY WHO BROUGHT LOVE, THE   SS
        CRISIS   ELWOOD, ROGER   OA
    CASSIDY'S SAUCER   SS NEW 68 AN
        FLYING SAUCERS IN FACT AND FICTION   SANTESSON, HANS S.   AN
    COMPUTER COPS   SS NEW 69 AN
        CRIME PREVENTION IN THE 30TH CENTURY   SANTESSON, HANS S.   AN
    IN THE STRAW   SS 72
        BEWARE MORE BEASTS   GHIDALIA, V.& ELWOOD   AN
    NIGHT OF THE MILLENNIUM
        OTHER SIDE OF TOMORROW, THE   ELWOOD, ROGER   OA
    UNNATURAL ACT   SS NEW 69 AN
        GENTLE INVADERS   SANTESSON, HANS S.   AN
    WOLFRAM HUNTERS, THE   SS SMM 64 03
        CHRONICLES OF A COMER AND OTHER RELIGIOUS SCIENCE FICTION
            STORIES   ELWOOD, ROGER   AN
        GODS FOR TOMORROW   SANTESSON, HANS S.   AN
        RULERS OF MEN   SANTESSON, HANS S.   AN

HOCKETT, CHARLES F.
    HOW TO LEARN MARTIAN   AR ASF 55 05
        COMING ATTRACTIONS   GREENBERG, MARTIN   NF

HODDER-WILLIAMS, C.
    FROM: FISTFUL OF DIGITS   EX HDS 68
        INSIDE INFORMATION   MOWSHOWITZ, ABBE   AN

HODGELL, PAT
    MATTER OF HONOR, A   SS
        CLARION SF   WILHELM, KATE   OA

HODGINS, RODERIC C.
    HISTORY OF DOCTOR FROST, THE   SS FSF 65 04
        BEST FROM FANTASY AND SCIENCE FICTION: 15
                                               FERMAN, EDWARD L.   AN

HODGSON, WILLIAM H.
    CREW OF THE LANCING, THE   SS
        BEWARE MORE BEASTS   GHIDALIA, V.& ELWOOD   AN
    DERELICT, THE (1914)   SS PFM 43 12
        SCIENCE FICTION GALAXY, THE   CONKLIN, GROFF   AN
    VOICE IN THE NIGHT, THE   SS BBM 07 11
        AVON FANTASY READER, THE   WOLLHEIM &ERNSBERGER   AN
        *BEYOND TIME AND SPACE   DERLETH, AUGUST   AN
        SCIENCE FICTION BY GASLIGHT   MOSKOWITZ, SAM   AN
    WILD MAN OF THE SEA, THE   SS
        TRAVELLERS BY NIGHT   DERLETH, AUGUST   OA

HODUS, MIKE
    DEAD END   SS ASF 67 05
        ANALOG 7   CAMPBELL, JOHN W. JR   AN

HOFFMAN, LEE
    LOST IN THE MARIGOLDS   NV C ORB 71 09
        ORBIT 9   KNIGHT, DAMON   OA
    SOUNDLESS EVENING   SS DVS 72 02
        AGAIN, DANGEROUS VISIONS   ELLISON, HARLAN   OA

HOFFMAN, LEE   (CONTINUED)
    EARTH IN TRANSIT   SCHWARTZ, SHEILA   AN

HOGG, THOMAS J.
    PARADISE LOST AT CAMBRIDGE   MS
    MATHEMATICAL MAGPIE, THE   FADIMAN, CLIFTON   AN

HOLBERG, LUDWIG
    TREE MEN OF POTU, THE (1741)   EX
    *BEYOND TIME AND SPACE   DERLETH, AUGUST   AN

HOLBROOKE, JOSEPH C.
    TA TA, THE (MUSIC)   SG C   62
    MATHEMATICAL MAGPIE, THE   FADIMAN, CLIFTON   AN

HOLDEN, FOX B.
    HERE LIE WE   NV   STS 53 06
    TALES OF OUTER SPACE   WOLLHEIM, DONALD A.   DA

HOLDEN, LARRY
    STORY OF A STRANGE RELATIVE   SS
    LONE STAR UNIVERSE   PROCTOR & UTLEY   OA

HOLDING, ELIZABETH S
    STRANGE CHILDREN, THE   SS   FSF 55 08
    ALONE BY NIGHT   CONGDON, MICHAEL&DON AN

HOLDSTOCK, ROBERT P.
    ASH, ASH   SS
    STOPWATCH   HAY, GEORGE   OA
    MICROCOSM   SS   NWR 72 20
    NEW WRITINGS IN SF. 20   CARNELL, JOHN   OA
    ON THE INSIDE   NV   NWR 76 28
    NEW WRITINGS IN SF. 28   BULMER, KENNETH   OA
    TRAVELLERS   NV
    ANDROMEDA I   WESTON, PETER   OA

HOLLAND, HESTER
    DORNER CORDAIANTHUS   SS   25
    ROOTS OF EVIL, THE   PARRY, MICHEL   AN

HOLLANDER, JOHN
    GREAT BEAR, THE   PM   58
    SPECULATIONS   SANDERS, THOMAS E.   AN

HOLLIS, H. H.
    EVERY DAY IN EVERY WAY   NV
    LONE STAR UNIVERSE   PROCTOR & UTLEY   OA
    STONED COUNSEL   SS   DVS 72 02
    AGAIN, DANGEROUS VISIONS   ELLISON, HARLAN   OA
    SWORD GAME   SS   GAL 68 04
    NEBULA AWARD STORIES NO. 4   ANDERSON, POUL   AN
    TOMORROW, AND TOMORROW, AND TOMORROW...
                                            HEINTZ/HERBERT/JOOS/ AN
    WORLD'S BEST SCIENCE FICTION: 1969   WOLLHEIM & CARR   AN
    TOO MANY PEOPLE   NV   GAL 71 01
    BEST SCIENCE FICTION FOR 1972   POHL, FREDERIK   AN

HOLLISTER, BERNARD C
    ANOTHER TOMORROW   AN L PFL 74
    YOU AND SCIENCE FICTION   AN L NTC 76
    A HUMANISTIC APPROACH TO SCIENCE FICTION
    EPILOG   MS
    YOU AND SCIENCE FICTION   HOLLISTER, BERNARD C AN
    INTRODUCTION   IN
    ANOTHER TOMORROW   HOLLISTER, BERNARD C AN
    YOU AND SCIENCE FICTION   HOLLISTER, BERNARD C AN
    WRITE SCIENCE FICTION? RIGHT   AR   74
    ANOTHER TOMORROW   HOLLISTER, BERNARD C AN

HOLLY, J. HUNTER   PSEUD. FOR JOAN C. HOLLY
    COME SEE THE LAST MAN CRY   NA
    TOMORROW: NEW WORLDS OF SCIENCE FICTION
                                            ELWOOD, ROGER   OA
    GRADUATED ROBOT, THE   SS
    GRADUATED ROBOT AND OTHER STORIES, THE ELWOOD, ROGER   OA
    OTHERS, THE   NV
    OTHER SIDE OF TOMORROW, THE   ELWOOD, ROGER   OA
    PSI CLONE   NA
    FUTURELOVE   ELWOOD, ROGER   OA

HOLLY, JOAN C.   ALSO AS   J. HUNTER HOLLY
    CHILD   SS   DEM 73
    DEMON KIND   ELWOOD, ROGER   OA
    GIFT OF NOTHING, THE   NV   WLK 73
    AND WALK NOW GENTLY THROUGH THE FIRE...
                                            ELWOOD, ROGER   OA
    CHRONICLES OF A COMER AND OTHER RELIGIOUS SCIENCE FICTION
    STORIES   ELWOOD, ROGER   AN
    PROPER STUDY, THE   SS
    LONG NIGHT OF WAITING AND OTHER STORIES
                                            ELWOOD, ROGER   OA

HOLMES, H. H.   PSEUD. FOR WILLIAM ANTHONY PARKER WHITE
    ROBINC   SS   ASF 43 09
    ROBOT AND THE MAN, THE   GREENBERG , MARTIN   AN

HOLMES, KENYON   PSEUD. FOR AUGUST DERLETH
    MAN WHO RODE THE SAUCER, THE   SS   NEW 52 AN
    FAR BOUNDARIES   DERLETH, AUGUST   AN

HOMER
    ODYSSEY, THE (EXCERPT)   EX
    3000 YEARS OF FANTASY AND SCIENCE FICTION
                                            DE CAMP, L. S.&C.   AN

HOOD, HUGH   SS   ESQ 60
    AFTER THE SIRENS
    MAN AGAINST TOMORROW   NOLAN, WILLIAM F.   AN

HOOPER, WALTER
    DARK TOWER AND OTHER STORIES, THE (LISTED UNDER C. S. LEWIS)
                                            EC H HBJ 77
    NOTE ON THE DARK TOWER, A   MS
    DARK TOWER AND OTHER STORIES, THE   LEWIS, C. S.   AC
    PREFACE   IN
    DARK TOWER AND OTHER STORIES, THE   LEWIS, C. S.   AC

HOOTON, EARNEST A.
    APOLOGY FOR MAN'S PHYSIQUE   AR
    APEMAN, SPACEMAN   STOVER & HARRISON   AN

HORN, HOLLOWAY
    OLD MAN, THE   SS   32
    OTHER SIDE OF THE CLOCK, THE   STERN, PHILIP VAN D. AN
    TRAVELERS IN TIME   STERN, PHILIP VAN D. AN

HOSKINS, ROBERT
    EDGE OF NEVER, THE   AN   FPR 73 06
    FAR-OUT PEOPLE, THE   AN   SIG 71 07
    FIRST STEP OUTWARD   AN   DEL 69 08
    FUTURE NOW, THE   AN   FCR 77 06
    INFINITY 1   OA   LAN 70
    INFINITY 2   OA   LAN 71
    INFINITY 3   OA   LAN 72
    INFINITY 4   OA   LAN 72
    INFINITY 5   OA   LAN 73
    LIBERATED FUTURE: VOYAGES INTO TOMORROW, THE AN FAW 74 12
    STARS AROUND US, THE   AN   SIG 70 03
    STRANGE TOMORROWS   AN   LAN 72
    TOMORROW 1   AN   SIG 71 06
    WONDERMAKERS   AN   FAW 72 05
    WONDERMAKERS 2   AN   FPR 74 02
    ALIEN AMONG US, THE   IN   INY 71 02
    INFINITY 2   HOSKINS, ROBERT   OA
    FUTURE OF THE FUTURE, THE   IN   INY 72 04
    INFINITY 4   HOSKINS, ROBERT   OA
    HOW TO BUILD TOMORROW   IN   INY 73 05
    INFINITY 5   HOSKINS, ROBERT   OA
    INTRODUCTION   IN
    FAR-OUT PEOPLE, THE   HOSKINS, ROBERT   AN
    FUTURE NOW, THE   HOSKINS, ROBERT   AN
    LIBERATED FUTURE: VOYAGES INTO TOMORROW, THE
                                            HOSKINS, ROBERT   AN
    STARS AROUND US, THE   HOSKINS, ROBERT   AN
    STRANGE TOMORROWS   HOSKINS, ROBERT   AN
    TOMORROW 1   HOSKINS, ROBERT   AN
    KELLEY'S EYE, THE   SS
    TOMORROW: NEW WORLDS OF SCIENCE FICTION
                                            ELWOOD, ROGER   OA
    MAN WHO LIKED, THE   SS   WOF 68 01
    EDGE OF NEVER, THE   HOSKINS, ROBERT   AN
    MOUNTAIN, THE   SS   75
    FUTURE NOW, THE   HOSKINS, ROBERT   AN
    POP GOES THE WEASEL   SS   FSF 75 04
    BEST SCIENCE FICTION STORIES OF THE YEAR (1975)
                                            DEL REY, LESTER   AN
    PRIZE OF WONDER, THE   IN
    WONDERMAKERS   HOSKINS, ROBERT   AN
    PROBLEM MAKERS, THE   NV   GAL 63 08
    FAR-OUT PEOPLE, THE   HOSKINS, ROBERT   AN
    PROLOGUE   IN
    FIRST STEP OUTWARD   HOSKINS, ROBERT   AN
    REACHING OUT OF TOMORROW   IN
    WONDERMAKERS 2   HOSKINS, ROBERT   AN
    TIME OF CHANGES, A   IN   INY 72 03
    INFINITY 3   HOSKINS, ROBERT   OA
    WORD FROM THE EDITOR, A   IN   INY 70 01
    INFINITY 1   HOSKINS, ROBERT   OA
    WORLD BEYOND, THE   IN
    EDGE OF NEVER, THE   HOSKINS, ROBERT   AN

HOUSEHOLD, GEOFFREY
    AS BEST WE CAN   SS   58
    NIGHT IN FUNLAND   BRONDFIELD, JEROME   AN
    LOST CONTINENT, THE   SS   SEP 60 09
    ANCIENT MYSTERIES READER, THE   HAINING, PETER   AN
    POST READER OF FANTASY AND SCIENCE FICTION
                                            SATURDAY EVE. POST   AN

HOUSEMAN, A. E.
    TO THINK THAT TWO AND TWO ARE FOUR   PM   40
    FANTASIA MATHEMATICA   FADIMAN, CLIFTON   AN

HOUSTON, JAMES D.
    GAS MASK   SS   NUG 64
    ANOTHER TOMORROW   HOLLISTER, BERNARD C AN
    CITY: 2000 A.D., THE   CLEM/GREENBERG/&   AN
    RUINS OF EARTH, THE   DISCH, THOMAS M.   AN
    10TH ANNUAL OF THE YEAR'S BEST S-F, THE
                                            MERRIL, JUDITH   AN

HOUSTON, LIBBY
    GHOST BREAD   PM   NWB 75 08
    NEW WORLDS EIGHT   BAILEY, HILARY   OA
    QUEEN LIES DYING, THE   PM   NWB 75 08
    NEW WORLDS EIGHT   BAILEY, HILARY   OA
    WEATHER CLOCK   PM   NWB 75 08
    NEW WORLDS EIGHT   BAILEY, HILARY   OA

HOWARD, HAYDEN   HOYLE, FRED

HOWARD, HAYDEN
  ESKIMO INVASION   NO   BAL 67
  DEATH AND BIRTH OF THE ANGAKOK, THE   NV   GAL 65 04
    ESKIMO INVASION   HOWARD, HAYDEN   NO
  ESKIMO INVASION, THE   NV   GAL 66 06
    ESKIMO INVASION   HOWARD, HAYDEN   NO
  MODERN PENITENTIARY, THE   NV   GAL 66 12
    ESKIMO INVASION   HOWARD, HAYDEN   NO
  OIL-MAD BUG-EYED MONSTERS   SS   GAL 70 06
    BEST SF: 1970   HARRISON & ALDISS   AN
  OUR MAN IN PEKING   NV   GAL 67 02
    ESKIMO INVASION   HOWARD, HAYDEN   NO
  PURPOSE OF LIFE, THE   NV   GAL 67 04
    ESKIMO INVASION   HOWARD, HAYDEN   NO
  TOO MANY ESKS   NV   GAL 66 10
    ESKIMO INVASION   HOWARD, HAYDEN   NO
  WHO IS HUMAN?   NV   GAL 66 08
    ESKIMO INVASION   HOWARD, HAYDEN   NO

HOWARD, IVAN
  ESCAPE TO EARTH   AN   BEL 63 09
  MASTERS OF SCIENCE FICTION   AN   BEL 64 10
  NOVELETS OF SCIENCE FICTION   AN   BEL 63
  NOW & BEYOND   AN   BEL 65 09
  RARE SCIENCE FICTION   AN   BEL 63 01
  THINGS   AN   BEL 64 02
  TIME UNTAMED   AN   BEL 67
  WAY OUT   AN   BEL 63 12
  WEIRD ONES, THE   AN   BEL 62 07
  6 AND THE SILENT SCREAM   AN   BEL 63 05

HOWARD, JAMES
  DIRECTOR, THE   NV   STG 74
    STRANGE GODS   ELWOOD, ROGER   OA

HOWARD, ROBERT E. AND L. SPRAGUE DE CAMP
  CONAN THE ADVENTURER   AC   LAN 66
  CONAN THE FREEBOOTER   AC   LAN 68
  CONAN THE USURPER   AC   LAN 67
  CONAN THE WARRIOR   AC   LAN 67
  TALES OF CONAN   AC H GNM 55

HOWARD, ROBERT E., L. SPRAGUE DE CAMP AND LIN CARTER
  CONAN   AC   LAN 67
  CONAN THE WANDERER   AC   LAN 68

HOWARD, ROBERT E., BJORN NYBERG AND L. SPRAGUE DE CAMP
  CONAN THE AVENGER   AC   LAN 68

HOWARD, ROBERT E.
  COMING OF CONAN, THE   AC H GNM 53
  CONAN THE BARBARIAN   AC H GNM 55
  KING CONAN   AC H GNM 53
  SWORD OF CONAN, THE   AC H GNM 55
  WOLFSHEAD   AC   LAN 68
  BEYOND THE BLACK RIVER   NA   WRT 35 05
    CONAN THE WARRIOR   HOWARD, R. & DE CAMP AC
    KING CONAN   HOWARD, ROBERT E.   AC
  BLACK COLOSSUS   SS   WRT 33 06
    CONAN THE BARBARIAN   HOWARD, ROBERT E.   AC
    CONAN THE FREEBOOTER   HOWARD, R. & DE CAMP AC
  BLACK STONE, THE   SS   WRT 31 11
    WOLFSHEAD   HOWARD, ROBERT E.   AC
  BLACK STRANGER, THE (SEE THE TREASURE OF TRANICOS)
                                                                 TC C
  BLONDE GODDESS OF BAL-SAGOTH, THE   NV   WRT 31 10
    SECOND AVON FANTASY READER, THE   WOLLHEIM &ERNSBERGER AN
  BLOOD-STAINED GOD, THE   NV   FUN 56 04
    TALES OF CONAN   HOWARD, R. & DE CAMP AC
  CAIRN ON THE HEADLAND, THE   SS   STT 33 01
    WOLFSHEAD   HOWARD, ROBERT E.   AC
  COMING OF BAST, THE   PM
    LONE STAR UNIVERSE   PROCTOR & UTLEY   OA
  CONAN, MAN OF DESTINY (SEE THE ROAD OF THE EAGLES)
                                                                 TC C
  DEAD REMEMBER, THE   SS   ARG 36 08
    HORROR TIMES TEN   NORTON, ALDEN H.   AN
  DEVIL IN IRON, THE   SS   WRT 34 08
    CONAN THE BARBARIAN   HOWARD, ROBERT E.   AC
    CONAN THE WANDERER   HOWARD, R./DE CAMP/& AC
  DRUMS OF TOMBALKU   SS C
    CONAN THE ADVENTURER   HOWARD, R. & DE CAMP AC
  FIRE OF ASSHURBANIPAL, THE   SS   WRT 36 12
    WOLFSHEAD   HOWARD, ROBERT E.   AC
  FLAME KNIFE, THE   SS
    CONAN THE WANDERER   HOWARD, R./DE CAMP/& AC
    TALES OF CONAN   HOWARD, R. & DE CAMP AC
  FROST-GIANT'S DAUGHTER, THE   SS C FMG 53 08
    COMING OF CONAN, THE   HOWARD, ROBERT E.   AC
  GARDEN OF FEAR, THE   SS   MVT 34 07
    GARDEN OF FEAR AND OTHER STORIES, THE   CRAWFORD, WILLIAM L. AN
  GOD IN THE BOWL, THE   SS   SSF 52 09
    COMING OF CONAN, THE   HOWARD, ROBERT E.   AC
    CONAN   HOWARD, R./DE CAMP/& AC
  HALL OF THE DEAD, THE   NV C FSF 67 02
    CONAN   HOWARD, R./DE CAMP/& AC
  HAND OF NERGAL, THE   SS C
    CONAN   HOWARD, R./DE CAMP/& AC
  HAWKS OVER EGYPT (SEE HAWKS OVER SHEM)   TC
  HAWKS OVER SHEM (FROM "HAWKS OVER EGYPT" BY REH.) NV C FUN 55 10
    CONAN THE FREEBOOTER   HOWARD, R. & DE CAMP AC
    TALES OF CONAN   HOWARD, R. & DE CAMP AC
  HORROR FROM THE MOUND, THE   SS   WRT 32 05
    WOLFSHEAD   HOWARD, ROBERT E.   AC
  HOUSE OF ARABU, THE   SS
    WOLFSHEAD   HOWARD, ROBERT E.   AC

HOWARD, ROBERT E.   (CONTINUED)
  HYBORIAN AGE, THE   AR   PHT 36
    COMING OF CONAN, THE   HOWARD, ROBERT E.   AC
  HYBORIAN AGE, THE   (PART 1)   AR   PHT 36
    CONAN   HOWARD, R./DE CAMP/& AC
  HYBORIAN AGE, THE   (PART 2)   AR   PHT 36
    CONAN THE AVENGER   HOWARD, R./NYBERG/& AC
  JEWELS OF GWAHLUR   SS   WRT 35 03
    CONAN THE WARRIOR   HOWARD, R. & DE CAMP AC
    KING CONAN   HOWARD, ROBERT E.   AC
  KING AND THE OAK, THE   PM
    COMING OF CONAN, THE   HOWARD, ROBERT E.   AC
  LETTER TO P. SCHUYLER MILLER   MS
    COMING OF CONAN, THE   HOWARD, ROBERT E.   AC
    CONAN   HOWARD, R./DE CAMP/& AC
  MIRRORS OF TUZUN THUNE, THE   SS   WRT 29 09
    COMING OF CONAN, THE   HOWARD, ROBERT E.   AC
  PEOPLE OF THE BLACK CIRCLE, THE   NA   WRT 34 09
    CONAN THE ADVENTURER   HOWARD, R. & DE CAMP AC
    SWORD OF CONAN, THE   HOWARD, ROBERT E.   AC
  PHOENIX ON THE SWORD, THE   SS   WRT 32 12
    CONAN THE USURPER   HOWARD, R. & DE CAMP AC
    KING CONAN   HOWARD, ROBERT E.   AC
  PIGEONS FROM HELL   NV   WRT 38 05
    WEIRD TALES   MARGULIES, LEO   AN
  POOL OF THE BLACK ONE, THE   SS   WRT 33 10
    CONAN THE ADVENTURER   HOWARD, R. & DE CAMP AC
    SWORD OF CONAN, THE   HOWARD, ROBERT E.   AC
  QUEEN OF THE BLACK COAST   SS   WRT 34 05
    COMING OF CONAN, THE   HOWARD, ROBERT E.   AC
  RED NAILS   NA   WRT 36 07
    CONAN THE WARRIOR   HOWARD, R. & DE CAMP AC
    SWORD OF CONAN, THE   HOWARD, ROBERT E.   AC
  ROAD OF THE EAGLES, THE (CONAN, MAN OF DESTINY) NV C FUN 55 12
    CONAN THE FREEBOOTER   HOWARD, R. & DE CAMP AC
    TALES OF CONAN   HOWARD, R. & DE CAMP AC
  ROGUES IN THE HOUSE   SS   WRT 34 01
    COMING OF CONAN, THE   HOWARD, ROBERT E.   AC
    CONAN   HOWARD, R./DE CAMP/& AC
  SCARLET CITADEL, THE   SS   WRT 33 01
    CONAN THE USURPER   HOWARD, R. & DE CAMP AC
    KING CONAN   HOWARD, ROBERT E.   AC
  SHADOW KINGDOM, THE   SS   WRT 29 08
    COMING OF CONAN, THE   HOWARD, ROBERT E.   AC
  SHADOWS IN THE MOONLIGHT   SS   WRT 34 04
    CONAN THE BARBARIAN   HOWARD, ROBERT E.   AC
    CONAN THE FREEBOOTER   HOWARD, R. & DE CAMP AC
  SHADOWS IN ZAMBOULA   NV   WRT 35 11
    CONAN THE BARBARIAN   HOWARD, ROBERT E.   AC
    CONAN THE WANDERER   HOWARD, R./DE CAMP/& AC
  SPELL OF SEVEN, THE   DE CAMP, L. SPRAGUE AN
  SLITHERING SHADOW, THE   SS   WRT 33 09
    CONAN THE ADVENTURER   HOWARD, R. & DE CAMP AC
    SWORD OF CONAN, THE   HOWARD, ROBERT E.   AC
  THING IN THE CRYPT, THE   SS
    CONAN   HOWARD, R./DE CAMP/& AC
  TOWER OF THE ELEPHANT, THE   SS   WRT 33 03
    COMING OF CONAN, THE   HOWARD, ROBERT E.   AC
    CONAN   HOWARD, R./DE CAMP/& AC
  TREASURE OF TRANICOS, THE (THE BLACK STRANGER) NA C FMG 53 03
    CONAN THE USURPER   HOWARD, R. & DE CAMP AC
    KING CONAN   HOWARD, ROBERT E.   AC
  VALLEY OF THE WORM, THE   SS   WRT 34 02
    WOLFSHEAD   HOWARD, ROBERT E.   AC
    WORLDS OF WEIRD   MARGULIES, LEO   AN
  WITCH FROM HELL'S KITCHEN, THE   NV   APR 52 18
    AVON FANTASY READER, THE   WOLLHEIM &ERNSBERGER AN
  WITCH SHALL BE BORN, A   SS   WRT 34 12
    CONAN THE BARBARIAN   HOWARD, ROBERT E.   AC
    CONAN THE FREEBOOTER   HOWARD, R. & DE CAMP AC
  WOLFSHEAD   SS   WRT 26 04
    WOLFSHEAD   HOWARD, ROBERT E.   AC
  WOLVES BEYOND THE BORDER   SS C
    CONAN THE USURPER   HOWARD, R. & DE CAMP AC

HOWELL, JOSEPH
  TRANSITION TROLLEY, THE   SS   SCS 73
    SHOWCASE   ELWOOD, ROGER   OA

HOWES, MARGARET
  MAP   MS
    BEST OF LEIGH BRACKETT, THE   BRACKETT, LEIGH   AC

HOYLE, FRED
  ELEMENT 79   AC H NAM 67
  A FOR ANDROMEDA   EX C SVN 62
    FROM FRANKENSTEIN TO ANDROMEDA   BROWN, JAMES GOLDIE AN
  AGENT 38   SS
    ELEMENT 79   HOYLE, FRED   AC
  AX, THE   SS
    ELEMENT 79   HOYLE, FRED   AC
  BLACK CLOUD, THE (EXCERPT)   EX   HEI 57
    EXPERT DREAMERS, THE   POHL, FREDERIK   AN
  BLACKMAIL   SS   FSF 67 02
    BEST SF: 1967   HARRISON & ALDISS   AN
    ELEMENT 79   HOYLE, FRED   AC
  CATTLE TRUCKS   SS
    ELEMENT 79   HOYLE, FRED   AC
  ELEMENT 79   SS
    ELEMENT 79   HOYLE, FRED   AC
  JUDGMENT OF APHRODITE, THE   SS
    ELEMENT 79   HOYLE, FRED   AC
  JURY OF FIVE, A   SS
    ELEMENT 79   HOYLE, FRED   AC
  MAGNETOSPHERE, THE   SS
    ELEMENT 79   HOYLE, FRED   AC

HOYLE, FRED   HYNE, C.J. CUTCLIFFE

HOYLE, FRED   (CONTINUED)
  MARTIANS, THE   SS
    ELEMENT 79   HOYLE, FRED   AC
  OPERATION, THE   SS
    ELEMENT 79   HOYLE, FRED   AC
  PLAY'S THE THING, A   SS
    ELEMENT 79   HOYLE, FRED   AC
  PYM MAKES HIS POINT   SS
    ELEMENT 79   HOYLE, FRED   AC
  SHORTSIGHTED   SS
    ELEMENT 79   HOYLE, FRED   AC
  WELCOME TO SLIPPAGE CITY   SS
    ELEMENT 79   HOYLE, FRED   AC
  ZOOMEN   SS   FSF 67 03
    ELEMENT 79   HOYLE, FRED   AC

HROLDA, JEAN
  EIGHT MISTRESSES, THE   SS   ESQ 37 08
    TIMELESS STORIES FOR TODAY AND TOMORROW
                                 BRADBURY, RAY   AN

HUBBARD, L. RON
  FROM DEATH TO THE STARS   AC H FPB 53
  KINGSLAYER, THE   AC H FPB 49
    ALSO IN "FROM DEATH TO THE STARS"
    ALSO AS "SEVEN STEPS TO THE ARBITER"
  OLE DOC METHUSELAH   AC   DAW 70
  SEVEN STEPS TO THE ARBITER   AC   MJR 75
    SEE "THE KINGSLAYER"
  BATTLE OF WIZARDS   SS   FBK 49 05
    WIZARDS AND WARLOCKS   GHIDALIA, VIC   AN
  BEAST, THE   SS   ASF 42 10
    KINGSLAYER, THE   HUBBARD, L. RON   AC
  BEHIND THE BLACK NEBULA (THE INVADERS)   NV   ASF 42 01
    TALES OF OUTER SPACE   WOLLHEIM, DONALD A. DA
  DANGEROUS DIMENSION, THE   SS   ASF 38 07
    FUTURES TO INFINITY   MOSKOWITZ, SAM   AN
  DEATH'S DEPUTY   NO   UNK 40 02
    FROM DEATH TO THE STARS   HUBBARD, L. RON   AC
  DEVIL'S RESCUE, THE   SS   UNK 40 10
    HELL HATH FURY   HAY, GEORGE   AN
  EXPENSIVE SLAVES, THE   SS   ASF 47 11
    OLE DOC METHUSELAH   HUBBARD, L. RON   AC
  GREAT AIR MONOPOLY, THE   NV   ASF 48 09
    OLE DOC METHUSELAH   HUBBARD, L. RON   AC
  HE DIDN'T LIKE CATS   SS   UNK 42 02
    ZACHERLEY'S VULTURE STEW   ZACHERLEY   AN
  HER MAJESTY'S ABERRATION   SS   ASF 48 03
    OLE DOC METHUSELAH   HUBBARD, L. RON   AC
  INVADERS, THE (ALSO AS BEHIND THE BLACK NEBULA) NV ASF 42 01
    KINGSLAYER, THE   HUBBARD, L. RON   AC
  KINGSLAYER, THE   AC   FPB 49
    FROM DEATH TO THE STARS   HUBBARD, L. RON   AC
  KINGSLAYER, THE   NO   FPB 49
    KINGSLAYER, THE   HUBBARD, L. RON   AC
  OLE DOC METHUSELAH   NV   ASF 47 10
    OLE DOC METHUSELAH   HUBBARD, L. RON   AC
  OLE MOTHER METHUSELAH   NV   ASF 50 01
    OLE DOC METHUSELAH   HUBBARD, L. RON   AC
  PLAGUE   NV   ASF 49 04
    OLE DOC METHUSELAH   HUBBARD, L. RON   AC
  PREFACE   IN
    KINGSLAYER, THE   HUBBARD, L. RON   AC
  PROFESSOR WAS A THIEF, THE   NV   ASF 40 02
    *MY BEST SCIENCE FICTION STORY MARGULIES & FRIEND AN
  SOUND INVESTMENT, A   NV   ASF 49 06
    OLE DOC METHUSELAH   HUBBARD, L. RON   AC
  TOUGH OLD MAN   SS   STS 50 11
    SPACE POLICE   NORTON, ANDRE   AN
  TRITON (THE UNDIGESTIBLE TRITON)   NO   UNK 40 04
    SCIENCE-FANTASY QUINTETTE   CRAWFORD, WILLIAM L. AN
  UNDIGESTIBLE TRITON, THE (SEE TRITON)   TC
  WHEN SHADOWS FALL   SS   STS 48 07
    *MEN AGAINST THE STARS   GREENBERG , MARTIN   AN
  WHY I SELECTED THE PROFESSOR WAS A THIEF   AI
    *MY BEST SCIENCE FICTION STORY MARGULIES & FRIEND AN

HUBBARD, P. M.
  BOTANY BAY   SS   FSF 55 02
    BEST FROM FANTASY AND SCIENCE FICTION: 5
                                 BOUCHER, ANTHONY   AN
  FREE FLIGHT   PM   FSF 56 04
    BEST FROM FANTASY AND SCIENCE FICTION: 6
                                 BOUCHER, ANTHONY   AN
  GOLDEN BRICK, THE   SS   FSF 63 01
    BEST FROM FANTASY AND SCIENCE FICTION: 13
                                 DAVIDSON, AVRAM   AN
  MANUSCRIPT FOUND IN A VACUUM (PUN 52 12)   SS   FSF 53 08
    BEST FROM FANTASY AND SCIENCE FICTION: 3
                                 BOUCHER & MCCOMAS   AN
  SPECIAL CONSENT   SS   FSF 63 10
    MARRIAGE AND THE FAMILY THROUGH SCIENCE FICTION
                                 CLEAR/WARRICK/&   AN

HUDSON, JEFFREY S.
  HALF-BAKED PUBLISHER'S DELIGHT   SS C IFS 74 08
    BEST FROM IF, THE VOLUME III
                                 BAEN, JAMES   AN

HUFFORD, LIZ
  BOOK LEARNERS, THE   SS   FSF 75 04
    BEST SCIENCE FICTION STORIES OF THE YEAR (1975)
                                 DEL REY, LESTER   AN
  TABLETS OF STONE   SS   ORB 70 08
    ORBIT 8   KNIGHT, DAMON   OA

HUGHES, RICHARD
  CART, THE   SS   34
    GRAVEYARD READER, THE   CONKLIN, GROFF   AN
  STRANGER, THE   SS   31
    SUPERNATURAL READER, THE   CONKLIN, G&L.   AN
  VANISHING MAN, THE   SS   26
    MATHEMATICAL MAGPIE, THE   FADIMAN, CLIFTON   AN

HUGHES, TED
  GHOST CRABS   PM   66
    HOLDING YOUR EIGHT HANDS   LUCIE-SMITH, EDWARD AN
    SCIENCE FICTION   BRODKIN & PEARSON   AN

HUGI, MAURICE G.   PSEUD. FOR ERIC FRANK RUSSELL
  MECHANICAL MICE   NV   ASF 41 01
    *ADVENTURES IN TIME AND SPACE HEALY & MCCOMAS   AN

HULL, E. MAYNE   (MRS. A. E. VAN VOGT)
            SEE ALSO   CO-AUTHOR A. E. VAN VOGT
  PLANETS FOR SALE   AC H FEL 54
  ABDICATION (ALSO AS THE INVISIBILITY GAMBIT) SS C ASF 43 04
    SCIENCE FICTION ROLL OF HONOR, THE POHL, FREDERIK AN
  BANKRUPTCY PROCEEDINGS   NV   ASF 46 08
    PLANETS FOR SALE   HULL, E. MAYNE   AC
  COMPETITION   SS   ASF 43 06
    *MEN AGAINST THE STARS   GREENBERG , MARTIN   AN
    PLANETS FOR SALE   HULL, E. MAYNE   AC
  CONTRACT, THE   NV   ASF 44 03
    PLANETS FOR SALE   HULL, E. MAYNE   AC
  DEBT, THE   NV   ASF 43 12
    PLANETS FOR SALE   HULL, E. MAYNE   AC
  ENTER THE PROFESSOR   SS   ASF 45 01
    PLANETS FOR SALE   HULL, E. MAYNE   AC
  FLIGHT THAT FAILED, THE   SS   ASF 42 12
    ADVENTURES IN DIMENSION   CONKLIN, GROFF   AN
    *SCIENCE FICTION ADVENTURES IN DIMENSION
                                 CONKLIN, GROFF   AN
  PATIENT, THE   SS   UNK 43 10
    OUT OF THE UNKNOWN   VAN VOGT & HULL   AC
    *SCIENCE FICTION ADVENTURES IN MUTATION CONKLIN, GROFF AN
  PLANETS FOR SALE   AC C FEL 54
    VAN VOGT OMNIBUS, A   VAN VOGT, A. E.   AC
  ULTIMATE WISH, THE   SS   UNK 43 02
    OUT OF THE UNKNOWN   VAN VOGT & HULL   AC
  WELLWISHER, THE   SS
    OUT OF THE UNKNOWN (ENGLISH EDITION ADDS:)
                                 VAN VOGT & HULL   AC
  WINGED MAN, THE   NO C ASF 44 05
    SCIENCE FICTION SPECIAL 4   ANONYMOUS   AN
  WISHES WE MAKE, THE   SS   UNK 43 06
    OUT OF THE UNKNOWN   VAN VOGT & HULL   AC

HULL, GERALD
  MONADIC UNIVERSE, THE   NV C INY 72 03
    INFINITY 3   HOSKINS, ROBERT   OA

HULL, PAUL E.
  MAGNETIC MARVIN   SS   YNW
    SCIENCE FICTION STORIES   BRADLEY, JOHANNA   AN

HURLBUT, KAATJE
  PASSAGE FROM THE STARS, A   SS   SEP 61 05
    7TH ANNUAL OF THE YEAR'S BEST S-F, THE MERRIL, JUDITH AN

HURLEY, RICHARD J.
  BEYOND BELIEF   AN   SBS 66 04
  WORD TO THE READER, A   IN
    TIME MACHINE AND OTHER STORIES, THE (PB)
                                 WELLS, H. G.   AC

HUTCHINS, ROY
  NOSTALGIA GENE, THE   SS   GAL 54 11
    BEST SF 6   CRISPIN, EDMUND   AN

HUTTON, AMY
  BEHOLDER'S EYE, THE   SS   CLR 71 01
    CLARION   WILSON, ROBIN SCOTT OA

HUXLEY, ALDOUS
  FROM "BRAVE NEW WORLD"   EX   WND 32
    TREASURY OF SCIENCE FICTION CLASSICS, THE
                                 KUEBLER, HAROLD W.   AN
  HATCHERY, THE (FROM BRAVE NEW WORLD)   EX   WND 32
    CHILDREN OF WONDER   TENN, WILLIAM   AN
  IN BONDAGE TO A CENTRAL AUTHORITY (FROM "BRAVE NEW WORLD")
                                             EX   WND 32
    ARMCHAIR SCIENCE READER, THE GORDON, I. & SORKIN AN
  YOUNG ARCHIMEDES   SS   24
    FANTASIA MATHEMATICA   FADIMAN, CLIFTON   AN

HUXLEY, JULIAN
  TISSUE-CULTURE KING, THE   SS   AMZ 27 08
    *BEST OF SCIENCE FICTION   CONKLIN, GROFF   AN
    GREAT SCIENCE FICTION BY SCIENTISTS CONKLIN, GROFF AN
    TIME PROBE: THE SCIENCES IN SF. CLARKE, ARTHUR C. AN

HYDE, GAVIN
  SPARKIE'S FALL   SS   STR 59 05
    STAR OF STARS   POHL, FREDERIK   AN
    STAR SCIENCE FICTION STORIES NO. 5 POHL, FREDERIK OA

HYNAM, JOHN   SEE PSEUD. JOHN KIPPAX

HYNE, C.J. CUTCLIFFE
  LIZARD, THE   SS   04
    ANCESTRAL VOICES   MENVILLE & REGINALD AN

IF, EDITORS OF
  BEST FROM IF, THE   VOLUME I   AN   AWD 73
  BEST FROM IF, THE   VOLUME II   AN   AWD 74

IMBERT, ENRIQUE A.
  LEGENDS FROM "THE CHESHIRE CAT" (TRANSLATED BY ISABEL READE)
                                                         SS
    NEW CONSTELLATIONS   DISCH & NAYLOR   OA

ING, DEAN
  MALF   NV
    ANALOG ANNUAL   BOVA, BEN   OA

INGLIS, JAMES
  NIGHT WATCH   SS   NWR 65 03
    BEST FROM NEW WRITINGS IN S-F FIRST SELECTION, THE
                                   CARNELL, JOHN   AN
    NEW WRITINGS IN SF. 3   CARNELL, JOHN   OA
    SPACE ODYSSEYS   ALDISS, BRIAN W.   AN

INOUYE, JON
  NIGHT TIDE, A   OC   RDN 76 12
  ARM   SS
    NIGHT TIDE, A   INOUYE, JON   OC
  COMIX   SS
    NIGHT TIDE, A   INOUYE, JON   OC
  CYB   SS
    NIGHT TIDE, A   INOUYE, JON   OC
  DOUBLE   PM
    NIGHT TIDE, A   INOUYE, JON   OC
  EPILOGUE   MS
    NIGHT TIDE, A   INOUYE, JON   OC
  ESCAPE ARTIST   SS
    NIGHT TIDE, A   INOUYE, JON   OC
  FAR PULSAR   SS
    NIGHT TIDE, A   INOUYE, JON   OC
  FAREWELL DREAM   SS
    NIGHT TIDE, A   INOUYE, JON   OC
  FINAL DINEB   SS
    NIGHT TIDE, A   INOUYE, JON   OC
  FROM CRIMSON CAME STARDUST   PM
    NIGHT TIDE, A   INOUYE, JON   OC
  GUIDELIGHT   SS
    NIGHT TIDE, A   INOUYE, JON   OC
  HOGARTH   SS
    NIGHT TIDE, A   INOUYE, JON   OC
  INVISIBLE JANITOR   SS
    NIGHT TIDE, A   INOUYE, JON   OC
  LAST MAN   SS
    NIGHT TIDE, A   INOUYE, JON   OC
  LETRON   SS
    NIGHT TIDE, A   INOUYE, JON   OC
  MATARAY, TOO   SS
    NIGHT TIDE, A   INOUYE, JON   OC
  MEGATON   SS
    NIGHT TIDE, A   INOUYE, JON   OC
  MINDSHIP   SS
    NIGHT TIDE, A   INOUYE, JON   OC
  MINDSPOT   SS
    NIGHT TIDE, A   INOUYE, JON   OC
  MYTH CHILD   SS
    NIGHT TIDE, A   INOUYE, JON   OC
  NEURO-GENERATION, THE   SS
    NIGHT TIDE, A   INOUYE, JON   OC
  NIGHT TIDE, A   SS
    NIGHT TIDE, A   INOUYE, JON   OC
  NIGHTSPAWN   SS
    NIGHT TIDE, A   INOUYE, JON   OC
  NOTHINK   SS
    NIGHT TIDE, A   INOUYE, JON   OC
  PROLOGUE   MS
    NIGHT TIDE, A   INOUYE, JON   OC
  RESTING GROUND   PM
    NIGHT TIDE, A   INOUYE, JON   OC
  ROBOT SLEEP   SS
    NIGHT TIDE, A   INOUYE, JON   OC
  SCOPE   SS
    NIGHT TIDE, A   INOUYE, JON   OC
  SMELL OF PULPS, THE   SS
    NIGHT TIDE, A   INOUYE, JON   OC
  SOJOURNER   SS
    NIGHT TIDE, A   INOUYE, JON   OC
  SPHERE   SS
    NIGHT TIDE, A   INOUYE, JON   OC
  SPHEROID OF ZANZOL   SS
    NIGHT TIDE, A   INOUYE, JON   OC
  STORY OF REJECTION, THE   SS
    NIGHT TIDE, A   INOUYE, JON   OC
  TURNTABLE   SS
    NIGHT TIDE, A   INOUYE, JON   OC
  UFO SPOTTED   SS
    NIGHT TIDE, A   INOUYE, JON   OC
  UGLY JAPANESE, THE   SS
    NIGHT TIDE, A   INOUYE, JON   OC
  VIDEO   PM
    NIGHT TIDE, A   INOUYE, JON   OC
  WINTER ARRIVAL   SS
    NIGHT TIDE, A   INOUYE, JON   OC
  WORK POEM, THE   PM
    NIGHT TIDE, A   INOUYE, JON   OC
  2076   SS
    NIGHT TIDE, A   INOUYE, JON   OC

IONESCO, EUGENE
  FLYING HIGH
                                                         SS   MAD 57 10

IONESCO, EUGENE   (CONTINUED)
  SF:58, THE YEAR'S GREATEST SCIENCE FICTION AND FANTASY
                                   MERRIL, JUDITH   AN

IRVING, WASHINGTON
  CONQUEST OF THE MOON, THE   SS
    ABC OF SCIENCE FICTION, AN   BOARDMAN, TOM JR.   AN
    TRANSFORMATIONS II   ROSELLE, DANIEL   AN

IRWIN, MARGARET
  EARLIER SERVICE, THE (1935)   SS   FSF 51 12
    BEST FROM FANTASY AND SCIENCE FICTION: 2
                                   BOUCHER & MCCOMAS   AN

ISAACS, LEONARD
  THRANGS AND OTHER WONDERS   PM   CLR 73 03
    CLARION III   WILSON, ROBIN SCOTT   OA

ISHERWOOD, C.
  I AM WAITING   SS   NYM 39 10
    TIMELESS STORIES FOR TODAY AND TOMORROW
                                   BRADBURY, RAY   AN

IVANOV, VSEVOLOD
  SISYPHUS, THE SON OF AEOLUS   SS
    VIEW FROM ANOTHER SHORE   ROTTENSTEINER, FRANZ AN

JACKSON, A. A., IV
  SUN UP   SS C   76
    FASTER THAN LIGHT   DANN & ZEBROWSKI   OA

JACKSON, CLIVE
  SWORDSMAN OF VARNIS, THE   SS   OWS 50 09
    *SCIENCE-FICTION CARNIVAL   BROWN, F. & REYNOLDS AN

JACKSON, IRENE
  EARTHBOUND   PM
    MARS, WE LOVE YOU   HIPOLITO & MCNELLY   AN

JACKSON, SHIRLEY
  BULLETIN   SS   FSF 54 03
    BEST FROM FANTASY AND SCIENCE FICTION: 4
                                   BOUCHER, ANTHONY   AN
    SCIENCE FACT/FICTION   FARRELL/GAGE/&   AN
  DAEMON LOVER, THE   NV   48
    OTHER DIMENSION, THE   ROSNER, SARA   AN
    TIMELESS STORIES FOR TODAY AND TOMORROW
                                   BRADBURY, RAY   AN
  OMEN, THE   SS   FSF 58 03
    BEST FROM FANTASY AND SCIENCE FICTION: 8
                                   BOUCHER, ANTHONY   AN
  ONE ORDINARY DAY, WITH PEANUTS   SS   FSF 55 01
    BEST FROM FANTASY AND SCIENCE FICTION: 5
                                   BOUCHER, ANTHONY   AN
    NIGHT IN FUNLAND   BRONDFIELD, JEROME   AN
    SCIENCE FICTION ARGOSY, A   KNIGHT, DAMON   AN
    SF: THE BEST OF THE BEST   MERRIL, JUDITH   AN
    SF: THE YEAR'S GREATEST SCIENCE FICTION AND FANTASY
                                   MERRIL, JUDITH   AN
  SUMMER PEOPLE, THE   SS   CHM 50
    CIRCUS OF DR. LAO AND OTHER IMPROBABLE STORIES
                                   BRADBURY, RAY   AN

JACOB, PIERS ANTHONY SEE PSEUD. PIERS ANTHONY

JACOBI, CARL
  PORTRAITS IN MOONLIGHT   AC H ARK 64
  CORBIE DOOR, THE   SS   WRT 47 05
    PORTRAITS IN MOONLIGHT   JACOBI, CARL   AC
  GENTLEMAN IS AN EPWA, THE   NV   NEW 53 AN
    NEW WORLDS FOR OLD   DERLETH, AUGUST   AN
    UNTRAVELLED WORLDS   BARTER & WILSON   AN
    *WORLDS OF TOMORROW   DERLETH, AUGUST   AN
  HISTORIAN, THE   SS
    PORTRAITS IN MOONLIGHT   JACOBI, CARL   AC
  INCIDENT AT THE GALLOPING HORSE   SS   WRT 48 11
    PORTRAITS IN MOONLIGHT   JACOBI, CARL   AC
  LA PRELLO PAPER, THE   SS   WRT 48 03
    PORTRAITS IN MOONLIGHT   JACOBI, CARL   AC
  LODANA   SS
    PORTRAITS IN MOONLIGHT   JACOBI, CARL   AC
  LONG VOYAGE, THE   SS   FUN 55 09
    PORTRAITS IN MOONLIGHT   JACOBI, CARL   AC
  LORENZO WATCH, THE   SS   WRT 48 01
    PORTRAITS IN MOONLIGHT   JACOBI, CARL   AC
  LOST STREET, THE (THE STREET THAT WASN'T THERE) SS C CMT 41 07
    *STRANGE PORTS OF CALL   DERLETH, AUGUST   AN
  MADE IN TANGANYIKA   SS   FUN 54 05
    PORTRAITS IN MOONLIGHT   JACOBI, CARL   AC
  MARTIAN CALENDAR, THE   SS   SPM 57 SP
    PORTRAITS IN MOONLIGHT   JACOBI, CARL   AC
  MATTHEW SOUTH AND COMPANY   SS   WRT 49 05
    PORTRAITS IN MOONLIGHT   JACOBI, CARL   AC
  PORTRAIT IN MOONLIGHT   SS   WRT 47 11
    PORTRAITS IN MOONLIGHT   JACOBI, CARL   AC
  SPANISH CAMERA, THE   SS   WRT 50 09
    PORTRAITS IN MOONLIGHT   JACOBI, CARL   AC
  STREET THAT WASN'T THERE, THE (ALSO AS THE LOST STREET)
                                                   SS C CMT 41 07
    CREATURES FROM BEYOND   CARR, TERRY   AN
  TEPONDICON   SS   PLS 46 WI
    FAR BOUNDARIES   DERLETH, AUGUST   AN
    PORTRAITS IN MOONLIGHT   JACOBI, CARL   AC
  UNPLEASANTNESS AT CARVER HOUSE, THE   SS
    TRAVELLERS BY NIGHT   DERLETH, AUGUST   OA

JACOBI, CARL   JAMESON, MALCOLM

JACOBI, CARL   (CONTINUED)
  WHITE PINNACLE, THE   SS
  *TIME TO COME   DERLETH, AUGUST   OA
  WITCHES IN THE CORNFIELD   SS
    PORTRAITS IN MOONLIGHT   JACOBI, CARL   AC

JACOBS, HARVEY
  EGG OF THE GLAK, AND OTHER STORIES, THE   AC H HPR 69
  ACCEPTING FOR WINKELMEYER   SS NWQ 73 05
    NEW WORLDS NO. 5   MOORCOCK & PLATT   OA
  BREAK IN THE WEATHER, A   SS
    EGG OF THE GLAK, AND OTHER STORIES, THE
                              JACOBS, HARVEY   AC
  DISTURBANCE OF THE PEACE, A   SS NWS 68 10
    EGG OF THE GLAK, AND OTHER STORIES, THE
                              JACOBS, HARVEY   AC
  DRESS REHEARSAL   SS FSF 74 07
    BEST SCIENCE FICTION STORIES OF THE YEAR (1974)
                              DEL REY, LESTER   AN
  EGG OF THE GLAK, THE   NV FSF 68 03
    BEST FROM FANTASY AND SCIENCE FICTION: 18
                              FERMAN, EDWARD L.   AN
    EGG OF THE GLAK, AND OTHER STORIES, THE
                              JACOBS, HARVEY   AC
  EPILOGUE (EPILOGUE FOR AN OFFICE PICNIC)   SS NWS 69 01
    EGG OF THE GLAK, AND OTHER STORIES, THE
                              JACOBS, HARVEY   AC
  GIRL WHO DREW THE GODS, THE   NV MAD 65 05
    EGG OF THE GLAK, AND OTHER STORIES, THE
                              JACOBS, HARVEY   AC
    11TH ANNUAL OF THE YEAR'S BEST S-F, THE
                              MERRIL, JUDITH   AN
  GRAVITY   SS NWS 69 08
    BEST SF STORIES FROM NEW WORLDS 6 MOORCOCK, MICHAEL AN
    DECADE THE 1960S   ALDISS & HARRISON   AN
  IN SECLUSION   SS NWS 68 02
    BEST SF STORIES FROM NEW WORLDS 4 MOORCOCK, MICHAEL AN
    EGG OF THE GLAK, AND OTHER STORIES, THE
                              JACOBS, HARVEY   AC
    SF12   MERRIL, JUDITH   AN
  LION'S SHARE, THE   SS PBY 61 09
    EGG OF THE GLAK, AND OTHER STORIES, THE
                              JACOBS, HARVEY   AC
  MAN WHO MADE A BABY, THE   SS NWQ 74 06
    NEW WORLDS NO. 6   PLATT & BAILEY   OA
  MUSICAL EDUCATION, A   SS
    EGG OF THE GLAK, AND OTHER STORIES, THE
                              JACOBS, HARVEY   AC
  REASONS OF HEALTH   SS
    EGG OF THE GLAK, AND OTHER STORIES, THE
                              JACOBS, HARVEY   AC
  THANKS FROM THE WHOLE BOUQUET   SS NUG 65 09
    SATAN'S PETS   GHIDALIA, VIC   AN
  TOOTH FAIRY, THE   SS NEW 73 AN
    MORE LITTLE MONSTERS   ELWOOD & GHIDALIA   AN
  TOY, THE   SS
    EGG OF THE GLAK, AND OTHER STORIES, THE
                              JACOBS, HARVEY   AC
  VOYAGE OF THE PEANUT, THE   SS PBY 59 06
    EGG OF THE GLAK, AND OTHER STORIES, THE
                              JACOBS, HARVEY   AC

JACOBS, SYLVIA
  PILOT AND THE BUSHMAN, THE   NV GAL 51 08
    *GALAXY READER OF SCIENCE FICTION GOLD, H. L. AN

JACOBSON, HELEN
  TRANSLATION   MS
    RUSSIAN SCIENCE FICTION, 1968 MAGIDOFF, ROBERT AN

JAFFRAY, NORMAN R.
  COWBOY LAMENT   PM FSF 54 01
    BEST FROM FANTASY AND SCIENCE FICTION: 4
                              BOUCHER, ANTHONY   AN

JAKES, JOHN W.
  BEST OF JOHN JAKES, THE   AC DAW 77 06
    EDITED BY MARTIN HARRY GREENBERG AND JOSEPH D. OLANDER
  FROM ON WHEELS   EX WPB 73
    BEST OF JOHN JAKES, THE   JAKES, JOHN W.   AC
  HERE IS THY STING   NV ORB 68 03
    BEST OF JOHN JAKES, THE   JAKES, JOHN W.   AC
    ORBIT   3   KNIGHT, DAMON   OA
  HIGHEST FORM OF LIFE, THE   SS AMZ 61 08
    BEST OF JOHN JAKES, THE   JAKES, JOHN W.   AC
  LOVE IS A PUNCH IN THE NOSE   SS BIZ 66 01
    BEST OF JOHN JAKES, THE   JAKES, JOHN W.   AC
  MACHINE   SS FSF 52 04
    BEST OF JOHN JAKES, THE   JAKES, JOHN W.   AC
    BEST SCIENCE-FICTION STORIES: 1953, THE
                              BLEILER & DIKTY   AN
    FRONTIERS IN SPACE   BLEILER & DIKTY   AN
  ONE RACE SHOW   NV GAL 62 08
    BEST OF JOHN JAKES, THE   JAKES, JOHN W.   AC
  POLITICAL MACHINE   SS AMZ 61 03
    BEST OF JOHN JAKES, THE   JAKES, JOHN W.   AC
  RANGING   SS FRS 68
    FARTHEST REACHES, THE   ELDER, JOSEPH   OA
    UNIVERSE AHEAD   ENGDAHL & ROBERSON   AN
  RECIDIVISM PREFERRED   SS AMZ 62 02
    BEST OF JOHN JAKES, THE   JAKES, JOHN W.   AC
  SELLERS OF THE DREAM, THE   NA GAL 63 06
    BEST OF JOHN JAKES, THE   JAKES, JOHN W.   AC
    FAR-OUT PEOPLE, THE   HOSKINS, ROBERT   AN
  SPECTRUM 4   AMIS & CONQUEST   AN
  TOMORROW, INC.   GREENBERG& OLANDER   AN

JAKES, JOHN W.   (CONTINUED)
  STRANGER WITH ROSES   PL INY 72 04
    INFINITY 4   HOSKINS, ROBERT   OA
    SIX SCIENCE FICTION PLAYS ELWOOD, ROGER   AN
  THERE'S NO VINISM LOKE CHAUVINISM   NV AMZ 65 04
    BEST OF JOHN JAKES, THE   JAKES, JOHN W.   AC
  UNDERFOLLOW   SS FSF 63 05
    STARS AROUND US, THE   HOSKINS, ROBERT   AN

JAKUBOWSKI, MAXIM
  SCIENCE FICTION STORY FOR JONI MITCHELL, A   NV
    NEW S.F., THE   JONES, LANGDON   OA

JAMES, CLIVE
  RISE OF AIRSTRIP ONE, THE   SS
    BEST SF: 1974   HARRISON & ALDISS   AN

JAMES, DANIEL B.
  INTEGRATION MODULE   NV ASF 73 01
    SOCIOLOGY THROUGH SCIENCE FICTION MILSTEAD/GREENBERG/& AN

JAMES, DANIEL LEWIS
  MOON OF DELIRIUM   SS ASF 40 01
    *POSSIBLE WORLDS OF SCIENCE FICTION CONKLIN, GROFF AN

JAMES, E. R.
  CLEVERJACKS AND THE MOONSTALKS, THE   SS
    WORLDS AT WAR   RAYER, FRANCIS G.   AN
  DODIE SLAMMED THE DOOR   SS
    WORLDS AT WAR   RAYER, FRANCIS G.   AN
  EMERGENCY WORKING   SS NWS 52 09
    GATEWAY TO TOMORROW   CARNELL, JOHN   AN
  SIX-FINGERED JACKS   SS NWS 62 06
    OUT OF THIS WORLD 4   WILLIAMS-ELLIS& OWEN AN

JAMES, EDWIN   PSEUD. FOR JAMES E. GUNN

JAMES, HENRY   PSEUD. FOR L. C. KELLENBERGER
  SIR EDMUND ORME   NV
    OTHER DIMENSION, THE   ROSNER, SARA   AN

JAMES, LAURENCE
  AND DUG THE DOG A TOMB   SS NWQ 72 03
    NEW WORLDS QUARTERLY NO. 3 MOORCOCK, MICHAEL OA
  ONLY MAN ON EARTH, THE   SS NWB 73 05
    NEW WORLDS QUARTERLY NO. 5 MOORCOCK, MICHAEL OA
  SQUARE ROOT OF MC, THE   SS NWR 73 22
    NEW WRITINGS IN SF. 22   BULMER, KENNETH   OA
  YOU GET LOTS OF YESTERDAYS, LOTS OF TOMORROWS, AND ONLY
    ONE TODAY   SS NWR 75 26
    NEW WRITINGS IN SF. 26   BULMER, KENNETH   OA

JAMES, M. R.
  CASTING THE RUNES   NV
    WIZARDS AND WARLOCKS   GHIDALIA, VIC   AN
  LOST HEARTS   SS   31
    EDGE OF NEVER, THE   HOSKINS, ROBERT   AN
    SUPERNATURAL READER, THE CONKLIN, G&L.   AN
  VIEW FROM A HILL, A   SS   26
    TRAVELERS IN TIME   STERN, PHILIP VAN D. AN

JAMES, PHILIP   PSEUD. FOR LESTER DEL REY AND JAMES H. BEARD
  CARILLON OF SKULLS   SS UNK 41 02
    ZACHERLEY'S MIDNIGHT SNACKS ZACHERLEY   AN

JAMESON, MALCOLM
  BULLARD OF THE SPACE PATROL   AC H WOR 51
    EDITED BY ANDRE NORTON, SECOND EDITION OMITS "THE BUREAUCRAT"
  ADMIRAL'S INSPECTION   NV ASF 40 04
    BULLARD OF THE SPACE PATROL JAMESON, MALCOLM AC
  ALIEN ENVOY   SS ASF 44 11
    ULTIMATE INVADER, AND OTHER SCIENCE FICTION, THE
                              WOLLHEIM, DONALD A. DA
  BLIND ALLEY   NV UNK 43 06
    GREAT STORIES OF SCIENCE FICTION LEINSTER, MURRAY AN
    ROD SERLING'S TRIPLE W: WITCHES, WARLOCKS AND WEREWOLVES
                              SERLING, ROD   AN
  BLIND MAN'S BUFF   NV ASF 44 10
    EVERY BOY'S BOOK OF OUTER SPACE STORIES
                              DIKTY, T. E.   AN
    *IMAGINATION UNLIMITED   BLEILER & DIKTY   AN
  BLOCKADE RUNNER (SLACKER'S PARADISE)   SS ASF 41 04
    BULLARD OF THE SPACE PATROL JAMESON, MALCOLM AC
  BRIMSTONE BILL   SS ASF 42 07
    BULLARD OF THE SPACE PATROL JAMESON, MALCOLM AC
  BULLARD REFLECTS   SS ASF 41 12
    BULLARD OF THE SPACE PATROL JAMESON, MALCOLM AC
    INFINITE ARENA, THE   CARR, TERRY   AN
    TREASURY OF GREAT SCIENCE FICTION, A VOL.2
                              BOUCHER, ANTHONY   AN
  BUREAUCRAT, THE   NV ASF 44 04
    BULLARD OF THE SPACE PATROL JAMESON, MALCOLM AC
  CHILDREN OF THE "BETSY B"   SS ASF 39 03
    *TREASURY OF SCIENCE FICTION, A CONKLIN, GROFF AN
  DOUBLED AND REDOUBLED   SS UNK 41 02
    UNKNOWN, THE   BENSEN, D. R.   AN
  HOBO GOD   SS ASF 44 09
    ALL ABOUT THE FUTURE   GREENBERG , MARTIN   AN
  LILIES OF LIFE (ALSO AS PLANET OF DOOM)   SS ASF 45 02
    *POSSIBLE WORLDS OF SCIENCE FICTION CONKLIN, GROFF AN
  ORDERS   SS ASF 45 12
    BULLARD OF THE SPACE PATROL JAMESON, MALCOLM AC
  PLANET OF DOOM (LILIES OF LIFE)   SS ASF 45 02
    PLANET OF DOOM AND OTHER STORIES ANONYMOUS   AN
  PRIDE   SS ASF 42 09
    *BEYOND HUMAN KEN   MERRIL, JUDITH   AN

JAMESON, MALCOLM   (CONTINUED)
  SLACKER'S PARADISE (SEE BLOCKADE RUNNER)   TC
  SORCERER'S APPRENTICE, THE   SS   ASF 41 12
    OPERATION FUTURE   CONKLIN, GROFF   AN
  SPACE WAR TACTICS   AR   ASF 39 11
    COMING ATTRACTIONS   GREENBERG , MARTIN   NF
  TRICKY TONNAGE   SS   ASF 44 12
    *BEST OF SCIENCE FICTION   CONKLIN, GROFF   AN
    WORLDS OF WONDER   HARRISON, HARRY   AN
  WHITE MUTINY   SS   ASF 40 10
    BULLARD OF THE SPACE PATROL   JAMESON, MALCOLM   AC

JANIFER, LAURENCE M. PSEUD. FOR LARRY M. HARRIS
  IMPOSSIBLE?   AC   BEL 68 08
  MASTERS' CHOICE   AN H SAS 66
    ALSO AS "18 GREAT SCIENCE FICTION STORIES"
  18 GREAT SCIENCE FICTION STORIES   AN   TMP 71 01
    SEE "MASTERS' CHOICE"
  ALL POSSIBLE WORLDS   SS
    BEYOND TIME   LEY, SANDRA   OA
  AMFORTAS   SS   OMG 73
    OMEGA   ELWOOD, ROGER   OA
  BIBLE AFTER THE APOCALYPSE, THE   SS   NDM 74 04
    NEW DIMENSIONS 4   SILVERBERG, ROBERT   OA
  BUT FIRST...   IN
    IMPOSSIBLE?   JANIFER, LAURENCE M. AC
  CHARLEY DE MILO   SS   ASF 60 06
    IMPOSSIBLE?   JANIFER, LAURENCE M. AC
  CIVIS OBIT   SS   DYS 75
    DYSTOPIAN VISIONS   ELWOOD, ROGER   OA
  ELEMENTARY   SS C FSF 64 09
    IMPOSSIBLE?   JANIFER, LAURENCE M. AC
  EXCERPTS FROM THE GALACTICK ALMANACK: MUSIC   FA   GAL 59 06
    IMPOSSIBLE?   JANIFER, LAURENCE M. AC
  EXPATRIATE   NV   CSM 53 11
    IMPOSSIBLE?   JANIFER, LAURENCE M. AC
  FEW MINUTES, A   SS   TTM 73
    TEN TOMORROWS   ELWOOD, ROGER   OA
  FIRE SALE   SS   FAN 64 09
    IMPOSSIBLE?   JANIFER, LAURENCE M. AC
  GIFT, THE   SS   DYS 75
    DYSTOPIAN VISIONS   ELWOOD, ROGER   OA
  IN THE BAG   SS   FSF 64 02
    ABC OF SCIENCE FICTION, AN   BOARDMAN, TOM JR.   AN
    IMPOSSIBLE?   JANIFER, LAURENCE M. AC
  LOST IN TRANSLATION   SS   ASF 61 08
    IMPOSSIBLE?   JANIFER, LAURENCE M. AC
  LOVE STORY   SS   FAN 63 05
    IMPOSSIBLE?   JANIFER, LAURENCE M. AC
  MAN WHO PLAYED TO LOSE, THE   SS   ASF 61 10
    IMPOSSIBLE?   JANIFER, LAURENCE M. AC
  OBEY THAT IMPULSE| SS   FUT 59 06
    IMPOSSIBLE?   JANIFER, LAURENCE M. AC
  PREFACE   IN
    MASTERS' CHOICE   JANIFER, LAURENCE M. AN
  QUESTION, THE   SS C FSF 63 03
    IMPOSSIBLE?   JANIFER, LAURENCE M. AC
  REPLACE THE HORSE   SS   FAN 59 01
    IMPOSSIBLE?   JANIFER, LAURENCE M. AC
  SIGHT GAG   SS   ASF 62 05
    IMPOSSIBLE?   JANIFER, LAURENCE M. AC
  STORY TIME   SS
    JOURNEY TO ANOTHER STAR AND OTHER STORIES
                                 ELWOOD, ROGER   OA
  SWORD OF FLOWERS   SS   FAN 62 08
    IMPOSSIBLE?   JANIFER, LAURENCE M. AC
  THINE ALABASTER CITIES GLEAM   SS   FUC 73
    FUTURE CITY   ELWOOD, ROGER   OA
  THREE EXCERPTS   SS
    IMPOSSIBLE?   JANIFER, LAURENCE M. AC
  WIZARD   SS   ASF 60 05
    IMPOSSIBLE?   JANIFER, LAURENCE M. AC

JANVIER, IVAN   PSEUD. FOR ALGIS J. BUDRYS
  THING   SS   FUN 55 03
    BEST SCIENCE FICTION STORIES AND NOVELS: 1956
                                 DIKTY, T. E.   AN

JANVIER, PAUL   PSEUD. FOR ALGIS J. BUDRYS

JARRY, ALFRED
  HOW TO CONSTRUCT A TIME MACHINE   SS
    TRAPS OF TIME, THE   MOORCOCK, MICHAEL   AN
  TWO TELEPATHIC LETTERS TO LORD KELVIN   SS   65
    11TH ANNUAL OF THE YEAR'S BEST S-F, THE
                                 MERRIL, JUDITH   AN

JARVIS, BOB
  TRUTH TEST   PM
    BEYOND THIS HORIZON   CARRELL, CHRISTOPHER OA

JAVOR, FRANK A.
  INTERVIEW   SS   ASF 63 11
    9TH ANNUAL OF THE YEAR'S BEST S-F, THE MERRIL, JUDITH AN

JEFFERS, DONNAN CALL
  MASK   SS   NDM 76 06
    NEW DIMENSIONS 6   SILVERBERG, ROBERT   OA

JEFFERS, ROBINSON
  SCIENCE   PM   25
    SPECULATIONS   SANDERS, THOMAS E.   AN

JENKINS, WILL F.   ALSO AS   MURRAY LEINSTER
  DEVIL'S HENCHMAN   SS   ARG 52 05
    SUPERNATURAL READER, THE   CONKLIN, G&L.   AN

JENKINS, WILL F.   (CONTINUED)
  DOOMSDAY DEFERRED   SS   SEP 49 09
    BEST SCIENCE-FICTION STORIES: 1950, THE
                                 BLEILER & DIKTY   AN
    BR-R-R-| CONKLIN, GROFF   AN
    FIRST CONTACT   KNIGHT, DAMON   AN
    POST READER OF FANTASY AND SCIENCE FICTION
                                 SATURDAY EVE. POST   AN
    SATURDAY EVENING POST FANTASY STORIES, THE
                                 FLES, BARTHOLD   AN
    STRANGE BEASTS AND UNNATURAL MONSTERS STERN, PHILIP VAN D. AN
  LITTLE TERROR, THE   SS   SEP 53 08
    MARRIAGE AND THE FAMILY THROUGH SCIENCE FICTION
                                 CLEAR/WARRICK/&   AN
    POST READER OF FANTASY AND SCIENCE FICTION
                                 SATURDAY EVE. POST   AN
    TOMORROW'S CHILDREN   ASIMOV, ISAAC   AN
  NIGHT DRIVE   SS   TDW 60
    *TWISTED   CONKLIN, GROFF   AN
  SYMBIOSIS   SS   COL 47 06
    GREAT STORIES OF SCIENCE FICTION LEINSTER, MURRAY AN
    *OTHER SIDE OF THE MOON, THE DERLETH, AUGUST   AN
    STORIES OF SCIENTIFIC IMAGINATION GALLANT, JOSEPH AN

JENNINGS, GARY
  MURKLE FOR JESSE, A   SS   FSF 65 07
    BEST FROM FANTASY AND SCIENCE FICTION: 15
                                 FERMAN, EDWARD L.   AN
  SOONER OR LATER OR NEVER NEVER   NV   FSF 72 05
    BEST FROM FANTASY AND SCIENCE FICTION: 20
                                 FERMAN, EDWARD L.   AN

JEROME, JEROME K.
  DANCING PARTNER, THE   SS   FFM 51 03
    FROM FRANKENSTEIN TO ANDROMEDA BROWN, JAMES GOLDIE AN
  PASSING OF THE THIRD FLOOR BACK   NV
    ODDBALLS, THE   GHIDALIA, VIC   AN

JESBY, EDWARD
  OGRE| NV   FSF 68 09
    BEST FROM FANTASY AND SCIENCE FICTION: 18
                                 FERMAN, EDWARD L.   AN
  SEA WRACK   NV   FSF 64 05
    SCIENCE FICTION ARGOSY, A   KNIGHT, DAMON   AN
    WORLD'S BEST SCIENCE FICTION: 1965 WOLLHEIM & CARR AN

JESCHKE, WOLFGANG
  KING AND THE DOLLMAKER, THE   NA   70
    BEST FROM THE REST OF THE WORLD, THE WOLLHEIM, DONALD A. AN
  LITTLE MORE THAN TWELVE MINUTES, A   NV   NWR 75 25
    NEW WRITINGS IN SF. 25   BULMER, KENNETH   OA

JESSEL, JOHN   PSEUD. FOR STANLEY G. WEINBAUM
  ADAPTIVE ULTIMATE, THE   NV   ASF 35 11
    OTHER WORLDS, THE   STONG, PHILIP D.   AN

JEWETT, SARAH ORNE
  WHITE HERON, A   SS
    ECO-FICTION   STADLER, JOHN   AN

JOBLING, PETER
  BUILDING BLOCKS   NV   NWB 75 08
    NEW WORLDS EIGHT   BAILEY, HILARY   OA

JOHANNESSON, OLOF
  FROM: THE TALE OF THE BIG COMPUTER   EX   GOL 68
    INSIDE INFORMATION   MOWSHOWITZ, ABBE   AN

JOHNSON, BILL
  STORMFALL   SS
    CLARION SF   WILHELM, KATE   OA

JOHNSON, DORIS
  TRANSLATION   MS
    RUSSIAN SCIENCE FICTION   MAGIDOFF, ROBERT   AN

JOHNSON, GEORGE CLAYTON
  ALL OF US ARE DYING   SS   ROG 61 10
    SF: AUTHORS' CHOICE 4   HARRISON, HARRY   AN
  FREEWAY, THE   SS   GAM 63 01
    MAN AGAINST TOMORROW   NOLAN, WILLIAM F.   AN
  HORNET, THE   SS   ROG 62 09
    FIEND IN YOU, THE   BEAUMONT, CHARLES   AN

JOHNSON, HUGH S.
  DAM, THE   SS   RBM 11 04
    SCIENCE FICTION BY GASLIGHT   MOSKOWITZ, SAM   AN

JOHNSON, JOSEPHINE
  NIGHT FLIGHT   SS   HRP 44 02
    TIMELESS STORIES FOR TODAY AND TOMORROW
                                 BRADBURY, RAY   AN

JOHNSON, LESLIE T.
  SEEKER OF TOMORROW   SN C ASF 37 07
    HISTORY OF THE SCIENCE FICTION MAGAZINE, THE PART 2 1936-1945
                                 ASHLEY, MICHAEL   AN
    SCIENCE FICTION OF THE 30'S   KNIGHT, DAMON   AN

JOHNSON, ROBERT B.
  FAR BELOW   SS   WRT 39 06
    EDITOR'S CHOICE IN SCIENCE FICTION MOSKOWITZ, SAM AN

JOHNSON, RONALD
  INVADERS, THE   PM   69
    HOLDING YOUR EIGHT HANDS   LUCIE-SMITH, EDWARD AN

JOHNSON, S. S.

JOHNSON, S. S.
HOUSE BY THE CRAB APPLE TREE, THE   NV   FSF 64 02
   BEST FROM FANTASY AND SCIENCE FICTION: 14
                                     DAVIDSON, AVRAM   AN

JOHNSON, VERA
DAY THEY CUT OFF THE POWER, THE   SS   NWR 75 27
   NEW WRITINGS IN SF. 27   BULMER, KENNETH   OA

JOHNSON, W. R.
EXCHANGE OF MEN   SS C STO 63 01
   NIGHT IN FUNLAND   BRONDFIELD, JEROME   AN

JOHNSTON, GEORGE
VALE, POLLINI| SS
   SECOND PACIFIC BOOK OF SCIENCE FICTION, THE
                                     BAXTER, JOHN   AN

JONAS, GERALD
IMAGINARY NUMBERS IN A REAL GARDEN   PM   FSF 65 04
   BEST FROM FANTASY AND SCIENCE FICTION: 16
                                     FERMAN, EDWARD L.   AN
SHAKER REVIVAL, THE   NV   GAL 70 02
   ALPHA 2   SILVERBERG, ROBERT   AN
   RUINS OF EARTH, THE   DISCH, THOMAS M.   AN
   SOCIOLOGY THROUGH SCIENCE FICTION MILSTEAD/GREENBERG/& AN
   WORLD'S BEST SCIENCE FICTION: 1971 WOLLHEIM & CARR   AN

JONES, ALICE ELEANOR
CREATED HE THEM   SS   FSF 55 06
   BEST FROM FANTASY AND SCIENCE FICTION: 5
                                     BOUCHER, ANTHONY   AN

JONES, EDDIE
SCIENCE FICTION COVER ILLUSTRATIONS   IL
   BEYOND THIS HORIZON   CARRELL, CHRISTOPHER OA

JONES, ELIS GWYN
WHEN THE ENGINES HAD TO STOP   SS   NEW 64 AN
   OUT OF THIS WORLD 4   WILLIAMS-ELLIS& OWEN AN

JONES, LANGDON
EYE OF THE LENS, THE   AC H MAC 72
NEW S.F., THE   OA H HUT 69
BIOGRAPHICAL NOTE ON LUDWIG VAN BEETHOVEN II   FA   NWS 68 10
   BEST SF STORIES FROM NEW WORLDS 5 MOORCOCK, MICHAEL   AN
COMING OF THE SUN, THE   SS   NWS 68 03
   EYE OF THE LENS, THE   JONES, LANGDON   AC
   SF: AUTHORS' CHOICE 3   HARRISON, HARRY   AN
EYE OF THE LENS, THE   SS   NWS 68 03
   BEST SF STORIES FROM NEW WORLDS 6 MOORCOCK, MICHAEL   AN
   EYE OF THE LENS, THE   JONES, LANGDON   AC
FLOWER-GATHERING   PM   NWS 69 06
   BEST SF STORIES FROM NEW WORLDS 7 MOORCOCK, MICHAEL   AN
GARDEN OF DELIGHTS, THE   NV   NWS 69 07
   EYE OF THE LENS, THE   JONES, LANGDON   AC
   NEW TOMORROWS, THE   SPINRAD, NORMAN   AN
GREAT CLOCK, THE   SS   NWS 66 03
   BEST SF STORIES FROM NEW WORLDS 3 MOORCOCK, MICHAEL   AN
   EYE OF THE LENS, THE   JONES, LANGDON   AC
   TRAPS OF TIME, THE   MOORCOCK, MICHAEL   AN
HALL OF MACHINES, THE   SS   NWS 68 03
   ENGLAND SWINGS SF   MERRIL, JUDITH   AN
   EYE OF THE LENS, THE   JONES, LANGDON   AC
   SPACE-TIME JOURNAL, THE   MERRIL, JUDITH   AN
I REMEMBER, ANITA   SS   NWS 64 10
   BEST OF NEW WORLDS, THE   MOORCOCK, MICHAEL   AN
INTRODUCTION   IN
   EYE OF THE LENS, THE   JONES, LANGDON   AC
MUSIC MAKERS, THE   SS   NWS 65 11
   BEST SF STORIES FROM NEW WORLDS NO. 1, THE
                                     MOORCOCK, MICHAEL   AN
SYMPHONY NO. 6 IN C MINOR "THE TRAGIC"- BY LUDWIG VAN
   BEETHOVEN II   FA   NWS 68 10
   EYE OF THE LENS, THE   JONES, LANGDON   AC
TIME MACHINE, THE   NV   ORB 69 05
   BEST FROM ORBIT, THE   KNIGHT, DAMON   AN
   EYE OF THE LENS, THE   JONES, LANGDON   AC
   ORBIT   5   KNIGHT, DAMON   OA
TRANSIENT   SS   NWS 65 12
   BEST SF STORIES FROM NEW WORLDS 4 MOORCOCK, MICHAEL   AN
TRANSPLANT   PM   NWS 69 10
   BEST SF STORIES FROM NEW WORLDS 7 MOORCOCK, MICHAEL   AN

JONES, LEROI
PLANETARY EXCHANGE   PM   69
   SPECULATIONS   SANDERS, THOMAS E.   AN

JONES, NEIL R.
DOOMSDAY ON AJIAT   AC   ACE 68
PLANET OF THE DOUBLE SUN   AC   ACE 67
SPACE WAR   AC   ACE 67
SUNLESS WORLD, THE   AC   ACE 67
TWIN WORLDS   AC   ACE 67
ACCELERATED WORLD, THE   NV   NEW 68 AC
   DOOMSDAY ON AJIAT   JONES, NEIL R.   AC
DOOMSDAY ON AJIAT   SS   AST 42 10
   DOOMSDAY ON AJIAT   JONES, NEIL R.   AC
HERMIT OF SATURN'S RING   SS   PLS 40 FL
   FLIGHT INTO SPACE   WOLLHEIM, DONALD A. AN
   HISTORY OF THE SCIENCE FICTION MAGAZINE, THE PART 2 1936-1945
                                     ASHLEY, MICHAEL   AN
IN THE METEORIC CLOUD   NV   NEW 68 AC
   DOOMSDAY ON AJIAT   JONES, NEIL R.   AC
INTO THE HYDROSPHERE   SS   AMZ 33 10
   SUNLESS WORLD, THE   JONES, NEIL R.   AC

JONES, RAYMOND F.

JONES, NEIL R.   (CONTINUED)
JAMESON SATELLITE, THE   SS   AMZ 31 07
   BEFORE THE GOLDEN AGE   ASIMOV, ISAAC   AN
   PLANET OF THE DOUBLE SUN   JONES, NEIL R.   AC
LABYRINTH   NV   AMZ 36 04
   SPACE WAR   JONES, NEIL R.   AC
METAL MOON, THE   NV   SSS 49 09
   DOOMSDAY ON AJIAT   JONES, NEIL R.   AC
MUSIC MONSTERS, THE   NV   AMZ 38 04
   TWIN WORLDS   JONES, NEIL R.   AC
ON THE PLANET FRAGMENT   NV   AMZ 37 10
   TWIN WORLDS   JONES, NEIL R.   AC
PLANET OF THE DOUBLE SUN   SS   AMZ 32 02
   PLANET OF THE DOUBLE SUN   JONES, NEIL R.   AC
RETURN OF THE TRIPEDS, THE   SS   AMZ 32 05
   PLANET OF THE DOUBLE SUN   JONES, NEIL R.   AC
SPACE WAR   NV   AMZ 35 07
   SPACE WAR   JONES, NEIL R.   AC
SUNLESS WORLD, THE   NV   AMZ 34 12
   SUNLESS WORLD, THE   JONES, NEIL R.   AC
TIME'S MAUSOLEUM   SS   AMZ 33 12
   SUNLESS WORLD, THE   JONES, NEIL R.   AC
TWIN WORLDS   NV   AMZ 37 04
   TWIN WORLDS   JONES, NEIL R.   AC
ZORA OF THE ZOROMES   NV   AMZ 35 03
   SPACE WAR   JONES, NEIL R.   AC

JONES, RAYMOND F.
NON-STATISTICAL MAN, THE   AC   BEL 64
THIS ISLAND EARTH   NO H SHS 52
TOYMAKER, THE   AC H FPB 51
ALIEN MACHINE, THE   NV   TWS 49 06
   THIS ISLAND EARTH   JONES, RAYMOND F.   NO
BOWL OF BISKIES MAKES A GROWING BOY, A   NV
   OTHER SIDE OF TOMORROW, THE   ELWOOD, ROGER   OA
CHILDREN'S HOUR, THE   NV   FAD 47 09
   TOYMAKER, THE   JONES, RAYMOND F.   AC
COLONISTS, THE   NV   IFS 54 06
   SECOND WORLD OF IF, THE   QUINN & WULFF   AN
CORRESPONDENCE COURSE   SS   ASF 45 04
   *ADVENTURES IN TIME AND SPACE   HEALY & MCCOMAS   AN
DEADLY HOST   SS   ASF 45 09
   TOYMAKER, THE   JONES, RAYMOND F.   AC
DISCONTINUITY   NV   ASF 50 10
   SEVEN COME INFINITY   CONKLIN, GROFF   AN
DOOMSDAY'S COLOR-PRESS   NV   FUT 52 11
   ESCAPE TO EARTH   HOWARD, IVAN   AN
FARTHEST HORIZON, THE   SS   ASF 52 04
   SPACE PIONEERS   NORTON, ANDRE   AN
   *STORIES FOR TOMORROW   SLOANE, WILLIAM   AN
FLAUNA   NV
   FAR SIDE OF TIME, THE   ELWOOD, ROGER   OA
FORECAST   NV   ASF 46 06
   TOYMAKER, THE   JONES, RAYMOND F.   AC
GARDENER, THE   SS   SFS 57 07
   NON-STATISTICAL MAN, THE   JONES, RAYMOND F.   AC
GIFT OF THE GODS, THE   NV   SFS 55 01
   LEARNING MAZE AND OTHER STORIES, THE ELWOOD, ROGER   OA
   THINGS   HOWARD, IVAN   AN
GREATER CONFLICT, THE   NV   TWS 50 02
   THIS ISLAND EARTH   JONES, RAYMOND F.   NO
INTERMISSION TIME   NV   SFQ 53 05
   NON-STATISTICAL MAN, THE   JONES, RAYMOND F.   AC
LAUGHING LION, THE   SS   SFT 73
   SCIENCE FICTION TALES   ELWOOD, ROGER   OA
LIGHTS OF MARS, THE   NV
   SCIENCE FICTION ADVENTURES FROM WAY OUT
                                     ELWOOD, ROGER   OA
LIONS OF ROME, THE   SS   FTP 73
   FLAME TREE PLANET   ELWOOD, ROGER   OA
MODEL SHOP, THE   SS   ASF 47 06
   TOYMAKER, THE   JONES, RAYMOND F.   AC
MOON IS DEATH, THE   SS   FUT 53 03
   NON-STATISTICAL MAN, THE   JONES, RAYMOND F.   AC
NOISE LEVEL   NV   ASF 52 12
   ASTOUNDING-ANALOG READER, THE VOLUME TWO
                                     HARRISON & ALDISS   AN
   BEST SF 5   CRISPIN, EDMUND   AN
   SPECTRUM 5   AMIS & CONQUEST   AN
   *STORIES FOR TOMORROW   SLOANE, WILLIAM   AN
NON-STATISTICAL MAN, THE   NA   SFS 56 05
   NON-STATISTICAL MAN, THE   JONES, RAYMOND F.   AC
PACER   NV
   FUTURE KIN   ELWOOD, ROGER   OA
PERSON FROM PORLOCK, THE   NV   ASF 47 08
   *TREASURY OF SCIENCE FICTION, A CONKLIN, GROFF   AN
PET   NV   FUQ 73
   FUTURE QUEST   ELWOOD, ROGER   OA
PETE CAN FIX IT   SS   ASF 47 02
   ADVENTURES IN DIMENSION   CONKLIN, GROFF   AN
   *SCIENCE FICTION ADVENTURES IN DIMENSION
                                     CONKLIN, GROFF   AN
PRODUCTION TEST   NV   ASF 49 10
   LOOKING FORWARD   LESSER, MILTON   AN
RAT RACE   SS   ASF 66 04
   ABOVE THE HUMAN LANDSCAPE   MCNELLY & STOVER   AN
   YOU AND SCIENCE FICTION   HOLLISTER, BERNARD C AN
REFLECTIONS FROM A STAR   SS
   SURVIVAL FROM INFINITY   ELWOOD, ROGER   OA
SHROUD OF SECRECY, THE   NV   TWS 49 12
   THIS ISLAND EARTH   JONES, RAYMOND F.   NO
STONE AND A SPEAR, A   NV   GAL 50 12
   OMNIBUS OF SCIENCE FICTION   CONKLIN, GROFF   AN
   STRANGE TRAVELS IN SCIENCE FICTION CONKLIN, GROFF   AN
TIME BROTHER   NV   COI 73
   CHILDREN OF INFINITY   ELWOOD, ROGER   OA

JONES, RAYMOND F.   (CONTINUED)
    TOOLS OF THE TRADE   NV   ASF 50 11
    SPACE, SPACE, SPACE   SLOANE, WILLIAM   AN
    TOYMAKER, THE   NV   ASF 46 09
    TOYMAKER, THE   JONES, RAYMOND F.   AC
    UTILITY   SS   ASF 44 07
    TOYMAKER, THE   JONES, RAYMOND F.   AC

JONES, ROGER
    ISLAND, THE   SS   SCF 65 02
    ENGLAND SWINGS SF   MERRIL, JUDITH   AN
    SPACE-TIME JOURNAL, THE   MERRIL, JUDITH   AN

JOOS, DONALD A.   SEE ALSO   CO-EDITOR BONNIE L. HEINTZ
    PREFACE   IN C
    TOMORROW, AND TOMORROW, AND TOMORROW...
                                   HEINTZ/HERBERT/JOOS/ AN

JORGENSSON, A. K.
    COMING-OF-AGE DAY   SS   SCF 65 09
    ABOVE THE HUMAN LANDSCAPE   MCNELLY & STOVER   AN
    DARK STARS   SILVERBERG, ROBERT   AN
    FUTURE POWER   DANN & DOZOIS   OA
    11TH ANNUAL OF THE YEAR'S BEST S-F, THE
                                   MERRIL, JUDITH   AN

JOURDAN, D. A.
    CHILDREN OF FORTUNE   NV   SFQ 57 02
    6 AND THE SILENT SCREAM   HOWARD, IVAN   AN

JOYCE, MICHAEL
    PERFORCE TO DREAM   SS
    BEST FANTASY STORIES   ALDISS, BRIAN W.   AN

JUSTER, NORTON
    MILO AND THE MATHEMAGICIAN   SS   61
    MATHEMATICAL MAGPIE, THE   FADIMAN, CLIFTON   AN

KAEMPFFERT, WALDEMAR
    DIMINISHING DRAFT, THE   SS   ASW 18 02
    *BIG BOOK OF SCIENCE FICTION   CONKLIN, GROFF   AN

KAFKA, FRANZ
    BURROW, THE   SS   46
    *TERROR IN THE MODERN VEIN   WOLLHEIM, DONALD A. AN
    IN THE PENAL COLONY   SS   48
    TIMELESS STORIES FOR TODAY AND TOMORROW
                                   BRADBURY, RAY   AN
    METAMORPHOSIS   NV   37
    WORLD OF WONDER   PRATT, FLETCHER   AN

KAGAN, NORMAN
    COUNTER ECOLOGY   SS
    TOMORROW TODAY   ZEBROWSKI, GEORGE   OA
    DREADFUL HAS ALREADY HAPPENED, THE   SS   NEW 71 AN
    RUINS OF EARTH, THE   DISCH, THOMAS M.   AN
    FOUR BRANDS OF IMPOSSIBLE   NV   FSF 64 09
    SCHOOL AND SOCIETY THROUGH SCIENCE FICTION
                                   OLANDER/GREENBERG/&   AN
    SCIENCE FICTION ARGOSY, A   KNIGHT, DAMON   AN
    WORLD'S BEST SCIENCE FICTION: 1965 WOLLHEIM & CARR   AN
    MATHENAUTS, THE   NV   IFS 64 07
    10TH ANNUAL OF THE YEAR'S BEST S-F, THE
                                   MERRIL, JUDITH   AN

KAHN, BERNARD I.
    COMMAND   NV   ASF 47 01
    GATES TO TOMORROW   NORTON, AN.&DONALDY AN
    SPACE SERVICE   NORTON, ANDRE   AN
    FOR THE PUBLIC   NV   ASF 46 12
    SPACE SERVICE   NORTON, ANDRE   AN

KALDOR, STEVE
    WHATEVER HAPPENED TO SUDEROV?   SS
    SECOND PACIFIC BOOK OF SCIENCE FICTION, THE
                                   BAXTER, JOHN   AN

KALETSKY, MILTON
    SPACE-SHIP DERBY   SS   SFQ 40 SU
    MOON CONQUERORS, THE   ANONYMOUS   AN

KANDEL, MICHAEL
    INTRODUCTION   IN
    MORTAL ENGINES   LEM, STANISLAW   AC

KANE, WILSON   PSEUD. FOR ROBERT BLOCH

KANIN, GARSON
    DAMNEDEST THING, THE   SS   ESQ 56 02
    SF:57, THE YEAR'S GREATEST SCIENCE FICTION AND FANTASY
                                   MERRIL, JUDITH   AN

KANTOR, MACKINLAY
    SECOND CHALLENGE, THE   SS   RDT 29
    FANTASTIC PULPS, THE   HAINING, PETER   AN

KAPP, COLIN
    AMBASSADOR TO VERDAMMT   SS   ASF 67 04
    WORLD'S BEST SCIENCE FICTION: 1968 WOLLHEIM & CARR   AN
    BLACK HOLE OF NEGRAV, THE   NV   NWR 75 25
    NEW WRITINGS IN SF. 25   BULMER, KENNETH   AN
    CASSIUS AND THE MIND-JAUNT   SS   NWR 75 27
    NEW WRITINGS IN SF. 27   BULMER, KENNETH   OA
    CLOUDBUILDERS, THE   NV   NWR 68 12
    NEW WRITINGS IN SF. 12   CARNELL, JOHN   OA

KAPP, COLIN   (CONTINUED)
    TOMORROW, AND TOMORROW, AND TOMORROW...
                                   HEINTZ/HERBERT/JOOS/ AN
    WORLD'S BEST SCIENCE FICTION: 1969 WOLLHEIM & CARR   AN
    GETAWAY FROM GETAWEHI   NA   NWR 69 16
    NEW WRITINGS IN SF. 16   CARNELL, JOHN   OA
    GOTTLOS   NV   ASF 69 11
    ANALOG 8   CAMPBELL, JOHN W. JR AN
    HUNGER OVER SWEET WATERS   NV   NWR 65 04
    NEW WRITINGS IN SF. 4   CARNELL, JOHN   OA
    IMAGINATION TRAP, THE   NV   NWR 67 10
    NEW WRITINGS IN SF. 8   CARNELL, JOHN   AN
    NEW WRITINGS IN SF. 10   CARNELL, JOHN   OA
    LAMBDA I   NV   NWS 62 12
    LAMBDA I AND OTHER STORIES   CARNELL, JOHN   AN
    MEPHISTO & THE ION EXPLORER   NV   IFS 74 10
    BEST FROM IF, THE VOLUME III BAEN, JAMES   AN
    NIGHT-FLAME, THE   NV   NWR 64 02
    BEST FROM NEW WRITINGS IN S-F FIRST SELECTION, THE
                                   CARNELL, JOHN   AN
    NEW WRITINGS IN SF. 2   CARNELL, JOHN   OA
    PEN AND THE DARK, THE   NV   NWR 66 08
    NEW WRITINGS IN SF. 7   CARNELL, JOHN   AN
    NEW WRITINGS IN SF. 8   CARNELL, JOHN   OA
    RAILWAYS UP ON CANNIS, THE   SS   NWS 59 10
    BEST OF NEW WORLDS, THE   MOORCOCK, MICHAEL   AN
    OUT OF THIS WORLD 2   WILLIAMS-ELLIS& OWEN AN
    SUBWAYS OF TAZOO, THE   NV   NWR 65 03
    BEST FROM NEW WRITINGS IN S-F FIRST SELECTION, THE
                                   CARNELL, JOHN   AN
    NEW WRITINGS IN SF. 3   CARNELL, JOHN   OA
    WHAT THE THUNDER SAID   SS   NWR 73 21
    NEW WRITINGS IN SF. 21   CARNELL, JOHN   OA
    WHICH WAY DO I GO FOR JERICHO?   NV   NWR 72 20
    NEW WRITINGS IN SF. 20   CARNELL, JOHN   OA

KARAGEORGE, MICHAEL PSEUD. FOR POUL ANDERSON

KARL, JEAN E.
    TURNING PLACE, THE   OC H DUT 76
    STORIES OF A FUTURE PAST
    ACCORD   NV
    TURNING PLACE, THE   KARL, JEAN E.   OC
    CATABILID CONQUEST   NV
    TURNING PLACE, THE   KARL, JEAN E.   OC
    CENTRAL QUESTION, A   NV
    TURNING PLACE, THE   KARL, JEAN E.   OC
    ENOUGH   SS
    TURNING PLACE, THE   KARL, JEAN E.   OC
    OUT OF THE FLICKER PATH   SS
    TURNING PLACE, THE   KARL, JEAN E.   OC
    OVER THE HILL   SS
    TURNING PLACE, THE   KARL, JEAN E.   OC
    QUIET AND A WHITE BUSH   SS
    TURNING PLACE, THE   KARL, JEAN E.   OC
    SOME NOTES ON SOURCES   MS
    TURNING PLACE, THE   KARL, JEAN E.   OC
    TALKAROUND, THE   SS
    TURNING PLACE, THE   KARL, JEAN E.   OC
    TURNING PLACE, THE   NV
    TURNING PLACE, THE   KARL, JEAN E.   OC

KASSON, HELEN W.
    PLEASE GO 'WAY AND LET ME SLEEP   SS   WRT 45 03
    GHOUL KEEPERS, THE   MARGULIES, LEO   AN

KATZ, HARVEY A., PATRICIA S. WARRICK AND MARTIN H. GREENBERG
    INTRODUCTORY PSYCHOLOGY THROUGH SCIENCE FICTION   AN L RAN 74

KATZ, HARVEY A.
    PREFACE   IN C
    INTRODUCTORY PSYCHOLOGY THROUGH SCIENCE FICTION
                                   KATZ/WARRICK/&   AN

KAWALEC, JULIAN
    I KILL MYSELF   SS   62
    TRANSFORMATIONS   ROSELLE, DANIEL   AN
    VINTAGE ANTHOLOGY OF SCIENCE FANTASY, THE
                                   CERF, CHRISTOPHER   AN

KAWIN, BRUCE
    FORM 5640: REPORT OF A MALFUNCTION   SS   DPM 67
    INSIDE INFORMATION   MOWSHOWITZ, ABBE   AN

KAZANTSEV, ALEXANDER
    MARTIAN, THE   SS
    SOVIET SCIENCE FICTION   ANONYMOUS   AN
    VISITOR FROM OUTER SPACE, A   SS
    SOVIET SCIENCE FICTION   ANONYMOUS   AN

KEARNS, WINN
    RAPE OF OOOOOOO, THE   SS
    NEW CONSTELLATIONS   DISCH & NAYLOR   OA

KEELER, HARRY S.
    JOHN JONES' DOLLAR   SS   BLC 15 08
    FANTASIA MATHEMATICA   FADIMAN, CLIFTON   AN
    *STRANGE PORTS OF CALL   DERLETH, AUGUST   AN

KEENE, DAY
    WHAT SO PROUDLY WE HAIL...   SS   IMG 50 12
    ADVENTURES IN DIMENSION   CONKLIN, GROFF   AN
    *SCIENCE FICTION ADVENTURES IN DIMENSION
                                   CONKLIN, GROFF   AN

KEIGHTLEY, DAVID H.

KEIGHTLEY, DAVID H. SEE PSEUD. NOEL KEYES

KEILTY, JAMES
  PEOPLE OF PRASHAD, THE   NV   QRK 71 02
    NEW IMPROVED SUN, THE   DISCH, THOMAS M.   AN
    QUARK/2   DELANY & HACKER   OA

KEITH, JOHN
  PLANET CALLED CERVANTES, A   SS   NWR 75 26
    NEW WRITINGS IN SF. 26   BULMER, KENNETH   OA

KELLEAM, JOSEPH E.
  EAGLES GATHER, THE   SS   ASF 42 04
    CROSSROADS IN TIME   CONKLIN, GROFF   AN
  RUST   SS   ASF 39 10
    GATES TO TOMORROW   NORTON, AN.&DONALDY   AN
    ROBOT AND THE MAN, THE   GREENBERG , MARTIN   AN

KELLENBERGER, L. C. SEE PSEUD. HENRY JAMES

KELLER, B. L.
  BIRDLIME   SS   FSF 71 03
    BEST FROM FANTASY AND SCIENCE FICTION: 20
                                   FERMAN, EDWARD L.   AN

KELLER, DAVID H. MD.
  FOLSOM FLINT AND OTHER CURIOUS TALES, THE   AC H ARK 69
  LIFE EVERLASTING AND OTHER TALES OF SCIENCE, FANTASY
    AND HORROR   AC H AVL 49
    EDITED BY SAM MOSKOWITZ
  TALES FROM UNDERWOOD   AC H PEL 52
  AIR LINES   SS   AMZ 30 01
    FOLSOM FLINT AND OTHER CURIOUS TALES, THE
                                   KELLER, DAVID H. MD. AC
  BIOLOGICAL EXPERIMENT, A   SS   AMZ 28 06
    TALES FROM UNDERWOOD   KELLER, DAVID H. MD. AC
  BONELESS HORROR, THE   SS   SWS 29 07
    LIFE EVERLASTING AND OTHER TALES OF SCIENCE, FANTASY
    AND HORROR   KELLER, DAVID H. MD. AC
  BRIDLE, THE   SS   WRT 42 09
    TALES FROM UNDERWOOD   KELLER, DAVID H. MD. AC
  CEREBRAL LIBRARY, THE   SS   AMZ 31 05
    LIFE EVERLASTING AND OTHER TALES OF SCIENCE, FANTASY
    AND HORROR   KELLER, DAVID H. MD. AC
  CHASM OF MONSTERS   SS   51
    FOLSOM FLINT AND OTHER CURIOUS TALES, THE
                                   KELLER, DAVID H. MD. AC
  CREATION UNFORGIVABLE   SS   WRT 30 04
    TALES FROM UNDERWOOD   KELLER, DAVID H. MD. AC
  DEAD WOMAN, THE (STE 39 04)   SS   FMG 34 04
    FOLSOM FLINT AND OTHER CURIOUS TALES, THE
                                   KELLER, DAVID H. MD. AC
    LIFE EVERLASTING AND OTHER TALES OF SCIENCE, FANTASY
    AND HORROR   KELLER, DAVID H. MD. AC
    TALES FROM UNDERWOOD   KELLER, DAVID H. MD. AC
  DOOR, THE   SS   ARS 49 SU
    TALES FROM UNDERWOOD   KELLER, DAVID H. MD. AC
  DOORBELL, THE   SS   WOS 34 06
    OMNIBUS OF SCIENCE FICTION   CONKLIN, GROFF   AN
    STRANGE ADVENTURES IN SCIENCE FICTION CONKLIN, GROFF AN
    TALES FROM UNDERWOOD   KELLER, DAVID H. MD. AC
  DUST IN THE HOUSE   SS   WRT 38 07
    FOLSOM FLINT AND OTHER CURIOUS TALES, THE
                                   KELLER, DAVID H. MD. AC
  FACE IN THE MIRROR, THE   SS
    LIFE EVERLASTING AND OTHER TALES OF SCIENCE, FANTASY
    AND HORROR   KELLER, DAVID H. MD. AC
  FEMININE METAMORPHOSIS, THE   NA   SWS 29 08
    WHEN WOMEN RULE   MOSKOWITZ, SAM   AN
  FINGERS IN THE SKY   SS   52
    FOLSOM FLINT AND OTHER CURIOUS TALES, THE
                                   KELLER, DAVID H. MD. AC
  FLYING FOOL, THE   SS   AMZ 29 07
    TALES FROM UNDERWOOD   KELLER, DAVID H. MD. AC
  FOLSOM FLINT, THE   SS   52
    FOLSOM FLINT AND OTHER CURIOUS TALES, THE
                                   KELLER, DAVID H. MD. AC
  FREE AS AIR   SS   AMZ 31 06
    TALES FROM UNDERWOOD   KELLER, DAVID H. MD. AC
  GOD WHEEL, THE   SS
    TALES FROM UNDERWOOD   KELLER, DAVID H. MD. AC
  GOLDEN BOUGH, THE   SS   MVT 34 WI
    GARDEN OF FEAR AND OTHER STORIES, THE CRAWFORD, WILLIAM L. AN
    TALES FROM UNDERWOOD   KELLER, DAVID H. MD. AC
  GOLDEN KEY, THE   SS   53
    FOLSOM FLINT AND OTHER CURIOUS TALES, THE
                                   KELLER, DAVID H. MD. AC
  HEREDITY   SS   47
    LIFE EVERLASTING AND OTHER TALES OF SCIENCE, FANTASY
    AND HORROR   KELLER, DAVID H. MD. AC
  IVY WAR, THE   SS   AMZ 30 05
    *BEST OF SCIENCE FICTION   CONKLIN, GROFF   AN
    ROOTS OF EVIL, THE   PARRY, MICHEL   AN
    TALES FROM UNDERWOOD   KELLER, DAVID H. MD. AC
  JELLY FISH, THE   SS   WRT 29 01
    TALES FROM UNDERWOOD   KELLER, DAVID H. MD. AC
  LANDSLIDE, THE   SS
    FOLSOM FLINT AND OTHER CURIOUS TALES, THE
                                   KELLER, DAVID H. MD. AC
  LIFE EVERLASTING   NA   AMZ 34 07
    LIFE EVERLASTING AND OTHER TALES OF SCIENCE, FANTASY
    AND HORROR   KELLER, DAVID H. MD. AC
  LITERARY CORKSCREW, THE   SS   WOS 34 03
    FROM OFF THIS WORLD   MARGULIES & FRIEND   AN
    TALES FROM UNDERWOOD   KELLER, DAVID H. MD. AC

KELLER, DAVID H. MD. (CONTINUED)
  LIVING MACHINE   SS   WOS 35 05
    EVERY BOY'S BOOK OF SCIENCE FICTION WOLLHEIM, DONALD A. AN
  LOST LANGUAGE, THE   SS   AMZ 34 01
    SCIENCE FICTION OF THE 30'S   KNIGHT, DAMON   AN
  MOON ARTIST, THE   SS   STI 41 06
    TALES FROM UNDERWOOD   KELLER, DAVID H. MD. AC
  NO MORE TOMORROWS   SS   AMZ 32 12
    LIFE EVERLASTING AND OTHER TALES OF SCIENCE, FANTASY
    AND HORROR   KELLER, DAVID H. MD. AC
  OPIUM EATER, THE   SS
    TALES FROM UNDERWOOD   KELLER, DAVID H. MD. AC
  PENT HOUSE, THE   SS   AMZ 32 02
    FOLSOM FLINT AND OTHER CURIOUS TALES, THE
                                   KELLER, DAVID H. MD. AC
  PERFUMED GARDEN, THE   SS
    TALES FROM UNDERWOOD   KELLER, DAVID H. MD. AC
  PIECE OF LINOLEUM, A (AS AMY WORTH)   SS   TST 33 12
    FOLSOM FLINT AND OTHER CURIOUS TALES, THE
                                   KELLER, DAVID H. MD. AC
    LIFE EVERLASTING AND OTHER TALES OF SCIENCE, FANTASY
    AND HORROR   KELLER, DAVID H. MD. AC
    TALES FROM UNDERWOOD   KELLER, DAVID H. MD. AC
  PSYCHOPHONIC NURSE, THE   NV   AMZ 28 11
    GREAT SCIENCE FICTION ABOUT DOCTORS CONKLIN, G&FABRICANT AN
    TALES FROM UNDERWOOD   KELLER, DAVID H. MD. AC
  QUESTION, THE   SS
    FOLSOM FLINT AND OTHER CURIOUS TALES, THE
                                   KELLER, DAVID H. MD. AC
  RAT RACKET, THE   SS   AMZ 31 11
    SATAN'S PETS   GHIDALIA, VIC   AN
  RED DEATH, THE   NV   COS 41 07
    FOLSOM FLINT AND OTHER CURIOUS TALES, THE
                                   KELLER, DAVID H. MD. AC
  REVOLT OF THE PEDESTRIANS, THE   SS   AMZ 28 02
    *BEYOND TIME AND SPACE   DERLETH, AUGUST   AN
    TALES FROM UNDERWOOD   KELLER, DAVID H. MD. AC
  SARAH   SS   52
    FOLSOM FLINT AND OTHER CURIOUS TALES, THE
                                   KELLER, DAVID H. MD. AC
  SERVICE FIRST   SS   AMQ 31 WI
    *OUTER REACHES, THE   DERLETH, AUGUST   AN
  STAR, THE   SS
    *BEACHHEADS IN SPACE   DERLETH, AUGUST   AN
  THING IN THE CELLAR, THE   SS   WRT 32 03
    FOLSOM FLINT AND OTHER CURIOUS TALES, THE
                                   KELLER, DAVID H. MD. AC
    LIFE EVERLASTING AND OTHER TALES OF SCIENCE, FANTASY
    AND HORROR   KELLER, DAVID H. MD. AC
    SUPERNATURAL READER, THE   CONKLIN, G&L.   AN
    TALES FROM UNDERWOOD   KELLER, DAVID H. MD. AC
    *TWISTED   CONKLIN, GROFF   AN
    WORLDS OF WEIRD   MARGULIES, LEO   AN
  THIRTY AND ONE, THE   SS   MAR 38 11
    LIFE EVERLASTING AND OTHER TALES OF SCIENCE, FANTASY
    AND HORROR   KELLER, DAVID H. MD. AC
  TIGER CAT   SS   WRT 37 10
    TALES FROM UNDERWOOD   KELLER, DAVID H. MD. AC
  TWENTIETH CENTURY HOMUNCULUS, A   NV   AMZ 30 02
    FANTASTIC PULPS, THE   HAINING, PETER   AN
  TWINS, THE   SS
    FOLSOM FLINT AND OTHER CURIOUS TALES, THE
                                   KELLER, DAVID H. MD. AC
  UNTO US A CHILD IS BORN   SS   AMZ 33 07
    FOLSOM FLINT AND OTHER CURIOUS TALES, THE
                                   KELLER, DAVID H. MD. AC
    LIFE EVERLASTING AND OTHER TALES OF SCIENCE, FANTASY
    AND HORROR   KELLER, DAVID H. MD. AC
  WHITE CITY, THE   SS   AMZ 35 05
    FOLSOM FLINT AND OTHER CURIOUS TALES, THE
                                   KELLER, DAVID H. MD. AC
  WORM, THE   SS   AMZ 29 03
    BEST OF AMAZING, THE   ROSS, JOSEPH   AN
    BR-R-R-| CONKLIN, GROFF   AN
    CREATURES FROM BEYOND   CARR, TERRY   AN
    *STRANGE PORTS OF CALL   DERLETH, AUGUST   AN
    TALES FROM UNDERWOOD   KELLER, DAVID H. MD. AC
  YEAST MEN, THE   SS   AMZ 28 04
    TALES FROM UNDERWOOD   KELLER, DAVID H. MD. AC

KELLER, TEDDY
  PLAGUE, THE   SS   ASF 61 02
    ANALOG 1   CAMPBELL, JOHN W. JR AN

KELLEY, DEFOREST
  INTRODUCTION TO THE WINGED DREAMERS   IN
    STAR TREK: THE NEW VOYAGES   MARSHAK, S&CULBREATH OA

KELLEY, LEO P.
  FANTASY: THE LITERATURE OF THE MARVELOUS   AN L MGH 74
  THEMES IN SCIENCE FICTION   AN L MGH 72
    A JOURNEY INTO WONDER
  COLD, THE FIRE OF THE PHOENIX   SS   PRT 71
    PROTOSTARS   GERROLD & GOLDIN   OA
  O'GRADY'S GIRL   SS   FSF 65 12
    FANTASY: THE LITERATURE OF THE MARVELOUS
                                   KELLEY, LEO P.   AN
  PREFACE   IN
    FANTASY: THE LITERATURE OF THE MARVELOUS
                                   KELLEY, LEO P.   AN
  TEACHING PRIME   SS   INY 72 03
    INFINITY 3   HOSKINS, ROBERT   OA
    SCHOOL AND SOCIETY THROUGH SCIENCE FICTION
                                   OLANDER/GREENBERG/&   AN
  TRAVELIN' MAN, THE   SS   FSF 70 09
    THEMES IN SCIENCE FICTION   KELLEY, LEO P.   AN

KELLY, FRANK K.
  INTO THE METEORITE ORBIT   SS   AMZ 33 12
    SCIENCE FICTION OF THE 30'S   KNIGHT, DAMON   AN

KELLY, WALT
  THINKERS, THE   CT   HAS 61 01
    6TH ANNUAL OF THE YEAR'S BEST S-F, THE MERRIL, JUDITH   AN

KEMP, EARL
  SCIENCE-FICTION BOOK INDEX, THE   MS
    BEST SCIENCE FICTION STORIES AND NOVELS: 1955
                                         DIKTY, T. E.   AN
    BEST SCIENCE FICTION STORIES AND NOVELS: 1956
                                         DIKTY, T. E.   AN
    BEST SCIENCE FICTION STORIES AND NOVELS: 9TH SERIES
                                         DIKTY, T. E.   AN

KENNEDY, X. J.
  SPACE: FOR MARTIN GREEN   PM
    SPECULATIONS   SANDERS, THOMAS E.   AN

KENT, KELVIN   PSEUD. FOR HENRY KUTTNER
  COMEDY OF ERAS, THE   SS   TWS 40 09
    OTHER WORLDS, THE   STONG, PHILIP D.   AN

KENT, MORGAN
  FAMILY PORTRAIT   SS   FAN 64 08
    10TH ANNUAL OF THE YEAR'S BEST S-F, THE
                                         MERRIL, JUDITH   AN

KENT, RUSSELL
  CRUISE OF THE S-900, THE   SS
    ADVENTURES TO COME   ESENWEIN, J. BERG   OA

KEPLER, JOHANNES
  MOON-VOYAGE, THE (FROM "SOMNIUM")   EX
    SCIENCE FICTION THROUGH THE AGES 1   EVANS, I. O.   AN
  SOMNIUM (1634)   EX
    *BEYOND TIME AND SPACE   DERLETH, AUGUST   AN

KERR, DAVID
  EPIPHANY FOR ALIENS   SS   DVS 72 02
    AGAIN, DANGEROUS VISIONS   ELLISON, HARLAN   OA

KERR, WALTER H.
  TREAT   PM   FSF 64 11
    BEST FROM FANTASY AND SCIENCE FICTION: 15
                                         FERMAN, EDWARD L.   AN

KERSH, GERALD
  MEN WITHOUT BONES   AC   PKB 62 01
  NIGHTSHADE & DAMNATIONS   AC   FGM 68
  ON AN ODD NOTE   AC   BAL 58
  APE AND THE MYSTERY, THE (THE MYSTERIOUS MONA LISA SMILE)
                                                      SS   SEP 48 06
    MEN WITHOUT BONES   KERSH, GERALD   AC
    NIGHTSHADE & DAMNATIONS   KERSH, GERALD   AC
  BARGAIN WITH CASHEL, A   SS   SEP 63 04
    9TH ANNUAL OF THE YEAR'S BEST S-F, THE MERRIL, JUDITH   AN
  BEGGARS' STONE, THE   SS   ESQ
    ON AN ODD NOTE   KERSH, GERALD   AC
  BONE FOR DEBUNKERS (THE KARMESIN AFFAIR)   SS   SEP 62 12
    NIGHTSHADE & DAMNATIONS   KERSH, GERALD   AC
  BRIGHTON MONSTER, THE (THE MONSTER)   SS   SEP 48 02
    NIGHTSHADE & DAMNATIONS   KERSH, GERALD   AC
    ON AN ODD NOTE   KERSH, GERALD   AC
  BUSTO IS A GHOST, TO MEAN TO GIVE US A FRIGHT!   SS
    NIGHTSHADE & DAMNATIONS   KERSH, GERALD   AC
  CLOCK WITHOUT HANDS   NV   COL 46 10
    MEN WITHOUT BONES   KERSH, GERALD   AC
  COPPER DAHLIA, THE   SS   53
    BEST SF 2   CRISPIN, EDMUND   AN
  CREWEL NEEDLE, THE   SS   ESQ
    ON AN ODD NOTE   KERSH, GERALD   AC
  DANCING DOLL, THE   SS
    MEN WITHOUT BONES   KERSH, GERALD   AC
  EPISTLE OF SIMPLE SIMON, THE   SS   TOM 47
    MEN WITHOUT BONES   KERSH, GERALD   AC
  EXTRAORDINARILY HORRIBLE DUMMY, THE (THE WHISPER) SS CMP 46 04
    ON AN ODD NOTE   KERSH, GERALD   AC
  EYE, THE (THE MURDERER'S EYE)   NV   SEP 57 03
    ON AN ODD NOTE   KERSH, GERALD   AC
  FANTASY OF A HUNTED MAN   SS
    ON AN ODD NOTE   KERSH, GERALD   AC
  FROZEN BEAUTY   SS   58
    NIGHTSHADE & DAMNATIONS   KERSH, GERALD   AC
    ON AN ODD NOTE   KERSH, GERALD   AC
  GENTLEMAN ALL IN BLACK, THE   SS   TDY
    ON AN ODD NOTE   KERSH, GERALD   AC
  HACK, THE   SS
    MEN WITHOUT BONES   KERSH, GERALD   AC
  IMAGINARY HEIR, THE (SEE THE SHADY LIFE OF ANNIBAL)
                                                      TC
  IN A ROOM WITHOUT WALLS   SS   ESQ
    MEN WITHOUT BONES   KERSH, GERALD   AC
  KARMESIN AFFAIR, THE (SEE BONE FOR DEBUNKERS)   TC
  KING WHO COLLECTED CLOCKS, THE (ROYAL IMPOSTOR)   NV   SEP 47 05
    NIGHTSHADE & DAMNATIONS   KERSH, GERALD   AC
  LADIES OR CLOTHES   SS   ESQ
    MEN WITHOUT BONES   KERSH, GERALD   AC
  LUCKY DAY FOR THE BOAR, A   SS   PBY 62 10
    NIGHTSHADE & DAMNATIONS   KERSH, GERALD   AC
  MADWOMAN, THE   SS
    MEN WITHOUT BONES   KERSH, GERALD   AC
  MEN WITHOUT BONES   SS   ESQ
    ANCIENT MYSTERIES READER, THE   HAINING, PETER   AN

KERSH, GERALD   (CONTINUED)
    MEN WITHOUT BONES   KERSH, GERALD   AC
    NIGHTSHADE & DAMNATIONS   KERSH, GERALD   AC
  MISTRESS OF PORCOSITO (SEE THE QUEEN OF PIG ISLAND)
                                                      TC
  MONSTER, THE (ALSO AS THE BRIGHTON MONSTER)   SS   SEP 48 02
    *OTHER SIDE OF THE MOON, THE   DERLETH, AUGUST   AN
  MURDERER'S EYE, THE (SEE THE EYE)   TC
  MYSTERIOUS MONA LISA SMILE, THE (SEE THE APE AND THE MYSTERY)
                                                      TC
  MYSTERY OF THE BOTTLE, THE (SEE THE OXOXOCO BOTTLE)
                                                      TC
  NOTE ON DANGER B   SS   SEP 47 04
    SATURDAY EVENING POST FANTASY STORIES, THE
                                         PLES, BARTHOLD   AN
  OXOXOCO BOTTLE, THE (THE MYSTERY OF THE BOTTLE)   NV   SEP 57 12
    MEN WITHOUT BONES   KERSH, GERALD   AC
  PROPHET WITHOUT HONOR   SS
    ON AN ODD NOTE   KERSH, GERALD   AC
  QUEEN OF PIG ISLAND, THE (MISTRESS OF PORCOSITO) SS   PBY 57 07
    NIGHTSHADE & DAMNATIONS   KERSH, GERALD   AC
    ON AN ODD NOTE   KERSH, GERALD   AC
  REFLECTIONS IN A TABLESPOON   SS
    ON AN ODD NOTE   KERSH, GERALD   AC
  RIVER OF RICHES   SS   SEP 58 03
    SF:59, THE YEAR'S GREATEST SCIENCE FICTION AND FANTASY
                                         MERRIL, JUDITH   AN
  ROYAL IMPOSTOR (SEE THE KING WHO COLLECTED CLOCKS)
                                                      TC
  SEED OF DESTRUCTION   SS   ESQ
    ON AN ODD NOTE   KERSH, GERALD   AC
  SHADY LIFE OF ANNIBAL, THE (THE IMAGINARY HEIR)   SS   SEP 59 04
    MEN WITHOUT BONES   KERSH, GERALD   AC
  SOMEWHERE NOT FAR FROM HERE   SS   PBY 65 03
    PLAYBOY'S STORIES OF THE SINISTER & STRANGE
                                         PLAYBOY, EDITORS OF   AN
    11TH ANNUAL OF THE YEAR'S BEST S-F, THE
                                         MERRIL, JUDITH   AN
  SYMPATHETIC SOUSE, THE   SS
    ON AN ODD NOTE   KERSH, GERALD   AC
  TERRIBLE RIDE OF COLONEL TESSIER, THE   NV   SEP 52 10
    MEN WITHOUT BONES   KERSH, GERALD   AC
  THICKER THAN WATER   NV
    MEN WITHOUT BONES   KERSH, GERALD   AC
  UNSAFE DEPOSIT BOX, THE   SS   SEP 62 04
    LIGHT FANTASTIC, THE   HARRISON, HARRY   AN
    POST READER OF FANTASY AND SCIENCE FICTION
                                         SATURDAY EVE. POST   AN
    8TH ANNUAL OF THE YEAR'S BEST S-F, THE MERRIL, JUDITH   AN
  VOICES IN THE DUST OF ANNAN   SS   SEP 47 09
    NIGHTSHADE & DAMNATIONS   KERSH, GERALD   AC
    SHOT IN THE DARK   MERRIL, JUDITH   AN
  WHATEVER HAPPENED TO CORPORAL CUCKOO? (1953)   NV   STR 54 03
    NIGHTSHADE & DAMNATIONS   KERSH, GERALD   AC
    ONE HUNDRED YEARS OF SCIENCE FICTION KNIGHT, DAMON   AN
    STAR OF STARS   POHL, FREDERICK   AN
    STAR SCIENCE FICTION STORIES NO. 3   POHL, FREDERICK   OA
  WHISPER, THE (SEE THE EXTRAORDINARILY HORRIBLE DUMMY)
                                                      TC

KESSLER, MERLE
  SOME ROOMS   SS   NWB 73 05
    NEW WORLDS QUARTERLY NO. 5   MOORCOCK, MICHAEL   OA

KETTLE, LEROY
  GREAT PLAN, THE   SS   NWR 76 28
    NEW WRITINGS IN SF. 28   BULMER, KENNETH   OA

KEVLES, BETTYANN
  MARS-STATION   SS
    TEEN-AGE SPACE ADVENTURES   FURMAN, A. L.   AN

KEY, EUGENE GEORGE
  MARS MOUNTAIN   AC H FNP 34
  EARTH SEES MARS   NV
    MARS MOUNTAIN   KEY, EUGENE GEORGE   AC
  LAKE TEMPEST   NV
    MARS MOUNTAIN   KEY, EUGENE GEORGE   AC
  MARS MOUNTAIN   NV
    MARS MOUNTAIN   KEY, EUGENE GEORGE   AC

KEYES, DANIEL
  CRAZY MARO   NV   FSF 60 04
    BEST FROM FANTASY AND SCIENCE FICTION: 10
                                         MILLS, ROBERT P.   AN
    THOSE WHO CAN: A SCIENCE FICTION READER
                                         WILSON, ROBIN SCOTT   AN
  FLOWERS FOR ALGERNON   SS   FSF 59 04
    BEST FROM FANTASY AND SCIENCE FICTION: 9
                                         MILLS, ROBERT P.   AN
    BEST SF 4   CRISPIN, EDMUND   AN
    HUGO WINNERS, THE (VOLUME 1)   ASIMOV, ISAAC   AN
    INTRODUCTORY PSYCHOLOGY THROUGH SCIENCE FICTION
                                         KATZ/WARRICK/&   AN
    LATE GREAT FUTURE, THE   FITZ GERALD & DILLON   AN
    NIGHT IN FUNLAND   BRONDFIELD, JEROME   AN
    STORIES FROM SCIENCE FICTION   DOHERTY, G. D.   AN
    5TH ANNUAL OF THE YEAR'S BEST S-F, THE MERRIL, JUDITH   AN
  HOW MUCH DOES A CHARACTER COST?   AR
    THOSE WHO CAN: A SCIENCE FICTION READER
                                         WILSON, ROBIN SCOTT   AN
  QUALITY OF MERCY, THE   NV   IFS 60 11
    FROZEN PLANET AND 4 OTHER SF NOVELLAS, THE
                                         ANONYMOUS   AN

KEYES, NOEL   KLEIN, GERARD

KEYES, NOEL   PSEUD. FOR DAVID H. KEIGHTLEY
  CONTACT   AN   PBK 63 05
    INTRODUCTION   IN
      CONTACT   KEYES, NOEL   AN

KEYES, THOM
  PERIOD OF GESTATION   SS   SCF 64 10
    BEST SF STORIES FROM NEW WORLDS 4 MOORCOCK, MICHAEL   AN
    SCIENCE FICTION HORIZONS NO. 1   BOARDMAN, TOM JR.   AN

KIDD, VIRGINIA   SEE ALSO   CO-EDITOR ROGER ELWOOD
  ABENDLANDES   PM   FUC 73
    FUTURE CITY   ELWOOD, ROGER   OA
  ASCENSION: A WORKDAY ARABESQUE   PM   ANA 70
    ALCHEMY AND ACADEME   MCCAFFREY, ANNE   OA
  BALLS: A MEDITATION AT THE GRAVESIDE   SS   QRK 71 03
    QUARK/3   DELANY & HACKER   OA
  CHOLOM   PM   STG 74
    STRANGE GODS   ELWOOD, ROGER   OA
  FLOWERING SEASON (KANGAROO COURT)   NV   ORB 66 01
    FUTURE NOW, THE   HOSKINS, ROBERT   AN
    INTRODUCTION   IN
      BEST OF JUDITH MERRIL, THE   MERRIL, JUDITH   AC
  KANGAROO COURT (ALSO AS FLOWERING SEASON) NV   ORB 66 01
    ORBIT 1   KNIGHT, DAMON   OA
  NIGHT AND MORNING OF THE IDIOT CHILD   PM   BER 74
    BERSERKERS, THE   ELWOOD, ROGER   OA
  ON THE WALL OF THE LODGE   NV C GAL 62 04
    DARK STARS   SILVERBERG, ROBERT AN

KILBURN, DAVID
  WEATHER FORECAST   PM   69
    HOLDING YOUR EIGHT HANDS   LUCIE-SMITH, EDWARD AN

KILWORTH, GARRY
  LET'S GO TO GOLGOTHA¦   SS
    GOLLANCZ - SUNDAY TIMES BEST SF STORIES
                                       ANONYMOUS   OA
  SOUL OF COLONEL 607, THE   SS
    GOLLANCZ - SUNDAY TIMES BEST SF STORIES
                                       ANONYMOUS   OA

KIMBERLY, GAIL
  FACE OF THE ENEMY, THE   NV
    SCIENCE FICTION ADVENTURES FROM WAY OUT
                                       ELWOOD, ROGER   OA
  FIRE FOUNTAIN, THE   NV   CTM 74 02
    CONTINUUM 2   ELWOOD, ROGER   OA
  HORSEMAN FROM HEL, THE   NV   BER 74
    BERSERKERS, THE   ELWOOD, ROGER   OA
  LADY BOUNTIFUL   SS
    LEARNING MAZE AND OTHER STORIES, THE ELWOOD, ROGER   OA
  MANY MANSIONS   SS   FTP 73
    FLAME TREE PLANET   ELWOOD, ROGER   OA
  MINNA IN THE NIGHT SKY   SS
    FAR SIDE OF TIME, THE   ELWOOD, ROGER   OA
  PEACE, LOVE, AND FOOD FOR THE HUNGRY   NV
    OTHER SIDE OF TOMORROW, THE   ELWOOD, ROGER   OA
  WHERE SUMMER SONG RINGS HOLLOW   SS   DYS 75
    DYSTOPIAN VISIONS   ELWOOD, ROGER   OA

KING, MAC
  FAMILY, THE   PM   NWQ 74 06
    NEW WORLDS NO. 6   PLATT & BAILEY   OA
  MY WRECK   PM   NWQ 74 06
    NEW WORLDS NO. 6   PLATT & BAILEY   OA
  RAISE   PM   NWQ 74 06
    NEW WORLDS NO. 6   PLATT & BAILEY   OA
  UNTITLED   PM   NWQ 74 06
    NEW WORLDS NO. 6   PLATT & BAILEY   OA
  WIND-DREAM   PM   NWQ 74 06
    NEW WORLDS NO. 6   PLATT & BAILEY   OA

KING, MARSHALL
  BEACH SCENE   SS   GAL 60 10
    6TH ANNUAL OF THE YEAR'S BEST S-F, THE MERRIL, JUDITH AN

KING, VALERIE
  GERANIUMS   SS C OMG 73
    BEST OF BARRY N. MALZBERG, THE   MALZBERG, BARRY N. AC
    OMEGA   ELWOOD, ROGER   OA

KING, VINCENT
  DEFENSE MECHANISM   NV   NWR 66 09
    NEW WRITINGS IN SF. 7   CARNELL, JOHN   AN
    NEW WRITINGS IN SF. 9   CARNELL, JOHN   OA
  DISCONTENT CONTINGENCY, THE   NV   NWR 71 19
    NEW WRITINGS IN SF. 19   CARNELL, JOHN   OA
  ETERNITY GAME, THE   NV   NWR 69 14
    NEW WRITINGS IN SF. 14   CARNELL, JOHN   OA
  REPORT FROM LINELOS   NV   NWR 69 15
    NEW WRITINGS IN SF. 15   CARNELL, JOHN   OA
  TESTAMENT   SS   NWR 68 13
    NEW WRITINGS IN SF. 9   CARNELL, JOHN   AN
    NEW WRITINGS IN SF. 13   CARNELL, JOHN   OA
  WALL TO END THE WORLD, THE   NV   NWR 68 11
    NEW WRITINGS IN SF. 8   CARNELL, JOHN   AN
    NEW WRITINGS IN SF. 11   CARNELL, JOHN   OA

KINGSTON, JOHN   PSEUD. FOR KEITH ROBERTS
  MANIPULATION   NV   NWR 65 03
    NEW WRITINGS IN SF. 3   CARNELL, JOHN   OA

KINSOLVING, MAY R.
  WALLS   NV
    SURVIVAL FROM INFINITY   ELWOOD, ROGER   OA

KIP, LEONARD
  SECRET OF APOLLONIUS SEPTRIO, THE   NV
    BATTLE OF THE MONSTERS AND OTHER STORIES, THE
                                       HARTWELL & CURREY   AN

KIPLING, RUDYARD
  AS EASY AS A. B. C.   NV   LOM 12 04
    SCIENCE FICTION GALAXY, THE   CONKLIN, GROFF   AN
    SPECULATIONS   SANDERS, THOMAS E. AN
    17 X INFINITY   CONKLIN, GROFF   AN
  BRUSHWOOD BOY, THE   SS   CNY 95 12
    PERCHANCE TO DREAM   KNIGHT, DAMON   AN
  FINEST STORY IN THE WORLD, THE   NV   CRV 91 07
    LIGHT FANTASTIC, THE   HARRISON, HARRY   AN
    TRAVELERS IN TIME   STERN, PHILIP VAN D. AN
    WORLD OF WONDER   PRATT, FLETCHER   AN
  MACDONOUGH'S SONG   PM   MPM 12 03
    17 X INFINITY   CONKLIN, GROFF   AN
  MARK OF THE BEAST, THE   SS   PIO 90 07
    BEWARE THE BEASTS   GHIDALIA, V.& ELWOOD AN
    ROD SERLING'S TRIPLE W: WITCHES, WARLOCKS AND WEREWOLVES
                                       SERLING, ROD   AN
    WORLD OF WONDER   PRATT, FLETCHER   AN
  THEY   NV   SCR 04
    LITTLE MONSTERS, THE   ELWOOD & GHIDALIA   AN
  UNPROFESSIONAL   SS   SRV 30 10
    IN DREAMS AWAKE   FIEDLER, LESLIE A. AN
  WIRELESS   SS   SCR 02 08
    JOURNEYS IN SCIENCE FICTION   LOUGHLIN, RICHARD L. AN
    MOONLIGHT TRAVELER, THE   STERN, PHILIP VAN D. AN
  WITH THE NIGHT MAIL   NV   MCS 05 11
    ONE HUNDRED YEARS OF SCIENCE FICTION KNIGHT, DAMON   AN
    VISIONS OF TOMORROW   ELWOOD, ROGER   AN
    WONDERMAKERS   HOSKINS, ROBERT   AN

KIPPAX, JOHN   PSEUD. FOR JOHN HYNAM
  BLOOD OFFERING   SS   SCF 61 06
    WEIRD SHADOWS FROM BEYOND   CARNELL, JOHN   AN
  DUSTY DEATH, THE   SS   NWS 58 11
    OUT OF THIS WORLD 2   WILLIAMS-ELLIS& OWEN AN
  FRIDAY   SS   NWS 59 02
    OUT OF THIS WORLD 1   WILLIAMS-ELLIS& OWEN AN
  NO CERTAIN ARMOUR   NV   NWR 74 24
    NEW WRITINGS IN SF. 24   BULMER, KENNETH   OA
  TIME WAGER, THE   SS   NWR 73 22
    NEW WRITINGS IN SF. 22   BULMER, KENNETH   OA

KIRBY, JACK
  FOREVER PEOPLE, THE   CT   70
    LOOKING AHEAD   ALLEN, D. & L.   AN

KIRBY, JOSH
  SCIENCE FICTION COVER ILLUSTRATIONS   IL
    BEYOND THIS HORIZON   CARRELL, CHRISTOPHER OA

KIRBY, RICHARD
  PSY FY PSYCHOLOGY AND SCIENCE FICTION   AR C
    BEYOND THIS HORIZON   CARRELL, CHRISTOPHER OA

KIRK, RUSSELL
  BALGRUMMO'S HELL   SS   FSF 67 07
    BEST FROM FANTASY AND SCIENCE FICTION: 17
                                       FERMAN, EDWARD L.   AN

KIRK, TIM
  EVISE, THE ZSOUCHMOID   IL
    WANDERING STARS   DANN, JACK M.   AN
  ILLUSTRATIONS   IL
    COMPLETE FEGHOOT, THE   BRIARTON, GRENDEL   AC
  PHOENIX WITHOUT ASHES   IL   76
    FASTER THAN LIGHT   DANN & ZEBROWSKI   OA

KIRKLAND, JACK
  WALL OF FIRE, THE   SS   BBM 32 07
    EDITOR'S CHOICE IN SCIENCE FICTION MOSKOWITZ, SAM   AN

KIRKUP, JAMES
  TEA IN A SPACE-SHIP   PM
    STARLIT CORRIDOR, THE   MANSFIELD, ROGER   AN

KIRS, ALEX
  BETTER THAN EVER   SS   FSF 65 03
    11TH ANNUAL OF THE YEAR'S BEST S-F, THE
                                       MERRIL, JUDITH   AN

KITA, MORIO
  EMPTY FIELD, THE (TRANSLATED BY TSURUTA & MERRIL) SS OMG 73
    OMEGA   ELWOOD, ROGER   OA

KLASS, MORTON
  IN THE BEGINNING   SS   ASF 54 07
    APEMAN, SPACEMAN   STOVER & HARRISON   AN
  KAPPA NU NEXUS, THE   SS C FSF 61 08
    13 ABOVE THE NIGHT   CONKLIN, GROFF   AN

KLASS, PHILIP   SEE PSEUD. WILLIAM TENN

KLEE, PAUL
  FOOL FROM THE DEPTHS   IL
    SCIENCE FICTION   BRODKIN & PEARSON   AN

KLEIN, GERARD
  MONSTER, THE   SS   58
    13 FRENCH SCIENCE-FICTION STORIES KNIGHT, DAMON   AN
  PARTY LINE   NV   73
    BEST FROM THE REST OF THE WORLD, THE WOLLHEIM, DONALD A. AN

KLEIN, GERARD   (CONTINUED)
    VALLEY OF ECHOES, THE   SS
    VIEW FROM ANOTHER SHORE   ROTTENSTEINER, FRANZ AN

KLEIN, SIDNEY
    TEETH OF DESPAIR, THE   SS C FSF 61 05
        SCIENCE FICTION ODDITIES   CONKLIN, GROFF   AN
        WHAT STRANGE STARS AND SKIES DAVIDSON, AVRAM   AC

KLEIN, T. E. D.
    EVENTS AT POROTH FARM, THE   NV
        YEAR'S BEST HORROR STORIES: SERIES II, THE
                                   DAVIS, RICHARD   AN
    RENAISSANCE MAN   SS SPC 74 02
    SPACE   2   DAVIS, RICHARD   OA
    S.F.   SS NEW 75 AN
        YEAR'S BEST HORROR STORIES: SERIES III, THE
                                   DAVIS, RICHARD   AN

KLINE, OTIS ADELBERT
    STOLEN CENTURIES   SS TWS 39 06
        EDITOR'S CHOICE IN SCIENCE FICTION MOSKOWITZ, SAM   AN
    VISION OF VENUS, A   SS AMZ 33 12
        SWORDSMEN IN THE SKY   WOLLHEIM, DONALD A.   AN

KLINE, T. F.
    SPACE POEM   PM BUL
        SECOND PACIFIC BOOK OF SCIENCE FICTION, THE
                                   BAXTER, JOHN   AN

KNEALE, NIGEL   PSEUD. FOR THOMAS NIGEL KNEALE
    JEREMY IN THE WIND   SS   50
        TIMELESS STORIES FOR TODAY AND TOMORROW
                                   BRADBURY, RAY   AN
    MINUKE   SS HRP 50 09
        SUPERNATURAL READER, THE   CONKLIN, G&L.   AN
    POND, THE   SS   50
        CIRCUS OF DR. LAO AND OTHER IMPROBABLE STORIES
                                   BRADBURY, RAY   AN

KNEALE, THOMAS NIGEL SEE PSEUD. NIGEL KNEALE

KNIGHT, DAMON
    BEST FROM ORBIT, THE   AN H BRK 75
    BEST OF DAMON KNIGHT, THE   AC H NDB 76
    BEYOND TOMORROW   AN H HPR 65
    CENTURY OF GREAT SHORT SCIENCE FICTION NOVELS, A AN H DCT 64
    CENTURY OF SCIENCE FICTION, A   AN H SAS 62
    CITIES OF WONDER   AN H DBL 66
    DARK SIDE, THE   AN H DBL 65
    DIMENSION X   AN H SAS 70
    FAR OUT   AC H SAS 61
    FIRST CONTACT   AN   PIN 71 11
    FIRST FLIGHT   AN   LAN 63
        MAIDEN VOYAGES IN SPACE AND TIME,
        ALSO AS "NOW BEGINS TOMORROW"
    GOLDEN ROAD, THE   AN H SAS 73
    IN DEEP   AC   BKM 63
        BRITISH EDITIONS OMIT "THE HANDLER"
    METAL SMILE, THE   AN   BEL 68
    NEBULA AWARD STORIES   AN H DBL 66
    NOW BEGINS TOMORROW   AN   LAN 69 11
        SEE "FIRST FLIGHT"
    OFF CENTER   DC   ACE 65
    OFF CENTRE   AC H GOL 69
    ONE HUNDRED YEARS OF SCIENCE FICTION   AN H SAS 68
    ORBIT   1   OA   BKM 66 10
    ORBIT   2   OA   BKM 67 09
    ORBIT   3   OA H PUT 68
    ORBIT   4   OA H PUT 68
    ORBIT   5   OA H PUT 69
    ORBIT   6   OA H PUT 70
    ORBIT   7   OA H PUT 70
    ORBIT   8   OA H PUT 70
    ORBIT   9   OA H PUT 71
    ORBIT   10   OA H PUT 72
    ORBIT   11   OA H PUT 73
    ORBIT   12   OA H PUT 73
    ORBIT   13   OA H PUT 74
    ORBIT   14   OA H HPR 74
    ORBIT   15   OA H HPR 74
    ORBIT   16   OA H HPR 75
    ORBIT   17   OA H HPR 75
    ORBIT   18   OA H HPR 76
    PERCHANCE TO DREAM   AN H DBL 72
    POCKETFUL OF STARS, A   AN H DBL 71
    SCIENCE FICTION ARGOSY, A   AN H SAS 72
    SCIENCE FICTION INVENTIONS   AN   LAN 67
    SCIENCE FICTION OF THE 30'S   AN H BML 75
    SHAPE OF THINGS, THE   AN   POP 67
    SHOCKING THING, A   AN   PKT 74 11
    THREE NOVELS   AC H DBL 67
    TOMORROW AND TOMORROW   AN H SAS 73
    TOMORROW X 4   AN   GMB 64
    TOWARD INFINITY   AN H SAS 68
    TURNING ON   AC H DBL 66
        ACE 67 EDITION OMITS STORY "THE HANDLER"
    WORLDS TO COME   AN H HPR 67
    13 FRENCH SCIENCE-FICTION STORIES   AN   BAN 65
        ABOUT THE AUTHORS   MS
            13 FRENCH SCIENCE-FICTION STORIES KNIGHT, DAMON   AN
    ANACHRON   SS IFS 54 01
        BEST OF DAMON KNIGHT, THE KNIGHT, DAMON   AC
        FAR OUT   KNIGHT, DAMON   AC
    ANALOGUES, THE   SS ASF 52 01
        BEST OF DAMON KNIGHT, THE KNIGHT, DAMON   AC

KNIGHT, DAMON   (CONTINUED)
    VINTAGE ANTHOLOGY OF SCIENCE FANTASY, THE
                                   CERF, CHRISTOPHER   AN
        13 GREAT STORIES OF SCIENCE FICTION CONKLIN, GROFF   AN
    ANCIENT MADNESS, AN (ALSO AS MARY)   NV GAL 64 06
        NINTH GALAXY READER, THE   POHL, FREDERIK   AN
    ANNOTATED "MASKS", A   SS PBY 68 07
        THOSE WHO CAN: A SCIENCE FICTION READER
                                   WILSON, ROBIN SCOTT AN
    ASK ME ANYTHING   NV GAL 51 05
        *GALAXY READER OF SCIENCE FICTION GOLD, H. L.   AN
        IN DEEP   KNIGHT, DAMON   AC
    AUTO-DA-FE   SS GAL 61 02
        TENTH GALAXY READER, THE   POHL, FREDERIK   AN
        TURNING ON   KNIGHT, DAMON   AC
    BABEL II   NV BEY 53 07
        BEST OF DAMON KNIGHT, THE KNIGHT, DAMON   AC
        FAR OUT   KNIGHT, DAMON   AC
        INFINITE JESTS   SILVERBERG, ROBERT   AN
        WORLDS OF SCIENCE FICTION, THE MILLS, ROBERT P.   AN
    BACKWARD, O TIME (THIS WAY TO THE REGRESS)   SS GAL 56 08
        BEST OF DAMON KNIGHT, THE KNIGHT, DAMON   AC
        TURNING ON   KNIGHT, DAMON   AC
    BE MY GUEST   NV FUN 58 09
        *OFF CENTER   KNIGHT, DAMON   DC
        OTHERS, THE   CARR, TERRY   AN
    BEACH WHERE TIME BEGAN, THE (SEE EXTEMPORE)   TC
    BEACHCOMBER   SS IMG 52 12
        IN DEEP   KNIGHT, DAMON   AC
    BIG PAT BOOM, THE   SS GAL 63 12
        BEST OF DAMON KNIGHT, THE KNIGHT, DAMON   AC
        SCIENCE FICTION HORIZONS NO. 1 BOARDMAN, TOM JR.   AN
        SEVENTH GALAXY READER, THE POHL, FREDERIK   AN
        TURNING ON   KNIGHT, DAMON   AC
    BOOK REVIEWS   BR ORB 74 14
        ORBIT 14   KNIGHT, DAMON   OA
    CABIN BOY   NV GAL 51 09
        BEST OF DAMON KNIGHT, THE KNIGHT, DAMON   AC
        FAR OUT   KNIGHT, DAMON   AC
        *GALAXY READER OF SCIENCE FICTION GOLD, H. L.   AN
        GREAT STORIES OF SPACE TRAVEL CONKLIN, GROFF   AN
        TOMORROW'S CHILDREN   ASIMOV, ISAAC   AN
    CATCH THAT MARTIAN   SS GAL 52 03
        INVADERS FROM SPACE   SILVERBERG, ROBERT   AN
        MARS, WE LOVE YOU   HIPOLITO & MCNELLY   AN
        *OFF CENTER   KNIGHT, DAMON   DC
        OMNIBUS OF SCIENCE FICTION CONKLIN, GROFF   AN
        STRANGE ADVENTURES IN SCIENCE FICTION CONKLIN, GROFF   AN
    CHARTING UTOPIA   AR CLR 71 01
        CLARION   WILSON, ROBIN SCOTT OA
    COLLECTOR'S ITEM (THE END OF THE SEARCH)   SS WOT 63 06
        TURNING ON   KNIGHT, DAMON   AC
    COUNTRY OF THE KIND, THE   SS FSF 56 02
        FUTURE POWER   DANN & DOZOIS   OA
        IN DEEP   KNIGHT, DAMON   AC
        LATE GREAT FUTURE, THE   FITZ GERALD & DILLON AN
        NEW DREAMS THIS MORNING   BLISH, JAMES   AN
        SCIENCE FICTION HALL OF FAME VOLUME 1 SILVERBERG, ROBERT   AN
        SF: THE YEAR'S GREATEST SCIENCE FICTION AND FANTASY
                                   MERRIL, JUDITH   AN
        YET MORE PENGUIN SCIENCE FICTION ALDISS, BRIAN W.   AN
    DEEP WELL OF THE UNCONSCIOUS- WELL, WELL..., THE AR CLR 73 03
        CLARION III   WILSON, ROBIN SCOTT OA
    DIO (ALSO AS THE DYING MAN)   SN INF 57 09
        ALPHA 4   SILVERBERG, ROBERT   AN
        5 UNEARTHLY VISIONS   CONKLIN, GROFF   AN
    DON'T LIVE IN THE PAST   NV GAL 51 06
        *GALAXY READER OF SCIENCE FICTION GOLD, H. L.   AN
        TURNING ON   KNIGHT, DAMON   AC
    DOUBLE MEANING   NA STS 53 01
        3 FROM OUT THERE   MARGULIES, LEO   AN
    DOWN THERE   SS NDM 73 03
        BEST OF DAMON KNIGHT, THE KNIGHT, DAMON   AC
        NEW DIMENSIONS 3   SILVERBERG, ROBERT   OA
    DULCIE AND DECORUM   NV GAL 55 03
        OFF CENTRE   KNIGHT, DAMON   AC
    DYING MAN, THE (DIO)   SN INF 57 09
        THREE NOVELS   KNIGHT, DAMON   AC
    EARLY YEARS, THE   SI
        SCIENCE FICTION OF THE 30'S KNIGHT, DAMON   AN
    END OF THE SEARCH, THE (SEE COLLECTOR'S ITEM) TC
    END, THE   SI
        SCIENCE FICTION OF THE 30'S KNIGHT, DAMON   AN
    ENEMY, THE   SS VSF 58 01
        BEST OF DAMON KNIGHT, THE KNIGHT, DAMON   AC
        FAR OUT   KNIGHT, DAMON   AC
    ENOUGH TIME (SEE TIME ENOUGH)   TC
    ERIPMAV   SS FSF 58 06
        BEST FROM FANTASY AND SCIENCE FICTION: 8
                                   BOUCHER, ANTHONY   AN
        BEST OF DAMON KNIGHT, THE KNIGHT, DAMON   AC
        TURNING ON   KNIGHT, DAMON   AC
    EXTEMPORE (THE BEACH WHERE TIME BEGAN)   SS INF 56 08
        BEST OF DAMON KNIGHT, THE KNIGHT, DAMON   AC
        FAR OUT   KNIGHT, DAMON   AC
    EYE FOR A WHAT?, AN   NV GAL 57 03
        ALIENS, THE   SILVERBERG, ROBERT   AN
        IN DEEP   KNIGHT, DAMON   AC
        WORLD THAT COULDN'T BE AND 8 OTHER SF NOVELETS
                                   GOLD, H. L.   AN
        WORLDS APART   WILLIAMS-ELLIS& OWEN AN
    FOREWORD   IN
        SCIENCE FICTION OF THE 30'S KNIGHT, DAMON   AN
    FOREWORD TO "COMMON TIME"   AR SFF 57
        MIRROR OF INFINITY, THE   SILVERBERG, ROBERT   AN

KNIGHT, DAMON   (CONTINUED)
  FOUR IN ONE   NV   GAL 53 02
    BEST SF 3   CRISPIN, EDMUND   AN
    GALAXY SCIENCE FICTION OMNIBUS   GOLD, H. L.   AN
    IN DEEP   KNIGHT, DAMON   AC
    OUT OF THIS WORLD 5   WILLIAMS-ELLIS& OWEN   AN
    SECOND GALAXY READER OF SCIENCE FICTION
                                      GOLD, H. L.   AN
    TO THE STARS   SILVERBERG, ROBERT   AN
  GOD'S NOSE   SS   ROG 64
    *OFF CENTER   KNIGHT, DAMON   DC
  GOODBYE, HENRY J. KOSTKOS, GOODBYE   AR   CLR 72 02
    CLARION II   WILSON, ROBIN SCOTT   OA
  HANDLER, THE   SS   ROG 60 08
    ABOVE THE HUMAN LANDSCAPE   MCNELLY & STOVER   AN
    ANOTHER TOMORROW   HOLLISTER, BERNARD C   AN
    BEST OF DAMON KNIGHT, THE   KNIGHT, DAMON   AC
    IN DEEP   KNIGHT, DAMON   AC
    SF: THE BEST OF THE BEST   MERRIL, JUDITH   AN
    TURNING ON   KNIGHT, DAMON   AC
    5TH ANNUAL OF THE YEAR'S BEST S-F, THE MERRIL, JUDITH   AN
  I SEE YOU   SS   FSF 76 11
    BEST SCIENCE FICTION OF THE YEAR, THE NO. 6
                                      CARR, TERRY   AN
    1977 ANNUAL WORLD'S BEST SF, THE WOLLHEIM, DONALD A.   AN
  IDIOT STICK   SS   STR 58 04
    BEYOND TOMORROW   HARDING, LEE   AN
    FAR OUT   KNIGHT, DAMON   AC
    STAR SCIENCE FICTION STORIES NO. 4 POHL, FREDERIK   OA
  IN THE BEGINNING   NV   FUT 53 01
    THINGS   HOWARD, IVAN   IN
  INTRODUCTION   IN
    BEST OF DAMON KNIGHT, THE   KNIGHT, DAMON   AC
    BEYOND TOMORROW   KNIGHT, DAMON   AN
    CASEY AGONISTES, AND OTHER S.F. & FANTASY STORIES
                                      MCKENNA, RICHARD M.   AC
    CENTURY OF SCIENCE FICTION, A   KNIGHT, DAMON   AN
    CITIES OF WONDER   KNIGHT, DAMON   AN
    DARK SIDE, THE   KNIGHT, DAMON   AN
    FIRST CONTACT   KNIGHT, DAMON   AN
    FIRST FLIGHT   KNIGHT, DAMON   AN
    GOLDEN ROAD, THE   KNIGHT, DAMON   AN
    NEBULA AWARD STORIES   KNIGHT, DAMON   AN
    ONE HUNDRED YEARS OF SCIENCE FICTION KNIGHT, DAMON   AN
    ORBIT   1   KNIGHT, DAMON   OA
    PAST THROUGH TOMORROW, THE   HEINLEIN, ROBERT A.   AC
    PERCHANCE TO DREAM   KNIGHT, DAMON   AN
    POCKETFUL OF STARS, A   KNIGHT, DAMON   AN
    SCIENCE FICTION ARGOSY, A   KNIGHT, DAMON   AN
    SCIENCE FICTION INVENTIONS   KNIGHT, DAMON   AN
    SHAPE OF THINGS, THE   KNIGHT, DAMON   AN
    TOMORROW X 4   KNIGHT, DAMON   AN
    TOWARD INFINITY   KNIGHT, DAMON   AN
    WORLDS TO COME   KNIGHT, DAMON   AN
    13 FRENCH SCIENCE-FICTION STORIES KNIGHT, DAMON   AN
  LAST WORD, THE   SS   SAT 57 02
    BEST OF DAMON KNIGHT, THE   KNIGHT, DAMON   AC
    FAR OUT   KNIGHT, DAMON   AC
  LIKELY STORY, A   SS   INF 56 02
    BEST OF DAMON KNIGHT, THE   KNIGHT, DAMON   AC
    TURNING ON   KNIGHT, DAMON   AC
  MAID TO MEASURE   SS   FSF 64 10
    ABC OF SCIENCE FICTION, AN   BOARDMAN, TOM JR.   AN
    TURNING ON   KNIGHT, DAMON   AC
  MAN IN THE JAR   SS   GAL 57 04
    ANOTHER WORLD   DOZOIS, GARDNER R.   AN
    BEST OF DAMON KNIGHT, THE   KNIGHT, DAMON   AC
    THIRD GALAXY READER, THE   GOLD, H. L.   AN
    TURNING ON   KNIGHT, DAMON   AC
  MARY (AN ANCIENT MADNESS)   NV   GAL 64 06
    BEST OF DAMON KNIGHT, THE   KNIGHT, DAMON   AC
    DAY IN THE LIFE, A   DOZOIS, GARDNER R.   AN
    TURNING ON   KNIGHT, DAMON   AC
  MASKS   SS   PBY 68 07
    AS TOMORROW BECOMES TODAY   SULLIVAN, CHARLES W.   AN
    BEST OF DAMON KNIGHT, THE   KNIGHT, DAMON   AC
    DARK STARS   SILVERBERG, ROBERT   AN
    HUMAN-MACHINES   SCORTIA & ZEBROWSKI   AN
    MASKS   PLAYBOY, EDITORS OF   AN
    NEW TOMORROWS, THE   SPINRAD, NORMAN   AN
    OFF CENTRE   KNIGHT, DAMON   AC
    POCKETFUL OF STARS, A   KNIGHT, DAMON   AN
    WORLD'S BEST SCIENCE FICTION: 1969 WOLLHEIM & CARR   AN
  MIDDLE PERIOD, THE   SI
    SCIENCE FICTION OF THE 30'S   KNIGHT, DAMON   AN
  MORE GOOD READING IN SCIENCE FICTION   MS
    WORLDS TO COME   KNIGHT, DAMON   AN
  NATURAL STATE   NA   GAL 54 01
    ALL ABOUT THE FUTURE   GREENBERG , MARTIN   AN
    HOT & COLD RUNNING CITIES   MCHARGUE, GEORGESS   AN
    THREE NOVELS   KNIGHT, DAMON   AC
    TIME WAITS FOR WINTHROP, AND FOUR OTHER SHORT NOVELS
                                      POHL, FREDERIK   AN
  NIGHT OF LIES, THE   SS   FSF 58 10
    TURNING ON   KNIGHT, DAMON   AC
  NOT WITH A BANG   SS   FSF 50 WS
    BEST OF DAMON KNIGHT, THE   KNIGHT, DAMON   AC
    *BIG BOOK OF SCIENCE FICTION   CONKLIN, GROFF   AN
    FAR OUT   KNIGHT, DAMON   AC
    FIFTY SHORT SCIENCE FICTION TALES ASIMOV & CONKLIN   AN
    SCIENCE FICTION FOR PEOPLE WHO HATE SCIENCE FICTION
                                      CARR, TERRY   AN
  ON THE WHEEL   SS   NOV 72 02
    NOVA 2   HARRISON, HARRY   OA
    SCIENCE FACT/FICTION   FARRELL/GAGE/&   AN

KNIGHT, DAMON   (CONTINUED)
  RULE GOLDEN   NV   SFA 54 06
    SIX GREAT SHORT SCIENCE FICTION NOVELS CONKLIN, GROFF   AN
    THREE NOVELS   KNIGHT, DAMON   AC
  SATISFACTION (SEE SEMPER FI)   TC
  SECOND-CLASS CITIZEN, THE   SS   IFS 63 11
    APEMAN, SPACEMAN   STOVER & HARRISON   AN
    *OFF CENTER   KNIGHT, DAMON   DC
  SEMPER FI (SATISFACTION)   SS   ASF 64 08
    BEST OF DAMON KNIGHT, THE   KNIGHT, DAMON   AC
    TURNING ON   KNIGHT, DAMON   AC
  SHALL THE DUST PRAISE THEE?   SS   DVS 67 01
    DANGEROUS VISIONS   ELLISON, HARLAN   OA
    OTHER WORLDS, OTHER GODS   MOHS, MAYO   AN
  SOMETHING THAT WORKS   AR
    CLARION SF   WILHELM, KATE   OA
  SORT OF INTRODUCTION, A   IN
    BEST FROM ORBIT, THE   KNIGHT, DAMON   AN
  SPECIAL DELIVERY   NV   GAL 54 04
    BEST OF DAMON KNIGHT, THE   KNIGHT, DAMON   AC
    FAR OUT   KNIGHT, DAMON   AC
    OPERATION FUTURE   CONKLIN, GROFF   AN
  STRANGER STATION   NV   FSF 56 12
    BUG-EYED MONSTERS   CHEETHAM, ANTHONY   AN
    EARTHMEN AND STRANGERS   SILVERBERG, ROBERT   AN
    IN DEEP   KNIGHT, DAMON   AC
    LOOKING AHEAD   ALLEN, D. & L.   AN
    MODERN SCIENCE FICTION   SPINRAD, NORMAN   AN
    SF: THE BEST OF THE BEST   MERRIL, JUDITH   AN
    SF:57, THE YEAR'S GREATEST SCIENCE FICTION AND FANTASY
                                      MERRIL, JUDITH   AN
    SPECTRUM 4   AMIS & CONQUEST   AN
  THEY SAY   MS
    ORBIT 14   KNIGHT, DAMON   OA
    ORBIT 15   KNIGHT, DAMON   OA
    ORBIT 16   KNIGHT, DAMON   OA
    ORBIT 17   KNIGHT, DAMON   OA
    ORBIT 18   KNIGHT, DAMON   OA
  THING OF BEAUTY   NV   GAL 58 09
    BEST OF DAMON KNIGHT, THE   KNIGHT, DAMON   AC
    FAR OUT   KNIGHT, DAMON   AC
    SIXTH GALAXY READER, THE   GOLD, H. L.   AN
  THIS WAY TO THE REGRESS (SEE BACKWARD, O TIME) TC
  TICKET TO ANYWHERE   NV   GAL 52 04
    DEEP SPACE   SILVERBERG, ROBERT   AN
    IN DEEP   KNIGHT, DAMON   AC
    SCIENCE FICTION SHOWCASE   KORNBLUTH, MARY   AN
  TIGER RIDE   SS C ASF 48 10
    SF: AUTHORS' CHOICE   HARRISON, HARRY   AN
  TIME ENOUGH (ENOUGH TIME)   SS   AMZ 60 07
    BEST OF DAMON KNIGHT, THE   KNIGHT, DAMON   AC
    FAR OUT   KNIGHT, DAMON   AC
  TO BE CONTINUED   SS   FSF 59 10
    OFF CENTRE   KNIGHT, DAMON   AC
  TO SERVE MAN   SS   GAL 50 11
    BEST OF DAMON KNIGHT, THE   KNIGHT, DAMON   AC
    BEST SCIENCE-FICTION STORIES: 1951, THE
                                      BLEILER & DIKTY   AN
    COSMIC LAUGHTER   HALDEMAN, JOE W.   AN
    FAR OUT   KNIGHT, DAMON   AC
    FRONTIERS IN SPACE   BLEILER & DIKTY   AN
    HISTORY OF THE SCIENCE FICTION MAGAZINE, THE PART 3 1946-1955
                                      ASHLEY, MICHAEL   AN
    MINDWORM, THE   ANONYMOUS   AN
  TO THE PURE   SS   NWS 66 10
    TURNING ON   KNIGHT, DAMON   AC
  WHAT ROUGH BEAST?   NV   FSF 59 02
    BEST FROM FANTASY AND SCIENCE FICTION: 9
                                      MILLS, ROBERT P.   AN
    *OFF CENTER   KNIGHT, DAMON   DC
  WORLD WITHOUT CHILDREN   NA   GAL 51 12
    5 GALAXY SHORT NOVELS   GOLD, H. L.   AN
  YOU'RE ANOTHER   NV   FSF 55 06
    BEST FROM FANTASY AND SCIENCE FICTION: 5
                                      BOUCHER, ANTHONY   AN
    FAR OUT   KNIGHT, DAMON   AC
    SPECIAL WONDER   MCCOMAS, J. FRANCIS   AN
    1971: THE YEAR IN SCIENCE FICTION AR
    NEBULA AWARD STORIES NO. 7   BIGGLE, LLOYD JR.   AN
    1973: THE YEAR IN SCIENCE FICTION AR
    NEBULA AWARD STORIES 9   WILHELM, KATE   AN

KNIGHT, DAVID C.
  AMAZING MRS. MIMMS, THE   SS   FUN 58 08
    FANTASTIC UNIVERSE OMNIBUS, THE SANTESSON, HANS S.   AN

KNIGHT, ERIC
  SAM SMALL'S BETTER HALF   SS   42
    MOONLIGHT TRAVELER, THE   STERN, PHILIP VAN D.   AN
  SAM SMALL'S TYKE   SS   42
    OUT OF THIS WORLD   FAST, JULIUS   AN

KNIGHT, NORMAN L.   SEE ALSO   CO-AUTHOR JAMES BLISH
  CRISIS IN UTOPIA   NO   ASF 40 07
    CRUCIBLE OF POWER, THE   GREENBERG , MARTIN   AN
    FIVE SCIENCE FICTION NOVELS   GREENBERG , MARTIN   AN
  PIPER OF DIS, THE   NV C GAL 66 08
    TORRENT OF FACES, A   BLISH & KNIGHT, N.   NO
  SHIPWRECKED HOTEL, THE   NV C GAL 65 08
    SCIENCE FICTION HORIZONS NO. 1   BOARDMAN, TOM JR.   AN
    TORRENT OF FACES, A   BLISH & KNIGHT, N.   NO
  SHORT-CIRCUITED PROBABILITY   SS   ASF 41 09
    *BEST OF SCIENCE FICTION   CONKLIN, GROFF   AN
  TO LOVE ANOTHER   NV C ASF 67 04
    TORRENT OF FACES, A   BLISH & KNIGHT, N.   NO

KNOX, CALVIN M.   KORNBLUTH, C. M.

KNOX, CALVIN M.   PSEUD. FOR ROBERT SILVERBERG
LEST WE FORGET THEE, EARTH   DN   ACE 58
  CHALICE OF DEATH   NO   SPA 57 06
    LEST WE FORGET THEE, EARTH   KNOX, CALVIN M. DN
  EARTH SHALL LIVE AGAIN   SN   SPA 57 12
    LEST WE FORGET THEE, EARTH   KNOX, CALVIN M. DN
  VENGEANCE OF THE SPACE ARMADAS   SN   SPA 58 03
    LEST WE FORGET THEE, EARTH   KNOX, CALVIN M. DN

KNOX, R. A.
SHORT CUTS TO SUCCESS   SS   SLP 17 11
  MATHEMATICAL MAGPIE, THE   FADIMAN, CLIFTON AN

KOCH, HOWARD
INVASION FROM INNER SPACE   NV   STR 59 06
  STAR SCIENCE FICTION STORIES NO. 6 POHL, FREDERIK OA
INVASION FROM MARS   PL   CBS 38 10
  ARMCHAIR SCIENCE READER, THE   GORDON, I. & SORKIN AN
  BUG-EYED MONSTERS   CHEETHAM, ANTHONY AN
  CONTACT   KEYES, NOEL   AN
  ENEMIES IN SPACE   CONKLIN, GROFF   AN
 *INVADERS OF EARTH   CONKLIN, GROFF   AN
  INVASION FROM MARS   WELLES, ORSON   AN
  SPECULATIONS   SANDERS, THOMAS E. AN
  TREASURY OF SCIENCE FICTION CLASSICS, THE
                                     KUEBLER, HAROLD W. AN

KOCH, KENNETH
ARTIST, THE   PM   62
  HOLDING YOUR EIGHT HANDS   LUCIE-SMITH, EDWARD AN
  SCIENCE FICTION: THE FUTURE   ALLEN, DICK   AN

KOESTLER, ARTHUR
AGE OF CLIMAX, THE (FROM "THE GHOST IN THE MACHINE")
                                                      EX   MAC 67
  SPECULATIONS   SANDERS, THOMAS E. AN
BOREDOM OF FANTASY, THE   AR   55
  SCIENCE FICTION: THE FUTURE   ALLEN, DICK   AN
CHIMERAS, THE   SS   PBY 69 05
  FULLY AUTOMATED LOVE LIFE OF HENRY KEANRIDGE
                                     PLAYBOY, EDITORS OF AN
ECHOES OF THE MIND   AR   ESQ 72 08
  SCIENCE FACT/FICTION   FARRELL/GAGE/&   AN
PYTHAGORAS AND THE PSYCHOANALYST   SS   43
  FANTASIA MATHEMATICA   FADIMAN, CLIFTON AN

KOLESNIKOV, LEONID
TRANSLATION   MS
  DESTINATION: AMALTHEIA   DIXON, RICHARD   AN

KOLUPAYEV, VICTOR
TICKET TO CHILDHOOD, A   SS   69
  AIR OF MARS AND OTHER STORIES, THE GINSBURG, MIRRA AN

KOONTZ, DEAN R.
SOFT COME THE DRAGONS   DC   ACE 70
ALTARBOY   SS   INY 72 03
  INFINITY 3   HOSKINS, ROBERT   OA
DARKNESS IN MY SOUL, A   NV   FAN 68 01
  SOFT COME THE DRAGONS   KOONTZ, DEAN R.   DC
DRAGON IN THE LAND   SS   VSF 69 08
  SOFT COME THE DRAGONS   KOONTZ, DEAN R.   DC
GRAYWORLD   SN   INY 73 05
  INFINITY 5   HOSKINS, ROBERT   OA
INTRODUCTION   IN
  SOFT COME THE DRAGONS   KOONTZ, DEAN R.   DC
KILLERBOT| (SEE A SEASON FOR FREEDOM)   TC
MOUSE IN THE WALLS OF THE GLOBAL VILLAGE, A SS   DVS 72 02
  AGAIN, DANGEROUS VISIONS   ELLISON, HARLAN   OA
MUSE   SS   FSF 69 09
  THEMES IN SCIENCE FICTION   KELLEY, LEO P.   AN
NIGHT OF THE STORM, THE   NV   CTM 74 01
  CONTINUUM 1   ELWOOD, ROGER   OA
NIGHTMARE GANG   SS   INY 70 01
  EDGE OF NEVER, THE   HOSKINS, ROBERT   AN
  INFINITY 1   HOSKINS, ROBERT   OA
OLLIE'S HANDS   SS   INY 72 04
  INFINITY 4   HOSKINS, ROBERT   OA
PSYCHEDELIC CHILDREN, THE   SS   FSF 68 07
  SOFT COME THE DRAGONS   KOONTZ, DEAN R.   DC
SEASON FOR FREEDOM, A (KILLERBOT|)   SS   GAL 69 05
  FUTURE NOW, THE   HOSKINS, ROBERT   AN
  SOFT COME THE DRAGONS   KOONTZ, DEAN R.   DC
SINLESS CHILD, THE   SS   FTP 73
  FLAME TREE PLANET   ELWOOD, ROGER   OA
SOFT COME THE DRAGONS   SS   FSF 67 08
  LIBERATED FUTURE: VOYAGES INTO TOMORROW, THE
                                     HOSKINS, ROBERT   AN
  SOFT COME THE DRAGONS   KOONTZ, DEAN R.   DC
TERRA PHOBIA   SS   NEW 73 AN
  ANDROIDS, TIME MACHINES AND BLUE GIRAFFES
                                     ELWOOD & GHIDALIA AN
THIRD HAND, A   NV   FSF 70 01
  SOFT COME THE DRAGONS   KOONTZ, DEAN R.   DC
TO BEHOLD THE SUN   SS   FSF 67 12
  SOFT COME THE DRAGONS   KOONTZ, DEAN R.   DC
TWELTH BED, THE   SS   FSF 68 08
  SOFT COME THE DRAGONS   KOONTZ, DEAN R.   DC
  WONDERMAKERS 2   HOSKINS, ROBERT   AN
UNDERCITY, THE   SS   FUC 73
  CITY: 2000 A.D., THE   CLEM/GREENBERG/& AN
  FUTURE CITY   ELWOOD, ROGER   OA
WAKE UP TO THUNDER   NV   COI 73
  CHILDREN OF INFINITY   ELWOOD, ROGER   OA
WE THREE   SS   FST 74
  FINAL STAGE   FERMAN & MALZBERG OA

KORNBLUTH, C. M.   ALSO AS   CECIL CORWIN AND SIMON EISNER
              SEE ALSO   CO-AUTHOR FREDERIK POHL
BEST OF C. M. KORNBLUTH, THE   AC H NDB 76
  EDITED BY FREDERIK POHL
BEST SCIENCE FICTION STORIES OF C. M. KORNBLUTH AC H FAB 68
EXPLORERS, THE   AC   BAL 54 08
MARCHING MORONS AND OTHER SCIENCE FICTION   AC   BAL 59 04
MILE BEYOND THE MOON, A   AC H DBL 58
MILE BEYOND THE MOON, A (11 OF 15)   AC   MCF 62
MINDWORM AND OTHER STORIES, THE   AC H JOS 55
THIRTEEN O'CLOCK AND OTHER ZERO HOURS   AC   DEL 70
  CECIL CORWIN STORIES, EDITED BY JAMES BLISH
ABOUT THE AUTHOR   MS
  BEST OF C. M. KORNBLUTH, THE   KORNBLUTH, C. M. AC
ADVENT ON CHANNEL TWELVE, THE   SS   STR 58 04
  BEST OF C. M. KORNBLUTH, THE   KORNBLUTH, C. M. AC
  STAR OF STARS   POHL, FREDERIK   AN
  STAR SCIENCE FICTION STORIES NO. 4 POHL, FREDERIK AN
ADVENTURER, THE   SS   SSF 53 05
  ASSIGNMENT IN TOMORROW   POHL, FREDERIK   AN
  BEST OF C. M. KORNBLUTH, THE   KORNBLUTH, C. M. AC
 *MILE BEYOND THE MOON, A   KORNBLUTH, C. M. AC
ALTAR AT MIDNIGHT, THE   SS   GAL 52 11
  BEST OF C. M. KORNBLUTH, THE   KORNBLUTH, C. M. AC
  BEST SCIENCE FICTION STORIES OF C. M. KORNBLUTH
                                     KORNBLUTH, C. M. AC
  BEST SF 2   CRISPIN, EDMUND   AN
  EXPLORERS, THE   KORNBLUTH, C. M. AC
  FIFTY SHORT SCIENCE FICTION TALES ASIMOV & CONKLIN AN
  MINDWORM AND OTHER STORIES, THE   KORNBLUTH, C. M. AC
  PRIZE SCIENCE FICTION   WOLLHEIM, DONALD A. AN
  SPECULATIONS   SANDERS, THOMAS E. AN
BEST FRIEND   SS C SSS 41 05
  WONDER EFFECT, THE   POHL, F. & KORNBLUTH AN
CITY IN THE SOFA, THE   SS   COS 41 07
  THIRTEEN O'CLOCK AND OTHER ZERO HOURS KORNBLUTH, C. M. AC
COSMIC CHARGE ACCOUNT, THE(ALSO AS THE COSMIC EXPENSE ACCOUNT)
                                                      NV   FSF 56 01
  MARCHING MORONS AND OTHER SCIENCE FICTION
                                     KORNBLUTH, C. M. AC
COSMIC EXPENSE ACCOUNT, THE (THE COSMIC CHARGE ACCOUNT)
                                                      NV   FSF 56 01
  BEST FROM FANTASY AND SCIENCE FICTION: 6
                                     BOUCHER, ANTHONY AN
  SF:57, THE YEAR'S GREATEST SCIENCE FICTION AND FANTASY
                                     MERRIL, JUDITH   AN
CRISIS!   SS   SFQ 42 SP
  THIRTEEN O'CLOCK AND OTHER ZERO HOURS KORNBLUTH, C. M. AC
CRITICAL MASS   NA C GAL 62 02
  EIGHTH GALAXY READER, THE   POHL, FREDERIK   AN
  WONDER EFFECT, THE   POHL, F. & KORNBLUTH AN
DOMINOES   SS   STR 53 01
  BEST OF C. M. KORNBLUTH, THE   KORNBLUTH, C. M. AC
  MARCHING MORONS AND OTHER SCIENCE FICTION
                                     KORNBLUTH, C. M. AC
  STAR SCIENCE FICTION STORIES   POHL, FREDERIK   OA
  VOYAGERS IN TIME   SILVERBERG, ROBERT AN
EDUCATION OF TIGRESS MACARDLE, THE   SS   VSF 57 07
  MARRIAGE AND THE FAMILY THROUGH SCIENCE FICTION
                                     CLEAR/WARRICK/&   AN
  NO LIMITS   FERMAN, JOSEPH W. AN
  13 ABOVE THE NIGHT   CONKLIN, GROFF   AN
ENGINEER, THE   SS C INF 56 02
  WONDER EFFECT, THE   POHL, F. & KORNBLUTH AC
EVENTS LEADING DOWN TO THE TRAGEDY, THE SS   FSF 58 01
 *MILE BEYOND THE MOON, A   KORNBLUTH, C. M. AC
EVERYBODY KNOWS JOE   SS   FUN 53 10
 *MILE BEYOND THE MOON, A   KORNBLUTH, C. M. AC
FRIEND TO MAN   SS   TSF 51 SP
  BEST OF C. M. KORNBLUTH, THE   KORNBLUTH, C. M. AC
  BEST SCIENCE FICTION STORIES OF C. M. KORNBLUTH
                                     KORNBLUTH, C. M. AC
  EXPLORERS, THE   KORNBLUTH, C. M. AC
  MINDWORM AND OTHER STORIES, THE   KORNBLUTH, C. M. AC
GENTLE DYING, A   SS C GAL 61 06
  WONDER EFFECT, THE   POHL, F. & KORNBLUTH AC
GIFT OF GARIGOLLI, THE   NV C GAL 74 08
  BEST FROM GALAXY, THE VOLUME III BAEN, JAMES   AN
  1975 ANNUAL WORLD'S BEST SF, THE   WOLLHEIM, DONALD A. AN
GOLDEN ROAD, THE   NV   STI 42 03
  THIRTEEN O'CLOCK AND OTHER ZERO HOURS KORNBLUTH, C. M. AC
GOMEZ   NV   NEW 54 AC
  BEST OF C. M. KORNBLUTH, THE   KORNBLUTH, C. M. AC
  BEST SCIENCE FICTION STORIES OF C. M. KORNBLUTH
                                     KORNBLUTH, C. M. AC
  EXPLORERS, THE   KORNBLUTH, C. M. AC
  MINDWORM AND OTHER STORIES, THE   KORNBLUTH, C. M. AC
  THEMES IN SCIENCE FICTION   KELLEY, LEO P.   AN
  TOMORROW AND TOMORROW   KNIGHT, DAMON   AN
  TREASURY OF GREAT SCIENCE FICTION, A VOL.1
                                     BOUCHER, ANTHONY AN
GOODLY CREATURES, THE   SS   FSF 52 12
  EXPLORERS, THE   KORNBLUTH, C. M. AC
  MINDWORM AND OTHER STORIES, THE   KORNBLUTH, C. M. AC
I NEVER AST NO FAVORS   SS   FSF 54 04
  BEST FROM FANTASY AND SCIENCE FICTION: 4
                                     BOUCHER, ANTHONY AN
  BEST SCIENCE FICTION STORIES OF C. M. KORNBLUTH
                                     KORNBLUTH, C. M. AC
  MARCHING MORONS AND OTHER SCIENCE FICTION
                                     KORNBLUTH, C. M. AC
KAZAM COLLECTS   SS   STI 41 06
 *MILE BEYOND THE MOON, A   KORNBLUTH, C. M. AC
  WORLDS FAR AND NEAR   CARR, TERRY   AN
LAST MAN LEFT IN THE BAR, THE   SS   INF 57 10
  ALPHA 1   SILVERBERG, ROBERT AN

KORNBLUTH, C. M.   (CONTINUED)
  BEST OF C. M. KORNBLUTH, THE   KORNBLUTH, C. M.   AC
 *MILE BEYOND THE MOON, A   KORNBLUTH, C. M.   AC
LITTLE BLACK BAG, THE   NV   ASF 50 07
  ASTOUNDING-ANALOG READER, THE VOLUME TWO
                                        HARRISON & ALDISS   AN
  BEST OF C. M. KORNBLUTH, THE   KORNBLUTH, C. M.   AC
  BEST SCIENCE FICTION STORIES OF C. M. KORNBLUTH
                                        KORNBLUTH, C. M.   AC
  BEYOND THE END OF TIME   POHL, FREDERIK   AN
  GREAT SCIENCE FICTION ABOUT DOCTORS   CONKLIN, G&FABRICANT   AN
  LIBERATED FUTURE: VOYAGES INTO TOMORROW,
                                        HOSKINS, ROBERT   AN
 *MILE BEYOND THE MOON, A   KORNBLUTH, C. M.   AC
  MINDWORM AND OTHER STORIES, THE   KORNBLUTH, C. M.   AC
  SCIENCE FICTION HALL OF FAME VOLUME 1 SILVERBERG, ROBERT   AN
  SCIENCE FICTION: THE GREAT YEARS   POHL, C. & F.   AN
  TIME PROBE: THE SCIENCES IN SF.   CLARKE, ARTHUR C.   AN
LUCKIEST MAN IN DENV, THE (AS SIMON EISNER)   SS   GAL 52 06
  ALPHA 7   SILVERBERG, ROBERT   AN
  BEST OF C. M. KORNBLUTH, THE   KORNBLUTH, C. M.   AC
  CITIES OF WONDER   KNIGHT, DAMON   AN
  HOT & COLD RUNNING CITIES   MCHARGUE, GEORGESS   AN
  MARCHING MORONS AND OTHER SCIENCE FICTION
                                        KORNBLUTH, C. M.   AC
  MINDWORM AND OTHER STORIES, THE   KORNBLUTH, C. M.   AC
  NIGHTMARE AGE   POHL, FREDERIK   AN
MAKE MINE MARS   NV   SPA 52 11
 *MILE BEYOND THE MOON, A   KORNBLUTH, C. M.   AC
MARCHING MORONS, THE   NV   GAL 51 04
  BEST OF C. M. KORNBLUTH, THE   KORNBLUTH, C. M.   AC
  BEST SCIENCE FICTION STORIES OF C. M. KORNBLUTH
                                        KORNBLUTH, C. M.   AC
  BEST SCIENCE-FICTION STORIES: 1952, THE
                                        BLEILER & DIKTY   AN
  DIMENSION X   KNIGHT, DAMON   AN
  LOOKING AHEAD   ALLEN, D. & L.   AN
  MARCHING MORONS AND OTHER SCIENCE FICTION
                                        KORNBLUTH, C. M.   AC
  MINDWORM AND OTHER STORIES, THE   KORNBLUTH, C. M.   AC
  MODERN SCIENCE FICTION   SPINRAD, NORMAN   AN
  NIGHTMARE AGE   POHL, FREDERIK   AN
  SCIENCE FICTION HALL OF FAME VOLUME 2A BOVA, BEN   AN
  SHADOW OF TOMORROW   POHL, FREDERIK   AN
  SPECTRUM 4   AMIS & CONQUEST   AN
MARS-TUBE   SS C AST 41 09
  WONDER EFFECT, THE   POHL, F. & KORNBLUTH   AC
MEDDLERS, THE   SS   SFA 53 09
 *MILE BEYOND THE MOON, A   KORNBLUTH, C. M.   AC
MEETING, THE   SS C FSF 72 11
  BEST SCIENCE FICTION OF THE YEAR, THE NO. 2
                                        CARR, TERRY   AN
  BEST SCIENCE FICTION STORIES OF THE YEAR (1972)
                                        DEL REY, LESTER   AN
MINDWORM, THE   SS   WBY 50 12
  BEST OF C. M. KORNBLUTH, THE   KORNBLUTH, C. M.   AC
  BEST SCIENCE FICTION STORIES OF C. M. KORNBLUTH
                                        KORNBLUTH, C. M.   AC
  BEST SCIENCE-FICTION STORIES: 1951, THE
                                        BLEILER & DIKTY   AN
  EXPLORERS, THE   KORNBLUTH, C. M.   AC
  MIND TO MIND   SILVERBERG, ROBERT   AN
  MINDWORM AND OTHER STORIES, THE   KORNBLUTH, C. M.   AC
  MINDWORM, THE   ANONYMOUS   AN
  ONE HUNDRED YEARS OF SCIENCE FICTION KNIGHT, DAMON   AN
MR. PACKER GOES TO HELL (SEE THIRTEEN O'CLOCK & MR. PACKER
  GOES TO HELL)   TC   STI 41 06
MS. FOUND IN A CHINESE FORTUNE COOKIE   SS   FSF 57 07
  BEST FROM FANTASY AND SCIENCE FICTION: 7
                                        BOUCHER, ANTHONY   AN
  MARCHING MORONS AND OTHER SCIENCE FICTION
                                        KORNBLUTH, C. M.   AC
  THIRTEEN O'CLOCK AND OTHER ZERO HOURS KORNBLUTH, C. M.   AC
  YET MORE PENGUIN SCIENCE FICTION   ALDISS, BRIAN W.   AN
MUTE INGLORIOUS TAM   SS C FSF 74 10
  BEST SCIENCE FICTION STORIES OF THE YEAR (1974)
                                        DEL REY, LESTER   AN
NIGHTMARE WITH ZEPPELINS   NV C GAL 58 12
  FIFTH GALAXY READER, THE   GOLD, H. L.   AN
  WONDER EFFECT, THE   POHL, F. & KORNBLUTH   AC
ONLY THING WE LEARN, THE   SS   STS 49 07
  BEST OF C. M. KORNBLUTH, THE   KORNBLUTH, C. M.   AC
  BEST SCIENCE FICTION STORIES OF C. M. KORNBLUTH
                                        KORNBLUTH, C. M.   AC
 *BIG BOOK OF SCIENCE FICTION   CONKLIN, GROFF   AN
  MARCHING MORONS AND OTHER SCIENCE FICTION
                                        KORNBLUTH, C. M.   AC
  SHAPE OF THINGS, THE   KNIGHT, DAMON   AN
PASSION PILLS   SS   NEW 58 AC
 *MILE BEYOND THE MOON, A   KORNBLUTH, C. M.   AC
QUAKER CANNON, THE   NV C ASF 61 08
  WONDER EFFECT, THE   POHL, F. & KORNBLUTH   AC
  7TH ANNUAL OF THE YEAR'S BEST S-F, THE MERRIL, JUDITH   AN
REAP THE DARK TIDE (SEE SHARK SHIP)   TC
REMORSEFUL, THE   SS   STR 53 02
  BEST OF C. M. KORNBLUTH, THE   KORNBLUTH, C. M.   AC
  MARCHING MORONS AND OTHER SCIENCE FICTION
                                        KORNBLUTH, C. M.   AC
  STAR SCIENCE FICTION STORIES NO. 2   POHL, FREDERIK   OA
REVERSIBLE REVOLUTIONS, THE   SS   COS 41 03
  THIRTEEN O'CLOCK AND OTHER ZERO HOURS KORNBLUTH, C. M.   AC
ROCKET OF 1955, THE   SS   STI 41 04
  BEST OF C. M. KORNBLUTH, THE   KORNBLUTH, C. M.   AC
  EXPLORERS, THE   KORNBLUTH, C. M.   AC
  MINDWORM AND OTHER STORIES, THE   KORNBLUTH, C. M.   AC
  THIRTEEN O'CLOCK AND OTHER ZERO HOURS KORNBLUTH, C. M.   AC

KORNBLUTH, C. M.   (CONTINUED)
  VINTAGE ANTHOLOGY OF SCIENCE FANTASY, THE
                                        CERF, CHRISTOPHER   AN
SHARK SHIP (REAP THE DARK TIDE)   NV   VAN 58 06
  BEST OF C. M. KORNBLUTH, THE   KORNBLUTH, C. M.   AC
  DARK STARS   SILVERBERG, ROBERT   AN
 *MILE BEYOND THE MOON, A   KORNBLUTH, C. M.   AC
  SCIENCE FICTION OMNIBUS ON POLLUTION, A
                                        ANONYMOUS   AN
  VOYAGES: SCENARIOS FOR A SHIP CALLED EARTH
                                        SAUER, ROB   AN
SILLY SEASON, THE   SS   FSF 50 FL
  BEST OF C. M. KORNBLUTH, THE   KORNBLUTH, C. M.   AC
  BEST SCIENCE FICTION STORIES OF C. M. KORNBLUTH
                                        KORNBLUTH, C. M.   AC
  EARTH IN PERIL, THE   WOLLHEIM, DONALD A.   DA
  FIRST CONTACT   KNIGHT, DAMON   AN
  INVADERS FROM SPACE   SILVERBERG, ROBERT   AN
  MARCHING MORONS AND OTHER SCIENCE FICTION
                                        KORNBLUTH, C. M.   AC
  MINDWORM AND OTHER STORIES, THE   KORNBLUTH, C. M.   AC
  TOMORROW, THE STARS   HEINLEIN, ROBERT A.   AN
  TWENTY YEARS OF FANTASY & SCIENCE FICTION
                                        FERMAN & MILLS   AN
SLAVE, THE   NV   SFA 57 09
 *MILE BEYOND THE MOON, A   KORNBLUTH, C. M.   AC
THAT SHARE OF GLORY   NV   ASF 52 01
  ALPHA 2   SILVERBERG, ROBERT   AN
  BEST SCIENCE FICTION STORIES OF C. M. KORNBLUTH
                                        KORNBLUTH, C. M.   AC
  EVERY BOY'S BOOK OF OUTER SPACE STORIES
                                        DIKTY, T. E.   AN
  EXPLORERS, THE   KORNBLUTH, C. M.   AC
  MINDWORM AND OTHER STORIES, THE   KORNBLUTH, C. M.   AC
  SPACE SERVICE   NORTON, ANDRE   AN
  WORLDS TO COME   KNIGHT, DAMON   AN
THEORY OF ROCKETRY   SS   FSF 58 07
  BEST FROM FANTASY AND SCIENCE FICTION: 8
                                        BOUCHER, ANTHONY   AN
  BEST SCIENCE FICTION STORIES OF C. M. KORNBLUTH
                                        KORNBLUTH, C. M.   AC
  MASTERS' CHOICE   JANIFER, LAURENCE M.   AN
THIRTEEN O'CLOCK   NV   STI 41 02
  EXPLORERS, THE   KORNBLUTH, C. M.   AC
THIRTEEN O'CLOCK & MR. PACKER GOES TO HELL   NV   STI 41 02
  THIRTEEN O'CLOCK AND OTHER ZERO HOURS KORNBLUTH, C. M.   AC
TIME BUM   SS   FAN 53 02
 *MILE BEYOND THE MOON, A   KORNBLUTH, C. M.   AC
TIME TRAVEL AND THE LAW   AR
  COMING ATTRACTIONS   GREENBERG, MARTIN   NF
TROUBLE IN TIME   SS C AST 40 12
  WONDER EFFECT, THE   POHL, F. & KORNBLUTH   AC
TWO DOOMS   NV   VSF 58 07
  BEST OF C. M. KORNBLUTH, THE   KORNBLUTH, C. M.   AC
  GREAT SHORT NOVELS OF SCIENCE FICTION SILVERBERG, ROBERT   AN
 *MILE BEYOND THE MOON, A   KORNBLUTH, C. M.   AC
UNFORTUNATE TOPOLOGIST, THE   PM   FSF 57 07
  BEST SCIENCE FICTION STORIES OF C. M. KORNBLUTH
                                        KORNBLUTH, C. M.   AC
  FANTASIA MATHEMATICA   FADIMAN, CLIFTON   AN
VIRGINIA   SS   VSF 58 03
 *MILE BEYOND THE MOON, A   KORNBLUTH, C. M.   AC
WHAT SORGHUM SAYS   SS   COS 41 05
  THIRTEEN O'CLOCK AND OTHER ZERO HOURS KORNBLUTH, C. M.   AC
WITH THESE HANDS   NV   GAL 51 12
  ALPHA 6   SILVERBERG, ROBERT   AN
  BEST OF C. M. KORNBLUTH, THE   KORNBLUTH, C. M.   AC
  BEST SCIENCE FICTION STORIES OF C. M. KORNBLUTH
                                        KORNBLUTH, C. M.   AC
  EXPLORERS, THE   KORNBLUTH, C. M.   AC
  FUTURE TENSE   CURTIS, RICHARD   AN
  MINDWORM AND OTHER STORIES, THE   KORNBLUTH, C. M.   AC
  NEW DREAMS THIS MORNING   BLISH, JAMES   AN
  SECOND ORBIT   DOHERTY, G. D.   AN
WORDS OF GURU, THE   SS   STI 41 06
  BEST OF C. M. KORNBLUTH, THE   KORNBLUTH, C. M.   AC
  CHILDREN OF WONDER   TENN, WILLIAM   AN
  GOLDEN ROAD, THE   KNIGHT, DAMON   AN
 *MILE BEYOND THE MOON, A   KORNBLUTH, C. M.   AC
WORLD OF MYRION FLOWERS, THE   SS C FSF 61 10
  HUMAN AND OTHER BEINGS   DEGRAEFF, ALLEN   AN
  THEMES IN SCIENCE FICTION   KELLEY, LEO P.   AN
  WONDER EFFECT, THE   POHL, F. & KORNBLUTH   AC

KORNBLUTH, MARY
  SCIENCE FICTION SHOWCASE   AN H DBL 59
    CURTIS PB EDITION OMITS STORY "MED SERVICE"

KORSHAK, MELVIN
  TRENDS IN MODERN SCIENCE-FICTION   IN
    BEST SCIENCE-FICTION STORIES: 1949, THE
                                        BLEILER & DIKTY   AN

KORZENIOWSKI, TEODOR SEE PSEUD. JOSEPH CONRAD

KRAPIVIV, VLADISLAV
  MEETING MY BROTHER   SS
    PATH INTO THE UNKNOWN   ANONYMOUS   AN

KRENKEL, R.
  ILLUSTRATIONS   IL
    TALES OF THREE PLANETS   BURROUGHS, EDGAR R.   AC

KREPPS, ROBERT W.
  ENORMOUS ROOM, THE   SN C AMZ 53 11
    WORLDS APART   WILLIAMS-ELLIS& OWEN   AN

KREPPS, ROBERT W.

KREPPS, ROBERT W.   (CONTINUED)
   YEAR'S BEST SCIENCE FICTION NOVELS: 1954
                                    BLEILER & DIKTY   AN
                                    SS FAD 49 07
   FIVE YEARS IN THE MARMALADE
      BEST SCIENCE-FICTION STORIES: 1950, THE
                                    BLEILER & DIKTY   AN

KRUSE, CLIFTON B.
   DR. LU-MIE   SS ASF 34 07
      EVERY BOY'S BOOK OF SCIENCE FICTION WOLLHEIM, DONALD A. AN

KUBILIUS, WALTER
   CARIDI SHALL NOT DIE   SS SFQ 41 WI
      INTO THE FOURTH DIMENSION   CUMMINGS, RAY   AN
   ETERNAL EARTHLING (SEE THE OTHER SIDE) TC
   OTHER SIDE, THE (ETERNAL EARTHLING) SS SSS 51 04
      BEST SCIENCE-FICTION STORIES: 1952, THE
                                    BLEILER & DIKTY   AN
                                    SS C FSM 52 FL
   SECOND CHANCE
      SPACE, SPACE, SPACE   SLOANE, WILLIAM   AN

KUEBLER, HAROLD W.
   TREASURY OF SCIENCE FICTION CLASSICS, THE AN H HAN 54
   INTRODUCTION   IN
      TREASURY OF SCIENCE FICTION CLASSICS, THE
                                    KUEBLER, HAROLD W.   AN

KUMIN, MAXINE W.
   TO AN ASTRONAUT DYING YOUNG   PM ATL 61 12
      7TH ANNUAL OF THE YEAR'S BEST S-F, THE MERRIL, JUDITH AN

KUMMER, FREDERICK A.
   FORGIVENESS OF TENCHU TAEN, THE SS ASF 38 11
      TRAVELLERS OF SPACE   GREENBERG, MARTIN   AN
                                    NA C TWS 50 02
   WHEN TIME WENT MAD
      SCIENCE FICTION: THE GREAT YEARS, VOL. II
                                    POHL, C. & F.   AN

KUNITZ, STANLEY
   FLIGHT OF APOLLO, THE   PM 69
      SCIENCE FICTION   BRODKIN & PEARSON   AN
      SPECULATIONS   SANDERS, THOMAS E.   AN

KUNOS, IGNAZ
   BOY WHO FOUND FEAR, THE   SS 07
      TALES BEYOND TIME   DE CAMP, L. S.&C.   AN

KUPFERBERG, TULI
   CINEMAGICIANS   PM ESR 66
      SF12   MERRIL, JUDITH   AN
   PERSONAL   SS ESR 66
      AS TOMORROW BECOMES TODAY   SULLIVAN, CHARLES W. AN
      SF12   MERRIL, JUDITH   AN
   W-A-V-E-R   PM ESR 66
      SF12   MERRIL, JUDITH   AN

KURLAND, MICHAEL J.
   ELEMENTARY   SS C FSF 64 09
      IMPOSSIBLE?   JANIFER, LAURENCE M. AC
   SMALL WORLD   NV TVW 73
      TWO VIEWS OF WONDER   SCORTIA & YARBRO   OA
   THINK ONLY THIS OF ME   NV GAL 73 11
      BEST SCIENCE FICTION STORIES OF THE YEAR (1973)
                                    DEL REY, LESTER   AN

KUROSAKA, BOB
   THOSE WHO CAN, DO   SS FSF 65 01
      11TH ANNUAL OF THE YEAR'S BEST S-F, THE
                                    MERRIL, JUDITH   AN

KUTTNER, HENRY AND C. L. MOORE
   NO BOUNDARIES   AC H BAL 55

KUTTNER, HENRY   ALSO AS
   KELVIN KENT, LAWRENCE O'DONNELL (WITH C. L. MOORE) AND LEWIS
   PADGETT (WITH C. L. MOORE)   AC BAL 53 07
   AHEAD OF TIME   AC MFL 65
   BEST OF HENRY KUTTNER 1, THE   AC MFL 66
   BEST OF HENRY KUTTNER 2, THE   AC H NDB 75
   BEST OF HENRY KUTTNER, THE   AC BAL 61
   BYPASS TO OTHERNESS   AN POP 67
   DR. CYCLOPS   AC BAL 62
   RETURN TO OTHERNESS   SS STS 46 FL
   ABSALOM
      BEST OF HENRY KUTTNER 1, THE KUTTNER, HENRY   AC
      BEST OF HENRY KUTTNER, THE   KUTTNER, HENRY   AC
      BYPASS TO OTHERNESS   KUTTNER, HENRY   AC
      TOMORROW, THE STARS   HEINLEIN, ROBERT A.   AN
      TRANSFORMATIONS   ROSELLE, DANIEL   AN
                                    NV FSF 51 06
   ANDROID (ALSO AS THOSE AMONG US)
      RETURN TO OTHERNESS   KUTTNER, HENRY   AC
                                    SS TWS 40 04
   BEAUTY AND THE BEAST
      CREATURES FROM BEYOND   CARR, TERRY   AN
      FUTURES TO INFINITY   MOSKOWITZ, SAM   AN
                                    NV TWS 47 06
   BIG NIGHT, THE (AS HUDSON HASTINGS)
      BEST OF HENRY KUTTNER 1, THE KUTTNER, HENRY   AC
      BEST OF HENRY KUTTNER, THE   KUTTNER, HENRY   AC
                                    NV SSS 49 01
   BLACK SUN RISES, THE
      SPACE MAGICIANS, THE   NORTON & MOSKOWITZ   AN
                                    SS FAN 53 03
   BY THESE PRESENTS
      AHEAD OF TIME   KUTTNER, HENRY   AC
                                    SS TWS 46 FL
   CALL HIM DEMON
      BEST OF HENRY KUTTNER 1, THE KUTTNER, HENRY   AC
      BYPASS TO OTHERNESS   KUTTNER, HENRY   AC
      DEVIL'S GENERATION, THE   GHIDALIA, VIC   AN
      *STRANGE PORTS OF CALL   DERLETH, AUGUST   AN

KUTTNER, HENRY   (CONTINUED)
                                    NV ASF 45 09
   CAMOUFLAGE   KUTTNER, HENRY   AC
      AHEAD OF TIME   SISSONS, MICHAEL   AN
      ASLEEP IN ARMAGEDDON   CRISPIN, EDMUND   AN
      BEST SF 6   SCORTIA & ZEBROWSKI   AN
      HUMAN-MACHINES   NV ASF 44 03
   CHILDREN'S HOUR, THE   CONKLIN, GROFF   AN
      FOUR FOR THE FUTURE   NV C ASF 44 03
   CHILDREN'S HOUR, THE
      TREASURY OF GREAT SCIENCE FICTION, A VOL.1
                                    BOUCHER, ANTHONY   AN
                                    NV ASF 43 03
   CLASH BY NIGHT   KUTTNER, HENRY   AC
      BEST OF HENRY KUTTNER 2, THE SS TWS 49 10
   COLD WAR   KUTTNER, HENRY   AC
      BEST OF HENRY KUTTNER 1, THE KUTTNER, HENRY   AC
      BEST OF HENRY KUTTNER, THE   KUTTNER, HENRY   AC
      BYPASS TO OTHERNESS   CONKLIN, GROFF   AN
      *SCIENCE FICTION ADVENTURES IN MUTATION SS STR 58 04
   CROSS OF CENTURIES, A
      OTHER WORLDS, OTHER GODS   MOHS, MAYO   AN
      STAR OF STARS   POHL, FREDERIK   AN
      STAR SCIENCE FICTION STORIES NO. 4 POHL, FREDERIK OA
   CURE, THE   SS C ASF 46 05
      SCIENCE FICTION ARGOSY, A   KNIGHT, DAMON   AN
   DARK ANGEL, THE   SS STS 46 03
      BYPASS TO OTHERNESS   KUTTNER, HENRY   AC
                                    SS SFQ 53 05
   DE PROFUNDIS (THE VISITORS)   KUTTNER, HENRY   AC
      AHEAD OF TIME   SS ASF 42 08
   DEADLOCK   KUTTNER, HENRY   AC
      AHEAD OF TIME   NV UNK 41 08
   DEVIL WE KNOW, THE   KUTTNER, HENRY   AC
      BEST OF HENRY KUTTNER 2, THE CAMPBELL, JOHN W. JR AN
      FROM UNKNOWN WORLDS   KUTTNER & MOORE   AC
      NO BOUNDARIES   SS STS 48 03
   DON'T LOOK NOW
      BEST OF HENRY KUTTNER 1, THE KUTTNER, HENRY   AC
      HISTORY OF THE SCIENCE FICTION MAGAZINE, THE PART 3 1946-1955
                                    ASHLEY, MICHAEL   AN
                                    JANIFER, LAURENCE M. AN
      MASTERS' CHOICE
      *MY BEST SCIENCE FICTION STORY MARGULIES & FRIEND AN
      SHAPE OF THINGS, THE   KNIGHT, DAMON   AN
                                    SS TWS 40 06
   DR. CYCLOPS
      DR. CYCLOPS   KUTTNER, HENRY   AN
                                    SS STS 47 07
   DREAM'S END   CROSSEN, KENDELL F.   AN
      *FUTURE TENSE
      PERCHANCE TO DREAM   KNIGHT, DAMON   AN
                                    NV SSF 52 05
   EGO MACHINE, THE
      BEST OF HENRY KUTTNER 1, THE KUTTNER, HENRY   AC
      RETURN TO OTHERNESS   KUTTNER, HENRY   AC
      *SCIENCE-FICTION CARNIVAL   BROWN, F. & REYNOLDS AN
                                    SS ASF 43 08
   ENDOWMENT POLICY
      BEST OF HENRY KUTTNER 2, THE KUTTNER, HENRY   AC
      BEST OF HENRY KUTTNER, THE   KUTTNER, HENRY   AC
                                    SS TWS 47 10
   EXIT THE PROFESSOR
      BEST OF HENRY KUTTNER 2, THE KUTTNER, HENRY   AC
      BEST OF HENRY KUTTNER, THE   KUTTNER, HENRY   AC
      NO BOUNDARIES   KUTTNER & MOORE   AC
                                    NV ASF 43 11
   GALLEGHER PLUS
      COSMIC LAUGHTER   HALDEMAN, JOE W.   AN
      RETURN TO OTHERNESS   KUTTNER, HENRY   AC
                                    SS ASF 43 05
   GHOST
      AHEAD OF TIME   KUTTNER, HENRY   AC
                                    NV UNK 41 10
   GNOME THERE WAS, A
      ALONE BY NIGHT   CONGDON, MICHAEL&DON AN
      BEST OF HENRY KUTTNER 1, THE KUTTNER, HENRY   AC
      BEST OF HENRY KUTTNER, THE   KUTTNER, HENRY   AC
                                    SS WRT 36 03
   GRAVEYARD RATS, THE
      GRAVEYARD READER, THE   CONKLIN, GROFF   AN
      OTHER WORLDS, THE   STONG, PHILIP D.   AN
                                    NV TWS 48 08
   HAPPY ENDING
      BEST SCIENCE-FICTION STORIES: 1949, THE
                                    BLEILER & DIKTY   AN
                                    KNIGHT, DAMON   AN
      BEYOND TOMORROW   NV GAL 53 07
   HOME IS THE HUNTER   KUTTNER, HENRY   AC
      AHEAD OF TIME   NV C NEW 55 AC
   HOME THERE'S NO RETURNING
      NO BOUNDARIES   KUTTNER & MOORE   AC
      SF: THE YEAR'S GREATEST SCIENCE FICTION AND FANTASY
                                    MERRIL, JUDITH   AN
                                    SS CHM 44 10
   HOUSING PROBLEM
      BEST OF HENRY KUTTNER 1, THE KUTTNER, HENRY   AC
      BEST OF HENRY KUTTNER, THE   KUTTNER, HENRY   AC
      BYPASS TO OTHERNESS   KUTTNER, HENRY   AC
      FANTASY: THE LITERATURE OF THE MARVELOUS
                                    KELLEY, LEO P.   AN
      TIMELESS STORIES FOR TODAY AND TOMORROW
                                    BRADBURY, RAY   AN
   INNOCENT EYE, THE   IN
      REVOLT IN 2100   HEINLEIN, ROBERT A.   AC
   IRON STANDARD, THE   SS ASF 43 12
      BEST OF HENRY KUTTNER 2, THE KUTTNER, HENRY   AC
      BEST OF HENRY KUTTNER, THE   KUTTNER, HENRY   AC
                                    SS ASF 47 05
   JESTING PILOT
      CITIES OF WONDER   KNIGHT, DAMON   AN
      CITY: 2000 A.D., THE   CLEM/GREENBERG/&   AN
                                    SS TWS 47 02
   JUKE-BOX
      BEST OF HENRY KUTTNER 1, THE KUTTNER, HENRY   AC
      RETURN TO OTHERNESS   KUTTNER, HENRY   AC
                                    SS ASF 45 11
   LINE TO TOMORROW
      BEST OF HENRY KUTTNER 2, THE KUTTNER, HENRY   AC
                                    SS TWS 46 FL
   LITTLE THINGS, THE
      BYPASS TO OTHERNESS   KUTTNER, HENRY   AC
                                    SS WRT 42 05
   MASQUERADE
      BEST OF HENRY KUTTNER 2, THE KUTTNER, HENRY   AC
                                    NV ASF 43 02
   MIMSY WERE THE BOROGOVES
      BEST OF HENRY KUTTNER 2, THE KUTTNER, HENRY   AC

KUTTNER, HENRY   (CONTINUED)
   BEST OF HENRY KUTTNER, THE   KUTTNER, HENRY   AC
   LITTLE MONSTERS, THE   ELWOOD & GHIDALIA   AN
MISGUIDED HALO, THE   SS   UNK 39 08
   BEST OF HENRY KUTTNER, THE   KUTTNER, HENRY   AC
   UNKNOWN, THE   BENSEN, D. R.   AN
NEAR MISS   SS   NEW 58 AN
   SF:58, THE YEAR'S GREATEST SCIENCE FICTION AND FANTASY
                                         MERRIL, JUDITH   AN
NOTHING BUT GINGERBREAD LEFT   SS   ASF 43 01
   BEST OF HENRY KUTTNER, THE   KUTTNER, HENRY   AC
   BYPASS TO OTHERNESS   KUTTNER, HENRY   AC
OR ELSE   SS   AMZ 53 09
   AHEAD OF TIME   KUTTNER, HENRY   AC
   BEST OF HENRY KUTTNER 1, THE   KUTTNER, HENRY   AC
   BEST OF HENRY KUTTNER, THE   KUTTNER, HENRY   AC
   BEST SF   CRISPIN, EDMUND   AN
OR ELSE   SS C AMZ 53 09
   NEVER IN THIS WORLD   STONE, IDELLA P.   AN
PIGGY BANK   NV   ASF 42 12
   INVASION OF THE ROBOTS   ELWOOD, ROGER   AN
   TREASURY OF GREAT SCIENCE FICTION, A VOL.2
                                         BOUCHER, ANTHONY   AN
PILE OF TROUBLE   SS   TWS 48 04
   AHEAD OF TIME   KUTTNER, HENRY   AC
   ZACHERLEY'S MIDNIGHT SNACKS   ZACHERLEY   AN
PIPER'S SON, THE   NV   ASF 45 02
   BEST OF HENRY KUTTNER 1, THE   KUTTNER, HENRY   AC
   BYPASS TO OTHERNESS   KUTTNER, HENRY   AC
PRIVATE EYE   NV   ASF 49 01
   BEST SCIENCE-FICTION STORIES: 1950, THE
                                         BLEILER & DIKTY   AN
   LIBERATED FUTURE: VOYAGES INTO TOMORROW, THE
                                         HOSKINS, ROBERT   AN
PRIVATE EYE   NV C ASF 49 01
   SCIENCE FICTION INVENTIONS   KNIGHT, DAMON   AN
PROUD ROBOT, THE   NV   ASF 43 10
   BEST OF HENRY KUTTNER 1, THE   KUTTNER, HENRY   AC
   BEST OF HENRY KUTTNER 1, THE   KUTTNER, HENRY   AC
   RETURN TO OTHERNESS   KUTTNER, HENRY   AC
SEE YOU LATER   SS   TWS 49 06
   BEST OF HENRY KUTTNER 1, THE   KUTTNER, HENRY   AC
   RETURN TO OTHERNESS   KUTTNER, HENRY   AC
SHOCK   SS   ASF 43 03
   AHEAD OF TIME   KUTTNER, HENRY   AC
   BEST OF HENRY KUTTNER 1, THE   KUTTNER, HENRY   AC
   *OUTER REACHES, THE   DERLETH, AUGUST   AN
SKY IS FALLING, THE   SS   PLS 50 FL
   RETURN TO OTHERNESS   KUTTNER, HENRY   AC
SPAWN OF DAGON   NV   WRT 38 07
   GHOUL KEEPERS, THE   MARGULIES, LEO   AN
SWORD OF TOMORROW   NV   TWS 45 FL
   GIANT ANTHOLOGY OF SCIENCE FICTION   MARGULIES & FRIEND   AN
THIS IS THE HOUSE   SS   ASF 46 02
   RETURN TO OTHERNESS   KUTTNER, HENRY   AC
THOSE AMONG US (ANDROID, AS C. H. LIDDELL) NV FSF 51 06
   PSEUDO PEOPLE, THE   NOLAN, WILLIAM F.   AN
THRESHOLD   SS   UNK 40 12
   CIRCUS OF DR. LAO AND OTHER IMPROBABLE STORIES
                                         BRADBURY, RAY   AN
   DEALS WITH THE DEVIL   DAVENPORT, BASIL   AN
TIME TRAP, THE   NO   MSS 38 11
   EVIL EARTHS   ALDISS, BRIAN W.   AN
TROPHY   SS   TWS 44 WI
   SAINT'S CHOICE OF IMPOSSIBLE CRIME, THE
                                         CHARTERIS, LESLIE   AN
TWO-HANDED ENGINE   SS   FSF 55 08
   BEST OF HENRY KUTTNER 2, THE   KUTTNER, HENRY   AC
   BEST OF HENRY KUTTNER, THE   KUTTNER, HENRY   AC
   DECADE THE 1950S   ALDISS & HARRISON   AN
   NO BOUNDARIES   KUTTNER & MOORE   AC
TWO-HANDED ENGINE   SS C FSF 55 08
   METAL SMILE, THE   KNIGHT, DAMON   AN
TWONKY, THE   SS   ASF 42 09
   BEST OF HENRY KUTTNER 2, THE   KUTTNER, HENRY   AC
   BEST OF HENRY KUTTNER, THE   KUTTNER, HENRY   AC
   SOULS IN METAL   ASHLEY, MICHAEL   AN
VINTAGE SEASON   NV   ASF 46 09
   NO BOUNDARIES   KUTTNER & MOORE   AC
   SPECTRUM 2   AMIS & CONQUEST   AN
VINTAGE SEASON   NV C ASF 46 09
   SCIENCE FICTION HALL OF FAME VOLUME 2A BOVA, BEN   AN
VISITORS, THE (SEE DE PROFUNDIS)   TC
VOICE OF THE LOBSTER, THE   NV   TWS 50 02
   ADVENTURES IN TOMORROW   CROSSEN, KENDELL F.   AN
   BEST OF HENRY KUTTNER 2, THE   KUTTNER, HENRY   AC
   BEST OF HENRY KUTTNER, THE   KUTTNER, HENRY   AC
WE GUARD THE BLACK PLANET!   NV   SSS 42 11
   MODERN MASTERPIECES OF SCIENCE FICTION MOSKOWITZ, SAM   AN
   PLANETS OF WONDER   CARR, TERRY   AN
   VORTEX BLASTERS, THE   MOSKOWITZ, SAM   AN
WHAT YOU NEED   SS   ASF 45 10
   BEST OF HENRY KUTTNER 2, THE   KUTTNER, HENRY   AC
   BEST OF HENRY KUTTNER, THE   KUTTNER, HENRY   AC
WHEN THE BOUGH BREAKS   NV   ASF 44 11
   BEST OF HENRY KUTTNER 2, THE   KUTTNER, HENRY   AC
WHEN THE EARTH LIVED   SS   TWS 37 10
   FROM OFF THIS WORLD   MARGULIES & FRIEND   AN
WHY I SELECTED DON'T LOOK NOW   AI
   *MY BEST SCIENCE FICTION STORY   MARGULIES & FRIEND   AN
WILD SURMISE, A   SS   STR 53 01
   BEST OF HENRY KUTTNER 2, THE   KUTTNER, HENRY   AC
WILD SURMISE, A   SS C STR 53 01
   STAR SCIENCE FICTION STORIES   POHL, FREDERIK   OA
YEAR DAY   SS   NEW 53 AC
   AHEAD OF TIME   KUTTNER, HENRY   AC

KUTTNER, HENRY   (CONTINUED)
   BEST OF HENRY KUTTNER 1, THE   KUTTNER, HENRY   AC
KUYKENDALL, ROGER
   WE DIDN'T DO ANYTHING WRONG, HARDLY   SS   ASF 59 05
   PROLOGUE TO ANALOG   CAMPBELL, JOHN W. JR   AN
   WORLDS OF WONDER   HARRISON, HARRY   AN
KYLE, DAVID A.
   FERRYMAN ON THE RIVER, THE   SS   NWR 68 13
      NEW WRITINGS IN SF. 13   CARNELL, JOHN   OA
   INTERSTELLAR ZOO, THE   AR
      TRAVELLERS OF SPACE   GREENBERG, MARTIN   AN
   SOME DREAMS COME IN PACKAGES   NV   NWR 71 18
      NEW WRITINGS IN SF. 18   CARNELL, JOHN   OA
   TOYS FOR DEBBIE   SS   IFS 65 12
      SECOND IF READER OF SCIENCE FICTION, THE
                                         POHL, FREDERIK   AN

LA FARGE, OLIVER
   JOHN THE REVELATOR   SS   FSF 51 02
      BEST FROM FANTASY AND SCIENCE FICTION 2 BOUCHER & MCCOMAS AN
   RESTING PLACE, THE   SS   NYM 54 10
      CIRCUS OF DR. LAO AND OTHER IMPROBABLE STORIES
                                         BRADBURY, RAY   AN
   SPUD AND COCHISE   NV   FSF 57 12
      DECADE OF FANTASY AND SCIENCE FICTION, A
                                         MILLS, ROBERT P.   AN

LA SPINA, GREYE
   ANTIMACASSAR, THE   SS   WRT 49 05
      LITTLE MONSTERS, THE   ELWOOD & GHIDALIA   AN
   TORTOISE-SHELL CAT, THE   SS   WRT 24 11
      BEWARE THE BEASTS   GHIDALIA, V.& ELWOOD   AN

LACH-SZYRMA, D. S.
   CANAL LIFE ON MARS   SS   CSL 90 04
      WORLDS APART   LOCKE, GEORGE   AN
   CORRESPONDING WITH THE PLANETS   SS   CSL 93 06
      WORLDS APART   LOCKE, GEORGE   AN
   IN THE ANTARCTIC REGIONS OF MARS   SS   CSL 87 04
      WORLDS APART   LOCKE, GEORGE   AN
   LETTERS FROM THE PLANETS   GR
      WORLDS APART   LOCKE, GEORGE   AN
   MERCURY   SS   CSL 87 10
      WORLDS APART   LOCKE, GEORGE   AN
   OUR SECOND VOYAGE TO MARS   SS   CSL 89 02
      WORLDS APART   LOCKE, GEORGE   AN
   PORTALS OF THE KING OF DAY, THE   SS   CSL 88 01
      WORLDS APART   LOCKE, GEORGE   AN
   QUEEN OF BEAUTY, OR THE PLANET OF LOVE, THE SS   CSL 87 08
      WORLDS APART   LOCKE, GEORGE   AN
   RUINED CITY IN THE MOON, A   SS   CSL 87 01
      WORLDS APART   LOCKE, GEORGE   AN
   TRIP TO JUPITER'S MOONLET, A   SS   CSL 91 12
      WORLDS APART   LOCKE, GEORGE   AN

LACK, G. L.
   ROBOT'S DOZEN   SS   NWR 67 10
      NEW WRITINGS IN SF. 8   CARNELL, JOHN   AN
      NEW WRITINGS IN SF. 10   CARNELL, JOHN   OA
   ROGUE LEONARDO   SS   NWR 64 02
      NEW WRITINGS IN SF. 2   CARNELL, JOHN   OA

LAFFERTY, R. A.
   DOES ANYONE ELSE HAVE SOMETHING FURTHER TO ADD? AC H SCB 74
   NINE HUNDRED GRANDMOTHERS   AC   ACE 70
   STRANGE DOINGS   AC H SCB 72
   ABOUT A SECRET CROCODILE   SS   GAL 70 08
      BEST FROM GALAXY, THE VOLUME I   GALAXY, EDITORS OF   AN
      DOES ANYONE ELSE HAVE SOMETHING FURTHER TO ADD?
                                         LAFFERTY, R. A.   AC
      SOCIAL PROBLEMS THROUGH SCIENCE FICTION
                                         GREENBERG/MILSTEAD/&   AN
   ADAM HAD THREE BROTHERS   SS   NMQ 69
      DOES ANYONE ELSE HAVE SOMETHING FURTHER TO ADD?
                                         LAFFERTY, R. A.   AC
      NEW WORLDS OF FANTASY NO. 3   CARR, TERRY   AN
   ALL BUT THE WORDS   SS   GAL 71 07
      STRANGE DOINGS   LAFFERTY, R. A.   AC
   ALL PIECES OF A RIVER SHORE   SS   ORB 70 08
      ALPHA 4   SILVERBERG, ROBERT   AN
      ORBIT 8   KNIGHT, DAMON   OA
      1972 ANNUAL WORLD'S BEST SF, THE   WOLLHEIM, DONALD A.   AN
   ALL THE PEOPLE   SS   GAL 61 04
      NINE HUNDRED GRANDMOTHERS   LAFFERTY, R. A.   AC
      STRANGE GIFTS   SILVERBERG, ROBERT   AN
   ALOYS   SS   GAL 61 08
      STRANGE DOINGS   LAFFERTY, R. A.   AC
   AMONG THE HAIRY EARTHMEN   SS   GAL 66 08
      ANOTHER WORLD   DOZOIS, GARDNER R.   AN
      EVIL EARTHS   ALDISS, BRIAN W.   AN
      NEBULA AWARD STORIES NO. 2   ALDISS & HARRISON   AN
   AND MAD UNDANCING BEARS   SS   BER 74
      BERSERKERS, THE   ELWOOD, ROGER   OA
   AND NAME MY NAME   SS   ORB 74 13
      BEST SCIENCE FICTION STORIES OF THE YEAR (1974)
                                         DEL REY, LESTER   AN
      ORBIT 13   KNIGHT, DAMON   OA
   AND READ THE FLESH BETWEEN THE LINES SS   UNI 74 04
      UNIVERSE 4   CARR, TERRY   AN
   AND WALK NOW GENTLY THROUGH THE FIRE... NV WLK 73
      AND WALK NOW GENTLY THROUGH THE FIRE...
                                         ELWOOD, ROGER   OA
   ANIMAL FAIR   NV   NDM 74 04
      NEW DIMENSIONS 4   SILVERBERG, ROBERT   OA

```
LAFFERTY, R. A.    (CONTINUED)
ASSAULT ON FAT MOUNTAIN                          SS
    BEYOND TIME                      LEY, SANDRA        OA
BARNABY'S CLOCK                                  SS  SCS 73
    SHOWCASE                         ELWOOD, ROGER      OA
BEEN A LONG, LONG TIME                           SS  FAN 70 12
    GALACTIC EMPIRES VOLUME ONE      ALDISS, BRIAN W.   AN
BOOMER FLATS                                     SS  IFS 71 08
    DOES ANYONE ELSE HAVE SOMETHING FURTHER TO ADD?
                                     LAFFERTY, R. A.    AC
BRAIN FEVER SEASON                               SS  UNI 77 07
    UNIVERSE 7                       CARR, TERRY        AN
BY THE SEASHORE                                  SS  GAL 73 11
    ANTIGRAV: COSMIC COMEDIES        STRICK, PHILIP     AN
    BEST FROM GALAXY, THE   VOLUME II  GALAXY, EDITORS OF  AN
CAMELS AND DROMEDARIES, CLEM                     SS  FSF 67 10
    STRANGE DOINGS                   LAFFERTY, R. A.    AC
CLIFF CLIMBERS, THE                              SS  QRK 70 01
    QUARK/1                          DELANY & HACKER    OA
CLIFFS THAT LAUGHED                              SS  MOH 69 03
    STRANGE DOINGS                   LAFFERTY, R. A.    AC
CONDILLAC'S STATUE                               SS  ANA 70
    ALCHEMY AND ACADEME              MCCAFFREY, ANNE    OA
CONFIGURATION OF THE NORTH SHORE                 SS  ORB 69 05
    ORBIT   5                        KNIGHT, DAMON      OA
CONTINUED ON NEXT ROCK                           NV  ORB 70 07
    BEST FROM ORBIT, THE             KNIGHT, DAMON      AN
    NEBULA AWARD STORIES   NO. 6     SIMAK, CLIFFORD D. AN
    ORBIT   7                        KNIGHT, DAMON      OA
    SPECULATIONS                     SANDERS, THOMAS E. AN
    STRANGE DOINGS                   LAFFERTY, R. A.    AC
    WORLD'S BEST SCIENCE FICTION: 1971  WOLLHEIM & CARR  AN
DAYS OF GRASS, DAYS OF STRAW                     SS  NDM 73 03
    NEW DIMENSIONS 3                 SILVERBERG, ROBERT OA
DORG                                             SS  ORB 72 10
    ORBIT  10                        KNIGHT, DAMON      OA
DREAM (DREAMWORLD)                               SS  GAL 62 06
    STRANGE DOINGS                   LAFFERTY, R. A.    AC
ENCASED IN ANCIENT RIND                          NV  QRK 71 03
    LIBERATED FUTURE: VOYAGES INTO TOMORROW, THE
                                     HOSKINS, ROBERT    AN
    QUARK/3                          DELANY & HACKER    OA
ENTIRE AND PERFECT CHRYSOLITE                    SS  ORB 70 06
    GOLDEN ROAD, THE                 KNIGHT, DAMON      AN
    ORBIT   6                        KNIGHT, DAMON      OA
    STRANGE DOINGS                   LAFFERTY, R. A.    AC
EUREMA'S DAM                                     SS  NDM 72 02
    BEST SCIENCE FICTION OF THE YEAR, THE NO. 2
                                     CARR, TERRY        AN
    BEST SCIENCE FICTION STORIES OF THE YEAR (1972)
                                     DEL REY, LESTER    AN
    NEW DIMENSIONS 2                 SILVERBERG, ROBERT OA
FLAMING DUCKS AND GIANT BREAD                    SS  ORB 74 15
    ORBIT  15                        KNIGHT, DAMON      OA
FOR ALL POOR FOLKS AT PICKETWIRE                 SS  EPC 75
    EPOCH                            ELWOOD & SILVERBERG OA
FOUR SIDES OF INFINITY                           GR
    FRONTIERS 2; THE NEW MIND        ELWOOD, ROGER      OA
FROG ON THE MOUNTAIN                             NV  NEW 70 AC
    NINE HUNDRED GRANDMOTHERS        LAFFERTY, R. A.    AC
FROM THE THUNDER COLT'S MOUTH                    NA
    IN THE WAKE OF MAN               ELWOOD, ROGER      OA
GINNY WRAPPED IN THE SUN                         SS  GAL 67 08
    MUTANTS                          SILVERBERG, ROBERT AN
    NINE HUNDRED GRANDMOTHERS        LAFFERTY, R. A.    AC
GOLDEN TRABANT                                   SS  IFS 66 05
    DOES ANYONE ELSE HAVE SOMETHING FURTHER TO ADD?
                                     LAFFERTY, R. A.    AC
GREAT DAY IN THE MORNING                         SS  ORB 75 17
    ORBIT  17                        KNIGHT, DAMON      OA
GROANING HINGES OF THE WORLD                     SS  NEW 71 AN
    DOES ANYONE ELSE HAVE SOMETHING FURTHER TO ADD?
                                     LAFFERTY, R. A.    AC
    RUINS OF EARTH, THE              DISCH, THOMAS M.   AN
GUESTING TIME                                    SS  IFS 65 05
    NINE HUNDRED GRANDMOTHERS        LAFFERTY, R. A.    AC
HAND WITH ONE HUNDRED FINGERS, THE               SS  ORB 76 18
    ORBIT  18                        KNIGHT, DAMON      OA
HANDS OF THE MAN                                 SS  INY 70 01
    INFINITY 1                       HOSKINS, ROBERT    OA
HEART GROW FONDER                                NV  FCR 75
    FUTURE CORRUPTION                ELWOOD, ROGER      OA
HELLACEOUS ROCKET OF HARRY O'DONOVAN, THE        SS  NMD 73
    FRONTIERS 2; THE NEW MIND        ELWOOD, ROGER      OA
HOG-BELLY HONEY                                  SS  FSF 65 09
    BEST FROM FANTASY AND SCIENCE FICTION: 15
                                     FERMAN, EDWARD L.  AN
    NINE HUNDRED GRANDMOTHERS        LAFFERTY, R. A.    AC
HOLE ON THE CORNER, THE                          SS  ORB 67 02
    BEST FROM ORBIT, THE             KNIGHT, DAMON      AN
    NINE HUNDRED GRANDMOTHERS        LAFFERTY, R. A.    AC
    ORBIT   2                        KNIGHT, DAMON      OA
TOMORROW, AND TOMORROW, AND TOMORROW...
                                     HEINTZ/HERBERT/JOOS/ AN
HOW THEY GAVE IT BACK                            SS  GAL 68 02
    DOES ANYONE ELSE HAVE SOMETHING FURTHER TO ADD?
                                     LAFFERTY, R. A.    AC
IN OUR BLOCK                                     SS  IFS 65 07
    NINE HUNDRED GRANDMOTHERS        LAFFERTY, R. A.    AC
    WORLD'S BEST SCIENCE FICTION: 1966  WOLLHEIM & CARR  AN
IN OUTRAGED STONE                                SS  TAL 73
    FRONTIERS 1; TOMORROW'S ALTERNATIVES  ELWOOD, ROGER  OA
IN THE GARDEN                                    SS  IFS 61 03
    DOES ANYONE ELSE HAVE SOMETHING FURTHER TO ADD?
                                     LAFFERTY, R. A.    AC

LAFFERTY, R. A.    (CONTINUED)
INCASED IN ANCIENT RIND                          NV  QRK 71 03
    STRANGE DOINGS                   LAFFERTY, R. A.    AC
INTERURBAN QUEEN                                 SS  ORB 70 08
    LOOKING AHEAD                    ALLEN, D. & L.     AN
    ORBIT   8                        KNIGHT, DAMON      OA
    SURVIVAL PRINTOUT                TOTAL EFFECT       AN
ISHMAEL INTO THE BARRENS                         NV  FFU 71
    FOUR FUTURES                     SILVERBERG, ROBERT AN
LAND OF THE GREAT HORSES                         SS  DVS 67 01
    DANGEROUS VISIONS                ELLISON, HARLAN    OA
    NINE HUNDRED GRANDMOTHERS        LAFFERTY, R. A.    OA
MAD MAN                                          SS  IFS 64 10
    DOES ANYONE ELSE HAVE SOMETHING FURTHER TO ADD?
                                     LAFFERTY, R. A.    AC
MAN UNDERNEATH, THE                              SS  IFS 71 01
    BEST SCIENCE FICTION STORIES OF THE YEAR (1971)
                                     DEL REY, LESTER    AN
    DOES ANYONE ELSE HAVE SOMETHING FURTHER TO ADD?
                                     LAFFERTY, R. A.    AC
MAN WHO NEVER WAS, THE                           SS  MOH 67 SU
    WORLD'S BEST SCIENCE FICTION: 1968  WOLLHEIM & CARR  AN
MAN WITH THE AURA, THE                           SS  WTS 74 10
    YEAR'S BEST HORROR STORIES: SERIES IV, THE
                                     PAGE, GERALD W.    AN
MAN WITH THE SPECKLED EYES, THE                  SS  FSF 64 12
    STRANGE DOINGS                   LAFFERTY, R. A.    AC
MAYBE JONES AND THE CITY                         SS
    DOES ANYONE ELSE HAVE SOMETHING FURTHER TO ADD?
                                     LAFFERTY, R. A.    AC
MOST FORGETABLE STORY IN THE WORLD, THE          SS
    LONG NIGHT OF WAITING AND OTHER STORIES
                                     ELWOOD, ROGER      OA
MR. HAMADRYAD                                    NV  STL 74 01
    STELLAR 1                        DEL REY, JUDY-LYNN OA
MUD VIOLET                                       SS  DEM 73
    DEMON KIND                       ELWOOD, ROGER      OA
NAME OF THE SNAKE                                SS  WOT 64 04
    NINE HUNDRED GRANDMOTHERS        LAFFERTY, R. A.    AC
NARROW VALLEY                                    SS  FSF 66 09
    EARTH IS THE STRANGEST PLANET    SILVERBERG, ROBERT AN
    NEW WORLDS OF FANTASY            CARR, TERRY        AN
    NINE HUNDRED GRANDMOTHERS        LAFFERTY, R. A.    AC
    OTHER DIMENSIONS                 SILVERBERG, ROBERT AN
    SF12                             MERRIL, JUDITH     AN
NINE HUNDRED GRANDMOTHERS                        SS  IFS 66 02
    ALPHA 3                          SILVERBERG, ROBERT AN
    NINE HUNDRED GRANDMOTHERS        LAFFERTY, R. A.    AC
    WORLD'S BEST SCIENCE FICTION: 1967  WOLLHEIM & CARR  AN
NOR LIMESTONE ISLANDS                            SS  UNI 71 01
    DOES ANYONE ELSE HAVE SOMETHING FURTHER TO ADD?
                                     LAFFERTY, R. A.    AC
    UNIVERSE 1                       CARR, TERRY        OA
OLD FOOT FORGOT                                  SS  ORB 70 07
    ORBIT   7                        KNIGHT, DAMON      OA
ONCE ON ARANEA                                   SS  NEW 72 AC
    STRANGE DOINGS                   LAFFERTY, R. A.    AC
ONE AT A TIME                                    SS  ORB 68 04
    NINE HUNDRED GRANDMOTHERS        LAFFERTY, R. A.    AC
    ORBIT   4                        KNIGHT, DAMON      OA
    WORLDS FAR AND NEAR              CARR, TERRY        AN
OR LITTLE DUCKS EACH DAY                         NV  DYS 75
    DYSTOPIAN VISIONS                ELWOOD, ROGER      OA
PARTHEN                                          SS  GAL 73 11
    BEST SCIENCE FICTION STORIES OF THE YEAR (1973)
                                     DEL REY, LESTER    AN
    BEST SF: 1973                    HARRISON & ALDISS  AN
    1974 ANNUAL WORLD'S BEST SF, THE WOLLHEIM, DONALD A. AN
PIG IN A POKEY                                   SS
    DOES ANYONE ELSE HAVE SOMETHING FURTHER TO ADD?
                                     LAFFERTY, R. A.    AC
POLICY AND CUSTOM OF THE CAMIROI                 SS  GAL 67 06
    AMERICAN GOVERNMENT THROUGH SCIENCE FICTION
                                     OLANDER/GREENBERG/& AN
    DARK STARS                       SILVERBERG, ROBERT AN
    NINE HUNDRED GRANDMOTHERS        LAFFERTY, R. A.    AC
PRIMARY EDUCATION OF THE CAMIROI                 SS  GAL 66 12
    AS TOMORROW BECOMES TODAY        SULLIVAN, CHARLES W. AN
    NINE HUNDRED GRANDMOTHERS        LAFFERTY, R. A.    AC
    SCHOOL AND SOCIETY THROUGH SCIENCE FICTION
                                     OLANDER/GREENBERG/& AN
    SF12                             MERRIL, JUDITH     AN
    SOCIOLOGY THROUGH SCIENCE FICTION  MILSTEAD/GREENBERG/& AN
PUDDLE ON THE FLOOR                              SS
    NEW CONSTELLATIONS               DISCH & NAYLOR     OA
RAINBIRD                                         SS  GAL 61 12
    BEYOND TOMORROW                  HARDING, LEE       AN
    SEVENTH GALAXY READER, THE       POHL, FREDERIK     AN
    STRANGE DOINGS                   LAFFERTY, R. A.    AC
RIDE A TIN CAN                                   SS  IFS 70 04
    STRANGE DOINGS                   LAFFERTY, R. A.    AC
    THIS SIDE OF INFINITY            CARR, TERRY        AN
RIVERS OF DAMASCUS                               NV  GAL 74 02
    BEST FROM GALAXY, THE   VOLUME III  BAEN, JAMES     AN
ROYAL LICORICE                                   SS  ORB 74 14
    ORBIT  14                        KNIGHT, DAMON      OA
SCORNER'S SEAT                                   NV  SVW 73
    SAVING WORLDS                    ELWOOD & KIDD      OA
SEVEN STORY DREAM                                SS
    DOES ANYONE ELSE HAVE SOMETHING FURTHER TO ADD?
                                     LAFFERTY, R. A.    AC
SEVEN-DAY TERROR                                 SS  IFS 62 03
    MASTERS' CHOICE                  JANIFER, LAURENCE M. AN
    NINE HUNDRED GRANDMOTHERS        LAFFERTY, R. A.    AC
    8TH ANNUAL OF THE YEAR'S BEST S-F, THE  MERRIL, JUDITH  AN
```

LAFFERTY, R. A.   LAUMER, KEITH

LAFFERTY, R. A.   (CONTINUED)
  SIX FINGERS OF TIME, THE   NV   IFS 60 09
    NINE HUNDRED GRANDMOTHERS   LAFFERTY, R. A.   AC
    OTHERS, THE   CARR, TERRY   AN
    6 FINGERS OF TIME AND 5 OTHER SCIENCE FICTION NOVELETS, THE
                                    ANONYMOUS   AN
  SKINNY PEOPLE OF LEPTOPHLEBO STREET, THE   SS   ORB 75 16
    ORBIT 16   KNIGHT, DAMON   OA
  SKY   SS   NDM 71 01
    NEBULA AWARD STORIES NO. 7   BIGGLE, LLOYD JR.   AN
    NEW DIMENSIONS 1   SILVERBERG, ROBERT   OA
  SLOW TUESDAY NIGHT   SS   GAL 65 04
    ABOVE THE HUMAN LANDSCAPE   MCNELLY & STOVER   AN
    BIO-FUTURES   SARGENT, PAMELA   AN
    DAY IN THE LIFE, A   DOZOIS, GARDNER R.   AN
    INFINITE JESTS   SILVERBERG, ROBERT   AN
    NINE HUNDRED GRANDMOTHERS   LAFFERTY, R. A.   AC
    NINTH GALAXY READER, THE   POHL, FREDERIK   AN
    SOCIOLOGY THROUGH SCIENCE FICTION MILSTEAD/GREENBERG/& AN
    11TH ANNUAL OF THE YEAR'S BEST S-F, THE
                                    MERRIL, JUDITH   AN
  SMOE AND THE IMPLICIT CLAY   NV   76
    FUTURE POWER   DANN & DOZOIS   OA
  SNUFFLES   NV   GAL 60 12
    BEST SF 7   CRISPIN, EDMUND   AN
    MIND PARTNER AND 8 OTHER NOVELETS FROM GALAXY
                                    GOLD, H. L.   AN
    NINE HUNDRED GRANDMOTHERS   LAFFERTY, R. A.   AC
  SODOM AND GOMORRAH, TEXAS   SS   GAL 62 12
    STRANGE DOINGS   LAFFERTY, R. A.   AC
  SPECIAL CONDITION IN SUMMIT CITY, A   SS   UNI 72 02
    UNIVERSE 2   CARR, TERRY   OA
  SYMPOSIUM   SS   OMG 73
    OMEGA   ELWOOD, ROGER   OA
  THIS GRAND CARCASS   SS   AMZ 68 11
    DOES ANYONE ELSE HAVE SOMETHING FURTHER TO ADD?
                                    LAFFERTY, R. A.   AC
  TOMORROW, AND TOMORROW, AND TOMORROW...   HEINTZ/HERBERT/JOOS/ AN
    WORLD'S BEST SCIENCE FICTION: 1969 WOLLHEIM & CARR   AN
  THROUGH OTHER EYES   SS   FUT 60 02
    MIND TO MIND   SILVERBERG, ROBERT   AN
    NINE HUNDRED GRANDMOTHERS   LAFFERTY, R. A.   AC
  THUS WE FRUSTRATE CHARLEMAGNE   SS   GAL 67 02
    ALPHA 1   SILVERBERG, ROBERT   AN
    AS TOMORROW BECOMES TODAY   SULLIVAN, CHARLES W. AN
    NINE HUNDRED GRANDMOTHERS   LAFFERTY, R. A.   AC
    TRANSFORMATIONS   ROSELLE, DANIEL   AN
    WORLD'S BEST SCIENCE FICTION: 1968 WOLLHEIM & CARR   AN
  TRANSCENDENT TIGERS, THE   SS   WOT 64 02
    STRANGE DOINGS   LAFFERTY, R. A.   AC
    YOUNG DEMONS   ELWOOD & GHIDALIA   AN
  TWO-HEADED LION OF CRIS BENEDETTI, THE   SS   NMD 73
    FRONTIERS 2; THE NEW MIND   ELWOOD, ROGER   OA
  UGLY SEA, THE   SS   LRV 60 FL
    NEW WORLDS OF FANTASY NO. 2   CARR, TERRY   AN
    STRANGE DOINGS   LAFFERTY, R. A.   AC
  ULTIMATE CREATURE, THE   SS   MOH 67 11
    DOES ANYONE ELSE HAVE SOMETHING FURTHER TO ADD?
                                    LAFFERTY, R. A.   AC
  UNGODLY MICE OF DOCTOR DRAKOS, THE   SS   NMD 73
    FRONTIERS 2; THE NEW MIND   ELWOOD, ROGER   OA
  WEIRDEST WORLD, THE   NV   GAL 61 06
    DOES ANYONE ELSE HAVE SOMETHING FURTHER TO ADD?
                                    LAFFERTY, R. A.   AC
  WHAT'S THE NAME OF THAT TOWN?   SS   GAL 64 10
    INSIDE INFORMATION   MOWSHOWITZ, ABBE   AN
    NINE HUNDRED GRANDMOTHERS   LAFFERTY, R. A.   AC
    SCIENCE FICTION ODDITIES   CONKLIN, GROFF   AN
  WHEN ALL THE LANDS POUR OUT AGAIN   SS   ORB 71 09
    ORBIT 9   KNIGHT, DAMON   OA
  WOLLY WORLD OF BARNABY SHEEN, THE   SS   NMD 73
    FRONTIERS 2; THE NEW MIND   ELWOOD, ROGER   OA
  WORLD ABOUNDING   NV   FSF 71 12
    STRANGE DOINGS   LAFFERTY, R. A.   AC
  WORLD AS WILL AND WALLPAPER, THE   SS   FUC 73
    BEST SCIENCE FICTION OF THE YEAR, THE NO. 3
                                    CARR, TERRY   AN
    FUTURE CITY   ELWOOD, ROGER   OA

LAISSING, W. K.   SEE PSEUD. DOLTON EDWARDS

LAKE, LEONARD M.
  ARE YOU RUN-DOWN, TIRED-   SS C UNK 42 10
    SUPERNATURAL READER, THE   CONKLIN, G&L.   AN

LAMONT, GIL
  MIRROR AT SUNSET, THE   SS   NDM 75 05
    NEW DIMENSIONS 5   SILVERBERG, ROBERT   OA

LAMPORT, FELICIA
  SIGH FOR CYBERNETICS, A   PM   HRP 61 01
    INSIDE INFORMATION   MOWSHOWITZ, ABBE   AN
    6TH ANNUAL OF THE YEAR'S BEST S-F, THE MERRIL, JUDITH   AN

LAMPTON, CHRIS
  BECKONING STAR   SS
    QUEST   BISCHOFF, DAVID   OA
  WEALTH OF THE SUN, THE   SS
    STRANGE ENCOUNTERS   BISCHOFF, DAVID   OA

LANDOLFI, TOMMASO
  GOGOL'S WIFE   SS   ENC 63
    SF12   MERRIL, JUDITH   AN
  (UNTITLED) (FROM CANCERQUEEN)   EX
    BEST SF: 1971   HARRISON & ALDISS   AN

LANG, ALLEN KIM
  BLIND MAN'S LANTERN   NV   ASF 62 12
    ANALOG 2   CAMPBELL, JOHN W. JR AN
  CINDERELLA STORY   SN   IFS 61 05
    FROZEN PLANET AND 4 OTHER SF NOVELLAS, THE
                                    ANONYMOUS   AN
  EEL BY THE TAIL, AN   SS   IMG 51 04
    *INVADERS OF EARTH   CONKLIN, GROFF   AN
    SPECULATIONS   SANDERS, THOMAS E.   AN
  GUEST EXPERT   SS   PLS 51 01
    EVIL EARTHS   ALDISS, BRIAN W.   AN
  THAW AND SERVE   SS   FSF 64 01
    BEST FROM FANTASY AND SCIENCE FICTION: 14
                                    DAVIDSON, AVRAM   AN
  WORLD IN A BOTTLE   NV   GAL 60 10
    ELSEWHERE AND ELSEWHEN   CONKLIN, GROFF   AN

LANG, ANDREW
  ROMANCE OF THE FIRST RADICAL, THE   SS   87
    ANCESTRAL VOICES   MENVILLE & REGINALD   AN

LANG, DANIEL
  MAN IN SPACE   AR   NYM 58 11
    SF:59, THE YEAR'S GREATEST SCIENCE FICTION AND FANTASY
                                    MERRIL, JUDITH   AN

LANG, NED   PSEUD. FOR ROBERT SHECKLEY

LANGART, DARREL T.   PSEUD. FOR RANDALL GARRETT
  WHAT THE LEFT HAND WAS DOING   NV   ASF 60 02
    5TH ANNUAL OF THE YEAR'S BEST S-F, THE MERRIL, JUDITH   AN

LANGDON, JOHN
  HERMIT ON BIKINI   SS   BBM 53 02
    PORTALS OF TOMORROW   DERLETH, AUGUST   AN

LANGELAAN, GEORGE
  FLY, THE   NV   PBY 57 06
    GHOULS, THE   HAINING, PETER   AN
    PLAYBOY BOOK OF SCIENCE FICTION AND FANTASY, THE
                                    PLAYBOY, EDITORS OF   AN
    SF:58, THE YEAR'S GREATEST SCIENCE FICTION AND FANTASY
                                    MERRIL, JUDITH   AN
  OTHER HAND, THE   SS   FSF 61 10
    *TWISTED   CONKLIN, GROFF   AN

LANGFORD, DAVID
  HEATWAVE   SS   NWR 75 27
    NEW WRITINGS IN SF. 27   BULMER, KENNETH   OA

LANGLEY, NOEL
  SCENE FOR SATAN   SS   SEP 47 01
    SATURDAY EVENING POST FANTASY STORIES, THE
                                    FLES, BARTHOLD   AN

LANIER, STERLING E.
  JOIN OUR GANG?   SS   ASF 61 05
    ANALOG 1   CAMPBELL, JOHN W. JR AN

LARIONOVA, OLGA
  TEMIRA   NV   71
    AIR OF MARS AND OTHER STORIES, THE GINSBURG, MIRRA   AN
  USELESS PLANET, THE   NV   67
    ULTIMATE THRESHOLD, THE   GINSBURG, MIRRA   AN

LASSWELL, HAROLD D.
  MEN IN SPACE   AR
    APEMAN, SPACEMAN   STOVER & HARRISON   AN

LASSWITZ, KURD
  UNIVERSAL LIBRARY, THE   SS   01
    FANTASIA MATHEMATICA   FADIMAN, CLIFTON   AN

LATHAM, PHILIP   PSEUD. FOR R. S. RICHARDSON
  BLINDNESS, THE   NV   ASF 46 07
    TIME PROBE: THE SCIENCES IN SF. CLARKE, ARTHUR C.   AN
  DIMPLE IN DRACO, THE   SS   ORB 67 02
    ORBIT 2   KNIGHT, DAMON   OA
  N DAY   SS   ASF 46 01
    *TREASURY OF SCIENCE FICTION, A CONKLIN, GROFF   AN
  ROSE-BOWL PLUTO HYPOTHESIS, THE   SS   ORB 69 05
    ORBIT 5   KNIGHT, DAMON   OA
  TO EXPLAIN MRS. THOMPSON   SS   ASF 51 11
    EXPERT DREAMERS, THE   POHL, FREDERIK   AN
  UNDER THE DRAGON'S TAIL   SS   ASF 66 12
    ON OUR WAY TO THE FUTURE   CARR, TERRY   AN
  XI EFFECT, THE   SS   ASF 50 01
    BEST SF   CRISPIN, EDMUND   AN
    DECADE THE 1940S   ALDISS & HARRISON   AN
    *IMAGINATION UNLIMITED   BLEILER & DIKTY   AN

LATHROP, GEORGE P.
  IN THE DEEP OF TIME   NV   EIM 97 03
    WORLDS APART   LOCKE, GEORGE   AN

LAUMER, KEITH
  BEST OF KEITH LAUMER, THE   AC   PKT 76 03
  BIG SHOW, THE   AC   ACE 72 10
  BOLO   AC H BKP 76
  DAY BEFORE FOREVER AND THUNDER HEAD, THE   AC H DBL 68
  ENVOY TO NEW WORLDS   AC   ACE 63
  FIVE FATES   AN H DBL 70
  GALACTIC DIPLOMAT   AC H DBL 65
  GREYLORN   AC   BKM 68 02
  IT'S A MAD, MAD, MAD GALAXY   AC   BKM 68 12
  NINE BY LAUMER   AC H DBL 67

LAUMER, KEITH   (CONTINUED)
ONCE THERE WAS A GIANT   AC H DBL 71
RETIEF OF THE CDT   AC H DBL 71
RETIEF: AMBASSADOR TO SPACE   AC H DBL 69
RETIEF: EMISSARY TO THE STARS   AC   DEL 75 12
TIMETRACKS   AC   BAL 72 04
UNDEFEATED, THE   AC   DEL 74 06
AIDE MEMOIRE   NV   IFS 62 07
  ENVOY TO NEW WORLDS   LAUMER, KEITH   AC
BAD DAY FOR VERMIN, A   SS   GAL 64 02
  EIGHTH GALAXY READER, THE   POHL, FREDERIK   AN
BALLOTS AND BANDITS   NV   IFS 70 09
  RETIEF OF THE CDT   LAUMER, KEITH   AC
BIG SHOW, THE   NV   GAL 68 02
  BIG SHOW, THE   LAUMER, KEITH   AC
BODY BUILDERS, THE   NV   GAL 66 08
  BEST OF KEITH LAUMER, THE   LAUMER, KEITH   AC
  INFINITE ARENA, THE   CARR, TERRY   AN
  IT'S A MAD, MAD, MAD GALAXY   LAUMER, KEITH   AC
BRASS GOD, THE (RETIEF, GOD SPEAKER)   NV   IFS 65 01
  GALACTIC DIPLOMAT   LAUMER, KEITH   AC
CASTLE OF LIGHT, THE   NV   IFS 64 10
  GALACTIC DIPLOMAT   LAUMER, KEITH   AC
CITY THAT GREW IN THE SEA, THE (SEE WICKER WONDERLAND)
                                                   TC
CLEAR AS MUD (SEE GRIME AND PUNISHMENT)   TC
COCOON   SS   FAN 62 12
  BEST OF KEITH LAUMER, THE   LAUMER, KEITH   AC
  NINE BY LAUMER   LAUMER, KEITH   AC
COMBAT UNIT (ALSO AS DINOCHROME)   SS   FSF 60 11
  BOLO   LAUMER, KEITH   AC
COURIER (THE FROZEN PLANET)   NV   IFS 61 09
  BOLO   LAUMER, KEITH   AC
  GALACTIC DIPLOMAT   LAUMER, KEITH   AC
CULTURAL EXCHANGE   NV   IFS 62 09
  ENVOY TO NEW WORLDS   LAUMER, KEITH   AC
DAM NUISANCE   NV   IFS 66 03
  RETIEF: AMBASSADOR TO SPACE   LAUMER, KEITH   AC
DAY BEFORE FOREVER, THE   SN   FSF 67 07
  DAY BEFORE FOREVER AND THUNDER HEAD, THE
                                    LAUMER, KEITH   AC
DESERT AND THE STARS, THE (SEE PROTEST NOTE)   TC
DEVIL YOU DON'T, THE   NV   ANA 70
  ALCHEMY AND ACADEME   MCCAFFREY, ANNE   OA
  BEST OF KEITH LAUMER, THE   LAUMER, KEITH   AC
  TIMETRACKS   LAUMER, KEITH   AC
DINOCHROME (COMBAT UNIT)   SS   FSF 60 11
  NINE BY LAUMER   LAUMER, KEITH   AC
DOORSTEP   SS   GAL 61 02
  BEST OF KEITH LAUMER, THE   LAUMER, KEITH   AC
  NINE BY LAUMER   LAUMER, KEITH   AC
DUNDERBIRD (SEE STREET SCENE)   TC C
END AS A HERO   NA   GAL 63 06
  NINE BY LAUMER   LAUMER, KEITH   AC
  UNDEFEATED, THE   LAUMER, KEITH   AC
EXCERPT FROM RETIEF & THE WARLORDS   EX   DBL 68
  RETIEF: EMISSARY TO THE STARS   LAUMER, KEITH   AC
EXTERMINATOR, THE   NV
  ONCE THERE WAS A GIANT   LAUMER, KEITH   AC
FIELD TEST   SS   ASF 76 03
  BOLO   LAUMER, KEITH   AC
FORBIDDEN CITY, THE (RETIEF, WAR CRIMINAL)   NV   IFS 67 04
  RETIEF: AMBASSADOR TO SPACE   LAUMER, KEITH   AC
FOREST IN THE SKY, THE   NV   IFS 67 02
  RETIEF: AMBASSADOR TO SPACE   LAUMER, KEITH   AC
  SECOND IF READER OF SCIENCE FICTION, THE
                                    POHL, FREDERIK   AN
FOUNDER'S DAY   NV   FSF 66 07
  ONCE THERE WAS A GIANT   LAUMER, KEITH   AC
FROZEN PLANET, THE (ALSO AS COURIER)   NV   IFS 61 09
  FROZEN PLANET AND 4 OTHER SF NOVELLAS, THE
                                    ANONYMOUS   AN
FURTHER SKY, THE (SEE THE OTHER SKY)   TC
GAMBLER'S WORLD (SEE PALACE REVOLUTION)   TC
GARBAGE INVASION, THE   NV   FSF 72 12
  RETIEF: EMISSARY TO THE STARS   LAUMER, KEITH   AC
GIANT KILLER   NV   IFS 65 09
  RETIEF: AMBASSADOR TO SPACE   LAUMER, KEITH   AC
GOOBEREALITY   NV   NEW 68 AC
  IT'S A MAD, MAD, MAD GALAXY   LAUMER, KEITH   AC
GOVERNOR OF GLAVE, THE (SEE NATIVE INTELLIGENCE)   TC
GREYLORN   NA   AMZ 59 04
  GREYLORN   LAUMER, KEITH   AC
GRIME AND PUNISHMENT (CLEAR AS MUD)   NV   IFS 67 08
  RETIEF: AMBASSADOR TO SPACE   LAUMER, KEITH   AC
HOOB MELON CRISIS, THE   NV   NEW 75 AC
  RETIEF: EMISSARY TO THE STARS   LAUMER, KEITH   AC
HYBRID   SS   FSF 61 11
  BEST OF KEITH LAUMER, THE   LAUMER, KEITH   AC
  DECADE THE 1960S   ALDISS & HARRISON   AN
  NINE BY LAUMER   LAUMER, KEITH   AC
IN THE QUEUE   SS   ORB 70 07
  BIG SHOW, THE   LAUMER, KEITH   AC
  NEBULA AWARD STORIES   NO. 6   SIMAK, CLIFFORD D.   AN
  ORBIT 7   KNIGHT, DAMON   OA
INTERNAL AFFAIR (RETIEF, INSIDER)   NV   INF 71 03
  RETIEF OF THE CDT   LAUMER, KEITH   AC
IT COULD BE ANYTHING (SEE A TRIP TO THE CITY)   TC
KING OF THE CITY, THE   NV   GAL 61 08
  GREYLORN   LAUMER, KEITH   AC
  SEVENTH GALAXY READER, THE   POHL, FREDERIK   AN
LAST COMMAND, THE   SS   ASF 67 01
  ANALOG 7   CAMPBELL, JOHN W. JR   AN
  BEST SF: 1967   HARRISON & ALDISS   AN
  BOLO   LAUMER, KEITH   AC
  COMBAT SF   DICKSON, GORDON R.   AN

LAUMER, KEITH   (CONTINUED)
  ONCE THERE WAS A GIANT   LAUMER, KEITH   AC
  POCKETFUL OF STARS, A   KNIGHT, DAMON   AN
  TALES OF TIME AND SPACE   OLNEY, ROSS R.   AN
  THEMES IN SCIENCE FICTION   KELLEY, LEO P.   AN
LAWGIVER, THE   SS   YRT 70
  BEST OF KEITH LAUMER, THE   LAUMER, KEITH   AC
  ONCE THERE WAS A GIANT   LAUMER, KEITH   AC
  TOMORROW, AND TOMORROW, AND TOMORROW...
                                    HEINTZ/HERBERT/JOOS/   AN
  YEAR 2000, THE   HARRISON, HARRY   OA
LIMITING VELOCITY OF ORTHODOXY, THE   AR   GAL 70 12
  FASTER THAN LIGHT   DANN & ZEBROWSKI   OA
LONG REMEMBERED THUNDER, THE   NV   WOT 63 04
  BEST SCIENCE FICTION FROM WORLDS OF TOMORROW, THE
                                    POHL, FREDERIK   AN
  NINE BY LAUMER   LAUMER, KEITH   AC
MADMEN FROM EARTH, THE (SEE POLICY)   TC
MECHANICAL ADVANTAGE (RETIEF, THE LONG-AWAITED MASTER)
                                                   NV   IFS 69 04
  RETIEF OF THE CDT   LAUMER, KEITH   AC
MESSAGE TO AN ALIEN   SS   ASF 70 06
  BIG SHOW, THE   LAUMER, KEITH   AC
MIGHTIEST QORN (SEE ULTIMATUM)   TC
MIND OUT OF TIME, THE   SS   FRS 68
  FARTHEST REACHES, THE   ELDER, JOSEPH   OA
  ONCE THERE WAS A GIANT   LAUMER, KEITH   AC
  TIMETRACKS   LAUMER, KEITH   AC
NATIVE INTELLIGENCE (THE GOVERNOR OF GLAVE)   NV   IFS 63 11
  GALACTIC DIPLOMAT   LAUMER, KEITH   AC
NEGOTIATORS, THE   SS   ASF 75 02
  RETIEF: EMISSARY TO THE STARS   LAUMER, KEITH   AC
NIGHT OF THE TROLLS, THE   SN   WOT 63 10
  BOLO   LAUMER, KEITH   AC
  GREYLORN   LAUMER, KEITH   AC
  UNDEFEATED, THE   LAUMER, KEITH   AC
OF DEATH WHAT DREAMS   NV   WOT 70 24
  FIVE FATES   LAUMER, KEITH   AN
ONCE THERE WAS A GIANT   SN   FSF 68 11
  ONCE THERE WAS A GIANT   LAUMER, KEITH   AC
OTHER SKY, THE (THE FURTHER SKY)   SN   AMZ 64 12
  GREYLORN   LAUMER, KEITH   AC
  TIMETRACKS   LAUMER, KEITH   AC
PALACE REVOLUTION (GAMBLER'S WORLD)   NV   IFS 61 11
  ENVOY TO NEW WORLDS   LAUMER, KEITH   AC
PIECEMAKERS, THE   NV   IFS 70 05
  RETIEF OF THE CDT   LAUMER, KEITH   AC
PIME DOESN'T CRAY   NV   IFS 71 01
  RETIEF OF THE CDT   LAUMER, KEITH   AC
PLACEMENT TEST   NV   AMZ 64 07
  BEST FROM AMAZING, THE   WHITE, TED   AN
  NINE BY LAUMER   LAUMER, KEITH   AC
PLAGUE, THE   NV   ASF 70 11
  ANALOG 9   BOVA, BEN   AN
  BIG SHOW, THE   LAUMER, KEITH   AC
  GATES TO TOMORROW   NORTON, AN.&DONALDY   AN
PLANET WRECKERS, THE   NV   WOT 67 02
  BEST OF KEITH LAUMER, THE   LAUMER, KEITH   AC
  IT'S A MAD, MAD, MAD GALAXY   LAUMER, KEITH   AC
POLICY (THE MADMAN FROM EARTH)   NV   IFS 62 03
  ENVOY TO NEW WORLDS   LAUMER, KEITH   AC
PRINCE AND THE PIRATE, THE   NV   IFS 64 09
  GALACTIC DIPLOMAT   LAUMER, KEITH   AC
PROTEST NOTE (THE DESERT AND THE STARS)   NV   IFS 62 11
  GALACTIC DIPLOMAT   LAUMER, KEITH   AC
PROTOCOL (THE YLLIAN WAY)   NV   IFS 62 01
  ENVOY TO NEW WORLDS   LAUMER, KEITH   AC
PROTOTAPH   SS   ASF 66 03
  ANALOG 6   CAMPBELL, JOHN W. JR   AN
  ONCE THERE WAS A GIANT   LAUMER, KEITH   AC
RELIC OF WAR, A   SS   ASF 69 10
  BEST OF KEITH LAUMER, THE   LAUMER, KEITH   AC
  BIG SHOW, THE   LAUMER, KEITH   AC
  BOLO   LAUMER, KEITH   AC
RETIEF OF THE RED-TAPE MOUNTAIN (SEE SEALED ORDERS)
                                                   TC
RETIEF, GOD SPEAKER (SEE THE BRASS GOD)   TC
RETIEF, INSIDER (SEE INTERNAL AFFAIR)   TC
RETIEF, THE LONG-AWAITED MASTER (SEE MECHANICAL ADVANTAGE)
                                                   TC
RETIEF, WAR CRIMINAL (SEE THE FORBIDDEN CITY)   TC
RIGHT TO RESIST, THE   SS   IFS 71 06
  AMERICAN GOVERNMENT THROUGH SCIENCE FICTION
                                    OLANDER/GREENBERG/&   AN
  BEST FROM IF, THE   VOLUME I   IF, EDITORS OF   AN
RIGHT TO REVOLT, THE   SS   IFS 71 06
  AMERICAN GOVERNMENT THROUGH SCIENCE FICTION
                                    OLANDER/GREENBERG/&   AN
  BEST FROM IF, THE   VOLUME I   IF, EDITORS OF   AN
SALINE SOLUTION   NV   IFS 63 03
  GALACTIC DIPLOMAT   LAUMER, KEITH   AC
SEALED ORDERS (RETIEF OF THE RED-TAPE MOUNTAIN)   NV   IFS 62 05
  ENVOY TO NEW WORLDS   LAUMER, KEITH   AC
SHORT HISTORY OF THE BOLO FIGHTING MACHINES, A   AR
  BOLO   LAUMER, KEITH   AC
STAR-SENT KNAVES, THE (ALSO AS THE TIME THIEVES)   NV   WOT 63 06
  IT'S A MAD, MAD, MAD GALAXY   LAUMER, KEITH   AC
STREET SCENE (DUNDERBIRD)   NV C GAL 69 01
  PARTNERS IN WONDER   ELLISON, HARLAN   OA
TEST TO DESTRUCTION   NV   DVS 67 01
  BIG SHOW, THE   LAUMER, KEITH   AC
  DANGEROUS VISIONS   ELLISON, HARLAN   OA
THREE BLIND MICE   NV   MWS 71
  MANY WORLDS OF SCIENCE FICTION, THE BOVA, BEN   OA
THUNDERHEAD   NV   GAL 67 04
  BEST OF KEITH LAUMER, THE   LAUMER, KEITH   AC

LAUMER, KEITH

LAUMER, KEITH   (CONTINUED)
    DAY BEFORE FOREVER AND THUNDER HEAD, THE
                                        LAUMER, KEITH   AC
    UNDEFEATED, THE   LAUMER, KEITH   AC
  TIME THIEVES, THE (THE STAR-SENT KNAVES)   NV WOT 63 06
    TIMETRACKS   LAUMER, KEITH   AC
  TIMESWEEPERS, THE   NV ASF 69 08
    TIMETRACKS   LAUMER, KEITH   AC
  TRICK OR TREATY   NV IFS 65 08
    IF READER OF SCIENCE FICTION, THE   POHL, FREDERIK   AN
    RETIEF: AMBASSADOR TO SPACE   LAUMER, KEITH   AC
  TRIP TO THE CITY, A (IT COULD BE ANYTHING) NV AMZ 63 01
    BEST FROM FANTASTIC, THE   WHITE, TED   AN
    NINE BY LAUMER   LAUMER, KEITH   AC
  TROUBLESHOOTER, THE   NV NEW 75 AC
    RETIEF: EMISSARY TO THE STARS   LAUMER, KEITH   AC
  TRUCE OR CONSEQUENCES   NV IFS 66 11
    RETIEF: AMBASSADOR TO SPACE   LAUMER, KEITH   AC
  ULTIMATUM (MIGHTIEST QORN)   NV IFS 63 07
    GALACTIC DIPLOMAT   LAUMER, KEITH   AC
    GATES TO TOMORROW   NORTON, AN.&DONALDY AN
  WALLS, THE   SS AMZ 63 03
    NINE BY LAUMER   LAUMER, KEITH   AC
  WAR WITH THE YUKKS, THE (WAR AGAINST THE YUKKS) NV GAL 65 04
    IT'S A MAD, MAD, MAD GALAXY   LAUMER, KEITH   AC
  WICKER WONDERLAND (THE CITY THAT GREW IN THE SEA) NV IFS 64 03
    GALACTIC DIPLOMAT   LAUMER, KEITH   AC
  WORLDMASTER   NV WOT 65 11
    ONCE THERE WAS A GIANT   LAUMER, KEITH   AC
    UNDEFEATED, THE   LAUMER, KEITH   AC
  WORLDS OF THE IMPERIUM (SELECTION FROM) EX FAN 61 02
    CENTURY OF SCIENCE FICTION, A   KNIGHT, DAMON   AN
  YLLIAN WAY, THE (SEE PROTOCOL)   TC

LAURANCE, ALICE
  CALL FROM KERLYANA   SS C ALC 73
    ALIEN CONDITION, THE   GOLDIN, STEPHEN   OA
  CHANCES ARE   SS PRT 71
    PROTOSTARS   GERROLD & GOLDIN   OA
  REPRISAL   SS GEN 72
    GENERATION   GERROLD, DAVID   OA

LAVIGNE, ROBERT
  SIX DRAWINGS   IL QRK 71 03
    QUARK/3   DELANY & HACKER   OA
  SIX MORE DRAWINGS   IL QRK 71 03
    QUARK/3   DELANY & HACKER   OA

LAVOND, PAUL DENNIS (PSEUDONYM)
  LURANI   PM UNK 40 02
    FROM UNKNOWN WORLDS   CAMPBELL, JOHN W. JR AN
  STAR OF THE UNDEAD (ROBERT A. W. LOWNDES) SS FBK 47 02
    MACHINE-GOD LAUGHS, THE   ANONYMOUS   AN

LAWLOR, HAROLD
  SILVER HIGHWAY, THE   SS WRT 46 05
    SUPERNATURAL READER, THE   CONKLIN, G&L.   AN

LAWRENCE, D. H.
  ROCKING-HORSE WINNER, THE   SS 33
    CHILDREN OF WONDER   TENN, WILLIAM   AN
    OTHER DIMENSION, THE   ROSNER, SARA   AN
    TRAVELERS IN TIME   STERN, PHILIP VAN D. AN

LAWRENCE, J. A.
  DESCENT OF MAN, THE   SS IFS 74 12
    BEST FROM IF, THE   VOLUME III   BAEN, JAMES   AN
  OPENING PROBLEM   NV GAL 74 07
    BEST FROM GALAXY, THE   VOLUME III BAEN, JAMES   AN
  TWINKLE, TWINKLE, LITTLE BAT   SS NDM 77 07
    NEW DIMENSIONS 7   SILVERBERG, ROBERT OA

LAWRENCE, JUDITH ANN
  GETTING ALONG   NV C DVS 72 02
    AGAIN, DANGEROUS VISIONS   ELLISON, HARLAN   OA

LAWRENCE, MARGERY
  TERROR OF ANERLY HOUSE SCHOOL, THE   SS
    TRAVELLERS BY NIGHT   DERLETH, AUGUST   OA

LAWSON, JACK B.
  COMPETITORS, THE   NV IFS 64 01
    WORLD'S BEST SCIENCE FICTION: 1965 WOLLHEIM & CARR   AN

LE FANU, J. SHERIDAN
  ACCOUNT OF SOME STRANGE DISTURBANCES IN AUNGIER ST
                                        NV
    EDGE OF NEVER, THE   HOSKINS, ROBERT   AN
  SIR DOMINICK'S BARGAIN   SS
    DEALS WITH THE DEVIL   DAVENPORT, BASIL   AN

LE GUIN, URSULA K.
  EARTHSEA   AC H GOL 77
  NEBULA AWARD STORIES 11   AN H HPR 77
  WINDS TWELVE QUARTERS, THE   AC H HPR 75
  APRIL IN PARIS   SS FAN 62 09
    BEST FROM FANTASTIC, THE   WHITE, TED   AN
    WINDS TWELVE QUARTERS, THE   LE GUIN, URSULA K. AC
  AUTHOR OF THE ACACIA SEEDS AND OTHER EXTRACTS FROM THE JOURNAL
    OF THE ASSOCIATION OF THERO   SS FOS 74
    BEST SCIENCE FICTION OF THE YEAR, THE NO. 4
                                        CARR, TERRY   AN
    FELLOWSHIP OF THE STARS   CARR, TERRY   OA
  DARKNESS BOX   SS FAN 63 11
    WINDS TWELVE QUARTERS, THE   LE GUIN, URSULA K. AC

LE GUIN, URSULA K.

LE GUIN, URSULA K.   (CONTINUED)
  DAY BEFORE THE REVOLUTION, THE   SS GAL 74 08
    BEST FROM GALAXY, THE   VOLUME III BAEN, JAMES   AN
    MORE WOMEN OF WONDER   SARGENT, PAMELA   AN
    NEBULA AWARD STORIES 10   GUNN, JAMES E.   AN
    WINDS TWELVE QUARTERS, THE   LE GUIN, URSULA K. AC
  DIARY OF THE ROSE, THE   NV 76
    BEST SCIENCE FICTION STORIES OF THE YEAR (1976)
                                        DOZOIS, GARDNER R. AN
    FUTURE POWER   DANN & DOZOIS   OA
  DIRECTION OF THE ROAD   SS ORB 73 12
    ORBIT 12   KNIGHT, DAMON   OA
    WINDS TWELVE QUARTERS, THE   LE GUIN, URSULA K. AC
  DOWRY OF THE ANGYAR, THE (ALSO AS SEMLEY'S NECKLACE)
                                        SS AMZ 64 09
    BEST FROM AMAZING, THE   WHITE, TED   AN
  END, THE (ALSO AS THINGS)   SS ORB 70 06
    BEST FROM ORBIT, THE   KNIGHT, DAMON   AN
    ORBIT 6   KNIGHT, DAMON   OA
  FARTHEST SHORE, THE   NO
    EARTHSEA   LE GUIN, URSULA K. AC
  FIELD OF VISION, THE   SS GAL 73 10
    BEST FROM GALAXY, THE   VOLUME II   GALAXY, EDITORS OF AN
    WINDS TWELVE QUARTERS, THE   LE GUIN, URSULA K. AC
  FIFTEEN VULTURES, THE STROP, AND THE OLD LADY AR CLR 72 02
    CLARION II   WILSON, ROBIN SCOTT OA
  FOREWORD   IN
    WINDS TWELVE QUARTERS, THE   LE GUIN, URSULA K. AC
  GOOD TRIP, THE   SS FAN 70 08
    WINDS TWELVE QUARTERS, THE   LE GUIN, URSULA K. AC
  INTRACOM   PL
    STOPWATCH   HAY, GEORGE   OA
  INTRODUCTION   IN
    NEBULA AWARD STORIES 11   LE GUIN, URSULA K. AN
  IS GENDER NECESSARY?   AR
    AURORA: BEYOND EQUALITY   MCINTYRE & ANDERSON OA
  MASTERS, THE   SS FAN 63 02
    WINDS TWELVE QUARTERS, THE   LE GUIN, URSULA K. AC
  MAZES   SS EPC 75
    EPOCH   ELWOOD & SILVERBERG OA
  NEW ATLANTIS, THE   NA NAL 75
    BEST SCIENCE FICTION OF THE YEAR, THE NO. 5
                                        CARR, TERRY   AN
  NEW ATLANTIS AND OTHER NOVELLAS OF S.F., THE
                                        SILVERBERG, ROBERT OA
  NINE LIVES   NV PBY 69 11
    AS TOMORROW BECOMES TODAY   SULLIVAN, CHARLES W. AN
    BEST SF: 1969   HARRISON & ALDISS   AN
    BEYOND TOMORROW   HARDING, LEE   AN
    BIO-FUTURES   SARGENT, PAMELA   AN
    DEAD ASTRONAUT, 10 STORIES OF SPACE FLIGHT, THE
                                        PLAYBOY, EDITORS OF AN
    IN DREAMS AWAKE   FIEDLER, LESLIE A. AN
    INTRODUCTORY PSYCHOLOGY THROUGH SCIENCE FICTION
                                        KATZ/WARRICK/&   AN
    MODERN SCIENCE FICTION   SPINRAD, NORMAN   AN
    NEBULA AWARD STORIES NO. 5   BLISH, JAMES   AN
    THOSE WHO CAN: A SCIENCE FICTION READER
                                        WILSON, ROBIN SCOTT AN
    WINDS TWELVE QUARTERS, THE   LE GUIN, URSULA K. AC
    WORLD'S BEST SCIENCE FICTION: 1970 WOLLHEIM & CARR   AN
  ON THEME   AR
    THOSE WHO CAN: A SCIENCE FICTION READER
                                        WILSON, ROBIN SCOTT AN
  ONES WHO WALK AWAY FROM OMELAS, THE   SS NDM 73 03
    BEST SCIENCE FICTION OF THE YEAR, THE NO. 3
                                        CARR, TERRY   AN
    NEW DIMENSIONS 3   SILVERBERG, ROBERT OA
    WINDS TWELVE QUARTERS, THE   LE GUIN, URSULA K. AC
  RULE OF NAMES, THE   SS FAN 64 04
    WINDS TWELVE QUARTERS, THE   LE GUIN, URSULA K. AC
  SCHRODINGER'S CAT   SS UNI 74 05
    UNIVERSE 5   CARR, TERRY   OA
  SEMLEY'S NECKLACE (DOWRY OF THE ANGYAR) SS AMZ 64 09
    WINDS TWELVE QUARTERS, THE   LE GUIN, URSULA K. AC
  STALIN IN THE SOUL, THE   AR 73
    FUTURE NOW, THE   HOSKINS, ROBERT   AN
  STARS BELOW, THE   SS ORB 74 14
    ANOTHER WORLD   DOZOIS, GARDNER R. AN
    ORBIT 14   KNIGHT, DAMON   OA
    WINDS TWELVE QUARTERS, THE   LE GUIN, URSULA K. AC
  THINGS (THE END)   SS ORB 70 06
    WINDS TWELVE QUARTERS, THE   LE GUIN, URSULA K. AC
  TOMBS OF ATUAN, THE   NO WOF 70 WI
    EARTHSEA   LE GUIN, URSULA K. AC
  TRIP TO THE HEAD, A   SS QRK 70 01
    LIBERATED FUTURE: VOYAGES INTO TOMORROW, THE
                                        HOSKINS, ROBERT   AN
    QUARK/1   DELANY & HACKER   OA
    WINDS TWELVE QUARTERS, THE   LE GUIN, URSULA K. AC
  URSULA MAJOR CONSTRUCT: OR, A FAR GREATER HORROR LOOMED, THE
                                        SS CLR 73 03
    CLARION III   WILSON, ROBIN SCOTT OA
  VASTER THAN EMPIRES AND MORE SLOW   NV NDM 71 01
    BEST SCIENCE FICTION OF THE YEAR, THE CARR, TERRY   AN
    EXPLORERS OF SPACE   SILVERBERG, ROBERT AN
    NEW DIMENSIONS 1   SILVERBERG, ROBERT OA
    WINDS TWELVE QUARTERS, THE   LE GUIN, URSULA K. AC
    WOMEN OF WONDER   SARGENT, PAMELA   AN
    WONDERMAKERS 2   HOSKINS, ROBERT   AN
  WINTER'S KING   NV ORB 69 05
    ORBIT 5   KNIGHT, DAMON   OA
    WINDS TWELVE QUARTERS, THE   LE GUIN, URSULA K. AC
  WIZARD OF EARTHSEA, A   NO
    EARTHSEA   LE GUIN, URSULA K. AC

LE GUIN, URSULA K. (CONTINUED)
    WORD FOR WORLD IS FOREST, THE   NV   DVS 72 02
        AGAIN, DANGEROUS VISIONS   ELLISON, HARLAN   OA
    WORD OF UNBINDING, THE   SS   FAN 64 01
        GOLDEN ROAD, THE   KNIGHT, DAMON   AN
        WINDS TWELVE QUARTERS, THE   LE GUIN, URSULA K.   AC

LE QUEX, WILLIAM
    GREAT WAR IN ENGLAND IN 1897, THE   NV
        BEFORE ARMAGEDDON   MOORCOCK, MICHAEL   AN

LEACOCK, STEPHEN
    A, B AND C- THE HUMAN ELEMENTS IN MATHEMATICS   AR   12
        MATHEMATICAL MAGPIE, THE   FADIMAN, CLIFTON   AN
    MAN IN ASBESTOS: AN ALLEGORY OF THE FUTURE, THE SS   41
        ASPECTS OF SCIENCE FICTION   DOHERTY, G. D.   AN
    MATHEMATICS FOR GOLFERS   AR   22
        MATHEMATICAL MAGPIE, THE   FADIMAN, CLIFTON   AN

LEAHY, JOHN M.
    VOICES FROM THE CLIFF   SS   WRT 25 05
        SCIENCE AND SORCERY   FORD, GARRET   AN

LEAVITT, HART DAY
    INTRODUCTION   IN
        INEXPERIENCED GHOST AND NINE OTHER STORIES, THE
                                        WELLS, H. G.   AC

LEBLANC, MAURICE
    INVISIBLE PRISONER, THE   SS
        INVISIBLE MEN   DAVENPORT, BASIL   AN

LECHTLINER, RUTH
    WINTER'S TALE, A   PM   69
        HOLDING YOUR EIGHT HANDS   LUCIE-SMITH, EDWARD   AN

LEE, CHRISTOPHER
    AFTERWORD   MS
        GHOULS, THE   HAINING, PETER   AN
    FOREWORD   IN
        YEAR'S BEST HORROR STORIES: SERIES II, THE
                                        DAVIS, RICHARD   AN

LEE, STANISLAW G.
    APOTHEM   MS   62
        MATHEMATICAL MAGPIE, THE   FADIMAN, CLIFTON   AN

LEE, TANITH
    TRUCE, THE   SS
        DAW SCIENCE FICTION READER, THE WOLLHEIM, DONALD A.   OA

LEE, WILLIAM M.
    JUNIOR ACHIEVEMENT   SS   ASF 62 07
        ANALOG 2   CAMPBELL, JOHN W. JR AN
        TOMORROW'S CHILDREN   ASIMOV, ISAAC   AN
    MESSAGE FROM CHARITY, A   SS   FSF 67 11
        NEW WORLDS OF FANTASY NO. 3   CARR, TERRY   AN
        THEMES IN SCIENCE FICTION   KELLEY, LEO P.   AN
    SEA HOME   NV   FSF 68 06
        BEST FROM FANTASY AND SCIENCE FICTION: 18
                                        FERMAN, EDWARD L.   AN

LEES, GENE
    STRANGER FROM SPACE   SS   SCP 54 03
        GATEWAY TO THE STARS   CARNELL, JOHN   AN

LEHRMAN, HERB
    REVOLT OF THE POTATO-PICKER   SS   FSF 66 07
        SOCIAL PROBLEMS THROUGH SCIENCE FICTION
                                        GREENBERG/MILSTEAD/& AN

LEIBER, FRITZ
    BEST OF FRITZ LEIBER, THE   AC H NDB 74
    BOOK OF FRITZ LEIBER, THE   AC   DAW 74 01
    MIND SPIDER AND OTHER STORIES, THE   DC   ACE 61
    MIND SPIDER AND OTHER STORIES, THE (ACE 76)   AC   ACE 76
    NIGHT MONSTERS   DC   ACE 69
    NIGHT OF THE WOLF, THE   AC   BAL 66 07
    NIGHT'S BLACK AGENTS   AC H ARK 47
        BALLANTINE 1961 EDITION OMITS "ADEPT'S GAMBIT"
    PAIL OF AIR, A   AC   BAL 64 07
    SECOND BOOK OF FRITZ LEIBER, THE   AC   DAW 75 09
    SECRET SONGS, THE   AC H HDV 68
    SHADOWS WITH EYES   AC   BAL 62 03
    SHIPS TO THE STARS   DC   ACE 64
    WORLDS OF FRITZ LEIBER, THE   AC   ACE 76 11
    YOU'RE ALL ALONE   AC   ACE 72
    ADEPT'S GAMBIT   SS   NEW 47 AC
        NIGHT'S BLACK AGENTS   LEIBER, FRITZ   AC
    AFTER SUCH KNOWLEDGE   AR   74
        BOOK OF FRITZ LEIBER, THE   LEIBER, FRITZ   AC
    AFTERWORD   MS
        BEST OF FRITZ LEIBER, THE   LEIBER, FRITZ   AC
    AMERICA THE BEAUTIFUL   SS   YRT 70
        BEST OF FRITZ LEIBER, THE   LEIBER, FRITZ   AC
        LATE GREAT FUTURE, THE   FITZ GERALD & DILLON AN
        RUINS OF EARTH, THE   DISCH, THOMAS M.   AN
        YEAR 2000, THE   HARRISON, HARRY   OA
    ANOTHER CASK OF WINE   SS   INY 72 04
        INFINITY 4   HOSKINS, ROBERT   OA
    ANSWERING SERVICE   SS   IFS 67 12
        BEST SF: 1967   HARRISON & ALDISS   AN
    APPOINTMENT IN TOMORROW (ALSO AS POOR SUPERMAN) NV   GAL 51 07
        BEST SCIENCE-FICTION STORIES: 1952, THE
                                        BLEILER & DIKTY   AN

LEIBER, FRITZ   (CONTINUED)
    AUTOMATIC PISTOL, THE   SS   WRT 40 05
        NIGHT'S BLACK AGENTS   LEIBER, FRITZ   AC
        UNEXPECTED, THE   MARGULIES, LEO   AN
    BAD DAY FOR SALES, A   SS   GAL 53 07
        BEST SCIENCE-FICTION STORIES: 1954, THE
                                        BLEILER & DIKTY   AN
        FIFTY SHORT SCIENCE FICTION TALES ASIMOV & CONKLIN   AN
        GALAXY SCIENCE FICTION OMNIBUS GOLD, H. L.   AN
        MEN AND MACHINES   SILVERBERG, ROBERT   AN
        NIGHTMARE AGE   POHL, FREDERIK   AN
        SECOND GALAXY READER OF SCIENCE FICTION
                                        GOLD, H. L.   AN
        SHADOW OF TOMORROW   POHL, FREDERIK   AN
    BAIT, THE   SS   73
        WORLDS OF FRITZ LEIBER, THE   LEIBER, FRITZ   AC
    BAZAAR OF THE BIZARRE   NV   SOI 63 08
        SPELL OF SEVEN, THE   DE CAMP, L. SPRAGUE   AN
    BE OF GOOD CHEER   SS   GAL 64 10
        RULERS OF MEN   SANTESSON, HANS S.   AN
        10TH ANNUAL OF THE YEAR'S BEST S-F, THE
                                        MERRIL, JUDITH   AN
    BEAT CLUSTER, THE   SS   GAL 61 10
        PAIL OF AIR, A   LEIBER, FRITZ   AC
        SEVENTH GALAXY READER, THE   POHL, FREDERIK   AN
        7TH ANNUAL OF THE YEAR'S BEST S-F, THE MERRIL, JUDITH
    BEAUTY AND THE BEASTS   SS   NEW 74 AC
        BOOK OF FRITZ LEIBER, THE   LEIBER, FRITZ   AC
    BELSEN EXPRESS   SS   NEW 75 AC
        SECOND BOOK OF FRITZ LEIBER, THE LEIBER, FRITZ   AC
    BIG ENGINE, THE   SS   GAL 62 02
        EIGHTH GALAXY READER, THE   POHL, FREDERIK   AN
    BIG HOLIDAY, THE   SS   FSF 53 01
        BEST OF FRITZ LEIBER, THE   LEIBER, FRITZ   AC
        BEST SCIENCE-FICTION STORIES: 1954, THE
                                        BLEILER & DIKTY   AN
    BIG TREK, THE   SS   FSF 57 10
        BEST FROM FANTASY AND SCIENCE FICTION: 7
                                        BOUCHER, ANTHONY   AN
        BEST OF FRITZ LEIBER, THE   LEIBER, FRITZ   AC
        SHIPS TO THE STARS   LEIBER, FRITZ   DC
    BIT OF THE DARK WORLD, A   NV   FAN 62 02
        SHADOWS WITH EYES   LEIBER, FRITZ   AC
    BLACK GONDOLIER, THE   NV   NEW 64 AN
        NIGHT MONSTERS   LEIBER, FRITZ   DC
    BLEAK SHORE, THE   SS   UNK 40 11
        HELL HATH FURY   HAY, GEORGE   AN
        UNKNOWN, THE   BENSEN, D. R.   AN
    BREAD OVERHEAD   NV   GAL 58 02
        PAIL OF AIR, A   LEIBER, FRITZ   AC
    BULLET WITH HIS NAME   NV   GAL 58 02
        WORLDS OF WHEN   CONKLIN, GROFF   AN
    BUMP, THE   SS   INY 72 04
        INFINITY 4   HOSKINS, ROBERT   OA
    BUSINESS OF KILLING   SS   ASF 44 09
        *SCIENCE FICTION ADVENTURES IN DIMENSION
                                        CONKLIN, GROFF   AN
    CASKET-DEMON, THE   SS   FAN 63 04
        NIGHT MONSTERS   LEIBER, FRITZ   DC
    CAT'S CRADLE   SS
        BOOK OF FRITZ LEIBER, THE   LEIBER, FRITZ   AC
    CATCH THAT ZEPPELIN   SS   FSF 75 03
        NEBULA AWARD STORIES 11   LE GUIN, URSULA K.   AN
        WORLDS OF FRITZ LEIBER, THE   LEIBER, FRITZ   AC
        1976 ANNUAL WORLD'S BEST SF, THE WOLLHEIM, DONALD A. AN
    COMING ATTRACTION   SS   GAL 50 11
        BEST OF FRITZ LEIBER, THE   LEIBER, FRITZ   AC
        BEST SCIENCE-FICTION STORIES: 1951, THE
                                        BLEILER & DIKTY   AN
        *GALAXY READER OF SCIENCE FICTION GOLD, H. L.   AN
        MASTERS' CHOICE   JANIFER, LAURENCE M. AN
        MODERN MASTERPIECES OF SCIENCE FICTION MOSKOWITZ, SAM AN
        PAIL OF AIR, A   LEIBER, FRITZ   AC
        SCIENCE FICTION HALL OF FAME VOLUME 1 SILVERBERG, ROBERT AN
        SECRET SONGS, THE   LEIBER, FRITZ   AC
        VORTEX BLASTERS, THE   MOSKOWITZ, SAM   AN
    CONJURE WIFE   SN   UNK 43 04
        WITCHES THREE   PRATT, FLETCHER   AN
    CRAZY ANNAOJ   SS   GAL 68 02
        BOOK OF FRITZ LEIBER, THE   LEIBER, FRITZ   AC
    CRAZY WOLF (SANITY)   SS   ASF 44 04
        NIGHT OF THE WOLF, THE   LEIBER, FRITZ   AC
    CREATURE FROM CLEVELAND DEPTHS, THE (ALSO AS THE LONE WOLF)
                                                     NA   GAL 62 12
        YOU'RE ALL ALONE   LEIBER, FRITZ   AC
    CYCLOPS   SS   WOT 65 09
        ON OUR WAY TO THE FUTURE   CARR, TERRY   AN
        WORLDS OF FRITZ LEIBER, THE   LEIBER, FRITZ   AC
    DAMNATION MORNING   SS   FAN 59 08
        *MIND SPIDER AND OTHER STORIES, THE LEIBER, FRITZ   DC
    DAY DARK, NIGHT BRIGHT   SS   INY 72 04
        INFINITY 4   HOSKINS, ROBERT   OA
    DEAD MAN, THE   NV   PNM 58 04
        SHADOWS WITH EYES   LEIBER, FRITZ   AC
    DEADLY MOON   NV   FAN 60 11
        SHIPS TO THE STARS   LEIBER, FRITZ   DC
    DEATH OF PRINCES, THE   NV   AMZ 76 06
        BEST SCIENCE FICTION OF THE YEAR, THE NO. 6
                                        CARR, TERRY   AN
    DEBUNKING THE I MACHINE   AR   49
        BOOK OF FRITZ LEIBER, THE   LEIBER, FRITZ   AC
    DEFENSE OF WEREWOLVES, A (FANTASY ON THE MARCH) AR   ARS 48 SP
        SECOND BOOK OF FRITZ LEIBER, THE LEIBER, FRITZ   AC
    DESKFUL OF GIRLS, A   NV   FSF 58 04
        BEST FROM FANTASY AND SCIENCE FICTION: 8
                                        BOUCHER, ANTHONY   AN

LEIBER, FRITZ

LEIBER, FRITZ   (CONTINUED)
    BEST OF FRITZ LEIBER, THE   LEIBER, FRITZ   AC
    DARK STARS   SILVERBERG, ROBERT   AN
    SHADOWS WITH EYES   LEIBER, FRITZ   AC
DESTINY TIMES THREE   SN   ASF 45 03
    FIVE SCIENCE FICTION NOVELS   GREENBERG, MARTIN   AN
DIARY IN THE SNOW   NV   NEW 47 AC
    NIGHT'S BLACK AGENTS   LEIBER, FRITZ   AC
DO YOU KNOW DAVE WENZEL?   SS   FOS 74
    FELLOWSHIP OF THE STARS   CARR, TERRY   OA
DR. ADAMS' GARDEN OF EVIL   SS   FAN 63 02
    ROOTS OF EVIL, THE   PARRY, MICHEL   AN
DR. KOMETEVSKY'S DAY   SS   GAL 52 02
    SHIPS TO THE STARS   LEIBER, FRITZ   DC
DREAMS OF ALBERT MORELAND, THE   NV   AFR 48 07
    NIGHT'S BLACK AGENTS   LEIBER, FRITZ   AC
    ODDBALLS, THE   GHIDALIA, VIC   AN
EERIEST RUINED DAWN WORLD, THE   SS
    IDES OF TOMORROW, THE   CARR, TERRY   OA
ENCHANTED FOREST, THE   SS   ASF 50 10
    BEST OF FRITZ LEIBER, THE   LEIBER, FRITZ   AC
    NEW WORLDS FOR OLD   DERLETH, AUGUST   AN
    SHIPS TO THE STARS   LEIBER, FRITZ   DC
    *WORLDS OF TOMORROW   DERLETH, AUGUST   AN
ENDFRAY OF THE OFAY   SS   IFS 69 03
    WORLDS OF FRITZ LEIBER, THE   LEIBER, FRITZ   AC
FAFHRD AND ME   AR   63
    SECOND BOOK OF FRITZ LEIBER, THE   LEIBER, FRITZ   AC
FANTASY ON THE MARCH (SEE A DEFENSE OF WEREWOLVES)
                                        TC
FANTASY: MANY MANSIONS AND HOVELS   AR   CLR 71 01
    CLARION   WILSON, ROBIN SCOTT OA
FAR REACH TO CYGNUS   SS   AMZ 65 02
    WORLDS OF FRITZ LEIBER, THE   LEIBER, FRITZ   AC
FOREWORD   IN
    BOOK OF FRITZ LEIBER, THE   LEIBER, FRITZ   AC
    MIND SPIDER AND OTHER STORIES, THE (ACE 76)
                                        LEIBER, FRITZ   AC
    SECOND BOOK OF FRITZ LEIBER, THE   LEIBER, FRITZ   AC
FOUR GHOSTS IN HAMLET   NV   FSF 65 01
    BEST FROM FANTASY AND SCIENCE FICTION: 15
                                        FERMAN, EDWARD L.   AN
    WORLDS FAR AND NEAR   CARR, TERRY   AN
    YOU'RE ALL ALONE   LEIBER, FRITZ   AC
FOXHOLES OF MARS, THE   SS   TWS 52 06
    BEST OF FRITZ LEIBER, THE   LEIBER, FRITZ   AC
    *BEYOND HUMAN KEN   MERRIL, JUDITH   AN
    PAIL OF AIR, A   LEIBER, FRITZ   AC
FRIENDS AND ENEMIES   SS   INF 57 04
    IF THIS GOES ON   NUETZEL, CHARLES   AN
    WORLDS OF FRITZ LEIBER, THE   LEIBER, FRITZ   AC
GAME FOR MOTEL ROOM   SS   FSF 63 03
    ALPHA 1   SILVERBERG, ROBERT   AN
    SCIENCE FICTION HORIZONS NO. 1   BOARDMAN, TOM JR.   AN
GIRL WITH THE HUNGRY EYES, THE   SS   49
    GIRL WITH THE HUNGRY EYES, AND OTHER STORIES, THE
                                        WOLLHEIM, DONALD A. OA
    SECRET SONGS, THE   LEIBER, FRITZ   AC
    *TERROR IN THE MODERN VEIN   WOLLHEIM, DONALD A. AN
GLOVE, THE   SS   WHS 75 03
    YEAR'S BEST HORROR STORIES: SERIES IV, THE
                                        PAGE, GERALD W.   AN
GOGGLES OF DR. DRAGONET, THE   SS   FAN 61 07
    WORLDS OF FRITZ LEIBER, THE   LEIBER, FRITZ   AC
GOLD, BLACK, AND SILVER   SS   QRK 71 02
    QUARK/2   DELANY & HACKER   OA
GONNA ROLL THE BONES   NV   DVS 67 01
    BEST OF FRITZ LEIBER, THE   LEIBER, FRITZ   AC
    DANGEROUS VISIONS   ELLISON, HARLAN   OA
    HUGO WINNERS, THE (VOLUME 2)   ASIMOV, ISAAC   AN
    NEBULA AWARD STORIES NO. 3   ZELAZNY, ROGER   AN
GOOD NEW DAYS, THE   SS   GAL 65 10
    BEST OF FRITZ LEIBER, THE   LEIBER, FRITZ   AC
    WORLD'S BEST SCIENCE FICTION: 1966 WOLLHEIM & CARR   AN
HATCHERY OF DREAMS   SS   FAN 61 11
    ROD SERLING'S TRIPLE W: WITCHES, WARLOCKS AND WEREWOLVES
                                        SERLING, ROD   AN
    WORLDS OF FRITZ LEIBER, THE   LEIBER, FRITZ   AC
HAUNTED FUTURE, THE (TRANQUILITY, OR ELSE!) NV   FAN 59 11
    DAY IN THE LIFE, A   DOZOIS, GARDNER R.   AN
    *MIND SPIDER AND OTHER STORIES, THE LEIBER, FRITZ   DC
HILL AND THE HOLE, THE   SS   UNK 42 08
    NIGHT'S BLACK AGENTS   LEIBER, FRITZ   AC
HITCH IN SPACE, A   SS   WOT 63 08
    BOOK OF FRITZ LEIBER, THE   LEIBER, FRITZ   AC
HOTTEST AND COLDEST MOLECULES   AR   SDG 52 03
    BOOK OF FRITZ LEIBER, THE   LEIBER, FRITZ   AC
HOUND, THE   SS   WRT 42 11
    BEWARE THE BEASTS   GHIDALIA, V.& ELWOOD AN
    NIGHT'S BLACK AGENTS   LEIBER, FRITZ   AC
I'M LOOKING FOR "JEFF"   SS   FAN 52 FL
    BEST FROM FANTASTIC, THE   WHITE, TED   AN
    NIGHT MONSTERS   LEIBER, FRITZ   DC
    TIME UNTAMED   HOWARD, IVAN   AN
ICON OF THE IMAGINATION   IN
    BEST SCIENCE-FICTION STORIES: 1954, THE
                                        BLEILER & DIKTY   AN
ILL MET IN LANKHMAR   SN   FSF 70 04
    NEBULA AWARD STORIES NO. 6   SIMAK, CLIFFORD D.   AN
IMPROPER AUTHORITIES, THE   SS   FAN 59 11
    WORLDS OF FRITZ LEIBER, THE   LEIBER, FRITZ   AC
INGMAR BERGMAN: FANTASY NOVELIST   BR   FAN 74 03
    SECOND BOOK OF FRITZ LEIBER, THE   LEIBER, FRITZ   AC
INHERITANCE, THE   SS   WRT 42 01
    NIGHT'S BLACK AGENTS   LEIBER, FRITZ   AC

LEIBER, FRITZ   (CONTINUED)
INNER CIRCLES, THE (ALSO AS THE WINTER FLIES) SS   FSF 67 10
    BEST FROM FANTASY AND SCIENCE FICTION: 17
                                        FERMAN, EDWARD L.   AN
    NEW WORLDS OF FANTASY NO. 3   CARR, TERRY   AN
INTRODUCTION   IN
    GLASS OF STARS, A   YOUNG, ROBERT F.   AC
    SECRET SONGS, THE   LEIBER, FRITZ   AC
    WORLDS OF FRITZ LEIBER, THE   LEIBER, FRITZ   AC
KINDERGARTEN   SS   FSF 63 04
    BOOK OF FRITZ LEIBER, THE   LEIBER, FRITZ   AC
KING LEAR   AR   34
    BOOK OF FRITZ LEIBER, THE   LEIBER, FRITZ   AC
KNIGHT TO MOVE (KNIGHT'S MOVE)   SS   BRD 65 12
    BOOK OF FRITZ LEIBER, THE   LEIBER, FRITZ   AC
LAST   SS   FSF 57 03
    ENDS OF TIME, THE   SILVERBERG, ROBERT   AN
    WORLDS OF FRITZ LEIBER, THE   LEIBER, FRITZ   AC
LAST LETTER, THE   SS   GAL 58 06
    FIFTH GALAXY READER, THE   GOLD, H. L.   AN
    PAIL OF AIR, A   LEIBER, FRITZ   AC
    WORLDS OF FRITZ LEIBER, THE   LEIBER, FRITZ   AC
LATER THAN YOU THINK   SS   GAL 50 10
    BEST SF 5   CRISPIN, EDMUND   AN
    EVIL EARTHS   ALDISS, BRIAN W.   AN
    FAR BOUNDARIES   DERLETH, AUGUST   AN
LET FREEDOM RING (SEE THE WOLF PACK)   TC
LION AND THE LAMB, THE   NV   ASF 50 09
    SECOND BOOK OF FRITZ LEIBER, THE   LEIBER, FRITZ   AC
LITTLE OLD MISS MACBETH   SS   FSF 58 12
    BEST OF FRITZ LEIBER, THE   LEIBER, FRITZ   AC
LONE WOLF, THE (THE CREATURE FROM CLEVELAND DEPTHS)
                                        NA   GAL 62 12
    NIGHT OF THE WOLF, THE   LEIBER, FRITZ   AC
LOTUS EATERS, THE   SS   FSF 72 10
    WORLDS OF FRITZ LEIBER, THE   LEIBER, FRITZ   AC
MAN WHO MADE FRIENDS WITH ELECTRICITY, THE SS   FSF 62 03
    BEST OF FRITZ LEIBER, THE   LEIBER, FRITZ   AC
    SECRET SONGS, THE   LEIBER, FRITZ   AC
    SHADOWS WITH EYES   LEIBER, FRITZ   AC
    8TH ANNUAL OF THE YEAR'S BEST S-F, THE MERRIL, JUDITH   AN
MAN WHO NEVER GREW YOUNG, THE   SS   AFR 49 09
    BEST OF FRITZ LEIBER, THE   LEIBER, FRITZ   AC
    DARK SIDE, THE   KNIGHT, DAMON   AN
    NIGHT'S BLACK AGENTS   LEIBER, FRITZ   AC
MARIANA   SS   FAN 60 02
    BEST OF FRITZ LEIBER, THE   LEIBER, FRITZ   AC
    SCIENCE FACT/FICTION   FARRELL/GAGE/&   AN
    SECRET SONGS, THE   LEIBER, FRITZ   AC
    SF: THE BEST OF THE BEST   MERRIL, JUDITH   AN
    5TH ANNUAL OF THE YEAR'S BEST S-F, THE MERRIL, JUDITH   AN
MASTERS OF MACE AND MAGIC   AR
    BOOK OF FRITZ LEIBER, THE   LEIBER, FRITZ   AC
MECHANICAL BRIDE, THE   PL   NEW 54 AN
    *SCIENCE FICTION THINKING MACHINES CONKLIN, GROFF   AN
    SECOND BOOK OF FRITZ LEIBER, THE   LEIBER, FRITZ   AC
    SIX SCIENCE FICTION PLAYS   ELWOOD, ROGER   AN
MIDNIGHT BY THE MORPHY WATCH   NV   IFS 74 08
    BEST FROM IF, THE VOLUME III   BAEN, JAMES   AN
MIDNIGHT IN THE MIRROR WORLD   SS   FAN 64 10
    MIND SPIDER AND OTHER STORIES, THE (ACE 76)
                                        LEIBER, FRITZ   AC
    NIGHT MONSTERS   LEIBER, FRITZ   DC
MIGHTY TIDES, THE (WHAT MAKES THE MIGHTY TIDES) AR   SDG 61 04
    SECOND BOOK OF FRITZ LEIBER, THE   LEIBER, FRITZ   AC
MIND SPIDER, THE   SS   FAN 59 11
    *MIND SPIDER AND OTHER STORIES, THE LEIBER, FRITZ   DC
MONSTERS AND MONSTER LOVERS   AR   FAN 65 03
    BOOK OF FRITZ LEIBER, THE   LEIBER, FRITZ   AC
MOON DUEL   SS   IFS 65 09
    11TH ANNUAL OF THE YEAR'S BEST S-F, THE
                                        MERRIL, JUDITH   AN
MOON IS GREEN, THE   SS   GAL 52 05
    BEST SCIENCE-FICTION STORIES: 1953, THE
                                        BLEILER & DIKTY   AN
    FRONTIERS IN SPACE   BLEILER & DIKTY   AN
    SECRET SONGS, THE   LEIBER, FRITZ   AC
MR. BAUER AND THE ATOMS   SS   WRT 46 01
    *STRANGE PORTS OF CALL   DERLETH, AUGUST   AN
MUTANT'S BROTHER, THE   SS   ASF 43 08
    CROSSROADS IN TIME   CONKLIN, GROFF   AN
MYSTERIOUS DOINGS IN THE METROPOLITAN MUSEUM SS   UNI 74 05
    UNIVERSE 5   CARR, TERRY   OA
    WORLDS OF FRITZ LEIBER, THE   LEIBER, FRITZ   AC
MYTHS MY GREAT-GRANDDAUGHTER TAUGHT ME SS   FSF 63 01
    SF: AUTHORS' CHOICE   HARRISON, HARRY   AN
    WORLDS OF FRITZ LEIBER, THE   LEIBER, FRITZ   AC
NICE GIRL WITH FIVE HUSBANDS   SS   GAL 51 04
    PAIL OF AIR, A   LEIBER, FRITZ   AC
    TIME CURVE, THE   MOSKOWITZ & ELWOOD   AN
    WORLDS OF FRITZ LEIBER, THE   LEIBER, FRITZ   AC
    13 ABOVE THE NIGHT   CONKLIN, GROFF   AN
NIGHT HE CRIED, THE   SS   STR 53 01
    BEST OF FRITZ LEIBER, THE   LEIBER, FRITZ   AC
    GALAXY OF GHOULS   MERRIL, JUDITH   AN
    GENTLE INVADERS   SANTESSON, HANS S.   AN
    STAR SCIENCE FICTION STORIES   POHL, FREDERIK   OA
NIGHT OF THE LONG KNIVES, THE (SEE THE WOLF PAIR) TC
NIGHT PASSAGE   NV   75
    WORLDS OF FRITZ LEIBER, THE   LEIBER, FRITZ   AC
NO GREAT MAGIC   SN   GAL 63 12
    SECRET SONGS, THE   LEIBER, FRITZ   AC
NUMBER OF THE BEAST, THE   NV   GAL 58 12
    *MIND SPIDER AND OTHER STORIES, THE LEIBER, FRITZ   DC
    SIXTH GALAXY READER, THE   GOLD, H. L.   AN

LEIBER, FRITZ   (CONTINUED)
  OLDEST SOLDIER, THE   NV   FSF 60 05
    ANOTHER WORLD   DOZOIS, GARDNER R.   AN
    *MIND SPIDER AND OTHER STORIES, THE LEIBER, FRITZ   DC
  ONE STATION OF THE WAY   SS   GAL 68 12
    BEST SF: 1968   HARRISON & ALDISS   AN
    ELEVENTH GALAXY READER, THE   POHL, FREDERIK   AN
  OUR SAUCER VACATION   AR   FUN 59 12
    FLYING SAUCERS IN FACT AND FICTION   SANTESSON, HANS S.   AN
    WORLDS OF FRITZ LEIBER, THE   LEIBER, FRITZ   AC
  PAIL OF AIR, A   SS   GAL 51 12
    BEST OF FRITZ LEIBER, THE   LEIBER, FRITZ   AC
    GALAXY SCIENCE FICTION OMNIBUS   GOLD, H. L.   AN
    GATES TO TOMORROW   NORTON, AN.&DONALDY   AN
    PAIL OF AIR, A   LEIBER, FRITZ   AC
    SECOND GALAXY READER OF SCIENCE FICTION
                                         GOLD, H. L.   AN
    SECRET SONGS, THE   LEIBER, FRITZ   AC
    SPACE PIONEERS   NORTON, ANDRE   AN
    SPECULATIONS   SANDERS, THOMAS E.   AN
    TOMORROW'S CHILDREN   ASIMOV, ISAAC   AN
    WINDOWS INTO TOMORROW   SILVERBERG, ROBERT   AN
    WORLDS OF WONDER   HARRISON, HARRY   AN
  PIPE DREAM   SS   IFS 59 02
    PAIL OF AIR, A   LEIBER, FRITZ   AC
    WORLDS OF FRITZ LEIBER, THE   LEIBER, FRITZ   AC
  POOR SUPERMAN (APPOINTMENT IN TOMORROW)   NV   GAL 51 07
    BEST OF FRITZ LEIBER, THE   LEIBER, FRITZ   AC
    TOMORROW, THE STARS   HEINLEIN, ROBERT A.   AN
  POWER OF THE PUPPETS, THE   SS   TMY 41 FL
    SHADOWS WITH EYES   LEIBER, FRITZ   AC
  PRINCESS IN THE TOWER 250,000 MILES HIGH, THE SS   NDM 77 07
    NEW DIMENSIONS 7   SILVERBERG, ROBERT   OA
  RITE OF SPRING, A   NV   UNI 77 07
    UNIVERSE 7   CARR, TERRY   OA
  RUMP-TITTY-TITTY-TUM-TAH-TEE   SS   FSF 58 05
    BEST OF FRITZ LEIBER, THE   LEIBER, FRITZ   AC
    PAIL OF AIR, A   LEIBER, FRITZ   AC
    SCIENCE FICTION ARGOSY, A   KNIGHT, DAMON   AN
    SCIENCE FICTION ODDITIES   CONKLIN, GROFF   AN
    SECRET SONGS, THE   LEIBER, FRITZ   AC
  SANITY (ALSO AS CRAZY WOLF)   SS   ASF 44 04
    BEST OF FRITZ LEIBER, THE   LEIBER, FRITZ   AC
    *BIG BOOK OF SCIENCE FICTION   CONKLIN, GROFF   AN
    ONE HUNDRED YEARS OF SCIENCE FICTION KNIGHT, DAMON   AN
    SCIENCE FICTION ROLL OF HONOR, THE   POHL, FREDERIK   AN
  SCHIZO JIMMIE   SS   SMM 60 02
    SHADOWS WITH EYES   LEIBER, FRITZ   AC
  SCREAM WOLF   SS   MSM 61 02
    SECOND BOOK OF FRITZ LEIBER, THE   LEIBER, FRITZ   AC
  SECRET SONGS, THE   SS   FSF 62 08
    PERCHANCE TO DREAM   KNIGHT, DAMON   AN
    SECRET SONGS, THE   LEIBER, FRITZ   AC
    SPECTRUM 4   AMIS & CONQUEST   AN
    STRANGE ECSTASIES   PARRY, MICHEL   AN
    SURVIVAL PRINTOUT   TOTAL EFFECT   AN
  SHIP OF SHADOWS   SN   FSF 69 07
    BEST FROM FANTASY AND SCIENCE FICTION, 25TH ANNIV.
                                         FERMAN, EDWARD L.   AN
    WORLD'S BEST SCIENCE FICTION: 1970   WOLLHEIM & CARR   AN
  SHIP SAILS AT MIDNIGHT, THE   NV   FAD 50 09
    BEST OF FRITZ LEIBER, THE   LEIBER, FRITZ   AC
    *OUTER REACHES, THE   DERLETH, AUGUST   AN
    SHIPS TO THE STARS   LEIBER, FRITZ   DC
  SMOKE GHOST   SS   UNK 41 10
    HUMAN?   MERRIL, JUDITH   AN
    NIGHT'S BLACK AGENTS   LEIBER, FRITZ   AC
    SECRET SONGS, THE   LEIBER, FRITZ   AC
  SNOWBANK ORBIT, THE   NV   IFS 62 09
    BEST SCIENCE FICTION FROM IF, THE   POHL, FREDERIK   AN
    SHIPS TO THE STARS   LEIBER, FRITZ   DC
  SPACE-TIME FOR SPRINGERS   SS   STR 58 04
    BEST OF FRITZ LEIBER, THE   LEIBER, FRITZ   AC
    SF: THE BEST OF THE BEST   MERRIL, JUDITH   AN
    SF:59, THE YEAR'S GREATEST SCIENCE FICTION AND FANTASY
                                         MERRIL, JUDITH   AN
    STAR OF STARS   POHL, FREDERIK   AN
    STAR SCIENCE FICTION STORIES NO. 4   POHL, FREDERIK   OA
  SPIDER MANSION   SS   WRT 42 09
    WEIRD TALES   MARGULIES, LEO   AN
  SPIDER, THE   SS   ROG 63 01
    BOOK OF FRITZ LEIBER, THE   LEIBER, FRITZ   AC
  SQUARE ROOT OF BRAIN, THE   SS   NWS 68 02
    BEST SF STORIES FROM NEW WORLDS 4   MOORCOCK, MICHAEL   AN
    WORLD'S BEST SCIENCE FICTION: 1969   WOLLHEIM & CARR   AN
  SUNKEN LAND, THE   SS   UNK 42 02
    NIGHT'S BLACK AGENTS   LEIBER, FRITZ   AC
  TABOO   SS   ASF 44 02
    JOURNEY TO INFINITY   GREENBERG, MARTIN   AN
  THIRTEENTH STEP, THE   SS   NEW 62 AN
    FIEND IN YOU, THE   BEAUMONT, CHARLES   AN
  THOSE WILD ALIEN WORDS: I   AR   NEW 74 AC
    BOOK OF FRITZ LEIBER, THE   LEIBER, FRITZ   AC
  THOSE WILD ALIEN WORDS: II   AR   NEW 75 AC
    SECOND BOOK OF FRITZ LEIBER, THE   LEIBER, FRITZ   AC
  THROUGH HYPERSPACE WITH BROWN JENKIN   AR   66
    SECOND BOOK OF FRITZ LEIBER, THE   LEIBER, FRITZ   AC
  TIME FIGHTER   SS   FUN 57 03
    PAIL OF AIR, A   LEIBER, FRITZ   AC
  TIME IN THE ROUND   NV   GAL 57 05
    THIRD GALAXY READER, THE   GOLD, H. L.   AN
  TO ARKHAM AND THE STARS   AR   66
    BOOK OF FRITZ LEIBER, THE   LEIBER, FRITZ   AC
  TRANQUILITY, OR ELSE! (SEE THE HAUNTED FUTURE)   TC
  TRAPPED IN THE SEA OF STARS   SS   NEW 75 AC
    SECOND BOOK OF FRITZ LEIBER, THE   LEIBER, FRITZ   AC

LEIBER, FRITZ   (CONTINUED)
  TRY AND CHANGE THE PAST   SS   ASF 58 03
    BEST OF FRITZ LEIBER, THE   LEIBER, FRITZ   AC
    *MIND SPIDER AND OTHER STORIES, THE LEIBER, FRITZ   DC
  WAIF   NV   74
    FAR SIDE OF TIME, THE   ELWOOD, ROGER   OA
    WORLDS OF FRITZ LEIBER, THE   LEIBER, FRITZ   AC
  WANTED- AN ENEMY   SS   ASF 45 02
    BEST OF FRITZ LEIBER, THE   LEIBER, FRITZ   AC
    *BEYOND TIME AND SPACE   DERLETH, AUGUST   AN
  WEIRD WORLD OF THE KNIGHT (TOPSY-TURVY WORLD OF..)   AR   CCR 60 01
    BOOK OF FRITZ LEIBER, THE   LEIBER, FRITZ   AC
  WHAT MAKES THE MIGHTY TIDES (SEE THE MIGHTY TIDES)
                                                         TC
  WHAT'S HE DOING IN THERE?   SS   GAL 57 12
    CONTACT   KEYES, NOEL   AN
    FOURTH GALAXY READER, THE   GOLD, H. L.   AN
    WORLDS OF FRITZ LEIBER, THE   LEIBER, FRITZ   AC
  WHEN THE CHANGE-WINDS BLOW   SS   FSF 64 08
    WORLD'S BEST SCIENCE FICTION: 1965   WOLLHEIM & CARR   AN
    WORLDS OF FRITZ LEIBER, THE   LEIBER, FRITZ   AC
  WHEN THE LAST GODS DIE   SS   FSF 51 12
    BOOK OF FRITZ LEIBER, THE   LEIBER, FRITZ   AC
    ENDS OF TIME, THE   SILVERBERG, ROBERT   AN
  WHISPERER RE-EXAMINED, THE   AR
    BOOK OF FRITZ LEIBER, THE   LEIBER, FRITZ   AC
  WINTER FLIES, THE (THE INNER CIRCLES)   SS   FSF 67 10
    POCKETFUL OF STARS, A   KNIGHT, DAMON   AN
    SECRET SONGS, THE   LEIBER, FRITZ   AC
    SP12   MERRIL, JUDITH   AN
  WOLF PACK, THE (LET FREEDOM RING)   SN   AMZ 50 04
    NIGHT OF THE WOLF, THE   LEIBER, FRITZ   AC
  WOLF PAIR, THE (THE NIGHT OF THE LONG KNIVES)   NA   AMZ 60 01
    NIGHT OF THE WOLF, THE   LEIBER, FRITZ   AC
  X MARKS THE PEDWALK   SS   WOT 63 04
    ABC OF SCIENCE FICTION, AN   BOARDMAN, TOM JR.   AN
    BEST SCIENCE FICTION FROM WORLDS OF TOMORROW, THE
                                         POHL, FREDERIK   AN
    NIGHTMARE AGE   POHL, FREDERIK   AN
    THEMES IN SCIENCE FICTION   KELLEY, LEO P.   AN
  YESTERDAY HOUSE   NV   GAL 52 08
    ALPHA 5   SILVERBERG, ROBERT   AN
    BOOK OF FRITZ LEIBER, THE   LEIBER, FRITZ   AC
  YOU'RE ALL ALONE   NO   FAD 50 07
    YOU'RE ALL ALONE   LEIBER, FRITZ   AC
  237 TALKING STATUES, ETC.   SS   FSF 63 09
    TWENTY YEARS OF FANTASY & SCIENCE FICTION
                                         FERMAN & MILLS   AN
    WORLDS OF FRITZ LEIBER, THE   LEIBER, FRITZ   AC
    9TH ANNUAL OF THE YEAR'S BEST S-F, THE MERRIL, JUDITH   AN
  64-SQUARE MADHOUSE, THE   NA   IFS 62 05
    IF READER OF SCIENCE FICTION, THE   POHL, FREDERIK   AN
    PAIL OF AIR, A   LEIBER, FRITZ   AC

LEIBSCHER, WALT
  DO ANDROIDS DREAM OF ELECTRIC LOVE?   SS   NEW 72 AN
    STRANGE BED FELLOWS   SCORTIA, THOMAS N.   AN

LEIF, EVELYN
  EVERY FOURTH HOUSE   SS   GEN 72
    GENERATION   GERROLD, DAVID   OA

LEIGH, STEPHEN
  MASK OF NIGHT ON HIS FACE, THE   SS
    FUTURE PASTIMES   EDELSTEIN, SCOTT   OA

LEIMERT, JOHN
  JOHN THOMAS'S CUBE   SS   ATL 45 08
    ARMCHAIR SCIENCE READER, THE   GORDON, I. & SORKIN   AN
    OMNIBUS OF SCIENCE FICTION   CONKLIN, GROFF   AN
    STRANGE TRAVELS IN SCIENCE FICTION   CONKLIN, GROFF   AN

LEINSTER, MURRAY   PSEUD. FOR WILLIAM F. JENKINS
  ALIENS, THE   AC   BKM 60 03
  BEST OF MURRAY LEINSTER, THE   AC   COR 76
    EDITED BY BRIAN DAVIS
  COLONIAL SURVEY   NO H GNM 56
    ALSO AS "THE PLANET EXPLORER"
  DOCTOR TO THE STARS   AC   PYR 64 03
  FORGOTTEN PLANET, THE   AC H GNM 54
  GET OFF MY WORLD!   AC   BEL 66 04
  GREAT STORIES OF SCIENCE FICTION   AN H RDM 51
  LAST SPACESHIP, THE   NO H FEL 49
  MONSTERS AND SUCH   AC   AVN 59
  MURRAY LEINSTER OMNIBUS, A   AC H SID 68
    ALSO IN "SCIENCE FICTION SPECIAL 7"
  OUT OF THIS WORLD   NO H AVL 58
  PLANET EXPLORER, THE   NO   AVN 57
    SEE "COLONIAL SURVEY"
  S.O.S. FROM THREE WORLDS   AC   ACE 66
  SIDEWISE IN TIME   AC H SHS 50
  TWISTS IN TIME   AC   AVN 60
  ALIENS, THE   NV   ASF 59 08
    ALIENS, THE   LEINSTER, MURRAY   AC
    OUT OF THIS WORLD 6   WILLIAMS-ELLIS& OWEN   AN
  AMBULANCE MADE TWO TRIPS, THE   SS   ASF 60 04
    NEVER IN THIS WORLD   STONE, IDELLA P.   AN
  ANTHROPOLOGICAL NOTE   NV   FSF 57 04
    ALIENS, THE   LEINSTER, MURRAY   AC
  ASSIGNMENT ON PASIK   SS   TWS 49 02
    ADVENTURES ON OTHER PLANETS   WOLLHEIM, DONALD A.   AN
  BOOMERANG CIRCUIT, THE   NV   TWS 47 06
    LAST SPACESHIP, THE   LEINSTER, MURRAY   NO
  CASE OF THE HOMICIDAL ROBOTS, THE   NV   FSF 61 08

LEINSTER, MURRAY

LEINSTER, MURRAY   (CONTINUED)
    ONCE AND FUTURE TALES FROM THE MAGAZINE OF FANTASY AND
        SCIENCE FICTION   FERMAN, EDWARD L.   AN
CASTAWAY, THE   NV   USF 53 06
    MONSTERS AND SUCH   LEINSTER, MURRAY   AC
CHECKPOINT LAMBDA (STOPOVER IN SPACE)   NO   AMZ 66 06
    MURRAY LEINSTER OMNIBUS, A   LEINSTER, MURRAY   AC
COMBAT TEAM (EXPLORATION TEAM)   NV   ASF 56 03
    COLONIAL SURVEY   LEINSTER, MURRAY   NO
CORIANIS DISASTER, THE   NV   SFS 60 05
    SEVEN COME INFINITY   CONKLIN, GROFF   AN
CRITICAL DIFFERENCE (SEE SOLAR CONSTANT)   TC
CURE FOR A YLITH   SS   STS 49 11
    OPERATION FUTURE   CONKLIN, GROFF   AN
DAY OF THE DEEPIES, THE   SS   FFM 47 10
    SHOT IN THE DARK   MERRIL, JUDITH   AN
DE PROFUNDIS   SS   TWS 45 WI
    BEST OF MURRAY LEINSTER, THE   LEINSTER, MURRAY   AC
    FAR BOUNDARIES   DERLETH, AUGUST   AN
    MONSTERS AND SUCH   LEINSTER, MURRAY   AC
    SIDEWISE IN TIME   LEINSTER, MURRAY   AC
DEAD CITY (ALSO AS MALIGNANT MARAUDER)   NV   TWS 46 SU
    TWISTS IN TIME   LEINSTER, MURRAY   AC
DEADLY DUST, THE   NV   TWS 47 08
    OUT OF THIS WORLD   LEINSTER, MURRAY   NO
DEAR CHARLES   SS   FSM 53 05
    TWISTS IN TIME   LEINSTER, MURRAY   AC
DEVIL OF EAST LUPTON, THE   SS   TWS 48 08
    BEST OF MURRAY LEINSTER, THE   LEINSTER, MURRAY   AC
    *OTHER SIDE OF THE MOON, THE   DERLETH, AUGUST   AN
DISCIPLINARY CIRCUIT, THE   NV   TWS 46 WI
    LAST SPACESHIP, THE   LEINSTER, MURRAY   NO
DOCTOR   NV   GAL 61 02
    WORLDS APART   WILLIAMS-ELLIS& OWEN AN
END, THE   NV   TWS 46 12
    TWISTS IN TIME   LEINSTER, MURRAY   AC
ETERNAL NOW, THE   NV   TWS 44 FL
    SHAPE OF THINGS, THE   KNIGHT, DAMON   AN
ETHICAL EQUATIONS, THE   SS   ASF 45 06
    BEST OF MURRAY LEINSTER, THE   LEINSTER, MURRAY   AC
    GIANTS UNLEASHED   CONKLIN, GROFF   AN
    *TREASURY OF SCIENCE FICTION, A   CONKLIN, GROFF   AN
EXPLORATION TEAM (ALSO AS COMBAT TEAM)   NV   ASF 56 03
    EXPLORERS OF SPACE   SILVERBERG, ROBERT   AN
    HUGO WINNERS, THE (VOLUME 1)   ASIMOV, ISAAC   AN
    SPECTRUM 3   AMIS & CONQUEST   AN
    TALES FROM THE GALAXIES   WILLIAMS-ELLIS& P.   AN
FIFTH-DIMENSION CATAPULT, THE   NV   ASF 31 01
    SCIENCE FICTION OF THE 30'S   KNIGHT, DAMON   AN
FIRST CONTACT   NV   ASF 45 05
    *ASTOUNDING SCIENCE FICTION ANTHOLOGY, THE
                                             CAMPBELL, JOHN W. JR AN
    ASTOUNDING-ANALOG READER, THE VOLUME ONE
                                             HARRISON & ALDISS   AN
    *BEST OF SCIENCE FICTION   CONKLIN, GROFF   AN
    CONTACT   KEYES, NOEL   AN
    *FIRST ASTOUNDING SCIENCE FICTION ANTHOLOGY, THE
                                             CAMPBELL, JOHN W. JR AN
    FIRST CONTACT   KNIGHT, DAMON   AN
    FIRST STEP OUTWARD   HOSKINS, ROBERT   AN
    SCIENCE FICTION HALL OF FAME VOLUME 1   SILVERBERG, ROBERT   AN
    *STORIES FOR TOMORROW   SLOANE, WILLIAM   AN
FOURTH-DIMENSIONAL DEMONSTRATOR, THE   SS   ASF 35 12
    FUTURE MAKERS, THE   HAINING, PETER   AN
    OTHER WORLDS, THE   STONG, PHILIP D.   AN
    SIDEWISE IN TIME   LEINSTER, MURRAY   AC
    TWISTS IN TIME   LEINSTER, MURRAY   AC
FUGITIVE FROM SPACE   NA   AMZ 54 05
    ALIENS, THE   LEINSTER, MURRAY   AC
GADGET HAD A GHOST, THE   NV   TWS 52 06
    YEAR'S BEST SCIENCE FICTION NOVELS: 1953
                                             BLEILER & DIKTY   AN
GRANDFATHERS' WAR, THE   SN   ASF 57 10
    DOCTOR TO THE STARS   LEINSTER, MURRAY   AC
GREGORY CIRCLE, THE   NV   TWS 47 04
    OUT OF THIS WORLD   LEINSTER, MURRAY   NO
HATE DISEASE, THE (SEE TALLIEN THREE)   TC
HISTORICAL NOTE   SS   ASF 51 02
    *ASTOUNDING SCIENCE FICTION ANTHOLOGY, THE
                                             CAMPBELL, JOHN W. JR AN
    ASTOUNDING TALES OF SPACE AND TIME   CAMPBELL, JOHN W. JR AN
    *SECOND ASTOUNDING SCIENCE FICTION ANTHOLOGY, THE
                                             CAMPBELL, JOHN W. JR AN
IF YOU WAS A MOKLIN   NV   GAL 51 09
    BEST OF MURRAY LEINSTER, THE   LEINSTER, MURRAY   AC
    *GALAXY READER OF SCIENCE FICTION   GOLD, H. L.   AN
    MONSTERS AND SUCH   LEINSTER, MURRAY   AC
INCIDENT ON CALYPSO   SS   STS 45 FL
    INVASION FROM MARS   WELLES, ORSON   AN
INTERFERENCE   SS   ASF 45 10
    BEST OF MURRAY LEINSTER, THE   LEINSTER, MURRAY   AC
INVADERS OF SPACE   NO   BRK 64
    MURRAY LEINSTER OMNIBUS, A   LEINSTER, MURRAY   AC
JEZEBEL   SS   STS 53 10
    PORTALS OF TOMORROW   DERLETH, AUGUST   AN
JOURNEY   SS   STR 53 01
    STAR SCIENCE FICTION STORIES   POHL, FREDERIK   OA
KEYHOLE   SS   TWS 51 12
    BEYOND BELIEF   HURLEY, RICHARD J.   AN
    CHILDREN OF WONDER   TENN, WILLIAM   AN
    MEN ON THE MOON   WOLLHEIM, DONALD A. DA
    SATAN'S PETS   GHIDALIA, VIC   AN
    TOMORROW, AND TOMORROW, AND TOMORROW...
                                             HEINTZ/HERBERT/JOOS/ AN
    TOMORROW, THE STARS   HEINLEIN, ROBERT A. AN
    WORLDS OF WONDER   HARRISON, HARRY   AN

LEINSTER, MURRAY   (CONTINUED)
LEADER, THE   SS   ASF 60 02
    14 GREAT TALES OF ESP   STONE, IDELLA P.   AN
LET'S CALL IT A HOBBY   IN
    GREAT STORIES OF SCIENCE FICTION   LEINSTER, MURRAY   AN
LIFE-WORK OF PROFESSOR MUNTZ, THE   SS   TWS 49 06
    BEST SCIENCE-FICTION STORIES: 1950, THE
                                             BLEILER & DIKTY   AN
    SCIENCE FICTION GALAXY, THE   CONKLIN, GROFF   AN
LOGIC NAMED JOE, A   SS   ASF 46 03
    DOORWAY INTO TIME   MOSKOWITZ, SAM   AN
    MODERN MASTERPIECES OF SCIENCE FICTION   MOSKOWITZ, SAM   AN
    *SCIENCE-FICTION CARNIVAL   BROWN, F. & REYNOLDS AN
    SIDEWISE IN TIME   LEINSTER, MURRAY   AC
    SOULS IN METAL   ASHLEY, MICHAEL   AN
LONELY PLANET, THE   NV   TWS 49 12
    BEYOND THE END OF TIME   POHL, FREDERIK   AN
    MONSTERS AND SUCH   LEINSTER, MURRAY   AC
LOST RACE, THE   NV   TWS 49 04
    *MY BEST SCIENCE FICTION STORY   MARGULIES & FRIEND   AN
MAD PLANET, THE   NA   ARG 20 06
    FORGOTTEN PLANET, THE   LEINSTER, MURRAY   AC
    UNDER THE MOONS OF MARS   MOSKOWITZ, SAM   AN
MALIGNANT MARAUDER (DEAD CITY)   NV   TWS 46 SU
    ULTIMATE INVADER, AND OTHER SCIENCE FICTION, THE
                                             WOLLHEIM, DONALD A. DA
MANLESS WORLDS, THE   NV   TWS 47 02
    LAST SPACESHIP, THE   LEINSTER, MURRAY   NO
MED SERVICE   SN   ASF 57 08
    SCIENCE FICTION SHOWCASE   KORNBLUTH, MARY   AN
MED SHIP MAN   NV   GAL 63 10
    DOCTOR TO THE STARS   LEINSTER, MURRAY   AC
MIDDLE OF THE WEEK AFTER NEXT, THE   SS   TWS 52 08
    BEST SCIENCE-FICTION STORIES: 1953, THE
                                             BLEILER & DIKTY   AN
    OUT OF THIS WORLD 1   WILLIAMS-ELLIS& OWEN AN
    *SCIENCE FICTION ADVENTURES IN DIMENSION
                                             CONKLIN, GROFF   AN
MOLE PIRATE, THE   SN   ASF 34 11
    THREE STORIES   MOSKOWITZ, SAM   AN
MURDER MADNESS   NO   ASF 30 05
    QUADRATIC   CRAWFORD, WILLIAM L. AN
MURRAY LEINSTER OMNIBUS, A   AC   SID 68
    SCIENCE FICTION SPECIAL 7   ANONYMOUS   AN
NAMELESS SOMETHING, THE   NV   TWS 47 06
    OUT OF THIS WORLD   LEINSTER, MURRAY   NO
NIGHTMARE PLANET   SN   SFP 53 06
    FORGOTTEN PLANET, THE   LEINSTER, MURRAY   AC
NOBODY SAW THE SHIP   SS   FUS 50 05
    *BIG BOOK OF SCIENCE FICTION   CONKLIN, GROFF   AN
    INVADERS FROM SPACE   SILVERBERG, ROBERT   AN
    MONSTERS AND SUCH   LEINSTER, MURRAY   AC
OPERATION TERROR   NO   BRK 62
    MURRAY LEINSTER OMNIBUS, A   LEINSTER, MURRAY   AC
OTHER NOW, THE   SS   GAL 51 03
    *GALAXY READER OF SCIENCE FICTION   GOLD, H. L.   AN
    ONE HUNDRED YEARS OF SCIENCE FICTION   KNIGHT, DAMON   AN
    TWISTS IN TIME   LEINSTER, MURRAY   AC
OTHER WORLD, THE   NA   STS 49 11
    6 GREAT SHORT NOVELS OF SCIENCE FICTION
                                             CONKLIN, GROFF   AN
OVERDRIVE   NV   STS 53 01
    ADVENTURES IN THE FAR FUTURE   WOLLHEIM, DONALD A. DA
PIPELINE TO PLUTO   SS   ASF 45 08
    BEST OF MURRAY LEINSTER, THE   LEINSTER, MURRAY   AC
    SCIENCE FICTION TERROR TALES   CONKLIN, GROFF   AN
PLAGUE   NV   ASF 44 02
    OMNIBUS OF SCIENCE FICTION   CONKLIN, GROFF   AN
    SCIENCE FICTION OMNIBUS   CONKLIN, GROFF   AN
    STRANGE ADVENTURES IN SCIENCE FICTION   CONKLIN, GROFF   AN
PLAGUE ON KRYDER II   NV   ASF 64 12
    S.O.S. FROM THREE WORLDS   LEINSTER, MURRAY   AC
PLANET OF SAND   NV   FFM 48 02
    GET OFF MY WORLD!   LEINSTER, MURRAY   AC
PLANTS, THE   SS   ASF 46 01
    *MEN AGAINST THE STARS   GREENBERG , MARTIN   AN
POLITICS   NV   AMZ 32 06
    FUTURE TENSE   CURTIS, RICHARD   AN
    MASTERS' CHOICE   JANIFER, LAURENCE M. AN
POWER, THE   SS   ASF 45 09
    HISTORY OF THE SCIENCE FICTION MAGAZINE, THE PART 2 1936-1945
                                             ASHLEY, MICHAEL   AN
    LOOKING FORWARD   LESSER, MILTON   AN
    *OUTER REACHES, THE   DERLETH, AUGUST   AN
    SIDEWISE IN TIME   LEINSTER, MURRAY   AC
PROPAGANDIST   SS   ASF 47 08
    GREAT STORIES OF SPACE TRAVEL   CONKLIN, GROFF   AN
    *POSSIBLE WORLDS OF SCIENCE FICTION   CONKLIN, GROFF   AN
    STORIES OF SCIENTIFIC IMAGINATION   GALLANT, JOSEPH   AN
PROXIMA CENTAURI   SN   ASF 35 03
    BEFORE THE GOLDEN AGE   ASIMOV, ISAAC   AN
    MONSTERS AND SUCH   LEINSTER, MURRAY   AC
    SIDEWISE IN TIME   LEINSTER, MURRAY   AC
QUARANTINE WORLD   SN   ASF 66 11
    S.O.S. FROM THREE WORLDS   LEINSTER, MURRAY   AC
QUEEN'S ASTROLOGER, THE   SS   TWS 49 10
    CROSSROADS IN TIME   CONKLIN, GROFF   AN
RED DUST, THE   NV   AAS 21 04
    FORGOTTEN PLANET, THE   LEINSTER, MURRAY   AC
RIBBON IN THE SKY   NV   ASF 57 06
    GREAT SCIENCE FICTION ABOUT DOCTORS   CONKLIN, G&FABRICANT AN
    S.O.S. FROM THREE WORLDS   LEINSTER, MURRAY   AC
ROGUE STAR   NV   NEW 60 AC
    TWISTS IN TIME   LEINSTER, MURRAY   AC
RUNAWAY SKYSCRAPER, THE   NV   ARG 19 02
    BEST OF AMAZING, THE   ROSS, JOSEPH   AN

LEINSTER, MURRAY   (CONTINUED)
  SAM, THIS IS YOU   NV   GAL 55 05
    BEST OF MURRAY LEINSTER, THE   LEINSTER, MURRAY   AC
    TWISTS IN TIME   LEINSTER, MURRAY   AC
  SAND DOOM   NV   ASF 55 12
    COLONIAL SURVEY   LEINSTER, MURRAY   NO
  SCRIMSHAW   SS   ASF 55 09
    BEST OF MURRAY LEINSTER, THE   LEINSTER, MURRAY   AC
  SECOND LANDING   NA   TWS 54 WI
    GET OFF MY WORLD¡   LEINSTER, MURRAY   AC
  SENTIMENTALISTS, THE   NV   GAL 53 04
    YEAR'S BEST SCIENCE FICTION NOVELS: 1954
                                     BLEILER & DIKTY   AN
  SIDEWISE IN TIME   SN   ASF 34 06
    BEFORE THE GOLDEN AGE   ASIMOV, ISAAC   AN
    SIDEWISE IN TIME   LEINSTER, MURRAY   AC
    WORLDS OF MAYBE   SILVERBERG, ROBERT   AN
  SKAG WITH THE QUEER HEAD   SS   MAR 51 08
    *SCIENCE FICTION ADVENTURES IN MUTATION CONKLIN, GROFF AN
  SKIT-TREE PLANET   SS   TWS 47 04
    ALIENS, THE   LEINSTER, MURRAY   AC
  SOLAR CONSTANT (CRITICAL DIFFERENCE)   NV   ASF 56 07
    COLONIAL SURVEY   LEINSTER, MURRAY   NO
  STRANGE CASE OF JOHN KINGMAN, THE   SS   ASF 48 05
    BEST SCIENCE-FICTION STORIES: 1949, THE
                                     BLEILER & DIKTY   AN
    GREAT STORIES OF SCIENCE FICTION LEINSTER, MURRAY   AN
  SWAMP WAS UPSIDE DOWN, THE   NV   ASF 56 09
    COLONIAL SURVEY   LEINSTER, MURRAY   NO
  SYMBIOSIS   SS   COL 47 06
    BEST OF MURRAY LEINSTER, THE   LEINSTER, MURRAY   AC
  TALLIEN THREE (THE HATE DISEASE)   NV   ASF 63 08
    DOCTOR TO THE STARS   LEINSTER, MURRAY   AC
  THING FROM THE SKY   SS   NEW 60 AC
    ALIENS, THE   LEINSTER, MURRAY   AC
  THINGS PASS BY   NV   TWS 45 SU
    EARTH IN PERIL, THE   WOLLHEIM, DONALD A.   DA
    GIANT ANTHOLOGY OF SCIENCE FICTION MARGULIES & FRIEND AN
  THIS STAR SHALL BE FREE   NV   SSS 49 11
    ASLEEP IN ARMAGEDDON   SISSONS, MICHAEL   AN
    *INVADERS OF EARTH   CONKLIN, GROFF   AN
    SPECULATIONS   SANDERS, THOMAS E.   AN
  TIME TO DIE   SS   ASF 47 01
    BEST OF MURRAY LEINSTER, THE   LEINSTER, MURRAY   AC
  TRANS-HUMAN, THE   SS   SPP 53 12
    MONSTERS AND SUCH   LEINSTER, MURRAY   AC
  WABBLER, THE   SS   ASF 42 10
    BEST SF 3   CRISPIN, EDMUND   AN
    *BEYOND HUMAN KEN   MERRIL, JUDITH   AN
    TIME PROBE: THE SCIENCES IN SF. CLARKE, ARTHUR C.   AN
  WEST WIND   NV   ASF 48 03
    3 IN 1   MARGULIES, LEO   AN
  WHITE SPOT   NV   STS 55 FL
    GET OFF MY WORLD¡   LEINSTER, MURRAY   AC
  WHY I SELECTED THE LOST RACE   AI
    *MY BEST SCIENCE FICTION STORY   MARGULIES & FRIEND   AN

LEM, STANISLAW
  CYBERIAD, THE   OC H SEA 74
  MORTAL ENGINES   AC H SEA 77 05
  ADVISERS OF KING HYDROPS, THE   SS   72
    MORTAL ENGINES   LEM, STANISLAW   AC
  ALTRUIZINE   NV
    CYBERIAD, THE   LEM, STANISLAW   OC
  AUTOMATTHEW'S FRIEND   NV   72
    MORTAL ENGINES   LEM, STANISLAW   AC
  COMPUTER THAT FOUGHT A DRAGON, THE   SS
    OTHER WORLDS, OTHER SEAS   SUVIN, DARKO   AN
  FIFTH SALLY, OR THE MISCHIEF OF KING BALERION, THE
                                                SS
    CYBERIAD, THE   LEM, STANISLAW   OC
  FIFTH SALLY(A), OR TRURL'S PRESCRIPTION   SS
    CYBERIAD, THE   LEM, STANISLAW   OC
  FIRST SALLY, OR THE TRAP OF GARGANTIUS, THE   SS
    CYBERIAD, THE   LEM, STANISLAW   OC
  FIRST SALLY(A), OR TRURL'S ELECTRONIC BARD, THE SS
    CYBERIAD, THE   LEM, STANISLAW   OC
  FOURTH SALLY, OR HOW TRURL BUILT A FEMFATALATRON TO SAVE
  PRINCE PANTAGOON..., THE   SS
    CYBERIAD, THE   LEM, STANISLAW   OC
  GOOD SHELLACKING, A   SS
    CYBERIAD, THE   LEM, STANISLAW   OC
  HOW ERG THE SELF-INDUCTING SLEW A PALEFACE   SS   72
    MORTAL ENGINES   LEM, STANISLAW   AC
  HOW MICROX AND GIGANT MADE THE UNIVERSE EXPAND SS   72
    MORTAL ENGINES   LEM, STANISLAW   AC
  HOW THE WORLD WAS SAVED   SS
    ANTIGRAV: COSMIC COMEDIES   STRICK, PHILIP   AN
    CYBERIAD, THE   LEM, STANISLAW   OC
  HUNT, THE   NV   73
    MORTAL ENGINES   LEM, STANISLAW   AC
  IN HOT PURSUIT OF HAPPINESS   NV
    VIEW FROM ANOTHER SHORE   ROTTENSTEINER, FRANZ AN
  KING GLOBARES AND THE SAGES   SS   72
    MORTAL ENGINES   LEM, STANISLAW   AC
  MASK, THE   SS
    MORTAL ENGINES   LEM, STANISLAW   AC
  PATROL, THE   NV
    OTHER WORLDS, OTHER SEAS   SUVIN, DARKO   AN
  PRINCE FERRIX AND PRINCESS CRYSTAL   SS
    CYBERIAD, THE   LEM, STANISLAW   OC
  SANATORIUM OF DR. VLIPERDIUS, THE   SS   71
    MORTAL ENGINES   LEM, STANISLAW   AC
  SECOND SALLY, OR THE OFFER OF KING KROOL, THE NV
    CYBERIAD, THE   LEM, STANISLAW   OC

LEM, STANISLAW   (CONTINUED)
  SEVENTH SALLY, OR HOW TRURL'S OWN PERFECTION LED TO
  NO GOOD, THE   SS
    CYBERIAD, THE   LEM, STANISLAW   OC
  SIXTH SALLY, OR HOW TRURL AND KLAPAUCIUS CREATED A DEMON OF
  THE SECOND KIND..., THE   NV
    CYBERIAD, THE   LEM, STANISLAW   OC
  TALE OF KING GNUFF, THE   SS   72
    MORTAL ENGINES   LEM, STANISLAW   AC
  TALE OF THE COMPUTER THAT FOUGHT A DRAGON   SS   72
    MORTAL ENGINES   LEM, STANISLAW   AC
  TALE OF THE THREE STORYTELLING MACHINES OF KING GENIUS
                                                NA
    CYBERIAD, THE   LEM, STANISLAW   OC
  THIRD SALLY, OR THE DRAGONS OF PROBABILITY, THE SS
    CYBERIAD, THE   LEM, STANISLAW   OC
  THIRTEENTH JOURNEY OF ION TICHY, THE   NV
    OTHER WORLDS, OTHER SEAS   SUVIN, DARKO   AN
  THREE ELECTROKNIGHTS, THE   SS   72
    MORTAL ENGINES   LEM, STANISLAW   AC
  TRURL'S MACHINE   SS
    CYBERIAD, THE   LEM, STANISLAW   OC
  TWENTY-FOURTH JOURNEY OF ION TICHY, THE   SS
    OTHER WORLDS, OTHER SEAS   SUVIN, DARKO   AN
  TWO MONSTERS   SS   72
    MORTAL ENGINES   LEM, STANISLAW   AC
  URANIUM EARPIECES   SS   72
    MORTAL ENGINES   LEM, STANISLAW   AC
  WHITE DEATH, THE   SS   72
    MORTAL ENGINES   LEM, STANISLAW   AC

LEMAN, GRAHAME
  CONVERSATIONAL MODE   SS   NWR 72 20
    BEST SCIENCE FICTION FOR 1972   POHL, FREDERIK   AN
    BEST SCIENCE FICTION OF THE YEAR, THE NO. 2
                                     CARR, TERRY   AN
  INFINITE JESTS   SILVERBERG, ROBERT AN
  NEW WRITINGS IN SF. 20   CARNELL, JOHN   OA
  DJANGO MAVERICK: 2051   SS   NWR 71 18
    NEW WRITINGS IN SF. 18   CARNELL, JOHN   OA
  WAGTAIL IN THE MORNING   SS   NWR 74 23
    NEW WRITINGS IN SF. 23   BULMER, KENNETH   OA
  WAY ERVING WENT, THE   SS   NWR 76 28
    NEW WRITINGS IN SF. 28   BULMER, KENNETH   OA

LEMON, DON MARK
  MANSION OF FORGETFULNESS, THE   SS   BLC 07 04
    SCIENCE FICTION BY GASLIGHT   MOSKOWITZ, SAM   AN

LENTINI, A.
  AUTUMNTIME   SS   GAL 71 11
    BEST SCIENCE FICTION STORIES OF THE YEAR (1971)
                                     DEL REY, LESTER   AN

LERMAN, RHODA
  CALL ME ISHTAR (EXCERPT)   EX   DBL 73
    NEW CONSTELLATIONS   DISCH & NAYLOR   OA

LERNET-HOLENIA, ALEX
  BARON BAGGE   SS
    BEST FANTASY STORIES   ALDISS, BRIAN W.   AN

LEROUX, GASTON
  PHANTOM OF THE OPERA   NA   11
    GHOULS, THE   HAINING, PETER   AN

LESLIE, DELIA
  LANDLORD, THE   SS   SFM 74 09
    BEST OF SCIENCE FICTION MONTHLY, THE SACKS, JANET   AN

LESLIE, NORMAN
  SIX HUNDRED FATHOMS   SS
    ADVENTURES TO COME   ESENWEIN, J. BERG   OA

LESSER, MILTON   ALSO AS   STEPHEN MARLOWE
  LOOKING FORWARD   AN H BCH 53
  "A" AS IN ANDROID   SS   FUT 51 05
    NOVELETS OF SCIENCE FICTION   HOWARD, IVAN   AN
  BLACK EYES AND THE DAILY GRIND   SS   IFS 52 03
    *STORIES FOR TOMORROW   SLOANE, WILLIAM   AN
  COLD NIGHT FOR CRYING, A   SS   IFS 54 12
    FIRST WORLD OF IF, THE   QUINN & WULFF   AN
  DO IT YOURSELF   SS   SFQ 57 11
    RARE SCIENCE FICTION   HOWARD, IVAN   AN
  ENNUI   SS   DSF 52 12
    WAY OUT   HOWARD, IVAN   AN
  EXTERRAN   SS   NEW 54 AN
    TOMORROW'S UNIVERSE   CAMPBELL, H. J.   AN
  INTRUDER ON THE RIM (SEE OPERATION ZERO)   TC
  NAME YOUR TIGER   NV   SFQ 57 05
    WEIRD ONES, THE   HOWARD, IVAN   AN
  OPERATION ZERO (INTRUDER ON THE RIM)   SS   OSF 54 09
    SANDS OF MARS AND OTHER STORIES, THE ANONYMOUS   AN
  PEN PAL   SS   GAL 51 07
    *INVADERS OF EARTH   CONKLIN, GROFF   AN
  SCIENCE FICTION COMES OF AGE   IN
    LOOKING FORWARD   LESSER, MILTON   AN

LESSING, DORIS
  MILD ATTACK OF LOCUSTS, A   SS   51
    VOYAGES: SCENARIOS FOR A SHIP CALLED EARTH
                                     SAUER, ROB   AN

LETTS, D.
  BEDTIME STORY, A   SS
    STOPWATCH   HAY, GEORGE   OA

LEVIN, IRA

LIVINGSTON, BERKELEY

LEVIN, IRA
  FROM:THIS PERFECT DAY   EX   RDM 70
    INSIDE INFORMATION   MOWSHOWITZ, ABBE   AN

LEVIN, SOL
  ILLUSTRATIONS   IL
    VENUS EQUILATERAL   SMITH, GEORGE O.   AC

LEWIS, AL
  LEIBER BIBLIOGRAPHY   MS   FSF 69 07
    BEST FROM FANTASY AND SCIENCE FICTION, 25TH ANNIV.
                        FERMAN, EDWARD L.   AN

LEWIS, ANTHONY R.
  REQUEST FOR PROPOSAL   SS   ASF 72 11
    AMERICAN GOVERNMENT THROUGH SCIENCE FICTION
                        OLANDER/GREENBERG/& AN

LEWIS, C. S.
  DARK TOWER AND OTHER STORIES, THE   AC H HBJ 77
    EDITED BY WALTER HOOPER
  ADVENTURE IN A SPACE SHIP (FROM "OUT OF THE SILENT PLANET")
                        EX   LNE 38
    SCIENCE IN FICTION   BAYLISS, A.E. & J.C. AN
  AFTER TEN YEARS   NV   66
    DARK TOWER AND OTHER STORIES, THE LEWIS, C. S.   AC
  DARK TOWER, THE (UNFINISHED)   NA   NEW 77 AC
    DARK TOWER AND OTHER STORIES, THE LEWIS, C. S.   AC
  EXPOSTULATION, AN   PM   FSF 59 06
    BEST FROM FANTASY AND SCIENCE FICTION: 9
                      MILLS, ROBERT P.   AN
  HOLDING YOUR EIGHT HANDS   LUCIE-SMITH, EDWARD AN
  SCIENCE FICTION THROUGH THE AGES 2 EVANS, I. O.   AN
  FLIGHT TO MALACANDRA (FROM "OUT OF THE SILENT PLANET")
                        EX   LNE 38
    ARMCHAIR SCIENCE READER, THE   GORDON, I. & SORKIN AN
  FORMS OF THINGS UNKNOWN   SS   66
    DARK TOWER AND OTHER STORIES, THE LEWIS, C. S.   AC
  MAN BORN BLIND, THE   SS   NEW 77 AC
    DARK TOWER AND OTHER STORIES, THE LEWIS, C. S.   AC
  MINISTERING ANGELS (SRV MAY 28, 1955)   SS   FSF 58 01
    BEST FROM FANTASY AND SCIENCE FICTION: 8
                      BOUCHER, ANTHONY AN
    DARK TOWER AND OTHER STORIES, THE LEWIS, C. S.   AC
  PERLANDRA (SELECTION)   EX   LNE 43
    ALL ABOUT VENUS   ALDISS, BRIAN W.   AN
    FAREWELL FANTASTIC VENUS   ALDISS & HARRISON   AN
  SHODDY LANDS, THE   SS   FSF 56 02
    BEST FROM FANTASY AND SCIENCE FICTION: 6
                      BOUCHER, ANTHONY AN
    DARK TOWER AND OTHER STORIES, THE LEWIS, C. S.   AC
  LATE GREAT FUTURE, THE   FITZ GERALD & DILLON AN
  LIGHT FANTASTIC, THE   HARRISON, HARRY   AN
  UNREAL ESTATES   MS C SFH 64 01
  SPECTRUM 4   AMIS & CONQUEST   AN

LEWIS, JACK
  WHO'S CRIBBING?   SS   STS 53 01
    BEST FROM STARTLING STORIES, THE MINES, SAMUEL   AN
    FIFTY SHORT SCIENCE FICTION TALES ASIMOV & CONKLIN AN
    SCIENCE FACT/FICTION   FARRELL/GAGE/&   AN

LEWIS, MYRON R.
  DUELING MACHINE, THE (SEE THE PERFECT WARRIOR) TC C
  MEN OF GOOD WILL   SS C GAL 64 06
    COMBAT SF   DICKSON, GORDON R. AN
  FORWARD IN TIME   BOVA, BEN   AC
  NOTES TO A SCIENCE FICTION WRITER BOVA, BEN   AC
  WORLD'S BEST SCIENCE FICTION: 1965 WOLLHEIM & CARR   AN
  PERFECT WARRIOR, THE (THE DUELING MACHINE) SN C ASF 63 05
  FORWARD IN TIME   BOVA, BEN   AC

LEWIS, OSCAR
  LOST YEARS, THE   EX   KNP 51
    TREASURY OF GREAT SCIENCE FICTION, A VOL.2
                      BOUCHER, ANTHONY AN

LEWIS, RICHARD O.
  DOCS, THE   SS   FSF 64 12
    SCHOOL AND SOCIETY THROUGH SCIENCE FICTION
                        OLANDER/GREENBERG/& AN

LEWIS, ROY
  EVOLUTION MAN, THE   SS   60
    APEMAN, SPACEMAN   STOVER & HARRISON AN

LEWIS, SINCLAIR
  GHOST PATROL, THE   SS   DSM 17
    FANTASTIC PULPS, THE   HAINING, PETER   AN

LEY, ARTHUR   SEE PSEUD. ARTHUR SELLINGS

LEY, OLGA
  CHECKMATE IN SIX MOVES   SS
    BEYOND TIME   LEY, SANDRA   OA

LEY, SANDRA
  BEYOND TIME   OA   PKT 76 10
    EDITOR'S NOTE   IN
  BEYOND TIME   LEY, SANDRA   OA

LEY, WILLY   ALSO AS   ROBERT WILLEY
  AT THE PERIHELION (SEE A MARTIAN ADVENTURE) TC
  CALLING ALL MARTIANS (SEE A LETTER TO THE MARTIANS)
                                    TC

LEY, WILLY   (CONTINUED)
  GEOGRAPHY FOR TIME TRAVELERS   AR   ASF 39 07
    COMING ATTRACTIONS   GREENBERG, MARTIN NF
  INTRODUCTION   IN
    *MEN AGAINST THE STARS   GREENBERG, MARTIN AN
    TRAVELLERS OF SPACE   GREENBERG, MARTIN AN
  LETTER TO THE MARTIANS, A (CALLING ALL MARTIANS) AR TWS 40 11
    COMING ATTRACTIONS   GREENBERG, MARTIN NF
  MARTIAN ADVENTURE, A (AT THE PERIHELION) SN ASF 37 02
    GREAT SCIENCE FICTION BY SCIENTISTS CONKLIN, GROFF   AN
  MEANING OF THE WORD "IMPOSSIBLE", THE AR
    SCIENCE FICTION ROLL OF HONOR, THE POHL, FREDERIK   AN
  POSTSCRIPT TO "THE UNIVERSAL LIBRARY" AR
    FANTASIA MATHEMATICA   FADIMAN, CLIFTON   AN
  SPACE WAR   AR   ASF 39 08
    COMING ATTRACTIONS   GREENBERG, MARTIN NF
  UNVEILING THE MYSTERY PLANET   AR
    FAREWELL FANTASTIC VENUS   ALDISS & HARRISON   AN
  V-2: ROCKET CARGO SHIP   AR   ASF 45 05
    *ADVENTURES IN TIME AND SPACE HEALY & MCCOMAS   AN
  WHERE DO WE GO FROM HERE?   AR NEW 58 AN
  SF:58, THE YEAR'S GREATEST SCIENCE FICTION AND FANTASY
                        MERRIL, JUDITH   AN
  YOUR LIFE IN 1977   AR
    IF THIS GOES ON   NUETZEL, CHARLES   AN

LEYSON, CAPT. BURR W
  SHAKE HANDS WITH THE MAN IN THE MOON SS   BLF 59
    TEEN-AGE OUTER SPACE STORIES   FURMAN, A. L.   AN
  TRAIL TO THE STARS   SS   BLF 50 02
    SCIENCE FICTION AND READER'S GUIDE BARROWS, MARJORIE AN

LICATA, TONY
  GREAT SCIENCE-FICTION   AN   TSB 65

LICHTENBERG, GEORGE
  APOTHEM   MS   59
    MATHEMATICAL MAGPIE, THE   FADIMAN, CLIFTON   AN

LICHTY
  GRIN AND BEAR IT   CT   PHS 72 06
    BEST SF: 1972
                      HARRISON & ALDISS AN

LIDDELL, C. H.   PSEUD. FOR HENRY KUTTNER

LIEF, EVELYN
  BED SHEETS ARE WHITE   SS   DVS 72 02
    AGAIN, DANGEROUS VISIONS   ELLISON, HARLAN   OA
  INSPECTOR, THE   SS   CLR 71 01
    CLARION   WILSON, ROBIN SCOTT OA

LIGHTNER, A. M.
  BEST FRIEND   SS   BLF 61
    BOYS' LIFE BOOK OF OUTER SPACE STORIES, THE
                      BOY'S LIFE, ED. OF AN
    TEEN-AGE SPACE ADVENTURES   FURMAN, A. L.   AN
  GREAT DAY FOR THE IRISH, A   SS   IFS 60 05
    TEEN-AGE SPACE ADVENTURES   FURMAN, A. L.   AN
  MARS JAR, THE   SS   66
    TEEN-AGE SPACE ADVENTURES   FURMAN, A. L.   AN
  NEW GAME, A   SS   BLF 59
    BOYS' LIFE BOOK OF OUTER SPACE STORIES, THE
                      BOY'S LIFE, ED. OF AN
    TEEN-AGE OUTER SPACE STORIES   FURMAN, A. L.   AN

LINDNER, ROBERT
  JET-PROPELLED COUCH, THE   AR   FSF 56 01
    BEST FANTASY STORIES   ALDISS, BRIAN W.   AN

LINDSAY, VACHEL
  EUCLID   PM   14
    FANTASIA MATHEMATICA   FADIMAN, CLIFTON   AN

LINEBARGER, PAUL M. SEE PSEUD. CORDWAINER SMITH

LINK
  GETTING TO KNOW YOU   PM   QRK 70 01
    QUARK/1   DELANY & HACKER   OA

LINNETT, PETER
  AND WHEN I DIE...   SS   NWR 74 24
    NEW WRITINGS IN SF. 24   BULMER, KENNETH   OA
  ZONE   SS   NWR 75 27
    NEW WRITINGS IN SF. 27   BULMER, KENNETH   OA

LISTER, R. P.
  SONG AGAINST CIRCLES, A   PM   NYM 61 05
    MATHEMATICAL MAGPIE, THE   FADIMAN, CLIFTON   AN

LITTKE, LAEL J.
  DEMON MACHINE, THE   SS
    STRANGE ENCOUNTERS   BISCHOFF, DAVID   OA
  FIRST FLIGHT OF SCAVENGER I, THE SS
    QUEST   BISCHOFF, DAVID   OA

LITTLE, MARGARET
  JAKE'S PICTURES   SS   ADS 75 01
    ARMADA SCI-FI ONE   DAVIS, RICHARD   OA
  LONELY ROBOT, THE   SS   ADS 75 01
    ARMADA SCI-FI ONE   DAVIS, RICHARD   OA

LIVINGSTON, BERKELEY SEE PSEUD.
  H. B. HICKEY (WITH HERB LIVINGSTON)

LIVINGSTON, HERB

LIVINGSTON, HERB   SEE PSEUD.
  H. B. HICKEY (WITH BERKELEY LIVINGSTON)

LLEWELLYN, RICHARD
  MOTHER AND THE DECIMAL POINT   SS   40
    FANTASIA MATHEMATICA   FADIMAN, CLIFTON   AN

LLOYD, DANIEL
  FOREWORD   IN
    NEW WRITINGS IN SF. 21   CARNELL, JOHN   OA

LO MEDICO, BRIAN T.
  HOLE IN JENNIFER'S ROOM, THE   SS
    MORE SCIENCE FICTION TALES   ELWOOD, ROGER   OA

LOCKE, DAVID M.
  POWER OF THE SENTENCE, THE   SS   FSF 71 04
    BEST SCIENCE FICTION STORIES OF THE YEAR (1971)
                                      DEL REY, LESTER   AN

LOCKE, GEORGE
  WORLDS APART   AN H CMK
    AN ANTHOLOGY OF INTERPLANETARY FICTION
  INTRODUCTION   IN
    WORLDS APART   LOCKE, GEORGE   AN

LOCKE, ROBERT DONALD
  DARK NUPTIAL   SS   TWS 53 02
    BEST FROM STARTLING STORIES, THE MINES, SAMUEL   AN
  DEMOTION   SS   ASF 52 09
    PRIZE SCIENCE FICTION   WOLLHEIM, DONALD A. AN

LOCKHARD, LEONARD   PSEUD. FOR THEODORE L. THOMAS
  LAGGING PROFESSION, THE   SF   ASF 61 01
    6TH ANNUAL OF THE YEAR'S BEST S-F, THE MERRIL, JUDITH   AN

LOHWATER, A. J.
  DEVIL A MATHEMATICIAN WOULD BE, THE   MS
    MATHEMATICAL MAGPIE, THE   FADIMAN, CLIFTON   AN

LONDON, JACK
  CURIOUS FRAGMENTS   AC H KNK 75
    EDITED BY DALE L. WALKER
  SCIENCE FICTION OF JACK LONDON, THE   AC H GRG 75
  CURIOUS FRAGMENT, A   SS   TTP 08 12
    CURIOUS FRAGMENTS   LONDON, JACK   AC
    SCIENCE FICTION OF JACK LONDON, THE LONDON, JACK   AC
  DREAM OF DEBS, THE   NV   ISR 09 01
    SCIENCE FICTION OF JACK LONDON, THE LONDON, JACK   AC
  ENEMY OF ALL THE WORLD, THE   SS   RBM 08 10
    CURIOUS FRAGMENTS   LONDON, JACK   AC
  EVEN UNTO DEATH   SS   EPM 00 07
    CURIOUS FRAGMENTS   LONDON, JACK   AC
  GOLIAH   NV   BOK 10 02
    CURIOUS FRAGMENTS   LONDON, JACK   AC
    SCIENCE FICTION OF JACK LONDON, THE LONDON, JACK   AC
  MINIONS OF MIDAS, THE   SS   PBS 01 05
    SCIENCE FICTION OF JACK LONDON, THE LONDON, JACK   AC
  RED ONE, THE   NV   CMP 18 10
    ANCESTRAL VOICES   MENVILLE & REGINALD AN
    CURIOUS FRAGMENTS   LONDON, JACK   AC
    SCIENCE FICTION OF JACK LONDON, THE LONDON, JACK   AC
    SPECTRUM OF WORLDS, A   CLARESON, THOMAS D. AN
  REJUVENATION OF MAJOR RATHBONE, THE   SS   CHJ 99 11
    CURIOUS FRAGMENTS   LONDON, JACK   AC
  RELIC OF THE PLIOCENE, A   SS   COL 01 01
    CURIOUS FRAGMENTS   LONDON, JACK   AC
    SCIENCE FICTION OF JACK LONDON, THE LONDON, JACK   AC
  SCARLET PLAGUE, THE   NA   LOM 12 06
    ASLEEP IN ARMAGEDDON   SISSONS, MICHAEL   AN
    CURIOUS FRAGMENTS   LONDON, JACK   AC
    OMNIBUS OF SCIENCE FICTION   CONKLIN, GROFF   AN
    OUT OF THIS WORLD   FAST, JULIUS   AN
    SCIENCE FICTION OF JACK LONDON, THE LONDON, JACK   AC
    STRANGE TRAVELS IN SCIENCE FICTION CONKLIN, GROFF   AN
  SHADOW AND THE FLASH, THE   SS   BOK 03 06
    CURIOUS FRAGMENTS   LONDON, JACK   AC
    INVISIBLE MEN   DAVENPORT, BASIL   AN
    SCIENCE FICTION OF JACK LONDON, THE LONDON, JACK   AC
  SHOT IN THE DARK   SS   HAM 11 03
    CURIOUS FRAGMENTS   MERRIL, JUDITH   AN
  STRENGTH OF THE STRONG, THE   SS   BLC 99 05
    CURIOUS FRAGMENTS   LONDON, JACK   AC
    SCIENCE FICTION OF JACK LONDON, THE LONDON, JACK   AC
  THOUSAND DEATHS, A
    BATTLE OF THE MONSTERS AND OTHER STORIES, THE
                                  HARTWELL & CURREY   AN
    CURIOUS FRAGMENTS   LONDON, JACK   AC
    FANTASTIC PULPS, THE   HAINING, PETER   AN
  UNPARALLELED INVASION, THE   SS   MCS 10 07
    CURIOUS FRAGMENTS   LONDON, JACK   AC
    SCIENCE FICTION OF JACK LONDON, THE LONDON, JACK   AC
    WONDERMAKERS   HOSKINS, ROBERT   AN
  WAR   SS   NAT 11 07
    CURIOUS FRAGMENTS   LONDON, JACK   AC
  WHEN THE WORLD WAS YOUNG   SS   SEP 10 09
    CURIOUS FRAGMENTS   LONDON, JACK   AC
    SCIENCE FICTION OF JACK LONDON, THE LONDON, JACK   AC
  WHO BELIEVES IN GHOSTS!   SS   HSA 95 10
    CURIOUS FRAGMENTS   LONDON, JACK   AC

LONG, AMELIA R.
  OMEGA   SS   AMZ 32 07
    END OF THE WORLD, THE   WOLLHEIM, DONALD A. AN
  REVERSE PHYLOGENY   SS   ASF 37 06
    ADVENTURES IN DIMENSION   CONKLIN, GROFF   AN

LONG, AMELIA R.   (CONTINUED)
  *SCIENCE FICTION ADVENTURES IN DIMENSION
                                  CONKLIN, GROFF   AN

LONG, FRANK BELKNAP
  DARK BEASTS, THE   AC   BEL 64 01
  EARLY LONG, THE   AC H DBL 75
  HORROR FROM THE HILLS, THE   AC   DIG 65
    SEE "ODD SCIENCE FICTION"
  HOUNDS OF TINDALOS, THE   AC H ARK 46
  HOUNDS OF TINDALOS, THE (9 OF 21)   AC   BEL 63 08
  JOHN CARSTAIRS: SPACE DETECTIVE   AC H FEL 49
  ODD SCIENCE FICTION   AC   BEL 64 08
    IN ENGLAND AS "THE HORROR FROM THE HILLS"
  RIM OF THE UNKNOWN   AC H ARK 72
  AND SOMEDAY TO MARS   SS   TWS 52 02
    EDITOR'S CHOICE IN SCIENCE FICTION MOSKOWITZ, SAM   AN
  BLACK DRUID, THE   SS   WRT 30 07
    *HOUNDS OF TINDALOS, THE   LONG, FRANK BELKNAP AC
  BODY-MASTERS, THE   SS   WRT 35 02
    WEIRD TALES   MARGULIES, LEO   AN
  BRIDGEHEAD (ALSO AS THE TEMPORAL TRANSGRESSOR) NV ASF 44 08
    *HOUNDS OF TINDALOS, THE   LONG, FRANK BELKNAP AC
  CENSUS TAKER, THE   SS   UNK 42 04
    DARK BEASTS, THE   LONG, FRANK BELKNAP AC
    EARLY LONG, THE   LONG, FRANK BELKNAP AC
    *HOUNDS OF TINDALOS, THE   LONG, FRANK BELKNAP AC
  CONES   NV   ASF 36 02
    *POSSIBLE WORLDS OF SCIENCE FICTION CONKLIN, GROFF   AN
    RIM OF THE UNKNOWN   LONG, FRANK BELKNAP AC
  COTTAGE TENANT   NV   FAN 75 04
    YEAR'S BEST HORROR STORIES: SERIES IV, THE
                                  PAGE, GERALD W.   AN
  COTTAGE, THE   SS   FUN 54 09
    RIM OF THE UNKNOWN   LONG, FRANK BELKNAP AC
  CRITTERS, THE   SS   ASF 45 11
    *OUTER REACHES, THE   DERLETH, AUGUST   AN
    RIM OF THE UNKNOWN   LONG, FRANK BELKNAP AC
  DARK BEASTS, THE   SS   MVT 34 07
    DARK BEASTS, THE   LONG, FRANK BELKNAP AC
    EARLY LONG, THE   LONG, FRANK BELKNAP AC
    *HOUNDS OF TINDALOS, THE   LONG, FRANK BELKNAP AC
  DARK VISION   SS   UNK 39 03
    EARLY LONG, THE   LONG, FRANK BELKNAP AC
    *HOUNDS OF TINDALOS, THE   LONG, FRANK BELKNAP AC
  DEATH-WATERS   SS   WRT 24 12
    DARK BEASTS, THE   LONG, FRANK BELKNAP AC
    EARLY LONG, THE   LONG, FRANK BELKNAP AC
    *HOUNDS OF TINDALOS, THE   LONG, FRANK BELKNAP AC
  ELEMENTAL, THE   SS   UNK 39 07
    EARLY LONG, THE   LONG, FRANK BELKNAP AC
    *HOUNDS OF TINDALOS, THE   LONG, FRANK BELKNAP AC
  ETHER ROBOTS, THE   NV   TWS 42 12
    JOHN CARSTAIRS: SPACE DETECTIVE LONG, FRANK BELKNAP AC
  FILCH   SS   ASF 45 03
    RIM OF THE UNKNOWN   LONG, FRANK BELKNAP AC
  FISHERMAN'S LUCK   SS   UNK 40 01
    EARLY LONG, THE   LONG, FRANK BELKNAP AC
    *HOUNDS OF TINDALOS, THE   LONG, FRANK BELKNAP AC
  FLAME MIDGET, THE   SS   ASF 36 12
    *BEST OF SCIENCE FICTION   CONKLIN, GROFF   AN
    DARK BEASTS, THE   LONG, FRANK BELKNAP AC
    EARLY LONG, THE   NORTON, AN.&DONALDY AN
    GATES TO TOMORROW   LONG, FRANK BELKNAP AC
    *HOUNDS OF TINDALOS, THE   LONG, FRANK BELKNAP AC
  FLAME OF LIFE, THE   SS   FUT 59 06
    ODD SCIENCE FICTION   LONG, FRANK BELKNAP AC
  FUZZY HEAD   SS   TWS 48 12
    RIM OF THE UNKNOWN   LONG, FRANK BELKNAP AC
  GALACTIC HERITAGE   SS   TWS 48 10
    MOLECULE MONSTERS, THE   ANONYMOUS   AN
  GIANT IN THE FOREST   SS   SFQ 55 02
    ODD SCIENCE FICTION   LONG, FRANK BELKNAP AC
  GIANTS IN THE SKY   SS   WRT 39 08
    WORLDS OF WEIRD   MARGULIES, LEO   AN
  GOLDEN CHILD   NV
    *HOUNDS OF TINDALOS, THE   LONG, FRANK BELKNAP AC
  GOOD TO BE A MARTIAN   SS   FUN 55 02
    RIM OF THE UNKNOWN   LONG, FRANK BELKNAP AC
  GRAB BAGS ARE DANGEROUS   SS   UNK 42 06
    EARLY LONG, THE   LONG, FRANK BELKNAP AC
    *HOUNDS OF TINDALOS, THE   LONG, FRANK BELKNAP AC
  GREAT COLD, THE   SS   ASF 35 02
    NEW WORLDS FOR OLD   DERLETH, AUGUST   AN
    RIM OF THE UNKNOWN   LONG, FRANK BELKNAP AC
    *WORLDS OF TOMORROW   DERLETH, AUGUST   AN
  GREEN GLORY   SS   ASF 35 01
    RIM OF THE UNKNOWN   LONG, FRANK BELKNAP AC
  GUEST IN THE HOUSE   SS   ASF 46 03
    RIM OF THE UNKNOWN   DERLETH, AUGUST   AN
    *STRANGE PORTS OF CALL   SN   WRT 31 01
  HORROR FROM THE HILLS, THE   LONG, FRANK BELKNAP AC
    ODD SCIENCE FICTION   SS   WRT 29 03
  HOUNDS OF TINDALOS, THE   LONG, FRANK BELKNAP AC
    EARLY LONG, THE   LONG, FRANK BELKNAP AC
    *HOUNDS OF TINDALOS, THE   PARRY, MICHEL   AN
    STRANGE ECSTASIES   SS   STS 48 05
  HOUSE OF RISING WINDS, THE   MARGULIES & FRIEND   AN
    *MY BEST SCIENCE FICTION STORY LONG, FRANK BELKNAP AC
    RIM OF THE UNKNOWN   SS   STS 48 11
  HUMPTY DUMPTY HAD A GREAT FALL   DERLETH, AUGUST   AN
    *BEYOND TIME AND SPACE   LONG, FRANK BELKNAP AC
    RIM OF THE UNKNOWN   SILVERBERG, ROBERT   AN
    STRANGE GIFTS   IN
  INTRODUCTION   LONG, FRANK BELKNAP AC
    EARLY LONG, THE

LONG, FRANK BELKNAP   LOVECRAFT, H. P.

LONG, FRANK BELKNAP (CONTINUED)
  INVASION   SS   STS 50 07
    FAR BOUNDARIES   DERLETH, AUGUST   AN
  IT WILL COME TO YOU   SS   UNK 42 12
    ALONE BY NIGHT   CONGDON, MICHAEL&DON   AN
    DARK BEASTS, THE   LONG, FRANK BELKNAP   AC
    EARLY LONG, THE   LONG, FRANK BELKNAP   AC
    *HOUNDS OF TINDALOS, THE   LONG, FRANK BELKNAP   AC
  LAST MEN, THE   SS   ASF 34 08
    RIM OF THE UNKNOWN   LONG, FRANK BELKNAP   AC
    SCIENCE FICTION OF THE 30'S   KNIGHT, DAMON   AN
  LESSON IN SURVIVAL   SS   TWS 52 12
    RIM OF THE UNKNOWN   LONG, FRANK BELKNAP   AC
  LITTLE MEN OF SPACE   SS   FUN 53 06
    RIM OF THE UNKNOWN   LONG, FRANK BELKNAP   AC
  MAN FROM TIME, THE   SS   FUN 54 03
    RIM OF THE UNKNOWN   LONG, FRANK BELKNAP   AC
  MAN OF DISTINCTION   SS   FUN 54 11
    RIM OF THE UNKNOWN   LONG, FRANK BELKNAP   AC
  MAN WITH A THOUSAND LEGS, THE   SS   WRT 27 08
    RIM OF THE UNKNOWN   LONG, FRANK BELKNAP   AC
  MATURITY NIGHT   SS   49
    GIRL WITH THE HUNGRY EYES, AND OTHER STORIES, THE
                                        WOLLHEIM, DONALD A.   OA
  MERCURIAN, THE   SS   PLS 41 WI
    FLIGHT INTO SPACE   WOLLHEIM, DONALD A.   AN
  MR. CAXTON DRAWS A MARTIAN BIRD   SS   FUN 54 07
    RIM OF THE UNKNOWN   LONG, FRANK BELKNAP   AC
  NIGHT-FEAR   SS   DSF 53 10
    NOVELETS OF SCIENCE FICTION   HOWARD, IVAN   AN
  OCEAN LEECH, THE   SS   WRT 25 01
    DARK BEASTS, THE   LONG, FRANK BELKNAP   AC
    EARLY LONG, THE   LONG, FRANK BELKNAP   AC
    *HOUNDS OF TINDALOS, THE   LONG, FRANK BELKNAP   AC
  PEEPER, THE   SS   WRT 44 03
    EARLY LONG, THE   LONG, FRANK BELKNAP   AC
    *HOUNDS OF TINDALOS, THE   LONG, FRANK BELKNAP   AC
  PLANTS MUST GROW   NV   TWS 41 10
    JOHN CARSTAIRS: SPACE DETECTIVE   LONG, FRANK BELKNAP   AC
  PLANTS MUST SLAY   SS   TWS 42 04
    JOHN CARSTAIRS: SPACE DETECTIVE   LONG, FRANK BELKNAP   AC
    SAINT'S CHOICE OF IMPOSSIBLE CRIME, THE
                                        CHARTERIS, LESLIE   AN
  PREVIEW   SS   FUN 56 01
    RIM OF THE UNKNOWN   LONG, FRANK BELKNAP   AC
  RED STORM ON JUPITER   SS   ASF 36 05
    FLIGHT INTO SPACE   WOLLHEIM, DONALD A.   AN
  REFUGEES, THE   SS   UNK 42 02
    DARK BEASTS, THE   LONG, FRANK BELKNAP   AC
    EARLY LONG, THE   LONG, FRANK BELKNAP   AC
    *HOUNDS OF TINDALOS, THE   LONG, FRANK BELKNAP   AC
  RIDDLE OF THE DEADLY PARADISE   NV   SFS 58 11
    6 AND THE SILENT SCREAM   HOWARD, IVAN   AN
  SATELLITE OF PERIL   NV   TWS 42 08
    JOHN CARSTAIRS: SPACE DETECTIVE   LONG, FRANK BELKNAP   AC
  SECOND NIGHT OUT   SS   WRT 33 10
    EARLY LONG, THE   LONG, FRANK BELKNAP   AC
    *HOUNDS OF TINDALOS, THE   LONG, FRANK BELKNAP   AC
  SNAPDRAGON   NV   TWS 41 12
    JOHN CARSTAIRS: SPACE DETECTIVE   LONG, FRANK BELKNAP   AC
  SPACE-EATERS, THE   NV   WRT 28 07
    EARLY LONG, THE   LONG, FRANK BELKNAP   AC
    *HOUNDS OF TINDALOS, THE   LONG, FRANK BELKNAP   AC
  SPECTACLES, THE   SS   FUN 56 04
    RIM OF THE UNKNOWN   LONG, FRANK BELKNAP   AC
  SPIRAL INTELLIGENCE, THE   SS   SFP 53 06
    RIM OF THE UNKNOWN   LONG, FRANK BELKNAP   AC
  STEP INTO MY GARDEN   SS   UNK 42 08
    DARK BEASTS, THE   LONG, FRANK BELKNAP   AC
    EARLY LONG, THE   LONG, FRANK BELKNAP   AC
    *HOUNDS OF TINDALOS, THE   LONG, FRANK BELKNAP   AC
    NIGHTMARE GARDEN   GHIDALIA, VIC   AN
  STITCH IN TIME, A   SS   SSS 40 03
    DARK BEASTS, THE   LONG, FRANK BELKNAP   AC
    *HOUNDS OF TINDALOS, THE   LONG, FRANK BELKNAP   AC
  TEMPORAL TRANSGRESSOR, THE (BRIDGEHEAD)   NV   ASF 44 08
    ULTIMATE INVADER, AND OTHER SCIENCE FICTION, THE
                                        WOLLHEIM, DONALD A.   DA
  TO FOLLOW KNOWLEDGE   SS   ASF 42 12
    ADVENTURES IN DIMENSION   CONKLIN, GROFF   AN
    *SCIENCE FICTION ADVENTURES IN DIMENSION
                                        CONKLIN, GROFF   AN
  TRAP, THE   SS   ASF 45 05
    RIM OF THE UNKNOWN   LONG, FRANK BELKNAP   AC
  TWO FACE   SS   WRT 50 03
    BEST SCIENCE-FICTION STORIES: 1951, THE
                                        BLEILER & DIKTY   AN
    MINDWORM, THE   ANONYMOUS   AN
  UNFINISHED, THE   SS   SSS 51 04
    SPACE ODYSSEYS   ALDISS, BRIAN W.   AN
  VISITOR FROM EGYPT, A   SS   WRT 30 09
    EARLY LONG, THE   LONG, FRANK BELKNAP   AC
    *HOUNDS OF TINDALOS, THE   LONG, FRANK BELKNAP   AC
  WHY I SELECTED THE HOUSE OF RISING WINDS   AI
    *MY BEST SCIENCE FICTION STORY   MARGULIES & FRIEND   AN
  WOBBLIES IN THE MOON   NV   TWS 43 06
    JOHN CARSTAIRS: SPACE DETECTIVE   LONG, FRANK BELKNAP   AC
  WORLD OF WULKINS, THE   SS   TWS 48 04
    *OTHER SIDE OF THE MOON, THE   DERLETH, AUGUST   AN
    RIM OF THE UNKNOWN   LONG, FRANK BELKNAP   AC

LONGDON, GEORGE   PSEUD. FOR FRANCIS G. RAYER
  OF THOSE WHO CAME   SS   FUN 53 06
    GATEWAY TO TOMORROW   CARNELL, JOHN   AN
    SPACE POLICE   NORTON, ANDRE   AN

LOOMIS, NOEL
  IF THE COURT PLEASES   NV   DSF 53 06
    ESCAPE TO EARTH   HOWARD, IVAN   AN
  LITTLE GREEN MAN   SS   DSF 53 03
    THINGS   HOWARD, IVAN   AN
  LONG DAWN, THE   SS   SSS 50 01
    *BIG BOOK OF SCIENCE FICTION   CONKLIN, GROFF   AN

LOPATE, PHILLIP
  WALKING BACKWARDS   SS   NWB 73 05
    NEW WORLDS QUARTERLY NO. 5   MOORCOCK, MICHAEL   OA

LORAN, MARTIN
  CASE OF THE PERJURED PLANET, THE   NV   ASF 67 11
    SECOND PACIFIC BOOK OF SCIENCE FICTION, THE
                                        BAXTER, JOHN   AN
  OUNCE OF DISSENSION, AN   SS   ASF 66 07
    OUT OF THIS WORLD 7   WILLIAMS-ELLIS& OWEN   AN
    PACIFIC BOOK OF AUSTRALIAN SCIENCE FICTION
                                        BAXTER, JOHN   AN

LORD, MINDRET
  DR. JACOBUS MELIFLORE'S LAST PATIENT   SS   FSF 53 11
    ZACHERLEY'S VULTURE STEW   ZACHERLEY   AN
  NAKED LADY   SS   WRT 34 09
    OTHER WORLDS, THE   STONG, PHILIP D.   AN
  PROBLEM FOR BIOGRAPHERS, A   SS   NEW 41 AN
    OTHER WORLDS, THE   STONG, PHILIP D.   AN

LORY, ROBERT
  HARVEST OF HOODWINKS, A   DC   ACE 70
  APPOINTMENT AT TEN O'CLOCK   SS   FSF 64 01
    HARVEST OF HOODWINKS, A   LORY, ROBERT   DC
  ARCHIMEDES' LEVER (THE COURTEOUS OF GHOOR)   SS   IFS 68 02
    HARVEST OF HOODWINKS, A   LORY, ROBERT   DC
  BECAUSE OF PURPLE ELEPHANTS   SS
    HARVEST OF HOODWINKS, A   LORY, ROBERT   DC
  COURTEOUS OF GHOOR, THE (SEE ARCHIMEDES' LEVER)   TC
  DEBUT   SS   66
    HARVEST OF HOODWINKS, A   LORY, ROBERT   DC
  FALL OF ALL-FATHER, THE   SS
    HARVEST OF HOODWINKS, A   LORY, ROBERT   DC
  FOREWORD   IN
    HARVEST OF HOODWINKS, A   LORY, ROBERT   DC
  FUTILITY IS ZUCK   SS
    HARVEST OF HOODWINKS, A   LORY, ROBERT   DC
  LOCATOR, THE   SS   FSF 68 02
    HARVEST OF HOODWINKS, A   LORY, ROBERT   DC
  MAR-TI-AN   SS   FSF 64 05
    HARVEST OF HOODWINKS, A   LORY, ROBERT   DC
  ONLY A GOD   SS
    HARVEST OF HOODWINKS, A   LORY, ROBERT   DC
  RECENT SEMIFINALS, THE   SS
    LONE STAR UNIVERSE   PROCTOR & UTLEY   OA
  ROLLING ROBERT   SS
    HARVEST OF HOODWINKS, A   LORY, ROBERT   DC
  RUNDOWN   SS   IFS 63 05
    SCIENCE FICTION ODDITIES   CONKLIN, GROFF   AN
  SNOWBIRD AND THE SEVEN WARFS   SS
    HARVEST OF HOODWINKS, A   LORY, ROBERT   DC
  STAR PARTY, THE   SS   FSF 64 09
    HARVEST OF HOODWINKS, A   LORY, ROBERT   DC
    WORLD'S BEST SCIENCE FICTION: 1965 WOLLHEIM & CARR   AN

LOTT, S. MAKEPEACE
  ESCAPE TO VENUS   SS   56
    ALL ABOUT VENUS   ALDISS, BRIAN W.   AN
    FAREWELL FANTASTIC VENUS   ALDISS & HARRISON   AN

LOUDEN, LEO
  GREEN BOY, THE   SS
    MIND ANGEL AND OTHER STORIES, THE   ELWOOD, ROGER   OA

LOUGHLIN, RICHARD L.
  JOURNEYS IN SCIENCE FICTION   AN H GLB 61

LOVECRAFT, H. P. AND AUGUST DRELETH
  SURVIVOR AND OTHER STORIES, THE   AC H ARK 57

LOVECRAFT, H. P.
  HAUNTER OF THE DARK, THE   AC H GOL 51
  ANCESTOR, THE   SS C
    FANTASY: THE LITERATURE OF THE MARVELOUS
                                        KELLEY, LEO P.   AN
    SURVIVOR AND OTHER STORIES, THE   LOVECRAFT & DERLETH   AC
  AT THE MOUNTAINS OF MADNESS   NO   ASF 36 02
    *STRANGE PORTS OF CALL   DERLETH, AUGUST   AN
  BEYOND THE WALL OF SLEEP   SS   WRT 38 03
    *OTHER SIDE OF THE MOON, THE   DERLETH, AUGUST   AN
  CALL OF CTHULHU, THE   NV   WRT 28 02
    ANCIENT MYSTERIES READER, THE   HAINING, PETER   AN
    HAUNTER OF THE DARK, THE   LOVECRAFT, H. P.   AC
  CATS OF ULTHAR, THE   SS   TRY 20 11
    BEWARE THE BEASTS   GHIDALIA, V.& ELWOOD   AN
    3000 YEARS OF FANTASY AND SCIENCE FICTION
                                        DE CAMP, L. S.&C.   AN
  CELEPHAIS   SS   MVT 34 05
    GARDEN OF FEAR AND OTHER STORIES, THE CRAWFORD, WILLIAM L.   AN
  COLOUR OUT OF SPACE, THE (ALSO AS MONSTER OF TERROR)
                                                       SS   AMZ 27 09
    HAUNTER OF THE DARK, THE   LOVECRAFT, H. P.   AC
    IN DREAMS AWAKE   FIEDLER, LESLIE A.   AN
    MASTERPIECES OF SCIENCE FICTION   MOSKOWITZ, SAM   AN
    OMNIBUS OF SCIENCE FICTION   CONKLIN, GROFF   AN
    SCIENCE FICTION OMNIBUS   CONKLIN, GROFF   AN
    STRANGE TRAVELS IN SCIENCE FICTION CONKLIN, GROFF   AN

LOVECRAFT, H. P.   (CONTINUED)
  COOL AIR   SS   TMM 28 03
    HORROR TIMES TEN   NORTON, ALDEN H.   AN
  DIARY OF ALONZO TYPER, THE   NV C WRT 38 02
    FANTASTIC PULPS, THE   HAINING, PETER   AN
  DREAM QUEST OF UNKNOWN KADATH, THE   NA   ARS 48 WI
    GOLDEN ROAD, THE   KNIGHT, DAMON   AN
  DUNWICH HORROR, THE   NV   WRT 29 04
    HAUNTER OF THE DARK, THE   LOVECRAFT, H. P.   AC
  FROM BEYOND   SS   WRT 38 02
    NEW WORLDS FOR OLD   DERLETH, AUGUST   AN
    *WORLDS OF TOMORROW   DERLETH, AUGUST   AN
  GABEL WINDOW, THE (THE MURKY GLASS)   SS C STN 57 05
    SURVIVOR AND OTHER STORIES, THE LOVECRAFT & DERLETH AC
  HARBOR WHISTLES   PM
    HOLDING YOUR EIGHT HANDS   LUCIE-SMITH, EDWARD   AN
  HAUNTER OF THE DARK, THE   NV   WRT 36 12
    HAUNTER OF THE DARK, THE   LOVECRAFT, H. P.   AC
  HE   SS   WRT 26 09
    *TERROR IN THE MODERN VEIN   WOLLHEIM, DONALD A.   AN
  HORROR FROM THE MIDDLE SPAN, THE   SS
    TRAVELLERS BY NIGHT   DERLETH, AUGUST   OA
  IN THE VAULT   SS   WRT 32 04
    OTHER WORLDS, THE   STONG, PHILIP D.   AN
  LAMP OF ALHAZRED, THE   SS C
    SURVIVOR AND OTHER STORIES, THE LOVECRAFT & DERLETH AC
  LETTER TO DONALD WOLLHEIM   MS
    COMING OF CONAN, THE   HOWARD, ROBERT E.   AC
  MONSTER OF TERROR (THE COLOUR OUT OF SPACE)   SS   AMZ 27 09
    GHOULS, THE   HAINING, PETER   AN
  MURKY GLASS, THE (SEE THE GABEL WINDOW)   TC C
  MUSIC OF ERICH ZANN, THE   SS   WRT 25 05
    HAUNTER OF THE DARK, THE   LOVECRAFT, H. P.   AC
  NYARLATHOTEP (1943)   PM   MOH 68 11
    HOLDING YOUR EIGHT HANDS   LUCIE-SMITH, EDWARD   AN
  OUTSIDER, THE   SS   WRT 26 04
    GRAVEYARD READER, THE   CONKLIN, GROFF   AN
    HAUNTER OF THE DARK, THE   LOVECRAFT, H. P.   AC
    SPECULATIONS   SANDERS, THOMAS E.   AN
  PEABODY HERITAGE, THE   NV C
    SURVIVOR AND OTHER STORIES, THE LOVECRAFT & DERLETH AC
  PICKMAN'S MODEL   SS   WRT 27 10
    HAUNTER OF THE DARK, THE   LOVECRAFT, H. P.   AC
  RATS IN THE WALLS, THE   SS   WRT 24 03
    HAUNTER OF THE DARK, THE   LOVECRAFT, H. P.   AC
  SHADOW OUT OF SPACE, THE   NV C
    SURVIVOR AND OTHER STORIES, THE LOVECRAFT & DERLETH AC
  SHADOW OUT OF TIME, THE   SN   ASF 36 06
    PORTABLE NOVELS OF SCIENCE   WOLLHEIM, DONALD A.   AN
  SHUNNED HOUSE, THE   NV   WRT 37 10
    *TWISTED   CONKLIN, GROFF   AN
  STRANGE HIGH HOUSE IN THE MIST, THE   SS   WRT 31 10
    WEIRD TALES   MARGULIES, LEO   AN
  SURVIVOR, THE   NV C WRT 54 07
    SURVIVOR AND OTHER STORIES, THE LOVECRAFT & DERLETH AC
  THING ON THE DOORSTEP, THE   NV   WRT 37 01
    HAUNTER OF THE DARK, THE   LOVECRAFT, H. P.   AC
  WENTWORTH'S DAY   SS C
    SURVIVOR AND OTHER STORIES, THE LOVECRAFT & DERLETH AC
  WHISPERER IN DARKNESS, THE   NV   WRT 31 08
    HAUNTER OF THE DARK, THE   LOVECRAFT, H. P.   AC
    STRANGE SIGNPOSTS   ELWOOD & MOSKOWITZ   AN
  WHITE APE, THE   SS   WRT 24 04
    ANDROIDS, TIME MACHINES AND BLUE GIRAFFES
                                     ELWOOD & GHIDALIA   AN

LOVELL, BERNARD
  SOME MYSTERIES OF VENUS RESOLVED   AR   TMS 67
    ALL ABOUT VENUS   ALDISS, BRIAN W.   AN
    FAREWELL FANTASTIC VENUS   ALDISS & HARRISON   AN

LOVIN, ROGER
  APOSTLE   SS   FTP 73
    FLAME TREE PLANET   ELWOOD, ROGER   OA
  INTRODUCTION: RELIGIOUS SCIENCE FICTION   IN
    FLAME TREE PLANET   ELWOOD, ROGER   OA

LOWELL, PERCIVAL
  MARS AS THE ABODE OF LIFE   AR
    MARS, WE LOVE YOU   HIPOLITO & MCNELLY   AN

LOWENKOPF, SHELLY
  ADDICT, THE   SS   NEW 65 AN
    PSEUDO PEOPLE, THE   NOLAN, WILLIAM F.   AN
  INTRODUCTION   IN
    WILDERNESS OF STARS, A   NOLAN, WILLIAM F.   AN

LOWNDES, ROBERT W.   ALSO AS   PAUL DENNIS LAVOND
  ABYSS, THE   SS   STI 41 02
    HISTORY OF THE SCIENCE FICTION MAGAZINE, THE PART 2 1936-1945
                                     ASHLEY, MICHAEL   AN
  DHACTWHU|- REMEMBER?   SS C SSS 49 04
    SCIENCE FICTION WORLDS OF FORREST J. ACKERMAN & FRIENDS
                                     ACKERMAN, FORREST J. AC
  HIGHWAY   SS   SFQ 42 FL
    LOOKING FORWARD   LESSER, MILTON   AN
  INHERITORS, THE   SS C FFS 42 10
    MORE TERROR IN THE MODERN VEIN   WOLLHEIM, DONALD A.   AN
    *TERROR IN THE MODERN VEIN   WOLLHEIM, DONALD A.   AN
  JAMES BLISH   AR   FSF 72 04
    BEST FROM FANTASY AND SCIENCE FICTION, 25TH ANNIV.
                                     FERMAN, EDWARD L.   AN

LOWRY, ROBERT
  CONSPIRACY, THE   SS   58
    FIEND IN YOU, THE   BEAUMONT, CHARLES   AN

LOXMITH, JOHN   PSEUD. FOR JOHN BRUNNER

LUCIAN OF SAMOSATA
  ANCIENT GULLIVER, AN (FROM "A TRUE HISTORY",165AD)
                                                  EX
    SCIENCE IN FICTION   BAYLISS, A.E. & J.C. AN
  FROM "A TRUE HISTORY" (165 A.D.)   EX
    PAST, PRESENT, AND FUTURE PERFECT WOLFE, J&FITZ GERALD AN
  INTERPLANETARY WARFARE (FROM "A TRUE HISTORY") EX
    SCIENCE FICTION THROUGH THE AGES 1 EVANS, I. O.   AN
  TRUE HISTORY, A (165 A.D.)   EX
    *BEYOND TIME AND SPACE   DERLETH, AUGUST   AN

LUCIE-SMITH, EDWARD
  HOLDING YOUR EIGHT HANDS   AN H DBL 69
  AFTERWARDS   PM   64
    HOLDING YOUR EIGHT HANDS   LUCIE-SMITH, EDWARD   AN
    SCIENCE FICTION   BRODKIN & PEARSON   AN
  ASTRONAUT (EXTRACT)   PM
    BEYOND THIS HORIZON   CARRELL, CHRISTOPHER OA
  IN THE FUTURE   PM   68
    HOLDING YOUR EIGHT HANDS   LUCIE-SMITH, EDWARD   AN
  INTRODUCTION   IN
    HOLDING YOUR EIGHT HANDS   LUCIE-SMITH, EDWARD   AN
  INTRODUCTION: POETRY AND SCIENCE FICTION   IN
    BEYOND THIS HORIZON   CARRELL, CHRISTOPHER OA
  MONSTER IN ART, THE   IN
    BEYOND THIS HORIZON   CARRELL, CHRISTOPHER OA

LUDWIG, EDWARD W.
  DRIVERS, THE   SS   IFS 56 03
    FIRST WORLD OF IF, THE   QUINN & WULFF   AN
  ROCKET MAN, THE   SS   OWS 51 05
    TALES BEYOND TIME   DE CAMP, L. S.&C.   AN

LUKODIANOV, ISAI
  FAREWELL ON THE SHORE, A   NV C
    RUSSIAN SCIENCE FICTION, 1969   MAGIDOFF, ROBERT   AN
  FORMULA FOR THE IMPOSSIBLE   SS C
    RUSSIAN SCIENCE FICTION, 1968   MAGIDOFF, ROBERT   AN

LUMLEY, BRIAN
  DAVID'S WORM   SS   71
    YEAR'S BEST HORROR STORIES: SERIES II, THE
                                     DAVIS, RICHARD   AN
  HAGGOPIAN   NV   FSF 73 06
    YEAR'S BEST HORROR STORIES: SERIES II, THE
                                     DAVIS, RICHARD   AN
  HOUSE OF CTHULHU, THE   SS   WHS 73
    YEAR'S BEST HORROR STORIES: SERIES III, THE
                                     DAVIS, RICHARD   AN
  NO WAY HOME   SS   FSF 75 09
    YEAR'S BEST HORROR STORIES: SERIES IV, THE
                                     PAGE, GERALD W.   AN
  SISTER CITY, THE   SS   70
    YEAR'S BEST HORROR STORIES, THE DAVIS, RICHARD   AN

LUMLEY, WILLIAM
  DIARY OF ALONZO TYPER, THE   NV C WRT 38 02
    FANTASTIC PULPS, THE   HAINING, PETER   AN

LUNAN, DUNCAN
  CONTACT WITH ANOTHER CIVILISATION   AR
    BEYOND THIS HORIZON   CARRELL, CHRISTOPHER OA

LUNDE, DAVID
  ONE ROAD TO DAMASCUS   SS C
    2076: THE AMERICAN TRICENTENNIAL BRYANT, EDWARD   OA

LUNDWALL, SAM J.
  NOBODY HERE BUT US SHADOWS   SS   GAL 75 08
    BEST FROM THE REST OF THE WORLD, THE WOLLHEIM, DONALD A. AN
  UTOPIA   AR   71
    LOOKING AHEAD   ALLEN, D. & L.   AN

LUPOFF, RICHARD A.
  AFTER THE DREAMTIME   NV   NDM 74 04
    NEW DIMENSIONS 4   SILVERBERG, ROBERT   OA
  FREEWAY FOR DRACULAS, A   NV   BER 74
    BERSERKERS, THE   ELWOOD, ROGER   OA
  MUSSPELSHEIM   NV   STG 74
    STRANGE GODS   ELWOOD, ROGER   OA
  PARTRIDGE PROJECT, THE   NA
    NO MIND OF MAN   SILVERBERG, ROBERT   OA
  SAIL THE TIDE OF MOURNING   SS   NDM 75 05
    BEST SCIENCE FICTION OF THE YEAR, THE NO. 5
                                     CARR, TERRY   AN
    NEW DIMENSIONS 5   SILVERBERG, ROBERT   OA
  SALTZMAN'S MADNESS   NV   FCR 75
    FUTURE CORRUPTION   ELWOOD, ROGER   OA
  WITH THE BENTFIN BOOMER BOYS ON LITTLE OLD NEW ALABAMA
                                                  NA   DVS 72 02
    AGAIN, DANGEROUS VISIONS   ELLISON, HARLAN   OA

LVOV, ARKADY
  SEVENTH FLOOR, THE   NA
    JOURNEY ACROSS THREE WORLDS   ANONYMOUS   AN

LYLE, DAVID
  HUMAN RACE HAS, MAYBE, THIRTY-FIVE YEARS LEFT, THE
                                                  AR   ESQ 67 09
    SCIENCE FICTION: THE FUTURE   ALLEN, DICK   AN

LYNCH, MAL
  AGE OF RETIREMENT   SS   ASF 54 04
    GALACTIC EMPIRES VOLUME ONE   ALDISS, BRIAN W.   AN

LYNE, STANDFORD
  STAR-GAZE POEM   PM   69
    SPECULATIONS   SANDERS, THOMAS E.   AN

LYNN, ELIZABETH A.
  WE ALL HAVE TO GO   SS
    FUTURE PASTIMES   EDELSTEIN, SCOTT   OA

LYON, LYMAN R.   PSEUD. FOR L. SPRAGUE DE CAMP

LYTLE, B. J.
  JAMEY'S VISITOR   SS
    GRADUATED ROBOT AND OTHER STORIES, THE ELWOOD, ROGER   OA
  MATTER OF CHOICE, A   SS
    SCIENCE FICTION ADVENTURES FROM WAY OUT
                                             ELWOOD, ROGER   OA
  OLD MAX   SS
    LONG NIGHT OF WAITING AND OTHER STORIES
                                             ELWOOD, ROGER   OA
  TUNNEL, THE   SS
    TUNNEL AND OTHER STORIES, THE   ELWOOD, ROGER   OA

LYTTON, EDWARD B.
  COMING RACE, THE (EXCERPT)   EX
    ANCIENT MYSTERIES READER, THE   HAINING, PETER   AN

MCALISTER, PATRICIA
  MAGICIAN'S SONG, THE   SS
    MISSING WORLD AND OTHER STORIES, THE   ELWOOD, ROGER   OA

MCALLISTER, BRUCE
  AND SO SAY ALL OF US   SS   IFS 69 09
    WORLD'S BEST SCIENCE FICTION: 1970   WOLLHEIM & CARR   AN
  ARRANGEMENT, THE   SS   SCS 73
    SHOWCASE   ELWOOD, ROGER   OA
  BENJI'S PENCIL   SS   FSF 69 03
    BEST FROM FANTASY AND SCIENCE FICTION: 19
                                             FERMAN, EDWARD L.   AN
  ECCE FEMINA!   NV   FSF 72 02
    ABOVE THE HUMAN LANDSCAPE   MCNELLY & STOVER   AN
  FACES OUTSIDE, THE   SS   IFS 63 07
    9TH ANNUAL OF THE YEAR'S BEST S-F, THE   MERRIL, JUDITH   AN
  MAN INSIDE, THE   SS   GAL 69 05
    BEST SF: 1969   HARRISON & ALDISS   AN
  PRIME-TIME TEASER   SS   FSF 68 12
    TWENTY YEARS OF FANTASY & SCIENCE FICTION
                                             FERMAN & MILLS   AN
  WORLD OF THE WARS   SS   NEW 71 AN
    MARS, WE LOVE YOU   HIPOLITO & MCNELLY   AN

MACAPP, C. C.   PSEUD. FOR CARROLL M. CAPPS
  AND ALL THE EARTH A GRAVE   SS   GAL 63 12
    EIGHTH GALAXY READER, THE   POHL, FREDERIK   AN
  FLASK OF FINE ARCTURAN, A   SS   GAL 65 02
    NINTH GALAXY READER, THE   POHL, FREDERIK   AN
  FOR EVERY ACTION   SS   AMZ 64 05
    WORLD'S BEST SCIENCE FICTION: 1965   WOLLHEIM & CARR   AN
  GUEST OF GANYMEDE, A   NV   WOT 63 06
    BEST SCIENCE FICTION FROM WORLDS OF TOMORROW, THE
                                             POHL, FREDERIK   AN
  IMPERSONATORS, THE   SS   IFS 67 01
    OUT OF THIS WORLD 7   WILLIAMS-ELLIS& OWEN AN
  PRIDE OF ISLANDS, A   NV   IFS 60 05
    6 FINGERS OF TIME AND 5 OTHER SCIENCE FICTION NOVELETS, THE
                                             ANONYMOUS   AN

MACBETH, GEORGE
  BEDTIME STORY   PM   63
    HOLDING YOUR EIGHT HANDS   LUCIE-SMITH, EDWARD AN
    STARLIT CORRIDOR, THE   MANSFIELD, ROGER   AN
  CIRCE UNDERSEA   PM   65
    HOLDING YOUR EIGHT HANDS   LUCIE-SMITH, EDWARD AN
    11TH ANNUAL OF THE YEAR'S BEST S-F, THE
                                             MERRIL, JUDITH   AN
  CRAB-APPLE CRISIS, THE   SS   NWS 66 10
    ANOTHER TOMORROW   HOLLISTER, BERNARD C AN
    HOLDING YOUR EIGHT HANDS   LUCIE-SMITH, EDWARD AN
    POLITICAL SCIENCE FICTION   GREENBERG& WARRICK   AN
    SCIENCE FICTION: THE FUTURE   ALLEN, DICK   AN
    SF12   MERRIL, JUDITH   AN
  FAST CAR WASH   SS
    NEW S.F., THE   JONES, LANGDON   OA
  LAMPS   PM
    BEYOND THIS HORIZON   CARRELL, CHRISTOPHER OA
  MOTHER SUPERIOR   PM   63
    HOLDING YOUR EIGHT HANDS   LUCIE-SMITH, EDWARD AN
  NEW SCIENCE FICTION, THE   AR C
    NEW S.F., THE   JONES, LANGDON   OA
  SILVER NEEDLE, THE   PM   NWS 67 01
    ENGLAND SWINGS SF   MERRIL, JUDITH   AN
    SPACE-TIME JOURNAL, THE   MERRIL, JUDITH   AN
  SOFT WORLD SEQUENCE, THE   PM   NWS 67 07
    BEST SF STORIES FROM NEW WORLDS 3   MOORCOCK, MICHAEL   AN

MCCAFFREY, ANNE
  ALCHEMY AND ACADEME   OA H DBL 70
  DRAGONFLIGHT   NO H WKR 69
  GET OFF THE UNICORN   AC   BAL 77 06
  SHIP WHO SANG, THE   AC H WKR 69
  TO RIDE PEGASUS   AC   BAL 73 08
  APPLE   NV   NEW 69 AN
    CRIME PREVENTION IN THE 30TH CENTURY   SANTESSON, HANS S.   AN
    GET OFF THE UNICORN   MCCAFFREY, ANNE   AC
    TO RIDE PEGASUS   MCCAFFREY, ANNE   AC
    YOUNG DEMONS   ELWOOD & GHIDALIA   AN

MCCAFFREY, ANNE   (CONTINUED)
  BRIDLE FOR PEGASUS, A   NV   ASF 73 07
    TO RIDE PEGASUS   MCCAFFREY, ANNE   AC
  CHANGELING   SS   NEW 77 AC
    GET OFF THE UNICORN   MCCAFFREY, ANNE   AC
  DAUGHTER   NV   MWS 71
    GET OFF THE UNICORN   MCCAFFREY, ANNE   AC
    MANY WORLDS OF SCIENCE FICTION, THE   BOVA, BEN   OA
  DRAGONRIDER   NA   ASF 67 12
    DRAGONFLIGHT   MCCAFFREY, ANNE   NO
    NEBULA AWARD STORIES NO. 4   ANDERSON, POUL   AN
  DRAMATIC MISSION   SN   ASF 69 06
    SHIP WHO SANG, THE   MCCAFFREY, ANNE   AC
  DULL DRUMS   NV   FUQ 73
    FUTURE QUEST   ELWOOD, ROGER   OA
    GET OFF THE UNICORN   MCCAFFREY, ANNE   AC
  FINDER'S FEEPER   SS   HOH 73 08
    GET OFF THE UNICORN   MCCAFFREY, ANNE   AC
  FOREWORD   IN
    ALCHEMY AND ACADEME   MCCAFFREY, ANNE   OA
  GREAT CANINE CHORUS, THE   SS   INY 70 01
    GET OFF THE UNICORN   MCCAFFREY, ANNE   AC
    INFINITY 1   HOSKINS, ROBERT   OA
  GREATEST LOVE, THE   NA
    FUTURELOVE   ELWOOD, ROGER   OA
  HONEYMOON   NV   NEW 77 AC
    GET OFF THE UNICORN   MCCAFFREY, ANNE   AC
  HORSE FROM A DIFFERENT SEA   SS   NEW 77 AC
    GET OFF THE UNICORN   MCCAFFREY, ANNE   AC
  INTRODUCTION   IN
    GET OFF THE UNICORN   MCCAFFREY, ANNE   AC
  KILLASHANDRA - CRYSTAL SINGER   NV   CTM 74 02
    CONTINUUM 2   ELWOOD, ROGER   OA
  KILLASHANDRA- CODA AND FINALE   NV   CTM 75 04
    CONTINUUM 4   ELWOOD, ROGER   OA
  LADY IN THE TOWER   SS   FSF 59 04
    GET OFF THE UNICORN   MCCAFFREY, ANNE   AC
  MEETING OF MINDS, A   NV   FSF 69 01
    GET OFF THE UNICORN   MCCAFFREY, ANNE   AC
    LIBERATED FUTURE: VOYAGES INTO TOMORROW, THE
                                             HOSKINS, ROBERT   AN
  MILEKEY MOUNTAIN   NV   CTM 74 03
    CONTINUUM 3   ELWOOD, ROGER   OA
  PARTNERED SHIP, THE   SS   NEW 69 AC
    SHIP WHO SANG, THE   MCCAFFREY, ANNE   AC
  PRELUDE TO A CRYSTAL SONG   NV   CTM 74 01
    CONTINUUM 1   ELWOOD, ROGER   OA
  PROPER SANTA CLAUS, A   SS   DEM 73
    DEMON KIND   ELWOOD, ROGER   OA
    GET OFF THE UNICORN   MCCAFFREY, ANNE   AC
  RABBEL-DOWSER   SS   OMG 73
    OMEGA   ELWOOD, ROGER   OA
  RESCUED GIRLS OF REFUGEE, THE   SS   TTM 73
    TEN TOMORROWS   ELWOOD, ROGER   OA
    VISIONS OF TOMORROW   ELWOOD, ROGER   AN
  SHIP WHO DISAPPEARED, THE (ALSO AS THE SHIP WHO DISSEMBLED)
                                                       NV   IFS 69 03
    VENUS FACTOR, THE   GHIDALIA, V.& ELWOOD AN
  SHIP WHO DISSEMBLED, THE (THE SHIP WHO DISAPPEARED)
                                                       NV   IFS 69 03
    SHIP WHO SANG, THE   MCCAFFREY, ANNE   AC
  SHIP WHO KILLED, THE   NV   GAL 66 10
    SHIP WHO SANG, THE   MCCAFFREY, ANNE   AC
  SHIP WHO MOURNED, THE   SS   ASF 66 03
    SHIP WHO SANG, THE   MCCAFFREY, ANNE   AC
  SHIP WHO SANG, THE   SS   FSF 61 04
    LOOKING AHEAD   ALLEN, D. & L.   AN
    SHIP WHO SANG, THE   MCCAFFREY, ANNE   AC
    WOMEN OF WONDER   SARGENT, PAMELA   AN
    7TH ANNUAL OF THE YEAR'S BEST S-F, THE   MERRIL, JUDITH   AN
  SMALLEST DRAGONBOY, THE   SS   SFT 73
    GET OFF THE UNICORN   MCCAFFREY, ANNE   AC
    SCIENCE FICTION TALES   ELWOOD, ROGER   OA
  THORNS OF BAREVI, THE   SS   70
    GET OFF THE UNICORN   MCCAFFREY, ANNE   AC
  TO RIDE PEGASUS   NV   NEW 73 AC
    TO RIDE PEGASUS   MCCAFFREY, ANNE   AC
  WEATHER ON WELLADAY   NV   GAL 69 03
    GET OFF THE UNICORN   MCCAFFREY, ANNE   AC
  WEYR SEARCH   SN   ASF 67 10
    ANALOG 7   CAMPBELL, JOHN W. JR AN
    DRAGONFLIGHT   MCCAFFREY, ANNE   NO
    HUGO WINNERS, THE (VOLUME 2)   ASIMOV, ISAAC   AN
    NEBULA AWARD STORIES NO. 3   ZELAZNY, ROGER   AN
  WOMANLY TALENT, A   SN   ASF 69 02
    TO RIDE PEGASUS   MCCAFFREY, ANNE   AC

MCCARDELL, ROY L.
  HYBRID HYPERBOREAN ANT, THE   SS   HAM 10 12
    SCIENCE FICTION BY GASLIGHT   MOSKOWITZ, SAM   AN

MCCLARY, THOMAS C.   SEE PSEUD. CALVIN PEREGOY

MCCLINTIC, WINONA
  ANTI-CLIMAX, THE   PM   FSF 56 01
    BEST FROM FANTASY AND SCIENCE FICTION: 6
                                             BOUCHER, ANTHONY   AN
  ANTIQUARY, THE   PM   FSF 53 07
    BEST FROM FANTASY AND SCIENCE FICTION: 3
                                             BOUCHER & MCCOMAS   AN
  BRIGHT DESTRUCTION   PM   FSF 56 06
    BEST FROM FANTASY AND SCIENCE FICTION: 6
                                             BOUCHER, ANTHONY   AN
  DOCTRINE OF ORIGINAL DESIGN, THE   PM   FSF 55 03
    BEST FROM FANTASY AND SCIENCE FICTION: 5
                                             BOUCHER, ANTHONY   AN

MCCLINTIC, WINONA   (CONTINUED)
  HIS MASTER'S VOICE   PM FSF 53 06
    BEST FROM FANTASY AND SCIENCE FICTION: 3
                                        BOUCHER & MCCOMAS   AN
  I WANT MY NAME IN THE TITLE   PM FSF 56 07
    BEST FROM FANTASY AND SCIENCE FICTION: 6
                                        BOUCHER, ANTHONY   AN
  IN THE DAYS OF OUR FATHERS   SS FSF 49 FL
    BEST FROM FANTASY AND SCIENCE FICTION BOUCHER & MCCOMAS
  TO GIVE THEM BEAUTY FOR ASHES   PM FSF 59 09
    BEST FROM FANTASY AND SCIENCE FICTION 9
                                        MILLS, ROBERT P.   AN
  TWO VOICES   PM FSF 53 06
    BEST FROM FANTASY AND SCIENCE FICTION: 3
                                        BOUCHER & MCCOMAS   AN
  UNQUIET GRAVE, THE   PM FSF 53 08
    BEST FROM FANTASY AND SCIENCE FICTION: 3
                                        BOUCHER & MCCOMAS   AN
  VALISE MACABRE   PM FSF 57 11
    BEST FROM FANTASY AND SCIENCE FICTION: 8
                                        BOUCHER, ANTHONY   AN
  YE PHANTASIE WRITER AND HIS CATTE   PM FSF 58 03
    BEST FROM FANTASY AND SCIENCE FICTION: 8
                                        BOUCHER, ANTHONY   AN
  1980 OVERTURES   PM FSF 55 04
    BEST FROM FANTASY AND SCIENCE FICTION: 5
                                        BOUCHER, ANTHONY   AN

MCCLOUD, RICHARD
  WIDENING CIRCLE, THE   SS NEW 72 AN
    STRANGE BED FELLOWS   SCORTIA, THOMAS N.   AN

MCCLOY, HELEN
  NUMBER TEN Q STREET   SS EQM 63 09
    WORLDS APART   WILLIAMS-ELLIS& OWEN AN

MCCLUSKY, THORP
  CONSIDERATE HOSTS, THE   SS WRT 39 12
    OTHER WORLDS, THE   STONG, PHILIP D.   AN
  CRAWLING HORROR, THE   NV WRT 36 11
    AVON FANTASY READER, THE   WOLLHEIM &ERNSBERGER AN

MCCOMAS, J. FRANCIS   SEE ALSO
    CO-EDITORS ANTHONY BOUCHER AND RAYMOND J. HEALY
              ALSO AS   WEBB MARLOWE
  SPECIAL WONDER   AN H RDM 70
    THE ANTHONY BOUCHER MEMORIAL ANTHOLOGY OF FANTASY AND
    SCIENCE FICTION
  BRAVE NEW WORD   SS FSF 54 09
    BEST FROM FANTASY AND SCIENCE FICTION: 4
                                        BOUCHER, ANTHONY   AN
                                        GREENBERG& OLANDER   AN
  TOMORROW, INC.
  CRIMINAL NEGLIGENCE   SS ASF 55 06
    SPACE, TIME & CRIME   DEFORD, MIRIAM ALLEN AN
  IN MEMORIAM- ANTHONY BOUCHER   MS
    NEBULA AWARD STORIES NO. 4   ANDERSON, POUL   AN
                                        IN
  INTRODUCTION
    SPECIAL WONDER   MCCOMAS, J. FRANCIS AN
  INTRODUCTION   IN C
    BEST FROM FANTASY AND SCIENCE FICTION BOUCHER & MCCOMAS AN
    BEST FROM FANTASY AND SCIENCE FICTION: 2
                                        BOUCHER & MCCOMAS   AN
    BEST FROM FANTASY AND SCIENCE FICTION: 3
                                        BOUCHER & MCCOMAS   AN
  SHOCK TREATMENT   NV FSF 56 04
    DECADE OF FANTASY AND SCIENCE FICTION, A
                                        MILLS, ROBERT P.   AN
    9 TALES OF SPACE AND TIME   HEALY, RAYMOND J.   OA

MCCONNELL, JAMES
  LEARNING THEORY   SS IFS 57 12
    GREAT SCIENCE FICTION BY SCIENTISTS CONKLIN, GROFF   AN
    INTRODUCTORY PSYCHOLOGY THROUGH SCIENCE FICTION
                                        KATZ/WARRICK/&   AN
  NOR DUST CORRUPT   SS IFS 57 02
    BEST SCIENCE FICTION STORIES AND NOVELS: 9TH SERIES
                                        DIKTY, T. E.   AN

MACCORMAC, JOHN
  ENCHANTED WEEKEND, THE   NO UNK 39 10
    FROM UNKNOWN WORLDS   CAMPBELL, JOHN W. JR AN

MCCORMACK, FORD
  HELL-BENT (CONTEST STORY)   SS FSF 51 06
    DEALS WITH THE DEVIL   DAVENPORT, BASIL   AN
  MARCH HARE MISSION   NV WBY 51 01
    TOWARD INFINITY   KNIGHT, DAMON   AN

MACCREIGH, JAMES   PSEUD. FOR FREDERIK POHL
  BIG MAN WITH THE GIRLS, A   SS C FUT 53 03
    ESCAPE TO EARTH   HOWARD, IVAN   AN
  HITCH IN TIME, A   SS TWS 47 06
    SHOT IN THE DARK   MERRIL, JUDITH   AN
  LET THE ANTS TRY   SS PLS 49 WI
    BEYOND THE END OF TIME   POHL, FREDERIK   AN
  LITTLE MAN ON THE SUBWAY, THE   SS C FBK 50 06
    EARLY ASIMOV, THE   ASIMOV, ISAAC   AC
    SCIENCE AND SORCERY   FORD, GARRET   AN
  WINGS OF THE LIGHTNING LAND   NV AST 41 11
    SCIENCE FICTION: THE GREAT YEARS   POHL, C. & F.   AN

MCCULLOUGH, KEN
  CHUCK BERRY, WON'T YOU PLEASE COME HOME?   SS DVS 72 02
    AGAIN, DANGEROUS VISIONS   ELLISON, HARLAN   OA

MCDANIEL, DAVE
  PROGNOSIS: TERMINAL   NV NEW 74 AN
    2020 VISION   POURNELLE, JERRY   AN

MACDONALD, ANSON   PSEUD. FOR ROBERT A. HEINLEIN
  BY HIS BOOTSTRAPS (ALSO AS THE TIME GATE)   NV ASF 41 10
    *ADVENTURES IN TIME AND SPACE   HEALY & MCCOMAS   AN
    ASTOUNDING-ANALOG READER, THE VOLUME ONE
                                        HARRISON & ALDISS   AN
  SOLUTION UNSATISFACTORY   NV ASF 41 05
    *BEST OF SCIENCE FICTION   CONKLIN, GROFF   AN

MACDONALD, JOHN D.
  ANNEX, THE   SS PBY 68 05
    BEST SF: 1968   HARRISON & ALDISS   AN
    LATE GREAT FUTURE, THE   FITZ GERALD & DILLON AN
    PLAYBOY'S STORIES OF THE SINISTER & STRANGE
                                        PLAYBOY, EDITORS OF AN
  BIG CONTEST, THE   SS WBY 50 12
    HUMAN?   MERRIL, JUDITH   AN
    WORLDS TO COME   KNIGHT, DAMON   AN
  CHILD IS CRYING, A   SS TWS 48 12
    SCIENCE FICTION GALAXY, THE   CONKLIN, GROFF   AN
    SHAPE OF THINGS, THE   KNIGHT, DAMON   AN
  COMMON DENOMINATOR   SS GAL 51 07
    *GALAXY READER OF SCIENCE FICTION   GOLD, H. L.   AN
  DANCE OF A NEW WORLD   SS ASF 48 09
    JOURNEY TO INFINITY   GREENBERG , MARTIN   AN
  ESCAPE TO CHAOS   NA SSS 51 06
    GALACTIC EMPIRES VOLUME TWO   ALDISS, BRIAN W.   AN
  FLAW   SS STS 49 01
    BEST SCIENCE-FICTION STORIES: 1950, THE
                                        BLEILER & DIKTY   AN
  GAME FOR BLONDES   SS GAL 52 10
    BEST SCIENCE-FICTION STORIES: 1953, THE
                                        BLEILER & DIKTY   AN
    SECOND GALAXY READER OF SCIENCE FICTION
                                        GOLD, H. L.   AN
  HALF-PAST ETERNITY   NV SSS 50 07
    HUMAN EQUATION, THE   NOLAN, WILLIAM F.   AN
  HUNTED, THE   SS SSS 49 07
    BEYOND THE END OF TIME   POHL, FREDERIK   AN
  INCUBATION   SS NEW 52 AN
    *FUTURE TENSE   CROSSEN, KENDELL F. AN
  LEGEND OF JOE LEE, THE   SS CMP 64
    10TH ANNUAL OF THE YEAR'S BEST S-F, THE
                                        MERRIL, JUDITH   AN
  MECHANICAL ANSWER   SS ASF 48 05
    ROBOT AND THE MAN, THE   GREENBERG , MARTIN   AN
  MINIATURE, THE   SS SSS 49 09
    *BIG BOOK OF SCIENCE FICTION   CONKLIN, GROFF   AN
  RING AROUND THE REDHEAD   SS STS 48 11
    ADVENTURES IN DIMENSION   CONKLIN, GROFF   AN
    *SCIENCE FICTION ADVENTURES IN DIMENSION
                                        CONKLIN, GROFF   AN
  SHADOW ON THE SAND   SN TWS 50 10
    STRANGE TOMORROWS   HOSKINS, ROBERT   AN
  SPECTATOR SPORT   SS TWS 50 02
    FIFTY SHORT SCIENCE FICTION TALES   ASIMOV & CONKLIN   AN
    OMNIBUS OF SCIENCE FICTION   CONKLIN, GROFF   AN
    SCIENCE FICTION OMNIBUS   CONKLIN, GROFF   AN
    STRANGE ADVENTURES IN SCIENCE FICTION CONKLIN, GROFF   AN
  SUSCEPTIBILITY   SS GAL 51 01
    *GALAXY READER OF SCIENCE FICTION   GOLD, H. L.   AN
  TROJAN HORSE LAUGH   NV ASF 49 08
    DIMENSION 4   CONKLIN, GROFF   AN
    TOMORROW 1   HOSKINS, ROBERT   AN

MACDONALD, PHILIP
  HUB (SOLITARY CONFINEMENT)   SS FSF 51 08
    BEST FROM FANTASY AND SCIENCE FICTION BOUCHER & MCCOMAS AN
  PRIVATE- KEEP OUT!   SS FSF 49 FL
    TWENTY YEARS OF FANTASY & SCIENCE FICTION
                                        FERMAN & MILLS   AN
    WORLD OF WONDER   PRATT, FLETCHER   AN
  SOLITARY CONFINEMENT (SEE HUB)   TC

MCDOWELL, EMMETT
  VEILED ISLAND   NV ASF 46 01
    *SCIENCE FICTION ADVENTURES IN MUTATION CONKLIN, GROFF   AN

MCEVOY, SETH
  WHICH IN THE WOOD DECAYS   SS ORB 75 17
    ORBIT 17   KNIGHT, DAMON   OA

MACFADYEN, A. JR.
  TIME DECELERATOR, THE   SS ASF 36 07
    CROSSROADS IN TIME   CONKLIN, GROFF   AN
    SCIENCE FICTION OF THE 30'S   KNIGHT, DAMON   AN

MACFARLANE, WALLACE
  CHANGING WOMAN   SS GAL 72 09
    1973 ANNUAL WORLD'S BEST SF, THE   WOLLHEIM, DONALD A. AN
  DEAD END   SS GAL 52 01
    *SCIENCE FICTION THINKING MACHINES CONKLIN, GROFF   AN
  FREE VACATION   SS ASF 67 01
    ANALOG 7   CAMPBELL, JOHN W. JR AN
  GARDENING NOTES FROM ALL OVER   SS ORB 74 13
    ORBIT 13   KNIGHT, DAMON   OA
  GRADUATION DAY   SS EPC 75
    EPOCH   ELWOOD & SILVERBERG OA
  HOW SHALL WE CONQUER?   SS NDM 73 03
    NEW DIMENSIONS 3   SILVERBERG, ROBERT   OA
  LAST LEAF, THE   SS ORB 71 09
    ORBIT 9   KNIGHT, DAMON   OA

MACFARLANE, WALLACE (CONTINUED)
  MERLIN STREET   NV INY 72 04
    INFINITY 4   HOSKINS, ROBERT   OA
  NO-WIND SPOTTED TIGER PLANET, THE   SS GAL 71 05
    BEST FROM GALAXY, THE VOLUME I   GALAXY, EDITORS OF   AN
  QUICKENING   SS GAL 73 09
    BEST FROM GALAXY, THE VOLUME II   GALAXY, EDITORS OF   AN
  ROBBIE AND DAVID AND LITTLE DAHL   SS GAL 72 05
    MORE LITTLE MONSTERS   ELWOOD & GHIDALIA   AN
  RUBAIYAT OF AMBROSE BAGLEY, THE   SS SFE 74 01
    SCIENCE FICTION EMPHASIS NO. 1   GERROLD, DAVID   OA
  TO MAKE A NEW NEANDERTHAL   SS ASF 71 09
    BEST SCIENCE FICTION STORIES OF THE YEAR (1971)
                                        DEL REY, LESTER   AN

MCGEE, JANE AGORN   SEE ALSO   CO-EDITOR BONNIE L. HEINTZ
  PREFACE   IN C
    TOMORROW, AND TOMORROW, AND TOMORROW...
                                        HEINTZ/HERBERT/JOOS/ AN

MCGIVERN, PATRICK
  NUMBER EIGHT   SS PBY 70 06
    FULLY AUTOMATED LOVE LIFE OF HENRY KEANRIDGE
                                        PLAYBOY, EDITORS OF AN

MACGREGOR, ELLEN
  MARS & MISS PICKERELL (FROM MISS P. GOES TO MARS) EX   51
    SCIENCE FICTION AND READER'S GUIDE BARROWS, MARJORIE   AN

MACGREGOR, JAMES M. SEE PSEUD. J. T. MCINTOSH

MCGREGOR, R. J.
  PERFECT GENTLEMAN, THE   SS STS 52 09
    BEST FROM STARTLING STORIES, THE   MINES, SAMUEL   AN

MCGUIRE, JOHN J.
  QUEEN'S MESSENGER, THE   SS ASF 57 05
    BEST SCIENCE FICTION STORIES AND NOVELS: 9TH SERIES
                                        DIKTY, T. E.   AN
  RETURN, THE   NV C ASF 54 01
    SCIENCE-FICTIONAL SHERLOCK HOLMES, THE COUNCIL OF FOUR   AN
  TO CATCH AN ALIEN   SS STR 59 06
    STAR SCIENCE FICTION STORIES NO. 6 POHL, FREDERIK   OA

MCGUIRE, PATRICK
  HER STRONG ENCHANTMENTS FAILING   AR
    MANY WORLDS OF POUL ANDERSON, THE   ANDERSON, POUL   AC

MCHALE, JOHN
  INTRODUCTION: TODAY'S TOMORROWS   IN
    TOMORROW TODAY   ZEBROWSKI, GEORGE   OA

MCHARGUE, GEORGESS
  HOT & COLD RUNNING CITIES   AN H HRW 74
  INTRODUCTION   IN
    HOT & COLD RUNNING CITIES   MCHARGUE, GEORGESS   AN

MACHEN, ARTHUR
  OPENING THE DOOR   SS   31
    TRAVELERS IN TIME   STERN, PHILIP VAN D. AN
  SHINING PYRAMID, THE   SS UKW 95 05
    ANCIENT MYSTERIES READER, THE   HAINING, PETER   AN
  WHITE PEOPLE, THE   NV HLK 04 01
    GOLDEN ROAD, THE   KNIGHT, DAMON   AN
  WHITE POWDER, THE   NV FFM 44 09
    STRANGE ECSTASIES   PARRY, MICHEL   AN

MACHT, NORMAN L.
  WAY OF LIFE, A   SS
    GOLLANCZ - SUNDAY TIMES BEST SF STORIES
                                        ANONYMOUS   OA

MCILWAIN, DAVID   SEE PSEUD. CHARLES ERIC MAINE

MCINTOSH, J. T.   PSEUD. FOR JAMES M. MACGREGOR
  ONE IN THREE HUNDRED   AC H DBL 54
  BLISS OF SOLITUDE, THE (HALLUCINATION ORBIT) NV GAL 52 01
    BEST SF 4   CRISPIN, EDMUND   AN
    GATEWAY TO TOMORROW   CARNELL, JOHN   AN
  BROKEN RECORD, THE   SS NWS 52 09
    BEST FROM NEW WORLDS SCIENCE FICTION, THE
                                        CARNELL, JOHN   AN
  FIRST LADY   NV GAL 53 06
    ANOTHER PART OF THE GALAXY   CONKLIN, GROFF   AN
    BEST SF   CRISPIN, EDMUND   AN
    MARRIAGE AND THE FAMILY THROUGH SCIENCE FICTION
                                        CLEAR/WARRICK/&   AN
  HALLUCINATION ORBIT (ALSO AS THE BLISS OF SOLITUDE)
                                                      NV GAL 52 01
    GALAXY SCIENCE FICTION OMNIBUS   GOLD, H. L.   AN
    SECOND GALAXY READER OF SCIENCE FICTION
                                        GOLD, H. L.   AN
  IMMORTALITY...FOR SOME   NV ASF 60 03
    12 GREAT CLASSICS OF SCIENCE FICTION CONKLIN, GROFF   AN
  MACHINE MADE   SS NWS 51 SU
    GIANTS UNLEASHED   CONKLIN, GROFF   AN
   *NO PLACE LIKE EARTH   CARNELL, JOHN   AN
    OUT OF THIS WORLD 2   WILLIAMS-ELLIS& OWEN AN
  MADE IN U.S.A.   NV GAL 53 04
    CONNOISSEUR'S S. F.   BOARDMAN, TOM JR.   AN
    CROSSROADS IN TIME   CONKLIN, GROFF   AN
    HUMAN AND OTHER BEINGS   DEGRAEFF, ALLEN   AN
  MIND ALONE   NA GAL 53 08
    5 GALAXY SHORT NOVELS   GOLD, H. L.   AN
  ONE IN A THOUSAND   SS FSF 54 01
    ONE IN THREE HUNDRED   MCINTOSH, J. T.   AC

MCINTOSH, J. T.   (CONTINUED)
  ONE IN THREE HUNDRED   NV FSF 53 02
    BEST SCIENCE-FICTION STORIES: 1954, THE
                                        BLEILER & DIKTY   AN
    ONE IN THREE HUNDRED   MCINTOSH, J. T.   AC
  ONE TOO MANY   SS FSF 54 09
    ONE IN THREE HUNDRED   MCINTOSH, J. T.   AC
  POOR PLANET   NV FSF 64 08
    SEVEN TRIPS THROUGH TIME AND SPACE CONKLIN, GROFF   AN
  STITCH IN TIME   SS SCF 52 FL
    GATEWAY TO THE STARS   CARNELL, JOHN   AN
  UNIT   NV NWS 57 02
    FIVE-ODD   CONKLIN, GROFF   AN
  VENUS MISSION   NV PLS 51 07
    HIDDEN PLANET, THE   WOLLHEIM, DONALD A. AN
  WRONG WORLD, THE   NV GAL 60 12
    ELSEWHERE AND ELSEWHEN   CONKLIN, GROFF   AN
  YOU WERE RIGHT, JOE   SS GAL 57 11
    FOURTH GALAXY READER, THE   GOLD, H. L.   AN

MCINTYRE, VONDA N. AND SUSAN J. ANDERSON
  AURORA: BEYOND EQUALITY   OA FGM 76 05

MCINTYRE, VONDA N.
  AZTECS   NA
    2076: THE AMERICAN TRICENTENNIAL   BRYANT, EDWARD   OA
  CAGES   SS QRK 71 04
    QUARK/4   DELANY & HACKER   OA
  CAN ANYTHING BE TAUGHT?   AR
    CLARION SF   WILHELM, KATE   OA
  GALACTIC CLOCK, THE   SS GEN 72
    GENERATION   GERROLD, DAVID   OA
  GENIUS FREAKS, THE   SS ORB 73 12
    ORBIT 12   KNIGHT, DAMON   OA
  MOUNTAINS OF SUNSET, THE MOUNTAINS OF DAWN, THE SS FSF 74 02
    BEST SCIENCE FICTION STORIES OF THE YEAR (1974)
                                        DEL REY, LESTER   AN
  OF MIST, AND GRASS, AND SAND   SS ASF 73 10
    BEST SCIENCE FICTION OF THE YEAR, THE NO. 3
                                        CARR, TERRY   AN
    LOOKING AHEAD   ALLEN, D. & L.   AN
    NEBULA AWARD STORIES 9   WILHELM, KATE   AN
    WOMEN OF WONDER   SARGENT, PAMELA   AN
  ONLY AT NIGHT   SS CLR 71 01
    CLARION   WILSON, ROBIN SCOTT OA
  POTENTIAL AND ACTUALITY IN SCIENCE FICTION   AR
    NEBULA AWARD STORIES 11   LE GUIN, URSULA K.   AN
  RECOURSE, INC.   SS ALT 74
    ALTERNATIES   GERROLD, DAVID   OA
  SCREWTOP   NA
    CRYSTAL SHIP, THE   SILVERBERG, ROBERT   OA
  SPECTRA   SS ORB 72 11
    ORBIT 11   KNIGHT, DAMON   OA
  THANATOS   SS   76
    FUTURE POWER   DANN & DOZOIS   OA
  WINGS   SS ALC 73
    ALIEN CONDITION, THE   GOLDIN, STEPHEN   OA

MACKAY, CHARLES
  WITCH TRIALS AND THE LAW (1841)   AR
    ROD SERLING'S TRIPLE W: WITCHES, WARLOCKS AND WEREWOLVES
                                        SERLING, ROD   AN

MACKELWORTH, R. W.
  EXPANDING MAN, THE   SS NWR 65 05
    NEW WRITINGS IN SF. 5   CARNELL, JOHN   OA
  FINAL SOLUTION   SS NWR 66 08
    NEW WRITINGS IN SF. 8   CARNELL, JOHN   OA
  TILT ANGLE   SS NWR 69 14
    NEW WRITINGS IN SF. 9   CARNELL, JOHN   AN
  TOUCH OF IMMORTALITY, A   SS NWR 66 07
    NEW WRITINGS IN SF. 7   CARNELL, JOHN   OA
  TWO RIVERS   NV NWR 70 17
    NEW WRITINGS IN SF. 17   CARNELL, JOHN   OA

MCKENNA, RICHARD
  NIGHT OF HOGGY DARN, THE   NV IFS 58 12
    ALPHA 7   SILVERBERG, ROBERT   AN

MCKENNA, RICHARD M.
  CASEY AGONISTES, AND OTHER S.F. & FANTASY STORIES AC H HPR 73
  BRAMBLE BUSH   NV ORB 68 03
    ORBIT 3   KNIGHT, DAMON   OA
  CASEY AGONISTES   SS FSF 58 09
    BEST FROM FANTASY AND SCIENCE FICTION: 9
                                        MILLS, ROBERT P.   AN
    CASEY AGONISTES, AND OTHER S.F. & FANTASY STORIES
                                        MCKENNA, RICHARD M. AC
    DARK SIDE, THE   KNIGHT, DAMON   AN
    SF: THE BEST OF THE BEST   MERRIL, JUDITH   AN
    SF:59, THE YEAR'S GREATEST SCIENCE FICTION AND FANTASY
                                        MERRIL, JUDITH   AN
    SHOCKING THING, A   KNIGHT, DAMON   AN
  FIDDLER'S GREEN   NV ORB 67 02
    CASEY AGONISTES, AND OTHER S.F. & FANTASY STORIES
                                        MCKENNA, RICHARD M. AC
    DIMENSION X   KNIGHT, DAMON   AN
    ORBIT 2   KNIGHT, DAMON   OA
  HUNTER, COME HOME   NV FSF 63 03
    BEST FROM FANTASY AND SCIENCE FICTION: 13
                                        DAVIDSON, AVRAM   AN
    CASEY AGONISTES, AND OTHER S.F. & FANTASY STORIES
                                        MCKENNA, RICHARD M. AC
    CENTURY OF GREAT SHORT SCIENCE FICTION NOVELS, A
                                        KNIGHT, DAMON   AN

MCKENNA, RICHARD M. (CONTINUED)
  MINE OWN WAYS   SS   FSF 60 02
    BEST FROM FANTASY AND SCIENCE FICTION: 10
                                         MILLS, ROBERT P.   AN
  CASEY AGONISTES, AND OTHER S.F. & FANTASY STORIES
                                         MCKENNA, RICHARD M. AC
  6TH ANNUAL OF THE YEAR'S BEST S-F, THE MERRIL, JUDITH   AN
  NIGHT OF HOGGY DARN, THE   NV   IFS 58 12
    TOMORROW X 4   KNIGHT, DAMON   AN
  SECRET PLACE, THE   SS   ORB 66 01
    BEST FROM ORBIT, THE   KNIGHT, DAMON   AN
  CASEY AGONISTES, AND OTHER S.F. & FANTASY STORIES
                                         MCKENNA, RICHARD M. AC
    NEBULA AWARD STORIES NO. 2   ALDISS & HARRISON   AN
    ORBIT 1   KNIGHT, DAMON   OA
  UNCLEAR CALL FOR LEE   SS   NEW 71 AN
    POCKETFUL OF STARS, A   KNIGHT, DAMON   AN

MACKENROTH, NANCY
  MOST BEAUTIFUL MUSIC, THE   SS
    LEARNING MAZE AND OTHER STORIES, THE ELWOOD, ROGER   OA
  TO SLEEP, PERCHANCE TO DREAM   SS   74
    FAR SIDE OF TIME, THE   ELWOOD, ROGER   OA
    GIFTS OF ASTI AND OTHER STORIES OF SCIENCE FICTION, THE
                                         ELWOOD, ROGER   AN

MCKENTY, JACK
  $1,000 A PLATE   SS   GAL 54 10
    FIFTH GALAXY READER, THE   GOLD, H. L.   AN

MACKENZIE, J. B.
  OVERPROOF   NV   ASF 65 10
    ANALOG 5   CAMPBELL, JOHN W. JR AN
    SEVEN TRIPS THROUGH TIME AND SPACE   CONKLIN, GROFF   AN
  THIN EDGE   SS   ASF 63 12
    ANALOG 3   CAMPBELL, JOHN W. JR AN

MCKETTRIG, SEATON   PSEUD. FOR RANDALL GARRETT
  AFTER A FEW WORDS   SS   ASF 62 10
    SCIENCE FICTION HORIZONS NO. 1   BOARDMAN, TOM JR.   AN
  WORLD BY THE TALE, A   SS   ASF 63 10
    ANALOG 3   CAMPBELL, JOHN W. JR AN

MCKIMMEY, JAMES
  EYES HAVE IT, THE   SS   IFS 53 11
    SPACE, TIME & CRIME   DEFORD, MIRIAM ALLEN AN
  INSPECTOR, THE   SS   FRS 68
    FARTHEST REACHES, THE   ELDER, JOSEPH   OA

MACKIN, EDWARD
  KEY TO CHAOS   NV   NWR 64 01
    NEW WRITINGS IN SF. 1   CARNELL, JOHN   OA
  TROUBLE WITH H.A.R.R.I., THE   SS   AUT 57 02
    SCIENCE FICTION ODDITIES   CONKLIN, GROFF   AN
  UNREMEMBERED, THE   SS   NWS 64 03
    WORLD'S BEST SCIENCE FICTION: 1965   WOLLHEIM & CARR   AN

MCKINLEY, MARY C.
  LIKE A DIAMOND IN THE SKY   SS
    LONG NIGHT OF WAITING AND OTHER STORIES
                                         ELWOOD, ROGER   OA

MCKNIGHT, JOHN P.
  PROLOG   SS   FSF 51 08
    FIFTY SHORT SCIENCE FICTION TALES   ASIMOV & CONKLIN   AN

MCLAUGHLIN, BERNARD
  SILENCE, THE   SS   STI 41 06
    GOLDEN ROAD, THE   KNIGHT, DAMON   AN
    MORE TERROR IN THE MODERN VEIN   WOLLHEIM, DONALD A. AN
    *TERROR IN THE MODERN VEIN   WOLLHEIM, DONALD A. AN

MCLAUGHLIN, DEAN
  HAWK AMONG THE SPARROWS   AC H SCB 76
  BROTHERHOOD OF KEEPERS, THE   NV   ASF 60 07
    HAWK AMONG THE SPARROWS   MCLAUGHLIN, DEAN   AC
    6TH ANNUAL OF THE YEAR'S BEST S-F, THE MERRIL, JUDITH   AN
  ENDORSEMENT, PERSONAL   SS   NOV 73 03
    NOVA 3   HARRISON, HARRY   OA
  FOR THOSE WHO FOLLOW AFTER   SS   ASF 51 07
    APEMAN, SPACEMAN   STOVER & HARRISON   AN
  HAWK AMONG THE SPARROWS   SN   ASF 68 07
    ANALOG 8   CAMPBELL, JOHN W. JR AN
    HAWK AMONG THE SPARROWS   MCLAUGHLIN, DEAN   AC
  PERMANENT IMPLOSION, THE   NV   ASF 64 02
    ANALOG 4   CAMPBELL, JOHN W. JR AN
    HAWK AMONG THE SPARROWS   MCLAUGHLIN, DEAN   AC
  TOUCHSTONE   SS   INY 72 03
    INFINITY 3   HOSKINS, ROBERT   OA
  TOURING THE WORKSHOP   IN
    HAWK AMONG THE SPARROWS   MCLAUGHLIN, DEAN   AC

MACLEAN, KATHERINE   ALSO AS   CHARLES DYE
  DIPLOIDS AND OTHER FLIGHTS OF FANCY, THE AC   AVN 62
  MISSING MAN, THE   NO   BKM 75
  AND BE MERRY... (ALSO AS THE PYRAMID IN THE DESERT)
                                           SS   ASF 50 02
    OMNIBUS OF SCIENCE FICTION   CONKLIN, GROFF   AN
    SCIENCE FICTION: THE GREAT YEARS, VOL. II
                                         POHL, C. & F.   AN
    TOWARD INFINITY   KNIGHT, DAMON   AN
  BRAIN WIPE   SS   NMD 73
    FRONTIERS 2: THE NEW MIND   ELWOOD, ROGER   OA
  CONTAGION   NV   GAL 50 10
    BEST SCIENCE-FICTION STORIES: 1951, THE
                                         BLEILER & DIKTY   AN

MACLEAN, KATHERINE   (CONTINUED)
    MINDWORM, THE   ANONYMOUS   AN
    *POSSIBLE WORLDS OF SCIENCE FICTION CONKLIN, GROFF   AN
    WOMEN OF WONDER   SARGENT, PAMELA   AN
  DEFENSE MECHANISM   SS   ASF 49 10
    BEYOND THE BARRIERS OF SPACE AND TIME MERRIL, JUDITH   AN
    *BIG BOOK OF SCIENCE FICTION   CONKLIN, GROFF   AN
    DIPLOIDS AND OTHER FLIGHTS OF FANCY, THE
                                         MACLEAN, KATHERINE AC
  DIPLOIDS, THE   NA   TWS 53 04
    DIPLOIDS AND OTHER FLIGHTS OF FANCY, THE
                                         MACLEAN, KATHERINE AC
  ECHO   SS   INY 70 01
    INFINITY 1   HOSKINS, ROBERT   OA
  FEAR HOUND   NV   ASF 68 05
    MISSING MAN, THE   MACLEAN, KATHERINE NO
    WORLD'S BEST SCIENCE FICTION: 1969   WOLLHEIM & CARR   AN
  FEEDBACK   SS   ASF 51 07
    CROSSROADS IN TIME   CONKLIN, GROFF   AN
    DIPLOIDS AND OTHER FLIGHTS OF FANCY, THE
                                         MACLEAN, KATHERINE AC
  FITTEST, THE   SS   WBY 51 01
    *BEYOND HUMAN KEN   MERRIL, JUDITH   AN
  GAMES   SS   GAL 53 03
    DIPLOIDS AND OTHER FLIGHTS OF FANCY, THE
                                         MACLEAN, KATHERINE AC
    OPERATION FUTURE   CONKLIN, GROFF   AN
    YOUNG DEMONS   ELWOOD & GHIDALIA   AN
  INCOMMUNICADO   NV   ASF 50 06
    DIPLOIDS AND OTHER FLIGHTS OF FANCY, THE
                                         MACLEAN, KATHERINE AC
    SIX GREAT SHORT SCIENCE FICTION NOVELS CONKLIN, GROFF   AN
  INTERBALANCE   SS   FSF 60 10
    BEST FROM FANTASY AND SCIENCE FICTION: 10
                                         MILLS, ROBERT P.   AN
  MISSING MAN, THE   NV   ASF 71 03
    ANALOG 9   BOVA, BEN   AN
    MISSING MAN, THE   MACLEAN, KATHERINE NO
    NEBULA AWARD STORIES NO. 7   BIGGLE, LLOYD JR.   AN
  ORIGIN OF THE SPECIES, THE   SS   NEW 53 AN
    CHILDREN OF WONDER   TENN, WILLIAM   AN
  OTHER, THE   SS   NWS 66 07
    NEW WORLDS OF FANTASY   CARR, TERRY   AN
    SF12   MERRIL, JUDITH   AN
    VOYAGES: SCENARIOS FOR A SHIP CALLED EARTH
                                         SAUER, ROB   AN
  PERCHANCE TO DREAM   SS   NEW 70 AN
    NEW WORLDS OF FANTASY NO. 2   CARR, TERRY   AN
  PICTURES DON'T LIE   SS   GAL 51 08
    ASPECTS OF SCIENCE FICTION   DOHERTY, G. D.   AN
    BEST SF   CRISPIN, EDMUND   AN
    DIPLOIDS AND OTHER FLIGHTS OF FANCY, THE
                                         MACLEAN, KATHERINE AC
    ENEMIES IN SPACE   CONKLIN, GROFF   AN
    INVADERS FROM SPACE   SILVERBERG, ROBERT AN
    *INVADERS OF EARTH   CONKLIN, GROFF   AN
    SPECULATIONS   SANDERS, THOMAS E. AN
  PYRAMID IN THE DESERT, THE (AND BE MERRY) SS ASF 50 02
    DIPLOIDS AND OTHER FLIGHTS OF FANCY, THE
                                         MACLEAN, KATHERINE AC
  RESCUE SQUAD FOR AHMED   NV   ASF 70 10
    MISSING MAN, THE   MACLEAN, KATHERINE NO
  SECOND GAME   NV C ASF 58 03
    GREAT SHORT NOVELS OF SCIENCE FICTION SILVERBERG, ROBERT AN
  SMALL WAR   SS   SVW 73
    SAVING WORLDS   ELWOOD & KIDD   OA
  SNOWBALL EFFECT, THE   SS   GAL 52 09
    DECADE THE 1950S   ALDISS & HARRISON   AN
    DIPLOIDS AND OTHER FLIGHTS OF FANCY, THE
                                         MACLEAN, KATHERINE AC
    GALAXY SCIENCE FICTION OMNIBUS   GOLD, H. L.   AN
    PENGUIN SCIENCE FICTION   ALDISS, BRIAN W.   AN
    SCIENCE FICTION INVENTIONS   KNIGHT, DAMON   AN
    SECOND GALAXY READER OF SCIENCE FICTION
                                         GOLD, H. L.   AN
  SYNDROME JOHNNY   SS   GAL 51 07
    SF: AUTHORS' CHOICE   HARRISON, HARRY   AN
  TROUBLE WITH TREATIES   NV C STR 59 05
    STAR SCIENCE FICTION STORIES NO. 5   POHL, FREDERIK   OA
  TROUBLE WITH YOU EARTH PEOPLE, THE   NV   AMZ 68 02
    LIBERATED FUTURE: VOYAGES INTO TOMORROW, THE
                                         HOSKINS, ROBERT   AN
  UNHUMAN SACRIFICE   NV   ASF 58 11
    ANTHROPOLOGY THROUGH SCIENCE FICTION MASON, C/GREENBERG/& AN
    CENTURY OF SCIENCE FICTION, A   KNIGHT, DAMON   AN
    GODS FOR TOMORROW   SANTESSON, HANS S. AN
    *SPECTRUM   AMIS & CONQUEST   AN

MACLENNAN, PHYLLIS
  THUS LOVE BETRAYS US   SS   FSF 72 09
    BEST FROM FANTASY AND SCIENCE FICTION: 20
                                         FERMAN, EDWARD L.   AN
    BEST SCIENCE FICTION STORIES OF THE YEAR (1972)
                                         DEL REY, LESTER   AN
    1973 ANNUAL WORLD'S BEST SF, THE   WOLLHEIM, DONALD A. AN

MCMAHON, JEREMIAH
  MR. SWIFT AND HIS REMARKABLE THING   SS   PBY
    FULLY AUTOMATED LOVE LIFE OF HENRY KEANRIDGE
                                         PLAYBOY, EDITORS OF AN

MACMANUS, S.
  TINKER OF TAMLACHT, THE   SS
    DEALS WITH THE DEVIL   DAVENPORT, BASIL   AN

MCMORROW, FRED

MCMORROW, FRED
BIG WHEEL, THE   SS   SEP 61 07
    POST READER OF FANTASY AND SCIENCE FICTION
                                            SATURDAY EVE. POST   AN

MCMORROW, THOMAS
MR. MURPHY OF NEW YORK   SS   SEP 30 03
    *BIG BOOK OF SCIENCE FICTION   CONKLIN, GROFF   AN
    ONE HUNDRED YEARS OF SCIENCE FICTION   KNIGHT, DAMON   AN

MCNAUGHTON, BRIAN J.
BLACK TOWER, THE   NV   C
    SHANADU   BRINEY, ROBERT E.   OA

MCNEAR, ROBERT
DEATH'S DOOR   SS   PBY 69 03
    MASKS   PLAYBOY, EDITORS OF   AN
    YEAR'S BEST HORROR STORIES, THE   DAVIS, RICHARD   AN

MCNELLY, WILLIS E. AND LEON E. STOVER
ABOVE THE HUMAN LANDSCAPE   AN H GYR 72
    A SOCIAL SCIENCE FICTION ANTHOLOGY

MCNELLY, WILLIS E.   SEE ALSO
    CO-EDITORS HARRY HARRISON AND JANE HIPOLITO
FOREWORD   IN   C
    MARS, WE LOVE YOU   HIPOLITO & MCNELLY   AN
FOREWORD TO "I HAVE NO MOUTH, AND I MUST SCREAM" IN
    MIRROR OF INFINITY, THE   SILVERBERG, ROBERT   AN
INTRODUCTION   IN   C
    ABOVE THE HUMAN LANDSCAPE   MCNELLY & STOVER   AN
LINGUISTIC RELATIVITY IN MIDDLE HIGH MARTIAN   AR   68
    MARS, WE LOVE YOU   HIPOLITO & MCNELLY   AN
SCIENCE FICTION AS CULTURE CRITICISM   AR   C
    ABOVE THE HUMAN LANDSCAPE   MCNELLY & STOVER   AN
SCIENCE FICTION NOVEL IN 1968, THE   IN
    NEBULA AWARD STORIES NO. 4   ANDERSON, POUL   AN
THINGS TO COME   IN   C
    SCIENCE FICTION NOVELLAS   HARRISON & MCNELLY   AN
VONNEGUT'S SLAUGHTERHOUSE-FIVE: SCIENCE FICTION AS
    OBJECTIVE CORRELATIVE   AR
    ABOVE THE HUMAN LANDSCAPE   MCNELLY & STOVER   AN

MACREADY, R. G.
PLANT-THING, THE   SS   WRT 25 07
    NIGHTMARE GARDEN   GHIDALIA, VIC   AN

M'INTOSH, J. T.   PSEUD. FOR JAMES M. MACGREGOR

MADDUX, RACHEL
FINAL CLEARANCE   SS   FSF 56 02
    BEST FROM FANTASY AND SCIENCE FICTION: 6
                                       BOUCHER, ANTHONY   AN

MADONIA, GAIL
ACID SOAP OPERA   SS   QRK 71 04
    QUARK/4   DELANY & HACKER   OA

MADSEN, SVEND AGE
GOOD RING, THE   SS
    VIEW FROM ANOTHER SHORE   ROTTENSTEINER, FRANZ   AN

MAGIDOFF, ROBERT
RUSSIAN SCIENCE FICTION   AN H NYU 64
RUSSIAN SCIENCE FICTION, 1968   AN H NYU 68
RUSSIAN SCIENCE FICTION, 1969   AN H NYU 69
INTRODUCTION   IN
    RUSSIAN SCIENCE FICTION   MAGIDOFF, ROBERT   AN
    RUSSIAN SCIENCE FICTION, 1968   MAGIDOFF, ROBERT   AN
PREFACE   IN
    RUSSIAN SCIENCE FICTION, 1969   MAGIDOFF, ROBERT   AN

MAGRITTE, RENE
CASTLE OF THE PYRENEES, THE   IL
    SCIENCE FICTION   BRODKIN & PEARSON   AN
ON THE THRESHOLD OF FREEDOM   IL
    SCIENCE FICTION   BRODKIN & PEARSON   AN

MAIEWSKI, SHIRLEY S.
MIND-SIFTER   NA
    STAR TREK: THE NEW VOYAGES   MARSHAK, S&CULBREATH   OA

MAILER, NORMAN
FROM "OF A FIRE ON THE MOON"   EX   69
    LOOKING AHEAD   ALLEN, D. & L.   AN

MAINE, CHARLES ERIC   PSEUD. FOR DAVID MCILWAIN
HIGHWAY J   NV   PLS 53 11
    OTHER WORLDS, OTHER TIMES   MOSKOWITZ & ELWOOD   AN

MALAMUD, BERNARD
JEWBIRD, THE   SS   REP 63 04
    WANDERING STARS   DANN, JACK M.   AN
    9TH ANNUAL OF THE YEAR'S BEST S-F, THE   MERRIL, JUDITH   AN

MALAVAL, SUZANNE
DEVIL'S GODDAUGHTER   SS   60
    13 FRENCH SCIENCE-FICTION STORIES KNIGHT, DAMON   AN

MALCOLM, DONALD
BETWEEN THE TIDES   NV   NWR 76 29
    NEW WRITINGS IN SF. 29   BULMER, KENNETH   OA
BIG DAY, THE   SS   NWR 71 18
    NEW WRITINGS IN SF. 18   CARNELL, JOHN   OA
ENEMY WITHIN, THE   NV   NWR 75 25
    NEW WRITINGS IN SF. 25   BULMER, KENNETH   OA

MALZBERG, BARRY N.

MALCOLM, DONALD   (CONTINUED)
POTENTIAL   NV   NWR 65 05
    NEW WRITINGS IN SF. 5   CARNELL, JOHN   OA
STRANGE AND TERRIBLE SEA, A   SS   NWR 74 24
    NEW WRITINGS IN SF. 24   BULMER, KENNETH   OA
TWICE BITTEN   SS   NWS 63 02
    OUT OF THIS WORLD 4   WILLIAMS-ELLIS& OWEN   AN

MALEC, ALEXANDER B.
EXTRAPOLASIS   AC H DBL 67
DIEHL   NV
    EXTRAPOLASIS   MALEC, ALEXANDER B.   AC
LANDMARK   SS
    EXTRAPOLASIS   MALEC, ALEXANDER B.   AC
MATAYAMA   SS   COQ 66 SU
    EXTRAPOLASIS   MALEC, ALEXANDER B.   AC
MONSIGNOR PRIMO MACINNO   SS
    EXTRAPOLASIS   MALEC, ALEXANDER B.   AC
ONCE WAS   NV
    EXTRAPOLASIS   MALEC, ALEXANDER B.   AC
OPAXTL   NV
    EXTRAPOLASIS   MALEC, ALEXANDER B.   AC
PROJECT INHUMANE   SS   COQ 64 SP
    EXTRAPOLASIS   MALEC, ALEXANDER B.   AC
    11TH ANNUAL OF THE YEAR'S BEST S-F, THE
                                       MERRIL, JUDITH   AN
PROOF POSITIVE   SS
    EXTRAPOLASIS   MALEC, ALEXANDER B.   AC
REMOTE INCIDENT   SS
    EXTRAPOLASIS   MALEC, ALEXANDER B.   AC
THING-THING   SS
    EXTRAPOLASIS   MALEC, ALEXANDER B.   AC
TO RELIEVE THE SANITY   SS
    EXTRAPOLASIS   MALEC, ALEXANDER B.   AC
10:01 A.M.   SS   ASF 66 03
    ANALOG 6   CAMPBELL, JOHN W. JR   AN
    EXTRAPOLASIS   MALEC, ALEXANDER B.   AC

MALKO, GEORGE
FLOWER KID CASHES IN, THE   SS   FSF 69 05
    FANTASY: THE LITERATURE OF THE MARVELOUS
                                       KELLEY, LEO P.   AN

MALLETTE, MOSE
SEVEN WONDERS OF THE UNIVERSE, THE   SS   FSF 66 08
    BEST FROM FANTASY AND SCIENCE FICTION: 16
                                       FERMAN, EDWARD L.   AN

MALONEY, RUSSELL
INFLEXIBLE LOGIC   SS   NYM 40 02
    FANTASIA MATHEMATICA   FADIMAN, CLIFTON   AN
    FANTASY: THE LITERATURE OF THE MARVELOUS
                                       KELLEY, LEO P.   AN
    TIMELESS STORIES FOR TODAY AND TOMORROW
                                       BRADBURY, RAY   AN

MALPASS, E. L.
RETURN OF THE MOON MAN (ALSO AS WHEN GRANDFATHER FLEW
    TO THE MOON)   SS   LOB 55 01
    AD 2500   WILSON, ANGUS   AN
STARLIT CORRIDOR, THE   MANSFIELD, ROGER   AN
    TALES OF SCIENCE FICTION   BALL, BRIAN N.   AN
WHEN GRANDFATHER FLEW TO THE MOON (RETURN OF THE MOON MAN)
                                                        SS   LOB 55 01
    SF:57, THE YEAR'S GREATEST SCIENCE FICTION AND FANTASY
                                       MERRIL, JUDITH   AN

MALSTROM, ROBERT C.
GREAT A, THE   SS   NDM 71 01
    NEW DIMENSIONS 1   SILVERBERG, ROBERT   OA

MALZBERG, BARRY N.   SEE ALSO   CO-EDITOR EDWARD L. FERMAN
                                ALSO AS
    K. M. O'DONNELL AND ROBIN SCHAEFFER
BEST OF BARRY N. MALZBERG, THE   AC   PKT 76 01
DOWN HERE IN THE DREAM QUARTER   AC H DBL 76
MANY WORLDS OF BARRY MALZBERG, THE   AC   POP 75
OUT FROM GANYMEDE   AC   WPB 74 12
AFTER THE GREAT SPACE WAR   SS   ALT 74
    DOWN HERE IN THE DREAM QUARTER   MALZBERG, BARRY N.   AC
AFTER THE UNFORTUNATE ACCIDENT   SS   NEW 75 AC
    MANY WORLDS OF BARRY MALZBERG, THE MALZBERG, BARRY N.   AC
AFTERWORD: ON THE NON-TRANSCENDENCE OF SPORT   MS
    ARENA: SPORTS SF   FERMAN & MALZBERG   AN
AGONY COLUMN   SS   EQM 71 12
    OUT FROM GANYMEDE   MALZBERG, BARRY N.   AC
AH, CARELESS, RAPTUROUS VAN VOGT!   IN
    BEST OF A. E. VAN VOGT, THE   VAN VOGT, A. E.   AC
ALLOWANCES   SS   FAN 72 08
    OUT FROM GANYMEDE   MALZBERG, BARRY N.   AC
AND STILL IN THE DARKNESS   SS   NEW 76 AC
    BEST OF BARRY N. MALZBERG, THE   MALZBERG, BARRY N.   AC
ART OF FICTION, THE   SS   MSM 72
    OUT FROM GANYMEDE   MALZBERG, BARRY N.   AC
AS IN A VISION APPREHENDED   SS   BER 74
    BERSERKERS, THE   ELWOOD, ROGER   OA
    BEST OF BARRY N. MALZBERG, THE   MALZBERG, BARRY N.   AC
AT THE INSTITUTE   SS   FAN 74 03
    BEST OF BARRY N. MALZBERG, THE   MALZBERG, BARRY N.   AC
BALLAD OF SLICK SID, THE   SS   INY 72 04
    DOWN HERE IN THE DREAM QUARTER   MALZBERG, BARRY N.   AC
    INFINITY 4   HOSKINS, ROBERT   OA
BATTERED-EARTH SYNDROME, THE   SS   SVW 73
    BEST OF BARRY N. MALZBERG, THE   MALZBERG, BARRY N.   AC
    SAVING WORLDS   ELWOOD & KIDD   OA

MALZBERG, BARRY N.   (CONTINUED)
  BEARING WITNESS   SS   FTP 73
    BEST OF BARRY N. MALZBERG, THE   MALZBERG, BARRY N.   AC
    FLAME TREE PLANET   ELWOOD, ROGER   OA
  BEYOND SLEEP   SS   EQM 70 11
    OUT FROM GANYMEDE   MALZBERG, BARRY N.   AC
  BREAKING IN   SS   FAN 72 06
    OUT FROM GANYMEDE   MALZBERG, BARRY N.   AC
  CAPTURING VANCE   IN
    BEST OF JACK VANCE, THE   VANCE, JACK   AC
  CAUSATION   SS   FSF 71 12
    OUT FROM GANYMEDE   MALZBERG, BARRY N.   AC
  CHRONICLES OF A COMER   SS   WLK 73
    MANY WORLDS OF BARRY MALZBERG, THE MALZBERG, BARRY N. AC
  CITY LIGHTS, CITY NIGHTS   SS   FUC 73
    BEST OF BARRY N. MALZBERG, THE   MALZBERG, BARRY N.   AC
  CLOSED SICILIAN   SS   FSF 73 11
    ARENA: SPORTS SF   FERMAN & MALZBERG   AN
    BEST OF BARRY N. MALZBERG, THE   MALZBERG, BARRY N.   AC
    MANY WORLDS OF BARRY MALZBERG, THE MALZBERG, BARRY N. AC
  CLOSING THE DEAL   SS   ASF 74 03
    BEST OF BARRY N. MALZBERG, THE   MALZBERG, BARRY N.   AC
  CONQUEST   SS   NDM 71 01
    BEST SF: 1971   HARRISON & ALDISS   AN
    NEW DIMENSIONS 1   SILVERBERG, ROBERT   OA
  CONQUEST OF MARS, THE   SS   NOV 72 02
    OUT FROM GANYMEDE   MALZBERG, BARRY N.   AC
  CONVERSATIONS AT LOTHAR'S   SS   COI 73
    CHILDREN OF INFINITY   ELWOOD, ROGER   OA
    LIBERATED FUTURE: VOYAGES INTO TOMORROW, THE
                                      HOSKINS, ROBERT   AN
  CULTURE LOCK   SS   FUC 73
    BEST OF BARRY N. MALZBERG, THE   MALZBERG, BARRY N.   AC
    FUTURE CITY   ELWOOD, ROGER   OA
  DARK OF KNIGHT   IN
    BEST OF DAMON KNIGHT, THE   KNIGHT, DAMON   AC
  DEATH TO THE KEEPER   NV   FSF 68 08
    MANY WORLDS OF BARRY MALZBERG, THE MALZBERG, BARRY N. AC
  DELIGHTFUL COMEDIC PREMISE, A   SS   FSF 74 02
    ANTIGRAV: COSMIC COMEDIES   STRICK, PHILIP   AN
    BEST OF BARRY N. MALZBERG, THE   MALZBERG, BARRY N.   AC
  DESTRUCTION AND EXCULPATION OF EARTH, THE   SS   NOV 73 03
    DOWN HERE IN THE DREAM QUARTER   MALZBERG, BARRY N.   AC
    NOVA 3   HARRISON, HARRY   OA
  DOWN HERE IN THE DREAM QUARTER   SS   AMZ 76 06
    DOWN HERE IN THE DREAM QUARTER   MALZBERG, BARRY N.   AC
  ELEPHANTS   SS   INY 71 02
    EDGE OF NEVER, THE   HOSKINS, ROBERT   AN
  EXPLORATION   SS   NEW 71 AN
    MARS, WE LOVE YOU   HIPOLITO & MCNELLY   AN
  FALCON AND THE FALCONEER, THE   SS   FSF 69 12
    SF: AUTHORS' CHOICE 3   HARRISON, HARRY   AN
    WONDERMAKERS 2   HOSKINS, ROBERT   AN
  FINAL WAR   NV   FSF 68 04
    FUTURE NOW, THE   HOSKINS, ROBERT   AN
    MANY WORLDS OF BARRY MALZBERG, THE MALZBERG, BARRY N. AC
  FIREDAY: FIRENIGHT   SS   74
    DOWN HERE IN THE DREAM QUARTER   MALZBERG, BARRY N.   AC
    FAR SIDE OF TIME, THE   ELWOOD, ROGER   OA
    GIFTS OF ASTI AND OTHER STORIES OF SCIENCE FICTION, THE
                                      ELWOOD, ROGER   AN
  FORM IN REMISSION (AS ROBIN SCHAEFFER)   SS   BER 74
    BEST OF BARRY N. MALZBERG, THE   MALZBERG, BARRY N.   AC
  GALAXY CALLED ROME, A   NV   FSF 75 07
    ALPHA 7   SILVERBERG, ROBERT   AN
    BEST SF: 75, THE NINTH ANNUAL   HARRISON & ALDISS   AN
    DOWN HERE IN THE DREAM QUARTER   MALZBERG, BARRY N.   AC
  GEHENNA   SS   GAL 71 03
    BEST SF: 1971   HARRISON & ALDISS   AN
    1972 ANNUAL WORLD'S BEST SF, THE WOLLHEIM, DONALD A. AN
  GERANIUMS   SS   C OMG 73
    BEST OF BARRY N. MALZBERG, THE   MALZBERG, BARRY N.   AC
    OMEGA   ELWOOD, ROGER   OA
  GETTING AROUND   SS   TAL 73
    BEST OF BARRY N. MALZBERG, THE   MALZBERG, BARRY N.   AC
  GOING DOWN   NV   DYS 75
    BEST OF BARRY N. MALZBERG, THE   MALZBERG, BARRY N.   AC
    DYSTOPIAN VISIONS   ELWOOD, ROGER   OA
  GUIDANCE   SS
    JOURNEY TO ANOTHER STAR AND OTHER STORIES
                                      ELWOOD, ROGER   OA
  HANGING (SEE LETTING IT ALL HANG OUT)   TC
  HARRY HARRISON: THE MAN WHO WALKED HOME   IN
    *BEST OF HARRY HARRISON, THE   HARRISON, HARRY   AC
  HELMET, THE   SS   FSF 73 09
    OUT FROM GANYMEDE   MALZBERG, BARRY N.   AC
  IN THE CUP   SS   SAW 72
    MANY WORLDS OF BARRY MALZBERG, THE MALZBERG, BARRY N. AC
    SIGNS AND WONDERS   ELWOOD, ROGER   OA
  IN THE STOCKS   SS   NDM 77 07
    NEW DIMENSIONS 7   SILVERBERG, ROBERT   OA
  INITIATION   SS   NEW 75 AC
    MANY WORLDS OF BARRY MALZBERG, THE MALZBERG, BARRY N. AC
  INSTITUTIONS   SS
    SURVIVAL FROM INFINITY   ELWOOD, ROGER   OA
  INTER ALIA   SS   INY 72 03
    INFINITY 3   HOSKINS, ROBERT   OA
    OUT FROM GANYMEDE   MALZBERG, BARRY N.   AC
  INTERCEPTOR, THE   SS   MSM 72
    OUT FROM GANYMEDE   MALZBERG, BARRY N.   AC
  INTRODUCTION   IN
    BEST OF BARRY N. MALZBERG, THE   MALZBERG, BARRY N.   AC
    BEST OF KEITH LAUMER, THE   LAUMER, KEITH   AC
    MANY WORLDS OF BARRY MALZBERG, THE MALZBERG, BARRY N. AC
    OUT FROM GANYMEDE   MALZBERG, BARRY N.   AC

MALZBERG, BARRY N.   (CONTINUED)
  INTRODUCTION   IN C
    FINAL STAGE   FERMAN & MALZBERG   OA
  INTRODUCTION TO THE SECOND EDITION   SS   NOV 73 03
    BEST OF BARRY N. MALZBERG, THE   MALZBERG, BARRY N.   AC
    NOVA 3   HARRISON, HARRY   OA
  INTRODUCTION: A SHORT ONE FOR THE BOYS IN THE BACK ROOM
                                      IN
    DOWN HERE IN THE DREAM QUARTER   MALZBERG, BARRY N.   AC
  INTRODUCTION: STARTING IN THE MIDDLE   IN
    MORE SCIENCE FICTION TALES   ELWOOD, ROGER   OA
  ISAIAH   SS   FAN 73 09
    DOWN HERE IN THE DREAM QUARTER   MALZBERG, BARRY N.   AC
  IT DOESN'T REALLY MATTER   SS
    GRADUATED ROBOT AND OTHER STORIES, THE ELWOOD, ROGER OA
  JANUARY, 1975   SS   ASF 75 01
    DOWN HERE IN THE DREAM QUARTER   MALZBERG, BARRY N.   AC
  LETTING IT ALL HANG OUT (HANGING)   SS   FAN 74 09
    BEST OF BARRY N. MALZBERG, THE   MALZBERG, BARRY N.   AC
  LEVITICUS: IN THE ARK   SS   EPC 75
    DOWN HERE IN THE DREAM QUARTER   MALZBERG, BARRY N.   AC
    EPOCH   ELWOOD & SILVERBERG OA
  LINKAGE   SS   DEM 73
    BEST OF BARRY N. MALZBERG, THE   MALZBERG, BARRY N.   AC
    DEMON KIND   ELWOOD, ROGER   OA
    OUT FROM GANYMEDE   MALZBERG, BARRY N.   AC
  MAKING IT ALL THE WAY INTO THE FUTURE ON GAXTON FALLS OF THE
  RED PLANET   SS   NOV 74 04
    NOVA 4   HARRISON, HARRY   OA
  MAKING IT THROUGH   SS   WLK 73
    AND WALK NOW GENTLY THROUGH THE FIRE...
                                      ELWOOD, ROGER   OA
    BEST OF BARRY N. MALZBERG, THE   MALZBERG, BARRY N.   AC
  MAKING IT TO GAXTON FALLS ON THE RED PLANET IN THE YEAR
  OF OUR LORD   SS   NOV 74 04
    DOWN HERE IN THE DREAM QUARTER   MALZBERG, BARRY N.   AC
  MAKING THE CONNECTIONS   SS   CTM 75 04
    CONTINUUM 4   ELWOOD, ROGER   OA
    DOWN HERE IN THE DREAM QUARTER   MALZBERG, BARRY N.   AC
  MAN IN THE POCKET, THE (THE MEN INSIDE)   NV   NDM 72 02
    BEST OF BARRY N. MALZBERG, THE   MALZBERG, BARRY N.   AC
  MANAGEMENT   SS   NEW 75 AC
    MANY WORLDS OF BARRY MALZBERG, THE MALZBERG, BARRY N. AC
  MEN INSIDE, THE (ALSO AS THE MAN IN THE POCKET) NV NDM 72 02
    NEW DIMENSIONS 2   SILVERBERG, ROBERT   OA
  NATURAL HISTORY   SS
    LONG NIGHT OF WAITING AND OTHER STORIES
                                      ELWOOD, ROGER   OA
  NETWORK   SS   FAN 74 01
    BEST OF BARRY N. MALZBERG, THE   MALZBERG, BARRY N.   AC
  NOTES FOR A NOVEL ABOUT THE FIRST SHIP EVER TO VENUS
                                      SS   UNI 71 01
    OUT FROM GANYMEDE   MALZBERG, BARRY N.   AC
    UNIVERSE 1   CARR, TERRY   OA
  NOTES JUST PRIOR TO THE FALL   SS   FSF 70 10
    BEST FROM FANTASY AND SCIENCE FICTION: 19
                                      FERMAN, EDWARD L.   AN
  NOTES LEADING DOWN TO THE CONQUEST (ALSO AS A RECKONING)
                                      SS   NDM 73 03
    NEW DIMENSIONS 3   SILVERBERG, ROBERT   OA
  NOTES LEADING DOWN TO THE EVENTS AT BEDLAM   SS   72
    DOWN HERE IN THE DREAM QUARTER   MALZBERG, BARRY N.   AC
  NOVEMBER 22, 1963   SS   NEW 74 AC
    OUT FROM GANYMEDE   MALZBERG, BARRY N.   AC
  ON ICE   SS   AMZ 73 01
    BEST OF BARRY N. MALZBERG, THE   MALZBERG, BARRY N.   AC
  ON THE AIR   SS   NDM 76 06
    NEW DIMENSIONS 6   SILVERBERG, ROBERT   OA
  ON THE CAMPAIGN TRAIL   SS   FCR 75
    DOWN HERE IN THE DREAM QUARTER   MALZBERG, BARRY N.   AC
    FUTURE CORRUPTION   ELWOOD, ROGER   OA
  OPENING FIRE   SS   NMD 73
    BEST OF BARRY N. MALZBERG, THE   MALZBERG, BARRY N.   AC
    FRONTIERS 2; THE NEW MIND   ELWOOD, ROGER   OA
  OUT FROM GANYMEDE   SS   NDM 72 02
    NEW DIMENSIONS 2   SILVERBERG, ROBERT   OA
    OUT FROM GANYMEDE   MALZBERG, BARRY N.   AC
  OVER THE LINE   SS   74
    BEST OF BARRY N. MALZBERG, THE   MALZBERG, BARRY N.   AC
    FUTURE KIN   ELWOOD, ROGER   OA
  OVERLOOKING   SS   AMZ 74 06
    BEST OF BARRY N. MALZBERG, THE   MALZBERG, BARRY N.   AC
  OVERSIGHT, AN   SS   STG 74
    BEST OF BARRY N. MALZBERG, THE   MALZBERG, BARRY N.   AC
  P.T.A. MEETS CHE GUEVARA, THE   SS   ALT 74
    ALTERNATIES   GERROLD, DAVID   AN
  PATER FAMILIAS   SS   C FSF 72 03
    BEST OF BARRY N. MALZBERG, THE   MALZBERG, BARRY N.   AC
    OUT FROM GANYMEDE   MALZBERG, BARRY N.   AC
  RAGE, PAIN, ALIENATION AND OTHER ASPECTS OF THE WRITING
  OF SCIENCE FICTION   AR   FSF 76 04
    DOWN HERE IN THE DREAM QUARTER   MALZBERG, BARRY N.   AC
  RECKONING, A (NOTES LEADING DOWN TO THE CONQUEST) SS NDM 73 03
    BEST OF BARRY N. MALZBERG, THE   MALZBERG, BARRY N.   AC
  RECOLLECTING ANDERSON   IN
    BEST OF POUL ANDERSON, THE   ANDERSON, POUL   AC
  RECONSTITUTION   SS   NEW 75 AC
    MANY WORLDS OF BARRY MALZBERG, THE MALZBERG, BARRY N. AC
  REDUNDANCY   SS   SWK 76 03
    DOWN HERE IN THE DREAM QUARTER   MALZBERG, BARRY N.   AC
  REPORT OF THE DEFENSE   SS   ETN 72
    OUT FROM GANYMEDE   MALZBERG, BARRY N.   AC
  REPORT TO HEADQUARTERS   SS   NDM 75 05
    DOWN HERE IN THE DREAM QUARTER   MALZBERG, BARRY N.   AC
    NEW DIMENSIONS 5   SILVERBERG, ROBERT   OA

MALZBERG, BARRY N.

MARSHALL, CHRIS

MALZBERG, BARRY N.   (CONTINUED)
  REVOLUTION (AS ROBIN SCHAEFFER)   SS   FUC 73
    BEST OF BARRY N. MALZBERG, THE   MALZBERG, BARRY N.   AC
  RUNNING AROUND   SS   OMG 73
    BEST OF BARRY N. MALZBERG, THE   MALZBERG, BARRY N.   AC
  OMEGA   ELWOOD, ROGER   OA
  SECOND SHORT SHORTEST FANTASY STORY EVER PUBLISHED
                                                 SS   FSF 73 03
    MANY WORLDS OF BARRY MALZBERG, THE MALZBERG, BARRY N.   AC
  SEDAN DEVILLE   SS   FSF 74 12
    DOWN HERE IN THE DREAM QUARTER   MALZBERG, BARRY N.   AC
  SEEKING ASSISTANCE   SS   FSF 76 04
    DOWN HERE IN THE DREAM QUARTER   MALZBERG, BARRY N.   AC
  SENSE OF THE FIRE, THE   NV   ESC 67
    OUT FROM GANYMEDE   MALZBERG, BARRY N.   AC
  SHORT RELIGIOUS NOVEL, A   SS   FSF 72 09
    OUT FROM GANYMEDE   MALZBERG, BARRY N.   AC
  SHOWING OFF REYNOLDS   IN
    BEST OF MACK REYNOLDS, THE   REYNOLDS, MACK   AC
  SOME NOTES TOWARD A USEABLE PAST   SS   NOV 72 02
    OUT FROM GANYMEDE   MALZBERG, BARRY N.   AC
  STATE OF THE ART   SS   NDM 74 04
    DOWN HERE IN THE DREAM QUARTER   MALZBERG, BARRY N.   AC
    NEW DIMENSIONS 4   SILVERBERG, ROBERT   OA
  STILL-LIFE (AS K. M. O'DONNELL)   SS   DVS 72 02
    OUT FROM GANYMEDE   MALZBERG, BARRY N.   AC
  STREAKING   SS   FCR 75
    DOWN HERE IN THE DREAM QUARTER   MALZBERG, BARRY N.   AC
  SUMMARY OF EVENTS LEADING UP TO BEDLAM, A   SS   72
    BEWARE MORE BEASTS   GHIDALIA, V.& ELWOOD AN
  TAPPING OUT   SS   FUQ 73
    BEST OF BARRY N. MALZBERG, THE   MALZBERG, BARRY N.   AC
    FUTURE QUEST   ELWOOD, ROGER   OA
  TERMINUS EST   SS   NOV 70 01
    *NOVA 1   HARRISON, HARRY   OA
  THINKING ABOUT SILVERBERG   IN
    BEST OF ROBERT SILVERBERG, THE   SILVERBERG, ROBERT   AC
  THIRTY-SEVEN NORTHWEST   SS   NEW 76 AC
    DOWN HERE IN THE DREAM QUARTER   MALZBERG, BARRY N.   AC
  THOSE WONDERFUL YEARS   SS   TAL 73
    BEST OF BARRY N. MALZBERG, THE   MALZBERG, BARRY N.   AC
    FRONTIERS 1; TOMORROW'S ALTERNATIVES ELWOOD, ROGER   OA
  TRACK TWO   SS   FAN 74 07
    BEST OF BARRY N. MALZBERG, THE   MALZBERG, BARRY N.   AC
  TRANSFER   SS   FAN 75 08
    DOWN HERE IN THE DREAM QUARTER   MALZBERG, BARRY N.   AC
  TRASHING   SS   INY 73 05
    DOWN HERE IN THE DREAM QUARTER   MALZBERG, BARRY N.   AC
    INFINITY 5   HOSKINS, ROBERT   OA
  TRIAL OF THE BLOOD   SS   BER 74
    BEST OF BARRY N. MALZBERG, THE   MALZBERG, BARRY N.   AC
  TRIPTYCH, A   SS   FSF 69 07
    ALPHA 1   SILVERBERG, ROBERT   AN
  TRUTH OF IT, THE   SS
    SCIENCE FICTION ADVENTURES FROM WAY OUT
                                       ELWOOD, ROGER   OA
  TRY AGAIN   SS   STG 74
    BEST OF BARRY N. MALZBERG, THE   MALZBERG, BARRY N.   AC
    STRANGE GODS   ELWOOD, ROGER   OA
  TWENTY SIXTY-ONE   SS   FSF 74 07
    BEST OF BARRY N. MALZBERG, THE   MALZBERG, BARRY N.   AC
  TWO ODYSSEYS INTO THE CENTER   SS   NOV 72 02
    NOVA 2   HARRISON, HARRY   OA
  UNCOUPLING   SS   DYS 75
    BEST OF BARRY N. MALZBERG, THE   MALZBERG, BARRY N.   AC
    DYSTOPIAN VISIONS   ELWOOD, ROGER   OA
  UNION FOREVER, THE   SS   SCS 73
    MANY WORLDS OF BARRY MALZBERG, THE MALZBERG, BARRY N.   AC
    OUT FROM GANYMEDE   MALZBERG, BARRY N.   AC
    SHOWCASE   ELWOOD, ROGER   OA
  UPS AND DOWNS   SS   EIO 73
    BEST OF BARRY N. MALZBERG, THE   MALZBERG, BARRY N.   AC
    EROS IN ORBIT   ELDER, JOSEPH   OA
  VIDI VICI VENI   SS   GEN 72
    GENERATION   GERROLD, DAVID   OA
  VOX POPULI   SS   EDG 73
    DOWN HERE IN THE DREAM QUARTER   MALZBERG, BARRY N.   AC
  WHAT THE BOARD SAID   SS   NEW 76 AC
    BEST OF BARRY N. MALZBERG, THE   MALZBERG, BARRY N.   AC
  WONDERFUL, ALL-PURPOSE TRANSMOGRIFIER, THE   SS   FST 74
    FINAL STAGE   FERMAN & MALZBERG   OA
  YAHRZEIT   SS   TTM 73
    TEN TOMORROWS   ELWOOD, ROGER   OA
  YEARBOOK, THE   SS   FSF 71 05
    OUT FROM GANYMEDE   MALZBERG, BARRY N.   AC

MANHATTAN, AVRO
  CRICKET BALL, THE   SS   FSF 55 10
    FIFTY SHORT SCIENCE FICTION TALES ASIMOV & CONKLIN   AN
    UNTRAVELLED WORLDS   BARTER & WILSON   AN

MANN, FRANCIS OSCAR
  DEVIL IN A CONVENT, THE   SS
    GHOULS, THE   HAINING, PETER   AN

MANNING, LAURENCE
  CITY OF THE LIVING DEAD, THE   NV C SWS 30 05
    SECOND AVON FANTASY READER, THE   WOLLHEIM &ERNSBERGER AN
  GOOD-BYE, ILHA¡   SS   NEW 52 AN
    *BEYOND HUMAN KEN   MERRIL, JUDITH   AN
    GIANTS UNLEASHED   CONKLIN, GROFF   AN
  LIVING GALAXY, THE   SS   WOS 34 09
    SCIENCE FICTION GALAXY, THE   CONKLIN, GROFF   AN
  MAN WHO AWOKE, THE   NV   WOS 33 03
    BEFORE THE GOLDEN AGE   ASIMOV, ISAAC   AN

MANSFIELD, ROGER
  STARLIT CORRIDOR, THE   AN H PGM 67
  INTRODUCTION   IN
    STARLIT CORRIDOR, THE   MANSFIELD, ROGER   AN

MARCUSE, KATHERINE
  TWENTY-FIRST CENTURY MOTHER   SS   AUT 54 01
    MARRIAGE AND THE FAMILY THROUGH SCIENCE FICTION
                                       CLEAR/WARRICK/&   AN

MARGROFF, ROBERT E.
  BOOK, THE   SS C ORB 70 08
    ORBIT 8   KNIGHT, DAMON   OA
  NAKED AND THE UNASHAMED, THE   SS   PRT 71
    PROTOSTARS   GERROLD & GOLDIN   OA

MARGULIES, LEO AND OSCAR J. FRIEND
  FROM OFF THIS WORLD   AN H MER 49
    GIANT ANTHOLOGY OF SCIENCE FICTION AN H MER 54
    DERIVATIVE ANTHOLOGY "RACE TO THE STARS"
  MY BEST SCIENCE FICTION STORY   AN H MER 49
  MY BEST SCIENCE FICTION STORY (12 OF 25)   AN   PKT 54 05
  RACE TO THE STARS   AN   CRS 58 10
    4 STORIES FROM "GIANT ANTHOLOGY OF SCIENCE FICTION"

MARGULIES, LEO
  GET OUT OF MY SKY   AN   CRS 60
  GHOUL KEEPERS, THE   AN   PYR 61
  THREE TIMES INFINITY   AN   GMB 58
  UNEXPECTED, THE   AN   PYR 61 02
  WEIRD TALES   AN   PYR 64 05
  WORLDS OF WEIRD   AN   PYR 65
  3 FROM OUT THERE   AN   CRS 59 03
  3 IN 1   AN   PYR 63 08
  INTRODUCTION   IN
    GHOUL KEEPERS, THE   MARGULIES, LEO   AN
    UNEXPECTED, THE   MARGULIES, LEO   AN
    WEIRD TALES   MARGULIES, LEO   AN
    3 IN 1   MARGULIES, LEO   AN
  INTRODUCTION   IN C
    *MY BEST SCIENCE FICTION STORY   MARGULIES & FRIEND   AN
  INTRODUCTION TO THE POCKET BOOK EDITION   IN C

MARKS, WINSTON K.
  CALL ME ADAM   SS   FSF 54 02
    OPERATION FUTURE   CONKLIN, GROFF   AN
  DOUBLE-TAKE (AS KEN WINNEY)   SS   SFA 53 12
    FIFTY SHORT SCIENCE FICTION TALES ASIMOV & CONKLIN   AN
  I'D GIVE A DOLLAR   SS   BEY 54 05
    BEYOND   ANONYMOUS   AN
  JOHN'S OTHER PRACTICE   SS   IMG 54 07
    BEST SCIENCE FICTION STORIES AND NOVELS: 1955
                                       DIKTY, T. E.   AN
  MATE IN TWO MOVES   NV   GAL 54 05
    GREAT SCIENCE FICTION ABOUT DOCTORS CONKLIN, G&FABRICANT AN
  WATER EATER, THE   SS   GAL 53 06
    SCIENCE FICTION ODDITIES   CONKLIN, GROFF   AN

MARLOWE, STEPHEN   PSEUD. FOR MILTON LESSER
  LION'S MOUTH   SS   FAD 52 06
    LOOKING FORWARD   LESSER, MILTON   AN

MARLOWE, WEBB   PSEUD. FOR J. FRANCIS MCCOMAS
  FLIGHT INTO DARKNESS   SS   ASF 43 02
    *ADVENTURES IN TIME AND SPACE   HEALY & MCCOMAS   AN

MARQUIS, DON
  GHOSTS (FROM ARCHIE AND MEHITABLE)   EX   27
    HUMAN?   MERRIL, JUDITH   AN

MARSDEN, BOB
  DEFINITION, THE   SS   NWS 68 07
    NEW TOMORROWS, THE   SPINRAD, NORMAN   AN

MARSH, JOYCE
  SPACE PEDLAR, THE   SS
    STRANGE WORLD OF SCIENCE FICTION   ANONYMOUS   OA

MARSH, RICHARD
  DISAPPEARANCE OF MRS. MACRECHAM, THE   NV
    WIZARDS AND WARLOCKS   GHIDALIA, VIC   AN

MARSH, WILLARD
  ETHICATORS, THE   SS   IFS 55 08
    SF: THE YEAR'S GREATEST SCIENCE FICTION AND FANTASY
                                       MERRIL, JUDITH   AN

MARSHAK, DAVID
  WATER   NV   NDM 76 06
    NEW DIMENSIONS 6   SILVERBERG, ROBERT   OA

MARSHAK, SONDRA AND MYRNA CULBREATH
  STAR TREK: THE NEW VOYAGES   OA   BAN 76 03

MARSHAK, SONDRA
  INTRODUCTION TO THE HUNTING   IN C
    STAR TREK: THE NEW VOYAGES   MARSHAK, S&CULBREATH OA
  INTRODUCTION: THE ONCE AND FUTURE VOYAGES   IN C
    STAR TREK: THE NEW VOYAGES   MARSHAK, S&CULBREATH OA

MARSHALL, CHRIS
  METAMORPHOSIS   IL C
    BEYOND THIS HORIZON   CARRELL, CHRISTOPHER OA

MARSHALL, EDISON T.
    WHO IS CHARLES AVISON?   SS   ARG 16 04
        SHOT IN THE DARK   MERRIL, JUDITH   AN

MARSHALL, LENORE
    I AM A   PM   69
        SCIENCE FICTION   BRODKIN & PEARSON   AN

MARTENSSON, BERTIL
    MODEST PROPOSAL, A   SS   NWQ 74 06
        NEW WORLDS NO. 6   PLATT & BAILEY   OA

MARTI-IBANEZ, FELIX
    NINA SOL   SS   FSF 63 05
        BEST FROM FANTASY AND SCIENCE FICTION: 13
                                 DAVIDSON, AVRAM   AN
    SENHOR ZUMBEIRA'S LEG   NV   FSF 62 12
        NEVER IN THIS WORLD   STONE, IDELLA P.   AN

MARTIN, GEORGE R. R.
    NEW VOICES IN SCIENCE FICTION   OA H MAC 77
    SONG FOR LYA, A   AC   AVN 76 02
    SONGS OF STARS AND SHADOWS   AC   PKT 77 07
        AND SEVEN TIMES NEVER KILL MAN   NV   ASF 75 07
            SONGS OF STARS AND SHADOWS MARTIN, GEORGE R. R. AC
    BEAST FOR NORN, A   NV
        ANDROMEDA I   WESTON, PETER   OA
    DARK, DARK WERE THE TUNNELS   SS   VTX 73 12
        SONG FOR LYA, A   MARTIN, GEORGE R. R. AC
    EXIT TO SAN BRETA, THE   SS   FAN 72 02
        SONG FOR LYA, A   MARTIN, GEORGE R. R. AC
    FAST-FRIEND   NV   76
        FASTER THAN LIGHT   DANN & ZEBROWSKI   OA
    "FOR A SINGLE YESTERDAY"   NV   EPC 75
        EPOCH   ELWOOD & SILVERBERG OA
        SONGS OF STARS AND SHADOWS MARTIN, GEORGE R. R. AC
    FTA   SS   ASF 74 05
        SONG FOR LYA, A   MARTIN, GEORGE R. R. AC
    HERO, THE   SS   GAL 71 02
        SONG FOR LYA, A   MARTIN, GEORGE R. R. AC
    IN THE HOUSE OF THE WORM   SS
        IDES OF TOMORROW, THE   CARR, TERRY   OA
    INTRODUCTION   IN
        SONGS OF STARS AND SHADOWS MARTIN, GEORGE R. R. AC
    LAST SUPER BOWL GAME, THE   NV   GLR 75 02
        RUN TO STARLIGHT, SPORTS THROUGH SCIENCE FICTION
                                 GREENBERG/OLANDER/& AN
    LONELY SONGS OF LAREN DORR, THE   SS   FAN 76 05
        SONGS OF STARS AND SHADOWS MARTIN, GEORGE R. R. AC
    MEATHOUSE MAN   SS   ORB 76 18
        BEST SCIENCE FICTION OF THE YEAR, THE NO. 6
                                 CARR, TERRY   AN
        ORBIT 18   KNIGHT, DAMON   OA
    MEN OF GREYWATER STATION   SS   AMZ 76 03
        SONGS OF STARS AND SHADOWS MARTIN, GEORGE R. R. AC
    NIGHT OF THE VAMPYRES, THE   NV   AMZ 75 05
        SONGS OF STARS AND SHADOWS MARTIN, GEORGE R. R. AC
    NIGHT SHIFT   SS   AMZ 73 01
        SONGS OF STARS AND SHADOWS MARTIN, GEORGE R. R. AC
    NOR THE MANY-COLORED FIRES OF A STAR RING   NV   76
        FASTER THAN LIGHT   DANN & ZEBROWSKI   OA
    OVERRIDE   NV   ASF 73 09
        SONG FOR LYA, A   MARTIN, GEORGE R. R. AC
    PATRICK HENRY, JUPITER, AND THE LITTLE RED BRICK SPACESHIP
                                                SS   AMZ 76 12
        SONGS OF STARS AND SHADOWS MARTIN, GEORGE R. R. AC
    RUN TO STARLIGHT   NV   AMZ 74 12
        INFINITE ARENA, THE   CARR, TERRY   AN
        RUN TO STARLIGHT, SPORTS THROUGH SCIENCE FICTION
                                 GREENBERG/OLANDER/& AN
    SONG FOR LYA, A   SS   FSF 75 09
        SONGS OF STARS AND SHADOWS MARTIN, GEORGE R. R. AC
    RUNNERS, THE   SS   ASF 72 12
        SECOND KIND OF LONELINESS, THE
        INTRODUCTORY PSYCHOLOGY THROUGH SCIENCE FICTION
                                 KATZ/WARRICK/&   AN
        SONG FOR LYA, A   MARTIN, GEORGE R. R. AC
    SLIDE SHOW   SS   OMG 73
        OMEGA   ELWOOD, ROGER   OA
        SONG FOR LYA, A   MARTIN, GEORGE R. R. AC
    SONG FOR LYA, A   NV   ASF 74 06
        SONG FOR LYA, A   MARTIN, GEORGE R. R. AC
        1975 ANNUAL WORLD'S BEST SF, THE WOLLHEIM, DONALD A. AN
    STARLADY   NV
        SCIENCE FICTION DISCOVERIES POHL, C. & F.   OA
    STONE CITY, THE   SS
        NEW VOICES IN SCIENCE FICTION MARTIN, GEORGE R. R. OA
    STORMS OF WINDHAVEN, THE   NV C ASF 75 05
        BEST SCIENCE FICTION OF THE YEAR, THE NO. 5
                                 CARR, TERRY   AN
        1976 ANNUAL WORLD'S BEST SF, THE WOLLHEIM, DONALD A. AN
    THIS TOWER OF ASHES   SS
        ANALOG ANNUAL   BOVA, BEN   OA
        SONGS OF STARS AND SHADOWS MARTIN, GEORGE R. R. AC
    WEEKEND IN A WAR ZONE   SS
        FUTURE PASTIMES   EDELSTEIN, SCOTT   OA
    WITH MORNING COMES MISTFALL   SS   ASF 73 05
        BEST SCIENCE FICTION STORIES OF THE YEAR (1973)
                                 DEL REY, LESTER   AN
                                 WILHELM, KATE   AN
        SONG FOR LYA, A   MARTIN, GEORGE R. R. AC

MARTIN, HAROLD
    SCAPE-GOAT OF LA JUSTICIA, THE   SS
        BATTLE FOR THE PACIFIC AND OTHER ADVENTURES AT SEA, THE
                                 ANONYMOUS   AN

MARTIN, LARRY W.
    LANDSCAPE WITH ALIENS   SS
        CLARION SF   WILHELM, KATE   OA

MARTIN, MARIO JR.
    HIDE AND SEEK   SS
        MORE SCIENCE FICTION TALES ELWOOD, ROGER   OA

MARTIN, WEBBER   PSEUD. FOR ROBERT SILVERBERG

MARTINO, JOSEPH P.
    NOT A PRISON MAKE   NV   ASF 66 09
        ANALOG 6   CAMPBELL, JOHN W. JR AN
        POLITICAL SCIENCE FICTION GREENBERG& WARRICK   AN
    PUSHBUTTON WAR   SS   ASF 60 08
        PROLOGUE TO ANALOG   CAMPBELL, JOHN W. JR AN
    TO CHANGE THEIR WAYS   NV   ASF 67 04
        OUT OF THIS WORLD 7   WILLIAMS-ELLIS& OWEN AN

MARTINSON, HARRY
    HADES AND EUCLID (TRANSLATED BY ROBERT BLY) SS   70
        NEW CONSTELLATIONS   DISCH & NAYLOR   OA

MARVELL, ANDREW   PSEUD. FOR HOWELL DAVIES
    MATHEMATICAL LOVE   PM   50
        FANTASIA MATHEMATICA   FADIMAN, CLIFTON   AN

MASEFIELD, JOHN
    DEVIL AND THE OLD MAN, THE   SS   13
        DEALS WITH THE DEVIL   DAVENPORT, BASIL   AN
    SEALMAN, THE (1913)   SS   FSF 55 07
        DECADE OF FANTASY AND SCIENCE FICTION, A
                                 MILLS, ROBERT P.   AN
        EDGE OF NEVER, THE   HOSKINS, ROBERT   AN

MASON, A. E. W.
    CLOCK, THE   SS   17
        TRAVELERS IN TIME   STERN, PHILIP VAN D. AN

MASON, CAROL, MARTIN H. GREENBERG, AND PATRICIA S. WARRICK
    ANTHROPOLOGY THROUGH SCIENCE FICTION   AN H SMP 74

MASON, CAROL
    PREFACE   IN C
        ANTHROPOLOGY THROUGH SCIENCE FICTION MASON, C/GREENBERG/& AN

MASON, DOUGLAS R.   ALSO AS   JOHN RANKINE
    ALGORA ONE SIX   SS   NWR 73 21
        NEW WRITINGS IN SF. 21   CARNELL, JOHN   OA
    ALL DONE BY MIRRORS   SS   NWR 69 16
        NEW WRITINGS IN SF. 16   CARNELL, JOHN   OA
    FOLLY TO BE WISE   SS   NWR 66 09
        NEW WRITINGS IN SF. 9   CARNELL, JOHN   OA
    MAN WHO MISSED THE FERRY, THE   SS   NWR 66 07
        NEW WRITINGS IN SF. 7   CARNELL, JOHN   AN
        NEW WRITINGS IN SF. 7   CARNELL, JOHN   OA
    THERE WAS THIS FELLA...   SS   NWR 68 11
        NEW WRITINGS IN SF. 11   CARNELL, JOHN   OA

MASON, JOHN KEITH
    ARCTIC RESCUE   SS
        TOMORROW: NEW WORLDS OF SCIENCE FICTION
                                 ELWOOD, ROGER   OA

MASSON, DAVID I.
    CALTRAPS OF TIME, THE   AC H FAB 68
    DOCTOR FAUSTA   NV
        STOPWATCH   HAY, GEORGE   OA
    LOST GROUND   SS   NWS 66 12
        BEST SF: 1968   HARRISON & ALDISS   AN
        CALTRAPS OF TIME, THE   MASSON, DAVID I.   AC
    MOUTH OF HELL   SS   NWS 66 01
        CALTRAPS OF TIME, THE   MASSON, DAVID I.   AC
    NOT SO CERTAIN   SS   NWS 67 07
        CALTRAPS OF TIME, THE   MASSON, DAVID I.   AC
    PSYCHOSMOSIS   SS   NWS 66 03
        CALTRAPS OF TIME, THE   MASSON, DAVID I.   AC
        DARK STARS   SILVERBERG, ROBERT   AN
        ENGLAND SWINGS SF   MERRIL, JUDITH   AN
        SPACE-TIME JOURNAL, THE MERRIL, JUDITH   AN
    TAKE IT OR LEAVE IT   SS   YRT 70
        YEAR 2000, THE   HARRISON, HARRY   OA
    TRANSFINITE CHOICE, THE   SS   NWS 66 08
        BEST SF STORIES FROM NEW WORLDS NO. 2, THE
                                 MOORCOCK, MICHAEL   AN
        CALTRAPS OF TIME, THE   MASSON, DAVID I.   AC
        SCIENCE FICTION HORIZONS NO. 1 BOARDMAN, TOM JR. AN
        SF: AUTHORS' CHOICE 3   HARRISON, HARRY   AN
    TRAVELER'S REST   SS   NWS 65 09
        CALTRAPS OF TIME, THE   MASSON, DAVID I.   AC
        TRAPS OF TIME, THE   MOORCOCK, MICHAEL   AN
        VOYAGERS IN TIME   SILVERBERG, ROBERT   AN
        WORLD'S BEST SCIENCE FICTION: 1966 WOLLHEIM & CARR AN
        11TH ANNUAL OF THE YEAR'S BEST S-F, THE
                                 MERRIL, JUDITH   AN
    TWO-TIMER, A   NV   NWS 66 02
        BEST SF STORIES FROM NEW WORLDS NO. 1, THE
                                 MOORCOCK, MICHAEL   AN
        CALTRAPS OF TIME, THE   MASSON, DAVID I.   AC

MATEYKO, G. M.
    ON HANDLING THE DATA   SS C ASF 59 09
        BEST SF 5   CRISPIN, EDMUND   AN

```
MATHESON, RICHARD                                                    MATHESON, RICHARD

MATHESON, RICHARD    ALSO AS    LOGAN SWANSON
BORN OF MAN AND WOMAN                            AC H CHB 54 03
    DERIVATIVE COLLECTION "THIRD FROM THE SUN"
    SHOCK II                                     AC     DEL 64 10
    SHOCK III                                    AC     DEL 66 03
    SHOCK WAVES                                  AC     DEL 70 10
    SHOCK!                                       AC     DEL 61 06
    SHORES OF SPACE, THE                         AC     BAN 57 02
    THIRD FROM THE SUN                           AC     BAN 55 02
        SELECTIONS FROM "BORN OF MAN AND WOMAN"
ADVANCE NOTICE                                   SS     ROG 59
    SHOCK WAVES                 MATHESON, RICHARD      AC
AFTERWORD                                        MS
    MAGIC MAN AND OTHER SCIENCE-FANTASY STORIES
                                BEAUMONT, CHARLES      AC
ASLEEP IN ARMAGEDDON                             NV     IFS 54 08
                                SISSONS, MICHAEL       AN
    SHORES OF SPACE, THE        MATHESON, RICHARD      AC
BIG SUPRISE (WHAT WAS IN THE BOX)                SS     EQM 59 04
    SHOCK II                    MATHESON, RICHARD      AC
BLOOD SON (DRINK MY RED BLOOD)                   SS     IMG 51 04
    SHORES OF SPACE, THE        MATHESON, RICHARD      AC
BORN OF MAN AND WOMAN                            SS     FSF 50 SU
    BEST SCIENCE-FICTION STORIES: 1951, THE
                                BLEILER & DIKTY        AN
    BORN OF MAN AND WOMAN       MATHESON, RICHARD      AC
    CHILDREN OF WONDER          TENN, WILLIAM          AN
    MINDWORM, THE               ANONYMOUS              AN
    SCIENCE FICTION HALL OF FAME VOLUME 1 SILVERBERG, ROBERT AN
    THIRD FROM THE SUN          MATHESON, RICHARD      AC
BROTHER TO THE MACHINE                           SS     IFS 52 11
    INVASION OF THE ROBOTS      ELWOOD, ROGER          AN
    SHOCK II                    MATHESON, RICHARD      AC
BUTTON, BUTTON                                   SS     PBY 70 06
    TRANSIT OF EARTH            PLAYBOY, EDITORS OF    AN
BY APPOINTMENT ONLY                              SS     PBY 70 04
    WEIRD SHOW                  PLAYBOY, EDITORS OF    AN
CHILDREN OF NOAH, THE                            SS     57
    SHOCK!                      MATHESON, RICHARD      AC
CLOTHS MAKE THE MAN                              SS     WBY 51 02
    SHORES OF SPACE, THE        MATHESON, RICHARD      AC
COME FYGURES, COME SHADOWES                      NV     NEW 70 AC
    SHOCK WAVES                 MATHESON, RICHARD      AC
CONQUEROR, THE                                   SS     54
    SHOCK WAVES                 MATHESON, RICHARD      AC
CREEPING TERROR, THE (A TOUCH OF GRAPEFRUIT)     SS     STR 59 05
    SHOCK!                      MATHESON, RICHARD      AC
CRESCENDO (SEE SHOCK WAVE)                        TC
CRICKETS                                         SS     SHK 60 05
    SHOCK II                    MATHESON, RICHARD      AC
CURIOUS CHILD, THE                               SS     FAN 54 06
    SHORES OF SPACE, THE        MATHESON, RICHARD      AC
DANCE OF THE DEAD                                SS     STR 54 03
    SHOCK!                      MATHESON, RICHARD      AC
    STAR OF STARS               POHL, FREDERIK         AN
    STAR SCIENCE FICTION STORIES NO. 3 POHL, FREDERIK  OA
DAY OF RECKONING                                 SS     MCB 60
    SHOCK WAVES                 MATHESON, RICHARD      AC
DEADLINE                                         SS     ROG 59
    SHOCK II                    MATHESON, RICHARD      AC
DEAR DIARY                                       SS     NEW 54 AN
    BORN OF MAN AND WOMAN       MATHESON, RICHARD      AC
    THIRD FROM THE SUN          MATHESON, RICHARD      AC
DEATH SHIP                                       NV     FSM 53 03
    SHOCK!                      MATHESON, RICHARD      AC
DESCENT                                          SS     IFS 54 05
    SHOCK II                    MATHESON, RICHARD      AC
DEUS EX MACHINA                                  SS     GAM 63 02
    SHOCK WAVES                 MATHESON, RICHARD      AC
DISAPPEARING ACT                                 SS     FSF 53 03
    BORN OF MAN AND WOMAN       MATHESON, RICHARD      AC
    THIRD FROM THE SUN          MATHESON, RICHARD      AC
DISINHERITORS, THE                               SS     FSM 53 01
    SHOCK III                   MATHESON, RICHARD      AC
DISTRIBUTOR, THE                                 SS     PBY 58 03
    SHOCK!                      MATHESON, RICHARD      AC
DOLL THAT DOES EVERYTHING, THE                   SS     FUN 54 12
    MORE LITTLE MONSTERS        ELWOOD & GHIDALIA      AN
    SHORES OF SPACE, THE        MATHESON, RICHARD      AC
DRESS OF WHITE SILK                              SS     FSF 51 10
    BEST FROM FANTASY AND SCIENCE FICTION BOUCHER & MCCOMAS AN
    BORN OF MAN AND WOMAN       MATHESON, RICHARD      AC
    THIRD FROM THE SUN          MATHESON, RICHARD      AC
DRINK MY RED BLOOD (SEE BLOOD SON)               TC
DRINK OF WATER, A                                SS     SGN 67
    SHOCK WAVES                 MATHESON, RICHARD      AC
DYING ROOM ONLY                                  SS     53
    SHOCK WAVES                 MATHESON, RICHARD      AC
EDGE, THE                                        SS     FSF 58 08
    SHOCK!                      MATHESON, RICHARD      AC
F--- (THE FOODLEGGER)                            SS     TWS 52 04
    BORN OF MAN AND WOMAN       MATHESON, RICHARD      AC
    THIRD FROM THE SUN          MATHESON, RICHARD      AC
FACES, THE (SEE GRAVEYARD SHIFT)                 TC
FINGER PRINTS                                    SS     NEW 62 AN
    FIEND IN YOU, THE           BEAUMONT, CHARLES      AN
    SHOCK WAVES                 MATHESON, RICHARD      AC
FINISHING TOUCHES, THE                           SS     NEW 70 AC
    SHOCK WAVES                 MATHESON, RICHARD      AC
FIRST ANNIVERSARY                                SS     PBY 60 07
    PLAYBOY BOOK OF HORROR AND THE SUPERNATURAL, THE
                                PLAYBOY, EDITORS OF    AN
    SHOCK III                   MATHESON, RICHARD      AC
FLOURISH OF STRUMPETS, A                         SS     PBY 56 11
    SHOCK II                    MATHESON, RICHARD      AC

MATHESON, RICHARD    (CONTINUED)
FOODLEGGER, THE (SEE F---)                       TC
FROM SHADOWED PLACES                             NV     FSF 60 10
    SHOCK II                    MATHESON, RICHARD      AC
FULL CIRCLE                                      SS     FUN 53 08
    BORN OF MAN AND WOMAN       MATHESON, RICHARD      AC
    SHOCK III                   MATHESON, RICHARD      AC
FUNERAL, THE                                     SS     FSF 55 04
    SHORES OF SPACE, THE        MATHESON, RICHARD      AC
GIRL OF MY DREAMS                                SS     FSF 63 10
    SHOCK III                   MATHESON, RICHARD      AC
GRAVEYARD SHIFT (THE FACES)                      SS     MCB 60
    SHOCK II                    MATHESON, RICHARD      AC
HOLIDAY MAN, THE                                 SS     FSF 57 07
    SHOCK!                      MATHESON, RICHARD      AC
    TWENTY YEARS OF FANTASY & SCIENCE FICTION
                                FERMAN & MILLS         AN
JAZZ MACHINE, THE                                PM     FSF 63 02
    SHOCK III                   MATHESON, RICHARD      AC
    9TH ANNUAL OF THE YEAR'S BEST S-F, THE MERRIL, JUDITH AN
LAST DAY, THE                                    SS     AMZ 53 05
    BEST SCIENCE-FICTION STORIES: 1954, THE
                                BLEILER & DIKTY        AN
    DECADE THE 1950S            ALDISS & HARRISON      AN
    HISTORY OF THE SCIENCE FICTION MAGAZINE, THE  PART 3 1946-1955
                                ASHLEY, MICHAEL        AN
    SHORES OF SPACE, THE        MATHESON, RICHARD      AC
LAZARUS II                                       SS     FSM 53 07
    SHOCK II                    MATHESON, RICHARD      AC
LEGION OF PLOTTERS                               SS     53
    SHOCK!                      MATHESON, RICHARD      AC
LEMMINGS                                         SS     FSF 58 01
    SHOCK!                      MATHESON, RICHARD      AC
LIKENESS OF JULIE, THE (AS LOGAN SWANSON)        SS     NEW 62 AN
    SHOCK II                    MATHESON, RICHARD      AC
LITTLE GIRL LOST                                 SS     AMZ 53 11
    SHORES OF SPACE, THE        MATHESON, RICHARD      AC
LONG DISTANCE CALL (SORRY, RIGHT NUMBER)         SS     BEY 53 11
    SHOCK!                      MATHESON, RICHARD      AC
LOVER, WHEN YOU'RE NEAR ME                       NV     GAL 52 05
    BEST SCIENCE-FICTION STORIES: 1953, THE
                                BLEILER & DIKTY        AN
    BORN OF MAN AND WOMAN       MATHESON, RICHARD      AC
    SECOND GALAXY READER OF SCIENCE FICTION
                                GOLD, H. L.            AN
    THIRD FROM THE SUN          MATHESON, RICHARD      AC
MAD HOUSE                                        NV     FAN 53 02
    BORN OF MAN AND WOMAN       MATHESON, RICHARD      AC
    THIRD FROM THE SUN          MATHESON, RICHARD      AC
MAN WHO MADE THE WORLD, THE                      SS     IMG 54 02
    SHOCK II                    MATHESON, RICHARD      AC
MANTAGE                                          NV     NEW 59 AN
    SCIENCE FICTION SHOWCASE    KORNBLUTH, MARY        AN
    SHOCK!                      MATHESON, RICHARD      AC
MISS STARDUST                                    SS     STS 55 SP
    SHOCK III                   MATHESON, RICHARD      AC
MOTHER BY PROTEST (ALSO AS TRESPASS)             NV     FAN 53 10
    DEVIL'S GENERATION, THE     GHIDALIA, VIC          AN
MUTE                                             NV     NEW 62 AN
    FIEND IN YOU, THE           BEAUMONT, CHARLES      AN
    SHOCK II                    MATHESON, RICHARD      AC
NIGHTMARE AT 20,000 FEET                         SS     NEW 62 AN
    ALONE BY NIGHT              CONGDON, MICHAEL&DON AN
    SHOCK III                   MATHESON, RICHARD      AC
NO SUCH THING AS A VAMPIRE                       SS     PBY 59 10
    PLAYBOY BOOK OF HORROR AND THE SUPERNATURAL, THE
                                PLAYBOY, EDITORS OF    AN
    SHOCK II                    MATHESON, RICHARD      AC
ONE FOR THE BOOKS                                NV     GAL 55 09
    SHOCK!                      MATHESON, RICHARD      AC
    UNTRAVELLED WORLDS          BARTER & WILSON        AN
    WORLD THAT COULDN'T BE AND 8 OTHER SF NOVELETS
                                GOLD, H. L.            AN
PATTERN FOR SURVIVAL                             SS     FSF 55 05
    BEST FROM FANTASY AND SCIENCE FICTION: 5
                                BOUCHER, ANTHONY       AN
    SHORES OF SPACE, THE        MATHESON, RICHARD      AC
PREY                                             SS     PBY 69 04
    SHOCK WAVES                 MATHESON, RICHARD      AC
    YEAR'S BEST HORROR STORIES, THE DAVIS, RICHARD     AN
RETURN                                           SS     TWS 51 10
    BORN OF MAN AND WOMAN       MATHESON, RICHARD      AC
    SHOCK III                   MATHESON, RICHARD      AC
SHIPSHAPE HOME                                   SS     GAL 52 07
    BORN OF MAN AND WOMAN       MATHESON, RICHARD      AC
    MORE TERROR IN THE MODERN VEIN WOLLHEIM, DONALD A. AN
    OMNIBUS OF SCIENCE FICTION  CONKLIN, GROFF         AN
    OTHERS, THE                 CARR, TERRY            AN
    STRANGE TRAVELS IN SCIENCE FICTION CONKLIN, GROFF  AN
    *TERROR IN THE MODERN VEIN  WOLLHEIM, DONALD A.    AN
    THIRD FROM THE SUN          MATHESON, RICHARD      AC
SHOCK WAVE (CRESCENDO)                           SS     GAM 63 01
    SHOCK III                   MATHESON, RICHARD      AC
SLAUGHTER HOUSE                                  NV     WRT 53 07
    SHOCK III                   MATHESON, RICHARD      AC
SORRY, RIGHT NUMBER (ALSO AS LONG DISTANCE CALL) SS  BEY 53 11
    ZACHERLEY'S MIDNIGHT SNACKS ZACHERLEY             AN
SPLENDID SOURCE, THE                             SS     PBY 56 05
    LAST TRAIN TO LIMBO         PLAYBOY, EDITORS OF    AN
    SHOCK!                      MATHESON, RICHARD      AC
SRL AD                                           SS     FSF 52 04
    BORN OF MAN AND WOMAN       MATHESON, RICHARD      AC
    *SCIENCE-FICTION CARNIVAL   BROWN, F. & REYNOLDS   AN
    THIRD FROM THE SUN          MATHESON, RICHARD      AC
STEEL                                            SS     FSF 56 05
    PSEUDO PEOPLE, THE          NOLAN, WILLIAM F.      AN
```

MATHESON, RICHARD

MERRIL, JUDITH

MATHESON, RICHARD   (CONTINUED)
  RUN TO STARLIGHT, SPORTS THROUGH SCIENCE FICTION
                              GREENBERG/OLANDER/&   AN
    SHORES OF SPACE, THE   MATHESON, RICHARD   AC
  TEST, THE   SS   FSF 54 11
    BEST FROM FANTASY AND SCIENCE FICTION: 4
                              BOUCHER, ANTHONY   AN
    FANTASY: THE LITERATURE OF THE MARVELOUS
                              KELLEY, LEO P.   AN
    IF THIS GOES ON   NUETZEL, CHARLES   AN
    SHORES OF SPACE, THE   MATHESON, RICHARD   AC
  THERESE   SS   68
    SHOCK WAVES   MATHESON, RICHARD   AC
  THING, THE   SS   MSS 51 05
    SHOCK WAVES   MATHESON, RICHARD   AC
  THIRD FROM THE SUN   SS   GAL 50 10
    BEYOND BELIEF   HURLEY, RICHARD J.   AN
    BORN OF MAN AND WOMAN   MATHESON, RICHARD   AC
    *GALAXY READER OF SCIENCE FICTION GOLD, H. L. AN
    THIRD FROM THE SUN   MATHESON, RICHARD   AC
  THROUGH CHANNELS   SS   FSF 51 04
    BORN OF MAN AND WOMAN   MATHESON, RICHARD   AC
    SCIENCE FICTION TERROR TALES CONKLIN, GROFF   AN
  'TIS THE SEASON TO BE JELLY SS   FSF 63 06
    SHOCK III   MATHESON, RICHARD   AC
  TO FIT THE CRIME   SS   FAN 52 12
    BORN OF MAN AND WOMAN   MATHESON, RICHARD   AC
    THIRD FROM THE SUN   MATHESON, RICHARD   AC
  TOUCH OF GRAPEFRUIT, A (ALSO AS THE CREEPING TERROR)
                              SS   STR 59 05
    STAR SCIENCE FICTION STORIES NO. 5 POHL, FREDERIK OA
  TRAVELER, THE   SS   FSF 62 02
    BORN OF MAN AND WOMAN   MATHESON, RICHARD   AC
    THIRD FROM THE SUN   MATHESON, RICHARD   AC
  TRESPASS (MOTHER BY PROTEST) NV   FAN 53 10
    SHORES OF SPACE, THE   MATHESON, RICHARD   AC
  VISIT TO SANTA CLAUS, A   SS   NEW 70 AC
    SHOCK WAVES   MATHESON, RICHARD   AC
  WAKER DREAMS, THE (ALSO AS WHEN THE WAKER SLEEPS) SS GAL 50 12
    *GALAXY READER OF SCIENCE FICTION GOLD, H. L. AN
  WEDDING, THE   SS   BEY 53 07
    BORN OF MAN AND WOMAN   MATHESON, RICHARD   AC
    THIRD FROM THE SUN   MATHESON, RICHARD   AC
  WET STRAW   SS   WRT 53 01
    SHOCK WAVES   MATHESON, RICHARD   AC
  WHAT WAS IN THE BOX (SEE BIG SUPRISE) TC
  WHEN DAY IS DUN   SS   FUN 54 05
    SHORES OF SPACE, THE   MATHESON, RICHARD   AC
  WHEN THE WAKER SLEEPS (THE WAKER DREAMS) SS GAL 50 12
    SHOCK III   MATHESON, RICHARD   AC
  WITCH WAR   SS   STS 51 07
    BEST SCIENCE-FICTION STORIES: 1952, THE
                              BLEILER & DIKTY   AN
    BORN OF MAN AND WOMAN   MATHESON, RICHARD   AC
    SHOCK III   MATHESON, RICHARD   AC
    THEMES IN SCIENCE FICTION KELLEY, LEO P.   AN

MATSCHAT, CECILE   SEE ALSO   CO-EDITOR LESTER DEL REY

MAUGHAM, W. SOMERSET
  LORD MOUNTDRAGO (DOCTOR AND PATIENT) SS   ITM 39 02
    MOONLIGHT TRAVELER, THE   STERN, PHILIP VAN D. AN
    PERCHANCE TO DREAM   KNIGHT, DAMON   AN
  MAGICIAN, THE   EX   HEI 08
    GHOULS, THE   HAINING, PETER   AN
  TAIPAN, THE   SS   PRS 22 10
    TRAVELERS IN TIME   STERN, PHILIP VAN D. AN

MAUROIS, ANDRE   PSEUD. FOR EMILE HERZOG
WEIGHER OF SOULS AND THE EARTH DWELLERS, THE AC H MAC 63
  EARTH DWELLERS, THE   NV   63
    WEIGHER OF SOULS AND THE EARTH DWELLERS, THE
                              MAUROIS, ANDRE   AC
  9TH ANNUAL OF THE YEAR'S BEST S-F, THE MERRIL, JUDITH AN
  INTRODUCTION   IN
    WEIGHER OF SOULS AND THE EARTH DWELLERS, THE
                              MAUROIS, ANDRE   AC
  WAR AGAINST THE MOON, THE (1928) SS   FSF 50 SU
    OMNIBUS OF SCIENCE FICTION CONKLIN, GROFF   OA
  WEIGHER OF SOULS, THE   NV   FFM 50 10
    FUTURES UNLIMITED   NORTON, ALDEN H.   AN
    WEIGHER OF SOULS AND THE EARTH DWELLERS, THE
                              MAUROIS, ANDRE   AC

MAXIMOV, HERMAN
  ULTIMATE THRESHOLD, THE   SS   65
    ULTIMATE THRESHOLD, THE   GINSBURG, MIRRA   AN

MAY, JULIAN C.   PSEUD. FOR JULIAN CHAIN MAY DIKTY
  DUNE ROLLER   NV   ASF 51 12
    ALPHA 7   SILVERBERG, ROBERT   AN
    *IMAGINATION UNLIMITED   BLEILER & DIKTY   AN
    *STORIES FOR TOMORROW   SLOANE, WILLIAM   AN
  STAR OF WONDER   SS   TWS 53 02
    EVERY BOY'S BOOK OF OUTER SPACE STORIES
                              DIKTY, T. E.   AN

MAYAN, EARL E.
  ILLUSTRATIONS   IL
    *ROD SERLING'S THE TWILIGHT ZONE SERLING, ROD OC

MAYNE, ISOBEL
  PLACE OF THE TIGRESS, THE   SS
    AD 2500   WILSON, ANGUS   AN

MEADE, L. T.
  WHERE THE AIR QUIVERED   SS C SND 98 12
    SCIENCE FICTION BY GASLIGHT MOSKOWITZ, SAM   AN

MEADLEY, ROBERT
  AMONG OTHER THINGS   SS   NWQ 73 09
    NEW WORLDS NO. 5   MOORCOCK & PLATT   OA
  CONVERSATIONS AT MA MAIA METRON SS   NWB 75 08
    NEW WORLDS EIGHT   BAILEY, HILARY   OA
  LOVE AT LOST SIGHT   SS   NWB 75 08
    NEW WORLDS EIGHT   BAILEY, HILARY   OA

MEADOWS, DENNIS L.
  FROM "THE LIMITS TO GROWTH"   AR C   72
    LOOKING AHEAD   ALLEN, D. & L.   AN

MEADOWS, DONELLA H.
  FROM "THE LIMITS TO GROWTH"   AR C   72
    LOOKING AHEAD   ALLEN, D. & L.   AN

MEADOWS, PATRICK
  COUNTERCOMMANDMENT   SS   ASF 65 12
    ANALOG 5   CAMPBELL, JOHN W. JR AN

MEECH, SHIRLEY
  SONNET FROM THE VULCAN: OMICRON CETI THREE   PM
    STAR TREK: THE NEW VOYAGES MARSHAK, S&CULBREATH OA

MEEK, CAPTAIN S. P.
  AWLO OF ULM   NV   AMZ 31 09
    BEFORE THE GOLDEN AGE   ASIMOV, ISAAC   AN
  SUBMICROSCOPIC   SS   AMZ 31 08
    BEFORE THE GOLDEN AGE   ASIMOV, ISAAC   AN

MELCHIOR, IB
  RACER, THE   SS   56
    IF THIS GOES ON   NUETZEL, CHARLES   AN

MELVILLE, HERMAN
  BELL-TOWER, THE (1855)   SS   PTM 55
    FUTURE PERFECT   FRANKLIN, H. BRUCE   AN
  TARTARUS OF MAIDS, THE   SS
    IN DREAMS AWAKE   FIEDLER, LESLIE A.   AN
    SPECULATIONS   SANDERS, THOMAS E.   AN

MENCKEN, J. B.
  APOTHEM (1715)   MS
    MATHEMATICAL MAGPIE, THE FADIMAN, CLIFTON   AN

MENDELSON, DREW
  MUSEUM PIECE   SS   NDM 75 05
    NEW DIMENSIONS 5   SILVERBERG, ROBERT   OA

MENVILLE, DOUGLAS AND R. REGINALD
  ANCESTRAL VOICES   AN H ANO 74

MERCER, JOHNNY
  SQUARE OF THE HYPOTENUSE, THE (LYRICS) SG C 58
    MATHEMATICAL MAGPIE, THE FADIMAN, CLIFTON   AN

MERCIER, LOUIS S.
  EARLY TIME-TRAVELER, AN (FROM "JOURNAL OF THE YEAR 2440",1795)
                              EX
    SCIENCE IN FICTION   BAYLISS, A.E. & J.C. AN

MEREDITH, RICHARD C.
  EARTHCOMING   NV   FIN 70
    FUTURE IS NOW, THE   NOLAN, WILLIAM F.   OA

MERLISS, R. R.
  STUTTERER, THE   NV   ASF 55 04
    SF: THE YEAR'S GREATEST SCIENCE FICTION AND FANTASY
                              MERRIL, JUDITH   AN

MERLYN, ARTHUR   PSEUD. FOR JAMES BLISH

MERRIL, JUDITH
  BEST OF JUDITH MERRIL, THE   AC WBK 76 01
  BEST OF SCIENCE FICTION 2, THE   AN MFL 64
    SEE "THE 7TH ANNUAL OF THE YEAR'S BEST S-F, THE"
  BEST OF SCIENCE FICTION 4, THE   AN MFL 65
    SEE "THE 8TH ANNUAL OF THE YEAR'S BEST S-F, THE"
  BEST OF SCIENCE FICTION 5, THE   AN MFL 66
    SEE "THE 5TH ANNUAL OF THE YEAR'S BEST S-F, THE"
  BEST OF SCIENCE FICTION, THE   AN MFL 63
    SEE "THE 6TH ANNUAL OF THE YEAR'S BEST S-F, THE"
  BEYOND HUMAN KEN   AN H RDM 52
  BEYOND HUMAN KEN (BRITISH)   AN H GRY 53
  BEYOND HUMAN KEN (SELECTIONS FROM)   AN PNN 54 06
  BEYOND THE BARRIERS OF SPACE AND TIME   AN H RDM 54
  DAUGHTERS OF EARTH   AC H DBL 68
  ENGLAND SWINGS SF   AN H DBL 68
    ENGLISH DERIVATIVE ANTHOLOGY "THE SPACE-TIME JOURNAL"
  GALAXY OF GHOULS   AN LIO 55 05
    ALSO AS "OFF THE BEATEN ORBIT"
  HUMAN?   AN LIO 54 04
  OFF THE BEATEN ORBIT   AN PYR 59
    SEE "GALAXY OF GHOULS"
  OUT OF BOUNDS   AC PYR 60 04
  SF: THE BEST OF THE BEST   AN H DCT 67
  SF: THE YEAR'S GREATEST SCIENCE FICTION AND FANTASY
                                          AN H GNM 56
  SF: THE YEAR'S GREATEST SCIENCE-FICTION AND FANTASY, FOURTH
    ANNUAL VOLUME   AN DEL 59 06
    SEE "SF:59"

MERRIL, JUDITH   MERWIN, SAM JR.

MERRIL, JUDITH   (CONTINUED)
SF: THE YEAR'S GREATEST SCIENCE-FICTION AND FANTASY, SECOND
  ANNUAL VOLUME   AN   DEL 57 06
    SEE "SF:57"
SF: THE YEAR'S GREATEST SCIENCE-FICTION AND FANTASY, THIRD
  ANNUAL VOLUME   AN   DEL 58 07
    SEE "SF:58"
SF:57, THE YEAR'S GREATEST SCIENCE FICTION AND FANTASY
                                        AN H GNM 57
SF:58, THE YEAR'S GREATEST SCIENCE FICTION AND FANTASY
                                        AN H GNM 58
SF:59, THE YEAR'S GREATEST SCIENCE FICTION AND FANTASY
                                        AN H GNM 59
SF12   AN H DCT 68
SHOT IN THE DARK   AN   BAN 50
SPACE-TIME JOURNAL, THE   AN   PTH 72
21 STORIES FROM "ENGLAND SWINGS SF"
SURVIVAL SHIP AND OTHER STORIES   AC   KAK 74
10TH ANNUAL OF THE YEAR'S BEST S-F, THE AN H DCT 65
11TH ANNUAL OF THE YEAR'S BEST S-F, THE AN H DCT 66
5TH ANNUAL OF THE YEAR'S BEST S-F, THE AN H SAS 60
  IN ENGLAND AS "THE BEST OF SCIENCE FICTION 5"
6TH ANNUAL OF THE YEAR'S BEST S-F, THE AN H SAS 61
  IN ENGLAND AS "THE BEST OF SCIENCE FICTION"
7TH ANNUAL OF THE YEAR'S BEST S-F, THE AN H SAS 62
  IN ENGLAND AS "THE BEST OF SCIENCE FICTION 2"
8TH ANNUAL OF THE YEAR'S BEST S-F, THE AN H SAS 63
  IN ENGLAND AS "THE BEST OF SCIENCE FICTION 4"
9TH ANNUAL OF THE YEAR'S BEST S-F, THE AN H SAS 64
AUCTION PIT   PM   46
  BEST OF JUDITH MERRIL, THE   MERRIL, JUDITH   AC
  SURVIVAL SHIP AND OTHER STORIES MERRIL, JUDITH   AC
BARRIER OF DREAD   SS   FUT 50 07
  JOURNEY TO INFINITY   GREENBERG , MARTIN AN
BIG MAN WITH THE GIRLS, A   SS C FUT 53 03
  ESCAPE TO EARTH   HOWARD, IVAN   AN
CONNECTION COMPLETED   SS   USF 54 SU
  OUT OF BOUNDS   MERRIL, JUDITH   AC
  SURVIVAL SHIP AND OTHER STORIES MERRIL, JUDITH   AC
DAUGHTERS OF EARTH   SN   52
  BEST OF JUDITH MERRIL, THE   MERRIL, JUDITH   AC
  DAUGHTERS OF EARTH   MERRIL, JUDITH   AC
  PETRIFIED PLANET, THE   CLARK, JOHN D.   OA
DEAD CENTER   NV   FSF 54 11
  BEST OF JUDITH MERRIL, THE   MERRIL, JUDITH   AC
  OUT OF BOUNDS   MERRIL, JUDITH   AC
  TREASURY OF GREAT SCIENCE FICTION, A VOL.2
                                   BOUCHER, ANTHONY   AN
DEATH CANNOT WITHER   NV   FSF 59 02
  OUT OF BOUNDS   MERRIL, JUDITH   AC
DEATH IS THE PENALTY   SS   ASF 49 01
  BEYOND THE END OF TIME   POHL, FREDERIK   AN
  SURVIVAL SHIP AND OTHER STORIES MERRIL, JUDITH   AC
DEEP DOWN DRAGON, THE   SS   GAL 61 08
  SEVENTH GALAXY READER, THE   POHL, FREDERIK   AN
  SURVIVAL SHIP AND OTHER STORIES MERRIL, JUDITH   AC
  13 ABOVE THE NIGHT   CONKLIN, GROFF   AN
EDITOR'S PREFACE   IN
  BEYOND THE BARRIERS OF SPACE AND TIME MERRIL, JUDITH AN
EXILE FROM SPACE   NV   FUN 56 11
  FANTASTIC UNIVERSE OMNIBUS, THE SANTESSON, HANS S. AN
  FLYING SAUCERS IN FACT AND FICTION SANTESSON, HANS S. AN
  SURVIVAL SHIP AND OTHER STORIES MERRIL, JUDITH   AC
FISH OUT OF WATER, MAN BESIDE HIMSELF   IN
  SF12   MERRIL, JUDITH   AN
FRITZ LEIBER   AR   FSF 69 07
  BEST FROM FANTASY AND SCIENCE FICTION, 25TH ANNIV.
                                   FERMAN, EDWARD L.   AN
HOMECALLING   NV   SFS 56 11
  DAUGHTERS OF EARTH   MERRIL, JUDITH   AC
HOW NEAR IS THE MOON?   AR   NEW 58 AN
  SF:58, THE YEAR'S GREATEST SCIENCE FICTION AND FANTASY
                                   MERRIL, JUDITH   AN
IN THE LAND OF UNBLIND   SS   FSP 74 10
  BEST OF JUDITH MERRIL, THE   MERRIL, JUDITH   AC
INTRODUCTION   IN
  ENGLAND SWINGS SF   MERRIL, JUDITH   AN
  ONCE AND FUTURE TALES FROM THE MAGAZINE OF FANTASY AND
    SCIENCE FICTION   FERMAN, EDWARD L.   AN
  PATH INTO THE UNKNOWN   ANONYMOUS   AN
  SF: THE BEST OF THE BEST   MERRIL, JUDITH   AN
  SF:58, THE YEAR'S GREATEST SCIENCE FICTION AND FANTASY
                                   MERRIL, JUDITH   AN
  SF:59, THE YEAR'S GREATEST SCIENCE FICTION AND FANTASY
                                   MERRIL, JUDITH   AN
  11TH ANNUAL OF THE YEAR'S BEST S-F, THE
                                   MERRIL, JUDITH   AN
  5TH ANNUAL OF THE YEAR'S BEST S-F, THE MERRIL, JUDITH AN
  6TH ANNUAL OF THE YEAR'S BEST S-F, THE MERRIL, JUDITH AN
LADY WAS A TRAMP, THE   SS   VSF 57 03
  BEST OF JUDITH MERRIL, THE   MERRIL, JUDITH   AC
  OUT OF BOUNDS   MERRIL, JUDITH   AC
  SURVIVAL SHIP AND OTHER STORIES MERRIL, JUDITH   AC
  VENUS FACTOR, THE   GHIDALIA, V.& ELWOOD AN
LONELY, THE   SS   WOT 63 10
  BEST OF JUDITH MERRIL, THE   MERRIL, JUDITH   AC
  SURVIVAL SHIP AND OTHER STORIES MERRIL, JUDITH   AC
PEEPING TOM   NV   STS 54 SP
  OUT OF BOUNDS   MERRIL, JUDITH   AC
  SURVIVAL SHIP AND OTHER STORIES MERRIL, JUDITH   AC
PREFACE   IN
  *BEYOND HUMAN KEN   MERRIL, JUDITH   AN
  SF: THE YEAR'S GREATEST SCIENCE FICTION AND FANTASY
                                   MERRIL, JUDITH   AN
PROJECT NURSEMAID   SN   FSF 55 10
  DAUGHTERS OF EARTH   MERRIL, JUDITH   AC

MERRIL, JUDITH   (CONTINUED)
SIX GREAT SHORT SCIENCE FICTION NOVELS CONKLIN, GROFF   AN
PROLOGUE   IN
  SURVIVAL SHIP AND OTHER STORIES MERRIL, JUDITH   AC
RAIN CHECK   NV   SFA 54 06
  CRIME PREVENTION IN THE 30TH CENTURY SANTESSON, HANS S. AN
ROCKETS TO WHERE?   AR   NEW 59 AN
  SF:59, THE YEAR'S GREATEST SCIENCE FICTION AND FANTASY
                                   MERRIL, JUDITH   AN
SHRINE OF TEMPTATION, THE   SS   FAN 62 04
  BEST OF JUDITH MERRIL, THE   MERRIL, JUDITH   AC
  DEVIL HIS DUE, THE   HILL, DOUGLAS   AN
  GODS FOR TOMORROW   SANTESSON, HANS S. AN
  SURVIVAL SHIP AND OTHER STORIES MERRIL, JUDITH   AC
SO PROUDLY WE HAIL   SS   STR 53 01
  STAR SCIENCE FICTION STORIES   POHL, FREDERIK   OA
  SURVIVAL SHIP AND OTHER STORIES MERRIL, JUDITH   AC
STORMY WEATHER   SS   STS 54 SU
  BEST OF JUDITH MERRIL, THE   MERRIL, JUDITH   AC
SUMMATION   MS
  10TH ANNUAL OF THE YEAR'S BEST S-F, THE
                                   MERRIL, JUDITH   AN
  11TH ANNUAL OF THE YEAR'S BEST S-F, THE
                                   MERRIL, JUDITH   AN
SUMMATION: S-F, 1961   MS
  7TH ANNUAL OF THE YEAR'S BEST S-F, THE MERRIL, JUDITH AN
SUMMATION: S-F, 1962   MS
  8TH ANNUAL OF THE YEAR'S BEST S-F, THE MERRIL, JUDITH AN
SUMMATION: S-F, 1963   MS
  9TH ANNUAL OF THE YEAR'S BEST S-F, THE MERRIL, JUDITH AN
SURVIVAL SHIP   SS   WBY 51 01
  ANTHROPOLOGY THROUGH SCIENCE FICTION MASON, C/GREENBERG/& AN
  SURVIVAL SHIP AND OTHER STORIES MERRIL, JUDITH   AN
  TOMORROW, THE STARS   HEINLEIN, ROBERT A. AN
  TRANSFORMATIONS   ROSELLE, DANIEL   AN
  YOU AND SCIENCE FICTION   HOLLISTER, BERNARD C AN
THAT ONLY A MOTHER   SS   ASF 48 06
  BEST OF JUDITH MERRIL, THE   MERRIL, JUDITH   AC
  CHILDREN OF WONDER   TENN, WILLIAM   AN
  FIRST FLIGHT   KNIGHT, DAMON   AN
  INTRODUCTORY PSYCHOLOGY THROUGH SCIENCE FICTION
                                   KATZ/WARRICK/&   AN
  OUT OF BOUNDS   MERRIL, JUDITH   AC
  SCIENCE FICTION HALL OF FAME VOLUME 1 SILVERBERG, ROBERT AN
  SPECULATIONS   SANDERS, THOMAS E. AN
  TRANSFORMATIONS   ROSELLE, DANIEL   AN
  WOMEN OF WONDER   SARGENT, PAMELA   AN
  WORLD OF WONDER   PRATT, FLETCHER   AN
THEODORE STURGEON   AR   FSF 62 09
  BEST FROM FANTASY AND SCIENCE FICTION, 25TH ANNIV.
                                   FERMAN, EDWARD L.   AN
WHOEVER YOU ARE   NV   STS 52 12
  BEST OF JUDITH MERRIL, THE   MERRIL, JUDITH   AC
  OUT OF BOUNDS   MERRIL, JUDITH   AC
  SURVIVAL SHIP AND OTHER STORIES MERRIL, JUDITH   AC
WISH UPON A STAR   SS   FSF 58 12
  BEST OF JUDITH MERRIL, THE   MERRIL, JUDITH   AC
  SURVIVAL SHIP AND OTHER STORIES MERRIL, JUDITH   AC
YEAR IN S-F, THE   MS
  6TH ANNUAL OF THE YEAR'S BEST S-F, THE MERRIL, JUDITH AN
YEAR'S S-F, THE, SUMMATION AND HONORABLE MENTIONS MS
  SF: THE YEAR'S GREATEST SCIENCE FICTION AND FANTASY
                                   MERRIL, JUDITH   AN
  SF:57, THE YEAR'S GREATEST SCIENCE FICTION AND FANTASY
                                   MERRIL, JUDITH   AN
  SF:58, THE YEAR'S GREATEST SCIENCE FICTION AND FANTASY
                                   MERRIL, JUDITH   AN
  SF:59, THE YEAR'S GREATEST SCIENCE FICTION AND FANTASY
                                   MERRIL, JUDITH   AN
  5TH ANNUAL OF THE YEAR'S BEST S-F, THE MERRIL, JUDITH AN

MERRITT, A.
FOX WOMAN & OTHER STORIES, THE   AC   AVN 49
DRONE, THE   SS   FMG 34 09
  FOX WOMAN & OTHER STORIES, THE   MERRITT, A.   AC
FOX WOMAN, THE   NV   46
  FOX WOMAN & OTHER STORIES, THE   MERRITT, A.   AC
LAST POET AND THE ROBOTS, THE   SS   FMG 34 04
  FOX WOMAN & OTHER STORIES, THE   MERRITT, A.   AC
MOON POOL, THE   NA   ASW 18 06
  ANCIENT MYSTERIES READER, THE   HAINING, PETER   AN
  UNDER THE MOONS OF MARS   MOSKOWITZ, SAM   AN
PEOPLE OF THE PIT, THE   NV   ASM 18 01
  FANTASTIC PULPS, THE   HAINING, PETER   AN
  FOX WOMAN & OTHER STORIES, THE   MERRITT, A.   AC
  MASTERPIECES OF SCIENCE FICTION MOSKOWITZ, SAM   AN
THREE LINES OF OLD FRENCH   SS   ASW 19 08
  ESCALES DANS L'INFINI   GALLET, GEORGES H. AN
  FUTURES UNLIMITED   NORTON, ALDEN H.   AN
THROUGH THE DRAGON GLASS   SS   ASW 17 11
  FOX WOMAN & OTHER STORIES, THE   MERRITT, A.   AC
WHEN OLD GODS WAKE   SS   AFR 48 07
  FOX WOMAN & OTHER STORIES, THE   MERRITT, A.   AC
WHITE ROAD, THE   SS   49
  FOX WOMAN & OTHER STORIES, THE   MERRITT, A.   AC
WOMEN OF THE WOOD, THE   SS   WRT 26 08
  FOX WOMAN & OTHER STORIES, THE   MERRITT, A.   AC
YHREE LINES OF OLD FRENCH   SS   ASW 19 08
  FOX WOMAN & OTHER STORIES, THE   MERRITT, A.   AC

MERWIN, SAM JR.
CARRIERS, THE   SS   TWS 49 02
  *MY BEST SCIENCE FICTION STORY   MARGULIES & FRIEND AN
EXILED FROM EARTH   SS   TWS 40 12
  ADVENTURES IN TOMORROW   CROSSEN, KENDELL F. AN

MERWIN, SAM JR.   MILLER, WALTER M. JR

MERWIN, SAM JR.   (CONTINUED)
  EXIT LINE   SS STS 50 09
    *POSSIBLE WORLDS OF SCIENCE FICTION   CONKLIN, GROFF   AN
  FINAL FIGURE, THE   NV DSF 54 01
    MASTERS OF SCIENCE FICTION   HOWARD, IVAN   AN
  JUDAS RAM   SS GAL 50 12
    *GALAXY READER OF SCIENCE FICTION   GOLD, H. L.   AN
  WHY I SELECTED THE CARRIERS   AI
    *MY BEST SCIENCE FICTION STORY   MARGULIES & FRIEND   AN

METCALF, JOHN
  NOT THERE   SS
    TRAVELLERS BY NIGHT   DERLETH, AUGUST   OA

METZGER, LOIS
  NO SPECIFIC TIME MENTIONED   SS
    CLARION SF   WILHELM, KATE   OA

MICHAEL, JOHN
  INHERITORS, THE   SS C FFS 42 10
    MORE TERROR IN THE MODERN VEIN   WOLLHEIM, DONALD A. AN
    *TERROR IN THE MODERN VEIN   WOLLHEIM, DONALD A. AN

MICHAUX, HENRI
  AND MORE CHANGES STILL   SS
    SF12   MERRIL, JUDITH   AN

MICHEL, JOHN   SEE PSEUD. HUGH RAYMOND

MIDDLETON, RICHARD
  SHEPHERD'S BOY   SS FSF 53 03
    BEST FROM FANTASY AND SCIENCE FICTION: 3
                                           BOUCHER & MCCOMAS   AN

MIESEL, SANDRA
  CHALLENGE AND RESPONSE   AR RVQ 70
    MANY WORLDS OF POUL ANDERSON, THE   ANDERSON, POUL   AC

MILES, HAMIS
  TRANSLATION   MS
    WEIGHER OF SOULS AND THE EARTH DWELLERS, THE
                                           MAUROIS, ANDRE   AC

MILES, JOSEPHINE
  SPEED   PM   60
    SCIENCE FACT/FICTION   FARRELL/GAGE/&   AN

MILLAR, JEFF
  TOTO, I HAVE A FEELING WE'RE NOT IN KANSAS ANYMORE
                                          SS ORB 75 17
    ORBIT 17   KNIGHT, DAMON   OA

MILLAY, EDNA ST. VINCENT
  EUCLID ALONE HAS LOOKED ON BEAUTY BARE PM   24
    FANTASIA MATHEMATICA   FADIMAN, CLIFTON   AN

MILLE, PIERRE
  AFTER THREE HUNDRED YEARS   SS   22
    13 FRENCH SCIENCE-FICTION STORIES   KNIGHT, DAMON   AN

MILLER, CHRIS
  PIPE DREAM   SS NLP 72 06
    STRANGE ECSTASIES   PARRY, MICHEL   AN

MILLER, JESSIE
  PHOENIX HOUSE   SS ORB 75 16
    ORBIT 16   KNIGHT, DAMON   OA
  PIGEON CITY   NV ASF 72 11
    SOCIOLOGY THROUGH SCIENCE FICTION   MILSTEAD/GREENBERG/& AN

MILLER, LION
  AVAILABLE DATA ON THE WORP REACTION, THE SS FSF 53 09
    BEST SF 3   CRISPIN, EDMUND   AN
    FIFTY SHORT SCIENCE FICTION TALES   ASIMOV & CONKLIN   AN
    13 GREAT STORIES OF SCIENCE FICTION   CONKLIN, GROFF   AN

MILLER, P. SCHUYLER
  TITAN, THE   AC H FPS 52
    BRITISH EDITION OMITS "THE ARRHENIUS HORROR"
  ARRHENIUS HORROR, THE   SS AMZ 31 09
    TITAN, THE   MILLER, P. SCHUYLER AC
  AS NEVER WAS   SS ASF 44 01
    *ADVENTURES IN TIME AND SPACE   HEALY & MCCOMAS   AN
    ALPHA 5   SILVERBERG, ROBERT   AN
    TITAN, THE   MILLER, P. SCHUYLER AC
  CAVE, THE   SS ASF 43 01
    CROSSROADS IN TIME   CONKLIN, GROFF   AN
    INTRODUCING SCIENCE FICTION   ALDISS, BRIAN W.   AN
    MARS, WE LOVE YOU   HIPOLITO & MCNELLY   AN
  CHRYSALIS, THE   SS ASF 36 04
    EARTH IS THE STRANGEST PLANET   SILVERBERG, ROBERT   AN
    *TREASURY OF SCIENCE FICTION, A   CONKLIN, GROFF   AN
  DAYDREAM   SS   49
    GIRL WITH THE HUNGRY EYES, AND OTHER STORIES, THE
                                           WOLLHEIM, DONALD A. OA
  FORGOTTEN (THE FORGOTTEN MAN OF SPACE) SS WOS 33 04
    *STRANGE PORTS OF CALL   DERLETH, AUGUST   AN
    TITAN, THE   MILLER, P. SCHUYLER AC
  FORGOTTEN MAN OF SPACE, THE (SEE FORGOTTEN) TC
  FROG, THE   SS UNK 42 10
    HELL HATH FURY   HAY, GEORGE   AN
  GLEEPS   SS ASF 43 07
    TITAN, THE   MILLER, P. SCHUYLER AC
  IN THE GOOD OLD SUMMERTIME   SS ASF 40 03
    TITAN, THE   MILLER, P. SCHUYLER AC

MILLER, P. SCHUYLER (CONTINUED)
  INFORMAL BIOGRAPHY OF CONAN THE CIMMERIAN, AN AR C
    COMING OF CONAN, THE   HOWARD, ROBERT E.   AC
  INTRODUCTION   IN
    TALES OF CONAN   HOWARD, R. & DE CAMP AC
  MAN FROM MARS, THE   SS WSQ 31 SU
    FROM OFF THIS WORLD   MARGULIES & FRIEND   AN
  OLD MAN MULLIGAN   NV ASF 40 12
    TITAN, THE   MILLER, P. SCHUYLER AC
  SANDS OF TIME, THE   SN ASF 37 04
    *ADVENTURES IN TIME AND SPACE   HEALY & MCCOMAS   AN
    GREAT SCIENCE FICTION STORIES   SMITH, CORDELIA T.   AN
    VOYAGERS IN TIME   SILVERBERG, ROBERT   AN
  SPAWN   SS WRT 39 08
    TITAN, THE   MILLER, P. SCHUYLER AC
  STATUS QUONDAM   NV NTS 51
    NEW TALES OF SPACE AND TIME   HEALY, RAYMOND J.   OA
  TETRAHEDRA OF SPACE   NV WOS 31 11
    BEFORE THE GOLDEN AGE   ASIMOV, ISAAC   AN
  THING ON OUTER SHOAL, THE   SS ASF 47 09
    *OTHER SIDE OF THE MOON, THE   DERLETH, AUGUST   AN
  TITAN, THE   NV MVT 34 WI
    TITAN, THE   MILLER, P. SCHUYLER AC
  TROUBLE ON TANTALUS   NV ASF 41 02
    ASTOUNDING-ANALOG READER, THE VOLUME ONE
                                           HARRISON & ALDISS   AN
    TRAVELLERS OF SPACE   GREENBERG , MARTIN   AN

MILLER, R. DEWITT
  SWENSON, DISPATCHER   NV GAL 56 04
    BEST SCIENCE FICTION STORIES AND NOVELS: 1956
                                           DIKTY, T. E.   AN
  WITHIN THE PYRAMID   SS ASF 37 03
    *ADVENTURES IN TIME AND SPACE   HEALY & MCCOMAS   AN
    MORE ADVENTURES IN TIME AND SPACE   HEALY & MCCOMAS   AN

MILLER, WALTER M. JR
  CANTICLE FOR LEIBOWITZ, A   NO H LIP 60
  CONDITIONALLY HUMAN   AC BAL 62
  VIEW FROM THE STARS, THE   AC BAL 65 01
  AND THE LIGHT IS RISEN   SN FSF 56 08
    CANTICLE FOR LEIBOWITZ, A   MILLER, WALTER M. JR NO
  ANYBODY ELSE LIKE ME? (COMMAND PERFORMANCE) NV GAL 52 11
    VIEW FROM THE STARS, THE   MILLER, WALTER M. JR AC
  BIG HUNGER, THE   SS ASF 52 10
    PRIZE SCIENCE FICTION   WOLLHEIM, DONALD A. AN
    SPACE ODYSSEYS   ALDISS, BRIAN W.   AN
    VIEW FROM THE STARS, THE   MILLER, WALTER M. JR AC
  BIG JOE AND THE NTH GENERATION (IT TAKES A THIEF) SS IFS 52 05
    VIEW FROM THE STARS, THE   MILLER, WALTER M. JR AC
  BLOOD BANK   NV ASF 52 06
    ALL ABOUT THE FUTURE   GREENBERG , MARTIN   AN
    VIEW FROM THE STARS, THE   MILLER, WALTER M. JR AC
  CANTICLE FOR LEIBOWITZ, A   NV FSF 55 04
    BEST FROM FANTASY AND SCIENCE FICTION: 5
                                           BOUCHER, ANTHONY   AN
    BEST SCIENCE FICTION STORIES AND NOVELS: 1956
                                           DIKTY, T. E.   AN
    CANTICLE FOR LEIBOWITZ, A   MILLER, WALTER M. JR NO
    NEW AWARENESS, THE   WARRICK & GREENBERG AN
    OTHER DIMENSION, THE   ROSNER, SARA   AN
    SOCIOLOGY THROUGH SCIENCE FICTION   MILSTEAD/GREENBERG/& AN
    VINTAGE ANTHOLOGY OF SCIENCE FANTASY, THE
                                           CERF, CHRISTOPHER   AN
  COMMAND PERFORMANCE (ALSO AS ANYBODY ELSE LIKE ME?)
                                          NV GAL 52 11
    BEST SCIENCE-FICTION STORIES: 1953, THE
                                           BLEILER & DIKTY   AN
    PENGUIN SCIENCE FICTION   ALDISS, BRIAN W.   AN
    SECOND GALAXY READER OF SCIENCE FICTION
                                           GOLD, H. L.   AN
  CONDITIONALLY HUMAN   NV GAL 52 02
    CONDITIONALLY HUMAN   MILLER, WALTER M. JR AC
    YEAR'S BEST SCIENCE FICTION NOVELS: 1953
                                           BLEILER & DIKTY   AN
  5 UNEARTHLY VISIONS   CONKLIN, GROFF   AN
  CRUCIFIXUS ETIAM   SS ASF 53 02
    ASLEEP IN ARMAGEDDON   SISSONS, MICHAEL   AN
    BEST SCIENCE-FICTION STORIES: 1954, THE
                                           BLEILER & DIKTY   AN
    HUMAN?   MERRIL, JUDITH   AN
    HUMAN-MACHINES   SCORTIA & ZEBROWSKI AN
    LATE GREAT FUTURE, THE   FITZ GERALD & DILLON AN
    SPECTRUM 5   AMIS & CONQUEST   AN
    TOMORROW'S WORLDS   SILVERBERG, ROBERT   AN
  TOMORROW, AND TOMORROW, AND TOMORROW...
                                           HEINTZ/HERBERT/JOOS/ AN
    VIEW FROM THE STARS, THE   MILLER, WALTER M. JR AC
  DARFSTELLER, THE   SN ASF 55 01
    CONDITIONALLY HUMAN   MILLER, WALTER M. JR AC
    HUGO WINNERS, THE (VOLUME 1)   ASIMOV, ISAAC   AN
  DARK BENEDICTION   SN FAD 51 09
    CONDITIONALLY HUMAN   MILLER, WALTER M. JR AC
  DEATH OF A SPACEMAN (ALSO AS MOMENTO HOMO) SS AMZ 54 03
    WILDERNESS OF STARS, A   NOLAN, WILLIAM F.   AN
  DUMB WAITER   NV ASF 52 04
    CITIES OF WONDER   KNIGHT, DAMON   AN
    *SCIENCE FICTION THINKING MACHINES   CONKLIN, GROFF   AN
    VIEW FROM THE STARS, THE   MILLER, WALTER M. JR AC
  HOOFER, THE   SS FUN 55 09
    SF: THE BEST OF THE BEST   MERRIL, JUDITH   AN
    SF: THE YEAR'S GREATEST SCIENCE FICTION AND FANTASY
                                           MERRIL, JUDITH   AN
  I MADE YOU   SS ASF 54 03
    EARTH IN TRANSIT   SCHWARTZ, SHEILA   AN
    INTRODUCING SCIENCE FICTION   ALDISS, BRIAN W.   AN

MILLER, WALTER M. JR (CONTINUED)
    METAL SMILE, THE   KNIGHT, DAMON   AN
    YET MORE PENGUIN SCIENCE FICTION   ALDISS, BRIAN W.
                                          SS   AMZ 53 07
I, DREAMER
    MAN AGAINST TOMORROW   NOLAN, WILLIAM F.   AN
    VIEW FROM THE STARS, THE   MILLER, WALTER M. JR AC
IZZARD AND THE MEMBRANE   NV   ASF 51 05
    YEAR'S BEST SCIENCE FICTION NOVELS: 1952
                                       BLEILER & DIKTY   AN
                                          NV   FSF 57 02
LAST CANTICLE, THE
    CANTICLE FOR LEIBOWITZ, A   MILLER, WALTER M. JR NO
LINEMAN, THE   SN   FSF 57 08
    WILDERNESS OF STARS, A   NOLAN, WILLIAM F.   AN
LITTLE CREEPS, THE   NV   AMZ 51 12
    LOOKING FORWARD   LESSER, MILTON   AN
MOMENTO HOMO (DEATH OF A SPACEMAN)   SS   AMZ 54 03
    BEST SCIENCE FICTION STORIES AND NOVELS: 1955
                                       DIKTY, T. E.   AN
    MASTERS' CHOICE   JANIFER, LAURENCE M. AN
    WORLDS OF SCIENCE FICTION, THE   MILLS, ROBERT P.   AN
NO MOON FOR ME   SS   ASF 52 09
    ABC OF SCIENCE FICTION, AN   BOARDMAN, TOM JR.   AN
    SPACE, SPACE, SPACE   SLOANE, WILLIAM   AN
SONG OF MARYA, THE (VENGEANCE FOR NIKOLAI) SS   VSF 57 03
    *TWISTED   CONKLIN, GROFF   AN
SOWER DOES NOT REAP, THE (SEE CRUCIFIXUS ETIAM) TC
                                          NV   IFS 54 05
TIES THAT BIND, THE
    SEA OF SPACE, A   NOLAN, WILLIAM F.   AN
TRIFLIN' MAN (ALSO AS YOU TRIFLIN' SKUNK!) SS   FUN 55 01
    GALAXY OF GHOULS   MERRIL, JUDITH   AN
VENGEANCE FOR NIKOLAI (ALSO AS THE SONG OF MARYA) SS VSF 57 03
    NO LIMITS   FERMAN, JOSEPH W.   AN
WILL, THE   SS   FAN 54 02
    BEST SCIENCE FICTION STORIES AND NOVELS: 1955
                                       DIKTY, T. E.   AN
    VIEW FROM THE STARS, THE   MILLER, WALTER M. JR AC
WOLF PACK   SS   FAN 53 10
    BEYOND THE BARRIERS OF SPACE AND TIME MERRIL, JUDITH   AN
YOU TRIFLIN' SKUNK! (TRIFLIN' MAN)   SS   FUN 55 01
    VIEW FROM THE STARS, THE   MILLER, WALTER M. JR AC

MILLS, ROBERT P.   SEE ALSO   CO-EDITOR EDWARD L. FERMAN
BEST FROM FANTASY AND SCIENCE FICTION: 9   AN H DBL 60
    ALSO AS "FLOWERS FOR ALGERNON AND OTHER STORIES"
    BRITISH EDITIONS OMIT FEGHOOTS,
    ACE PB EDITION OMITS FEGHOOTS AND POEMS
BEST FROM FANTASY AND SCIENCE FICTION: 10   AN H DBL 61
BEST FROM FANTASY AND SCIENCE FICTION: 11   AN H DBL 62
BEST FROM FANTASY AND SCIENCE FICTION: 11 (BRITISH)
                                              AN   PTH 66
DECADE OF FANTASY AND SCIENCE FICTION, A   AN H DBL 60
FLOWERS FOR ALGERNON AND OTHER STORIES   AN   ACE 60
    SEE "BEST FROM FANTASY AND SCIENCE FICTION: 9"
WORLDS OF SCIENCE FICTION, THE   AN   PBK 63
    INTRODUCTION   IN
    DECADE OF FANTASY AND SCIENCE FICTION, A
                                       MILLS, ROBERT P.   AN
    WORLDS OF SCIENCE FICTION, THE   MILLS, ROBERT P.   AN
LAST SHALL BE FIRST, THE   SS   FSF 58 08
    DECADE OF FANTASY AND SCIENCE FICTION, A
                                       MILLS, ROBERT P.   AN

MILSTEAD, JOHN W., MARTIN H. GREENBERG, JOSEPH D. OLANDER
    AND PATRICIA S. WARRICK
SOCIOLOGY THROUGH SCIENCE FICTION   AN H SMP 74

MILSTEAD, JOHN W.   SEE ALSO   CO-EDITOR MARTIN HARRY GREENBERG
    INTRODUCTION   IN C
    SOCIAL PROBLEMS THROUGH SCIENCE FICTION
                                       GREENBERG/MILSTEAD/& AN
    SOCIOLOGY THROUGH SCIENCE FICTION MILSTEAD/GREENBERG/& AN

MINES, SAMUEL
BEST FROM STARTLING STORIES, THE   AN H HLT 53
    ALSO AS "STARTLING STORIES" AND "MOMENT WITHOUT TIME"
MOMENT WITHOUT TIME   AN H SBB 56
    SEE "THE BEST FROM STARTLING STORIES"
STARTLING STORIES   AN H CAS 54
    SEE "THE BEST FROM STARTLING STORIES"
    BLUEPRINT FOR TOMORROW   IN
    BEST FROM STARTLING STORIES, THE   MINES, SAMUEL   AN

MINOR, HORACE M.
    BODY RITUAL AMONG THE NACIREMA   FA   ANT 66 03
    APEMAN, SPACEMAN   STOVER & HARRISON   AN

MIRO, JOAN
    PERSON THROWING A STONE AT A BIRD   IL
    SCIENCE FICTION   BRODKIN & PEARSON   AN

MIRRIELEES, EDITH
    FOREWORD   IN
    WORLD OF WONDER   PRATT, FLETCHER   AN

MITCHELL, ADRIAN
    DISCOVERY   PM
    BEYOND THIS HORIZON   CARRELL, CHRISTOPHER OA

MITCHELL, EDWARD PAGE
CRYSTAL MAN, THE   AC H DBL 73
    ABLEST MAN IN THE WORLD, THE   SS   SUN 79 05
    CRYSTAL MAN, THE   MITCHELL, EDWARD P. AC
BACK FROM THAT BOURNE   SS   SUN 74 12
    CRYSTAL MAN, THE   MITCHELL, EDWARD P. AC
BALLOON TREE, THE   SS   SUN 83 02
    CRYSTAL MAN, THE   MITCHELL, EDWARD P. AC

MITCHELL, EDWARD P.   (CONTINUED)
    CASE OF THE DOW TWINS, THE   SS   SUN 77 04
    CRYSTAL MAN, THE   MITCHELL, EDWARD P. AC
CAVE OF THE SPLURGLES, THE   SS   SUN 77 07
    CRYSTAL MAN, THE   MITCHELL, EDWARD P. AC
CLOCK THAT WENT BACKWARDS, THE   SS   SUN 81 01
    CRYSTAL MAN, THE   MITCHELL, EDWARD P. AC
CRYSTAL MAN, THE   SS   SUN 81 01
    CRYSTAL MAN, THE   MITCHELL, EDWARD P. AC
DAY AMONG THE LIARS, A   SS   SUN 85 08
    CRYSTAL MAN, THE   MITCHELL, EDWARD P. AC
DEVIL'S FUNERAL, THE   SS   SUN 79 03
    CRYSTAL MAN, THE   MITCHELL, EDWARD P. AC
DEVILISH RAT, THE   SS   SUN 78 01
    CRYSTAL MAN, THE   MITCHELL, EDWARD P. AC
EXCHANGING THEIR SOULS   SS   SUN 77 04
    CRYSTAL MAN, THE   MITCHELL, EDWARD P. AC
EXTRAORDINARY WEDDING, AN   SS   SUN 78 01
    CRYSTAL MAN, THE   MITCHELL, EDWARD P. AC
FACTS IN THE RATCLIFF CASE, THE   SS   SUN 79 03
    CRYSTAL MAN, THE   MITCHELL, EDWARD P. AC
FLYING WEATHERCOCK, THE   SS   SUN 84 04
    CRYSTAL MAN, THE   MITCHELL, EDWARD P. AC
INSIDE OF THE EARTH, THE   SS   SUN 76 03
    CRYSTAL MAN, THE   MITCHELL, EDWARD P. AC
LAST CRUISE OF THE JUDAS ISCARIOT, THE   SS   SUN 82 04
    CRYSTAL MAN, THE   MITCHELL, EDWARD P. AC
LEGENDARY SHIP, THE   SS   SUN 85 05
    CRYSTAL MAN, THE   MITCHELL, EDWARD P. AC
MAN WITHOUT A BODY, THE   SS   SUN 77 03
    CRYSTAL MAN, THE   MITCHELL, EDWARD P. AC
OLD SQUIDS AND LITTLE SPELLER   SS   SUN 85 07
    CRYSTAL MAN, THE   MITCHELL, EDWARD P. AC
OUR WAR WITH MONACO   SS   SUN 80 03
    CRYSTAL MAN, THE   MITCHELL, EDWARD P. AC
PAIN EPICURES, THE   SS   SUN 78 08
    CRYSTAL MAN, THE   MITCHELL, EDWARD P. AC
PROFESSOR'S EXPERIMENT, THE   SS   SUN 80 02
    CRYSTAL MAN, THE   MITCHELL, EDWARD P. AC
SENATOR'S DAUGHTER, THE   SS   SUN 79 07
    CRYSTAL MAN, THE   MITCHELL, EDWARD P. AC
SHADOW ON THE FANCHER TWINS, THE   SS   SUN 86 01
    CRYSTAL MAN, THE   MITCHELL, EDWARD P. AC
SOUL SPECTROSCOPE, THE   SS   SUN 75 12
    CRYSTAL MAN, THE   MITCHELL, EDWARD P. AC
STORY OF THE DELUGE, THE   SS   SUN 75 04
    CRYSTAL MAN, THE   MITCHELL, EDWARD P. AC
TACHYPOMP, THE   SS   SCR 74 03
    CRYSTAL MAN, THE   MITCHELL, EDWARD P. AC
    FANTASIA MATHEMATICA   FADIMAN, CLIFTON   AN
TERRIBLE VOYAGE OF THE TOAD, THE   SS   SUN 78 10
    CRYSTAL MAN, THE   MITCHELL, EDWARD P. AC
UNCOMMON SORT OF SPECTRE, AN   SS   SUN 79 03
    CRYSTAL MAN, THE   MITCHELL, EDWARD P. AC
WONDERFUL COROT, THE   SS   SUN 81 12
    CRYSTAL MAN, THE   MITCHELL, EDWARD P. AC

MITCHELL, J. A.
    LAST AMERICAN, THE   SS   SCR 89 06
    FAR BOUNDARIES   DERLETH, AUGUST   AN

MITCHELL, SILAS W.
    WAS HE DEAD? (1870)   NV   ATL 70 01
    FUTURE PERFECT   FRANKLIN, H. BRUCE   AN

MITCHISON, NAOMI
    AFTER THE ACCIDENT   SS   YRT 70
    YEAR 2000, THE   HARRISON, HARRY   OA
    FACTORY, THE   SS   NOV 73 03
    NOVA 3   HARRISON, HARRY   OA
    MARY AND JOE   SS   NOV 70 01
    *NOVA 1   HARRISON & ALDISS   AN
    MISS OMEGA RAVEN   SS   NOV 72 02
    BEST SCIENCE FICTION OF THE YEAR, THE NO. 2
                                       CARR, TERRY   AN
    NOVA 2   HARRISON, HARRY   OA
    OUT OF THE WATERS   SS   NOV 74 04
    NOVA 4   HARRISON, HARRY   OA
    VALLEY OF THE BUSHES   SS
    ANDROMEDA I   WESTON, PETER   OA

MITSKEVICH, A. P.   SEE PSEUD. ANATOLY DNIEPROV

MITSUSE, RYU
    SUNSET, 2217 AD, THE (TRANSLATED BY TETSU YANO AND
    JUDITH MERRIL)   NV
    BEST SCIENCE FICTION FOR 1972   POHL, FREDERIK   AN

MOHLER, WILL
    JOURNEY OF TEN THOUSAND MILES   SS   FSF 63 03
    ONCE AND FUTURE TALES FROM THE MAGAZINE OF FANTASY AND
    SCIENCE FICTION   FERMAN, EDWARD L.   AN

MOHS, MAYO
    OTHER WORLDS, OTHER GODS   AN H DBL 71
    SCIENCE FICTION AND THE WORLD OF RELIGION   IN
    OTHER WORLDS, OTHER GODS   MOHS, MAYO   AN

MONIG, CHRISTOPHER   PSEUD. FOR KENDELL F. CROSSEN
    LOVE STORY   SS   NEW 52 AN
    *FUTURE TENSE   CROSSEN, KENDELL F.   AN

MONROE, LYLE   PSEUD. FOR ROBERT A. HEINLEIN
    BEYOND DOUBT   SS C AST 41 04
    POLITICAL SCIENCE FICTION   GREENBERG& WARRICK   AN

```
MONROE, LYLE        (CONTINUED)
   COLUMBUS WAS A DOPE                          SS    STS 47 05
      TRAVELLERS OF SPACE         GREENBERG , MARTIN    AN

MONTALVO, GARCIA O.
   QUEEN OF CALIFORNIA, THE (1510, TRANSLATION AND NOTES BY
   EDWARD EVERETT HALE)                         NV
      WHEN WOMEN RULE             MOSKOWITZ, SAM        AN

MONTELEONE, THOMAS F
   BREATH'S A WARE THAT WILL NOT KEEP           SS    DYS 75
      DYSTOPIAN VISIONS           ELWOOD, ROGER         OA
   CHICAGO                                      SS    FUC 73
      CITY: 2000 A.D., THE        CLEM/GREENBERG/&      AN
      FUTURE CITY                 ELWOOD, ROGER         OA
   THING FROM ENNIS ROCK, THE                   SS
      MORE SCIENCE FICTION TALES  ELWOOD, ROGER         OA

MONTGOMERY, R. BRUCE SEE PSEUD. EDMUND CRISPIN

MOORCOCK, MICHAEL AND CHARLES PLATT
   NEW WORLDS NO. 5                             OA L EQN 73

MOORCOCK, MICHAEL    ALSO AS    JAMES COLVIN
   BEFORE ARMAGEDDON                            AN H ALL 75
      AN ANTHOLOGY OF VICTORIAN AND EDWARDIAN IMAGINATIVE FICTION
      PUBLISHED BEFORE 1914
   BEST OF NEW WORLDS, THE                      AN    CPT 65
   BEST SF STORIES FROM NEW WORLDS NO. 1, THE   AN    BKM 67
   BEST SF STORIES FROM NEW WORLDS NO. 2, THE   AN    BKM 68
   BEST SF STORIES FROM NEW WORLDS 3            AN    BKM 68
   BEST SF STORIES FROM NEW WORLDS 4            AN    BKM 69
   BEST SF STORIES FROM NEW WORLDS 5            AN    BKM 69
   BEST SF STORIES FROM NEW WORLDS 6            AN    BKM 70
   BEST SF STORIES FROM NEW WORLDS 7            AN    PTH 71
   BEST SF STORIES FROM NEW WORLDS 8            AN    PTH 74
   FINAL PROGRAMME, THE                         NO    AVN 68
   INNER LANDSCAPE, THE                         AN H ALS 69
   LEGENDS FROM THE END OF TIME                 AC H HPR 76
   LIVES AND TIMES OF JERRY CORNELIUS, THE      AC H ALB 76
   MOORCOCK'S BOOK OF MARTYRS                   AC   QRT 76
   NEW WORLDS QUARTERLY NO. 1                   OA    BKM 71 09
   NEW WORLDS QUARTERLY NO. 2                   OA    BKM 71 12
   NEW WORLDS QUARTERLY NO. 3                   OA    BKM 72 03
   NEW WORLDS QUARTERLY NO. 4                   OA    BKM 72 06
   NEW WORLDS QUARTERLY NO. 5                   OA    SPH 73
   TIME DWELLER, THE                            AC H HDV 69
   TRAPS OF TIME, THE                           AN H RPW 68
   AFTERWORD                                    MS    NWQ 73 05
      NEW WORLDS NO. 5            MOORCOCK & PLATT      OA
   ANCIENT SHADOWS                              NV    NWB 75 09
      LEGENDS FROM THE END OF TIME MOORCOCK, MICHAEL    AC
      NEW WORLDS NINE             BAILEY, HILARY        OA
   APOCALYPSE: SOME SCENES FROM EUROPEAN LIFE, AN  NV  BMR 73
      BAD MOON RISING             DISCH, THOMAS M.      OA
   BEHOLD THE MAN                               NV    NWS 66 09
      MOORCOCK'S BOOK OF MARTYRS  MOORCOCK, MICHAEL     AC
      NEBULA AWARD STORIES  NO. 3 ZELAZNY, ROGER        AN
      NEW AWARENESS, THE          WARRICK & GREENBERG   AN
      WORLD'S BEST SCIENCE FICTION: 1967  WOLLHEIM & CARR  AN
   CONSUMING PASSION                            SS    NWS 66 04
      TIME DWELLER, THE           MOORCOCK, MICHAEL     AC
   DEAD SINGER, A                               NV    74
      BEST SF: 75, THE NINTH ANNUAL  HARRISON & ALDISS  AN
      MOORCOCK'S BOOK OF MARTYRS  MOORCOCK, MICHAEL     AC
   DEAD SINGERS                                 SS    INK 71
      LIVES AND TIMES OF JERRY CORNELIUS, THE
                                  MOORCOCK, MICHAEL     AC
   DEEP FIX, THE (AS JAMES COLVIN)              NV    SCF 64 04
      TIME DWELLER, THE           MOORCOCK, MICHAEL     AC
   DELHI DIVISION, THE                          SS    NWS 68 12
      BEST SF STORIES FROM NEW WORLDS 6  MOORCOCK, MICHAEL  AN
      LIVES AND TIMES OF JERRY CORNELIUS, THE
                                  MOORCOCK, MICHAEL     AC
   ENTROPY CIRCUIT, THE                         SS    74
      LIVES AND TIMES OF JERRY CORNELIUS, THE
                                  MOORCOCK, MICHAEL     AC
   ENVIRONMENT PROBLEM                          SS    SPC 73 01
      SPACE  1                    DAVIS, RICHARD        OA
   ESCAPE FROM EVENING                          NV    NWS 65 03
      TIME DWELLER, THE           MOORCOCK, MICHAEL     AC
   FLUX                                         NV    NWS 63 07
      LAMBDA I AND OTHER STORIES  CARNELL, JOHN         AN
      MOORCOCK'S BOOK OF MARTYRS  MOORCOCK, MICHAEL     AC
      VOYAGERS IN TIME            SILVERBERG, ROBERT    AN
   FOR THOMAS TOMPION                           SS
      NEW S.F., THE               JONES, LANGDON        OA
   FURTHER INFORMATION                          SS    NWS 65 12
      FINAL PROGRAMME, THE        MOORCOCK, MICHAEL     NO
   GOLDEN BARGE, THE (AS WILLIAM BARCLAY)       SS    NWS 65 10
      TIME DWELLER, THE           MOORCOCK, MICHAEL     AC
   GOOD-BYE, MIRANDA                            SS    NWS 64 08
      MOORCOCK'S BOOK OF MARTYRS  MOORCOCK, MICHAEL     AC
   GREAT CONQUEROR, THE                         NV    SCF 63 04
      MOORCOCK'S BOOK OF MARTYRS  MOORCOCK, MICHAEL     AC
   IN MEMORIAM- MERVYN PEAKE                    MS
      NEBULA AWARD STORIES  NO. 4 ANDERSON, POUL        AN
   INTRODUCTION                                 IN
      BEFORE ARMAGEDDON           MOORCOCK, MICHAEL     AN
      BEST SF STORIES FROM NEW WORLDS NO. 1, THE
                                  MOORCOCK, MICHAEL     AN
      BEST SF STORIES FROM NEW WORLDS NO. 2, THE
                                  MOORCOCK, MICHAEL     AN
      BEST SF STORIES FROM NEW WORLDS 3  MOORCOCK, MICHAEL  AN
      BEST SF STORIES FROM NEW WORLDS 4  MOORCOCK, MICHAEL  AN
      BEST SF STORIES FROM NEW WORLDS 5  MOORCOCK, MICHAEL  AN


MOORCOCK, MICHAEL    (CONTINUED)
   BEST SF STORIES FROM NEW WORLDS 6  MOORCOCK, MICHAEL     A#
   BEST SF STORIES FROM NEW WORLDS 7  MOORCOCK, MICHAEL     A#
   MOORCOCK'S BOOK OF MARTYRS  MOORCOCK, MICHAEL     A#
   NEW WORLDS QUARTERLY NO. 1  MOORCOCK, MICHAEL     O.
   NEW WORLDS QUARTERLY NO. 3  MOORCOCK, MICHAEL     O.
   NEW WORLDS QUARTERLY NO. 5  MOORCOCK, MICHAEL     O.
   TRAPS OF TIME, THE          MOORCOCK, MICHAEL     A
   ISLANDS                                      NV    NWS 63
      MOORCOCK'S BOOK OF MARTYRS  MOORCOCK, MICHAEL     A#
   KEEPING PERSPECTIVE                          MS
      NEW WORLDS QUARTERLY NO. 2  MOORCOCK, MICHAEL     O.
   KINGS IN DARKNESS                            NV    SCF 62 0#
      SPELL OF SEVEN, THE         DE CAMP, L. SPRAGUE   A
   LONGFORD CUP, THE                            SS    PNT 73
      LIVES AND TIMES OF JERRY CORNELIUS, THE
                                  MOORCOCK, MICHAEL     A#
   MAL DEAN                                     AR    NWB 75 0#
      NEW WORLDS EIGHT            BAILEY, HILARY        O.
   MASTER OF CHAOS                              SS    FAN 64 0#
      WEIRD SHADOWS FROM BEYOND   CARNELL, JOHN         A#
   MOUNTAIN, THE                                SS    NWS 65 0.
      ENGLAND SWINGS SF           MERRIL, JUDITH        A
      TIME DWELLER, THE           MOORCOCK, MICHAEL     A#
   NATURE OF THE CATASTROPHE, THE               SS    NWS 70 0
      DECADE THE 1960S            ALDISS & HARRISON     A#
      LIVES AND TIMES OF JERRY CORNELIUS, THE
                                  MOORCOCK, MICHAEL     AC
   PALE ROSES                                   NV    NWQ 74 0#
      BEST SCIENCE FICTION OF THE YEAR, THE NO. 4
                                  CARR, TERRY           A#
      LEGENDS FROM THE END OF TIME  MOORCOCK, MICHAEL   A#
      NEW WORLDS NO. 6            PLATT & BAILEY        O#
   PEKING JUNCTION, THE                         SS
      LIVES AND TIMES OF JERRY CORNELIUS, THE
                                  MOORCOCK, MICHAEL     A#
      NEW S.F., THE               JONES, LANGDON        O#
   PHASE THREE                                  SS    NWS 66 03
      FINAL PROGRAMME, THE        MOORCOCK, MICHAEL     NO
   PLEASURE GARDEN OF FELIPE SAGITTARIUS, THE   SS    NWS 65 09
      MODERN SCIENCE FICTION      SPINRAD, NORMAN       A#
      NEW TOMORROWS, THE          SPINRAD, NORMAN       A#
      TIME DWELLER, THE           MOORCOCK, MICHAEL     A#
   PREFACE                                      IN
      NEW S.F., THE               JONES, LANGDON        O#
   PRELIMINARY DATA                             SS    NWS 65 08
      FINAL PROGRAMME, THE        MOORCOCK, MICHAEL     NO
   RUINS, THE (AS JAMES COLVIN)                 SS    NWS 66 04
      TIME DWELLER, THE           MOORCOCK, MICHAEL     A#
   SEA WOLVES                                   SS    SAG 70
      LIVES AND TIMES OF JERRY CORNELIUS, THE
                                  MOORCOCK, MICHAEL     AC
      SCIENCE AGAINST MAN         CHEETHAM, ANTHONY     O#
   SINGING CITADEL, THE                         NV    63
      DEVIL HIS DUE, THE          HILL, DOUGLAS         A#
   SUNSET PERSPECTIVE, THE                      SS    71
      LIVES AND TIMES OF JERRY CORNELIUS, THE
                                  MOORCOCK, MICHAEL     AC
   SWASTIKA SET-UP, THE                         NV    72
      LIVES AND TIMES OF JERRY CORNELIUS, THE
                                  MOORCOCK, MICHAEL     AC
   TANK TRAPEZE, THE                            SS    NWS 69 01
      BEST SF STORIES FROM NEW WORLDS 7  MOORCOCK, MICHAEL  A#
      LIVES AND TIMES OF JERRY CORNELIUS, THE
                                  MOORCOCK, MICHAEL     AC
      SF: AUTHORS' CHOICE 3       HARRISON, HARRY       A#
   TIME DWELLER, THE                            SS    NWS 64 02
      BEST OF NEW WORLDS, THE     MOORCOCK, MICHAEL     A#
      TIME DWELLER, THE           MOORCOCK, MICHAEL     A#
   VOORTREKKER                                  NV    QRK 71 0#
      LIVES AND TIMES OF JERRY CORNELIUS, THE
                                  MOORCOCK, MICHAEL     AC
      QUARK/4                     DELANY & HACKER       OA
   WAITING FOR THE END OF TIME...               SS    VOT 70
      MOORCOCK'S BOOK OF MARTYRS  MOORCOCK, MICHAEL     AC
   WHITE STARS                                  NV    NWB 75 08
      LEGENDS FROM THE END OF TIME  MOORCOCK, MICHAEL   AC
      NEW WORLDS EIGHT            BAILEY, HILARY        OA
   WOLF                                         SS    66
      TIME DWELLER, THE           MOORCOCK, MICHAEL     AC

MOORE, C. L.      SEE ALSO   CO-AUTHOR HENRY KUTTNER
                  ALSO AS
      LAWRENCE O'DONNELL AND LEWIS PADGETT (BOTH WITH HENRY KUTTNER)
   BEST OF C. L. MOORE, THE                     AC H NDB 75
      EDITED BY LESTER DEL REY
   JIREL OF JOIRY                               AC    PBK 69 08
   JUDGEMENT NIGHT                              AC H GNM 52
   NORTHWEST OF EARTH                           AC H GNM 54
   SHAMBLEAU AND OTHERS                         AC H GNM 53
      BRITISH CONSUL EDITION OMITS "JIREL MEETS MAGIC"
   SHAMBLEAU AND OTHERS (3 OF 7)                AC    GAN 58 31
      AFTERWORD: FOOTNOTE TO "SHAMBLEAU"... AND OTHERS MS
      BEST OF C. L. MOORE, THE    MOORE, C. L.          AC
   BLACK GOD'S KISS                             NV    WRT 34 10
      BEST OF C. L. MOORE, THE    MOORE, C. L.          AC
      JIREL OF JOIRY              MOORE, C. L.          AC
      *SHAMBLEAU AND OTHERS       MOORE, C. L.          AC
   BLACK GOD'S SHADOW                           NV    WRT 34 12
      JIREL OF JOIRY              MOORE, C. L.          AC
      *SHAMBLEAU AND OTHERS       MOORE, C. L.          AC
   BLACK THIRST                                 NV    WRT 34 04
      AVON FANTASY READER, THE    WOLLHEIM &ERNSBERGER  AN
      BEST OF C. L. MOORE, THE    MOORE, C. L.          AC
      *SHAMBLEAU AND OTHERS       MOORE, C. L.          AC
```

MOORE, C. L.   (CONTINUED)
  BRIGHT ILLUSION, THE   NV ASF 34 10
    BEST OF C. L. MOORE, THE   MOORE, C. L.   AC
    MASTERS' CHOICE   JANIFER, LAURENCE M. AN
  CHILDREN'S HOUR, THE   NV C ASF 44 03
    TREASURY OF GREAT SCIENCE FICTION, A VOL.1
                                      BOUCHER, ANTHONY   AN
  CODE, THE   NV ASF 45 07
    JUDGEMENT NIGHT   MOORE, C. L.   AC
  COLD GRAY GOD, THE   SS WRT 35 10
    NORTHWEST OF EARTH   MOORE, C. L.   AC
  CURE, THE   SS C ASF 46 05
    SCIENCE FICTION ARGOSY, A   KNIGHT, DAMON   AN
  DAEMON   NV FFM 46 10
    BEST OF C. L. MOORE, THE   MOORE, C. L.   AC
  DARK LAND, THE   NV WRT 36 01
    JIREL OF JOIRY   MOORE, C. L.   AC
    NORTHWEST OF EARTH   MOORE, C. L.   AC
    VENUS FACTOR, THE   GHIDALIA, V.& ELWOOD AN
  DOORWAY INTO TIME   SS FFM 43 09
    DOORWAY INTO TIME   MOSKOWITZ, SAM   AN
    MODERN MASTERPIECES OF SCIENCE FICTION MOSKOWITZ, SAM   AN
  DUST OF GODS   NV WRT 34 08
    NORTHWEST OF EARTH   MOORE, C. L.   AC
    PLANETS OF WONDER   CARR, TERRY   AN
  FRUIT OF KNOWLEDGE   NV UNK 40 10
    BEST OF C. L. MOORE, THE   MOORE, C. L.   AC
  GREATER THAN GODS   NV ASF 39 07
    BEST OF C. L. MOORE, THE   MOORE, C. L.   AC
  HEIR APPARENT   NV ASF 50 07
    JUDGEMENT NIGHT   MOORE, C. L.   AC
  HELLSGARDE   SS WRT 39 04
    JIREL OF JOIRY   MOORE, C. L.   AC
    NORTHWEST OF EARTH   MOORE, C. L.   AC
  HOME THERE'S NO RETURNING   NV NEW 55 AC
    ASLEEP IN ARMAGEDDON   SISSONS, MICHAEL   AN
  HOME THERE'S NO RETURNING   NV C NEW 55 AC
    NO BOUNDARIES   KUTTNER & MOORE   AC
    SF: THE YEAR'S GREATEST SCIENCE FICTION AND FANTASY
                                      MERRIL, JUDITH   AN
  JIREL MEETS MAGIC   NV WRT 35 07
    JIREL OF JOIRY   MOORE, C. L.   AC
    MORE WOMEN OF WONDER   SARGENT, PAMELA   AN
    *SHAMBLEAU AND OTHERS   MOORE, C. L.   AC
  JUDGEMENT NIGHT   NA ASF 43 08
    JUDGEMENT NIGHT   MOORE, C. L.   AC
  JUHLI   SS WRT 35 03
    NORTHWEST OF EARTH   MOORE, C. L.   AC
  LOST PARADISE   SS WRT 36 07
    NORTHWEST OF EARTH   MOORE, C. L.   AC
  NO WOMAN BORN   NV ASF 44 12
    BEST OF C. L. MOORE, THE   MOORE, C. L.   AC
    BEST SF   CRISPIN, EDMUND   AN
    GREAT STORIES OF SCIENCE FICTION LEINSTER, MURRAY   AN
    HUMAN-MACHINES   SCORTIA & ZEBROWSKI   AN
    TOMORROW X 4   KNIGHT, DAMON   AN
    *TREASURY OF SCIENCE FICTION, A   CONKLIN, GROFF   AN
  OR ELSE   SS C AMZ 53 09
    NEVER IN THIS WORLD   STONE, IDELLA P.   AN
  PARADISE STREET   NV ASF 50 09
    JUDGEMENT NIGHT   MOORE, C. L.   AC
  PRIVATE EYE   NV C ASF 49 01
    SCIENCE FICTION INVENTIONS   KNIGHT, DAMON   AN
  PROMISED LAND   NV ASF 50 02
    JUDGEMENT NIGHT   MOORE, C. L.   AC
  SCARLET DREAM   NV WRT 34 05
    *FUTURE TENSE   CROSSEN, KENDELL F.   AN
    *SHAMBLEAU AND OTHERS   MOORE, C. L.   AC
  SHAMBLEAU   NV WRT 33 11
    ADVENTURES IN TOMORROW   CROSSEN, KENDELL F.   AN
    BEST OF C. L. MOORE, THE   MOORE, C. L.   AC
    ESCALES DANS L'INFINI   GALLET, GEORGES H.   AN
    SECOND AVON FANTASY READER, THE   WOLLHEIM &ERNSBERGER AN
    *SHAMBLEAU AND OTHERS   MOORE, C. L.   AC
  THERE SHALL BE DARKNESS   NV ASF 42 02
    JOURNEY TO INFINITY   GREENBERG , MARTIN   AN
  TREE OF LIFE, THE   NV WRT 36 10
    FANTASTIC PULPS, THE   HAINING, PETER   AN
    *SHAMBLEAU AND OTHERS   MOORE, C. L.   AC
  TRYST IN TIME   NV ASF 36 12
    BEST OF C. L. MOORE, THE   MOORE, C. L.   AC
  TWO-HANDED ENGINE   SS C FSF 55 08
    METAL SMILE, THE   KNIGHT, DAMON   AN
  VINTAGE SEASON   NV ASF 46 09
    BEST OF C. L. MOORE, THE   MOORE, C. L.   AC
  VINTAGE SEASON   NV C ASF 46 09
    SCIENCE FICTION HALL OF FAME VOLUME 2A BOVA, BEN AN
  WEREWOMAN   NV LVS 38 WI
    EDGE OF NEVER, THE   HOSKINS, ROBERT   AN
  WILD SURMISE, A   SS C STR 53 01
    STAR SCIENCE FICTION STORIES   POHL, FREDERIK   OA
  YVALA   SS WRT 36 02
    NORTHWEST OF EARTH   MOORE, C. L.   AC

MOORE, HAL R.
  SEA BRIGHT   SS FSF 65 09
    BEST FROM FANTASY AND SCIENCE FICTION: 15
                                      FERMAN, EDWARD L.   AN

MOORE, PATRICK
  INTRODUCTION: ASTRONOMY TODAY AND TOMORROW   IN
    BEYOND THIS HORIZON   CARRELL, CHRISTOPHER OA

MOORE, RAYLYN
  DIFFERENT DRUMMER, A   SS FSF 71 02

MOORE, RAYLYN   (CONTINUED)
  BEST FROM FANTASY AND SCIENCE FICTION: 20
                                      FERMAN, EDWARD L.   AN
    SCHOOL AND SOCIETY THROUGH SCIENCE FICTION
                                      OLANDER/GREENBERG/&   AN
  FUN PALACE   SS ORB 75 17
    ORBIT 17   KNIGHT, DAMON   OA
  IF SOMETHING BEGINS   SS
    WORLDS FAR AND NEAR   CARR, TERRY   AN
  MODULAR STORY, A   SS ORB 76 18
    ORBIT 18   KNIGHT, DAMON   OA
  POVERELLO   SS PTP 73
    FLAME TREE PLANET   ELWOOD, ROGER   OA
  THAUMATURGE   SS BER 74
    BERSERKERS, THE   ELWOOD, ROGER   OA
  TRIGONONOMY   NV SCS 73
    SHOWCASE   ELWOOD, ROGER   OA
  WHERE HAVE ALL THE FOLLOWERS GONE?   SS BMR 73
    BAD MOON RISING   DISCH, THOMAS M.   OA

MOORE, WARD
  ADJUSTMENT   NV FSF 57 05
    BEST FROM FANTASY AND SCIENCE FICTION: 7
                                      BOUCHER, ANTHONY   AN
    INTRODUCTORY PSYCHOLOGY THROUGH SCIENCE FICTION
                                      KATZ/WARRICK/&   AN
  CLASS WITH DR. CHANG, A   SS
    BEYOND TIME   LEY, SANDRA   OA
  COLD PEACE, THE (SEE IT BECOMES NECESSARY)   TC
  DOMINIONS BEYOND (THE SECOND TRIP TO MARS)   SS SEP 54 08
    BEST SCIENCE FICTION STORIES AND NOVELS: 1955
                                      DIKTY, T. E.   AN
    WONDERMAKERS 2   HOSKINS, ROBERT   AN
  DURANCE   SS EPC 75
    EPOCH   ELWOOD & SILVERBERG   OA
  FELLOW WHO MARRIED THE MAXILL GIRL, THE   NV FSF 60 02
    BEST FROM FANTASY AND SCIENCE FICTION: 10
                                      MILLS, ROBERT P.   AN
    6TH ANNUAL OF THE YEAR'S BEST S-F, THE MERRIL, JUDITH AN
  FLYING DUTCHMAN   SS FSF 56 09
    ADVENTURES IN TOMORROW   CROSSEN, KENDELL F.   AN
  FRANK MERRIWELL IN THE WHITE HOUSE   NV GAL 73 11
    AMERICAN GOVERNMENT THROUGH SCIENCE FICTION
                                      OLANDER/GREENBERG/&   AN
  IT BECOMES NECESSARY (THE COLD PEACE)   SS GNT 61
    7TH ANNUAL OF THE YEAR'S BEST S-F, THE MERRIL, JUDITH AN
  LOT   NV FSF 53 05
    BEST FROM FANTASY AND SCIENCE FICTION: 3
                                      BOUCHER & MCCOMAS   AN
    BEST SCIENCE-FICTION STORIES: 1954, THE
                                      BLEILER & DIKTY   AN
    EARTH IN TRANSIT   SCHWARTZ, SHEILA   AN
    PENGUIN SCIENCE FICTION   ALDISS, BRIAN W.   AN
  LOT'S DAUGHTER   NV FSF 54 10
    DECADE OF FANTASY AND SCIENCE FICTION, A
                                      MILLS, ROBERT P.   AN
  NO MAN PURSUETH   NV FSF 56 04
    BEST FROM FANTASY AND SCIENCE FICTION: 6
                                      BOUCHER, ANTHONY   AN
  PEACEBRINGER (SWORD OF PEACE)   SS AMZ 50 03
    *BIG BOOK OF SCIENCE FICTION   CONKLIN, GROFF   AN
  REBEL   SS FSF 62 02
    NEVER IN THIS WORLD   STONE, IDELLA P.   AN
  SECOND TRIP TO MARS, THE (ALSO AS DOMINIONS BEYOND)
                                                     SS SEP 54 08
    POST READER OF FANTASY AND SCIENCE FICTION
                                      SATURDAY EVE. POST   AN
  SWORD OF PEACE (SEE PEACEBRINGER)   TC
  WE THE PEOPLE   SS SFQ 52 05
    *FUTURE TENSE   CROSSEN, KENDELL F.   AN

MORE, SIR THOMAS
  FROM "UTOPIA" (1516)   EX
    PAST, PRESENT, AND FUTURE PERFECT WOLFE, J&FITZ GERALD AN
  UTOPIA (1516)   EX
    *BEYOND TIME AND SPACE   DERLETH, AUGUST   AN

MORGAN, CHRIS
  FROM ALKAID ASCENDING   SS
    GOLLANCZ - SUNDAY TIMES BEST SF STORIES
                                      ANONYMOUS   OA
  SO PROUDLY WE CLING   SS
    GOLLANCZ - SUNDAY TIMES BEST SF STORIES
                                      ANONYMOUS   OA

MORGAN, DAN
  CANARY   SS NWR 72 20
    NEW WRITINGS IN SF. 20   CARNELL, JOHN   OA
  EMRETH   SS NWR 65 03
    NEW WRITINGS IN SF. 3   CARNELL, JOHN   OA
  FIRST DAY OF THE REST OF YOUR LIFE, THE   SS SFM 74 05
    BEST OF SCIENCE FICTION MONTHLY, THE SACKS, JANET   AN
  PARKING PROBLEM   SS NWR 65 04
    NEW WRITINGS IN SF. 4   CARNELL, JOHN   OA
  YOUNG TOM   SS NWR 76 29
    NEW WRITINGS IN SF. 29   BULMER, KENNETH   OA

MORGAN, EDWIN
  FROM THE DOMAIN OF ARNHEIM   PM   68
    HOLDING YOUR EIGHT HANDS   LUCIE-SMITH, EDWARD   AN
  IN SOBIESKI'S SHIELD   PM   68
    HOLDING YOUR EIGHT HANDS   LUCIE-SMITH, EDWARD   AN
  OFF COURSE   PM   67
    SCIENCE FICTION   BRODKIN & PEARSON   AN
  POLYFILLA   PM
    BEYOND THIS HORIZON   CARRELL, CHRISTOPHER OA

MORGAN, EDWIN   (CONTINUED)
  SPACE SONNET   PM
    BEYOND THIS HORIZON   CARRELL, CHRISTOPHER OA
  TWILIGHT OF A TYRANNY   PM
    BEYOND THIS HORIZON   CARRELL, CHRISTOPHER OA

MORLEY, CHRISTOPHER
  CIRCLE, THE   PM
    FANTASIA MATHEMATICA   FADIMAN, CLIFTON   AN
  TO A MISSING MEMBER OF A FAMILY GROUP OF TERMS IN AN
    ALGEBRAIC FORMULA   PM   50
    MATHEMATICAL MAGPIE, THE   FADIMAN, CLIFTON   AN

MORPHETT, TONY
  LITTERBUG   NV   FSF 69 07
    BEST FROM FANTASY AND SCIENCE FICTION: 19
                                 FERMAN, EDWARD L.   AN
    BEYOND TOMORROW   HARDING, LEE   AN
    SCIENCE FICTION   BRODKIN & PEARSON   AN

MORRIS, GOUVERNEUR
  BACK THERE IN THE GRASS   SS   22
    WORLD OF WONDER   PRATT, FLETCHER   AN

MORRIS, VIC
  BLUE DANUBE   NA
    GOLLANCZ - SUNDAY TIMES BEST SF STORIES
                                 ANONYMOUS   OA

MORRISON, D. A. C.
  ANOTHER ANTIGONE   SS
    AD 2500   WILSON, ANGUS   AN

MORRISON, WILLIAM   PSEUD. FOR JOSEPH SAMACHSON
  BEDSIDE MANNOR   NV   GAL 54 05
    GREAT SCIENCE FICTION ABOUT DOCTORS CONKLIN, G&FABRICANT AN
  COUNTRY DOCTOR   NV   STR 53 01
    STAR OF STARS   POHL, FREDERIK   AN
    STAR SCIENCE FICTION STORIES POHL, FREDERIK   OA
    WHERE DO WE GO FROM HERE?   ASIMOV, ISAAC   AN
    ZOO 2000   YOLEN, JANE   AN
  FEAST OF DEMONS, A   NV   GAL 58 03
    EXPERT DREAMERS, THE   POHL, FREDERIK   AN
    FIFTH GALAXY READER, THE   GOLD, H. L.   AN
  INNER WORLDS, THE   NV   FSF 54 04
    BEST SCIENCE FICTION STORIES AND NOVELS: 1955
                                 DIKTY, T. E.   AN
  MODEL OF A JUDGE, THE   SS   GAL 53 10
    BEST SCIENCE-FICTION STORIES: 1954, THE
                                 BLEILER & DIKTY   AN
    THIRD GALAXY READER, THE   GOLD, H. L.   AN
  SACK, THE   SS   ASF 50 09
    SCIENCE FACT/FICTION   FARRELL/GAGE/&   AN
    SCIENCE FICTION: THE GREAT YEARS, VOL. II
                                 POHL, C. & F.   AN
    TOMORROW, THE STARS   HEINLEIN, ROBERT A. AN
  SHIPPING CLERK   SS   GAL 52 06
    13 GREAT STORIES OF SCIENCE FICTION CONKLIN, GROFF AN
  SLY BUNGERHOP, THE   NV   GAL 57 09
    MIND PARTNER AND 8 OTHER NOVELETS FROM GALAXY
                                 GOLD, H. L.   AN

MORROW, W. C.
  HIS UNCONQUERABLE ENEMY   SS   97
    HORROR TIMES TEN   NORTON, ALDEN H.   AN
  MONSTER MAKER, THE   NV
    BATTLE OF THE MONSTERS AND OTHER STORIES, THE
                                 HARTWELL & CURREY   AN

MORTLOCK, BILL
  APOTHEM   MS   59
    MATHEMATICAL MAGPIE, THE   FADIMAN, CLIFTON   AN

MOSKOWITZ, SAM AND ROGER ELWOOD
  HUMAN ZERO, THE   AN   TWR 67
  OTHER WORLDS, OTHER TIMES   AN   MBB 69
  TIME CURVE, THE   AN   TWR 68

MOSKOWITZ, SAM   SEE ALSO
  CO-EDITORS ROGER ELWOOD AND ALDEN H. NORTON
  COMING OF THE ROBOTS, THE   AN   CLB 63
  DOORWAY INTO TIME   AN   MBB 66
    AND OTHER STORIES FROM MODERN MASTERPIECES OF SCIENCE FICTION
  EDITOR'S CHOICE IN SCIENCE FICTION   AN H MBR 54
  EXPLORING OTHER WORLDS   AN   CLB 63
  FUTURES TO INFINITY   AN   PYR 70 09
  LIFE EVERLASTING AND OTHER TALES OF SCIENCE, FANTASY & HORROR
    (LISTED UNDER DAVID KELLER)   EC H AVL 47
  MARTIAN ODYSSEY AND OTHER SCIENCE FICTION TALES, A (LISTED
    UNDER STANLEY G. WEINBAUM)   EC H HYP 74
  MARTIAN ODYSSEY, A (LISTED UNDER STANLEY G. WEINBAUM)
                                               EC   LAN 62
  MASTERPIECES OF SCIENCE FICTION   AN H WOR 66
  MICROCOSMIC GOD   AN   MBB 65
    AND OTHER STORIES FROM MODERN MASTERPIECES OF SCIENCE FICTION
  MODERN MASTERPIECES OF SCIENCE FICTION   AN H WOR 65
    DERIVATIVE ANTHOLOGIES "DOORWAY INTO TIME", "MICROCOSMIC GOD"
    AND "THE VORTEX BLASTERS"
  MOON ERA, THE   AN H DBL 67
    SEE "THREE STORIES"
  SCIENCE FICTION BY GASLIGHT   AN H WOR 68
    A HISTORY AND ANTHOLOGY OF SCIENCE FICTION
    IN THE POPULAR MAGAZINES 1891 TO 1911
  SENSE OF WONDER, A   AN H SID 67
    SEE "THREE STORIES"
  THREE STORIES   AN H DBL 67

    ALSO AS "THE MOON ERA" AND "A SENSE OF WONDER"
  UNDER THE MOONS OF MARS   AN H HRW 70
  VORTEX BLASTERS, THE   AN   MBB 65
    AND OTHER STORIES FROM MODERN MASTERPIECES OF SCIENCE FICTION
  WHEN WOMEN RULE   AN H WKR 72
  COLORFUL SCIENCE FICTION WORLDS OF ALDEN H. NORTON
                                               IN
    AWARD SCIENCE FICTION READER NORTON, ALDEN H.   AN
  DAWN OF FAME: THE CAREER OF STANLEY G. WEINBAUM AR   SAT 59 05
    MARTIAN ODYSSEY AND OTHER SCIENCE FICTION TALES, A
                                 WEINBAUM, STANLEY G. AC
  DEATH OF A DINOSAUR   SS   AMZ 56 08
    TIME CURVE, THE   MOSKOWITZ & ELWOOD AN
  FORGOTTEN CREATOR OF WEIRD TALES, THE   IN
    WORLDS OF WEIRD   MARGULIES, LEO   AN
  GOLDEN PYRAMID, THE   SS   FUN 56 11
    FANTASTIC UNIVERSE OMNIBUS, THE SANTESSON, HANS S. AN
  HISTORY OF "THE SCIENTIFIC ROMANCE" IN THE MUNSEY MAGAZINES,
    1912-1920, A   AR
    UNDER THE MOONS OF MARS   MOSKOWITZ, SAM   AN
  INTRODUCTION   IN
    COMING OF THE ROBOTS, THE   MOSKOWITZ, SAM   AN
    DOORWAY INTO TIME   MOSKOWITZ, SAM   AN
    EXPLORING OTHER WORLDS   MOSKOWITZ, SAM   AN
    LIFE EVERLASTING AND OTHER TALES OF SCIENCE, FANTASY
    AND HORROR   KELLER, DAVID H. MD. AC
    MODERN MASTERPIECES OF SCIENCE FICTION MOSKOWITZ, SAM AN
  INTRODUCTION   IN C
    SPACE MAGICIANS, THE   NORTON & MOSKOWITZ AN
  INTRODUCTION: A HISTORY OF SCIENCE FICTION IN THE POPULAR
    MAGAZINES, 1891-1911   IN
    SCIENCE FICTION BY GASLIGHT MOSKOWITZ, SAM   AN
  LOST CHORD, THE   SS   NEW 53 AN
    SCIENCE AND SORCERY   FORD, GARRET   AN
  LOST GIANT OF AMERICAN SCIENCE FICTION- A BIOGRAPHICAL
    PERSPECTIVE   AR
    CRYSTAL MAN, THE   MITCHELL, EDWARD P. AC
  MAN OF THE STARS   SS   PLS 41 WI
    EXPLORING OTHER WORLDS   MOSKOWITZ, SAM   AN
  OTHER SIDE OF THE CURTAIN- A REFLECTION OF THE FUTURE, THE
                                               IN C
    STRANGE SIGNPOSTS   ELWOOD & MOSKOWITZ AN
  PREFACE   IN
    SCIENCE FICTION BY GASLIGHT MOSKOWITZ, SAM   AN
    UNDER THE MOONS OF MARS   MOSKOWITZ, SAM   AN
  "PSYCHO"-LOGICAL BLOCH   AR   AMZ 62 12
    BOGEY MEN   BLOCH, ROBERT   AC
  SENSE OF WONDER, THE   IN
    THREE STORIES   MOSKOWITZ, SAM   AN
  STURGEON BIBLIOGRAPHY   MS   FSF 62 09
    BEST FROM FANTASY AND SCIENCE FICTION, 25TH ANNIV.
                                 FERMAN, EDWARD L.   AN
  WAY BACK, THE   NV   CMT 41 01
    FUTURES TO INFINITY   MOSKOWITZ, SAM   AN
  WHEN WOMEN RULE   AR   IFS 67 08
    WHEN WOMEN RULE   MOSKOWITZ, SAM   AN
  WONDERS OF WEINBAUM, THE   IN
    MARTIAN ODYSSEY, A   WEINBAUM, STANLEY G. AC

MOUDY, WALTER F.
  SEARCH FOR MAN, THE   NA
    IN THE WAKE OF MAN   ELWOOD, ROGER   OA
  SURVIVOR, THE   NV   AMZ 65 05
    POLITICAL SCIENCE FICTION   GREENBERG& WARRICK AN
    THEMES IN SCIENCE FICTION   KELLEY, LEO P.   AN
    11TH ANNUAL OF THE YEAR'S BEST S-F, THE
                                 MERRIL, JUDITH   AN

MOWSHOWITZ, ABBE
  INSIDE INFORMATION   AN L ADW 77
    COMPUTERS IN FICTION
  PREFACE   IN
    INSIDE INFORMATION   MOWSHOWITZ, ABBE   AN

MROZEK, SLAWOMIR
  UGUPU BIRD, THE   SS   68
    BEST SF: 1970   HARRISON & ALDISS   AN

MUDGETT, HERMAN W.   PSEUD. FOR WILLIAM ANTHONY PARKER WHITE
  GLASS OF THE FUTURE, THE   PM   FSF 55 01
    BEST FROM FANTASY AND SCIENCE FICTION: 5
                                 BOUCHER, ANTHONY   AN
  NAMING OF NAMES, THE   PM   FSF 53 10
    BEST FROM FANTASY AND SCIENCE FICTION: 3
                                 BOUCHER & MCCOMAS   AN
  REPORT ON THE SEXUAL BEHAVIOR OF THE EXTRA-SENSORY PERCEPTOR
                                               PM   FSF 54 08
    BEST FROM FANTASY AND SCIENCE FICTION: 4
                                 BOUCHER, ANTHONY   AN
  SILENT, UPON TWO PEAKS   PM   FSF 55 07
    BEST FROM FANTASY AND SCIENCE FICTION: 5
                                 BOUCHER, ANTHONY   AN

MUIR, EDWIN
  HORSES, THE   PM   60
    LOOKING AHEAD   ALLEN, D. & L.   AN

MULLEN, RICHARD D.
  EARTHMANIST CULTURE, THE   AR   68
    CITIES IN FLIGHT   BLISH, JAMES   AC

MUNDIS, JERROLD J.
  CHRISTMAS IN WATSON HOLLOW   SS
    NEW CONSTELLATIONS   DISCH & NAYLOR   OA
  DO IT FOR MOMMA   SS   NEW 71 AN
    RUINS OF EARTH, THE   DISCH, THOMAS M.   AN

UNDIS, JERROLD J.   NESVADBA, JOSEF

UNDIS, JERROLD J.   (CONTINUED)
LUGER IS A 9MM AUTOMATIC HANDGUN WITH A PARABELLUM ACTION, THE
                                        SS   NWS 69 03
   BEST SF STORIES FROM NEW WORLDS 6   MOORCOCK, MICHAEL   AN

UNN, H. WARNER
BLACK CAPTAIN, THE   SS   75
   YEAR'S BEST HORROR STORIES: SERIES IV, THE
                                        PAGE, GERALD W.   AN

UNRO, H. H.   ALSO AS   SAKI
GABRIEL-ERNEST   SS   30
   SUPERNATURAL READER, THE   CONKLIN, G&L.   AN

UNRO, JOHN
TRIP TO VENUS, A (1897)   SS   97
   FAREWELL FANTASTIC VENUS   ALDISS & HARRISON   AN

UNRO, KIRK
"CAP'N IL'S" CLOSEST CALL   SS
   BATTLE FOR THE PACIFIC AND OTHER ADVENTURES AT SEA, THE
                                        ANONYMOUS   AN

URPHY, ROBERT
FALLOUT ISLAND   SS   SEP 62 03
   POST READER OF FANTASY AND SCIENCE FICTION
                                        SATURDAY EVE. POST   AN
PHANTOM SETTER, THE   SS   SEP 61 06
   OTHER SIDE OF THE CLOCK, THE   STERN, PHILIP VAN D. AN
   POST READER OF FANTASY AND SCIENCE FICTION
                                        SATURDAY EVE. POST   AN

URPHY, SHIRLEY R.
MOONCUP, THE   NV
   ANYWHERE, ANYWHEN   ENGDAHL, SYLVIA   OA

URRAY, ROBERT
REPLACEMENT, THE   SS   FSF 60 02
   BEST FROM FANTASY AND SCIENCE FICTION: 10
                                        MILLS, ROBERT P.   AN

URRY, JOHN M.   SEE PSEUD. RICHARD COWPER

USLIN, E.
ROBOT HUMOR   SS C
   RUSSIAN SCIENCE FICTION, 1969   MAGIDOFF, ROBERT   AN

YERS, HOWARD L.
MISINFORMATION   SS   ASF 72 04
   SOCIOLOGY THROUGH SCIENCE FICTION MILSTEAD/GREENBERG/& AN
OTHER WAY AROUND, THE   NV   INY 71 02
   INFINITY 2   HOSKINS, ROBERT   OA
OUT, WITH   SS   ASF 72 06
   ANALOG 9   BOVA, BEN   AN
   BEST SF: 1972   HARRISON & ALDISS   AN

ADLER, MAGGIE
PILL, THE   SS   FAN 72 04
   YOU AND SCIENCE FICTION   HOLLISTER, BERNARD C AN
SECRET, THE   SS   CLR 71 01
   CLARION   WILSON, ROBIN SCOTT OA

ARAYAN, R. K.
BREATH OF LUCIFER, A   SS   PBY 69 07
   MASKS   PLAYBOY, EDITORS OF AN

ASH, OGDEN
TALE OF THE THIRTEENTH FLOOR, A   PM   FSF 55 07
   DECADE OF FANTASY AND SCIENCE FICTION, A
                                        MILLS, ROBERT P.   AN

ATHAN, ROBERT
DIGGING THE WEANS   FA   HRP 56 11
   SF:57, THE YEAR'S GREATEST SCIENCE FICTION AND FANTASY
                                        MERRIL, JUDITH   AN
ENCOUNTER IN THE PAST   SS   FSF 67 07
   BEST FROM FANTASY AND SCIENCE FICTION: 17
                                        FERMAN, EDWARD L.   AN
PRIDE OF CARROTS, A   NV   FSF 59 12
   SCIENCE FICTION ODDITIES   CONKLIN, GROFF   AN

AYLOR, CHARLES   SEE ALSO   CO-EDITOR THOMAS M. DISCH
REPAIRING THE OFFICE   NV   NEW 75 AN
   NEW IMPROVED SUN, THE   DISCH, THOMAS M.   AN
WE ARE DAINTY LITTLE PEOPLE   SS   BMR 73
   BAD MOON RISING   DISCH, THOMAS M.   OA

EAL, H. C.
WHO SHALL DWELL...   SS   PBY 62 07
   LAST TRAIN TO LIMBO   PLAYBOY, EDITORS OF AN
   PLAYBOY BOOK OF SCIENCE FICTION AND FANTASY, THE
                                        PLAYBOY, EDITORS OF   AN
   THEMES IN SCIENCE FICTION   KELLEY, LEO P.   AN

EARING, H. JR.
SINISTER RESEARCHES OF C. P. RANSOM, THE   AC H DBL 54
ACTINIC ACTOR, THE (SEE THE ACTINIC GHOST)   TC
ACTINIC GHOST, THE (THE ACTINIC ACTOR)   SS   FSF 52 04
   SINISTER RESEARCHES OF C. P. RANSOM, THE
                                        NEARING, H. JR.   AC
AESTHETIC DECAPITATIONS, THE   SS   NEW 54 AC
   SINISTER RESEARCHES OF C. P. RANSOM, THE
                                        NEARING, H. JR.   AC
AWARD, THE (EPILOGUE)   MS
   SINISTER RESEARCHES OF C. P. RANSOM, THE
                                        NEARING, H. JR.   AC

NEARING, H. JR.   (CONTINUED)
CEREBRATIVE PSITTACOID, THE   SS   FSF 53 08
   BEST SF   CRISPIN, EDMUND   AN
DILEMMA, THE (PROLOGUE)   MS
   SINISTER RESEARCHES OF C. P. RANSOM, THE
                                        NEARING, H. JR.   AC
FACETITIOUS PENTANGLE, THE   SS   FSF 52 09
   SINISTER RESEARCHES OF C. P. RANSOM, THE
                                        NEARING, H. JR.   AC
HERMENEUTICAL DOUGHNUT, THE   SS   NEW 54 AC
   MATHEMATICAL MAGPIE, THE   FADIMAN, CLIFTON   AN
   SINISTER RESEARCHES OF C. P. RANSOM, THE
                                        NEARING, H. JR.   AC
HYPERSPHERICAL BASKETBALL, THE   SS   FSF 51 12
   BEST FROM FANTASY AND SCIENCE FICTION: 2
                                        BOUCHER & MCCOMAS   AN
   SINISTER RESEARCHES OF C. P. RANSOM, THE
                                        NEARING, H. JR.   AC
MALADJUSTED CLASSROOM, THE   SS   FSF 53 06
   BEST FROM FANTASY AND SCIENCE FICTION: 3
                                        BOUCHER & MCCOMAS   AN
MALIGNANT ORGAN, THE   SS   FSF 53 03
   SINISTER RESEARCHES OF C. P. RANSOM, THE
                                        NEARING, H. JR.   AC
MATHEMATICAL VOODOO, THE   SS   FSF 51 04
   BEST FROM FANTASY AND SCIENCE FICTION BOUCHER & MCCOMAS   AN
   FANTASIA MATHEMATICA   FADIMAN, CLIFTON   AN
   SINISTER RESEARCHES OF C. P. RANSOM, THE
                                        NEARING, H. JR.   AC
POETRY MACHINE, THE   SS   FSF 50 FL
   SINISTER RESEARCHES OF C. P. RANSOM, THE
                                        NEARING, H. JR.   AC
UNIDENTIFIED AMAZON, THE   SS   FSF 52 12
   SINISTER RESEARCHES OF C. P. RANSOM, THE
                                        NEARING, H. JR.   AC

NELSON, ALAN
NARAPOIA (THE ORIGIN OF NARAPOIA, WDG 48 04) SS   FSF 51 04
   BEST FROM FANTASY AND SCIENCE FICTION BOUCHER & MCCOMAS   AN
   FIFTY SHORT SCIENCE FICTION TALES   ASIMOV & CONKLIN   AN
ORIGIN OF NARAPOIA, THE (SEE NARAPOIA)   TC
SHOPDROPPER, THE   SS   FSF 55 01
   GREAT SCIENCE FICTION ABOUT DOCTORS   CONKLIN, G&FABRICANT AN
SILENZIA   SS   FSF 53 09
   17 X INFINITY   CONKLIN, GROFF   AN
SOAP OPERA   SS   FSF 53 04
   13 GREAT STORIES OF SCIENCE FICTION   CONKLIN, GROFF   AN

NELSON, RADELL F.   SEE PSEUD. RAY NELSON

NELSON, RAY   PSEUD. FOR RADELL F. NELSON
EIGHT O'CLOCK IN THE MORNING   SS   FSF 63 11
   BEST FROM FANTASY AND SCIENCE FICTION: 13
                                        DAVIDSON, AVRAM   AN
   OTHERS, THE   CARR, TERRY   AN
   TALES OF TERROR FROM OUTER SPACE   CHETWYND-HAYES, R.   AN
   9TH ANNUAL OF THE YEAR'S BEST S-F, THE MERRIL, JUDITH   AN
TIME TRAVEL FOR PEDESTRIANS   SS   DVS 72 02
   AGAIN, DANGEROUS VISIONS   ELLISON, HARLAN   OA

NEMEROV, HOWARD
EXCHANGE OF MEN   SS C STO 63 01
   NIGHT IN FUNLAND   BRONDFIELD, JEROME   AN

NESBIT, EDITH
PAVILION, THE   SS   23
   SUPERNATURAL READER, THE   CONKLIN, G&L.   AN
THREE DRUGS, THE   SS   10
   BEFORE ARMAGEDDON   MOORCOCK, MICHAEL   AN

NESVADBA, JOSEF
IN THE FOOTSTEPS OF THE ABOMINABLE SNOWMAN   AC   70
   SEE "THE LOST FACE"
LOST FACE, THE   AC H TAP 71
   BEST SCIENCE FICTION FROM CZECHOSLOVAKIA
   IN ENGLAND AS "IN THE FOOTSTEPS OF THE ABOMINABLE SNOWMAN"
   ALL BUT FIRST AND THIRD STORIES ARE IN "VAMPIRES LTD."
                                               AC   VNS 64
   SEE "THE LOST FACE"
CAPTAIN NEMO'S LAST ADVENTURE   NV   73
   BEST SF: 1973   HARRISON & ALDISS   AN
   VIEW FROM ANOTHER SHORE   ROTTENSTEINER, FRANZ AN
CHEMICAL FORMULA OF DESTINY, THE   SS   64
   LOST FACE, THE   NESVADBA, JOSEF   AC
DEATH OF AN APEMAN, THE   NV
   LOST FACE, THE   NESVADBA, JOSEF   AC
DOCTOR MOREAU'S OTHER ISLAND   SS   64
   LOST FACE, THE   NESVADBA, JOSEF   AC
EXPEDITION IN THE OPPOSITE DIRECTION   NV   64
   LOST FACE, THE   NESVADBA, JOSEF   AC
IN THE FOOTSTEPS OF THE ABOMINABLE SNOWMAN NV   64
   LOST FACE, THE   NESVADBA, JOSEF   AC
INVENTER OF HIS OWN UNDOING   NV   64
   LOST FACE, THE   NESVADBA, JOSEF   AC
LAST SECRET WEAPON OF THE THIRD REICH, THE SS   64
   10TH ANNUAL OF THE YEAR'S BEST S-F, THE
                                        MERRIL, JUDITH   AN
LOST FACE, THE   NV   64
   BEST SF: 1970   HARRISON & ALDISS   AN
   LOST FACE, THE   NESVADBA, JOSEF   AC
TRIAL NOBODY EVER HEARD OF, THE   SS
   LOST FACE, THE   NESVADBA, JOSEF   AC
VAMPIRES LTD.   SS   64
   OTHER WORLDS, OTHER SEAS   SUVIN, DARKO   AN
   WORLD'S BEST SCIENCE FICTION: 1965   WOLLHEIM & CARR   AN

NEVILLE, KRIS   NIVEN, LARR

NEVILLE, KRIS
  MISSION: MANSTOP   AC   LEI 71 10
    BALLENGER'S PEOPLE   SS   GAL 67 04
      ON OUR WAY TO THE FUTURE   CARR, TERRY   AN
    BETTYANN   NV   NTS 51
      GIFTS OF ASTI AND OTHER STORIES OF SCIENCE FICTION, THE
                                           ELWOOD, ROGER   AN
      NEW TALES OF SPACE AND TIME   HEALY, RAYMOND J.   OA
     *STORIES FOR TOMORROW   SLOANE, WILLIAM   AN
      STRANGE GIFTS   SILVERBERG, ROBERT   AN
      YOUNG DEMONS   ELWOOD & GHIDALIA   AN
    BETTYANN'S CHILDREN   SS   DEM 73
      DEMON KIND   ELWOOD, ROGER   OA
    COLD WAR   SS   ASF 49 10
     *ASTOUNDING SCIENCE FICTION ANTHOLOGY, THE
                                           CAMPBELL, JOHN W. JR AN
      FIRST STEP OUTWARD   HOSKINS, ROBERT   AN
     *SECOND ASTOUNDING SCIENCE FICTION ANTHOLOGY, THE
                                           CAMPBELL, JOHN W. JR AN
    DOMINANT SPECIES   SS   ORB 71 09
      ORBIT 9   KNIGHT, DAMON   OA
    EXPERIMENTAL STATION (THE FIRST)   SS   SSS 50 09
      MISSION: MANSTOP   NEVILLE, KRIS   AC
     *SCIENCE FICTION ADVENTURES IN MUTATION CONKLIN, GROFF   AN
      FIRST, THE (SEE EXPERIMENTAL STATION)   TC
    FOREST OF ZIL, THE   SS   AMZ 67 12
      BEST SF: 1967   HARRISON & ALDISS   AN
    FRANCHISE   SS   ASF 51 02
     *STORIES FOR TOMORROW   SLOANE, WILLIAM   AN
    FROM THE GOVERNMENT PRINTING OFFICE   SS   DVS 67 01
      DANGEROUS VISIONS   ELLISON, HARLAN   OA
    GRATITUDE GUARANTEED   SS C FSF 53 08
      PORTALS OF TOMORROW   DERLETH, AUGUST   AN
      TWENTY YEARS OF FANTASY & SCIENCE FICTION
                                           FERMAN & MILLS   AN
    HOLD BACK TOMORROW   SS   IMG 51 09
     *IMAGINATION UNLIMITED   BLEILER & DIKTY   AN
    HUNT THE HUNTER   SS   GAL 51 06
      MISSION: MANSTOP   NEVILLE, KRIS   AC
    IT PAYS TO ADVERTISE   SS   FSF 53 06
      TOMORROW'S UNIVERSE   CAMPBELL, H. J.   AN
    MARGINAL ERROR   SS   TWS 53 06
      MISSION: MANSTOP   NEVILLE, KRIS   AC
    MISSION: MANSTOP (MISSION)   NV   FSF 53 04
      MISSION: MANSTOP   NEVILLE, KRIS   AC
    NEW APPLES IN THE GARDEN   SS   ASF 63 07
      NIGHTMARE AGE   POHL, FREDERIK   AN
      ONE HUNDRED YEARS OF SCIENCE FICTION KNIGHT, DAMON   AN
    NIGHT OF THE NICKEL BEER, THE   SS   ESC 67
      NEW WORLDS OF FANTASY NO. 2   CARR, TERRY   AN
    OLD MAN HENDERSON   SS   FSF 51 06
      BEST FROM FANTASY AND SCIENCE FICTION BOUCHER & MCCOMAS   AN
      SPECIAL WONDER   MCCOMAS, J. FRANCIS   AN
      UNIVERSE AHEAD   ENGDAHL & ROBERSON   AN
    OVERTURE   SS   NTL 54
      9 TALES OF SPACE AND TIME   HEALY, RAYMOND J.   OA
    PACEM EST   SS C INY 70 01
      BEST SF: 1970   HARRISON & ALDISS   AN
      IN THE POCKET AND OTHER S-F STORIES O'DONNELL, K. M.   DC
      INFINITY 1   HOSKINS, ROBERT   OA
    PATER FAMILIAS   SS C FSF 72 03
      BEST OF BARRY N. MALZBERG, THE   MALZBERG, BARRY N.   AC
      OUT FROM GANYMEDE   MALZBERG, BARRY N.   AC
    PRICE OF SIMERYL, THE   NV   ASF 66 12
      FAR-OUT PEOPLE, THE   HOSKINS, ROBERT   AN
    QUALITY OF THE PRODUCT, THE   SS C SVW 73
      SAVING WORLDS   ELWOOD & KIDD   OA
    SHAMAR'S WAR   NV   GAL 64 02
      SEVEN TRIPS THROUGH TIME AND SPACE   CONKLIN, GROFF   AN
    SPECIAL DELIVERY   NO   IMG 52 01
      MAN AGAINST TOMORROW   NOLAN, WILLIAM F.   AN
    SURVIVAL PROBLEMS   SS   UNI 74 05
      UNIVERSE 5   CARR, TERRY   OA
    TAKE TWO QUIGGIES   NV   FSF 50 12
      MISSION: MANSTOP   NEVILLE, KRIS   AC
    TOY, THE   SS   IMG 52 12
      MISSION: MANSTOP   NEVILLE, KRIS   AC
    UNDERGROUND MOVEMENT   SS   FSF 52 06
     *BEYOND HUMAN KEN   MERRIL, JUDITH   AN
      MISSION: MANSTOP   NEVILLE, KRIS   AC
    WORSHIP NIGHT   SS   FSF 53 11
      SEA OF SPACE, A   NOLAN, WILLIAM F.   AN

NEVILLE, LIL
  QUALITY OF THE PRODUCT, THE   SS C SVW 73
    SAVING WORLDS   ELWOOD & KIDD   OA

NEWCOMB, SIMON
  END OF THE WORLD, THE   SS
    BATTLE OF THE MONSTERS AND OTHER STORIES, THE
                                           HARTWELL & CURREY   AN
  THAT MASON-DIXON LINE   MS
    MATHEMATICAL MAGPIE, THE   FADIMAN, CLIFTON   AN

NEWMAN, LOUIS
  LICENSE TO STEAL   FA   GAL 59 08
    SIXTH GALAXY READER, THE   GOLD, H. L.   AN

NEYROUD, GERALD E.
  TERRA-VENUSIAN WAR OF 1979, THE   SS   FSF 59 12
    SCIENCE FICTION ODDITIES   CONKLIN, GROFF   AN

NICHOLLS, PETER
  INTRODUCTION: AN ABC OF BRITISH SCIENCE FICTION- APOCALYPSE,
    BLEAKNESS, CATASTROPHE   IN
      BEYOND THIS HORIZON   CARRELL, CHRISTOPHER OA

NICHOLLS, PETER   (CONTINUED)
  1975: THE YEAR IN SCIENCE FICTION, OR LET'S HEAR IT FOR THE
    DECLINE AND FALL OF THE...   AR
    NEBULA AWARD STORIES 11   LE GUIN, URSULA K.   A

NICHOLS, NICHELLE
  INTRODUCTION TO THE ENCHANTED POOL   IN
    STAR TREK: THE NEW VOYAGES   MARSHAK, S&CULBREATH O

NICHOLSON, JOHN
  LITTLE GREEN MEN   AR   FUN 58 0
    FLYING SAUCERS IN FACT AND FICTION   SANTESSON, HANS S.   A

NIELSEN, LIN
  IN THE GREENHOUSE   SS   CLR 72 0
    CLARION II   WILSON, ROBIN SCOTT O
  WHEN PAPPY ISN'T THERE   SS   CLR 73 0
    CLARION III   WILSON, ROBIN SCOTT O

NIELSEN, NIELS E.
  PLANET FOR SALE   SS   64
    BEST FROM THE REST OF THE WORLD, THE   WOLLHEIM, DONALD A. A

NIGHTINGALE, CHARLES
  PLANTING TIME   SS C NEW 76 A
    ANTIGRAV: COSMIC COMEDIES   STRICK, PHILIP   A
    GALACTIC EMPIRES VOLUME ONE   ALDISS, BRIAN W.   A

NIMOY, LEONARD
  INTRODUCTION TO NI VAR   IN
    STAR TREK: THE NEW VOYAGES   MARSHAK, S&CULBREATH O

NIMS, JOHN FREDERICK
  A.D. 2267   PM   67
    SCIENCE FICTION   BRODKIN & PEARSON   A

NISSENSON, HUGH
  MISSION, THE   SS   PBY 64 1
    FIEND, THE   PLAYBOY, EDITORS OF A
    PLAYBOY BOOK OF SCIENCE FICTION AND FANTASY, THE
                                           PLAYBOY, EDITORS OF A

NIVEN, LARRY
  ALL THE MYRIAD WAYS   AC   BAL 71 06
  FLIGHT OF THE HORSE, THE   AC   BAL 73 09
  HOLE IN SPACE, A   AC   BAL 74 06
  LONG ARM OF GIL HAMILTON, THE   AC   BAL 76 02
  NEUTRON STAR   AC   BAL 68 04
  SHAPE OF SPACE, THE   AC   BAL 69 09
  TALES OF KNOWN SPACE: THE UNIVERSE OF LARRY NIVEN AC   BAL 75 08
  WORLD OUT OF TIME, A   NO H HRW 76
    AFTERTHOUGHTS   MS
      TALES OF KNOWN SPACE: THE UNIVERSE OF LARRY NIVEN
                                           NIVEN, LARRY   AC
    AFTERWORD   MS
      FLIGHT OF THE HORSE, THE   NIVEN, LARRY   AC
    AFTERWORD: THE LAST WORD ABOUT SF: DETECTIVES   MS
      LONG ARM OF GIL HAMILTON, THE   NIVEN, LARRY   AC
    ALIBI MACHINE, THE   SS   VTX 73 06
      ANTIGRAV: COSMIC COMEDIES   STRICK, PHILIP   A
      HOLE IN SPACE, A   NIVEN, LARRY   AC
    ALL THE BRIDGES RUSTING   NV   VTX 73 08
      HOLE IN SPACE, A   NIVEN, LARRY   AC
    ALL THE MYRIAD WAYS   SS   GAL 68 10
      ALL THE MYRIAD WAYS   NIVEN, LARRY   AC
      WORLDS OF MAYBE   SILVERBERG, ROBERT   AC
    ARM   NA   EPC 75
      EPOCH   ELWOOD & SILVERBERG ON
      LONG ARM OF GIL HAMILTON, THE   NIVEN, LARRY   AC
    AT THE BOTTOM OF A HOLE   NV   GAL 66 12
      SHAPE OF SPACE, THE   NIVEN, LARRY   AC
      TALES OF KNOWN SPACE: THE UNIVERSE OF LARRY NIVEN
                                           NIVEN, LARRY   AC
    AT THE CORE   NV   IFS 66 11
      NEUTRON STAR   NIVEN, LARRY   AC
      SECOND IF READER OF SCIENCE FICTION, THE
                                           POHL, FREDERIK   AN
    BECALMED IN HELL   SS   FSF 65 07
      ALL THE MYRIAD WAYS   NIVEN, LARRY   AC
      NEBULA AWARD STORIES   KNIGHT, DAMON   AN
      SCIENCE FICTION ARGOSY, A   KNIGHT, DAMON   AN
      TALES OF KNOWN SPACE: THE UNIVERSE OF LARRY NIVEN
                                           NIVEN, LARRY   AC
      TWENTY YEARS OF FANTASY & SCIENCE FICTION
                                           FERMAN & MILLS   AN
      WORLD'S BEST SCIENCE FICTION: 1966   WOLLHEIM & CARR   AN
    BIGGER THAN WORLDS   AR   ASF 74 03
      HOLE IN SPACE, A   NIVEN, LARRY   AC
    BIRD IN THE HAND   SS   FSF 70 10
      FLIGHT OF THE HORSE, THE   NIVEN, LARRY   AC
      WORLD'S BEST SCIENCE FICTION: 1971   WOLLHEIM & CARR   AN
    BORDERED IN BLACK   SS   FSF 66 04
      SF: AUTHORS' CHOICE 3   HARRISON, HARRY   AN
      SHAPE OF SPACE, THE   NIVEN, LARRY   AN
    BORDERLAND OF SOL, THE   NV   ASF 75 0
      TALES OF KNOWN SPACE: THE UNIVERSE OF LARRY NIVEN
                                           NIVEN, LARRY   AC
    CHILDREN OF THE STATE   NO   GAL 76 09
      WORLD OUT OF TIME, A   NIVEN, LARRY   NO
    CLOAK OF ANARCHY   NV   ASF 72 03
      BEST SCIENCE FICTION STORIES OF THE YEAR (1972)
                                           DEL REY, LESTER   AN
      TALES OF KNOWN SPACE: THE UNIVERSE OF LARRY NIVEN
                                           NIVEN, LARRY   AC
    2020 VISION   POURNELLE, JERRY   AN

NIVEN, LARRY

NOLAN, WILLIAM F.

NIVEN, LARRY   (CONTINUED)
COLDEST PLACE, THE   SS   IFS 64 12
  TALES OF KNOWN SPACE: THE UNIVERSE OF LARRY NIVEN
                                          NIVEN, LARRY   AC
CONVERGENT SERIES (THE LONG NIGHT)   SS   FSF 67 03
  SHAPE OF SPACE, THE   NIVEN, LARRY   AC
DEADLIER WEAPON, THE   SS   EQM 68 06
  SHAPE OF SPACE, THE   NIVEN, LARRY   AC
DEATH BY ECSTASY (THE ORGANLEGGERS)   NV   GAL 69 01
  LONG ARM OF GIL HAMILTON, THE   NIVEN, LARRY   AC
  SHAPE OF SPACE, THE   NIVEN, LARRY   AC
  WORLD'S BEST SCIENCE FICTION: 1970   WOLLHEIM & CARR   AN
DEATH IN A CAGE   SS   NEW 73 AC
  FLIGHT OF THE HORSE, THE   NIVEN, LARRY   AC
DECEIVERS, THE (SEE INTENT TO DECEIVE)   TC
DEFENSELESS DEAD, THE   NV   TTM 73
  LONG ARM OF GIL HAMILTON, THE   NIVEN, LARRY   AC
  TEN TOMORROWS   ELWOOD, ROGER   OA
DOWN AND OUT   NV   GAL 76 02
  BEST FROM GALAXY, THE VOLUME IV   BAEN, JAMES   AN
  WORLD OUT OF TIME, A   NIVEN, LARRY   NO
DRY RUN   SS   FSF 68 05
  SHAPE OF SPACE, THE   NIVEN, LARRY   AC
ETHICS OF MADNESS, THE   NV   IFS 67 04
  NEUTRON STAR   NIVEN, LARRY   AC
EXERCISE IN SPECULATION: THE THEORY AND PRACTICE OF
  TELEPORTATION   AR   GAL 69 03
  ALL THE MYRIAD WAYS   NIVEN, LARRY   AC
EYE OF AN OCTOPUS   SS   GAL 66 02
  TALES OF KNOWN SPACE: THE UNIVERSE OF LARRY NIVEN
                                          NIVEN, LARRY   AC
FLASH CROWD   NA   TTT 73
  FLIGHT OF THE HORSE, THE   NIVEN, LARRY   AC
  THREE TRIPS IN TIME AND SPACE   SILVERBERG, ROBERT   OA
FLATLANDER   NV   IFS 67 03
  NEUTRON STAR   NIVEN, LARRY   AC
  SEVEN TRIPS THROUGH TIME AND SPACE   CONKLIN, GROFF   AN
FLIGHT OF THE HORSE, THE (GET A HORSE!)   SS   FSF 69 10
  FLIGHT OF THE HORSE, THE   NIVEN, LARRY   AC
FOR A FOGGY NIGHT   SS   FSF 71 07
  ALL THE MYRIAD WAYS   NIVEN, LARRY   AC
FOURTH PROFESSION, THE   NV   QRK 71 04
  BEST SCIENCE FICTION OF THE YEAR, THE   CARR, TERRY   AN
  HOLE IN SPACE, A   NIVEN, LARRY   AC
  QUARK/4   DELANY & HACKER   OA
  1972 ANNUAL WORLD'S BEST SF, THE   WOLLHEIM, DONALD A.   AN
GET A HORSE! (ALSO AS THE FLIGHT OF THE HORSE)   SS   FSF 69 10
  BEST FROM FANTASY AND SCIENCE FICTION: 19
                                          FERMAN, EDWARD L.   AN
GRENDEL   NV   NEW 68 AC
  NEUTRON STAR   NIVEN, LARRY   AC
HANDICAP (ALSO AS THE HANDICAPPED)   NV   GAL 67 12
  WORLD'S BEST SCIENCE FICTION: 1968   WOLLHEIM & CARR   AN
HANDICAPPED, THE (HANDICAP)   NV   GAL 67 12
  NEUTRON STAR   NIVEN, LARRY   AC
HOLE MAN, THE   SS   ASF 74 01
  BEST SCIENCE FICTION OF THE YEAR, THE NO. 4
                                          CARR, TERRY   AN
  HOLE IN SPACE, A   NIVEN, LARRY   AC
HOW THE HEROES DIE   NV   GAL 66 10
  SHAPE OF SPACE, THE   NIVEN, LARRY   AC
  TALES OF KNOWN SPACE: THE UNIVERSE OF LARRY NIVEN
                                          NIVEN, LARRY   AC
INCONSTANT MOON   NV   NEW 71 AC
  ALL THE MYRIAD WAYS   NIVEN, LARRY   AC
  BEST SCIENCE FICTION FOR 1972   POHL, FREDERIK   AN
INTENT TO DECEIVE (THE DECEIVERS)   SS   GAL 68 04
  TALES OF KNOWN SPACE: THE UNIVERSE OF LARRY NIVEN
                                          NIVEN, LARRY   AC
INTRODUCTION: MY UNIVERSE AND WELCOME TO IT!   IN
  TALES OF KNOWN SPACE: THE UNIVERSE OF LARRY NIVEN
                                          NIVEN, LARRY   AC
JIGSAW MAN, THE   SS   DVS 67 01
  ALL THE MYRIAD WAYS   NIVEN, LARRY   AC
  DANGEROUS VISIONS   ELLISON, HARLAN   OA
  TALES OF KNOWN SPACE: THE UNIVERSE OF LARRY NIVEN
                                          NIVEN, LARRY   AC
KIND OF MURDER, A   SS   ASF 74 04
  HOLE IN SPACE, A   NIVEN, LARRY   AC
LAST DAYS OF THE PERMANENT FLOATING RIOT CLUB, THE
                                                 SS   NEW 74 AC
  HOLE IN SPACE, A   NIVEN, LARRY   AC
LEVIATHAN!   SS   PBY 70 08
  FLIGHT OF THE HORSE, THE   NIVEN, LARRY   AC
  LAST TRAIN TO LIMBO   PLAYBOY, EDITORS OF   AN
LIKE BANQUO'S GHOST   SS   IFS 68 09
  SHAPE OF SPACE, THE   NIVEN, LARRY   AC
LONG NIGHT, THE (SEE CONVERGENT SERIES)   TC
MAN OF STEEL- WOMAN OF KLEENEX   AR   NEW 71 AC
  ALL THE MYRIAD WAYS   NIVEN, LARRY   AC
MEDDLER, THE   NV   FSF 68 10
  SHAPE OF SPACE, THE   NIVEN, LARRY   AC
MISTAKE   SS   STL 76 02
  STELLAR 2   DEL REY, JUDY-LYNN   OA
NEUTRON STAR   NV   IFS 66 10
  HUGO WINNERS, THE (VOLUME 2)   ASIMOV, ISAAC   AN
  NEUTRON STAR   NIVEN, LARRY   AC
  SPECULATIONS   SANDERS, THOMAS E.   AN
  WHERE DO WE GO FROM HERE?   ASIMOV, ISAAC   AN
NOT LONG BEFORE THE END   SS   FSF 69 04
  ALL THE MYRIAD WAYS   NIVEN, LARRY   AC
  GOLDEN ROAD, THE   KNIGHT, DAMON   AN
  NEBULA AWARD STORIES NO. 5   BLISH, JAMES   AN
ONE FACE   NV   GAL 65 06
  SHAPE OF SPACE, THE   NIVEN, LARRY   AC

NIVEN, LARRY   (CONTINUED)
ORGANLEGGERS, THE (SEE DEATH BY ECSTACY)   TC
PASSERBY   SS   GAL 69 09
  ALL THE MYRIAD WAYS   NIVEN, LARRY   AC
PLAYTHING   SS   IFS 74 08
  BEST FROM IF, THE VOLUME III   BAEN, JAMES   AN
RAMMER   NV   GAL 71 11
  BEST FROM GALAXY, THE VOLUME I   GALAXY, EDITORS OF   AN
  BEST SCIENCE FICTION STORIES OF THE YEAR (1971)
                                          DEL REY, LESTER   AN
  HOLE IN SPACE, A   NIVEN, LARRY   AC
  WORLD OUT OF TIME, A   NIVEN, LARRY   NO
RELIC OF EMPIRE, A   NV   IFS 66 12
  NEUTRON STAR   NIVEN, LARRY   AC
SAFE AT ANY SPEED   SS   FSF 67 05
  SHAPE OF SPACE, THE   NIVEN, LARRY   AC
  TALES OF KNOWN SPACE: THE UNIVERSE OF LARRY NIVEN
                                          NIVEN, LARRY   AC
SINGULARITIES MAKE ME NERVOUS   SS   STL 74 01
  STELLAR 1   DEL REY, JUDY-LYNN   OA
SOFT WEAPON, THE   NV   IFS 67 02
  NEUTRON STAR   NIVEN, LARRY   AC
THEORY AND PRACTICE OF TIME TRAVEL, THE   AR   NEW 71 AC
  ALL THE MYRIAD WAYS   NIVEN, LARRY   AC
  LOOKING AHEAD   ALLEN, D. & L.   AN
THERE IS A TIDE   NV   GAL 68 07
  HOLE IN SPACE, A   NIVEN, LARRY   AC
  TALES OF KNOWN SPACE: THE UNIVERSE OF LARRY NIVEN
                                          NIVEN, LARRY   AC
THERE'S A WOLF IN MY TIME MACHINE   SS   FSF 71 06
  FLIGHT OF THE HORSE, THE   NIVEN, LARRY   AC
  ZOO 2000   YOLEN, JANE   AN
TIMELINE FOR KNOWN SPACE   MS
  TALES OF KNOWN SPACE: THE UNIVERSE OF LARRY NIVEN
                                          NIVEN, LARRY   AC
UNFINISHED STORY NO. 1   SS   FSF 70 12
  ALL THE MYRIAD WAYS   NIVEN, LARRY   AC
UNFINISHED STORY NO. 2   SS   NEW 71 AC
  ALL THE MYRIAD WAYS   NIVEN, LARRY   AC
WAIT IT OUT   SS   FUP 68
  ALL THE MYRIAD WAYS   NIVEN, LARRY   AC
  TALES OF KNOWN SPACE: THE UNIVERSE OF LARRY NIVEN
                                          NIVEN, LARRY   AC
  TOMORROW'S WORLDS   SILVERBERG, ROBERT   AN
WARRIORS, THE   NV   IFS 66 02
  SHAPE OF SPACE, THE   NIVEN, LARRY   AC
  TALES OF KNOWN SPACE: THE UNIVERSE OF LARRY NIVEN
                                          NIVEN, LARRY   AC
WHAT CAN YOU SAY ABOUT CHOCOLATE COVERED MANHOLE COVERS?
                                                 SS   NEW 71 AC
  ALL THE MYRIAD WAYS   NIVEN, LARRY   AC
WHAT GOOD IS A GLASS DAGGER?   NV   FSF 72 09
  FLIGHT OF THE HORSE, THE   NIVEN, LARRY   AC
WRONG-WAY STREET   SS   GAL 65 04
  FIRST FLIGHTS TO THE MOON   CLEMENT, HAL   AN
  NINTH GALAXY READER, THE   POHL, FREDERIK   AN
  VOYAGERS IN TIME   SILVERBERG, ROBERT   AN
$16,940.00   SS   AHM 74
  HOLE IN SPACE, A   NIVEN, LARRY   AC

NOAKES, DONALD
LONG SILENCE, THE   SS   ASF 72 03
  BEST SCIENCE FICTION STORIES OF THE YEAR (1972)
                                          DEL REY, LESTER   AN

NODVIK, STAN
POSTPONED CURE, THE   SS   VTX 74 06
  BEST SCIENCE FICTION STORIES OF THE YEAR (1974)
                                          DEL REY, LESTER   AN

NOLAN, WILLIAM F.   ALSO AS   FRANK ANMAR
ALIEN HORIZONS   AC   PKT 74 08
ALMOST HUMAN   AN H SVN 66
  SEE "THE PSEUDO-PEOPLE"
FUTURE IS NOW, THE   OA H SHB 70
HUMAN EQUATION, THE   AN H SHB 71
IMPACT-20   AC   PBK 63 11
MAN AGAINST TOMORROW   AN   AVN 65 12
PSEUDO PEOPLE, THE   AN H SHB 65
  IN ENGLAND AS "ALMOST HUMAN"
SEA OF SPACE, A   AN   BAN 70 05
WILDERNESS OF STARS, A   AN H SHB 69
3 TO THE HIGHEST POWER   AN   AVN 68 02
ALFRED BESTER   AR
  HUMAN EQUATION, THE   NOLAN, WILLIAM F.   AN
AMAZON KICK, THE   SS   ROG 59
  IMPACT-20   NOLAN, WILLIAM F.   AC
AND MILES TO GO BEFORE I SLEEP   SS   INF 58 08
  IMPACT-20   NOLAN, WILLIAM F.   AC
  MAN AGAINST TOMORROW   NOLAN, WILLIAM F.   AN
  WONDERMAKERS 2   HOSKINS, ROBERT   AN
BEAUTIFUL DOLL CAPER, THE   SS   NUG 56
  IMPACT-20   NOLAN, WILLIAM F.   AC
BRADBURY BIBLIOGRAPHY   MS   FSF 63 05
  BEST FROM FANTASY AND SCIENCE FICTION, 25TH ANNIV.
                                          FERMAN, EDWARD L.   AN
CHAD OLIVER   AR
  3 TO THE HIGHEST POWER   NOLAN, WILLIAM F.   AN
CHAD OLIVER'S COLLECTED SCIENCE FICTION: A BASIC CHECKLIST
                                                 MS
  EDGE OF FOREVER, THE   OLIVER, CHAD   AC
COINCIDENCE   SS   BER 74
  BERSERKERS, THE   ELWOOD, ROGER   OA
DARENDINGER BUILD-UP, THE   SS   PBY 56 06
  IMPACT-20   NOLAN, WILLIAM F.   AC

NOLAN, WILLIAM F.   (CONTINUED)
  DARK ENCOUNTER   SS   59
    IMPACT-20   NOLAN, WILLIAM F.   AC
  DAY THE GORF TOOK OVER, THE (GORF¡ GORF¡ GORF¡) SS INY 71 02
    ALIEN HORIZONS   NOLAN, WILLIAM F.   AC
  DEATH DOUBLE   SS   NEW 63 AC
    IMPACT-20   NOLAN, WILLIAM F.   AC
  DUTCH   SS   58
    IMPACT-20   NOLAN, WILLIAM F.   AC
  EDITOR'S POSTSCRIPT   MS
    WILDERNESS OF STARS, A   NOLAN, WILLIAM F.   AN
  EDITOR'S PREFACE   IN
    HUMAN EQUATION, THE   NOLAN, WILLIAM F.   AN
    SEA OF SPACE, A   NOLAN, WILLIAM F.   AN
  EDITOR'S PREFACE: A IS FOR ANDROID   IN
    PSEUDO PEOPLE, THE   NOLAN, WILLIAM F.   AN
  END WITH NO PERHAPS, THE   SS   NEW 63 AC
    IMPACT-20   NOLAN, WILLIAM F.   AC
  FASTERFASTER¡ (THE FASTERFASTER AFFAIR) SS   NEW 65 AN
    ALIEN HORIZONS   NOLAN, WILLIAM F.   AC
  FROM THE OTHER SIDE OF THE MASK   IN
    ALIEN HORIZONS   NOLAN, WILLIAM F.   AC
  FULL OF, MOSTLY, BAGELS AND CREAM CHEESE SS   NEW 74 AC
    ALIEN HORIZONS   NOLAN, WILLIAM F.   AC
  FULL QUOTA   SS   FUN 58 04
    IMPACT-20   NOLAN, WILLIAM F.   AC
  GIRL WHO WASN'T THERE, THE   SS C GAM 63 01
    SCIENCE FICTION WORLDS OF FORREST J. ACKERMAN & FRIENDS
                                  ACKERMAN, FORREST J. AC
  GORF¡ GORF¡ GORF¡ (ALSO AS THE DAY THE GORF TOOK OVER)
                                           SS   INY 71 02
    INFINITY 2   HOSKINS, ROBERT   OA
  HAPPILY EVER AFTER   SS   GAM 65 04
    ALIEN HORIZONS   NOLAN, WILLIAM F.   AC
    WILDERNESS OF STARS, A   NOLAN, WILLIAM F.   AN
  HE KILT IT WITH A STICK   SS   FSF 68 02
    ALIEN HORIZONS   NOLAN, WILLIAM F.   AC
    SPECIAL WONDER   MCCOMAS, J. FRANCIS AN
  INTO THE LION'S DEN   SS   56
    IMPACT-20   NOLAN, WILLIAM F.   AC
  INTRODUCTION   IN
    FUTURE IS NOW, THE   NOLAN, WILLIAM F.   OA
    MAN AGAINST TOMORROW   NOLAN, WILLIAM F.   AN
  JENNY AMONG THE ZEEBS (AS FRANK ANMAR)   SS   FIN 70
    ALIEN HORIZONS   NOLAN, WILLIAM F.   AC
  JOHN D. MACDONALD   AR
    HUMAN EQUATION, THE   NOLAN, WILLIAM F.   AN
  JOY OF LIVING, THE   SS   IFS 54 08
    ALIEN HORIZONS   NOLAN, WILLIAM F.   AC
    IMPACT-20   NOLAN, WILLIAM F.   AC
    PSEUDO PEOPLE, THE   NOLAN, WILLIAM F.   AN
  KELLY, FREDRIC MICHAEL: 1928-1987   SS   INY 73 05
    ALIEN HORIZONS   NOLAN, WILLIAM F.   AC
    INFINITY 5   HOSKINS, ROBERT   OA
  LAP OF THE PRIMITIVE, THE   SS   FUN 58 10
    IMPACT-20   NOLAN, WILLIAM F.   AC
    SEA OF SPACE, A   NOLAN, WILLIAM F.   AN
  LAST THREE MONTHS, THE   SS   RAT 63
    ALIEN HORIZONS   NOLAN, WILLIAM F.   AC
  LAWBREAKER (VIOLATION)   SS   FUC 73
    ALIEN HORIZONS   NOLAN, WILLIAM F.   AC
  LEIGH BRACKETT & RAY BRADBURY   AR
    HUMAN EQUATION, THE   NOLAN, WILLIAM F.   AN
  MARTIANS AND THE LEADFOOT, THE   SS   SCJ 57
    IMPACT-20   NOLAN, WILLIAM F.   AC
  MATING OF THIRDBURT, THE   SS   NEW 74 AC
    ALIEN HORIZONS   NOLAN, WILLIAM F.   AC
  NOBODY, THAT'S WHO   SS   NEW 63 AC
    IMPACT-20   NOLAN, WILLIAM F.   AC
  OF TIME AND TEXAS   SS   FUN 56 11
    IMPACT-20   NOLAN, WILLIAM F.   AC
  ONE OF THOSE DAYS   SS   FSF 62 05
    FIEND IN YOU, THE   BEAUMONT, CHARLES   AN
    IMPACT-20   NOLAN, WILLIAM F.   AC
  8TH ANNUAL OF THE YEAR'S BEST S-F, THE   MERRIL, JUDITH AN
  PAPA'S PLANET   SS   PBY 68 04
    ALIEN HORIZONS   NOLAN, WILLIAM F.   AC
    FAR-OUT PEOPLE, THE   HOSKINS, ROBERT   AN
    LAST TRAIN TO LIMBO   PLAYBOY, EDITORS OF AN
  PARTY, THE   SS   PBY 67 04
    ALIEN HORIZONS   NOLAN, WILLIAM F.   AC
    PLAYBOY BOOK OF HORROR AND THE SUPERNATURAL, THE
                                  PLAYBOY, EDITORS OF AN
    WEIRD SHOW   PLAYBOY, EDITORS OF AN
  PHILIP K. DICK   AR
    HUMAN EQUATION, THE   NOLAN, WILLIAM F.   AN
  PIGEON   SS   57
    IMPACT-20   NOLAN, WILLIAM F.   AC
  PROMISES TO KEEP: A SCIENCE FICTION DRAMA SS   NEW 74 AC
    ALIEN HORIZONS   NOLAN, WILLIAM F.   AC
  PUBLIC LOVES A JOHNNY, THE   SS   NEW 63 AC
    IMPACT-20   NOLAN, WILLIAM F.   AC
  RAY BRADBURY   AR
    3 TO THE HIGHEST POWER   NOLAN, WILLIAM F.   AN
  RAY BRADBURY   AR   FSF 63 05
    BEST FROM FANTASY AND SCIENCE FICTION, 25TH ANNIV.
                                  FERMAN, EDWARD L.   AN
  SMALL WORLD OF LEWIS STILLMAN, THE (SMALL WORLD) SS FUN 57 08
    IMPACT-20   NOLAN, WILLIAM F.   AC
  SOLUTION (TO SERVE THE SHIP)   SS   GAM 63 01
    ALIEN HORIZONS   NOLAN, WILLIAM F.   AC
  STARBLOOD   SS   INY 72 04
    ALIEN HORIZONS   NOLAN, WILLIAM F.   AC
    INFINITY 4   HOSKINS, ROBERT   OA
  THEODORE STURGEON   AR
    3 TO THE HIGHEST POWER   NOLAN, WILLIAM F.   AN

NOLAN, WILLIAM F.   (CONTINUED)
  TO SERVE THE SHIP (ALSO AS SOLUTION)   SS   GAM 63 01
    IMPACT-20   NOLAN, WILLIAM F.   AC
  TOE TO TIP, TIP TO TOE, PIP-POP AS YOU GO SS   FIN 70
    ALIEN HORIZONS   NOLAN, WILLIAM F.   AC
    FUTURE IS NOW, THE   NOLAN, WILLIAM F.   OA
  UNDERDWELLER, THE (SMALL WORLD)   SS   FUN 57 08
    ALIEN HORIZONS   NOLAN, WILLIAM F.   AC
  VIOLATION (ALSO AS LAWBREAKER)   SS   FUC 73
    FUTURE CITY   ELWOOD, ROGER   OA
  WORLDS OF CHAD OLIVER: A BIOGRAPHICAL INTRODUCTION
                                           IN
    EDGE OF FOREVER, THE   OLIVER, CHAD   AC
  WORLDS OF MONTY WILLSON, THE   SS   AMZ 71 07
    ALIEN HORIZONS   NOLAN, WILLIAM F.   AC

NORBERT, W.   PSEUD. FOR NORBERT WIENER
  BRAIN, THE   SS   TEN 52 04
    CROSSROADS IN TIME   CONKLIN, GROFF   AN
  MIRACLE OF THE BROOM CLOSET, THE   SS   TEN 52 04
    EXPERT DREAMERS, THE   POHL, FREDERIK   AN

NORTH, ANDREW   PSEUD. FOR ALICE MARY NORTON

NORTHRUP, EDWIN F.
  OFF FOR THE MOON (FROM "ZERO TO EIGHTY") EX   37
    SCIENCE IN FICTION   BAYLISS, A.E. & J.C. AN

NORTON, ALDEN H. AND SAM MOSKOWITZ
  SPACE MAGICIANS, THE   AN   PYR 71 01

NORTON, ALDEN H.
  AWARD SCIENCE FICTION READER   AN   AWD 66
  FUTURES UNLIMITED   AN   PYR 69 06
  HORROR TIMES TEN   AN   BKM 67 06
  INTRODUCTION   IN
    HORROR TIMES TEN   NORTON, ALDEN H.   AN
  INTRODUCTION   IN C
    SPACE MAGICIANS, THE   NORTON & MOSKOWITZ AN

NORTON, ALICE MARY   SEE PSEUD. ANDRE NORTON AND ANDREW NORTH

NORTON, ANDRE AND ERNESTINE DONALDY
  GATES TO TOMORROW   AN H ATH 73

NORTON, ANDRE   PSEUD. FOR ALICE MARY NORTON
  BOOK OF ANDRE NORTON, THE   AC   DAW 75 10
    SEE "THE MANY WORLDS OF ANDRE NORTON"
  BULLARD OF THE SPACE PATROL (LISTED UNDER MALCOLM JAMESON)
                                           EC H WOR 51
  MANY WORLDS OF ANDRE NORTON, THE   AC H CHL 74
    EDITED BY ROGER ELWOOD, ALSO AS "THE BOOK OF ANDRE NORTON"
  SPACE PIONEERS   AN H WOR 54
  SPACE POLICE   AN H WOR 56
  SPACE SERVICE   AN H WOR 53
  ALL CATS ARE GRAY (AS ANDREW NORTH)   SS   FUN 53 08
    MANY WORLDS OF ANDRE NORTON, THE NORTON, ANDRE   AC
    MANY WORLDS OF SCIENCE FICTION, THE BOVA, BEN   OA
    ZOO 2000   YOLEN, JANE   AN
  AUTHOR'S INTRODUCTION TO THIS EDITION OF FUR MAGIC
                                           AI
    DAW SCIENCE FICTION READER, THE WOLLHEIM, DONALD A. OA
  DESIRABLE LAKESIDE RESIDENCE   SS   SVW 73
    SAVING WORLDS   ELWOOD & KIDD   OA
  FUR MAGIC   NO   WOR 68
    DAW SCIENCE FICTION READER, THE WOLLHEIM, DONALD A. OA
  GIFTS OF ASTI, THE   SS   FBK 48 03
    GIFTS OF ASTI AND OTHER STORIES OF SCIENCE FICTION, THE
                                  ELWOOD, ROGER   AN
    MANY WORLDS OF ANDRE NORTON, THE NORTON, ANDRE   AC
    TIME CURVE, THE   MOSKOWITZ & ELWOOD AN
  INTRODUCTION   IN
    BULLARD OF THE SPACE PATROL   JAMESON, MALCOLM   AC
    SPACE POLICE   NORTON, ANDRE   AN
    SPACE SERVICE   NORTON, ANDRE   AN
  INTRODUCTION   IN C
    GATES TO TOMORROW   NORTON, AN.&DONALDY AN
  LONDON BRIDGE   SS   FSF 73 10
    MANY WORLDS OF ANDRE NORTON, THE NORTON, ANDRE   AC
  LONG LIVE LORD KOR¡   SN   WOF 70 02
    MANY WORLDS OF ANDRE NORTON, THE NORTON, ANDRE   AC
  LONG NIGHT OF WAITING, THE   SS   73
    LONG NIGHT OF WAITING AND OTHER STORIES
                                  ELWOOD, ROGER   OA
    MANY WORLDS OF ANDRE NORTON, THE NORTON, ANDRE   AC
  MOUSETRAP   SS   FSF 54 06
    BEST SCIENCE FICTION STORIES AND NOVELS: 1955
                                  DIKTY, T. E.   AN
    MANY WORLDS OF ANDRE NORTON, THE NORTON, ANDRE   AC
  NORTON BIBLIOGRAPHY   MS
    MANY WORLDS OF ANDRE NORTON, THE NORTON, ANDRE   AC
  ON WRITING FANTASY   AR   DIP 71 11
    MANY WORLDS OF ANDRE NORTON, THE NORTON, ANDRE   AC
  PEOPLE OF THE CRATER, THE   NV   FBK 47 01
    ALIEN EARTH AND OTHER STORIES ELWOOD & MOSKOWITZ AN
    SWORDSMEN IN THE SKY   WOLLHEIM, DONALD A. AN
  PREFACE   IN
    SPACE PIONEERS   NORTON, ANDRE   AN
  TEDDI   NV
    SCIENCE FICTION ADVENTURES FROM WAY OUT
                                  ELWOOD, ROGER   OA
  TOADS OF GRIMMERDALE, THE   NV   FLS 73 02
    MANY WORLDS OF ANDRE NORTON, THE NORTON, ANDRE   AC

NORTON, HENRY

O'BRIEN, FITZ-JAMES

NORTON, HENRY
    MAN IN THE MOON, THE   SS   ASF 43 02
        ENEMIES IN SPACE   CONKLIN, GROFF   AN
        *INVADERS OF EARTH   CONKLIN, GROFF   AN

NORTON, RALPH
    WARP   SS   MAY 68
        YEAR'S BEST HORROR STORIES, THE DAVIS, RICHARD   AN

NORWOOD, RICK
    OMNIA TRISTE   SS   CLR 72 02
        CLARION II   WILSON, ROBIN SCOTT   OA

NOURSE, ALAN E.
    BEYOND INFINITY   AC   COR 64
        SEE "TIGER BY THE TAIL"
    COUNTERFEIT MAN, THE   AC H MCK 63
    PSI-HIGH AND OTHERS   AC H MCK 67
    RX FOR TOMORROW   AC H MCK 71
    TIGER BY THE TAIL   AC H MCK 61
        AND OTHER SCIENCE FICTION STORIES
        IN ENGLAND AS "BEYOND INFINITY"
    BRAMBLE BUSH   SS   IFS 57 08
        RX FOR TOMORROW   NOURSE, ALAN E.   AC
    BRIGHTSIDE CROSSING   NV   GAL 56 01
        BEYOND TOMORROW   KNIGHT, DAMON   AN
        TIGER BY THE TAIL   NOURSE, ALAN E.   AC
        WORLD THAT COULDN'T BE AND 8 OTHER SF NOVELETS
                                       GOLD, H. L.   AN
    CANVAS BAG, THE   SS   FSF 55 04
        COUNTERFEIT MAN, THE   NOURSE, ALAN E.   AC
        SPECIAL WONDER   MCCOMAS, J. FRANCIS   AN
    CIRCUS   SS
        COUNTERFEIT MAN, THE   NOURSE, ALAN E.   AC
    COFFIN CURE, THE   SS   GAL 57 04
        BEST SF 7   CRISPIN, EDMUND   AN
        SCIENCE FICTION ODDITIES   CONKLIN, GROFF   AN
        TIGER BY THE TAIL   NOURSE, ALAN E.   AC
    COMPLEAT CONSUMATORS, THE   SS   FSF 64 04
        BEST FROM FANTASY AND SCIENCE FICTION: 14
                                       DAVIDSON, AVRAM   AN
        MARRIAGE AND THE FAMILY THROUGH SCIENCE FICTION
                                       CLEAR/WARRICK/&   AN
    CONTAMINATION CREW   SS   IFS 58 02
        RX FOR TOMORROW   NOURSE, ALAN E.   AC
    COUNTERFEIT (ALSO AS THE COUNTERFEIT MAN)   NV   TWS 52 08
        MORE PENGUIN SCIENCE FICTION   ALDISS, BRIAN W.   AN
    COUNTERFEIT MAN, THE (COUNTERFEIT)   NV   TWS 52 08
        COUNTERFEIT MAN, THE   NOURSE, ALAN E.   AC
    DARK DOOR, THE   NV   GAL 53 12
        COUNTERFEIT MAN, THE   NOURSE, ALAN E.   AC
    EXPERT TOUCH, THE   NV   FSF 55 11
        COUNTERFEIT MAN, THE   NOURSE, ALAN E.   AC
        SF: AUTHORS' CHOICE 2   HARRISON, HARRY   AN
    FAMILY RESEMBLANCE   SS   ASF 53 04
        ABC OF SCIENCE FICTION, AN   BOARDMAN, TOM JR.   AN
        GREAT SCIENCE FICTION ABOUT DOCTORS CONKLIN, G&FABRICANT AN
        *SCIENCE FICTION ADVENTURES IN MUTATION CONKLIN, GROFF AN
        TIGER BY THE TAIL   NOURSE, ALAN E.   AC
    FREE AGENT (SIXTY-YEAR EXTENSION)   NV   PLS 54 05
        RX FOR TOMORROW   NOURSE, ALAN E.   AC
    GIFT FOR NUMBERS, A   SS   SUP 58 08
        RX FOR TOMORROW   NOURSE, ALAN E.   AC
    GRAND ROUNDS   SS   FUN 55 08
        RX FOR TOMORROW   NOURSE, ALAN E.   AC
    HARD BARGAIN   SS   PBY 58 05
        PLAYBOY BOOK OF SCIENCE FICTION AND FANTASY, THE
                                       PLAYBOY, EDITORS OF   AN
    HEIR APPARENT   SS   IMG 53 10
        RX FOR TOMORROW   NOURSE, ALAN E.   AC
    HIGH THRESHOLD   SS   ASF 51 03
        OMNIBUS OF SCIENCE FICTION   CONKLIN, GROFF   AN
        STRANGE TRAVELS IN SCIENCE FICTION CONKLIN, GROFF   AN
    IMAGE OF THE GODS, THE   SS   OSF 54 09
        COUNTERFEIT MAN, THE   NOURSE, ALAN E.   AC
        PLANET OF DOOM AND OTHER STORIES ANONYMOUS   AN
    IN SHEEP'S CLOTHING   SS   FSM 52 11
        RX FOR TOMORROW   NOURSE, ALAN E.   AC
    LAST HOUSE CALL, THE   SS   NEW 71 AC
        RX FOR TOMORROW   NOURSE, ALAN E.   AC
    LETTER OF THE LAW   SS   IFS 54 01
        TIGER BY THE TAIL   NOURSE, ALAN E.   AC
    LINK, THE   SS   IFS 54 06
        COUNTERFEIT MAN, THE   NOURSE, ALAN E.   AC
    LOVE THY VIMP   SS   FSF 52 04
        TIGER BY THE TAIL   NOURSE, ALAN E.   AC
    MARTYR, THE   NV   FUN 57 01
        PSI-HIGH AND OTHERS   NOURSE, ALAN E.   AC
    MEETING OF THE BOARD   SS   IFS 55 10
        COUNTERFEIT MAN, THE   NOURSE, ALAN E.   AC
    MIRACLE TOO MANY, A   SS C FSF 64 09
        10TH ANNUAL OF THE YEAR'S BEST S-F, THE
                                       MERRIL, JUDITH   AN
    MIRROR, MIRROR (THE MIRROR)   NV   FAN 60 06
        PSI-HIGH AND OTHERS   NOURSE, ALAN E.   AC
    MY FRIEND BOBBY   SS   OSF 54 03
        COUNTERFEIT MAN, THE   NOURSE, ALAN E.   AC
    NATIVE SOIL, THE   SS   FUN 57 07
        TIGER BY THE TAIL   NOURSE, ALAN E.   AC
    NIGHTMARE BROTHER   NV   ASF 53 02
        SCIENCE FICTION TERROR TALES   CONKLIN, GROFF   AN
        SPACE, SPACE, SPACE   SLOANE, WILLIAM   AN
        TIGER BY THE TAIL   NOURSE, ALAN E.   AC
        UNIVERSE AHEAD   ENGDAHL & ROBERSON   AN
    NIZE KITTY   SS

NOURSE, ALAN E.   (CONTINUED)
    TOMORROW: NEW WORLDS OF SCIENCE FICTION
                                       ELWOOD, ROGER   OA
    OUNCE OF CURE, AN   SS   IMT 55 11
        COUNTERFEIT MAN, THE   NOURSE, ALAN E.   AC
    PLAGUE!   SS   NEW 71 AC
        RX FOR TOMORROW   NOURSE, ALAN E.   AC
    PROBLEM   SS   GAL 56 10
        TIGER BY THE TAIL   NOURSE, ALAN E.   AC
    PSI-HIGH   NV
        PSI-HIGH AND OTHERS   NOURSE, ALAN E.   AC
    RX   SS   IFS 57 10
        RX FOR TOMORROW   NOURSE, ALAN E.   AC
    SECOND SIGHT   SS   FUN 56 04
        COUNTERFEIT MAN, THE   NOURSE, ALAN E.   AC
    SIXTY-YEAR EXTENSION (SEE FREE AGENT)   TC
    SYMPTOMATICUS MEDICUS   SS   USF 54 09
        RX FOR TOMORROW   NOURSE, ALAN E.   AC
    TIGER BY THE TAIL   SS   GAL 51 11
        ADVENTURES IN DIMENSION   CONKLIN, GROFF   AN
        FIFTY SHORT SCIENCE FICTION TALES ASIMOV & CONKLIN   AN
        *SCIENCE FICTION ADVENTURES IN DIMENSION
                                       CONKLIN, GROFF   AN
        SECOND GALAXY READER OF SCIENCE FICTION
                                       GOLD, H. L.   AN
        TIGER BY THE TAIL   NOURSE, ALAN E.   AC

NOVOTNY, JOHN
    ON CAMERA   SS   FSP 56 04
        SCIENCE FICTION ODDITIES   CONKLIN, GROFF   AN
    TRICK OR TWO, A   SS   FSF 57 07
        DECADE OF FANTASY AND SCIENCE FICTION, A
                                       MILLS, ROBERT P.   AN

NUETZEL, CHARLES   ALSO AS   GEORGE FREDERIC
    IF THIS GOES ON   AN   BCA 65
        STORY "ALMOST THE END OF THE WORLD" BY RAY BRADBURY LISTED
        IN CONTENTS AND ON COVER BUT NOT IN BOOK
    IMAGES OF TOMORROW   AC   POW 69 03
        COUNT DOWN TO DOOM   SS C FMS 66
        SCIENCE FICTION WORLDS OF FORREST J. ACKERMAN & FRIENDS
                                       ACKERMAN, FORREST J. AC
    ERSATZ, THE   SS
        IMAGES OF TOMORROW   NUETZEL, CHARLES   AC
    GOOD DOCTOR, THE   SS
        IMAGES OF TOMORROW   NUETZEL, CHARLES   AC
    GROOVY HOMO SAP, THE (HOMO SAP)   SS
        IMAGES OF TOMORROW   NUETZEL, CHARLES   AC
    GUIDED TOUR   SS
        IMAGES OF TOMORROW   NUETZEL, CHARLES   AC
    HOMO SAP, THE ALSO AS THE GROOVY HOMO SAP)   SS
        IF THIS GOES ON   NUETZEL, CHARLES   AN
    HUNGER PANGS   SS
        IMAGES OF TOMORROW   NUETZEL, CHARLES   AC
    IMAGES OF MAN   SS
        IMAGES OF TOMORROW   NUETZEL, CHARLES   AC
    JUDGMENT, THE   SS
        IMAGES OF TOMORROW   NUETZEL, CHARLES   AC
    NOVA INCIDENT, THE   SS
        IMAGES OF TOMORROW   NUETZEL, CHARLES   AC
    PLANET OF THE LOVE FEAST   SS
        IMAGES OF TOMORROW   NUETZEL, CHARLES   AC
    PREFACE   IN
        IF THIS GOES ON   NUETZEL, CHARLES   AN
    ROYAL LESSON   SS
        IMAGES OF TOMORROW   NUETZEL, CHARLES   AC
    VERY CULTURED TASTE, A (AS GEORGE FREDERIC)   SS   60
        IMAGES OF TOMORROW   NUETZEL, CHARLES   AC
    WORD TO THE WISE   SS
        IMAGES OF TOMORROW   NUETZEL, CHARLES   AC
    WORLD THAT WOMB MADE, THE   SS
        IMAGES OF TOMORROW   NUETZEL, CHARLES   AC

NULISCH, HARRY
    WHAT HAPPENED TO SERGEANT MASURO?   NV   64
        WORLD'S BEST SCIENCE FICTION: 1965 WOLLHEIM & CARR   AN

NUTT, CHARLES   SEE PSEUD. CHARLES BEAUMONT

NUTTALL, JEFF
    POEM   PM   69
        HOLDING YOUR EIGHT HANDS   LUCIE-SMITH, EDWARD   AN

NYBERG, BJORN   SEE ALSO   CO-AUTHOR ROBERT E. HOWARD
    CONAN THE VICTORIOUS (SEE THE RETURN OF CONAN) TC C
    RETURN OF CONAN, THE (EXPANDED FROM "CONAN THE VICTORIOUS",
        PUBLISHED BY GNOME, 1957)   NO C FUN 57 09
        CONAN THE AVENGER   HOWARD, R./NYBERG/& AC

NYE, CASSANDRA
    DRUMBLE   SS   NEW 75 AN
        NEW IMPROVED SUN, THE   DISCH, THOMAS M.   AN

O'BRIEN, CLANCY
    GENERATION GAPS   SS   ASF 72 09
        SOCIOLOGY THROUGH SCIENCE FICTION MILSTEAD/GREENBERG/& AN
    MATTER OF FREEDOMS, A   SS   FTP 73
        FLAME TREE PLANET   ELWOOD, ROGER   OA

O'BRIEN, D. W.
    TRUTH IS A PLAGUE   SS   AMZ 40 02
        OTHER WORLDS, THE   STONG, PHILIP D.   AN

O'BRIEN, FITZ-JAMES
    CHILD THAT LOVED A GRAVE, THE   SS
        GRAVEYARD READER, THE   CONKLIN, GROFF   AN

O'BRIEN, FITZ-JAMES (CONTINUED)
  DIAMOND LENS, THE (1858)   NV ATL 58 01
    FUTURE PERFECT   FRANKLIN, H. BRUCE   AN
  LOST ROOM, THE   SS WBT 29 10
    SUPERNATURAL READER, THE   CONKLIN, G&L.   AN
  WHAT WAS IT? (1859)   SS HRP 59 03
    CENTURY OF SCIENCE FICTION, A   KNIGHT, DAMON AN
    INVISIBLE MEN   DAVENPORT, BASIL   AN
  WONDERSMITH, THE (1859, FSF 50 12)   NV ATL 59 10
    MASTERPIECES OF SCIENCE FICTION   MOSKOWITZ, SAM AN

O'DONNELL, K. M.   PSEUD. FOR BARRY N. MALZBERG
  FINAL WAR AND OTHER FANTASIES   DC ACE 69
  IN THE POCKET AND OTHER S-F STORIES   DC ACE 71
  UNIVERSE DAY   NO AVN 71 04
  ADDENDUM   SS NEW 71 DC
    IN THE POCKET AND OTHER S-F STORIES   O'DONNELL, K. M.   DC
  AH, FAIR URANUS   SS NEW 71 DC
    IN THE POCKET AND OTHER S-F STORIES   O'DONNELL, K. M.   DC
  AS BETWEEN GENERATIONS   SS FAN 70 10
    IN THE POCKET AND OTHER S-F STORIES   O'DONNELL, K. M.   DC
  ASCENSION, THE   SS FAN 69 04
    FINAL WAR AND OTHER FANTASIES   O'DONNELL, K. M.   IN
  AUTHOR'S INTRODUCTION   IN
    IN THE POCKET AND OTHER S-F STORIES   O'DONNELL, K. M.   DC
  BAT   SS NEW 71 DC
    IN THE POCKET AND OTHER S-F STORIES   O'DONNELL, K. M.   DC
  BY RIGHT OF SUCCESSION   SS IFS 69 10
    FINAL WAR AND OTHER FANTASIES   O'DONNELL, K. M.   DC
  CHRONICLES OF A COMER   SS WLK 73
    AND WALK NOW GENTLY THROUGH THE FIRE...
                              ELWOOD, ROGER   OA
    CHRONICLES OF A COMER AND OTHER RELIGIOUS SCIENCE FICTION
    STORIES   ELWOOD, ROGER   AN
  CITY LIGHTS, CITY NIGHTS   SS FUC 73
    FUTURE CITY   ELWOOD, ROGER   OA
  COP-OUT   SS ESC 68
    FAR-OUT PEOPLE, THE   HOSKINS, ROBERT   AN
    FINAL WAR AND OTHER FANTASIES   O'DONNELL, K. M.   DC
  DEATH TO THE KEEPER   NV FSF 68 08
    FINAL WAR AND OTHER FANTASIES   O'DONNELL, K. M.   DC
  ELEPHANTS   SS INY 71 02
    INFINITY 2   HOSKINS, ROBERT   OA
    UNIVERSE DAY   O'DONNELL, K. M.   NO
  FALCON AND THE FALCONEER, THE   SS FSF 69 12
    IN THE POCKET AND OTHER S-F STORIES   O'DONNELL, K. M.   DC
  FINAL WAR   NV FSF 68 04
    BEST FROM FANTASY AND SCIENCE FICTION: 18
                              FERMAN, EDWARD L.   AN
    BEST SF: 1968   HARRISON & ALDISS   AN
    FINAL WAR AND OTHER FANTASIES   O'DONNELL, K. M.   DC
  GEHENNA   SS GAL 71 03
    IN THE POCKET AND OTHER S-F STORIES   O'DONNELL, K. M.   DC
  GETTING AROUND   SS TAL 73
    FRONTIERS 1: TOMORROW'S ALTERNATIVES   ELWOOD, ROGER   OA
  HOW I TAKE THEIR MEASURE   SS FSF 69 01
    FINAL WAR AND OTHER FANTASIES   O'DONNELL, K. M.   DC
    SOCIAL PROBLEMS THROUGH SCIENCE FICTION
                              GREENBERG/MILSTEAD/&   AN
  IDEA, THE   SS NEW 71 DC
    IN THE POCKET AND OTHER S-F STORIES   O'DONNELL, K. M.   DC
  IN THE POCKET   SS NOV 70 01
    IN THE POCKET AND OTHER S-F STORIES   O'DONNELL, K. M.   DC
    *NOVA 1   HARRISON, HARRY   OA
  INTRODUCTION   IN
    FINAL WAR AND OTHER FANTASIES   O'DONNELL, K. M.   DC
  IT WASN'T MY FAULT   SS
    MISSING WORLD AND OTHER STORIES, THE   ELWOOD, ROGER   OA
  JULY 24, 1970   SS VSF 69 05
    IN THE POCKET AND OTHER S-F STORIES   O'DONNELL, K. M.   DC
  MAJOR INCITEMENT TO RIOT, THE   SS FAN 69 02
    FINAL WAR AND OTHER FANTASIES   O'DONNELL, K. M.   DC
  MAKING TITAN   SS FSF 70 07
    UNIVERSE DAY   O'DONNELL, K. M.   NO
  MARKET IN ALIENS, THE   SS GAL 68 11
    FINAL WAR AND OTHER FANTASIES   O'DONNELL, K. M.   DC
    FIRST STEP OUTWARD   HOSKINS, ROBERT   AN
  NEW RAPPACCINI, THE   SS FAN 70 12
    IN THE POCKET AND OTHER S-F STORIES   O'DONNELL, K. M.   DC
  NOTES JUST PRIOR TO THE FALL   SS FSF 70 10
    IN THE POCKET AND OTHER S-F STORIES   O'DONNELL, K. M.   DC
  OATEN   SS FAN 68 10
    FINAL WAR AND OTHER FANTASIES   O'DONNELL, K. M.   DC
  OVERSIGHT   SS STG 74
    STRANGE GODS   ELWOOD, ROGER   OA
  PACEM EST   SS INY 70 01
    UNIVERSE DAY   O'DONNELL, K. M.   NO
  PACEM EST   SS C INY 70 01
    BEST SF: 1970   HARRISON & ALDISS   AN
    IN THE POCKET AND OTHER S-F STORIES   O'DONNELL, K. M.   DC
    INFINITY 1   HOSKINS, ROBERT   OA
  QUESTION OF SLANT, A   SS
    IN THE POCKET AND OTHER S-F STORIES   O'DONNELL, K. M.   DC
  SOULSONG TO THE SAD, SILLY, SOARING SIXTIES, A   SS FAN 71 02
    IN THE POCKET AND OTHER S-F STORIES   O'DONNELL, K. M.   DC
  STILL-LIFE   SS DVS 72 02
    AGAIN, DANGEROUS VISIONS   ELLISON, HARLAN   OA
  STREAKING   SS FCR 75
    FUTURE CORRUPTION   ELWOOD, ROGER   OA
  TERMINUS EST   SS NOV 70 01
    UNIVERSE DAY   O'DONNELL, K. M.   NO
  TRIAL OF THE BLOOD   SS BER 74
    BERSERKERS, THE   ELWOOD, ROGER   OA
  TRIPTYCH, A   SS FSF 69 07
    FINAL WAR AND OTHER FANTASIES   O'DONNELL, K. M.   DC
    UNIVERSE DAY   O'DONNELL, K. M.   NO

O'DONNELL, K. M.   (CONTINUED)
  TWO ODYSSEYS INTO THE CENTER   SS NOV 72 02
    UNIVERSE DAY   O'DONNELL, K. M.   NO
  WE'RE COMING THROUGH THE WINDOW   SS GAL 67 08
    FINAL WAR AND OTHER FANTASIES   O'DONNELL, K. M.   DC
  WHAT TIME WAS THAT?   SS IFS 69 12
    IN THE POCKET AND OTHER S-F STORIES   O'DONNELL, K. M.   DC

O'DONNELL, LAWRENCE PSEUD. FOR HENRY KUTTNER AND C. L. MOORE
  CLASH BY NIGHT   NV ASF 43 03
    *ASTOUNDING SCIENCE FICTION ANTHOLOGY, THE
                              CAMPBELL, JOHN W. JR AN
    ASTOUNDING-ANALOG READER, THE VOLUME ONE
                              HARRISON & ALDISS   AN
    FIRST ASTOUNDING SCIENCE FICTION ANTHOLOGY, THE (PB)
                              CAMPBELL, JOHN W. JR AN
    *SECOND ASTOUNDING SCIENCE FICTION ANTHOLOGY, THE
                              CAMPBELL, JOHN W. JR AN
  VINTAGE SEASON   NV ASF 46 09
    ASTOUNDING-ANALOG READER, THE VOLUME ONE
                              HARRISON & ALDISS   AN
    *TREASURY OF SCIENCE FICTION, A   CONKLIN, GROFF   AN

O'DONNEVAN, FINN   PSEUD. FOR ROBERT SHECKLEY
  GUN WITHOUT A BANG, THE   NV GAL 58 06
    FOURTH GALAXY READER, THE   GOLD, H. L.   AN
  WIND IS RISING, A   SS GAL 57 07
    THIRD GALAXY READER, THE   GOLD, H. L.   AN

O'HARA, KENNETH   PSEUD. FOR BRYCE WALTON
  MATING OF THE MOONS, THE   SS OSF 54 02
    PLANET OF DOOM AND OTHER STORIES   ANONYMOUS   AN

O'LEARY, TIMOTHY J.
  PRELIMINARY INVESTIGATION OF AN EARLY MAN SITE IN THE DELAWARE
  RIVER VALLEY   FA C
    APEMAN, SPACEMAN   STOVER & HARRISON   AN

O'NEIL, DENNIS
  AFTER THEY'VE SEEN PAREE   SS GEN 72
    GENERATION   GERROLD, DAVID   OA
  ANNIE MAE: A LOVE STORY   SS
    FAR SIDE OF TIME, THE   ELWOOD, ROGER   OA
  NOONDAY DEVIL   SS SVW 73
    SAVING WORLDS   ELWOOD & KIDD   OA

O'NEILL, SCOTT
  MARTIAN SEXPOT   AC JAD 63
  AND THEY'RE ALL EXACTLY TWENTY-SIX YEARS OLD   SS
    MARTIAN SEXPOT   O'NEILL, SCOTT   AC
  DEAR MAVIS   SS
    MARTIAN SEXPOT   O'NEILL, SCOTT   AC
  I TELL YOU, AL   SS
    MARTIAN SEXPOT   O'NEILL, SCOTT   AC
  INSTANT MAIDS OF MARS, THE   SS
    MARTIAN SEXPOT   O'NEILL, SCOTT   AC
  SPEAKING OF GANYMEDE   SS
    MARTIAN SEXPOT   O'NEILL, SCOTT   AC
  WORLD'S GREATEST SALESMAN, THE   SS
    MARTIAN SEXPOT   O'NEILL, SCOTT   AC

O'QUINN, VITHALDAS H PSEUD. FOR HANS STEFAN SANTESSON
  DAY WILL COME..., THE   MS
    FANTASTIC UNIVERSE OMNIBUS, THE   SANTESSON, HANS S.   AN
  FLOWERS OF VENUS, THE   MS
    FANTASTIC UNIVERSE OMNIBUS, THE   SANTESSON, HANS S.   AN

OBOLER, ARCH
  AND ADAM BEGOT   SS 42
    OUT OF THIS WORLD   FAST, JULIUS   AN

OBTULOWICZ, MAREK
  COUNT D'UNADIX   SS NWQ 73 05
    NEW WORLDS NO. 5   MOORCOCK & PLATT   OA
  FIRST OF TWO RAPED PROSPECTS, THE   SS NWQ 72 04
    NEW WORLDS QUARTERLY NO. 4   MOORCOCK, MICHAEL   OA
  MAN OF LETTERS, A   SS QRK 71 04
    QUARK/4   DELANY & HACKER   OA
  TROJAK   SS QRK 71 02
    QUARK/2   DELANY & HACKER   OA

OFFUTT, ANDREW J.
  BLACK SORCERER OF THE BLACK CASTLE, THE   SS NEW 74 AN
    COSMIC LAUGHTER   HALDEMAN, JOE W.   AN
  BLACKSWORD   NV GAL 59 12
    MIND PARTNER AND 8 OTHER NOVELETS FROM GALAXY
                              GOLD, H. L.   AN
  BOOK, THE   SS C ORB 70 08
    ORBIT 8   KNIGHT, DAMON   OA
  ENCHANTE   SS
    TOMORROW: NEW WORLDS OF SCIENCE FICTION
                              ELWOOD, ROGER   OA
  FOR VALUE RECEIVED   SS DVS 72 02
    AGAIN, DANGEROUS VISIONS   ELLISON, HARLAN   OA
  GREENHOUSE DEFECT, THE   NA
    STELLAR SHORT NOVELS   DEL REY, JUDY-LYNN OA
  MEANWHILE, WE ELIMINATE   SS FUC 73
    FUTURE CITY   ELWOOD, ROGER   OA
  MY COUNTRY, RIGHT OR WRONG   SS PRT 71
    PROTOSTARS   GERROLD & GOLDIN   OA
  POPULATION IMPLOSION   NV IFS 67 07
    AS TOMORROW BECOMES TODAY   SULLIVAN, CHARLES W.   AN
    WORLD'S BEST SCIENCE FICTION: 1968   WOLLHEIM & CARR   AN

OGILVY, G. S.

ORGILL, MICHAEL

OGILVY, G. S.
  FOR ALL PRACTICAL PURPOSES   PM
    FANTASIA MATHEMATICA   FADIMAN, CLIFTON   AN

OKHOTNIKOV, VADIM
  FICTION MACHINES, THE   SS
    OUT OF THIS WORLD 5   WILLIAMS-ELLIS& OWEN AN
    RUSSIAN SCIENCE FICTION   MAGIDOFF, ROBERT   AN

OLANDER, JOSEPH D., MARTIN H. GREENBERG AND
  PATRICIA S. WARRICK
  AMERICAN GOVERNMENT THROUGH SCIENCE FICTION   AN L RAN 74
  SCHOOL AND SOCIETY THROUGH SCIENCE FICTION   AN L RAN 74

OLANDER, JOSEPH D.   SEE ALSO
  CO-EDITORS V. CLEAR, R. CLEM, M. H. GREENBERG, AND J. MILSTEAD
  INTRODUCTION   IN C
    BEST OF JOHN JAKES, THE   JAKES, JOHN W.   AC
  MARRIAGE AND THE FAMILY THROUGH SCIENCE FICTION
                           CLEAR/WARRICK/&   AN
  RUN TO STARLIGHT, SPORTS THROUGH SCIENCE FICTION
                       GREENBERG/OLANDER/&   AN
  SCHOOL AND SOCIETY THROUGH SCIENCE FICTION
                       OLANDER/GREENBERG/&   AN
  SOCIAL PROBLEMS THROUGH SCIENCE FICTION
                       GREENBERG/MILSTEAD/& AN
  SOCIOLOGY THROUGH SCIENCE FICTION   MILSTEAD/GREENBERG/& AN
  TOMORROW, INC.   GREENBERG& OLANDER   AN
  INTRODUCTION: WHY THE CITY   IN C
    CITY: 2000 A.D., THE   CLEM/GREENBERG/&   AN
  PREFACE   IN C
    AMERICAN GOVERNMENT THROUGH SCIENCE FICTION
                       OLANDER/GREENBERG/&   AN

OLDALE, PETER
  PROBLEM CHILD   SS   VOT 70 06
    YEAR'S BEST HORROR STORIES, THE   DAVIS, RICHARD   AN

OLIVER, CHAD   PSEUD. FOR C. OLIVER SYMMES
  ANOTHER KIND   AC H BAL 55
  EDGE OF FOREVER, THE   AC H SHB 71
  AFTERTHOUGHTS   MS
    EDGE OF FOREVER, THE   OLIVER, CHAD   AC
  ANT AND THE EYE, THE   NV   ASF 53 04
    EDGE OF FOREVER, THE   OLIVER, CHAD   AC
    *STORIES FOR TOMORROW   SLOANE, WILLIAM   AN
  ANY MORE AT HOME LIKE YOU?   SS   STR 54 03
    STAR SCIENCE FICTION STORIES NO. 3   POHL, FREDERIK   OA
  ARTIFACT   NV   FSF 55 06
    ANOTHER KIND   OLIVER, CHAD   AC
  BETWEEN THE THUNDER AND THE SUN   NV   FSF 57 05
    BEST FROM FANTASY AND SCIENCE FICTION: 7
                       BOUCHER, ANTHONY   AN
  BLOOD'S A ROVER   NV   ASF 52 05
    DEEP SPACE   SILVERBERG, ROBERT   AN
    OPERATION FUTURE   CONKLIN, GROFF   AN
  BOY NEXT DOOR, THE   SS   FSF 51 06
    HUMAN?   MERRIL, JUDITH   AN
  CARAVANS UNLIMITED: MONITOR   NV   CTM 75 04
    CONTINUUM 4   ELWOOD, ROGER   OA
  CARAVANS UNLIMITED: STABILITY   NV   CTM 74 02
    CONTINUUM 2   ELWOOD, ROGER   OA
  COMMUNITY STUDY   NV
    LONE STAR UNIVERSE   PROCTOR & UTLEY   OA
  CONTROLLED EXPERIMENT   SS   OSF 54 11
    SPACE STATION 42 AND OTHER STORIES   ANONYMOUS   AN
  DIDN'T HE RAMBLE   SS   FSF 57 04
    BEST SCIENCE FICTION STORIES AND NOVELS: 9TH SERIES
                       DIKTY, T. E.   AN
    EDGE OF FOREVER, THE   OLIVER, CHAD   AC
  END OF THE LINE   NV   FSF 65 01
    ONCE AND FUTURE TALES FROM THE MAGAZINE OF FANTASY AND
    SCIENCE FICTION   FERMAN, EDWARD L.   AN
  FAR FROM THIS EARTH   SS   YRT 70
    ANTHROPOLOGY THROUGH SCIENCE FICTION   MASON, C/GREENBERG/& AN
    THEMES IN SCIENCE FICTION   KELLEY, LEO P.   AN
    YEAR 2000, THE   HARRISON, HARRY   OA
  FIELD EXPEDIENT   NV   ASF 55 01
    EDGE OF FOREVER, THE   OLIVER, CHAD   AC
    HIDDEN PLANET, THE   WOLLHEIM, DONALD A.   AN
  FINAL EXAM   SS   FAN 52 11
    ABC OF SCIENCE FICTION, AN   BOARDMAN, TOM JR.   AN
    BEST FROM FANTASTIC, THE   WHITE, TED   AN
  FIRST TO THE STARS (STARDUST)   NV   ASF 52 07
    EDGE OF FOREVER, THE   OLIVER, CHAD   AC
  FRIEND TO MAN, A (LET ME LIVE IN A HOUSE)   NV   USF 54 03
    EDGE OF FOREVER, THE   OLIVER, CHAD   AC
  GIFT, THE   NV
    FUTURE KIN   ELWOOD, ROGER   OA
  GUARDIAN SPIRIT (SEE THE MARGINAL MAN)   TC
  GUESTS OF CHANCE, THE   SS C INF 56 06
    NIGHT RIDE AND OTHER JOURNEYS   BEAUMONT, CHARLES   AC
  HANDS ACROSS SPACE (ALSO AS SCIENTIFIC METHOD)   SS   SFP 53 08
    HUMAN ZERO, THE   MOSKOWITZ & ELWOOD   AN
  KING OF THE HILL   SS   DVS 72 02
    AGAIN, DANGEROUS VISIONS   ELLISON, HARLAN   OA
  LAST WORD, THE   SS C FSF 55 04
    BEST FROM FANTASY AND SCIENCE FICTION: 5
                       BOUCHER, ANTHONY   AN
    EVIL EARTHS   ALDISS, BRIAN W.   AN
  LET ME LIVE IN A HOUSE (ALSO AS A FRIEND TO MAN) NV   USF 54 03
    SCIENCE FICTION TERROR TALES   CONKLIN, GROFF   AN
  LIFE GAME, THE   NV   TWS 53 06
    PSEUDO PEOPLE, THE   NOLAN, WILLIAM F.   AN
  MARGINAL MAN, THE (GUARDIAN SPIRIT)   NV   FSF 58 04
    3 TO THE HIGHEST POWER   NOLAN, WILLIAM F.   AN

OLIVER, CHAD   (CONTINUED)
  MIDDLE MAN, THE   NV   CTM 74 03
    CONTINUUM 3   ELWOOD, ROGER   OA
  MOTHER OF NECESSITY, THE   SS   NEW 55 AC
    ABOVE THE HUMAN LANDSCAPE   MCNELLY & STOVER   AN
    ANOTHER KIND   OLIVER, CHAD   AC
    GREAT SCIENCE FICTION BY SCIENTISTS   CONKLIN, GROFF   AN
  NIGHT   SS   IFS 55 03
    ANOTHER KIND   OLIVER, CHAD   AC
  NORTH WIND   SS   FSF 56 03
    FAR-OUT PEOPLE, THE   HOSKINS, ROBERT   AN
    WILDERNESS OF STARS, A   NOLAN, WILLIAM F.   AN
  OF COURSE   SS   ASF 54 05
    APEMAN, SPACEMAN   STOVER & HARRISON   AN
    BEST SCIENCE FICTION STORIES AND NOVELS: 1955
                       DIKTY, T. E.   AN
    SOCIOLOGY THROUGH SCIENCE FICTION   MILSTEAD/GREENBERG/& AN
  PILGRIMAGE   SS   FSF 58 02
    SPECIAL WONDER   MCCOMAS, J. FRANCIS   AN
  RITE OF PASSAGE   NV   ASF 54 04
    ANOTHER KIND   OLIVER, CHAD   AC
    SEVEN COME INFINITY   CONKLIN, GROFF   AN
  SCIENTIFIC METHOD (HANDS ACROSS SPACE)   SS   SFP 53 08
    ANOTHER KIND   OLIVER, CHAD   AC
  SECOND NATURE   NV   FUQ 73
    FUTURE QUEST   ELWOOD, ROGER   OA
    GIFTS OF ASTI AND OTHER STORIES OF SCIENCE FICTION, THE
                       ELWOOD, ROGER   AN
  SHAKA!   NV   CTM 74 01
    CONTINUUM 1   ELWOOD, ROGER   OA
  SHORE OF TOMORROW, THE   NV   STS 53 03
    TOMORROW'S UNIVERSE   CAMPBELL, H. J.   AN
  STAR ABOVE IT, A   SS   NEW 55 AC
    ANOTHER KIND   OLIVER, CHAD   AC
  STARDUST (ALSO AS FIRST TO THE STARS)   NV   ASF 52 07
    ADVENTURES IN THE FAR FUTURE   WOLLHEIM, DONALD A.   DA
  STICK FOR HARRY EDDINGTON, A   SS   FSF 65 08
    SF: AUTHORS' CHOICE 2   HARRISON, HARRY   AN
  SUBVERSIVES, THE (SEE WIN THE WORLD)   TC
  TECHNICAL ADVISOR   SS   FSF 53 02
    CROSSROADS IN TIME   CONKLIN, GROFF   AN
  TRANSFORMER   SS   FSF 54 11
    ANOTHER KIND   OLIVER, CHAD   AC
    MAN AGAINST TOMORROW   NOLAN, WILLIAM F.   AN
  TRANSFUSION   NV   ASF 59 06
    EDGE OF FOREVER, THE   OLIVER, CHAD   AC
    WORLDS OF WHEN   CONKLIN, GROFF   AN
  WIN THE WORLD (THE SUBVERSIVES)   SS   STS 52 02
    LOOKING FORWARD   LESSER, MILTON   AN
  WIND BLOWS FREE, THE   NV   FSF 57 07
    SEA OF SPACE, A   NOLAN, WILLIAM F.   AN

OLIVER, GEORGE   SEE PSEUD. OLIVER ONIONS

OLIVER, J. T.
  PEACEFUL MARTIAN, THE   SS   FBK 51 08
    SCIENCE AND SORCERY   FORD, GARRET   AN

OLIVER, OWEN
  BLACK SHADOW, THE   SS   CSL 03 02
    WORLDS APART   LOCKE, GEORGE   AN

OLIVER, SYMMES C.   SEE PSEUD. CHAD OLIVER

OLIVIER, OLIVIER
  TWELVE DRAWINGS   IL   QRK 71 04
    QUARK/4   DELANY & HACKER   OA

OLMSTEAD, DVORA
  TEARDROP, THE   SS   CLR 73 03
    CLARION III   WILSON, ROBIN SCOTT OA

OLNEY, ROSS R.
  TALES OF TIME AND SPACE   AN H WPC 69
    YESTERDAY'S FANTASY, TODAY'S FACT- AN INTRODUCTION
                                IN
      TALES OF TIME AND SPACE   OLNEY, ROSS R.   AN

OLSEN, ALFRED J. JR. SEE PSEUD. BOB OLSEN

OLSEN, BOB   PSEUD. FOR ALFRED J. OLSEN, JR.
  FOUR-DIMENSIONAL ROLLER-PRESS, THE   SS   AMZ 27 06
    EVERY BOY'S BOOK OF SCIENCE FICTION   WOLLHEIM, DONALD A. AN

OLSEN, ROBERT R.
  PALEONTOLOGY: AN EXPERIMENTAL SCIENCE   SS   ASF 74 08
    BEST SF: 1974   HARRISON & ALDISS   AN

ONIONS, OLIVER   PSEUD. FOR GEORGE OLIVER
  PHANTAS   SS   11
    GOLDEN ROAD, THE   KNIGHT, DAMON   AN
    MOONLIGHT TRAVELER, THE   STERN, PHILIP VAN D. AN
    TRAVELERS IN TIME   STERN, PHILIP VAN D. AN

ONSPAUGH, CARL
  EINE KLEINE NACHTMUSIK   SS C FSF 65 06
    BEST OF FREDRIC BROWN, THE   BROWN, FREDRIC   AC
    PARADOX LOST, AND 12 OTHER GREAT S.F. STORIES
                       BROWN, FREDRIC   AC

ORGILL, MICHAEL
  FABER-MASTER   NV
    WORLD NAMED CLEOPATRA, A   ANDERSON, POUL   OA
  MANY RUBICONS   NV
    BEYOND TIME   LEY, SANDRA   OA

ORGILL, MICHAEL   (CONTINUED)
    MIND ANGEL, THE   SS
        MIND ANGEL AND OTHER STORIES, THE   ELWOOD, ROGER   OA
    SMALLEST STARSHIP, THE   SS
        TUNNEL AND OTHER STORIES, THE   ELWOOD, ROGER   OA

ORR, WILLIAM F.
    EUCLID ALONE   NV   ORB 75 16
        ORBIT 16   KNIGHT, DAMON   OA
    MOUTH IS FOR EATING, THE   SS   ORB 74 13
        ORBIT 13   KNIGHT, DAMON   OA

ORTON, ARTHUR W.
    FOUR-FACED VISITORS OF EZEKIEL, THE   SS   ASF 61 03
        ENCOUNTERS WITH ALIENS   EARLEY, GEORGE W.   AN

ORWELL, GEORGE   PSEUD. FOR ERIC BLAIR
    APOTHEM   MS   45
        MATHEMATICAL MAGPIE, THE   FADIMAN, CLIFTON   AN

OSBORNE, ROBERTSON
    ACTION ON AZURA (ALSO AS CONTACT, INCORPORATED)   NV   PLS 49 FL
        TRAVELLERS OF SPACE   GREENBERG , MARTIN   AN
    CONTACT, INCORPORATED (ACTION ON AZURA)   NV   PLS 49 FL
        *BIG BOOK OF SCIENCE FICTION   CONKLIN, GROFF   AN

OSSIAN, JOHN
    LET IT RING   SS   INY 72 03
        INFINITY 3   HOSKINS, ROBERT   OA

OTTUM, BOB JR.
    ADO ABOUT NOTHING   SS   FSF 65 03
        11TH ANNUAL OF THE YEAR'S BEST S-F, THE
                                                MERRIL, JUDITH   AN

OWEN, MABLY   SEE ALSO   CO-EDITOR AMABEL WILLIAMS-ELLIS

OWINGS, MARK
    BLISH BIBLIOGRAPHY   MS   FSF 72 04
        BEST FROM FANTASY AND SCIENCE FICTION, 25TH ANNIV.
                                                FERMAN, EDWARD L.   AN

OWSLEY, CLIFF
    CONFESSIONS OF THE FIRST NUMBER   SS   SRV 63
        9TH ANNUAL OF THE YEAR'S BEST S-F, THE MERRIL, JUDITH   AN

OZICK, CYNTHIA
    PAGAN RABBI, THE   NV   66
        BEST SF: 1971   HARRISON & ALDISS   AN

PAALEN, WOLFGANG
    ALIENS, THE   IL
        SCIENCE FICTION   BRODKIN & PEARSON   AN

PACINI, KATHLEEN
    GIFT FROM EARTH   SS   YNW
        SCIENCE FICTION STORIES   BRADLEY, JOHANNA   AN

PADGETT, LEWIS   PSEUD. FOR HENRY KUTTNER AND C. L. MOORE
    GNOME THERE WAS, A   AC H SAS 50
    LINE TO TOMORROW AND OTHER STORIES OF FANTASY AND SCIENCE
        FICTION   AC   BAN 54 08
    MUTANT   AC H GNM 53
    ROBOTS HAVE NO TAILS   AC H GNM 52
    TOMORROW AND TOMORROW AND THE FAIRY CHESSMEN   AC H GNM 51
    BEGGARS IN VELVET   NV   ASF 45 12
        MUTANT   PADGETT, LEWIS   AC
    COMPLIMENTS OF THE AUTHOR   NV   UNK 42 10
        GNOME THERE WAS, A   PADGETT, LEWIS   AC
        LINE TO TOMORROW AND OTHER STORIES OF FANTASY AND SCIENCE
        FICTION   PADGETT, LEWIS   AC
    CURE, THE   SS   ASF 46 05
        GNOME THERE WAS, A   PADGETT, LEWIS   AC
        *OTHER SIDE OF THE MOON, THE   DERLETH, AUGUST   AN
    DARK ANGEL, THE   SS   STS 46 03
        SHOT IN THE DARK   MERRIL, JUDITH   AN
    DEADLOCK   SS   ASF 42 08
        ROBOT AND THE MAN, THE   GREENBERG , MARTIN AN
    ENDOWMENT POLICY   SS   ASF 43 08
        ADVENTURES IN DIMENSION   CONKLIN, GROFF   AN
        *SCIENCE FICTION ADVENTURES IN DIMENSION
                                                CONKLIN, GROFF   AN
    EX MACHINA   NV   ASF 48 04
        BEST SCIENCE-FICTION STORIES: 1949, THE
                                                BLEILER & DIKTY   AN
        ROBOTS HAVE NO TAILS   PADGETT, LEWIS   AC
    EXIT THE PROFESSOR   SS   TWS 47 10
        GNOME THERE WAS, A   PADGETT, LEWIS   AC
    FAIRY CHESSMEN, THE   SN   ASF 46 01
        TOMORROW AND TOMORROW AND THE FAIRY CHESSMEN
                                                PADGETT, LEWIS   AC
    GALLEGHER PLUS   NV   ASF 43 11
        ROBOTS HAVE NO TAILS   PADGETT, LEWIS   AC
    GNOME THERE WAS, A   NV   UNK 41 10
        *BEYOND HUMAN KEN   MERRIL, JUDITH   AN
        GNOME THERE WAS, A   PADGETT, LEWIS   AC
        LINE TO TOMORROW AND OTHER STORIES OF FANTASY AND SCIENCE
        FICTION   PADGETT, LEWIS   AC
    HUMPTY DUMPTY   NV   ASF 53 09
        MUTANT   PADGETT, LEWIS   AC
    IRON STANDARD, THE   SS   ASF 43 12
        *MEN AGAINST THE STARS   GREENBERG , MARTIN AN
    JESTING PILOT   SS   ASF 47 05
        GNOME THERE WAS, A   PADGETT, LEWIS   AC
    LINE TO TOMORROW   SS   ASF 45 11

PADGETT, LEWIS   (CONTINUED)
        LINE TO TOMORROW AND OTHER STORIES OF FANTASY AND SCIENCE
        FICTION   PADGETT, LEWIS   AC
        NEW WORLDS FOR OLD   DERLETH, AUGUST   AN
        *WORLDS OF TOMORROW   DERLETH, AUGUST   AN
    LION AND THE UNICORN, THE   NV   ASF 45 07
        MUTANT   PADGETT, LEWIS   AC
    MARGIN FOR ERROR   NV   ASF 47 11
        *BIG BOOK OF SCIENCE FICTION   CONKLIN, GROFF   AN
    MIMSY WERE THE BOROGOVES   NV   ASF 43 02
        GNOME THERE WAS, A   PADGETT, LEWIS   AC
        SCIENCE FICTION HALL OF FAME VOLUME 1   SILVERBERG, ROBERT AN
        *TREASURY OF SCIENCE FICTION, A   CONKLIN, GROFF   AN
        UBERWINDUNG VON RAUM UND ZEIT   GUNTHER, GOTTHARD   AN
    OPEN SECRET   SS   ASF 43 04
        GREAT STORIES OF SCIENCE FICTION   LEINSTER, MURRAY   AN
    PIPER'S SON, THE   NV   ASF 45 02
        *BEST OF SCIENCE FICTION   CONKLIN, GROFF   AN
        CHILDREN OF WONDER   TENN, WILLIAM   AN
        MUTANT   PADGETT, LEWIS   AC
    PRIVATE EYE   NV   ASF 49 01
        LINE TO TOMORROW AND OTHER STORIES OF FANTASY AND SCIENCE
        FICTION   PADGETT, LEWIS   AC
        MIRROR OF INFINITY, THE   SILVERBERG, ROBERT AN
    TOMORROW, AND TOMORROW, AND TOMORROW...
                                            HEINTZ/HERBERT/JOOS/   AN
    PROJECT   SS   ASF 47 04
        OPERATION FUTURE   CONKLIN, GROFF   AN
    PROUD ROBOT, THE   NV   ASF 43 10
        *ADVENTURES IN TIME AND SPACE   HEALY & MCCOMAS   AN
        MORE ADVENTURES IN TIME AND SPACE   HEALY & MCCOMAS   AN
        ROBOTS HAVE NO TAILS   PADGETT, LEWIS   AC
    RAIN CHECK   SS   ASF 46 07
        GNOME THERE WAS, A   PADGETT, LEWIS   AC
    SEE YOU LATER   SS   TWS 49 06
        GNOME THERE WAS, A   PADGETT, LEWIS   AC
    THIS IS THE HOUSE   SS   ASF 46 02
        GNOME THERE WAS, A   PADGETT, LEWIS   AC
    THREE BLIND MICE   NV   ASF 45 06
        MUTANT   PADGETT, LEWIS   AC
    TIME LOCKER   SS   ASF 43 01
        *ADVENTURES IN TIME AND SPACE   HEALY & MCCOMAS   AN
        ROBOTS HAVE NO TAILS   PADGETT, LEWIS   AC
    TOMORROW AND TOMORROW   SN   ASF 47 01
        TOMORROW AND TOMORROW AND THE FAIRY CHESSMEN
                                                PADGETT, LEWIS   AC
    TWONKY, THE   SS   ASF 42 09
        *ADVENTURES IN TIME AND SPACE   HEALY & MCCOMAS   AN
        GNOME THERE WAS, A   PADGETT, LEWIS   AC
        LINE TO TOMORROW AND OTHER STORIES OF FANTASY AND SCIENCE
        FICTION   PADGETT, LEWIS   AC
        MEN AND MACHINES   SILVERBERG, ROBERT AN
    WE KILL PEOPLE   NV   ASF 46 03
        LOOKING FORWARD   LESSER, MILTON   AN
    WHAT YOU NEED   SS   ASF 45 10
        GNOME THERE WAS, A   PADGETT, LEWIS   AC
        LINE TO TOMORROW AND OTHER STORIES OF FANTASY AND SCIENCE
        FICTION   PADGETT, LEWIS   AC
        OMNIBUS OF SCIENCE FICTION   CONKLIN, GROFF   AN
    WHEN THE BOUGH BREAKS   NV   ASF 44 11
        *ASTOUNDING SCIENCE FICTION ANTHOLOGY, THE
                                                CAMPBELL, JOHN W. JR AN
        *BEYOND TIME AND SPACE   DERLETH, AUGUST   AN
        LINE TO TOMORROW AND OTHER STORIES OF FANTASY AND SCIENCE
        FICTION   PADGETT, LEWIS   AC
        TOMORROW'S CHILDREN   ASIMOV, ISAAC   AN
    WORLD IS MINE, THE   NV   ASF 43 06
        ROBOTS HAVE NO TAILS   PADGETT, LEWIS   AC

PADGETT, RON
    COLD TURKEY   SS C BMR 73
        BAD MOON RISING   DISCH, THOMAS M.   OA

PAGE, GERALD W.
    YEAR'S BEST HORROR STORIES: SERIES IV, THE   AN   DAW 76 11
    GUARDIAN ANGEL   SS   NWR 66 09
        NEW WRITINGS IN SF. 9   CARNELL, JOHN   OA
    HAPPY MAN, THE   NV   ASF 63 03
        INTRODUCING SCIENCE FICTION   ALDISS, BRIAN W.   AN
        STARLIT CORRIDOR, THE   MANSFIELD, ROGER   AN
    INTRODUCTION   IN
        YEAR'S BEST HORROR STORIES: SERIES IV, THE
                                                PAGE, GERALD W.   AN
    MERCYSHIP, THE   SS   SPC 73 01
        SPACE 1   DAVIS, RICHARD   OA
    SPACEMEN LIVE FOREVER   SS   NWR 66 08
        NEW WRITINGS IN SF. 8   CARNELL, JOHN   OA
    WAYGIFT   SS
        FUTURE PASTIMES   EDELSTEIN, SCOTT   OA

PAGE, NORVELL W.
    BUT WITHOUT HORNS   SN   UNK 40 06
        CRUCIBLE OF POWER, THE   GREENBERG , MARTIN AN
        FIVE SCIENCE FICTION NOVELS   GREENBERG , MARTIN AN

PAGE, WILL A.
    AIR SERPENT, THE   SS   RBM 11 04
        SCIENCE FICTION BY GASLIGHT   MOSKOWITZ, SAM   AN

PAIGE, LEO
    HOW HIGH ON THE LADDER?   SS   FBK 50 07
        SCIENCE AND SORCERY   FORD, GARRET   AN

PAINE, J. LINCOLN
    DREISTEIN CASE, THE   SS   FSF 58 06
        13 ABOVE THE NIGHT   CONKLIN, GROFF   AN

PALLANDER, EDWIN
    WHEELS OF DR. GINOCHIO GYVES, THE   SS C CSL 99 09
        WORLDS APART   LOCKE, GEORGE   AN

PALMER, CHARLES H.
    CITIZEN 504   SS   ARG 96 12
        SCIENCE FICTION BY GASLIGHT   MOSKOWITZ, SAM   AN

PALTOCK, ROBERT
    HUMAN MUTANT, THE (FROM "THE LIFE AND ADVENTURES OF
        PETER WILKINS")   EX
        SCIENCE FICTION THROUGH THE AGES 1 EVANS, I. O.   AN

PANGBORN, EDGAR
    GOOD NEIGHBORS AND OTHER STRANGERS   AC H MAC 72
    ANGEL'S EGG   NV   GAL 51 06
        ALPHA 4   SILVERBERG, ROBERT   AN
        BEST SF 2   CRISPIN, EDMUND   AN
        CENTURY OF SCIENCE FICTION, A   KNIGHT, DAMON   AN
        ENEMIES IN SPACE   CONKLIN, GROFF   AN
        GOOD NEIGHBORS AND OTHER STRANGERS PANGBORN, EDGAR   AC
        *INVADERS OF EARTH   CONKLIN, GROFF   AN
    BETTER MOUSEHOLE, A   SS   GAL 65 10
        GOOD NEIGHBORS AND OTHER STRANGERS PANGBORN, EDGAR   AC
        ON OUR WAY TO THE FUTURE   CARR, TERRY   AN
    CHILDREN'S CRUSADE, THE   NV   CTM 74 01
        CONTINUUM 1   ELWOOD, ROGER   OA
    DARIUS   SS
        GOOD NEIGHBORS AND OTHER STRANGERS PANGBORN, EDGAR   AC
    FRESHMAN ANGLE, THE   NV   TTM 73
        TEN TOMORROWS   ELWOOD, ROGER   OA
    GOLDEN HORN, THE   NV   FSF 62 02
        BEST FROM FANTASY AND SCIENCE FICTION: 12
                                            DAVIDSON, AVRAM   AN
    GOOD NEIGHBORS   SS   GAL 60 06
        GOOD NEIGHBORS AND OTHER STRANGERS PANGBORN, EDGAR   AC
    HARPER CONAN & SINGER DAVID   NV
        TOMORROW TODAY   ZEBROWSKI, GEORGE   OA
    LEGEND OF HOMBAS, THE   NV   CTM 74 02
        CONTINUUM 2   ELWOOD, ROGER   OA
    LONGTOOTH   NV   FSF 70 01
        BEST FROM FANTASY AND SCIENCE FICTION: 19
                                            FERMAN, EDWARD L.   AN
        GOOD NEIGHBORS AND OTHER STRANGERS PANGBORN, EDGAR   AC
        NEW WORLDS OF FANTASY NO. 3   CARR, TERRY   AN
    MAM SOLA'S HOUSE   NV   CTM 75 04
        CONTINUUM 4   ELWOOD, ROGER   OA
    MAXWELL'S MONKEY   SS   GAL 64 10
        GOOD NEIGHBORS AND OTHER STRANGERS PANGBORN, EDGAR   AC
    MOUNT CHARITY   NV   UNI 71 01
        NEBULA AWARD STORIES NO. 7   BIGGLE, LLOYD JR.   AN
        UNIVERSE 1   CARR, TERRY   AN
    MUSIC MASTER OF BABYLON, THE   NV   GAL 54 11
        BEST SF 7   CRISPIN, EDMUND   AN
        NEW DREAMS THIS MORNING   BLISH, JAMES   AN
        WORLD THAT COULDN'T BE AND 8 OTHER SF NOVELETS
                                            GOLD, H. L.   AN
    MY BROTHER LEOPOLD   NV   73
        EXALTATION OF STARS, AN   CARR, TERRY   OA
    NIGHT WIND, THE   SS   UNI 74 05
        UNIVERSE 5   CARR, TERRY   OA
    PICKUP FOR OLYMPUS   SS   NEW 53 AN
        GOOD NEIGHBORS AND OTHER STRANGERS PANGBORN, EDGAR   AC
        SUPERNATURAL READER, THE   CONKLIN, G&L.   AN
    PONSONBY CASE, THE   SS
        GOOD NEIGHBORS AND OTHER STRANGERS PANGBORN, EDGAR   AC
    RED HILLS OF SUMMER, THE   NV   FSF 59 09
        ANOTHER PART OF THE GALAXY   CONKLIN, GROFF   AN
    TIGER BOY   NV   UNI 72 02
        UNIVERSE 2   CARR, TERRY   OA
    WITCHES OF NUPAL, THE   NV   CTM 74 03
        CONTINUUM 3   ELWOOD, ROGER   OA
    WOGGLEBEAST   SS   FSF 65 01
        GOOD NEIGHBORS AND OTHER STRANGERS PANGBORN, EDGAR   AC
    WORLD IS A SPHERE, THE   NV   UNI 73 03
        UNIVERSE 3   CARR, TERRY   OA
    WRENS IN GRAMPA'S WHISKERS, THE   SS   FSF 60 04
        GOOD NEIGHBORS AND OTHER STRANGERS PANGBORN, EDGAR   AC

PANSHIN, ALEXEI
    FAREWELL TO YESTERDAY'S TOMORROW   AC H PUT 75
    ARPAD   SS   QRK 71 02
        FAREWELL TO YESTERDAY'S TOMORROW   PANSHIN, ALEXEI   AC
    QUARK/2   DELANY & HACKER   OA
    DESTINY OF MILTON GOMRATH, THE   SS   ASF 67 12
        FAR-OUT PEOPLE, THE   HOSKINS, ROBERT   AN
        FAREWELL TO YESTERDAY'S TOMORROW   PANSHIN, ALEXEI   AC
        OTHER DIMENSIONS   SILVERBERG, ROBERT   AN
    FAREWELL TO YESTERDAY'S TOMORROW   AR C GAL 74 06
        FAREWELL TO YESTERDAY'S TOMORROW   PANSHIN, ALEXEI   AC
    FOREWORD TO "ALL YOU ZOMBIES-"   IN
        MIRROR OF INFINITY, THE   SILVERBERG, ROBERT   AN
    HOW CAN WE SINK WHEN WE CAN FLY?   NV   FFU 71
        BEST SCIENCE FICTION OF THE YEAR, THE CARR, TERRY   AN
        FAREWELL TO YESTERDAY'S TOMORROW   PANSHIN, ALEXEI   AC
        FOUR FUTURES   SILVERBERG, ROBERT   OA
    HOW GEORGES DUCHAMPS DISCOVERED A PLOT TO TAKE OVER THE WORLD
                                                    SS   FAN 71 04
        FAREWELL TO YESTERDAY'S TOMORROW   PANSHIN, ALEXEI   AC
    LADY SUNSHINE AND THE MAGOON OF BEATUS   NA C EPC 75
        EPOCH   ELWOOD & SILVERBERG   OA
    NOW I'M WATCHING ROGER   SS   ORB 72 10
        FAREWELL TO YESTERDAY'S TOMORROW   PANSHIN, ALEXEI   AC
        ORBIT 10   KNIGHT, DAMON   OA
    ONE SUNDAY IN NEPTUNE   SS   NEW 69 AN
        FAREWELL TO YESTERDAY'S TOMORROW   PANSHIN, ALEXEI   AC

PANSHIN, ALEXEI   (CONTINUED)
    TOMORROW'S WORLDS   SILVERBERG, ROBERT   AN
    WORLD'S BEST SCIENCE FICTION: 1970   WOLLHEIM & CARR   AN
    PREFACE   IN
        FAREWELL TO YESTERDAY'S TOMORROW   PANSHIN, ALEXEI   AC
    RITE OF PASSAGE   NO   ACE 68
        SCIENCE FICTION SPECIAL 5   ANONYMOUS   AN
    SENSE OF DIRECTION, A   SS   AMZ 69 11
        DAYS AFTER TOMORROW, THE   SANTESSON, HANS S.   AN
        FAREWELL TO YESTERDAY'S TOMORROW   PANSHIN, ALEXEI   AC
    SHORT SF IN 1968   AR
        NEBULA AWARD STORIES NO. 5   BLISH, JAMES   AN
    SKY BLUE   SS C AMZ 72 03
        BEST SCIENCE FICTION OF THE YEAR, THE NO. 2
                                            CARR, TERRY   AN
        FAREWELL TO YESTERDAY'S TOMORROW   PANSHIN, ALEXEI   AC
    SONS OF PROMETHEUS, THE   NV   ASF 66 10
        FAREWELL TO YESTERDAY'S TOMORROW   PANSHIN, ALEXEI   AC
    WHAT'S YOUR EXCUSE?   SS   FAN 69 08
        FAREWELL TO YESTERDAY'S TOMORROW   PANSHIN, ALEXEI   AC
    WHEN THE VERTICAL WORLD BECOMES HORIZONTAL   SS   UNI 74 04
        FAREWELL TO YESTERDAY'S TOMORROW   PANSHIN, ALEXEI   AC
        UNIVERSE 4   CARR, TERRY   OA

PANSHIN, CORY
    FAREWELL TO YESTERDAY'S TOMORROW   AR C GAL 74 06
        FAREWELL TO YESTERDAY'S TOMORROW   PANSHIN, ALEXEI   AC
    LADY SUNSHINE AND THE MAGOON OF BEATUS   NA C EPC 75
        EPOCH   ELWOOD & SILVERBERG   OA
    SKY BLUE   SS C AMZ 72 03
        BEST SCIENCE FICTION OF THE YEAR, THE NO. 2
                                            CARR, TERRY   AN
        FAREWELL TO YESTERDAY'S TOMORROW   PANSHIN, ALEXEI   AC

PAREDES, HORACIO V.
    POPULATION CONTROL, 1986   SS   ATS 70 04
        VOYAGES: SCENARIOS FOR A SHIP CALLED EARTH
                                            SAUER, ROB   AN

PARIS, MATTHEW
    JOURNAL OF BODLEY CLIVE, THE   SS   NWB 75 09
        NEW WORLDS NINE   BAILEY, HILARY   OA

PARKER, RICHARD
    WHEELBARROW BOY, THE   SS   FSF 53 03
        GALAXY OF GHOULS   MERRIL, JUDITH   AN

PARKES, LUCAS   PSEUD. FOR
    JOHN BEYNON HARRIS (JOHN WYNDHAM PARKES LUCAS BEYNON HARRIS)
    MOON, THE   SS
        OUT OF THIS WORLD 7   WILLIAMS-ELLIS& OWEN AN

PARNOV, YEREMEY
    HE WHO LEAVES NO TRACE   NV C   63
        ULTIMATE THRESHOLD, THE   GINSBURG, MIRRA   AN
    LAST DOOR TO AIYA   SS C ISF 68 06
        LAST DOOR TO AIYA   GINSBURG, MIRRA   AN
    MYSTERY OF GREEN CROSSING   SS C
        RUSSIAN SCIENCE FICTION, 1968   MAGIDOFF, ROBERT   AN
    SNOWBALL, THE   SS C
        JOURNEY ACROSS THREE WORLDS   ANONYMOUS   AN
    WHITE PILOT, THE   NV C   69
        AIR OF MARS AND OTHER STORIES, THE GINSBURG, MIRRA   AN

PARR, CHRISTIE
    SOUTH GATE SEA   SS   ADS 75 02
        ARMADA SCI-FI TWO   DAVIS, RICHARD   OA
    WAIT, THE   NV   ADS 75 01
        ARMADA SCI-FI ONE   DAVIS, RICHARD   OA

PARRA (Y FIGUEREDO)
    TOTENBUCH   SS   DVS 72 02
        AGAIN, DANGEROUS VISIONS   ELLISON, HARLAN   OA

PARRY, MICHEL
    ROOTS OF EVIL, THE   AN H TAP 76
    STRANGE ECSTASIES   AN   PIN 74 10
    INTRODUCTION   IN
        ROOTS OF EVIL, THE   PARRY, MICHEL   AN
        STRANGE ECSTASIES   PARRY, MICHEL   AN

PARTINGTON, CHARLES
    DEBRIS OF RECENT LIVES, THE   SS   NWR 75 25
        NEW WRITINGS IN SF. 25   BULMER, KENNETH   OA
    IN THE COMA CONDITION   SS   NWR 76 29
        NEW WRITINGS IN SF. 29   BULMER, KENNETH   OA
    NARRATIVE OF MASKS   SS   NWB 75 09
        NEW WORLDS NINE   BAILEY, HILARY   OA
    SPORTING ON APTERYX   SS   NWR 74 23
        NEW WRITINGS IN SF. 23   BULMER, KENNETH   OA

PATCHEN, KENNETH
    WOULDN'T YOU AFTER A JAUNT OF 964,000,000,000,000 MILLION
        MILES?   PM   NDR 49
        HOLDING YOUR EIGHT HANDS   LUCIE-SMITH, EDWARD   AN

PATTEN, BRIAN
    PERHAPS WHERE HE IS ONLY LOVING ROCKETS CAN LAND PM   69
        HOLDING YOUR EIGHT HANDS   LUCIE-SMITH, EDWARD   AN
    SMALL DRAGON, A   PM   69
        HOLDING YOUR EIGHT HANDS   LUCIE-SMITH, EDWARD   AN

PAUL, BARBARA
    ANSWER "AFFIRMATIVE" OR "NEGATIVE"   SS   ASF 72 04
        ANALOG 9   BOVA, BEN   AN

PAUL, ELLIOT
  MATHEMATICS CHEZ MADAME MARIETTE   MS   42
    MATHEMATICAL MAGPIE, THE   FADIMAN, CLIFTON   AN

PAUL, FRANK R.
  MAN FROM VENUS, THE   SS
    FAREWELL FANTASTIC VENUS   ALDISS & HARRISON   AN
  SCIENCE WONDER STORIES COVER   IL
    BEYOND THIS HORIZON   CARRELL, CHRISTOPHER OA
  SF, THE SPIRIT OF YOUTH   AR   39
    SCIENCE FICTION ROLL OF HONOR, THE   POHL, FREDERICK   AN

PAUL, HERB
  ANGEL WITH PURPLE HAIR, THE   SS   FSF 50 12
    SUPERNATURAL READER, THE   CONKLIN, G&L.   AN

PAULI, WOLFGANG
  ON THE RELATIVITY OF TIME   AR   49
    SCIENCE FACT/FICTION   FARRELL/GAGE/&   AN

PAULSEN, KATHRYN
  TWENTY-EIGHTH DAY, THE   SS
    NEW CONSTELLATIONS   DISCH & NAYLOR   OA

PAYES, RACHEL COSGROVE
  AND THE POWER...   SS   WLK 73
    AND WALK NOW GENTLY THROUGH THE FIRE...
                                      ELWOOD, ROGER   OA
  COME TAKE A DIP WITH ME IN THE GENETIC POOL   SS   DYS 75
    DYSTOPIAN VISIONS   ELWOOD, ROGER   OA
  DEAF LISTENER   SS   ALC 73
    ALIEN CONDITION, THE   GOLDIN, STEPHEN   OA
  GORGONS, THE   SS
    QUEST   BISCHOFF, DAVID   OA
  GRANDMA WAS NEVER LIKE THIS   SS   NEW 73 AN
    ANDROIDS, TIME MACHINES AND BLUE GIRAFFES
                                      ELWOOD & GHIDALIA   AN
  HALF LIFE   SS   COI 73
    CHILDREN OF INFINITY   ELWOOD, ROGER   OA
  IN HIS OWN IMAGE   SS   STG 74
    STRANGE GODS   ELWOOD, ROGER   OA

PEAKE, MERVYN
  BOY IN DARKNESS   NV   56
    INNER LANDSCAPE, THE   MOORCOCK, MICHAEL   AN
    SOMETIME, NEVER   ANONYMOUS   OA
  DANSE MACABRE   SS   SCF 63 10
    WEIRD SHADOWS FROM BEYOND   CARNELL, JOHN   AN
  SAME TIME, SAME PLACE   SS   SCF 63 08
    WEIRD SHADOWS FROM BEYOND   CARNELL, JOHN   AN

PEARL, CLINTON
  CRASH ALERT   SS   59
    TEEN-AGE OUTER SPACE STORIES   FURMAN, A. L.   AN
  SPACE SECRET   SS   58
    TEEN-AGE OUTER SPACE STORIES   FURMAN, A. L.   AN

PEARSON, ELIZABETH J SEE ALSO   CO-EDITOR SYLVIA Z. BRODKIN

PEARSON, MARTIN   PSEUD. FOR DONALD A. WOLLHEIM
  AJAX OF AJAX   SS   FUT 42 08
    FLIGHT INTO SPACE   WOLLHEIM, DONALD A.   AN
  EMBASSY, THE   SS   ASF 42 03
    BEYOND THE END OF TIME   POHL, FREDERICK   AN
    *TREASURY OF SCIENCE FICTION, A   CONKLIN, GROFF   AN
  MASK OF DEMETER   SS C FSF 53 01
    PRIZE SCIENCE FICTION   WOLLHEIM, DONALD A.   AN
  MILLIONTH YEAR, THE   SS   SFS 43 04
    ADVENTURES IN THE FAR FUTURE   WOLLHEIM, DONALD A.   DA

PEARSON, MICHAEL   SEE ALSO   CO-EDITOR AMABEL WILLIAMS-ELLIS
  PREFACE   IN C
    TALES FROM THE GALAXIES   WILLIAMS-ELLIS& P.   AN

PEART, NOEL
  SPUD FAILURE DEFINITE   SS
    AD 2500   WILSON, ANGUS   AN

PEASE, M. C.
  PATH OF DARKNESS   SS   SFS 55 03
    MASTERS OF SCIENCE FICTION   HOWARD, IVAN   AN
  RIPENESS   NV   SFS 55 01
    RARE SCIENCE FICTION   HOWARD, IVAN   AN
  TELESTASSIS   SS   SFS 55 05
    NOW & BEYOND   HOWARD, IVAN   AN
  TEMPLE OF DESPAIR   NV   DSF 53 10
    ESCAPE TO EARTH   HOWARD, IVAN   AN

PECK, RICHARD E.
  GANTLET   SS   ORB 72 10
    BEST SF: 1971   HARRISON & ALDISS   AN
    CITY: 2000 A.D., THE   CLEM/GREENBERG/&   AN
    ORBIT 10   KNIGHT, DAMON   OA

PEDERSEN, CON
  PUSHOVER PLANET   SS   FSF 63 06
    OUT OF THIS WORLD 5   WILLIAMS-ELLIS& OWEN AN

PEDLER, KIT
  LONG-TERM RESIDENTS, THE   SS
    YEAR'S BEST HORROR STORIES: SERIES II, THE
                                      DAVIS, RICHARD   AN

PEIRCE, HAYFORD
  HIGH YIELD BONDAGE   NV   GAL 75 08

PEIRCE, HAYFORD   (CONTINUED)
    BEST SCIENCE FICTION STORIES OF THE YEAR (1975)
                                      DEL REY, LESTER   AN
  MAIL SUPREMACY   SS   ASF 75 03
    BEST SCIENCE FICTION STORIES OF THE YEAR (1975)
                                      DEL REY, LESTER   AN

PENDEN, WILLIAM
  NIGHT IN FUNLAND   SS   60
    NIGHT IN FUNLAND   BRONDFIELD, JEROME   AN

PENMAN, THOMAS
  BANKS OF THE NILE, THE   NV C NWR 76 28
    NEW WRITINGS IN SF. 28   BULMER, KENNETH   OA
  SEAFARER, THE   SS C NWR 75 26
    NEW WRITINGS IN SF. 26   BULMER, KENNETH   OA

PENNEY, ROGER
  SIX DRAWINGS   IL   QRK 71 02
    QUARK/2   DELANY & HACKER   OA

PERCY, H. R.
  LETTER FROM AMERICA   SS
    BEYOND TIME   LEY, SANDRA   OA

PEREGOY, CALVIN   PSEUD. FOR THOMAS C. MCCLARY
  TERRIBLE SENSE, THE   SS   ASF 38 08
    *BEST OF SCIENCE FICTION   CONKLIN, GROFF   AN

PERKINS, F. B.
  DEVIL-PUZZLERS   SS
    DEALS WITH THE DEVIL   DAVENPORT, BASIL   AN

PERKINS, LAWRENCE A.
  HIDDEN EARS, THE   SS   ASF 69 01
    ANALOG 8   CAMPBELL, JOHN W. JR AN

PERRIN, JEFFERY
  JUST A MATTER OF TIME   SS   GAL 73 07
    BEST FROM GALAXY, THE VOLUME II GALAXY, EDITORS OF   AN

PERSKY, STAN
  FROM "THE DAY"   EX   QRK 71 04
    QUARK/4   DELANY & HACKER   OA

PETAJA, EMIL
  STARDRIFT AND OTHER FANTASTIC FLOTSAM   AC H FPB 71
  ANSWER, THE   SS   IMG 51 09
    STARDRIFT AND OTHER FANTASTIC FLOTSAM PETAJA, EMIL   AC
  BE A WINGDINGER, EARN BIG MONEY   SS
    STARDRIFT AND OTHER FANTASTIC FLOTSAM PETAJA, EMIL   AC
  CUBE IN A DODECAGON GARDEN (SEE DODECAGON GARDEN) TC
  DARK BALCONY, THE   SS   FAD 51 02
    STARDRIFT AND OTHER FANTASTIC FLOTSAM PETAJA, EMIL   AC
  DARK HOLLOW   SS   MOH 66 WI
    STARDRIFT AND OTHER FANTASTIC FLOTSAM PETAJA, EMIL   AC
  DODECAGON GARDEN (CUBE IN A DODECAGON GARDEN) SS   SWY 70 06
    STARDRIFT AND OTHER FANTASTIC FLOTSAM PETAJA, EMIL   AC
  DOG'S BEST FRIEND, A   SS
    STARDRIFT AND OTHER FANTASTIC FLOTSAM PETAJA, EMIL   AC
  FOUND OBJECTS   SS
    STARDRIFT AND OTHER FANTASTIC FLOTSAM PETAJA, EMIL   AC
  HUNGER (THE HUNGRY GHOST)   SS   WRT 50 03
    STARDRIFT AND OTHER FANTASTIC FLOTSAM PETAJA, EMIL   AC
  HUNGRY GHOST, THE (SEE HUNGER)   TC
  IN MEMORIAM- FRANK OWEN   MS
    NEBULA AWARD STORIES NO. 4   ANDERSON, POUL   AN
  MAN WHO HATED WAR, THE (SEE PEACEMONGER)   TC
  MILLION-MILE HUNT (SEE MOON FEVER)   TC
  MOON FEVER (MILLION-MILE HUNT)   SS   IFS 65 03
    STARDRIFT AND OTHER FANTASTIC FLOTSAM PETAJA, EMIL   AC
  ONLY GONE BEFORE   SS   MOH 68 03
    STARDRIFT AND OTHER FANTASTIC FLOTSAM PETAJA, EMIL   AC
  PATTERN FOR PLUNDER   NV
    STARDRIFT AND OTHER FANTASTIC FLOTSAM PETAJA, EMIL   AC
  PEACEMONGER (THE MAN WHO HATED WAR)   SS   AMZ 44 12
    STARDRIFT AND OTHER FANTASTIC FLOTSAM PETAJA, EMIL   AC
  SKYDRIFT (SEE STARDRIFT)   TC
  STARDRIFT (SKYDRIFT)   SS   WRT 49 11
    STARDRIFT AND OTHER FANTASTIC FLOTSAM PETAJA, EMIL   AC
  TERRIBLE QUICK SWORD   SS   SAW 72
    SIGNS AND WONDERS   ELWOOD, ROGER   OA
  WHERE IS THY STING   SS   FSF 67 05
    STARDRIFT AND OTHER FANTASTIC FLOTSAM PETAJA, EMIL   AC

PETHEBRIDGE, DENIS
  SPACE: THE THIRD MILLENNIUM   PM
    STARLIT CORRIDOR, THE   MANSFIELD, ROGER   AN

PETRACCA, JOSEPH
  TOLLIVER'S TRAVELS   NV C NTS 51
    NEW TALES OF SPACE AND TIME   HEALY, RAYMOND J.   OA

PEYTON, GREEN   PSEUD. FOR G. PEYTON WERTENBAKER
  SHIP THAT TURNED ASIDE, THE   SS   AMZ 30 03
    *BIG BOOK OF SCIENCE FICTION   CONKLIN, GROFF   AN

PHELAN, R. C.
  SOMETHING INVENTED ME   SS   REP 60 10
    6TH ANNUAL OF THE YEAR'S BEST S-F, THE MERRIL, JUDITH AN

PHILLIFENT, JOHN T.   ALSO AS   JOHN RACKHAM
  AIM FOR THE HEEL   NV   ASF 67 07
    ANALOG 7   CAMPBELL, JOHN W. JR AN
  ETHICAL QUOTIENT   SN   ASF 62 10
    ANALOG 2   CAMPBELL, JOHN W. JR AN

PHILLIFENT, JOHN T.

PHILLIFENT, JOHN T.   (CONTINUED)
  OWE ME   SS   ASF 74 05
    TOMORROW, INC.   GREENBERG& OLANDER   AN

PHILLIPS, A. M.
  DEATH OF THE MOON, THE   SS   AMZ 29 02
    FLIGHT INTO SPACE   WOLLHEIM, DONALD A.   AN
  EXTRA BRICKLAYER, THE   SS   UNK 40 09
    HELL HATH FURY   HAY, GEORGE   AN
  TIME-TRAVEL HAPPENS¡   AR   UNK 39 12
    *ADVENTURES IN TIME AND SPACE HEALY & MCCOMAS   AN

PHILLIPS, LOUIS
  LOP-EARED CAT THAT DEVOURED PHILADELPHIA, THE   SS
    BEST SF: 75, THE NINTH ANNUAL HARRISON & ALDISS AN

PHILLIPS, PETER
  AT NO EXTRA COST   SS   MSS 51 08
    BEST SCIENCE-FICTION STORIES: 1952, THE
                               BLEILER & DIKTY   AN
  C/O MR. MAKEPEACE   SS   FSF 54 02
  DARK SIDE, THE   KNIGHT, DAMON   AN
  OPERATION FUTURE   CONKLIN, GROFF   AN
  COUNTER CHARM   SS   SLN 51 SP
    FIFTY SHORT SCIENCE FICTION TALES ASIMOV & CONKLIN AN
    OMNIBUS OF SCIENCE FICTION CONKLIN, GROFF   AN
  DREAMS ARE SACRED   SS   ASF 48 09
    ASTOUNDING-ANALOG READER, THE VOLUME TWO
                               HARRISON & ALDISS   AN
    *IMAGINATION UNLIMITED   BLEILER & DIKTY   AN
    SPECTRUM 3   AMIS & CONQUEST   AN
  FIELD STUDY   SS   GAL 51 04
    *GALAXY READER OF SCIENCE FICTION GOLD, H. L.   AN
  LOST MEMORY   SS   GAL 52 05
    COMING OF THE ROBOTS, THE MOSKOWITZ, SAM   AN
    CONTACT   KEYES, NOEL   AN
    GALAXY SCIENCE FICTION OMNIBUS GOLD, H. L.   AN
    GATEWAY TO TOMORROW   CARNELL, JOHN   AN
    SCIENCE FICTION TERROR TALES CONKLIN, GROFF   AN
    SECOND GALAXY READER OF SCIENCE FICTION
                               GOLD, H. L.   AN
    THEMES IN SCIENCE FICTION KELLEY, LEO P.   AN
  MANNA   NV   ASF 49 02
    *BIG BOOK OF SCIENCE FICTION CONKLIN, GROFF   AN
    SCIENCE FICTION ARGOSY, A KNIGHT, DAMON   AN
  PLAGAIRIST   NV   NWS 50 SU
    *FUTURE TENSE   CROSSEN, KENDELL F.   AN
  SHE WHO LAUGHS...   SS   GAL 52 04
    ASSIGNMENT IN TOMORROW   POHL, FREDERICK   AN
  UNIVERSITY   NV   GAL 53 04
    SECOND GALAXY READER OF SCIENCE FICTION
                               GOLD, H. L.   AN
  UNKNOWN QUANTITY   SS   NWS 49 05
    BEST FROM NEW WORLDS SCIENCE FICTION, THE
                               CARNELL, JOHN   AN
    *NO PLACE LIKE EARTH   CARNELL, JOHN   AN
  WARNING, THE   SS   FSF 53 09
    BEYOND THE BARRIERS OF SPACE AND TIME MERRIL, JUDITH   AN

PHILLIPS, R. A. J.
  DAY IN THE LIFE OF KELVIN THROOP, A   SS   ASF 64 07
    ANALOG 4   CAMPBELL, JOHN W. JR   AN

PHILLIPS, ROG   PSEUD. FOR ROGER P. GRAHAM
  GAME PRESERVE   SS   IFS 57 10
    SF:58, THE YEAR'S GREATEST SCIENCE FICTION AND FANTASY
                               MERRIL, JUDITH   AN
  YELLOW PILL, THE   SS   ASF 58 10
    ASTOUNDING-ANALOG READER, THE VOLUME TWO
                               HARRISON & ALDISS   AN
    BEST SF 4   CRISPIN, EDMUND   AN
    INTRODUCTORY PSYCHOLOGY THROUGH SCIENCE FICTION
                               KATZ/WARRICK/&   AN
    SCIENCE FICTION   BRODKIN & PEARSON   AN
    SF:59, THE YEAR'S GREATEST SCIENCE FICTION AND FANTASY
                               MERRIL, JUDITH   AN

PHILLIPS, VIC
  ONCE AROUND THE MOON   NV   ASF 37 06
    FIRST FLIGHTS TO THE MOON CLEMENT, HAL   AN

PICARD, DON
  GATO-O   NV   SFE 74 01
    SCIENCE FICTION EMPHASIS NO. 1 GERROLD, DAVID   OA

PICKENS, THOMAS
  DING DONG, THE WITCH IS WELL   SS   INY 72 04
    INFINITY 4   HOSKINS, ROBERT   OA
  ROUTINE PATROL ACTIVITY   SS   ALC 73
    ALIEN CONDITION, THE   GOLDIN, STEPHEN   OA

PIERCE, J. J.
  BEST OF CORDWAINER SMITH, THE (LISTED UNDER CORDWAINER SMITH)
                                                 EC   BAL 75
  CORDWAINER SMITH: THE SHAPER OF MYTHS   IN
    BEST OF CORDWAINER SMITH, THE SMITH, CORDWAINER AC
  TIMELINE FROM THE INSTRUMENTALITY OF MANKIND   MS
    BEST OF CORDWAINER SMITH, THE SMITH, CORDWAINER AC

PIERCE, JOHN R.   ALSO AS   J. J. COUPLING
  HIGHER THINGS, THE   SS   NOV 70 01
    *NOVA 1   HARRISON, HARRY   OA
  INVARIANT   SS   ASF 44 04
    *ASTOUNDING SCIENCE FICTION ANTHOLOGY, THE
                               CAMPBELL, JOHN W. JR AN

PIERCE, JOHN R.   (CONTINUED)
  *FIRST ASTOUNDING SCIENCE FICTION ANTHOLOGY, THE
                               CAMPBELL, JOHN W. JR AN
    SCIENCE FICTION INVENTIONS KNIGHT, DAMON   AN
  JOHN SZE'S FUTURE   SS   NEW 62 AN
    GREAT SCIENCE FICTION BY SCIENTISTS CONKLIN, GROFF   AN
  RIME OF THE ANCIENT SF AUTHOR,OF CONVENTIONS AND RECOLLECTIONS
                                                 PM   68
    BEST SF: 1968   HARRISON & ALDISS   AN
  SEE NO EVIL   SS   NEW 66 AN
    SCIENCE FICTION ODDITIES CONKLIN, GROFF   AN

PIERCY, MARGE
  DEATH OF SAPPHO, THE   NV
    2076: THE AMERICAN TRICENTENNIAL BRYANT, EDWARD   OA
  WOMAN ON THE EDGE OF TIME   NV
    AURORA: BEYOND EQUALITY   MCINTYRE & ANDERSON OA

PIERIK, ROBERT
  LEFT-HANDED BOY, THE   NV
    ANYWHERE, ANYWHEN   ENGDAHL, SYLVIA   OA

PINCKARD, TERRI E.
  HATE, THE   SS   WTS 71 01
    YEAR'S BEST HORROR STORIES, THE DAVIS, RICHARD   AN

PINKNEY, DOROTHY C.
  FULL CIRCLE   PM   FSF 56 12
    BEST FROM FANTASY AND SCIENCE FICTION: 7
                               BOUCHER, ANTHONY   AN

PIPER, H. BEAM
  GENESIS   NV   FUT 51 09
    SHADOW OF TOMORROW   POHL, FREDERIK   AN
  HE WALKED AROUND THE HORSES   NV   ASF 48 04
    ASPECTS OF SCIENCE FICTION DOHERTY, G. D.   AN
    BEST SF 3   CRISPIN, EDMUND   AN
    SCIENCE FICTION ARGOSY, A KNIGHT, DAMON   AN
    SCIENCE FICTION THROUGH THE AGES 2 EVANS, I. O. AN
    WORLD OF WONDER   PRATT, FLETCHER   AN
  LAST ENEMY   NV   ASF 50 08
    *ASTOUNDING SCIENCE FICTION ANTHOLOGY, THE
                               CAMPBELL, JOHN W. JR AN
  MINISTRY OF DISTURBANCE   NV   ASF 58 12
    SEVEN TRIPS THROUGH TIME AND SPACE CONKLIN, GROFF   AN
  OMNILINGUAL   NV   ASF 57 02
    APEMAN, SPACEMAN   STOVER & HARRISON   AN
    DAYS AFTER TOMORROW, THE SANTESSON, HANS S.   AN
    GREAT SCIENCE FICTION STORIES ABOUT MARS
                               DIKTY, T. E.   AN
    MARS, WE LOVE YOU   HIPOLITO & MCNELLY   AN
    PROLOGUE TO ANALOG   CAMPBELL, JOHN W. JR AN
    SCIENCE FICTION NOVELLAS HARRISON & MCNELLY   AN
    TOMORROW, AND TOMORROW, AND TOMORROW...
                               HEINTZ/HERBERT/JOOS/   AN
    WHERE DO WE GO FROM HERE? ASIMOV, ISAAC   AN
  OPERATION RSVP   SS   AMZ 51 01
    WORLD OF WONDER   PRATT, FLETCHER   AN
  POLICE OPERATION   NV   ASF 48 07
    SPACE POLICE   NORTON, ANDRE   AN
  RETURN, THE   NV C ASF 54 01
    SCIENCE-FICTIONAL SHERLOCK HOLMES, THE COUNCIL OF FOUR
  TIME AND TIME AGAIN   SS   ASF 47 04
    *TREASURY OF SCIENCE FICTION, A CONKLIN, GROFF   AN
    UBERWINDUNG VON RAUM UND ZEIT GUNTHER, GOTTHARD AN
  ULLR UPRISING   NA   SSF 53 02
    PETRIFIED PLANET, THE   CLARK, JOHN D.   OA

PISERCHIA, DORIS
  BRILLIANT CURIOSITY, A   NV   ORB 75 16
    ORBIT 16   KNIGHT, DAMON   OA
  DEATHRIGHTS DEFERRED   SS
    SCIENCE FICTION DISCOVERIES POHL, C. & F.   OA
  HALF THE KINGDOM   SS   ORB 73 12
    ORBIT 12   KNIGHT, DAMON   OA
  IDIO   SS   ORB 74 13
    ORBIT 13   KNIGHT, DAMON   OA
  LIMITED ACCOMMODATIONS   SS
    CRISIS   ELWOOD, ROGER   OA
  NAKED AND AFRAID I GO   SS   ORB 74 13
    ORBIT 13   KNIGHT, DAMON   OA
  PALE HANDS   SS   ORB 74 15
    ORBIT 15   KNIGHT, DAMON   OA
  QUARANTINE   SS   GAL 73 09
    BEST FROM GALAXY, THE   VOLUME II GALAXY, EDITORS OF AN
  SHELTERING DREAM   SS   IFS 72 02
    BEST SCIENCE FICTION FOR 1972 POHL, FREDERICK   AN
  TYPICAL DAY, A   SS   GAL 74 03
    BEST SF: 1974   HARRISON & ALDISS   AN

PLACHTA, DANNIE
  LAST INN ON THE ROAD, THE   SS C NWS 67 10
    BEST SF STORIES FROM NEW WORLDS 5 MOORCOCK, MICHAEL AN
  MAN FROM WHEN, THE   SS   IFS 66 07
    WORLD'S BEST SCIENCE FICTION: 1967 WOLLHEIM & CARR AN

PLANCHAT, HENRY-LUC
  PRISON OF CLAY, PRISON OF STEEL   SS   ORB 75 16
    ORBIT 16   KNIGHT, DAMON   OA
  SEVERAL WAYS, AND THE SUN   NV   NDM 77 07
    NEW DIMENSIONS 7   SILVERBERG, ROBERT   OA

PLATH, SYLVIA
  MUSHROOMS   PM   60
    SCIENCE FICTION   BRODKIN & PEARSON   AN

PLATO
  ATLANTIS (370 B.C.)   EX
  *BEYOND TIME AND SPACE   DERLETH, AUGUST   AN
  FROM "CRITIAS, OR THE ISLAND OF ATLANTIS" (370 B.C.)
                                                        EX
  PAST, PRESENT, AND FUTURE PERFECT   WOLFE, J&FITZ GERALD AN
  SOCRATES AND THE SLAVE   SS
  FANTASIA MATHEMATICA   FADIMAN, CLIFTON   AN
  TIMAIOS (EXCERPT)   EX
  3000 YEARS OF FANTASY AND SCIENCE FICTION
                                  DE CAMP, L. S.&C.   AN
  VANISHED CIVILIZATION, THE (FROM "TIMAIOS" AND "CRITIAS")
                                                        EX
  SCIENCE FICTION THROUGH THE AGES 1   EVANS, I. O.   AN

PLATT, CHARLES AND HILARY BAILEY
NEW WORLDS NO. 6   OA L EQN 74

PLATT, CHARLES   SEE ALSO   CO-EDITOR MICHAEL MOORCOCK
  ATTACK-ESCAPE, AN INTERVIEW WITH ALFRED BESTER   AR   NWQ 72 04
  NEW WORLDS QUARTERLY NO. 4   MOORCOCK, MICHAEL   OA
  CLEANSING OF THE SYSTEM, A   SS   NWQ 72 03
  NEW WORLDS QUARTERLY NO. 3   MOORCOCK, MICHAEL   OA
  COLDNESS, THE   SS   NWQ 73 05
  NEW WORLDS NO. 5   MOORCOCK & PLATT   OA
  DIRECTION   SS
  NEW S.F., THE   JONES, LANGDON   OA
  DISASTER STORY, THE   AR   NWS 66 03
  BEST SF STORIES FROM NEW WORLDS 3   MOORCOCK, MICHAEL AN
  FAMILY LITERATURE   SS   NWB 73 05
  NEW WORLDS QUARTERLY NO. 5   MOORCOCK, MICHAEL   OA
  INTRODUCTION   IN
  NEW WORLDS NO. 5   MOORCOCK & PLATT   OA
  NEW WORLDS NO. 6   PLATT & BAILEY   OA
  LONE ZONE   SS   NWS 65 07
  BEST SF STORIES FROM NEW WORLDS 7   MOORCOCK, MICHAEL AN
  MOTIVATION CHART   SS   NWB 73 05
  NEW WORLDS QUARTERLY NO. 5   MOORCOCK, MICHAEL   OA
  NEW YORK TIMES   SS   ORB 72 11
  ORBIT 11   KNIGHT, DAMON   OA
  NORMAN VS. AMERICA   CT   QRK 71 04
  QUARK/4   DELANY & HACKER   OA
  RODENT LABORATORY, THE   SS   NWS 66 08
  BEST SF STORIES FROM NEW WORLDS 5   MOORCOCK, MICHAEL AN
  TOTAL EXPERIENCE KICK, THE   SS   NWS 66 12
  BEST SF STORIES FROM NEW WORLDS NO. 2, THE
                                  MOORCOCK, MICHAEL   AN
  ENGLAND SWINGS SF   MERRIL, JUDITH   AN
  THEMES IN SCIENCE FICTION   KELLEY, LEO P.   AN

PLAUGER, P. J.
  CHILD OF ALL AGES   SS   ASF 75 03
  BEST SCIENCE FICTION OF THE YEAR, THE NO. 5
                                  CARR, TERRY   AN
  BEST SCIENCE FICTION STORIES OF THE YEAR (1975)
                                  DEL REY, LESTER   AN
  NEBULA AWARD STORIES 11   LE GUIN, URSULA K.   AN
  1976 ANNUAL WORLD'S BEST SF, THE   WOLLHEIM, DONALD A. AN
  FIGHTING MADNESS   NO
  ANALOG ANNUAL   BOVA, BEN   OA
  HERE BE DRAGONS   SS
  AURORA: BEYOND EQUALITY   MCINTYRE & ANDERSON   OA

PLAYBOY, EDITORS OF
DEAD ASTRONAUT, 10 STORIES OF SPACE FLIGHT, THE   AN   PBP 71
FIEND, THE   AN   PBP 71
FROM THE "S" FILE   AN   PBP 71
FULLY AUTOMATED LOVE LIFE OF HENRY KEANRIDGE   AN   PBP 71
LAST TRAIN TO LIMBO   AN   PBP 71
MASKS   AN   PBP 71
PLAYBOY BOOK OF HORROR AND THE SUPERNATURAL, THE   AN H PBP 67
PLAYBOY BOOK OF SCIENCE FICTION AND FANTASY, THE   AN H PBP 66
PLAYBOY'S STORIES OF THE SINISTER & STRANGE   AN   PBP 69
TRANSIT OF EARTH   AN   PBP 71
WEIRD SHOW   AN   PBP 71
  PREFACE   IN
  DEAD ASTRONAUT, 10 STORIES OF SPACE FLIGHT, THE
                                  PLAYBOY, EDITORS OF AN
  FIEND, THE   PLAYBOY, EDITORS OF AN
  FROM THE "S" FILE   PLAYBOY, EDITORS OF AN
  FULLY AUTOMATED LOVE LIFE OF HENRY KEANRIDGE
                                  PLAYBOY, EDITORS OF AN
  LAST TRAIN TO LIMBO   PLAYBOY, EDITORS OF AN
  MASKS   PLAYBOY, EDITORS OF AN
  PLAYBOY BOOK OF HORROR AND THE SUPERNATURAL, THE
                                  PLAYBOY, EDITORS OF AN
  PLAYBOY BOOK OF SCIENCE FICTION AND FANTASY, THE
                                  PLAYBOY, EDITORS OF AN
  PLAYBOY'S STORIES OF THE SINISTER & STRANGE
                                  PLAYBOY, EDITORS OF AN
  SAGITTARIUS   RUSSELL, RAY   AC
  WEIRD SHOW   PLAYBOY, EDITORS OF AN

PLUNKETT, EDWARD J. SEE PSEUD. LORD DUNSANY

PODOLNY, ROMAN
  INVASION   SS   66
  ULTIMATE THRESHOLD, THE   GINSBURG, MIRRA   AN
  TALES OF THE DISTANT PAST   SS
  RUSSIAN SCIENCE FICTION, 1968   MAGIDOFF, ROBERT   AN

POE, EDGAR ALLEN
  BALLOON-HOAX, THE   SS   SUN 44 04
  PAST, PRESENT, AND FUTURE PERFECT   WOLFE, J&FITZ GERALD AN
  WONDERMAKERS   HOSKINS, ROBERT   AN

POE, EDGAR ALLEN   (CONTINUED)
CONQUEST OF THE AIR, THE (FROM "THE BALLOON HOAX")
                                       EX   SUN 44 04
  SCIENCE FICTION THROUGH THE AGES 1   EVANS, I. O.   AN
  CONVERSATION OF EIROS AND CHARMION, THE SS   BGM 39 12
  ECO-FICTION   STADLER, JOHN   AN
  IN DREAMS AWAKE   FIEDLER, LESLIE A.   AN
  TREASURY OF SCIENCE FICTION CLASSICS, THE
                                  KUEBLER, HAROLD W.   AN
  DESCENT INTO THE MAELSTROM, A   SS   GLG 41 05
  ARMCHAIR SCIENCE READER, THE   GORDON, I. & SORKIN   AN
  JOURNEYS IN SCIENCE FICTION   LOUGHLIN, RICHARD L.   AN
  FACTS IN THE CASE OF M. VALDEMAR   SS   AWR 45 12
  FUTURE PERFECT   FRANKLIN, H. BRUCE   AN
  GREAT SCIENCE FICTION ABOUT DOCTORS CONKLIN, G&FABRICANT AN
  SHOT IN THE DARK   MERRIL, JUDITH   AN
  HANS PHAALL- A TALE   SS   SLM 35 06
  MASTERPIECES OF SCIENCE FICTION   MOSKOWITZ, SAM   AN
  KING PEST   SS   SLM 35 09
  ANDROIDS, TIME MACHINES AND BLUE GIRAFFES
                                  ELWOOD & GHIDALIA   AN
  LUNATICS, THE (THE SYSTEM OF DOCTOR TARR & PROFESSOR FEATHER)
                                       SS   GLG 45 11
  GHOULS, THE   HAINING, PETER   AN
  MELLONTA TAUTA   SS   GDY 49 02
  FUTURE PERFECT   FRANKLIN, H. BRUCE   AN
  SPECULATIONS   SANDERS, THOMAS E.   AN
  STRANGE SIGNPOSTS   ELWOOD & MOSKOWITZ   AN
  METZENGERSTEIN   SS   SLM 36 02
  BEWARE THE BEASTS   GHIDALIA, V.& ELWOOD   AN
  MS FOUND IN A BOTTLE   SS   BSV 33 11
  ANCIENT MYSTERIES READER, THE   HAINING, PETER   AN
  OBLONG BOX, THE   SS   GDY 44 09
  GHOULS, THE   HAINING, PETER   AN
  SONNET: TO SCIENCE (1829)   PM   29
  SPECULATIONS   SANDERS, THOMAS E.   AN
  SYSTEM OF DOCTOR TARR & PROFESSOR FEATHER, THE (SEE THE
  LUNATICS)   TC
  TALE OF THE RAGGED MOUNTAINS, A   SS   GDY 44 04
  *BEST OF SCIENCE FICTION   CONKLIN, GROFF   AN
  FUTURE PERFECT   FRANKLIN, H. BRUCE   AN
  TELL-TALE HEART, THE   SS   POI 43 01
  *TWISTED   CONKLIN, GROFF   AN
  THOUSAND-AND-SECOND TALE OF SCHEHERAZADE, THE SS GDY 45 02
  *BEYOND TIME AND SPACE   DERLETH, AUGUST   AN
  WILLIAM WILSON (1839)   NV   GFT 39 09
  MOONLIGHT TRAVELER, THE   STERN, PHILIP VAN D.   AN
  OTHER DIMENSION, THE   ROSNER, SARA   AN
  X+1   PM
  FANTASIA MATHEMATICA   FADIMAN, CLIFTON   AN

POHL, CAROL AND FREDERIK
JUPITER   AN   BAL 73 12
SCIENCE FICTION DISCOVERIES   OA   BAN 76 08
SCIENCE FICTION: THE GREAT YEARS   AN   ACE 73 01
SCIENCE FICTION: THE GREAT YEARS, VOL. II   AN   ACE 76

POHL, CAROL
  INTRODUCTION   IN C
  SCIENCE FICTION: THE GREAT YEARS, VOL. II
                                  POHL, C. & F.   AN
  INTRODUCTION (A DIALOGUE)   IN C
  SCIENCE FICTION DISCOVERIES   POHL, C. & F.   OA
  INTRODUCTION THE SECOND   IN
  SCIENCE FICTION: THE GREAT YEARS   POHL, C. & F.   AN
  JUPITER AT LAST   IN C
  JUPITER   POHL, C. & F.   AN

POHL, FREDERIK AND C. M. KORNBLUTH
WONDER EFFECT, THE   AC   BAL 62

POHL, FREDERIK   SEE ALSO   CO-EDITOR CAROL POHL
                     ALSO AS
     PAUL FLEHR, JAMES MACCREIGH AND CHARLES SATTERFIELD
ABOMINABLE EARTHMAN, THE   AC   BAL 63
ALTERNATING CURRENTS   AC   BAL 56
ASSIGNMENT IN TOMORROW   AN H HAN 54
BEST OF C. M. KORNBLUTH, THE (LISTED UNDER C. M. KORNBLUTH)
                                       EC H NDB 76
BEST OF FREDERIK POHL, THE   AC H NDB 75
  EDITED BY LESTER DEL REY
BEST SCIENCE FICTION FOR 1972   AN   ACE 72 09
BEST SCIENCE FICTION FROM IF, THE   AN D GPC 64
BEST SCIENCE FICTION FROM WORLDS OF TOMORROW, THE AN D GPC 64
BEYOND THE END OF TIME   AN H DBL 52
CASE AGAINST TOMORROW, THE   AC   BAL 57 05
DAY MILLION   AC   BAL 70 06
DIGITS AND DASTARDS   AC   BAL 66 06
DOOR TO ANYWHERE   AN   CUR 67
  SEE "THE TENTH GALAXY READER"
EARLY POHL, THE   AC H DBL 76
EIGHTH GALAXY READER, THE   AN H DBL 65
  ALSO AS "FINAL ENCOUNTER"
ELEVENTH GALAXY READER, THE   AN H DBL 69
EXPERT DREAMERS, THE   AN H DBL 62
FINAL ENCOUNTER   AN   CUR 65
  SEE "THE EIGHTH GALAXY READER"
FREDERIK POHL OMNIBUS, THE   AC H GOL 66
GOLD AT STARBOW'S END, THE   AC   BAL 72 08
IF READER OF SCIENCE FICTION, THE   AN H DBL 66
IN THE PROBLEM PIT   AC   BAN 76 06
MAN WHO ATE THE WORLD, THE   AC   BAL 60
NIGHTMARE AGE   AN   BAL 70 10
NINTH GALAXY READER, THE   AN H DBL 66 02
SCIENCE FICTION ROLL OF HONOR, THE   AN H RDM 75
SECOND IF READER OF SCIENCE FICTION, THE   AN H DBL 68

POHL, FREDERIK

POHL, FREDERIK   (CONTINUED)
  SEVENTH GALAXY READER, THE   AN H DBL 64
  SHADOW OF TOMORROW   AN H DBL 53
  STAR FOURTEEN   AN H WHW 66
    SEE "STAR OF STARS"
  STAR OF STARS   AN   BAL 60
    IN ENGLAND AS "STAR FOURTEEN"
  STAR SCIENCE FICTION STORIES   OA H BAL 53
  STAR SCIENCE FICTION STORIES NO. 2   OA H BAL 53
  STAR SCIENCE FICTION STORIES NO. 3   OA H BAL 54
  STAR SCIENCE FICTION STORIES NO. 4   OA   BAL 58
  STAR SCIENCE FICTION STORIES NO. 5   OA   BAL 59
  STAR SCIENCE FICTION STORIES NO. 6   OA   BAL 59
  STAR SHORT NOVELS   OA   BAL 54 10
  TENTH GALAXY READER, THE   AN H DBL 67
    ALSO AS "DOOR TO ANYWHERE"
  TIME WAITS FOR WINTHROP, AND FOUR OTHER SHORT NOVELS
                                                      AN H DBL 62
  TOMORROW TIMES SEVEN   AC   BAL 59 07
  TURN LEFT AT THURSDAY   AC   BAL 61 03
ABOMINABLE EARTHMAN, THE   SS   GAL 61 10
  ABOMINABLE EARTHMAN, THE   POHL, FREDERIK   AC
AFTERWORD   MS   FUC 73
  BEST SCIENCE FICTION STORIES OF THE YEAR (1973)
                                    DEL REY, LESTER   AN
  FUTURE CITY   ELWOOD, ROGER   OA
APPRECIATION, AN   IN
  BEST OF C. M. KORNBLUTH, THE   KORNBLUTH, C. M.   AC
BEST FRIEND   SS C SSS 41 05
  WONDER EFFECT, THE   POHL, F. & KORNBLUTH AC
BITTEREST PILL, THE (ALSO AS THE RICHEST MAN IN LEVITTOWN)
                                                      SS   GAL 59 04
  ABC OF SCIENCE FICTION, AN   BOARDMAN, TOM JR.   AN
  FIFTH GALAXY READER, THE   GOLD, H. L.   AN
CALL ME MILLION   SS   WOF 70 02
  GOLD AT STARBOW'S END, THE   POHL, FREDERIK   AC
CANDLE LIGHTER, THE   SS   GAL 55 03
  CASE AGAINST TOMORROW, THE   POHL, FREDERIK   AC
CELEBRATED NO-HIT INNING, THE   SS   FUN 56 09
  CASE AGAINST TOMORROW, THE   POHL, FREDERIK   AC
  RUN TO STARLIGHT, SPORTS THROUGH SCIENCE FICTION
                                    GREENBERG/OLANDER/& AN
CENSUS TAKERS, THE   SS   FSF 56 02
  BEST FROM FANTASY AND SCIENCE FICTION: 6
                                    BOUCHER, ANTHONY   AN
  BEST OF FREDERIK POHL, THE   POHL, FREDERIK   AC
  CASE AGAINST TOMORROW, THE   POHL, FREDERIK   AC
  NIGHTMARE AGE   POHL, FREDERIK   AN
  SCIENCE FACT/FICTION   FARRELL/GAGE/&   AN
  YOU AND SCIENCE FICTION   HOLLISTER, BERNARD C AN
CHILDREN OF NIGHT, THE   NV   GAL 64 10
  BEST OF FREDERIK POHL, THE   POHL, FREDERIK   AC
  BEST SF 7   CRISPIN, EDMUND   AN
  DIGITS AND DASTARDS   POHL, FREDERIK   AC
  NINTH GALAXY READER, THE   POHL, FREDERIK   AN
CONSPIRACY ON CALLISTO   SS   PLS 43 WI
  EARLY POHL, THE   POHL, FREDERIK   AC
CRITICAL MASS   NA C GAL 62 02
  EIGHTH GALAXY READER, THE   POHL, FREDERIK   AN
  WONDER EFFECT, THE   POHL, F. & KORNBLUTH AC
DAUGHTERS OF ETERNITY   SS   AST 42 03
  EARLY POHL, THE   POHL, FREDERIK   AC
DAY AFTER THE DAY THE MARTIANS CAME, THE (ALSO AS THE DAY
  THE MARTIANS CAME)   SS   DVS 67 01
  DANGEROUS VISIONS   ELLISON, HARLAN   OA
DAY MILLION   SS   ROG 66 02
  ALPHA 3   SILVERBERG, ROBERT   AN
  BEST OF FREDERIK POHL, THE   POHL, FREDERIK   AC
  BIO-FUTURES   SARGENT, PAMELA   AN
  DAY MILLION   POHL, FREDERIK   AC
  DECADE THE 1960S   ALDISS & HARRISON   AN
  MARRIAGE AND THE FAMILY THROUGH SCIENCE FICTION
                                    CLEAR/WARRICK/&   AN
  NEBULA AWARD STORIES NO. 2   ALDISS & HARRISON   AN
  SCIENCE FICTION ARGOSY, A   KNIGHT, DAMON   AN
  SCIENCE FICTION: THE FUTURE   ALLEN, DICK   AN
  SF: AUTHORS' CHOICE   HARRISON, HARRY   AN
  THOSE WHO CAN: A SCIENCE FICTION READER
                                    WILSON, ROBIN SCOTT AN
  WORLD'S BEST SCIENCE FICTION: 1967 WOLLHEIM & CARR   AN
DAY OF THE BOOMER DUKES, THE   SS   FUT 56 30
  FREDERIK POHL OMNIBUS, THE   POHL, FREDERIK   AC
  MASTERS OF SCIENCE FICTION   HOWARD, IVAN   AN
  TOMORROW TIMES SEVEN   POHL, FREDERIK   AC
DAY THE ICICLE WORKS CLOSED, THE   NV   GAL 60 02
  BEST OF FREDERIK POHL, THE   POHL, FREDERIK   AC
  FREDERIK POHL OMNIBUS, THE   POHL, FREDERIK   AC
  MAN WHO ATE THE WORLD, THE   POHL, FREDERIK   AC
DAY THE MARTIANS CAME, THE (THE DAY AFTER THE DAY THE MARTIANS
  CAME)   SS   DVS 67 01
  BEST OF FREDERIK POHL, THE   POHL, FREDERIK   AC
  DAY MILLION   POHL, FREDERIK   AC
DEADLY MISSION OF PHINEAS SNODGRASS, THE   SS   GAL 62 06
  DAY MILLION   POHL, FREDERIK   AC
  IN THE PROBLEM PIT   POHL, FREDERIK   AC
DOOMSHIP   NA C IFS 73 04
  1974 ANNUAL WORLD'S BEST SF, THE WOLLHEIM, DONALD A.   AN
DOUBLE-CROSS   SS   PLS 44 WI
  EARLY POHL, THE   POHL, FREDERIK   AC
DWELLER IN THE ICE, THE   SS   SSS 41 01
  EARLY POHL, THE   POHL, FREDERIK   AC
EARTH EIGHTEEN   FA   GAL 64 04
  DIGITS AND DASTARDS   POHL, FREDERIK   AC
EARTH, FAREWELL| SS   AST 43 02
  EARLY POHL, THE   POHL, FREDERIK   AC

POHL, FREDERIK   (CONTINUED)
  EDITOR'S NOTE   IN
    STAR SCIENCE FICTION STORIES   POHL, FREDERIK   OA
    STAR SCIENCE FICTION STORIES NO. 2 POHL, FREDERIK   OA
    STAR SCIENCE FICTION STORIES NO. 3 POHL, FREDERIK   OA
  ELEGY TO A DEAD PLANET: LUNA   PM   AMZ 37 10
    EARLY POHL, THE   POHL, FREDERIK   AC
  ENGINEER, THE   SS C INF 56 02
    WONDER EFFECT, THE   POHL, F. & KORNBLUTH AC
  ENJOY, ENJOY   SS   POS 74
    FELLOWSHIP OF THE STARS   CARR, TERRY   OA
  EVERYBODY'S HAPPY BUT ME| (SEE WHAT TO DO TILL THE ANALYST
    COMES)   TC
  FANTASY IN SCIENCE FICTION- NO   IN
    WALL AROUND THE WORLD, THE   COGSWELL, THEODORE R AC
  FATHER OF THE STARS   SS   IFS 64 11
    BEST OF FREDERIK POHL, THE   POHL, FREDERIK   AC
    DIGITS AND DASTARDS   POHL, FREDERIK   AC
    IF READER OF SCIENCE FICTION, THE POHL, FREDERIK   AN
  FIEND, THE   SS   PBY 64 04
    BEST FROM NEW WRITINGS IN S-F FIRST SELECTION, THE
                                    CARNELL, JOHN   AN
    DIGITS AND DASTARDS   POHL, FREDERIK   AC
    FIEND, THE   PLAYBOY, EDITORS OF AN
    NEW WRITINGS IN SF. 3   CARNELL, JOHN   OA
    PLAYBOY BOOK OF SCIENCE FICTION AND FANTASY, THE
                                    PLAYBOY, EDITORS OF AN
  FIVE HELLS OF ORION, THE   NV   IFS 63 01
    BEST SCIENCE FICTION FROM IF, THE POHL, FREDERIK   AN
    DIGITS AND DASTARDS   POHL, FREDERIK   AC
  FOR C. M. KORNBLUTH   MS
    SCIENCE FICTION SHOWCASE   KORNBLUTH, MARY   AN
  FOREWORD   IN
    AMERICAN GOVERNMENT THROUGH SCIENCE FICTION
                                    OLANDER/GREENBERG/& AN
    EXPLORERS, THE   KORNBLUTH, C. M.   AN
  GAME-PLAYING LITERATURE, THE   AR   CLR 71 01
    CLARION   WILSON, ROBIN SCOTT OA
  GENTLE DYING, A   SS C GAL 61 06
    WONDER EFFECT, THE   POHL, F. & KORNBLUTH AC
  GENTLE VENUSIAN, THE (THE GENTLEST UNPEOPLE)   NV   GAL 58 06
    TOMORROW TIMES SEVEN   POHL, FREDERIK   AC
  GENTLEST UNPEOPLE, THE (ALSO AS THE GENTLE VENUSIAN)
                                                      NV   GAL 58 06
    FOURTH GALAXY READER, THE   GOLD, H. L.   AN
  GHOST MAKER, THE   SS   BEY 54 01
    ALTERNATING CURRENTS   POHL, FREDERIK   AC
    BEYOND   ANONYMOUS   AN
  GIFT OF GARIGOLLI, THE   NV C GAL 74 08
    BEST FROM GALAXY, THE VOLUME III BAEN, JAMES   AN
    1975 ANNUAL WORLD'S BEST SF, THE WOLLHEIM, DONALD A. AN
  GOLD AT THE STARBOW'S END, THE   NV   ASF 72 03
    ANALOG 9   BOVA, BEN   AN
    BEST SCIENCE FICTION FOR 1972   POHL, FREDERIK   AN
    GOLD AT STARBOW'S END, THE   POHL, FREDERIK   AC
    1973 ANNUAL WORLD'S BEST SF, THE WOLLHEIM, DONALD A. AN
  GOLDEN AGES GONE AWAY   AR   CLR 72 02
    CLARION II   WILSON, ROBIN SCOTT OA
    IN THE PROBLEM PIT   POHL, FREDERIK   AC
  GRANDY DEVIL   SS   GAL 55 06
    ALTERNATING CURRENTS   POHL, FREDERIK   AC
    BEST OF FREDERIK POHL, THE   POHL, FREDERIK   AC
    THOSE WHO CAN: A SCIENCE FICTION READER
                                    WILSON, ROBIN SCOTT AN
  GROWING UP IN EDGE CITY   SS   EPC 75
    EPOCH   ELWOOD & SILVERBERG OA
  GUEST EDITORIAL   ED   IFS 74 06
    BEST FROM IF, THE VOLUME II   IF, EDITORS OF   AN
  HAPPY BIRTHDAY, DEAR JESUS   SS   NEW 56 01
    ALTERNATING CURRENTS   POHL, FREDERIK   AC
    BEST OF FREDERIK POHL, THE   POHL, FREDERIK   AC
  HATED, THE   SS   GAL 58 01
    BEST OF FREDERIK POHL, THE   POHL, FREDERIK   AC
    FIRST STEP OUTWARD   HOSKINS, ROBERT   AN
    TURN LEFT AT THURSDAY   POHL, FREDERIK   AC
  HAUNTED CORPSE, THE   SS   GAL 57 01
    FREDERIK POHL OMNIBUS, THE   POHL, FREDERIK   AC
    THIRD GALAXY READER, THE   GOLD, H. L.   AN
    TOMORROW TIMES SEVEN   POHL, FREDERIK   AC
  HIGHWAYMAN OF THE VOID   NV   PLS 44 FL
    EARLY POHL, THE   POHL, FREDERIK   AC
  HOW TO COUNT ON YOUR FINGERS   AR   SFS 56 09
    BEST OF FREDERIK POHL, THE   POHL, FREDERIK   AC
    COMING ATTRACTIONS   GREENBERG , MARTIN   NF
    DIGITS AND DASTARDS   POHL, FREDERIK   AC
  I PLINGLOT, WHO YOU?   NV   GAL 59 02
    FREDERIK POHL OMNIBUS, THE   POHL, FREDERIK   AC
    INFINITE JESTS   SILVERBERG, ROBERT   AN
    TURN LEFT AT THURSDAY   POHL, FREDERIK   AC
  I REMEMBER A WINTER   SS   ORB 72 11
    IN THE PROBLEM PIT   POHL, FREDERIK   AC
    ORBIT 11   KNIGHT, DAMON   OA
  IN THE PROBLEM PIT   NA   FSF 73 09
    IN THE PROBLEM PIT   POHL, FREDERIK   AC
  INTRODUCTION   IN
    ASSIGNMENT IN TOMORROW   POHL, FREDERIK   AN
    BEST SCIENCE FICTION FOR 1972   POHL, FREDERIK   AN
    BEYOND THE END OF TIME   POHL, FREDERIK   AN
    BEYOND TIME   LEY, SANDRA   OA
    BODYGUARD AND 4 OTHER SHORT SF NOVELS FROM GALAXY
                                    GOLD, H. L.   AN
    DAY MILLION   POHL, FREDERIK   AN
    DIGITS AND DASTARDS   POHL, FREDERIK   AC
    EARLY POHL, THE   POHL, FREDERIK   AC
    ELEVENTH GALAXY READER, THE   POHL, FREDERIK   AN
    EXPERT DREAMERS, THE   POHL, FREDERIK   AN

POHL, FREDERIK

POHL, FREDERIK   (CONTINUED)
  FRONTIERS 2; THE NEW MIND   ELWOOD, ROGER   OA
  IF READER OF SCIENCE FICTION, THE   POHL, FREDERIK   AN
  NIGHTMARE AGE   POHL, FREDERIK   AN
  NINTH GALAXY READER, THE   POHL, FREDERIK   AN
  SCIENCE FICTION ROLL OF HONOR, THE   POHL, FREDERIK   AN
  SECOND IF READER OF SCIENCE FICTION, THE
                POHL, FREDERIK   AN
  SEVENTH GALAXY READER, THE   POHL, FREDERIK   AN
  SHADOW OF TOMORROW   POHL, FREDERIK   AN
  STAR OF STARS   POHL, FREDERIK   AN
  STAR SHORT NOVELS   POHL, FREDERIK   OA
  WONDER EFFECT, THE   POHL, F. & KORNBLUTH AC
                IN C
INTRODUCTION
  SCIENCE FICTION: THE GREAT YEARS, VOL. II
                POHL, C. & F.   AN
                IN C
INTRODUCTION (A DIALOGUE)
  SCIENCE FICTION DISCOVERIES   POHL, C. & F.   OA
                IN
INTRODUCTION THE FIRST
  SCIENCE FICTION: THE GREAT YEARS   POHL, C. & F.   AN
INTRODUCTION: SCIENCE-FICTION GAMES
  IN THE PROBLEM PIT   POHL, FREDERIK   AC
                NV   AST 41 04
IT'S A YOUNG WORLD
  DAY MILLION   POHL, FREDERIK   AC
  EARLY POHL, THE   POHL, FREDERIK   AC
                IN C
JUPITER AT LAST
  JUPITER   POHL, C. & F.   AN
                SS   AST 41 02
KING'S EYE, THE
  EARLY POHL, THE   POHL, FREDERIK   AC
                NA   GAL 58 01
KNIGHTS OF ARTHUR, THE
  FREDERIK POHL OMNIBUS, THE   POHL, FREDERIK   AC
  TOMORROW TIMES SEVEN   POHL, FREDERIK   AC
                NV C WRT 50 09
LEGAL RITES
  BR-R-R-!   CONKLIN, GROFF   AN
  EARLY ASIMOV, THE   ASIMOV, ISAAC   AC
  EDGE OF NEVER, THE   HOSKINS, ROBERT   AN
  UNEXPECTED, THE   MARGULIES, LEO   AN
                SS   PLS 49 WI
LET THE ANTS TRY
  ALTERNATING CURRENTS   POHL, FREDERIK   AC
  IN THE PROBLEM PIT   POHL, FREDERIK   AC
  MUTANTS   SILVERBERG, ROBERT   AN
                SS   IFS 59 07
LIFE AND A HALF, A
  ABOMINABLE EARTHMAN, THE   POHL, FREDERIK   AC
  BEST SF 6   CRISPIN, EDMUND   AN
                SS   PBY 66 12
LOVEMAKING (ALSO AS MAKING LOVE)
  FIEND, THE   PLAYBOY, EDITORS OF AN
                SS   PBY 66 12
MAKING LOVE (LOVEMAKING)
  DAY MILLION   POHL, FREDERIK   AC
                NV   GAL 56 11
MAN WHO ATE THE WORLD, THE
  FREDERIK POHL OMNIBUS, THE   POHL, FREDERIK   AC
  IN THE PROBLEM PIT   POHL, FREDERIK   AC
  MAN WHO ATE THE WORLD, THE   POHL, FREDERIK   AC
  SCIENCE FICTION SHOWCASE   KORNBLUTH, MARY   AN
                NV   GAL 55 07
MAPMAKERS, THE
  ALTERNATING CURRENTS   POHL, FREDERIK   AC
                NA   GAL 58 06
MARS BY MOONLIGHT
  FREDERIK POHL OMNIBUS, THE   POHL, FREDERIK   AC
  TURN LEFT AT THURSDAY   POHL, FREDERIK   AC
                SS C AST 41 09
MARS-TUBE
  WONDER EFFECT, THE   POHL, F. & KORNBLUTH AC
MARTIAN IN THE ATTIC, THE   SS   IFS 60 07
  BEST OF FREDERIK POHL, THE   POHL, FREDERIK   AC
  TURN LEFT AT THURSDAY   POHL, FREDERIK   AC
                FA   GAL 62 02
MARTIAN STAR-GAZERS, THE
  ABOMINABLE EARTHMAN, THE   POHL, FREDERIK   AC
  8TH ANNUAL OF THE YEAR'S BEST S-F, THE MERRIL, JUDITH   AN
                SS C FSF 72 11
MEETING, THE
  BEST SCIENCE FICTION OF THE YEAR, THE NO. 2
                CARR, TERRY   AN
  BEST SCIENCE FICTION STORIES OF THE YEAR (1972)
                DEL REY, LESTER   AN
                NA   IFS 72 08
MERCHANTS OF VENUS, THE
  BEST SCIENCE FICTION FOR 1973   ACKERMAN, FORREST J. AN
  FUTURE NOW, THE   HOSKINS, ROBERT   AN
  GOLD AT STARBOW'S END, THE   POHL, FREDERIK   AC
                NA   GAL 54 04
MIDAS PLAGUE, THE
  ALL ABOUT THE FUTURE   GREENBERG, MARTIN   AN
  BEST OF FREDERIK POHL, THE   POHL, FREDERIK   AC
  CASE AGAINST TOMORROW, THE   POHL, FREDERIK   AC
  NIGHTMARE AGE   POHL, FREDERIK   AN
  SCIENCE FICTION HALL OF FAME VOLUME 2B BOVA, BEN   AN
  *SPECTRUM   AMIS & CONQUEST   AN
                SS   GAL 55 05
MIDDLE OF NOWHERE, THE
  FREDERIK POHL OMNIBUS, THE   POHL, FREDERIK   AC
  TOMORROW TIMES SEVEN   POHL, FREDERIK   AC
                SS C FSF 74 10
MUTE INGLORIOUS TAM
  BEST SCIENCE FICTION STORIES OF THE YEAR (1974)
                DEL REY, LESTER   AN
                NA   GAL 57 02
MY LADY GREEN SLEEVES
  CASE AGAINST TOMORROW, THE   POHL, FREDERIK   AC
  HUMAN AND OTHER BEINGS   DEGRAEFF, ALLEN   AN
                NV C GAL 58 12
NIGHTMARE WITH ZEPPELINS
  FIFTH GALAXY READER, THE   GOLD, H. L.   AN
  WONDER EFFECT, THE   POHL, F. & KORNBLUTH AC
                AR FSF 62 12
ON BINARY DIGITS AND HUMAN HABITS
  DIGITS AND DASTARDS   POHL, FREDERIK   AC
                AR
ON VELOCITY EXERCISES
  THOSE WHO CAN: A SCIENCE FICTION READER
                WILSON, ROBIN SCOTT AN
                IN
PINCH OF STARDUST, A
  STAR SCIENCE FICTION STORIES NO. 4   POHL, FREDERIK   OA
                SS   PBY 62 06
PUNCH
  ABOMINABLE EARTHMAN, THE   POHL, FREDERIK   AC
  BEST OF FREDERIK POHL, THE   POHL, FREDERIK   AC
  FULLY AUTOMATED LOVE LIFE OF HENRY KEANRIDGE
                PLAYBOY, EDITORS OF AN

POHL, FREDERIK   (CONTINUED)
  PLAYBOY BOOK OF SCIENCE FICTION AND FANTASY, THE
                PLAYBOY, EDITORS OF AN
  SCIENCE FICTION ODDITIES   CONKLIN, GROFF   AN
                SS   GAL 55 02
PYTHIAS
  ALTERNATING CURRENTS   POHL, FREDERIK   AC
                NV C ASF 61 08
QUAKER CANNON, THE
  WONDER EFFECT, THE   POHL, F. & KORNBLUTH AC
  7TH ANNUAL OF THE YEAR'S BEST S-F, THE MERRIL, JUDITH   AN
                SS   FUN 55 10
RAFFERTY'S REASONS
  ALTERNATING CURRENTS   POHL, FREDERIK   AC
  IN THE PROBLEM PIT   POHL, FREDERIK   AC
RICHEST MAN IN LEVITTOWN, THE (THE BITTEREST PILL)
                SS   GAL 59 04
  BEST OF FREDERIK POHL, THE   POHL, FREDERIK   AC
  TURN LEFT AT THURSDAY   POHL, FREDERIK   AC
                SS   FSF 72 06
SAD SOLARIAN SCREENWRITER SAM
  GOLD AT STARBOW'S END, THE   POHL, FREDERIK   AC
                SS   PBY 69 01
SCHEMATIC MAN, THE
  BEST SF: 1969   HARRISON & ALDISS   AN
  DAY MILLION   POHL, FREDERIK   AC
  IN THE PROBLEM PIT   POHL, FREDERIK   AC
                NV   GAL 58 08
SEVEN DEADLY VIRTUES, THE
  FREDERIK POHL OMNIBUS, THE   POHL, FREDERIK   AC
  TURN LEFT AT THURSDAY   POHL, FREDERIK   AC
                AR   CLR 71 01
SF: THE GAME-PLAYING LITERATURE
  IN THE PROBLEM PIT   POHL, FREDERIK   AC
                SS   FSF 72 07
SHAFFERY AMONG THE IMMORTALS
  BEST FROM FANTASY AND SCIENCE FICTION: 20
                FERMAN, EDWARD L.   AN
  GOLD AT STARBOW'S END, THE   POHL, FREDERIK   AC
  NEBULA AWARD STORIES 8   ASIMOV, ISAAC   AN
                AR   73
SHAPE OF SCIENCE FICTION TO COME, THE
  BEST SCIENCE FICTION FOR 1973   ACKERMAN, FORREST J. AN
                NV   SFQ 57 02
SMALL LORDS
  DAY MILLION   POHL, FREDERIK   AC
  WEIRD ONES, THE   HOWARD, IVAN   AN
                SS   GAL 59 12
SNOWMEN, THE
  BEST OF FREDERIK POHL, THE   POHL, FREDERIK   AC
  FREDERIK POHL OMNIBUS, THE   POHL, FREDERIK   AC
  MAN WHO ATE THE WORLD, THE   POHL, FREDERIK   AC
                SS   GAL 73 11
SOME JOYS UNDER THE STARS (THE STAR)
  IN THE PROBLEM PIT   POHL, FREDERIK   AC
                SS   PBY 67 11
SPEED TRAP
  BEST OF FREDERIK POHL, THE   POHL, FREDERIK   AC
  DAY MILLION   POHL, FREDERIK   AC
  TRANSIT OF EARTH   PLAYBOY, EDITORS OF AN
STAR, THE (SEE SOME JOYS UNDER THE STARS)
                TC
SURVIVAL KIT   NV   GAL 57 05
  FREDERIK POHL OMNIBUS, THE   POHL, FREDERIK   AC
  TOMORROW TIMES SEVEN   POHL, FREDERIK   AC
                SS   GAL 55 04
TARGET ONE
  ALTERNATING CURRENTS   POHL, FREDERIK   AC
                SS   GAL 58 08
THIRD OFFENSE (AS CHARLES SATTERFIELD)
  SPACE, TIME & CRIME   DEFORD, MIRIAM ALLEN AN
  TURN LEFT AT THURSDAY   POHL, FREDERIK   AC
                SS   GAL 62 08
THREE PORTRAITS AND A PRAYER
  ABOMINABLE EARTHMAN, THE   POHL, FREDERIK   AC
  BEST OF FREDERIK POHL, THE   POHL, FREDERIK   AC
  LATE GREAT FUTURE, THE   FITZ GERALD & DILLON AN
  SEVENTH GALAXY READER, THE   POHL, FREDERIK   AN
                SS   FSF 59 04
TO SEE ANOTHER MOUNTAIN
  IN THE PROBLEM PIT   POHL, FREDERIK   AC
  TOMORROW TIMES SEVEN   POHL, FREDERIK   AC
                SS C AST 40 12
TROUBLE IN TIME
  WONDER EFFECT, THE   POHL, F. & KORNBLUTH AC
                NV   GAL 55 01
TUNNEL UNDER THE WORLD, THE
  ALTERNATING CURRENTS   POHL, FREDERIK   AC
  BEST OF FREDERIK POHL, THE   POHL, FREDERIK   AC
  MORE PENGUIN SCIENCE FICTION   ALDISS, BRIAN W.   AN
  TENTH GALAXY READER, THE   POHL, FREDERIK   AN
  TOMORROW, INC.   GREENBERG& OLANDER   AN
                NV   IFS 65 09
UNDER TWO MOONS
  DAY MILLION   POHL, FREDERIK   AC
  SECOND IF READER OF SCIENCE FICTION, THE
                POHL, FREDERIK   AN
VARIETIES OF THE SCIENCE-FICTION EXPERIENCE, THE IN
  EIGHTH GALAXY READER, THE   POHL, FREDERIK   AN
                NV   GAL 59 08
WAGING OF THE PEACE, THE
  FREDERIK POHL OMNIBUS, THE   POHL, FREDERIK   AC
  MAN WHO ATE THE WORLD, THE   POHL, FREDERIK   AC
                SS   SFS 56 07
WAPSHOT'S DEMON
  CASE AGAINST TOMORROW, THE   POHL, FREDERIK   AC
  NOW & BEYOND   HOWARD, IVAN   AN
                NV   GAL 59 10
WAY UP YONDER
  DAY MILLION   POHL, FREDERIK   AC
                SS   GAL 58 07
WE NEVER MENTION AUNT NORA (AS PAUL FLEHR)
  ABOMINABLE EARTHMAN, THE   POHL, FREDERIK   AC
  BEST OF FREDERIK POHL, THE   POHL, FREDERIK   AC
  WONDERMAKERS 2   HOSKINS, ROBERT   AN
                SS   FST 74
WE PURCHASE PEOPLE
  BEST SCIENCE FICTION OF THE YEAR, THE NO. 4
                CARR, TERRY   AN
  FINAL STAGE   FERMAN & MALZBERG   OA
WHAT THE AUTHOR HAS TO SAY ABOUT ALL THIS   MS
  BEST OF FREDERIK POHL, THE   POHL, FREDERIK   AC
WHAT TO DO TILL THE ANALYST COMES (EVERYBODY'S HAPPY BUT ME!)
                SS   IMG 56 02
  ALTERNATING CURRENTS   POHL, FREDERIK   AC
  IN THE PROBLEM PIT   POHL, FREDERIK   AC
  SPECULATIONS   SANDERS, THOMAS E.   AN
  STRANGE ECSTASIES   PARRY, MICHEL   AN
  YOU AND SCIENCE FICTION   HOLLISTER, BERNARD C AN
  17 X INFINITY   CONKLIN, GROFF   AN
                NA   GAL 59 06
WHATEVER COUNTS
  ABOMINABLE EARTHMAN, THE   POHL, FREDERIK   AC

POHL, FREDERIK   PRATT, FLETCHER

POHL, FREDERIK   (CONTINUED)
  BODYGUARD AND 4 OTHER SHORT SF NOVELS FROM GALAXY
                                                GOLD, H. L.   AN
  WITH REDFERN ON CAPELLA XII (AS CHAS. SATTERFIELD)
                                          NV   GAL 55 11
    DIGITS AND DASTARDS   POHL, FREDERIK   AC
    STARS AROUND US, THE   HOSKINS, ROBERT   AN
  WIZARDS OF PUNG'S CORNERS, THE   NV   GAL 58 10
    AS TOMORROW BECOMES TODAY   SULLIVAN, CHARLES W. AN
    CONNOISSEUR'S S. F.   BOARDMAN, TOM JR.   AN
    FREDERIK POHL OMNIBUS, THE   POHL, FREDERIK   AC
    MAN WHO ATE THE WORLD, THE   POHL, FREDERIK   AC
  WORLD OF MYRION FLOWERS, THE   SS C FSF 61 10
    HUMAN AND OTHER BEINGS   DEGRAEFF, ALLEN   AN
    THEMES IN SCIENCE FICTION   KELLEY, LEO P.   AN
    WONDER EFFECT, THE   POHL, F. & KORNBLUTH AC

POLESHCHUK, A.
  HOMER'S SECRET   SS
    LAST DOOR TO AIYA   GINSBURG, MIRRA   AN

POLLACK, RACHEL
  BLACK ROSE AND WHITE ROSE   SS   NWQ 74 06
    NEW WORLDS NO. 6   PLATT & BAILEY   OA
  IS YOUR CHILD USING DRUGS?   SS   NDM 76 06
    NEW DIMENSIONS 6   SILVERBERG, ROBERT OA
  TUBS OF SLAW   SS   NWQ 73 05
    NEW WORLDS NO. 5   MOORCOCK & PLATT   OA

POLLACK, RICHARD A.
  PANDORA'S BUST   SS   NWQ 71 02
    NEW WORLDS QUARTERLY NO. 2 MOORCOCK, MICHAEL   OA

POLLOCK, FRANK L.
  FINIS   SS   ARG 06 06
    SCIENCE FICTION BY GASLIGHT MOSKOWITZ, SAM   AN

POLYA, G.
  APOTHEM   MS   45
    MATHEMATICAL MAGPIE, THE   FADIMAN, CLIFTON   AN

POPE, ALEXANDER
  FROM "THE DUNCIAD" (1728)   PM   DPS 28 05
    MATHEMATICAL MAGPIE, THE   FADIMAN, CLIFTON   AN

POPE, CARL
  LETTER TO THOSE WHO SEE NO THREAT, A   AR
    VOYAGES: SCENARIOS FOR A SHIP CALLED EARTH
                                 SAUER, ROB   AN

PORGES, ARTHUR
  DEVIL AND SIMON FLAGG, THE   SS FSF 54 08
    DEALS WITH THE DEVIL   DAVENPORT, BASIL   AN
    FANTASIA MATHEMATICA   FADIMAN, CLIFTON   AN
  EMERGENCY OPERATION   SS FSF 56 05
    GREAT SCIENCE FICTION ABOUT DOCTORS   CONKLIN, G&FABRICANT AN
  FLY, THE   SS FSF 52 09
    BEST SCIENCE-FICTION STORIES: 1953, THE
                               BLEILER & DIKTY   AN
    BEST SF 6   CRISPIN, EDMUND   AN
  *BEYOND HUMAN KEN   MERRIL, JUDITH   AN
    FIFTY SHORT SCIENCE FICTION TALES ASIMOV & CONKLIN AN
  GUILTY AS CHARGED   SS NEW 55 AN
    BEST SCIENCE FICTION STORIES AND NOVELS: 1955
                               DIKTY, T. E.   AN
    SOCIOLOGY THROUGH SCIENCE FICTION MILSTEAD/GREENBERG/& AN
  MOP-UP   SS FSF 53 07
    GALAXY OF GHOULS   MERRIL, JUDITH   AN
  PROBLEM CHILD   SS ASF 64 04
    10TH ANNUAL OF THE YEAR'S BEST S-F, THE
                               MERRIL, JUDITH   AN
  RATS, THE   SS MSW 51 02
    BEST SCIENCE-FICTION STORIES: 1952, THE
                               BLEILER & DIKTY   AN
    FRONTIERS IN SPACE   BLEILER & DIKTY   AN
  RESCUER, THE   SS ASF 62 07
    ASTOUNDING-ANALOG READER, THE VOLUME TWO
                               HARRISON & ALDISS AN
    YET MORE PENGUIN SCIENCE FICTION ALDISS, BRIAN W.   AN
  RUUM, THE   SS FSF 53 10
    BEST SF   CRISPIN, EDMUND   AN
    FROM FRANKENSTEIN TO ANDROMEDA BROWN, JAMES GOLDIE AN
    GREAT SCIENCE-FICTION   LICATA, TONY   AN
    OUT OF THIS WORLD 1   WILLIAMS-ELLIS& OWEN AN
    STARS AND UNDER, THE   CRISPIN, EDMUND   AN
    TALES OF TERROR FROM OUTER SPACE CHETWYND-HAYES, R. AN
  $1.98   SS FSF 54 05
    BEST FROM FANTASY AND SCIENCE FICTION: 4
                               BOUCHER, ANTHONY   AN

PORGES, PAUL PETER
  CARTOON   CT   ALM 55 07
    MATHEMATICAL MAGPIE, THE   FADIMAN, CLIFTON   AN

PORTER, PETER
  TO START A CONTROVERSY   PM   64
    HOLDING YOUR EIGHT HANDS   LUCIE-SMITH, EDWARD AN
  YOUR ATTENTION PLEASE   PM   PMP 62 02
    HOLDING YOUR EIGHT HANDS   LUCIE-SMITH, EDWARD AN

PORTER, WILLIAM SYDNEY
        SEE PSEUD. O. HENRY

POSNER, RICHARD
  JACOB'S BUG   SS   TAL 73
    FRONTIERS 1: TOMORROW'S ALTERNATIVES ELWOOD, ROGER   OA

POSNER, RICHARD   (CONTINUED)
  ONE DAY IN THE WAR   SS INY 72 03
    INFINITY 3   HOSKINS, ROBERT   OA
  RUNNING, THE   SS NEW 73 AN
    ANDROIDS, TIME MACHINES AND BLUE GIRAFFES
                               ELWOOD & GHIDALIA   AN
    VISIONS OF TOMORROW   ELWOOD, ROGER   AN
  VACATION   NV NMD 73
    FRONTIERS 2: THE NEW MIND   ELWOOD, ROGER   OA

POULIN, A. JR.
  COMING, THE   PM   63
    SPECULATIONS   SANDERS, THOMAS E. AN

POURNELLE, JERRY
  HIGH JUSTICE   AC PKT 77 05
  MERCENARY, THE   NO PKT 77 02
  2020 VISION   AN AVN 74 02
  CONSORT   SS ASF 75 08
    HIGH JUSTICE   POURNELLE, JERRY   AC
  DO WE LIVE IN A GOLDEN AGE?   IN
    2020 VISION   POURNELLE, JERRY   AN
  ENFORCER   NV FSF 74 06
    HIGH JUSTICE   POURNELLE, JERRY   AC
  EXTREME PREJUDICE   NV ASF 74 07
    HIGH JUSTICE   POURNELLE, JERRY   AC
  HIGH JUSTICE   NV ASF 74 03
    HIGH JUSTICE   POURNELLE, JERRY   AC
  HIS TRUTH GOES MARCHING ON   SS NEW 75 AN
    COMBAT SF   DICKSON, GORDON R. AN
  LIFE AMONG THE ASTEROIDS   AR GAL 75 07
    BEST FROM GALAXY, THE VOLUME IV BAEN, JAMES   AN
  MATTER OF SOVEREIGNTY, A   NV ASF 72 01
    HIGH JUSTICE   POURNELLE, JERRY   AC
  MERCENARY   NV ASF 72 07
    MERCENARY, THE   POURNELLE, JERRY   NO
  PEACE WITH HONOR   NV ASF 71 05
    MERCENARY, THE   POURNELLE, JERRY   NO
  POWER TO THE PEOPLE   SS ASF 72 08
    HIGH JUSTICE   POURNELLE, JERRY   AC
  PREFACE   IN
    2020 VISION   POURNELLE, JERRY   AN
  SILENT LEGES   SS
    NEW VOICES IN SCIENCE FICTION   MARTIN, GEORGE R. R. OA
  SWORD AND SCEPTRE   NA ASF 73 05
    MERCENARY, THE   POURNELLE, JERRY   NO
  TINKER   NA GAL 75 07
    BEST FROM GALAXY, THE VOLUME IV BAEN, JAMES   AN
    HIGH JUSTICE   POURNELLE, JERRY   AC

POWERS, J. F.
  LOOK HOW THE FISH LIVE   SS REP 57 10
    ECO-FICTION   STADLER, JOHN   AN

POWERS, RICHARD GID
  INTRODUCTION   IN
    SCIENCE FICTION OF FRANK R. STOCKTON, THE
                                STOCKTON, FRANK R. AC
    SCIENCE FICTION OF JACK LONDON, THE LONDON, JACK   AC

POWERS, WILLIAM T.
  ALLEGORY   SS ASF 53 04
    13 GREAT STORIES OF SCIENCE FICTION CONKLIN, GROFF   AN
  METEOR   SS ASF 50 09
    *ASTOUNDING SCIENCE FICTION ANTHOLOGY, THE
                                CAMPBELL, JOHN W. JR AN

POYER, JOE
  MISSION "RED CLASH"   NV ASF 65 12
    ANALOG 5   CAMPBELL, JOHN W. JR AN

PRAGNELL, FESTUS
  MACHINE-GOD LAUGHS, THE   NV FBK 47 02
    MACHINE-GOD LAUGHS, THE   ANONYMOUS   AN

PRATCHETT, TERRY
  HADES BUSINESS, THE   SS SCF 63 08
    .UNFRIENDLY FUTURE, THE   BOARDMAN, TOM JR.   AN

PRATT, FLETCHER   SEE ALSO   CO-AUTHOR L. SPRAGUE DE CAMP
  DOUBLE IN SPACE   AC H DBL 51
  DOUBLE JEOPARDY   AC H DBL 52
  WITCHES THREE   AN H TWN 52
  WORLD OF WONDER   AN H TWN 51
  ALL THAT GLITTERS   SS C NEW 53 AC
    TALES FROM GAVAGAN'S BAR   DE CAMP, L. S.&PRATT AC
  ANCESTRAL AMETHYST, THE   SS C FSF 52 08
    TALES FROM GAVAGAN'S BAR   DE CAMP, L. S.&PRATT AC
  ASYLUM SATELLITE (SEE PROJECT EXCELSIOR)   TC
  BEASTS OF BOURBON   SS C FSF 51 10
    TALES FROM GAVAGAN'S BAR   DE CAMP, L. S.&PRATT AC
  BETTER MOUSETRAP, THE   SS C FSF 50 12
    TALES FROM GAVAGAN'S BAR   DE CAMP, L. S.&PRATT AC
  BLACK BALL, THE   SS C FSF 52 10
    BEST FROM FANTASY AND SCIENCE FICTION: 2
                                BOUCHER & MCCOMAS   AN
    TALES FROM GAVAGAN'S BAR   DE CAMP, L. S.&PRATT AC
  BLUE STAR, THE   NA NEW 52 AN
    WITCHES THREE   PRATT, FLETCHER   AN
  CAVEAT EMPTOR   SS C WRT 53 03
    DEALS WITH THE DEVIL   DAVENPORT, BASIL   AN
    TALES FROM GAVAGAN'S BAR   DE CAMP, L. S.&PRATT AC
  CITY OF THE LIVING DEAD, THE   NV C SWS 30 05
    SECOND AVON FANTASY READER, THE WOLLHEIM &ERNSBERGER AN
  CORPUS DELECTABLE   SS C NEW 53 AC
    TALES FROM GAVAGAN'S BAR   DE CAMP, L. S.&PRATT AC

PRATT, FLETCHER   (CONTINUED)
  DIME BRINGS YOU SUCCESS, A   SS C NEW 53 AC
    TALES FROM GAVAGAN'S BAR   DE CAMP, L. S.&PRATT AC
  DOCTOR GRIMSHAW'S SANITARIUM   SS   AMZ 34 05
    *MY BEST SCIENCE FICTION STORY   MARGULIES & FRIEND   AN
  DOUBLE JEOPARDY   NO   TWS 52 04
    DOUBLE JEOPARDY   PRATT, FLETCHER   AC
  ELEPHAS FRUMENTI   SS C FSF 50 WS
    BEST FROM FANTASY AND SCIENCE FICTION BOUCHER & MCCOMAS AN
    TALES FROM GAVAGAN'S BAR   DE CAMP, L. S.&PRATT AC
  EVE OF ST. JOHN, THE   SS C NEW 53 AC
    TALES FROM GAVAGAN'S BAR   DE CAMP, L. S.&PRATT AC
  GIFT OF GOD, THE   SS C FSF 50 WS
    BEST FROM FANTASY AND SCIENCE FICTION BOUCHER & MCCOMAS AN
    TALES FROM GAVAGAN'S BAR   DE CAMP, L. S.&PRATT AC
  GIN COMES IN BOTTLES   SS C NEW 53 AC
    TALES FROM GAVAGAN'S BAR   DE CAMP, L. S.&PRATT AC
  GREEN THUMB, THE   SS C FSF 53 02
    TALES FROM GAVAGAN'S BAR   DE CAMP, L. S.&PRATT AC
  HERE, PUTZI| SS C NEW 53 AC
    TALES FROM GAVAGAN'S BAR   DE CAMP, L. S.&PRATT AC
  HORMONES   SS   STR 53 02
    STAR SCIENCE FICTION STORIES NO. 2 POHL, FREDERIK   OA
  INTRODUCTION   IN
    *BEYOND HUMAN KEN   MERRIL, JUDITH   AN
  JOURNEY TO INFINITY   GREENBERG, MARTIN   AN
  LONG VIEW, THE   NA   STS 52 12
    PETRIFIED PLANET, THE   CLARK, JOHN D.   OA
  LOVE-NEST, THE   SS C NEW 53 AC
    TALES FROM GAVAGAN'S BAR   DE CAMP, L. S.&PRATT AC
  MORE THAN SKIN DEEP   SS C FSF 51 04
    TALES FROM GAVAGAN'S BAR   DE CAMP, L. S.&PRATT AC
  MY BROTHER'S KEEPER   SS C NEW 53 AC
    TALES FROM GAVAGAN'S BAR   DE CAMP, L. S.&PRATT AC
  NATURE OF IMAGINATIVE LITERATURE, THE   IN
    WORLD OF WONDER   PRATT, FLETCHER   AN
  NO FORWARDING ADDRESS   SS C NEW 53 AC
    TALES FROM GAVAGAN'S BAR   DE CAMP, L. S.&PRATT AC
  OFFICIAL RECORD   NV   SSF 52 09
    ASSIGNMENT IN TOMORROW   POHL, FREDERIK   AN
  PALIMPSEST OF ST. AUGUSTINE, THE   SS C NEW 53 AC
    TALES FROM GAVAGAN'S BAR   DE CAMP, L. S.&PRATT AC
  PARDON MY MISTAKE   SS   TWS 46 12
    *OUTER REACHES, THE   DERLETH, AUGUST   AN
  PROJECT EXCELSIOR (ASYLUM SATELLITE)   NO   TWS 51 10
    DOUBLE IN SPACE   PRATT, FLETCHER   AC
  RAPE OF THE LOCK, THE   SS C FSF 52 02
    TALES FROM GAVAGAN'S BAR   DE CAMP, L. S.&PRATT AC
  ROGER BACON FORMULA, THE   SS   AMZ 29 01
    *BIG BOOK OF SCIENCE FICTION   CONKLIN, GROFF   AN
  SECOND CHANCE   SS C FSM 52 FL
    SPACE, SPACE, SPACE   SLOANE, WILLIAM   AN
  SQUARE CUBE LAW, THE   NV   TWS 52 06
    DOUBLE JEOPARDY   PRATT, FLETCHER   AC
  STONE OF THE SAGES, THE   SS C NEW 53 AC
    TALES FROM GAVAGAN'S BAR   DE CAMP, L. S.&PRATT AC
  THING IN THE WOODS, THE   SS C AMZ 35 02
    OMNIBUS OF SCIENCE FICTION   CONKLIN, GROFF   AN
  UNTIMELY TOPPER, THE   SS C FSF 53 07
    BEST FROM FANTASY AND SCIENCE FICTION: 3
                                      BOUCHER & MCCOMAS   AN
  WANDERER'S RETURN, THE   NO   TWS 51 12
    DOUBLE IN SPACE   PRATT, FLETCHER   AC
  WEISSENBROCH SPECTACLES, THE   SS C FSF 54 11
    INVISIBLE MEN   DAVENPORT, BASIL   AN
  WHEN THE NIGHT WIND HOWLS   SS C WRT 51 11
    GHOUL KEEPERS, THE   MARGULIES, LEO   AN
    TALES FROM GAVAGAN'S BAR   DE CAMP, L. S.&PRATT AC
  WHERE TO, PLEASE?   SS C WRT 52 09
    TALES FROM GAVAGAN'S BAR   DE CAMP, L. S.&PRATT AC
  WHY I SELECTED DOCTOR GRIMSHAW'S SANITARIUM   AI
    *MY BEST SCIENCE FICTION STORY   MARGULIES & FRIEND   AN

PRENTICE, PATRICK H.
  WELCOME TO THE TRICENTENNIAL   NV
    2076: THE AMERICAN TRICENTENNIAL BRYANT, EDWARD   OA

PRESSLIE, ROBERT
  ANOTHER WORD FOR MAN   SS   NWS 58 12
    BEST OF NEW WORLDS, THE   MOORCOCK, MICHAEL   AN
    OUT OF THIS WORLD 2   WILLIAMS-ELLIS& OWEN AN
  DAY BEFORE NEVER, THE   NV   NWR 65 06
    NEW WRITINGS IN SF. 6   CARNELL, JOHN   OA
  DIAL "O" FOR OPERATOR   SS   SCF 58 02
    OTHER SIDE OF THE CLOCK, THE   STERN, PHILIP VAN D. AN
    WEIRD SHADOWS FROM BEYOND   CARNELL, JOHN   AN
  NIGHT OF THE SEVENTH FINGER, THE   SS   NWR 66 07
    NEW WRITINGS IN SF. 7   CARNELL, JOHN   AN
    NEW WRITINGS IN SF. 7   CARNELL, JOHN   OA
    TALES OF TERROR FROM OUTER SPACE CHETWYND-HAYES, R.   AN

PRESTON, L. E.
  DOLLHOUSE, THE   SS   YNW
    SCIENCE FICTION STORIES   BRADLEY, JOHANNA   AN

PRICE, D. M.
  AS A DROP   PM   FUC 73
    FUTURE CITY   ELWOOD, ROGER   OA
  BILLENNIUM: A NOTE TO DEADCAT   PM   SVW 73
    SAVING WORLDS   ELWOOD & KIDD   OA
  STARFISH   PM   SVW 73
    SAVING WORLDS   ELWOOD & KIDD   OA

PRICE, E. HOFFMANN
  APPRENTICE MAGICIAN   SS   WRT 39 08
    WIZARDS AND WARLOCKS   GHIDALIA, VIC   AN

PRICE, E. HOFFMANN   (CONTINUED)
  DESERT ROMANCE (SHADOW GUIDE)   SS
    STRANGE LOVE STORIES   ANONYMOUS   AN
  EVE WAS A SNAKE (SNAKE GODDESS)   SS   STE 39 08
    STRANGE LOVE STORIES   ANONYMOUS   AN
  LOVECRAFT CONTROVERSY- WHY?, THE   AR   NEW 76 AN
    YEAR'S BEST HORROR STORIES: SERIES IV, THE
                                      PAGE, GERALD W.   AN
  SHADOW GUIDE (SEE DESERT ROMANCE)   TC
  SNAKE GODDESS (SEE EVE WAS A SNAKE)   TC

PRICE, ROGER
  INQUIRY CONCERNING THE CURVATURE OF THE EARTH'S SURFACE
                                      SS   MON 59 WI
    5TH ANNUAL OF THE YEAR'S BEST S-F, THE MERRIL, JUDITH AN
  J.G. (FROM "J.G. THE UPRIGHT APE")   EX   60
    6TH ANNUAL OF THE YEAR'S BEST S-F, THE MERRIL, JUDITH AN

PRICE, VINCENT
  INTRODUCTION   IN
    GHOULS, THE   HAINING, PETER   AN

PRIEST, CHRISTOPHER
  REAL-TIME WORLD   AC H NLB 74
  BREEDING GROUND   SS   VOT 70 01
    REAL-TIME WORLD   PRIEST, CHRISTOPHER AC
  DOUBLE CONSUMMATION   SS   70
    REAL-TIME WORLD   PRIEST, CHRISTOPHER AC
  ERSATZ WINE, THE   SS   NWS 67 02
    BEST SF STORIES FROM NEW WORLDS 6 MOORCOCK, MICHAEL   AN
  FIRE STORM   SS   QRK 70 01
    QUARK/1   DELANY & HACKER   OA
    REAL-TIME WORLD   PRIEST, CHRISTOPHER AC
  HEAD AND THE HAND, THE   SS   NWQ 72 03
    BEST SF: 1972   HARRISON & ALDISS   AN
    NEW WORLDS QUARTERLY NO. 3   MOORCOCK, MICHAEL   OA
    REAL-TIME WORLD   PRIEST, CHRISTOPHER AC
  INFINITE SUMMER, AN   NV
    ANDROMEDA I   WESTON, PETER   OA
    BEST SCIENCE FICTION OF THE YEAR, THE NO. 6
                                      CARR, TERRY   AN
  INTERROGATOR, THE   NV   NWR 69 15
    NEW WRITINGS IN SF. 15   CARNELL, JOHN   OA
  INTRODUCTION   IN
    REAL-TIME WORLD   PRIEST, CHRISTOPHER AC
  INVERTED WORLD, THE   EX   FAB 74
    BEYOND THIS HORIZON   CARRELL, CHRISTOPHER OA
  INVERTED WORLD, THE   NV   NWR 73 22
    NEW WRITINGS IN SF. 22   BULMER, KENNETH   OA
  INVISIBLE MEN, THE   SS
    STOPWATCH   HAY, GEORGE   OA
  MEN OF GOOD VALUE   SS   NWR 75 26
    NEW WRITINGS IN SF. 26   BULMER, KENNETH   OA
  PERIHELION MAN, THE   NV   NWR 69 16
    NEW WRITINGS IN SF. 16   CARNELL, JOHN   OA
    REAL-TIME WORLD   PRIEST, CHRISTOPHER AC
  REAL-TIME WORLD   NV   NWR 71 19
    NEW WRITINGS IN SF. 19   CARNELL, JOHN   OA
    REAL-TIME WORLD   PRIEST, CHRISTOPHER AC
    1972 ANNUAL WORLD'S BEST SF, THE WOLLHEIM, DONALD A. AN
  RUN, THE   SS   IMP 66 05
    ENGLAND SWINGS SF   MERRIL, JUDITH   AN
    REAL-TIME WORLD   PRIEST, CHRISTOPHER AC
    SPACE-TIME JOURNAL, THE   MERRIL, JUDITH   AN
  SENTENCE IN BINARY CODE   SS   FAN 71 08
    REAL-TIME WORLD   PRIEST, CHRISTOPHER AC
  TRANSPLANT   SS   IFS 74 02
    REAL-TIME WORLD   PRIEST, CHRISTOPHER AC
  WOMAN NAKED, A   SS   SFM 74 01
    BEST OF SCIENCE FICTION MONTHLY, THE SACKS, JANET   AN
    REAL-TIME WORLD   PRIEST, CHRISTOPHER AC

PRIESTLEY, J. B.
  OTHER PLACE, THE   AC H HPR 53
  DEMON KING, THE   SS   34
    GALAXY OF GHOULS   MERRIL, JUDITH   AN
  GRAY ONES, THE   SS
    OTHER PLACE, THE   PRIESTLEY, J. B.   AC
  GUEST OF HONOR   SS
    OTHER PLACE, THE   PRIESTLEY, J. B.   AC
  INTRODUCTION   IN
    OF TIME AND STARS   CLARKE, ARTHUR C.   AC
  LEADINGTON INCIDENT, THE   SS
    OTHER PLACE, THE   PRIESTLEY, J. B.   AC
  LOOK AFTER THE STRANGE GIRL (THE STRANGE GIRL)   SS   FSF 54 01
    OTHER PLACE, THE   PRIESTLEY, J. B.   AC
    OTHER SIDE OF THE CLOCK, THE   STERN, PHILIP VAN D. AN
  MR. STRENBERRY'S TALE   SS   34
    OTHER PLACE, THE   PRIESTLEY, J. B.   AC
    TRAVELERS IN TIME   STERN, PHILIP VAN D. AN
    TREASURY OF SCIENCE FICTION CLASSICS, THE
                                      KUEBLER, HAROLD W.   AN
  NIGHT SEQUENCE   SS   FSF 56 03
    OTHER PLACE, THE   PRIESTLEY, J. B.   AC
  OTHER PLACE, THE   SS
    OTHER PLACE, THE   PRIESTLEY, J. B.   AC
  STATUES, THE   SS
    OTHER PLACE, THE   PRIESTLEY, J. B.   AC
  STRANGE GIRL, THE (SEE LOOK AFTER THE STRANGE GIRL)
                                      TC
  UNCLE PHIL ON TV   SS   FSF 55 10
    OTHER PLACE, THE   PRIESTLEY, J. B.   AC

PRIESTLEY, LEE
  SIGN AMONG THE STARS   SS   58
    TEEN-AGE OUTER SPACE STORIES   FURMAN, A. L.   AN

PROCTOR, GEORGE W. AN   RAPHAEL, RICK

PROCTOR, GEORGE W. AND STEVEN UTLEY
    LONE STAR UNIVERSE   OA H HDL 76
        SPECULATIVE FICTION & FANTASY FROM TEXAS

PROCTOR, GEORGE W.
    MIGRATION, THE   SS
        LONE STAR UNIVERSE   PROCTOR & UTLEY   OA

PRONZINI, BILL
    EVERGREEN LIBRARY, THE   SS C VSF 70 05
        WONDERMAKERS 2   HOSKINS, ROBERT   AN
    HUNGARIAN CINCH, THE   NV NEW 76 AN
        ARENA: SPORTS SF   FERMAN & MALZBERG   AN
    IT'S SO WONDERFUL HERE   SS
        SCIENCE FICTION ADVENTURES FROM WAY OUT
                                     ELWOOD, ROGER   OA
    OUR TIMES   SS SWK 72 04
        FUTURE NOW, THE   HOSKINS, ROBERT   AN
    PAXTON'S WORLD   SS FCR 75
        FUTURE CORRUPTION   ELWOOD, ROGER   OA

PUMILIA, JOSEPH F.
    AND DEATH ONCE DEAD   SS
        LONE STAR UNIVERSE   PROCTOR & UTLEY   OA
    FOREVER STAND THE STONES   SS   75
        YEAR'S BEST HORROR STORIES: SERIES IV, THE
                                     PAGE, GERALD W.   AN
    HUNG LIKE AN ELEPHANT   SS C ALT 74
        ALTERNATES   GERROLD, DAVID   OA
    PORTER OF HELL-GATE, THE   SS GEN 72
        GENERATION   GERROLD, DAVID   OA
    WILLOWISP   SS SFE 74 01
        SCIENCE FICTION EMPHASIS NO. 1 GERROLD, DAVID   OA

PURDOM, TOM
    GREENPLACE   SS FSF 64 11
        WORLD'S BEST SCIENCE FICTION: 1965 WOLLHEIM & CARR AN
    HOLY GRAIL, THE   SS STR 59 06
        STAR SCIENCE FICTION STORIES NO. 6 POHL, FREDERIK OA
    MOONCHILD   NV FUQ 73
        FUTURE QUEST   ELWOOD, ROGER   OA
    TOYS   SS ASF 67 10
        CRIME PREVENTION IN THE 30TH CENTURY SANTESSON, HANS S. AN
        THIS SIDE OF INFINITY   CARR, TERRY   AN
    WAR OF PASSION, A   SS FIN 70
        FUTURE IS NOW, THE   NOLAN, WILLIAM F.   OA

PURDY, KEN W.
    CONVERT, THE   SS PBY 70 03
        WEIRD SHOW   PLAYBOY, EDITORS OF AN
    DANNOLD CHEQUE, THE   SS PBY 69 09
        BEST SF: 1969   HARRISON & ALDISS   AN
    FOR THE RICH THEY SING- SOMETIMES   SS PBY 62 05
        PLAYBOY BOOK OF HORROR AND THE SUPERNATURAL, THE
                                     PLAYBOY, EDITORS OF AN
    GOLDEN FROG, THE   NV PBY 63 01
        PLAYBOY'S STORIES OF THE SINISTER & STRANGE
                                     PLAYBOY, EDITORS OF AN
    IN THE MATTER OF THE ASSASSIN MEREFIRS   SS ASF 72 11
        BEST SF: 1972   HARRISON & ALDISS   AN
    NOISE, THE   SS PBY 59 03
        INTRODUCTORY PSYCHOLOGY THROUGH SCIENCE FICTION
                                     KATZ/WARRICK/&   AN
        PLAYBOY BOOK OF SCIENCE FICTION AND FANTASY, THE
                                     PLAYBOY, EDITORS OF AN
    UNTITLED   SS PBY 66 10
        MASKS   PLAYBOY, EDITORS OF AN

QUATTROCCHI, FRANK
    HE HAD A BIG HEART   SS FSF 55 03
        ABC OF SCIENCE FICTION, AN   BOARDMAN, TOM JR.   AN

QUENEAU, RAYMOND
    THREE MATHEMATICAL DIVERSIONS   AR   58
        MATHEMATICAL MAGPIE, THE   FADIMAN, CLIFTON   AN

QUILLER-COUCH, A. T.
    NEW BALLAD OF SIR PATRICK SPENS, A   PM
        FANTASIA MATHEMATICA   FADIMAN, CLIFTON   AN

QUINN, JAMES L. AND EVE WULFF
    FIRST WORLD OF IF, THE   AN D QUI 57
    SECOND WORLD OF IF, THE   AN D QUI 58

QUINN, SEABURY
    BLOOD-FLOWER, THE   NV WRT 27 03
        NIGHTMARE GARDEN   GHIDALIA, VIC   AN
    CLAIR DE LUNE   NV WRT 47 11
        GHOUL KEEPERS, THE   MARGULIES, LEO   AN
    HOUSE WHERE TIME STOOD STILL, THE   SS WRT 39 03
        OTHER WORLDS, THE   STONG, PHILIP D.   AN
    ROADS   SS WRT 38 01
        WORLDS OF WEIRD   MARGULIES, LEO   AN
    SUICIDE CHAPEL   NV WRT 38 06
        FANTASTIC PULPS, THE   HAINING, PETER   AN

RABELAIS, FRANCIS
    PHALANSTERY OF THELEME, THE (1534)   EX
        *BEYOND TIME AND SPACE   DERLETH, AUGUST   AN

RACKHAM, JOHN   PSEUD. FOR JOHN T. PHILLIFENT
    ADVANTAGE   NV NWR 65 06
        NEW WRITINGS IN SF. 6   CARNELL, JOHN   OA
    CATHARSIS   SS NWR 68 11
        NEW WRITINGS IN SF. 11   CARNELL, JOHN   OA

RACKHAM, JOHN   (CONTINUED)
    COMPUTER'S MATE   SS NWR 66 08
        NEW WRITINGS IN SF. 8   CARNELL, JOHN   OA
    DIVIDED HOUSE, THE   SS NWR 68 13
        NEW WRITINGS IN SF. 13   CARNELL, JOHN   OA
    HALTED VILLAGE, THE   NV NWR 75 25
        NEW WRITINGS IN SF. 25   BULMER, KENNETH   OA
    HEAL THYSELF   SS NWR 75 27
        NEW WRITINGS IN SF. 27   BULMER, KENNETH   OA
    HELL-PLANET   NV NWR 64 02
        NEW WRITINGS IN SF. 2   CARNELL, JOHN   OA
    LAST SALAMANDER, THE   SS NWS 63 07
        LAMBDA I AND OTHER STORIES   CARNELL, JOHN   AN
    POSEIDON PROJECT   NA NWR 66 09
        NEW WRITINGS IN SF. 9   CARNELL, JOHN   OA
    STOOP TO CONQUER   SS NWR 71 19
        NEW WRITINGS IN SF. 19   CARNELL, JOHN   OA
    WISE CHILD   SS NWR 73 22
        NEW WRITINGS IN SF. 22   BULMER, KENNETH   OA

RADFORD, JOHN
    PSY FY PSYCHOLOGY AND SCIENCE FICTION   AR C
        BEYOND THIS HORIZON   CARRELL, CHRISTOPHER OA

RALPH, JULIAN
    MY BORROWED TORPEDO-BOAT   SS
        BATTLE FOR THE PACIFIC AND OTHER ADVENTURES AT SEA, THE
                                     ANONYMOUS   AN

RAMSAY, KATHRYN
    NIGHT AT THE FAIR, A   SS
        FUTURE PASTIMES   EDELSTEIN, SCOTT   OA

RANDALL, MARTA
    MEGAN'S WORLD   NA
        CRYSTAL SHIP, THE   SILVERBERG, ROBERT   OA
    SCARAB IN THE CITY OF TIME, A   SS NDM 75 05
        NEW DIMENSIONS 5   SILVERBERG, ROBERT   OA
    SECRET RIDER   NV NDM 76 06
        NEW DIMENSIONS 6   SILVERBERG, ROBERT   OA
    STATE OF THE ART ON ALYSSUM, THE   SS NDM 77 07
        NEW DIMENSIONS 7   SILVERBERG, ROBERT   OA

RANDALL, ROBERT   PSEUD. FOR
    RANDALL GARRETT AND ROBERT SILVERBERG
    SHROUDED PLANET, THE   AC H GNM 58
        CHOSEN PEOPLE, THE   NV ASF 56 06
            SHROUDED PLANET, THE   RANDALL, ROBERT   AC
        FALSE PROPHET   NV ASF 56 12
            SHROUDED PLANET, THE   RANDALL, ROBERT   AC
        PROMISED LAND, THE   NV ASF 56 08
            SHROUDED PLANET, THE   RANDALL, ROBERT   AC

RANDERS, JORGEN
    FROM "THE LIMITS TO GROWTH"   AR C   72
        LOOKING AHEAD   ALLEN, D. & L.   AN

RANDOLPH, V.
    THREE WISHES, THE   SS
        DEALS WITH THE DEVIL   DAVENPORT, BASIL   AN

RANKINE, JOHN   PSEUD. FOR DOUGLAS R. MASON
    FLIGHT OF A PLASTIC BEE   SS NWR 68 11
        NEW WRITINGS IN SF. 11   CARNELL, JOHN   OA
    IMAGE OF DESTRUCTION   NV NWR 67 10
        NEW WRITINGS IN SF. 10   CARNELL, JOHN   OA
    MAIDEN VOYAGE   NV NWR 64 02
        NEW WRITINGS IN SF. 2   CARNELL, JOHN   OA
    SIX CUBED PLUS 1   NV NWR 66 07
        NEW WRITINGS IN SF. 7   CARNELL, JOHN   AN
        NEW WRITINGS IN SF. 7   CARNELL, JOHN   OA
    TWO'S COMPANY   SS NWR 64 01
        NEW WRITINGS IN SF. 1   CARNELL, JOHN   OA
        SOCIOLOGY THROUGH SCIENCE FICTION MILSTEAD/GREENBERG/& AN
    WORM IN THE BUD   SS NWR 68 12
        NEW WRITINGS IN SF. 12   CARNELL, JOHN   OA

RANKINE, W. J. M.
    MATHEMATICIAN IN LOVE, THE (1874)   PM
        MATHEMATICAL MAGPIE, THE   FADIMAN, CLIFTON   AN

RANSOM, JAMES
    FRED ONE   SS FSF 64 04
        BEST FROM FANTASY AND SCIENCE FICTION: 14
                                     DAVIDSON, AVRAM   AN

RAPHAEL, RICK
    THIRST QUENCHERS, THE   AC H GOL 65
        FILBERT IS A NUT, A   SS ASF 59 11
            PROLOGUE TO ANALOG   CAMPBELL, JOHN W. JR AN
        GUTTERSNIPE   NV ASF 64 11
            THIRST QUENCHERS, THE   RAPHAEL, RICK   AC
        MAILMAN COMETH, THE   NV ASF 65 02
            THIRST QUENCHERS, THE   RAPHAEL, RICK   AC
        MAKE MINE HOMOGENIZED   NV ASF 60 04
            NEVER IN THIS WORLD   STONE, IDELLA P.   AN
        ODD MAN IN   NV
            THIRST QUENCHERS, THE   RAPHAEL, RICK   AC
        SONNY   SS ASF 63 04
            ANALOG 3   CAMPBELL, JOHN W. JR AN
            10TH ANNUAL OF THE YEAR'S BEST S-F, THE
                                     MERRIL, JUDITH   AN
        THIRST QUENCHERS, THE   NV ASF 63 09
            THIRST QUENCHERS, THE   RAPHAEL, RICK   AC

RASPE, RUDOLPH
  ADVENTURES OF BARON MUNCHAUSEN, THE   EX
    FROM FRANKENSTEIN TO ANDROMEDA   BROWN, JAMES GOLDIE AN

RAWORTH, TOM
  AH THE POETRY OF MISS PARROT'S FEET DEMONSTRATING THE TANGO
                                PM   68
    HOLDING YOUR EIGHT HANDS   LUCIE-SMITH, EDWARD AN

RAY, JEAN   SEE PSEUD. JOHN FLANDERS

RAY, ROBERT
  CRAVING FOR BLACKNESS, THE (SEE THE HEART OF BLACKNESS)
                         TC
  HEART OF BLACKNESS, THE (THE CRAVING FOR BLACKNESS)
                       SS NWS 62 09
    OUT OF THIS WORLD 6   WILLIAMS-ELLIS& OWEN AN
  PSYCHEDELIC FLIGHT   SS GEN 72
    GENERATION   GERROLD, DAVID   OA

RAYER, FRANCIS G.   ALSO AS   GEORGE LONGDON
  WORLDS AT WAR   AN TPS
  FEARFUL BANNER   SS
    WORLDS AT WAR   RAYER, FRANCIS G. AN
  PRISON TRAP   SS NWS 51 SU
    LAURIE'S SPACE ANNUAL   ANONYMOUS   AN
  SANDS OUR ABODE   SS NWS 59 06
    OUT OF THIS WORLD 3   WILLIAMS-ELLIS& OWEN AN

RAYMOND, HUGH   PSEUD. FOR JOHN MICHEL
  SPOKESMAN FOR TERRA   SS STI 41 06
  SHOT IN THE DARK   MERRIL, JUDITH   AN

READY, W. B.
  DEVLIN   SS FSF 53 04
    BEST FROM FANTASY AND SCIENCE FICTION: 3
                   BOUCHER & MCCOMAS AN

REAMY, TOM
  BEYOND THE CLEFT   NV NOV 74 04
    NOVA 4   HARRISON, HARRY   OA
  DINOSAURS   NV NDM 76 06
    NEW DIMENSIONS 6   SILVERBERG, ROBERT OA
  SAN DIEGO LIGHTFOOT SUE   NV FSF 75 08
    NEBULA AWARD STORIES 11   LE GUIN, URSULA K. AN
  STING!   PL   75
    SIX SCIENCE FICTION PLAYS   ELWOOD, ROGER   AN
  SWEETWATER FACTOR, THE   SS
    LONE STAR UNIVERSE   PROCTOR & UTLEY   OA
  TWILLA   NV FSF 74 09
    NEBULA AWARD STORIES 10   GUNN, JAMES E.   AN
  UNDER THE HOLLYWOOD SIGN   SS ORB 75 17
    ORBIT 17   KNIGHT, DAMON   OA

REAVES, J. MICHAEL
  BREATH OF DRAGONS, THE   SS CLR 73 03
    CLARION III   WILSON, ROBIN SCOTT OA
  PASSION PLAY   SS UNI 74 05
    UNIVERSE 5   CARR, TERRY   OA

REDD, DAVID
  MAMMOTH HUNTERS, THE   SS NWB 73 05
    NEW WORLDS QUARTERLY NO. 5 MOORCOCK, MICHAEL OA
  PRISONERS OF PARADISE   SS NWS 66 10
    NEW WORLDS QUARTERLY NO. 1 MOORCOCK, MICHAEL OA
    SCIENCE FICTION   BRODKIN & PEARSON AN
  QUIET KIND OF MADNESS, A   NV FSF 68 05
    NEW WORLDS OF FANTASY NO. 2 CARR, TERRY   AN
  SUNDOWN   NV FSF 67 12
    BEST FROM FANTASY AND SCIENCE FICTION: 18
                   FERMAN, EDWARD L. AN
    THIS SIDE OF INFINITY   CARR, TERRY   AN

REDGROVE, PETER
  CASE, THE   PM NWS 66 01
    11TH ANNUAL OF THE YEAR'S BEST S-F, THE
                   MERRIL, JUDITH   AN
  IDEA OF ENTROPY AT MAENPORTH BEACH, THE PM   67
    ENGLAND SWINGS SF   MERRIL, JUDITH   AN
  SPACE-TIME JOURNAL, THE   MERRIL, JUDITH   AN
                     SS PRV 63 29
  MR. WATERMAN
    HOLDING YOUR EIGHT HANDS LUCIE-SMITH, EDWARD AN
    9TH ANNUAL OF THE YEAR'S BEST S-F, THE MERRIL, JUDITH AN
  TWELVEMONTH, A   SS NYT
    BEST SF: 75, THE NINTH ANNUAL HARRISON & ALDISS AN
  WIZARD'S NEW MEETING, THE   PM   69
    HOLDING YOUR EIGHT HANDS LUCIE-SMITH, EDWARD AN

REED, CLIFFORD C.
  MARTIAN ENTERPRISE   AC DIG 62
                     SN SFB 59 07
    CHILDREN OF THE STARS   REED, CLIFFORD C.   AC
    FORGOTTEN KNOWLEDGE   SN SFB 59 11
    MARTIAN ENTERPRISE   REED, CLIFFORD C.   AC
    ROAD BACK, THE   SN SFB 60 02
    MARTIAN ENTERPRISE   REED, CLIFFORD C.   AC

REED, KIT
  ACROSS THE BAR   SS ORB 71 09
    ORBIT 9   KNIGHT, DAMON   OA
  AT CENTRAL   SS   67
    SF: AUTHORS' CHOICE 3   HARRISON, HARRY   AN
  AUTOMATIC TIGER   SS FSF 64 03
    BEST FROM FANTASY AND SCIENCE FICTION: 14
                   DAVIDSON, AVRAM   AN

REED, KIT   (CONTINUED)
  10TH ANNUAL OF THE YEAR'S BEST S-F, THE
               MERRIL, JUDITH   AN
                SS FSF 64 06
  CYNOSURE
    MARRIAGE AND THE FAMILY THROUGH SCIENCE FICTION
                CLEAR/WARRICK/&   AN
  FOOD FARM, THE   SS ORB 67 02
    ALPHA 6   SILVERBERG, ROBERT AN
    ORBIT 2   KNIGHT, DAMON   OA
    SF12   MERRIL, JUDITH   AN
    VOYAGES: SCENARIOS FOR A SHIP CALLED EARTH
                SAUER, ROB   AN
    WOMEN OF WONDER   SARGENT, PAMELA   AN
  GOLDEN ACRES   NV   68
    ABOVE THE HUMAN LANDSCAPE MCNELLY & STOVER   AN
    AS TOMORROW BECOMES TODAY SULLIVAN, CHARLES W. AN
    BEST SF: 1968   HARRISON & ALDISS AN
    SOCIAL PROBLEMS THROUGH SCIENCE FICTION
              GREENBERG/MILSTEAD/& AN
    VOYAGES: SCENARIOS FOR A SHIP CALLED EARTH
                SAUER, ROB   AN
  GREAT ESCAPE TOURS, INC.   SS FST 74
    FINAL STAGE   FERMAN & MALZBERG OA
  IN BEHALF OF THE PRODUCT   SS BMR 73
    BAD MOON RISING   DISCH, THOMAS M.   OA
    MARRIAGE AND THE FAMILY THROUGH SCIENCE FICTION
                CLEAR/WARRICK/&   AN
                SS FSF 61 04
  JUDAS BOMB
    BEST SF 6   CRISPIN, EDMUND   AN
    7TH ANNUAL OF THE YEAR'S BEST S-F, THE MERRIL, JUDITH AN
  NEW YOU, THE   SS FSF 62 09
    MARRIAGE AND THE FAMILY THROUGH SCIENCE FICTION
                CLEAR/WARRICK/&   AN
                SS NWS 67 01
  SISOHPROMATEM
    BEST SF STORIES FROM NEW WORLDS NO. 2, THE
                MOORCOCK, MICHAEL AN
  SONGS OF WAR   NV NOV 74 04
    BEST SF: 1974   HARRISON & ALDISS AN
    NOVA 4   HARRISON, HARRY   OA
  VINE, THE   SS FSF 67 11
    ANTHROPOLOGY THROUGH SCIENCE FICTION MASON, C/GREENBERG/& AN
    BEST SF: 1967   HARRISON & ALDISS AN
    MARRIAGE AND THE FAMILY THROUGH SCIENCE FICTION
                CLEAR/WARRICK/&   AN
  NIGHTMARE GARDEN   GHIDALIA, VIC   AN
  WAIT, THE   SS FSF 58 04
    APEMAN, SPACEMAN   STOVER & HARRISON AN
    BEST FROM FANTASY AND SCIENCE FICTION: 8
                BOUCHER, ANTHONY   AN
  WINSTON   SS ORB 69 05
    ORBIT 5   KNIGHT, DAMON   OA
  WINTER   SS ARG 70
    YEAR'S BEST HORROR STORIES, THE DAVIS, RICHARD   AN

REEDS, F. ANTON   SEE PSEUD. ANTHONY RIKER

REESE, JOHN
  DOUBLE EXPOSURE   SS PBY 65 02
    PLAYBOY BOOK OF HORROR AND THE SUPERNATURAL, THE
                PLAYBOY, EDITORS OF AN
    WEIRD SHOW   PLAYBOY, EDITORS OF AN
                SS SEP 49 02
  RAINMAKER
    TOMORROW, THE STARS   HEINLEIN, ROBERT A. AN
  SYMBOLIC LOGIC OF MURDER, THE SS EQM 60 10
    MATHEMATICAL MAGPIE, THE   FADIMAN, CLIFTON   AN

REEVE, ARTHUR B.
  SILENT BULLET, THE   AC H DOM 12
  ARTIFICIAL PARADISE   SS
    SILENT BULLET, THE   REEVE, ARTHUR B.   AC
  AZURE RING, THE   SS SCD 30 05
    SILENT BULLET, THE   REEVE, ARTHUR B.   AC
  BACTERIOLOGICAL DETECTIVE, THE SS SCD 30 02
    SILENT BULLET, THE   REEVE, ARTHUR B.   AC
  BLACK HAND, THE   SS
    SILENT BULLET, THE   REEVE, ARTHUR B.   AC
  DEADLY TUBE, THE   SS
    SILENT BULLET, THE   REEVE, ARTHUR B.   AC
  DIAMOND MAKER, THE   SS AMD 30 06
    SILENT BULLET, THE   REEVE, ARTHUR B.   AC
  SCIENTIFIC CRACKSMAN, THE   SS AMD 30 08
    SILENT BULLET, THE   REEVE, ARTHUR B.   AC
  SEISMOGRAPH ADVENTURE, THE   SS SCD 30 03
    SILENT BULLET, THE   REEVE, ARTHUR B.   AC
  SILENT BULLET, THE   SS
    SILENT BULLET, THE   REEVE, ARTHUR B.   AC
  "SPONTANEOUS COMBUSTION"   SS
    SILENT BULLET, THE   REEVE, ARTHUR B.   AC
  STEEL DOOR, THE   SS SCD 30 04
    SILENT BULLET, THE   REEVE, ARTHUR B.   AC
  TERROR IN THE AIR   SS
    SILENT BULLET, THE   REEVE, ARTHUR B.   AC

REEVES, ROSSER
  E=MC2   PM FSF 61 09
    *BEST FROM FANTASY AND SCIENCE FICTION: 11
                MILLS, ROBERT P.   AN
                PM FSF 61 09
  EFFIGY
    *BEST FROM FANTASY AND SCIENCE FICTION: 11
                MILLS, ROBERT P.   AN
                PM FSF 60 12
  INFINITY
    BEST FROM FANTASY AND SCIENCE FICTION: 10
                MILLS, ROBERT P.   AN

REGINALD, R.   SEE ALSO   CO-EDITOR DOUGLAS MENVILLE

REID, JULIA
  PROBABILITY STORM   NV   UNI 77 07
    UNIVERSE 7   CARR, TERRY   OA

REINES, DONALD F.
  INTERPLANETARY COPYRIGHT (THE SHAPE OF COPYRIGHT TO COME)
                                              AR   FSF 53 04
    COMING ATTRACTIONS   GREENBERG , MARTIN   NF
  SHAPE OF COPYRIGHT TO COME, THE (SEE INTERPLANETARY COPYRIGHT)
                                                    TC

RENARD, JULES
  APOTHEM   MS
    MATHEMATICAL MAGPIE, THE   FADIMAN, CLIFTON   AN

RENCELAW, BRIAN   PSEUD. FOR RAY RUSSELL
  SKIN-DEEP   SS   PBY 63 06
    DEAD ASTRONAUT, 10 STORIES OF SPACE FLIGHT, THE
                                    PLAYBOY, EDITORS OF AN

REPP, ED EARL
  RADIUM POOL, THE   AC H FPB 49
    ALSO IN "SCIENCE-FANTASY QUINTETTE"
  STELLAR MISSILES, THE   AC H FPB 49
    BATTLE OF WIZARDS   SS
      RADIUM POOL, THE   REPP, ED EARL   AC
    BUCCANEER OF THE STAR SEAS (SEE THE QUEST OF THE IMMORTAL)
                                                    TC
    KLEON OF THE GOLDEN SUN   SS   FBK 50 07
      SCIENCE AND SORCERY   FORD, GARRET   AN
    PHANTOM OF TERROR, THE   SS   AMZ 33 04
      RADIUM POOL, THE   REPP, ED EARL   AC
    QUEST OF THE IMMORTAL, THE (BUCCANEER OF THE STAR SEAS)
                                              SS   PLS 40 FL
      STELLAR MISSILES, THE   REPP, ED EARL   AC
    RADIUM POOL, THE   AC   FPB 49
      SCIENCE-FANTASY QUINTETTE   CRAWFORD, WILLIAM L. AN
    RADIUM POOL, THE   NV   SWS 29 08
      RADIUM POOL, THE   REPP, ED EARL   AC
    RED DIMENSION, THE   SS   SWS 30 01
      RADIUM POOL, THE   REPP, ED EARL   AC
    SECOND MISSILE, THE   NV   AMZ 30 12
      STELLAR MISSILES, THE   REPP, ED EARL   AC
    STELLAR MISSILE, THE   SS   SWS 29 11
      STELLAR MISSILES, THE   REPP, ED EARL   AC

REPTON, HUMPHREY
  FROM A PRIVATE MAD-HOUSE (1787)   SS   VAR 87
    FAR BOUNDARIES   DERLETH, AUGUST   AN

REYNOLDS, DALLAS M. SEE PSEUD. MACK REYNOLDS

REYNOLDS, MACK   SEE ALSO   CO-EDITOR FREDRIC BROWN
                    PSEUD. FOR DALLAS MCCORD REYNOLDS
  BEST OF MACK REYNOLDS, THE   AC   PKT 76 04
  DEPRESSION OR BUST   DN   ACE 74
    ADVENTURE OF THE BALL OF NOSTRADAMUS, THE SS C FSF 55 06
      SCIENCE-FICTIONAL SHERLOCK HOLMES, THE COUNCIL OF FOUR
                                                    AN
    ADVENTURE OF THE EXTRATERRESTRIAL, THE   NV   ASF 65 07
      ANALOG 5   CAMPBELL, JOHN W. JR AN
      BEST OF MACK REYNOLDS, THE   REYNOLDS, MACK   AC
    ADVENTURE OF THE SNITCH IN TIME, THE   SS C FSF 53 07
      SCIENCE-FICTIONAL SHERLOCK HOLMES, THE COUNCIL OF FOUR
                                                    AN
      SPACE, TIME & CRIME   DEFORD, MIRIAM ALLEN AN
    ALBATROSS   SS   IMG 55 04
      BEST OF MACK REYNOLDS, THE   REYNOLDS, MACK   AC
      ENCOUNTERS WITH ALIENS   EARLEY, GEORGE W.   AN
    AMONG THE BAD BABOONS   NV   GAL 68 08
      ELEVENTH GALAXY READER, THE POHL, FREDERIK   AN
      NIGHTMARE AGE   POHL, FREDERIK   AN
    AND THOU BESIDE ME   SS   FSF 54 04
      *SCIENCE FICTION ADVENTURES IN MUTATION CONKLIN, GROFF AN
    BLACK SHEEP ASTRAY   NV   AMA 73
      ASTOUNDING   HARRISON, HARRY   OA
    BUCK AND THE GENTS FROM SPACE   NV
      SCIENCE FICTION ADVENTURES FROM WAY OUT
                                  ELWOOD, ROGER   OA
    BURNT TOAST   SS   PBY 55 11
      BEST OF MACK REYNOLDS, THE   REYNOLDS, MACK   AC
      PLAYBOY BOOK OF HORROR AND THE SUPERNATURAL, THE
                                  PLAYBOY, EDITORS OF AN
    BUSINESS, AS USUAL, THE   SS   FSF 52 06
      BEST OF MACK REYNOLDS, THE   REYNOLDS, MACK   AC
      CENTURY OF SCIENCE FICTION, A KNIGHT, DAMON   AN
      FIFTY SHORT SCIENCE FICTION TALES ASIMOV & CONKLIN AN
      NEW WORLDS FOR OLD   DERLETH, AUGUST   AN
      TIMES 4 (ABRIDGED STORIES) ALLEN, VIRGINIA F. AN
      *WORLDS OF TOMORROW   DERLETH, AUGUST   AN
    CARTOONIST   SS C
      NIGHTMARES AND GEEZENSTACKS BROWN, FREDRIC   AC
    CITY'S END   NV   FUQ 73
      CITY: 2000 A.D., THE   CLEM/GREENBERG/&   AN
      FUTURE QUEST   ELWOOD, ROGER   OA
    COLD WAR...CONTINUED, THE   NV   NOV 73 03
      NOVA 3   HARRISON, HARRY   OA
    COME IN, SPACEPORT   SS   GOM 74
      BEST OF MACK REYNOLDS, THE   REYNOLDS, MACK   AC
    COMPOUND INTEREST   SS   FSF 56 08
      BEST OF MACK REYNOLDS, THE   REYNOLDS, MACK   AC
      SF: THE BEST OF THE BEST   MERRIL, JUDITH   AN
      SF:57, THE YEAR'S GREATEST SCIENCE FICTION AND FANTASY
                                  MERRIL, JUDITH   AN
    CRIMINAL IN UTOPIA   NV   GAL 68 10
      BEST SF: 1968   HARRISON & ALDISS   AN

REYNOLDS, MACK   (CONTINUED)
    TOMORROW, INC.   GREENBERG& OLANDER AN
  D. P. FROM TOMORROW   SS   OSF 53 FL
    PORTALS OF TOMORROW   DERLETH, AUGUST   AN
  DARK INTERLUDE   SS C GAL 51 01
    BEST SCIENCE-FICTION STORIES: 1952, THE
                                  BLEILER & DIKTY   AN
    FRONTIERS IN SPACE   BLEILER & DIKTY   AN
    *GALAXY READER OF SCIENCE FICTION GOLD, H. L.   AN
    HUMAN AND OTHER BEINGS   DEGRAEFF, ALLEN   AN
    NIGHTMARES AND GEEZENSTACKS   BROWN, FREDRIC   AC
  DEPRESSION...OR BUST   SS   ASF 67 08
    DEPRESSION OR BUST   REYNOLDS, MACK   DN
  DISCORD MAKERS, THE   SS   OTW 50 07
    *INVADERS OF EARTH   CONKLIN, GROFF   AN
  DOWN THE RIVER   SS   STS 50 09
    BEST OF MACK REYNOLDS, THE   REYNOLDS, MACK   AC
    GALACTIC EMPIRES VOLUME TWO   ALDISS, BRIAN W.   AN
  EARTHLINGS GO HOME!   SS   ROG 62 08
    BEST OF MACK REYNOLDS, THE   REYNOLDS, MACK   AC
    8TH ANNUAL OF THE YEAR'S BEST S-F, THE MERRIL, JUDITH AN
  ENEMY WITHIN, THE   SS   ASF 67 04
    BEST OF MACK REYNOLDS, THE   REYNOLDS, MACK   AC
  EXPEDITER   SS   ASF 63 05
    DEPRESSION OR BUST   REYNOLDS, MACK   DN
  FAD   SS   ASF 65 04
    BEST OF MACK REYNOLDS, THE   REYNOLDS, MACK   AC
    DEPRESSION OR BUST   REYNOLDS, MACK   DN
  FARMER   NV   GAL 61 06
    WORLDS OF WHEN   CONKLIN, GROFF   AN
  FIESTA BRAVA   SN   ASF 67 09
    ANALOG 7   CAMPBELL, JOHN W. JR AN
  FREEDOM   NV   ASF 61 02
    BEST OF MACK REYNOLDS, THE   REYNOLDS, MACK   AC
    POLITICAL SCIENCE FICTION   GREENBERG& WARRICK AN
    7TH ANNUAL OF THE YEAR'S BEST S-F, THE MERRIL, JUDITH AN
  GENERATION GAP   NV
    FUTURE KIN   ELWOOD, ROGER   OA
  GENUS TRAITOR   NV   ASF 64 08
    ANALOG 4   CAMPBELL, JOHN W. JR AN
  GOOD INDIAN   SS   ASF 62 09
    ANALOG 2   CAMPBELL, JOHN W. JR AN
    BEST OF MACK REYNOLDS, THE   REYNOLDS, MACK   AC
  GUN FOR HIRE   SS   ASF 60 12
    SPECIAL WONDER   MCCOMAS, J. FRANCIS AN
  HUNTED ONES, THE   NV   SFS 59 11
    WEIRD ONES, THE   HOWARD, IVAN   AN
  I'M A STRANGER HERE MYSELF   SS   AMZ 60 12
    14 GREAT TALES OF ESP   STONE, IDELLA P.   AN
  ISOLATIONIST   SS   FAD 50 04
    *BIG BOOK OF SCIENCE FICTION CONKLIN, GROFF   AN
  MAN IN THE MOON, THE   SS   AMZ 50 07
    LOOKING FORWARD   LESSER, MILTON   AN
  MARTIANS AND THE COYS, THE   SS   IMG 51 06
    GENTLE INVADERS   SANTESSON, HANS S. AN
    *SCIENCE-FICTION CARNIVAL   BROWN, F. & REYNOLDS AN
  ME AND FLAPJACK AND THE MARTIANS   SS C ASF 52 12
    NIGHTMARES AND GEEZENSTACKS   BROWN, FREDRIC   AC
  NO RETURN FROM ELBA   SS   FAN 53 10
    BEST OF MACK REYNOLDS, THE   REYNOLDS, MACK   AC
  PACIFIST   SS   FSF 64 01
    BEST OF MACK REYNOLDS, THE   REYNOLDS, MACK   AC
    POLITICAL SCIENCE FICTION   GREENBERG& WARRICK AN
    10TH ANNUAL OF THE YEAR'S BEST S-F, THE
                                  MERRIL, JUDITH   AN
  POTENTIAL ENEMY   SS   OSF 54 02
    BEYOND THE STARS AND OTHER STORIES ANONYMOUS   AN
    PREFACE   IN
      SCIENCE-FICTION CARNIVAL (11 OF 13) BROWN, F. & REYNOLDS AN
  PRONE   SS   FSF 54 09
    BEST OF MACK REYNOLDS, THE   REYNOLDS, MACK   AC
    WORLDS OF WONDER   HARRISON, HARRY   AN
    13 ABOVE THE NIGHT   CONKLIN, GROFF   AN
  RADICAL CENTER   NV   ASF 67 03
    AMERICAN GOVERNMENT THROUGH SCIENCE FICTION
                                  OLANDER&GREENBERG/& AN
  RETALIATION (TIME OF WAR)   SS   IFS 65 11
    .SF: AUTHORS' CHOICE   HARRISON, HARRY   AN
  REVOLUTION   NV   ASF 60 05
    BEST OF MACK REYNOLDS, THE   REYNOLDS, MACK   AC
  RUSSKIES GO HOME!   SS   FSF 60 11
    UNFRIENDLY FUTURE, THE   BOARDMAN, TOM JR.   AN
  SECOND ADVENT   SS   IFS 74 06
    BEST OF MACK REYNOLDS, THE   REYNOLDS, MACK   AC
  SPACEMAN ON A SPREE   NV   WOT 63 06
    BEST OF MACK REYNOLDS, THE   REYNOLDS, MACK   AC
  SPOOKY   SS
    KILLER PLANTS AND OTHER STORIES, THE ELWOOD, ROGER OA
  SUBVERSIVE   SS   ASF 62 12
    BEST OF MACK REYNOLDS, THE   REYNOLDS, MACK   AC
    DECADE THE 1960S   ALDISS & HARRISON   AN
    SCIENCE FICTION HORIZONS NO. 1 BOARDMAN, TOM JR. AN
  SURVIVAL, A.D. 2000   SS
    SURVIVAL FROM INFINITY   ELWOOD, ROGER   OA
  SURVIVOR   SS   ASF 66 07
    BEST OF MACK REYNOLDS, THE   REYNOLDS, MACK   AC
  UTOPIAN   SS   YRT 70
    BEST OF MACK REYNOLDS, THE   REYNOLDS, MACK   AC
    TOMORROW, AND TOMORROW, AND TOMORROW...
                                  HEINTZ/HERBERT/JOOS/ AN
    YEAR 2000, THE   HARRISON, HARRY   OA
  VISITOR   NV
    TOMORROW TODAY   ZEBROWSKI, GEORGE   OA
  YOUR SOUL COMES C.O.D.   SS   FAD 52 03
    BEST OF MACK REYNOLDS, THE   REYNOLDS, MACK   AC

RHYLICK, FRANK   ROBERTS, KEITH

RHYLICK, FRANK   SEE PSEUD. FRANK RILEY

RICE, ALLISON   PSEUD. FOR JANE RICE AND RUTH ALLISON
  LOOLIES ARE HERE, THE   SS   ORB 66 01
    BEST FROM ORBIT, THE   KNIGHT, DAMON   AN
    ORBIT 1   KNIGHT, DAMON   OA

RICE, CHARLES D.
  CUPID WITH AN ADDING MACHINE   SS   TWK 60 09
    MATHEMATICAL MAGPIE, THE   FADIMAN, CLIFTON   AN

RICE, ELMER L.
  FROM: THE ADDING MACHINE   EX   DBL 22
    INSIDE INFORMATION   MOWSHOWITZ, ABBE   AN

RICE, JANE   ALSO AS   ALLISON RICE (WITH RUTH ALLISON)
  CREST OF THE WAVE, THE   SS   UNK 41 06
    UNKNOWN 5, THE   BENSEN, D. R.   AN
  IDOL OF THE FLIES, THE   SS   UNK 42 06
    CHILDREN OF WONDER   TENN, WILLIAM   AN
  RAINBOW GOLD, THE   SS   FSF 59 12
    BEST FROM FANTASY AND SCIENCE FICTION: 10
                                   MILLS, ROBERT P.   AN
  REFUGEE, THE   SS   UNK 43 10
    FROM UNKNOWN WORLDS   CAMPBELL, JOHN W. JR AN
  HELL HATH FURY   HAY, GEORGE   AN
  WILLOW TREE, THE   SS   FSF 59 02
    BEST FROM FANTASY AND SCIENCE FICTION: 9
                                   MILLS, ROBERT P.   AN

RICHARDS, NELSON
  SCIENCE STEALS A MARCH   SS
    ADVENTURES TO COME   ESENWEIN, J. BERG   OA

RICHARDSON, MAURICE
  WAY OUT IN THE CONTINUUM   SS   HOR
    BEST SF 7   CRISPIN, EDMUND   AN

RICHARDSON, R. S.   ALSO AS   PHILIP LATHAM
  KID ANDERSON   SS   SPM 57 SP
    GREAT SCIENCE FICTION BY SCIENTISTS   CONKLIN, GROFF   AN
  SPACE FIX   AR   ASF 43 03
    COMING ATTRACTIONS   GREENBERG, MARTIN   NF

RICHMOND, LEIGH   SEE ALSO   CO-AUTHOR WALT RICHMOND
  COWS CAN'T EAT GRASS   SS C ASF 67 08
    POSITIVE CHARGE   RICHMOND, W. & L.   DC
  I, BEM   SS C ASF 64 06
    POSITIVE CHARGE   RICHMOND, W. & L.   DC
  IF THE SABOT FITS...   SS C ASF 68 02
    POSITIVE CHARGE   RICHMOND, W. & L.   DC
  M'LORD IS THE SHEPHERD   SS C IFS 65 09
    POSITIVE CHARGE   RICHMOND, W. & L.   DC
  POPPA NEEDS SHORTS   SS C ASF 64 01
    ABOVE THE HUMAN LANDSCAPE   MCNELLY & STOVER   AN
    9TH ANNUAL OF THE YEAR'S BEST S-F, THE MERRIL, JUDITH   AN
  PROLOGUE TO...AN ANALOGUE   NV   ASF 61 06
    ANALOG 1   CAMPBELL, JOHN W. JR AN
  PROLOGUE TO...AN ANALOGUE   NV C ASF 61 06
    POSITIVE CHARGE   RICHMOND, W. & L.   DC
  SHORTS WING   SS C NEW 70 DC
    POSITIVE CHARGE   RICHMOND, W. & L.   DC
  SHORTSITE   SS C ASF 64 04
    POSITIVE CHARGE   RICHMOND, W. & L.   DC
  SHORTSTACK   SS C ASF 64 12
    ELSEWHERE AND ELSEWHEN   CONKLIN, GROFF   AN
    POSITIVE CHARGE   RICHMOND, W. & L.   DC
    THEMES IN SCIENCE FICTION   KELLEY, LEO P.   AN

RICHMOND, WALT AND LEIGH
  POSITIVE CHARGE   DC   ACE 70

RICHMOND, WALT
  COWS CAN'T EAT GRASS   SS C ASF 67 08
    POSITIVE CHARGE   RICHMOND, W. & L.   DC
  I, BEM   SS C ASF 64 06
    POSITIVE CHARGE   RICHMOND, W. & L.   DC
  IF THE SABOT FITS...   SS C ASF 68 02
    POSITIVE CHARGE   RICHMOND, W. & L.   DC
  M'LORD IS THE SHEPHERD   SS C IFS 65 09
    POSITIVE CHARGE   RICHMOND, W. & L.   DC
  POPPA NEEDS SHORTS   SS C ASF 64 01
    ABOVE THE HUMAN LANDSCAPE   MCNELLY & STOVER   AN
    9TH ANNUAL OF THE YEAR'S BEST S-F, THE MERRIL, JUDITH   AN
  PROLOGUE TO...AN ANALOGUE   NV C ASF 61 06
    POSITIVE CHARGE   RICHMOND, W. & L.   DC
  SHORTS WING   SS C NEW 70 DC
    POSITIVE CHARGE   RICHMOND, W. & L.   DC
  SHORTSITE   SS C ASF 64 04
    POSITIVE CHARGE   RICHMOND, W. & L.   DC
  SHORTSTACK   SS C ASF 64 12
    ELSEWHERE AND ELSEWHEN   CONKLIN, GROFF   AN
    POSITIVE CHARGE   RICHMOND, W. & L.   DC
    THEMES IN SCIENCE FICTION   KELLEY, LEO P.   AN

RICHTER, CONRAD
  DOCTOR HANRAY'S SECOND CHANCE   SS   SEP 50 01
    POST READER OF FANTASY AND SCIENCE FICTION
                                   SATURDAY EVE. POST   AN
    SATURDAY EVENING POST FANTASY STORIES, THE
                                   FLES, BARTHOLD   AN
  SINISTER JOURNEY   SS   SEP 53 09
    POST READER OF FANTASY AND SCIENCE FICTION
                                   SATURDAY EVE. POST   AN

RICKETTS, MARTIN I.
  GREEN FUSE, THE   SS   NWR 75 25
    NEW WRITINGS IN SF. 25   BULMER, KENNETH   OA
  NEW CANUTE   SS   NWR 74 24
    NEW WRITINGS IN SF. 24   BULMER, KENNETH   OA

RIDENOUR, DR. LOUIS
  PILOT LIGHTS OF THE APOCALYPSE   SS   FOR 46 10
    GREAT SCIENCE FICTION BY SCIENTISTS   CONKLIN, GROFF   AN

RIKER, ANTHONY   PSEUD. FOR F. ANTON REEDS
  AUNT ELSIE'S STAIRWAY (SEE BETWEEN TWO WORLDS)   TC
  BETWEEN TWO WORLDS (AUNT ELSIE'S STAIRWAY)   SS   OSP 54 11
    SPACE STATION 42 AND OTHER STORIES   ANONYMOUS   AN

RILEY, DAVE
  AFTER NIGHTFALL   SS   70
    YEAR'S BEST HORROR STORIES, THE   DAVIS, RICHARD   AN

RILEY, FRANK   PSEUD. FOR FRANK RHYLICK
  CYBER AND JUSTICE HOLMES, THE   SS   IFS 55 03
    BEST SCIENCE FICTION STORIES AND NOVELS: 1956
                                   DIKTY, T. E.   AN
    FIRST WORLD OF IF, THE   QUINN & WULFF   AN

ROBB, STEWART
  LETTER FROM A HIGHER CRITIC   SS   ASF 66 11
    ANALOG 6   CAMPBELL, JOHN W. JR AN

ROBBINS, CLARENCE A. SEE PSEUD. TOD ROBBINS

ROBBINS, TOD   PSEUD. FOR CLARENCE AARON ROBBINS
  FREAKS (SPURS)   SS
    GHOULS, THE   HAINING, PETER   AN
  SPURS (SEE FREAKS)   TC

ROBERSON, RICK   SEE ALSO   CO-EDITOR SYLVIA ENGDAHL
  ASTORIA INCIDENT, THE   NV
    ANYWHERE, ANYWHEN   ENGDAHL, SYLVIA   OA
  BECKONING TRAIL, THE   NV C NEW 76 03
    UNIVERSE AHEAD   ENGDAHL & ROBERSON   AN
  CLOUDLAB, THE   NV   NEW 76 AN
    UNIVERSE AHEAD   ENGDAHL & ROBERSON   AN
  INTRODUCTION   IN
    UNIVERSE AHEAD   ENGDAHL & ROBERSON   AN

ROBERTS, FRANK
  HAPPENING, A   SS
    SECOND PACIFIC BOOK OF SCIENCE FICTION, THE
                                   BAXTER, JOHN   AN
  IT COULD BE YOU   SS   SSI 64
    PACIFIC BOOK OF AUSTRALIAN SCIENCE FICTION
                                   BAXTER, JOHN   AN
    10TH ANNUAL OF THE YEAR'S BEST S-F, THE
                                   MERRIL, JUDITH   AN

ROBERTS, JANE
  CHESTNUT BEADS, THE   NV   FSF 57 10
    ROD SERLING'S TRIPLE W: WITCHES, WARLOCKS AND WEREWOLVES
                                   SERLING, ROD   AN

ROBERTS, KEITH   ALSO AS   ALISTAIR BEVAN AND JOHN KINGSTON
  GRAIN KINGS, THE   AC H HUT 76
  MACHINES AND MEN   AC H HUT 73
  PASSING OF THE DRAGONS, THE   AC   BKM 77 04
  PAVANE   NO H DBL 68
  BEAUTIFUL ONE, THE   NV   NWQ 73 05
    NEW WORLDS NO. 5   MOORCOCK & PLATT   OA
  BOULTER'S CANARIES   NV   NWR 65 03
    MACHINES AND MEN   ROBERTS, KEITH   AC
    NEW WRITINGS IN SF. 3   CARNELL, JOHN   OA
    PASSING OF THE DRAGONS, THE   ROBERTS, KEITH   AC
  BREAKDOWN   SS   IMP 66 10
    MACHINES AND MEN   ROBERTS, KEITH   AC
  BROTHER JOHN   NV   IMP 66 05
    PAVANE   ROBERTS, KEITH   NO
  CORANDA   SS   NWS 67 01
    BEST SF STORIES FROM NEW WORLDS 3   MOORCOCK, MICHAEL AN
    PASSING OF THE DRAGONS, THE   ROBERTS, KEITH   AC
    WORLD'S BEST SCIENCE FICTION: 1968 WOLLHEIM & CARR   AN
  CORFE GATE   NV   IMP 66 07
    PAVANE   ROBERTS, KEITH   NO
  DEEPS, THE   SS   ORB 66 01
    HOT & COLD RUNNING CITIES   MCHARGUE, GEORGESS   AN
    MACHINES AND MEN   ROBERTS, KEITH   AC
    ORBIT 1   KNIGHT, DAMON   OA
    PASSING OF THE DRAGONS, THE   ROBERTS, KEITH   AC
  EASTERN WINDOWS, THE   SS   NEW 67 AN
    DEVIL HIS DUE, THE   HILL, DOUGLAS   AN
  ESCAPISM   SS   SCF 64 10
    MACHINES AND MEN   ROBERTS, KEITH   AC
  GOD HOUSE, THE   NV   NWQ 71 01
    NEW WORLDS QUARTERLY NO. 1   MOORCOCK, MICHAEL   OA
  GRAIN KINGS, THE   NV   NWQ 72 03
    GRAIN KINGS, THE   ROBERTS, KEITH   AC
    NEW WORLDS QUARTERLY NO. 3   MOORCOCK, MICHAEL   OA
    PASSING OF THE DRAGONS, THE   ROBERTS, KEITH   AC
  I LOSE MEDEA (AS ALISTAIR BEVAN)   SS   NWQ 72 03
    GRAIN KINGS, THE   ROBERTS, KEITH   AC
    PASSING OF THE DRAGONS, THE   ROBERTS, KEITH   AC
  INNER WHEEL, THE   NV   NWR 65 06
    NEW WRITINGS IN SF. 6   CARNELL, JOHN   OA
  LADY ANNE, THE (SEE THE LADY MARGARET)   TC
  LADY MARGARET, THE (THE LADY ANNE)   NV   IMP 66 04
    DAY IN THE LIFE, A   DOZOIS, GARDNER R.   AN
    PAVANE   ROBERTS, KEITH   NO

ROBERTS, KEITH

ROCKLYNNE, ROSS

ROBERTS, KEITH   (CONTINUED)
  LAKE OF TUONELA, THE   NV NWR 74 23
    GRAIN KINGS, THE   ROBERTS, KEITH   AC
    NEW WRITINGS IN SF. 23   BULMER, KENNETH   OA
    PASSING OF THE DRAGONS, THE   ROBERTS, KEITH   AC
  LORDS AND LADIES   NV IMP 66 06
    PAVANE   ROBERTS, KEITH   NO
  MANIPULATION   NV NWR 65 03
    MACHINES AND MEN   ROBERTS, KEITH   AC
  MANSCARER   NV NWR 66 07
    DECADE THE 1960S   ALDISS & HARRISON   AN
    ENGLAND SWINGS SF   MERRIL, JUDITH   AN
    MACHINES AND MEN   ROBERTS, KEITH   AC
    NEW WRITINGS IN SF. 7   CARNELL, JOHN   OA
    PASSING OF THE DRAGONS, THE   ROBERTS, KEITH   AC
    SPACE-TIME JOURNAL, THE   MERRIL, JUDITH   AN
  MINISTRY OF CHILDREN, THE   NV NWB 75 09
    NEW WORLDS NINE   BAILEY, HILARY   OA
  MONKEY AND PRU AND SAL   SS NWQ 71 02
    NEW WORLDS QUARTERLY NO. 2   MOORCOCK, MICHAEL   OA
  PACE THAT KILLS, THE   NV IMP 66 05
    MACHINES AND MEN   ROBERTS, KEITH   AC
  PASSING OF THE DRAGONS, THE   NV NWR 73 21
    GRAIN KINGS, THE   ROBERTS, KEITH   AC
    NEW WRITINGS IN SF. 21   CARNELL, JOHN   OA
    PASSING OF THE DRAGONS, THE   ROBERTS, KEITH   AC
  SCARLET LADY, THE   NV IMP 66 08
    NEW WORLDS OF FANTASY NO. 2   CARR, TERRY   AN
  SIGNALLER, THE   NV IMP 66 03
    ANOTHER WORLD   DOZOIS, GARDNER R.   AN
    PAVANE   ROBERTS, KEITH   NO
  SUB-LIM   NV NWR 65 04
    MACHINES AND MEN   ROBERTS, KEITH   AC
    NEW WRITINGS IN SF. 4   CARNELL, JOHN   OA
  SYNTH   SS NWR 66 08
    MACHINES AND MEN   ROBERTS, KEITH   AC
    NEW WRITINGS IN SF. 8   CARNELL, JOHN   OA
    PASSING OF THE DRAGONS, THE   ROBERTS, KEITH   AC
  THERAPY 2000   SS NWR 69 15
    MACHINES AND MEN   ROBERTS, KEITH   AC
    NEW WRITINGS IN SF. 15   CARNELL, JOHN   OA
    PASSING OF THE DRAGONS, THE   ROBERTS, KEITH   AC
    WORLD'S BEST SCIENCE FICTION: 1970   WOLLHEIM & CARR   AN
  TIMOTHY   SS IMP 66 09
    NEW WORLDS OF FANTASY   CARR, TERRY   AN
  TRUSTIE TREE, THE   SS NWB 73 05
    GRAIN KINGS, THE   ROBERTS, KEITH   AC
    NEW WORLDS QUARTERLY NO. 5   MOORCOCK, MICHAEL   OA
  WEIHNACHTABEND   NV NWQ 72 04
    BEST SF: 1972   HARRISON & ALDISS   AN
    NEW WORLDS QUARTERLY NO. 4   MOORCOCK, MICHAEL   OA
  WEIHNACHTSABEND (WEIHNACHTABEND)   NV NWQ 72 04
    GRAIN KINGS, THE   ROBERTS, KEITH   AC
    PASSING OF THE DRAGONS, THE   ROBERTS, KEITH   AC
  WHITE BOAT, THE   SS NWS 66 12
    GRAIN KINGS, THE   ROBERTS, KEITH   AC
    PASSING OF THE DRAGONS, THE   ROBERTS, KEITH   AC
    PAVANE   ROBERTS, KEITH   NO

ROBERTS, MICHAEL
  NOTE ON THETA, PHI, AND PSI   PM NSM 35 03
    MATHEMATICAL MAGPIE, THE   FADIMAN, CLIFTON   AN

ROBERTS, MORLEY
  ANTICIPATOR, THE (1898)   SS   98
    TRAVELERS IN TIME   STERN, PHILIP VAN D. AN

ROBERTS, WILLO DAVIS
  PERSONAGE OF ROYAL BLOOD, A   SS TVW 73
    TWO VIEWS OF WONDER   SCORTIA & YARBRO   OA

ROBERTSON, MORGAN
  BATTLE OF THE MONSTERS, THE   SS   99
    BATTLE OF THE MONSTERS AND OTHER STORIES, THE
                                  HARTWELL & CURREY   AN
   *BEYOND TIME AND SPACE   DERLETH, AUGUST   AN
  BEYOND THE SPECTRUM   SS   14
    ANCESTRAL VOICES   MENVILLE & REGINALD   AN

ROBIDA, ALBERT
  LIFE IN THE TWENTIETH CENTURY (1883)   IL
    BEYOND THIS HORIZON   CARRELL, CHRISTOPHER OA

ROBIN, RALPH
  BUDDING EXPLORER   SS FSF 52 09
    BEST FROM FANTASY AND SCIENCE FICTION: 2
                                  BOUCHER & MCCOMAS   AN
  PLEASANT DREAMS   SS GAL 51 10
    OMNIBUS OF SCIENCE FICTION   CONKLIN, GROFF   AN
    STRANGE TRAVELS IN SCIENCE FICTION   CONKLIN, GROFF   AN

ROBINETT, STEPHEN
  HELBENT 4   NV GAL 75 10
    BEST FROM GALAXY, THE VOLUME IV   BAEN, JAMES   AN
    BEST SCIENCE FICTION STORIES OF THE YEAR (1975)
                                  DEL REY, LESTER   AN
    1976 ANNUAL WORLD'S BEST SF, THE   WOLLHEIM, DONALD A. AN
  LINGUIST, THE (AS TAK HALLUS)   SS GAL 75 02
    BEST SF: 75, THE NINTH ANNUAL   HARRISON & ALDISS AN

ROBINSON, FRANK M.
  DREAM STREET   SS IMT 55 03
    BEST SCIENCE FICTION STORIES AND NOVELS: 1956
                                  DIKTY, T. E.   AN
    DAYS AFTER TOMORROW, THE   SANTESSON, HANS S.   AN
    6 FROM WORLDS BEYOND   DIKTY, T. E.   AN

ROBINSON, FRANK M.   (CONTINUED)
  "EAST WIND, WEST WIND"   NV NOV 72 02
    CITY: 2000 A.D., THE   CLEM/GREENBERG/&   AN
    NOVA 2   HARRISON, HARRY   OA
    SCIENCE FICTION NOVELLAS   HARRISON & MCNELLY   AN
  FIRE AND THE SWORD, THE   NV GAL 51 08
   *IMAGINATION UNLIMITED   BLEILER & DIKTY   AN
    SF: AUTHORS' CHOICE 4   HARRISON, HARRY   AN
  GIRLS FROM EARTH, THE   NV GAL 52 01
    BEST SCIENCE-FICTION STORIES: 1953, THE
                                  BLEILER & DIKTY   AN
    MARRIAGE AND THE FAMILY THROUGH SCIENCE FICTION
                                  CLEAR/WARRICK/&   AN
   *STORIES FOR TOMORROW   SLOANE, WILLIAM   AN
  HUNTING SEASON, THE   SN ASF 51 11
    YEAR'S BEST SCIENCE FICTION NOVELS: 1952
                                  BLEILER & DIKTY   AN
  LIFE IN THE DAY OF, A   SS PBY 69 06
    WEIRD SHOW   PLAYBOY, EDITORS OF   AN
  OCEANS ARE WIDE, THE   SN SST 54 04
    YEAR'S BEST SCIENCE FICTION NOVELS: 1954
                                  BLEILER & DIKTY   AN
  ONE THOUSAND MILES UP   SS SST 54 04
    BEST SCIENCE FICTION STORIES AND NOVELS: 1955
                                  DIKTY, T. E.   AN
  QUIZ GAME   SS ASF 53 06
    GENTLE INVADERS   SANTESSON, HANS S.   AN
  RELUCTANT HEROES, THE   NV GAL 51 01
    EVERY BOY'S BOOK OF OUTER SPACE STORIES
                                  DIKTY, T. E.   AN
   *GALAXY READER OF SCIENCE FICTION   GOLD, H. L.   AN
    GREAT SCIENCE FICTION STORIES ABOUT THE MOON
                                  DIKTY, T. E.   AN
    MEN ON THE MOON   WOLLHEIM, DONALD A.   DA
  ROVER I WILL BE, A   SS C
    EVERY BOY'S BOOK OF OUTER SPACE STORIES
                                  DIKTY, T. E.   AN
  SANTA CLAUS PLANET, THE   SS NEW 51 AN
    BEST SCIENCE-FICTION STORIES: 1951, THE
                                  BLEILER & DIKTY   AN
    MINDWORM, THE   ANONYMOUS   AN
  TWO WEEKS IN AUGUST   SS GAL 51 02
    FIFTY SHORT SCIENCE FICTION TALES   ASIMOV & CONKLIN AN
  WRECK OF THE SHIP JOHN B., THE   NV PBY 67 06
    BEST SF: 1967   HARRISON & ALDISS   AN
    DEAD ASTRONAUT, 10 STORIES OF SPACE FLIGHT, THE
                                  PLAYBOY, EDITORS OF   AN

ROBINSON, KIM S.
  COMING BACK TO DIXIELAND   SS ORB 76 18
    ORBIT 18   KNIGHT, DAMON   OA
  IN PIERSON'S ORCHESTRA   SS ORB 76 18
    ORBIT 18   KNIGHT, DAMON   OA
  THING ITSELF, THE   SS
    CLARION SF   WILHELM, KATE   OA

ROBINSON, SPIDER
  CALLAHAN'S CROSSTIME SALOON   AC ACE 77 06
    CENTIPEDE'S DILEMMA, THE   SS
    CALLAHAN'S CROSSTIME SALOON   ROBINSON, SPIDER   AC
  FOREWORD   IN
    CALLAHAN'S CROSSTIME SALOON   ROBINSON, SPIDER   AC
  GUY WITH THE EYES, THE   SS ASF 73 02
    CALLAHAN'S CROSSTIME SALOON   ROBINSON, SPIDER   AC
  HALF AN OAF   NV
    ANALOG ANNUAL   BOVA, BEN   OA
  JUST DESSERT   SS
    CALLAHAN'S CROSSTIME SALOON   ROBINSON, SPIDER   AC
  LAW OF CONSERVATION OF PAIN, THE   NV VTX 74 12
    CALLAHAN'S CROSSTIME SALOON   ROBINSON, SPIDER   AC
  OVERDOSE   SS GAL 75 09
    BEST FROM GALAXY, THE VOLUME IV   BAEN, JAMES   AN
  TIME-TRAVELER, THE   NV ASF 74 04
    CALLAHAN'S CROSSTIME SALOON   ROBINSON, SPIDER   AC
  TWO HEADS ARE BETTER THAN ONE   SS ASF 75 05
    CALLAHAN'S CROSSTIME SALOON   ROBINSON, SPIDER   AC
  UNNATURAL CAUSES   NV ASF 75 10
    CALLAHAN'S CROSSTIME SALOON   ROBINSON, SPIDER   AC
  "VOICE IS HEARD IN RAMAH..., A"   SS ASF 75 11
    CALLAHAN'S CROSSTIME SALOON   ROBINSON, SPIDER   AC
  WONDERFUL CONSPIRACY, THE   SS
    CALLAHAN'S CROSSTIME SALOON   ROBINSON, SPIDER   AC

ROBISON, NANCY L.
  SPACE-SHUTTLE TRIP, A   SS YNW
    SCIENCE FICTION STORIES   BRADLEY, JOHANNA   AN

ROBLES, EDWARD G.
  SEE?   SS GAL 54 06
    FIFTY SHORT SCIENCE FICTION TALES   ASIMOV & CONKLIN AN

ROCKLIN, R. L.   SEE PSEUD. ROSS ROCKLYNNE

ROCKLYNNE, ROSS   PSEUD. FOR R. L. ROCKLIN
  MEN AND THE MIRROR, THE   AC ACE 73 02
  SUN DESTROYERS, THE   DC ACE 73 03
  ABYSS OF DARKNESS   NV AST 42 12
    SUN DESTROYERS, THE   ROCKLYNNE, ROSS   DC
  AND THEN THERE WAS ONE   SS ASF 40 02
    MEN AND THE MIRROR, THE   ROCKLYNNE, ROSS   AC
  AT THE CENTER OF GRAVITY   SS ASF 36 06
    EXPLORING OTHER WORLDS   MOSKOWITZ, SAM   AN
    MEN AND THE MIRROR, THE   ROCKLYNNE, ROSS   AC
  BACKFIRE   SS ASF 43 01
    OMNIBUS OF SCIENCE FICTION   CONKLIN, GROFF   AN

ROCKLYNNE, ROSS   (CONTINUED)
  BOTTLED MEN, THE   NV   ASF 46 06
    MEN AND THE MIRROR, THE   ROCKLYNNE, ROSS   AC
  CHING WITCH¡   SS   DVS 72 02
    AGAIN, DANGEROUS VISIONS   ELLISON, HARLAN   OA
  DAUGHTER OF DARKNESS   NA   AST 41 11
    SUN DESTROYERS, THE   ROCKLYNNE, ROSS   DC
  DIVERSIFAL, THE   SS   PLS 51 03
    BEST OF PLANET STORIES NO. 1, THE BRACKETT, LEIGH   AN
  EMPRESS OF MARS, THE   NV   FAD 39 05
    SPACE ODYSSEYS   ALDISS, BRIAN W.   AN
  FIND THE FACE   SS   GAL 68 09
    ELEVENTH GALAXY READER, THE   POHL, FREDERIK   AN
  IMMORTAL, THE   SS   CMT 41 03
    TOMORROW'S UNIVERSE   CAMPBELL, H. J.   AN
  INTO THE DARKNESS   NV   AST 40 06
    FUTURES UNLIMITED   NORTON, ALDEN H.   AN
    SUN DESTROYERS, THE   ROCKLYNNE, ROSS   DC
  JACKDAW   NV   ASF 42 08
    *BEST OF SCIENCE FICTION   CONKLIN, GROFF   AN
  JAYWALKER   SS   GAL 50 12
    FIRST STEP OUTWARD   HOSKINS, ROBERT   AN
    *GALAXY READER OF SCIENCE FICTION GOLD, H. L.   AN
  JUPITER TRAP   SS   ASF 37 08
    MEN AND THE MIRROR, THE   ROCKLYNNE, ROSS   AC
  MEN AND THE MIRROR, THE   NV   ASF 38 07
    BEFORE THE GOLDEN AGE   ASIMOV, ISAAC   AN
    MEN AND THE MIRROR, THE   ROCKLYNNE, ROSS   AC
  PRESSURE   SS   ASF 39 06
    *IMAGINATION UNLIMITED   BLEILER & DIKTY   AN
  QUIETUS   SS   ASF 40 09
    *ADVENTURES IN TIME AND SPACE   HEALY & MCCOMAS   AN
  RANDY-TANDY MAN   SS   UNI 73 03
    UNIVERSE 3   CARR, TERRY   OA
  REBEL OF THE DARKNESS (REVOLT OF THE DEVIL STAR) NV IMG 51 02
    SUN DESTROYERS, THE   ROCKLYNNE, ROSS   DC
  REVOLT OF THE DEVIL STAR (SEE REBEL OF THE DARKNESS)
                                                      TC
  THEY FLY SO HIGH   SS   AMZ 52 06
    HISTORY OF THE SCIENCE FICTION MAGAZINE, THE   PART 3 1946-1955
                                     ASHLEY, MICHAEL   AN
    MEN AND THE MIRROR, THE   ROCKLYNNE, ROSS   AC
  TIME WANTS A SKELETON   NV   ASF 41 06
    ASTOUNDING-ANALOG READER, THE VOLUME ONE
                                     HARRISON & ALDISS   AN
  WINNER TAKE ALL   NV
    *TIME TO COME   DERLETH, AUGUST   OA

RODDENBERRY, GENE
  FOREWORD   IN
    STAR TREK: THE NEW VOYAGES   MARSHAK, S&CULBREATH   OA

RODDENBERRY, MAJEL BARRETT
  INTRODUCTION TO VISIT TO A WEIRD PLANET REVISITED IN
    STAR TREK: THE NEW VOYAGES   MARSHAK, S&CULBREATH   OA

RODMAN, HOWARD
  MAN WHO WENT TO THE MOON- TWICE, THE   SS   DVS 67 01
    DANGEROUS VISIONS   ELLISON, HARLAN   OA

ROGERS, ALVA
  IN MEMORIAM- EDISON MARSHALL   MS
    NEBULA AWARD STORIES   NO. 4   ANDERSON, POUL   AN

ROGERS, ANGELA
  WHAT HAPPENED TO WILLIAM COOMBES   SS   NWR 76 28
    NEW WRITINGS IN SF. 28   BULMER, KENNETH   OA

ROGERS, IVIR
  FOREWORD TO "THE LIBRARY OF BABEL"   IN
    MIRROR OF INFINITY, THE   SILVERBERG, ROBERT   AN

ROGERS, JOEL T.
  BEYOND SPACE AND TIME   SS   SSS 50 09
    TREASURY OF GREAT SCIENCE FICTION, A VOL.1
                                     BOUCHER, ANTHONY   AN
  MOMENT WITHOUT TIME   NV   TWS 52 04
    BEST FROM STARTLING STORIES, THE MINES, SAMUEL   AN
  NO MATTER WHERE YOU GO   NV   FSF 59 02
    BEST FROM FANTASY AND SCIENCE FICTION: 9
                                     MILLS, ROBERT P.   AN

ROGERS, KAY
  EXPERIMENT   SS   FSF 53 02
    BEST FROM FANTASY AND SCIENCE FICTION: 3
                                     BOUCHER & MCCOMAS   AN

ROGERS, NORMAN L.
  CHARTING A BETTER VOYAGE- ZPG   AR
    VOYAGES: SCENARIOS FOR A SHIP CALLED EARTH
                                     SAUER, ROB   AN

ROGOZ, ADRIAN
  ALTAR OF THE RANDOM GODS, THE   SS
    VIEW FROM ANOTHER SHORE   ROTTENSTEINER, FRANZ AN

ROHMER, SAX   PSEUD. FOR ARTHUR SARSFIELD WARD
  CURSE OF A THOUSAND KISSES, THE   SS   AFR 48 07
    SECOND AVON FANTASY READER, THE WOLLHEIM &ERNSBERGER AN
  VALLEY OF THE SORCERESS, THE   SS
    ANCIENT MYSTERIES READER, THE   HAINING, PETER   AN

ROHRER, ROBERT
  KEEP THEM HAPPY   SS   FSF 65 04
    BEST FROM FANTASY AND SCIENCE FICTION: 15
                                     FERMAN, EDWARD L.   AN

ROHRER, ROBERT   (CONTINUED)
  MAN WHO FOUND PROTEUS, THE   SS   FAN 64 11
    10TH ANNUAL OF THE YEAR'S BEST S-F, THE
                                     MERRIL, JUDITH   AN

ROMANS, R. H.
  MOON CONQUERORS, THE   NO   SFQ 40 SU
    MOON CONQUERORS, THE   ANONYMOUS   AN

ROME, DAVID
  PARKY   SS   SCF 61 08
    7TH ANNUAL OF THE YEAR'S BEST S-F, THE MERRIL, JUDITH   AN
  REPRESENTATIVE   SS   NWR 68 13
    NEW WRITINGS IN SF. 13   CARNELL, JOHN   OA
  ROBINSON   SS
    SECOND PACIFIC BOOK OF SCIENCE FICTION, THE
                                     BAXTER, JOHN   AN
  THERE'S A STARMAN IN WARD 7   SS   NWS 65 01
    11TH ANNUAL OF THE YEAR'S BEST S-F, THE
                                     MERRIL, JUDITH   AN
  THEY SHALL REAP   NV   NWR 68 12
    NEW WRITINGS IN SF. 8   CARNELL, JOHN   AN
    NEW WRITINGS IN SF. 12   CARNELL, JOHN   OA

RONAN, COLIN
  MAN'S EXPANDING VIEW OF SPACE   AR
    BEYOND THIS HORIZON   CARRELL, CHRISTOPHER OA

ROONEY, GRACE
  TEETH   SS   ORB 74 13
    ORBIT 13   KNIGHT, DAMON   OA

ROSE, MARK
  WE WOULD SEE A SIGN   SS   NEW 64 AN
    SPECTRUM 3   AMIS & CONQUEST   AN

ROSELLE, DANIEL
  TRANSFORMATIONS   AN   FPR 73 12
    UNDERSTANDING WORLD HISTORY THROUGH SCIENCE FICTION
  TRANSFORMATIONS II   AN   FAW 74 11
    UNDERSTANDING AMERICAN HISTORY THROUGH SCIENCE FICTION
  INTRODUCTION   IN
    TRANSFORMATIONS II   ROSELLE, DANIEL   AN

ROSMOND, BABETTE
  ARE YOU RUN-DOWN, TIRED-   SS C UNK 42 10
    SUPERNATURAL READER, THE   CONKLIN, G&L.   AN
  ERROR HURLED   NO
    SCIENCE FICTION DISCOVERIES   POHL, C. & F.   OA

ROSNER, SARA
  OTHER DIMENSION, THE   AN   SBS 72 11

ROSNY, J. H. (AINE)
  ANOTHER WORLD (1895)   NV   RVP 95
    CENTURY OF SCIENCE FICTION, A   KNIGHT, DAMON   AN
  SHAPES, THE   SS
    ONE HUNDRED YEARS OF SCIENCE FICTION KNIGHT, DAMON   AN

ROSOKHOVATSKY, IGOR
  DESERT ENCOUNTER   SS
    RUSSIAN SCIENCE FICTION, 1968   MAGIDOFF, ROBERT   AN
  ONE LESS   SS   66
    ULTIMATE THRESHOLD, THE   GINSBURG, MIRRA   AN
  WHEN YOU RETURN   NV   67
    ULTIMATE THRESHOLD, THE   GINSBURG, MIRRA   AN

ROSS, JOSEPH   PSEUD. FOR JOSEPH WROCZ
  BEST OF AMAZING, THE   AN H DBL 67
  FOREWORD   IN
    BEST OF AMAZING, THE   ROSS, JOSEPH   AN

ROTHMAN, MILTON A.   ALSO AS   LEE GREGOR
  FUSION   NV   STL 74 01
    STELLAR 1   DEL REY, JUDY-LYNN   OA
  GETTING TOGETHER   SS   GAL 72 03
    BEST FROM GALAXY, THE VOLUME I GALAXY, EDITORS OF   AN
    BEST SCIENCE FICTION FOR 1973   ACKERMAN, FORREST J.   AN
  HEAVY PLANET   SS   ASF 39 08
    JUPITER   POHL, C. & F.   AN
    WHERE DO WE GO FROM HERE?   ASIMOV, ISAAC   AN
    WORLDS OF WONDER   HARRISON, HARRY   AN

ROTSLER, WILLIAM
  BEST SF: 1972   CT
    BEST SF: 1972   HARRISON & ALDISS   AN
  BOHASSIAN LEARNS   SS   AMZ 71 07
    SCHOOL AND SOCIETY THROUGH SCIENCE FICTION
                                     OLANDER/GREENBERG/& AN
  EPIC   NV
    FUTURE PASTIMES   EDELSTEIN, SCOTT   OA
  KONG PAPERS, THE   SS C KNT 73 04
    PARTNERS IN WONDER   ELLISON, HARLAN   AC
  PATRON OF THE ARTS   NV   UNI 72 02
    BEST SCIENCE FICTION OF THE YEAR, THE NO. 2
                                     CARR, TERRY   AN
    BEST SCIENCE FICTION STORIES OF THE YEAR (1972)
                                     DEL REY, LESTER   AN
    NEBULA AWARD STORIES   8   ASIMOV, ISAAC   AN
    UNIVERSE 2   CARR, TERRY   OA

ROTTENSTEINER, FRANZ
  VIEW FROM ANOTHER SHORE   AN H SEA 73
  INTRODUCTION   IN
    VIEW FROM ANOTHER SHORE   ROTTENSTEINER, FRANZ AN

ROUNDS, EMMA   RUSSELL, ERIC FRANK

ROUNDS, EMMA
  PLANE GEOMETRY   PM   25
    FANTASIA MATHEMATICA   FADIMAN, CLIFTON   AN
ROUSSEAU, VICTOR   PSEUD. FOR VICTOR ROUSSEAU EMANUEL
  CRY FROM BEYOND, A   NV   STT 31 09
    FANTASTIC PULPS, THE   HAINING, PETER   AN
RUBIN, RICK
  WINTER IN THIS LATITUDE   NV   PBY 62 12
    MASKS   PLAYBOY, EDITORS OF   AN
RUBY, B. F.
  THING IN THE WOODS, THE   SS C AMZ 35 02
    OMNIBUS OF SCIENCE FICTION   CONKLIN, GROFF   AN
RUD, A. M.
  OOZE   NV   WRT 23 03
    MOON TERROR, THE   BIRCH, A. G.   AN
RUHEN, OLAF
  IMMORTAL, THE   SS
    SECOND PACIFIC BOOK OF SCIENCE FICTION, THE
                       BAXTER, JOHN   AN
RUNYON, CHARLES W.
  DREAM PATROL   SS   FSF 70 02
    BEST FROM FANTASY AND SCIENCE FICTION: 19
                       FERMAN, EDWARD L.   AN
  SWEET HELEN   SS   FSF 69 09
    TWENTY YEARS OF FANTASY & SCIENCE FICTION
                       FERMAN & MILLS   AN
RUSH, NORMAN
  CLOSING WITH NATURE   SS   MRV 70
    RUINS OF EARTH, THE   DISCH, THOMAS M.   AN
  FIGHTING FASCISM   SS   BMR 73
    BAD MOON RISING   DISCH, THOMAS M.   OA
  RIDING   SS   BMR 73
    BAD MOON RISING   DISCH, THOMAS M.   OA
RUSS, J. J.
  AURELIA   SS   FCR 75
    FUTURE CORRUPTION   ELWOOD, ROGER   OA
  M IS FOR THE MANY   SS   UNI 74 05
    UNIVERSE 5   CARR, TERRY   OA
RUSS, JOANNA
  ALYX   AC H GRG 76 06
  ADVENTURESS, THE (ALSO AS BLUESTOCKING)   NV   ORB 67 02
    ORBIT 2   KNIGHT, DAMON   OA
  BARBARIAN, THE   NV   ORB 68 03
    ALYX   RUSS, JOANNA   AC
  ANOTHER WORLD   DOZOIS, GARDNER R.   AN
    ORBIT 3   KNIGHT, DAMON   OA
  BLUESTOCKING (THE ADVENTURESS)   NV   ORB 67 02
    ALYX   RUSS, JOANNA   AC
  CORRUPTION   SS
    AURORA: BEYOND EQUALITY MCINTYRE & ANDERSON   OA
  DADDY'S GIRL   SS   NWB 75 09
    NEW WORLDS NINE   BAILEY, HILARY   OA
  EXISTENCE   SS   EPC 75
    EPOCH   ELWOOD & SILVERBERG   OA
  EXPERIMENTER, THE   NV   GAL 75 10
    BEST FROM GALAXY, THE VOLUME IV BAEN, JAMES   AN
  FEW THINGS I KNOW ABOUT WHILEAWAY, A (FROM "THE FEMALE MAN")
                                                   EX   BAN 75
    NEW IMPROVED SUN, THE   DISCH, THOMAS M.   AN
  GENRE   AR   CLR 71 01
    CLARION   WILSON, ROBIN SCOTT   OA
  GLEEPSITE   SS   ORB 71 09
    BEST FROM ORBIT, THE   KNIGHT, DAMON   AN
    ORBIT 9   KNIGHT, DAMON   OA
  1972 ANNUAL WORLD'S BEST SF, THE WOLLHEIM, DONALD A.   AN
  HE-MAN ETHOS IN SCIENCE FICTION, THE   AR   CLR 72 02
    CLARION II   WILSON, ROBIN SCOTT   OA
  I GAVE HER SACK AND SHERRY (ALSO AS I THOUGHT SHE WAS AFEARED
    TILL SHE STROKED MY BEARD)   NV   ORB 67 02
    BEST FROM ORBIT, THE   KNIGHT, DAMON   AN
    ORBIT 2   KNIGHT, DAMON   OA
  I THOUGHT SHE WAS AFEARED TILL SHE STROKED MY BEARD (I GAVE
    HER SACK AND SHERRY)   NV   ORB 67 02
    ALYX   RUSS, JOANNA   AC
  INTRODUCTION   IN
    TALES AND STORIES   SHELLEY, MARY W.   AC
  MAN WHO COULD NOT SEE DEVILS, THE   SS   ANA 70
    ALCHEMY AND ACADEME   MCCAFFREY, ANNE   OA
    THOSE WHO CAN: A SCIENCE FICTION READER
                       WILSON, ROBIN SCOTT   AN
  MY BOAT   SS   FSF 76 01
    1977 ANNUAL WORLD'S BEST SF, THE WOLLHEIM, DONALD A.   AN
  MY DEAR EMILY   NV   FSF 62 07
    BEST FROM FANTASY AND SCIENCE FICTION: 12
                       DAVIDSON, AVRAM   AN
  NOBODY'S HOME   SS   NDM 72 02
    BEST SCIENCE FICTION OF THE YEAR, THE NO. 2
                       CARR, TERRY   AN
    NEW DIMENSIONS 2   SILVERBERG, ROBERT   OA
    WOMEN OF WONDER   SARGENT, PAMELA   AN
  OLD FASHIONED GIRL, AN   SS   FST 74
    FINAL STAGE   FERMAN & MALZBERG   OA
  ON SETTING   AR
    THOSE WHO CAN: A SCIENCE FICTION READER
                       WILSON, ROBIN SCOTT   AN
  PASSAGES   AR   GAL 74 01
    BEST FROM GALAXY, THE VOLUME III BAEN, JAMES   AN

RUSS, JOANNA   (CONTINUED)
  PICNIC ON PARADISE   NO   ACE 68
    ALYX   RUSS, JOANNA   AC
  POOR MAN, BEGGER MAN   NV   UNI 71 01
    NEBULA AWARD STORIES NO. 7 BIGGLE, LLOYD JR.   AN
    UNIVERSE 1   CARR, TERRY   OA
  REASONABLE PEOPLE   SS   ORB 74 14
    ORBIT 14   KNIGHT, DAMON   OA
  SECOND INQUISITION, THE   NV   ORB 70 06
    ALYX   RUSS, JOANNA   AC
    IN DREAMS AWAKE   FIEDLER, LESLIE A.   AN
    MORE WOMEN OF WONDER   SARGENT, PAMELA   AN
    NEBULA AWARD STORIES NO. 6 SIMAK, CLIFFORD D.   AN
    ORBIT 6   KNIGHT, DAMON   OA
  SOUL OF A SERVANT, THE   SS   SCS 73
    SHOWCASE   ELWOOD, ROGER   OA
  THIS NIGHT, AT MY FIRE   SS   EPO 66 WI
    POCKETFUL OF STARS, A   KNIGHT, DAMON   AN
  USEFUL PHRASES FOR THE TOURIST   SS   UNI 72 02
    FUTURE PASTIMES   EDELSTEIN, SCOTT   OA
    INFINITE JESTS   SILVERBERG, ROBERT   AN
    UNIVERSE 2   CARR, TERRY   OA
  VIEW FROM THE WINDOW, THE   NV   QRK 70 01
    QUARK/1   DELANY & HACKER   OA
  WHEN IT CHANGED   SS   DVS 72 02
    AGAIN, DANGEROUS VISIONS ELLISON, HARLAN   OA
    MARRIAGE AND THE FAMILY THROUGH SCIENCE FICTION
                       CLEAR/WARRICK/&   AN
    NEBULA AWARD STORIES 8 ASIMOV, ISAAC   AN
  WINDOW DRESSING   SS   NEW 70 01
    NEW WORLDS OF FANTASY NO. 2 CARR, TERRY   AN
  ZANZIBAR CAT, THE   SS   QRK 71 03
    QUARK/3   DELANY & HACKER   OA

RUSSELL, BERTRAND
  DR. SOUTHPORT VULPES'S NIGHTMARE (FROM "NIGHTMARES OF
    EMINENT PERSONS")   EX
    ARMCHAIR SCIENCE READER, THE   GORDON, I. & SORKIN   AN
  MATHEMATICIAN'S NIGHTMARE: THE VISION OF PROFESSOR SQUAREPUNT
                                                   SS   55
    MATHEMATICAL MAGPIE, THE   FADIMAN, CLIFTON   AN
  PLANETARY EFFULGENCE   SS   61
    8TH ANNUAL OF THE YEAR'S BEST S-F, THE MERRIL, JUDITH   AN

RUSSELL, ERIC FRANK   ALSO AS   MAURICE G. HUGI
  DARK TIDES   AC H DOB 62
  DEEP SPACE   AC H FPS 54
    BANTAM 1955 EDITION OMITS "FIRST PERSON SINGULAR"
  FAR STARS   AC H DOB 61
  LIKE NOTHING ON EARTH   AC H DOB 75
  MEN, MARTIANS AND MACHINES   AC H DOB 55
  SIX WORLDS YONDER   DC ACE 58
  SOMEWHERE A VOICE   AC H DOB 65
  AFTERNOON OF A FAHN (ALSO AS RAINBOW'S END)   SS   IMG 51 04
    ALIEN WORLDS   ELWOOD, ROGER   AN
  ALLAMAGOOSA   SS   ASF 55 05
    FAR STARS   RUSSELL, ERIC FRANK   AC
    GREAT STORIES OF SPACE TRAVEL CONKLIN, GROFF   AN
    HUGO WINNERS, THE (VOLUME 1) ASIMOV, ISAAC   AN
    SECOND ORBIT   DOHERTY, G. D.   AN
    TALES OF SCIENCE FICTION BALL, BRIAN N.   AN
  AND STILL IT MOVES   AR   ASF 57 06
    14 GREAT TALES OF ESP   STONE, IDELLA P.   AN
  AND THEN THERE WERE NONE   NV   ASF 51 06
    SCIENCE FICTION HALL OF FAME VOLUME 2A BOVA, BEN   AN
    SCIENCE FICTION: THE GREAT YEARS POHL, C. & F.   AN
    *STORIES FOR TOMORROW   SLOANE, WILLIAM   AN
    YEAR'S BEST SCIENCE FICTION NOVELS: 1952
                       BLEILER & DIKTY   AN
  APPOINTMENT AT NOON   SS   AMZ 54 03
    FIFTY SHORT SCIENCE FICTION TALES ASIMOV & CONKLIN   AN
  ARMY COMES TO VENUS, THE   NV   FUN 59 05
    GODS FOR TOMORROW   SANTESSON, HANS S.   AN
  BASIC RIGHT   NV   ASF 58 04
    GIANTS UNLEASHED   CONKLIN, GROFF   AN
  BIG SHOT, THE   SS   WRT 49 01
    UNEXPECTED, THE   MARGULIES, LEO   AN
  BITTER END   SS   SFP 53 12
    DARK TIDES   RUSSELL, ERIC FRANK   AC
    SPACE MAGICIANS, THE   NORTON & MOSKOWITZ   AN
  TOMORROW, AND TOMORROW, AND TOMORROW...
                       HEINTZ/HERBERT/JOOS/   AN
    UNTRAVELLED WORLDS   BARTER & WILSON   AN
  BOOMERANG (A GREAT DEAL OF POWER)   SS   FUN 53 08
    INVASION OF THE ROBOTS   ELWOOD, ROGER   AN
    *SCIENCE FICTION THINKING MACHINES CONKLIN, GROFF   AN
  CASE FOR EARTH, THE   SS   FUT 58 04
    NOW & BEYOND   HOWARD, IVAN   AN
  COSMIC RELIC, THE   NV   FAN 61 06
    HUMAN ZERO, THE   MOSKOWITZ & ELWOOD   AN
  DEAR DEVIL   NV   OWS 50 05
    *BIG BOOK OF SCIENCE FICTION CONKLIN, GROFF   AN
    CREATURES FROM BEYOND   CARR, TERRY   AN
    EARTHMEN AND STRANGERS   SILVERBERG, ROBERT   AN
    GENTLE INVADERS   SANTESSON, HANS S.   AN
    SOMEWHERE A VOICE   RUSSELL, ERIC FRANK   AC
    SPACE, SPACE, SPACE   SLOANE, WILLIAM   AN
  DESIGN FOR GREAT DAY (SEE THE ULTIMATE INVADER) TC
  DIABOLOGIC   SS   ASF 55 03
    CONNOISSEUR'S S. F.   BOARDMAN, TOM JR.   AN
    FAR STARS   RUSSELL, ERIC FRANK   AC
    SIX WORLDS YONDER   RUSSELL, ERIC FRANK   DC
  DISPLACED PERSON   SS   WRT 48 09
    SOMEWHERE A VOICE   RUSSELL, ERIC FRANK   AC
    WORLDS FAR AND NEAR   CARR, TERRY   AN

RUSSELL, ERIC FRANK   RUSSELL, RAY

RUSSELL, ERIC FRANK   (CONTINUED)
  EARLY BIRD   NV SFS 57 11
    MASTERS OF SCIENCE FICTION   HOWARD, IVAN   AN
  EXPOSURE   SS ASF 50 07
    LIKE NOTHING ON EARTH   RUSSELL, ERIC FRANK   AC
    OPERATION FUTURE   CONKLIN, GROFF   AN
  FAST FALLS THE EVENTIDE   SS ASF 52 05
    BEST SCIENCE-FICTION STORIES: 1953, THE
                                   BLEILER & DIKTY   AN
  FIRST PERSON SINGULAR   NV TWS 50 10
    DEEP SPACE   RUSSELL, ERIC FRANK   AC
  GLASS EYE, THE   SS ASF 49 03
    *BEYOND HUMAN KEN   MERRIL, JUDITH   AN
  GREAT DEAL OF POWER, A (SEE BOOMERANG)   TC
  GREAT RADIO PERIL, THE   SS ASF 37 04
    ABOVE THE HUMAN LANDSCAPE   MCNELLY & STOVER   AN
  HEAV'N, HEAV'N   SS FUT 56 30
    NOW & BEYOND   HOWARD, IVAN   AN
  HOBBYIST   NV ASF 47 09
    *ASTOUNDING SCIENCE FICTION ANTHOLOGY, THE
                                   CAMPBELL, JOHN W. JR AN
    ASTOUNDING TALES OF SPACE AND TIME   CAMPBELL, JOHN W. JR AN
    BEST SF 4   CRISPIN, EDMUND   AN
    DECADE THE 1940S   ALDISS & HARRISON   AN
    *FIRST ASTOUNDING SCIENCE FICTION ANTHOLOGY, THE
                                   CAMPBELL, JOHN W. JR AN
    LIKE NOTHING ON EARTH   RUSSELL, ERIC FRANK   AC
  HOMO SAPS   SS ASF 41 12
    DEEP SPACE   RUSSELL, ERIC FRANK   AC
  I AM NOTHING   SS ASF 52 07
    BEST SCIENCE-FICTION STORIES: 1953, THE
                                   BLEILER & DIKTY   AN
    FRONTIERS IN SPACE   BLEILER & DIKTY   AN
    SOMEWHERE A VOICE   RUSSELL, ERIC FRANK   AC
  I HEAR YOU CALLING   SS SCF 54 12
    DARK TIDES   RUSSELL, ERIC FRANK   AC
  I'M A STRANGER HERE MYSELF   SS OWS 52 03
    DARK TIDES   RUSSELL, ERIC FRANK   AC
  ILLUSIONARIES, THE   SS PLS 51 11
    SPACE PIONEERS   NORTON, ANDRE   AN
  IMPULSE   SS ASF 38 09
    *INVADERS OF EARTH   CONKLIN, GROFF   AN
    *TWISTED   CONKLIN, GROFF   AN
  INTO YOUR TENT I'LL CREEP   SS ASF 57 09
    BEST SCIENCE FICTION STORIES AND NOVELS: 9TH SERIES
                                   DIKTY, T. E.   AN
    LIKE NOTHING ON EARTH   RUSSELL, ERIC FRANK   AC
    SIX WORLDS YONDER   RUSSELL, ERIC FRANK   DC
  INTRODUCTION   IN
    DARK TIDES   RUSSELL, ERIC FRANK   AC
  JAY SCORE   SS ASF 41 05
    MEN, MARTIANS AND MACHINES   RUSSELL, ERIC FRANK   AC
    TOMORROW, THE STARS   HEINLEIN, ROBERT A.   AN
  LAST BLAST   NV ASF 52 11
    DEEP SPACE   RUSSELL, ERIC FRANK   AC
  LATE NIGHT FINAL   NV ASF 48 12
    *ASTOUNDING SCIENCE FICTION ANTHOLOGY, THE
                                   CAMPBELL, JOHN W. JR AN
    ASTOUNDING TALES OF SPACE AND TIME   CAMPBELL, JOHN W. JR AN
    *SECOND ASTOUNDING SCIENCE FICTION ANTHOLOGY, THE
                                   CAMPBELL, JOHN W. JR AN
  LEGWORK   NV ASF 56 04
    FAR STARS   RUSSELL, ERIC FRANK   AC
    5 UNEARTHLY VISIONS   CONKLIN, GROFF   AN
  LITTLE OIL, A   NV GAL 52 10
    DEEP SPACE   RUSSELL, ERIC FRANK   AC
    SCIENCE FICTION THROUGH THE AGES 2   EVANS, I. O.   AN
  LOVE STORY   SS ASF 57 08
    ABC OF SCIENCE FICTION, AN   BOARDMAN, TOM JR.   AN
  MATTER OF INSTINCT, A   SS
    DARK TIDES   RUSSELL, ERIC FRANK   AC
  ME AND MY SHADOW   SS SRS 40 02
    DARK TIDES   RUSSELL, ERIC FRANK   AC
  MECHANICAL MICE, THE (AS MAURICE G. HUGI)   NV ASF 41 01
    LIKE NOTHING ON EARTH   RUSSELL, ERIC FRANK   AC
  MECHANISTRIA   NV ASF 42 01
    MEN, MARTIANS AND MACHINES   RUSSELL, ERIC FRANK   AC
  MESMERICA   NV NEW 56 AC
    MEN, MARTIANS AND MACHINES   RUSSELL, ERIC FRANK   AC
  METAMORPHOSITE   NV ASF 46 12
    *BEACHHEADS IN SPACE   DERLETH, AUGUST   AN
    JOURNEY TO INFINITY   GREENBERG , MARTIN   AN
  MINOR INGREDIENT   SS ASF 56 03
    PROLOGUE TO ANALOG   CAMPBELL, JOHN W. JR AN
  MUTEN   SS ASF 48 10
    *SCIENCE-FICTION CARNIVAL   BROWN, F. & REYNOLDS   AN
  NOTHING NEW   SS ASF 55 01
    LIKE NOTHING ON EARTH   RUSSELL, ERIC FRANK   AC
    SIX WORLDS YONDER   RUSSELL, ERIC FRANK   DC
  NOW INHALE   NV ASF 59 04
    13 ABOVE THE NIGHT   CONKLIN, GROFF   AN
  P.S.   SS NEB 58 05
    FAR STARS   RUSSELL, ERIC FRANK   AC
  PANIC BUTTON   SS ASF 59 11
    SEVEN COME INFINITY   CONKLIN, GROFF   AN
  PLUS X   NV ASF 56 06
    FOUR FOR THE FUTURE   CONKLIN, GROFF   AN
  PONDERER, THE   SS WRT 48 11
    DARK TIDES   RUSSELL, ERIC FRANK   AC
  PRESENT FROM JOE, A   SS ASF 49 02
    BEST SF   CRISPIN, EDMUND   AN
    SCIENCE FICTION   BURTON, S. H.   AN
  RAINBOW'S END (AFTERNOON OF A FAHN)   SS IMG 51 04
    DEEP SPACE   RUSSELL, ERIC FRANK   AC
  RHYTHM OF THE RATS   SS WRT 50 07
    DARK TIDES   RUSSELL, ERIC FRANK   AC

RUSSELL, ERIC FRANK   (CONTINUED)
  SEAT OF OBLIVION   SS ASF 41 11
    SOMEWHERE A VOICE   RUSSELL, ERIC FRANK   AC
  SECOND GENESIS   SS 51
    DEEP SPACE   RUSSELL, ERIC FRANK   AC
    NEW WRITINGS IN SF. 9   CARNELL, JOHN   OA
  SEEKER OF TOMORROW   SN C ASF 37 07
    HISTORY OF THE SCIENCE FICTION MAGAZINE, THE PART 2 1936-1945
                                   ASHLEY, MICHAEL   AN
    SCIENCE FICTION OF THE 30'S   KNIGHT, DAMON   AN
  SIN OF HYACINTH PEUCH, THE   NV FAN 52 FL
    DARK TIDES   RUSSELL, ERIC FRANK   AC
    OTHER WORLDS, OTHER TIMES   MOSKOWITZ & ELWOOD   AN
  SOLE SOLUTION   SS FUN 56 04
    DARK TIDES   RUSSELL, ERIC FRANK   AC
    PENGUIN SCIENCE FICTION   ALDISS, BRIAN W.   AN
  SOMEWHERE A VOICE   NV OWS 53 01
    SOMEWHERE A VOICE   RUSSELL, ERIC FRANK   AC
  SPIRO (VENTURER OF THE MARTIAN MIMICS)   NV WRT 47 03
    *OTHER SIDE OF THE MOON, THE   DERLETH, AUGUST   AN
  STILL LIFE (STUDY IN STILL LIFE)   SS ASF 59 01
    ANOTHER PART OF THE GALAXY   CONKLIN, GROFF   AN
  STUDY IN STILL LIFE (SEE STILL LIFE)   TC
  SYMBIOTICA   NV ASF 43 10
    *ADVENTURES IN TIME AND SPACE HEALY & MCCOMAS   AN
    MEN, MARTIANS AND MACHINES   RUSSELL, ERIC FRANK   AC
  TAKE A SEAT   SS STS 52 05
    HUMAN?   MERRIL, JUDITH   AN
  TEST PIECE   SS OWS 51 03
    HUMAN AND OTHER BEINGS   DEGRAEFF, ALLEN   AN
    OMNIBUS OF SCIENCE FICTION   CONKLIN, GROFF   AN
    SCIENCE FICTION OMNIBUS   CONKLIN, GROFF   AN
  THIS ONE'S ON ME   SS NEB 53 FL
    DARK TIDES   RUSSELL, ERIC FRANK   AC
    *SCIENCE FICTION ADVENTURES IN MUTATION CONKLIN, GROFF AN
  TIELINE   SS ASF 55 07
    SIX WORLDS YONDER   RUSSELL, ERIC FRANK   DC
    SOMEWHERE A VOICE   RUSSELL, ERIC FRANK   AC
  TIMELESS ONES, THE   SS SFQ 52 11
    FAR STARS   RUSSELL, ERIC FRANK   AC
    PRIZE SCIENCE FICTION   WOLLHEIM, DONALD A.   AN
  TIMID TIGER, THE   SS ASF 47 02
    DEEP SPACE   RUSSELL, ERIC FRANK   AC
  TOP SECRET   SS ASF 56 08
    SIX WORLDS YONDER   RUSSELL, ERIC FRANK   DC
  U-TURN   SS ASF 50 04
    SOMEWHERE A VOICE   RUSSELL, ERIC FRANK   AC
  ULTIMA THULE   SS ASF 51 10
    BEST SF 7   CRISPIN, EDMUND   AN
    LIKE NOTHING ON EARTH   RUSSELL, ERIC FRANK   AC
    LOOKING FORWARD   LESSER, MILTON   AN
  ULTIMATE INVADER, THE (DESIGN FOR GREAT-DAY) NO PLS 53 01
    ULTIMATE INVADER, AND OTHER SCIENCE FICTION, THE
                                   WOLLHEIM, DONALD A.   DA
  UNDECIDED, THE   NV ASF 49 04
    DEEP SPACE   RUSSELL, ERIC FRANK   AC
  VENTURER OF THE MARTIAN MIMICS (SEE SPIRO)   TC TOW 40 FL
  WAITABITS, THE   NV ASF 55 07
    ASTOUNDING-ANALOG READER, THE VOLUME TWO
                                   HARRISON & ALDISS   AN
    BEST SF 6   CRISPIN, EDMUND   AN
    FAR STARS   RUSSELL, ERIC FRANK   AC
    SIX WORLDS YONDER   RUSSELL, ERIC FRANK   DC
  WISEL   SS
    DARK TIDES   RUSSELL, ERIC FRANK   AC
  WITH A BLUNT INSTRUMENT   SS UNK 41 12
    DARK TIDES   RUSSELL, ERIC FRANK   AC
  WITNESS, THE   SS OWS 51 09
    DEEP SPACE   RUSSELL, ERIC FRANK   AC
    MODERN MASTERPIECES OF SCIENCE FICTION MOSKOWITZ, SAM AN
    VORTEX BLASTERS, THE   MOSKOWITZ, SAM   AN

RUSSELL, RAY   ALSO AS   BRIAN BENCELAW AND ROGER THORNE
  SAGITTARIUS   AC PBP 71
  SARDONICUS AND OTHER STORIES   AC BAL 61
  ACTOR, THE   SS PBY 60 03
    SARDONICUS AND OTHER STORIES   RUSSELL, RAY   AC
  BETTER MAN, THE   SS PBY 66 07
    FIEND, THE   PLAYBOY, EDITORS OF   AN
    WILDERNESS OF STARS, A   NOLAN, WILLIAM F.   AN
  BOOKED SOLID   SS 61
    SARDONICUS AND OTHER STORIES   RUSSELL, RAY   AC
  CAGE, THE   SS 59
    SARDONICUS AND OTHER STORIES   RUSSELL, RAY   AC
  COMET WINE   NV PBY 67 03
    NEW WORLDS OF FANTASY   CARR, TERRY   AN
    PLAYBOY BOOK OF HORROR AND THE SUPERNATURAL, THE
                                   PLAYBOY, EDITORS OF   AN
    SAGITTARIUS   RUSSELL, RAY   AC
  DARWIN SAMPLER, THE   SS FIN 70
    FUTURE IS NOW, THE   NOLAN, WILLIAM F.   OA
  EXPLOITS OF ARGO, THE (ALSO AS THE LONG NIGHT) SS ROG 61 04
    SARDONICUS AND OTHER STORIES   RUSSELL, RAY   AC
  HERE COMES JOHN HENRY   SS PBY 68 09
    DEAD ASTRONAUT, 10 STORIES OF SPACE FLIGHT, THE
                                   PLAYBOY, EDITORS OF   AN
  HIS FATHER'S HOUSE   SS IFS 60 03
    SARDONICUS AND OTHER STORIES   RUSSELL, RAY   AC
  I AM RETURNING   SS 61
    SARDONICUS AND OTHER STORIES   RUSSELL, RAY   AC
  SEA OF SPACE, A   NOLAN, WILLIAM F.   AN
  INCOMMUNICADO   SS FSF 57 11
    SARDONICUS AND OTHER STORIES   RUSSELL, RAY   AC
  LAST WILL AND TESTAMENT   SS 55
    SARDONICUS AND OTHER STORIES   RUSSELL, RAY   AC

RUSSELL, RAY   (CONTINUED)
  LONDON CALLING   SS   61
    SARDONICUS AND OTHER STORIES   RUSSELL, RAY   AC
  LONG NIGHT, THE (THE EXPLOITS OF ARGO)   SS   ROG 61 04
    7TH ANNUAL OF THE YEAR'S BEST S-F, THE MERRIL, JUDITH   AN
  MONTAGE   SS   PBY 58 10
    SARDONICUS AND OTHER STORIES   RUSSELL, RAY   AC
  MOST PRIMATIVE, THE   SS   FUC 73
    FUTURE CITY   ELWOOD, ROGER   OA
  NAKED IN XANADU   NV   PBY 64 11
    SAGITTARIUS   RUSSELL, RAY   AC
  NIGHT IN THE BYZANTINE PALACE, A   SS   PBY
    SAGITTARIUS   RUSSELL, RAY   AC
  OUNCE OF PREVENTION   SS   PBY 60 09
    SAGITTARIUS   RUSSELL, RAY   AC
    SARDONICUS AND OTHER STORIES   RUSSELL, RAY   AC
  PLEASURE WAS OURS, THE   SS   IMG 55 05
    SARDONICUS AND OTHER STORIES   RUSSELL, RAY   AC
  PUT THEM ALL TOGETHER, THEY SPELL MONSTER   SS   PBY 56 10
    FULLY AUTOMATED LOVE LIFE OF HENRY KEANRIDGE
                                      PLAYBOY, EDITORS OF AN
    SF:57, THE YEAR'S GREATEST SCIENCE FICTION AND FANTASY
                                      MERRIL, JUDITH   AN
  RIPPLES   SS   PBY 67 10
    PLAYBOY'S STORIES OF THE SINISTER & STRANGE
                                      PLAYBOY, EDITORS OF AN
    SAGITTARIUS   RUSSELL, RAY   AC
  ROOM, THE   SS   PBY 61 02
    MAN AGAINST TOMORROW   NOLAN, WILLIAM F.   AN
    PLAYBOY BOOK OF SCIENCE FICTION AND FANTASY, THE
                                      PLAYBOY, EDITORS OF AN
    SAGITTARIUS   RUSSELL, RAY   AC
    SARDONICUS AND OTHER STORIES   RUSSELL, RAY   AC
  ROSEBUD, THE   SS   FSF 59 08
    SARDONICUS AND OTHER STORIES   RUSSELL, RAY   AC
  SAGITTARIUS   NA   PBY 62 03
    SAGITTARIUS   RUSSELL, RAY   AC
  SARDONICUS   NA   PBY 61 01
    PLAYBOY BOOK OF HORROR AND THE SUPERNATURAL, THE
                                      PLAYBOY, EDITORS OF AN
    SAGITTARIUS   RUSSELL, RAY   AC
    SARDONICUS AND OTHER STORIES   RUSSELL, RAY   AC
  SPACE OPERA   SS   PBY 61 12
    FULLY AUTOMATED LOVE LIFE OF HENRY KEANRIDGE
                                      PLAYBOY, EDITORS OF AN
  SWORD OF LAERTES, THE   SS   59
    SARDONICUS AND OTHER STORIES   RUSSELL, RAY   AC
  TAKE A DEEP BREATH   SS   TIG 56
    SARDONICUS AND OTHER STORIES   RUSSELL, RAY   AC
  XONG OF XUXAN   SS   PBY 70 10
    CRISIS   ELWOOD, ROGER   OA
    WEIRD SHOW   PLAYBOY, EDITORS OF AN
    WONDERMAKERS 2   HOSKINS, ROBERT   AN

RUSSELL, WILLIAM M.
  THREE BROTHERS, THE   SS   LOB 54 12
    AD 2500   WILSON, ANGUS   AN

RYMER, G. A.
  ATAVISTS, THE   SS
    AD 2500   WILSON, ANGUS   AN

RYNAS, STEPHEN A.   SEE PSEUD. STEPHEN ARR

SAARI, OLIVER E.
  SITTING DUCK   SS   ASF 52 01
    EVERY BOY'S BOOK OF OUTER SPACE STORIES
                                      DIKTY, T. E.   AN
  UNDER THE SAND-SEAS   SS   SSS 41 01
    GREAT SCIENCE FICTION STORIES ABOUT MARS
                                      DIKTY, T. E.   AN

SABAH, VICTOR
  IMAGINARY JOURNEY TO THE MOON, AN   SS   NEW 72 AN
    BEST SF: 1972   HARRISON & ALDISS   AN

SABERHAGEN, FRED
  BERSERKER   AC   BAL 67 01
  BOOK OF SABERHAGEN, THE   AC   DAW 75 01
  BERSERKER'S PREY (SEE PRESSURE)   TC
  CALENDARS   SS   GAL 74 01
    BOOK OF SABERHAGEN, THE   SABERHAGEN, FRED   AC
  DEEP SPACE   SS
    BOOK OF SABERHAGEN, THE   SABERHAGEN, FRED   AC
  FACE OF THE DEEP, THE   SS   IFS 66 09
    BERSERKER   SABERHAGEN, FRED   AC
  FORTRESS SHIP (ALSO AS WITHOUT A THOUGHT)   SS   IFS 63 01
    9TH ANNUAL OF THE YEAR'S BEST S-F, THE MERRIL, JUDITH   AN
  GOODLIFE   NV   WOT 63 12
    BERSERKER   SABERHAGEN, FRED   AC
  IN THE TEMPLE OF MARS   NV   IFS 66 04
    BERSERKER   SABERHAGEN, FRED   AC
  INHUMAN ERROR (SEE WHAT DO YOU WANT ME TO DO TO PROVE
    IM HUMAN STOP)   TC
  LIFE HATER, THE (ALSO AS THE PEACEMAKER)   SS   IFS 64 08
    IF READER OF SCIENCE FICTION, THE POHL, FREDERIK   AN
  LONG WAY HOME, THE   SS   GAL 61 06
    BOOK OF SABERHAGEN, THE   SABERHAGEN, FRED   AC
  MASQUE OF THE RED SHIFT   NV   IFS 65 11
    BERSERKER   SABERHAGEN, FRED   AC
    SECOND IF READER OF SCIENCE FICTION, THE
                                      POHL, FREDERIK   AN
    WORLD'S BEST SCIENCE FICTION: 1966 WOLLHEIM & CARR   AN
  MR. JESTER   SS   IFS 66 01
    BERSERKER   SABERHAGEN, FRED   AC

SABERHAGEN, FRED   (CONTINUED)
  PATRON OF THE ARTS   SS   IFS 65 08
    BERSERKER   SABERHAGEN, FRED   AC
    COMBAT SF   DICKSON, GORDON R.   AN
  PEACEMAKER, THE (THE LIFE HATER)   SS   IFS 64 08
    BERSERKER   SABERHAGEN, FRED   AC
  PLANETEER   NV   GAL 61 04
    BOOK OF SABERHAGEN, THE   SABERHAGEN, FRED   AC
  PRESSURE (BERSERKER'S PREY)   SS   IFS 67 06
    BOOK OF SABERHAGEN, THE   SABERHAGEN, FRED   AC
  SEVEN DOORS TO EDUCATION   NV   IFS 61 05
    BOOK OF SABERHAGEN, THE   SABERHAGEN, FRED   AC
  SIGN OF THE WOLF   SS   IFS 65 05
    BERSERKER   SABERHAGEN, FRED   AC
  STARSONG   SS   IFS 68 01
    BOOK OF SABERHAGEN, THE   SABERHAGEN, FRED   AC
    WORLD'S BEST SCIENCE FICTION: 1969 WOLLHEIM & CARR   AN
  STONE PLACE   NV   IFS 65 03
    BERSERKER   SABERHAGEN, FRED   AC
  TO MARK THE YEAR ON AZLAROC   SS
    SCIENCE FICTION DISCOVERIES   POHL, C. & F.   OA
  VOLUME PAA-PYX   SS   GAL 61 02
    BOOK OF SABERHAGEN, THE   SABERHAGEN, FRED   AC
  WHAT DO YOU WANT ME TO DO TO PROVE IM HUMAN STOP (INHUMAN
    ERROR)   SS   ASF 74 10
    BOOK OF SABERHAGEN, THE   SABERHAGEN, FRED   AC
  WHAT T AND I DID   SS   IFS 65 04
    BERSERKER   SABERHAGEN, FRED   AC
  WINGS OUT OF SHADOW   NV   IFS 74 04
    BEST FROM IF, THE VOLUME II   IF, EDITORS OF   AN
  WITHOUT A THOUGHT (FORTRESS SHIP)   SS   IFS 63 01
    BERSERKER   SABERHAGEN, FRED   AC
    MEN AND MACHINES   SILVERBERG, ROBERT   AN
  YOUNG GIRL AT AN OPEN HALF-DOOR   SS   FSF 68 11
    BOOK OF SABERHAGEN, THE   SABERHAGEN, FRED   AC
    THEMES IN SCIENCE FICTION   KELLEY, LEO P.   AN

SACKETT, SAM
  HAIL TO THE CHIEF   SN   FUT 54 06
    AMERICAN GOVERNMENT THROUGH SCIENCE FICTION
                                      OLANDER/GREENBERG/& AN
    WEIRD ONES, THE   HOWARD, IVAN   AN

SACKS, JANET
  BEST OF SCIENCE FICTION MONTHLY, THE   AN H NLB 75
  INTRODUCTION   IN
    BEST OF SCIENCE FICTION MONTHLY, THE SACKS, JANET   AN

SAFRONOV, Y.
  THREAD OF LIFE   SS
    RUSSIAN SCIENCE FICTION, 1968   MAGIDOFF, ROBERT   AN

SAGAN, CARL
  DIRECT CONTACT AMONG GALACTIC CIVILIZATIONS   AR C   66
    SURVIVAL PRINTOUT   TOTAL EFFECT   AN
  INTELLIGENT LIFE IN THE UNIVERSE   AR   66
    ALL ABOUT VENUS   ALDISS, BRIAN W.   AN
    FAREWELL FANTASTIC VENUS   ALDISS & HARRISON   AN

SAIL, LAWRENCE
  AFTER WEIGHTLESSNESS   PM   74
    BEST SF: 1974   HARRISON & ALDISS   AN
  CYMBAL PLAYER   PM   CND 72
    BEST SF: 1972   HARRISON & ALDISS   AN
  FISHERMAN   PM   NSM 71
    BEST SF: 1971   HARRISON & ALDISS   AN
  PICTURE BY KLEE, A   PM
    BEST SF: 1974   HARRISON & ALDISS   AN
  REPORT FROM THE PLANET PROTEUS   PM   CND 72
    BEST SF: 1972   HARRISON & ALDISS   AN

SAKI   PSEUD. FOR H. H. MUNRO
  GABRIEL-ERNEST   SS   30
    ALONE BY NIGHT   CONGDON, MICHAEL&DON AN
  LAURA   SS   14
    BEWARE MORE BEASTS   GHIDALIA, V.& ELWOOD AN
    OUT OF THIS WORLD   FAST, JULIUS   AN
  MUSIC ON THE HILL, THE   SS   12
    MOONLIGHT TRAVELER, THE   STERN, PHILIP VAN D. AN
  OPEN WINDOW, THE   SS   14
    CHILDREN OF WONDER   TENN, WILLIAM   AN
  SREDNI VASHTAR   SS
    SPECULATIONS   SANDERS, THOMAS E.   AN
    YOUNG DEMONS   ELWOOD & GHIDALIA   AN
  STORY-TELLER, THE   SS
    BEST FANTASY STORIES   ALDISS, BRIAN W.   AN
  TOBERMORY   SS
    JOURNEYS IN SCIENCE FICTION   LOUGHLIN, RICHARD L. AN
  TOYS OF PEACE, THE   SS
    ECO-FICTION   STADLER, JOHN   AN

SALLIS, JAMES
  FEW LAST WORDS, A   AC H MAC 70
  SHORES BENEATH, THE   AN   AVN 71 08
  AND THEN THE DARK-   SS   69
    FEW LAST WORDS, A   SALLIS, JAMES   AC
  ANXIETY IN THE EYES OF THE CRICKET   SS
    FEW LAST WORDS, A   SALLIS, JAMES   AC
    NEW S.F., THE   JONES, LANGDON   OA
  AT THE FITTING SHOP   SS   DVS 72 02
    AGAIN, DANGEROUS VISIONS   ELLISON, HARLAN   OA
  BINARIES   SS   ORB 71 09
    BEST FROM ORBIT, THE   KNIGHT, DAMON   AN
    ORBIT 9   KNIGHT, DAMON   OA
  BUBBLES   SS   NWS 68 10
    FEW LAST WORDS, A   SALLIS, JAMES   AC

SALLIS, JAMES   (CONTINUED)
  CREATION OF BENNIE GOOD, THE   SS   ORB 70 06
    FEW LAST WORDS, A   SALLIS, JAMES   AC
    ORBIT 6   KNIGHT, DAMON   OA
  DELTA FLIGHT 281   SS   ALT 74
    ALTERNATIVES   GERROLD, DAVID   OA
  DOUCEMENT, S'IL VOUS PLAIT   SS   ORB 72 11
    ORBIT 11   KNIGHT, DAMON   OA
  ECHO   SS   BER 74
    BERSERKERS, THE   ELWOOD, ROGER   OA
  ENCLAVE   SS   70
    FEW LAST WORDS, A   SALLIS, JAMES   AC
  FACES & HANDS   NV   NOV 70 01
    FEW LAST WORDS, A   SALLIS, JAMES   AC
    *NOVA 1   HARRISON, HARRY   OA
  FEW LAST WORDS, A   SS   ORB 68 04
    FEW LAST WORDS, A   SALLIS, JAMES   AC
    ORBIT 4   KNIGHT, DAMON   OA
    POCKETFUL OF STARS, A   KNIGHT, DAMON   AN
  FIELD   SS   QRK 71 03
    QUARK/3   DELANY & HACKER   OA
  FIRST FEW KINDS OF TRUTH, THE   SS   ALT 74
    ALTERNATIVES   GERROLD, DAVID   OA
  FLOORS OF HIS HEART, THE   SS
    FEW LAST WORDS, A   SALLIS, JAMES   AC
  FRONT & CENTAUR   SS   NWS 70 03
    FEW LAST WORDS, A   SALLIS, JAMES   AC
  HISTORY MAKERS, THE   SS   ORB 69 05
    FEW LAST WORDS, A   SALLIS, JAMES   AC
    ORBIT 5   KNIGHT, DAMON   OA
  INSECT MEN OF BOSTON   SS   NWQ 74 06
    NEW WORLDS NO. 6   PLATT & BAILEY   OA
  INTRODUCTION   IN
    CLARION II   WILSON, ROBIN SCOTT OA
  INVASION OF DALLAS, THE   SS
    LONE STAR UNIVERSE   PROCTOR & UTLEY   OA
  JANE CRYING   SS   70
    FEW LAST WORDS, A   SALLIS, JAMES   AC
  JEREMIAD   SS   NWS 69 02
    FEW LAST WORDS, A   SALLIS, JAMES   AC
  JIM AND MARY G   SS   ORB 70 07
    BEST FROM ORBIT, THE   KNIGHT, DAMON   AN
    FEW LAST WORDS, A   SALLIS, JAMES   AC
    ORBIT 7   KNIGHT, DAMON   OA
  KAZOO   SS   NWS 67 08
    BEST SF STORIES FROM NEW WORLDS 3 MOORCOCK, MICHAEL   AN
    FEW LAST WORDS, A   SALLIS, JAMES   AC
  KETTLE OF STARS   SS
    FEW LAST WORDS, A   SALLIS, JAMES   AC
  LETTER TO A YOUNG POET   SS   ORB 68 03
    FEW LAST WORDS, A   SALLIS, JAMES   AC
    ORBIT 3   KNIGHT, DAMON   OA
  MENSURATION   PM   QRK 71 02
    QUARK/2   DELANY & HACKER   OA
  MY FRIEND ZARATHUSTRA   SS   ORB 74 13
    ORBIT 13   KNIGHT, DAMON   OA
  OCCASIONS   SS   70
    FEW LAST WORDS, A   SALLIS, JAMES   AC
  ONE ROAD TO DAMASCUS   SS C
    2076: THE AMERICAN TRICENTENNIAL BRYANT, EDWARD   OA
  ONLY THE WORDS ARE DIFERENT   SS   ORB 71 09
    ORBIT 9   KNIGHT, DAMON   OA
  OPENING OF THE TERRAN BALLET, THE   SS   70
    FEW LAST WORDS, A   SALLIS, JAMES   AC
  SLICE OF THE UNIVERSE   SS   FAN 69 02
    FEW LAST WORDS, A   SALLIS, JAMES   AC
  WRITER AS TEACHER, THE   AR   CLR 72 02
    CLARION II   WILSON, ROBIN SCOTT OA
  53RD AMERICAN DREAM   SS   DVS 72 02
    AGAIN, DANGEROUS VISIONS   ELLISON, HARLAN   OA

SALOMON, LOUIS B.
  UNIVAC TO UNIVAC   PM   HRP 58 03
    ANOTHER TOMORROW   HOLLISTER, BERNARD C AN
    INSIDE INFORMATION   MOWSHOWITZ, ABBE   AN

SAMACHSON, JOSEPH   SEE PSEUD. WILLIAM MORRISON

SAMALMAN, ALEXANDER
  LIFE ON THE MOON   SS   TWS 46 12
    SHOT IN THE DARK   MERRIL, JUDITH   AN

SAMARIS, LUCAS
  UNTITLED BOX NO. 3   IL
    SCIENCE FICTION   BRODKIN & PEARSON   AN

SAMBROT, WILLIAM
  ISLAND OF FEAR AND OTHER SCIENCE FICTION   AC   PMA 63 03
  CATHARTIC   SS   SAT 57 08
    ISLAND OF FEAR AND OTHER SCIENCE FICTION
                                 SAMBROT, WILLIAM   AC
  CATHEDRAL OF MARS (SEE A DISTANT SHRINE)   TC
  CONTROL SOMNAMBULE   SS   PBY 62 05
    FROM THE "S" FILE   PLAYBOY, EDITORS OF AN
    ISLAND OF FEAR AND OTHER SCIENCE FICTION
                                 SAMBROT, WILLIAM   AC
    TRANSIT OF EARTH   PLAYBOY, EDITORS OF AN
  CREATURE OF THE SNOWS   SS   SEP 60 10
    ANCIENT MYSTERIES READER, THE HAINING, PETER   AN
    ISLAND OF FEAR AND OTHER SCIENCE FICTION
                                 SAMBROT, WILLIAM   AC
    UNTRAVELLED WORLDS   BARTER & WILSON   AN
    6TH ANNUAL OF THE YEAR'S BEST S-F, THE MERRIL, JUDITH   AN
  DEADLY DECISION   SS   EXT 58
    ISLAND OF FEAR AND OTHER SCIENCE FICTION
                                 SAMBROT, WILLIAM   AC

SAMBROT, WILLIAM   (CONTINUED)
  DISTANT SHRINE, A (CATHEDRAL OF MARS)   SS   SEP 61 06
    ISLAND OF FEAR AND OTHER SCIENCE FICTION
                                 SAMBROT, WILLIAM   AC
  FOOTBALL MAJORS AT PACIFIC U. (SEE THE SECRET OF THE
    TERRIBLE TITANS)   TC
  INVASION¡   SS   SEP 56 07
    ISLAND OF FEAR AND OTHER SCIENCE FICTION
                                 SAMBROT, WILLIAM   AC
  ISLAND OF FEAR   SS   SEP 58 01
    ISLAND OF FEAR AND OTHER SCIENCE FICTION
                                 SAMBROT, WILLIAM   AC
    POST READER OF FANTASY AND SCIENCE FICTION
                                 SATURDAY EVE. POST   AN
  LEPRECHAUN   SS   ESC 62
    8TH ANNUAL OF THE YEAR'S BEST S-F, THE MERRIL, JUDITH AN
  MAN WHO KNEW, THE   SS   TIG 57
    ISLAND OF FEAR AND OTHER SCIENCE FICTION
                                 SAMBROT, WILLIAM   AC
  NIGHT OF THE LEOPARD   NV   67
    NEW AWARENESS, THE   WARRICK & GREENBERG AN
    SOCIAL PROBLEMS THROUGH SCIENCE FICTION
                                 GREENBERG/MILSTEAD/& AN
  NINE DAYS TO DIE (STORY OF AN ATOMIC-AGE ORDEAL) SS SEP 60 07
    ISLAND OF FEAR AND OTHER SCIENCE FICTION
                                 SAMBROT, WILLIAM   AC
  REPORT TO THE PEOPLE   SS   BBM 33
    ISLAND OF FEAR AND OTHER SCIENCE FICTION
                                 SAMBROT, WILLIAM   AC
  SECOND EXPERIMENT, THE   SS
    ISLAND OF FEAR AND OTHER SCIENCE FICTION
                                 SAMBROT, WILLIAM   AC
  SECRET OF THE TERRIBLE TITANS, THE (FOOTBALL MAJORS AT
    PACIFIC U.)   SS   CMP 59 10
    ISLAND OF FEAR AND OTHER SCIENCE FICTION
                                 SAMBROT, WILLIAM   AC
  SON OF EVE, A   SS   MRM 59
    ISLAND OF FEAR AND OTHER SCIENCE FICTION
                                 SAMBROT, WILLIAM   AC
  SPACE SECRET   SS   SEP 59 02
    ISLAND OF FEAR AND OTHER SCIENCE FICTION
                                 SAMBROT, WILLIAM   AC
    POST READER OF FANTASY AND SCIENCE FICTION
                                 SATURDAY EVE. POST   AN
  STORY OF AN ATOMIC-AGE ORDEAL (SEE NINE DAYS TO DIE)
                                                 TC

SANDBURG, CARL
  ARITHMETIC   PM   50
    FANTASIA MATHEMATICA   FADIMAN, CLIFTON   AN

SANDERS, THOMAS E.
  SPECULATIONS   AN L GLN 73
  ESSAY, AN EXPLANATION, AND AN EXCERPT, AN   SI
    SPECULATIONS   SANDERS, THOMAS E.   AN
  FICTION   SI
    SPECULATIONS   SANDERS, THOMAS E.   AN
  INTRODUCTION   IN
    SPECULATIONS   SANDERS, THOMAS E.   AN
  POETRY   SI
    SPECULATIONS   SANDERS, THOMAS E.   AN
  PREFACE   IN
    SPECULATIONS   SANDERS, THOMAS E.   AN

SANDERS, WINSTON P. PSEUD. FOR POUL ANDERSON
  BARNACLE BULL   SS   ASF 60 09
    ANALOG 1   CAMPBELL, JOHN W. JR AN
  INDUSTRIAL REVOLUTION   SN   ASF 63 09
    ANALOG 3   CAMPBELL, JOHN W. JR AN
  PACT   SS   FSF 59 08
    BEST FROM FANTASY AND SCIENCE FICTION: 9
                                 MILLS, ROBERT P.   AN
  SAY IT WITH FLOWERS   SS   ASF 65 09
    ANALOG 5   CAMPBELL, JOHN W. JR AN
  WORD TO SPACE, THE   SS   FSF 60 09
    OTHER WORLDS, OTHER GODS   MOHS, MAYO   AN

SANDERSON, IVAN T.
  INTRODUCTION   IN
    ENCOUNTERS WITH ALIENS   EARLEY, GEORGE W.   AN
  NOW MEET THE NONTERRESTRIAL   AR   FUN 59 01
    FLYING SAUCERS IN FACT AND FICTION SANTESSON, HANS S. AN

SANDRELLI, SANDRO
  SCYTHE, THE   SS   63
    BEST FROM THE REST OF THE WORLD, THE WOLLHEIM, DONALD A. AN

SANSOM, WILLIAM
  VERTICAL LADDER, THE   SS   60
    NIGHT IN FUNLAND   BRONDFIELD, JEROME   AN
  WITNESSES, THE   SS   44
    TIMELESS STORIES FOR TODAY AND TOMORROW
                                 BRADBURY, RAY   AN

SANTAYANA, GEORGE
  MAP OF ENGLAND AND THE ABSOLUTE, THE   SS   20
    MATHEMATICAL MAGPIE, THE   FADIMAN, CLIFTON   AN

SANTESSON, HANS STEFAN
            ALSO AS   VITHALDAS H. O'QUINN
  CRIME PREVENTION IN THE 30TH CENTURY   AN H WLK 69
  DAYS AFTER TOMORROW, THE   AN H LBR 71
  FANTASTIC UNIVERSE OMNIBUS, THE   AN H PRH 60
  FLYING SAUCERS IN FACT AND FICTION   AN   LAN 68
  GENTLE INVADERS   AN   BEL 69 05
  GODS FOR TOMORROW   AN   AWD 67

SANTESSON, HANS S.

SANTESSON, HANS S.   (CONTINUED)
RULERS OF MEN   AN   PYR 65
  INTRODUCTION   IN
    CRIME PREVENTION IN THE 30TH CENTURY   SANTESSON, HANS S.   AN
    FLYING SAUCERS IN FACT AND FICTION   SANTESSON, HANS S.   AN
    GENTLE INVADERS   SANTESSON, HANS S.   AN
    GODS FOR TOMORROW   SANTESSON, HANS S.   AN
    RULERS OF MEN   SANTESSON, HANS S.   AN

SANTOS, DOMINGO   PSEUD. FOR PEDRO DOMINGO
ROUND AND ROUND AND ROUND AGAIN   NV   70
  BEST FROM THE REST OF THE WORLD, THE   WOLLHEIM, DONALD A.   AN
SONG OF INFINITY, THE   SS   NWR 69 14
  NEW WRITINGS IN SF. 14   CARNELL, JOHN   OA

SAPARIN, VICTOR
MAGIC SHOES, THE   SS
  RUSSIAN SCIENCE FICTION   MAGIDOFF, ROBERT   AN
TRIAL OF TANTALUS, THE   NV
  MORE SOVIET SCIENCE FICTION   ANONYMOUS   AN

SARGENT, PAMELA
BIO-FUTURES   AN   VNT 76 06
CLONED LIVES   NO   FGM 76 06
MORE WOMEN OF WONDER   AN   VNT 76 08
STARSHADOWS   AC   ACE 77 06
WOMEN OF WONDER   AN   VNT 75 01
AUNT ELVIRA'S ZOO   SS
  NIGHT OF THE SPHINX AND OTHER STORIES   ELWOOD, ROGER   OA
BOND AND FREE   NV   FSF 74 06
  STARSHADOWS   SARGENT, PAMELA   AC
CLONE SISTER   NV   EIO 73
  CLONED LIVES   SARGENT, PAMELA   NO
  EROS IN ORBIT   ELDER, JOSEPH   OA
MARRIAGE AND THE FAMILY THROUGH SCIENCE FICTION
                                           CLEAR/WARRICK/&   AN
  STARSHADOWS   SARGENT, PAMELA   AC
DARKNESS OF DAY   SS C CTM 74 03
  CONTINUUM 3   ELWOOD, ROGER   OA
DESERT PLACES   SS   UNI 74 04
  STARSHADOWS   SARGENT, PAMELA   AC
  UNIVERSE 4   CARR, TERRY   OA
FATHER   SN   AMZ 74 02
  CLONED LIVES   SARGENT, PAMELA   NO
FRIEND FROM THE STARS   SS
  MISSING WORLD AND OTHER STORIES, THE   ELWOOD, ROGER   OA
GATHER BLUE ROSES   SS   FSF 72 02
  STARSHADOWS   SARGENT, PAMELA   AC
  WANDERING STARS   DANN, JACK M.   AN
IF EVER I SHOULD LEAVE YOU (REVISED)   SS   IFS 74 02
  STARSHADOWS   SARGENT, PAMELA   AC
IMT   SS   TVW 73
  STARSHADOWS   SARGENT, PAMELA   AC
  TWO VIEWS OF WONDER   SCORTIA & YARBRO   OA
INTRODUCTION   IN
  BIO-FUTURES   SARGENT, PAMELA   AN
  MORE WOMEN OF WONDER   SARGENT, PAMELA   AN
INVISIBLE GIRL, THE   SS
  KILLER PLANTS AND OTHER STORIES, THE   ELWOOD, ROGER   OA
JULIO 204   SS   NWQ 72 03
  NEW WORLDS QUARTERLY NO. 3   MOORCOCK, MICHAEL   OA
  STARSHADOWS   SARGENT, PAMELA   AC
MATTHEW   SS   TTM 73
  TEN TOMORROWS   ELWOOD, ROGER   OA
OASIS   SS   PRT 71
  PROTOSTARS   GERROLD & GOLDIN   OA
OTHER PERCEIVER, THE   SS   UNI 72 02
  STARSHADOWS   SARGENT, PAMELA   AC
  UNIVERSE 2   CARR, TERRY   OA
SENSE OF DIFFERENCE, A   SS   WLK 73
  AND WALK NOW GENTLY THROUGH THE FIRE...
                                           ELWOOD, ROGER   OA
  CLONED LIVES   SARGENT, PAMELA   NO
SHADOWS   NV   FOS 74
  FELLOWSHIP OF THE STARS   CARR, TERRY   OA
  STARSHADOWS   SARGENT, PAMELA   AC
WEAPONS   SS C DYS 75
  DYSTOPIAN VISIONS   ELWOOD, ROGER   OA
WOMEN IN SCIENCE FICTION   IN
  WOMEN OF WONDER   SARGENT, PAMELA   AN

SAROYAN, WILLIAM
HUMMINGBIRD THAT LIVED THROUGH WINTER, THE   SS   44
  ECO-FICTION   STADLER, JOHN   AN

SATTERFIELD, CHARLES PSEUD. FOR FREDERIK POHL
WITH REDFERN ON CAPELLA XII   NV   GAL 55 11
  MIND PARTNER AND 8 OTHER NOVELETS FROM GALAXY
                                           GOLD, H. L.   AN

SATURDAY EVE. POST
POST READER OF FANTASY AND SCIENCE FICTION   AN H DBL 64

SAUER, ROB
VOYAGES: SCENARIOS FOR A SHIP CALLED EARTH   AN   BAL 71 04

SAUNDERS, BUDDY
VOICE AND BITTER WEEPING, A   SS C GAL 73 07
  BEST FROM GALAXY, THE   VOLUME II   GALAXY, EDITORS OF   AN

SAUNDERS, JAKE
BACK TO THE STONE AGE   SS
  BEST SCIENCE FICTION STORIES OF THE YEAR (1976)
                                           DOZOIS, GARDNER R.   AN
  LONE STAR UNIVERSE   PROCTOR & UTLEY   OA

SAVAGE, ARTHUR D.
BUTTERFLY KISS, THE (SEE THE LAST WAR)   TC
LAST WAR, THE (THE BUTTERFLY KISS)   SS   OSF 54 02
  PLANET OF DOOM AND OTHER STORIES   ANONYMOUS   AN

SAVCHENKO, VLADIMIR
PROFESSOR BERN'S AWAKENING   SS
  SOVIET SCIENCE FICTION   ANONYMOUS   AN

SAXTON, COLIN
DAY, THE   SS   SVW 73
  SAVING WORLDS   ELWOOD & KIDD   OA

SAXTON, JOSEPHINE
ELOUISE AND THE DOCTORS OF THE PLANET PERGAMON   SS   DVS 72 02
  AGAIN, DANGEROUS VISIONS   ELLISON, HARLAN   OA
HEADS AFRICA TAILS AMERICA   SS   ORB 71 09
  ORBIT 9   KNIGHT, DAMON   OA
IN MEMORIAM, JEANNIE   SS
  STOPWATCH   HAY, GEORGE   OA
NATURE BOY   SS   QRK 71 03
  QUARK/3   DELANY & HACKER   OA
NE DEJA VU PAS   SS   67
  ENGLAND SWINGS SF   MERRIL, JUDITH   AN
  SPACE-TIME JOURNAL, THE   MERRIL, JUDITH   AN
POWER OF TIME, THE   NV   NDM 71 01
  MORE WOMEN OF WONDER   SARGENT, PAMELA   AN
  NEW DIMENSIONS 1   SILVERBERG, ROBERT   OA
TRIUMPHANT HEAD, THE   SS   ANA 70
  ALCHEMY AND ACADEME   MCCAFFREY, ANNE   OA
WALL, THE   SS   SCF 65 11
  BEST SF STORIES FROM NEW WORLDS 7   MOORCOCK, MICHAEL   OA
  FANTASY: THE LITERATURE OF THE MARVELOUS
                                           KELLEY, LEO P.   AN
  11TH ANNUAL OF THE YEAR'S BEST S-F, THE
                                           MERRIL, JUDITH   AN

SAYE, LEE
MORNING RUSH OR HAPPY BIRTHDAY, DEAR LEAH, THE   SS   TAL 73
  FRONTIERS 1; TOMORROW'S ALTERNATIVES ELWOOD, ROGER   OA
NO ROOM FOR THE WANDERER   SS   ALT 74
  ALTERNATIES   GERROLD, DAVID   OA

SCARFF, WILLIAM   PSEUD. FOR ALGIS J. BUDRYS

SCHACHNER, NAT
PAST, PRESENT AND FUTURE   SN   ASF 37 09
  BEFORE THE GOLDEN AGE   ASIMOV, ISAAC   AN
SHINING ONE, THE   SS   ASF 37 05
  VISIONS OF TOMORROW   ELWOOD, ROGER   AN
ULTIMATE METAL, THE   NV   ASF 35 02
  *BEST OF SCIENCE FICTION   CONKLIN, GROFF   AN

SCHAEFFER, ROBIN   PSEUD. FOR BARRY N. MALZBERG
FORM IN REMISSION   SS   BER 74
  BERSERKERS, THE   ELWOOD, ROGER   OA
MEETING THE ALIENS ON ALGOL IV   SS
  SURVIVAL FROM INFINITY   ELWOOD, ROGER   OA
REVOLUTION   SS   FUC 73
  FUTURE CITY   ELWOOD, ROGER   OA
TRIPPERS, THE   SS
  LONG NIGHT OF WAITING AND OTHER STORIES
                                           ELWOOD, ROGER   OA

SCHAFHAUSER, CHARLES
GLEEB FOR EARTH, A   SS   GAL 53 05
  GALAXY SCIENCE FICTION OMNIBUS   GOLD, H. L.   AN
  SECOND GALAXY READER OF SCIENCE FICTION
                                           GOLD, H. L.   AN
I'M YOURS   SS   PBY 54 12
  PLAYBOY BOOK OF HORROR AND THE SUPERNATURAL, THE
                                           PLAYBOY, EDITORS OF AN
  WEIRD SHOW   PLAYBOY, EDITORS OF AN

SCHAUB, MARY H.
SERPENTINE   NV
  SURVIVAL FROM INFINITY   ELWOOD, ROGER   OA

SCHENCK, HILBERT JR.
ED LEAR WASN'T SO CRAZY| PM   FSF 60 06
  6TH ANNUAL OF THE YEAR'S BEST S-F, THE   MERRIL, JUDITH   AN
ME   PM   FSF 59 08
  BEST FROM FANTASY AND SCIENCE FICTION: 9
                                           MILLS, ROBERT P.   AN
  MATHEMATICAL MAGPIE, THE   FADIMAN, CLIFTON   AN
  5TH ANNUAL OF THE YEAR'S BEST S-F, THE   MERRIL, JUDITH   AN
PUN IN ORBIT   PM   NEW 62 AN
  MATHEMATICAL MAGPIE, THE   FADIMAN, CLIFTON   AN
SNIP SNIP   PM   FSF 59 09
  MATHEMATICAL MAGPIE, THE   FADIMAN, CLIFTON   AN
WOCKYJABBER   PM   FSF 60 05
  MATHEMATICAL MAGPIE, THE   FADIMAN, CLIFTON   AN

SCHERE, MOSES
BARGAIN IN BODIES, A   SS   UNK 43 06
  DEALS WITH THE DEVIL   DAVENPORT, BASIL   AN

SCHIAPARELLI, G. V.
REPORT ON CANALI   AR
  MARS, WE LOVE YOU   HIPOLITO & MCNELLY   AN

SCHJELDAHL, PETER
FOR APOLLO 11   PM   BMR 73
  BAD MOON RISING   DISCH, THOMAS M.   OA
HO CHI MINH ELEGY   PM   BMR 73
  BAD MOON RISING   DISCH, THOMAS M.   OA

SCHMIDT, STANLEY
  LOST NEWTON   NV ASF 70 09
    ANTHROPOLOGY THROUGH SCIENCE FICTION   MASON, C/GREENBERG/& AN
    SOCIOLOGY THROUGH SCIENCE FICTION   MILSTEAD/GREENBERG/& AN
  MAY THE BEST MAN WIN   SS ASF 71 03
    AMERICAN GOVERNMENT THROUGH SCIENCE FICTION
                                        OLANDER/GREENBERG/& AN

SCHMITZ, JAMES H.
  AGENT OF VEGA   AC H GNM 60
  NICE DAY FOR SCREAMING, AND OTHER TALES OF THE HUB AC H CHL 65
  PRIDE OF MONSTERS, A   AC H MAC 70
  TELZEY TOY, THE   NO DAW 73 12
  AGENT OF VEGA   NV ASF 49 07
    AGENT OF VEGA   SCHMITZ, JAMES H. AC
    SPACE POLICE   NORTON, ANDRE   AN
  BALANCED ECOLOGY   SS ASF 65 03
    ABOVE THE HUMAN LANDSCAPE   MCNELLY & STOVER   AN
    ANALOG 5   CAMPBELL, JOHN W. JR AN
    BUG-EYED MONSTERS   CHEETHAM, ANTHONY AN
    NEBULA AWARD STORIES   KNIGHT, DAMON   AN
    NICE DAY FOR SCREAMING, AND OTHER TALES OF THE HUB
                                  SCHMITZ, JAMES H. AC
  CARETAKER   SS GAL 53 07
    GALAXY SCIENCE FICTION OMNIBUS GOLD, H. L.   AN
    SECOND GALAXY READER OF SCIENCE FICTION
                                  GOLD, H. L.   AN
  COMPANY PLANET   NV ASF 71 05
    TELZEY TOY, THE   SCHMITZ, JAMES H. NO
  COMPULSION   NV ASF 70 06
    TELZEY TOY, THE   SCHMITZ, JAMES H. NO
  END OF THE LINE, THE   NV ASF 51 07
    SPACE PIONEERS   NORTON, ANDRE   AN
    TO THE STARS   SILVERBERG, ROBERT AN
    TOMORROW 1   HOSKINS, ROBERT   AN
  GOBLIN NIGHT   NV ASF 65 04
    ON OUR WAY TO THE FUTURE   CARR, TERRY   AN
  GONE FISHING   NV ASF 61 05
    FIVE-ODD   CONKLIN, GROFF   AN
  GRANDPA   SS ASF 55 02
    ASTOUNDING-ANALOG READER, THE VOLUME TWO
                                  HARRISON & ALDISS AN
    DECADE THE 1950S   ALDISS & HARRISON AN
    PENGUIN SCIENCE FICTION   ALDISS, BRIAN W.   AN
    SCIENCE FICTION BESTIARY, THE SILVERBERG, ROBERT AN
    SPECTRUM 5   AMIS & CONQUEST   AN
    TIME PROBE: THE SCIENCES IN SF. CLARKE, ARTHUR C. AN
  GREENFACE   NV UNK 43 08
    CIRCUS OF DR. LAO AND OTHER IMPROBABLE STORIES
                                  BRADBURY, RAY   AN
    PRIDE OF MONSTERS, A   SCHMITZ, JAMES H. AC
  ILLUSIONISTS, THE (SPACE FEAR)   NV ASF 51 03
    AGENT OF VEGA   SCHMITZ, JAMES H. AC
  INCIDENT ON ROUTE 12, AN   SS IFS 62 01
    BEST SCIENCE FICTION FROM IF, THE POHL, FREDERIK AN
  INTRODUCTION   IN
    PRIDE OF MONSTERS, A   SCHMITZ, JAMES H. AC
  JUST CURIOUS   SS 68
    SF: AUTHORS' CHOICE 2   HARRISON, HARRY   AN
  LION LOOSE   SN ASF 61 10
    PRIDE OF MONSTERS, A   SCHMITZ, JAMES H. AC
  MACHMEN, THE   SS ASF 64 09
    NICE DAY FOR SCREAMING, AND OTHER TALES OF THE HUB
                                  SCHMITZ, JAMES H. AC
  NICE DAY FOR SCREAMING, A   SS ASF 65 01
    NICE DAY FOR SCREAMING, AND OTHER TALES OF THE HUB
                                  SCHMITZ, JAMES H. AC
  NOVICE   NV ASF 62 06
    ANALOG 2   CAMPBELL, JOHN W. JR AN
    MIND TO MIND   SILVERBERG, ROBERT AN
    TOMORROW'S CHILDREN   ASIMOV, ISAAC   AN
  OTHER LIKENESS, THE   SS ASF 62 07
    NICE DAY FOR SCREAMING, AND OTHER TALES OF THE HUB
                                  SCHMITZ, JAMES H. AC
  PLANET OF FORGETTING   NV GAL 65 02
    WORLD'S BEST SCIENCE FICTION: 1966 WOLLHEIM & CARR AN
  PORK CHOP TREE, THE   SS ASF 65 02
    PRIDE OF MONSTERS, A   SCHMITZ, JAMES H. AC
  RESEARCH ALPHA   SN C IFS 65 07
    MORE THAN SUPERHUMAN   VAN VOGT, A. E.   AC
  RESIDENT WITCH   NV ASF 70 05
    TELZEY TOY, THE   SCHMITZ, JAMES H. NO
    THIS SIDE OF INFINITY   CARR, TERRY   AN
  ROGUE PSI   NV AMZ 62 08
    BEST FROM AMAZING, THE   WHITE, TED   AN
  SEARCHER, THE   SN ASF 66 02
    PRIDE OF MONSTERS, A   SCHMITZ, JAMES H. AC
  SECOND NIGHT OF SUMMER   SS GAL 50 12
    AGENT OF VEGA   SCHMITZ, JAMES H. AC
    *POSSIBLE WORLDS OF SCIENCE FICTION CONKLIN, GROFF AN
  SPACE FEAR (SEE THE ILLUSIONISTS)   TC
  SPACEMASTER   NV NWR 65 03
    NEW WRITINGS IN SF. 3   CARNELL, JOHN   OA
  STAR HYACINTHS, THE (SEE THE TANGLED WEB)   TC
  TANGLED WEB, THE (THE STAR HYACINTHS)   SS AMZ 61 12
    NICE DAY FOR SCREAMING, AND OTHER TALES OF THE HUB
                                  SCHMITZ, JAMES H. AC
  TELZEY TOY, THE   NV ASF 71 01
    TELZEY TOY, THE   SCHMITZ, JAMES H. NO
  THESE ARE THE ARTS   SS FSF 62 09
    14 GREAT TALES OF ESP   STONE, IDELLA P.   AN
  TROUBLE TIDE   NV ASF 65 05
    ELSEWHERE AND ELSEWHEN   CONKLIN, GROFF   AN
  TRUTH ABOUT CUSHGAR, THE   NV ASF 50 11
    AGENT OF VEGA   SCHMITZ, JAMES H. AC

SCHMITZ, JAMES H.   (CONTINUED)
  WE DON'T WANT ANY TROUBLE   SS GAL 53 0
    ASSIGNMENT IN TOMORROW   POHL, FREDERIK   A
    FIFTY SHORT SCIENCE FICTION TALES ASIMOV & CONKLIN A
  WHERE THE TIME WENT   SS IFS 68 1
    ANDROIDS, TIME MACHINES AND BLUE GIRAFFES
                                  ELWOOD & GHIDALIA   A
  WINDS OF TIME, THE   NV ASF 62 0
    NICE DAY FOR SCREAMING, AND OTHER TALES OF THE HUB
                                  SCHMITZ, JAMES H. AC
    PRIDE OF MONSTERS, A   SCHMITZ, JAMES H. AC
  WITCHES OF KARRES, THE   NV ASF 49 12
    *ASTOUNDING SCIENCE FICTION ANTHOLOGY, THE
                                  CAMPBELL, JOHN W. JR AN
    *FIRST ASTOUNDING SCIENCE FICTION ANTHOLOGY, THE
                                  CAMPBELL, JOHN W. JR AN
    SCIENCE FICTION HALL OF FAME VOLUME 2B BOVA, BEN A
    SECOND ASTOUNDING SCIENCE FICTION ANTHOLOGY, THE (PB)
                                  CAMPBELL, JOHN W. JR A
    TOWARD INFINITY   KNIGHT, DAMON   A

SCHNIRRING, ALICEMARY
  CHILD'S PLAY   SS WRT 42 0
    CHILDREN OF WONDER   TENN, WILLIAM   AN

SCHNITZLER, ARTHUR
  LEINBACH'S PROOF   PM 31
    FANTASIA MATHEMATICA   FADIMAN, CLIFTON   AN

SCHOENFELD, HOWARD
  BUILT DOWN LOGICALLY   SS FSF 51 12
    FIFTY SHORT SCIENCE FICTION TALES ASIMOV & CONKLIN AN
  BUILT UP LOGICALLY (THE UNIVERSAL TANCEA, RET 49 WI)
                                                      SS FSF 50 P
    BEST FROM FANTASY AND SCIENCE FICTION BOUCHER & MCCOMAS AN
    MORE PENGUIN SCIENCE FICTION ALDISS, BRIAN W.   AN
    SCIENCE FICTION ARGOSY, A   KNIGHT, DAMON   AN
    SPECIAL WONDER   MCCOMAS, J. FRANCIS AN
  UNIVERSAL TANCEA, THE (SEE BUILT UP LOGICALLY)   TC

SCHOEPFLIN, HARL V. SEE PSEUD. HARL VINCENT

SCHOLES, ROBERT
  AS THE WALL CRUMBLES   AR NEW 75 AN
    NEBULA AWARD STORIES 10   GUNN, JAMES E.   AN

SCHOLZ, CARTER
  CLOSED CIRCUIT   SS
    CLARION SF   WILHELM, KATE   OA
  EVE OF THE LAST APOLLO, THE   SS ORB 76 18
    ORBIT 18   KNIGHT, DAMON   OA
  NINTH SYMPHONY OF LUDWIG VAN BEETHOVEN AND OTHER LOST SONGS
                                                      NV UNI 77 07
    UNIVERSE 7   CARR, TERRY   OA

SCHORER, MARK
  IN THE LEFT WING   SS C WRT 32 06
    WIZARDS AND WARLOCKS   GHIDALIA, VIC   AN
  RETURN OF ANDREW BENTLEY, THE   SS C WRT 33 09
    OTHER WORLDS, THE   STONG, PHILIP D.   AN

SCHRADER, STEVEN
  COHEN DOG EXCLUSION ACT, THE   SS NEW 71 AN
    BEST SF: 1971   HARRISON & ALDISS AN
    ECO-FICTION   STADLER, JOHN   AN

SCHRAMM, WILBUR
  VOICE IN THE EARPHONES, THE   SS SEP 47 05
    POST READER OF FANTASY AND SCIENCE FICTION
                                  SATURDAY EVE. POST AN
    SATURDAY EVENING POST FANTASY STORIES, THE
                                  FLES, BARTHOLD   AN

SCHULTZ, CHARLES M.
  PEANUTS   CT 64
    APEMAN, SPACEMAN   STOVER & HARRISON AN

SCHWARTZ, SHEILA
  EARTH IN TRANSIT   AN LLL 76 1
  INTRODUCTION   IN
    EARTH IN TRANSIT   SCHWARTZ, SHEILA   AN

SCHWEITZER, BRITT
  EN PASSANT   SS HBK 60 12
    NEW WORLDS OF FANTASY NO. 2   CARR, TERRY   AN

SCORTIA, THOMAS N. AND CHELSEA QUINN YARBRO
  TWO VIEWS OF WONDER   OA BAL 73 12

SCORTIA, THOMAS N. AND GEORGE ZEBROWSKI
  HUMAN-MACHINES   AN VNT 75 11

SCORTIA, THOMAS N.
  CAUTION! INFLAMMABLE!   AC H DBL 75 07
  STRANGE BED FELLOWS   AN H RDM 72
  ALIEN NIGHT   NV SFA 57 08
    GET OUT OF MY SKY   MARGULIES, LEO   AN
  ARMAGEDDON TAPES, THE- TAPE I   SS CTM 74 01
    CONTINUUM 1   ELWOOD, ROGER   OA
  ARMAGEDDON TAPES, THE- TAPE II   NV CTM 74 02
    CONTINUUM 2   ELWOOD, ROGER   OA
  ARMAGEDDON TAPES, THE- TAPE III   NV CTM 74 03
    CONTINUUM 3   ELWOOD, ROGER   OA
  ARMAGEDDON TAPES, THE- TAPE IV   SS CTM 75 04
    CONTINUUM 4   ELWOOD, ROGER   OA

SCORTIA, THOMAS N.   SELLINGS, ARTHUR

SCORTIA, THOMAS N.   (CONTINUED)
  BLOOD BROTHER   SS
    FUTURE KIN   ELWOOD, ROGER   OA
  BOMB IN THE BATHTUB, THE   SS   GAL 57 02
    CAUTION| INFLAMMABLE| SCORTIA, THOMAS N.   AC
    COSMIC LAUGHTER   HALDEMAN, JOE W.   AN
    FOURTH GALAXY READER, THE   GOLD, H. L.   AN
  BY THE TIME I GET TO PHOENIX   SS   INY 72 04
    BEST SCIENCE FICTION FOR 1973   ACKERMAN, FORREST J.   AN
    CAUTION| INFLAMMABLE| SCORTIA, THOMAS N.   AC
    INFINITY 4   HOSKINS, ROBERT   OA
  CAUTION| INFLAMMABLE| (THE END OF THE LINE) SS   FAN 55 02
    CAUTION| INFLAMMABLE| SCORTIA, THOMAS N.   AC
  END OF THE LINE, THE (SEE CAUTION| INFLAMMABLE|) TC
  FALL OUT ONE   SS   MSM 72 03
    CAUTION| INFLAMMABLE| SCORTIA, THOMAS N.   AC
  FINAL EXAM   SS
    OTHER SIDE OF TOMORROW, THE   ELWOOD, ROGER   OA
  FLOWERING NARCISSUS   SS   EIO 73
    CAUTION| INFLAMMABLE| SCORTIA, THOMAS N.   AC
    EROS IN ORBIT   ELDER, JOSEPH   OA
  GEE, WURLITZER| IT'S A DAD| SS   DAP 71 06
    CAUTION| INFLAMMABLE| SCORTIA, THOMAS N.   AC
  GODDESS OF THE CATS, THE   SS   72
    CAUTION| INFLAMMABLE| SCORTIA, THOMAS N.   AC
  ICEBOX BLONDE, THE   SS   ROG 59 06
    CAUTION| INFLAMMABLE| SCORTIA, THOMAS N.   AC
    MARRIAGE AND THE FAMILY THROUGH SCIENCE FICTION
                                        CLEAR/WARRICK/&   AN
    STRANGE BED FELLOWS   SCORTIA, THOMAS N.   AN
  INTRODUCTION: "UNHOLY MARRIAGE": THE CYBORG IN SCIENCE FICTION
                                               IN C
    HUMAN-MACHINES   SCORTIA & ZEBROWSKI   AN
  JOHN ROBERTS AND THE DRAGON'S EGG   SS   FUN 57 08
    CAUTION| INFLAMMABLE| SCORTIA, THOMAS N.   AC
  JUDAS FISH   SS   YRT 70
    CAUTION| INFLAMMABLE| SCORTIA, THOMAS N.   AC
    YEAR 2000, THE   HARRISON, HARRY   OA
  LAST WAR, THE   SS   NEW 75 AC
    CAUTION| INFLAMMABLE| SCORTIA, THOMAS N.   AC
  MORALITY   SS   FAN 69 12
    CAUTION| INFLAMMABLE| SCORTIA, THOMAS N.   AC
  OLD, OLD DEATH IN NEW, NEW VENICE   SS   NEW 75 AC
    CAUTION| INFLAMMABLE| SCORTIA, THOMAS N.   AC
  PREMIER'S LADY, THE   SS   NEW 75 AC
    CAUTION| INFLAMMABLE| SCORTIA, THOMAS N.   AC
  SEA CHANGE (ALSO AS THE SHORES OF NIGHT)   SS   ASF 56 06
    CAUTION| INFLAMMABLE| SCORTIA, THOMAS N.   AC
    HUMAN-MACHINES   SCORTIA & ZEBROWSKI   AN
    SPACE OPERA   ALDISS, BRIAN W.   AN
  SHORES OF NIGHT, THE (EXPANDED FROM "SEA CHANGE") SS ASF 56 06
    BEST SCIENCE FICTION STORIES AND NOVELS: 1956
                                        DIKTY, T. E.   AN
    6 FROM WORLDS BEYOND   DIKTY, T. E.   AN
  TARRYING   SS   FTP 73
    FLAME TREE PLANET   ELWOOD, ROGER   OA
  THIS IS: AN INTRODUCTION   IN
    MONADIC UNIVERSE, THE   ZEBROWSKI, GEORGE   AC
  THOU GOOD AND FAITHFUL   NV   TVW 73
    BEST SCIENCE FICTION STORIES OF THE YEAR (1973)
                                        DEL REY, LESTER   AN
    TWO VIEWS OF WONDER   SCORTIA & YARBRO   OA
  THOUGH A SPARROW FALL   SS   ASF 65 07
    CAUTION| INFLAMMABLE| SCORTIA, THOMAS N.   AC
  TOWER, THE   SS   COI 73
    CHILDREN OF INFINITY   ELWOOD, ROGER   OA
  "VIVE LAQUELLE DIFFERENCE?"   IN C
    TWO VIEWS OF WONDER   SCORTIA & YARBRO   OA
  WEARIEST RIVER, THE   NV   FUC 73
    BIO-FUTURES   SARGENT, PAMELA   AN
    CAUTION| INFLAMMABLE| SCORTIA, THOMAS N.   AC
    FUTURE CITY   ELWOOD, ROGER   OA
    VISIONS OF TOMORROW   ELWOOD, ROGER   AN
  WHEN YOU HEAR THE TONE   SS   GAL 71 01
    BEST SCIENCE FICTION STORIES OF THE YEAR (1971)
                                        DEL REY, LESTER   AN
    CAUTION| INFLAMMABLE   SCORTIA, THOMAS N.   AC
  "WHERE HAVE ALL THE DEFLOWERERS GONE?"   IN
    STRANGE BED FELLOWS   SCORTIA, THOMAS N.   AN
  WOMAN'S RIB   SS   GAL 72 07
    BEST SCIENCE FICTION STORIES OF THE YEAR (1972)
                                        DEL REY, LESTER   AN
    CAUTION| INFLAMMABLE| SCORTIA, THOMAS N.   AC
    MARRIAGE AND THE FAMILY THROUGH SCIENCE FICTION
                                        CLEAR/WARRICK/&   AN
  WORM IN THE ROSE, THE   SS   SWK 72 05
    CAUTION| INFLAMMABLE| SCORTIA, THOMAS N.   AC
  WORM, THE   NV   72
    BEWARE MORE BEASTS   GHIDALIA, V.& ELWOOD AN

SCOTT, JODY
  GO FOR BAROQUE   SS   FSF 61 06
    *BEST FROM FANTASY AND SCIENCE FICTION: 11
                                        MILLS, ROBERT P.   AN

SCOTT, MARTIN   PSEUD. FOR RICHARD GEHMAN

SCOTT, ROBIN S.   PSEUD. FOR ROBIN SCOTT WILSON
  BIG CONNECTION, THE   SS   NOV 70 01
    *NOVA 1   HARRISON, HARRY   OA
  EARLY WARNING   SS   ASF 66 06
    ANALOG 6   CAMPBELL, JOHN W. JR AN
  LAST TRAIN TO KANKAKEE   SS   DVS 72 02
    AGAIN, DANGEROUS VISIONS   ELLISON, HARLAN   OA
  MAYBE JEAN-BAPTISTE PIERRE ANTOINE DE MONET, CHEVALIER DE LAM-
  ARCK,WAS A LITTLE BIT RIGHT   SS   ORB 70 06

SCOTT, ROBIN S.   (CONTINUED)
    ORBIT 6   KNIGHT, DAMON   OA
  WHO NEEDS INSURANCE?   NV   ASF 66 04
    NEBULA AWARD STORIES NO. 2   ALDISS & HARRISON   AN

SCOTT, WALTER
  SECRET WEAPON (FROM "COUNT ROBERT OF PARIS")   EX
    SCIENCE FICTION THROUGH THE AGES 1 EVANS, I. O.   AN

SEABRIGHT, IDRIS   PSEUD. FOR MARGARET ST. CLAIR
  ALTRUISTS, THE   SS   FSF 53 11
    PORTALS OF TOMORROW   DERLETH, AUGUST   AN
  BRIGHTNESS FALLS FROM THE AIR (CONTEST STORY) SS FSF 51 04
    BEST SCIENCE-FICTION STORIES: 1952, THE
                                        BLEILER & DIKTY   AN
    GALACTIC EMPIRES VOLUME ONE   ALDISS, BRIAN W.   AN
  CAUSES, THE   SS   FSF 52 06
    DECADE OF FANTASY AND SCIENCE FICTION, A
                                        MILLS, ROBERT P.   AN
  EGG A MONTH FROM ALL OVER, AN   SS   FSF 52 10
    FIFTY SHORT SCIENCE FICTION TALES   ASIMOV & CONKLIN   AN
    HUMAN?   MERRIL, JUDITH   AN
    VINTAGE ANTHOLOGY OF SCIENCE FANTASY, THE
                                        CERF, CHRISTOPHER   AN
  HOLE IN THE MOON, THE   SS   FSF 52 02
    BEST FROM FANTASY AND SCIENCE FICTION: 2
                                        BOUCHER & MCCOMAS   AN
  LISTENING CHILD, THE   SS   FSF 50 12
    BEST FROM FANTASY AND SCIENCE FICTION BOUCHER & MCCOMAS   AN
  MAN WHO SOLD ROPE TO THE GNOLES, THE   SS   FSF 51 10
    *BEYOND HUMAN KEN   MERRIL, JUDITH   AN
  NEW RITUAL   SS   FSF 53 01
    BEST FROM FANTASY AND SCIENCE FICTION: 3
                                        BOUCHER & MCCOMAS   AN
  SHORT IN THE CHEST   SS   FUN 54 07
    ALPHA 6   SILVERBERG, ROBERT   AN
    METAL SMILE, THE   KNIGHT, DAMON   AN
    OPERATION FUTURE   CONKLIN, GROFF   AN
    17 X INFINITY   CONKLIN, GROFF   AN
  WHITE GODDESS   SS   FSF 56 07
    BR-R-R-| CONKLIN, GROFF   AN
  WINES OF EARTH, THE   SS   FSF 57 09
    BEST FROM FANTASY AND SCIENCE FICTION: 7
                                        BOUCHER, ANTHONY   AN

SEAGER, ALLAN
  COLORLESS IN LIMESTONE CAVERNS   SS   PBY 69 11
    MASKS   PLAYBOY, EDITORS OF AN

SEAMARK   PSEUD. FOR AUSTIN J. SMALL
  AVENGING RAY, THE   EX   30
    SCIENCE IN FICTION   BAYLISS, A.E. & J.C. AN

SELL, WILLIAM
  OTHER TRACKS   NV   ASF 38 10
    *SCIENCE FICTION ADVENTURES IN DIMENSION
                                        CONKLIN, GROFF   AN

SELLINGS, ARTHUR   PSEUD. FOR ARTHUR LEY
  LONG EUREKA, THE   AC H DOB 68
  TIME TRANSFER   AC H JOS 56
  TIME TRANSFER (11 OF 16)   AC   CPT 66
  AGE OF KINDNESS, THE   SS   GAL 54 11
    *TIME TRANSFER   SELLINGS, ARTHUR   AC
  AWAKENING, THE   SS
    *TIME TRANSFER   SELLINGS, ARTHUR   AC
  BIRTHRIGHT   SS   NWS 56 11
    LONG EUREKA, THE   SELLINGS, ARTHUR   AC
  BLANK FORM   SS   GAL 58 07
    FOURTH GALAXY READER, THE   GOLD, H. L.   AN
    LONG EUREKA, THE   SELLINGS, ARTHUR   AC
  CATEGORICAL IMPERATIVE (THE CATEGORY INVENTORS) NV GAL 56 02
    *TIME TRANSFER   SELLINGS, ARTHUR   AC
    WINDOW ON THE FUTURE   HILL, DOUGLAS   AN
  CATEGORY INVENTORS, THE (SEE CATEGORICAL IMPERATIVE)
                                               TC
  CONTROL ROOM   SS
    *TIME TRANSFER   SELLINGS, ARTHUR   AC
  ESCAPE MECHANISM   SS   FUN 55 08
    *TIME TRANSFER   SELLINGS, ARTHUR   AC
  FIGMENT, THE   SS   FUN 55 02
    *TIME TRANSFER   SELLINGS, ARTHUR   AC
  FROM UP THERE   SS
    *TIME TRANSFER   SELLINGS, ARTHUR   AC
  GIFTS OF THE GODS   NV   NWR 66 09
    NEW WRITINGS IN SF. 7   CARNELL, JOHN   AN
    NEW WRITINGS IN SF. 9   CARNELL, JOHN   OA
  HAUNTING, THE   SS   AUT 53 10
    *TIME TRANSFER   SELLINGS, ARTHUR   AC
  HOMECOMING   SS
    LONG EUREKA, THE   SELLINGS, ARTHUR   AC
  JUKEBOX   SS   FUN 55 12
    *TIME TRANSFER   SELLINGS, ARTHUR   AC
  KEY OF THE DOOR, THE   SS   NWS 67 03
    NEW WORLDS QUARTERLY NO. 2   MOORCOCK, MICHAEL   OA
  LAST TIME AROUND, THE   NV   NWR 68 12
    NEW WRITINGS IN SF. 9   CARNELL, JOHN   AN
    NEW WRITINGS IN SF. 12   CARNELL, JOHN   OA
    WORLD'S BEST SCIENCE FICTION: 1971 WOLLHEIM & CARR   AN
  LONG EUREKA, THE   SS   SCF 59 08
    LONG EUREKA, THE   SELLINGS, ARTHUR   AC
  MISSION, THE   SS
    AD 2500   WILSON, ANGUS   AN
  ONE ACROSS   SS   GAL 56 05
    LONG EUREKA, THE   SELLINGS, ARTHUR   AC

SELLINGS, ARTHUR   (CONTINUED)
  OUTSTRETCHED HAND, THE   SS   NWS 59 05
    BEST OF NEW WORLDS, THE   MOORCOCK, MICHAEL   AN
  PENTAGRAM   SS   SAT 58 10
    *TIME TRANSFER   SELLINGS, ARTHUR   AC
  PROXIES, THE   SS   IFS 55 10
    *TIME TRANSFER   SELLINGS, ARTHUR   AC
  SCENE SHIFTER, THE   SS   STR 59 05
    LONG EUREKA, THE   SELLINGS, ARTHUR   AC
    STAR SCIENCE FICTION STORIES NO. 5 POHL, FREDERIK   OA
  SOLILOQUY   SS
    *TIME TRANSFER   SELLINGS, ARTHUR   AC
  START IN LIFE, A   SS   GAL 54 09
    INTRODUCING SCIENCE FICTION   ALDISS, BRIAN W.   AN
    *TIME TRANSFER   SELLINGS, ARTHUR   AC
  THAT EVENING SUN GO DOWN   SS   NWS 66 09
    GODS FOR TOMORROW   SANTESSON, HANS S.   AN
  TIME TRANSFER   SS
    *TIME TRANSFER   SELLINGS, ARTHUR   AC
  TRADE-IN   SS
    LONG EUREKA, THE   SELLINGS, ARTHUR   AC
  TRANSFER, THE   SS
    *TIME TRANSFER   SELLINGS, ARTHUR   AC
  TRIAL, THE   NV   NWR 69 15
    NEW WRITINGS IN SF. 15   CARNELL, JOHN   OA
  VERBAL AGREEMENT   NV   GAL 56 09
    LONG EUREKA, THE   SELLINGS, ARTHUR   AC
  WELL TRAINED HEROES, THE   NV   GAL 64 06
    LONG EUREKA, THE   SELLINGS, ARTHUR   AC
  WORDLESS ONES, THE   SS
    *TIME TRANSFER   SELLINGS, ARTHUR   AC

SENARENS, LOUIS P.
  FRANK READE JUNIOR'S AIR WONDER (1876)   SS   BNY 76
    ANDROIDS, TIME MACHINES AND BLUE GIRAFFES
                                       ELWOOD & GHIDALIA   AN
    STRANGE SIGNPOSTS   ELWOOD & MOSKOWITZ   AN
  LOST IN A COMET'S TAIL, OR, FRANK READE JR'S STRANGE ADVENTURE
    IN HIS NEW AIRSHIP   SS   FRL 95 12
    MASTERPIECES OF SCIENCE FICTION   MOSKOWITZ, SAM   AN

SENTRY, JOHN A.   PSEUD. FOR ALGIS J. BUDRYS

SERLING, ROD
  FROM THE TWILIGHT ZONE   AC H NDB 62
  MORE STORIES FROM THE TWILIGHT ZONE   OC   BAN 61 04
  NEW STORIES FROM THE TWILIGHT ZONE   OC   BAN 62 05
  NIGHT GALLERY   OC   BAN 71 11
  NIGHT GALLERY 2   OC   BAN 72 12
  ROD SERLING'S THE TWILIGHT ZONE   OC H GRS 63
  ROD SERLING'S THE TWILIGHT ZONE (CHILLING STORIES FROM)
                                                      OC   TMP 65 08
  ROD SERLING'S TRIPLE W: WITCHES, WARLOCKS AND WEREWOLVES
                                                      AN   BAN 63 05
  ROD SERLING'S TWILIGHT ZONE REVISITED   OC H GRS 64
  STORIES FROM THE TWILIGHT ZONE   OC   BAN 60 04
  AVENGING GHOST, THE   SA
    *ROD SERLING'S THE TWILIGHT ZONE   SERLING, ROD   OC
  BACK THERE   SA
    *ROD SERLING'S THE TWILIGHT ZONE   SERLING, ROD   OC
  BEYOND THE RIM   SA
    ROD SERLING'S TWILIGHT ZONE REVISITED SERLING, ROD   OC
  BIG, TALL WISH, THE   SA
    FROM THE TWILIGHT ZONE   SERLING, ROD   AC
    MORE STORIES FROM THE TWILIGHT ZONE SERLING, ROD   OC
  CLEAN KILLS AND OTHER TROPHIES   SA
    NIGHT GALLERY   SERLING, ROD   OC
  COLLECTOR'S ITEMS   SA
    NIGHT GALLERY 2   SERLING, ROD   OC
  CURSE OF SEVEN TOWERS, THE   SA
    *ROD SERLING'S THE TWILIGHT ZONE   SERLING, ROD   OC
  DEAD MAN'S CHEST   SA
    *ROD SERLING'S THE TWILIGHT ZONE   SERLING, ROD   OC
  DEATH'S MASQUERADE   SA
    *ROD SERLING'S THE TWILIGHT ZONE   SERLING, ROD   OC
  DIFFERENT ONES, THE   SA
    NIGHT GALLERY 2   SERLING, ROD   OC
  DOES THE NAME GRIMSBY DO ANYTHING TO YOU?   SA
    NIGHT GALLERY   SERLING, ROD   OC
  DUST   SA
    FROM THE TWILIGHT ZONE   SERLING, ROD   AC
    MORE STORIES FROM THE TWILIGHT ZONE SERLING, ROD   OC
  ESCAPE CLAUSE   SA
    FROM THE TWILIGHT ZONE   SERLING, ROD   AC
    STORIES FROM THE TWILIGHT ZONE   SERLING, ROD   OC
  FEVER, THE   SA
    STORIES FROM THE TWILIGHT ZONE   SERLING, ROD   OC
  FOREWORD   IN
    ROD SERLING'S THE TWILIGHT ZONE (CHILLING STORIES FROM)
                                       SERLING, ROD   OC
    ROD SERLING'S TWILIGHT ZONE REVISITED SERLING, ROD   OC
  GHOST OF JOLLY ROGER, THE   SA
    ROD SERLING'S TWILIGHT ZONE REVISITED SERLING, ROD   OC
  GHOST OF THE DIXIE BELLE, THE   SA
    ROD SERLING'S TWILIGHT ZONE REVISITED SERLING, ROD   OC
  GHOST OF TICONDEROGA, THE   SA
    *ROD SERLING'S THE TWILIGHT ZONE   SERLING, ROD   OC
  GHOST TRAIN, THE   SA
    ROD SERLING'S TWILIGHT ZONE REVISITED SERLING, ROD   OC
  GHOST-TOWN GHOST, THE   SA
    *ROD SERLING'S THE TWILIGHT ZONE   SERLING, ROD   OC
  HOUSE ON THE SQUARE, THE   SA
    *ROD SERLING'S THE TWILIGHT ZONE   SERLING, ROD   OC
  INTRODUCTION   IN
    ROD SERLING'S TRIPLE W: WITCHES, WARLOCKS AND WEREWOLVES
                                       SERLING, ROD   AN

SERLING, ROD   (CONTINUED)
  JUDGMENT NIGHT   SA
    *ROD SERLING'S THE TWILIGHT ZONE   SERLING, ROD   OC
  LINDEMANN'S CATCH   SA
    NIGHT GALLERY 2   SERLING, ROD   OC
  LONELY, THE   SA
    FROM THE TWILIGHT ZONE   SERLING, ROD   AC
    MORE STORIES FROM THE TWILIGHT ZONE SERLING, ROD   OC
  MAKE ME LAUGH   SA
    NIGHT GALLERY   SERLING, ROD   OC
  MAN IN THE BOTTLE, THE   SA
    ROD SERLING'S TWILIGHT ZONE REVISITED SERLING, ROD   OC
  MAN WHO DROPPED BY, THE   SA
    ROD SERLING'S TWILIGHT ZONE REVISITED SERLING, ROD   OC
  MESSIAH ON MOTT STREET, THE   SA
    NIGHT GALLERY 2   SERLING, ROD   OC
  MIDNIGHT SUN, THE   SA
    FROM THE TWILIGHT ZONE   SERLING, ROD   AC
    NEW STORIES FROM THE TWILIGHT ZONE SERLING, ROD   OC
  MIGHTY CASEY, THE   SA
    FROM THE TWILIGHT ZONE   SERLING, ROD   AC
    STORIES FROM THE TWILIGHT ZONE   SERLING, ROD   OC
  MIRROR IMAGE, THE   SA
    ROD SERLING'S TWILIGHT ZONE REVISITED SERLING, ROD   OC
  MONSTERS ARE DUE ON MAPLE STREET, THE   SA
    FROM THE TWILIGHT ZONE   SERLING, ROD   AC
    STORIES FROM THE TWILIGHT ZONE   SERLING, ROD   OC
  MR. DINGLE, THE STRONG   SA
    FROM THE TWILIGHT ZONE   SERLING, ROD   AC
    MORE STORIES FROM THE TWILIGHT ZONE SERLING, ROD   OC
  NIGHT OF THE MEEK   SA
    NEW STORIES FROM THE TWILIGHT ZONE SERLING, ROD   OC
  ODYSSEY OF FLIGHT 33, THE   SA
    FROM THE TWILIGHT ZONE   SERLING, ROD   AC
    MORE STORIES FROM THE TWILIGHT ZONE SERLING, ROD   OC
  PAMELA'S VOICE   SA
    NIGHT GALLERY   SERLING, ROD   OC
  PURPLE TESTAMENT, THE   SA
    ROD SERLING'S TWILIGHT ZONE REVISITED SERLING, ROD   OC
  RETURN FROM OBLIVION   SA
    *ROD SERLING'S THE TWILIGHT ZONE   SERLING, ROD   OC
  RIDDLE OF THE CRYPT, THE   SA
    *ROD SERLING'S THE TWILIGHT ZONE   SERLING, ROD   OC
  RIP VAN WINKLE CAPER, THE   SA
    FROM THE TWILIGHT ZONE   SERLING, ROD   AC
    NEW STORIES FROM THE TWILIGHT ZONE SERLING, ROD   OC
  SHELTER, THE   SA
    FROM THE TWILIGHT ZONE   SERLING, ROD   AC
    NEW STORIES FROM THE TWILIGHT ZONE SERLING, ROD   OC
  SHOWDOWN WITH RANCE MCGREW   SA
    NEW STORIES FROM THE TWILIGHT ZONE SERLING, ROD   OC
  SOLE SURVIVOR, THE   SA
    NIGHT GALLERY   SERLING, ROD   OC
  STOP AT WILLOUGHBY, A   SA
    MORE STORIES FROM THE TWILIGHT ZONE SERLING, ROD   OC
  SUGGESTION   SA
    NIGHT GALLERY 2   SERLING, ROD   OC
  THEY'RE TEARING DOWN TIM RILEY'S BAR   SA
    NIGHT GALLERY   SERLING, ROD   OC
  THING ABOUT MACHINES, A   SA
    MORE STORIES FROM THE TWILIGHT ZONE SERLING, ROD   OC
  THIRTEENTH STORY, THE   SA
    *ROD SERLING'S THE TWILIGHT ZONE   SERLING, ROD   OC
  TIGER GOD, THE   SA
    *ROD SERLING'S THE TWILIGHT ZONE   SERLING, ROD   OC
  TWO LIVE GHOSTS   SA
    ROD SERLING'S TWILIGHT ZONE REVISITED SERLING, ROD   OC
  WALKING DISTANCE   SA
    FROM THE TWILIGHT ZONE   SERLING, ROD   AC
    STORIES FROM THE TWILIGHT ZONE   SERLING, ROD   OC
  WHERE IS EVERYBODY?   SA
    FROM THE TWILIGHT ZONE   SERLING, ROD   AC
    STORIES FROM THE TWILIGHT ZONE   SERLING, ROD   OC
  WHOLE TRUTH, THE   SA
    FROM THE TWILIGHT ZONE   SERLING, ROD   AC
    NEW STORIES FROM THE TWILIGHT ZONE SERLING, ROD   OC

SERVISS, GARRETT P.
  EDISON'S CONQUEST OF MARS (ABRIDGED)   SS   NYE 98 01
    TREASURY OF SCIENCE FICTION CLASSICS, THE
                                       KUEBLER, HAROLD W.   AN

SHAARA, MICHAEL
  ALL THE WAY BACK   SS   ASF 52 07
    GALACTIC EMPIRES VOLUME ONE   ALDISS, BRIAN W.   AN
  BOOK, THE   NV   GAL 53 11
    ELSEWHERE AND ELSEWHEN   CONKLIN, GROFF   AN
  GRENVILLE'S PLANET   SS   FSF 52 10
    BEST SF 3   CRISPIN, EDMUND   AN
    UNTRAVELLED WORLDS   BARTER & WILSON   AN
  MAN OF DISTINCTION   SS   GAL 56 10
    FOURTH GALAXY READER, THE   GOLD, H. L.   AN
  ORPHANS OF THE VOID   NV   GAL 52 06
    ALPHA 7   SILVERBERG, ROBERT   AN
    SHADOW OF TOMORROW   POHL, FREDERIK   AN
  SOLDIER BOY   NV   GAL 53 07
    *SCIENCE FICTION THINKING MACHINES CONKLIN, GROFF   AN
  2066: ELECTION DAY   SS   ASF 56 12
    BEST SCIENCE FICTION STORIES AND NOVELS: 9TH SERIES
                                       DIKTY, T. E.   AN
    POLITICAL SCIENCE FICTION   GREENBERG& WARRICK   AN

SHACKLETON, C. C.   PSEUD. FOR BRIAN W. ALDISS
  ULTIMATE CONSTRUCTION   SS   TBT 67
    BEST SF: 1967   HARRISON & ALDISS   AN

SHALLIT, JOSEPH   SHECKLEY, ROBERT

SHALLIT, JOSEPH
  WONDER CHILD   NV FAN 53 01
    BEST SCIENCE-FICTION STORIES: 1954, THE
                                        BLEILER & DIKTY   AN

SHAMIR, MOSHE
  DOCTOR SCHMIDT   SS   52
    VOYAGES: SCENARIOS FOR A SHIP CALLED EARTH
                                        SAUER, ROB   AN

SHANGO, J. R.
  MATTER OF ETHICS, A   SS FSF 54 11
    GREAT SCIENCE FICTION ABOUT DOCTORS CONKLIN, G&FABRICANT AN

SHANKS, EDWARD
  RECEPTIVE BOSOM, THE   PM
    FANTASIA MATHEMATICA   FADIMAN, CLIFTON   AN

SHAPIRO, NEIL
  JOURNEY OF THE SOUL   NV
    TOMORROW: NEW WORLDS OF SCIENCE FICTION
                                        ELWOOD, ROGER   OA

SHAPLEY, HARLOW
  ON LETHAL CLOUDS   AR
    POISON BELT, THE   DOYLE, ARTHUR CONAN AC

SHARKEY, JACK
  CONVERSATION WITH A BUG   SS PBY 61 10
    FROM THE "S" FILE   PLAYBOY, EDITORS OF AN
  FINAL INGREDIENT, THE   SS FSF 60 08
    ROD SERLING'S TRIPLE W: WITCHES, WARLOCKS AND WEREWOLVES
                                        SERLING, ROD   AN
  MULTUM IN PARVO   SS GNT 59 12
    5TH ANNUAL OF THE YEAR'S BEST S-F, THE MERRIL, JUDITH   AN
  POOL, THE   SS PBY 64 11
    FROM THE "S" FILE   PLAYBOY, EDITORS OF AN
  TO EACH HIS OWN   SS IFS 60 01
    6 FINGERS OF TIME AND 5 OTHER SCIENCE FICTION NOVELETS, THE
                                        ANONYMOUS   AN
  TRADE-IN   SS FSF 64 06
    BEST FROM FANTASY AND SCIENCE FICTION: 14
                                        DAVIDSON, AVRAM   AN
  TWERLIK, THE   SS WOT 64 06
    10TH ANNUAL OF THE YEAR'S BEST S-F, THE
                                        MERRIL, JUDITH   AN

SHARNIK, JOHN S.
  LIMITS OF WALTER HORTON, THE   SS CHM 54
    CIRCUS OF DR. LAO AND OTHER IMPROBABLE STORIES
                                        BRADBURY, RAY   AN

SHARP, D. D.
  ETERNAL MAN, THE   SS SWS 29 08
    FROM OFF THIS WORLD   MARGULIES & FRIEND   AN
    HISTORY OF THE SCIENCE FICTION MAGAZINE, THE PART 1 1926-1935
                                        ASHLEY, MICHAEL   AN
    *TREASURY OF SCIENCE FICTION, A   CONKLIN, GROFF   AN

SHATNER, WILLIAM
  INTRODUCTION TO MIND-SIFTER   IN
    STAR TREK: THE NEW VOYAGES   MARSHAK, S&CULBREATH OA

SHAW, BOB
COSMIC KALEIDOSCOPE   AC H GOL 76
OTHER DAYS, OTHER EYES   NO ACE 72 07
TOMORROW LIES IN AMBUSH   AC ACE 73 02
    ENGLISH EDITION (GOL 73) OMITS STORIES "STORMSEEKER"
    AND "ELEMENT OF CHANCE"
  ALTAR EGOES   SS
    BEYOND THIS HORIZON   CARRELL, CHRISTOPHER OA
  AND ISLES WHERE GOOD MEN LIE   SS NWS 65 10
    TOMORROW LIES IN AMBUSH   SHAW, BOB   AC
  APPOINTMENT ON PRILA   SS ASF 68 08
    BEST SF: 1968   HARRISON & ALDISS   AN
    WORLDS OF WONDER   HARRISON, HARRY   AN
  BRINK, THE   SS FAN 76
    COSMIC KALEIDOSCOPE   SHAW, BOB   AC
  BURDEN OF PROOF   SS ASF 67 05
    ANALOG 7   CAMPBELL, JOHN W. JR AN
    OTHER DAYS, OTHER EYES   SHAW, BOB   NO
  CALL ME DUMBO   NV IFS 66 12
    TOMORROW LIES IN AMBUSH   SHAW, BOB   AC
  COMMUNICATION   NV FAN 70 06
    TOMORROW LIES IN AMBUSH   SHAW, BOB   AC
  COSMIC COCKTAIL PARTY, THE (HAROLD WILSON AT THE COSMIC
    COCKTAIL PARTY)   SS SAG 70
    TOMORROW LIES IN AMBUSH   SHAW, BOB   AC
  DARK ICARUS (ALSO AS A LITTLE NIGHT FLYING)   SS SFM 74 04
    BEST OF SCIENCE FICTION MONTHLY, THE SACKS, JANET   AN
    BEST SCIENCE FICTION OF THE YEAR, THE NO. 4
                                        CARR, TERRY   AN
  DOME OF MANY-COLORED GLASS, A   SS FAN 72 04
    OTHER DAYS, OTHER EYES   SHAW, BOB   NO
  ELEMENT OF CHANCE   SS GAL 69 10
    TOMORROW LIES IN AMBUSH   SHAW, BOB   AC
  FULL MEMBER OF THE CLUB, A   NV GAL 74 07
    COSMIC KALEIDOSCOPE   SHAW, BOB   AC
    1975 ANNUAL WORLD'S BEST SF, THE   WOLLHEIM, DONALD A. AN
  GIACONDA CAPER, THE   NV   76
    COSMIC KALEIDOSCOPE   SHAW, BOB   AC
  HAPPIEST DAY OF YOUR LIFE, THE   SS ASF 70 10
    TOMORROW LIES IN AMBUSH   SHAW, BOB   AC
  HAROLD WILSON AT THE COSMIC COCKTAIL PARTY (ALSO AS THE
    COSMIC COCKTAIL PARTY)   SS SAG 70
    SCIENCE AGAINST MAN   CHEETHAM, ANTHONY   OA

SHAW, BOB   (CONTINUED)
  INVASION OF PRIVACY   NV AMZ 70 07
    TALES OF TERROR FROM OUTER SPACE   CHETWYND-HAYES, R.   AN
    TOMORROW LIES IN AMBUSH   SHAW, BOB   AC
    WORLD'S BEST SCIENCE FICTION: 1971   WOLLHEIM & CARR   AN
  LIGHT OF OTHER DAYS   SS ASF 66 08
    ABOVE THE HUMAN LANDSCAPE   MCNELLY & STOVER   AN
    ALPHA 6   SILVERBERG, ROBERT   AN
    ANALOG 6   CAMPBELL, JOHN W. JR AN
    NEBULA AWARD STORIES NO. 2   ALDISS & HARRISON   AN
    OTHER DAYS, OTHER EYES   SHAW, BOB   NO
    SCIENCE FICTION ARGOSY, A   KNIGHT, DAMON   AN
    SCIENCE FICTION: THE FUTURE   ALLEN, DICK   AN
    SF12   MERRIL, JUDITH   AN
    WORLD'S BEST SCIENCE FICTION: 1967   WOLLHEIM & CARR   AN
  LITTLE NIGHT FLYING, A (DARK ICARUS)   NV IFS 74 08
    BEST FROM IF, THE VOLUME III   BAEN, JAMES   AN
    COSMIC KALEIDOSCOPE   SHAW, BOB   AC
  OTHER DAYS, OTHER EYES   NA AMZ 72 05
    OTHER DAYS, OTHER EYES   SHAW, BOB   NO
  PILOT PLANT   NV NWS 66 05
    TOMORROW LIES IN AMBUSH   SHAW, BOB   AC
  REPEAT PERFORMANCE   SS FSF 71 02
    TOMORROW LIES IN AMBUSH   SHAW, BOB   AC
  RETROACTIVE   NV UNI 72 02
    UNIVERSE 2   CARR, TERRY   OA
  SILENT PARTNERS, THE   SS NEB 59 06
    COSMIC KALEIDOSCOPE   SHAW, BOB   AC
  SKIRMISH ON A SUMMER MORNING   NA   76
    COSMIC KALEIDOSCOPE   SHAW, BOB   AC
  STORMSEEKER   SS GAL 72 01
    TOMORROW LIES IN AMBUSH   SHAW, BOB   AC
  TELEMART THREE   SS IFS 70 03
    TOMORROW LIES IN AMBUSH   SHAW, BOB   AC
  UNCOMIC BOOK HORROR STORY, AN   SS SFM 75 10
    COSMIC KALEIDOSCOPE   SHAW, BOB   AC
  UNREASONABLE FACSIMILE   SS
    COSMIC KALEIDOSCOPE   SHAW, BOB   AC
    LONG NIGHT OF WAITING AND OTHER STORIES
                                        ELWOOD, ROGER   OA
  WALTZ OF THE BODYSNATCHERS   NV
    ANDROMEDA I   WESTON, PETER   OA
    COSMIC KALEIDOSCOPE   SHAW, BOB   AC
  WEAPONS OF ISHER II, THE   SS AMZ 71 05
    TOMORROW LIES IN AMBUSH   SHAW, BOB   AC
  WHAT TIME DO YOU CALL THIS?   SS AMZ 71 09
    TOMORROW LIES IN AMBUSH   SHAW, BOB   AC

SHAW, GEORGE BERNARD
  CREATIVE EVOLUTION (FROM PREFACE TO "BACK TO METHUSELAH")
                                                         EX
    ARMCHAIR SCIENCE READER, THE   GORDON, I. & SORKIN AN

SHAW, IRWIN
  MANNICHON SOLUTION, THE   NV PBY 67 12
    PLAYBOY'S STORIES OF THE SINISTER & STRANGE
                                        PLAYBOY, EDITORS OF AN
  WHISPERS IN BEDLAM   NA PBY 69 02
    ARENA: SPORTS SF   FERMAN & MALZBERG   AN

SHAW, LAO
  EVERYBODYOVSKYISM IN CAT CITY   SS
    APEMAN, SPACEMAN   STOVER & HARRISON   AN

SHAW, LARRY T.
  GREAT SCIENCE FICTION ADVENTURES   AN LAN 63
  SIMWORTHY'S CIRCUS   SS WBY 50 12
    *SCIENCE-FICTION CARNIVAL   BROWN, F. & REYNOLDS AN

SHCHERBAKOV, VLADIMIR
  WE PLAYED UNDER YOUR WINDOW   SS   66
    ULTIMATE THRESHOLD, THE   GINSBURG, MIRRA   AN

SHECKLEY, ROBERT   ALSO AS   FINN O'DONNEVAN
  CAN YOU FEEL ANYTHING WHEN I DO THIS?, AND OTHER STORIES
                                                         AC H DBL 71
        IN ENGLAND AS "THE SAME TO YOU DOUBLED"
  CITIZEN IN SPACE   AC BAL 55 12
  NOTIONS: UNLIMITED   AC BAN 60 06
  PEOPLE TRAP AND OTHER PITFALLS, THE   AC DEL 68 12
  PILGRIMAGE TO EARTH   AC BAN 57 10
  ROBERT SHECKLEY OMNIBUS, THE   AC H GOL 73
        EDITED BY ROBERT CONQUEST
  SAME TO YOU DOUBLED AND OTHER STORIES, THE   AC PAN 74
        SEE "CAN YOU FEEL ANYTHING WHEN I DO THIS?"
  SHARDS OF SPACE   AC BAN 62 07
  STORE OF INFINITY   AC BAN 60 11
  UNTOUCHED BY HUMAN HANDS   AC H BAL 54 03
  UNTOUCHED BY HUMAN HANDS (BRITISH)   AC FSP 67
  ACADEMY, THE   NV IFS 54 08
    PILGRIMAGE TO EARTH   SHECKLEY, ROBERT   AC
  ACCOUNTANT, THE   SS FSF 54 07
    BEST FROM FANTASY AND SCIENCE FICTION: 4
                                        BOUCHER, ANTHONY   AN
    CITIZEN IN SPACE   SHECKLEY, ROBERT   AC
    TOMORROW'S CHILDREN   ASIMOV, ISAAC   AN
  ALL THE THINGS YOU ARE   SS GAL 56 07
    PILGRIMAGE TO EARTH   SHECKLEY, ROBERT   AC
  ALONE AT LAST   SS INF 57 02
    SHARDS OF SPACE   SHECKLEY, ROBERT   AC
  ALTAR, THE   SS FAN 53 08
    *UNTOUCHED BY HUMAN HANDS   SHECKLEY, ROBERT   AC
  ASK A FOOLISH QUESTION   SS SFS 53 01
    CITIZEN IN SPACE   SHECKLEY, ROBERT   AC
    ROBERT SHECKLEY OMNIBUS, THE   SHECKLEY, ROBERT   AC
    6 AND THE SILENT SCREAM   HOWARD, IVAN   AN

SHECKLEY, ROBERT   (CONTINUED)
ASPECTS OF LANGRANAK   SS   NEW 71 AC
  CAN YOU FEEL ANYTHING WHEN I DO THIS?, AND OTHER STORIES
                                     SHECKLEY, ROBERT   AC
BAD MEDICINE   NV   GAL 56 07
  PILGRIMAGE TO EARTH   SHECKLEY, ROBERT   AC
  ROBERT SHECKLEY OMNIBUS, THE   SHECKLEY, ROBERT   AC
  SF: AUTHORS' CHOICE 4   HARRISON, HARRY   AN
BATTLE, THE   SS   IFS 54 09
  CITIZEN IN SPACE   SHECKLEY, ROBERT   AC
  FIRST WORLD OF IF, THE   QUINN & WULFF   AN
  ROBERT SHECKLEY OMNIBUS, THE   SHECKLEY, ROBERT   AC
BESIDE STILL WATERS   SS   AMZ 53 11
  *UNTOUCHED BY HUMAN HANDS   SHECKLEY, ROBERT   AC
BODY, THE   SS   GAL 56 01
  PILGRIMAGE TO EARTH   SHECKLEY, ROBERT   AC
BUDGET PLANET   EX   FSF 68 03
  BEST SF: 1968   HARRISON & ALDISS   AN
CAN YOU FEEL ANYTHING WHEN I DO THIS?   SS   PBY 69 08
  CAN YOU FEEL ANYTHING WHEN I DO THIS?, AND OTHER STORIES
                                     SHECKLEY, ROBERT   AC
  FIEND, THE   PLAYBOY, EDITORS OF   AN
  FROM THE "S" FILE   PLAYBOY, EDITORS OF   AN
  SCIENCE FICTION ARGOSY, A   KNIGHT, DAMON   AN
CARRIER   NV   IFS 54 04
  WILDERNESS OF STARS, A   NOLAN, WILLIAM F.   AN
CITIZEN IN SPACE (SPY STORY)   SS   PBY 55 09
  CITIZEN IN SPACE   SHECKLEY, ROBERT   AC
CORDLE TO ONION TO CARROT   SS   PBY 69 12
  CAN YOU FEEL ANYTHING WHEN I DO THIS?, AND OTHER STORIES
                                     SHECKLEY, ROBERT   AC
  FROM THE "S" FILE   PLAYBOY, EDITORS OF   AN
COST OF LIVING   SS   GAL 52 12
  *UNTOUCHED BY HUMAN HANDS   SHECKLEY, ROBERT   AC
CRUEL EQUATIONS, THE   SS   BOA
  CAN YOU FEEL ANYTHING WHEN I DO THIS?, AND OTHER STORIES
                                     SHECKLEY, ROBERT   AC
DAWN INVADER   SS   FSF 57 03
  ALIEN WORLDS   ELWOOD, ROGER   AN
  NOTIONS: UNLIMITED   SHECKLEY, ROBERT   AC
DEADHEAD   SS   GAL 55 07
  PILGRIMAGE TO EARTH   SHECKLEY, ROBERT   AC
DEATHS OF BEN BAXTER, THE   NV   GAL 57 07
  STORE OF INFINITY   SHECKLEY, ROBERT   AC
DEMONS, THE   SS   FNF 53 02
  *UNTOUCHED BY HUMAN HANDS   SHECKLEY, ROBERT   AC
DIPLOMATIC IMMUNITY   NV   GAL 53 08
  PEOPLE TRAP AND OTHER PITFALLS, THE SHECKLEY, ROBERT   AC
DISPOSAL SERVICE   SS   BBM 55
  PILGRIMAGE TO EARTH   SHECKLEY, ROBERT   AC
DOCTOR ZOMBIE AND HIS FURRY LITTLE FRIENDS   SS   NEW 71 AC
  BEST SF: 1971   HARRISON & ALDISS   AN
  CAN YOU FEEL ANYTHING WHEN I DO THIS?, AND OTHER STORIES
                                     SHECKLEY, ROBERT   AC
DOUBLE INDEMNITY   NV   GAL 57 10
  NOTIONS: UNLIMITED   SHECKLEY, ROBERT   AC
DOWN THE DIGESTIVE TRACT AND INTO THE COSMOS WITH MANTRA,
  TANTRA, AND SPECKLEBANG   SS   GAL 71 02
  CAN YOU FEEL ANYTHING WHEN I DO THIS?, AND OTHER STORIES
                                     SHECKLEY, ROBERT   AC
DREAMWORLD   SS   NEW 68 AC
  PEOPLE TRAP AND OTHER PITFALLS, THE SHECKLEY, ROBERT   AC
EARLY MODEL   NV   GAL 56 08
  DECADE THE 1950S   ALDISS & HARRISON   AN
  PILGRIMAGE TO EARTH   SHECKLEY, ROBERT   AC
EARTH, AIR, FIRE AND WATER   SS   ASF 55 07
  PILGRIMAGE TO EARTH   SHECKLEY, ROBERT   AC
END CITY   SS   GAL 74 05
  BEST FROM GALAXY, THE   VOLUME III BAEN, JAMES   AN
FEAR IN THE NIGHT   SS   TDW 52
  PILGRIMAGE TO EARTH   SHECKLEY, ROBERT   AC
FEEDING TIME   SS   FNF 53 02
  NOTIONS: UNLIMITED   SHECKLEY, ROBERT   AC
FISHING SEASON   SS   TWS 53 08
  PEOPLE TRAP AND OTHER PITFALLS, THE SHECKLEY, ROBERT   AC
  *TERROR IN THE MODERN VEIN   WOLLHEIM, DONALD A.   AN
FOOL'S MATE   SS   ASF 53 03
  METAL SMILE, THE   KNIGHT, DAMON   AN
  SHARDS OF SPACE   SHECKLEY, ROBERT   AC
FOREVER (AS NED LANG)   SS   GAL 59 02
  SHARDS OF SPACE   SHECKLEY, ROBERT   AC
FORTUNATE PERSON (SEE THE LUCKIEST MAN IN THE WORLD)
                                     TC
FROM: JOURNEY BEYOND TOMORROW   EX   DEL 62
  INSIDE INFORMATION   MOWSHOWITZ, ABBE   AN
  INSIDE INFORMATION   MOWSHOWITZ, ABBE   AN
GAME: FIRST SCHEMATIC   SS   NEW 71 AC
  CAN YOU FEEL ANYTHING WHEN I DO THIS?, AND OTHER STORIES
                                     SHECKLEY, ROBERT   AC
GHOST V   SS   GAL 54 10
  PEOPLE TRAP AND OTHER PITFALLS, THE SHECKLEY, ROBERT   AC
  ROBERT SHECKLEY OMNIBUS, THE   SHECKLEY, ROBERT   AC
GIRLS AND NUGENT MILLER, THE   SS   FSF 60 03
  SHARDS OF SPACE   SHECKLEY, ROBERT   AC
GRAY FLANNEL ARMOR   SS   GAL 57 11
  NOTIONS: UNLIMITED   SHECKLEY, ROBERT   AC
GUN WITHOUT A BANG, THE   NV   GAL 58 06
  SCIENCE FACT/FICTION   FARRELL/GAGE/&   AN
  STORE OF INFINITY   SHECKLEY, ROBERT   AC
  WONDERMAKERS 2   HOSKINS, ROBERT   AN
HANDS OFF   NV   GAL 54 04
  CITIZEN IN SPACE   SHECKLEY, ROBERT   AC
HISTORY OF THE SCIENCE FICTION MAGAZINE, THE   PART 3 1946-1955
                                     ASHLEY, MICHAEL   AN
  ROBERT SHECKLEY OMNIBUS, THE   SHECKLEY, ROBERT   AC

SHECKLEY, ROBERT   (CONTINUED)
HOLDOUT   SS   FSF 57 12
  HUMAN AND OTHER BEINGS   DEGRAEFF, ALLEN   AN
  NOTIONS: UNLIMITED   SHECKLEY, ROBERT   AC
  THEMES IN SCIENCE FICTION   KELLEY, LEO P.   AN
HOUR OF BATTLE, THE   SS   SSF 53 09
  FUTURE MAKERS, THE   HAINING, PETER   AN
HUMAN MAN'S BURDEN   SS   GAL 56 09
  PILGRIMAGE TO EARTH   SHECKLEY, ROBERT   AC
  12 GREAT CLASSICS OF SCIENCE FICTION CONKLIN, GROFF   AN
HUMORS, THE (JOIN NOW)   NA   GAL 58 12
  STORE OF INFINITY   SHECKLEY, ROBERT   AC
HUNTING PROBLEM   SS   GAL 55 09
  CITIZEN IN SPACE   SHECKLEY, ROBERT   AC
  ROBERT SHECKLEY OMNIBUS, THE   SHECKLEY, ROBERT   AC
  STORIES FROM SCIENCE FICTION   DOHERTY, G. D.   AN
I SEE A MAN SITTING IN A CHAIR,AND THE CHAIR IS BITING HIS LEG
                                               NV C FSF 68 01
  PARTNERS IN WONDER   ELLISON, HARLAN   AC
IF THE RED SLAYER   SS   AMZ 59 07
  STORE OF INFINITY   SHECKLEY, ROBERT   AC
IMMORTALITY INC. (TIME KILLER)   NO   GAL 58 10
  ROBERT SHECKLEY OMNIBUS, THE   SHECKLEY, ROBERT   AC
IMPACTED MAN, THE   SS   ASF 52 12
  *UNTOUCHED BY HUMAN HANDS   SHECKLEY, ROBERT   AC
IN A LAND OF CLEAR COLORS   NV
  NEW CONSTELLATIONS   DISCH & NAYLOR   OA
JOIN NOW (SEE THE HUMORS)   TC
KEEP YOUR SHAPE (SEE SHAPE)   TC
KING'S WISHES, THE   SS   FSF 53 07
  *UNTOUCHED BY HUMAN HANDS   SHECKLEY, ROBERT   AC
LANGUAGE OF LOVE, THE   SS   GAL 57 05
  NOTIONS: UNLIMITED   SHECKLEY, ROBERT   AC
LAST WEAPON, THE   SS   STR 53 01
  PEOPLE TRAP AND OTHER PITFALLS, THE SHECKLEY, ROBERT   AC
  STAR SCIENCE FICTION STORIES   POHL, FREDERIK   OA
LAXIAN KEY, THE   SS   GAL 54 11
  PEOPLE TRAP AND OTHER PITFALLS, THE SHECKLEY, ROBERT   AC
LEECH, THE   SS   GAL 52 12
  NOTIONS: UNLIMITED   SHECKLEY, ROBERT   AC
  SCIENCE FICTION TERROR TALES   CONKLIN, GROFF   AN
LIFEBOAT MUTINY, THE   SS   GAL 55 04
  PILGRIMAGE TO EARTH   SHECKLEY, ROBERT   AC
LOVE, INCORPORATED (ALSO AS PILGRIMAGE TO EARTH) SS PBY 56 09
  FIEND, THE   PLAYBOY, EDITORS OF   AN
  INTRODUCTORY PSYCHOLOGY THROUGH SCIENCE FICTION
                                     KATZ/WARRICK/&   AN
  MARRIAGE AND THE FAMILY THROUGH SCIENCE FICTION
                                     CLEAR/WARRICK/&   AN
  PLAYBOY BOOK OF SCIENCE FICTION AND FANTASY, THE
                                     PLAYBOY, EDITORS OF   AN
LUCKIEST MAN IN THE WORLD, THE (FORTUNATE PERSON) SS FUN 55 02
  CITIZEN IN SPACE   SHECKLEY, ROBERT   AC
MEETING OF THE MINDS   NA   GAL 60 02
  OUT OF THIS WORLD 7   WILLIAMS-ELLIS& OWEN   AN
  SHARDS OF SPACE   SHECKLEY, ROBERT   AC
MILK RUN   SS   GAL 54 09
  PILGRIMAGE TO EARTH   SHECKLEY, ROBERT   AC
MINIMUM MAN, THE   NV   GAL 58 06
  FOURTH GALAXY READER, THE   GOLD, H. L.   AN
  STORE OF INFINITY   SHECKLEY, ROBERT   AC
MNEMONE, THE   SS   NEW 71 AC
  CAN YOU FEEL ANYTHING WHEN I DO THIS?, AND OTHER STORIES
                                     SHECKLEY, ROBERT   AC
MONSTERS, THE   SS   FSF 53 03
  ANTHROPOLOGY THROUGH SCIENCE FICTION MASON, C/GREENBERG/& AN
  BEST SF 5   CRISPIN, EDMUND   AN
  STARLIT CORRIDOR, THE   MANSFIELD, ROGER   AN
  *UNTOUCHED BY HUMAN HANDS   SHECKLEY, ROBERT   AC
MORNING AFTER   NV   GAL 57 11
  NOTIONS: UNLIMITED   SHECKLEY, ROBERT   AC
MOUNTAIN WITHOUT A NAME, THE   SS   NEW 55 AC
  CITIZEN IN SPACE   SHECKLEY, ROBERT   AC
NATIVE PROBLEM, THE   NV   GAL 56 12
  NOTIONS: UNLIMITED   SHECKLEY, ROBERT   AC
NECESSARY THING, THE   SS   GAL 55 06
  PEOPLE TRAP AND OTHER PITFALLS, THE SHECKLEY, ROBERT   AC
NEVER-ENDING WESTERN MOVIE, THE   SS
  SCIENCE FICTION DISCOVERIES   POHL, C. & F.   OA
NOTES ON THE PERCEPTION OF IMAGINARY DIFFERENCES SS NEW 71 AC
  CAN YOU FEEL ANYTHING WHEN I DO THIS?, AND OTHER STORIES
                                     SHECKLEY, ROBERT   AC
ODOR OF THOUGHT, THE   SS   STR 53 02
  PEOPLE TRAP AND OTHER PITFALLS, THE SHECKLEY, ROBERT   AC
  STAR SCIENCE FICTION STORIES NO. 2 POHL, FREDERIK   OA
  TALES FROM THE GALAXIES   WILLIAMS-ELLIS& P.   AN
ONE MAN'S POISON (SEE UNTOUCHED BY HUMAN HANDS) TC
OPERATING INSTRUCTIONS   SS   ASF 53 05
  BEYOND THE BARRIERS OF SPACE AND TIME MERRIL, JUDITH   AN
PARADISE II   SS   NWS 55 07
  NOTIONS: UNLIMITED   SHECKLEY, ROBERT   AC
  *TIME TO COME   DERLETH, AUGUST   OA
PAS DE TROIS OF THE CHEF AND THE WAITER AND THE CUSTOMER
  (THREE SINNERS IN THE...)   SS   PBY 71 08
  CAN YOU FEEL ANYTHING WHEN I DO THIS?, AND OTHER STORIES
                                     SHECKLEY, ROBERT   AC
PEOPLE TRAP, THE   SS   FSF 68 06
  BEST FROM FANTASY AND SCIENCE FICTION: 18
                                     FERMAN, EDWARD L.   AN
  PEOPLE TRAP AND OTHER PITFALLS, THE SHECKLEY, ROBERT   AC
  SOCIAL PROBLEMS THROUGH SCIENCE FICTION
                                     GREENBERG/MILSTEAD/&   AN
PERFECT WOMAN, THE   SS   AMZ 54 01
  FIFTY SHORT SCIENCE FICTION TALES ASIMOV & CONKLIN   AN
  TOMORROW, AND TOMORROW, AND TOMORROW...
                                     HEINTZ/HERBERT/JOOS/   AN

SHECKLEY, ROBERT

SHELLEY, MARY W.

SHECKLEY, ROBERT   (CONTINUED)
    PETRIFIED WORLD, THE   SS   IFS 68 02
        CAN YOU FEEL ANYTHING WHEN I DO THIS?, AND OTHER STORIES
                                        SHECKLEY, ROBERT   AC
    NEW WORLDS OF FANTASY NO. 2   CARR, TERRY   AN
    PILGRIMAGE TO EARTH (LOVE, INCORPORATED)   SS   PBY 56 09
        PILGRIMAGE TO EARTH   SHECKLEY, ROBERT   AC
        ROBERT SHECKLEY OMNIBUS, THE   SHECKLEY, ROBERT   AC
        *SPECTRUM   AMIS & CONQUEST   AN
    PLAGUE CIRCUIT   SS   NEW 71 AC
        CAN YOU FEEL ANYTHING WHEN I DO THIS?, AND OTHER STORIES
                                        SHECKLEY, ROBERT   AC
    POTENTIAL   SS   ASF 53 11
        ASTOUNDING-ANALOG READER, THE VOLUME TWO
                                        HARRISON & ALDISS   AN
        PORTALS OF TOMORROW   DERLETH, AUGUST   AN
        SHARDS OF SPACE   SHECKLEY, ROBERT   AC
    PRIZE OF PERIL, THE   SS   FSF 58 05
        ROBERT SHECKLEY OMNIBUS, THE   SHECKLEY, ROBERT   AC
        SECOND ORBIT   DOHERTY, G. D.   AN
        SF: THE BEST OF THE BEST   MERRIL, JUDITH   AN
        SF:59, THE YEAR'S GREATEST SCIENCE FICTION AND FANTASY
                                        MERRIL, JUDITH   AN
        SOCIAL PROBLEMS THROUGH SCIENCE FICTION
                                        GREENBERG/MILSTEAD/& AN
        STORE OF INFINITY   SHECKLEY, ROBERT   AC
    PROOF OF THE PUDDING   SS   GAL 52 08
        GALAXY OF GHOULS   MERRIL, JUDITH   AN
        PEOPLE TRAP AND OTHER PITFALLS, THE SHECKLEY, ROBERT AC
    PROSPECTOR'S SPECIAL   NV   GAL 59 12
        SHARDS OF SPACE   SHECKLEY, ROBERT   AC
    PROTECTION   SS   GAL 56 04
        PILGRIMAGE TO EARTH   SHECKLEY, ROBERT   AC
        THIRD GALAXY READER, THE   GOLD, H. L.   AN
    REDFERN'S LABYRINTH   SS   NEW 68 AC
        PEOPLE TRAP AND OTHER PITFALLS, THE SHECKLEY, ROBERT AC
    RESTRICTED AREA   SS   AMZ 53 07
        PEOPLE TRAP AND OTHER PITFALLS, THE SHECKLEY, ROBERT AC
        SEA OF SPACE, A   NOLAN, WILLIAM F.   AN
    RITUAL (STRANGE RITUAL)   SS   CLM 53
        *UNTOUCHED BY HUMAN HANDS   SHECKLEY, ROBERT   AC
    SAME TO YOU DOUBLED, THE   SS   PBY 70 03
        CAN YOU FEEL ANYTHING WHEN I DO THIS?, AND OTHER STORIES
                                        SHECKLEY, ROBERT   AC
        FROM THE "S" FILE   PLAYBOY, EDITORS OF   AN
    SEVENTH VICTIM   SS   GAL 53 04
        ABOVE THE HUMAN LANDSCAPE   MCNELLY & STOVER   AN
        INTRODUCTORY PSYCHOLOGY THROUGH SCIENCE FICTION
                                        KATZ/WARRICK/&   AN
        MAN AGAINST TOMORROW   NOLAN, WILLIAM F.   AN
        *UNTOUCHED BY HUMAN HANDS   SHECKLEY, ROBERT   AC
    SHALL WE HAVE A LITTLE TALK?   NV   GAL 65 10
        PEOPLE TRAP AND OTHER PITFALLS, THE SHECKLEY, ROBERT AC
    SHAPE (KEEP YOUR SHAPE)   NV   GAL 53 11
        ALPHA 7   SILVERBERG, ROBERT   AN
        GATES TO TOMORROW   NORTON, AN.&DONALDY   AN
        *UNTOUCHED BY HUMAN HANDS   SHECKLEY, ROBERT   AC
    SKULKING PERMIT   NV   GAL 54 12
        CITIZEN IN SPACE   SHECKLEY, ROBERT   AC
    SLAVES OF TIME   NV   NOV 74 04
        NOVA 4   HARRISON, HARRY   OA
    SLOW SEASON, THE   SS   FSF 54 10
        SHARDS OF SPACE   SHECKLEY, ROBERT   AC
    SOMETHING FOR NOTHING   SS   GAL 54 06
        CITIZEN IN SPACE   SHECKLEY, ROBERT   AC
        ROBERT SHECKLEY OMNIBUS, THE   SHECKLEY, ROBERT   AC
        TOMORROW, INC.   GREENBERG& OLANDER   AN
        VINTAGE ANTHOLOGY OF SCIENCE FANTASY, THE
                                        CERF, CHRISTOPHER   AN
    SPECIAL EXHIBIT, THE   SS   ESQ 53 10
        SHARDS OF SPACE   SHECKLEY, ROBERT   AC
    SPECIALIST   SS   GAL 53 05
        AS TOMORROW BECOMES TODAY   SULLIVAN, CHARLES W. AN
        CONTACT   KEYES, NOEL   AN
        MIRROR OF INFINITY, THE   SILVERBERG, ROBERT   AN
        ROBERT SHECKLEY OMNIBUS, THE   SHECKLEY, ROBERT   AC
        SECOND GALAXY READER OF SCIENCE FICTION
                                        GOLD, H. L.   AN
        TALES OF TERROR FROM OUTER SPACE CHETWYND-HAYES, R. AN
        TOMORROW, AND TOMORROW, AND TOMORROW...
                                        HEINTZ/HERBERT/JOOS/ AN
        *UNTOUCHED BY HUMAN HANDS   SHECKLEY, ROBERT   AC
    SPY STORY (ALSO AS CITIZEN IN SPACE)   SS   PBY 55 09
        DEAD ASTRONAUT, 10 STORIES OF SPACE FLIGHT, THE
                                        PLAYBOY, EDITORS OF   AN
        PLAYBOY BOOK OF SCIENCE FICTION AND FANTASY, THE
                                        PLAYBOY, EDITORS OF   AN
    STARTING FROM SCRATCH   SS   FSF 70 11
        BEST FROM FANTASY AND SCIENCE FICTION: 19
                                        FERMAN, EDWARD L.   AN
        CAN YOU FEEL ANYTHING WHEN I DO THIS?, AND OTHER STORIES
                                        SHECKLEY, ROBERT   AC
    STORE OF THE WORLDS, THE (THE WORLD OF HEART'S DESIRE)
                                                      SS   PBY 59 09
        MORE PENGUIN SCIENCE FICTION   ALDISS, BRIAN W.   AN
        ROBERT SHECKLEY OMNIBUS, THE   SHECKLEY, ROBERT   AC
        STORE OF INFINITY   SHECKLEY, ROBERT   AC
    STRANGE RITUAL (SEE RITUAL)   TC
    STREET OF DREAMS, FEET OF CLAY   NV   GAL 68 02
        CITY: 2000 A.D., THE   CLEM/GREENBERG/&   AN
        LIBERATED FUTURE: VOYAGES INTO TOMORROW, THE
                                        HOSKINS, ROBERT   AN
        SPECULATIONS   SANDERS, THOMAS E.   AN
        TOMORROW, AND TOMORROW, AND TOMORROW...
                                        HEINTZ/HERBERT/JOOS/ AN
        WANDERING STARS   DANN, JACK M.   AN

SHECKLEY, ROBERT   (CONTINUED)
        WORLD'S BEST SCIENCE FICTION: 1969 WOLLHEIM & CARR   AN
    SUBSISTENCE LEVEL   SS   GAL 54 08
        SHARDS OF SPACE   SHECKLEY, ROBERT   AC
    SUPPLIANT IN SPACE, A   NV   GAL 73 11
        BEST FROM GALAXY, THE VOLUME II GALAXY, EDITORS OF AN
        1974 ANNUAL WORLD'S BEST SF, THE WOLLHEIM, DONALD A. AN
    SWEEPER OF LORAY, THE   SS   GAL 59 04
        SHARDS OF SPACE   SHECKLEY, ROBERT   AC
    TAILPIPE TO DISASTER   SS   FSF
        CAN YOU FEEL ANYTHING WHEN I DO THIS?, AND OTHER STORIES
                                        SHECKLEY, ROBERT   AC
    THIEF IN TIME, A   NV   GAL 54 07
        CITIZEN IN SPACE   SHECKLEY, ROBERT   AC
        TIMES 4 (ABRIDGED STORIES)   ALLEN, VIRGINIA F.   AN
    TICKET TO TRANAI, A   NA   GAL 55 10
        CITIZEN IN SPACE   SHECKLEY, ROBERT   AC
        ROBERT SHECKLEY OMNIBUS, THE   SHECKLEY, ROBERT   AC
    TRAP   SS   GAL 56 02
        PILGRIMAGE TO EARTH   SHECKLEY, ROBERT   AC
    TRIPLICATION   SS   PBY 59 05
        FROM THE "S" FILE   PLAYBOY, EDITORS OF   AN
        STORE OF INFINITY   SHECKLEY, ROBERT   AC
    TRIPOUT   SS   BOA
        CAN YOU FEEL ANYTHING WHEN I DO THIS?, AND OTHER STORIES
                                        SHECKLEY, ROBERT   AC
    UNTOUCHED BY HUMAN HANDS (ONE MAN'S POISON)   SS   GAL 53 12
        GATES TO TOMORROW   NORTON, AN.&DONALDY   AN
        *UNTOUCHED BY HUMAN HANDS   SHECKLEY, ROBERT   AC
    VICTIM FROM SPACE, THE   NV   GAL 57 04
        PEOPLE TRAP AND OTHER PITFALLS, THE SHECKLEY, ROBERT AC
    WARM   SS   GAL 53 06
        GALAXY SCIENCE FICTION OMNIBUS GOLD, H. L.   AN
        SECOND GALAXY READER OF SCIENCE FICTION
                                        GOLD, H. L.   AN
        *UNTOUCHED BY HUMAN HANDS   SHECKLEY, ROBERT   AC
    WATCHBIRD   NV   GAL 53 02
        NOTIONS: UNLIMITED   SHECKLEY, ROBERT   AC
        SHADOW OF TOMORROW   POHL, FREDERIK   AN
        UNTOUCHED BY HUMAN HANDS (BRITISH) SHECKLEY, ROBERT AC
    WE ARE ALONE   SS   FUT 52 11
        ESCAPE TO EARTH   HOWARD, IVAN   AN
    WELCOME TO THE STANDARD NIGHTMARE   SS   NOV 73 03
        BEST SF: 1973   HARRISON & ALDISS   AN
        NOVA 3   HARRISON, HARRY   OA
    WIND IS RISING, A   SS   GAL 57 07
        NOTIONS: UNLIMITED   SHECKLEY, ROBERT   AC
    WORLD OF HEART'S DESIRE, THE (ALSO AS THE STORE OF THE WORLDS)
                                                      SS   PBY 59 09
        FROM THE "S" FILE   PLAYBOY, EDITORS OF   AN
    ZIRN LEFT UNGUARDED, THE JENGHIK PALACE IN FLAMES,
    JOHN WESTERLY DEAD   SS   NOV 72 02
        NOVA 2   HARRISON, HARRY   OA
        SPACE OPERA   ALDISS, BRIAN W.   AN

SHEFNER, VADIM
    MODEST GENIUS, A   SS
        RUSSIAN SCIENCE FICTION, 1969   MAGIDOFF, ROBERT   AN
        VIEW FROM ANOTHER SHORE   ROTTENSTEINER, FRANZ AN
        1974 ANNUAL WORLD'S BEST SF, THE WOLLHEIM, DONALD A. AN

SHELDON, ALICE   SEE PSEUD.
    RACCOONA SHELDON AND JAMES TIPTREE, JR.

SHELDON, RACCOONA   PSEUD. FOR ALICE SHELDON
    ANGEL FIX   NV   IFS 74 08
        BEST FROM IF, THE VOLUME III   BAEN, JAMES   AN
    YOUR FACES, O MY SISTERS! YOUR FACES FILLED OF LIGHT!
                                                      SS
        AURORA: BEYOND EQUALITY   MCINTYRE & ANDERSON   OA

SHELDON, WALT
    CHORE FOR A SPACEMAN   SS   TWS 50 12
        SPACE SERVICE   NORTON, ANDRE   AN
    HUNTERS, THE   SS   STS 52 03
        FIFTY SHORT SCIENCE FICTION TALES ASIMOV & CONKLIN   AN
    I, THE UNSPEAKABLE   NV   GAL 51 04
        ‡GALAXY READER OF SCIENCE FICTION GOLD, H. L.   AN

SHELLEY, MARY W.
    TALES AND STORIES   AC H GRG 75
        REPRINT OF 1891 EDITION PUBLISHED BY WM. PATERSON & CO, LONDON
    BROTHER AND SISTER, THE   NV   KPS 33
        TALES AND STORIES   SHELLEY, MARY W.   AC
    DREAM, THE   SS   KPS 32
        TALES AND STORIES   SHELLEY, MARY W.   AC
    ELDER SON, THE   NV   35
        TALES AND STORIES   SHELLEY, MARY W.   AC
    EUPHRASIA   SS   KPS 39
        TALES AND STORIES   SHELLEY, MARY W.   AC
    EVIL EYE, THE   NV   KPS 30
        TALES AND STORIES   SHELLEY, MARY W.   AC
    FALSE RHYME, THE   SS   KPS 30
        TALES AND STORIES   SHELLEY, MARY W.   AC
    FERDINANDO EBOLI   NV   KPS 29
        TALES AND STORIES   SHELLEY, MARY W.   AC
    FRANKENSTEIN, OR, THE MODERN PROMETHEUS   EX   WRT 32 05
        FROM FRANKENSTEIN TO ANDROMEDA BROWN, JAMES GOLDIE   AN
    FROM "FRANKENSTEIN, OR THE MODERN PROMETHEUS" (1818)
                                                      EX   WRT 32 05
        PAST, PRESENT, AND FUTURE PERFECT WOLFE, J&FITZ GERALD AN
    FROM "THE LAST MAN" (1826)   EX
        PAST, PRESENT, AND FUTURE PERFECT WOLFE, J&FITZ GERALD AN
    INVISIBLE GIRL, THE   SS   KPS 33
        TALES AND STORIES   SHELLEY, MARY W.   AC

SHELLEY, MARY W.   (CONTINUED)
  LAST MAN, THE (1826)   EX
    SPECULATIONS   SANDERS, THOMAS E.   AN
    STRANGE SIGNPOSTS   ELWOOD & MOSKOWITZ   AN
    VISIONS OF TOMORROW   ELWOOD, ROGER   AN
  MORTAL IMMORTAL, THE (1834)   SS   KPS 34
    MASTERPIECES OF SCIENCE FICTION   MOSKOWITZ, SAM   AN
    TALES AND STORIES   SHELLEY, MARY W.   AC
  MOURNER, THE   NV   KPS 30
    TALES AND STORIES   SHELLEY, MARY W.   AC
  PARVENUE, THE   SS   KPS 37
    TALES AND STORIES   SHELLEY, MARY W.   AC
  PILGRIMS, THE   NV   KPS 38
    TALES AND STORIES   SHELLEY, MARY W.   AC
  POLE, THE   NV   CMG 32 08
    TALES AND STORIES   SHELLEY, MARY W.   AC
  RECALCITRANT ROBOT, THE (FROM "FRANKENSTEIN")   EX
    SCIENCE FICTION THROUGH THE AGES 1 EVANS, I. O.   AN
  SWISS PEASANT, THE   NV   KPS 31
    TALES AND STORIES   SHELLEY, MARY W.   AC
  TALE OF THE PASSIONS: OR, THE DEATH OF DESPINA, A NV LIB 22 01
    TALES AND STORIES   SHELLEY, MARY W.   AC
  TRANSFORMATION   NV   KPS 31
    TALES AND STORIES   SHELLEY, MARY W.   AC

SHELTON, JERRY
  CULTURE   NV   ASF 44 09
    APEMAN, SPACEMAN   STOVER & HARRISON   AN
   *BIG BOOK OF SCIENCE FICTION   CONKLIN, GROFF   AN

SHELTON, WILLIAM ROY
  MOON CRAZY   SS   SEP
    POST READER OF FANTASY AND SCIENCE FICTION
                                      SATURDAY EVE. POST   AN

SHEPLEY, JOHN
  GORILLA SUIT   SS   FSF 58 05
    BEST FROM FANTASY AND SCIENCE FICTION: 8
                                      BOUCHER, ANTHONY   AN
  THREE FOR CARNIVAL   SS   FSF 66 05
    BEST FROM FANTASY AND SCIENCE FICTION: 16
                                      FERMAN, EDWARD L.   AN

SHERRED, T. L.
  FIRST PERSON, PECULIAR   AC   BAL 72 01
  BOUNTY   SS   DVS 72 02
    AGAIN, DANGEROUS VISIONS   ELLISON, HARLAN   OA
    SOCIAL PROBLEMS THROUGH SCIENCE FICTION
                                      GREENBERG/MILSTEAD/& AN
  CUE FOR QUIET   NA   SSF 53 05
    FIRST PERSON, PECULIAR   SHERRED, T. L.   AC
  CURE, GUARANTEED   NV   FUT 54 08
    FIRST PERSON, PECULIAR   SHERRED, T. L.   AC
  E FOR EFFORT   NV   ASF 47 05
   *ASTOUNDING SCIENCE FICTION ANTHOLOGY, THE
                                      CAMPBELL, JOHN W. JR AN
    ASTOUNDING TALES OF SPACE AND TIME CAMPBELL, JOHN W. JR AN
   *BIG BOOK OF SCIENCE FICTION   CONKLIN, GROFF   AN
    CENTURY OF GREAT SHORT SCIENCE FICTION NOVELS, A
                                      KNIGHT, DAMON   AN
    FIRST ASTOUNDING SCIENCE FICTION ANTHOLOGY, THE (PB)
                                      CAMPBELL, JOHN W. JR AN
    FIRST PERSON, PECULIAR   SHERRED, T. L.   AC
    SCIENCE FICTION HALL OF FAME VOLUME 2B BOVA, BEN   AN
   *SECOND ASTOUNDING SCIENCE FICTION ANTHOLOGY, THE
                                      CAMPBELL, JOHN W. JR AN
  EYE FOR INIQUITY   NV   BEY 53 07
    DARK SIDE, THE   KNIGHT, DAMON   AN
    FIRST PERSON, PECULIAR   SHERRED, T. L.   AC
    PORTALS OF TOMORROW   DERLETH, AUGUST   AN

SHIEL, M. P.
  PLACE OF PAIN, THE   SS   APR 51 16
    MASTERPIECES OF SCIENCE FICTION   MOSKOWITZ, SAM   AN

SHIPPEY, TOM
  MODERN VIEW OF SCIENCE FICTION, A   AR
    BEYOND THIS HORIZON   CARRELL, CHRISTOPHER OA

SHIRAS, WILMAR H.
  CHILDREN OF THE ATOM   AC H GNM 53
  BACKWARD, TURN BACKWARD   NV   NEW 70 AN
    NEW WORLDS OF FANTASY NO. 2   CARR, TERRY   AN
  CHILDREN OF THE ATOM   NV   NEW 53 AC
    CHILDREN OF THE ATOM   SHIRAS, WILMAR H.   AC
  IN HIDING   NV   ASF 48 11
    ARMCHAIR SCIENCE READER, THE   GORDON, I. & SORKIN AN
    BEST SCIENCE-FICTION STORIES: 1949, THE
                                      BLEILER & DIKTY   AN
    CHILDREN OF THE ATOM   SHIRAS, WILMAR H.   AC
    CHILDREN OF WONDER   TENN, WILLIAM   AN
    GREAT SCIENCE FICTION STORIES   SMITH, CORDELIA T.   AN
    GREAT STORIES OF SCIENCE FICTION LEINSTER, MURRAY   AN
    SCIENCE FICTION FOR PEOPLE WHO HATE SCIENCE FICTION
                                      CARR, TERRY   AN
    SCIENCE FICTION HALL OF FAME VOLUME 2B BOVA, BEN   AN
   *STORIES FOR TOMORROW   SLOANE, WILLIAM   AN
    TOWARD INFINITY   KNIGHT, DAMON   AN
  NEW FOUNDATIONS   NV   ASF 50 03
    CHILDREN OF THE ATOM   SHIRAS, WILMAR H.   AC
  OPENING DOORS   NV   ASF 49 03
    BEST SCIENCE-FICTION STORIES: 1950, THE
                                      BLEILER & DIKTY   AN
    CHILDREN OF THE ATOM   SHIRAS, WILMAR H.   AC
  PROBLEMS   NV   NEW 53 AC
    CHILDREN OF THE ATOM   SHIRAS, WILMAR H.   AC

SHIRLEY, JOHN
  ALMOST EMPTY ROOMS, THE   NV   NDM 77 07
    NEW DIMENSIONS 7   SILVERBERG, ROBERT   OA
  UNDER THE GENERATOR   NV   UNI 76 06
    UNIVERSE 6   CARR, TERRY   OA
  UNEASY CHRYSALIDS, OUR MEMORIES   SS   EPC 75
    EPOCH   ELWOOD & SILVERBERG   OA
  WORD "RANDOM", DELIBERATELY REPEATED, THE   SS   CLR 73 03
    CLARION III   WILSON, ROBIN SCOTT   OA

SHKLOVSKII, I. S.
  DIRECT CONTACT AMONG GALACTIC CIVILIZATIONS   AR C   66
    SURVIVAL PRINTOUT   TOTAL EFFECT   AN

SHOFNER, PHILIP
  PITY THE POOR OUTDATED MAN   NV   NOV 73 03
    NOVA 3   HARRISON, HARRY   OA

SHORE, WILMA
  BULLETIN FROM THE TRUSTEES, A   SS   FSF 64 08
    BEST FROM FANTASY AND SCIENCE FICTION: 14
                                      DAVIDSON, AVRAM   AN
    VOYAGERS IN TIME   SILVERBERG, ROBERT   AN
  GOODBYE AMANDA JEAN   SS   GAL 70 07
    ALPHA 2   SILVERBERG, ROBERT   AN
  IS IT THE END OF THE WORLD?   SS   FSF 72 03
    BEST FROM FANTASY AND SCIENCE FICTION: 20
                                      FERMAN, EDWARD L.   AN

SHUTE, NEVIL
  THOSE ABOUT TO DIE (FROM "ON THE BEACH")   EX
    SCIENCE FICTION THROUGH THE AGES 2 EVANS, I. O.   AN

SIDNEY, KATHLEEN M.
  ANTHROPOLOGIST, THE   SS   ORB 75 17
    ORBIT 17   KNIGHT, DAMON   OA
  TEACHER, THE   SS   ORB 76 18
    ORBIT 18   KNIGHT, DAMON   OA
  TRADERS, THE   NV
    CLARION SF   WILHELM, KATE   OA

SILVERBERG, BARBARA
  DEADLOCK   NV C ASF 59 01
    SHORES OF TOMORROW, THE   SILVERBERG, ROBERT   AC

SILVERBERG, ROBERT   ALSO AS
    CALVIN M. KNOX AND ROBERT RANDALL (WITH RANDALL GARRETT)
              SEE ALSO   CO-EDITOR ROGER ELWOOD
  ALIENS, THE   AN H NEL 76
  ALPHA 1   AN   BAL 70 09
  ALPHA 2   AN   BAL 71 11
  ALPHA 3   AN   BAL 72 10
  ALPHA 4   AN   BAL 73 10
  ALPHA 5   AN   BAL 74 08
  ALPHA 6   AN   BKM 76 04
  ALPHA 7   AN   BKM 77 07
  BEST OF ROBERT SILVERBERG, THE   AC   PKT 76 02
  BEYOND CONTROL   AN H NEL 72
  BORN WITH THE DEAD   AC H RDM 74
  CALLIBRATED ALLIGATOR AND OTHER SCIENCE FICTION STORIES, THE
                                                  AC H HRW 69
  CAPRICORN GAMES   AC H RDM 76
  CHAINS OF THE SEA   OA H NDB 73
  CRYSTAL SHIP, THE   OA H NEL 76
  CUBE ROOT OF UNCERTAINTY, THE   AC H MAC 70
  DARK STARS   AN   BAL 69 12
  DAY THE SUN STOOD STILL, THE   OA H NEL 72
  DEEP SPACE   AN H NDB 73
  DIMENSION THIRTEEN   AC   BAL 69 05
  EARTH IS THE STRANGEST PLANET   AN H NEL 77
  EARTH'S OTHER SHADOW   AC   SIG 73 06
  EARTHMEN AND STRANGERS   AN H MDT 66
  ENDS OF TIME, THE   AN H HAW 70
  EXPLORERS OF SPACE   AN H NEL 75
  FEAST OF ST. DIONYSUS, THE   AC H SCB 75 03
  FOUR FUTURES   OA H HAW 71
  GODLING, GO HOME!   AC   BEL 64 06
  GREAT SHORT NOVELS OF SCIENCE FICTION   AN   BAL 70 07
  INFINITE JESTS   AN H CHL 74
  INVADERS FROM SPACE   AN H HAW 72
  MEN AND MACHINES   AN H MDT 68
  MIND TO MIND   AN H NEL 71
  MIRROR OF INFINITY, THE   AN H HPR 70
  MOONFERNS & STARSONGS   AC   BAL 71 06
  MUTANTS   AN H NDB 74
  NEEDLE IN A TIMESTACK   AC   BAL 66 11
  NEW ATLANTIS AND OTHER NOVELLAS OF S.F., THE   OA H HAW 74
  NEW DIMENSIONS 1   OA H DBL 71
  NEW DIMENSIONS 2   OA H DBL 72
  NEW DIMENSIONS 3   OA   SIG 74 02
  NEW DIMENSIONS 4   OA   SIG 74 10
  NEW DIMENSIONS 5   OA H HPR 75
  NEW DIMENSIONS 6   OA H HPR 76
  NEW DIMENSIONS 7   OA H HPR 77
  NEXT STOP THE STARS   DC   ACE 62
  NO MIND OF MAN   OA H HAW 73
  OTHER DIMENSIONS   AN H HAW 73
  PARSECS AND PARABLES   AC H DBL 70
  REALITY TRIP, THE   AC   BAL 72 03
  SCIENCE FICTION BESTIARY, THE   AN H NEL 71
  SCIENCE FICTION HALL OF FAME VOLUME 1   AN H DBL 70
  SHORES OF TOMORROW, THE   AC H NEL 70
  STRANGE GIFTS   AN H NEL 75
  SUNDANCE AND OTHER SCIENCE FICTION STORIES   AC H NEL 74
  SUNRISE ON MERCURY AND OTHER SCIENCE FICTION STORIES
                                                  OA L NDB 75

SILVERBERG, ROBERT (CONTINUED)
THREADS OF TIME — OA H NDB 74
THREE FOR TOMORROW — OA H MDT 69
THREE TRIPS IN TIME AND SPACE — OA H HAW 73
TO OPEN THE SKY — NO BAL 67 05
TO THE STARS — AN H HAW 71
TO WORLDS BEYOND — AC H CHL 65
TOMORROW'S WORLDS — AN H MDT 69
UNFAMILIAR TERRITORY — AC H SCB 73
VALLEY BEYOND TIME — AC DEL 73 01
VOYAGERS IN TIME — AN H MDT 67
WINDOWS INTO TOMORROW — AN H HAW 74
WORLD INSIDE, THE — NO H DBL 71
WORLDS OF MAYBE — AN H NEL 70
ABSOLUTELY INFLEXIBLE — SS FUN 56 07
CUBE ROOT OF UNCERTAINTY, THE — SILVERBERG, ROBERT AC
NEEDLE IN A TIMESTACK — SILVERBERG, ROBERT AC
VOYAGERS IN TIME — SILVERBERG, ROBERT AN
AFTER THE MYTHS WENT HOME — SS FSF 69 11
ANOTHER WORLD — DOZOIS, GARDNER R. AN
MOONFERNS & STARSONGS — SILVERBERG, ROBERT AC
SUNRISE ON MERCURY AND OTHER SCIENCE FICTION STORIES — SILVERBERG, ROBERT OA
TOMORROW, AND TOMORROW, AND TOMORROW... — HEINTZ/HERBERT/JOOS/ AN
WORLD'S BEST SCIENCE FICTION: 1970 — WOLLHEIM & CARR AN
ALAREE — SS STN 58 03
EARTHMEN AND STRANGERS — SILVERBERG, ROBERT AN
SUNRISE ON MERCURY AND OTHER SCIENCE FICTION STORIES — SILVERBERG, ROBERT OA
ALL THE WAY UP, ALL THE WAY DOWN — NV GAL 71 07
WORLD INSIDE, THE — SILVERBERG, ROBERT NO
ARTIFACT BUSINESS, THE — SS FUN 57 04
CALLIBRATED ALLIGATOR AND OTHER SCIENCE FICTION STORIES, THE — SILVERBERG, ROBERT AC
TIME PROBE: THE SCIENCES IN SF. — CLARKE, ARTHUR C. AN
AS IS — NV WOF 68 01
INTO THE UNKNOWN — CARR, TERRY AN
AT THE END OF DAYS — SS NWS 65 09
ENDS OF TIME, THE — SILVERBERG, ROBERT AN
BIRDS OF A FEATHER — NV GAL 58 11
NEEDLE IN A TIMESTACK — SILVERBERG, ROBERT AC
SUNRISE ON MERCURY AND OTHER SCIENCE FICTION STORIES — SILVERBERG, ROBERT OA
TALES OF TIME AND SPACE — OLNEY, ROSS R. AN
BLACK IS BEAUTIFUL — SS YRT 70
ABOVE THE HUMAN LANDSCAPE — MCNELLY & STOVER AN
BEST SF: 1970 — HARRISON & ALDISS AN
CITY: 2000 A.D., THE — CLEM/GREENBERG/& AN
REALITY TRIP, THE — SILVERBERG, ROBERT AC
SPECULATIONS — SANDERS, THOMAS E. AN
YEAR 2000, THE — HARRISON, HARRY OA
BLAZE OF GLORY — SS GAL 57 08
CALLIBRATED ALLIGATOR AND OTHER SCIENCE FICTION STORIES, THE — SILVERBERG, ROBERT AC
NEXT STOP THE STARS — SILVERBERG, ROBERT DC
BLUE FIRE — NV GAL 65 06
TO OPEN THE SKY — SILVERBERG, ROBERT NO
BORN WITH THE DEAD — NA FSF 74 04
BEST SCIENCE FICTION OF THE YEAR, THE NO. 4 — CARR, TERRY AN
BORN WITH THE DEAD — SILVERBERG, ROBERT AC
NEBULA AWARD STORIES 10 — GUNN, JAMES E. AN
BRECKENRIDGE AND THE CONTINUUM — NV SCS 73
BEST SCIENCE FICTION OF THE YEAR, THE NO. 3 — CARR, TERRY AN
CAPRICORN GAMES — SILVERBERG, ROBERT AC
SHOWCASE — ELWOOD, ROGER OA
BRIDE NINETY-ONE — SS IFS 67 09
DIMENSION THIRTEEN — SILVERBERG, ROBERT AC
BY THE SEAWALL — SS IFS 67 01
DIMENSION THIRTEEN — SILVERBERG, ROBERT AC
CALIBAN — SS INY 72 03
BEST SCIENCE FICTION OF THE YEAR, THE NO. 2 — CARR, TERRY AN
INFINITY 3 — HOSKINS, ROBERT OA
REALITY TRIP, THE — SILVERBERG, ROBERT AC
UNFAMILIAR TERRITORY — SILVERBERG, ROBERT AC
CALIBRATED ALLIGATOR, THE — NV ASF 60 02
CALLIBRATED ALLIGATOR AND OTHER SCIENCE FICTION STORIES, THE — SILVERBERG, ROBERT AC
CAPRICORN GAMES — SS 74
CAPRICORN GAMES — SILVERBERG, ROBERT AC
FAR SIDE OF TIME, THE — ELWOOD, ROGER OA
CAUGHT IN THE ORGAN DRAFT — SS WLK 73
AND WALK NOW GENTLY THROUGH THE FIRE... — ELWOOD, ROGER OA
SUNDANCE AND OTHER SCIENCE FICTION STORIES — SILVERBERG, ROBERT AC
UNFAMILIAR TERRITORY — SILVERBERG, ROBERT AC
WONDERMAKERS 2 — HOSKINS, ROBERT AN
YOU AND SCIENCE FICTION — HOLLISTER, BERNARD C AN
CERTAINTY — SS ASF 59 11
TO WORLDS BEYOND — SILVERBERG, ROBERT AC
COLLECTING TEAM — SS AUT 57 06
EXPLORERS OF SPACE — SILVERBERG, ROBERT AN
MOONFERNS & STARSONGS — SILVERBERG, ROBERT AC
SCIENCE FICTION BESTIARY, THE — SILVERBERG, ROBERT AN
TO WORLDS BEYOND — SILVERBERG, ROBERT AC
COMPANY STORE — SS STR 59 05
STAR SCIENCE FICTION STORIES NO. 5 — POHL, FREDERIK OA
SUNRISE ON MERCURY AND OTHER SCIENCE FICTION STORIES — SILVERBERG, ROBERT OA
TOMORROW, INC. — GREENBERG& OLANDER AN
COUNTERPART — NV FUN 59 10
PARSECS AND PARABLES — SILVERBERG, ROBERT AC

SILVERBERG, ROBERT (CONTINUED)
DARK COMPANION — NV AMZ 61 01
DIMENSION THIRTEEN — SILVERBERG, ROBERT AC
DAY THE FOUNDER DIED, THE — SS
CRISIS — ELWOOD, ROGER OA
SHORES OF TOMORROW, THE — SILVERBERG, ROBERT AC
DEADLOCK — NV C ASF 59 01
SHORES OF TOMORROW, THE — SILVERBERG, ROBERT AC
DELIVERY GUARANTEED — SS SFS 59 02
CALLIBRATED ALLIGATOR AND OTHER SCIENCE FICTION STORIES, THE — SILVERBERG, ROBERT AC
DESICCATOR, THE — SS SFS 56 05
GODLING, GO HOME! — SILVERBERG, ROBERT AC
DOUBLE DARE — SS GAL 56 11
CUBE ROOT OF UNCERTAINTY, THE — SILVERBERG, ROBERT AC
FIFTH GALAXY READER, THE — GOLD, H. L. AN
TO WORLDS BEYOND — SILVERBERG, ROBERT AC
DYBBUK OF MAZEL TOV IV, THE — SS NEW 74 AN
CAPRICORN GAMES — SILVERBERG, ROBERT AC
WANDERING STARS — DANN, JACK M. AN
WORLDS FAR AND NEAR — CARR, TERRY AN
EDITOR'S INTRODUCTION — IN
THREE FOR TOMORROW — SILVERBERG, ROBERT OA
EN ROUTE TO EARTH — SS SFQ 57 08
DIMENSION THIRTEEN — SILVERBERG, ROBERT AC
EVE AND THE TWENTY-THREE ADAMS — SS VSF 58 03
DIMENSION THIRTEEN — SILVERBERG, ROBERT AC
FANGS OF THE TREES, THE — NV FSF 68 10
EARTH'S OTHER SHADOW — SILVERBERG, ROBERT AC
NIGHTMARE GARDEN — GHIDALIA, VIC AN
PARSECS AND PARABLES — SILVERBERG, ROBERT AC
FEAST OF ST. DIONYSUS, THE — NV 73
EXALTATION OF STARS, AN — CARR, TERRY OA
FEAST OF ST. DIONYSUS, THE — SILVERBERG, ROBERT AC
FINAL CHALLENGE, THE — SS INF 56 08
SHORES OF TOMORROW, THE — SILVERBERG, ROBERT AC
FLAME AND THE HAMMER, THE — NO SFA 57 09
VALLEY BEYOND TIME — SILVERBERG, ROBERT AC
FLIES — SS DVS 67 01
BEST OF ROBERT SILVERBERG, THE — SILVERBERG, ROBERT AC
DANGEROUS VISIONS — ELLISON, HARLAN OA
EARTH'S OTHER SHADOW — SILVERBERG, ROBERT AC
PARSECS AND PARABLES — SILVERBERG, ROBERT AC
FORCE OF MORTALITY — SS FUT 57 FL
GODLING, GO HOME! — SILVERBERG, ROBERT AC
FOREWORD — IN
NO MIND OF MAN — SILVERBERG, ROBERT OA
THREE TRIPS IN TIME AND SPACE — SILVERBERG, ROBERT OA
FOUR, THE — SS SFS 58 08
DIMENSION THIRTEEN — SILVERBERG, ROBERT AC
GETTING ACROSS — NV FUC 73
CAPRICORN GAMES — SILVERBERG, ROBERT AC
FUTURE CITY — ELWOOD, ROGER OA
GODLING, GO HOME! — SS SFS 57 01
GODLING, GO HOME! — SILVERBERG, ROBERT AC
GOING — NA FFU 71
BORN WITH THE DEAD — SILVERBERG, ROBERT AC
FOUR FUTURES — SILVERBERG, ROBERT OA
GOING DOWN SMOOTH — SS GAL 68 08
INTRODUCTORY PSYCHOLOGY THROUGH SCIENCE FICTION — KATZ/WARRICK/& AN
MOONFERNS & STARSONGS — SILVERBERG, ROBERT AC
NEW TOMORROWS, THE — SPINRAD, NORMAN AN
PARSECS AND PARABLES — SILVERBERG, ROBERT AC
WORLD'S BEST SCIENCE FICTION: 1969 — WOLLHEIM & CARR AN
GOOD NEWS FROM THE VATICAN — SS UNI 71 01
BEST OF ROBERT SILVERBERG, THE — SILVERBERG, ROBERT AC
BEST SCIENCE FICTION STORIES OF THE YEAR (1971) — DEL REY, LESTER AN
NEBULA AWARD STORIES NO. 7 — BIGGLE, LLOYD JR. AN
NEW AWARENESS, THE — WARRICK & GREENBERG AN
SOCIAL PROBLEMS THROUGH SCIENCE FICTION — GREENBERG/MILSTEAD/& AN
UNFAMILIAR TERRITORY — SILVERBERG, ROBERT AC
UNIVERSE 1 — CARR, TERRY OA
GREAT KLADNAR RACE, THE (AS RICHARD GREER) — SS C AMZ 56 12
INFINITE ARENA, THE — CARR, TERRY AN
HALFWAY HOUSE — SS IFS 66 11
CUBE ROOT OF UNCERTAINTY, THE — SILVERBERG, ROBERT AC
DIMENSION THIRTEEN — SILVERBERG, ROBERT AC
HAPPY DAY IN 2381, A — SS NOV 70 01
CITY: 2000 A.D., THE — CLEM/GREENBERG/& AN
DAY IN THE LIFE, A — DOZOIS, GARDNER R. AN
EARTH IN TRANSIT — SCHWARTZ, SHEILA AN
MOONFERNS & STARSONGS — SILVERBERG, ROBERT AC
*NOVA 1 — HARRISON, HARRY OA
SURVIVAL PRINTOUT — TOTAL EFFECT AN
HAWKSBILL STATION — NV GAL 67 08
BEST OF ROBERT SILVERBERG, THE — SILVERBERG, ROBERT AC
BEST SF: 1967 — HARRISON & ALDISS AN
DECADE THE 1960S — ALDISS & HARRISON AN
GIFTS OF ASTI AND OTHER STORIES OF SCIENCE FICTION, THE — ELWOOD, ROGER AN
REALITY TRIP, THE — SILVERBERG, ROBERT AC
WORLD'S BEST SCIENCE FICTION: 1968 — WOLLHEIM & CARR AN
HI DIDDLE DIDDLE! — NV ASF 59 02
SUNRISE ON MERCURY AND OTHER SCIENCE FICTION STORIES — SILVERBERG, ROBERT OA
WORLDS OF WONDER — HARRISON, HARRY AN
HIDDEN TALENT — NV IFS 57 04
EARTH'S OTHER SHADOW — SILVERBERG, ROBERT AC
HIS BROTHER'S WEEPER — NV FUN 59 03
NEEDLE IN A TIMESTACK — SILVERBERG, ROBERT AC
HIS HEAD IN THE CLOUDS — SS SFS 57 09
CALLIBRATED ALLIGATOR AND OTHER SCIENCE FICTION STORIES, THE — SILVERBERG, ROBERT AC

SILVERBERG, ROBERT (CONTINUED)
  HOLE IN THE AIR   SS   AMZ 56 01
    DEVIL'S GENERATION, THE   GHIDALIA, VIC   AN
  HOPPER   NV   INF 56 10
    NEXT STOP THE STARS   SILVERBERG, ROBERT   DC
  HOW IT WAS WHEN THE PAST WENT AWAY   NA   TFT 69
    EARTH'S OTHER SHADOW   SILVERBERG, ROBERT   AC
    THREE FOR TOMORROW   SILVERBERG, ROBERT   OA
  HUNT THE SPACE-WITCH¡   SN   SFA 58 01
    GREAT SCIENCE FICTION ADVENTURES SHAW, LARRY T.   AN
  IN ENTROPY'S JAWS   NV   INY 71 02
    BEST SCIENCE FICTION OF THE YEAR, THE CARR, TERRY   AN
    INFINITY 2   HOSKINS, ROBERT   OA
    MODERN SCIENCE FICTION   SPINRAD, NORMAN   AN
    REALITY TRIP, THE   SILVERBERG, ROBERT   AC
    UNFAMILIAR TERRITORY   SILVERBERG, ROBERT   AC
  IN THE BEGINNING   SS   SAG 70
    SCIENCE AGAINST MAN   CHEETHAM, ANTHONY   OA
  IN THE GROUP   SS   EIO 73
    EROS IN ORBIT   ELDER, JOSEPH   OA
    UNFAMILIAR TERRITORY   SILVERBERG, ROBERT   AC
  IN THE HOUSE OF DOUBLE MINDS   SS   VTX 74 06
    FEAST OF ST. DIONYSUS, THE   SILVERBERG, ROBERT   AC
  INTRODUCTION   IN
    ALIENS, THE   SILVERBERG, ROBERT   AN
    ALPHA 1   SILVERBERG, ROBERT   AN
    ALPHA 2   SILVERBERG, ROBERT   AN
    ALPHA 3   SILVERBERG, ROBERT   AN
    ALPHA 4   SILVERBERG, ROBERT   AN
    ALPHA 5   SILVERBERG, ROBERT   AN
    ALPHA 6   SILVERBERG, ROBERT   AN
    ALPHA 7   SILVERBERG, ROBERT   AN
    BEYOND CONTROL   SILVERBERG, ROBERT   AN
    CHAINS OF THE SEA   SILVERBERG, ROBERT   OA
    CRYSTAL SHIP, THE   SILVERBERG, ROBERT   OA
    CUBE ROOT OF UNCERTAINTY, THE   SILVERBERG, ROBERT   AC
    DARK STARS   SILVERBERG, ROBERT   AN
    DAY THE SUN STOOD STILL, THE   SILVERBERG, ROBERT   OA
    DEEP SPACE   SILVERBERG, ROBERT   AN
    EARTH IS THE STRANGEST PLANET   SILVERBERG, ROBERT   AN
    EARTHMEN AND STRANGERS   SILVERBERG, ROBERT   AN
    ENDS OF TIME, THE   SILVERBERG, ROBERT   AN
    EXPLORERS OF SPACE   SILVERBERG, ROBERT   AN
    GREAT SHORT NOVELS OF SCIENCE FICTION SILVERBERG, ROBERT   AN
    INFINITE JESTS   SILVERBERG, ROBERT   AN
    INVADERS FROM SPACE   SILVERBERG, ROBERT   AN
    IRRATIONAL NUMBERS   EFFINGER, GEO. ALEC   AC
    MEN AND MACHINES   SILVERBERG, ROBERT   AN
    MIND TO MIND   SILVERBERG, ROBERT   AN
    MIRROR OF INFINITY, THE   SILVERBERG, ROBERT   AN
    MUTANTS   SILVERBERG, ROBERT   AN
    NEW ATLANTIS AND OTHER NOVELLAS OF S.F., THE
                                      SILVERBERG, ROBERT   OA
    NEW DIMENSIONS 1   SILVERBERG, ROBERT   OA
    NEW DIMENSIONS 2   SILVERBERG, ROBERT   OA
    NEW DIMENSIONS 3   SILVERBERG, ROBERT   OA
    NEW DIMENSIONS 7   SILVERBERG, ROBERT   OA
    OTHER DIMENSIONS   SILVERBERG, ROBERT   AN
    SCIENCE FICTION BESTIARY, THE   SILVERBERG, ROBERT   AN
    SCIENCE FICTION HALL OF FAME VOLUME 1 SILVERBERG, ROBERT   AN
    STRANGE GIFTS   SILVERBERG, ROBERT   AN
    THREADS OF TIME   SILVERBERG, ROBERT   OA
    THREE TRIPS IN TIME AND SPACE   SILVERBERG, ROBERT   OA
    TO THE STARS   SILVERBERG, ROBERT   AN
    TOMORROW'S WORLDS   SILVERBERG, ROBERT   AN
    VALLEY BEYOND TIME   SILVERBERG, ROBERT   AC
    VOYAGERS IN TIME   SILVERBERG, ROBERT   AN
    WINDOWS INTO TOMORROW   SILVERBERG, ROBERT   AN
    WORLDS OF MAYBE   SILVERBERG, ROBERT   AN
  INTRODUCTION   IN C
    EPOCH   ELWOOD & SILVERBERG   OA
  INTRODUCTION TO "SUNDANCE"   AR
    THOSE WHO CAN: A SCIENCE FICTION READER
                                      WILSON, ROBIN SCOTT   AN
  IRON CHANCELLOR, THE   NV   GAL 58 05
    BEYOND CONTROL   SILVERBERG, ROBERT   AN
    CUBE ROOT OF UNCERTAINTY, THE   SILVERBERG, ROBERT   AC
    NEEDLE IN A TIMESTACK   SILVERBERG, ROBERT   AC
  ISHMAEL IN LOVE   SS   FSF 70 07
    EARTH'S OTHER SHADOW   SILVERBERG, ROBERT   AC
    PARSECS AND PARABLES   SILVERBERG, ROBERT   AC
    WORLD'S BEST SCIENCE FICTION: 1971 WOLLHEIM & CARR   AN
  ISOLATIONISTS, THE   SS   SFS 58 11
    SHORES OF TOMORROW, THE   SILVERBERG, ROBERT   AC
  JOURNEY'S END (THE SEED OF EARTH)   SS   SUP 58 04
    DIMENSION THIRTEEN   SILVERBERG, ROBERT   AC
  KING OF THE GOLDEN RIVER, THE   SS   GAL 67 12
    DIMENSION THIRTEEN   SILVERBERG, ROBERT   AC
  LAZARUS COME FORTH¡   NV   GAL 66 04
    TO OPEN THE SKY   SILVERBERG, ROBERT   NO
  LONELY ONE, THE   SS   FSF 56 07
    GODLING, GO HOME¡   SILVERBERG, ROBERT   AC
  LUNATIC PLANET, THE   SS   AMZ 57 11
    ODDBALLS, THE   GHIDALIA, VIC   AN
  MACAULEY CIRCUIT, THE   SS   FUN 56 08
    MEN AND MACHINES   SILVERBERG, ROBERT   AN
    SUNRISE ON MERCURY AND OTHER SCIENCE FICTION STORIES
                                      SILVERBERG, ROBERT   OA
  MAN IN THE MAZE, THE   NO   IFS 68 04
    SCIENCE FICTION SPECIAL 4   ANONYMOUS   AN
  MAN OF TALENT, A (MAN WITH TALENT)   NV   FUT 56 WI
    MOONFERNS & STARSONGS   SILVERBERG, ROBERT   AC
    NEW DREAMS THIS MORNING   BLISH, JAMES   AN
  MAN WHO CAME BACK, THE   SS   GAL 74 12
    BEST SCIENCE FICTION STORIES OF THE YEAR (1974)
                                      DEL REY, LESTER   AN

SILVERBERG, ROBERT (CONTINUED)
  MAN WHO NEVER FORGOT, THE   SS   FSF 58 02
    MUTANTS   SILVERBERG, ROBERT   AN
    PARSECS AND PARABLES   SILVERBERG, ROBERT   AN
  MAN WITH TALENT, THE   SS   FUT 56 WI
    GODLING, GO HOME¡   SILVERBERG, ROBERT   AC
  MANY MANSIONS   NV   UNI 73 03
    UNFAMILIAR TERRITORY   SILVERBERG, ROBERT   AC
    UNIVERSE 3   CARR, TERRY   OA
  MIND FOR BUSINESS   SS   ASF 56 09
    TO WORLDS BEYOND   SILVERBERG, ROBERT   AC
  MISFIT   SS   SUP 57 12
    TO WORLDS BEYOND   SILVERBERG, ROBERT   AC
  MS. FOUND IN AN ABANDONED TIME MACHINE   SS   TTM 73
    CAPRICORN GAMES   SILVERBERG, ROBERT   AC
    TEN TOMORROWS   ELWOOD, ROGER   OA
    VISIONS OF TOMORROW   ELWOOD, ROGER   AN
  MUGWUMP FOUR   NV   GAL 59 08
    CALLIBRATED ALLIGATOR AND OTHER SCIENCE FICTION STORIES, THE
                                      SILVERBERG, ROBERT   AC
    CUBE ROOT OF UNCERTAINTY, THE   SILVERBERG, ROBERT   AC
    OTHER DIMENSIONS   SILVERBERG, ROBERT   AN
  MUTANT WEAPON, THE   SS   NEW 73 AN
    ANDROIDS, TIME MACHINES AND BLUE GIRAFFES
                                      ELWOOD & GHIDALIA   AN
    UNFAMILIAR TERRITORY   SILVERBERG, ROBERT   AC
  NEIGHBOR   SS   GAL 64 08
    CUBE ROOT OF UNCERTAINTY, THE   SILVERBERG, ROBERT   AC
    SUNDANCE AND OTHER SCIENCE FICTION STORIES
                                      SILVERBERG, ROBERT   AC
  NEUTRAL PLANET   SS   SFS 57 07
    GODLING, GO HOME¡   SILVERBERG, ROBERT   AC
    SUNDANCE AND OTHER SCIENCE FICTION STORIES
                                      SILVERBERG, ROBERT   AC
  NEW MEN FOR MARS   NV   SUP 57 06
    TO WORLDS BEYOND   SILVERBERG, ROBERT   AC
  NIGHTWINGS   NV   GAL 68 09
    BEST OF ROBERT SILVERBERG, THE   SILVERBERG, ROBERT   AC
    ELEVENTH GALAXY READER, THE   POHL, FREDERIK   AN
    HUGO WINNERS, THE (VOLUME 2)   ASIMOV, ISAAC   AN
    INVADERS FROM SPACE   SILVERBERG, ROBERT   AN
    MOONFERNS & STARSONGS   SILVERBERG, ROBERT   AC
  (NOW+N), (NOW-N)   NV   NOV 72 02
    INFINITE JESTS   SILVERBERG, ROBERT   AN
    NOVA 2   HARRISON, HARRY   OA
    UNFAMILIAR TERRITORY   SILVERBERG, ROBERT   AC
  OLD MAN, THE   SS   IMG 57 04
    TO WORLDS BEYOND   SILVERBERG, ROBERT   AC
  ONE-WAY JOURNEY   NV   INF 57 11
    PARSECS AND PARABLES   SILVERBERG, ROBERT   AC
  OPEN THE SKY (SEE TO OPEN THE SKY)   TC
  OUTBREEDERS, THE   SS   FUN 59 09
    PARSECS AND PARABLES   SILVERBERG, ROBERT   AC
    SUNDANCE AND OTHER SCIENCE FICTION STORIES
                                      SILVERBERG, ROBERT   AC
  OVERLORD'S THUMB, THE   NV   INF 58 03
    SUNDANCE AND OTHER SCIENCE FICTION STORIES
                                      SILVERBERG, ROBERT   AC
    TO WORLDS BEYOND   SILVERBERG, ROBERT   AC
  OZYMANDIAS   SS   INF 58 11
    REALITY TRIP, THE   SILVERBERG, ROBERT   AC
    TO THE STARS   SILVERBERG, ROBERT   AN
    TO WORLDS BEYOND   SILVERBERG, ROBERT   AC
  PAIN PEDDLERS, THE   SS   GAL 63 08
    NEEDLE IN A TIMESTACK   SILVERBERG, ROBERT   AC
    SUNDANCE AND OTHER SCIENCE FICTION STORIES
                                      SILVERBERG, ROBERT   AC
    WINDOWS INTO TOMORROW   SILVERBERG, ROBERT   AN
  PASSENGERS   SS   ORB 68 04
    BEST FROM ORBIT, THE   KNIGHT, DAMON   AN
    BEST OF ROBERT SILVERBERG, THE   SILVERBERG, ROBERT   AC
    CUBE ROOT OF UNCERTAINTY, THE   SILVERBERG, ROBERT   AC
    MOONFERNS & STARSONGS   SILVERBERG, ROBERT   AC
    NEBULA AWARD STORIES NO. 5   BLISH, JAMES   AN
    ORBIT   4   KNIGHT, DAMON   OA
  PASSPORT TO SIRIUS   SS   IFS 58 04
    NEEDLE IN A TIMESTACK   SILVERBERG, ROBERT   AC
    SUNDANCE AND OTHER SCIENCE FICTION STORIES
                                      SILVERBERG, ROBERT   AC
  PLEASURE OF OUR COMPANY, THE (ALSO AS THE PLEASURE OF
    THEIR COMPANY)   NV   INY 70 01
    INFINITY 1   HOSKINS, ROBERT   OA
  PLEASURE OF THEIR COMPANY, THE (THE PLEASURE OF OUR COMPANY)
                                                           NV   INY 70 01
    MOONFERNS & STARSONGS   SILVERBERG, ROBERT   AC
  POINT OF FOCUS   SS   ASF 58 08
    CALLIBRATED ALLIGATOR AND OTHER SCIENCE FICTION STORIES, THE
                                      SILVERBERG, ROBERT   AC
    OUT OF THIS WORLD 7   WILLIAMS-ELLIS& OWEN   AN
  PRECEDENT   NV   ASF 57 12
    CALLIBRATED ALLIGATOR AND OTHER SCIENCE FICTION STORIES, THE
                                      SILVERBERG, ROBERT   AC
  PRIME COMMANDMENT   SS   SFS 58 01
    DIMENSION THIRTEEN   SILVERBERG, ROBERT   AC
  PUSH NO MORE   NV   NEW 72 AN
    STRANGE BED FELLOWS   SCORTIA, THOMAS N.   AN
    UNFAMILIAR TERRITORY   SILVERBERG, ROBERT   AC
  QUICK FREEZE   SS   SFQ 57 05
    RARE SCIENCE FICTION   HOWARD, IVAN   AN
    SHORES OF TOMORROW, THE   SILVERBERG, ROBERT   AC
  REALITY TRIP, THE   NV   IFS 70 05
    BEST FROM IF, THE   VOLUME I   IF, EDITORS OF   AN
    REALITY TRIP, THE   SILVERBERG, ROBERT   AC
    THIS SIDE OF INFINITY   CARR, TERRY   AN
  RINGING THE CHANGES   SS   ANA 70
    ALCHEMY AND ACADEME   MCCAFFREY, ANNE   OA

SILVERBERG, ROBERT   SIMAK, CLIFFORD D.

SILVERBERG, ROBERT   (CONTINUED)
    REALITY TRIP, THE   SILVERBERG, ROBERT   AC
ROAD TO NIGHTFALL   NV   FUN 58 07
    BEST OF ROBERT SILVERBERG, THE   SILVERBERG, ROBERT   AC
    DARK STARS   SILVERBERG, ROBERT   AN
    FANTASTIC UNIVERSE OMNIBUS, THE   SANTESSON, HANS S.   AN
    PARSECS AND PARABLES   SILVERBERG, ROBERT   AC
SCHWARTZ BETWEEN THE GALAXIES   SS   STL 74 01
    FEAST OF ST. DIONYSUS, THE   SILVERBERG, ROBERT   AC
    STELLAR 1   DEL REY, JUDY-LYNN   OA
SCIENCE FICTION HALL OF FAME, THE   SS   INY 73 05
    CAPRICORN GAMES   SILVERBERG, ROBERT   AC
    INFINITY 5   HOSKINS, ROBERT   OA
SEA OF FACES, A   SS   UNI 74 04
    CAPRICORN GAMES   SILVERBERG, ROBERT   AC
    UNIVERSE 4   CARR, TERRY   OA
SEED OF EARTH, THE (SEE JOURNEY'S END)   TC
SHADOW OF WINGS, THE   SS   IFS 63 07
    CUBE ROOT OF UNCERTAINTY, THE   SILVERBERG, ROBERT   AC
    NEEDLE IN A TIMESTACK   SILVERBERG, ROBERT   AC
SHIP-SISTER, STAR-SISTER   NV   TAL 73
    CAPRICORN GAMES   SILVERBERG, ROBERT   AC
    FRONTIERS 1: TOMORROW'S ALTERNATIVES ELWOOD, ROGER   OA
SHRINES OF EARTH, THE   SS   ASF 57 11
    REALITY TRIP, THE   SILVERBERG, ROBERT   AC
SILENT COLONY, THE   SS   FUT 54 10
    CREATURES FROM BEYOND   CARR, TERRY   AN
    GODLING, GO HOME¦   SILVERBERG, ROBERT   AC
    SHORES OF TOMORROW, THE   SILVERBERG, ROBERT   AC
SIXTH PALACE, THE   SS   GAL 65 02
    BEST OF ROBERT SILVERBERG, THE   SILVERBERG, ROBERT   AC
    CUBE ROOT OF UNCERTAINTY, THE   SILVERBERG, ROBERT   AC
    DEEP SPACE   SILVERBERG, ROBERT   AN
    NEEDLE IN A TIMESTACK   SILVERBERG, ROBERT   AC
SLAVES OF THE STAR GIANTS   NA   SPA 57 02
    NEXT STOP THE STARS   SILVERBERG, ROBERT   DC
SOLITARY   SS   FUT 57 SP
    DIMENSION THIRTEEN   SILVERBERG, ROBERT   AC
    GODLING, GO HOME¦   SILVERBERG, ROBERT   AC
SOME NOTES ON THE PREDYNASTIC EPOCH   SS   BMR 73
    BAD MOON RISING   DISCH, THOMAS M.   OA
    UNFAMILIAR TERRITORY   SILVERBERG, ROBERT   AC
SOMETHING WILD IS LOOSE   NV   MWS 71
    EARTH'S OTHER SHADOW   SILVERBERG, ROBERT   AC
    MANY WORLDS OF SCIENCE FICTION, THE BOVA, BEN   OA
    MIND TO MIND   SILVERBERG, ROBERT   AN
    SUNDANCE AND OTHER SCIENCE FICTION STORIES
                                        SILVERBERG, ROBERT   AC
SONG THE ZOMBIE SANG, THE   SS C CMP 70 12
    EARTH'S OTHER SHADOW   SILVERBERG, ROBERT   AC
    PARTNERS IN WONDER   ELLISON, HARLAN   AC
SONGS OF SUMMER, THE   SS   SFS 56 09
    MOONFERNS & STARSONGS   SILVERBERG, ROBERT   AC
    NEXT STOP THE STARS   SILVERBERG, ROBERT   DC
SOUND DECISION   NV C ASF 56 10
    DAYS AFTER TOMORROW, THE   SANTESSON, HANS S.   AN
    PROLOGUE TO ANALOG   CAMPBELL, JOHN W. JR AN
    SHORES OF TOMORROW, THE   SILVERBERG, ROBERT   AC
SPACEROGUE (AS WEBBER MARTIN)   SN   INF 58 11
    VALLEY BEYOND TIME   SILVERBERG, ROBERT   AC
STRESS PATTERN   NV   ASF 60 01
    SHORES OF TOMORROW, THE   SILVERBERG, ROBERT   AC
SUNDANCE   SS   FSF 69 06
    ALIENS, THE   SILVERBERG, ROBERT   AN
    BEST FROM FANTASY AND SCIENCE FICTION: 19
                                        FERMAN, EDWARD L.   AN
    BEST OF ROBERT SILVERBERG, THE   SILVERBERG, ROBERT   AC
    BEYOND TOMORROW   HARDING, LEE   AN
    CUBE ROOT OF UNCERTAINTY, THE   SILVERBERG, ROBERT   AC
    ON OUR WAY TO THE FUTURE   CARR, TERRY   AN
    SPECTRUM OF WORLDS, A   CLARESON, THOMAS D. AN
    SPECULATIONS   SANDERS, THOMAS E.   AN
    SUNDANCE AND OTHER SCIENCE FICTION STORIES
                                        SILVERBERG, ROBERT   AC
    THOSE WHO CAN: A SCIENCE FICTION READER
                                        WILSON, ROBIN SCOTT AN
    TOMORROW, AND TOMORROW, AND TOMORROW...
                                        HEINTZ/HERBERT/JOOS/ AN
SUNRISE ON MERCURY   SS   SFS 57 05
    FIRST STEP OUTWARD   HOSKINS, ROBERT   AN
    MORE ADVENTURES ON OTHER PLANETS   WOLLHEIM, DONALD A. AN
    PARSECS AND PARABLES   SILVERBERG, ROBERT   AC
    SUNRISE ON MERCURY AND OTHER SCIENCE FICTION STORIES
                                        SILVERBERG, ROBERT   OA
    TOMORROW'S WORLDS   SILVERBERG, ROBERT   AN
    TOMORROW, AND TOMORROW, AND TOMORROW...
                                        HEINTZ/HERBERT/JOOS/ AN
THERE WAS AN OLD WOMAN-   SS   INF 58 11
    NEEDLE IN A TIMESTACK   SILVERBERG, ROBERT   AC
    SUNRISE ON MERCURY AND OTHER SCIENCE FICTION STORIES
                                        SILVERBERG, ROBERT   OA
THERE'S NO PLACE LIKE SPACE   NV   SFS 59 05
    GODLING, GO HOME¦   SILVERBERG, ROBERT   AC
THIS IS THE ROAD   NA
    FEAST OF ST. DIONYSUS, THE   SILVERBERG, ROBERT   AC
    NO MIND OF MAN   SILVERBERG, ROBERT   OA
THOMAS THE PROCLAIMER   NA
    BORN WITH THE DEAD   SILVERBERG, ROBERT   AC
    DAY THE SUN STOOD STILL, THE   SILVERBERG, ROBERT   OA
THROWBACKS, THE   NV   GAL 70 07
    WORLD INSIDE, THE   SILVERBERG, ROBERT   NO
TIME-HOPPERS, THE   NO   DBL 67
    SCIENCE FICTION SPECIAL 3   ANONYMOUS   AN
TO BE CONTINUED   SS   ASF 56 05
    MOONFERNS & STARSONGS   SILVERBERG, ROBERT   AC
    STRANGE GIFTS   SILVERBERG, ROBERT   AN

SILVERBERG, ROBERT   (CONTINUED)
TO OPEN THE SKY (OPEN THE SKY)   NV   GAL 66 06
    TO OPEN THE SKY   SILVERBERG, ROBERT   NO
TO SEE THE INVISIBLE MAN   SS   WOT 63 04
    ANOTHER TOMORROW   HOLLISTER, BERNARD C AN
    BEST OF ROBERT SILVERBERG, THE   SILVERBERG, ROBERT   AC
    EARTH IN TRANSIT   SCHWARTZ, SHEILA   AN
    EARTH'S OTHER SHADOW   SILVERBERG, ROBERT   AC
    NEEDLE IN A TIMESTACK   SILVERBERG, ROBERT   AC
    SF: AUTHORS' CHOICE 2   HARRISON, HARRY   AN
TO THE DARK STAR   SS   FRS 68
    BEST SF: 1968   HARRISON & ALDISS   AN
    CUBE ROOT OF UNCERTAINTY, THE   SILVERBERG, ROBERT   AC
    EARTH'S OTHER SHADOW   SILVERBERG, ROBERT   AC
    FARTHEST REACHES, THE   ELDER, JOSEPH   OA
TRANSLATION ERROR   SS   ASF 59 03
    CUBE ROOT OF UNCERTAINTY, THE   SILVERBERG, ROBERT   AC
    TRANSFORMATIONS II   ROSELLE, DANIEL   AN
    WORLDS OF MAYBE   SILVERBERG, ROBERT   AN
TRIPS   NV   FST 74
    FEAST OF ST. DIONYSUS, THE   SILVERBERG, ROBERT   AC
    FINAL STAGE   FERMAN & MALZBERG   OA
VALLEY BEYOND TIME   SN   SPA 57 12
    VALLEY BEYOND TIME   SILVERBERG, ROBERT   AC
VENUS TRAP   SS   FUT 56 30
    NOW & BEYOND   HOWARD, IVAN   AN
WAGES OF DEATH, THE   NV   IFS 58 08
    VALLEY BEYOND TIME   SILVERBERG, ROBERT   AC
WARM MAN   SS   FSF 57 05
    BEST OF ROBERT SILVERBERG, THE   SILVERBERG, ROBERT   AC
    DIMENSION THIRTEEN   SILVERBERG, ROBERT   AC
    NEXT STOP THE STARS   SILVERBERG, ROBERT   DC
    SPECIAL WONDER   MCCOMAS, J. FRANCIS AN
WARRIORS OF LIGHT, THE   NV   GAL 65 12
    TO OPEN THE SKY   SILVERBERG, ROBERT   NO
WE ARE WELL ORGANIZED   NV   GAL 70 12
    WORLD INSIDE, THE   SILVERBERG, ROBERT   NO
WE KNOW WHO WE ARE   SS   AMZ 70 07
    MOONFERNS & STARSONGS   SILVERBERG, ROBERT   AC
WHAT WE LEARNED FROM THIS MORNING'S NEWSPAPER SS INY 72 04
    BEST SCIENCE FICTION FOR 1973   ACKERMAN, FORREST J. AN
    INFINITY 4   HOSKINS, ROBERT   OA
    UNFAMILIAR TERRITORY   SILVERBERG, ROBERT   AC
WHEN WE WENT TO SEE THE END OF THE WORLD   SS UNI 72 02
    BEST SCIENCE FICTION OF THE YEAR, THE NO. 2
                                        CARR, TERRY   AN
    BEST SCIENCE FICTION STORIES OF THE YEAR (1972)
                                        DEL REY, LESTER   AN
    EARTH IS THE STRANGEST PLANET   SILVERBERG, ROBERT   AN
    FUTURE PASTIMES   EDELSTEIN, SCOTT   OA
    LATE GREAT FUTURE, THE   FITZ GERALD & DILLON AN
    NEBULA AWARD STORIES 8   ASIMOV, ISAAC   AN
    UNFAMILIAR TERRITORY   SILVERBERG, ROBERT   AC
    UNIVERSE 2   CARR, TERRY   OA
WHERE THE CHANGED ONES GO   NV   GAL 66 02
    TO OPEN THE SKY   SILVERBERG, ROBERT   NO
WHO IS TIPTREE, WHAT IS HE?   IN
    WARM WORLDS AND OTHERWISE   TIPTREE, JAMES JR.   AC
WHY?   SS   SFS 57 11
    CALLIBRATED ALLIGATOR AND OTHER SCIENCE FICTION STORIES, THE
                                        SILVERBERG, ROBERT   AC
    GODLING, GO HOME¦   SILVERBERG, ROBERT   AC
WIND AND THE RAIN, THE   SS   SVW 73
    BEST SF: 1973   HARRISON & ALDISS   AN
    FUTURE NOW, THE   HOSKINS, ROBERT   AN
    SAVING WORLDS   ELWOOD & KIDD   OA
    UNFAMILIAR TERRITORY   SILVERBERG, ROBERT   AC
WORLD HE LEFT BEHIND, THE   SS   NEB 59 02
    GODLING, GO HOME¦   SILVERBERG, ROBERT   AC
WORLD OF A THOUSAND COLORS   SS   SUP 57 06
    DIMENSION THIRTEEN   SILVERBERG, ROBERT   AC
WORLD OUTSIDE, THE   NA   GAL 70 10
    WORLD INSIDE, THE   SILVERBERG, ROBERT   NO

SILVERSTEIN, SHEL
    DISTORTION, THE   CT   PBY 60 05
    6TH ANNUAL OF THE YEAR'S BEST S-F, THE MERRIL, JUDITH   AN

SIMAK, CLIFFORD D.
ALIENS FOR NEIGHBOURS   AC H FAB 61
    9 STORIES FROM "THE WORLDS OF CLIFFORD SIMAK"
ALL THE TRAPS OF EARTH AND OTHER STORIES   AC H DBL 62
    IN ENGLAND AS "THE NIGHT OF THE PUUDLY"
ALL THE TRAPS OF EARTH AND OTHER STORIES (BRITISH PB 2)
                                            AC   FSP 64
ALL THE TRAPS OF EARTH AND OTHER STORIES (6 OF 9) AC MCF 63
BEST SCIENCE FICTION STORIES OF CLIFFORD D. SIMAK AC H FAB LM
CITY   NO H GNM 52 05
NEBULA AWARD STORIES NO. 6   AN H DBL 71 12
NIGHT OF THE PUUDLY, THE   AC   FSP 64
    5 STORIES FROM "ALL THE TRAPS OF EARTH"
OTHER WORLDS OF CLIFFORD SIMAK   AC   AVN 62
    6 STORIES FROM "THE WORLDS OF CLIFFORD SIMAK"
SO BRIGHT THE VISION   DC   ACE 68
STRANGERS IN THE UNIVERSE   AC H SAS 56
STRANGERS IN THE UNIVERSE (BRITISH)   AC H FAB 58
STRANGERS IN THE UNIVERSE (7 OF 11)   AC   BKM 57 09
WORLDS OF CLIFFORD SIMAK, THE   AC H SAS 60
    DERIVATIVE COLLECTION "OTHER WORLDS OF CLIFFORD SIMAK"
    IN ENGLAND AS "ALIENS FOR NEIGHBOURS"
WORLDS OF CLIFFORD SIMAK, THE (BRITISH PB) AC   FSP 63
WORLDS OF CLIFFORD SIMAK, THE (6 OF 12)   AC   AVN 61
WORLDS WITHOUT END   AC   BEL 64 04
AESOP   NV   ASF 47 12
    CITY   SIMAK, CLIFFORD D.   NO

SIMAK, CLIFFORD D.   SIMAK, CLIFFORD D.

SIMAK, CLIFFORD D.   (CONTINUED)
  ALL THE TRAPS OF EARTH   SS   FSF 60 03
  *ALL THE TRAPS OF EARTH AND OTHER STORIES
                                          SIMAK, CLIFFORD D.   AC
  BEST SCIENCE FICTION STORIES OF CLIFFORD D. SIMAK
                                          SIMAK, CLIFFORD D.   AC
AND THE TRUTH SHALL MAKE YOU FREE (ALSO AS THE ANSWERS)
                                               SS   FUT 53 03
  NOVELETS OF SCIENCE FICTION   HOWARD, IVAN   AN
ANSWERS, THE (AND THE TRUTH SHALL MAKE YOU FREE) SS FUT 53 03
  *STORIES FOR TOMORROW   SLOANE, WILLIAM   AN
  *STRANGERS IN THE UNIVERSE   SIMAK, CLIFFORD D.   AC
ASTEROID OF GOLD, THE   SS   WOS 32 11
  EVERY BOY'S BOOK OF SCIENCE FICTION   WOLLHEIM, DONALD A. AN
  HISTORY OF THE SCIENCE FICTION MAGAZINE, THE PART 1 1926-1935
                                          ASHLEY, MICHAEL   AN
AUTUMN LAND, THE   NV   FSF 71 10
  SF: AUTHORS' CHOICE 4   HARRISON, HARRY   AN
BATHE YOUR BEARINGS IN BLOOD (SEE SKIRMISH)   TC
BEACHHEAD (YOU'LL NEVER GO HOME AGAIN)   SS   PAD 51 07
  *BEACHHEADS IN SPACE   DERLETH, AUGUST   AN
  EXPLORERS OF SPACE   SILVERBERG, ROBERT   AN
  *STRANGERS IN THE UNIVERSE   SIMAK, CLIFFORD D.   AC
BIG FRONT YARD, THE   NV   ASF 58 10
  HUGO WINNERS, THE (VOLUME 1)   ASIMOV, ISAAC   AN
  SCIENCE FICTION HALL OF FAME VOLUME 2B BOVA, BEN   AN
  *WORLDS OF CLIFFORD SIMAK, THE   SIMAK, CLIFFORD D.   AC
BIRCH CLUMP CYLINDER, THE   NV   STL 74 01
  BEST SCIENCE FICTION STORIES OF THE YEAR (1974)
                                          DEL REY, LESTER   AN
  STELLAR 1   DEL REY, JUDY-LYNN   OA
CALL FROM BEYOND, THE   NV   SSS 50 05
  SPACE MAGICIANS, THE   NORTON & MOSKOWITZ   AN
CARBON COPY   NA   GAL 57 12
  ALIENS FOR NEIGHBOURS   SIMAK, CLIFFORD D.   AC
  OTHER WORLDS OF CLIFFORD SIMAK   SIMAK, CLIFFORD D.   AC
  *WORLDS OF CLIFFORD SIMAK, THE   SIMAK, CLIFFORD D.   AC
CENSUS   NV   ASF 44 09
  CITY   SIMAK, CLIFFORD D.   NO
CITY   NV   ASF 44 05
  ASTOUNDING-ANALOG READER, THE VOLUME ONE
                                          HARRISON & ALDISS   AN
  CITY   SIMAK, CLIFFORD D.   NO
  SCIENCE FICTION OMNIBUS ON POLLUTION, A
                                          ANONYMOUS   AN
CIVILIZATION GAME, THE   NV   GAL 58 11
  MIND PARTNER AND 8 OTHER NOVELETS FROM GALAXY
                                          GOLD, H. L.   AN
  TOMORROW 1   HOSKINS, ROBERT   AN
CONDITION OF EMPLOYMENT   SS   GAL 60 04
  *ALL THE TRAPS OF EARTH AND OTHER STORIES
                                          SIMAK, CLIFFORD D.   AC
  NIGHT OF THE PUUDLY, THE   SIMAK, CLIFFORD D.   AC
CONSTRUCTION SHACK   SS   IFS 73 02
  BEST FROM IF, THE VOLUME II   IF, EDITORS OF   AN
  BEST SCIENCE FICTION STORIES OF THE YEAR (1973)
                                          DEL REY, LESTER   AN
  1974 ANNUAL WORLD'S BEST SF, THE   WOLLHEIM, DONALD A. AN
CONTRAPTION   SS   STR 53 01
  STAR SCIENCE FICTION STORIES   POHL, FREDERIK   OA
  *STRANGERS IN THE UNIVERSE   SIMAK, CLIFFORD D.   AC
COURTESY   SS   ASF 51 08
  CROSSROADS IN TIME   CONKLIN, GROFF   AN
  SPACE, SPACE, SPACE   SLOANE, WILLIAM   AN
CRYING JAG   NV   GAL 60 02
  *ALL THE TRAPS OF EARTH AND OTHER STORIES
                                          SIMAK, CLIFFORD D.   AC
  BEST SCIENCE FICTION STORIES OF CLIFFORD D. SIMAK
                                          SIMAK, CLIFFORD D.   AC
  NIGHT OF THE PUUDLY, THE   SIMAK, CLIFFORD D.   AC
DAY OF TRUCE   NV   GAL 63 02
  DEVIL'S GENERATION, THE   GHIDALIA, VIC   AN
  NIGHTMARE AGE   POHL, FREDERIK   AN
  YOU AND SCIENCE FICTION   HOLLISTER, BERNARD C AN
DEATH IN THE HOUSE, A   NV   GAL 59 10
  AS TOMORROW BECOMES TODAY   SULLIVAN, CHARLES W. AN
  SF: THE BEST OF THE BEST   MERRIL, JUDITH   AN
  5TH ANNUAL OF THE YEAR'S BEST S-F, THE MERRIL, JUDITH   AN
DEATH SCENE   SS   INF 57 10
  ALIENS FOR NEIGHBOURS   SIMAK, CLIFFORD D.   AC
  OTHER WORLDS OF CLIFFORD SIMAK   SIMAK, CLIFFORD D.   AC
  *WORLDS OF CLIFFORD SIMAK, THE   SIMAK, CLIFFORD D.   AC
DESERTION   SS   ASF 44 11
  BEYOND TOMORROW   KNIGHT, DAMON   AN
  *BIG BOOK OF SCIENCE FICTION   CONKLIN, GROFF   AN
  CITY   SIMAK, CLIFFORD D.   NO
  GALAXY OF GHOULS   MERRIL, JUDITH   AN
  JUPITER   POHL, C. & F.   AN
  SPECTRUM OF WORLDS, A   CLARESON, THOMAS D. AN
  SURVIVAL PRINTOUT   TOTAL EFFECT   AN
  TOMORROW'S WORLDS   SILVERBERG, ROBERT   AN
  TOMORROW, AND TOMORROW, AND TOMORROW...
                                          HEINTZ/HERBERT/JOOS/ AN
  UBERWINDUNG VON RAUM UND ZEIT   GUNTHER, GOTTHARD   AN
DROP DEAD   NV   GAL 56 07
  *ALL THE TRAPS OF EARTH AND OTHER STORIES
                                          SIMAK, CLIFFORD D.   AC
  SCIENCE FICTION BESTIARY, THE   SILVERBERG, ROBERT   AN
DUSTY ZEBRA   NV   GAL 54 09
  ALIENS FOR NEIGHBOURS   SIMAK, CLIFFORD D.   AC
  OTHER WORLDS OF CLIFFORD SIMAK   SIMAK, CLIFFORD D.   AC
  *WORLDS OF CLIFFORD SIMAK, THE   SIMAK, CLIFFORD D.   AC
EARTH FOR INSPIRATION   SS   TWS 41 04
  COMING OF THE ROBOTS, THE   MOSKOWITZ, SAM   AN
EPILOG   SS   AMA 73
  ASTOUNDING   HARRISON, HARRY   OA

SIMAK, CLIFFORD D.   (CONTINUED)
  ETERNITY LOST   NV   ASF 49 07
  *ASTOUNDING SCIENCE FICTION ANTHOLOGY, THE
                                          CAMPBELL, JOHN W. JR AN
  BEST SCIENCE-FICTION STORIES: 1950, THE
                                          BLEILER & DIKTY   AN
  POLITICAL SCIENCE FICTION   GREENBERG& WARRICK   AN
  SECOND ASTOUNDING SCIENCE FICTION ANTHOLOGY, THE (PB)
                                          CAMPBELL, JOHN W. JR AN
FENCE, THE   SS   SSP 52 09
  ABC OF SCIENCE FICTION, AN   BOARDMAN, TOM JR.   AN
  *STRANGERS IN THE UNIVERSE   SIMAK, CLIFFORD D.   AC
FINAL GENTLEMAN   NV   FSF 60 01
  SIX GREAT SHORT SCIENCE FICTION NOVELS CONKLIN, GROFF   AN
FOREWORD   IN
  FUTURE CITY   ELWOOD, ROGER   OA
FOUNDING FATHER   SS   GAL 57 05
  BEST SCIENCE FICTION STORIES OF CLIFFORD D. SIMAK
                                          SIMAK, CLIFFORD D.   AC
  OTHER WORLDS OF CLIFFORD SIMAK   SIMAK, CLIFFORD D.   AC
  *WORLDS OF CLIFFORD SIMAK, THE   SIMAK, CLIFFORD D.   AC
FULL CYCLE   NA   SFS 55 11
  WORLDS WITHOUT END   SIMAK, CLIFFORD D.   AC
GALACTIC CHEST   NV   SFS 56 09
  SO BRIGHT THE VISION   SIMAK, CLIFFORD D.   DC
  3 IN 1   MARGULIES, LEO   AN
GHOST OF A MODEL T, THE   NV   EPC 75
  EPOCH   ELWOOD & SILVERBERG OA
GLEANERS   SN   IFS 60 03
  FROZEN PLANET AND 4 OTHER SF NOVELLAS, THE
                                          ANONYMOUS   AN
GOLDEN BUGS, THE   NV   FSF 60 06
  SEVEN COME INFINITY   CONKLIN, GROFF   AN
  SO BRIGHT THE VISION   SIMAK, CLIFFORD D.   DC
GOOD NIGHT, MR. JAMES   NV   GAL 51 03
  *ALL THE TRAPS OF EARTH AND OTHER STORIES
                                          SIMAK, CLIFFORD D.   AC
  *GALAXY READER OF SCIENCE FICTION   GOLD, H. L.   AN
  *OUTER REACHES, THE   DERLETH, AUGUST   AN
GREEN THUMB   NV   GAL 54 07
  ALIENS FOR NEIGHBOURS   SIMAK, CLIFFORD D.   AC
  BEST SF 5   CRISPIN, EDMUND   AN
  OTHER WORLDS OF CLIFFORD SIMAK   SIMAK, CLIFFORD D.   AC
  ROOTS OF EVIL, THE   PARRY, MICHEL   AN
  *WORLDS OF CLIFFORD SIMAK, THE   SIMAK, CLIFFORD D.   AC
HOBBIES   NV   ASF 46 11
  CITY   SIMAK, CLIFFORD D.   NO
HONORABLE OPPONENT   SS   GAL 56 08
  ALIENS FOR NEIGHBOURS   SIMAK, CLIFFORD D.   AC
  THIRD GALAXY READER, THE   GOLD, H. L.   AN
  *WORLDS OF CLIFFORD SIMAK, THE   SIMAK, CLIFFORD D.   AC
HOW-2   NV   GAL 54 11
  BEST SCIENCE FICTION STORIES AND NOVELS: 1955
                                          DIKTY, T. E.   AN
  BODYGUARD AND 4 OTHER SHORT SF NOVELS FROM GALAXY
                                          GOLD, H. L.   AN
  5 TALES FROM TOMORROW   DIKTY, T. E.   AN
HUDDLING PLACE   SS   ASF 44 07
  CITY   SIMAK, CLIFFORD D.   NO
  DECADE THE 1940S   ALDISS & HARRISON   AN
  MICROCOSMIC GOD   MOSKOWITZ, SAM   AN
  MODERN MASTERPIECES OF SCIENCE FICTION MOSKOWITZ, SAM   AN
  SCIENCE FICTION HALL OF FAME VOLUME 1   SILVERBERG, ROBERT   AN
I AM CRYING ALL INSIDE   SS   GAL 69 08
  SOULS IN METAL   ASHLEY, MICHAEL   AN
IDIOT'S CRUSADE   SS   GAL 54 10
  ALIENS FOR NEIGHBOURS   SIMAK, CLIFFORD D.   AC
  OTHER WORLDS OF CLIFFORD SIMAK   SIMAK, CLIFFORD D.   AC
  *WORLDS OF CLIFFORD SIMAK, THE   SIMAK, CLIFFORD D.   AC
IMMIGRANT   SN   ASF 54 03
  BEST SCIENCE FICTION STORIES OF CLIFFORD D. SIMAK
                                          SIMAK, CLIFFORD D.   AC
  GALACTIC EMPIRES VOLUME ONE   ALDISS, BRIAN W.   AN
  *STRANGERS IN THE UNIVERSE   SIMAK, CLIFFORD D.   AC
INSTALLMENT PLAN   NA   GAL 59 02
  *ALL THE TRAPS OF EARTH AND OTHER STORIES
                                          SIMAK, CLIFFORD D.   AC
  NIGHT OF THE PUUDLY, THE   SIMAK, CLIFFORD D.   AC
INTRODUCTION   IN
  NEBULA AWARD STORIES NO. 6   SIMAK, CLIFFORD D.   AN
JACKPOT   NV   GAL 56 10
  ALIENS FOR NEIGHBOURS   SIMAK, CLIFFORD D.   AC
  *WORLDS OF CLIFFORD SIMAK, THE   SIMAK, CLIFFORD D.   AC
JUNKYARD   NV   GAL 53 05
  GALAXY SCIENCE FICTION OMNIBUS   GOLD, H. L.   AN
  SECOND GALAXY READER OF SCIENCE FICTION
                                          GOLD, H. L.   AN
KINDERGARTEN   NV   GAL 53 07
  PORTALS OF TOMORROW   DERLETH, AUGUST   AN
  *STRANGERS IN THE UNIVERSE   SIMAK, CLIFFORD D.   AC
LEG. FORST.   NV   INF 58 04
  SO BRIGHT THE VISION   SIMAK, CLIFFORD D.   DC
LIMITING FACTOR   SS   STS 49 11
  BEYOND THE STARS AND OTHER STORIES   ANONYMOUS   AN
  CONTACT   KEYES, NOEL   AN
  *POSSIBLE WORLDS OF SCIENCE FICTION   CONKLIN, GROFF   AN
  *SPECTRUM   AMIS & CONQUEST   AN
LOBBY   SS   ASF 44 04
  *BEST OF SCIENCE FICTION   CONKLIN, GROFF   AN
LOOT OF TIME, THE   NV   TWS 38 12
  ALIEN EARTH AND OTHER STORIES   ELWOOD & MOSKOWITZ   AN
LOST STREET, THE (THE STREET THAT WASN'T THERE) SS C CMT 41 07
  *STRANGE PORTS OF CALL   DERLETH, AUGUST   AN
LULU   NV   GAL 57 06
  BEST SCIENCE FICTION STORIES OF CLIFFORD D. SIMAK
                                          SIMAK, CLIFFORD D.   AC

SIMAK, CLIFFORD D.   SLADEK, JOHN T.

SIMAK, CLIFFORD D.   (CONTINUED)
  *WORLDS OF CLIFFORD SIMAK, THE   SIMAK, CLIFFORD D.   AC
MADNESS FROM MARS   SS   TWS 39 04
  ALIEN WORLDS   ELWOOD, ROGER   AN
MARATHON PHOTOGRAPH, THE   NA   TOT 74
  THREADS OF TIME   SILVERBERG, ROBERT   OA
MASQUERADE (SEE OPERATION MERCURY)   TC
MIRAGE   NV
  *STRANGERS IN THE UNIVERSE   SIMAK, CLIFFORD D.   AC
MR. MEEK PLAYS POLO   SS   PLS 44 FL
  INFINITE ARENA, THE   CARR, TERRY   AN
NEIGHBOR   NV   ASF 54 06
  ALIENS FOR NEIGHBOURS   SIMAK, CLIFFORD D.   AC
  BEST SCIENCE FICTION STORIES OF CLIFFORD D. SIMAK
                                     SIMAK, CLIFFORD D.   AC
  SPACE   1   DAVIS, RICHARD   OA
  *WORLDS OF CLIFFORD SIMAK, THE   SIMAK, CLIFFORD D.   AC
NEW FOLKS' HOME   SS   ASF 63 07
  ANALOG 3   CAMPBELL, JOHN W. JR AN
  BEST SCIENCE FICTION STORIES OF CLIFFORD D. SIMAK
                                     SIMAK, CLIFFORD D.   AC
  PAST, PRESENT, AND FUTURE PERFECT WOLFE, J&FITZ GERALD AN
NIGHT OF THE PUUDLY, THE (GOOD NIGHT, MR. JAMES) NV GAL 51 03
  NIGHT OF THE PUUDLY, THE   SIMAK, CLIFFORD D.   AC
NO LIFE OF THEIR OWN   NA   GAL 59 08
  *ALL THE TRAPS OF EARTH AND OTHER STORIES
                                     SIMAK, CLIFFORD D.   AC
  TOMORROW'S CHILDREN   ASIMOV, ISAAC   AN
OGRE   NV   ASF 44 01
  ADVENTURES ON OTHER PLANETS   WOLLHEIM, DONALD A. AN
OPERATION MERCURY (MASQUERADE)   NV   ASF 41 03
  TALES OF OUTER SPACE   WOLLHEIM, DONALD A. DA
OPERATION STINKY   NV   GAL 57 04
  ALIENS FOR NEIGHBOURS   SIMAK, CLIFFORD D.   AC
  *WORLDS OF CLIFFORD SIMAK, THE   SIMAK, CLIFFORD D.   AC
OVER THE RIVER AND THROUGH THE WOODS   SS   AMZ 65 05
  TIME CURVE, THE   MOSKOWITZ & ELWOOD   AN
  WORLD'S BEST SCIENCE FICTION: 1966 WOLLHEIM & CARR   AN
PARADISE   SS   ASF 46 06
  CITY   SIMAK, CLIFFORD D.   NO
PROJECT MASTODON   NV   GAL 55 03
  *ALL THE TRAPS OF EARTH AND OTHER STORIES
                                     SIMAK, CLIFFORD D.   AC
  NIGHT OF THE PUUDLY, THE   SIMAK, CLIFFORD D.   AC
RETROGRADE EVOLUTION   NV   SFP 53 04
  *STRANGERS IN THE UNIVERSE   SIMAK, CLIFFORD D.   AC
RIM OF THE DEEP   NV   ASF 40 05
  FUTURES TO INFINITY   MOSKOWITZ, SAM   AN
SECOND CHILDHOOD   SS   GAL 51 02
  *GALAXY READER OF SCIENCE FICTION GOLD, H. L.   AN
  *STORIES FOR TOMORROW   SLOANE, WILLIAM   AN
SENIOR CITIZEN   SS   FSF 75 10
  BEST SCIENCE FICTION STORIES OF THE YEAR (1975)
                                     DEL REY, LESTER   AN
SHADOW SHOW   NV   FSF 53 11
  *STRANGERS IN THE UNIVERSE   SIMAK, CLIFFORD D.   AC
  VINTAGE ANTHOLOGY OF SCIENCE FANTASY, THE
                                     CERF, CHRISTOPHER   AN
SHADOW WORLD   NV   GAL 57 09
  5 UNEARTHLY VISIONS   CONKLIN, GROFF   AN
SHIPSHAPE MIRACLE, THE   NV   IFS 63 01
  BEST SCIENCE FICTION FROM IF, THE POHL, FREDERIK   AN
SHOTGUN CURE   SS   FSF 61 01
  *BEST FROM FANTASY AND SCIENCE FICTION: 11
                                     MILLS, ROBERT P.   AN
SIMPLE WAY   SS
  CITY   SIMAK, CLIFFORD D.   NO
SITTERS, THE   NV   GAL 58 04
  *ALL THE TRAPS OF EARTH AND OTHER STORIES
                                     SIMAK, CLIFFORD D.   AC
SKIRMISH (BATHE YOUR BEARINGS IN BLOOD)   SS   AMZ 50 12
  PENGUIN SCIENCE FICTION   ALDISS, BRIAN W.   AN
  *SCIENCE FICTION THINKING MACHINES CONKLIN, GROFF   AN
  *STRANGERS IN THE UNIVERSE   SIMAK, CLIFFORD D.   AC
SO BRIGHT THE VISION   NV   FUN 56 08
  SO BRIGHT THE VISION   SIMAK, CLIFFORD D.   DC
SPACEMAN'S VAN GOGH, THE   SS   SFS 56 03
  WORLDS WITHOUT END   SIMAK, CLIFFORD D.   AC
STREET THAT WASN'T THERE, THE (ALSO AS THE LOST STREET)
                                     SS C CMT 41 07
  CREATURES FROM BEYOND   CARR, TERRY   AN
TARGET GENERATION   NV
  *STRANGERS IN THE UNIVERSE   SIMAK, CLIFFORD D.   AC
THING IN THE STONE, THE   NV   IFS 70 03
  WORLD'S BEST SCIENCE FICTION: 1971 WOLLHEIM & CARR   AN
TO WALK A CITY'S STREET   SS   INY 72 03
  INFINITY 3   HOSKINS, ROBERT   OA
  1973 ANNUAL WORLD'S BEST SF, THE   WOLLHEIM, DONALD A. AN
TOOLS   NV   ASF 42 07
  *TREASURY OF SCIENCE FICTION, A   CONKLIN, GROFF   AN
TROUBLE WITH TYCHO, THE   NA   AMZ 60 10
  ACE SCIENCE FICTION READER   WOLLHEIM, DONALD A. AN
UNIVAC: 2200   SS   TAL 73
  FRONTIERS 1: TOMORROW'S ALTERNATIVES ELWOOD, ROGER   OA
UNSILENT SPRING   NV C STL 76 02
  STELLAR 2   DEL REY, JUDY-LYNN   OA
WORLD OF THE RED SUN, THE   SS   WOS 31 12
  BEFORE THE GOLDEN AGE   ASIMOV, ISAAC   AN
WORLD THAT COULDN'T BE, THE   NV   GAL 58 01
  WORLD THAT COULDN'T BE AND 8 OTHER SF NOVELETS
                                     GOLD, H. L.   AN
WORLDS WITHOUT END   NA   FUT 56 WI
  WORLDS WITHOUT END   SIMAK, CLIFFORD D.   AC
WORRYWORT   SS   GAL 53 09
  BEST SF 2   CRISPIN, EDMUND   AN
  OPERATION FUTURE   CONKLIN, GROFF   AN

SIMAK, CLIFFORD D.   (CONTINUED)
  YOU'LL NEVER GO HOME AGAIN (ALSO AS BEACHHEAD) SS FAD 51 07
  AWARD SCIENCE FICTION READER   NORTON, ALDEN H.   AN
  TIME UNTAMED   HOWARD, IVAN   AN

SIMAK, RICHARD S.
  UNSILENT SPRING   NV C STL 76 02
  STELLAR 2   DEL REY, JUDY-LYNN   OA

SIME, SIDNEY H.
  TA TA, THE (JINGLES)   SG C   62
  MATHEMATICAL MAGPIE, THE   FADIMAN, CLIFTON   AN

SIMMONS, HERBERT A.
  ONE NIGHT STAND   SS   GAM 63 01
  SEA OF SPACE, A   NOLAN, WILLIAM F.   AN

SIMNETT, JOHN
  PROSPECTS FOR GENETIC ENGINEERING IN MAN   AR
  BEYOND THIS HORIZON   CARRELL, CHRISTOPHER OA

SIMONDS, BRUCE
  SEARCH, THE   PM   FSF 64 06
  10TH ANNUAL OF THE YEAR'S BEST S-F, THE
                                     MERRIL, JUDITH   AN

SIMONS, WALTON
  COLD TOMORROWS   SS
  QUEST   BISCHOFF, DAVID   OA

SIMPSON, ALAN
  TWENTY-THIRD PSALM— MODERN STYLE, THE   PM   WUM 61
  INSIDE INFORMATION   MOWSHOWITZ, ABBE   AN

SIMPSON, DONALD
  CONTINUOUS LANDSCAPE   AR   QRK 71 03
  QUARK/3   DELANY & HACKER   OA

SINCLAIR, CLIVE
  UNCLE VLAD   SS   TRV 73
  YEAR'S BEST HORROR STORIES: SERIES III, THE
                                     DAVIS, RICHARD   AN

SINCLAIR, MAY
  NATURE OF THE EVIDENCE, THE   SS   FOR 23 05
  STRANGE BEASTS AND UNNATURAL MONSTERS STERN, PHILIP VAN D. AN
  SUPERNATURAL READER, THE   CONKLIN, G&L.   AN

SINCLAIR, UPTON
  AUTHOR'S ADVENTURE   SS   POM 04
  FANTASTIC PULPS, THE   HAINING, PETER   AN

SINGER, ISAAC B.
  JACHID AND JACHIDAH   SS   64
  SCIENCE FICTION: THE FUTURE   ALLEN, DICK   AN
  JACHID AND JECHIDAH   SS   64
  WANDERING STARS   DANN, JACK M.   AN
  YACHID AND YECHIDA   SS   64
  10TH ANNUAL OF THE YEAR'S BEST S-F, THE
                                     MERRIL, JUDITH   AN

SISK, JOHN P.
  FUTURE OF PREDICTION, THE   AR   CMM 70
  SCIENCE FICTION: THE FUTURE   ALLEN, DICK   AN

SISSONS, MICHAEL
  ASLEEP IN ARMAGEDDON   AN   PTH 62 06

SKAL, DAVE
  AMBIENCE   SS   ORB 75 16
  ORBIT 16   KNIGHT, DAMON   OA
  CHAINS   SS   CLR 71 01
  CLARION   WILSON, ROBIN SCOTT OA
  CRAYOLA   SS   CLR 72 02
  CLARION II   WILSON, ROBIN SCOTT OA
  MOTHERS, THE MOTHERS, HOW EERILY IT SOUNDS, THE SS
  AURORA: BEYOND EQUALITY   MCINTYRE & ANDERSON OA
  THEY COPE   SS   ORB 72 11
  ORBIT 11   KNIGHT, DAMON   OA
  WHEN WE WERE GOOD   SS   ORB 75 17
  ORBIT 17   KNIGHT, DAMON   OA

SKINNER, B. F.
  FROM. "WALDEN TWO" (CHAPTER 29)   EX   48
  PAST, PRESENT, AND FUTURE PERFECT WOLFE, J&FITZ GERALD AN
  INSTEAD OF THE CROSS, THE LOLLIPOP (FROM "WALDEN 2")
                                              EX   48
  NEW IMPROVED SUN, THE   DISCH, THOMAS M.   AN

SKY, KATHLEEN
  LAMENT OF THE KEEKU BIRD   SS   ALC 73
  ALIEN CONDITION, THE   GOLDIN, STEPHEN   OA
  ONE ORDINARY DAY, WITH BOX   SS   GEN 72
  GENERATION   GERROLD, DAVID   OA

SLADEK, JOHN T.
  ATHEIST'S BARGAIN, THE   SS C NEW 67 AN
  DEVIL HIS DUE, THE   HILL, DOUGLAS   AN
  BILL GETS HEP TO GOD!   SS   NWB 73 05
  NEW WORLDS QUARTERLY NO. 5   MOORCOCK, MICHAEL   OA
  COMMUNICANTS, THE   NA
  NEW S.F., THE   JONES, LANGDON   OA
  DANNY'S NEW FRIENDS FROM DENEB   SS C
  WHITE FANG GOES DINGO AND OTHER FUNNY S.F. STORIES
                                     DISCH, THOMAS M.   AC

SLADEK, JOHN T.   (CONTINUED)
   DISCOVERY OF THE NULLITRON, THE   FA C GAL 67 02
   WHITE FANG GOES DINGO AND OTHER FUNNY S.F. STORIES
                                          DISCH, THOMAS M.   AC
   ELEPHANT WITH WOODEN LEG   SS GAL 75 06
      ANTIGRAV: COSMIC COMEDIES   STRICK, PHILIP   AN
      BEST FROM GALAXY, THE VOLUME IV   BAEN, JAMES   AN
   FLATLAND   SS NWB 73 05
      NEW WORLDS QUARTERLY NO. 5   MOORCOCK, MICHAEL   OA
   GREAT WALL OF MEXICO, THE   NV BMR 73
      BAD MOON RISING   DISCH, THOMAS M.   OA
   HAMMER OF EVIL, THE   SS NWB 75 09
      NEW WORLDS NINE   BAILEY, HILARY   OA
   HAPPY BREED, THE   SS DVS 67 01
      DANGEROUS VISIONS   ELLISON, HARLAN   OA
   HEAVENS BELOW: FIFTEEN UTOPIAS   SS NEW 75 AN
      NEW IMPROVED SUN, THE   DISCH, THOMAS M.   AN
   INTERSTATE, THE   SS QRK 71 02
      QUARK/2   DELANY & HACKER   OA
   KINDLY ONES, THE   SS NWQ 74 06
      NEW WORLDS NO. 6   PLATT & BAILEY   OA
   LOCKED ROOM, THE   SS NWQ 72 04
      NEW WORLDS QUARTERLY NO. 4   MOORCOCK, MICHAEL   OA
   LOVE NEST   PM 69
      HOLDING YOUR EIGHT HANDS   LUCIE-SMITH, EDWARD AN
   MAN FROM NOT-YET, THE   SS PBY 68 06
      FROM THE "S" FILE   PLAYBOY, EDITORS OF AN
   MAN WHO DEVOURED BOOKS, THE   SS IFS 71 01
      INTRODUCTORY PSYCHOLOGY THROUGH SCIENCE FICTION
                                          KATZ/WARRICK/&
   MASTERSON AND THE CLERKS   SS NWS 67 09
      BEST SF STORIES FROM NEW WORLDS 4   MOORCOCK, MICHAEL   AN
      SHORES BENEATH, THE   SALLIS, JAMES   AN
   MYSTERY DIET OF THE GODS: A REVELATION   SS C SWK 76 10
      NEW CONSTELLATIONS   DISCH & NAYLOR   OA
   NAME (PLEASE PRINT):   SS NWB 73 05
      NEW WORLDS QUARTERLY NO. 5   MOORCOCK, MICHAEL   OA
   PEMBERLY'S START-AFRESH CALLIOPE OR, THE NEW PROTEUS
                                            SS NWQ 71 01
      NEW WORLDS QUARTERLY NO. 1   MOORCOCK, MICHAEL   OA
   POETS OF MILLGROVE IOWA, THE   SS NWS 66 11
      BEST SF STORIES FROM NEW WORLDS NO. 2, THE
                                          MOORCOCK, MICHAEL   AN
   PURLOINED BUTTER, THE   SS NWQ 72 03
      NEW WORLDS QUARTERLY NO. 3   MOORCOCK, MICHAEL   OA
   SECRET OF THE OLD CUSTARD, THE (THE BABE IN THE OVEN)
                                            SS IFS 66 11
      ALPHA 6   SILVERBERG, ROBERT AN
   SHORT, HAPPY WIFE OF MANSARD ELIOT, THE SS NWQ 71 01
      NEW WORLDS QUARTERLY NO. 1   MOORCOCK, MICHAEL   OA
   STEAM-DRIVEN BOY, THE   SS NOV 72 02
      NOVA 2   HARRISON, HARRY   OA
   TREASURE OF THE HAUNTED RAMBLER, THE   PM 69
      HOLDING YOUR EIGHT HANDS   LUCIE-SMITH, EDWARD AN
   1937 A.D.!   SS NWS 67 07
      BEST SF: 1967   HARRISON & ALDISS   AN
   198-, A TALE OF "TOMORROW"   SS NWS 70 01
      NEW TOMORROWS, THE   SPINRAD, NORMAN   AN

SLATEN, JEFF
   BIOLOGICAL REVOLUTION, THE   SS C
      2076: THE AMERICAN TRICENTENNIAL   BRYANT, EDWARD   OA

SLESAR, HENRY
   AFTER   SS PBY 60 06
      FROM THE "S" FILE   PLAYBOY, EDITORS OF AN
      PLAYBOY BOOK OF SCIENCE FICTION AND FANTASY, THE
                                          PLAYBOY, EDITORS OF AN
   BEFORE THE TALENT DIES   SS VSF 57 09
      NO LIMITS   FERMAN, JOSEPH W.   AN
   CANDIDATE, THE   SS ROG 61
      FIEND IN YOU, THE   BEAUMONT, CHARLES   AN
   CHIEF   SS PBY 60 06
      SCIENCE FICTION   BRODKIN & PEARSON   AN
      6TH ANNUAL OF THE YEAR'S BEST S-F, THE MERRIL, JUDITH   AN
   EXAMINATION DAY   SS PBY 58 02
      FROM THE "S" FILE   PLAYBOY, EDITORS OF AN
      INSIDE INFORMATION   MOWSHOWITZ, ABBE   AN
      SCHOOL AND SOCIETY THROUGH SCIENCE FICTION
                                          OLANDER/GREENBERG/& AN
   I DO NOT LIKE THEE, DR. FELDMAN   SS PBY 59 06
      WEIRD SHOW   PLAYBOY, EDITORS OF AN
   INVISIBLE MAN MURDER CASE, THE   SS FAN 58 05
      INVISIBLE MEN   DAVENPORT, BASIL   AN
   JAM, THE   SS PBY 58 11
      FROM THE "S" FILE   PLAYBOY, EDITORS OF AN
      PLAYBOY BOOK OF HORROR AND THE SUPERNATURAL, THE
                                          PLAYBOY, EDITORS OF AN
   LEGACY OF TERROR   SS AMZ 58 11
      SATAN'S PETS   GHIDALIA, VIC   AN
   MAN WITH THE GREEN NOSE, THE (SEE SURVIVOR NO. 1) TC C
   MELODRAMINE   SS PBY 65 08
      FROM THE "S" FILE   PLAYBOY, EDITORS OF AN
   MY FATHER THE CAT   SS FUN 57 12
      FANTASTIC UNIVERSE OMNIBUS, THE   SANTESSON, HANS S. AN
   SURVIVOR NO. 1 (THE MAN WITH THE GREEN NOSE) SS C KNV 59 09
      PARTNERS IN WONDER   ELLISON, HARLAN   AC
   VICTORY PARADE   SS PBY 57 04
      FROM THE "S" FILE   PLAYBOY, EDITORS OF AN
      SCIENCE FICTION   BRODKIN & PEARSON   AN

SLOANE, WILLIAM
   RIM OF MORNING, THE   AC H DOM 64
   SPACE, SPACE, SPACE   AN H WAT 53
   STORIES FOR TOMORROW   AN H PKW 54 06
   STORIES FOR TOMORROW (BRITISH)   AN H EYR 55

SLOANE, WILLIAM   (CONTINUED)
   ABOUT THIS BOOK   IN
      *STORIES FOR TOMORROW   SLOANE, WILLIAM   AN
   EDGE OF RUNNING WATER, THE   NA
   RIM OF MORNING, THE   SLOANE, WILLIAM   AC
   INTRODUCTION   IN
      SPACE, SPACE, SPACE   SLOANE, WILLIAM   AN
   LET NOTHING YOU DISMAY   SS NEW 55 AN
      *STORIES FOR TOMORROW   SLOANE, WILLIAM   AN
   TO WALK THE NIGHT   NO PSY 37
      RIM OF MORNING, THE   SLOANE, WILLIAM   AC

SMALL, AUSTIN J.   SEE PSEUD. SEAMARK

SMITH, CLARK ASHTON
   OTHER DIMENSIONS   AC H ARK 70
   OUT OF SPACE AND TIME   AC H NSP 71
   TALES OF SCIENCE AND SORCERY   AC H ARK 64
   ADVENTURE IN FUTURITY, AN   NV WOS 31 04
      OTHER DIMENSIONS   SMITH, CLARK ASHTON AC
   AMAZING PLANET, THE   NV WSQ 31 SU
      OTHER DIMENSIONS   SMITH, CLARK ASHTON AC
   BEYOND THE SINGING FLAME   SS WOS 31 11
      FROM OFF THIS WORLD   MARGULIES & FRIEND AN
   CHAIN OF AFORGOMON, THE   SS WRT 35 12
      OUT OF SPACE AND TIME   SMITH, CLARK ASHTON AC
   CITY OF THE SINGING FLAME, THE   SS WOS 31 07
      FROM OFF THIS WORLD   MARGULIES & FRIEND AN
      *OTHER SIDE OF THE MOON, THE   DERLETH, AUGUST   AN
      OUT OF SPACE AND TIME   SMITH, CLARK ASHTON AC
   DARK EIDOLON, THE   NV WRT 35 01
      OUT OF SPACE AND TIME   SMITH, CLARK ASHTON AC
      SPELL OF SEVEN, THE   DE CAMP, L. SPRAGUE AN
   DEATH OF ILALOTHA, THE   SS WRT 37 09
      OUT OF SPACE AND TIME   SMITH, CLARK ASHTON AC
   DIMENSION OF CHANCE, THE   NV WOS 32 11
      OTHER DIMENSIONS   SMITH, CLARK ASHTON AC
   DOUBLE SHADOW, THE   SS WRT 39 02
      OUT OF SPACE AND TIME   SMITH, CLARK ASHTON AC
   END OF THE STORY, THE   NV WRT 30 05
      OUT OF SPACE AND TIME   SMITH, CLARK ASHTON AC
   FROM THE CRYPTS OF MEMORY   SS 22
      OUT OF SPACE AND TIME   SMITH, CLARK ASHTON AC
   GHOST OF MOHAMMED DIN, THE   SS OVL 10 11
      OTHER DIMENSIONS   SMITH, CLARK ASHTON AC
   GHOUL, THE   SS FFN 34 01
      OTHER DIMENSIONS   SMITH, CLARK ASHTON AC
   GREAT GOD AWTO, THE   SS TWS 40 02
      TALES OF SCIENCE AND SORCERY   SMITH, CLARK ASHTON AC
   IMMEASURABLE HORROR, THE   SS WRT 31 09
      OTHER DIMENSIONS   SMITH, CLARK ASHTON AC
   IMMORTALS OF MERCURY, THE   NV 32
      TALES OF SCIENCE AND SORCERY   SMITH, CLARK ASHTON AC
   INVISIBLE CITY, THE   SS WOS 32 06
      OTHER DIMENSIONS   SMITH, CLARK ASHTON AC
   JUSTICE OF THE ELEPHANT, THE   SS ORI 31 08
      OTHER DIMENSIONS   SMITH, CLARK ASHTON AC
   KINGDOM OF THE WORM, THE (SEE A TALE OF SIR JOHN MAUNDEVILLE)
                                            TC
   KISS OF ZORAIDA, THE   SS MGC 33 07
      OTHER DIMENSIONS   SMITH, CLARK ASHTON AC
   LAST HIEROGLYPH, THE   SS WRT 35 04
      OUT OF SPACE AND TIME   SMITH, CLARK ASHTON AC
   MAHOUT, THE   SS BLC 11 08
      OTHER DIMENSIONS   SMITH, CLARK ASHTON AC
   MAKER OF GARGOYLES, THE   SS WRT 32 08
      TALES OF SCIENCE AND SORCERY   SMITH, CLARK ASHTON AC
   MALAY KRISE, THE   SS OVL 10 10
      OTHER DIMENSIONS   SMITH, CLARK ASHTON AC
   MANDRAKES, THE   SS WRT 33 02
      OTHER DIMENSIONS   SMITH, CLARK ASHTON AC
   MAROONED IN ANDROMEDA   NV WOS 30 10
      OTHER DIMENSIONS   SMITH, CLARK ASHTON AC
   MASTER OF THE ASTEROID   SS WOS 32 10
      *STRANGE PORTS OF CALL   DERLETH, AUGUST   AC
      TALES OF SCIENCE AND SORCERY   SMITH, CLARK ASHTON AC
   METAMORPHOSIS OF EARTH, THE   NV WRT 51 09
      *BEACHHEADS IN SPACE   DERLETH, AUGUST   AN
      FROM OTHER WORLDS   DERLETH, AUGUST   AN
      OTHER DIMENSIONS   SMITH, CLARK ASHTON AC
   MONSTER OF THE PROPHECY, THE   NV WRT 32 01
      OUT OF SPACE AND TIME   SMITH, CLARK ASHTON AC
   MONSTERS IN THE NIGHT (A PROPHECY OF MONSTERS) SS FSF 54 10
      OTHER DIMENSIONS   SMITH, CLARK ASHTON AC
   MORTHYLLA   SS WRT 53 05
      TALES OF SCIENCE AND SORCERY   SMITH, CLARK ASHTON AC
   MOTHER OF TOADS   SS WRT 38 07
      TALES OF SCIENCE AND SORCERY   SMITH, CLARK ASHTON AC
      WORLDS OF WEIRD   MARGULIES, LEO   AN
   MURDER IN THE FOURTH DIMENSION   SS AMD 30 10
      TALES OF SCIENCE AND SORCERY   SMITH, CLARK ASHTON AC
   NECROMANTIC TALE, THE   SS WRT 31 01
      OTHER DIMENSIONS   SMITH, CLARK ASHTON AC
      WIZARDS AND WARLOCKS   GHIDALIA, VIC   AN
   NIGHT IN MALNEANT, A   SS WRT 39 09
      EDGE OF NEVER, THE   HOSKINS, ROBERT   AN
      OUT OF SPACE AND TIME   SMITH, CLARK ASHTON AC
   OFFERING TO THE MOON, AN   SS WRT 53 09
      ANCIENT MYSTERIES READER, THE   HAINING, PETER   AN
      OTHER DIMENSIONS   SMITH, CLARK ASHTON AC
   PHOENIX   SS
      BEYOND BELIEF   HURLEY, RICHARD J. AN
      OTHER DIMENSIONS   SMITH, CLARK ASHTON AC
      *TIME TO COME   DERLETH, AUGUST   OA
   PLANET ENTITY, THE (SEE SEEDLING OF MARS) TC

SMITH, CLARK ASHTON

SMITH, CLARK ASHTON (CONTINUED)
PLUTONIAN DRUG, THE   SS   AMZ 34 09
 *OUTER REACHES, THE   DERLETH, AUGUST   AN
  STRANGE ECSTASIES   PARRY, MICHEL   AN
POWER OF THE HYPERBOREA, THE (SEE THE THEFT OF THE
 THIRTY-NINE GIRDLES)   TC
PROPHECY OF MONSTERS, A (SEE MONSTERS IN THE NIGHT)
                                                   TC
RAJA AND THE TIGER, THE   SS   BLC 12 02
 OTHER DIMENSIONS   SMITH, CLARK ASHTON AC
RENDEZVOUS IN AVEROIGNE, A   SS   WRT 31 04
 OUT OF SPACE AND TIME   SMITH, CLARK ASHTON AC
RESURRECTION OF THE RATTLESNAKE, THE   SS   WRT 31 10
 OTHER DIMENSIONS   SMITH, CLARK ASHTON AC
RETURN OF THE SORCERER, THE   NV   STT 31 09
 OUT OF SPACE AND TIME   SMITH, CLARK ASHTON AC
ROOT OF AMPOI, THE   SS   ARS 49 SP
 TALES OF SCIENCE AND SORCERY   SMITH, CLARK ASHTON AC
SADASTOR   SS   WRT 30 07
 OUT OF SPACE AND TIME   SMITH, CLARK ASHTON AC
SCHIZOID CREATOR   SS   FNF 53 11
 TALES OF SCIENCE AND SORCERY   SMITH, CLARK ASHTON AC
SECOND INTERMENT, THE   SS   STT 33 01
 OUT OF SPACE AND TIME   SMITH, CLARK ASHTON AC
SEED FROM THE SEPULCHRE, THE   SS   WRT 33 10
 ROOTS OF EVIL, THE   PARRY, MICHEL   AN
 TALES OF SCIENCE AND SORCERY   SMITH, CLARK ASHTON AC
SEEDLING OF MARS (THE PLANET ENTITY)   NV   WSQ 31 PL
 TALES OF SCIENCE AND SORCERY   SMITH, CLARK ASHTON AC
SHADOWS, THE   SS   22
 OUT OF SPACE AND TIME   SMITH, CLARK ASHTON AC
SOMETHING NEW   SS   TST 24 08
 OTHER DIMENSIONS   SMITH, CLARK ASHTON AC
SUPERNUMERARY CORPSE, THE   SS   WRT 32 11
 OTHER DIMENSIONS   SMITH, CLARK ASHTON AC
SYMPOSIUM OF THE GORGON   SS   FUN 58 10
 TALES OF SCIENCE AND SORCERY   SMITH, CLARK ASHTON AC
TALE OF SIR JOHN MAUNDEVILLE, A (THE KINGDOM OF THE WORM)
                                             SS   FFN 33 10
 OTHER DIMENSIONS   SMITH, CLARK ASHTON AC
TESTAMENT OF ATHAMMAUS, THE   NV   WRT 32 10
 OUT OF SPACE AND TIME   SMITH, CLARK ASHTON AC
THEFT OF THE THIRTY-NINE GIRDLES, THE (THE POWER OF THE
 HYPERBOREA)   SS   STN 58 03
 TALES OF SCIENCE AND SORCERY   SMITH, CLARK ASHTON AC
THIRTEEN PHANTASMS   SS   FFN 36 03
 OTHER DIMENSIONS   SMITH, CLARK ASHTON AC
TOLD IN THE DESERT   SS   64
 OTHER DIMENSIONS   SMITH, CLARK ASHTON AC
TOMB-SPAWN, THE   SS   WRT 34 05
 TALES OF SCIENCE AND SORCERY   SMITH, CLARK ASHTON AC
UBBO-SATHLA   SS   WRT 33 07
 OUT OF SPACE AND TIME   SMITH, CLARK ASHTON AC
 SECOND AVON FANTASY READER, THE WOLLHEIM &ERNSBERGER AN
UNCHARTED ISLE, THE   SS   WRT 30 11
 *MY BEST SCIENCE FICTION STORY MARGULIES & FRIEND   AN
 OUT OF SPACE AND TIME   SMITH, CLARK ASHTON AC
VAULTS OF YOH-VOMBIS, THE   NV   WRT 32 05
 OUT OF SPACE AND TIME   SMITH, CLARK ASHTON AC
VENUS OF AZOMBEII, THE   NV   WRT 31 06
 OTHER DIMENSIONS   SMITH, CLARK ASHTON AC
VOYAGE TO SFANOMOE, A   SS   WRT 31 08
 *BEYOND TIME AND SPACE   DERLETH, AUGUST   AN
WEIRD OF AVOOSL WUTHOQQUAN, THE   SS   WRT 32 06
 OUT OF SPACE AND TIME   SMITH, CLARK ASHTON AC
WHY I SELECTED UNCHARTED ISLE   AI
 *MY BEST SCIENCE FICTION STORY MARGULIES & FRIEND   AN

SMITH, CORDELIA T.
BEST SCIENCE FICTION STORIES 3, THE   AN   MFL 64
 SEE "GREAT SCIENCE FICTION STORIES"
GREAT SCIENCE FICTION STORIES   AN   DEL 64 02
 IN ENGLAND AS "THE BEST SCIENCE FICTION STORIES 3"
 INTRODUCTION   IN
  GREAT SCIENCE FICTION STORIES SMITH, CORDELIA T.   AN

SMITH, CORDWAINER   PSEUD. FOR PAUL M. A. LINEBARGER
BEST OF CORDWAINER SMITH, THE   AC   BAL 75
 EDITED BY J. J. PIERCE
QUEST OF THE THREE WORLDS   NO   ACE 66
SPACE LORDS   AC   PYR 65 05
STARDREAMER   AC   BEA 71 08
YOU WILL NEVER BE THE SAME   AC   BKM 63
ALPHA RALPHA BOULEVARD   NV   FSF 61 06
 *BEST FROM FANTASY AND SCIENCE FICTION: 11
                                 MILLS, ROBERT P.   AN
 BEST OF CORDWAINER SMITH, THE   SMITH, CORDWAINER   AC
 ENDS OF TIME, THE   SILVERBERG, ROBERT   AN
 YOU WILL NEVER BE THE SAME   SMITH, CORDWAINER   AC
ANGERHELM   NV   STR 59 06
 STAR SCIENCE FICTION STORIES NO. 6 POHL, FREDERIK   OA
 STARDREAMER   SMITH, CORDWAINER   AC
BALLAD OF LOST C'MELL, THE   NV   GAL 62 10
 BEST OF CORDWAINER SMITH, THE   SMITH, CORDWAINER   AC
 SCIENCE FICTION HALL OF FAME VOLUME 2A BOVA, BEN   AN
 SPACE LORDS   SMITH, CORDWAINER   AC
 12 GREAT CLASSICS OF SCIENCE FICTION CONKLIN, GROFF   AN
BURNING OF THE BRAIN, THE   SS   IFS 58 10
 ALPHA 2   SILVERBERG, ROBERT   AN
 BEST OF CORDWAINER SMITH, THE   SMITH, CORDWAINER   AC
 YOU WILL NEVER BE THE SAME   SMITH, CORDWAINER   AC
CRIME AND THE GLORY OF COMMANDER SUZDAL, THE SS   AMZ 64 05
 BEST OF CORDWAINER SMITH, THE   SMITH, CORDWAINER   AC
 GALACTIC EMPIRES VOLUME ONE   ALDISS, BRIAN W.   AN
 SEVEN TRIPS THROUGH TIME AND SPACE CONKLIN, GROFF   AN
 STARDREAMER   SMITH, CORDWAINER   AC

SMITH, EDWARD E. PHD

SMITH, CORDWAINER   (CONTINUED)
DEAD LADY OF CLOWN TOWN, THE   SN   GAL 64 08
 BEST OF CORDWAINER SMITH, THE   SMITH, CORDWAINER   AC
 SPACE LORDS   SMITH, CORDWAINER   AC
DOWN TO A SUNLESS SEA   NV   FSF 75 10
 BEST SCIENCE FICTION OF THE YEAR, THE NO. 5
                                 CARR, TERRY   AN
DRUNKBOAT   NV   AMZ 63 10
 SPACE LORDS   SMITH, CORDWAINER   AC
 9TH ANNUAL OF THE YEAR'S BEST S-F, THE MERRIL, JUDITH   AN
EPILOGUE   MS
 SPACE LORDS   SMITH, CORDWAINER   AC
FIFE OF BODIDHARMA, THE   SS   FAN 59 06
 STARDREAMER   SMITH, CORDWAINER   AC
FROM GUSTIBLES PLANET   SS   IFS 62 07
 BEST SCIENCE FICTION FROM IF, THE POHL, FREDERIK   AN
GAME OF RAT AND DRAGON, THE   NV   GAL 55 10
 AS TOMORROW BECOMES TODAY   SULLIVAN, CHARLES W. AN
 BEST OF CORDWAINER SMITH, THE   SMITH, CORDWAINER   AC
 BEST SCIENCE FICTION STORIES AND NOVELS: 1956
                                 DIKTY, T. E.   AN
 BEST SF 3   CRISPIN, EDMUND   AN
 MIRROR OF INFINITY, THE   SILVERBERG, ROBERT   AN
 SCIENCE FICTION ARGOSY, A   KNIGHT, DAMON   AN
 THIRD GALAXY READER, THE   GOLD, H. L.   AN
 YOU WILL NEVER BE THE SAME   SMITH, CORDWAINER   AC
 6 FROM WORLDS BEYOND   DIKTY, T. E.   AN
GOLDEN THE SHIP WAS- OH! OH! OH!   SS   AMZ 59 04
 BEST OF CORDWAINER SMITH, THE   SMITH, CORDWAINER   AC
 YOU WILL NEVER BE THE SAME   SMITH, CORDWAINER   AC
GOOD FRIENDS, THE   SS   WOT 63 10
 BEST SCIENCE FICTION FROM WORLDS OF TOMORROW, THE
                                 POHL, FREDERIK   AN
 STARDREAMER   SMITH, CORDWAINER   AC
LADY WHO SAILED THE SOUL, THE   NV   GAL 60 04
 BEST OF CORDWAINER SMITH, THE   SMITH, CORDWAINER   AC
 MIND PARTNER AND 8 OTHER NOVELETS FROM GALAXY
                                 GOLD, H. L.   AN
 YOU WILL NEVER BE THE SAME   SMITH, CORDWAINER   AC
MARK ELF   SS   STN 57 05
 YOU WILL NEVER BE THE SAME   SMITH, CORDWAINER   AC
MOTHER HITTON'S LITTUL KITTONS   NV   GAL 61 06
 BEST OF CORDWAINER SMITH, THE   SMITH, CORDWAINER   AC
 BEYOND TOMORROW   HARDING, LEE   AN
 SPACE LORDS   SMITH, CORDWAINER   AC
NO, NO, NOT ROGOV!   SS   IFS 59 02
 SCIENCE FICTION INVENTIONS   KNIGHT, DAMON   AN
 SF: THE BEST OF THE BEST   MERRIL, JUDITH   AN
 YOU WILL NEVER BE THE SAME   SMITH, CORDWAINER   AC
 5TH ANNUAL OF THE YEAR'S BEST S-F, THE MERRIL, JUDITH   AN
ON THE GEM PLANET   NV   GAL 63 10
 ANOTHER WORLD   DOZOIS, GARDNER R.   AN
 QUEST OF THE THREE WORLDS   SMITH, CORDWAINER   NO
 SEVENTH GALAXY READER, THE   POHL, FREDERIK   AN
ON THE SAND PLANET   NV   AMZ 65 12
 QUEST OF THE THREE WORLDS   SMITH, CORDWAINER   NO
ON THE STORM PLANET   SN   GAL 65 02
 DAY IN THE LIFE, A   DOZOIS, GARDNER R.   AN
 QUEST OF THE THREE WORLDS   SMITH, CORDWAINER   NO
PLANET NAMED SHAYOL, A   NA   GAL 61 10
 BEST OF CORDWAINER SMITH, THE   SMITH, CORDWAINER   AC
 SPACE LORDS   SMITH, CORDWAINER   AC
 SPECTRUM 4   AMIS & CONQUEST   AN
 7TH ANNUAL OF THE YEAR'S BEST S-F, THE MERRIL, JUDITH   AN
PROLOGUE   MS
 SPACE LORDS   SMITH, CORDWAINER   AC
SCANNERS LIVE IN VAIN   NA   FBK 50 06
 BEST OF CORDWAINER SMITH, THE   SMITH, CORDWAINER   AC
 BEYOND THE END OF TIME   POHL, FREDERIK   AN
 DECADE THE 1950S   ALDISS & HARRISON   AN
 SCIENCE AND SORCERY   FORD, GARRET   AN
 SCIENCE FICTION HALL OF FAME VOLUME 1 SILVERBERG, ROBERT AN
 SURVIVAL PRINTOUT   TOTAL EFFECT   AN
 YOU WILL NEVER BE THE SAME   SMITH, CORDWAINER   AC
THINK BLUE, COUNT TWO   NA   GAL 63 02
 ELSEWHERE AND ELSEWHEN   CONKLIN, GROFF   AN
 STARDREAMER   SMITH, CORDWAINER   AC
THREE TO A GIVEN STAR   NV   GAL 65 10
 QUEST OF THE THREE WORLDS   SMITH, CORDWAINER   NO
UNDER OLD EARTH   NV   GAL 66 02
 ALPHA 3   SILVERBERG, ROBERT   AN
 BEST OF CORDWAINER SMITH, THE   SMITH, CORDWAINER   AC
 STARDREAMER   SMITH, CORDWAINER   AC
WESTERN SCIENCE IS SO WONDERFUL   SS   IFS 58 12
 STARDREAMER   SMITH, CORDWAINER   AC
WHEN THE PEOPLE FELL   SS   GAL 59 04
 FIFTH GALAXY READER, THE   GOLD, H. L.   AN
 STARDREAMER   SMITH, CORDWAINER   AC

SMITH, EDWARD E. PHD
BEST OF E. E. 'DOC' SMITH, THE   AC H WEI 75
ATLANTIS (FROM TRIPLANETARY)   EX   AMZ 34 01
 JOURNEY TO INFINITY   GREENBERG, MARTIN   AN
FROM "THE SKYLARK OF SPACE"   EX   AMZ 28 08
 SCIENCE FICTION ROLL OF HONOR, THE POHL, FREDERIK   AN
GALACTIC PATROL   EX   ASF 37 09
 SPACE ODYSSEYS   ALDISS, BRIAN W.   AN
IMPERIAL STARS, THE   SN   IFS 64 05
 BEST OF E. E. 'DOC' SMITH, THE SMITH, EDWARD E. PHD AC
LORD TEDRIC   NV   USF 54 03
 BEST OF E. E. 'DOC' SMITH, THE SMITH, EDWARD E. PHD AC
PIRATES OF SPACE (FROM TRIPLANETARY)   EX   AMZ 34 01
 BEST OF E. E. 'DOC' SMITH, THE SMITH, EDWARD E. PHD AC
ROBOT NEMESIS (WHAT A COURSE!, PART 13 OF COSMOS, FMG 34)
                                             SS   TWS 39 06
 BEST OF E. E. 'DOC' SMITH, THE SMITH, EDWARD E. PHD AC

SMITH, EDWARD E. PHD (CONTINUED)
  SUBSPACE SURVIVORS   NV ASF 60 07
    BEST OF E. E. 'DOC' SMITH, THE   SMITH, EDWARD E. PHD AC
  TEDRIC   SS OWS 53 03
    BEST OF E. E. 'DOC' SMITH, THE   SMITH, EDWARD E. PHD AC
  TO THE FAR REACHES OF SPACE (FROM THE SKYLARK OF SPACE)
                                                            EX AMZ 28 08
    BEST OF E. E. 'DOC' SMITH, THE   SMITH, EDWARD E. PHD AC
  VORTEX BLASTER, THE   SS CMT 41 07
    BEST OF E. E. 'DOC' SMITH, THE   SMITH, EDWARD E. PHD AC
    MODERN MASTERPIECES OF SCIENCE FICTION MOSKOWITZ, SAM   AN
  VORTEX BLASTERS, THE   MOSKOWITZ, SAM   AN

SMITH, EVELYN E.
  BAXBR DAXBR   SS FSF 56 09
    BEST SF 4   CRISPIN, EDMUND   AN
    JOURNEYS IN SCIENCE FICTION   LOUGHLIN, RICHARD L. AN
    OUT OF THIS WORLD 3   WILLIAMS-ELLIS& OWEN AN
    *TIME TO COME   DERLETH, AUGUST   OA
  CALLIOPE AND GHERKIN AND THE YANKEE DOODLE THING NV FSF 69 03
    BEST FROM FANTASY AND SCIENCE FICTION: 19
                                         FERMAN, EDWARD L. AN
  DAY IN THE SUBURBS, A   SS FSF 60 09
    SOCIOLOGY THROUGH SCIENCE FICTION   MILSTEAD/GREENBERG/& AN
  HARDEST BARGAIN, THE   NV GAL 57 06
    BEYOND BELIEF   HURLEY, RICHARD J. AN
  MIND PARTNER AND 8 OTHER NOVELETS FROM GALAXY
                                         GOLD, H. L.   AN
  LAST OF THE SPODE, THE   SS FSF 53 06
    17 X INFINITY   CONKLIN, GROFF   AN
  MARTIAN AND THE MAGICIAN, THE   SS FSF 52 11
    FIFTY SHORT SCIENCE FICTION TALES   ASIMOV & CONKLIN   AN
  NOT FIT FOR CHILDREN   SS GAL 53 05
    GALAXY SCIENCE FICTION OMNIBUS   GOLD, H. L.   AN
    SECOND GALAXY READER OF SCIENCE FICTION
                                         GOLD, H. L.   AN
  ONCE A GREECH   NV GAL 57 04
    WORLD THAT COULDN'T BE AND 8 OTHER SF NOVELETS
                                         GOLD, H. L.   AN
  SOFTLY WHILE YOU'RE SLEEPING   SS FSF 61 04
    *BEST FROM FANTASY AND SCIENCE FICTION: 11
                                         MILLS, ROBERT P.   AN
  TEA TRAY IN THE SKY   SS GAL 52 09
    GALAXY SCIENCE FICTION OMNIBUS   GOLD, H. L.   AN
    SECOND GALAXY READER OF SCIENCE FICTION
                                         GOLD, H. L.   AN
  VILBAR PARTY, THE   SS GAL 55 01
    HUMAN AND OTHER BEINGS   DEGRAEFF, ALLEN   AN
    THIRD GALAXY READER, THE   GOLD, H. L.   AN

SMITH, GEORGE HENRY
  FLAME TREE PLANET   NV FTP 73
    FLAME TREE PLANET   ELWOOD, ROGER   OA
  IN THE IMAGICON   SS GAL 66 02
    NEBULA AWARD STORIES NO. 2   ALDISS & HARRISON AN

SMITH, GEORGE HUDSON
  LAST CRUSADE, THE   SS IFS 55 02
    FIRST WORLD OF IF, THE   QUINN & WULFF   AN
    THIS SIDE OF INFINITY   CARR, TERRY   AN
  OUTCASTS, THE   SS SFS 58 09
    NOW & BEYOND   HOWARD, IVAN   AN

SMITH, GEORGE O.
  COMPLETE VENUS EQUILATERAL, THE   AC BAL 76 11
    IN ENGLAND (ORBIT, 1977) AS "VENUS EQUILATERAL"
  VENUS EQUILATERAL   AC H PRM 47
  AMATEUR IN CHANCERY   SS GAL 61 10
    EXPERT DREAMERS, THE   POHL, FREDERIK   AN
  BEAM PIRATE   NV ASF 44 10
    COMPLETE VENUS EQUILATERAL, THE   SMITH, GEORGE O.   AC
    VENUS EQUILATERAL   SMITH, GEORGE O.   AC
  CALLING THE EMPRESS   NV ASF 43 06
    COMPLETE VENUS EQUILATERAL, THE   SMITH, GEORGE O.   AC
    VENUS EQUILATERAL   SMITH, GEORGE O.   AC
  COSMIC JACKPOT, THE   SS TWS 48 10
    *SCIENCE-FICTION CARNIVAL   BROWN, F. & REYNOLDS AN
  COUNTER FOIL   NV ASF 64 04
    MEN AND MACHINES   SILVERBERG, ROBERT AN
  EPILOGUE: IDENTITY (IDENTITY)   NV ASF 45 11
    COMPLETE VENUS EQUILATERAL, THE   SMITH, GEORGE O.   AC
  EXTERNAL TRIANGLE, THE (INTERLUDE)   NV AMA 73
    COMPLETE VENUS EQUILATERAL, THE   SMITH, GEORGE O.   AC
  FIRING LINE   NV ASF 44 12
    COMPLETE VENUS EQUILATERAL, THE   SMITH, GEORGE O.   AC
    VENUS EQUILATERAL   SMITH, GEORGE O.   AC
  IDENTITY (SEE EPILOGUE: IDENTITY)   TC
  INTERLUDE (ALSO AS THE EXTERNAL TRIANGLE)   NV AMA 73
    ASTOUNDING   HARRISON, HARRY   OA
  LONG WAY, THE   NV ASF 44 04
    COMPLETE VENUS EQUILATERAL, THE   SMITH, GEORGE O.   AC
    VENUS EQUILATERAL   SMITH, GEORGE O.   AC
  LOST ART   NV ASF 43 12
    COMPLETE VENUS EQUILATERAL, THE   SMITH, GEORGE O.   AC
    MARS, WE LOVE YOU   HIPOLITO & MCNELLY AN
  TREASURY OF GREAT SCIENCE FICTION, A VOL.2
                                         BOUCHER, ANTHONY   AN
  MAD HOLIDAY   NV NEW 47 AC
    COMPLETE VENUS EQUILATERAL, THE   SMITH, GEORGE O.   AC
    VENUS EQUILATERAL   SMITH, GEORGE O.   AC
  OFF THE BEAM   NV ASF 44 02
    COMPLETE VENUS EQUILATERAL, THE   SMITH, GEORGE O.   AC
    VENUS EQUILATERAL   SMITH, GEORGE O.   AC
  PANDORA'S MILLIONS   NV ASF 45 06
    COMPLETE VENUS EQUILATERAL, THE   SMITH, GEORGE O.   AC
    VENUS EQUILATERAL   SMITH, GEORGE O.   AC

SMITH, GEORGE O.   (CONTINUED)
  QRM-INTERPLANETARY   NV ASF 42 10
    COMPLETE VENUS EQUILATERAL, THE   SMITH, GEORGE O.   AC
    FUTURE TENSE   CURTIS, RICHARD   AN
    VENUS EQUILATERAL   SMITH, GEORGE O.   AC
  RECOIL   NV ASF 43 11
    COMPLETE VENUS EQUILATERAL, THE   SMITH, GEORGE O.   AC
    VENUS EQUILATERAL   SMITH, GEORGE O.   AC
  SPECIAL DELIVERY   NV ASF 45 03
    COMPLETE VENUS EQUILATERAL, THE   SMITH, GEORGE O.   AC
    VENUS EQUILATERAL   SMITH, GEORGE O.   AC
  VOCATION   SS ASF 45 04
    CROSSROADS IN TIME   CONKLIN, GROFF   AN

SMITH, H. ALLEN
  ACHIEVEMENT OF H. T. WENSEL, THE   SS SRV 60 05
    MATHEMATICAL MAGPIE, THE   FADIMAN, CLIFTON   AN

SMITH, LADY ELEANOR
  NO SHIPS PASS   NV CSL 32 04
    OTHER SIDE OF THE CLOCK, THE   STERN, PHILIP VAN D. AN
    TRAVELERS IN TIME   STERN, PHILIP VAN D. AN

SMITH, LOWELL KENT
  ERNIE   SS ORB 74 15
    ORBIT 15   KNIGHT, DAMON   OA

SMITH, PHILIP H.
  MIRACLE TOO MANY, A   SS C FSF 64 09
    10TH ANNUAL OF THE YEAR'S BEST S-F, THE
                                         MERRIL, JUDITH   AN

SMITH, RITCHIE
  BANKS OF THE NILE, THE   NV C NWR 76 28
    NEW WRITINGS IN SF. 28   BULMER, KENNETH   OA
  SEAFARER, THE   SS C NWR 75 26
    NEW WRITINGS IN SF. 26   BULMER, KENNETH   OA

SMITH, RON
  HORROR STORY SHORTER BY ONE LETTER THAN THE SHORTEST HORROR
    STORY EVER WRITTEN, A   SS FSF 57 07
    BEST FROM FANTASY AND SCIENCE FICTION: 7
                                         BOUCHER, ANTHONY   AN
  I DON'T MIND   SS FSF 56 10
    BEST FROM FANTASY AND SCIENCE FICTION: 6
                                         BOUCHER, ANTHONY   AN
  STRONG ATTRACTION   SS NEW 68 AN
    PACIFIC BOOK OF AUSTRALIAN SCIENCE FICTION
                                         BAXTER, JOHN   AN

SMITTER, WESSEL H.
  HAND, THE   SS STO 47 02
    TIMELESS STORIES FOR TODAY AND TOMORROW
                                         BRADBURY, RAY   AN

SMYTH, ROBIN
  VOYAGE OF THE MORNING STAR, THE   SS
    STRANGE WORLD OF SCIENCE FICTION   ANONYMOUS   OA

SNYDER, GARY
  SMOKEY THE BEAR SUTRA, THE   SS SVW 73
    SAVING WORLDS   ELWOOD & KIDD   OA

SODDY, FREDERICK
  HEXLET, THE   PM NTR 36 12
    MATHEMATICAL MAGPIE, THE   FADIMAN, CLIFTON   AN
  KISS PRECISE, THE   SS NTR 36 06
    MATHEMATICAL MAGPIE, THE   FADIMAN, CLIFTON   AN

SOHL, JERRY
  BEFORE A LIVE AUDIENCE   SS FCR 75
    FUTURE CORRUPTION   ELWOOD, ROGER   OA
  I AM ALEPPO   NV NMD 73
    FRONTIERS 2: THE NEW MIND   ELWOOD, ROGER   OA

SOLT, MARY ELLEN
  MOONSHOT SONNET   IL
    SCIENCE FICTION   BRODKIN & PEARSON AN

SONNEMANN, W. K.
  COUNCIL OF THE DRONES, THE   NV AMZ 36 10
    SCIENCE FICTION OF THE 30'S   KNIGHT, DAMON   AN

SONTAG, SUSAN
  IMAGINATION OF DISASTER, THE   AR   65
    SCIENCE FICTION: THE FUTURE   ALLEN, DICK   AN

SORKIN, SOPHIE   SEE ALSO CO-EDITOR ISABEL S. GORDON

SOUTO, MARCIAL
  MIRROR IMAGE (SEE TIME TO CHANGE)   TC C
  TIME TO CHANGE (MIRROR IMAGE)   SS C   68
    SCIENCE FICTION WORLDS OF FORREST J. ACKERMAN & FRIENDS
                                         ACKERMAN, FORREST J. AC

SPALDING, WILLIAM   PSEUD. FOR RAY BRADBURY

SPALTEN, RONA
  LIBERATION   SS NWQ 74 06
    NEW WORLDS NO. 6   PLATT & BAILEY   OA

SPARK, MURIEL
  PORTOBELLO ROAD, THE   NV CMP 58
    7TH ANNUAL OF THE YEAR'S BEST S-F, THE MERRIL, JUDITH   AN

SPEARMAN, F. H.
  LOST VOICE, THE   SS
    BATTLE FOR THE PACIFIC AND OTHER ADVENTURES AT SEA, THE
                                                      ANONYMOUS   AN

SPENCER, PAUL
  IN MEMORIAM: DAVID HENRY KELLER   MS
    FOLSOM FLINT AND OTHER CURIOUS TALES, THE
                                                      KELLER, DAVID H. MD. AC

SPENCER, WILLIAM
  CYCLOPS PATROL, THE   SS   NWR 71 18
    NEW WRITINGS IN SF. 18   CARNELL, JOHN   OA
  ETERNAL MACHINES, THE   SS   NWR 64 02
    BEST FROM NEW WRITINGS IN S-F FIRST SELECTION, THE
                                     CARNELL, JOHN   AN
    NEW WRITINGS IN SF.   2   CARNELL, JOHN   OA
  HORIZONTAL MAN   SS   NWR 65 06
    NEW WRITINGS IN SF.   6   CARNELL, JOHN   OA
  LONG MEMORY, THE   SS   NWR 66 09
    NEW WRITINGS IN SF.   7   CARNELL, JOHN   AN
    NEW WRITINGS IN SF.   9   CARNELL, JOHN   OA

SPINRAD, NORMAN
  LAST HURRAH OF THE GOLDEN HORDE, THE   AC H DBL 70
  MODERN SCIENCE FICTION   AN   ANC 74
  NEW TOMORROWS, THE   AN   BEL 71
  NO DIRECTION HOME   AC   PKT 75 05
  AGE OF INVENTION, THE   SS   FSF 66 07
    BEST FROM FANTASY AND SCIENCE FICTION: 16
                                     FERMAN, EDWARD L.   AN
    LAST HURRAH OF THE GOLDEN HORDE, THE SPINRAD, NORMAN   AC
    TOMORROW, INC.   GREENBERG& OLANDER   AN
  ALL THE SOUNDS OF THE RAINBOW   NV   VTX 73 06
    NO DIRECTION HOME   SPINRAD, NORMAN   AC
  BIG FLASH, THE   NV   ORB 69 05
    BEST FROM ORBIT, THE   KNIGHT, DAMON   AN
    NO DIRECTION HOME   SPINRAD, NORMAN   AC
    ORBIT 5   KNIGHT, DAMON   OA
    SOCIAL PROBLEMS THROUGH SCIENCE FICTION
                                     GREENBERG/MILSTEAD/&   AN
    VOYAGES: SCENARIOS FOR A SHIP CALLED EARTH
                                     SAUER, ROB   AN
    WORLD'S BEST SCIENCE FICTION: 1970 WOLLHEIM & CARR   AN
  CARCINOMA ANGELS   SS   DVS 67 01
    ABOVE THE HUMAN LANDSCAPE   MCNELLY & STOVER   AN
    ALPHA 4   SILVERBERG, ROBERT   AN
    DANGEROUS VISIONS   ELLISON, HARLAN   OA
    FANTASY: THE LITERATURE OF THE MARVELOUS
                                     KELLEY, LEO P.   AN
    LAST HURRAH OF THE GOLDEN HORDE, THE SPINRAD, NORMAN   AC
  CHILD OF MIND, A   SS   AMZ 65 01
    LAST HURRAH OF THE GOLDEN HORDE, THE SPINRAD, NORMAN   AC
  CONSPIRACY, THE   SS   NWS 69 02
    NO DIRECTION HOME   SPINRAD, NORMAN   AC
  DEAD END   SS   GAL 69 11
    LAST HURRAH OF THE GOLDEN HORDE, THE SPINRAD, NORMAN   AC
  DEATHWATCH   SS   PBY 65 11
    FROM THE "S" FILE   PLAYBOY, EDITORS OF   AN
    LAST HURRAH OF THE GOLDEN HORDE, THE SPINRAD, NORMAN   AC
  ENTROPIC GANG BANG CAPER, THE   SS   NWS 69 08
    LAST HURRAH OF THE GOLDEN HORDE, THE SPINRAD, NORMAN   AC
  EQUALIZER, THE   SS   ASF 64 12
    LAST HURRAH OF THE GOLDEN HORDE, THE SPINRAD, NORMAN   AC
    ONE HUNDRED YEARS OF SCIENCE FICTION KNIGHT, DAMON   AN
  ERSATZ EGO, THE (YOUR NAME SHALL BE...DARKNESS)   SS   AMZ 64 11
    LAST HURRAH OF THE GOLDEN HORDE, THE SPINRAD, NORMAN   AC
  EYE OF THE STORM (SEE IN THE EYE OF THE STORM)   TC
  FOREWORD   IN
    MODERN SCIENCE FICTION   SPINRAD, NORMAN   AN
  FRONTIERS OF EDGEVILLE, THE   IN
    OVER THE EDGE   ELLISON, HARLAN   AC
  FULL FLOWERING, THE   SI
    MODERN SCIENCE FICTION   SPINRAD, NORMAN   AN
  GOLDEN AGE, THE   SI
    MODERN SCIENCE FICTION   SPINRAD, NORMAN   AN
  HEIRLOOM   SS   LST 72
    NO DIRECTION HOME   SPINRAD, NORMAN   AC
  HEROES DIE BUT ONCE   SS   IFS 69 12
    NO DIRECTION HOME   SPINRAD, NORMAN   AC
  IN THE EYE OF THE STORM (EYE OF THE STORM)   SS   IFS 74 02
    NO DIRECTION HOME   SPINRAD, NORMAN   AC
  INTRODUCTION- MODERN SCIENCE FICTION   IN
    MODERN SCIENCE FICTION   SPINRAD, NORMAN   AN
  IT'S A BIRD, IT'S A PLANE| SS   GNT 67
    COSMIC LAUGHTER   HALDEMAN, JOE W.   AN
    LAST HURRAH OF THE GOLDEN HORDE, THE SPINRAD, NORMAN   AC
  LAST HURRAH OF THE GOLDEN HORDE, THE   SS   NWS 69 07
    BEST SF STORIES FROM NEW WORLDS 5 MOORCOCK, MICHAEL   AN
    DECADE THE 1960S   ALDISS & HARRISON   AN
    LAST HURRAH OF THE GOLDEN HORDE, THE SPINRAD, NORMAN   AC
    NEW TOMORROWS, THE   SPINRAD, NORMAN   AN
    SF: AUTHORS' CHOICE 3   HARRISON, HARRY   AN
  LAST OF THE ROMANY, THE   SS   ASF 63 05
    LAST HURRAH OF THE GOLDEN HORDE, THE SPINRAD, NORMAN   AC
    THEMES IN SCIENCE FICTION   KELLEY, LEO P.   AN
    WINDOWS INTO TOMORROW   SILVERBERG, ROBERT   AN
  LOST CONTINENT, THE   NV   SAG 70
    ALPHA 6   SILVERBERG, ROBERT   AN
    NO DIRECTION HOME   SPINRAD, NORMAN   AC
    SCIENCE AGAINST MAN   CHEETHAM, ANTHONY   OA
  NATIONAL PASTIME, THE   NV   NOV 73 03
    BEST SCIENCE FICTION STORIES OF THE YEAR (1973)
                                     DEL REY, LESTER   AN
    FUTURE PASTIMES   EDELSTEIN, SCOTT   OA
    NO DIRECTION HOME   SPINRAD, NORMAN   AC

SPINRAD, NORMAN   (CONTINUED)
  NOVA 3   HARRISON, HARRY   OA
    RUN TO STARLIGHT, SPORTS THROUGH SCIENCE FICTION
                                     GREENBERG/OLANDER/&   AN
  NEUTRAL GROUND   SS   FSF 66 11
    LAST HURRAH OF THE GOLDEN HORDE, THE SPINRAD, NORMAN   AC
  NEW TOMORROWS, THE   IN
    NEW TOMORROWS, THE   SPINRAD, NORMAN   AN
  NIGHT IN ELF HILL, A   SS   FRS 68
    FARTHEST REACHES, THE   ELDER, JOSEPH   OA
    LAST HURRAH OF THE GOLDEN HORDE, THE SPINRAD, NORMAN   AC
  NO DIRECTION HOME   SS   NWQ 71 02
    BEST SCIENCE FICTION OF THE YEAR, THE CARR, TERRY   AN
    BEST SF: 1971   HARRISON & ALDISS   AN
    MODERN SCIENCE FICTION   SPINRAD, NORMAN   AN
    NEW WORLDS QUARTERLY NO. 2   MOORCOCK, MICHAEL   OA
    NO DIRECTION HOME   SPINRAD, NORMAN   AC
    SOCIAL PROBLEMS THROUGH SCIENCE FICTION
                                     GREENBERG/MILSTEAD/&   AN
  ONCE MORE, WITH FEELING   SS   KNT 69
    LAST HURRAH OF THE GOLDEN HORDE, THE SPINRAD, NORMAN   AC
  OUTWARD BOUND   NV   ASF 64 03
    LAST HURRAH OF THE GOLDEN HORDE, THE SPINRAD, NORMAN   AC
  POSTWAR AWAKENING, THE   SI
    MODERN SCIENCE FICTION   SPINRAD, NORMAN   AN
  RIDING THE TORCH   NA   TOT 74
    THREADS OF TIME   SILVERBERG, ROBERT   OA
  RULES OF THE ROAD, THE   SS   GAL 64 12
    FIRST STEP OUTWARD   HOSKINS, ROBERT   AN
    LAST HURRAH OF THE GOLDEN HORDE, THE SPINRAD, NORMAN   AC
  SUBJECTIVITY   SS   ASF 64 01
    ANALOG 4   CAMPBELL, JOHN W. JR   AN
    LAST HURRAH OF THE GOLDEN HORDE, THE SPINRAD, NORMAN   AC
    STRANGE ECSTASIES   PARRY, MICHEL   AN
  TECHNICALITY   SS   ASF 66 08
    LAST HURRAH OF THE GOLDEN HORDE, THE SPINRAD, NORMAN   AC
  THING OF BEAUTY, A   SS   ASF 73 01
    BEST SCIENCE FICTION FOR 1973   ACKERMAN, FORREST J.   AN
    BEST SCIENCE FICTION STORIES OF THE YEAR (1973)
                                     DEL REY, LESTER   AN
    NEBULA AWARD STORIES 9   WILHELM, KATE   AN
    NO DIRECTION HOME   SPINRAD, NORMAN   AC
    2020 VISION   POURNELLE, JERRY   AN
  WEED OF TIME, THE   SS   ANA 70
    ALCHEMY AND ACADEME   MCCAFFREY, ANNE   OA
    NO DIRECTION HOME   SPINRAD, NORMAN   AC
    1974 ANNUAL WORLD'S BEST SF, THE WOLLHEIM, DONALD A.   AN
  WORLD OF GRAY   SS   DEM 73
    DEMON KIND   ELWOOD, ROGER   OA
  YOUR NAME SHALL BE...DARKNESS (SEE THE ERSATZ EGO)
                                                      TC

SPOFFORD, HARRIET P.
  RAY OF DISPLACEMENT, THE   SS   MPM 03 10
    SCIENCE FICTION BY GASLIGHT   MOSKOWITZ, SAM   AN

SPRINGER, SHERWOOD
  EPITAPH IN AVALON   PM   FSF 54 07
    BEST FROM FANTASY AND SCIENCE FICTION: 4
                                     BOUCHER, ANTHONY   AN
  EPITAPH NEAR MOONPORT   PM   FSF 54 01
    BEST FROM FANTASY AND SCIENCE FICTION: 4
                                     BOUCHER, ANTHONY   AN
  NO LAND OF NOD   SS   TWS 52 12
    BEST FROM STARTLING STORIES, THE MINES, SAMUEL   AN
    IF THIS GOES ON   NUETZEL, CHARLES   AN
    MARRIAGE AND THE FAMILY THROUGH SCIENCE FICTION
                                     CLEAR/WARRICK/&   AN
  SOME FACTS ABOUT ROBOTS II (SEE MORE FACTS ABOUT ROBOTS)
                                                      TC

SQUARE, A   PSEUD. FOR EDWIN A. ABBOTT

ST. CLAIR, ERIC
  OLSEN AND THE GULL   SS   FSF 64 09
    BEST FROM FANTASY AND SCIENCE FICTION: 14
                                     DAVIDSON, AVRAM   AN

ST. CLAIR, MARGARET ALSO AS   IDRIS SEABRIGHT
  CHANGE THE SKY AND OTHER STORIES   AC   ACE 74
  THREE WORLDS OF FUTURITY   DC   ACE 64
  AGE OF PROPHECY, THE   NA   FUT 51 03
    CHANGE THE SKY AND OTHER STORIES ST. CLAIR, MARGARET   AC
    *SCIENCE FICTION ADVENTURES IN MUTATION CONKLIN, GROFF AN
  ALTRUISTS, THE   SS   FSF 53 11
    CHANGE THE SKY AND OTHER STORIES ST. CLAIR, MARGARET   AC
  ASKING   SS   FSF 55 11
    CHANGE THE SKY AND OTHER STORIES ST. CLAIR, MARGARET   AC
  BEAULIEU   SS   FSF 57 07
    CHANGE THE SKY AND OTHER STORIES ST. CLAIR, MARGARET   AC
  BRENDA   SS   WRT 54 03
    MORE LITTLE MONSTERS   ELWOOD & GHIDALIA   AN
    *TWISTED   CONKLIN, GROFF   AN
  BRIGHTNESS FALLS FROM THE AIR (CONTEST STORY)   SS   FSF 51 04
    SPECIAL WONDER   MCCOMAS, J. FRANCIS   AN
  CHANGE THE SKY   SS   FSF 55 03
    CHANGE THE SKY AND OTHER STORIES ST. CLAIR, MARGARET   AC
  CHILD OF VOID   SS   SSS 49 11
    *INVADERS OF EARTH   CONKLIN, GROFF   AN
    TOMORROW'S CHILDREN   ASIMOV, ISAAC   AN
  COUNTER CHARM, THE   SS   FFM 49 08
    ANDROIDS, TIME MACHINES AND BLUE GIRAFFES
                                     ELWOOD & GHIDALIA   AN
  DEATH OF EACH DAY, THE   SS   FSF 58 04
    CHANGE THE SKY AND OTHER STORIES ST. CLAIR, MARGARET   AC

ST. CLAIR, MARGARET   STARZL, R. F.

ST. CLAIR, MARGARET (CONTINUED)
  EGG A MONTH FROM ALL OVER, AN   SS FSF 52 10
    CHANGE THE SKY AND OTHER STORIES   ST. CLAIR, MARGARET AC
  EVERLASTING FOOD, THE   NV TWS 50 12
    THREE WORLDS OF FUTURITY   ST. CLAIR, MARGARET DC
  FORT IRON   SS SFQ 55 11
    CHANGE THE SKY AND OTHER STORIES   ST. CLAIR, MARGARET AC
  GARDENER, THE   SS TWS 49 10
    ROOTS OF EVIL, THE   PARRY, MICHEL   AN
    *WORLDS OF TOMORROW   DERLETH, AUGUST   AN
  GODDESS ON THE STREET CORNER, THE   SS BEY 53 09
    CHANGE THE SKY AND OTHER STORIES   ST. CLAIR, MARGARET AC
  GRAVEYARD SHIFT   SS FSF 59 02
    CHANGE THE SKY AND OTHER STORIES   ST. CLAIR, MARGARET AC
  HORRER HOWCE   SS GAL 56 07
    FOURTH GALAXY READER, THE   GOLD, H. L.   AN
  IDRIS' PIG (THE SACRED MARTIAN PIG)   NV STS 49 10
    THREE WORLDS OF FUTURITY   ST. CLAIR, MARGARET DC
  ISLAND OF THE HANDS, THE   SS WRT 52 09
    THREE WORLDS OF FUTURITY   ST. CLAIR, MARGARET DC
  LAZARUS   SS STS 55 FL
    CHANGE THE SKY AND OTHER STORIES   ST. CLAIR, MARGARET AC
  MARRIAGE MANUAL   SS STS 54 FL
    CHANGE THE SKY AND OTHER STORIES   ST. CLAIR, MARGARET AC
  MRS. HAWK   SS WRT 50 07
    UNEXPECTED, THE   MARGULIES, LEO   AN
  NUSE MAN, THE   SS GAL 60 02
    SIXTH GALAXY READER, THE   GOLD, H. L.   AN
  OLD-FASHIONED BIRD CHRISTMAS, AN   NV GAL 61 12
    CHANGE THE SKY AND OTHER STORIES   ST. CLAIR, MARGARET AC
    SEVENTH GALAXY READER, THE   POHL, FREDERIK   AN
  PILLOWS, THE   SS TWS 50 06
    *POSSIBLE WORLDS OF SCIENCE FICTION CONKLIN, GROFF   AN
  SANDS OF MARS AND OTHER STORIES, THE   ANONYMOUS   AN
  PROTT   SS GAL 53 01
    BEST SF   CRISPIN, EDMUND   AN
    SCIENCE FICTION TERROR TALES   CONKLIN, GROFF   AN
  QUIS CUSTODIET...   SS STS 48 07
    SCIENCE FICTION GALAXY, THE   CONKLIN, GROFF   AN
  RAGES, THE (RATIONS OF TANTALUS)   NV FUN 54 07
    THREE WORLDS OF FUTURITY   ST. CLAIR, MARGARET DC
  RATIONS OF TANTALUS (ALSO AS THE RAGES)   NV FUN 54 07
    WORLDS OF WHEN   CONKLIN, GROFF   AN
  ROBERTA   SS GAL 62 10
    THREE WORLDS OF FUTURITY   ST. CLAIR, MARGARET DC
  SACRED MARTIAN PIG, THE (SEE IDRIS' PIG)   TC
  SHORE LEAVE   SS
    CHANGE THE SKY AND OTHER STORIES   ST. CLAIR, MARGARET AC
  STAWDUST   SS FSF 56 09
    CHANGE THE SKY AND OTHER STORIES   ST. CLAIR, MARGARET AC
  THEN FLY OUR GREETINGS   SS STS 51 03
    CHANGE THE SKY AND OTHER STORIES   ST. CLAIR, MARGARET AC
  THIRSTY GOD   SS FSF 53 03
    CHANGE THE SKY AND OTHER STORIES   ST. CLAIR, MARGARET AC
    CROSSROADS IN TIME   CONKLIN, GROFF   AN
  WINES OF EARTH, THE   SS FSF 57 09
    CHANGE THE SKY AND OTHER STORIES   ST. CLAIR, MARGARET AC

ST. JOHN, J. ALLEN
  ILLUSTRATIONS   IL
    LAND THAT TIME FORGOT, THE   BURROUGHS, EDGAR R. NO
    MOON MAID, THE   BURROUGHS, EDGAR R. NO
    SAVAGE PELLUCIDAR   BURROUGHS, EDGAR R. NO
    THREE MARTIAN NOVELS   BURROUGHS, EDGAR R. AC
    THREE SCIENCE FICTION NOVELS   BURROUGHS, EDGAR R. AC

ST. JOHN, PHILIP   PSEUD. FOR LESTER DEL REY
  ANYTHING   SS UNK 39 10
    FROM UNKNOWN WORLDS   CAMPBELL, JOHN W. JR AN

STABLEFORD, BRIAN M.
  CAPTAIN FAGAN DIED ALONE   SS
    DAW SCIENCE FICTION READER, THE   WOLLHEIM, DONALD A. OA
  CRADLE OF THE SUN   NO
    SCIENCE FICTION SPECIAL 5   ANONYMOUS   AN
  ENGINEER AND THE EXECUTIONER, THE   NV AMZ 75 05
    1976 ANNUAL WORLD'S BEST SF, THE   WOLLHEIM, DONALD A. AN
  EVOLUTION OF SCIENCE FICTION, THE   AR
    BEYOND THIS HORIZON   CARRELL, CHRISTOPHER OA
  JUDAS STORY   SS NEW 75 AN
    YEAR'S BEST HORROR STORIES: SERIES III, THE
                                       DAVIS, RICHARD   AN
  SUN'S TEARS, THE   SS AMZ 74 10
    1975 ANNUAL WORLD'S BEST SF, THE   WOLLHEIM, DONALD A. AN

STADLER, JOHN
  ECO-FICTION   AN WSP 71 04
  PREFACE   IN
    ECO-FICTION   STADLER, JOHN   AN

STAFFORD, WILLIAM
  TOWARD THE SPACE AGE   PM   70
    SCIENCE FACT/FICTION   FARRELL/GAGE/&   AN

STALL, MICHAEL
  FIVE DOORS, THE   SS NWR 74 23
    NEW WRITINGS IN SF. 23   BULMER, KENNETH   OA
  MANGANON   NV NWR 76 28
    NEW WRITINGS IN SF. 28   BULMER, KENNETH   OA
  RICE BRANDY   NV NWR 75 25
    NEW WRITINGS IN SF. 25   BULMER, KENNETH   OA

STANCIC, MILJENKO
  DEAD CHILD, THE   IL
    SCIENCE FICTION   BRODKIN & PEARSON   AN

STANDISH, ROBERT   PSEUD. FOR DIGBY GEORGE GERAHTY
  TEST-TUBE TERROR   SS SEP 58 09
    POST READER OF FANTASY AND SCIENCE FICTION
                                       SATURDAY EVE. POST   AN

STANGLAND, A. G.
  ANCIENT BRAIN, THE   SS SWS 29 10
    FROM OFF THIS WORLD   MARGULIES & FRIEND   AN

STANLEY, GEORGE
  ORION   SS QRK 70 01
    QUARK/1   DELANY & HACKER   OA
  TO THE CHILD WHOSE BIRTH WILL CHANGE THE WAY THE UNIVERSE
    WORKS   PM QRK 71 03
    QUARK/3   DELANY & HACKER   OA

STANTON, L. JEROME
  GLITCH, THE   NV C GAL 74 06
    ANTIGRAV: COSMIC COMEDIES   STRICK, PHILIP   AN
    BEST FROM GALAXY, THE VOLUME III BAEN, JAMES   AN

STANTON, WILL
  AS LONG AS YOU'RE HERE   SS FSF 63 07
    TWENTY YEARS OF FANTASY & SCIENCE FICTION
                                       FERMAN & MILLS   AN
  BARNEY   SS FSF 51 02
    BEST FROM FANTASY AND SCIENCE FICTION BOUCHER & MCCOMAS AN
    FIFTY SHORT SCIENCE FICTION TALES ASIMOV & CONKLIN   AN
  DODGER FAN   SS FSF 57 06
    ARENA: SPORTS SF   FERMAN & MALZBERG   AN
    BEST FROM FANTASY AND SCIENCE FICTION: 7
                                       BOUCHER, ANTHONY   AN
    NEVER IN THIS WORLD   STONE, IDELLA P.   AN
    RUN TO STARLIGHT, SPORTS THROUGH SCIENCE FICTION
                                       GREENBERG/OLANDER/& AN
  GUMDROP KING, THE   SS FSF 62 08
    BEST FROM FANTASY AND SCIENCE FICTION: 12
                                       DAVIDSON, AVRAM   AN
  LAST PRESENT, THE   SS FSF 56 08
    BEST FROM FANTASY AND SCIENCE FICTION: 6
                                       BOUCHER, ANTHONY   AN
  YOU ARE WITH IT!   SS FSF 61 12
    CENTURY OF SCIENCE FICTION, A   KNIGHT, DAMON   AN

STANYUKOVICH, KIRILL
  GOLUB-YAVAN, THE   SS
    DESTINATION: AMALTHEIA   DIXON, RICHARD   AN

STAPLEDON, OLAF
  TO THE END OF TIME   AC H FKW 53
    THE BEST OF OLAF STAPLEDON, EDITED BY BASIL DAVENPORT
  WORLDS OF WONDER   AC H FPB 49
  DEATH INTO LIFE   NO MTH 46
    WORLDS OF WONDER   STAPLEDON, OLAF   AC
  FLAMES, THE   NO SKW 47
    TO THE END OF TIME   STAPLEDON, OLAF   AC
    WORLDS OF WONDER   STAPLEDON, OLAF   AC
  FLYING MEN, THE (FROM "LAST AND FIRST MEN") EX MTH 30
    *BEYOND TIME AND SPACE   DERLETH, AUGUST   AN
  HUMANITY ON VENUS (FROM "LAST AND FIRST MEN") EX MTH 30
    MASTERPIECES OF SCIENCE FICTION   MOSKOWITZ, SAM   AN
  LAST AND FIRST MEN   EX MTH 30
    ALL ABOUT VENUS   ALDISS, BRIAN W.   AN
    FAREWELL FANTASTIC VENUS   ALDISS & HARRISON   AN
    WORLDS APART   WILLIAMS-ELLIS& OWEN AN
  LAST AND FIRST MEN   NO MTH 30
    TO THE END OF TIME   STAPLEDON, OLAF   AC
  LAST TERRESTRIALS, THE (FROM "LAST AND FIRST MEN")
                                             EX MTH 30
    TREASURY OF SCIENCE FICTION CLASSICS, THE
                                       KUEBLER, HAROLD W.   AN
  MARTIANS, THE (FROM "LAST AND FIRST MEN") EX MTH 30
    TREASURY OF SCIENCE FICTION CLASSICS, THE
                                       KUEBLER, HAROLD W.   AN
  ODD JOHN   NO MTH 35
    PORTABLE NOVELS OF SCIENCE   WOLLHEIM, DONALD A. AN
    TO THE END OF TIME   STAPLEDON, OLAF   AC
  ODD JOHN (SELECTION FROM)   EX MTH 35
    CENTURY OF SCIENCE FICTION, A   KNIGHT, DAMON   AN
  OLD MAN IN A NEW WORLD   NO ALN 44
    WORLDS OF WONDER   STAPLEDON, OLAF   AC
  SIRIUS   NO SKW 44
    TO THE END OF TIME   STAPLEDON, OLAF   AC
  STAR MAKER, THE   NO MTH 37
    TO THE END OF TIME   STAPLEDON, OLAF   AC
  WORLD OF SOUND, A   SS SFM 74 11
    BEST OF SCIENCE FICTION MONTHLY, THE SACKS, JANET   AN
  WORLDS OF WONDER   AC FPB 49
    QUADRATIC   CRAWFORD, WILLIAM L. AN

STARRETT, VINCENT
  PENELOPE   NV WRT 23 05
    MOON TERROR, THE   BIRCH, A. G.   AN
  SORT OF INTRODUCTION, A   IN
    BEST SCIENCE-FICTION STORIES: 1950, THE
                                       BLEILER & DIKTY   AN

STARZL, R. F.
  HORNETS OF SPACE   SS WOS 30 11
    FROM OFF THIS WORLD   MARGULIES & FRIEND   AN
  OUT OF THE SUB-UNIVERSE   SS ASQ 28 SU
    HISTORY OF THE SCIENCE FICTION MAGAZINE, THE PART 1 1926-1935
                                       ASHLEY, MICHAEL   AN
  RADIANT ENEMIES, THE   SS ARG 34 02
    EXPLORING OTHER WORLDS   MOSKOWITZ, SAM   AN

STEARNS, CHARLES A.   STOCKTON, FRANK R.

STEARNS, CHARLES A.
  PASTORAL AFFAIR   SS   GAL 59 02
    FIFTH GALAXY READER, THE   GOLD, H. L.   AN

STECHER, L. J. JR.   PSEUD. FOR JOSEPH WESLEY
  ELEPHANT FOR THE PRINKIP, AN   SS   GAL 60 08
    TENTH GALAXY READER, THE   POHL, FREDERICK   AN
  MAN IN A QUANDARY   SS   GAL 58 07
    FOURTH GALAXY READER, THE   GOLD, H. L.   AN
  PERFECT ANSWER   SS   GAL 58 06
    FIFTH GALAXY READER, THE   GOLD, H. L.   AN

STEIGER, BRAD
  BETTER RAT TRAP, A   SS   NEW 65 AN
    GREAT SCIENCE-FICTION   LICATA, TONY   AN

STEINBECK, JOHN
  SAINT KATY THE VIRGIN   SS   38
    TIMELESS STORIES FOR TODAY AND TOMORROW
                                          BRADBURY, RAY   AN
  SHORT-SHORT STORY OF MANKIND, THE   SS   PBY 58 04
    PENGUIN SCIENCE FICTION   ALDISS, BRIAN W.   AN
    SF:59, THE YEAR'S GREATEST SCIENCE FICTION AND FANTASY
                                          MERRIL, JUDITH   AN
  TURTLE, THE (FROM "THE GRAPES OF WRATH")   EX   39
    ECO-FICTION   STADLER, JOHN   AN

STEINBERG, SAUL
  ALLIGATOR WALKING LINE   CT   60
    MATHEMATICAL MAGPIE, THE   FADIMAN, CLIFTON   AN
  MAN IN CUBE   CT   NYM 60 09
    MATHEMATICAL MAGPIE, THE   FADIMAN, CLIFTON   AN
  QUESTION MARK ON A SEESAW   CT   NYM 60 07
    MATHEMATICAL MAGPIE, THE   FADIMAN, CLIFTON   AN

STEPHENS, FRANCES
  PROJECT D   SS   SPC 74 02
    SPACE   2   DAVIS, RICHARD   OA

STEPHENS, JAMES
  DESIRE   SS   28
    MOONLIGHT TRAVELER, THE   STERN, PHILIP VAN D. AN
  ETCHED IN MOONLIGHT   SS   28
    TRAVELERS IN TIME   STERN, PHILIP VAN D. AN
  THREEPENNY-PIECE, THE (1913)   SS   FSF 51 06
    BEST FROM FANTASY AND SCIENCE FICTION BOUCHER & MCCOMAS   AN

STEPHENS, JOHN
  AMUSED VISITOR   SS   NEW 68 AN
    FLYING SAUCERS IN FACT AND FICTION   SANTESSON, HANS S.   AN

STEPHENS, KEVIN
  METAMORPHOSIS   IL C
    BEYOND THIS HORIZON   CARRELL, CHRISTOPHER OA

STEPHENS, ROSEMARY
  ANIMAL, THE   SS
    UNIVERSE AHEAD   ENGDAHL & ROBERSON   AN

STEPHENSON, ANDREW M
  GIANT KILLERS, THE   NV
    ANDROMEDA I   WESTON, PETER   OA

STERBA, MONICA
  CYPRIAN'S ROOM   NV   FSF 67 05
    BEST FROM FANTASY AND SCIENCE FICTION: 17
                                          FERMAN, EDWARD L.   AN

STERLING, BRUCE
  MAN-MADE SELF   SS
    LONE STAR UNIVERSE   PROCTOR & UTLEY   OA

STERN, DONNEL
  DIGGERS, THE   SS   CLR 73 03
    CLARION III   WILSON, ROBIN SCOTT OA
  MOLTEN CORE   SS   CLR 73 03
    CLARION III   WILSON, ROBIN SCOTT OA

STERN, PHILIP VAN DOREN
  GREAT TALES OF FANTASY AND IMAGINATION   AN   PKT 54 11
    SEE "THE MOONLIGHT TRAVELER"
  MOONLIGHT TRAVELER, THE   AN H DBL 43 05
    ALSO AS "GREAT TALES OF FANTASY AND IMAGINATION"
  OTHER SIDE OF THE CLOCK, THE   AN H VNR 69
  STRANGE BEASTS AND UNNATURAL MONSTERS   AN   FCR 68 08
  TRAVELERS IN TIME   AN H DBL 47 07
  GREATEST GIFT, THE   SS   43
    OTHER SIDE OF THE CLOCK, THE   STERN, PHILIP VAN D. AN
  INTRODUCTION   IN
    MOONLIGHT TRAVELER, THE   STERN, PHILIP VAN D. AN
    OTHER SIDE OF THE CLOCK, THE   STERN, PHILIP VAN D. AN
    STRANGE BEASTS AND UNNATURAL MONSTERS STERN, PHILIP VAN D. AN

STERNBACH, RICK
  ABOUT THE COVER   MS
    TALES OF KNOWN SPACE: THE UNIVERSE OF LARRY NIVEN
                                          NIVEN, LARRY   AC

STERNBERG, JACQUES
  FUTURE WITHOUT FUTURE   OC H SEA 73
  EPHEMERA, THE   SS
    FUTURE WITHOUT FUTURE   STERNBERG, JACQUES   OC
  FIN DE SIECLE   NO
    FUTURE WITHOUT FUTURE   STERNBERG, JACQUES   OC
  FUTURE WITHOUT FUTURE   SS
    FUTURE WITHOUT FUTURE   STERNBERG, JACQUES   OC

STERNBERG, JACQUES   (CONTINUED)
  VACATION   SS
    FUTURE WITHOUT FUTURE   STERNBERG, JACQUES   OC
  VERY SINCERELY YOURS   NV
    FUTURE WITHOUT FUTURE   STERNBERG, JACQUES   OC

STERNIG, LARRY
  CLUTCH OF MORPHEUS   NV   TWS 46 WI
    TALES OF TIME AND SPACE   OLNEY, ROSS R.   AN
  TOTAL RECALL   SS   PLS 46 FL
    TEEN-AGE SPACE ADVENTURES   FURMAN, A. L.   AN
  VENUSIAN INVADER   SS   PLS 45 WI
    TEEN-AGE SPACE ADVENTURES   FURMAN, A. L.   AN

STEVENS, FRANCIS   PSEUD. FOR GERTRUDE BENNETT
  FRIEND ISLAND   SS   ASW 18 09
    UNDER THE MOONS OF MARS   MOSKOWITZ, SAM   AN

STEVENS, JAMES
  AND I FOR AN EYE   SS
    2076: THE AMERICAN TRICENTENNIAL   BRYANT, EDWARD   OA
  BIRTHDAY BOY, THE   SS   GEN 72
    GENERATION   GERROLD, DAVID   OA
  SYN   SS
    TOMORROW TODAY   ZEBROWSKI, GEORGE   OA

STEVENS, ROWAN
  BATTLE FOR THE PACIFIC, THE   SS
    BATTLE FOR THE PACIFIC AND OTHER ADVENTURES AT SEA, THE
                                          ANONYMOUS   AN
    BATTLE OF THE MONSTERS AND OTHER STORIES, THE
                                          HARTWELL & CURREY   AN

STEVENSON, LYNNDA
  NORMAN: FRIENDS AND OTHER STRANGERS   SS   CLR 71 01
    CLARION   WILSON, ROBIN SCOTT OA

STEVENSON, ROBERT LOUIS
  BODY SNATCHER, THE   SS
    GHOULS, THE   HAINING, PETER   AN
  BOTTLE IMP, THE   SS   BAW 91 03
    MOONLIGHT TRAVELER, THE   STERN, PHILIP VAN D. AN
  STRANGE CASE OF DR. JEKYLL AND MR. HYDE   SN   85
    CENTURY OF GREAT SHORT SCIENCE FICTION NOVELS, A
                                          KNIGHT, DAMON   AN

STEWART, DOUGLAS
  FROM: RUTHERFORD   PM
    SECOND PACIFIC BOOK OF SCIENCE FICTION, THE
                                          BAXTER, JOHN   AN

STEWART, WILL   PSEUD. FOR JACK WILLIAMSON
  SEETEE SHIP   AC H GNM 51
  COLLISION ORBIT   NV   ASF 42 07
    SEETEE SHIP   STEWART, WILL   AC
  MINUS SIGN   SN   ASF 42 11
    SEETEE SHIP   STEWART, WILL   AC
  OPPOSITES- REACT!   SN   ASF 43 01
    SEETEE SHIP   STEWART, WILL   AC

STICKGOLD, BOB
  SUSIE'S REALITY   NV   IFS 73 06
    BEST FROM IF, THE   VOLUME II   IF, EDITORS OF   AN
    INTRODUCTORY PSYCHOLOGY THROUGH SCIENCE FICTION
                                          KATZ/WARRICK/&   AN

STILSON, CHARLES B.
  POLARIS OF THE SNOWS   NV   ASW 15 12
    UNDER THE MOONS OF MARS   MOSKOWITZ, SAM   AN

STIMSON, FREDERIC J.
  DR. MATERIALISMUS   SS   SCR 90 08
    FUTURE PERFECT   FRANKLIN, H. BRUCE   AN

STINE, G. HARRY   ALSO AS   LEE CORREY
  HOW TO THINK A SCIENCE FICTION STORY (EXCERPT)   AR   ASF 61 05
    6TH ANNUAL OF THE YEAR'S BEST S-F, THE MERRIL, JUDITH   AN
  SPUTNIK: ONE REASON WHY WE LOST   AR   FSF 58 01
    SF:58, THE YEAR'S GREATEST SCIENCE FICTION AND FANTASY
                                          MERRIL, JUDITH   AN

STIRLING, YATES JR.
  BATTLE OFF THE HOOK, THE   SS
    BATTLE FOR THE PACIFIC AND OTHER ADVENTURES AT SEA, THE
                                          ANONYMOUS   AN
  BOMBARDMENT OF THE GOLDEN GATE, THE   SS
    BATTLE FOR THE PACIFIC AND OTHER ADVENTURES AT SEA, THE
                                          ANONYMOUS   AN
  CRUISE OF A COMMERCE DESTROYER, THE   SS
    BATTLE FOR THE PACIFIC AND OTHER ADVENTURES AT SEA, THE
                                          ANONYMOUS   AN
  FIGHT IN THE FOG, A   SS
    BATTLE FOR THE PACIFIC AND OTHER ADVENTURES AT SEA, THE
                                          ANONYMOUS   AN

STOCKHAM, RICHARD
  VALLEY, THE   SS   IFS 54 06
    EVIL EARTHS   ALDISS, BRIAN W.   AN

STOCKTON, FRANK R.
  SCIENCE FICTION OF FRANK R. STOCKTON, THE   AC H GRG 76 06
  AMOS KILBRIGHT: HIS ADSCITITIOUS EXPERIENCES   NA   AMR 88 04
    SCIENCE FICTION OF FRANK R. STOCKTON, THE
                                          STOCKTON, FRANK R.   AC
  GREAT STONE OF SARDIS, THE   NO   HPM 97 11

STOCKTON, FRANK R.   STUART, WILLIAM W.

STOCKTON, FRANK R.   (CONTINUED)
    SCIENCE FICTION OF FRANK R. STOCKTON, THE
                                             STOCKTON, FRANK R.   AC
    GREAT WAR SYNDICATE, THE (ABRIDGED)   NV   OAW 88 12
    *BEST OF SCIENCE FICTION   CONKLIN, GROFF   AN
    KNIFE THAT KILLED PO HANCY, THE   NV   93
    SCIENCE FICTION OF FRANK R. STOCKTON, THE
                                             STOCKTON, FRANK R.   AC
    MY TERMINAL MORAINE   NV   OAW 92 04
    SCIENCE FICTION OF FRANK R. STOCKTON, THE
                                             STOCKTON, FRANK R.   AC
    MY TRANSLATOPHONE   NV   HBZ 00 10
    SCIENCE FICTION OF FRANK R. STOCKTON, THE
                                             STOCKTON, FRANK R.   AC
    TALE OF NEGATIVE GRAVITY, A   NV   CNY 84 11
    *BEYOND TIME AND SPACE   DERLETH, AUGUST   AN
    JOURNEYS IN SCIENCE FICTION   LOUGHLIN, RICHARD L. AN
    SCIENCE FICTION OF FRANK R. STOCKTON, THE
                                             STOCKTON, FRANK R.   AC
    WATER-DEVIL, THE (1874)   NV   SCR 74 10
    SCIENCE FICTION OF FRANK R. STOCKTON, THE
                                             STOCKTON, FRANK R.   AC

STOKER, BRAM
    DRACULA'S DAUGHTER (DRACULA'S GUEST)   SS   WRT 27 12
    GHOULS, THE   HAINING, PETER   AN
    JUDGE'S HOUSE, THE   SS
    STRANGE BEASTS AND UNNATURAL MONSTERS   STERN, PHILIP VAN D. AN
    SQUAW, THE   SS   93
    BEWARE THE BEASTS   GHIDALIA, V.& ELWOOD AN

STOKES, MALCOM
    HERITAGE, THE   CT
    TALES FROM THE GALAXIES   WILLIAMS-ELLIS& P.   AN

STONE, IDELLA PURNELL
    NEVER IN THIS WORLD   AN   FGM 71 04
    14 GREAT TALES OF ESP   AN   FGM 69 11
    INTRODUCTION   IN
    NEVER IN THIS WORLD   STONE, IDELLA P.   AN

STONE, LESLIE F.   (MRS WILLIAM SILVERBERG)
    CONQUEST OF GOLA, THE   SS   WOS 31 04
    *BEST OF SCIENCE FICTION   CONKLIN, GROFF   AN
    HUMAN PETS OF MARS, THE   NV   AMZ 36 10
    BEFORE THE GOLDEN AGE   ASIMOV, ISAAC   AN
    RAPE OF THE SOLAR SYSTEM, THE   SS   AMZ 34 12
    FLIGHT INTO SPACE   WOLLHEIM, DONALD A. AN

STONES, JONATHAN
    ALPHA IN OMEGA   SS
    AD 2500   WILSON, ANGUS   AN

STONEY, LELAND
    VILLAGE, THE   PM   QRK 71 02
    QUARK/2   DELANY & HACKER   OA

STONG, PHILIP D.
    OTHER WORLDS, THE   AN H FNK 41
    ALSO AS "25 MODERN STORIES OF MYSTERY AND IMAGINATION"
    25 MODERN STORIES OF MYSTERY AND IMAGINATION   AN H GCB 42
    SEE "THE OTHER WORLDS"
    FOREWORD   IN
    OTHER WORLDS, THE   STONG, PHILIP D.   AN

STOPA, JON
    KIDDY-LIB   NV   EIO 73
    EROS IN ORBIT   ELDER, JOSEPH   OA

STOUT, TIM
    "FLAP"   SS   ADS 75 01
    ARMADA SCI-FI ONE   DAVIS, RICHARD   OA
    "HAPPY LANDINGS, PROFESSOR|"   SS   ADS 75 02
    ARMADA SCI-FI TWO   DAVIS, RICHARD   OA
    LIVING FOSSIL   SS   SPC 74 02
    SPACE 2   DAVIS, RICHARD   OA
    WAKE UP DEAD   SS   NEW 75 AN
    YEAR'S BEST HORROR STORIES: SERIES III, THE
                                             DAVIS, RICHARD   AN

STOVER, LEON E. AND HARRY HARRISON
    APEMAN, SPACEMAN   AN H DBL 68
    ANTHROPOLOGICAL SCIENCE FICTION

STOVER, LEON E.   SEE ALSO   CO-EDITOR WILLIS E. MCNELLY
    AFTERWORD   MS
    APEMAN, SPACEMAN   STOVER & HARRISON   AN
    APEMAN, SPACEMAN- OR 2001'S ANSWER TO THE WORLD RIDDLE
                                                   AR
    ABOVE THE HUMAN LANDSCAPE   MCNELLY & STOVER   AN
    INTRODUCTION   IN C
    ABOVE THE HUMAN LANDSCAPE   MCNELLY & STOVER   AN
    APEMAN, SPACEMAN   STOVER & HARRISON   AN
    SCIENCE FICTION AS CULTURE CRITICISM   AR C
    ABOVE THE HUMAN LANDSCAPE   MCNELLY & STOVER   AN
    WHAT WE HAVE HERE IS TOO MUCH COMMUNICATION   SS   ORB 71 09
    ABOVE THE HUMAN LANDSCAPE   MCNELLY & STOVER   AN
    ORBIT 9   KNIGHT, DAMON   OA
    2001: A SPACE ODYSSEY- REVIEW 4   MR   AMZ 69 03
    BEST SF: 1968   HARRISON & ALDISS   AN

STRAUS, RALPH
    MOST MADDENING STORY IN THE WORLD   SS   37
    MOONLIGHT TRAVELER, THE   STERN, PHILIP VAN D. AN

STREET, CLAIRE EDWIN
    MYSTERIOUS GEM, THE   SS   SFT 73
    SCIENCE FICTION TALES   ELWOOD, ROGER   OA
    TO THE WORLD OF ZZZD   SS
    TUNNEL AND OTHER STORIES, THE   ELWOOD, ROGER   OA

STRETE, CRAIG
    BLEEDING MAN, THE   NV   GAL 74 12
    1975 ANNUAL WORLD'S BEST SF, THE   WOLLHEIM, DONALD A. AN
    HORSE OF A DIFFERENT TECHNICOLOR, A   SS   GAL 75 01
    BEST FROM GALAXY, THE VOLUME IV   BAEN, JAMES   AN
    TIME DEER   SS   IFS 74 12
    BEST FROM IF, THE VOLUME III   BAEN, JAMES   AN
    BEST SF: 1974   HARRISON & ALDISS   AN
    NEBULA AWARD STORIES 11   LE GUIN, URSULA K.   AN
    WHO WAS THE FIRST OSCAR TO WIN A NEGRO?   SS   ORB 76 18
    ORBIT 18   KNIGHT, DAMON   OA
    WHY HAS THE VIRGIN MARY NEVER ENTERED THE WIGWAM OF
    STANDING BEAR?   SS
    AURORA: BEYOND EQUALITY   MCINTYRE & ANDERSON OA

STRIBLING, T. S.
    GREEN SPLOTCHES, THE   NV   ADV 20 01
    POCKET BOOK OF SCIENCE-FICTION, THE   WOLLHEIM, DONALD A. AN

STRICK, PHILIP
    ANTIGRAV: COSMIC COMEDIES   AN H HUT 76 01
    BUG-EYED SCREEN, THE   AR
    BEYOND THIS HORIZON   CARRELL, CHRISTOPHER OA
    INTRODUCTION   IN
    ANTIGRAV: COSMIC COMEDIES   STRICK, PHILIP   AN

STRINGER, DAVID
    ACCLIMATIZATION   NV   NWR 65 05
    NEW WRITINGS IN SF. 5   CARNELL, JOHN   OA
    HIGH EIGHT   NV   NWR 65 04
    BEST FROM NEW WRITINGS IN S-F FIRST SELECTION, THE
                                             CARNELL, JOHN   AN
    NEW WRITINGS IN SF. 4   CARNELL, JOHN   OA

STRUGATSKY, ARKADY
    DESTINATION: AMALTHEIA   SS C
    DESTINATION: AMALTHEIA   DIXON, RICHARD   AN
    EMERGENCY CASE, AN   SS C
    PATH INTO THE UNKNOWN   ANONYMOUS   AN
    GIGANTIC FLUCTUATION, THE   NO C
    JOURNEY ACROSS THREE WORLDS   ANONYMOUS   AN
    SIX MATCHES   SS C
    MORE SOVIET SCIENCE FICTION   ANONYMOUS   AN
    SPONTANEOUS REFLEX   SS AMZ 59 05
    SOVIET SCIENCE FICTION   ANONYMOUS   AN
    WANDERERS AND TRAVELERS   SS   ISF 67 11
    PATH INTO THE UNKNOWN   ANONYMOUS   AN
    WHITE CONE OF THE ALAID, THE   SS C
    LAST DOOR TO AIYA   GINSBURG, MIRRA   AN

STRUGATSKY, BORIS
    DESTINATION: AMALTHEIA   SS C
    DESTINATION: AMALTHEIA   DIXON, RICHARD   AN
    EMERGENCY CASE, AN   SS C
    PATH INTO THE UNKNOWN   ANONYMOUS   AN
    GIGANTIC FLUCTUATION, THE   NO C
    JOURNEY ACROSS THREE WORLDS   ANONYMOUS   AN
    SIX MATCHES   SS C
    MORE SOVIET SCIENCE FICTION   ANONYMOUS   AN
    SPONTANEOUS REFLEX   SS AMZ 59 05
    SOVIET SCIENCE FICTION   ANONYMOUS   AN
    WHITE CONE OF THE ALAID, THE   SS C
    LAST DOOR TO AIYA   GINSBURG, MIRRA   AN

STRUTHER, JAN   PSEUD. FOR JOYCE MAXTONE GRAHAM
    COBBLER, COBBLER, MEND MY SHOE   SS   WRV 29 11
    MOONLIGHT TRAVELER, THE   STERN, PHILIP VAN D. AN
    MINIVER PROBLEM, THE   AR   40
    MATHEMATICAL MAGPIE, THE   FADIMAN, CLIFTON   AN
    UGLY SISTER (LMR 35 12)   SS   FSF 52 02
    BEST FROM FANTASY AND SCIENCE FICTION: 2
                                             BOUCHER & MCCOMAS   AN

STUART, DON A.   PSEUD. FOR JOHN W. CAMPBELL, JR.
    ATOMIC POWER   SS   ASF 34 12
    *BEST OF SCIENCE FICTION   CONKLIN, GROFF   AN
    FORGETFULNESS   SN   ASF 37 06
    *ADVENTURES IN TIME AND SPACE   HEALY & MCCOMAS   AN
    ASTOUNDING-ANALOG READER, THE VOLUME ONE
                                             HARRISON & ALDISS   AN
    CITIES OF WONDER   KNIGHT, DAMON   AN
    TWILIGHT   SS   ASF 34 11
    BEYOND TOMORROW   KNIGHT, DAMON   AN
    POCKET BOOK OF SCIENCE-FICTION, THE   WOLLHEIM, DONALD A. AN
    WHO GOES THERE?   NV   ASF 38 08
    *ADVENTURES IN TIME AND SPACE   HEALY & MCCOMAS   AN
    TOWARD INFINITY   KNIGHT, DAMON   AN

STUART, JESSE
    SPLIT CHERRY TREE   SS
    ARMCHAIR SCIENCE READER, THE   GORDON, I. & SORKIN AN

STUART, WILLIAM W.
    HUSBAND FOR MY WIFE, A   SS   GAL 60 08
    SIXTH GALAXY READER, THE   GOLD, H. L.   AN
    INSIDE JOHN BARTH   NV   GAL 60 06
    FIFTH GALAXY READER, THE   GOLD, H. L.   AN
    LITTLE MAN WHO WASN'T QUITE, THE   NV   GAL 61 12
    *TWISTED   CONKLIN, GROFF   AN

STUART, WILLIAM W.   STURGEON, THEODORE

STUART, WILLIAM W. (CONTINUED)
  STAR-CROSSED LOVER   NV GAL 62 04
    12 GREAT CLASSICS OF SCIENCE FICTION CONKLIN, GROFF   AN

STUBBS, HARRY C.   SEE PSEUD. HAL CLEMENT

STURGEON, THEODORE
  ALIENS 4   AC   AVN 59
  BEYOND   AC   AVN 60
  CASE AND THE DREAMER   AC H NDB 74
  CAVIAR   AC H BAL 55 11
    ALSO IN "SCIENCE FICTION SPECIAL 3"
  E PLURIBUS UNICORN   AC H ABE 53
  JOYOUS INVASION, THE   AC H GOL 65
  MORE THAN HUMAN   NO H FSY 53
  NOT WITHOUT SORCERY   AC   BAL 61 06
    8 STORIES FROM "WITHOUT SORCERY"
  STARSHINE   AC   PYR 66 12
  STURGEON IN ORBIT   AC   PYR 64 02
  STURGEON IS ALIVE AND WELL...   AC H PUT 71
  THUNDER AND ROSES   AC H JOS 57
    8 STORIES FROM "A WAY HOME"
  TO HERE AND THE EASEL   AC H GOL 73
  TOUCH OF STRANGE, A   AC H DBL 58
  TOUCH OF STRANGE, A (7 OF 9)   AC   BRK 59
  WAY HOME, A   AC H FKW 55
    EDITED BY GROFF CONKLIN
    ENGLISH DERIVATIVE COLLECTION "THUNDER AND ROSES"
  WAY HOME, A (9 OF 11)   AC   PYR 56
    EDITED BY GROFF CONKLIN
  WITHOUT SORCERY   AC H PRM 48
    DERIVATIVE COLLECTION "NOT WITHOUT SORCERY"
  WORLDS OF THEODORE STURGEON, THE   AC   ACE 72
  ABOUT JOHN CAMPBELL   MS
    WHO GOES THERE? AND OTHER STORIES CAMPBELL, JOHN W. JR AC
  ABREACTION   SS   WRT 48 07
    BEYOND   STURGEON, THEODORE AC
    FUTURE MAKERS, THE   HAINING, PETER   AN
  AFFAIR WITH A GREEN MONKEY   SS   VSF 57 05
    MODERN SCIENCE FICTION   SPINRAD, NORMAN   AN
    *TOUCH OF STRANGE, A   STURGEON, THEODORE AC
  AGNES, ACCENT AND ACCESS   SS   GAL 73 10
    BEST FROM GALAXY, THE VOLUME II   GALAXY, EDITORS OF AN
  AND MY FEAR IS GREAT   NA   BEY 53 07
    THUNDER AND ROSES   STURGEON, THEODORE AC
    *WAY HOME, A   STURGEON, THEODORE AC
  AND NOW THE NEWS...   SS   FSF 56 12
    BEST FROM FANTASY AND SCIENCE FICTION: 6
                                       BOUCHER, ANTHONY   AN
    INTRODUCTORY PSYCHOLOGY THROUGH SCIENCE FICTION
                                       KATZ/WARRICK/&   AN
    MASTERS' CHOICE   JANIFER, LAURENCE M. AN
    SECOND ORBIT   DOHERTY, G. D.   AN
    TOMORROW AND TOMORROW   KNIGHT, DAMON   AN
    VINTAGE ANTHOLOGY OF SCIENCE FANTASY, THE
                                       CERF, CHRISTOPHER   AN
  ARTNAN PROCESS   NV   ASF 41 06
    NOT WITHOUT SORCERY   STURGEON, THEODORE AC
    STARSHINE   STURGEON, THEODORE AC
    WITHOUT SORCERY   STURGEON, THEODORE AC
  ATOMIC MONUMENT, THE (MEMORIAL)   SS C ASF 46 04
    SCIENCE FICTION WORLDS OF FORREST J. ACKERMAN & FRIENDS
                                       ACKERMAN, FORREST J. AC
  BABY IS THREE   NA   GAL 52 10
    CHILDREN OF WONDER   TENN, WILLIAM   AN
    MORE THAN HUMAN   STURGEON, THEODORE NO
    SCIENCE FICTION HALL OF FAME VOLUME 2A BOVA, BEN   AN
  BEWARE THE FURY (SEE EXTRAPOLATION)   TC
  BIANCA'S HANDS   SS   ARB 47 05
    E PLURIBUS UNICORN   STURGEON, THEODORE AC
    SHOCKING THING, A   KNIGHT, DAMON   AN
  BLABBERMOUTH   SS   AMZ 47 02
    CAVIAR   STURGEON, THEODORE AC
  BONES, THE   SS   UNK 43 08
    BEYOND   STURGEON, THEODORE AC
  BRAT   SS   UNK 41 12
    NOT WITHOUT SORCERY   STURGEON, THEODORE AC
    WITHOUT SORCERY   STURGEON, THEODORE AC
  BRIGHT SEGMENT   NV   NEW 55 AC
    CAVIAR   STURGEON, THEODORE AC
  BROWNSHOES   SS   KNT 69
    STURGEON IS ALIVE AND WELL...   STURGEON, THEODORE AC
  BULKHEAD (WHO?)   NV   GAL 55 03
    SF: THE BEST OF THE BEST   MERRIL, JUDITH   AN
    SF: THE YEAR'S GREATEST SCIENCE FICTION AND FANTASY
                                       MERRIL, JUDITH   AN
    THUNDER AND ROSES   STURGEON, THEODORE AC
    *WAY HOME, A   STURGEON, THEODORE AC
  BUTYL AND THE BREATHER   NV   ASF 40 10
    NOT WITHOUT SORCERY   STURGEON, THEODORE AC
    WITHOUT SORCERY   STURGEON, THEODORE AC
  CACTUS DANCE   NV   LSW 54 10
    ALIENS 4   STURGEON, THEODORE AC
  CARGO   NV   UNK 40 11
    NOT WITHOUT SORCERY   STURGEON, THEODORE AC
    WITHOUT SORCERY   STURGEON, THEODORE AC
  CASE AND THE DREAMER   NV   GAL 73 01
    CASE AND THE DREAMER   STURGEON, THEODORE AC
  CAVE OF HISTORY, THE   SS
    ANCIENT MYSTERIES READER, THE   HAINING, PETER   AN
    ENCOUNTERS WITH ALIENS   EARLEY, GEORGE W.   AN
  CAVIAR   AC   BAL 55 11
    SCIENCE FICTION SPECIAL 3   ANONYMOUS   AN
  CELLMATE   SS   WRT 47 01
    E PLURIBUS UNICORN   STURGEON, THEODORE AC

STURGEON, THEODORE (CONTINUED)
  CHROMIUM HELMET, THE   NV   ASF 46 06
    GREAT STORIES OF SCIENCE FICTION   LEINSTER, MURRAY   AN
    SCIENCE FICTION INVENTIONS   KNIGHT, DAMON   AN
  CLAUSTROPHILE, THE   NV   GAL 56 08
    FOUR FOR THE FUTURE   CONKLIN, GROFF   AN
  CLINIC, THE   SS   STR 53 02
    STAR SCIENCE FICTION STORIES NO. 2 POHL, FREDERIK   OA
  COMEDIAN'S CHILDREN, THE   NV   VSF 58 05
    ALIENS 4   STURGEON, THEODORE AC
    JOYOUS INVASION, THE   STURGEON, THEODORE AC
    NO LIMITS   FERMAN, JOSEPH W.   AN
    SF:59, THE YEAR'S GREATEST SCIENCE FICTION AND FANTASY
                                       MERRIL, JUDITH   AN
    STRANGE TOMORROWS   HOSKINS, ROBERT   AN
  COMPLETELY AUTOMATIC   SS   ASF 41 02
    *POSSIBLE WORLDS OF SCIENCE FICTION CONKLIN, GROFF   AN
  CRATE   SS   70
    STURGEON IS ALIVE AND WELL...   STURGEON, THEODORE AC
    TOMORROW, AND TOMORROW, AND TOMORROW...
                                       HEINTZ/HERBERT/JOOS/ AN
  CRIME FOR LLEWELLYN, A   NV   NEW 58 AC
    *TOUCH OF STRANGE, A   STURGEON, THEODORE AC
  DARK ROOM, THE   NV   FAN 53 08
    TIME UNTAMED   HOWARD, IVAN   AN
  DAZED   NV   GAL 71 09
    NEW AWARENESS, THE   WARRICK & GREENBERG AN
  DEADLY RATIO, THE (SEE IT WASN'T SYZYGY)   TC
  DERM FOOL   SS   UNK 40 03
    CROSSROADS IN TIME   CONKLIN, GROFF   AN
    STARSHINE   STURGEON, THEODORE AC
  DIE, MAESTRO, DIE¡   NV   DDT 49 05
    E PLURIBUS UNICORN   STURGEON, THEODORE AC
  EDUCATION OF DRUSILLA STRANGE, THE   NV   GAL 54 03
    OPERATION FUTURE   CONKLIN, GROFF   AN
  ETHER BREATHER   SS   ASF 39 09
    FIRST FLIGHT   KNIGHT, DAMON   AN
    NOT WITHOUT SORCERY   STURGEON, THEODORE AC
    WITHOUT SORCERY   STURGEON, THEODORE AC
  EXTRAPOLATION (BEWARE THE FURY)   SS   FAN 54 04
    STURGEON IN ORBIT   STURGEON, THEODORE AC
  FABULOUS IDIOT, THE   NV   NEW 53 NO
    MORE THAN HUMAN   STURGEON, THEODORE NO
  FAREWELL TO EDEN   SS   NEW 49 AC
    INVASION FROM MARS   WELLES, ORSON   AN
    *OUTER REACHES, THE   DERLETH, AUGUST   AN
  FEAR IS A BUSINESS   SS   FSF 56 08
    DECADE OF FANTASY AND SCIENCE FICTION, A
                                       MILLS, ROBERT P.   AN
    ENCOUNTERS WITH ALIENS   EARLEY, GEORGE W.   AN
  FLUFFY   SS   WRT 47 03
    E PLURIBUS UNICORN   STURGEON, THEODORE AC
  FOREWORD   IN
    LONG NIGHT OF WAITING AND OTHER STORIES
                                       ELWOOD, ROGER   OA
    STURGEON IS ALIVE AND WELL...   STURGEON, THEODORE AC
  FROM PLYNCK TO PLANCK   SF   IFS 62 01
    WORLDS OF THEODORE STURGEON, THE   STURGEON, THEODORE AC
  GHOST OF A CHANCE (THE GREEN EYED MONSTER)   SS   UNK 43 06
    CAVIAR   STURGEON, THEODORE AC
  GIRL HAD GUTS, THE   SS   VSF 57 01
    *TOUCH OF STRANGE, A   STURGEON, THEODORE AC
  GIRL WHO KNEW WHAT THEY MENT, THE   SS   70
    STURGEON IS ALIVE AND WELL...   STURGEON, THEODORE AC
  GOD IN A GARDEN, A   SS   UNK 39 10
    OTHER WORLDS, THE   STONG, PHILIP D.   AN
  GOLDEN EGG, THE   NV   UNK 41 08
    *SCIENCE FICTION THINKING MACHINES CONKLIN, GROFF   AN
  GOLDEN HELIX, THE   NA   TWS 54 SU
    THREE TIMES INFINITY   MARGULIES, LEO   AN
  GRANNY WON'T KNIT   NA   GAL 54 05
    ALL ABOUT THE FUTURE   GREENBERG , MARTIN AN
    5 GALAXY SHORT NOVELS   GOLD, H. L.   AN
  GRAVEYARD READER, THE   SS   SCF 58 10
    FANTASY: THE LITERATURE OF THE MARVELOUS
                                       KELLEY, LEO P.   AN
    GRAVEYARD READER, THE   CONKLIN, GROFF   AN
    TO HERE AND THE EASEL   STURGEON, THEODORE AC
    WEIRD SHADOWS FROM BEYOND   CARNELL, JOHN   AN
    WORLDS OF THEODORE STURGEON, THE   STURGEON, THEODORE AC
  GREEN EYED MONSTER, THE (SEE GHOST OF A CHANCE) TC
  HAG SELEEN, THE   SS   UNK 42 12
    UNKNOWN 5, THE   BENSEN, D. R.   AN
  HAUNT, THE   SS   UNK 41 04
    STARSHINE   STURGEON, THEODORE AC
  HEART, THE   SS   OWS 55 05
    STURGEON IN ORBIT   STURGEON, THEODORE AC
  HELIX THE CAT   NV   AMA 73
    ASTOUNDING   HARRISON, HARRY   OA
  HOW TO KILL AUNTY   NV   MSM 61 03
    STARSHINE   STURGEON, THEODORE AC
  HURKLE IS A HAPPY BEAST, THE   SS   FSF 49 FL
    BEST SCIENCE-FICTION STORIES: 1950, THE
                                       BLEILER & DIKTY   AN
    FIRST CONTACT   KNIGHT, DAMON   AN
    SCIENCE FICTION BESTIARY, THE   SILVERBERG, ROBERT AN
    SCIENCE FICTION GALAXY, THE   CONKLIN, GROFF   AN
    SCIENCE FICTION ROLL OF HONOR, THE POHL, FREDERIK   AN
    THUNDER AND ROSES   STURGEON, THEODORE AC
    *WAY HOME, A   STURGEON, THEODORE AC
    ZOO 2000   YOLEN, JANE   AN
  HURRICANE TRIO   NV   GAL 55 04
    *WAY HOME, A   STURGEON, THEODORE AC
  IF ALL MEN WERE BROTHERS, WOULD YOU LET ONE MARRY YOUR SISTER?
                                               NA   DVS 67 01
    CASE AND THE DREAMER   STURGEON, THEODORE AC

STURGEON, THEODORE (CONTINUED)
  DANGEROUS VISIONS   ELLISON, HARLAN   OA
INCUBI OF PARALLEL X, THE   NA PLS 51 09
  STURGEON IN ORBIT   STURGEON, THEODORE   AC
INTRODUCTION   IN
  BEYOND THE BARRIERS OF SPACE AND TIME   MERRIL, JUDITH   AN
  CAUTION| INFLAMMABLE| SCORTIA, THOMAS N.   AC
  FOUR FOR TOMORROW   ZELAZNY, ROGER   AC
  OUT OF BOUNDS   MERRIL, JUDITH   AC
  STURGEON IN ORBIT   STURGEON, THEODORE   AC
  YOUNG DEMONS   ELWOOD & GHIDALIA   AN
INTRODUCTION: ALL THE EFFINGERS AT ONCE   IN
  MIXED FEELINGS   EFFINGER, GEO. ALEC AC
INTRODUCTION: THE WONDER-FULL AGE   IN
  SCIENCE FICTION TALES   ELWOOD, ROGER   OA
IT   NV UNK 40 08
  BR-R-R-| CONKLIN, GROFF   AN
  CREATURES FROM BEYOND   CARR, TERRY   AN
  DARK SIDE, THE   KNIGHT, DAMON   AN
  NOT WITHOUT SORCERY   STURGEON, THEODORE   AC
  WITHOUT SORCERY   STURGEON, THEODORE   AC
IT OPENS THE SKY   NV VSF 57 11
  *TOUCH OF STRANGE, A   STURGEON, THEODORE   AC
IT WAS NOTHING- REALLY| SS   69
  ANTIGRAV: COSMIC COMEDIES   STRICK, PHILIP   AN
  STURGEON IS ALIVE AND WELL...   STURGEON, THEODORE   AC
IT WASN'T SYZYGY (THE DEADLY RATIO)   NV WRT 48 01
  E PLURIBUS UNICORN   STURGEON, THEODORE   AC
IT'S YOU| SS KNT 69
  STURGEON IS ALIVE AND WELL...   STURGEON, THEODORE   AC
JORRY'S GAP   SS KNT 69
  STURGEON IS ALIVE AND WELL...   STURGEON, THEODORE   AC
KILLDOZER| SN ASF 44 11
  ALIENS 4   STURGEON, THEODORE   AC
  *BEST OF SCIENCE FICTION   CONKLIN, GROFF   AN
  SPECTRUM 3   AMIS & CONQUEST   AN
  WONDERMAKERS   HOSKINS, ROBERT   AN
LARGO   SS FAD 47 07
  BEYOND   STURGEON, THEODORE   AC
LAST LAUGH (SEE SPECIAL APTITUDE)   TC
LIKE YOUNG   SS FSF 60 03
  BEYOND   STURGEON, THEODORE   AC
LOVE OF HEAVEN, THE   SS ASF 48 11
  *SCIENCE FICTION ADVENTURES IN MUTATION   CONKLIN, GROFF   AN
MAKE ROOM FOR ME   NV FAD 51 05
  STURGEON IN ORBIT   STURGEON, THEODORE   AC
MAN WHO LEARNED LOVING, THE   SS FSF 69 10
  BEST FROM FANTASY AND SCIENCE FICTION: 19 FERMAN, EDWARD L.   AN
  NEBULA AWARD STORIES NO. 5   BLISH, JAMES   AN
  NEW AWARENESS, THE   WARRICK & GREENBERG AN
MAN WHO LOST THE SEA, THE   SS FSF 59 10
  BEST FROM FANTASY AND SCIENCE FICTION: 9 MILLS, ROBERT P.   AN
  BEYOND BELIEF   HURLEY, RICHARD J.   AN
  FIRST STEP OUTWARD   HOSKINS, ROBERT   AN
  TOWARD INFINITY   KNIGHT, DAMON   AN
  5TH ANNUAL OF THE YEAR'S BEST S-F, THE   MERRIL, JUDITH   AN
MARTIAN AND THE MORON, THE   NV WRT 49 03
  GHOUL KEEPERS, THE   MARGULIES, LEO   AN
  NEW WORLDS FOR OLD   DERLETH, AUGUST   AN
  *WORLDS OF TOMORROW   DERLETH, AUGUST   AN
MATURITY   NV ASF 47 02
  WITHOUT SORCERY   STURGEON, THEODORE   AC
  WORLDS OF THEODORE STURGEON, THE   STURGEON, THEODORE   AC
  6 GREAT SHORT NOVELS OF SCIENCE FICTION   CONKLIN, GROFF   AN
MEDUSA   SS ASF 42 02
  CAVIAR   STURGEON, THEODORE   AC
MEMORIAL (SEE ALSO ATOMIC MEMORIAL)   SS ASF 46 04
  HISTORY OF THE SCIENCE FICTION MAGAZINE, THE PART 3 1946-1955
                                            ASHLEY, MICHAEL   AN
  *OTHER SIDE OF THE MOON, THE   DERLETH, AUGUST   AN
  SCIENCE FICTION TERROR TALES   CONKLIN, GROFF   AN
  WITHOUT SORCERY   STURGEON, THEODORE   AC
  WORLDS OF THEODORE STURGEON, THE   STURGEON, THEODORE   AC
MEMORY   NV TWS 48 08
  ADVENTURES IN TOMORROW   CROSSEN, KENDELL F. AN
MEWHU'S JET   NV ASF 46 11
  *BIG BOOK OF SCIENCE FICTION   CONKLIN, GROFF   AN
  SCIENCE FICTION: THE GREAT YEARS, VOL. II POHL, C. & F.   AN
  THUNDER AND ROSES   STURGEON, THEODORE   AC
  *WAY HOME, A   STURGEON, THEODORE   AC
MICROCOSMIC GOD   NV ASF 41 04
  CAVIAR   STURGEON, THEODORE   AC
  GIANTS UNLEASHED   CONKLIN, GROFF   AN
  MICROCOSMIC GOD   MOSKOWITZ, SAM   AN
  MODERN MASTERPIECES OF SCIENCE FICTION   MOSKOWITZ, SAM   AN
  POCKET BOOK OF SCIENCE-FICTION, THE   WOLLHEIM, DONALD A. AN
  SCIENCE FICTION HALL OF FAME VOLUME 1   SILVERBERG, ROBERT   AN
  WITHOUT SORCERY   STURGEON, THEODORE   AC
MINORITY REPORT   SS ASF 49 06
  *BEYOND TIME AND SPACE   DERLETH, AUGUST   AN
  THUNDER AND ROSES   STURGEON, THEODORE   AC
  *WAY HOME, A   STURGEON, THEODORE   AC
MORALITY   NV NEW 53 NO
  MORE THAN HUMAN   STURGEON, THEODORE   NO
MORE THAN HUMAN   NO FSY 52
  SCIENCE FICTION ARGOSY, A   KNIGHT, DAMON   AN
MOVER, THE SHAKER, THE   IN
  I HAVE NO MOUTH, AND I MUST SCREAM   ELLISON, HARLAN   AC
MR. COSTELLO, HERO   NV GAL 53 12
  ABOVE THE HUMAN LANDSCAPE   MCNELLY & STOVER   AN
  ASSIGNMENT IN TOMORROW   POHL, FREDERICK   AN
  CONNOISSEUR'S S. F.   BOARDMAN, TOM JR.   AN

STURGEON, THEODORE (CONTINUED)
  *TOUCH OF STRANGE, A   STURGEON, THEODORE   AC
MUSIC, THE   SS NEW 53 AC
  E PLURIBUS UNICORN   STURGEON, THEODORE   AC
NAIL AND THE ORACLE, THE   NV PBY 65 10
  FROM THE "S" FILE   PLAYBOY, EDITORS OF AN
  PLAYBOY BOOK OF SCIENCE FICTION AND FANTASY, THE
                                            PLAYBOY, EDITORS OF AN
NEBULA AWARD S. F., 1965-1970, THE FICTION   MS
  NEBULA AWARD STORIES NO. 7   BIGGLE, LLOYD JR.   AN
NECESSARY AND SUFFICIENT   SS GAL 71 04
  BEST FROM GALAXY, THE VOLUME I   GALAXY, EDITORS OF   AN
NEED   NV NEW 60 AC
  BEYOND   STURGEON, THEODORE   AC
NEVER UNDERESTIMATE...   SS IFS 52 03
  OMNIBUS OF SCIENCE FICTION   CONKLIN, GROFF   AN
  STRANGE ADVENTURES IN SCIENCE FICTION   CONKLIN, GROFF   AN
  17 X INFINITY   CONKLIN, GROFF   AN
NIGHTMARE ISLAND   NV UNK 41 06
  BEYOND   STURGEON, THEODORE   AC
OCCAM'S SCALPEL   NV IFS 71 08
  BEST FROM IF, THE VOLUME I   IF, EDITORS OF   AN
  BEST SCIENCE FICTION OF THE YEAR, THE   CARR, TERRY   AN
  BEST SCIENCE FICTION STORIES OF THE YEAR (1971)
  1972 ANNUAL WORLD'S BEST SF, THE   WOLLHEIM, DONALD A. AN
ONE FOOT AND THE GRAVE   NV WRT 49 09
  3 TO THE HIGHEST POWER   NOLAN, WILLIAM F.   AN
OTHER CELIA, THE   NV GAL 57 03
  ONE HUNDRED YEARS OF SCIENCE FICTION   KNIGHT, DAMON   AN
  *TOUCH OF STRANGE, A   STURGEON, THEODORE   AC
OTHER MAN, THE   NA GAL 56 09
  SF:57, THE YEAR'S GREATEST SCIENCE FICTION AND FANTASY
                                            MERRIL, JUDITH   AN
  WORLDS OF THEODORE STURGEON, THE   STURGEON, THEODORE   AC
PATTERNS OF DORNE, THE   SS   70
  STURGEON IS ALIVE AND WELL...   STURGEON, THEODORE   AC
PERFECT HOST, THE   NV WRT 48 11
  *BEYOND HUMAN KEN   MERRIL, JUDITH   AN
  TO HERE AND THE EASEL   STURGEON, THEODORE   AC
  WORLDS OF THEODORE STURGEON, THE   STURGEON, THEODORE   AC
POD AND THE BARRIER, THE   NA GAL 57 09
  STARSHINE   STURGEON, THEODORE   AC
  *TOUCH OF STRANGE, A   STURGEON, THEODORE   AC
POKER FACE   SS ASF 41 03
  NOT WITHOUT SORCERY   STURGEON, THEODORE   AC
  WITHOUT SORCERY   STURGEON, THEODORE   AC
PREFACE   IN
  NOT WITHOUT SORCERY   STURGEON, THEODORE   AC
PRODIGY   SS ASF 49 04
  CAVIAR   STURGEON, THEODORE   AC
PROFESSOR'S TEDDY-BEAR, THE   SS WRT 48 03
  E PLURIBUS UNICORN   STURGEON, THEODORE   AC
  UNEXPECTED, THE   MARGULIES, LEO   AN
RULE OF THREE   NV GAL 51 01
  *GALAXY READER OF SCIENCE FICTION   GOLD, H. L.   AN
RUNESMITH   SS C FSF 70 05
  PARTNERS IN WONDER   ELLISON, HARLAN   AN
SAUCER OF LONELINESS   SS GAL 53 02
  E PLURIBUS UNICORN   STURGEON, THEODORE   AC
  FLYING SAUCERS IN FACT AND FICTION   SANTESSON, HANS S.   AN
  GALAXY SCIENCE FICTION OMNIBUS   GOLD, H. L.   AN
  SECOND GALAXY READER OF SCIENCE FICTION
                                            GOLD, H. L.   AN
  WORLDS OF SCIENCE FICTION, THE   MILLS, ROBERT P.   AN
SCARS   SS ZGW 49 05
  E PLURIBUS UNICORN   STURGEON, THEODORE   AC
SEX OPPOSITE, THE   SS FAN 52 FL
  E PLURIBUS UNICORN   STURGEON, THEODORE   AC
SHADOW, SHADOW, ON THE WALL   SS IMG 51 02
  CAVIAR   STURGEON, THEODORE   AC
  OTHER WORLDS, OTHER TIMES   MOSKOWITZ & ELWOOD   AN
SHOTTLE BOP   SS UNK 41 02
  EDGE OF NEVER, THE   HOSKINS, ROBERT   AN
  INVISIBLE MEN   DAVENPORT, BASIL   AN
  SUPERNATURAL READER, THE   CONKLIN, G&L.   AN
  TO HERE AND THE EASEL   STURGEON, THEODORE   AC
  WITHOUT SORCERY   STURGEON, THEODORE   AC
  WORLDS OF THEODORE STURGEON, THE   STURGEON, THEODORE   AC
SILKEN-SWIFT, THE   SS FSF 53 11
  E PLURIBUS UNICORN   STURGEON, THEODORE   AC
SKILLS OF XANADU, THE   NV GAL 56 07
  ALPHA 5   SILVERBERG, ROBERT   AN
  TO HERE AND THE EASEL   STURGEON, THEODORE   AC
  WORLDS OF THEODORE STURGEON, THE   STURGEON, THEODORE   AC
  13 GREAT STORIES OF SCIENCE FICTION   CONKLIN, GROFF   AN
SKY WAS FULL OF SHIPS, THE   SS TWS 47 06
  SHAPE OF THINGS, THE   KNIGHT, DAMON   AN
  SHOT IN THE DARK   MERRIL, JUDITH   AN
  WORLDS OF THEODORE STURGEON, THE   STURGEON, THEODORE   AC
SLOW SCULPTURE   NV GAL 70 02
  NEBULA AWARD STORIES NO. 6   SIMAK, CLIFFORD D.   AN
  SPECULATIONS   SANDERS, THOMAS E.   AN
  STURGEON IS ALIVE AND WELL...   STURGEON, THEODORE   AC
  WORLD'S BEST SCIENCE FICTION: 1971   WOLLHEIM & CARR   AN
SPECIAL APTITUDE (LAST LAUGH)   SS OWS 51 03
  *WAY HOME, A   STURGEON, THEODORE   AC
STARS ARE THE STYX, THE   NV GAL 50 10
  *GALAXY READER OF SCIENCE FICTION   GOLD, H. L.   AN
SUICIDE   SS KNT 70
  STURGEON IS ALIVE AND WELL...   STURGEON, THEODORE   AC
TAKE CARE OF JOEY   SS   70
  STURGEON IS ALIVE AND WELL...   STURGEON, THEODORE   AC
TALENT   SS BEY 53 09
  BEYOND   ANONYMOUS   AN
  FIFTY SHORT SCIENCE FICTION TALES   ASIMOV & CONKLIN   AN

STURGEON, THEODORE   SZILARD, LEO

STURGEON, THEODORE (CONTINUED)
    ZACHERLEY'S MIDNIGHT SNACKS   ZACHERLEY   AN
                                            SS   FFM 48 10
    THAT LOW
        SCIENCE FICTION SHOWCASE   KORNBLUTH, MARY   AN
    THERE IS NO DEFENSE   NV   ASF 48 02
        TO HERE AND THE EASEL   STURGEON, THEODORE AC
        WORLDS OF THEODORE STURGEON, THE STURGEON, THEODORE AC
        3 IN 1   MARGULIES, LEO   AN
    THUNDER AND ROSES   SS   ASF 47 11
       *ASTOUNDING SCIENCE FICTION ANTHOLOGY, THE
                                         CAMPBELL, JOHN W. JR AN
        ASTOUNDING TALES OF SPACE AND TIME CAMPBELL, JOHN W. JR AN
        ASTOUNDING-ANALOG READER, THE VOLUME TWO
                                         HARRISON & ALDISS   AN
       *FIRST ASTOUNDING SCIENCE FICTION ANTHOLOGY, THE
                                         CAMPBELL, JOHN W. JR AN
       *MY BEST SCIENCE FICTION STORY   MARGULIES & FRIEND AN
       *STRANGE PORTS OF CALL   DERLETH, AUGUST   AN
        THUNDER AND ROSES   STURGEON, THEODORE AC
       *WAY HOME, A   STURGEON, THEODORE AC
    TINY AND THE MONSTER   NV   ASF 47 05
       *INVADERS OF EARTH   CONKLIN, GROFF   AN
        THUNDER AND ROSES   STURGEON, THEODORE AC
       *WAY HOME, A   STURGEON, THEODORE AC
    TO HERE AND THE EASEL   SN   SSN 54
        STAR SHORT NOVELS   POHL, FREDERIK   OA
        STURGEON IS ALIVE AND WELL...   STURGEON, THEODORE AC
        TO HERE AND THE EASEL   STURGEON, THEODORE AC
    TO MARRY MEDUSA   NA   GAL 58 08
        JOYOUS INVASION, THE   STURGEON, THEODORE AC
    TIME WAITS FOR WINTHROP, AND FOUR OTHER SHORT NOVELS
                                         POHL, FREDERIK   AN
    TOUCH OF STRANGE, A   SS   FSF 58 01
       *TOUCH OF STRANGE, A   STURGEON, THEODORE AC
        TWENTY YEARS OF FANTASY & SCIENCE FICTION
                                         FERMAN & MILLS   AN
    TOUCH OF YOUR HAND, THE   NA   GAL 53 09
       *TOUCH OF STRANGE, A   STURGEON, THEODORE AC
    TRAVELING CRAG, THE   NV   FAD 51 07
        AWARD SCIENCE FICTION READER   NORTON, ALDEN H.   AN
    TWINK   SS   GAL 55 08
        CAVIAR   STURGEON, THEODORE AC
    TWO PERCENT INSPIRATION   SS   ASF 41 10
        NOT WITHOUT SORCERY   STURGEON, THEODORE AC
        WITHOUT SORCERY   STURGEON, THEODORE AC
    ULTIMATE EGOIST, THE   NV   UNK 41 02
        HUMAN?   MERRIL, JUDITH   AN
        WITHOUT SORCERY   STURGEON, THEODORE AC
    UNCLE FREMMIS   SS   KNT 70
        STURGEON IS ALIVE AND WELL...   STURGEON, THEODORE AC
    UNITE AND CONQUER   NV   ASF 48 10
        JOURNEY TO INFINITY   GREENBERG, MARTIN   AN
       *WAY HOME, A   STURGEON, THEODORE AC
    WAGES OF SYNERGY, THE   NV   STS 53 08
        BEST FROM STARTLING STORIES, THE MINES, SAMUEL   AN
        STURGEON IN ORBIT   STURGEON, THEODORE AC
    WAY HOME, A   SS   AMZ 53 05
        THUNDER AND ROSES   STURGEON, THEODORE AC
       *WAY HOME, A   STURGEON, THEODORE AC
    WAY OF THINKING, A   NV   AMZ 53 11
        E PLURIBUS UNICORN   STURGEON, THEODORE AC
        GALAXY OF GHOULS   MERRIL, JUDITH   AN
    WHAT DEAD MEN TELL   NV   ASF 49 11
       *IMAGINATION UNLIMITED   BLEILER & DIKTY   AN
    WHEN YOU CARE, WHEN YOU LOVE   NV   FSF 62 09
        BEST FROM FANTASY AND SCIENCE FICTION, 25TH ANNIV.
                                         FERMAN, EDWARD L.   AN
        CASE AND THE DREAMER   STURGEON, THEODORE AC
        ONCE AND FUTURE TALES FROM THE MAGAZINE OF FANTASY AND
            SCIENCE FICTION   FERMAN, EDWARD L.   AN
    WHEN YOU'RE SMILING   NV   GAL 55 01
        BEST SF 2   CRISPIN, EDMUND   AN
    WHY I SELECTED THUNDER AND ROSES   AI
       *MY BEST SCIENCE FICTION STORY   MARGULIES & FRIEND AN
    WHY?   AR   CLR 73 03
        CLARION III   WILSON, ROBIN SCOTT OA
    (WIDGET), THE (WADGET), AND BOFF, THE   SN   FSF 55 11
        ALIENS 4   STURGEON, THEODORE AC
        JOYOUS INVASION, THE   STURGEON, THEODORE AC
        TREASURY OF GREAT SCIENCE FICTION, A VOL.1
                                         BOUCHER, ANTHONY   AN
    WON'T YOU WALK?   NV   ASF 56 01
        DIMENSION 4   CONKLIN, GROFF   AN
    WORLD WELL LOST, THE   SS   USF 53 06
        E PLURIBUS UNICORN   STURGEON, THEODORE AC
        SOCIAL PROBLEMS THROUGH SCIENCE FICTION
                                         GREENBERG/MILSTEAD/& AN
        STARSHINE   STURGEON, THEODORE AC
        STRANGE BED FELLOWS   SCORTIA, THOMAS N. AN
       *TWISTED   CONKLIN, GROFF   AN
    YESTERDAY WAS MONDAY   SS   UNK 41 06
        FROM UNKNOWN WORLDS   CAMPBELL, JOHN W. JR AN
       *SCIENCE FICTION ADVENTURES IN DIMENSION
                                         CONKLIN, GROFF   AN
        UNKNOWN, THE   BENSEN, D. R.   AN

STYRON, WILLIAM
    PIE IN THE SKY   SS   NEW 66 AN
        VINTAGE ANTHOLOGY OF SCIENCE FANTASY, THE
                                         CERF, CHRISTOPHER   AN

SUDBERY, TONY
    SCIENCE OF FICTION? A SURVEY OF ATTITUDES   AR
        BEYOND THIS HORIZON   CARRELL, CHRISTOPHER OA

SUGGS, ROBERT C.
    KON-TIKI MYTH, THE   AR   60
        APEMAN, SPACEMAN   STOVER & HARRISON   AN

SULLIVAN, CHARLES W.
    AS TOMORROW BECOMES TODAY   AN L PRH 74
        AFTERWORD   MS
            AS TOMORROW BECOMES TODAY   SULLIVAN, CHARLES W. AN
        INTRODUCTION   IN
            AS TOMORROW BECOMES TODAY   SULLIVAN, CHARLES W. AN
        PREFACE   IN
            AS TOMORROW BECOMES TODAY   SULLIVAN, CHARLES W. AN

SULLIVAN, JAMES F.
    IMPOSSIBILITY, A STUDY OF REASON AND SCIENCE SS   00
        ANCESTRAL VOICES   MENVILLE & REGINALD AN

SULLIVAN, JEAN
    MORE I CANNOT WISH YOU   SS   CLR 73 03
        CLARION III   WILSON, ROBIN SCOTT OA

SUTHERLAND, HERB
    BLOND KID, THE   SS
        AD 2500   WILSON, ANGUS   AN

SUTHERLAND, JAMES
    AT THE SECOND SOLSTICE   SS   CLR 72 02
        CLARION II   WILSON, ROBIN SCOTT OA
    BESIDE STILL WATERS   SS C GEN 72
        GENERATION   GERROLD, DAVID   OA
    SWORDS OF IFTHAN   SS   OMG 73
        OMEGA   ELWOOD, ROGER   OA

SUTTON, JEFF
    AFTER IXMAL   SS   AMZ 62 10
        SPACE OPERA   ALDISS, BRIAN W.   AN
    FORERUNNER   SS   NEW 73 AN
        ANDROIDS, TIME MACHINES AND BLUE GIRAFFES
                                         ELWOOD & GHIDALIA   AN

SUTTON, LEE
    SOUL MATE   SS   FSF 59 06
        BEST FROM FANTASY AND SCIENCE FICTION: 9
                                         MILLS, ROBERT P.   AN
        OTHER WORLDS, OTHER GODS   MOHS, MAYO   AN

SUVIN, DARKO
    OTHER WORLDS, OTHER SEAS   AN H RDM 70
        PREFACE   IN
            OTHER WORLDS, OTHER SEAS   SUVIN, DARKO   AN
    SF NOVEL IN 1969, THE   AR
        NEBULA AWARD STORIES NO. 5   BLISH, JAMES   AN

SWAN, VIRGINIA
    AUNT CASSIE   SS   NEW 41 AN
        OTHER WORLDS, THE   STONG, PHILIP D.   AN

SWANN, THOMAS B.
    MANOR OF ROSES, THE   SN   FSF 66 11
        ONCE AND FUTURE TALES FROM THE MAGAZINE OF FANTASY AND
            SCIENCE FICTION   FERMAN, EDWARD L.   AN

SWANSON, LOGAN   PSEUD. FOR RICHARD MATHESON
    LIKENESS OF JULIE, THE   SS   NEW 62 AN
        ALONE BY NIGHT   CONGDON, MICHAEL&DON AN

SWENSON, MAY
    EARTH WILL NOT LET GO   PM   70
        SPECULATIONS   SANDERS, THOMAS E. AN
    ORBITER 5 SHOWS HOW EARTH LOOKS FROM THE MOON PM SOU 69
        SCIENCE FACT/FICTION   FARRELL/GAGE/&   AN
        SCIENCE FICTION   BRODKIN & PEARSON   AN
    SOUTHBOUND ON THE FREEWAY   PM   NYM 63 02
        ANOTHER TOMORROW   HOLLISTER, BERNARD C AN

SWIFT, JONATHAN
    FLYING ISLAND, THE (FROM "THE THIRD VOYAGE OF GULLIVER", 1726)
                                            EX
        SCIENCE IN FICTION   BAYLISS, A.E. & J.C. AN
    FROM "GULLIVER'S TRAVELS"   EX
        PAST, PRESENT, AND FUTURE PERFECT WOLFE, J&FITZ GERALD AN
    LAPUTA (FROM "GULLIVER'S TRAVELS", 1726) EX
       *BEYOND TIME AND SPACE   DERLETH, AUGUST   AN
    LAPUTAN PROJECTS (FROM "GULLIVER'S TRAVELS") EX
        ARMCHAIR SCIENCE READER, THE   GORDON, I. & SORKIN AN
    SATIRICAL SCIENCE FICTION (FROM "GULLIVER'S TRAVELS")
                                            EX
        SCIENCE FICTION THROUGH THE AGES 1 EVANS, I. O.   AN

SWISHER, ROBERT D.
    LETTER   MS   ASF 38 11
        MEN AND THE MIRROR, THE   ROCKLYNNE, ROSS   AC

SYNGE, J. L.
    EUCLID AND THE BRIGHT BOY   SS
        MATHEMATICAL MAGPIE, THE   FADIMAN, CLIFTON   AN
    O'BRIEN'S TABLE   SS   51
        MATHEMATICAL MAGPIE, THE   FADIMAN, CLIFTON   AN
    TENDING TO INFINITY   PM   57
        MATHEMATICAL MAGPIE, THE   FADIMAN, CLIFTON   AN

SZILARD, LEO
    VOICE OF THE DOLPHINS, AND OTHER STORIES, THE AC H SAS 61
    CALLING ALL STARS   SS   61
        VOICE OF THE DOLPHINS, AND OTHER STORIES, THE
                                         SZILARD, LEO   AC

SZILARD, LEO   (CONTINUED)
   GRAND CENTRAL TERMINAL   SS   UCM 52 06
      GREAT SCIENCE FICTION BY SCIENTISTS CONKLIN, GROFF   AN
   MARK GABLE FOUNDATION, THE   SS   61
      EXPERT DREAMERS, THE   POHL, FREDERIK   AN
      LIGHT FANTASTIC, THE   HARRISON, HARRY   AN
      VOICE OF THE DOLPHINS, AND OTHER STORIES, THE
                                          SZILARD, LEO   AC
   MY TRIAL AS A WAR CRIMINAL   SS   UCL 49 FL
      VOICE OF THE DOLPHINS, AND OTHER STORIES, THE
                                          SZILARD, LEO   AC
      7TH ANNUAL OF THE YEAR'S BEST S-F, THE MERRIL, JUDITH   AN
   REPORT ON "GRAND CENTRAL TERMINAL"   SS   UCM 52 06
      VOICE OF THE DOLPHINS, AND OTHER STORIES, THE
                                          SZILARD, LEO   AC
   VOICE OF THE DOLPHINS, THE   SS
      VOICE OF THE DOLPHINS, AND OTHER STORIES, THE
                                          SZILARD, LEO   AC

TAFOYA, ALFONSO
   BIRDS OF PREY   PM   NWQ 74 06
      NEW WORLDS NO. 6   PLATT & BAILEY   OA
   MY MISTRESS   PM   NWQ 74 06
      NEW WORLDS NO. 6   PLATT & BAILEY   OA
   PASTORAL, A   PM   NWQ 74 06
      NEW WORLDS NO. 6   PLATT & BAILEY   OA

TAINE, JOHN   PSEUD. FOR ERIC TEMPLE BELL
   THREE SCIENCE FICTION NOVELS   AC L DOV 64
   BEFORE THE DAWN (ALSO IN FFM 46 02)   NO   WMW 34
      PORTABLE NOVELS OF SCIENCE   WOLLHEIM, DONALD A.   AN
   GREATEST ADVENTURE, THE (SEE THE GREATEST GAME)   TC
   PURPLE SAPPHIRE, THE   NO   DUT 24
      THREE SCIENCE FICTION NOVELS   TAINE, JOHN   AC
   TIME STREAM, THE   NO   WOS 31 12
      THREE SCIENCE FICTION NOVELS   TAINE, JOHN   AC
   ULTIMATE CATALYST, THE   NV   TWS 39 06
      *BEST OF SCIENCE FICTION   CONKLIN, GROFF   AN
      *MY BEST SCIENCE FICTION STORY   MARGULIES & FRIEND   AN
   WHY I SELECTED THE ULTIMATE CATALYST   AI
      *MY BEST SCIENCE FICTION STORY   MARGULIES & FRIEND   AN

TAKEI, GEORGE
   INTRODUCTION TO THE FACE ON THE BARROOM FLOOR   IN
      STAR TREK: THE NEW VOYAGES   MARSHAK, S&CULBREATH OA

TALL, STEPHEN   PSEUD. FOR COMPTON N. CROOK
   STARDUST VOYAGES, THE   AC   BKM 75 10
   ALLISON, CARMICHAEL AND TATTERSALL   NV   GAL 70 04
      BEST FROM GALAXY, THE   VOLUME I   GALAXY, EDITORS OF   AN
   BEAR WITH THE KNOT ON HIS TAIL, THE   NV   FSF 71 05
      BEST FROM FANTASY AND SCIENCE FICTION: 20
                                          FERMAN, EDWARD L.   AN
      STARDUST VOYAGES, THE   TALL, STEPHEN   AC
      1972 ANNUAL WORLD'S BEST SF, THE   WOLLHEIM, DONALD A.   AN
   BIRDS FLY SOUTH IN WINTER   NV   GAL 71 11
      STARDUST VOYAGES, THE   TALL, STEPHEN   AC
   FOREWORD   IN
      STARDUST VOYAGES, THE   TALL, STEPHEN   AC
   GODS ON OLYMPUS, THE   NA   IFS 72 10
      STARDUST VOYAGES, THE   TALL, STEPHEN   AC
   INVADERS, THE   NV   IFS 73 08
      STARDUST VOYAGES, THE   TALL, STEPHEN   AC
   MUSHROOM WORLD   NA   FSF 74 11
      STARDUST VOYAGES, THE   TALL, STEPHEN   AC
   STAR CALLED CYRENE, A (70 LIGHT-YEARS FROM SOL)   NV   WOT 66 11
      STARDUST VOYAGES, THE   TALL, STEPHEN   AC
   70 LIGHT-YEARS FROM SOL (SEE A STAR CALLED CYRENE)
                                          TC

TANGUY, YVES
   LARGE PAINTING WHICH IS A LANDSCAPE, A   IL
      SCIENCE FICTION   BRODKIN & PEARSON   AN
   MAMA, PAPA IS WOUNDED| IL
      SCIENCE FICTION   BRODKIN & PEARSON   AN

TANNER, CHARLES R.
   ANGUS MACAULIFFE AND THE GOWDEN TOOCH   SS   OWS 51 03
      SUPERNATURAL READER, THE   CONKLIN, G&L.   AN
   OUT OF THE JAR   SS   STI 41 02
      ZACHERLEY'S VULTURE STEW   ZACHERLEY   AN
   TUMITHAK IN SHAWM   NV   AMZ 33 06
      BEFORE THE GOLDEN AGE   ASIMOV, ISAAC   AN
   TUMITHAK OF THE CORRIDORS   NV   AMZ 32 01
      BEFORE THE GOLDEN AGE   ASIMOV, ISAAC   AN

TARKINGTON, BOOTH
   VEILED FEMINISTS OF ATLANTIS, THE   SS   FRM 26 03
      WHEN WOMEN RULE   MOSKOWITZ, SAM   AN

TASSONE, G. L.
   ROOM 312   SS   PBY 67 08
      PLAYBOY'S STORIES OF THE SINISTER & STRANGE
                                          PLAYBOY, EDITORS OF AN

TATE, PETER
   SEAGULLS UNDER GLASS AND OTHER STORIES   AC H DBL 75
   BEYOND THE WEEDS (THE POST-MORTEM PEOPLE)   SS   NWS 66 03
      SF12   MERRIL, JUDITH   AN
   CRUMBLING HOLLYWOOD MANSION, CRUMBLING HOLLYWOOD MAN (PROTEST)
                                                       SS   GAL 74 02
      SEAGULLS UNDER GLASS AND OTHER STORIES TATE, PETER   AC
   DAY THE WIND DIED, THE   NV   FSF 69 03
      SEAGULLS UNDER GLASS AND OTHER STORIES TATE, PETER   AC
   DAYLENGTH TALKING BLUES   SS
      SEAGULLS UNDER GLASS AND OTHER STORIES TATE, PETER   AC

TATE, PETER   (CONTINUED)
   DEAR WITCH HAZEL, MY BIRDS WON'T FLY   NV
      SEAGULLS UNDER GLASS AND OTHER STORIES TATE, PETER   AC
   FIFTH PERSON SINGULAR   SS   NWS 66 05
      NEW WORLDS QUARTERLY NO. 2   MOORCOCK, MICHAEL   OA
   GLOOM PATTERN, THE   SS   NWS 66 06
      SEAGULLS UNDER GLASS AND OTHER STORIES TATE, PETER   AC
   MAINCHANCE   NV   ANA 70
      ALCHEMY AND ACADEME   MCCAFFREY, ANNE   OA
      ANDROIDS, TIME MACHINES AND BLUE GIRAFFES
                                          ELWOOD & GHIDALIA   AN
      SEAGULLS UNDER GLASS AND OTHER STORIES TATE, PETER   AC
   MARS PASTORALE   SS   NWS 67 08
      BEST SF STORIES FROM NEW WORLDS 5 MOORCOCK, MICHAEL   AN
      SEAGULLS UNDER GLASS AND OTHER STORIES TATE, PETER   AC
   POST-MORTEM PEOPLE, THE (ALSO AS BEYOND THE WEEDS)
                                                       SS   NWS 66 03
      BEST SF STORIES FROM NEW WORLDS 3 MOORCOCK, MICHAEL   AN
      SEAGULLS UNDER GLASS AND OTHER STORIES TATE, PETER   AC
      THEMES IN SCIENCE FICTION   KELLEY, LEO P.   AN
   PROTEST (SEE CRUMBLING HOLLYWOOD MANSION, CRUMBLING
      HOLLYWOOD MAN)   TC
   SAME AUTUMN IN A DIFFERENT PARK   SS   FAN 67 09
      ENGLAND SWINGS SF   MERRIL, JUDITH   AN
      SEAGULLS UNDER GLASS AND OTHER STORIES TATE, PETER   AC
      SPACE-TIME JOURNAL, THE   MERRIL, JUDITH   AN
   SEAGULLS UNDER GLASS   SS
      SEAGULLS UNDER GLASS AND OTHER STORIES TATE, PETER   AC
   SKYHAMMER   SS
      SEAGULLS UNDER GLASS AND OTHER STORIES TATE, PETER   AC
   WELCOME TO THE LAND OF SMILES   SS
      SEAGULLS UNDER GLASS AND OTHER STORIES TATE, PETER   AC

TAVES, ERNEST
   MAYFLOWER ONE   NV   GAL 72 11
      BEST FROM GALAXY, THE   VOLUME II GALAXY, EDITORS OF   AN

TAYLOR, BERNARD
   FORGET-ME-NOT   SS   NEW 75 AN
      YEAR'S BEST HORROR STORIES: SERIES III, THE
                                          DAVIS, RICHARD   AN

TAYLOR, JOHN
   END OF THE UNIVERSE?, THE   AR   LIS 71 09
      BEYOND THIS HORIZON   CARRELL, CHRISTOPHER OA
   SURVIVAL OF THE FITTEST   PL
      BEYOND THIS HORIZON   CARRELL, CHRISTOPHER OA

TAYLOR, ROBERT
   SENSE OF BEAUTY, A   SS   FSF 68 08
      SF: AUTHORS' CHOICE 4   HARRISON, HARRY   AN

TEICHNER, ALBERT
   CHRISTLINGS   SS   ORB 72 10
      ORBIT 10   KNIGHT, DAMON   OA
   FANTASY'S PROFESSION   SS   ORB 74 13
      ORBIT 13   KNIGHT, DAMON   OA
   JUNKMAKERS, THE   NV   IFS 61 07
      6 FINGERS OF TIME AND 5 OTHER SCIENCE FICTION NOVELETS, THE
                                          ANONYMOUS   AN

TELEMAQUE, HERVE
   PIEGE   IL
      SCIENCE FICTION   BRODKIN & PEARSON   AN

TELFAIR, DAVID
   IN A QUART OF WATER   SS   ANA 70
      ALCHEMY AND ACADEME   MCCAFFREY, ANNE   OA

TEMPLE, WILLARD
   ETERNAL DUFFER, THE   SS   SEP 46 01
      SATURDAY EVENING POST FANTASY STORIES, THE
                                          FLES, BARTHOLD   AN

TEMPLE, WILLIAM F.
   COCO-TALK   SS   NWR 66 07
      NEW WRITINGS IN SF. 7   CARNELL, JOHN   OA
   COUNTER-TRANSFERENCE   NV   TWS 52 04
      BEST SCIENCE-FICTION STORIES: 1953, THE
                                          BLEILER & DIKTY   AN
   DATE TO REMEMBER, A   SS   TWS 49 08
      *INVADERS OF EARTH   CONKLIN, GROFF   AN
      SPECULATIONS   SANDERS, THOMAS E.   AN
   EXPLORERS OF MARS   SS
      AUTHENTIC BOOK OF SPACE   CAMPBELL, H. J.   AN
   FORGET-ME-NOT   NV   OWS 50 09
      BEST SCIENCE-FICTION STORIES: 1951, THE
                                          BLEILER & DIKTY   AN
   NICHE IN TIME, A   SS   ASF 64 05
      WORLD'S BEST SCIENCE FICTION: 1965 WOLLHEIM & CARR   AN
   SMILE OF THE SPHINX, THE   SS   TOW 38 FL
      ESCALES DANS L'INFINI   GALLET, GEORGES H.   AN
   TWO SHADOWS, THE   NV   STS 51 03
      BEST SCIENCE-FICTION STORIES: 1952, THE
                                          BLEILER & DIKTY   AN
      *NO PLACE LIKE EARTH   CARNELL, JOHN   AN
   UNDISCOVERED COUNTRY, THE   SS   NEB 58 10
      SEA OF SPACE, A   NOLAN, WILLIAM F.   AN
   UNPICKER, THE   SS   NEW 73 AN
      ANDROIDS, TIME MACHINES AND BLUE GIRAFFES
                                          ELWOOD & GHIDALIA   AN
   WAY OF ESCAPE   SS   TWS 48 06
      ADVENTURES IN DIMENSION   CONKLIN, GROFF   AN
      *SCIENCE FICTION ADVENTURES IN DIMENSION
                                          CONKLIN, GROFF   AN

TEMPLE, WILLIAM F.

TEMPLE, WILLIAM F.   (CONTINUED)
  WHISPERING GALLERY, THE   SS   FUN 53 10
    ZACHERLEY'S MIDNIGHT SNACKS   ZACHERLEY   AN
  4-SIDED TRIANGLE, THE   NV   AMZ 39 11
    HISTORY OF THE SCIENCE FICTION MAGAZINE, THE PART 2 1936-1945
                                       ASHLEY, MICHAEL   AN

TENN, WILLIAM   PSEUD. FOR PHILIP KLASS
  CHILDREN OF WONDER   AN H SAS 53
    ALSO AS "OUTSIDERS: CHILDREN OF WONDER"
  HUMAN ANGLE, THE   AC   BAL 56 08
  OF ALL POSSIBLE WORLDS   AC   BAL 55
  OUTSIDERS: CHILDREN OF WONDER   AN   PMA 54
    SEE "CHILDREN OF WONDER"
  SEVEN SEXES, THE   AC   BAL 68 06
  SQUARE ROOT OF MAN, THE   AC   BAL 68 06
  TIME IN ADVANCE   AC   BAN 58 06
  WOODEN STAR, THE   AC   BAL 68 06
  ALEXANDER THE BAIT   SS   ASF 46 05
    OMNIBUS OF SCIENCE FICTION   CONKLIN, GROFF   AN
    SQUARE ROOT OF MAN, THE   TENN, WILLIAM   AC
  AUTHOR'S NOTE   IN
    SEVEN SEXES, THE   TENN, WILLIAM   AC
    SQUARE ROOT OF MAN, THE   TENN, WILLIAM   AC
    WOODEN STAR, THE   TENN, WILLIAM   AC
  BERNIE THE FAUST   NV   PBY 63 11
    BEST FROM NEW WRITINGS IN S-F FIRST SELECTION, THE
                                       CARNELL, JOHN   AN
    NEW WRITINGS IN SF. 4   CARNELL, JOHN   OA
    PLAYBOY BOOK OF SCIENCE FICTION AND FANTASY, THE
                                       PLAYBOY, EDITORS OF AN
    SCIENCE FICTION ARGOSY, A   KNIGHT, DAMON   AN
    SEVEN SEXES, THE   TENN, WILLIAM   AC
    TRANSIT OF EARTH   PLAYBOY, EDITORS OF AN
    9TH ANNUAL OF THE YEAR'S BEST S-F, THE MERRIL, JUDITH
  BETELGEUSE BRIDGE   SS   GAL 51 04
    *GALAXY READER OF SCIENCE FICTION GOLD, H. L.   AN
    TOMORROW, THE STARS   HEINLEIN, ROBERT A. AN
    WOODEN STAR, THE   TENN, WILLIAM   AC
  BROOKLYN PROJECT   SS   PLS 48 FL
    SHOT IN THE DARK   MERRIL, JUDITH   AN
    VOYAGERS IN TIME   SILVERBERG, ROBERT   AN
    WOODEN STAR, THE   TENN, WILLIAM   AC
    17 X INFINITY   CONKLIN, GROFF   AN
  CHILD'S PLAY   NV   ASF 47 03
    *ASTOUNDING SCIENCE FICTION ANTHOLOGY, THE
                                       CAMPBELL, JOHN W. JR AN
    ASTOUNDING-ANALOG READER, THE VOLUME TWO
                                       HARRISON & ALDISS   AN
    BEYOND CONTROL   SILVERBERG, ROBERT   AN
    *FIRST ASTOUNDING SCIENCE FICTION ANTHOLOGY, THE
                                       CAMPBELL, JOHN W. JR AN
    GALAXY OF GHOULS   MERRIL, JUDITH   AN
    SECOND ASTOUNDING SCIENCE FICTION ANTHOLOGY, THE (PB)
                                       CAMPBELL, JOHN W. JR AN
    SEVEN SEXES, THE   TENN, WILLIAM   AC
    *TREASURY OF SCIENCE FICTION, A   CONKLIN, GROFF   AN
    WORLD OF WONDER   PRATT, FLETCHER   AN
  CONFUSION CARGO   SS   PLS 48 SP
    SQUARE ROOT OF MAN, THE   TENN, WILLIAM   AC
  CONSULATE   SS   TWS 48 06
    SQUARE ROOT OF MAN, THE   TENN, WILLIAM   AC
  CUSTODIAN, THE   NV   IFS 53 11
    MASTERS' CHOICE   JANIFER, LAURENCE M. AN
    OF ALL POSSIBLE WORLDS   TENN, WILLIAM   AC
  DARK STAR, THE   SS   GAL 57 09
    WOODEN STAR, THE   TENN, WILLIAM   AC
  DESERTER, THE   SS   STR 53 01
    BUG-EYED MONSTERS   CHEETHAM, ANTHONY   AN
    STAR SCIENCE FICTION STORIES   POHL, FREDERIK   OA
    WOODEN STAR, THE   TENN, WILLIAM   AC
  DID YOUR COFFEE TASTE FUNNY THIS MORNING? (SEE LEMON-GREEN
    SPAGHETTI-LOUD DYNAMITE-..)   TC
  DISCOVERY OF MORNIEL MATHAWAY, THE   SS   GAL 55 10
    HUMAN ANGLE, THE   TENN, WILLIAM   AC
  DOWN AMONG THE DEAD MEN   NV   GAL 54 06
    ALPHA 6   SILVERBERG, ROBERT   AN
    EVIL EARTHS   ALDISS, BRIAN W.   AN
    HUMAN AND OTHER BEINGS   DEGRAEFF, ALLEN   AN
    OF ALL POSSIBLE WORLDS   TENN, WILLIAM   AC
  EASTWARD HO!   SS   FSF 58 10
    ALPHA 4   SILVERBERG, ROBERT   AN
    BEST FROM FANTASY AND SCIENCE FICTION: 9
                                       MILLS, ROBERT P.   AN
    WONDERMAKERS 2   HOSKINS, ROBERT   AN
    WOODEN STAR, THE   TENN, WILLIAM   AC
    YET MORE PENGUIN SCIENCE FICTION ALDISS, BRIAN W.   AN
  ERRAND BOY   SS   ASF 47 06
    CHILDREN OF WONDER   TENN, WILLIAM   AC
    SEVEN SEXES, THE   TENN, WILLIAM   AC
  EVERYBODY LOVES IRVING BOMMER   SS   FAD 51 08
    OF ALL POSSIBLE WORLDS   TENN, WILLIAM   AC
  FIREWATER   SN   ASF 52 02
    ALIENS, THE   SILVERBERG, ROBERT   AN
    STRANGE TOMORROWS   HOSKINS, ROBERT   AN
    TIME IN ADVANCE   TENN, WILLIAM   AC
    YEAR'S BEST SCIENCE FICTION NOVELS: 1953
                                       BLEILER & DIKTY   AN
  FLAT-EYED MONSTER, THE   NV   GAL 55 08
    HUMAN ANGLE, THE   TENN, WILLIAM   AC
  FLIRGLEFLIP (THE REMARKABLE FLIRGLEFLIP)   SS   FAD 50 05
    OF ALL POSSIBLE WORLDS   TENN, WILLIAM   AC
  GENERATION OF NOAH   SS   SUS 51 SP
    BEST SCIENCE-FICTION STORIES: 1952, THE
                                       BLEILER & DIKTY   AN
    FRONTIERS IN SPACE   BLEILER & DIKTY   AN

TENN, WILLIAM

TENN, WILLIAM   (CONTINUED)
    WOODEN STAR, THE   TENN, WILLIAM   AC
  HOUSE DUTIFUL, THE   SS   ASF 48 04
    *BEYOND HUMAN KEN   MERRIL, JUDITH   AN
    SEVEN SEXES, THE   TENN, WILLIAM   AC
  HUMAN ANGLE, THE   SS   FFM 48 10
    HUMAN ANGLE, THE   TENN, WILLIAM   AC
  INTRODUCTION   IN
    CHILDREN OF WONDER   TENN, WILLIAM   AN
  IONIAN CIRCLE, THE   SS   TWS 49 08
    TRAVELLERS OF SPACE   GREENBERG, MARTIN   AN
  IT ENDS WITH A FLICKER (OF ALL POSSIBLE WORLDS) SS GAL 56 12
    WOODEN STAR, THE   TENN, WILLIAM   AC
  JESTER, THE   SS   TWS 51 08
    *SCIENCE FICTION THINKING MACHINES CONKLIN, GROFF   AN
    SQUARE ROOT OF MAN, THE   TENN, WILLIAM   AC
  LAST BOUNCE, THE   NV   FAD 50 09
    SQUARE ROOT OF MAN, THE   TENN, WILLIAM   AC
  LEMON-GREEN SPAGHETTI-LOUD DYNAMITE-DRIBBLE DAY (DID YOUR COFFE
    TASTE FUNNY THIS MORNING?)   SS   CAV 67 01
    SQUARE ROOT OF MAN, THE   TENN, WILLIAM   AC
  LIBERATION OF EARTH, THE   SS   FUT 53 05
    INVADERS FROM SPACE   SILVERBERG, ROBERT   AN
    LIBERATED FUTURE: VOYAGES INTO TOMORROW, THE
                                       HOSKINS, ROBERT   AN
    MORE PENGUIN SCIENCE FICTION   ALDISS, BRIAN W.   AN
    OF ALL POSSIBLE WORLDS   TENN, WILLIAM   AC
    SCIENCE FICTION: THE GREAT YEARS POHL, C. & F.   AN
    STARLIT CORRIDOR, THE   MANSFIELD, ROGER   AN
    TOMORROW AND TOMORROW   KNIGHT, DAMON   AN
  LISBON CUBED   NV   GAL 58 10
    WOODEN STAR, THE   TENN, WILLIAM   AC
  MALTED MILK MONSTER, THE   NV   GAL 59 08
    SEVEN SEXES, THE   TENN, WILLIAM   AC
  MAN OF FAMILY, A   SS
    HUMAN ANGLE, THE   TENN, WILLIAM   AC
  MASCULINIST REVOLT, THE   NV   FSF 65 08
    ONCE AND FUTURE TALES FROM THE MAGAZINE OF FANTASY AND
      SCIENCE FICTION   FERMAN, EDWARD L.   AN
    WOODEN STAR, THE   TENN, WILLIAM   AC
  ME, MYSELF, AND I   SS   PLS 47 WI
    OF ALL POSSIBLE WORLDS   TENN, WILLIAM   AC
  MISTRESS SARY   SS   WRT 47 05
    SEVEN SEXES, THE   TENN, WILLIAM   AC
  MY MOTHER WAS A WITCH   SS   66
    SQUARE ROOT OF MAN, THE   TENN, WILLIAM   AC
  NULL-P   SS   WBY 51 01
    *SPECTRUM   AMIS & CONQUEST   AN
    STARS AND UNDER, THE   CRISPIN, EDMUND   AN
    WOODEN STAR, THE   TENN, WILLIAM   AC
    *WORLDS OF TOMORROW   DERLETH, AUGUST   AN
  OF ALL POSSIBLE WORLDS (SEE IT ENDS WITH A FLICKER)
                                                 TC
  ON THE FICTION IN SCIENCE FICTION   IN   SFA 54 03
    OF ALL POSSIBLE WORLDS   TENN, WILLIAM   AC
  ON VENUS, HAVE WE GOT A RABBI   NV   NEW 74 AN
    BEST SCIENCE FICTION OF THE YEAR, THE NO. 4
                                       CARR, TERRY   AN
    WANDERING STARS   DANN, JACK M.   AN
  PARTY OF THE TWO PARTS   NV   GAL 54 08
    CRIME PREVENTION IN THE 30TH CENTURY SANTESSON, HANS S. AN
    GENTLE INVADERS   SANTESSON, HANS S.   AN
    HUMAN ANGLE, THE   TENN, WILLIAM   AC
  PROJECT HUSH   SS   GAL 54 02
    ABC OF SCIENCE FICTION, AN   BOARDMAN, TOM JR.   AN
    FIFTY SHORT SCIENCE FICTION TALES ASIMOV & CONKLIN   AN
    HUMAN ANGLE, THE   TENN, WILLIAM   AC
  REMARKABLE FLIRGLEFLIP, THE (SEE FLIRGLEFLIP) TC
  SANCTUARY   SS   GAL 57 12
    SEVEN SEXES, THE   TENN, WILLIAM   AC
  SERVANT PROBLEM, THE   NV   GAL 55 04
    HUMAN ANGLE, THE   TENN, WILLIAM   AC
    SEVEN COME INFINITY   CONKLIN, GROFF   AN
  SHE ONLY GOES OUT AT NIGHT   SS   FUN 56 10
    FANTASTIC UNIVERSE OMNIBUS, THE   SANTESSON, HANS S.   AN
    SQUARE ROOT OF MAN, THE   TENN, WILLIAM   AC
  SICKNESS, THE   NV   INF 55 11
    OUT OF THIS WORLD 6   WILLIAMS-ELLIS& OWEN AN
    TIME IN ADVANCE   TENN, WILLIAM   AC
    TOMORROW 1   HOSKINS, ROBERT   AN
  TENANTS, THE   SS   FSF 54 04
    OF ALL POSSIBLE WORLDS   TENN, WILLIAM   AC
  TIME IN ADVANCE   NV   GAL 56 08
    INTRODUCING SCIENCE FICTION   ALDISS, BRIAN W.   AN
    TIME IN ADVANCE   TENN, WILLIAM   AC
  TIME WAITS FOR WINTHROP (ALSO AS WINTHROP WAS STUBBORN)
                                                 NA   GAL 57 08
    TIME WAITS FOR WINTHROP, AND FOUR OTHER SHORT NOVELS
                                       POHL, FREDERIK   AN
  VENUS AND THE SEVEN SEXES   NV   49
    GIRL WITH THE HUNGRY EYES, AND OTHER STORIES, THE
                                       WOLLHEIM, DONALD A. OA
    INFINITE JESTS   SILVERBERG, ROBERT   AN
    *SCIENCE-FICTION CARNIVAL   BROWN, F. & REYNOLDS AN
    SEVEN SEXES, THE   TENN, WILLIAM   AC
  VENUS IS A MAN'S WORLD   NV   GAL 51 07
    *GALAXY READER OF SCIENCE FICTION GOLD, H. L.   AN
    GIANTS UNLEASHED   CONKLIN, GROFF   AN
    SQUARE ROOT OF MAN, THE   TENN, WILLIAM   AC
  WEDNESDAY'S CHILD   SS   FUN 56 01
    HUMAN ANGLE, THE   TENN, WILLIAM   AC
    WEIRD SHADOWS FROM BEYOND   CARNELL, JOHN   AN
  WILL YOU WALK A LITTLE FASTER?   SS   MAR 51 11
    *INVADERS OF EARTH   CONKLIN, GROFF   AN
    WOODEN STAR, THE   TENN, WILLIAM   AC

TENN, WILLIAM   TIME MAGAZINE

TENN, WILLIAM   (CONTINUED)
  WINTHROP WAS STUBBORN (TIME WAITS FOR WINTHROP)   NA   GAL 57 08
    OUT OF THIS WORLD 5   WILLIAMS-ELLIS& OWEN AN
    TIME IN ADVANCE   TENN, WILLIAM   AC

TENNANT, EMMA
  CRACK, THE   NV   NWB 73 05
    NEW WORLDS QUARTERLY NO. 5   MOORCOCK, MICHAEL   OA

TESLER, O.
  CARTOON   CT   SME
    BEST SF: 1972   HARRISON & ALDISS   AN

TEVIS, WALTER S. JR.
  BIG BOUNCE, THE   SS   GAL 58 02
    WHERE DO WE GO FROM HERE?   ASIMOV, ISAAC   AN
  FAR FROM HOME   SS   FSF 58 12
    BEST FROM FANTASY AND SCIENCE FICTION: 9
                                       MILLS, ROBERT P.   AN
  IFTH OF OOFTH, THE   SS   GAL 57 04
    SCIENCE FACT/FICTION   FARRELL/GAGE/&   AN
    SIXTH GALAXY READER, THE   GOLD, H. L.   AN

THARP, BEEBE
  HARP THAT CONQUERED HELL, THE   SS
    NEW CONSTELLATIONS   DISCH & NAYLOR   OA

THAYER, FRANK D.
  FAMILY TREE   SS
    TRAVELLERS BY NIGHT   DERLETH, AUGUST   OA

THEALL, DONALD F.
  INTRODUCTION   IN
    SURVIVAL SHIP AND OTHER STORIES   MERRIL, JUDITH   AC

THELWELL
  INSTRUCTOR   CT   PUN 61 01
    6TH ANNUAL OF THE YEAR'S BEST S-F, THE MERRIL, JUDITH   AN

THOLE, KAREL
  SCIENCE FICTION COVER ILLUSTRATIONS   IL
    BEYOND THIS HORIZON   CARRELL, CHRISTOPHER OA

THOMAS, D. M.
  HEAD-RAPE, THE   PM   NWS 68 03
    BEST SF STORIES FROM NEW WORLDS 4 MOORCOCK, MICHAEL   AN
  HOLDING YOUR EIGHT HANDS   LUCIE-SMITH, EDWARD   AN
  HOSPITAL OF TRANSPLANTED HEARTS   SS   NWS 69 01
    BEST SF: 1969   HARRISON & ALDISS   AN
  MISSIONARY   PM   PMP 68 11
    HOLDING YOUR EIGHT HANDS   LUCIE-SMITH, EDWARD   AN
  NIGHT-MARRIAGE   PM   NWQ 73 05
    NEW WORLDS NO. 5   MOORCOCK & PLATT   OA
  NOTES TOWARD A SUPREME SCIENCE FICTION   PM
    BEYOND THIS HORIZON   CARRELL, CHRISTOPHER OA
  SEEKING A SUITABLE DONOR   SS
    NEW S.F., THE   JONES, LANGDON   OA
  SONORAN POEMS   SS   NWB 73 05
    NEW WORLDS QUARTERLY NO. 5   MOORCOCK, MICHAEL   OA
  SPECTRUM, THE   PM   NWS 69 02
    BEST SF STORIES FROM NEW WORLDS 5 MOORCOCK, MICHAEL   AN
  TITHONUS   PM   PMP 68 11
    HOLDING YOUR EIGHT HANDS   LUCIE-SMITH, EDWARD   AN
    SCIENCE FICTION: THE FUTURE   ALLEN, DICK   AN

THOMAS, GILBERT
  LUANA   SS   FSF 66 09
    BEST FROM FANTASY AND SCIENCE FICTION: 16
                                       FERMAN, EDWARD L.   AN
    SF12   MERRIL, JUDITH   AN

THOMAS, JOHN B.
  PUBLISH AND PERISH   SS   IFS 68 06
    SCHOOL AND SOCIETY THROUGH SCIENCE FICTION
                                       OLANDER/GREENBERG/&   AN
  RETURN TO A HOSTILE PLANET   SS   STG 74
    STRANGE GODS   ELWOOD, ROGER   OA

THOMAS, THEODORE L.   ALSO AS   LEONARD LOCKHARD
  CLONE, THE   SS   FAN 59 12
    SHOCKING THING, A   KNIGHT, DAMON   AN
  DAY OF SUCCESSION   SS   ASF 59 08
    CENTURY OF SCIENCE FICTION, A   KNIGHT, DAMON   AN
  DECEMBER 28TH   SS   PBY 59 12
    LAST TRAIN TO LIMBO   PLAYBOY, EDITORS OF   AN
    PLAYBOY BOOK OF SCIENCE FICTION AND FANTASY, THE
                                       PLAYBOY, EDITORS OF   AN
  DOCTOR, THE   SS   ORB 67 02
    ALPHA 1   SILVERBERG, ROBERT   AN
    BEST FROM ORBIT, THE   KNIGHT, DAMON   AN
    ORBIT 2   KNIGHT, DAMON   OA
  EARLY BIRD   SS C AMA 73
    ASTOUNDING   HARRISON, HARRY   OA
    BEST SF: 1973   HARRISON & ALDISS   AN
  FAR LOOK, THE   NV   ASF 56 08
    LOOKING AHEAD   ALLEN, D. & L.   AN
    SCIENCE FICTION NOVELLAS   HARRISON & MCNELLY   AN
    SF:57, THE YEAR'S GREATEST SCIENCE FICTION AND FANTASY
                                       MERRIL, JUDITH   AN
    SPECTRUM 5   AMIS & CONQUEST   AN
  INTRUDER, THE   SS   FSF 61 02
    POCKETFUL OF STARS, A   KNIGHT, DAMON   AN
  LONELY MAN, THE   NV   GAL 63 04
    EIGHTH GALAXY READER, THE   POHL, FREDERICK   AN
  SATELLITE PASSAGE   SS   IFS 58 12
    SF: THE BEST OF THE BEST   MERRIL, JUDITH   AN

THOMAS, THEODORE L.   (CONTINUED)
    SF:59, THE YEAR'S GREATEST SCIENCE FICTION AND FANTASY
                                       MERRIL, JUDITH   AN
  TEST   SS   FSF 62 04
    BEST FROM FANTASY AND SCIENCE FICTION: 12
                                       DAVIDSON, AVRAM   AN
  WEATHER MAN, THE   SN   ASF 62 06
    ANALOG 2   CAMPBELL, JOHN W. JR AN
    ASTOUNDING-ANALOG READER, THE VOLUME TWO
                                       HARRISON & ALDISS   AN
    DAYS AFTER TOMORROW, THE   SANTESSON, HANS S.   AN
    TIME PROBE: THE SCIENCES IN SF.   CLARKE, ARTHUR C.   AN
  WEATHER ON THE SUN, THE   NV   ORB 70 08
    ORBIT 8   KNIGHT, DAMON   OA

THOMPSON, DON
  WORLDS ENOUGH   SS
    BEYOND TIME   LEY, SANDRA   OA

THOMPSON, J. C.
  RIGHT MAN FOR THE RIGHT JOB, THE   SS   62
    SHOCKING THING, A   KNIGHT, DAMON   AN

THOMPSON, R. W.
  ULTIMATE HORROR, THE   AR
    LOOKING AHEAD   ALLEN, D. & L.   AN

THOMPSON, WILL
  NO ONE BELIEVED ME   SS   SEP 48 04
    BEYOND THE BARRIERS OF SPACE AND TIME   MERRIL, JUDITH   AN

THORNE, ROGER   PSEUD. FOR RAY RUSSELL
  TAKE A DEEP BREATH   SS   TIG 56
    SF:57, THE YEAR'S GREATEST SCIENCE FICTION AND FANTASY
                                       MERRIL, JUDITH   AN

THORP, RODERICK
  SUNBURST   SS   ORB 70 06
    ORBIT 6   KNIGHT, DAMON   OA

THURBER, JAMES
  FRIEND TO ALEXANDER, A   SS   NYM 42 01
    PERCHANCE TO DREAM   KNIGHT, DAMON   AN
    TRAVELERS IN TIME   STERN, PHILIP VAN D. AN
  INTERVIEW WITH A LEMMING   SS   43
    BEST SF: 1967   HARRISON & ALDISS   AN
    SHOT IN THE DARK   MERRIL, JUDITH   AN
    ZOO 2000   YOLEN, JANE   AN

THURSTON, ROBERT
  ANACONDA   SS   CLR 71 01
    CLARION   WILSON, ROBIN SCOTT   OA
  GET FDR!   SS   CLR 72 02
    CLARION II   WILSON, ROBIN SCOTT   OA
  GOOD LIFE, THE   SS   CLR 72 02
    CLARION II   WILSON, ROBIN SCOTT   OA
  GOOD-BYE, SHELLEY, SHIRLEY, CHARLOTTE, CHARLENE   SS   ORB 72 11
    ORBIT 11   KNIGHT, DAMON   OA
  HIPPIE-DIP FILE, THE   SS   FSF 71 03
    SOCIAL PROBLEMS THROUGH SCIENCE FICTION
                                       GREENBERG/MILSTEAD/& AN
  JACK AND BETTY   SS   ORB 75 16
    ORBIT 16   KNIGHT, DAMON   OA
  KINGMAKERS   SS
    NEW VOICES IN SCIENCE FICTION   MARTIN, GEORGE R. R. OA
  LAST DESPERATE HOUR, THE   SS   CLR 71 01
    CLARION   WILSON, ROBIN SCOTT   OA
  PUNCHLINE (STOP ME BEFORE I TELL MORE)   SS   ORB 71 09
    CLARION II   WILSON, ROBIN SCOTT   OA
  SHE/HER   SS   INY 73 05
    INFINITY 5   HOSKINS, ROBERT   OA
  STOP ME BEFORE I TELL MORE (ALSO AS PUNCHLINE)   SS   ORB 71 09
    ORBIT 9   KNIGHT, DAMON   OA
  THEODORA AND THEODORA   SS   NDM 75 05
    NEW DIMENSIONS 5   SILVERBERG, ROBERT   OA
  UP AGAINST THE WALL   SS   AMZ 73 08
    SCHOOL AND SOCIETY THROUGH SCIENCE FICTION
                                       OLANDER/GREENBERG/&   AN
  WHEELS   SS   CLR 71 01
    CLARION   WILSON, ROBIN SCOTT   OA

TIGRINA   PSEUD. FOR EDYTHE EIDE
  GIRL WHO WASN'T THERE, THE   SS C GAM 63 01
    SCIENCE FICTION WORLDS OF FORREST J. ACKERMAN & FRIENDS
                                       ACKERMAN, FORREST J. AC
  LADY TAKES A POWDER, THE   SS C INS 53
    SCIENCE FICTION WORLDS OF FORREST J. ACKERMAN & FRIENDS
                                       ACKERMAN, FORREST J. AC

TILLEY, ROBERT J.
  SOMETHING ELSE   SS   FSF 65 10
    BEST FROM FANTASY AND SCIENCE FICTION: 15
                                       FERMAN, EDWARD L.   AN
    TWENTY YEARS OF FANTASY & SCIENCE FICTION
                                       FERMAN & MILLS   AN
    11TH ANNUAL OF THE YEAR'S BEST S-F, THE
                                       MERRIL, JUDITH   AN
  "WILLIE'S BLUES"   NV   FSF 72 05
    1973 ANNUAL WORLD'S BEST SF, THE   WOLLHEIM, DONALD A.   AN

TIME MAGAZINE
  NO WAY OUT, NO WAY BACK   AR   TIM 69
    SCIENCE FICTION: THE FUTURE   ALLEN, DICK   AN

TIMPERLEY, ROSEMARY
    COMPUTER THAT FELL IN LOVE, THE   SS   ADS 75 02
        ARMADA SCI-FI TWO   DAVIS, RICHARD   OA
    MR. NOBODY   SS   ADS 75 01
        ARMADA SCI-FI ONE   DAVIS, RICHARD   OA

TINCROWDER, LEO Q.
    OSIRIS ON CRUTCHES   SS C NDM 76 06
        NEW DIMENSIONS 6   SILVERBERG, ROBERT   OA

TIPTREE, JAMES JR.   PSEUD. FOR ALICE SHELDON
    TEN THOUSAND LIGHT-YEARS FROM HOME   AC   ACE 73 07
    WARM WORLDS AND OTHERWISE   AC   BAL 75 02
    ALL THE KINDS OF YES (FILOMENA & GREG & RIKKI-TIKKI & BARLOW &
        THE ALIEN)   NV   NDM 72 02
        WARM WORLDS AND OTHERWISE   TIPTREE, JAMES JR.   AC
    AMBERJACK   SS   GEN 72
        GENERATION   GERROLD, DAVID   OA
        WARM WORLDS AND OTHERWISE   TIPTREE, JAMES JR.   AC
    AND I AWOKE AND FOUND ME HERE ON THE COLD HILL'S SIDE
                                                            SS   FSF 72 03
        SPACE ODYSSEYS   ALDISS, BRIAN W.   AN
        TEN THOUSAND LIGHT-YEARS FROM HOME   TIPTREE, JAMES JR.   AC
    AND I HAVE COME UPON THIS PLACE BY LOST WAYS   NV   NOV 72 02
        NEW AWARENESS, THE   WARRICK & GREENBERG AN
        NOVA 2   HARRISON, HARRY   OA
        WARM WORLDS AND OTHERWISE   TIPTREE, JAMES JR.   AC
    BEAM US HOME   SS   GAL 69 04
        ANOTHER WORLD   DOZOIS, GARDNER R.   AN
        TEN THOUSAND LIGHT-YEARS FROM HOME   TIPTREE, JAMES JR.   AC
    BIRTH OF A SALESMAN   SS   ASF 68 03
        TEN THOUSAND LIGHT-YEARS FROM HOME   TIPTREE, JAMES JR.   AC
    FAITHFUL TO THEE, TERRA, IN OUR FASHION (PARAMUTUEL PLANET)
                                                            NV   GAL 69 01
        TEN THOUSAND LIGHT-YEARS FROM HOME   TIPTREE, JAMES JR.   AC
    FAULT   SS   FAN 68 08
        WARM WORLDS AND OTHERWISE   TIPTREE, JAMES JR.   AC
    FILOMENA & GREG & RIKKI-TIKKI & BARLOW & THE ALIEN (ALSO AS
        ALL THE KINDS OF YES)   NV   NDM 72 02
        NEW DIMENSIONS 2   SILVERBERG, ROBERT   OA
    FOREVER TO A HUDSON BAY BLANKET   SS   FAN 72 08
        TEN THOUSAND LIGHT-YEARS FROM HOME   TIPTREE, JAMES JR.   AC
    GIRL WHO WAS PLUGGED IN, THE   NV   NDM 73 03
        NEW DIMENSIONS 3   SILVERBERG, ROBERT   OA
        WARM WORLDS AND OTHERWISE   TIPTREE, JAMES JR.   AC
    HELP (PUPA KNOWS BEST)   NV   IFS 68 10
        TEN THOUSAND LIGHT-YEARS FROM HOME   TIPTREE, JAMES JR.   AC
    HER SMOKE ROSE UP FOREVER   NV   FST 74
        FINAL STAGE   FERMAN & MALZBERG   OA
    HOUSTON, HOUSTON, DO YOU READ?   NA
        AURORA: BEYOND EQUALITY   MCINTYRE & ANDERSON OA
        1977 ANNUAL WORLD'S BEST SF, THE   WOLLHEIM, DONALD A. AN
    I'LL BE WAITING FOR YOU WHEN THE SWIMMING POOL IS EMPTY
                                                            SS   PRT 71
        BEST SCIENCE FICTION STORIES OF THE YEAR (1971)
                                             DEL REY, LESTER   AN
        PROTOSTARS   GERROLD & GOLDIN   OA
        TEN THOUSAND LIGHT-YEARS FROM HOME   TIPTREE, JAMES JR.   AC
    I'M TOO BIG BUT I LOVE TO PLAY   NV   AMZ 70 03
        TEN THOUSAND LIGHT-YEARS FROM HOME   TIPTREE, JAMES JR.   AC
    LAST FLIGHT OF DR. AIN, THE   SS   GAL 69 03
        SF: AUTHORS' CHOICE 4   HARRISON, HARRY   AN
        WARM WORLDS AND OTHERWISE   TIPTREE, JAMES JR.   AC
    LOVE IS THE PLAN THE PLAN IS DEATH   SS   ALC 73
        ALIEN CONDITION, THE   GOLDIN, STEPHEN   OA
        NEBULA AWARD STORIES 9   WILHELM, KATE   AN
        WARM WORLDS AND OTHERWISE   TIPTREE, JAMES JR.   AC
    MAMMA COME HOME (THE MOTHER SHIP)   NV   IFS 68 06
        TEN THOUSAND LIGHT-YEARS FROM HOME   TIPTREE, JAMES JR.   AC
    MAN DOORS SAID HELLO TO, THE   SS   WOF 70 WI
        TEN THOUSAND LIGHT-YEARS FROM HOME   TIPTREE, JAMES JR.   AC
    MAN WHO WALKED HOME, THE   NV   AMZ 72 05
        BEST SCIENCE FICTION STORIES OF THE YEAR (1972)
                                             DEL REY, LESTER   AN
        LOOKING AHEAD   ALLEN, D. & L.   AN
        TEN THOUSAND LIGHT-YEARS FROM HOME   TIPTREE, JAMES JR.   AC
        1973 ANNUAL WORLD'S BEST SF, THE   WOLLHEIM, DONALD A. AN
    MILK OF PARADISE, THE   SS   DVS 72 02
        AGAIN, DANGEROUS VISIONS   ELLISON, HARLAN   OA
        WARM WORLDS AND OTHERWISE   TIPTREE, JAMES JR.   AC
    MOMENTARY TASTE OF BEING, A   NA   NAL 75
        NEW ATLANTIS AND OTHER NOVELLAS OF S.F., THE
                                             SILVERBERG, ROBERT   OA
    MOTHER IN THE SKY WITH DIAMONDS   NV   GAL 71 03
        BEST SCIENCE FICTION FOR 1972   POHL, FREDERIK   AN
        TEN THOUSAND LIGHT-YEARS FROM HOME   TIPTREE, JAMES JR.   AC
    MOTHER SHIP, THE (SEE MAMMA COME HOME)   TC
    NIGHTBLOOMING SAURIAN, THE   SS   IFS 70 05
        BEST FROM IF, THE VOLUME I   IF, EDITORS OF   AN
        WARM WORLDS AND OTHERWISE   TIPTREE, JAMES JR.   AC
    ON THE LAST AFTERNOON   NA   AMZ 72 11
        WARM WORLDS AND OTHERWISE   TIPTREE, JAMES JR.   AC
    PAINWISE   NV   FSF 72 02
        ALPHA 6   SILVERBERG, ROBERT   AN
        BEST SCIENCE FICTION OF THE YEAR, THE NO. 2
                                             CARR, TERRY   AN
        TEN THOUSAND LIGHT-YEARS FROM HOME   TIPTREE, JAMES JR.   AC
    PARAMUTUEL PLANET (SEE FAITHFUL TO THEE, TERRA, IN OUR FASHION)
                                                            TC
    PEACEFULNESS OF VIVYAN, THE   SS   AMZ 71 07
        TEN THOUSAND LIGHT-YEARS FROM HOME   TIPTREE, JAMES JR.   AC
    PSYCHOLOGIST WHO WOULDN'T DO AWFUL THINGS TO RATS, THE
                                                            NV   NDM 76 06
        BEST SCIENCE FICTION OF THE YEAR, THE NO. 6
                                             CARR, TERRY   AN
        NEW DIMENSIONS 6   SILVERBERG, ROBERT   OA

TIPTREE, JAMES JR.   (CONTINUED)
    PUPA KNOWS BEST (SEE HELP)   TC
    SHE WAITS FOR ALL MEN BORN   SS   76
        FUTURE POWER   DANN & DOZOIS   OA
    SNOWS ARE MELTED, THE SNOWS ARE GONE, THE   SS   VSF 69 11
        BEST SF: 1969   HARRISON & ALDISS   AN
        TEN THOUSAND LIGHT-YEARS FROM HOME   TIPTREE, JAMES JR.   AC
    THROUGH A LASS DARKLY   SS   GEN 72
        GENERATION   GERROLD, DAVID   OA
        WARM WORLDS AND OTHERWISE   TIPTREE, JAMES JR.   AC
    WOMEN MEN DON'T SEE, THE   NV   FSF 73 12
        BEST SCIENCE FICTION OF THE YEAR, THE NO. 3
                                             CARR, TERRY   AN
        BEST SF: 1974   HARRISON & ALDISS   AN
        WARM WORLDS AND OTHERWISE   TIPTREE, JAMES JR.   AC
    YOUR HAPLOID HEART   NV   ASF 69 09
        WORLD'S BEST SCIENCE FICTION: 1970   WOLLHEIM & CARR   AN

TOFTE, ARTHUR
    ALONE IN SPACE   SS   SFT 73
        SCIENCE FICTION TALES   ELWOOD, ROGER   OA
    BERSERKS, THE   SS   BER 74
        BERSERKERS, THE   ELWOOD, ROGER   OA
    CAPTURED¦   SS
        STRANGE ENCOUNTERS   BISCHOFF, DAVID   OA
    FATEFUL FIRST DAY ON XENE   NV   NEW 72 AN
        TEEN-AGE SPACE ADVENTURES   FURMAN, A. L.   AN
    SPEEDERS, THE   SS
        OTHER SIDE OF TOMORROW, THE   ELWOOD, ROGER   OA
    SURVIVAL ON A PRIMATIVE PLANET   NV
        SURVIVAL FROM INFINITY   ELWOOD, ROGER   OA
    TERRAFIED   NV   COI 73
        CHILDREN OF INFINITY   ELWOOD, ROGER   OA
    THIRST FOR BLOOD, A   NV
        MORE SCIENCE FICTION TALES   ELWOOD, ROGER   OA
    WHEN THE COLD CAME   SS
        NIGHT OF THE SPHINX AND OTHER STORIES ELWOOD, ROGER   OA

TOKUNAGA, LAURA
    BEHIND THE WALLS   SS   NWQ 73 05
        NEW WORLDS NO. 5   MOORCOCK & PLATT   OA

TOMAN, MICHAEL D.
    SHARDS OF DIVINITY   SS   SFE 74 01
        SCIENCE FICTION EMPHASIS NO. 1   GERROLD, DAVID   OA

TOMAN, NIKOLAY
    DEBATE ON SF- MOSCOW 1965, A   SS
        OTHER WORLDS, OTHER SEAS   SUVIN, DARKO   AN

TOMERLIN, JOHN
    SIDE BY SIDE   SS   PBY 64 09
        PLAYBOY BOOK OF HORROR AND THE SUPERNATURAL, THE
                                             PLAYBOY, EDITORS OF AN

TOMKINS, CALVIN
    VIRGINIA   SS   PBY 67 03
        PLAYBOY BOOK OF HORROR AND THE SUPERNATURAL, THE
                                             PLAYBOY, EDITORS OF AN

TOMPKINS, PETER
    LOVE AMONG THE CABBAGES   AR C HRP 72 11
        SCIENCE FACT/FICTION   FARRELL/GAGE/&   AN

TOOMEY, ROBERT E. JR
    LOST IN THE MARIGOLDS   NV C ORB 71 09
        ORBIT 9   KNIGHT, DAMON   OA
    RE-CREATION, THE   SS   GEN 72
        GENERATION   GERROLD, DAVID   OA

TOTAL EFFECT
    SURVIVAL PRINTOUT   AN   VNT 73
        PRINTOUT   IN
        SURVIVAL PRINTOUT   TOTAL EFFECT   AN

TOWNES, ROBERT S.
    PROBLEM FOR EMMY   SS   STS 52 06
        *SCIENCE FICTION THINKING MACHINES   CONKLIN, GROFF   AN

TOZER, D. C.
    PLANETARY SURFACES AND INTERIORS   AR
        BEYOND THIS HORIZON   CARRELL, CHRISTOPHER OA

TRACEY, ROBYN
    SIREN SINGERS   SS
        SECOND PACIFIC BOOK OF SCIENCE FICTION, THE
                                             BAXTER, JOHN   AN

TRANSUE, JACOB
    THIS CORRUPTIBLE   NV   ORB 68 04
        ORBIT 4   KNIGHT, DAMON   OA

TRAVERN, B.
    NEW GOD WAS BORN, A   AR
        ANCIENT MYSTERIES READER, THE   HAINING, PETER   AN

TRAVERS, ANDREW
    PENULTIMATE TRIP, THE   SS   SAG 70
        SCIENCE AGAINST MAN   CHEETHAM, ANTHONY   OA

TREMAINE, F. ORLIN   ALSO AS   WARNER VAN LORNE
    TRUE CONFESSION   SS   TWS 40 02
        COMING OF THE ROBOTS, THE   MOSKOWITZ, SAM   AN

TREVES, FREDERICK
ELEPHANT MAN, THE SS 23
STRANGE BEASTS AND UNNATURAL MONSTERS STERN, PHILIP VAN D. AN

TSCHIRGI, ROBERT D.
SINGULAR CASE OF EXTREME ELECTROLYTE BALANCE ASSOCIATED WITH
FOLIE A DEUX FA 65
11TH ANNUAL OF THE YEAR'S BEST S-F, THE
MERRIL, JUDITH AN

TSIOLKOVSKY, K.
ON THE MOON SS
RUSSIAN SCIENCE FICTION MAGIDOFF, ROBERT AN

TUBB, E. C. ALSO AS CHARLES GREY
ALIEN DUST NO H BDM 55
SCATTER OF STARDUST, A DC ACE 72
TEN FROM TOMORROW AC H HDV 66
ALIEN DUST SS NWS 53 01
ALIEN DUST TUBB, E. C. NO
ANNE SS NWS 66 01
SCATTER OF STARDUST, A TUBB, E. C. DC
BELLS OF ACHERON, THE SS SCF 57 04
SCATTER OF STARDUST, A TUBB, E. C. DC
ENCHANTER'S ENCOUNTER NV SCF 59 12
SCATTER OF STARDUST, A TUBB, E. C. DC
EVANE SS NWR 73 22
NEW WRITINGS IN SF. 22 BULMER, KENNETH OA
1974 ANNUAL WORLD'S BEST SF, THE WOLLHEIM, DONALD A. AN
EYES OF SILENCE, THE SS INF 57 04
SCATTER OF STARDUST, A TUBB, E. C. DC
FACE TO INFINITY SS NWR 76 28
NEW WRITINGS IN SF. 28 BULMER, KENNETH OA
FRESH GUY SS SCF 58 06
SF:59, THE YEAR'S GREATEST SCIENCE FICTION AND FANTASY
MERRIL, JUDITH AN
SPECULATIONS SANDERS, THOMAS E. AN
TEN FROM TOMORROW TUBB, E. C. AC
WEIRD SHADOWS FROM BEYOND CARNELL, JOHN AN
GREATER THAN INFINITY SS NWS 60 11
TEN FROM TOMORROW TUBB, E. C. AC
HOME IS THE HERO SS NWS 52 05
ALIEN DUST TUBB, E. C. NO
GATEWAY TO TOMORROW CARNELL, JOHN AN
J IS FOR JEANNE SS NWS 65 12
11TH ANNUAL OF THE YEAR'S BEST S-F, THE
MERRIL, JUDITH AN
LAST DAY OF SUMMER, THE SS SCF 55 02
SF: THE YEAR'S GREATEST SCIENCE FICTION AND FANTASY
MERRIL, JUDITH AN
TEN FROM TOMORROW TUBB, E. C. AC
LAST OF THE MORTICIANS SS GAL 59 10
TEN FROM TOMORROW TUBB, E. C. AC
LAZARUS SS
BEYOND THIS HORIZON CARRELL, CHRISTOPHER OA
LITTLE GIRL LOST SS NWS 55 10
SCATTER OF STARDUST, A TUBB, E. C. DC
LUCIFER! SS VOT 69 11
YEAR'S BEST HORROR STORIES, THE DAVIS, RICHARD AN
MADE TO BE BROKEN SS NWR 74 23
NEW WRITINGS IN SF. 23 BULMER, KENNETH OA
MEN ONLY SS NWS 52 07
ALIEN DUST TUBB, E. C. NO
MING VASE, THE SS ASF 63 05
TEN FROM TOMORROW TUBB, E. C. AC
9TH ANNUAL OF THE YEAR'S BEST S-F, THE MERRIL, JUDITH AN
MISTAKEN IDENTITY SS SPC 73 01
SPACE 1 DAVIS, RICHARD OA
NEW EXPERIENCE SS NWS 64 10
BEST OF NEW WORLDS, THE MOORCOCK, MICHAEL AN
OPERATION MARS NO NEB 54 12
ALIEN DUST TUBB, E. C. NO
PIEBALD HORSE SS ASF 60 11
TEN FROM TOMORROW TUBB, E. C. AC
PISTOL POINT SS NWS 53 06
ALIEN DUST TUBB, E. C. NO
RANDOM SAMPLE SS NWR 76 29
NEW WRITINGS IN SF. 29 BULMER, KENNETH OA
RETURN VISIT SS SCF 58 04
DEVIL HIS DUE, THE HILL, DOUGLAS AN
SCATTER OF STARDUST, A TUBB, E. C. DC
ROCKETS AREN'T HUMAN SS NWS 53 03
BEST FROM NEW WORLDS SCIENCE FICTION, THE
CARNELL, JOHN AN
SEEKERS, THE SS NWR 65 06
NEW WRITINGS IN SF. 6 CARNELL, JOHN OA
SENSE OF PROPORTION NV NEB 58 07
DIMENSION 4 CONKLIN, GROFF AN
TEN FROM TOMORROW TUBB, E. C. AC
WINDOW ON THE FUTURE HILL, DOUGLAS AN
SHRINE, THE (AS ALAN GUTHRIE) SS NWS 60 02
SCATTER OF STARDUST, A TUBB, E. C. DC
SURVIVAL DEMANDS SS NWS 60 02
SCATTER OF STARDUST, A TUBB, E. C. DC
TELL THE TRUTH SS ASF 59 12
TEN FROM TOMORROW TUBB, E. C. AC
UNFORTUNATE PURCHASE SS SCF 54 03
GATEWAY TO THE STARS CARNELL, JOHN AN
VIGIL SS GAL 56 11
TEN FROM TOMORROW TUBB, E. C. AC
WAGER, THE NV SCF 55 11
HISTORY OF THE SCIENCE FICTION MAGAZINE, THE PART 3 1946-1955
ASHLEY, MICHAEL AN
WITHOUT BUGLES SS NWS 52 01
ALIEN DUST TUBB, E. C. NO

TUBB, E. C. (CONTINUED)
WORM IN THE WOODWORK NV ASF 62 01
TEN FROM TOMORROW TUBB, E. C. AC

TUCKER, ARTHUR W. SEE PSEUD. BOB TUCKER AND WILSON TUCKER

TUCKER, BOB PSEUD. FOR ARTHUR WILSON TUCKER
TOURIST TRADE, THE SS WBY 51 01
TOMORROW, THE STARS HEINLEIN, ROBERT A. AN

TUCKER, LOUIS
CUBIC CITY, THE SS SWS 29 09
FROM OFF THIS WORLD MARGULIES & FRIEND AN

TUCKER, WILSON PSEUD. FOR ARTHUR WILSON TUCKER
SCIENCE FICTION SUBTREASURY, THE AC H RIN 54 09
ALSO AS "TIME: X"
TIME: X AC BAN 55 12
SEE "THE SCIENCE FICTION SUBTREASURY"
ABLE TO ZEBRA SS FSF 53 03
SCIENCE FICTION SUBTREASURY, THE TUCKER, WILSON AC
EXIT SS AST 43 04
EDITOR'S CHOICE IN SCIENCE FICTION MOSKOWITZ, SAM AN
SCIENCE FICTION SUBTREASURY, THE TUCKER, WILSON AC
GENTLEMEN- THE QUEEN! SS SFQ 42 FL
SCIENCE FICTION SUBTREASURY, THE TUCKER, WILSON AC
HOME IS WHERE THE WRECK IS SS USF 54 05
SCIENCE FICTION SUBTREASURY, THE TUCKER, WILSON AC
INTRODUCTION IN
SCIENCE FICTION SUBTREASURY, THE TUCKER, WILSON AC
JOB IS ENDED, THE SS OWS 50 11
SCIENCE FICTION SUBTREASURY, THE TUCKER, WILSON AC
MCMLV SS USF 54 11
SCIENCE FICTION SUBTREASURY, THE TUCKER, WILSON AC
MOUNTAIN JUSTICE (SEE THE MOUNTAINEER) TC
MOUNTAINEER, THE (MOUNTAIN JUSTICE) SS FND 53 12
SCIENCE FICTION SUBTREASURY, THE TUCKER, WILSON AC
MY BROTHER'S WIFE SS FSF 51 02
SCIENCE FICTION SUBTREASURY, THE TUCKER, WILSON AC
STREET WALKER, THE SS
SCIENCE FICTION SUBTREASURY, THE TUCKER, WILSON AC
TIME EXPOSURES NV UNI 71 01
UNIVERSE 1 CARR, TERRY OA
TO A RIPE OLD AGE SS FSF 52 12
SHADOW OF TOMORROW POHL, FREDERIK AN
TOURIST TRADE, THE SS WBY 51 01
BEST SCIENCE-FICTION STORIES: 1952, THE
BLEILER & DIKTY AN
WAYFARING STRANGERS, THE SS FWS 52 FL
SCIENCE FICTION SUBTREASURY, THE TUCKER, WILSON AC

TURNER, STEPHEN C.
LOOKING BACK SS
QUEST BISCHOFF, DAVID OA

TUSHNET, LEONARD
AUNT JENNIE'S TONIC SS FSF 71 12
ANTHROPOLOGY THROUGH SCIENCE FICTION MASON, C/GREENBERG/& AN
1972 ANNUAL WORLD'S BEST SF, THE WOLLHEIM, DONALD A. AN
GIFTS FROM THE UNIVERSE SS FSF 68 05
BEST FROM FANTASY AND SCIENCE FICTION: 18
FERMAN, EDWARD L. AN
IN RE GLOVER SS DVS 72 02
AGAIN, DANGEROUS VISIONS ELLISON, HARLAN OA
BIO-FUTURES SARGENT, PAMELA AN
PLAGUE OF CARS, A SS NDM 71 01
NEW DIMENSIONS 1 SILVERBERG, ROBERT OA

TUTTLE, LISA
CHANGELINGS SS GAL 75 03
BEST SF: 75, THE NINTH ANNUAL HARRISON & ALDISS AN
FAMILY MONKEY, THE SS
NEW VOICES IN SCIENCE FICTION MARTIN, GEORGE R. R. OA
I HAVE HEARD THE MERMAIDS SS
SURVIVAL FROM INFINITY ELWOOD, ROGER OA
STORMS OF WINDHAVEN, THE NV C ASF 75 05
BEST SCIENCE FICTION OF THE YEAR, THE NO. 5
CARR, TERRY AN
1976 ANNUAL WORLD'S BEST SF, THE WOLLHEIM, DONALD A. AN
STRANGER IN THE HOUSE SS CLR 72 02
CLARION II WILSON, ROBIN SCOTT OA
TILL HUMAN VOICES WAKE US... SS CLR 73 03
CLARION III WILSON, ROBIN SCOTT OA
WOMAN WAITING NV
LONE STAR UNIVERSE PROCTOR & UTLEY OA

TWAIN, MARK PSEUD. FOR SAMUEL L. CLEMENS
CONNECTICUT YANKEE IN KING ARTHUR'S COURT, A EX HRP 89
STORIES OF SCIENTIFIC IMAGINATION GALLANT, JOSEPH AN
EXTRACT FROM CAPTAIN STORMFIELD'S VISIT TO HEAVEN EX HRP 07 12
GOLDEN ROAD, THE KNIGHT, DAMON AN
FROM THE "LONDON TIMES" OF 1904 SS CNY 98 11
CENTURY OF SCIENCE FICTION, A KNIGHT, DAMON AN
FUTURE PERFECT FRANKLIN, H. BRUCE AN
FROM- A CONNECTICUT YANKEE IN KING ARTHUR'S COURT EX HRP 89
PAST, PRESENT, AND FUTURE PERFECT WOLFE, J&FITZ GERALD AN
SOLD TO SATAN SS
LIGHT FANTASTIC, THE HARRISON, HARRY AN
THREE THOUSAND YEARS AMONG THE MICROBES SS
IN DREAMS AWAKE FIEDLER, LESLIE A. AN
TWO EXTRACTS EX
MATHEMATICAL MAGPIE, THE FADIMAN, CLIFTON AN

TYRE, RICHARD H.
NOTE TO TEACHERS AND PARENTS:, A IN
CITIZEN IN SPACE SHECKLEY, ROBERT AC

UNTERMEYER, L.

UNTERMEYER, L.
  EINSTEIN: A PARODY IN THE MANNER OF EDW-N MARKH-M SS   26
    MATHEMATICAL MAGPIE, THE   FADIMAN, CLIFTON   AN

UPDIKE, JOHN
  CHASTE PLANET, THE   SS   75
    BEST SF: 75, THE NINTH ANNUAL   HARRISON & ALDISS   AN
  DANCE OF THE SOLIDS, THE   PM   SAM 69 01
    ALCHEMY AND ACADEME   MCCAFFREY, ANNE   OA
  DURING THE JURASSIC   SS   TRV 66 SU
    SF12   MERRIL, JUDITH   AN

UPSON, WILLIAM H.
  A. BOTTS AND THE MOEBIUS STRIP   SS   SEP 45 12
    FANTASIA MATHEMATICA   FADIMAN, CLIFTON   AN
  PAUL BUNYAN VERSUS THE CONVEYOR BELT   SS   FTM 49
    MATHEMATICAL MAGPIE, THE   FADIMAN, CLIFTON   AN

URBAN, HELEN M.
  FINER BREED, THE   SS   FSF 56 03
    ABC OF SCIENCE FICTION, AN   BOARDMAN, TOM JR.   AN

URWIN, IRIS
  TRANSLATION   MS
    LOST FACE, THE   NESVADBA, JOSEF   AC

UTLEY, STEVEN   SEE ALSO   CO-EDITOR GEORGE W. PROCTOR
  BLACK AS THE PIT, FROM POLE TO POLE   NV C NDM 77 07
    NEW DIMENSIONS 7   SILVERBERG, ROBERT   OA
  CUSTER'S LAST JUMP   NV C UNI 76 06
    BEST SCIENCE FICTION OF THE YEAR, THE NO. 6
                                      CARR, TERRY   AN
    BEST SCIENCE FICTION STORIES OF THE YEAR (1976)
                                      DOZOIS, GARDNER R.   AN
    UNIVERSE 6   CARR, TERRY   OA
  GHOST SEAS   SS
    LONE STAR UNIVERSE   PROCTOR & UTLEY   OA
  HUNG LIKE AN ELEPHANT   SS C ALT 74
    ALTERNATIVES   GERROLD, DAVID   OA
  LOCAL ALLOSAURUS, THE   PM   NDM 75 05
    NEW DIMENSIONS 5   SILVERBERG, ROBERT   OA
  PREDATORS   SS
    IDES OF TOMORROW, THE   CARR, TERRY   OA
  SIC TRANSIT...?, A SHAGGY HAIRLESS-DOG STORY   SS C STL 76 02
    STELLAR 2   DEL REY, JUDY-LYNN   OA
  SPORT   PM   CND 73
    BEST SF: 1973   HARRISON & ALDISS   AN
  WOMB, WITH A VIEW   SS   ALT 74
    ALTERNATIVES   GERROLD, DAVID   OA

VAN ALM, AIDAN
  PICKUP   SS   FUN 60 01
    FLYING SAUCERS IN FACT AND FICTION SANTESSON, HANS S.   AN

VAN DOREN, MARK
  STRANGE GIRL, THE   SS   62
    WORLDS OF SCIENCE FICTION, THE   MILLS, ROBERT P.   AN

VAN DRESSER, PETER
  BY VIRTUE OF CIRCUMFERENCE   SS   AMB 37 11
    YEAR AFTER TOMORROW, THE   DEL REY, L/MATSCHAT/ AN
  PLUM DUFF   SS   AMB 35 12
    YEAR AFTER TOMORROW, THE   DEL REY, L/MATSCHAT/ AN
  ROCKET TO THE SUN   SS   AMB 39 07
    YEAR AFTER TOMORROW, THE   DEL REY, L/MATSCHAT/ AN

VAN LAERHOVEN, BOB
  LONG TIME AGO, NOT FORGOTTEN   SS   NWR 75 27
    NEW WRITINGS IN SF. 27   BULMER, KENNETH   OA

VAN LOGGEM, MANUEL
  CALL OF THE WILD, THE   SS   NWR 76 28
    NEW WRITINGS IN SF. 28   BULMER, KENNETH   OA
  PAIRPUPPETS   SS   74
    BEST FROM THE REST OF THE WORLD, THE WOLLHEIM, DONALD A. AN

VAN LORNE, WARNER   PSEUD. FOR F. ORLIN TREMAINE
  UPPER LEVEL ROAD, THE   SS   ASF 35 08
    *BEST OF SCIENCE FICTION   CONKLIN, GROFF   AN

VAN SCYOC, SYDNEY J.
  DEATHSONG   NA   GAL 74 02
    1975 ANNUAL WORLD'S BEST SF, THE WOLLHEIM, DONALD A.   AN
  MNARRA MOBILIS   NV   IFS 73 06
    BEST FROM IF, THE VOLUME II   IF, EDITORS OF   AN
  SWEET SISTER, GREEN BROTHER   NA   GAL 73 12
    BEST FROM GALAXY, THE VOLUME III BAEN, JAMES   AN
  VISIT TO CLEVELAND GENERAL, A   SS   GAL 68 10
    SOCIAL PROBLEMS THROUGH SCIENCE FICTION
                                      GREENBERG/MILSTEAD/& AN
    WORLD'S BEST SCIENCE FICTION: 1969 WOLLHEIM & CARR   AN
  WHEN PETALS FALL   NV   TVW 73
    BEST SF: 1974   HARRISON & ALDISS   AN
    TWO VIEWS OF WONDER   SCORTIA & YARBRO   OA

VAN VOGT, A. E. AND E. MAYNE HULL
  OUT OF THE UNKNOWN   AC H FPB 48
    IN ENGLAND AS "THE SEA THING AND OTHER STORIES"
  OUT OF THE UNKNOWN (ENGLISH EDITION ADDS:)   AC H SID 70

VAN VOGT, A. E.
  AWAY AND BEYOND   AC H PEL 52
  AWAY AND BEYOND (7 OF 9)   AC   BKM 59 02
  BEAST, THE   NO H DBL 63
    ALSO IN "A VAN VOGT OMNIBUS"
  BEST OF A. E. VAN VOGT, THE   AC   PKT 76 07

                                                  VAN VOGT, A. E.

VAN VOGT, A. E.   (CONTINUED)
  BEST OF A. E. VAN VOGT, THE (BRITISH)   AC H SID 74 05
    EDITED BY ANGUS WELLS
  BLAL, THE   AC   ZEB 76 08
    SEE "MONSTERS"
  BOOK OF VAN VOGT, THE   AC   DAW 72
  DESTINATION: UNIVERSE¦   AC H PEL 52
  EMPIRE OF THE ATOM   NO H SHS 57
  FAR-OUT WORLDS OF A. E. VAN VOGT, THE   AC   ACE 68
  M 33 IN ANDROMEDA   AC   PBK 71 04
  MASTERS OF TIME   AC H FPS 50
  MISSION TO THE STARS   NO   BKM 71 03
    SEE "THE MIXED MEN"
  MISSION: INTERPLANETARY   NO   NAM 52
    SEE "THE VOYAGE OF THE SPACE BEAGLE"
  MIXED MEN, THE   NO H GNM 52
    ALSO AS "MISSION TO THE STARS"
  MONSTERS   AC   PKT 65
    EDITED BY FORREST J. ACKERMAN, ALSO AS "THE BLAL"
  MORE THAN SUPERHUMAN   AC   DEL 71 05
  PROXY INTELLIGENCE AND OTHER MIND BENDERS   AC   PBK 71 01
  QUEST FOR THE FUTURE   NO   ACE 70
  ROGUE SHIP   NO H DBL 65
  SILKIE, THE   NO   ACE 69
  TRIAD   AC H SAS 51
  TWISTED MEN, THE   DC   ACE 64
  VAN VOGT OMNIBUS, A   AC H SID 67
  VOYAGE OF THE SPACE BEAGLE, THE   NO H SAS 50
    IN "TRIAD"
    ALSO AS "MISSION: INTERPLANETARY"
  WAR AGAINST THE RULL, THE   NO H SAS 59 09
  WEAPON SHOPS OF ISHER, THE   NO H GBG 51
    ALSO IN "A TREASURY OF GREAT SCIENCE FICTION VOL. 1"
  WORLDS OF A. E. VAN VOGT, THE   AC   ACE 74 01
  ABDICATION (ALSO AS THE INVISIBILITY GAMBIT)   SS C ASF 43 04
    SCIENCE FICTION ROLL OF HONOR, THE POHL, FREDERICK   AN
  ALL THE LOVING ANDROIDS   NV   NEW 71 AC
    MORE THAN SUPERHUMAN   VAN VOGT, A. E.   AC
  ALL WE HAVE ON THIS PLANET   SS
    BEST OF A. E. VAN VOGT, THE   VAN VOGT, A. E.   AC
    STOPWATCH   HAY, GEORGE   OA
  ASYLUM   NV   ASF 42 05
    *ADVENTURES IN TIME AND SPACE   HEALY & MCCOMAS   AN
    *AWAY AND BEYOND   VAN VOGT, A. E.   AC
  AUTOMATON   SS   OWS 50 09
    ADVENTURES IN TOMORROW   CROSSEN, KENDELL F.   AN
    ALIEN EARTH AND OTHER STORIES   ELWOOD & MOSKOWITZ   AN
    FAR-OUT WORLDS OF A. E. VAN VOGT, THE VAN VOGT, A. E.   AC
    SPECULATIONS   SANDERS, THOMAS E.   AN
    WORLDS OF A. E. VAN VOGT, THE   VAN VOGT, A. E.   AC
  BARBARIAN, THE   NV   ASF 47 12
    BOOK OF VAN VOGT, THE   VAN VOGT, A. E.   AC
    EMPIRE OF THE ATOM   VAN VOGT, A. E.   NO
  BEAST, THE   NO   DBL 63
    VAN VOGT OMNIBUS, A   VAN VOGT, A. E.   AC
  BEAST, THE   NV   ASF 43 11
    BEAST, THE   VAN VOGT, A. E.   NO
  BEING AN EXAMINATION OF THE PONSIAN AND HOLMESIAN SECRET
    DEDUCTIVE SYSTEMS   AR   71
    BEST OF A. E. VAN VOGT, THE   VAN VOGT, A. E.   AC
  BLACK DESTROYER   NV   ASF 39 07
    *ADVENTURES IN TIME AND SPACE   HEALY & MCCOMAS   AN
    FIRST FLIGHT   KNIGHT, DAMON   AN
    SCIENCE FICTION NOVELLAS   HARRISON & MCNELLY   AN
    VOYAGE OF THE SPACE BEAGLE, THE   VAN VOGT, A. E.   NO
  BOOK OF PTATH, THE   NO   UNK 43 10
    VAN VOGT OMNIBUS, A   VAN VOGT, A. E.   AC
  CAN OF PAINT, A   SS   ASF 44 09
    DESTINATION: UNIVERSE¦   VAN VOGT, A. E.   AC
  CARTHING   SS   QRK 70 01
    QUARK/1   DELANY & HACKER   OA
  CATAAAAA, THE   SS   PBK 70 01
    BEST OF A. E. VAN VOGT, THE (BRITISH) VAN VOGT, A. E.   AC
    FAR-OUT WORLDS OF A. E. VAN VOGT, THE VAN VOGT, A. E.   AC
    WORLDS OF A. E. VAN VOGT, THE   VAN VOGT, A. E.   AC
  CENTAURUS II   NV   ASF 47 06
    ROGUE SHIP   VAN VOGT, A. E.   NO
  CHANGELING, THE (ALSO AS THE WONDERFUL MAN)   NA   ASF 44 04
    MASTERS OF TIME   VAN VOGT, A. E.   AC
  CHILD OF THE GODS   NV   ASF 46 08
    EMPIRE OF THE ATOM   VAN VOGT, A. E.   NO
  CHILDREN OF TOMORROW   NO   70
    SCIENCE FICTION SPECIAL 6   ANONYMOUS   AN
  CHRONICLER, THE (ALSO AS SIEGE OF THE UNSEEN)   NA   ASF 46 10
    FIVE SCIENCE FICTION NOVELS   GREENBERG , MARTIN   AN
  CO-OPERATE- OR ELSE¦   NV   ASF 42 04
    DECADE THE 1940S   ALDISS & HARRISON   AN
    *OUTER REACHES, THE   DERLETH, AUGUST   AN
    WAR AGAINST THE RULL, THE   VAN VOGT, A. E.   NO
  CONCEALMENT   SS   ASF 43 09
    GALACTIC EMPIRES VOLUME TWO   ALDISS, BRIAN W.   AN
    MIXED MEN, THE   VAN VOGT, A. E.   NO
    MONSTERS   VAN VOGT, A. E.   AC
  CONFESSION, THE   SS   NEW 72 AC
    BOOK OF VAN VOGT, THE   VAN VOGT, A. E.   AC
  DEAR PEN PAL   SS   ARS 49 WI
    BEST OF A. E. VAN VOGT, THE (BRITISH) VAN VOGT, A. E.   AC
    DESTINATION: UNIVERSE¦   VAN VOGT, A. E.   AC
    FAR BOUNDARIES   DERLETH, AUGUST   AN
  DEFENSE   SS   AFR 47 04
    DESTINATION: UNIVERSE¦   VAN VOGT, A. E.   AC
  DISCORD IN SCARLET   NV   ASF 39 12
    M 33 IN ANDROMEDA   VAN VOGT, A. E.   AC
    VOYAGE OF THE SPACE BEAGLE, THE   VAN VOGT, A. E.   NO
  DON'T HOLD YOUR BREATH   SS   SVW 73
    BEST OF A. E. VAN VOGT, THE   VAN VOGT, A. E.   AC

VAN VOGT, A. E.   (CONTINUED)
    SAVING WORLDS   ELWOOD & KIDD   OA
DORMANT   SS   STS 48 11
    ASPECTS OF SCIENCE FICTION   DOHERTY, G. D.   AN
    BEST FROM STARTLING STORIES, THE   MINES, SAMUEL   AN
    BEST SF   CRISPIN, EDMUND   AN
    DESTINATION: UNIVERSE| VAN VOGT, A. E.   AC
    SHAPE OF THINGS, THE   KNIGHT, DAMON   AN
EARTH KILLERS, THE   NV   SSS 49 04
    FAR-OUT WORLDS OF A. E. VAN VOGT, THE VAN VOGT, A. E.   AC
    IF THIS GOES ON   NUETZEL, CHARLES   AN
    TWISTED MEN, THE   VAN VOGT, A. E.   DC
    WORLDS OF A. E. VAN VOGT, THE   VAN VOGT, A. E.   AC
ENCHANTED VILLAGE (ALSO AS THE SANDS OF MARS) SS   OWS 50 07
    ANTHROPOLOGY THROUGH SCIENCE FICTION   MASON, C/GREENBERG/&   AN
    ASLEEP IN ARMAGEDDON   SISSONS, MICHAEL   AN
    DESTINATION: UNIVERSE| VAN VOGT, A. E.   AC
    HOT & COLD RUNNING CITIES   MCHARGUE, GEORGESS   AN
    MICROCOSMIC GOD   MOSKOWITZ, SAM   AN
    MODERN MASTERPIECES OF SCIENCE FICTION MOSKOWITZ, SAM   AN
    MODERN SCIENCE FICTION   SPINRAD, NORMAN   AN
    MONSTERS   VAN VOGT, A. E.   AC
    *POSSIBLE WORLDS OF SCIENCE FICTION   CONKLIN, GROFF   AN
    SCIENCE FICTION   BRODKIN & PEARSON   AN
ENEMY OF THE SILKIE   NV   IFS 67 10
    SILKIE, THE   VAN VOGT, A. E.   NO
ERSATZ ETERNAL   NV   NEW 72 AC
    BEST SCIENCE FICTION FOR 1973   ACKERMAN, FORREST J.   AN
    BOOK OF VAN VOGT, THE   VAN VOGT, A. E.   AC
EXPENDABLES, THE   NV   IFS 63 09
    BEST OF A. E. VAN VOGT, THE (BRITISH) VAN VOGT, A. E.   AC
    BEST SCIENCE FICTION FROM IF, THE   POHL, FREDERIK   AN
    M 33 IN ANDROMEDA   VAN VOGT, A. E.   AC
    ROGUE SHIP   VAN VOGT, A. E.   NO
    WORLDS OF A. E. VAN VOGT, THE   VAN VOGT, A. E.   AC
FAR CENTAURUS   SS   ASF 44 01
    DEEP SPACE   SILVERBERG, ROBERT   AN
    DESTINATION: UNIVERSE| VAN VOGT, A. E.   AC
    GREAT STORIES OF SPACE TRAVEL   CONKLIN, GROFF   AN
    *MEN AGAINST THE STARS   GREENBERG, MARTIN   AN
    QUEST FOR THE FUTURE   VAN VOGT, A. E.   NO
    SPECTRUM OF WORLDS, A   CLARESON, THOMAS D.   AN
    *STRANGE PORTS OF CALL   DERLETH, AUGUST   AN
FILM LIBRARY   SS   ASF 46 07
    *AWAY AND BEYOND   VAN VOGT, A. E.   AC
    QUEST FOR THE FUTURE   VAN VOGT, A. E.   NO
FINAL COMMAND   SS   ASF 49 11
    MONSTERS   VAN VOGT, A. E.   AC
    ROBOT AND THE MAN, THE   GREENBERG, MARTIN   AN
FINAL COMMENT   MS
    BEST OF A. E. VAN VOGT, THE   VAN VOGT, A. E.   AC
FIRST MARTIAN, THE (THIS JOE)   SS   39
    FAR-OUT WORLDS OF A. E. VAN VOGT, THE VAN VOGT, A. E.   AC
    GREAT SCIENCE FICTION STORIES ABOUT MARS
                                           DIKTY, T. E.   AN
    WORLDS OF A. E. VAN VOGT, THE   VAN VOGT, A. E.   AC
FLIGHT THAT FAILED, THE (SEE REBIRTH: EARTH) TC
FULFILLMENT   NV   NTS 51
    FAR-OUT WORLDS OF A. E. VAN VOGT, THE VAN VOGT, A. E.   AC
    NEW TALES OF SPACE AND TIME   HEALY, RAYMOND J.   OA
    WORLDS OF A. E. VAN VOGT, THE   VAN VOGT, A. E.   AC
    YET MORE PENGUIN SCIENCE FICTION   ALDISS, BRIAN W.   AN
FUTURE PERFECT   SS   VTX 73 08
    BEST OF A. E. VAN VOGT, THE   VAN VOGT, A. E.   AC
    2020 VISION   POURNELLE, JERRY   AN
GHOST, THE   NV   UNK 42 08
    OUT OF THE UNKNOWN   VAN VOGT & HULL   AC
    ZACHERLEY'S MIDNIGHT SNACKS   ZACHERLEY   AN
GREAT ENGINE, THE   NV   ASF 43 07
    *AWAY AND BEYOND   VAN VOGT, A. E.   AC
    BEAST, THE   VAN VOGT, A. E.   NO
GREAT JUDGE, THE   SS   FBK 48 03
    *AWAY AND BEYOND   VAN VOGT, A. E.   AC
    FIFTY SHORT SCIENCE FICTION TALES   ASIMOV & CONKLIN   AN
    TIME CURVE, THE   MOSKOWITZ & ELWOOD   AN
GREEN FOREST, THE   NV   ASF 49 06
    BEST OF A. E. VAN VOGT, THE (BRITISH) VAN VOGT, A. E.   AC
    FUTURES TO INFINITY   MOSKOWITZ, SAM   AN
    WAR AGAINST THE RULL, THE   VAN VOGT, A. E.   NO
GRYB, THE (REPETITION)   NV   ASF 40 04
    PROXY INTELLIGENCE AND OTHER MIND BENDERS
                                           VAN VOGT, A. E.   AC
HAND OF THE GODS   NV   ASF 46 12
    BEST OF A. E. VAN VOGT, THE (BRITISH) VAN VOGT, A. E.   AC
    EMPIRE OF THE ATOM   VAN VOGT, A. E.   NO
HARMONIZER, THE   SS   ASF 44 11
    *AWAY AND BEYOND   VAN VOGT, A. E.   AC
HEIR APPARENT (SEE HEIR UNAPPARENT)   TC
HEIR UNAPPARENT (HEIR APPARENT)   SS   ASF 45 06
    *AWAY AND BEYOND   VAN VOGT, A. E.   AC
    M 33 IN ANDROMEDA   VAN VOGT, A. E.   AC
    SF: AUTHORS' CHOICE 2   HARRISON, HARRY   AN
HIM   SS   SPW 69 01
    MORE THAN SUPERHUMAN   VAN VOGT, A. E.   AC
HOME OF THE GODS   NV   ASF 47 04
    BEST OF A. E. VAN VOGT, THE   VAN VOGT, A. E.   AC
    EMPIRE OF THE ATOM   VAN VOGT, A. E.   NO
HUMAN OPERATORS, THE   NV C FSF 71 01
    BEST SCIENCE FICTION STORIES OF THE YEAR (1971)
                                           DEL REY, LESTER   AN
    PARTNERS IN WONDER   ELLISON, HARLAN   AC
HUMANS, GO HOME| NV   GAL 69 09
    MORE THAN SUPERHUMAN   VAN VOGT, A. E.   AC
INTRODUCTION   IN
    BEST OF A. E. VAN VOGT, THE (BRITISH) VAN VOGT, A. E.   AC
    PSEUDO PEOPLE, THE   NOLAN, WILLIAM F.   AN

VAN VOGT, A. E.   (CONTINUED)
    INVISIBILITY GAMBIT, THE (ABDICATION) SS   ASF 43 04
    PROXY INTELLIGENCE AND OTHER MIND BENDERS
                                           VAN VOGT, A. E.   AC
ITSELF| SS   GAM 63 01
    FAR-OUT WORLDS OF A. E. VAN VOGT, THE VAN VOGT, A. E.   AC
    HUMAN ZERO, THE   MOSKOWITZ & ELWOOD   AN
    WORLDS OF A. E. VAN VOGT, THE   VAN VOGT, A. E.   AC
JUGGERNAUT   SS   ASF 44 08
    BEST OF A. E. VAN VOGT, THE (BRITISH) VAN VOGT, A. E.   AC
    *TREASURY OF SCIENCE FICTION, A   CONKLIN, GROFF   AN
LAUGH, CLONE, LAUGH   SS C NEW 69 AC
    MORE THAN SUPERHUMAN   VAN VOGT, A. E.   AC
    SCIENCE FICTION WORLDS OF FORREST J. ACKERMAN & FRIENDS
                                           ACKERMAN, FORREST J.   AC
LETTER FROM THE STARS   SS   OTW 50 07
    BEYOND THE END OF TIME   POHL, FREDERIK   AN
    EARTH IN PERIL, THE   WOLLHEIM, DONALD A.   DA
LOST: FIFTY SUNS   NV   NEW 52 NO
    BOOK OF VAN VOGT, THE   VAN VOGT, A. E.   AC
    MIXED MEN, THE   VAN VOGT, A. E.   NO
M 33 IN ANDROMEDA   SS   ASF 43 08
    M 33 IN ANDROMEDA   VAN VOGT, A. E.   AC
    TOMORROW'S UNIVERSE   CAMPBELL, H. J.   AN
MASTERS OF TIME (RECRUITING STATION)   NV   ASF 42 03
    MASTERS OF TIME   VAN VOGT, A. E.   AC
MIXED MEN, THE   NV   ASF 45 01
    MIXED MEN, THE   VAN VOGT, A. E.   NO
MONSTER, THE (ALSO AS RESURRECTION)   SS   ASF 48 08
    BEST OF A. E. VAN VOGT, THE (BRITISH) VAN VOGT, A. E.   AC
    DESTINATION: UNIVERSE| VAN VOGT, A. E.   AC
NOT ONLY DEAD MEN   SS   ASF 42 11
    BUG-EYED MONSTERS   CHEETHAM, ANTHONY   AN
    *INVADERS OF EARTH   CONKLIN, GROFF   AN
    MONSTERS   VAN VOGT, A. E.   AC
NOT THE FIRST   SS   ASF 41 04
    FAR-OUT WORLDS OF A. E. VAN VOGT, THE VAN VOGT, A. E.   AC
    WORLDS OF A. E. VAN VOGT, THE   VAN VOGT, A. E.   AC
PLANETS FOR SALE   AC C FEL 54
    VAN VOGT OMNIBUS, A   VAN VOGT, A. E.   AC
PROBLEM PROFESSOR, THE (PROJECT SPACESHIP) SS   TWS 49 08
    PROXY INTELLIGENCE AND OTHER MIND BENDERS
                                           VAN VOGT, A. E.   AC
PROCESS   SS   FSF 50 12
    BEST SCIENCE-FICTION STORIES: 1951, THE
                                           BLEILER & DIKTY   AN
    FAR-OUT WORLDS OF A. E. VAN VOGT, THE VAN VOGT, A. E.   AC
    FRONTIERS IN SPACE   BLEILER & DIKTY   AN
    MINDWORM, THE   ANONYMOUS   AN
    WORLDS OF A. E. VAN VOGT, THE   VAN VOGT, A. E.   AC
PROJECT- SPACESHIP (ALSO AS THE PROBLEM PROFESSOR)
                                           NV   TWS 49 08
    *MY BEST SCIENCE FICTION STORY   MARGULIES & FRIEND   AN
PROLOGUE TO "THE SILKIE"   EX   IFS 64 07
    BEST OF A. E. VAN VOGT, THE   VAN VOGT, A. E.   AC
PROXY INTELLIGENCE, THE   SN   IFS 68 10
    BEST OF A. E. VAN VOGT, THE   VAN VOGT, A. E.   AC
    BEST OF A. E. VAN VOGT, THE (BRITISH) VAN VOGT, A. E.   AC
    PROXY INTELLIGENCE AND OTHER MIND BENDERS
                                           VAN VOGT, A. E.   AC
PURPOSE, THE   NV   ASF 45 05
    FAR-OUT WORLDS OF A. E. VAN VOGT, THE VAN VOGT, A. E.   AC
    WORLDS OF A. E. VAN VOGT, THE   VAN VOGT, A. E.   AC
QUEST FOR THE FUTURE   NO   ACE 70
    SCIENCE FICTION SPECIAL 8   ANONYMOUS   AN
RAT AND THE SNAKE, THE   SS   WTS 71 01
    BOOK OF VAN VOGT, THE   VAN VOGT, A. E.   AC
REBIRTH: EARTH (THE FLIGHT THAT FAILED)   SS   ASF 42 12
    PROXY INTELLIGENCE AND OTHER MIND BENDERS
                                           VAN VOGT, A. E.   AC
RECRUITING STATION (ALSO AS MASTERS OF TIME) NV   ASF 42 03
    OMNIBUS OF SCIENCE FICTION   CONKLIN, GROFF   AN
    STRANGE ADVENTURES IN SCIENCE FICTION CONKLIN, GROFF   AN
REFLECTED MEN, THE   NV   GAL 71 02
    MORE THAN SUPERHUMAN   VAN VOGT, A. E.   AC
    WORLDS OF A. E. VAN VOGT, THE   VAN VOGT, A. E.   AC
REPETITION (ALSO AS THE GRYB)   NV   ASF 40 04
    *BEACHHEADS IN SPACE   DERLETH, AUGUST   AN
    WAR AGAINST THE RULL, THE   VAN VOGT, A. E.   NO
REPLICATORS, THE   NV   IFS 65 02
    FAR-OUT WORLDS OF A. E. VAN VOGT, THE VAN VOGT, A. E.   AC
    WORLDS OF A. E. VAN VOGT, THE   VAN VOGT, A. E.   AC
RESEARCH ALPHA   SN C IFS 65 07
    MORE THAN SUPERHUMAN   VAN VOGT, A. E.   AC
RESURRECTION (THE MONSTER)   SS   ASF 48 08
    IN DREAMS AWAKE   FIEDLER, LESLIE A.   AN
    INVADERS FROM SPACE   SILVERBERG, ROBERT   AN
    MONSTERS   VAN VOGT, A. E.   AC
    *OTHER SIDE OF THE MOON, THE   DERLETH, AUGUST   AN
    SPECTRUM 2   AMIS & CONQUEST   AN
    TOWARD INFINITY   KNIGHT, DAMON   AN
    UBERWINDUNG VON RAUM UND ZEIT   GUNTHER, GOTTHARD   AN
ROGUE SHIP (ALSO AS THE TWISTED MEN)   NV   SSS 50 03
    GIANT ANTHOLOGY OF SCIENCE FICTION   MARGULIES & FRIEND   AN
    ROGUE SHIP   VAN VOGT, A. E.   NO
    TOMORROW AND TOMORROW   KNIGHT, DAMON   AN
RULERS, THE   SS   ASF 44 03
    DESTINATION: UNIVERSE| VAN VOGT, A. E.   AC
RULL, THE   NV   ASF 48 05
    ADVENTURES ON OTHER PLANETS   WOLLHEIM, DONALD A.   AN
    BEST OF A. E. VAN VOGT, THE   VAN VOGT, A. E.   AC
    SCIENCE FICTION: THE GREAT YEARS, VOL. II
                                           POHL, C. & F.   AN
    TRAVELLERS OF SPACE   GREENBERG, MARTIN   AN
    WAR AGAINST THE RULL, THE   VAN VOGT, A. E.   NO

VAN VOGT, A. E.

VANCE, JACK

VAN VOGT, A. E.   (CONTINUED)
SANDS OF MARS, THE (ENCHANTED VILLAGE)   SS   OWS 50 07
  SANDS OF MARS AND OTHER STORIES, THE   ANONYMOUS   AN
SEA THING, THE   NV   UNK 40 01
  MONSTERS   VAN VOGT, A. E.   AC
  OUT OF THE UNKNOWN   VAN VOGT & HULL   AC
SEARCH, THE   NV   ASF 43 01
  *BEST OF SCIENCE FICTION   CONKLIN, GROFF   AN
  DESTINATION: UNIVERSE| VAN VOGT, A. E.   AC
  QUEST FOR THE FUTURE   VAN VOGT, A. E.   NO
SECOND SOLUTION, THE   SS   ASF 42 10
  *AWAY AND BEYOND   VAN VOGT, A. E.   AC
  WAR AGAINST THE RULL, THE   VAN VOGT, A. E.   NO
SECRET UNATTAINABLE   NV   ASF 42 07
SEESAW, THE   SS   ASF 41 07
  *BEYOND TIME AND SPACE   DERLETH, AUGUST   AN
  BEYOND TOMORROW   KNIGHT, DAMON   AN
  WEAPON SHOPS OF ISHER, THE   VAN VOGT, A. E.   NO
SEMANTICS OF TWENTY-FIRST CENTURY SCIENCE, THE   AR
  BEST OF A. E. VAN VOGT, THE   VAN VOGT, A. E.   AC
SHIP OF DARKNESS   SS   FBK 47 02
  AWARD SCIENCE FICTION READER   NORTON, ALDEN H.   AN
  FAR-OUT WORLDS OF A. E. VAN VOGT, THE   VAN VOGT, A. E.   AC
  WORLDS OF A. E. VAN VOGT, THE   VAN VOGT, A. E.   AC
SIEGE OF THE UNSEEN (THE CHRONICLER)   NA   ASF 46 10
  M 33 IN ANDROMEDA   VAN VOGT, A. E.   AC
SILKIE, THE   NV   IFS 64 07
  IF READER OF SCIENCE FICTION, THE   POHL, FREDERIK   AN
  SILKIE, THE   VAN VOGT, A. E.   NO
SILKIES IN SPACE   NV   IFS 66 05
  BEST OF A. E. VAN VOGT, THE (BRITISH)   VAN VOGT, A. E.   AC
  SILKIE, THE   VAN VOGT, A. E.   AC
SLAN   NO   ASF 40 09
  TRIAD   VAN VOGT, A. E.   AC
SON IS BORN, A   SS   ASF 46 05
  EMPIRE OF THE ATOM   VAN VOGT, A. E.   NO
SOUND OF WILD LAUGHTER, THE   NV   NEW 72 AC
  BOOK OF VAN VOGT, THE   VAN VOGT, A. E.   AC
SOUND, THE   NV   ASF 50 02
  DESTINATION: UNIVERSE| VAN VOGT, A. E.   AC
  WAR AGAINST THE RULL, THE   VAN VOGT, A. E.   NO
STAR-SAINT, THE   NV   PLS 51 03
  PROXY INTELLIGENCE AND OTHER MIND BENDERS
                                       VAN VOGT, A. E.   AC
  TWISTED MEN, THE   VAN VOGT, A. E.   DC
STORM, THE   NV   ASF 43 10
  ASTOUNDING-ANALOG READER, THE VOLUME ONE
                                       HARRISON & ALDISS   AN
  BEST OF A. E. VAN VOGT, THE (BRITISH)   VAN VOGT, A. E.   AC
  MIXED MEN, THE   VAN VOGT, A. E.   NO
  SPACE OPERA   ALDISS, BRIAN W.   AN
  WORLDS OF A. E. VAN VOGT, THE   VAN VOGT, A. E.   AC
THIS JOE (SEE THE FIRST MARTIAN)   TC
TIMED CLOCK, THE   SS   NEW 72 AC
  BOOK OF VAN VOGT, THE   VAN VOGT, A. E.   AC
TWISTED MEN, THE (ROGUE SHIP)   NV   SSS 50 03
  TWISTED MEN, THE   VAN VOGT, A. E.   DC
ULTRA MAN, THE   NV   WOT 66 05
  FAR-OUT WORLDS OF A. E. VAN VOGT, THE   VAN VOGT, A. E.   AC
  WORLDS OF A. E. VAN VOGT, THE   VAN VOGT, A. E.   AC
VAULT OF THE BEAST   NV   ASF 40 08
  *ASTOUNDING SCIENCE FICTION ANTHOLOGY, THE
                                       CAMPBELL, JOHN W. JR   AN
  *AWAY AND BEYOND   VAN VOGT, A. E.   AC
  BEST OF A. E. VAN VOGT, THE (BRITISH)   VAN VOGT, A. E.   AC
  FIRST ASTOUNDING SCIENCE FICTION ANTHOLOGY, THE (PB)
                                       CAMPBELL, JOHN W. JR   AN
  MONSTERS   VAN VOGT, A. E.   AC
  *OTHER SIDE OF THE MOON, THE   DERLETH, AUGUST   AN
  *SECOND ASTOUNDING SCIENCE FICTION ANTHOLOGY, THE
                                       CAMPBELL, JOHN W. JR   AN
                                       AR   65
VIOLENT MAN, THE
  BEST OF A. E. VAN VOGT, THE   VAN VOGT, A. E.   AC
VOYAGE OF THE SPACE BEAGLE, THE   NO   SAS 50
  TRIAD   VAN VOGT, A. E.   AC
WAR OF NERVES   SS   OWS 50 05
  BEST OF A. E. VAN VOGT, THE   VAN VOGT, A. E.   AC
  BEST OF A. E. VAN VOGT, THE (BRITISH)   VAN VOGT, A. E.   AC
  MONSTERS   VAN VOGT, A. E.   AC
  VOYAGE OF THE SPACE BEAGLE, THE   VAN VOGT, A. E.   NO
WEAPON SHOP, THE   NV   ASF 42 12
  *ADVENTURES IN TIME AND SPACE   HEALY & MCCOMAS   AN
  BEST OF A. E. VAN VOGT, THE (BRITISH)   VAN VOGT, A. E.   AC
  M 33 IN ANDROMEDA   VAN VOGT, A. E.   AC
  SCIENCE FICTION HALL OF FAME VOLUME 1   SILVERBERG, ROBERT   AN
  WEAPON SHOPS OF ISHER, THE   VAN VOGT, A. E.   NO
WEAPON SHOPS OF ISHER, THE   NA   TWS 49 02
  WEAPON SHOPS OF ISHER, THE   VAN VOGT, A. E.   NO
WEAPON SHOPS OF ISHER, THE   NO   GBG 51
  TREASURY OF GREAT SCIENCE FICTION, A VOL.1
                                       BOUCHER, ANTHONY   AN
                                       AI
WHY I SELECTED PROJECT- SPACESHIP
  *MY BEST SCIENCE FICTION STORY   MARGULIES & FRIEND   AN
WINGED MAN, THE   NO C ASF 44 05
  SCIENCE FICTION SPECIAL 4   ANONYMOUS   AN
WITCH, THE   SS   UNK 43 02
  OUT OF THE UNKNOWN   VAN VOGT & HULL   AC
  ZACHERLEY'S VULTURE STEW   ZACHERLEY   AN
WONDERFUL MAN, THE (THE CHANGELING)   SN   ASF 44 04
  BEAST, THE   VAN VOGT, A. E.   NO
WORLD OF NULL A, THE   NO   ASF 45 08
  TRIAD   VAN VOGT, A. E.   AC

VANCE, JACK
BEST OF JACK VANCE, THE   AC   PKT 76 05
DYING EARTH, THE   OC   HIL 50
EIGHT FANTASMS AND MAGICS   AC H MAC 69
FUTURE TENSE   AC   BAL 64 06
MANY WORLDS OF MAGNUS RIDOLPH, THE   DC   ACE 66
MOON MOTH AND OTHER STORIES, THE   AC H DOB 76
  SEE "THE WORLD BETWEEN AND OTHER STORIES"
WORLD BETWEEN AND OTHER STORIES, THE   DC   ACE 65
  IN ENGLAND AS "THE MOON MOTH AND OTHER STORIES"
WORLDS OF JACK VANCE, THE   AC   ACE 73 12
  ABERCROMBIE STATION   NA   TWS 52 02
    BEST OF JACK VANCE, THE   VANCE, JACK   AC
  ASSAULT ON A CITY   NV   UNI 74 04
    UNIVERSE 4   CARR, TERRY   OA
  AUGMENTED AGENT, THE (I-C-A-BEM)   NV   AMZ 61 10
    BEST FROM AMAZING, THE   WHITE, TED   AN
  BRAIN OF THE GALAXY   NV   WBY 51 02
    WORLD BETWEEN AND OTHER STORIES, THE   VANCE, JACK   DC
    WORLDS OF JACK VANCE, THE   VANCE, JACK   AC
  BRAINS OF EARTH, THE   NA   66
    WORLDS OF JACK VANCE, THE   VANCE, JACK   AC
  CIL (THE EYES OF THE OVERWORLD)   NV
    EIGHT FANTASMS AND MAGICS   VANCE, JACK   AC
  COUPE DE GRACE   NV
    MANY WORLDS OF MAGNUS RIDOLPH, THE   VANCE, JACK   DC
    WORLDS OF JACK VANCE, THE   VANCE, JACK   AC
  DEVIL ON SALVATION BLUFF, THE   NV   STR 54 03
    STAR SCIENCE FICTION STORIES NO. 3   POHL, FREDERIK   OA
    WORLD BETWEEN AND OTHER STORIES, THE   VANCE, JACK   DC
    WORLDS OF JACK VANCE, THE   VANCE, JACK   AC
  DODKIN'S JOB   NV   ASF 59 10
    FUTURE TENSE   VANCE, JACK   AC
    WINDOWS INTO TOMORROW   SILVERBERG, ROBERT   AN
  DOGTOWN TOURIST AGENCY, THE   NO   EPC 75
    EPOCH   ELWOOD & SILVERBERG   OA
  DP| NV   AVS 53 04
    BEST SCIENCE-FICTION STORIES: 1954, THE
                                       BLEILER & DIKTY   AN
    POLITICAL SCIENCE FICTION   GREENBERG& WARRICK   AN
  DRAGON MASTERS, THE   SN   GAL 62 08
    HUGO WINNERS, THE (VOLUME 2)   ASIMOV, ISAAC   AN
  DREAMER, THE (THE ENCHANTED PRINCESS)   SS   OSF 54 11
    SPACE STATION 42 AND OTHER STORIES   ANONYMOUS   AN
  ENCHANTED PRINCESS, THE (SEE THE DREAMER)   TC
  EYES OF THE OVERWORLD, THE (SEE CIL)   TC
  FOREWORD   IN
    EIGHT FANTASMS AND MAGICS   VANCE, JACK   AC
  GATEWAY TO STRANGENESS (SEE SAIL 25)   TC
  GIFT OF GAB, THE   NV   ASF 55 09
    ALPHA 3   SILVERBERG, ROBERT   AN
    BEST SF 3   CRISPIN, EDMUND   AN
    FUTURE TENSE   VANCE, JACK   AC
    OUT OF THIS WORLD 2   WILLIAMS-ELLIS& OWEN   AN
  GREEN MAGIC   SS   FSF 63 06
    BEST FROM FANTASY AND SCIENCE FICTION: 13
                                       DAVIDSON, AVRAM   AN
    SPECIAL WONDER   MCCOMAS, J. FRANCIS   AN
  GUYAL OF SFERE   NV   50
    DYING EARTH, THE   VANCE, JACK   OC
    EIGHT FANTASMS AND MAGICS   VANCE, JACK   AC
    ENDS OF TIME, THE   SILVERBERG, ROBERT   AN
  HARD LUCK DIGGINGS   SS   STS 48 07
    *POSSIBLE WORLDS OF SCIENCE FICTION   CONKLIN, GROFF   AN
  HOWLING BOUNDERS, THE   NV   STS 49 03
    MANY WORLDS OF MAGNUS RIDOLPH, THE   VANCE, JACK   DC
    WORLDS OF WONDER   HARRISON, HARRY   AN
  I'LL BUILD YOUR DREAM CASTLE   SS   ASF 47 09
    GREAT STORIES OF SPACE TRAVEL   CONKLIN, GROFF   AN
  I-C-A-BEM (SEE THE AUGMENTED AGENT)   TC
  KING OF THIEVES, THE   NV   STS 49 11
    LOOKING FORWARD   LESSER, MILTON   AN
    MANY WORLDS OF MAGNUS RIDOLPH, THE   VANCE, JACK   DC
    WORLDS OF JACK VANCE, THE   VANCE, JACK   AC
  KOKOD WARRIORS, THE   NV   TWS 52 10
    MANY WORLDS OF MAGNUS RIDOLPH, THE   VANCE, JACK   DC
    WORLDS OF JACK VANCE, THE   VANCE, JACK   AC
  LAST CASTLE, THE   NV   GAL 66 04
    ACE SCIENCE FICTION READER   WOLLHEIM, DONALD A.   AN
    BEST OF JACK VANCE, THE   VANCE, JACK   AC
    HUGO WINNERS, THE (VOLUME 2)   ASIMOV, ISAAC   AN
    NEBULA AWARD STORIES NO. 2   ALDISS & HARRISON   AN
  LIANE THE WAYFARER   NV   50
    DYING EARTH, THE   VANCE, JACK   OC
  MAZIRIAN THE MAGICIAN   SS   50
    DYING EARTH, THE   VANCE, JACK   OC
    SPELL OF SEVEN, THE   DE CAMP, L. SPRAGUE   AN
  MEN OF THE TEN BOOKS   SS   STS 51 03
    BEST SCIENCE-FICTION STORIES: 1952, THE
                                       BLEILER & DIKTY   AN
    OUT OF THIS WORLD 1   WILLIAMS-ELLIS& OWEN   AN
  MEN RETURN, THE   SS   INF 57 07
    ALPHA 2   SILVERBERG, ROBERT   AN
    EIGHT FANTASMS AND MAGICS   VANCE, JACK   AC
    EVIL EARTHS   ALDISS, BRIAN W.   AN
    WORLD BETWEEN AND OTHER STORIES, THE   VANCE, JACK   DC
    WORLDS OF JACK VANCE, THE   VANCE, JACK   AC
  MIRACLE-WORKERS, THE   SN   ASF 58 07
    EIGHT FANTASMS AND MAGICS   VANCE, JACK   AC
  MITR, THE   SS   53
    SPACE OPERA   ALDISS, BRIAN W.   AN
  MOON MOTH, THE   NA   GAL 61 08
    ALPHA 1   SILVERBERG, ROBERT   AN
    BEST OF JACK VANCE, THE   VANCE, JACK   AC
    SCIENCE FICTION HALL OF FAME VOLUME 2B   BOVA, BEN   AN
    WORLD BETWEEN AND OTHER STORIES, THE   VANCE, JACK   DC

VANCE, JACK   (CONTINUED)
    WORLDS OF JACK VANCE, THE   VANCE, JACK   AC
NEW PRIME, THE   NV
    EIGHT FANTASMS AND MAGICS   VANCE, JACK   AC
NOISE   SS   STS 52 08
    BEST FROM STARTLING STORIES, THE   MINES, SAMUEL   AN
    DEEP SPACE   SILVERBERG, ROBERT   AN
    EIGHT FANTASMS AND MAGICS   VANCE, JACK   AC
POTTERS OF FIRSK, THE   SS   ASF 50 05
    TIME PROBE: THE SCIENCES IN SF.   CLARKE, ARTHUR C.   AN
PREFACE TO THE COLLECTION   IN
    BEST OF JACK VANCE, THE   VANCE, JACK   AC
RUMFUDDLE   NA   TTT 73
    BEST OF JACK VANCE, THE   VANCE, JACK   AC
    BEST SCIENCE FICTION OF THE YEAR, THE NO. 3
                                          CARR, TERRY   AN
    THREE TRIPS IN TIME AND SPACE   SILVERBERG, ROBERT   OA
SAIL 25 (GATEWAY TO STRANGENESS)   NV   AMZ 62 08
    BEST OF JACK VANCE, THE   VANCE, JACK   AC
    FUTURE TENSE   VANCE, JACK   AC
SPA OF THE STARS, THE   NV   STS 50 07
    MANY WORLDS OF MAGNUS RIDOLPH, THE   VANCE, JACK   DC
SUB-STANDARD SARDINES   SS   STS 49 01
    SPACE POLICE   NORTON, ANDRE   AN
SULWEN'S PLANET   SS   FRS 68
    FARTHEST REACHES, THE   ELDER, JOSEPH   OA
T'SAIS   NV   50
    DYING EARTH, THE   VANCE, JACK   OC
TELEK   SN   ASF 52 01
    EIGHT FANTASMS AND MAGICS   VANCE, JACK   AC
    GREAT SHORT NOVELS OF SCIENCE FICTION SILVERBERG, ROBERT   AN
TURJAN OF MIIR   NV   50
    DYING EARTH, THE   VANCE, JACK   OC
ULAN DHOR ENDS A DREAM   NV   50
    DYING EARTH, THE   VANCE, JACK   OC
ULLWARD'S RETREAT   NV   GAL 58 12
    BEST OF JACK VANCE, THE   VANCE, JACK   AC
    FUTURE TENSE   VANCE, JACK   AC
    SF: AUTHORS' CHOICE 4   HARRISON, HARRY   AN
UNSPEAKABLE MCINCH, THE   NV   STS 48 11
    MANY WORLDS OF MAGNUS RIDOLPH, THE   VANCE, JACK   DC
WHEN THE FIVE MOONS RISE   NV   CSM 54 03
    EIGHT FANTASMS AND MAGICS   VANCE, JACK   AC
WINNER LOSE ALL   SS   GAL 51 12
    OMNIBUS OF SCIENCE FICTION   CONKLIN, GROFF   AN
WORLD BETWEEN, THE   NV
    WORLD BETWEEN AND OTHER STORIES, THE VANCE, JACK   DC
    WORLDS OF JACK VANCE, THE   VANCE, JACK   AC

VARDEMAN, ROBERT E.
    BIOLOGICAL REVOLUTION, THE   SS   C
    2076: THE AMERICAN TRICENTENNIAL   BRYANT, EDWARD   OA

VARLEY, JOHN
    AIR RAID   SS   76
    BEST SCIENCE FICTION STORIES OF THE YEAR (1976)
                                          DOZOIS, GARDNER R.   AN
    IN THE BOWL   NV   FSF 75 12
    BEST SCIENCE FICTION OF THE YEAR, THE NO. 5
                                          CARR, TERRY   AN
    M&M SEEN AS A LOW-YIELD THERMONUCLEAR DEVICE, THE SS   ORB 76 18
    ORBIT 18   KNIGHT, DAMON   OA
    OVERDRAWN AT THE MEMORY BANK   NV   GAL 76 05
    1977 ANNUAL WORLD'S BEST SF, THE   WOLLHEIM, DONALD A.   AN
    PHANTOM OF KANSAS, THE   NV   GAL 76 02
    BEST SCIENCE FICTION OF THE YEAR, THE NO. 6
                                          CARR, TERRY   AN
    RETROGRADE SUMMER   NV   FSF 75 02
    BEST SCIENCE FICTION OF THE YEAR, THE NO. 5
                                          CARR, TERRY   AN

VARSHAVSKY, ILYA
    BIOCURRENTS, BIOCURRENTS...   SS
    OTHER WORLDS, OTHER SEAS   SUVIN, DARKO   AN
    CADET PLOSHKIN   NV
    JOURNEY ACROSS THREE WORLDS   ANONYMOUS   AN
    CONFLICT, THE   SS
    PATH INTO THE UNKNOWN   ANONYMOUS   AN
    ESCAPE   SS   73
    BEST SF: 1973   HARRISON & ALDISS   AN
    IN MAN'S OWN IMAGE   SS
    RUSSIAN SCIENCE FICTION, 1968   MAGIDOFF, ROBERT   AN
    LECTURES ON PARAPSYCHOLOGY   SS
    OTHER WORLDS, OTHER SEAS   SUVIN, DARKO   AN
    NONEATRINS, THE   SS
    OTHER WORLDS, OTHER SEAS   SUVIN, DARKO   AN
    OUT IN SPACE   SS
    LAST DOOR TO AIYA   GINSBURG, MIRRA   AN
    PRELIMINARY RESEARCH   SS   65
    ULTIMATE THRESHOLD, THE   GINSBURG, MIRRA   AN
    RAID TAKES PLACE AT MIDNIGHT, A   SS
    RUSSIAN SCIENCE FICTION, 1969   MAGIDOFF, ROBERT   AN
    ROBBIE   SS
    PATH INTO THE UNKNOWN   ANONYMOUS   AN
    SOMP   SS
    OTHER WORLDS, OTHER SEAS   SUVIN, DARKO   AN

VASILYEV, MIKHAIL
    FLYING FLOWERS   SS
    DESTINATION: AMALTHEIA   DIXON, RICHARD   AN
    RUSSIAN SCIENCE FICTION   MAGIDOFF, ROBERT   AN

VEILLOT, CLAUDE
    FIRST DAYS OF MAY, THE (FCT 60 05)   SS   FSF 61 12
    CENTURY OF SCIENCE FICTION, A   KNIGHT, DAMON   AN
    TALES OF TERROR FROM OUTER SPACE   CHETWYND-HAYES, R.   AN

VEILLOT, CLAUDE   (CONTINUED)
    LITTLE MORE CAVIAR?, A   SS   63
    13 FRENCH SCIENCE-FICTION STORIES   KNIGHT, DAMON   AN

VEITCH, TOM
    SEXUAL SONG, A   SS   QRK 71 03
    QUARK/3   DELANY & HACKER   OA

VENEZIS, ELIAS
    SEA GULLS, THE   SS   55
    NIGHT IN FUNLAND   BRONDFIELD, JEROME   AN

VERNE, JULES
    JULES VERNE- MASTER OF SCIENCE FICTION   AC H SID 56
    EDITED BY I. O. EVANS
    NOVELS   AC H GOL 29
    EDITED BY H. C. HARWOOD
    OMNIBUS, THE   AC H LIP 31
    YESTERDAY AND TOMORROW   AC H ARC 64
    EDITED BY I. O. EVANS
    ANTARCTIC MYSTERY, AN (THE MYSTERY OF ARTHUR GORDON PYM, 1897)
                                              EX   97
    JULES VERNE- MASTER OF SCIENCE FICTION VERNE, JULES   AC
    AROUND THE WORLD IN EIGHTY DAYS (1873)   NO
    NOVELS   VERNE, JULES   AC
    OMNIBUS, THE   VERNE, JULES   AC
    BEGUM'S FORTUNE, THE (1879)   EX
    ANDROIDS, TIME MACHINES AND BLUE GIRAFFES
                                          ELWOOD & GHIDALIA   AN
    JULES VERNE- MASTER OF SCIENCE FICTION VERNE, JULES   AC
    STRANGE SIGNPOSTS   ELWOOD & MOSKOWITZ   AN
    VISIONS OF TOMORROW   ELWOOD, ROGER   AN
    BLOCKADE RUNNERS, THE   NA
    NOVELS   VERNE, JULES   AC
    OMNIBUS, THE   VERNE, JULES   AC
    CAPTAIN NEMO'S THUNDERBOLT (FROM "20,000 LEAGUES UNDER
    THE SEA", 1873)   EX   GMS 73
    SCIENCE IN FICTION   BAYLISS, A.E. & J.C. AN
    CHILD OF THE CAVERN, THE (1877)   EX
    JULES VERNE- MASTER OF SCIENCE FICTION VERNE, JULES   AC
    CLIPPER OF THE CLOUDS, THE   EX   86
    JULES VERNE- MASTER OF SCIENCE FICTION VERNE, JULES   AC
    DR. OX'S EXPERIMENT (1874)   SS   AMZ 26 08
    *BEYOND TIME AND SPACE   DERLETH, AUGUST   AN
    DR. TRIFULGAS   SS   SND 92 07
    BEFORE ARMAGEDDON   MOORCOCK, MICHAEL   AN
    DROPPED FROM THE CLOUDS (THE MYSTERIOUS ISLAND, 1875)
                                              EX
    JULES VERNE- MASTER OF SCIENCE FICTION VERNE, JULES   AC
    ETERNAL ADAM, THE (1905)   NV   STN 57 03
    MASTERPIECES OF SCIENCE FICTION   MOSKOWITZ, SAM   AN
    YESTERDAY AND TOMORROW   VERNE, JULES   AC
    EXPRESS OF THE FUTURE, AN   SS   SND 95 01
    SCIENCE FICTION BY GASLIGHT   MOSKOWITZ, SAM   AN
    FATE OF JEAN MORENAS, THE   SS
    YESTERDAY AND TOMORROW   VERNE, JULES   AC
    FIVE WEEKS IN A BALLOON (1863)   EX
    JULES VERNE- MASTER OF SCIENCE FICTION VERNE, JULES   AC
    FLOATING ISLAND, THE (1895)   EX
    JULES VERNE- MASTER OF SCIENCE FICTION VERNE, JULES   AC
    FLOATING ISLAND, THE (1895)   NO
    NOVELS   VERNE, JULES   AC
    FOR THE FLAG (1896)   EX
    JULES VERNE- MASTER OF SCIENCE FICTION VERNE, JULES   AC
    FROM "TWENTY THOUSAND LEAGUES UNDER THE SEA" (1873)
                                              EX
    PAST, PRESENT, AND FUTURE PERFECT   WOLFE, G&FITZ GERALD AN
    FROM THE EARTH TO THE MOON (1865)   EX
    JULES VERNE- MASTER OF SCIENCE FICTION VERNE, JULES   AC
    FROM THE EARTH TO THE MOON AND A TRIP AROUND IT (1865)
                                              NO
    OMNIBUS, THE   VERNE, JULES   AC
    FRRITT-FLACC (1884)   SS   FSF 59 11
    YESTERDAY AND TOMORROW   VERNE, JULES   AC
    GIL BRALTAR (1857)   SS   FSF 58 07
    BEST FROM FANTASY AND SCIENCE FICTION: 8
                                          BOUCHER, ANTHONY   AN
    YESTERDAY AND TOMORROW   VERNE, JULES   AC
    HECTOR SERVADAC (1877)   EX
    JULES VERNE- MASTER OF SCIENCE FICTION VERNE, JULES   AC
    HECTOR SERVADAC (1877)   NO
    NOVELS   VERNE, JULES   AC
    IDEAL CITY, AN   SS
    YESTERDAY AND TOMORROW   VERNE, JULES   AC
    IN THE TWENTY NINTH CENTURY (ARS 49 SU)   SS   FRM 89 02
    YESTERDAY AND TOMORROW   VERNE, JULES   AC
    IN THE YEAR 2889 (ARS 49 SU)   SS   FRM 89 02
    *BIG BOOK OF SCIENCE FICTION   CONKLIN, GROFF   AN
    INTO SPACE   NV
    GREAT SCIENCE FICTION STORIES   SMITH, CORDELIA T.   AN
    INTO THE UNKNOWN (FROM "20,000 LEAGUES UNDER THE SEA")
                                              EX   GMS 73
    SCIENCE FICTION THROUGH THE AGES 1   EVANS, I. O.   AN
    JOURNEY TO THE CENTER OF THE EARTH, A (1864) EX   AMZ 26 05
    FROM FRANKENSTEIN TO ANDROMEDA   BROWN, JAMES GOLDIE   AN
    JULES VERNE- MASTER OF SCIENCE FICTION VERNE, JULES   AC
    JOURNEY TO THE CENTER OF THE EARTH, A (1864) NO   AMZ 26 05
    JOURNEYS IN SCIENCE FICTION   LOUGHLIN, RICHARD L. AN
    MR. RAY SHARP AND MISS ME FLAT (1893)   SS
    YESTERDAY AND TOMORROW   VERNE, JULES   AC
    NAUTILUS REACHES THE POLE, THE (FROM "20,000 LEAGUES
    UNDER THE SEA")   EX   GMS 73
    ARMCHAIR SCIENCE READER, THE   GORDON, I. & SORKIN   AN
    ROUND THE MOON (1870)   EX
    JULES VERNE- MASTER OF SCIENCE FICTION VERNE, JULES   AC

VERNE, JULES   (CONTINUED)
  ROUND THE MOON (1870)   NO
    TREASURY OF SCIENCE FICTION CLASSICS, THE
                                        KUEBLER, HAROLD W.   AN
  SECRET OF THE ISLAND, THE (THE MYSTERIOUS ISLAND, 1875)
                                                     EX
    JULES VERNE- MASTER OF SCIENCE FICTION VERNE, JULES   AC
  STEAM HOUSE, THE (1880)   EX   SCB 81
    JULES VERNE- MASTER OF SCIENCE FICTION VERNE, JULES   AC
  TEN HOURS HUNTING   SS
    YESTERDAY AND TOMORROW   VERNE, JULES   AC
  TWENTY THOUSAND LEAGUES UNDER THE SEA (1873)   EX   GMS 73
    CENTURY OF SCIENCE FICTION, A   KNIGHT, DAMON   AN
    JULES VERNE- MASTER OF SCIENCE FICTION VERNE, JULES   AC
  TWENTY THOUSAND LEAGUES UNDER THE SEA (1873)   NO   GMS 73
    NOVELS   VERNE, JULES   AC
    OMNIBUS, THE   VERNE, JULES   AC

VERNON, ROGER LEE
  SPACE FRONTIERS, THE   AC   SIG 55 08
  BATTLE   SS
    SPACE FRONTIERS, THE   VERNON, ROGER LEE AC
  CHESS CIVILIZATION, THE   SS
    SPACE FRONTIERS, THE   VERNON, ROGER LEE AC
  CITY AND THE SHIP, THE   NV
    SPACE FRONTIERS, THE   VERNON, ROGER LEE AC
  DEATH SEEKERS, THE   NV
    SPACE FRONTIERS, THE   VERNON, ROGER LEE AC
  INCIDENT IN SPACE   SS
    SPACE FRONTIERS, THE   VERNON, ROGER LEE AC
  PLANT WORLD, THE   SS
    SPACE FRONTIERS, THE   VERNON, ROGER LEE AC
  POPULATION CRISIS: 2550   SS
    SPACE FRONTIERS, THE   VERNON, ROGER LEE AC
  STOP WATCH, THE   SS
    SPACE FRONTIERS, THE   VERNON, ROGER LEE AC
  XENOPHOBIA   NV
    SPACE FRONTIERS, THE   VERNON, ROGER LEE AC

VIAN, BORIS
  DEAD FISH, THE   SS   55
    13 FRENCH SCIENCE-FICTION STORIES   KNIGHT, DAMON   AN

VICKERS, BRIAN
  CODED SUN GAME, THE   NA   QRK 71 03
    QUARK/3   DELANY & HACKER   OA

VIDAL, GORE
  VISIT TO A SMALL PLANET   PL   55
    JOURNEYS IN SCIENCE FICTION   LOUGHLIN, RICHARD L. AN

VINCENT, HARL   PSEUD. FOR HARL VINCENT SCHOEPFLIN
  LIFE INSIDE A WALL   SS   SFQ 40 SU
    MOON CONQUERORS, THE   ANONYMOUS   AN
  PROWLER OF THE WASTELANDS   SS   ASF 35 04
    STRANGE SIGNPOSTS   ELWOOD & MOSKOWITZ AN
  REX   SS   ASF 34 06
    COMING OF THE ROBOTS, THE   MOSKOWITZ, SAM   AN

VINGE, JOAN D.
  CRYSTAL SHIP, THE   NA
    CRYSTAL SHIP, THE   SILVERBERG, ROBERT OA
  MOTHER AND CHILD   NA   ORB 75 16
    ORBIT 16   KNIGHT, DAMON   OA
  PEDDLER'S APPRENTICE, THE   NV C ASF 75 08
    BEST SCIENCE FICTION STORIES OF THE YEAR (1975)
                                          DEL REY, LESTER   AN
    1976 ANNUAL WORLD'S BEST SF, THE   WOLLHEIM, DONALD A. AN
  TIN SOLDIER   NA   ORB 74 14
    MORE WOMEN OF WONDER   SARGENT, PAMELA   AN
    ORBIT 14   KNIGHT, DAMON   OA

VINGE, VERNOR
  APARTMENT   SS   NWS 65 06
    WORLD'S BEST SCIENCE FICTION: 1966   WOLLHEIM & CARR   AN
  BOMB SCARE   SS   ASF 70 11
    TOMORROW, AND TOMORROW, AND TOMORROW...
                                          HEINTZ/HERBERT/JOOS/ AN
  BOOKWORM, RUN| NV   ASF 66 03
    ANALOG 6   CAMPBELL, JOHN W. JR AN
  GRIMM'S STORY   NA   ORB 68 04
    ORBIT 4   KNIGHT, DAMON   OA
  LONG SHOT   SS   ASF 72 08
    BEST SCIENCE FICTION STORIES OF THE YEAR (1972)
                                          DEL REY, LESTER   AN
    1973 ANNUAL WORLD'S BEST SF, THE   WOLLHEIM, DONALD A. AN
  PEDDLER'S APPRENTICE, THE   NV C ASF 75 08
    BEST SCIENCE FICTION STORIES OF THE YEAR (1975)
                                          DEL REY, LESTER   AN
    1976 ANNUAL WORLD'S BEST SF, THE   WOLLHEIM, DONALD A. AN
  SCIENCE FAIR, THE   SS   ORB 71 09
    ORBIT 9   KNIGHT, DAMON   OA
  WHIRLIGIG OF TIME, THE   SS   STL 74 01
    STELLAR 1   DEL REY, JUDY-LYNN OA

VIVIAN, THOMAS J.
  TILTING ISLAND, THE   SS C EVB 09 09
    SCIENCE FICTION BY GASLIGHT   MOSKOWITZ, SAM   AN

VOISKUNSKY, YEVGENY
  FAREWELL ON THE SHORE, A   NV C
    RUSSIAN SCIENCE FICTION, 1969   MAGIDOFF, ROBERT   AN
  FORMULA FOR THE IMPOSSIBLE   SS C
    RUSSIAN SCIENCE FICTION, 1968   MAGIDOFF, ROBERT   AN

VOLTAIRE   PSEUD. FOR FRANCOIS MARIE AROUET
  MICROMEGAS   NV
    PAST, PRESENT, AND FUTURE PERFECT   WOLFE, J&FITZ GERALD AN
  VISITORS FROM OUTER SPACE (FROM "MICROMEGAS")   EX
    SCIENCE FICTION THROUGH THE AGES 1   EVANS, I. O.   AN

VOM SCHEIDT, JURGEN
  BLINDNESS   SS   SFM 74 09
    BEST OF SCIENCE FICTION MONTHLY, THE   SACKS, JANET   AN

VON WALD, E. G.
  HEMEAC   SS   GAL 68 08
    AS TOMORROW BECOMES TODAY   SULLIVAN, CHARLES W. AN
    EARTH IN TRANSIT   SCHWARTZ, SHEILA   AN
    SCIENCE FICTION   BRODKIN & PEARSON AN
    TOMORROW, AND TOMORROW, AND TOMORROW...
                                          HEINTZ/HERBERT/JOOS/ AN
    WORLD'S BEST SCIENCE FICTION: 1969   WOLLHEIM & CARR   AN

VONNEGUT, KURT JR.
  CANARY IN A CAT HOUSE   AC   PAW 61 09
  WELCOME TO THE MONKEY HOUSE   AC H DCT 68
  ADAM   SS   CMP 54 04
    WELCOME TO THE MONKEY HOUSE   VONNEGUT, KURT JR. AC
  ALL THE KING'S HORSES   SS   COL 51 02
    CANARY IN A CAT HOUSE   VONNEGUT, KURT JR. AC
    WELCOME TO THE MONKEY HOUSE   VONNEGUT, KURT JR. AC
  BIG SPACE FUCK, THE   SS   DVS 72 02
    AGAIN, DANGEROUS VISIONS   ELLISON, HARLAN   OA
  BIG TRIP UP YONDER, THE (ALSO AS TOMORROW AND TOMORROW
    AND TOMORROW)   SS   GAL 54 01
    ASSIGNMENT IN TOMORROW   POHL, FREDERIK   AN
  D.P.   SS   LHJ 53 08
    CANARY IN A CAT HOUSE   VONNEGUT, KURT JR. AC
    WELCOME TO THE MONKEY HOUSE   VONNEGUT, KURT JR. AC
  DEER IN THE WORKS   SS   ESQ 55 04
    CANARY IN A CAT HOUSE   VONNEGUT, KURT JR. AC
    RUINS OF EARTH, THE   DISCH, THOMAS M.   AN
    WELCOME TO THE MONKEY HOUSE   VONNEGUT, KURT JR. AC
  EPICAC   SS   COL 50 11
    SCIENCE FACT/FICTION   FARRELL/GAGE/&   AN
    THEMES IN SCIENCE FICTION   KELLEY, LEO P.   AN
    WELCOME TO THE MONKEY HOUSE   VONNEGUT, KURT JR. AC
  EUPHIO QUESTION, THE   SS   COL 51 05
    CANARY IN A CAT HOUSE   VONNEGUT, KURT JR. AC
    WELCOME TO THE MONKEY HOUSE   VONNEGUT, KURT JR. AC
  FORTITUDE   SS   PBY 68 09
    HUMAN-MACHINES   SCORTIA & ZEBROWSKI AN
    MASKS   PLAYBOY, EDITORS OF AN
  FOSTER PORTFOLIO, THE   SS   COL 51 09
    CANARY IN A CAT HOUSE   VONNEGUT, KURT JR. AC
    WELCOME TO THE MONKEY HOUSE   VONNEGUT, KURT JR. AC
  FROM: PLAYER PIANO   EX   HRW 52
    INSIDE INFORMATION   MOWSHOWITZ, ABBE   AN
  GO BACK TO YOUR PRECIOUS WIFE AND SON   SS   LHJ 62 07
    WELCOME TO THE MONKEY HOUSE   VONNEGUT, KURT JR. AC
  HAL IRWIN'S MAGIC LAMP   SS   CMP 57 06
    CANARY IN A CAT HOUSE   VONNEGUT, KURT JR. AC
  HARRISON BERGERON   SS   FSF 61 10
    ABC OF SCIENCE FICTION, AN   BOARDMAN, TOM JR. AN
    *BEST FROM FANTASY AND SCIENCE FICTION: 11
                                          MILLS, ROBERT P.   AN
    BEST SF 7   CRISPIN, EDMUND   AN
    DECADE THE 1960S   ALDISS & HARRISON AN
    SCIENCE FICTION   BRODKIN & PEARSON AN
    SCIENCE FICTION: THE FUTURE   ALLEN, DICK   AN
    STARLIT CORRIDOR, THE   MANSFIELD, ROGER   AN
    WELCOME TO THE MONKEY HOUSE   VONNEGUT, KURT JR. AC
  HYANNIS PORT STORY, THE   SS   NEW 68 AC
    WELCOME TO THE MONKEY HOUSE   VONNEGUT, KURT JR. AC
  KID NOBODY COULD HANDLE, THE   SS   SEP 55 09
    WELCOME TO THE MONKEY HOUSE   VONNEGUT, KURT JR. AC
  LIE, THE   SS   SEP 62 02
    WELCOME TO THE MONKEY HOUSE   VONNEGUT, KURT JR. AC
  LONG WALK TO FOREVER   SS   LHJ 60 08
    WELCOME TO THE MONKEY HOUSE   VONNEGUT, KURT JR. AC
  MANNED MISSILES, THE   SS   CMP 58 07
    CANARY IN A CAT HOUSE   VONNEGUT, KURT JR. AC
    WELCOME TO THE MONKEY HOUSE   VONNEGUT, KURT JR. AC
  MISS TEMPTATION   SS   SEP 56 04
    WELCOME TO THE MONKEY HOUSE   VONNEGUT, KURT JR. AC
  MORE STATELY MANSIONS   SS   COL 51 12
    CANARY IN A CAT HOUSE   VONNEGUT, KURT JR. AC
    WELCOME TO THE MONKEY HOUSE   VONNEGUT, KURT JR. AC
  MY NAME IS EVERYONE (SEE WHO AM I THIS TIME?)   TC
  NEW DICTIONARY (THE RANDOM HOUSE DICTIONARY)   BR   NYT 66 10
    WELCOME TO THE MONKEY HOUSE   VONNEGUT, KURT JR. AC
  NEXT DOOR   SS   CMP 55 04
    WELCOME TO THE MONKEY HOUSE   VONNEGUT, KURT JR. AC
  PREFACE   IN
    WELCOME TO THE MONKEY HOUSE   VONNEGUT, KURT JR. AC
  RANDOMHOUSE DICTIONARY, THE (SEE NEW DICTIONARY)   TC
  REPORT ON THE BARNHOUSE EFFECT   SS   COL 50 02
    CANARY IN A CAT HOUSE   VONNEGUT, KURT JR. AC
    JOURNEYS IN SCIENCE FICTION   LOUGHLIN, RICHARD L. AN
    SPECULATIONS   SANDERS, THOMAS E. AN
    TOMORROW, THE STARS   HEINLEIN, ROBERT A. AN
    WELCOME TO THE MONKEY HOUSE   VONNEGUT, KURT JR. AC
  TOM EDISON'S SHAGGY DOG   SS   COL 53 03
    CANARY IN A CAT HOUSE   VONNEGUT, KURT JR. AC
    WELCOME TO THE MONKEY HOUSE   VONNEGUT, KURT JR. AC
  TOMORROW AND TOMORROW AND TOMORROW (THE BIG TRIP UP YONDER)
                                                     SS   GAL 54 01
    CANARY IN A CAT HOUSE   VONNEGUT, KURT JR. AC
    CONNOISSEUR'S S. F.   BOARDMAN, TOM JR. AN
    ECO-FICTION   STADLER, JOHN   AN

VONNEGUT, KURT JR.   WANDREI, DONALD

VONNEGUT, KURT JR.   (CONTINUED)
    LOOKING AHEAD   ALLEN, D. & L.   AN
    WELCOME TO THE MONKEY HOUSE   VONNEGUT, KURT JR. AC
  UNREADY TO WEAR   SS GAL 53 04
    CANARY IN A CAT HOUSE   VONNEGUT, KURT JR. AC
    SECOND GALAXY READER OF SCIENCE FICTION
                                       GOLD, H. L.   AN
    WELCOME TO THE MONKEY HOUSE   VONNEGUT, KURT JR. AC
  WELCOME TO THE MONKEY HOUSE   SS PBY 68 01
    FIEND, THE   PLAYBOY, EDITORS OF AN
    PAST, PRESENT, AND FUTURE PERFECT WOLFE, J&FITZ GERALD AN
    PLAYBOY'S STORIES OF THE SINISTER & STRANGE
                                       PLAYBOY, EDITORS OF AN
    WELCOME TO THE MONKEY HOUSE   VONNEGUT, KURT JR. AC
    WORLD'S BEST SCIENCE FICTION: 1969 WOLLHEIM & CARR   AN
  WHERE I LIVE (YOU'VE NEVER BEEN TO BARNSTABLE?) AR VTR 64 10
    WELCOME TO THE MONKEY HOUSE   VONNEGUT, KURT JR. AC
  WHO AM I THIS TIME? (MY NAME IS EVERYONE) SS SEP 61 12
    WELCOME TO THE MONKEY HOUSE   VONNEGUT, KURT JR. AC
    YOU AND SCIENCE FICTION   HOLLISTER, BERNARD C AN
  YOU'VE NEVER BEEN TO BARNSTABLE? (SEE WHERE I LIVE)
                                       TC
  2 B R 0 2 B   SS IFS 62 01
    BEST SCIENCE FICTION FROM IF, THE POHL, FREDERIK   AN

WADSWORTH, PHYLLIS M
  OVERMIND   NO SID 67
    SCIENCE FICTION SPECIAL 3   ANONYMOUS   AN

WAKEFIELD, H.RUSSELL
  ANIMALS IN THE CASE, THE   SS   62
    SATAN'S PETS   GHIDALIA, VIC   AN
  DEATH OF A BUMBLEBEE   SS
    TRAVELLERS BY NIGHT   DERLETH, AUGUST   OA

WALDE, A. A.
  BIRCHER   NV IFS 66 07
    WORLD'S BEST SCIENCE FICTION: 1967 WOLLHEIM & CARR   AN

WALDROP, F. N.
  TOMORROW'S CHILDREN   NV C ASF 47 03
    MUTANTS   SILVERBERG, ROBERT AN
    *TREASURY OF SCIENCE FICTION, A   CONKLIN, GROFF   AN

WALDROP, HOWARD
  BLACK AS THE PIT, FROM POLE TO POLE   NV C NDM 77 07
    NEW DIMENSIONS 7   SILVERBERG, ROBERT OA
  CUSTER'S LAST JUMP   NV C UNI 76 06
    BEST SCIENCE FICTION OF THE YEAR, THE NO. 6
                                       CARR, TERRY   AN
    BEST SCIENCE FICTION STORIES OF THE YEAR (1976)
                                       DOZOIS, GARDNER R. AN
    UNIVERSE 6   CARR, TERRY   OA
  MARY MARGARET ROAD-GRADER   SS ORB 76 18
    BEST SCIENCE FICTION STORIES OF THE YEAR (1976)
                                       DOZOIS, GARDNER R. AN
    ORBIT 18   KNIGHT, DAMON   OA
  MY SWEET LADY JO   SS UNI 74 04
    UNIVERSE 4   CARR, TERRY   OA
  SIC TRANSIT...?, A SHAGGY HAIRLESS-DOG STORY SS C STL 76 02
    STELLAR 2   DEL REY, JUDY-LYNN OA
  SUN UP   SS C   76
    FASTER THAN LIGHT   DANN & ZEBROWSKI   OA
  UNSLEEPING BEAUTY AND THE BEAST   SS
    LONE STAR UNIVERSE   PROCTOR & UTLEY   OA
  VOICE AND BITTER WEEPING, A   SS C GAL 73 07
    BEST FROM GALAXY, THE   VOLUME II GALAXY, EDITORS OF AN

WALKER, DALE L.
  CURIOUS FRAGMENTS (LISTED UNDER JACK LONDON) EC H KNK 75

WALLACE, F. L.
  ACCIDENTAL FLIGHT   NA GAL 52 04
    TIME WAITS FOR WINTHROP, AND FOUR OTHER SHORT NOVELS
                                       POHL, FREDERIK   AN
  BIG ANCESTOR   NV GAL 54 11
    FIVE-ODD   CONKLIN, GROFF   AN
    GALACTIC EMPIRES VOLUME TWO   ALDISS, BRIAN W.   AN
  BOLDEN'S PETS   NV GAL 55 10
    GREAT SCIENCE FICTION ABOUT DOCTORS CONKLIN, G&FABRICANT AN
  DELAY IN TRANSIT   NA GAL 52 09
    BODYGUARD AND 4 OTHER SHORT SF NOVELS FROM GALAXY
                                       GOLD, H. L.   AN
  END AS A WORLD   SS GAL 55 09
    THIRD GALAXY READER, THE   GOLD, H. L.   AN
  GROWING SEASON   NV IFS 59 07
    FROZEN PLANET AND 4 OTHER SF NOVELLAS, THE
                                       ANONYMOUS   AN
  IMPOSSIBLE VOYAGE HOME, THE   NV GAL 54 08
    *SCIENCE FICTION ADVENTURES IN MUTATION CONKLIN, GROFF AN
  MEZZEROW LOVES COMPANY   NV GAL 56 06
    WORLD THAT COULDN'T BE AND 8 OTHER SF NOVELETS
                                       GOLD, H. L.   AN
  STUDENT BODY   NV GAL 53 03
    CROSSROADS IN TIME   CONKLIN, GROFF   AN
    GALAXY SCIENCE FICTION OMNIBUS   GOLD, H. L.   AN
    SECOND GALAXY READER OF SCIENCE FICTION
                                       GOLD, H. L.   AN
    SPECTRUM 5   AMIS & CONQUEST   AN
    VOYAGES: SCENARIOS FOR A SHIP CALLED EARTH
                                       SAUER, ROB   AN
  TANGLE HOLD   NA GAL 53 06
    5 GALAXY SHORT NOVELS   GOLD, H. L.   AN

WALLACE, ROBERT
  LIVING DOLL, A   SS HRP 64 01
    10TH ANNUAL OF THE YEAR'S BEST S-F, THE
                                       MERRIL, JUDITH   AN

WALLACE, ROBIN E.
  CANIS FAMILIARIS   SS C
    FUTURE PASTIMES   EDELSTEIN, SCOTT   OA

WALLIS, GEORGE C.
  GREAT SACRIFICE, THE   SS LON 03 06
    WORLDS APART   LOCKE, GEORGE   AN

WALLMANN, JEFFREY
  EVERGREEN LIBRARY, THE   SS C VSF 70 05
    WONDERMAKERS 2   HOSKINS, ROBERT   AN

WALPOLE, HORACE
  SATURNIA CELIA (1903)   SS FSF 57 04
    DECADE OF FANTASY AND SCIENCE FICTION, A
                                       MILLS, ROBERT P.   AN

WALSH, BUTHRAM
  CASE OF OMEGA SMITH, THE   SS
    AD 2500   WILSON, ANGUS   AN

WALSH, GEORGE E.
  CAPTAIN SAMPSON'S QUEER CARGO   SS
    BATTLE FOR THE PACIFIC AND OTHER ADVENTURES AT SEA, THE
                                       ANONYMOUS   AN
    PRIVATE OR PRIVATEER?   SS
    BATTLE FOR THE PACIFIC AND OTHER ADVENTURES AT SEA, THE
                                       ANONYMOUS   AN

WALTER, W. GREY
  SINGERS, THE   SS   56
    EXPERT DREAMERS, THE   POHL, FREDERIK   AN

WALTERS, DAVID H.
  SENTENCED TO A SCHEHRRAZADEAN DEATH   SS NWR 76 29
    NEW WRITINGS IN SF. 29   BULMER, KENNETH   OA

WALTON, BRYCE   ALSO AS   KENNETH O'HARA
  HAPPY HERD, THE   NV IFS 56 10
    SECOND WORLD OF IF, THE   QUINN & WULFF   AN
  MARY ANONYMOUS   SS PLS 54 SU
    EARTH IN PERIL, THE   WOLLHEIM, DONALD A. DA
  TO EACH HIS STAR   SS SSF 52 05
    SPACE ODYSSEYS   ALDISS, BRIAN W.   AN
  TOO LATE FOR ETERNITY   NO STS 55 SP
    DR. CYCLOPS   KUTTNER, HENRY   AN

WALTON, HARRY
  EPISODE ON DHEE MINOR   SS ASF 39 10
    TRAVELLERS OF SPACE   GREENBERG , MARTIN AN
  HOUSING SHORTAGE   SS ASF 47 01
    *TREASURY OF SCIENCE FICTION, A   CONKLIN, GROFF   AN
  INTELLIGENCE TEST   SS SFP 53 05
    CONTACT   KEYES, NOEL   AN
  SCHEDULE   SS ASF 45 06
    *MEN AGAINST THE STARS   GREENBERG , MARTIN AN

WANDREI, DONALD
  EYE AND THE FINGER   AC H ARK 44
  STRANGE HARVEST   AC H ARK 65
  ATOM SMASHER, THE   SS ASF 34 04
    STRANGE HARVEST   WANDREI, DONALD   AC
  BLACK FOG   SS TWS 37 02
    EYE AND THE FINGER   WANDREI, DONALD   AC
  BLINDING SHADOWS   SS ASF 34 05
    *BEACHHEADS IN SPACE   DERLETH, AUGUST   AN
    EYE AND THE FINGER   WANDREI, DONALD   AC
  CHUCKLER, THE   SS
    STRANGE HARVEST   WANDREI, DONALD   AC
  COLOSSUS   NV ASF 34 01
    BEFORE THE GOLDEN AGE   ASIMOV, ISAAC   AN
    *BEYOND TIME AND SPACE   DERLETH, AUGUST   AN
  CRATER, THE   SS
    TRAVELLERS BY NIGHT   DERLETH, AUGUST   OA
  CRYSTAL BULLET, THE   SS WRT 41 03
    EYE AND THE FINGER   WANDREI, DONALD   AC
    *STRANGE PORTS OF CALL   DERLETH, AUGUST   AN
  DESTROYING HORDE, THE   SS WRT 35 06
    STRANGE HARVEST   WANDREI, DONALD   AC
  EARTH MINUS   NV ASF 35 09
    EYE AND THE FINGER   WANDREI, DONALD   AC
  EYE AND THE FINGER   SS
    EYE AND THE FINGER   WANDREI, DONALD   AC
  FINALITY UNLIMITED   SN ASF 36 09
    EYE AND THE FINGER   WANDREI, DONALD   AC
    *OUTER REACHES, THE   DERLETH, AUGUST   AN
  FIRE VAMPIRES, THE   SS WRT 33 02
    STRANGE HARVEST   WANDREI, DONALD   AC
  FRAGMENT OF A DREAM   SS
    EYE AND THE FINGER   WANDREI, DONALD   AC
  GIANT-PLASM   SS WRT 39 02
    STRANGE HARVEST   WANDREI, DONALD   AC
  GREEN FLAME, THE   SS WRT 30 07
    STRANGE HARVEST   WANDREI, DONALD   AC
  INFINITY ZERO   SS ASF 36 10
    FAR BOUNDARIES   DERLETH, AUGUST   AN
    STRANGE HARVEST   WANDREI, DONALD   AC
  IT WILL GROW ON YOU   SS
    EYE AND THE FINGER   WANDREI, DONALD   AC
  LADY IN GRAY, THE   SS WRT 33 12
    EYE AND THE FINGER   WANDREI, DONALD   AC

WANDREI, DONALD   WEINBAUM, STANLEY G.

WANDREI, DONALD   (CONTINUED)
  LIFE CURRENT   SS   ASF 35 04
    STRANGE HARVEST   WANDREI, DONALD   AC
  LIVES OF ALFRED KRAMER, THE   SS   WRT 32 12
    EYE AND THE FINGER   WANDREI, DONALD   AC
  MAN WHO NEVER LIVED, THE   SS   ASF 34 03
    STRANGE HARVEST   WANDREI, DONALD   AC
  MESSENGERS, THE   SS
    EYE AND THE FINGER   WANDREI, DONALD   AC
  MONSTER FROM NOWHERE, THE   SS   ARG 35 11
    EYE AND THE FINGER   WANDREI, DONALD   AC
  MURRAY'S LIGHT   SS   ASF 35 06
    STRANGE HARVEST   WANDREI, DONALD   AC
  NERVELESS MAN, THE   SS   ASF 34 07
    EYE AND THE FINGER   WANDREI, DONALD   AC
  NIGHTMARE   SS
    STRANGE HARVEST   WANDREI, DONALD   AC
  ON THE THRESHOLD OF ETERNITY   SS
    EYE AND THE FINGER   WANDREI, DONALD   AC
  PAINTED MIRROR, THE   SS   AFR 49 09
    EYE AND THE FINGER   WANDREI, DONALD   AC
    SECOND AVON FANTASY READER, THE WOLLHEIM &ERNSBERGER AN
  PURSUERS, THE   SS
    EYE AND THE FINGER   WANDREI, DONALD   AC
  RED BRAIN, THE   SS   WRT 27 10
    EYE AND THE FINGER   WANDREI, DONALD   AC
  SCIENTIST DIVIDES, A   SS   ASF 34 09
    *BEST OF SCIENCE FICTION   CONKLIN, GROFF   AN
    EYE AND THE FINGER   WANDREI, DONALD   AC
  SOMETHING FROM ABOVE   NV   WRT 30 12
    *OTHER SIDE OF THE MOON, THE   DERLETH, AUGUST   AN
    STRANGE HARVEST   WANDREI, DONALD   AC
  SPAWN OF THE SEA   NV   WRT 33 05
    STRANGE HARVEST   WANDREI, DONALD   AC
  STRANGE HARVEST   NV   WRT 53 05
    NIGHTMARE GARDEN   GHIDALIA, VIC   AN
    STRANGE HARVEST   WANDREI, DONALD   AC
    *WORLDS OF TOMORROW   DERLETH, AUGUST   AN
  TREE MEN OF M'BWA, THE   SS   WRT 32 02
    EYE AND THE FINGER   WANDREI, DONALD   AC
  TRIP TO INFINITY, A   NV
    STRANGE HARVEST   WANDREI, DONALD   AC
  UNEASY LIE THE DROWNED   NV   WRT 37 12
    STRANGE HARVEST   WANDREI, DONALD   AC
  WITCH-MAKERS, THE   SS   ARG 36 05
    EYE AND THE FINGER   WANDREI, DONALD   AC
  WOMAN AT THE WINDOW   SS
    EYE AND THE FINGER   WANDREI, DONALD   AC

WANDREI, HOWARD E.   ALSO AS
    HOWARD W. GRAHAM AND H. W. GUERNSEY
  GOD-BOX, THE   SS   ASF 34 04
    *STRANGE PORTS OF CALL   DERLETH, AUGUST   AN

WARD, ARTHUR S.   SEE PSEUD. SAX ROHMER

WARD, CHARLES W.
  PRELIMINARY INVESTIGATION OF AN EARLY MAN SITE IN THE DELAWARE
    RIVER VALLEY   FA C
    APEMAN, SPACEMAN   STOVER & HARRISON   AN

WARDEN, ANTHON
  TIMESPRAWL   SS   INY 71 02
    INFINITY 2   HOSKINS, ROBERT   OA

WARLAND, ALAN
  BABY DREAMS   SS   SFQ 41 WI
    INTO THE FOURTH DIMENSION   CUMMINGS, RAY   AN

WARRICK, PATRICIA S. AND MARTIN HARRY GREENBERG
  NEW AWARENESS, THE   AN H DCT 75

WARRICK, PATRICIA S. SEE ALSO
    CO-EDITORS V. CLEAR, M. H. GREENBERG, H. KATZ, C. MASON,
    J. MILSTEAD AND J. OLANDER
  INTRODUCTION   IN C
    MARRIAGE AND THE FAMILY THROUGH SCIENCE FICTION
                                     CLEAR/WARRICK/&   AN
    NEW AWARENESS, THE   WARRICK & GREENBERG AN
    POLITICAL SCIENCE FICTION   GREENBERG& WARRICK   AN
    RUN TO STARLIGHT, SPORTS THROUGH SCIENCE FICTION
                                     GREENBERG/OLANDER/& AN
    SCHOOL AND SOCIETY THROUGH SCIENCE FICTION
                                     OLANDER/GREENBERG/& AN
    SOCIAL PROBLEMS THROUGH SCIENCE FICTION
                                     GREENBERG/MILSTEAD/& AN
    SOCIOLOGY THROUGH SCIENCE FICTION MILSTEAD/GREENBERG/& AN
  PREFACE   IN C
    AMERICAN GOVERNMENT THROUGH SCIENCE FICTION
                                     OLANDER/GREENBERG/& AN
    ANTHROPOLOGY THROUGH SCIENCE FICTION MASON, C/GREENBERG/& AN
    INTRODUCTORY PSYCHOLOGY THROUGH SCIENCE FICTION
                                     KATZ/WARRICK/&   AN
    NEW AWARENESS, THE   WARRICK & GREENBERG AN
    POLITICAL SCIENCE FICTION   GREENBERG& WARRICK   AN

WATERLOO, STANLEY
  CHRISTMAS 200,000 B.C. (1887)   SS   87
    FUTURE PERFECT   FRANKLIN, H. BRUCE   AN
  LOVE AND THE TRIANGLE   SS   99
    ANCESTRAL VOICES   MENVILLE & REGINALD AN

WATKINS, JOAN N.
  MAGIC TRICK   SS   YNW
    SCIENCE FICTION STORIES   BRADLEY, JOHANNA   AN

WATKINS, WILLIAM JON
  LIKE SNOW-HUMPED FIELDS AFRAID OF RAIN   PM
    2076: THE AMERICAN TRICENTENNIAL BRYANT, EDWARD   OA
  TWO POEMS   PM   CND 73
    BEST SF: 1973   HARRISON & ALDISS   AN

WATSON, IAN
  EA 5000: REPORT ON THE EFFECTS OF RIOT GAS SS
    STOPWATCH   HAY, GEORGE   OA
  EVENT HORIZON, THE   NV   76
    FASTER THAN LIGHT   DANN & ZEBROWSKI   OA
  GHOSTS OF LUNA, THE   SS   NWQ 74 06
    NEW WORLDS NO. 6   PLATT & BAILEY   OA
  PROGRAMMED LOVE STORY   SS   TRV 74
    BEST SF: 1974   HARRISON & ALDISS   AN
  SITTING ON A STARWOOD STOOL   SS   SFM 74 10
    BEST OF SCIENCE FICTION MONTHLY, THE SACKS, JANET   AN
  THY BLOOD LIKE MILK   NV   NWQ 73 05
    NEW WORLDS NO. 5   MOORCOCK & PLATT   OA
  TO THE PUMP ROOM WITH JANE   SS   NWR 75 26
    NEW WRITINGS IN SF. 26   BULMER, KENNETH   OA

WATSON, RAYMOND
  TWENTY-FIVE MILES ALOFT   SS
    ADVENTURES TO COME   ESENWEIN, J. BERG   OA

WEBB, LELAND
  MAN FOR THE MOON, A   SS   PBY 60 08
    DEAD ASTRONAUT, 10 STORIES OF SPACE FLIGHT, THE
                                     PLAYBOY, EDITORS OF AN
    PLAYBOY BOOK OF SCIENCE FICTION AND FANTASY, THE
                                     PLAYBOY, EDITORS OF AN

WEBB, RON
  GIRL WITH THE HUNDRED PROOF EYES, THE   SS   FSF 64 07
    BEST FROM FANTASY AND SCIENCE FICTION: 14
                                     DAVIDSON, AVRAM   AN

WEBB, VIC
  TWO PEOPLE WITHIN THE DESIGN   SS
    CLARION SF   WILHELM, KATE   OA

WEBB, W. T.
  FOR WHAT PURPOSE?   SS   NWR 68 11
    NEW WRITINGS IN SF. 11   CARNELL, JOHN   OA

WEBBERT, JAMES
  HAGGARD HONEYMOON   NV C NWR 64 01
    NEW WRITINGS IN SF. 1   CARNELL, JOHN   OA

WEHRLE, JOE JR.
  BANDEMAR, THE   SS   CLR 71 01
    CLARION   WILSON, ROBIN SCOTT OA

WEINBAUM, STANLEY G. ALSO AS   JOHN JESSEL
  BEST OF STANLEY G. WEINBAUM, THE   AC   BAL 74
  DAWN OF FLAME   AC H CHR 36
    THE WEINBAUM MEMORIAL VOLUME
  MARTIAN ODYSSEY AND OTHER SCIENCE FICTION TALES, A AC H HYP 74
    EDITED BY SAM MOSKOWITZ
  MARTIAN ODYSSEY AND OTHERS, A   AC H FPS 49
  MARTIAN ODYSSEY, A   AC   LAN 62
    AND OTHER CLASSICS OF SCIENCE FICTION, EDITED BY SAM MOSKOWITZ
  RED PERI, THE   AC H FPS 52
  ADAPTIVE ULTIMATE, THE   NV   ASF 35 11
    BEST OF STANLEY G. WEINBAUM, THE WEINBAUM, STANLEY G. AC
    DAWN OF FLAME   WEINBAUM, STANLEY G. AC
    MARTIAN ODYSSEY AND OTHER SCIENCE FICTION TALES, A
                                     WEINBAUM, STANLEY G. AC
    MARTIAN ODYSSEY AND OTHERS, A   WEINBAUM, STANLEY G. AC
    MARTIAN ODYSSEY, A   WEINBAUM, STANLEY G. AC
  AUTOBIOGRAPHICAL SKETCH OF STANLEY G. WEINBAUM, A MS
    MARTIAN ODYSSEY AND OTHER SCIENCE FICTION TALES, A
                                     WEINBAUM, STANLEY G. AC
  BRINK OF INFINITY, THE   SS   TWS 36 12
    MARTIAN ODYSSEY AND OTHER SCIENCE FICTION TALES, A
                                     WEINBAUM, STANLEY G. AC
    MARTIAN ODYSSEY, A   WEINBAUM, STANLEY G. AC
    RED PERI, THE   WEINBAUM, STANLEY G. AC
  CIRCLE OF ZERO, THE   SS   TWS 36 08
    HISTORY OF THE SCIENCE FICTION MAGAZINE, THE   PART 2 1936-1945
                                     ASHLEY, MICHAEL   AN
    MARTIAN ODYSSEY AND OTHER SCIENCE FICTION TALES, A
                                     WEINBAUM, STANLEY G. AC
    MARTIAN ODYSSEY AND OTHERS, A   WEINBAUM, STANLEY G. AC
  DAWN OF FLAME   NV   TWS 39 06
    DAWN OF FLAME   WEINBAUM, STANLEY G. AC
  FLIGHT ON TITAN   NV   ASF 35 01
    MARTIAN ODYSSEY AND OTHER SCIENCE FICTION TALES, A
                                     WEINBAUM, STANLEY G. AC
    RED PERI, THE   WEINBAUM, STANLEY G. AC
  GRAPH   SS   FMG 36 09
    MARTIAN ODYSSEY AND OTHER SCIENCE FICTION TALES, A
                                     WEINBAUM, STANLEY G. AC
  IDEAL, THE   NV   WOS 35 09
    BEST OF STANLEY G. WEINBAUM, THE WEINBAUM, STANLEY G. AC
    MARTIAN ODYSSEY AND OTHER SCIENCE FICTION TALES, A
                                     WEINBAUM, STANLEY G. AC
    MARTIAN ODYSSEY AND OTHERS, A   WEINBAUM, STANLEY G. AC
  IDEAL, THE (SELECTION FROM)   EX   WOS 35 09
    CENTURY OF SCIENCE FICTION, A   KNIGHT, DAMON   AN
  LAST MARTIAN, THE   PM
    MARTIAN ODYSSEY AND OTHER SCIENCE FICTION TALES, A
                                     WEINBAUM, STANLEY G. AC
  LOTUS EATERS, THE   NV   ASF 35 04
    BEST OF STANLEY G. WEINBAUM, THE WEINBAUM, STANLEY G. AC

WEINBAUM, STANLEY G.   WELLMAN, MANLY WADE

WEINBAUM, STANLEY G. (CONTINUED)   WEINER, GUY
  *BEYOND TIME AND SPACE   DERLETH, AUGUST   AN   PARALLEL DEVELOPMENT, THE   SS
   DAWN OF FLAME   WEINBAUM, STANLEY G. AC   STRANGE WORLD OF SCIENCE FICTION ANONYMOUS   OA
   HIDDEN PLANET, THE   WOLLHEIM, DONALD A.   AN
   MARTIAN ODYSSEY AND OTHER SCIENCE FICTION TALES, A   WEINER, NORBERT   ALSO AS   W. NORBERT
                             WEINBAUM, STANLEY G. AC   BRAIN, THE   SS   TEN 52 04
   MARTIAN ODYSSEY AND OTHERS, A WEINBAUM, STANLEY G. AC   GREAT SCIENCE FICTION BY SCIENTISTS CONKLIN, GROFF   AN
   MARTIAN ODYSSEY, A   WEINBAUM, STANLEY G. AC
   MASTERPIECES OF SCIENCE FICTION MOSKOWITZ, SAM   AN   WEINSTEIN, RICHARD S
   UBERWINDUNG VON RAUM UND ZEIT GUNTHER, GOTTHARD AN   OCEANS AWAY   NA
MAD MOON, THE   NV ASF 35 12   STELLAR SHORT NOVELS   DEL REY, JUDY-LYNN   OA
   BEST OF STANLEY G. WEINBAUM, THE WEINBAUM, STANLEY G. AC
   DAWN OF FLAME   WEINBAUM, STANLEY G. AC   WEISS, ALAN
   EXPLORING OTHER WORLDS   MOSKOWITZ, SAM   AN   SATANESQUE   SS   LMF 74
   JUPITER   POHL, C. & F.   AN   YEAR'S BEST HORROR STORIES: SERIES III, THE
   MARTIAN ODYSSEY AND OTHER SCIENCE FICTION TALES, A   DAVIS, RICHARD   AN
                             WEINBAUM, STANLEY G. AC
   MARTIAN ODYSSEY AND OTHERS, A WEINBAUM, STANLEY G. AC WEISS, GEORGE HENRY   SEE PSEUD. FRANCIS FLAGG
   SCIENCE FICTION OF THE 30'S KNIGHT, DAMON   AN
MARTIAN ODYSSEY, A   NV WOS 34 07   WEISSMAN, BARRY
   ANTHROPOLOGY THROUGH SCIENCE FICTION MASON, C/GREENBERG/& AN AND WATCH THE SMOG ROLL IN...   SS   PRT 71
   BEST OF STANLEY G. WEINBAUM, THE WEINBAUM, STANLEY G. AC   PROTOSTARS   GERROLD & GOLDIN   OA
   DAWN OF FLAME   WEINBAUM, STANLEY G. AC
   ESCALES DANS L'INFINI   GALLET, GEORGES H.   AN   WELLEN, EDWARD
   FROM OFF THIS WORLD   MARGULIES & FRIEND   AN   ANDROIDS DON'T CRY   SS   FSF 73 05
   MARS, WE LOVE YOU   HIPOLITO & MCNELLY   AN   BEST SCIENCE FICTION STORIES OF THE YEAR (1973)
   MARTIAN ODYSSEY AND OTHER SCIENCE FICTION TALES, A   DEL REY, LESTER   AN
                             WEINBAUM, STANLEY G. AC   DEADLY GAME, THE   SS   IFS 62 05
   MARTIAN ODYSSEY AND OTHERS, A WEINBAUM, STANLEY G. AC   8TH ANNUAL OF THE YEAR'S BEST S-F, THE MERRIL, JUDITH AN
   MARTIAN ODYSSEY, A   WEINBAUM, STANLEY G. AC   DOWN BY THE OLD MAELSTROM   SS   ORB 72 11
   POCKET BOOK OF SCIENCE-FICTION, THE WOLLHEIM, DONALD A. AN   ORBIT 11   KNIGHT, DAMON   AN
   SCIENCE FICTION BESTIARY, THE SILVERBERG, ROBERT AN   "END, THE"   SS   ORB 74 15
   SCIENCE FICTION HALL OF FAME VOLUME 1 SILVERBERG, ROBERT AN   ORBIT 15   KNIGHT, DAMON   OA
   WHERE DO WE GO FROM HERE? ASIMOV, ISAAC   AN   I.O.U.   NV   IFS 61 03
   3000 YEARS OF FANTASY AND SCIENCE FICTION   6 FINGERS OF TIME AND 5 OTHER SCIENCE FICTION NOVELETS, THE
                             DE CAMP, L. S.&C.   AN   ANONYMOUS   AN
PARASITE PLANET   NV ASF 35 02   LATEST FROM SIGMA CORVI, THE   SS   ALC 73
   BEFORE THE GOLDEN AGE   ASIMOV, ISAAC   AN   ALIEN CONDITION, THE GOLDIN, STEPHEN   OA
   BEST OF STANLEY G. WEINBAUM, THE WEINBAUM, STANLEY G. AC   ORIGINS OF GALACTIC ETIQUETTE   FA   GAL 53 10
   FLIGHT INTO SPACE   WOLLHEIM, DONALD A.   AN   ALL ABOUT THE FUTURE GREENBERG , MARTIN   AN
   MARTIAN ODYSSEY AND OTHER SCIENCE FICTION TALES, A   ORIGINS OF GALACTIC LAW   FA   GAL 53 04
                             WEINBAUM, STANLEY G. AC   ALL ABOUT THE FUTURE GREENBERG , MARTIN   AN
   MARTIAN ODYSSEY AND OTHERS, A WEINBAUM, STANLEY G. AC   ORIGINS OF GALACTIC MEDICINE   FA   GAL 53 12
PLANET OF DOUBT, THE   NV ASF 35 10   ALL ABOUT THE FUTURE GREENBERG , MARTIN   AN
   MARTIAN ODYSSEY AND OTHER SCIENCE FICTION TALES, A   ORIGINS OF GALACTIC SLANG   FA   GAL 52 07
                             WEINBAUM, STANLEY G. AC   ALL ABOUT THE FUTURE GREENBERG , MARTIN   AN
   MARTIAN ODYSSEY AND OTHERS, A WEINBAUM, STANLEY G. AC   THESE OUR ACTORS   SS   INY 70 01
   MORE ADVENTURES ON OTHER PLANETS WOLLHEIM, DONALD A. AN   INFINITY 1   HOSKINS, ROBERT   OA
   TOMORROW'S WORLDS   SILVERBERG, ROBERT   AN   TITLE   SS   ORB 74 15
POINT OF VIEW, THE   SS WOS 36 01   ORBIT 15   KNIGHT, DAMON   OA
   MARTIAN ODYSSEY AND OTHER SCIENCE FICTION TALES, A   TOO LONG AT THE FAIR   SS   NOV 74 04
                             WEINBAUM, STANLEY G. AC   NOVA 4   HARRISON, HARRY   OA
   MARTIAN ODYSSEY AND OTHERS, A WEINBAUM, STANLEY G. AC
PROTEUS ISLAND   SN ASF 36 08   WELLER, ANTHONY
   BEST OF STANLEY G. WEINBAUM, THE WEINBAUM, STANLEY G. AC   ANTIQUITY   PM   INY 72 03
   MARTIAN ODYSSEY AND OTHER SCIENCE FICTION TALES, A   INFINITY 3   HOSKINS, ROBERT   OA
                             WEINBAUM, STANLEY G. AC
   MARTIAN ODYSSEY, A   WEINBAUM, STANLEY G. AC   WELLES, ORSON
   RED PERI, THE   WEINBAUM, STANLEY G. AC   INVASION FROM MARS   AN   DEL 49
PYGMALION'S SPECTACLES   SS WOS 35 06   CAN A MARTIAN HELP IT IF HE'S COLORED GREEN? IN
   BEST OF STANLEY G. WEINBAUM, THE WEINBAUM, STANLEY G. AC   INVASION FROM MARS WELLES, ORSON   AN
   MARTIAN ODYSSEY AND OTHER SCIENCE FICTION TALES, A   INTRODUCTION   IN
                             WEINBAUM, STANLEY G. AC   SF: THE YEAR'S GREATEST SCIENCE FICTION AND FANTASY
   MARTIAN ODYSSEY AND OTHERS, A WEINBAUM, STANLEY G. AC   MERRIL, JUDITH   AN
RED PERI, THE   SN ASF 35 11
   DAWN OF FLAME   WEINBAUM, STANLEY G. AC   WELLMAN, MANLY WADE
   MARTIAN ODYSSEY AND OTHER SCIENCE FICTION TALES, A   WHO FEARS THE DEVIL?   AC H ARK 63
                             WEINBAUM, STANLEY G. AC   ADVENTURE OF THE MARTIAN CLIENT, THE SS C FSF 69 12
   RED PERI, THE   WEINBAUM, STANLEY G. AC   WONDERMAKERS 2   HOSKINS, ROBERT   AN
REDEMPTION CAIRN   NV ASF 36 03   CALL ME FROM THE VALLEY (SEE DUMB SUPPER) TC
   BEST OF STANLEY G. WEINBAUM, THE WEINBAUM, STANLEY G. AC   COME INTO MY PARLOR   SS   49
   MARTIAN ODYSSEY AND OTHER SCIENCE FICTION TALES, A   GIRL WITH THE HUNGRY EYES, AND OTHER STORIES, THE
                             WEINBAUM, STANLEY G. AC   WOLLHEIM, DONALD A.   OA
   RED PERI, THE   WEINBAUM, STANLEY G. AC   ROOTS OF EVIL, THE PARRY, MICHEL   AN
REVOLUTION OF 1950   NA AMZ 38 10   DESRICK ON YANDRO, THE   SS   FSF 52 06
   MARTIAN ODYSSEY AND OTHER SCIENCE FICTION TALES, A   BEST FROM FANTASY AND SCIENCE FICTION: 2
                             WEINBAUM, STANLEY G. AC   BOUCHER & MCCOMAS   AN
   RED PERI, THE   WEINBAUM, STANLEY G. AC   WHO FEARS THE DEVIL? WELLMAN, MANLY WADE AC
SHIFTING SEAS   NV AMZ 37 04   DEVIL IS NOT MOCKED, THE   SS   UNK 43 06
   BEST OF STANLEY G. WEINBAUM, THE WEINBAUM, STANLEY G. AC   ZACHERLEY'S VULTURE STEW ZACHERLEY   AN
   MARTIAN ODYSSEY AND OTHER SCIENCE FICTION TALES, A   DUMB SUPPER (CALL ME FROM THE VALLEY) SS   FSF 54 03
                             WEINBAUM, STANLEY G. AC   WHO FEARS THE DEVIL? WELLMAN, MANLY WADE AC
   RED PERI, THE   WEINBAUM, STANLEY G. AC   ISLAND IN THE SKY   NV   TWS 41 10
SMOTHERED SEAS   NV ASF 36 01   GIANT ANTHOLOGY OF SCIENCE FICTION MARGULIES & FRIEND AN
   MARTIAN ODYSSEY AND OTHER SCIENCE FICTION TALES, A   KELPIE, THE   SS   WRT 36 07
                             WEINBAUM, STANLEY G. AC   AVON FANTASY READER, THE WOLLHEIM &ERNSBERGER AN
   RED PERI, THE   WEINBAUM, STANLEY G. AC   LITTLE BLACK TRAIN, THE   SS   FSF 54 08
VALLEY OF DREAMS   NV WOS 34 11   BEST FROM FANTASY AND SCIENCE FICTION: 4
   BEST OF STANLEY G. WEINBAUM, THE WEINBAUM, STANLEY G. AC   BOUCHER, ANTHONY   AN
   FROM OFF THIS WORLD   MARGULIES & FRIEND   AN   WHO FEARS THE DEVIL? WELLMAN, MANLY WADE AC
   MARTIAN ODYSSEY AND OTHER SCIENCE FICTION TALES, A   MEN AGAINST THE STARS   NV   ASF 38 06
                             WEINBAUM, STANLEY G. AC   EVERY BOY'S BOOK OF OUTER SPACE STORIES
   MARTIAN ODYSSEY AND OTHERS, A WEINBAUM, STANLEY G. AC   DIKTY, T. E.   AN
WORLDS OF IF, THE   SS WOS 35 08   *MEN AGAINST THE STARS GREENBERG , MARTIN   AN
   BEST OF STANLEY G. WEINBAUM, THE WEINBAUM, STANLEY G. AC   NINE YARDS OF OTHER CLOTH   SS   FSF 58 07
   DAWN OF FLAME   WEINBAUM, STANLEY G. AC   WHO FEARS THE DEVIL? WELLMAN, MANLY WADE AC
   MARTIAN ODYSSEY AND OTHER SCIENCE FICTION TALES, A   O UGLY BIRD!   SS   FSF 51 12
                             WEINBAUM, STANLEY G. AC   EDGE OF NEVER, THE HOSKINS, ROBERT   AN
   MARTIAN ODYSSEY AND OTHERS, A WEINBAUM, STANLEY G. AC   GALAXY OF GHOULS   MERRIL, JUDITH   AN
   OTHER DIMENSIONS   SILVERBERG, ROBERT   AN   WHO FEARS THE DEVIL? WELLMAN, MANLY WADE AC
                                                         OLD DEVLINS WAS A-WAITING   SS   FSF 57 02
WEINER, ANDREW   WHO FEARS THE DEVIL? WELLMAN, MANLY WADE AC
  EMPIRE OF THE SUN   SS DVS 72 02   ON THE HILLS AND EVERYWHERE   SS   FSF 56 01
   AGAIN, DANGEROUS VISIONS   ELLISON, HARLAN   OA   WHO FEARS THE DEVIL? WELLMAN, MANLY WADE AC
                                                         ONE OTHER   SS   FSF 53 08
                                                           WHO FEARS THE DEVIL? WELLMAN, MANLY WADE AC

WELLMAN, MANLY WADE   WELLS, H. G.

WELLMAN, MANLY WADE   (CONTINUED)   WELLS, H. G.
  PITHECANTHROPUS REJECTUS   SS   ASF 38 01   BEST SCIENCE FICTION STORIES OF H. G. WELLS   AC L DOV 66
    SCIENCE FICTION OF THE 30'S   KNIGHT, DAMON   AN   BEST STORIES OF H. G. WELLS   AC   BAL 60 08
  SCHOOL FOR THE UNSPEAKABLE   SS   WRT 37 09   COUNTRY OF THE BLIND, THE   AC H NEL 13
    OTHER WORLDS, THE   STONG, PHILIP D.   AN   DOOR IN THE WALL, THE   AC H KEN 11
  SHIVER IN THE PINES   SS   FSF 55 02   INEXPERIENCED GHOST AND NINE OTHER STORIES, THE AC   BAN 65 02
    WHO FEARS THE DEVIL?   WELLMAN, MANLY WADE AC   PLATTNER STORY AND OTHERS, THE   AC H MTH 97
  SONG OF THE SLAVES, THE   SS   WRT 40 03   SEVEN FAMOUS NOVELS BY H. G. WELLS   AC H KNP 34
    OTHER WORLDS, THE   STONG, PHILIP D.   AN   ALSO AS "SEVEN SCIENCE FICTION NOVELS"
  SPACE STATION NO. 1   SS   ARG 36 10   SEVEN SCIENCE FICTION NOVELS   AC H DOV 50
    ESCALES DANS L'INFINI   GALLET, GEORGES H. AN   SEE "SEVEN FAMOUS NOVELS BY H. G. WELLS"
   *MY BEST SCIENCE FICTION STORY MARGULIES & FRIEND AN   SHORT STORIES OF H. G. WELLS, THE   AC H BEN 27
  VALLEY WAS STILL, THE   SS   WRT 39 08   STOLEN BACILLUS AND OTHER INCIDENTS, THE   AC H MTH 95
    UNEXPECTED, THE   MARGULIES, LEO   AN   TALES OF SPACE AND TIME   AC H HPR 99
  VANDY, VANDY   SS   FSF 53 03   THIRTY STRANGE STORIES   AC H ANL 97
    BEST FROM FANTASY AND SCIENCE FICTION: 3   TIME MACHINE AND OTHER STORIES, THE   AC H HLT 95
                                  BOUCHER & MCCOMAS AN   TIME MACHINE AND OTHER STORIES, THE (PB)   AC   SBS 63
    WHO FEARS THE DEVIL?   WELLMAN, MANLY WADE AC   TWELVE STORIES AND A DREAM   AC H MCM 03
  WALK LIKE A MOUNTAIN   SS   FSF 55 06   TWENTY-EIGHT SCIENCE FICTION STORIES   AC H DOV 52
    DECADE OF FANTASY AND SCIENCE FICTION, A   WAR OF THE WORLDS, THE TIME MACHINE AND SELECTED SHORT STORIES
                                  MILLS, ROBERT P.   AN   AC H PLM 63
    WHO FEARS THE DEVIL?   WELLMAN, MANLY WADE AC   3 PROPHETIC SCIENCE FICTION NOVELS OF H. G. WELLS AC L DOV 60
  WHEN IT WAS MOONLIGHT   SS   UNK 40 02   ADVENT OF THE FLYING MAN, THE (SEE THE FLYING MAN)
    UNKNOWN, THE   BENSEN, D. R.   AN   TC
  WHY I SELECTED SPACE STATION NO. 1   AI   AEPYORNIS ISLAND   SS   PMB 94 12
   *MY BEST SCIENCE FICTION STORY MARGULIES & FRIEND AN   BEST SCIENCE FICTION STORIES OF H. G. WELLS
  WONDER AS I WANDER   SS   FSF 62 03   WELLS, H. G.   AC
    WHO FEARS THE DEVIL?   WELLMAN, MANLY WADE AC   COUNTRY OF THE BLIND, THE   WELLS, H. G.   AC
                                                              JOURNEYS IN SCIENCE FICTION LOUGHLIN, RICHARD L. AN
WELLMAN, WADE   SHORT STORIES OF H. G. WELLS, THE   WELLS, H. G. AC
  ADVENTURE OF THE MARTIAN CLIENT, THE SS C FSF 69 12   STOLEN BACILLUS AND OTHER INCIDENTS, THE
    WONDERMAKERS 2   HOSKINS, ROBERT   AN   WELLS, H. G.   AC
                                                              STRANGE BEASTS AND UNNATURAL MONSTERS STERN, PHILIP VAN D. AN
WELLS, ANGUS   THIRTY STRANGE STORIES   WELLS, H. G.   AC
  BEST OF A. E. VAN VOGT, THE (LISTED UNDER A. E. VAN VOGT)   TWENTY-EIGHT SCIENCE FICTION STORIES WELLS, H. G. AC
                                     EC H SID 74 05   APPLE, THE   SS   IDL 96 10
  BEST OF FRANK HERBERT, THE (LISTED UNDER FRANK HERBERT)   BEST SCIENCE FICTION STORIES OF H. G. WELLS
                                     EC H SID 75   WELLS, H. G.   AC
  BEST OF ISAAC ASIMOV, THE (LISTED UNDER ISAAC ASIMOV)   INEXPERIENCED GHOST AND NINE OTHER STORIES, THE
                                     EC H SID 73   WELLS, H. G.   AC
                                                              PLATTNER STORY AND OTHERS, THE   WELLS, H. G.   AC
WELLS, BASIL   SHORT STORIES OF H. G. WELLS, THE   WELLS, H. G. AC
  DOORWAYS TO SPACE   AC H FPB 51   THIRTY STRANGE STORIES   WELLS, H. G.   AC
  PLANETS OF ADVENTURE   AC H FPB 49   ARGONAUTS OF THE AIR, THE   SS   PMY 95
    ALIENS, THE   SS   BEST STORIES OF H. G. WELLS WELLS, H. G.   AC
      DOORWAYS TO SPACE   WELLS, BASIL   AC   PLATTNER STORY AND OTHERS, THE   WELLS, H. G.   AC
    BARREN WORLD   SS   SHORT STORIES OF H. G. WELLS, THE   WELLS, H. G. AC
      DOORWAYS TO SPACE   WELLS, BASIL   AC   THIRTY STRANGE STORIES   WELLS, H. G.   AC
    CAVERNS OF ITH   SS   FBK 47 02   TWENTY-EIGHT SCIENCE FICTION STORIES WELLS, H. G. AC
      PLANETS OF ADVENTURE   WELLS, BASIL   AC   AT A WINDOW (SEE THROUGH A WINDOW)   TC
    CHAIR, THE   SS   ATOMIC BOMB, THE (FROM "THE WORLD SET FREE")   EX
      DOORWAYS TO SPACE   WELLS, BASIL   AC   SCIENCE FICTION THROUGH THE AGES 2 EVANS, I. O. AN
    CHRYSALID   SS   BARDLET'S ROMANCE, A (SEE IN THE MODERN VEIN: AN UNSYMPATHETIC
      DOORWAYS TO SPACE   WELLS, BASIL   AC   LOVE STORY)   TC
    CONQUEST   SS   BEAUTIFUL SUIT, THE (A MOONLIGHT FABLE)   SS   COL 09 04
      DOORWAYS TO SPACE   WELLS, BASIL   AC   COUNTRY OF THE BLIND, THE   WELLS, H. G.   AC
    CRUSADER (AS GENE ELLERMAN)   SS   FBK 49 05   SHORT STORIES OF H. G. WELLS, THE   WELLS, H. G. AC
      MACHINE-GOD LAUGHS, THE   ANONYMOUS   AN   *TIME MACHINE AND OTHER STORIES, THE WELLS, H. G. AC
      PLANETS OF ADVENTURE   WELLS, BASIL   AC   BULLA, THE (SEE THE RECONCILLIATION)   TC
    ELFIN HILLS, THE   SS   CATASTROPHE, A   SS   NBG 95 08
      DOORWAYS TO SPACE   WELLS, BASIL   AC   PLATTNER STORY AND OTHERS, THE   WELLS, H. G.   AC
    EMPIRE OF THE DUST   SS   FBK 49 05   SHORT STORIES OF H. G. WELLS, THE   WELLS, H. G. AC
      PLANETS OF ADVENTURE   WELLS, BASIL   AC   THIRTY STRANGE STORIES   WELLS, H. G.   AC
    EXILES OF THE FORBIDDEN PLANET   SS   CHANGE, THE (FROM "IN THE DAYS OF THE COMET")   EX   CMP 05 12
      DOORWAYS TO SPACE   WELLS, BASIL   AC   NEW IMPROVED SUN, THE   DISCH, THOMAS M.   AN
    GATEWAYS   SS   CHRONIC ARGONAUTS, THE   NV   SSJ 88 04
      PLANETS OF ADVENTURE   WELLS, BASIL   AC   ANDROIDS, TIME MACHINES AND BLUE GIRAFFES
    HAIRY ONES, THE   SS   ELWOOD & GHIDALIA   AN
      PLANETS OF ADVENTURE   WELLS, BASIL   AC   SPECULATIONS   SANDERS, THOMAS E.   AN
    KNIGHT FOR MISS MERKINS, A   SS   FBK 51 07   STRANGE SIGNPOSTS   ELWOOD & MOSKOWITZ   AN
      PLANETS OF ADVENTURE   WELLS, BASIL   AC   VISIONS OF TOMORROW   ELWOOD, ROGER   AN
    LORD OF THE DESERT PLANET   SS   CONE, THE   SS   UCN 95 09
      DOORWAYS TO SPACE   WELLS, BASIL   AC   COUNTRY OF THE BLIND, THE   WELLS, H. G.   AC
    LURKERS OF BURM, THE   SS   DOOR IN THE WALL, THE   WELLS, H. G.   AC
      DOORWAYS TO SPACE   WELLS, BASIL   AC   PLATTNER STORY AND OTHERS, THE   WELLS, H. G.   AC
    MARTYR FROM MARS   SS   SHORT STORIES OF H. G. WELLS, THE   WELLS, H. G. AC
      DOORWAYS TO SPACE   WELLS, BASIL   AC   THIRTY STRANGE STORIES   WELLS, H. G.   AC
    PLANET OF NEW MEN   SS   COUNTRY OF THE BLIND, THE   SS   SND 04 04
      PLANETS OF ADVENTURE   WELLS, BASIL   AC   COUNTRY OF THE BLIND, THE   WELLS, H. G.   AC
    PLANET OF THE MIST   SS   DOOR IN THE WALL, THE   WELLS, H. G.   AC
      DOORWAYS TO SPACE   WELLS, BASIL   AC   INEXPERIENCED GHOST AND NINE OTHER STORIES, THE
    POWER FOR THE DARM   SS   FBK 50 06   WELLS, H. G.   AC
      PLANETS OF ADVENTURE   WELLS, BASIL   AC   MASTERPIECES OF SCIENCE FICTION MOSKOWITZ, SAM   AN
    PRISON RATS (AS GENE ELLERMAN)   SS   FBK 48 04   SCIENCE FICTION: THE FUTURE ALLEN, DICK   AN
      PLANETS OF ADVENTURE   WELLS, BASIL   AC   SHORT STORIES OF H. G. WELLS, THE   WELLS, H. G. AC
    QUEST OF THIG   SS   PLS 42 FL   *TIME MACHINE AND OTHER STORIES, THE WELLS, H. G. AC
      BEST OF PLANET STORIES NO. 1, THE BRACKETT, LEIGH AN   TWENTY-EIGHT SCIENCE FICTION STORIES WELLS, H. G. AC
      PLANETS OF ADVENTURE   WELLS, BASIL   AC   CROQUET PLAYER, THE   EX   36
    REBELLION ON VENUS   SS   *TERROR IN THE MODERN VEIN   WOLLHEIM, DONALD A.   AN
      DOORWAYS TO SPACE   WELLS, BASIL   AC   CRYSTAL EGG, THE   SS   NRV 97 05
    SCRAMBLED WORLD   SS   PLS 47 SP   ASPECTS OF SCIENCE FICTION   DOHERTY, G. D.   AN
      PLANETS OF ADVENTURE   WELLS, BASIL   AC   BEST SCIENCE FICTION STORIES OF H. G. WELLS
    SINGER, THE   SS   WELLS, H. G.   AC
      DOORWAYS TO SPACE   WELLS, BASIL   AC   BEST STORIES OF H. G. WELLS WELLS, H. G.   AC
    SPACE WOMAN   SS   CENTURY OF SCIENCE FICTION, A KNIGHT, DAMON   AN
      DOORWAYS TO SPACE   WELLS, BASIL   AC   COUNTRY OF THE BLIND, THE   WELLS, H. G.   AC
    SUDDEN FOREST, THE   SS   IN DREAMS AWAKE   FIEDLER, LESLIE A.   AN
      DOORWAYS TO SPACE   WELLS, BASIL   AC   SHORT STORIES OF H. G. WELLS, THE   WELLS, H. G. AC
    SWIFT PEOPLE, THE   SS   FUT 43 02   *STRANGE PORTS OF CALL   DERLETH, AUGUST   AN
      PLANETS OF ADVENTURE   WELLS, BASIL   AC   TALES OF SPACE AND TIME   WELLS, H. G.   AC
    TWISTED MEN, THE   SS   TWENTY-EIGHT SCIENCE FICTION STORIES WELLS, H. G. AC
      PLANETS OF ADVENTURE   WELLS, BASIL   AC   VISIONS OF TOMORROW   ELWOOD, ROGER   AN
    WALL OF DARKNESS   SS   FBK 48 04   WAR OF THE WORLDS, THE TIME MACHINE AND SELECTED SHORT STORIES
      PLANETS OF ADVENTURE   WELLS, BASIL   AC   WELLS, H. G.   AC
  WORLD OF MISTERS (AS GENE ELLERMAN)   SS   FBK 50 06   DEAL IN OSTRICHES, A   SS   PMB 94
    PLANETS OF ADVENTURE   WELLS, BASIL   AC   SHORT STORIES OF H. G. WELLS, THE   WELLS, H. G. AC

```
WELLS, H. G.        (CONTINUED)
   STOLEN BACILLUS AND OTHER INCIDENTS, THE
                                           WELLS, H. G.         AC
   THIRTY STRANGE STORIES                  WELLS, H. G.         AC
DIAMOND MAKER, THE                                    SS  PMB 94
   BEST SCIENCE FICTION STORIES OF H. G. WELLS
                                           WELLS, H. G.         AC
   DOOR IN THE WALL, THE                   WELLS, H. G.         AC
   SHORT STORIES OF H. G. WELLS, THE       WELLS, H. G.         AC
   STOLEN BACILLUS AND OTHER INCIDENTS, THE
                                           WELLS, H. G.         AC
DOOR IN THE WALL, THE                                 SS  DCH 06 07
   COUNTRY OF THE BLIND, THE               WELLS, H. G.         AC
   DOOR IN THE WALL, THE                   WELLS, H. G.         AC
   SHORT STORIES OF H. G. WELLS, THE       WELLS, H. G.         AC
   *TIME MACHINE AND OTHER STORIES, THE    WELLS, H. G.         AC
DREAM OF ARMAGEDDON, A                                NV  BAW 01
   BEST SCIENCE FICTION STORIES OF H. G. WELLS
                                           WELLS, H. G.         AC
   BEST STORIES OF H. G. WELLS             WELLS, H. G.         AC
   COUNTRY OF THE BLIND, THE               WELLS, H. G.         AC
   DOOR IN THE WALL, THE                   WELLS, H. G.         AC
   SHORT STORIES OF H. G. WELLS, THE       WELLS, H. G.         AC
   TWELVE STORIES AND A DREAM              WELLS, H. G.         AC
   TWENTY-EIGHT SCIENCE FICTION STORIES    WELLS, H. G.         AC
EMPIRE OF THE ANTS, THE                               SS  SND 05 12
   COUNTRY OF THE BLIND, THE               WELLS, H. G.         AC
   EARTH IS THE STRANGEST PLANET           SILVERBERG, ROBERT   AN
   SHORT STORIES OF H. G. WELLS, THE       WELLS, H. G.         AC
   *TIME MACHINE AND OTHER STORIES, THE    WELLS, H. G.         AC
   TWENTY-EIGHT SCIENCE FICTION STORIES    WELLS, H. G.         AC
EXPERIMENTAL FARM, THE (FROM "THE FOOD OF THE GODS")
                                           EX  PRS 03 12
   SCIENCE IN FICTION                      BAYLISS, A.E. & J.C. AN
FILMER                                                SS  GRP 01
   BEST SCIENCE FICTION STORIES OF H. G. WELLS
                                           WELLS, H. G.         AC
   SHORT STORIES OF H. G. WELLS, THE       WELLS, H. G.         AC
   TWELVE STORIES AND A DREAM              WELLS, H. G.         AC
   TWENTY-EIGHT SCIENCE FICTION STORIES    WELLS, H. G.         AC
FIRST MEN IN THE MOON, THE                            NO  SND 00 11
   PORTABLE NOVELS OF SCIENCE              WOLLHEIM, DONALD A.  AN
   SEVEN FAMOUS NOVELS BY H. G. WELLS      WELLS, H. G.         AC
FLOWERING OF THE STRANGE ORCHID, THE (ALSO AS THE STRANGE
   ORCHID)                                            SS  PMB 94 08
   COUNTRY OF THE BLIND, THE               WELLS, H. G.         AC
   INEXPERIENCED GHOST AND NINE OTHER STORIES, THE
                                           WELLS, H. G.         AC
   NIGHTMARE GARDEN                        GHIDALIA, VIC        AN
   ROOTS OF EVIL, THE                      PARRY, MICHEL        AN
   SHORT STORIES OF H. G. WELLS, THE       WELLS, H. G.         AC
   STOLEN BACILLUS AND OTHER INCIDENTS, THE
                                           WELLS, H. G.         AC
   TWENTY-EIGHT SCIENCE FICTION STORIES    WELLS, H. G.         AC
FLYING MAN, THE (THE ADVENT OF THE FLYING MAN)  SS  PGZ 93 12
   SHORT STORIES OF H. G. WELLS, THE       WELLS, H. G.         AC
   STOLEN BACILLUS AND OTHER INCIDENTS, THE
                                           WELLS, H. G.         AC
FOOD OF THE GODS, THE                                 NO  PRS 03 12
   SEVEN FAMOUS NOVELS BY H. G. WELLS      WELLS, H. G.         AC
FROM "THE TIME MACHINE"                               EX  NRV 95 01
   SCIENCE FICTION: THE FUTURE             ALLEN, DICK          AN
FROM: A MODERN UTOPIA                                 EX       05
   INSIDE INFORMATION                      MOWSHOWITZ, ABBE     AN
GRISLY FOLK, THE                                      AR  SRY 21 04
   ANCIENT MYSTERIES READER, THE           HAINING, PETER       AN
   SHORT STORIES OF H. G. WELLS, THE       WELLS, H. G.         AC
HAMMERPOUND PARK BURGLARY, THE                        SS  PMB 94
   SHORT STORIES OF H. G. WELLS, THE       WELLS, H. G.         AC
   STOLEN BACILLUS AND OTHER INCIDENTS, THE
                                           WELLS, H. G.         AC
IN THE ABYSS                                          SS  PRS 96 08
   BEST SCIENCE FICTION STORIES OF H. G. WELLS
                                           WELLS, H. G.         AC
   FIRST CONTACT                           KNIGHT, DAMON        AN
   PLATTNER STORY AND OTHERS, THE          WELLS, H. G.         AC
   POCKET BOOK OF SCIENCE-FICTION, THE     WOLLHEIM, DONALD A.  AN
   SHORT STORIES OF H. G. WELLS, THE       WELLS, H. G.         AC
   THIRTY STRANGE STORIES                  WELLS, H. G.         AC
   TWENTY-EIGHT SCIENCE FICTION STORIES    WELLS, H. G.         AC
   WAR OF THE WORLDS, THE TIME MACHINE AND SELECTED SHORT STORIES
                                           WELLS, H. G.         AC
IN THE AVU OBSERVATORY                                SS  PMB 94 08
   BEST SCIENCE FICTION STORIES OF H. G. WELLS
                                           WELLS, H. G.         AC
   BEWARE THE BEASTS                       GHIDALIA, V.& ELWOOD AN
   COUNTRY OF THE BLIND, THE               WELLS, H. G.         AC
   SHORT STORIES OF H. G. WELLS, THE       WELLS, H. G.         AC
   STOLEN BACILLUS AND OTHER INCIDENTS, THE
                                           WELLS, H. G.         AC
   THIRTY STRANGE STORIES                  WELLS, H. G.         AC
   TWENTY-EIGHT SCIENCE FICTION STORIES    WELLS, H. G.         AC
   WAR OF THE WORLDS, THE TIME MACHINE AND SELECTED SHORT STORIES
                                           WELLS, H. G.         AC
IN THE DAYS OF THE COMET                              NO  DCH 05
   SEVEN FAMOUS NOVELS BY H. G. WELLS      WELLS, H. G.         AC
IN THE MODERN VEIN: AN UNSYMPATHETIC LOVE STORY (A BARDLET'S
   ROMANCE)                                           SS  TTH 94 03
   PLATTNER STORY AND OTHERS, THE          WELLS, H. G.         AC
   SHORT STORIES OF H. G. WELLS, THE       WELLS, H. G.         AC
   THIRTY STRANGE STORIES                  WELLS, H. G.         AC
INEXPERIENCED GHOST, THE(THE STORY OF THE INEXPERIENCED GHOST)
                                           SS  SND 02 03
   INEXPERIENCED GHOST AND NINE OTHER STORIES, THE
                                           WELLS, H. G.         AC
   SHORT STORIES OF H. G. WELLS, THE       WELLS, H. G.         AC

WELLS, H. G.        (CONTINUED)
   TWELVE STORIES AND A DREAM              WELLS, H. G.         AC
INVISIBLE MAN, THE                                    SN  PRS 97 06
   BEST SCIENCE FICTION STORIES OF H. G. WELLS
                                           WELLS, H. G.         AC
   CENTURY OF GREAT SHORT SCIENCE FICTION NOVELS, A
                                           KNIGHT, DAMON        AN
   SEVEN FAMOUS NOVELS BY H. G. WELLS      WELLS, H. G.         AC
ISLAND OF DR. MOREAU, THE                             NO  SRV 95 01
   SEVEN FAMOUS NOVELS BY H. G. WELLS      WELLS, H. G.         AC
JILTING OF JANE, THE                                  SS       97
   COUNTRY OF THE BLIND, THE               WELLS, H. G.         AC
   PLATTNER STORY AND OTHERS, THE          WELLS, H. G.         AC
   SHORT STORIES OF H. G. WELLS, THE       WELLS, H. G.         AC
   THIRTY STRANGE STORIES                  WELLS, H. G.         AC
JIMMY GOGGLES THE GOD                                 SS  GRP 98 12
   COUNTRY OF THE BLIND, THE               WELLS, H. G.         AC
   SHORT STORIES OF H. G. WELLS, THE       WELLS, H. G.         AC
   TWELVE STORIES AND A DREAM              WELLS, H. G.         AC
LAND IRONCLADS, THE                                   NV  SND 03 12
   BEST STORIES OF H. G. WELLS             WELLS, H. G.         AC
   FUTURE TENSE                            CURTIS, RICHARD      AN
   SCIENCE FICTION BY GASLIGHT             MOSKOWITZ, SAM       AN
   SHORT STORIES OF H. G. WELLS, THE       WELLS, H. G.         AC
   *TIME MACHINE AND OTHER STORIES, THE    WELLS, H. G.         AC
   TWENTY-EIGHT SCIENCE FICTION STORIES    WELLS, H. G.         AC
   VISIONS OF TOMORROW                     ELWOOD, ROGER        AN
   WONDERMAKERS                            HOSKINS, ROBERT      AN
LITTLE MOTHER UP THE MORDERBEN, THE                   SS  SND 10 04
   SHORT STORIES OF H. G. WELLS, THE       WELLS, H. G.         AC
LORD OF THE DYNAMOS, THE                              SS  PMB 94 09
   BEST SCIENCE FICTION STORIES OF H. G. WELLS
                                           WELLS, H. G.         AC
   BEST STORIES OF H. G. WELLS             WELLS, H. G.         AC
   COUNTRY OF THE BLIND, THE               WELLS, H. G.         AC
   DOOR IN THE WALL, THE                   WELLS, H. G.         AC
   SHORT STORIES OF H. G. WELLS, THE       WELLS, H. G.         AC
   STOLEN BACILLUS AND OTHER INCIDENTS, THE
                                           WELLS, H. G.         AC
   STORIES FROM SCIENCE FICTION            DOHERTY, G. D.       AN
   THIRTY STRANGE STORIES                  WELLS, H. G.         AC
LOST INHERITANCE, THE                                 SS       97
   PLATTNER STORY AND OTHERS, THE          WELLS, H. G.         AC
   SHORT STORIES OF H. G. WELLS, THE       WELLS, H. G.         AC
   THIRTY STRANGE STORIES                  WELLS, H. G.         AC
MAGIC SHOP, THE                                       SS  SND 03 06
   BEST STORIES OF H. G. WELLS             WELLS, H. G.         AC
   COUNTRY OF THE BLIND, THE               WELLS, H. G.         AC
   INEXPERIENCED GHOST AND NINE OTHER STORIES, THE
                                           WELLS, H. G.         AC
   SHORT STORIES OF H. G. WELLS, THE       WELLS, H. G.         AC
   TWELVE STORIES AND A DREAM              WELLS, H. G.         AC
   TWENTY-EIGHT SCIENCE FICTION STORIES    WELLS, H. G.         AC
MAN OF THE YEAR MILLION, THE                          SS  PMB 93
   APEMAN, SPACEMAN                        STOVER & HARRISON    AN
MAN WHO COULD WORK MIRACLES, THE                      SS  ILN 98 07
   BEST SCIENCE FICTION STORIES OF H. G. WELLS
                                           WELLS, H. G.         AC
   BEST STORIES OF H. G. WELLS             WELLS, H. G.         AC
   COUNTRY OF THE BLIND, THE               WELLS, H. G.         AC
   INEXPERIENCED GHOST AND NINE OTHER STORIES, THE
                                           WELLS, H. G.         AC
   MOONLIGHT TRAVELER, THE                 STERN, PHILIP VAN D. AN
   ODDBALLS                                GHIDALIA, VIC        AN
   SCIENCE FACT/FICTION                    FARRELL/GAGE/&       AN
   SHORT STORIES OF H. G. WELLS, THE       WELLS, H. G.         AC
   TALES OF SPACE AND TIME                 WELLS, H. G.         AC
   TIME MACHINE AND OTHER STORIES, THE (PB)
                                           WELLS, H. G.         AC
   TWENTY-EIGHT SCIENCE FICTION STORIES    WELLS, H. G.         AC
MARI TERRIBLE                                         SS       97
   THIRTY STRANGE STORIES                  WELLS, H. G.         AC
MEN LIKE GODS                                         NO  HRS 22 11
   TWENTY-EIGHT SCIENCE FICTION STORIES    WELLS, H. G.         AC
MISS WINCHELSEA'S HEART                               SS  QUN 98 10
   COUNTRY OF THE BLIND, THE               WELLS, H. G.         AC
   SHORT STORIES OF H. G. WELLS, THE       WELLS, H. G.         AC
   TWELVE STORIES AND A DREAM              WELLS, H. G.         AC
MOONLIGHT FABLE, THE (ALSO AS THE BEAUTIFUL SUIT) SS  COL 09 04
   DOOR IN THE WALL, THE                   WELLS, H. G.         AC
MOTH, THE (A MOTH- GENUS NOVO)                        SS  PGZ 95 03
   COUNTRY OF THE BLIND, THE               WELLS, H. G.         AC
   SHORT STORIES OF H. G. WELLS, THE       WELLS, H. G.         AC
   STOLEN BACILLUS AND OTHER INCIDENTS, THE
                                           WELLS, H. G.         AC
   THIRTY STRANGE STORIES                  WELLS, H. G.         AC
MR. BRISHER'S TREASURE                                SS  SND 99 04
   SHORT STORIES OF H. G. WELLS, THE       WELLS, H. G.         AC
   TWELVE STORIES AND A DREAM              WELLS, H. G.         AC
MR. LEDBETTER'S VACATION                              SS  SND 98 10
   SHORT STORIES OF H. G. WELLS, THE       WELLS, H. G.         AC
   TWELVE STORIES AND A DREAM              WELLS, H. G.         AC
MR. SKELMERSDALE IN FAIRYLAND                         SS  SND 01
   BEST STORIES OF H. G. WELLS             WELLS, H. G.         AC
   SHORT STORIES OF H. G. WELLS, THE       WELLS, H. G.         AC
   TWELVE STORIES AND A DREAM              WELLS, H. G.         AC
MY FIRST AEROPLANE                                    SS  SND 10 01
   SHORT STORIES OF H. G. WELLS, THE       WELLS, H. G.         AC
NEW ACCELERATOR, THE                                  SS  SND 01 12
   BEST SCIENCE FICTION STORIES OF H. G. WELLS
                                           WELLS, H. G.         AC
   BEST STORIES OF H. G. WELLS             WELLS, H. G.         AC
   *BEYOND TIME AND SPACE                  DERLETH, AUGUST      AN
   COUNTRY OF THE BLIND, THE               WELLS, H. G.         AC
   INVISIBLE MEN                           DAVENPORT, BASIL     AN
   MASTERS' CHOICE                         JANIFER, LAURENCE M. AN
```

WELLS, H. G.   WELLS, H. G.

WELLS, H. G.   (CONTINUED)
   SHORT STORIES OF H. G. WELLS, THE   WELLS, H. G.   AC
   STRANGE ECSTASIES   PARRY, MICHEL   AN
   TWELVE STORIES AND A DREAM   WELLS, H. G.   AC
   TWENTY-EIGHT SCIENCE FICTION STORIES   WELLS, H. G.   AC
   3000 YEARS OF FANTASY AND SCIENCE FICTION
                                          DE CAMP, L. S.&C.   AN
                                          SS
OBLITERATED MAN, THE
   COUNTRY OF THE BLIND, THE   WELLS, H. G.   AC
                                          SS   24
PEARL OF LOVE, THE
   SHORT STORIES OF H. G. WELLS, THE   WELLS, H. G.   AC
   *TIME MACHINE AND OTHER STORIES, THE   WELLS, H. G.   AC
                                          SS   18
PETER LEARNS ARITHMETIC
   FANTASIA MATHEMATICA   FADIMAN, CLIFTON   AN
                                          SS   NRV 96 04
PLATTNER STORY, THE
   BEST SCIENCE FICTION STORIES OF H. G. WELLS
                                          WELLS, H. G.   AC
   BEST STORIES OF H. G. WELLS   WELLS, H. G.   AC
   COUNTRY OF THE BLIND, THE   WELLS, H. G.   AC
   PLATTNER STORY AND OTHERS, THE   WELLS, H. G.   AC
   SHORT STORIES OF H. G. WELLS, THE   WELLS, H. G.   AC
   THIRTY STRANGE STORIES   WELLS, H. G.   AC
   TWENTY-EIGHT SCIENCE FICTION STORIES   WELLS, H. G.   AC
                                          SS   NBG 95 05
POLLOCK AND THE PORROH MAN
   INEXPERIENCED GHOST AND NINE OTHER STORIES, THE
                                          WELLS, H. G.   AC
   PLATTNER STORY AND OTHERS, THE   WELLS, H. G.   AC
   SHORT STORIES OF H. G. WELLS, THE   WELLS, H. G.   AC
   THIRTY STRANGE STORIES   WELLS, H. G.   AC
                                          SS   BAW 96 12
PURPLE PILEUS, THE
   BEST SCIENCE FICTION STORIES OF H. G. WELLS
                                          WELLS, H. G.   AC
   COUNTRY OF THE BLIND, THE   WELLS, H. G.   AC
   INEXPERIENCED GHOST AND NINE OTHER STORIES, THE
                                          WELLS, H. G.   AC
   PLATTNER STORY AND OTHERS, THE   WELLS, H. G.   AC
   SHORT STORIES OF H. G. WELLS, THE   WELLS, H. G.   AC
   THIRTY STRANGE STORIES   WELLS, H. G.   AC
                                          SS   PRS 96 07
RAJAH'S TREASURE, THE
   THIRTY STRANGE STORIES   WELLS, H. G.   AC
                                          SS   WSL 95 12
RECONCILIATION, THE (THE BULLA)
   SHORT STORIES OF H. G. WELLS, THE   WELLS, H. G.   AC
   THIRTY STRANGE STORIES   WELLS, H. G.   AC
                                          SS   IDL 96 03
RED ROOM, THE
   COUNTRY OF THE BLIND, THE   WELLS, H. G.   AC
   PLATTNER STORY AND OTHERS, THE   WELLS, H. G.   AC
   SHORT STORIES OF H. G. WELLS, THE   WELLS, H. G.   AC
   THIRTY STRANGE STORIES   WELLS, H. G.   AC
   WAR OF THE WORLDS, THE TIME MACHINE AND SELECTED SHORT STORIES
                                          WELLS, H. G.   AC
REMARKABLE CASE OF DAVIDSON'S EYES, THE   SS   PMB 95 03
   *BEST OF SCIENCE FICTION   CONKLIN, GROFF   AN
   COUNTRY OF THE BLIND, THE   WELLS, H. G.   AC
   SHORT STORIES OF H. G. WELLS, THE   WELLS, H. G.   AC
   STOLEN BACILLUS AND OTHER INCIDENTS, THE
                                          WELLS, H. G.   AC
   TWENTY-EIGHT SCIENCE FICTION STORIES   WELLS, H. G.   AC
SAD STORY OF A DRAMATIC CRITIC, THE   SS   BON 15
   PLATTNER STORY AND OTHERS, THE   WELLS, H. G.   AC
   SHORT STORIES OF H. G. WELLS, THE   WELLS, H. G.   AC
   THIRTY STRANGE STORIES   WELLS, H. G.   AC
                                          SS   WSL 96 12
SEA-RAIDERS, THE
   ASPECTS OF SCIENCE FICTION   DOHERTY, G. D.   AN
   BEST SCIENCE FICTION STORIES OF H. G. WELLS
                                          WELLS, H. G.   AC
   BEST STORIES OF H. G. WELLS   WELLS, H. G.   AC
   COUNTRY OF THE BLIND, THE   WELLS, H. G.   AC
   PLATTNER STORY AND OTHERS, THE   WELLS, H. G.   AC
   SHORT STORIES OF H. G. WELLS, THE   WELLS, H. G.   AC
   SPECTRUM OF WORLDS, A   CLARESON, THOMAS D. AN
   THIRTY STRANGE STORIES   WELLS, H. G.   AC
   TWENTY-EIGHT SCIENCE FICTION STORIES   WELLS, H. G.   AC
SLIP UNDER THE KNIFE (ALSO AS UNDER THE KNIFE) SS NRV 96 01
   THIRTY STRANGE STORIES   WELLS, H. G.   AC
                                          SS   YBK 96 01
SLIP UNDER THE MICROSCOPE, A
   COUNTRY OF THE BLIND, THE   WELLS, H. G.   AC
   INEXPERIENCED GHOST AND NINE OTHER STORIES, THE
                                          WELLS, H. G.   AC
   PLATTNER STORY AND OTHERS, THE   WELLS, H. G.   AC
   SHORT STORIES OF H. G. WELLS, THE   WELLS, H. G.   AC
   THIRTY STRANGE STORIES   WELLS, H. G.   AC
                                          NO   VIK 37
STAR BEGOTTEN
   TWENTY-EIGHT SCIENCE FICTION STORIES   WELLS, H. G.   AC
                                          SS   GRP 97 12
STAR, THE
   BEST SCIENCE FICTION STORIES OF H. G. WELLS
                                          WELLS, H. G.   AC
   BEST STORIES OF H. G. WELLS   WELLS, H. G.   AC
   COUNTRY OF THE BLIND, THE   WELLS, H. G.   AC
   DOOR IN THE WALL, THE   WELLS, H. G.   AC
   EARTH IN PERIL, THE   WOLLHEIM, DONALD A. DA
   FROM FRANKENSTEIN TO ANDROMEDA   BROWN, JAMES GOLDIE AN
   GREAT SCIENCE FICTION STORIES   SMITH, CORDELIA T. AN
   MIRROR OF INFINITY, THE   SILVERBERG, ROBERT AN
   *OTHER SIDE OF THE MOON, THE   DERLETH, AUGUST   AN
   PAST, PRESENT, AND FUTURE PERFECT   WOLFE, J&FITZ GERALD AN
   SCIENCE IN FICTION   BAYLISS, A.E. & J.C. AN
   SECOND ORBIT   DOHERTY, G. D.   AN
   SHORT STORIES OF H. G. WELLS, THE   WELLS, H. G.   AC
   SHOT IN THE DARK   MERRIL, JUDITH   AN
   TALES OF SPACE AND TIME   WELLS, H. G.   AC
TOMORROW, AND TOMORROW, AND TOMORROW...
                                          HEINTZ/HERBERT/JOOS/ AN
   TREASURY OF SCIENCE FICTION CLASSICS, THE
                                          KUEBLER, HAROLD W. AN
   TWENTY-EIGHT SCIENCE FICTION STORIES   WELLS, H. G.   AC

WELLS, H. G.   (CONTINUED)
   STOLEN BACILLUS, THE   SS   PMB 94 06
   COUNTRY OF THE BLIND, THE   WELLS, H. G.   AC
   GREAT SCIENCE FICTION STORIES   SMITH, CORDELIA T. AN
   SHORT STORIES OF H. G. WELLS, THE   WELLS, H. G.   AC
   STOLEN BACILLUS AND OTHER INCIDENTS, THE
                                          WELLS, H. G.   AC
   THIRTY STRANGE STORIES   WELLS, H. G.   AC
   TWENTY-EIGHT SCIENCE FICTION STORIES   WELLS, H. G.   AC
STOLEN BODY, THE   SS   SND 98 11
   INEXPERIENCED GHOST AND NINE OTHER STORIES, THE
                                          WELLS, H. G.   AC
   SHORT STORIES OF H. G. WELLS, THE   WELLS, H. G.   AC
   TWELVE STORIES AND A DREAM   WELLS, H. G.   AC
   TWENTY-EIGHT SCIENCE FICTION STORIES   WELLS, H. G.   AC
STORY OF DAVIDSON'S EYES, THE   SS   PMB 95 03
   BEST SCIENCE FICTION STORIES OF H. G. WELLS
                                          WELLS, H. G.   AC
   THIRTY STRANGE STORIES   WELLS, H. G.   AC
STORY OF THE DAYS TO COME, A   NA   PGZ 97
   BEST STORIES OF H. G. WELLS   WELLS, H. G.   AC
   SHORT STORIES OF H. G. WELLS, THE   WELLS, H. G.   AC
   TALES OF SPACE AND TIME   WELLS, H. G.   AC
   TWENTY-EIGHT SCIENCE FICTION STORIES   WELLS, H. G.   AC
   3 PROPHETIC SCIENCE FICTION NOVELS OF H. G. WELLS
                                          WELLS, H. G.   AC
STORY OF THE INEXPERIENCED GHOST, THE (SEE THE INEXPERIENCED
GHOST)   TC
STORY OF THE LAST TRUMP, THE   SS   BON 15
   SHORT STORIES OF H. G. WELLS, THE   WELLS, H. G.   AC
STORY OF THE LATE MR. ELVESHAM, THE   SS   IDL 96 05
   BEST STORIES OF H. G. WELLS   WELLS, H. G.   AC
   COUNTRY OF THE BLIND, THE   WELLS, H. G.   AC
   DARK SIDE, THE   KNIGHT, DAMON   AN
   OTHER SIDE OF THE CLOCK, THE   STERN, PHILIP VAN D. AN
   PLATTNER STORY AND OTHERS, THE   WELLS, H. G.   AC
   SHORT STORIES OF H. G. WELLS, THE   WELLS, H. G.   AC
   THIRTY STRANGE STORIES   WELLS, H. G.   AC
   TWENTY-EIGHT SCIENCE FICTION STORIES   WELLS, H. G.   AC
   WAR OF THE WORLDS, THE TIME MACHINE AND SELECTED SHORT STORIES
                                          WELLS, H. G.   AC
STORY OF THE STONE AGE, A   NA   IDL 97 05
   SHORT STORIES OF H. G. WELLS, THE   WELLS, H. G.   AC
   TALES OF SPACE AND TIME   WELLS, H. G.   AC
   TWENTY-EIGHT SCIENCE FICTION STORIES   WELLS, H. G.   AC
STRANGE ORCHID, THE (THE FLOWERING OF THE STRANGE ORCHID)
                                          SS   PMB 94 08
   BEST SCIENCE FICTION STORIES OF H. G. WELLS
                                          WELLS, H. G.   AC
   THIRTY STRANGE STORIES   WELLS, H. G.   AC
TEMPTATION OF HARRINGAY, THE   SS   SJG 95 02
   HUMAN?   MERRIL, JUDITH   AN
   SHORT STORIES OF H. G. WELLS, THE   WELLS, H. G.   AC
   STOLEN BACILLUS AND OTHER INCIDENTS, THE
                                          WELLS, H. G.   AC
THROUGH A WINDOW (AT A WINDOW)   SS   BAW 94 08
   SHORT STORIES OF H. G. WELLS, THE   WELLS, H. G.   AC
   STOLEN BACILLUS AND OTHER INCIDENTS, THE
                                          WELLS, H. G.   AC
TIME MACHINE, THE   NA   NRV 95 01
   SCIENCE FICTION HALL OF FAME VOLUME 2A BOVA, BEN   AN
   SEVEN FAMOUS NOVELS BY H. G. WELLS   WELLS, H. G.   AC
   SHORT STORIES OF H. G. WELLS, THE   WELLS, H. G.   AC
   *TIME MACHINE AND OTHER STORIES, THE   WELLS, H. G.   AC
   TIMES 4 (ABRIDGED STORIES)   ALLEN, VIRGINIA F. AN
   TRAVELERS IN TIME   STERN, PHILIP VAN D. AN
   TREASURY OF SCIENCE FICTION CLASSICS, THE
                                          KUEBLER, HAROLD W. AN
   WAR OF THE WORLDS, THE TIME MACHINE AND SELECTED SHORT STORIES
                                          WELLS, H. G.   AC
   3 PROPHETIC SCIENCE FICTION NOVELS OF H. G. WELLS
                                          WELLS, H. G.   AC
TIME MACHINE, THE (CHAPTER XI, XII-PART) EX   NRV 95 01
   VOYAGERS IN TIME   SILVERBERG, ROBERT AN
TIME MACHINE, THE (SELECTION FROM)   EX   NRV 95 01
   CENTURY OF SCIENCE FICTION, A   KNIGHT, DAMON   AN
TREASURE IN THE FOREST, THE   SS   PMB 94
   COUNTRY OF THE BLIND, THE   WELLS, H. G.   AC
   SHORT STORIES OF H. G. WELLS, THE   WELLS, H. G.   AC
   STOLEN BACILLUS AND OTHER INCIDENTS, THE
                                          WELLS, H. G.   AC
   THIRTY STRANGE STORIES   WELLS, H. G.   AC
TRIUMPHS OF A TAXIDERMIST, THE   SS   PGZ 94
   SHORT STORIES OF H. G. WELLS, THE   WELLS, H. G.   AC
   STOLEN BACILLUS AND OTHER INCIDENTS, THE
                                          WELLS, H. G.   AC
   THIRTY STRANGE STORIES   WELLS, H. G.   AC
TRUTH ABOUT PYECRAFT, THE   SS   SND 03 04
   BEST STORIES OF H. G. WELLS   WELLS, H. G.   AC
   COUNTRY OF THE BLIND, THE   WELLS, H. G.   AC
   GOLDEN ROAD, THE   KNIGHT, DAMON   AN
   SCIENCE FICTION AND READER'S GUIDE   BARROWS, MARJORIE   AN
   SHORT STORIES OF H. G. WELLS, THE   WELLS, H. G.   AC
   TWELVE STORIES AND A DREAM   WELLS, H. G.   AC
   TWENTY-EIGHT SCIENCE FICTION STORIES   WELLS, H. G.   AC
   WAR OF THE WORLDS, THE TIME MACHINE AND SELECTED SHORT STORIES
                                          WELLS, H. G.   AC
UNDER THE KNIFE (SLIP UNDER THE KNIFE)   SS   NRV 96 01
   COUNTRY OF THE BLIND, THE   WELLS, H. G.   AC
   PERCHANCE TO DREAM   KNIGHT, DAMON   AN
   PLATTNER STORY AND OTHERS, THE   WELLS, H. G.   AC
   SHORT STORIES OF H. G. WELLS, THE   WELLS, H. G.   AC
   TWENTY-EIGHT SCIENCE FICTION STORIES   WELLS, H. G.   AC
VALLEY OF SPIDERS, THE   SS   PRS 03 03
   BEST STORIES OF H. G. WELLS   WELLS, H. G.   AC
   COUNTRY OF THE BLIND, THE   WELLS, H. G.   AC

WELLS, H. G.   (CONTINUED)
    SHORT STORIES OF H. G. WELLS, THE   WELLS, H. G.   AC
    TWELVE STORIES AND A DREAM   WELLS, H. G.   AC
    TWENTY-EIGHT SCIENCE FICTION STORIES   WELLS, H. G.   AC
    WAR OF THE WORLDS, THE TIME MACHINE AND SELECTED SHORT STORIES
                                             WELLS, H. G.   AC
  VISION OF JUDGEMENT, A   SS   BUT 99 09
    COUNTRY OF THE BLIND, THE   WELLS, H. G.   AC
    LOOKING AHEAD   ALLEN, D. & L.   AN
    OUT OF THIS WORLD   FAST, JULIUS   AN
    SHORT STORIES OF H. G. WELLS, THE   WELLS, H. G.   AC
   *TIME MACHINE AND OTHER STORIES, THE   WELLS, H. G.   AC
  WAR OF THE WORLDS, THE   EX   PRS 97 04
    FROM FRANKENSTEIN TO ANDROMEDA   BROWN, JAMES GOLDIE   AN
  WAR OF THE WORLDS, THE   NA   PRS 97 04
    MARS, WE LOVE YOU   HIPOLITO & MCNELLY   AN
    SEVEN FAMOUS NOVELS BY H. G. WELLS   WELLS, H. G.   AC
    WAR OF THE WORLDS, THE TIME MACHINE AND SELECTED SHORT STORIES
                                             WELLS, H. G.   AC
  WHEN THE SLEEPER WAKES   NO   HPR 99
    3 PROPHETIC SCIENCE FICTION NOVELS OF H. G. WELLS
                                             WELLS, H. G.   AC

WELLS, KEITH
  CAT AND THE COIN, THE   NV   NWR 75 25
    NEW WRITINGS IN SF. 25   BULMER, KENNETH   OA
  TIME OF MIND, A   SS   NWR 75 27
    NEW WRITINGS IN SF. 27   BULMER, KENNETH   OA

WELLS, ROBERT
  BLUE THEME AND FUGUE   SS   SFM 74 02
    BEST OF SCIENCE FICTION MONTHLY, THE   SACKS, JANET   AN
  FRONTIER INCIDENT   SS   NWR 71 18
    NEW WRITINGS IN SF. 18   CARNELL, JOHN   OA
  MACHINE THAT WAS LONELY, THE   SS
    AD 2500   WILSON, ANGUS   AN

WENSKES, HELMUT
  DALIS ASCENSION   IL
    BEYOND THIS HORIZON   CARRELL, CHRISTOPHER OA
  GREED   IL
    BEYOND THIS HORIZON   CARRELL, CHRISTOPHER OA
  PHILOSOPHERS STONE   IL
    BEYOND THIS HORIZON   CARRELL, CHRISTOPHER OA
  STAGE SET   IL
    BEYOND THIS HORIZON   CARRELL, CHRISTOPHER OA

WENTZ, ELMA
  BEYOND DOUBT   SS C AST 41 04
    BEYOND THE END OF TIME   POHL, FREDERIK   AN
    POLITICAL SCIENCE FICTION   GREENBERG& WARRICK   AN

WERTENBAKER, G. P.   ALSO AS   GREEN PEYTON
  COMING OF THE ICE, THE   SS   AMZ 26 06
    HISTORY OF THE SCIENCE FICTION MAGAZINE, THE PART 1 1926-1935
                                             ASHLEY, MICHAEL   AN

WESLEY, JOSEPH   ALSO AS   L. J. STECHER, JR.
  WOMB TO TOMB   SS   ASF 69 08
    ANALOG 8   CAMPBELL, JOHN W. JR AN
    BEST SF: 1969   HARRISON & ALDISS   AN

WEST, D.
  PIT, THE   NA
    GOLLANCZ - SUNDAY TIMES BEST SF STORIES
                                             ANONYMOUS   OA

WEST, JESSAMYN
  LITTLE MEN   SN   SSN 54
    STAR SHORT NOVELS   POHL, FREDERIK   OA

WEST, JOHN ANTHONY
  CASE HISTORY, A   SS   73
    SHOCKING THING, A   KNIGHT, DAMON   AN
  GEORGE   SS   FSF 61 06
   *BEST FROM FANTASY AND SCIENCE FICTION: 11
                                             MILLS, ROBERT P.   AN
  GLADYS'S GREGORY   SS   FSF 63 02
    ARENA: SPORTS SF   FERMAN & MALZBERG   AN
    TWENTY YEARS OF FANTASY & SCIENCE FICTION
                                             FERMAN & MILLS   AN

WEST, MICHAEL
  POPPIN' FRESH   SS
    CLARION SF   WILHELM, KATE   OA

WEST, WALLACE
  BIRD OF TIME, THE   NO H GNM 59
  OUTPOSTS IN SPACE   AC H AVL 62
  BIRD OF TIME, THE   NO   TWS 52 08
    BIRD OF TIME, THE   WEST, WALLACE   NO
  CAPTIVE AUDIENCE   NO   TWS 53 06
    BIRD OF TIME, THE   WEST, WALLACE   NO
  DAWNINGSBURGH   SS   GAL 62 06
    EIGHTH GALAXY READER, THE   POHL, FREDERIK   AN
  EN ROUTE TO PLUTO   SS   ASF 36 08
   *BEST OF SCIENCE FICTION   CONKLIN, GROFF   AN
    BIRD OF TIME, THE   WEST, WALLACE   NO
  GLIMPSES OF THE MOON   NV   ASF 65 06
    GREAT SCIENCE FICTION STORIES ABOUT THE MOON
                                             DIKTY, T. E.   AN
  HAUNTED CENTENNIAL   NV   FUT 58 02
    OUTPOSTS IN SPACE   WEST, WALLACE   AC
  LAST MAN, THE   NV   AMZ 29 02
    POCKET BOOK OF SCIENCE-FICTION, THE   WOLLHEIM, DONALD A.   AN
    WHEN WOMEN RULE   MOSKOWITZ, SAM   AN

WEST, WALLACE   (CONTINUED)
    LISTEN, CHILDREN, LISTEN   SS   FUN 53 10
    GRAVEYARD READER, THE   CONKLIN, GROFF   AN
    ZACHERLEY'S MIDNIGHT SNACKS   ZACHERLEY   AN
  LURE OF POLARIS, THE   SS   TWS 49 10
    BIRD OF TIME, THE   WEST, WALLACE   NO
  MOON DANCE   NV   SFQ 54 11
    OUTPOSTS IN SPACE   WEST, WALLACE   AC
  MOON MADNESS   SS   WRT 31 08
    OUTPOSTS IN SPACE   WEST, WALLACE   AC
  NO WAR TOMORROW   NO   SFQ 51 05
    OUTPOSTS IN SPACE   WEST, WALLACE   AC
  OUTLAW   SS
    OUTPOSTS IN SPACE   WEST, WALLACE   AC
  SCULPTORS OF LIFE   SS   ASF 39 12
   *SCIENCE FICTION THINKING MACHINES   CONKLIN, GROFF   AN

WESTLAKE, DONALD E.
  EARTHMAN'S BURDEN, THE   NA   GAL 62 10
    ELSEWHERE AND ELSEWHEN   CONKLIN, GROFF   AN
  QUESTION, THE   SS C FSF 63 03
  IMPOSSIBLE?   JANIFER, LAURENCE M. AC
  WINNER, THE   SS   NOV 70 01
    ANOTHER TOMORROW   HOLLISTER, BERNARD C AN
    EARTH IN TRANSIT   SCHWARTZ, SHEILA   AN
   *NOVA 1   HARRISON, HARRY   OA
    SCIENCE FICTION   BRODKIN & PEARSON   AN
    TOMORROW, AND TOMORROW, AND TOMORROW...
                                             HEINTZ/HERBERT/JOOS/ AN

WESTON, PETER
  ANDROMEDA I   OA   FPL 76
  INTRODUCTION   IN
    ANDROMEDA I   WESTON, PETER   OA
  INTRODUCTION: A NEW WAY OF EXPRESSION   IN
    BEYOND THIS HORIZON   CARRELL, CHRISTOPHER OA

WHARTON, EDITH
  AFTERWARD   NV   CNY 10 01
    OTHER DIMENSION, THE   ROSNER, SARA   AN

WHARTON, THOM LEE
  BYSTANDER, THE   SS   ORB 70 08
    BEST FROM ORBIT, THE   KNIGHT, DAMON   AN
    ORBIT 8   KNIGHT, DAMON   OA

WHELPLEY, J. D.
  ATOMS OF CHLADNI, THE (1859)   SS   HRP 59
    FUTURE PERFECT   FRANKLIN, H. BRUCE   AN

WHEWELL, DR. WILLIAM
  NO POWER ON EARTH   PM
    FANTASIA MATHEMATICA   FADIMAN, CLIFTON   AN
  VERSE   PM C 25
    MATHEMATICAL MAGPIE, THE   FADIMAN, CLIFTON   AN

WHITE, CECIL B.   PSEUD. FOR WILLIAM H. CHRISTIE
  RETREAT TO MARS, THE   SS   AMZ 27 08
   *BEST OF SCIENCE FICTION   CONKLIN, GROFF   AN

WHITE, DON
  PEGGY AND PETER GO TO THE MOON   SS   FSF 63 02
    BEST FROM FANTASY AND SCIENCE FICTION: 13
                                             DAVIDSON, AVRAM   AN

WHITE, E. B.
  DOOR, THE   SS   NYM 39
    LIGHT FANTASTIC, THE   HARRISON, HARRY   AN
  HOUR OF LETDOWN, THE   SS   FSF 52 08
    CIRCUS OF DR. LAO AND OTHER IMPROBABLE STORIES
                                             BRADBURY, RAY   AN
    OUT OF THIS WORLD 5   WILLIAMS-ELLIS& OWEN AN
  MORNING OF THE DAY THEY DID IT, THE   SS   NYM 50 02
    ARMCHAIR SCIENCE READER, THE   GORDON, I. & SORKIN AN
    PAST, PRESENT, AND FUTURE PERFECT   WOLFE, J&FITZ GERALD AN
    TREASURY OF GREAT SCIENCE FICTION, A VOL.2
                                             BOUCHER, ANTHONY   AN
  SUPREMACY OF URUGUAY, THE   SS   NYM 33 11
    ECO-FICTION   STADLER, JOHN   AN
    TIMELESS STORIES FOR TODAY AND TOMORROW
                                             BRADBURY, RAY   AN

WHITE, EDWARD LUCAS
  AMINIA   SS   27
    SECOND AVON FANTASY READER, THE   WOLLHEIM &ERNSBERGER AN
  HOUSE OF THE NIGHTMARE, THE   SS   TTB 19 09
    BEWARE THE BEASTS   GHIDALIA, V.& ELWOOD AN
  LUKUNDOO   SS   WRT 25 11
    SHOCKING THING, A   KNIGHT, DAMON   AN

WHITE, FRED M.
  PURPLE TERROR, THE   SS   SND 99 09
    SCIENCE FICTION BY GASLIGHT   MOSKOWITZ, SAM   AN

WHITE, JAMES
  ALIENS AMONG US, THE   AC   BAL 69 03
  DEADLY LITTER   NO   BAL 64 10
  HOSPITAL STATION   AC   BAL 62
  MAJOR OPERATION   NO   BAL 71 02
  MONSTERS AND MEDICS   AC   BAL 77 03
  ANSWER CAME THERE NONE   SS   GAL 74 01
    BEST FROM GALAXY, THE VOLUME III   BAEN, JAMES   AN
    MONSTERS AND MEDICS   WHITE, JAMES   AC
  APPRENTICE, THE   NV   NWS 60 10
    MONSTERS AND MEDICS   WHITE, JAMES   AC
    OUT OF THIS WORLD 3   WILLIAMS-ELLIS& OWEN AN

WHITE, JAMES   (CONTINUED)
  ASSISTED PASSAGE   SS   NWS 53 01
    GATEWAY TO THE STARS   CARNELL, JOHN   AN
  BLOOD BROTHER   NV   NWR 69 14
    MAJOR OPERATION   WHITE, JAMES   NO
    NEW WRITINGS IN SF. 14   CARNELL, JOHN   OA
  CHRISTMAS TREASON   NV   FSF 62 01
    SPACE 1   DAVIS, RICHARD   OA
    8TH ANNUAL OF THE YEAR'S BEST S-F, THE MERRIL, JUDITH AN
  COMMUTER   SS   NWR 73 21
    NEW WRITINGS IN SF. 21   CARNELL, JOHN   OA
  CONSPIRATORS, THE   NV   NWS 54 06
    ALIENS AMONG US, THE   WHITE, JAMES   AC
    MIND TO MIND   SILVERBERG, ROBERT   AN
    *SCIENCE FICTION ADVENTURES IN MUTATION CONKLIN, GROFF AN
  COUNTER SECURITY   NV   FSF 63 02
    MONSTERS AND MEDICS   WHITE, JAMES   AC
    13 ABOVE THE NIGHT   CONKLIN, GROFF   AN
  COUNTERCHARM   SS   NWS 60 11
    ALIENS AMONG US, THE   WHITE, JAMES   AC
    ALIENS, THE   SILVERBERG, ROBERT   AN
  CROSSFIRE   SS   NWS 53 06
    BEST FROM NEW WORLDS SCIENCE FICTION, THE
                                    CARNELL, JOHN   AN
  CUSTOM FITTING   NV   STL 76 02
    STELLAR 2   DEL REY, JUDY-LYNN   OA
  DEADLY LITTER   NV   SFB 60 02
    DEADLY LITTER   WHITE, JAMES   NO
  DOGFIGHT   NV   NWS 59 03
    MONSTERS AND MEDICS   WHITE, JAMES   AC
  FAST TRIP   SS   FSF 63 04
    OUT OF THIS WORLD 6   WILLIAMS-ELLIS& OWEN AN
  GRAPELINER   NV   NWS 59 11
    DEADLY LITTER   WHITE, JAMES   NO
  IDEAL CAPTAIN, THE   NV   NWS 58 08
    DEADLY LITTER   WHITE, JAMES   NO
  IN LOVING MEMORY   SS   NEB 56 01
    MONSTERS AND MEDICS   WHITE, JAMES   AC
  INTRODUCTION: REALITY IN SCIENCE FICTION   IN
    MONSTERS AND MEDICS   WHITE, JAMES   AC
  INVADER   NV   NWR 66 07
    MAJOR OPERATION   WHITE, JAMES   NO
    NEW WRITINGS IN SF. 7   CARNELL, JOHN   OA
  LIGHTS OUTSIDE THE WINDOWS, THE   NV   NWS 57 02
    DEADLY LITTER   WHITE, JAMES   NO
  MAJOR OPERATION   NV   NWR 71 18
    MAJOR OPERATION   WHITE, JAMES   NO
    NEW WRITINGS IN SF. 18   CARNELL, JOHN   OA
  MEATBALL   NV   NWR 69 16
    MAJOR OPERATION   WHITE, JAMES   NO
    NEW WRITINGS IN SF. 16   CARNELL, JOHN   OA
  MEDIC (O'MARA'S ORPHAN).   NV   NWS 60 01
    HOSPITAL STATION   WHITE, JAMES   AC
  NUISANCE VALUE   SS   ASF 75 10
    MONSTERS AND MEDICS   WHITE, JAMES   AC
  O'MARA'S ORPHAN (ALSO AS MEDIC)   NV   NWS 60 01
    WORLDS APART   WILLIAMS-ELLIS& OWEN AN
  OCCUPATION: WARRIOR   SN   SFA 59 03
    ALIENS AMONG US, THE   WHITE, JAMES   AC
  OUT-PATIENT   NV   NWS 60 06
    HOSPITAL STATION   WHITE, JAMES   AC
  RED ALERT   NV   NWS 56 01
    ALIENS AMONG US, THE   WHITE, JAMES   AC
  RESIDENT PHYSICIAN   NV   NWS 61 09
    GALACTIC EMPIRES VOLUME ONE   ALDISS, BRIAN W.   AN
  SCAVENGERS, THE   SS   ASF 53 10
    ALIENS AMONG US, THE   WHITE, JAMES   AC
  SECOND ENDING   NA   FAN 61 06
    MONSTERS AND MEDICS   WHITE, JAMES   AC
  SECTOR GENERAL   NV   NWS 57 11
    HOSPITAL STATION   WHITE, JAMES   AC
  SPACEBIRD   SS   NWR 73 22
    NEW WRITINGS IN SF. 22   BULMER, KENNETH   OA
  TABLEAU   NV   NWS 58 05
    ALIENS AMONG US, THE   WHITE, JAMES   AC
    BEST OF NEW WORLDS, THE   MOORCOCK, MICHAEL   AN
  TO KILL OR CURE   SS   NWS 57 04
    ALIENS AMONG US, THE   WHITE, JAMES   AC
  TROUBLE WITH EMILY, THE   NV   NWS 58 11
    HOSPITAL STATION   WHITE, JAMES   AC
    OUT OF THIS WORLD 2   WILLIAMS-ELLIS& OWEN AN
  VERTIGO   NV   NWR 68 12
    MAJOR OPERATION   WHITE, JAMES   NO
    NEW WRITINGS IN SF. 12   CARNELL, JOHN   OA
  VISITOR AT LARGE   NV   NWS 59 06
    HOSPITAL STATION   WHITE, JAMES   AC

WHITE, M. E.
  POWER OF POSITIVE THINKING, THE   SS   NDR 64 18
    10TH ANNUAL OF THE YEAR'S BEST S-F, THE
                                    MERRIL, JUDITH   AN

WHITE, TED
  BEST FROM AMAZING, THE   AN   MAN 73
  BEST FROM FANTASTIC, THE   AN   MAN 73
  DANDY   SS   DEM 73
    DEMON KIND   ELWOOD, ROGER   OA
  FOREWORD   IN
    BEST FROM FANTASTIC, THE   WHITE, TED   AN
  PHOENIX   SS C AMZ 63 02
    BEST FROM AMAZING, THE   WHITE, TED   AN
  STELLA   SS   WLK 73
    AND WALK NOW GENTLY THROUGH THE FIRE...
                                    ELWOOD, ROGER   OA
    GIFTS OF ASTI AND OTHER STORIES OF SCIENCE FICTION, THE
                                    ELWOOD, ROGER   AN

WHITE, WILLIAM A. P. SEE PSEUD.
  ANTHONY BOUCHER, H. H. HOLMES AND HERMAN W. MUDGETT

WHITEHILL, JOSEPH
  IN THE HOUSE, ANOTHER   SS   FSF 60 04
    6TH ANNUAL OF THE YEAR'S BEST S-F, THE MERRIL, JUDITH AN

WHITLEY, GEORGE   PSEUD. FOR A. BERTRAM CHANDLER
  ALL LACED UP   SS   NWS 61 11
    LAMBDA I AND OTHER STORIES   CARNELL, JOHN   AN
  CASTAWAY   SS   WBT 47 11
    *NO PLACE LIKE EARTH   CARNELL, JOHN   AN
  CHANGE OF HEART   SS   NWS 61 09
    8TH ANNUAL OF THE YEAR'S BEST S-F, THE MERRIL, JUDITH AN
  TIE THAT BINDS, THE   SS   FUN 58 06
    ENCOUNTERS WITH ALIENS   EARLEY, GEORGE W.   AN

WHITMAN, WALT
  WHEN I HEARD THE LEARN'D ASTRONOMER   PM
    SPECULATIONS   SANDERS, THOMAS E.   AN

WHITTEMORE, REED
  PROJECTION, A   PM   67
    SCIENCE FICTION   BRODKIN & PEARSON   AN

WHYBROW, GEOFFREY
  HITCH HIKE TO PARADISE   SS
    AD 2500   WILSON, ANGUS   AN

WILBUR, RICHARD
  ADVICE TO A PROPHET   PM   59
    SCIENCE FICTION: THE FUTURE   ALLEN, DICK   AN

WILCOX, DON
  SMALLEST MOON, THE   SS   BLF
    BOYS' LIFE BOOK OF OUTER SPACE STORIES, THE
                                    BOY'S LIFE, ED. OF   AN
  VOYAGE THAT LASTED SIX HUNDRED YEARS, THE   NV   AMZ 40 10
    LOOKING FORWARD   LESSER, MILTON   AN

WILDE, NIALL
  DIVVIL WITH THE WOMEN, A   SS   FSF 60 01
    BEST FROM FANTASY AND SCIENCE FICTION: 10
                                    MILLS, ROBERT P.   AN

WILDE, OSCAR
  CANTERVILLE GHOST, THE   SS   CSR 87 03
    OUT OF THIS WORLD   FAST, JULIUS   AN

WILDER, CHERRY
  ARK OF JAMES CARLYLE, THE   SS   NWR 74 24
    BEYOND TOMORROW   HARDING, LEE   AN
    NEW WRITINGS IN SF. 24   BULMER, KENNETH   OA
  DOUBLE SUMMER TIME   NV   NWR 76 29
    NEW WRITINGS IN SF. 29   BULMER, KENNETH   OA
  PHOBOS TRANSCRIPTS, THE   SS   NWR 75 26
    NEW WRITINGS IN SF. 26   BULMER, KENNETH   OA

WILDING, MICHAEL
  MAN OF SLOW FEELINGS, THE   SS
    SECOND PACIFIC BOOK OF SCIENCE FICTION, THE
                                    BAXTER, JOHN   AN

WILHELM, KATE
  ANDOVER AND THE ANDROID   AC H DOB 66
    SEE "THE MILE-LONG SPACESHIP"
  CLARION SF   OA   BKM 77 01
  DOWNSTAIRS ROOM AND OTHER SPECULATIVE FICTION, THE AC H HPR 68
  INFINITY BOX, THE   AC H HPR 75
  MILE-LONG SPACESHIP, THE   AC   BKM 63 12
    IN ENGLAND AS "ANDOVER AND THE ANDROID"
  NEBULA AWARD STORIES 9   AN H HPR 74
  A IS FOR AUTOMATION   SS   FUT 59 10
    MILE-LONG SPACESHIP, THE   WILHELM, KATE   AC
  ANDOVER AND THE ANDROID   SS   NEW 63 AC
    MILE-LONG SPACESHIP, THE   WILHELM, KATE   AC
  APOSTOLIC TRAVELERS, THE   SS   NEW 63 AC
    MILE-LONG SPACESHIP, THE   WILHELM, KATE   AC
  APRIL FOOL'S DAY FOREVER   NV   ORB 70 07
    INFINITY BOX, THE   WILHELM, KATE   AC
    ORBIT 7   KNIGHT, DAMON   OA
  BABY, YOU WERE GREAT   SS   ORB 67 02
    ALPHA 5   SILVERBERG, ROBERT   AN
    BEST FROM ORBIT, THE   KNIGHT, DAMON   AN
    DOWNSTAIRS ROOM AND OTHER SPECULATIVE FICTION, THE
                                    WILHELM, KATE   AC
    ORBIT 2   KNIGHT, DAMON   OA
    WOMEN OF WONDER   SARGENT, PAMELA   AN
  BROTHER TO DRAGONS, A COMPANION OF OWLS, A   NV   ORB 74 14
    ORBIT 14   KNIGHT, DAMON   OA
  CASE OF DESPERATION, A (SEE THE FEEL OF DESPERATION)
                                    TC
  CHOSEN, THE   SS   ORB 70 06
    ORBIT 6   KNIGHT, DAMON   OA
  COLD DARK NIGHT WITH SNOW, A   SS   ORB 70 06
    ORBIT 6   KNIGHT, DAMON   OA
  COUNTDOWN   SS   NEW 68 AC
    DOWNSTAIRS ROOM AND OTHER SPECULATIVE FICTION, THE
                                    WILHELM, KATE   AC
  DOWNSTAIRS ROOM, THE   SS   NEW 68 AC
    DOWNSTAIRS ROOM AND OTHER SPECULATIVE FICTION, THE
                                    WILHELM, KATE   AC
  ENCOUNTER, THE   NV   ORB 70 08
    BEST FROM ORBIT, THE   KNIGHT, DAMON   AN
    NEBULA AWARD STORIES NO. 7   BIGGLE, LLOYD JR.   AN
    ORBIT 8   KNIGHT, DAMON   OA

WILHELM, KATE   WILLIAMS, JONATHAN

WILHELM, KATE   (CONTINUED)
  FEAR IS A COLD BLACK   NV   NEW 63 AC
    MILE-LONG SPACESHIP, THE   WILHELM, KATE   AC
  FEEL OF DESPERATION, THE (A CASE OF DESPERATION) SS   AHM 64
    DOWNSTAIRS ROOM AND OTHER SPECULATIVE FICTION, THE
                                      WILHELM, KATE   AC
  FUNERAL, THE   NV   DVS 72 02
    AGAIN, DANGEROUS VISIONS   ELLISON, HARLAN   OA
    INFINITY BOX, THE   WILHELM, KATE   AC
    MORE WOMEN OF WONDER   SARGENT, PAMELA   AN
  FUSION BOMB, THE   NV   ORB 72 10
    INFINITY BOX, THE   WILHELM, KATE   AC
    ORBIT 10   KNIGHT, DAMON   OA
  GIFT FROM THE STARS   SS   FUT 58 12
    MILE-LONG SPACESHIP, THE   WILHELM, KATE   AC
  HOUNDS, THE   NV   NEW 74 AN
    SHOCKING THING, A   KNIGHT, DAMON
  HOW MANY MILES TO BABYLON?   SS   NEW 68 AC
    DOWNSTAIRS ROOM AND OTHER SPECULATIVE FICTION, THE
                                      WILHELM, KATE   AC
                                                  NA   ORB 71 09
    INFINITY BOX, THE   WILHELM, KATE   AC
    ORBIT 9   KNIGHT, DAMON   OA
  INTRODUCTION   IN
    CLARION SF   WILHELM, KATE   OA
    DOWNSTAIRS ROOM AND OTHER SPECULATIVE FICTION, THE
                                      WILHELM, KATE   AC
    INFINITY BOX, THE   WILHELM, KATE   AC
    NEBULA AWARD STORIES 9   WILHELM, KATE   AN
  JENNY WITH WINGS   SS   NEW 63 AC
    GOLDEN ROAD, THE   KNIGHT, DAMON   AN
    MILE-LONG SPACESHIP, THE   WILHELM, KATE   AC
  LADIES AND GENTLEMEN, THIS IS YOUR CRISIS SS   ORB 76 18
    BEST SCIENCE FICTION STORIES OF THE YEAR (1976)
                                      DOZOIS, GARDNER R.   AN
    ORBIT 18   KNIGHT, DAMON   OA
  LAST DAYS OF THE CAPTAIN, THE   SS   AMZ 62 11
    MILE-LONG SPACESHIP, THE   WILHELM, KATE   AC
  MAN OF LETTERS   SS   NEW 75 AC
    INFINITY BOX, THE   WILHELM, KATE   AC
  MAN WITHOUT A PLANET, THE   SS   FSF 62 07
    BEST FROM FANTASY AND SCIENCE FICTION: 12
                                      DAVIDSON, AVRAM   AN
    MILE-LONG SPACESHIP, THE   WILHELM, KATE   AC
  MILE-LONG SPACESHIP, THE   SS   ASF 57 04
    BEST SCIENCE FICTION STORIES AND NOVELS: 9TH SERIES
                                      DIKTY, T. E.   AN
    BEYOND TOMORROW   KNIGHT, DAMON   AN
    MILE-LONG SPACESHIP, THE   WILHELM, KATE   AC
  MOST BEAUTIFUL WOMAN IN THE WORLD, THE SS   NEW 68 AC
    DOWNSTAIRS ROOM AND OTHER SPECULATIVE FICTION, THE
                                      WILHELM, KATE   AC
  NO LIGHT IN THE WINDOW   SS   NEW 63 AC
    MILE-LONG SPACESHIP, THE   WILHELM, KATE   AC
  ON POINT OF VIEW   AR
    THOSE WHO CAN: A SCIENCE FICTION READER
                                      WILSON, ROBIN SCOTT AN
  ON THE ROAD TO HONEYVILLE   SS   ORB 72 11
    ORBIT 11   KNIGHT, DAMON   OA
  ONE FOR THE ROAD   SS   FUN 59 07
    MILE-LONG SPACESHIP, THE   WILHELM, KATE   AC
  PERCHANCE TO DREAM   SS   NEW 68 AC
    DOWNSTAIRS ROOM AND OTHER SPECULATIVE FICTION, THE
                                      WILHELM, KATE   AC
  PLANET STORY   SS   EPC 75
    EPOCH   ELWOOD & SILVERBERG   OA
  PLANNERS, THE   SS   ORB 68 03
    BEST FROM ORBIT, THE   KNIGHT, DAMON   AN
    BIO-FUTURES   SARGENT, PAMELA   AN
    DOWNSTAIRS ROOM AND OTHER SPECULATIVE FICTION, THE
                                      WILHELM, KATE   AC
    NEBULA AWARD STORIES NO. 4   ANDERSON, POUL   AN
    ORBIT 3   KNIGHT, DAMON   OA
    THOSE WHO CAN: A SCIENCE FICTION READER
                                      WILSON, ROBIN SCOTT AN
  PLAUSIBLE IMPROBABLE, THE   SS   NEW 68 AC
    DOWNSTAIRS ROOM AND OTHER SPECULATIVE FICTION, THE
                                      WILHELM, KATE   AC
  RED CANARY, THE   SS   ORB 73 12
    INFINITY BOX, THE   WILHELM, KATE   AC
    ORBIT 12   KNIGHT, DAMON   OA
  SCREAM, THE   NV   ORB 74 13
    BEST SF: 1974   HARRISON & ALDISS   AN
    ORBIT 13   KNIGHT, DAMON   OA
  SIRLOIN AND WHITE WINE   SS   NEW 68 AC
    DOWNSTAIRS ROOM AND OTHER SPECULATIVE FICTION, THE
                                      WILHELM, KATE   AC
  SOMERSET DREAMS   NV   ORB 69 05
    ORBIT 5   KNIGHT, DAMON   OA
    SCIENCE FICTION ARGOSY, A   KNIGHT, DAMON   AN
  SOMETHING HAPPENS   AR   CLR 71 01
    CLARION   WILSON, ROBIN SCOTT OA
  SOURCE, THE   AR   CLR 73 03
    CLARION III   WILSON, ROBIN SCOTT OA
  STARAS FLONDERANS   SS   ORB 66 01
    ORBIT 1   KNIGHT, DAMON   OA
  TIME PIECE, THE   NV   NEW 75 AC
    INFINITY BOX, THE   WILHELM, KATE   AC
  TIME TO KEEP, A   SS   FSF 62 01
    DOWNSTAIRS ROOM AND OTHER SPECULATIVE FICTION, THE
                                      WILHELM, KATE   AC
  UNBIRTHDAY PARTY   SS   NEW 68 AC
    DOWNSTAIRS ROOM AND OTHER SPECULATIVE FICTION, THE
                                      WILHELM, KATE   AC
  VILLAGE, THE   SS   BMR 73
    BAD MOON RISING   DISCH, THOMAS M.   OA

WILHELM, KATE   (CONTINUED)
  INFINITY BOX, THE   WILHELM, KATE   AC
  WHATEVER HAPPENED TO THE OLMECS?   SS   FSF 73 10
    BEST SCIENCE FICTION STORIES OF THE YEAR (1973)
                                      DEL REY, LESTER   AN
  WHEN THE MOON WAS RED   SS   AMZ 60 09
    DOWNSTAIRS ROOM AND OTHER SPECULATIVE FICTION, THE
                                      WILHELM, KATE   AC
  WHERE HAVE YOU BEEN, BILLY BOY, BILLY BOY? SS   QRK 71 03
    INFINITY BOX, THE   WILHELM, KATE   AC
    QUARK/3   DELANY & HACKER   OA
  WHERE LATE THE SWEET BIRDS SANG   NA   ORB 74 15
    ORBIT 15   KNIGHT, DAMON   OA
  WHY IS IT SO HARD?   AR   CLR 72 02
    CLARION II   WILSON, ROBIN SCOTT OA
  WINDSONG   NV   ORB 68 04
    DOWNSTAIRS ROOM AND OTHER SPECULATIVE FICTION, THE
                                      WILHELM, KATE   AC
    ORBIT 4   KNIGHT, DAMON   OA
    POCKETFUL OF STARS, A   KNIGHT, DAMON   AN

WILKINS, PERCY H.
  IS THERE LIFE ON THE MOON?   AR   CYE 53 01
    SCIENCE FICTION AND READER'S GUIDE BARROWS, MARJORIE   AN

WILLEFORD, CHARLES
  MACHINE IN WARD ELEVEN, THE   NO   BEL 63 06
    ALECTRYOMANCER, THE   NV   AHM
      MACHINE IN WARD ELEVEN, THE   WILLEFORD, CHARLES   NO
    JAKE'S JOURNAL   NV
      MACHINE IN WARD ELEVEN, THE   WILLEFORD, CHARLES   NO
    "JUST LIKE ON TELEVISION-"   SS
      MACHINE IN WARD ELEVEN, THE   WILLEFORD, CHARLES   NO
    LETTER TO A.A. (ALMOST ANYBODY), A   SS
      MACHINE IN WARD ELEVEN, THE   WILLEFORD, CHARLES   NO
  MACHINE IN WARD ELEVEN, THE   NV   PBY 61 03
    MACHINE IN WARD ELEVEN, THE   WILLEFORD, CHARLES   NO
    PLAYBOY BOOK OF HORROR AND THE SUPERNATURAL, THE
                                      PLAYBOY, EDITORS OF AN
    WEIRD SHOW   PLAYBOY, EDITORS OF AN
  SELECTED INCIDENTS (THE SIN OF INTEGRITY)   SS   GNT
    MACHINE IN WARD ELEVEN, THE   WILLEFORD, CHARLES   NO
  SIN OF INTEGRITY, THE (SEE SELECTED INCIDENTS) TC

WILLEY, ROBERT   PSEUD. FOR WILLY LEY
  INVASION, THE   NV   SSS 40 09
    BEYOND BELIEF   HURLEY, RICHARD J.   AN
    EXPERT DREAMERS, THE   POHL, FREDERIK   AN

WILLIAMS-ELLIS, AMABEL AND MABLY OWEN
  OUT OF THIS WORLD 1   AN H BLK 60
  OUT OF THIS WORLD 2   AN H BLK 61
  OUT OF THIS WORLD 3   AN H BLK 61
  OUT OF THIS WORLD 4   AN H BLK 64
  OUT OF THIS WORLD 5   AN H BLK 65
  OUT OF THIS WORLD 6   AN H BLK 67
  OUT OF THIS WORLD 7   AN H BLK 68
  WORLDS APART   AN H BLK 66

WILLIAMS-ELLIS, AMABEL AND MICHAEL PEARSON
  TALES FROM THE GALAXIES   AN   PPL 73

WILLIAMS-ELLIS, AMABEL
  CHANGELING   SS   NEW 64 AN
    OUT OF THIS WORLD 4   WILLIAMS-ELLIS& OWEN AN
  MISS INMAN AND THE KLOOTS   NV   NEW 73 AN
    TALES FROM THE GALAXIES   WILLIAMS-ELLIS& P.   AN
  PREFACE   IN C
    TALES FROM THE GALAXIES   WILLIAMS-ELLIS& P.   AN

WILLIAMS, BEN A.
  COCONUTS   SS
    MATHEMATICAL MAGPIE, THE   FADIMAN, CLIFTON   AN

WILLIAMS, DAVID N.
  GIVE MY REGARDS TO THE CZAR   SS   CLR 73 03
    CLARION III   WILSON, ROBIN SCOTT OA

WILLIAMS, ERIC C.
  GARDEN OF PARIS, THE   SS   NEW 65 AN
    STRANGE BEASTS AND UNNATURAL MONSTERS STERN, PHILIP VAN D. AN
    WEIRD SHADOWS FROM BEYOND   CARNELL, JOHN   AN
  SUNOUT   NV   NWR 65 05
    NEW WRITINGS IN SF. 5   CARNELL, JOHN   OA

WILLIAMS, JAY
  ASA RULE, THE   SS   FSF 56 06
    BEST FROM FANTASY AND SCIENCE FICTION: 6
                                      BOUCHER, ANTHONY   AN
  FALSE IMAGE   SS   ASF 58 10
    14 GREAT TALES OF ESP   STONE, IDELLA P.   AN
  SEED OF VIOLENCE, THE   SN   FUN 58 11
    UNFRIENDLY FUTURE, THE   BOARDMAN, TOM JR.   AN
  SOMEBODY TO PLAY WITH   SS   FSF 61 05
  *BEST FROM FANTASY AND SCIENCE FICTION: 11
                                      MILLS, ROBERT P.   AN

WILLIAMS, JOHN
  NO SALE   SS
    SECOND PACIFIC BOOK OF SCIENCE FICTION, THE
                                      BAXTER, JOHN   AN

WILLIAMS, JONATHAN
  EVERYBODY'S HOMESICK SOLDIER BOY   PM   62
    HOLDING YOUR EIGHT HANDS   LUCIE-SMITH, EDWARD AN

WILLIAMS, RALPH
  BERTHA (SEE DOORWAY IN THE SKY)   TC
  BUSINESS AS USUAL, DURING ALTERATIONS   NV   ASF 58 07
    ONE HUNDRED YEARS OF SCIENCE FICTION   KNIGHT, DAMON   AN
    PROLOGUE TO ANALOG   CAMPBELL, JOHN W. JR AN
    TOMORROW, INC.   GREENBERG& OLANDER   AN
  DOORWAY IN THE SKY (BERTHA)   NV   ASF 54 01
    TALES OF OUTER SPACE   WOLLHEIM, DONALD A. DA
  EMERGENCY LANDING   SS   ASF 40 07
    *BIG BOOK OF SCIENCE FICTION   CONKLIN, GROFF   AN
    FIFTY SHORT SCIENCE FICTION TALES   ASIMOV & CONKLIN   AN
  HEAD HUNTERS, THE   SS   ASF 51 10
    OMNIBUS OF SCIENCE FICTION   CONKLIN, GROFF   AN
    *STORIES FOR TOMORROW   SLOANE, WILLIAM   AN
    TALES OF TERROR FROM OUTER SPACE   CHETWYND-HAYES, R.   AN
  PAX GALACTICA   SS   ASF 52 11
    SPACE POLICE   NORTON, ANDRE   AN

WILLIAMS, ROBERT MOORE
                  ALSO AS   JOHN S. BROWNING
  TO THE END OF TIME AND OTHER STORIES   DC   ACE 60
  VOID BEYOND, AND OTHER STORIES, THE   DC   ACE 58
  WHEN TWO WORLDS MEET   AC   CUR 70
    STORIES OF MEN ON MARS
  AUROCHS CAME WALKING   SS   FSF 53 12
    WHEN TWO WORLDS MEET   WILLIAMS, ROBERT M. AC
  CASTAWAY   SS   ASF 41 02
    *INVADERS OF EARTH   CONKLIN, GROFF   AN
  CHALLENGE, THE   SS   TWS 50 10
    VOID BEYOND, AND OTHER STORIES, THE   WILLIAMS, ROBERT M. DC
  FINAL FRONTIER, THE   SS   SSS 50 01
    VOID BEYOND, AND OTHER STORIES, THE   WILLIAMS, ROBERT M. DC
    WHEN TWO WORLDS MEET   WILLIAMS, ROBERT M. AC
  FLIGHT OF THE DAWN STAR   SS   ASF 38 03
    *TREASURY OF SCIENCE FICTION, A   CONKLIN, GROFF   AN
  HOMEWARD BOUND   SS   STS 49 11
    TO THE END OF TIME AND OTHER STORIES   WILLIAMS, ROBERT M. DC
  LIKE ALARM BELLS RINGING   SS   AMZ 47 01
    TO THE END OF TIME AND OTHER STORIES   WILLIAMS, ROBERT M. DC
  NOW COMES TOMORROW   NO   71
    SCIENCE FICTION SPECIAL 6   ANONYMOUS   AN
  ON PAIN OF DEATH   NV   ASF 42 06
    WHEN TWO WORLDS MEET   WILLIAMS, ROBERT M. AC
  PIPING DEATH, THE   SS   UNK 39 05
    ZACHERLEY'S MIDNIGHT SNACKS   ZACHERLEY   AN
  RED DEATH OF MARS, THE   NV   ASF 40 07
    *MEN AGAINST THE STARS   GREENBERG, MARTIN   AN
    MORE ADVENTURES ON OTHER PLANETS   WOLLHEIM, DONALD A. AN
    YEAR AFTER TOMORROW, THE   DEL REY, L/MATSCHAT/ AN
  REFUGE FOR TONIGHT   NV   BBM 49 03
    BEST SCIENCE-FICTION STORIES: 1950, THE
                                           BLEILER & DIKTY   AN
    VOID BEYOND, AND OTHER STORIES, THE   WILLIAMS, ROBERT M. DC
  ROBOTS RETURN   SS   ASF 38 09
    *ADVENTURES IN TIME AND SPACE   HEALY & MCCOMAS   AN
    ANTHROPOLOGY THROUGH SCIENCE FICTION   MASON, C/GREENBERG/& AN
    ROBOT AND THE MAN, THE   GREENBERG, MARTIN   AN
  SEEKERS, THE   SS   STS 48 05
    FLIGHT INTO SPACE   WOLLHEIM, DONALD A. AN
  SOUND OF BUGLES, THE   SS   STS 49 03
    ADVENTURES ON OTHER PLANETS   WOLLHEIM, DONALD A. AN
    GREAT SCIENCE FICTION STORIES ABOUT MARS
                                           DIKTY, T. E.   AN
    WHEN TWO WORLDS MEET   WILLIAMS, ROBERT M. AC
  STUBBORN MEN, THE   SS   SSS 48 11
    VOID BEYOND, AND OTHER STORIES, THE   WILLIAMS, ROBERT M. DC
  TO THE END OF TIME   SS   SSS 50 07
    TO THE END OF TIME AND OTHER STORIES   WILLIAMS, ROBERT M. DC
  VOID BEYOND, THE   NV   TWS 51 04
    VOID BEYOND, AND OTHER STORIES, THE   WILLIAMS, ROBERT M. DC
  WEAPON, THE   SS   AMZ 47 07
    VOID BEYOND, AND OTHER STORIES, THE   WILLIAMS, ROBERT M. DC
  WHEN THE SPOILERS CAME   NV   PLS 52 05
    TO THE END OF TIME AND OTHER STORIES   WILLIAMS, ROBERT M. DC
    WHEN TWO WORLDS MEET   WILLIAMS, ROBERT M. AC
  WHEN TWO WORLDS MEET   NV   AMZ 50 04
    WHEN TWO WORLDS MEET   WILLIAMS, ROBERT M. AC
  WHERE TALL TOWERS GLEAM   SS   FAD 50 08
    TO THE END OF TIME AND OTHER STORIES   WILLIAMS, ROBERT M. DC

WILLIAMS, TENNESSEE PSEUD. FOR THOMAS LANIER WILLIAMS
  RECLUSE AND HIS GUEST, A   SS   PBY 70 01
  WEIRD SHOW   PLAYBOY, EDITORS OF AN

WILLIAMS, THOMAS L. SEE PSEUD. TENNESSEE WILLIAMS

WILLIAMS, WILLIAM C.
  HEEL & TOE TO THE END   PM   62
    SPECULATIONS   SANDERS, THOMAS E.   AN

WILLIAMSON, IAN
  CHEMICAL PLANT   SS   NWS 50 WI
    CONTACT   KEYES, NOEL   AN
    *NO PLACE LIKE EARTH   CARNELL, JOHN   AN
    OUT OF THIS WORLD 1   WILLIAMS-ELLIS& OWEN AN

WILLIAMSON, JACK   ALSO AS   WILL STEWART
  EARLY WILLIAMSON, THE   AC H DBL 75
  PANDORA EFFECT, THE   AC   ACE 69
  PEOPLE MACHINES   AC   ACE 71
  SEETEE SHIP/SEETEE SHOCK   AC   LAN
  TRIAL OF TERRA, THE   NO   ACE 62
    AFTERWORD ABOUT THEME   MS
      PEOPLE MACHINES   WILLIAMSON, JACK   AC
    AUTHOR'S INTRODUCTION   IN
      PANDORA EFFECT, THE   WILLIAMSON, JACK   AC

WILLIAMSON, JACK   (CONTINUED)
    AUTHOR'S INTRODUCTION- WITH HINTS FOR DESIGN AND ASSEMBLY
                                                         IN
      PEOPLE MACHINES   WILLIAMSON, JACK   AC
  BORN OF THE SUN   NV   ASF 34 03
    BEFORE THE GOLDEN AGE   ASIMOV, ISAAC   AN
  BREAKDOWN   NV   ASF 42 01
    JOURNEY TO INFINITY   GREENBERG, MARTIN   AN
    PEOPLE MACHINES   WILLIAMSON, JACK   AC
  COLD GREEN EYE, THE   SS   FAN 53 03
    PANDORA EFFECT, THE   WILLIAMSON, JACK   AC
    SCIENCE FICTION SHOWCASE   KORNBLUTH, MARY   AN
  COSMIC EXPRESS, THE   SS   AMZ 30 11
    EARLY WILLIAMSON, THE   WILLIAMSON, JACK   AC
    PANDORA EFFECT, THE   WILLIAMSON, JACK   AC
    STRANGE SIGNPOSTS   ELWOOD & MOSKOWITZ   AN
  CRUCIBLE OF POWER, THE   NV   ASF 39 02
    CRUCIBLE OF POWER, THE   GREENBERG, MARTIN   AN
    FIVE SCIENCE FICTION NOVELS   GREENBERG, MARTIN   AN
  DEAD SPOT, THE   NV   MAR 38 11
    HISTORY OF THE SCIENCE FICTION MAGAZINE, THE PART 2 1936-1945
                                           ASHLEY, MICHAEL   AN
  DEAD STAR STATION   SS   ASF 33 11
    EARLY WILLIAMSON, THE   WILLIAMSON, JACK   AC
  DOOM FROM PLANET 4, THE   SS   ASF 31 07
    EARLY WILLIAMSON, THE   WILLIAMSON, JACK   AC
  DOOMSHIP   NA C IFS 73 04
    1974 ANNUAL WORLD'S BEST SF, THE   WOLLHEIM, DONALD A. AN
  EQUALIZER, THE   NV   ASF 47 03
    PANDORA EFFECT, THE   WILLIAMSON, JACK   AC
  FOREWORD TO "THE STAR"   IN
    MIRROR OF INFINITY, THE   SILVERBERG, ROBERT   AN
  GIRL FROM MARS, THE (FIRST OF "SCIENCE FICTION SERIES")
                                                         EX   29
    EARLY WILLIAMSON, THE   WILLIAMSON, JACK   AC
  GREATEST INVENTION, THE   NV   ASF 51 07
    STRANGE TOMORROWS   HOSKINS, ROBERT   AN
  GUINEVERE FOR EVERYBODY   SS   STR 54 03
    PANDORA EFFECT, THE   WILLIAMSON, JACK   AC
    STAR SCIENCE FICTION STORIES NO. 3   POHL, FREDERIK   OA
  HAPPIEST CREATURE, THE   SS   STR 53 02
    PANDORA EFFECT, THE   WILLIAMSON, JACK   AC
    STAR OF STARS   POHL, FREDERIK   AN
    STAR SCIENCE FICTION STORIES NO. 2   POHL, FREDERIK   OA
    TRIAL OF TERRA, THE   WILLIAMSON, JACK   NO
  HIGHEST DIVE, THE   SS   SFM 76 01
    BEST SCIENCE FICTION OF THE YEAR, THE NO. 6
                                           CARR, TERRY   AN
  HINDSIGHT   SS   ASF 40 05
    *ASTOUNDING SCIENCE FICTION ANTHOLOGY, THE
                                           CAMPBELL, JOHN W. JR AN
    ASTOUNDING TALES OF SPACE AND TIME   CAMPBELL, JOHN W. JR AN
    FIRST ASTOUNDING SCIENCE FICTION ANTHOLOGY, THE (PB)
                                           CAMPBELL, JOHN W. JR AN
    PEOPLE MACHINES   WILLIAMSON, JACK   AC
  IN THE SCARLET STAR   SS   AMZ 33 03
    EVERY BOY'S BOOK OF SCIENCE FICTION   WOLLHEIM, DONALD A. AN
  INTRODUCTION   IN
    EARLY WILLIAMSON, THE   WILLIAMSON, JACK   AC
  JAMBOREE   SS   GAL 69 12
    PEOPLE MACHINES   WILLIAMSON, JACK   AC
    THOSE WHO CAN: A SCIENCE FICTION READER
                                           WILSON, ROBIN SCOTT AN
    YOUNG DEMONS   ELWOOD & GHIDALIA   AN
  MAN DOWN   NV   ASF 52 03
    TRIAL OF TERRA, THE   WILLIAMSON, JACK   NO
  MAN FROM OUTSIDE, THE   SS   ASF 51 03
    *BEACHHEADS IN SPACE   DERLETH, AUGUST   AN
    FROM OTHER WORLDS   DERLETH, AUGUST   AN
    LOOKING FORWARD   LESSER, MILTON   AN
    PEOPLE MACHINES   WILLIAMSON, JACK   AC
    TRIAL OF TERRA, THE   WILLIAMSON, JACK   NO
  MASKED WORLD, THE   SS   WOT 63 10
    BEST SCIENCE FICTION FROM WORLDS OF TOMORROW, THE
                                           POHL, FREDERIK   AN
    PEOPLE MACHINES   WILLIAMSON, JACK   AC
  METAL MAN, THE   SS   AMZ 28 12
    ANDROIDS, TIME MACHINES AND BLUE GIRAFFES
                                           ELWOOD & GHIDALIA   AN
    BEST OF AMAZING, THE   ROSS, JOSEPH   AN
    EARLY WILLIAMSON, THE   WILLIAMSON, JACK   AC
    PANDORA EFFECT, THE   WILLIAMSON, JACK   AC
    SPECTRUM OF WORLDS, A   CLARESON, THOMAS D. AN
  METEOR GIRL, THE   SS   ASF 31 03
    EARLY WILLIAMSON, THE   WILLIAMSON, JACK   AC
  MOON ERA, THE   NV   WOS 32 02
    BEFORE THE GOLDEN AGE   ASIMOV, ISAAC   AN
    THREE STORIES   MOSKOWITZ, SAM   AN
  NON-STOP TO MARS   NV   ARG 39 02
    GREAT SCIENCE FICTION STORIES ABOUT MARS
                                           DIKTY, T. E.   AN
    PEOPLE MACHINES   WILLIAMSON, JACK   AC
  OPERATION: GRAVITY   SS   SPP 53 10
    PEOPLE MACHINES   WILLIAMSON, JACK   AC
  PEDDLER'S NOSE, THE   SS   ASF 51 04
    ASSIGNMENT IN TOMORROW   POHL, FREDERIK   AN
    PEOPLE MACHINES   WILLIAMSON, JACK   AC
    STARS AROUND US, THE   HOSKINS, ROBERT   AN
  PLANET FOR PLUNDERING, A   NA   GAL 62 04
    TRIAL OF TERRA, THE   WILLIAMSON, JACK   NO
  PLOTTING "JAMBOREE"   AR
    THOSE WHO CAN: A SCIENCE FICTION READER
                                           WILSON, ROBIN SCOTT AN
  PLUTONIAN TERROR, THE   SS   WRT 33 10
    EARLY WILLIAMSON, THE   WILLIAMSON, JACK   AC

WILLIAMSON, JACK   WILSON, ROBIN SCOTT

WILLIAMSON, JACK   (CONTINUED)
  SALVAGE IN SPACE   SS   ASF 33 03
    EARLY WILLIAMSON, THE   WILLIAMSON, JACK   AC
  SEETEE SHIP   NO   SAS 50
    SEETEE SHIP/SEETEE SHOCK   WILLIAMSON, JACK   AC
  SEETEE SHOCK   NO   ASF 49 02
    SEETEE SHIP/SEETEE SHOCK   WILLIAMSON, JACK   AC
  STAR BRIGHT   NV   AEG 39 11
    *MY BEST SCIENCE FICTION STORY   MARGULIES & FRIEND   AN
  PEOPLE MACHINES   WILLIAMSON, JACK   AC
    STRANGE LOVE STORIES   ANONYMOUS   AN
  SUN MAKER, THE   NV   TWS 40 06
    GIANT ANTHOLOGY OF SCIENCE FICTION MARGULIES & FRIEND AN
    RACE TO THE STARS   MARGULIES & FRIEND   AN
  TERROR OUT OF TIME   SS   ASF 33 12
    TIME CURVE, THE   MOSKOWITZ & ELWOOD   AN
  THROUGH THE PURPLE CLOUD   SS   WOS 31 05
    EARLY WILLIAMSON, THE   WILLIAMSON, JACK   AC
    FROM OFF THIS WORLD   MARGULIES & FRIEND   AN
  TWELVE HOURS TO LIVE!   SS   WOS 31 08
    EARLY WILLIAMSON, THE   WILLIAMSON, JACK   AC
  "WE AIN'T BEGGARS"   SS
    EARLY WILLIAMSON, THE   WILLIAMSON, JACK   AC
  WHY I SELECTED STAR BRIGHT   AI
    *MY BEST SCIENCE FICTION STORY   MARGULIES & FRIEND   AN
  WITH FOLDED HANDS...   NV   ASF 47 07
    DOORWAY INTO TIME   MOSKOWITZ, SAM   AN
    INVASION OF THE ROBOTS   ELWOOD, ROGER   AN
    MEN AND MACHINES   SILVERBERG, ROBERT   AN
    MODERN MASTERPIECES OF SCIENCE FICTION MOSKOWITZ, SAM AN
    PANDORA EFFECT, THE   WILLIAMSON, JACK   AC
    SCIENCE FICTION HALL OF FAME VOLUME 2A BOVA, BEN   AN
    *TREASURY OF SCIENCE FICTION, A CONKLIN, GROFF   AN
  WOLVES OF DARKNESS   NA   STT 32 01
    BEWARE MORE BEASTS   GHIDALIA, V.& ELWOOD AN

WILSON, ANGUS
  AD 2500   AN H HEI 55
    THE OBSERVER PRIZE STORIES 1954
  MUMMY TO THE RESCUE   SS
    BEST FANTASY STORIES   ALDISS, BRIAN W.   AN

WILSON, CARTER
  BRIEF, SWINGING CAREER OF DAN AND JUDY SMYTHE, THE
                                                  SS   FSF 70 04
    BEST FROM FANTASY AND SCIENCE FICTION: 19
                                     FERMAN, EDWARD L.   AN

WILSON, GAHAN
                                                  SS   DVS 72 02
    AGAIN, DANGEROUS VISIONS   ELLISON, HARLAN   OA
  CARTOONS   CT   FSF
    BEST FROM FANTASY AND SCIENCE FICTION: 20
                                     FERMAN, EDWARD L.   AN
  FIVE CARTOONS   CT   FSF 65
    BEST FROM FANTASY AND SCIENCE FICTION: 15
                                     FERMAN, EDWARD L.   AN
  FIVE CARTOONS   CT   FSF 68
    BEST FROM FANTASY AND SCIENCE FICTION: 18
                                     FERMAN, EDWARD L.   AN
  FOUR CARTOONS   CT   FSF 67
    BEST FROM FANTASY AND SCIENCE FICTION: 17
                                     FERMAN, EDWARD L.   AN
  GAHAN WILSON HORROR MOVIE POCKET COMPUTER, THE MS   NLP 74 05
    BEST SF: 1974   HARRISON & ALDISS   AN
  M-1   SS   FSF 70 02
    TWENTY YEARS OF FANTASY & SCIENCE FICTION
                                     FERMAN & MILLS   AN
  MANUSCRIPT OF DR. ARNESS, THE   SS   PBY 66 08
    FANTASY: THE LITERATURE OF THE MARVELOUS
                                     KELLEY, LEO P.   AN
    PLAYBOY BOOK OF HORROR AND THE SUPERNATURAL, THE
                                     PLAYBOY, EDITORS OF   AN
  SCIENCE FICTION HORROR MOVIE POCKET COMPUTER, THE MS NLP 71 11
    BEST SF: 1971   HARRISON & ALDISS   AN
  SEA WAS WET AS WET COULD BE, THE   SS   PBY 67 05
    FANTASY: THE LITERATURE OF THE MARVELOUS
                                     KELLEY, LEO P.   AN
    PLAYBOY BOOK OF HORROR AND THE SUPERNATURAL, THE
                                     PLAYBOY, EDITORS OF   AN
  SIX CARTOONS   CT   FSF 66
    BEST FROM FANTASY AND SCIENCE FICTION: 16
                                     FERMAN, EDWARD L.   AN
  SIX CARTOONS   CT   FSF 70
    BEST FROM FANTASY AND SCIENCE FICTION: 19
                                     FERMAN, EDWARD L.   AN

WILSON, JOHN ANTHONY SEE PSEUD. ANTHONY BURGESS

WILSON, JOHN FLEMING
  REJECTED PLANET, THE   SS   PRS 12 06
    WORLDS APART   LOCKE, GEORGE   AN

WILSON, R.   SEE ALSO   CO-EDITOR ALAN FRANK BARTER
  FOREWORD   IN C
    UNTRAVELLED WORLDS   BARTER & WILSON   AN

WILSON, RICHARD
  THOSE IDIOTS FROM EARTH   AC   BAL 57
  TIME OUT FOR TOMORROW   AC   BAL 62
  ABUNDANCE OF GOOD THINGS, AN (HAVE IT YOUR OWN WAY)
                                                  SS   AMZ 54 05
    TIME OUT FOR TOMORROW   WILSON, RICHARD   AC
  BACK TO JULIE   SS   GAL 54 05
    ASSIGNMENT IN TOMORROW   POHL, FREDERIK   AN

WILSON, RICHARD   (CONTINUED)
  BEST POSSIBLE WORLD, THE   SS   NWS 60 09
    TIME OUT FOR TOMORROW   WILSON, RICHARD   AC
  BIG FIX, THE   NV   INF 56 08
    STRANGE ECSTASIES   PARRY, MICHEL   AN
    TIME OUT FOR TOMORROW   WILSON, RICHARD   AC
  CARSON EFFECT, THE   SS   WOT 64 11
    10TH ANNUAL OF THE YEAR'S BEST S-F, THE
                                     MERRIL, JUDITH   AN
  DENY THE SLAKE   SS   INF 57 04
    SPECIAL WONDER   MCCOMAS, J. FRANCIS   AN
  DON'T FENCE ME IN   SS   FSF 56 04
    THOSE IDIOTS FROM EARTH   WILSON, RICHARD   AC
  EIGHT BILLION, THE   SS   FSF 65 07
    BEST FROM FANTASY AND SCIENCE FICTION: 15
                                     FERMAN, EDWARD L.   AN
  FRIEND OF THE FAMILY   SS   STR 53 02
    STAR SCIENCE FICTION STORIES NO. 2 POHL, FREDERIK   OA
  HAVE IT YOUR OWN WAY (SEE AN ABUNDANCE OF GOOD THINGS)
                                                  TC
  HOAXTERS, THE   NV   GAL 52 06
    THOSE IDIOTS FROM EARTH   WILSON, RICHARD   AC
  HONOR   SS   SFQ 56 02
    HUMAN AND OTHER BEINGS   DEGRAEFF, ALLEN   AN
    THOSE IDIOTS FROM EARTH   WILSON, RICHARD   AC
  IF YOU WERE THE ONLY-   SS   GAL 53 06
    TENTH GALAXY READER, THE   POHL, FREDERIK   AN
  IN-BETWEENS, THE (SEE THE UBIQUITOUS YOU)   TC
  INHABITED, THE   NV   GAL 53 01
    THOSE IDIOTS FROM EARTH   WILSON, RICHARD   AC
  IT'S COLD OUTSIDE   NV   IFS 56 12
    THOSE IDIOTS FROM EARTH   WILSON, RICHARD   AC
  JUST CALL ME IRISH   SS   FUT 58 06
    TIME OUT FOR TOMORROW   WILSON, RICHARD   AC
  KILL ME WITH KINDNESS   SS   GAL 58 01
    FOURTH GALAXY READER, THE   GOLD, H. L.   AN
  KIN (SHOW YOUR MIGHT)   SS   FUN 56 05
    TIME OUT FOR TOMORROW   WILSON, RICHARD   AC
  LOCUS FOCUS, THE   SS   SFQ 57 08
    TIME OUT FOR TOMORROW   WILSON, RICHARD   AC
  LONELY ROAD   SS   FSF 56 09
    THOSE IDIOTS FROM EARTH   WILSON, RICHARD   AC
  LOVE   SS   FSF 52 06
    HUMAN AND OTHER BEINGS   DEGRAEFF, ALLEN   AN
    SHADOW OF TOMORROW   POHL, FREDERIK   AN
    THOSE IDIOTS FROM EARTH   WILSON, RICHARD   AC
  MAN SPEKITH, A   NV   GAL 69 05
    WORLD'S BEST SCIENCE FICTION: 1970 WOLLHEIM & CARR   AN
  MAN WORKING   SS   STR 58 04
    STAR SCIENCE FICTION STORIES NO. 4 POHL, FREDERIK   OA
  MOTHER TO THE WORLD   NV   ORB 68 03
    BEST FROM ORBIT, THE   KNIGHT, DAMON   AN
    NEBULA AWARD STORIES   NO. 4   ANDERSON, POUL   AN
    ORBIT   3   KNIGHT, DAMON   OA
  PRESS CONFERENCE (VISITOR FROM THE VOID)   SS   AMZ 53 11
    FLYING SAUCERS IN FACT AND FICTION SANTESSON, HANS S. AN
    THOSE IDIOTS FROM EARTH   WILSON, RICHARD   AC
  QRM   SS   FSF 57 04
    TIME OUT FOR TOMORROW   WILSON, RICHARD   AC
  SEE ME NOT   NV   IMP 67 02
    WORLD'S BEST SCIENCE FICTION: 1968 WOLLHEIM & CARR   AN
  SHOW YOUR MIGHT (SEE KIN)   TC
  SUCCESS STORY (SEE 88 BEATS 266)   TC
  THOSE IDIOTS FROM EARTH   SS   NEW 57 AC
    THOSE IDIOTS FROM EARTH   WILSON, RICHARD   AC
  TIME OUT FOR TOMORROW   SS   SCF 57 12
    TIME OUT FOR TOMORROW   WILSON, RICHARD   AC
  TRAVELING COMPANION WANTED (SEE THE TUNNEL UNDER THE WORLD)
                                                  TC
  TUNNEL UNDER THE WORLD, THE (TRAVELING COMPANION WANTED)
                                                  SS   GAL 59 06
    TIME OUT FOR TOMORROW   WILSON, RICHARD   AC
  UBIQUITOUS YOU, THE (THE IN-BETWEENS)   SS   FUT 57 SP
    TIME OUT FOR TOMORROW   WILSON, RICHARD   AC
  VENUS PAPERS, THE   SS   FSF 58 03
    ENCOUNTERS WITH ALIENS   EARLEY, GEORGE W.   AN
  VISITOR FROM THE VOID (SEE PRESS CONFERENCE)   TC
  VOICE OF THE DIAPHRAGM, THE   SS   GAL 58 05
    TIME OUT FOR TOMORROW   WILSON, RICHARD   AC
  WASP (THE WASP)   SS   PAN 54 06
    TIME OUT FOR TOMORROW   WILSON, RICHARD   AC
  WATCHERS IN THE GLADE, THE   NV   GAL 64 08
    NINTH GALAXY READER, THE   POHL, FREDERIK   AN
  88 BEATS 266 (SUCCESS STORY)   SS   FUN 57 02
    THOSE IDIOTS FROM EARTH   WILSON, RICHARD   AC

WILSON, ROBERT H.
  OUT AROUND RIGEL   SS   ASF 31 12
    SCIENCE FICTION OF THE 30'S   KNIGHT, DAMON   AN

WILSON, ROBIN SCOTT ALSO AS   ROBIN S. SCOTT
  CLARION   OA   SIG 71 06
  CLARION II   OA   SIG 72 06
  CLARION III   OA   SIG 73 10
  THOSE WHO CAN: A SCIENCE FICTION READER   AN   MNT 73 09
    CHARACTER: THE DETERMINANT OF INCIDENT   SI
      THOSE WHO CAN: A SCIENCE FICTION READER
                                     WILSON, ROBIN SCOTT   AN
    FOR A WHILE THERE, HERBERT MARCUSE, I THOUGHT YOU WERE MAYBE
    RIGHT ABOUT ALIENATION AND   SS   FSF 72 07
      THOSE WHO CAN: A SCIENCE FICTION READER
                                     WILSON, ROBIN SCOTT   AN
  GONE FISHIN'   SS   FSF 70 10
    BEST FROM FANTASY AND SCIENCE FICTION: 19
                                     FERMAN, EDWARD L.   AN
    BEST SF: 1970   HARRISON & ALDISS   AN

WILSON, ROBIN SCOTT   WOLFE, GENE

WILSON, ROBIN SCOTT (CONTINUED)
  INTRODUCTION   IN
    CLARION   WILSON, ROBIN SCOTT OA
    CLARION III   WILSON, ROBIN SCOTT OA
  INTRODUCTION: TO THE READER   IN
    THOSE WHO CAN: A SCIENCE FICTION READER
                                 WILSON, ROBIN SCOTT AN
  PLOT: THE TANGELED WEB   SI
    THOSE WHO CAN: A SCIENCE FICTION READER
                                 WILSON, ROBIN SCOTT AN
  POINT OF VIEW: THE QUICK-CHANGE ARTIST IN THE TYPE
                                        AR
    THOSE WHO CAN: A SCIENCE FICTION READER
                                 WILSON, ROBIN SCOTT AN
  POINT OF VIEW: WHO'S MINDING THE STORE SI
    THOSE WHO CAN: A SCIENCE FICTION READER
                                 WILSON, ROBIN SCOTT AN
  PREFACE   IN
    CLARION II   WILSON, ROBIN SCOTT OA
  SETTING: A LOCAL HABITATION AND A NAME SI
    THOSE WHO CAN: A SCIENCE FICTION READER
                                 WILSON, ROBIN SCOTT AN
  SOMETHING NEW UNDER THE SUN   IN
    WONDERMAKERS   HOSKINS, ROBERT   AN
  STYLE: THE DRESS OF THOUGHT   SI
    THOSE WHO CAN: A SCIENCE FICTION READER
                                 WILSON, ROBIN SCOTT AN
  TERRIFIC PLAY OF FORCES NATURAL AND HUMAN, THE AR CLR 71 01
    CLARION   WILSON, ROBIN SCOTT OA
  THEME: TO MEAN INTENSELY   SI
    THOSE WHO CAN: A SCIENCE FICTION READER
                                 WILSON, ROBIN SCOTT AN

WILSON, ROBLEY JR.
  STAY AT THE OCEAN, A   SS   69
    ECO-FICTION   STADLER, JOHN   AN

WINN, PIP
  RIGHT OFF THE MAP   SS   ORB 70 08
    ORBIT   8   KNIGHT, DAMON   OA

WINNEY, KEN   PSEUD. FOR WINSTON K. MARKS

WINSOR, FREDERICK
  THREE VERSES   PM   58
    MATHEMATICAL MAGPIE, THE   FADIMAN, CLIFTON   AN
  VERSE   PM   58
    MATHEMATICAL MAGPIE, THE   FADIMAN, CLIFTON   AN

WINTER, JOSEPH A. MD
  EXPEDITION MERCY   NV   ASF 48 11
    GREAT SCIENCE FICTION ABOUT DOCTORS CONKLIN, G&FABRICANT AN
  EXPEDITION POLYCHROME   NV   ASF 49 01
    GATES TO TOMORROW   NORTON, AN.&DONALDY   AN
    SPACE SERVICE   NORTON, ANDRE   AN

WINTERBOTHAM, R. R.
  FOURTH DYNASTY, THE   SS   ASF 36 12
    OMNIBUS OF SCIENCE FICTION   CONKLIN, GROFF   AN

WINTLE, W. J.
  LIFE IN OUR NEW CENTURY   SS   HRM 01 01
    BEFORE ARMAGEDDON   MOORCOCK, MICHAEL   AN

WISE, DAVID
  ACHIEVEMENTS   SS   NDM 75 05
    NEW DIMENSIONS 5   SILVERBERG, ROBERT   OA
  AT THE ACCIDENT   SS
    FUTURE PASTIMES   EDELSTEIN, SCOTT   OA
  FLAT HATTER   SS   CLR 73 03
    CLARION III   WILSON, ROBIN SCOTT OA
  SERVANTS   SS   CLR 73 03
    CLARION III   WILSON, ROBIN SCOTT OA

WISSNER, ROBERT
  FROZEN ASSETS   SS   CLR 72 02
    CLARION II   WILSON, ROBIN SCOTT OA
  NOTES ON A RESTLESS URGE   SS   CLR 72 02
    CLARION II   WILSON, ROBIN SCOTT OA
  SAY GOODBYE TO THE WORLD'S LAST BROTHEL SS CLR 73 03
    CLARION III   WILSON, ROBIN SCOTT OA

WODHAMS, JACK
  HELMET OF HADES, THE   SS   NWR 68 11
    NEW WRITINGS IN SF. 11   CARNELL, JOHN   OA
  THERE IS A CROOKED MAN   SN   ASF 67 02
    ANALOG 7   CAMPBELL, JOHN W. JR AN
    PACIFIC BOOK OF AUSTRALIAN SCIENCE FICTION
                                 BAXTER, JOHN   AN

WOLF, GARY K.
  BRIDGE BUILDER, THE   SS   ORB 74 14
    ORBIT 14   KNIGHT, DAMON   OA
  DISSOLVE   SS   ORB 72 11
    ORBIT 11   KNIGHT, DAMON   OA
  THERAPY   SS   ORB 74 13
    ORBIT 13   KNIGHT, DAMON   OA

WOLF, LEONARD
  MORE FACTS ABOUT ROBOTS (SOME FACTS ABOUT ROBOTS II)
                                        PM   FSF 54 01
    BEST FROM FANTASY AND SCIENCE FICTION: 4
                                 BOUCHER, ANTHONY   AN
  SOME FACTS ABOUT ROBOTS   PM   FSF 54 07
    BEST FROM FANTASY AND SCIENCE FICTION: 4
                                 BOUCHER, ANTHONY   AN

WOLF, LEONARD   (CONTINUED)
  SOME FACTS ABOUT ROBOTS I   PM   FSF 53 11
    BEST FROM FANTASY AND SCIENCE FICTION: 3
                                 BOUCHER & MCCOMAS   AN

WOLFE, BERNARD
  BISQUIT POSITION, THE   NV   DVS 72 02
    AGAIN, DANGEROUS VISIONS   ELLISON, HARLAN   OA
  DOT AND DASH BIRD, THE   SS   PBY 64 12
    PLAYBOY BOOK OF SCIENCE FICTION AND FANTASY, THE
                                 PLAYBOY, EDITORS OF AN
  GIRL WITH RAPID EYE MOVEMENTS, THE   NV   DVS 72 02
    AGAIN, DANGEROUS VISIONS   ELLISON, HARLAN   OA
  NEVER ENDING PENNY, THE   SS   PBY 60 09
    PLAYBOY BOOK OF SCIENCE FICTION AND FANTASY, THE
                                 PLAYBOY, EDITORS OF AN
    6TH ANNUAL OF THE YEAR'S BEST S-F, THE MERRIL, JUDITH AN
  SELF PORTRAIT   NV   GAL 51 11
    ROBOT AND THE MAN, THE   GREENBERG , MARTIN   AN
    SECOND GALAXY READER OF SCIENCE FICTION
                                 GOLD, H. L.   AN
  TOMORROW AND TOMORROW   KNIGHT, DAMON   AN

WOLFE, GENE
  FIFTH HEAD OF CERBERUS, THE   AC H SCB 72
  AGAINST THE LAFAYETTE ESCADRILLE   SS   DVS 72 02
    AGAIN, DANGEROUS VISIONS   ELLISON, HARLAN   OA
  ALIEN STONES   NV   ORB 72 11
    ORBIT 11   KNIGHT, DAMON   OA
  ARTICLE ABOUT HUNTING, AN   SS   SVW 73
    SAVING WORLDS   ELWOOD & KIDD   OA
  BEAUTYLAND   SS   SVW 73
    SAVING WORLDS   ELWOOD & KIDD   OA
  BEECH HILL   SS   INY 72 03
    INFINITY 3   HOSKINS, ROBERT   OA
  BELLMAN'S WONDER RING, THE   AR
    CLARION SF   WILHELM, KATE   OA
  BLUE MOUSE, THE   SS   MWS 71
    MANY WORLDS OF SCIENCE FICTION, THE BOVA, BEN   OA
  CAR SINISTER   SS   FSF 70 01
    BEST SF: 1970   HARRISON & ALDISS   AN
  CHANGELING, THE   SS   ORB 68 03
    BEST FROM ORBIT, THE   KNIGHT, DAMON   AN
    ORBIT   3   KNIGHT, DAMON   OA
  CIVIS LAPVTVS SVM   SS   DYS 75
    DYSTOPIAN VISIONS   ELWOOD, ROGER   OA
  CONTINUING WESTWARD   SS   ORB 73 12
    ORBIT 12   KNIGHT, DAMON   OA
  CUES   SS
    FAR SIDE OF TIME, THE   ELWOOD, ROGER   OA
  DARK OF THE JUNE, THE   SS   CTM 74 01
    CONTINUUM 1   ELWOOD, ROGER   OA
  DEATH OF DOCTOR ISLAND, THE   NV   UNI 73 03
    BEST SCIENCE FICTION OF THE YEAR, THE NO. 3
                                 CARR, TERRY   AN
    NEBULA AWARD STORIES 9   WILHELM, KATE   AN
    .UNIVERSE 3   CARR, TERRY   OA
  DEATH OF HYLE, THE   SS   CTM 74 02
    CONTINUUM 2   ELWOOD, ROGER   OA
  EYEBEM   SS   ORB 70 07
    ORBIT   7   KNIGHT, DAMON   OA
    THEMES IN SCIENCE FICTION   KELLEY, LEO P.   AN
  EYEFLASH MIRACLES, THE   NA   76
    BEST SCIENCE FICTION OF THE YEAR, THE NO. 6
                                 CARR, TERRY   AN
    FUTURE POWER   DANN & DOZOIS   OA
  FEATHER TIGERS   SS
    WORLDS FAR AND NEAR   CARR, TERRY   AN
  FIFTH HEAD OF CERBERUS, THE   NV   ORB 72 10
    BEST SCIENCE FICTION OF THE YEAR, THE NO. 2
                                 CARR, TERRY   AN
    FIFTH HEAD OF CERBERUS, THE WOLFE, GENE   AC
    NEBULA AWARD STORIES 8   ASIMOV, ISAAC   AN
    ORBIT 10   KNIGHT, DAMON   OA
  FORLESEN   NV   ORB 74 14
    ORBIT 14   KNIGHT, DAMON   OA
  FROM THE NOTEBOOK OF DOCTOR STEIN   SS   CTM 74 03
    -CONTINUUM 3   ELWOOD, ROGER   OA
  GOING TO THE BEACH   SS   SCS 73
    SHOWCASE   ELWOOD, ROGER   OA
  HEADLESS MAN, THE   SS   UNI 72 02
    UNIVERSE 2   CARR, TERRY   OA
  HERO AS WERWOLF, THE   SS   NEW 75 AN
    BEST SCIENCE FICTION OF THE YEAR, THE NO. 5
                                 CARR, TERRY   AN
    NEW IMPROVED SUN, THE   DISCH, THOMAS M.   AN
  HORARS OF WAR, THE   SS   NOV 70 01
    COMBAT SF   DICKSON, GORDON R.   AN
    *NOVA 1   HARRISON, HARRY   OA
    POCKETFUL OF STARS, A   KNIGHT, DAMON   AN
  HOUR OF TRUST   NV   BMR 73
    BAD MOON RISING   DISCH, THOMAS M.   OA
  HOW THE WHIP CAME BACK   SS   ORB 70 06
    ORBIT   6   KNIGHT, DAMON   OA
  ISLAND OF DOCTOR DEATH AND OTHER STORIES, THE SS ORB 70 07
    BEST FROM ORBIT, THE   KNIGHT, DAMON   AN
    NEBULA AWARD STORIES NO. 6 SIMAK, CLIFFORD D.   AN
    ORBIT   7   KNIGHT, DAMON   OA
  IT'S VERY CLEAN   SS   GEN 72
    GENERATION   GERROLD, DAVID   OA
  LA BEFANA   SS   GAL 73 01
    BEST FROM GALAXY, THE VOLUME II GALAXY, EDITORS OF AN
    BEST SF: 1973   HARRISON & ALDISS   AN
  LOCO PARENTIS   SS   DVS 72 02
    AGAIN, DANGEROUS VISIONS   ELLISON, HARLAN   OA

WOLFE, GENE   WOLLHEIM, DONALD A.

WOLFE, GENE   (CONTINUED)
   MARVELOUS BRASS CHESSPLAYING AUTOMATON, THE   NV   UNI 77 07
      UNIVERSE 7   CARR, TERRY   OA
   MELTING   SS   ORB 74 15
      ORBIT 15   KNIGHT, DAMON   OA
   METHOD BIT IN "B", A   SS   ORB 70 08
      ORBIT 8   KNIGHT, DAMON   OA
   MORNING-GLORY   SS   ANA 70
      ALCHEMY AND ACADEME   MCCAFFREY, ANNE   OA
   PACKERHAUS METHOD, THE   SS   INY 70 01
      INFINITY 1   HOSKINS, ROBERT   OA
   PAUL'S TREEHOUSE   SS   ORB 69 05
      ORBIT 5   KNIGHT, DAMON   OA
   PERITONITIS   SS   TAL 73
      FRONTIERS 1: TOMORROW'S ALTERNATIVES ELWOOD, ROGER   OA
   REMEMBRANCE TO COME   SS   ORB 70 06
      ORBIT 6   KNIGHT, DAMON   OA
   ROBOT'S STORY   SS   DVS 72 02
      AGAIN, DANGEROUS VISIONS   ELLISON, HARLAN   OA
   RUBBER BEND, THE   NV   UNI 74 05
      UNIVERSE 5   CARR, TERRY   OA
   SILHOUETTE   NA   NAL 75
      NEW ATLANTIS AND OTHER NOVELLAS OF S.F., THE
                                        SILVERBERG, ROBERT   OA
   SONYA, CRANE WESSLEMAN, AND KITTEE   SS   ORB 70 08
      ORBIT 8   KNIGHT, DAMON   OA
   "STORY, A" BY JOHN V. MARSCH   NV
      FIFTH HEAD OF CERBERUS, THE   WOLFE, GENE   AC
   STRAW   SS   GAL 75 01
      ANOTHER WORLD   DOZOIS, GARDNER R.   AN
   THAG   SS   CTM 75 04
      CONTINUUM 4   ELWOOD, ROGER   OA
   THREE MILLION SQUARE MILES   SS   NEW 71 AN
      RUINS OF EARTH, THE   DISCH, THOMAS M.   AN
   TOY THEATER, THE   SS   ORB 71 09
      ORBIT 9   KNIGHT, DAMON   OA
   TRACKING SONG   NA
      IN THE WAKE OF MAN   ELWOOD, ROGER   OA
   TRIP, TRAP   NV   ORB 67 02
      ORBIT 2   KNIGHT, DAMON   OA
   V.R.T.   NV
      FIFTH HEAD OF CERBERUS, THE   WOLFE, GENE   AC
   WESTWIND   SS   IFS 73 08
      BEST FROM IF, THE VOLUME II   IF, EDITORS OF   AN
   WHEN I WAS MING THE MERCILESS   SS
      IDES OF TOMORROW, THE   CARR, TERRY   OA

WOLFE, JACK C. AND GREGORY FITZ GERALD
PAST, PRESENT, AND FUTURE PERFECT   AN   FPR 73 08

WOLFE, JACK C.
   INTRODUCTION   IN C
      PAST, PRESENT, AND FUTURE PERFECT WOLFE, J&FITZ GERALD AN
   PREFACE   IN C
      PAST, PRESENT, AND FUTURE PERFECT WOLFE, J&FITZ GERALD AN

WOLFE, MARI
   HOMELAND (THE STATUE)   NV   IFS 53 01
      *STORIES FOR TOMORROW   SLOANE, WILLIAM   AN

WOLFE, THOMAS
   THREE FINGERS   SS
      NEW CONSTELLATIONS   DISCH & NAYLOR   OA

WOLLHEIM, DONALD A. AND TERRY CARR
   WORLD'S BEST SCIENCE FICTION: 1965   AN   ACE 65
   WORLD'S BEST SCIENCE FICTION: 1966   AN   ACE 66
   WORLD'S BEST SCIENCE FICTION: 1967   AN   ACE 67
   WORLD'S BEST SCIENCE FICTION: 1968   AN   ACE 68
   WORLD'S BEST SCIENCE FICTION: 1969   AN   ACE 69
   WORLD'S BEST SCIENCE FICTION: 1970   AN   ACE 70
   WORLD'S BEST SCIENCE FICTION: 1971   AN   ACE 71

WOLLHEIM, DONALD A. AND GEORGE ERNSBERGER
   AVON FANTASY READER, THE   AN   AVN 68
   SECOND AVON FANTASY READER, THE   AN   AVN 69

WOLLHEIM, DONALD A. ALSO AS   DAVID GRINNELL AND MARTIN PEARSON
   ACE SCIENCE FICTION READER   AN   ACE 71
      IN ENGLAND AS "TRILOGY OF THE FUTURE"
   ADVENTURES IN THE FAR FUTURE   DA   ACE 54
   ADVENTURES ON OTHER PLANETS   DA   ACE 55
   BEST FROM THE REST OF THE WORLD, THE   AN H DBL 76
   DAW SCIENCE FICTION READER, THE   OA H DAW 76 07
   EARTH IN PERIL, THE   DA   ACE 57
   END OF THE WORLD, THE   AN   ACE 56
   EVERY BOY'S BOOK OF SCIENCE FICTION   AN H FEL 51
   FLIGHT INTO SPACE   AN H FEL 50
   GIRL WITH THE HUNGRY EYES, AND OTHER STORIES, THE OA AVN 49
   HIDDEN PLANET, THE   AN   ACE 59
   MEN ON THE MOON   DA   ACE 58
   MORE ADVENTURES ON OTHER PLANETS   AN   ACE 63
   MORE TERROR IN THE MODERN VEIN   AN   DIG 61
      7 STORIES FROM "TERROR IN THE MODERN VEIN"
   POCKET BOOK OF SCIENCE-FICTION, THE   AN   PKT 43 03
   PORTABLE NOVELS OF SCIENCE   AN H VIK 45
   PRIZE SCIENCE FICTION   AN H MBR 53
      IN ENGLAND AS "PRIZE STORIES OF SPACE AND TIME"
   PRIZE STORIES OF SPACE AND TIME   AN H WEI 53
      SEE "PRIZE SCIENCE FICTION"
   SWORDSMEN IN THE SKY   AN   ACE 64
   TALES OF OUTER SPACE   DA   ACE 54
   TERROR IN THE MODERN VEIN   AN H HAN 55 04
      ENGLISH DERIVATIVE ANTHOLOGY "MORE TERROR IN THE MODERN VEIN"
   TERROR IN THE MODERN VEIN (BRITISH PB)   AN   DIG 61
   TRILOGY OF THE FUTURE   AN H SID 62

   SEE "ACE SCIENCE FICTION READER"
   TWO DOZEN DRAGON EGGS   AC   POW 69 09
   ULTIMATE INVADER, AND OTHER SCIENCE FICTION, THE DA   ACE 54
   WORLD'S BEST SF SHORT STORIES NO. 1, THE   AN H ELM 75
      SEE "THE 1974 ANNUAL WORLD'S BEST SF"
   WORLD'S BEST SF SHORT STORIES NO. 2, THE   AN H ELM 76
      SEE "THE 1975 ANNUAL WORLD'S BEST SF"
   1972 ANNUAL WORLD'S BEST SF, THE   AN H DAW 72
   1973 ANNUAL WORLD'S BEST SF, THE   AN H DAW 73
   1974 ANNUAL WORLD'S BEST SF, THE   AN H DAW 74
      IN ENGLAND AS "THE WORLD'S BEST SF SHORT STORIES NO. 1"
   1975 ANNUAL WORLD'S BEST SF, THE   AN   DAW 75
      IN ENGLAND AS "THE WORLD'S BEST SF SHORT STORIES NO. 2"
   1976 ANNUAL WORLD'S BEST SF, THE   AN   DAW 76 05
   1977 ANNUAL WORLD'S BEST SF, THE   AN   DAW 77 05
      WITH ARTHUR W. SAHA
   ADVANCE POST IN THE WAR BETWEEN THE SEXES, AN SS
      TWO DOZEN DRAGON EGGS   WOLLHEIM, DONALD A. AC
   AQUELLA   SS   AFR 48 07
      IF THIS GOES ON   NUETZEL, CHARLES   AN
   BABYLON: 70 M. (SEE HOW MANY MILES TO BABYLON?) TC
   BONES   SS   STI 41 02
      ZACHERLEY'S VULTURE STEW   ZACHERLEY   AN
   DISGUISE   SS   OWS 53 02
      *STORIES FOR TOMORROW   SLOANE, WILLIAM   AN
      TWO DOZEN DRAGON EGGS   WOLLHEIM, DONALD A. AC
   DOORSLAMMER   SS   MOH 63 11
      TWO DOZEN DRAGON EGGS   WOLLHEIM, DONALD A. AC
   EGG FROM ALPHA CENTAURI, THE   SS
      TWO DOZEN DRAGON EGGS   WOLLHEIM, DONALD A. AC
   EIN BLICK IN DIE ZUKUNFT   SS
      TWO DOZEN DRAGON EGGS   WOLLHEIM, DONALD A. AC
   EMBASSY, THE   SS   ASF 42 03
      MARS, WE LOVE YOU   HIPOLITO & MCNELLY   AN
   EXTENDING THE HOLDINGS   SS   FSF 51 04
      TWO DOZEN DRAGON EGGS   WOLLHEIM, DONALD A. AC
   FEMININE FRACTION, THE   SS   MOH 64 11
      TWO DOZEN DRAGON EGGS   WOLLHEIM, DONALD A. AC
   GANYMEDE HOUSE   SS   OSF 53 01
      TWO DOZEN DRAGON EGGS   WOLLHEIM, DONALD A. AC
   GARRISON, THE   SS   MOH 65 04
      TWO DOZEN DRAGON EGGS   WOLLHEIM, DONALD A. AC
   GIVE HER HELL   SS
      TWO DOZEN DRAGON EGGS   WOLLHEIM, DONALD A. AC
   HOW MANY MILES TO BABYLON? (BABYLON: 70 M.)   SS   MOH 63 08
      TWO DOZEN DRAGON EGGS   WOLLHEIM, DONALD A. AC
   IN MEMORIAM- A. A. WYN   MS
      NEBULA AWARD STORIES NO. 4   ANDERSON, POUL   AN
   INTRODUCTION   IN
      ACE SCIENCE FICTION READER   WOLLHEIM, DONALD A.   AN
      BEST FROM THE REST OF THE WORLD, THE WOLLHEIM, DONALD A. AN
      DAW SCIENCE FICTION READER, THE   WOLLHEIM, DONALD A.   OA
      HIDDEN PLANET, THE   WOLLHEIM, DONALD A.   AN
      MANY WORLDS OF ANDRE NORTON, THE NORTON, ANDRE   AC
      MEN ON THE MOON   WOLLHEIM, DONALD A.   DA
      MORE ADVENTURES ON OTHER PLANETS WOLLHEIM, DONALD A.   AN
      POCKET BOOK OF SCIENCE-FICTION, THE WOLLHEIM, DONALD A. AN
      PORTABLE NOVELS OF SCIENCE   WOLLHEIM, DONALD A.   AN
      PRIZE SCIENCE FICTION   WOLLHEIM, DONALD A.   AN
      TWO DOZEN DRAGON EGGS   WOLLHEIM, DONALD A.   AC
      1972 ANNUAL WORLD'S BEST SF, THE WOLLHEIM, DONALD A.   AN
      1973 ANNUAL WORLD'S BEST SF, THE WOLLHEIM, DONALD A.   AN
      1974 ANNUAL WORLD'S BEST SF, THE WOLLHEIM, DONALD A.   AN
      1975 ANNUAL WORLD'S BEST SF, THE WOLLHEIM, DONALD A.   AN
      1976 ANNUAL WORLD'S BEST SF, THE WOLLHEIM, DONALD A.   AN
      1977 ANNUAL WORLD'S BEST SF, THE WOLLHEIM, DONALD A.   AN
   INTRODUCTION   IN C
      WORLD'S BEST SCIENCE FICTION: 1965 WOLLHEIM & CARR   AN
      WORLD'S BEST SCIENCE FICTION: 1966 WOLLHEIM & CARR   AN
      WORLD'S BEST SCIENCE FICTION: 1967 WOLLHEIM & CARR   AN
      WORLD'S BEST SCIENCE FICTION: 1968 WOLLHEIM & CARR   AN
      WORLD'S BEST SCIENCE FICTION: 1969 WOLLHEIM & CARR   AN
      WORLD'S BEST SCIENCE FICTION: 1970 WOLLHEIM & CARR   AN
      WORLD'S BEST SCIENCE FICTION: 1971 WOLLHEIM & CARR   AN
   LANDRAGON   SS
      TWO DOZEN DRAGON EGGS   WOLLHEIM, DONALD A. AC
   LAST STAND OF A SPACE GRENADIER   SS   SFQ 54 02
      TWO DOZEN DRAGON EGGS   WOLLHEIM, DONALD A. AC
   LYSENKO MAZE, THE   SS   FSF 54 07
      INTRODUCTORY PSYCHOLOGY THROUGH SCIENCE FICTION
                                        KATZ/WARRICK/&   AN
      TWO DOZEN DRAGON EGGS   WOLLHEIM, DONALD A. AC
   MALICE AFORETHOUGHT   SS   FSF 52 11
      TWO DOZEN DRAGON EGGS   WOLLHEIM, DONALD A. AC
   MIMIC   SS   AST 42 12
      CREATURES FROM BEYOND   CARR, TERRY   AN
      MORE TERROR IN THE MODERN VEIN   WOLLHEIM, DONALD A.   AN
      *TERROR IN THE MODERN VEIN   WOLLHEIM, DONALD A.   AN
      TWO DOZEN DRAGON EGGS   WOLLHEIM, DONALD A. AC
   PLANET PASSAGE   SS   FUT 42 10
      FLIGHT INTO SPACE   WOLLHEIM, DONALD A.   AN
      STORIES OF SCIENTIFIC IMAGINATION GALLANT, JOSEPH   AN
   POETESS AND THE 21 GRAY-HAIRED CADAVERS, THE   SS
      TWO DOZEN DRAGON EGGS   WOLLHEIM, DONALD A. AC
   RAG THING, THE   SS   FSF 51 10
      TWO DOZEN DRAGON EGGS   WOLLHEIM, DONALD A. AC
   ROAD TO ROME   SS   FUT 53 07
      TWO DOZEN DRAGON EGGS   WOLLHEIM, DONALD A. AC
   RULES OF THE GAME, THE   SS   NWR 73 22
      NEW WRITINGS IN SF. 22   BULMER, KENNETH   OA
   SANTA RIDES A SAUCER   SS
      TWO DOZEN DRAGON EGGS   WOLLHEIM, DONALD A. AC
   SHOO, FLY¡   SS
      TWO DOZEN DRAGON EGGS   WOLLHEIM, DONALD A. AC
   STORM WARNING   SS   FUT 42 10
      INVADERS FROM SPACE   SILVERBERG, ROBERT   AN

WOLLHEIM, DONALD A.   WYNDHAM, JOHN

WOLLHEIM, DONALD A. (CONTINUED)
  *INVADERS OF EARTH   CONKLIN, GROFF   AN
    TWO DOZEN DRAGON EGGS   WOLLHEIM, DONALD A.   AC
  TOP SECRET   SS   FSF 50 FL
    TWO DOZEN DRAGON EGGS   WOLLHEIM, DONALD A.   AC
  UP THERE   SS   SFQ 42 SU
    HISTORY OF THE SCIENCE FICTION MAGAZINE, THE   PART 2 1936-1945
                                         ASHLEY, MICHAEL   AN
  WEB SIXTY-FOUR   SS
    TWO DOZEN DRAGON EGGS   WOLLHEIM, DONALD A.   AC

WOOD, EDWARD W.
  LOAD OF TROUBLE   SS   BLF
    BOYS' LIFE BOOK OF OUTER SPACE STORIES, THE
                                         BOY'S LIFE, ED. OF   AN

WOOD, MARGARET
  KNITTING, THE   SS
    AD 2500   WILSON, ANGUS   AN

WOOD, RAMSEY
  SAMUEL F. MAYNARD AND ANTHROPOLOGIC DEMONOGRAPHY SS   NEW 67 AN
    DEVIL HIS DUE, THE   HILL, DOUGLAS   AN

WOOD, WALTER
  SUBMARINED   SS   PBS 05 02
    SCIENCE FICTION BY GASLIGHT   MOSKOWITZ, SAM   AN

WOODCOTT, KEITH   PSEUD. FOR JOHN BRUNNER

WOODROW, WILLIAM
  MEEK, THE   SS   NWQ 71 02
    NEW WORLDS QUARTERLY NO. 2   MOORCOCK, MICHAEL   OA
  SIMON   SS   NWQ 72 04
    NEW WORLDS QUARTERLY NO. 4   MOORCOCK, MICHAEL   OA

WOODS, P. F.   PSEUD. FOR BARRINGTON J. BAYLEY
  COUNTENANCE, THE   SS   NWS 64 01
    BEST SF STORIES FROM NEW WORLDS NO. 2, THE
                                         MOORCOCK, MICHAEL   AN
  INTEGRITY   SS   NWS 64 10
    BEST SF STORIES FROM NEW WORLDS 3   MOORCOCK, MICHAEL   AN

WORDSWORTH, WILLIAM
  GEOMETRY (1805)   PM
    MATHEMATICAL MAGPIE, THE   FADIMAN, CLIFTON   AN

WORTH, AMY   PSEUD. FOR DAVID H. KELLER, MD.

WORTHINGTON, WILL
  FOOD GOES IN THE TOP, THE   SS   SCF 61 08
    DECADE THE 1960S   ALDISS & HARRISON   AN
    UNFRIENDLY FUTURE, THE   BOARDMAN, TOM JR.   AN
  PLENITUDE   SS   FSF 59 11
    AS TOMORROW BECOMES TODAY   SULLIVAN, CHARLES W. AN
    HOT & COLD RUNNING CITIES   MCHARGUE, GEORGESS   AN
    SF: THE BEST OF THE BEST   MERRIL, JUDITH   AN
    5TH ANNUAL OF THE YEAR'S BEST S-F, THE MERRIL, JUDITH   AN
  WHO DREAMS OF IVY   SS   FSF 60 11
    BEST FROM FANTASY AND SCIENCE FICTION: 10
                                         MILLS, ROBERT P.   AN

WRIGHT, FARNSWORTH
  ADVENTURE IN THE FOURTH DIMENSION, AN NV   WRT 23 10
    MOON TERROR, THE   BIRCH, A. G.   AN

WRIGHT, GARY
  MIRROR OF ICE   SS   GAL 67 06
    ARENA: SPORTS SF   FERMAN & MALZBERG   AN
    BEST SF: 1967   HARRISON & ALDISS   AN
    NEBULA AWARD STORIES   NO. 3   ZELAZNY, ROGER   AN
    WORLDS OF WONDER   HARRISON, HARRY   AN

WRIGHT, LAN   PSEUD. FOR LIONEL P. WRIGHT
  OPERATION EXODUS   SS   NWS 52 01
    GATEWAY TO THE STARS   CARNELL, JOHN   AN

WRIGHT, LIONEL P.   SEE PSEUD. LAN WRIGHT

WRIGHT, R. GLENN
  SCIENCE FICTION, ARCHETYPES, AND THE FUTURE   AR   CLR 73 03
    CLARION III   WILSON, ROBIN SCOTT   OA

WRIGHT, S. FOWLER
  NEW GODS LEAD, THE   AC H JAR 32
    ALSO IN "THE THRONE OF SATURN"
  THRONE OF SATURN, THE   AC H ARK 49
  WITCHFINDER, THE   AC H BFT 46
  APPEAL   SS
    NEW GODS LEAD, THE   WRIGHT, S. FOWLER   AC
  AUTOMATA   NV   WRT 29 09
    NEW GODS LEAD, THE   WRIGHT, S. FOWLER   AC
  AUTOMATA: I   SS   WRT 29 09
    *SCIENCE FICTION THINKING MACHINES   CONKLIN, GROFF   AN
  AUTOMATA: II   SS   WRT 29 09
    *SCIENCE FICTION THINKING MACHINES   CONKLIN, GROFF   AN
  AUTOMATA: III   SS   WRT 29 09
    *SCIENCE FICTION THINKING MACHINES   CONKLIN, GROFF   AN
  BETTER CHOICE, THE   SS   NEW 55 AN
    *SCIENCE FICTION ADVENTURES IN MUTATION CONKLIN, GROFF   AN
  BRAIN   SS   32
    *ADVENTURES IN TIME AND SPACE   HEALY & MCCOMAS   AN
    NEW GODS LEAD, THE   WRIGHT, S. FOWLER   AC
  BURGLAR'S AID   SS
    WITCHFINDER, THE   WRIGHT, S. FOWLER   AC

WRIGHT, S. FOWLER   (CONTINUED)
  CARROTS   SS
    WITCHFINDER, THE   WRIGHT, S. FOWLER   AC
  CHOICE   SS
    NEW GODS LEAD, THE   WRIGHT, S. FOWLER   AC
  CONGO CAT, THE   SS
    WITCHFINDER, THE   WRIGHT, S. FOWLER   AC
  JUSTICE   SS
    NEW GODS LEAD, THE   WRIGHT, S. FOWLER   AC
  NEW GODS LEAD, THE   AC   JAR 32
    THRONE OF SATURN, THE   WRIGHT, S. FOWLER   AC
  OBVIOUSLY SUICIDE   SS   SUS 51 SP
    BEYOND THE END OF TIME   POHL, FREDERIK   AN
    FIFTY SHORT SCIENCE FICTION TALES   ASIMOV & CONKLIN   AN
  ORIGINAL SIN   SS   AFR 50 13
    *OTHER SIDE OF THE MOON, THE   DERLETH, AUGUST   AN
    THRONE OF SATURN, THE   WRIGHT, S. FOWLER   AC
    WITCHFINDER, THE   WRIGHT, S. FOWLER   AC
  P.N. 40   SS
    NEW GODS LEAD, THE   WRIGHT, S. FOWLER   AC
  PROOF   SS
    NEW GODS LEAD, THE   WRIGHT, S. FOWLER   AC
  QUESTION OF E.D.D., A   SS
    WITCHFINDER, THE   WRIGHT, S. FOWLER   AC
  RAT, THE   SS   WRT 29 03
    NEW GODS LEAD, THE   WRIGHT, S. FOWLER   AC
    TREASURY OF SCIENCE FICTION CLASSICS, THE
                                         KUEBLER, HAROLD W.   AN
  RULE, THE   SS
    NEW GODS LEAD, THE   WRIGHT, S. FOWLER   AC
  STATUS   SS
    WITCHFINDER, THE   WRIGHT, S. FOWLER   AC
  TEMPERATURE OF GEHENNA SUE, THE   SS
    THRONE OF SATURN, THE   WRIGHT, S. FOWLER   AC
    WITCHFINDER, THE   WRIGHT, S. FOWLER   AC
  TERROR OF WILLIAM STICKERS, THE   SS
    WITCHFINDER, THE   WRIGHT, S. FOWLER   AC
  THIS NIGHT   SS
    NEW GODS LEAD, THE   WRIGHT, S. FOWLER   AC
  WHO ELSE BUT SHE?   SS
    WITCHFINDER, THE   WRIGHT, S. FOWLER   AC
  WITCHFINDER, THE   SS
    WITCHFINDER, THE   WRIGHT, S. FOWLER   AC

WRIGHT, SEWELL P.
  INFRA-MEDIANS, THE   SS   ASF 31 12
    EVERY BOY'S BOOK OF SCIENCE FICTION WOLLHEIM, DONALD A.   AN

WROCZ, JOSEPH   SEE PSEUD. JOSEPH ROSS

WULFF, EVE   SEE ALSO   CO-EDITOR JAMES L. QUINN

WYAL, PG
  CASTLE ON THE CRAG, THE   SS   FAN 69 02
    BEST SF: 1969   HARRISON & ALDISS   AN
  FREAK, THE   SS   FSF 69 04
    AMERICAN GOVERNMENT THROUGH SCIENCE FICTION
                                         OLANDER/GREENBERG/&   AN
  HOTSY-TOTSY MACHINE, THE   SS
    FUTURE PASTIMES   EDELSTEIN, SCOTT   OA
  NEWSOCRATS: CONFESSIONS OF A EUNICH DREAMER, THE SS
    FUTURE PASTIMES   EDELSTEIN, SCOTT   OA
  SIDE EFFECT   NV   PRT 71
    PROTOSTARS   GERROLD & GOLDIN   OA

WYLIE, DIRK   (PSEUDONYM)
  WHEN TIME WENT MAD   NA C TWS 50 02
    SCIENCE FICTION: THE GREAT YEARS, VOL. II
                                         POHL, C. & F.   AN

WYLIE, PHILIP
  ANSWER, THE   NV   SEP 55 05
    POST READER OF FANTASY AND SCIENCE FICTION
                                         SATURDAY EVE. POST   AN
  BLUNDER   SS   COL 46 01
    SHOT IN THE DARK   MERRIL, JUDITH   AN
    *STRANGE PORTS OF CALL   DERLETH, AUGUST   AN
  FROM "WHEN WORLDS COLLIDE"   EX C LIP 32
    TREASURY OF SCIENCE FICTION CLASSICS, THE
                                         KUEBLER, HAROLD W.   AN
  JUNGLE JOURNEY (THE PARADISE CRATER)   SS   BBM 45 10
    MASTERPIECES OF SCIENCE FICTION   MOSKOWITZ, SAM   AN
  PARADISE CRATER, THE (SEE JUNGLE JOURNEY)   TC

WYNDHAM & PARKES
  OUTWARD URGE, THE   AC   BAL 59
    ONLY LATER EDITIONS CONTAIN "THE EMPTYNESS OF SPACE"

WYNDHAM, JOHN AND LUCAS PARKS

WYNDHAM, JOHN   PSEUD. FOR
    JOHN BEYNON HARRIS (JOHN WYNDHAM PARKES LUCAS BEYNON HARRIS)
  BEST OF JOHN WYNDHAM, THE   AC   SPH 73
  CONSIDER HER WAYS AND OTHERS   AC H JOS 61
  INFINITE MOMENT, THE   AC   BAL 61
  JIZZLE   AC H DOB 54
  JOHN WYNDHAM OMNIBUS, THE   AC H SAS 65
  MAN FROM BEYOND AND OTHER STORIES, THE AC H JOS 75
  SEEDS OF TIME, THE   AC H JOS 56
  TALES OF GOOSEFLESH AND LAUGHTER   AC   BAL 56 12
  WANDERERS OF TIME   AC   CNT 73
  ADAPTATION   SS   ASF 49 07
    BEST OF JOHN WYNDHAM, THE   WYNDHAM, JOHN   AC
    MAN FROM BEYOND AND OTHER STORIES, THE WYNDHAM, JOHN   AC
    MICROCOSMIC GOD   MOSKOWITZ, SAM   AN
    MODERN MASTERPIECES OF SCIENCE FICTION MOSKOWITZ, SAM   AN

WYNDHAM, JOHN   (CONTINUED)
AFFAIR OF THE HEART   SS
  JIZZLE   WYNDHAM, JOHN   AC
AND THE WALLS CAME TUMBLING DOWN   SS   STS 51 05
  *BEACHHEADS IN SPACE   DERLETH, AUGUST   AN
  FROM OTHER WORLDS   DERLETH, AUGUST   AN
  MAN FROM BEYOND AND OTHER STORIES, THE WYNDHAM, JOHN   AC
AND THE WALLS CAME TUMBLING DOWN, THE   SS   STS 51 05
  BEST OF JOHN WYNDHAM, THE   WYNDHAM, JOHN   AC
ASTEROIDS, 2194, THE (THE EMPTYNESS OF SPACE, NWS 60 11)
                                                  SS   AMZ 61 01
  STORIES FROM SCIENCE FICTION   DOHERTY, G. D.   AN
  7TH ANNUAL OF THE YEAR'S BEST S-F, THE MERRIL, JUDITH   AN
BARGAIN FROM BRUNSWICK (SEE A PRESENT FROM BRUNSWICK)
                                                  TC
CHILD OF POWER   NV   FSB 39 03
  WANDERERS OF TIME   WYNDHAM, JOHN   AC
CHINESE PUZZLE (A STRAY FROM CATHAY)   NV   FNF 53 08
  JIZZLE   WYNDHAM, JOHN   AC
  TALES OF GOOSEFLESH AND LAUGHTER   WYNDHAM, JOHN   AC
CHRONOCLASM, THE   NV   STR 53 01
  OTHER SIDE OF THE CLOCK, THE   STERN, PHILIP VAN D.   AN
  SEEDS OF TIME, THE   WYNDHAM, JOHN   AC
  STAR SCIENCE FICTION STORIES   POHL, FREDERIK   OA
CHRYSALIDS, THE (RE-BIRTH)   NO   BAL 55
  JOHN WYNDHAM OMNIBUS, THE   WYNDHAM, JOHN   AC
CLOSE BEHIND HIM   SS   FAN 53 02
  ABC OF SCIENCE FICTION, AN   BOARDMAN, TOM JR.   AN
  BEST OF JOHN WYNDHAM, THE   WYNDHAM, JOHN   AC
  MAN FROM BEYOND AND OTHER STORIES, THE WYNDHAM, JOHN   AC
COMPASSION CIRCUIT   SS   FUN 54 12
  SEEDS OF TIME, THE   WYNDHAM, JOHN   AC
  SPECTRUM 4   AMIS & CONQUEST   AN
  TALES OF GOOSEFLESH AND LAUGHTER   WYNDHAM, JOHN   AC
  13 GREAT STORIES OF SCIENCE FICTION   CONKLIN, GROFF   AN
CONFIDENCE TRICK   SS   FAN 53 08
  JIZZLE   WYNDHAM, JOHN   AC
  TALES OF GOOSEFLESH AND LAUGHTER   WYNDHAM, JOHN   AC
CONSIDER HER WAYS   NV   56
  BEST SF 5   CRISPIN, EDMUND   AN
  CONSIDER HER WAYS AND OTHERS   WYNDHAM, JOHN   AC
  INFINITE MOMENT, THE   WYNDHAM, JOHN   AC
  SCIENCE FICTION ARGOSY, A   KNIGHT, DAMON   AN
  SOMETIME, NEVER   ANONYMOUS   OA
  WORLDS APART   WILLIAMS-ELLIS& OWEN   AN
DAY OF THE TRIFFIDS, THE (REVOLT OF THE TRIFFIDS) EX   COL 51 01
  FROM FRANKENSTEIN TO ANDROMEDA   BROWN, JAMES GOLDIE   AN
DAY OF THE TRIFFIDS, THE (REVOLT OF THE TRIFFIDS) NO   COL 51 01
  JOHN WYNDHAM OMNIBUS, THE   WYNDHAM, JOHN   AC
DERELICT OF SPACE   NV   FSB 39 03
  WANDERERS OF TIME   WYNDHAM, JOHN   AC
DUMB MARTIAN   NV   GAL 52 07
  BEST OF JOHN WYNDHAM, THE   WYNDHAM, JOHN   AC
  BEST SF   CRISPIN, EDMUND   AN
  GATEWAY TO TOMORROW   CARNELL, JOHN   AN
  MAN FROM BEYOND AND OTHER STORIES, THE WYNDHAM, JOHN   AC
  OUT OF THIS WORLD 3   WILLIAMS-ELLIS& OWEN   AN
  SEEDS OF TIME, THE   WYNDHAM, JOHN   AC
EMPTYNESS OF SPACE, THE (ALSO AS THE ASTEROIDS, 2194)
                                                  SS   NWS 60 11
  BEST OF JOHN WYNDHAM, THE   WYNDHAM, JOHN   AC
  MAN FROM BEYOND AND OTHER STORIES, THE WYNDHAM, JOHN   AC
  *OUTWARD URGE, THE   WYNDHAM & PARKES   AC
ESMERALDA   SS
  JIZZLE   WYNDHAM, JOHN   AC
ETERNAL EVE, THE   NV   AMZ 50 09
  TIME UNTAMED   HOWARD, IVAN   AN
EXILES ON ASPERUS   NV   WSQ 33 WI
  THREE STORIES   MOSKOWITZ, SAM   AN
FOR ALL THE NIGHT   NV   NWS 58 04
  *OUTWARD URGE, THE   WYNDHAM & PARKES   AC
HEAVEN SCENT   SS
  JIZZLE   WYNDHAM, JOHN   AC
  TALES OF GOOSEFLESH AND LAUGHTER   WYNDHAM, JOHN   AC
HOW DO I DO?   SS   BEY 53 09
  INFINITE MOMENT, THE   WYNDHAM, JOHN   AC
  JIZZLE   WYNDHAM, JOHN   AC
IDIOT'S DELIGHT   NV   NWS 58 06
  *OUTWARD URGE, THE   WYNDHAM & PARKES   AC
INTRODUCTION   IN
  BEST FROM NEW WORLDS SCIENCE FICTION, THE
                                        CARNELL, JOHN   AN
JIZZLE (REVISED FROM COL 49 01)   SS   FSF 52 02
  BEST FROM FANTASY AND SCIENCE FICTION: 2
                                        BOUCHER & MCCOMAS   AN
  JIZZLE   WYNDHAM, JOHN   AC
  TALES OF GOOSEFLESH AND LAUGHTER   WYNDHAM, JOHN   AC
KRAKEN WAKES, THE (THE THINGS FROM THE DEEP)   NO   EVB 53
  JOHN WYNDHAM OMNIBUS, THE   WYNDHAM, JOHN   AC
LAST LUNARIANS, THE   SS   TOW 38 SU
  WANDERERS OF TIME   WYNDHAM, JOHN   AC
LONG SPOON, A   SS   60
  CONSIDER HER WAYS AND OTHERS   WYNDHAM, JOHN   AC
  DEVIL HIS DUE, THE   HILL, DOUGLAS   AN
LOOK NATURAL, PLEASE¡   SS
  JIZZLE   WYNDHAM, JOHN   AC
LOST MACHINE, THE   SS   AMZ 32 04
  BEST OF JOHN WYNDHAM, THE   WYNDHAM, JOHN   AC
  COMING OF THE ROBOTS, THE   MOSKOWITZ, SAM   AN
  MAN FROM BEYOND AND OTHER STORIES, THE WYNDHAM, JOHN   AC
MAN FROM BEYOND, THE   NV   WOS 34 09
  ALIEN WORLDS   ELWOOD, ROGER   AN
  BEST OF JOHN WYNDHAM, THE   WYNDHAM, JOHN   AC
  MAN FROM BEYOND AND OTHER STORIES, THE WYNDHAM, JOHN   AC
METEOR (PHONEY METEOR)   SS   AMZ 41 03
  SEEDS OF TIME, THE   WYNDHAM, JOHN   AC

WYNDHAM, JOHN   (CONTINUED)
  TALES OF SCIENCE FICTION   BALL, BRIAN N.   AN
  UNTRAVELLED WORLDS   BARTER & WILSON   AN
MORE SPINNED AGAINST   SS   FNF 53 06
  JIZZLE   WYNDHAM, JOHN   AC
  TALES OF GOOSEFLESH AND LAUGHTER   WYNDHAM, JOHN   AC
NEVER ON MARS   SS   FUN 54 01
  GATEWAY TO THE STARS   CARNELL, JOHN   AN
NO PLACE LIKE EARTH (TYRANT AND SLAVE-GIRL ON VENUS)
                                                  NV   NWS 51 SP
  OUT OF THIS WORLD 1   WILLIAMS-ELLIS& OWEN   AN
ODD   SS
  CONSIDER HER WAYS AND OTHERS   WYNDHAM, JOHN   AC
  INFINITE MOMENT, THE   WYNDHAM, JOHN   AC
OH, WHERE, NOW, IS PEGGY MACRAFFERTY?   SS
  CONSIDER HER WAYS AND OTHERS   WYNDHAM, JOHN   AC
OPERATION PEEP (ALSO AS PAWLEY'S PEEPHOLES)   SS   SUS 51 SU
  BEYOND THE END OF TIME   POHL, FREDERIK   AN
  TIME CURVE, THE   MOSKOWITZ & ELWOOD   AN
OPPOSITE NUMBERS   SS   NWS 54 04
  SEEDS OF TIME, THE   WYNDHAM, JOHN   AC
  TALES OF GOOSEFLESH AND LAUGHTER   WYNDHAM, JOHN   AC
PAWLEY'S PEEPHOLES (OPERATION PEEP)   SS   SCF 51 WI
  BEST OF JOHN WYNDHAM, THE   WYNDHAM, JOHN   AC
  ESCALES DANS L'INFINI   GALLET, GEORGES H.   AN
  MAN FROM BEYOND AND OTHER STORIES, THE WYNDHAM, JOHN   AC
  SEEDS OF TIME, THE   WYNDHAM, JOHN   AC
  STARLIT CORRIDOR, THE   MANSFIELD, ROGER   AN
PERFECT CREATURE, THE (ALSO AS UNA, FSF 53 01)   NV   TOW 37 01
  BEST OF JOHN WYNDHAM, THE   WYNDHAM, JOHN   AC
  MAN FROM BEYOND AND OTHER STORIES, THE WYNDHAM, JOHN   AC
  SHADOW OF TOMORROW   POHL, FREDERIK   AN
PERFORCE TO DREAM   SS   BEY 54 01
  BEYOND THE BARRIERS OF SPACE AND TIME MERRIL, JUDITH   AN
  JIZZLE   WYNDHAM, JOHN   AC
PILLAR TO POST   NV   GAL 51 12
  GALAXY SCIENCE FICTION OMNIBUS   GOLD, H. L.   AN
  SECOND GALAXY READER OF SCIENCE FICTION
                                        GOLD, H. L.   AN
  SEEDS OF TIME, THE   WYNDHAM, JOHN   AC
PRESENT FROM BRUNSWICK, A (BARGAIN FROM BRUNSWICK)
                                                  SS   FSF 51 06
  JIZZLE   WYNDHAM, JOHN   AC
  TALES OF GOOSEFLESH AND LAUGHTER   WYNDHAM, JOHN   AC
PUFF-BALL MENACE, THE   NV   TOW 38 SU
  WANDERERS OF TIME   WYNDHAM, JOHN   AC
RANDOM QUEST   NV   NEW 61 AC
  AS TOMORROW BECOMES TODAY   SULLIVAN, CHARLES W.   AN
  CONSIDER HER WAYS AND OTHERS   WYNDHAM, JOHN   AC
  INFINITE MOMENT, THE   WYNDHAM, JOHN   AC
  VINTAGE ANTHOLOGY OF SCIENCE FANTASY, THE
                                        CERF, CHRISTOPHER   AN
RE-BIRTH (ALSO AS THE CHRYSALIDS)   NO   BAL 55
  TREASURY OF GREAT SCIENCE FICTION, A VOL.1
                                        BOUCHER, ANTHONY   AN
RED STUFF, THE   NV   MSS 51 02
  BEST OF JOHN WYNDHAM, THE   WYNDHAM, JOHN   AC
  MAN FROM BEYOND AND OTHER STORIES, THE WYNDHAM, JOHN   AC
  TALES FROM THE GALAXIES   WILLIAMS-ELLIS& P.   AN
RESERVATION DEFERRED   SS   FAN 53 06
  JIZZLE   WYNDHAM, JOHN   AC
REVOLT OF THE TRIFFIDS (SEE THE DAY OF THE TRIFFIDS)
                                                  TC
SPACE IS A PROVINCE OF BRAZIL   NV   NWS 58 09
  *OUTWARD URGE, THE   WYNDHAM & PARKES   AC
STITCH IN TIME, A   SS   FSF 61 03
  CONSIDER HER WAYS AND OTHERS   WYNDHAM, JOHN   AC
  INFINITE MOMENT, THE   WYNDHAM, JOHN   AC
STRAY FROM CATHAY, A (SEE CHINESE PUZZLE)   TC
SURVIVAL   NV   TWS 52 02
  BEST SCIENCE-FICTION STORIES: 1953, THE
                                        BLEILER & DIKTY   AN
  FRONTIERS IN SPACE   BLEILER & DIKTY   AN
  *NO PLACE LIKE EARTH   CARNELL, JOHN   AN
  SEEDS OF TIME, THE   WYNDHAM, JOHN   AC
TECHNICAL SLIP (ARS 49 WI)   SS   IMG 50 12
  INTO THE UNKNOWN   CARR, TERRY   AN
  JIZZLE   WYNDHAM, JOHN   AC
THIN GNAT-VOICES, THE   NV   NWS 58 07
  *OUTWARD URGE, THE   WYNDHAM & PARKES   AC
THINGS FROM THE DEEP, THE (SEE THE KRAKEN WAKES)   TC
TIME OUT   NV
  INFINITE MOMENT, THE   WYNDHAM, JOHN   AC
TIME TO REST   SS   ARS 49 WI
  SEEDS OF TIME, THE   WYNDHAM, JOHN   AC
TRIFFID, THE (FROM "THE DAY OF THE TRIFFIDS")   EX   COL 51 01
  SCIENCE IN FICTION   BAYLISS, A.E. & J.C.   AN
TROJAN BEAM, THE   NV   FSB 39 02
  BEST OF JOHN WYNDHAM, THE   WYNDHAM, JOHN   AC
  MAN FROM BEYOND AND OTHER STORIES, THE WYNDHAM, JOHN   AC
TYRANT AND SLAVE-GIRL ON VENUS (SEE NO PLACE LIKE EARTH)
                                                  TC
UNA (THE PERFECT CREATURE, TOW 37 01)   NV   FSF 53 01
  BEST SF 2   CRISPIN, EDMUND   AN
  JIZZLE   WYNDHAM, JOHN   AC
  TALES OF GOOSEFLESH AND LAUGHTER   WYNDHAM, JOHN   AC
VENGEANCE BY PROXY   SS   STE 40 02
  BEST OF JOHN WYNDHAM, THE   WYNDHAM, JOHN   AC
  MAN FROM BEYOND AND OTHER STORIES, THE WYNDHAM, JOHN   AC
VENUS ADVENTURE, THE   SS   WOS 32 05
  SPACE MAGICIANS, THE   NORTON & MOSKOWITZ   AN
WANDERERS OF TIME   NV   TOW 41 WI
  WANDERERS OF TIME   WYNDHAM, JOHN   AC
WHEEL, THE   SS   STS 52 01
  JIZZLE   WYNDHAM, JOHN   AC
  TALES OF GOOSEFLESH AND LAUGHTER   WYNDHAM, JOHN   AC

WYNDHAM, JOHN

WYNDHAM, JOHN   (CONTINUED)
  WILD FLOWER   SS   FUN 55 11
    SEEDS OF TIME, THE   WYNDHAM, JOHN   AC
    TALES OF GOOSEFLESH AND LAUGHTER WYNDHAM, JOHN   AC
  WISE CHILD   SS   PBY 67 05
    PLAYBOY'S STORIES OF THE SINISTER & STRANGE
                                     PLAYBOY, EDITORS OF   AN

XERXES, B. T. H.
  THREE LIMERICKS   PM
    ABC OF SCIENCE FICTION, AN   BOARDMAN, TOM JR.   AN

XLEBNIKOV, A.
  HUMAN FRAILTY   SS
    RUSSIAN SCIENCE FICTION, 1969   MAGIDOFF, ROBERT   AN

YACO, MURRAY F.
  WINNING OF THE GREAT AMERICAN GREENING REVOLUTION SS ORB 74 14
    ORBIT 14   KNIGHT, DAMON   OA

YARBRO, CHELSEA QUINN
            SEE ALSO   CO-EDITOR THOMAS N. SCORTIA
  DEAD IN IRONS   NV   76
    FASTER THAN LIGHT   DANN & ZEBROWSKI   OA
  EVERYTHING THAT BEGINS WITH AN "M"   SS   GEN 72
    GENERATION   GERROLD, DAVID   OA
  FALSE DAWN   SS   NEW 72 AN
    STRANGE BED FELLOWS   SCORTIA, THOMAS N.   AN
    WOMEN OF WONDER   SARGENT, PAMELA   AN
  FELLINI BEGGAR, THE   SS
    BEYOND TIME   LEY, SANDRA   OA
  FROG POND   SS   GAL 71 03
    ANTHROPOLOGY THROUGH SCIENCE FICTION MASON, C/GREENBERG/& AN
    YOU AND SCIENCE FICTION   HOLLISTER, BERNARD C   AN
  INTO MY OWN   SS
    TOMORROW TODAY   ZEBROWSKI, GEORGE   OA
  TIME OF THE FOURTH HORSEMAN, A   NV   INY 72 03
    INFINITY 3   HOSKINS, ROBERT   OA
  UN BEL DI   NV   TVW 73
    TWO VIEWS OF WONDER   SCORTIA & YARBRO   OA
  "VIVE LAQUELLE DIFFERENCE?"   IN C
    TWO VIEWS OF WONDER   SCORTIA & YARBRO   OA

YAROV, ROMAIN
  FOUNDING OF CIVILIZATION, THE   SS   ISF 68 06
    OTHER WORLDS, OTHER SEAS   SUVIN, DARKO   AN
    RUSSIAN SCIENCE FICTION, 1968   MAGIDOFF, ROBERT   AN

YATES, R. F.
  ADRIFT ON THE SEA OF SPACE   AR
    LAURIE'S SPACE ANNUAL   ANONYMOUS   AN
  AND SO TO THE MOON   AR
    LAURIE'S SPACE ANNUAL   ANONYMOUS   AN
  WHAT MAKES ROCKETS ROCKET?   AR
    LAURIE'S SPACE ANNUAL   ANONYMOUS   AN

YEFREMOV, IVAN
  MEETING OVER TUSCARORA AND OTHER ADVENTURE TALES, A
                                                  AC H HUT 46
    STORIES   AC H FLP 54
  ALLERGORKHOY-KHORKHOV (THE MONSTROUS WORM)   SS
    MEETING OVER TUSCARORA AND OTHER ADVENTURE TALES, A
                                     YEFREMOV, IVAN   AC
  BARE MOUNTAIN BENEATH THE MOON   SS
    MEETING OVER TUSCARORA AND OTHER ADVENTURE TALES, A
                                     YEFREMOV, IVAN   AC
  COR SERPENTIS   NV
    RUSSIAN SCIENCE FICTION   MAGIDOFF, ROBERT   AN
  FOREWORD   IN
    STORIES   YEFREMOV, IVAN   AC
  HEART OF THE SERPENT, THE   NV
    MORE SOVIET SCIENCE FICTION   ANONYMOUS   AN
  IN THE STEPS OF THE ANCIENT MINERS   SS
    MEETING OVER TUSCARORA AND OTHER ADVENTURE TALES, A
                                     YEFREMOV, IVAN   AC
  LAKE OF THE MOUNTAIN SPIRITS, THE   SS
    MEETING OVER TUSCARORA AND OTHER ADVENTURE TALES, A
                                     YEFREMOV, IVAN   AC
    STORIES   YEFREMOV, IVAN   AC
  MEETING OVER THE TUSCARORA   SS
    STORIES   YEFREMOV, IVAN   AC
  MEETING OVER TUSCARORA, A   SS
    MEETING OVER TUSCARORA AND OTHER ADVENTURE TALES, A
                                     YEFREMOV, IVAN   AC
  MOON MOUNTAIN   SS
    STORIES   YEFREMOV, IVAN   AC
  NUR-I-DESHT OBSERVATORY, THE   SS
    STORIES   YEFREMOV, IVAN   AC
  OLGOI-KHORKHOI   SS
    STORIES   YEFREMOV, IVAN   AC
  SHADOWS OF THE PAST   SS
    RUSSIAN SCIENCE FICTION   MAGIDOFF, ROBERT   AN
    STORIES   YEFREMOV, IVAN   AC
  STELLAR SHIPS   SS
    STORIES   YEFREMOV, IVAN   AC
  WHITE HORN   SS
    STORIES   YEFREMOV, IVAN   AC

YEMTSEV, MIKHAIL
  HE WHO LEAVES NO TRACE   NV C   63
    ULTIMATE THRESHOLD, THE   GINSBURG, MIRRA   AN
  LAST DOOR TO AIYA   SS C ISF 68 06
    LAST DOOR TO AIYA   GINSBURG, MIRRA   AN
  MYSTERY OF GREEN CROSSING   SS C
    RUSSIAN SCIENCE FICTION, 1968   MAGIDOFF, ROBERT   AN

YOUNG, ROBERT F.

YEMTSEV, MIKHAIL   (CONTINUED)
  SNOWBALL, THE   SS C
    JOURNEY ACROSS THREE WORLDS   ANONYMOUS   AN
  WHITE PILOT, THE   NV C   69
    AIR OF MARS AND OTHER STORIES, THE GINSBURG, MIRRA   AN

YEP, LAURENCE
  EDDYSTONE LIGHT, THE   NV   DEM 73
    DEMON KIND   ELWOOD, ROGER   OA
  ELECTRIC NEON MERMAID, THE   NV   QRK 71 02
    QUARK/2   DELANY & HACKER   OA
  IN A SKY OF DAEMONS   NV   PRT 71
    PROTOSTARS   GERROLD & GOLDIN   OA
  LOOKING-GLASS SEA   SS   NEW 72 AN
    STRANGE BED FELLOWS   SCORTIA, THOMAS N.   AN
  MY FRIEND KLATU   NV   SAW 72
    SIGNS AND WONDERS   ELWOOD, ROGER   OA
    VISIONS OF TOMORROW   ELWOOD, ROGER   AN
  SELCHEY KIDS, THE   NV   IFS 68 02
    WORLD'S BEST SCIENCE FICTION: 1969 WOLLHEIM & CARR   AN

YIN, LESLIE CHARLES SEE PSEUD. LESLIE CHARTERIS

YOLEN, JANE
  ZOO 2000   AN H SEA 73
  INTRODUCTION   IN
    ZOO 2000   YOLEN, JANE   AN

YORE, MARY JANE
  TEAMWORK   SS
    ADRIFT IN SPACE AND OTHER STORIES ELWOOD, ROGER   OA

YOUD, CHRISTOPHER   ALSO AS   JOHN CHRISTOPHER
  CHRISTMAS TREE (ALSO AS CHRISTMAS ROSES)   SS   ASF 49 02
    TRAVELLERS OF SPACE   GREENBERG , MARTIN   AN

YOUNG, PETER
  MAN MANIFOLD   SS
    AD 2500   WILSON, ANGUS   AN

YOUNG, ROBERT F.
  GLASS OF STARS, A   AC H HWF 68
  WORLDS OF ROBERT F. YOUNG, THE   AC H SAS 65
  ADDED INDUCEMENT   SS   FSF 57 03
    WORLDS OF ROBERT F. YOUNG, THE   YOUNG, ROBERT F.   AC
  BOY MEETS DYEVITZA   SS   AMZ 62 10
    GLASS OF STARS, A   YOUNG, ROBERT F.   AC
  CHROME PASTURES   NV   IFS 56 04
    SECOND WORLD OF IF, THE   QUINN & WULFF   AN
  CLAY SUBURB   SS   AMZ 75 11
    BEST SCIENCE FICTION OF THE YEAR, THE NO. 5
                                     CARR, TERRY   AN
  COURTS OF JAMSHYD, THE   SS   INF 57 09
    WORLDS OF ROBERT F. YOUNG, THE   YOUNG, ROBERT F.   AC
  DANDELION GIRL, THE   SS   SEP 61 04
    WORLDS OF ROBERT F. YOUNG, THE   YOUNG, ROBERT F.   AC
    7TH ANNUAL OF THE YEAR'S BEST S-F, THE MERRIL, JUDITH   AN
  DOLL-FRIEND (SEE JUKE DOLL)   TC
  DRINK OF DARKNESS, A   SS   FAN 62 07
    WORLDS OF ROBERT F. YOUNG, THE   YOUNG, ROBERT F.   AC
  EMILY AND THE BARDS SUBLIME   SS   FSF 56 07
    WORLDS OF ROBERT F. YOUNG, THE   YOUNG, ROBERT F.   AC
  FLYING PAN   SS   FSF 56 11
    WORLDS OF ROBERT F. YOUNG, THE   YOUNG, ROBERT F.   AC
  FUGITIVES, THE   SS
    GLASS OF STARS, A   YOUNG, ROBERT F.   AC
  GARDEN IN THE FOREST, THE   SS   ASF 53 09
    OPERATION FUTURE   CONKLIN, GROFF   AN
    14 GREAT TALES OF ESP   STONE, IDELLA P.   AN
  GHOSTS   SS   IFS 73 02
    BEST SCIENCE FICTION STORIES OF THE YEAR (1973)
                                     DEL REY, LESTER   AN
  GIRL WHO MADE TIME STOP, THE   SS   SEP 61 04
    WORLDS OF ROBERT F. YOUNG, THE   YOUNG, ROBERT F.   AC
  GODDESS IN GRANITE   NV   FSF 57 09
    BEST FROM FANTASY AND SCIENCE FICTION: 7
                                     BOUCHER, ANTHONY   AN
    WORLDS OF ROBERT F. YOUNG, THE   YOUNG, ROBERT F.   AC
  GROWN-UP PEOPLE'S FEET, THE   SS   FUN 55 06
    GLASS OF STARS, A   YOUNG, ROBERT F.   AC
  HOPSOIL   SS   FSF 61 01
    WORLDS OF ROBERT F. YOUNG, THE   YOUNG, ROBERT F.   AC
  JUKE DOLL (DOLL-FRIEND)   SS   AMZ 59 07
    PSEUDO PEOPLE, THE   NOLAN, WILLIAM F.   AN
  JUNGLE DOCTOR   NV   STS 55 FL
    BEST SCIENCE FICTION STORIES AND NOVELS: 1956
                                     DIKTY, T. E.   AN
    6 FROM WORLDS BEYOND   DIKTY, T. E.   AN
  L'ARC DE JEANNE   NV   FSF 66 01
    GLASS OF STARS, A   YOUNG, ROBERT F.   AC
  LITTLE DOG GONE   NV   WOT 64 02
    BEST SCIENCE FICTION FROM WORLDS OF TOMORROW, THE
                                     POHL, FREDERIK   AN
    GLASS OF STARS, A   YOUNG, ROBERT F.   AC
  LITTLE RED SCHOOLHOUSE   SS   GAL 56 03
    WORLDS OF ROBERT F. YOUNG, THE   YOUNG, ROBERT F.   AC
  NINE EYES HAVE SEEN THE GLORY (REDEMPTION)   NV   AMZ 63 07
    GLASS OF STARS, A   YOUNG, ROBERT F.   AC
  NEITHER DO THEY REAP   NV
    GLASS OF STARS, A   YOUNG, ROBERT F.   AC
  NIKITA EISENHOWER JONES   NV   FSF 60 08
    BEST FROM FANTASY AND SCIENCE FICTION: 10
                                     MILLS, ROBERT P.   AN
  NOT TO BE OPENED-   NV   ASF 50 01
    BEST SCIENCE-FICTION STORIES: 1951, THE
                                     BLEILER & DIKTY   AN

YOUNG, ROBERT F.   (CONTINUED)
    MINDWORM, THE   ANONYMOUS   AN
        OGRESS, THE   SS   FIN 70
        FUTURE IS NOW, THE   NOLAN, WILLIAM F.   OA
    ON THE RIVER   SS   FAN 65 01
        GLASS OF STARS, A   YOUNG, ROBERT F.   AC
    ONE LOVE HAVE I   SS   IFS 55 04
        SEA OF SPACE, A   NOLAN, WILLIAM F.   AN
        THEMES IN SCIENCE FICTION   KELLEY, LEO P.   AN
    OTHER KIDS, THE   SS   FUN 56 03
        ENCOUNTERS WITH ALIENS   EARLEY, GEORGE W.   AN
    PATTERN FOR PENELOPE, A   SS   IFS 54 10
        FIRST WORLD OF IF, THE   QUINN & WULFF   AN
    PRODUCTION PROBLEM   SS   FSF 59 06
        WORLDS OF ROBERT F. YOUNG, THE   YOUNG, ROBERT F.   AC
    PROMISED PLANET   SS   IFS 55 12
        WORLDS OF ROBERT F. YOUNG, THE   YOUNG, ROBERT F.   AC
    PYRAMID PROJECT, THE (THE SPHINX)   NV   AMZ 64 06
        GLASS OF STARS, A   YOUNG, ROBERT F.   AC
    REDEMPTION (SEE MINE EYES HAVE SEEN THE GLORY)   TC
                                                 NV   FUN 59 09
    ROBOT SON
        GODS FOR TOMORROW   SANTESSON, HANS S.   AN
    ROMANCE IN A 21ST CENTURY USED CAR LOT   SS   FSF 60 11
        WORLDS OF ROBERT F. YOUNG, THE   YOUNG, ROBERT F.   AC
    SPHINX, THE (SEE THE PYRAMID PROJECT)   TC
    STAR MOTHER   SS   AMZ 59 01
        GLASS OF STARS, A   YOUNG, ROBERT F.   AC
    STARS ARE CALLING, MR. KEATS, THE   SS   AMZ 59 06
        WORLDS OF ROBERT F. YOUNG, THE   YOUNG, ROBERT F.   AC
    STARSCAPE WITH FRIEZE OF DREAMS   SS   ORB 70 08
        ORBIT   8   KNIGHT, DAMON   OA
    SUBURBAN FRONTIERS   SS   ASF 50 02
        *SCIENCE FICTION ADVENTURES IN DIMENSION
                                          CONKLIN, GROFF   AN
    THIRTY DAYS HAD SEPTEMBER   SS   FSF 57 10
        ABC OF SCIENCE FICTION, AN   BOARDMAN, TOM JR.   AN
        GLASS OF STARS, A   YOUNG, ROBERT F.   AC
        12 GREAT CLASSICS OF SCIENCE FICTION   CONKLIN, GROFF   AN
    TO FELL A TREE   NV   FSF 59 07
        DECADE OF FANTASY AND SCIENCE FICTION, A
                                          MILLS, ROBERT P.   AN
        GLASS OF STARS, A   YOUNG, ROBERT F.   AC
    WHEN TIME WAS NEW   NV   IFS 64 12
        IF READER OF SCIENCE FICTION, THE POHL, FREDERIK   AN
    WISH UPON A STAR   SS   FUN 56 12
        GLASS OF STARS, A   YOUNG, ROBERT F.   AC
    WRITTEN IN THE STARS   SS   VSF 57 09
        WORLDS OF ROBERT F. YOUNG, THE   YOUNG, ROBERT F.   AC
    YEARS, THE   SS   GAL 72 09
        BEST SF: 1972   HARRISON & ALDISS   AN
    YOUR GHOST WILL WALK...   SS   FSF 57 07
        WORLDS OF ROBERT F. YOUNG, THE   YOUNG, ROBERT F.   AC

ZABELIN, IGOR
    VALLEY OF THE FOUR CROSSES, THE   SS
        DESTINATION: AMALTHEIA   DIXON, RICHARD   AN

ZACHERLE, JOHN   SEE PSEUD. ZACHERLEY

ZACHERLEY   PSEUD. FOR JOHN ZACHERLE
    ZACHERLEY'S MIDNIGHT SNACKS   AN   BAL 60
    ZACHERLEY'S VULTURE STEW   AN   BAL 60

ZAGAT, ARTHUR LEO
    LANSON SCREEN, THE   NV   TWS 36 12
        *BEST OF SCIENCE FICTION   CONKLIN, GROFF   AN

ZEBROWSKI, GEORGE   SEE ALSO
    CO-EDITORS JACK M. DANN AND THOMAS N. SCORTIA
    MONADIC UNIVERSE, THE   AC   ACE 77 03
    TOMORROW TODAY   OA L UPR 75
    ADRIFT IN SPACE   SS
        ADRIFT IN SPACE AND OTHER STORIES ELWOOD, ROGER   OA
    AFTERWORD   MS
        SPACE BEYOND, THE   CAMPBELL, JOHN W. JR   OC
    ASSASSINS OF AIR   SS   FUC 73
        FUTURE CITY   ELWOOD, ROGER   OA
        MONADIC UNIVERSE, THE   ZEBROWSKI, GEORGE   AC
    CLIOMETRICON, THE   SS   AMZ 75 05
        BEYOND TIME   LEY, SANDRA   OA
        MONADIC UNIVERSE, THE   ZEBROWSKI, GEORGE   AC
    DARKNESS OF DAY   SS C CTM 74 03
        CONTINUUM 3   ELWOOD, ROGER   OA
    FACES FORWARD   SS C DYS 75
        DYSTOPIAN VISIONS   ELWOOD, ROGER   OA
    FIRST LOVE, FIRST FEAR   SS   NEW 72 AN
        MONADIC UNIVERSE, THE   ZEBROWSKI, GEORGE   AC
        STRANGE BED FELLOWS   SCORTIA, THOMAS N.   AN
    FLOWER THAT MISSED THE MORNING, THE   SS C
        KILLER PLANTS AND OTHER STORIES, THE ELWOOD, ROGER   OA
    FOUNTAIN OF FORCE   SS C INY 72 04
        INFINITY 4   HOSKINS, ROBERT   OA
    HEATHEN GOD   SS   FSF 71 01
        MONADIC UNIVERSE, THE   ZEBROWSKI, GEORGE   AC
        NEBULA AWARD STORIES   NO. 7   BIGGLE, LLOYD JR.   AN
    HISTORY MACHINE, THE   SS   NWQ 72 03
        MONADIC UNIVERSE, THE   ZEBROWSKI, GEORGE   AC
        NEW WORLDS QUARTERLY NO. 3   MOORCOCK, MICHAEL   OA
    INTERPOSE   SS   INY 73 05
        INFINITY 5   HOSKINS, ROBERT   OA
        MONADIC UNIVERSE, THE   ZEBROWSKI, GEORGE   AC
    INTRODUCTION: "UNHOLY MARRIAGE": THE CYBORG IN SCIENCE FICTION
                                                 IN C
        HUMAN-MACHINES   SCORTIA & ZEBROWSKI   AN
    INTRODUCTION: DREAMING AGAIN   IN C
        FASTER THAN LIGHT   DANN & ZEBROWSKI   OA

ZEBROWSKI, GEORGE   (CONTINUED)
    JOURNEY TO ANOTHER STAR   SS
        JOURNEY TO ANOTHER STAR AND OTHER STORIES
                                          ELWOOD, ROGER   OA
    LISTEN, LOVE   SS C NWQ 71 02
        NEW WORLDS QUARTERLY NO. 2   MOORCOCK, MICHAEL   OA
    MONADIC UNIVERSE, THE   NV   INY 72 03
        MONADIC UNIVERSE, THE   ZEBROWSKI, GEORGE   AC
    MONADIC UNIVERSE, THE   NV C INY 72 03
        INFINITY 3   HOSKINS, ROBERT   OA
    OD   SS C OMG 73
        OMEGA   ELWOOD, ROGER   OA
    PARKS OF REST AND CULTURE   SS   SVW 73
        MONADIC UNIVERSE, THE   ZEBROWSKI, GEORGE   AC
        SAVING WORLDS   ELWOOD & KIDD   OA
    ROPE OF GLASS   SS   TVW 73
        MONADIC UNIVERSE, THE   ZEBROWSKI, GEORGE   AC
        TWO VIEWS OF WONDER   SCORTIA & YARBRO   OA
    STANCE OF SPLENDOUR   SS   NWQ 73 05
        MONADIC UNIVERSE, THE   ZEBROWSKI, GEORGE   AC
        NEW WORLDS NO. 5   MOORCOCK & PLATT   OA
    STARCROSSED   SS   EIO 73
        EROS IN ORBIT   ELDER, JOSEPH   OA
        HUMAN-MACHINES   SCORTIA & ZEBROWSKI   AN
        MONADIC UNIVERSE, THE   ZEBROWSKI, GEORGE   AC
    THIRTY-THREE AND ONE-THIRD   SS C
        LONG NIGHT OF WAITING AND OTHER STORIES
                                          ELWOOD, ROGER   OA
    WATER SCULPTOR OF STATION 233, THE   SS   INY 70 01
        INFINITY 1   HOSKINS, ROBERT   OA
        MONADIC UNIVERSE, THE   ZEBROWSKI, GEORGE   AC
    WAYSIDE WORLD   NV
        WORLD NAMED CLEOPATRA, A   ANDERSON, POUL   OA
    WEAPONS   SS C DYS 75
        DYSTOPIAN VISIONS   ELWOOD, ROGER   OA
    WHATEVER GODS THERE BE: SPACE-TIME AND DEITY IN SF
                                                 IN   STG 74
        STRANGE GODS   ELWOOD, ROGER   OA
    YELLOWHEAD   SS C
        NEW CONSTELLATIONS   DISCH & NAYLOR   OA

ZELAZNY, ROGER
    DOORS OF HIS FACE, THE LAMPS OF HIS MOUTH, THE   AC H DBL 71
    FOUR FOR TOMORROW   AC   ACE 67 03
        IN ENGLAND AS "A ROSE FOR ECCLESIASTES"
    MY NAME IS LEGION   AC   BAL 76 04
    NEBULA AWARD STORIES   NO. 3   AN H DBL 68 12
    ROSE FOR ECCLESIASTES, A   AC H HDV 69
        SEE "FOUR FOR TOMORROW"
    AFTERWORD   MS
        NEBULA AWARD STORIES   NO. 3   ZELAZNY, ROGER   AN
    ANGEL, DARK ANGEL   SS   GAL 67 08
        FAR-OUT PEOPLE, THE   HOSKINS, ROBERT   AN
    AUTO-DA-FE   SS   DVS 67 01
        DANGEROUS VISIONS   ELLISON, HARLAN   OA
        FANTASY: THE LITERATURE OF THE MARVELOUS
                                          KELLEY, LEO P.   AN
        VOYAGES: SCENARIOS FOR A SHIP CALLED EARTH
                                          SAUER, ROB   AN
    COLLECTOR'S FEVER   SS   GAL 64 06
        DOORS OF HIS FACE, THE LAMPS OF HIS MOUTH, THE
                                          ZELAZNY, ROGER   AC
    COME TO ME NOT IN WINTER'S WHITE   SS C FSF 69 10
        PARTNERS IN WONDER   ELLISON, HARLAN   AC
    COMES NOW THE POWER   SS   MOH 66 WI
        BEYOND TOMORROW   HARDING, LEE   AN
    CORRIDA   SS   68
        DOORS OF HIS FACE, THE LAMPS OF HIS MOUTH, THE
                                          ZELAZNY, ROGER   AC
    DEVIL CAR   SS   GAL 65 06
        ANOTHER TOMORROW   HOLLISTER, BERNARD C AN
        DECADE THE 1960S   ALDISS & HARRISON   AN
        DOORS OF HIS FACE, THE LAMPS OF HIS MOUTH, THE
                                          ZELAZNY, ROGER   AC
        TENTH GALAXY READER, THE   POHL, FREDERIK   AN
    DIVINE MADNESS   SS   MOH 66 SU
        DOORS OF HIS FACE, THE LAMPS OF HIS MOUTH, THE
                                          ZELAZNY, ROGER   AC
        NEW WORLDS OF FANTASY   CARR, TERRY   AN
        TRAPS OF TIME, THE   MOORCOCK, MICHAEL   AN
    DOORS OF HIS FACE, THE LAMPS OF HIS MOUTH, THE   NV   FSF 65 03
        BEST FROM FANTASY AND SCIENCE FICTION: 15
                                          FERMAN, EDWARD L.   AN
        BEST SF   7   CRISPIN, EDMUND   AN
        DOORS OF HIS FACE, THE LAMPS OF HIS MOUTH, THE
                                          ZELAZNY, ROGER   AC
        FOUR FOR TOMORROW   ZELAZNY, ROGER   AC
        NEBULA AWARD STORIES   KNIGHT, DAMON   AN
        RUN TO STARLIGHT, SPORTS THROUGH SCIENCE FICTION
                                          GREENBERG/OLANDER/&   AN
    ENGINE AT HEARTSPRING'S CENTER, THE   SS   ASF 74 07
        BEST SCIENCE FICTION OF THE YEAR, THE NO. 4
                                          CARR, TERRY   AN
        NEBULA AWARD STORIES 10   GUNN, JAMES E.   AN
    EVE OF RUMOKO, THE   NA   TFT 69
        MY NAME IS LEGION   ZELAZNY, ROGER   AC
        THREE FOR TOMORROW   SILVERBERG, ROBERT   OA
    FOR A BREATH I TARRY   NV   NWS 66 03
        ALPHA 1   SILVERBERG, ROBERT   AN
        BEST SF STORIES FROM NEW WORLDS NO. 2, THE
                                          MOORCOCK, MICHAEL   AN
        MODERN SCIENCE FICTION   SPINRAD, NORMAN   AN
        SURVIVAL PRINTOUT   TOTAL EFFECT   AN
        WORLD'S BEST SCIENCE FICTION: 1967 WOLLHEIM & CARR   AN
    FORCE THAT THROUGH THE CIRCUIT DRIVES THE CURRENT, THE
                                                 SS

ZELAZNY, ROGER   (CONTINUED)
    SCIENCE FICTION DISCOVERIES   POHL, C. & F.   OA
                                           NV   AMZ 65 06
    FURIES, THE
      FOUR FOR TOMORROW   ZELAZNY, ROGER   AC
GAME OF BLOOD AND DUST, THE   SS   GAL 75 04
    BEST FROM GALAXY, THE   VOLUME IV   BAEN, JAMES   AN
                                           NV   FAN 64 03
GRAVEYARD HEART, THE
    FOUR FOR TOMORROW   ZELAZNY, ROGER   AC
    GREAT SHORT NOVELS OF SCIENCE FICTION SILVERBERG, ROBERT   AN
    SHORES BENEATH, THE   SALLIS, JAMES   AN
GREAT SLOW KINGS, THE   SS   WOT 63 12
    ABC OF SCIENCE FICTION, AN   BOARDMAN, TOM JR.   AN
    DOORS OF HIS FACE, THE LAMPS OF HIS MOUTH, THE
                                           ZELAZNY, ROGER   AC
    STARS AROUND US, THE   HOSKINS, ROBERT   AN
HE WHO SHAPES   NV   AMZ 65 01
    NEBULA AWARD STORIES   KNIGHT, DAMON   AN
HOME IS THE HANGMAN   NV   ASF 75 11
    MY NAME IS LEGION   ZELAZNY, ROGER   AC
    NEBULA AWARD STORIES 11   LE GUIN, URSULA K.   AN
IN PRAISE OF HIS SPIRITS NOBLE AND OTHERWISE   IN
    FROM THE LAND OF FEAR   ELLISON, HARLAN   AC
INTRODUCTION   IN
    NEBULA AWARD STORIES NO. 3   ZELAZNY, ROGER   AN
KEYS TO DECEMBER, THE   SS   NWS 66 08
    BEST SF STORIES FROM NEW WORLDS NO. 1, THE
                                           MOORCOCK, MICHAEL   AN
    DOORS OF HIS FACE, THE LAMPS OF HIS MOUTH, THE
                                           ZELAZNY, ROGER   AC
    TO THE STARS   SILVERBERG, ROBERT   AN
    WORLD'S BEST SCIENCE FICTION: 1967   WOLLHEIM & CARR   AN
KING SOLOMON'S RING   SS   FAN 63 10
    ON OUR WAY TO THE FUTURE   CARR, TERRY   AN
'KJWALLL'KJE'K'KOOTHAILLL'KJE'K   NA   73
    EXALTATION OF STARS, AN   CARR, TERRY   OA
    MY NAME IS LEGION   ZELAZNY, ROGER   AC
LAST INN ON THE ROAD, THE   SS C NWS 67 10
    BEST SF STORIES FROM NEW WORLDS 5   MOORCOCK, MICHAEL   AN
LOVE IS AN IMAGINARY NUMBER   SS   NWS 66 01
    DOORS OF HIS FACE, THE LAMPS OF HIS MOUTH, THE
                                           ZELAZNY, ROGER   AC
LUCIFER   SS   WOT 64 06
    DOORS OF HIS FACE, THE LAMPS OF HIS MOUTH, THE
                                           ZELAZNY, ROGER   AC
MALATESTA COLLECTION, THE   SS   FAN 63 04
    BEST FROM FANTASTIC, THE   WHITE, TED   AN
MAN WHO LOVED THE FAIOLI, THE   SS   GAL 67 06
    DOORS OF HIS FACE, THE LAMPS OF HIS MOUTH, THE
                                           ZELAZNY, ROGER   AC
    SF: AUTHORS' CHOICE 4   HARRISON, HARRY   AN
    WORLD'S BEST SCIENCE FICTION: 1968   WOLLHEIM & CARR   AN
MISFIT, THE   NV   AMZ 63 10
    BEST FROM AMAZING, THE   WHITE, TED   AN
MONSTER AND THE MAIDEN, THE   SS   GAL 64 12
    DOORS OF HIS FACE, THE LAMPS OF HIS MOUTH, THE
                                           ZELAZNY, ROGER   AC
    NINTH GALAXY READER, THE   POHL, FREDERIK   AN
    WONDERMAKERS 2   HOSKINS, ROBERT   AN
MUSEUM PIECE, A   SS   FAN 63 06
    DOORS OF HIS FACE, THE LAMPS OF HIS MOUTH, THE
                                           ZELAZNY, ROGER   AC
    NEW WORLDS OF FANTASY NO. 2   CARR, TERRY   AN
ROSE FOR ECCLESIASTES, A   NV   FSF 63 11
    BEST FROM FANTASY AND SCIENCE FICTION: 14
                                           DAVIDSON, AVRAM   AN
    DOORS OF HIS FACE, THE LAMPS OF HIS MOUTH, THE
                                           ZELAZNY, ROGER   AC
    FOUR FOR TOMORROW   ZELAZNY, ROGER   AC

NEW AWARENESS, THE   WARRICK & GREENBERG   AN
SCIENCE FICTION HALL OF FAME VOLUME 1   SILVERBERG, ROBERT   AN
SCIENCE FICTION: THE FUTURE   ALLEN, DICK   AN
10TH ANNUAL OF THE YEAR'S BEST S-F, THE
                                           MERRIL, JUDITH   AN
STAINLESS STEEL LEECH, THE   SS   AMZ 63 04
    NEW WORLDS OF FANTASY NO. 3   CARR, TERRY   AN
THIS MOMENT OF THE STORM   NV   FSF 66 06
    BEST FROM FANTASY AND SCIENCE FICTION: 16
                                           FERMAN, EDWARD L.   AN
    DAY IN THE LIFE, A   DOZOIS, GARDNER R.   AN
    DOORS OF HIS FACE, THE LAMPS OF HIS MOUTH, THE
                                           ZELAZNY, ROGER   AC
THIS MORTAL MOUNTAIN   NV   IFS 67 03
    DOORS OF HIS FACE, THE LAMPS OF HIS MOUTH, THE
                                           ZELAZNY, ROGER   AC
    THIS SIDE OF INFINITY   CARR, TERRY   AN

ZELIKOVICH, E.
    DANGEROUS INVENTION, A   SS
    RUSSIAN SCIENCE FICTION   MAGIDOFF, ROBERT   AN

ZHURAVLEVA, VALENTINA
    ASTRONAUT, THE   SS
    DESTINATION: AMALTHEIA   DIXON, RICHARD   AN
    OUT OF THIS WORLD 4   WILLIAMS-ELLIS& OWEN   AN
    RUSSIAN SCIENCE FICTION   MAGIDOFF, ROBERT   AN
    BRAT, THE   SS   67
    AIR OF MARS AND OTHER STORIES, THE   GINSBURG, MIRRA   AN
    STONE FROM THE STARS   SS
    MORE SOVIET SCIENCE FICTION   ANONYMOUS   AN
    STORM   SS
    RUSSIAN SCIENCE FICTION, 1968   MAGIDOFF, ROBERT   AN

ZICREE, MARC SCOTT
    LEADER OF THE CLUB, THE   SS
    CLARION SF   WILHELM, KATE   OA
ZINDEL, PAUL
    LET ME HEAR YOU WHISPER   PL   SVM 70
    SIX SCIENCE FICTION PLAYS   ELWOOD, ROGER   AN

ZIRUL, ARTHUR
    BEAUTIFUL THINGS, THE   SS   FUN 58 05
    SF:59, THE YEAR'S GREATEST SCIENCE FICTION AND FANTASY
                                           MERRIL, JUDITH   AN

ZOLINE, PAMELA A.
    HEAT DEATH OF THE UNIVERSE, THE   SS   NWS 67 07
    BEST SF STORIES FROM NEW WORLDS 3   MOORCOCK, MICHAEL   AN
    DECADE THE 1960S   ALDISS & HARRISON   AN
    ENGLAND SWINGS SF   MERRIL, JUDITH   AN
    MIRROR OF INFINITY, THE   SILVERBERG, ROBERT   AN
    VOYAGES: SCENARIOS FOR A SHIP CALLED EARTH
                                           SAUER, ROB   AN
    HOLLAND OF THE MIND, THE   NV
    NEW S.F., THE   JONES, LANGDON   OA

ZORIN, LEO
    APOCALYPSE MACHINE, THE   SS   NWS 68 12
    BEST SF STORIES FROM NEW WORLDS 7   MOORCOCK, MICHAEL   AN

ZOSS, JOEL
    VALVE TRANSCRIPT, THE   SS   NWS 68 04
    BEST SF STORIES FROM NEW WORLDS 4   MOORCOCK, MICHAEL   AN

ZUBKOV, E.
    ROBOT HUMOR   SS C
    RUSSIAN SCIENCE FICTION, 1969   MAGIDOFF, ROBERT   AN

Story Index

```
                              WILSON, GAHAN      SS  DVS 72 02
AGAIN, DANGEROUS VISIONS       ELLISON, HARLAN            OA
A FOR ANDROMEDA                ELLIOT, JOHN
                 AND HOYLE, FRED           EX C SVN 62 AN
  FROM FRANKENSTEIN TO ANDROMEDA  BROWN, JAMES GOLDIE  AN
A IS FOR AUTOMATION            WILHELM, KATE      SS  FUT 59 10
  MILE-LONG SPACESHIP, THE        WILHELM, KATE             AC
"A" AS IN ANDROID              LESSER, MILTON     SS  FUT 51 05
  NOVELETS OF SCIENCE FICTION     HOWARD, IVAN              AN
A. BOTTS AND THE MOEBIUS STRIP UPSON, WILLIAM H.  SS  SEP 45 12
  FANTASIA MATHEMATICA            FADIMAN, CLIFTON          AN
A.D. 2267                      NIMS, JOHN FREDERICK PM     67
  SCIENCE FICTION                 BRODKIN & PEARSON         AN
A-W-F, UNLIMITED               HERBERT, FRANK     NV  GAL 61 06
  WORLDS OF FRANK HERBERT, THE    HERBERT, FRANK            AC
  17 X INFINITY                   CONKLIN, GROFF            AN
A, B AND C- THE HUMAN ELEMENTS IN MATHEMATICS
                              LEACOCK, STEPHEN   AR        12
  MATHEMATICAL MAGPIE, THE        FADIMAN, CLIFTON          AN
AARDVARK OF DESPAIR, THE       COVER, ARTHUR BYRON NV
  PLATYPUS OF DOOM AND OTHER NIHILISTS, THE
                              COVER, ARTHUR BYRON          OC
ABATTOIR EFFECT, THE           BLISH, JAMES       SS  NEW 61 AC
  SO CLOSE TO HOME               BLISH, JAMES              AC
ABDICATION (ALSO AS THE INVISIBILITY GAMBIT)
                              HULL, E. MAYNE
                 AND VAN VOGT, A. E.   SS C ASF 43 04
  SCIENCE FICTION ROLL OF HONOR, THE  POHL, FREDERIK       AN
ABDUCTION OF ABNER GREER, THE  BOND, NELSON S.    SS  BBM 41 06
  NIGHTMARES AND DAYDREAMS        BOND, NELSON S.           AN
  *SCIENCE-FICTION CARNIVAL       BROWN, F. & REYNOLDS AN
ABENDLANDES                    KIDD, VIRGINIA     PM  FUC 73
  FUTURE CITY                     ELWOOD, ROGER             OA
ABERCROMBIE STATION            VANCE, JACK        NA  TWS 52 02
  BEST OF JACK VANCE, THE         VANCE, JACK               AC
ABLE TO ZEBRA                  TUCKER, WILSON     SS  FSF 53 03
  SCIENCE FICTION SUBTREASURY, THE TUCKER, WILSON           AC
ABLEST MAN IN THE WORLD, THE   MITCHELL, EDWARD P. SS SUN 79 05
  CRYSTAL MAN, THE                MITCHELL, EDWARD P.       AC
ABNORMALS, THE (SEE THE DISCARDED)
                              ELLISON, HARLAN    TC
ABOMINABLE                     BROWN, FREDRIC     SS  DUD 60 03
  BEST OF FREDRIC BROWN, THE      BROWN, FREDRIC            AC
  NIGHTMARES AND GEEZENSTACKS     BROWN, FREDRIC            AC
  6TH ANNUAL OF THE YEAR'S BEST S-F, THE  MERRIL, JUDITH   AN
ABOMINABLE EARTHMAN, THE       POHL, FREDERIK     NV  GAL 61 10
  ABOMINABLE EARTHMAN, THE        POHL, FREDERIK            AC
ABOMINABLE MR. GUNN, THE       GRAVES, ROBERT     SS
  MATHEMATICAL MAGPIE, THE        FADIMAN, CLIFTON          AN
ABOUT A SECRET CROCODILE       LAFFERTY, R. A.    SS  GAL 70 08
  BEST FROM GALAXY, THE  VOLUME I  GALAXY, EDITORS OF       AN
  DOES ANYONE ELSE HAVE SOMETHING FURTHER TO ADD?
                              LAFFERTY, R. A.             AC
  SOCIAL PROBLEMS THROUGH SCIENCE FICTION GREENBERG/MILSTEAD/& AN
ABOUT BILL NOLAN              BRADBURY, RAY      IN
  IMPACT-20                       NOLAN, WILLIAM F.         AC
ABOUT H. G. WELLS: BIOGRAPHICAL NOTES
                              MISC. MATERIAL     MS
  WAR OF THE WORLDS, THE TIME MACHINE AND SELECTED SHORT STORIES
                              WELLS, H. G.              AC
ABOUT JOHN CAMPBELL            STURGEON, THEODORE MS
  WHO GOES THERE? AND OTHER STORIES  CAMPBELL, JOHN W. JR AC
ABOUT THE AUTHOR               ACKERMAN, FORREST J. IN
  WORLDS OF A. E. VAN VOGT, THE   VAN VOGT, A. E.           AC
ABOUT THE AUTHOR               KORNBLUTH, C. M.   MS
  BEST OF C. M. KORNBLUTH, THE    KORNBLUTH, C. M.          AC
ABOUT THE AUTHORS              MISC. MATERIAL     MS
  AURORA: BEYOND EQUALITY         MCINTYRE & ANDERSON      OA
  BEST SCIENCE-FICTION STORIES: 1950, THE  BLEILER & DIKTY  AN
  BEST SCIENCE-FICTION STORIES: 1951, THE  BLEILER & DIKTY  AN
  BEST SCIENCE-FICTION STORIES: 1952, THE  BLEILER & DIKTY  AN
  BEST SCIENCE-FICTION STORIES: 1953, THE  BLEILER & DIKTY  AN
  BEST SCIENCE-FICTION STORIES: 1954, THE  BLEILER & DIKTY  AN
  BIO-FUTURES                     SARGENT, PAMELA          AN
  MORE WOMEN OF WONDER             SARGENT, PAMELA          AN
  STAR SHORT NOVELS                POHL, FREDERIK           OA
  TOMORROW TODAY                   ZEBROWSKI, GEORGE        OA
  WORLD NAMED CLEOPATRA, A         ANDERSON, POUL           OA
ABOUT THE AUTHORS              KNIGHT, DAMON      MS
  13 FRENCH SCIENCE-FICTION STORIES  KNIGHT, DAMON          AN
ABOUT THE COVER                STERNBACH, RICK    MS
  TALES OF KNOWN SPACE: THE UNIVERSE OF LARRY NIVEN
                              NIVEN, LARRY              AC
ABOUT THE EDITOR               MISC. MATERIAL     MS
  CHILDREN OF WONDER              TENN, WILLIAM             AN
  MORE WOMEN OF WONDER             SARGENT, PAMELA          AN
  OTHER WORLDS, OTHER SEAS         SUVIN, DARKO             AN
ABOUT THIS BOOK                SLOANE, WILLIAM    IN
  *STORIES FOR TOMORROW           SLOANE, WILLIAM           AN
ABOUT WILLIAM TENN             MISC. MATERIAL     MS
  OF ALL POSSIBLE WORLDS          TENN, WILLIAM             AC
ABREACTION                     STURGEON, THEODORE SS  WRT 48 07
  BEYOND                          STURGEON, THEODORE        AC
  FUTURE MAKERS, THE              HAINING, PETER            AN
ABSALOM                        KUTTNER, HENRY     SS  STS 46 PL
  BEST OF HENRY KUTTNER 1, THE    KUTTNER, HENRY            AC
  BEST OF HENRY KUTTNER, THE      KUTTNER, HENRY            AC
  BYPASS TO OTHERNESS             KUTTNER, HENRY            AC
  TOMORROW, THE STARS             HEINLEIN, ROBERT A.       AN
  TRANSFORMATIONS                 ROSELLE, DANIEL           AN
ABSOLUTE AT LARGE, THE         CAPEK, KAREL       SN  MAC 27
  CENTURY OF GREAT SHORT SCIENCE FICTION NOVELS, A
                              KNIGHT, DAMON             AN
ABSOLUTE ULTIMATE INVENTION, THE
                              BARR, STEPHEN      SS  INY 70 01
  INFINITY 1                      HOSKINS, ROBERT           OA

ABSOLUTELY INFLEXIBLE          SILVERBERG, ROBERT SS  FUN 56 07
  CUBE ROOT OF UNCERTAINTY, THE   SILVERBERG, ROBERT        AC
  NEEDLE IN A TIMESTACK            SILVERBERG, ROBERT        AC
  VOYAGERS IN TIME                 SILVERBERG, ROBERT        AN
ABSOLUTELY PERFECT MURDER, THE DEFORD, MIRIAM ALLEN SS FSF 65 02
  XENOGENESIS                      DEFORD, MIRIAM ALLEN     AC
ABSORBING THE MIRACULOUS       HARRISON, M. JOHN  BR  NWQ 74 06
  NEW WORLDS NO. 6                PLATT & BAILEY            AN
ABUNDANCE OF GOOD THINGS, AN (HAVE IT YOUR OWN WAY)
                              WILSON, RICHARD    SS  AMZ 54 05
  TIME OUT FOR TOMORROW           WILSON, RICHARD           AC
ABYSS OF DARKNESS              ROCKLYNNE, ROSS    NV  AST 42 12
  SUN DESTROYERS, THE             ROCKLYNNE, ROSS           DC
ABYSS, THE                     ANDREYEV, LEONID   SS       43
  SHOCKING THING, A               KNIGHT, DAMON             AN
ABYSS, THE                     LOWNDES, ROBERT W. SS  STI 41 02
  HISTORY OF THE SCIENCE FICTION MAGAZINE, THE  PART 2 1936-1945
                              ASHLEY, MICHAEL           AN
ACADEMY, THE                   ELY, DAVID         SS  PBY 65 06
  FANTASY: THE LITERATURE OF THE MARVELOUS KELLEY, LEO P.  AN
  PLAYBOY BOOK OF HORROR AND THE SUPERNATURAL, THE
                              PLAYBOY, EDITORS OF AN
  WEIRD SHOW                      PLAYBOY, EDITORS OF AN
ACADEMY, THE                   SHECKLEY, ROBERT   NV  IFS 54 08
  PILGRIMAGE TO EARTH             SHECKLEY, ROBERT          AC
ACCELERATED WORLD, THE         JONES, NEIL R.     NV  NEW 68 05
  DOOMSDAY ON AJIAT               JONES, NEIL R.            AC
ACCEPTING FOR WINKELMEYER      JACOBS, HARVEY     SS  NWQ 73 05
  NEW WORLDS NO. 5                MOORCOCK & PLATT          AN
ACCIDENT VERTIGO               ELMSLIE, KENWARD   PV  PRV 71 50
  RUINS OF EARTH, THE             DISCH, THOMAS M.          AN
ACCIDENTAL FLIGHT              WALLACE, F. L.     NA  GAL 52 04
  TIME WAITS FOR WINTHROP, AND FOUR OTHER SHORT NOVELS
                              POHL, FREDERIK            AN
ACCIDENTS OF A COUNTRY ROAD    DIONNE, ROGER      SS  PBY 70 11
  WEIRD SHOW                      PLAYBOY, EDITORS OF AN
ACCLIMATIZATION               STRINGER, DAVID    NV  NWR 65 05
  NEW WRITINGS IN SF. 5           CARNELL, JOHN             OA
ACCOLADE                       GREY, CHARLES      SS  NWR 74 23
  NEW WRITINGS IN SF. 23          BULMER, KENNETH           OA
ACCORD                         KARL, JEAN E.      NV
  TURNING PLACE, THE              KARL, JEAN E.             OC
ACCORDING TO HIS ABILITIES     HARRISON, HARRY    SS  AMZ 64 05
  TWO TALES AND EIGHT TOMORROWS   HARRISON, HARRY           AC
ACCOUNT OF SOME STRANGE DISTURBANCES IN AUNGIER ST
                              LE FANU, J. SHERIDAN NV
  EDGE OF NEVER, THE              HOSKINS, ROBERT           AN
ACCOUNTANT, THE                SHECKLEY, ROBERT   SS  FSF 54 07
  BEST FROM FANTASY AND SCIENCE FICTION: 4
                              BOUCHER, ANTHONY          AN
  CITIZEN IN SPACE                SHECKLEY, ROBERT          AC
  TOMORROW'S CHILDREN             ASIMOV, ISAAC             AN
ACCURSED GALAXY, THE           HAMILTON, EDMOND   SS  ASF 35 07
  BEFORE THE GOLDEN AGE           ASIMOV, ISAAC             AN
  BEST OF EDMOND HAMILTON, THE    HAMILTON, EDMOND          AC
  HORROR ON THE ASTEROID AND OTHER TALES OF PLANETARY HORROR
                              HAMILTON, EDMOND          AC
ACE 167                        ARNASON, ELEANOR   SS  ORB 74 15
                              KNIGHT, DAMON             OA
ACHIEVEMENT OF H. T. WENSEL, THE
                              SMITH, H. ALLEN    SS  SRV 60 05
  MATHEMATICAL MAGPIE, THE        FADIMAN, CLIFTON          AN
ACHIEVEMENTS                   WISE, DAVID        SS  NDM 75 05
  NEW DIMENSIONS 5                SILVERBERG, ROBERT        OA
ACID SOAP OPERA                MADONIA, GAIL      SS  QRK 71 04
  QUARK/4                         DELANY & HACKER           OA
ACROSS PARIS                   AYME, MARCEL       SS
  WALKER THROUGH WALLS, THE       AYME, MARCEL              AC
ACROSS THE BAR                 REED, KIT          SS  ORB 71 09
  ORBIT  9                        KNIGHT, DAMON             OA
"ACT III. SCENE V. ANOTHER PART OF THE FOREST"
                              CONKLIN, GROFF     IN
  ANOTHER PART OF THE GALAXY      CONKLIN, GROFF            AN
ACTINIC ACTOR, THE (SEE THE ACTINIC GHOST)
                              NEARING, H. JR.    TC
ACTINIC GHOST, THE (THE ACTINIC ACTOR)
                              NEARING, H. JR.    SS  FSF 52 04
  SINISTER RESEARCHES OF C. P. RANSOM, THE NEARING, H. JR.  AC
ACTION FROM A DISTANCE (FROM "RALPH 124C 41+")
                              GERNSBACK, HUGO    EX  MEL 11 04
  SCIENCE FICTION THROUGH THE AGES 2  EVANS, I. O.          AN
ACTION ON AZURA (ALSO AS CONTACT, INCORPORATED)
                              OSBORNE, ROBERTSON NV  PLS 49 FL
  TRAVELLERS OF SPACE            GREENBERG , MARTIN  AN
ACTOR, THE                     RUSSELL, RAY       SS  PBY 60 03
  SARDONICUS AND OTHER STORIES    RUSSELL, RAY              AC
AD ASTRA                       HARRISON, HARRY    SS  VTX 74 08
  BEST SCIENCE FICTION STORIES OF THE YEAR (1974)
                              DEL REY, LESTER           AN
AD ASTRA                       HENDERSON, ZENNA   SS  NEW 71 AC
  HOLDING WONDER                  HENDERSON, ZENNA          AC
ADAM                           VONNEGUT, KURT JR. SS  CMP 54 04
  WELCOME TO THE MONKEY HOUSE     VONNEGUT, KURT JR.        AC
ADAM AND EVE AND PINCH ME       COPPARD, A. E.     SS       21
  CHILDREN OF WONDER              TENN, WILLIAM             AN
  MOONLIGHT TRAVELER, THE         STERN, PHILIP VAN D. AN
ADAM AND NO EVE                BESTER, ALFRED     SS  ASF 41 09
  *ADVENTURES IN TIME AND SPACE   HEALY & MCCOMAS           AN
  BEYOND CONTROL                  SILVERBERG, ROBERT        AN
  MORE ADVENTURES IN TIME AND SPACE  HEALY & MCCOMAS        AN
  STAR LIGHT, STAR BRIGHT          BESTER, ALFRED           AC
  STARBURST                        BESTER, ALFRED           AC
ADAM FROST                     AANDAHL, VANCE     SS  PBY 62 04
  FIEND, THE                      PLAYBOY, EDITORS OF AN
ADAM HAD THREE BROTHERS        LAFFERTY, R. A.    SS  NMQ 69
```

DOES ANYONE ELSE HAVE SOMETHING FURTHER TO ADD?
    LAFFERTY, R. A.   AC
  NEW WORLDS OF FANTASY NO. 3 CARR, TERRY   AN
ADAM LINK IN BUSINESS BINDER, EANDO SS AMZ 40 01
  ADAM LINK- ROBOT BINDER, EANDO AC
ADAM LINK SAVES THE WORLD BINDER, EANDO SS AMZ 42 04
  ADAM LINK- ROBOT BINDER, EANDO AC
ADAM LINK'S VENGEANCE BINDER, EANDO NV AMZ 40 02
  ADAM LINK- ROBOT BINDER, EANDO AC
  OTHER WORLDS, THE STONG, PHILIP D. AN
ADAM LINK, CHAMPION ATHLETE BINDER, EANDO SS AMZ 40 07
  ADAM LINK- ROBOT BINDER, EANDO AC
ADAM LINK, ROBOT DETECTIVE BINDER, EANDO SS AMZ 40 05
  ADAM LINK- ROBOT BINDER, EANDO AC
ADAPTATION FELDSTEIN, ALBERT B. MS
  AUTUMN PEOPLE, THE BRADBURY, RAY AC
  TOMORROW MIDNIGHT BRADBURY, RAY AC
ADAPTATION GIBSON, WALTER B. MS
  *ROD SERLING'S THE TWILIGHT ZONE SERLING, ROD OC
  ROD SERLING'S TWILIGHT ZONE REVISITED SERLING, ROD SS ASF 49 07
ADAPTATION WYNDHAM, JOHN SS ASF 49 07
  BEST OF JOHN WYNDHAM, THE WYNDHAM, JOHN AC
  MAN FROM BEYOND AND OTHER STORIES, THE WYNDHAM, JOHN AC
  MICROCOSMIC GOD MOSKOWITZ, SAM AN
  MODERN MASTERPIECES OF SCIENCE FICTION MOSKOWITZ, SAM AN
ADAPTIVE ULTIMATE, THE JESSEL, JOHN NV ASF 35 11
  OTHER WORLDS, THE STONG, PHILIP D. AN
ADAPTIVE ULTIMATE, THE WEINBAUM, STANLEY G. NV ASF 35 11
  BEST OF STANLEY G. WEINBAUM, THE WEINBAUM, STANLEY G. AC
  DAWN OF FLAME WEINBAUM, STANLEY G. AC
  MARTIAN ODYSSEY AND OTHER SCIENCE FICTION TALES, A
    WEINBAUM, STANLEY G. AC
  MARTIAN ODYSSEY AND OTHERS, A WEINBAUM, STANLEY G. AC
  MARTIAN ODYSSEY, A WEINBAUM, STANLEY G. AC
ADDED INDUCEMENT YOUNG, ROBERT F. SS FSF 57 03
  WORLDS OF ROBERT F. YOUNG, THE YOUNG, ROBERT F. AC
ADDENDUM O'DONNELL, K. M. SS NEW 71 DC
  IN THE POCKET AND OTHER S-F STORIES O'DONNELL, K. M. DC
ADDICT, THE LOWENKOPF, SHELLY SS NEW 65 AN
  PSEUDO PEOPLE, THE NOLAN, WILLIAM F. AN
ADDITIONAL FEGHOOT PUNS (LAST IN BSJ)
    BRIARTON, GRENDEL MS
  COMPLETE FEGHOOT, THE BRIARTON, GRENDEL AC
ADDITIONAL SIGNIFICANT WORKS OF SPECULATIVE FICTION
    MISC. MATERIAL MS
  MODERN SCIENCE FICTION SPINRAD, NORMAN AN
ADEPT'S GAMBIT LEIBER, FRITZ SS NEW 47 AC
  NIGHT'S BLACK AGENTS LEIBER, FRITZ AC
ADJUSTED, THE BULMER, KENNETH SS FSF 66 06
  BEST FROM FANTASY AND SCIENCE FICTION: 16
    FERMAN, EDWARD L. AN
  MARRIAGE AND THE FAMILY THROUGH SCIENCE FICTION
    CLEAR/WARRICK/& AN
ADJUSTMENT MOORE, WARD NV FSF 57 05
  BEST FROM FANTASY AND SCIENCE FICTION: 7
    BOUCHER, ANTHONY AN
  INTRODUCTORY PSYCHOLOGY THROUGH SCIENCE FICTION
    KATZ/WARRICK/& AN
ADJUSTMENT TEAM DICK, PHILIP K. NV OSF 54 09
  BOOK OF PHILIP K. DICK, THE DICK, PHILIP K. AC
  SANDS OF MARS AND OTHER STORIES, THE ANONYMOUS AN
ADMIRAL'S INSPECTION JAMESON, MALCOLM NV ASF 40 04
  BULLARD OF THE SPACE PATROL JAMESON, MALCOLM AC
ADMIRALTY ANDERSON, POUL SN FSF 65 06
  STAR FOX, THE ANDERSON, POUL AC
ADO ABOUT NOTHING OTTUM, BOB JR. SS FSF 65 03
  11TH ANNUAL OF THE YEAR'S BEST S-F, THE MERRIL, JUDITH SS
ADRIFT IN SPACE ZEBROWSKI, GEORGE SS
  ADRIFT IN SPACE AND OTHER STORIES ELWOOD, ROGER OA
ADRIFT JUST OFF THE ISLETS OF LANGERHANS: LATITUDE 38° 54' N,
LONGITUDE 77° 00' 13" W ELLISON, HARLAN NV FSF 74 10
  DEATHBIRD STORIES ELLISON, HARLAN AC
ADRIFT ON THE FREEWAY BRYANT, EDWARD SS QRK 70 01
  AMONG THE DEAD BRYANT, EDWARD AC
  QUARK/1 DELANY & HACKER OA
ADRIFT ON THE POLICY LEVEL DAVIS, CHAN SS STR 59 05
  ABOVE THE HUMAN LANDSCAPE MCNELLY & STOVER AN
  EXPERT DREAMERS, THE POHL, FREDERIK AN
  POLITICAL SCIENCE FICTION GREENBERG& WARRICK AN
  STAR SCIENCE FICTION STORIES NO. 5 POHL, FREDERIK OA
ADRIFT ON THE SEA OF SPACE YATES, R. F. AR
  LAURIE'S SPACE ANNUAL ANONYMOUS AN
ADVANCE NOTICE MATHESON, RICHARD SS ROG 59
  SHOCK WAVES MATHESON, RICHARD AC
ADVANCE POST IN THE WAR BETWEEN THE SEXES, AN
    WOLLHEIM, DONALD A. SS
  TWO DOZEN DRAGON EGGS WOLLHEIM, DONALD A. AC
ADVANTAGE RACKHAM, JOHN NV NWR 65 06
  NEW WRITINGS IN SF. 6 CARNELL, JOHN OA
ADVENT OF THE FLYING MAN, THE (SEE THE FLYING MAN)
    WELLS, H. G. TC
ADVENT ON CHANNEL TWELVE, THE KORNBLUTH, C. M. SS STR 58 04
  BEST OF C. M. KORNBLUTH, THE KORNBLUTH, C. M. AC
  STAR OF STARS POHL, FREDERIK AN
  STAR SCIENCE FICTION STORIES NO. 4 POHL, FREDERIK OA
ADVENTURE IN A SPACE SHIP (FROM "OUT OF THE SILENT PLANET")
    LEWIS, C. S. EX LNE 38
  SCIENCE IN FICTION BAYLISS, A.E. & J.C. AN
ADVENTURE IN FUTURITY, AN SMITH, CLARK ASHTON NV WOS 31 04
  OTHER DIMENSIONS SMITH, CLARK ASHTON AC
ADVENTURE IN THE FOURTH DIMENSION, AN
    WRIGHT, FARNSWORTH NV WRT 23 10
  MOON TERROR, THE BIRCH, A. G. AN
ADVENTURE IN THE YOLLA BOLLY MIDDLE EEL WILDERNESS, AN
    AANDAHL, VANCE NV FSF 69 08

BEST FROM FANTASY AND SCIENCE FICTION: 19
    FERMAN, EDWARD L. AN
ADVENTURE OF THE BALL OF NOSTRADAMUS, THE
    DERLETH, AUGUST
    AND REYNOLDS, MACK SS C FSF 55 06
  SCIENCE-FICTIONAL SHERLOCK HOLMES, THE COUNCIL OF FOUR AN
ADVENTURE OF THE EXTRATERRESTRIAL, THE
    REYNOLDS, MACK NV ASF 65 07
  ANALOG 5 CAMPBELL, JOHN W. JR AN
  BEST OF MACK REYNOLDS, THE REYNOLDS, MACK AC
ADVENTURE OF THE MARTIAN CLIENT, THE
    WELLMAN, MANLY WADE
    AND WELLMAN, WADE SS C FSF 69 12
  WONDERMAKERS 2 HOSKINS, ROBERT AN
ADVENTURE OF THE MISPLACED HOUND, THE
    ANDERSON, POUL
    AND DICKSON, GORDON R. NV C USF 53 12
  EARTHMAN'S BURDEN ANDERSON, P.&DICKSON AC
  SCIENCE-FICTIONAL SHERLOCK HOLMES, THE COUNCIL OF FOUR AN
ADVENTURE OF THE SNITCH IN TIME, THE
    DERLETH, AUGUST
    AND REYNOLDS, MACK SS C FSF 53 07
  SCIENCE-FICTIONAL SHERLOCK HOLMES, THE COUNCIL OF FOUR AN
  SPACE, TIME & CRIME DEFORD, MIRIAM ALLEN AN
ADVENTURER, THE KORNBLUTH, C. M. SS SSF 53 05
  ASSIGNMENT IN TOMORROW POHL, FREDERIK AN
  BEST OF C. M. KORNBLUTH, THE KORNBLUTH, C. M. AC
  *MILE BEYOND THE MOON, A KORNBLUTH, C. M. AC
ADVENTURES OF BARON MUNCHAUSEN, THE
    RASPE, RUDOLPH EX
  FROM FRANKENSTEIN TO ANDROMEDA BROWN, JAMES GOLDIE AN
ADVENTURES ON MARS ELAM, RICHARD M. JR. SS STP 52 12
  SCIENCE FICTION AND READER'S GUIDE BARROWS, MARJORIE AN
ADVENTURESS, THE (ALSO AS BLUESTOCKING)
    RUSS, JOANNA NV ORB 67 02
  ORBIT 2 KNIGHT, DAMON OA
ADVICE TO A PROPHET WILBUR, RICHARD PM 59
  SCIENCE FICTION: THE FUTURE ALLEN, DICK AN
ADVISERS OF KING HYDROPS, THE LEM, STANISLAW SS 72
  MORTAL ENGINES LEM, STANISLAW AC
AELUROPHOBE BROWN, FREDRIC SS DUD 62
  PARADOX LOST, AND 12 OTHER GREAT S.F. STORIES
    BROWN, FREDRIC AC
AEPYORNIS ISLAND WELLS, H. G. SS PMB 94 12
  BEST SCIENCE FICTION STORIES OF H. G. WELLS
    WELLS, H. G. AC
  COUNTRY OF THE BLIND, THE WELLS, H. G. AC
  JOURNEYS IN SCIENCE FICTION LOUGHLIN, RICHARD L. AN
  SHORT STORIES OF H. G. WELLS, THE WELLS, H. G. AC
  STOLEN BACILLUS AND OTHER INCIDENTS, THE WELLS, H. G. AC
  STRANGE BEASTS AND UNNATURAL MONSTERS STERN, PHILIP VAN D. AN
  THIRTY STRANGE STORIES WELLS, H. G. AC
  TWENTY-EIGHT SCIENCE FICTION STORIES WELLS, H. G. AC
AESOP SIMAK, CLIFFORD D. NV ASF 47 12
  CITY SIMAK, CLIFFORD D. NO
AESTHETIC DECAPITATIONS, THE NEARING, H. JR. SS NEW 54 AN
  SINISTER RESEARCHES OF C. P. RANSOM, THE NEARING, H. JR. AC
AESTHETICS OF THE MOON ANDERSON, JACK PM
  SCIENCE FACT/FICTION FARRELL/GAGE/& AN
AFFAIR OF THE BRAINS, THE GILMORE, ANTHONY NV ASF 32 03
  SPACE HAWK GILMORE, ANTHONY AC
AFFAIR OF THE HEART WYNDHAM, JOHN SS
  JIZZLE WYNDHAM, JOHN AC
AFFAIR WITH A GREEN MONKEY STURGEON, THEODORE SS VSF 57 05
  MODERN SCIENCE FICTION SPINRAD, NORMAN AN
  *TOUCH OF STRANGE, A STURGEON, THEODORE AC
AFFAIR WITH GENIUS, AN GREEN, JOSEPH SS FSF 69 03
  AFFAIR WITH GENIUS, AN GREEN, JOSEPH AC
AFFLUENCE OF EDWIN LOLLARD, THE
    DISCH, THOMAS M. SS NWR 67 10
  NEW WRITINGS IN SF. 10 CARNELL, JOHN OA
  WHITE FANG GOES DINGO AND OTHER FUNNY S.F. STORIES
    DISCH, THOMAS M. AC
AFTER SLESAR, HENRY SS PBY 60 06
  FROM THE "S" FILE PLAYBOY, EDITORS OF AN
  PLAYBOY BOOK OF SCIENCE FICTION AND FANTASY, THE
    PLAYBOY, EDITORS OF AN
AFTER A FEW WORDS GARRETT, RANDALL SS ASF 62 10
  ASTOUNDING-ANALOG READER, THE VOLUME TWO HARRISON & ALDISS AN
AFTER A FEW WORDS MCKETTRIG, SEATON SS ASF 62 10
  SCIENCE FICTION HORIZONS NO. 1 BOARDMAN, TOM JR. AN
AFTER A JUDGMENT DAY HAMILTON, EDMOND SS FSF 63 12
  BEST OF EDMOND HAMILTON, THE HAMILTON, EDMOND AC
AFTER DEATH BEER, PATRICIA PM NSM 72
  BEST SF: 1972 HARRISON & ALDISS AN
AFTER IXMAL SUTTON, JEFF SS AMZ 62 10
  SPACE OPERA ALDISS, BRIAN W. AN
AFTER KING KONG FELL FARMER, PHILIP JOSE SS OMG 73
  BEST SF: 1974 HARRISON & ALDISS AN
  NEBULA AWARD STORIES 10 GUNN, JAMES E. AN
  OMEGA ELWOOD, ROGER OA
AFTER MATH FARLEY, RALPH MILNE AR
  OMNIBUS OF TIME, THE FARLEY, RALPH MILNE AC
AFTER NIGHTFALL RILEY, DAVE SS 70
  YEAR'S BEST HORROR STORIES, THE DAVIS, RICHARD AN
AFTER SUCH KNOWLEDGE LEIBER, FRITZ AR 74
  BOOK OF FRITZ LEIBER, THE LEIBER, FRITZ AC
AFTER TEN YEARS LEWIS, C. S. NV 66
  DARK TOWER AND OTHER STORIES, THE LEWIS, C. S. AC
AFTER THE ACCIDENT MITCHISON, NAOMI SS YRT 70
  YEAR 2000, THE HARRISON, HARRY OA
AFTER THE DREAMTIME LUPOFF, RICHARD A. NV NDM 74 04
  NEW DIMENSIONS 4 SILVERBERG, ROBERT OA
AFTER THE GREAT SPACE WAR MALZBERG, BARRY N. SS ALT 74
  DOWN HERE IN THE DREAM QUARTER MALZBERG, BARRY N. AC

AFTER THE MYTHS WENT HOME

AFTER THE MYTHS WENT HOME   SILVERBERG, ROBERT   SS   FSF 69 11
  ANOTHER WORLD   DOZOIS, GARDNER R.   AN
  MOONFERNS & STARSONGS   SILVERBERG, ROBERT   AC
  SUNRISE ON MERCURY AND OTHER SCIENCE FICTION STORIES
                                     SILVERBERG, ROBERT   OA
  TOMORROW, AND TOMORROW, AND TOMORROW... HEINTZ/HERBERT/JOOS/   AN
  WORLD'S BEST SCIENCE FICTION: 1970 WOLLHEIM & CARR   AN
AFTER THE SIRENS   HOOD, HUGH   SS   ESQ 60
  MAN AGAINST TOMORROW   NOLAN, WILLIAM F.   AN
AFTER THE UNFORTUNATE ACCIDENT MALZBERG, BARRY N.   SS   NEW 75 AC
  MANY WORLDS OF BARRY MALZBERG, THE MALZBERG, BARRY N.   AC
AFTER THEY'VE SEEN PAREE   O'NEIL, DENNIS   SS   GEN 72
  GENERATION   GERROLD, DAVID   OA
AFTER THREE HUNDRED YEARS   MILLE, PIERRE   SS   22
  13 FRENCH SCIENCE-FICTION STORIES   KNIGHT, DAMON   AN
AFTER WEIGHTLESSNESS   SAIL, LAWRENCE   PM   74
  BEST SF: 1974   HARRISON & ALDISS   AN
AFTER YOU, MR. HENDERSON   DERLETH, AUGUST   SS   SRS 40 06
  NOT LONG FOR THIS WORLD   DERLETH, AUGUST   AC
AFTERGLOW, THE   ENGLAND, GEORGE A.   NO   CSB 13 06
  DARKNESS AND DAWN   ENGLAND, GEORGE A.   NO
AFTERNOON OF A FAHN (ALSO AS RAINBOW'S END)
                          RUSSELL, ERIC FRANK   SS   IMG 51 04
  ALIEN WORLDS   ELWOOD, ROGER   AN
AFTERNOON WITH A DEAD BUS   GERROLD, DAVID   PRT 71
  FANTASY: THE LITERATURE OF THE MARVELOUS KELLEY, LEO P.   AN
  PROTOSTARS   GERROLD & GOLDIN   OA
AFTERTHOUGHT   FYFE, H. B.   SS   FUS 51 01
  *BEYOND HUMAN KEN   MERRIL, JUDITH   AN
AFTERTHOUGHTS   NIVEN, LARRY   MS
  TALES OF KNOWN SPACE: THE UNIVERSE OF LARRY NIVEN
                                     NIVEN, LARRY   AC
AFTERTHOUGHTS   OLIVER, CHAD   MS
  EDGE OF FOREVER, THE   OLIVER, CHAD   AC
AFTERTHOUGHTS BY THE AUTHOR DICK, PHILIP K.   MS
  BEST OF PHILIP K. DICK, THE   DICK, PHILIP K.   AC
AFTERWARD   WHARTON, EDITH   NV   CNY 10 01
  OTHER DIMENSION, THE   ROSNER, SARA   AN
AFTERWARDS   LUCIE-SMITH, EDWARD PM   64
  HOLDING YOUR EIGHT HANDS   LUCIE-SMITH, EDWARD   AN
  SCIENCE FICTION   BRODKIN & PEARSON   AN
AFTERWORD   ACKERMAN, FORREST J. MS
  BEST SCIENCE FICTION FOR 1973   ACKERMAN, FORREST J.   AN
AFTERWORD   ASHLEY, MICHAEL   MS
  SOULS IN METAL   ASHLEY, MICHAEL   AN
AFTERWORD   BRACKETT, LEIGH   MS
  BEST OF LEIGH BRACKETT, THE   BRACKETT, LEIGH   AC
AFTERWORD   FAST, HOWARD   MS
  TIME AND THE RIDDLE   FAST, HOWARD   AC
AFTERWORD   HAMILTON, EDMOND   MS
  BEST OF EDMOND HAMILTON, THE   HAMILTON, EDMOND   AC
AFTERWORD   HARRISON, HARRY   MS
  LIGHT FANTASTIC, THE   HARRISON, HARRY   AN
  NOVA 4   HARRISON, HARRY   OA
AFTERWORD   LEE, CHRISTOPHER   MS
  GHOULS, THE   HAINING, PETER   AN
AFTERWORD   LEIBER, FRITZ   MS
  BEST OF FRITZ LEIBER, THE   LEIBER, FRITZ   AC
AFTERWORD   MATHESON, RICHARD   MS
  MAGIC MAN AND OTHER SCIENCE-FANTASY STORIES
                                     BEAUMONT, CHARLES   AC
AFTERWORD   MOORCOCK, MICHAEL   MS   NWQ 73 05
  NEW WORLDS NO. 5   MOORCOCK & PLATT   OA
AFTERWORD   NIVEN, LARRY   MS
  FLIGHT OF THE HORSE, THE   NIVEN, LARRY   AC
AFTERWORD   POHL, FREDERIK   MS   FUC 73
  BEST SCIENCE FICTION STORIES OF THE YEAR (1973)
                                     DEL REY, LESTER   AN
  FUTURE CITY   ELWOOD, ROGER   OA
AFTERWORD   STOVER, LEON E.   MS
  APEMAN, SPACEMAN   STOVER & HARRISON   AN
AFTERWORD   SULLIVAN, CHARLES W. MS
  AS TOMORROW BECOMES TODAY   SULLIVAN, CHARLES W.   AN
AFTERWORD   ZEBROWSKI, GEORGE   MS
  SPACE BEYOND, THE   CAMPBELL, JOHN W. JR   OC
AFTERWORD   ZELAZNY, ROGER   MS
  NEBULA AWARD STORIES   NO. 3   ZELAZNY, ROGER   AN
AFTERWORD ABOUT THEME   WILLIAMSON, JACK   MS
  PEOPLE MACHINES   WILLIAMSON, JACK   AC
AFTERWORD: A DAY IN THE LIFE-STYLE OF...
                          ALDISS, BRIAN W.   MS
  BEST SF: 1971   HARRISON & ALDISS   AN
AFTERWORD: FOOTNOTE TO "SHAMBLEAU"... AND OTHERS
                          MOORE, C. L.   MS
  BEST OF C. L. MOORE, THE   MOORE, C. L.   AC
AFTERWORD: ON THE NON-TRANSCENDENCE OF SPORT
                          MALZBERG, BARRY N.   MS
  ARENA: SPORTS SF   FERMAN & MALZBERG   AN
AFTERWORD: OUR MANY ROADS TO THE STARS
                          ANDERSON, POUL   AE   GAL 75 09
  FASTER THAN LIGHT   DANN & ZEBROWSKI   OA
AFTERWORD: POSTSCRIPTUM   CAMPBELL, MRS. JOHN MS
  *BEST OF JOHN W. CAMPBELL, THE   CAMPBELL, JOHN W. JR AC
AFTERWORD: SCIENCE FICTION ON THE TITANIC
                          ALDISS, BRIAN W.   MS
  BEST SF: 75, THE NINTH ANNUAL   HARRISON & ALDISS   AN
AFTERWORD: THE EPIC OF SPACE BY E. E. 'DOC' SMITH
                          MISC. MATERIAL   MS
  BEST OF E. E. 'DOC' SMITH, THE   SMITH, EDWARD E. PHD AC
AFTERWORD: THE GALAXY BEGINS AT HOME
                          ALDISS, BRIAN W.   MS
  BEST SF: 1974   HARRISON & ALDISS   AN
AFTERWORD: THE LAST WORD ABOUT SF| DETECTIVES
                          NIVEN, LARRY   MS
  LONG ARM OF GIL HAMILTON, THE   NIVEN, LARRY   AC

ALEXANDER THE BAIT

AFTERWORD: THE WIZARD AND THE PLUMBER
                          ALDISS, BRIAN W.   MS
  BEST SF: 1973   HARRISON & ALDISS   AN
AFTERWORD: THE YEAR OF THE BIG SPRING CLEAN
                          ALDISS, BRIAN W.   MS
  BEST SF: 1972   HARRISON & ALDISS   AN
AGAINST AUTHORITY   DEFORD, MIRIAM ALLEN NV   FSF 66 02
  VENUS FACTOR, THE   GHIDALIA, V.& ELWOOD   AN
AGAINST THE FALL OF NIGHT CLARKE, ARTHUR C.   NO   STS 48 11
  LION OF COMARRE AND AGAINST THE FALL OF NIGHT
                                     CLARKE, ARTHUR C.   AC
AGAINST THE LAFAYETTE ESCADRILLE
                          WOLFE, GENE   SS   DVS 72 02
  AGAIN, DANGEROUS VISIONS   ELLISON, HARLAN   OA
AGAINST THE ODDS (SEE THE ODDS AGAINST YOU)
AGAINST THE ODDS   BRUNNER, JOHN   TC
AGE OF CLIMAX, THE (FROM "THE GHOST IN THE MACHINE")
                          KOESTLER, ARTHUR   EX   MAC 67
  SPECULATIONS   SANDERS, THOMAS E.   AN
AGE OF INVENTION, THE   SPINRAD, NORMAN   SS   FSF 66 07
  BEST FROM FANTASY AND SCIENCE FICTION: 16
                                     FERMAN, EDWARD L.   AN
  LAST HURRAH OF THE GOLDEN HORDE, THE   SPINRAD, NORMAN   AC
  TOMORROW, INC.   GREENBERG& OLANDER   AN
AGE OF KINDNESS, THE   SELLINGS, ARTHUR   SS   GAL 54 11
  *TIME TRANSFER   SELLINGS, ARTHUR   AC
AGE OF LIBRA, THE   EDELSTEIN, SCOTT   SS
  SCIENCE FICTION DISCOVERIES   POHL, C. & F.   OA
AGE OF PROPHECY, THE   ST. CLAIR, MARGARET NA   FUT 51 03
  CHANGE THE SKY AND OTHER STORIES   ST. CLAIR, MARGARET   AC
  *SCIENCE FICTION ADVENTURES IN MUTATION CONKLIN, GROFF   AN
AGE OF RETIREMENT   LYNCH, MAL   SS   ASF 54 04
  GALACTIC EMPIRES VOLUME ONE   ALDISS, BRIAN W.   AN
AGE OF WISDOM, THE   BOULLE, PIERRE   SS
  TIME OUT OF MIND   BOULLE, PIERRE   OC
AGENT OF VEGA   SCHMITZ, JAMES H.   NV   ASF 49 07
  AGENT OF VEGA   SCHMITZ, JAMES H.   AC
  SPACE POLICE   NORTON, ANDRE   AN
AGENT 38   HOYLE, FRED   SS
  ELEMENT 79   HOYLE, FRED   AC
AGENT, THE   HILL, RICHARD   SS
  FUTURE PASTIMES   EDELSTEIN, SCOTT   OA
AGNES, ACCENT AND ACCESS   STURGEON, THEODORE   SS   GAL 73 10
  BEST FROM GALAXY, THE   VOLUME II   GALAXY, EDITORS OF   AN
AGONY COLUMN   MALZBERG, BARRY N.   SS   EQM 71 12
  OUT FROM GANYMEDE   MALZBERG, BARRY N.   AC
AH THE POETRY OF MISS PARROT'S FEET DEMONSTRATING THE TANGO
                          RAWORTH, TOM   PM   68
  HOLDING YOUR EIGHT HANDS   LUCIE-SMITH, EDWARD   AN
AH, CARELESS, RAPTUROUS VAN VOGT|
                          MALZBERG, BARRY N.   IN
  BEST OF A. E. VAN VOGT, THE   VAN VOGT, A. E.   AC
AH, FAIR URANUS   O'DONNELL, K. M.   SS   NEW 71 DC
  IN THE POCKET AND OTHER S-F STORIES O'DONNELL, K. M.   DC
AHEAD (THE FAILED MEN)   ALDISS, BRIAN W.   SS   SCF 56 05
  *BEST SCIENCE FICTION STORIES OF BRIAN W. ALDISS
                                     ALDISS, BRIAN W.   AC
AIDE MEMOIRE   LAUMER, KEITH   NV   IFS 62 07
  ENVOY TO NEW WORLDS   LAUMER, KEITH   AC
AIM FOR THE HEEL   PHILLIFENT, JOHN T. NV   ASF 67 07
  ANALOG 7   CAMPBELL, JOHN W. JR   AN
AIMEZ-VOUS HOLMAN HUNT?   ALDISS, BRIAN W.   EPC 75
  EPOCH   ELWOOD & SILVERBERG   OA
AIR LINES   KELLER, DAVID H. MD. SS   AMZ 30 01
  FOLSOM FLINT AND OTHER CURIOUS TALES, THE
                                     KELLER, DAVID H. MD.   AC
AIR OF MARS, THE   BILENKIN, DMITRY   SS   69
  AIR OF MARS AND OTHER STORIES, THE GINSBURG, MIRRA   AN
AIR RAID   VARLEY, JOHN   SS   76
  BEST SCIENCE FICTION STORIES OF THE YEAR (1976)
                                     DOZOIS, GARDNER R.   AN
AIR SERPENT, THE   PAGE, WILL A.   SS   RBM 11 04
  SCIENCE FICTION BY GASLIGHT   MOSKOWITZ, SAM   AN
AJAX OF AJAX   PEARSON, MARTIN   SS   FUT 42 08
  FLIGHT INTO SPACE   WOLLHEIM, DONALD A.   AN
AJERI DIARY, THE   DEFORD, MIRIAM ALLEN SS   FSF 68 03
  XENOGENESIS   DEFORD, MIRIAM ALLEN   AC
AL   EMSHWILLER, CAROL   SS   ORB 72 10
  BEST FROM ORBIT, THE   KNIGHT, DAMON   AN
  JOY IN OUR CAUSE   EMSHWILLER, CAROL   AC
  ORBIT 10   KNIGHT, DAMON   OA
AL HADDON'S LAMP   BOND, NELSON S.   NV   UNK 42 06
  NIGHTMARES AND DAYDREAMS   BOND, NELSON S.   AC
ALANNAH   DERLETH, AUGUST   SS   WRT 45 03
  MR. GEORGE AND OTHER ODD PERSONS   DERLETH, AUGUST   AC
ALAREE   SILVERBERG, ROBERT   SS   STN 58 03
  EARTHMEN AND STRANGERS   SILVERBERG, ROBERT   AN
  SUNRISE ON MERCURY AND OTHER SCIENCE FICTION STORIES
                                     SILVERBERG, ROBERT   OA
ALAS, ALL THINKING| BATES, HARRY   SN   ASF 35 06
  *IMAGINATION UNLIMITED   BLEILER & DIKTY   AN
  OTHER WORLDS, THE   STONG, PHILIP D.   AN
  SCIENCE FICTION OF THE 30'S   KNIGHT, DAMON   AN
ALBATROSS   REYNOLDS, MACK   SS   IMG 55 04
  BEST OF MACK REYNOLDS, THE   REYNOLDS, MACK   AC
  ENCOUNTERS WITH ALIENS   EARLEY, GEORGE W.   AN
ALBATROSS (DARIO FINELLI) FOSTER, ALAN DEAN   SA   SLG 76 06
  STAR TREK LOG SIX   FOSTER, ALAN DEAN   AC
ALCHEMY   DE COURCY, DOROTHY
                          AND DE COURCY, JOHN SS C OTW 50 12
  FAREWELL FANTASTIC VENUS   ALDISS & HARRISON   AN
ALECTRYOMANCER, THE   WILLEFORD, CHARLES   NV   AHM
  MACHINE IN WARD ELEVEN, THE   WILLEFORD, CHARLES   NO
ALEXANDER THE BAIT   TENN, WILLIAM   SS   ASF 46 05
  OMNIBUS OF SCIENCE FICTION   CONKLIN, GROFF   AN
  SQUARE ROOT OF MAN, THE   TENN, WILLIAM   AC

```
ALFRED BESTER                          NOLAN, WILLIAM F.    AR
  HUMAN EQUATION, THE                  NOLAN, WILLIAM F.    AN
ALGORA ONE SIX                         MASON, DOUGLAS R.   SS   NWR 73 21
  NEW WRITINGS IN SF. 21               CARNELL, JOHN        OA
ALIBI MACHINE, THE                     NIVEN, LARRY        SS   VTX 73 06
  ANTIGRAV: COSMIC COMEDIES            STRICK, PHILIP       AN
  HOLE IN SPACE, A                     NIVEN, LARRY         AC
ALIEN                                  DEL REY, LESTER     SS   STR 54 03
  STAR SCIENCE FICTION STORIES NO. 3   POHL, FREDERIK       OA
ALIEN AGONY, AN (THE STREETS OF ASHKELON)
                                       HARRISON, HARRY     SS   NWS 62 09
  MORE PENGUIN SCIENCE FICTION         ALDISS, BRIAN W.     AN
ALIEN AMONG US, THE                    HOSKINS, ROBERT     IN   INY 71 02
  INFINITY 2                           HOSKINS, ROBERT      OA
ALIEN DUST                             TUBB, E. C.         SS   NWS 53 01
  ALIEN DUST                           TUBB, E. C.          NO
ALIEN EARTH                            HAMILTON, EDMOND    SS   TWS 49 04
  ALIEN EARTH AND OTHER STORIES        ELWOOD & MOSKOWITZ   AN
  BEST OF EDMOND HAMILTON, THE         HAMILTON, EDMOND     AC
ALIEN ENEMY, THE (AS MICHAEL KARAGEORGE)
                                       ANDERSON, POUL      SS   ASF 68 11
  QUEEN OF AIR AND DARKNESS AND OTHER STORIES, THE
                                       ANDERSON, POUL       AC
ALIEN ENVOY                            JAMESON, MALCOLM    SS   ASF 44 11
  ULTIMATE INVADER, AND OTHER SCIENCE FICTION, THE
                                       WOLLHEIM, DONALD A.  DA
ALIEN MACHINE, THE                     JONES, RAYMOND F.   NV   TWS 49 06
  THIS ISLAND EARTH                    JONES, RAYMOND F.    NO
ALIEN NIGHT                            SCORTIA, THOMAS N.  NV   SPA 57 08
  GET OUT OF MY SKY                    MARGULIES, LEO       AN
ALIEN STONES                           WOLFE, GENE         NV   ORB 72 11
  ORBIT 11                             KNIGHT, DAMON        OA
ALIEN VIEWPOINT, THE                   GEIS, RICHARD E.    AR   IFS 74 10
  BEST FROM IF, THE  VOLUME III        BAEN, JAMES          AN
ALIENS AREN'T WANTED                   CUMMINGS, M. A.     SS
  EXILE AND OTHER TALES OF FANTASY     CUMMINGS, M. A.      OC
ALIENS, THE                            LEINSTER, MURRAY    NV   ASF 59 08
  ALIENS, THE                          LEINSTER, MURRAY     AC
  OUT OF THIS WORLD  6                 WILLIAMS-ELLIS& OWEN AN
ALIENS, THE                            PAALEN, WOLFGANG    IL
  SCIENCE FICTION                      BRODKIN & PEARSON    AN
ALIENS, THE                            WELLS, BASIL        SS
  DOORWAYS TO SPACE                    WELLS, BASIL         AC
ALL                                    CAMPBELL, JOHN W. JR SN
  SPACE BEYOND, THE                    CAMPBELL, JOHN W. JR OC
ALL ABOUT "THE THING" (PARODIES TOSSED)
                                       GARRETT, RANDALL    PM   SFS 56 05
  SF:57, THE YEAR'S GREATEST SCIENCE FICTION AND FANTASY
                                       MERRIL, JUDITH       AN
ALL ADAM AGAIN                         FAIRFAX, JOHN       PM
  BEYOND THIS HORIZON                  CARRELL, CHRISTOPHER OA
ALL AT ONE POINT                       CALVINO, ITALO      SS
  COSMICOMICS                          CALVINO, ITALO       OC
ALL BUT THE WORDS                      LAFFERTY, R. A.     SS   GAL 71 07
  STRANGE DOINGS                       LAFFERTY, R. A.      AC
ALL CATS ARE GRAY (AS ANDREW NORTH)
                                       NORTON, ANDRE       SS   FUN 53 08
  MANY WORLDS OF ANDRE NORTON, THE     NORTON, ANDRE        AC
  MANY WORLDS OF SCIENCE FICTION, THE  BOVA, BEN            OA
  ZOO 2000                             YOLEN, JANE          AN
ALL DONE BY MIRRORS                    MASON, DOUGLAS R.   SS   NWR 69 16
  NEW WRITINGS IN SF. 16               CARNELL, JOHN        OA
ALL FOR LOVE (BY WAY OF MARS)          GOULART, RON        SS   WOT 65 03
  BROKE DOWN ENGINE AND OTHER TROUBLES WITH MACHINES
                                       GOULART, RON         AC
ALL GOOD BEMS                          BROWN, FREDRIC      SS   TWS 49 04
  SPACE ON MY HANDS                    BROWN, FREDRIC       AC
ALL HALLOWS                            DE LA MARE, WALTER  SS   26
  MOONLIGHT TRAVELER, THE              STERN, PHILIP VAN D. AN
ALL IN GOOD TIME                       BINDER, EANDO       SS   SAW 72
  SIGNS AND WONDERS                    ELWOOD, ROGER        OA
ALL IN GOOD TIME                       DEFORD, MIRIAM ALLEN SS  FSF 60 07
  XENOGENESIS                          DEFORD, MIRIAM ALLEN AC
ALL IN THE MIND                        CLEAVER, PAMELA     SS   ADS 75 02
  ARMADA SCI-FI TWO                    DAVIS, RICHARD       OA
ALL LACED UP                           CHANDLER, A. BERTRAM SS NWS 61 11
  PACIFIC BOOK OF AUSTRALIAN SCIENCE FICTION
                                       BAXTER, JOHN         AN
ALL LACED UP                           WHITLEY, GEORGE     SS   NWS 61 11
  LAMBDA I AND OTHER STORIES           CARNELL, JOHN        AN
ALL MAD, EXCEPT ME                     BURKE, JONATHAN F.  SS
  EXODUS FROM ELYSIUM                  BURKE, JONATHAN F.   AC
ALL MY YESTERDAYS                      BRODERICK, DAMIEN   SS   65
  PACIFIC BOOK OF AUSTRALIAN SCIENCE FICTION
                                       BAXTER, JOHN         AN
ALL OF THEM WERE EMPTY                 GERROLD, DAVID      SS   NEW 72 AC
  GENERATION                           GERROLD, DAVID       OA
  WITH A FINGER IN MY I                GERROLD, DAVID       AC
ALL OF US ARE DYING                    JOHNSON, GEORGE C.  SS   ROG 61 10
  SF: AUTHORS' CHOICE 4                HARRISON, HARRY      AN
ALL ON A GOLDEN AFTERNOON              BLOCH, ROBERT       NV   FSF 56 06
  *BLOOD RUNS COLD                     BLOCH, ROBERT        AC
ALL OUR YESTERDAYS (JEAN LISETTE AROESTE)
                                       BLISH, JAMES        SA   STK 71 04
  STAR TREK  4                         BLISH, JAMES         OC
ALL PIECES OF A RIVER SHORE            LAFFERTY, R. A.     SS   ORB 70 08
  ALPHA 4                              SILVERBERG, ROBERT   AN
  ORBIT  8                             KNIGHT, DAMON        OA
  1972 ANNUAL WORLD'S BEST SF, THE     WOLLHEIM, DONALD A.  AN
ALL POSSIBLE WORLDS                    JANIFER, LAURENCE M. SS
  BEYOND TIME                          LEY, SANDRA          OA
ALL ROADS                              FARNSWORTH, MONA    SS   UNK 40 08
  EDITOR'S CHOICE IN SCIENCE FICTION   MOSKOWITZ, SAM       AN
ALL SUMMER IN A DAY                    BRADBURY, RAY       SS   FSF 54 03
  BEST FROM FANTASY AND SCIENCE FICTION:  4
                                       BOUCHER, ANTHONY     AN
    MEDICINE FOR MELANCHOLY, A         BRADBURY, RAY        AC
    SPACE OPERA                        ALDISS, BRIAN W.     AN
    TOMORROW'S CHILDREN                ASIMOV, ISAAC        AN
    VOYAGES: SCENARIOS FOR A SHIP CALLED EARTH
                                       SAUER, ROB           AN
  YOU AND SCIENCE FICTION              HOLLISTER, BERNARD C AN
ALL THAT GLITTERS                      DE CAMP, L. SPRAGUE
    AND PRATT, FLETCHER                             SS C NEW 53 AC
  TALES FROM GAVAGAN'S BAR             DE CAMP, L. S.&PRATT AC
ALL THAT GLITTERS (VENTURE TO THE MOON)
                                       CLARKE, ARTHUR C.        FSF 57 01
  OTHER SIDE OF THE SKY, THE           CLARKE, ARTHUR C.    AC
ALL THAT MONEY CAN BUY (THE DEVIL AND DANIEL WEBSTER)
                                       BENET, STEPHEN V.   NV   SEP 36 10
  GHOULS, THE                          HAINING, PETER       AN
ALL THE BRIDGES RUSTING                NIVEN, LARRY        NV   VTX 73 08
  HOLE IN SPACE, A                     NIVEN, LARRY         AC
ALL THE COLORS OF THE RAINBOW          BRACKETT, LEIGH     SS   VSF 57 11
  HALFLING AND OTHER STORIES, THE      BRACKETT, LEIGH      AC
  HUMAN AND OTHER BEINGS               DEGRAEFF, ALLEN      AN
  NO LIMITS                            FERMAN, JOSEPH W.    AN
ALL THE KINDS OF YES (FILOMENA & GREG & RIKKI-TIKKI & BARLOW &
  THE ALIEN)                           TIPTREE, JAMES JR.  NV   NDM 72 02
  WARM WORLDS AND OTHERWISE            TIPTREE, JAMES JR.   AC
ALL THE KING'S HORSES                  VONNEGUT, KURT JR.  SS   COL 51 02
  CANARY IN A CAT HOUSE                VONNEGUT, KURT JR.   AC
  WELCOME TO THE MONKEY HOUSE          VONNEGUT, KURT JR.   AC
ALL THE KING'S MEN                     BAYLEY, BARRINGTON J NV NWS 65 03
  BEST OF NEW WORLDS, THE              MOORCOCK, MICHAEL    AN
  BEST SF STORIES FROM NEW WORLDS 7    MOORCOCK, MICHAEL    AN
  ENGLAND SWINGS SF                    MERRIL, JUDITH       AN
ALL THE LAST WARS AT ONCE             EFFINGER, GEO. ALEC SS  UNI 71 01
  BEST SCIENCE FICTION OF THE YEAR, THE CARR, TERRY         AN
  INTRODUCTORY PSYCHOLOGY THROUGH SCIENCE FICTION
                                       KATZ/WARRICK/&       AN
  MIXED FEELINGS                       EFFINGER, GEO. ALEC  AC
  UNIVERSE 1                           CARR, TERRY          OA
  WINDOWS INTO TOMORROW                SILVERBERG, ROBERT   AN
ALL THE LOVING ANDROIDS                VAN VOGT, A. E.     NV   NEW 71 AC
  MORE THAN SUPERHUMAN                 VAN VOGT, A. E.      AC
ALL THE MYRIAD WAYS                    NIVEN, LARRY        SS   GAL 68 10
  ALL THE MYRIAD WAYS                  NIVEN, LARRY         AC
  WORLDS OF MAYBE                      SILVERBERG, ROBERT   AN
ALL THE PEOPLE                         LAFFERTY, R. A.     SS   GAL 61 04
  NINE HUNDRED GRANDMOTHERS            LAFFERTY, R. A.      AC
  STRANGE GIFTS                        SILVERBERG, ROBERT   AN
ALL THE SOUNDS OF FEAR                 ELLISON, HARLAN     SS   SDM 62 07
  ALONE AGAINST TOMORROW               ELLISON, HARLAN      AC
  ELLISON WONDERLAND                   ELLISON, HARLAN      AC
  *LOVE AIN'T NOTHING BUT SEX MISSPELLED ELLISON, HARLAN    AC
  8TH ANNUAL OF THE YEAR'S BEST S-F, THE MERRIL, JUDITH     AN
ALL THE SOUNDS OF THE RAINBOW          SPINRAD, NORMAN     NV   VTX 73 06
  NO DIRECTION HOME                    SPINRAD, NORMAN      AC
ALL THE TEA IN CHINA                   BRETNOR, REGINALD   SS   FSF 61 05
  7TH ANNUAL OF THE YEAR'S BEST S-F, THE MERRIL, JUDITH     AN
ALL THE THINGS YOU ARE                 SHECKLEY, ROBERT    SS   GAL 56 07
  PILGRIMAGE TO EARTH                  SHECKLEY, ROBERT     AC
ALL THE TIME IN THE WORLD              CLARKE, ARTHUR C.   SS   STS 52 07
  OF TIME AND STARS                    CLARKE, ARTHUR C.    AC
  OTHER SIDE OF THE SKY, THE           CLARKE, ARTHUR C.    AC
  PRIZE SCIENCE FICTION                WOLLHEIM, DONALD A.  AN
  TALES OF TIME AND SPACE              OLNEY, ROSS R.       AN
ALL THE TRAPS OF EARTH                 SIMAK, CLIFFORD D.  SS   FSF 60 03
  *ALL THE TRAPS OF EARTH AND OTHER STORIES SIMAK, CLIFFORD D. AC
  BEST SCIENCE FICTION STORIES OF CLIFFORD D. SIMAK
                                       SIMAK, CLIFFORD D.   AC
ALL THE TROUBLES OF THE WORLD          ASIMOV, ISAAC       SS   SUP 58 04
  FUTURE NOW, THE                      HOSKINS, ROBERT      AN
  IF THIS GOES ON                      NUETZEL, CHARLES     AN
  NINE TOMORROWS                       ASIMOV, ISAAC        AC
  OUT OF THIS WORLD  6                 WILLIAMS-ELLIS& OWEN AN
ALL THE WAY BACK                       SHAARA, MICHAEL     SS   ASF 52 07
  GALACTIC EMPIRES VOLUME ONE          ALDISS, BRIAN W.     AN
ALL THE WAY UP, ALL THE WAY DOWN
                                       SILVERBERG, ROBERT  NV   GAL 71 07
                                       SILVERBERG, ROBERT   NO
  WORLD INSIDE, THE                    SILVERBERG, ROBERT   NO
ALL THE WORLD'S TEARS                  ALDISS, BRIAN W.    SS   NEB 57 05
  BOOK OF BRIAN ALDISS, THE            ALDISS, BRIAN W.     AC
  CANOPY OF TIME, THE                  ALDISS, BRIAN W.     AC
  GALAXIES LIKE GRAINS OF SAND         ALDISS, BRIAN W.     AC
ALL THOSE ENDURING OLD CHARMS          ALDISS, BRIAN W.    SS   NWR 74 23
  NEW WRITINGS IN SF. 23               BULMER, KENNETH      OA
ALL WATCHED OVER BY MACHINES OF LOVING GRACE
                                       BRAUTIGAN, RICHARD  PM   68
  INSIDE INFORMATION                   MOWSHOWITZ, ABBE     AN
  SCIENCE FACT/FICTION                 FARRELL/GAGE/&       AN
ALL WE HAVE ON THIS PLANET             VAN VOGT, A. E.     SS
  BEST OF A. E. VAN VOGT, THE          VAN VOGT, A. E.      AC
  STOPWATCH                            HAY, GEORGE          OA
ALL YOU CAN EAT                        BILKER, AUDREY L.
    AND BILKER, HARVEY L.                            NV C COI 73
  CHILDREN OF INFINITY                 ELWOOD, ROGER        OA
ALL YOU ZOMBIES—                       HEINLEIN, ROBERT A. SS   FSF 59 03
  AS TOMORROW BECOMES TODAY            SULLIVAN, CHARLES W. AN
  BEST FROM FANTASY AND SCIENCE FICTION: 9
                                       MILLS, ROBERT P.     AN
  BEST OF ROBERT HEINLEIN, THE         HEINLEIN, ROBERT A.  AC
  MIRROR OF INFINITY, THE              SILVERBERG, ROBERT   AN
  SURVIVAL PRINTOUT                    TOTAL EFFECT         AN
  UNPLEASANT PROFESSION OF JONATHAN HOAG, THE
                                       HEINLEIN, ROBERT A.  AC
  WORLDS OF SCIENCE FICTION, THE       MILLS, ROBERT P.     AN
ALLAMAGOOSA                            RUSSELL, ERIC FRANK SS   ASF 55 05
  FAR STARS                            RUSSELL, ERIC FRANK  AC
  GREAT STORIES OF SPACE TRAVEL        CONKLIN, GROFF       AN
  HUGO WINNERS, THE (VOLUME 1)         ASIMOV, ISAAC        AN
```

ALLAMAGOOSA

SECOND ORBIT — DOHERTY, G. D. — AN
TALES OF SCIENCE FICTION — BALL, BRIAN N. — AN
ALLEGIANCES — BISHOP, MICHAEL — NA — GAL 75 02
BEST FROM GALAXY, THE   VOLUME IV — BAEN, JAMES — AN
1976 ANNUAL WORLD'S BEST SF, THE — WOLLHEIM, DONALD A. — AN
ALLEGORY — POWERS, WILLIAM T. — SS — ASF 53 04
13 GREAT STORIES OF SCIENCE FICTION — CONKLIN, GROFF — AN
ALLERGORKHOY-KHORKHOV (THE MONSTROUS WORM) — YEFREMOV, IVAN — SS
MEETING OVER TUSCARORA AND OTHER ADVENTURE TALES, A — YEFREMOV, IVAN — AC
ALLEY MAN, THE — FARMER, PHILIP JOSE — NV — FSF 59 06
ALLEY GOD, THE — FARMER, PHILIP JOSE — AC
BOOK OF PHILIP JOSE FARMER, THE — FARMER, PHILIP JOSE — AC
ALLIGATOR WALKING LINE — STEINBERG, SAUL — CT — 60
MATHEMATICAL MAGPIE, THE — FADIMAN, CLIFTON — AN
ALLISON, CARMICHAEL AND TATTERSALL — TALL, STEPHEN — NV — GAL 70 04
BEST FROM GALAXY, THE   VOLUME I — GALAXY, EDITORS OF — AN
ALLOWANCES — MALZBERG, BARRY N. — SS — GEN 72 08
OUT FROM GANYMEDE — MALZBERG, BARRY N. — AC
ALMOST EMPTY ROOMS, THE — SHIRLEY, JOHN — NV — NDM 77 07
NEW DIMENSIONS 7 — SILVERBERG, ROBERT — OA
ALMOST HUMAN (AS TARLETON FISKE) — BLOCH, ROBERT — SS — FAD 43 06
HISTORY OF THE SCIENCE FICTION MAGAZINE, THE   PART 2 1936-1945 — ASHLEY, MICHAEL — AN
INVASION OF THE ROBOTS — ELWOOD, ROGER — AN
*MY BEST SCIENCE FICTION STORY — MARGULIES & FRIEND — AN
ALMOST THE END OF THE WORLD — BRADBURY, RAY — SS — REP 57 12
DAY IT RAINED FOREVER, THE — BRADBURY, RAY — AC
MACHINERIES OF JOY, THE — BRADBURY, RAY — AC
ALMUSSEN'S COMET (THE SEVEN SLEEPERS) — BARNES, ARTHUR K. — NV — TWS 40 05
INTERPLANETARY HUNTER — BARNES, ARTHUR K. — AC
ALONE AT LAST — SHECKLEY, ROBERT — SS — INF 57 02
SHARDS OF SPACE — SHECKLEY, ROBERT — AC
ALONE IN SPACE — TOFTE, ARTHUR — SS — SFT 73
SCIENCE FICTION TALES — ELWOOD, ROGER — OA
ALONG THE SCENIC ROUTE (DOGFIGHT ON 101) — ELLISON, HARLAN — SS — AMZ 69 09
BEAST THAT SHOUTED LOVE AT THE HEART OF THE WORLD, THE — ELLISON, HARLAN — AC
DEATHBIRD STORIES — ELLISON, HARLAN — AC
ALOYS — LAFFERTY, R. A. — SS — GAL 61 08
STRANGE DOINGS — LAFFERTY, R. A. — AC
ALPHA IN OMEGA — STONES, JONATHAN — SS
AD 2500 — WILSON, ANGUS — AN
ALPHA RALPHA BOULEVARD — SMITH, CORDWAINER — NV — FSF 61 06
*BEST FROM FANTASY AND SCIENCE FICTION: 11 — MILLS, ROBERT P. — AN
BEST OF CORDWAINER SMITH, THE — SMITH, CORDWAINER — AC
ENDS OF TIME, THE — SILVERBERG, ROBERT — AN
YOU WILL NEVER BE THE SAME — SMITH, CORDWAINER — AC
ALTAR AT MIDNIGHT, THE — KORNBLUTH, C. M. — SS — GAL 52 11
BEST OF C. M. KORNBLUTH, THE — KORNBLUTH, C. M. — AC
BEST SCIENCE FICTION STORIES OF C. M. KORNBLUTH — KORNBLUTH, C. M. — AC
BEST SF 2 — CRISPIN, EDMUND — AN
EXPLORERS, THE — KORNBLUTH, C. M. — AC
FIFTY SHORT SCIENCE FICTION TALES — ASIMOV & CONKLIN — AN
MINDWORM AND OTHER STORIES, THE — KORNBLUTH, C. M. — AC
PRIZE SCIENCE FICTION — WOLLHEIM, DONALD A. — AN
SPECULATIONS — SANDERS, THOMAS E. — AN
ALTAR EGOES — SHAW, BOB — SS
BEYOND THIS HORIZON — CARRELL, CHRISTOPHER — OA
ALTAR OF ASCONEL — BRUNNER, JOHN — NO — IFS 65 04
INTERSTELLAR EMPIRE — BRUNNER, JOHN — AC
ALTAR OF THE RANDOM GODS, THE — ROGOZ, ADRIAN — SS
VIEW FROM ANOTHER SHORE — ROTTENSTEINER, FRANZ — AN
ALTAR, THE — SHECKLEY, ROBERT — SS — FAN 53 08
*UNTOUCHED BY HUMAN HANDS — SHECKLEY, ROBERT — AC
ALTARBOY — KOONTZ, DEAN R. — SS — INY 72 03
INFINITY 3 — HOSKINS, ROBERT — OA
ALTER EGO — CORREA, HUGO — SS — FSF 67 07
INTRODUCTORY PSYCHOLOGY THROUGH SCIENCE FICTION — KATZ/WARRICK/& — AN
ALTERNATE UNIVERSE I — DISCH, THOMAS M. — PM
BEYOND TIME — LEY, SANDRA — OA
ALTERNATE UNIVERSE II — DISCH, THOMAS M. — PM
BEYOND TIME — LEY, SANDRA — OA
ALTERNATE UNIVERSE III — DISCH, THOMAS M. — PM
BEYOND TIME — LEY, SANDRA — OA
ALTERNATES, THE — GIRARD, JAMES P. — NV — NDM 76 06
NEW DIMENSIONS 6 — SILVERBERG, ROBERT — OA
ALTERNATIVE FACTOR, THE (DON INGALLS) — BLISH, JAMES — SA — STK 74 10
STAR TREK 10 — BLISH, JAMES — OC
ALTERNATIVE FUTURES: THE PRESENT AS FUTURE — ALLEN, DICK — SI
SCIENCE FICTION: THE FUTURE — ALLEN, DICK — AN
ALTERNATIVE, THE — BARING, MAURICE — SS — 25
TRAVELERS IN TIME — STERN, PHILIP VAN D. — AN
ALTRUISTS, THE — SEABRIGHT, IDRIS — SS — FSF 53 11
PORTALS OF TOMORROW — DERLETH, AUGUST — AN
ALTRUISTS, THE — ST. CLAIR, MARGARET — SS — FSF 53 11
CHANGE THE SKY AND OTHER STORIES — ST. CLAIR, MARGARET — AC
ALTRUIZINE — LEM, STANISLAW — NV
CYBERIAD, THE — LEM, STANISLAW — OC
ALWAYS SOMEBODY THERE — ALDISS, BRIAN W. — SS
TOMORROW: NEW WORLDS OF SCIENCE FICTION — ELWOOD, ROGER — OA
AMATEUR IN CHANCERY — SMITH, GEORGE O. — SS — GAL 61 10
EXPERT DREAMERS, THE — POHL, FREDERIK — AN
AMAZING MRS. MIMMS, THE — KNIGHT, DAVID C. — SS — FUN 58 08
FANTASTIC UNIVERSE OMNIBUS, THE — SANTESSON, HANS S. — AN

ANCIENT BRAIN, THE

AMAZING PLANET, THE — SMITH, CLARK ASHTON — NV — WSQ 31 SU
OTHER DIMENSIONS — SMITH, CLARK ASHTON — AC
AMAZON KICK, THE — NOLAN, WILLIAM F. — SS — ROG 59
IMPACT-20 — NOLAN, WILLIAM F. — AC
AMAZONS, THE (500 B.C.) — HERODOTUS — AR
WHEN WOMEN RULE — MOSKOWITZ, SAM — AN
AMBASSADOR TO VERDAMMT — KAPP, COLIN — SS — ASF 67 04
WORLD'S BEST SCIENCE FICTION: 1968 — WOLLHEIM & CARR — AN
AMBASSADORS FROM VENUS, THE — CROSSEN, KENDELL F. — NV — PLS 52 03
*BEACHHEADS IN SPACE — DERLETH, AUGUST — AN
FROM OTHER WORLDS — DERLETH, AUGUST — AN
AMBASSADORS OF FLESH, THE (SEE WARRIORS FROM NOWHERE) — ANDERSON, POUL — TC
AMBASSADORS, THE — BOUCHER, ANTHONY — SS — STS 52 06
FIFTY SHORT SCIENCE FICTION TALES — ASIMOV & CONKLIN — AN
*FUTURE TENSE — CROSSEN, KENDELL F. — AN
GALAXY OF GHOULS — MERRIL, JUDITH — AN
SHAPE OF THINGS, THE — KNIGHT, DAMON — AN
AMBERGRIS ELEMENT, THE (MARGARET ARMEN) — FOSTER, ALAN DEAN — SA — SLG 75 05
STAR TREK LOG FIVE — FOSTER, ALAN DEAN — OC
AMBERJACK — TIPTREE, JAMES JR. — SS — GEN 72
GENERATION — GERROLD, DAVID — QA
WARM WORLDS AND OTHERWISE — TIPTREE, JAMES JR. — AC
AMBIENCE — SKAL, DAVE — SS — ORB 75 16
ORBIT 16 — KNIGHT, DAMON — OA
AMBIGUITIES OF YESTERDAY, THE — EKLUND, GORDON — SS
FAR SIDE OF TIME, THE — ELWOOD, ROGER — OA
AMBITION — BADE, WILLIAM L. — NV — GAL 51 10
*SCIENCE FICTION ADVENTURES IN DIMENSION — CONKLIN, GROFF — AN
AMBULANCE MADE TWO TRIPS, THE — LEINSTER, MURRAY — SS — ASF 60 04
NEVER IN THIS WORLD — STONE, IDELLA P. — AN
AMEN AND OUT — ALDISS, BRIAN W. — SS — NWS 66 08
BOOK OF BRIAN ALDISS, THE — ALDISS, BRIAN W. — AC
WORLD'S BEST SCIENCE FICTION: 1967 — WOLLHEIM & CARR — AN
AMERICA THE BEAUTIFUL — LEIBER, FRITZ — SS — YRT 70
BEST OF FRITZ LEIBER, THE — LEIBER, FRITZ — AC
LATE GREAT FUTURE, THE — FITZ GERALD & DILLON — AN
RUINS OF EARTH, THE — DISCH, THOMAS M. — AN
YEAR 2000, THE — HARRISON, HARRY — OA
AMERICAN DEAD — HARRISON, HARRY — SS — YRT 70
YEAR 2000, THE — HARRISON, HARRY — OA
AMFORTAS — JANIFER, LAURENCE M. — SS — OMG 73
OMEGA — ELWOOD, ROGER — OA
AMINIA — WHITE, EDWARD LUCAS — SS — 27
SECOND AVON FANTASY READER, THE — WOLLHEIM & ERNSBERGER — AN
AMOK TIME (THEODORE STURGEON) — BLISH, JAMES — SA — STK 69 03
STAR TREK 3 — BLISH, JAMES — OC
AMONG OTHER THINGS — MEADLEY, ROBERT — SS — NWQ 73 05
NEW WORLDS NO. 5 — MOORCOCK & PLATT — OA
AMONG THE BAD BABOONS — REYNOLDS, MACK — NV — GAL 68 08
ELEVENTH GALAXY READER, THE — POHL, FREDERIK — AN
NIGHTMARE AGE — POHL, FREDERIK — AN
AMONG THE DANGS (EXCERPT) — ELLIOTT, GEORGE P. — EX — ESQ 58 06
7TH ANNUAL OF THE YEAR'S BEST S-F, THE — MERRIL, JUDITH — AN
AMONG THE DEAD — BRYANT, EDWARD — SS — QRK 71 02
AMONG THE DEAD — BRYANT, EDWARD — AC
QUARK/2 — DELANY & HACKER — OA
AMONG THE HAIRY EARTHMEN — LAFFERTY, R. A. — SS — GAL 66 08
ANOTHER WORLD — DOZOIS, GARDNER R. — AN
EVIL EARTHS — ALDISS, BRIAN W. — AN
NEBULA AWARD STORIES NO. 2 — ALDISS & HARRISON — AN
AMONG THE METAL-AND-PEOPLE PEOPLE — BUNCH, DAVID R. — SS — NDM 74 04
NEW DIMENSIONS 4 — SILVERBERG, ROBERT — OA
AMONG THE MOUNTAINS — DANN, JACK M. — NV
WORLD NAMED CLEOPATRA, A — ANDERSON, POUL — OA
AMONG THIEVES — ANDERSON, POUL — NV — ASF 57 06
STRANGERS FROM EARTH — ANDERSON, POUL — AC
AMOS KILBRIGHT: HIS ADSCITITIOUS EXPERIENCES — STOCKTON, FRANK R. — NA — AMR 88 04
SCIENCE FICTION OF FRANK R. STOCKTON, THE — STOCKTON, FRANK R. — AC
AMULET, THE — DICKSON, GORDON R. — SS — FSF 59 04
ROD SERLING'S TRIPLE W: WITCHES, WARLOCKS AND WEREWOLVES — SERLING, ROD — AN
AMUSED VISITOR — STEPHENS, JOHN — SS — NEW 68 04
FLYING SAUCERS IN FACT AND FICTION — SANTESSON, HANS S. — AN
ANACHRON — KNIGHT, DAMON — SS — IFS 54 01
BEST OF DAMON KNIGHT, THE — KNIGHT, DAMON — AC
FAR OUT — KNIGHT, DAMON — AC
ANACONDA — THURSTON, ROBERT — SS — CLR 71 01
CLARION — WILSON, ROBIN SCOTT — OA
ANALOG 1 — CAMPBELL, JOHN W. JR — AN — DBL 63
ANALOG ANTHOLOGY — CAMPBELL, JOHN W. JR — AN
ANALOG 2 — CAMPBELL, JOHN W. JR — AN — DBL 64
ANALOG ANTHOLOGY — CAMPBELL, JOHN W. JR — AN
ANALOGUES, THE — KNIGHT, DAMON — SS — ASF 52 01
BEST OF DAMON KNIGHT, THE — KNIGHT, DAMON — AC
VINTAGE ANTHOLOGY OF SCIENCE FANTASY, THE — CERF, CHRISTOPHER — AN
13 GREAT STORIES OF SCIENCE FICTION — CONKLIN, GROFF — AN
ANARCHIST: OR, THE DOOM OF THE GREAT CITY, THE — FAWCETT, DOUGLAS — SS
WORLDS APART — WILLIAMS-ELLIS & OWEN — AN
ANCESTOR, THE — DERLETH, AUGUST
AND LOVECRAFT, H. P. — SS C
FANTASY: THE LITERATURE OF THE MARVELOUS — KELLEY, LEO P. — AN
SURVIVOR AND OTHER STORIES, THE — LOVECRAFT & DERLETH — AC
ANCESTRAL AMETHYST, THE — DE CAMP, L. SPRAGUE
AND PRATT, FLETCHER — SS C — FSF 52 08
TALES FROM GAVAGAN'S BAR — DE CAMP, L. S. & PRATT — AC
ANCIENT BRAIN, THE — STANGLAND, A. G. — SS — SWS 29 10
FROM OFF THIS WORLD — MARGULIES & FRIEND — AN

ANCIENT GODS, THE (SEE WORLD WITHOUT STARS)
    ANDERSON, POUL   TC
ANCIENT GULLIVER, AN (FROM "A TRUE HISTORY",165AD)
    LUCIAN OF SAMOSATA   EX
  SCIENCE IN FICTION   BAYLISS, A.E. & J.C. AN
ANCIENT MADNESS, AN (ALSO AS MARY)
    KNIGHT, DAMON   NV GAL 64 06
  NINTH GALAXY READER, THE   POHL, FREDERIK   AN
ANCIENT SHADOWS MOORCOCK, MICHAEL NV NWB 75 09
  LEGENDS FROM THE END OF TIME MOORCOCK, MICHAEL AC
  NEW WORLDS NINE   BAILEY, HILARY   OA
ANCIENT, MY ENEMY DICKSON, GORDON R. NV IFS 69 12
  ANCIENT, MY ENEMY   DICKSON, GORDON R.   AC
AND A LITTLE CHILD- HENDERSON, ZENNA SS FSF 59 10
  ANYTHING BOX, THE   HENDERSON, ZENNA   AC
AND A STAR TO STEER HER BY CORREY, LEE NV ASF 53 06
  EVERY BOY'S BOOK OF OUTER SPACE STORIES DIKTY, T. E. AN
AND ADAM BEGOT   OBOLER, ARCH   SS   42
  OUT OF THIS WORLD   FAST, JULIUS   AN
AND ALL THE EARTH A GRAVE MACAPP, C. C. SS GAL 63 12
  EIGHTH GALAXY READER, THE POHL, FREDERIK   AN
AND BE MERRY... (ALSO AS THE PYRAMID IN THE DESERT)
    MACLEAN, KATHERINE SS ASF 50 02
  OMNIBUS OF SCIENCE FICTION CONKLIN, GROFF   AN
  SCIENCE FICTION: THE GREAT YEARS, VOL. II
    POHL, C. & F.   AN
  TOWARD INFINITY   KNIGHT, DAMON   AN
AND DEATH ONCE DEAD PUMILIA, JOSEPH F. SS
  LONE STAR UNIVERSE PROCTOR & UTLEY   OA
AND DON'T FORGET THE ONE RED ROSE
    DAVIDSON, AVRAM SS PBY 75 09
  YEAR'S BEST HORROR STORIES: SERIES IV, THE
    PAGE, GERALD W.   AN
AND DRAGONS IN THE SKY COOK, GLEN NV CLR 72 02
  CLARION II   WILSON, ROBIN SCOTT OA
AND DUG THE DOG A TOMB JAMES, LAURENCE SS NWQ 72 03
  NEW WORLDS QUARTERLY NO. 3 MOORCOCK, MICHAEL OA
AND HE BUILT A CROOKED HOUSE HEINLEIN, ROBERT A. SS ASF 41 02
  AS TOMORROW BECOMES TODAY SULLIVAN, CHARLES W. AN
  BEST OF ROBERT HEINLEIN, THE HEINLEIN, ROBERT A. AC
  FANTASIA MATHEMATICA FADIMAN, CLIFTON   AN
  INTRODUCTORY PSYCHOLOGY THROUGH SCIENCE FICTION
    KATZ/WARRICK/&   AN
  OTHER DIMENSIONS SILVERBERG, ROBERT AN
  OTHER SIDE OF THE CLOCK, THE STERN, PHILIP VAN D. AN
  POCKET BOOK OF SCIENCE-FICTION, THE WOLLHEIM, DONALD A. AN
  SCIENCE FICTION BRODKIN & PEARSON AN
  TIME PROBE: THE SCIENCES IN SF. CLARKE, ARTHUR C. AN
  UNPLEASANT PROFESSION OF JONATHAN HOAG, THE
    HEINLEIN, ROBERT A. AC
  WHERE DO WE GO FROM HERE? ASIMOV, ISAAC AN
AND I AWOKE AND FOUND ME HERE ON THE COLD HILL'S SIDE
    TIPTREE, JAMES JR. SS FSF 72 03
  SPACE ODYSSEYS ALDISS, BRIAN W. AN
  TEN THOUSAND LIGHT-YEARS FROM HOME TIPTREE, JAMES JR. AC
AND I FOR AN EYE STEVENS, JAMES· SS
  2076: THE AMERICAN TRICENTENNIAL BRYANT, EDWARD OA
AND I HAVE COME UPON THIS PLACE BY LOST WAYS
    TIPTREE, JAMES JR. NV NOV 72 02
  NEW AWARENESS, THE WARRICK & GREENBERG AN
  NOVA 2   HARRISON, HARRY OA
  WARM WORLDS AND OTHERWISE TIPTREE, JAMES JR. AC
AND ISLES WHERE GOOD MEN LIE SHAW, BOB SS NWS 65 10
  TOMORROW LIES IN AMBUSH SHAW, BOB AC
AND IT COMES OUT HERE DEL REY, LESTER SS GAL 51 02
  MORTALS AND MONSTERS DEL REY, LESTER AC
  OTHER SIDE OF THE CLOCK, THE STERN, PHILIP VAN D. AN
  *SCIENCE FICTION ADVENTURES IN DIMENSION CONKLIN, GROFF AN
  VOYAGERS IN TIME SILVERBERG, ROBERT AN
AND IT WILL SERVE US RIGHT ASIMOV, ISAAC AR PSY 69 04
  SCIENCE FICTION BRODKIN & PEARSON AN
AND LO! THE BIRD BOND, NELSON S. SS BBM 50 09
  EARTH IS THE STRANGEST PLANET SILVERBERG, ROBERT AN
  FAR BOUNDARIES DERLETH, AUGUST AN
  NO TIME LIKE THE FUTURE BOND, NELSON S. AC
AND MAD UNDANCING BEARS LAFFERTY, R. A. SS BER 74
  BERSERKERS, THE ELWOOD, ROGER OA
AND MADLY TEACH BIGGLE, LLOYD JR. NV FSF 66 05
  BEST FROM FANTASY AND SCIENCE FICTION: 16
    FERMAN, EDWARD L.   AN
  GALAXY OF STRANGERS, A BIGGLE, LLOYD JR. AC
AND MILES TO GO BEFORE I SLEEP NOLAN, WILLIAM F. SS INF 58 08
  IMPACT-20   NOLAN, WILLIAM F. AC
  MAN AGAINST TOMORROW NOLAN, WILLIAM F. AN
  WONDERMAKERS 2 HOSKINS, ROBERT AN
AND MORE CHANGES STILL MICHAUX, HENRI SS
  SF12   MERRIL, JUDITH   AN
AND MY FEAR IS GREAT STURGEON, THEODORE NA BEY 53 07
  THUNDER AND ROSES STURGEON, THEODORE AC
  *WAY HOME, A STURGEON, THEODORE AC
AND NAME MY NAME LAFFERTY, R. A. SS ORB 74 13
  BEST SCIENCE FICTION STORIES OF THE YEAR (1974)
    DEL REY, LESTER   AN
  ORBIT 13   KNIGHT, DAMON   OA
AND NOT QUITE HUMAN HENSLEY, JOE L. SS BEY 53 09
  ROD SERLING'S TRIPLE W: WITCHES, WARLOCKS AND WEREWOLVES
    SERLING, ROD   AN
AND NOW THE NEWS... STURGEON, THEODORE SS FSF 56 12
  BEST FROM FANTASY AND SCIENCE FICTION: 6
    BOUCHER, ANTHONY   AN
  INTRODUCTORY PSYCHOLOGY THROUGH SCIENCE FICTION
    KATZ/WARRICK/&   AN
  MASTERS' CHOICE JANIFER, LAURENCE M. AN
  SECOND ORBIT DOHERTY, G. D. AN
  TOMORROW AND TOMORROW KNIGHT, DAMON AN

VINTAGE ANTHOLOGY OF SCIENCE FANTASY, THE
    CERF, CHRISTOPHER   AN
AND NOW YOU DON'T ASIMOV, ISAAC NO ASF 49 11
  SECOND FOUNDATION ASIMOV, ISAAC NO
AND READ THE FLESH BETWEEN THE LINES
    LAFFERTY, R. A. SS UNI 74 04
  UNIVERSE 4 CARR, TERRY OA
AND SEVEN TIMES NEVER KILL MAN MARTIN, GEORGE R. R. NV ASF 75 07
  SONGS OF STARS AND SHADOWS MARTIN, GEORGE R. R. AC
AND SO DIED RIABOUCHINSKA BRADBURY, RAY SS SDM 53 06
  MACHINERIES OF JOY, THE BRADBURY, RAY AC
AND SO SAY ALL OF US MCALLISTER, BRUCE SS IFS 69 09
  WORLD'S BEST SCIENCE FICTION: 1970 WOLLHEIM & CARR AN
AND SO TO THE MOON YATES, R. F. AR
  LAURIE'S SPACE ANNUAL ANONYMOUS AN
AND SO WHITE WITCH VALLEY BUNCH, DAVID R. SS
  MODERAN BUNCH, DAVID R. AC
AND SOME WERE SAVAGES BLISH, JAMES NV AMZ 60 11
  ANYWHEN BLISH, JAMES AC
AND SOMEDAY TO MARS LONG, FRANK BELKNAP SS TWS 52 02
  EDITOR'S CHOICE IN SCIENCE FICTION MOSKOWITZ, SAM AN
AND STILL IN THE DARKNESS MALZBERG, BARRY N. SS NEW 76 AC
  BEST OF BARRY N. MALZBERG, THE MALZBERG, BARRY N. AC
AND STILL IT MOVES RUSSELL, ERIC FRANK AR ASF 57 06
  14 GREAT TALES OF ESP STONE, IDELLA P. AN
AND THE DARKNESS (OMEGA AND THE WOLF GIRL)
    DEL REY, LESTER SS OTW 50 07
  EARLY DEL REY DEL REY, LESTER AC
AND THE GODS LAUGHED BROWN, FREDRIC SS TIS 53 FL
  HONEYMOON IN HELL BROWN, FREDRIC AC
AND THE LIGHT IS RISEN MILLER, WALTER M. JR SN FSF 56 08
  CANTICLE FOR LEIBOWITZ, A MILLER, WALTER M. JR NO
AND THE MOON BE STILL AS BRIGHT
    BRADBURY, RAY SS TWS 48 06
  BEST SCIENCE-FICTION STORIES: 1949, THE BLEILER & DIKTY AN
  MARTIAN CHRONICLES, THE BRADBURY, RAY AC
AND THE POWER... PAYES, RACHEL C. SS WLK 73
  AND WALK NOW GENTLY THROUGH THE FIRE... ELWOOD, ROGER OA
AND THE ROCK CRIED OUT (THE MILLIONTH MURDER)
    BRADBURY, RAY SS MHT 53 09
  DAY IT RAINED FOREVER, THE BRADBURY, RAY AC
  FAHRENHEIT 451 BRADBURY, RAY AC
  VINTAGE BRADBURY, THE BRADBURY, RAY AC
AND THE SAILOR, HOME FROM THE SEA (FOREVER VOYAGE)
    BRADBURY, RAY SS SEP 60 01
  MACHINERIES OF JOY, THE BRADBURY, RAY AC
AND THE SEA LIKE MIRRORS BENFORD, GREGORY SS DVS 72 02
  AGAIN, DANGEROUS VISIONS ELLISON, HARLAN OA
AND THE STAGNATION OF THE HEART
    ALDISS, BRIAN W. SS NWS 68 12
  FOUR FOR THE FUTURE HARRISON, HARRY AN
  MOMENT OF ECLIPSE, THE ALDISS, BRIAN W. AC
  THIS SIDE OF INFINITY CARR, TERRY AN
AND THE TRUTH (DEAD RINGER) DEL REY, LESTER SS GAL 56 11
  MORTALS AND MONSTERS DEL REY, LESTER AC
AND THE TRUTH SHALL MAKE YOU FREE (ALSO AS THE ANSWERS)
    SIMAK, CLIFFORD D. SS FUT 53 03
  NOVELETS OF SCIENCE FICTION HOWARD, IVAN AN
AND THE WALLS CAME TUMBLING DOWN
    WYNDHAM, JOHN SS STS 51 05
  *BEACHHEADS IN SPACE DERLETH, AUGUST AN
  FROM OTHER WORLDS DERLETH, AUGUST AN
  MAN FROM BEYOND AND OTHER STORIES, THE WYNDHAM, JOHN AC
AND THE WALLS CAME TUMBLING DOWN, THE
    WYNDHAM, JOHN SS STS 51 05
  BEST OF JOHN WYNDHAM, THE WYNDHAM, JOHN AC
AND THEN SHE FOUND HIM... BUDRYS, ALGIS SS VSF 57 07
  BUDRYS' INFERNO BUDRYS, ALGIS AC
  NO LIMITS FERMAN, JOSEPH W. AN
AND THEN THE COVER WAS BARE ACKERMAN, FORREST J. S.
  SCIENCE FICTION WORLDS OF FORREST J. ACKERMAN & FRIENDS
    ACKERMAN, FORREST J. AC
AND THEN THE DARK- SALLIS, JAMES SS 69
  FEW LAST WORDS, A SALLIS, JAMES AC
AND THEN THERE WAS ONE ROCKLYNNE, ROSS SS ASF 40 02
  MEN AND THE MIRROR, THE ROCKLYNNE, ROSS AC
AND THEN THERE WAS PEACE DICKSON, GORDON R. SS IFS 62 09
  DANGER- HUMAN DICKSON, GORDON R. AC
AND THEN THERE WERE NONE RUSSELL, ERIC FRANK NV ASF 51 06
  SCIENCE FICTION HALL OF FAME VOLUME 2A BOVA, BEN AN
  SCIENCE FICTION: THE GREAT YEARS POHL, C. & F. AN
  *STORIES FOR TOMORROW SLOANE, WILLIAM AN
  YEAR'S BEST SCIENCE FICTION NOVELS: 1952 BLEILER & DIKTY AN
AND THEY'RE ALL EXACTLY TWENTY-SIX YEARS OLD
    O'NEILL, SCOTT SS
  MARTIAN SEXPOT O'NEILL, SCOTT AC
AND THIS DID DANTE DO BRADBURY, RAY SS NOV 70 01
  *NOVA 1 HARRISON, HARRY OA
AND THOU BESIDE ME REYNOLDS, MACK SS FSF 54 04
  *SCIENCE FICTION ADVENTURES IN MUTATION CONKLIN, GROFF AN
AND THREE TO GET READY GOLD, H. L. SS FAN 52 SU
  OLD DIE RICH AND OTHER SCIENCE FICTION, THE
    GOLD, H. L. AC
AND US, TOO, I GUESS EFFINGER, GEO. ALEC NA CHN 73
  CHAINS OF THE SEA SILVERBERG, ROBERT OA
  IRRATIONAL NUMBERS EFFINGER, GEO. ALEC AC
AND WALK NOW GENTLY THROUGH THE FIRE...
    LAFFERTY, R. A. NV WLK 73
  AND WALK NOW GENTLY THROUGH THE FIRE... ELWOOD, ROGER OA
AND WATCH THE SMOG ROLL IN... WEISSMAN, BARRY SS PRT 71
  PROTOSTARS GERROLD & GOLDIN OA
AND WHEN I DIE... LINNETT, PETER SS NWR 74 24
  NEW WRITINGS IN SF. 24 BULMER, KENNETH OA
AND YET SO FAR (CONDEMNED TO DEATH)
    ANDERSON, POUL SS FUN 59 10
  ORBIT UNLIMITED ANDERSON, POUL NO

ANDERSON BIBLIOGRAPHY

ANDERSON BIBLIOGRAPHY   MISC. MATERIAL   MS   FSF 71 04
  BEST FROM FANTASY AND SCIENCE FICTION, 25TH ANNIV.
                                     FERMAN, EDWARD L.   AN
ANDOVER AND THE ANDROID   WILHELM, KATE   SS   NEW 63 AC
  MILE-LONG SPACESHIP, THE   WILHELM, KATE   AC
ANDRE NORTON: LOSS OF FAITH   BROOKS, RICK   AR   DIP 71 11
  MANY WORLDS OF ANDRE NORTON, THE   NORTON, ANDRE   AC
ANDREW   GLOECKNER, CAROLYN SS   FCR 75
  FUTURE CORRUPTION   ELWOOD, ROGER   OA
ANDREW WHITE- 2028 (THE ANSWER)
                            GUNN, JAMES E.   NV   GAL 72 01
  LISTENERS, THE   GUNN, JAMES E.   NO
ANDROID (ALSO AS THOSE AMONG US)
                            KUTTNER, HENRY   NV   FSF 51 06
  RETURN TO OTHERNESS   KUTTNER, HENRY   AC
ANDROIDS DON'T CRY   WELLEN, EDWARD   SS   FSF 73 05
  BEST SCIENCE FICTION STORIES OF THE YEAR (1973)
                            DEL REY, LESTER   AN
ANGEL FIX   SHELDON, RACCOONA   NV   IFS 74 08
  BEST FROM IF, THE VOLUME III   BAEN, JAMES   AN
ANGEL OF TRUTH   EKLUND, GORDON   NV   EPC 75
  EPOCH   ELWOOD & SILVERBERG   OA
ANGEL WAS A YANKEE, THE   BENET, STEPHEN V.   SS   MCL 40 10
  *BEYOND HUMAN KEN   MERRIL, JUDITH   AN
ANGEL WITH PURPLE HAIR, THE PAUL, HERB   SS   FSF 50 12
  SUPERNATURAL READER, THE   CONKLIN, G&L.   AN
ANGEL'S EGG   PANGBORN, EDGAR   NV   GAL 51 06
  ALPHA 4   SILVERBERG, ROBERT   AN
  BEST SF 2   CRISPIN, EDMUND   AN
  CENTURY OF SCIENCE FICTION, A   KNIGHT, DAMON   AN
  ENEMIES IN SPACE   CONKLIN, GROFF   AN
  GOOD NEIGHBORS AND OTHER STRANGERS PANGBORN, EDGAR   AC
  *INVADERS OF EARTH   CONKLIN, GROFF   AN
ANGEL, DARK ANGEL   ZELAZNY, ROGER   SS   GAL 67 08
  FAR-OUT PEOPLE, THE   HOSKINS, ROBERT   AN
ANGELA'S SATYR   CLEEVE, BRIAN   SS   SEP 62 11
  8TH ANNUAL OF THE YEAR'S BEST S-F, THE MERRIL, JUDITH   AN
ANGELIC ANGLEWORM, THE   BROWN, FREDRIC   NV   UNK 43 02
  ANGELS AND SPACESHIPS   BROWN, FREDRIC   AC
  DAYMARES   BROWN, FREDRIC   AC
ANGELS IN THE JETS   BIXBY, JEROME   SS   FAN 52 FL
  ASSIGNMENT IN TOMORROW   POHL, FREDERIK   AN
  BEST FROM FANTASTIC, THE   WHITE, TED   AN
  SPACE BY THE TAIL   BIXBY, JEROME   AC
ANGELS UNAWARES   HENDERSON, ZENNA   NV   FSF 66 03
  PEOPLE: NO DIFFERENT FLESH, THE HENDERSON, ZENNA   AC
ANGERHELM   SMITH, CORDWAINER   NV   STR 59 06
  STAR SCIENCE FICTION STORIES NO. 6 POHL, FREDERIK   OA
  STARDREAMER   SMITH, CORDWAINER   AC
ANGOULEME   DISCH, THOMAS M.   SS   NWQ 71 01
  BEST SF: 1971   HARRISON & ALDISS   AN
  NEW WORLDS QUARTERLY NO. 1   MOORCOCK, MICHAEL   OA
  334   DISCH, THOMAS M.   NO
ANGUS MACAULIFFE AND THE GOWDEN TOOCH
                            TANNER, CHARLES R.   SS   OWS 51 03
  SUPERNATURAL READER, THE   CONKLIN, G&L.   AN
ANIMAL   EMSHWILLER, CAROL   SS   ORB 68 04
  JOY IN OUR CAUSE   EMSHWILLER, CAROL   AC
  ORBIT 4   KNIGHT, DAMON   OA
ANIMAL FAIR   LAFFERTY, R. A.   NV   NDM 74 04
  NEW DIMENSIONS 4   SILVERBERG, ROBERT   OA
ANIMAL FAIR, THE   BESTER, ALFRED   NV   FSF 72 10
  BEST FROM FANTASY AND SCIENCE FICTION: 20
                            FERMAN, EDWARD L.   AN
ANIMAL FAIR, THE   BLOCH, ROBERT   SS   PBY 71 05
  COLD CHILLS   BLOCH, ROBERT   AC
  YEAR'S BEST HORROR STORIES: SERIES II, THE
                            DAVIS, RICHARD   AN
ANIMAL-CRACKER PLOT, THE   DE CAMP, L. SPRAGUE SS   ASF 49 07
  CONTINENT MAKERS AND OTHER TALES OF THE VIAGENS
                            DE CAMP, L. SPRAGUE   AC
ANIMAL, THE   STEPHENS, ROSEMARY   SS
  UNIVERSE AHEAD   ENGDAHL & ROBERSON   AN
ANIMALS IN THE CASE, THE   WAKEFIELD, H. RUSSELL SS   62
  SATAN'S PETS   GHIDALIA, VIC   AN
ANIMATORS, THE   BOUNDS, SYDNEY J.   SS   NEW 75 AN
  TALES OF TERROR FROM OUTER SPACE CHETWYND-HAYES, R.   AN
ANNE   TUBB, E. C.   SS   NWS 66 01
  SCATTER OF STARDUST, A   TUBB, E. C.   DC
ANNEX, THE   MACDONALD, JOHN D.   SS   PBY 68 05
  BEST SF: 1968   HARRISON & ALDISS   AN
  LATE GREAT FUTURE, THE   FITZ GERALD & DILLON   AN
  PLAYBOY'S STORIES OF THE SINISTER & STRANGE
                            PLAYBOY, EDITORS OF   AN
ANNIE MAE: A LOVE STORY   O'NEIL, DENNIS   SS
  FAR SIDE OF TIME, THE   ELWOOD, ROGER   OA
ANNIVERSARY   ASIMOV, ISAAC   SS   AMZ 59 03
  ASIMOV'S MYSTERIES   ASIMOV, ISAAC   AC
  BEST OF AMAZING, THE   ROSS, JOSEPH   AN
  BEST OF ISAAC ASIMOV, THE   ASIMOV, ISAAC   AC
ANNOTATED "MASKS", A   KNIGHT, DAMON   SS   PBY 68 07
  THOSE WHO CAN: A SCIENCE FICTION READER WILSON, ROBIN SCOTT AN
ANOMALY OF THE EMPTY MAN, THE BOUCHER, ANTHONY SS   FSF 52 04
  FAR AND AWAY   BOUCHER, ANTHONY   AC
  SCIENCE-FICTIONAL SHERLOCK HOLMES, THE COUNCIL OF FOUR   AN
ANOTHER ANTIGONE   MORRISON, D. A. C.   SS
  AD 2500   WILSON, ANGUS   AN
ANOTHER CASK OF WINE   LEIBER, FRITZ   SS   INY 72 04
  INFINITY 4   HOSKINS, ROBERT   OA
ANOTHER LITTLE BOY   ALDISS, BRIAN W.   SS   NWS 66 09
  BEST SCIENCE FICTION STORIES OF BRIAN W. ALDISS (REVISED)
                            ALDISS, BRIAN W.   AC
  BEST SF STORIES FROM NEW WORLDS NO. 2, THE
                            MOORCOCK, MICHAEL   AN
ANOTHER WORD FOR MAN   PRESSLIE, ROBERT   SS   NWS 58 12
  BEST OF NEW WORLDS, THE   MOORCOCK, MICHAEL   AN

APE AND THE MYSTERY, THE (THE MYSTERIOUS MONA LISA SMILE)

  OUT OF THIS WORLD 2   WILLIAMS-ELLIS& OWEN   AN
ANOTHER WORLD (1895)   ROSNY, J. H. (AINE) NV   RVP 95
  CENTURY OF SCIENCE FICTION, A   KNIGHT, DAMON   AN
ANOTHER WORLD BEGINS (SEE THE CUNNING OF THE BEAST)
                            BOND, NELSON S.   TC
ANSWER   BROWN, FREDRIC   SS   NEW 54 AC
  ANGELS AND SPACESHIPS   BROWN, FREDRIC   AC
  BEST OF FREDRIC BROWN, THE   BROWN, FREDRIC   AC
  BEST SF 3   CRISPIN, EDMUND   AN
  INSIDE INFORMATION   MOWSHOWITZ, ABBE   AN
  METAL SMILE, THE   KNIGHT, DAMON   AN
  STARS AND UNDER, THE   CRISPIN, EDMUND   AN
ANSWER   CLEMENT, HAL   SS   ASF 47 04
  *SCIENCE FICTION THINKING MACHINES CONKLIN, GROFF   AN
ANSWER "AFFIRMATIVE" OR "NEGATIVE"
                            PAUL, BARBARA   SS   ASF 72 04
  ANALOG 9   BOVA, BEN   AN
ANSWER CAME THERE NONE   WHITE, JAMES   SS   GAL 74 01
  BEST FROM GALAXY, THE VOLUME III BAEN, JAMES   AN
  MONSTERS AND MEDICS   WHITE, JAMES   AC
ANSWER, THE   CARR, TERRY   SS   TAL 73
  FRONTIERS 1; TOMORROW'S ALTERNATIVES ELWOOD, ROGER   OA
ANSWER, THE   PETAJA, EMIL   SS   IMG 51 09
  STARDRIFT AND OTHER FANTASTIC FLOTSAM PETAJA, EMIL   AC
ANSWER, THE   WYLIE, PHILIP   NV   SEP 55 05
  POST READER OF FANTASY AND SCIENCE FICTION
                            SATURDAY EVE. POST   AN
ANSWER, THE (SEE ANDREW WHITE- 2028)
                            GUNN, JAMES E.   TC
ANSWERING SERVICE   LEIBER, FRITZ   SS   IFS 67 12
  BEST SF: 1967   HARRISON & ALDISS   AN
ANSWERS, THE (AND THE TRUTH SHALL MAKE YOU FREE)
                            SIMAK, CLIFFORD D.   SS   FUT 53 03
  *STORIES FOR TOMORROW   SLOANE, WILLIAM   AN
  *STRANGERS IN THE UNIVERSE   SIMAK, CLIFFORD D.   AC
ANT AND THE EYE, THE   OLIVER, CHAD   NV   ASF 53 04
  EDGE OF FOREVER, THE   OLIVER, CHAD   AC
  *STORIES FOR TOMORROW   SLOANE, WILLIAM   AN
ANTAEUS   DEAL, BORDEN   61
  NIGHT IN FUNLAND   BRONDFIELD, JEROME   AN
ANTARCTIC MYSTERY, AN (THE MYSTERY OF ARTHUR GORDON PYM, 1897)
                            VERNE, JULES   EX   97
  JULES VERNE- MASTER OF SCIENCE FICTION VERNE, JULES   AC
ANTHEM   BEAUMONT, CHARLES   SS   NEW 58 AC
  YONDER   BEAUMONT, CHARLES   AC
ANTHEM SPRINTERS, THE (THE QUEEN'S OWN EVADERS)
                            BRADBURY, RAY   SS   PBY 63 06
  MACHINERIES OF JOY, THE   BRADBURY, RAY   AC
  VINTAGE BRADBURY, THE   BRADBURY, RAY   AC
ANTHROPOLOGICAL NOTE   LEINSTER, MURRAY   NV   FSF 57 04
  ALIENS, THE   LEINSTER, MURRAY   AC
ANTHROPOLOGIST, THE   SIDNEY, KATHLEEN M. SS   ORB 75 17
  ORBIT 17   KNIGHT, DAMON   OA
ANTI-CLIMAX, THE   MCCLINTIC, WINONA   PM   FSF 56 01
  BEST FROM FANTASY AND SCIENCE FICTION: 6
                            BOUCHER, ANTHONY   AN
ANTICIPATOR, THE (1898)   ROBERTS, MORLEY   98
  TRAVELERS IN TIME   STERN, PHILIP VAN D.   AN
ANTIMACASSAR, THE   LA SPINA, GREYE   SS   WRT 49 05
  LITTLE MONSTERS, THE   ELWOOD & GHIDALIA   AN
ANTIQUARY, THE   MCCLINTIC, WINONA   PM   FSF 53 07
  BEST FROM FANTASY AND SCIENCE FICTION: 3
                            BOUCHER & MCCOMAS   AN
ANTIQUITY   WELLER, ANTHONY   PM   INY 72 03
  INFINITY 3   HOSKINS, ROBERT   OA
ANTRIM HILLS, THE   BROXON, MILDRED D.   NV
  AURORA: BEYOND EQUALITY   MCINTYRE & ANDERSON   OA
ANXIETY IN THE EYES OF THE CRICKET
                            SALLIS, JAMES   SS
  FEW LAST WORDS, A   SALLIS, JAMES   AC
  NEW S.F.   JONES, LANGDON   OA
ANY FRIEND OF NICHOLAS NICKLEBY'S IS A FRIEND OF MINE
  (THE BEST OF TIMES)   BRADBURY, RAY   NV   MCC 66 01
  I SING THE BODY ELECTRIC   BRADBURY, RAY   AC
ANY MORE AT HOME LIKE YOU? OLIVER, CHAD   SS   STR 54 03
  STAR SCIENCE FICTION STORIES NO. 3 POHL, FREDERIK   OA
ANY RESEMBLANCE TO MAGIC   BINDER, EANDO   SS
  LONG NIGHT OF WAITING AND OTHER STORIES ELWOOD, ROGER   OA
ANYBODY ELSE LIKE ME? (COMMAND PERFORMANCE)
                            MILLER, WALTER M. JR NV   GAL 52 11
  VIEW FROM THE STARS, THE   MILLER, WALTER M. JR   AC
ANYTHING   DEL REY, LESTER   SS   UNK 39 10
  EARLY DEL REY   DEL REY, LESTER   AC
ANYTHING   ST. JOHN, PHILIP   SS   UNK 39 10
  FROM UNKNOWN WORLDS   CAMPBELL, JOHN W. JR   AN
ANYTHING BOX   HENDERSON, ZENNA   SS   FSF 56 10
  ANYTHING BOX, THE   HENDERSON, ZENNA   AC
  GOLDEN ROAD, THE   KNIGHT, DAMON   AN
  SF: THE BEST OF THE BEST   MERRIL, JUDITH   AN
  SF:57, THE YEAR'S GREATEST SCIENCE FICTION AND FANTASY
                            MERRIL, JUDITH   AN
ANYTHING FOR LAUGHS (SEE JOKER FOR HIRE)
                            GOULART, RON   TC
APARTMENT HUNTING   BILKER, AUDREY L.
                            AND BILKER, HARVEY L. SS C FUC 73
  FUTURE CITY   ELWOOD, ROGER   OA
APARTNESS   VINGE, VERNOR   SS   NWS 65 06
  WORLD'S BEST SCIENCE FICTION: 1966 WOLLHEIM & CARR   AN
APE ABOUT THE HOUSE, AN   CLARKE, ARTHUR C.   SS   DUD 62
  OF TIME AND STARS   CLARKE, ARTHUR C.   AC
  TALES OF TEN WORLDS   CLARKE, ARTHUR C.   AC
APE AND THE MYSTERY, THE (THE MYSTERIOUS MONA LISA SMILE)
                            KERSH, GERALD   SS   SEP 48 06
  MEN WITHOUT BONES   KERSH, GERALD   AC
  NIGHTSHADE & DAMNATIONS   KERSH, GERALD   AC

APE CYCLE, THE

APE CYCLE, THE   HARRIS, CLARE WINGER SS   WSQ 30 SP
  AWAY FROM THE HERE AND NOW   HARRIS, CLARE WINGER   AC
APEMAN, SPACEMAN- OR 2001'S ANSWER TO THE WORLD RIDDLE
                                  STOVER, LEON E.   AR
  ABOVE THE HUMAN LANDSCAPE   MCNELLY & STOVER   AN
APERTURE MOMENT, THE   ALDISS, BRIAN W.   GR EPC 75
  EPOCH   ELWOOD & SILVERBERG   OA
APOCALYPSE MACHINE, THE   ZORIN, LEO   SS NWS 68 12
  BEST SF STORIES FROM NEW WORLDS 7   MOORCOCK, MICHAEL   AN
APOCALYPSE: SOME SCENES FROM EUROPEAN LIFE, AN
                                  MOORCOCK, MICHAEL   NV BMR 73
  BAD MOON RISING   DISCH, THOMAS M.   OA
APOLLO   DICKEY, JAMES   PM LIF 69
  SPECULATIONS   SANDERS, THOMAS E.   AN
APOLLO   DISCH, THOMAS M.   SS
  GETTING INTO DEATH AND OTHER STORIES DISCH, THOMAS M.   AC
APOLOGY FOR MAN'S PHYSIQUE   HOOTON, EARNEST A.   AR
  APEMAN, SPACEMAN   STOVER & HARRISON   AN
APOLOGY TO INKY   GREEN, ROBERT M. JR. NV FSF 66 01
  BEST FROM FANTASY AND SCIENCE FICTION: 16
                                  FERMAN, EDWARD L.   AN
SCIENCE FICTION ARGOSY, A   KNIGHT, DAMON   AN
APOSTLE   LOVIN, ROGER   SS FTP 73
  FLAME TREE PLANET   ELWOOD, ROGER   OA
APOSTLE TO ALPHA   BALKE, BETTY T.   SS EPS 66 01
  GODS FOR TOMORROW   SANTESSON, HANS S.   AN
APOSTOLIC TRAVELERS, THE   WILHELM, KATE   SS NEW 63 AC
  MILE-LONG SPACESHIP, THE   WILHELM, KATE   AC
APOTHEM   ANONYMOUS   MS
  MATHEMATICAL MAGPIE, THE   FADIMAN, CLIFTON   AN
APOTHEM   CARROLL, LEWIS   MS   96
  MATHEMATICAL MAGPIE, THE   FADIMAN, CLIFTON   AN
APOTHEM   CHURCHILL, WINSTON MS
  MATHEMATICAL MAGPIE, THE   FADIMAN, CLIFTON   AN
APOTHEM   DE CONDILLAC, E. B. MS
  MATHEMATICAL MAGPIE, THE   FADIMAN, CLIFTON   AN
APOTHEM   GOETHE, J. V.   MS
  MATHEMATICAL MAGPIE, THE   FADIMAN, CLIFTON   AN
APOTHEM   LEE, STANISLAW G.   MS   62
  MATHEMATICAL MAGPIE, THE   FADIMAN, CLIFTON   AN
APOTHEM   LICHTENBERG, GEORGE MS   59
  MATHEMATICAL MAGPIE, THE   FADIMAN, CLIFTON   AN
APOTHEM   MORTLOCK, BILL   MS   59
  MATHEMATICAL MAGPIE, THE   FADIMAN, CLIFTON   AN
APOTHEM   ORWELL, GEORGE   MS   45
  MATHEMATICAL MAGPIE, THE   FADIMAN, CLIFTON   AN
APOTHEM   POLYA, G.   MS   45
  MATHEMATICAL MAGPIE, THE   FADIMAN, CLIFTON   AN
APOTHEM   RENARD, JULES   MS
  MATHEMATICAL MAGPIE, THE   FADIMAN, CLIFTON   AN
APOTHEM (1715)   MENCKEN, J. B.   MS
  MATHEMATICAL MAGPIE, THE   FADIMAN, CLIFTON   AN
APOTHEM (1872)   DEMORGAN, AUGUSTUS MS
  MATHEMATICAL MAGPIE, THE   FADIMAN, CLIFTON   AN
APOTHEOSIS OF KI, THE   DEFORD, MIRIAM ALLEN SS FSF 56 12
  ELSEWHERE, ELSEWHEN, ELSEHOW   DEFORD, MIRIAM ALLEN   AC
  SPECIAL WONDER   MCCOMAS, J. FRANCIS   AN
APPEAL   WRIGHT, S. FOWLER   SS
  NEW GODS LEAD, THE   WRIGHT, S. FOWLER   AC
APPEARANCE OF LIFE   ALDISS, BRIAN W.   SS   76
  ANDROMEDA I   WESTON, PETER   OA
  1977 ANNUAL WORLD'S BEST SF, THE WOLLHEIM, DONALD A.   AN
APPEARANCE OF MAN, THE   BERESFORD, JOHN D. PL   21
  *OTHER SIDE OF THE MOON, THE   DERLETH, AUGUST   AN
APPENDICES   MISC. MATERIAL   MS
  FANTASTIC PULPS, THE   HAINING, PETER   AN
  HISTORY OF THE SCIENCE FICTION MAGAZINE, THE PART 1 1926-1935
                                  ASHLEY, MICHAEL   AN
  HISTORY OF THE SCIENCE FICTION MAGAZINE, THE PART 2 1936-1945
                                  ASHLEY, MICHAEL   AN
  HISTORY OF THE SCIENCE FICTION MAGAZINE, THE PART 3 1946-1955
                                  ASHLEY, MICHAEL   AN
APPENDIX   MISC. MATERIAL   MS
  EARLY DEL REY   DEL REY, LESTER   AC
APPENDIX AND THE SPECTACLES, THE
                                  BREUER, MILES J. MD. SS AMZ 28 12
  MATHEMATICAL MAGPIE, THE   FADIMAN, CLIFTON   AN
  SCIENCE FICTION GALAXY, THE   CONKLIN, GROFF   AN
APPENDIX OF THEMES   MISC. MATERIAL   MS
  TWO VIEWS OF WONDER   SCORTIA & YARBRO   OA
APPENDIX: MY HUNDRED BOOKS   ASIMOV, ISAAC   MS
  OPUS 100   ASIMOV, ISAAC   AC
APPENDIX: THE HUGO AWARDS   MISC. MATERIAL   MS
  HUGO WINNERS, THE (VOLUME 1)   ASIMOV, ISAAC   AN
APPLE   BAXTER, JOHN   SS NWR 67 10
  NEW WRITINGS IN SF. 8   CARNELL, JOHN   AN
  NEW WRITINGS IN SF. 10   CARNELL, JOHN   OA
  SECOND PACIFIC BOOK OF SCIENCE FICTION, THE
                                  BAXTER, JOHN   AN
  ZOO 2000   YOLEN, JANE   AN
APPLE   MCCAFFREY, ANNE   NV NEW 69 AN
  CRIME PREVENTION IN THE 30TH CENTURY SANTESSON, HANS S. AN
  GET OFF THE UNICORN   MCCAFFREY, ANNE   AC
  TO RIDE PEGASUS   MCCAFFREY, ANNE   AC
  YOUNG DEMONS   ELWOOD & GHIDALIA   AN
APPLE FOR THE TEACHER, AN   BURKE, JONATHAN F. SS NEB 55 04
  ALIEN LANDSCAPES   BURKE, JONATHAN F.   AC
APPLE, THE   WELLS, H. G.   SS IDL 96 10
  BEST SCIENCE FICTION STORIES OF H. G. WELLS
                                  WELLS, H. G.   AC
  INEXPERIENCED GHOST AND NINE OTHER STORIES, THE
                                  WELLS, H. G.   AC
  PLATTNER STORY AND OTHERS, THE WELLS, H. G.   AC
  SHORT STORIES OF H. G. WELLS, THE WELLS, H. G.   AC
  THIRTY STRANGE STORIES   WELLS, H. G.   AC

APPLE, THE (MAX EHRLICH & GENE L. COON)
                                  BLISH, JAMES   SA STK 72 06
  STAR TREK   6   BLISH, JAMES   OC
APPOINTMENT AT NOON   RUSSELL, ERIC FRANK SS AMZ 54 03
  FIFTY SHORT SCIENCE FICTION TALES ASIMOV & CONKLIN   AN
APPOINTMENT AT TEN O'CLOCK   LORY, ROBERT   SS FSF 64 01
  HARVEST OF HOODWINKS, A   LORY, ROBERT   DC
APPOINTMENT IN TOMORROW (ALSO AS POOR SUPERMAN)
                                  LEIBER, FRITZ   NV GAL 51 07
  BEST SCIENCE-FICTION STORIES: 1952, THE BLEILER & DIKTY AN
APPOINTMENT ON PRILA   SHAW, BOB   SS ASF 68 08
  BEST SF: 1968   HARRISON & ALDISS   AN
  WORLDS OF WONDER   HARRISON, HARRY   AN
APPRECIATION, AN   POHL, FREDERIK   IN
  BEST OF C. M. KORNBLUTH, THE   KORNBLUTH, C. M.   AC
APPRENTICE GOD, THE   DEFORD, MIRIAM ALLEN PM WOT 64 04
  BEST SCIENCE FICTION FROM WORLDS OF TOMORROW, THE
                                  POHL, FREDERIK   AN
APPRENTICE MAGICIAN   PRICE, E. HOFFMANN SS WRT 39 08
  WIZARDS AND WARLOCKS   GHIDALIA, VIC   AN
APPRENTICE, THE   WHITE, JAMES   NV NWS 60 10
  MONSTERS AND MEDICS   WHITE, JAMES   AC
  OUT OF THIS WORLD 3   WILLIAMS-ELLIS& OWEN   AN
APPROACHING ELLISON   CRICHTON, MICHAEL   MS
  APPROACHING OBLIVION   ELLISON, HARLAN   AC
APRES NOUS   DAVIDSON, AVRAM   SS FSF 60 03
  BEST FROM FANTASY AND SCIENCE FICTION: 10
                                  MILLS, ROBERT P.   AN
  STRANGE SEAS AND SHORES   DAVIDSON, AVRAM   AC
APRIL FOOL'S DAY FOREVER   WILHELM, KATE   NV ORB 70 07
  INFINITY BOX, THE   WILHELM, KATE   AC
  ORBIT   7   KNIGHT, DAMON   OA
APRIL IN PARIS   LE GUIN, URSULA K. SS FAN 62 09
  BEST FROM FANTASTIC, THE   WHITE, TED   AC
  WINDS TWELVE QUARTERS, THE   LE GUIN, URSULA K.   AC
APRIL WITCH, THE   BRADBURY, RAY   SS SEP 52 04
  *GOLDEN APPLES OF THE SUN   BRADBURY, RAY   AC
AQUAMAN   BULMER, KENNETH   SS SPC 74 02
  SPACE   2   DAVIS, RICHARD   OA
AQUATIC UNCLE, THE   CALVINO, ITALO   SS
  COSMICOMICS   CALVINO, ITALO   OC
AQUELLA   WOLLHEIM, DONALD A. SS AFR 48 07
  IF THIS GOES ON   NUETZEL, CHARLES   AN
ARARAT   HENDERSON, ZENNA   SS FSF 52 10
  BEST SCIENCE-FICTION STORIES: 1953, THE BLEILER & DIKTY AN
  FRONTIERS IN SPACE   BLEILER & DIKTY   AN
  OUT OF THIS WORLD 3   WILLIAMS-ELLIS& OWEN   AN
  PILGRIMAGE: THE BOOK OF THE PEOPLE HENDERSON, ZENNA   AC
  UNIVERSE AHEAD   ENGDAHL & ROBERSON   AN
  14 GREAT TALES OF ESP   STONE, IDELLA P.   AN
ARCHETYPICAL HOLMES, THE   ANDERSON, POUL   AR BSJ 68 09
  HOMEBREW   ANDERSON, POUL   AC
ARCHIMEDES' LEVER (THE COURTEOUS OF GHOOR)
                                  LORY, ROBERT   SS IFS 68 02
  HARVEST OF HOODWINKS, A   LORY, ROBERT   DC
ARCS & SECANTS   MISC. MATERIAL   MS
  ORBIT 12   KNIGHT, DAMON   OA
  ORBIT 13   KNIGHT, DAMON   OA
  ORBIT 14   KNIGHT, DAMON   OA
  ORBIT 15   KNIGHT, DAMON   OA
  ORBIT 16   KNIGHT, DAMON   OA
  ORBIT 17   KNIGHT, DAMON   OA
  ORBIT 18   KNIGHT, DAMON   OA
ARCTIC RESCUE   MASON, JOHN KEITH   SS
  TOMORROW: NEW WORLDS OF SCIENCE FICTION ELWOOD, ROGER   OA
ARE YOU LISTENING?   ELLISON, HARLAN   SS AMZ 58 12
  ALONE AGAINST TOMORROW   ELLISON, HARLAN   AC
  BEAST THAT SHOUTED LOVE AT THE HEART OF THE WORLD, THE
                                  ELLISON, HARLAN   AC
  INTO THE UNKNOWN   CARR, TERRY   AN
ARE YOU RUN-DOWN, TIRED-   LAKE, LEONARD M.
  AND ROSMOND, BABETTE   SS C UNK 42 10
  SUPERNATURAL READER, THE   CONKLIN, G&L.   AN
ARE YOU TOO LATE OR WAS I TOO EARLY
                                  COLLIER, JOHN   SS NYM 51 04
  GOLDEN ROAD, THE   KNIGHT, DAMON   AN
ARE YOUR HOME GROWN VEGETABLES RADIOACTIVE?
                                  BRENNAN, KATHLEEN   SS
  STOPWATCH   HAY, GEORGE   OA
ARENA   BROWN, FREDRIC   NV ASF 44 06
  ALIENS, THE   SILVERBERG, ROBERT   AN
  ANTHROPOLOGY THROUGH SCIENCE FICTION MASON, C/GREENBERG/& AN
  ARENA: SPORTS SF   FERMAN & MALZBERG   AN
  BEST OF FREDRIC BROWN, THE   BROWN, FREDRIC   AC
  *BIG BOOK OF SCIENCE FICTION   CONKLIN, GROFF   AN
  BUG-EYED MONSTERS   CHEETHAM, ANTHONY   AN
  DECADE THE 1940S   ALDISS & HARRISON   AN
  HONEYMOON IN HELL   BROWN, FREDRIC   AC
  INTRODUCING SCIENCE FICTION   ALDISS, BRIAN W.   AN
  SCIENCE FICTION HALL OF FAME VOLUME 1 SILVERBERG, ROBERT AN
  SCIENCE FICTION TERROR TALES   CONKLIN, GROFF   AN
  TOMORROW, AND TOMORROW, AND TOMORROW... HEINTZ/HERBERT/JOOS/ AN
ARENA (GENE L. COON)   BLISH, JAMES   SA STK 68 OC
  STAR TREK   2   BLISH, JAMES   OC
ARGONAUTS OF THE AIR, THE   WELLS, H. G.   SS PMY 95
  BEST STORIES OF H. G. WELLS   WELLS, H. G.   AC
  PLATTNER STORY AND OTHERS, THE WELLS, H. G.   AC
  SHORT STORIES OF H. G. WELLS, THE WELLS, H. G.   AC
  THIRTY STRANGE STORIES   WELLS, H. G.   AC
  TWENTY-EIGHT SCIENCE FICTION STORIES WELLS, H. G.   AC
ARIEL   ELWOOD, ROGER   SS NDM 74 04
  NEW DIMENSIONS 4   SILVERBERG, ROBERT   OA
  VISIONS OF TOMORROW   ELWOOD, ROGER   AN
ARISTOTLE AND THE GUN   DE CAMP, L. SPRAGUE NV ASF 58 02
  ALPHA 3   SILVERBERG, ROBERT   AN

ARISTOTLE AND THE GUN
  GUN FOR DINOSAUR AND OTHER IMAGINATIVE TALES
                          DE CAMP, L. SPRAGUE   AC
ARITHMETIC   SANDBURG, CARL   PM   50
  FANTASIA MATHEMATICA   FADIMAN, CLIFTON   AN
ARK OF JAMES CARLYLE, THE WILDER, CHERRY   SS   NWR 74 24
  BEYOND TOMORROW   HARDING, LEE   AN
  NEW WRITINGS IN SF. 24 BULMER, KENNETH   OA
ARM   INOUYE, JON   SS
  NIGHT TIDE, A   INOUYE, JON   OC
ARM   NIVEN, LARRY   NA   EPC 75
  EPOCH   ELWOOD & SILVERBERG OA
  LONG ARM OF GIL HAMILTON, THE NIVEN, LARRY AC
ARM OF THE LAW   HARRISON, HARRY   SS   FUN 58 08
  WAR WITH THE ROBOTS   HARRISON, HARRY   AC
ARMADILLO OF DESTRUCTION, THE COVER, ARTHUR BYRON NV
  PLATYPUS OF DOOM AND OTHER NIHILISTS, THE
                          COVER, ARTHUR BYRON OC
ARMAGEDDON   BROWN, FREDRIC   SS   UNK 41 08
  ANGELS AND SPACESHIPS BROWN, FREDRIC   AC
  BEST OF FREDRIC BROWN, THE BROWN, FREDRIC AC
  EDGE OF NEVER, THE   HOSKINS, ROBERT   AN
  UNKNOWN, THE   BENSEN, D. R.   AN
ARMAGEDDON TAPES, THE- TAPE I SCORTIA, THOMAS N. NV CTM 74 01
  CONTINUUM 1   ELWOOD, ROGER   OA
ARMAGEDDON TAPES, THE- TAPE II SCORTIA, THOMAS N. NV CTM 74 02
  CONTINUUM 2   ELWOOD, ROGER   OA
ARMAGEDDON TAPES, THE- TAPE III
                        SCORTIA, THOMAS N. NV CTM 74 03
  CONTINUUM 3   ELWOOD, ROGER   OA
ARMAGEDDON TAPES, THE- TAPE IV SCORTIA, THOMAS N. SS CTM 75 04
  CONTINUUM 4   ELWOOD, ROGER   OA
ARMAJA DAS   HALDEMAN, JOE W.   SS   76
  BEST SCIENCE FICTION STORIES OF THE YEAR (1976)
                          DOZOIS, GARDNER R. AN
ARMAMENTS RACE   CLARKE, ARTHUR C.   SS   ADV 54 04
  ACROSS THE SEA OF STARS CLARKE, ARTHUR C. AC
  TALES FROM THE WHITE HART CLARKE, ARTHUR C. AC
ARMY COMES TO VENUS, THE RUSSELL, ERIC FRANK NV FUN 59 05
  GODS FOR TOMORROW   SANTESSON, HANS S. AN
AROUND THE WORLD IN EIGHTY DAYS (1873)
                        VERNE, JULES   NO
  NOVELS   VERNE, JULES   AC
  OMNIBUS, THE   VERNE, JULES   AC
ARPAD   PANSHIN, ALEXEI   SS   QRK 71 02
  FAREWELL TO YESTERDAY'S TOMORROW PANSHIN, ALEXEI AC
  QUARK/2   DELANY & HACKER   OA
ARRANGEMENT, THE   MCALLISTER, BRUCE   SS   SCS 73
  SHOWCASE   ELWOOD, ROGER   OA
ARRHENIUS HORROR, THE MILLER, P. SCHUYLER SS   AMZ 31 09
  TITAN, THE   MILLER, P. SCHUYLER AC
ARSENAL PORT   ANDERSON, POUL   SN   FSF 65 04
  STAR FOX, THE   ANDERSON, POUL   AC
ARSONS OF DESIRE, THE HARRISON, WILLIAM   SS   72
  ROLLERBALL   HARRISON, WILLIAM AC
ART OF FICTION, THE   MALZBERG, BARRY N.   SS   MSM 72
  OUT FROM GANYMEDE   MALZBERG, BARRY N. AC
ART-WORK (SEE A WORK OF ART) BLISH, JAMES TC
ARTICLE ABOUT HUNTING, AN WOLFE, GENE   SS   SVW 73
  SAVING WORLDS   ELWOOD & KIDD   OA
ARTICLES   MISC. MATERIAL   AR
  AUTHENTIC BOOK OF SPACE CAMPBELL, H. J.   AN
ARTIFACT   OLIVER, CHAD   NV   FSF 55 06
  ANOTHER KIND   OLIVER, CHAD   AC
ARTIFACT BUSINESS, THE SILVERBERG, ROBERT SS   FUN 57 04
  CALLIBRATED ALLIGATOR AND OTHER SCIENCE FICTION STORIES, THE
                          SILVERBERG, ROBERT AC
  TIME PROBE: THE SCIENCES IN SF. CLARKE, ARTHUR C. AN
ARTIFICIAL MAN, THE   HARRIS, CLARE WINGER SS   WSQ 29 FL
  AWAY FROM THE HERE AND NOW HARRIS, CLARE WINGER AC
ARTIFICIAL PARADISE   REEVE, ARTHUR B.   SS
  SILENT BULLET, THE   REEVE, ARTHUR B.   AC
ARTIST OF THE BEAUTIFUL, THE (1844)
                        HAWTHORNE, NATHANIEL NV DMR 44 06
  FUTURE PERFECT   FRANKLIN, H. BRUCE AN
  LOOKING AHEAD   ALLEN, D. & L.   AN
ARTIST UNKNOWN   BROUN, HEYWOOD   SS   41
  GOLDEN ROAD, THE   KNIGHT, DAMON   AN
ARTIST, THE   KOCH, KENNETH   PM   62
  HOLDING YOUR EIGHT HANDS LUCIE-SMITH, EDWARD AN
  SCIENCE FICTION: THE FUTURE ALLEN, DICK   AN
ARTNAN PROCESS   STURGEON, THEODORE NV   ASF 41 06
  NOT WITHOUT SORCERY   STURGEON, THEODORE AC
  STARSHINE   STURGEON, THEODORE AC
  WITHOUT SORCERY   STURGEON, THEODORE AC
AS A DROP   PRICE, D. M.   PM   FUC 73
  FUTURE CITY   ELWOOD, ROGER   OA
AS BEST WE CAN   HOUSEHOLD, GEOFFREY SS   58
  NIGHT IN FUNLAND   BRONDFIELD, JEROME AN
AS BETWEEN GENERATIONS O'DONNELL, K. M.   SS   FAN 70 10
  IN THE POCKET AND OTHER S-F STORIES O'DONNELL, K. M. DC
AS EASY AS A. B. C.   KIPLING, RUDYARD   NV   LOM 12 04
  SCIENCE FICTION GALAXY, THE CONKLIN, GROFF AN
  SPECULATIONS   SANDERS, THOMAS E. AN
  17 X INFINITY   CONKLIN, GROFF   AN
AS FOR OUR FATAL CONTINUITY... ALDISS, BRIAN W. SS   NWQ 72 03
  BEST SF: 1972   HARRISON & ALDISS AN
  BOOK OF BRIAN ALDISS, THE ALDISS, BRIAN W. AC
  NEW WORLDS QUARTERLY NO. 3 MOORCOCK, MICHAEL OA
AS IN A VISION APPREHENDED MALZBERG, BARRY N. SS   BER 74
  BERSERKERS, THE   ELWOOD, ROGER   OA
  BEST OF BARRY N. MALZBERG, THE MALZBERG, BARRY N. AC
AS IS   SILVERBERG, ROBERT NV   WOF 68 01
  INTO THE UNKNOWN   CARR, TERRY   AN
AS LONG AS YOU'RE HERE STANTON, WILL   SS   FSF 63 07
  TWENTY YEARS OF FANTASY & SCIENCE FICTION
                          FERMAN & MILLS   AN

AS NEVER WAS   MILLER, P. SCHUYLER SS   ASF 44 01
  *ADVENTURES IN TIME AND SPACE HEALY & MCCOMAS AN
  ALPHA 5   SILVERBERG, ROBERT AN
  TITAN, THE   MILLER, P. SCHUYLER AC
AS SIMPLE AS THAT   HENDERSON, ZENNA   SS   NEW 71 AC
  HOLDING WONDER   HENDERSON, ZENNA   AC
AS THE WALL CRUMBLES SCHOLES, ROBERT   AR   NEW 75 AN
  NEBULA AWARD STORIES 10 GUNN, JAMES E.   AN
ASA RULE, THE   WILLIAMS, JAY   SS   FSF 56 06
  BEST FROM FANTASY AND SCIENCE FICTION: 6
                          BOUCHER, ANTHONY   AN
ASCENSION: A WORKDAY ARABESQUE KIDD, VIRGINIA PM ANA 70
  ALCHEMY AND ACADEME   MCCAFFREY, ANNE   OA
ASCENSION, THE   O'DONNELL, K. M.   SS   FAN 69 04
  FINAL WAR AND OTHER FANTASIES O'DONNELL, K. M. DC
ASCLEPIUS HAS PAWS   BROXON, MILDRED D. SS   CLR 73 03
  CLARION III   WILSON, ROBIN SCOTT AN
ASH CIRCUS, THE   HARRISON, M. JOHN   SS   NWS 69 04
  BEST SF STORIES FROM NEW WORLDS 7 MOORCOCK, MICHAEL AN
ASH, ASH   HOLDSTOCK, ROBERT P. SS
  STOPWATCH   HAY, GEORGE   OA
ASHES ALL MY LUST   EFFINGER, GEO. ALEC NV   FOS 74
  FELLOWSHIP OF THE STARS CARR, TERRY   OA
ASIAN SHORE, THE   DISCH, THOMAS M.   NV   ORB 70 06
  BEST SF: 1970   HARRISON & ALDISS AN
  *GETTING INTO DEATH   DISCH, THOMAS M.   AC
  ORBIT 6   KNIGHT, DAMON   OA
  SCIENCE FICTION NOVELLAS HARRISON & MCNELLY AN
  SHORES BENEATH, THE   SALLIS, JAMES   AN
ASIMOV BIBLIOGRAPHY   MISC. MATERIAL   MS   FSF 66 10
  BEST FROM FANTASY AND SCIENCE FICTION, 25TH ANNIV.
                          FERMAN, EDWARD L. AN
ASK A FOOLISH QUESTION SHECKLEY, ROBERT   SS   SFS 53 01
  CITIZEN IN SPACE   SHECKLEY, ROBERT   AC
  ROBERT SHECKLEY OMNIBUS, THE SHECKLEY, ROBERT AC
  6 AND THE SILENT SCREAM HOWARD, IVAN   AN
ASK AND IT MAY BE GIVEN DAVIS, WESLEY FORD SS   FSF 71 10
  NEW AWARENESS, THE   WARRICK & GREENBERG AN
ASK ME ANYTHING   KNIGHT, DAMON   NV   GAL 51 05
  *GALAXY READER OF SCIENCE FICTION GOLD, H. L. AN
  IN DEEP   KNIGHT, DAMON   AC
ASKING   ST. CLAIR, MARGARET SS   FSF 55 11
  CHANGE THE SKY AND OTHER STORIES ST. CLAIR, MARGARET AC
ASLEEP IN ARMAGEDDON (ALSO AS PERCHANCE TO DREAM)
                        BRADBURY, RAY   SS   PLS 48 WI
  ASLEEP IN ARMAGEDDON   SISSONS, MICHAEL   AN
  BEYOND THE STARS AND OTHER STORIES ANONYMOUS AN
  *POSSIBLE WORLDS OF SCIENCE FICTION CONKLIN, GROFF AN
ASLEEP: WITH STILL HANDS (THE SLEEPER WITH STILL HANDS)
                        ELLISON, HARLAN   NV   IFS 68 07
  BEAST THAT SHOUTED LOVE AT THE HEART OF THE WORLD, THE
                          ELLISON, HARLAN   AC
ASPECT OF ENVIRONMENT DAVISON, L.   SS   NWR 70 17
  NEW WRITINGS IN SF. 17 CARNELL, JOHN   OA
ASPECTS OF LANGRANAK SHECKLEY, ROBERT   SS   NEW 71 AC
  CAN YOU FEEL ANYTHING WHEN I DO THIS?, AND OTHER STORIES
                          SHECKLEY, ROBERT   AC
ASSASSINATION OF JOHN FITZGERALD KENNEDY CONSIDERED AS A
  DOWNHILL MOTOR RACE, THE BALLARD, J. G. SS   NWS 67 02
  AMERICAN GOVERNMENT THROUGH SCIENCE FICTION
                          OLANDER/GREENBERG/& AN
  BEST SF: 1967   HARRISON & ALDISS AN
  DAY OF FOREVER, THE   BALLARD, J. G.   AG
  DECADE THE 1960S   ALDISS & HARRISON AN
  ENGLAND SWINGS SF   MERRIL, JUDITH   AN
  LOVE & NAPALM: EXPORT U.S.A. BALLARD, J. G. AC
ASSASSINATION OF THE MAYOR, THE
                        DISCH, THOMAS M.   SS   NWB 73 05
  NEW WORLDS QUARTERLY NO. 5 MOORCOCK, MICHAEL OA
ASSASSINATION WEAPON, THE BALLARD, J. G. SS   NWS 66 04
  BEST SF STORIES FROM NEW WORLDS NO. 1, THE
                          MOORCOCK, MICHAEL AN
  LOVE & NAPALM: EXPORT U.S.A. BALLARD, J. G. AC
ASSASSINS OF AIR   ZEBROWSKI, GEORGE   SS   FUC 73
  FUTURE CITY   ELWOOD, ROGER   OA
  MONADIC UNIVERSE, THE ZEBROWSKI, GEORGE AC
ASSAULT ON A CITY   VANCE, JACK   NV   UNI 74 04
  UNIVERSE 4   CARR, TERRY   OA
ASSAULT ON FAT MOUNTAIN LAFFERTY, R. A.   SS
  BEYOND TIME   LEY, SANDRA   OA
ASSAULT ON NEW DREAMERS, AN ELLISON, HARLAN IN   DVS 72 02
  AGAIN, DANGEROUS VISIONS ELLISON, HARLAN AN
ASSIGNMENT IN ALDEBARAN CROSSEN, KENDELL F. NV   TWS 53 02
  YEAR'S BEST SCIENCE FICTION NOVELS: 1954 BLEILER & DIKTY AN
ASSIGNMENT ON PASIK   LEINSTER, MURRAY   SS   TWS 49 02
  ADVENTURES ON OTHER PLANETS WOLLHEIM, DONALD A. AN
ASSIGNMENT: EARTH (GENE RODDENBERRY & ART WALLACE)
                        BLISH, JAMES   SA   STK 69 03
  STAR TREK 3   BLISH, JAMES   OC
ASSISTED PASSAGE   WHITE, JAMES   SS   NWS 53 01
  GATEWAY TO THE STARS   CARNELL, JOHN   AN
ASSUMPTION UNJUSTIFIED CLEMENT, HAL   NV   ASF 46 10
  CROSSROADS IN TIME   CONKLIN, GROFF   AN
  NATIVES OF SPACE   CLEMENT, HAL   AC
ASTEROID OF FEAR   GALLUN, RAYMOND Z. NV   PLS 51 03
  SPACE PIONEERS   NORTON, ANDRE   AN
ASTEROID OF GOLD, THE SIMAK, CLIFFORD D. SS   WOS 32 11
  EVERY BOY'S BOOK OF SCIENCE FICTION WOLLHEIM, DONALD A. AN
  HISTORY OF THE SCIENCE FICTION MAGAZINE, THE PART 1 1926-1935
                          ASHLEY, MICHAEL   AN
ASTEROIDS, 2194, THE (THE EMPTYNESS OF SPACE, NWS 60 11)
                        WYNDHAM, JOHN   SS   AMZ 61 01
  STORIES FROM SCIENCE FICTION DOHERTY, G. D. AN
  7TH ANNUAL OF THE YEAR'S BEST S-F, THE MERRIL, JUDITH AN
ASTORIA INCIDENT, THE ROBERSON, RICK   NV
  ANYWHERE, ANYWHEN   ENGDAHL, SYLVIA   OA

ASTRONAUT (EXTRACT)   LUCIE-SMITH, EDWARD PM
  BEYOND THIS HORIZON   CARRELL, CHRISTOPHER OA
ASTRONAUT, THE   ZHURAVLEVA,VALENTINA SS
  DESTINATION: AMALTHEIA   DIXON, RICHARD   AN
  OUT OF THIS WORLD 4   WILLIAMS-ELLIS& OWEN   AN
  RUSSIAN SCIENCE FICTION   MAGIDOFF, ROBERT   AN
ASTRONOMY AND ART: PAINTINGS EARLY, DAVID   IL
  BEYOND THIS HORIZON   CARRELL, CHRISTOPHER OA
ASYLUM   BULLOCK, ALICE   SS FUT 54 08
  RARE SCIENCE FICTION   HOWARD, IVAN   AN
ASYLUM   VAN VOGT, A. E.   NV ASF 42 05
  *ADVENTURES IN TIME AND SPACE   HEALY & MCCOMAS   AN
  *AWAY AND BEYOND   VAN VOGT, A. E.   AC
ASYLUM SATELLITE (SEE PROJECT EXCELSIOR)
                           PRATT, FLETCHER   TC
AT A WINDOW (SEE THROUGH A WINDOW)
                           WELLS, H. G.   TC
AT CENTRAL   REED, KIT   SS   67
  SF: AUTHORS' CHOICE 3   HARRISON, HARRY   AN
AT DAYBREAK   CALVINO, ITALO   SS
  COSMICOMICS   CALVINO, ITALO   OC
AT DEATH'S END   BLISH, JAMES   NV ASF 54 05
  YEAR 2018| BLISH, JAMES   NO
AT LAST, THE TRUE STORY OF FRANKENSTEIN
                           HARRISON, HARRY   SS FSF 63
  *BEST OF HARRY HARRISON, THE   HARRISON, HARRY   AC
AT NO EXTRA COST   PHILLIPS, PETER   SS MSS 51 08
  BEST SCIENCE-FICTION STORIES: 1952, THE BLEILER & DIKTY AN
AT THE ACCIDENT   WISE, DAVID   SS
  FUTURE PASTIMES   EDELSTEIN, SCOTT   OA
AT THE BOTTOM OF A HOLE   NIVEN, LARRY   NV GAL 66 12
  SHAPE OF SPACE, THE   NIVEN, LARRY   AC
  TALES OF KNOWN SPACE: THE UNIVERSE OF LARRY NIVEN
                                   NIVEN, LARRY   AC
AT THE BOTTOM OF THE GARDEN CAMPTON, DAVID   NV ADS 75 01
  ARMADA SCI-FI ONE   DAVIS, RICHARD   OA
AT THE BRAN FOUNDRY   EFFINGER, GEO. ALEC SS NDM 73 03
  IRRATIONAL NUMBERS   EFFINGER, GEO. ALEC   AC
  NEW DIMENSIONS 3   SILVERBERG, ROBERT   OA
AT THE CENTER OF GRAVITY   ROCKLYNNE, ROSS   SS ASF 36 06
  EXPLORING OTHER WORLDS   MOSKOWITZ, SAM   AN
  MEN AND THE MIRROR, THE   ROCKLYNNE, ROSS   AC
AT THE CORE   NIVEN, LARRY   NV IFS 66 11
  NEUTRON STAR   NIVEN, LARRY   AC
  SECOND IF READER OF SCIENCE FICTION, THE POHL, FREDERIK AN
AT THE EARTH'S CORE   BURROUGHS, EDGAR R. NO ASW 14 04
  THREE SCIENCE FICTION NOVELS   BURROUGHS, EDGAR R.   AC
AT THE END OF DAYS   SILVERBERG, ROBERT SS NWS 65 09
  ENDS OF TIME, THE   SILVERBERG, ROBERT   AN
AT THE END OF THE ORBIT   CLARKE, ARTHUR C.   NV IFS 61 11
  EXPERT DREAMERS, THE   POHL, FREDERIK   AN
AT THE FITTING SHOP   SALLIS, JAMES   SS DVS 72 02
  AGAIN, DANGEROUS VISIONS   ELLISON, HARLAN   OA
AT THE INSTITUTE   MALZBERG, BARRY N. SS FAN 74 03
  BEST OF BARRY N. MALZBERG, THE   MALZBERG, BARRY N.   AC
AT THE MOUNTAINS OF MADNESS LOVECRAFT, H. P.   NO ASF 36 02
  *STRANGE PORTS OF CALL   DERLETH, AUGUST   AN
AT THE MOUSE CIRCUS   ELLISON, HARLAN   SS NDM 71 01
  BEST SCIENCE FICTION FOR 1972   POHL, FREDERIK   AN
  DEATHBIRD STORIES   ELLISON, HARLAN   AC
  MODERN SCIENCE FICTION   SPINRAD, NORMAN   AN
  NEW DIMENSIONS 1   SILVERBERG, ROBERT   OA
AT THE PERIHELION (SEE A MARTIAN ADVENTURE)
                           LEY, WILLY   TC
AT THE POST   GOLD, H. L.   NV GAL 53 10
  OLD DIE RICH AND OTHER SCIENCE FICTION, THE
                                   GOLD, H. L.   AC
AT THE SECOND SOLSTICE   SUTHERLAND, JAMES   SS CLR 72 02
  CLARION II   WILSON, ROBIN SCOTT   OA
ATAVIST, THE   FRITCH, CHARLES E. SS
  HORSES' ASTEROID   FRITCH, CHARLES E.   AC
ATAVISTS, THE   RYMER, G. A.   SS
  AD 2500   WILSON, ANGUS   AN
ATHEIST'S BARGAIN, THE   DISCH, THOMAS X.
                           AND SLADEK, JOHN T. SS C NEW 67 AN
  DEVIL HIS DUE, THE   HILL, DOUGLAS   AN
ATLANTIS (FROM TRIPLANETARY) SMITH, EDWARD E. PhD EX AMZ 34 01
  JOURNEY TO INFINITY   GREENBERG , MARTIN   AN
ATLANTIS (370 B.C.)   PLATO   EX
  *BEYOND TIME AND SPACE   DERLETH, AUGUST   AN
ATOM BOMB IS TWENTY-FIVE THIS YEAR, THE
                           BRUNNER, JOHN   PM STY 70
  BOOK OF JOHN BRUNNER, THE   BRUNNER, JOHN   AC
ATOM SMASHER, THE   WANDREI, DONALD   SS ASF 34 04
  STRANGE HARVEST   WANDREI, DONALD   AC
ATOMIC BOMB, THE (FROM "THE WORLD SET FREE")
                           WELLS, H. G.   EX
  SCIENCE FICTION THROUGH THE AGES 2 EVANS, I. O.   AN
ATOMIC MONUMENT, THE (MEMORIAL)
                           ACKERMAN, FORREST J.
                           AND STURGEON, THEODORE SS C ASF 46 04
  SCIENCE FICTION WORLDS OF FORREST J. ACKERMAN & FRIENDS
                                   ACKERMAN, FORREST J. AC
ATOMIC POWER   STUART, DON A.   SS ASF 34 12
  *BEST OF SCIENCE FICTION   CONKLIN, GROFF   AN
ATOMS OF CHLADNI, THE (1859) WHELPLEY, J. D.   SS HRP 59
  FUTURE PERFECT   FRANKLIN, H. BRUCE   AN
ATROCITY EXHIBITION, THE   BALLARD, J. G.   SS NWS 66 09
  LOVE & NAPALM: EXPORT U.S.A.   BALLARD, J. G.   AC
ATROPHY   HILL, ERNEST   SS NWR 65 06
  NEW WRITINGS IN SF. 6   CARNELL, JOHN   OA
ATTACK-ESCAPE, AN INTERVIEW WITH ALFRED BESTER
                           PLATT, CHARLES   AR NWQ 72 04
  NEW WORLDS QUARTERLY NO. 4   MOORCOCK, MICHAEL   OA

ATTIC VOICE, THE (SEE NIGHTSOUND)
                           BUDRYS, ALGIS   TC
ATTITUDE   CLEMENT, HAL   NV ASF 43 09
  TRAVELLERS OF SPACE   GREENBERG , MARTIN   AN
ATTITUDES   FARMER, PHILIP JOSE NV FSF 53 10
  BEST FROM FANTASY AND SCIENCE FICTION: 3
                                   BOUCHER & MCCOMAS   AN
AUCTION PIT   MERRIL, JUDITH   PM   46
  BEST OF JUDITH MERRIL, THE   MERRIL, JUDITH   AC
  SURVIVAL SHIP AND OTHER STORIES MERRIL, JUDITH   AC
AUDITION: SOON TO BE A MAJOR PRODUCTION
                           BRYANT, EDWARD   SS INY 72 04
  INFINITY 4   HOSKINS, ROBERT   OA
AUGMENTED AGENT, THE (I-C-A-BEM)
                           VANCE, JACK   NV AMZ 61 10
  BEST FROM AMAZING, THE   WHITE, TED   AN
AUGUST HEAT   HARVEY, WILLIAM F. SS   28
  NIGHT IN FUNLAND   BRONDFIELD, JEROME   AN
  OTHER SIDE OF THE CLOCK, THE   STERN, PHILIP VAN D. AN
  TRAVELERS IN TIME   STERN, PHILIP VAN D. AN
AUGUST 2026: THERE WILL COME SOFT RAINS
                           BRADBURY, RAY   SS COL 50 05
  IN DREAMS AWAKE   FIEDLER, LESLIE A.   AN
AUNT AGATHA   BUCK, DORIS PITKIN SS FSF 52 10
  SPECIAL WONDER   MCCOMAS, J. FRANCIS   AN
AUNT CASSIE   SWAN, VIRGINIA   SS NEW 41 10
  OTHER WORLDS, THE   STONG, PHILIP D.   AN
AUNT ELSIE'S STAIRWAY (SEE BETWEEN TWO WORLDS)
                           RIKER, ANTHONY   TC
AUNT ELVIRA'S ZOO   SARGENT, PAMELA   SS
  NIGHT OF THE SPHINX AND OTHER STORIES ELWOOD, ROGER   OA
AUNT JENNIE'S TONIC   TUSHNET, LEONARD   SS FSF 71 12
  ANTHROPOLOGY THROUGH SCIENCE FICTION MASON, C/GREENBERG/& AN
  1972 ANNUAL WORLD'S BEST SF, THE WOLLHEIM, DONALD A.   AN
AUNT MILLICENT AT THE RACES GUTTRIDGE, LEN   SS FSF 65 04
  BEST FROM FANTASY AND SCIENCE FICTION: 15
                                   FERMAN, EDWARD L.   AN
AURELIA   RUSS, J. J.   SS FCR 75
  FUTURE CORRUPTION   ELWOOD, ROGER   OA
AUROCHS CAME WALKING   WILLIAMS, ROBERT M. SS FSF 53 12
  WHEN TWO WORLDS MEET   WILLIAMS, ROBERT M.   AC
AURORA IN ZENITH   ABBOTT, GORDON   SS NWQ 73 05
  NEW WORLDS NO. 5   MOORCOCK & PLATT   OA
AUTHOR OF THE ACACIA SEEDS AND OTHER EXTRACTS FROM THE JOURNAL
  OF THE ASSOCIATION OF THERO LE GUIN, URSULA K. SS FOS 74
  BEST SCIENCE FICTION OF THE YEAR, THE NO. 4
                                   CARR, TERRY   AN
  FELLOWSHIP OF THE STARS   CARR, TERRY   OA
AUTHOR'S ADVENTURE   SINCLAIR, UPTON   SS POM 04
  FANTASTIC PULPS, THE   HAINING, PETER   AN
AUTHOR'S INTRODUCTION   O'DONNELL, K. M.   IN
  IN THE POCKET AND OTHER S-F STORIES O'DONNELL, K. M.   DC
AUTHOR'S INTRODUCTION   WILLIAMSON, JACK   IN
  PANDORA EFFECT, THE   WILLIAMSON, JACK   AC
AUTHOR'S INTRODUCTION TO THIS EDITION OF FUR MAGIC·
                           NORTON, ANDRE   AI
  DAW SCIENCE FICTION READER, THE WOLLHEIM, DONALD A.   OA
AUTHOR'S INTRODUCTION- WITH HINTS FOR DESIGN AND ASSEMBLY
                           WILLIAMSON, JACK   IN
  PEOPLE MACHINES   WILLIAMSON, JACK   AC
AUTHOR'S NOTE   DE CAMP, L. SPRAGUE IN
  CONTINENT MAKERS AND OTHER TALES OF THE VIAGENS
                                   DE CAMP, L. SPRAGUE AC
AUTHOR'S NOTE   TENN, WILLIAM   IN
  SEVEN SEXES, THE   TENN, WILLIAM   AC
  SQUARE ROOT OF MAN, THE   TENN, WILLIAM   AC
  WOODEN STAR, THE   TENN, WILLIAM   AC
AUTHOR'S ORDEAL, THE   ASIMOV, ISAAC   PM SFQ 57 05
  EARTH IS ROOM ENOUGH   ASIMOV, ISAAC   AC
AUTHOR| AUTHOR| ASIMOV, ISAAC   NV NEW 64 04
  EARLY ASIMOV, THE   ASIMOV, ISAAC   AC
  UNKNOWN 5, THE   BENSEN, D. R.   AC
AUTHOR, AUTHOR   DAVIDSON, AVRAM   SS FSF 59 07
  OR ALL THE SEAS WITH OYSTERS   DAVIDSON, AVRAM   AC
AUTHORS, THE   MISC. MATERIAL   MS
  NEBULA AWARD STORIES 9   WILHELM, KATE   AN
  NEW WORLDS NO. 6   PLATT & BAILEY   OA
  NEW WORLDS QUARTERLY NO. 1   MOORCOCK, MICHAEL   OA
  NEW WORLDS QUARTERLY NO. 2   MOORCOCK, MICHAEL   OA
  NEW WORLDS QUARTERLY NO. 3   MOORCOCK, MICHAEL   OA
  NEW WORLDS QUARTERLY NO. 4   MOORCOCK, MICHAEL   OA
  NEW WORLDS QUARTERLY NO. 5   MOORCOCK, MICHAEL   OA
  SURVIVAL PRINTOUT   TOTAL EFFECT   AN
AUTO-ANCESTRAL FRACTURE   ALDISS, BRIAN W.   NV NWS 67 12
  SF: AUTHORS' CHOICE 2   HARRISON, HARRY   OA
AUTO-APOTHEOSIS   HADEN-GUEST, ANTHONY PM DTM 72
  BEST SF: 1973   HARRISON & ALDISS   AN
AUTO-DA-FE   KNIGHT, DAMON   SS GAL 61 02
  TENTH GALAXY READER, THE   POHL, FREDERIK   AN
  TURNING ON   KNIGHT, DAMON   AC
AUTO-DA-FE   ZELAZNY, ROGER   SS DVS 67 01
  DANGEROUS VISIONS   ELLISON, HARLAN   OA
  FANTASY: THE LITERATURE OF THE MARVELOUS KELLEY, LEO P. AC
  VOYAGES: SCENARIOS FOR A SHIP CALLED EARTH
                                   SAUER, ROB   AN
AUTOBIOGRAPHICAL SKETCH OF STANLEY G. WEINBAUM, THE
                           WEINBAUM, STANLEY G. MS
  MARTIAN ODYSSEY AND OTHER SCIENCE FICTION TALES, A
                                   WEINBAUM, STANLEY G. AC
AUTOBIOGRAPHY   EMSHWILLER, CAROL   SS
  JOY IN OUR CAUSE   EMSHWILLER, CAROL   AC
AUTOFAC   DICK, PHILIP K.   NV GAL 55 11
  BEST OF PHILIP K. DICK, THE   DICK, PHILIP K.   AC
  BEYOND CONTROL   SILVERBERG, ROBERT   AN
  RUINS OF EARTH, THE   DISCH, THOMAS M.   AN
  SCIENCE FACT/FICTION   FARRELL/GAGE/&   AN

AUTOFAC

VARIABLE MAN, THE	DICK, PHILIP K.			AC
AUTOMATA	WRIGHT, S. FOWLER	NV	WRT 29	09
NEW GODS LEAD, THE	WRIGHT, S. FOWLER			AC
AUTOMATA: I	WRIGHT, S. FOWLER	SS	WRT 29	09
*SCIENCE FICTION THINKING MACHINES	CONKLIN, GROFF			AN
AUTOMATA: II	WRIGHT, S. FOWLER	SS	WRT 29	09
*SCIENCE FICTION THINKING MACHINES	CONKLIN, GROFF			AN
AUTOMATA: III	WRIGHT, S. FOWLER	SS	WRT 29	09
*SCIENCE FICTION THINKING MACHINES	CONKLIN, GROFF			AN
AUTOMATIC PISTOL, THE	LEIBER, FRITZ	SS	WRT 40	05
NIGHT'S BLACK AGENTS	LEIBER, FRITZ			AC
UNEXPECTED, THE	MARGULIES, LEO			AN
AUTOMATIC TIGER	REED, KIT	SS	FSF 64	03
BEST FROM FANTASY AND SCIENCE FICTION: 14				
	DAVIDSON, AVRAM			AN
10TH ANNUAL OF THE YEAR'S BEST S-F, THE	MERRIL, JUDITH			AN
AUTOMATON	VAN VOGT, A. E.	SS	OWS 50	09
ADVENTURES IN TOMORROW	CROSSEN, KENDELL F.			AN
ALIEN EARTH AND OTHER STORIES	ELWOOD & MOSKOWITZ			AN
FAR-OUT WORLDS OF A. E. VAN VOGT, THE	VAN VOGT, A. E.			AC
SPECULATIONS	SANDERS, THOMAS E.			AN
WORLDS OF A. E. VAN VOGT, THE	VAN VOGT, A. E.			AC
AUTOMATTHEW'S FRIEND	LEM, STANISLAW	NV		72
MORTAL ENGINES	LEM, STANISLAW			AC
AUTOPSY IN TRANSIT	CHAPMAN, STEVE	SS	ORB 75	17
ORBIT 17	KNIGHT, DAMON			OA
AUTUMN LAND, THE	SIMAK, CLIFFORD D.	NV	FSF 71	10
SF: AUTHORS' CHOICE 4	HARRISON, HARRY			AN
AUTUMNTIME	LENTINI, A.	SS	GAL 71	11
BEST SCIENCE FICTION STORIES OF THE YEAR (1971)				
	DEL REY, LESTER			AN
AVAILABLE DATA ON THE WORP REACTION, THE				
	MILLER, LION	SS	FSF 53	09
BEST SF 3	CRISPIN, EDMUND			AN
FIFTY SHORT SCIENCE FICTION TALES	ASIMOV & CONKLIN			AN
13 GREAT STORIES OF SCIENCE FICTION	CONKLIN, GROFF			AN
AVENGING GHOST, THE	SERLING, ROD	SA		
*ROD SERLING'S THE TWILIGHT ZONE	SERLING, ROD			OC
AVENGING RAY, THE	SEAMARK	EX		30
SCIENCE IN FICTION	BAYLISS, A.E. & J.C.			AN
AWAKENING, THE	CLARKE, ARTHUR C.	SS	ZEN 42	02
ABC OF SCIENCE FICTION, AN	BOARDMAN, TOM JR.			AN
BEST OF ARTHUR C. CLARKE: 1937-1971, THE	CLARKE, ARTHUR C.			AC
ENDS OF TIME, THE	SILVERBERG, ROBERT			AN
PRELUDE TO MARS	CLARKE, ARTHUR C.			AC
REACH FOR TOMORROW	CLARKE, ARTHUR C.			AC
AWAKENING, THE	SELLINGS, ARTHUR	SS		
*TIME TRANSFER	SELLINGS, ARTHUR			AC
AWARD WINNING SCIENCE FICTION, 1965-1974				
	MISC. MATERIAL	MS		
NEBULA AWARD STORIES 10	GUNN, JAMES E.			AN
AWARD, THE (EPILOGUE)	NEARING, H. JR.	MS		
SINISTER RESEARCHES OF C. P. RANSOM, THE	NEARING, H. JR.			AC
AWFUL LOT OF COPY, AN	ALDISS, BRIAN W.	MS		
BEST SF: 1969	HARRISON & ALDISS			AN
AWLO OF ULM	MEEK, CAPTAIN S. P.	NV	AMZ 31	09
BEFORE THE GOLDEN AGE	ASIMOV, ISAAC			AN
AX, THE	HOYLE, FRED	SS		
ELEMENT 79	HOYLE, FRED			AC
AXOLOTL (ALSO AS DEEP SPACE)	ABERNATHY, ROBERT	SS	FSF 54	01
BEST SCIENCE FICTION STORIES AND NOVELS: 1955				
	DIKTY, T. E.			AN
AYE, AND GOMORRAH...	DELANY, SAMUEL R.	SS	DVS 67	01
DANGEROUS VISIONS	ELLISON, HARLAN			OA
DRIFTGLASS	DELANY, SAMUEL R.			AC
MODERN SCIENCE FICTION	SPINRAD, NORMAN			AN
NEBULA AWARD STORIES NO. 3	ZELAZNY, ROGER			AN
AZTECS	MCINTYRE, VONDA N.	NA		
2076: THE AMERICAN TRICENTENNIAL	BRYANT, EDWARD			OA
AZURE RING, THE	REEVE, ARTHUR B.	SS	SCD 30	05
SILENT BULLET, THE	REEVE, ARTHUR B.			AC
B + M - PLANET 4	HEARD, GERALD	NV	NTS 51	
NEW TALES OF SPACE AND TIME	HEALY, RAYMOND J.			OA
B.C.	HART, JOHNNY	CT	NYH 61	08
MATHEMATICAL MAGPIE, THE	FADIMAN, CLIFTON			AN
BAA BAA BLOCKSHEEP	HARRISON, M. JOHN	SS	NWS 68	11
BEST SF STORIES FROM NEW WORLDS 6	MOORCOCK, MICHAEL			AN
BABEL II	KNIGHT, DAMON	NV	BEY 53	07
BEST OF DAMON KNIGHT, THE	KNIGHT, DAMON			AC
FAR OUT	KNIGHT, DAMON			AC
INFINITE JESTS	SILVERBERG, ROBERT			AN
WORLDS OF SCIENCE FICTION, THE	MILLS, ROBERT P.			AN
BABY DREAMS	WARLAND, ALAN	SS	SFQ 41	WI
INTO THE FOURTH DIMENSION	CUMMINGS, RAY			AN
BABY IS THREE	STURGEON, THEODORE	NA	GAL 52	10
CHILDREN OF WONDER	TENN, WILLIAM			AN
MORE THAN HUMAN	STURGEON, THEODORE			NO
SCIENCE FICTION HALL OF FAME VOLUME 2A	BOVA, BEN			AN
BABY KILLERS	ELLIOTT, ROSE B.	SS	NEW 52	AN
*FUTURE TENSE	CROSSEN, KENDELL F.			AN
BABY MAKES TWO	CONWAY, GERARD F.	SS	CLR 73	03
CLARION III	WILSON, ROBIN SCOTT			OA
BABY ON NEPTUNE, A	BREUER, MILES J. MD.			
	AND HARRIS, CLARE WINGER SS C AMZ 29			12
AWAY FROM THE HERE AND NOW	HARRIS, CLARE WINGER			AC
FLIGHT INTO SPACE	WOLLHEIM, DONALD A.			AN
BABY, YOU WERE GREAT	WILHELM, KATE	SS	ORB 67	02
ALPHA 5	SILVERBERG, ROBERT			AN
BEST FROM ORBIT, THE	KNIGHT, DAMON			AN
DOWNSTAIRS ROOM AND OTHER SPECULATIVE FICTION, THE				
	WILHELM, KATE			AC
ORBIT 2	KNIGHT, DAMON			OA
WOMEN OF WONDER	SARGENT, PAMELA			AN
BABYLON: 70 M. (SEE HOW MANY MILES TO BABYLON?)				
	WOLLHEIM, DONALD A.	TC		

BALLAD OF LOST C'MELL, THE

BACK FROM THAT BOURNE	MITCHELL, EDWARD P.	SS	SUN 74	12
CRYSTAL MAN, THE	MITCHELL, EDWARD P.			AC
BACK OF OUR HEADS, THE	BARR, STEPHEN	NV	GAL 58	07
13 ABOVE THE NIGHT	CONKLIN, GROFF			AN
BACK THERE	SERLING, ROD	SA		
*BACK SERLING'S THE TWILIGHT ZONE	SERLING, ROD			OC
BACK THERE IN THE GRASS	MORRIS, GOUVERNEUR	SS		22
WORLD OF WONDER	PRATT, FLETCHER			AN
BACK TO JULIE	WILSON, RICHARD	SS	GAL 54	05
ASSIGNMENT IN TOMORROW	POHL, FREDERIK			AN
BACK TO THE DRAWING BOARDS	ELLISON, HARLAN	SS	FUN 58	08
ELLISON WONDERLAND	ELLISON, HARLAN			AC
FROM THE LAND OF FEAR	ELLISON, HARLAN			AC
TOUCH OF INFINITY, A	ELLISON, HARLAN			DC
BACK TO THE STONE AGE	SAUNDERS, JAKE	SS		
BEST SCIENCE FICTION STORIES OF THE YEAR (1976)				
	DOZOIS, GARDNER R.			AN
LONE STAR UNIVERSE	PROCTOR & UTLEY			OA
BACK WORD	BLOCH, ROBERT	MS		
DRAGONS AND NIGHTMARES	BLOCH, ROBERT			AC
BACKFIRE	ROCKLYNNE, ROSS	SS	ASF 43	01
OMNIBUS OF SCIENCE FICTION	CONKLIN, GROFF			AN
BACKTRACKED	FILER, BURT K.	SS	FSF 68	06
AS TOMORROW BECOMES TODAY	SULLIVAN, CHARLES W.			AN
WORLD'S BEST SCIENCE FICTION: 1969	WOLLHEIM & CARR			AN
BACKWARD, INTO BEASTS EVOLVING	ALLEN, DICK	PM		
BEST SF: 1974	HARRISON & ALDISS			AN
BACKWARD, O TIME (THIS WAY TO THE REGRESS)				
	KNIGHT, DAMON	SS	GAL 56	08
BEST OF DAMON KNIGHT, THE	KNIGHT, DAMON			AC
TURNING ON	KNIGHT, DAMON			AC
BACKWARD, TURN BACKWARD	SHIRAS, WILMAR H.	NV	NEW 70	AN
NEW WORLDS OF FANTASY NO. 2	CARR, TERRY			AN
BACKWARDNESS	ANDERSON, POUL	SS	FSF 58	03
BEST FROM FANTASY AND SCIENCE FICTION: 8				
	BOUCHER, ANTHONY			AN
SCHOOL AND SOCIETY THROUGH SCIENCE FICTION				
	OLANDER/GREENBERG/&			AN
BACTERIOLOGICAL DETECTIVE, THE	REEVE, ARTHUR B.	SS	SCD 30	02
SILENT BULLET, THE	REEVE, ARTHUR B.			AC
BACULAR CLOCK, THE	BOND, NELSON S.	SS	BBM 42	07
MR. MERGENTHWIRKER'S LOBBIES AND OTHER FANTASTIC TALES				
	BOND, NELSON S.			AC
BAD DAY FOR SALES, A	LEIBER, FRITZ	SS	GAL 53	07
BEST SCIENCE-FICTION STORIES: 1954, THE	BLEILER & DIKTY			AN
FIFTY SHORT SCIENCE FICTION TALES	ASIMOV & CONKLIN			AN
GALAXY SCIENCE FICTION OMNIBUS	GOLD, H. L.			AN
MEN AND MACHINES	SILVERBERG, ROBERT			AN
NIGHTMARE AGE	POHL, FREDERIK			AN
SECOND GALAXY READER OF SCIENCE FICTION	GOLD, H. L.			AN
SHADOW OF TOMORROW	POHL, FREDERIK			AN
BAD DAY FOR VERMIN, A	LAUMER, KEITH	SS	GAL 64	02
EIGHTH GALAXY READER, THE	POHL, FREDERIK			AN
BAD LIFE, THE	BIXBY, JEROME	NA	GAL 63	02
SPACE BY THE TAIL	BIXBY, JEROME			AC
BAD MEDICINE	SHECKLEY, ROBERT	NV	GAL 56	07
PILGRIMAGE TO EARTH	SHECKLEY, ROBERT			AC
ROBERT SHECKLEY OMNIBUS, THE	SHECKLEY, ROBERT			AC
SF: AUTHORS' CHOICE 4	HARRISON, HARRY			AN
BAD NEWS AND THE GOOD, THE	ASIMOV, ISAAC	IN		
BEYOND TOMORROW	HARDING, LEE			AN
BADINAGE	GOULART, RON	SS	NEW 65	AN
NUTZENBOLTS	GOULART, RON			AC
PSEUDO PEOPLE, THE	NOLAN, WILLIAM F.			AN
BADMAN	BRUNNER, JOHN	SS	NWS 60	03
NO FUTURE IN IT	BRUNNER, JOHN			AC
OUT OF THIS WORLD 5	WILLIAMS-ELLIS& OWEN			AN
BAIT	CLOUGH, ROY L.	SS	ASF 51	06
SPACE POLICE	NORTON, ANDRE			AN
BAIT PRINCIPLE, THE	HARRISON, M. JOHN	SS	NWS 70	02
BEST SF STORIES FROM NEW WORLDS 8	MOORCOCK, MICHAEL			AN
MACHINE IN SHAFT TEN AND OTHER STORIES, THE				
	HARRISON, M. JOHN			AC
BAIT, THE	LEIBER, FRITZ	SS		73
WORLDS OF FRITZ LEIBER, THE	LEIBER, FRITZ			AC
BAKED BEAN FACTORY, THE	BUTTERWORTH, MICHAEL SS	NWS 67	10
ENGLAND SWINGS SF	MERRIL, JUDITH			AN
SPACE-TIME JOURNAL, THE	MERRIL, JUDITH			AN
BALAAM	BOUCHER, ANTHONY	SS	NTL 54	
BEST SF 4	CRISPIN, EDMUND			AN
FAR AND AWAY	BOUCHER, ANTHONY			AC
GODS FOR TOMORROW	SANTESSON, HANS S.			AN
OTHER WORLDS, OTHER GODS	MOHS, MAYO			AN
9 TALES OF SPACE AND TIME	HEALY, RAYMOND J.			OA
BALANCE	CHRISTOPHER, JOHN	SS	NWS 51	SP
BEST SCIENCE-FICTION STORIES: 1952, THE	BLEILER & DIKTY			AN
*NO PLACE LIKE EARTH	CARNELL, JOHN			AN
BALANCE OF TERROR (PAUL SCHNEIDER)				
	BLISH, JAMES	SA	STK 67	01
STAR TREK	BLISH, JAMES			OC
BALANCED ECOLOGY	SCHMITZ, JAMES H.	SS	ASF 65	03
ABOVE THE HUMAN LANDSCAPE	MCNELLY & STOVER			AN
ANALOG 5	CAMPBELL, JOHN W. JR			AN
BUG-EYED MONSTERS	CHEETHAM, ANTHONY			AN
NEBULA AWARD STORIES	KNIGHT, DAMON			AN
NICE DAY FOR SCREAMING, AND OTHER TALES OF THE HUB				
	SCHMITZ, JAMES H.			AC
BALD-HEADED MIRAGE, THE	BLOCH, ROBERT	SS	AMZ 60	06
ANCIENT MYSTERIES READER, THE	HAINING, PETER			AN
FEAR TODAY, GONE TOMORROW	BLOCH, ROBERT			AC
BALGRUMMO'S HELL	KIRK, RUSSELL	SS	FSF 67	07
BEST FROM FANTASY AND SCIENCE FICTION: 17				
	FERMAN, EDWARD L.			AN
BALLAD OF LOST C'MELL, THE	SMITH, CORDWAINER	NV	GAL 62	10
BEST OF CORDWAINER SMITH, THE	SMITH, CORDWAINER			AC
SCIENCE FICTION HALL OF FAME VOLUME 2A	BOVA, BEN			AN

BALLAD OF LOST C'MELL, THE
  SPACE LORDS   SMITH, CORDWAINER AC
  12 GREAT CLASSICS OF SCIENCE FICTION CONKLIN, GROFF AN
BALLAD OF LUNA LIL, THE   BOUNDS, SYDNEY J. SS NWR 69 14
  NEW WRITINGS IN SF. 14   CARNELL, JOHN   OA
BALLAD OF SLICK SID, THE   MALZBERG, BARRY N. SS INY 72 04
  DOWN HERE IN THE DREAM QUARTER MALZBERG, BARRY N. AC
  INFINITY 4   HOSKINS, ROBERT   OA
"BALLAD OF TEDDY HART, THE" BRUNNER, JOHN SG NEW 76 04
  BOOK OF JOHN BRUNNER, THE   BRUNNER, JOHN   AC
BALLAD OF THE SHOSHONU   DICKSON, GORDON R. SG NEW 61 AN
  6TH ANNUAL OF THE YEAR'S BEST S-F, THE MERRIL, JUDITH AN
BALLADE OF AN ARTIFICIAL SATELLITE
                ANDERSON, POUL   PM FSF 58 10
  FIFTY SHORT SCIENCE FICTION TALES ASIMOV & CONKLIN AN
  HOMEBREW   ANDERSON, POUL   AC
BALLENGER'S PEOPLE   NEVILLE, KRIS SS GAL 67 04
  ON OUR WAY TO THE FUTURE   CARR, TERRY   AN
BALLOON TREE, THE   MITCHELL, EDWARD P. SS SUN 83 02
  CRYSTAL MAN, THE   MITCHELL, EDWARD P. AC
BALLOON-HOAX, THE   POE, EDGAR ALLEN SS SUN 44 04
  PAST, PRESENT, AND FUTURE PERFECT WOLFE, J&FITZ GERALD AN
  WONDERMAKERS   HOSKINS, ROBERT   AN
BALLOON, THE   BARTHELME, DONALD SS NYM 66 04
  SCIENCE FICTION: THE FUTURE   ALLEN, DICK   AN
  SF12   MERRIL, JUDITH   AN
BALLOTS AND BANDITS   LAUMER, KEITH   NV IFS 70 09
  RETIEF OF THE CDT   LAUMER, KEITH   AC
BALLS: A MEDITATION AT THE GRAVESIDE
                KIDD, VIRGINIA   SS QRK 71 03
  QUARK/3   DELANY & HACKER OA
BALU   DERLETH, AUGUST   SS WRT 49 01
  MR. GEORGE AND OTHER ODD PERSONS DERLETH, AUGUST   AC
BANDEMAR, THE   WEHRLE, JOE JR. SS CLR 71 01
  CLARION   WILSON, ROBIN SCOTT OA
BANKRUPTCY PROCEEDINGS HULL, E. MAYNE   NV ASF 46 08
  PLANETS FOR SALE   HULL, E. MAYNE   AC
BANKS OF THE NILE, THE   PENMAN, THOMAS
         AND SMITH, RITCHIE   NV C NWR 76 28
  NEW WRITINGS IN SF. 28   BULMER, KENNETH   OA
BARBARIAN, THE   ANDERSON, POUL   SS FSF 56 05
  BEST FROM FANTASY AND SCIENCE FICTION: 6
                BOUCHER, ANTHONY   AN
  BEST OF POUL ANDERSON, THE ANDERSON, POUL   AC
  ODDBALLS   GHIDALIA, VIC   AN
BARBARIAN, THE   RUSS, JOANNA   NV ORB 68 03
  ALIX   RUSS, JOANNA   AC
  ANOTHER WORLD   DOZOIS, GARDNER R. AN
  ORBIT 3   KNIGHT, DAMON   OA
BARBARIAN, THE   VAN VOGT, A. E. NV ASF 47 12
  BOOK OF VAN VOGT, THE   VAN VOGT, A. E.   AC
  EMPIRE OF THE ATOM   VAN VOGT, A. E.   NO
BARD'S TALE, THE   DIXON, TERRY   SS INY 72 03
  INFINITY 3   HOSKINS, ROBERT   OA
BARDLET'S ROMANCE, A (SEE IN THE MODERN VEIN: AN UNSYMPATHETIC
  LOVE STORY)   WELLS, H. G.   TC
BARE MOUNTAIN BENEATH THE MOON YEFREMOV, IVAN   SS
  MEETING OVER TUSCARORA AND OTHER ADVENTURE TALES, A
                YEFREMOV, IVAN   AC
BARGAIN FROM BRUNSWICK (SEE A PRESENT FROM BRUNSWICK)
                WYNDHAM, JOHN   TC
BARGAIN IN BODIES, A SCHERE, MOSES   SS UNK 43 06
  DEALS WITH THE DEVIL   DAVENPORT, BASIL   AN
BARGAIN IN CASHEL, A KERSH, GERALD   SS SEP 63 04
  9TH ANNUAL OF THE YEAR'S BEST S-F, THE MERRIL, JUDITH AN
BARGAIN, THE   CARTMILL, CLEVE SS UNK 42 08
  UNKNOWN 5, THE   BENSEN, D. R.   AN
BARNABY'S CLOCK   LAFFERTY, R. A. SS SCS 73
  SHOWCASE   ELWOOD, ROGER   OA
BARNACLE BULL   SANDERS, WINSTON P. SS ASF 60 09
  ANALOG 1   CAMPBELL, JOHN W. JR AN
BARNEY   STANTON, WILL   SS FSF 51 02
  BEST FROM FANTASY AND SCIENCE FICTION BOUCHER & MCCOMAS AN
  FIFTY SHORT SCIENCE FICTION TALES ASIMOV & CONKLIN AN
BARON BAGGE   LERNET-HOLENIA, ALEX SS
  BEST FANTASY STORIES   ALDISS, BRIAN W.   AN
BARON MUNCHAUSEN'S SCIENTIFIC ADVENTURES (HOW THE MARTIAN
  CANALS ARE BUILT)   GERNSBACK, HUGO SS ELX 16 11
  FANTASTIC PULPS, THE   HAINING, PETER   AN
BARREN WORLD   WELLS, BASIL   SS
  DOORWAYS TO SPACE   WELLS, BASIL   AC
BARRIER   BOUCHER, ANTHONY NV ASF 42 09
  SPECTRUM 4   AMIS & CONQUEST   AN
  6 GREAT SHORT NOVELS OF SCIENCE FICTION CONKLIN, GROFF AN
BARRIER OF DREAD   MERRIL, JUDITH SS FUT 50 07
  JOURNEY TO INFINITY   GREENBERG, MARTIN AN
BARTHOLOMEW & SON (AND THE FISH-GIRL)
          CONEY, MICHAEL G. NV NWR 75 27
  NEW WRITINGS IN SF. 27   BULMER, KENNETH   OA
BASIC RIGHT   RUSSELL, ERIC FRANK NV ASF 58 04
  GIANTS UNLEASHED   CONKLIN, GROFF   AN
BASILEIKON: SUMMER DAVIDSON, AVRAM SS QRK 71 04
  QUARK/4   DELANY & HACKER OA
BASILISK   DAVIDSON, AVRAM NV NEW 67 AN
  NEW WORLDS OF FANTASY   CARR, TERRY   AN
BASILISK   ELLISON, HARLAN SS FSF 72 08
  DEATHBIRD STORIES   ELLISON, HARLAN   AC
BASILISK, THE   BLACK, D. M.   PM   69
  HOLDING YOUR EIGHT HANDS LUCIE-SMITH, EDWARD AN
BASIS FOR NEGOTIATION ALDISS, BRIAN W. NV NWS 62 01
  AIRS OF EARTH, THE   ALDISS, BRIAN W.   AC
  *BEST SCIENCE FICTION STORIES OF BRIAN W. ALDISS
                ALDISS, BRIAN W.   AC
  BRIAN ALDISS OMNIBUS, A   ALDISS, BRIAN W.   AC
  LAMBDA I AND OTHER STORIES CARNELL, JOHN   AN
BAT   O'DONNELL, K. M. SS NEW 71 DC
  IN THE POCKET AND OTHER S-F STORIES O'DONNELL, K. M. DC

BEAR WITH THE KNOT ON HIS TAIL, THE

BATHE YOUR BEARINGS IN BLOOD (SEE SKIRMISH)
                SIMAK, CLIFFORD D. TC
BATTERED-EARTH SYNDROME, THE MALZBERG, BARRY N. SS SVW 73
  BEST OF BARRY N. MALZBERG, THE MALZBERG, BARRY N. AC
  SAVING WORLDS   ELWOOD & KIDD   OA
BATTERY OF HATE, THE CAMPBELL, JOHN W. JR SS AMZ 33 11
  SCIENCE FICTION OF THE 30'S KNIGHT, DAMON   AN
BATTLE   VERNON, ROGER LEE SS
  SPACE FRONTIERS, THE   VERNON, ROGER LEE   AC
BATTLE FOR THE PACIFIC, THE STEVENS, ROWAN AN
  BATTLE FOR THE PACIFIC AND OTHER ADVENTURES AT SEA, THE
                ANONYMOUS   AN
  BATTLE OF THE MONSTERS AND OTHER STORIES, THE
                HARTWELL & CURREY AN
BATTLE HUM AND THE BOJE GERROLD, DAVID NV NEW 72 AC
  WITH A FINGER IN MY I   GERROLD, DAVID   AC
BATTLE OF DORKING, THE CHESNEY, G. T.   NA
  BEFORE ARMAGEDDON   MOORCOCK, MICHAEL AN
BATTLE OF THE BELLS, THE BIXBY, JEROME   SS IMG 54 09
  SPACE BY THE TAIL   BIXBY, JEROME   AC
BATTLE OF THE MONSTERS, THE ROBERTSON, MORGAN SS   99
  BATTLE OF THE MONSTERS AND OTHER STORIES, THE
                HARTWELL & CURREY AN
  *BEYOND TIME AND SPACE   DERLETH, AUGUST   AN
BATTLE OF THE S...S, THE ELLIOTT, BRUCE SS NEW 52 AN
  *FUTURE TENSE   CROSSEN, KENDELL F. AN
BATTLE OF THE UNBORN (ALSO AS STRUGGLE IN THE WOMB)
                BLISH, JAMES   SS FUT 50 05
  *SCIENCE FICTION ADVENTURES IN MUTATION CONKLIN, GROFF AN
BATTLE OF WIZARDS HUBBARD, L. RON SS FBK 49 05
  WIZARDS AND WARLOCKS   GHIDALIA, VIC   AN
BATTLE OF WIZARDS REPP, ED EARL   SS
  RADIUM POOL, THE   REPP, ED EARL   AC
BATTLE OFF THE HOOK, THE STIRLING, YATES JR. SS
  BATTLE FOR THE PACIFIC AND OTHER ADVENTURES AT SEA, THE
                ANONYMOUS   OC
BATTLE WITHOUT BANNERS ELLISON, HARLAN SS NEW 64 AC
  FROM THE LAND OF FEAR   ELLISON, HARLAN   AC
  *LOVE AIN'T NOTHING BUT SEX MISSPELLED ELLISON, HARLAN AC
BATTLE WON   BUNCH, DAVID R.   SS
  MODERAN   BUNCH, DAVID R.   AC
BATTLE, THE   SHECKLEY, ROBERT SS IFS 54 09
  CITIZEN IN SPACE   SHECKLEY, ROBERT   AC
  FIRST WORLD OF IF, THE   QUINN & WULFF   AN
  ROBERT SHECKLEY OMNIBUS, THE SHECKLEY, ROBERT   AC
BATTLEFIELD (HIS FIRST DAY AT WAR)
                ELLISON, HARLAN SS STM 58 11
  ELLISON WONDERLAND   ELLISON, HARLAN   AC
  WINDOWS INTO TOMORROW   SILVERBERG, ROBERT AN
BAXBR DAXBR   SMITH, EVELYN E. SS FSF 56 09
  BEST SF 4   CRISPIN, EDMUND   AN
  JOURNEYS IN SCIENCE FICTION LOUGHLIN, RICHARD L. AN
  OUT OF THIS WORLD 3   WILLIAMS-ELLIS& OWEN AN
  *TIME TO COME   DERLETH, AUGUST   OA
BAYNTER'S IMP   DERLETH, AUGUST SS WRT 43 09
  ALONE BY NIGHT   CONGDON, MICHAEL&DON AN
  NOT LONG FOR THIS WORLD DERLETH, AUGUST   AC
BAZAAR OF THE BIZARRE LEIBER, FRITZ   NV SOI 63 08
  SPELL OF SEVEN, THE   DE CAMP, L. SPRAGUE AN
BE A WINGDINGER, EARN BIG MONEY
                PETAJA, EMIL   SS
  STARDRIFT AND OTHER FANTASTIC FLOTSAM PETAJA, EMIL   AC
BE MERRY   BUDRYS, ALGIS   NV IFS 66 12
  ON OUR WAY TO THE FUTURE CARR, TERRY   AN
BE MY GUEST   KNIGHT, DAMON   NV FUN 58 09
  *OFF CENTER   KNIGHT, DAMON   DC
  OTHERS, THE   CARR, TERRY   AN
BE OF GOOD CHEER   LEIBER, FRITZ   SS GAL 64 10
  RULERS OF MEN   SANTESSON, HANS S. AN
  10TH ANNUAL OF THE YEAR'S BEST S-F, THE MERRIL, JUDITH AN
BEACH MURDERS, THE (CONFETTI ROYALE, ROG 66 01)
                BALLARD, J. G.   SS NWS 69 04
  BEST SF STORIES FROM NEW WORLDS 7 MOORCOCK, MICHAEL AN
  LOW-FLYING AIRCRAFT AND OTHER STORIES BALLARD, J. G. AC
BEACH SCENE   KING, MARSHALL   SS GAL 60 10
  6TH ANNUAL OF THE YEAR'S BEST S-F, THE MERRIL, JUDITH AN
BEACH WHERE TIME BEGAN, THE (SEE EXTEMPORE)
                KNIGHT, DAMON   TC
BEACH, THE   BAXTER, JOHN   SS NWR 68 13
  NEW WRITINGS IN SF. 13   CARNELL, JOHN   OA
  PACIFIC BOOK OF AUSTRALIAN SCIENCE FICTION
                BAXTER, JOHN   AN
BEACHCOMBER   KNIGHT, DAMON   SS IMG 52 12
  IN DEEP   KNIGHT, DAMON   AC
BEACHHEAD (YOU'LL NEVER GO HOME AGAIN)
                SIMAK, CLIFFORD D. SS FAD 51 07
  *BEACHHEADS IN SPACE   DERLETH, AUGUST   AN
  EXPLORERS OF SPACE   SILVERBERG, ROBERT AN
  *STRANGERS IN THE UNIVERSE SIMAK, CLIFFORD D. AN
BEACHHEAD IN UTOPIA BIGGLE, LLOYD JR. SS OMG 73
  OMEGA   ELWOOD, ROGER   OA
BEAM PIRATE   SMITH, GEORGE O. NV ASF 44 10
  COMPLETE VENUS EQUILATERAL, THE SMITH, GEORGE O. AC
  VENUS EQUILATERAL   SMITH, GEORGE O.   AC
BEAM US HOME   TIPTREE, JAMES JR. SS GAL 69 04
  ANOTHER WORLD   DOZOIS, GARDNER R. AN
  TEN THOUSAND LIGHT-YEARS FROM HOME TIPTREE, JAMES JR. AC
BEANSTALK   BLISH, JAMES   NA NEW 52 AN
  *FUTURE TENSE   CROSSEN, KENDELL F. AN
BEAR POSSIBILITY   BROWN, FREDRIC   SS
  NIGHTMARES AND GEEZENSTACKS BROWN, FREDRIC   AC
BEAR WITH THE KNOT ON HIS TAIL, THE
                TALL, STEPHEN   NV FSF 71 05
  BEST FROM FANTASY AND SCIENCE FICTION: 20
                FERMAN, EDWARD L.   AN
  STARDUST VOYAGES, THE   TALL, STEPHEN   AC

Title / Collection	Author	Type	Mag	Yr	No
1972 ANNUAL WORLD'S BEST SF, THE	WOLLHEIM, DONALD A.	AN			
BEARING WITNESS	MALZBERG, BARRY N.	SS	FTP	73	
BEST OF BARRY N. MALZBERG, THE	MALZBERG, BARRY N.	AC			
FLAME TREE PLANET	ELWOOD, ROGER	OA			
BEAST FOR NORN, A	MARTIN, GEORGE R. R.	NV			
ANDROMEDA I	WESTON, PETER	OA			
BEAST FROM 20,000 FATHOMS, THE (ALSO AS THE FOGHORN)					
	BRADBURY, RAY	SS	SEP	51	06
GHOULS, THE	HAINING, PETER	AN			
BEAST IN VIEW	DEFORD, MIRIAM ALLEN	SS	OMG	73	
OMEGA	ELWOOD, ROGER	OA			
BEAST OF THE VOID, A	GALLUN, RAYMOND Z.	SS	ASF	36	09
ESCALES DANS L'INFINI	GALLET, GEORGES H.	AN			
BEAST THAT SHOUTED LOVE AT THE HEART OF THE WORLD, THE					
	ELLISON, HARLAN	NV	GAL	68	06
BEAST THAT SHOUTED LOVE AT THE HEART OF THE WORLD, THE					
	ELLISON, HARLAN	AC			
DARK STARS	SILVERBERG, ROBERT	AN			
HUGO WINNERS, THE (VOLUME 2)	ASIMOV, ISAAC	AN			
BEAST WITH FIVE FINGERS, THE	HARVEY, WILLIAM F.	NV			
GHOULS, THE	HAINING, PETER	AN			
BEAST-JEWEL OF MARS, THE	BRACKETT, LEIGH	SS	PLS	55	SP
COMING OF THE TERRANS, THE	BRACKETT, LEIGH	NO			
BEAST, THE	HUBBARD, L. RON	SS	ASF	42	10
KINGSLAYER, THE	HUBBARD, L. RON	AC			
BEAST, THE	VAN VOGT, A. E.	NO	DBL	63	
VAN VOGT OMNIBUS, A	VAN VOGT, A. E.	AC			
BEAST, THE	VAN VOGT, A. E.	NV	ASF	43	11
BEAST, THE	VAN VOGT, A. E.	NO			
BEASTS OF BARSAC, THE	BLOCH, ROBERT	SS	WRT	44	07
LIVING DEMONS, THE	BLOCH, ROBERT	AC			
BEASTS OF BOURBON	DE CAMP, L. SPRAGUE				
AND PRATT, FLETCHER		SS C	FSF	51	10
TALES FROM GAVAGAN'S BAR	DE CAMP, L. S.&PRATT	AC			
BEAT CLUSTER, THE	LEIBER, FRITZ	SS	GAL	61	10
PAIL OF AIR, A	LEIBER, FRITZ	AC			
SEVENTH GALAXY READER, THE	POHL, FREDERIK	AN			
7TH ANNUAL OF THE YEAR'S BEST S-F, THE	MERRIL, JUDITH	AN			
BEAULIEU	ST. CLAIR, MARGARET	SS	FSF	57	07
CHANGE THE SKY AND OTHER STORIES	ST. CLAIR, MARGARET	AC			
BEAUTIFUL BREW, THE	GUNN, JAMES E.	NV	BEY	54	09
BEYOND	ANONYMOUS	AN			
WITCHING HOUR, THE	GUNN, JAMES E.	AC			
BEAUTIFUL DOLL CAPER, THE	NOLAN, WILLIAM F.	SS	NUG	56	
IMPACT-20	NOLAN, WILLIAM F.	AC			
BEAUTIFUL ONE IS HERE, THE (SEE I SING THE BODY ELECTRIC)					
	BRADBURY, RAY	TC			
BEAUTIFUL ONE, THE	ROBERTS, KEITH	NV	NWQ	73	05
NEW WORLDS NO. 5	MOORCOCK & PLATT	OA			
BEAUTIFUL PEOPLE, THE (ALSO AS THE BEAUTIFUL WOMAN)					
	BEAUMONT, CHARLES	SS	IFS	52	09
YONDER	BEAUMONT, CHARLES	AC			
BEAUTIFUL SUIT, THE (A MOONLIGHT FABLE)					
	WELLS, H. G.	SS	COL	09	04
COUNTRY OF THE BLIND, THE	WELLS, H. G.	AC			
SHORT STORIES OF H. G. WELLS, THE	WELLS, H. G.	AC			
*TIME MACHINE AND OTHER STORIES, THE	WELLS, H. G.	AC			
BEAUTIFUL THINGS, THE	ZIRUL, ARTHUR	SS	FUN	58	05
SF:59, THE YEAR'S GREATEST SCIENCE FICTION AND FANTASY					
	MERRIL, JUDITH	AN			
BEAUTIFUL WOMAN, THE (THE BEAUTIFUL PEOPLE)					
	BEAUMONT, CHARLES	SS	IFS	52	09
PRIZE SCIENCE FICTION	WOLLHEIM, DONALD A.	AN			
BEAUTIFUL, BEAUTIFUL, BEAUTIFUL!					
	FRIEDMAN, STUART	SS	FUT	52	03
FIFTY SHORT SCIENCE FICTION TALES	ASIMOV & CONKLIN	AN			
*WORLDS OF TOMORROW	DERLETH, AUGUST	AN			
BEAUTY AND THE BEAST	KUTTNER, HENRY	SS	TWS	40	04
CREATURES FROM BEYOND	CARR, TERRY	AN			
FUTURES TO INFINITY	MOSKOWITZ, SAM	AN			
BEAUTY AND THE BEASTS	LEIBER, FRITZ	SS	NEW	74	AC
BOOK OF FRITZ LEIBER, THE	LEIBER, FRITZ	AC			
BEAUTY'S BEAST	BLOCH, ROBERT	SS	WRT	41	05
LIVING DEMONS, THE	BLOCH, ROBERT	AC			
BEAUTYLAND	WOLFE, GENE	SS	SVW	73	
SAVING WORLDS	ELWOOD & KIDD	OA			
BECALMED IN HELL	NIVEN, LARRY	SS	FSF	65	07
ALL THE MYRIAD WAYS	NIVEN, LARRY	AC			
NEBULA AWARD STORIES	KNIGHT, DAMON	AN			
SCIENCE FICTION ARGOSY, A	KNIGHT, DAMON	AC			
TALES OF KNOWN SPACE: THE UNIVERSE OF LARRY NIVEN					
	NIVEN, LARRY	AC			
TWENTY YEARS OF FANTASY & SCIENCE FICTION					
	FERMAN & MILLS	AN			
WORLD'S BEST SCIENCE FICTION: 1966	WOLLHEIM & CARR	AN			
BECAUSE OF PURPLE ELEPHANTS	LORY, ROBERT	SS			
HARVEST OF HOODWINKS, A	LORY, ROBERT	DC			
BECKONING STAR	LAMPTON, CHRIS	SS			
QUEST	BISCHOFF, DAVID	OA			
BECKONING TRAIL, THE	ENGDAHL, SYLVIA				
AND ROBERSON, RICK		NV C	NEW	76	AN
UNIVERSE AHEAD	ENGDAHL & ROBERSON	AN			
BED SHEETS ARE WHITE	LIEF, EVELYN	SS	DVS	72	02
AGAIN, DANGEROUS VISIONS	ELLISON, HARLAN	AN			
BEDSIDE MANNOR	MORRISON, WILLIAM	NV	GAL	54	05
GREAT SCIENCE FICTION ABOUT DOCTORS	CONKLIN, G&FABRICANT	AN			
BEDTIME STORY	MACBETH, GEORGE	PM		63	
HOLDING YOUR EIGHT HANDS	LUCIE-SMITH, EDWARD	AN			
STARLIT CORRIDOR, THE	MANSFIELD, ROGER	AN			
BEDTIME STORY, A	LETTS, D.	SS			
STOPWATCH	HAY, GEORGE	OA			
BEECH HILL	WOLFE, GENE	SS	INY	72	04
INFINITY 3	HOSKINS, ROBERT	OA			
BEELZEBUB	BLOCH, ROBERT	SS	PBY	63	12
CHAMBER OF HORRORS	BLOCH, ROBERT	AC			
PLAYBOY BOOK OF HORROR AND THE SUPERNATURAL, THE					
	PLAYBOY, EDITORS OF	AN			
BEEN A LONG, LONG TIME	LAFFERTY, R. A.	SS	FAN	70	12
GALACTIC EMPIRES VOLUME ONE	ALDISS, BRIAN W.	AN			
BEEP	BLISH, JAMES	NV	GAL	54	02
*GALACTIC CLUSTER	BLISH, JAMES	AC			
GALACTIC EMPIRES VOLUME TWO	ALDISS, BRIAN W.	AN			
SPACE POLICE	NORTON, ANDRE	AN			
*STORIES FOR TOMORROW	SLOANE, WILLIAM	AN			
BEES FROM BORNEO, THE	GRAY, WILL H.	SS	AMZ	31	02
OMNIBUS OF SCIENCE FICTION	CONKLIN, GROFF	AN			
BEES OF KNOWLEDGE, THE	BAYLEY, BARRINGTON J	NV	NWB	75	08
NEW WORLDS EIGHT	BAILEY, HILARY	OA			
1976 ANNUAL WORLD'S BEST SF, THE	WOLLHEIM, DONALD A.	AN			
BEETLES	BLOCH, ROBERT	SS	WRT	38	12
*OPENER OF THE WAY, THE	BLOCH, ROBERT	AC			
YOURS TRULY, JACK THE RIPPER	BLOCH, ROBERT	AC			
BEFORE A LIVE AUDIENCE	SOHL, JERRY	SS	FCR	75	
FUTURE CORRUPTION	ELWOOD, ROGER	OA			
BEFORE EDEN	CLARKE, ARTHUR C.	SS	AMZ	61	06
ALL ABOUT VENUS	ALDISS, BRIAN W.	AN			
DOORWAY INTO TIME	MOSKOWITZ, SAM	AN			
FAREWELL FANTASTIC VENUS	ALDISS & HARRISON	AN			
MODERN MASTERPIECES OF SCIENCE FICTION	MOSKOWITZ, SAM	AN			
NINE BILLION NAMES OF GOD, THE	CLARKE, ARTHUR C.	AC			
STARLIT CORRIDOR, THE	MANSFIELD, ROGER	AN			
TALES OF TEN WORLDS	CLARKE, ARTHUR C.	AC			
TOMORROW'S WORLDS	SILVERBERG, ROBERT	AN			
YET MORE PENGUIN SCIENCE FICTION	ALDISS, BRIAN W.	AN			
3000 YEARS OF FANTASY AND SCIENCE FICTION					
	DE CAMP, L. S.&C.	AN			
BEFORE THE CURTAIN...	BOUCHER, ANTHONY	IN			
TREASURY OF GREAT SCIENCE FICTION, A VOL.1					
	BOUCHER, ANTHONY	AN			
BEFORE THE DAWN (ALSO IN FFM 46 02)					
	TAINE, JOHN	NO	WMW	34	
PORTABLE NOVELS OF SCIENCE	WOLLHEIM, DONALD A.	AN			
BEFORE THE TALENT DIES	SLESAR, HENRY	SS	VSF	57	09
NO LIMITS	FERMAN, JOSEPH W.	AN			
BEFORE THE TRIFFIDS...	GILLINGS, WALTER	IN			
WANDERERS OF TIME	WYNDHAM, JOHN	AC			
BEGGAR ON DUBLIN BRIDGE, THE (SEE THE BEGGAR ON O'CONNELL					
BRIDGE)	BRADBURY, RAY	TC			
BEGGAR ON O'CONNELL BRIDGE, THE (THE BEGGAR ON DUBLIN BRIDGE)					
	BRADBURY, RAY	SS	SEP	61	01
MACHINERIES OF JOY, THE	BRADBURY, RAY	AC			
BEGGARS IN VELVET	PADGETT, LEWIS	NV	ASF	45	12
MUTANT	PADGETT, LEWIS	AC			
BEGGARS' STONE, THE	KERSH, GERALD	SS	ESQ		
ON AN ODD NOTE	KERSH, GERALD	AC			
BEGIN AGAIN	CHRISTOPHER, JOHN	SS	ESQ		
TWENTY-SECOND CENTURY, THE	CHRISTOPHER, JOHN	AC			
BEGINNING OF APRIL OR THE END OF MARCH, THE					
	DISCH, THOMAS M.	SS	FSF	71	02
*GETTING INTO DEATH	DISCH, THOMAS M.	AC			
BEGINNINGS, THE	FIEDLER, LESLIE A.	SI			
IN DREAMS AWAKE	FIEDLER, LESLIE A.	AN			
BEGUM'S FORTUNE, THE (1879)	VERNE, JULES	EX			
ANDROIDS, TIME MACHINES AND BLUE GIRAFFES					
	ELWOOD & GHIDALIA	AN			
JULES VERNE- MASTER OF SCIENCE FICTION	VERNE, JULES	AC			
STRANGE SIGNPOSTS	ELWOOD & MOSKOWITZ	AN			
VISIONS OF TOMORROW	ELWOOD, ROGER	AN			
BEHIND THE ATE BALL (SEE A MARTIAN ODDITY)					
	ACKERMAN, FORREST J.	TC			
BEHIND THE BLACK NEBULA (THE INVADERS)					
	HUBBARD, L. RON	NV	ASF	42	01
TALES OF OUTER SPACE	WOLLHEIM, DONALD A.	DA			
BEHIND THE SANDRAT HOAX	ANVIL, CHRISTOPHER	NV	GAL	68	10
ELEVENTH GALAXY READER, THE	POHL, FREDERIK	AN			
BEHIND THE WALLS	TOKUNAGA, LAURA	SS	NWQ	73	05
NEW WORLDS NO. 5	MOORCOCK & PLATT	OA			
BEHOLD IT WAS A DREAM (1873)	BROUGHTON, RHODA	SS			
BEYOND THE BARRIERS OF SPACE AND TIME	MERRIL, JUDITH	AN			
BEHOLD THE MAN	MOORCOCK, MICHAEL	NV	NWS	66	09
MOORCOCK'S BOOK OF MARTYRS	MOORCOCK, MICHAEL	AC			
NEBULA AWARD STORIES NO. 3	ZELAZNY, ROGER	AN			
NEW AWARENESS, THE	WARRICK & GREENBERG	AN			
WORLD'S BEST SCIENCE FICTION: 1967	WOLLHEIM & CARR	AN			
BEHOLDER'S EYE, THE	HUTTON, AMY	SS	CLR	71	01
CLARION	WILSON, ROBIN SCOTT	OA			
BEING	MATHESON, RICHARD	NV	IFS	54	08
ASLEEP IN ARMAGEDDON	SISSONS, MICHAEL	AN			
SHORES OF SPACE, THE	MATHESON, RICHARD	AC			
BEING AN EXAMINATION OF THE PONSIAN AND HOLMESIAN SECRET					
DEDUCTIVE SYSTEMS	VAN VOGT, A. E.	AR		71	
BEST OF A. E. VAN VOGT, THE	VAN VOGT, A. E.	AC			
BEING MACHINE, THE (THE MIND BOMB)					
	HERBERT, FRANK	NV	IFS	69	10
BEST OF FRANK HERBERT, THE	HERBERT, FRANK	AC			
BELIEF	ASIMOV, ISAAC	NV	ASF	53	10
BEYOND THE BARRIERS OF SPACE AND TIME	MERRIL, JUDITH	AN			
PROLOGUE TO ANALOG	CAMPBELL, JOHN W. JR	AN			
THROUGH A GLASS, CLEARLY	ASIMOV, ISAAC	AC			
14 GREAT TALES OF ESP	STONE, IDELLA P.	AN			
BELIEVING CHILD, THE	HENDERSON, ZENNA	SS	FSF	70	06
HOLDING WONDER	HENDERSON, ZENNA	AC			
BELL-TOWER, THE (1855)	MELVILLE, HERMAN	SS	PTM	55	
FUTURE PERFECT	FRANKLIN, H. BRUCE	AN			
BELLA GOES TO THE DARK TOWER	BAILEY, HILARY	SS	NWQ	73	05
NEW WORLDS NO. 5	MOORCOCK & PLATT	OA			
BELLES LETTRES, 2272	CORWIN, NORMAN		FIN	70	
FUTURE IS NOW, THE	NOLAN, WILLIAM F.	OA			
BELLMAN'S WONDER RING, THE	WOLFE, GENE	AR			
CLARION SF	WILHELM, KATE	OA			

BELLS OF ACHERON, THE   TUBB, E. C.   SS   SCF 57 04
  SCATTER OF STARDUST, A   TUBB, E. C.   DC
BELOVED HEAD, A   BENEDIKT, MICHAEL   PM   69
  HOLDING YOUR EIGHT HANDS   LUCIE-SMITH, EDWARD   AN
BELSEN EXPRESS   LEIBER, FRITZ   SS   NEW 75 AC
  SECOND BOOK OF FRITZ LEIBER, THE   LEIBER, FRITZ   AC
BEND OF TIME, THE   DANTON, WILLIAM   SS
  MORE SCIENCE FICTION TALES   ELWOOD, ROGER   OA
BENEATH STILL WATERS   CONEY, MICHAEL G.   SS   IFS 71 01
  MONITOR FOUND IN ORBIT   CONEY, MICHAEL G.   AC
BENEFACTOR OF HUMANITY, A   FARRELL, JAMES T.   SS   SSI 58
  10TH ANNUAL OF THE YEAR'S BEST S-F, THE MERRIL, JUDITH AN
BENJI'S PENCIL   MCALLISTER, BRUCE   SS   FSF 69 03
  BEST FROM FANTASY AND SCIENCE FICTION: 19
                               FERMAN, EDWARD L.   AN
BERNIE THE FAUST   TENN, WILLIAM   NV   PBY 63 11
  BEST FROM NEW WRITINGS IN S-F FIRST SELECTION, THE
                               CARNELL, JOHN   AN
  NEW WRITINGS IN SF. 4   CARNELL, JOHN   OA
  PLAYBOY BOOK OF SCIENCE FICTION AND FANTASY, THE
                               PLAYBOY, EDITORS OF   AN
  SCIENCE FICTION ARGOSY, A   KNIGHT, DAMON   AN
  SEVEN SEXES, THE   TENN, WILLIAM   AC
  TRANSIT OF EARTH   PLAYBOY, EDITORS OF   AN
  9TH ANNUAL OF THE YEAR'S BEST S-F, THE MERRIL, JUDITH   AN
BEROM   BERRYMAN, JOHN   NV   ASF 51 01
  *IMAGINATION UNLIMITED   BLEILER & DIKTY   AN
BERSERKER'S PREY (SEE PRESSURE)
                               SABERHAGEN, FRED   TC
BERSERKS, THE   TOFTE, ARTHUR   SS   BER 74
  BERSERKERS, THE   ELWOOD, ROGER   OA
BERTHA (SEE DOORWAY IN THE SKY)
                               WILLIAMS, RALPH   TC
BERTRAND RUSSELL'S DREAM   HARDY, G. H.   PM   48
  FANTASIA MATHEMATICA   FADIMAN, CLIFTON   AN
BESIDE STILL WATERS   SHECKLEY, ROBERT   SS   AMZ 53 11
  *UNTOUCHED BY HUMAN HANDS   SHECKLEY, ROBERT   AC
BESIDE STILL WATERS   BRYANT, EDWARD
  AND SUTHERLAND, JAMES   SS C GEN 72
  GENERATION   GERROLD, DAVID   OA
BEST FRIEND   LIGHTNER, A. M.   SS   BLF 61
  TEEN-AGE SPACE ADVENTURES   FURMAN, A. L.   AN
  BOYS' LIFE BOOK OF OUTER SPACE STORIES, THE
                               BOY'S LIFE, ED. OF   AN
BEST FRIEND   KORNBLUTH, C. M.
  AND POHL, FREDERICK   SS C SSS 41 05
  WONDER EFFECT, THE   POHL, F. & KORNBLUTH AC
BEST HOLIDAY I EVER HAD, THE CROSS, JOHN KEIR   SS
  LAURIE'S SPACE ANNUAL   ANONYMOUS   AN
BEST OF ALL POSSIBLE WORLDS   BRADBURY, RAY   SS   PBY 60 08
  MACHINERIES OF JOY, THE   BRADBURY, RAY   AC
BEST OF TIMES, THE (SEE ANY FRIEND OF NICHOLAS NICKLEBY'S IS A
  FRIEND OF MINE)   BRADBURY, RAY   TC
BEST POLICY, THE   GARRETT, RANDALL   SS   ASF 57 07
  EARTHMEN AND STRANGERS   SILVERBERG, ROBERT   AN
BEST POSSIBLE WORLD, THE   WILSON, RICHARD   SS   NWS 60 09
  TIME OUT FOR TOMORROW   WILSON, RICHARD   AC
BEST SCIENCE-FICTION STORIES: 1949, THE
                               BLEILER & DIKTY   AN   FEL 49 08
  SCIENCE FICTION OMNIBUS   BLEILER & DIKTY   AN
BEST SCIENCE-FICTION STORIES: 1950, THE
                               BLEILER & DIKTY   AN   FEL 50 08
  SCIENCE FICTION OMNIBUS   BLEILER & DIKTY   AN
BEST SF: 1972   ROTSLER, WILLIAM   CT
  BEST SF: 1972   HARRISON & ALDISS   AN
BEST-LAID SCHEME, THE   DE CAMP, L. SPRAGUE SS   ASF 41 02
  WHEELS OF IF, THE   DE CAMP, L. SPRAGUE   AC
BETELGEUSE BRIDGE   TENN, WILLIAM   SS   GAL 51 04
  *GALAXY READER OF SCIENCE FICTION   GOLD, H. L.   AN
  TOMORROW, THE STARS   HEINLEIN, ROBERT A.   AN
  WOODEN STAR, THE   TENN, WILLIAM   AC
BETSY BLAKE WILL LIVE FOREVER (SEE IS BETSY BLAKE STILL ALIVE)
                               BLOCH, ROBERT   TC
BETTER BET, THE   BRODE, ANTHONY   PM   FSF 58 02
  BEST FROM FANTASY AND SCIENCE FICTION: 8
                               BOUCHER, ANTHONY   AN
BETTER CHOICE, THE   WRIGHT, S. FOWLER   SS   NEW 55 AN
  *SCIENCE FICTION ADVENTURES IN MUTATION CONKLIN, GROFF AN
BETTER DUMB THAN DEAD   BINDER, EANDO   SS
  JOURNEY TO ANOTHER STAR AND OTHER STORIES
                               ELWOOD, ROGER   OA
BETTER MAN, THE   RUSSELL, RAY   SS   PBY 66 07
  FIEND, THE   PLAYBOY, EDITORS OF   AN
  WILDERNESS OF STARS, A   NOLAN, WILLIAM F.   AN
BETTER MOUSEHOLE, A   PANGBORN, EDGAR   SS   GAL 65 10
  GOOD NEIGHBORS AND OTHER STRANGERS PANGBORN, EDGAR   AC
  ON OUR WAY TO THE FUTURE   CARR, TERRY   AN
BETTER MOUSETRAP, A   BRUNNER, JOHN   NV   IFS 63 11
  IF READER OF SCIENCE FICTION, THE   POHL, FREDERICK   AN
  NOT BEFORE TIME   BRUNNER, JOHN   AC
  *OUT OF MY MIND   BRUNNER, JOHN   AC
BETTER MOUSETRAP, THE   DE CAMP, L. SPRAGUE
  AND PRATT, FLETCHER   SS C FSF 50 12
  TALES FROM GAVAGAN'S BAR   DE CAMP, L. S.&PRATT AC
BETTER PART OF WISDOM, THE   BRADBURY, RAY   SS
  LONG AFTER MIDNIGHT   BRADBURY, RAY   AC
BETTER RAT TRAP, A   STEIGER, BRAD   SS   NEW 65 AN
  GREAT SCIENCE-FICTION   LICATA, TONY   AN
BETTER THAN EVER   KIRS, ALEX   SS   FSF 65 03
  11TH ANNUAL OF THE YEAR'S BEST S-F, THE MERRIL, JUDITH AN
BETTYANN   NEVILLE, KRIS   NV   NTS 51
  GIFTS OF ASTI AND OTHER STORIES OF SCIENCE FICTION, THE
                               ELWOOD, ROGER   AN
  NEW TALES OF SPACE AND TIME HEALY, RAYMOND J.   OA
  *STORIES FOR TOMORROW   SLOANE, WILLIAM   AN
  STRANGE GIFTS   SILVERBERG, ROBERT   AN

  YOUNG DEMONS   ELWOOD & GHIDALIA   AN
BETTYANN'S CHILDREN   NEVILLE, KRIS   SS   DEM 73
  DEMON KIND   ELWOOD, ROGER   OA
BETWEEN THE DARK AND THE DAYLIGHT
                               BUDRYS, ALGIS   SS   INF 58 10
  BUDRYS' INFERNO   BUDRYS, ALGIS   AC
BETWEEN THE MINUTE AND THE HOUR
                               BURRAGE, A. M.   SS   27
  TRAVELERS IN TIME   STERN, PHILIP VAN D. AN
BETWEEN THE THUNDER AND THE SUN
                               OLIVER, CHAD   NV   FSF 57 05
  BEST FROM FANTASY AND SCIENCE FICTION: 7
                               BOUCHER, ANTHONY   AN
BETWEEN THE TIDES   MALCOLM, DONALD   NV   NWR 76 29
  NEW WRITINGS IN SF. 29   BULMER, KENNETH   OA
BETWEEN TWO WORLDS (AUNT ELSIE'S STAIRWAY)
                               RIKER, ANTHONY   SS   OSP 54 11
  SPACE STATION 42 AND OTHER STORIES ANONYMOUS   AN
BEWARE THE FURY (SEE EXTRAPOLATION)
                               STURGEON, THEODORE   TC
BEYOND ASTRONAUT   FAIRFAX, JOHN   PM   69
  HOLDING YOUR EIGHT HANDS   LUCIE-SMITH, EDWARD AN
BEYOND BEDLAM   GUIN, WYMAN   NA   GAL 51 08
  *GALAXY READER OF SCIENCE FICTION GOLD, H. L.   AN
  GREAT SHORT NOVELS OF SCIENCE FICTION SILVERBERG, ROBERT AN
  LIVING WAY OUT   GUIN, WYMAN   AC
  SPECTRUM 2   AMIS & CONQUEST   AN
BEYOND DOUBT   HEINLEIN, ROBERT A.
  MONROE, LYLE
  AND WENTZ, ELMA   SS C AST 41 04
  BEYOND THE END OF TIME   POHL, FREDERICK   AN
  POLITICAL SCIENCE FICTION   GREENBERG& WARRICK   AN
BEYOND INFINITY   CARR, ROBERT S.   NV   NEW 51 AC
  BEYOND INFINITY   CARR, ROBERT S.   AC
BEYOND LIES THE WUB   DICK, PHILIP K.   SS   PLS 52 07
  ALPHA 3   SILVERBERG, ROBERT   AN
  BEST OF PHILIP K. DICK, THE DICK, PHILIP K.   AC
  PRESERVING MACHINE, THE   DICK, PHILIP K.   AC
BEYOND OUR NARROW SKIES   BRACKETT, LEIGH   IN
  BEST OF PLANET STORIES NO. 1, THE BRACKETT, LEIGH   AN
BEYOND SLEEP   MALZBERG, BARRY N.   SS   EQM 70 11
  OUT FROM GANYMEDE   MALZBERG, BARRY N.   AC
BEYOND SPACE AND TIME   ROGERS, JOEL T.   SS   SSS 50 09
  TREASURY OF GREAT SCIENCE FICTION, A VOL.1
                               BOUCHER, ANTHONY   AN
BEYOND THE BLACK RIVER   HOWARD, ROBERT E.   NA   WRT 35 05
  CONAN THE WARRIOR   HOWARD, R. & DE CAMP AC
  KING CONAN   HOWARD, ROBERT E.   AC
BEYOND THE CLEFT   REAMY, TOM   NV   NOV 74 04
  NOVA 4   HARRISON, HARRY   OA
BEYOND THE FARTHEST STAR (INCLUDES UNPUBLISHED SEQUEL,
  TANGOR RETURNS)   BURROUGHS, EDGAR R. NV   BBM 42 01
  TALES OF THREE PLANETS   BURROUGHS, EDGAR R.   AC
BEYOND THE FARTHEST STAR (SAMUEL A. PEEPLES)
                               FOSTER, ALAN DEAN   SA   SLG 74 0?
  STAR TREK LOG ONE   FOSTER, ALAN DEAN   OC
BEYOND THE GAME   AANDAHL, VANCE   SS   FSF 68 05
  ARENA: SPORTS SF   FERMAN & MALZBERG   AN
  BEST FROM FANTASY AND SCIENCE FICTION: 18
                               FERMAN, EDWARD L.   AN
  INTO THE UNKNOWN   CARR, TERRY   AN
  TRANSFORMATIONS II   ROSELLE, DANIEL   AN
BEYOND THE GREAT OBLIVION   ENGLAND, GEORGE A.   NO   CSB 13 01
  DARKNESS AND DAWN   ENGLAND, GEORGE A.   OC
BEYOND THE RIM   SERLING, ROD   SA
  ROD SERLING'S TWILIGHT ZONE REVISITED SERLING, ROD   OC
BEYOND THE SAND RIVER RANGE BRYANT, EDWARD   SS   INY 72 03
  INFINITY 3   HOSKINS, ROBERT   OA
BEYOND THE SINGING FLAME   SMITH, CLARK ASHTON SS   WOS 31 11
  FROM OFF THIS WORLD   MARGULIES & FRIEND   AN
BEYOND THE SPECTRUM   ROBERTSON, MORGAN   SS   14
  ANCESTRAL VOICES   MENVILLE & REGINALD   AN
BEYOND THE STARS (SPACE RATING)
                               BERRYMAN, JOHN   SS   ASF 39 10
  BEYOND THE STARS AND OTHER STORIES ANONYMOUS   AN
BEYOND THE THRESHOLD   DERLETH, AUGUST   NV   WRT 41 09
  BEWARE MORE BEASTS   GHIDALIA, V.& ELWOOD AN
BEYOND THE WALL OF SLEEP   LOVECRAFT, H. P.   SS   WRT 38 03
  *OTHER SIDE OF THE MOON, THE DERLETH, AUGUST   AN
BEYOND THE WEEDS (THE POST-MORTEM PEOPLE)
                               TATE, PETER   SS   NWS 66 03
  SF12   MERRIL, JUDITH   AN
BEYOND THIRTY   BURROUGHS, EDGAR R. NV   AAM 16 02
  BEYOND THIRTY & THE MAN-EATER BURROUGHS, EDGAR R.   AC
BEYOND THIS HORIZON   HEINLEIN, ROBERT A. NO   ASF 42 04
  ROBERT HEINLEIN OMNIBUS, A HEINLEIN, ROBERT A.   AC
BIANCA'S HANDS   STURGEON, THEODORE   SS   ARB 47 05
  E PLURIBUS UNICORN   STURGEON, THEODORE   AC
  SHOCKING THING, A   KNIGHT, DAMON   AN
BIBLE AFTER THE APOCALYPSE, THE
                               JANIFER, LAURENCE M. SS   NDM 74 04
  NEW DIMENSIONS 4   SILVERBERG, ROBERT   OA
BIBLIOGRAPHICAL NOTE   CLARKE, ARTHUR C.   IN
  OTHER SIDE OF THE SKY, THE CLARKE, ARTHUR C.   AC
BIBLIOGRAPHY   MISC. MATERIAL   MS
  ANOTHER TOMORROW   HOLLISTER, BERNARD C AN
  AS TOMORROW BECOMES TODAY   SULLIVAN, CHARLES W. AN
  BEST OF A. E. VAN VOGT, THE (BRITISH) VAN VOGT, A. E. AC
  BEST OF ARTHUR C. CLARKE: 1937-1971, THE CLARKE, ARTHUR C. AC
  BEST OF E. E. 'DOC' SMITH, THE SMITH, EDWARD E. PHD   AC
  BEST OF FRANK HERBERT, THE HERBERT, FRANK   AC
  BEST OF JOHN W. CAMPBELL, THE (BRITISH) CAMPBELL, JOHN W. JR AC
  BEST OF ROBERT HEINLEIN, THE HEINLEIN, ROBERT A.   AC
  *BEYOND HUMAN KEN   MERRIL, JUDITH   AN
  FANTASTIC PULPS, THE   HAINING, PETER   AN

BIBLIOGRAPHY

HISTORY OF THE SCIENCE FICTION MAGAZINE, THE   PART 2 1936-1945
                                        ASHLEY, MICHAEL   AN
HISTORY OF THE SCIENCE FICTION MAGAZINE, THE   PART 3 1946-1955
                                        ASHLEY, MICHAEL   AN
INSIDE INFORMATION   MOWSHOWITZ, ABBE   AN
INTRODUCTORY PSYCHOLOGY THROUGH SCIENCE FICTION
                                        KATZ/WARRICK/&   AN
JULES VERNE- MASTER OF SCIENCE FICTION VERNE, JULES   AC
SCIENCE FICTION OF THE 30'S   KNIGHT, DAMON   AN
SCIENCE FICTION THROUGH THE AGES 1   EVANS, I. O.   AN
BIBLIOGRAPHY   BISHOP, GERALD   MS
BEST OF ISAAC ASIMOV, THE   ASIMOV, ISAAC   AC
BEST OF JOHN WYNDHAM, THE   WYNDHAM, JOHN   AC
BIBLIOGRAPHY OF MUTATION STORIES
                    MISC. MATERIAL   MS
*SCIENCE FICTION ADVENTURES IN MUTATION CONKLIN, GROFF   AN
BIBLIOGRAPHY OF PRINCIPAL NONFICTION WORKS CONSULTED
                    MISC. MATERIAL   MS
ALL ABOUT VENUS   ALDISS, BRIAN W.   AN
BIBLIOGRAPHY OF ROBOT FICTION, A
                    MISC. MATERIAL   MS
PSEUDO PEOPLE, THE   NOLAN, WILLIAM F.   AN
BIBLIOGRAPHY: BOOKS BY ARTHUR C. CLARKE
                    MISC. MATERIAL   MS
OF TIME AND STARS   CLARKE, ARTHUR C.   AC
BIBLIOGRAPHY: THE CRITICAL LITERATURE OF S. F., A
                    MISC. MATERIAL   MS
MIRROR OF INFINITY, THE   SILVERBERG, ROBERT   AN
BIBLIOGRAPHY: THE WORLDS OF LARRY NIVEN
                    MISC. MATERIAL   MS
TALES OF KNOWN SPACE: THE UNIVERSE OF LARRY NIVEN
                                        NIVEN, LARRY   AC
BICENTENNIAL MAN, THE   ASIMOV, ISAAC NV   STL 76 02
BEST SCIENCE FICTION OF THE YEAR, THE NO. 6
                                        CARR, TERRY   AN
BICENTENNIAL MAN AND OTHER STORIES, THE ASIMOV, ISAAC   AC
STELLAR 2   DEL REY, JUDY-LYNN   OA
1977 ANNUAL WORLD'S BEST SF, THE   WOLLHEIM, DONALD A.   AN
BIG ANCESTOR   WALLACE, F. L.   NV   GAL 54 11
FIVE-ODD   CONKLIN, GROFF   AN
GALACTIC EMPIRES VOLUME TWO   ALDISS, BRIAN W.   AN
BIG AND THE LITTLE, THE ASIMOV, ISAAC NV   ASF 44 08
FOUNDATION   ASIMOV, ISAAC   NO
BIG ANT, THE (SEE THE LARGE ANT)
                      FAST, HOWARD   TC
BIG BLACK AND WHITE GAME, THE BRADBURY, RAY SS AMM 45 08
*GOLDEN APPLES OF THE SUN   BRADBURY, RAY   AC
BIG BOUNCE, THE   TEVIS, WALTER S. JR. SS GAL 58 02
WHERE DO WE GO FROM HERE?   ASIMOV, ISAAC   AN
BIG CONNECTION, THE   SCOTT, ROBIN S. SS   NOV 70 01
*NOVA 1   HARRISON, HARRY   OA
BIG CONTEST, THE   MACDONALD, JOHN D. SS WBY 50 12
HUMAN?   MERRIL, JUDITH   AN
WORLDS TO COME   KNIGHT, DAMON   AN
BIG DAY, THE   MALCOLM, DONALD SS   NWR 71 04
NEW WRITINGS IN SF. 18   CARNELL, JOHN   OA
BIG ENGINE, THE   LEIBER, FRITZ   SS   GAL 62 02
EIGHTH GALAXY READER, THE   POHL, FREDERIK   AN
BIG FIX, THE   WILSON, RICHARD NV   INF 56 08
STRANGE ECSTASIES   PARRY, MICHEL   AN
TIME OUT FOR TOMORROW   WILSON, RICHARD   AC
BIG FLASH, THE   SPINRAD, NORMAN NV   ORB 69 05
BEST FROM ORBIT, THE   KNIGHT, DAMON   AN
NO DIRECTION HOME   SPINRAD, NORMAN   AC
ORBIT 5   KNIGHT, DAMON   OA
SOCIAL PROBLEMS THROUGH SCIENCE FICTION GREENBERG/MILSTEAD/& AN
VOYAGES: SCENARIOS FOR A SHIP CALLED EARTH
                                        SAUER, ROB   AN
WORLD'S BEST SCIENCE FICTION: 1970   WOLLHEIM & CARR   AN
BIG FRONT YARD, THE   SIMAK, CLIFFORD D. NV ASF 58 10
HUGO WINNERS, THE (VOLUME 1)   ASIMOV, ISAAC   AN
SCIENCE FICTION HALL OF FAME VOLUME 2B BOVA, BEN   AN
*WORLDS OF CLIFFORD SIMAK, THE   SIMAK, CLIFFORD D.   AC
BIG GAME (WRITTEN 11/18/41) ASIMOV, ISAAC SS NEW 74 01
BEFORE THE GOLDEN AGE   ASIMOV, ISAAC   AN
BIG GAME HUNT   CLARKE, ARTHUR C. SS   54
PRELUDE TO MARS   CLARKE, ARTHUR C.   AC
TALES FROM THE WHITE HART   CLARKE, ARTHUR C.   AC
BIG HOLIDAY, THE   LEIBER, FRITZ   SS   FSF 53 01
BEST OF FRITZ LEIBER, THE   LEIBER, FRITZ   AN
BEST SCIENCE-FICTION STORIES: 1954, THE BLEILER & DIKTY   AN
BIG HUNGER, THE   MILLER, WALTER M. JR SS ASF 52 10
PRIZE SCIENCE FICTION   WOLLHEIM, DONALD A.   AN
SPACE ODYSSEYS   ALDISS, BRIAN W.   AN
VIEW FROM THE STARS, THE   MILLER, WALTER M. JR AC
BIG JOE AND THE NTH GENERATION (IT TAKES A THIEF)
                      MILLER, WALTER M. JR SS IFS 52 05
VIEW FROM THE STARS, THE   MILLER, WALTER M. JR SS
BIG KICK, THE   BLOCH, ROBERT   SS   ROG 59 07
*BLOOD RUNS COLD   BLOCH, ROBERT   AC
BIG LEAP, THE   FRITCH, CHARLES E. SS IFS 55 02
HORSES' ASTEROID   FRITCH, CHARLES E.   AC
BIG MAN WITH THE GIRLS, A MACCREIGH, JAMES
                      AND MERRIL, JUDITH SS C FUT 53 03
ESCAPE TO EARTH   HOWARD, IVAN   AN
BIG NIGHT, THE (AS HUDSON HASTINGS)
                      KUTTNER, HENRY   NV   TWS 47 06
BEST OF HENRY KUTTNER 1, THE   KUTTNER, HENRY   AC
BEST OF HENRY KUTTNER, THE   KUTTNER, HENRY   AC
BIG PAT BOOM, THE   KNIGHT, DAMON   SS   GAL 63 12
BEST OF DAMON KNIGHT, THE   KNIGHT, DAMON   AC
SCIENCE FICTION HORIZONS NO. 1   BOARDMAN, TOM JR.   AN
SEVENTH GALAXY READER, THE   POHL, FREDERIK   AN
TURNING ON   KNIGHT, DAMON   AC
BIG RAIN, THE   ANDERSON, POUL   SN   ASF 54 10
ALL ABOUT VENUS   ALDISS, BRIAN W.   AN

FAREWELL FANTASTIC VENUS   ALDISS & HARRISON   AN
BIG SAM   DAVIDSON, AVRAM SS   ANA 70
ALCHEMY AND ACADEME   MCCAFFREY, ANNE   OA
NEW WORLDS OF FANTASY NO. 3   CARR, TERRY   AN
BIG SAM WAS MY FRIEND ELLISON, HARLAN SS   SFA 58 03
I HAVE NO MOUTH, AND I MUST SCREAM   ELLISON, HARLAN   AC
BIG SHOT, THE   RUSSELL, ERIC FRANK SS WRT 49 01
UNEXPECTED, THE   MARGULIES, LEO   AN
BIG SHOW, THE   LAUMER, KEITH   NV   GAL 68 02
BIG SHOW, THE   LAUMER, KEITH   AC
BIG SISTER   ALDISS, BRIAN W. SI
ALL ABOUT VENUS   ALDISS, BRIAN W.   AN
BIG SLEEP, THE   ACKERMAN, FORREST J. SS   50
SCIENCE FICTION WORLDS OF FORREST J. ACKERMAN & FRIENDS
                                        ACKERMAN, FORREST J. AC
BIG SOUND, THE   BAYLEY, BARRINGTON J SS SFB 62 02
BEST SF STORIES FROM NEW WORLDS 8   MOORCOCK, MICHAEL   AN
BIG SPACE FUCK, THE   VONNEGUT, KURT JR. SS DVS 72 02
AGAIN, DANGEROUS VISIONS   ELLISON, HARLAN   OA
BIG STINK, THE   COGSWELL, THEODORE R SS IFS 54 07
HUMAN AND OTHER BEINGS   DEGRAEFF, ALLEN   AN
BIG SUPRISE (WHAT WAS IN THE BOX)
                       MATHESON, RICHARD SS EQM 59 04
SHOCK II   MATHESON, RICHARD   AC
BIG SWORD   ASH, PAUL   NV   ASF 58 10
ANOTHER PART OF THE GALAXY   CONKLIN, GROFF   AN
SPECTRUM 5   AMIS & CONQUEST   AN
BIG TREK, THE   LEIBER, FRITZ   SS   FSF 57 10
BEST FROM FANTASY AND SCIENCE FICTION: 7
                                        BOUCHER, ANTHONY   AN
BEST OF FRITZ LEIBER, THE   LEIBER, FRITZ   AC
SHIPS TO THE STARS   LEIBER, FRITZ   DC
BIG TRIP UP YONDER, THE (ALSO AS TOMORROW AND TOMORROW
AND TOMORROW)   VONNEGUT, KURT JR. SS GAL 54 01
ASSIGNMENT IN TOMORROW   POHL, FREDERIK   AN
BIG WHEEL, THE   GUNN, JAMES E.   SS   FUN 56 09
STATION IN SPACE   GUNN, JAMES E.   AC
BIG WHEEL, THE   MCMORROW, FRED   SS   SEP 61 07
POST READER OF FANTASY AND SCIENCE FICTION
                                        SATURDAY EVE. POST   AN
BIG, BIG, BIG   ASIMOV, ISAAC   IN
SPACE BEYOND, THE   CAMPBELL, JOHN W. JR OC
BIG, TALL WISH, THE   SERLING, ROD   SA
FROM THE TWILIGHT ZONE   SERLING, ROD   AC
MORE STORIES FROM THE TWILIGHT ZONE   SERLING, ROD   OC
BIG, WIDE, WONDERFUL WORLD FRITCH, CHARLES E. SS FSF 58 03
CRAZY MIXED-UP PLANET   FRITCH, CHARLES E.   AN
FIEND IN YOU, THE   BEAUMONT, CHARLES   AN
YEAR'S BEST HORROR STORIES: SERIES III, THE
                                        DAVIS, RICHARD   AN
BIGGER THAN WORLDS   NIVEN, LARRY   AR   ASF 74 03
HOLE IN SPACE, A   NIVEN, LARRY   AC
BIGGEST GAME, THE (AS KEITH WOODCOTT)
                       BRUNNER, JOHN   SS   SCF 56 02
FROM THIS DAY FORWARD   BRUNNER, JOHN   AC
BILL FOR DELIVERY   ANVIL, CHRISTOPHER SS ASF 64 11
WORLD'S BEST SCIENCE FICTION: 1965   WOLLHEIM & CARR   AN
BILL GETS HEP TO GOD   SLADEK, JOHN T. SS   NWB 73 05
NEW WORLDS QUARTERLY NO. 5   MOORCOCK, MICHAEL   OA
BILLENIUM   BALLARD, J. G.   SS   NWS 61 11
BEST OF J. G. BALLARD, THE   BALLARD, J. G.   AC
BEST SF 6   CRISPIN, EDMUND   AN
BILLENIUM   BALLARD, J. G.   AC
CHRONOPOLIS AND OTHER STORIES   BALLARD, J. G.   AC
CITIES OF WONDER   KNIGHT, DAMON   AN
CITY: 2000 A.D., THE   CLEM/GREENBERG/&   AN
EARTH IN TRANSIT   SCHWARTZ, SHEILA   AN
FUTURE TENSE   CURTIS, RICHARD   AN
OUT OF THIS WORLD 4   WILLIAMS-ELLIS& OWEN AN
SOCIAL PROBLEMS THROUGH SCIENCE FICTION GREENBERG/MILSTEAD/& AN
STARS AND UNDER, THE   CRISPIN, EDMUND   AN
TERMINAL BEACH (BRITISH VERSION)   BALLARD, J. G.   AC
VOYAGES: SCENARIOS FOR A SHIP CALLED EARTH
                                        SAUER, ROB   AN
WINDOWS INTO TOMORROW   SILVERBERG, ROBERT   AN
YOU AND SCIENCE FICTION   HOLLISTER, BERNARD C AN
BILLENNIUM: A NOTE TO DEADCAT PRICE, D. M. PM SVW 73
SAVING WORLDS   ELWOOD & KIDD   OA
BILLIARD BALL, THE   ASIMOV, ISAAC   NV   IFS 67 03
ASIMOV'S MYSTERIES   ASIMOV, ISAAC   AC
BEST OF ISAAC ASIMOV, THE   ASIMOV, ISAAC   AC
SECOND IF READER OF SCIENCE FICTION, THE POHL, FREDERIK   AN
WORLD'S BEST SCIENCE FICTION: 1968   WOLLHEIM & CARR   AN
BINARIES   SALLIS, JAMES   SS   ORB 71 09
BEST FROM ORBIT, THE   KNIGHT, DAMON   AN
ORBIT 9   KNIGHT, DAMON   OA
BINARY JUSTICE   BIRELEY, RICHARD SS   ORB 75 16
ORBIT 16   KNIGHT, DAMON   OA
BINDLESTIFF   BLISH, JAMES   NV   ASF 50 12
EARTHMAN, COME HOME   BLISH, JAMES   NO
BIOCURRENTS, BIOCURRENTS... VARSHAVSKY, ILYA SS
OTHER WORLDS, OTHER SEAS   SUVIN, DARKO   AN
BIOGRAPHICAL NOTE ON LUDWIG VAN BEETHOVEN II
                       JONES, LANGDON   FA   NWS 68 10
BEST SF STORIES FROM NEW WORLDS 5   MOORCOCK, MICHAEL   AN
BIOGRAPHICAL NOTES   MISC. MATERIAL   MS
HOLDING YOUR EIGHT HANDS   LUCIE-SMITH, EDWARD   AN
BIOGRAPHIES OF AUTHORS MISC. MATERIAL   MS
SCIENCE FACT/FICTION   FARRELL/GAGE/&   AN
BIOGRAPHY OF AN UNCIRCUMCISED MAN (INCLUDING INTERVIEW)
                       EMSHWILLER, CAROL SS
JOY IN OUR CAUSE   EMSHWILLER, CAROL   AC
BIOGRAPHY PROJECT, THE DELL, DUDLEY   SS   GAL 51 09
*GALAXY READER OF SCIENCE FICTION   GOLD, H. L.   AN
BIOGRAPHY PROJECT, THE GOLD, H. L.   SS   GAL 51 09

OLD DIE RICH AND OTHER SCIENCE FICTION, THE
                                    GOLD, H. L.   AC
BIOLOGICAL EXPERIMENT, A   KELLER, DAVID H. MD. SS   AMZ 28 06
TALES FROM UNDERWOOD   KELLER, DAVID H. MD. AC
BIOLOGICAL REVOLUTION, THE SLATEN, JEFF
  AND VARDEMAN, ROBERT E. SS C
2076: THE AMERICAN TRICENTENNIAL BRYANT, EDWARD   OA
BIRCH CLUMP CYLINDER, THE   SIMAK, CLIFFORD D.   NV   STL 74 01
BEST SCIENCE FICTION STORIES OF THE YEAR (1974)
                            DEL REY, LESTER   AN
STELLAR 1   DEL REY, JUDY-LYNN   OA
BIRCHER   WALDE, A. A.   NV   IFS 66 07
WORLD'S BEST SCIENCE FICTION: 1967 WOLLHEIM & CARR   AN
BIRD IN THE HAND   NIVEN, LARRY   SS   FSF 70 10
FLIGHT OF THE HORSE, THE   NIVEN, LARRY   AC
WORLD'S BEST SCIENCE FICTION: 1971 WOLLHEIM & CARR   AN
BIRD LOVER, THE   GREEN, JOSEPH   NV   SCS 73
SHOWCASE   ELWOOD, ROGER   OA
BIRD MAN OF MODERAN, THE   BUNCH, DAVID R. SS
MODERAN   BUNCH, DAVID R.   AC
BIRD OF PREY   BOND, NELSON S. SS   BBM 49 08
NIGHTMARES AND DAYDREAMS   BOND, NELSON S.   AC
BIRD OF PREY   COLLIER, JOHN   SS   41
SUPERNATURAL READER, THE   CONKLIN, G&L.   AN
BIRD OF TIME, THE   WEST, WALLACE   NO   TWS 52 08
BIRD OF TIME, THE   WEST, WALLACE   NO
BIRD-BRAINED NAVIGATOR, THE CHANDLER, A. BERTRAM NV IFS 68 06
RIM GODS, THE   CHANDLER, A. BERTRAM DC
BIRDLIME   KELLER, B. L.   SS   FSF 71 03
BEST FROM FANTASY AND SCIENCE FICTION: 20
                            FERMAN, EDWARD L.   AN
BIRDS CAN'T COUNT   CLINGERMAN, MILDRED SS FSF 55 02
BEST FROM FANTASY AND SCIENCE FICTION: 5
                            BOUCHER, ANTHONY   AN
CUPFUL OF SPACE, A   CLINGERMAN, MILDRED AC
SF: THE YEAR'S GREATEST SCIENCE FICTION AND FANTASY
                            MERRIL, JUDITH   AN
BIRDS FLY SOUTH IN WINTER   TALL, STEPHEN   NV   GAL 71 11
STARDUST VOYAGES, THE   TALL, STEPHEN   AC
BIRDS OF A FEATHER   SILVERBERG, ROBERT NV GAL 58 11
NEEDLE IN A TIMESTACK   SILVERBERG, ROBERT   AC
SUNRISE ON MERCURY AND OTHER SCIENCE FICTION STORIES
                            SILVERBERG, ROBERT   OA
TALES OF TIME AND SPACE   OLNEY, ROSS R.   AN
BIRDS OF PREY   TAFOYA, ALFONSO PM   NWQ 74 06
NEW WORLDS NO. 6   PLATT & BAILEY   OA
BIRDS, THE   DISCH, THOMAS M. SS   73
BEST SF: 1973   HARRISON & ALDISS   AN
GETTING INTO DEATH AND OTHER STORIES DISCH, THOMAS M. AC
BIRDS, THE   DU MAURIER, DAPHNE NV GHK 52 10
ECO-FICTION   STADLER, JOHN   AN
RUINS OF EARTH, THE   DISCH, THOMAS M.   AN
STRANGE BEASTS AND UNNATURAL MONSTERS STERN, PHILIP VAN D. AN
YOU AND SCIENCE FICTION   HOLLISTER, BERNARD C AN
BIRDSEED FOR OUR FEATHERED FANS
                            CLUTE, JOHN   BR   NWQ 74 06
NEW WORLDS NO. 6   PLATT & BAILEY   OA
BIRKETT'S TWELFTH CORPSE   DERLETH, AUGUST SS   SRS 40 08
NOT LONG FOR THIS WORLD   DERLETH, AUGUST   AC
BIRTH OF A BUTTERFLY   GREEN, JOSEPH   SS   NWR 67 10
NEW WRITINGS IN SF. 8   CARNELL, JOHN   AN
NEW WRITINGS IN SF. 10   CARNELL, JOHN   OA
BIRTH OF A NOTION   ASIMOV, ISAAC   SS   AMZ 76 06
BICENTENNIAL MAN AND OTHER STORIES, THE ASIMOV, ISAAC AC
BIRTH OF A SALESMAN   TIPTREE, JAMES JR. SS ASF 68 03
TEN THOUSAND LIGHT-YEARS FROM HOME TIPTREE, JAMES JR. AC
BIRTHDAY BOY, THE   STEVENS, JAMES   SS   GEN 72
GENERATION   GERROLD, DAVID   OA
BIRTHDAY PRESENT   FRITCH, CHARLES E. SS SCF 55 09
CRAZY MIXED-UP PLANET   FRITCH, CHARLES E.   AC
MAN AGAINST TOMORROW   NOLAN, WILLIAM F.   AN
BIRTHMARK, THE (1843)   HAWTHORNE, NATHANIEL SS PIO 43 03
FUTURE PERFECT   FRANKLIN, H. BRUCE   AN
JOURNEYS IN SCIENCE FICTION LOUGHLIN, RICHARD L. AN
PAST, PRESENT, AND FUTURE PERFECT WOLFE, J&FITZ GERALD AN
BIRTHRIGHT   ANDERSON, POUL   NV   ASF 70 02
SOCIOLOGY THROUGH SCIENCE FICTION MILSTEAD/GREENBERG/& AN
BIRTHRIGHT   SELLINGS, ARTHUR SS   NWS 56 11
LONG EUREKA, THE   SELLINGS, ARTHUR   AC
BISHOP'S GAMBIT   DERLETH, AUGUST SS   AFR 47 03
MR. GEORGE AND OTHER ODD PERSONS DERLETH, AUGUST   AC
BISQUIT POSITION, THE   WOLFE, BERNARD   NV   DVS 72 02
AGAIN, DANGEROUS VISIONS   ELLISON, HARLAN   OA
BIT OF THE DARK WORLD, A   LEIBER, FRITZ   NV   FAN 62 02
SHADOWS WITH EYES   LEIBER, FRITZ   AC
BITCHING IT   DORMAN, SONYA   SS   QRK 71 02
QUARK/2   DELANY & HACKER   OA
BITING DOWN HARD ON TRUTH   EFFINGER, GEO. ALEC NV ORB 74 15
IRRATIONAL NUMBERS   EFFINGER, GEO. ALEC AC
ORBIT 15   KNIGHT, DAMON   OA
BITTER BREAD, THE   ANDERSON, POUL   NV   ASF 75 12
BEST SCIENCE FICTION STORIES OF THE YEAR (1975)
                            DEL REY, LESTER   AN
BITTER END   RUSSELL, ERIC FRANK SS SFP 53 12
DARK TIDES   RUSSELL, ERIC FRANK AC
SPACE MAGICIANS, THE   NORTON & MOSKOWITZ   AN
TOMORROW, AND TOMORROW, AND TOMORROW... HEINTZ/HERBERT/JOOS/ AN
UNTRAVELLED WORLDS   BARTER & WILSON   AN
BITTEREST PILL, THE (ALSO AS THE RICHEST MAN IN LEVITTOWN)
                            POHL, FREDERIK   SS   GAL 59 04
ABC OF SCIENCE FICTION, AN BOARDMAN, TOM JR.   AN
FIFTH GALAXY READER, THE   GOLD, H. L.   AN
BLABBERMOUTH   STURGEON, THEODORE SS AMZ 47 02
CAVIAR   STURGEON, THEODORE   AC
BLACK AND WHITE   BRADLEY, MARION Z. SS AMZ 62 11
DARK INTRUDER & OTHER STORIES, THE BRADLEY, MARION Z. DC

BLACK AS THE PIT, FROM POLE TO POLE
                            UTLEY, STEVEN
  AND WALDROP, HOWARD   NV C NDM 77 07
NEW DIMENSIONS 7   SILVERBERG, ROBERT   OA
BLACK BALL, THE   DE CAMP, L. SPRAGUE
  AND PRATT, FLETCHER   SS C FSF 52 1?
BEST FROM FANTASY AND SCIENCE FICTION: 2
                            BOUCHER & MCCOMAS   AN
TALES FROM GAVAGAN'S BAR   DE CAMP, L. S.&PRATT AC
BLACK BARGAIN   BLOCH, ROBERT   SS   WRT 42 05
LIVING DEMONS, THE   BLOCH, ROBERT   AC
BLACK CAPTAIN, THE   MUNN, H. WARNER SS   75
YEAR'S BEST HORROR STORIES: SERIES IV, THE
                            PAGE, GERALD W.   AN
BLACK CATS   HASTINGS, CHRISTEL PM UNK 40 12
FROM UNKNOWN WORLDS   CAMPBELL, JOHN W. JR AN
BLACK CHARLIE   DICKSON, GORDON R. SS GAL 54 04
DANGER- HUMAN   DICKSON, GORDON R.   AC
FIFTH GALAXY READER, THE   GOLD, H. L.   AN
ONE HUNDRED YEARS OF SCIENCE FICTION KNIGHT, DAMON   AN
BLACK CLOUD, THE (EXCERPT) HOYLE, FRED   EX   HEI 57
EXPERT DREAMERS, THE   POHL, FREDERIK   AN
BLACK COLOSSUS   HOWARD, ROBERT E. SS WRT 33 06
CONAN THE BARBARIAN   HOWARD, ROBERT E.   AC
CONAN THE FREEBOOTER   HOWARD, R. & DE CAMP AC
BLACK COUNTRY   BEAUMONT, CHARLES NV PBY 54 09
HUNGER AND OTHER STORIES, THE BEAUMONT, CHARLES   AC
MAGIC MAN AND OTHER SCIENCE-FANTASY STORIES
                            BEAUMONT, CHARLES   AC
PLAYBOY BOOK OF HORROR AND THE SUPERNATURAL, THE
                            PLAYBOY, EDITORS OF AN
BLACK DESTROYER   VAN VOGT, A. E. NV   ASF 39 07
*ADVENTURES IN TIME AND SPACE HEALY & MCCOMAS   AN
FIRST FLIGHT   KNIGHT, DAMON   AN
SCIENCE FICTION NOVELLAS   HARRISON & MCNELLY   AN
VOYAGE OF THE SPACE BEAGLE, THE VAN VOGT, A. E. OA
BLACK DRUID, THE   LONG, FRANK BELKNAP SS WRT 30 07
*HOUNDS OF TINDALOS, THE   LONG, FRANK BELKNAP AN
BLACK EYES AND THE DAILY GRIND LESSER, MILTON SS IFS 52 02
*STORIES FOR TOMORROW   SLOANE, WILLIAM   AN
BLACK FERRIS, THE   BRADBURY, RAY   SS   WRT 48 0?
DARK SIDE, THE   KNIGHT, DAMON   AN
DEVIL'S GENERATION, THE   GHIDALIA, VIC   AN
BLACK FOG   WANDREI, DONALD SS   TWS 37 0?
EYE AND THE FINGER   WANDREI, DONALD   AC
BLACK FRIAR OF THE FLAME   ASIMOV, ISAAC   NV   PLS 42 S?
EARLY ASIMOV, THE   ASIMOV, ISAAC   AC
BLACK GLAK, THE   HARRISON, M. JOHN AR NWQ 72 0?
NEW WORLDS QUARTERLY NO. 3 MOORCOCK, MICHAEL   O?
BLACK GOD'S KISS   MOORE, C. L.   NV   WRT 34 0?
BEST OF C. L. MOORE, THE   MOORE, C. L.   A?
JIREL OF JOIRY   MOORE, C. L.   A?
*SHAMBLEAU AND OTHERS   MOORE, C. L.   A?
BLACK GOD'S SHADOW   MOORE, C. L.   NV   WRT 34 1?
JIREL OF JOIRY   MOORE, C. L.   A?
*SHAMBLEAU AND OTHERS   MOORE, C. L.   A?
BLACK GONDOLIER, THE   LEIBER, FRITZ   NV   NEW 64 A?
NIGHT MONSTERS   LEIBER, FRITZ   D?
BLACK HAND, THE   REEVE, ARTHUR B. SS
SILENT BULLET, THE   REEVE, ARTHUR B.   A?
BLACK HOLE   FRANCIS, NIGEL   SS   NWB 75 0?
NEW WORLDS EIGHT   BAILEY, HILARY   O?
BLACK HOLE OF NEGRAV, THE   KAPP, COLIN   NV   NWR 75 2?
NEW WRITINGS IN SF. 25   BULMER, KENNETH   O?
BLACK IS BEAUTIFUL   SILVERBERG, ROBERT SS YRT 70
ABOVE THE HUMAN LANDSCAPE   MCNELLY & STOVER   A?
BEST SF: 1970   HARRISON & ALDISS   A?
CITY: 2000 A.D., THE   CLEM/GREENBERG/&   A?
REALITY TRIP, THE   SILVERBERG, ROBERT   A?
SPECULATIONS   SANDERS, THOMAS E.   A?
YEAR 2000, THE   HARRISON, HARRY   A?
BLACK KISS, THE   BLOCH, ROBERT   SS   WRT 37 0?
SECOND AVON FANTASY READER, THE WOLLHEIM &ERNSBERGER A?
BLACK PIRATES OF BARSOOM   BURROUGHS, EDGAR R. NV AMZ 41 0?
LLANA OF GATHOL   BURROUGHS, EDGAR R. N?
BLACK PITS OF LUNA, THE   HEINLEIN, ROBERT A. SS SEP 48 0?
GREEN HILLS OF EARTH, THE   HEINLEIN, ROBERT A. A?
PAST THROUGH TOMORROW, THE HEINLEIN, ROBERT A. A?
*POSSIBLE WORLDS OF SCIENCE FICTION CONKLIN, GROFF A?
SCIENCE FICTION AND READER'S GUIDE BARROWS, MARJORIE A?
STORIES OF SCIENTIFIC IMAGINATION GALLANT, JOSEPH A?
TOMORROW'S WORLDS   SILVERBERG, ROBERT   A?
BLACK RETRIEVER, THE   FINNEY, CHARLES G. SS FSF 58 1?
ROD SERLING'S TRIPLE W: WITCHES, WARLOCKS AND WEREWOLVES
                            SERLING, ROD   A?
BLACK ROSE AND WHITE ROSE   POLLACK, RACHEL SS   NWQ 74 0?
NEW WORLDS NO. 6   PLATT & BAILEY   O?
BLACK SHADOW, THE   OLIVER, OWEN   SS   CSL 03 0?
WORLDS APART   LOCKE, GEORGE   A?
BLACK SHEEP ASTRAY   REYNOLDS, MACK   NV   AMA 73
ASTOUNDING   HARRISON, HARRY   O?
BLACK SORCERER OF THE BLACK CASTLE, THE
                            OFFUTT, ANDREW J. SS NEW 74 0?
COSMIC LAUGHTER   HALDEMAN, JOE W.   A?
BLACK STAR PASSES, THE   CAMPBELL, JOHN W. JR NA AMQ 30 F?
BLACK STAR PASSES, THE   CAMPBELL, JOHN W. JR A?
JOHN W. CAMPBELL ANTHOLOGY: THREE NOVELS CAMPBELL, JOHN W. G?
BLACK STONE, THE   HOWARD, ROBERT E. SS WRT 31 1?
WOLFSHEAD   HOWARD, ROBERT E.   A?
BLACK STRANGER, THE (SEE THE TREASURE OF TRANICOS)
                            DE CAMP, L. SPRAGUE
  AND HOWARD, ROBERT E.   TC C
BLACK SUN   ETCHISON, DENNIS SS   ORB 74 1?
ORBIT 13   KNIGHT, DAMON   O?
BLACK SUN RISES, THE   KUTTNER, HENRY   NV   SSS 49 0?
SPACE MAGICIANS, THE   NORTON & MOSKOWITZ

BLACK SUNDAY (THE VLY)

BLACK SUNDAY (THE VLY)   GOGOL, NIKOLAI   NV
  GHOULS, THE   HAINING, PETER   AN
BLACK TEARS   CARTER, LIN
                                AND DE CAMP, L. SPRAGUE SS C
  CONAN THE WANDERER   HOWARD, R./DE CAMP/& AC
BLACK THIRST   MOORE, C. L.   NV WRT 34 04
  AVON FANTASY READER, THE   WOLLHEIM &ERNSBERGER AN
  BEST OF C. L. MOORE, THE   MOORE, C. L.   AC
  *SHAMBLEAU AND OTHERS   MOORE, C. L.   AC
BLACK TOWER, THE   DUANE, ANDREW
                                AND MCNAUGHTON, BRIAN J. NV C
  SHANADU   BRINEY, ROBERT E.   OA
BLACKMAIL   HOYLE, FRED   SS FSF 67 02
  BEST SF: 1967   HARRISON & ALDISS   AN
  ELEMENT 79   HOYLE, FRED   AC
BLACKSWORD   OFFUTT, ANDREW J. NV GAL 59 12
  MIND PARTNER AND 8 OTHER NOVELETS FROM GALAXY
                                GOLD, H. L.   AN
BLANK   ELLISON, HARLAN SS INF 57 06
  OVER THE EDGE   ELLISON, HARLAN   AC
BLANK FORM   SELLINGS, ARTHUR SS GAL 58 07
  FOURTH GALAXY READER, THE   GOLD, H. L.   AN
  LONG EUREKA, THE   SELLINGS, ARTHUR   AC
BLANK!   ASIMOV, ISAAC   SS INF 57 06
  BUY JUPITER AND OTHER STORIES ASIMOV, ISAAC   AC
  HAVE YOU SEEN THESE?   ASIMOV, ISAAC   AC
BLASPHEMERS, THE   FARMER, PHILIP JOSE NV GAL 64 04
  DOWN IN THE BLACK GANG AND OTHER STORIES FARMER, PHILIP JOSE AC
BLAST, THE   CLOETE, STUART   NV COL 47 04
  6 GREAT SHORT NOVELS OF SCIENCE FICTION CONKLIN, GROFF AN
BLASTOFF   BONFIGLIOLI, KYRIL SS   64
  ENGLAND SWINGS SF   MERRIL, JUDITH   AN
  SPACE-TIME JOURNAL, THE   MERRIL, JUDITH   AN
BLAZE OF GLORY   GARRETT, RANDALL PM FSF 55 12
  BEST FROM FANTASY AND SCIENCE FICTION: 6
                                BOUCHER, ANTHONY   AN
BLAZE OF GLORY   SILVERBERG, ROBERT SS GAL 57 08
  CALLIBRATED ALLIGATOR AND OTHER SCIENCE FICTION STORIES, THE
                                SILVERBERG, ROBERT   AC
  NEXT STOP THE STARS   SILVERBERG, ROBERT   DC
BLEAK AND BARREN LAND, THE   DICKSON, GORDON R. NV SPS 53 02
  ANCIENT, MY ENEMY   DICKSON, GORDON R.   AC
BLEAK SHORE, THE   LEIBER, FRITZ   SS UNK 40 11
  HELL HATH FURY   HAY, GEORGE   AN
  UNKNOWN, THE   BENSEN, D. R.   AN
BLEEDING MAN, THE   STRETE, CRAIG   NV GAL 74 12
  1975 ANNUAL WORLD'S BEST SF, THE WOLLHEIM, DONALD A. AN
BLEEDING STONES   ELLISON, HARLAN SS VTX 73 04
  DEATHBIRD STORIES   ELLISON, HARLAN   AC
BLEMISH   CHRISTOPHER, JOHN SS AUT 53 11
  TWENTY-SECOND CENTURY, THE   CHRISTOPHER, JOHN   AC
BLESSED ARE THE MEEK   DERLETH, AUGUST SS WRT 48 11
  MR. GEORGE AND OTHER ODD PERSONS DERLETH, AUGUST   AC
BLESSEDNESS OF SAINTS, A   ANDERSON, POUL   AR VPG 62 04
  HOMEBREW   ANDERSON, POUL   AC
BLIGHT, THE   COX, ARTHUR JEAN NV
  *TIME TO COME   DERLETH, AUGUST   OA
BLIGHTED PROFILE   ALDISS, BRIAN W. SS SCF 58 06
  CANOPY OF TIME, THE   ALDISS, BRIAN W.   AC
  NO TIME LIKE TOMORROW   ALDISS, BRIAN W.   AC
BLIND ALLEY   ASIMOV, ISAAC   SS ASF 45 03
  *BEST OF SCIENCE FICTION   CONKLIN, GROFF   AN
  EARLY ASIMOV, THE   ASIMOV, ISAAC   AC
  GREAT STORIES OF SPACE TRAVEL CONKLIN, GROFF   AN
BLIND ALLEY   JAMESON, MALCOLM NV UNK 43 06
  GREAT STORIES OF SCIENCE FICTION LEINSTER, MURRAY   AN
  ROD SERLING'S TRIPLE W: WITCHES, WARLOCKS AND WEREWOLVES
                                SERLING, ROD   AN
BLIND BIRD, BLIND BIRD, GO AWAY FROM ME!
                                ELLISON, HARLAN SS KNT 63 07
  *LOVE AIN'T NOTHING BUT SEX MISSPELLED ELLISON, HARLAN AC
BLIND LIGHTNING   ELLISON, HARLAN SS FUN 56 06
  ALONE AGAINST TOMORROW   ELLISON, HARLAN   AC
  EARTHMEN AND STRANGERS   SILVERBERG, ROBERT   AN
  OVER THE EDGE   ELLISON, HARLAN   AC
  TOUCH OF INFINITY, A   ELLISON, HARLAN   DC
BLIND MAN'S BUFF   GIESY, J. U.   SS ASW 20 01
  ESCALES DANS L'INFINI   GALLET, GEORGES H.   AN
BLIND MAN'S BUFF   JAMESON, MALCOLM NV ASF 44 10
  EVERY BOY'S BOOK OF OUTER SPACE STORIES DIKTY, T. E. AN
  *IMAGINATION UNLIMITED   BLEILER & DIKTY   AN
BLIND MAN'S LANTERN   LANG, ALLEN KIM NV ASF 62 12
  ANALOG 2   CAMPBELL, JOHN W. JR   AN
BLIND PILOT, THE (TRANSLATED BY DAMON KNIGHT)
                                HENNEBERG, CHARLES SS FSF 60 01
  BEST FROM FANTASY AND SCIENCE FICTION: 10
                                MILLS, ROBERT P.   AN
  FIRST CONTACT   KNIGHT, DAMON   AN
  13 FRENCH SCIENCE-FICTION STORIES KNIGHT, DAMON   AN
BLIND SPOT, THE   FLINT, HOMER EON
                                AND HALL, AUSTIN NV C AAS 21 05
  UNDER THE MOONS OF MARS   MOSKOWITZ, SAM   AN
BLINDING SHADOWS   WANDREI, DONALD SS ASF 34 05
  *BEACHHEADS IN SPACE   DERLETH, AUGUST   AN
  EYE AND THE FINGER   WANDREI, DONALD   AC
BLINDMAN'S WORLD, THE (1886)   BELLAMY, EDWARD SS ATL 86
  *BEYOND TIME AND SPACE   DERLETH, AUGUST   AN
  FUTURE PERFECT   FRANKLIN, H. BRUCE   AN
BLINDNESS   CAMPBELL, JOHN W. JR SS ASF 35 03
  *BEST OF JOHN W. CAMPBELL, THE CAMPBELL, JOHN W. JR AC
  *MY BEST SCIENCE FICTION STORY MARGULIES & FRIEND   AN
  WHO GOES THERE?   CAMPBELL, JOHN W. JR   AC
  WHO GOES THERE? AND OTHER STORIES CAMPBELL, JOHN W. JR AC
BLINDNESS   VOM SCHEIDT, JURGEN SS SFM 74 09
  BEST OF SCIENCE FICTION MONTHLY, THE SACKS, JANET   AN

BLUESTOCKING (THE ADVENTURESS)

BLINDNESS, THE   LATHAM, PHILIP   NV ASF 46 07
  TIME PROBE: THE SCIENCES IN SF. CLARKE, ARTHUR C.   AN
BLISH BIBLIOGRAPHY   OWINGS, MARK   MS FSF 72 04
  BEST FROM FANTASY AND SCIENCE FICTION, 25TH ANNIV.
                                FERMAN, EDWARD L.   AN
BLISS OF SOLITUDE, THE (HALLUCINATION ORBIT)
                                MCINTOSH, J. T. NV GAL 52 01
  BEST SF 4   CRISPIN, EDMUND   AN
  GATEWAY TO TOMORROW   CARNELL, JOHN   AN
BLOCK THAT METAPHOR   BLOCH, ROBERT   SS GAL 58 10
  ATOMS AND EVIL   BLOCH, ROBERT   AC
BLOCKADE RUNNER (SLACKER'S PARADISE)
                                JAMESON, MALCOLM SS ASF 41 04
  BULLARD OF THE SPACE PATROL   JAMESON, MALCOLM   AC
BLOCKADE RUNNERS, THE   VERNE, JULES   NA
  NOVELS   VERNE, JULES   AC
  OMNIBUS, THE   VERNE, JULES   AC
BLOND KID, THE   SUTHERLAND, HERB SS
  AD 2500   WILSON, ANGUS   AN
BLONDE GODDESS OF BAL-SAGOTH, THE
                                HOWARD, ROBERT E. NV WRT 31 10
  SECOND AVON FANTASY READER, THE WOLLHEIM &ERNSBERGER AN
BLOOD   BROWN, FREDRIC   SS FSF 55 02
  GALAXY OF GHOULS   MERRIL, JUDITH   AN
  HONEYMOON IN HELL   BROWN, FREDRIC   AC
BLOOD BANK   MILLER, WALTER M. JR NV ASF 52 06
  ALL ABOUT THE FUTURE   GREENBERG, MARTIN   AN
  VIEW FROM THE STARS, THE   MILLER, WALTER M. JR   AC
BLOOD BROTHER   BEAUMONT, CHARLES SS PBY 61 04
  PLAYBOY BOOK OF SCIENCE FICTION AND FANTASY, THE
                                PLAYBOY, EDITORS OF   AN
BLOOD BROTHER   SCORTIA, THOMAS N. SS
  FUTURE KIN   ELWOOD, ROGER   OA
BLOOD BROTHER   WHITE, JAMES   NV NWR 69 14
  MAJOR OPERATION   WHITE, JAMES   NO
  NEW WRITINGS IN SF. 14   CARNELL, JOHN   OA
BLOOD LANDS   COPPEL, ALFRED   SS DSF 52 12
  WAY OUT   HOWARD, IVAN   AN
BLOOD OF TYRANTS   BOVA, BEN   NV AMZ 70 05
  FORWARD IN TIME   BOVA, BEN   AC
BLOOD OFFERING   KIPPAX, JOHN   SS SCF 61 06
  WEIRD SHADOWS FROM BEYOND   CARNELL, JOHN   AN
BLOOD SON (DRINK MY RED BLOOD) MATHESON, RICHARD SS IMG 51 04
  SHORES OF SPACE, THE   MATHESON, RICHARD   AC
BLOOD/THOUGHTS   ELLISON, HARLAN   IN
  NO DOORS, NO WINDOWS (STORIES REWRITTEN) ELLISON, HARLAN AC
BLOOD'S A ROVER   OLIVER, CHAD   NV ASF 52 05
  DEEP SPACE   SILVERBERG, ROBERT   AN
  OPERATION FUTURE   CONKLIN, GROFF   AN
BLOOD'S HORIZON, THE   ATTANASIO, A. A. NV NDM 77 07
  NEW DIMENSIONS 7   SILVERBERG, ROBERT   OA
BLOOD-FLOWER, THE   QUINN, SEABURY   NV WRT 27 03
  NIGHTMARE GARDEN   GHIDALIA, VIC   AN
BLOOD-STAINED GOD, THE   HOWARD, ROBERT E. NV FUN 56 04
  TALES OF CONAN   HOWARD, R. & DE CAMP   AC
BLOODED ON ARACHNE   BISHOP, MICHAEL NV EPC 75
  EPOCH   ELWOOD & SILVERBERG   OA
BLOODMOBILE   FRITCH, CHARLES E. SS
  HORSES' ASTEROID   FRITCH, CHARLES E.   AC
BLOODSTREAM   BRUNNER, JOHN   SS VTX 74 06
  BOOK OF JOHN BRUNNER, THE   BRUNNER, JOHN   AC
BLOODSTREAM   FISHER, LOU   SS EPC 75
  EPOCH   ELWOOD & SILVERBERG   OA
BLOWUP BLUES   COGSWELL, THEODORE R SG   60
  6TH ANNUAL OF THE YEAR'S BEST S-F, THE MERRIL, JUDITH AN
BLOWUPS HAPPEN   HEINLEIN, ROBERT A. NV ASF 40 09
  *ASTOUNDING SCIENCE FICTION ANTHOLOGY, THE
                                CAMPBELL, JOHN W. JR   AN
  *BEST OF SCIENCE FICTION   CONKLIN, GROFF   AN
  BEST SF 2   CRISPIN, EDMUND   AN
  *FIRST ASTOUNDING SCIENCE FICTION ANTHOLOGY, THE
                                CAMPBELL, JOHN W. JR   AN
  *MAN WHO SOLD THE MOON, THE   HEINLEIN, ROBERT A.   AC
  PAST THROUGH TOMORROW, THE   HEINLEIN, ROBERT A.   AC
  WORLDS OF ROBERT A. HEINLEIN, THE HEINLEIN, ROBERT A. AC
BLUE BOTTLE, THE (DEATH WISH)   BRADBURY, RAY   SS PLS 50 FL
  LONG AFTER MIDNIGHT   BRADBURY, RAY   AC
  SEA OF SPACE, A   NOLAN, WILLIAM F.   AN
BLUE CLOUD, THE   DOGGE, MARY   SS
  AUTHENTIC BOOK OF SPACE   CAMPBELL, H. J.   AN
BLUE DANUBE   MORRIS, VIC   NA
  GOLLANCZ - SUNDAY TIMES BEST SF STORIES ANONYMOUS   OA
BLUE FIRE   SILVERBERG, ROBERT NV GAL 65 06
  TO OPEN THE SKY   SILVERBERG, ROBERT   NO
BLUE GIRAFFE, THE   DE CAMP, L. SPRAGUE NV ASF 39 08
  *ADVENTURES IN TIME AND SPACE HEALY & MCCOMAS   AN
  ANDROIDS, TIME MACHINES AND BLUE GIRAFFES
                                ELWOOD & GHIDALIA   AN
  ESCALES DANS L'INFINI   GALLET, GEORGES H.   AN
  SCIENCE FICTION BESTIARY, THE SILVERBERG, ROBERT   AN
  WORLD OF WONDER   PRATT, FLETCHER   AN
BLUE LENSES, THE   DU MAURIER, DAPHNE NV   59
  OTHERS, THE   CARR, TERRY   AN
BLUE MOUSE, THE   WOLFE, GENE   SS MWS 71
  MANY WORLDS OF SCIENCE FICTION, THE BOVA, BEN   OA
BLUE SPECTACLES, THE   DERLETH, AUGUST SS WRT 49 07
  MR. GEORGE AND OTHER ODD PERSONS DERLETH, AUGUST   AC
BLUE STAR, THE   PRATT, FLETCHER NA NEW 52 14
  WITCHES THREE   PRATT, FLETCHER   AN
BLUE THEME AND FUGUE   WELLS, ROBERT   SS SFM 74 02
  BEST OF SCIENCE FICTION MONTHLY, THE SACKS, JANET   AN
BLUEPRINT FOR TOMORROW   MINES, SAMUEL   IN
  BEST FROM STARTLING STORIES, THE MINES, SAMUEL   AN
BLUESTOCKING (THE ADVENTURESS) RUSS, JOANNA   NV ORB 67 02
  ALYX   RUSS, JOANNA   AC

BLUFF OF THE HAWK, THE   GILMORE, ANTHONY   SS   ASF 32 05
  SPACE HAWK   GILMORE, ANTHONY   AC
BLUNDER   WYLIE, PHILIP   SS   COL 46 01
  SHOT IN THE DARK   MERRIL, JUDITH   AN
  *STRANGE PORTS OF CALL   DERLETH, AUGUST   AN
BLUNDER ENLIGHTENING   DRYFOOS, DAVE   NV   DSF 52 12
  WAY OUT   HOWARD, IVAN   AN
BLURB KING, THE   HARRISON, WILLIAM   SS   71
  ROLLERBALL   HARRISON, WILLIAM   AC
BODIES   DISCH, THOMAS M.   NV   QRK 71 04
  QUARK/4   DELANY & HACKER   OA
  334   DISCH, THOMAS M.   NO
BODY BUILDERS, THE   LAUMER, KEITH   NV   GAL 66 08
  BEST OF KEITH LAUMER, THE   LAUMER, KEITH   AC
  INFINITE ARENA, THE   CARR, TERRY   AN
  IT'S A MAD, MAD, MAD GALAXY LAUMER, KEITH   AN
BODY RITUAL AMONG THE NACIREMA MINOR, HORACE M.   FA   ANT 66 03
  APEMAN, SPACEMAN   STOVER & HARRISON   AN
BODY SNATCHER, THE   STEVENSON, ROBERT L. SS
  GHOULS, THE   HAINING, PETER   AN
BODY-MASTERS, THE   LONG, FRANK BELKNAP SS   WRT 35 02
  WEIRD TALES   MARGULIES, LEO   AN
BODY, THE   SHECKLEY, ROBERT   SS   GAL 56 01
  PILGRIMAGE TO EARTH   SHECKLEY, ROBERT   AC
BODYGUARD   GRIMM, CHRISTOPHER   NA   GAL 56 02
  BODYGUARD AND 4 OTHER SHORT SF NOVELS FROM GALAXY
                              GOLD, H. L.   AN
BOGEY MAN WILL GET YOU, THE   BLOCH, ROBERT   SS   WRT 46 03
  SKULL OF THE MARQUIS DE SADE, THE BLOCH, ROBERT   AC
BOHASSIAN LEARNS   ROTSLER, WILLIAM   SS   AMZ 71 07
  SCHOOL AND SOCIETY THROUGH SCIENCE FICTION
                              OLANDER/GREENBERG/&   AN
BOLDEN'S PETS   WALLACE, F. L.   NV   GAL 55 10
  GREAT SCIENCE FICTION ABOUT DOCTORS CONKLIN, G&FABRICANT AN
BOMB IN THE BATHTUB, THE   SCORTIA, THOMAS N.   SS   GAL 57 02
  CAUTION! INFLAMMABLE!   SCORTIA, THOMAS N.   AC
  COSMIC LAUGHTER   HALDEMAN, JOE W.   AN
  FOURTH GALAXY READER, THE   GOLD, H. L.   AN
BOMB SCARE   VINGE, VERNOR   SS   ASF 70 11
  TOMORROW, AND TOMORROW, AND TOMORROW... HEINTZ/HERBERT/JOOS/ AN
BOMBARDMENT OF THE GOLDEN GATE, THE
                              STIRLING, YATES JR. SS
  BATTLE FOR THE PACIFIC AND OTHER ADVENTURES AT SEA, THE
                              ANONYMOUS   AN
BOND AND FREE   SARGENT, PAMELA   NV   FSF 74 06
  STARSHADOWS   SARGENT, PAMELA   AC
BONE FOR DEBUNKERS (THE KARMESIN AFFAIR)
                              KERSH, GERALD   SS   SEP 62 12
  NIGHTSHADE & DAMNATIONS   KERSH, GERALD   AC
BONE OF CONTENTION   DISCH, THOMAS M.   SS   AHM 66
  *ONE HUNDRED AND TWO H-BOMBS DISCH, THOMAS M.   AC
  WHITE FANG GOES DINGO AND OTHER FUNNY S.F. STORIES
                              DISCH, THOMAS M.   AC
BONELESS HORROR, THE   KELLER, DAVID H. MD. SS   SWS 29 07
  LIFE EVERLASTING AND OTHER TALES OF SCIENCE, FANTASY
  AND HORROR   KELLER, DAVID H. MD.   AC
BONES   WOLLHEIM, DONALD A. SS   STI 41 02
  ZACHERLEY'S VULTURE STEW   ZACHERLEY   AN
BONES OF BERTRAND RUSSELL, THE ALDISS, BRIAN W.   SS   NWR 76 28
  NEW WRITINGS IN SF. 28   BULMER, KENNETH   OA
BONES, THE   STURGEON, THEODORE   SS   UNK 43 08
  BEYOND   STURGEON, THEODORE   AC
BONUS BABY   GOTSCHALK, FELIX C. SS   SPE 74 01
  SCIENCE FICTION EMPHASIS NO. 1 GERROLD, DAVID   OA
BOOK LEARNERS, THE   HUFFORD, LIZ   SS   FSF 75 04
  BEST SCIENCE FICTION STORIES OF THE YEAR (1975)
                              DEL REY, LESTER   AN
BOOK OF PTATH, THE   VAN VOGT, A. E.   NO   UNK 43 10
  VAN VOGT OMNIBUS, A   VAN VOGT, A. E.   AC
BOOK REVIEWS   KNIGHT, DAMON   BR   ORB 74 14
  ORBIT 14   KNIGHT, DAMON   OA
BOOK, THE   MARGROFF, ROBERT E.
  AND OFFUTT, ANDREW J.   SS C ORB 70 08
  ORBIT 8   KNIGHT, DAMON   OA
BOOK, THE   SHAARA, MICHAEL   NV   GAL 53 11
  ELSEWHERE AND ELSEWHEN   CONKLIN, GROFF   AN
BOOKED SOLID   RUSSELL, RAY   SS   61
  SARDONICUS AND OTHER STORIES RUSSELL, RAY   AC
BOOKMOBILE   HARNESS, CHARLES L. SS   IFS 68 11
  SCHOOL AND SOCIETY THROUGH SCIENCE FICTION
                              OLANDER/GREENBERG/&   AN
BOOKS   BOUCHER, ANTHONY   MS
  7TH ANNUAL OF THE YEAR'S BEST S-F, THE MERRIL, JUDITH   AN
  8TH ANNUAL OF THE YEAR'S BEST S-F, THE MERRIL, JUDITH   AN
  9TH ANNUAL OF THE YEAR'S BEST S-F, THE MERRIL, JUDITH   AN
BOOKSHOP, THE   BOND, NELSON S.   SS
  MR. MERGENTHWIRKER'S LOBBIES AND OTHER FANTASTIC TALES
                              BOND, NELSON S.   AC
BOOKWORM, RUN!   VINGE, VERNOR   NV   ASF 66 03
  ANALOG 6   CAMPBELL, JOHN W. JR AN
BOOMER FLATS   LAFFERTY, R. A.   SS   IFS 71 08
  DOES ANYONE ELSE HAVE SOMETHING FURTHER TO ADD?
                              LAFFERTY, R. A.   AC
BOOMERANG (A GREAT DEAL OF POWER)
                              RUSSELL, ERIC FRANK SS   FUN 53 08
  INVASION OF THE ROBOTS   ELWOOD, ROGER   AN
  *SCIENCE FICTION THINKING MACHINES CONKLIN, GROFF   AN
BOOMERANG CIRCUIT, THE   LEINSTER, MURRAY   NV   TWS 47 06
  LAST SPACESHIP, THE   LEINSTER, MURRAY   NO
BOONA ON SCANCIA   HENDERSON, ZENNA   SS   NEW 71 AC
  HOLDING WONDER   HENDERSON, ZENNA   AC
BORDERED IN BLACK   NIVEN, LARRY   SS   FSF 66 04
  SF: AUTHORS' CHOICE 3   HARRISON, HARRY   AN
  SHAPE OF SPACE, THE   NIVEN, LARRY   AC
BORDERLAND OF SOL, THE   NIVEN, LARRY   NV   ASF 75 01

  TALES OF KNOWN SPACE: THE UNIVERSE OF LARRY NIVEN
                              NIVEN, LARRY   AC
BOREDOM OF FANTASY, THE   KOESTLER, ARTHUR   AR   55
  SCIENCE FICTION: THE FUTURE ALLEN, DICK   AN
BORN OF MAN AND WOMAN   MATHESON, RICHARD   SS   FSF 50 SU
  BEST SCIENCE-FICTION STORIES: 1951, THE BLEILER & DIKTY   AN
  BORN OF MAN AND WOMAN   MATHESON, RICHARD   AC
  CHILDREN OF WONDER   TENN, WILLIAM   AN
  MINDWORM, THE   ANONYMOUS   AN
  SCIENCE FICTION HALL OF FAME VOLUME 1 SILVERBERG, ROBERT AN
  THIRD FROM THE SUN   MATHESON, RICHARD   AC
BORN OF THE SUN   WILLIAMSON, JACK   NV   ASF 34 03
  BEFORE THE GOLDEN AGE   ASIMOV, ISAAC   AN
BORN TO EXILE   EISENSTEIN, PHYLLIS NV   FSF 71 08
  BEST FROM FANTASY AND SCIENCE FICTION: 20
                              FERMAN, EDWARD L.   AN
BORN WITH THE DEAD   SILVERBERG, ROBERT   NA   FSF 74 04
  BEST SCIENCE FICTION OF THE YEAR, THE NO. 4
                              CARR, TERRY   AN
  BORN WITH THE DEAD   SILVERBERG, ROBERT   AC
  NEBULA AWARD STORIES 10   GUNN, JAMES E.   AN
BOTANY BAY   HUBBARD, P. M.   SS   FSF 55 02
  BEST FROM FANTASY AND SCIENCE FICTION: 5
                              BOUCHER, ANTHONY   AN
BOTTICELLI HORROR, THE   BIGGLE, LLOYD JR.   NV   FAN 60 03
  METALLIC MUSE, THE   BIGGLE, LLOYD JR.   AC
BOTTLE FULL OF KISMET, A   DAVIDSON, AVRAM   SS
  STRANGE SEAS AND SHORES   DAVIDSON, AVRAM   AC
BOTTLE IMP, THE   STEVENSON, ROBERT L. SS   BAW 91 03
  MOONLIGHT TRAVELER, THE   STERN, PHILIP VAN D.   AN
BOTTLED MEN, THE   ROCKLYNNE, ROSS   NV   ASF 46 06
  MEN AND THE MIRROR, THE   ROCKLYNNE, ROSS   AC
BOTTOMLESS GRAVE, A   BIERCE, AMBROSE   SS
  GRAVEYARD READER, THE   CONKLIN, GROFF   AN
BOTTOMLESS PIT   HIGH, PHILIP E.   SS   NWS 63 03
  OUT OF THIS WORLD 5   WILLIAMS-ELLIS& OWEN AN
BOULTER'S CANARIES   ROBERTS, KEITH   NV   NWR 65 03
  MACHINES AND MEN   ROBERTS, KEITH   AC
  NEW WRITINGS IN SF. 3   CARNELL, JOHN   OA
  PASSING OF THE DRAGONS, THE ROBERTS, KEITH   AC
BOUNTY   SHERRED, T. L.   SS   DVS 72 02
  AGAIN, DANGEROUS VISIONS   ELLISON, HARLAN   OA
  SOCIAL PROBLEMS THROUGH SCIENCE FICTION GREENBERG/MILSTEAD/& AN
BOUNTY HUNTER, THE   DAVIDSON, AVRAM   SS   FUN 58 03
  FANTASTIC UNIVERSE OMNIBUS, THE SANTESSON, HANS S.   AN
  GALACTIC EMPIRES VOLUME TWO ALDISS, BRIAN W.   AN
  WHAT STRANGE STARS AND SKIES DAVIDSON, AVRAM   AC
BOWL BIGGER THAN EARTH, A   FARMER, PHILIP JOSE NV   IFS 67 09
  DOWN IN THE BLACK GANG AND OTHER STORIES FARMER, PHILIP JOSE AC
BOWL OF BISKIES MAKES A GROWING BOY, A
                              JONES, RAYMOND F.   NV
  OTHER SIDE OF TOMORROW, THE ELWOOD, ROGER   OA
BOX, THE   BLISH, JAMES   SS   TWS 49 04
  BEYOND CONTROL   SILVERBERG, ROBERT   AN
  OMNIBUS OF SCIENCE FICTION CONKLIN, GROFF   AN
  SHAPE OF THINGS, THE   KNIGHT, DAMON   AN
  SO CLOSE TO HOME   BLISH, JAMES   AC
  STRANGE ADVENTURES IN SCIENCE FICTION CONKLIN, GROFF   AN
BOY AND HIS DOG, A   ELLISON, HARLAN   NV   NWS 69 04
  AS TOMORROW BECOMES TODAY   SULLIVAN, CHARLES W. A.   AN
  BEAST THAT SHOUTED LOVE AT THE HEART OF THE WORLD, THE
                              ELLISON, HARLAN   AC
  BEST SF STORIES FROM NEW WORLDS 8 MOORCOCK, MICHAEL   AN
  NEBULA AWARD STORIES NO. 5 BLISH, JAMES   AN
  WORLD'S BEST SCIENCE FICTION: 1970 WOLLHEIM & CARR   AN
BOY DAVID, THE   COOPER, EDMUND   SS
  VOICES IN THE DARK   COOPER, EDMUND   AC
BOY IN DARKNESS   PEAKE, MERVYN   NV   56
  INNER LANDSCAPE, THE   MOORCOCK, MICHAEL   AN
  SOMETIME, NEVER   ANONYMOUS   OA
BOY MEETS DYEVITZA   YOUNG, ROBERT F.   SS   AMZ 62 10
  GLASS OF STARS, A   YOUNG, ROBERT F.   AC
BOY NEXT DOOR, THE   OLIVER, CHAD   SS   FSF 51 06
  HUMAN?   MERRIL, JUDITH   AN
BOY WHO BROUGHT LOVE, THE   HOCH, EDWARD D.   SS
  CRISIS   ELWOOD, ROGER   OA
BOY WHO FOUND FEAR, THE   KUNOS, IGNAZ   SS   07
  TALES BEYOND TIME   DE CAMP, L. S.&C.   AN
BOY, THE   GOR, GENNADY   SS
  PATH INTO THE UNKNOWN   ANONYMOUS   AN
BOYS, RAISE GIANT MUSHROOMS IN YOUR CELLAR (COME INTO MY
  CELLAR)   BRADBURY, RAY   SS   GAL 62 10
  MACHINERIES OF JOY, THE   BRADBURY, RAY   AC
BRACE YOURSELF FOR ANOTHER ICE AGE
                              COLLIGAN, DOUGLAS   AR   SDG 73 02
  SCIENCE FACT/FICTION   FARRELL/GAGE/&   AN
BRADBURY BIBLIOGRAPHY   NOLAN, WILLIAM F.   MS   FSF 63 05
  BEST FROM FANTASY AND SCIENCE FICTION, 25TH ANNIV.
                              FERMAN, EDWARD L.   AN
BRAIN   WRIGHT, S. FOWLER   SS   32
  *ADVENTURES IN TIME AND SPACE HEALY & MCCOMAS   AN
  NEW GODS LEAD, THE   WRIGHT, S. FOWLER   AC
BRAIN CHILD (INVISIBLE BOY)   COOPER, EDMUND   SS   SEP 56 06
  TOMORROW'S GIFT   COOPER, EDMUND   AC
BRAIN FEVER SEASON   LAFFERTY, R. A.   SS   UNI 77 07
  UNIVERSE 7   CARR, TERRY   OA
BRAIN OF THE GALAXY   VANCE, JACK   NV   WBY 51 02
  WORLD BETWEEN AND OTHER STORIES, THE VANCE, JACK   DC
  WORLDS OF JACK VANCE, THE   VANCE, JACK   AC
BRAIN PIRATES, THE   CAMPBELL, JOHN W. JR SS   TWS 38 10
  PLANETEERS, THE   CAMPBELL, JOHN W. JR NO
BRAIN STEALERS OF MARS, THE   CAMPBELL, JOHN W. JR SS   TWS 36 12
  ALIEN WORLDS   ELWOOD, ROGER   AN
  BEFORE THE GOLDEN AGE   ASIMOV, ISAAC   AN
  PLANETEERS, THE   CAMPBELL, JOHN W. JR DC

```
BRAIN WAVE                        ANDERSON, POUL        NO   BAL 54
  TREASURY OF GREAT SCIENCE FICTION, A VOL.2
                                  BOUCHER, ANTHONY           AN
BRAIN WIPE                        MACLEAN, KATHERINE    SS   NMD 73
  FRONTIERS 2: THE NEW MIND       ELWOOD, ROGER              OA
BRAIN, THE                        NORBERT, W.           SS   TEN 52 04
  CROSSROADS IN TIME              CONKLIN, GROFF             AN
BRAIN, THE                        WEINER, NORBERT       SS   TEN 52 04
  GREAT SCIENCE FICTION BY SCIENTISTS  CONKLIN, GROFF        AN
BRAINS OF EARTH, THE              VANCE, JACK           NA   66
  WORLDS OF JACK VANCE, THE       VANCE, JACK                AC
BRAKE                             ANDERSON, POUL        NV   ASF 57 08
  BEYOND THE BEYOND               ANDERSON, POUL             AC
BRAMBLE BUSH                      MCKENNA, RICHARD M.   NV   ORB 68 03
  ORBIT  3                        KNIGHT, DAMON              OA
BRAMBLE BUSH                      NOURSE, ALAN E.       SS   IFS 57 08
  RX FOR TOMORROW                 NOURSE, ALAN E.            AC
BRASS AND GOLD, OR HORSE AND ZEPPELIN IN BEVERLY HILLS
                                  FARMER, PHILIP JOSE   QRK 71 04
  BOOK OF PHILIP JOSE FARMER, THE FARMER, PHILIP JOSE        AC
                                  DELANY & HACKER            OA
  QUARK/4
BRASS GOD, THE (RETIEF, GOD SPEAKER)
                                  LAUMER, KEITH         NV   IFS 65 01
  GALACTIC DIPLOMAT               LAUMER, KEITH              AC
BRAT                              STURGEON, THEODORE    SS   UNK 41 12
  NOT WITHOUT SORCERY             STURGEON, THEODORE         AC
  WITHOUT SORCERY                 STURGEON, THEODORE         AC
BRAT,                            ZHURAVLEVA,VALENTINA SS    67
  AIR OF MARS AND OTHER STORIES, THE  GINSBURG, MIRRA        AN
BRAVE NEW WORD                    MCCOMAS, J. FRANCIS   SS   FSF 54 09
  BEST FROM FANTASY AND SCIENCE FICTION: 4
                                  BOUCHER, ANTHONY           AN
  TOMORROW, INC.                  GREENBERG& OLANDER         AN
BRAVE NEWER WORLD                 HARRISON, HARRY       NV   FFU 71
  *BEST OF HARRY HARRISON, THE    HARRISON, HARRY            AC
  FOUR FUTURES                    SILVERBERG, ROBERT         OA
BRAVE SALT                        HILL, RICHARD         SS   QRK 71 03
  QUARK/3                         DELANY & HACKER            OA
BRAVE TO BE A KING                ANDERSON, POUL        NV   FSF 59 08
  GUARDIANS OF TIME               ANDERSON, POUL             AC
BRAZEN LOCKED ROOM, THE (ALSO AS GIMMICKS THREE)
                                  ASIMOV, ISAAC         SS   FSF 56 11
  DEALS WITH THE DEVIL            DAVENPORT, BASIL           AN
  SPECIAL WONDER                  MCCOMAS, J. FRANCIS        AN
BREAD AND CIRCUSES (GENE RODDENBERRY & G. L. COON)
                                  BLISH, JAMES          SA   STK 75 11
  STAR TREK 11                    BLISH, JAMES               OC
BREAD OVERHEAD                    LEIBER, FRITZ         NV   GAL 58 02
  PAIL OF AIR, A                  LEIBER, FRITZ              AC
BREAK                             BOSTON, BRUCE         SS   NWQ 74 06
  NEW WORLDS NO. 6                PLATT & BAILEY             OA
BREAK IN THE WEATHER, A           JACOBS, HARVEY        SS
  EGG OF THE GLAK, AND OTHER STORIES, THE  JACOBS, HARVEY    AC
BREAK THE DOOR OF HELL            BRUNNER, JOHN         NV   IMP 66 04
  NEW WORLDS OF FANTASY           CARR, TERRY                AN
  TRAVELER IN BLACK, THE          BRUNNER, JOHN              AC
BREAKAWAY HOUSE                   GOULART, RON          SS   FSF 66 05
  GHOST BREAKER                   GOULART, RON               DC
BREAKDOWN                         ROBERTS, KEITH        SS   IMP 66 10
  MACHINES AND MEN                ROBERTS, KEITH             AC
BREAKDOWN                         WILLIAMSON, JACK      NV   ASF 42 01
  JOURNEY TO INFINITY             GREENBERG , MARTIN         AN
  PEOPLE MACHINES                 WILLIAMSON, JACK           AC
BREAKFAST AT TWILIGHT             DICK, PHILIP K.       SS   AMZ 54 07
  BEST OF PHILIP K. DICK, THE     DICK, PHILIP K.            AC
  BOOK OF PHILIP K. DICK, THE     DICK, PHILIP K.            AC
BREAKING IN                       MALZBERG, BARRY N.    SS   FAN 72 06
  OUT FROM GANYMEDE               MALZBERG, BARRY N.         AC
BREAKING POINT                    CHRISTOPHER, JOHN     SS   NWS 52 05
  TWENTY-SECOND CENTURY, THE      CHRISTOPHER, JOHN          AC
BREAKING POINT                    GUNN, JAMES E.        NV   SSP 53 03
  BREAKING POINT                  GUNN, JAMES E.             AC
BREAKING STRAIN (THIRTY SECONDS - THIRTY DAYS)
                                  CLARKE, ARTHUR C.     NV   TWS 49 12
  ACROSS THE SEA OF STARS         CLARKE, ARTHUR C.          AC
  EXPEDITION TO EARTH             CLARKE, ARTHUR C.          AC
  *NO PLACE LIKE EARTH            CARNELL, JOHN              AN
  OUT OF THIS WORLD 1             WILLIAMS-ELLIS& OWEN       AN
BREAKOUT IN ECOL 2                BUNCH, DAVID R.       SS   NOV 73 03
  NOVA 3                          HARRISON, HARRY            OA
BREATH OF DRAGONS, THE            REAVES, J. MICHAEL    SS   CLR 73 03
  CLARION III                     WILSON, ROBIN SCOTT        OA
BREATH OF LUCIFER, A              NARAYAN, R. K.        SS   PBY 69 07
  MASKS                           PLAYBOY, EDITORS OF        AN
BREATH'S A WARE THAT WILL NOT KEEP
                                  MONTELEONE, THOMAS F  SS   DYS 75
  DYSTOPIAN VISIONS               ELWOOD, ROGER              OA
BREATHES THERE A MAN              FRITCH, CHARLES E.    SS   RKS 53 07
  HORSES' ASTEROID                FRITCH, CHARLES E.         AC
BRECKENRIDGE AND THE CONTINUUM SILVERBERG, ROBERT     NV   SCS 73
  BEST SCIENCE FICTION OF THE YEAR, THE NO. 3
                                  CARR, TERRY                AN
  CAPRICORN GAMES                 SILVERBERG, ROBERT         AC
  SHOWCASE                        ELWOOD, ROGER              OA
BREEDING GROUND                   PRIEST, CHRISTOPHER   SS   VOT 70 01
  REAL-TIME WORLD                 PRIEST, CHRISTOPHER        AC
BREEDS THERE A MAN...?            ASIMOV, ISAAC         NV   ASF 51 06
  *BEACHHEADS IN SPACE            DERLETH, AUGUST            AN
  FROM OTHER WORLDS               DERLETH, AUGUST            AN
  NIGHTFALL AND OTHER STORIES     ASIMOV, ISAAC              AC
  THROUGH A GLASS, CLEARLY        ASIMOV, ISAAC              AC
BRENDA                            ST. CLAIR, MARGARET   SS   WRT 54 03
  MORE LITTLE MONSTERS            ELWOOD & GHIDALIA          AN
  *TWISTED                        CONKLIN, GROFF             AN
BRIAN IN THE DREAMING SEAT        BRENNERT, ALAN        SS
  CLARION SF                      WILHELM, KATE              OA
```

```
BRICK MOON, THE (1869, INCLUDES SEQUEL "LIFE IN THE
  BRICK MOON" ATL 70 02)          HALE, EDWARD EVERETT NA   ATL 69 10
  MASTERPIECES OF SCIENCE FICTION MOSKOWITZ, SAM            AN
BRIDE NINETY-ONE                  SILVERBERG, ROBERT    SS   IFS 67 09
  DIMENSION THIRTEEN              SILVERBERG, ROBERT         AC
BRIDGE                            BLISH, JAMES          NV   ASF 52 02
  ASTOUNDING-ANALOG READER, THE VOLUME TWO HARRISON & ALDISS AN
  JUPITER                         POHL, C. & F.              AN
  SPECTRUM  2                     AMIS & CONQUEST            AN
  YEAR 2018!                      BLISH, JAMES               NO
BRIDGE BUILDER, THE               WOLF, GARY K.         SS   ORB 74 14
  ORBIT 14                        KNIGHT, DAMON              OA
BRIDGE CROSSING                   DRYFOOS, DAVE         SS   GAL 51 05
  BEYOND THE END OF TIME          POHL, FREDERIK             AN
BRIDGE OF SIGHS, THE              DERLETH, AUGUST       SS   WRT 31 09
  NOT LONG FOR THIS WORLD         DERLETH, AUGUST            AC
BRIDGEHEAD (ALSO AS THE TEMPORAL TRANSGRESSOR)
                                  LONG, FRANK BELKNAP   NV   ASF 44 08
  *HOUNDS OF TINDALOS, THE        LONG, FRANK BELKNAP        AC
BRIDLE AND SADDLE                 ASIMOV, ISAAC         NV   ASF 42 06
  FOUNDATION                      ASIMOV, ISAAC              NO
  *MEN AGAINST THE STARS          GREENBERG , MARTIN         AN
BRIDLE FOR PEGASUS, A             MCCAFFREY, ANNE       NV   ASF 73 07
  TO RIDE PEGASUS                 MCCAFFREY, ANNE            AC
BRIDLE SHOWER (SEE SECRET WEAPON)
                                  BIGGLE, LLOYD JR.          TC
BRIDLE, THE                       KELLER, DAVID H. MD.  SS   WRT 42 09
  TALES FROM UNDERWOOD            KELLER, DAVID H. MD.       AC
BRIEF, SWINGING CAREER OF DAN AND JUDY SMYTHE, THE
                                  WILSON, CARTER        SS   FSF 70 04
  BEST FROM FANTASY AND SCIENCE FICTION: 19
                                  FERMAN, EDWARD L.          AN
BRIGHT ARE THE STARS THAT SHINE, DARK IS THE SKY
                                  ETCHISON, DENNIS      SS   NWR 68 11
  NEW WRITINGS IN SF. 11          CARNELL, JOHN              OA
BRIGHT BEARD                      BROWN, FREDRIC        SS
  NIGHTMARES AND GEEZENSTACKS     BROWN, FREDRIC             AC
BRIGHT DESTRUCTION                MCCLINTIC, WINONA     PM   FSF 56 06
  BEST FROM FANTASY AND SCIENCE FICTION: 6
                                  BOUCHER, ANTHONY           AN
BRIGHT EYES                       ELLISON, HARLAN       SS   FAN 65 04
  ALONE AGAINST TOMORROW          ELLISON, HARLAN            AC
  *PAINGOD AND OTHER DELUSIONS    ELLISON, HARLAN            AC
BRIGHT ILLUSION, THE              MOORE, C. L.          NV   ASF 34 10
  BEST OF C. L. MOORE, THE        MOORE, C. L.               AC
  MASTERS' CHOICE                 JANIFER, LAURENCE M.       AN
BRIGHT SEGMENT                    STURGEON, THEODORE    NV   NEW 55 AC
  CAVIAR                          STURGEON, THEODORE         AC
BRIGHTNESS FALLS FROM THE AIR (CONTEST STORY)
                                  SEABRIGHT, IDRIS      SS   FSF 51 04
  BEST SCIENCE-FICTION STORIES: 1952, THE BLEILER & DIKTY   AN
  GALACTIC EMPIRES VOLUME ONE     ALDISS, BRIAN W.           AN
BRIGHTNESS FALLS FROM THE AIR (CONTEST STORY)
                                  ST. CLAIR, MARGARET   SS   FSF 51 04
  SPECIAL WONDER                  MCCOMAS, J. FRANCIS        AN
BRIGHTON MONSTER, THE (THE MONSTER)
                                  KERSH, GERALD         SS   SEP 48 02
  NIGHTSHADE & DAMNATIONS         KERSH, GERALD              AC
  ON AN ODD NOTE                  KERSH, GERALD              AC
BRIGHTSIDE CROSSING               NOURSE, ALAN E.       NV   GAL 56 01
  BEYOND TOMORROW                 KNIGHT, DAMON              AN
  TIGER BY THE TAIL               NOURSE, ALAN E.            AC
  WORLD THAT COULDN'T BE AND 8 OTHER SF NOVELETS
                                  GOLD, H. L.                AN
BRILLIANT CURIOSITY, A            PISERCHIA, DORIS      NV   ORB 75 16
  ORBIT 16                        KNIGHT, DAMON              OA
BRILLO                            BOVA, BEN
                                  AND ELLISON, HARLAN   NV C ASF 70 08
  PARTNERS IN WONDER              ELLISON, HARLAN            AC
BRIMSTONE BILL                    JAMESON, MALCOLM      SS   ASF 42 07
  BULLARD OF THE SPACE PATROL     JAMESON, MALCOLM           AC
BRINGER WITH THE WINDOW, THE (LAMIA MUTABLE)
                                  HARRISON, M. JOHN     SS   DVS 72 02
  MACHINE IN SHAFT TEN AND OTHER STORIES, THE
                                  HARRISON, M. JOHN          AC
BRINK OF INFINITY, THE            WEINBAUM, STANLEY G. SS    TWS 36 12
  MARTIAN ODYSSEY AND OTHER SCIENCE FICTION TALES, A
                                  WEINBAUM, STANLEY G. AC
  MARTIAN ODYSSEY, A              WEINBAUM, STANLEY G. AC
  RED PERI, THE                   WEINBAUM, STANLEY G. AC
BRINK, THE                        SHAW, BOB             SS   FAN 76
  COSMIC KALEIDOSCOPE             SHAW, BOB                  AC
BRINKMANSHIP                      ELLISON, HARLAN       IN
  OVER THE EDGE                   ELLISON, HARLAN            AC
BRITISH INTERPLANETARY SOCIETY, THE
                                  MISC. MATERIAL        MS
  LAURIE'S SPACE ANNUAL           ANONYMOUS                  AN
BROKE AND HUNGRY, NO PLACE TO GO (SEE BROKE DOWN ENGINE)
                                  GOULART, RON               TC
BROKE DOWN ENGINE (BROKE AND HUNGRY, NO PLACE TO GO)
                                  GOULART, RON          SS   GAL 69 11
  BROKE DOWN ENGINE AND OTHER TROUBLES WITH MACHINES
                                  GOULART, RON               AC
BROKEN FIELD, THE                 FRANCIS, NIGEL        SS   NWB 75 08
  NEW WORLDS EIGHT                BAILEY, HILARY             OA
BROKEN RECORD, THE                MCINTOSH, J. T.       SS   NWS 52 09
  BEST FROM NEW WORLDS SCIENCE FICTION, THE
                                  CARNELL, JOHN              AN
BRONZE PARROT, THE                FREEMAN, AUSTIN       SS   24
  SHOT IN THE DARK                MERRIL, JUDITH             AN
BROOKLYN PROJECT                  TENN, WILLIAM         SS   PLS 48 FL
  SHOT IN THE DARK                MERRIL, JUDITH             AN
  VOYAGERS IN TIME                SILVERBERG, ROBERT         AN
  WOODEN STAR, THE                TENN, WILLIAM              AC
  17 X INFINITY                   CONKLIN, GROFF             AN
```

BROOMSTICK RIDE-   BLOCH, ROBERT   SS   SUP 57 12
  BOGEY MEN   BLOCH, ROBERT   AC
BROTHER AND SISTER, THE   SHELLEY, MARY W.   NV   KPS 33
  TALES AND STORIES   SHELLEY, MARY W.   AC
BROTHER JOHN   ROBERTS, KEITH   NV   IMP 66 05
  PAVANE   ROBERTS, KEITH   NO
BROTHER TO DRAGONS, A COMPANION OF OWLS, A
                             WILHELM, KATE   NV   ORB 74 14
  ORBIT 14   KNIGHT, DAMON   OA
BROTHER TO THE MACHINE   MATHESON, RICHARD SS   IFS 52 11
  INVASION OF THE ROBOTS   ELWOOD, ROGER   AN
  SHOCK II   MATHESON, RICHARD   AC
BROTHERHOOD OF KEEPERS, THE   MCLAUGHLIN, DEAN   NV   ASF 60 07
  HAWK AMONG THE SPARROWS   MCLAUGHLIN, DEAN   AN
  6TH ANNUAL OF THE YEAR'S BEST S-F, THE MERRIL, JUDITH   AN
BROTHERS   DICKSON, GORDON R. NV   AMA 73
  ASTOUNDING   HARRISON, HARRY   OA
BROTHERS BEYOND THE VOID   FAIRMAN, PAUL W.   SS   FAD 52 03
  *WORLDS OF TOMORROW   DERLETH, AUGUST   AN
BROTHERS, THE   DANCE, CLIFTON JR. SS   FSF 52 06
  GREAT SCIENCE FICTION ABOUT DOCTORS CONKLIN, G&FABRICANT AN
BROWN PACKAGE, THE   FAIRMAN, PAUL W.   SS
  FORGETFUL ROBOT, THE   FAIRMAN, PAUL W.   OC
BROWN ROBERT   CARR, TERRY   SS   FSF 62 07
  ALPHA 6   SILVERBERG, ROBERT   AN
  LIGHT AT THE END OF THE UNIVERSE, THE CARR, TERRY   AC
BROWNSHOES   STURGEON, THEODORE SS   KNT 69
  STURGEON IS ALIVE AND WELL... STURGEON, THEODORE   AC
BRUSHWOOD BOY, THE   KIPLING, RUDYARD   SS   CNY 95 12
  PERCHANCE TO DREAM   KNIGHT, DAMON   AN
BUBBLE-DOME HOMES   BUNCH, DAVID R.   SS
  MODERAN   BUNCH, DAVID R.   AC
BUBBLES   SALLIS, JAMES   SS   NWS 68 10
  FEW LAST WORDS, A   SALLIS, JAMES   AC
BUCCANEER OF THE STAR SEAS (SEE THE QUEST OF THE IMMORTAL)
                             REPP, ED EARL   TC
BUCK AND THE GENTS FROM SPACE REYNOLDS, MACK   NV
  SCIENCE FICTION ADVENTURES FROM WAY OUT ELWOOD, ROGER   OA
BUCK FEVER   BEAUMONT, CHARLES SS   NEW 60 AC
  NIGHT RIDE AND OTHER JOURNEYS BEAUMONT, CHARLES   AC
BUDDING EXPLORER   ROBIN, RALPH   SS   FSF 52 09
  BEST FROM FANTASY AND SCIENCE FICTION: 2
                             BOUCHER & MCCOMAS   AN
BUDGET PLANET   SHECKLEY, ROBERT   EX   FSF 68 03
  BEST SF: 1968   HARRISON & ALDISS   AN
BUG-EYED SCREEN, THE   STRICK, PHILIP   AR
  BEYOND THIS HORIZON   CARRELL, CHRISTOPHER   OA
BUILD ME A MOUNTAIN   BOVA, BEN   SS   NEW 74 AN
  2020 VISION   POURNELLE, JERRY   AN
BUILD-UP (ALSO AS THE CONCENTRATION CITY)
                             BALLARD, J. G.   SS   NWS 57 01
  AS TOMORROW BECOMES TODAY   SULLIVAN, CHARLES W.   AN
  BILLENIUM   BALLARD, J. G.   AC
  CHRONOPOLIS AND OTHER STORIES BALLARD, J. G.   AC
  CONNOISSEUR'S S. F.   BOARDMAN, TOM JR.   AN
BUILDER, THE   DICK, PHILIP K.   SS   AMZ 54 01
  HANDFUL OF DARKNESS, A   DICK, PHILIP K.   AC
BUILDING BLOCKS   JOBLING, PETER   NV   NWB 75 08
  NEW WORLDS EIGHT   BAILEY, HILARY   OA
BUILDING ON THE LINE   DICKSON, GORDON R. NV   GAL 68 11
  STAR ROAD, THE   DICKSON, GORDON R.   AC
BUILT DOWN LOGICALLY   SCHOENFELD, HOWARD SS FSF 51 12
  FIFTY SHORT SCIENCE FICTION TALES ASIMOV & CONKLIN   AN
BUILT UP LOGICALLY (THE UNIVERSAL TANCEA, RET 49 WI)
                             SCHOENFELD, HOWARD SS   FSF 50 FL
  BEST FROM FANTASY AND SCIENCE FICTION BOUCHER & MCCOMAS   AN
  MORE PENGUIN SCIENCE FICTION ALDISS, BRIAN W.   AN
  SCIENCE FICTION ARGOSY, A   KNIGHT, DAMON   AN
  SPECIAL WONDER   MCCOMAS, J. FRANCIS   AN
BULKHEAD (WHO?)   STURGEON, THEODORE NV   GAL 55 03
  SF: THE BEST OF THE BEST   MERRIL, JUDITH   AN
  SF: THE YEAR'S GREATEST SCIENCE FICTION AND FANTASY
                             MERRIL, JUDITH   AN
  THUNDER AND ROSES   STURGEON, THEODORE   AC
  *WAY HOME, A   STURGEON, THEODORE   AC
BULLA, THE (SEE THE RECONCILLIATION)
                             WELLS, H. G.   TC
BULLARD REFLECTS   JAMESON, MALCOLM   SS   ASF 41 12
  BULLARD OF THE SPACE PATROL JAMESON, MALCOLM   AC
  INFINITE ARENA, THE   CARR, TERRY   AN
  TREASURY OF GREAT SCIENCE FICTION, A VOL.2
                             BOUCHER, ANTHONY   AN
BULLET WITH HIS NAME   LEIBER, FRITZ   NV   GAL 58 07
  WORLDS OF WHEN   CONKLIN, GROFF   AN
BULLETIN   JACKSON, SHIRLEY   SS   FSF 54 03
  BEST FROM FANTASY AND SCIENCE FICTION: 4
                             BOUCHER, ANTHONY   AN
  SCIENCE FACT/FICTION   FARRELL/GAGE/&   AN
BULLETIN FROM THE TRUSTEES, A SHORE, WILMA   SS   FSF 64 08
  BEST FROM FANTASY AND SCIENCE FICTION: 14
                             DAVIDSON, AVRAM   AN
  VOYAGERS IN TIME   SILVERBERG, ROBERT   AN
BUMBERBOOM   DAVIDSON, AVRAM   NV   FSF 66 12
  BEST FROM FANTASY AND SCIENCE FICTION: 17
                             FERMAN, EDWARD L.   AN
  WORLD'S BEST SCIENCE FICTION: 1967 WOLLHEIM & CARR   AN
BUMP, THE   LEIBER, FRITZ   SS   INY 72 04
  INFINITY 4   HOSKINS, ROBERT   OA
BURDEN OF PROOF   SHAW, BOB   SS   ASF 67 05
  ANALOG 7   CAMPBELL, JOHN W. JR   AN
  OTHER DAYS, OTHER EYES   SHAW, BOB   NO
BUREAU OF SLICK TRICKS   FYFE, H. B.   SS   ASF 48 12
  TRAVELLERS OF SPACE   GREENBERG, MARTIN   AN
BUREAUCRAT, THE   JAMESON, MALCOLM   NV   ASF 44 04
  BULLARD OF THE SPACE PATROL JAMESON, MALCOLM   AC

BURGER CREATURE   CHAPMAN, STEVE   SS   ORB 73 12
  ORBIT 12   KNIGHT, DAMON   OA
  YEAR'S BEST HORROR STORIES: SERIES III, THE
                             DAVIS, RICHARD   AN
BURGLAR'S AID   WRIGHT, S. FOWLER SS
  WITCHFINDER, THE   WRIGHT, S. FOWLER   AC
BURN WITCH, BURN   ACKERMAN, FORREST J. SS SEX 58
  SCIENCE FICTION WORLDS OF FORREST J. ACKERMAN & FRIENDS
                             ACKERMAN, FORREST J.   AC
BURNING BRIDGE, THE   ANDERSON, POUL   NV   ASF 60 01
  ORBIT UNLIMITED   ANDERSON, POUL   NO
BURNING BRIGHT   BROWNING, JOHN S. SS   ASF 48 07
  ROBOT AND THE MAN, THE   GREENBERG, MARTIN   AN
BURNING MAN, THE   BRADBURY, RAY   SS
  LONG AFTER MIDNIGHT   BRADBURY, RAY   AC
BURNING OF THE BRAIN, THE   SMITH, CORDWAINER SS   IFS 58 10
  ALPHA 2   SILVERBERG, ROBERT   AN
  BEST OF CORDWAINER SMITH, THE SMITH, CORDWAINER   AC
  YOU WILL NEVER BE THE SAME SMITH, CORDWAINER   AC
BURNING QUESTION   ALDISS, BRIAN W.   SS   FSF 66 12
  POLITICAL SCIENCE FICTION   GREENBERG& WARRICK   AN
BURNING SPEAR   DENTON, KIT   SS   FSF 64 02
  PACIFIC BOOK OF AUSTRALIAN SCIENCE FICTION
                             BAXTER, JOHN   AN
BURNING WORLD, THE   BUDRYS, ALGIS   NV   INF 57 07
  UNEXPECTED DIMENSION, THE   BUDRYS, ALGIS   AC
BURNING, THE   COGSWELL, THEODORE R SS FSF 60 07
  POCKETFUL OF STARS, A   KNIGHT, DAMON   AN
  WALL AROUND THE WORLD, THE COGSWELL, THEODORE R   AC
BURNT TOAST   REYNOLDS, MACK   SS   PBY 55 11
  BEST OF MACK REYNOLDS, THE REYNOLDS, MACK   AC
  PLAYBOY BOOK OF HORROR AND THE SUPERNATURAL, THE
                             PLAYBOY, EDITORS OF   AN
BURNT UMBER   COOPER, EDMUND   SS
  VOICES IN THE DARK   COOPER, EDMUND   AC
BURROW, THE   KAFKA, FRANZ   SS   46
  *TERROR IN THE MODERN VEIN WOLLHEIM, DONALD A.   AN
BUS STATION   EARLS, WILLIAM   SS   CLR 73 03
  CLARION III   WILSON, ROBIN SCOTT   OA
BUSBY'S PETRIFIED WOMAN   EISELEY, LOREN   SS   HRP 48 11
  CIRCUS OF DR. LAO AND OTHER IMPROBABLE STORIES
                             BRADBURY, RAY   AN
BUSINESS AS USUAL, DURING ALTERATIONS
                             WILLIAMS, RALPH   NV   ASF 58 07
  ONE HUNDRED YEARS OF SCIENCE FICTION KNIGHT, DAMON   AN
  PROLOGUE TO ANALOG   CAMPBELL, JOHN W. JR AN
  TOMORROW, INC.   GREENBERG& OLANDER   AN
BUSINESS OF KILLING   LEIBER, FRITZ   SS   ASF 44 09
  *SCIENCE FICTION ADVENTURES IN DIMENSION CONKLIN, GROFF AN
BUSINESS, AS USUAL, THE   REYNOLDS, MACK   SS   FSF 52 06
  BEST OF MACK REYNOLDS, THE REYNOLDS, MACK   AC
  CENTURY OF SCIENCE FICTION, A KNIGHT, DAMON   AN
  FIFTY SHORT SCIENCE FICTION TALES ASIMOV & CONKLIN   AN
  NEW WORLDS FOR OLD   DERLETH, AUGUST   AN
  TIMES 4 (ABRIDGED STORIES) ALLEN, VIRGINIA F.   AN
  *WORLDS OF TOMORROW   DERLETH, AUGUST   AN
BUSTO IS A GHOST, TO MEAN TO GIVE US A FRIGHT|
                             KERSH, GERALD   SS
  NIGHTSHADE & DAMNATIONS   KERSH, GERALD   AC
BUT AS A SOLDIER, FOR HIS COUNTRY
                             GOLDIN, STEPHEN   SS   UNI 74 05
  UNIVERSE 5   CARR, TERRY   OA
BUT FIRST...   JANIFER, LAURENCE M. IN
  IMPOSSIBLE?   JANIFER, LAURENCE M.   AC
BUT SOFT, WHAT LIGHT...   EMSHWILLER, CAROL SS   FSF 66 07
  SF: AUTHORS' CHOICE 4   HARRISON, HARRY   AN
BUT WHAT IF WE TRIED IT?   BOVA, BEN   AR   76
  FASTER THAN LIGHT   DANN & ZEBROWSKI   AN
BUT WHO CAN REPLACE A MAN?   ALDISS, BRIAN W.   SS   INF 58 06
  MEN AND MACHINES   SILVERBERG, ROBERT   AN
  OUT OF THIS WORLD 2   WILLIAMS-ELLIS& OWEN   AN
  TALES OF SCIENCE FICTION   BALL, BRIAN N.   AN
BUT WITHOUT HORNS   PAGE, NORVELL W.   SN   UNK 40 06
  CRUCIBLE OF POWER, THE   GREENBERG, MARTIN   AN
  FIVE SCIENCE FICTION NOVELS GREENBERG, MARTIN   AN
BUT WITHOUT ORFICES   ALDISS, BRIAN W.   SS   EPC 75
  EPOCH   ELWOOD & SILVERBERG   AN
BUTCH   ANDERSON, POUL   NV   NWS 55 07
  *TIME TO COME   DERLETH, AUGUST   AN
BUTCHER'S BILL, THE   DRAKE, DAVID   NV   GAL 74 11
  COMBAT SF   DICKSON, GORDON R.   AN
BUTTERFLIES   ESCHER, M. C.   IL
  SCIENCE FICTION   BRODKIN & PEARSON   AN
BUTTERFLIES WERE EAGLE-BIG THAT DAY, THE
                             BUNCH, DAVID R.   SS
  MODERAN   BUNCH, DAVID R.   AC
BUTTERFLIES, THE   COOPER, EDMUND   SS
  NEWS FROM ELSEWHERE   COOPER, EDMUND   AC
  TOMORROW'S GIFT   COOPER, EDMUND   AC
  UNBORN TOMORROW   COOPER, EDMUND   AN
BUTTERFLY KISS, THE (SEE THE LAST WAR)
                             SAVAGE, ARTHUR D.   TC
BUTTERFLYS OF BEAUTY, THE   GREEN, JOSEPH   NV   FSF 71 06
  CONSCIENCE INTERPLANETARY   GREEN, JOSEPH   NO
BUTTON, BUTTON   ASIMOV, ISAAC   SS   STS 53 01
  BUY JUPITER AND OTHER STORIES ASIMOV, ISAAC   AC
  13 ABOVE THE NIGHT   CONKLIN, GROFF   AN
BUTTON, BUTTON   BOND, NELSON S.   SS
  NO TIME LIKE THE FUTURE   BOND, NELSON S.   AC
BUTTON, BUTTON   MATHESON, RICHARD SS   PBY 70 06
  TRANSIT OF EARTH   PLAYBOY, EDITORS OF   AN
BUTYL AND THE BREATHER   STURGEON, THEODORE NV   ASF 40 10
  NOT WITHOUT SORCERY   STURGEON, THEODORE   AC
  WITHOUT SORCERY   STURGEON, THEODORE   AC
BUY JUPITER| ASIMOV, ISAAC   SS   VSF 58 05
  BUY JUPITER AND OTHER STORIES ASIMOV, ISAAC   AC

BUY JUPITER   CALORIES

NO LIMITS   FERMAN, JOSEPH W.   AN
BUY ME A WOOFL   CUMMINGS, M. A.   SS
 EXILE AND OTHER TALES OF FANTASY   CUMMINGS, M. A.   OC
BY ANY OTHER NAME (D. C. FONTANA & JEROME BIXBY)
                              BLISH, JAMES   SA STK 72 06
 STAR TREK   6   BLISH, JAMES   OC
BY APPOINTMENT ONLY   MATHESON, RICHARD   SS PBY 70 04
 WEIRD SHOW   PLAYBOY, EDITORS OF   AN
BY HIS BOOTSTRAPS (ALSO AS THE TIME GATE)
                              HEINLEIN, ROBERT A.   NV ASF 41 10
 GIANT ANTHOLOGY OF SCIENCE FICTION   MARGULIES & FRIEND   AN
 MENACE FROM EARTH, THE   HEINLEIN, ROBERT A.   AC
 *SPECTRUM   AMIS & CONQUEST   AN
BY HIS BOOTSTRAPS (ALSO AS THE TIME GATE)
                              MACDONALD, ANSON   NV ASF 41 10
 *ADVENTURES IN TIME AND SPACE   HEALY & MCCOMAS   AN
 ASTOUNDING-ANALOG READER, THE VOLUME ONE HARRISON & ALDISS   AN
BY JUPITER   ELAM, RICHARD M. JR. SS BLF 51
 TEEN-AGE SCIENCE FICTION STORIES   ELAM, RICHARD M. JR.   AC
BY NEW HEARTH FIRES   DICKSON, GORDON R.   SS ASF 59 01
 MUTANTS   DICKSON, GORDON R.   AC
BY RIGHT OF SUCCESSION   O'DONNELL, K. M.   IFS 69 10
 FINAL WAR AND OTHER FANTASIES   O'DONNELL, K. M.   DC
BY ROCKET TO THE MOON   DERLETH, AUGUST   NV VTA 65
 HARRIGAN'S FILE   DERLETH, AUGUST   AC
BY TENNYSON OUT OF DISNEY   HARRISON, M. JOHN   SS NWQ 71 02
 NEW WORLDS QUARTERLY NO. 2   MOORCOCK, MICHAEL   OA
BY THE BOOK   HERBERT, FRANK   NV ASF 66 08
 BEST OF FRANK HERBERT, THE   HERBERT, FRANK   AC
 WORLDS OF FRANK HERBERT, THE   HERBERT, FRANK   AC
BY THE FALLS   HARRISON, HARRY   SS IFS 70 01
 BEST FROM IF, THE   VOLUME I   IF, EDITORS OF   AN
 *BEST OF HARRY HARRISON, THE   HARRISON, HARRY   AC
 NEBULA AWARD STORIES   NO. 6   SIMAK, CLIFFORD D.   AN
 NEW WORLDS OF FANTASY NO. 2   CARR, TERRY   AN
 SF: AUTHORS' CHOICE 3   HARRISON, HARRY   AN
BY THE NAME OF MAN (SUBSTITUTE GOD, FUN 58 08)
                              BRUNNER, JOHN   NV NEB 56 07
 MORE ADVENTURES ON OTHER PLANETS   WOLLHEIM, DONALD A.   AN
BY THE SEASHORE   LAFFERTY, R. A.   SS GAL 73 11
 ANTIGRAV: COSMIC COMEDIES   STRICK, PHILIP   AN
 BEST FROM GALAXY, THE   VOLUME II   GALAXY, EDITORS OF   AN
BY THE SEAWALL   SILVERBERG, ROBERT   SS IFS 67 01
 DIMENSION THIRTEEN   SILVERBERG, ROBERT   AC
BY THE TIME I GET TO PHOENIX SCORTIA, THOMAS N.   SS INY 72 04
 BEST SCIENCE FICTION FOR 1973   ACKERMAN, FORREST J.   AN
 CAUTION| INFLAMMABLE| SCORTIA, THOMAS N.   AC
 INFINITY 4   HOSKINS, ROBERT   OA
BY THE WATERS OF BABYLON (THE PLACE OF THE GODS)
                              BENET, STEPHEN V.   SS SEP 37 07
 ARMCHAIR SCIENCE READER, THE   GORDON, I. & SORKIN   AN
 CITIES OF WONDER   KNIGHT, DAMON   AN
 POCKET BOOK OF SCIENCE-FICTION, THE   WOLLHEIM, DONALD A.   AN
 SCIENCE FICTION   BRODKIN & PEARSON   AN
 SPECTRUM OF WORLDS, A   CLARESON, THOMAS D.   AN
 SPECULATIONS   SANDERS, THOMAS E.   AN
BY THESE PRESENTS   KUTTNER, HENRY   SS FAN 53 03
 AHEAD OF TIME   KUTTNER, HENRY   AC
BY VIRTUE OF CIRCUMFERENCE   VAN DRESSER, PETER   SS AMB 37 11
 YEAR AFTER TOMORROW, THE   DEL REY, L/MATSCHAT/   AN
BY WAY OF INTRODUCTION   BLOCH, ROBERT   IN
 OPENER OF THE WAY, THE (BRITISH PB)   BLOCH, ROBERT   AC
BY WAY OF MARS (SEE ALL FOR LOVE)
                              GOULART, RON   TC
BYSTANDER, THE   WHARTON, THOM LEE   SS ORB 70 08
 BEST FROM ORBIT, THE   KNIGHT, DAMON   AN
 ORBIT 8   KNIGHT, DAMON   AN
C/O MR. MAKEPEACE   PHILLIPS, PETER   SS FSF 54 02
 DARK SIDE, THE   KNIGHT, DAMON   AN
 OPERATION FUTURE   CONKLIN, GROFF   AN
C. M. KORNBLUTH: A MEMORIAL BIBLIOGRAPHY
                              BOUCHER, ANTHONY   MS FSF 58 07
 BEST FROM FANTASY AND SCIENCE FICTION: 8
                                           BOUCHER, ANTHONY   AN
C-CHUTE, THE   ASIMOV, ISAAC   NV GAL 51 10
 BEST OF ISAAC ASIMOV, THE   ASIMOV, ISAAC   AC
 GALAXY SCIENCE FICTION OMNIBUS   GOLD, H. L.   AN
 NIGHTFALL AND OTHER STORIES   ASIMOV, ISAAC   AC
 SECOND GALAXY READER OF SCIENCE FICTION   GOLD, H. L.   AN
 SHADOW OF TOMORROW   POHL, FREDERIK   AN
 THROUGH A GLASS, CLEARLY   ASIMOV, ISAAC   AC
CABBAGE PATCH, THE   COGSWELL, THEODORE R SS FSF 57 12
 SHOCKING THING, A   KNIGHT, DAMON   AN
 THIRD EYE, THE   COGSWELL, THEODORE R   AC
CABIN BOY   KNIGHT, DAMON   NV GAL 51 09
 BEST OF DAMON KNIGHT, THE   KNIGHT, DAMON   AC
 FAR OUT   KNIGHT, DAMON   AC
 *GALAXY READER OF SCIENCE FICTION   GOLD, H. L.   AN
 GREAT STORIES OF SPACE TRAVEL   CONKLIN, GROFF   AN
 TOMORROW'S CHILDREN   ASIMOV, ISAAC   AN
CABINET DECISION (FROM "WHO IS MY NEIGHBOUR")
                              BALCHIN, NIGEL   EX
 ARMCHAIR SCIENCE READER, THE   GORDON, I. & SORKIN   AN
CABINET OF OLIVER NAYLOR, THE BAYLEY, BARRINGTON J SS NWB 76 10
 1977 ANNUAL WORLD'S BEST SF, THE   WOLLHEIM, DONALD A.   AN
CABLES PARTING| (NOT SF)   HAIL, STEVE   SS
 MOLECULE MONSTERS, THE   ANONYMOUS   AN
CACTUS DANCE   STURGEON, THEODORE   NV LSW 54 10
 ALIENS 4   STURGEON, THEODORE   AC
CADET PLOSHKIN   VARSHAVSKY, ILYA   NV
 JOURNEY ACROSS THREE WORLDS   ANONYMOUS   AN
CAGE OF BRASS   DELANY, SAMUEL R.   SS IFS 68 06
 DRIFTGLASS   DELANY, SAMUEL R.   AC
CAGE OF SAND, THE   BALLARD, J. G.   SS NWS 62 06
 BEST OF J. G. BALLARD, THE   BALLARD, J. G.   AC
 CHRONOPOLIS AND OTHER STORIES   BALLARD, J. G.   AC

 DARK STARS   SILVERBERG, ROBERT   AN
 *FOUR-DIMENSIONAL NIGHTMARE, THE   BALLARD, J. G.   AC
 PASSPORT TO ETERNITY   BALLARD, J. G.   AC
 RUINS OF EARTH, THE   DISCH, THOMAS M.   AN
CAGE, THE   CHANDLER, A. BERTRAM SS FSF 57 06
 ANTHROPOLOGY THROUGH SCIENCE FICTION   MASON, C/GREENBERG/&   AN
 BEST FROM FANTASY AND SCIENCE FICTION: 7
                                           BOUCHER, ANTHONY   AN
 YET MORE PENGUIN SCIENCE FICTION   ALDISS, BRIAN W.   AN
 12 GREAT CLASSICS OF SCIENCE FICTION   CONKLIN, GROFF   AN
CAGE, THE   RUSSELL, RAY   SS   59
 SARDONICUS AND OTHER STORIES   RUSSELL, RAY   AC
CAGES   MCINTYRE, VONDA N.   SS QRK 71 04
 QUARK/4   DELANY & HACKER   OA
CAIN N   HARGREAVES, H. A.   NV NWR 72 20
 NEW WRITINGS IN SF. 20   CARNELL, JOHN   AN
CAIRN ON THE HEADLAND, THE   HOWARD, ROBERT E.   SS STT 33 01
 WOLFSHEAD   HOWARD, ROBERT E.   AC
CAKE CHRONICLE, THE   AHERN, MICHAEL   SS NWB 73 05
 NEW WORLDS QUARTERLY NO. 5   MOORCOCK, MICHAEL   OA
CALENDARS   SABERHAGEN, FRED   SS GAL 74 01
 BOOK OF SABERHAGEN, THE   SABERHAGEN, FRED   AC
CALIBAN   SILVERBERG, ROBERT   SS INY 72 03
 BEST SCIENCE FICTION OF THE YEAR, THE NO. 2
                                           CARR, TERRY   AN
 INFINITY 3   HOSKINS, ROBERT   OA
 REALITY TRIP, THE   SILVERBERG, ROBERT   AC
 UNFAMILIAR TERRITORY   SILVERBERG, ROBERT   AC
CALIBRATED ALLIGATOR, THE   SILVERBERG, ROBERT   NV ASF 60 02
 CALLIBRATED ALLIGATOR AND OTHER SCIENCE FICTION STORIES, THE
                                           SILVERBERG, ROBERT   AC
CALL FROM BEYOND, THE   SIMAK, CLIFFORD D.   SS SSS 50 05
 SPACE MAGICIANS, THE   NORTON & MOSKOWITZ   AN
CALL FROM KERLYANA   CARLSON, WILLIAM
                          AND LAURANCE, ALICE   SS C ALC 73
 ALIEN CONDITION, THE   GOLDIN, STEPHEN   OA
CALL HIM DEMON   KUTTNER, HENRY   SS TWS 46 FL
 BEST OF HENRY KUTTNER 1, THE   KUTTNER, HENRY   AC
 BYPASS TO OTHERNESS   KUTTNER, HENRY   AC
 DEVIL'S GENERATION, THE   GHIDALIA, VIC   AN
 *STRANGE PORTS OF CALL   DERLETH, AUGUST   AN
CALL HIM LORD   DICKSON, GORDON R.   SS ASF 66 05
 ANALOG 6   CAMPBELL, JOHN W. JR   AN
 BEYOND TOMORROW   HARDING, LEE   AN
 DANGER- HUMAN   DICKSON, GORDON R.   AC
 NEBULA AWARD STORIES   NO. 2   ALDISS & HARRISON   AN
 POLITICAL SCIENCE FICTION   GREENBERG& WARRICK   AN
CALL ME ADAM   MARKS, WINSTON K.   SS FSF 54 02
 OPERATION FUTURE   CONKLIN, GROFF   AN
CALL ME DUMBO   SHAW, BOB   NV IFS 66 12
 TOMORROW LIES IN AMBUSH   SHAW, BOB   AC
CALL ME FROM THE VALLEY (SEE DUMB SUPPER)
                              WELLMAN, MANLY WADE   TC
CALL ME ISHTAR (EXCERPT)   LERMAN, RHODA   EX DBL 73
 NEW CONSTELLATIONS   DISCH & NAYLOR   OA
CALL ME JOE   ANDERSON, POUL   NV ASF 57 04
 ALPHA 2   SILVERBERG, ROBERT   AN
 ASTOUNDING-ANALOG READER, THE VOLUME TWO HARRISON & ALDISS   AN
 BEST SCIENCE FICTION STORIES AND NOVELS: 9TH SERIES
                                           DIKTY, T. E.   AN
 BIO-FUTURES   SARGENT, PAMELA   AN
 CENTURY OF SCIENCE FICTION, A   KNIGHT, DAMON   AN
 JUPITER   POHL, C. & F.   AN
 SCIENCE FICTION HALL OF FAME VOLUME 2A   BOVA, BEN   AN
 SCIENCE FICTION NOVELLAS   HARRISON & MCNELLY   AN
 SPECTRUM 3   AMIS & CONQUEST   AN
CALL ME MILLION   POHL, FREDERIK   SS WOF 70 02
 GOLD AT STARBOW'S END, THE   POHL, FREDERIK   AC
CALL ME MISTER   BRODE, ANTHONY   PM FSF 59 02
 BEST FROM FANTASY AND SCIENCE FICTION: 9
                                           MILLS, ROBERT P.   AN
CALL OF CTHULHU, THE   LOVECRAFT, H. P.   NV WRT 28 02
 ANCIENT MYSTERIES READER, THE   HAINING, PETER   AN
 HAUNTER OF THE DARK, THE   LOVECRAFT, H. P.   AC
CALL OF THE STARS, THE (THE OTHER SIDE OF THE SKY)
                              CLARKE, ARTHUR C.   SS INF 57 10
 NINE BILLION NAMES OF GOD, THE   CLARKE, ARTHUR C.   AC
 OTHER SIDE OF THE SKY, THE   CLARKE, ARTHUR C.   AC
CALL OF THE WILD, THE   VAN LOGGEM, MANUEL   SS NWR 76 28
 NEW WRITINGS IN SF. 28   BULMER, KENNETH   OA
CALLAHAN AND THE WHEELIES   BARR, STEPHEN   NV FSF 60 08
 SCIENCE FICTION ODDITIES   CONKLIN, GROFF   AN
CALLING ALL MARTIANS (SEE A LETTER TO THE MARTIANS)
                              LEY, WILLY   TC
CALLING ALL STARS   SZILARD, LEO   SS   61
 VOICE OF THE DOLPHINS, AND OTHER STORIES, THE
                                           SZILARD, LEO   AC
CALLING DR. CLOCKWORK   GOULART, RON   SS AMZ 65 03
 ANDROIDS, TIME MACHINES AND BLUE GIRAFFES
                                           ELWOOD & GHIDALIA   AN
 AS TOMORROW BECOMES TODAY   SULLIVAN, CHARLES W.   AN
 BROKE DOWN ENGINE AND OTHER TROUBLES WITH MACHINES
                                           GOULART, RON   AC
 WORLD'S BEST SCIENCE FICTION: 1966   WOLLHEIM & CARR   AN
CALLING THE EMPRESS   SMITH, GEORGE O.   NV ASF 43 06
 COMPLETE VENUS EQUILATERAL, THE   SMITH, GEORGE O.   AC
 VENUS EQUILATERAL   SMITH, GEORGE O.   AC
CALLIOPE AND GHERKIN AND THE YANKEE DOODLE THING
                              SMITH, EVELYN E.   NV FSF 69 03
 BEST FROM FANTASY AND SCIENCE FICTION: 19
                                           FERMAN, EDWARD L.   AN
CALLISTAN MENACE, THE   ASIMOV, ISAAC   SS AST 40 04
 EARLY ASIMOV, THE   ASIMOV, ISAAC   AC
 FUTURES UNLIMITED   NORTON, ALDEN H.   AN
CALORIES   DE CAMP, L. SPRAGUE SS TST 51 SP
 SPRAGUE DE CAMP'S NEW ANTHOLOGY   DE CAMP, L. SPRAGUE   AC

CAMBRIDGE, 1:58 A.M.   BENFORD, GREGORY   SS   EPC 75
  EPOCH   ELWOOD & SILVERBERG   OA
CAMELS AND DROMEDARIES, CLEM LAFFERTY, R. A.   SS   FSF 67 10
  STRANGE DOINGS   LAFFERTY, R. A.   AC
CAMOUFLAGE   KUTTNER, HENRY   NV   ASF 45 09
  AHEAD OF TIME   KUTTNER, HENRY   AC
  ASLEEP IN ARMAGEDDON   SISSONS, MICHAEL   AN
  BEST SF 6   CRISPIN, EDMUND   AN
  HUMAN-MACHINES   SCORTIA & ZEBROWSKI   AN
CAN A MARTIAN HELP IT IF HE'S COLORED GREEN?
                              WELLES, ORSON   IN
  INVASION FROM MARS   WELLES, ORSON   AN
CAN ANYTHING BE TAUGHT?   MCINTYRE, VONDA N.   AR
  CLARION SF   WILHELM, KATE   OA
CAN OF PAINT, A   VAN VOGT, A. E.   SS   ASF 44 09
  DESTINATION: UNIVERSE| VAN VOGT, A. E.   AC
CAN SUCH BEAUTY BE?   BIXBY, JEROME   SS   BEY 53 09
  BEYOND   ANONYMOUS   AN
CAN YOU FEEL ANYTHING WHEN I DO THIS?
                              SHECKLEY, ROBERT   SS   PBY 69 08
  CAN YOU FEEL ANYTHING WHEN I DO THIS?, AND OTHER STORIES
                                SHECKLEY, ROBERT   AC
  FIEND, THE   PLAYBOY, EDITORS OF   AN
  FROM THE "S" FILE   PLAYBOY, EDITORS OF   AN
  SCIENCE FICTION ARGOSY, A   KNIGHT, DAMON   AN
CANAL BUILDERS, THE   ABERNATHY, ROBERT   SS   ASF 45 01
  EVERY BOY'S BOOK OF OUTER SPACE STORIES DIKTY, T. E.   AN
CANAL LIFE ON MARS   LACH-SZYRMA, D. S.   CSL 90 04
  WORLDS APART   LOCKE, GEORGE   AN
CANARY   MORGAN, DAN   IN   NWR 72 20
  NEW WRITINGS IN SF. 20   CARNELL, JOHN   OA
CANDIDATE, THE   SLESAR, HENRY   SS   ROG 61
  FIEND IN YOU, THE   BEAUMONT, CHARLES   AN
CANDLE LIGHTER, THE   POHL, FREDERIK   SS   GAL 55 03
  CASE AGAINST TOMORROW, THE   POHL, FREDERIK   AC
CANIS FAMILIARIS   BRONSON, DONNA
                                AND WALLACE, ROBIN E. SS C
  FUTURE PASTIMES   EDELSTEIN, SCOTT   OA
CANTALOUPES AND KANGAROOS   CARO, DENNIS R.   SS   CLR 73 03
  CLARION III   WILSON, ROBIN SCOTT   OA
CANTATA 140 (SEE THE CRACK IN SPACE)
                              DICK, PHILIP K.   TC   FSF 64 07
CANTERVILLE GHOST, THE   WILDE, OSCAR   SS   CSR 87 03
  OUT OF THIS WORLD   FAST, JULIUS   AN
CANTICLE FOR LEIBOWITZ, A   MILLER, WALTER M. JR NV   FSF 55 04
  BEST FROM FANTASY AND SCIENCE FICTION: 5
                                BOUCHER, ANTHONY   AN
  BEST SCIENCE FICTION STORIES AND NOVELS: 1956
                                DIKTY, T. E.   AN
  CANTICLE FOR LEIBOWITZ, A   MILLER, WALTER M. JR NO
  NEW AWARENESS, THE   WARRICK & GREENBERG   AN
  OTHER DIMENSION, THE   ROSNER, SARA   AN
  SOCIOLOGY THROUGH SCIENCE FICTION MILSTEAD/GREENBERG/& AN
  VINTAGE ANTHOLOGY OF SCIENCE FANTASY, THE
                                CERF, CHRISTOPHER   AN
CANVAS BAG, THE   NOURSE, ALAN E.   SS   FSF 55 04
  COUNTERFEIT MAN, THE   NOURSE, ALAN E.   AC
  SPECIAL WONDER   MCCOMAS, J. FRANCIS   AN
"CAP'N IL'S" CLOSEST CALL   MUNRO, KIRK   SS
  BATTLE FOR THE PACIFIC AND OTHER ADVENTURES AT SEA, THE
                                ANONYMOUS   AN
CAPRICORN GAMES   SILVERBERG, ROBERT   SS   74
  CAPRICORN GAMES   SILVERBERG, ROBERT   AC
  FAR SIDE OF TIME, THE   ELWOOD, ROGER   OA
CAPTAIN BEDLAM   HARRISON, HARRY   SS   SFA 57 12
  TWO TALES AND EIGHT TOMORROWS HARRISON, HARRY   AC
CAPTAIN FAGAN DIED ALONE   STABLEFORD, BRIAN M. SS
  DAW SCIENCE FICTION READER, THE WOLLHEIM, DONALD A.   OA
CAPTAIN HONARIO HARRPLAYER, R.N.
                              HARRISON, HARRY   SS   FSF 63 03
  BEST FROM FANTASY AND SCIENCE FICTION: 13
                                DAVIDSON, AVRAM   AN
  *BEST OF HARRY HARRISON, THE HARRISON, HARRY   AC
  SPECTRUM OF WORLDS, A   CLARESON, THOMAS D.   AN
  TWO TALES AND EIGHT TOMORROWS HARRISON, HARRY   AC
CAPTAIN NEMO'S LAST ADVENTURE NESVADBA, JOSEF   NV   73
  BEST SF: 1973   HARRISON & ALDISS   AN
  VIEW FROM ANOTHER SHORE   ROTTENSTEINER, FRANZ   AN
CAPTAIN NEMO'S THUNDERBOLT (FROM "20,000 LEAGUES UNDER
  THE SEA", 1873)   VERNE, JULES   EX   GMS 73
  SCIENCE IN FICTION   BAYLISS, A.E. & J.C.   AN
CAPTAIN OF THE "POLE STAR", THE
                              DOYLE, ARTHUR CONAN NV   94
  HORROR TIMES TEN   NORTON, ALDEN H.   AN
CAPTAIN SAMPSON'S QUEER CARGO WALSH, GEORGE E.   SS
  BATTLE FOR THE PACIFIC AND OTHER ADVENTURES AT SEA, THE
                                ANONYMOUS   AN
CAPTAIN WYXTPTHLL'S FLYING SAUCER (SEE TROUBLE WITH
  THE NATIVES)   CLARKE, ARTHUR C.   TC
CAPTAIN'S DAUGHTER, THE (STRANGE COMPULSION)
                              FARMER, PHILIP JOSE SN   SFP 53 10
  ALLEY GOD, THE   FARMER, PHILIP JOSE   AC
CAPTIVE AUDIENCE   GRIFFITH, ANN WARREN SS   FSF 53 08
  BEST FROM FANTASY AND SCIENCE FICTION: 3
                                BOUCHER & MCCOMAS   AN
  TOMORROW, INC.   GREENBERG& OLANDER   AN
CAPTIVE AUDIENCE   WEST, WALLACE   NO   TWS 53 06
  BIRD OF TIME, THE   WEST, WALLACE   NO
CAPTIVE DJINN, THE   ANVIL, CHRISTOPHER   SS   ASF 65 05
  WORLD'S BEST SCIENCE FICTION: 1966 WOLLHEIM & CARR   AN
CAPTIVE MARKET   DICK, PHILIP K.   SS   IFS 55 04
  FIRST WORLD OF IF, THE   QUINN & WULFF   AN
  PRESERVING MACHINE, THE   DICK, PHILIP K.   AC
  TOMORROW, INC.   GREENBERG& OLANDER   AN
CAPTIVES, THE   CHAIN, JULIAN   NV   ASF 53 01
  APEMAN, SPACEMAN   STOVER & HARRISON   AN

CAPTIVITY   HENDERSON, ZENNA   SS   FSF 58 06
  BEST FROM FANTASY AND SCIENCE FICTION: 8
                                BOUCHER, ANTHONY   AN
  PILGRIMAGE: THE BOOK OF THE PEOPLE HENDERSON, ZENNA   AC
  WORLDS APART   WILLIAMS-ELLIS& OWEN   AN
CAPTIVITY, THE   FINNEY, CHARLES G.   SS   FSF 61 10
  *BEST FROM FANTASY AND SCIENCE FICTION: 11
                                MILLS, ROBERT P.   AN
CAPTURED CROSS-SECTION, THE   BREUER, MILES J. MD. SS   AMZ 29 02
  FANTASIA MATHEMATICA   FADIMAN, CLIFTON   AN
  OTHER DIMENSIONS   SILVERBERG, ROBERT   AN
CAPTURED| TOFTE, ARTHUR   SS
  STRANGE ENCOUNTERS   BISCHOFF, DAVID   OA
CAPTURING VANCE   MALZBERG, BARRY N.   IN
  BEST OF JACK VANCE, THE   VANCE, JACK   AC
CAR POOL   BROWN, ROSEL GEORGE NV   IFS 59 07
  HANDFUL OF TIME, A   BROWN, ROSEL GEORGE   AC
CAR SINISTER   WOLFE, GENE   SS   FSF 70 01
  BEST OF 1970   HARRISON & ALDISS   AN
CARAVANS UNLIMITED: MONITOR   OLIVER, CHAD   NV   CTM 75 04
  CONTINUUM 4   ELWOOD, ROGER   OA
CARAVANS UNLIMITED: STABILITY OLIVER, CHAD   NV   CTM 74 02
  CONTINUUM 2   ELWOOD, ROGER   OA
CARBON COPY   SIMAK, CLIFFORD D.   NA   GAL 57 12
  ALIENS FOR NEIGHBOURS   SIMAK, CLIFFORD D.   AC
  OTHER WORLDS OF CLIFFORD SIMAK SIMAK, CLIFFORD D.   AC
  *WORLDS OF CLIFFORD SIMAK, THE SIMAK, CLIFFORD D.   AC
CARCINOMA ANGELS   SPINRAD, NORMAN   SS   DVS 67 01
  ABOVE THE HUMAN LANDSCAPE   MCNELLY & STOVER   AN
  ALPHA 4   SILVERBERG, ROBERT   AN
  DANGEROUS VISIONS   ELLISON, HARLAN   OA
  FANTASY: THE LITERATURE OF THE MARVELOUS KELLEY, LEO P. AN
  LAST HURRAH OF THE GOLDEN HORDE, THE SPINRAD, NORMAN   AC
CARDIAC ARREST   ALDISS, BRIAN W.   NV   FAN 70 12
  BOOK OF BRIAN ALDISS, THE   ALDISS, BRIAN W.   AC
CAREFULLY OBSERVED WOMEN   ALDISS, BRIAN W.   SS   NWR 75 26
  NEW WRITINGS IN SF. 26   BULMER, KENNETH   OA
CARELESS LOVE (ALSO AS PUSH-BUTTON PASSION)
                              FRIBORG, ALBERT C.   SS   FSF 54 07
  BEST FROM FANTASY AND SCIENCE FICTION: 4
                                BOUCHER, ANTHONY   AN
  BEST SCIENCE FICTION STORIES AND NOVELS: 1955
                                DIKTY, T. E.   AN
CARETAKER   SCHMITZ, JAMES H.   SS   GAL 53 07
  GALAXY SCIENCE FICTION OMNIBUS GOLD, H. L.   AN
  SECOND GALAXY READER OF SCIENCE FICTION GOLD, H. L.   AN
CARGO   STURGEON, THEODORE   NV   UNK 40 11
  NOT WITHOUT SORCERY   STURGEON, THEODORE   AC
  WITHOUT SORCERY   STURGEON, THEODORE   AC
CARIDI SHALL NOT DIE   KUBILIUS, WALTER   SS   SFQ 41 WI
  INTO THE FOURTH DIMENSION   CUMMINGS, RAY   AN
CARILLON OF SKULLS   BEARD, JAMES H.
                                AND DEL REY, LESTER SS C UNK 41 02
  EARLY DEL REY   DEL REY, LESTER   AC
CARILLON OF SKULLS   JAMES, PHILIP   SS   UNK 41 02
  ZACHERLEY'S MIDNIGHT SNACKS   ZACHERLEY   AN
CARNIVAL OF MADNESS (SEE USHER II)
                              BRADBURY, RAY   TC
CARRIER   SHECKLEY, ROBERT   NV   IFS 54 07
  WILDERNESS OF STARS, A   NOLAN, WILLIAM F.   AN
CARRIERS, THE   MERWIN, SAM JR.   SS   TWS 49 02
  *MY BEST SCIENCE FICTION STORY MARGULIES & FRIEND   AN
CARRION COUNTRY   ALDISS, BRIAN W.   SS   NWS 58 11
  NO TIME LIKE TOMORROW   ALDISS, BRIAN W.   AC
CARROTS   WRIGHT, S. FOWLER   SS
  WITCHFINDER, THE   WRIGHT, S. FOWLER   AC
CARSON EFFECT, THE   WILSON, RICHARD   SS   WOT 64 11
  10TH ANNUAL OF THE YEAR'S BEST S-F, THE MERRIL, JUDITH AN
CART, THE   HUGHES, RICHARD   SS   34
  GRAVEYARD READER, THE   CONKLIN, GROFF   AN
CARTHAGE: REFLECTIONS OF A MARTIAN
                              HERBERT, FRANK   PM   NEW 71 03
  MARS, WE LOVE YOU   HIPOLITO & MCNELLY   AN
CARTHING   VAN VOGT, A. E.   SS   QRK 70 01
  QUARK/1   DELANY & HACKER   OA
CARTOON   DEAN, ABNER   CT   47
  MATHEMATICAL MAGPIE, THE   FADIMAN, CLIFTON   AN
CARTOON   DEMARE, LEO   CT   MNS 58
  MATHEMATICAL MAGPIE, THE   FADIMAN, CLIFTON   AN
CARTOON   DUNN, ALAN   CT   SRV 55 03
  MATHEMATICAL MAGPIE, THE   FADIMAN, CLIFTON   AN
CARTOON   FRANKFORT, JAMES   CT   VLG 61 10
  MATHEMATICAL MAGPIE, THE   FADIMAN, CLIFTON   AN
CARTOON   FRUCH, A.   CT   NYM 58 12
  MATHEMATICAL MAGPIE, THE   FADIMAN, CLIFTON   AN
CARTOON   PORGES, PAUL PETER   CT   ALM 55 07
  MATHEMATICAL MAGPIE, THE   FADIMAN, CLIFTON   AN
CARTOON   TESLER, O.   CT   SME
  BEST SF: 1972   HARRISON & ALDISS   AN
CARTOONIST   BROWN, FREDRIC
                                AND REYNOLDS, MACK   SS C
  NIGHTMARES AND GEEZENSTACKS   BROWN, FREDRIC   AC
CARTOONS   WILSON, GAHAN   CT   FSF
  BEST FROM FANTASY AND SCIENCE FICTION: 20
                                FERMAN, EDWARD L.   AN
CARTWRIGHT'S CAMERA (SEE JOHNNY CARTWRIGHT'S CAMERA)
                              BOND, NELSON S.   TC
CASABLANCA   DISCH, THOMAS M.   NV   67
  ALPHA 4   SILVERBERG, ROBERT   AN
  FUN WITH YOUR NEW HEAD   DISCH, THOMAS M.   AC
CASE AND THE DREAMER   STURGEON, THEODORE   NV   GAL 73 01
  CASE AND THE DREAMER   STURGEON, THEODORE   AC
CASE FOR EARTH, THE   RUSSELL, ERIC FRANK SS   FUT 58 04
  NOW & BEYOND   HOWARD, IVAN   AN
CASE HISTORY, A   WEST, JOHN ANTHONY   SS   73
  SHOCKING THING, A   KNIGHT, DAMON   AN

CASE OF CONSCIENCE, A

CASE OF CONSCIENCE, A   BLISH, JAMES   SN   IPS 53 09
   BEST SF   CRISPIN, EDMUND   AN
CASE OF DESPERATION, A (SEE THE FEEL OF DESPERATION)
                                 WILHELM, KATE   TC
CASE OF IDENTITY, A   GARRETT, RANDALL   NV   ASF 64 09
   ANALOG 4   CAMPBELL, JOHN W. JR AN
CASE OF OMEGA SMITH, THE   WALSH, BUTHRAM   SS
   AD 2500   WILSON, ANGUS   AN
CASE OF PTOMAINE, A (SEE MEALTIME)
                                 ELLISON, HARLAN   TC
CASE OF THE DOW TWINS, THE   MITCHELL, EDWARD P.   SS   SUN 77 04
   CRYSTAL MAN, THE   MITCHELL, EDWARD P.   AC
CASE OF THE HOMOCIDAL ROBOTS, THE
                                 LEINSTER, MURRAY   NV   FSF 61 08
   ONCE AND FUTURE TALES FROM THE MAGAZINE OF FANTASY AND
      SCIENCE FICTION   FERMAN, EDWARD L.   AN
CASE OF THE MOTHER-IN-LAW OF PEARL, THE
                                 DAVIDSON, AVRAM   NV   FAN 75 10
   ENQUIRIES OF DOCTOR ESZTERHAZY, THE DAVIDSON, AVRAM   NO
CASE OF THE PERJURED PLANET, THE
                                 LORAN, MARTIN   NV   ASF 67 11
   SECOND PACIFIC BOOK OF SCIENCE FICTION, THE
                                 BAXTER, JOHN   AN
CASE OF THE SNORING HEIR, THE (SEE SLEEPING BEAUTY)
                                 CLARKE, ARTHUR C.   TC
CASE, THE   REDGROVE, PETER   PM   NWS 66 01
   11TH ANNUAL OF THE YEAR'S BEST S-F, THE MERRIL, JUDITH
                                                           AN
CASEY AGONISTES   MCKENNA, RICHARD M.   SS   FSF 58 09
   BEST FROM FANTASY AND SCIENCE FICTION: 9
                                 MILLS, ROBERT P.   AN
   CASEY AGONISTES, AND OTHER S.F. & FANTASY STORIES
                                 MCKENNA, RICHARD M.   AC
   DARK SIDE, THE   KNIGHT, DAMON   AN
   SF: THE BEST OF THE BEST   MERRIL, JUDITH   AN
   SF:59, THE YEAR'S GREATEST SCIENCE FICTION AND FANTASY
                                 MERRIL, JUDITH   AN
   SHOCKING THING, A   KNIGHT, DAMON   AN
CASKET-DEMON, THE   LEIBER, FRITZ   SS   FAN 63 04
   NIGHT MONSTERS   LEIBER, FRITZ   DC
CASSIDY'S SAUCER   HOCH, EDWARD D.   SS   NEW 68 AN
   FLYING SAUCERS IN FACT AND FICTION SANTESSON, HANS S.   AN
CASSIUS AND THE MIND-JAUNT   KAPP, COLIN   SS   NWR 75 27
   NEW WRITINGS IN SF. 27   BULMER, KENNETH   OA
CAST AND CREDITS   MISC. MATERIAL   MS
   GHOULS, THE   HAINING, PETER   AN
CASTAWAY   CHANDLER, A. BERTRAM SS   WRT 47 11
   *SCIENCE FICTION ADVENTURES IN DIMENSION CONKLIN, GROFF AN
CASTAWAY   CLARKE, ARTHUR C.   SS   FSB 47 04
   BEST OF ARTHUR C. CLARKE: 1937-1971, THE CLARKE, ARTHUR C.
                                                           AC
   FUTURE MAKERS, THE   HAINING, PETER   AN
   STRANGE SIGNPOSTS   ELWOOD & MOSKOWITZ   AN
CASTAWAY   HAMILTON, EDMOND   SS   68
   BEST OF EDMOND HAMILTON, THE   HAMILTON, EDMOND   AC
   WHAT'S IT LIKE OUT THERE? AND OTHER STORIES
                                 HAMILTON, EDMOND   AC
CASTAWAY   WHITLEY, GEORGE   SS   WRT 47 11
   *NO PLACE LIKE EARTH   CARNELL, JOHN   AN
CASTAWAY   WILLIAMS, ROBERT M.   SS   ASF 41 02
   *INVADERS OF EARTH   CONKLIN, GROFF   AN
CASTAWAY, THE   BOND, NELSON S.   SS   PLS 40 WI
   INVASION FROM MARS   WELLES, ORSON   AN
CASTAWAY, THE   FRITCH, CHARLES E.   SS   GAM 63 02
   WILDERNESS OF STARS, A   NOLAN, WILLIAM F.   AN
CASTAWAY, THE   LEINSTER, MURRAY   NV   USF 53 06
   MONSTERS AND SUCH   LEINSTER, MURRAY   AC
CASTING THE RUNES   JAMES, M. R.   NV
   WIZARDS AND WARLOCKS   GHIDALIA, VIC   AN
CASTLE IN THE STARS   CARR, TERRY   SS
   TOMORROW: NEW WORLDS OF SCIENCE FICTION ELWOOD, ROGER   OA
CASTLE OF LIGHT, THE   LAUMER, KEITH   NV   IFS 64 10
   GALACTIC DIPLOMAT   LAUMER, KEITH   AC
CASTLE OF THE PYRENEES, THE   MAGRITTE, RENE   IL
   SCIENCE FICTION   BRODKIN & PEARSON   AN
CASTLE ON THE CRAG, THE   WYAL, PG   SS   FAN 69 02
   BEST SF: 1969   HARRISON & ALDISS   AN
CASTLE SCENE WITH PENITENTS   ALDISS, BRIAN W.   SS   ORB 73 12
   ORBIT 12   KNIGHT, DAMON   OA
CAT "I AM", THE   HEARD, H. F.   SS
   GREAT FOG AND OTHER WEIRD TALES, THE HEARD, H. F.   OC
CAT AND THE COIN, THE   WELLS, KEITH   NV   NWR 75 25
   NEW WRITINGS IN SF. 25   BULMER, KENNETH   OA
CAT BURGLAR   BROWN, FREDRIC   SS
   NIGHTMARES AND GEEZENSTACKS   BROWN, FREDRIC   AC
CAT WHO LIKED THRILLERS, THE CUMMINGS, M. A.   SS
   EXILE AND OTHER TALES OF FANTASY CUMMINGS, M. A.   OC
CAT'S CRADLE   LEIBER, FRITZ   SS
   BOOK OF FRITZ LEIBER, THE   LEIBER, FRITZ   AC
CAT, THE   BENSON, E. F.   SS   12
   SATAN'S PETS   GHIDALIA, VIC   AN
CATAAAAA, THE   VAN VOGT, A. E.   SS   FBK 47 01
   BEST OF A. E. VAN VOGT, THE (BRITISH) VAN VOGT, A. E.   AC
   FAR-OUT WORLDS OF A. E. VAN VOGT, THE VAN VOGT, A. E.   AC
   WORLDS OF A. E. VAN VOGT, THE VAN VOGT, A. E.   AC
CATABILID CONQUEST   KARL, JEAN E.   NV
   TURNING PLACE, THE   KARL, JEAN E.   OC
CATASTROPHE, A   WELLS, H. G.   SS   NBG 95 08
   PLATTNER STORY AND OTHERS, THE WELLS, H. G.   AC
   SHORT STORIES OF H. G. WELLS, THE WELLS, H. G.   AC
   THIRTY STRANGE STORIES   WELLS, H. G.   AC
CATCH THAT MARTIAN   KNIGHT, DAMON   SS ·GAL 52 03
   INVADERS FROM SPACE   SILVERBERG, ROBERT   AN
   MARS, WE LOVE YOU   HIPOLITO & MCNELLY   AN
   *OFF CENTER   KNIGHT, DAMON   DC
   OMNIBUS OF SCIENCE FICTION   CONKLIN, GROFF   AN
   STRANGE ADVENTURES IN SCIENCE FICTION CONKLIN, GROFF   AN

CELESTIAL OMNIBUS, THE

CATCH THAT RABBIT   ASIMOV, ISAAC   SS   ASF 44 02
   I, ROBOT   ASIMOV, ISAAC   AC
CATCH THAT ZEPPELIN¡   LEIBER, FRITZ   SS   FSF 75 03
   NEBULA AWARD STORIES 11   LE GUIN, URSULA K.   AN
   WORLDS OF FRITZ LEIBER, THE   LEIBER, FRITZ   AN
   1976 ANNUAL WORLD'S BEST SF, THE WOLLHEIM, DONALD A.   AN
CATCH, THE   DICKSON, GORDON R.   SS   ASF 59 04
   STAR ROAD, THE   DICKSON, GORDON R.   AC
CATEGORICAL IMPERATIVE (THE CATEGORY INVENTORS)
                                 SELLINGS, ARTHUR   NV   GAL 56 02
   *TIME TRANSFER   SELLINGS, ARTHUR   AC
   WINDOW ON THE FUTURE   HILL, DOUGLAS   AN
CATEGORY INVENTORS, THE (SEE CATEGORICAL IMPERATIVE)
                                 SELLINGS, ARTHUR   TC
CATEGORY PHOENIX   ELLANBY, BOYD   NA   GAL 52 05
   YEAR'S BEST SCIENCE FICTION NOVELS: 1953 BLEILER & DIKTY AN
CATHADONIAN ODYSSEY   BISHOP, MICHAEL   SS   FSF 74 09
   1975 ANNUAL WORLD'S BEST SF, THE WOLLHEIM, DONALD A.   AN
CATHARSIS   RACKHAM, JOHN   SS   NWR 68 11
   NEW WRITINGS IN SF. 11   CARNELL, JOHN   OA
CATHARTIC   SAMBROT, WILLIAM   SS   SAT 57 08
   ISLAND OF FEAR AND OTHER SCIENCE FICTION SAMBROT, WILLIAM AC
CATHEDRAL OF MARS (SEE A DISTANT SHRINE)
                                 SAMBROT, WILLIAM   TC
CATMAN   ELLISON, HARLAN   NV   FST 74
   APPROACHING OBLIVION   ELLISON, HARLAN   AC
   FINAL STAGE   FERMAN & MALZBERG   OA
CATNIP   BLOCH, ROBERT   SS   WRT 48 03
   NIGHTMARES   BLOCH, ROBERT   AC
   PLEASANT DREAMS   BLOCH, ROBERT   AC
CATO THE MARTIAN   FAST, HOWARD   SS   FSF 60 06
   EDGE OF TOMORROW, THE   FAST, HOWARD   AC
   SPECULATIONS   SANDERS, THOMAS E.   AN
   17 X INFINITY   CONKLIN, GROFF   AN
CATS OF ULTHAR, THE   LOVECRAFT, H. P.   SS   TRY 20 11
   BEWARE THE BEASTS   GHIDALIA, V.& ELWOOD   AN
   3000 YEARS OF FANTASY AND SCIENCE FICTION
                                 DE CAMP, L. S.&C.   AN
CATSPAW (ROBERT BLOCH)   BLISH, JAMES   SA   STK 72 08
   STAR TREK   8   BLISH, JAMES   OC
CATTLE TRUCKS   HOYLE, FRED   SS
   ELEMENT 79   HOYLE, FRED   AC
CAUGHT IN THE ORGAN DRAFT   SILVERBERG, ROBERT   SS   WLK 73
   AND WALK NOW GENTLY THROUGH THE FIRE... ELWOOD, ROGER   OA
   SUNDANCE AND OTHER SCIENCE FICTION STORIES
                                 SILVERBERG, ROBERT   AC
   UNFAMILIAR TERRITORY   SILVERBERG, ROBERT   AC
   WONDERMAKERS 2   HOSKINS, ROBERT   AN
   YOU AND SCIENCE FICTION   HOLLISTER, BERNARD C   AN
CAULDRON OF LIFE, THE (THE CAULDRON)
                                 ESHBACH, LLOYD A.   SS   SRS 40 04
   TYRANT OF TIME, THE   ESHBACH, LLOYD A.   AC
CAUSATION   MALZBERG, BARRY N.   SS   FSF 71 12
   OUT FROM GANYMEDE   MALZBERG, BARRY N.   AC
CAUSES, THE   SEABRIGHT, IDRIS   SS   FSF 52 06
   DECADE OF FANTASY AND SCIENCE FICTION, A MILLS, ROBERT P. AN
CAUSEWAY, THE   HARRISON, M. JOHN   SS   NWQ 71 02
   MACHINE IN SHAFT TEN AND OTHER STORIES, THE
                                 HARRISON, M. JOHN   AC
   NEW WORLDS QUARTERLY NO. 2   MOORCOCK, MICHAEL   OA
CAUTION¡ INFLAMMABLE¡ (THE END OF THE LINE)
                                 SCORTIA, THOMAS N.   SS   FAN 55 02
   CAUTION¡ INFLAMMABLE¡   SCORTIA, THOMAS N.   AC
CAVE GIRL, THE   BURROUGHS, EDGAR R.   NO   ASM 13 07
   CAVE GIRL, THE   BURROUGHS, EDGAR R.   AC
CAVE MAN, THE   BURROUGHS, EDGAR R.   NO   ASW 17 03
   CAVE GIRL, THE   BURROUGHS, EDGAR R.   AC
CAVE OF HISTORY, THE   STURGEON, THEODORE   SS
   ANCIENT MYSTERIES READER, THE HAINING, PETER   AN
   ENCOUNTERS WITH ALIENS   EARLEY, GEORGE W.   AN
CAVE OF NIGHT, THE   GUNN, JAMES E.   SS   GAL 55 02
   SF: THE YEAR'S GREATEST SCIENCE FICTION AND FANTASY
                                 MERRIL, JUDITH   AN
   SOME DREAMS ARE NIGHTMARES   GUNN, JAMES E.   AC
   STATION IN SPACE   GUNN, JAMES E.   AC
   WHERE DO WE GO FROM HERE?   ASIMOV, ISAAC   AN
CAVE OF THE SPLURGLES, THE   MITCHELL, EDWARD P.   SS   SUN 77 07
   CRYSTAL MAN, THE   MITCHELL, EDWARD P.   AC
CAVE, THE   MILLER, P. SCHUYLER   SS   ASF 43 01
   CROSSROADS IN TIME   CONKLIN, GROFF   AN
   INTRODUCING SCIENCE FICTION   ALDISS, BRIAN W.   AN
   MARS, WE LOVE YOU   HIPOLITO & MCNELLY   AN
CAVEAT EMPTOR   DE CAMP, L. SPRAGUE
                                 AND PRATT, FLETCHER   SS C WRT 53 03
   DEALS WITH THE DEVIL   DAVENPORT, BASIL   AN
   TALES FROM GAVAGAN'S BAR   DE CAMP, L. S.&PRATT   AC
CAVERNS OF ITH   WELLS, BASIL   SS   FBK 47 02
   PLANETS OF ADVENTURE   WELLS, BASIL   AC
CAVES OF STEEL, THE   ASIMOV, ISAAC   NO   GAL 53 10
   *REST OF THE ROBOTS, THE   ASIMOV, ISAAC   AC
CAVIAR   STURGEON, THEODORE   AC   BAL 55 11
   SCIENCE FICTION SPECIAL 3   ANONYMOUS   AN
CEASE FIRE   HERBERT, FRANK   SS   ASF 58 01
   CENTURY OF SCIENCE FICTION, A KNIGHT, DAMON   AN
CEASELESS STONES, THE   DAVIDSON, AVRAM   NV
   ENQUIRIES OF DOCTOR ESZTERHAZY, THE DAVIDSON, AVRAM   NO
CELEBRATED NO-HIT INNING, THE POHL, FREDERIK   SS   FUN 56 09
   CASE AGAINST TOMORROW, THE   POHL, FREDERIK   AC
   RUN TO STARLIGHT, SPORTS THROUGH SCIENCE FICTION
                                 GREENBERG/OLANDER/&   AN
CELEPHAIS   LOVECRAFT, H. P.   SS   MVT 34 05
   GARDEN OF FEAR AND OTHER STORIES, THE CRAWFORD, WILLIAM L. AN
CELESTIAL BLUEPRINT, THE   FARMER, PHILIP JOSE SS FUN 54 07
   CELESTIAL BLUEPRINT, THE   FARMER, PHILIP JOSE   DC
CELESTIAL OMNIBUS, THE   FORSTER, E. M.   SS   23
   MOONLIGHT TRAVELER, THE   STERN, PHILIP VAN D.   AN

CELLARS, THE   CAMPBELL, J. RAMSEY SS
  TRAVELLERS BY NIGHT   DERLETH, AUGUST   OA
CELLMATE   STURGEON, THEODORE   SS   WRT 47 01
  E PLURIBUS UNICORN   STURGEON, THEODORE   AC
CENSORS, THE   BURKE, JONATHAN F.   SS   AUT 54 01
  ALIEN LANDSCAPES   BURKE, JONATHAN F.   AC
CENSUS   SIMAK, CLIFFORD D.   NV   ASF 44 09
  CITY   SIMAK, CLIFFORD D.   NO
CENSUS TAKER, THE   LONG, FRANK BELKNAP SS   UNK 42 04
  DARK BEASTS, THE   LONG, FRANK BELKNAP   AC
  EARLY LONG, THE   LONG, FRANK BELKNAP   AC
  *HOUNDS OF TINDALOS, THE   LONG, FRANK BELKNAP   AC
CENSUS TAKERS, THE   POHL, FREDERIK   SS   FSF 56 02
  BEST FROM FANTASY AND SCIENCE FICTION: 6
                                  BOUCHER, ANTHONY   AN
  BEST OF FREDERIK POHL, THE   POHL, FREDERIK   AC
  CASE AGAINST TOMORROW, THE   POHL, FREDERIK   AC
  NIGHTMARE AGE   POHL, FREDERIK   AN
  SCIENCE FACT/FICTION   FARRELL/GAGE/&   AN
  YOU AND SCIENCE FICTION   HOLLISTER, BERNARD C   AN
CENTAURUS II   VAN VOGT, A. E.   NV   ASF 47 06
  ROGUE SHIP   VAN VOGT, A. E.   NO
CENTIPEDE'S DILEMMA, THE   ROBINSON, SPIDER   SS
  CALLAHAN'S CROSSTIME SALOON   ROBINSON, SPIDER   AC
CENTRAL QUESTION, A   KARL, JEAN E.   NV
  TURNING PLACE, THE   KARL, JEAN E.   OC
CENTURY JUMPER (A TRAVELLER IN TIME)
                                  DERLETH, AUGUST   SS   OSF 54 02
  BEYOND THE STARS AND OTHER STORIES ANONYMOUS   AN
CEPHALOTRON (ALSO AS FUN WITH YOUR NEW HEAD)
                                  DISCH, THOMAS M.   SS   PBY 66 12
  TRANSIT OF EARTH   PLAYBOY, EDITORS OF AN
CEPHES 5   FAST, HOWARD   SS
  TOUCH OF INFINITY, A   FAST, HOWARD   OC
CEREBRAL LIBRARY, THE   KELLER, DAVID H. MD. SS   AMZ 31 05
  LIFE EVERLASTING AND OTHER TALES OF SCIENCE, FANTASY
  AND HORROR   KELLER, DAVID H. MD.   AC
CEREBRATIVE PSITTACOID, THE   NEARING, H. JR.   SS   FSF 53 08
  BEST SF   CRISPIN, EDMUND   AN
CERTAIN SOLDIER, A   HARRIS, CLARE WINGER SS   WRT 27 11
  AWAY FROM THE HERE AND NOW   HARRIS, CLARE WINGER   AC
CERTAINTY   SILVERBERG, ROBERT   SS   ASF 59 11
  TO WORLDS BEYOND   SILVERBERG, ROBERT   AC
CERTIFICATE, THE   DAVIDSON, AVRAM   SS   FSF 59 03
  DECADE OF FANTASY AND SCIENCE FICTION, A MILLS, ROBERT P. AN
  STRANGE SEAS AND SHORES   DAVIDSON, AVRAM   AC
CHAD OLIVER   NOLAN, WILLIAM F.   AR
  3 TO THE HIGHEST POWER   NOLAN, WILLIAM F.   AN
CHAD OLIVER SF/FANTASY INDEX, A
                                  MISC. MATERIAL   MS
  3 TO THE HIGHEST POWER   NOLAN, WILLIAM F.   AN
CHAD OLIVER'S COLLECTED SCIENCE FICTION: A BASIC CHECKLIST
                                  NOLAN, WILLIAM F.   MS
  EDGE OF FOREVER, THE   OLIVER, CHAD   AC
CHAIN OF AFORGOMON, THE   SMITH, CLARK ASHTON SS   WRT 35 12
  OUT OF SPACE AND TIME   SMITH, CLARK ASHTON   AC
CHAIN OF COMMAND   ARR, STEPHEN   SS   GAL 54 05
  *SCIENCE FICTION ADVENTURES IN MUTATION CONKLIN, GROFF   AN
CHAIN OF LOGIC (LOGIC)   ANDERSON, POUL   NV   ASF 47 07
  TWILIGHT WORLD   ANDERSON, POUL   NO
CHAIN OF LOVE, THE   CLIFF, CATHERINE   SS   55
  13 FRENCH SCIENCE-FICTION STORIES KNIGHT, DAMON   AN
CHAIN REACTION   ELLANBY, BOYD   NV   GAL 56 09
  EXPERT DREAMERS, THE   POHL, FREDERIK   AN
CHAIN REACTION (AS JOHN A. SENTRY)
                                  BUDRYS, ALGIS   NV   ASF 57 04
  SIX GREAT SHORT SCIENCE FICTION NOVELS CONKLIN, GROFF   AN
CHAINS   SKAL, DAVE   SS   CLR 71 01
  CLARION   WILSON, ROBIN SCOTT   OA
CHAINS OF SHAMBALLAH   CARTER, LIN
  AND DE CAMP, L. SPRAGUE SS C
  CONAN   HOWARD, R./DE CAMP/& AC
CHAINS OF THE SEA   DOZOIS, GARDNER R.   NA   CHN 73
  CHAINS OF THE SEA   SILVERBERG, ROBERT   OA
CHAIR, THE   WELLS, BASIL   SS
  DOORWAYS TO SPACE   WELLS, BASIL   AC
CHALICE OF DEATH   KNOX, CALVIN M.   NO   SFA 57 06
  LEST WE FORGET THEE, EARTH   KNOX, CALVIN M.   DN
CHALLENGE AND RESPONSE   MIESEL, SANDRA   AR   RVQ 70
  MANY WORLDS OF POUL ANDERSON, THE ANDERSON, POUL   AC
CHALLENGE, THE   WILLIAMS, ROBERT M. SS   TWS 50 10
  VOID BEYOND, AND OTHER STORIES, THE WILLIAMS, ROBERT M. DC
CHAMELEON   GOULART, RON   SS   FSF 64 09
  CHAMELEON CORPS & OTHER SHAPE CHANGERS, THE
                                  GOULART, RON   AC
CHAMELEON, THE   EISENBERG, LARRY   SS   FSF 70 03
  AMERICAN GOVERNMENT THROUGH SCIENCE FICTION
                                  OLANDER/GREENBERG/& AN
  BEST LAID SCHEMES, THE   EISENBERG, LARRY   AC
CHANCES ARE   LAURANCE, ALICE   SS   PRT 71
  PROTOSTARS   GERROLD & GOLDIN   OA
CHANGE OF HEART   BLOCH, ROBERT   SS   ARS 48 FL
  ATOMS AND EVIL   BLOCH, ROBERT   AC
CHANGE OF HEART   WHITLEY, GEORGE   SS   NWS 61 09
  8TH ANNUAL OF THE YEAR'S BEST S-F, THE MERRIL, JUDITH   AN
CHANGE OVER   GOULART, RON   SS   NEW 72 AC
  CHAMELEON CORPS & OTHER SHAPE CHANGERS, THE
                                  GOULART, RON   AC
CHANGE THE SKY   ST. CLAIR, MARGARET SS   FSF 55 03
  CHANGE THE SKY AND OTHER STORIES ST. CLAIR, MARGARET   AC
CHANGE, THE (FROM "IN THE DAYS OF THE COMET")
                                  WELLS, H. G.   EX   CMP 05 12
  NEW IMPROVED SUN, THE   DISCH, THOMAS M.   AN
CHANGELING   BRADBURY, RAY   SS   SSS 49 07
  PSEUDO PEOPLE, THE   NOLAN, WILLIAM F.   AN

CHANGELING   MCCAFFREY, ANNE   SS   NEW 77 AC
  GET OFF THE UNICORN   MCCAFFREY, ANNE   AC
CHANGELING   WILLIAMS-ELLIS, A.   SS   NEW 64 AC
  OUT OF THIS WORLD 4   WILLIAMS-ELLIS& OWEN AN
CHANGELING, THE   WOLFE, GENE   SS   ORB 68 03
  BEST FROM ORBIT, THE   KNIGHT, DAMON   AN
  ORBIT 3   KNIGHT, DAMON   OA
CHANGELING, THE (ALSO AS THE WONDERFUL MAN)
                                  VAN VOGT, A. E.   NA   ASF 44 04
  MASTERS OF TIME   VAN VOGT, A. E.   AC
CHANGELING, THE (JOHN MEREDYTH LUCAS)
                                  BLISH, JAMES   SA   STK 72 07
  STAR TREK 7   BLISH, JAMES   OC
CHANGELINGS   TUTTLE, LISA   SS   GAL 75 03
  BEST SF: 75, THE NINTH ANNUAL   HARRISON & ALDISS   AN
CHANGING OF THE GODS   CARR, TERRY   NV   INY 73 05
  INFINITY 5   HOSKINS, ROBERT   OA
  LIGHT AT THE END OF THE UNIVERSE, THE CARR, TERRY   AC
CHANGING WOMAN   MACFARLANE, WALLACE SS   GAL 72 09
  1973 ANNUAL WORLD'S BEST SF, THE WOLLHEIM, DONALD A.   AN
CHAPEL OF EASE, THE   HEARD, H. F.   NV
  LOST CAVERN AND OTHER TALES OF THE FANTASTIC, THE
                                  HEARD, H. F.   AC
CHAPTER ENDS, THE   ANDERSON, POUL   NV   DSF 54 01
  ADVENTURES IN THE FAR FUTURE   WOLLHEIM, DONALD A.   DA
  NOVELETS OF SCIENCE FICTION   HOWARD, IVAN   AN
CHAPTER OF REVELATION, THE   ANDERSON, POUL   NA
  DAY THE SUN STOOD STILL, THE   SILVERBERG, ROBERT   OA
CHARACTER: THE DETERMINANT OF INCIDENT
                                  WILSON, ROBIN SCOTT SI
  THOSE WHO CAN: A SCIENCE FICTION READER WILSON, ROBIN SCOTT AN
CHARISMA LEAK   GOTSCHALK, FELIX C. NV   NDM 76 06
  NEW DIMENSIONS 6   SILVERBERG, ROBERT   OA
CHARLEY   CHAPDELAINE, PERRY A SS
  STOPWATCH   HAY, GEORGE   OA
CHARLEY DE MILO   JANIFER, LAURENCE M. SS   ASF 60 06
  IMPOSSIBLE?   JANIFER, LAURENCE M. AC
CHARLIE X (SEE CHARLIE'S LAW)   BLISH, JAMES   TC
CHARLIE'S LAW (CHARLIE X, FONTANA & RODDENBERRY)
                                  BLISH, JAMES   SA   STK 67 01
  STAR TREK   BLISH, JAMES   OC
CHARTING A BETTER VOYAGE- ZPG   ROGERS, NORMAN L.   AR
  VOYAGES: SCENARIOS FOR A SHIP CALLED EARTH
                                  SAUER, ROB   AN
CHARTING UTOPIA   KNIGHT, DAMON   AR   CLR 71 01
  CLARION   WILSON, ROBIN SCOTT   OA
CHASE OUR BLUES AWAY   EFFINGER, GEO. ALEC SS   NDM 76 06
  NEW DIMENSIONS 6   SILVERBERG, ROBERT   OA
CHASM OF MONSTERS   KELLER, DAVID H. MD. SS   51
  FOLSOM FLINT AND OTHER CURIOUS TALES, THE
                                  KELLER, DAVID H. MD. AC
CHASTE PLANET, THE   UPDIKE, JOHN   SS   75
  BEST SF: 75, THE NINTH ANNUAL   HARRISON & ALDISS   AN
CHATTING WITH COMPUTERS (REVISED)
                                  EVANS, CHRISTOPHER AR   DSP 73 10
  BEYOND THIS HORIZON   CARRELL, CHRISTOPHER OA
CHEATERS, THE   BLOCH, ROBERT   NV   WRT 47 11
  EDGE OF NEVER, THE   HOSKINS, ROBERT   AN
  FANTASY: THE LITERATURE OF THE MARVELOUS KELLEY, LEO P.   AN
  MORE NIGHTMARES   BLOCH, ROBERT   AC
  PLEASANT DREAMS   BLOCH, ROBERT   AC
CHECK YOUR UNDERSTANDING   MISC. MATERIAL   MS
  JOURNEYS IN SCIENCE FICTION   LOUGHLIN, RICHARD L. AN
CHECKMATE IN SIX MOVES   LEY, OLGA   SS
  BEYOND TIME   LEY, SANDRA   OA
CHECKPOINT LAMBDA (STOPOVER IN SPACE)
                                  LEINSTER, MURRAY   NO   AMZ 66 06
  MURRAY LEINSTER OMNIBUS, A   LEINSTER, MURRAY   AC
CHEERY SOUL, THE (1945)   BOWEN, ELIZABETH   SS   FSF 52 04
  BEST FROM FANTASY AND SCIENCE FICTION: 2
                                  BOUCHER & MCCOMAS   AN
CHEMICAL FORMULA OF DESTINY, THE
                                  NESVADBA, JOSEF   SS   64
  LOST FACE, THE   NESVADBA, JOSEF   AC
CHEMICAL PLANT   WILLIAMSON, IAN   SS   NWS 50 WI
  CONTACT   KEYES, NOEL   AN
  *NO PLACE LIKE EARTH   CARNELL, JOHN   AN
  OUT OF THIS WORLD 1   WILLIAMS-ELLIS& OWEN AN
CHESS CIVILIZATION, THE   VERNON, ROGER LEE   SS
  SPACE FRONTIERS, THE   VERNON, ROGER LEE   AC
CHESSMEN OF MARS, THE   BURROUGHS, EDGAR R. NO   AAS 22 02
  THREE MARTIAN NOVELS   BURROUGHS, EDGAR R.   AC
CHESSPLAYERS, THE   HARNESS, CHARLES L. SS   FSF 53 10
  ROSE, THE   HARNESS, CHARLES L.   AC
  SCIENCE FICTION ODDITIES   CONKLIN, GROFF   AN
CHESTNUT BEADS, THE   ROBERTS, JANE   NV   FSF 57 10
  ROD SERLING'S TRIPLE W: WITCHES, WARLOCKS AND WEREWOLVES
                                  SERLING, ROD   AN
CHICAGO   MONTELEONE, THOMAS F SS   FUC 73
  CITY: 2000 A.D., THE   CLEM/GREENBERG/&   AN
  FUTURE CITY   ELWOOD, ROGER   AN
CHICKEN ICARUS (A DREAM OF FLYING)
                                  EMSHWILLER, CAROL   SS   CAV 66
  JOY IN OUR CAUSE   EMSHWILLER, CAROL   AC
  SF12   MERRIL, JUDITH   AN
CHICKEN OR THE EGG-HEAD, THE   FENTON, FRANK   SS   NTL 54
  9 TALES OF SPACE AND TIME   HEALY, RAYMOND J.   OA
CHIEF   SLESAR, HENRY   SS   PBY 60 06
  SCIENCE FICTION   BRODKIN & PEARSON   AN
  6TH ANNUAL OF THE YEAR'S BEST S-F, THE MERRIL, JUDITH   AN
CHILD   HOLLY, JOAN C.   SS   DEM 73
  DEMON KIND   ELWOOD, ROGER   OA
CHILD BY CHRONOS   HARNESS, CHARLES L. SS   FSF 53 06
  BEST FROM FANTASY AND SCIENCE FICTION: 3
                                  BOUCHER & MCCOMAS   AN

CHILD DREAMS, THE   DORMAN, SONYA   PM
  WOMEN OF WONDER   SARGENT, PAMELA   AN
CHILD IS CRYING, A   MACDONALD, JOHN D. SS TWS 48 12
  SCIENCE FICTION GALAXY, THE   CONKLIN, GROFF   AN
  SHAPE OF THINGS, THE   KNIGHT, DAMON   AN
CHILD OF ALL AGES   PLAUGER, P. J.   SS ASF 75 03
  BEST SCIENCE FICTION OF THE YEAR, THE NO. 5
                                 CARR, TERRY   AN
  BEST SCIENCE FICTION STORIES OF THE YEAR (1975)
                                 DEL REY, LESTER   AN
  NEBULA AWARD STORIES 11   LE GUIN, URSULA K.   AN
  1976 ANNUAL WORLD'S BEST SF, THE WOLLHEIM, DONALD A. AN
CHILD OF MIND, A   SPINRAD, NORMAN   SS AMZ 65 01
  LAST HURRAH OF THE GOLDEN HORDE, THE SPINRAD, NORMAN AC
CHILD OF POWER   WYNDHAM, JOHN   NV FSB 39 03
  WANDERERS OF TIME   WYNDHAM, JOHN   AC
CHILD OF THE CAVERN, THE (1877)
                                 VERNE, JULES   EX
  JULES VERNE- MASTER OF SCIENCE FICTION VERNE, JULES   AC
CHILD OF THE GODS   VAN VOGT, A. E.   NV ASF 46 08
  EMPIRE OF THE ATOM   VAN VOGT, A. E.   NO
CHILD OF THE SUN   BRACKETT, LEIGH   SS PLS 42 SP
  MORE ADVENTURES ON OTHER PLANETS WOLLHEIM, DONALD A. AN
CHILD OF THE WINDS   HAMILTON, EDMOND   SS WRT 36 05
  BEST OF EDMOND HAMILTON, THE   HAMILTON, EDMOND   AC
CHILD OF VOID   ST. CLAIR, MARGARET SS SSS 49 11
  *INVADERS OF EARTH   CONKLIN, GROFF   AN
  TOMORROW'S CHILDREN   ASIMOV, ISAAC   AN
CHILD THAT LOVED A GRAVE, THE O'BRIEN, FITZ-JAMES SS
  GRAVEYARD READER, THE   CONKLIN, GROFF   AN
CHILD WHO BELIEVED, THE   AMUNDSON, GRACE   SS SEP 50 12
  SATURDAY EVENING POST FANTASY STORIES, THE
                                 FLES, BARTHOLD   AN
CHILD'S PLAY   SCHNIRRING,ALICEMARY SS WRT 42 03
  CHILDREN OF WONDER   TENN, WILLIAM   AN
CHILD'S PLAY   TENN, WILLIAM   NV ASF 47 03
  *ASTOUNDING SCIENCE FICTION ANTHOLOGY, THE
                                 CAMPBELL, JOHN W. JR AN
  ASTOUNDING-ANALOG READER, THE VOLUME TWO HARRISON & ALDISS AN
  BEYOND CONTROL   SILVERBERG, ROBERT   AN
  *FIRST ASTOUNDING SCIENCE FICTION ANTHOLOGY, THE
                                 CAMPBELL, JOHN W. JR AN
  GALAXY OF GHOULS   MERRIL, JUDITH   AN
  SECOND ASTOUNDING SCIENCE FICTION ANTHOLOGY, THE (PB)
                                 CAMPBELL, JOHN W. JR AN
  SEVEN SEXES, THE   TENN, WILLIAM   AC
  *TREASURY OF SCIENCE FICTION, A CONKLIN, GROFF   AN
  WORLD OF WONDER   PRATT, FLETCHER   AN
CHILD'S PLAY (SEE UNCLE SAM'S CHILDREN)
                                 EISENBERG, LARRY   TC
CHILDHOOD OF THE HUMAN HERO, THE
                                 EMSHWILLER, CAROL   SS SCS 73
  JOY IN OUR CAUSE   EMSHWILLER, CAROL   AC
  NEBULA AWARD STORIES 9   WILHELM, KATE   AN
  SHOWCASE   ELWOOD, ROGER   OA
CHILDHOOD'S END (EXPANDED FROM "GUARDIAN ANGEL")
                                 CLARKE, ARTHUR C.   NO NWS 50 WI
  ACROSS THE SEA OF STARS   CLARKE, ARTHUR C.   AC
  ARTHUR C. CLARKE OMNIBUS, AN   CLARKE, ARTHUR C.   AC
CHILDREN IN HIDING (SEE SIEZURE)
                                 BRUNNER, JOHN   TC
CHILDREN OF FORTUNE   ANDERSON, POUL   NV NEW 61 NO
  TWILIGHT WORLD   ANDERSON, POUL   NO
CHILDREN OF FORTUNE   JOURDAN, D. A.   NV SFQ 57 02
  6 AND THE SILENT SCREAM   HOWARD, IVAN   AN
CHILDREN OF NIGHT, THE   POHL, FREDERIK   NV GAL 64 10
  BEST OF FREDERIK POHL, THE   POHL, FREDERIK   AC
  BEST SF 7   CRISPIN, EDMUND   AN
  DIGITS AND DASTARDS   POHL, FREDERIK   AC
  NINTH GALAXY READER, THE   POHL, FREDERIK   AN
CHILDREN OF NOAH, THE   MATHESON, RICHARD   SS   57
  SHOCK!   MATHESON, RICHARD   AC
CHILDREN OF THE "BETSY B"   JAMESON, MALCOLM   SS ASF 39 03
  *TREASURY OF SCIENCE FICTION, A CONKLIN, GROFF   AN
CHILDREN OF THE ATOM   SHIRAS, WILMAR H.   NV NEW 53 AC
  CHILDREN OF THE ATOM   SHIRAS, WILMAR H.   AC
CHILDREN OF THE STARS   REED, CLIFFORD C.   SN SFB 59 07
  MARTIAN ENTERPRISE   REED, CLIFFORD C.   AC
CHILDREN OF THE STATE   NIVEN, LARRY   NO GAL 76 09
  WORLD OUT OF TIME, A   NIVEN, LARRY   NO
CHILDREN OF TOMORROW   VAN VOGT, A. E.   NO   70
  SCIENCE FICTION SPECIAL 6   ANONYMOUS   AN
CHILDREN'S CRUSADE, THE   PANGBORN, EDGAR   NV CTM 74 01
  CONTINUUM 1   ELWOOD, ROGER   OA
CHILDREN'S HOUR, THE   JONES, RAYMOND F.   NV FAD 47 09
  TOYMAKER, THE   JONES, RAYMOND F.   AC
CHILDREN'S HOUR, THE   KUTTNER, HENRY   NV ASF 44 03
  FOUR FOR THE FUTURE   CONKLIN, GROFF   AN
CHILDREN'S HOUR, THE   KUTTNER, HENRY
                              AND MOORE, C. L.   NV C ASF 44 03
  TREASURY OF GREAT SCIENCE FICTION, A VOL.1
                                 BOUCHER, ANTHONY   AN
CHILDREN'S HOUR, THE (AS WALLACE EDMONDSON)
                                 ELLISON, HARLAN   SS FUN 58 07
  NO DOORS, NO WINDOWS (STORIES REWRITTEN) ELLISON, HARLAN AC
CHILDREN, THE   DEFORD, MIRIAM ALLEN SS STS 52 12
  XENOGENESIS   DEFORD, MIRIAM ALLEN   AC
CHIMERAS, THE   KOESTLER, ARTHUR   SS PBY 69 05
  FULLY AUTOMATED LOVE LIFE OF HENRY KEANRIDGE
                                 PLAYBOY, EDITORS OF   AN
CHINESE BOXES, THE   CHARNOCK, GRAHAM   SS ORB 70 08
  ORBIT 8   KNIGHT, DAMON   OA
CHINESE PUZZLE (A STRAY FROM CATHAY)
                                 WYNDHAM, JOHN   NV FNF 53 08
  JIZZLE   WYNDHAM, JOHN   AC
  TALES OF GOOSEFLESH AND LAUGHTER WYNDHAM, JOHN   AC

CHING WITCH!   ROCKLYNNE, ROSS   SS DVS 72 02
  AGAIN, DANGEROUS VISIONS   ELLISON, HARLAN   OA
CHOCOLATE EGG, THE   DISCH, THOMAS M.   SS
  *GETTING INTO DEATH   DISCH, THOMAS M.   AC
CHOICE   WRIGHT, S. FOWLER   SS
  NEW GODS LEAD, THE   WRIGHT, S. FOWLER   AC
CHOICE, THE   HILTON-YOUNG, WAYLAND SS PUN 52 03
  FIFTY SHORT SCIENCE FICTION TALES ASIMOV & CONKLIN   AN
  OMNIBUS OF SCIENCE FICTION   CONKLIN, GROFF   AN
  SPECTRUM 4   AMIS & CONQUEST   AN
  STRANGE ADVENTURES IN SCIENCE FICTION CONKLIN, GROFF AN
  VOYAGES: SCENARIOS FOR A SHIP CALLED EARTH
                                 SAUER, ROB   AN
CHOLOM   KIDD, VIRGINIA   PM STG 74
  STRANGE GODS   ELWOOD, ROGER   OA
CHORE FOR A SPACEMAN   SHELDON, WALT   SS TWS 50 12
  SPACE SERVICE   NORTON, ANDRE   AN
CHOSEN PEOPLE, THE   RANDALL, ROBERT   NV ASF 56 06
  SHROUDED PLANET, THE   RANDALL, ROBERT   AC
CHOSEN, THE   WILHELM, KATE   SS ORB 70 06
  ORBIT 6   KNIGHT, DAMON   OA
CHRIST, OLD STUDENT IN A NEW SCHOOL
                                 BRADBURY, RAY   PM DVS 72 02
  AGAIN, DANGEROUS VISIONS   ELLISON, HARLAN   OA
CHRISTLINGS   TEICHNER, ALBERT   SS ORB 72 10
  ORBIT 10   KNIGHT, DAMON   OA
CHRISTMAS IN WATSON HOLLOW   MUNDIS, JERROLD J. SS
  NEW CONSTELLATIONS   DISCH & NAYLOR   OA
CHRISTMAS ON GANYMEDE   ASIMOV, ISAAC   SS STS 42 01
  ADVENTURES IN TOMORROW   CROSSEN, KENDELL F.   AN
  EARLY ASIMOV, THE   ASIMOV, ISAAC   AC
CHRISTMAS PRESENT   CAMPBELL, J. RAMSEY SS BBC 69 12
  YEAR'S BEST HORROR STORIES: SERIES IV, THE
                                 PAGE, GERALD W.   AN
CHRISTMAS PRESENT, THE   DICKSON, GORDON R. SS FSF 58 01
  STAR ROAD, THE   DICKSON, GORDON R.   AC
  UNIVERSE AHEAD   ENGDAHL & ROBERSON   AN
CHRISTMAS ROSES (CHRISTMAS TREE)
                                 CHRISTOPHER, JOHN   SS ASF 49 02
  TWENTY-SECOND CENTURY, THE   CHRISTOPHER, JOHN   AC
CHRISTMAS TREASON   WHITE, JAMES   NV FSF 62 01
  SPACE 1   DAVIS, RICHARD   OA
  8TH ANNUAL OF THE YEAR'S BEST S-F, THE MERRIL, JUDITH AN
CHRISTMAS TREE (ALSO AS CHRISTMAS ROSES)
                                 YOUD, CHRISTOPHER   SS ASF 49 02
  TRAVELLERS OF SPACE   GREENBERG , MARTIN   AN
CHRISTMAS TROMBONE   BANKS, RAYMOND E.   SS FSF 54 01
  BEST SCIENCE FICTION STORIES AND NOVELS: 1955
                                 DIKTY, T. E.   AN
CHRISTMAS 200,000 B.C. (1887) WATERLOO, STANLEY   SS   87
  FUTURE PERFECT   FRANKLIN, H. BRUCE   AN
CHRISTUS APOLLO   BRADBURY, RAY   PM NEW 69 AC
  I SING THE BODY ELECTRIC   BRADBURY, RAY   AC
CHRISTUS APOLLO (SELECTION)   BRADBURY, RAY   PM NEW 69 AC
  OTHER WORLDS, OTHER GODS   MOHS, MAYO   AC
CHROME PASTURES   YOUNG, ROBERT F.   NV IFS 56 04
  SECOND WORLD OF IF, THE   QUINN & WULFF   AN
CHROMIUM HELMET, THE   STURGEON, THEODORE NV ASF 46 06
  GREAT STORIES OF SCIENCE FICTION LEINSTER, MURRAY   AN
  SCIENCE FICTION INVENTIONS   KNIGHT, DAMON   AN
CHRONIC ARGONAUTS, THE   WELLS, H. G.   NV SSJ 88 04
  ANDROIDS, TIME MACHINES AND BLUE GIRAFFES
                                 ELWOOD & GHIDALIA   AN
  SPECULATIONS   SANDERS, THOMAS E.   AN
  STRANGE SIGNPOSTS   ELWOOD & MOSKOWITZ   AN
  VISIONS OF TOMORROW   ELWOOD, ROGER   AN
CHRONICLE OF BLACKTON, A   BAILEY, HILARY   SS NWQ 72 03
  NEW WORLDS QUARTERLY NO. 3   MOORCOCK, MICHAEL   OA
CHRONICLER, THE (ALSO AS SIEGE OF THE UNSEEN)
                                 VAN VOGT, A. E.   NA ASF 46 10
  FIVE SCIENCE FICTION NOVELS   GREENBERG , MARTIN   AN
CHRONICLES OF A COMET   MALZBERG, BARRY N. SS WLK 73
  MANY WORLDS OF BARRY MALZBERG, THE MALZBERG, BARRY N. AC
CHRONICLES OF A COMET   O'DONNELL, K. M.   SS WLK 73
  AND WALK NOW GENTLY THROUGH THE FIRE... ELWOOD, ROGER OA
  CHRONICLES OF A COMET AND OTHER RELIGIOUS SCIENCE FICTION
  STORIES   ELWOOD, ROGER   AN
CHRONIUS OF THE D.F.C. (SEE D.F.C.)
                                 BIGGLE, LLOYD JR.   TC
CHRONOCLASM, THE   WYNDHAM, JOHN   NV STR 53 01
  OTHER SIDE OF THE CLOCK, THE   STERN, PHILIP VAN D. AN
  SEEDS OF TIME, THE   WYNDHAM, JOHN   AC
  STAR SCIENCE FICTION STORIES   POHL, FREDERIK   OA
CHRONOKINESIS OF JONATHAN HULL, THE
                                 BOUCHER, ANTHONY   SS ASF 46 06
  GREAT STORIES OF SCIENCE FICTION LEINSTER, MURRAY   AN
CHRONOLOGY OF CITIES IN FLIGHT BLISH, JAMES   MS
  YEAR 2018!   BLISH, JAMES   NO
CHRONOLOGY OF SCIENCE FICTION, A
                                 MISC. MATERIAL   MS
  LOOKING AHEAD   ALLEN, D. & L.   AN
CHRONOPOLIS   BALLARD, J. G.   NV NWS 60 06
  BEST OF J. G. BALLARD, THE   BALLARD, J. G.   AC
  BILLENIUM   BALLARD, J. G.   AC
  CHRONOPOLIS AND OTHER STORIES BALLARD, J. G.   AC
  *FOUR-DIMENSIONAL NIGHTMARE, THE BALLARD, J. G.   AC
  VINTAGE ANTHOLOGY OF SCIENCE FANTASY, THE
                                 CERF, CHRISTOPHER   AN
CHRYSALID   WELLS, BASIL   SS
  DOORWAYS TO SPACE   WELLS, BASIL   AC
CHRYSALIDS, THE (RE-BIRTH)   WYNDHAM, JOHN   NO BAL 55
  JOHN WYNDHAM OMNIBUS, THE   WYNDHAM, JOHN   AC
CHRYSALIS   BRADBURY, RAY   SS AMZ 46 07
  S IS FOR SPACE   BRADBURY, RAY   AC
CHRYSALIS, THE   MILLER, P. SCHUYLER SS ASF 36 04
  EARTH IS THE STRANGEST PLANET SILVERBERG, ROBERT   AN

CHRYSALIS, THE   CLINIC, THE

*TREASURY OF SCIENCE FICTION, A   CONKLIN, GROFF   AN
CHRYSTALLIZATION OF THE MYTH   BARFOOT, JOHN   SS   ORB 72 11
   ORBIT 11   KNIGHT, DAMON   OA
CHUCK BERRY, WON'T YOU PLEASE COME HOME?
                                MCCULLOUGH, KEN   SS   DVS 72 02
   AGAIN, DANGEROUS VISIONS   ELLISON, HARLAN   OA
CHUCKLER, THE   WANDREI, DONALD   SS
   STRANGE HARVEST   WANDREI, DONALD   AC
CHURCH OF SAINT SATAN AND PANDAEMONS, THE
                                DAVIDSON, AVRAM   NV FAN 75 12
   ENQUIRIES OF DOCTOR ESZTERHAZY, THE DAVIDSON, AVRAM   NO
CICERONES, THE   AICKMAN, ROBERT   SS
   TRAVELLERS BY NIGHT   DERLETH, AUGUST   OA
CIL (THE EYES OF THE OVERWORLD)
                                VANCE, JACK   NV
   EIGHT FANTASMS AND MAGICS   VANCE, JACK   AC
CINDERELLA STORY   LANG, ALLEN KIM   SN IFS 61 05
   FROZEN PLANET AND 4 OTHER SF NOVELLAS, THE
                                ANONYMOUS   AN
CINDERELLA STORY (WHEN THE SHOE FITS)
                                GUNN, JAMES E.   SS VAN 58 06
   BREAKING POINT   GUNN, JAMES E.   AC
CINEMAGICIANS   KUPFERBERG, TULI   PM ESR 66
   SF12   MERRIL, JUDITH   AN
CIRCE UNDERSEA   MACBETH, GEORGE   PM   65
   HOLDING YOUR EIGHT HANDS   LUCIE-SMITH, EDWARD   AN
   11TH ANNUAL OF THE YEAR'S BEST S-F, THE MERRIL, JUDITH   AN
CIRCLE AND THE SQUARE, THE   DEKKER, THOMAS   PM
   FANTASIA MATHEMATICA   FADIMAN, CLIFTON   AN
CIRCLE OF ZERO, THE   WEINBAUM, STANLEY G. SS TWS 36 08
   HISTORY OF THE SCIENCE FICTION MAGAZINE, THE PART 2 1936-1945
                                ASHLEY, MICHAEL   AN
   MARTIAN ODYSSEY AND OTHER SCIENCE FICTION TALES, A
                                WEINBAUM, STANLEY G. AC
   MARTIAN ODYSSEY AND OTHERS, A WEINBAUM, STANLEY G. AC
CIRCLE, THE   MORLEY, CHRISTOPHER PM
   FANTASIA MATHEMATICA   FADIMAN, CLIFTON   AN
CIRCUIT RIDERS, THE   FITZPATRICK, R. C. SS ASF 62 04
   ANALOG 2   CAMPBELL, JOHN W. JR AN
   8TH ANNUAL OF THE YEAR'S BEST S-F, THE MERRIL, JUDITH   AN
CIRCULAR RUINS, THE (TRANSLATED BY JAMES E. IRBY)
                                BORGES, JORGE LUIS SS   62
   LIGHT FANTASTIC, THE   HARRISON, HARRY   AN
   PERCHANCE TO DREAM   KNIGHT, DAMON   AN
   11TH ANNUAL OF THE YEAR'S BEST S-F, THE MERRIL, JUDITH AN
CIRCULARIZATION OF CONDENSED CONVENTIONAL STRAIGHT-LINE
   WORD-IMAGE STRUCTURES   BUTTERWORTH, MICHAEL SS NWS 69 07
   NEW TOMORROWS, THE   SPINRAD, NORMAN   AN
CIRCULATION OF THE BLOOD, THE ALDISS, BRIAN W.   NV IMP 66 03
   FOUR FOR THE FUTURE   HARRISON, HARRY   AN
   MOMENT OF ECLIPSE, THE   ALDISS, BRIAN W.   AC
   WINDOW ON THE FUTURE   HILL, DOUGLAS   AN
CIRCUS   HAWKINS, PETER   SS SCF 52 FL
   GATEWAY TO THE STARS   CARNELL, JOHN   AN
CIRCUS   NOURSE, ALAN E.   SS
   COUNTERFEIT MAN, THE   NOURSE, ALAN E.   AC
CIRCUS OF DR. LAO, THE   FINNEY, CHARLES G. NA   35
   CIRCUS OF DR. LAO AND OTHER IMPROBABLE STORIES
                                BRADBURY, RAY   AN
CISTERN, THE   BRADBURY, RAY   SS MAD 47 05
   *DARK CARNIVAL   BRADBURY, RAY   AC
   *OCTOBER COUNTRY, THE   BRADBURY, RAY   AC
   SMALL ASSASSIN, THE   BRADBURY, RAY   AC
CITADEL OF LOST AGES, THE   BRACKETT, LEIGH   NV TWS 50 12
   HALFLING AND OTHER STORIES, THE BRACKETT, LEIGH   AC
CITIZEN BACILLUS   BRUNNER, JOHN   PM   69
   HOLDING YOUR EIGHT HANDS   LUCIE-SMITH, EDWARD   AN
CITIZEN IN SPACE (SPY STORY)   SHECKLEY, ROBERT   SS PBY 55 09
   CITIZEN IN SPACE   SHECKLEY, ROBERT   AC
CITIZEN 504   PALMER, CHARLES H. SS ARG 96 12
   SCIENCE FICTION BY GASLIGHT MOSKOWITZ, SAM   AN
CITY   SIMAK, CLIFFORD D. NV ASF 44 05
   ASTOUNDING-ANALOG READER, THE VOLUME ONE HARRISON & ALDISS AN
   CITY   SIMAK, CLIFFORD D.   NO
   SCIENCE FICTION OMNIBUS ON POLLUTION, A ANONYMOUS   AN
CITY AND THE SHIP, THE   VERNON, ROGER LEE NV
   SPACE FRONTIERS, THE   VERNON, ROGER LEE   AC
CITY AND THE STARS, THE   CLARKE, ARTHUR C. NO HBW 56
   FROM THE OCEAN, FROM THE STARS CLARKE, ARTHUR C.   AC
CITY IN THE SOFA, THE   KORNBLUTH, C. M.   SS COS 41 07
   THIRTEEN O'CLOCK AND OTHER ZERO HOURS KORNBLUTH, C. M. AC
CITY LIGHTS, CITY NIGHTS   MALZBERG, BARRY N. SS FUC 73
   BEST OF BARRY N. MALZBERG, THE MALZBERG, BARRY N.   AC
CITY LIGHTS, CITY NIGHTS   O'DONNELL, K. M.   SS FUC 73
   FUTURE CITY   ELWOOD, ROGER   OA
CITY OF DREAD, THE   ESHBACH, LLOYD A. SS
   TYRANT OF TIME, THE   ESHBACH, LLOYD A.   AC
CITY OF FORCE, THE   GALOUYE, DANIEL F. NA GAL 59 04
   BODYGUARD AND 4 OTHER SHORT SF NOVELS FROM GALAXY
                                GOLD, H. L.   AN
CITY OF MACHINES (SEE THE MAD MACHINES)
                                ARNOLD, FRANK EDWARD TC
CITY OF PENETRATING LIGHT, THE DISCH, THOMAS M.   SS
   FUN WITH YOUR NEW HEAD   DISCH, THOMAS M.   AC
CITY OF THE LIVING DEAD, THE   MANNING, LAURENCE
                                AND PRATT, FLETCHER NV C SWS 30 05
   SECOND AVON FANTASY READER, THE WOLLHEIM &ERNSBERGER AN
CITY OF THE LOST ONES (ENCHANTRESS OF VENUS)
                                BRACKETT, LEIGH   NV PLS 49 FL
   RACE TO THE STARS   MARGULIES & FRIEND   AN
CITY OF THE MUMMIES, THE   BURROUGHS, EDGAR R. NV AMZ 41 03
   LLANA OF GATHOL   BURROUGHS, EDGAR R.   NO
CITY OF THE SINGING FLAME, THE SMITH, CLARK ASHTON SS WOS 31 07
   FROM OFF THIS WORLD   MARGULIES & FRIEND   AN
   *OTHER SIDE OF THE MOON, THE DERLETH, AUGUST   AN
   OUT OF SPACE AND TIME   SMITH, CLARK ASHTON AC

CITY OF THE SUN, THE (1623) CAMPANELLA, G. D.   EX
   *BEYOND TIME AND SPACE   DERLETH, AUGUST   AN
CITY OF THE TIGER   BRUNNER, JOHN   SN SCF 58 12
   WHOLE MAN, THE   BRUNNER, JOHN   NO
CITY OF YESTERDAY   CARR, TERRY   SS IFS 67 12
   BEYOND CONTROL   SILVERBERG, ROBERT   AN
   EARTH IN TRANSIT   SCHWARTZ, SHEILA   AN
CITY ON THE EDGE OF FOREVER, THE
                                ELLISON, HARLAN   PL NBC 67 04
   SIX SCIENCE FICTION PLAYS   ELWOOD, ROGER   AN
CITY ON THE EDGE OF FOREVER, THE (HARLAN ELLISON)
                                BLISH, JAMES   SA STK 68 04
   STAR TREK 2   BLISH, JAMES   OC
CITY ON VENUS, A   GADE, HENRY   SS
   FAREWELL FANTASTIC VENUS   ALDISS & HARRISON   AN
CITY THAT GREW IN THE SEA, THE (SEE WICKER WONDERLAND)
                                LAUMER, KEITH   TC
CITY THAT LOVES YOU, THE   BANKS, RAYMOND E. SS GAL 69 03
   HOT & COLD RUNNING CITIES   MCHARGUE, GEORGESS   AN
CITY'S END   REYNOLDS, MACK   NV FUQ 73
   CITY: 2000 A.D., THE   CLEM/GREENBERG/&
   FUTURE QUEST   ELWOOD, ROGER   OA
CITY, DYING, THE   BERTIN, EDDY C.   SS NWR 68 13
   NEW WRITINGS IN SF. 9   CARNELL, JOHN   AN
   NEW WRITINGS IN SF. 13   CARNELL, JOHN   OA
CITY, THE   DOLAN, MIKE   SS
   SANTANA MORNING AND OTHER STORIES DOLAN, MIKE   OC
CITY, THE (PURPOSE)   BRADBURY, RAY   SS STS 50 07
   *ILLUSTRATED MAN, THE   BRADBURY, RAY   AC
CIVIL SERVICE SERVANT, A (THE FAIRLY CIVIL SERVANT)
                                HARRISON, HARRY   SS GAL 67 12
   PRIME NUMBER   HARRISON, HARRY   AC
CIVILIZATION GAME, THE   SIMAK, CLIFFORD D. NV GAL 58 11
   MIND PARTNER AND 8 OTHER NOVELETS FROM GALAXY
                                GOLD, H. L.   AN
   TOMORROW 1   HOSKINS, ROBERT   AN
CIVILIZED (WE'RE CIVILIZED) APOSTOLIDES, ALEX
                                AND CLIFTON, MARK   SS C GAL 53 08
   PORTALS OF TOMORROW   DERLETH, AUGUST   AN
CIVIS LAPVTVS SVM   WOLFE, GENE   SS DYS 75
   DYSTOPIAN VISIONS   ELWOOD, ROGER   OA
CIVIS OBIT   JANIFER, LAURENCE M. SS DYS 75
   DYSTOPIAN VISIONS   ELWOOD, ROGER   OA
CLAIR DE LUNE   QUINN, SEABURY   NV WRT 47 11
   GHOUL KEEPERS, THE   MARGULIES, LEO   AN
CLAM OF CATASTROPHE, THE   COVER, ARTHUR BYRON NV
   PLATYPUS OF DOOM AND OTHER NIHILISTS, THE
                                COVER, ARTHUR BYRON OC
CLARK ASHTON SMITH: MASTER OF FANTASY
                                MISC. MATERIAL   IN
   OUT OF SPACE AND TIME   SMITH, CLARK ASHTON AC
CLASH BY NIGHT   KUTTNER, HENRY   NV ASF 43 03
   BEST OF HENRY KUTTNER 2, THE KUTTNER, HENRY   AC
CLASH BY NIGHT   O'DONNELL, LAWRENCE NV ASF 43 03
   *ASTOUNDING SCIENCE FICTION ANTHOLOGY, THE
                                CAMPBELL, JOHN W. JR AN
   ASTOUNDING-ANALOG READER, THE VOLUME ONE HARRISON & ALDISS AN
   FIRST ASTOUNDING SCIENCE FICTION ANTHOLOGY, THE (PB)
                                CAMPBELL, JOHN W. JR AN
   *SECOND ASTOUNDING SCIENCE FICTION ANTHOLOGY, THE
                                CAMPBELL, JOHN W. JR AN
CLASH OF CYMBOLS, A (SEE THE TRIUMPH OF TIME)
                                BLISH, JAMES   TC
CLASS WITH DR. CHANG, A   MOORE, WARD   SS
   BEYOND TIME   LEY, SANDRA   OA
CLASSIC AFFAIR, A   BEAUMONT, CHARLES SS PBY 55
   MAGIC MAN AND OTHER SCIENCE-FANTASY STORIES
                                BEAUMONT, CHARLES   AC
   NIGHT RIDE AND OTHER JOURNEYS BEAUMONT, CHARLES   AC
CLASSICAL QUERY COMPOSED WHILE SHAMPOOING
                                BUCK, DORIS PITKIN PM FSF 59 07
   BEST FROM FANTASY AND SCIENCE FICTION: 9
                                MILLS, ROBERT P.   AN
CLAUSTROPHILE, THE   STURGEON, THEODORE NV GAL 56 08
   FOUR FOR THE FUTURE   CONKLIN, GROFF   AN
CLAY SUBURB   YOUNG, ROBERT F.   SS AMZ 75 11
   BEST SCIENCE FICTION OF THE YEAR, THE NO. 5
                                CARR, TERRY   AN
CLEAN KILLS AND OTHER TROPHIES SERLING, ROD   SA
   NIGHT GALLERY   SERLING, ROD   OC
CLEANSING OF THE SYSTEM, A   PLATT, CHARLES   SS NWQ 72 03
   NEW WORLDS QUARTERLY NO. 3 MOORCOCK, MICHAEL   OA
CLEAR AS MUD (SEE GRIME AND PUNISHMENT)
                                LAUMER, KEITH   TC
CLEAR DAY IN THE MOTOR CITY, A ARNASON, ELEANOR SS NWQ 73 05
   NEW IMPROVED SUN, THE   DISCH, THOMAS M.   AN
   NEW WORLDS NO. 5   MOORCOCK & PLATT   OA
CLERICAL ERROR   CLIFTON, MARK   NV ASF 56 02
   BEST SCIENCE FICTION STORIES AND NOVELS: 1956
                                DIKTY, T. E.   AN
CLEVERJACKS AND THE MOONSTALKS, THE
                                JAMES, E. R.   SS
   WORLDS AT WAR   RAYER, FRANCIS G.   AN
CLIFF CLIMBERS, THE   LAFFERTY, R. A.   SS QRK 70 01
   QUARK/1   DELANY & HACKER   OA
CLIFFS THAT LAUGHED   LAFFERTY, R. A.   SS MOH 69 03
   STRANGE DOINGS   LAFFERTY, R. A.   AC
CLIMACTERIC   DAVIDSON, AVRAM   SS FSF 60 08
   STRANGE SEAS AND SHORES   DAVIDSON, AVRAM   AC
CLIMATIC THREAT, THE   GRIBBIN, DR. JOHN AR
   ANALOG ANNUAL   BOVA, BEN   OA
CLIMBING WAVE, THE   BRADLEY, MARION Z. NV FSF 55 02
   IF THIS GOES ON   NUETZEL, CHARLES   AN
CLINIC, THE   STURGEON, THEODORE SS STR 53 02
   STAR SCIENCE FICTION STORIES NO. 2 POHL, FREDERIK   OA

CLIOMETRICON, THE

```
CLIOMETRICON, THE            ZEBROWSKI, GEORGE    SS    AMZ 75 05
  BEYOND TIME                LEY, SANDRA                      OA
  MONADIC UNIVERSE, THE      ZEBROWSKI, GEORGE                AC
CLIPPER OF THE CLOUDS, THE   VERNE, JULES         EX        86
  JULES VERNE- MASTER OF SCIENCE FICTION  VERNE, JULES        AC
CLOAK FROM MESSER LANDO, A   DERLETH, AUGUST      SS    WRT 34 09
  NOT LONG FOR THIS WORLD    DERLETH, AUGUST                  AC
CLOAK OF AESIR               CAMPBELL, JOHN W. JR NV   ASF 39 03
  *BEST OF JOHN W. CAMPBELL, THE  CAMPBELL, JOHN W. JR        AC
  CLOAK OF AESIR             CAMPBELL, JOHN W. JR             AC
  WHO GOES THERE? AND OTHER STORIES  CAMPBELL, JOHN W. JR     AC
CLOAK OF ANARCHY             NIVEN, LARRY         NV   ASF 72 03
  BEST SCIENCE FICTION STORIES OF THE YEAR (1972)
                            DEL REY, LESTER                   AN
  TALES OF KNOWN SPACE: THE UNIVERSE OF LARRY NIVEN
                            NIVEN, LARRY                      AC
  2020 VISION                POURNELLE, JERRY                 AN
CLOAK, THE                   BLOCH, ROBERT        SS    UNK 39 05
  FROM UNKNOWN WORLDS        CAMPBELL, JOHN W. JR             AN
  HELL HATH FURY             HAY, GEORGE                      AN
  *OPENER OF THE WAY, THE    BLOCH, ROBERT                    AC
  YOURS TRULY, JACK THE RIPPER  BLOCH, ROBERT                 AC
CLOCK THAT WENT BACKWARDS, THE MITCHELL, EDWARD P.  SS  SUN 81 01
  CRYSTAL MAN, THE           MITCHELL, EDWARD P.              AC
CLOCK WITHOUT HANDS          KERSH, GERALD        NV   COL 46 10
  MEN WITHOUT BONES          KERSH, GERALD                    AC
CLOCK, THE                   MASON, A. E. W.      SS        17
  TRAVELERS IN TIME          STERN, PHILIP VAN D.             AN
CLONE SISTER                 SARGENT, PAMELA      NV   EIO 73
  CLONED LIVES               SARGENT, PAMELA                  NO
  EROS IN ORBIT              ELDER, JOSEPH                    OA
  MARRIAGE AND THE FAMILY THROUGH SCIENCE FICTION
                            CLEAR/WARRICK/&                   AN
  STARSHADOWS                SARGENT, PAMELA                  AC
CLONE, THE                   THOMAS, THEODORE L.  SS    FAN 59 12
  SHOCKING THING, A          KNIGHT, DAMON                    AN
CLOSE BEHIND HIM             WYNDHAM, JOHN        SS    FAN 53 02
  ABC OF SCIENCE FICTION, AN BOARDMAN, TOM JR.                AN
  BEST OF JOHN WYNDHAM, THE  WYNDHAM, JOHN                    AC
  MAN FROM BEYOND AND OTHER STORIES, THE  WYNDHAM, JOHN       AC
CLOSED CIRCUIT               SCHOLZ, CARTER       SS
  CLARION SF                 WILHELM, KATE                    OA
CLOSED DOOR, THE             CROSSEN, KENDELL F.  SS    AMZ 53 09
  SPACE POLICE               NORTON, ANDRE                    AN
CLOSED SICILIAN              MALZBERG, BARRY N.   SS    FSF 73 11
  ARENA: SPORTS SF           FERMAN & MALZBERG                AN
  BEST OF BARRY N. MALZBERG, THE  MALZBERG, BARRY N.          AC
  MANY WORLDS OF BARRY MALZBERG, THE  MALZBERG, BARRY N.      AC
CLOSEST SCHOOL, THE          HENDERSON, ZENNA     SS    FAN 60 04
  HOLDING WONDER             HENDERSON, ZENNA                 AC
CLOSING THE DEAL             MALZBERG, BARRY N.   SS    ASF 74 03
  BEST OF BARRY N. MALZBERG, THE  MALZBERG, BARRY N.          AC
CLOSING WITH NATURE          RUSH, NORMAN         SS    MRV 70
  RUINS OF EARTH, THE        DISCH, THOMAS M.                 AN
CLOTHS MAKE THE MAN          MATHESON, RICHARD    SS    WBY 51 02
  SHORES OF SPACE, THE       MATHESON, RICHARD                AC
CLOUD MINERS, THE (ARMEN, GERROLD & CRAWFORD)
                            BLISH, JAMES         SA    STK 72 06
  STAR TREK   6              BLISH, JAMES                     OC
CLOUD-SCULPTORS OF CORAL D, THE
                            BALLARD, J. G.       SS    FSF 67 12
  BEST FROM FANTASY AND SCIENCE FICTION: 18
                            FERMAN, EDWARD L.                 AN
  NEBULA AWARD STORIES  NO. 3  ZELAZNY, ROGER                 AN
  SF12                       MERRIL, JUDITH                   AN
  *VERMILLION SANDS          BALLARD, J. G.                   AC
CLOUDBUILDERS, THE           KAPP, COLIN          NV   NWR 68 12
  NEW WRITINGS IN SF. 12     CARNELL, JOHN                    OA
  TOMORROW, AND TOMORROW, AND TOMORROW...  HEINTZ/HERBERT/JOOS/ AN
  WORLD'S BEST SCIENCE FICTION: 1969  WOLLHEIM & CARR         AN
CLOUDED JUDGEMENTS           ALDISS, BRIAN W.     SI
  ALL ABOUT VENUS            ALDISS, BRIAN W.                 AN
CLOUDLAB, THE                ROBERSON, RICK       NV   NEW 76 AN
  UNIVERSE AHEAD             ENGDAHL & ROBERSON               AN
CLUB SECRETARY               DUNSANY, LORD        SS        34
  OUT OF THIS WORLD          FAST, JULIUS                     AN
CLUTCH OF MORPHEUS           STERNIG, LARRY       NV   TWS 46 WI
  TALES OF TIME AND SPACE    OLNEY, ROSS R.                   AN
CO-OPERATE- OR ELSE|         VAN VOGT, A. E.      SS    ASF 42 04
  DECADE THE 1940S           ALDISS & HARRISON                AN
  *OUTER REACHES, THE        DERLETH, AUGUST                  AN
  WAR AGAINST THE RULL, THE  VAN VOGT, A. E.                  NO
COBBLER, COBBLER, MEND MY SHOE STRUTHER, JAN     SS    WRV 29 11
  MOONLIGHT TRAVELER, THE    STERN, PHILIP VAN D.             AN
COCO-TALK                    TEMPLE, WILLIAM F.   SS    NWR 66 07
  NEW WRITINGS IN SF. 7      CARNELL, JOHN                    OA
COCONUTS                     WILLIAMS, BEN A.     SS
  MATHEMATICAL MAGPIE, THE   FADIMAN, CLIFTON                 AN
COCOON                       LAUMER, KEITH        SS    FAN 62 12
  BEST OF KEITH LAUMER, THE  LAUMER, KEITH                    AC
  NINE BY LAUMER             LAUMER, KEITH                    AC
COCOON, THE                  GOODWIN, JOHN B. L.  SS    STO 46 10
  STRANGE BEASTS AND UNNATURAL MONSTERS  STERN, PHILIP VAN D. AN
  TIMELESS STORIES FOR TODAY AND TOMORROW  BRADBURY, RAY      AN
CODE, THE                    MOORE, C. L.         NV   ASF 45 07
  JUDGEMENT NIGHT            MOORE, C. L.                     AC
CODED SUN GAME, THE          VICKERS, BRIAN       NA   QRK 71 03
  QUARK/3                    DELANY & HACKER                  OA
CODEMUS                      BRINGSVAERD, TOR AGE SS        68
  BEST FROM THE REST OF THE WORLD, THE  WOLLHEIM, DONALD A.   AN
COFFIN CURE, THE             NOURSE, ALAN E.      SS    GAL 57 04
  BEST SF 7                  CRISPIN, EDMUND                  AN
  SCIENCE FICTION ODDITIES   CONKLIN, GROFF                   AN
  TIGER BY THE TAIL          NOURSE, ALAN E.                  AC
```

COLLECTOR'S ITEMS

```
COFFIN, THE (WAKE FOR THE LIVING)
                            BRADBURY, RAY        SS    DMN 47 09
  AUTUMN PEOPLE, THE         BRADBURY, RAY                    AC
  *DARK CARNIVAL             BRADBURY, RAY                    AC
COG, THE                     FRITCH, CHARLES E.   SS    ASF 53 02
  CRAZY MIXED-UP PLANET      FRITCH, CHARLES E.               AC
COHEN DOG EXCLUSION ACT, THE SCHRADER, STEVEN     SS    NEW 71 AN
  BEST SF: 1971              HARRISON & ALDISS                AN
  ECO-FICTION                STADLER, JOHN                    AN
COILS                        BARFOOT, JOHN        SS    ORB 74 13
  ORBIT 13                   KNIGHT, DAMON                    OA
COIN COLLECTOR, THE (THE OTHER WIFE)
                            FINNEY, JACK         SS    SEP 60 01
  I LOVE GALESBURG IN THE SPRINGTIME  FINNEY, JACK            AC
COINCIDENCE                  NOLAN, WILLIAM F.    SS    BER 74
  BERSERKERS, THE            ELWOOD, ROGER                    OA
COINCIDENCE DAY              BRUNNER, JOHN        SS    ASF 65 02
  ANALOG 5                   CAMPBELL, JOHN W. JR             AN
  NOT BEFORE TIME            BRUNNER, JOHN                    AC
  TIME-JUMP                  BRUNNER, JOHN                    AC
COLD DARK NIGHT WITH SNOW, A WILHELM, KATE        SS    ORB 70 06
  ORBIT 6                    KNIGHT, DAMON                    OA
COLD EQUATIONS, THE          GODWIN, TOM          NV   ASF 54 08
  ASPECTS OF SCIENCE FICTION  DOHERTY, G. D.                  AN
  ASTOUNDING-ANALOG READER, THE VOLUME TWO  HARRISON & ALDISS AN
  BEST SCIENCE FICTION STORIES AND NOVELS: 1955
                            DIKTY, T. E.                      AN
  BEST SF 3                  CRISPIN, EDMUND                  AN
  BEYOND THE STARS AND OTHER STORIES  ANONYMOUS               AN
  IN DREAMS AWAKE            FIEDLER, LESLIE A.               AN
  MASTERS' CHOICE            JANIFER, LAURENCE M.             AN
  MODERN SCIENCE FICTION     SPINRAD, NORMAN                  AN
  NEW AWARENESS, THE         WARRICK & GREENBERG              AN
  SCIENCE FICTION HALL OF FAME VOLUME 1  SILVERBERG, ROBERT   AN
  SCIENCE FICTION THROUGH THE AGES 2  EVANS, I. O.            AN
  THEMES IN SCIENCE FICTION  KELLEY, LEO P.                   AN
  3000 YEARS OF FANTASY AND SCIENCE FICTION
                            DE CAMP, L. S.&C.                 AN
  5 TALES FROM TOMORROW      DIKTY, T. E.                     AN
COLD FRIEND                  ELLISON, HARLAN      SS    GAL 73 10
  APPROACHING OBLIVION       ELLISON, HARLAN                  AC
  BEST FROM GALAXY, THE  VOLUME II  GALAXY, EDITORS OF        AN
COLD FRONT                   CLEMENT, HAL         NV   ASF 46 07
  *MEN AGAINST THE STARS     GREENBERG, MARTIN                AN
COLD GRAY GOD, THE           MOORE, C. L.         SS    WRT 35 10
  NORTHWEST OF EARTH         MOORE, C. L.                     AC
COLD GREEN EYE, THE          WILLIAMSON, JACK     SS    FAN 53 03
  PANDORA EFFECT, THE        WILLIAMSON, JACK                 AC
  SCIENCE FICTION SHOWCASE   KORNBLUTH, MARY                  AN
COLD NIGHT FOR CRYING, A     LESSER, MILTON       SS    IFS 54 12
  FIRST WORLD OF IF, THE     QUINN & WULFF                    AN
COLD PEACE, THE (SEE IT BECOMES NECESSARY)
                            MOORE, WARD                       TC
COLD STORAGE                 CASTELL, DAPHNE      SS
  GOLLANCZ - SUNDAY TIMES BEST SF STORIES  ANONYMOUS          OA
COLD TOMORROWS               SIMONS, WALTON       SS
  QUEST                      BISCHOFF, DAVID                  OA
COLD TURKEY                  GALLUP, DICK
            AND PADGETT, RON    SS C  BMR 73
  BAD MOON RISING            DISCH, THOMAS M.                 AN
COLD VICTORY                 ANDERSON, POUL       SS    FSF 57 05
  7 CONQUESTS                ANDERSON, POUL                   AC
COLD WAR                     CLARKE, ARTHUR C.    SS    SAT 57 04
  PRELUDE TO MARS            CLARKE, ARTHUR C.                AC
  TALES FROM THE WHITE HART  CLARKE, ARTHUR C.                AC
COLD WAR                     KUTTNER, HENRY       SS    TWS 49 10
  BEST OF HENRY KUTTNER 1, THE  KUTTNER, HENRY                AC
  BEST OF HENRY KUTTNER, THE  KUTTNER, HENRY                  AC
  BYPASS TO OTHERNESS        KUTTNER, HENRY                   AC
  *SCIENCE FICTION ADVENTURES IN MUTATION  CONKLIN, GROFF     AN
COLD WAR                     NEVILLE, KRIS        SS    ASF 49 10
  *ASTOUNDING SCIENCE FICTION ANTHOLOGY, THE
                            CAMPBELL, JOHN W. JR             AN
  FIRST STEP OUTWARD         HOSKINS, ROBERT                  AN
  *SECOND ASTOUNDING SCIENCE FICTION ANTHOLOGY, THE
                            CAMPBELL, JOHN W. JR             AN
COLD WAR...CONTINUED, THE    REYNOLDS, MACK       NV   NOV 73 03
  NOVA 3                     HARRISON, HARRY                  OA
COLD WIND AND THE WARM, THE  BRADBURY, RAY        SS    HRP 64 07
  I SING THE BODY ELECTRIC   BRADBURY, RAY                    AC
COLD, COLD BOX, THE          FAST, HOWARD         SS    FSF 59 07
  EDGE OF TOMORROW, THE      FAST, HOWARD                     AC
  OUT OF THIS WORLD 7        WILLIAMS-ELLIS& OWEN             AN
COLD, THE FIRE OF THE PHOENIX KELLEY, LEO P.      SS    PRT 71
  PROTOSTARS                 GERROLD & GOLDIN                 OA
COLDEST PLACE, THE           NIVEN, LARRY         SS    IFS 64 12
  TALES OF KNOWN SPACE: THE UNIVERSE OF LARRY NIVEN
                            NIVEN, LARRY                      AC
COLDNESS, THE                PLATT, CHARLES       SS    NWQ 73 05
  NEW WORLDS NO. 5           MOORCOCK & PLATT                 OA
COLLECTING TEAM              SILVERBERG, ROBERT   SS    AUT 57 06
  EXPLORERS OF SPACE         SILVERBERG, ROBERT               AN
  MOONFERNS & STARSONGS      SILVERBERG, ROBERT               AC
  SCIENCE FICTION BESTIARY, THE  SILVERBERG, ROBERT           AN
  TO WORLDS BEYOND           SILVERBERG, ROBERT               AC
COLLECTOR OF STONES, A       DERLETH, AUGUST      SS    WRT 46 11
  NOT LONG FOR THIS WORLD    DERLETH, AUGUST                  AC
COLLECTOR'S FEVER            ZELAZNY, ROGER       SS    GAL 64 06
  DOORS OF HIS FACE, THE LAMPS OF HIS MOUTH, THE
                            ZELAZNY, ROGER                    AC
COLLECTOR'S ITEM (THE END OF THE SEARCH)
                            KNIGHT, DAMON        SS    WOT 63 06
  TURNING ON                 KNIGHT, DAMON                    AC
COLLECTOR'S ITEMS            SERLING, ROD         SA
  NIGHT GALLERY 2            SERLING, ROD                     OC
```

COLLECTOR, THE   HEARD, H. F.   SS   FSF 51 08
  BEST FROM FANTASY AND SCIENCE FICTION   BOUCHER & MCCOMAS   AN
COLLECTORS, THE   DANCEY, MAX
  AND DEWEY, G. GORDON   SS C AMZ 53 07
  BEST SCIENCE-FICTION STORIES: 1954, THE BLEILER & DIKTY   AN
COLLISION ORBIT   STEWART, WILL   NV   ASF 42 07
  SEETEE SHIP   STEWART, WILL   AC
COLONIAL   CHRISTOPHER, JOHN   NV   ASF 49 04
  OUT OF THIS WORLD 5   WILLIAMS-ELLIS& OWEN AN
  TWENTY-SECOND CENTURY, THE   CHRISTOPHER, JOHN   AC
COLONISTS, THE   JONES, RAYMOND F.   NV   IFS 54 06
  SECOND WORLD OF IF, THE   QUINN & WULFF   AN
COLONY   DICK, PHILIP K.   NV   GAL 53 06
  BEST OF PHILIP K. DICK, THE   DICK, PHILIP K.   AC
  HANDFUL OF DARKNESS, A   DICK, PHILIP K.   AC
  SPACE OPERA   ALDISS, BRIAN W.   AN
COLONY, THE   DEFORD, MIRIAM ALLEN SS FSF 66 05
  ELSEWHERE, ELSEWHEN, ELSEHOW   DEFORD, MIRIAM ALLEN   AC
COLORFUL CHARACTER, THE   DE CAMP, L. SPRAGUE SS   TWS 49 12
  SPRAGUE DE CAMP'S NEW ANTHOLOGY   DE CAMP, L. SPRAGUE   AC
COLORFUL SCIENCE FICTION WORLDS OF ALDEN H. NORTON
                              MOSKOWITZ, SAM   IN
  AWARD SCIENCE FICTION READER   NORTON, ALDEN H.   AN
COLORLESS IN LIMESTONE CAVERNS SEAGER, ALLAN   SS   PBY 69 11
  MASKS   PLAYBOY, EDITORS OF   AN
COLORS OF FEAR, THE   CARR, TERRY   SS   NDM 74 04
  LIGHT AT THE END OF THE UNIVERSE, THE CARR, TERRY   AC
  NEW DIMENSIONS 4   SILVERBERG, ROBERT   OA
COLORS, THE   DISCH, THOMAS M.   SS   NWS 68 12
  *GETTING INTO DEATH   DISCH, THOMAS M.   AC
COLOSSUS   WANDREI, DONALD   NV   ASF 34 01
  BEFORE THE GOLDEN AGE   ASIMOV, ISAAC   AN
  *BEYOND TIME AND SPACE   DERLETH, AUGUST   AN
COLOUR OUT OF SPACE, THE (ALSO AS MONSTER OF TERROR)
                              LOVECRAFT, H. P.   SS   AMZ 27 09
  HAUNTER OF THE DARK, THE   LOVECRAFT, H. P.   AC
  IN DREAMS AWAKE   FIEDLER, LESLIE A.   AN
  MASTERPIECES OF SCIENCE FICTION   MOSKOWITZ, SAM   AN
  OMNIBUS OF SCIENCE FICTION   CONKLIN, GROFF   AN
  SCIENCE FICTION OMNIBUS   CONKLIN, GROFF   AN
  STRANGE TRAVELS IN SCIENCE FICTION CONKLIN, GROFF   AN
COLUMBUS ON ST. DOMENICA   COTTON, JOHN   PM   72
  BEST SF: 1972   HARRISON & ALDISS   AN
COLUMBUS WAS A DOPE   HEINLEIN, ROBERT A. SS   STS 47 05
  FIFTY SHORT SCIENCE FICTION TALES ASIMOV & CONKLIN   AN
  FUTURE MAKERS, THE   HAINING, PETER   AN
  MENACE FROM EARTH, THE   HEINLEIN, ROBERT A.   AC
  SCIENCE FICTION: THE GREAT YEARS, VOL. II
                              POHL, C. & F.   AN
COLUMBUS WAS A DOPE   MONROE, LYLE   SS   STS 47 05
  TRAVELLERS OF SPACE   GREENBERG , MARTIN   AN
COMBAT SF: INTRODUCTION   DICKSON, GORDON R. IN
  COMBAT SF   DICKSON, GORDON R.   AN
COMBAT TEAM (EXPLORATION TEAM) LEINSTER, MURRAY   NV   ASF 56 03
  COLONIAL SURVEY   LEINSTER, MURRAY   NO
COMBAT UNIT (ALSO AS DINOCHROME)
                              LAUMER, KEITH   SS   FSF 60 11
  BOLO   LAUMER, KEITH   AC
COME AND GO MAD   BROWN, FREDRIC   NV   WRT 49 07
  BEST OF FREDRIC BROWN, THE   BROWN, FREDRIC   AC
  DAYMARES   BROWN, FREDRIC   AC
  SPACE ON MY HANDS   BROWN, FREDRIC   AC
  UNEXPECTED, THE   MARGULIES, LEO   AN
COME FYGURES, COME SHADOWES   MATHESON, RICHARD   NV   NEW 70 AC
  SHOCK WAVES   MATHESON, RICHARD   AC
COME IN, SPACEPORT   REYNOLDS, MACK   SS   GOM 74
  BEST OF MACK REYNOLDS, THE   REYNOLDS, MACK   AC
COME INTO MY CELLAR (ALSO AS BOYS, RAISE GIANT MUSHROOMS
  IN YOUR CELLAR)   BRADBURY, RAY   SS   GAL 62 10
  NIGHTMARE GARDEN   GHIDALIA, VIC   AN
  S IS FOR SPACE   BRADBURY, RAY   AC
  SEVENTH GALAXY READER, THE   POHL, FREDERIK   AN
  17 X INFINITY   CONKLIN, GROFF   AN
COME INTO MY PARLOR   FRITCH, CHARLES E. SS   SFA 53 02
  CRAZY MIXED-UP PLANET   FRITCH, CHARLES E.   AC
COME INTO MY PARLOR   WELLMAN, MANLY WADE SS   49
  GIRL WITH THE HUNGRY EYES, AND OTHER STORIES, THE
                              WOLLHEIM, DONALD A. OA
  ROOTS OF EVIL, THE   PARRY, MICHEL   AN
COME LADY DEATH   BEAGLE, PETER S.   SS   ATL 63 09
  NEW WORLDS OF FANTASY   CARR, TERRY   AN
COME ON, WAGON!   HENDERSON, ZENNA   SS   FSF 51 12
  ANYTHING BOX, THE   HENDERSON, ZENNA   AC
  BEST FROM FANTASY AND SCIENCE FICTION: 2
                              BOUCHER & MCCOMAS   AN
COME SEE THE LAST MAN CRY   HOLLY, J. HUNTER   NA
  TOMORROW: NEW WORLDS OF SCIENCE FICTION ELWOOD, ROGER   OA
COME SING THE MOONS OF MORAVENN
                              BRACKETT, LEIGH   NV
  OTHER SIDE OF TOMORROW, THE   ELWOOD, ROGER   OA
COME TAKE A DIP WITH ME IN THE GENETIC POOL
                              PAYES, RACHEL C.   SS   DYS 75
  DYSTOPIAN VISIONS   ELWOOD, ROGER   OA
COME TO ME NOT IN WINTER'S WHITE
                              ELLISON, HARLAN
  AND ZELAZNY, ROGER   SS C FSF 69 10
  PARTNERS IN WONDER   ELLISON, HARLAN   AC
COME TO VENUS MELANCHOLY   DISCH, THOMAS M.   SS   FSF 65 11
  ALPHA 3   SILVERBERG, ROBERT   AN
  BEST SF 7   CRISPIN, EDMUND   AN
  FUN WITH YOUR NEW HEAD   DISCH, THOMAS M.   AC
  LATE GREAT FUTURE, THE   FITZ GERALD & DILLON   AN
COME UP AND SEE ME   CASTELL, DAPHNE   SS   ANA 70
  ALCHEMY AND ACADEME   MCCAFFREY, ANNE   AN
COMEDIAN'S CHILDREN, THE   STURGEON, THEODORE NV   VSF 58 05
  ALIENS 4   STURGEON, THEODORE   AC

JOYOUS INVASION, THE   STURGEON, THEODORE   AC
NO LIMITS   FERMAN, JOSEPH W.   AN
SF:59, THE YEAR'S GREATEST SCIENCE FICTION AND FANTASY
                                  MERRIL, JUDITH   AN
  STRANGE TOMORROWS   HOSKINS, ROBERT   AN
COMEDY OF ERAS, THE   KENT, KELVIN   SS   TWS 40 09
  OTHER WORLDS, THE   STONG, PHILIP D.   AN
COMES NOW THE POWER   ZELAZNY, ROGER   SS   MOH 66 WI
  BEYOND TOMORROW   HARDING, LEE   AN
COMET DRIVERS, THE   HAMILTON, EDMOND NV   WRT 30 02
  CRASHING SUNS   HAMILTON, EDMOND   AC
COMET WINE   RUSSELL, RAY   NV   PBY 67 03
  NEW WORLDS OF FANTASY   CARR, TERRY   AN
  PLAYBOY BOOK OF HORROR AND THE SUPERNATURAL, THE
                                  PLAYBOY, EDITORS OF   AN
  SAGITTARIUS   RUSSELL, RAY   AC
COMFORT ME, MY ROBOT BLOCH, ROBERT   SS   IMG 55 01
  ATOMS AND EVIL   BLOCH, ROBERT   AC
COMIC INFERNO   ALDISS, BRIAN W. NA   GAL 63 02
  BOOK OF BRIAN ALDISS, THE   ALDISS, BRIAN W.   AC
  EIGHTH GALAXY READER, THE   POHL, FREDERIK   AN
  SCIENCE FICTION HORIZONS NO. 1 BOARDMAN, TOM JR.   AN
COMING ATTRACTION   LEIBER, FRITZ   SS   GAL 50 11
  BEST OF FRITZ LEIBER, THE   LEIBER, FRITZ   AC
  BEST SCIENCE-FICTION STORIES: 1951, THE BLEILER & DIKTY AN
  *GALAXY READER OF SCIENCE FICTION GOLD, H. L.   AN
  MASTERS' CHOICE   JANIFER, LAURENCE M.   AN
  MODERN MASTERPIECES OF SCIENCE FICTION MOSKOWITZ, SAM   AN
  PAIL OF AIR, A   LEIBER, FRITZ   AC
  SCIENCE FICTION HALL OF FAME VOLUME 1 SILVERBERG, ROBERT AN
  SECRET SONGS, THE   LEIBER, FRITZ   AC
  VORTEX BLASTERS, THE   MOSKOWITZ, SAM   AN
COMING BACK TO DIXIELAND ROBINSON, KIM S. SS   ORB 76 18
  ORBIT 18   KNIGHT, DAMON   AN
COMING FROM BEHIND   HARRISON, M. JOHN SS   NWQ 73 05
  MACHINE IN SHAFT TEN AND OTHER STORIES, THE
                                  HARRISON, M. JOHN   AC
  NEW WORLDS NO. 5   MOORCOCK & PLATT   OA
COMING OF BAST, THE   HOWARD, ROBERT E. PM
  LONE STAR UNIVERSE   PROCTOR & UTLEY   OA
COMING OF THE ICE, THE WERTENBAKER, G. P. SS   AMZ 26 06
  HISTORY OF THE SCIENCE FICTION MAGAZINE, THE PART 1 1926-1935
                                  ASHLEY, MICHAEL   AN
COMING OF THE SUN, THE JONES, LANGDON SS   NWS 68 03
  EYE OF THE LENS, THE   JONES, LANGDON   AC
  SF: AUTHORS' CHOICE 3   HARRISON, HARRY   AN
COMING OF THE UNCONSCIOUS, THE BALLARD, J. G. BR NWS 66 07
  OVERLOADED MAN, THE   BALLARD, J. G.   AC
COMING RACE, THE (EXCERPT) LYTTON, EDWARD B. EX
  ANCIENT MYSTERIES READER, THE   HAINING, PETER   AN
COMING TO LIFE   HARRISON, M. JOHN MS   NWB 75 08
  NEW WORLDS EIGHT   BAILEY, HILARY   OA
COMING-OF-AGE DAY   JORGENSSON, A. K. SS   SCF 65 09
  ABOVE THE HUMAN LANDSCAPE   MCNELLY & STOVER   OA
  DARK STARS   SILVERBERG, ROBERT   AN
  FUTURE POWER   DANN & DOZOIS   OA
  11TH ANNUAL OF THE YEAR'S BEST S-F, THE MERRIL, JUDITH AN
COMING, THE   POULIN, A. JR.   PM   63
  SPECULATIONS   SANDERS, THOMAS E.   AN
COMIX   INOUYE, JON   SS
  NIGHT TIDE, A   INOUYE, JON   OC
COMMAND   KAHN, BERNARD I. NV   ASF 47 01
  GATES TO TOMORROW   NORTON, AN.&DONALD   AN
  SPACE SERVICE   NORTON, ANDRE   AN
COMMAND PERFORMANCE (ALSO AS ANYBODY ELSE LIKE ME?)
                      MILLER, WALTER M. JR NV GAL 52 11
  BEST SCIENCE-FICTION STORIES: 1953, THE BLEILER & DIKTY AN
  PENGUIN SCIENCE FICTION   ALDISS, BRIAN W.   AN
  SECOND GALAXY READER OF SCIENCE FICTION GOLD, H. L.   AN
COMMAND, THE   DE CAMP, L. SPRAGUE SS ASF 38 10
  DOORWAY INTO TIME   MOSKOWITZ, SAM   AN
  MODERN MASTERPIECES OF SCIENCE FICTION MOSKOWITZ, SAM   AN
COMMANDO RAID   HARRISON, HARRY   SS   NEW 70 AC
  PRIME NUMBER   HARRISON, HARRY   AC
COMMENCEMENT NIGHT   ASHBY, RICHARD   SS   ASF 53 08
  GIANTS UNLEASHED   CONKLIN, GROFF   AN
  SPECTRUM 5   AMIS & CONQUEST   AN
COMMENT ON FONDLY FAHRENHEIT BESTER, ALFRED   AR
  LIGHT FANTASTIC, THE   BESTER, ALFRED   AC
COMMITTEE OF THE WHOLE HERBERT, FRANK NV   GAL 65 04
  BEST OF FRANK HERBERT, THE   HERBERT, FRANK   AC
  SCIENCE FICTION INVENTIONS   KNIGHT, DAMON   AN
  WORLDS OF FRANK HERBERT, THE   HERBERT, FRANK   AN
COMMON DENOMINATOR   MACDONALD, JOHN D. SS GAL 51 07
  *GALAXY READER OF SCIENCE FICTION GOLD, H. L.   AN
COMMON SENSE   HEINLEIN, ROBERT A. NV ASF 41 10
  ORPHANS OF THE SKY   HEINLEIN, ROBERT A.   NO
COMMON TIME   BLISH, JAMES   SS   SFQ 53 08
  *BEST SCIENCE FICTION STORIES OF JAMES BLISH
                                  BLISH, JAMES   AC
  *GALACTIC CLUSTER   BLISH, JAMES   AC
  MIRROR OF INFINITY, THE   SILVERBERG, ROBERT   AN
  SECOND ORBIT   DOHERTY, G. D.   AN
  SHADOW OF TOMORROW   POHL, FREDERIK   AN
  SURVIVAL PRINTOUT   TOTAL EFFECT   AN
  TO THE STARS   SILVERBERG, ROBERT   AN
  YET MORE PENGUIN SCIENCE FICTION ALDISS, BRIAN W.   AN
COMMUNICANTS, THE   SLADEK, JOHN T.   NA
  NEW S.F., THE   JONES, LANGDON   AN
COMMUNICATION   SHAW, BOB   NV   FAN 70 06
  TOMORROW LIES IN AMBUSH   SHAW, BOB   AC
COMMUNICATORS, THE   ANDERSON, POUL   SN   INY 70 01
  INFINITY 1   HOSKINS, ROBERT   OA
COMMUNITY STUDY   OLIVER, CHAD   NV
  LONE STAR UNIVERSE   PROCTOR & UTLEY   OA

```
COMMUTER                     WHITE, JAMES       SS  NWR 73 21
  NEW WRITINGS IN SF. 21            CARNELL, JOHN        OA
COMMUTER'S PROBLEM           ELLISON, HARLAN    SS  FUN 57 06
  ELLISON WONDERLAND               ELLISON, HARLAN      AC
COMMUTER, THE                DICK, PHILIP K.    SS  AMZ 53 09
  BEYOND TOMORROW                  HARDING, LEE         AN
  BOOK OF PHILIP K. DICK, THE      DICK, PHILIP K.      AC
COMPANY PLANET               SCHMITZ, JAMES H.  NV  ASF 71 05
  TELZEY TOY, THE                  SCHMITZ, JAMES H.    NO
COMPANY STORE                SILVERBERG, ROBERT SS  STR 59 05
  STAR SCIENCE FICTION STORIES NO. 5  POHL, FREDERIK    OA
  SUNRISE ON MERCURY AND OTHER SCIENCE FICTION STORIES
                                   SILVERBERG, ROBERT   OA
                                   GREENBERG& OLANDER   AN
  TOMORROW, INC.
COMPASS, THE                 CORMAN, CID        PM       67
  SPECULATIONS                     SANDERS, THOMAS E.   AN
COMPASSION CIRCUIT           WYNDHAM, JOHN      SS  FUN 54 12
  SEEDS OF TIME, THE               WYNDHAM, JOHN        AC
  SPECTRUM 4                       AMIS & CONQUEST      AN
  TALES OF GOOSEFLESH AND LAUGHTER WYNDHAM, JOHN        AC
  13 GREAT STORIES OF SCIENCE FICTION  CONKLIN, GROFF   AN
COMPETITION                  HULL, E. MAYNE     SS  ASF 43 06
  *MEN AGAINST THE STARS           GREENBERG , MARTIN   AN
  PLANETS FOR SALE                 HULL, E. MAYNE       AC
COMPETITORS, THE             LAWSON, JACK B.    NV  IFS 64 01
  WORLD'S BEST SCIENCE FICTION: 1965  WOLLHEIM & CARR   AN
COMPLEAT CONSUMATORS, THE    NOURSE, ALAN E.    SS  FSF 64 04
  BEST FROM FANTASY AND SCIENCE FICTION: 14
                                   DAVIDSON, AVRAM      AN
  MARRIAGE AND THE FAMILY THROUGH SCIENCE FICTION
                                   CLEAR/WARRICK/&      AN
COMPLEAT WEREWOLF, THE       BOUCHER, ANTHONY   NV  UNK 42 04
  *BEYOND HUMAN KEN                MERRIL, JUDITH       AN
  COMPLEAT WEREWOLF, THE           BOUCHER, ANTHONY     AC
  FROM UNKNOWN WORLDS              CAMPBELL, JOHN W. JR AN
COMPLETE FATHER, A           BUNCH, DAVID R.    SS  FAN 60 01
  MODERAN                          BUNCH, DAVID R.      AC
COMPLETE SHORT STORIES, THE  DISCH, THOMAS M.   GR
  *GETTING INTO DEATH              DISCH, THOMAS M.     AC
COMPLETELY AUTOMATIC         STURGEON, THEODORE SS  ASF 41 02
  *POSSIBLE WORLDS OF SCIENCE FICTION CONKLIN, GROFF    AN
COMPLIMENTS OF THE AUTHOR    PADGETT, LEWIS     NV  UNK 42 10
  GNOME THERE WAS, A               PADGETT, LEWIS       AC
  LINE TO TOMORROW AND OTHER STORIES OF FANTASY AND SCIENCE
  FICTION                          PADGETT, LEWIS       AC
COMPOUND B                   FINK, DAVID H. MD. NV  NTL 54
  GREAT SCIENCE FICTION ABOUT DOCTORS CONKLIN, G&FABRICANT AN
  9 TALES OF SPACE AND TIME        HEALY, RAYMOND J.    OA
COMPOUND INTEREST            REYNOLDS, MACK     SS  FSF 56 08
  BEST OF MACK REYNOLDS, THE       REYNOLDS, MACK       AC
  SF: THE BEST OF THE BEST         MERRIL, JUDITH       AN
  SF:57, THE YEAR'S GREATEST SCIENCE FICTION AND FANTASY
                                   MERRIL, JUDITH       AN
COMPULSION                   SCHMITZ, JAMES H.  NV  ASF 70 06
  TELZEY TOY, THE                  SCHMITZ, JAMES H.    NO
COMPUTER COPS                HOCH, EDWARD D.    SS  NEW 69 04
  CRIME PREVENTION IN THE 30TH CENTURY SANTESSON, HANS S. AN
COMPUTER THAT FELL IN LOVE, THE
                             TIMPERLEY, ROSEMARY SS ADS 75 02
  ARMADA SCI-FI TWO                DAVIS, RICHARD       OA
COMPUTER THAT FOUGHT A DRAGON, THE
                             LEM, STANISLAW     SS
  OTHER WORLDS, OTHER SEAS         SUVIN, DARKO         AN
COMPUTER'S MATE              RACKHAM, JOHN      SS  NWR 66 08
  NEW WRITINGS IN SF.  8           CARNELL, JOHN        OA
COMPUTER- 2118, THE (THE REPLY)
                             GUNN, JAMES E.     NV  GAL 72 05
  LISTENERS, THE                   GUNN, JAMES E.       NO
COMPUTERS DON'T ARGUE        DICKSON, GORDON R. SS  ASF 65 09
  ANALOG 5                         CAMPBELL, JOHN W. JR AN
  ASTOUNDING-ANALOG READER, THE VOLUME TWO HARRISON & ALDISS AN
  DECADE THE 1960S                 ALDISS & HARRISON    AN
  NEBULA AWARD STORIES             KNIGHT, DAMON        AN
  TRANSFORMATIONS II               ROSELLE, DANIEL      AN
  WONDERMAKERS 2                   HOSKINS, ROBERT      AN
  YOU AND SCIENCE FICTION          HOLLISTER, BERNARD C AN
COMSAT ANGELS, THE           BALLARD, J. G.     SS  IFS 68 12
  LOW-FLYING AIRCRAFT AND OTHER STORIES BALLARD, J. G.  AC
CONAN THE VICTORIOUS (SEE THE RETURN OF CONAN)
                             DE CAMP, L. SPRAGUE
                             AND NYBERG, BJORN  TC C
CONAN, MAN OF DESTINY (SEE THE ROAD OF THE EAGLES)
                             DE CAMP, L. SPRAGUE
                             AND HOWARD, ROBERT E.  TC C
CONCEALMENT                  VAN VOGT, A. E.    SS  ASF 43 09
  GALACTIC EMPIRES VOLUME TWO      ALDISS, BRIAN W.     AN
  MIXED MEN, THE                   VAN VOGT, A. E.      NO
  MONSTERS                         VAN VOGT, A. E.      AC
CONCENTRATION CITY, THE (BUILD-UP)
                             BALLARD, J. G.     SS  NWS 57 01
  BEST OF J. G. BALLARD, THE       BALLARD, J. G.       AC
  DISASTER AREA, THE               BALLARD, J. G.       AC
CONCERNING SCIENCE FICTION   CAMPBELL, JOHN W. JR IN
  *BEST OF SCIENCE FICTION         CONKLIN, GROFF       AN
CONCERNING STORIES NEVER WRITTEN: POSTSCRIPT
                             HEINLEIN, ROBERT A.  MS
  REVOLT IN 2100                   HEINLEIN, ROBERT A.  AC
CONCRETE MIXER, THE          BRADBURY, RAY      SS  TWS 49 04
  *ILLUSTRATED MAN, THE            BRADBURY, RAY        AC
CONDEMNED TO DEATH (SEE AND YET SO FAR)
                             ANDERSON, POUL     TC
CONDILLAC'S STATUE           LAFFERTY, R. A.    SS  ANA 70
  ALCHEMY AND ACADEME              MCCAFFREY, ANNE      OA
CONDITION OF EMPLOYMENT      SIMAK, CLIFFORD D. SS  GAL 60 04
  *ALL THE TRAPS OF EARTH AND OTHER STORIES SIMAK, CLIFFORD D. AC
  NIGHT OF THE PUUDLY, THE         SIMAK, CLIFFORD D.   AC

CONDITIONALLY HUMAN          MILLER, WALTER M. JR NV GAL 52 02
  CONDITIONALLY HUMAN              MILLER, WALTER M. JR AC
  YEAR'S BEST SCIENCE FICTION NOVELS: 1953 BLEILER & DIKTY AN
  5 UNEARTHLY VISIONS              CONKLIN, GROFF       AN
CONDITIONED REFLEX           DOZOIS, GARDNER R. SS  GEN 72
  GENERATION                       GERROLD, DAVID       OA
CONDITIONED REFLEX (MIND OF TOMORROW)
                             DEL REY, LESTER    SS  FUT 51 05
  EARLY DEL REY                    DEL REY, LESTER      AC
CONE, THE                    WELLS, H. G.       SS  UCN 95 09
  COUNTRY OF THE BLIND, THE        WELLS, H. G.         AC
  DOOR IN THE WALL, THE            WELLS, H. G.         AC
  PLATTNER STORY AND OTHERS, THE   WELLS, H. G.         AC
  SHORT STORIES OF H. G. WELLS, THE WELLS, H. G.        AC
  THIRTY STRANGE STORIES           WELLS, H. G.         AC
CONES                        LONG, FRANK BELKNAP NV ASF 36 02
  *POSSIBLE WORLDS OF SCIENCE FICTION CONKLIN, GROFF    AN
  RIM OF THE UNKNOWN               LONG, FRANK BELKNAP  AC
CONFESSION, THE              VAN VOGT, A. E.    SS  NEW 72 AC
  BOOK OF VAN VOGT, THE            VAN VOGT, A. E.      AC
CONFESSIONS                  GOULART, RON       NV  FSF 70 08
  BEST FROM FANTASY AND SCIENCE FICTION: 19
                                   FERMAN, EDWARD L.    AN
  WHAT'S BECOME OF SCREWLOOSE? AND OTHER INQUIRIES
                                   GOULART, RON         AC
  WORLD'S BEST SCIENCE FICTION: 1971 WOLLHEIM & CARR    AN
CONFESSIONS OF A SCIENCE FICTION ADDICT
                             ACKERMAN, FORREST J. AR AFT 57
  SCIENCE FICTION WORLDS OF FORREST J. ACKERMAN & FRIENDS
                                   ACKERMAN, FORREST J. AC
CONFESSIONS OF THE FIRST NUMBER
                             OWSLEY, CLIFF      SS  SRV 63
  9TH ANNUAL OF THE YEAR'S BEST S-F, THE  MERRIL, JUDITH   AN
CONFETTI ROYALE (SEE THE BEACH MURDERS)
                             BALLARD, J. G.     TC  ROG 66 01
CONFIDENCE TRICK             WYNDHAM, JOHN      SS  FAN 53 08
  JIZZLE                           WYNDHAM, JOHN        AC
  TALES OF GOOSEFLESH AND LAUGHTER WYNDHAM, JOHN        AC
CONFIGURATION OF THE NORTH SHORE
                             LAFFERTY, R. A.    SS  ORB 69 05
  ORBIT  5                         KNIGHT, DAMON        OA
CONFLICT, THE                VARSHAVSKY, ILYA   SS
  PATH INTO THE UNKNOWN            ANONYMOUS            AN
CONFLUENCE                   ALDISS, BRIAN W.   SS  FUN 67 08
  MOMENT OF ECLIPSE, THE           ALDISS, BRIAN W.     AC
  SF12                             MERRIL, JUDITH       AN
CONFUSION CARGO              TENN, WILLIAM      SS  PLS 48 SP
  SQUARE ROOT OF MAN, THE          TENN, WILLIAM        AC
CONGEALING THE ICE TRUST     BISHOP, H. G.      SS  NBM 07 12
  SCIENCE FICTION BY GASLIGHT      MOSKOWITZ, SAM       AN
CONGO CAT, THE               WRIGHT, S. FOWLER  SS
  WITCHFINDER, THE                 WRIGHT, S. FOWLER    AC
CONGRUENT PEOPLE, THE        BUDRYS, ALGIS      SS  STR 53 02
  STAR SCIENCE FICTION STORIES NO. 2 POHL, FREDERIK     OA
CONJURE WIFE                 LEIBER, FRITZ      SN  UNK 43 04
  WITCHES THREE                    PRATT, FLETCHER      AN
CONNECTICUT YANKEE IN KING ARTHUR'S COURT, A
                             TWAIN, MARK        EX  HRP 89
  STORIES OF SCIENTIFIC IMAGINATION GALLANT, JOSEPH     AN
CONNECTION COMPLETED         MERRIL, JUDITH     SS  USF 54 SU
  OUT OF BOUNDS                    MERRIL, JUDITH       AC
  SURVIVAL SHIP AND OTHER STORIES  MERRIL, JUDITH       AC
CONQUEROR                    EISENBERG, LARRY   SS  IFS 67 10
  BEST LAID SCHEMES, THE           EISENBERG, LARRY     AC
CONQUEROR'S ISLE             BOND, NELSON S.    SS  BBM 46 06
  MR. MERGENTHWIRKER'S LOBBIES AND OTHER FANTASTIC TALES
                                   BOND, NELSON S.      AC
  NO TIME LIKE THE FUTURE          BOND, NELSON S.      AC
  *OTHER SIDE OF THE MOON, THE     DERLETH, AUGUST      AN
  STORIES OF SCIENTIFIC IMAGINATION GALLANT, JOSEPH     AN
  WORLD OF WONDER                  PRATT, FLETCHER      AN
CONQUEROR, THE               CLIFTON, MARK      SS  ASF 52 08
  BEST SCIENCE-FICTION STORIES: 1953, THE BLEILER & DIKTY AN
  MUTANTS                          SILVERBERG, ROBERT   AN
  OMNIBUS OF SCIENCE FICTION       CONKLIN, GROFF       AN
CONQUEROR, THE               MATHESON, RICHARD  SS       54
  SHOCK WAVES                      MATHESON, RICHARD    AC
CONQUEST                     BOUCHER, ANTHONY   SS  STR 53 02
  STAR SCIENCE FICTION STORIES NO. 2 POHL, FREDERIK     OA
CONQUEST                     MALZBERG, BARRY N. SS  NDM 71 01
  BEST SF: 1971                    HARRISON & ALDISS    AN
  NEW DIMENSIONS 1                 SILVERBERG, ROBERT   OA
CONQUEST                     WELLS, BASIL       SS
  DOORWAYS TO SPACE                WELLS, BASIL         AC
CONQUEST OF GOLA, THE        STONE, LESLIE F.   SS  WOS 31 04
  *BEST OF SCIENCE FICTION         CONKLIN, GROFF       AN
CONQUEST OF LIFE             BINDER, EANDO      SS  TWS 37 08
  ANTON YORK, IMMORTAL             BINDER, EANDO        AC
  FROM OFF THIS WORLD              MARGULIES & FRIEND   AN
CONQUEST OF MARS, THE        MALZBERG, BARRY N. SS  NOV 72 02
  OUT FROM GANYMEDE                MALZBERG, BARRY N.   AC
CONQUEST OF THE AIR, THE (FROM "THE BALLOON HOAX")
                             POE, EDGAR ALLEN   EX  SUN 44 04
  SCIENCE FICTION THROUGH THE AGES 1 EVANS, I. O.       AN
CONQUEST OF THE MOON, THE    IRVING, WASHINGTON SS
  ABC OF SCIENCE FICTION, AN        BOARDMAN, TOM JR.   AN
  TRANSFORMATIONS II               ROSELLE, DANIEL      AN
CONQUEST OF TWO WORLDS, A    HAMILTON, EDMOND   NV  WOS 32 02
  BEST OF EDMOND HAMILTON, THE     HAMILTON, EDMOND     AC
  EVERY BOY'S BOOK OF SCIENCE FICTION WOLLHEIM, DONALD A. AN
CONSCIENCE OF THE KING, THE (BARRY TRIVERS)
                             BLISH, JAMES       SA  STK 67 01
  STAR TREK                        BLISH, JAMES         OC
CONSIDER HER WAYS            WYNDHAM, JOHN      NV       56
  BEST SF 5                        CRISPIN, EDMUND      AN
  CONSIDER HER WAYS AND OTHERS     WYNDHAM, JOHN        AC
```

INFINITE MOMENT, THE   WYNDHAM, JOHN   AC
SCIENCE FICTION ARGOSY, A   KNIGHT, DAMON   AN
SOMETIME, NEVER   ANONYMOUS   OA
WORLDS APART   WILLIAMS-ELLIS& OWEN   AN
CONSIDERATE HOSTS, THE   MCCLUSKY, THORP   SS   WRT 39 12
OTHER WORLDS, THE   STONG, PHILIP D.   AN
CONSORT   POURNELLE, JERRY SS   ASF 75 08
HIGH JUSTICE   POURNELLE, JERRY   AC
CONSPIRACY   CHRISTOPHER, JOHN SS   AUT 55 01
GATEWAY TO THE STARS   CARNELL, JOHN   AN
CONSPIRACY ON CALLISTO   POHL, FREDERIK   SS   PLS 43 WI
EARLY POHL, THE   POHL, FREDERIK   AC
CONSPIRACY, THE   LOWRY, ROBERT   SS   58
FIEND IN YOU, THE   BEAUMONT, CHARLES   AN
CONSPIRACY, THE   SPINRAD, NORMAN   SS   NWS 69 02
NO DIRECTION HOME   SPINRAD, NORMAN   AC
CONSPIRATORS, THE   WHITE, JAMES   NV   NWS 54 06
ALIENS AMONG US, THE   WHITE, JAMES   AC
MIND TO MIND   SILVERBERG, ROBERT   AN
*SCIENCE FICTION ADVENTURES IN MUTATION CONKLIN, GROFF   AN
CONSTANT READER   BLOCH, ROBERT   SS   USF 53 06
ATOMS AND EVIL   BLOCH, ROBERT   AC
SCIENCE FACT/FICTION   FARRELL/GAGE/&   AN
SPACE MAGICIANS, THE   NORTON & MOSKOWITZ   AN
CONSTITUTION IN E FLAT   CARTER, PAUL A.   SS   GEN 72
GENERATION   GERROLD, DAVID   OA
CONSTRUCTION SHACK   SIMAK, CLIFFORD D. SS IFS 73 02
BEST FROM IF, THE VOLUME II   IF, EDITORS OF   AN
BEST SCIENCE FICTION STORIES OF THE YEAR (1973)
                                        DEL REY, LESTER   AN
1974 ANNUAL WORLD'S BEST SF, THE   WOLLHEIM, DONALD A.   AN
CONSULATE   TENN, WILLIAM   SS   TWS 48 06
SQUARE ROOT OF MAN, THE   TENN, WILLIAM   AC
CONSUMER'S REPORT (NO GUN TO THE VICTOR)
                            COGSWELL, THEODORE R SS IMG 55 10
SF: AUTHORS' CHOICE   HARRISON, HARRY   AN
VOYAGES: SCENARIOS FOR A SHIP CALLED EARTH
                                        SAUER, ROB   AN
YOU AND SCIENCE FICTION   HOLLISTER, BERNARD C   AN
CONSUMING PASSION   MOORCOCK, MICHAEL SS   NWS 66 04
TIME DWELLER, THE   MOORCOCK, MICHAEL   AC
CONTACT   BROWN, FREDRIC   SS
NIGHTMARES AND GEEZENSTACKS   BROWN, FREDRIC   AC
CONTACT BETWEEN EQUALS   BUDRYS, ALGIS   SS   VSF 58 07
BUDRYS' INFERNO   BUDRYS, ALGIS   AC
SF: AUTHORS' CHOICE 2   HARRISON, HARRY   AN
CONTACT MAN   HARRISON, HARRY   SS   66
PRIME NUMBER   HARRISON, HARRY   AC
CONTACT POINT   COGSWELL, GEORGE RAE
                    AND COGSWELL, THEODORE R PL C   75
SIX SCIENCE FICTION PLAYS   ELWOOD, ROGER   AN
CONTACT WITH ANOTHER CIVILISATION
                            LUNAN, DUNCAN   AR
BEYOND THIS HORIZON   CARRELL, CHRISTOPHER OA
CONTACT, INCORPORATED (ACTION ON AZURA)
                            OSBORNE, ROBERTSON NV PLS 49 FL
*BIG BOOK OF SCIENCE FICTION   CONKLIN, GROFF   AN
CONTACT, THE   COLIN, VLADIMIR   SS
OTHER WORLDS, OTHER SEAS   SUVIN, DARKO   AN
CONTAGION   MACLEAN, KATHERINE NV GAL 50 10
BEST SCIENCE-FICTION STORIES: 1951, THE BLEILER & DIKTY   AN
MINDWORM, THE   ANONYMOUS   AN
*POSSIBLE WORLDS OF SCIENCE FICTION   CONKLIN, GROFF   AN
WOMEN OF WONDER   SARGENT, PAMELA   AN
CONTAMINATION CREW   NOURSE, ALAN E.   SS   IFS 58 02
RX FOR TOMORROW   NOURSE, ALAN E.   AC
CONTENTMENT, SATISFACTION, CHEER, WELL-BEING, GLADNESS, JOY,
COMFORT, AND NOT HAVING... EFFINGER, GEO. ALEC NV   76
FUTURE POWER   DANN & DOZOIS   OA
CONTENTS OF THE DEAD MAN'S POCKETS
                            FINNEY, JACK   NV   NEW 57 AC
NIGHT IN FUNLAND   BRONDFIELD, JEROME   AN
THIRD LEVEL, THE   FINNEY, JACK   AC
CONTEST, THE   DISCH, THOMAS M. SS   NWS 67 03
BEST SF STORIES FROM NEW WORLDS NO. 2, THE
                                        MOORCOCK, MICHAEL   AN
FUN WITH YOUR NEW HEAD   DISCH, THOMAS M.   AC
CONTINENT MAKERS, THE   DE CAMP, L. SPRAGUE NA TWS 51 04
CONTINENT MAKERS AND OTHER TALES OF THE VIAGENS
                            DE CAMP, L. SPRAGUE   AC
CONTINUED ON NEXT ROCK   LAFFERTY, R. A.   NV   ORB 70 07
BEST FROM ORBIT, THE   KNIGHT, DAMON   AN
NEBULA AWARD STORIES NO. 6   SIMAK, CLIFFORD D.   AN
ORBIT 7   KNIGHT, DAMON   OA
SPECULATIONS   SANDERS, THOMAS E.   AN
STRANGE DOINGS   LAFFERTY, R. A.   AC
WORLD'S BEST SCIENCE FICTION: 1971   WOLLHEIM & CARR   AN
CONTINUING WESTWARD   WOLFE, GENE   SS   ORB 73 12
ORBIT 12   KNIGHT, DAMON   OA
CONTINUOUS LANDSCAPE   SIMPSON, DONALD   AR   QRK 71 03
QUARK/3   DELANY & HACKER   OA
CONTRABAND COW, THE   DE CAMP, L. SPRAGUE SS ASF 42 07
WHEELS OF IF, THE   DE CAMP, L. SPRAGUE   AC
CONTRACT, THE   HULL, E. MAYNE   NV   ASF 44 03
PLANETS FOR SALE   HULL, E. MAYNE   AC
CONTRAPTION   SIMAK, CLIFFORD D. SS STR 53 01
STAR SCIENCE FICTION STORIES   POHL, FREDERIK   OA
*STRANGERS IN THE UNIVERSE   SIMAK, CLIFFORD D.   AC
CONTRIBUTORS   MISC. MATERIAL   MS
CHRONICLES OF A COMER AND OTHER RELIGIOUS SCIENCE FICTION
STORIES   ELWOOD, ROGER   AN
CONTRIBUTORS TO PLENUM FOUR, THE
                            BISHOP, MICHAEL   SS   NDM 75 05
NEW DIMENSIONS 5   SILVERBERG, ROBERT   OA
CONTRIBUTORS' NOTES   MISC. MATERIAL   MS
QUARK/1   DELANY & HACKER   OA

QUARK/3   DELANY & HACKER   OA
CONTRIBUTORS, THE   MISC. MATERIAL   MS
FASTER THAN LIGHT   DANN & ZEBROWSKI   OA
CONTROL ROOM   SELLINGS, ARTHUR SS
*TIME TRANSFER   SELLINGS, ARTHUR   AC
CONTROL SOMNAMBULE   SAMBROT, WILLIAM SS   PBY 62 05
FROM THE "S" FILE   PLAYBOY, EDITORS OF   AN
ISLAND OF FEAR AND OTHER SCIENCE FICTION SAMBROT, WILLIAM   AN
TRANSIT OF EARTH   PLAYBOY, EDITORS OF   AN
CONTROLLED EXPERIMENT   OLIVER, CHAD   SS   OSF 54 11
SPACE STATION 42 AND OTHER STORIES   ANONYMOUS   AN
CONVENIENT MONSTER, THE   CHARTERIS, LESLIE SS
ANCIENT MYSTERIES READER, THE   HAINING, PETER   AN
CONVENTIONAL ENDING   COGSWELL, THEODORE R SS FUT 54 10
THIRD EYE, THE   COGSWELL, THEODORE R   AC
CONVERGENT SERIES (THE LONG NIGHT)
                            NIVEN, LARRY   SS   FSF 67 03
SHAPE OF SPACE, THE   NIVEN, LARRY   AC
CONVERSATION OF EIROS AND CHARMION, THE
                            POE, EDGAR ALLEN SS   BGM 39 12
ECO-FICTION   STADLER, JOHN   AN
IN DREAMS AWAKE   FIEDLER, LESLIE A.   AN
TREASURY OF SCIENCE FICTION CLASSICS, THE
                                        KUEBLER, HAROLD W.   AN
CONVERSATION ON A STARSHIP IN WARPDRIVE
                            BROSNAN, JOHN   SS   NEW 76 AN
ANTIGRAV: COSMIC COMEDIES   STRICK, PHILIP   AN
CONVERSATION WITH A BUG   SHARKEY, JACK   SS   PBY 61 10
FROM THE "S" FILE   PLAYBOY, EDITORS OF   AN
CONVERSATIONAL MODE   LEMAN, GRAHAME   SS   NWR 72 20
BEST SCIENCE FICTION FOR 1972   POHL, FREDERIK   AN
BEST SCIENCE FICTION OF THE YEAR, THE NO. 2
                                        CARR, TERRY   AN
INFINITE JESTS   SILVERBERG, ROBERT   AN
NEW WRITINGS IN SF. 20   CARNELL, JOHN   OA
CONVERSATIONS AT LOTHAR'S   MALZBERG, BARRY N. SS COI 73
CHILDREN OF INFINITY   ELWOOD, ROGER   OA
LIBERATED FUTURE: VOYAGES INTO TOMORROW, THE
                                        HOSKINS, ROBERT   AN
CONVERSATIONS AT MA MAIA METRON
                            MEADLEY, ROBERT   SS   NWB 75 08
NEW WORLDS EIGHT   BAILEY, HILARY   OA
CONVERT, THE   PURDY, KEN W.   SS   PBY 70 03
WEIRD SHOW   PLAYBOY, EDITORS OF   AN
CONVICTION   ALDISS, BRIAN W. SS   NWS 56 09
SPACE, TIME AND NATHANIEL   ALDISS, BRIAN W.   AC
COOK'S TALE, A   HARRISON, WILLIAM NV   66
ROLLERBALL   HARRISON, WILLIAM   AC
COOKIE LADY, THE   DICK, PHILIP K.   SS   FNP 53 06
HANDFUL OF DARKNESS, A   DICK, PHILIP K.   AC
COOL AIR   LOVECRAFT, H. P. SS   TMM 28 03
HORROR TIMES TEN   NORTON, ALDEN H.   AC
COP-OUT   O'DONNELL, K. M. SS   ESC 68
FAR-OUT PEOPLE, THE   HOSKINS, ROBERT   AN
FINAL WAR AND OTHER FANTASIES   O'DONNELL, K. M.   DC
COPPER DAHLIA, THE   KERSH, GERALD   SS   53
BEST SF 2   CRISPIN, EDMUND   AN
COPPERSMITH, THE   DEL REY, LESTER   SS   UNK 39 09
*AND SOME WERE HUMAN   DEL REY, LESTER   AC
ROBOTS AND CHANGELINGS   DEL REY, LESTER   AC
COPSTATE   GOULART, RON   SS   FSF 69 05
CHAMELEON CORPS & OTHER SHAPE CHANGERS, THE
                                        GOULART, RON   AC
COR SERPENTIS   YEFREMOV, IVAN   NV
RUSSIAN SCIENCE FICTION   MAGIDOFF, ROBERT   AN
CORA AND THE GREAT WIDE WORLD OVER THERE (SEE THE GREAT WIDE
WORLD OVER THERE)   BRADBURY, RAY   TC
CORANDA   ROBERTS, KEITH   SS   NWS 67 01
BEST SF STORIES FROM NEW WORLDS 3   MOORCOCK, MICHAEL   AC
PASSING OF THE DRAGONS, THE   ROBERTS, KEITH   AC
WORLD'S BEST SCIENCE FICTION: 1968   WOLLHEIM & CARR   AN
CORBIE DOOR, THE   JACOBI, CARL   SS   WRT 47 05
PORTRAITS IN MOONLIGHT   JACOBI, CARL   AC
CORDLE TO ONION TO CARROT   SHECKLEY, ROBERT SS   PBY 69 12
CAN YOU FEEL ANYTHING WHEN I DO THIS?, AND OTHER STORIES
                                        SHECKLEY, ROBERT   AC
FROM THE "S" FILE   PLAYBOY, EDITORS OF   AN
CORDWAINER SMITH: THE SHAPER OF MYTHS
                            PIERCE, J. J.   IN
BEST OF CORDWAINER SMITH, THE   SMITH, CORDWAINER   AC
CORFE GATE   ROBERTS, KEITH   NV   IMP 66 07
PAVANE   ROBERTS, KEITH   NO
CORIANIS DISASTER, THE   LEINSTER, MURRAY NV   SFS 60 05
SEVEN COME INFINITY   CONKLIN, GROFF   AN
CORNER FOR LUCIA, A   DERLETH, AUGUST   SS   WRT 53 05
HARRIGAN'S FILE   DERLETH, AUGUST   AC
CORNER IN LIGHTNING, A   GRIFFITH, GEORGE SS   PRS 98 03
ANCESTRAL VOICES   MENVILLE & REGINALD   AN
GAMBLES WITH DESTINY   GRIFFITH, GEORGE   AC
SCIENCE FICTION BY GASLIGHT   MOSKOWITZ, SAM   AN
CORNZAN THE MIGHTY   DE CAMP, L. SPRAGUE SS FUT 55 28
GUN FOR DINOSAUR AND OTHER IMAGINATIVE TALES
                                        DE CAMP, L. SPRAGUE   AC
CORONA   DELANY, SAMUEL R. SS   FSF 67 10
BEST FROM FANTASY AND SCIENCE FICTION: 17
                                        FERMAN, EDWARD L.   AN
DRIFTGLASS   DELANY, SAMUEL R.   AC
LOOKING AHEAD   ALLEN, D. & L.   AC
CORPSE   ELLISON, HARLAN   SS   FSF 72 01
DEATHBIRD STORIES   ELLISON, HARLAN   AC
CORPUS DELECTABLE   DE CAMP, L. SPRAGUE
                    AND PRATT, FLETCHER   SS C NEW 53 AC
TALES FROM GAVAGAN'S BAR   DE CAMP, L. S.&PRATT   AC
CORRESPONDENCE COURSE   JONES, RAYMOND F. SS   ASF 45 04
*ADVENTURES IN TIME AND SPACE   HEALY & MCCOMAS   AN

CORRESPONDING WITH THE PLANETS   CRAZY ANNAOJ

```
CORRESPONDING WITH THE PLANETS LACH-SZYRMA, D. S.    SS   CSL 93 06
  WORLDS APART                     LOCKE, GEORGE             AN
CORRIDA                       ZELAZNY, ROGER      SS        68
  DOORS OF HIS FACE, THE LAMPS OF HIS MOUTH, THE
                                ZELAZNY, ROGER              AC
CORRIDA (BY RAINER MARIA RILKE, TRANSLATION)
                              BRUNNER, JOHN       PM    CHP 73
  BOOK OF JOHN BRUNNER, THE        BRUNNER, JOHN             AC
CORRUPTION                    RUSS, JOANNA        SS
  AURORA: BEYOND EQUALITY          MCINTYRE & ANDERSON   OA
CORRUPTION OF METALS          DORMAN, SONYA       PM
  2076: THE AMERICAN TRICENTENNIAL BRYANT, EDWARD           OA
COSMIC CASANOVA               CLARKE, ARTHUR C.   SS   VSF 58 05
  OTHER SIDE OF THE SKY, THE       CLARKE, ARTHUR C.         AC
COSMIC CHARGE ACCOUNT, THE(ALSO AS THE COSMIC EXPENSE ACCOUNT)
                              KORNBLUTH, C. M.    NV   FSF 56 01
  MARCHING MORONS AND OTHER SCIENCE FICTION
                              KORNBLUTH, C. M.          AC
COSMIC CLOUD, THE             HAMILTON, EDMOND    NV   WRT 30 11
  CRASHING SUNS                    HAMILTON, EDMOND          AC
COSMIC COCKTAIL PARTY, THE (HAROLD WILSON AT THE COSMIC
  COCKTAIL PARTY)             SHAW, BOB           SS   SAG 70
  TOMORROW LIES IN AMBUSH          SHAW, BOB                 AC
COSMIC EXPENSE ACCOUNT, THE (THE COSMIC CHARGE ACCOUNT)
                              KORNBLUTH, C. M.    NV   FSF 56 01
  BEST FROM FANTASY AND SCIENCE FICTION: 6
                              BOUCHER, ANTHONY          AN
  SF:57, THE YEAR'S GREATEST SCIENCE FICTION AND FANTASY
                              MERRIL, JUDITH            AN
COSMIC EXPRESS, THE           WILLIAMSON, JACK    SS   AMZ 30 11
  EARLY WILLIAMSON, THE            WILLIAMSON, JACK          AC
  PANDORA EFFECT, THE              WILLIAMSON, JACK          AC
  STRANGE SIGNPOSTS                ELWOOD & MOSKOWITZ        AN
COSMIC JACKPOT, THE           SMITH, GEORGE O.    SS   TWS 48 10
  *SCIENCE-FICTION CARNIVAL        BROWN, F. & REYNOLDS  AN
COSMIC MEGILLAH, THE          CONRAD, EARL        SS
  DA VINCI MACHINE, THE            CONRAD, EARL              OC
COSMIC POACHERS, THE          DICK, PHILIP K.     SS   IMG 53 07
  ALIEN WORLDS                     ELWOOD, ROGER             AN
COSMIC RELIC, THE             RUSSELL, ERIC FRANK NV   FAN 61 06
  HUMAN ZERO, THE                  MOSKOWITZ & ELWOOD        AN
COST OF LIVING                SHECKLEY, ROBERT    SS   GAL 52 12
  *UNTOUCHED BY HUMAN HANDS        SHECKLEY, ROBERT          AC
COTTAGE TENANT                LONG, FRANK BELKNAP NV   FAN 75 04
  YEAR'S BEST HORROR STORIES: SERIES IV, THE
                              PAGE, GERALD W.           AN
COTTAGE, THE                  LONG, FRANK BELKNAP SS   FUN 54 09
  RIM OF THE UNKNOWN               LONG, FRANK BELKNAP       AC
COTTONWOOD TREE, THE          DISCH, THOMAS M.    SS
  *GETTING INTO DEATH              DISCH, THOMAS M.          AC
COUNCIL OF THE DRONES, THE    SONNEMANN, W. K.    NV   AMZ 36 10
  SCIENCE FICTION OF THE 30'S      KNIGHT, DAMON             AN
COUNT D'UNADIX                OBTULOWICZ, MAREK   SS   NWQ 73 05
  NEW WORLDS NO. 5                 MOORCOCK & PLATT          OA
COUNT DOWN TO DOOM            ACKERMAN, FORREST J.
                              AND NUETZEL, CHARLES  SS C FMS 66
  SCIENCE FICTION WORLDS OF FORREST J. ACKERMAN & FRIENDS
                              ACKERMAN, FORREST J. AC
COUNTDOWN                     WILHELM, KATE       SS   NEW 68 AC
  DOWNSTAIRS ROOM AND OTHER SPECULATIVE FICTION, THE
                              WILHELM, KATE             AC
COUNTDOWN, THE                HAASE, JOHN         SS   NYM 61 10
  7TH ANNUAL OF THE YEAR'S BEST S-F, THE  MERRIL, JUDITH  AN
COUNTENANCE, THE              WOODS, P. F.        NV   NWS 64 01
  BEST SF STORIES FROM NEW WORLDS NO. 2, THE
                              MOORCOCK, MICHAEL         AN
COUNTER CHARM                 PHILLIPS, PETER     SS   SLN 51 SP
  FIFTY SHORT SCIENCE FICTION TALES    ASIMOV & CONKLIN  AN
  OMNIBUS OF SCIENCE FICTION       CONKLIN, GROFF            AN
COUNTER CHARM, THE            ST. CLAIR, MARGARET SS   FFM 49 08
  ANDROIDS, TIME MACHINES AND BLUE GIRAFFES
                              ELWOOD & GHIDALIA         AN
COUNTER ECOLOGY               KAGAN, NORMAN       SS
  TOMORROW TODAY                   ZEBROWSKI, GEORGE         OA
COUNTER FOIL                  SMITH, GEORGE O.    NV   ASF 64 04
  MEN AND MACHINES                 SILVERBERG, ROBERT        AN
COUNTER SECURITY              WHITE, JAMES        NV   FSF 63 02
  MONSTERS AND MEDICS              WHITE, JAMES              AC
  13 ABOVE THE NIGHT               CONKLIN, GROFF            AN
COUNTER-TRANSFERENCE          TEMPLE, WILLIAM F.  NV   TWS 52 04
  BEST SCIENCE-FICTION STORIES: 1953, THE BLEILER & DIKTY AN
COUNTERCHARM                  WHITE, JAMES        SS   NWS 60 11
  ALIENS AMONG US, THE             WHITE, JAMES              AN
  ALIENS, THE                      SILVERBERG, ROBERT        AN
COUNTERCOMMANDMENT            MEADOWS, PATRICK    SS   ASF 65 12
  ANALOG 7                         CAMPBELL, JOHN W. JR      AN
COUNTERFEIT (ALSO AS THE COUNTERFEIT MAN)
                              NOURSE, ALAN E.     NV   TWS 52 08
  MORE PENGUIN SCIENCE FICTION     ALDISS, BRIAN W.          AN
COUNTERFEIT MAN, THE (COUNTERFEIT)
                              NOURSE, ALAN E.     NV   TWS 52 08
  COUNTERFEIT MAN, THE             NOURSE, ALAN E.           AC
COUNTERPART                   SILVERBERG, ROBERT  NV   FUN 59 10
  PARSECS AND PARABLES             SILVERBERG, ROBERT        AC
COUNTERPOINT                  HALDEMAN, JOE W.    SS   ORB 72 11
  ORBIT 11                         KNIGHT, DAMON             OA
COUNTERPOINT OF VIEW, THE     HEIDENRY, JOHN      MS   DVS 72 02
  AGAIN, DANGEROUS VISIONS         ELLISON, HARLAN           OA
COUNTERSPY                    EDWARDS, KELLEY     SS   ASF 53 12
  BEST SF 3                        CRISPIN, EDMUND           AN
COUNTESS KATHLEEN O'SHEA      ANONYMOUS           SS
  DEALS WITH THE DEVIL             DAVENPORT, BASIL          AN
COUNTRY BOY, THE              EDMONDSON, G. C.    SS   FSF 61 05
  STRANGER THAN YOU THINK          EDMONDSON, G. C.          DC
COUNTRY DOCTOR                MORRISON, WILLIAM   NV   STR 53 01
  STAR OF STARS                    POHL, FREDERIK            AN

  STAR SCIENCE FICTION STORIES     POHL, FREDERIK            OA
  WHERE DO WE GO FROM HERE?        ASIMOV, ISAAC             AN
  ZOO 2000                         YOLEN, JANE               AN
COUNTRY OF THE BLIND, THE     WELLS, H. G.        SS   SND 04 04
  COUNTRY OF THE BLIND, THE        WELLS, H. G.              AC
  DOOR IN THE WALL, THE            WELLS, H. G.              AC
  INEXPERIENCED GHOST AND NINE OTHER STORIES, THE
                              WELLS, H. G.              AC
  MASTERPIECES OF SCIENCE FICTION  MOSKOWITZ, SAM            AN
  SCIENCE FICTION: THE FUTURE      ALLEN, DICK               AN
  SHORT STORIES OF H. G. WELLS, THE WELLS, H. G.             AC
  *TIME MACHINE AND OTHER STORIES, THE  WELLS, H. G.         AC
  TWENTY-EIGHT SCIENCE FICTION STORIES  WELLS, H. G.         AC
COUNTRY OF THE KIND, THE      KNIGHT, DAMON       SS   FSF 56 02
  FUTURE POWER                     DANN & DOZOIS             OA
  IN DEEP                          KNIGHT, DAMON             AC
  LATE GREAT FUTURE, THE           FITZ GERALD & DILLON  AN
  NEW DREAMS THIS MORNING          BLISH, JAMES              AN
  SCIENCE FICTION HALL OF FAME VOLUME 1  SILVERBERG, ROBERT AN
  SF: THE YEAR'S GREATEST SCIENCE FICTION AND FANTASY
                              MERRIL, JUDITH            AN
  YET MORE PENGUIN SCIENCE FICTION ALDISS, BRIAN W.          AN
COUNTRY OF THE STRONG, THE    ETCHISON, DENNIS    SS   SEV 62
  NEW WRITINGS IN SF. 4            CARNELL, JOHN             OA
COUPE DE GRACE                VANCE, JACK         NV
  MANY WORLDS OF MAGNUS RIDOLPH, THE  VANCE, JACK            DC
  WORLDS OF JACK VANCE, THE        VANCE, JACK               AC
COURIER (THE FROZEN PLANET)   LAUMER, KEITH       NV   IFS 61 09
  BOLO                             LAUMER, KEITH             AC
  GALACTIC DIPLOMAT                LAUMER, KEITH             AC
COURIER OF CHAOS              ANDERSON, POUL      NV   FUT 53 03
  THINGS                           HOWARD, IVAN              AN
COURSE OF LOGIC, THE          DEL REY, LESTER     SS   IFS 63 09
  MORTALS AND MONSTERS             DEL REY, LESTER           AC
COURT MARTIAL (D. M. MANKIEWICZ & S. CARABATSOS)
                              BLISH, JAMES        SA   STK 68 02
  STAR TREK  2                     BLISH, JAMES              OC
COURT OF TARTARY, THE         CARAVAN, T. P.      SS   FSF 63 12
  BEST FROM FANTASY AND SCIENCE FICTION: 14
                              DAVIDSON, AVRAM           AN
COURTEOUS OF GHOOR, THE (SEE ARCHIMEDES' LEVER)
                              LORY, ROBERT        TC
COURTESY                      SIMAK, CLIFFORD D.  SS   ASF 51 08
  CROSSROADS IN TIME               CONKLIN, GROFF            AN
  SPACE, SPACE, SPACE              SLOANE, WILLIAM           AN
COURTS OF JAMSHYD, THE        YOUNG, ROBERT F.    SS   INF 57 09
  WORLDS OF ROBERT F. YOUNG, THE   YOUNG, ROBERT F.          AC
COUSIN LEN'S WONDERFUL ADJECTIVE CELLAR
                              FINNEY, JACK        SS
  BEST FANTASY STORIES             ALDISS, BRIAN W.          AN
  THIRD LEVEL, THE                 FINNEY, JACK              AC
COVENTRY                      HEINLEIN, ROBERT A. NV   ASF 40 07
  BEYOND TOMORROW                  KNIGHT, DAMON             AN
  PAST THROUGH TOMORROW, THE       HEINLEIN, ROBERT A.       AC
  REVOLT IN 2100                   HEINLEIN, ROBERT A.       AC
  '6 GREAT SHORT NOVELS OF SCIENCE FICTION CONKLIN, GROFF  AN
COWBOY LAMENT                 JAFFRAY, NORMAN R.  PM   FSF 54 01
  BEST FROM FANTASY AND SCIENCE FICTION: 4
                              BOUCHER, ANTHONY          AN
COWBOYS, INDIANS              BRYANT, EDWARD      SS   ALT 74
  ALTERNATIES                      GERROLD, DAVID            OA
COWS CAN'T EAT GRASS          RICHMOND, LEIGH
                              AND RICHMOND, WALT  SS C ASF 67 08
  POSITIVE CHARGE                  RICHMOND, W. & L.         DC
CRAB-APPLE CRISIS, THE        MACBETH, GEORGE     SS   NWS 66 10
  ANOTHER TOMORROW                 HOLLISTER, BERNARD C      AN
  HOLDING YOUR EIGHT HANDS         LUCIE-SMITH, EDWARD       AN
  POLITICAL SCIENCE FICTION        GREENBERG& WARRICK        AN
  SCIENCE FICTION: THE FUTURE      ALLEN, DICK               AN
  SF12                             MERRIL, JUDITH            AN
CRABS TAKE OVER THE ISLAND    DNIEPROV, ANATOLY   SS   ISF 68 06
  RUSSIAN SCIENCE FICTION, 1969    MAGIDOFF, ROBERT          AN
  SCIENCE FACT/FICTION             FARRELL/GAGE/&            AN
CRACK IN SPACE, THE (CANTATA 140, FSF 64 07)
                              DICK, PHILIP K.     NO   ACE 66
  PHILIP K. DICK OMNIBUS, A        DICK, PHILIP K.           AC
CRACK, THE                    TENNANT, EMMA       NV   NWB 73 05
  NEW WORLDS QUARTERLY NO. 5       MOORCOCK, MICHAEL         OA
CRACKPOTS, THE                ELLISON, HARLAN     NV   IFS 56 06
  *PAINGOD AND OTHER DELUSIONS     ELLISON, HARLAN           AC
CRADLE OF THE SUN             STABLEFORD, BRIAN M. NO
  SCIENCE FICTION SPECIAL 5        ANONYMOUS                 AN
CRASH ALERT                   PEARL, CLINTON      SS        59
  TEEN-AGE OUTER SPACE STORIES     FURMAN, A. L.             AN
CRASH!                        BALLARD, J. G.      SS   ICA 69
  LOVE & NAPALM: EXPORT U.S.A.     BALLARD, J. G.            AC
CRASHING SUNS                 HAMILTON, EDMOND    NV   WRT 28 08
  CRASHING SUNS                    HAMILTON, EDMOND          AC
CRATE                         STURGEON, THEODORE  SS        70
  STURGEON IS ALIVE AND WELL...    STURGEON, THEODORE        AC
  TOMORROW, AND TOMORROW, AND TOMORROW... HEINTZ/HERBERT/JOOS/ AN
CRATER, THE                   WANDREI, DONALD     SS
  TRAVELLERS BY NIGHT              DERLETH, AUGUST           OA
CRAVING FOR BLACKNESS, THE (SEE THE HEART OF BLACKNESS)
                              RAY, ROBERT         TC
CRAWLERS, THE                 DICK, PHILIP K.     SS   IMG 54 07
  PRESERVING MACHINE, THE          DICK, PHILIP K.           AC
  YOU AND SCIENCE FICTION          HOLLISTER, BERNARD C      AN
CRAWLING HORROR, THE          MCCLUSKY, THORP     NV   WRT 36 11
  AVON FANTASY READER, THE         WOLLHEIM &ERNSBERGER      AN
CRAYFISH, THE                 HEARD, H. F.        SS
  GREAT FOG AND OTHER WEIRD TALES, THE  HEARD, H. F.         OC
CRAYOLA                       SKAL, DAVE          SS   CLR 72 02
  CLARION II                       WILSON, ROBIN SCOTT       OA
CRAZY ANNAOJ                  LEIBER, FRITZ       SS   GAL 68 02
  BOOK OF FRITZ LEIBER, THE        LEIBER, FRITZ             AC
```

CRAZY JOEY   APOSTOLIDES, ALEX
                                AND CLIFTON, MARK   SS C·ASF 53 08
  BEYOND THE BARRIERS OF SPACE AND TIME   MERRIL, JUDITH   AN
CRAZY MARO   KEYES, DANIEL   NV   FSP 60 04
  BEST FROM FANTASY AND SCIENCE FICTION: 10
                                MILLS, ROBERT P.   AN
  THOSE WHO CAN: A SCIENCE FICTION READER WILSON, ROBIN SCOTT AN
CRAZY WOLF (SANITY)   LEIBER, FRITZ   SS   ASF 44 04
  NIGHT OF THE WOLF, THE   LEIBER, FRITZ   AC
CRAZY, MIXED-UP PLANET   FRITCH, CHARLES E. NV FUN 55 08
  CRAZY MIXED-UP PLANET   FRITCH, CHARLES E.   AC
CREATED HE THEM   JONES, ALICE ELEANOR SS   FSP 55 06
  BEST FROM FANTASY AND SCIENCE FICTION: 5
                                BOUCHER, ANTHONY   AN
CREATION OF A FUTURE WORLD IN THE TRACER
                                HERBST, STEVE   SS   ORB 74 13
  ORBIT 13   KNIGHT, DAMON   OA
CREATION OF BENNIE GOOD, THE   SALLIS, JAMES   SS   ORB 70 06
  FEW LAST WORDS, A   SALLIS, JAMES   AC
  ORBIT 6   KNIGHT, DAMON   AN
CREATION UNFORGIVABLE   KELLER, DAVID H. MD. SS WRT 30 04
  TALES FROM UNDERWOOD   KELLER, DAVID H. MD.   AC
CREATIVE EVOLUTION (FROM PREFACE TO "BACK TO METHUSELAH")
                                SHAW, GEORGE BERNARD   EX
  ARMCHAIR SCIENCE READER, THE GORDON, I. & SORKIN   AN
CREATORS, THE   GREEN, JOSEPH   SS   NWR 64 02
  BEST FROM NEW WRITINGS IN S-F FIRST SELECTION, THE
                                CARNELL, JOHN   AN
  NEW WRITINGS IN SF. 2   CARNELL, JOHN   OA
CREATURE FROM CLEVELAND DEPTHS, THE (ALSO AS THE LONE WOLF)
                                LEIBER, FRITZ   NA   GAL 62 12
  YOU'RE ALL ALONE   LEIBER, FRITZ   AC
CREATURE OF THE SNOWS   SAMBROT, WILLIAM SS   SEP 60 10
  ANCIENT MYSTERIES READER, THE HAINING, PETER   AN
  ISLAND OF FEAR AND OTHER SCIENCE FICTION SAMBROT, WILLIAM AC
  UNTRAVELLED WORLDS   BARTER & WILSON   AN
  6TH ANNUAL OF THE YEAR'S BEST S-F, THE   MERRIL, JUDITH AN
CREATURES THAT TIME FORGOT, THE (SEE FROST AND FIRE)
                                BRADBURY, RAY   TC
CREDO   BLISH, JAMES   IN
  BEST SF: 1967   HARRISON & ALDISS   AN
CREEPING TERROR, THE (A TOUCH OF GRAPEFRUIT)
                                MATHESON, RICHARD SS   STR 59 05
  SHOCK!   MATHESON, RICHARD   AC
CRESCENDO (SEE SHOCK WAVE)   MATHESON, RICHARD   TC
CREST OF THE WAVE, THE   RICE, JANE   SS   UNK 41 06
  UNKNOWN 5, THE   BENSEN, D. R.   AN
CREW OF THE LANCING, THE   HODGSON, WILLIAM H. SS
  BEWARE MORE BEASTS   GHIDALIA, V.& ELWOOD   AN
CREWEL NEEDLE, THE   KERSH, GERALD   SS   ESQ
  ON AN ODD NOTE   KERSH, GERALD   AC
CRIB CIRCUIT, THE   DEFORD, MIRIAM ALLEN SS FSP 69 11
  ELSEWHERE, ELSEWHEN, ELSEHOW DEFORD, MIRIAM ALLEN   AC
CRICKET BALL, THE   MANHATTAN, AVRO SS   FSP 55 10
  FIFTY SHORT SCIENCE FICTION TALES   ASIMOV & CONKLIN AN
  UNTRAVELLED WORLDS   BARTER & WILSON   AN
CRICKETS   MATHESON, RICHARD SS   SHK 60 05
  SHOCK II   MATHESON, RICHARD   AC
CRIME AND THE GLORY OF COMMANDER SUZDAL, THE
                                SMITH, CORDWAINER SS   AMZ 64 05
  BEST OF CORDWAINER SMITH, THE SMITH, CORDWAINER   AC
  GALACTIC EMPIRES VOLUME ONE   ALDISS, BRIAN W.   AN
  SEVEN TRIPS THROUGH TIME AND SPACE CONKLIN, GROFF   AN
  STARDREAMER   SMITH, CORDWAINER   AC
CRIME FOR LLEWELLYN, A   STURGEON, THEODORE NV NEW 58 AC
  *TOUCH OF STRANGE, A   STURGEON, THEODORE   AC
CRIME IN RHYME (SEE RHYME NEVER PAYS)
                                BLOCH, ROBERT   TC
CRIME MACHINE   BLOCH, ROBERT   SS   GAL 61 10
  FEAR TODAY, GONE TOMORROW   BLOCH, ROBERT   AC
  SEVENTH GALAXY READER, THE   POHL, FREDERIK   AN
CRIME ON MARS (SEE TROUBLE WITH TIME)
                                CLARKE, ARTHUR C.   TC
CRIME THERAPIST, THE   BRADLEY, MARION Z. SS FUT 54 10
  DARK INTRUDER & OTHER STORIES, THE   BRADLEY, MARION Z. DC
CRIMINAL ACT, A   HARRISON, HARRY SS   ASF 67 01
  *BEST OF HARRY HARRISON, THE HARRISON, HARRY   AC
  PRIME NUMBER   HARRISON, HARRY   AC
CRIMINAL IN UTOPIA   REYNOLDS, MACK   NV   GAL 68 10
  BEST SF: 1968   HARRISON & ALDISS   AN
  TOMORROW, INC.   GREENBERG& OLANDER   AN
CRIMINAL NEGLIGENCE   MCCOMAS, J. FRANCIS SS ASF 55 06
  SPACE, TIME & CRIME   DEFORD, MIRIAM ALLEN   AN
CRIMINAL RECORD   ALDISS, BRIAN W. SS   SCF 54 07
  SPACE, TIME AND NATHANIEL   ALDISS, BRIAN W.   AC
CRIMINAL, THE   GORES, JOE   SS   ADM 70 12
  STRANGE BED FELLOWS   SCORTIA, THOMAS N.   AN
CRISIS   GRENDON, EDWARD SS   ASF 51 06
  *INVADERS OF EARTH   CONKLIN, GROFF   AN
CRISIS IN UTOPIA   KNIGHT, NORMAN L. NO ASF 40 07
  CRUCIBLE OF POWER, THE   GREENBERG, MARTIN   AN
  FIVE SCIENCE FICTION NOVELS   GREENBERG, MARTIN   AN
CRISIS!   KORNBLUTH, C. M. SS   SFQ 42 SP
  THIRTEEN O'CLOCK AND OTHER ZERO HOURS KORNBLUTH, C. M. AC
CRISIS, 1999   BROWN, FREDRIC   SS   EQM 49 08
  SPACE ON MY HANDS   BROWN, FREDRIC   AC
  SPACE, TIME & CRIME   DEFORD, MIRIAM ALLEN   AN
CRITICAL ANGLE   CHANDLER, A. BERTRAM SS FSP·58 11
  FIRST FLIGHTS TO THE MOON   CLEMENT, HAL   AN
CRITICAL DIFFERENCE (SEE SOLAR CONSTANT)
                                LEINSTER, MURRAY   TC
CRITICAL FACTOR   CLEMENT, HAL   SS   STR 53 02
  STAR SCIENCE FICTION STORIES NO. 2 POHL, FREDERIK   OA
CRITICAL MASS   KORNBLUTH, C. M.
                                AND POHL, FREDERIK NA C GAL 62 02
  EIGHTH GALAXY READER, THE   POHL, FREDERIK   AN

WONDER EFFECT, THE   POHL, F. & KORNBLUTH   AC
CRITICAL MASS (ORIGINAL VERSION IN LILLIPUT MARCH 1949)
                                CLARKE, ARTHUR C. SS SPM 57 08
  PRELUDE TO MARS   CLARKE, ARTHUR C.   AC
  TALES FROM THE WHITE HART   CLARKE, ARTHUR C.   AC
CRITICAL METHODS: SPECULATIVE FICTION
                                DELANY, SAMUEL R. AR QRK 70 01
  QUARK/1   DELANY & HACKER   OA
CRITICAL PATH   COLES, DAVID   SS   NWR 71 19
  NEW WRITINGS IN SF. 19   CARNELL, JOHN   OA
CRITICAL WORKS ABOUT SCIENCE FICTION
                                MISC. MATERIAL   MS
  SCIENCE FICTION NOVELLAS   HARRISON & MCNELLY   AN
CRITIQUE OF IMPURE REASON, THE ANDERSON, POUL   NV   IPS 62 11
  NEVER IN THIS WORLD   STONE, IDELLA P.   AN
  TIME AND STARS   ANDERSON, POUL   AC
CRITTERS, THE   LONG, FRANK BELKNAP SS ASF 45 11
  *OUTER REACHES, THE   DERLETH, AUGUST   AN
  RIM OF THE UNKNOWN   LONG, FRANK BELKNAP   AC
CROATOAN   ELLISON, HARLAN SS   FSP 75 05
  BEST SCIENCE FICTION OF THE YEAR, THE NO. 5
                                CARR, TERRY   AN
CROOKED MAN, THE   BEAUMONT, CHARLES SS   PBY 55 08
  FIEND, THE   PLAYBOY, EDITORS OF   AN
  HUNGER AND OTHER STORIES, THE BEAUMONT, CHARLES   AC
  MAGIC MAN AND OTHER SCIENCE-FANTASY STORIES
                                BEAUMONT, CHARLES   AC
  PLAYBOY BOOK OF SCIENCE FICTION AND FANTASY, THE
                                PLAYBOY, EDITORS OF   AN
CROQUET PLAYER, THE   WELLS, H. G.   EX   36
  *TERROR IN THE MODERN VEIN   WOLLHEIM, DONALD A.   AN
CROSS OF CENTURIES, A   KUTTNER, HENRY   SS   STR 58 04
  OTHER WORLDS, OTHER GODS   MOHS, MAYO   AN
  STAR OF STARS   POHL, FREDERIK   AN
  STAR SCIENCE FICTION STORIES NO. 4 POHL, FREDERIK   OA
CROSS OF FIRE   DEL REY, LESTER SS   WRT 39 05
  EARLY DEL REY   DEL REY, LESTER   AC
CROSS THE BORDER, CLOSE THE GAP
                                FIEDLER, LESLIE A. AR
  LOOKING AHEAD   ALLEN, D. & L.   AN
CROSSFIRE   WHITE, JAMES   SS   NWS 53 06
  BEST FROM NEW WORLDS SCIENCE FICTION, THE
                                CARNELL, JOHN   AN
CROSSOVER   BUTLER, OCTAVIA E. SS CLR 71 01
  CLARION   WILSON, ROBIN SCOTT   OA
CROSSWORD   BRUNNER, JOHN   MS
  BOOK OF JOHN BRUNNER, THE   BRUNNER, JOHN   AC
CROWD, THE   BRADBURY, RAY   SS   WRT 43 05
  *DARK CARNIVAL   BRADBURY, RAY   AC
  *OCTOBER COUNTRY, THE   BRADBURY, RAY   AC
  SMALL ASSASSIN, THE   BRADBURY, RAY   AC
  *TERROR IN THE MODERN VEIN   WOLLHEIM, DONALD A.   AN
CROWDED CITIES OF PATAGONIA, THE
                                ALDISS, BRIAN W. PL   NWB 75 09
  NEW WORLDS NINE   BAILEY, HILARY   OA
CROWN JEWELS OF JERUSALEM, OR, THE TELL-TALE HEAD, THE
                                DAVIDSON, AVRAM NV   FSP 75 08
  ENQUIRIES OF DOCTOR ESZTERHAZY, THE DAVIDSON, AVRAM NO
CROWNING GLORY   HENDERSON, ZENNA SS   NEW 71 05
  HOLDING WONDER   HENDERSON, ZENNA   AC
CRUCIBLE OF POWER, THE   WILLIAMSON, JACK NV   ASF 39 02
  CRUCIBLE OF POWER, THE   GREENBERG, MARTIN   AN
  FIVE SCIENCE FICTION NOVELS   GREENBERG, MARTIN   AN
CRUCIFIXUS ETIAM   MILLER, WALTER M. JR SS ASF 53 02
  ASLEEP IN ARMAGEDDON   SISSONS, MICHAEL   AN
  BEST SCIENCE-FICTION STORIES: 1954, THE BLEILER & DIKTY AN
  HUMAN?   MERRIL, JUDITH   AN
  HUMAN-MACHINES   SCORTIA & ZEBROWSKI   AN
  LATE GREAT FUTURE, THE   FITZ GERALD & DILLON   AN
  SPECTRUM 5   AMIS & CONQUEST   AN
  TOMORROW'S WORLDS   SILVERBERG, ROBERT   AN
  TOMORROW AND TOMORROW, AND TOMORROW... HEINTZ/HERBERT/JOOS/ AN
  VIEW FROM THE STARS, THE   MILLER, WALTER M. JR   AC
CRUEL EQUATIONS, THE   SHECKLEY, ROBERT SS   BOA
  CAN YOU FEEL ANYTHING WHEN I DO THIS?, AND OTHER STORIES
                                SHECKLEY, ROBERT   AC
CRUEL SKY, THE   CLARKE, ARTHUR C. SS
  WIND FROM THE SUN, THE   CLARKE, ARTHUR C.   AC
CRUELTY   DE CLES, JON   SS   NEW 71 05
  SPECIAL WONDER   MCCOMAS, J. FRANCIS   AN
CRUISE OF A COMMERCE DESTROYER, THE
                                STIRLING, YATES JR. SS
  BATTLE FOR THE PACIFIC AND OTHER ADVENTURES AT SEA, THE
                                ANONYMOUS   AN
CRUISE OF THE S-900, THE   KENT, RUSSELL   SS
  ADVENTURES TO COME   ESENWEIN, J. BERG   OA
CRUMBLING HOLLYWOOD MANSION, CRUMBLING HOLLYWOOD MAN (PROTEST)
                                TATE, PETER   SS   GAL 74 02
  SEAGULLS UNDER GLASS AND OTHER STORIES TATE, PETER AC
CRUSADE   CLARKE, ARTHUR C. SS FRS 68
  FARTHEST REACHES, THE   ELDER, JOSEPH   OA
  WIND FROM THE SUN, THE   CLARKE, ARTHUR C.   AC
CRUSADER (AS GENE ELLERMAN)   WELLS, BASIL   SS   FBK 49 05
  MACHINE-GOD LAUGHS, THE   ANONYMOUS   AN
  PLANETS OF ADVENTURE   WELLS, BASIL   AC
CRY FROM BEYOND, A   ROUSSEAU, VICTOR NV   STT 31 09
  FANTASTIC PULPS, THE   HAINING, PETER   AN
CRY HOPE, CRY FURY!   BALLARD, J. G.   SS   FSP 67 10
  *VERMILLION SANDS   BALLARD, J. G.   AC
CRYER OF CRYSTAL, THE   GREEN, JOSEPH   SS   ASF 71 10
  CONSCIENCE INTERPLANETARY   GREEN, JOSEPH   NO
CRYING JAG   SIMAK, CLIFFORD D. NV GAL 60 02
  *ALL THE TRAPS OF EARTH AND OTHER STORIES SIMAK, CLIFFORD D. AC
  BEST SCIENCE FICTION STORIES OF CLIFFORD D. SIMAK
                                SIMAK, CLIFFORD D.   AC
  NIGHT OF THE PUUDLY, THE   SIMAK, CLIFFORD D.   AC

CRYSTAL BULLET, THE   WANDREI, DONALD   SS   WRT 41 03
  EYE AND THE FINGER   WANDREI, DONALD   AC
  *STRANGE PORTS OF CALL   DERLETH, AUGUST   AN
CRYSTAL CASTLE, THE   GERROLD, DAVID   SS   NEW 72 AC
  WITH A FINGER IN MY I   GERROLD, DAVID   AC
CRYSTAL EGG, THE   WELLS, H. G.   SS   NRV 97 05
  ASPECTS OF SCIENCE FICTION   DOHERTY, G. D.   AN
  BEST SCIENCE FICTION STORIES OF H. G. WELLS
                            WELLS, H. G.   AC
  BEST STORIES OF H. G. WELLS   WELLS, H. G.   AC
  CENTURY OF SCIENCE FICTION, A KNIGHT, DAMON   AN
  COUNTRY OF THE BLIND, THE WELLS, H. G.   AC
  IN DREAMS AWAKE   FIEDLER, LESLIE A.   AN
  SHORT STORIES OF H. G. WELLS, THE WELLS, H. G.   AC
  *STRANGE PORTS OF CALL   DERLETH, AUGUST   AN
  TALES OF SPACE AND TIME   WELLS, H. G.   AC
  TWENTY-EIGHT SCIENCE FICTION STORIES WELLS, H. G.   AC
  VISIONS OF TOMORROW   ELWOOD, ROGER   AN
  WAR OF THE WORLDS, THE TIME MACHINE AND SELECTED SHORT STORIES
                            WELLS, H. G.   AC
CRYSTAL MAN, THE   MITCHELL, EDWARD P. SS   SUN 81 01
  CRYSTAL MAN, THE   MITCHELL, EDWARD D.   AC
CRYSTAL SHIP, THE   VINGE, JOAN D.   NA
  CRYSTAL SHIP, THE   SILVERBERG, ROBERT   OA
CUBE IN A DODECAGON GARDEN (SEE DODECAGON GARDEN)
                           PETAJA, EMIL   TC
CUBIC CITY, THE   TUCKER, LOUIS   SS   SWS 29 09
  FROM OFF THIS WORLD   MARGULIES & FRIEND   AN
CUE FOR QUIET   SHERRED, T. L.   NA   SSF 53 05
  FIRST PERSON, PECULIAR   SHERRED, T. L.   AC
CUES   WOLFE, GENE   SS
  FAR SIDE OF TIME, THE   ELWOOD, ROGER   OA
CULTURAL EXCHANGE   LAUMER, KEITH   NV   IFS 62 09
  ENVOY TO NEW WORLDS   LAUMER, KEITH   AC
CULTURAL SIDE EFFECT, A   ALDISS, BRIAN W.   SS   FST 74
  FINAL STAGE   FERMAN & MALZBERG   OA
CULTURE   SHELTON, JERRY   NV   ASF 44 09
  APEMAN, SPACEMAN   STOVER & HARRISON   AN
  *BIG BOOK OF SCIENCE FICTION CONKLIN, GROFF   AN
CULTURE FOR THE PLANETS   FAIRMAN, PAUL W.   SS
  FORGETFUL ROBOT, THE   FAIRMAN, PAUL W.   OC
CULTURE LOCK   MALZBERG, BARRY N.   SS   FUC 73
  BEST OF BARRY N. MALZBERG, THE MALZBERG, BARRY N.   AC
  FUTURE CITY   ELWOOD, ROGER   OA
CULVER CITY ARITHMATIC EXERCISE PAPER
                           ANONYMOUS   MS   NYM 61 02
  MATHEMATICAL MAGPIE, THE FADIMAN, CLIFTON   AN
CUNNING OF THE BEAST, THE (ANOTHER WORLD BEGINS)
                           BOND, NELSON S.   SS   BBM 42 11
  NO TIME LIKE THE FUTURE   BOND, NELSON S.   AC
  OTHER WORLDS, OTHER GODS MOHS, MAYO   AN
  *STRANGE PORTS OF CALL   DERLETH, AUGUST   AN
  31ST OF FEBRUARY, THE   BOND, NELSON S.   AC
CUP, THE   HEARD, H. F.   NV
  LOST CAVERN AND OTHER TALES OF THE FANTASTIC, THE
                           HEARD, H. F.   AC
CUPID WITH AN ADDING MACHINE RICE, CHARLES D.   SS   TWK 60 09
  MATHEMATICAL MAGPIE, THE FADIMAN, CLIFTON   AN
CURATE'S FRIEND, THE   FORSTER, E. M.   SS   47
  SUPERNATURAL READER, THE CONKLIN, G&L.   AN
CURATIVE TELEPATH   BRUNNER, JOHN   NV   FUN 59 12
  WHOLE MAN, THE   BRUNNER, JOHN   NO
CURE FOR A YLITH   LEINSTER, MURRAY   SS   STS 49 11
  OPERATION FUTURE   CONKLIN, GROFF   AN
CURE, GUARANTEED   SHERRED, T. L.   NV   FUT 54 08
  FIRST PERSON, PECULIAR   SHERRED, T. L.   AC
CURE, THE   BLOCH, ROBERT   SS   PBY 57 10
  *BLOOD RUNS COLD   BLOCH, ROBERT   AC
CURE, THE   PADGETT, LEWIS   SS   ASF 46 05
  GNOME THERE WAS, A   PADGETT, LEWIS   AC
  *OTHER SIDE OF THE MOON, THE DERLETH, AUGUST   AN
CURE, THE   KUTTNER, HENRY
                           AND MOORE, C. L.   SS C ASF 46 05
  SCIENCE FICTION ARGOSY, A KNIGHT, DAMON   AN
CURFEW TOLLS, THE   BENET, STEPHEN V.   SS   SEP 35 10
  MOONLIGHT TRAVELER, THE   STERN, PHILIP VAN D.   AN
CURIOUS CASE OF BENJAMIN BUTTON, THE
                           FITZGERALD, F. SCOTT SS   COL 22 05
  TRAVELERS IN TIME   STERN, PHILIP VAN D.   AN
  TREASURY OF SCIENCE FICTION CLASSICS, THE
                           KUEBLER, HAROLD W.   AN
CURIOUS CHILD, THE   MATHESON, RICHARD   SS   FAN 54 06
  SHORES OF SPACE, THE   MATHESON, RICHARD   AC
CURIOUS FRAGMENT, A   LONDON, JACK   SS   TTP 08 12
  CURIOUS FRAGMENTS   LONDON, JACK   AC
  SCIENCE FICTION OF JACK LONDON, THE LONDON, JACK   AC
CURRENTS OF SPACE, THE   ASIMOV, ISAAC   NO   ASF 52 10
  TRIANGLE   ASIMOV, ISAAC   AC
CURSE OF A THOUSAND KISSES, THE
                           ROHMER, SAX   SS   AFR 48 07
  SECOND AVON FANTASY READER, THE WOLLHEIM &ERNSBERGER AN
CURSE OF SEVEN TOWERS, THE SERLING, ROD   SA
  *ROD SERLING'S THE TWILIGHT ZONE SERLING, ROD   OC
CURSE OF YIG, THE   BISHOP, ZEALIA BROWN SS   WRT 29 11
  SECOND AVON FANTASY READER, THE WOLLHEIM &ERNSBERGER AN
CURSE, A   AUDEN, W. H.   PM   DTM 72
  BEST SF: 1973   HARRISON & ALDISS   AN
CURSE, THE   CLARKE, ARTHUR C.   SS   CSM 53 09
  FROM FRANKENSTEIN TO ANDROMEDA BROWN, JAMES GOLDIE AN
  NINE BILLION NAMES OF GOD, THE CLARKE, ARTHUR C.   AC
  PRELUDE TO MARS   CLARKE, ARTHUR C.   AC
  REACH FOR TOMORROW   CLARKE, ARTHUR C.   AC
CURTAINS   EFFINGER, GEO. ALEC   SS   FSF 74 08
  IRRATIONAL NUMBERS   EFFINGER, GEO. ALEC   AC
CUSTER'S LAST JUMP   UTLEY, STEVEN
                           AND WALDROP, HOWARD   NV C UNI 76 06

BEST SCIENCE FICTION OF THE YEAR, THE NO. 6
                           CARR, TERRY   AN
BEST SCIENCE FICTION STORIES OF THE YEAR (1976)
                           DOZOIS, GARDNER R.   AN
UNIVERSE 6   CARR, TERRY   OA
CUSTODIAN, THE   TENN, WILLIAM   NV   IFS 53 11
  MASTERS' CHOICE   JANIFER, LAURENCE M.   AN
  OF ALL POSSIBLE WORLDS   TENN, WILLIAM   AC
CUSTODIANS, THE   COWPER, RICHARD   NV   FSF 75 10
  BEST SF: 75, THE NINTH ANNUAL HARRISON & ALDISS   AN
  CUSTODIANS AND OTHER STORIES, THE COWPER, RICHARD   AC
  1976 ANNUAL WORLD'S BEST SF, THE WOLLHEIM, DONALD A. AN
CUSTOM FITTING   WHITE, JAMES   NV   STL 76 02
  STELLAR 2   DEL REY, JUDY-LYNN   OA
CUSTOMERS, THE   BEAUMONT, CHARLES   SS   NEW 57 AC
  HUNGER AND OTHER STORIES, THE BEAUMONT, CHARLES   AC
CWACC STRIKES AGAIN   DEMPSEY, HANK   NV   ASF 66 06
  ANALOG 6   CAMPBELL, JOHN W. JR   AN
CYB   INOUYE, JON   SS
  NIGHT TIDE, A   INOUYE, JON   OC
CYBER AND JUSTICE HOLMES, THE RILEY, FRANK   SS   IFS 55 03
  BEST SCIENCE FICTION STORIES AND NOVELS: 1956
                           DIKTY, T. E.   AN
  FIRST WORLD OF IF, THE   QUINN & WULFF   AN
CYBERNETIC TABERNACLE JOB, THE GOULART, RON   NV   INY 72 03
  INFINITY 3   HOSKINS, ROBERT   OA
  ODD JOB NO. 101   GOULART, RON   AC
CYCLOPS   HEARD, H. F.   SS   NEW 52 AN
  *FUTURE TENSE   CROSSEN, KENDELL F.   AN
CYCLOPS   LEIBER, FRITZ   SS   WOT 65 09
  ON OUR WAY TO THE FUTURE CARR, TERRY   AN
  WORLDS OF FRITZ LEIBER, THE LEIBER, FRITZ   AC
CYCLOPS PATROL, THE   SPENCER, WILLIAM   SS   NWR 71 18
  NEW WRITINGS IN SF. 18   CARNELL, JOHN   OA
CYMBAL PLAYER   SAIL, LAWRENCE   PM   CND 72
  BEST SF: 1972   HARRISON & ALDISS   AN
CYNOSURE   REED, KIT   SS   FSF 64 06
  MARRIAGE AND THE FAMILY THROUGH SCIENCE FICTION
                           CLEAR/WARRICK/&   AN
CYPRIAN'S ROOM   STERBA, MONICA   NV   FSF 67 05
  BEST FROM FANTASY AND SCIENCE FICTION: 17
                           FERMAN, EDWARD L.   AN
D. P. FROM TOMORROW   REYNOLDS, MACK   SS   OSF 53 FL
  PORTALS OF TOMORROW   DERLETH, AUGUST   AN
D.F.C. (CHRONIUS OF THE D.F.C.)
                           BIGGLE, LLOYD JR.   SS   IFS 57 02
  RULE OF THE DOOR AND OTHER FANCIFUL REGULATIONS
                           BIGGLE, LLOYD JR.   AC
D.P.   VONNEGUT, KURT JR.   SS   LHJ 53 08
  CANARY IN A CAT HOUSE   VONNEGUT, KURT JR.   AC
  WELCOME TO THE MONKEY HOUSE VONNEGUT, KURT JR.   AC
DA VINCI MACHINE, THE   CONRAD, EARL   SS
  DA VINCI MACHINE, THE   CONRAD, EARL   OC
DADDY'S GIRL   RUSS, JOANNA   SS   NWB 75 09
  NEW WORLDS NINE   BAILEY, HILARY   OA
DAEDALUS (1855)   BULFINCH, THOMAS   SS
  JOURNEYS IN SCIENCE FICTION LOUGHLIN, RICHARD L.   A
DAEMON   MOORE, C. L.   NV   FFM 46 10
  BEST OF C. L. MOORE, THE MOORE, C. L.   AC
DAEMON LOVER, THE   JACKSON, SHIRLEY   NV   48
  OTHER DIMENSION, THE   ROSNER, SARA   AN
  TIMELESS STORIES FOR TODAY AND TOMORROW BRADBURY, RAY AN
DAFFODIL RETURNS THE SMILE, THE
                           ALDISS, BRIAN W.   SS   NWR 75 26
  NEW WRITINGS IN SF. 26   BULMER, KENNETH   OA
DAGGER OF THE MIND (S. BAR-DAVID)
                           BLISH, JAMES   SA   STK 67 01
  STAR TREK   BLISH, JAMES   OC
DAGON   DAVIDSON, AVRAM   SS   FSF 59 10
  BEST FROM FANTASY AND SCIENCE FICTION: 9
                           MILLS, ROBERT P.   AN
  OR ALL THE SEAS WITH OYSTERS DAVIDSON, AVRAM   AC
DAISIES (TRIPLICATE TWISTEROO) BROWN, FREDRIC   SS   PBY 57 03
  ANGELS AND SPACESHIPS   BROWN, FREDRIC   AC
DALIS ASCENSION   WENSKES, HELMUT   IL
  BEYOND THIS HORIZON   CARRELL, CHRISTOPHER   OA
DAM NUISANCE   LAUMER, KEITH   NV   IFS 66 03
  RETIEF: AMBASSADOR TO SPACE LAUMER, KEITH   AC
DAM, THE   JOHNSON, HUGH S.   SS   RBM 11 04
  SCIENCE FICTION BY GASLIGHT MOSKOWITZ, SAM   AN
DAMECHILD   ETCHISON, DENNIS   SS   FIN 70
  FUTURE IS NOW, THE   NOLAN, WILLIAM F.   OA
DAMNATION MORNING   LEIBER, FRITZ   SS   FAN 59 08
  *MIND SPIDER AND OTHER STORIES, THE LEIBER, FRITZ   DC
DAMNED THING, THE (1893)   BIERCE, AMBROSE   SS   WRT 23 09
  SPECTRUM OF WORLDS, A   CLARESON, THOMAS D.   AN
  TREASURY OF SCIENCE FICTION CLASSICS, THE
                           KUEBLER, HAROLD W.   AN
DAMNEDEST THING, THE   KANIN, GARSON   SS   ESQ 56 02
  SF:57, THE YEAR'S GREATEST SCIENCE FICTION AND FANTASY
                           MERRIL, JUDITH   AN
DANCE OF A NEW WORLD   MACDONALD, JOHN D.   SS   ASF 48 09
  JOURNEY TO INFINITY   GREENBERG, MARTIN   AN
DANCE OF THE CATS   GREEN, JOSEPH   SS   NWS 65 12
  AFFAIR WITH GENIUS, AN   GREEN, JOSEPH   AC
DANCE OF THE CHANGER AND THE THREE, THE
                           CARR, TERRY   SS   FRS 68
  BUG-EYED MONSTERS   CHEETHAM, ANTHONY   AN
  DEEP SPACE   SILVERBERG, ROBERT   AN
  FARTHEST REACHES, THE   ELDER, JOSEPH   OA
  LIGHT AT THE END OF THE UNIVERSE, THE CARR, TERRY   AC
  NEBULA AWARD STORIES NO. 4 ANDERSON, POUL   AN
  WORLD'S BEST SCIENCE FICTION: 1969 WOLLHEIM & CARR AN
DANCE OF THE DEAD   MATHESON, RICHARD   SS   STR 54 03
  SHOCK!   MATHESON, RICHARD   AC
  STAR OF STARS   POHL, FREDERIK   AN

```
STAR SCIENCE FICTION STORIES NO. 3      POHL, FREDERIK         OA
DANCE OF THE SOLIDS, THE       UPDIKE, JOHN      PM  SAM 69 01
ALCHEMY AND ACADEME            MCCAFFREY, ANNE         OA
DANCING DOLL, THE              KERSH, GERALD     SS
MEN WITHOUT BONES              KERSH, GERALD           AC
DANCING GERONTIUS              HARDING, LEE      SS  VOT 69 12
SECOND PACIFIC BOOK OF SCIENCE FICTION, THE
                               BAXTER, JOHN            AN
DANCING GIRL OF GANYMEDE, THE  BRACKETT, LEIGH   SS  TWS 50 02
AWARD SCIENCE FICTION READER   NORTON, ALDEN H.        AN
HALFLING AND OTHER STORIES, THE     BRACKETT, LEIGH    AC
DANCING PARTNER, THE           JEROME, JEROME K. SS  FFM 51 03
FROM FRANKENSTEIN TO ANDROMEDA      BROWN, JAMES GOLDIE AN
DANDELION GIRL, THE            YOUNG, ROBERT F.  SS  SEP 61 04
WORLDS OF ROBERT F. YOUNG, THE      YOUNG, ROBERT F.   AC
7TH ANNUAL OF THE YEAR'S BEST S-F, THE  MERRIL, JUDITH  AN
DANDELION WINE                 BRADBURY, RAY     SS  GOR 53 06
DANDELION WINE                 BRADBURY, RAY           NO
VINTAGE BRADBURY, THE          BRADBURY, RAY           AC
DANDY                          WHITE, TED        SS  DEM 73
DEMON KIND                     ELWOOD, ROGER           OA
DANGER IN THE VOID             FRITCH, CHARLES E. SS INF 54 08
HORSES' ASTEROID               FRITCH, CHARLES E.      AC
DANGER: RELIGION! (MATRIX)  ALDISS, BRIAN W.  TC  SCF 62 10
INNER LANDSCAPE, THE           MOORCOCK, MICHAEL       AN
NEANDERTHAL PLANET             ALDISS, BRIAN W.        AC
SALIVA TREE AND OTHER STRANGE GROWTHS, THE
                               ALDISS, BRIAN W.        AC
UNFRIENDLY FUTURE, THE         BOARDMAN, TOM JR.       AN
DANGER- HUMAN!                 DICKSON, GORDON R. SS ASF 57 12
DANGER- HUMAN                  DICKSON, GORDON R.      AC
MUTANTS                        DICKSON, GORDON R.      AC
STRANGE GIFTS                  SILVERBERG, ROBERT      AN
DANGER! CHILD AT LARGE         COTTRELL, C. L.   NV  STR 59 06
STAR SCIENCE FICTION STORIES NO. 6   POHL, FREDERIK    OA
DANGEROUS DIMENSION, THE       HUBBARD, L. RON   SS  ASF 38 07
FUTURES TO INFINITY            MOSKOWITZ, SAM          AN
DANGEROUS FLAGS                DISCH, THOMAS M.  SS  FAN 64 08
*ONE HUNDRED AND TWO H-BOMBS        DISCH, THOMAS M.   AC
WHITE FANG GOES DINGO AND OTHER FUNNY S.F. STORIES
                               DISCH, THOMAS M.        AC
DANGEROUS INVENTION, A         ZELIKOVICH, E.    SS
RUSSIAN SCIENCE FICTION        MAGIDOFF, ROBERT        AN
DANIEL WHITE FOR THE GREATER GOOD
                               ELLISON, HARLAN   SS  ROG 61 03
*LOVE AIN'T NOTHING BUT SEX MISSPELLED  ELLISON, HARLAN  AC
DANNOLD CHEQUE, THE            PURDY, KEN W.     SS  PBY 69 09
BEST SF: 1969                  HARRISON & ALDISS       AN
DANNY'S NEW FRIENDS FROM DENEB DISCH, THOMAS M.
                               AND SLADEK, JOHN T.  SS C
WHITE FANG GOES DINGO AND OTHER FUNNY S.F. STORIES
                               DISCH, THOMAS M.        AC
DANSE MACABRE                  PEAKE, MERVYN     SS  SCF 63 10
WEIRD SHADOWS FROM BEYOND      CARNELL, JOHN           AN
DARENDINGER BUILD-UP, THE      NOLAN, WILLIAM F. SS  PBY 56 06
IMPACT-20                      NOLAN, WILLIAM F.       AC
DARFSTELLER, THE               MILLER, WALTER M. JR SN ASF 55 01
CONDITIONALLY HUMAN            MILLER, WALTER M. JR    AC
HUGO WINNERS, THE (VOLUME 1)   ASIMOV, ISAAC           AN
DARIUS                         PANGBORN, EDGAR   SS
GOOD NEIGHBORS AND OTHER STRANGERS  PANGBORN, EDGAR    AC
DARK ANGEL, THE                KUTTNER, HENRY    SS  STS 46 03
BYPASS TO OTHERNESS            KUTTNER, HENRY          AC
DARK ANGEL, THE                PADGETT, LEWIS    SS  STS 46 03
SHOT IN THE DARK               MERRIL, JUDITH          AN
DARK BALCONY, THE              PETAJA, EMIL      SS  FAD 51 02
STARDRIFT AND OTHER FANTASTIC FLOTSAM  PETAJA, EMIL    AC
DARK BEASTS, THE               LONG, FRANK BELKNAP SS MVT 34 07
DARK BEASTS, THE               LONG, FRANK BELKNAP     AC
EARLY LONG, THE                LONG, FRANK BELKNAP     AC
*HOUNDS OF TINDALOS, THE       LONG, FRANK BELKNAP     AC
DARK BENEDICTION               MILLER, WALTER M. JR SN FAD 51 09
CONDITIONALLY HUMAN            MILLER, WALTER M. JR    AC
DARK CAME OUT TO PLAY, THE (SEE STEVIE AND THE DARK)
                               HENDERSON, ZENNA  TC
DARK COMPANION                 SILVERBERG, ROBERT NV AMZ 61 01
DIMENSION THIRTEEN             SILVERBERG, ROBERT      AC
DARK CONCEPTION                ADAMS, LOUIS J. A. SS FSF 64 11
BEST FROM FANTASY AND SCIENCE FICTION: 14
                               DAVIDSON, AVRAM         AN
DARK DEMON, THE                BLOCH, ROBERT     SS  WRT 36 11
MORE NIGHTMARES                BLOCH, ROBERT           AC
*OPENER OF THE WAY, THE        BLOCH, ROBERT           AC
DARK DOOR, THE                 BOND, NELSON S.   SS  BBM 52 05
NIGHTMARES AND DAYDREAMS       BOND, NELSON S.         AC
DARK DOOR, THE                 NOURSE, ALAN E.   NV  GAL 53 12
COUNTERFEIT MAN, THE           NOURSE, ALAN E.         AC
DARK EIDOLON, THE              SMITH, CLARK ASHTON NV WRT 35 01
OUT OF SPACE AND TIME          SMITH, CLARK ASHTON     AC
SPELL OF SEVEN, THE            DE CAMP, L. SPRAGUE     AN
DARK ENCOUNTER                 NOLAN, WILLIAM F. SS  59
IMPACT-20                      NOLAN, WILLIAM F.       AC
DARK HOLLOW                    PETAJA, EMIL      SS  MOH 66 WI
STARDRIFT AND OTHER FANTASTIC FLOTSAM  PETAJA, EMIL    AC
DARK ICARUS (ALSO AS A LITTLE NIGHT FLYING)
                               SHAW, BOB         SS  SFM 74 04
BEST OF SCIENCE FICTION MONTHLY, THE  SACKS, JANET     AN
BEST SCIENCE FICTION OF THE YEAR, THE NO. 4
                               CARR, TERRY             AN
DARK INTERLUDE                 BROWN, FREDRIC
                               AND REYNOLDS, MACK  SS C GAL 51 01
BEST SCIENCE-FICTION STORIES: 1952, THE  BLEILER & DIKTY  AN
FRONTIERS IN SPACE             BLEILER & DIKTY         AN
*GALAXY READER OF SCIENCE FICTION    GOLD, H. L.        AN
HUMAN AND OTHER BEINGS         DEGRAEFF, ALLEN         AN
NIGHTMARES AND GEEZENSTACKS    BROWN, FREDRIC          AC

DARK INTRUDER, THE (MEASURELESS TO MAN)
                               BRADLEY, MARION Z. NV AMZ 62 12
DARK INTRUDER & OTHER STORIES, THE  BRADLEY, MARION Z. DC
DARK LAND, THE                 MOORE, C. L.      NV  WRT 36 01
JIREL OF JOIRY                 MOORE, C. L.            AC
NORTHWEST OF EARTH             MOORE, C. L.            AC
VENUS FACTOR, THE              GHIDALIA, V.& ELWOOD    AN
DARK MISSION                   DEL REY, LESTER   SS  ASF 40 07
*AND SOME WERE HUMAN           DEL REY, LESTER         AC
GREAT SCIENCE-FICTION          LICATA, TONY            AN
MARS, WE LOVE YOU              HIPOLITO & MCNELLY      AN
*TREASURY OF SCIENCE FICTION, A     CONKLIN, GROFF     AN
DARK MUSIC, THE                BEAUMONT, CHARLES SS  PBY 56 12
HUNGER AND OTHER STORIES, THE  BEAUMONT, CHARLES       AC
MAGIC MAN AND OTHER SCIENCE-FANTASY STORIES
                               BEAUMONT, CHARLES       AC
PLAYBOY'S STORIES OF THE SINISTER & STRANGE
                               PLAYBOY, EDITORS OF     AN
DARK NIGHT OF THE SOUL, THE (GENIUS HEAP)
                               BLISH, JAMES      SS  GAL 56 08
NEW DREAMS THIS MORNING        BLISH, JAMES            AN
DARK NUPTIAL                   LOCKE, ROBERT DONALD SS TWS 53 02
BEST FROM STARTLING STORIES, THE  MINES, SAMUEL        AN
DARK OF KNIGHT                 MALZBERG, BARRY N.  IN
BEST OF DAMON KNIGHT, THE      KNIGHT, DAMON           AC
DARK OF THE JUNE, THE          WOLFE, GENE       SS  CTM 74 01
CONTINUUM 1                    ELWOOD, ROGER           OA
DARK ROOM, THE                 STURGEON, THEODORE NV FAN 53 08
TIME UNTAMED                   HOWARD, IVAN            AN
DARK SIDE OF THE EARTH, THE    BESTER, ALFRED    AC  SIG 64 05
ALFRED BESTER OMNIBUS, AN      BESTER, ALFRED          AC
DARK SOUL OF THE NIGHT, THE    ALDISS, BRIAN W.  SS
IDES OF TOMORROW, THE          CARR, TERRY             OA
DARK STAR, THE                 TENN, WILLIAM     SS  GAL 57 09
WOODEN STAR, THE               TENN, WILLIAM           AC
DARK THEY WERE AND GOLEM-EYED  ALDISS, BRIAN W.  SI
EVIL EARTHS                    ALDISS, BRIAN W.        AN
DARK THEY WERE, AND GOLDEN-EYED (THE NAMING OF NAMES)
                               BRADBURY, RAY     SS  TWS 49 08
DAY IT RAINED FOREVER, THE     BRADBURY, RAY           AC
MEDICINE FOR MELANCHOLY, A     BRADBURY, RAY           AC
OTHER DIMENSION, THE           ROSNER, SARA            AN
S IS FOR SPACE                 BRADBURY, RAY           AC
SCIENCE FICTION                BURTON, S. H.           AN
DARK TOWER, THE (UNFINISHED)   LEWIS, C. S.      NA  NEW 77 01
DARK TOWER AND OTHER STORIES, THE  LEWIS, C. S.        AC
DARK VISION                    LONG, FRANK BELKNAP SS UNK 39 03
EARLY LONG, THE                LONG, FRANK BELKNAP     AC
*HOUNDS OF TINDALOS, THE       LONG, FRANK BELKNAP     AC
DARK, DARK WERE THE TUNNELS    MARTIN, GEORGE R. R. SS VTX 73 12
SONG FOR LYA, A                MARTIN, GEORGE R. R.    AC
DARKNESS (TRANSLATED BY LEO L. BARROW)
                               CARNEIRO, ANDRE   SS  NOV 72 02
BEST SF: 1972                  HARRISON & ALDISS       AN
NOVA 2                         HARRISON, HARRY         OA
DARKNESS AND DAWN              ENGLAND, GEORGE A. NO CSB 12 01
DARKNESS AND DAWN              ENGLAND, GEORGE A.      NO
UNDER THE MOONS OF MARS        MOSKOWITZ, SAM          AN
DARKNESS BOX                   LE GUIN, URSULA K. SS FAN 63 11
WINDS TWELVE QUARTERS, THE     LE GUIN, URSULA K.      AC
DARKNESS IN MY SOUL, A         KOONTZ, DEAN R.   NV  FAN 68 01
SOFT COME THE DRAGONS          KOONTZ, DEAN R.         DC
DARKNESS OF DAY                SARGENT, PAMELA
                               AND ZEBROWSKI, GEORGE SS C CTM 74 03
CONTINUUM 3                    ELWOOD, ROGER           OA
DARKSIDE CROSSING              BLISH, JAMES      NV  GAL 70 12
BEST FROM GALAXY, THE  VOLUME I   GALAXY, EDITORS OF   AN
DARLING ADOLPH                 BRADBURY, RAY     SS
LONG AFTER MIDNIGHT            BRADBURY, RAY           AC
DARWIN SAMPLER, THE            RUSSELL, RAY      SS  FIN 70
FUTURE IS NOW, THE             NOLAN, WILLIAM F.       OA
DARWINIAN POOL ROOM            ASIMOV, ISAAC     SS  GAL 50 10
BUY JUPITER AND OTHER STORIES  ASIMOV, ISAAC           AC
DASH OF SPRING, A              FINNEY, JACK      SS
THIRD LEVEL, THE               FINNEY, JACK            AC
DASIES (TRIPLICATE TWISTEROO)  BROWN, FREDRIC    SS  PBY 57 03
ROOTS OF EVIL, THE             PARRY, MICHEL           AN
DATE TO REMEMBER, A            TEMPLE, WILLIAM F. SS TWS 49 08
*INVADERS OF EARTH             CONKLIN, GROFF          AN
SPECULATIONS                   SANDERS, THOMAS E.      AN
DAUGHTER                       FARMER, PHILIP JOSE SS TWS 54 WI
STRANGE RELATIONS              FARMER, PHILIP JOSE     AC
DAUGHTER                       MCCAFFREY, ANNE   NV  MWS 71
GET OFF THE UNICORN            MCCAFFREY, ANNE         AC
MANY WORLDS OF SCIENCE FICTION, THE  BOVA, BEN         OA
DAUGHTER OF DARKNESS           ROCKLYNNE, ROSS   NA  AST 41 11
SUN DESTROYERS, THE            ROCKLYNNE, ROSS         DC
DAUGHTER OF ROSES              ADAM, HELEN       PM  QRK 70 01
QUARK/1                        DELANY & HACKER         OA
DAUGHTER OF THE TREE, THE      DEFORD, MIRIAM ALLEN SS FSF 51 08
STRANGE BED FELLOWS            SCORTIA, THOMAS N.      AN
XENOGENESIS                    DEFORD, MIRIAM ALLEN    AC
DAUGHTERS OF EARTH             MERRIL, JUDITH    SN  52
BEST OF JUDITH MERRIL, THE     MERRIL, JUDITH          AC
DAUGHTERS OF EARTH             MERRIL, JUDITH          AC
PETRIFIED PLANET, THE          CLARK, JOHN D.          OA
DAUGHTERS OF ETERNITY          POHL, FREDERIK    SS  AST 42 03
EARLY POHL, THE                POHL, FREDERIK          AC
DAVEY JONES' AMBASSADOR        GALLUN, RAYMOND Z. NV ASF 35 12
*BEST OF SCIENCE FICTION       CONKLIN, GROFF          AN
HISTORY OF THE SCIENCE FICTION MAGAZINE, THE  PART 1 1926-1935
                               ASHLEY, MICHAEL         AN
SCIENCE FICTION OF THE 30'S    KNIGHT, DAMON           AN
DAVID'S DADDY                  BROWN, ROSEL GEORGE SS FAN 60 06
6TH ANNUAL OF THE YEAR'S BEST S-F, THE  MERRIL, JUDITH  AN
```

DAVID'S WORM   LUMLEY, BRIAN   SS   71
   YEAR'S BEST HORROR STORIES: SERIES II, THE
                                DAVIS, RICHARD   AN
DAVY JONES' AMBASSADOR   GALLUN, RAYMOND Z.   NV ASF 35 12
   EARTH IS THE STRANGEST PLANET   SILVERBERG, ROBERT AN
DAWN ATTACK   COPEMAN, BERGER   SS
   ADVENTURES TO COME   ESENWEIN, J. BERG   OA
DAWN BREAKS OVER CRAKOW   DISCH, THOMAS M.   SS
   *GETTING INTO DEATH   DISCH, THOMAS M.   AC
DAWN INVADER   SHECKLEY, ROBERT   SS FSF 57 03
   ALIEN WORLDS   ELWOOD, ROGER   AN
   NOTIONS: UNLIMITED   SHECKLEY, ROBERT   AC
DAWN OF FAME: THE CAREER OF STANLEY G. WEINBAUM
                                MOSKOWITZ, SAM   AR SAT 59 05
   MARTIAN ODYSSEY AND OTHER SCIENCE FICTION TALES, A
                                     WEINBAUM, STANLEY G. AC
DAWN OF FLAME   WEINBAUM, STANLEY G. NV TWS 39 06
   DAWN OF FLAME   WEINBAUM, STANLEY G. AC
DAWN OF REASON, THE   BEARD, JAMES H.   PM UNK 39 10
   FROM UNKNOWN WORLDS   CAMPBELL, JOHN W. JR AN
DAWNINGSBURGH   WEST, WALLACE   SS GAL 62 06
   EIGHTH GALAXY READER, THE   POHL, FREDERIK   AN
DAY AFTER THE DAY THE MARTIANS CAME, THE (ALSO AS THE DAY
   THE MARTIANS CAME)   POHL, FREDERIK   SS DVS 67 01
   DANGEROUS VISIONS   ELLISON, HARLAN   OA
DAY AMONG THE LIARS, A   MITCHELL, EDWARD P.   SS SUN 85 08
   CRYSTAL MAN, THE   MITCHELL, EDWARD P. AC
DAY AT THE BEACH   EMSHWILLER, CAROL   SS FSF 59 08
   ABC OF SCIENCE FICTION, AN   BOARDMAN, TOM JR.   AN
   FANTASY: THE LITERATURE OF THE MARVELOUS KELLEY, LEO P. AN
   SF: THE BEST OF THE BEST   MERRIL, JUDITH   AN
   5TH ANNUAL OF THE YEAR'S BEST S-F, THE MERRIL, JUDITH AN
DAY BEFORE FOREVER, THE   LAUMER, KEITH   SN FSF 67 07
   DAY BEFORE FOREVER AND THUNDER HEAD, THE LAUMER, KEITH AC
DAY BEFORE NEVER, THE   PRESSLIE, ROBERT   NV NWR 65 06
   NEW WRITINGS IN SF. 6   CARNELL, JOHN   OA
DAY BEFORE THE REVOLUTION, THE LE GUIN, URSULA K.   SS GAL 74 08
   BEST FROM GALAXY, THE   VOLUME III BAEN, JAMES   AN
   MORE WOMEN OF WONDER   SARGENT, PAMELA   AN
   NEBULA AWARD STORIES 10   GUNN, JAMES E.   AN
   WINDS TWELVE QUARTERS, THE   LE GUIN, URSULA K. AC
DAY DARK, NIGHT BRIGHT   LEIBER, FRITZ   SS INY 72 04
   INFINITY 4   HOSKINS, ROBERT   OA
DAY EQUALITY BROKE OUT, THE   ALDISS, BRIAN W.   MS
   BEST SF: 1970   HARRISON & ALDISS   AN
DAY EUTERPE DIED, THE   DISCH, THOMAS M.   PM   69
   HOLDING YOUR EIGHT HANDS   LUCIE-SMITH, EDWARD AN
DAY FOR WAVING, A   CLINGERMAN, MILDRED   SS FSF 57 08
   CUPFUL OF SPACE, A   CLINGERMAN, MILDRED AC
DAY IN THE LIFE OF KELVIN THROOP, A
                                PHILLIPS, R. A. J.   SS ASF 64 07
   ANALOG 4   CAMPBELL, JOHN W. JR AN
DAY IN THE LIFE OF THE ARTIST, A
                                DISCH, THOMAS M.   SS
   *GETTING INTO DEATH   DISCH, THOMAS M.   AC
DAY IN THE SOUTH QUAD, A   GOTSCHALK, FELIX C.   SS NDM 75 05
   NEW DIMENSIONS 5   SILVERBERG, ROBERT OA
DAY IN THE SUBURBS, A   SMITH, EVELYN E.   SS FSF 60 09
   SOCIOLOGY THROUGH SCIENCE FICTION   MILSTEAD/GREENBERG/& AN
DAY IS DONE, THE   DEL REY, LESTER   SS ASF 39 05
   *AND SOME WERE HUMAN   DEL REY, LESTER   AC
   OPERATION FUTURE   CONKLIN, GROFF   AN
   SCIENCE FICTION OF THE 30'S   KNIGHT, DAMON   AN
   WHERE DO WE GO FROM HERE?   ASIMOV, ISAAC   AN
DAY IT RAINED FOREVER, THE   BRADBURY, RAY   SS HRP 57 07
   DAY IT RAINED FOREVER, THE   BRADBURY, RAY   AC
   MEDICINE FOR MELANCHOLY, A   BRADBURY, RAY   AC
DAY MILLION   POHL, FREDERIK   SS ROG 66 02
   ALPHA 3   SILVERBERG, ROBERT AN
   BEST OF FREDERIK POHL, THE   POHL, FREDERIK   AC
   BIO-FUTURES   SARGENT, PAMELA   AN
   DAY MILLION   POHL, FREDERIK   AC
   DECADE THE 1960S   ALDISS & HARRISON   AN
   MARRIAGE AND THE FAMILY THROUGH SCIENCE FICTION
                                     CLEAR/WARRICK/&   AN
   NEBULA AWARD STORIES   NO. 2   ALDISS & HARRISON   AN
   SCIENCE FICTION ARGOSY, A   KNIGHT, DAMON   AN
   SCIENCE FICTION: THE FUTURE   ALLEN, DICK   AN
   SF: AUTHORS' CHOICE   HARRISON, HARRY   AN
   THOSE WHO CAN: A SCIENCE FICTION READER WILSON, ROBIN SCOTT AN
   WORLD'S BEST SCIENCE FICTION: 1967 WOLLHEIM & CARR AN
DAY OF BURNING (SUPERNOVA)   ANDERSON, POUL   SN ASF 67 01
   BEYOND THE BEYOND   ANDERSON, POUL   AC
   MANY WORLDS OF POUL ANDERSON, THE   ANDERSON, POUL   AC
DAY OF DEATH, THE (SEE EL DIA DE MUERTE)
                                BRADBURY, RAY   TC
DAY OF FOREVER, THE   BALLARD, J. G.   SS NWS 67 01
   BEST OF J. G. BALLARD, THE   BALLARD, J. G.   AC
   DAY OF FOREVER, THE   BALLARD, J. G.   AC
   IMPOSSIBLE MAN, THE   BALLARD, J. G.   AC
DAY OF JUDGMENT   HAMILTON, EDMOND   SS WRT 46 09
   BEST OF EDMOND HAMILTON, THE   HAMILTON, EDMOND   AC
DAY OF RECKONING   MATHESON, RICHARD   SS MCB 60
   SHOCK WAVES   MATHESON, RICHARD   AC
DAY OF SUCCESSION   THOMAS, THEODORE L.   SS ASF 59 08
   CENTURY OF SCIENCE FICTION, A   KNIGHT, DAMON   AN
DAY OF THE BIG TEST, THE   GOTSCHALK, FELIX C.   NV   76
   FUTURE POWER   DANN & DOZOIS   OA
DAY OF THE BOOMER DUKES, THE   POHL, FREDERIK   SS FUT 56 30
   FREDERIK POHL OMNIBUS, THE   POHL, FREDERIK   AC
   MASTERS OF SCIENCE FICTION   HOWARD, IVAN   AN
   TOMORROW TIMES SEVEN   POHL, FREDERIK   AC
DAY OF THE BUTTERFLIES, THE   BRADLEY, MARION Z.   SS
   DAW SCIENCE FICTION READER, THE WOLLHEIM, DONALD A. OA
DAY OF THE DEEPIES, THE   LEINSTER, MURRAY   SS FFM 47 10
   SHOT IN THE DARK   MERRIL, JUDITH   AN

DAY OF THE DOOMED KING   ALDISS, BRIAN W.   SS SCF 65 11
   SALIVA TREE AND OTHER STRANGE GROWTHS, THE
                                ALDISS, BRIAN W.   AC
DAY OF THE DOVE (JEROME BIXBY) BLISH, JAMES   SA STK 75 11
   STAR TREK 11   BLISH, JAMES   OC
DAY OF THE DRAGON, THE   ENDORE, GUY   NV AFR 47 02
   ZOO 2000   YOLEN, JANE   AN
DAY OF THE GREEN VELVET CLOAK, THE
                                CLINGERMAN, MILDRED   SS FSF 58 07
   CUPFUL OF SPACE, A   CLINGERMAN, MILDRED AC
DAY OF THE HUNTERS   ASIMOV, ISAAC   SS FUT 50 11
   BUY JUPITER AND OTHER STORIES   ASIMOV, ISAAC   AC
   HAVE YOU SEEN THESE?   ASIMOV, ISAAC   AC
DAY OF THE TRIFFIDS, THE (REVOLT OF THE TRIFFIDS)
                                WYNDHAM, JOHN   EX COL 51 01
   FROM FRANKENSTEIN TO ANDROMEDA   BROWN, JAMES GOLDIE AN
DAY OF THE TRIFFIDS, THE (REVOLT OF THE TRIFFIDS)
                                WYNDHAM, JOHN   NO COL 51 01
   JOHN WYNDHAM OMNIBUS, THE   WYNDHAM, JOHN   AC
DAY OF TRUCE   SIMAK, CLIFFORD D.   NV GAL 63 02
   DEVIL'S GENERATION, THE   GHIDALIA, VIC   AN
   NIGHTMARE AGE   POHL, FREDERIK   AN
   YOU AND SCIENCE FICTION   HOLLISTER, BERNARD C AN
DAY OF WRATH, A   GANSOVSKY, SEVER   SS
   PATH INTO THE UNKNOWN   ANONYMOUS   AN
DAY ON DEATH HIGHWAY, A   ELLIOTT, H. CHANDLER   NV GAL 63 10
   EIGHTH GALAXY READER, THE   POHL, FREDERIK   AN
DAY REMBRANDT WENT PUBLIC, THE AUERBACH, ARNOLD M.   SS HRP 62 07
   FUTURE TENSE   CURTIS, RICHARD   AN
   8TH ANNUAL OF THE YEAR'S BEST S-F, THE MERRIL, JUDITH AN
DAY THE FLAG FELL, THE   ELAM, RICHARD M. JR.   SS
   TEEN-AGE SCIENCE FICTION STORIES   ELAM, RICHARD M. JR. AC
DAY THE FOUNDER DIED, THE   SILVERBERG, ROBERT   SS
   CRISIS   ELWOOD, ROGER   OA
   SHORES OF TOMORROW, THE   SILVERBERG, ROBERT AC
DAY THE GORF TOOK OVER, THE (GORF! GORF! GORF!)
                                NOLAN, WILLIAM F.   SS INY 71 02
   ALIEN HORIZONS   NOLAN, WILLIAM F.   AC
DAY THE ICICLE WORKS CLOSED, THE
                                POHL, FREDERIK   NV GAL 60 02
   BEST OF FREDERIK POHL, THE   POHL, FREDERIK   AC
   FREDERIK POHL OMNIBUS, THE   POHL, FREDERIK   AC
   MAN WHO ATE THE WORLD, THE   POHL, FREDERIK   AC
DAY THE MARTIANS CAME, THE (THE DAY AFTER THE DAY THE MARTIANS
   CAME)   POHL, FREDERIK   SS DVS 67 01
   BEST OF FREDERIK POHL, THE   POHL, FREDERIK   AC
   DAY MILLION   POHL, FREDERIK   AC
DAY THE WIND DIED, THE   TATE, PETER   NV FSF 69 03
   SEAGULLS UNDER GLASS AND OTHER STORIES TATE, PETER AC
DAY THEY CUT OFF THE POWER, THE
                                JOHNSON, VERA   SS NWR 75 27
   NEW WRITINGS IN SF. 27   BULMER, KENNETH   OA
DAY THEY GOT BOSTON, THE   GOLD, HERBERT   SS FSF 61 09
   POLITICAL SCIENCE FICTION   GREENBERG& WARRICK AN
   17 X INFINITY   CONKLIN, GROFF   AN
DAY WE CELEBRATE, THE   BOND, NELSON S.   SS ASF 41 01
   *POSSIBLE WORLDS OF SCIENCE FICTION CONKLIN, GROFF AN
DAY WE EMBARKED FOR CYTHERA, THE
                                ALDISS, BRIAN W.   SS NWQ 71 01
   MOMENT OF ECLIPSE, THE   ALDISS, BRIAN W.   AC
   NEW WORLDS QUARTERLY NO. 1   MOORCOCK, MICHAEL   OA
DAY WE EMBARKED FOR CYTHERA, THE
                                COUZYN, JENI   PM
   BEYOND THIS HORIZON   CARRELL, CHRISTOPHER OA
DAY WILL COME..., THE   O'QUINN, VITHALDAS H MS
   FANTASTIC UNIVERSE OMNIBUS, THE SANTESSON, HANS S. AN
DAY, THE   SAXTON, COLIN   SS SVW 73
   SAVING WORLDS   ELWOOD & KIDD   OA
DAYBROKE   BLOCH, ROBERT   SS SMG 58 01
   *BLOOD RUNS COLD   BLOCH, ROBERT   AC
   SCIENCE FICTION ROLL OF HONOR, THE POHL, FREDERIK   AN
   STAR OF STARS   POHL, FREDERIK   AN
DAYDREAM   MILLER, P. SCHUYLER   SS   49
   GIRL WITH THE HUNGRY EYES, AND OTHER STORIES, THE
                                WOLLHEIM, DONALD A.   OA
DAYLENGTH TALKING BLUES   TATE, PETER   SS
   SEAGULLS UNDER GLASS AND OTHER STORIES TATE, PETER AC
DAYMARE   BROWN, FREDRIC   NV TWS 43 FL
   DAYMARES   BROWN, FREDRIC   AC
   SAINT'S CHOICE OF IMPOSSIBLE CRIME, THE CHARTERIS, LESLIE AN
   SPACE ON MY HANDS   BROWN, FREDRIC   AC
DAYS OF GRASS, DAYS OF STRAW   LAFFERTY, R. A.   SS NDM 73 03
   NEW DIMENSIONS 3   SILVERBERG, ROBERT OA
DAYS OF PERKY PAT, THE   DICK, PHILIP K.   NV AMZ 63 12
   BEST OF PHILIP K. DICK, THE   DICK, PHILIP K.   AC
DAZED   STURGEON, THEODORE   NV GAL 71 09
   NEW AWARENESS, THE   WARRICK & GREENBERG AN
DE PROFUNDIS   LEINSTER, MURRAY   SS TWS 45 WI
   BEST OF MURRAY LEINSTER, THE   LEINSTER, MURRAY   AC
   FAR BOUNDARIES   DERLETH, AUGUST   AN
   MONSTERS AND SUCH   LEINSTER, MURRAY   AC
   SIDEWISE IN TIME   LEINSTER, MURRAY   AC
DE PROFUNDIS (THE VISITORS)   KUTTNER, HENRY   SS SFQ 53 05
   AHEAD OF TIME   KUTTNER, HENRY   AC
DEAD ASTRONAUT, THE   BALLARD, J. G.   SS PBY 68 05
   DEAD ASTRONAUT, 10 STORIES OF SPACE FLIGHT, THE
                                PLAYBOY, EDITORS OF   AN
   LOW-FLYING AIRCRAFT AND OTHER STORIES BALLARD, J. G. AC
DEAD CENTER   MERRIL, JUDITH   NV FSF 54 11
   BEST OF JUDITH MERRIL, THE   MERRIL, JUDITH   AC
   OUT OF BOUNDS   MERRIL, JUDITH   AC
   TREASURY OF GREAT SCIENCE FICTION, A VOL.2
                                BOUCHER, ANTHONY   AN
DEAD CHILD, THE   STANCIC, MILJENKO   IL
   SCIENCE FICTION   BRODKIN & PEARSON   AN

DEAD CITY (ALSO AS MALIGNANT MARAUDER)

DEAD CITY (ALSO AS MALIGNANT MARAUDER)
              LEINSTER, MURRAY   NV TWS 46 SU
  TWISTS IN TIME   LEINSTER, MURRAY   AC
DEAD END   HODUS, MIKE   SS ASF 67 05
  ANALOG 7   CAMPBELL, JOHN W. JR AN
DEAD END   MACFARLANE, WALLACE SS GAL 52 01
  *SCIENCE FICTION THINKING MACHINES CONKLIN, GROFF   AN
DEAD END   SPINRAD, NORMAN   SS GAL 69 11
  LAST HURRAH OF THE GOLDEN HORDE, THE SPINRAD, NORMAN   AC
DEAD FISH, THE   VIAN, BORIS   SS   55
  13 FRENCH SCIENCE-FICTION STORIES KNIGHT, DAMON   AN
DEAD HAND   ASIMOV, ISAAC   NV ASF 45 04
  FOUNDATION AND EMPIRE   ASIMOV, ISAAC   NO
DEAD IN IRONS   YARBRO, CHELSEA Q. NV   76
  FASTER THAN LIGHT   DANN & ZEBROWSKI   OA
DEAD KNOWLEDGE   CAMPBELL, JOHN W. JR NV ASF 38 01
  WHO GOES THERE?   CAMPBELL, JOHN W. JR AC
DEAD LADY OF CLOWN TOWN, THE SMITH, CORDWAINER SN GAL 64 08
  BEST OF CORDWAINER SMITH, THE   SMITH, CORDWAINER AC
  SPACE LORDS   SMITH, CORDWAINER AC
DEAD LETTER   BROWN, FREDRIC   SS
  NIGHTMARES AND GEEZENSTACKS   BROWN, FREDRIC   AC
DEAD MAN'S CHEST   SERLING, ROD   SA
  *ROD SERLING'S THE TWILIGHT ZONE SERLING, ROD   OC
DEAD MAN'S SHOES   DERLETH, AUGUST   SS WRT 46 03
  MR. GEORGE AND OTHER ODD PERSONS DERLETH, AUGUST   AC
DEAD MAN, THE   BRADBURY, RAY   SS WRT 45 07
  BLOCH AND BRADBURY   BRADBURY & BLOCH   AC
  *DARK CARNIVAL   BRADBURY, RAY   AC
  SMALL ASSASSIN, THE   BRADBURY, RAY   AC
DEAD MAN, THE   LEIBER, FRITZ   NV PNM 58 04
  SHADOWS WITH EYES   LEIBER, FRITZ   AC
DEAD PAST, THE   ASIMOV, ISAAC   NV ASF 56 04
  BEST OF ISAAC ASIMOV, THE   ASIMOV, ISAAC   AC
  BEYOND CONTROL   SILVERBERG, ROBERT AN
  EARTH IS ROOM ENOUGH   ASIMOV, ISAAC   AC
  FIVE-ODD   CONKLIN, GROFF   AN
DEAD PLANET, THE   HAMILTON, EDMOND   SS STS 46 SP
  EXPLORING OTHER WORLDS   MOSKOWITZ, SAM   AN
  *WORLDS OF TOMORROW   DERLETH, AUGUST   AN
DEAD REMEMBER, THE HOWARD, ROBERT E. SS ARG 36 08
  HORROR TIMES TEN   NORTON, ALDEN H.   AC
DEAD RINGER (ALSO AS AND THE TRUTH)
         DEL REY, LESTER   SS GAL 56 11
  THIRD GALAXY READER, THE   GOLD, H. L.   AN
DEAD RUN   CARTMILL, CLEVE   NV TWS 50 02
  SPACE SCAVENGERS, THE   CARTMILL, CLEVE   NO
DEAD SINGER, A   MOORCOCK, MICHAEL NV   74
  BEST SF: 75, THE NINTH ANNUAL HARRISON & ALDISS   AN
  MOORCOCK'S BOOK OF MARTYRS   MOORCOCK, MICHAEL AC
DEAD SINGERS   MOORCOCK, MICHAEL SS INK 71
  LIVES AND TIMES OF JERRY CORNELIUS, THE MOORCOCK, MICHAEL AC
DEAD SPOT, THE   WILLIAMSON, JACK   NV MAR 38 11
  HISTORY OF THE SCIENCE FICTION MAGAZINE, THE PART 2 1936-1945
         ASHLEY, MICHAEL   AN
DEAD STAR STATION WILLIAMSON, JACK   SS ASF 33 11
  EARLY WILLIAMSON, THE   WILLIAMSON, JACK   AC
DEAD TO THE WORLD HARGREAVES, H. A. SS NWR 68 11
  NEW WRITINGS IN SF. 8   CARNELL, JOHN   AN
  NEW WRITINGS IN SF. 11   CARNELL, JOHN   OA
DEAD VALLEY, THE   CRAM, RALPH ADAMS SS   95
  HORROR TIMES TEN   NORTON, ALDEN H.   AN
DEAD WOMAN, THE (STE 39 04) KELLER, DAVID H. MD. SS FMG 34 04
  FOLSOM FLINT AND OTHER CURIOUS TALES, THE
         KELLER, DAVID H. MD. AC
  LIFE EVERLASTING AND OTHER TALES OF SCIENCE, FANTASY
   AND HORROR   KELLER, DAVID H. MD. AC
  TALES FROM UNDERWOOD   KELLER, DAVID H. MD. AC
DEAD-END DOCTOR   BLOCH, ROBERT   SS GAL 56 02
  ATOMS AND EVIL   BLOCH, ROBERT   AC
DEADHEAD   SHECKLEY, ROBERT SS GAL 55 07
  PILGRIMAGE TO EARTH   SHECKLEY, ROBERT   AC
DEADLIER WEAPON, THE NIVEN, LARRY   SS EQM 68 06
  SHAPE OF SPACE, THE   NIVEN, LARRY   AC
DEADLIEST ART, THE   BLOCH, ROBERT   SS BMM 58 11
  KING OF TERRORS, THE   BLOCH, ROBERT   AC
  TALES IN A JUGULAR VEIN   BLOCH, ROBERT   AC
DEADLINE   CARTMILL, CLEVE   NV ASF 44 03
  *BEST OF SCIENCE FICTION   CONKLIN, GROFF   AN
DEADLINE   MATHESON, RICHARD SS ROG 59
  SHOCK II   MATHESON, RICHARD   AC
DEADLINE SUNDAY GALOUYE, DANIEL F. NV IMG 55 10
  LAST LEAP AND OTHER STORIES OF THE SUPER-MIND, THE
         GALOUYE, DANIEL F.   AC
DEADLOCK   KUTTNER, HENRY   SS ASF 42 08
  AHEAD OF TIME   KUTTNER, HENRY   AC
DEADLOCK   PADGETT, LEWIS   SS ASF 42 08
  ROBOT AND THE MAN, THE   GREENBERG, MARTIN AN
DEADLOCK   SILVERBERG, BARBARA
        AND SILVERBERG, ROBERT NV C ASF 59 01
  SHORES OF TOMORROW, THE   SILVERBERG, ROBERT AC
DEADLY DECISION SAMBROT, WILLIAM SS EXT 58
  ISLAND OF FEAR AND OTHER SCIENCE FICTION SAMBROT, WILLIAM AC
DEADLY DUST, THE LEINSTER, MURRAY NV TWS 47 08
  OUT OF THIS WORLD   LEINSTER, MURRAY   NO
DEADLY GAME, THE WELLEN, EDWARD SS IFS 62 05
  8TH ANNUAL OF THE YEAR'S BEST S-F, THE MERRIL, JUDITH AN
DEADLY HOST   JONES, RAYMOND F. SS ASF 45 09
  TOYMAKER, THE   JONES, RAYMOND F.   AC
DEADLY JOKER, THE (SEE IMPRACTICAL JOKER)
         BLOCH, ROBERT   TC
DEADLY LITTER   WHITE, JAMES   NV SFB 60 02
  DEADLY LITTER   WHITE, JAMES   NO
DEADLY MISSION OF PHINEAS SNODGRASS, THE
         POHL, FREDERIK   SS GAL 62 06
  DAY MILLION   POHL, FREDERIK   AC

DEATH MODULE, THE (ALSO AS NOTES TOWARD A MENTAL BREAKDOWN)

  IN THE PROBLEM PIT   POHL, FREDERIK   AC
DEADLY MOON   LEIBER, FRITZ   NV FAN 60 11
  SHIPS TO THE STARS   LEIBER, FRITZ   DC
DEADLY RATIO, THE (SEE IT WASN'T SYZYGY)
         STURGEON, THEODORE TC
DEADLY TUBE, THE   REEVE, ARTHUR B.   SS
  SILENT BULLET, THE   REEVE, ARTHUR B.   AC
DEADLY WILL TO WIN, THE (SEE A DEATH IN THE COUNTRY)
         BEAUMONT, CHARLES TC
DEADLY YEARS, THE (DAVID P. HARMON)
         BLISH, JAMES   SA STK 72 07
  STAR TREK 7   BLISH, JAMES   OC
DEAF LISTENER   PAYES, RACHEL C.   SS ALC 73
  ALIEN CONDITION, THE   GOLDIN, STEPHEN   OA
DEAL FROM THE BOTTOM ELLISON, HARLAN SS ROG 60 01
  ELLISON WONDERLAND   ELLISON, HARLAN   AC
DEAL IN OSTRICHES, A WELLS, H. G.   SS PMB 94
  SHORT STORIES OF H. G. WELLS, THE WELLS, H. G.   AC
  STOLEN BACILLUS AND OTHER INCIDENTS, THE WELLS, H. G.   AC
  THIRTY STRANGE STORIES   WELLS, H. G.   AC
DEAL WITH THE DEVIL, A DUNSANY, LORD   SS   48
  DEALS WITH THE DEVIL   DAVENPORT, BASIL   AN
DEAR AUNT ANNIE   EKLUND, GORDON   NV FAN 70 04
  WORLD'S BEST SCIENCE FICTION: 1971 WOLLHEIM & CARR   AN
DEAR CHARLES   LEINSTER, MURRAY SS FSM 53 05
  TWISTS IN TIME   LEINSTER, MURRAY   AC
DEAR DEVIL   RUSSELL, ERIC FRANK NV OWS 50 05
  *BIG BOOK OF SCIENCE FICTION   CONKLIN, GROFF   AN
  CREATURES FROM BEYOND   CARR, TERRY   AN
  EARTHMEN AND STRANGERS   SILVERBERG, ROBERT AN
  GENTLE INVADERS   SANTESSON, HANS S. AN
  SOMEWHERE A VOICE   RUSSELL, ERIC FRANK AC
  SPACE, SPACE, SPACE   SLOANE, WILLIAM   AN
DEAR DIARY   MATHESON, RICHARD SS NEW 54 AC
  BORN OF MAN AND WOMAN   MATHESON, RICHARD AC
  THIRD FROM THE SUN   MATHESON, RICHARD AC
DEAR MAVIS   O'NEILL, SCOTT   SS
  MARTIAN SEXPOT   O'NEILL, SCOTT   AC
DEAR PEN PAL   VAN VOGT, A. E. SS ARS 49 WI
  BEST OF A. E. VAN VOGT, THE (BRITISH) VAN VOGT, A. E. AC
  DESTINATION: UNIVERSE!   VAN VOGT, A. E.   AC
  FAR BOUNDARIES   DERLETH, AUGUST   AC
DEAR WITCH HAZEL, MY BIRDS WON'T FLY
         TATE, PETER   NV
  SEAGULLS UNDER GLASS AND OTHER STORIES TATE, PETER   AC
DEATH AND BIRTH OF THE ANGAKOK, THE
         HOWARD, HAYDEN NV GAL 65 04
  ESKIMO INVASION   HOWARD, HAYDEN   NO
DEATH AND DESIGNATION AMONG THE ASADI
         BISHOP, MICHAEL   NA IFS 73 02
  BEST FROM IF, THE VOLUME II   IF, EDITORS OF   AN
  1974 ANNUAL WORLD'S BEST SF, THE WOLLHEIM, DONALD A. AN
DEATH AND THE MAIDEN BRADBURY, RAY   SS FSF 60 03
  MACHINERIES OF JOY, THE   BRADBURY, RAY   AC
DEATH AND THE SENATOR CLARKE, ARTHUR C. NV ASF 61 05
  BEST OF ARTHUR C. CLARKE: 1937-1971, THE CLARKE, ARTHUR C. AC
  NINE BILLION NAMES OF GOD, THE   CLARKE, ARTHUR C.   AC
  POLITICAL SCIENCE FICTION   GREENBERG& WARRICK AN
  TALES OF TEN WORLDS   CLARKE, ARTHUR C.   AC
  WORLDS OF WHEN   CONKLIN, GROFF   AN
DEATH AND THE SENSPERIENCE POET
         GREEN, JOSEPH   SS NWR 70 17
  NEW WRITINGS IN SF. 17   CARNELL, JOHN   OA
DEATH AND THE SINGLE GIRL DISCH, THOMAS M. SS
  GETTING INTO DEATH AND OTHER STORIES DISCH, THOMAS M. AC
DEATH BETWEEN THE STARS BRADLEY, MARION Z. SS FUN 56 03
  DARK INTRUDER & OTHER STORIES, THE BRADLEY, MARION Z. DC
DEATH BY ECSTASY (THE ORGANLEGGERS)
         NIVEN, LARRY   NV GAL 69 01
  LONG ARM OF GIL HAMILTON, THE   NIVEN, LARRY   AC
  SHAPE OF SPACE, THE   NIVEN, LARRY   AC
  WORLD'S BEST SCIENCE FICTION: 1970 WOLLHEIM & CARR   AN
DEATH CANNOT WITHER MERRIL, JUDITH   NV FSF 59 02
  OUT OF BOUNDS   MERRIL, JUDITH   AC
DEATH DO US PART   BRUNNER, JOHN   SS SCF 55 11
  TIME-JUMP   BRUNNER, JOHN   AC
DEATH DOUBLE   NOLAN, WILLIAM F. SS NEW 63 AC
  IMPACT-20   NOLAN, WILLIAM F.   AC
DEATH DUST, THE   HARVEY, FRANK   SS SEP 59 08
  POST READER OF FANTASY AND SCIENCE FICTION
         SATURDAY EVE. POST   AN
DEATH FROM THE STARS HILLIARD, A. ROWLEY NV WOS 31 10
  SCIENCE FICTION GALAXY, THE   CONKLIN, GROFF   AN
DEATH IN A CAGE   NIVEN, LARRY   SS NEW 73 AC
  FLIGHT OF THE HORSE, THE   NIVEN, LARRY   AC
DEATH IN COVENTRY, A GREEN, JOSEPH   SS DYS 75
  DYSTOPIAN VISIONS   ELWOOD, ROGER   OA
DEATH IN THE COUNTRY, A (THE DEADLY WILL TO WIN)
         BEAUMONT, CHARLES SS PBY 57 11
  MAGIC MAN AND OTHER SCIENCE-FANTASY STORIES
         BEAUMONT, CHARLES AC
  NIGHT RIDE AND OTHER JOURNEYS   BEAUMONT, CHARLES AC
DEATH IN THE HOUSE, A SIMAK, CLIFFORD D. NV GAL 59 10
  AS TOMORROW BECOMES TODAY   SULLIVAN, CHARLES W. AN
  SF: THE BEST OF THE BEST   MERRIL, JUDITH   AN
  5TH ANNUAL OF THE YEAR'S BEST S-F, THE MERRIL, JUDITH AN
DEATH INTO LIFE   STAPLEDON, OLAF   NO MTH 46
  WORLDS OF WONDER   STAPLEDON, OLAF   AC
DEATH IS THE PENALTY MERRIL, JUDITH   SS ASF 49 01
  BEYOND THE END OF TIME   POHL, FREDERIK   AN
  SURVIVAL SHIP AND OTHER STORIES   MERRIL, JUDITH   AC
DEATH MARCH   BUDRYS, ALGIS   NV ASF 56 10
  BEST SF 6   CRISPIN, EDMUND   AN
DEATH MODULE, THE (ALSO AS NOTES TOWARD A MENTAL BREAKDOWN)
         BALLARD, J. G.   SS NWS 67 07
  BEST SF STORIES FROM NEW WORLDS 5 MOORCOCK, MICHAEL AN

DEATH OF A BUMBLEBEE   WAKEFIELD, H.RUSSELL SS
  TRAVELLERS BY NIGHT   DERLETH, AUGUST   OA
DEATH OF A CITY   HERBERT, FRANK   SS   FUC 73
  FUTURE CITY   ELWOOD, ROGER   OA
DEATH OF A DINOSAUR   MOSKOWITZ, SAM   SS   AMZ 56 08
  TIME CURVE, THE   MOSKOWITZ & ELWOOD   AN
DEATH OF A PLANET   ANONYMOUS   CT
  LAURIE'S SPACE ANNUAL   ANONYMOUS   AN
DEATH OF A SENSITIVE   BATES, HARRY   NV   SFP 53 05
  EDITOR'S CHOICE IN SCIENCE FICTION MOSKOWITZ, SAM   AN
DEATH OF A SPACEMAN (ALSO AS MOMENTO HOMO)
                            MILLER, WALTER M. JR SS AMZ 54 03
  WILDERNESS OF STARS, A   NOLAN, WILLIAM F.   AN
DEATH OF AN APEMAN, THE   NESVADBA, JOSEF   NV
  LOST FACE, THE   NESVADBA, JOSEF   AC
DEATH OF ARCHIMEDES, THE   CAPEK, KAREL   SS   49
  FANTASIA MATHEMATICA   FADIMAN, CLIFTON   AN
DEATH OF DOCTOR ISLAND, THE WOLFE, GENE   NV   UNI 73 03
  BEST SCIENCE FICTION OF THE YEAR, THE NO. 3
                                 CARR, TERRY   AN
  NEBULA AWARD STORIES 9   WILHELM, KATE   AN
  UNIVERSE 3   CARR, TERRY   OA
DEATH OF EACH DAY, THE   ST. CLAIR, MARGARET SS   FSF 58 04
  CHANGE THE SKY AND OTHER STORIES ST. CLAIR, MARGARET AC
DEATH OF HYLE, THE   WOLFE, GENE   SS   CTM 74 02
  CONTINUUM 2   ELWOOD, ROGER   OA
DEATH OF ILALOTHA, THE   SMITH, CLARK ASHTON SS   WRT 37 09
  OUT OF SPACE AND TIME   SMITH, CLARK ASHTON   AC
DEATH OF MAN, THE   FULTHORPE, DOUGLAS SS   SFM 74 05
  BEST OF SCIENCE FICTION MONTHLY, THE SACKS, JANET   AN
DEATH OF PRINCES, THE   LEIBER, FRITZ   NV   AMZ 76 06
  BEST SCIENCE FICTION OF THE YEAR, THE NO. 6
                                 CARR, TERRY   AN
DEATH OF SAPPHO, THE   PIERCY, MARGE   NV
  2076: THE AMERICAN TRICENTENNIAL BRYANT, EDWARD   OA
DEATH OF SOCRATES, THE   DISCH, THOMAS M.   NV
  334   DISCH, THOMAS M.   NO
DEATH OF THE MOON, THE   PHILLIPS, A. M.   SS   AMZ 29 02
  FLIGHT INTO SPACE   WOLLHEIM, DONALD A.   AN
DEATH OF THE SEA, THE   GIRONELLA, JOSE MARIA SS   64
  VINTAGE ANTHOLOGY OF SCIENCE FANTASY, THE
                                 CERF, CHRISTOPHER   AN
DEATH ON THE MOUNTAIN   BROWN, FREDRIC   SS
  NIGHTMARES AND GEEZENSTACKS   BROWN, FREDRIC   AC
DEATH OR CONSEQUENCES   DORMAN, SONYA   SS
  TOMORROW: NEW WORLDS OF SCIENCE FICTION ELWOOD, ROGER OA
DEATH RIDES THE SPACEWAYS   ACKERMAN, FORREST J. SS
  AUTHENTIC BOOK OF SPACE   CAMPBELL, H. J.   AN
DEATH SCENE   SIMAK, CLIFFORD D. SS   INF 57 10
  ALIENS FOR NEIGHBOURS   SIMAK, CLIFFORD D.   AC
  OTHER WORLDS OF CLIFFORD SIMAK SIMAK, CLIFFORD D.   AC
  *WORLDS OF CLIFFORD SIMAK, THE SIMAK, CLIFFORD D.   AC
DEATH SEEKERS, THE   VERNON, ROGER LEE   NV
  SPACE FRONTIERS, THE   VERNON, ROGER LEE   AC
DEATH SENTENCE   ASIMOV, ISAAC   SS   ASF 43 11
  EARLY ASIMOV, THE   ASIMOV, ISAAC   AC
  *OUTER REACHES, THE   DERLETH, AUGUST   AN
DEATH SENTENCE (SEE SENTENCE OF DEATH)
                            CHRISTOPHER, JOHN   TC
DEATH SHIP   MATHESON, RICHARD   NV   FSM 53 03
  SHOCK!   MATHESON, RICHARD   AC
DEATH TO THE KEEPER   MALZBERG, BARRY N. NV   FSF 68 08
  MANY WORLDS OF BARRY MALZBERG, THE MALZBERG, BARRY N. AC
DEATH TO THE KEEPER   O'DONNELL, K. M.   NV   FSF 68 08
  FINAL WAR AND OTHER FANTASIES O'DONNELL, K. M.   DC
DEATH WATCH   COOPER, EDMUND   SS
  TOMORROW CAME   COOPER, EDMUND   AC
DEATH WISH (SEE THE BLUE BOTTLE)
                            BRADBURY, RAY   TC
DEATH'S DEPUTY   HUBBARD, L. RON   NO   UNK 40 02
  FROM DEATH TO THE STARS   HUBBARD, L. RON   AC
DEATH'S DOOR   MCNEAR, ROBERT   SS   PBY 69 03
  MASKS   PLAYBOY, EDITORS OF   AN
  YEAR'S BEST HORROR STORIES, THE DAVIS, RICHARD   AN
DEATH'S MASQUERADE   SERLING, ROD   SA
  *ROD SERLING'S THE TWILIGHT ZONE SERLING, ROD   OC
DEATH-BY-RAIN (SEE THE LONG RAIN)
                            BRADBURY, RAY   TC
DEATH-TRAP, THE   DAULTON, GEORGE   SS   PRS 08 03
  SCIENCE FICTION BY GASLIGHT   MOSKOWITZ, SAM   AN
DEATH-WATERS   LONG, FRANK BELKNAP SS   WRT 24 12
  DARK BEASTS, THE   LONG, FRANK BELKNAP   AC
  EARLY LONG, THE   LONG, FRANK BELKNAP   AC
  *HOUNDS OF TINDALOS, THE   LONG, FRANK BELKNAP   AC
DEATHBIRD, THE   ELLISON, HARLAN   NV   FSF 73 03
  BEST FROM FANTASY AND SCIENCE FICTION: 20
                                 FERMAN, EDWARD L.   AN
  BEST SCIENCE FICTION OF THE YEAR, THE NO. 3
                                 CARR, TERRY   AN
  DEATHBIRD STORIES   ELLISON, HARLAN   AC
  NEBULA AWARD STORIES 9   WILHELM, KATE   AN
  1974 ANNUAL WORLD'S BEST SF, THE WOLLHEIM, DONALD A. AN
DEATHRIGHTS DEFERRED   PISERCHIA, DORIS   SS
  SCIENCE FICTION DISCOVERIES   POHL, C. & F.   OA
DEATHS OF BEN BAXTER, THE   SHECKLEY, ROBERT   NV   GAL 57 07
  STORE OF INFINITY   SHECKLEY, ROBERT   AC
DEATHSONG   VAN SCYOC, SYDNEY J. NA   GAL 74 02
  1975 ANNUAL WORLD'S BEST SF, THE WOLLHEIM, DONALD A. AN
DEATHWATCH   SPINRAD, NORMAN   SS   PBY 65 11
  FROM THE "S" FILE   PLAYBOY, EDITORS OF   AN
  LAST HURRAH OF THE GOLDEN HORDE, THE SPINRAD, NORMAN AC
DEATHWORLD   HARRISON, HARRY   NO   ASF 60 01
  DEATHWORLD TRILOGY, THE   HARRISON, HARRY   AC
DEATHWORLD 2 (THE ETHICAL ENGINEER)
                            HARRISON, HARRY   NO   ASF 63 07
  DEATHWORLD TRILOGY, THE   HARRISON, HARRY   AC

DEATHWORLD 3 (THE HORSE BARBARIANS)
                            HARRISON, HARRY   NO   ASF 68 02
  DEATHWORLD TRILOGY, THE   HARRISON, HARRY   AC
DEBATE ON SF- MOSCOW 1965, A TOMAN, NIKOLAY   SS
  OTHER WORLDS, OTHER SEAS   SUVIN, DARKO   AN
DEBRIS OF RECENT LIVES, THE PARTINGTON, CHARLES NWR 75 25
  NEW WRITINGS IN SF. 25   BULMER, KENNETH   OA
DEBT, THE   HULL, E. MAYNE   NV   ASF 43 12
  PLANETS FOR SALE   HULL, E. MAYNE   AC
DEBUNKING THE I MACHINE   LEIBER, FRITZ   AR   49
  BOOK OF FRITZ LEIBER, THE   LEIBER, FRITZ   AC
DEBUT   EMSHWILLER, CAROL   SS   ORB 70 06
  ORBIT 6   KNIGHT, DAMON   OA
DEBUT   LORY, ROBERT   SS   66
  HARVEST OF HOODWINKS, A   LORY, ROBERT   DC
DECADENCE (TRANSLATED BY RICHARD HOWARD)
                            GARY, ROMAIN   SS   SGA 64
  10TH ANNUAL OF THE YEAR'S BEST S-F, THE MERRIL, JUDITH AN
DECEIVERS, THE (SEE INTENT TO DECEIVE)
                            NIVEN, LARRY   TC
DECEMBER 28TH   THOMAS, THEODORE L. SS   PBY 59 12
  LAST TRAIN TO LIMBO   PLAYBOY, EDITORS OF   AN
  PLAYBOY BOOK OF SCIENCE FICTION AND FANTASY, THE
                                 PLAYBOY, EDITORS OF   AN
DECISION MAKERS, THE   GREEN, JOSEPH   NV   GAL 65 04
  AFFAIR WITH GENIUS, AN   GREEN, JOSEPH   AC
  AS TOMORROW BECOMES TODAY   SULLIVAN, CHARLES W.   AN
  CONSCIENCE INTERPLANETARY   GREEN, JOSEPH   NO
  WORLD'S BEST SCIENCE FICTION: 1966 WOLLHEIM & CARR   AN
DECOY   CHRISTOPHER, JOHN   SS   SFS 55 07
  TWENTY-SECOND CENTURY, THE   CHRISTOPHER, JOHN   AC
DEEP DOWN DRAGON, THE   MERRIL, JUDITH   SS   GAL 61 08
  SEVENTH GALAXY READER, THE   POHL, FREDERIK   AN
  SURVIVAL SHIP AND OTHER STORIES MERRIL, JUDITH   AC
  13 ABOVE THE NIGHT   CONKLIN, GROFF   AN
DEEP END   BALLARD, J. G.   SS   NWS 61 05
  CHRONOPOLIS AND OTHER STORIES BALLARD, J. G.   AC
  TERMINAL BEACH (BRITISH VERSION) BALLARD, J. G.   AC
  VOICES OF TIME AND OTHER STORIES, THE BALLARD, J. G. AC
DEEP FIX, THE   COLVIN, JAMES   NV   SCF 64 04
  DEEP FIX, THE   COLVIN, JAMES   AC
DEEP FIX, THE (AS JAMES COLVIN)
                            MOORCOCK, MICHAEL   NV   SCF 64 04
  TIME DWELLER, THE   MOORCOCK, MICHAEL   AC
DEEP RANGE, THE (ARB 54 04) CLARKE, ARTHUR C.   NO   STR 54 03
  FROM THE OCEAN, FROM THE STARS CLARKE, ARTHUR C.   AC
DEEP RANGE, THE (ARB 54 04) CLARKE, ARTHUR C.   NO   STR 54 03
  BEYOND TOMORROW   KNIGHT, DAMON   AN
  FROM FRANKENSTEIN TO ANDROMEDA BROWN, JAMES GOLDIE   AN
  GIANTS UNLEASHED   CONKLIN, GROFF   AN
  STAR OF STARS   POHL, FREDERICK   AN
  STAR SCIENCE FICTION STORIES NO. 3 POHL, FREDERICK   OA
  WHERE DO WE GO FROM HERE?   ASIMOV, ISAAC   AN
  ZOO 2000   YOLEN, JANE   AN
DEEP SPACE   SABERHAGEN, FRED   SS
  BOOK OF SABERHAGEN, THE   SABERHAGEN, FRED   AC
DEEP SPACE (AXOLOTL)   ABERNATHY, ROBERT   SS   FSF 54 01
  5 TALES FROM TOMORROW   DIKTY, T. E.   AN
DEEP WELL OF THE UNCONSCIOUS- WELL, WELL..., THE
                            KNIGHT, DAMON   AR   CLR 73 03
  CLARION III   WILSON, ROBIN SCOTT   AN
DEEP, THE   ASIMOV, ISAAC   NV   GAL 52 12
  BEST OF ISAAC ASIMOV, THE   ASIMOV, ISAAC   AC
  MARTIAN WAY AND OTHER STORIES, THE ASIMOV, ISAAC   AC
DEEPER THAN DARKNESS   ELLISON, HARLAN   NV   INF 57 04
  ALONE AGAINST TOMORROW   ELLISON, HARLAN   AC
  *PAINGOD AND OTHER DELUSIONS   ELLISON, HARLAN   AC
DEEPER THAN THE DARKNESS   BENFORD, GREGORY   NV   FSF 69 04
  SOCIOLOGY THROUGH SCIENCE FICTION MILSTEAD/GREENBERG/& AN
DEEPEST BLUE IN THE WORLD, THE DORMAN, SONYA   SS   FSF 64 09
  SF: AUTHORS' CHOICE 3   HARRISON, HARRY   AN
DEEPS, THE   ROBERTS, KEITH   SS   ORB 66 01
  HOT & COLD RUNNING CITIES   MCHARGUE, GEORGESS   AN
  MACHINES AND MEN   ROBERTS, KEITH   AC
  ORBIT 1   KNIGHT, DAMON   OA
  PASSING OF THE DRAGONS, THE   ROBERTS, KEITH   AC
DEER IN THE WORKS   VONNEGUT, KURT JR. SS   ESQ 55 04
  CANARY IN A CAT HOUSE   VONNEGUT, KURT JR.   AC
  RUINS OF EARTH, THE   DISCH, THOMAS M.   AN
  WELCOME TO THE MONKEY HOUSE   VONNEGUT, KURT JR.   AC
DEFENDERS, THE   DICK, PHILIP K.   NV   GAL 53 01
  BOOK OF PHILIP K. DICK, THE   DICK, PHILIP K.   AC
  INVASION OF THE ROBOTS   ELWOOD, ROGER   AN
DEFENESTRATION OF ERMINTRUDE INCH, THE
                            CLARKE, ARTHUR C.   SS
  TALES FROM THE WHITE HART   CLARKE, ARTHUR C.   AC
DEFENSE   VAN VOGT, A. E.   SS   AFR 47 04
  DESTINATION: UNIVERSE!   VAN VOGT, A. E.   AC
DEFENSE MECHANISM   KING, VINCENT   NV   NWR 66 09
  NEW WRITINGS IN SF. 7   CARNELL, JOHN   AN
  NEW WRITINGS IN SF. 9   CARNELL, JOHN   OA
DEFENSE MECHANISM   MACLEAN, KATHERINE SS   ASF 49 10
  BEYOND THE BARRIERS OF SPACE AND TIME MERRIL, JUDITH AN
  *BIG BOOK OF SCIENCE FICTION   CONKLIN, GROFF   AN
  DIPLOIDS AND OTHER FLIGHTS OF FANCY, THE MACLEAN, KATHERINE AC
DEFENSE OF WEREWOLVES, A (FANTASY ON THE MARCH)
                            LEIBER, FRITZ   AR   ARS 48 SP
  SECOND BOOK OF FRITZ LEIBER, THE LEIBER, FRITZ   AC
DEFENSELESS DEAD, THE   NIVEN, LARRY   NV   TTM 73
  LONG ARM OF GIL HAMILTON, THE NIVEN, LARRY   AC
  TEN TOMORROWS   ELWOOD, ROGER   OA
DEFENSIVE BOMBER, THE   DEMPSEY, HANK   SS   NOV 73 03
  NOVA 3   HARRISON, HARRY   OA
DEFINITION, THE   MARSDEN, BOB   SS   NWS 68 07
  NEW TOMORROWS, THE   SPINRAD, NORMAN   AN

DELAY IN TRANSIT   WALLACE, F. L.   NA   GAL 52 09
   BODYGUARD AND 4 OTHER SHORT SF NOVELS FROM GALAXY
                               GOLD, H. L.   AN
DELEGATE FROM GUAPANGA, THE   GUIN, WYMAN   NV   GAL 64 08
   AMERICAN GOVERNMENT THROUGH SCIENCE FICTION
                               OLANDER/GREENBERG/&   AN
   LIVING WAY OUT   GUIN, WYMAN   AC
DELENDA EST   ANDERSON, POUL   NV   FSF 55 12
   GUARDIANS OF TIME   ANDERSON, POUL   AC
   WORLDS OF MAYBE   SILVERBERG, ROBERT   AN
DELENDA EST CARTHAGO   FAIRMAN, PAUL W.   SS
   FORGETFUL ROBOT, THE   FAIRMAN, PAUL W.   OC
DELHI DIVISION, THE   MOORCOCK, MICHAEL   SS   NWS 68 12
   BEST SF STORIES FROM NEW WORLDS 6   MOORCOCK, MICHAEL   AN
   LIVES AND TIMES OF JERRY CORNELIUS, THE MOORCOCK, MICHAEL   AC
DELICIOUS CIRCLE, A   ALDISS, BRIAN W.   PL   NWB 75 09
   NEW WORLDS NINE   BAILEY, HILARY   OA
DELIGHTFUL COMEDIC PREMISE, A MALZBERG, BARRY N.   SS   FSF 74 02
   ANTIGRAV: COSMIC COMEDIES   STRICK, PHILIP   AN
   BEST OF BARRY N. MALZBERG, THE   MALZBERG, BARRY N.   AC
DELILAH AND THE SPACE-RIGGER   HEINLEIN, ROBERT A.   SS   BBM 49 12
   GREEN HILLS OF EARTH, THE   HEINLEIN, ROBERT A.   AC
   PAST THROUGH TOMORROW, THE HEINLEIN, ROBERT A.   AC
DELIVERY GUARANTEED   SILVERBERG, ROBERT   SS   SFS 59 02
   CALLIBRATED ALLIGATOR AND OTHER SCIENCE FICTION STORIES, THE
                               SILVERBERG, ROBERT   AC
DELTA AT SUNSET, THE   BALLARD, J. G.   SS   NEW 64 AC
   IMPOSSIBLE MAN, THE   BALLARD, J. G.   AC
   TERMINAL BEACH (BRITISH VERSION) BALLARD, J. G.   AC
DELTA FLIGHT 281   SALLIS, JAMES   SS   ALT 74
   ALTERNATIES   GERROLD, DAVID   OA
DELUGE   HENDERSON, ZENNA   NV   FSF 63 10
   BEST FROM FANTASY AND SCIENCE FICTION: 13
                               DAVIDSON, AVRAM   AN
   PEOPLE: NO DIFFERENT FLESH, THE   HENDERSON, ZENNA   AC
DELUSION FOR A DRAGON SLAYER   ELLISON, HARLAN   SS   KNT 66 09
   DEATHBIRD STORIES   ELLISON, HARLAN   AC
   I HAVE NO MOUTH, AND I MUST SCREAM   ELLISON, HARLAN   AC
   *LOVE AIN'T NOTHING BUT SEX MISSPELLED   ELLISON, HARLAN   AC
DEMI-URGE, THE   DISCH, THOMAS M.   SS   AMZ 63 06
   *ONE HUNDRED AND TWO H-BOMBS   DISCH, THOMAS M.   AC
   WHITE FANG GOES DINGO AND OTHER FUNNY S.F. STORIES
                               DISCH, THOMAS M.   AC
DEMOBILIZATION   COWIE, GEORGE R.   SS   VOX 47
   SCIENCE AND SORCERY   FORD, GARRET   AN
DEMOISELLE D'YS, THE   CHAMBERS, ROBERT W.   SS   WRT 28 08
   EDITOR'S CHOICE IN SCIENCE FICTION   MOSKOWITZ, SAM   AN
DEMOLISHED MAN, THE   BESTER, ALFRED   NO   GAL 52 01
   ALFRED BESTER OMNIBUS, AN   BESTER, ALFRED   AC
   SCIENCE FICTION ARGOSY, A   KNIGHT, DAMON   AN
DEMON KING, THE   PRIESTLEY, J. B.   SS   34
   GALAXY OF GHOULS   MERRIL, JUDITH   AN
DEMON MACHINE, THE   LITTKE, LAEL J.   SS
   STRANGE ENCOUNTERS   BISCHOFF, DAVID   OA
DEMONS, THE   SHECKLEY, ROBERT   SS   FNF 53 02
   *UNTOUCHED BY HUMAN HANDS   SHECKLEY, ROBERT   AC
DEMOTION   LOCKE, ROBERT DONALD   SS   ASF 52 09
   PRIZE SCIENCE FICTION   WOLLHEIM, DONALD A.   AN
DENKIRK   DRAKE, DAVID   SS
   TRAVELLERS BY NIGHT   DERLETH, AUGUST   AN
DENY THE SLAKE   WILSON, RICHARD   SS   INF 57 04
   SPECIAL WONDER   MCCOMAS, J. FRANCIS   AN
DEPRESSION...OR BUST   REYNOLDS, MACK   SS   ASF 67 08
   DEPRESSION...OR BUST   REYNOLDS, MACK   DN
DERELICT   GALLUN, RAYMOND Z.   SS   ASF 35 10
   COMING OF THE ROBOTS, THE   MOSKOWITZ, SAM   AN
DERELICT OF SPACE   WYNDHAM, JOHN   NV   FSB 39 03
   WANDERERS OF TIME   WYNDHAM, JOHN   AC
DERELICT, THE (1914)   HODGSON, WILLIAM H.   SS   FFM 43 12
   SCIENCE FICTION GALAXY, THE CONKLIN, GROFF   AN
DERM FOOL   STURGEON, THEODORE   SS   UNK 40 03
   CROSSROADS IN TIME   CONKLIN, GROFF   AN
   STARSHINE   STURGEON, THEODORE   AC
DERMUCHE   AYME, MARCEL   SS
   WALKER THROUGH WALLS, THE   AYME, MARCEL   AC
DESCENDING   DISCH, THOMAS M.   SS   FAN 64 07
   DECADE THE 1960S   ALDISS & HARRISON   AN
   FUN WITH YOUR NEW HEAD   DISCH, THOMAS M.   AC
   MODERN SCIENCE FICTION   SPINRAD, NORMAN   AN
   10TH ANNUAL OF THE YEAR'S BEST S-F, THE   MERRIL, JUDITH   AN
DESCENT   MATHESON, RICHARD   SS   IFS 54 05
   SHOCK II   MATHESON, RICHARD   AC
DESCENT INTO THE MAELSTROM, A POE, EDGAR ALLEN   SS   GLG 41 05
   ARMCHAIR SCIENCE READER, THE   GORDON, I. & SORKIN   AN
   JOURNEYS IN SCIENCE FICTION   LOUGHLIN, RICHARD L.   AN
DESCENT OF MAN, THE   LAWRENCE, J. A.   SS   IFS 74 12
   BEST FROM IF, THE   VOLUME III   BAEN, JAMES   AN
DESCENT OF THE WEST END, THE   DISCH, THOMAS M.   SS   NWS 67 03
   BEST SF STORIES FROM NEW WORLDS NO. 2, THE
                               MOORCOCK, MICHAEL   AN
   WHITE FANG GOES DINGO AND OTHER FUNNY S.F. STORIES
                               DISCH, THOMAS M.   AC
DESERT AND THE STARS, THE (SEE PROTEST NOTE)
                               LAUMER, KEITH   TC
DESERT ENCOUNTER   ROSOKHOVATSKY, IGOR   SS
   RUSSIAN SCIENCE FICTION, 1968   MAGIDOFF, ROBERT   AN
DESERT PLACES   SARGENT, PAMELA   SS   UNI 74 04
   STARSHADOWS   SARGENT, PAMELA   AC
   UNIVERSE 4   CARR, TERRY   OA
DESERT ROMANCE (SHADOW GUIDE) PRICE, E. HOFFMANN   SS
   STRANGE LOVE STORIES   ANONYMOUS   AN
DESERTER, THE   TENN, WILLIAM   SS   STR 53 01
   BUG-EYED MONSTERS   CHEETHAM, ANTHONY   AN
   STAR SCIENCE FICTION STORIES   POHL, FREDERICK   OA
   WOODEN STAR, THE   TENN, WILLIAM   AC

DESERTION   SIMAK, CLIFFORD D.   SS   ASF 44 11
   BEYOND TOMORROW   KNIGHT, DAMON   AN
   *BIG BOOK OF SCIENCE FICTION   CONKLIN, GROFF   AN
   CITY   SIMAK, CLIFFORD D.   NO
   GALAXY OF GHOULS   MERRIL, JUDITH   AN
   JUPITER   POHL, C. & F.   AN
   SPECTRUM OF WORLDS, A   CLARESON, THOMAS D.   AN
   SURVIVAL PRINTOUT   TOTAL EFFECT   AN
   TOMORROW'S WORLDS   SILVERBERG, ROBERT   AN
   TOMORROW, AND TOMORROW, AND TOMORROW... HEINTZ/HERBERT/JOOS/ AN
   UBERWINDUNG VON RAUM UND ZEIT   GUNTHER, GOTTHARD   AN
DESICCATOR, THE   SILVERBERG, ROBERT   SS   SFS 56 05
   GODLING, GO HOME!   SILVERBERG, ROBERT   AC
DESIGN FOR GREAT DAY (SEE THE ULTIMATE INVADER)
                               RUSSELL, ERIC FRANK   TC
DESIRABLE LAKESIDE RESIDENCE   NORTON, ANDRE   SS   SVW 73
   SAVING WORLDS   ELWOOD & KIDD   AN
DESIRE   STEPHENS, JAMES   SS   28
   MOONLIGHT TRAVELER, THE   STERN, PHILIP VAN D.   AN
DESKFUL OF GIRLS, A   LEIBER, FRITZ   NV   FSF 58 04
   BEST FROM FANTASY AND SCIENCE FICTION: 8
                               BOUCHER, ANTHONY   AN
   BEST OF FRITZ LEIBER, THE   LEIBER, FRITZ   AC
   DARK STARS   SILVERBERG, ROBERT   AC
   SHADOWS WITH EYES   LEIBER, FRITZ   AC
DESMOND'S DINOSAUR   CAMPTON, DAVID   SS   ADS 75 02
   ARMADA SCI-FI TWO   DAVIS, RICHARD   OA
DESRICK ON YANDRO, THE   WELLMAN, MANLY WADE   SS   FSF 52 06
   BEST FROM FANTASY AND SCIENCE FICTION: 2
                               BOUCHER & MCCOMAS   AN
   WHO FEARS THE DEVIL?   WELLMAN, MANLY WADE   AC
DESTINATION MOON   HEINLEIN, ROBERT A.   NV   SSM 50 09
   THREE TIMES INFINITY   MARGULIES, LEO   AN
DESTINATION: AMALTHEIA   STRUGATSKY, ARKADY
                               AND STRUGATSKY, BORIS SS C
   DESTINATION: AMALTHEIA   DIXON, RICHARD   AN
DESTINATIONS, PREMONITIONS AND THE NATURE OF ANXIETY
                               EMSHWILLER, CAROL   SS
   JOY IN OUR CAUSE   EMSHWILLER, CAROL   AC
DESTINIES OF THE STARS   ARRHENIUS, SVANTE   AR   18
   ALL ABOUT VENUS   ALDISS, BRIAN W.   AN
   FAREWELL FANTASTIC VENUS   ALDISS & HARRISON   AN
DESTINY OF MILTON GOMRATH, THE PANSHIN, ALEXEI   SS   ASF 67 03
   FAR-OUT PEOPLE, THE   HOSKINS, ROBERT   AN
   FAREWELL TO YESTERDAY'S TOMORROW   PANSHIN, ALEXEI   AC
   OTHER DIMENSIONS   SILVERBERG, ROBERT   AN
DESTINY TIMES THREE   LEIBER, FRITZ   SN   ASF 45 03
   FIVE SCIENCE FICTION NOVELS GREENBERG, MARTIN   AN
DESTROYING HORDE, THE   WANDREI, DONALD   SS   WRT 35 06
   STRANGE HARVEST   WANDREI, DONALD   AC
DESTRUCT BUTTON   HARVEY, FRANK   SS   ARG 59
   AIR FORCE!   HARVEY, FRANK   AC
DESTRUCTION AND EXCULPATION OF EARTH, THE
                               MALZBERG, BARRY N.   SS   NOV 73 03
   DOWN HERE IN THE DREAM QUARTER   MALZBERG, BARRY N.   AC
   NOVA 3   HARRISON, HARRY   OA
DETAILS   ANDERSON, POUL   SS   IFS 56 10
   7 CONQUESTS   ANDERSON, POUL   AC
DETECTIVE AND THE SENATOR, THE DERLETH, AUGUST   SS   SDM 53 08
   HARRIGAN'S FILE   DERLETH, AUGUST   AC
DEUS EX MACHINA   MATHESON, RICHARD   SS   GAM 63 02
   SHOCK WAVES   MATHESON, RICHARD   AC
DEVALUATION OF THE SYMBOL, THE BROWN, ROSEL GEORGE   SS   NEW 63 AC
   HANDFUL OF TIME, A   BROWN, ROSEL GEORGE   AC
DEVIL A MATHEMATICIAN WOULD BE, THE
                               LOHWATER, A. J.   MS
   MATHEMATICAL MAGPIE, THE   FADIMAN, CLIFTON   AN
DEVIL AND DANIEL WEBSTER, THE (ALSO AS ALL THAT MONEY CAN BUY)
                               BENET, STEPHEN V.   NV   SEP 36 10
   DEALS WITH THE DEVIL   DAVENPORT, BASIL   AN
DEVIL AND DEMOCRACY, THE   CLEEVE, BRIAN   SS   FSF 66 11
   BEST FROM FANTASY AND SCIENCE FICTION: 17
                               FERMAN, EDWARD L.   AN
DEVIL AND MR. CHIPS, THE (THE RAT THAT COULD SPEAK)
                               DICKENS, CHARLES   SS   FSF 51 08
   DEALS WITH THE DEVIL   DAVENPORT, BASIL   AN
DEVIL AND SIMON FLAGG, THE   PORGES, ARTHUR   SS   FSF 54 08
   DEALS WITH THE DEVIL   DAVENPORT, BASIL   AN
   FANTASIA MATHEMATICA   FADIMAN, CLIFTON   AN
DEVIL AND THE DEEP BLUE SEA, THE
                               CHILSON, ROBERT   SS
   BEYOND TIME   LEY, SANDRA   OA
DEVIL AND THE OLD MAN, THE   MASEFIELD, JOHN   SS   13
   DEALS WITH THE DEVIL   DAVENPORT, BASIL   AN
DEVIL CAR   ZELAZNY, ROGER   SS   GAL 65 06
   ANOTHER TOMORROW   HOLLISTER, BERNARD C   AN
   DECADE THE 1960S   ALDISS & HARRISON   AN
   DOORS OF HIS FACE, THE LAMPS OF HIS MOUTH, THE
                               ZELAZNY, ROGER   AC
   TENTH GALAXY READER, THE   POHL, FREDERIK   AN
DEVIL IN A CONVENT, THE   MANN, FRANCIS OSCAR   SS
   GHOULS, THE   HAINING, PETER   AN
DEVIL IN IRON, THE   HOWARD, ROBERT E.   SS   WRT 34 08
   CONAN THE BARBARIAN   HOWARD, ROBERT E.   AC
   CONAN THE WANDERER   HOWARD, R./DE CAMP/&   AC
DEVIL IN THE DARK, THE (GENE L. COON)
                               BLISH, JAMES   SA   STK 71 04
   STAR TREK 4   BLISH, JAMES   OC
DEVIL IS NOT MOCKED, THE   WELLMAN, MANLY WADE   SS   UNK 43 06
   ZACHERLEY'S VULTURE STEW   ZACHERLEY   AN
DEVIL MAKES THE LAW, THE (SEE MAGIC, INC.)
                               HEINLEIN, ROBERT A.   TC
DEVIL OF A DRUMMER   BAILEY, HILARY   SS   NEW 67 AN
   DEVIL HIS DUE, THE   HILL, DOUGLAS   AN
DEVIL OF EAST LUPTON, THE   LEINSTER, MURRAY   SS   TWS 48 08
   BEST OF MURRAY LEINSTER, THE   LEINSTER, MURRAY   AC

DEVIL OF EAST LUPTON, THE

*OTHER SIDE OF THE MOON, THE   DERLETH, AUGUST   AN
DEVIL ON SALVATION BLUFF, THE VANCE, JACK   NV   STR 54 03
  STAR SCIENCE FICTION STORIES NO. 3   POHL, FREDERIK   OA
  WORLD BETWEEN AND OTHER STORIES, THE VANCE, JACK   DC
  WORLDS OF JACK VANCE, THE   VANCE, JACK   AC
DEVIL TO PAY, THE   BOND, NELSON S.   SS   BBM 51 02
  NIGHTMARES AND DAYDREAMS   BOND, NELSON S.   AC
DEVIL WAS SICK, THE   ELLIOTT, BRUCE   SS   FSF 51 04
  ADVENTURES IN TOMORROW   CROSSEN, KENDELL F. AN
  DEALS WITH THE DEVIL   DAVENPORT, BASIL   AN
DEVIL WE KNOW, THE   KUTTNER, HENRY   NV   UNK 41 08
  BEST OF HENRY KUTTNER 2, THE   KUTTNER, HENRY   AC
  FROM UNKNOWN WORLDS   CAMPBELL, JOHN W. JR AN
  NO BOUNDARIES   KUTTNER & MOORE   AC
DEVIL YOU DON'T, THE   LAUMER, KEITH   NV   ANA 70
  ALCHEMY AND ACADEME   MCCAFFREY, ANNE   OA
  BEST OF KEITH LAUMER, THE   LAUMER, KEITH   AC
  TIMETRACKS   LAUMER, KEITH   AC
DEVIL'S FUNERAL, THE   MITCHELL, EDWARD P. SS SUN 79 03
  CRYSTAL MAN, THE   MITCHELL, EDWARD P. AC
DEVIL'S GODDAUGHTER   MALAVAL, SUZANNE   SS   60
  13 FRENCH SCIENCE-FICTION STORIES   KNIGHT, DAMON   AN
DEVIL'S HENCHMAN   JENKINS, WILL F.   SS   ARG 52 05
  SUPERNATURAL READER, THE   CONKLIN, G&L.   AN
DEVIL'S INVENTION, THE (SEE ODDY AND ID)
                          BESTER, ALFRED   TC
DEVIL'S RESCUE, THE   HUBBARD, L. RON   SS   UNK 40 10
  HELL HATH FURY   HAY, GEORGE   AN
DEVIL'S TICKET, THE   BLOCH, ROBERT   SS   WRT 44 09
  SKULL OF THE MARQUIS DE SADE, THE   BLOCH, ROBERT   AC
DEVIL-PUZZLERS   PERKINS, F. B.   SS
  DEALS WITH THE DEVIL   DAVENPORT, BASIL   AN
DEVIL, GEORGE, AND ROSIE, THE COLLIER, JOHN SS   34
  DEALS WITH THE DEVIL   DAVENPORT, BASIL   AN
DEVILISH RAT, THE   MITCHELL, EDWARD P. SS SUN 78 01
  CRYSTAL MAN, THE   MITCHELL, EDWARD P. AC
DEVLIN   READY, W. B.   SS   FSF 53 04
  BEST FROM FANTASY AND SCIENCE FICTION: 3
                          BOUCHER & MCCOMAS   AN
DEVOLUTION   HAMILTON, EDMOND   SS   AMZ 36 12
  BEFORE THE GOLDEN AGE   ASIMOV, ISAAC   AN
DHACTWHU|- REMEMBER?   ACKERMAN, FORREST J.
                 AND LOWNDES, ROBERT W. SS C SSS 49 04
  SCIENCE FICTION WORLDS OF FORREST J. ACKERMAN & FRIENDS
                          ACKERMAN, FORREST J. AC
DIABOLICAL DRUG, THE   HARRIS, CLARE WINGER SS AMZ 29 05
  AWAY FROM THE HERE AND NOW   HARRIS, CLARE WINGER AC
DIABOLICAL WEAPON, THE   BOULLE, PIERRE   SS
  TIME OUT OF MIND   BOULLE, PIERRE   OC
DIABOLOGIC   RUSSELL, ERIC FRANK SS ASF 55 03
  CONNOISSEUR'S S. F.   BOARDMAN, TOM JR.   AN
  FAR STARS   RUSSELL, ERIC FRANK AC
  SIX WORLDS YONDER   RUSSELL, ERIC FRANK DC
DIAGRAMS FOR THREE ENIGMATIC STORIES
                          ALDISS, BRIAN W.   GR   FST 74
  FINAL STAGE   FERMAN & MALZBERG   OA
DIAL "F" FOR FRANKENSTEIN CLARKE, ARTHUR C. SS   PBY 65 01
  LAST TRAIN TO LIMBO   PLAYBOY, EDITORS OF AN
  PLAYBOY BOOK OF SCIENCE FICTION AND FANTASY, THE
                          PLAYBOY, EDITORS OF AN
  WIND FROM THE SUN, THE   CLARKE, ARTHUR C.   AC
DIAL "O" FOR OPERATOR   PRESSLIE, ROBERT   SS   SCF 58 02
  OTHER SIDE OF THE CLOCK, THE   STERN, PHILIP VAN D. AN
  WEIRD SHADOWS FROM BEYOND   CARNELL, JOHN   AN
DIALOGUE   ANDERSON, POUL   NV   76
  FASTER THAN LIGHT   DANN & ZEBROWSKI   OA
DIAMOND AS BIG AS THE RITZ, THE
                          FITZGERALD, F. SCOTT SS   22
  MOONLIGHT TRAVELER, THE   STERN, PHILIP VAN D. AN
DIAMOND LENS, THE (1858)   O'BRIEN, FITZ-JAMES NV ATL 58 01
  FUTURE PERFECT   FRANKLIN, H. BRUCE   AN
DIAMOND MAKER, THE   REEVE, ARTHUR B.   SS   AMD 30 06
  SILENT BULLET, THE   REEVE, ARTHUR B.   AC
DIAMOND MAKER, THE   WELLS, H. G.   SS   PMB 94
  BEST SCIENCE FICTION STORIES OF H. G. WELLS
                          WELLS, H. G.   AC
  DOOR IN THE WALL, THE   WELLS, H. G.   AC
  SHORT STORIES OF H. G. WELLS, THE   WELLS, H. G.   AC
  STOLEN BACILLUS AND OTHER INCIDENTS, THE WELLS, H. G.   AC
DIARY IN THE SNOW   LEIBER, FRITZ   NV   NEW 47 AC
  NIGHT'S BLACK AGENTS   LEIBER, FRITZ   AC
DIARY OF A MADMAN, THE   DE MAUPASSANT, GUY SS
  *TWISTED   CONKLIN, GROFF   AN
DIARY OF ALONZO TYPER, THE LOVECRAFT, H. P.
                 AND LUMLEY, WILLIAM NV C WRT 38 02
  FANTASTIC PULPS, THE   HAINING, PETER   AN
DIARY OF THE ROSE, THE   LE GUIN, URSULA K. NV   76
  BEST SCIENCE FICTION STORIES OF THE YEAR (1976)
                          DOZOIS, GARDNER R.   AN
  FUTURE POWER   DANN & DOZOIS   OA
DID YOUR COFFEE TASTE FUNNY THIS MORNING? (SEE LEMON-GREEN
  SPAGHETTI-LOUD DYNAMITE-..) TENN, WILLIAM   TC
DIDN'T HE RAMBLE   OLIVER, CHAD   SS   FSF 57 04
  BEST SCIENCE FICTION STORIES AND NOVELS: 9TH SERIES
                          DIKTY, T. E.   AN
  EDGE OF FOREVER, THE   OLIVER, CHAD   AC
DIE SPANGE (BY STEFAN GEORGE, TRANSLATION)
                          BRUNNER, JOHN   PM   NEW 76 AC
  BOOK OF JOHN BRUNNER, THE   BRUNNER, JOHN   AC
DIE-HARD, THE   BESTER, ALFRED   SS   NEW 58 AC
  STARBURST   BESTER, ALFRED   AC
DIE, MAESTRO, DIE| STURGEON, THEODORE NV DDT 49 05
  E PLURIBUS UNICORN   STURGEON, THEODORE   AC
DIE, SHADOW| BUDRYS, ALGIS   NV   IFS 63 05
  BEST SCIENCE FICTION FROM IF, THE   POHL, FREDERIK   AN
  SECOND IF READER OF SCIENCE FICTION, THE POHL, FREDERIK AN

DIEHL   MALEC, ALEXANDER B. NV
  EXTRAPOLASIS   MALEC, ALEXANDER B. AC
DIFFERENT DRUMMER, A   MOORE, RAYLYN   SS   FSF 71 02
  BEST FROM FANTASY AND SCIENCE FICTION: 20
                          FERMAN, EDWARD L.   AN
  SCHOOL AND SOCIETY THROUGH SCIENCE FICTION
                          OLANDER/GREENBERG/& AN
DIFFERENT KICK, OR HOW TO GET HIGH WITHOUT ACTUALLY GOING
  INTO ORBIT, A   BRUNNER, JOHN   AR   NIE 65
  BOOK OF JOHN BRUNNER, THE   BRUNNER, JOHN   AC
DIFFERENT ONES, THE   SERLING, ROD   SA
  NIGHT GALLERY 2   SERLING, ROD   OC
DIFFERENT PURPOSE, A   BENNETT, KEM   SS   FSF 58 11
  BEST FROM FANTASY AND SCIENCE FICTION: 9
                          MILLS, ROBERT P.   AN
DIG THAT CRAZY GRAVE| BLOCH, ROBERT   SS   EQM 57 06
  *BLOOD RUNS COLD   BLOCH, ROBERT   AC
DIGGERS, THE   STERN, DONNEL   SS   CLR 73 03
  CLARION III   WILSON, ROBIN SCOTT OA
DIGGING THE WEANS   NATHAN, ROBERT   FA   HRP 56 11
  SF:57, THE YEAR'S GREATEST SCIENCE FICTION AND FANTASY
                          MERRIL, JUDITH   AN
DILEMMA, THE (PROLOGUE)   NEARING, H. JR.   MS
  SINISTER RESEARCHES OF C. P. RANSOM, THE NEARING, H. JR. AC
DILOPS ARE COMING, THE   FARLEY, CAROL   NV
  ANYWHERE, ANYWHEN   ENGDAHL, SYLVIA   OA
DIME BRINGS YOU SUCCESS, A DE CAMP, L. SPRAGUE
                 AND PRATT, FLETCHER SS C NEW 53 AC
  TALES FROM GAVAGAN'S BAR   DE CAMP, L. S.&PRATT AC
DIMENSION OF CHANCE, THE   SMITH, CLARK ASHTON NV WOS 32 11
  OTHER DIMENSIONS   SMITH, CLARK ASHTON AC
DIMINISHING DRAFT, THE   KAEMPFFERT, WALDEMAR SS ASW 18 02
  *BIG BOOK OF SCIENCE FICTION   CONKLIN, GROFF   AN
DIMPLE IN DRACO, THE   LATHAM, PHILIP   SS   ORB 67 02
  ORBIT 2   KNIGHT, DAMON   OA
DING DONG, THE WITCH IS WELL PICKENS, THOMAS SS   INY 72 04
  INFINITY 4   HOSKINS, ROBERT   OA
DINGBAT   GOULART, RON   NV   IFS 73 12
  NUTZENBOLTS   GOULART, RON   AC
DINNER AT DAWN   BRADBURY, RAY   SS   EVW 54 02
  DANDELION WINE   BRADBURY, RAY   NO
DINNER AT HELEN'S   CARLSON, WILLIAM   SS   NEW 72 AN
  STRANGE BED FELLOWS   SCORTIA, THOMAS N.   AN
DINNER AT IMOLA, A   DERLETH, AUGUST   SS   WRT 29 04
  NOT LONG FOR THIS WORLD   DERLETH, AUGUST   AC
DINOCHROME (COMBAT UNIT)   LAUMER, KEITH   SS   FSF 60 11
  NINE BY LAUMER   LAUMER, KEITH   AC
DINOSAURS   REAMY, TOM   NV   NDM 76 06
  NEW DIMENSIONS 6   SILVERBERG, ROBERT   OA
DINOSAURS, THE   CALVINO, ITALO   SS
  COSMICOMICS   CALVINO, ITALO   OC
DIO (ALSO AS THE DYING MAN) KNIGHT, DAMON   SN   INF 57 09
  ALPHA 4   SILVERBERG, ROBERT   AN
  5 UNEARTHLY VISIONS   CONKLIN, GROFF   AN
DIPLOIDS   MACLEAN, KATHERINE NA   TWS 53 04
  DIPLOIDS AND OTHER FLIGHTS OF FANCY, THE MACLEAN, KATHERINE AC
DIPLOMATIC COOP   GALOUYE, DANIEL F. SS   STR 59 05
  SF: AUTHORS' CHOICE 2   HARRISON, HARRY   AN
  STAR SCIENCE FICTION STORIES NO. 5 POHL, FREDERIK   OA
DIPLOMATIC IMMUNITY   SHECKLEY, ROBERT   NV   GAL 53 08
  PEOPLE TRAP AND OTHER PITFALLS, THE SHECKLEY, ROBERT   AC
DIPTEROID PHENOMENON, THE ANDERSON, POUL   SS
  FOUR FOR THE FUTURE   HARRISON, HARRY   AN
DIRECT CONTACT AMONG GALACTIC CIVILIZATIONS
                          SAGAN, CARL
                 AND SHKLOVSKII, I. S. AR C   66
  SURVIVAL PRINTOUT   TOTAL EFFECT   AN
DIRECTION   PLATT, CHARLES   SS
  NEW S.F., THE   JONES, LANGDON   OA
DIRECTION OF THE ROAD   LE GUIN, URSULA K. SS   ORB 73 12
  ORBIT 12   KNIGHT, DAMON   OA
  WINDS TWELVE QUARTERS, THE   LE GUIN, URSULA K.   AC
DIRECTOR, THE   HOWARD, JAMES   NV   STG 74
  STRANGE GODS   ELWOOD, ROGER   OA
DIRTY WAR, THE   BUNCH, DAVID R.   SS
  FUTURE PASTIMES   EDELSTEIN, SCOTT   OA
DISAPPEARANCE OF MRS. MACRECHAM, THE
                          MARSH, RICHARD   NV
  WIZARDS AND WARLOCKS   GHIDALIA, VIC   AN
DISAPPEARING ACT   BESTER, ALFRED   SS   STR 53 02
  CONNOISSEUR'S S. F.   BOARDMAN, TOM JR.   AN
  LIGHT FANTASTIC, THE   BESTER, ALFRED   AC
  OTHER DIMENSIONS   SILVERBERG, ROBERT   AN
  POLITICAL SCIENCE FICTION   GREENBERG& WARRICK   AN
  SCIENCE FACT/FICTION   FARRELL/GAGE/&   AN
  STAR OF STARS   POHL, FREDERIK   AN
  STAR SCIENCE FICTION STORIES NO. 2 POHL, FREDERIK   OA
  STARBURST   BESTER, ALFRED   AC
  STARLIT CORRIDOR, THE   MANSFIELD, ROGER   AN
DISAPPEARING ACT   MATHESON, RICHARD SS   FSF 53 03
  BORN OF MAN AND WOMAN   MATHESON, RICHARD   AC
  THIRD FROM THE SUN   MATHESON, RICHARD   AC
DISASSEMBLY LINE   COGSWELL, THEODORE R SS BEY 54 07
  THIRD EYE, THE   COGSWELL, THEODORE R AC
DISASTER STORY, THE   PLATT, CHARLES   AR   NWS 66 03
  BEST SF STORIES FROM NEW WORLDS 3   MOORCOCK, MICHAEL   AN
DISCARDED, THE (THE ABNORMALS) ELLISON, HARLAN SS FAN 59 04
  ALONE AGAINST TOMORROW   ELLISON, HARLAN   AC
  *PAINGOD AND OTHER DELUSIONS   ELLISON, HARLAN   AC
DISCIPLINARY CIRCUIT, THE LEINSTER, MURRAY   NV   TWS 46 WI
  LAST SPACESHIP, THE   LEINSTER, MURRAY   NO
DISCONTENT CONTINGENCY, THE KING, VINCENT   NV   NWR 71 19
  NEW WRITINGS IN SF. 19   CARNELL, JOHN   OA
DISCONTINUITY   JONES, RAYMOND F. NV   ASF 50 10
  SEVEN COME INFINITY   CONKLIN, GROFF   AN

DISCORD IN SCARLET

DISCORD IN SCARLET   VAN VOGT, A. E.   NV   ASF 39 12
   M 33 IN ANDROMEDA   VAN VOGT, A. E.   AC
   VOYAGE OF THE SPACE BEAGLE, THE   VAN VOGT, A. E.   NO
DISCORD MAKERS, THE   REYNOLDS, MACK   SS   OTW 50 07
   *INVADERS OF EARTH   CONKLIN, GROFF   AN
DISCOVERY   MITCHELL, ADRIAN   PM
   BEYOND THIS HORIZON   CARRELL, CHRISTOPHER OA
DISCOVERY IN THE WOODS, A   GREENE, GRAHAM   NV   63
   PAST, PRESENT, AND FUTURE PERFECT WOLFE, J&FITZ GERALD AN
   SPECULATIONS   SANDERS, THOMAS E.   AN
DISCOVERY OF MORNIEL MATHAWAY, THE
                                 TENN, WILLIAM   SS   GAL 55 10
   HUMAN ANGLE, THE   TENN, WILLIAM   AC
DISCOVERY OF THE NULLITRON, THE
                                 DISCH, THOMAS M.
                                 AND SLADEK, JOHN T. FA C GAL 67 02
   WHITE FANG GOES DINGO AND OTHER FUNNY S.F. STORIES
                                 DISCH, THOMAS M.   AC
DISCUSSION QUESTIONS   MISC. MATERIAL   MS
   SCIENCE FACT/FICTION   FARRELL/GAGE/&   AN
DISGUISE   WOLLHEIM, DONALD A. SS   OWS 53 02
   *STORIES FOR TOMORROW   SLOANE, WILLIAM   AN
   TWO DOZEN DRAGON EGGS   WOLLHEIM, DONALD A.   AC
DISHONESTIES OF A LONELY FILLING STATION
                                 ALDISS, BRIAN W.   PL   NWB 75 09
   NEW WORLDS NINE   BAILEY, HILARY   OA
DISINHERITED, THE (ALSO AS HOME)
                                 ANDERSON, POUL   SS   ORB 66 01
   ORBIT 1   KNIGHT, DAMON   OA
DISINHERITING PARTY, THE   CLUTE, JOHN   NV   NWB 73 05
   NEW WORLDS QUARTERLY NO. 5   MOORCOCK, MICHAEL   OA
DISINHERITORS, THE   MATHESON, RICHARD   SS   FSM 53 01
   SHOCK III   MATHESON, RICHARD   AC
DISINTEGRATING SKY, THE   ANDERSON, POUL   NV   FUN 53 08
   STRANGERS FROM EARTH   ANDERSON, POUL   AC
DISINTEGRATION   BUTTERWORTH, MICHAEL SS NWQ 73 05
   NEW WORLDS NO. 5   MOORCOCK & PLATT   OA
DISINTEGRATION MACHINE, THE   DOYLE, ARTHUR CONAN SS   CMP 28
   JOURNEYS IN SCIENCE FICTION   LOUGHLIN, RICHARD L. AN
   MARACOT DEEP AND OTHER STORIES, THE DOYLE, ARTHUR CONAN AC
   POISON BELT, THE   DOYLE, ARTHUR CONAN   AC
   WONDERMAKERS   HOSKINS, ROBERT   AN
DISPATCHER, THE   GREEN, GERALD   NV   PBY 67 08
   PLAYBOY'S STORIES OF THE SINISTER & STRANGE
                                 PLAYBOY, EDITORS OF   AN
DISPLACED PERSON   RUSSELL, ERIC FRANK SS   WRT 48 09
   SOMEWHERE A VOICE   RUSSELL, ERIC FRANK   AC
   WORLDS FAR AND NEAR   CARR, TERRY   AN
DISPLAYING THE FLAG   DISCH, THOMAS M.
   *GETTING INTO DEATH   DISCH, THOMAS M.   AC
DISPOSAL   GOULART, RON   SS   VSF 70 02
   BROKE DOWN ENGINE AND OTHER TROUBLES WITH MACHINES
                                 GOULART, RON   AC
   CITY: 2000 A.D., THE   CLEM/GREENBERG/&   AN
DISPOSAL SERVICE   SHECKLEY, ROBERT   SS   BBM 55
   PILGRIMAGE TO EARTH   SHECKLEY, ROBERT   AC
DISPOSAL UNIT MAN, THE   ALEXANDER, DAVID   SS   NWS 63 08
   WINDOW ON THE FUTURE   HILL, DOUGLAS   AN
DISPUTED AUTHORSHIP, A (1895)   BANGS, JOHN KENDRICK SS
   OUT OF THIS WORLD   FAST, JULIUS   AN
DISQUALIFIED   FONTENAY, CHARLES L. SS IFS 54 09
   FIRST WORLD OF IF, THE   QUINN & WULFF   AN
DISSOLVE   WOLF, GARY K.   SS   ORB 72 11
   ORBIT 11   KNIGHT, DAMON   OA
DISTANCE OF THE MOON, THE   CALVINO, ITALO   SS
   COSMICOMICS   CALVINO, ITALO   OC
DISTANT SHRINE, A (CATHEDRAL OF MARS)
                                 SAMBROT, WILLIAM   SS   SEP 61 06
   ISLAND OF FEAR AND OTHER SCIENCE FICTION SAMBROT, WILLIAM AC
DISTANT SOUND OF ENGINES, THE   BUDRYS, ALGIS   SS   FSF 59 03
   UNEXPECTED DIMENSION, THE   BUDRYS, ALGIS   AC
DISTORTION, THE   SILVERSTEIN, SHEL   CT   PBY 60 05
   6TH ANNUAL OF THE YEAR'S BEST S-F, THE MERRIL, JUDITH   AN
DISTRIBUTOR, THE   MATHESON, RICHARD   SS   PBY 58 03
   SHOCK!   MATHESON, RICHARD   AC
DISTURBANCE OF THE PEACE, A   JACOBS, HARVEY   SS   NWS 68 10
   EGG OF THE GLAK, AND OTHER STORIES, THE JACOBS, HARVEY   AC
DIVERSIFAL, THE   ROCKLYNNE, ROSS   SS   PLS 51 03
   BEST OF PLANET STORIES NO. 1, THE BRACKETT, LEIGH   AN
DIVIDED HOUSE, THE   RACKHAM, JOHN   SS   NWR 68 13
   NEW WRITINGS IN SF. 13   CARNELL, JOHN   OA
DIVINE MADNESS   ZELAZNY, ROGER   SS   MOH 66 SU
   DOORS OF HIS FACE, THE LAMPS OF HIS MOUTH, THE
                                 ZELAZNY, ROGER   AC
   NEW WORLDS OF FANTASY   CARR, TERRY   AN
   TRAPS OF TIME, THE   MOORCOCK, MICHAEL   AN
DIVVIL WITH THE WOMEN, A   WILDE, NIALL   SS   FSF 60 01
   BEST FROM FANTASY AND SCIENCE FICTION: 10
                                 MILLS, ROBERT P.   AN
DJANGO MAVERICK: 2051   LEMAN, GRAHAME   SS   NWR 71 18
   NEW WRITINGS IN SF. 18   CARNELL, JOHN   OA
DNA   ACKERSON, DUANE   PM
   BEST SF: 1974   HARRISON & ALDISS   AN
DO ANDROIDS DREAM OF ELECTRIC LOVE?
                                 LEIBSCHER, WALT   SS   NEW 72 AN
   STRANGE BED FELLOWS   SCORTIA, THOMAS N.   AN
DO IT FOR MOMMA   MUNDIS, JERROLD J. SS   NEW 71 AN
   RUINS OF EARTH, THE   DISCH, THOMAS M.   AN
DO IT YOURSELF   LESSER, MILTON   SS   SFQ 57 11
   RARE SCIENCE FICTION   HOWARD, IVAN   AN
DO WE LIVE IN A GOLDEN AGE?   POURNELLE, JERRY   IN
   2020 VISION   POURNELLE, JERRY   AN
DO YOU KNOW DAVE WENZEL?   LEIBER, FRITZ   SS   FOS 74
   FELLOWSHIP OF THE STARS   CARR, TERRY   OA
DO-IT-YOURSELF   ELLISON, HARLAN
                                 AND HENSLEY, JOE L. SS C ROG 61 02

ELLISON WONDERLAND   ELLISON, HARLAN   AC
DOCS, THE   LEWIS, RICHARD O.   SS   FSF 64 12
   SCHOOL AND SOCIETY THROUGH SCIENCE FICTION
                                 OLANDER/GREENBERG/&   AN
DOCTOR   LEINSTER, MURRAY   NV   GAL 61 02
   WORLDS APART   WILLIAMS-ELLIS& OWEN AN
DOCTOR FAUSTA   MASSON, DAVID I.   NV
   STOPWATCH   HAY, GEORGE   OA
DOCTOR FAUSTUS   ANONYMOUS   SS
   DEALS WITH THE DEVIL   DAVENPORT, BASIL   AN
DOCTOR GRIMSHAW'S SANITARIUM   PRATT, FLETCHER   SS   AMZ 34 05
   *MY BEST SCIENCE FICTION STORY   MARGULIES & FRIEND   AN
DOCTOR HANRAY'S SECOND CHANCE   RICHTER, CONRAD   SS   SEP 50 01
   POST READER OF FANTASY AND SCIENCE FICTION
                                 SATURDAY EVE. POST   AN
   SATURDAY EVENING POST FANTASY STORIES, THE
                                 FLES, BARTHOLD   AN
DOCTOR MOREAU'S OTHER ISLAND   NESVADBA, JOSEF   SS   64
   LOST FACE, THE   NESVADBA, JOSEF   AC
DOCTOR SCHMIDT   SHAMIR, MOSHE   SS   52
   VOYAGES: SCENARIOS FOR A SHIP CALLED EARTH
                                 SAUER, ROB   AN
DOCTOR ZOMBIE AND HIS FURRY LITTLE FRIENDS
                                 SHECKLEY, ROBERT   SS   NEW 71 AC
   BEST SF: 1971   HARRISON & ALDISS   AN
   CAN YOU FEEL ANYTHING WHEN I DO THIS?, AND OTHER STORIES
                                 SHECKLEY, ROBERT   AC
DOCTOR, THE   THOMAS, THEODORE L. SS   ORB 67 02
   ALPHA 1   SILVERBERG, ROBERT   AN
   BEST FROM ORBIT, THE   KNIGHT, DAMON   AN
   ORBIT 2   KNIGHT, DAMON   OA
DOCTRINE OF ORIGINAL DESIGN, THE
                                 MCCLINTIC, WINONA   PM   FSF 55 03
   BEST FROM FANTASY AND SCIENCE FICTION: 5
                                 BOUCHER, ANTHONY   AN
DODECAGON GARDEN (CUBE IN A DODECAGON GARDEN)
                                 PETAJA, EMIL   SS   SWY 70 06
   STARDRIFT AND OTHER FANTASTIC FLOTSAM PETAJA, EMIL   AC
DODGER FAN   STANTON, WILL   SS   FSF 57 06
   ARENA: SPORTS SF   FERMAN & MALZBERG   AN
   BEST FROM FANTASY AND SCIENCE FICTION: 7
                                 BOUCHER, ANTHONY   AN
   NEVER IN THIS WORLD   STONE, IDELLA P.   AN
   RUN TO STARLIGHT, SPORTS THROUGH SCIENCE FICTION
                                 GREENBERG/OLANDER/&   AN
DODIE SLAMMED THE DOOR   JAMES, E. R.   SS
   WORLDS AT WAR   RAYER, FRANCIS G.   AN
DODKIN'S JOB   VANCE, JACK   NV   ASF 59 10
   FUTURE TENSE   VANCE, JACK   AC
   WINDOWS INTO TOMORROW   SILVERBERG, ROBERT   AN
DOES A BEE CARE?   ASIMOV, ISAAC   SS   IFS 57 06
   BUY JUPITER AND OTHER STORIES   ASIMOV, ISAAC   AC
   OTHER WORLDS, OTHER TIMES   MOSKOWITZ & ELWOOD   AN
DOES THE NAME GRIMSBY DO ANYTHING TO YOU?
                                 SERLING, ROD   SA
   NIGHT GALLERY   SERLING, ROD   OC
DOG EAT DOG   FEIFFER, JULES   CT   63
   9TH ANNUAL OF THE YEAR'S BEST S-F, THE MERRIL, JUDITH   AN
DOG IN A FISHERMAN'S NET   DELANY, SAMUEL R.   SS   QRK 71 03
   DRIFTGLASS   DELANY, SAMUEL R.   AC
   QUARK/3   DELANY & HACKER   OA
DOG IS DEAD   EMSHWILLER, CAROL   SS
   JOY IN OUR CAUSE   EMSHWILLER, CAROL   AC
DOG STAR (MOONDOG)   CLARKE, ARTHUR C.   SS   GAL 62 04
   NINE BILLION NAMES OF GOD, THE   CLARKE, ARTHUR C.   AC
   SCIENCE FICTION ROLL OF HONOR, THE POHL, FREDERIK   AN
   TALES OF TEN WORLDS   CLARKE, ARTHUR C.   AC
DOG'S BEST FRIEND, A   PETAJA, EMIL   SS
   STARDRIFT AND OTHER FANTASTIC FLOTSAM PETAJA, EMIL   AC
DOGFIGHT   WHITE, JAMES   NV   NWS 59 03
   MONSTERS AND MEDICS   WHITE, JAMES   AC
DOGFIGHT ON 101 (SEE ALONG THE SCENIC ROUTE)
                                 ELLISON, HARLAN   TC
DOGMAN OF ISLINGTON   BAILEY, HILARY   SS   QRK 70 01
   INTO THE UNKNOWN   CARR, TERRY   AN
   QUARK/1   DELANY & HACKER   OA
DOGS OF DOCTOR DWANN, THE   HAMILTON, EDMOND   NV   WRT 32 10
   SATAN'S PETS   GHIDALIA, VIC   AN
DOGTOWN TOURIST AGENCY, THE   VANCE, JACK   NO   EPC 75
   EPOCH   ELWOOD & SILVERBERG   OA
DOING LENNON   BENFORD, GREGORY   SS   ASF 75 04
   BEST SCIENCE FICTION OF THE YEAR, THE NO. 5
                                 CARR, TERRY   OA
DOLL   GREENHOUGH, TERRY   SS
   ANDROMEDA I   WESTON, PETER   OA
DOLL THAT DOES EVERYTHING, THE   MATHESON, RICHARD   SS   FUN 54 12
   MORE LITTLE MONSTERS   ELWOOD & GHIDALIA   AN
   SHORES OF SPACE, THE   MATHESON, RICHARD   AC
DOLL-FRIEND (SEE JUKE DOLL)   YOUNG, ROBERT F.   TC
DOLL-HOUSE, THE   CROSS, JAMES   SS   DVS 67 01
   DANGEROUS VISIONS   ELLISON, HARLAN   OA
   FANTASY: THE LITERATURE OF THE MARVELOUS KELLEY, LEO P.   AN
DOLLHOUSE, THE   PRESTON, L. E.   SS   YNW
   SCIENCE FICTION STORIES   BRADLEY, JOHANNA   AN
DOLPHIN'S WAY   DICKSON, GORDON R. SS   ASF 64 06
   DANGER- HUMAN   DICKSON, GORDON R.   AC
DOME OF MANY-COLORED GLASS, A   SHAW, BOB   SS   FAN 72 04
   OTHER DAYS, OTHER EYES   SHAW, BOB   NO
DOME, THE   BROWN, FREDRIC   SS   TWS 51 08
   HONEYMOON IN HELL   BROWN, FREDRIC   AC
DOMESTIC CRISIS 2017   BRUNNER, JOHN   PM   TRB 74 03
   BOOK OF JOHN BRUNNER, THE   BRUNNER, JOHN   AC
DOMINANT SPECIES   NEVILLE, KRIS   SS   ORB 71 09
   ORBIT 9   KNIGHT, DAMON   OA

DOMINIONS BEYOND (THE SECOND TRIP TO MARS)
                    MOORE, WARD   SS   SEP 54 08
  BEST SCIENCE FICTION STORIES AND NOVELS: 1955
                    DIKTY, T. E.   AN
  WONDERMAKERS 2   HOSKINS, ROBERT   AN
DOMINOES   KORNBLUTH, C. M.   SS   STR 53 01
  BEST OF C. M. KORNBLUTH, THE   KORNBLUTH, C. M. AC
  MARCHING MORONS AND OTHER SCIENCE FICTION
                    KORNBLUTH, C. M.   AC
  STAR SCIENCE FICTION STORIES   POHL, FREDERIK   OA
  VOYAGERS IN TIME   SILVERBERG, ROBERT   AN
DON JONES   ANDERSON, POUL
      AND DICKSON, GORDON R.   NV C NEW 57 AC
  EARTHMAN'S BURDEN   ANDERSON, P.&DICKSON   AC
DON SLOW AND HIS ELECTRIC GIRL GETTER
                    BRAND, THOMAS   SS   EIO 73
  EROS IN ORBIT   ELDER, JOSEPH   OA
DON'T FENCE ME IN   WILSON, RICHARD   SS   FSF 56 04
  THOSE IDIOTS FROM EARTH   WILSON, RICHARD   AC
DON'T HOLD YOUR BREATH   VAN VOGT, A. E.   SS   SVW 73
  BEST OF A. E. VAN VOGT, THE   VAN VOGT, A. E.   AC
  SAVING WORLDS   ELWOOD & KIDD   OA
DON'T LIVE IN THE PAST   KNIGHT, DAMON   NV   GAL 51 06
  *GALAXY READER OF SCIENCE FICTION   GOLD, H. L. AN
                    KNIGHT, DAMON   AN
  TURNING ON   KNIGHT, DAMON   AN
DON'T LOOK NOW   KUTTNER, HENRY   SS   STS 48 03
  BEST OF HENRY KUTTNER 1, THE   KUTTNER, HENRY   AC
  HISTORY OF THE SCIENCE FICTION MAGAZINE, THE PART 3 1946-1955
                    ASHLEY, MICHAEL   AN
  MASTERS' CHOICE   JANIFER, LAURENCE M.   AN
  *MY BEST SCIENCE FICTION STORY   MARGULIES & FRIEND AN
  SHAPE OF THINGS, THE   KNIGHT, DAMON   AN
DON'T TAKE IT TO HEART   GOLD, H. L.   SS   FAN 53 08
  OLD DIE RICH AND OTHER SCIENCE FICTION, THE
                    GOLD, H. L.   AC
DON'T WASH THE CARATS   FARMER, PHILIP JOSE SS ORB 68 03
  BEST FROM ORBIT, THE   KNIGHT, DAMON   AN
  BOOK OF PHILIP JOSE FARMER, THE   FARMER, PHILIP JOSE AC
  MODERN SCIENCE FICTION   SPINRAD, NORMAN   AN
  ORBIT 3   KNIGHT, DAMON   OA
DON'T YOU REMEMBER?   CUMMINGS, M. A.   SS
  EXILE AND OTHER TALES OF FANTASY   CUMMINGS, M. A. OC
DONE WITHOUT EAGLES   DEL REY, LESTER   SS   ASF 40 08
  EARLY DEL REY   DEL REY, LESTER   AC
DONOR   GUNN, JAMES E.   NV   FAN 60 11
  IMMORTALS, THE   GUNN, JAMES E.   NO
DOODAD   BRADBURY, RAY   SS   ASF 43 09
  ALIEN EARTH AND OTHER STORIES   ELWOOD & MOSKOWITZ AN
  STRANGE SIGNPOSTS   ELWOOD & MOSKOWITZ   AN
DOOM FROM PLANET 4, THE   WILLIAMSON, JACK SS ASF 31 07
  EARLY WILLIAMSON, THE   WILLIAMSON, JACK   AC
DOOM OF LONDON, THE   BARR, ROBERT   SS   IDL 92 11
  SCIENCE FICTION BY GASLIGHT   MOSKOWITZ, SAM   AN
DOOMSDAY DEFERRED   JENKINS, WILL F.   SS   SEP 49 09
  BEST SCIENCE-FICTION STORIES: 1950, THE BLEILER & DIKTY AN
  BR-R-R-!   CONKLIN, GROFF   AN
  FIRST CONTACT   KNIGHT, DAMON   AN
  POST READER OF FANTASY AND SCIENCE FICTION
                    SATURDAY EVE. POST   AN
  SATURDAY EVENING POST FANTASY STORIES, THE
                    FLES, BARTHOLD   AN
  STRANGE BEASTS AND UNNATURAL MONSTERS   STERN, PHILIP VAN D. AN
DOOMSDAY MACHINE, THE (NORMAN SPINRAD)
                    BLISH, JAMES   SA   STK 69 03
  STAR TREK 3   BLISH, JAMES   OC
DOOMSDAY ON AJIAT   JONES, NEIL R.   SS   AST 42 10
  DOOMSDAY ON AJIAT   JONES, NEIL R.   AC
DOOMSDAY STORY, THE   COOPER, EDMUND   SS
  TOMORROW CAME   COOPER, EDMUND   AC
DOOMSDAY'S COLOR-PRESS   JONES, RAYMOND F. NV   FUT 52 11
  ESCAPE TO EARTH   HOWARD, IVAN   AN
DOOMSHIP   POHL, FREDERIK
      AND WILLIAMSON, JACK   NA C IFS 73 04
  1974 ANNUAL WORLD'S BEST SF, THE   WOLLHEIM, DONALD A. AN
DOOR IN THE WALL, THE   WELLS, H. G.   SS   DCH 06 07
  COUNTRY OF THE BLIND, THE   WELLS, H. G.   AC
  DOOR IN THE WALL, THE   WELLS, H. G.   AC
  SHORT STORIES OF H. G. WELLS, THE   WELLS, H. G. AC
  *TIME MACHINE AND OTHER STORIES, THE   WELLS, H. G. AC
DOOR TO ANYWHERE   ANDERSON, POUL   NV   GAL 66 12
  TENTH GALAXY READER, THE   POHL, FREDERIK   AN
DOOR, THE   KELLER, DAVID H. MD. SS ARS 49 SU
  TALES FROM UNDERWOOD   KELLER, DAVID H. MD.   AC
DOOR, THE   WHITE, E. B.   SS   NYM 39
  LIGHT FANTASTIC, THE   HARRISON, HARRY   AN
DOORBELL, THE   KELLER, DAVID H. MD. SS WOS 34 06
  OMNIBUS OF SCIENCE FICTION   CONKLIN, GROFF   AN
  STRANGE ADVENTURES IN SCIENCE FICTION   CONKLIN, GROFF AN
  TALES FROM UNDERWOOD   KELLER, DAVID H. MD.   AC
DOORS OF HIS FACE, THE LAMPS OF HIS MOUTH, THE
                    ZELAZNY, ROGER   NV   FSF 65 03
  BEST FROM FANTASY AND SCIENCE FICTION: 15
                    FERMAN, EDWARD L.   AN
  BEST SF 7   CRISPIN, EDMUND   AN
  DOORS OF HIS FACE, THE LAMPS OF HIS MOUTH, THE
                    ZELAZNY, ROGER   AC
  FOUR FOR TOMORROW   ZELAZNY, ROGER   AC
  NEBULA AWARD STORIES   KNIGHT, DAMON   AN
  RUN TO STARLIGHT, SPORTS THROUGH SCIENCE FICTION
                    GREENBERG/OLANDER/&   AN
DOORSLAMMER   WOLLHEIM, DONALD A. SS MOH 63 11
  TWO DOZEN DRAGON EGGS   WOLLHEIM, DONALD A.   AC
DOORSTEP   LAUMER, KEITH   SS   GAL 61 02
  BEST OF KEITH LAUMER, THE   LAUMER, KEITH   AC
  NINE BY LAUMER   LAUMER, KEITH   AC

DOORSTOP, THE   BRETNOR, REGINALD   SS   ASF 56 11
  SF:57, THE YEAR'S GREATEST SCIENCE FICTION AND FANTASY
                    MERRIL, JUDITH   AN
DOORWAY IN THE SKY (BERTHA)   WILLIAMS, RALPH   NV ASF 54 01
  TALES OF OUTER SPACE   WOLLHEIM, DONALD A.   DA
DOORWAY INTO TIME   MOORE, C. L.   SS   FFM 43 09
  DOORWAY INTO TIME   MOSKOWITZ, SAM   AN
  MODERN MASTERPIECES OF SCIENCE FICTION   MOSKOWITZ, SAM AN
DORG   LAFFERTY, R. A.   SS   ORB 72 10
  ORBIT 10   KNIGHT, DAMON   OA
DORMANT   VAN VOGT, A. E.   SS   STS 48 11
  ASPECTS OF SCIENCE FICTION   DOHERTY, G. D.   AN
  BEST FROM STARTLING STORIES, THE   MINES, SAMUEL AN
  BEST SF   CRISPIN, EDMUND   AN
  DESTINATION: UNIVERSE!   VAN VOGT, A. E.   AC
  SHAPE OF THINGS, THE   KNIGHT, DAMON   AN
DORNER CORDAIANTHUS   HOLLAND, HESTER   25
  ROOTS OF EVIL, THE PARRY, MICHEL   AN
DORSAI!   DICKSON, GORDON R. NO   ASF 59 05
  THREE TO DORSAI!   DICKSON, GORDON R.   AC
DOT AND DASH BIRD, THE   WOLFE, BERNARD   SS   PBY 64 12
  PLAYBOY BOOK OF SCIENCE FICTION AND FANTASY, THE
                    PLAYBOY, EDITORS OF   AN
DOUBLE   INOUYE, JON   PM
  NIGHT TIDE, A   INOUYE, JON   OC
DOUBLE CONSUMMATION   PRIEST, CHRISTOPHER SS   70
  REAL-TIME WORLD   PRIEST, CHRISTOPHER   AC
DOUBLE DARE   SILVERBERG, ROBERT SS   GAL 56 11
  CUBE ROOT OF UNCERTAINTY, THE   SILVERBERG, ROBERT AC
  FIFTH GALAXY READER, THE   GOLD, H. L.   AN
  TO WORLDS BEYOND   SILVERBERG, ROBERT   AN
DOUBLE DOME   BANKS, RAYMOND E.   SS   GAL 57 05
  HUMAN AND OTHER BEINGS   DEGRAEFF, ALLEN   AN
DOUBLE DYED VILLAINS, THE   ANDERSON, POUL   NV ASF 49 09
  TRAVELLERS OF SPACE   GREENBERG, MARTIN   AN
DOUBLE EXPOSURE   REESE, JOHN   SS   PBY 65 02
  PLAYBOY BOOK OF HORROR AND THE SUPERNATURAL, THE
                    PLAYBOY, EDITORS OF   AN
  WEIRD SHOW   PLAYBOY, EDITORS OF   AN
DOUBLE INDEMNITY   SHECKLEY, ROBERT   NV   GAL 57 10
  NOTIONS: UNLIMITED SHECKLEY, ROBERT   AC
DOUBLE JEOPARDY   PRATT, FLETCHER   NO   TWS 52 04
  DOUBLE JEOPARDY   PRATT, FLETCHER   AC
DOUBLE MEANING   KNIGHT, DAMON   NA   STS 53 01
  3 FROM OUT THERE   MARGULIES, LEO   AN
DOUBLE MINDS, THE   CAMPBELL, JOHN W. JR NV TWS 37 08
  BEST OF JOHN W. CAMPBELL, THE (BRITISH)   CAMPBELL, JOHN W. JR AC
  PLANETEERS, THE   CAMPBELL, JOHN W. JR   DC
DOUBLE SHADOW, THE   SMITH, CLARK ASHTON SS WRT 39 02
  OUT OF SPACE AND TIME   SMITH, CLARK ASHTON   AC
DOUBLE STANDARD   BROWN, FREDRIC   SS   PBY 63
  FIEND, THE   PLAYBOY, EDITORS OF   AN
  PARADOX LOST, AND 12 OTHER GREAT S.F. STORIES
                    BROWN, FREDRIC   AC
  9TH ANNUAL OF THE YEAR'S BEST S-F, THE   MERRIL, JUDITH AN
DOUBLE STAR (EXCERPT)   HEINLEIN, ROBERT A. EX ASF 56 02
  MARS, WE LOVE YOU   HIPOLITO & MCNELLY   AN
DOUBLE SUMMER TIME   WILDER, CHERRY   NV   NWR 76 29
  NEW WRITINGS IN SF. 29   BULMER, KENNETH   OA
DOUBLE TAKE   FINNEY, JACK   SS   PBY 65 04
  PLAYBOY BOOK OF SCIENCE FICTION AND FANTASY, THE
                    PLAYBOY, EDITORS OF   AN
DOUBLE TIME   BAYLEY, BARRINGTON J SS NWS 62 07
  BEST SF STORIES FROM NEW WORLDS 8   MOORCOCK, MICHAEL AN
DOUBLE TRAGEDY (SEE DOUBLE-CROSS)
                    BLOCH, ROBERT   TC
DOUBLE WHAMMY   BLOCH, ROBERT   SS   FAN 70 02
  COLD CHILLS   BLOCH, ROBERT   AC
  YEAR'S BEST HORROR STORIES, THE   DAVIS, RICHARD AN
DOUBLE WHAMMY (SEE NATURALLY AND VOODOO)
                    BROWN, FREDRIC   TC
DOUBLE-CROSS   POHL, FREDERIK   SS   PLS 44 WI
  EARLY POHL, THE   POHL, FREDERIK   AC
DOUBLE-CROSS (DOUBLE TRAGEDY)   BLOCH, ROBERT   SS MSM 59 10
  TALES IN A JUGULAR VEIN   BLOCH, ROBERT   AC
DOUBLE-EDGED ROPE, THE   BIGGLE, LLOYD JR.   SS ASF 67 06
  GALAXY OF STRANGERS, A   BIGGLE, LLOYD JR.   AC
DOUBLE-TAKE (AS KEN WINNEY)   MARKS, WINSTON K.   SS SPA 53 12
  FIFTY SHORT SCIENCE FICTION TALES   ASIMOV & CONKLIN AN
DOUBLE, DOUBLE, TOIL AND TROUBLE
                    CANTINE, HOLLEY   SS   FSF 60 01
  BEST FROM FANTASY AND SCIENCE FICTION: 10
                    MILLS, ROBERT P.   AN
  6TH ANNUAL OF THE YEAR'S BEST S-F, THE   MERRIL, JUDITH AN
DOUBLED AND REDOUBLED   JAMESON, MALCOLM   SS UNK 41 02
  UNKNOWN, THE   BENSEN, D. R.   AN
DOUBLED IN BRASS   DEL REY, LESTER   SS   UNK 40 01
  EARLY DEL REY   DEL REY, LESTER   AC
DOUCEMENT, S'IL VOUS PLAIT   SALLIS, JAMES   SS ORB 72 11
  ORBIT 11   KNIGHT, DAMON   AN
DOUGHNUT JOCKEY   FENNEL, ERIC   SS   BBM 48 05
  BEST SCIENCE-FICTION STORIES: 1949, THE BLEILER & DIKTY AN
DOWN AMONG THE DEAD MEN   TENN, WILLIAM   NV GAL 54 06
  ALPHA 6   SILVERBERG, ROBERT   AN
  EVIL EARTHS   ALDISS, BRIAN W.   AN
  HUMAN AND OTHER BEINGS   DEGRAEFF, ALLEN   AN
  OF ALL POSSIBLE WORLDS   TENN, WILLIAM   AC
DOWN AND OUT   GOULART, RON   SS   FSF 73 08
  NUTZENBOLTS   GOULART, RON   AC
DOWN AND OUT   NIVEN, LARRY   NV   GAL 76 02
  BEST FROM GALAXY, THE VOLUME IV   BAEN, JAMES AN
  WORLD OUT OF TIME, A   NIVEN, LARRY   NO
DOWN BY THE OLD MAELSTROM   WELLEN, EDWARD   SS ORB 72 11
  ORBIT 11   KNIGHT, DAMON   OA
DOWN HERE IN THE DREAM QUARTER MALZBERG, BARRY N. SS AMZ 76 06
  DOWN HERE IN THE DREAM QUARTER   MALZBERG, BARRY N.   AC

DOWN IN THE BLACK GANG   FARMER, PHILIP JOSE NV   IFS 69 03
  DOWN IN THE BLACK GANG AND OTHER STORIES FARMER, PHILIP JOSE   AC
DOWN IN THE DARK (AS ELLIS HART)
                                ELLISON, HARLAN   SS   ABR 67 30
  NO DOORS, NO WINDOWS (STORIES REWRITTEN) ELLISON, HARLAN   AC
DOWN THE BLUE HOLE   HARRISON, WILLIAM SS   73
  ROLLERBALL   HARRISON, WILLIAM   AC
DOWN THE DIGESTIVE TRACT AND INTO THE COSMOS WITH MANTRA,
  TANTRA, AND SPECKLEBANG   SHECKLEY, ROBERT   SS   GAL 71 02
  CAN YOU FEEL ANYTHING WHEN I DO THIS?, AND OTHER STORIES
                                SHECKLEY, ROBERT   AC
DOWN THE RIVER   REYNOLDS, MACK   SS   STS 50 09
  BEST OF MACK REYNOLDS, THE   REYNOLDS, MACK   AC
  GALACTIC EMPIRES VOLUME TWO   ALDISS, BRIAN W.   AN
DOWN THE UP ESCALATION   ALDISS, BRIAN W.   SS   LOM 67
  MOMENT OF ECLIPSE, THE   ALDISS, BRIAN W.   AC
  NEW TOMORROWS, THE   SPINRAD, NORMAN   AN
DOWN THERE   KNIGHT, DAMON   SS   NDM 73 03
  BEST OF DAMON KNIGHT, THE   KNIGHT, DAMON   AC
  NEW DIMENSIONS 3   SILVERBERG, ROBERT   OA
DOWN TO A SUNLESS SEA   SMITH, CORDWAINER NV   FSF 75 10
  BEST SCIENCE FICTION OF THE YEAR, THE NO. 5
                                CARR, TERRY   AN
DOWN TO EARTH   HARRISON, HARRY   SS   AMZ 63 11
  PRIME NUMBER   HARRISON, HARRY   AC
DOWN WILL COME THE SKY   BOND, NELSON S.   SS   USF 53 06
  NIGHTMARES AND DAYDREAMS   BOND, NELSON S.   AC
DOWNSTAIRS ROOM, THE   WILHELM, KATE   SS   NEW 68 AC
  DOWNSTAIRS ROOM AND OTHER SPECULATIVE FICTION, THE
                                WILHELM, KATE   AC
DOWNWIND FROM GETTYSBURG   BRADBURY, RAY   SS   PBY 69 06
  I SING THE BODY ELECTRIC   BRADBURY, RAY   AC
DOWRY OF THE ANGYAR, THE (ALSO AS SEMLEY'S NECKLACE)
                                LE GUIN, URSULA K. SS   AMZ 64 09
  BEST FROM AMAZING, THE   WHITE, TED   AN
DP!   VANCE, JACK   NV   AVS 53 04
  BEST SCIENCE-FICTION STORIES: 1954, THE BLEILER & DIKTY   AN
  POLITICAL SCIENCE FICTION   GREENBERG& WARRICK   AN
DR. ADAMS' GARDEN OF EVIL   LEIBER, FRITZ   SS   FAN 63 02
  ROOTS OF EVIL, THE   PARRY, MICHEL   AN
DR. BIRDMOUSE   BRETNOR, REGINALD SS   FAN 62 04
  STRANGE BED FELLOWS   SCORTIA, THOMAS N.   AN
DR. CYCLOPS   KUTTNER, HENRY   SS   TWS 40 06
  DR. CYCLOPS   KUTTNER, HENRY   AN
DR. FUDDLE'S FINGERS   BOND, NELSON S.   SS
  MR. MERGENTHWIRKER'S LOBBIES AND OTHER FANTASTIC TALES
                                BOND, NELSON S.   AC
DR. FUTURITY (TIME PAWN, TWS 54 SU)
                                DICK, PHILIP K.   DN   ACE 60
  PHILIP K. DICK OMNIBUS, A   DICK, PHILIP K.   AC
DR. GELABIUS   BAILEY, HILARY   SS   NWS 68 04
  BEST SF STORIES FROM NEW WORLDS 4 MOORCOCK, MICHAEL   AN
  ENGLAND SWINGS SF   MERRIL, JUDITH   AN
  SPACE-TIME JOURNAL, THE   MERRIL, JUDITH   AN
DR. JACOBUS MELIFLORE'S LAST PATIENT
                                LORD, MINDRET   SS   FSF 53 11
  ZACHERLEY'S VULTURE STEW   ZACHERLEY   AN
DR. KOMETEVSKY'S DAY   LEIBER, FRITZ   SS   GAL 52 02
  SHIPS TO THE STARS   LEIBER, FRITZ   DC
DR. LU-MIE   KRUSE, CLIFTON B. SS   ASF 34 07
  EVERY BOY'S BOOK OF SCIENCE FICTION WOLLHEIM, DONALD A.   AN
DR. MATERIALISMUS   STIMSON, FREDERIC J. SS   SCR 90 08
  FUTURE PERFECT   FRANKLIN, H. BRUCE   AN
DR. MORRIS GOLDPEPPER RETURNS   DAVIDSON, AVRAM SS GAL 62 12
  STRANGE SEAS AND SHORES   DAVIDSON, AVRAM   AC
DR. OX'S EXPERIMENT (1874)   VERNE, JULES   SS   AMZ 26 08
  *BEYOND TIME AND SPACE   DERLETH, AUGUST   AN
DR. SOUTHPORT VULPES'S NIGHTMARE (FROM "NIGHTMARES OF
  EMINENT PERSONS")   RUSSELL, BERTRAND   EX
  ARMCHAIR SCIENCE READER, THE GORDON, I. & SORKIN   AN
DR. TRIFULGAS   VERNE, JULES   SS   SND 92 07
  BEFORE ARMAGEDDON   MOORCOCK, MICHAEL   AN
DRACULA'S DAUGHTER (DRACULA'S GUEST)
                                STOKER, BRAM   SS   WRT 27 12
  GHOULS, THE   HAINING, PETER   AN
DRAGON IN THE LAND   KOONTZ, DEAN R.   SS   VSF 69 08
  SOFT COME THE DRAGONS   KOONTZ, DEAN R.   DC
DRAGON IN THE SEA (UNDER PRESSURE)
                                HERBERT, FRANK   EX   ASF 55 11
  BEST OF FRANK HERBERT, THE   HERBERT, FRANK   AC
DRAGON MASTERS, THE   VANCE, JACK   SN   GAL 62 08
  HUGO WINNERS, THE (VOLUME 2) ASIMOV, ISAAC   AN
DRAGON, THE   BRADBURY, RAY   SS   FSF 56 03
  DAY IT RAINED FOREVER, THE   BRADBURY, RAY   AC
  MEDICINE FOR MELANCHOLY, A   BRADBURY, RAY   AC
  R IS FOR ROCKET   BRADBURY, RAY   AC
DRAGONRIDER   MCCAFFREY, ANNE   NA   ASF 67 12
  DRAGONFLIGHT   MCCAFFREY, ANNE   NO
  NEBULA AWARD STORIES NO. 4   ANDERSON, POUL   AN
DRAMATIC MISSION   MCCAFFREY, ANNE   SN   ASF 69 06
  SHIP WHO SANG, THE   MCCAFFREY, ANNE   AC
DRAW, THE   BIXBY, JEROME   SS   AMZ 54 03
  SPACE BY THE TAIL   BIXBY, JEROME   AC
DREAD EMPIRE   BRUNNER, JOHN   SN   FAN 71 04
  TRAVELER IN BLACK, THE   BRUNNER, JOHN   AC
DREADED BLACK PLANET, THE   ANONYMOUS   CT
  LAURIE'S SPACE ANNUAL   ANONYMOUS   AN
DREADFUL HAS ALREADY HAPPENED, THE
                                KAGAN, NORMAN   SS   NEW 71 AN
  RUINS OF EARTH, THE   DISCH, THOMAS M.   AN
DREAM (DREAMWORLD)   LAFFERTY, R. A.   SS   GAL 62 06
  STRANGE DOINGS   LAFFERTY, R. A.   AC
DREAM AT NOONDAY, A   DOZOIS, GARDNER R. SS   ORB 70 07
  ORBIT   7   KNIGHT, DAMON   OA
DREAM DONE GREEN   FOSTER, ALAN DEAN SS   FOS 74

BEST SCIENCE FICTION STORIES OF THE YEAR (1974)
                                DEL REY, LESTER   AN
  FELLOWSHIP OF THE STARS   CARR, TERRY   OA
DREAM MAKERS, THE   BLOCH, ROBERT   NV   BEY 53 06
  MORE TERROR IN THE MODERN VEIN WOLLHEIM, DONALD A.   AN
  PLEASANT DREAMS   BLOCH, ROBERT   AC
  *TERROR IN THE MODERN VEIN   WOLLHEIM, DONALD A.   AN
  YOURS TRULY, JACK THE RIPPER BLOCH, ROBERT   AC
DREAM OF A RIDICULOUS MAN, THE DOSTOEVSKY, FYODOR SS
  PERCHANCE TO DREAM   KNIGHT, DAMON   AN
DREAM OF ARMAGEDDON, A   WELLS, H. G.   NV   BAW 01
  BEST SCIENCE FICTION STORIES OF H. G. WELLS
                                WELLS, H. G.   AC
  BEST STORIES OF H. G. WELLS   WELLS, H. G.   AC
  COUNTRY OF THE BLIND, THE   WELLS, H. G.   AC
  DOOR IN THE WALL, THE   WELLS, H. G.   AC
  SHORT STORIES OF H. G. WELLS, THE WELLS, H. G.   AC
  TWELVE STORIES AND A DREAM   WELLS, H. G.   AC
  TWENTY-EIGHT SCIENCE FICTION STORIES WELLS, H. G.   AC
DREAM OF DEBS, THE   LONDON, JACK   NV   ISR 09 05
  SCIENCE FICTION OF JACK LONDON, THE LONDON, JACK   AC
DREAM OF DISTANCE   ANONYMOUS   MS   67
  ALL ABOUT VENUS   ALDISS, BRIAN W.   AN
  FAREWELL FANTASTIC VENUS   ALDISS & HARRISON   AN
DREAM OF FLYING, A (SEE CHICKEN ICARUS)
                                EMSHWILLER, CAROL TC
DREAM OF VICTORY   BUDRYS, ALGIS   NV   AMZ 53 09
  BUDRYS' INFERNO   BUDRYS, ALGIS   AC
DREAM PATROL   RUNYON, CHARLES W. SS   FSF 70 02
  BEST FROM FANTASY AND SCIENCE FICTION: 19
                                FERMAN, EDWARD L.   AN
DREAM PILLS, THE   DAVIS, F. H.   SS   20
  STRANGE ECSTASIES   PARRY, MICHEL   AN
DREAM QUEST OF UNKNOWN KADATH, THE
                                LOVECRAFT, H. P.   NA   ARS 48 WI
  GOLDEN ROAD, THE   KNIGHT, DAMON   AN
DREAM STREET   ROBINSON, FRANK M. SS   IMT 55 03
  BEST SCIENCE FICTION STORIES AND NOVELS: 1956
                                DIKTY, T. E.   AN
  DAYS AFTER TOMORROW, THE   SANTESSON, HANS S.   AN
  6 FROM WORLDS BEYOND   DIKTY, T. E.   AN
DREAM'S END   KUTTNER, HENRY   SS   STS 47 03
  *FUTURE TENSE   CROSSEN, KENDELL F.   AN
  PERCHANCE TO DREAM   KNIGHT, DAMON   AN
DREAM, THE   SHELLEY, MARY W.   SS   KPS 32
  TALES AND STORIES   SHELLEY, MARY W.   AC
DREAMER'S WORLD   HAMILTON, EDMOND   NV   WRT 41 11
  WHAT'S IT LIKE OUT THERE? AND OTHER STORIES
                                HAMILTON, EDMOND   AC
DREAMER, THE   COPPEL, ALFRED   SS   FSF 52 04
  BEST SCIENCE-FICTION STORIES: 1953, THE BLEILER & DIKTY   AN
DREAMER, THE (THE ENCHANTED PRINCESS)
                                VANCE, JACK   SS   OSF 54 11
  SPACE STATION 42 AND OTHER STORIES ANONYMOUS   AN
DREAMERS ON THE BARRICADES   ELLISON, HARLAN   AR   CLR 71 01
  CLARION   WILSON, ROBIN SCOTT   OA
DREAMING IS A PRIVATE THING   ASIMOV, ISAAC   SS   FSF 55 12
  EARTH IS ROOM ENOUGH   ASIMOV, ISAAC   AC
  FANTASY: THE LITERATURE OF THE MARVELOUS KELLEY, LEO P.   AN
  NEW DREAMS THIS MORNING   BLISH, JAMES   AN
  SCIENCE FICTION INVENTIONS   KNIGHT, DAMON   AN
  SF: THE BEST OF THE BEST   MERRIL, JUDITH   AN
  SF: THE YEAR'S GREATEST SCIENCE FICTION AND FANTASY
                                MERRIL, JUDITH   AN
  TOMORROW, INC.   GREENBERG& OLANDER   AN
DREAMS ARE SACRED   PHILLIPS, PETER   SS   ASF 48 09
  ASTOUNDING-ANALOG READER, THE VOLUME TWO HARRISON & ALDISS   AN
  *IMAGINATION UNLIMITED   BLEILER & DIKTY   AN
  SPECTRUM   3   AMIS & CONQUEST   AN
DREAMS OF ALBERT MORELAND, THE LEIBER, FRITZ   NV   AFR 48 07
  NIGHT'S BLACK AGENTS   LEIBER, FRITZ   AC
  ODDBALLS, THE   GHIDALIA, VIC   AN
DREAMSMAN, THE   DICKSON, GORDON R. SS   STR 59 06
  STAR SCIENCE FICTION STORIES NO. 6 POHL, FREDERIK   OA
  5TH ANNUAL OF THE YEAR'S BEST S-F, THE MERRIL, JUDITH   AN
DREAMWORLD   ASIMOV, ISAAC   SS   FSF 55 11
  BEST FROM FANTASY AND SCIENCE FICTION: 5
                                BOUCHER, ANTHONY   AN
  NEVER IN THIS WORLD   STONE, IDELLA P.   AN
  OPUS 100   ASIMOV, ISAAC   AN
DREAMWORLD   SHECKLEY, ROBERT   SS   NEW 68 AC
  PEOPLE TRAP AND OTHER PITFALLS, THE SHECKLEY, ROBERT   AC
DREISTEIN CASE, THE   PAINE, J. LINCOLN SS   FSF 58 10
  13 ABOVE THE NIGHT   CONKLIN, GROFF   AN
DRESS OF WHITE SILK   MATHESON, RICHARD SS   FSF 51 10
  BEST FROM FANTASY AND SCIENCE FICTION BOUCHER & MCCOMAS   AN
  BORN OF MAN AND WOMAN   MATHESON, RICHARD   AC
  THIRD FROM THE SUN   MATHESON, RICHARD   AC
DRESS REHEARSAL   JACOBS, HARVEY   SS   FSF 74 07
  BEST SCIENCE FICTION STORIES OF THE YEAR (1974)
                                DEL REY, LESTER   AN
DRIFTGLASS   DELANY, SAMUEL R. NV   IFS 67 06
  DAY IN THE LIFE, A   DOZOIS, GARDNER R.   AN
  DRIFTGLASS   DELANY, SAMUEL R.   AC
  NEW TOMORROWS, THE   SPINRAD, NORMAN   AN
  SPECTRUM OF WORLDS, A   CLARESON, THOMAS D.   AN
  SURVIVAL PRINTOUT   TOTAL EFFECT   AN
  WORLD'S BEST SCIENCE FICTION: 1968 WOLLHEIM & CARR   AN
DRIFTING SNOW, THE   DERLETH, AUGUST   SS   WRT 39 02
  NOT LONG FOR THIS WORLD   DERLETH, AUGUST   AC
  WEIRD TALES   MARGULIES, LEO   AN
DRINK ENTIRE: AGAINST THE MADNESS OF CROWDS
                                BRADBURY, RAY   SS   GLR
  LONG AFTER MIDNIGHT   BRADBURY, RAY   AC

```
DRINK MY RED BLOOD (SEE BLOOD SON)
                    MATHESON, RICHARD    TC
DRINK OF DARKNESS, A     YOUNG, ROBERT F.     SS    FAN 62 07
  WORLDS OF ROBERT F. YOUNG, THE     YOUNG, ROBERT F.          AC
DRINK OF WATER, A     MATHESON, RICHARD     SS    SGN 67
  SHOCK WAVES     MATHESON, RICHARD          AC
DRIVERS, THE     LUDWIG, EDWARD W.     SS    IFS 56 03
  FIRST WORLD OF IF, THE     QUINN & WULFF          AN
DROMENON     HEARD, H. F.     SS
  GREAT FOG AND OTHER WEIRD TALES, THE     HEARD, H. F.          OC
DRONE, THE     MERRITT, A.     SS    FMG 34 09
  FOX WOMAN & OTHER STORIES, THE     MERRITT, A.          AC
DROP DEAD     SIMAK, CLIFFORD D.     NV    GAL 56 07
  *ALL THE TRAPS OF EARTH AND OTHER STORIES SIMAK, CLIFFORD D.          AC
  SCIENCE FICTION BESTIARY, THE     SILVERBERG, ROBERT          AN
DROP, THE     CHRISTOPHER, JOHN     SS    GAL 53 03
  GATEWAY TO TOMORROW     CARNELL, JOHN          AN
DROPPED FROM THE CLOUDS (THE MYSTERIOUS ISLAND, 1875)
                    VERNE, JULES     EX
  JULES VERNE- MASTER OF SCIENCE FICTION     VERNE, JULES          AC
DROWNED GIANT, THE (SOUVENIR)     BALLARD, J. G.     SS    PBY 65 05
  CHRONOPOLIS AND OTHER STORIES     BALLARD, J. G.          AC
  IMPOSSIBLE MAN, THE     BALLARD, J. G.          AC
  INTO THE UNKNOWN     CARR, TERRY          AN
  NEBULA AWARD STORIES     KNIGHT, DAMON          AN
  TERMINAL BEACH (BRITISH VERSION)     BALLARD, J. G.          AC
  11TH ANNUAL OF THE YEAR'S BEST S-F, THE     MERRIL, JUDITH          AN
DROWNED WORLD, THE (ENLARGED)     BALLARD, J. G.     NO    SFB 62 01
  DROWNED WORLD AND THE WIND FROM NOWHERE, THE
                    BALLARD, J. G.          AC
DRUIDIC DOOM, THE     BLOCH, ROBERT     SS    WRT 36 04
  BLOCH AND BRADBURY     BRADBURY & BLOCH          AC
DRUM LOLLIPOP, THE     DANN, JACK M.     SS    ORB 72 11
  ORBIT 11     KNIGHT, DAMON          OA
DRUMBLE     NYE, CASSANDRA     SS    NEW 75 AN
  NEW IMPROVED SUN, THE     DISCH, THOMAS M.          AN
DRUMMER BOY OF SHILOH, THE     BRADBURY, RAY     SS    SEP 60 04
  MACHINERIES OF JOY, THE     BRADBURY, RAY          AC
  TRANSFORMATIONS II     ROSELLE, DANIEL          AN
DRUMS OF TOMBALKU     DE CAMP, L. SPRAGUE
                    AND HOWARD, ROBERT E.     SS C
  CONAN THE ADVENTURER     HOWARD, R. & DE CAMP          AC
DRUNKBOAT     SMITH, CORDWAINER     NV    AMZ 63 10
  SPACE LORDS     SMITH, CORDWAINER          AC
  9TH ANNUAL OF THE YEAR'S BEST S-F, THE     MERRIL, JUDITH          AN
DRY RUN     NIVEN, LARRY     SS    FSF 68 05
  SHAPE OF SPACE, THE     NIVEN, LARRY          AC
DUCKWORTH'S FOREVER     EISENBERG, LARRY     SS    NEW 71 AC
  BEST LAID SCHEMES, THE     EISENBERG, LARRY          AC
DUCKWORTH'S IQ SOUP (IQ SOUP)     EISENBERG, LARRY     SS    VSF 69 11
  BEST LAID SCHEMES, THE     EISENBERG, LARRY          AC
DUE PROCESS     BUDRYS, ALGIS     SS    ASF 60 02
  12 GREAT CLASSICS OF SCIENCE FICTION     CONKLIN, GROFF          AN
DUEL ON SYRTIS     ANDERSON, POUL     SS    PLS 51 03
  BEST OF PLANET STORIES NO. 1, THE     BRACKETT, LEIGH          AN
  STRANGERS FROM EARTH     ANDERSON, POUL          AC
DUELING MACHINE, THE (SEE THE PERFECT WARRIOR)
                    BOVA, BEN
                    AND LEWIS, MYRON R.     TC C
DUET FOR ONE FINGER     COOPER, EDMUND     SS
  VOICES IN THE DARK     COOPER, EDMUND          AC
DULCIE AND DECORUM     KNIGHT, DAMON     NV    GAL 55 03
  OFF CENTRE     KNIGHT, DAMON          AC
DULL DRUMS     MCCAFFREY, ANNE     NV    FUQ 73
  FUTURE QUEST     ELWOOD, ROGER          OA
  GET OFF THE UNICORN     MCCAFFREY, ANNE          AC
DUMB MARTIAN     WYNDHAM, JOHN     NV    GAL 52 07
  BEST OF JOHN WYNDHAM, THE     WYNDHAM, JOHN          AC
  BEST SF     CRISPIN, EDMUND          AN
  GATEWAY TO TOMORROW     CARNELL, JOHN          AN
  MAN FROM BEYOND AND OTHER STORIES, THE     WYNDHAM, JOHN          AC
  OUT OF THIS WORLD 3     WILLIAMS-ELLIS& OWEN          AN
  SEEDS OF TIME, THE     WYNDHAM, JOHN          AC
DUMB SHOW     ALDISS, BRIAN W.     SS    NEB 56 12
  ASPECTS OF SCIENCE FICTION     DOHERTY, G. D.          AN
  *BEST SCIENCE FICTION STORIES OF BRIAN W. ALDISS
                    ALDISS, BRIAN W.          AC
  SPACE, TIME AND NATHANIEL     ALDISS, BRIAN W.          AC
DUMB SUPPER (CALL ME FROM THE VALLEY)
                    WELLMAN, MANLY WADE     SS    FSF 54 03
  WHO FEARS THE DEVIL?     WELLMAN, MANLY WADE          AC
DUMB WAITER     MILLER, WALTER M. JR     NV    ASF 52 04
  CITIES OF WONDER     KNIGHT, DAMON          AN
  *SCIENCE FICTION THINKING MACHINES     CONKLIN, GROFF          AN
  VIEW FROM THE STARS, THE     MILLER, WALTER M. JR          AC
DUNDERBIRD (SEE STREET SCENE)     ELLISON, HARLAN     TC C
DUNDERBIRD (SEE STREET SCENE)     LAUMER, KEITH
DUNE     HERBERT, FRANK     EX    CHL 65
  BEST OF FRANK HERBERT, THE     HERBERT, FRANK          AC
DUNE ROLLER     MAY, JULIAN C.     NV    ASF 51 12
  ALPHA 7     SILVERBERG, ROBERT          AN
  *IMAGINATION UNLIMITED     BLEILER & DIKTY          AN
  *STORIES FOR TOMORROW     SLOANE, WILLIAM          AN
DUNE'S EDGE     BRYANT, EDWARD     SS    ORB 72 11
  AMONG THE DEAD     BRYANT, EDWARD          AC
  ORBIT 11     KNIGHT, DAMON          OA
DUNWICH HORROR, THE     LOVECRAFT, H. P.     NV    WRT 29 04
  HAUNTER OF THE DARK, THE     LOVECRAFT, H. P.          AC
DURANCE     MOORE, WARD     SS    EPC 75
  EPOCH     ELWOOD & SILVERBERG          OA
DURING THE JURASSIC     UPDIKE, JOHN     SS    TRV 66 SU
  SF12     MERRIL, JUDITH          AN
DUSK OF IDOLS, A     BLISH, JAMES     NV    AMZ 61 03
  ANYWHEN     BLISH, JAMES          AC
DUST     ESHBACH, LLOYD A.     SS    MSS 39 08
  SCIENCE FICTION ROLL OF HONOR, THE     POHL, FREDERICK          AN

DUST     SERLING, ROD     SA
  FROM THE TWILIGHT ZONE     SERLING, ROD          AC
  MORE STORIES FROM THE TWILIGHT ZONE     SERLING, ROD          AC
DUST IN THE HOUSE     KELLER, DAVID H. MD. SS    WRT 38 07
  FOLSOM FLINT AND OTHER CURIOUS TALES, THE
                    KELLER, DAVID H. MD.          AC
DUST OF DEATH, THE     ASIMOV, ISAAC     SS    VSF 57 01
  ASIMOV'S MYSTERIES     ASIMOV, ISAAC          AC
DUST OF EVENING, THE     CRAIS, ROBERT     SS
  2076: THE AMERICAN TRICENTENNIAL     BRYANT, EDWARD          OA
DUST OF GODS     MOORE, C. L.     NV    WRT 34 08
  NORTHWEST OF EARTH     MOORE, C. L.          AC
  PLANETS OF WONDER     CARR, TERRY          AN
DUST RAG     CLEMENT, HAL     SS    ASF 56 09
  SMALL CHANGES     CLEMENT, HAL          AN
  WHERE DO WE GO FROM HERE?     ASIMOV, ISAAC          AN
DUSTY DEATH, THE     KIPPAX, JOHN     SS    NWS 58 11
  OUT OF THIS WORLD  2     WILLIAMS-ELLIS& OWEN          AN
DUSTY ZEBRA     SIMAK, CLIFFORD D.     NV    GAL 54 09
  ALIENS FOR NEIGHBOURS     SIMAK, CLIFFORD D.          AC
  OTHER WORLDS OF CLIFFORD SIMAK     SIMAK, CLIFFORD D.          AC
  *WORLDS OF CLIFFORD SIMAK, THE     SIMAK, CLIFFORD D.          AC
DUTCH     NOLAN, WILLIAM F.     SS    58
  IMPACT-20     NOLAN, WILLIAM F.          AC
DWARF, THE     AYME, MARCEL     SS
  WALKER THROUGH WALLS, THE     AYME, MARCEL          AC
DWARF, THE     BRADBURY, RAY     SS    FAN 54 01
  *OCTOBER COUNTRY, THE     BRADBURY, RAY          AC
  VINTAGE BRADBURY, THE     BRADBURY, RAY          AC
DWELLER IN THE ICE, THE     POHL, FREDERIK     SS    SSS 41 01
  EARLY POHL, THE     POHL, FREDERIK          AC
DWELLER IN TWO WORLDS, A     GOR, GENNADY     SS
  RUSSIAN SCIENCE FICTION, 1968     MAGIDOFF, ROBERT          AN
DWELLERS IN SILENCE (THE LONG YEARS)
                    BRADBURY, RAY     SS    MCL 48 09
  BEST SCIENCE-FICTION STORIES: 1950, THE     BLEILER & DIKTY          AN
DWELLERS IN THE DUST     ACKERMAN, FORREST J.     SS    FBK 48 04
  SCIENCE FICTION WORLDS OF FORREST J. ACKERMAN & FRIENDS
                    ACKERMAN, FORREST J.          AC
DWINDLING SPHERE, THE     HAWKINS, WILLIAM     SS    ASF 40 03
  MASTERS' CHOICE     JANIFER, LAURENCE M.          AN
DWINDLING YEARS, THE     DEL REY, LESTER     SS    GAL 56 01
  MORTALS AND MONSTERS     DEL REY, LESTER          AC
DYBBUK DOLLS, THE     DANN, JACK M.     SS    NDM 75 05
  NEW DIMENSIONS 5     SILVERBERG, ROBERT          AN
DYBBUK OF MAZEL TOV IV, THE     SILVERBERG, ROBERT     SS    NEW 74 AN
  CAPRICORN GAMES     SILVERBERG, ROBERT          AC
  WANDERING STARS     DANN, JACK M.          AN
  WORLDS FAR AND NEAR     CARR, TERRY          AN
DYING MAN, THE (DIO)     KNIGHT, DAMON     SN    INF 57 09
  THREE NOVELS     KNIGHT, DAMON          AC
DYING NIGHT, THE     ASIMOV, ISAAC     SS    FSF 56 07
  ASIMOV'S MYSTERIES     ASIMOV, ISAAC          AC
  BEST OF ISAAC ASIMOV, THE     ASIMOV, ISAAC          AC
  NINE TOMORROWS     ASIMOV, ISAAC          AC
DYING ROOM ONLY     MATHESON, RICHARD     SS    53
  SHOCK WAVES     MATHESON, RICHARD          AC
DYNAMO     DOLAN, MIKE     SS
  SANTANA MORNING AND OTHER STORIES     DOLAN, MIKE          OC
E FOR EFFORT     SHERRED, T. L.     NV    ASF 47 05
  *ASTOUNDING SCIENCE FICTION ANTHOLOGY, THE
                    CAMPBELL, JOHN W. JR    AN
  ASTOUNDING TALES OF SPACE AND TIME     CAMPBELL, JOHN W. JR    AN
  *BIG BOOK OF SCIENCE FICTION     CONKLIN, GROFF          AN
  CENTURY OF GREAT SHORT SCIENCE FICTION NOVELS, A
                    KNIGHT, DAMON          AN
  FIRST ASTOUNDING SCIENCE FICTION ANTHOLOGY, THE (PB)
                    CAMPBELL, JOHN W. JR    AN
  FIRST PERSON, PECULIAR     SHERRED, T. L.          AC
  SCIENCE FICTION HALL OF FAME VOLUME 2B     BOVA, BEN          AN
  *SECOND ASTOUNDING SCIENCE FICTION ANTHOLOGY, THE
                    CAMPBELL, JOHN W. JR    AN
E OF HER VOICE, THE     ALDISS, BRIAN W.     SS    NWR 73 22
  NEW WRITINGS IN SF. 22     BULMER, KENNETH          OA
E=MC2     BISHOP, MORRIS     PM    NYM 46
  MATHEMATICAL MAGPIE, THE     FADIMAN, CLIFTON          AN
  SPECULATIONS     SANDERS, THOMAS E.          AN
E=MC2     BOULLE, PIERRE     NV
  TIME OUT OF MIND     BOULLE, PIERRE          OC
E=MC2     REEVES, ROSSER     PM    FSF 61 09
  *BEST FROM FANTASY AND SCIENCE FICTION: 11
                    MILLS, ROBERT P.          AN
EA 5000: REPORT ON THE EFFECTS OF RIOT GAS
                    WATSON, IAN     SS
  STOPWATCH     HAY, GEORGE          OA
EACH AN EXPLORER     ASIMOV, ISAAC     SS    FUT 56 30
  BUY JUPITER AND OTHER STORIES     ASIMOV, ISAAC          AC
  EXPLORERS OF SPACE     SILVERBERG, ROBERT          AN
  ODDBALLS, THE     GHIDALIA, VIC          AN
  SF:57, THE YEAR'S GREATEST SCIENCE FICTION AND FANTASY
                    MERRIL, JUDITH          AN
EAGER DRAGON, THE     BLOCH, ROBERT     NV    WRT 43 01
  DRAGONS AND NIGHTMARES     BLOCH, ROBERT          AC
EAGLES GATHER, THE     KELLEAM, JOSEPH E.     SS    ASF 42 04
  CROSSROADS IN TIME     CONKLIN, GROFF          AN
EAR-FRIEND, THE     BANKS, RAYMOND E.     NV    SFS 55 03
  6 AND THE SILENT SCREAM     HOWARD, IVAN          AN
EARLIER SERVICE, THE (1935)     IRWIN, MARGARET     SS    FSF 51 12
  BEST FROM FANTASY AND SCIENCE FICTION: 2
                    BOUCHER & MCCOMAS          AN
EARLY BIRD     RUSSELL, ERIC FRANK     NV    SFS 57 11
  MASTERS OF SCIENCE FICTION     HOWARD, IVAN          AN
EARLY BIRD     COGSWELL, THEODORE R
                    AND THOMAS, THEODORE L.     SS C    AMA 73
  ASTOUNDING     HARRISON, HARRY          OA
  BEST SF: 1973     HARRISON & ALDISS          AN
```

EARLY MODEL   SHECKLEY, ROBERT   NV   GAL 56 08
  DECADE THE 1950S   ALDISS & HARRISON   AN
  PILGRIMAGE TO EARTH   SHECKLEY, ROBERT   AC
EARLY TIME-TRAVELER, AN (FROM "JOURNAL OF THE YEAR 2440", 1795)
                            MERCIER, LOUIS S.   EX
  SCIENCE IN FICTION   BAYLISS, A.E. & J.C.   AN
EARLY TO BED   EFFINGER, GEO. ALEC SS   CLR 72 02
  CLARION II   WILSON, ROBIN SCOTT   OA
EARLY WARNING   SCOTT, ROBIN S.   SS   ASF 66 06
  ANALOG 6   CAMPBELL, JOHN W. JR   AN
EARLY YEARS, THE   KNIGHT, DAMON   SI
  SCIENCE FICTION OF THE 30'S   KNIGHT, DAMON   AN
EARTH DWELLERS, THE   MAUROIS, ANDRE   NV   63
  WEIGHER OF SOULS AND THE EARTH DWELLERS, THE
                            MAUROIS, ANDRE   AC
  9TH ANNUAL OF THE YEAR'S BEST S-F, THE MERRIL, JUDITH   AN
EARTH EIGHTEEN   POHL, FREDERIK   FA   GAL 64 04
  DIGITS AND DASTARDS   POHL, FREDERIK   AC
EARTH FOR INSPIRATION   SIMAK, CLIFFORD D. SS   TWS 41 04
  COMING OF THE ROBOTS, THE   MOSKOWITZ, SAM   AN
EARTH IS A MAN, THE   ECHAURREN, ROBERTO IL
  SCIENCE FICTION   BRODKIN & PEARSON   AN
EARTH KILLERS, THE   VAN VOGT, A. E.   NV   SSS 49 04
  FAR-OUT WORLDS OF A. E. VAN VOGT, THE VAN VOGT, A. E.   AC
  IF THIS GOES ON   NUETZEL, CHARLES   AN
  TWISTED MEN, THE   VAN VOGT, A. E.   DC
  WORLDS OF A. E. VAN VOGT, THE VAN VOGT, A. E.   AC
EARTH MEN, THE   BRADBURY, RAY   SS   TWS 48 08
  MARTIAN CHRONICLES, THE   BRADBURY, RAY   AC
  *OTHER SIDE OF THE MOON, THE   DERLETH, AUGUST   AN
  TOWARD INFINITY   KNIGHT, DAMON   AN
EARTH MINUS   WANDREI, DONALD   NV   ASF 35 09
  EYE AND THE FINGER   WANDREI, DONALD   AC
EARTH MOTHER   GLOECKNER, CAROLYN SS   74
  BEST SCIENCE FICTION STORIES OF THE YEAR (1974)
                            DEL REY, LESTER   AN
  LONG NIGHT OF WAITING AND OTHER STORIES ELWOOD, ROGER   OA
EARTH SEES MARS   KEY, EUGENE GEORGE NV
  MARS MOUNTAIN   KEY, EUGENE GEORGE   AC
EARTH SHALL LIVE AGAIN   KNOX, CALVIN M.   SN   SFA 57 12
  LEST WE FORGET THEE, EARTH   KNOX, CALVIN M.   DN
EARTH WILL NOT LET GO   SWENSON, MAY   PM   70
  SPECULATIONS   SANDERS, THOMAS E.   AN
EARTH'S HOLOCAUST   HAWTHORNE, NATHANIEL SS GLG 44 05
  CIRCUS OF DR. LAO AND OTHER IMPROBABLE STORIES
                            BRADBURY, RAY   AN
  SCIENCE FICTION: THE FUTURE   ALLEN, DICK   AN
  SPECULATIONS   SANDERS, THOMAS E.   AN
EARTH'S NATURAL SATELLITE   DIKTY, T. E.   IN
  GREAT SCIENCE FICTION STORIES ABOUT THE MOON
                            DIKTY, T. E.   AN
EARTH-BRAIN, THE   HAMILTON, EDMOND   SS   WRT 32 04
  HORROR ON THE ASTEROID AND OTHER TALES OF PLANETARY HORROR
                            HAMILTON, EDMOND   AC
EARTH, AIR, FIRE AND WATER SHECKLEY, ROBERT   SS   ASF 55 07
  PILGRIMAGE TO EARTH   SHECKLEY, ROBERT   AC
EARTH, FAREWELL!   POHL, FREDERIK   SS   AST 43 02
  EARLY POHL, THE   POHL, FREDERIK   AC
EARTHBLOSSOM   FAST, JON   SS
  NEW CONSTELLATIONS   DISCH & NAYLOR   OA
EARTHBOUND   JACKSON, IRENE   PM
  MARS, WE LOVE YOU   HIPOLITO & MCNELLY   AN
EARTHCOMING   MEREDITH, RICHARD C. NV FIN 70
  FUTURE IS NOW, THE   NOLAN, WILLIAM F.   OA
EARTHLIGHT   CLARKE, ARTHUR C.   NO   TWS 51 08
  ACROSS THE SEA OF STARS   CLARKE, ARTHUR C.   AC
  ARTHUR C. CLARKE SECOND OMNIBUS, AN CLARKE, ARTHUR C.   AC
EARTHLINGS GO HOME!   REYNOLDS, MACK   SS   ROG 62 08
  BEST OF MACK REYNOLDS, THE   REYNOLDS, MACK   AC
  8TH ANNUAL OF THE YEAR'S BEST S-F, THE MERRIL, JUDITH   AN
EARTHMAN'S BURDEN, THE   WESTLAKE, DONALD E. NA   GAL 62 10
  ELSEWHERE AND ELSEWHEN   CONKLIN, GROFF   AN
EARTHMAN, BEWARE!   ANDERSON, POUL   NV   SSS 51 06
  HISTORY OF THE SCIENCE FICTION MAGAZINE, THE PART 3 1946-1955
                            ASHLEY, MICHAEL   AN
  STRANGERS FROM EARTH   ANDERSON, POUL   AC
EARTHMAN, COME HOME   BLISH, JAMES   NO   PUT 55
  CITIES IN FLIGHT   BLISH, JAMES   AC
EARTHMAN, COME HOME   BLISH, JAMES   NV   ASF 53 11
  EARTHMAN, COME HOME   BLISH, JAMES   NO
  SCIENCE FICTION HALL OF FAME VOLUME 2B BOVA, BEN   AN
EARTHMANIST CULTURE, THE   MULLEN, RICHARD D. AR   68
  CITIES IN FLIGHT   BLISH, JAMES   AC
EARTHMEN BEARING GIFTS   BROWN, FREDRIC   SS   GAL 60 06
  BEST OF FREDRIC BROWN, THE   BROWN, FREDRIC   AC
  SCIENCE FACT/FICTION   FARRELL/GAGE/&   AN
  SEVENTH GALAXY READER, THE   POHL, FREDERIK   AN
  12 GREAT CLASSICS OF SCIENCE FICTION CONKLIN, GROFF   AN
EARTHWOMAN   BRETNOR, REGINALD   SS   FSF 67 08
  MARRIAGE AND THE FAMILY THROUGH SCIENCE FICTION
                            CLEAR/WARRICK/&   AN
"EAST WIND, WEST WIND"   ROBINSON, FRANK M. NV NOV 72 02
  CITY: 2000 A.D., THE   CLEM/GREENBERG/&   AN
  NOVA 2   HARRISON, HARRY   OA
  SCIENCE FICTION NOVELLAS   HARRISON & MCNELLY   AN
EASTER EGGS (ALSO AS THOSE MEN FROM MARS)
                            CARR, ROBERT S.   NV   SEP 49 09
  BEST SCIENCE-FICTION STORIES: 1950, THE BLEILER & DIKTY AN
EASTERN WINDOWS, THE   ROBERTS, KEITH   SS   NEW 67 AN
  DEVIL HIS DUE, THE   HILL, DOUGLAS   AN
EASTWARD HO!   TENN, WILLIAM   SS   FSF 58 10
  ALPHA 4   SILVERBERG, ROBERT   AN
  BEST FROM FANTASY AND SCIENCE FICTION: 9
                            MILLS, ROBERT P.   AN
  WONDERMAKERS 2   HOSKINS, ROBERT   AN
  WOODEN STAR, THE   TENN, WILLIAM   AC

YET MORE PENGUIN SCIENCE FICTION   ALDISS, BRIAN W.   AN
EASY MONEY   HAMILTON, EDMOND   SS   TWS 38 04
  BEST OF EDMOND HAMILTON, THE   HAMILTON, EDMOND   AC
EASY WAY OUT, THE   BRUNNER, JOHN   NV   IFS 71 06
  BEST SCIENCE FICTION FOR 1972 POHL, FREDERIK   AN
EASY WAY OUT, THE   CORREY, LEE   SS   ASF 66 04
  ANALOG 6   CAMPBELL, JOHN W. JR   AN
EAT, DRINK, AND BE MERRY   GIRAD, DIAN   SS   NEW 74 AN
  2020 VISION   POURNELLE, JERRY   AN
EATING IT   HARRISON, WILLIAM   SS   70
  ROLLERBALL   HARRISON, WILLIAM   AN
ECCE FEMINA!   MCALLISTER, BRUCE   NV   FSF 72 02
  ABOVE THE HUMAN LANDSCAPE   MCNELLY & STOVER   AN
ECHINOMASTUS CONTENTII   FAST, HOWARD   SS
  TIME AND THE RIDDLE   FAST, HOWARD   AC
ECHO   MACLEAN, KATHERINE SS   INY 70 01
  INFINITY 1   HOSKINS, ROBERT   AN
ECHO   SALLIS, JAMES   SS   BER 74
  BERSERKERS, THE   ELWOOD, ROGER   AN
ECHOES OF THE MIND   KOESTLER, ARTHUR   AR   ESQ 72 08
  SCIENCE FACT/FICTION   FARRELL/GAGE/&   AN
ECLIPSE   HEARD, H. F.   SS
  GREAT FOG AND OTHER WEIRD TALES, THE HEARD, H. F.   OC
ECO-CATASTROPHE!   EHRLICH, DR. PAUL R. SS RAM 69 09
  BEST SF: 1969   HARRISON & ALDISS   AN
  NIGHTMARE AGE   POHL, FREDERIK   AN
ECOWARENESS   ELLISON, HARLAN   SS   NEW 74 AC
  APPROACHING OBLIVION   ELLISON, HARLAN   AC
ECSTASY MACHINE OR PROFESSOR A'GLEY IN ANTIMATTERLAND, THE
                            CONRAD, EARL   NA
  DA VINCI MACHINE, THE   CONRAD, EARL   OC
ED EMSHWILLER   MISC. MATERIAL   MS
  AGAIN, DANGEROUS VISIONS   ELLISON, HARLAN   OA
ED LEAR WASN'T SO CRAZY!   SCHENCK, HILBERT JR. PM FSF 60 06
  6TH ANNUAL OF THE YEAR'S BEST S-F, THE MERRIL, JUDITH   AN
EDDIE, YOU'RE MY FRIEND   ELLISON, HARLAN   SS   KNT 75
  NO DOORS, NO WINDOWS (STORIES REWRITTEN) ELLISON, HARLAN AC
EDDYSTONE LIGHT, THE   YEP, LAURENCE   NV   DEM 73
  DEMON KIND   ELWOOD, ROGER   OA
EDGE OF RUNNING WATER, THE SLOANE, WILLIAM   NA
  RIM OF MORNING, THE   SLOANE, WILLIAM   AC
EDGE OF THE SEA, THE   BUDRYS, ALGIS   SS   VSP 58 03
  DECADE THE 1950S   ALDISS & HARRISON   AN
  INTRODUCING SCIENCE FICTION   ALDISS, BRIAN W.   AN
  SF:58, THE YEAR'S GREATEST SCIENCE FICTION AND FANTASY
                            MERRIL, JUDITH   AN
  WORLDS TO COME   KNIGHT, DAMON   AN
EDGE OF TOMORROW, THE (OMITS STORY "THE FIRST MEN")
                            FAST, HOWARD   AC BAN 61 06
  TIME AND THE RIDDLE   FAST, HOWARD   AC
EDGE, THE   MATHESON, RICHARD   SS   FSF 58 08
  SHOCK!   MATHESON, RICHARD   AC
EDIFICE COMPLEX   BLOCH, ROBERT   SS   ESC 58 02
  ATOMS AND EVIL   BLOCH, ROBERT   AC
EDISON'S CONQUEST OF MARS (ABRIDGED)
                            SERVISS, GARRETT P. SS   NYE 98 01
  TREASURY OF SCIENCE FICTION CLASSICS, THE
                            KUEBLER, HAROLD W.   AN
EDITOR'S FOREWORD   HAINING, PETER   IN
  GHOULS, THE   HAINING, PETER   IN
EDITOR'S INTRODUCTION   ELWOOD, ROGER   IN
  ALIEN WORLDS   ELWOOD, ROGER   AN
EDITOR'S INTRODUCTION   SILVERBERG, ROBERT IN
  THREE FOR TOMORROW   SILVERBERG, ROBERT   OA
EDITOR'S NOTE   CROSSEN, KENDELL F. IN
  ADVENTURES IN TOMORROW   CROSSEN, KENDELL F.   AN
EDITOR'S NOTE   ELWOOD, ROGER   IN
  SURVIVAL FROM INFINITY   ELWOOD, ROGER   IN
EDITOR'S NOTE   GINSBURG, MIRRA   IN
  AIR OF MARS AND OTHER STORIES, THE GINSBURG, MIRRA   AN
EDITOR'S NOTE   LEY, SANDRA   IN
  BEYOND TIME   LEY, SANDRA   OA
EDITOR'S NOTE   POHL, FREDERIK   IN
  STAR SCIENCE FICTION STORIES   POHL, FREDERIK   OA
  STAR SCIENCE FICTION STORIES NO. 2 POHL, FREDERIK   OA
  STAR SCIENCE FICTION STORIES NO. 3 POHL, FREDERIK   OA
EDITOR'S POSTSCRIPT   NOLAN, WILLIAM F.   MS
  WILDERNESS OF STARS, A   NOLAN, WILLIAM F.   AN
EDITOR'S PREFACE   EARLEY, GEORGE W.   IN
  ENCOUNTERS WITH ALIENS   EARLEY, GEORGE W.   AN
EDITOR'S PREFACE   ELWOOD, ROGER   IN
  FUTURE CORRUPTION   ELWOOD, ROGER   OA
EDITOR'S PREFACE   MERRIL, JUDITH   IN
  BEYOND THE BARRIERS OF SPACE AND TIME MERRIL, JUDITH   AN
EDITOR'S PREFACE   NOLAN, WILLIAM F.   IN
  HUMAN EQUATION, THE   NOLAN, WILLIAM F.   AN
  SEA OF SPACE, A   NOLAN, WILLIAM F.   AN
EDITOR'S PREFACE: A IS FOR ANDROID
                            NOLAN, WILLIAM F.   IN
  PSEUDO PEOPLE, THE   NOLAN, WILLIAM F.   AN
EDITORIAL   DELANY, SAMUEL R.
                            AND HACKER, MARILYN ED C QRK 70 01
  QUARK/1   DELANY & HACKER   OA
EDITORIAL   HARRISON, HARRY   ED
  BEST SF: 1974   HARRISON & ALDISS   AN
EDITORS' PREFACE   BLEILER, EVERETT F. IN C
  BEST SCIENCE-FICTION STORIES: 1954, THE BLEILER & DIKTY AN
EDITORS' PREFACE   DIKTY, T. E.   IN C
  BEST SCIENCE-FICTION STORIES: 1954, THE BLEILER & DIKTY AN
EDITORS, THE   MISC. MATERIAL   MS
  SURVIVAL PRINTOUT   TOTAL EFFECT   AN
EDUCATION OF DRUSILLA STRANGE, THE
                            STURGEON, THEODORE NV   GAL 54 03
  OPERATION FUTURE   CONKLIN, GROFF   AN

EDUCATION OF TIGRESS MACARDLE, THE
    KORNBLUTH, C. M.   SS   VSF 57 07
  MARRIAGE AND THE FAMILY THROUGH SCIENCE FICTION
    CLEAR/WARRICK/&   AN
  NO LIMITS   FERMAN, JOSEPH W.   AN
  13 ABOVE THE NIGHT   CONKLIN, GROFF   AN
EDUCATIONAL   BUNCH, DAVID R.   SS
  MODERAN   BUNCH, DAVID R.   AC
EDUCATIONAL RELEVANCE OF SCIENCE FICTION, THE
    BRUNNER, JOHN   AR   PHE 71 06
  BOOK OF JOHN BRUNNER, THE   BRUNNER, JOHN   AC
EEL BY THE TAIL, AN   LANG, ALLEN KIM   SS   IMG 51 04
  *INVADERS OF EARTH   CONKLIN, GROFF   AN
  SPECULATIONS   SANDERS, THOMAS E.   AN
EEL, THE   DEFORD, MIRIAM ALLEN   SS   GAL 58 04
  CRIME PREVENTION IN THE 30TH CENTURY   SANTESSON, HANS S.   AN
  ELSEWHERE, ELSEWHEN, ELSEHOW   DEFORD, MIRIAM ALLEN   AC
  FIFTH GALAXY READER, THE   GOLD, H. L.   AN
EERIEST RUINED DAWN WORLD, THE LEIBER, FRITZ   SS
  IDES OF TOMORROW, THE   CARR, TERRY   OA
EFFECTIVES, THE   HENDERSON, ZENNA   SS   WOT 65 05
  HOLDING WONDER   HENDERSON, ZENNA   AC
EFFIGY   REEVES, ROSSER   PM   FSF 61 09
  *BEST FROM FANTASY AND SCIENCE FICTION: 11
    MILLS, ROBERT P.   AN
EGG A MONTH FROM ALL OVER, AN SEABRIGHT, IDRIS   SS   FSF 52 10
  FIFTY SHORT SCIENCE FICTION TALES   ASIMOV & CONKLIN   AN
  HUMAN?   MERRIL, JUDITH   AN
  VINTAGE ANTHOLOGY OF SCIENCE FANTASY, THE
    CERF, CHRISTOPHER   AN
EGG A MONTH FROM ALL OVER, AN ST. CLAIR, MARGARET   SS   FSF 52 10
  CHANGE THE SKY AND OTHER STORIES   ST. CLAIR, MARGARET   AC
EGG AND ASHES   HERBERT, FRANK   SS   IFS 60 11
  BEST OF FRANK HERBERT, THE   HERBERT, FRANK   AC
  BEST SCIENCE FICTION FROM IF, THE   POHL, FREDERIK   AN
EGG FROM ALPHA CENTAURI, THE WOLLHEIM, DONALD A.   SS
  TWO DOZEN DRAGON EGGS   WOLLHEIM, DONALD A.   AC
EGG OF THE GLAK, THE   JACOBS, HARVEY   NV   FSF 68 03
  BEST FROM FANTASY AND SCIENCE FICTION: 18
    FERMAN, EDWARD L.   AN
EGG OF THE GLAK, AND OTHER STORIES, THE JACOBS, HARVEY   AC
EGG, THE   DE CAMP, L. SPRAGUE   SS   SAT 56 10
  GUN FOR DINOSAUR AND OTHER IMAGINATIVE TALES
    DE CAMP, L. SPRAGUE   AC
EGG, THE   FAST, HOWARD   SS
  TOUCH OF INFINITY, A   FAST, HOWARD   OC
EGGHEAD   BLOCH, ROBERT   SS   FUN 58 07
  ATOMS AND EVIL   BLOCH, ROBERT   AC
EGGS AND I, THE   ACKERMAN, FORREST J. IN
  TWO DOZEN DRAGON EGGS   WOLLHEIM, DONALD A.   AC
EGO MACHINE, THE   KUTTNER, HENRY   NV   SSF 52 05
  BEST OF HENRY KUTTNER 1, THE   KUTTNER, HENRY   AC
  RETURN TO OTHERNESS   KUTTNER, HENRY   AC
  *SCIENCE-FICTION CARNIVAL   BROWN, F. & REYNOLDS AN
EGO TRIP   BLOCH, ROBERT   SS   PNT 72 03
  COLD CHILLS   BLOCH, ROBERT   AC
EGYPTIAN HORNET, AN   BLACKWOOD, ALGERNON SS   17
  BR-R-R-| CONKLIN, GROFF   AN
EIGHT BILLION, THE   WILSON, RICHARD   SS   FSF 65 07
  BEST FROM FANTASY AND SCIENCE FICTION: 15
    FERMAN, EDWARD L.   AN
EIGHT MISTRESSES, THE   HROLDA, JEAN   SS   ESQ 37 08
  TIMELESS STORIES FOR TODAY AND TOMORROW BRADBURY, RAY   AN
EIGHT O'CLOCK IN THE MORNING NELSON, RAY   SS   FSF 63 11
  BEST FROM FANTASY AND SCIENCE FICTION: 13
    DAVIDSON, AVRAM   AN
  OTHERS, THE   CARR, TERRY   AN
  TALES OF TERROR FROM OUTER SPACE   CHETWYND-HAYES, R.   AN
  9TH ANNUAL OF THE YEAR'S BEST S-F, THE MERRIL, JUDITH   AN
EIN BLICK IN DIE ZUKUNFT WOLLHEIM, DONALD A.   SS
  TWO DOZEN DRAGON EGGS   WOLLHEIM, DONALD A.   AC
EINE KLEINE NACHTMUSIK   BROWN, FREDRIC
  AND ONSPAUGH, CARL   SS C FSF 65 06
  BEST OF FREDRIC BROWN, THE   BROWN, FREDRIC   AC
  PARADOX LOST, AND 12 OTHER GREAT S.F. STORIES
    BROWN, FREDRIC   AC
EINSTEIN INSHOOT, THE BOND, NELSON S.   SS   ASF 38 11
  MR. MERGENTHWIRKER'S LOBBIES AND OTHER FANTASTIC TALES
    BOND, NELSON S.   AC
EINSTEIN: A PARODY IN THE MANNER OF EDW-N MARKH-M
    UNTERMEYER, L.   SS   26
  MATHEMATICAL MAGPIE, THE   FADIMAN, CLIFTON   AN
EL DIA DE MUERTE (THE DAY OF DEATH)
    BRADBURY, RAY   SS   TCH 47 FL
  MACHINERIES OF JOY, THE   BRADBURY, RAY   AC
ELAAN OF TROYIUS (JOHN MEREDYTH LUCAS)
    BLISH, JAMES   SA   STK 72 07
  STAR TREK 7   BLISH, JAMES   OC
ELDER SON, THE   SHELLEY, MARY W.   NV   35
  TALES AND STORIES   SHELLEY, MARY W.   AC
ELECTED SILENCE (SILENCE) BRUNNER, JOHN   NV   GAL 59 10
  NO FUTURE IN IT   BRUNNER, JOHN   AC
ELECTRIC ANT, THE   DICK, PHILIP K.   NV   FSF 69 10
  BEST OF PHILIP K. DICK, THE   DICK, PHILIP K.   AC
  BEST SF: 1969   HARRISON & ALDISS   AN
  DECADE THE 1960S   ALDISS & HARRISON   AN
  WINDOWS INTO TOMORROW   SILVERBERG, ROBERT   AN
ELECTRIC NEON MERMAID, THE YEP, LAURENCE   NV   QRK 71 02
  QUARK/2   DELANY & HACKER   OA
ELECTRONIC CONCERT   DEUTSCH, BABETTE   PM   63
  SCIENCE FICTION   BRODKIN & PEARSON   AN
ELECTRONIC TAPE FOUND IN A BOTTLE
    CABRAL, OLGA   PM
  SCIENCE FACT/FICTION   FARRELL/GAGE/&   AN
ELEGY   BEAUMONT, CHARLES SS IMG 53 02
  SCIENCE FACT/FICTION   FARRELL/GAGE/&   AN

SEA OF SPACE, A   NOLAN, WILLIAM F.   AN
ELEGY FOR JANIS JOPLIN HACKER, MARILYN   PM   BMR 73
  BAD MOON RISING   DISCH, THOMAS M.   OA
ELEGY TO A DEAD PLANET: LUNA POHL, FREDERIK   PM   AMZ 37 10
  EARLY POHL, THE   POHL, FREDERIK   AC
ELEMENT OF CHANCE   SHAW, BOB   SS   GAL 69 10
  TOMORROW LIES IN AMBUSH   SHAW, BOB   AC
ELEMENT 79   HOYLE, FRED   SS
  ELEMENT 79   HOYLE, FRED   AC
ELEMENTAL, THE   LONG, FRANK BELKNAP SS UNK 39 07
  EARLY LONG, THE   LONG, FRANK BELKNAP   AC
  *HOUNDS OF TINDALOS, THE   LONG, FRANK BELKNAP   AC
ELEMENTARY   JANIFER, LAURENCE M.
  AND KURLAND, MICHAEL J. SS C FSF 64 09
  IMPOSSIBLE?   JANIFER, LAURENCE M. AC
ELEPHANT CIRCUIT, THE (SEE THE MAN WHO TRAVELED IN ELEPHANTS)
    HEINLEIN, ROBERT A.   TC
ELEPHANT FOR THE PRINKIP, AN STECHER, L. J. JR. SS GAL 60 08
  TENTH GALAXY READER, THE   POHL, FREDERIK   AN
ELEPHANT MAN, THE   TREVES, FREDERICK   SS   23
  STRANGE BEASTS AND UNNATURAL MONSTERS STERN, PHILIP VAN D. AN
ELEPHANT WITH WOODEN LEG SLADEK, JOHN T.   SS   GAL 75 06
  ANTIGRAV: COSMIC COMEDIES   STRICK, PHILIP   AN
  BEST FROM GALAXY, THE VOLUME IV BAEN, JAMES   AN
ELEPHANTS   MALZBERG, BARRY N. SS INY 71 02
  EDGE OF NEVER, THE   HOSKINS, ROBERT   AN
ELEPHANTS   O'DONNELL, K. M. SS INY 71 02
  INFINITY 2   HOSKINS, ROBERT   OA
  UNIVERSE DAY   O'DONNELL, K. M.   NO
ELEPHAS FRUMENTI   DE CAMP, L. SPRAGUE
  AND PRATT, FLETCHER SS C FSF 50 WS
  BEST FROM FANTASY AND SCIENCE FICTION BOUCHER & MCCOMAS AN
  TALES FROM GAVAGAN'S BAR   DE CAMP, L. S.&PRATT AC
ELFIN HILLS, THE   WELLS, BASIL   SS
  DOORWAYS TO SPACE   WELLS, BASIL   AC
ELIMINATION   CAMPBELL, JOHN W. JR SS ASF 36 05
  *BEST OF JOHN W. CAMPBELL, THE   CAMPBELL, JOHN W. JR AC
  WHO GOES THERE?   CAMPBELL, JOHN W. JR AC
ELIXER FOR THE EMPEROR, THE BRUNNER, JOHN SS FAN 64 11
  FROM THIS DAY FORWARD   BRUNNER, JOHN   AC
ELLISON'S GRAMMATICAL GUIDE AND GLOSSARY FOR GOYIM
    ELLISON, HARLAN   MS
  WANDERING STARS   DANN, JACK M.   AN
ELOUISE AND THE DOCTORS OF THE PLANET PERGAMON
    SAXTON, JOSEPHINE SS DVS 72 02
  AGAIN, DANGEROUS VISIONS   ELLISON, HARLAN   OA
ELSEWHEN   BOUCHER, ANTHONY NV ASF 43 01
  FAR AND AWAY   BOUCHER, ANTHONY   AC
ELSEWHEN (ELSEWHERE) HEINLEIN, ROBERT A. NV ASF 41 09
  ASSIGNMENT IN ETERNITY   HEINLEIN, ROBERT A.   AC
ELSEWHERE (SEE ELSEWHEN) HEINLEIN, ROBERT A. TC
ELSEWHERE AND OTHERWISE BLACKWOOD, ALGERNON SS 36
  TRAVELERS IN TIME   STERN, PHILIP VAN D. AN
ELTONIAN PYRAMID   DEXTER, RALPH W. MS SCM 52 10
  APEMAN, SPACEMAN   STOVER & HARRISON   AN
EMANCIPATION: A ROMANCE OF THE TIMES TO COME
    DISCH, THOMAS M.   NV NDM 71 01
  BIO-FUTURES   SARGENT, PAMELA   AN
  NEW DIMENSIONS 1   SILVERBERG, ROBERT   OA
  334   DISCH, THOMAS M.   NO
EMBASSY, THE   PEARSON, MARTIN SS ASF 42 03
  BEYOND THE END OF TIME   POHL, FREDERIK   AN
  *TREASURY OF SCIENCE FICTION, A CONKLIN, GROFF   AN
EMBASSY, THE   WOLLHEIM, DONALD A. SS ASF 42 03
  MARS, WE LOVE YOU   HIPOLITO & MCNELLY   AN
EMBROIDERY   BRADBURY, RAY SS MAR 51 11
  *GOLDEN APPLES OF THE SUN   BRADBURY, RAY   AC
EMERGENCY CASE, AN   STRUGATSKY, ARKADY
  AND STRUGATSKY, BORIS SS C
  PATH INTO THE UNKNOWN   ANONYMOUS   AN
EMERGENCY LANDING   WILLIAMS, RALPH SS ASF 40 07
  *BIG BOOK OF SCIENCE FICTION   CONKLIN, GROFF   AN
  FIFTY SHORT SCIENCE FICTION TALES ASIMOV & CONKLIN   AN
EMERGENCY OPERATION   PORGES, ARTHUR SS FSF 56 05
  GREAT SCIENCE FICTION ABOUT DOCTORS CONKLIN, G&FABRICANT AN
EMERGENCY RATIONS   COGSWELL, THEODORE R SS IMG 53 09
  WALL AROUND THE WORLD, THE   COGSWELL, THEODORE R AC
EMERGENCY SOCIETY   FRITH, UTA SS NEW 76 AN
  ANTIGRAV: COSMIC COMEDIES   STRICK, PHILIP   AN
EMERGENCY WORKING   JAMES, E. R. SS NWS 52 09
  GATEWAY TO TOMORROW   CARNELL, JOHN   AN
EMILY AND THE BARDS SUBLIME YOUNG, ROBERT F. SS FSF 56 07
  WORLDS OF ROBERT F. YOUNG, THE   YOUNG, ROBERT F.   AC
EMISSARY   FRITCH, CHARLES E. SS FNF 53 06
  CRAZY MIXED-UP PLANET   FRITCH, CHARLES E.   AC
EMISSARY FROM HAMELIN   ELLISON, HARLAN   SS
  2076: THE AMERICAN TRICENTENNIAL BRYANT, EDWARD   OA
EMISSARY, THE   BRADBURY, RAY SS NEW 47 AC
  *DARK CARNIVAL   BRADBURY, RAY   AC
  *OCTOBER COUNTRY, THE   BRADBURY, RAY   AC
EMPATH, THE (JOYCE MUSKAT) BLISH, JAMES SA STK 74 10
  STAR TREK 10   BLISH, JAMES   OC
EMPEROR'S FAN, THE   DE CAMP, L. SPRAGUE NV AMA 73
  ASTOUNDING   HARRISON, HARRY   OA
EMPIRE OF T'ANG LANG, THE FOSTER, ALAN DEAN SS ALC 73
  ALIEN CONDITION, THE   GOLDIN, STEPHEN   OA
EMPIRE OF THE ANTS, THE WELLS, H. G. SS SND 05 12
  COUNTRY OF THE BLIND, THE   WELLS, H. G.   AC
  EARTH IS THE STRANGEST PLANET SILVERBERG, ROBERT   AN
  SHORT STORIES OF H. G. WELLS, THE WELLS, H. G.   AC
  *TIME MACHINE AND OTHER STORIES, THE WELLS, H. G.   AC
  TWENTY-EIGHT SCIENCE FICTION STORIES WELLS, H. G.   AC
EMPIRE OF THE DUST   WELLS, BASIL SS FBK 49 05
  PLANETS OF ADVENTURE   WELLS, BASIL   AC
EMPIRE OF THE SUN   WEINER, ANDREW SS DVS 72 02
  AGAIN, DANGEROUS VISIONS   ELLISON, HARLAN   OA

EMPIRE STAR   DELANY, SAMUEL R.   NO   ACE 66
  ACE SCIENCE FICTION READER   WOLLHEIM, DONALD A.   AN
EMPLOYMENT (AS LYMAN R. LYON) DE CAMP, L. SPRAGUE SS   ASF 39 05
*IMAGINATION UNLIMITED   BLEILER & DIKTY   AN
  SCIENCE FICTION INVENTIONS   KNIGHT, DAMON   AN
EMPRESS OF MARS, THE   ROCKLYNNE, ROSS   NV   FAD 39 05
  SPACE ODYSSEYS   ALDISS, BRIAN W.   AN
  (TRANSLATED BY TSURUTA & MERRIL)
EMPTY FIELD, THE (TRANSLATED BY TSURUTA & MERRIL)
                               KITA, MORIO   SS   OMG 73
  OMEGA   ELWOOD, ROGER   OA
EMPTY ROOM, THE   DISCH, THOMAS M.   SS   NWS 67 03
  BEST SF STORIES FROM NEW WORLDS NO. 2, THE
                                          MOORCOCK, MICHAEL   AN
  FUN WITH YOUR NEW HEAD   DISCH, THOMAS M.   AC
EMPTYNESS OF SPACE, THE (ALSO AS THE ASTEROIDS, 2194)
                               WYNDHAM, JOHN   SS   NWS 60 11
  BEST OF JOHN WYNDHAM, THE   WYNDHAM, JOHN   AC
  MAN FROM BEYOND AND OTHER STORIES, THE WYNDHAM, JOHN   AC
  *OUTWARD URGE, THE   WYNDHAM & PARKES   AC
EMRETH   MORGAN, DAN   SS   NWR 65 03
  NEW WRITINGS IN SF. 3   CARNELL, JOHN   OA
EN LA NOCHE (TORRID SACRIFICE) BRADBURY, RAY   SS   CAV 52 11
  *GOLDEN APPLES OF THE SUN   BRADBURY, RAY   AC
EN PASSANT   SCHWEITZER, BRITT   SS   HBK 60 12
  NEW WORLDS OF FANTASY NO. 2   CARR, TERRY   AN
EN ROUTE TO EARTH   SILVERBERG, ROBERT   SS   SFQ 57 08
  DIMENSION THIRTEEN   SILVERBERG, ROBERT   AC
EN ROUTE TO PLUTO   WEST, WALLACE   SS   ASF 36 08
  *BEST OF SCIENCE FICTION   CONKLIN, GROFF   AN
  BIRD OF TIME, THE   WEST, WALLACE   NO
ENCASED IN ANCIENT RIND   LAFFERTY, R. A.   NV   QRK 71 03
  LIBERATED FUTURE: VOYAGES INTO TOMORROW, THE
                                          HOSKINS, ROBERT   AN
                                          DELANY & HACKER   OA
  QUARK/3   OFFUTT, ANDREW J.   SS
ENCHANTE
  TOMORROW: NEW WORLDS OF SCIENCE FICTION ELWOOD, ROGER   OA
ENCHANTED FOREST, THE   LEIBER, FRITZ   SS   ASF 50 10
  BEST OF FRITZ LEIBER, THE   LEIBER, FRITZ   AC
  NEW WORLDS FOR OLD   DERLETH, AUGUST   AN
  SHIPS TO THE STARS   LEIBER, FRITZ   DC
  *WORLDS OF TOMORROW   DERLETH, AUGUST   AN
ENCHANTED PENCIL, THE   BOND, NELSON S.   SS
  31ST OF FEBRUARY, THE   BOND, NELSON S.   AC
ENCHANTED POOL, THE   ERICSON, MARCIA   NV
  STAR TREK: THE NEW VOYAGES   MARSHAK, S&CULBREATH   OA
ENCHANTED PRINCE, THE (SEE THE PRINCESS' CARILLON)
                               DISCH, THOMAS M.   TC
ENCHANTED PRINCESS, THE (SEE THE DREAMER)
                               VANCE, JACK   TC
ENCHANTED VILLAGE (ALSO AS THE SANDS OF MARS)
                               VAN VOGT, A. E.   SS   OWS 50 07
  ANTHROPOLOGY THROUGH SCIENCE FICTION   MASON, C/GREENBERG/&   AN
  ASLEEP IN ARMAGEDDON   SISSONS, MICHAEL   AN
  DESTINATION: UNIVERSE!   VAN VOGT, A. E.   AC
  HOT & COLD RUNNING CITIES   MCHARGUE, GEORGESS   AN
  MICROCOSMIC GOD   MOSKOWITZ, SAM   AN
  MODERN MASTERPIECES OF SCIENCE FICTION MOSKOWITZ, SAM   AN
  MODERN SCIENCE FICTION   SPINRAD, NORMAN   AN
  MONSTERS   VAN VOGT, A. E.   AC
  *POSSIBLE WORLDS OF SCIENCE FICTION   CONKLIN, GROFF   AN
  SCIENCE FICTION   BRODKIN & PEARSON   AN
ENCHANTED WEEKEND, THE   MACCORMAC, JOHN   NO   UNK 39 10
  FROM UNKNOWN WORLDS   CAMPBELL, JOHN W. JR   AN
ENCHANTER'S ENCOUNTER   TUBB, E. C.   NV   SCF 59 12
  SCATTER OF STARDUST, A   TUBB, E. C.   DC
ENCHANTMENT   EMMETT, ELIZABETH   SS   SEP 60 10
  6TH ANNUAL OF THE YEAR'S BEST S-F, THE MERRILL, JUDITH   AN
ENCHANTRESS OF VENUS (ALSO AS CITY OF THE LOST ONES)
                               BRACKETT, LEIGH   NV   PLS 49 FL
  BEST OF LEIGH BRACKETT, THE   BRACKETT, LEIGH   AC
  GIANT ANTHOLOGY OF SCIENCE FICTION   MARGULIES & FRIEND   AN
  HALFLING AND OTHER STORIES, THE   BRACKETT, LEIGH   AC
ENCLAVE   SALLIS, JAMES   SS   70
  FEW LAST WORDS, A   SALLIS, JAMES   AC
ENCOUNTER AT DAWN (ENCOUNTER IN THE DAWN)
                               CLARKE, ARTHUR C.   SS   AMZ 53 07
  ACROSS THE SEA OF STARS   CLARKE, ARTHUR C.   AC
  NINE BILLION NAMES OF GOD, THE   CLARKE, ARTHUR C.   AC
  OF TIME AND STARS   CLARKE, ARTHUR C.   AC
ENCOUNTER IN A LONELY PLACE   HERBERT, FRANK   SS   NEW 73 AC
  BOOK OF FRANK HERBERT, THE   HERBERT, FRANK   AC
ENCOUNTER IN THE DAWN (SEE ENCOUNTER AT DAWN AND EXPEDITION
  TO EARTH)   CLARKE, ARTHUR C.   TC
ENCOUNTER IN THE PAST   NATHAN, ROBERT   SS   FSF 67 07
  BEST FROM FANTASY AND SCIENCE FICTION: 17
                                          FERMAN, EDWARD L.   AN
ENCOUNTER WITH A CARNIVORE   GREEN, JOSEPH   SS   EPC 75
  EPOCH   ELWOOD & SILVERBERG   OA
ENCOUNTER WITH A HICK   BRAND, JONATHAN   SS   DVS 67 01
  DANGEROUS VISIONS   ELLISON, HARLAN   AN
ENCOUNTER, THE   WILHELM, KATE   NV   ORB 70 08
  BEST FROM ORBIT, THE   KNIGHT, DAMON   AN
  NEBULA AWARD STORIES NO. 7   BIGGLE, LLOYD JR   AN
  ORBIT 8   KNIGHT, DAMON   OA
ENCOUNTER, THE (SEE THE VENUS HUNTERS)
                               BALLARD, J. G.   TC
END AS A HERO   LAUMER, KEITH   NA   GAL 63 06
  NINE BY LAUMER   LAUMER, KEITH   AC
  UNDEFEATED, THE   LAUMER, KEITH   AC
END AS A WORLD   WALLACE, F. L.   SS   GAL 55 09
  THIRD GALAXY READER, THE   GOLD, H. L.   AN
END CITY   SHECKLEY, ROBERT   SS   GAL 74 05
  BEST FROM GALAXY, THE VOLUME III   BAEN, JAMES   AN
END GAME   HALDEMAN, JOE W.   NV   ASF 75 01
  BEST SF: 75, THE NINTH ANNUAL   HARRISON & ALDISS   AN
  FOREVER WAR, THE   HALDEMAN, JOE W.   NO

  NEBULA AWARD STORIES 11   LE GUIN, URSULA K.   AN
END OF SUMMER, THE   BUDRYS, ALGIS   NV   ASF 54 11
  PENGUIN SCIENCE FICTION   ALDISS, BRIAN W.   AN
  UNEXPECTED DIMENSION, THE   BUDRYS, ALGIS   AC
END OF THE BEGINNING, THE (NEXT STOP: THE STARS)
                               BRADBURY, RAY   SS   MCL 56 10
  DAY IT RAINED FOREVER, THE   BRADBURY, RAY   AC
  MEDICINE FOR MELANCHOLY, A   BRADBURY, RAY   AC
  R IS FOR ROCKET   BRADBURY, RAY   AC
  SCIENCE FICTION SHOWCASE   KORNBLUTH, MARY   AN
END OF THE JOURNEY, THE (SEE M81: URSA MAJOR)
                               COOPER, EDMUND   TC
END OF THE LINE   OLIVER, CHAD   NV   FSF 65 01
  ONCE AND FUTURE TALES FROM THE MAGAZINE OF FANTASY AND
  SCIENCE FICTION   FERMAN, EDWARD L.   AN
END OF THE LINE, THE   SCHMITZ, JAMES H.   NV   ASF 51 07
  SPACE PIONEERS   NORTON, ANDRE   AN
  TO THE STARS   SILVERBERG, ROBERT   AN
  TOMORROW 1   HOSKINS, ROBERT   AN
END OF THE LINE, THE (SEE CAUTION! INFLAMMABLE!)
                               SCORTIA, THOMAS N.   TC
END OF THE PARTY, THE (1947)   GREENE, GRAHAM   SS   WBY 50 12
  CHILDREN OF WONDER   TENN, WILLIAM   AN
  LIGHT FANTASTIC, THE   HARRISON, HARRY   AN
  PERCHANCE TO DREAM   KNIGHT, DAMON   AN
END OF THE RACE, THE   BERMEL, ALBERT   SS   GAL 64 04
  EIGHTH GALAXY READER, THE   POHL, FREDERIK   AN
END OF THE SEARCH, THE (SEE COLLECTOR'S ITEM)
                               KNIGHT, DAMON   TC
END OF THE STORY, THE   SMITH, CLARK ASHTON NV   WRT 30 05
  OUT OF SPACE AND TIME   SMITH, CLARK ASHTON   AC
END OF THE UNIVERSE?, THE   TAYLOR, JOHN   AR   LIS 71 09
  BEYOND THIS HORIZON   CARRELL, CHRISTOPHER   OA
END OF THE WORLD, THE   FARLEY, RALPH MILNE SS
  OMNIBUS OF TIME, THE   FARLEY, RALPH MILNE   AC
END OF THE WORLD, THE   NEWCOMB, SIMON   SS
  BATTLE OF THE MONSTERS AND OTHER STORIES, THE
                                          HARTWELL & CURREY   AN
END OF WINTER, THE (SEE GO AND BEHOLD THEM)
                               BUDRYS, ALGIS   TC
END TO COMPLACENCY, AN   COLE, BARRY   PM   69
  HOLDING YOUR EIGHT HANDS   LUCIE-SMITH, EDWARD   AN
END WITH NO PERHAPS, THE   NOLAN, WILLIAM F.   SS   NEW 63 AC
  IMPACT-20   NOLAN, WILLIAM F.   AC
END-GAME   BALLARD, J. G.   SS   NWS 63 06
  CHRONOPOLIS AND OTHER STORIES   BALLARD, J. G.   AC
  SF: AUTHORS' CHOICE   HARRISON, HARRY   AN
  TERMINAL BEACH (AMERICAN VERSION)   BALLARD, J. G.   AC
  TERMINAL BEACH (BRITISH VERSION)   BALLARD, J. G.   AC
END, THE   BROWN, FREDRIC   SS   NEW 61 AC
  BEST OF FREDRIC BROWN, THE   BROWN, FREDRIC   AC
  NIGHTMARES AND GEEZENSTACKS   BROWN, FREDRIC   AC
END, THE   KNIGHT, DAMON   SI
  SCIENCE FICTION OF THE 30'S   KNIGHT, DAMON   AN
END, THE   LEINSTER, MURRAY   NV   TWS 46 12
  TWISTS IN TIME   LEINSTER, MURRAY   AC
END, THE (ALSO AS THINGS)   LE GUIN, URSULA K.   SS   ORB 70 06
  BEST FROM ORBIT, THE   KNIGHT, DAMON   AN
  ORBIT 6   KNIGHT, DAMON   OA
"END, THE"   WELLEN, EDWARD   SS   ORB 74 15
  ORBIT 15   KNIGHT, DAMON   OA
ENDFRAY OF THE OFAY   LEIBER, FRITZ   SS   IFS 69 03
  WORLDS OF FRITZ LEIBER, THE   LEIBER, FRITZ   AC
ENDLESS DIMENSIONS   ARNOLD, FRANK EDWARD NV
  WINGS ACROSS TIME   ARNOLD, FRANK EDWARD   AC
ENDOCHRONIC PROPERTIES OF RESUBLIMATED THIOTIMOLINE, THE
                               ASIMOV, ISAAC   FA   ASF 48 03
  EARLY ASIMOV, THE   ASIMOV, ISAAC   AC
ENDORSEMENT, PERSONAL   MCLAUGHLIN, DEAN   SS   NOV 73 03
  NOVA 3   HARRISON, HARRY   OA
ENDOWMENT POLICY   KUTTNER, HENRY   SS   ASF 43 08
  BEST OF HENRY KUTTNER 2, THE   KUTTNER, HENRY   AN
  BEST OF HENRY KUTTNER, THE   KUTTNER, HENRY   AC
ENDOWMENT POLICY   PADGETT, LEWIS   SS   ASF 43 08
  ADVENTURES IN DIMENSION   CONKLIN, GROFF   AC
  *SCIENCE FICTION ADVENTURES IN DIMENSION CONKLIN, GROFF   AN
ENEMIES IN SPACE (TRANSLATED BY WILLY LEY)
                               GRUNERT, KARL   SS   07
  *INVADERS OF EARTH   CONKLIN, GROFF   AN
ENEMY OF ALL THE WORLD, THE   LONDON, JACK   SS   RBM 08 10
  CURIOUS FRAGMENTS   LONDON, JACK   AC
ENEMY OF THE SILKIE   VAN VOGT, A. E.   NV   IFS 67 10
  SILKIE, THE   VAN VOGT, A. E.   NO
ENEMY PLANET, THE   GALLERY, D. V.   SS   SEP 50 09
  SATURDAY EVENING POST FANTASY STORIES, THE
                                          FLES, BARTHOLD   AN
ENEMY WITHIN, THE   MALCOLM, DONALD   NV   NWR 75 25
  NEW WRITINGS IN SF. 25   BULMER, KENNETH   OA
ENEMY WITHIN, THE   REYNOLDS, MACK   SS   ASF 67 04
  BEST OF MACK REYNOLDS, THE   REYNOLDS, MACK   AC
ENEMY WITHIN, THE (RICHARD MATHESON)
                               BLISH, JAMES   SA   STK 72 08
                                          BLISH, JAMES   OC
  STAR TREK 8
ENEMY YOU KILLED, MY FRIEND, THE
                               BREADY, RICHARD S.   SS
                                          WILHELM, KATE   OA
  CLARION SF
ENEMY, THE   KNIGHT, DAMON   SS   VSF 58 01
  BEST OF DAMON KNIGHT, THE   KNIGHT, DAMON   AC
  FAR OUT   KNIGHT, DAMON   AC
ENFORCER   POURNELLE, JERRY   NV   FSF 74 06
  HIGH JUSTICE   POURNELLE, JERRY   AC
ENGINE AT HEARTSPRING'S CENTER, THE
                               ZELAZNY, ROGER   SS   ASF 74 07
  BEST SCIENCE FICTION OF THE YEAR, THE NO. 4
                                          CARR, TERRY   AN
  NEBULA AWARD STORIES 10   GUNN, JAMES E.   AN

ENGINEER AND THE EXECUTIONER, THE   ESCAPE MECHANISM

ENGINEER AND THE EXECUTIONER, THE
                    STABLEFORD, BRIAN M. NV   AMZ 75 05
  1976 ANNUAL WORLD'S BEST SF, THE   WOLLHEIM, DONALD A. AN
ENGINEER'S YELL   ANONYMOUS   PM
  MATHEMATICAL MAGPIE, THE   FADIMAN, CLIFTON   AN
ENGINEER, THE   GREEN, JOSEPH   SS NWS 62 02
  AFFAIR WITH GENIUS, AN   GREEN, JOSEPH   AC
ENGINEER, THE   KORNBLUTH, C. M.
                    AND POHL, FREDERIK SS C INF 56 02
  WONDER EFFECT, THE   POHL, F. & KORNBLUTH AC
ENIGMATIC SAINT, THE   BOULLE, PIERRE   NV
  TIME OUT OF MIND   BOULLE, PIERRE   OC
ENJOY, ENJOY   POHL, FREDERIK   SS FOS 74
  FELLOWSHIP OF THE STARS   CARR, TERRY   OA
ENLIGHTENED ONES, THE   COOPER, EDMUND   NV FUN 59 01
  NEWS FROM ELSEWHERE   COOPER, EDMUND   AC
  TOMORROW'S GIFT   COOPER, EDMUND   AC
  UNBORN TOMORROW   COOPER, EDMUND   AC
ENNUI   LESSER, MILTON   SS DSF 52 12
  WAY OUT   HOWARD, IVAN   AN
ENOCH   BLOCH, ROBERT   SS WRT 46 09
  ALONE BY NIGHT   CONGDON, MICHAEL&DON AN
  HORROR-7   BLOCH, ROBERT   AC
  PLEASANT DREAMS   BLOCH, ROBERT   AC
ENOCH SOAMES   BEERBOHM, MAX   NV CNY 16 05
  DEALS WITH THE DEVIL   DAVENPORT, BASIL   AN
  MOONLIGHT TRAVELER, THE   STERN, PHILIP VAN D. AN
  TRAVELERS IN TIME   STERN, PHILIP VAN D. AN
ENORMOUS RADIO, THE   CHEEVER, JOHN   SS NYM 47 05
  LIGHT FANTASTIC, THE   HARRISON, HARRY   AN
  TIMELESS STORIES FOR TODAY AND TOMORROW BRADBURY, RAY AN
ENORMOUS ROOM, THE   GOLD, H. L.
                    AND KREPPS, ROBERT W. SN C AMZ 53 11
  WORLDS APART   WILLIAMS-ELLIS& OWEN AN
  YEAR'S BEST SCIENCE FICTION NOVELS: 1954 BLEILER & DIKTY AN
ENOUGH   KARL, JEAN E.   SS
  TURNING PLACE, THE   KARL, JEAN E.   OC
ENOUGH ROPE   ANDERSON, POUL   NV ASF 53 07
  FOUR FOR THE FUTURE   CONKLIN, GROFF   AN
ENOUGH TIME (SEE TIME ENOUGH) KNIGHT, DAMON   TC
ENTER A PILGRIM   DICKSON, GORDON R. SS ASF 74 08
  BEST SCIENCE FICTION STORIES OF THE YEAR (1974)
                    DEL REY, LESTER   AN
ENTER THE FANATIC, STAGE CENTER
                    ELLISON, HARLAN SS ADM 66 07
  OVER THE EDGE   ELLISON, HARLAN   AC
ENTER THE PROFESSOR   HULL, E. MAYNE   SS ASF 45 01
  PLANETS FOR SALE   HULL, E. MAYNE   AC
ENTERPRISE INCIDENT, THE (D. C. FONTANA)
                    BLISH, JAMES   SA STK 71 04
  STAR TREK 4   BLISH, JAMES   OC
ENTIRE AND PERFECT CHRYSOLITE LAFFERTY, R. A. SS ORB 70 06
  GOLDEN ROAD, THE   KNIGHT, DAMON   AN
  ORBIT 6   KNIGHT, DAMON   OA
  STRANGE DOINGS   LAFFERTY, R. A.   AC
ENTITY STRIKES TWICE, THE, BURKE, JONATHAN F. SS
  EXODUS FROM ELYSIUM   BURKE, JONATHAN F.   AC
ENTITY TRAP   BROWN, FREDRIC   SS
  NIGHTMARES AND GEEZENSTACKS   BROWN, FREDRIC   AC
ENTROPIC GANG BANG CAPER, THE SPINRAD, NORMAN SS NWS 69 08
  LAST HURRAH OF THE GOLDEN HORDE, THE   SPINRAD, NORMAN AC
ENTROPY CIRCUIT, THE   MOORCOCK, MICHAEL SS   74
  LIVES AND TIMES OF JERRY CORNELIUS, THE MOORCOCK, MICHAEL AC
ENVIRONMENT   GEIER, CHESTER S. SS ASF 44 05
  OMNIBUS OF SCIENCE FICTION   CONKLIN, GROFF   AN
  STRANGE ADVENTURES IN SCIENCE FICTION CONKLIN, GROFF   AN
ENVIRONMENT PROBLEM   MOORCOCK, MICHAEL SS SPC 73 01
  SPACE 1   DAVIS, RICHARD   OA
ENVOI   ALDISS, BRIAN W. MS
  SPACE OPERA   ALDISS, BRIAN W.   AN
ENVOY EXTRAORDINARY   GOLDING, WILLIAM NV   56
  SOMETIME, NEVER   ANONYMOUS   OA
EOHIPPUS   EMSHWILLER, CAROL SS TRV
  JOY IN OUR CAUSE   EMSHWILLER, CAROL   AC
EPHEMERA, THE   STERNBERG, JACQUES SS
  FUTURE WITHOUT FUTURE   STERNBERG, JACQUES   OC
EPHONY'S SPECTACLES   GRANOSKI, CLARENCE SS SFQ 41 WI
  INTO THE FOURTH DIMENSION   CUMMINGS, RAY   AN
EPIC   ROTSLER, WILLIAM NV
  FUTURE PASTIMES   EDELSTEIN, SCOTT   OA
EPICAC   VONNEGUT, KURT JR. SS COL 50 11
  SCIENCE FACT/FICTION   FARRELL/GAGE/&   AN
  THEMES IN SCIENCE FICTION   KELLEY, LEO P.   AN
  WELCOME TO THE MONKEY HOUSE   VONNEGUT, KURT JR.   AC
EPIGRAMMATA LXV (BY DECIMUS MAGNUS AUSONIUS,TRANS)
                    BRUNNER, JOHN   PM NEW 76 AC
  BOOK OF JOHN BRUNNER, THE   BRUNNER, JOHN   AC
EPIGRAPH (FROM "THE SCIENCE IN SCIENCE FICTION")
                    BLISH, JAMES   EX VCT 75 SU
  FASTER THAN LIGHT   DANN & ZEBROWSKI   OA
EPILIGUE   DICKSON, GORDON R. MS
  THREE TO DORSAI| DICKSON, GORDON R.   AC
EPILOG   HOLLISTER, BERNARD C MS
  YOU AND SCIENCE FICTION   HOLLISTER, BERNARD C AN
EPILOG   SIMAK, CLIFFORD D. SS AMA 73
  ASTOUNDING   HARRISON, HARRY   OA
EPILOGUE   ALDISS, BRIAN W. MS
  GALACTIC EMPIRES VOLUME TWO   ALDISS, BRIAN W.   AN
EPILOGUE   ANDERSON, POUL   MS
  TALES OF THE FLYING MOUNTAINS ANDERSON, POUL   AC
EPILOGUE   ANDERSON, POUL   SN ASF 62 03
  ENDS OF TIME, THE   SILVERBERG, ROBERT   AN
  MANY WORLDS OF POUL ANDERSON, THE ANDERSON, POUL AC
  TIME AND STARS   ANDERSON, POUL   AC
EPILOGUE   BRADBURY, RAY   MS   51
  *ILLUSTRATED MAN, THE   BRADBURY, RAY   AC

EPILOGUE   CHORON, JACQUES   MS
  WEIGHER OF SOULS AND THE EARTH DWELLERS, THE
                    MAUROIS, ANDRE   AC
EPILOGUE   INOUYE, JON   MS
  NIGHT TIDE, A   INOUYE, JON   OC
EPILOGUE   SMITH, CORDWAINER MS
  SPACE LORDS   SMITH, CORDWAINER   AC
EPILOGUE (EPILOGUE FOR AN OFFICE PICNIC)
                    JACOBS, HARVEY   SS NWS 69 01
  EGG OF THE GLAK, AND OTHER STORIES, THE JACOBS, HARVEY AC
EPILOGUE: IDENTITY (IDENTITY) SMITH, GEORGE O. NV ASF 45 11
  COMPLETE VENUS EQUILATERAL, THE   SMITH, GEORGE O. AC
EPILOGUE: THE FUTURE OF SCIENCE FICTION
                    BILKER, AUDREY L. MS C
  LONG NIGHT OF WAITING AND OTHER STORIES ELWOOD, ROGER OA
EPILOGUE: THE FUTURE OF SCIENCE FICTION
                    BILKER, HARVEY L. MS C
  LONG NIGHT OF WAITING AND OTHER STORIES ELWOOD, ROGER OA
EPIPHANY FOR ALIENS   KERR, DAVID   SS DVS 72 02
  AGAIN, DANGEROUS VISIONS   ELLISON, HARLAN   OA
EPISODE ON CAIN STREET   BRENNAN, JOSEPH P. SS
  TRAVELLERS BY NIGHT   DERLETH, AUGUST   OA
EPISODE ON DHEE MINOR   WALTON, HARRY   SS ASF 39 10
  TRAVELLERS OF SPACE   GREENBERG , MARTIN   AN
EPISTLE OF SIMPLE SIMON, THE KERSH, GERALD   SS TOM 47
  MEN WITHOUT BONES   KERSH, GERALD   AC
EPITAPH IN AVALON   SPRINGER, SHERWOOD PM FSF 54 07
  BEST FROM FANTASY AND SCIENCE FICTION: 4
                    BOUCHER, ANTHONY   AN
EPITAPH NEAR MOONPORT   SPRINGER, SHERWOOD PM FSF 54 01
  BEST FROM FANTASY AND SCIENCE FICTION: 4
                    BOUCHER, ANTHONY   AN
EPITHALAMIUM   BUCK, DORIS PITKIN PM FSF 58 01
  BEST FROM FANTASY AND SCIENCE FICTION: 8
                    BOUCHER, ANTHONY   AN
EQUALIZER, THE   SPINRAD, NORMAN SS ASF 64 12
  LAST HURRAH OF THE GOLDEN HORDE, THE   SPINRAD, NORMAN AC
  ONE HUNDRED YEARS OF SCIENCE FICTION   KNIGHT, DAMON   AN
EQUALIZER, THE   WILLIAMSON, JACK NV ASF 47 03
  PANDORA EFFECT, THE   WILLIAMSON, JACK   AC
EQUATOR   ALDISS, BRIAN W. NA NWS 58 09
  FUTURE MAKERS, THE   HAINING, PETER   AN
EQUIVOCATION   CUNNINGHAM, BEN   IL
  SCIENCE FICTION   BRODKIN & PEARSON   AN
EREM   ANFILOV, GLEB   SS   63
  BEST SF: 1970   HARRISON & ALDISS   AN
  ULTIMATE THRESHOLD, THE   GINSBURG, MIRRA   AN
ERGOT SHOW, THE   ALDISS, BRIAN W. SS NOV 72 02
  ANTIGRAV: COSMIC COMEDIES   STRICK, PHILIP   AN
  NOVA 2   HARRISON, HARRY   OA
ERIPMAV   KNIGHT, DAMON   SS FSF 58 06
  BEST FROM FANTASY AND SCIENCE FICTION: 8
                    BOUCHER, ANTHONY   AN
  BEST OF DAMON KNIGHT, THE   KNIGHT, DAMON   AC
  TURNING ON   KNIGHT, DAMON   AC
ERNEST AND THE MACHINE GOD ELLISON, HARLAN NV KNT 68 01
  DEATHBIRD STORIES   ELLISON, HARLAN   AC
  *LOVE AIN'T NOTHING BUT SEX MISSPELLED ELLISON, HARLAN AC
  OVER THE EDGE   ELLISON, HARLAN   AC
ERNIE   SMITH, LOWELL KENT SS ORB 74 15
  ORBIT 15   KNIGHT, DAMON   AC
EROGENOUS ZONE, THE   CHARNOCK, GRAHAM SS NWS 69 07
  BEST SF STORIES FROM NEW WORLDS 8 MOORCOCK, MICHAEL AN
EROTOPHOBIA   ELLISON, HARLAN SS PNT 71 08
  APPROACHING OBLIVION   ELLISON, HARLAN   AC
ERRAND BOY   TENN, WILLIAM   SS ASF 47 06
  CHILDREN OF WONDER   TENN, WILLIAM   AN
  SEVEN SEXES, THE   TENN, WILLIAM   AC
ERRAND OF MERCY (GENE L. COON) BLISH, JAMES   SA STK 68 02
  STAR TREK 2   BLISH, JAMES   OC
ERROR HURLED   ROSMOND, BABETTE NO
  SCIENCE FICTION DISCOVERIES   POHL, C. & F.   OA
ERSATZ EGO, THE (YOUR NAME SHALL BE...DARKNESS)
                    SPINRAD, NORMAN SS AMZ 64 11
  LAST HURRAH OF THE GOLDEN HORDE, THE   SPINRAD, NORMAN AC
ERSATZ ETERNAL   VAN VOGT, A. E. NV NEW 72 AC
  BEST SCIENCE FICTION FOR 1973 ACKERMAN, FORREST J. AN
  BOOK OF VAN VOGT, THE   VAN VOGT, A. E.   AC
ERSATZ WINE, THE   PRIEST, CHRISTOPHER SS NWS 67 02
  BEST SF STORIES FROM NEW WORLDS 6 MOORCOCK, MICHAEL AN
ERSATZ, THE   NUETZEL, CHARLES SS
  IMAGES OF TOMORROW   NUETZEL, CHARLES   AC
ESCAPE   ERNST, PAUL   SS WRT 38 07
  OTHER WORLDS, THE   STONG, PHILIP D.   AN
ESCAPE   VARSHAVSKY, ILYA SS   73
  BEST SF: 1973   HARRISON & ALDISS   AN
ESCAPE (PARADOXICAL ESCAPE) ASIMOV, ISAAC   SS ASF 45 08
  I, ROBOT   ASIMOV, ISAAC   AC
ESCAPE ARTIST   INOUYE, JON   SS
  NIGHT TIDE, A   INOUYE, JON   OC
ESCAPE CLAUSE   SERLING, ROD   SA
  FROM THE TWILIGHT ZONE   SERLING, ROD   AC
  STORIES FROM THE TWILIGHT ZONE SERLING, ROD   OC
ESCAPE FELICITY   HERBERT, FRANK   SS ASF 66 06
  WORLDS OF FRANK HERBERT, THE HERBERT, FRANK   AC
ESCAPE FROM EVENING   MOORCOCK, MICHAEL NV NWS 65 03
  TIME DWELLER, THE   MOORCOCK, MICHAEL   AC
ESCAPE FROM ORBIT   ANDERSON, POUL   NV AMZ 62 10
  TIME AND STARS   ANDERSON, POUL   AC
ESCAPE IS NO ACCIDENT   EMSHWILLER, CAROL SS
  2076: THE AMERICAN TRICENTENNIAL BRYANT, EDWARD   OA
ESCAPE MECHANISM   FRITCH, CHARLES E. SS IFS 55 04
  HORSES' ASTEROID   FRITCH, CHARLES E.   AC
ESCAPE MECHANISM   SELLINGS, ARTHUR SS FUN 55 08
  *TIME TRANSFER   SELLINGS, ARTHUR   AC

ESCAPE THE MORNING

ESCAPE THE MORNING   ANDERSON, POUL   SS   BLF 66 11
  WORLDS OF WONDER   HARRISON, HARRY   AN
ESCAPE TO CHAOS   MACDONALD, JOHN D. NA   SSS 51 06
  GALACTIC EMPIRES VOLUME TWO   ALDISS, BRIAN W.   AN
ESCAPE TO EARTH   BANISTER, MANLY   NV   SFQ 57 11
  ESCAPE TO EARTH   HOWARD, IVAN   AN
ESCAPE TO VENUS   LOTT, S. MAKEPEACE SS   56
  ALL ABOUT VENUS   ALDISS, BRIAN W.   AN
  FAREWELL FANTASTIC VENUS   ALDISS & HARRISON   AN
ESCAPE TO YESTERDAY BURKS, ARTHUR J.   SS   NEW 53 AN
  SCIENCE AND SORCERY   FORD, GARRET   AN
ESCAPE VELOCITY   BALL, BRIAN N.   SS
  TALES OF SCIENCE FICTION   BALL, BRIAN N.   AN
ESCAPE, THE   CAMPBELL, JOHN W. JR NV   ASF 35 05
  CLOAK OF AESIR   CAMPBELL, JOHN W. JR   AC
ESCAPEMENT   BALLARD, J. G.   SS   NWS 56 12
  OVERLOADED MAN, THE   BALLARD, J. G.   AC
  PASSPORT TO ETERNITY   BALLARD, J. G.   AC
ESCAPING, THE   BUNCH, DAVID R.   SS   DVS 67 01
  DANGEROUS VISIONS   ELLISON, HARLAN   OA
ESCAPISM   ROBERTS, KEITH   SS   SCF 64 10
  MACHINES AND MEN   ROBERTS, KEITH   AC
ESCAPIST, THE   B., E. D.   PM   FSF 53 02
  BEST FROM FANTASY AND SCIENCE FICTION: 3
                                      BOUCHER & MCCOMAS   AN
ESIDARAP OT PIRT DNUOR (SEE ROUND TRIP TO ESIDARAP)
                    BIGGLE, LLOYD JR.   TC
ESKIMO INVASION, THE HOWARD, HAYDEN   NV   GAL 66 06
  ESKIMO INVASION   HOWARD, HAYDEN   NO
ESMERALDA   CASTELL, DAPHNE   SS
  GOLLANCZ - SUNDAY TIMES BEST SF STORIES ANONYMOUS   OA
ESMERALDA   CONEY, MICHAEL G.   SS   GAL 72 01
  MONITOR FOUND IN ORBIT   CONEY, MICHAEL G.   AC
ESMERALDA   WYNDHAM, JOHN   SS
  JIZZLE   WYNDHAM, JOHN   AC
ESSAY ON STURGEON   CONKLIN, GROFF   IN
  E PLURIBUS UNICORN   STURGEON, THEODORE   AC
ESSAY: A LITERATURE OF COMFORT HARRISON, M. JOHN BR NWQ 71 01
  NEW WORLDS QUARTERLY NO. 1   MOORCOCK, MICHAEL   OA
ESSAY, AN EXPLANATION, AND AN EXCERPT, AN
                    SANDERS, THOMAS E. SI
  SPECULATIONS   SANDERS, THOMAS E.   AN
ET IN ARCADIA EGO (ALSO AS THE PLANET ARCADIA)
                    DISCH, THOMAS M.   SS   QRK 71 02
  QUARK/2   DELANY & HACKER   OA
  SF: AUTHORS' CHOICE 4   HARRISON, HARRY   AN
ETAOIN SHRDLU   BROWN, FREDRIC   SS   UNK 42 02
  ANGELS AND SPACESHIPS   BROWN, FREDRIC   AC
  BEST OF FREDRIC BROWN, THE   BROWN, FREDRIC   AC
  STORIES FROM SCIENCE FICTION   DOHERTY, G. D.   AN
  WORLD OF WONDER   PRATT, FLETCHER   AN
ETCHED IN MOONLIGHT STEPHENS, JAMES   SS   28
  TRAVELERS IN TIME   STERN, PHILIP VAN D.   AN
ETERNAL ADAM, THE (1905) VERNE, JULES   NV   STN 57 03
  MASTERPIECES OF SCIENCE FICTION   MOSKOWITZ, SAM   AN
  YESTERDAY AND TOMORROW   VERNE, JULES   AC
ETERNAL DUFFER, THE TEMPLE, WILLARD   SS   SEP 46 01
  SATURDAY EVENING POST FANTASY STORIES, THE
                                      FLES, BARTHOLD   AN
ETERNAL EARTHLING (SEE THE OTHER SIDE)
                    KUBILIUS, WALTER   TC
ETERNAL EVE, THE   WYNDHAM, JOHN   NV   AMZ 50 09
  TIME UNTAMED   HOWARD, IVAN   AN
ETERNAL LOVER, THE BURROUGHS, EDGAR R. NV   ASW 14 03
  ETERNAL LOVER, THE   BURROUGHS, EDGAR R.   AC
ETERNAL MACHINES, THE SPENCER, WILLIAM SS   NWR 64 02
  BEST FROM NEW WRITINGS IN S-F FIRST SELECTION, THE
                                      CARNELL, JOHN   AN
  NEW WRITINGS IN SF. 2   CARNELL, JOHN   OA
ETERNAL MAN, THE   SHARP, D. D.   SS   SWS 29 08
  FROM OFF THIS WORLD   MARGULIES & FRIEND   AN
  HISTORY OF THE SCIENCE FICTION MAGAZINE, THE PART 1 1926-1935
                                      ASHLEY, MICHAEL   AN
*TREASURY OF SCIENCE FICTION, A   CONKLIN, GROFF   AN
ETERNAL NOW, THE   LEINSTER, MURRAY   NV   TWS 44 FL
  SHAPE OF THINGS, THE   KNIGHT, DAMON   AN
ETERNAL THEME OF EXILE, THE ALDISS, BRIAN W. SS NWR 74 23
  NEW WRITINGS IN SF. 23   BULMER, KENNETH   OA
ETERNITY GAME, THE KING, VINCENT   NV   NWR 69 14
  NEW WRITINGS IN SF. 14   CARNELL, JOHN   OA
ETERNITY LOST   SIMAK, CLIFFORD D. NV   ASF 49 07
*ASTOUNDING SCIENCE FICTION ANTHOLOGY, THE
                                      CAMPBELL, JOHN W. JR   AN
  BEST SCIENCE-FICTION STORIES: 1950, THE BLEILER & DIKTY   AN
  POLITICAL SCIENCE FICTION   GREENBERG& WARRICK   AN
  SECOND ASTOUNDING SCIENCE FICTION ANTHOLOGY, THE (PB)
                                      CAMPBELL, JOHN W. JR   AN
ETERNITY: A NIGHTMARE CARROLL, LEWIS   PM   93
  FANTASIA MATHEMATICA   FADIMAN, CLIFTON   AN
ETHER BREATHER   STURGEON, THEODORE SS   ASF 39 09
  FIRST FLIGHT   KNIGHT, DAMON   AN
  NOT WITHOUT SORCERY   STURGEON, THEODORE   AC
  WITHOUT SORCERY   STURGEON, THEODORE   AC
ETHER ROBOTS, THE   LONG, FRANK BELKNAP NV   TWS 42 12
  JOHN CARSTAIRS: SPACE DETECTIVE   LONG, FRANK BELKNAP   AC
ETHICAL ENGINEER, THE (SEE DEATHWORLD 2)
                    HARRISON, HARRY   TC
ETHICAL EQUATIONS, THE LEINSTER, MURRAY SS   ASF 45 06
  BEST OF MURRAY LEINSTER, THE   LEINSTER, MURRAY   AC
  GIANTS UNLEASHED   CONKLIN, GROFF   AN
*TREASURY OF SCIENCE FICTION, A   CONKLIN, GROFF   AN
ETHICAL QUOTIENT   PHILLIFENT, JOHN T. SN   ASF 62 10
  ANALOG 2   CAMPBELL, JOHN W. JR   AN
ETHICATORS, THE   MARSH, WILLARD   SS   IFS 55 08
  SF: THE YEAR'S GREATEST SCIENCE FICTION AND FANTASY
                                      MERRIL, JUDITH   AN

EVERYBODY'S HAPPY BUT ME! (SEE WHAT TO DO TILL THE ANALYS?

ETHICS OF MADNESS, THE NIVEN, LARRY   NV   IPS 67 0?
  NEUTRON STAR   NIVEN, LARRY   AC
EUCLID   LINDSAY, VACHEL   PM   14
  FANTASIA MATHEMATICA   FADIMAN, CLIFTON   AN
EUCLID ALONE   ORR, WILLIAM F.   NV   ORB 75 16
  ORBIT 16   KNIGHT, DAMON   OA
EUCLID ALONE HAS LOOKED ON BEAUTY BARE
                    MILLAY, EDNA ST. V. PM   24
  FANTASIA MATHEMATICA   FADIMAN, CLIFTON   AN
EUCLID AND THE BRIGHT BOY SYNGE, J. L. SS
  MATHEMATICAL MAGPIE, THE   FADIMAN, CLIFTON   AN
EULER, DIDEROT, ALGEBRA AND GOD (1872)
                    DEMORGAN, AUGUSTUS MS
  MATHEMATICAL MAGPIE, THE   FADIMAN, CLIFTON   AN
EUPHIO QUESTION, THE VONNEGUT, KURT JR. SS   COL 51 05
  CANARY IN A CAT HOUSE   VONNEGUT, KURT JR.   AC
  WELCOME TO THE MONKEY HOUSE   VONNEGUT, KURT JR.   AC
EUPHRASIA   SHELLEY, MARY W.   SS   KPS 39
  TALES AND STORIES   SHELLEY, MARY W.   AC
EUREMA'S DAM   LAFFERTY, R. A.   SS   NDM 72 07
  BEST SCIENCE FICTION OF THE YEAR, THE NO. 2
                                      CARR, TERRY   AN
  BEST SCIENCE FICTION STORIES OF THE YEAR (1972)
                                      DEL REY, LESTER   AN
  NEW DIMENSIONS 2   SILVERBERG, ROBERT   OA
EUROPE AFTER THE RAIN ERNST, MAX   IL
  SCIENCE FICTION   BRODKIN & PEARSON   AN
EUTOPIA   ANDERSON, POUL   SS   DVS 67 0?
  DANGEROUS VISIONS   ELLISON, HARLAN   OA
  PAST, PRESENT, AND FUTURE PERFECT   WOLFE, J&FITZ GERALD   AN
EVANE   TUBB, E. C.   SS   NWR 73 22
  NEW WRITINGS IN SF. 22   BULMER, KENNETH   OA
  1974 ANNUAL WORLD'S BEST SF, THE   WOLLHEIM, DONALD A.   AN
EVE AND THE TWENTY-THREE ADAMS SILVERBERG, ROBERT SS VSF 58 03
  DIMENSION THIRTEEN   SILVERBERG, ROBERT   AC
EVE OF RUMOKO, THE ZELAZNY, ROGER   NA   TFT 69
  MY NAME IS LEGION   ZELAZNY, ROGER   AC
  THREE FOR TOMORROW   SILVERBERG, ROBERT   AC
EVE OF ST. JOHN, THE DE CAMP, L. SPRAGUE
                    AND PRATT, FLETCHER SS   C NEW 53 AN
  TALES FROM GAVAGAN'S BAR   DE CAMP, L. S.&PRATT   AC
EVE OF THE LAST APOLLO, THE SCHOLZ, CARTER SS ORB 76 18
  ORBIT 18   KNIGHT, DAMON   OA
EVE TIMES FOUR   ANDERSON, POUL   NV   FAN 50 04
  BEST FROM FANTASTIC, THE   WHITE, TED   AN
  TIME AND STARS   ANDERSON, POUL   AC
EVE WAS A SNAKE (SNAKE GODDESS)
                    PRICE, E. HOFFMANN SS   STE 39 08
  STRANGE LOVE STORIES   ANONYMOUS   AN
EVEN CHANCE   BRUNNER, JOHN   SS   ASF 65 11
  FROM THIS DAY FORWARD   BRUNNER, JOHN   AC
EVEN UNTO DEATH   LONDON, JACK   SS   EPM 00 07
  CURIOUS FRAGMENTS   LONDON, JACK   AC
EVENING PRIMROSE (1941) COLLIER, JOHN   SS   APR 47 03
  FANTASY: THE LITERATURE OF THE MARVELOUS KELLEY, LEO P.   AN
  OUT OF THIS WORLD   FAST, JULIUS   AN
  WORLDS OF SCIENCE FICTION, THE   MILLS, ROBERT P.   AN
EVENSONG   DEL REY, LESTER   SS   DVS 67 01
  DANGEROUS VISIONS   ELLISON, HARLAN   OA
  OTHER WORLDS, OTHER GODS   MOHS, MAYO   AN
EVENT HORIZON, THE WATSON, IAN   NV   76
  FASTER THAN LIGHT   DANN & ZEBROWSKI   OA
EVENTS AT POROTH FARM, THE KLEIN, T. E. D. NV
  YEAR'S BEST HORROR STORIES: SERIES II, THE
                                      DAVIS, RICHARD   AN
EVENTS LEADING DOWN TO THE TRAGEDY, THE
                    KORNBLUTH, C. M.   SS   FSF 58 0?
  *MILE BEYOND THE MOON, A   KORNBLUTH, C. M.   AC
EVENTS WITNESSED FROM A CITY HARRISON, M. JOHN SS
  MACHINE IN SHAFT TEN AND OTHER STORIES, THE
                                      HARRISON, M. JOHN   AC
EVER-BRANCHING TREE, THE HARRISON, HARRY SS   SAG 70
  *BEST OF HARRY HARRISON, THE   HARRISON, HARRY   AC
  SCHOOL AND SOCIETY THROUGH SCIENCE FICTION
                                      OLANDER/GREENBERG/&   AN
  SCIENCE AGAINST MAN   CHEETHAM, ANTHONY   OA
EVEREST   ASIMOV, ISAAC   SS   USF 53 12
  BUY JUPITER AND OTHER STORIES   ASIMOV, ISAAC   AC
  HAVE YOU SEEN THESE?   ASIMOV, ISAAC   AC
EVERGREEN   ALDISS, BRIAN W.   NV   FSF 61 12
  LONG AFTERNOON OF EARTH, THE   ALDISS, BRIAN W.   NC
EVERGREEN LIBRARY, THE PRONZINI, BILL
                    AND WALLMANN, JEFFREY SS C VSF 70 05
  WONDERMAKERS 2   HOSKINS, ROBERT   AN
EVERLASTING FOOD, THE ST. CLAIR, MARGARET NV TWS 50 12
  THREE WORLDS OF FUTURITY   ST. CLAIR, MARGARET   DC
EVERY DAY IN EVERY WAY HOLLIS, H. H.   NV
  LONE STAR UNIVERSE   PROCTOR & UTLEY   OA
EVERY DAY IS CHRISTMAS GUNN, JAMES E.   NV   SUP 57 02
  FUTURE IMPERFECT   GUNN, JAMES E.   AC
EVERY FOURTH HOUSE   LEIF, EVELYN   SS   GEN 72
  GENERATION   GERROLD, DAVID   OA
EVERYBODY A WINNER, THE BARKER CRIED
                    GRANT, C. L.   SS   ORB 74 13
  ORBIT 13   KNIGHT, DAMON   OA
EVERYBODY KNOWS JOE KORNBLUTH, C. M.   SS   FUN 53 10
  *MILE BEYOND THE MOON, A   KORNBLUTH, C. M.   AC
EVERYBODY LOVES IRVING BOMMER TENN, WILLIAM SS FAD 51 08
  OF ALL POSSIBLE WORLDS   TENN, WILLIAM   AC
EVERYBODY LOVES: IN A CIRCULAR MOTION
                    GILDEN, MEL   SS   CLR 73 03
  CLARION III   WILSON, ROBIN SCOTT   OA
EVERYBODY'S HAPPY BUT ME! (SEE WHAT TO DO TILL THE ANALYST
  COMES)   POHL, FREDERIK   TC

EVERYBODY'S HOMESICK SOLDIER BOY
               WILLIAMS, JONATHAN PM   62
  HOLDING YOUR EIGHT HANDS   LUCIE-SMITH, EDWARD AN
EVERYBODYOVSKYISM IN CAT CITY SHAW, LAO   SS
  APEMAN, SPACEMAN   STOVER & HARRISON   AN
EVERYDAY LIFE IN THE LATER ROMAN EMPIRE
               DISCH, THOMAS M. NV BMR 73
  BAD MOON RISING   DISCH, THOMAS M.   OA
  334   DISCH, THOMAS M.   NO
EVERYTHING THAT BEGINS WITH AN "M"
               YARBRO, CHELSEA Q. SS GEN 72
  GENERATION   GERROLD, DAVID   OA
EVIDENCE   ASIMOV, ISAAC SS ASF 46 09
  I, ROBOT   ASIMOV, ISAAC   AC
  POLITICAL SCIENCE FICTION   GREENBERG& WARRICK   AN
  PSEUDO PEOPLE, THE   NOLAN, WILLIAM F.   AN
EVIDENCE, THE   HARDING, LEE SS NWS 64 08
  PACIFIC BOOK OF AUSTRALIAN SCIENCE FICTION
               BAXTER, JOHN   AN
EVIL EYE, THE   GILLESPIE, ALFRED NV SEP 66 01
  NEW WORLDS OF FANTASY   CARR, TERRY   AN
EVIL EYE, THE   SHELLEY, MARY W. NV KPS 30
  TALES AND STORIES   SHELLEY, MARY W.   AC
EVISE, THE ZSOUCHMOID   KIRK, TIM   IL
  WANDERING STARS   DANN, JACK M.   AN
EVITABLE CONFLICT, THE   ASIMOV, ISAAC NV ASF 50 06
  I, ROBOT   ASIMOV, ISAAC   AC
EVOLUTION MAN, THE   LEWIS, ROY   SS   60
  APEMAN, SPACEMAN   STOVER & HARRISON   AN
EVOLUTION OF A SCIENCE FICTION WRITER, THE
               BRUNNER, JOHN   AR FDN 72 01
  BOOK OF JOHN BRUNNER, THE   BRUNNER, JOHN   AC
EVOLUTION OF SCIENCE FICTION, THE
               STABLEFORD, BRIAN M. AR
  BEYOND THIS HORIZON   CARRELL, CHRISTOPHER OA
EVOLUTION'S END   ARTHUR, ROBERT SS TWS 41 04
  ADVENTURES IN TOMORROW   CROSSEN, KENDELL F. AN
  NEW AWARENESS, THE   WARRICK & GREENBERG AN
EVOLUTIONARY MONSTROSITY, THE HARRIS, CLARE WINGER SS AMQ 29 WI
  AWAY FROM THE HERE AND NOW HARRIS, CLARE WINGER AC
EX MACHINA   PADGETT, LEWIS   NV ASF 48 04
  BEST SCIENCE-FICTION STORIES: 1949, THE BLEILER & DIKTY AN
  ROBOTS HAVE NO TAILS   PADGETT, LEWIS   AC
EXALTED, THE   DE CAMP, L. SPRAGUE NV ASF 40 11
  *ASTOUNDING SCIENCE FICTION ANTHOLOGY, THE
               CAMPBELL, JOHN W. JR AN
EXAMINATION DAY   EKLUND, GORDON   NV
  OTHER SIDE OF TOMORROW, THE ELWOOD, ROGER   OA
EXAMINATION DAY   SLESAR, HENRY SS PBY 58 02
  FROM THE "S" FILE   PLAYBOY, EDITORS OF AN
  INSIDE INFORMATION   MOWSHOWITZ, ABBE   AN
  SCHOOL AND SOCIETY THROUGH SCIENCE FICTION
               OLANDER/GREENBERG/& AN
EXAMINATION, THE   GOTSCHALK, FELIX C. SS NDM 74 04
  NEW DIMENSIONS 4   SILVERBERG, ROBERT OA
EXCERPT FROM A SOCIAL HISTORY OF THE 20TH CENTURY
               BRUNNER, JOHN   SS   70
  BOOK OF JOHN BRUNNER, THE   BRUNNER, JOHN   AC
EXCERPT FROM RETIEF & THE WARLORDS
               LAUMER, KEITH   EX DBL 68
  RETIEF: EMISSARY TO THE STARS LAUMER, KEITH   AC
EXCERPTS FROM THE GALACTICK ALMANACK: MUSIC
            JANIFER, LAURENCE M. FA GAL 59 06
  IMPOSSIBLE?   JANIFER, LAURENCE M. AC
EXCHANGE OF MEN   JOHNSON, W. R.
         AND NEMEROV, HOWARD SS C STO 63 01
  NIGHT IN FUNLAND   BRONDFIELD, JEROME   AN
EXCHANGING THEIR SOULS   MITCHELL, EDWARD P. SS SUN 77 04
  CRYSTAL MAN, THE   MITCHELL, EDWARD P. AC
EXCLUSIVE INTERVIEW WITH LORD GREYSTOKE, AN (TARZAN LIVES)
             FARMER, PHILIP JOSE SS ESQ 72 04
  BOOK OF PHILIP JOSE FARMER, THE FARMER, PHILIP JOSE AC
EXECUTIONER'S BEAUTIFUL DAUGHTER, THE
               CARTER, ANGELA   SS
  BEST SF: 1974   HARRISON & ALDISS   AN
EXECUTIONER, THE   BUDRYS, ALGIS NV ASF 56 01
  *SPECTRUM   AMIS & CONQUEST   AN
  UNEXPECTED DIMENSION, THE   BUDRYS, ALGIS   AC
EXERCISE IN SPECULATION: THE THEORY AND PRACTICE OF
  TELEPORTATION   NIVEN, LARRY   AR GAL 69 03
  ALL THE MYRIAD WAYS   NIVEN, LARRY   AC
EXHIBIT PIECE   DICK, PHILIP K. SS IFS 54 08
  HANDFUL OF DARKNESS, A   DICK, PHILIP K.   AC
EXHIBITION, THE   EDELSTEIN, SCOTT SS NOV 73 03
  BEST OF SCIENCE FICTION MONTHLY, THE SACKS, JANET   AN
  NOVA 3   HARRISON, HARRY   OA
EXILE   COLE, EVERETT B. SN ASF 54 01
  BEST SCIENCE FICTION STORIES AND NOVELS: 1955
               DIKTY, T. E.   AN
  5 TALES FROM TOMORROW   DIKTY, T. E.   AN
EXILE   CUMMINGS, M. A. SN
  EXILE AND OTHER TALES OF FANTASY CUMMINGS, M. A.   OC
EXILE   HAMILTON, EDMOND SS SSS 43 05
  BEST OF EDMOND HAMILTON, THE HAMILTON, EDMOND   AN
  LOOKING FORWARD   LESSER, MILTON   AN
EXILE FROM SPACE   MERRIL, JUDITH NV FUN 56 11
  FANTASTIC UNIVERSE OMNIBUS, THE SANTESSON, HANS S. AN
  FLYING SAUCERS IN FACT AND FICTION SANTESSON, HANS S. AN
  SURVIVAL SHIP AND OTHER STORIES MERRIL, JUDITH   AC
EXILE IS OUR LOT   ALDISS, BRIAN W. SI
  SPACE OPERA   ALDISS, BRIAN W.   AN
EXILE OF THE EONS   CLARKE, ARTHUR C. SS SSS 50 03
  AWARD SCIENCE FICTION READER NORTON, ALDEN H.   AN
  EXPEDITION TO EARTH   CLARKE, ARTHUR C. AC
  FUTURES UNLIMITED   NORTON, ALDEN H.   AN
  PRELUDE TO MARS   CLARKE, ARTHUR C. AC

EXILE TO HELL   ASIMOV, ISAAC   SS ASF 68 05
  BUY JUPITER AND OTHER STORIES ASIMOV, ISAAC   AC
  FAR-OUT PEOPLE, THE   HOSKINS, ROBERT   AN
EXILE, THE   COPPEL, ALFRED SS ASF 52 10
  *STORIES FOR TOMORROW   SLOANE, WILLIAM   AN
EXILED FROM EARTH   MERWIN, SAM JR. SS TWS 40 12
  ADVENTURES IN TOMORROW   CROSSEN, KENDELL F. AN
EXILES OF THE FORBIDDEN PLANET WELLS, BASIL SS
  DOORWAYS TO SPACE   WELLS, BASIL   AC
EXILES OF TOMORROW   BRADLEY, MARION Z. SS FUN 55 03
  DARK INTRUDER & OTHER STORIES, THE BRADLEY, MARION Z. DC
EXILES ON ASPERUS   WYNDHAM, JOHN NV WSQ 33 WI
  THREE STORIES   MOSKOWITZ, SAM   AN
EXILES, THE (THE MAD WIZARDS OF MARS, MCL 49 09)
               BRADBURY, RAY   SS FSF 50 WS
  *BEYOND TIME AND SPACE   DERLETH, AUGUST   AN
  *ILLUSTRATED MAN, THE   BRADBURY, RAY   AC
  R IS FOR ROCKET   BRADBURY, RAY   AC
EXISTENCE   RUSS, JOANNA SS EPC 75
  EPOCH   ELWOOD & SILVERBERG OA
EXIT   TUCKER, WILSON SS AST 43 04
  EDITOR'S CHOICE IN SCIENCE FICTION MOSKOWITZ, SAM   AN
  SCIENCE FICTION SUBTREASURY, THE TUCKER, WILSON   AC
EXIT FROM CITY 5   BAYLEY, BARRINGTON J NV NWQ 71 01
  NEW WORLDS QUARTERLY NO. 1   MOORCOCK, MICHAEL   OA
EXIT LINE   MERWIN, SAM JR. SS STS 50 09
  *POSSIBLE WORLDS OF SCIENCE FICTION CONKLIN, GROFF   AN
EXIT THE PROFESSOR   KUTTNER, HENRY SS TWS 47 10
  BEST OF HENRY KUTTNER 2, THE KUTTNER, HENRY   AC
  BEST OF HENRY KUTTNER, THE   KUTTNER, HENRY   AC
  NO BOUNDARIES   KUTTNER & MOORE   AC
EXIT THE PROFESSOR   PADGETT, LEWIS SS TWS 47 10
  GNOME THERE WAS, A   PADGETT, LEWIS   AC
EXIT TO SAN BRETA, THE   MARTIN, GEORGE R. R. SS FAN 72 02
  SONG FOR LYA, A   MARTIN, GEORGE R. R. AC
EXODUS FROM ELYSIUM   BURKE, JONATHAN F. SN
  EXODUS FROM ELYSIUM   BURKE, JONATHAN F. AC
EXPANDING MAN, THE   MACKELWORTH, R. W. SS NWR 65 05
  NEW WRITINGS IN SF. 5   CARNELL, JOHN   OA
EXPATRIATE   JANIFER, LAURENCE M. NV CSM 53 11
  IMPOSSIBLE?   JANIFER, LAURENCE M. AC
EXPEDITER   REYNOLDS, MACK SS ASF 63 05
  DEPRESSION OR BUST   REYNOLDS, MACK   DN
EXPEDITION   BOUCHER, ANTHONY SS TWS 43 08
  *BEST OF SCIENCE FICTION   CONKLIN, GROFF   AN
  COMPLEAT WEREWOLF, THE   BOUCHER, ANTHONY   AC
  INVASION FROM MARS   WELLES, ORSON   AN
  MARS, WE LOVE YOU   HIPOLITO & MCNELLY AN
EXPEDITION   BROWN, FREDRIC SS FSF 57 02
  BEST FROM FANTASY AND SCIENCE FICTION: 7
               BOUCHER, ANTHONY   AN
  FANTASIA MATHEMATICA   FADIMAN, CLIFTON   AN
  NIGHTMARES AND GEEZENSTACKS BROWN, FREDRIC   AC
EXPEDITION IN THE OPPOSITE DIRECTION
               NESVADBA, JOSEF   NV   64
  LOST FACE, THE   NESVADBA, JOSEF   AC
EXPEDITION MERCY   WINTER, JOSEPH A. MD NV ASF 48 11
  GREAT SCIENCE FICTION ABOUT DOCTORS CONKLIN, G&FABRICANT AN
EXPEDITION PLUTO   ELAM, RICHARD M. JR. NV
  TEEN-AGE SUPER SCIENCE STORIES ELAM, RICHARD M. JR. AC
EXPEDITION POLYCHROME   WINTER, JOSEPH A. MD NV ASF 49 01
  GATES TO TOMORROW   NORTON, AN.&DONALDY AN
  SPACE SERVICE   NORTON, ANDRE   AN
EXPEDITION TO EARTH   CLARKE, ARTHUR C. AC BAL 53 12
  ARTHUR C. CLARKE OMNIBUS, AN CLARKE, ARTHUR C. AC
EXPEDITION TO EARTH (ENCOUNTER IN THE DAWN)
               CLARKE, ARTHUR C. SS AMZ 53 07
  EXPEDITION TO EARTH   CLARKE, ARTHUR C. AC
EXPENDABLE   DICK, PHILIP K. SS FSF 53 07
  BEST OF PHILIP K. DICK, THE   DICK, PHILIP K.   AC
  HANDFUL OF DARKNESS, A   DICK, PHILIP K.   AC
  SCIENCE FICTION SHOWCASE   KORNBLUTH, MARY   AN
EXPENDABLES, THE   VAN VOGT, A. E. NV IFS 63 09
  BEST OF A. E. VAN VOGT, THE (BRITISH) VAN VOGT, A. E. AC
  BEST SCIENCE FICTION FROM IF, THE POHL, FREDERIK   AN
  M 33 IN ANDROMEDA   VAN VOGT, A. E.   NO
  ROGUE SHIP   VAN VOGT, A. E.   AC
  WORLDS OF A. E. VAN VOGT, THE VAN VOGT, A. E.   AC
EXPENSIVE DELICATE SHIP, THE ALDISS, BRIAN W. SS NOV 73 03
  NOVA 3   HARRISON, HARRY   OA
EXPENSIVE SLAVES, THE   HUBBARD, L. RON SS ASF 47 11
  OLE DOC METHUSELAH   HUBBARD, L. RON   AC
EXPERIMENT   ROGERS, KAY   SS FSF 53 02
  BEST FROM FANTASY AND SCIENCE FICTION: 3
               BOUCHER & MCCOMAS   AN
EXPERIMENT (TWO TIMER)   BROWN, FREDRIC SS GAL 54 02
  BEST OF FREDRIC BROWN, THE   BROWN, FREDRIC   AC
  HONEYMOON IN HELL   BROWN, FREDRIC   AC
EXPERIMENT IN AUTOBIOGRAPHY GOULART, RON SS FSF 66 07
  BEST FROM FANTASY AND SCIENCE FICTION: 16
               FERMAN, EDWARD L.   AN
EXPERIMENT IN GYRO-HATS, AN BUTLER, ELLIS PARKER SS HAM 10 06
  SCIENCE FICTION BY GASLIGHT MOSKOWITZ, SAM   AN
EXPERIMENTAL FARM, THE (FROM "THE FOOD OF THE GODS")
               WELLS, H. G.   EX PRS 03 12
  SCIENCE IN FICTION   BAYLISS, A.E. & J.C. AN
EXPERIMENTAL STATION (THE FIRST)
               NEVILLE, KRIS   SS SSS 50 09
  MISSION: MANSTOP   NEVILLE, KRIS   AC
  *SCIENCE FICTION ADVENTURES IN MUTATION CONKLIN, GROFF AN
EXPERIMENTER, THE   RUSS, JOANNA NV GAL 75 10
  BEST FROM GALAXY, THE VOLUME IV BAEN, JAMES   AN
EXPERT TOUCH, THE   NOURSE, ALAN E. NV FSF 55 11
  COUNTERFEIT MAN, THE   NOURSE, ALAN E.   AC
  SF: AUTHORS' CHOICE 2   HARRISON, HARRY   AN

EXPLODING STARS   CALDER, NIGEL   AR   69
   SURVIVAL PRINTOUT   TOTAL EFFECT   AN
EXPLOITERS' END   CAUSEY, JAMES   SS   OSF 54 02
   BEYOND THE STARS AND OTHER STORIES   ANONYMOUS   AN
EXPLOITS OF ARGO, THE (ALSO AS THE LONG NIGHT)
                               RUSSELL, RAY   SS   ROG 61 04
   SARDONICUS AND OTHER STORIES   RUSSELL, RAY   AC
EXPLORATION   MALZBERG, BARRY N.   SS   NEW 71 AN
   MARS, WE LOVE YOU   HIPOLITO & MCNELLY   AN
EXPLORATION OF SPACE, THE   BAYLEY, BARRINGTON J SS NWQ 72 04
   NEW WORLDS QUARTERLY NO. 4   MOORCOCK, MICHAEL   OA
EXPLORATION TEAM (ALSO AS COMBAT TEAM)
                               LEINSTER, MURRAY   NV   ASF 56 03
   EXPLORERS OF SPACE   SILVERBERG, ROBERT   AN
   HUGO WINNERS, THE (VOLUME 1)   ASIMOV, ISAAC   AN
   SPECTRUM 3   AMIS & CONQUEST   AN
   TALES FROM THE GALAXIES   WILLIAMS-ELLIS& P.   AN
EXPLORERS OF MARS   TEMPLE, WILLIAM F.   SS
   AUTHENTIC BOOK OF SPACE   CAMPBELL, H. J.   AN
EXPLORING THE PLANETS   FIRSOFF, V. A.   AR   SID 64
   ALL ABOUT VENUS   ALDISS, BRIAN W.   AN
   FAREWELL FANTASTIC VENUS   ALDISS & HARRISON   AN
EXPOSTULATION, AN   LEWIS, C. S.   PM   FSF 59 06
   BEST FROM FANTASY AND SCIENCE FICTION: 9
                                        MILLS, ROBERT P.   AN
   HOLDING YOUR EIGHT HANDS   LUCIE-SMITH, EDWARD   AN
   SCIENCE FICTION THROUGH THE AGES 2   EVANS, I. O.   AN
EXPOSURE   RUSSELL, ERIC FRANK SS   ASF 50 07
   LIKE NOTHING ON EARTH   RUSSELL, ERIC FRANK   AC
   OPERATION FUTURE   CONKLIN, GROFF   AN
EXPRESS OF THE FUTURE, AN   VERNE, JULES   SS   SND 95 01
   SCIENCE FICTION BY GASLIGHT   MOSKOWITZ, SAM   AN
EXTEMPORE (THE BEACH WHERE TIME BEGAN)
                               KNIGHT, DAMON   SS   INF 56 08
   BEST OF DAMON KNIGHT, THE   KNIGHT, DAMON   AC
   FAR OUT   KNIGHT, DAMON   AC
EXTENDING THE HOLDINGS   GRINNELL, DAVID   SS   FSF 51 04
   BEST SCIENCE-FICTION STORIES: 1952, THE BLEILER & DIKTY   AN
   FIRST FLIGHTS TO THE MOON   CLEMENT, HAL   AN
EXTENDING THE HOLDINGS   WOLLHEIM, DONALD A. SS   FSF 51 04
   TWO DOZEN DRAGON EGGS   WOLLHEIM, DONALD A.   AC
EXTENSION CORD, THE   DISCH, THOMAS M.   SS
   *GETTING INTO DEATH   DISCH, THOMAS M.   AC
EXTERMINATOR, THE   LAUMER, KEITH   NV
   ONCE THERE WAS A GIANT   LAUMER, KEITH   AC
EXTERNAL TRIANGLE, THE (INTERLUDE)
                               SMITH, GEORGE O.   NV   AMA 73
   COMPLETE VENUS EQUILATERAL, THE   SMITH, GEORGE O.   AC
EXTERRAN   LESSER, MILTON   SS   NEW 54 AN
   TOMORROW'S UNIVERSE   CAMPBELL, H. J.   AN
EXTINCTION BY SUBTRACTION   BALL, W. W. R.   MS
   MATHEMATICAL MAGPIE, THE   FADIMAN, CLIFTON   AN
EXTINCTION OF CONFIDENCE, THE EXERCISE OF HONESTY
                               CONNER, MICHAEL   SS
   NEW CONSTELLATIONS   DISCH & NAYLOR   OA
EXTRA BRICKLAYER, THE   PHILLIPS, A. M.   SS   UNK 40 09
   HELL HATH FURY   HAY, GEORGE   AN
EXTRA PASSENGER, THE   DERLETH, AUGUST   SS   WRT 47 01
   MR. GEORGE AND OTHER ODD PERSONS   DERLETH, AUGUST   AC
EXTRA SENSORY PERFECTION   GERNSBACK, HUGO   SS
   MASTERPIECES OF SCIENCE FICTION   MOSKOWITZ, SAM   AN
EXTRACT FROM CAPTAIN STORMFIELD'S VISIT TO HEAVEN
                               TWAIN, MARK   EX   HRP 07 12
   GOLDEN ROAD, THE   KNIGHT, DAMON   AN
EXTRAORDINARILY HORRIBLE DUMMY, THE (THE WHISPER)
                               KERSH, GERALD   SS   CMP 46 04
   ON AN ODD NOTE   KERSH, GERALD   AC
EXTRAORDINARY WEDDING, AN   MITCHELL, EDWARD P. SS   SUN 78 01
   CRYSTAL MAN, THE   MITCHELL, EDWARD P.   AC
EXTRAPOLATION (BEWARE THE FURY)
                               STURGEON, THEODORE   SS   FAN 54 04
   STURGEON IN ORBIT   STURGEON, THEODORE   AC
EXTRATERRESTRIAL TRILOGY ON TERRAN SELF-DESTRUCTION
                               EBERHART, SHERI   PM   GAL 61 08
   7TH ANNUAL OF THE YEAR'S BEST S-F, THE MERRIL, JUDITH   AN
EXTREME PREJUDICE   POURNELLE, JERRY   NV   ASF 74 07
   HIGH JUSTICE   POURNELLE, JERRY   AC
EYE AND THE FINGER   WANDREI, DONALD   SS
   EYE AND THE FINGER   WANDREI, DONALD   AC
EYE FOR A WHAT?, AN   KNIGHT, DAMON   NV   GAL 57 03
   ALIENS, THE   SILVERBERG, ROBERT   AN
   IN DEEP   KNIGHT, DAMON   AC
   WORLD THAT COULDN'T BE AND 8 OTHER SF NOVELETS
                                        GOLD, H. L.   AN
   WORLDS APART   WILLIAMS-ELLIS& OWEN AN
EYE FOR AN EYE   BIGGLE, LLOYD JR.   NV
   FAR SIDE OF TIME, THE   ELWOOD, ROGER   OA
   GALAXY OF STRANGERS, A   BIGGLE, LLOYD JR.   AC
EYE FOR HISTORY, AN   DERLETH, AUGUST   SS
   HARRIGAN'S FILE   DERLETH, AUGUST   AC
EYE FOR INIQUITY   SHERRED, T. L.   NV   BEY 53 07
   DARK SIDE, THE   KNIGHT, DAMON   AN
   FIRST PERSON, PECULIAR   SHERRED, T. L.   AC
   PORTALS OF TOMORROW   DERLETH, AUGUST   AN
EYE OF AN OCTOPUS   NIVEN, LARRY   SS   GAL 66 02
   TALES OF KNOWN SPACE: THE UNIVERSE OF LARRY NIVEN
                                        NIVEN, LARRY   AC
EYE OF TANDYLA, THE   DE CAMP, L. SPRAGUE NV   FAD 51 05
   TIME UNTAMED   HOWARD, IVAN   AN
   TRITONIAN RING, THE   DE CAMP, L. SPRAGUE   AC
EYE OF THE BEHOLDER   FILER, BURT K.   SS   DVS 72 02
   AGAIN, DANGEROUS VISIONS   ELLISON, HARLAN   OA
EYE OF THE BEHOLDER, THE   BRUNNER, JOHN   SS   FUN 57 01
   NOT BEFORE TIME   BRUNNER, JOHN   AC
   *OUT OF MY MIND   BRUNNER, JOHN   AC

EYE OF THE LENS, THE   JONES, LANGDON   SS   NWS 68 03
   BEST SF STORIES FROM NEW WORLDS 6   MOORCOCK, MICHAEL   AN
EYE OF THE LENS, THE   JONES, LANGDON   AC
EYE OF THE STORM (SEE IN THE EYE OF THE STORM)
                               SPINRAD, NORMAN   TC
EYE, THE (THE MURDERER'S EYE) KERSH, GERALD   NV   SEP 57 03
   ON AN ODD NOTE   KERSH, GERALD   AC
EYEBALL OF THE SUN   CHILDS, BERNARD   IL
   SCIENCE FICTION   BRODKIN & PEARSON   AN
EYEBEM   WOLFE, GENE   SS   ORB 70 07
   ORBIT 7   KNIGHT, DAMON   OA
   THEMES IN SCIENCE FICTION   KELLEY, LEO P.   AN
EYEFLASH MIRACLES, THE   WOLFE, GENE   NA   76
   BEST SCIENCE FICTION OF THE YEAR, THE NO. 6
                                        CARR, TERRY   AN
   FUTURE POWER   DANN & DOZOIS   OA
EYES DO MORE THAN SEE   ASIMOV, ISAAC   SS   FSF 65 04
   BEST FROM FANTASY AND SCIENCE FICTION: 15
                                        FERMAN, EDWARD L.   AN
   NIGHTFALL AND OTHER STORIES   ASIMOV, ISAAC   AC
   11TH ANNUAL OF THE YEAR'S BEST S-F, THE MERRIL, JUDITH   AN
EYES HAVE IT, THE   GARRETT, RANDALL   NV   ASF 64 01
   RULERS OF MEN   SANTESSON, HANS S.   AN
EYES HAVE IT, THE   MCKIMMEY, JAMES   SS   IFS 53 11
   SPACE, TIME & CRIME   DEFORD, MIRIAM ALLEN AN
EYES OF A WOMAN- FROM A PORTRAIT BY PICASSO
                               CONESA, LISA   PM
   BEST SF: 1974   HARRISON & ALDISS   AN
EYES OF DUST   ELLISON, HARLAN   SS   ROG 59 12
   ALONE AGAINST TOMORROW   ELLISON, HARLAN   AC
   I HAVE NO MOUTH, AND I MUST SCREAM   ELLISON, HARLAN   AC
EYES OF ONYX   BRYANT, EDWARD   SS   PRT 71
   NEW AWARENESS, THE   WARRICK & GREENBERG   AN
   PROTOSTARS   GERROLD & GOLDIN   OA
EYES OF SILENCE, THE   TUBB, E. C.   SS   INF 57 04
   SCATTER OF STARDUST, A   TUBB, E. C.   DC
EYES OF THE MUMMY, THE   BLOCH, ROBERT   SS   WRT 38 04
   HOUSE OF THE HATCHET, THE   BLOCH, ROBERT   AC
   *OPENER OF THE WAY, THE   BLOCH, ROBERT   AC
   YOURS TRULY, JACK THE RIPPER   BLOCH, ROBERT   AC
EYES OF THE OVERWORLD, THE (SEE CIL)
                               VANCE, JACK   TC
EYES, THE   HASSE, HENRY   SS   FBK 51 08
   SCIENCE AND SORCERY   FORD, GARRET   AN
F & SF AND I   ASIMOV, ISAAC   IN
   TWENTY YEARS OF FANTASY & SCIENCE FICTION
                                        FERMAN & MILLS   AN
F Y I   BLISH, JAMES   SS   STR 53 02
   BEYOND THIS HORIZON   CARRELL, CHRISTOPHER OA
   MATHEMATICAL MAGPIE, THE   FADIMAN, CLIFTON   AN
   SO CLOSE TO HOME   BLISH, JAMES   AC
   STAR SCIENCE FICTION STORIES NO. 2   POHL, FREDERIK   AN
F.O.B. VENUS   BLOCH, ROBERT   SS   FAN 58 11
   FEAR TODAY, GONE TOMORROW   BLOCH, ROBERT   AC
F.O.B. VENUS   BOND, NELSON S.   SS   FAD 39 11
   LANCELOT BIGGS: SPACEMAN   BOND, NELSON S.   AC
F--- (THE FOODLEGGER)   MATHESON, RICHARD   SS   TWS 52 04
   BORN OF MAN AND WOMAN   MATHESON, RICHARD   AC
   THIRD FROM THE SUN   MATHESON, RICHARD   AC
F (X) = (11/15/67) X=HER, F(X)≠0 EFFINGER, GEO. ALEC SS NDM 72 02
   MIXED FEELINGS   EFFINGER, GEO. ALEC   AC
   NEW DIMENSIONS 2   SILVERBERG, ROBERT   OA
FABER-MASTER   ORGILL, MICHAEL   NV
   WORLD NAMED CLEOPATRA, A   ANDERSON, POUL   OA
FABLE, A   ANONYMOUS   PM   MAG 54 38
   FANTASIA MATHEMATICA   FADIMAN, CLIFTON   OA
FABLES (THE FROG PRINCE & MICKEY MOUSE)
                               DIEFENDORF, DAVID   SS   NYT 75 12
   NEW CONSTELLATIONS   DISCH & NAYLOR   OA
FABULOUS IDIOT, THE   STURGEON, THEODORE   NV   NEW 53 NO
   MORE THAN HUMAN   STURGEON, THEODORE   NO
FACE IN THE MIRROR, THE   KELLER, DAVID H. MD. SS
   LIFE EVERLASTING AND OTHER TALES OF SCIENCE, FANTASY
   AND HORROR   KELLER, DAVID H. MD. AC
FACE IN THE PHOTO, THE (TIME HAS NO BOUNDARIES)
                               FINNEY, JACK   SS   SEP 62 10
   I LOVE GALESBURG IN THE SPRINGTIME   FINNEY, JACK   AC
   TIMES 4 (ABRIDGED STORIES)   ALLEN, VIRGINIA F.   AN
   8TH ANNUAL OF THE YEAR'S BEST S-F, THE MERRIL, JUDITH   AN
FACE OF HELENE BOURNOUW, THE   ELLISON, HARLAN   SS   CLG 60 10
   DEATHBIRD STORIES   ELLISON, HARLAN   AC
   *LOVE AIN'T NOTHING BUT SEX MISSPELLED ELLISON, HARLAN   AC
FACE OF THE DEEP, THE   SABERHAGEN, FRED   SS   IFS 66 09
   BERSERKER   SABERHAGEN, FRED   AC
FACE OF THE ENEMY, THE   KIMBERLY, GAIL   NV
   SCIENCE FICTION ADVENTURES FROM WAY OUT ELWOOD, ROGER   OA
FACE ON THE BARROOM FLOOR, THE, THE ARNASON, ELEANOR
                               AND BERMAN, RUTH   NV C
   STAR TREK: THE NEW VOYAGES   MARSHAK, S&CULBREATH OA
FACE TO INFINITY   TUBB, E. C.   SS   NWR 76 28
   NEW WRITINGS IN SF. 28   BULMER, KENNETH   OA
FACELESS GOD, THE   BLOCH, ROBERT   SS   WRT 36 05
   *OPENER OF THE WAY, THE   BLOCH, ROBERT   AC
   YOURS TRULY, JACK THE RIPPER   BLOCH, ROBERT   AC
FACES & HANDS   SALLIS, JAMES   NV   NOV 70 01
   FEW LAST WORDS, A   SALLIS, JAMES   AC
   *NOVA 1   HARRISON, HARRY   OA
FACES FORWARD   DANN, JACK M.
                               AND ZEBROWSKI, GEORGE SS C DYS 75
   DYSTOPIAN VISIONS   ELWOOD, ROGER   OA
FACES OUTSIDE, THE   MCALLISTER, BRUCE   SS   IFS 63 07
   9TH ANNUAL OF THE YEAR'S BEST S-F, THE MERRIL, JUDITH   AN
FACES, THE (SEE GRAVEYARD SHIFT)
                               MATHESON, RICHARD   TC
FACETITIOUS PENTANGLE, THE   NEARING, H. JR.   SS   FSF 52 09
   SINISTER RESEARCHES OF C. P. RANSOM, THE NEARING, H. JR. AC

FACTORY, THE   MITCHISON, NAOMI   SS   NOV 73 03
  NOVA 3   HARRISON, HARRY   OA
FACTS IN THE CASE OF M. VALDEMAR
                                      POE, EDGAR ALLEN   SS   AWR 45 12
  FUTURE PERFECT   FRANKLIN, H. BRUCE   AN
  GREAT SCIENCE FICTION ABOUT DOCTORS CONKLIN, G&FABRICANT   AN
  SHOT IN THE DARK   MERRIL, JUDITH   AN
FACTS IN THE RATCLIFF CASE, THE
                                      MITCHELL, EDWARD P.   SS   SUN 79 03
  CRYSTAL MAN, THE   MITCHELL, EDWARD P.   AC
FACTS OF LIFE, THE   HILLMAN, MARTIN   SS
  WINDOW ON THE FUTURE   HILL, DOUGLAS   AN
FACTSHEET SIX   BRUNNER, JOHN   NV   GAL 68 07
  FROM THIS DAY FORWARD   BRUNNER, JOHN   AC
FAD   REYNOLDS, MACK   SS   ASF 65 04
  BEST OF MACK REYNOLDS, THE   REYNOLDS, MACK   AC
  DEPRESSION OR BUST   REYNOLDS, MACK   DN
FAED-OUT   DAVIDSON, AVRAM   SS   FSF 63 10
  WHAT STRANGE STARS AND SKIES   DAVIDSON, AVRAM   AC
FAEX DELENDA EST   COGSWELL, THEODORE R PM   CND 72
  BEST SF: 1972   HARRISON & ALDISS   AN
FAFHRD AND ME   LEIBER, FRITZ   AR   63
  SECOND BOOK OF FRITZ LEIBER, THE   LEIBER, FRITZ   AC
FAHRENHEIT 451 (EXPANSION OF "THE FIREMAN")
                                      BRADBURY, RAY   NO   GAL 51 02
  FAHRENHEIT 451   BRADBURY, RAY   AC
FAILED MEN, THE   ALDISS, BRIAN W.   SS   SCF 56 05
  NO TIME LIKE TOMORROW   ALDISS, BRIAN W.   AC
  SPACE, TIME AND NATHANIEL   ALDISS, BRIAN W.   AC
FAIR (AS KEITH WOODCOTT)   BRUNNER, JOHN   SS   NWS 56 03
  NO FUTURE IN IT   BRUNNER, JOHN   AC
  SF: AUTHORS' CHOICE 4   HARRISON, HARRY   AN
FAIR EXCHANGE, A   ANDERSON, POUL   NV   CTM 74 03
  CONTINUUM 3   ELWOOD, ROGER   OA
FAIR LADY   BEAUMONT, CHARLES   SS   NEW 57 AC
  HUNGER AND OTHER STORIES, THE   BEAUMONT, CHARLES   AC
  MAGIC MAN AND OTHER SCIENCE-FANTASY STORIES
                                      BEAUMONT, CHARLES   AC
FAIR TRADE   DAVIDSON, AVRAM   SS   FSF 60 07
  WHAT STRANGE STARS AND SKIES   DAVIDSON, AVRAM   AC
FAIR WARNING   BRUNNER, JOHN   SS   ASF 64 05
  NOT BEFORE TIME   BRUNNER, JOHN   AC
  *OUT OF MY MIND   BRUNNER, JOHN   AC
FAIR YOUNG WILLOWY TREE, THE   COPPARD, A. E.   SS
  ECO-FICTION   STADLER, JOHN   AN
FAIRLY CIVIL SERVANT, THE (SEE A CIVIL SERVICE SERVANT)
                                      HARRISON, HARRY   TC
FAIRY CHESSMEN, THE   PADGETT, LEWIS   SN   ASF 46 01
  TOMORROW AND TOMORROW AND THE FAIRY CHESSMEN
                                      PADGETT, LEWIS   AC
FAIRY TALE   BRUNNER, JOHN   SS   VOT 70 07
  FROM THIS DAY FORWARD   BRUNNER, JOHN   AC
FAITH OF OUR FATHERS   DICK, PHILIP K.   NV   DVS 67 01
  ALPHA 2   SILVERBERG, ROBERT   AN
  BEST OF PHILIP K. DICK, THE   DICK, PHILIP K.   AC
  DANGEROUS VISIONS   ELLISON, HARLAN   OA
  MODERN SCIENCE FICTION   SPINRAD, NORMAN   AN
FAITHFUL TO THEE, TERRA, IN OUR FASHION (PARAMUTUEL PLANET)
                                      TIPTREE, JAMES JR.   NV   GAL 69 01
  TEN THOUSAND LIGHT-YEARS FROM HOME   TIPTREE, JAMES JR.   AC
FAITHFUL   DEL REY, LESTER   SS   ASF 38 04
  *AND SOME WERE HUMAN   DEL REY, LESTER   AC
  EARLY DEL REY   DEL REY, LESTER   AC
  FIRST FLIGHT   KNIGHT, DAMON   AN
"FAITHLESS JACK THE SPACEMAN"   BRUNNER, JOHN   SG   NEW 76 AC
  BOOK OF JOHN BRUNNER, THE   BRUNNER, JOHN   AC
FALCON AND THE FALCONEER, THE MALZBERG, BARRY N. SS   FSF 69 12
  SF: AUTHORS' CHOICE 3   HARRISON, HARRY   AN
  WONDERMAKERS 2   HOSKINS, ROBERT   AN
FALCON AND THE FALCONEER, THE O'DONNELL, K. M.   SS   FSF 69 12
  IN THE POCKET AND OTHER S-F STORIES O'DONNELL, K. M.   DC
FALCON CHASE   COOPER, EDMUND   SS
  TOMORROW'S GIFT   COOPER, EDMUND   AC
FALL OF ALL-FATHER, THE   LORY, ROBERT   SS
  HARVEST OF HOODWINKS, A   LORY, ROBERT   DC
FALL OF FRENCHY STEINER, THE BAILEY, HILARY   NV   NWS 64 08
  BEST OF NEW WORLDS, THE   MOORCOCK, MICHAEL   AN
  BEST SF STORIES FROM NEW WORLDS 8   MOORCOCK, MICHAEL   AN
  SF12   MERRIL, JUDITH   AN
FALL OF KNIGHT   CHANDLER, A. BERTRAM SS   FUN 58 06
  FANTASTIC UNIVERSE OMNIBUS, THE   SANTESSON, HANS S.   AN
  RULERS OF MEN   SANTESSON, HANS S.   AN
FALL OF MOONDUST, A   CLARKE, ARTHUR C.   NO   GOL 61
  ARTHUR C. CLARKE SECOND OMNIBUS, AN CLARKE, ARTHUR C.   AC
FALL OUT ONE   SCORTIA, THOMAS N.   SS   MSM 72 03
  CAUTION: INFLAMMABLE!   SCORTIA, THOMAS N.   AC
FALLING TORCH   BUDRYS, ALGIS   NV   VSF 58 01
  FALLING TORCH, THE   BUDRYS, ALGIS   NO
FALLOUT ISLAND   MURPHY, ROBERT   SS   SEP 62 03
  POST READER OF FANTASY AND SCIENCE FICTION
                                      SATURDAY EVE. POST   AN
FALSE DAWN   CHANDLER, A. BERTRAM NV   ASF 46 10
  JOURNEY TO INFINITY   GREENBERG, MARTIN   AN
FALSE DAWN   YARBRO, CHELSEA Q.   SS   NEW 72 AN
  STRANGE BED FELLOWS   SCORTIA, THOMAS N.   AN
  WOMEN OF WONDER   SARGENT, PAMELA   AN
FALSE IMAGE   WILLIAMS, JAY   SS   ASF 58 10
  14 GREAT TALES OF ESP   STONE, IDELLA P.   AN
FALSE PROPHET   RANDALL, ROBERT   NV   ASF 56 12
  SHROUDED PLANET, THE   RANDALL, ROBERT   AC
FALSE RHYME, THE   SHELLEY, MARY W.   SS   KPS 30
  TALES AND STORIES   SHELLEY, MARY W.   AC
FAME   COX, ARTHUR JEAN   SS   ORB 70 06
  ORBIT 6   KNIGHT, DAMON   OA
FAMILY LITERATURE   PLATT, CHARLES   SS   NWB 73 05
  NEW WORLDS QUARTERLY NO. 5   MOORCOCK, MICHAEL   OA

FAMILY MONKEY, THE   TUTTLE, LISA   SS
  NEW VOICES IN SCIENCE FICTION   MARTIN, GEORGE R. R.   OA
FAMILY PORTRAIT   KENT, MORGAN   SS   FAN 64 08
  10TH ANNUAL OF THE YEAR'S BEST S-F, THE MERRIL, JUDITH   AN
FAMILY RESEMBLANCE   NOURSE, ALAN E.   SS   ASF 53 04
  ABC OF SCIENCE FICTION, AN   BOARDMAN, TOM JR.   AN
  GREAT SCIENCE FICTION ABOUT DOCTORS CONKLIN, G&FABRICANT   AN
  *SCIENCE FICTION ADVENTURES IN MUTATION CONKLIN, GROFF   AN
  TIGER BY THE TAIL   NOURSE, ALAN E.   AC
FAMILY TREE   THAYER, FRANK D.   SS
  TRAVELLERS BY NIGHT   DERLETH, AUGUST   OA
FAMILY WINTER OF 1986, THE GOTSCHALK, FELIX C. SS   ORB 76 18
  ORBIT 18   KNIGHT, DAMON   OA
FAMILY, THE   KING, MAC   PM   NWQ 74 06
  NEW WORLDS NO. 6   PLATT & BAILEY   OA
FAMOUS FIRST WORDS   HARRISON, HARRY   SS   FSF 65 01
  PRIME NUMBER   HARRISON, HARRY   AC
FANGS OF THE TREES, THE   SILVERBERG, ROBERT   NV   FSF 68 10
  EARTH'S OTHER SHADOW   SILVERBERG, ROBERT   AC
  NIGHTMARE GARDEN   GHIDALIA, VIC   AN
  PARSECS AND PARABLES   SILVERBERG, ROBERT   AC
FANTASY AND/OR SCIENCE FICTION BOUCHER, ANTHONY   IN
  WALL AROUND THE WORLD, THE   COGSWELL, THEODORE R AC
FANTASY IN SCIENCE FICTION- NO POHL, FREDERICK   IN
  WALL AROUND THE WORLD, THE   COGSWELL, THEODORE R AC
FANTASY OF A HUNTED MAN   KERSH, GERALD   SS
  ON AN ODD NOTE   KERSH, GERALD   AC
FANTASY ON THE MARCH (SEE A DEFENSE OF WEREWOLVES)
                                      LEIBER, FRITZ   TC
FANTASY: MANY MANSIONS AND HOVELS
                                      LEIBER, FRITZ   AR   CLR 71 01
  CLARION   WILSON, ROBIN SCOTT   OA
FANTASY'S PROFESSION   TEICHNER, ALBERT   SS   ORB 74 13
  ORBIT 13   KNIGHT, DAMON   OA
FAQ'   ELLIOTT, GEORGE P.   SS   FSF 61 11
  WORLDS OF SCIENCE FICTION, THE   MILLS, ROBERT P.   AN
FAR BELOW   JOHNSON, ROBERT B.   SS   WRT 39 06
  EDITOR'S CHOICE IN SCIENCE FICTION   MOSKOWITZ, SAM   AN
FAR CENTAURUS   VAN VOGT, A. E.   SS   ASF 44 01
  DEEP SPACE   SILVERBERG, ROBERT   AN
  DESTINATION: UNIVERSE!   VAN VOGT, A. E.   AC
  GREAT STORIES OF SPACE TRAVEL   CONKLIN, GROFF   AN
  *MEN AGAINST THE STARS   GREENBERG, MARTIN   AN
  QUEST FOR THE FUTURE   VAN VOGT, A. E.   NO
  SPECTRUM OF WORLDS, A   CLARESON, THOMAS D.   AN
  *STRANGE PORTS OF CALL   DERLETH, AUGUST   AN
FAR FROM HOME   TEVIS, WALTER S. JR. SS   FSF 58 12
  BEST FROM FANTASY AND SCIENCE FICTION: 9
                                      MILLS, ROBERT P.   AN
FAR FROM THIS EARTH   OLIVER, CHAD   SS   YRT 70
  ANTHROPOLOGY THROUGH SCIENCE FICTION MASON, C/GREENBERG/& AN
  THEMES IN SCIENCE FICTION   KELLEY, LEO P.   AN
  YEAR 2000, THE   HARRISON, HARRY   OA
FAR LOOK, THE   THOMAS, THEODORE L.   NV   ASF 56 08
  LOOKING AHEAD   ALLEN, D. & L.   AN
  SCIENCE FICTION NOVELLAS   HARRISON & MCNELLY   AN
  SF:57, THE YEAR'S GREATEST SCIENCE FICTION AND FANTASY
                                      MERRIL, JUDITH   AN
                                      AMIS & CONQUEST   AN
  SPECTRUM 5   CONQUEST, ROBERT   PM   69
FAR OUT   LUCIE-SMITH, EDWARD   AN
  HOLDING YOUR EIGHT HANDS   INOUYE, JON   SS
FAR PULSAR   INOUYE, JON   OC
  NIGHT TIDE, A   LEIBER, FRITZ   SS   AMZ 65 02
FAR REACH TO CYGNUS   LEIBER, FRITZ   AC
  WORLDS OF FRITZ LEIBER, THE
FAR-OUT PHILOSOPHER OF SCIENCE FICTION, THE
                                      ACKERMAN, FORREST J. AR   49
  SCIENCE FICTION WORLDS OF FORREST J. ACKERMAN & FRIENDS
                                      ACKERMAN, FORREST J. AC
FAREWELL DREAM   INOUYE, JON   SS
  NIGHT TIDE, A   INOUYE, JON   OC
FAREWELL ON THE SHORE, A   LUKODIANOV, ISAI
                                      AND VOISKUNSKY, YEVGENY NV C
  RUSSIAN SCIENCE FICTION, 1969   MAGIDOFF, ROBERT   AN
FAREWELL TO EDEN   STURGEON, THEODORE   SS   NEW 49 AN
  INVASION FROM MARS   WELLES, ORSON   AN
  *OUTER REACHES, THE   DERLETH, AUGUST   AN
FAREWELL TO THE MASTER   BATES, HARRY   NV   ASF 40 10
  *ADVENTURES IN TIME AND SPACE   HEALY & MCCOMAS   AN
  ASTOUNDING-ANALOG READER, THE VOLUME ONE HARRISON & ALDISS   AN
FAREWELL TO THE RIVIERA   DISCH, THOMAS M.   SS
  *GETTING INTO DEATH   DISCH, THOMAS M.   AC
FAREWELL TO YESTERDAY'S TOMORROW
                                      PANSHIN, ALEXEI
                                      AND PANSHIN, CORY   AR C GAL 74 06
  FAREWELL TO YESTERDAY'S TOMORROW   PANSHIN, ALEXEI   AC
FARMER   REYNOLDS, MACK   NV   GAL 61 06
  WORLDS OF WHEN   CONKLIN, GROFF   AN
FARRELL AND LILA THE WEREWOLF BEAGLE, PETER S.   SS   GUA 69
  NEW WORLDS OF FANTASY NO. 3   CARR, TERRY   AN
FARTHEST HORIZON, THE   JONES, RAYMOND F.   SS   ASF 52 04
  SPACE PIONEERS   NORTON, ANDRE   AN
  *STORIES FOR TOMORROW   SLOANE, WILLIAM   AN
FARTHEST SHORE, THE   LE GUIN, URSULA K.   NO
  EARTHSEA   LE GUIN, URSULA K.   AC
FASCINATING STRANGER, THE FESSIER, MICHAEL   NV   SEP 48 05
  GREAT STORIES OF SCIENCE FICTION   LEINSTER, MURRAY   AN
FAST CAR WASH   MACBETH, GEORGE   SS
  NEW S.F., THE   JONES, LANGDON   OA
FAST FALLS THE EVENTIDE   RUSSELL, ERIC FRANK   SS   ASF 52 05
  BEST SCIENCE-FICTION STORIES: 1953, THE BLEILER & DIKTY   AN
FAST TRIP   WHITE, JAMES   SS   FSF 63 04
  OUT OF THIS WORLD 6   WILLIAMS-ELLIS& OWEN AN
FAST-FRIEND   MARTIN, GEORGE R. R. NV   76
  FASTER THAN LIGHT   DANN & ZEBROWSKI   OA

FASTERFASTER AFFAIR, THE   ANMAR, FRANK   SS   NEW 65 AN
  PSEUDO PEOPLE, THE   NOLAN, WILLIAM F.   AN
FASTERFASTER (THE FASTERFASTER AFFAIR)
                               NOLAN, WILLIAM F.   SS   NEW 65 AN
  ALIEN HORIZONS   NOLAN, WILLIAM F.   AC
FASTEST DRAW, THE (SEE THE MARVELOUS MARSHAL)
                               EISENBERG, LARRY   TC
FASTEST GUN DEAD, THE   GROW, JULIAN F.   SS   IFS 61 03
  7TH ANNUAL OF THE YEAR'S BEST S-F, THE   MERRIL, JUDITH   AN
FAT CHANCE   BLOCH, ROBERT   SS   KHM 60 08
  CHAMBER OF HORRORS   BLOCH, ROBERT   AC
  KING OF TERRORS, THE   BLOCH, ROBERT   AC
FATAL ERROR   BROWN, FREDRIC   SS
  NIGHTMARES AND GEEZENSTACKS   BROWN, FREDRIC   AC
FATAL FULFILLMENT, THE   ANDERSON, POUL   SN   FSF 70 03
  BEST OF POUL ANDERSON, THE   ANDERSON, POUL   AC
  FIVE FATES   LAUMER, KEITH   AN
FATE OF JEAN MORENAS, THE   VERNE, JULES   SS
  YESTERDAY AND TOMORROW   VERNE, JULES   AC
FATE OF THE POSEIDONIA, THE   HARRIS, CLARE WINGER SS   AMZ 27 06
  AWAY FROM THE HERE AND NOW   HARRIS, CLARE WINGER   AC
FATEFUL FIRST DAY ON XENE   TOFTE, ARTHUR   NV   NEW 72 AN
  TEEN-AGE SPACE ADVENTURES   FURMAN, A. L.   AN
FATHER   FARMER, PHILIP JOSE   NV   FSF 55 07
  STRANGE RELATIONS   FARMER, PHILIP JOSE   AC
FATHER   SARGENT, PAMELA   SN   AMZ 74 02
  CLONED LIVES   SARGENT, PAMELA   NO
FATHER OF SCIENCE FICTION, THE ASIMOV, ISAAC   IN   AMA 73
  ASTOUNDING   HARRISON, HARRY   OA
FATHER OF THE STARS   POHL, FREDERIK   SS   IFS 64 11
  BEST OF FREDERIK POHL, THE   POHL, FREDERIK   AC
  DIGITS AND DASTARDS   POHL, FREDERIK   AC
  IF READER OF SCIENCE FICTION, THE   POHL, FREDERIK   AC
FATHER'S IN THE BASEMENT   FARMER, PHILIP JOSE   SS   ORB 72 11
  BOOK OF PHILIP JOSE FARMER, THE   FARMER, PHILIP JOSE   AC
  ORBIT 11   KNIGHT, DAMON   OA
FATHER-THING, THE   DICK, PHILIP K.   SS   FSF 54 12
  BEST OF PHILIP K. DICK, THE   DICK, PHILIP K.   AC
  SOCIAL PROBLEMS THROUGH SCIENCE FICTION GREENBERG/MILSTEAD/& AN
  THEMES IN SCIENCE FICTION   KELLEY, LEO P.   AN
  TOMORROW'S CHILDREN   ASIMOV, ISAAC   AN
  TREASURY OF GREAT SCIENCE FICTION, A VOL.1
                               BOUCHER, ANTHONY   AN
FATHER, DEAR FATHER (OH FATHER OF MINE)
                               BEAUMONT, CHARLES   SS   VSF 57 01
  NIGHT RIDE AND OTHER JOURNEYS BEAUMONT, CHARLES   AC
FAULT   TIPTREE, JAMES JR.   SS   FAN 68 08
  WARM WORLDS AND OTHERWISE   TIPTREE, JAMES JR.   AC
FAULTY REGISTER   GORES, JOE   SS   TVW 73
  TWO VIEWS OF WONDER   SCORTIA & YARBRO   OA
FAUN, THE   ANDERSON, POUL   SS   BLF 68 09
  QUEEN OF AIR AND DARKNESS AND OTHER STORIES, THE
                               ANDERSON, POUL   AC
FEAR HOUND   MACLEAN, KATHERINE   NV   ASF 68 05
  MISSING MAN, THE   MACLEAN, KATHERINE   NO
  WORLD'S BEST SCIENCE FICTION: 1969   WOLLHEIM & CARR   AN
FEAR IN THE NIGHT   SHECKLEY, ROBERT   SS   TDW 52
  PILGRIMAGE TO EARTH   SHECKLEY, ROBERT   AC
FEAR IS A BUSINESS   STURGEON, THEODORE   SS   FSF 56 08
  DECADE OF FANTASY AND SCIENCE FICTION, A   MILLS, ROBERT P.   AN
  ENCOUNTERS WITH ALIENS   EARLEY, GEORGE W.   AN
FEAR IS A COLD BLACK   WILHELM, KATE   NV   NEW 63 AC
  MILE-LONG SPACESHIP, THE   WILHELM, KATE   AC
FEAR PLANET, THE   BLOCH, ROBERT   SS   SSS 43 02
  ALIEN WORLDS   ELWOOD, ROGER   AN
  FAR BOUNDARIES   DERLETH, AUGUST   AN
FEARFUL BANNER   RAYER, FRANCIS G.   SS
  WORLDS AT WAR   RAYER, FRANCIS G.   AN
FEARSOME FABLE   ELLIOTT, BRUCE   SS   FSF 51 02
  BEST FROM FANTASY AND SCIENCE FICTION   BOUCHER & MCCOMAS   AN
  FANTASIA MATHEMATICA   FADIMAN, CLIFTON   AN
FEASIBILITY PLAN, THE   CONRAD, EARL   SS
  DA VINCI MACHINE, THE   CONRAD, EARL   OC
FEAST   ELWOOD, ROGER   SS   FCR 75
  FUTURE CORRUPTION   ELWOOD, ROGER   OA
FEAST IN THE ABBEY, THE   BLOCH, ROBERT   SS   WRT 35 01
  HOUSE OF THE HATCHET, THE   BLOCH, ROBERT   AC
  MORE NIGHTMARES   BLOCH, ROBERT   AC
  *OPENER OF THE WAY, THE   BLOCH, ROBERT   AC
FEAST OF DEMONS, A   MORRISON, WILLIAM   NV   GAL 58 03
  EXPERT DREAMERS, THE   POHL, FREDERIK   AN
  FIFTH GALAXY READER, THE   GOLD, H. L.   AN
FEAST OF ST. DIONYSUS, THE   SILVERBERG, ROBERT   NV   73
  EXALTATION OF STARS, AN   CARR, TERRY   OA
  FEAST OF ST. DIONYSUS, THE   SILVERBERG, ROBERT   AC
FEATHER TIGERS   WOLFE, GENE   SS
  WORLDS FAR AND NEAR   CARR, TERRY   AN
FEATHERBED ON CHLYNTHA   DEFORD, MIRIAM ALLEN SS   VSF 57 11
  XENOGENESIS   DEFORD, MIRIAM ALLEN   AC
FEATHERBEDDERS, THE   HERBERT, FRANK   NV   ASF 67 08
  ANALOG 7   CAMPBELL, JOHN W. JR   AN
  WORLDS OF FRANK HERBERT, THE HERBERT, FRANK   AC
FEATHERED FRIEND (THE OTHER SIDE OF THE SKY)
                               CLARKE, ARTHUR C.   SS   INF 57 09
  OF TIME AND STARS   CLARKE, ARTHUR C.   AC
  OTHER SIDE OF THE SKY, THE   CLARKE, ARTHUR C.   AC
FEATHERS FROM THE WINGS OF AN ANGEL
                               DISCH, THOMAS M.   SS   NWS 71 03
  *GETTING INTO DEATH   DISCH, THOMAS M.   AC
  NEW WORLDS QUARTERLY NO. 2   MOORCOCK, MICHAEL   OA
FEATHERTOP (SEE PURITAN PASSIONS)
                               HAWTHORNE, NATHANIEL   TC
FEEDBACK   MACLEAN, KATHERINE   SS   ASF 51 07
  CROSSROADS IN TIME   CONKLIN, GROFF   AN
  DIPLOIDS AND OTHER FLIGHTS OF FANCY, THE MACLEAN, KATHERINE   AC

FEEDING TIME   GUNN, JAMES E.   SS   ASF 55 08
  FUTURE IMPERFECT   GUNN, JAMES E.   AC
FEEDING TIME   SHECKLEY, ROBERT   SS   FNF 53 02
  NOTIONS: UNLIMITED   SHECKLEY, ROBERT   AC
FEEL OF DESPERATION, THE (A CASE OF DESPERATION)
                               WILHELM, KATE   SS   AHM 64
  DOWNSTAIRS ROOM AND OTHER SPECULATIVE FICTION, THE
                               WILHELM, KATE   AC
FEELING OF POWER, THE   ASIMOV, ISAAC   SS   IFS 58 02
  INSIDE INFORMATION   MOWSHOWITZ, ABBE   AN
  MATHEMATICAL MAGPIE, THE   FADIMAN, CLIFTON   AN
  NINE TOMORROWS   ASIMOV, ISAAC   AC
  OPUS 100   ASIMOV, ISAAC   AC
  PAST, PRESENT, AND FUTURE PERFECT   WOLFE, J&FITZ GERALD   AN
  SCIENCE FICTION THROUGH THE AGES 2   EVANS, I. O.   AN
  SPECTRUM 2   AMIS & CONQUEST   AN
  STARS AROUND US, THE   HOSKINS, ROBERT   AN
FEGHOOT I   BRUNNER, JOHN   SS   FSF 62 06
  BOOK OF JOHN BRUNNER, THE   BRUNNER, JOHN   AC
FEGHOOT II   BRUNNER, JOHN   SS   NEW 76 AC
  BOOK OF JOHN BRUNNER, THE   BRUNNER, JOHN   AC
FEGHOOT III   BRUNNER, JOHN   SS   NEW 76 AC
  BOOK OF JOHN BRUNNER, THE   BRUNNER, JOHN   AC
FEIGMAN'S BEARD   DERLETH, AUGUST   SS   WRT 34 11
  NOT LONG FOR THIS WORLD   DERLETH, AUGUST   AC
FELLINI BEGGAR, THE   YARBRO, CHELSEA Q.   SS
  BEYOND TIME   LEY, SANDRA   ON
FELLOW WHO MARRIED THE MAXILL GIRL, THE
                               MOORE, WARD   NV   FSF 60 02
  BEST FROM FANTASY AND SCIENCE FICTION: 10
                               MILLS, ROBERT P.   AN
  6TH ANNUAL OF THE YEAR'S BEST S-F, THE   MERRIL, JUDITH   AN
FELONY   CAUSEY, JAMES   SS   GAL 54 07
  BEST SCIENCE FICTION STORIES AND NOVELS: 1955
                               DIKTY, T. E.   AN
FEMININE DEMYSTIFICATION   HARPER, JO ANN   PM
  2076: THE AMERICAN TRICENTENNIAL   BRYANT, EDWARD   OA
FEMININE FRACTION, THE   WOLLHEIM, DONALD A.   SS   MOH 64 11
  TWO DOZEN DRAGON EGGS   WOLLHEIM, DONALD A.   AC
FEMININE INTUITION   ASIMOV, ISAAC   NV   FSF 69 10
  BICENTENNIAL MAN AND OTHER STORIES, THE ASIMOV, ISAAC   AC
  TWENTY YEARS OF FANTASY & SCIENCE FICTION
                               FERMAN & MILLS   AN
FEMININE METAMORPHOSIS, THE   KELLER, DAVID H. MD. NA   SWS 29 08
  WHEN WOMEN RULE   MOSKOWITZ, SAM   AN
FEMINISM AND SCIENCE FICTION: BEYOND BEMS AND BOOBS
                               ANDERSON, SUSAN J.   IN
  AURORA: BEYOND EQUALITY   MCINTYRE & ANDERSON   OA
FENCE, THE   SIMAK, CLIFFORD D.   SS   SSF 52 09
  ABC OF SCIENCE FICTION, AN   BOARDMAN, TOM JR.   AN
  *STRANGERS IN THE UNIVERSE   SIMAK, CLIFFORD D.   AC
FERDINANDO EBOLI   SHELLEY, MARY W.   NV   KPS 29
  TALES AND STORIES   SHELLEY, MARY W.   AC
FERGUSON'S CAPSULES   DERLETH, AUGUST   SS
  HARRIGAN'S FILE   DERLETH, AUGUST   AC
FERRYMAN ON THE RIVER, THE   KYLE, DAVID A.   SS   NWR 68 13
  NEW WRITINGS IN SF. 13   CARNELL, JOHN   OA
FESSENDEN'S WORLDS   HAMILTON, EDMOND   SS   WRT 37 04
  BEST OF EDMOND HAMILTON, THE HAMILTON, EDMOND   AC
  *BEYOND TIME AND SPACE   DERLETH, AUGUST   AN
FEVER DREAM   BRADBURY, RAY   SS   WRT 48 09
  BLOCH AND BRADBURY   BRADBURY & BLOCH   AC
  DAY IT RAINED FOREVER, THE   BRADBURY, RAY   AC
  MEDICINE FOR MELANCHOLY, A   BRADBURY, RAY   AC
  VINTAGE BRADBURY, THE   BRADBURY, RAY   AC
FEVER, THE   SERLING, ROD   SA
  STORIES FROM THE TWILIGHT ZONE   SERLING, ROD   OC
FEW KINDRED SPIRITS, A   CHRISTOPHER, JOHN   SS   FSF 65 11
  BEST FROM FANTASY AND SCIENCE FICTION: 16
                               FERMAN, EDWARD L.   AN
FEW LAST WORDS, A   SALLIS, JAMES   SS   ORB 68 04
  FEW LAST WORDS, A   SALLIS, JAMES   AC
  ORBIT 4   KNIGHT, DAMON   OA
  POCKETFUL OF STARS, A   KNIGHT, DAMON   OA
FEW MILES, A   FARMER, PHILIP JOSE   NV   FSF 60 10
  DOWN IN THE BLACK GANG AND OTHER STORIES FARMER, PHILIP JOSE AC
FEW MINUTES, A   JANIFER, LAURENCE M. SS   TTM 73
  TEN TOMORROWS   ELWOOD, ROGER   OA
FEW THINGS I KNOW ABOUT WHILEAWAY, A (FROM "THE FEMALE MAN")
                               RUSS, JOANNA   EX   BAN 75
  NEW IMPROVED SUN, THE   DISCH, THOMAS M.   AN
FICTION   GRANT, ALLAN   PM   UNK 41 02
  FROM UNKNOWN WORLDS   CAMPBELL, JOHN W. JR   AN
FICTION   SANDERS, THOMAS E.   SI
  SPECULATIONS   SANDERS, THOMAS E.   AN
FICTION MACHINES, THE   OKHOTNIKOV, VADIM   SS
  OUT OF THIS WORLD 5   WILLIAMS-ELLIS & OWEN   AN
  RUSSIAN SCIENCE FICTION   MAGIDOFF, ROBERT   AN
FIDDLE ESS   GILLETTE, GLEN L.   NV
  LONE STAR UNIVERSE   PROCTOR & UTLEY   AN
FIDDLER'S FEE, THE   BLOCH, ROBERT   SS   WRT 40 07
  MORE NIGHTMARES   BLOCH, ROBERT   AC
  *OPENER OF THE WAY, THE   BLOCH, ROBERT   AC
FIDDLER'S GREEN   MCKENNA, RICHARD M.   NV   ORB 67 02
  CASEY AGONISTES, AND OTHER S.F. & FANTASY STORIES
                               MCKENNA, RICHARD M.   AN
  DIMENSION X   KNIGHT, DAMON   AN
  ORBIT 2   KNIGHT, DAMON   OA
FIELD   SALLIS, JAMES   SS   QRK 71 03
  QUARK/3   DELANY & HACKER   OA
FIELD EXPEDIENT   OLIVER, CHAD   NV   ASF 55 01
  EDGE OF FOREVER, THE   OLIVER, CHAD   AC
  HIDDEN PLANET, THE   WOLLHEIM, DONALD A.   AN
FIELD OF VISION, THE   LE GUIN, URSULA K.   SS   GAL 73 10
  BEST FROM GALAXY, THE   VOLUME II   GALAXY, EDITORS OF   AN
  WINDS TWELVE QUARTERS, THE   LE GUIN, URSULA K.   AC

FIELD STUDY   PHILLIES, PETER   SS   GAL 51 04
*GALAXY READER OF SCIENCE FICTION   GOLD, H. L.   AN
FIELD TEST   LAUMER, KEITH   SS   ASF 76 03
  BOLO   LAUMER, KEITH   AC
FIEND, THE   POHL, FREDERIK   SS   PBY 64 04
  BEST FROM NEW WRITINGS IN S-F FIRST SELECTION, THE
                                       CARNELL, JOHN   AN
  DIGITS AND DASTARDS   POHL, FREDERIK   AC
  FIEND, THE   PLAYBOY, EDITORS OF   AN
  NEW WRITINGS IN SF. 3   CARNELL, JOHN   OA
  PLAYBOY BOOK OF SCIENCE FICTION AND FANTASY, THE
                                       PLAYBOY, EDITORS OF   AN
FIESTA BRAVA   REYNOLDS, MACK   SN   ASF 67 09
  ANALOG 7   CAMPBELL, JOHN W. JR AN
FIFE OF BODIDHARMA, THE   SMITH, CORDWAINER   SS   FAN 59 06
  STARDREAMER   SMITH, CORDWAINER   AC
FIFTEEN MILES   BOVA, BEN   SS   FSF 67 05
  BEST SF: 1967   HARRISON & ALDISS   AN
  FORWARD IN TIME   BOVA, BEN   AC
  NOTES TO A SCIENCE FICTION WRITER   BOVA, BEN   AC
  POCKETFUL OF STARS, A   KNIGHT, DAMON   AN
FIFTEEN VULTURES, THE STROP, AND THE OLD LADY
                                       LE GUIN, URSULA K.   AR   CLR 72 02
  CLARION II   WILSON, ROBIN SCOTT   OA
FIFTEENTH WIND OF MARCH, THE   BLAND, FREDERICK   NV   FSF 62 06
  ONCE AND FUTURE TALES FROM THE MAGAZINE OF FANTASY AND
  SCIENCE FICTION   FERMAN, EDWARD L.   AN
FIFTH COMMANDMENT   BRUNNER, JOHN   SS   VOT 70 03
  FROM THIS DAY FORWARD   BRUNNER, JOHN   AC
FIFTH DIMENSION   HARRIS, CLARE WINGER SS   AMZ 28 12
  AWAY FROM THE HERE AND NOW   HARRIS, CLARE WINGER AC
FIFTH FREEDOM   DEL REY, LESTER   SS   ASF 43 05
  EARLY DEL REY   DEL REY, LESTER   AC
FIFTH HEAD OF CERBERUS, THE   WOLFE, GENE   NV   ORB 72 10
  BEST SCIENCE FICTION OF THE YEAR, THE NO. 2
                                       CARR, TERRY   AN
  FIFTH HEAD OF CERBERUS, THE   WOLFE, GENE   AC
  NEBULA AWARD STORIES 8   ASIMOV, ISAAC   AN
  ORBIT 10   KNIGHT, DAMON   OA
FIFTH PERSON SINGULAR   TATE, PETER   SS   NWS 66 05
  NEW WORLDS QUARTERLY NO. 2   MOORCOCK, MICHAEL   OA
FIFTH SALLY, OR THE MISCHIEF OF KING BALERION, THE
                                       LEM, STANISLAW   SS
  CYBERIAD, THE   LEM, STANISLAW   OC
FIFTH SALLY (A), OR TRURL'S PRESCRIPTION
                                       LEM, STANISLAW   SS
  CYBERIAD, THE   LEM, STANISLAW   OC
FIFTH-DIMENSION CATAPULT, THE   LEINSTER, MURRAY   NV   ASF 31 01
  SCIENCE FICTION OF THE 30'S   KNIGHT, DAMON   AN
FIFTY YEARS OF WONDER   BRACKETT, LEIGH   IN
  BEST OF EDMOND HAMILTON, THE   HAMILTON, EDMOND   AC
FIGHT IN THE FOG, A   STIRLING, YATES JR. SS
  BATTLE FOR THE PACIFIC AND OTHER ADVENTURES AT SEA, THE
                                       ANONYMOUS   AN
FIGHTING DIVISION   GARRETT, RANDALL   SS   ASF 65 08
  ANALOG 5   CAMPBELL, JOHN W. JR AN
FIGHTING FASCISM   RUSH, NORMAN   SS   BMR 73
  BAD MOON RISING   DISCH, THOMAS M.   OA
FIGHTING MADNESS   PLAUGER, P. J.   NO
  ANALOG ANNUAL   BOVA, BEN   OA
FIGHTING MAN OF MARS, A   BURROUGHS, EDGAR R. NO   BBM 30 04
  PRINCESS OF MARS AND A FIGHTING MAN OF MARS, A
                                       BURROUGHS, EDGAR R.   AC
FIGHTING PHILOSOPHER   COLE, EVERETT B.   NV   ASF 54 04
  PHILOSOPHICAL CORPS, THE   COLE, EVERETT B.   AC
FIGHTING SPIRIT   GALOUYE, DANIEL F.   NV   GAL 60 12
  LAST LEAP AND OTHER STORIES OF THE SUPER-MIND, THE
                                       GALOUYE, DANIEL F.   AC
FIGMENT, THE   SELLINGS, ARTHUR   SS   FUN 55 02
  *TIME TRANSFER   SELLINGS, ARTHUR   AC
FIGURE, THE   GRENDON, EDWARD   SS   ASF 47 07
  FIFTY SHORT SCIENCE FICTION TALES   ASIMOV & CONKLIN   AN
  *TREASURY OF SCIENCE FICTION, A   CONKLIN, GROFF   AN
FILBERT IS A NUT, A   RAPHAEL, RICK   SS   ASF 59 11
  PROLOGUE TO ANALOG   CAMPBELL, JOHN W. JR AN
FILCH   LONG, FRANK BELKNAP SS   ASF 45 03
  RIM OF THE UNKNOWN   LONG, FRANK BELKNAP   AC
FILE ON THE PLAGUE   BRYANT, EDWARD   SS   NLP 71 04
  AMONG THE DEAD   BRYANT, EDWARD   AC
FILL IN THE BLANK   GOULART, RON   SS   FSF 67 05
  BEST FROM FANTASY AND SCIENCE FICTION: 17
                                       FERMAN, EDWARD L.   AN
  GHOST BREAKER   GOULART, RON   DC
FILLING US UP   HARRISON, M. JOHN   SS   NWQ 73 05
  NEW WORLDS NO. 5   MOORCOCK & PLATT   OA
FILM LIBRARY   VAN VOGT, A. E.   SS   ASF 46 07
  *AWAY AND BEYOND   VAN VOGT, A. E.   AC
  QUEST FOR THE FUTURE   VAN VOGT, A. E.   NO
FILM OF DEATH   CAMPBELL, J. SCOTT   SS   ASF 48 03
  EVIL EARTHS   ALDISS, BRIAN W.   AN
FILMER   WELLS, H. G.   SS   GRP 01
  BEST SCIENCE FICTION STORIES OF H. G. WELLS
                                       WELLS, H. G.   AC
  SHORT STORIES OF H. G. WELLS, THE   WELLS, H. G.   AC
  TWELVE STORIES AND A DREAM   WELLS, H. G.   AC
  TWENTY-EIGHT SCIENCE FICTION STORIES WELLS, H. G.   AC
FILOMENA & GREG & RIKKI-TIKKI & BARLOW & THE ALIEN (ALSO AS
  ALL THE KINDS OF YES)   TIPTREE, JAMES JR.   NV   NDM 72 02
  NEW DIMENSIONS 2   SILVERBERG, ROBERT   OA
FIN DE SIECLE   STERNBERG, JACQUES   NO
  FUTURE WITHOUT FUTURE   STERNBERG, JACQUES   OC
FINAL AUDIT   DISCH, THOMAS M.   SS   FAN 63 07
  *ONE HUNDRED AND TWO H-BOMBS   DISCH, THOMAS M.   AC
  WHITE FANG GOES DINGO AND OTHER FUNNY S.F. STORIES
                                       DISCH, THOMAS M.   AC

FINAL BATTLE   HARRISON, HARRY   SS   NEW 70 AC
  PRIME NUMBER   HARRISON, HARRY   AC
FINAL CHALLENGE, THE   SILVERBERG, ROBERT   SS   INF 56 08
  SHORES OF TOMORROW, THE   SILVERBERG, ROBERT   AC
FINAL CLEARENCE   MADDUX, RACHEL   SS   FSF 56 02
  BEST FROM FANTASY AND SCIENCE FICTION: 6
                                       BOUCHER, ANTHONY   AN
FINAL COMMAND   VAN VOGT, A. E.   SS   ASF 49 11
  MONSTERS   VAN VOGT, A. E.   AC
  ROBOT AND THE MAN, THE   GREENBERG, MARTIN   AN
FINAL COMMENT   VAN VOGT, A. E.   MS
  BEST OF A. E. VAN VOGT, THE   VAN VOGT, A. E.   AC
FINAL DECISION, THE   BUNCH, DAVID R.   SS   AMZ 61 02
  MODERAN   BUNCH, DAVID R.   AC
FINAL DINEB   INOUYE, JON   SS
  NIGHT TIDE, A   INOUYE, JON   OC
FINAL ENCOUNTER   HARRISON, HARRY   NV   GAL 64 04
  EIGHTH GALAXY READER, THE   POHL, FREDERIK   AN
  GALACTIC EMPIRES VOLUME TWO   ALDISS, BRIAN W.   AN
  TWO TALES AND EIGHT TOMORROWS   HARRISON, HARRY   AC
FINAL EXAM   OLIVER, CHAD   SS   FAN 52 11
  ABC OF SCIENCE FICTION, AN   BOARDMAN, TOM JR.   AN
  BEST FROM FANTASTIC, THE   WHITE, TED   AN
FINAL EXAM   SCORTIA, THOMAS N.   SS
  OTHER SIDE OF TOMORROW, THE   ELWOOD, ROGER   OA
FINAL FIGURE, THE   MERWIN, SAM JR.   NV   DSF 54 01
  MASTERS OF SCIENCE FICTION   HOWARD, IVAN   AN
FINAL FLOWER   COOK, STEPHEN   SS   NEW 68 AN
  PACIFIC BOOK OF AUSTRALIAN SCIENCE FICTION
                                       BAXTER, JOHN   AN
FINAL FRONTIER, THE   WILLIAMS, ROBERT M. SS   SSS 50 01
  VOID BEYOND, AND OTHER STORIES, THE WILLIAMS, ROBERT M.   DC
  WHEN TWO WORLDS MEET   WILLIAMS, ROBERT M.   AC
FINAL GENTLEMAN   SIMAK, CLIFFORD D.   NV   FSF 60 01
  SIX GREAT SHORT SCIENCE FICTION NOVELS CONKLIN, GROFF   AN
FINAL INGREDIENT, THE   SHARKEY, JACK   SS   FSF 60 08
  ROD SERLING'S TRIPLE W: WITCHES, WARLOCKS AND WEREWOLVES
                                       SERLING, ROD   AN
FINAL PERFORMANCE   BLOCH, ROBERT   NV   SHK 60 09
  *BLOOD RUNS COLD   BLOCH, ROBERT   AC
FINAL REPORT   BOND, NELSON S.   PM   FUN 58 01
  NIGHTMARES AND DAYDREAMS   BOND, NELSON S.   AC
FINAL SCEPTRE, A LASTING CROWN, A (ALSO AS HENRY THE NINTH)
                                       BRADBURY, RAY   SS   FSF 69 10
  TWENTY YEARS OF FANTASY & SCIENCE FICTION
                                       FERMAN & MILLS   AN
FINAL SHTICK   ELLISON, HARLAN   SS   ROG 60 08
  *LOVE AIN'T NOTHING BUT SEX MISSPELLED ELLISON, HARLAN   AC
FINAL SOLUTION   MACKELWORTH, R. W.   SS   NWR 66 08
  NEW WRITINGS IN SF. 8   CARNELL, JOHN   OA
FINAL TROPHY   ELLISON, HARLAN   NV   SUP 57 06
  OVER THE EDGE   ELLISON, HARLAN   AC
  TOUCH OF INFINITY, A   ELLISON, HARLAN   DC
FINAL WAR   MALZBERG, BARRY N.   NV   FSF 68 04
  FUTURE NOW, THE   HOSKINS, ROBERT   AN
  MANY WORLDS OF BARRY MALZBERG, THE   MALZBERG, BARRY N.   AC
FINAL WAR   O'DONNELL, K. M.   NV   FSF 68 04
  BEST FROM FANTASY AND SCIENCE FICTION: 18
                                       FERMAN, EDWARD L.   AN
  BEST SF: 1968   HARRISON & ALDISS   AN
  FINAL WAR AND OTHER FANTASIES   O'DONNELL, K. M.   DC
FINALITY UNLIMITED   WANDREI, DONALD   SN   ASF 36 09
  EYE AND THE FINGER   WANDREI, DONALD   AC
  *OUTER REACHES, THE   DERLETH, AUGUST   AN
FIND THE FACE   ROCKLYNNE, ROSS   SS   GAL 68 09
  ELEVENTH GALAXY READER, THE   POHL, FREDERIK   AN
FIND THE LADY   FISK, NICHOLAS   SS   NDM 75 05
  NEW DIMENSIONS 5   SILVERBERG, ROBERT   OA
FINDER'S FEEPER   MCCAFFREY, ANNE   SS   HOH 73 08
  GET OFF THE UNICORN   MCCAFFREY, ANNE   AC
FINER BREED, THE   URBAN, HELEN M.   SS   FSF 56 03
  ABC OF SCIENCE FICTION, AN   BOARDMAN, TOM JR.   AN
FINEST HUNTER IN THE WORLD, THE
                                       HARRISON, HARRY   SS   NEW 70 AC
  PRIME NUMBER   HARRISON, HARRY   AC
FINEST STORY IN THE WORLD, THE   KIPLING, RUDYARD   NV   CRV 91 07
  LIGHT FANTASTIC, THE   HARRISON, HARRY   AN
  TRAVELERS IN TIME   STERN, PHILIP VAN D.   AN
  WORLD OF WONDER   PRATT, FLETCHER   AN
FINGER PRINTS   MATHESON, RICHARD   SS   NEW 62 AN
  FIEND IN YOU, THE   BEAUMONT, CHARLES   AN
  SHOCK WAVES   MATHESON, RICHARD   AC
FINGERS IN THE SKY   KELLER, DAVID H. MD. SS   52
  FOLSOM FLINT AND OTHER CURIOUS TALES, THE
                                       KELLER, DAVID H. MD.   AC
FINIS   POLLOCK, FRANK L.   SS   ARG 06 06
  SCIENCE FICTION BY GASLIGHT   MOSKOWITZ, SAM   AN
FINISHED   DE CAMP, L. SPRAGUE SS   ASF 49 11
  CONTINENT MAKERS AND OTHER TALES OF THE VIAGENS
                                       DE CAMP, L. SPRAGUE   AC
FINISHING TOUCH   CHANDLER, A. BERTRAM SS   NWS 52 07
  GATEWAY TO TOMORROW   CARNELL, JOHN   AN
FINISHING TOUCHES, THE   MATHESON, RICHARD   SS   NEW 70 AC
  SHOCK WAVES   MATHESON, RICHARD   AC
FIRE AND THE SWORD, THE   ROBINSON, FRANK M.   NV   GAL 51 08
  *IMAGINATION UNLIMITED   BLEILER & DIKTY   AN
  SF: AUTHORS' CHOICE 4   HARRISON, HARRY   AN
FIRE BALLOONS, THE (IN THIS SIGN)
                                       BRADBURY, RAY   SS   IMG 51 04
  BEST SF   CRISPIN, EDMUND   AN
  CONTACT   KEYES, NOEL   AN
  *ILLUSTRATED MAN, THE   BRADBURY, RAY   AC
  MARTIAN CHRONICLES, THE (BRITISH SFBC, ADDS:)
                                       BRADBURY, RAY   AC
  NEW AWARENESS, THE   WARRICK & GREENBERG   AN
  SILVER LOCUSTS, THE   BRADBURY, RAY   AC

FIRE BALLOONS, THE (IN THIS SIGN)   "FLAP"

SPECIAL WONDER   MCCOMAS, J. FRANCIS   AN
FIRE BORN, THE   DUANE, TOBY   NV
  SHANADU   BRINEY, ROBERT E.   OA
FIRE FOUNTAIN, THE   KIMBERLY, GAIL   NV CTM 74 02
  CONTINUUM 2   ELWOOD, ROGER   OA
FIRE OF ASSHURBANIPAL, THE HOWARD, ROBERT E. SS WRT 36 12
  WOLFSHEAD   HOWARD, ROBERT E.   AC
FIRE SALE   JANIFER, LAURENCE M. SS FAN 64 09
  IMPOSSIBLE?   JANIFER, LAURENCE M.   AC
FIRE STORM   PRIEST, CHRISTOPHER SS QRK 70 01
  QUARK/1   DELANY & HACKER   OA
  REAL-TIME WORLD   PRIEST, CHRISTOPHER   AC
FIRE VAMPIRES, THE   WANDREI, DONALD SS WRT 33 02
  STRANGE HARVEST   WANDREI, DONALD   AC
FIREDAY: FIRENIGHT   MALZBERG, BARRY N. SS 74
  DOWN HERE IN THE DREAM QUARTER   MALZBERG, BARRY N. AC
  FAR SIDE OF TIME, THE   ELWOOD, ROGER   OA
  GIFTS OF ASTI AND OTHER STORIES OF SCIENCE FICTION, THE
                        ELWOOD, ROGER   AN
FIREMAN, THE (SEE FAHRENHEIT 451)
                        BRADBURY, RAY   TC
FIREPROOF   CLEMENT, HAL   SS ASF 49 03
  DECADE THE 1940S   ALDISS & HARRISON   AN
  SMALL CHANGES   CLEMENT, HAL   AC
FIRES OF NIGHT, THE ETCHISON, DENNIS SS NEW 65 05
  PSEUDO PEOPLE, THE   NOLAN, WILLIAM F.   AN
FIRES WITHIN, THE   CLARKE, ARTHUR C. SS FSB 47 08
  ACROSS THE SEA OF STARS   CLARKE, ARTHUR C. AC
  HISTORY OF THE SCIENCE FICTION MAGAZINE, THE PART 3 1946-1955
                        ASHLEY, MICHAEL   AN
  NEW WORLDS FOR OLD   DERLETH, AUGUST   AN
  OF TIME AND STARS   CLARKE, ARTHUR C.   AC
  REACH FOR TOMORROW   CLARKE, ARTHUR C.   AC
  SCIENCE FICTION GALAXY, THE CONKLIN, GROFF AN
  *WORLDS OF TOMORROW   DERLETH, AUGUST   AN
FIREWATER   TENN, WILLIAM   SN ASF 52 02
  ALIENS, THE   SILVERBERG, ROBERT   AN
  STRANGE TOMORROWS   HOSKINS, ROBERT   AN
  TIME IN ADVANCE   TENN, WILLIAM   AC
  YEAR'S BEST SCIENCE FICTION NOVELS: 1953 BLEILER & DIKTY AN
FIRING LINE   SMITH, GEORGE O. NV ASF 44 12
  COMPLETE VENUS EQUILATERAL, THE   SMITH, GEORGE O. AC
  VENUS EQUILATERAL   SMITH, GEORGE O.   AC
FIRST ANNIVERSARY   MATHESON, RICHARD SS PBY 60 07
  PLAYBOY BOOK OF HORROR AND THE SUPERNATURAL, THE
                        PLAYBOY, EDITORS OF AN
  SHOCK III   MATHESON, RICHARD   AN
FIRST CONTACT   LEINSTER, MURRAY NV ASF 45 05
  *ASTOUNDING SCIENCE FICTION ANTHOLOGY, THE
                        CAMPBELL, JOHN W. JR AN
  ASTOUNDING-ANALOG READER, THE VOLUME ONE HARRISON & ALDISS AN
  *BEST OF SCIENCE FICTION   CONKLIN, GROFF   AN
  CONTACT   KEYES, NOEL   AN
  *FIRST ASTOUNDING SCIENCE FICTION ANTHOLOGY, THE
                        CAMPBELL, JOHN W. JR AN
  FIRST CONTACT   KNIGHT, DAMON   AN
  FIRST STEP OUTWARD   HOSKINS, ROBERT   AN
  SCIENCE FICTION HALL OF FAME VOLUME 1 SILVERBERG, ROBERT AN
  *STORIES FOR TOMORROW SLOANE, WILLIAM   AN
FIRST DAY OF THE REST OF YOUR LIFE, THE
                        MORGAN, DAN   SS SFM 74 05
  BEST OF SCIENCE FICTION MONTHLY, THE SACKS, JANET AN
FIRST DAYS OF MAY, THE (FCT 60 05)
                        VEILLOT, CLAUDE SS FSF 61 12
  CENTURY OF SCIENCE FICTION, A KNIGHT, DAMON AN
  TALES OF TERROR FROM OUTER SPACE CHETWYND-HAYES, R. AN
FIRST DIG   DEFORD, MIRIAM ALLEN SS FSF 59 05
  ELSEWHERE, ELSEWHEN, ELSEHOW DEFORD, MIRIAM ALLEN AC
FIRST FEW KINDS OF TRUTH, THE SALLIS, JAMES SS ALT 74
  ALTERNATES   GERROLD, DAVID   OA
FIRST FLIGHT OF SCAVENGER I, THE
                        LITTKE, LAEL J.   SS
  QUEST   BISCHOFF, DAVID   OA
FIRST GORILLA ON THE MOON, THE BUTLER, BILL PM NEW 68 AN
  ENGLAND SWINGS SF   MERRIL, JUDITH   AN
  SPACE-TIME JOURNAL, THE MERRIL, JUDITH   AN
FIRST LADY   MCINTOSH, J. T. NV GAL 53 06
  ANOTHER PART OF THE GALAXY CONKLIN, GROFF   AN
  BEST SF   CRISPIN, EDMUND   AN
  MARRIAGE AND THE FAMILY THROUGH SCIENCE FICTION
                        CLEAR/WARRICK/&   AN
FIRST LAW   ASIMOV, ISAAC   SS FUN 56 10
  FANTASTIC UNIVERSE OMNIBUS, THE SANTESSON, HANS S. AN
  *REST OF THE ROBOTS, THE ASIMOV, ISAAC   AC
FIRST LESSON   CLINGERMAN, MILDRED SS FSF 56 12
  CUPFUL OF SPACE, A   CLINGERMAN, MILDRED   AC
  DECADE OF FANTASY AND SCIENCE FICTION, A MILLS, ROBERT P. AN
FIRST LIGHT ON A DARKLING PLAIN
                        GREEN, JOSEPH   SS NWR 71 19
  NEW WRITINGS IN SF. 19   CARNELL, JOHN   OA
FIRST LOVE   BIGGLE, LLOYD JR. SS AMZ 59 09
  GALAXY OF STRANGERS, A   BIGGLE, LLOYD JR.   AC
FIRST LOVE, FIRST FEAR   ZEBROWSKI, GEORGE SS NEW 72 04
  MONADIC UNIVERSE, THE   ZEBROWSKI, GEORGE   AC
  STRANGE BED FELLOWS   SCORTIA, THOMAS N. AN
FIRST LOVE, THE   ANDERSON, POUL   PM ARA 60 12
  HOMEBREW   ANDERSON, POUL   AC
FIRST MAN INTO SPACE, THE ELAM, RICHARD M. JR. NV
  TEEN-AGE SUPER SCIENCE STORIES ELAM, RICHARD M. JR. AC
FIRST MARTIAN, THE   COOPER, EDMUND   SS
  TOMORROW CAME   COOPER, EDMUND   AC
  VOICES IN THE DARK   COOPER, EDMUND   AC
FIRST MARTIAN, THE (THIS JOE) VAN VOGT, A. E. SS 39
  FAR-OUT WORLDS OF A. E. VAN VOGT, THE VAN VOGT, A. E. AC
  GREAT SCIENCE FICTION STORIES ABOUT MARS DIKTY, T. E. AN
  WORLDS OF A. E. VAN VOGT, THE VAN VOGT, A. E. AC

FIRST MEN IN THE MOON, THE WELLS, H. G. NO SND 00 11
  PORTABLE NOVELS OF SCIENCE   WOLLHEIM, DONALD A. AN
  SEVEN FAMOUS NOVELS BY H. G. WELLS WELLS, H. G. AN
FIRST MEN, THE   FAST, HOWARD   NV FSF 60 02
  EDGE OF TOMORROW, THE   FAST, HOWARD   AC
  INTRODUCTORY PSYCHOLOGY THROUGH SCIENCE FICTION
                        KATZ/WARRICK/&   AN
  MORE PENGUIN SCIENCE FICTION ALDISS, BRIAN W. AN
  SCHOOL AND SOCIETY THROUGH SCIENCE FICTION
                        OLANDER/GREENBERG/& AN
  WORLDS OF SCIENCE FICTION, THE   MILLS, ROBERT P. AN
FIRST MISSION   CARLSON, WILLIAM   NV
  LONG NIGHT OF WAITING AND OTHER STORIES ELWOOD, ROGER OA
FIRST NIGHT OF LENT, THE BRADBURY, RAY SS PBY 56 03
  MEDICINE FOR MELANCHOLY, A BRADBURY, RAY   AC
FIRST OF TWO RAPED PROSPECTS, THE
                        OBTULOWICZ, MAREK SS NWQ 72 04
  NEW WORLDS QUARTERLY NO. 4 MOORCOCK, MICHAEL OA
FIRST PERSON SINGULAR   RUSSELL, ERIC FRANK NV TWS 50 10
  DEEP SPACE   RUSSELL, ERIC FRANK   AC
FIRST PERSPECTIVES   ALLEN, DICK   SI
  SCIENCE FICTION: THE FUTURE ALLEN, DICK   AN
FIRST SALLY, OR THE TRAP OF GARGANTIUS, THE
                        LEM, STANISLAW   SS
  CYBERIAD, THE   LEM, STANISLAW   OC
FIRST SALLY(A), OR TRURL'S ELECTRONIC BARD, THE
                        LEM, STANISLAW   SS
  CYBERIAD, THE   LEM, STANISLAW   OC
FIRST STAGE: MOON   HETSCHEL, DICK   SS IFS 54 12
  FIRST WORLD OF IF, THE   QUINN & WULFF   AN
FIRST STRIKE   BLISH, JAMES   SS FSF 53 06
  SO CLOSE TO HOME   BLISH, JAMES   AC
FIRST TIME MACHINE   BROWN, FREDRIC   SS EQM 55 09
  HONEYMOON IN HELL   BROWN, FREDRIC   AC
FIRST TO SERVE   BUDRYS, ALGIS   SS ASF 54 05
  METAL SMILE, THE   KNIGHT, DAMON   AN
  UNEXPECTED DIMENSION, THE BUDRYS, ALGIS   AC
FIRST TO THE STARS (STARDUST) OLIVER, CHAD NV ASF 52 07
  EDGE OF FOREVER, THE   OLIVER, CHAD   AC
FIRST, THE   BOUCHER, ANTHONY SS FSF 52 10
  FAR AND AWAY   BOUCHER, ANTHONY   AC
FIRST, THE (SEE EXPERIMENTAL STATION)
                        NEVILLE, KRIS   TC
FISH OUT OF WATER, MAN BESIDE HIMSELF
                        MERRIL, JUDITH   IN
  SF12   MERRIL, JUDITH   AN
FISH STORY   BROWN, FREDRIC   SS
  NIGHTMARES AND GEEZENSTACKS BROWN, FREDRIC AC
FISH STORY   CHARTERIS, LESLIE SS BBM 53 11
  GALAXY OF GHOULS   MERRIL, JUDITH   AN
FISHERMAN   SAIL, LAWRENCE   PM NSM 71
  BEST SF: 1971   HARRISON & ALDISS   AN
FISHERMAN'S LUCK   LONG, FRANK BELKNAP SS UNK 40 07
  EARLY LONG, THE   LONG, FRANK BELKNAP   AC
  *HOUNDS OF TINDALOS, THE LONG, FRANK BELKNAP AC
FISHING SEASON   SHECKLEY, ROBERT SS TWS 53 08
  PEOPLE TRAP AND OTHER PITFALLS, THE SHECKLEY, ROBERT AC
  *TERROR IN THE MODERN VEIN WOLLHEIM, DONALD A. AN
FITTEST, THE   MACLEAN, KATHERINE SS WBY 51 01
  *BEYOND HUMAN KEN   MERRIL, JUDITH   AN
FIVE CARTOONS   WILSON, GAHAN   CT FSF 65
  BEST FROM FANTASY AND SCIENCE FICTION: 15
                        FERMAN, EDWARD L. AN
FIVE CARTOONS   WILSON, GAHAN   CT FSF 68
  BEST FROM FANTASY AND SCIENCE FICTION: 18
                        FERMAN, EDWARD L. AN
FIVE DOORS, THE   STALL, MICHAEL   SS NWR 74 23
  NEW WRITINGS IN SF. 23   BULMER, KENNETH   OA
FIVE DRAWINGS   FROST, NEMI   IL QRK 71 02
  QUARK/2   DELANY & HACKER   OA
FIVE HELLS OF ORION, THE POHL, FREDERIK NV IFS 63 01
  BEST SCIENCE FICTION FROM IF, THE POHL, FREDERIK AN
  DIGITS AND DASTARDS   POHL, FREDERIK   AC
FIVE LIVES OF ROBERT JORDAN, THE
                        BOND, NELSON S.   SS
  31ST OF FEBRUARY, THE   BOND, NELSON S.   AC
FIVE WEEKS IN A BALLOON (1863) VERNE, JULES EX
  JULES VERNE- MASTER OF SCIENCE FICTION VERNE, JULES AC
FIVE YEARS IN THE MARMALADE KREPPS, ROBERT W. SS FAD 49 07
  BEST SCIENCE-FICTION STORIES: 1950, THE BLEILER & DIKTY AN
FIVE-DIMENSIONAL SUGAR CUBE, THE
                        DEELEY, ROGER   SS PRT 71
  PROTOSTARS   GERROLD & GOLDIN   AN
FLAME AND THE HAMMER, THE SILVERBERG, ROBERT NO SFA 57 09
  VALLEY BEYOND TIME   SILVERBERG, ROBERT   AC
FLAME KNIFE, THE   HOWARD, ROBERT E. SS
  CONAN THE WANDERER   HOWARD, R./DE CAMP/& AC
  TALES OF CONAN   HOWARD, R. & DE CAMP AC
FLAME MIDGET, THE   LONG, FRANK BELKNAP SS ASF 36 12
  *BEST OF SCIENCE FICTION   CONKLIN, GROFF   AN
  DARK BEASTS, THE   LONG, FRANK BELKNAP   AC
  EARLY LONG, THE   LONG, FRANK BELKNAP   AC
  GATES TO TOMORROW   NORTON, AN.&DONALDY AN
  *HOUNDS OF TINDALOS, THE LONG, FRANK BELKNAP AC
FLAME OF LIFE, THE   LONG, FRANK BELKNAP SS FUT 59 06
  ODD SCIENCE FICTION   LONG, FRANK BELKNAP   AC
FLAME TREE PLANET   SMITH, GEORGE HENRY NV FTP 73
  FLAME TREE PLANET   ELWOOD, ROGER   OA
FLAMES, THE   STAPLEDON, OLAF   NO SKW 47
  TO THE END OF TIME   STAPLEDON, OLAF   AC
  WORLDS OF WONDER   STAPLEDON, OLAF   AC
FLAMING DUCKS AND GIANT BREAD LAFFERTY, R. A. SS ORB 74 15
  ORBIT 15   KNIGHT, DAMON   OA
"FLAP"   STOUT, TIM   SS ADS 75 01
  ARMADA SCI-FI ONE   DAVIS, RICHARD   OA

FLASH CROWD   NIVEN, LARRY   NA   TTT 73
  FLIGHT OF THE HORSE, THE   NIVEN, LARRY   AC
  THREE TRIPS IN TIME AND SPACE   SILVERBERG, ROBERT   OA
FLASH POINT   DOZOIS, GARDNER R. NV   ORB 74 13
  ORBIT 13   KNIGHT, DAMON   OA
FLASK OF FINE ARCTURAN, A   MACAPP, C. C.   SS   GAL 65 02
  NINTH GALAXY READER, THE   POHL, FREDERIK   AN
FLAT HATTER   WISE, DAVID   SS   CLR 73 03
  CLARION III   WILSON, ROBIN SCOTT   OA
FLAT TIGER   DICKSON, GORDON R. SS   GAL 56 03
  DANGER- HUMAN   DICKSON, GORDON R.   AC
FLAT-EYED MONSTER, THE   TENN, WILLIAM   NV   GAL 55 08
  HUMAN ANGLE, THE   TENN, WILLIAM   AC
FLATLAND   SLADEK, JOHN T.   SS   NWB 73 05
  NEW WORLDS QUARTERLY NO. 5   MOORCOCK, MICHAEL   OA
FLATLAND: TWO EXCERPTS   ABBOTT, EDWIN A.   EX   SEE 84
  WONDERMAKERS   HOSKINS, ROBERT   AN
FLATLANDER   NIVEN, LARRY   NV   IFS 67 03
  NEUTRON STAR   NIVEN, LARRY   AC
  SEVEN TRIPS THROUGH TIME AND SPACE   CONKLIN, GROFF   AN
FLAUNA   JONES, RAYMOND F.   NV
  FAR SIDE OF TIME, THE   ELWOOD, ROGER   OA
FLAW   MACDONALD, JOHN D. SS   STS 49 01
  BEST SCIENCE-FICTION STORIES: 1950, THE BLEILER & DIKTY   AN
FLESH-MAN FROM FAR WIDE, THE   BUNCH, DAVID R.   SS   AMZ 59 11
  MODERAN   BUNCH, DAVID R.   AC
FLIES   ASIMOV, ISAAC   SS   FSF 53 06
  NIGHTFALL AND OTHER STORIES   ASIMOV, ISAAC   AC
  SCIENCE FICTION TERROR TALES   CONKLIN, GROFF   AN
FLIES   SILVERBERG, ROBERT SS   DVS 67 01
  BEST OF ROBERT SILVERBERG, THE   SILVERBERG, ROBERT   AC
  DANGEROUS VISIONS   ELLISON, HARLAN   OA
  EARTH'S OTHER SHADOW   SILVERBERG, ROBERT   AC
  PARSECS AND PARABLES   SILVERBERG, ROBERT   AC
FLIGHT INTO DARKNESS   MARLOWE, WEBB   SS   ASF 43 02
  *ADVENTURES IN TIME AND SPACE   HEALY & MCCOMAS   AN
FLIGHT OF A PLASTIC BEE   RANKINE, JOHN   SS   NWR 68 11
  NEW WRITINGS IN SF. 11   CARNELL, JOHN   OA
FLIGHT OF APOLLO, THE   KUNITZ, STANLEY   PM   69
  SCIENCE FICTION   BRODKIN & PEARSON   AN
  SPECULATIONS   SANDERS, THOMAS E.   AN
FLIGHT OF RAVENS, A   BRADBURY, RAY   SS   CFQ 52 WI
  MACHINERIES OF JOY, THE   BRADBURY, RAY   AC
FLIGHT OF THE CENTAURUS   ELAM, RICHARD M. JR. SS
  TEEN-AGE SUPER SCIENCE STORIES   ELAM, RICHARD M. JR. AC
FLIGHT OF THE DAWN STAR   WILLIAMS, ROBERT M. SS   ASF 38 03
  *TREASURY OF SCIENCE FICTION, A   CONKLIN, GROFF   AN
FLIGHT OF THE HORSE, THE (GET A HORSE!)
                                         NIVEN, LARRY   SS   FSF 69 10
  FLIGHT OF THE HORSE, THE   NIVEN, LARRY   AC
FLIGHT ON TITAN   WEINBAUM, STANLEY G. NV ASF 35 01
  MARTIAN ODYSSEY AND OTHER SCIENCE FICTION TALES, A
                                         WEINBAUM, STANLEY G.   AC
  RED PERI, THE   WEINBAUM, STANLEY G.   AC
FLIGHT THAT FAILED, THE   HULL, E. MAYNE   SS   ASF 42 12
  ADVENTURES IN DIMENSION   CONKLIN, GROFF   AN
  *SCIENCE FICTION ADVENTURES IN DIMENSION CONKLIN, GROFF   AN
FLIGHT THAT FAILED, THE (SEE REBIRTH: EARTH)
                                         VAN VOGT, A. E.   TC
FLIGHT TO FOREVER   ANDERSON, POUL   NV   SSS 50 11
  YEAR'S BEST SCIENCE FICTION NOVELS: 1952 BLEILER & DIKTY   AN
FLIGHT TO MALACANDRA (FROM "OUT OF THE SILENT PLANET")
                                         LEWIS, C. S.   EX   LNE 38
  ARMCHAIR SCIENCE READER, THE   GORDON, I. & SORKIN   AN
FLIGHT USELESS, INEXORABLE THE PURSUIT
                                         DISCH, THOMAS M.   SS
  FUN WITH YOUR NEW HEAD   DISCH, THOMAS M.   AC
  NEW TOMORROWS, THE   SPINRAD, NORMAN   AN
FLINTIES, THE   EVANS, I. O.   SS
  SCIENCE FICTION THROUGH THE AGES 2   EVANS, I. O.   AN
FLIRGLEFLIP (THE REMARKABLE FLIRGLEFLIP)
                                         TENN, WILLIAM   SS   FAD 50 05
  OF ALL POSSIBLE WORLDS   TENN, WILLIAM   AC
FLOATING ISLAND, THE (1895)   VERNE, JULES   EX
  JULES VERNE- MASTER OF SCIENCE FICTION   VERNE, JULES   AC
FLOATING ISLAND, THE (1895)   VERNE, JULES   NO
  NOVELS   VERNE, JULES   AC
FLOORS OF HIS HEART, THE   SALLIS, JAMES   SS
  FEW LAST WORDS, A   SALLIS, JAMES   AC
FLORAL TRIBUTE   BLOCH, ROBERT   SS   WRT 49 07
  DEVIL'S GENERATION, THE   GHIDALIA, VIC   AN
FLOURISH OF STRUMPETS, A   MATHESON, RICHARD   SS   PBY 56 11
  SHOCK II   MATHESON, RICHARD   AC
FLOWER ARRANGEMENT   BROWN, ROSEL GEORGE SS   GAL 59 12
  SIXTH GALAXY READER, THE   GOLD, H. L.   AN
FLOWER KID CASHES IN, THE   MALKO, GEORGE   SS   FSF 69 05
  FANTASY: THE LITERATURE OF THE MARVELOUS KELLEY, LEO P.   AN
FLOWER THAT MISSED THE MORNING, THE
                                         DANN, JACK M.
                                         AND ZEBROWSKI, GEORGE SS C
  KILLER PLANTS AND OTHER STORIES, THE   ELWOOD, ROGER   OA
FLOWER-GATHERING   JONES, LANGDON   PM   NWS 69 06
  BEST SF STORIES FROM NEW WORLDS 7   MOORCOCK, MICHAEL   AN
FLOWERED THUNDERMUG, THE   BESTER, ALFRED   NV
  DARK SIDE OF THE EARTH, THE   BESTER, ALFRED   AC
  HUMAN EQUATION, THE   NOLAN, WILLIAM F.   AN
FLOWERING NARCISSUS   SCORTIA, THOMAS N. SS   EIO 73
  CAUTION! INFLAMMABLE!   SCORTIA, THOMAS N.   AC
  EROS IN ORBIT   ELDER, JOSEPH   OA
FLOWERING OF THE STRANGE ORCHID, THE (ALSO AS THE STRANGE
ORCHID)   WELLS, H. G.   SS   PMB 94 08
  COUNTRY OF THE BLIND, THE   WELLS, H. G.   AC
  INEXPERIENCED GHOST AND NINE OTHER STORIES, THE
                                         WELLS, H. G.   AC
  NIGHTMARE GARDEN   GHIDALIA, VIC   AN
  ROOTS OF EVIL, THE   PARRY, MICHEL   AN

  SHORT STORIES OF H. G. WELLS, THE   WELLS, H. G.   AC
  STOLEN BACILLUS AND OTHER INCIDENTS, THE WELLS, H. G.   AC
  TWENTY-EIGHT SCIENCE FICTION STORIES   WELLS, H. G.   AC
FLOWERING SEASON (KANGAROO COURT)
                                         KIDD, VIRGINIA   NV   ORB 66 01
  FUTURE NOW, THE   HOSKINS, ROBERT   AN
FLOWERS FOR ALGERNON   KEYES, DANIEL   SS   FSF 59 04
  BEST FROM FANTASY AND SCIENCE FICTION: 9
                                         MILLS, ROBERT P.   AN
  BEST SF 4   CRISPIN, EDMUND   AN
  HUGO WINNERS, THE (VOLUME 1)   ASIMOV, ISAAC   AN
  INTRODUCTORY PSYCHOLOGY THROUGH SCIENCE FICTION
                                         KATZ/WARRICK/&   AN
  LATE GREAT FUTURE, THE   FITZ GERALD & DILLON AN
  NIGHT IN FUNLAND   BRONDFIELD, JEROME   AN
  STORIES FROM SCIENCE FICTION   DOHERTY, G. D.   AN
  5TH ANNUAL OF THE YEAR'S BEST S-F, THE   MERRIL, JUDITH   AN
FLOWERS OF THE FOREST, THE   ALDISS, BRIAN W.   SS   SCF 57 08
  WEIRD SHADOWS FROM BEYOND   CARNELL, JOHN   AN
FLOWERS OF VENUS, THE   O'QUINN, VITHALDAS H MS
  FANTASTIC UNIVERSE OMNIBUS, THE   SANTESSON, HANS S.   AN
FLUFFY   STURGEON, THEODORE SS   WRT 47 03
  E PLURIBUS UNICORN   STURGEON, THEODORE   AC
FLUX   MOORCOCK, MICHAEL   NV   NWS 63 07
  LAMBDA I AND OTHER STORIES   CARNELL, JOHN   AN
  MOORCOCK'S BOOK OF MARTYRS   MOORCOCK, MICHAEL   AC
  VOYAGERS IN TIME   SILVERBERG, ROBERT   AN
FLY, THE   LANGELAAN, GEORGE   NV   PBY 57 06
  GHOULS, THE   HAINING, PETER   AN
  PLAYBOY BOOK OF SCIENCE FICTION AND FANTASY, THE
                                         PLAYBOY, EDITORS OF   AN
  SF:58, THE YEAR'S GREATEST SCIENCE FICTION AND FANTASY
                                         MERRIL, JUDITH   AN
FLY, THE   PORGES, ARTHUR   SS   FSF 52 09
  BEST SCIENCE-FICTION STORIES: 1953, THE BLEILER & DIKTY   AN
  BEST SF 6   CRISPIN, EDMUND   AN
  *BEYOND HUMAN KEN   MERRIL, JUDITH   AN
  FIFTY SHORT SCIENCE FICTION TALES   ASIMOV & CONKLIN   AN
FLYING CHAUCER   BRODE, ANTHONY   PM   FSF 56 03
  BEST FROM FANTASY AND SCIENCE FICTION: 6
                                         BOUCHER, ANTHONY   AN
FLYING DUTCHMAN   MOORE, WARD   SS   FSF 56 09
  ADVENTURES IN TOMORROW   CROSSEN, KENDELL F.   AN
FLYING FLOWERS   VASILYEV, MIKHAIL   AN
  DESTINATION: AMALTHEIA   DIXON, RICHARD   AN
  RUSSIAN SCIENCE FICTION   MAGIDOFF, ROBERT   AN
FLYING FOOL, THE   KELLER, DAVID H. MD. SS AMZ 29 07
  TALES FROM UNDERWOOD   KELLER, DAVID H. MD. AC
FLYING HIGH   IONESCO, EUGENE   SS   MAD 57 10
  SF:58, THE YEAR'S GREATEST SCIENCE FICTION AND FANTASY
                                         MERRIL, JUDITH   AN
FLYING ISLAND, THE (FROM "THE THIRD VOYAGE OF GULLIVER", 1726)
                                         SWIFT, JONATHAN   EX
  SCIENCE IN FICTION   BAYLISS, A.E. & J.C. AN
FLYING MACHINE, THE   BRADBURY, RAY   SS   NEW 53 AC
  *GOLDEN APPLES OF THE SUN   BRADBURY, RAY   AC
  S IS FOR SPACE   BRADBURY, RAY   AC
FLYING MAN, THE (THE ADVENT OF THE FLYING MAN)
                                         WELLS, H. G.   SS   PGZ 93 12
  SHORT STORIES OF H. G. WELLS, THE   WELLS, H. G.   AC
  STOLEN BACILLUS AND OTHER INCIDENTS, THE WELLS, H. G.   AC
FLYING MEN, THE (FROM "LAST AND FIRST MEN")
                                         STAPLEDON, OLAF   BX   MTH 30
  *BEYOND TIME AND SPACE   DERLETH, AUGUST   AN
FLYING PAN   YOUNG, ROBERT F.   SS   FSF 56 11
  WORLDS OF ROBERT F. YOUNG, THE   YOUNG, ROBERT F.   AC
FLYING SAUCER MYTH, THE   DEL REY, LESTER   AR   FUN 57 08
  FLYING SAUCERS IN FACT AND FICTION   SANTESSON, HANS S.   AN
FLYING SAUCERS - PEOPLE AND REALITY
                                         BEER, LIONEL   AR
  BEYOND THIS HORIZON   CARRELL, CHRISTOPHER OA
FLYING TEACUP   GOHMAN, FRED   SS   53
  TEEN-AGE OUTER SPACE STORIES   FURMAN, A. L.   AN
FLYING WEATHERCOCK, THE   MITCHELL, EDWARD P. SS   SUN 84 04
  CRYSTAL MAN, THE   MITCHELL, EDWARD P.   AC
FOG   GAULT, WILLIAM C.   SS   TWS 51 06
  TALES OF TIME AND SPACE   OLNEY, ROSS R.   AN
FOG HORN, THE (THE BEAST FROM 20,000 FATHOMS)
                                         BRADBURY, RAY   SS   SEP 51 06
  *GOLDEN APPLES OF THE SUN   BRADBURY, RAY   AC
  R IS FOR ROCKET   BRADBURY, RAY   AC
  SPECULATIONS   SANDERS, THOMAS E.   AN
  VINTAGE BRADBURY, THE   BRADBURY, RAY   AC
FOG, THE   DOLAN, MIKE   SS
  SANTANA MORNING AND OTHER STORIES   DOLAN, MIKE   OC
FOGHORN, THE   ATHERTON, GERTRUDE SS
  VENUS FACTOR, THE   GHIDALIA, V.& ELWOOD AN
FOGHORN, THE   BRADBURY, RAY   PL   SEP 51 06
  PILLAR OF FIRE AND OTHER PLAYS   BRADBURY, RAY   AC
FOLLOWING YONDER STAR   HOAGLAND, RICHARD C. AR IFS 74 12
  BEST FROM IF, THE VOLUME III   BAEN, JAMES   AN
FOLLY TO BE WISE   MASON, DOUGLAS R.   SS   NWR 66 09
  NEW WRITINGS IN SF. 9   CARNELL, JOHN   OA
FOLSOM FLINT, THE   KELLER, DAVID H. MD. SS   52
  FOLSOM FLINT AND OTHER CURIOUS TALES, THE
                                         KELLER, DAVID H. MD. AC
FONDLY FAHRENHEIT   BESTER, ALFRED   SS   FSF 54 08
  BEST FROM FANTASY AND SCIENCE FICTION: 4
                                         BOUCHER, ANTHONY   AN
  LIGHT FANTASTIC, THE   BESTER, ALFRED   AC
  SCIENCE FICTION HALL OF FAME VOLUME 1   SILVERBERG, ROBERT   AN
  SF: AUTHORS' CHOICE 2   HARRISON, HARRY   AN
  SHOCKING THING, A   KNIGHT, DAMON   AN
  SPECTRUM 3   AMIS & CONQUEST   AN
  STARBURST   BESTER, ALFRED   AC
  STARS AROUND US, THE   HOSKINS, ROBERT   AN

```
SURVIVAL PRINTOUT                 TOTAL EFFECT          AN      FOR WHAT PURPOSE?          WEBB, W. T.        SS  NWR 68 11
FOOD FARM, THE          REED, KIT        SS  ORB 67 02        NEW WRITINGS IN SF. 11       CARNELL, JOHN             OA
  ALPHA 6                           SILVERBERG, ROBERT   AN    FOR YOU, THE POSSESSED     BURKE, JONATHAN F.   SS  AUT 53 12
  ORBIT   2                         KNIGHT, DAMON        OA      ALIEN LANDSCAPES             BURKE, JONATHAN F.        AC
  SF12                              MERRIL, JUDITH       AN    FORBIDDEN CITY, THE (RETIEF, WAR CRIMINAL)
  VOYAGES: SCENARIOS FOR A SHIP CALLED EARTH                          LAUMER, KEITH        NV  IFS 67 04
                                    SAUER, ROB           AN      RETIEF: AMBASSADOR TO SPACE  LAUMER, KEITH             AC
  WOMEN OF WONDER                   SARGENT, PAMELA      AN    FORBIDDEN FRUIT            BERGER, MICHAEL      SS  YNW
FOOD GOES IN THE TOP, THE   WORTHINGTON, WILL  SS  SCF 61 08      SCIENCE FICTION STORIES      BRADLEY, JOHANNA          AN
  DECADE THE 1960S                  ALDISS & HARRISON    AN    FORBIDDEN PLANET          CHANDLER, A. BERTRAM SS  FUN 59 07
  UNFRIENDLY FUTURE, THE            BOARDMAN, TOM JR.    AN      BEYOND THE GALACTIC RIM      CHANDLER, A. BERTRAM      DC
FOOD OF THE GODS, THE    CLARKE, ARTHUR C.  SS  PBY 64 05    FORCE OF MORTALITY         SILVERBERG, ROBERT   SS  FUT 57 FL
  LAST TRAIN TO LIMBO               PLAYBOY, EDITORS OF  AN      GODLING, GO HOME!            SILVERBERG, ROBERT        AC
  WIND FROM THE SUN, THE            CLARKE, ARTHUR C.    AC    FORCE THAT THROUGH THE CIRCUIT DRIVES THE CURRENT, THE
FOOD OF THE GODS, THE    WELLS, H. G.       NO  PRS 03 12                            ZELAZNY, ROGER       SS
  SEVEN FAMOUS NOVELS BY H. G. WELLS  WELLS, H. G.       AN      SCIENCE FICTION DISCOVERIES  POHL, C. & F.             OA
FOOD TO ALL FLESH        HENDERSON, ZENNA   SS  FSF 53 12    FORECAST                   JONES, RAYMOND F.    NV  ASF 46 06
  ANYTHING BOX, THE                 HENDERSON, ZENNA     AC      TOYMAKER, THE                JONES, RAYMOND F.         AC
  BEST SF 3                         CRISPIN, EDMUND      AN    FOREIGN HAND TIE, THE      GARRETT, RANDALL     NV  ASF 61 12
  STARS AND UNDER, THE              CRISPIN, EDMUND      AN      14 GREAT TALES OF ESP        STONE, IDELLA P.          AN
FOODLEGGER, THE (SEE F---)  MATHESON, RICHARD  TC            FOREIGNER, THE             BLAKE, E. MICHAEL    SS  INY 72 04
FOOL FROM THE DEPTHS     KLEE, PAUL         IL              INFINITY 4                   HOSKINS, ROBERT           AN
  SCIENCE FICTION                   BRODKIN & PEARSON    AN    FORERUNNER                 SUTTON, JEFF         SS  NEW 73 AN
FOOL'S ERRAND           DEL REY, LESTER    SS  SFQ 51 11      ANDROIDS, TIME MACHINES AND BLUE GIRAFFES
  EARLY DEL REY                     DEL REY, LESTER      AC                                 ELWOOD & GHIDALIA         AN
FOOL'S MATE             ELLIN, STANLEY     SS  SEM 48        FOREST IN THE SKY, THE     LAUMER, KEITH        NV  IFS 67 02
  FIEND IN YOU, THE                 BEAUMONT, CHARLES    AN      RETIEF: AMBASSADOR TO SPACE  LAUMER, KEITH             AC
FOOL'S MATE             SHECKLEY, ROBERT   SS  ASF 53 03      SECOND IF READER OF SCIENCE FICTION, THE  POHL, FREDERICK  AN
  METAL SMILE, THE                  KNIGHT, DAMON        AN    FOREST OF ZIL, THE         NEVILLE, KRIS        SS  AMZ 67 12
  SHARDS OF SPACE                   SHECKLEY, ROBERT     AC      BEST SF: 1967                HARRISON & ALDISS         AN
FOOT IN THE DOOR, A     FRIEDMAN, BRUCE JAY SS  PBY 60 10    FOREVER (AS NED LANG)      SHECKLEY, ROBERT     SS  GAL 59 02
  FULLY AUTOMATED LOVE LIFE OF HENRY KEANRIDGE                    SHARDS OF SPACE              SHECKLEY, ROBERT          AC
                          PLAYBOY, EDITORS OF  AN             FOREVER AND AMEN           BLOCH, ROBERT        SS  WLK 73
  PLAYBOY BOOK OF SCIENCE FICTION AND FANTASY, THE               AND WALK NOW GENTLY THROUGH THE FIRE... ELWOOD, ROGER  OA
                          PLAYBOY, EDITORS OF  AN               BEST SCIENCE FICTION FOR 1973  ACKERMAN, FORREST J.  AN
FOOTBALL MAJORS AT PACIFIC U. (SEE THE SECRET OF THE            COLD CHILLS                  BLOCH, ROBERT             AC
  TERRIBLE TITANS)                  SAMBROT, WILLIAM     TC      GIFTS OF ASTI AND OTHER STORIES OF SCIENCE FICTION, THE
FOOTPRINTS              GILBERT, ROBERT E. SS  FBK 51 08                                  ELWOOD, ROGER             AN
  SCIENCE AND SORCERY               FORD, GARRET         AN    FOREVER AND THE EARTH      BRADBURY, RAY        SS  PLS 50 SP
FOR A BREATH I TARRY     ZELAZNY, ROGER     NV  NWS 66 03     *BIG BOOK OF SCIENCE FICTION  CONKLIN, GROFF            AN
  ALPHA 1                           SILVERBERG, ROBERT   AN      LONG AFTER MIDNIGHT          BRADBURY, RAY             AC
  BEST SF STORIES FROM NEW WORLDS NO. 2, THE                   FOREVER PEOPLE, THE        KIRBY, JACK          CT     70
                          MOORCOCK, MICHAEL    AN               LOOKING AHEAD                ALLEN, D. & L.            AN
  MODERN SCIENCE FICTION            SPINRAD, NORMAN      AN    FOREVER STAND THE STONES   PUMILIA, JOSEPH F.   SS     75
  SURVIVAL PRINTOUT                 TOTAL EFFECT         AN      YEAR'S BEST HORROR STORIES: SERIES IV, THE
  WORLD'S BEST SCIENCE FICTION: 1967  WOLLHEIM & CARR    AN                                 PAGE, GERALD W.           AN
FOR A FOGGY NIGHT       NIVEN, LARRY       SS  FSF 71 07    FOREVER TO A HUDSON BAY BLANKET
  ALL THE MYRIAD WAYS               NIVEN, LARRY         AC                                 TIPTREE, JAMES JR.   SS  FAN 72 08
"FOR A SINGLE YESTERDAY" MARTIN, GEORGE R. R. NV  EPC 75      TEN THOUSAND LIGHT-YEARS FROM HOME  TIPTREE, JAMES JR.   AC
  EPOCH                             ELWOOD & SILVERBERG  OA    FOREVER VOYAGE (SEE AND THE SAILOR, HOME FROM THE SEA)
  SONGS OF STARS AND SHADOWS        MARTIN, GEORGE R. R. AC                                 BRADBURY, RAY
FOR A WHILE THERE, HERBERT MARCUSE, I THOUGHT YOU WERE MAYBE  FOREWARD                   ANDERSON, POUL       SS
  RIGHT ABOUT ALIENATION AND  WILSON, ROBIN SCOTT  SS  FSF 72 07  HOMEBREW                   ANDERSON, POUL            AC
  THOSE WHO CAN: A SCIENCE FICTION READER  WILSON, ROBIN SCOTT  AN  FOREWORD             ALDISS, BRIAN W.     IN
FOR ALL POOR FOLKS AT PICKETWIRE                               ALL ABOUT VENUS              ALDISS, BRIAN W.          AN
                          LAFFERTY, R. A.    SS  EPC 75      FOREWORD                   ANDERSON, POUL       IN
  EPOCH                             ELWOOD & SILVERBERG  OA      QUEEN OF AIR AND DARKNESS AND OTHER STORIES, THE
FOR ALL PRACTICAL PURPOSES  OGILVY, G. S.      PM                                           ANDERSON, POUL            AC
  FANTASIA MATHEMATICA              FADIMAN, CLIFTON     AN    7 CONQUESTS                  ANDERSON, POUL            AC
FOR ALL THE NIGHT       WYNDHAM, JOHN      NV  NWS 58 04    FOREWORD                   ASIMOV, ISAAC        IN
 *OUTWARD URGE, THE                 WYNDHAM & PARKES     AC      ADRIFT IN SPACE AND OTHER STORIES  ELWOOD, ROGER      OA
FOR APOLLO 11           SCHJELDAHL, PETER  PM  BMR 73        GRADUATED ROBOT AND OTHER STORIES, THE  ELWOOD, ROGER    OA
  BAD MOON RISING                   DISCH, THOMAS M.     OA    JOURNEY TO ANOTHER STAR AND OTHER STORIES
FOR C. M. KORNBLUTH     POHL, FREDERIK     MS                                              ELWOOD, ROGER             OA
  SCIENCE FICTION SHOWCASE          KORNBLUTH, MARY      AN    KILLER PLANTS AND OTHER STORIES, THE  ELWOOD, ROGER    OA
FOR EVERY ACTION        MACAPP, C. C.      SS  AMZ 64 05    MIND ANGEL AND OTHER STORIES, THE  ELWOOD, ROGER      OA
  WORLD'S BEST SCIENCE FICTION: 1965  WOLLHEIM & CARR    AN    MISSING WORLD AND OTHER STORIES, THE  ELWOOD, ROGER    OA
FOR FURTHER READING     MISC. MATERIAL     MS              NIGHT OF THE SPHINX AND OTHER STORIES  ELWOOD, ROGER      OA
  SCIENCE FICTION                   BURTON, S. H.        AN    TUNNEL AND OTHER STORIES, THE  ELWOOD, ROGER          OA
FOR G.O.D.'S SAKE       GERROLD, DAVID     NV  GAL 72 07    UNKNOWN, THE                 BENSEN, D. R.             AN
  WHEN HARLIE WAS ONE               GERROLD, DAVID       NO    FOREWORD                   BARTER, ALAN FRANK   IN C
FOR I AM A JEALOUS PEOPLE!  DEL REY, LESTER    SN  SSN 54      UNTRAVELLED WORLDS           BARTER & WILSON           AN
  GODS AND GOLEMS                   DEL REY, LESTER      AC    FOREWORD                   BOARDMAN, TOM JR.    IN
  STAR SHORT NOVELS                 POHL, FREDERIK       OA      SCIENCE FICTION HORIZONS NO. 1  BOARDMAN, TOM JR.   AN
FOR LOVE                BUDRYS, ALGIS      NV  GAL 62 06    FOREWORD                   BRADBURY, RAY        IN
  ALPHA 7                           SILVERBERG, ROBERT   AN      AUTUMN PEOPLE, THE           BRADBURY, RAY             AC
  SEVENTH GALAXY READER, THE        POHL, FREDERIK       AN    MAGIC MAN AND OTHER SCIENCE-FANTASY STORIES
FOR MEN MUST WORK (AUJ 55 08)  BRYNING, FRANK B.  SS  FUN 56 02                            BEAUMONT, CHARLES         AC
  PACIFIC BOOK OF AUSTRALIAN SCIENCE FICTION                    TOMORROW MIDNIGHT            BRADBURY, RAY             AC
                          BAXTER, JOHN         AN            FOREWORD                   BRONDFIELD, JEROME   IN
FOR THE BLOOD IS THE LIFE  CRAWFORD, F. MARION  SS        11    NIGHT IN FUNLAND             BRONDFIELD, JEROME        AN
  ALONE BY NIGHT                    CONGDON, MICHAEL&DON AN    FOREWORD                   BULMER, KENNETH      IN
  SUPERNATURAL READER, THE          CONKLIN, G&L.        AN      NEW WRITINGS IN SF. 22       BULMER, KENNETH           OA
FOR THE DURATION        ANDERSON, POUL     SS  VSF 57 09      NEW WRITINGS IN SF. 23       BULMER, KENNETH           OA
  STRANGERS FROM EARTH              ANDERSON, POUL       AC      NEW WRITINGS IN SF. 24       BULMER, KENNETH           OA
FOR THE FLAG (1896)     VERNE, JULES       EX                NEW WRITINGS IN SF. 25       BULMER, KENNETH           OA
  JULES VERNE- MASTER OF SCIENCE FICTION  VERNE, JULES     AC    NEW WRITINGS IN SF. 26       BULMER, KENNETH           OA
FOR THE PUBLIC          KAHN, BERNARD I.   NV  ASF 46 12      NEW WRITINGS IN SF. 27       BULMER, KENNETH           OA
  SPACE SERVICE                     NORTON, ANDRE        AN      NEW WRITINGS IN SF. 28       BULMER, KENNETH           OA
FOR THE RICH THEY SING- SOMETIMES                              NEW WRITINGS IN SF. 29       BULMER, KENNETH           OA
                          PURDY, KEN W.      SS  PBY 62 05    FOREWORD                   CAMPBELL, JOHN W. JR IN
  PLAYBOY BOOK OF HORROR AND THE SUPERNATURAL, THE              FROM UNKNOWN WORLDS          CAMPBELL, JOHN W. JR AN
                          PLAYBOY, EDITORS OF  AN            FOREWORD                   CARNELL, JOHN        IN
FOR THE SAKE OF GRACE    ELGIN, SUZETTE HADEN NV  FSF 69 05    BEST FROM NEW WORLDS SCIENCE FICTION, THE
  TOMORROW AND TOMORROW, AND TOMORROW...  HEINTZ/HERBERT/JOOS/ AN                            CARNELL, JOHN             AN
  WORLD'S BEST SCIENCE FICTION: 1970  WOLLHEIM & CARR    AN    BEST FROM NEW WRITINGS IN S-F FIRST SELECTION, THE
FOR THE WORLD IS HOLLOW AND I HAVE TOUCHED THE SKY                                          CARNELL, JOHN             AN
  (RIK VOLLAERTS)          BLISH, JAMES       SA  STK 72 08    LAMBDA I AND OTHER STORIES   CARNELL, JOHN             AN
  STAR TREK   8                     BLISH, JAMES         OC    NEW WRITINGS IN SF.  1       CARNELL, JOHN             AN
FOR THOMAS TOMPION      MOORCOCK, MICHAEL  SS              NEW WRITINGS IN SF.  2       CARNELL, JOHN             OA
  NEW S.F., THE                     JONES, LANGDON       OA    NEW WRITINGS IN SF.  3       CARNELL, JOHN             OA
FOR THOSE WHO FOLLOW AFTER  MCLAUGHLIN, DEAN   SS  ASF 51 07    NEW WRITINGS IN SF.  4       CARNELL, JOHN             OA
  APEMAN, SPACEMAN                  STOVER & HARRISON    AN      NEW WRITINGS IN SF.  5       CARNELL, JOHN             OA
FOR VALUE RECEIVED      OFFUTT, ANDREW J.  SS  DVS 72 02    NEW WRITINGS IN SF.  6       CARNELL, JOHN             OA
  AGAIN, DANGEROUS VISIONS          ELLISON, HARLAN      OA    NEW WRITINGS IN SF.  7       CARNELL, JOHN             AN
                                                              NEW WRITINGS IN SF.  7       CARNELL, JOHN             OA
```

FOREWORD   FORGETFULNESS

FOREWORD
  NEW WRITINGS IN SF. 8   CARNELL, JOHN   AN
  NEW WRITINGS IN SF. 8   CARNELL, JOHN   OA
  NEW WRITINGS IN SF. 9   CARNELL, JOHN   AN
  NEW WRITINGS IN SF. 9   CARNELL, JOHN   OA
  NEW WRITINGS IN SF. 10   CARNELL, JOHN   OA
  NEW WRITINGS IN SF. 11   CARNELL, JOHN   OA
  NEW WRITINGS IN SF. 12   CARNELL, JOHN   OA
  NEW WRITINGS IN SF. 13   CARNELL, JOHN   OA
  NEW WRITINGS IN SF. 14   CARNELL, JOHN   OA
  NEW WRITINGS IN SF. 15   CARNELL, JOHN   OA
  NEW WRITINGS IN SF. 16   CARNELL, JOHN   OA
  NEW WRITINGS IN SF. 17   CARNELL, JOHN   OA
  NEW WRITINGS IN SF. 18   CARNELL, JOHN   OA
  NEW WRITINGS IN SF. 19   CARNELL, JOHN   OA
  NEW WRITINGS IN SF. 20   CARNELL, JOHN   OA
FOREWORD   CLARKE, ARTHUR C.   IN
  AUTHENTIC BOOK OF SPACE   CAMPBELL, H. J.   AN
  OF TIME AND STARS   CLARKE, ARTHUR C.   AC
  PRELUDE TO MARS   CLARKE, ARTHUR C.   AC
  THREE FOR TOMORROW   SILVERBERG, ROBERT   OA
FOREWORD   COON, CARLETON S.   IN
  APEMAN, SPACEMAN   STOVER & HARRISON   AN
FOREWORD   CRISPIN, EDMUND   IN
  BEST SF 6   CRISPIN, EDMUND   AN
  BEST SF 7   CRISPIN, EDMUND   AN
FOREWORD   DE CAMP, L. SPRAGUE IN
  WHEELS OF IF, THE   DE CAMP, L. SPRAGUE AC
FOREWORD   DEL REY, LESTER   IN
  *AND SOME WERE HUMAN   DEL REY, LESTER   AC
  DAY THE SUN STOOD STILL, THE   SILVERBERG, ROBERT   OA
  YEAR AFTER TOMORROW, THE   DEL REY, L/MATSCHAT/ AN
FOREWORD   DELANY, SAMUEL R.   IN C
  QUARK/3   DELANY & HACKER   OA
FOREWORD   DERLETH, AUGUST   IN
  NOT LONG FOR THIS WORLD   DERLETH, AUGUST   AC
  *OUTER REACHES, THE   DERLETH, AUGUST   AN
  *TIME TO COME   DERLETH, AUGUST   OA
FOREWORD   DOLAN, MIKE   IN
  SANTANA MORNING AND OTHER STORIES DOLAN, MIKE   OC
FOREWORD   EHRLICH, ANNE H.   IN C
  VOYAGES: SCENARIOS FOR A SHIP CALLED EARTH
                                     SAUER, ROB   AN
FOREWORD   EHRLICH, DR. PAUL R. IN C
  VOYAGES: SCENARIOS FOR A SHIP CALLED EARTH
                                     SAUER, ROB   AN
FOREWORD   ELDER, JOSEPH   IN
  FARTHEST REACHES, THE   ELDER, JOSEPH   OA
FOREWORD   ELWOOD, ROGER   IN
  CHILDREN OF INFINITY   ELWOOD, ROGER   OA
  CHRONICLES OF A COMER AND OTHER RELIGIOUS SCIENCE FICTION
    STORIES   ELWOOD, ROGER   AN
  FAR SIDE OF TIME, THE   ELWOOD, ROGER   OA
FOREWORD   ENGDAHL, SYLVIA   IN
  ANYWHERE, ANYWHEN   ENGDAHL, SYLVIA   OA
FOREWORD   ERNSBERGER, GEORGE   IN
  AVON FANTASY READER, THE   WOLLHEIM &ERNSBERGER AN
  SECOND AVON FANTASY READER, THE   WOLLHEIM &ERNSBERGER AN
FOREWORD   FARMER, PHILIP JOSE IN
  BOOK OF PHILIP JOSE FARMER, THE   FARMER, PHILIP JOSE AC
FOREWORD   FAST, HOWARD   IN
  TIME AND THE RIDDLE   FAST, HOWARD   AC
FOREWORD   GILLINGS, WALTER   IN
  BEST OF E. E. 'DOC' SMITH, THE   SMITH, EDWARD E. PHD AC
FOREWORD   GREENBERG , MARTIN   IN
  ALL ABOUT THE FUTURE   GREENBERG , MARTIN   AN
  JOURNEY TO INFINITY   GREENBERG , MARTIN   AN
  *MEN AGAINST THE STARS   GREENBERG , MARTIN   AN
  ROBOT AND THE MAN, THE   GREENBERG , MARTIN   AN
  TRAVELLERS OF SPACE   GREENBERG , MARTIN   AN
FOREWORD   GUREVICH, G.   IN
  JOURNEY ACROSS THREE WORLDS   ANONYMOUS   AN
FOREWORD   HACKER, MARILYN   IN C
  QUARK/3   DELANY & HACKER   OA
FOREWORD   HIPOLITO, JANE   IN C
  MARS, WE LOVE YOU   HIPOLITO & MCNELLY   AN
FOREWORD   KNIGHT, DAMON   IN
  SCIENCE FICTION OF THE 30'S   KNIGHT, DAMON   AN
FOREWORD   LE GUIN, URSULA K.   IN
  WINDS TWELVE QUARTERS, THE   LE GUIN, URSULA K.   AC
FOREWORD   LEE, CHRISTOPHER   IN
  YEAR'S BEST HORROR STORIES: SERIES II, THE
                                     DAVIS, RICHARD   AN
FOREWORD   LEIBER, FRITZ   IN
  BOOK OF FRITZ LEIBER, THE   LEIBER, FRITZ   AC
  MIND SPIDER AND OTHER STORIES, THE (ACE 76)
                                     LEIBER, FRITZ   AC
  SECOND BOOK OF FRITZ LEIBER, THE   LEIBER, FRITZ   AC
FOREWORD   LLOYD, DANIEL   IN
  NEW WRITINGS IN SF. 21   CARNELL, JOHN   OA
FOREWORD   LORY, ROBERT   IN
  HARVEST OF HOODWINKS, A   LORY, ROBERT   DC
FOREWORD   MCCAFFREY, ANNE   IN
  ALCHEMY AND ACADEME   MCCAFFREY, ANNE   OA
FOREWORD   MCNELLY, WILLIS H.   IN
  MARS, WE LOVE YOU   HIPOLITO & MCNELLY   AN
FOREWORD   MIRRIELEES, EDITH   IN
  WORLD OF WONDER   PRATT, FLETCHER   AN
FOREWORD   POHL, FREDERIK   IN
  AMERICAN GOVERNMENT THROUGH SCIENCE FICTION
                                     OLANDER/GREENBERG/& AN
  EXPLORERS, THE   KORNBLUTH, C. M.   AC
FOREWORD   ROBINSON, SPIDER   IN
  CALLAHAN'S CROSSTIME SALOON   ROBINSON, SPIDER   AC
FOREWORD   RODDENBERRY, GENE   IN
  STAR TREK: THE NEW VOYAGES   MARSHAK, S&CULBREATH OA

FOREWORD   ROSS, JOSEPH   IN
  BEST OF AMAZING, THE   ROSS, JOSEPH   AN
FOREWORD   SERLING, ROD   IN
  ROD SERLING'S THE TWILIGHT ZONE (CHILLING STORIES FROM)
                                     SERLING, ROD   OC
  ROD SERLING'S TWILIGHT ZONE REVISITED SERLING, ROD   OC
FOREWORD   SILVERBERG, ROBERT   IN
  NO MIND OF MAN   SILVERBERG, ROBERT   OA
  THREE TRIPS IN TIME AND SPACE   SILVERBERG, ROBERT   OA
FOREWORD   SIMAK, CLIFFORD D.   IN
  FUTURE CITY   ELWOOD, ROGER   OA
FOREWORD   SPINRAD, NORMAN   IN
  MODERN SCIENCE FICTION   SPINRAD, NORMAN   AN
FOREWORD   STONG, PHILIP D.   IN
  OTHER WORLDS, THE   STONG, PHILIP D.   AN
FOREWORD   STURGEON, THEODORE   IN
  LONG NIGHT OF WAITING AND OTHER STORIES ELWOOD, ROGER OA
  STURGEON IS ALIVE AND WELL...   STURGEON, THEODORE   AC
FOREWORD   TALL, STEPHEN   IN
  STARDUST VOYAGES, THE   TALL, STEPHEN   AC
FOREWORD   VANCE, JACK   IN
  EIGHT FANTASMS AND MAGICS   VANCE, JACK   AC
FOREWORD   WHITE, TED   IN
  BEST FROM FANTASTIC, THE   WHITE, TED   AN
FOREWORD   WILSON, R.   IN C
  UNTRAVELLED WORLDS   BARTER & WILSON   AN
FOREWORD   YEFREMOV, IVAN   IN
  STORIES   YEFREMOV, IVAN   AC
FOREWORD TO "ALL YOU ZOMBIES-" PANSHIN, ALEXEI   IN
  MIRROR OF INFINITY, THE   SILVERBERG, ROBERT   AN
FOREWORD TO "COMMON TIME"   KNIGHT, DAMON   AR   SFF 57
  MIRROR OF INFINITY, THE   SILVERBERG, ROBERT   AN
FOREWORD TO "I HAVE NO MOUTH, AND I MUST SCREAM"
                             MCNELLY, WILLIS E.   IN
  MIRROR OF INFINITY, THE   SILVERBERG, ROBERT   AN
FOREWORD TO "NIGHTFALL"   HARRISON, HARRY   IN
  MIRROR OF INFINITY, THE   SILVERBERG, ROBERT   AN
FOREWORD TO "PRIVATE EYE"   BLISH, JAMES   IN
  MIRROR OF INFINITY, THE   SILVERBERG, ROBERT   AN
FOREWORD TO "SPECIALIST"   CONQUEST, ROBERT   IN
  MIRROR OF INFINITY, THE   SILVERBERG, ROBERT   AN
FOREWORD TO "THE GAME OF RAT AND DRAGON"
                             AMIS, KINGSLEY   IN
  MIRROR OF INFINITY, THE   SILVERBERG, ROBERT   AN
FOREWORD TO "THE HEAT DEATH OF THE UNIVERSE"
                             ALDISS, BRIAN W.   IN
  MIRROR OF INFINITY, THE   SILVERBERG, ROBERT   AN
FOREWORD TO "THE LIBRARY OF BABEL"
                             ROGERS, IVER   IN
  MIRROR OF INFINITY, THE   SILVERBERG, ROBERT   AN
FOREWORD TO "THE SENTINEL"   CLARESON, THOMAS D. IN
  MIRROR OF INFINITY, THE   SILVERBERG, ROBERT   AN
FOREWORD TO "THE STAR"   WILLIAMSON, JACK   IN
  MIRROR OF INFINITY, THE   SILVERBERG, ROBERT   AN
FOREWORD TO "THE SUBLIMINAL MAN"
                             FRANKLIN, H. BRUCE   AR   70
  MIRROR OF INFINITY, THE   SILVERBERG, ROBERT   AN
FOREWORD TO "TWILIGHT"   BUDRYS, ALGIS   IN
  MIRROR OF INFINITY, THE   SILVERBERG, ROBERT   AN
FOREWORD 1- THE SECOND REVOLUTION
                             ASIMOV, ISAAC   IN DVS 67 01
  DANGEROUS VISIONS   ELLISON, HARLAN   OA
FOREWORD 2- HARLAN AND I   ASIMOV, ISAAC   IN DVS 67 01
  DANGEROUS VISIONS   ELLISON, HARLAN   OA
FOREWORD: A SPATE OF CHANGES DEL REY, LESTER   IN
  BEST SCIENCE FICTION STORIES OF THE YEAR (1973)
                                     DEL REY, LESTER   AN
FOREWORD: ALTERNATE POSSIBILITIES
                             DEL REY, LESTER   IN
  BEST SCIENCE FICTION STORIES OF THE YEAR (1971)
                                     DEL REY, LESTER   AN
FOREWORD: FIFTY YEARS OF SCIENCE FICTION
                             DEL REY, LESTER   IN
  BEST SCIENCE FICTION STORIES OF THE YEAR (1975)
                                     DEL REY, LESTER   AN
FOREWORD: FOUR THEMES FOR FOUR FUTURES
                             ASIMOV, ISAAC   IN   FFU 71
  FOUR FUTURES   SILVERBERG, ROBERT   OA
FOREWORD: MAN OF A THOUSAND FACES
                             GOULART, RON   IN
  CHAMELEON CORPS & OTHER SHAPE CHANGERS, THE
                                     GOULART, RON   AC
FOREWORD: POPULAR MECHANICS GOULART, RON   IN
  NUTZENBOLTS   GOULART, RON   AC
FOREWORD: THE SENSE OF WONDER DEL REY, LESTER   IN
  BEST SCIENCE FICTION STORIES OF THE YEAR (1974)
                                     DEL REY, LESTER   AN
FOREWORD: THE SPICE OF VARIETY DEL REY, LESTER   IN
  BEST SCIENCE FICTION STORIES OF THE YEAR (1972)
                                     DEL REY, LESTER   AN
FOREWORD- WHY READ SCIENCE FICTION?
                             ASIMOV, ISAAC   IN
  3000 YEARS OF FANTASY AND SCIENCE FICTION
                                     DE CAMP, L. S.&C.   AN
FORGET-ME-NOT   TAYLOR, BERNARD   SS   NEW 75 AN
  YEAR'S BEST HORROR STORIES: SERIES III, THE
                                     DAVIS, RICHARD   AN
FORGET-ME-NOT   TEMPLE, WILLIAM F.   NV OWS 50 09
  BEST SCIENCE-FICTION STORIES: 1951, THE BLEILER & DIKTY AN
FORGETFULNESS   CAMPBELL, JOHN W. JR SN   ASF 37 06
  *BEST OF JOHN W. CAMPBELL, THE   CAMPBELL, JOHN W. JR AC
  CLOAK OF AESIR   CAMPBELL, JOHN W. JR AC
FORGETFULNESS   STUART, DON A.   SN   ASF 37 06
  *ADVENTURES IN TIME AND SPACE   HEALY & MCCOMAS   AN
  ASTOUNDING-ANALOG READER, THE VOLUME ONE HARRISON & ALDISS AN
  CITIES OF WONDER   KNIGHT, DAMON   AN

FORGIVE US OUR DEBTS (ALSO AS RECESSIONAL)
                              DEL REY, LESTER   SS   FUT 52 05
   MASTERS OF SCIENCE FICTION   HOWARD, IVAN   AN
FORGIVENESS OF TENCHU TAEN, THE
                              KUMMER, FREDERICK A. SS   ASF 38 11
   TRAVELLERS OF SPACE   GREENBERG , MARTIN   AN
FORGOTTEN (THE FORGOTTEN MAN OF SPACE)
                              MILLER, P. SCHUYLER SS   WOS 33 04
   *STRANGE PORTS OF CALL   DERLETH, AUGUST   AN
   TITAN, THE   MILLER, P. SCHUYLER   AC
FORGOTTEN CREATOR OF WEIRD TALES, THE
                              MOSKOWITZ, SAM   IN
   WORLDS OF WEIRD   MARGULIES, LEO   AN
FORGOTTEN ENEMY, THE   CLARKE, ARTHUR C.   SS   NWS 49 05
   MORE PENGUIN SCIENCE FICTION   ALDISS, BRIAN W.   AN
   OF TIME AND STARS   CLARKE, ARTHUR C.   AC
   PRELUDE TO MARS   CLARKE, ARTHUR C.   AC
   REACH FOR TOMORROW   CLARKE, ARTHUR C.   AC
   SCIENCE FACT/FICTION   FARRELL/GAGE/&   AN
   SF: AUTHORS' CHOICE 4   HARRISON, HARRY   AN
   STARS AND UNDER, THE   CRISPIN, EDMUND   AN
   *STORIES FOR TOMORROW   SLOANE, WILLIAM   AN
FORGOTTEN KNOWLEDGE   REED, CLIFFORD C.   SN   SFB 59 11
   MARTIAN ENTERPRISE   REED, CLIFFORD C.   AC
FORGOTTEN MAN OF SPACE, THE (SEE FORGOTTEN)
                              MILLER, P. SCHUYLER TC
FORGOTTEN WORLD   HAMILTON, EDMOND   NV   TWS 46 WI
   GIANT ANTHOLOGY OF SCIENCE FICTION   MARGULIES & FRIEND   AN
   RACE TO THE STARS   MARGULIES & FRIEND   AN
FORLESEN   WOLFE, GENE   NV   ORB 74 14
   ORBIT 14   KNIGHT, DAMON   OA
FORM IN REMISSION   SCHAEFFER, ROBIN   SS   BER 74
   BERSERKERS, THE   ELWOOD, ROGER   OA
FORM IN REMISSION (AS ROBIN SCHAEFFER)
                              MALZBERG, BARRY N.   SS   BER 74
   BEST OF BARRY N. MALZBERG, THE MALZBERG, BARRY N.   AC
FORM OF SPACE, THE   CALVINO, ITALO   SS
   COSMICOMICS   CALVINO, ITALO   OC
FORM 5640: REPORT OF A MALFUNCTION
                              KAWIN, BRUCE   SS   DPM 67
   INSIDE INFORMATION   MOWSHOWITZ, ABBE   AN
FORMS OF THINGS UNKNOWN   LEWIS, C. S.   SS   66
   DARK TOWER AND OTHER STORIES, THE   LEWIS, C. S.   AC
FORMULA FOR IMMORTALITY   DNIEPROV, ANATOLY   NV   63
   ULTIMATE THRESHOLD, THE   GINSBURG, MIRRA   AN
FORMULA FOR THE IMPOSSIBLE   LUKODIANOV, ISAI
                     AND VOISKUNSKY, YEVGENY SS C
   RUSSIAN SCIENCE FICTION, 1968   MAGIDOFF, ROBERT   AN
FORSAKING ALL OTHERS   DEL REY, LESTER   SS   UNK 39 08
   *AND SOME WERE HUMAN   DEL REY, LESTER   AC
FORT IRON   ST. CLAIR, MARGARET SS   SFQ 55 11
   CHANGE THE SKY AND OTHER STORIES   ST. CLAIR, MARGARET   AC
FORTITUDE   VONNEGUT, KURT JR.   SS   PBY 68 09
   HUMAN-MACHINES   SCORTIA & ZEBROWSKI   AN
   MASKS   PLAYBOY, EDITORS OF   AN
FORTRESS SHIP (ALSO AS WITHOUT A THOUGHT)
                              SABERHAGEN, FRED   SS   IFS 63 01
   9TH ANNUAL OF THE YEAR'S BEST S-F, THE   MERRILL, JUDITH   AN
FORTUNATE PERSON (SEE THE LUCKIEST MAN IN THE WORLD)
                              SHECKLEY, ROBERT   TC
FORTUNE HUNTER   ANDERSON, POUL   SS   INY 72 04
   BEST SCIENCE FICTION OF THE YEAR, THE NO. 2
                              CARR, TERRY   AN
   INFINITY 4   HOSKINS, ROBERT   OA
FORTY YEARS OF C. L. MOORE   DEL REY, LESTER   IN
   BEST OF C. L. MOORE, THE   MOORE, C. L.   AC
FOSTER PORTFOLIO, THE   VONNEGUT, KURT JR.   SS   COL 51 09
   CANARY IN A CAT HOUSE   VONNEGUT, KURT JR.   AC
   WELCOME TO THE MONKEY HOUSE   VONNEGUT, KURT JR.   AC
FOSTER, YOU'RE DEAD   DICK, PHILIP K.   NV   STR 54 03
   BEST OF PHILIP K. DICK, THE   DICK, PHILIP K.   AC
   STAR SCIENCE FICTION STORIES NO. 3   POHL, FREDERIK   OA
FOUND OBJECTS   PETAJA, EMIL   SS
   STARDRIFT AND OTHER FANTASTIC FLOTSAM   PETAJA, EMIL   AC
FOUNDATION   ASIMOV, ISAAC   NO   GNM 51
   FOUNDATION TRILOGY, THE   ASIMOV, ISAAC   AC
FOUNDATION   ASIMOV, ISAAC   NV   ASF 42 05
   FOUNDATION   ASIMOV, ISAAC   NO
   GALACTIC EMPIRES VOLUME ONE   ALDISS, BRIAN W.   AN
FOUNDATION AND EMPIRE   ASIMOV, ISAAC   NO   GNM 52
   FOUNDATION TRILOGY, THE   ASIMOV, ISAAC   AC
FOUNDATION OF SCIENCE FICTION SUCCESS, THE
                              ASIMOV, ISAAC   PM   FSF 54 10
   BEST FROM FANTASY AND SCIENCE FICTION: 4
                              BOUCHER, ANTHONY   AN
   EARTH IS ROOM ENOUGH   ASIMOV, ISAAC   AC
FOUNDER'S DAY   LAUMER, KEITH   NV   FSF 66 07
   ONCE THERE WAS A GIANT   LAUMER, KEITH   AC
FOUNDING FATHER   ASIMOV, ISAAC   SS   GAL 65 10
   BUY JUPITER AND OTHER STORIES   ASIMOV, ISAAC   AC
   SCIENCE FACT/FICTION   FARRELL/GAGE/&   AN
   SF: AUTHORS' CHOICE   HARRISON, HARRY   AN
   THEMES IN SCIENCE FICTION   KELLEY, LEO P.   AN
FOUNDING FATHER   BONE, J. F.   NA   GAL 62 04
   13 ABOVE THE NIGHT   CONKLIN, GROFF   AN
FOUNDING FATHER   SIMAK, CLIFFORD D.   SS   GAL 57 05
   BEST SCIENCE FICTION STORIES OF CLIFFORD D. SIMAK
                              SIMAK, CLIFFORD D.   AC
   OTHER WORLDS OF CLIFFORD SIMAK SIMAK, CLIFFORD D.   AC
   *WORLDS OF CLIFFORD SIMAK, THE SIMAK, CLIFFORD D.   AC
FOUNDING FATHERS   BLOCH, ROBERT   SS   FUN 56 07
   TALES IN A JUGULAR VEIN   BLOCH, ROBERT   AC
FOUNDING OF CIVILIZATION, THE   YAROV, ROMAIN   SS   ISF 68 06
   OTHER WORLDS, OTHER SEAS   SUVIN, DARKO   AN
   RUSSIAN SCIENCE FICTION, 1968   MAGIDOFF, ROBERT   AN

FOUNDLING STARS, THE   CLEMENT, HAL   SS   IFS 66 08
   SECOND IF READER OF SCIENCE FICTION, THE POHL, FREDERIK   AN
   SMALL CHANGES   CLEMENT, HAL   AC
FOUNTAIN OF FORCE   CARRINGTON, GRANT
                     AND ZEBROWSKI, GEORGE SS C INY 72 04
   INFINITY 4   HOSKINS, ROBERT   OA
FOUNTAIN, THE   BOND, NELSON S.   SN   UNK 41 06
   MR. MERGENTHWIRKER'S LOBBIES AND OTHER FANTASTIC TALES
                              BOND, NELSON S.   AC
FOUR BRANDS OF IMPOSSIBLE   KAGAN, NORMAN   NV   FSF 64 09
   SCHOOL AND SOCIETY THROUGH SCIENCE FICTION
                              OLANDER/GREENBERG/&   AN
   SCIENCE FICTION ARGOSY, A   KNIGHT, DAMON   AN
   WORLD'S BEST SCIENCE FICTION: 1965   WOLLHEIM & CARR   AN
FOUR CARTOONS   WILSON, GAHAN   CT   FSF 67
   BEST FROM FANTASY AND SCIENCE FICTION: 17
                              FERMAN, EDWARD L.   AN
FOUR GHOSTS IN HAMLET   LEIBER, FRITZ   NV   FSF 65 01
   BEST FROM FANTASY AND SCIENCE FICTION: 15
                              FERMAN, EDWARD L.   AN
   WORLDS FAR AND NEAR   CARR, TERRY   AN
   YOU'RE ALL ALONE   LEIBER, FRITZ   AC
FOUR IN ONE   KNIGHT, DAMON   NV   GAL 53 02
   BEST SF 3   CRISPIN, EDMUND   AN
   GALAXY SCIENCE FICTION OMNIBUS GOLD, H. L.   AN
   IN DEEP   KNIGHT, DAMON   AC
   OUT OF THIS WORLD 5   WILLIAMS-ELLIS& OWEN   AN
   SECOND GALAXY READER OF SCIENCE FICTION GOLD, H. L. AN
   TO THE STARS   SILVERBERG, ROBERT   AN
FOUR SIDES OF INFINITY   LAFFERTY, R. A.   GR
   FRONTIERS 2: THE NEW MIND   ELWOOD, ROGER   OA
FOUR-COLOR PROBLEM   BAYLEY, BARRINGTON J NV   NWQ 71 02
   NEW WORLDS QUARTERLY NO. 2   MOORCOCK, MICHAEL   AN
FOUR-DIMENSIONAL ROLLER-PRESS, THE
                              OLSEN, BOB   SS   AMZ 27 06
   EVERY BOY'S BOOK OF SCIENCE FICTION   WOLLHEIM, DONALD A.   AN
FOUR-DIMENSIONAL SPACE (1885) ANONYMOUS   AR   NTR 85
   FUTURE PERFECT   FRANKLIN, H. BRUCE   AN
FOUR-FACED VISITORS OF EZEKIEL, THE
                              ORTON, ARTHUR W.   SS   ASF 61 03
   ENCOUNTERS WITH ALIENS   EARLEY, GEORGE W.   AN
FOUR-HOUR FUGUE, THE   BESTER, ALFRED   SS   ASF 74 06
   BEST SF: 1974   HARRISON & ALDISS   AN
   LIGHT FANTASTIC, THE   BESTER, ALFRED   AC
   1975 ANNUAL WORLD'S BEST SF, THE   WOLLHEIM, DONALD A.   AN
FOUR, THE   SILVERBERG, ROBERT   SS   SFS 58 08
   DIMENSION THIRTEEN   SILVERBERG, ROBERT   AC
FOURTEEN STATIONS ON THE NORTHERN LINE
                              GORDON, GILES   SS
   NEW S.F., THE   JONES, LANGDON   OA
FOURTH DYNASTY, THE   WINTERBOTHAM, R. R. SS   ASF 36 12
   OMNIBUS OF SCIENCE FICTION   CONKLIN, GROFF   AN
FOURTH POWER, THE   BRUNNER, JOHN   NV   NWS 60 04
   *OUT OF MY MIND   BRUNNER, JOHN   AC
FOURTH PROFESSION, THE   NIVEN, LARRY   NV   QRK 71 04
   BEST SCIENCE FICTION OF THE YEAR, THE   CARR, TERRY   AN
   HOLE IN SPACE, A   NIVEN, LARRY   AC
   QUARK/4   DELANY & HACKER   OA
   1972 ANNUAL WORLD'S BEST SF, THE   WOLLHEIM, DONALD A.   AN
FOURTH SALLY, OR HOW TRURL BUILT A FEMFATALATRON TO SAVE
   PRINCE PANTAGOON..., THE   LEM, STANISLAW   SS
   CYBERIAD, THE   LEM, STANISLAW   OC
FOURTH-DIMENSIONAL DEMONSTRATOR, THE
                              LEINSTER, MURRAY   SS   ASF 35 12
   FUTURE MAKERS, THE   HAINING, PETER   AN
   OTHER WORLDS, THE   STONG, PHILIP D.   AN
   SIDEWISE IN TIME   LEINSTER, MURRAY   AC
   TWISTS IN TIME   LEINSTER, MURRAY   AC
FOWLING, THE   BULMER, KENNETH   EX
   BEYOND THIS HORIZON   CARRELL, CHRISTOPHER   OA
FOX AND THE FOREST, THE (TO THE FUTURE)
                              BRADBURY, RAY   SS   COL 50 05
   BEST SCIENCE-FICTION STORIES: 1951, THE BLEILER & DIKTY   AN
   FRONTIERS IN SPACE   BLEILER & DIKTY   AN
   *ILLUSTRATED MAN, THE   BRADBURY, RAY   AC
   MINDWORM, THE   ANONYMOUS   AN
   VINTAGE BRADBURY, THE   BRADBURY, RAY   AC
FOX WOMAN, THE   MERRITT, A.   NV   46
   FOX WOMAN & OTHER STORIES, THE MERRITT, A.   AC
FOXHOLES OF MARS, THE   LEIBER, FRITZ   SS   TWS 52 06
   BEST OF FRITZ LEIBER, THE   LEIBER, FRITZ   AC
   *BEYOND HUMAN KEN   MERRIL, JUDITH   AN
   PAIL OF AIR, A   LEIBER, FRITZ   AC
FRAGMENT OF A DREAM   WANDREI, DONALD   SS
   EYE AND THE FINGER   WANDREI, DONALD   AC
FRAGMENTARY BLUE   DANN, JACK M.   NV   FAN 75 04
   FUTURE PASTIMES   EDELSTEIN, SCOTT   OA
FRANCES HARKINS   GOGGIN, RICHARD   SS   FSF 52 12
   SPECULATIONS   SANDERS, THOMAS E.   AN
   17 X INFINITY   CONKLIN, GROFF   AN
FRANCHISE   ASIMOV, ISAAC   SS   IFS 55 08
   ALIEN EARTH AND OTHER STORIES   ELWOOD & MOSKOWITZ   AN
   EARTH IS ROOM ENOUGH   ASIMOV, ISAAC   AC
   FIRST WORLD OF IF, THE   QUINN & WULFF   AN
   INSIDE INFORMATION   MOWSHOWITZ, ABBE   AN
   POLITICAL SCIENCE FICTION   GREENBERG& WARRICK   AN
FRANCHISE   NEVILLE, KRIS   SS   ASF 51 02
   *STORIES FOR TOMORROW   SLOANE, WILLIAM   AN
FRANK MERRIWELL IN THE WHITE HOUSE
                              MOORE, WARD   NV   GAL 73 11
   AMERICAN GOVERNMENT THROUGH SCIENCE FICTION
                              OLANDER/GREENBERG/&   AN
FRANK READE JUNIOR'S AIR WONDER (1876)
                              SENARENS, LOUIS P.   SS   BNY 76
   ANDROIDS, TIME MACHINES AND BLUE GIRAFFES
                              ELWOOD & GHIDALIA   AN

FRANK READE JUNIOR'S AIR WONDER (1876)
  STRANGE SIGNPOSTS   ELWOOD & MOSKOWITZ   AN
FRANKENSTEIN   COLOMBO, JOHN ROBERT PM   69
  HOLDING YOUR EIGHT HANDS   LUCIE-SMITH, EDWARD   AN
FRANKENSTEIN UNLIMITED   HIGHSTONE, H. A.   SS ASF 36 12
  FAR BOUNDARIES   DERLETH, AUGUST   AN
FRANKENSTEIN, OR, THE MODERN PROMETHEUS
            SHELLEY, MARY W.   EX WRT 32 05
  FROM FRANKENSTEIN TO ANDROMEDA BROWN, JAMES GOLDIE AN
"FRANZ KAFKA" BY JORGE LUIS BORGES
          GREENBERG , ALVIN   SS NAR 70 08
  BEST SF: 1970   HARRISON & ALDISS   AN
FRAYED STRING ON THE STRETCHED FOREFINGER OF TIME, THE
          BIGGLE, LLOYD JR. SS FSF 71 05
  BEST SCIENCE FICTION OF THE YEAR, THE CARR, TERRY   AN
FREAK SHOW   DEFORD, MIRIAM ALLEN SS FUN 58 02
  ELSEWHERE, ELSEWHEN, ELSEHOW DEFORD, MIRIAM ALLEN AC
  GENTLE INVADERS   SANTESSON, HANS S.   AN
FREAK, THE   WYAL, PG   SS FSF 69 04
  AMERICAN GOVERNMENT THROUGH SCIENCE FICTION
          OLANDER/GREENBERG/& AN
FREAKS (SPURS)   ROBBINS, TOD   SS
  GHOULS, THE   HAINING, PETER   AN
FRED ONE   RANSOM, JAMES   SS FSF 64 04
  BEST FROM FANTASY AND SCIENCE FICTION: 14
          DAVIDSON, AVRAM   AN
FREE AGENT (SIXTY-YEAR EXTENSION)
          NOURSE, ALAN E.   NV PLS 54 05
  RX FOR TOMORROW   NOURSE, ALAN E.   AC
FREE AS AIR   KELLER, DAVID H. MD. SS AMZ 31 06
  TALES FROM UNDERWOOD KELLER, DAVID H. MD. AC
FREE AT LAST   GOULART, RON   SS INY 73 05
  INFINITY 5   HOSKINS, ROBERT   OA
  NUTZENBOLTS   GOULART, RON   AC
FREE CITY BLUES   EKLUND, GORDON   NV UNI 73 03
  UNIVERSE 3   CARR, TERRY   OA
FREE DIRT   BEAUMONT, CHARLES SS FSF 55 05
  GRAVEYARD READER, THE CONKLIN, GROFF   AN
  HUNGER AND OTHER STORIES, THE BEAUMONT, CHARLES AC
  TWENTY YEARS OF FANTASY & SCIENCE FICTION
          FERMAN & MILLS   AN
FREE FLIGHT   HUBBARD, P. M.   PM FSF 56 04
  BEST FROM FANTASY AND SCIENCE FICTION: 6
          BOUCHER, ANTHONY   AN
FREE MEN   HEINLEIN, ROBERT A. NV NEW 66 AC
  WORLDS OF ROBERT A. HEINLEIN, THE HEINLEIN, ROBERT A. AC
FREE PASS TO THE CARNIVAL, A EFFINGER, GEO. ALEC SS FSF 71 05
  CLARION   WILSON, ROBIN SCOTT OA
FREE VACATION   MACFARLANE, WALLACE SS ASF 67 10
  ANALOG 7   CAMPBELL, JOHN W. JR AN
FREEDOM   REYNOLDS, MACK   NV ASF 61 02
  BEST OF MACK REYNOLDS, THE REYNOLDS, MACK   AC
  POLITICAL SCIENCE FICTION GREENBERG& WARRICK AN
  7TH ANNUAL OF THE YEAR'S BEST S-F, THE MERRIL, JUDITH AN
FREEDOM OF SPACE (THE OTHER SIDE OF THE SKY)
          CLARKE, ARTHUR C. SS INF 57 10
  OTHER SIDE OF THE SKY, THE CLARKE, ARTHUR C.   AC
FREEWAY FOR DRACULAS, A LUPOFF, RICHARD A. NV BER 74 05
  BERSERKERS, THE   ELWOOD, ROGER   OA
FREEWAY, THE   JOHNSON, GEORGE C. SS GAM 63 01
  MAN AGAINST TOMORROW NOLAN, WILLIAM F.   AN
FRESH GUY   TUBB, E. C.   SS SCF 58 06
  SF:59, THE YEAR'S GREATEST SCIENCE FICTION AND FANTASY
          MERRIL, JUDITH   AN
  SPECULATIONS   SANDERS, THOMAS E.   AN
  TEN FROM TOMORROW   TUBB, E. C.   AC
  WEIRD SHADOWS FROM BEYOND CARNELL, JOHN   AN
FRESHMAN ANGLE, THE   PANGBORN, EDGAR   NV TTM 73
  TEN TOMORROWS   ELWOOD, ROGER   OA
FRICTIONAL LOSSES   CAMPBELL, JOHN W. JR NV ASF 36 07
  WHO GOES THERE?   CAMPBELL, JOHN W. JR AC
FRIDAY   KIPPAX, JOHN   SS NWS 59 02
  OUT OF THIS WORLD 1   WILLIAMS-ELLIS& OWEN AN
FRIDAY'S CHILD (D. C. FONTANA) BLISH, JAMES SA STK 69 03
  STAR TREK 3   BLISH, JAMES   OC
FRIEND FROM THE STARS SARGENT, PAMELA SS
  MISSING WORLD AND OTHER STORIES, THE ELWOOD, ROGER   OA
FRIEND ISLAND   STEVENS, FRANCIS SS ASW 18 09
  UNDER THE MOONS OF MARS MOSKOWITZ, SAM   AN
FRIEND OF THE FAMILY WILSON, RICHARD SS STR 53 02
  STAR SCIENCE FICTION STORIES NO. 2 POHL, FREDERIK OA
FRIEND TO ALEXANDER, A THURBER, JAMES SS NYM 42 01
  PERCHANCE TO DREAM   KNIGHT, DAMON   AN
  TRAVELERS IN TIME   STERN, PHILIP VAN D. AN
FRIEND TO MAN   KORNBLUTH, C. M. SS TSF 51 SP
  BEST OF C. M. KORNBLUTH, THE KORNBLUTH, C. M.   AC
  BEST SCIENCE FICTION STORIES OF C. M. KORNBLUTH
          KORNBLUTH, C. M.   AC
  EXPLORERS, THE   KORNBLUTH, C. M.   AC
  MINDWORM AND OTHER STORIES, THE KORNBLUTH, C. M. AC
FRIEND TO MAN, A   ELLISON, HARLAN SS FUN 59 10
  FROM THE LAND OF FEAR ELLISON, HARLAN   AC
FRIEND TO MAN, A (LET ME LIVE IN A HOUSE)
          OLIVER, CHAD   NV USF 54 03
  EDGE OF FOREVER, THE OLIVER, CHAD   AC
FRIENDLY DEMON, THE (1726) DEFOE, DANIEL SS FSF 51 02
  BEST FROM FANTASY AND SCIENCE FICTION BOUCHER & MCCOMAS AN
FRIENDLY MAN, THE   DICKSON, GORDON R. SS ASF 51 02
  ANCIENT, MY ENEMY   DICKSON, GORDON R.   AC
FRIENDS AND ENEMIES LEIBER, FRITZ   SS INF 57 04
  IF THIS GOES ON   NUETZEL, CHARLES   AN
  WORLDS OF FRITZ LEIBER, THE LEIBER, FRITZ   AC
FRIENDS?   GHIDALIA, ROBERTA SS NEW 73 AN
  MORE LITTLE MONSTERS ELWOOD & GHIDALIA   AN
FRIGHTENED TREE, THE (PROTECTIVE MIMICRY)
          BUDRYS, ALGIS   SS GAL 53 02
  ASSIGNMENT IN TOMORROW POHL, FREDERIK   AN

FRITZ LEIBER   MERRIL, JUDITH   AR FSF 69 07
  BEST FROM FANTASY AND SCIENCE FICTION, 25TH ANNIV.
          FERMAN, EDWARD L.   AN
FRITZCHEN   BEAUMONT, CHARLES SS OSF 53 01
  *TERROR IN THE MODERN VEIN WOLLHEIM, DONALD A. AN
  YONDER   BEAUMONT, CHARLES   AC
FROG ON THE MOUNTAIN LAFFERTY, R. A.   NV NEW 70 AC
  NINE HUNDRED GRANDMOTHERS LAFFERTY, R. A.   AC
FROG POND   YARBRO, CHELSEA Q. SS GAL 71 03
  ANTHROPOLOGY THROUGH SCIENCE FICTION MASON, C/GREENBERG/& AN
  YOU AND SCIENCE FICTION HOLLISTER, BERNARD C AN
FROG, THE   MILLER, P. SCHUYLER SS UNK 42 10
  HELL HATH FURY   HAY, GEORGE   AN
FROM "A TRUE HISTORY" (165 A.D.)
          LUCIAN OF SAMOSATA   EX
  PAST, PRESENT, AND FUTURE PERFECT WOLFE, J&FITZ GERALD AN
FROM "A VOYAGE TO THE MOON" (1650)
          DE BERGERAC, CYRANO EX
  PAST, PRESENT, AND FUTURE PERFECT WOLFE, J&FITZ GERALD AN
FROM "ASIMOV'S BIOGRAPHICAL ENCYCLOPEDIA OF SCIENCE"
          ASIMOV, ISAAC   AR DBL 64
  OPUS 100   ASIMOV, ISAAC   AC
FROM "ASIMOV'S GUIDE TO THE BIBLE"
          ASIMOV, ISAAC   AR DBL 68
  OPUS 100   ASIMOV, ISAAC   AC
FROM "BIOCHEMISTRY AND HUMAN METABOLISM"
          ASIMOV, ISAAC   AR WMW 52
  OPUS 100   ASIMOV, ISAAC   AC
FROM "BRAVE NEW WORLD" HUXLEY, ALDOUS   EX WND 32
  TREASURY OF SCIENCE FICTION CLASSICS, THE
          KUEBLER, HAROLD W.   AN
FROM "CRITIAS, OR THE ISLAND OF ATLANTIS" (370 B.C.)
          PLATO   EX
  PAST, PRESENT, AND FUTURE PERFECT WOLFE, J&FITZ GERALD AN
FROM "EREWHON, OR OVER THE RANGE" (1872)
          BUTLER, SAMUEL   EX
  PAST, PRESENT, AND FUTURE PERFECT WOLFE, J&FITZ GERALD AN
FROM "FOUR-DIMENSIONAL SPACE" (1896)
          BOSTWICK, ARTHUR E. AR NSR 96
  FUTURE PERFECT   FRANKLIN, H. BRUCE   AN
FROM "FRANKENSTEIN, OR THE MODERN PROMETHEUS" (1818)
          SHELLEY, MARY W.   EX WRT 32 05
  PAST, PRESENT, AND FUTURE PERFECT WOLFE, J&FITZ GERALD AN
FROM "GALAXIES"   ASIMOV, ISAAC   AR FOL 68
  OPUS 100   ASIMOV, ISAAC   AC
FROM "GULLIVER'S TRAVELS" SWIFT, JONATHAN   EX
  PAST, PRESENT, AND FUTURE PERFECT WOLFE, J&FITZ GERALD AN
FROM "I, ROBOT"   ASIMOV, ISAAC   EX GNM 50
  OPUS 100   ASIMOV, ISAAC   AC
FROM "ISAAC ASIMOV EXPLAINS" (FORCE FIELDS)
          ASIMOV, ISAAC   AR SDG 68
  OPUS 100   ASIMOV, ISAAC   AC
FROM "ISAAC ASIMOV EXPLAINS" (IRRESISTABLE FORCE)
          ASIMOV, ISAAC   AR SDG 68
  OPUS 100   ASIMOV, ISAAC   AC
FROM "LIAR!"   ASIMOV, ISAAC   EX ASF 41 05
  OPUS 100   ASIMOV, ISAAC   AC
FROM "LOOKING BACKWARD" BELLAMY, EDWARD   EX TIC 88
  PAST, PRESENT, AND FUTURE PERFECT WOLFE, J&FITZ GERALD AN
FROM "LUCKIE STARR AND THE MOONS OF JUPITER"
          ASIMOV, ISAAC   EX DBL 57
  OPUS 100   ASIMOV, ISAAC   AC
FROM "LUCKIE STARR AND THE OCEANS OF VENUS"
          ASIMOV, ISAAC   EX DBL 54
  OPUS 100   ASIMOV, ISAAC   AC
FROM "NEW ATLANTIS" (1624) BACON, FRANCIS   EX
  PAST, PRESENT, AND FUTURE PERFECT WOLFE, J&FITZ GERALD AN
FROM "OF A FIRE ON THE MOON" MAILER, NORMAN   EX   69
  LOOKING AHEAD   ALLEN, D. & L.   AN
FROM "ONLY A TRILLION" ASIMOV, ISAAC   AR ABE 57
  OPUS 100   ASIMOV, ISAAC   AC
FROM "PHOTOSYNTHESIS" ASIMOV, ISAAC   AR BAS 68
  OPUS 100   ASIMOV, ISAAC   AC
FROM "QUICK AND EASY MATH" ASIMOV, ISAAC   AR HMF 64
  OPUS 100   ASIMOV, ISAAC   AC
FROM "RUNAROUND"   ASIMOV, ISAAC   EX ASF 42 03
  OPUS 100   ASIMOV, ISAAC   AC
FROM "STRANGE PLAYFELLOW" ASIMOV, ISAAC   EX SSS 40 09
  OPUS 100   ASIMOV, ISAAC   AC
FROM "SUPERNUTRON"   ASIMOV, ISAAC   EX AST 41 09
  OPUS 100   ASIMOV, ISAAC   AC
FROM "THE CALLISTAN MENACE" ASIMOV, ISAAC EX AST 40 04
  OPUS 100   ASIMOV, ISAAC   AC
FROM "THE CHEMICALS OF LIFE" ASIMOV, ISAAC AR ABE 54
  OPUS 100   ASIMOV, ISAAC   AC
FROM "THE CITY OF THE SUN" (1623)
          CAMPANELLA, G. D.   EX
  PAST, PRESENT, AND FUTURE PERFECT WOLFE, J&FITZ GERALD AN
FROM "THE DAY"   PERSKY, STAN   EX QRK 71 04
  QUARK/4   DELANY & HACKER   OA
FROM "THE DEAD HAND" ASIMOV, ISAAC   EX ASF 45 04
  OPUS 100   ASIMOV, ISAAC   AC
FROM "THE DUNCIAD" (1728) POPE, ALEXANDER   PM DPS 28 05
  MATHEMATICAL MAGPIE, THE FADIMAN, CLIFTON   AN
FROM "THE EGYPTIANS" ASIMOV, ISAAC   AR HMF 67
  OPUS 100   ASIMOV, ISAAC   AC
FROM "THE FALL OF JAPAN" CRAIG, WILLIAM   AR   67
  LOOKING AHEAD   ALLEN, D. & L.   AN
FROM "THE GREEKS"   ASIMOV, ISAAC   AR HMF 65
  OPUS 100   ASIMOV, ISAAC   AC
FROM "THE INTELLIGENT MAN'S GUIDE TO SCIENCE"
          ASIMOV, ISAAC   AR BAS 60
  OPUS 100   ASIMOV, ISAAC   AC
FROM "THE KINETICS OF THE REACTION INACTIVATION OF TYROSINASE
  DURING ITS CATALYSIS OF.." ASIMOV, ISAAC AR   48
  OPUS 100   ASIMOV, ISAAC   AC

```
FROM "THE LAST MAN" (1826)    SHELLEY, MARY W.    EX
  PAST, PRESENT, AND FUTURE PERFECT    WOLFE, J&FITZ GERALD AN
FROM "THE LIMITS TO GROWTH"   BEHRENS, WILLIAM W.
                              MEADOWS, DENNIS L.
                              MEADOWS, DONELLA H.
                              AND RANDERS, JORGEN   AR C   72
  LOOKING AHEAD               ALLEN, D. & L.        AN
FROM "THE MARTIAN WAY"        ASIMOV, ISAAC    EX  GAL 52 11
  OPUS 100                    ASIMOV, ISAAC         AC
FROM "THE NEAR EAST"          ASIMOV, ISAAC    AR  HMF 68
  OPUS 100                    ASIMOV, ISAAC         AC
FROM "THE NOBLE GASSES"       ASIMOV, ISAAC    AR  BAS 66
  OPUS 100                    ASIMOV, ISAAC         AC
FROM "THE NUTRINO"            ASIMOV, ISAAC    AR  DBL 66
  OPUS 100                    ASIMOV, ISAAC         AC
FROM "THE PERFECT MACHINE"    ASIMOV, ISAAC    AR  SJR 68 10
  OPUS 100                    ASIMOV, ISAAC         AC
FROM "THE POISON BELT"        DOYLE, ARTHUR CONAN EX SND 13 03
  PAST, PRESENT, AND FUTURE PERFECT    WOLFE, J&FITZ GERALD AN
FROM "THE REALM OF NUMBERS"   ASIMOV, ISAAC    AR  HMF 59
  OPUS 100                    ASIMOV, ISAAC         AC
FROM "THE ROMAN REPUBLIC"     ASIMOV, ISAAC    AR  HMF 66
  OPUS 100                    ASIMOV, ISAAC         AC
FROM "THE SKYLARK OF SPACE"   SMITH, EDWARD E. PHD EX AMZ 28 08
  SCIENCE FICTION ROLL OF HONOR, THE    POHL, FREDERICK  AN
FROM "THE SOUND OF PANTING"   ASIMOV, ISAAC    AR  ASP 55 06
  OPUS 100                    ASIMOV, ISAAC         AC
FROM "THE TIME MACHINE"       WELLS, H. G.     EX  NRV 95 01
  SCIENCE FICTION: THE FUTURE ALLEN, DICK           AN
FROM "THE UNIVERSE"           ASIMOV, ISAAC    AR  WKR 66
  OPUS 100                    ASIMOV, ISAAC         AC
FROM "THE WELLSPRINGS OF LIFE" ASIMOV, ISAAC   AR  ABE 60
  OPUS 100                    ASIMOV, ISAAC         AC
FROM "THERE'S NOTHING LIKE A GOOD FOUNDATION"
                              ASIMOV, ISAAC    AR      67
  OPUS 100                    ASIMOV, ISAAC         AC
FROM "TWENTY THOUSAND LEAGUES UNDER THE SEA" (1873)
                              VERNE, JULES     EX
  PAST, PRESENT, AND FUTURE PERFECT    WOLFE, J&FITZ GERALD AN
FROM "UTOPIA" (1516)          MORE, SIR THOMAS EX
  PAST, PRESENT, AND FUTURE PERFECT    WOLFE, J&FITZ GERALD AN
FROM "VIEW FROM AMALTHEA"     ASIMOV, ISAAC    AR  FSF 68 12
  OPUS 100                    ASIMOV, ISAAC         AC
FROM "WALDEN TWO" (CHAPTER 29) SKINNER, B. F.  EX      48
  PAST, PRESENT, AND FUTURE PERFECT    WOLFE, J&FITZ GERALD AN
FROM "WHEN WORLDS COLLIDE"    BALMER, EDWIN
                              AND WYLIE, PHILIP EX C LIP 32
  TREASURY OF SCIENCE FICTION CLASSICS, THE
                              KUEBLER, HAROLD W.    AN
FROM "WORDS FROM HISTORY"     ASIMOV, ISAAC    AR  HMF 68
  OPUS 100                    ASIMOV, ISAAC         AC
FROM "WORDS OF SCIENCE"       ASIMOV, ISAAC    AR  HMF 59
  OPUS 100                    ASIMOV, ISAAC         AC
FROM "WORDS ON THE MAP"       ASIMOV, ISAAC    AR  HMF 62
  OPUS 100                    ASIMOV, ISAAC         AC
FROM A PRIVATE MAD-HOUSE (1787)
                              REPTON, HUMPHREY SS  VAR 87
  FAR BOUNDARIES              DERLETH, AUGUST       AN
FROM ALKAID ASCENDING         MORGAN, CHRIS    SS
  GOLLANCZ - SUNDAY TIMES BEST SF STORIES  ANONYMOUS   OA
FROM ALL OF US                BAUER, GERALD M. SS  NMD 73
  FRONTIERS 2; THE NEW MIND   ELWOOD, ROGER         OA
FROM AN ECCLESIASTICAL CHRONICLE
                              HEATH-STUBBS, JOHN PM
  HOLDING YOUR EIGHT HANDS    LUCIE-SMITH, EDWARD   AN
FROM BEYOND                   LOVECRAFT, H. P. SS  WRT 38 02
  NEW WORLDS FOR OLD          DERLETH, AUGUST       AN
  *WORLDS OF TOMORROW         DERLETH, AUGUST       AN
"FROM CARIBOU TO CARRY NATION" EDMONDSON, G. C. SS FSF 59 11
  STRANGER THAN YOU THINK     EDMONDSON, G. C.      DC
FROM CRIMSON CAME STARDUST    INOUYE, JON      PM
  NIGHT TIDE, A               INOUYE, JON           OC
FROM DARKNESS TO DARKNESS     CARR, TERRY      SS  DEM 73
  DEMON KIND                  ELWOOD, ROGER         OA
FROM FANATICISM, OR FOR REWARD HARRISON, HARRY SS ASF 69 03
  *BEST OF HARRY HARRISON, THE HARRISON, HARRY      AC
  ONE STEP FROM EARTH         HARRISON, HARRY       AC
FROM GUSTIBLES PLANET         SMITH, CORDWAINER SS IFS 62 07
  BEST SCIENCE FICTION FROM IF, THE    POHL, FREDERICK  AN
FROM ON WHEELS                JAKES, JOHN W.   EX  WPB 73
  BEST OF JOHN JAKES, THE     JAKES, JOHN W.        AC
FROM PLYNCK TO PLANCK         STURGEON, THEODORE SF IFS 62 01
  WORLDS OF THEODORE STURGEON, THE    STURGEON, THEODORE AC
FROM SCIENCE FICTION TO SCIENCE FACT: THE UNIVERSE
                              MISC. MATERIAL   MS
  SF:59, THE YEAR'S GREATEST SCIENCE FICTION AND FANTASY
                              MERRIL, JUDITH        AN
FROM SEA TO SHINING SEA       ELA, JONATHAN    FA  SCL 72
  BEST SF: 1972               HARRISON & ALDISS     AN
FROM SHADOWED PLACES          MATHESON, RICHARD NV FSF 60 10
  SHOCK II                    MATHESON, RICHARD     AC
FROM THE "LONDON TIMES" OF 1904
                              TWAIN, MARK      SS  CNY 98 11
  CENTURY OF SCIENCE FICTION, A KNIGHT, DAMON       AN
  FUTURE PERFECT              FRANKLIN, H. BRUCE    AN
FROM THE CRYPTS OF MEMORY     SMITH, CLARK ASHTON SS   22
  OUT OF SPACE AND TIME       SMITH, CLARK ASHTON   AC
FROM THE DOMAIN OF ARNHEIM    MORGAN, EDWIN    PM      68
  HOLDING YOUR EIGHT HANDS    LUCIE-SMITH, EDWARD   AN
FROM THE EARTH TO THE MOON (1865)
                              VERNE, JULES     EX
  JULES VERNE- MASTER OF SCIENCE FICTION  VERNE, JULES  AC
FROM THE EARTH TO THE MOON AND A TRIP AROUND IT (1865)
                              VERNE, JULES     NO
  OMNIBUS, THE                VERNE, JULES          AC

FROM THE GOVERNMENT PRINTING OFFICE
                              NEVILLE, KRIS    SS  DVS 67 01
  DANGEROUS VISIONS           ELLISON, HARLAN       OA
FROM THE NOTEBOOK OF DOCTOR STEIN
                              WOLFE, GENE      SS  CTM 74 03
  CONTINUUM 3                 ELWOOD, ROGER         OA
FROM THE OTHER SIDE OF THE MASK
                              NOLAN, WILLIAM F. IN
  ALIEN HORIZONS              NOLAN, WILLIAM F.     AC
FROM THE THUNDER COLT'S MOUTH LAFFERTY, R. A.  NA
  IN THE WAKE OF MAN          ELWOOD, ROGER         OA
FROM THE TOWER OF ERIDU       FEHRENBACH, T. R. SS
  LONE STAR UNIVERSE          PROCTOR & UTLEY       OA
"FROM THIS DAY FOREWORD", AS IT WERE, A
                              BRUNNER, JOHN    IN
  FROM THIS DAY FORWARD       BRUNNER, JOHN         AC
FROM TWO UNIVERSES           BUCK, DORIS PITKIN PM FSF 64 12
  BEST FROM FANTASY AND SCIENCE FICTION: 15
                              FERMAN, EDWARD L.     AN
FROM UP THERE                 SELLINGS, ARTHUR SS
  *TIME TRANSFER              SELLINGS, ARTHUR      AC
FROM: A MODERN UTOPIA         WELLS, H. G.     EX      05
  INSIDE INFORMATION          MOWSHOWITZ, ABBE      AN
FROM: FISTFUL OF DIGITS       HODDER-WILLIAMS, C. EX HDS 68
  INSIDE INFORMATION          MOWSHOWITZ, ABBE      AN
FROM: GILES GOAT-BOY          BARTH, JOHN      EX  DBL 66
  INSIDE INFORMATION          MOWSHOWITZ, ABBE      AN
FROM: JOURNEY BEYOND TOMORROW SHECKLEY, ROBERT EX DEL 62
  INSIDE INFORMATION          MOWSHOWITZ, ABBE      AN
  INSIDE INFORMATION          MOWSHOWITZ, ABBE      AN
FROM: NOVA                    DELANY, SAMUEL R. EX DBL 68
  INSIDE INFORMATION          MOWSHOWITZ, ABBE      AN
FROM: PLAYER PIANO            VONNEGUT, KURT JR. EX HRW 52
  INSIDE INFORMATION          MOWSHOWITZ, ABBE      AN
FROM: RUTHERFORD              STEWART, DOUGLAS PM
  SECOND PACIFIC BOOK OF SCIENCE FICTION, THE
                              BAXTER, JOHN          AN
FROM: THE ADDING MACHINE      RICE, ELMER L.   EX  DBL 22
  INSIDE INFORMATION          MOWSHOWITZ, ABBE      AN
FROM: THE CITY AND THE STARS  CLARKE, ARTHUR C. EX HBW 56
  INSIDE INFORMATION          MOWSHOWITZ, ABBE      AN
FROM: THE MOON IS A HARSH MISTRESS
                              HEINLEIN, ROBERT A. EX IFS 65 12
  INSIDE INFORMATION          MOWSHOWITZ, ABBE      AN
FROM: THE STEEL CROCODILE     COMPTON, D. G.   EX  ACE 70
  INSIDE INFORMATION          MOWSHOWITZ, ABBE      AN
FROM: THE TALE OF THE BIG COMPUTER
                              JOHANNESSON, OLOF EX GOL 68
  INSIDE INFORMATION          MOWSHOWITZ, ABBE      AN
FROM: THE 480                 BURDICK, EUGENE  EX  MGH 64
  INSIDE INFORMATION          MOWSHOWITZ, ABBE      AN
FROM:THE JAGGED ORBIT         BRUNNER, JOHN    EX  ACE 69
  INSIDE INFORMATION          MOWSHOWITZ, ABBE      AN
FROM:THIS PERFECT DAY         LEVIN, IRA       EX  RDM 70
  INSIDE INFORMATION          MOWSHOWITZ, ABBE      AN
FROM- A CONNECTICUT YANKEE IN KING ARTHUR'S COURT
                              TWAIN, MARK      EX  HRP 89
  PAST, PRESENT, AND FUTURE PERFECT    WOLFE, J&FITZ GERALD AN
FRONT & CENTAUR               SALLIS, JAMES    SS  NWS 70 03
  FEW LAST WORDS, A           SALLIS, JAMES         AC
FRONTIER INCIDENT             WELLS, ROBERT    SS  NWR 71 18
  NEW WRITINGS IN SF. 18      CARNELL, JOHN         OA
FRONTIERS OF EDGEVILLE, THE   SPINRAD, NORMAN  IN
  OVER THE EDGE               ELLISON, HARLAN       OA
FRONTISPIECE                  GILDEN, STEPHEN  MS  QRK 70 01
  QUARK/1                     DELANY & HACKER       OA
FROST AND FIRE (THE CREATURES THAT TIME FORGOT)
                              BRADBURY, RAY    NV  PLS 46 FL
  R IS FOR ROCKET             BRADBURY, RAY         AC
FROST-GIANT'S DAUGHTER, THE   DE CAMP, L. SPRAGUE
                              AND HOWARD, ROBERT E. SS C FMG 53 08
  COMING OF CONAN, THE        HOWARD, ROBERT E.     AC
FROZEN ASSETS                 WISSNER, ROBERT  SS  CLR 72 07
  CLARION II                  WILSON, ROBIN SCOTT   OA
FROZEN BEAUTY                 KERSH, GERALD    SS      58
  NIGHTSHADE & DAMNATIONS     KERSH, GERALD         AC
  ON AN ODD NOTE              KERSH, GERALD         AC
FROZEN FEAR                   BLOCH, ROBERT    SS  WRT 46 11
  CHAMBER OF HORRORS          BLOCH, ROBERT         AC
FROZEN PLANET, THE (ALSO AS COURIER)
                              LAUMER, KEITH    NV  IFS 61 09
  FROZEN PLANET AND 4 OTHER SF NOVELLAS, THE
                              ANONYMOUS             AN
FRRITT-FLACC (1884)           VERNE, JULES     SS  FSF 59 11
  YESTERDAY AND TOMORROW      VERNE, JULES          AC
FRUIT AT THE BOTTOM OF THE BOWL, THE (TOUCH AND GO)
                              BRADBURY, RAY    SS  DBM 48 11
  *GOLDEN APPLES OF THE SUN   BRADBURY, RAY         AC
  VINTAGE BRADBURY, THE       BRADBURY, RAY         AC
FRUIT OF KNOWLEDGE            MOORE, C. L.     NV  UNK 40 10
  BEST OF C. L. MOORE, THE    MOORE, C. L.          AC
FRUITING BODY                 BROWN, ROSEL GEORGE NV FSF 62 08
  HANDFUL OF TIME, A          BROWN, ROSEL GEORGE   AC
  ONCE AND FUTURE TALES FROM THE MAGAZINE OF FANTASY AND
  SCIENCE FICTION             FERMAN, EDWARD L.     AN
FTA                           MARTIN, GEORGE R. R. SS ASF 74 05
  SONG FOR LYA, A             MARTIN, GEORGE R. R.  AC
FUEL FOR THE FUTURE           HATCHER, JACK    AR  ASF 40 03
  COMING ATTRACTIONS          GREENBERG, MARTIN     NF
FUGITIVE FROM SPACE           LEINSTER, MURRAY NA  AMZ 54 05
  ALIENS, THE                 LEINSTER, MURRAY      AC
FUGITIVES, THE                YOUNG, ROBERT F. SS
  GLASS OF STARS, A           YOUNG, ROBERT F.      AC
FULFILLMENT                   VAN VOGT, A. E.  NV  NTS 51
  FAR-OUT WORLDS OF A. E. VAN VOGT, THE  VAN VOGT, A. E.  AC
  NEW TALES OF SPACE AND TIME HEALY, RAYMOND J.     OA
```

FULFILLMENT   GAME PRESERVE

WORLDS OF A. E. VAN VOGT, THE   VAN VOGT, A. E.   AC
YET MORE PENGUIN SCIENCE FICTION   ALDISS, BRIAN W.   AN
FULL CIRCLE   MATHESON, RICHARD   SS   FUN 53 08
BORN OF MAN AND WOMAN   MATHESON, RICHARD   AC
SHOCK III   MATHESON, RICHARD   AC
FULL CIRCLE   PINKNEY, DOROTHY C.   PM   FSF 56 12
BEST FROM FANTASY AND SCIENCE FICTION: 7
                                     BOUCHER, ANTHONY   AN
FULL CYCLE   SIMAK, CLIFFORD D.   NA   SFS 55 11
WORLDS WITHOUT END   SIMAK, CLIFFORD D.   AC
FULL FLOWERING, THE   SPINRAD, NORMAN   SI
MODERN SCIENCE FICTION   SPINRAD, NORMAN   AN
FULL MEMBER OF THE CLUB, A   SHAW, BOB   NV   GAL 74 07
COSMIC KALEIDOSCOPE   SHAW, BOB   AC
1975 ANNUAL WORLD'S BEST SF, THE   WOLLHEIM, DONALD A.   AN
FULL MOON   CUMMINGS, M. A.   SS
EXILE AND OTHER TALES OF FANTASY   CUMMINGS, M. A.   OC
FULL OF, MOSTLY, BAGELS AND CREAM CHEESE
                             NOLAN, WILLIAM F. SS   NEW 74   AC
ALIEN HORIZONS   NOLAN, WILLIAM F.   AC
FULL QUOTA   NOLAN, WILLIAM F. SS   FUN 58 04
IMPACT-20   NOLAN, WILLIAM F.   AC
FULL SUN   ALDISS, BRIAN W.   SS   ORB 67 02
CREATURES FROM BEYOND   CARR, TERRY   AN
INSIDE INFORMATION   MOWSHOWITZ, ABBE   AN
ORBIT   2   KNIGHT, DAMON   OA
WORLD'S BEST SCIENCE FICTION: 1968   WOLLHEIM & CARR   AN
FULLNESS OF TIME, THE   BRUNNER, JOHN   NV   SFA 62 07
TIMES WITHOUT NUMBER   BRUNNER, JOHN   NO
FULLY AUTOMATED LOVE LIFE OF HENRY KEANRIDGE, THE
                             DRYER, STAN   NV   PBY 68 07
FULLY AUTOMATED LOVE LIFE OF HENRY KEANRIDGE
                                     PLAYBOY, EDITORS OF   AN
FUN PALACE   MOORE, RAYLYN   SS   ORB 75 17
ORBIT 17   KNIGHT, DAMON   OA
FUN THEY HAD, THE (NEA 51 12) ASIMOV, ISAAC SS   FSF 54 02
AS TOMORROW BECOMES TODAY   SULLIVAN, CHARLES W.   AN
BEST OF ISAAC ASIMOV, THE   ASIMOV, ISAAC   AC
CONNOISSEUR'S S. F.   BOARDMAN, TOM JR.   AN
EARTH IS ROOM ENOUGH   ASIMOV, ISAAC   AC
FIFTY SHORT SCIENCE FICTION TALES   ASIMOV & CONKLIN   AN
JOURNEYS IN SCIENCE FICTION   LOUGHLIN, RICHARD L.   AN
OPERATION FUTURE   CONKLIN, GROFF   AN
UNTRAVELLED WORLDS   BARTER & WILSON   AN
FUN WITH YOUR NEW HEAD (CEPHALOTRON)
                             DISCH, THOMAS M. SS   PBY 66 12
FUN WITH YOUR NEW HEAD   DISCH, THOMAS M.   AC
FUNERAL SERVICE   CONWAY, GERARD F. SS   UNI 72 02
UNIVERSE 2   CARR, TERRY   OA
FUNERAL, THE   MATHESON, RICHARD SS   FSF 55 04
SHORES OF SPACE, THE   MATHESON, RICHARD   AC
FUNERAL, THE   WILHELM, KATE   NV   DVS 72 02
AGAIN, DANGEROUS VISIONS   ELLISON, HARLAN   OA
INFINITY BOX, THE   WILHELM, KATE   AC
MORE WOMEN OF WONDER   SARGENT, PAMELA   AN
FUNES THE MEMORIOUS   BORGES, JORGE LUIS   62
NEW WORLDS OF FANTASY NO. 3   CARR, TERRY   AN
FUNNEL OF GOD, THE   BLOCH, ROBERT   NV   FAN 60 01
FEAR TODAY, GONE TOMORROW   BLOCH, ROBERT   AC
FUR MAGIC   NORTON, ANDRE   NO   WOR 68
DAW SCIENCE FICTION READER, THE   WOLLHEIM, DONALD A.   OA
FURIES, THE   ZELAZNY, ROGER   NV   AMZ 65 06
FOUR FOR TOMORROW   ZELAZNY, ROGER   AC
FURTHER INFORMATION   MOORCOCK, MICHAEL SS   NWS 65 12
FINAL PROGRAMME, THE   MOORCOCK, MICHAEL   NO
FURTHER READING   MISC. MATERIAL   MS
BIO-FUTURES   SARGENT, PAMELA   AN
MORE WOMEN OF WONDER   SARGENT, PAMELA   AN
FURTHER READINGS   MISC. MATERIAL   MS
NEW AWARENESS, THE   WARRICK & GREENBERG   AN
FURTHER SKY, THE (SEE THE OTHER SKY)
                             LAUMER, KEITH   TC
FUSION   ROTHMAN, MILTON A. NV   STL 74 01
STELLAR 1   DEL REY, JUDY-LYNN   OA
FUSION BOMB, THE   WILHELM, KATE   NV   ORB 72 10
INFINITY BOX, THE   WILHELM, KATE   AC
ORBIT 10   KNIGHT, DAMON   OA
FUTILITY IS ZUCK   LORY, ROBERT   SS
HARVEST OF HOODWINKS, A   LORY, ROBERT   DC
FUTURE IS OURS, THE   DENTINGER, STEPHEN SS   NEW 69 AN
CRIME PREVENTION IN THE 30TH CENTURY SANTESSON, HANS S.   AN
FUTURE MAKERS, THE   HAINING, PETER   AN   BEL 71 05
SCIENCE FICTION SPECIAL 5   ANONYMOUS   AN
FUTURE OF PREDICTION, THE SISK, JOHN P.   AR   CMM 70
SCIENCE FICTION: THE FUTURE   ALLEN, DICK   AN
FUTURE OF SCIENCE: PROMETHEUS, APOLLO, ATHENA, THE
                             BOVA, BEN   AR
NEBULA AWARD STORIES 9   WILHELM, KATE   AN
FUTURE OF THE FUTURE, THE HOSKINS, ROBERT IN   INY 72 04
INFINITY 4   HOSKINS, ROBERT   OA
FUTURE OF THE RACES OF MAN, THE
                             COON, CARLETON S. AR   65
APEMAN, SPACEMAN   STOVER & HARRISON   AN
FUTURE ON A CHIPPED PLATE, THE ALDISS, BRIAN W. NV NWB 73 05
NEW WORLDS QUARTERLY NO. 5   MOORCOCK, MICHAEL   OA
FUTURE PERFECT   VAN VOGT, A. E.   NV   VTX 73 08
BEST OF A. E. VAN VOGT, THE   VAN VOGT, A. E.   AC
2020 VISION   POURNELLE, JERRY   AN
FUTURE SPORTSMAN'S MANUAL, THE ACKERSON, DUANE   SS
FUTURE PASTIMES   EDELSTEIN, SCOTT   OA
FUTURE WITHOUT FUTURE   STERNBERG, JACQUES SS
FUTURE WITHOUT FUTURE   STERNBERG, JACQUES   OC
FUTURE, THE   ALLEN, DICK   SI
SCIENCE FICTION: THE FUTURE   ALLEN, DICK   AN
FUZZY HEAD   LONG, FRANK BELKNAP SS   TWS 48 12
RIM OF THE UNKNOWN   LONG, FRANK BELKNAP   AC

G. I. SPARROW   GIANNATTASIO, GERARD SS NWQ 74 06
NEW WORLDS NO. 6   PLATT & BAILEY   OA
G.B.K. - A MANY FLAVORED BIRD ELLISON, HARLAN SS ROG 62 06
*LOVE AIN'T NOTHING BUT SEX MISSPELLED ELLISON, HARLAN   AC
G.B.S.-MARK V   BRADBURY, RAY   SS
LONG AFTER MIDNIGHT   BRADBURY, RAY   AC
GABEL WINDOW, THE (THE MURKY GLASS)
                             DERLETH, AUGUST
                             AND LOVECRAFT, H. P. SS C STN 57 05
SURVIVOR AND OTHER STORIES, THE   LOVECRAFT & DERLETH   AC
GABRIEL-ERNEST   MUNRO, H. H.   SS   30
SUPERNATURAL READER, THE   CONKLIN, G&L.   AN
GABRIEL-ERNEST   SAKI   SS   30
ALONE BY NIGHT   CONGDON, MICHAEL&DON   AN
GADGET HAD A GHOST, THE   LEINSTER, MURRAY   NV   TWS 52 06
YEAR'S BEST SCIENCE FICTION NOVELS: 1953 BLEILER & DIKTY   AN
GADGET VS. TREND   ANVIL, CHRISTOPHER SS ASF 62 12
ANOTHER TOMORROW   HOLLISTER, BERNARD C   AN
SOCIOLOGY THROUGH SCIENCE FICTION   MILSTEAD/GREENBERG/&   AN
SPECTRUM 4   AMIS & CONQUEST   AN
GAHAN WILSON HORROR MOVIE POCKET COMPUTER, THE
                             WILSON, GAHAN   MS   NLP 74 05
BEST SF: 1974   HARRISON & ALDISS   AN
GALACTIC CALABASH, THE   EDMONDSON, G. C.   SS   FSF 60 01
SCIENCE FICTION ODDITIES   CONKLIN, GROFF   AN
STRANGER THAN YOU THINK   EDMONDSON, G. C.   DC
GALACTIC CHEST   SIMAK, CLIFFORD D. NV SFS 56 09
SO BRIGHT THE VISION   SIMAK, CLIFFORD D.   DC
3 IN 1   MARGULIES, LEO   AN
GALACTIC CLOCK, THE   MCINTYRE, VONDA N. SS GEN 72
GENERATION   GERROLD, DAVID   OA
GALACTIC CONSUMER REPORT NO. 1: INEXPENSIVE TIME MACHINES
                             BRUNNER, JOHN   FA   GAL 65 12
TIME-JUMP   BRUNNER, JOHN   AC
GALACTIC CONSUMER REPORT NO. 2: AUTOMATIC TWIN-TUBE WISHING
MACHINES   BRUNNER, JOHN   FA   GAL 66 06
TIME-JUMP   BRUNNER, JOHN   AC
GALACTIC CONSUMER REPORT NO. 3: A SURVEY OF THE MEMBERSHIP
                             BRUNNER, JOHN   FA   GAL 67 12
TIME-JUMP   BRUNNER, JOHN   AC
GALACTIC HERITAGE   LONG, FRANK BELKNAP SS TWS 48 10
MOLECULE MONSTERS, THE   ANONYMOUS   AN
GALACTIC LOVEPOEM   HENRI, ADRIAN   PM   68
HOLDING YOUR EIGHT HANDS   LUCIE-SMITH, EDWARD   AN
GALACTIC LOVEPOEM TWO   MISC. MATERIAL   PM
BEYOND THIS HORIZON   CARRELL, CHRISTOPHER   OA
GALACTIC PATROL   SMITH, EDWARD E. PHD EX ASF 37 09
SPACE ODYSSEYS   ALDISS, BRIAN W.   AN
GALAXY CALLED ROME, A   MALZBERG, BARRY N. NV FSF 75 07
ALPHA 7   SILVERBERG, ROBERT   AN
BEST SF: 75, THE NINTH ANNUAL   HARRISON & ALDISS   AN
DOWN HERE IN THE DREAM QUARTER   MALZBERG, BARRY N.   AC
GALILEO SEVEN, THE (S. WINCELBERG & O. CRAWFORD)
                             BLISH, JAMES   SA   STK 74 10
STAR TREK 10   BLISH, JAMES   OC
GALLANT LADY, THE   FAIRMAN, PAUL W.   SS
FORGETFUL ROBOT, THE   FAIRMAN, PAUL W.   OC
GALLEGHER PLUS   KUTTNER, HENRY   NV   ASF 43 11
COSMIC LAUGHTER   HALDEMAN, JOE W.   AN
RETURN TO OTHERNESS   KUTTNER, HENRY   AC
GALLEGHER PLUS   PADGETT, LEWIS   NV   ASF 43 11
ROBOTS HAVE NO TAILS   PADGETT, LEWIS   AC
GALLEY SLAVE   ASIMOV, ISAAC   NV   GAL 57 12
*REST OF THE ROBOTS, THE   ASIMOV, ISAAC   AC
SIX GREAT SHORT SCIENCE FICTION NOVELS CONKLIN, GROFF   AN
TIME WAITS FOR WINTHROP, AND FOUR OTHER SHORT NOVELS
                                     POHL, FREDERIK   AN
GALTON WHISTLE, THE (ULTRASONIC GOD)
                             DE CAMP, L. SPRAGUE NV FUT 51 07
CONTINENT MAKERS AND OTHER TALES OF THE VIAGENS
                                     DE CAMP, L. SPRAGUE   AC
GAMBLER'S WORLD (SEE PALACE REVOLUTION)
                             LAUMER, KEITH   TC
GAMBLING DEVICE   HERBERT, FRANK   SS   NEW 73 AC
BOOK OF FRANK HERBERT, THE   HERBERT, FRANK   AC
GAME   BARTHELME, DONALD SS   NYM 65 07
11TH ANNUAL OF THE YEAR'S BEST S-F, THE MERRIL, JUDITH   AN
GAME FOR BLONDES   MACDONALD, JOHN D. SS GAL 52 10
BEST SCIENCE-FICTION STORIES: 1953, THE BLEILER & DIKTY   AN
SECOND GALAXY READER OF SCIENCE FICTION GOLD, H. L.   AN
GAME FOR MOTEL ROOM   LEIBER, FRITZ   SS   FSF 63 03
ALPHA 1   SILVERBERG, ROBERT   AN
SCIENCE FICTION HORIZONS NO. 1   BOARDMAN, TOM JR.   AN
GAME OF BLOOD AND DUST, THE ZELAZNY, ROGER   SS   GAL 75 04
BEST FROM GALAXY, THE VOLUME IV   BAEN, JAMES   AN
GAME OF FUTURES- AN INTRODUCTION, A
                             DEL REY, LESTER   IN
CHILDREN OF INFINITY   ELWOOD, ROGER   OA
GAME OF GLORY, THE   ANDERSON, POUL   NV   VSF 58 03
FLANDRY OF TERRA   ANDERSON, POUL   AC
GAME OF GOD, THE (SEGREGATION) ALDISS, BRIAN W. NV NWS 58 07
AIRS OF EARTH, THE   ALDISS, BRIAN W.   AC
STARSWARM   ALDISS, BRIAN W.   AC
GAME OF RAT AND DRAGON, THE SMITH, CORDWAINER NV GAL 55 10
AS TOMORROW BECOMES TODAY   SULLIVAN, CHARLES W.   AN
BEST OF CORDWAINER SMITH, THE   SMITH, CORDWAINER   AC
BEST SCIENCE FICTION STORIES AND NOVELS: 1956
                                     DIKTY, T. E.   AN
BEST SF 3   CRISPIN, EDMUND   AN
MIRROR OF INFINITY, THE   SILVERBERG, ROBERT   AN
SCIENCE FICTION ARGOSY, A   KNIGHT, DAMON   AN
THIRD GALAXY READER, THE   GOLD, H. L.   AN
YOU WILL NEVER BE THE SAME   SMITH, CORDWAINER   AC
6 FROM WORLDS BEYOND   DIKTY, T. E.   AN
GAME PRESERVE   PHILLIPS, ROG   SS   IFS 57 10

GAME PRESERVE   GESTURE OF FAREWELL

SF:58, THE YEAR'S GREATEST SCIENCE FICTION AND FANTASY
                                   MERRIL, JUDITH   AN
GAME: FIRST SCHEMATIC   SHECKLEY, ROBERT   SS   NEW 71 AC
  CAN YOU FEEL ANYTHING WHEN I DO THIS?, AND OTHER STORIES
                                   SHECKLEY, ROBERT   AC
GAME-PLAYING LITERATURE, THE POHL, FREDERIK AR CLR 71 01
  CLARION   WILSON, ROBIN SCOTT   OA
GAMES   MACLEAN, KATHERINE SS GAL 53 03
  DIPLOIDS AND OTHER FLIGHTS OF FANCY, THE MACLEAN, KATHERINE AC
  OPERATION FUTURE   CONKLIN, GROFF   AN
  YOUNG DEMONS   ELWOOD & GHIDALIA   AN
GAMES WITHOUT END   CALVINO, ITALO   SS
  COSMICOMICS   CALVINO, ITALO   OC
GAMESMAN   BONE, J. F.   NV
  CRISIS   ELWOOD, ROGER   OA
GANDOLPHUS   BOUCHER, ANTHONY   SS   FSF 56 12
  DECADE OF FANTASY AND SCIENCE FICTION, A MILLS, ROBERT P. AN
GANTLET   PECK, RICHARD E.   SS   ORB 72 10
  BEST SF: 1971   HARRISON & ALDISS   AN
  CITY: 2000 A.D., THE   CLEM/GREENBERG/&   AN
  ORBIT 10   KNIGHT, DAMON   OA
GANYMEDE HOUSE   WOLLHEIM, DONALD A. SS OSF 53 01
  TWO DOZEN DRAGON EGGS   WOLLHEIM, DONALD A.   AC
GARBAGE COLLECTOR, THE   BRADBURY, RAY   SS   NAT 53 10
  *GOLDEN APPLES OF THE SUN   BRADBURY, RAY   AC
GARBAGE INVASION, THE   LAUMER, KEITH   NV   FSF 72 12
  RETIEF: EMISSARY TO THE STARS   LAUMER, KEITH   AC
GARDEN IN THE FOREST, THE YOUNG, ROBERT F. SS ASF 53 09
  OPERATION FUTURE   CONKLIN, GROFF   AN
  14 GREAT TALES OF ESP   STONE, IDELLA P.   AN
GARDEN IN THE VOID   ANDERSON, POUL   NV   GAL 52 05
  EXPLORING OTHER WORLDS   MOSKOWITZ, SAM   AN
GARDEN OF DELIGHTS, THE JONES, LANGDON   NV   NWS 69 07
  EYE OF THE LENS, THE   JONES, LANGDON   AC
  NEW TOMORROWS, THE   SPINRAD, NORMAN   AN
GARDEN OF FEAR, THE   HOWARD, ROBERT E. SS   MVT 34 07
  GARDEN OF FEAR AND OTHER STORIES, THE CRAWFORD, WILLIAM L. AN
GARDEN OF FORKING PATHS, THE BORGES, JORGE LUIS SS   62
  TRAPS OF TIME, THE   MOORCOCK, MICHAEL   AN
GARDEN OF PARIS, THE   WILLIAMS, ERIC C. SS   NEW 65 AN
  STRANGE BEASTS AND UNNATURAL MONSTERS STERN, PHILIP VAN D. AN
  WEIRD SHADOWS FROM BEYOND   CARNELL, JOHN   AN
GARDEN OF TIME, THE   BALLARD, J. G.   SS   FSF 62 02
  BEST FROM FANTASY AND SCIENCE FICTION: 12
                                   DAVIDSON, AVRAM   AN
  BEST OF J. G. BALLARD, THE   BALLARD, J. G.   AC
  BEYOND TOMORROW   HARDING, LEE   AN
  BILLENIUM   BALLARD, J. G.   AC
  CHRONOPOLIS AND OTHER STORIES   BALLARD, J. G.   AC
  *FOUR-DIMENSIONAL NIGHTMARE, THE BALLARD, J. G.   AC
  INTRODUCING SCIENCE FICTION   ALDISS, BRIAN W.   AN
  SPECULATIONS   SANDERS, THOMAS E.   AN
GARDEN, THE   GOR, GENNADY   SS   68
  AIR OF MARS AND OTHER STORIES, THE GINSBURG, MIRRA   AN
  RUSSIAN SCIENCE FICTION, 1969   MAGIDOFF, ROBERT   AN
GARDENER, THE   JONES, RAYMOND F. SS   SFS 57 07
  NON-STATISTICAL MAN, THE   JONES, RAYMOND F.   AC
GARDENER, THE   ST. CLAIR, MARGARET SS TWS 49 10
  ROOTS OF EVIL, THE   PARRY, MICHEL   AN
  *WORLDS OF TOMORROW   DERLETH, AUGUST   AN
GARDENERS, THE   BENVENISTE, ASA   PM   68
  HOLDING YOUR EIGHT HANDS   LUCIE-SMITH, EDWARD   AN
GARDENING NOTES FROM ALL OVER MACFARLANE, WALLACE SS ORB 74 13
  ORBIT 13   KNIGHT, DAMON   OA
GARRISON, THE   WOLLHEIM, DONALD A. SS MOH 65 04
  TWO DOZEN DRAGON EGGS   WOLLHEIM, DONALD A.   AC
GAS MASK   HOUSTON, JAMES D. SS   NUG 64
  ANOTHER TOMORROW   HOLLISTER, BERNARD C AN
  CITY: 2000 A.D., THE   CLEM/GREENBERG/&   AN
  RUINS OF EARTH, THE   DISCH, THOMAS M.   AN
  10TH ANNUAL OF THE YEAR'S BEST S-F, THE MERRIL, JUDITH AN
GATEWAY TO DARKNESS   BROWN, FREDRIC   NV   SSS 49 11
  DAYMARES   BROWN, FREDRIC   AC
  GIANT ANTHOLOGY OF SCIENCE FICTION MARGULIES & FRIEND AN
GATEWAY TO STRANGENESS (SEE SAIL 25)
                         VANCE, JACK   TC
GATEWAYS   WELLS, BASIL   SS
  PLANETS OF ADVENTURE   WELLS, BASIL   AC
GATHER BLUE ROSES   SARGENT, PAMELA   SS   FSF 72 02
  STARSHADOWS   SARGENT, PAMELA   AC
  WANDERING STARS   DANN, JACK M.   AN
GATHI   DEFORD, MIRIAM ALLEN SS FSF 58 06
  XENOGENESIS   DEFORD, MIRIAM ALLEN AC
GATO-O   PICARD, DON   NV   SPE 74 01
  SCIENCE FICTION EMPHASIS NO. 1   GERROLD, DAVID   OA
GAY DECEIVER, THE   CLINGERMAN, MILDRED SS NEW 61 AC
  CUPFUL OF SPACE, A   CLINGERMAN, MILDRED   AC
GEE, ISN'T HE THE CUTEST LITTLE THING?
                         COVER, ARTHUR BYRON SS ALC 73
  ALIEN CONDITION, THE   GOLDIN, STEPHEN   OA
GEE, WURLITZER! IT'S A DAD! SCORTIA, THOMAS N. SS DAP 71 06
  CAUTION! INFLAMMABLE!   SCORTIA, THOMAS N.   AC
GEEVER'S FLIGHT   FRITCH, CHARLES E. SS NEW 65 AN
  PSEUDO PEOPLE, THE   NOLAN, WILLIAM F.   AN
GEEZENSTACKS, THE   BROWN, FREDRIC   SS   WRT 43 09
  BEST OF FREDRIC BROWN, THE   BROWN, FREDRIC   AC
  NIGHTMARES AND GEEZENSTACKS   BROWN, FREDRIC   AC
GEHENNA   MALZBERG, BARRY N. SS   GAL 71 03
  BEST SF: 1971   HARRISON & ALDISS   AN
  1972 ANNUAL WORLD'S BEST SF, THE WOLLHEIM, DONALD A.   AN
GEHENNA   O'DONNELL, K. M.   SS   GAL 71 03
  IN THE POCKET AND OTHER S-F STORIES O'DONNELL, K. M. DC
GENE-HIVE (JOURNEY TO THE INTERIOR)
                         ALDISS, BRIAN W.   NV   NEB 58 05
  CANOPY OF TIME, THE   ALDISS, BRIAN W.   AC
  GALAXIES LIKE GRAINS OF SAND   ALDISS, BRIAN W.   AC

GENERAL HARDY'S PROFESSION   FAST, HOWARD   SS
  TOUCH OF INFINITY, A   FAST, HOWARD   OC
GENERAL ZAPPED AN ANGEL, THE FAST, HOWARD   OC   MOR 70
  TIME AND THE RIDDLE   FAST, HOWARD   AC
GENERAL ZAPPED AN ANGEL, THE FAST, HOWARD   SS
  GENERAL ZAPPED AN ANGEL, THE   FAST, HOWARD   OC
  POLITICAL SCIENCE FICTION   GREENBERG& WARRICK AN
GENERALIZED NONFICTION BIBLIOGRAPHY
                         MISC. MATERIAL   MS
  VOYAGES: SCENARIOS FOR A SHIP CALLED EARTH
                                    SAUER, ROB   AN
GENERATION GAP   REYNOLDS, MACK   NV
  FUTURE KIN   ELWOOD, ROGER   OA
GENERATION GAPS   O'BRIEN, CLANCY   SS   ASF 72 09
  SOCIOLOGY THROUGH SCIENCE FICTION MILSTEAD/GREENBERG/& AN
GENERATION OF NOAH   TENN, WILLIAM   SS   SUS 51 SP
  BEST SCIENCE-FICTION STORIES: 1952, THE BLEILER & DIKTY AN
  FRONTIERS IN SPACE   BLEILER & DIKTY   AN
  WOODEN STAR, THE   TENN, WILLIAM   AC
GENERATIONS OF AMERICA, THE BALLARD, J. G. SS NWS 68 10
  LOVE & NAPALM: EXPORT U.S.A.   BALLARD, J. G.   AC
GENESIS   PIPER, H. BEAM   NV   FUT 51 09
  SHADOW OF TOMORROW   POHL, FREDERIK   AN
GENETIC CODA   DISCH, THOMAS M.   SS   FAN 64 06
  *ONE HUNDRED AND TWO H-BOMBS   DISCH, THOMAS M.   AC
  WHITE FANG GOES DINGO AND OTHER FUNNY S.F. STORIES
                                    DISCH, THOMAS M.   AC
GENETIC FAUX PAS   BILKER, HARVEY L. SS   RLS 65 03
  STRANGE BED FELLOWS   SCORTIA, THOMAS N.   AN
GENIUS   ANDERSON, POUL   NV   ASF 48 12
  BEST SCIENCE-FICTION STORIES: 1949, THE BLEILER & DIKTY AN
  GIANTS UNLEASHED   CONKLIN, GROFF   AN
GENIUS FOR A YEAR, A   GRIFFITH, GEORGE   SS
  GAMBLES WITH DESTINY   GRIFFITH, GEORGE   AC
GENIUS FREAKS, THE   MCINTYRE, VONDA N. SS   ORB 73 12
  ORBIT 12   KNIGHT, DAMON   OA
GENIUS HEAP, THE (ALSO AS THE DARK NIGHT OF THE SOUL)
                         BLISH, JAMES   SS   GAL 56 08
  SIXTH GALAXY READER, THE   GOLD, H. L.   AN
GENIUS OF LANCELOT BIGGS, THE BOND, NELSON S. SS FAD 40 06
  LANCELOT BIGGS: SPACEMAN   BOND, NELSON S.   AC
GENIUS OF THE SPECIES   BRETNOR, REGINALD SS   FSF 56 06
  9 TALES OF SPACE AND TIME   HEALY, RAYMOND J.   OA
GENIUS, THE   BARTHELME, DONALD SS   NYM 71 02
  BEST SF: 1971   HARRISON & ALDISS   AN
GENRE   RUSS, JOANNA   AR   CLR 71 01
  CLARION   WILSON, ROBIN SCOTT OA
GENTLE ASSASSIN, THE   BALLARD, J. G.   SS   NWS 61 12
  BILLENIUM   BALLARD, J. G.   AC
  DAY OF FOREVER, THE   BALLARD, J. G.   AC
GENTLE BRAIN, THE   ALLPORT, ARTHUR   SS   SFQ 40 SU
  MOON CONQUERORS, THE   ANONYMOUS   AN
GENTLE CAPTIVE, THE   GODWIN, TOM   SS   SAW 72
  SIGNS AND WONDERS   ELWOOD, ROGER   OA
  VISIONS OF TOMORROW   ELWOOD, ROGER   AN
GENTLE DYING, A   KORNBLUTH, C. M.
                         AND POHL, FREDERIK SS C GAL 61 06
  WONDER EFFECT, THE   POHL, F. & KORNBLUTH AC
GENTLE VENUSIAN, THE (THE GENTLEST UNPEOPLE)
                         POHL, FREDERIK   NV   GAL 58 06
  TOMORROW TIMES SEVEN   POHL, FREDERIK   AC
GENTLE VULTURES, THE   ASIMOV, ISAAC   SS   SUP 57 12
  CONTACT   KEYES, NOEL   AN
  EARTHMEN AND STRANGERS   SILVERBERG, ROBERT   AN
  NINE TOMORROWS   ASIMOV, ISAAC   AC
GENTLEMAN ALL IN BLACK, THE KERSH, GERALD   SS TDY
  ON AN ODD NOTE   KERSH, GERALD   AC
GENTLEMAN FROM PRAGUE, A DERLETH, AUGUST   SS   WRT 44 11
  MR. GEORGE AND OTHER ODD PERSONS DERLETH, AUGUST   AC
GENTLEMAN IS AN EPWA, THE JACOBI, CARL   NV   NEW 53 AN
  NEW WORLDS FOR OLD   DERLETH, AUGUST   AN
  UNTRAVELLED WORLDS   BARTER & WILSON   AN
  *WORLDS OF TOMORROW   DERLETH, AUGUST   AN
GENTLEMEN- THE QUEEN!   TUCKER, WILSON   SS   SFQ 42 FL
  SCIENCE FICTION SUBTREASURY, THE TUCKER, WILSON   AC
GENTLEMEN, BE SEATED!   HEINLEIN, ROBERT A. SS ARG 48 05
  FIRST STEP OUTWARD   HOSKINS, ROBERT   AN
  GREEN HILLS OF EARTH, THE   HEINLEIN, ROBERT A. AC
  PAST THROUGH TOMORROW, THE   HEINLEIN, ROBERT A. AC
  SHOT IN THE DARK   MERRIL, JUDITH   AN
GENTLEST UNPEOPLE, THE (ALSO AS THE GENTLE VENUSIAN)
                         POHL, FREDERIK   NV   GAL 58 06
  FOURTH GALAXY READER, THE   GOLD, H. L.   AN
GENUINE ARTICLE, THE   COLE, ADRIAN   SS   BER 74
  BERSERKERS, THE   ELWOOD, ROGER   AN
GENUS TRAITOR   REYNOLDS, MACK   NV   ASF 64 08
  ANALOG 4   CAMPBELL, JOHN W. JR AN
GEOGRAPHY FOR TIME TRAVELERS LEY, WILLY   AR   ASF 39 07
  COMING ATTRACTIONS   GREENBERG , MARTIN   NF
GEOMETRY (1805)   WORDSWORTH, WILLIAM PM
  MATHEMATICAL MAGPIE, THE   FADIMAN, CLIFTON   AN
GEORGE   WEST, JOHN ANTHONY SS FSF 61 06
  *BEST FROM FANTASY AND SCIENCE FICTION: 11
                                    MILLS, ROBERT P.   AN
GEORGE THOMAS- 2027 (THE VOICES)
                         GUNN, JAMES E.   NV   FSF 72 09
  LISTENERS, THE   GUNN, JAMES E.   NO
GERANIUMS   KING, VALERIE
                         AND MALZBERG, BARRY N. SS C OMG 73
  BEST OF BARRY N. MALZBERG, THE   MALZBERG, BARRY N.   AC
  OMEGA   ELWOOD, ROGER   AN
GESTURE OF FAREWELL   ALDISS, BRIAN W.   SS   NWS 57 07
  INTRODUCING SCIENCE FICTION   ALDISS, BRIAN W.   AN
  NO TIME LIKE TOMORROW   ALDISS, BRIAN W.   AN

GET A HORSE! (ALSO AS THE FLIGHT OF THE HORSE)
　　　　　　　　　NIVEN, LARRY　　　SS　FSF 69 10
　BEST FROM FANTASY AND SCIENCE FICTION: 19
　　　　　　　　　FERMAN, EDWARD L.　　AN
GET FDR!　　　　　THURSTON, ROBERT　SS　CLR 72 02
　CLARION II　　　WILSON, ROBIN SCOTT　OA
GET OUT OF MY SKY　BLISH, JAMES　　SN　ASF 57 01
　GET OUT OF MY SKY　MARGULIES, LEO　　AN
GET RICH QUICK　　CUMMINGS, M. A.　SS
　EXILE AND OTHER TALES OF FANTASY　CUMMINGS, M. A.　OC
GETAWAY FROM GETAWEHI　KAPP, COLIN　NA　NWR 69 16
　NEW WRITINGS IN SF. 16　CARNELL, JOHN　　OA
GETTING ACROSS　　SILVERBERG, ROBERT　NV　FUC 73
　CAPRICORN GAMES　SILVERBERG, ROBERT　AC
　FUTURE CITY　　　ELWOOD, ROGER　　OA
GETTING ALONG　　BLISH, JAMES
　　　AND LAWRENCE, JUDITH ANN　NV C DVS 72 02
　AGAIN, DANGEROUS VISIONS　ELLISON, HARLAN　OA
GETTING AROUND　　MALZBERG, BARRY N.　SS　TAL 73
　BEST OF BARRY N. MALZBERG, THE　MALZBERG, BARRY N.　AC
GETTING AROUND　　O'DONNELL, K. M.　SS　TAL 73
　FRONTIERS 1: TOMORROW'S ALTERNATIVES　ELWOOD, ROGER　OA
GETTING INTO DEATH　DISCH, THOMAS M.　NV
　*GETTING INTO DEATH　DISCH, THOMAS M.　AC
GETTING OFF　　　CROSS, RONALD A.　SS
　FUTURE PASTIMES　EDELSTEIN, SCOTT　　OA
GETTING REGULAR　　BUNCH, DAVID R.　SS　AMZ 60 08
　MODERAN　　　　BUNCH, DAVID R.　　AC
GETTING THROUGH SUNDAY SOMEHOW BRADBURY, RAY　SS
　LONG AFTER MIDNIGHT　BRADBURY, RAY　　AC
GETTING TO KNOW YOU　LINK　　　　PM　QRK 70 01
　QUARK/1　　　DELANY & HACKER　　OA
GETTING TOGETHER　ROTHMAN, MILTON A.　SS　GAL 72 03
　BEST FROM GALAXY, THE　VOLUME I　GALAXY, EDITORS OF　AN
　BEST SCIENCE FICTION FOR 1973　ACKERMAN, FORREST J.　AN
GHETTO　　　　ANDERSON, POUL　　NV　FSF 54 05
　WILDERNESS OF STARS, A　NOLAN, WILLIAM F.　AN
GHOST　　　　KUTTNER, HENRY　　SS　ASF 43 05
　AHEAD OF TIME　KUTTNER, HENRY　　AC
GHOST BREAD　　　HOUSTON, LIBBY　　PM　NWB 75 08
　NEW WORLDS EIGHT　BAILEY, HILARY　　OA
GHOST CRABS　　　HUGHES, TED　　PM　66
　HOLDING YOUR EIGHT HANDS　LUCIE-SMITH, EDWARD　AN
　SCIENCE FICTION　BRODKIN & PEARSON　　AN
GHOST FLEET　　　ANVIL, CHRISTOPHER　SS　ASF 61 02
　STARS AROUND US, THE　HOSKINS, ROBERT　　AN
GHOST MAKER, THE　POHL, FREDERIK　　SS　BEY 54 04
　ALTERNATING CURRENTS　POHL, FREDERIK　AC
　BEYOND　　　ANONYMOUS　　　　AN
GHOST OF A CHANCE (THE GREEN EYED MONSTER)
　　　　　　　STURGEON, THEODORE　SS　UNK 43 06
　CAVIAR　　　STURGEON, THEODORE　AC
GHOST OF A MODEL T, THE　SIMAK, CLIFFORD D.　NV　EPC 75
　EPOCH　　　ELWOOD & SILVERBERG　OA
GHOST OF AN APPREHENSION, THE　CLARK, WALTER VAN T.　AR　PSP 49 SU
　SPECULATIONS　SANDERS, THOMAS E.　AN
GHOST OF JOLLY ROGER, THE　SERLING, ROD　SA
　ROD SERLING'S TWILIGHT ZONE REVISITED　SERLING, ROD　OC
GHOST OF LANCELOT BIGGS, THE　BOND, NELSON S.　SS　WRT 42 01
　LANCELOT BIGGS: SPACEMAN　BOND, NELSON S.　AC
GHOST OF ME, THE　BOUCHER, ANTHONY　SS　UNK 42 06
　BEYOND THE BARRIERS OF SPACE AND TIME　MERRIL, JUDITH　AN
　COMPLEAT WEREWOLF, THE　BOUCHER, ANTHONY　AC
GHOST OF MOHAMMED DIN, THE　SMITH, CLARK ASHTON　OVL 10 11
　OTHER DIMENSIONS　SMITH, CLARK ASHTON　AC
GHOST OF THE DIXIE BELLE, THE　SERLING, ROD　SA
　ROD SERLING'S TWILIGHT ZONE REVISITED　SERLING, ROD　OC
GHOST OF TICONDEROGA, THE　SERLING, ROD　SA
　*ROD SERLING'S THE TWILIGHT ZONE　SERLING, ROD　OC
GHOST PATROL, THE　GOULART, RON　　SS　FSF 68 10
　GHOST BREAKER　GOULART, RON　　DC
GHOST PATROL, THE　LEWIS, SINCLAIR　SS　DSM 17
　FANTASTIC PULPS, THE　HAINING, PETER　　AN
GHOST SEAS　　　UTLEY, STEVEN　　SS
　LONE STAR UNIVERSE　PROCTOR & UTLEY　OA
GHOST SHIP OF SPACE, THE　ELAM, RICHARD M. JR.　NV
　TEEN-AGE SUPER SCIENCE STORIES　ELAM, RICHARD M. JR.　AC
GHOST TRAIN, THE　SERLING, ROD　　SA
　ROD SERLING'S TWILIGHT ZONE REVISITED　SERLING, ROD　OC
GHOST V　　　SHECKLEY, ROBERT　SS　GAL 54 10
　PEOPLE TRAP AND OTHER PITFALLS, THE　SHECKLEY, ROBERT　AC
　ROBERT SHECKLEY OMNIBUS, THE　SHECKLEY, ROBERT　AC
GHOST WRITER, THE　BLOCH, ROBERT　　SS　WRT 40 05
　BOGEY MEN　　BLOCH, ROBERT　　AC
GHOST WRITER, THE　EFFINGER, GEO. ALEC SS　UNI 73 03
　MIXED FEELINGS　EFFINGER, GEO. ALEC　AC
　UNIVERSE 3　　CARR, TERRY　　OA
GHOST-TOWN GHOST, THE　SERLING, ROD　SA
　*ROD SERLING'S THE TWILIGHT ZONE　SERLING, ROD　OC
GHOST, THE　　　VAN VOGT, A. E.　NV　UNK 42 08
　OUT OF THE UNKNOWN　VAN VOGT & HULL　AC
　ZACHERLEY'S MIDNIGHT SNACKS　ZACHERLEY　AN
GHOSTS　　　YOUNG, ROBERT F.　SS　IFS 73 02
　BEST SCIENCE FICTION STORIES OF THE YEAR (1973)
　　　　　　　DEL REY, LESTER　　AN
GHOSTS (FROM ARCHIE AND MEHITABEL)
　　　　　　　MARQUIS, DON　　EX　27
　HUMAN?　　　MERRIL, JUDITH　　AN
GHOSTS OF LUNA, THE　WATSON, IAN　　SS　NWQ 74 06
　NEW WORLDS NO. 6　PLATT & BAILEY　　OA
GHOUL SQUAD, THE　HARRISON, HARRY　SS　ASF 69 06
　PRIME NUMBER　HARRISON, HARRY　　AC
GHOUL, THE　　　HARRISON, HARRY　SS
　FOUR FOR THE FUTURE　HARRISON, HARRY　AN
GHOUL, THE　　　SMITH, CLARK ASHTON　SS　FFN 34 01
　OTHER DIMENSIONS　SMITH, CLARK ASHTON　AC

GIACONDA CAPER, THE　SHAW, BOB　　NV　76
　COSMIC KALEIDOSCOPE　SHAW, BOB　　AC
GIANT IN THE EARTH　COLLADAY, MORRISON　SS　WOS 33 04
　*BEST OF SCIENCE FICTION　CONKLIN, GROFF　　AN
GIANT IN THE FOREST　LONG, FRANK BELKNAP　SS　SFQ 55 02
　ODD SCIENCE FICTION　LONG, FRANK BELKNAP　AC
GIANT KILLER　　CHANDLER, A. BERTRAM　NV　ASF 45 10
　ASTOUNDING-ANALOG READER, THE VOLUME ONE　HARRISON & ALDISS　AN
　GREAT SHORT NOVELS OF SCIENCE FICTION　SILVERBERG, ROBERT　AN
　WORLD OF WONDER　PRATT, FLETCHER　　AN
GIANT KILLER　　LAUMER, KEITH　　NV　IFS 65 09
　RETIEF: AMBASSADOR TO SPACE　LAUMER, KEITH　AC
GIANT KILLERS, THE　STEPHENSON, ANDREW M　NV
　ANDROMEDA 1　WESTON, PETER　　AN
GIANT METEOR IMPACT　ENEVER, J. E.　AR　ASF 66 03
　ANALOG 6　　CAMPBELL, JOHN W. JR　AN
GIANT-PLASM　　WANDREI, DONALD　SS　WRT 39 02
　STRANGE HARVEST　WANDREI, DONALD　　AC
GIANTS IN THE SKY　LONG, FRANK BELKNAP　SS　WRT 39 08
　WORLDS OF WEIRD　MARGULIES, LEO　　AN
GIBEREL, THE　　BUCK, DORIS PITKIN　SS　NDM 71 01
　NEBULA AWARD STORIES　NO. 7　BIGGLE, LLOYD JR.　AN
　NEW DIMENSIONS 1　SILVERBERG, ROBERT　OA
GIFT FOR NUMBERS, A　NOURSE, ALAN E.　SS　SUP 58 08
　RX FOR TOMORROW　NOURSE, ALAN E.　　AC
GIFT FROM EARTH　PACINI, KATHLEEN　SS　YNW
　SCIENCE FICTION STORIES　BRADLEY, JOHANNA　AN
GIFT FROM THE STARS　WILHELM, KATE　SS　FUT 58 12
　MILE-LONG SPACESHIP, THE　WILHELM, KATE　AC
GIFT OF GAB, THE　VANCE, JACK　　NV　ASF 55 09
　ALPHA 3　　SILVERBERG, ROBERT　AN
　BEST SF 3　CRISPIN, EDMUND　　AN
　FUTURE TENSE　VANCE, JACK　　AC
　OUT OF THIS WORLD 2　WILLIAMS-ELLIS& OWEN　AN
GIFT OF GARIGOLLI, THE　KORNBLUTH, C. M.
　　　AND POHL, FREDERIK　NV C GAL 74 08
　BEST FROM GALAXY, THE　VOLUME III　BAEN, JAMES　AN
　1975 ANNUAL WORLD'S BEST SF, THE　WOLLHEIM, DONALD A.　AN
GIFT OF GOD, THE　DE CAMP, L. SPRAGUE
　　　AND PRATT, FLETCHER　SS C FSF 50 WS
　BEST FROM FANTASY AND SCIENCE FICTION　BOUCHER & MCCOMAS　AN
　TALES FROM GAVAGAN'S BAR　DE CAMP, L. S.&PRATT　AC
GIFT OF NOTHING, THE　HOLLY, JOAN C.　NV　WLK 73
　AND WALK NOW GENTLY THROUGH THE FIRE...　ELWOOD, ROGER　OA
　CHRONICLES OF A COMER AND OTHER RELIGIOUS SCIENCE FICTION
　STORIES　　　ELWOOD, ROGER　　AN
GIFT OF THE GODS, THE　JONES, RAYMOND F.　NV　SFS 55 01
　LEARNING MAZE AND OTHER STORIES, THE　ELWOOD, ROGER　OA
　THINGS　　　HOWARD, IVAN　　AN
GIFT, THE　　　BRADBURY, RAY　　SS　FAN 59 07
　DAY IT RAINED FOREVER, THE　BRADBURY, RAY　AC
　MEDICINE FOR MELANCHOLY, A　BRADBURY, RAY　AC
　R IS FOR ROCKET　BRADBURY, RAY　　AC
GIFT, THE　　　JANIFER, LAURENCE M.　SS　DYS 75
　DYSTOPIAN VISIONS　ELWOOD, ROGER　　OA
GIFT, THE　　　OLIVER, CHAD　　NV
　FUTURE KIN　ELWOOD, ROGER　　OA
GIFTS FROM THE UNIVERSE　TUSHNET, LEONARD　SS　FSF 68 05
　BEST FROM FANTASY AND SCIENCE FICTION: 18
　　　　　　　FERMAN, EDWARD L.　　AN
GIFTS OF ASTI, THE　NORTON, ANDRE　SS　FBK 48 03
　GIFTS OF ASTI AND OTHER STORIES OF SCIENCE FICTION, THE
　　　　　　　ELWOOD, ROGER　　AN
　MANY WORLDS OF ANDRE NORTON, THE　NORTON, ANDRE　AC
　TIME CURVE, THE　MOSKOWITZ & ELWOOD　AN
GIFTS OF THE GODS　SELLINGS, ARTHUR　NV　NWR 66 09
　NEW WRITINGS IN SF. 7　CARNELL, JOHN　　AN
　NEW WRITINGS IN SF. 9　CARNELL, JOHN　　OA
GIGANTIC FLUCTUATION, THE　STRUGATSKY, ARKADY
　　　AND STRUGATSKY, BORIS　NO C
　JOURNEY ACROSS THREE WORLDS　ANONYMOUS　　AN
GIGOLO　　　GOULART, RON　　SS　FSF 72 08
　MARRIAGE AND THE FAMILY THROUGH SCIENCE FICTION
　　　　　　　CLEAR/WARRICK/&　　AN
　NUTZENBOLTS　GOULART, RON　　AC
GIL BRALTAR (1857)　VERNE, JULES　　SS　FSF 58 07
　BEST FROM FANTASY AND SCIENCE FICTION: 8
　　　　　　　BOUCHER, ANTHONY　　AN
　YESTERDAY AND TOMORROW　VERNE, JULES　AC
GILEAD　　　HENDERSON, ZENNA　SS　FSF 54 08
　PILGRIMAGE: THE BOOK OF THE PEOPLE　HENDERSON, ZENNA　AC
　TOMORROW'S CHILDREN　ASIMOV, ISAAC　　AN
　YOU AND SCIENCE FICTION　HOLLISTER, BERNARD C　AN
GIMMICKS THREE (THE BRAZEN LOCKED ROOM)
　　　　　　　ASIMOV, ISAAC　SS　FSF 56 11
　EARTH IS ROOM ENOUGH　ASIMOV, ISAAC　AC
GIN COMES IN BOTTLES　DE CAMP, L. SPRAGUE
　　　AND PRATT, FLETCHER　SS C NEW 53 AC
　TALES FROM GAVAGAN'S BAR　DE CAMP, L. S.&PRATT　AC
GINGER STAR, THE　BRACKETT, LEIGH　NO　IFS 74 02
　BOOK OF SKAITH, THE　BRACKETT, LEIGH　AC
GINNY WRAPPED IN THE SUN　LAFFERTY, R. A.　SS　GAL 67 08
　MUTANTS　　SILVERBERG, ROBERT　AN
　NINE HUNDRED GRANDMOTHERS　LAFFERTY, R. A.　AC
GIOCONDA OF THE TWILIGHT NOON, THE
　　　　　　　BALLARD, J. G.　SS　NEW 64 AC
　IMPOSSIBLE MAN, THE　BALLARD, J. G.　AC
　TERMINAL BEACH (BRITISH VERSION)　BALLARD, J. G.　AC
GIRL AND ROBOT WITH FLOWERS　ALDISS, BRIAN W.　SS　NWS 65 09
　BEST SCIENCE FICTION STORIES OF BRIAN W. ALDISS (REVISED)
　　　　　　　ALDISS, BRIAN W.　　AC
　SALIVA TREE AND OTHER STRANGE GROWTHS, THE
　　　　　　　ALDISS, BRIAN W.　　AC
GIRL FROM MARS, THE　BLOCH, ROBERT　SS　FAD 50 03
　LIVING DEMONS, THE　BLOCH, ROBERT　　AC
　TALES OF TERROR FROM OUTER SPACE　CHETWYND-HAYES, R.　AN

GIRL FROM MARS, THE (FIRST OF "SCIENCE FICTION SERIES")
                         WILLIAMSON, JACK   EX   29
  EARLY WILLIAMSON, THE   WILLIAMSON, JACK   AC
GIRL HAD GUTS, THE   STURGEON, THEODORE SS   VSF 57 01
  *TOUCH OF STRANGE, A   STURGEON, THEODORE   AC
GIRL IN THE GOLDEN ATOM, THE CUMMINGS, RAY NA   ASW 19 03
  GIANT ANTHOLOGY OF SCIENCE FICTION MARGULIES & FRIEND   AN
  UNDER THE MOONS OF MARS   MOSKOWITZ, SAM   AN
GIRL IN THE TRU-DREAM, THE ALDISS, BRIAN W. SS   FST 74
  FINAL STAGE   FERMAN & MALZBERG   OA
GIRL NOTHING HAPPENS TO, THE BULYCHEV, KIRILL   SS
  JOURNEY ACROSS THREE WORLDS   ANONYMOUS   AN
GIRL OF MY DREAMS   MATHESON, RICHARD   SS   FSF 63 10
  SHOCK III   MATHESON, RICHARD   AC
GIRL WHO DREW THE GODS, THE JACOBS, HARVEY   NV   MAD 65 05
  EGG OF THE GLAK, AND OTHER STORIES, THE JACOBS, HARVEY   AC
  11TH ANNUAL OF THE YEAR'S BEST S-F, THE MERRIL, JUDITH   AN
GIRL WHO KNEW WHAT THEY MENT, THE
                         STURGEON, THEODORE SS   70
  STURGEON IS ALIVE AND WELL...   STURGEON, THEODORE   AC
GIRL WHO MADE TIME STOP, THE YOUNG, ROBERT F. SS   SEP 61 04
  WORLDS OF ROBERT F. YOUNG, THE   YOUNG, ROBERT F.   AC
GIRL WHO WAS PLUGGED IN, THE TIPTREE, JAMES JR. NV NDM 73 03
  NEW DIMENSIONS 3   SILVERBERG, ROBERT   OA
  WARM WORLDS AND OTHERWISE   TIPTREE, JAMES JR.   AC
GIRL WHO WASN'T THERE, THE ACKERMAN, FORREST J.
                         FRITCH, CHARLES E.
                         NOLAN, WILLIAM F.
                         AND TIGRINA   SS C GAM 63 01
  SCIENCE FICTION WORLDS OF FORREST J. ACKERMAN & FRIENDS
                         ACKERMAN, FORREST J.   AC
GIRL WITH RAPID EYE MOVEMENTS, THE
                         WOLFE, BERNARD   NV   DVS 72 02
  AGAIN, DANGEROUS VISIONS   ELLISON, HARLAN   OA
GIRL WITH THE GREEN GLASS EYES, THE
                         CUMMINGS, M. A.   SS
  EXILE AND OTHER TALES OF FANTASY CUMMINGS, M. A.   OC
GIRL WITH THE HUNDRED PROOF EYES, THE
                         WEBB, RON   SS   FSF 64 07
  BEST FROM FANTASY AND SCIENCE FICTION: 14
                         DAVIDSON, AVRAM   AN
GIRL WITH THE HUNGRY EYES, THE LEIBER, FRITZ SS   49
  GIRL WITH THE HUNGRY EYES, AND OTHER STORIES, THE
                         WOLLHEIM, DONALD A.   OA
  SECRET SONGS, THE   LEIBER, FRITZ   AC
  *TERROR IN THE MODERN VEIN   WOLLHEIM, DONALD A.   AN
GIRLS AND NUGENT MILLER, THE SHECKLEY, ROBERT SS   FSF 60 03
  SHARDS OF SPACE   SHECKLEY, ROBERT   AC
GIRLS FROM EARTH, THE   ROBINSON, FRANK M. NV   GAL 52 01
  BEST SCIENCE-FICTION STORIES: 1953, THE BLEILER & DIKTY   AN
  MARRIAGE AND THE FAMILY THROUGH SCIENCE FICTION
                         CLEAR/WARRICK/&   AN
  *STORIES FOR TOMORROW   SLOANE, WILLIAM   AN
GIRLS WHO WERE REALLY BUILT, THE (NEOSHO'S CHOICEST)
                         GUNN, JAMES E.   SS   FAN 58 06
  FUTURE IMPERFECT   GUNN, JAMES E.   AC
GIT ALONG!   DE CAMP, L. SPRAGUE SS   ASF 50 08
  CONTINENT MAKERS AND OTHER TALES OF THE VIAGENS
                         DE CAMP, L. SPRAGUE   AC
  *OUTER REACHES, THE   DERLETH, AUGUST   AN
GIVE HER HELL   WOLLHEIM, DONALD A. SS
  TWO DOZEN DRAGON EGGS   WOLLHEIM, DONALD A.   AC
GIVE MY REGARDS TO THE CZAR WILLIAMS, DAVID N. SS   CLR 73 03
  CLARION III   WILSON, ROBIN SCOTT   OA
GLADYS'S GREGORY   WEST, JOHN ANTHONY SS   FSF 63 02
  ARENA: SPORTS SF   FERMAN & MALZBERG   AN
  TWENTY YEARS OF FANTASY & SCIENCE FICTION
                         FERMAN & MILLS   AN
GLANCE AHEAD: BEING A CHRISTMAS TALE OF A.D. 3568, A
                         BANGS, JOHN KENDRICK SS   01
  ANCESTRAL VOICES   MENVILLE & REGINALD   AN
GLANCE AT THE PAST, A   BUNCH, DAVID R.   SS   FAN 70 10
  MODERAN   BUNCH, DAVID R.   AC
GLASS EYE, THE   CROSS, JOHN KEIR   SS   46
  TIMELESS STORIES FOR TODAY AND TOMORROW BRADBURY, RAY   AN
GLASS EYE, THE   RUSSELL, ERIC FRANK SS   ASF 49 03
  *BEYOND HUMAN KEN   MERRIL, JUDITH   AN
GLASS OF THE FUTURE, THE MUDGETT, HERMAN W. PM   FSF 55 01
  BEST FROM FANTASY AND SCIENCE FICTION: 5
                         BOUCHER, ANTHONY   AN
GLEANERS   SIMAK, CLIFFORD D. SN   IFS 60 03
  FROZEN PLANET AND 4 OTHER SF NOVELLAS, THE
                         ANONYMOUS   AN
GLEEB FOR EARTH, A   SCHAFHAUSER, CHARLES SS   GAL 53 05
  GALAXY SCIENCE FICTION OMNIBUS   GOLD, H. L.   AN
  SECOND GALAXY READER OF SCIENCE FICTION GOLD, H. L.   AN
GLEEPS   MILLER, P. SCHUYLER SS   ASF 43 07
  TITAN, THE   MILLER, P. SCHUYLER   AC
GLEEPSITE   RUSS, JOANNA   SS   ORB 71 09
  BEST FROM ORBIT, THE   KNIGHT, DAMON   AN
  ORBIT 9   KNIGHT, DAMON   OA
  1972 ANNUAL WORLD'S BEST SF, THE WOLLHEIM, DONALD A.   AN
GLIMPSE OF MARY, A   GYLES, GORDON A.   SS   SAW 72
  SIGNS AND WONDERS   ELWOOD, ROGER   OA
GLIMPSE OF THE SINLESS STAR, A GRIFFITH, GEORGE SS   PRS 00 03
  WORLDS APART   LOCKE, GEORGE   AN
GLIMPSES OF THE MOON   WEST, WALLACE   NV   ASF 65 06
  GREAT SCIENCE FICTION STORIES ABOUT THE MOON
                         DIKTY, T. E.   AN
GLITCH, THE   BLISH, JAMES
                         AND STANTON, L. JEROME NV C GAL 74 06
  ANTIGRAV: COSMIC COMEDIES   STRICK, PHILIP   AN
  BEST FROM GALAXY, THE VOLUME III BAEN, JAMES   AN
GLOATING PLACE, THE   BLOCH, ROBERT   SS   ROG 59 06
  *BLOOD RUNS COLD   BLOCH, ROBERT   AC

GLOOM PATTERN, THE   TATE, PETER   SS   NWS 66 0
  SEAGULLS UNDER GLASS AND OTHER STORIES TATE, PETER   A
GLOSSARY   MISC. MATERIAL   MS
  GREAT SCIENCE FICTION STORIES ABOUT THE MOON
                         DIKTY, T. E.   A
  INTRODUCING SCIENCE FICTION   ALDISS, BRIAN W.   A
  SCIENCE FICTION   BURTON, S. H.   A
GLOVE, THE   LEIBER, FRITZ   SS   WHS 75 0
  YEAR'S BEST HORROR STORIES: SERIES IV, THE
                         PAGE, GERALD W.   A
GM EFFECT, THE   HERBERT, FRANK   SS   ASF 65 0
  WORLDS OF FRANK HERBERT, THE   HERBERT, FRANK   A
GNARLY MAN, THE   DE CAMP, L. SPRAGUE NV   UNK 39 0
  HUMAN?   MERRIL, JUDITH   A
  UNKNOWN, THE   BENSEN, D. R.   A
  WHEELS OF IF, THE   DE CAMP, L. SPRAGUE   A
GNOME THERE WAS, A   KUTTNER, HENRY   NV   UNK 41 0
  ALONE BY NIGHT   CONGDON, MICHAEL&DON   A
  BEST OF HENRY KUTTNER 1, THE   KUTTNER, HENRY   A
  BEST OF HENRY KUTTNER, THE   KUTTNER, HENRY   A
GNOME THERE WAS, A   PADGETT, LEWIS   NV   UNK 41 0
  *BEYOND HUMAN KEN   MERRIL, JUDITH   A
  GNOME THERE WAS, A   PADGETT, LEWIS   A
  LINE TO TOMORROW AND OTHER STORIES OF FANTASY AND SCIENCE
  FICTION   PADGETT, LEWIS   A
GNOMEBODY   ELLISON, HARLAN   SS   AMZ 56 1
  ELLISON WONDERLAND   ELLISON, HARLAN   A
GNURRS COME FROM THE VOODVORK OUT, THE
                         BRETNOR, REGINALD   SS   FSF 50 0
  BEST SCIENCE-FICTION STORIES: 1951, THE BLEILER & DIKTY   A
  SCIENCE FICTION BESTIARY, THE   SILVERBERG, ROBERT   A
  SPECIAL WONDER   MCCOMAS, J. FRANCIS   A
GO AND BEHOLD THEM (THE END OF WINTER, AS WILLIAM SCARFF)
                         BUDRYS, ALGIS   SS   VSF 58 0
  UNEXPECTED DIMENSION, THE   BUDRYS, ALGIS   A
GO BACK TO YOUR PRECIOUS WIFE AND SON
                         VONNEGUT, KURT JR. SS   LHJ 62 0
  WELCOME TO THE MONKEY HOUSE   VONNEGUT, KURT JR.   A
GO FOR BAROQUE   SCOTT, JODY   SS   FSF 61 0
  *BEST FROM FANTASY AND SCIENCE FICTION: 11
                         MILLS, ROBERT P.   A
GO, GO, GO, SAID THE BIRD DORMAN, SONYA   SS   DVS 67 0
  DANGEROUS VISIONS   ELLISON, HARLAN   O
GOAL TENDING   BLAKE, E. MICHAEL   NV   75
  RUN TO STARLIGHT, SPORTS THROUGH SCIENCE FICTION
                         GREENBERG/OLANDER/&   A
GOAT SONG   ANDERSON, POUL   NV   FSF 72 0
  HOMEWARD AND BEYOND   ANDERSON, POUL   A
  NEBULA AWARD STORIES 8   ASIMOV, ISAAC   A
  1973 ANNUAL WORLD'S BEST SF, THE WOLLHEIM, DONALD A.   A
GOBLIN NIGHT   SCHMITZ, JAMES H.   NV   ASF 65 0
  ON OUR WAY TO THE FUTURE   CARR, TERRY   A
GOD AND THE MACHINE   BALCHIN, NIGEL   SS   51
  FANTASIA MATHEMATICA   FADIMAN, CLIFTON   A
GOD BUSINESS, THE   FARMER, PHILIP JOSE NA   BEY 54 0
  ALLEY GOD, THE   FARMER, PHILIP JOSE   A
GOD GRANTE THAT SHE LYE STILLE ASQUITH, CYNTHIA NV   31
  VENUS FACTOR, THE   GHIDALIA, V.& ELWOOD   A
GOD HOUSE, THE   ROBERTS, KEITH   NV   NWQ 71 0
  NEW WORLDS QUARTERLY NO. 1   MOORCOCK, MICHAEL   O
GOD IN A GARDEN, A   STURGEON, THEODORE SS   UNK 39 1
  OTHER WORLDS, THE   STONG, PHILIP D.   A
GOD IN THE BOWL, THE   HOWARD, ROBERT E.   SS   SSF 52 0
  COMING OF CONAN, THE   HOWARD, ROBERT E.   A
  CONAN   HOWARD, R./DE CAMP/&   A
GOD MACHINE, THE   GERROLD, DAVID   NV   GAL 70 0
  WHEN HARLIE WAS ONE   GERROLD, DAVID   A
GOD OF LIGHT (SEE THE LIGHT FROM BEYOND)
                         ESHBACH, LLOYD A.   TC
GOD OF THE PLAYBACK   DENTINGER, STEPHEN SS   NEW 67 0
  GODS FOR TOMORROW   SANTESSON, HANS S.   A
GOD THAT SCIENCE MADE, THE (SEE THE PLACE OF ORCHIDS)
                         ESHBACH, LLOYD A.   TC
GOD WHEEL, THE   KELLER, DAVID H. MD. SS
  TALES FROM UNDERWOOD   KELLER, DAVID H. MD.   A
GOD'S NOSE   KNIGHT, DAMON   SS   ROG 64
  *OFF CENTER   KNIGHT, DAMON   D
GOD-BOX, THE   DERLETH, AUGUST   SS   WRT 45 0
  NOT LONG FOR THIS WORLD   DERLETH, AUGUST   A
GOD-BOX, THE   WANDREI, HOWARD E. SS   ASF 34 0
  *STRANGE PORTS OF CALL   DERLETH, AUGUST   A
GODDESS IN GRANITE   YOUNG, ROBERT F.   NV   FSF 57 0
  BEST FROM FANTASY AND SCIENCE FICTION: 7
                         BOUCHER, ANTHONY   A
  WORLDS OF ROBERT F. YOUNG, THE   YOUNG, ROBERT F.   A
GODDESS OF FIRE   BURROUGHS, EDGAR R. NV   FAD 41 0
  ESCAPE ON VENUS   BURROUGHS, EDGAR R.   A
GODDESS OF THE CATS, THE SCORTIA, THOMAS N. SS   72
  CAUTION! INFLAMMABLE!   SCORTIA, THOMAS N.   A
GODDESS OF WISDOM, THE   BLOCH, ROBERT   SS   FUN 54 0
  FEAR TODAY, GONE TOMORROW   BLOCH, ROBERT   A
GODDESS ON THE STREET CORNER, THE
                         ST. CLAIR, MARGARET SS   BEY 53 0
  CHANGE THE SKY AND OTHER STORIES ST. CLAIR, MARGARET   A
GODLIKE MACHINES, THE   ALDISS, BRIAN W.   SI
  SPACE OPERA   ALDISS, BRIAN W.   A
GODLING, GO HOME!   SILVERBERG, ROBERT SS   SFS 57 0
  GODLING, GO HOME!   SILVERBERG, ROBERT   A
GODS ARE NOT MOCKED, THE BLOCH, ROBERT   SS   EQM 68 0
  COLD CHILLS   BLOCH, ROBERT   A
  FEAR TODAY, GONE TOMORROW   BLOCH, ROBERT   A
GODS ON OLYMPUS, THE   TALL, STEPHEN   NA   IFS 72 0
  STARDUST VOYAGES, THE   TALL, STEPHEN   A
GODS THEMSELVES THROW INCENSE, THE
                         HARRISON, HARRY   SS   IMP 66 0
  FOUR FOR THE FUTURE   HARRISON, HARRY   A

GOGGLES OF DR. DRAGONET, THE   LEIBER, FRITZ   SS   FAN 61 07
WORLDS OF FRITZ LEIBER, THE   LEIBER, FRITZ   AC
GOGOL'S WIFE   LANDOLFI, TOMMASO   SS   ENC 63
SF12   MERRIL, JUDITH   AN
GOING   SILVERBERG, ROBERT   NA   FFU 71
BORN WITH THE DEAD   SILVERBERG, ROBERT   AC
FOUR FUTURES   SILVERBERG, ROBERT   OA
GOING DOWN   MALZBERG, BARRY N.   NV   DYS 75
BEST OF BARRY N. MALZBERG, THE   MALZBERG, BARRY N.   AC
DYSTOPIAN VISIONS   ELWOOD, ROGER   OA
GOING DOWN SMOOTH   SILVERBERG, ROBERT   SS   GAL 68 08
INTRODUCTORY PSYCHOLOGY THROUGH SCIENCE FICTION   KATZ/WARRICK/&   AN
MOONFERNS & STARSONGS   SILVERBERG, ROBERT   AC
NEW TOMORROWS, THE   SPINRAD, NORMAN   AN
PARSECS AND PARABLES   SILVERBERG, ROBERT   AC
WORLD'S BEST SCIENCE FICTION: 1969   WOLLHEIM & CARR   AN
GOING TO THE BEACH   WOLFE, GENE   SS   SCS 73
SHOWCASE   ELWOOD, ROGER   OA
GOING UP| (FROM THE ARTICLE "SPACE TRAVEL")   DRISCOLL, DENNIS   AR   BLF 57 05
SF:58, THE YEAR'S GREATEST SCIENCE FICTION AND FANTASY   MERRIL, JUDITH   AN
GOING WEST   BRYANT, EDWARD   SS   ORB 74 13
ORBIT 13   KNIGHT, DAMON   OA
GOLD AT THE STARBOW'S END, THE   POHL, FREDERIK   NV   ASF 72 03
ANALOG 9   BOVA, BEN   AN
BEST SCIENCE FICTION FOR 1972   POHL, FREDERIK   AN
GOLD AT STARBOW'S END, THE   POHL, FREDERIK   AC
1973 ANNUAL WORLD'S BEST SF, THE   WOLLHEIM, DONALD A.   AN
GOLD STANDARD, THE   CHARTERIS, LESLIE   SS   33
SAINT'S CHOICE OF IMPOSSIBLE CRIME, THE   CHARTERIS, LESLIE   AN
GOLD-MAKERS, THE (1932)   HALDANE, J. B. S.   SS   EQM 52 10
GREAT SCIENCE FICTION BY SCIENTISTS   CONKLIN, GROFF   AN
GOLD, BLACK, AND SILVER   LEIBER, FRITZ   SS   QRK 71 02
QUARK/2   DELANY & HACKER   OA
GOLDEN ACRES   REED, KIT   NV   68
ABOVE THE HUMAN LANDSCAPE   MCNELLY & STOVER   AN
AS TOMORROW BECOMES TODAY   SULLIVAN, CHARLES W.   AN
BEST SF: 1968   HARRISON & ALDISS   AN
SOCIAL PROBLEMS THROUGH SCIENCE FICTION   GREENBERG/MILSTEAD/&   AN
VOYAGES: SCENARIOS FOR A SHIP CALLED EARTH   SAUER, ROB   AN
GOLDEN AGE, THE   CONQUEST, ROBERT   PM   69
HOLDING YOUR EIGHT HANDS   LUCIE-SMITH, EDWARD   AN
GOLDEN AGE, THE   FIEDLER, LESLIE A.   SI
IN DREAMS AWAKE   FIEDLER, LESLIE A.   AN
GOLDEN AGE, THE   SPINRAD, NORMAN   SI
MODERN SCIENCE FICTION   SPINRAD, NORMAN   AN
GOLDEN AGES GONE AWAY   POHL, FREDERIK   AR   CLR 72 02
CLARION II   WILSON, ROBIN SCOTT   OA
IN THE PROBLEM PIT   POHL, FREDERIK   AC
GOLDEN APPLES OF THE SUN   BRADBURY, RAY   AC   DBL 53
TWICE 22   BRADBURY, RAY   AC
GOLDEN APPLES OF THE SUN, THE   BRADBURY, RAY   SS   PLS 53 11
*GOLDEN APPLES OF THE SUN   BRADBURY, RAY   AC
R IS FOR ROCKET   BRADBURY, RAY   AC
STORIES FROM SCIENCE FICTION   DOHERTY, G. D.   AN
GOLDEN BARGE, THE (AS WILLIAM BARCLAY)   MOORCOCK, MICHAEL   SS   NWS 65 10
TIME DWELLER, THE   MOORCOCK, MICHAEL   AC
GOLDEN BOUGH, THE   KELLER, DAVID H. MD.   SS   MVT 34 WI
GARDEN OF FEAR AND OTHER STORIES, THE   CRAWFORD, WILLIAM L.   AN
TALES FROM UNDERWOOD   KELLER, DAVID H. MD.   AC
GOLDEN BRICK, THE   HUBBARD, P. M.   SS   FSF 63 01
BEST FROM FANTASY AND SCIENCE FICTION: 13   DAVIDSON, AVRAM   AN
GOLDEN BUGS, THE   SIMAK, CLIFFORD D.   NV   FSF 60 06
SEVEN COME INFINITY   CONKLIN, GROFF   AN
SO BRIGHT THE VISION   SIMAK, CLIFFORD D.   DC
GOLDEN CHILD   LONG, FRANK BELKNAP   NV
*HOUNDS OF TINDALOS, THE   LONG, FRANK BELKNAP   AC
GOLDEN CITY, THE   FARLEY, RALPH MILNE   EX   ARG 33 05
OMNIBUS OF TIME, THE   FARLEY, RALPH MILNE   AC
GOLDEN EFFECT, THE   DOLAN, MIKE   SS
SANTANA MORNING AND OTHER STORIES   DOLAN, MIKE   OC
GOLDEN EGG, THE   STURGEON, THEODORE   NV   UNK 41 08
*SCIENCE FICTION THINKING MACHINES   CONKLIN, GROFF   AN
GOLDEN FROG, THE   PURDY, KEN W.   NV   PBY 63 01
PLAYBOY'S STORIES OF THE SINISTER & STRANGE   PLAYBOY, EDITORS OF   AN
GOLDEN HELIX, THE   STURGEON, THEODORE   NA   TWS 54 SU
THREE TIMES INFINITY   MARGULIES, LEO   AN
GOLDEN HORN, THE   PANGBORN, EDGAR   NV   FSF 62 02
BEST FROM FANTASY AND SCIENCE FICTION: 12   DAVIDSON, AVRAM   AN
GOLDEN KEY, THE   KELLER, DAVID H. MD.   SS   53
FOLSOM FLINT AND OTHER CURIOUS TALES, THE   KELLER, DAVID H. MD.   AC
GOLDEN KITE, THE SILVER WIND, THE   BRADBURY, RAY   SS   EPO 53 WI
*GOLDEN APPLES OF THE SUN   BRADBURY, RAY   AC
GOLDEN LEMONS, THE   DISCH, THOMAS M.   SS
*GETTING INTO DEATH   DISCH, THOMAS M.   AC
GOLDEN LOTUS, A LEGEND, THE   GRESHNOV, M.   SS
LAST DOOR TO AIYA   GINSBURG, MIRRA   AN
GOLDEN MAN, THE   DICK, PHILIP K.   NV   IFS 54 04
BEYOND THE BARRIERS OF SPACE AND TIME   MERRIL, JUDITH   AN
EVIL EARTHS   ALDISS, BRIAN W.   AN
STRANGE GIFTS   SILVERBERG, ROBERT   AN
GOLDEN PYRAMID, THE   MOSKOWITZ, SAM   SS   FUN 56 11
FANTASTIC UNIVERSE OMNIBUS, THE   SANTESSON, HANS S.   AN
GOLDEN ROAD, THE   KORNBLUTH, C. M.   NV   STI 42 03
THIRTEEN O'CLOCK AND OTHER ZERO HOURS   KORNBLUTH, C. M.   AC

GOLDEN THE SHIP WAS- OH| OH| OH| SMITH, CORDWAINER   SS   AMZ 59 04
BEST OF CORDWAINER SMITH, THE   SMITH, CORDWAINER   AC
YOU WILL NEVER BE THE SAME   SMITH, CORDWAINER   AC
GOLDEN TRABANT   LAFFERTY, R. A.   SS   IFS 66 05
DOES ANYONE ELSE HAVE SOMETHING FURTHER TO ADD?   LAFFERTY, R. A.   AC
GOLDFISH BOWL   HEINLEIN, ROBERT A.   NV   ASF 42 03
APEMAN, SPACEMAN   STOVER & HARRISON   AN
*BEST OF SCIENCE FICTION   CONKLIN, GROFF   AN
FIRST CONTACT   KNIGHT, DAMON   AN
MENACE FROM EARTH, THE   HEINLEIN, ROBERT A.   AC
TOMORROW, AND TOMORROW, AND TOMORROW...   HEINTZ/HERBERT/JOOS/   AN
GOLEM, THE   DAVIDSON, AVRAM   SS   FSF 55 03
BEST FROM FANTASY AND SCIENCE FICTION: 5   BOUCHER, ANTHONY   AN
DARK SIDE, THE   KNIGHT, DAMON   AN
GREAT SCIENCE-FICTION   LICATA, TONY   AN
MASTERS' CHOICE   JANIFER, LAURENCE M.   AN
OR ALL THE SEAS WITH OYSTERS   DAVIDSON, AVRAM   AC
SF: THE BEST OF THE BEST   MERRIL, JUDITH   AN
SF: THE YEAR'S GREATEST SCIENCE FICTION AND FANTASY   MERRIL, JUDITH   AN
WANDERING STARS   DANN, JACK M.   AN
GOLIAH   LONDON, JACK   NV   BOK 10 02
CURIOUS FRAGMENTS   LONDON, JACK   AC
SCIENCE FICTION OF JACK LONDON, THE   LONDON, JACK   AC
GOLUB-YAVAN, THE   STANYUKOVICH, KIRILL SS
DESTINATION: AMALTHEIA   DIXON, RICHARD   AN
GOMEZ   KORNBLUTH, C. M.   NV   NEW 54 03
BEST OF C. M. KORNBLUTH, THE   KORNBLUTH, C. M.   AC
BEST SCIENCE FICTION STORIES OF C. M. KORNBLUTH   KORNBLUTH, C. M.   AC
EXPLORERS, THE   KORNBLUTH, C. M.   AC
MINDWORM AND OTHER STORIES, THE   KORNBLUTH, C. M.   AC
THEMES IN SCIENCE FICTION   KELLEY, LEO P.   AN
TOMORROW AND TOMORROW   KNIGHT, DAMON   AN
TREASURY OF GREAT SCIENCE FICTION, A VOL.1   BOUCHER, ANTHONY   AN
GONE ARE THE LUPO   HICKEY, H. B.   SS   QRK 70 01
QUARK/1   DELANY & HACKER   OA
WORLD'S BEST SCIENCE FICTION: 1971   WOLLHEIM & CARR   AN
GONE AWAY   COPPARD, A. E.   SS   46
MORE TERROR IN THE MODERN VEIN   WOLLHEIM, DONALD A.   AN
*TERROR IN THE MODERN VEIN   WOLLHEIM, DONALD A.   AN
GONE DOGS, THE   HERBERT, FRANK   SS   AMZ 54 11
BOOK OF FRANK HERBERT, THE   HERBERT, FRANK   AC
GONE FISHIN'   WILSON, ROBIN SCOTT   SS   FSF 70 10
BEST FROM FANTASY AND SCIENCE FICTION: 19   FERMAN, EDWARD L.   AN
BEST SF: 1970   HARRISON & ALDISS   AN
GONE FISHING   SCHMITZ, JAMES H.   NV   ASF 61 05
FIVE-ODD   CONKLIN, GROFF   AN
GONE TO THE DOGS (HENRY MARTINDALE, GREAT DANE)   DEFORD, MIRIAM ALLEN SS   BEY 54 03
ELSEWHERE, ELSEWHEN, ELSEHOW   DEFORD, MIRIAM ALLEN   AC
GONNA ROLL THE BONES   LEIBER, FRITZ   NV   DVS 67 01
BEST OF FRITZ LEIBER, THE   LEIBER, FRITZ   AC
DANGEROUS VISIONS   ELLISON, HARLAN   OA
HUGO WINNERS, THE (VOLUME 2)   ASIMOV, ISAAC   AN
NEBULA AWARD STORIES NO. 3   ZELAZNY, ROGER   AN
GOOBEREALITY   LAUMER, KEITH   NV   NEW 68 AC
IT'S A MAD, MAD, MAD GALAXY   LAUMER, KEITH   AC
GOOBERS, THE   DAVIDSON, AVRAM   SS   SWK 65 11
STRANGE SEAS AND SHORES   DAVIDSON, AVRAM   AC
GOOD DOCTOR, THE   NUETZEL, CHARLES   SS
IMAGES OF TOMORROW   NUETZEL, CHARLES   AC
GOOD DOG, THE   BIXBY, JEROME   SS   FAN 54 02
SPACE BY THE TAIL   BIXBY, JEROME   AC
GOOD FRIENDS, THE   SMITH, CORDWAINER   SS   WOT 63 10
BEST SCIENCE FICTION FROM WORLDS OF TOMORROW, THE   POHL, FREDERIK   AN
STARDREAMER   SMITH, CORDWAINER   AC
GOOD IMAGINATION, A   BLOCH, ROBERT   SS   SUS 56 01
KING OF TERRORS, THE   BLOCH, ROBERT   AC
GOOD INDIAN   REYNOLDS, MACK   SS   ASF 62 09
ANALOG 2   CAMPBELL, JOHN W. JR   AN
BEST OF MACK REYNOLDS, THE   REYNOLDS, MACK   AC
GOOD KNIGHT'S WORK, A   BLOCH, ROBERT   NV   UNK 41 10
DRAGONS AND NIGHTMARES   BLOCH, ROBERT   AC
GOOD LIFE, THE   THURSTON, ROBERT   SS   CLR 72 02
CLARION II   WILSON, ROBIN SCOTT   OA
GOOD NEIGHBORS   PANGBORN, EDGAR   SS   GAL 60 06
GOOD NEIGHBORS AND OTHER STRANGERS   PANGBORN, EDGAR   AC
GOOD NEW DAYS, THE   LEIBER, FRITZ   SS   GAL 65 10
BEST OF FRITZ LEIBER, THE   LEIBER, FRITZ   AC
WORLD'S BEST SCIENCE FICTION: 1966   WOLLHEIM & CARR   AN
GOOD NEWS FROM THE VATICAN   SILVERBERG, ROBERT   UNI 71 01
BEST OF ROBERT SILVERBERG, THE   SILVERBERG, ROBERT   AC
BEST SCIENCE FICTION STORIES OF THE YEAR (1971)   DEL REY, LESTER   AN
NEBULA AWARD STORIES NO. 7   BIGGLE, LLOYD JR.   AN
NEW AWARENESS, THE   WARRICK & GREENBERG   AN
SOCIAL PROBLEMS THROUGH SCIENCE FICTION   GREENBERG/MILSTEAD/&   AN
UNFAMILIAR TERRITORY   SILVERBERG, ROBERT   AC
UNIVERSE 1   CARR, TERRY   OA
GOOD NIGHT, MR. JAMES   SIMAK, CLIFFORD D.   NV   GAL 51 03
*ALL THE TRAPS OF EARTH AND OTHER STORIES SIMAK, CLIFFORD D.   AC
*GALAXY READER OF SCIENCE FICTION   GOLD, H. L.   AN
*OUTER REACHES, THE   DERLETH, AUGUST   AN
GOOD.NIGHT, SOPHIE   ALDANI, LINO   NV
VIEW FROM ANOTHER SHORE   ROTTENSTEINER, FRANZ AN
GOOD OLD DAYS, THE   DANN, JACK M.   SS
JOURNEY TO ANOTHER STAR AND OTHER STORIES   ELWOOD, ROGER   OA

GOOD PROVIDER, THE   GROSS, MARION   SS   FSF 52 09
  FIFTY SHORT SCIENCE FICTION TALES   ASIMOV & CONKLIN   AN
  SCIENCE FACT/FICTION   FARRELL/GAGE/&   AN
  *SCIENCE FICTION ADVENTURES IN DIMENSION CONKLIN, GROFF AN
  THEMES IN SCIENCE FICTION   KELLEY, LEO P.   AN
GOOD RING, THE   MADSEN, SVEND AGE   SS
  VIEW FROM ANOTHER SHORE   ROTTENSTEINER, FRANZ AN
GOOD SHELLACKING, A   LEM, STANISLAW   SS
  CYBERIAD, THE   LEM, STANISLAW   OC
GOOD SHIP ERASMUS, THE   HARRISON, WILLIAM   SS   71
  ROLLERBALL   HARRISON, WILLIAM   AC
GOOD TO BE A MARTIAN   LONG, FRANK BELKNAP SS   FUN 55 02
  RIM OF THE UNKNOWN   LONG, FRANK BELKNAP AC
GOOD TRIP, THE   LE GUIN, URSULA K.   SS   FAN 70 08
  WINDS TWELVE QUARTERS, THE   LE GUIN, URSULA K. AC
GOOD-BY, GRANDMA   BRADBURY, RAY   SS   SEP 57 05
  DANDELION WINE   BRADBURY, RAY   NO
GOOD-BYE, ILHA¡   MANNING, LAURENCE   SS   NEW 52 05
  *BEYOND HUMAN KEN   MERRIL, JUDITH   AN
  GIANTS UNLEASHED   CONKLIN, GROFF   AN
GOOD-BYE, MIRANDA   MOORCOCK, MICHAEL   SS   NWS 64 08
  MOORCOCK'S BOOK OF MARTYRS   MOORCOCK, MICHAEL   AC
GOOD-BYE, SHELLEY, SHIRLEY, CHARLOTTE, CHARLENE
                           THURSTON, ROBERT   SS   ORB 72 11
  ORBIT 11   KNIGHT, DAMON   OA
GOODBYE AMANDA JEAN   SHORE, WILMA   SS   GAL 70 07
  ALPHA 2   SILVERBERG, ROBERT AN
GOODBYE, HENRY J. KOSTKOS, GOODBYE
                           KNIGHT, DAMON   AR   CLR 72 02
  CLARION II   WILSON, ROBIN SCOTT OA
GOODLIFE   SABERHAGEN, FRED   NV   WOT 63 12
  BERSERKER   SABERHAGEN, FRED   AC
GOODLY CREATURES, THE   KORNBLUTH, C. M.   SS   FSF 52 12
  EXPLORERS, THE   KORNBLUTH, C. M.   AC
  MINDWORM AND OTHER STORIES, THE   KORNBLUTH, C. M.   AC
GORF¡ GORF¡ GORF¡ (ALSO AS THE DAY THE GORF TOOK OVER)
                           NOLAN, WILLIAM F.   SS   INY 71 02
  INFINITY 2   HOSKINS, ROBERT   OA
GORGIAS   CARLSSON, PEDER   SS   NWQ 73 05
  NEW WORLDS NO. 5   MOORCOCK & PLATT   OA
GORGON'S HEAD, THE   BACON, GERTRUDE   SS
  TRANSFORMATIONS   ROSELLE, DANIEL   AN
GORGON'S HEAD, THE   BAKER, DOROTHY   SS   SND 99 12
  HORROR TIMES TEN   NORTON, ALDEN H.   AN
GORGONS, THE   PAYES, RACHEL C.   SS
  QUEST   BISCHOFF, DAVID   OA
GORILLA SUIT   SHEPLEY, JOHN   SS   FSF 58 05
  BEST FROM FANTASY AND SCIENCE FICTION: 8
                                       BOUCHER, ANTHONY   AN
GORMAN   FARBER, JERRY   SS   69
  BEST SF: 1970   HARRISON & ALDISS   AN
  SCHOOL AND SOCIETY THROUGH SCIENCE FICTION
                                       OLANDER/GREENBERG/& AN
GOSLIN DAY   DAVIDSON, AVRAM   SS   ORB 70 06
  ORBIT 6   KNIGHT, DAMON   OA
  WANDERING STARS   DANN, JACK M.   AN
GOSTAK AND THE DOSHES, THE BREUER, MILES J. MD. SS AMZ 30 03
  ADVENTURES IN DIMENSION   CONKLIN, GROFF   AN
  GREAT SCIENCE FICTION BY SCIENTISTS CONKLIN, GROFF   AN
  *SCIENCE FICTION ADVENTURES IN DIMENSION CONKLIN, GROFF AN
GOTTLOS   KAPP, COLIN   NV   ASF 69 11
  ANALOG 8   CAMPBELL, JOHN W. JR AN
GOVERNOR OF GLAVE, THE (SEE NATIVE INTELLIGENCE)
                           LAUMER, KEITH   TC
GRAB BAGS ARE DANGEROUS   LONG, FRANK BELKNAP   SS   UNK 42 06
  EARLY LONG, THE   LONG, FRANK BELKNAP AC
  *HOUNDS OF TINDALOS, THE   LONG, FRANK BELKNAP AC
GRADUATED ROBOT, THE   HOLLY, J. HUNTER   SS
  GRADUATED ROBOT AND OTHER STORIES, THE ELWOOD, ROGER   OA
GRADUATION DAY   MACFARLANE, WALLACE   SS   EPC 75
  EPOCH   ELWOOD & SILVERBERG OA
GRAIN KINGS, THE   ROBERTS, KEITH   NV   NWQ 72 03
  GRAIN KINGS, THE   ROBERTS, KEITH   AC
  NEW WORLDS QUARTERLY NO. 3   MOORCOCK, MICHAEL   OA
  PASSING OF THE DRAGONS, THE   ROBERTS, KEITH   AC
GRAND CENTRAL TERMINAL   SZILARD, LEO   SS   UCM 52 06
  GREAT SCIENCE FICTION BY SCIENTISTS CONKLIN, GROFF   AN
GRAND ROUNDS   NOURSE, ALAN E.   SS   FUN 55 08
  RX FOR TOMORROW   NOURSE, ALAN E.   AC
GRANDFATHERS' WAR, THE   LEINSTER, MURRAY   SN   ASF 57 10
  DOCTOR TO THE STARS   LEINSTER, MURRAY   AC
GRANDMA WAS NEVER LIKE THIS PAYES, RACHEL C.   SS   NEW 73 AN
  ANDROIDS, TIME MACHINES AND BLUE GIRAFFES
                                       ELWOOD & GHIDALIA   AN
GRANDMA'S LIE SOAP   ABERNATHY, ROBERT   SS   FUN 56 02
  SF:57, THE YEAR'S GREATEST SCIENCE FICTION AND FANTASY
                                       MERRIL, JUDITH   AN
GRANDPA   SCHMITZ, JAMES H.   SS   ASF 55 02
  ASTOUNDING-ANALOG READER, THE VOLUME TWO HARRISON & ALDISS AN
  DECADE THE 1950S   ALDISS & HARRISON   AN
  PENGUIN SCIENCE FICTION   ALDISS, BRIAN W.   AN
  SCIENCE FICTION BESTIARY, THE   SILVERBERG, ROBERT AN
  SPECTRUM 5   AMIS & CONQUEST   AN
  TIME PROBE: THE SCIENCES IN SF.   CLARKE, ARTHUR C.   AN
GRANDY DEVIL   POHL, FREDERIK   SS   GAL 55 06
  ALTERNATING CURRENTS   POHL, FREDERIK   AC
  BEST OF FREDERIK POHL, THE   POHL, FREDERIK   AC
  THOSE WHO CAN: A SCIENCE FICTION READER WILSON, ROBIN SCOTT AN
GRANNY WON'T KNIT   STURGEON, THEODORE   NA   GAL 54 05
  ALL ABOUT THE FUTURE   GREENBERG, MARTIN   AN
  5 GALAXY SHORT NOVELS   GOLD, H. L.   AN
GRANNY'S BIRTHDAY   BROWN, FREDRIC   SS
  NIGHTMARES AND GEEZENSTACKS   BROWN, FREDRIC   AC
GRANTHA SIGHTING, THE   DAVIDSON, AVRAM   SS   FSF 58 04
  BEST FROM FANTASY AND SCIENCE FICTION: 8
                                       BOUCHER, ANTHONY   AN

  ENCOUNTERS WITH ALIENS   EARLEY, GEORGE W.   AN
  OR ALL THE SEAS WITH OYSTERS   DAVIDSON, AVRAM   AC
GRAPELINER   WHITE, JAMES   NV   NWS 59 11
  DEADLY LITTER   WHITE, JAMES   NO
GRAPH   WEINBAUM, STANLEY G. SS   FMG 36 09
  MARTIAN ODYSSEY AND OTHER SCIENCE FICTION TALES, A
                                       WEINBAUM, STANLEY G. AC
GRASS, THE   DOLAN, MIKE   SS
  SANTANA MORNING AND OTHER STORIES   DOLAN, MIKE   AC
GRASSHOPPER TIME   EKLUND, GORDON   SS   FSF 72 03
  BEST SCIENCE FICTION OF THE YEAR, THE NO. 2
                                       CARR, TERRY   AN
GRATITUDE (PROPERTY OF VENUS) DE CAMP, L. SPRAGUE NV GAL 55 07
  GUN FOR DINOSAUR AND OTHER IMAGINATIVE TALES
                                       DE CAMP, L. SPRAGUE AC
GRATITUDE GUARANTEED   BRETNOR, REGINALD
                           AND NEVILLE, KRIS   SS C FSF 53 08
  PORTALS OF TOMORROW   DERLETH, AUGUST   AN
  TWENTY YEARS OF FANTASY & SCIENCE FICTION
                                       FERMAN & MILLS   AN
GRATITUDE, OR, THE SERPENT'S TOOTH
                           DISCH, THOMAS M.   SS
  *GETTING INTO DEATH   DISCH, THOMAS M.   AC
GRAVEYARD HEART, THE   ZELAZNY, ROGER   NV   FAN 64 03
  FOUR FOR TOMORROW   ZELAZNY, ROGER   AC
  GREAT SHORT NOVELS OF SCIENCE FICTION SILVERBERG, ROBERT AN
  SHORES BENEATH, THE   SALLIS, JAMES   AN
GRAVEYARD RATS, THE   KUTTNER, HENRY   SS   WRT 36 03
  GRAVEYARD READER, THE   CONKLIN, GROFF   AN
  OTHER WORLDS, THE   STONG, PHILIP D.   AN
GRAVEYARD READER, THE   STURGEON, THEODORE   SS   SCF 58 10
  FANTASY: THE LITERATURE OF THE MARVELOUS KELLEY, LEO P. AN
  GRAVEYARD READER, THE   CONKLIN, GROFF   AN
  TO HERE AND THE EASEL   STURGEON, THEODORE AC
  WEIRD SHADOWS FROM BEYOND   CARNELL, JOHN   AN
  WORLDS OF THEODORE STURGEON, THE   STURGEON, THEODORE AC
GRAVEYARD SHIFT   ST. CLAIR, MARGARET   SS   FSF 59 02
  CHANGE THE SKY AND OTHER STORIES   ST. CLAIR, MARGARET AC
GRAVEYARD SHIFT (THE FACES) MATHESON, RICHARD   SS   MCB 60
  SHOCK II   MATHESON, RICHARD   AC
GRAVITY   JACOBS, HARVEY   SS   NWS 69 08
  BEST SF STORIES FROM NEW WORLDS 6   MOORCOCK, MICHAEL   AN
  DECADE THE 1960S   ALDISS & HARRISON   AN
GRAVITY IS A THING   ANONYMOUS   AR
  LAURIE'S SPACE ANNUAL   ANONYMOUS   AN
GRAVITY PROFESSOR   CUMMINGS, RAY   SS   AAS 21 05
  EVERY BOY'S BOOK OF SCIENCE FICTION WOLLHEIM, DONALD A. AN
GRAY FLANNEL ARMOR   SHECKLEY, ROBERT   SS   GAL 57 11
  NOTIONS: UNLIMITED   SHECKLEY, ROBERT   AC
GRAY ONES, THE   PRIESTLEY, J. B.   SS
  OTHER PLACE, THE   PRIESTLEY, J. B.   AC
GRAYWORLD   KOONTZ, DEAN R.   SN   INY 73 05
  INFINITY 5   HOSKINS, ROBERT   OA
GREAT A, THE   MALSTROM, ROBERT C.   SS   NDM 71 01
  NEW DIMENSIONS 1   SILVERBERG, ROBERT OA
GREAT AIR MONOPOLY, THE   HUBBARD, L. RON   NV   ASF 48 09
  OLE DOC METHUSELAH   HUBBARD, L. RON   AC
GREAT AMERICAN NUDE, THE   BALLARD, J. G.   SS   AMB 68 SU
  LOVE & NAPALM: EXPORT U.S.A.   BALLARD, J. G.   AC
GREAT AUTOMATIC GRAMMATISATOR, THE
                           DAHL, ROALD   SS   53
  VINTAGE ANTHOLOGY OF SCIENCE FANTASY, THE
                                       CERF, CHRISTOPHER   AN
GREAT BEAR, THE   HOLLANDER, JOHN   PM   58
  SPECULATIONS   SANDERS, THOMAS E. AN
GREAT CANINE CHORUS, THE   MCCAFFREY, ANNE   SS   INY 70 01
  GET OFF THE UNICORN   MCCAFFREY, ANNE   AC
  INFINITY 1   HOSKINS, ROBERT   OA
GREAT CHAIN OF BEING WHAT?, THE
                           ALDISS, BRIAN W.   SS   NWR 73 22
  NEW WRITINGS IN SF. 22   BULMER, KENNETH   OA
GREAT CLOCK, THE   JONES, LANGDON   SS   NWS 66 03
  BEST SF STORIES FROM NEW WORLDS 3   MOORCOCK, MICHAEL   AN
  EYE OF THE LENS, THE   JONES, LANGDON   AC
  TRAPS OF TIME, THE   MOORCOCK, MICHAEL   AN
GREAT COLD, THE   LONG, FRANK BELKNAP   SS   ASF 35 02
  NEW WORLDS FOR OLD   DERLETH, AUGUST   AN
  RIM OF THE UNKNOWN   LONG, FRANK BELKNAP AC
  *WORLDS OF TOMORROW   DERLETH, AUGUST   AN
GREAT COLLISION OF MONDAY LAST, THE
                           BRADBURY, RAY   SS   CON 58 01
  MEDICINE FOR MELANCHOLY, A   BRADBURY, RAY   AC
GREAT CONQUEROR, THE   MOORCOCK, MICHAEL   NV   SCF 63 04
  MOORCOCK'S BOOK OF MARTYRS   MOORCOCK, MICHAEL   AC
GREAT CRELLIN COMET, THE   GRIFFITH, GEORGE   SS
  GAMBLES WITH DESTINY   GRIFFITH, GEORGE   AC
GREAT DAY FOR THE IRISH, A LIGHTNER, A. M.   SS   IFS 60 05
  TEEN-AGE SPACE ADVENTURES   FURMAN, A. L.   AN
GREAT DAY IN THE MORNING   LAFFERTY, R. A.   SS   ORB 75 17
  ORBIT 17   KNIGHT, DAMON   OA
GREAT DEAL OF POWER, A (SEE BOOMERANG)
                           RUSSELL, ERIC FRANK   TC
GREAT DEVON MYSTERY, THE   HEALY, RAYMOND J.   SS   NTL 54
  9 TALES OF SPACE AND TIME   HEALY, RAYMOND J.   OA
GREAT ENGINE, THE   VAN VOGT, A. E.   NV   ASF 43 07
  *AWAY AND BEYOND   VAN VOGT, A. E.   NO
  BEAST, THE   VAN VOGT, A. E.   AC
GREAT ESCAPE TOURS, INC.   REED, KIT   SS   FST 74
  FINAL STAGE   FERMAN & MALZBERG   AN
GREAT FIRE, THE   BRADBURY, RAY   SS   SEV 49 03
  *GOLDEN APPLES OF THE SUN   BRADBURY, RAY   AC
GREAT FOG, THE   HEARD, H. F.   SS   44
  GREAT FOG AND OTHER WEIRD TALES, THE HEARD, H. F.   OC
  *TREASURY OF SCIENCE FICTION, A   CONKLIN, GROFF   AN
GREAT GOD AWTO, THE   SMITH, CLARK ASHTON   SS   TWS 40 02
  TALES OF SCIENCE AND SORCERY   SMITH, CLARK ASHTON AC

GREAT INTELLECT BOOM, THE   ANVIL, CHRISTOPHER   SS   ASF 69 07
  SCHOOL AND SOCIETY THROUGH SCIENCE FICTION
                                   OLANDER/GREENBERG/&   AN
  SOCIAL PROBLEMS THROUGH SCIENCE FICTION GREENBERG/MILSTEAD/& AN
GREAT IS DIANA   DAVIDSON, AVRAM   SS   FSF 58 08
  OR ALL THE SEAS WITH OYSTERS   DAVIDSON, AVRAM   AC
GREAT JUDGE, THE   VAN VOGT, A. E.   SS   FBK 48 03
  *AWAY AND BEYOND   VAN VOGT, A. E.   AC
  FIFTY SHORT SCIENCE FICTION TALES ASIMOV & CONKLIN   AN
  TIME CURVE, THE   MOSKOWITZ & ELWOOD   AN
GREAT KEINPLATZ EXPERIMENT, THE
                                   DOYLE, ARTHUR CONAN   SS   WRT 36 10
  *BEST OF SCIENCE FICTION   CONKLIN, GROFF   AN
  GREAT SCIENCE FICTION ABOUT DOCTORS CONKLIN, G&FABRICANT AN
GREAT KLADNAR RACE, THE (AS RICHARD GREER)
                                   GARRETT, RANDALL
                   AND SILVERBERG, ROBERT   SS C AMZ 56 12
  INFINITE ARENA, THE   CARR, TERRY   AN
GREAT LOST DISCOVERIES I - INVISIBILITY
                                   BROWN, FREDRIC   SS
  NIGHTMARES AND GEEZENSTACKS   BROWN, FREDRIC   AC
GREAT LOST DISCOVERIES II - INVULNERABILITY
                                   BROWN, FREDRIC   SS
  NIGHTMARES AND GEEZENSTACKS   BROWN, FREDRIC   AC
GREAT LOST DISCOVERIES III - IMMORTALITY
                                   BROWN, FREDRIC   SS   NEW 61 AC
  NIGHTMARES AND GEEZENSTACKS   BROWN, FREDRIC   AC
GREAT NEBRASKA SEA, THE   DANZIG, ALLAN   FA   GAL 63 08
  SPECTRUM 4   AMIS & CONQUEST   AN
  9TH ANNUAL OF THE YEAR'S BEST S-F, THE MERRIL, JUDITH   AN
GREAT PLAN, THE   KETTLE, LEROY   SS   NWR 76 28
  NEW WRITINGS IN SF. 28   BULMER, KENNETH   OA
GREAT RADIO PERIL, THE   RUSSELL, ERIC FRANK   SS   ASF 37 04
  ABOVE THE HUMAN LANDSCAPE   MCNELLY & STOVER   AN
GREAT SACRIFICE, THE   WALLIS, GEORGE C.   SS   LOM 03 06
  WORLDS APART   LOCKE, GEORGE   AN
GREAT SLOW KINGS, THE   ZELAZNY, ROGER   SS   WOT 63 12
  ABC OF SCIENCE FICTION, AN   BOARDMAN, TOM JR.   AN
  DOORS OF HIS FACE, THE LAMPS OF HIS MOUTH, THE
                                   ZELAZNY, ROGER   AC
  STARS AROUND US, THE   HOSKINS, ROBERT   AN
GREAT STONE OF SARDIS, THE   STOCKTON, FRANK R.   NO   HPM 97 11
  SCIENCE FICTION OF FRANK R. STOCKTON, THE
                                   STOCKTON, FRANK R.   AC
GREAT SUPERSONIC ZEPPELIN RACE, THE
                                   BOVA, BEN   NV
  FAR SIDE OF TIME, THE   ELWOOD, ROGER   OA
GREAT WALL OF MEXICO, THE   SLADEK, JOHN T.   NV   BMR 73
  BAD MOON RISING   DISCH, THOMAS M.   OA
GREAT WAR IN ENGLAND IN 1897, THE
                                   LE QUEX, WILLIAM   NV
  BEFORE ARMAGEDDON   MOORCOCK, MICHAEL   AN
GREAT WAR SYNDICATE, THE (ABRIDGED)
                                   STOCKTON, FRANK R.   NV   OAW 88 12
  *BEST OF SCIENCE FICTION   CONKLIN, GROFF   AN
GREAT WIDE WORLD OVER THERE, THE (CORA AND THE GREAT WIDE
  WORLD OVER THERE)   BRADBURY, RAY   SS   MCL 52 08
  *GOLDEN APPLES OF THE SUN   BRADBURY, RAY   AC
GREATER CONFLICT, THE   JONES, RAYMOND F.   NV   TWS 50 02
  THIS ISLAND EARTH   JONES, RAYMOND F.   NO
GREATER THAN GODS   MOORE, C. L.   NV   ASF 39 07
  BEST OF C. L. MOORE, THE   MOORE, C. L.   AC
GREATER THAN INFINITY   TUBB, E. C.   SS   NWS 60 11
  TEN FROM TOMORROW   TUBB, E. C.   AC
GREATER THING, THE   GODWIN, TOM   NV   ASF 54 02
  MORE PENGUIN SCIENCE FICTION   ALDISS, BRIAN W.   AN
GREATEST ADVENTURE, THE (SEE THE GREATEST GAME)
                                   TAINE, JOHN   TC
GREATEST ASSET, THE   ASIMOV, ISAAC   SS   ASF 72 01
  BEST SCIENCE FICTION STORIES OF THE YEAR (1972)
                                   DEL REY, LESTER   AN
  BUY JUPITER AND OTHER STORIES   ASIMOV, ISAAC   AC
GREATEST CAR IN THE WORLD, THE HARRISON, HARRY   SS   NWS 66 10
  PRIME NUMBER   HARRISON, HARRY   AC
GREATEST GIFT, THE   STERN, PHILIP VAN D. SS   43
  OTHER SIDE OF THE CLOCK, THE   STERN, PHILIP VAN D.   AN
GREATEST INVENTION, THE   WILLIAMSON, JACK   NV   ASF 51 07
  STRANGE TOMORROWS   HOSKINS, ROBERT   AN
GREATEST LOVE, THE   MCCAFFREY, ANNE   NA
  FUTURELOVE   ELWOOD, ROGER   OA
GREATEST TELEVISION SHOW ON EARTH, THE
                                   BALLARD, J. G.   SS   ABT 72 WI
  LOW-FLYING AIRCRAFT AND OTHER STORIES BALLARD, J. G.   AC
GREATEST TERTIAN, THE   BOUCHER, ANTHONY   SS   NEW 52 AN
  ENEMIES IN SPACE   CONKLIN, GROFF   AN
  *INVADERS OF EARTH   CONKLIN, GROFF   AN
  SCIENCE-FICTIONAL SHERLOCK HOLMES, THE COUNCIL OF FOUR   AN
GREED   WENSKES, HELMUT   IL
  BEYOND THIS HORIZON   CARRELL, CHRISTOPHER OA
GREEN BOY, THE   LOUDEN, LEO   SS
  MIND ANGEL AND OTHER STORIES, THE ELWOOD, ROGER   OA
GREEN CAT, THE   CARTMILL, CLEVE   SS   WBY 51 01
  *OUTER REACHES, THE   DERLETH, AUGUST   AN
GREEN EYED MONSTER, THE (SEE GHOST OF A CHANCE)
                                   STURGEON, THEODORE   TC
GREEN FINGERS (VENTURE TO THE MOON)
                                   CLARKE, ARTHUR C.   SS   FSF 57 01
  DAYS AFTER TOMORROW, THE   SANTESSON, HANS S.   AN
  OF TIME AND STARS   CLARKE, ARTHUR C.   AC
  OTHER SIDE OF THE SKY, THE   CLARKE, ARTHUR C.   AC
GREEN FIVE RENEGADE   HARRISON, M. JOHN   NV   NWR 69 14
  NEW WRITINGS IN SF. 14   CARNELL, JOHN   OA
GREEN FLAME, THE   WANDREI, DONALD   SS   WRT 30 07
  STRANGE HARVEST   WANDREI, DONALD   AC
GREEN FOREST, THE   VAN VOGT, A. E.   NV   ASF 49 06
  BEST OF A. E. VAN VOGT, THE (BRITISH) VAN VOGT, A. E.   AC

FUTURES TO INFINITY   MOSKOWITZ, SAM   AN
WAR AGAINST THE RULL, THE   VAN VOGT, A. E.   NO
GREEN FUSE, THE   RICKETTS, MARTIN I.   SS   NWR 75 25
  NEW WRITINGS IN SF. 25   BULMER, KENNETH   OA
GREEN GLORY   LONG, FRANK BELKNAP   SS   ASF 35 01
  RIM OF THE UNKNOWN   LONG, FRANK BELKNAP   AC
GREEN HILLS OF EARTH, THE, A   HEINLEIN, ROBERT A.   AC   SHS 51
  ROBERT HEINLEIN OMNIBUS, A   HEINLEIN, ROBERT A.   AC
GREEN HILLS OF EARTH, THE   HEINLEIN, ROBERT A.   SS   SEP 47 02
  BEST OF ROBERT HEINLEIN, THE   HEINLEIN, ROBERT A.   AC
  GREEN HILLS OF EARTH, THE   HEINLEIN, ROBERT A.   AC
  IN DREAMS AWAKE   FIEDLER, LESLIE A.   AN
  INVASION FROM MARS   WELLES, ORSON   AN
  *MY BEST SCIENCE FICTION STORY   MARGULIES & FRIEND   AN
  PAST THROUGH TOMORROW, THE   HEINLEIN, ROBERT A.   AC
  POST READER OF FANTASY AND SCIENCE FICTION
                                   SATURDAY EVE. POST   AN
  SCIENCE FICTION: THE FUTURE   ALLEN, DICK   AN
  SPECULATIONS   SANDERS, THOMAS E.   AN
  *STRANGE PORTS OF CALL   DERLETH, AUGUST   AN
GREEN MACHINE, THE   BRADBURY, RAY   SS   ARG 51 03
  DANDELION WINE   BRADBURY, RAY   NO
GREEN MAGIC   VANCE, JACK   SS   FSF 63 06
  BEST FROM FANTASY AND SCIENCE FICTION: 13
                                   DAVIDSON, AVRAM   AN
  SPECIAL WONDER   MCCOMAS, J. FRANCIS   AN
GREEN MORNING, THE   BRADBURY, RAY   SS   NEW 51 AC
  MARTIAN CHRONICLES, THE   BRADBURY, RAY   AC
GREEN PATCHES (MISBEGOTTEN MISSIONARY)
                                   ASIMOV, ISAAC   SS   GAL 50 11
  NIGHTFALL AND OTHER STORIES   ASIMOV, ISAAC   AC
  SCIENCE FICTION   BRODKIN & PEARSON   AN
GREEN SPLOTCHES, THE   STRIBLING, T. S.   NV   ADV 20 01
  POCKET BOOK OF SCIENCE-FICTION, THE WOLLHEIM, DONALD A. AN
GREEN THOUGHTS   COLLIER, JOHN   SS   31
  POCKET BOOK OF SCIENCE-FICTION, THE WOLLHEIM, DONALD A. AN
  ROOTS OF EVIL, THE   PARRY, MICHEL   AN
  SCIENCE FICTION ARGOSY, A   KNIGHT, DAMON   AN
GREEN THUMB   GUNN, JAMES E.   NV   IFS 57 04
  BREAKING POINT   GUNN, JAMES E.   AC
GREEN THUMB   SIMAK, CLIFFORD D.   NV   GAL 54 07
  ALIENS FOR NEIGHBOURS   SIMAK, CLIFFORD D.   AC
  BEST SF 5   CRISPIN, EDMUND   AN
  OTHER WORLDS OF CLIFFORD SIMAK   SIMAK, CLIFFORD D.   AC
  ROOTS OF EVIL, THE   PARRY, MICHEL   AN
  *WORLDS OF CLIFFORD SIMAK, THE   SIMAK, CLIFFORD D.   AC
GREEN THUMB, THE   ANDERSON, POUL   SS   SFQ 53 02
  MASTERS OF SCIENCE FICTION   HOWARD, IVAN   AN
GREEN THUMB, THE   DE CAMP, L. SPRAGUE
                   AND PRATT, FLETCHER   SS C FSF 53 02
  TALES FROM GAVAGAN'S BAR   DE CAMP, L. S.&PRATT   AC
GREEN TORTURE, THE   HILLIARD, A. ROWLEY   SS   WOS 31 03
  FROM OFF THIS WORLD   MARGULIES & FRIEND   AN
GREEN WINE FOR DREAMING   BRADBURY, RAY   SS   NEW 57 NO
  VINTAGE BRADBURY, THE   BRADBURY, RAY   AC
GREENFACE   SCHMITZ, JAMES H.   NV   UNK 43 08
  CIRCUS OF DR. LAO AND OTHER IMPROBABLE STORIES
                                   BRADBURY, RAY   AN
  PRIDE OF MONSTERS, A   SCHMITZ, JAMES H.   AC
GREENHOUSE DEFECT, THE   OFFUTT, ANDREW J.   NA
  STELLAR SHORT NOVELS   DEL REY, JUDY-LYNN   OA
GREENPLACE   PURDOM, TOM   SS   FSF 64 11
  WORLD'S BEST SCIENCE FICTION: 1965 WOLLHEIM & CARR   AN
GREENSLAVES   HERBERT, FRANK   NV   AMZ 65 03
  BUG-EYED MONSTERS   CHEETHAM, ANTHONY   AN
  ON OUR WAY TO THE FUTURE   CARR, TERRY   AN
GREGORY CIRCLE, THE   LEINSTER, MURRAY   NV   TWS 47 04
  OUT OF THIS WORLD   LEINSTER, MURRAY   NO
GRENDEL   NIVEN, LARRY   NV   NEW 68 AC
  NEUTRON STAR   NIVEN, LARRY   AC
GRENVILLE'S PLANET   SHAARA, MICHAEL   SS   FSF 52 10
  BEST SF 3   CRISPIN, EDMUND   AN
  UNTRAVELLED WORLDS   BARTER & WILSON   AN
GREYLORN   LAUMER, KEITH   NA   AMZ 59 04
  GREYLORN   LAUMER, KEITH   AC
GREYSPUN'S GIFT   BARRETT, NEAL JR.   SS   WOT 70 WI
  WORLD'S BEST SCIENCE FICTION: 1971 WOLLHEIM & CARR   AN
GRIEF OF BAGDAD   BARNES, ARTHUR K.   SS   TWS 43 06
  *MY BEST SCIENCE FICTION STORY   MARGULIES & FRIEND   AN
GRIME AND PUNISHMENT (CLEAR AS MUD)
                                   LAUMER, KEITH   NV   IFS 67 08
  RETIEF: AMBASSADOR TO SPACE   LAUMER, KEITH   AC
GRIMM'S STORY   VINGE, VERNOR   NA   ORB 68 04
  ORBIT 4   KNIGHT, DAMON   OA
GRIN AND BEAR IT   LICHTY   CT   PHS 72 06
  BEST SF: 1972   HARRISON & ALDISS   AN
GRINNING GHOUL, THE   BLOCH, ROBERT   SS   WRT 36 06
  BLOCH AND BRADBURY   BRADBURY & BLOCH   AC
GRIPES OF WRAITH, THE   BOND, NELSON S.   SS
  31ST OF FEBRUARY, THE   BOND, NELSON S.   AC
GRISLY FOLK, THE   WELLS, H. G.   AR   SRY 21 04
  ANCIENT MYSTERIES READER, THE   HAINING, PETER   AN
  SHORT STORIES OF H. G. WELLS, THE WELLS, H. G.   AC
GROANING HINGES OF THE WORLD LAFFERTY, R. A.   SS   NEW 71 AC
  DOES ANYONE ELSE HAVE SOMETHING FURTHER TO ADD?
                                   LAFFERTY, R. A.   AC
  RUINS OF EARTH, THE   DISCH, THOMAS M.   AN
GROOVY HOMO SAP, THE (HOMO SAP)
                                   NUETZEL, CHARLES   SS
  IMAGES OF TOMORROW   NUETZEL, CHARLES   AC
GROSS LOVE STORY, A   COVER, ARTHUR BYRON SS   ALT 74
  ALTERNATES   GERROLD, DAVID   OA
GROWING SEASON   WALLACE, F. L.   NV   IFS 59 07
  FROZEN PLANET AND 4 OTHER SF NOVELLAS, THE
                                   ANONYMOUS   AN

GROWING UP IN EDGE CITY

GROWING UP IN EDGE CITY   POHL, FREDERIK   SS   EPC 75
  EPOCH   ELWOOD & SILVERBERG   OA
GROWN-UP PEOPLE'S FEET, THE   YOUNG, ROBERT F.   SS   FUN 55 06
  GLASS OF STARS, A   YOUNG, ROBERT F.   AC
GRUNDER, THE   HENDERSON, ZENNA   SS   IMG 53 06
  ANYTHING BOX, THE   HENDERSON, ZENNA   AC
GRYB, THE (REPETITION)   VAN VOGT, A. E.   NV   ASF 40 04
  PROXY INTELLIGENCE AND OTHER MIND BENDERS
                                     VAN VOGT, A. E.   AC
GUARDIAN ANGEL   PAGE, GERALD W.   SS   NWR 66 09
  NEW WRITINGS IN SF. 9   CARNELL, JOHN   OA
GUARDIAN ANGEL (SEE CHILDHOOD'S END, REWRITTEN BY JAMES BLISH)
                               CLARKE, ARTHUR C.   TC   FFM 50 04
GUARDIAN SPIRIT (SEE THE MARGINAL MAN)
                               OLIVER, CHAD   TC
GUEST EDITORIAL   POHL, FREDERIK   ED   IFS 74 06
  BEST OF IF, THE VOLUME II   IF, EDITORS OF   AN
GUEST EXPERT   LANG, ALLEN KIM   SS   PLS 51 01
  EVIL EARTHS   ALDISS, BRIAN W.   AN
GUEST IN THE HOUSE   LONG, FRANK BELKNAP SS   ASF 46 03
  RIM OF THE UNKNOWN   LONG, FRANK BELKNAP AC
  *STRANGE PORTS OF CALL   DERLETH, AUGUST   AN
GUEST OF GANYMEDE, A   MACAPP, C. C.   NV   WOT 63 06
  BEST SCIENCE FICTION FROM WORLDS OF TOMORROW, THE
                                   POHL, FREDERIK   AN
GUEST OF HONOR   PRIESTLEY, J. B.   SS
  OTHER PLACE, THE   PRIESTLEY, J. B.   AC
GUESTING TIME   LAFFERTY, R. A.   SS   IFS 65 05
  NINE HUNDRED GRANDMOTHERS   LAFFERTY, R. A.   AC
GUESTS OF CHANCE, THE   BEAUMONT, CHARLES
                               AND OLIVER, CHAD   SS C INF 56 06
  NIGHT RIDE AND OTHER JOURNEYS   BEAUMONT, CHARLES   AC
GUIDANCE   MALZBERG, BARRY N. SS
  JOURNEY TO ANOTHER STAR AND OTHER STORIES
                                   ELWOOD, ROGER   OA
GUIDED MAN, THE   DE CAMP, L. SPRAGUE NV   STS 52 10
  GUN FOR DINOSAUR AND OTHER IMAGINATIVE TALES
                                   DE CAMP, L. SPRAGUE AC
GUIDED TOUR   NUETZEL, CHARLES   SS
  IMAGES OF TOMORROW   NUETZEL, CHARLES   AC
GUIDELIGHT   INOUYE, JON   SS
  NIGHT TIDE, A   INOUYE, JON   OC
GUILTY AS CHARGED   PORGES, ARTHUR   SS   NEW 55 AN
  BEST SCIENCE FICTION STORIES AND NOVELS: 1955
                                   DIKTY, T. E.   AN
  SOCIOLOGY THROUGH SCIENCE FICTION MILSTEAD/GREENBERG/& AN
GUINEVERE FOR EVERYBODY   WILLIAMSON, JACK   SS   STR 54 03
  PANDORA EFFECT, THE   WILLIAMSON, JACK   AC
  STAR SCIENCE FICTION STORIES NO. 3 POHL, FREDERIK   OA
GULF   HEINLEIN, ROBERT A. SN   ASF 49 11
  ASSIGNMENT IN ETERNITY   HEINLEIN, ROBERT A. AC
  CENTURY OF GREAT SHORT SCIENCE FICTION NOVELS, A
                                   KNIGHT, DAMON   AN
GUMDROP KING, THE   STANTON, WILL   SS   FSF 62 08
  BEST FROM FANTASY AND SCIENCE FICTION: 12
                                   DAVIDSON, AVRAM   AN
GUN FOR DINOSAUR, A   DE CAMP, L. SPRAGUE NV   GAL 56 03
  GUN FOR DINOSAUR AND OTHER IMAGINATIVE TALES
                                   DE CAMP, L. SPRAGUE AC
  TIME CURVE, THE   MOSKOWITZ & ELWOOD   AN
  WORLD THAT COULDN'T BE AND 8 OTHER SF NOVELETS
                                   GOLD, H. L.   AN
  3000 YEARS OF FANTASY AND SCIENCE FICTION
                                   DE CAMP, L. S.&C.   AN
GUN FOR HIRE   REYNOLDS, MACK   SS   ASF 60 12
  SPECIAL WONDER   MCCOMAS, J. FRANCIS AN
GUN WITHOUT A BANG, THE   O'DONNEVAN, FINN   NV   GAL 58 06
  FOURTH GALAXY READER, THE   GOLD, H. L.   AN
GUN WITHOUT A BANG, THE   SHECKLEY, ROBERT   NV   GAL 58 06
  SCIENCE FACT/FICTION   FARRELL/GAGE/&   AN
  STORE OF INFINITY   SHECKLEY, ROBERT   AC
  WONDERMAKERS 2   HOSKINS, ROBERT   AN
GUT IN PERIL   DARNAY, ARSEN   SS   IFS 74 12
  BEST OF IF, THE VOLUME III   BAEN, JAMES   AN
GUTTERSNIPE   RAPHAEL, RICK   NV   ASF 64 11
  THIRST QUENCHERS, THE   RAPHAEL, RICK   AC
GUY WITH THE EYES, THE   ROBINSON, SPIDER   SS   ASF 73 02
  CALLAHAN'S CROSSTIME SALOON   ROBINSON, SPIDER   AC
GUYAL OF SFERE   VANCE, JACK   NV   50
  DYING EARTH, THE   VANCE, JACK   OC
  EIGHT FANTASMS AND MAGICS   VANCE, JACK   AC
  ENDS OF TIME, THE   SILVERBERG, ROBERT   AN
GYPSY   ANDERSON, POUL   SS   ASF 50 01
  EVERY BOY'S BOOK OF OUTER SPACE STORIES DIKTY, T. E. AN
  STRANGERS FROM EARTH   ANDERSON, POUL   AC
  TO THE STARS   SILVERBERG, ROBERT   AN
H. G. WELLS   AMIS, KINGSLEY   IN
  WAR OF THE WORLDS, THE TIME MACHINE AND SELECTED SHORT STORIES
                                   WELLS, H. G.   AC
H. G. WELLS: EXPONENT OF EXTRAPOLATION
                               CLARKE, I. F.   AR   FTS 70 06
  BEYOND THIS HORIZON   CARRELL, CHRISTOPHER OA
"H-BOMBS' THUNDER, THE"   BRUNNER, JOHN   SG   SNG 58 10
  BOOK OF JOHN BRUNNER, THE   BRUNNER, JOHN   AC
HABIT   DEL REY, LESTER   SS   ASF 39 11
  EARLY DEL REY   DEL REY, LESTER   AC
  JUPITER   POHL, C. & F.   AN
HABITS OF THE RIGELIAN NIGHTFOX
                               BIANCHI, ED   SS   IFS 71 12
  BEST FROM IF, THE VOLUME I IF, EDITORS OF   AN
HACK, THE   KERSH, GERALD   SS
  MEN WITHOUT BONES   KERSH, GERALD   AC
HADES AND EUCLID (TRANSLATED BY ROBERT BLY)
                               MARTINSON, HARRY   SS   70
  NEW CONSTELLATIONS   DISCH & NAYLOR   OA

HADES BUSINESS, THE   PRATCHETT, TERRY   SS   SCF 63 08
  UNFRIENDLY FUTURE, THE   BOARDMAN, TOM JR.   AN
HADJ   ELLISON, HARLAN   SS   SPA 56 12
  ELLISON WONDERLAND   ELLISON, HARLAN   AC
HAG SELEEN, THE   STURGEON, THEODORE SS   UNK 42 12
  UNKNOWN 5, THE   BENSEN, D. R.   AN
HAGGARD HONEYMOON   GREEN, JOSEPH
                               AND WEBBERT, JAMES NV C NWR 64 01
  NEW WRITINGS IN SF. 1   CARNELL, JOHN   OA
HAGGOPIAN   LUMLEY, BRIAN   NV   FSF 73 06
  YEAR'S BEST HORROR STORIES: SERIES II, THE
                                   DAVIS, RICHARD   AN
HAIL AND FAREWELL   BRADBURY, RAY   SS   TDY 53 03
  *GOLDEN APPLES OF THE SUN   BRADBURY, RAY   AC
  S IS FOR SPACE   BRADBURY, RAY   AC
  VINTAGE BRADBURY, THE   BRADBURY, RAY   AC
HAIL TO THE CHIEF   CORES, LUCY   NV
  BEYOND TIME   LEY, SANDRA   OA
HAIL TO THE CHIEF   GARRETT, RANDALL   SS   ASF 62
  AMERICAN GOVERNMENT THROUGH SCIENCE FICTION
                                   OLANDER/GREENBERG/& AN
HAIL TO THE CHIEF   SACKETT, SAM   SN   FUT 54 06
  AMERICAN GOVERNMENT THROUGH SCIENCE FICTION
                                   OLANDER/GREENBERG/& AN
  WEIRD ONES, THE   HOWARD, IVAN   AN
HAIR OF THE DOG   BEAUMONT, CHARLES   SS   OSF 54 03
  YONDER   BEAUMONT, CHARLES   AC
HAIR-RAISING ADVENTURE   BROWN, ROSEL GEORGE SS   STR 59 05
  STAR SCIENCE FICTION STORIES NO. 5 POHL, FREDERIK   OA
HAIRY ONES, THE   WELLS, BASIL   SS
  PLANETS OF ADVENTURE   WELLS, BASIL   AC
HAL IRWIN'S MAGIC LAMP   VONNEGUT, KURT JR. SS   CMP 57 06
  CANARY IN A CAT HOUSE   VONNEGUT, KURT JR.   AC
HALCYON IN A MIRROR AT MIDNIGHT
                               BRADFIELD, SCOTT   SS
  FUTURE PASTIMES   EDELSTEIN, SCOTT   OA
HALF A HOKA- POUL ANDERSON   DICKSON, GORDON R. AR   59
  SCIENCE-FICTIONAL SHERLOCK HOLMES, THE COUNCIL OF FOUR AN
HALF AN OAF   ROBINSON, SPIDER   NV
  ANALOG ANNUAL   BOVA, BEN   OA
HALF LIFE   PAYES, RACHEL C.   SS   COI 73
  CHILDREN OF INFINITY   ELWOOD, ROGER   OA
HALF PAIR, THE   CHANDLER, A. BERTRAM SS   NWS 57 11
  PENGUIN SCIENCE FICTION   ALDISS, BRIAN W.   AN
HALF THE KINGDOM   PISERCHIA, DORIS   SS   ORB 73 12
  ORBIT 12   KNIGHT, DAMON   OA
HALF-BAKED PUBLISHER'S DELIGHT ASIMOV, ISAAC
                               AND HUDSON, JEFFREY S. SS C IFS 74 08
  BEST FROM IF, THE VOLUME III   BAEN, JAMES   AN
HALF-BREED   ASIMOV, ISAAC   SS   AST 40 02
  EARLY ASIMOV, THE   ASIMOV, ISAAC   AC
  SPACE MAGICIANS, THE   NORTON & MOSKOWITZ   AN
  TOMORROW, AND TOMORROW, AND TOMORROW... HEINTZ/HERBERT/JOOS/ AN
HALF-BREEDS ON VENUS   ASIMOV, ISAAC   SS   AST 40 10
  EARLY ASIMOV, THE   ASIMOV, ISAAC   AC
HALF-PAST ETERNITY   MACDONALD, JOHN D. NV   SSS 50 07
  HUMAN EQUATION, THE   NOLAN, WILLIAM F.   AN
HALFLING, THE   BRACKETT, LEIGH   SS   AST 43 02
  HALFLING AND OTHER STORIES, THE BRACKETT, LEIGH   AC
  SHOT IN THE DARK   MERRIL, JUDITH   AN
HALFWAY HOUSE   SILVERBERG, ROBERT SS   IFS 66 11
  CUBE ROOT OF UNCERTAINTY, THE   SILVERBERG, ROBERT   AC
  DIMENSION THIRTEEN   SILVERBERG, ROBERT   AC
HALL OF FAME (KINGSOLVING'S PLANET IRREGULARS)
                               CHANDLER, A. BERTRAM NV GAL 69 07
  ALTERNATE ORBITS   CHANDLER, A. BERTRAM DC
HALL OF MACHINES, THE   JONES, LANGDON   SS   NWS 68 03
  ENGLAND SWINGS SF   MERRIL, JUDITH   AN
  EYE OF THE LENS, THE   JONES, LANGDON   AC
  SPACE-TIME JOURNAL, THE   MERRIL, JUDITH   AN
HALL OF MIRRORS   BROWN, FREDRIC   SS   GAL 53 12
  ASSIGNMENT IN TOMORROW   POHL, FREDERIK   AN
  BEST OF FREDRIC BROWN, THE   BROWN, FREDRIC   AC
  HONEYMOON IN HELL   BROWN, FREDRIC   AC
HALL OF THE DEAD, THE   DE CAMP, L. SPRAGUE
                               AND HOWARD, ROBERT E. NV C FSF 67 02
  CONAN   HOWARD, R./DE CAMP/& AC
HALLOWEEN STORY   FITZ GERALD, GREGORY SS BTH 73
  YEAR'S BEST HORROR STORIES: SERIES III, THE
                                   DAVIS, RICHARD   AN
HALLUCINATION ORBIT (ALSO AS THE BLISS OF SOLITUDE)
                               MCINTOSH, J. T.   NV   GAL 52 01
  GALAXY SCIENCE FICTION OMNIBUS   GOLD, H. L.   AN
  SECOND GALAXY READER OF SCIENCE FICTION GOLD, H. L. AN
HALLUCINATION, THE   BOULLE, PIERRE   SS
  TIME OUT OF MIND   BOULLE, PIERRE   OC
HALO   CLEMENT, HAL   NV   GAL 52 10
  SHADOW OF TOMORROW   POHL, FREDERIK   AN
  SMALL CHANGES   CLEMENT, HAL   AC
HALTED VILLAGE, THE   RACKHAM, JOHN   NV   NWR 75 25
  NEW WRITINGS IN SF. 25   BULMER, KENNETH   OA
HAMMER OF EVIL, THE   SLADEK, JOHN T.   SS   NWB 75 09
  NEW WORLDS NINE   BAILEY, HILARY   OA
HAMMERPOUND PARK BURGLARY, THE WELLS, H. G.   SS   PMB 94
  SHORT STORIES OF H. G. WELLS, THE WELLS, H. G.   AC
  STOLEN BACILLUS AND OTHER INCIDENTS, THE WELLS, H. G. AC
HAND OF NERGAL, THE   CARTER, LIN
                               AND HOWARD, ROBERT E. SS C
  CONAN   HOWARD, R./DE CAMP/& AC
HAND OF THE GODS   VAN VOGT, A. E.   NV   ASF 46 12
  BEST OF A. E. VAN VOGT, THE (BRITISH) VAN VOGT, A. E. AC
  EMPIRE OF THE ATOM   VAN VOGT, A. E.   NO
HAND WITH ONE HUNDRED FINGERS, THE
                               LAFFERTY, R. A.   SS   ORB 76 18
  ORBIT 18   KNIGHT, DAMON   OA

HAND, THE   SMITTER, WESSEL H.   SS   STO 47 02
  TIMELESS STORIES FOR TODAY AND TOMORROW BRADBURY, RAY   AN
HANDFUL OF SILVER, A   COUNSELMAN, MARY E. SS
  TRAVELLERS BY NIGHT   DERLETH, AUGUST   OA
HANDFUL OF STARS, A   ANDERSON, POUL   NA AMZ 59 06
  AGENT OF THE TERRAN EMPIRE   ANDERSON, POUL   AC
HANDICAP (ALSO AS THE HANDICAPPED)
                                 NIVEN, LARRY   NV GAL 67 12
  WORLD'S BEST SCIENCE FICTION: 1968 WOLLHEIM & CARR   AN
HANDICAPPED, THE (HANDICAP)   NIVEN, LARRY   NV GAL 67 12
  NEUTRON STAR   NIVEN, LARRY   AC
HANDLER, THE   BRADBURY, RAY   SS WRT 47 01
  AUTUMN PEOPLE, THE   BRADBURY, RAY   AC
  BLOCH AND BRADBURY   BRADBURY & BLOCH   AC
  BR-R-R-!   CONKLIN, GROFF   AN
  *DARK CARNIVAL   BRADBURY, RAY   AC
  SMALL ASSASSIN, THE   BRADBURY, RAY   AC
  UNEXPECTED, THE   MARGULIES, LEO   AN
HANDLER, THE   KNIGHT, DAMON   SS ROG 60 08
  ABOVE THE HUMAN LANDSCAPE   MCNELLY & STOVER   AN
  ANOTHER TOMORROW   HOLLISTER, BERNARD C AN
  BEST OF DAMON KNIGHT, THE   KNIGHT, DAMON   AC
  IN DEEP   KNIGHT, DAMON   AC
  SF: THE BEST OF THE BEST   MERRIL, JUDITH   AN
  TURNING ON   KNIGHT, DAMON   AC
  5TH ANNUAL OF THE YEAR'S BEST S-F, THE MERRIL, JUDITH   AN
HANDS ACROSS SPACE (ALSO AS SCIENTIFIC METHOD)
                                 OLIVER, CHAD   SS SFP 53 08
  HUMAN ZERO, THE   MOSKOWITZ & ELWOOD   AN
HANDS ACROSS THE DEEP   ELAM, RICHARD M. JR. SS
  TEEN-AGE SCIENCE FICTION STORIES ELAM, RICHARD M. JR.   AC
HANDS OF THE MAN   LAFFERTY, R. A.   SS INY 70 01
  INFINITY 1   HOSKINS, ROBERT   OA
HANDS OFF   SHECKLEY, ROBERT NV GAL 54 04
  CITIZEN IN SPACE   SHECKLEY, ROBERT   AC
  HISTORY OF THE SCIENCE FICTION MAGAZINE, THE PART 3 1946-1955
                                 ASHLEY, MICHAEL   AN
  ROBERT SHECKLEY OMNIBUS, THE   SHECKLEY, ROBERT   AC
HANDS   BAXTER, JOHN   SS NWR 65 06
  NEW WRITINGS IN SF. 6   CARNELL, JOHN   OA
HANDS, THE   DOLAN, MIKE   SS
  SANTANA MORNING AND OTHER STORIES DOLAN, MIKE   OC
HANG HEAD, VANDAL!   CLIFTON, MARK   SS AMZ 62 04
  8TH ANNUAL OF THE YEAR'S BEST S-F, THE MERRIL, JUDITH   AN
HANGED MAN, THE   BRYANT, EDWARD   SS CLR 72 02
  AMONG THE DEAD   BRYANT, EDWARD   AC
  CLARION II   WILSON, ROBIN SCOTT OA
HANGING (SEE LETTING IT ALL HANG OUT)
                                 MALZBERG, BARRY N.   TC
HANS PHAALL- A TALE   POE, EDGAR ALLEN SS SLM 35 06
  MASTERPIECES OF SCIENCE FICTION MOSKOWITZ, SAM   AN
HANS SCHNAP'S SPY-GLASS   ERCKMANN-CHATRIAN SS
  STRANGE SIGNPOSTS   ELWOOD & MOSKOWITZ   AN
HAPPENING, A   ROBERTS, FRANK   SS
  SECOND PACIFIC BOOK OF SCIENCE FICTION, THE
                                 BAXTER, JOHN   AN
HAPPIEST CREATURE, THE   WILLIAMSON, JACK SS STR 53 02
  PANDORA EFFECT, THE   WILLIAMSON, JACK   AC
  STAR OF STARS   POHL, FREDERIK   AN
  STAR SCIENCE FICTION STORIES NO. 2 POHL, FREDERIK   OA
  TRIAL OF TERRA, THE   WILLIAMSON, JACK   NO
HAPPIEST DAY OF YOUR LIFE, THE   SHAW, BOB   SS ASF 70 10
  TOMORROW LIES IN AMBUSH   SHAW, BOB   AC
HAPPILY EVER AFTER   NOLAN, WILLIAM F. SS GAM 65 04
  ALIEN HORIZONS   NOLAN, WILLIAM F.   AC
  WILDERNESS OF STARS, A   NOLAN, WILLIAM F.   AN
HAPPINESS MACHINE, THE (ALSO AS THE TIME MACHINE)
                                 BRADBURY, RAY   SS SEP 57 09
  DANDELION WINE   BRADBURY, RAY   NO
HAPPY BIRTHDAY, DEAR JESUS   POHL, FREDERIK   SS NEW 56 AC
  ALTERNATING CURRENTS   POHL, FREDERIK   AC
  BEST OF FREDERIK POHL, THE   POHL, FREDERIK   AC
HAPPY BREED, THE   SLADEK, JOHN T.   SS DVS 67 01
  DANGEROUS VISIONS   ELLISON, HARLAN   OA
HAPPY DAY IN 2381, A   SILVERBERG, ROBERT SS NOV 70 01
  CITY: 2000 A.D., THE   CLEM/GREENBERG/&   AN
  DAY IN THE LIFE, A   DOZOIS, GARDNER R.   AN
  EARTH IN TRANSIT   SCHWARTZ, SHEILA   AN
  MOONFERNS & STARSONGS   SILVERBERG, ROBERT   AC
  *NOVA 1   HARRISON, HARRY   OA
  SURVIVAL PRINTOUT   TOTAL EFFECT   AN
HAPPY ENDING   KUTTNER, HENRY   NV TWS 48 08
  BEST SCIENCE-FICTION STORIES: 1949, THE BLEILER & DIKTY   AN
  BEYOND TOMORROW   KNIGHT, DAMON   AN
HAPPY FAMILIES ALL LIKE SCRABBLE
                                 DISCH, THOMAS M. SS
  *GETTING INTO DEATH   DISCH, THOMAS M.   AC
HAPPY HERD, THE   WALTON, BRYCE   NV IFS 56 10
  SECOND WORLD OF IF, THE   QUINN & WULFF   AN
"HAPPY LANDINGS, PROFESSOR!"   STOUT, TIM   SS ADS 75 02
  ARMADA SCI-FI TWO   DAVIS, RICHARD   OA
HAPPY MAN, THE   PAGE, GERALD W.   NV ASF 63 03
  INTRODUCING SCIENCE FICTION   ALDISS, BRIAN W.   AN
  STARLIT CORRIDOR, THE   MANSFIELD, ROGER   AN
HAPPY STORY, THE   DISCH, THOMAS M. SS
  *GETTING INTO DEATH   DISCH, THOMAS M.   AC
  WHITE FANG GOES DINGO AND OTHER FUNNY S.F. STORIES
                                 DISCH, THOMAS M.   AC
HARBOR WHISTLES   LOVECRAFT, H. P. PM
  HOLDING YOUR EIGHT HANDS   LUCIE-SMITH, EDWARD AN
HARD BARGAIN   NOURSE, ALAN E.   SS PBY 58 05
  PLAYBOY BOOK OF SCIENCE FICTION AND FANTASY, THE
                                 PLAYBOY, EDITORS OF AN
HARD LUCK DIGGINGS   VANCE, JACK   SS STS 48 07
  *POSSIBLE WORLDS OF SCIENCE FICTION CONKLIN, GROFF   AN

HARD TIMES   EFFINGER, GEO. ALEC SS AMZ 73 03
  IRRATIONAL NUMBERS   EFFINGER, GEO. ALEC   AC
HARD WAY, THE   BARCLAY, ALAN   SS NWS 53 06
  BEST FROM NEW WORLDS SCIENCE FICTION, THE
                                 CARNELL, JOHN   AN
HARDCASTLE   GOULART, RON   SS NEW 71 AC
  ANTIGRAV: COSMIC COMEDIES   STRICK, PHILIP   AN
  INSIDE INFORMATION   MOWSHOWITZ, ABBE   AN
  WHAT'S BECOME OF SCREWLOOSE? AND OTHER INQUIRIES
                                 GOULART, RON   AC
HARDEST BARGAIN, THE   SMITH, EVELYN E. NV GAL 57 06
  BEYOND BELIEF   HURLEY, RICHARD J.   AN
  MIND PARTNER AND 8 OTHER NOVELETS FROM GALAXY
                                 GOLD, H. L.   AN
HARMONIZER, THE   VAN VOGT, A. E.   SS ASF 44 11
  *AWAY AND BEYOND   VAN VOGT, A. E.   AC
HARMONY AGGRO, THE   CLEAVER, PAMELA   SS SPC 74 02
  SPACE 2   DAVIS, RICHARD   OA
HAROLD WILSON AT THE COSMIC COCKTAIL PARTY (ALSO AS THE
  COSMIC COCKTAIL PARTY)   SHAW, BOB   SS SAG 70
  SCIENCE AGAINST MAN   CHEETHAM, ANTHONY   OA
HARP THAT CONQUERED HELL, THE   THARP, BEEBE   SS
  NEW CONSTELLATIONS   DISCH & NAYLOR   OA
HARPER CONAN & SINGER DAVID   PANGBORN, EDGAR   NV
  TOMORROW TODAY   ZEBROWSKI, GEORGE   OA
HARPERS OF TITAN, THE   HAMILTON, EDMOND SS STS 50 09
  DR. CYCLOPS   KUTTNER, HENRY   AN
HARRIET   GOLDIN, STEPHEN
                                 AND HENSEL, C. F. SS C TAL 73
  FRONTIERS 1: TOMORROW'S ALTERNATIVES ELWOOD, ROGER   OA
HARRISON BERGERON   VONNEGUT, KURT JR. SS FSF 61 10
  ABC OF SCIENCE FICTION, AN   BOARDMAN, TOM JR.   AN
  *BEST FROM FANTASY AND SCIENCE FICTION: 11
                                 MILLS, ROBERT P.   AN
  BEST SF 7   CRISPIN, EDMUND   AN
  DECADE THE 1960S   ALDISS & HARRISON   AN
  SCIENCE FICTION   BRODKIN & PEARSON   AN
  SCIENCE FICTION: THE FUTURE   ALLEN, DICK   AN
  STARLIT CORRIDOR, THE   MANSFIELD, ROGER   AN
  WELCOME TO THE MONKEY HOUSE   VONNEGUT, KURT JR.   AC
HARRY AMONG THE ALIENS   ANONYMOUS   SS
  STRANGE WORLD OF SCIENCE FICTION ANONYMOUS   OA
HARRY BORDEN'S NAVAL MONSTER   HENDERSON, WILLIAM J SS
  BATTLE FOR THE PACIFIC AND OTHER ADVENTURES AT SEA, THE
                                 ANONYMOUS   AN
  BATTLE OF THE MONSTERS AND OTHER STORIES, THE
                                 HARTWELL & CURREY   AN
HARRY HARRISON: THE MAN WHO WALKED HOME
                                 MALZBERG, BARRY N. IN
  *BEST OF HARRY HARRISON, THE   HARRISON, HARRY   AC
HARRY THE HARE   HEMESATH, JAMES B. SS DVS 72 02
  AGAIN, DANGEROUS VISIONS   ELLISON, HARLAN   OA
HARRY THE TAILOR   DORMAN, SONYA   SS CMP 61
  POCKETFUL OF STARS, A   KNIGHT, DAMON   AN
HAS ANYONE SEEN THIS HORSEMAN?   BUNCH, DAVID R.   SS
  MODERAN   BUNCH, DAVID R.   AC
HASHISH MAN, THE   DUNSANY, LORD   SS FFM 45 12
  FUTURES UNLIMITED   NORTON, ALDEN H.   AN
HAT ACT, THE   COOVER, ROBERT   SS PBY 68 02
  MASKS   PLAYBOY, EDITORS OF   AN
HAT TRICK, THE   BROWN, FREDRIC   SS UNK 43 02
  ANGELS AND SPACESHIPS   BROWN, FREDRIC   AC
HATCHERY OF DREAMS   LEIBER, FRITZ   SS FAN 61 11
  ROD SERLING'S TRIPLE W: WITCHES, WARLOCKS AND WEREWOLVES
                                 SERLING, ROD   AN
  WORLDS OF FRITZ LEIBER, THE   LEIBER, FRITZ   AC
HATCHERY, THE (FROM BRAVE NEW WORLD)
                                 HUXLEY, ALDOUS   EX WND 32
  CHILDREN OF WONDER   TENN, WILLIAM   AN
HATE (AT THE END OF THE ORBIT)   CLARKE, ARTHUR C. NV IFS 61 11
  BEST OF ARTHUR C. CLARKE: 1937-1971, THE CLARKE, ARTHUR C. AC
  TALES OF TEN WORLDS   CLARKE, ARTHUR C.   AC
HATE DISEASE, THE (SEE TALLIEN THREE)
                                 LEINSTER, MURRAY TC
HATE IS A SANDPAPER ICE CUBE WITH POLKA DOTS OF LOVE ON IT
                                 DIXON, TERRY   SS FIN 70
  FUTURE IS NOW, THE   NOLAN, WILLIAM F.   OA
HATE, THE   PINCKARD, TERRI E. SS WTS 71 01
  YEAR'S BEST HORROR STORIES, THE DAVIS, RICHARD   AN
HATED, THE   FLEHR, PAUL   SS GAL 58 01
  FOURTH GALAXY READER, THE   GOLD, H. L.   AN
HATED, THE   POHL, FREDERIK   SS GAL 58 01
  BEST OF FREDERIK POHL, THE   POHL, FREDERIK   AC
  FIRST STEP OUTWARD   HOSKINS, ROBERT   AN
  TURN LEFT AT THURSDAY   POHL, FREDERIK   AC
HAUNT, THE   STURGEON, THEODORE SS UNK 41 04
  STARSHINE   STURGEON, THEODORE   AC
HAUNTED CENTENNIAL   WEST, WALLACE   NV FUT 58 02
  OUTPOSTS IN SPACE   WEST, WALLACE   AC
HAUNTED CORPSE, THE   POHL, FREDERIK   SS GAL 57 01
  FREDERIK POHL OMNIBUS, THE   POHL, FREDERIK   AC
  THIRD GALAXY READER, THE   GOLD, H. L.   AN
  TOMORROW TIMES SEVEN   POHL, FREDERIK   AC
HAUNTED FUTURE, THE (TRANQUILITY, OR ELSE!)
                                 LEIBER, FRITZ   NV FAN 59 11
  DAY IN THE LIFE, A   DOZOIS, GARDNER R.   AN
  *MIND SPIDER AND OTHER STORIES, THE LEIBER, FRITZ   DC
HAUNTED SPACESUIT, THE (WHO'S THERE?)
                                 CLARKE, ARTHUR C. SS NWS 58 11
  FIFTY SHORT SCIENCE FICTION TALES ASIMOV & CONKLIN   AN
HAUNTED VILLAGE, THE   DICKSON, GORDON R. NV FSF 61 08
  *BEST FROM FANTASY AND SCIENCE FICTION: 11
                                 MILLS, ROBERT P.   AN
HAUNTER OF THE DARK, THE   LOVECRAFT, H. P. NV WRT 36 12
  HAUNTER OF THE DARK, THE   LOVECRAFT, H. P.   AC

HAUNTING OF THE NEW, THE   BRADBURY, RAY   SS   VOB 69 10
  I SING THE BODY ELECTRIC   BRADBURY, RAY   AC
HAUNTING, THE   SELLINGS, ARTHUR   SS   AUT 53 10
  *TIME TRANSFER   SELLINGS, ARTHUR   AC
HAUNTS OF THE VERY RICH   BROWN, T. K. III   NV   PBY 71 05
  YEAR'S BEST HORROR STORIES: SERIES II, THE
                          DAVIS, RICHARD   AN
HAVE I GOT A CHOCOLATE BAR FOR YOU¡
                          BRADBURY, RAY   SS   PNT 73 10
  LONG AFTER MIDNIGHT   BRADBURY, RAY   AC
HAVE IT YOUR OWN WAY (SEE AN ABUNDANCE OF GOOD THINGS)
                          WILSON, RICHARD   TC
HAVE YOUR HATREDS READY (SEE SECRET OF A MIGHTY CITY)
                          ALDISS, BRIAN W.   TC
HAWK AMONG THE SPARROWS   MCLAUGHLIN, DEAN   SN   ASF 68 07
  ANALOG 8   CAMPBELL, JOHN W. JR   AN
  HAWK AMONG THE SPARROWS   MCLAUGHLIN, DEAN   AC
HAWK CARSE   GILMORE, ANTHONY   NV   ASF 31 11
  SPACE HAWK   GILMORE, ANTHONY   AC
HAWKS OVER EGYPT (SEE HAWKS OVER SHEM)
                          HOWARD, ROBERT E.   TC
HAWKS OVER SHEM (FROM "HAWKS OVER EGYPT" BY REH.)
                          DE CAMP, L. SPRAGUE
                          AND HOWARD, ROBERT E.   NV C FUN 55 10
  CONAN THE FREEBOOTER   HOWARD, R. & DE CAMP   AC
  TALES OF CONAN   HOWARD, R. & DE CAMP   AC
HAWKSBILL STATION   SILVERBERG, ROBERT   NV   GAL 67 08
  BEST OF ROBERT SILVERBERG, THE   SILVERBERG, ROBERT   AC
  BEST SF: 1967   HARRISON & ALDISS   AN
  DECADE THE 1960S   ALDISS & HARRISON   AN
  GIFTS OF ASTI AND OTHER STORIES OF SCIENCE FICTION, THE
                          ELWOOD, ROGER   AN
  REALITY TRIP, THE   SILVERBERG, ROBERT   AC
  WORLD'S BEST SCIENCE FICTION: 1968   WOLLHEIM & CARR   AN
HAZING, THE   ASIMOV, ISAAC   SS   TWS 42 10
  EARLY ASIMOV, THE   ASIMOV, ISAAC   AC
HE   LOVECRAFT, H. P.   SS   WRT 26 09
  *TERROR IN THE MODERN VEIN   WOLLHEIM, DONALD A.   AN
HE DIDN'T LIKE CATS   HUBBARD, L. RON   SS   UNK 42 02
  ZACHERLEY'S VULTURE STEW   ZACHERLEY   AN
HE HAD A BIG HEART   QUATTROCCHI, FRANK   SS   FSF 55 03
  ABC OF SCIENCE FICTION, AN   BOARDMAN, TOM JR.   AN
HE KILT IT WITH A STICK   NOLAN, WILLIAM F.   SS   FSF 68 02
  ALIEN HORIZONS   NOLAN, WILLIAM F.   AC
  SPECIAL WONDER   MCCOMAS, J. FRANCIS   AN
HE SHALL COME   DERLETH, AUGUST   SS   MSP 29 12
  NOT LONG FOR THIS WORLD   DERLETH, AUGUST   AC
HE THAT HATH WINGS   HAMILTON, EDMOND   SS   WRT 38 07
  BEST OF EDMOND HAMILTON, THE   HAMILTON, EDMOND   AC
  WORLDS OF WEIRD   MARGULIES, LEO   AN
HE THOUGHT HE SAW ELECTRONS SWIFT
                          DINGLE, HERBERT   PM
  FANTASIA MATHEMATICA   FADIMAN, CLIFTON   AN
HE WALKED AROUND THE HORSES   PIPER, H. BEAM   NV   ASF 48 04
  ASPECTS OF SCIENCE FICTION   DOHERTY, G. D.   AN
  BEST SF 3   CRISPIN, EDMUND   AN
  SCIENCE FICTION ARGOSY, A   KNIGHT, DAMON   AN
  SCIENCE FICTION THROUGH THE AGES 2   EVANS, I. O.   AN
  WORLD OF WONDER   PRATT, FLETCHER   AN
HE WHO LEAVES NO TRACE   PARNOV, YEREMEY
                          AND YEMTSEV, MIKHAIL   NV C   63
  ULTIMATE THRESHOLD, THE   GINSBURG, MIRRA   AN
HE WHO SHAPES   ZELAZNY, ROGER   NV   AMZ 65 01
  NEBULA AWARD STORIES   KNIGHT, DAMON   AN
HE WHO SHRANK   HASSE, HENRY   NV   AMZ 36 08
  *ADVENTURES IN TIME AND SPACE   HEALY & MCCOMAS   AN
  BEFORE THE GOLDEN AGE   ASIMOV, ISAAC   AN
HE-MAN ETHOS IN SCIENCE FICTION, THE
                          RUSS, JOANNA   AR   CLR 72 02
  CLARION II   WILSON, ROBIN SCOTT   OA
HEAD   BELLING, RUDOLPH   IL
  SCIENCE FICTION   BRODKIN & PEARSON   AN
HEAD AND THE HAND, THE   PRIEST, CHRISTOPHER   SS   NWQ 72 03
  BEST SF: 1972   HARRISON & ALDISS   AN
  NEW WORLDS QUARTERLY NO. 3   MOORCOCK, MICHAEL   OA
  REAL-TIME WORLD   PRIEST, CHRISTOPHER   AC
HEAD HUNTER, THE (THE HEAD MAN)
                          BLOCH, ROBERT   SS   FIF 50 06
  CHAMBER OF HORRORS   BLOCH, ROBERT   AC
HEAD HUNTERS, THE   WILLIAMS, RALPH   SS   ASF 51 10
  OMNIBUS OF SCIENCE FICTION   CONKLIN, GROFF   AN
  *STORIES FOR TOMORROW   SLOANE, WILLIAM   AN
  TALES OF TERROR FROM OUTER SPACE   CHETWYND-HAYES, R.   AN
HEAD MAN, THE (SEE THE HEAD HUNTER)
                          BLOCH, ROBERT   TC
HEAD THUMPING THE TROOPS   BUNCH, DAVID R.   SS
  MODERAN   BUNCH, DAVID R.   AC
HEAD-RAPE, THE   THOMAS, D. M.   PM   NWS 68 03
  BEST SF STORIES FROM NEW WORLDS 4   MOORCOCK, MICHAEL   AN
  HOLDING YOUR EIGHT HANDS   LUCIE-SMITH, EDWARD   AN
HEAD, THE   BLOCH, ROBERT   SS
  IDES OF TOMORROW, THE   CARR, TERRY   OA
HEADLESS MAN, THE   WOLFE, GENE   SS   UNI 72 02
  UNIVERSE 2   CARR, TERRY   OA
HEADNOTES   FRENKEL, JAMES   MS
  BEST FROM IF, THE   VOLUME I   IF, EDITORS OF   AN
HEADPIECE, THE   BRADBURY, RAY   SS   LIL 58 05
  DAY IT RAINED FOREVER, THE   BRADBURY, RAY   AC
  MEDICINE FOR MELANCHOLY, A   BRADBURY, RAY   AC
HEADS AFRICA TAILS AMERICA   SAXTON, JOSEPHINE   SS   ORB 71 09
  ORBIT 9   KNIGHT, DAMON   OA
HEAL THYSELF   RACKHAM, JOHN   SS   NWR 75 27
  NEW WRITINGS IN SF. 27   BULMER, KENNETH   OA
HEART GROW FONDER   LAFFERTY, R. A.   NV   FCR 75
  FUTURE CORRUPTION   ELWOOD, ROGER   OA

HEART OF BLACKNESS, THE (THE CRAVING FOR BLACKNESS)
                          RAY, ROBERT   SS   NWS 62 09
  OUT OF THIS WORLD 6   WILLIAMS-ELLIS& OWEN   AN
HEART OF THE SERPENT, THE   YEFREMOV, IVAN   NV
  MORE SOVIET SCIENCE FICTION   ANONYMOUS   AN
HEART ON THE OTHER SIDE, THE   GAMOW, GEORGE   SS
  EXPERT DREAMERS, THE   POHL, FREDERIK   AN
HEART, THE   STURGEON, THEODORE   SS   OWS 55 05
  STURGEON IN ORBIT   STURGEON, THEODORE   AC
HEARTBURN   CALISHER, HORTENSE   SS   AMM 51 01
  TIMELESS STORIES FOR TODAY AND TOMORROW   BRADBURY, RAY   AN
HEARTLAND   HASFORD, GUSTAV   SS   ORB 75 16
  ORBIT 16   KNIGHT, DAMON   OA
HEARTS AND ENGINES (SOLDIERS RUNNING)
                          ALDISS, BRIAN W.   SS   NWS 60 06
  STARSWARM   ALDISS, BRIAN W.   AC
HEAT DEATH OF THE UNIVERSE, THE
                          ZOLINE, PAMELA A.   SS   NWS 67 07
  BEST SF STORIES FROM NEW WORLDS 3   MOORCOCK, MICHAEL   AN
  DECADE THE 1960S   ALDISS & HARRISON   AN
  ENGLAND SWINGS SF   MERRIL, JUDITH   AN
  MIRROR OF INFINITY, THE   SILVERBERG, ROBERT   AN
  VOYAGES: SCENARIOS FOR A SHIP CALLED EARTH
                          SAUER, ROB   AN
HEATHEN GOD   ZEBROWSKI, GEORGE   SS   FSF 71 01
  MONADIC UNIVERSE, THE   ZEBROWSKI, GEORGE   AC
  NEBULA AWARD STORIES   NO. 7   BIGGLE, LLOYD JR.   AN
HEATWAVE   LANGFORD, DAVID   SS   NWR 75 27
  NEW WRITINGS IN SF. 27   BULMER, KENNETH   OA
HEAV'N, HEAV'N   RUSSELL, ERIC FRANK   SS   FUT 56 30
  NOW & BEYOND   HOWARD, IVAN   AN
HEAVEN MAKERS, THE   HERBERT, FRANK   EX   AMZ 67 04
  BEST OF FRANK HERBERT, THE   HERBERT, FRANK   AC
HEAVEN SCENT   WYNDHAM, JOHN   SS
  JIZZLE   WYNDHAM, JOHN   AC
  TALES OF GOOSEFLESH AND LAUGHTER   WYNDHAM, JOHN   AC
HEAVENS BELOW: FIFTEEN UTOPIAS SLADEK, JOHN T.   SS   NEW 75 16
  NEW IMPROVED SUN, THE   DISCH, THOMAS M.   AN
HEAVY DUTY (AS HANK DEMPSEY)   HARRISON, HARRY   SS   ASF 70 05
  ONE STEP FROM EARTH   HARRISON, HARRY   AC
HEAVY METAL   BISCHOFF, DAVE   SS
  FUTURE PASTIMES   EDELSTEIN, SCOTT   OA
HEAVY PLANET   GREGOR, LEE   SS   ASF 39 08
  *ADVENTURES IN TIME AND SPACE   HEALY & MCCOMAS   AN
  EXPERT DREAMERS, THE   POHL, FREDERIK   AN
  MORE ADVENTURES IN TIME AND SPACE   HEALY & MCCOMAS   AN
HEAVY PLANET   ROTHMAN, MILTON A.   SS   ASF 39 08
  JUPITER   POHL, C. & F.   AN
  WHERE DO WE GO FROM HERE?   ASIMOV, ISAAC   AN
  WORLDS OF WONDER   HARRISON, HARRY   AN
HEAVY-SET   BRADBURY, RAY   SS   PBY 64 10
  I SING THE BODY ELECTRIC   BRADBURY, RAY   AC
  PLAYBOY BOOK OF HORROR AND THE SUPERNATURAL, THE
                          PLAYBOY, EDITORS OF   AN
HECTOR SERVADAC (1877)   VERNE, JULES   EX
  JULES VERNE- MASTER OF SCIENCE FICTION   VERNE, JULES   AC
HECTOR SERVADAC (1877)   VERNE, JULES   NO
  NOVELS   VERNE, JULES   AC
HEDONIST, THE (NAME YOUR PLEASURE)
                          GUNN, JAMES E.   NA   TWS 55 WI
  SOME DREAMS ARE NIGHTMARES   GUNN, JAMES E.   AC
HEEL & TOE TO THE END   WILLIAMS, WILLIAM C. PM   62
  SPECULATIONS   SANDERS, THOMAS E.   AN
HEIGHT OF THE SCREAM, THE   CAMPBELL, J. RAMSEY   EX
  BEYOND THIS HORIZON   CARRELL, CHRISTOPHER   OA
HEIL¡   HEINLEIN, ROBERT A.   SS   FUF 40 04
  FUTURES TO INFINITY   MOSKOWITZ, SAM   AN
HEIR APPARENT   MOORE, C. L.   NV   ASF 50 07
  JUDGEMENT NIGHT   MOORE, C. L.   AC
HEIR APPARENT   NOURSE, ALAN E.   SS   IMG 53 10
  RX FOR TOMORROW   NOURSE, ALAN E.   AC
HEIR APPARENT (SEE HEIR UNAPPARENT)
                          VAN VOGT, A. E.   TC
HEIR UNAPPARENT (HEIR APPARENT)
                          VAN VOGT, A. E.   SS   ASF 45 06
  *AWAY AND BEYOND   VAN VOGT, A. E.   AC
  M 33 IN ANDROMEDA   VAN VOGT, A. E.   AC
  SF: AUTHORS' CHOICE 2   HARRISON, HARRY   AN
HEIRLOOM   SPINRAD, NORMAN   SS   LST 72
  NO DIRECTION HOME   SPINRAD, NORMAN   AC
HEIRS APPARENT   ABERNATHY, ROBERT   NV   FSF 54 06
  BEST FROM FANTASY AND SCIENCE FICTION: 4
                          BOUCHER, ANTHONY   AN
  BEST SCIENCE FICTION STORIES AND NOVELS: 1955
                          DIKTY, T. E.   AN
HELBENT 4   ROBINETT, STEPHEN   NV   GAL 75 10
  BEST FROM GALAXY, THE   VOLUME IV   BAEN, JAMES   AN
  BEST SCIENCE FICTION STORIES OF THE YEAR (1975)
                          DEL REY, LESTER   AN
  1976 ANNUAL WORLD'S BEST SF, THE   WOLLHEIM, DONALD A.   AN
HELEN O'LOY   DEL REY, LESTER   SS   ASF 38 12
  *AND SOME WERE HUMAN   DEL REY, LESTER   AC
  ASSIGNMENT IN TOMORROW   POHL, FREDERIK   AN
  *BEYOND HUMAN KEN   MERRIL, JUDITH   AN
  COMING OF THE ROBOTS, THE   MOSKOWITZ, SAM   AN
  IN DREAMS AWAKE   FIEDLER, LESLIE A.   AN
  MASTERS' CHOICE   JANIFER, LAURENCE M.   AN
  MODERN SCIENCE FICTION   SPINRAD, NORMAN   AN
  SCIENCE FICTION HALL OF FAME VOLUME 1   SILVERBERG, ROBERT   AN
  SOULS IN METAL   ASHLEY, MICHAEL   AN
  3000 YEARS OF FANTASY AND SCIENCE FICTION
                          DE CAMP, L. S.&C.   AN
HELIX THE CAT   STURGEON, THEODORE   NV   AMA 73
  ASTOUNDING   HARRISON, HARRY   OA
HELL HATH FURY   CARTMILL, CLEVE   SN   UNK 43 08
  HELL HATH FURY   HAY, GEORGE   AN

HELL IS FOREVER   HIDING PLACE

HELL IS FOREVER   BESTER, ALFRED   SN   UNK 42 08
  LIGHT FANTASTIC, THE   BESTER, ALFRED   AC
  UNKNOWN 5, THE   BENSEN, D. R.   AN
HELL-BENT (CONTEST STORY)   MCCORMACK, FORD   SS   FSF 51 06
  DEALS WITH THE DEVIL   DAVENPORT, BASIL   AN
HELL-FIRE   ASIMOV, ISAAC   SS   FUN 56 05
  EARTH IS ROOM ENOUGH   ASIMOV, ISAAC   AC
HELL-PLANET   RACKHAM, JOHN   NV   NWR 64 02
  NEW WRITINGS IN SF. 2   CARNELL, JOHN   OA
HELLACEOUS ROCKET OF HARRY O'DONOVAN, THE
                            LAFFERTY, R. A.   SS   NMD 73
  FRONTIERS 2; THE NEW MIND ELWOOD, ROGER   OA
HELLO, WALLS AND FENCES   BATES, RUSSELL L.   SS   INY 73 05
  INFINITY 5   HOSKINS, ROBERT   OA
HELLSGARDE   MOORE, C. L.   SS   WRT 39 04
  JIREL OF JOIRY   MOORE, C. L.   AC
  NORTHWEST OF EARTH   MOORE, C. L.   AC
HELLVILLE U.S.A.   GRIFFITH, GEORGE   SS
  GAMBLES WITH DESTINY   GRIFFITH, GEORGE   AC
HELMET OF HADES, THE   WODHAMS, JACK   SS   NWR 68 11
  NEW WRITINGS IN SF. 11   CARNELL, JOHN   OA
HELMET, THE   MALZBERG, BARRY N. SS   FSF 73 09
  OUT FROM GANYMEDE   MALZBERG, BARRY N.   AC
HELP (PUPA KNOWS BEST)   TIPTREE, JAMES JR. NV   IFS 68 10
  TEN THOUSAND LIGHT-YEARS FROM HOME   TIPTREE, JAMES JR.   AC
HELP STAMP OUT CHESNEY   GOULART, RON   SS   NEW 71 DC
  GHOST BREAKER   GOULART, RON   DC
HELP! I AM DR. MORRIS GOLDPEPPER
                            DAVIDSON, AVRAM   NV   GAL 57 07
  INFINITE JESTS   SILVERBERG, ROBERT   AN
  OR ALL THE SEAS WITH OYSTERS   DAVIDSON, AVRAM   AC
  THIRD GALAXY READER, THE   GOLD, H. L.   AN
HELPING HAND   DEL REY, LESTER   NV   STR 58 04
  STAR SCIENCE FICTION STORIES NO. 4   POHL, FREDERIK   AN
HELPING HAND, THE   ANDERSON, POUL   NV   ASF 50 05
  GREAT STORIES OF SPACE TRAVEL   CONKLIN, GROFF   AN
  POLITICAL SCIENCE FICTION GREENBERG& WARRICK   AN
  *POSSIBLE WORLDS OF SCIENCE FICTION   CONKLIN, GROFF   AN
  STARS AROUND US, THE   HOSKINS, ROBERT   AN
HEMEAC   VON WALD, E. G.   SS   GAL 68 08
  AS TOMORROW BECOMES TODAY SULLIVAN, CHARLES W.   AN
  EARTH IN TRANSIT   SCHWARTZ, SHEILA   AN
  SCIENCE FICTION   BRODKIN & PEARSON   AN
  TOMORROW, AND TOMORROW, AND TOMORROW...   HEINTZ/HERBERT/JOOS/   AN
  WORLD'S BEST SCIENCE FICTION: 1969   WOLLHEIM & CARR   AN
HEMINGWAY IN SPACE   AMIS, KINGSLEY   SS   PUN 60 12
  DECADE THE 1960S   ALDISS & HARRISON   AN
  6TH ANNUAL OF THE YEAR'S BEST S-F, THE   MERRIL, JUDITH   AN
HENRY KUTTNER: A NEGLECTED MASTER
                            BRADBURY, RAY   IN   75
  BEST OF HENRY KUTTNER, THE KUTTNER, HENRY   AC
HENRY MARTINDALE, GREAT DANE (SEE GONE TO THE DOGS)
                            DEFORD, MIRIAM ALLEN TC
HENRY THE NINTH (FINAL SCEPTRE, A LASTING CROWN)
                            BRADBURY, RAY   SS   FSF 69 10
  I SING THE BODY ELECTRIC   BRADBURY, RAY   AC
HER MAJESTY'S ABERRATION   HUBBARD, L. RON   SS   ASF 48 03
  OLE DOC METHUSELAH   HUBBARD, L. RON   AC
HER SMOKE ROSE UP FOREVER   TIPTREE, JAMES JR. NV   FST 74
  FINAL STAGE   FERMAN & MALZBERG   OA
HER STRONG ENCHANTMENTS FAILING
                            MCGUIRE, PATRICK   AR
  MANY WORLDS OF POUL ANDERSON, THE   ANDERSON, POUL   AC
HERBERT GEORGE MORLEY ROBERTS WELLS, ESQ.
                            CLARKE, ARTHUR C.   ED   IFS 67 12
  WIND FROM THE SUN, THE   CLARKE, ARTHUR C.   AC
HERE BE DRAGONS   PLAUGER, P. J.   SS
  AURORA: BEYOND EQUALITY   MCINTYRE & ANDERSON   OA
HERE COMES JOHN HENRY   RUSSELL, RAY   SS   PBY 68 09
  DEAD ASTRONAUT, 10 STORIES OF SPACE FLIGHT, THE
                            PLAYBOY, EDITORS OF AN
HERE I AM AGAIN   ASIMOV, ISAAC   IN
  HUGO WINNERS, THE (VOLUME 2)   ASIMOV, ISAAC   AN
HERE IS THY STING   JAKES, JOHN W.   NV   ORB 68 03
  BEST OF JOHN JAKES, THE   JAKES, JOHN W.   AC
  ORBIT 3   KNIGHT, DAMON   OA
HERE LIE WE   HOLDEN, FOX B.   NV   STS 53 06
  TALES OF OUTER SPACE   WOLLHEIM, DONALD A.   DA
HERE THERE BE TYGERS   BRADBURY, RAY   SS   NTS 51
  DAY IT RAINED FOREVER, THE BRADBURY, RAY   AC
  NEW TALES OF SPACE AND TIME   HEALY, RAYMOND J.   OA
  R IS FOR ROCKET   BRADBURY, RAY   AC
  TOMORROW, AND TOMORROW, AND TOMORROW...   HEINTZ/HERBERT/JOOS/ AN
HERE'S A HEALTH UNTO HIS MAJESTY
                            DEELEY, ROGER   SS   GEN 72
  GENERATION   GERROLD, DAVID   OA
HERE, DAEMOS!   DERLETH, AUGUST   SS   WRT 42 03
  BEWARE THE BEASTS   GHIDALIA, V.& ELWOOD   AN
HERE, PUTZI!   DE CAMP, L. SPRAGUE
                            AND PRATT, FLETCHER SS C NEW 53 AC
  TALES FROM GAVAGAN'S BAR   DE CAMP, L. S.&PRATT   AC
HERE, THERE, AND EVERYWHERE BUSBY, F. M.   SS   CLR 72 02
  CLARION II   WILSON, ROBIN SCOTT   OA
HEREAFTER, INC.   DEL REY, LESTER   SS   UNK 41 12
  *AND SOME WERE HUMAN   DEL REY, LESTER   AC
HEREDITY   ASIMOV, ISAAC   SS   AST 41 04
  BEYOND THE END OF TIME   POHL, FREDERIK   AN
  EARLY ASIMOV, THE   ASIMOV, ISAAC   AC
HEREDITY   KELLER, DAVID H. SS   47
  LIFE EVERLASTING AND OTHER TALES OF SCIENCE, FANTASY
    AND HORROR   KELLER, DAVID H. MD.   AC
HERESIES OF THE HUGE GOD   ALDISS, BRIAN W.   FA   GAL 66 08
  BEST SF 7   CRISPIN, EDMUND   AN
  DARK STARS   SILVERBERG, ROBERT   AN
  EVIL EARTHS   ALDISS, BRIAN W.   AN
  INFINITE JESTS   SILVERBERG, ROBERT   AN

  INVADERS FROM SPACE   SILVERBERG, ROBERT   AN
  MOMENT OF ECLIPSE, THE   ALDISS, BRIAN W.   AC
  TALES OF TERROR FROM OUTER SPACE   CHETWYND-HAYES, R.   AN
  TENTH GALAXY READER, THE   POHL, FREDERIK   AN
HERESIES OF THE HUGE GOD   COUZYN, JENI   PM
  BEYOND THIS HORIZON   CARRELL, CHRISTOPHER OA
HERITAGE   ABERNATHY, ROBERT   NV   ASF 42 06
  OMNIBUS OF SCIENCE FICTION CONKLIN, GROFF   AN
HERITAGE   HARNESS, CHARLES L. SS   FSF 50 FL
  TOMORROW'S UNIVERSE   CAMPBELL, H. J.   AN
HERITAGE, THE   STOKES, MALCOM   CT
  TALES FROM THE GALAXIES   WILLIAMS-ELLIS& P.   AN
HERMENEUTICAL DOUGHNUT, THE NEARING, H. JR.   SS   NEW 54 AC
  MATHEMATICAL MAGPIE, THE   FADIMAN, CLIFTON   AN
  SINISTER RESEARCHES OF C. P. RANSOM, THE NEARING, H. JR.   AC
HERMIT OF SATURN'S RING   JONES, NEIL R.   SS   PLS 40 FL
  FLIGHT INTO SPACE   WOLLHEIM, DONALD A.   AN
  HISTORY OF THE SCIENCE FICTION MAGAZINE, THE PART 2 1936-1945
                            ASHLEY, MICHAEL   AN
HERMIT ON BIKINI   LANGDON, JOHN   SS   BBM 53 02
  PORTALS OF TOMORROW   DERLETH, AUGUST   AN
HERMIT, THE   HARRISON, WILLIAM   SS   68
  ROLLERBALL   HARRISON, WILLIAM   AC
HERO   GOLD, H. L.   SS   TWS 39 10
  OLD DIE RICH AND OTHER SCIENCE FICTION, THE
                            GOLD, H. L.   AC
HERO   HALDEMAN, JOE W.   NV   ASF 72 06
  ANALOG 9   BOVA, BEN   AN
  BEST SCIENCE FICTION OF THE YEAR, THE NO. 2
                            CARR, TERRY   AN
  BEST SF: 1972   HARRISON & ALDISS   AN
  FOREVER WAR, THE   HALDEMAN, JOE W.   NO
HERO AS WERWOLF, THE   WOLFE, GENE   SS   NEW 75 AN
  BEST SCIENCE FICTION OF THE YEAR, THE NO. 5
                            CARR, TERRY   AN
  NEW IMPROVED SUN, THE   DISCH, THOMAS M.   AN
HERO'S LIFE, A (ALSO AS A STYLE IN TREASON)
                            BLISH, JAMES   NV   IMP 66 03
  FOUR FOR THE FUTURE   HARRISON, HARRY   AN
HERO, THE   HILL, ERNEST   SS   NWR 70 17
  NEW WRITINGS IN SF. 17   CARNELL, JOHN   OA
HERO, THE   MARTIN, GEORGE R. R. SS GAL 71 02
  SONG FOR LYA, A   MARTIN, GEORGE R. R.   AC
HEROES ARE MADE (SEE THE SHERIFF OF CANYON GULCH)
                            ANDERSON, POUL
                            AND DICKSON, GORDON R.   TC C
HEROES DIE BUT ONCE   SPINRAD, NORMAN   SS   IFS 69 12
  NO DIRECTION HOME   SPINRAD, NORMAN   AC
HEROIC FEAT, THE   DNIEPROV, ANATOLY   SS
  RUSSIAN SCIENCE FICTION, 1968   MAGIDOFF, ROBERT   AN
HERRINGS   ANDERSON, POUL   MS   59
  HOMEBREW   ANDERSON, POUL   AC
HERTFORD MANUSCRIPT, THE   COWPER, RICHARD   NV   FSF 76 10
  CUSTODIANS AND OTHER STORIES, THE   COWPER, RICHARD   AC
  1977 ANNUAL WORLD'S BEST SF, THE   WOLLHEIM, DONALD A.   AN
HEXAMINATION   DAVIS, CHAN   SS   NOV 70 01
  *NOVA 1   HARRISON, HARRY   OA
HEXER, THE   GUERNSEY, H. W.   SS   UNK 39 06
  FROM UNKNOWN WORLDS   CAMPBELL, JOHN W. JR.   AN
HEXLET, THE   SODDY, FREDERICK   PM   NTR 36 12
  MATHEMATICAL MAGPIE, THE   FADIMAN, CLIFTON   AN
HEY! LOOK AT ME!   FINNEY, JACK   SS   PBY 62 09
  I LOVE GALESBURG IN THE SPRINGTIME   FINNEY, JACK   AC
  PLAYBOY BOOK OF HORROR AND THE SUPERNATURAL, THE
                            PLAYBOY, EDITORS OF AN
HI DIDDLE DIDDLE!   SILVERBERG, ROBERT NV   ASF 59 02
  SUNRISE ON MERCURY AND OTHER SCIENCE FICTION STORIES
                            SILVERBERG, ROBERT   OA
  WORLDS OF WONDER   HARRISON, HARRY   AN
HIBBIE, THE   ALEXANDER, JAMES   SS
  GOLLANCZ - SUNDAY TIMES BEST SF STORIES ANONYMOUS   AN
HIBITED MAN, THE   DE CAMP, L. SPRAGUE SS   TWS 49 10
  *MY BEST SCIENCE FICTION STORY   MARGULIES & FRIEND   AN
  SHAPE OF THINGS, THE   KNIGHT, DAMON   AN
HICKORY, DICKORY, KEROUAC (AS MARTIN SCOTT)
                            GEHMAN, RICHARD   SS   PBY 58 03
  FANTASY: THE LITERATURE OF THE MARVELOUS KELLEY, LEO P.   AN
  SF: THE BEST OF THE BEST   MERRIL, JUDITH   AN
  SF:59, THE YEAR'S GREATEST SCIENCE FICTION AND FANTASY
                            MERRIL, JUDITH   AN
HIDDEN EARS, THE   PERKINS, LAWRENCE A. SS ASF 69 01
  ANALOG 8   CAMPBELL, JOHN W. JR.   AN
HIDDEN TALENT   SILVERBERG, ROBERT NV   IFS 57 04
  EARTH'S OTHER SHADOW   SILVERBERG, ROBERT   AC
HIDDEN UNIVERSE, THE   FARLEY, RALPH MILNE EX   AMZ 39 11
  OMNIBUS OF TIME, THE   FARLEY, RALPH MILNE   AC
HIDDEN UNIVERSE, THE   FARLEY, RALPH MILNE NO   AMZ 39 11
  STRANGE WORLDS   FARLEY, RALPH MILNE   AC
HIDE AND SEEK   CLARKE, ARTHUR C.   SS   ASF 49 09
  ACROSS THE SEA OF STARS   CLARKE, ARTHUR C.   AC
  ASTOUNDING-ANALOG READER, THE VOLUME TWO HARRISON & ALDISS AN
  BEST OF ARTHUR C. CLARKE: 1937-1971, THE CLARKE, ARTHUR C. AC
  EXPEDITION TO EARTH   CLARKE, ARTHUR C.   AC
  GATEWAY TO TOMORROW   CARNELL, JOHN   AN
  NINE BILLION NAMES OF GOD, THE   CLARKE, ARTHUR C.   AC
  OF TIME AND STARS   CLARKE, ARTHUR C.   AC
  SPACE, SPACE, SPACE   SLOANE, WILLIAM   AN
  TALES OF SCIENCE FICTION   BALL, BRIAN N.   AN
HIDE AND SEEK   MARTIN, MARIO JR.   SS
  MORE SCIENCE FICTION TALES ELWOOD, ROGER   OA
HIDE AND SEEK (CACHE-CACHE BY GERARD KLEIN, TRANS)
                            BRUNNER, JOHN   SS   73
  BOOK OF JOHN BRUNNER, THE BRUNNER, JOHN   AC
HIDING PLACE   ANDERSON, POUL   NV   ASF 61 03
  BEST OF POUL ANDERSON, THE ANDERSON, POUL   AC
  TRADER TO THE STARS   ANDERSON, POUL   AC

HIGH BANK   CLINGAN, C. C.   SS
  FUTURE PASTIMES   EDELSTEIN, SCOTT   OA
HIGH BARBARY   DURRELL, LAWRENCE SS   MAD 61 09
  7TH ANNUAL OF THE YEAR'S BEST S-F, THE MERRIL, JUDITH   AN
HIGH EIGHT   STRINGER, DAVID   NV NWR 65 04
  BEST FROM NEW WRITINGS IN S-F FIRST SELECTION, THE
                                 CARNELL, JOHN   AN
  NEW WRITINGS IN SF. 4   CARNELL, JOHN   AN
HIGH JACK AND DAME   CARTMILL, CLEVE   NV   TWS 49 10
  SPACE SCAVENGERS, THE   CARTMILL, CLEVE   NO
HIGH JUSTICE   POURNELLE, JERRY   NV   ASF 74 03
  HIGH JUSTICE   POURNELLE, JERRY   AC
HIGH ONES, THE   ANDERSON, POUL   NV   INF 58 06
  HORN OF TIME, THE   ANDERSON, POUL   AC
HIGH PRIEST   BONE, J. F.   SS   STG 74
  STRANGE GODS   ELWOOD, ROGER   OA
  VISIONS OF TOMORROW   ELWOOD, ROGER   AN
HIGH THRESHOLD   NOURSE, ALAN E.   SS   ASF 51 03
  OMNIBUS OF SCIENCE FICTION   CONKLIN, GROFF   AN
  STRANGE TRAVELS IN SCIENCE FICTION CONKLIN, GROFF   AN
HIGH TREASON   ANDERSON, POUL   SS   IMP 66 03
  FOUR FOR THE FUTURE   HARRISON, HARRY   AN
HIGH WEIR   DELANY, SAMUEL R. NV   IFS 68 10
  DRIFTGLASS   DELANY, SAMUEL R.   AC
  WONDERMAKERS 2   HOSKINS, ROBERT   AN
HIGH YIELD BONDAGE   PEIRCE, HAYFORD   NV   GAL 75 08
  BEST SCIENCE FICTION STORIES OF THE YEAR (1975)
                                 DEL REY, LESTER   AN
HIGHER THINGS, THE   PIERCE, JOHN R.   SS   NOV 70 01
  *NOVA 1   HARRISON, HARRY   OA
HIGHEST DIVE, THE   WILLIAMSON, JACK   SS   SFM 76 01
  BEST SCIENCE FICTION OF THE YEAR, THE NO. 6
                                 CARR, TERRY   AN
HIGHEST FORM OF LIFE, THE   JAKES, JOHN W.   SS   AMZ 61 08
  BEST OF JOHN JAKES, THE   JAKES, JOHN W.   AN
HIGHWAY   LOWNDES, ROBERT W. SS   SFQ 42 FL
  LOOKING FORWARD   LESSER, MILTON   AN
HIGHWAY J   MAINE, CHARLES ERIC NV PLS 53 11
  OTHER WORLDS, OTHER TIMES   MOSKOWITZ & ELWOOD   AN
HIGHWAY, THE (AS LEONARD SPALDING)
                                 BRADBURY, RAY   SS   CPY 50 SP
  ABOVE THE HUMAN LANDSCAPE   MCNELLY & STOVER   AN
  *ILLUSTRATED MAN, THE   BRADBURY, RAY   AN
HIGHWAYMAN OF THE VOID   POHL, FREDERIK   NV   PLS 44 FL
  EARLY POHL, THE   POHL, FREDERIK   AC
HILDA   HICKEY, H. B.   SS   FSF 52 09
  FIFTY SHORT SCIENCE FICTION TALES ASIMOV & CONKLIN AN
  OPERATION FUTURE   CONKLIN, GROFF   AN
HILIFTER   DICKSON, GORDON R. SS   ASF 63 02
  ANALOG 3   CAMPBELL, JOHN W. JR AN
  SPECULATIONS   SANDERS, THOMAS E.   AN
  STAR ROAD, THE   DICKSON, GORDON R.   AC
HILL AND THE HOLE, THE   LEIBER, FRITZ   SS   UNK 42 08
  NIGHT'S BLACK AGENTS   LEIBER, FRITZ   AC
HIM   VAN VOGT, A. E.   SS   SPW 69 01
  MORE THAN SUPERHUMAN   VAN VOGT, A. E.   AC
HINDSIGHT   WILLIAMSON, JACK   SS   ASF 40 05
  *ASTOUNDING SCIENCE FICTION ANTHOLOGY, THE
                                 CAMPBELL, JOHN W. JR AN
  ASTOUNDING TALES OF SPACE AND TIME CAMPBELL, JOHN W. JR AN
  FIRST ASTOUNDING SCIENCE FICTION ANTHOLOGY, THE (PB)
                                 CAMPBELL, JOHN W. JR AN
  PEOPLE MACHINES   WILLIAMSON, JACK   AC
HINDSIGHT: 480 SECONDS   ELLISON, HARLAN   SS   FUC 73
  APPROACHING OBLIVION   ELLISON, HARLAN   AC
  FUTURE CITY   ELWOOD, ROGER   OA
HIPPIE-DIP FILE, THE   THURSTON, ROBERT   SS   FSF 71 03
  SOCIAL PROBLEMS THROUGH SCIENCE FICTION GREENBERG/MILSTEAD/& AN
HIS BROTHER'S KEEPER   SILVERBERG, ROBERT NV   FUN 59 03
  NEEDLE IN A TIMESTACK   SILVERBERG, ROBERT   AC
HIS FATHER'S HOUSE   RUSSELL, RAY   SS   IFS 60 01
  SARDONICUS AND OTHER STORIES   RUSSELL, RAY   AC
HIS FIRST DAY AT WAR (SEE BATTLEFIELD)
                                 ELLISON, HARLAN   TC
HIS HEAD IN THE CLOUDS   SILVERBERG, ROBERT SS   SFS 57 09
  CALLIBRATED ALLIGATOR AND OTHER SCIENCE FICTION STORIES, THE
                                 SILVERBERG, ROBERT   AC
HIS MASTER'S VOICE   MCCLINTIC, WINONA PM   FSF 53 06
  BEST FROM FANTASY AND SCIENCE FICTION: 3
                                 BOUCHER & MCCOMAS   AN
HIS OWN KIND   DISCH, THOMAS M.   SS   NEW 70 01
  NEW WORLDS OF FANTASY NO. 2   CARR, TERRY   AN
HIS TRUTH GOES MARCHING ON   POURNELLE, JERRY   SS   NEW 75 AN
  COMBAT SF   DICKSON, GORDON R.   AN
HIS UNCONQUERABLE ENEMY   MORROW, W. C.   SS   97
  HORROR TIMES TEN   NORTON, ALDEN H.   AN
HISTORIAN, THE   JACOBI, CARL   SS
  PORTRAITS IN MOONLIGHT   JACOBI, CARL   AC
HISTORICAL NOTE   LEINSTER, MURRAY   SS   ASF 51 02
  *ASTOUNDING SCIENCE FICTION ANTHOLOGY, THE
                                 CAMPBELL, JOHN W. JR AN
  ASTOUNDING TALES OF SPACE AND TIME CAMPBELL, JOHN W. JR AN
  *SECOND ASTOUNDING SCIENCE FICTION ANTHOLOGY, THE
                                 CAMPBELL, JOHN W. JR AN
HISTORY   ASIMOV, ISAAC   SS   SSS 41 03
  EARLY ASIMOV, THE   ASIMOV, ISAAC   AC
HISTORY LESSON   CLARKE, ARTHUR C. SS   STS 49 05
  ACROSS THE SEA OF STARS   CLARKE, ARTHUR C.   AN
  ANOTHER TOMORROW   HOLLISTER, BERNARD C AN
  BEST OF ARTHUR C. CLARKE: 1937-1971, THE CLARKE, ARTHUR C. AC
  BEYOND BELIEF   HURLEY, RICHARD J.   AN
  EARTH IN TRANSIT   SCHWARTZ, SHEILA   AN
  EXPEDITION TO EARTH   CLARKE, ARTHUR C.   AC
  GREAT SCIENCE FICTION STORIES   SMITH, CORDELIA T.   AN
  GREAT SCIENCE-FICTION   LICATA, TONY   AN
  OMNIBUS OF SCIENCE FICTION   CONKLIN, GROFF   AN

SCIENCE FICTION OMNIBUS   CONKLIN, GROFF   AN
SCIENCE FICTION: THE FUTURE   ALLEN, DICK   AN
TRANSFORMATIONS II   ROSELLE, DANIEL   AN
HISTORY MACHINE, THE   ZEBROWSKI, GEORGE SS   NWQ 72 03
  MONADIC UNIVERSE, THE   ZEBROWSKI, GEORGE   AC
  NEW WORLDS QUARTERLY NO. 3   MOORCOCK, MICHAEL   OA
HISTORY MAKERS, THE   SALLIS, JAMES   SS   ORB 69 05
  FEW LAST WORDS, A   SALLIS, JAMES   AC
  ORBIT 5   KNIGHT, DAMON   OA
HISTORY OF "THE SCIENTIFIC ROMANCE" IN THE MUNSEY MAGAZINES,
  1912-1920, A   MOSKOWITZ, SAM   AR
  UNDER THE MOONS OF MARS   MOSKOWITZ, SAM   AN
HISTORY OF BRITISH SCIENCE FICTION MAGAZINES, A
                                 HARBOTTLE, PHILIP   AR
  BEYOND THIS HORIZON   CARRELL, CHRISTOPHER OA
HISTORY OF DOCTOR FROST, THE   HODGINS, RODERIC C. SS FSF 65 04
  BEST FROM FANTASY AND SCIENCE FICTION: 15
                                 FERMAN, EDWARD L.   AN
HITCH HIKE TO PARADISE   WHYBROW, GEOFFREY SS
  AD 2500   WILSON, ANGUS   AN
HITCH IN SPACE, A   LEIBER, FRITZ   SS   WOT 63 08
  BOOK OF FRITZ LEIBER, THE   LEIBER, FRITZ   AC
HITCH IN TIME, A   MACCREIGH, JAMES   SS   TWS 47 06
  SHOT IN THE DARK   MERRIL, JUDITH   AN
HO CHI MINH ELEGY   SCHJELDAHL, PETER PM   BMR 73
  BAD MOON RISING   DISCH, THOMAS M.   OA
HOARD OF THE GIBBELINS, THE   DUNSANY, LORD   SS   AFR 47 04
  SPELL OF SEVEN, THE   DE CAMP, L. SPRAGUE   AN
HOAX   GUNN, JAMES E.   NV   IFS 55 12
  STATION IN SPACE   GUNN, JAMES E.   AC
HOAXTERS, THE   WILSON, RICHARD   NV   GAL 52 06
  THOSE IDIOTS FROM EARTH   WILSON, RICHARD   AC
HOBBIES   SIMAK, CLIFFORD D. NV   ASF 46 11
  CITY   SIMAK, CLIFFORD D.   NO
HOBBYIST   BROWN, FREDRIC   SS   PBY 61 05
  NIGHTMARES AND GEEZENSTACKS   BROWN, FREDRIC   AC
HOBBYIST   RUSSELL, ERIC FRANK NV ASF 47 09
  *ASTOUNDING SCIENCE FICTION ANTHOLOGY, THE
                                 CAMPBELL, JOHN W. JR AN
  ASTOUNDING TALES OF SPACE AND TIME CAMPBELL, JOHN W. JR AN
  BEST SF 4   CRISPIN, EDMUND   AN
  DECADE THE 1940S   ALDISS & HARRISON   AN
  *FIRST ASTOUNDING SCIENCE FICTION ANTHOLOGY, THE
                                 CAMPBELL, JOHN W. JR AN
  LIKE NOTHING ON EARTH   RUSSELL, ERIC FRANK   AC
HOBO GOD   JAMESON, MALCOLM   SS   ASF 44 09
  ALL ABOUT THE FUTURE   GREENBERG, MARTIN   AN
HOBO JUNGLE   GOULART, RON   NV   FSF 70 06
  WHAT'S BECOME OF SCREWLOOSE? AND OTHER INQUIRIES
                                 GOULART, RON   AC
HOBSON'S CHOICE   BESTER, ALFRED   SS   FSF 52 08
  BEST FROM FANTASY AND SCIENCE FICTION: 2
                                 BOUCHER & MCCOMAS   AN
  BEST SF 2   CRISPIN, EDMUND   AN
  INFINITE JESTS   SILVERBERG, ROBERT   AN
  STAR LIGHT, STAR BRIGHT   BESTER, ALFRED   AC
  STARBURST   BESTER, ALFRED   AC
  TOMORROW AND TOMORROW   KNIGHT, DAMON   AN
HODSON'S CAPER   CONRAD, EARL   SS
  DA VINCI MACHINE, THE   CONRAD, EARL   OC
HOG-BELLY HONEY   LAFFERTY, R. A.   SS   FSF 65 09
  BEST FROM FANTASY AND SCIENCE FICTION: 15
                                 FERMAN, EDWARD L.   AN
  NINE HUNDRED GRANDMOTHERS   LAFFERTY, R. A.   AC
HOGARTH   INOUYE, JON   SS
  NIGHT TIDE, A   INOUYE, JON   OC
HOITY-TOITY   BELAYEV, ALEXANDER NV
  SOVIET SCIENCE FICTION   ANONYMOUS   AN
HOLD BACK TOMORROW   NEVILLE, KRIS   SS   IMG 51 09
  *IMAGINATION UNLIMITED   BLEILER & DIKTY   AN
HOLD MY HAND, MY LOVE¦   CONEY, MICHAEL G. SS   WOT 71 SP
  MONITOR FOUND IN ORBIT   CONEY, MICHAEL G.   AC
HOLD YOUR FIRE   EISENBERG, LARRY   SS   NEW 71 01
  BEST LAID SCHEMES, THE   EISENBERG, LARRY   AC
HOLDHOLTZER'S BOX   BUNCH, DAVID R.   SS   PRT 71
  PROTOSTARS   GERROLD & GOLDIN   OA
HOLDOUT   SHECKLEY, ROBERT   SS   FSF 57 12
  HUMAN AND OTHER BEINGS   DEGRAEFF, ALLEN   AN
  NOTIONS: UNLIMITED   SHECKLEY, ROBERT   AC
  THEMES IN SCIENCE FICTION   KELLEY, LEO P.   AN
HOLE IN JENNIFER'S ROOM, THE   LO MEDICO, BRIAN T. SS
  MORE SCIENCE FICTION TALES   ELWOOD, ROGER   OA
HOLE IN THE AIR   SILVERBERG, ROBERT SS   AMZ 56 01
  DEVIL'S GENERATION, THE   GHIDALIA, VIC   AN
HOLE IN THE FLOOR, THE   FAST, HOWARD   SS
  TOUCH OF INFINITY, A   FAST, HOWARD   OC
HOLE IN THE MOON, THE   SEABRIGHT, IDRIS   SS   FSF 52 02
  BEST FROM FANTASY AND SCIENCE FICTION: 2
                                 BOUCHER & MCCOMAS   AN
HOLE IN THE SKY   COX, IRVING E. JR. NV
  *TIME TO COME   DERLETH, AUGUST   OA
HOLE MAN, THE   NIVEN, LARRY   SS   ASF 74 01
  BEST SCIENCE FICTION OF THE YEAR, THE NO. 4
                                 CARR, TERRY   AN
  HOLE IN SPACE, A   NIVEN, LARRY   AC
HOLE ON THE CORNER, THE   LAFFERTY, R. A.   SS   ORB 67 02
  BEST FROM ORBIT, THE   KNIGHT, DAMON   AN
  NINE HUNDRED GRANDMOTHERS   LAFFERTY, R. A.   AC
  ORBIT 2   KNIGHT, DAMON   OA
  TOMORROW, AND TOMORROW, AND TOMORROW... HEINTZ/HERBERT/JOOS/& AN
HOLE, THE   DOLAN, MIKE   SS
  SANTANA MORNING AND OTHER STORIES DOLAN, MIKE   OC
HOLES AROUND MARS, THE   BIXBY, JEROME   SS   GAL 54 01
  DECADE THE 1950S   ALDISS & HARRISON   AN
  GREAT STORIES OF SPACE TRAVEL   CONKLIN, GROFF   AN
  OPERATION FUTURE   CONKLIN, GROFF   AN

HOLES AROUND MARS, THE

WHERE DO WE GO FROM HERE?	ASIMOV, ISAAC		AN		
HOLIDAY	BRADBURY, RAY	SS	ARS 49	FL	
FAR BOUNDARIES	DERLETH, AUGUST		AN		
HOLIDAY MAN, THE	MATHESON, RICHARD	SS	FSF 57	07	
SHOCK!	MATHESON, RICHARD		AC		
TWENTY YEARS OF FANTASY & SCIENCE FICTION
	FERMAN & MILLS		AN		
HOLLAND OF THE MIND, THE	ZOLINE, PAMELA A.	NV			
NEW S.F., THE	JONES, LANGDON		OA		
HOLMES-GINSBOOK DEVICE, THE	ASIMOV, ISAAC	SS	IFS 68	12	
OPUS 100	ASIMOV, ISAAC		AC		
HOLY GRAIL, THE	PURDOM, TOM	SS	STR 59	06	
STAR SCIENCE FICTION STORIES NO. 6	POHL, FREDERIK		OA		
HOLY TERROR, A	BIERCE, AMBROSE	SS	91		
*TWISTED	CONKLIN, GROFF		AN		
HOME (THE DISINHERITED)	ANDERSON, POUL	SS	ORB 66	01	
FUTURE NOW, THE	HOSKINS, ROBERT		AN		
QUEEN OF AIR AND DARKNESS AND OTHER STORIES, THE
	ANDERSON, POUL	SS		AC	
HOME AGAIN, HOME AGAIN	EKLUND, GORDON	SS	QRK 71	03	
QUARK/3	DELANY & HACKER		OA		
HOME AWAY FROM HOME, A	BLOCH, ROBERT	SS	AHM 61	06	
KING OF TERRORS, THE	BLOCH, ROBERT		AC		
TALES IN A JUGULAR VEIN	BLOCH, ROBERT		AC		
HOME FROM THE SHORE	DICKSON, GORDON R.	NA	GAL 63	02	
MUTANTS	DICKSON, GORDON R.		AC		
8TH ANNUAL OF THE YEAR'S BEST S-F, THE	MERRIL, JUDITH		AN		
HOME IS THE HANGMAN	ZELAZNY, ROGER	NV	ASF 75	11	
MY NAME IS LEGION	ZELAZNY, ROGER		AC		
NEBULA AWARD STORIES 11	LE GUIN, URSULA K.		AN		
HOME IS THE HERO	TUBB, E. C.	SS	NWS 52	05	
ALIEN DUST	TUBB, E. C.		NO		
GATEWAY TO TOMORROW	CARNELL, JOHN		AN		
HOME IS THE HUNTER	KUTTNER, HENRY	NV	GAL 53	07	
AHEAD OF TIME	KUTTNER, HENRY		AC		
HOME IS WHERE THE WRECK IS	TUCKER, WILSON	SS	USF 54	05	
SCIENCE FICTION SUBTREASURY, THE	TUCKER, WILSON		AC		
HOME OF THE GODS	VAN VOGT, A. E.	NV	ASF 47	04	
BEST OF A. E. VAN VOGT, THE	VAN VOGT, A. E.		NO		
EMPIRE OF THE ATOM	VAN VOGT, A. E.		NO		
HOME SWEET GERIATRIC DOME	GOTSCHALK, FELIX C.	SS	NDM 77	07	
NEW DIMENSIONS 7	SILVERBERG, ROBERT		OA		
HOME THERE'S NO RETURNING	MOORE, C. L.	NV	NEW 55	AC	
ASLEEP IN ARMAGEDDON	SISSONS, MICHAEL		AN		
HOME THERE'S NO RETURNING	KUTTNER, HENRY
	AND MOORE, C. L.	NV C	NEW 55	AC	
NO BOUNDARIES	KUTTNER & MOORE		AC		
SF: THE YEAR'S GREATEST SCIENCE FICTION AND FANTASY
	MERRIL, JUDITH		AN		
HOMECALLING	MERRIL, JUDITH	NV	SFS 56	11	
DAUGHTERS OF EARTH	MERRIL, JUDITH		AC		
HOMECOMING	SELLINGS, ARTHUR	SS			
LONG EUREKA, THE	SELLINGS, ARTHUR		AC		
HOMECOMING, THE	BRADBURY, RAY	SS	MAD 46	10	
*DARK CARNIVAL	BRADBURY, RAY		AC		
GALAXY OF GHOULS	MERRIL, JUDITH		AN		
*OCTOBER COUNTRY, THE	BRADBURY, RAY		AC		
HOMELAND (THE STATUE)	WOLFE, MARI	NV	IFS 53	01	
*STORIES FOR TOMORROW	SLOANE, WILLIAM		AN		
HOMELESS ONE, THE	COPPARD, A. E.	SS	46		
TRAVELERS IN TIME	STERN, PHILIP VAN D.		AN		
HOMER'S SECRET	POLESHCHUK, A.	SS			
LAST DOOR TO AIYA	GINSBURG, MIRRA		AN		
HOMEWARD BOUND	GRIFFITH, GEORGE	SS	PRS 00	06	
WORLDS APART	LOCKE, GEORGE		AN		
HOMEWARD BOUND	WILLIAMS, ROBERT M.	SS	STS 49	11	
TO THE END OF TIME AND OTHER STORIES	WILLIAMS, ROBERT M.		DC		
HOMEY ATMOSPHERE	GALOUYE, DANIEL F.	SS	GAL 61	04	
ABC OF SCIENCE FICTION, AN	BOARDMAN, TOM JR.		AN		
HOMING INSTINCT OF JOE VARGO, THE
	BARR, STEPHEN	SS	FSF 59	12	
*SPECTRUM	AMIS & CONQUEST		AN		
HOMO AQUATICUS (SEE THE HORN OF TIME THE HUNTER)
	ANDERSON, POUL	TC			
HOMO SAP, THE ALSO AS THE GROOVY HOMO SAP)
	NUETZEL, CHARLES	SS			
IF THIS GOES ON	NUETZEL, CHARLES		AN		
HOMO SAPS	RUSSELL, ERIC FRANK	SS	ASF 41	12	
DEEP SPACE	RUSSELL, ERIC FRANK		AC		
HOMO SOL	ASIMOV, ISAAC	SS	ASF 40	09	
EARLY ASIMOV, THE	ASIMOV, ISAAC		AC		
OMNIBUS OF SCIENCE FICTION	CONKLIN, GROFF		AN		
SCIENCE FICTION OMNIBUS	CONKLIN, GROFF		AN		
HONEST DAY'S WORK, AN	HARRISON, HARRY	NV	NWR 73	22	
*BEST OF HARRY HARRISON, THE	HARRISON, HARRY		AC		
NEW WRITINGS IN SF. 22	BULMER, KENNETH		OA		
HONEYMOON	FRITCH, CHARLES E.	SS	VOR 53	05	
HORSES' ASTEROID	FRITCH, CHARLES E.		AC		
HONEYMOON	MCCAFFREY, ANNE	NV	NEW 77	AC	
GET OFF THE UNICORN	MCCAFFREY, ANNE		AC		
HONEYMOON IN BEDLAM	BOND, NELSON S.	SS	WRT 41	01	
LANCELOT BIGGS: SPACEMAN	BOND, NELSON S.		AC		
HONEYMOON IN HELL	BROWN, FREDRIC	NV	GAL 50	11	
DAYMARES	BROWN, FREDRIC		AC		
*GALAXY READER OF SCIENCE FICTION	GOLD, H. L.		AN		
GREAT SCIENCE FICTION STORIES ABOUT THE MOON
	DIKTY, T. E.		AN		
HONEYMOON IN HELL	BROWN, FREDRIC		AN		
HONEYMOON IN SPACE, A	GRIFFITH, GEORGE	EX	PRS 00	01	
FAREWELL FANTASTIC VENUS	ALDISS & HARRISON		AN		
SPACE OPERA	ALDISS, BRIAN W.		AN		
HONOR	WILSON, RICHARD	SS	SFQ 56	02	
HUMAN AND OTHER BEINGS	DEGRAEFF, ALLEN		AN		
THOSE IDIOTS FROM EARTH	WILSON, RICHARD		AC		
HONOR ROLL, THE	MISC. MATERIAL	MS			
MASTERS' CHOICE	JANIFER, LAURENCE M.		AN		

HORSES, THE

HONORABLE DEATH, AN	DICKSON, GORDON R.	NV	GAL 61	02	
ALPHA 6	SILVERBERG, ROBERT		AN		
DANGER- HUMAN	DICKSON, GORDON R.		AC		
POCKETFUL OF STARS, A	KNIGHT, DAMON		AN		
HONORABLE ENEMIES	ANDERSON, POUL	NV	FUT 51	05	
AGENT OF THE TERRAN EMPIRE	ANDERSON, POUL		AC		
WAY OUT	HOWARD, IVAN		AN		
HONORABLE MENTIONS	MISC. MATERIAL	MS			
BEST SCIENCE FICTION OF THE YEAR, THE NO. 2
	CARR, TERRY		AN		
BEST SCIENCE FICTION OF THE YEAR, THE NO. 3
	CARR, TERRY		AN		
10TH ANNUAL OF THE YEAR'S BEST S-F, THE	MERRIL, JUDITH		AN		
6TH ANNUAL OF THE YEAR'S BEST S-F, THE	MERRIL, JUDITH		AN		
7TH ANNUAL OF THE YEAR'S BEST S-F, THE	MERRIL, JUDITH		AN		
8TH ANNUAL OF THE YEAR'S BEST S-F, THE	MERRIL, JUDITH		AN		
9TH ANNUAL OF THE YEAR'S BEST S-F, THE	MERRIL, JUDITH		AN		
HONORABLE MENTIONS- 1974	CARR, TERRY		MS		
BEST SCIENCE FICTION OF THE YEAR, THE NO. 4
	CARR, TERRY		AN		
HONORABLE OPPONENT	SIMAK, CLIFFORD D.	SS	GAL 56	08	
ALIENS FOR NEIGHBOURS	SIMAK, CLIFFORD D.		AC		
THIRD GALAXY READER, THE	GOLD, H. L.		AN		
*WORLDS OF CLIFFORD SIMAK, THE	SIMAK, CLIFFORD D.		AC		
HOOB MELON CRISIS, THE	LAUMER, KEITH	NV	NEW 75	AC	
RETIEF: EMISSARY TO THE STARS	LAUMER, KEITH		AC		
HOOFER, THE	MILLER, WALTER M. JR	SS	FUN 55	09	
SF: THE BEST OF THE BEST	MERRIL, JUDITH		AN		
SF: THE YEAR'S GREATEST SCIENCE FICTION AND FANTASY
	MERRIL, JUDITH		AN		
HOOP, THE	FAST, HOWARD	SS	FSF 72	10	
TOUCH OF INFINITY, A	FAST, HOWARD		OC		
HOP-FRIEND	CARR, TERRY	SS	FSF 62	11	
ALIENS, THE	SILVERBERG, ROBERT		AN		
BEST FROM FANTASY AND SCIENCE FICTION: 12
	DAVIDSON, AVRAM		AN		
FIRST STEP OUTWARD	HOSKINS, ROBERT		AN		
LIGHT AT THE END OF THE UNIVERSE, THE	CARR, TERRY		AC		
POCKETFUL OF STARS, A	KNIGHT, DAMON		AN		
HOPPER	SILVERBERG, ROBERT	NV	INF 56	10	
NEXT STOP THE STARS	SILVERBERG, ROBERT		DC		
HOPSOIL	YOUNG, ROBERT F.	SS	FSF 61	01	
WORLDS OF ROBERT F. YOUNG, THE	YOUNG, ROBERT F.		AC		
HORARS OF WAR, THE	WOLFE, GENE	SS	NOV 70	01	
COMBAT SF	DICKSON, GORDON R.		OA		
*NOVA 1	HARRISON, HARRY		OA		
POCKETFUL OF STARS, A	KNIGHT, DAMON		AN		
HORIZONTAL MAN	SPENCER, WILLIAM	SS	NWR 65	06	
NEW WRITINGS IN SF. 6	CARNELL, JOHN		OA		
HORLA, THE (1886)	DE MAUPASSANT, GUY	SS	WRT 26	08	
ANDROIDS, TIME MACHINES AND BLUE GIRAFFES
	ELWOOD & GHIDALIA		AN		
HORMONES	PRATT, FLETCHER	SS	STR 53	02	
STAR SCIENCE FICTION STORIES NO. 2	POHL, FREDERIK		OA		
HORN OF PLENTY, THE	GRIGORIEV, VLADIMIR	SS	GAL 69	12	
ULTIMATE THRESHOLD, THE	GINSBURG, MIRRA		AN		
HORN OF TIME THE HUNTER, THE (HOMO AQUATICUS)
	ANDERSON, POUL	SS	AMZ 63	09	
BEST FROM AMAZING, THE	WHITE, TED		AN		
HORN OF TIME, THE	ANDERSON, POUL		AC		
WONDERMAKERS 2	HOSKINS, ROBERT		AN		
HORNET, THE	JOHNSON, GEORGE C.	SS	ROG 62	09	
FIEND IN YOU, THE	BEAUMONT, CHARLES		AN		
HORNETS OF SPACE	STARZL, R. F.	SS	WOS 30	11	
FROM OFF THIS WORLD	MARGULIES & FRIEND		AN		
HORRER HOWCE	ST. CLAIR, MARGARET	SS	GAL 56	07	
FOURTH GALAXY READER, THE	GOLD, H. L.		AN		
HORROR FROM THE HILLS, THE	LONG, FRANK BELKNAP	SN	WRT 31	01	
ODD SCIENCE FICTION	LONG, FRANK BELKNAP		AC		
HORROR FROM THE MIDDLE SPAN, THE
	LOVECRAFT, H. P.	SS			
TRAVELLERS BY NIGHT	DERLETH, AUGUST		OA		
HORROR FROM THE MOUND, THE	HOWARD, ROBERT E.	SS	WRT 32	05	
WOLFSHEAD	HOWARD, ROBERT E.		AC		
HORROR OF THE HEIGHTS, THE	DOYLE, ARTHUR CONAN	SS	EVB 13	11	
FUTURES UNLIMITED	NORTON, ALDEN H.		AN		
HORROR ON THE ASTEROID	HAMILTON, EDMOND	SS	WRT 33	09	
HORROR ON THE ASTEROID AND OTHER TALES OF PLANETARY HORROR
	HAMILTON, EDMOND		AC		
HORROR STORY SHORTER BY ONE LETTER THAN THE SHORTEST HORROR
STORY EVER WRITTEN, A	SMITH, RON	SS	FSF 57	07	
BEST FROM FANTASY AND SCIENCE FICTION: 7
	BOUCHER, ANTHONY		AN		
HORSE BARBARIANS, THE (SEE DEATHWORLD 3)
	HARRISON, HARRY	TC			
HORSE FROM A DIFFERENT SEA	MCCAFFREY, ANNE	SS	NEW 77	AC	
GET OFF THE UNICORN	MCCAFFREY, ANNE		AC		
HORSE OF A DIFFERENT TECHNICOLOR, A
	STRETE, CRAIG	SS	GAL 75	01	
BEST FROM GALAXY, THE VOLUME IV	BAEN, JAMES		AN		
HORSE OF AIR	DOZOIS, GARDNER R.	SS	ORB 70	08	
BEST FROM ORBIT, THE	KNIGHT, DAMON		AN		
NEBULA AWARD STORIES NO. 7	BIGGLE, LLOYD JR.		AN		
ORBIT 8	KNIGHT, DAMON		OA		
HORSE RACE	BROWN, FREDRIC	SS			
NIGHTMARES AND GEEZENSTACKS	BROWN, FREDRIC		AC		
HORSE WITH ONE LEG, THE	EFFINGER, GEO. ALEC	SS	NEW 74	AN	
WORLDS FAR AND NEAR	CARR, TERRY		AN		
HORSEMAN FROM HEL, THE	KIMBERLY, GAIL	NV	BER 74		
BERSERKERS, THE	ELWOOD, ROGER		OA		
HORSES' ASTEROID	FRITCH, CHARLES E.	SS	58		
HORSES' ASTEROID	FRITCH, CHARLES E.		AC		
HORSES, THE	MUIR, EDWIN	PM	60		
LOOKING AHEAD	ALLEN, D. & L.		AN		

```
HOSPITAL OF TRANSPLANTED HEARTS
                              THOMAS, D. M.        SS   NWS 69 01
  BEST SF: 1969               HARRISON & ALDISS        AN
HOST AGE         BRUNNER, JOHN        NV   NWS 56 01
  ENTRY TO ELSEWHEN (STORIES REVISED)  BRUNNER, JOHN      AC
HOSTESS          ASIMOV, ISAAC        SS   GAL 51 05
  *GALAXY READER OF SCIENCE FICTION   GOLD, H. L.        AN
  NIGHTFALL AND OTHER STORIES        ASIMOV, ISAAC       AC
HOT ARGUMENT     GARRETT, RANDALL     PM   FSF 60 02
  5TH ANNUAL OF THE YEAR'S BEST S-F, THE  MERRIL, JUDITH  AN
HOT PLANET       CLEMENT, HAL         NV   GAL 63 08
  EIGHTH GALAXY READER, THE           POHL, FREDERIK      AN
  SPECTRUM 4                          AMIS & CONQUEST     AN
  9TH ANNUAL OF THE YEAR'S BEST S-F, THE  MERRIL, JUDITH  AN
HOT POTATO       BUDRYS, ALGIS        SS   ASF 57 07
  FALLING TORCH, THE                  BUDRYS, ALGIS       NO
HOT POTATO       FILER, BURT K.       SS   MWS 71
  BEST SCIENCE FICTION STORIES OF THE YEAR (1971)
                              DEL REY, LESTER          AN
  MANY WORLDS OF SCIENCE FICTION, THE  BOVA, BEN          OA
HOTHOUSE         ALDISS, BRIAN W.     NV   FSF 61 02
  LONG AFTERNOON OF EARTH, THE        ALDISS, BRIAN W.    NO
  MUTANTS                             SILVERBERG, ROBERT  AN
  OUT OF THIS WORLD 4                 WILLIAMS-ELLIS& OWEN AN
HOTHOUSE PLANET (SEE VENUS)  BARNES, ARTHUR K.    TC
HOTSY-TOTSY MACHINE, THE     WYAL, PG              SS
  FUTURE PASTIMES                     EDELSTEIN, SCOTT    OA
HOTTEST AND COLDEST MOLECULES LEIBER, FRITZ       AR   SDG 52 03
  BOOK OF FRITZ LEIBER, THE           LEIBER, FRITZ       AC
HOTTEST PIECE OF REAL ESTATE IN THE SOLAR SYSTEM, THE
  (SEE SUMMERTIME ON ICARUS)  CLARKE, ARTHUR C.    TC
HOUND, THE       LEIBER, FRITZ        SS   WRT 42 11
  BEWARE THE BEASTS                   GHIDALIA, V.& ELWOOD AN
  NIGHT'S BLACK AGENTS                LEIBER, FRITZ       AC
HOUNDS OF SKAITH, THE        BRACKETT, LEIGH      NO   BAL 74 10
  BOOK OF SKAITH, THE                 BRACKETT, LEIGH     AC
HOUNDS OF TINDALOS, THE      LONG, FRANK BELKNAP SS   WRT 29 03
  EARLY LONG, THE                     LONG, FRANK BELKNAP AC
  *HOUNDS OF TINDALOS, THE            LONG, FRANK BELKNAP AC
  STRANGE ECSTASIES                   PARRY, MICHEL       AN
HOUNDS, THE      WILHELM, KATE        NV   NEW 74 AN
  SHOCKING THING, A                   KNIGHT, DAMON       AN
HOUR AFTER WESTERLY, THE     COATES, ROBERT M.    SS   NYM 47 11
  TIMELESS STORIES FOR TODAY AND TOMORROW  BRADBURY, RAY  AN
HOUR OF BATTLE, THE          SHECKLEY, ROBERT     SS   SSF 53 09
  FUTURE MAKERS, THE                  HAINING, PETER      AN
HOUR OF LETDOWN, THE         WHITE, E. B.         SS   FSF 52 08
  CIRCUS OF DR. LAO AND OTHER IMPROBABLE STORIES
                              BRADBURY, RAY            AN
  OUT OF THIS WORLD 5                 WILLIAMS-ELLIS& OWEN AN
HOUR OF TRUST     WOLFE, GENE         NV   BMR 73
  BAD MOON RISING                     DISCH, THOMAS M.    OA
HOUSE             BARFOOT, JOHN       SS   ORB 75 17
  ORBIT 17                            KNIGHT, DAMON       OA
HOUSE BY THE CRAB APPLE TREE, THE
                              JOHNSON, S. S.       NV   FSF 64 02
  BEST FROM FANTASY AND SCIENCE FICTION: 14
                              DAVIDSON, AVRAM          AN
HOUSE BY THE SEA, THE         ARNASON, ELEANOR    SS   ORB 75 16
  ORBIT 16                            KNIGHT, DAMON       AN
HOUSE DUTIFUL, THE           TENN, WILLIAM        SS   ASF 48 04
  *BEYOND HUMAN KEN                   MERRIL, JUDITH      AN
  SEVEN SEXES, THE                    TENN, WILLIAM       AC
HOUSE IN THE TWILIGHT ZONE, THE  ACKERMAN, FORREST J. AR
  SCIENCE FICTION WORLDS OF FORREST J. ACKERMAN & FRIENDS
                              ACKERMAN, FORREST J. AC
HOUSE IN THE VALLEY, THE     DERLETH, AUGUST      NV   WRT 53 07
  ANDROIDS, TIME MACHINES AND BLUE GIRAFFES
                              ELWOOD & GHIDALIA        AN
HOUSE OF ARABU, THE          HOWARD, ROBERT E.    SS
  WOLFSHEAD                           HOWARD, ROBERT E.   AC
HOUSE OF CTHULHU, THE        LUMLEY, BRIAN        SS   WHS 73
  YEAR'S BEST HORROR STORIES: SERIES III, THE
                              DAVIS, RICHARD           AN
HOUSE OF ECSTASY, THE        FARLEY, RALPH MILNE SS   WRT 38 04
  OTHER WORLDS, THE                   STONG, PHILIP D.    AN
HOUSE OF RISING WINDS, THE   LONG, FRANK BELKNAP SS   STS 48 05
  *MY BEST SCIENCE FICTION STORY      MARGULIES & FRIEND  AN
  RIM OF THE UNKNOWN                  LONG, FRANK BELKNAP AC
HOUSE OF THE HATCHET, THE    BLOCH, ROBERT        SS   WRT 41 01
  HOUSE OF THE HATCHET, THE           BLOCH, ROBERT       AC
  *OPENER OF THE WAY, THE             BLOCH, ROBERT       AC
  YOURS TRULY, JACK THE RIPPER        BLOCH, ROBERT       AC
HOUSE OF THE NIGHTMARE, THE  WHITE, EDWARD LUCAS  SS   TTB 19 09
  BEWARE THE BEASTS                   GHIDALIA, V.& ELWOOD AN
HOUSE ON STILLCROFT STREET, THE
                              BRENNAN, JOSEPH P.   SS   AHM 75 06
  YEAR'S BEST HORROR STORIES: SERIES IV, THE
                              PAGE, GERALD W.          AN
HOUSE ON THE SQUARE, THE     SERLING, ROD         SA
  *ROD SERLING'S THE TWILIGHT ZONE    SERLING, ROD        OC
HOUSE RULE        ANDERSON, POUL      SS   NEW 76 AC
  HOMEBREW                            ANDERSON, POUL      AC
HOUSE THAT JULES BUILT, THE  ALDISS, BRIAN W.     MS
  BEST SF: 1968                       HARRISON & ALDISS   AN
HOUSE THE BLAKENEYS BUILT, THE DAVIDSON, AVRAM    SS   FSF 65 01
  ANTHROPOLOGY THROUGH SCIENCE FICTION  MASON, C/GREENBERG/& AN
  BEST FROM FANTASY AND SCIENCE FICTION: 15
                              FERMAN, EDWARD L.        AN
  STRANGE SEAS AND SHORES             DAVIDSON, AVRAM     AC
HOUSE WHERE TIME STOOD STILL, THE
                              QUINN, SEABURY       SS   WRT 39 03
  OTHER WORLDS, THE                   STONG, PHILIP D.    AN
HOUSE, THE        BROWN, FREDRIC      SS   FAN 60 08
  NIGHTMARES AND GEEZENSTACKS         BROWN, FREDRIC      AC

HOUSING PROBLEM   KUTTNER, HENRY      SS   CHM 44 10
  BEST OF HENRY KUTTNER 1, THE        KUTTNER, HENRY      AC
  BEST OF HENRY KUTTNER, THE          KUTTNER, HENRY      AC
  BYPASS TO OTHERNESS                 KUTTNER, HENRY      AC
  FANTASY: THE LITERATURE OF THE MARVELOUS KELLEY, LEO P. AN
  TIMELESS STORIES FOR TODAY AND TOMORROW BRADBURY, RAY   AN
HOUSING SHORTAGE  WALTON, HARRY       SS   ASF 47 01
  *TREASURY OF SCIENCE FICTION, A     CONKLIN, GROFF      AN
HOUSTON, HOUSTON, DO YOU READ? TIPTREE, JAMES JR.  NA
  AURORA: BEYOND EQUALITY             MCINTYRE & ANDERSON OA
  1977 ANNUAL WORLD'S BEST SF, THE    WOLLHEIM, DONALD A. AN
HOW ALLIED        CLIFTON, MARK       NV   ASF 57 03
  ELSEWHERE AND ELSEWHEN              CONKLIN, GROFF      AN
HOW BEAUTIFUL WITH BANNERS   BLISH, JAMES         SS   ORB 66 01
  ANYWHEN                             BLISH, JAMES        AC
  BEST SCIENCE FICTION STORIES OF JAMES BLISH (REVISED)
                              BLISH, JAMES             AC
  LATE GREAT FUTURE, THE              FITZ GERALD & DILLON AN
  ORBIT 1                             KNIGHT, DAMON       OA
  SCIENCE FICTION ROLL OF HONOR, THE  POHL, FREDERIK      AN
HOW BRIGHT THE STARS         BRACKETT, LEIGH      SS   FTP 73
  FLAME TREE PLANET                   ELWOOD, ROGER       OA
HOW CAN WE SINK WHEN WE CAN FLY?
                              PANSHIN, ALEXEI      NV   FFU 71
  BEST SCIENCE FICTION OF THE YEAR, THE  CARR, TERRY      AN
  FAREWELL TO YESTERDAY'S TOMORROW    PANSHIN, ALEXEI     AC
  FOUR FUTURES                        SILVERBERG, ROBERT  OA
HOW DEEP THE GROOVES         FARMER, PHILIP JOSE SS   AMZ 63 02
  DOWN IN THE BLACK GANG AND OTHER STORIES FARMER, PHILIP JOSE AC
HOW DO I DO?      WYNDHAM, JOHN       SS   BEY 53 09
  INFINITE MOMENT, THE                WYNDHAM, JOHN       AC
  JIZZLE                              WYNDHAM, JOHN       AC
HOW DO YOU KNOW YOU CAN'T WRITE SCIENCE FICTION?
                              GOLD, H. L.          IN
  WORLD THAT COULDN'T BE AND 8 OTHER SF NOVELETS
                              GOLD, H. L.              AN
HOW ERG THE SELF-INDUCTING SLEW A PALEFACE
                              LEM, STANISLAW       SS   72
  MORTAL ENGINES                      LEM, STANISLAW      AC
HOW FEAR DEPARTED FROM THE LONG GALLERY
                              BENSON, E. F.        SS   12
  LITTLE MONSTERS, THE                ELWOOD & GHIDALIA   AN
HOW GEORGES DUCHAMPS DISCOVERED A PLOT TO TAKE OVER THE WORLD
                              PANSHIN, ALEXEI      SS   FAN 71 04
  FAREWELL TO YESTERDAY'S TOMORROW    PANSHIN, ALEXEI     AC
HOW HIGH ON THE LADDER?      PAIGE, LEO           SS   FBK 50 07
  SCIENCE AND SORCERY                 FORD, GARRET        AN
HOW I TAKE THEIR MEASURE     O'DONNELL, K. M.     SS   FSF 69 01
  FINAL WAR AND OTHER FANTASIES       O'DONNELL, K. M.    DC
  SOCIAL PROBLEMS THROUGH SCIENCE FICTION  GREENBERG/MILSTEAD/& AN
HOW IT ENDED      BUNCH, DAVID R.     SS   AMZ 69 01
  MODERAN                             BUNCH, DAVID R.     AC
HOW IT FELT       EFFINGER, GEO. ALEC SS   UNI 74 05
  IRRATIONAL NUMBERS                  EFFINGER, GEO. ALEC AC
  UNIVERSE 5                          CARR, TERRY         OA
HOW IT WAS WHEN THE PAST WENT AWAY
                              SILVERBERG, ROBERT   NA   TFT 69
  EARTH'S OTHER SHADOW                SILVERBERG, ROBERT  AC
  THREE FOR TOMORROW                  SILVERBERG, ROBERT  OA
HOW LIKE A GOD    BLOCH, ROBERT       SS   GAL 69 04
  COLD CHILLS                         BLOCH, ROBERT       AC
HOW MANY MILES TO BABYLON?   WILHELM, KATE        SS   NEW 68 AC
  DOWNSTAIRS ROOM AND OTHER SPECULATIVE FICTION, THE
                              WILHELM, KATE            AC
HOW MANY MILES TO BABYLON? (BABYLON: 70 M.)
                              WOLLHEIM, DONALD A.  SS   MOH 63 08
  TWO DOZEN DRAGON EGGS               WOLLHEIM, DONALD A. AC
HOW MICROX AND GIGANT MADE THE UNIVERSE EXPAND
                              LEM, STANISLAW       SS   72
  MORTAL ENGINES                      LEM, STANISLAW      AC
HOW MUCH DOES A CHARACTER COST?
                              KEYES, DANIEL        AR
  THOSE WHO CAN: A SCIENCE FICTION READER  WILSON, ROBIN SCOTT AN
HOW MUCH SHALL WE BET?       CALVINO, ITALO       SS
  COSMICOMICS                         CALVINO, ITALO      OC
HOW NEAR IS THE MOON?        MERRIL, JUDITH       AR   NEW 58 AN
  SF:58, THE YEAR'S GREATEST SCIENCE FICTION AND FANTASY
                              MERRIL, JUDITH           AN
HOW SCIENCE FICTION SAVED ME FROM A LIFE OF CRIME
                              ELLISON, HARLAN      IN
  I HAVE NO MOUTH, AND I MUST SCREAM  ELLISON, HARLAN     AC
HOW SHALL WE CONQUER?        MACFARLANE, WALLACE  SS   NDM 73 03
  NEW DIMENSIONS 3                    SILVERBERG, ROBERT  AN
HOW SHARPER THAN A SERPENT'S TOOTH (RUSSELL BATES &DAVID WISE)
                              FOSTER, ALAN DEAN    SA   SLG 76 06
  STAR TREK LOG SIX                   FOSTER, ALAN DEAN   OC
HOW THE CONSOLATIONS OF PHILOSOPHY WORKED OUT IN ACTUAL
  PRACTICE                   HADEN-GUEST, ANTHONY PM   69
  HOLDING YOUR EIGHT HANDS            LUCIE-SMITH, EDWARD AN
HOW THE HEROES DIE           NIVEN, LARRY         NV   GAL 66 10
  SHAPE OF SPACE, THE                 NIVEN, LARRY        AC
  TALES OF KNOWN SPACE: THE UNIVERSE OF LARRY NIVEN
                              NIVEN, LARRY             AC
HOW THE OLD WORLD DIED       HARRISON, HARRY      SS   GAL 64 10
  NINTH GALAXY READER, THE            POHL, FREDERIK      AN
HOW THE WHIP CAME BACK       WOLFE, GENE          SS   ORB 70 06
  ORBIT 6                             KNIGHT, DAMON       OA
HOW THE WORLD WAS SAVED      LEM, STANISLAW       SS
  ANTIGRAV: COSMIC COMEDIES           STRICK, PHILIP      AN
  CYBERIAD, THE                       LEM, STANISLAW      OC
HOW THEY GAVE IT BACK        LAFFERTY, R. A.      SS   GAL 68 02
  DOES ANYONE ELSE HAVE SOMETHING FURTHER TO ADD?
                              LAFFERTY, R. A.          AC
HOW THEY TOOK CARE OF SOUL IN A LAST DAY FOR A NON-BEGINNING
                              BUNCH, DAVID R.      SS
  MODERAN                             BUNCH, DAVID R.     AC
```

HOW TO BE A SOLDIER (SOLDIERS RUNNING)
      ALDISS, BRIAN W. SS NWS 60 06
 AIRS OF EARTH, THE ALDISS, BRIAN W. AC
HOW TO BE ETHNIC IN ONE EASY LESSON
      ANDERSON, POUL NV FUQ 73
 FUTURE QUEST ELWOOD, ROGER OA
HOW TO BUILD TOMORROW HOSKINS, ROBERT IN INY 73 05
 INFINITY 5 HOSKINS, ROBERT OA
HOW TO CONSTRUCT A TIME MACHINE
      JARRY, ALFRED SS
 TRAPS OF TIME, THE MOORCOCK, MICHAEL AN
HOW TO COUNT ON YOUR FINGERS POHL, FREDERIK AR SPS 56 09
 BEST OF FREDERIK POHL, THE POHL, FREDERIK AC
 COMING ATTRACTIONS GREENBERG, MARTIN NF
 DIGITS AND DASTARDS POHL, FREDERIK AC
HOW TO KILL AUNTY STURGEON, THEODORE NV MSM 61 03
 STARSHINE STURGEON, THEODORE AC
HOW TO LEARN MARTIAN HOCKETT, CHARLES F. AR ASF 55 05
 COMING ATTRACTIONS GREENBERG, MARTIN NF
HOW TO THINK A SCIENCE FICTION STORY (EXCERPT)
      STINE, G. HARRY AR ASF 61 05
 6TH ANNUAL OF THE YEAR'S BEST S-F, THE MERRIL, JUDITH AN
HOW WE SAVED THE HUMAN RACE GERROLD, DAVID NV NEW 72 04
 WITH A FINGER IN MY I GERROLD, DAVID AC
HOW XMAS GHOSTS ARE MADE BUNCH, DAVID R. SS ALT 74
 ALTERNATIES GERROLD, DAVID OA
HOW-2 SIMAK, CLIFFORD D. NV GAL 54 11
 BEST SCIENCE FICTION STORIES AND NOVELS: 1955
      DIKTY, T. E. AN
 BODYGUARD AND 4 OTHER SHORT SF NOVELS FROM GALAXY
      GOLD, H. L. AN
 5 TALES FROM TOMORROW DIKTY, T. E. AN
HOWLING BOUNDERS, THE VANCE, JACK NV STS 49 03
 MANY WORLDS OF MAGNUS RIDOLPH, THE VANCE, JACK DC
 WORLDS OF WONDER HARRISON, HARRY AN
HOWLING MAN, THE BEAUMONT, CHARLES SS NEW 60 AC
 EDGE, THE BEAUMONT, CHARLES AC
 NIGHT RIDE AND OTHER JOURNEYS BEAUMONT, CHARLES AC
HUB (SOLITARY CONFINEMENT) MACDONALD, PHILIP SS FSF 51 08
 BEST FROM FANTASY AND SCIENCE FICTION BOUCHER & MCCOMAS AN
HUDDLING PLACE SIMAK, CLIFFORD D. SS ASF 44 07
 CITY SIMAK, CLIFFORD D. NO
 DECADE THE 1940S ALDISS & HARRISON AN
 MICROCOSMIC GOD MOSKOWITZ, SAM AN
 MODERN MASTERPIECES OF SCIENCE FICTION MOSKOWITZ, SAM AN
 SCIENCE FICTION HALL OF FAME VOLUME 1 SILVERBERG, ROBERT AN
HUGE BEAST CARTMILL, CLEVE SS FSF 50 SU
 BEST FROM FANTASY AND SCIENCE FICTION BOUCHER & MCCOMAS AN
HUGO AWARDS MISC. MATERIAL MS
 NEBULA AWARD STORIES 8 ASIMOV, ISAAC AN
HUMAN ANGLE, THE TENN, WILLIAM SS FFM 48 10
 HUMAN ANGLE, THE TENN, WILLIAM AC
HUMAN FACTOR, THE ELY, DAVID SS SEP 63 11
 SCIENCE FACT/FICTION FARRELL/GAGE/& AN
HUMAN FRAILTY XLEBNIKOV, A. SS
 RUSSIAN SCIENCE FICTION, 1969 MAGIDOFF, ROBERT AN
HUMAN IS DICK, PHILIP K. SS STS 55 WI
 BEST OF PHILIP K. DICK, THE DICK, PHILIP K. AC
HUMAN MAN'S BURDEN SHECKLEY, ROBERT SS GAL 56 09
 PILGRIMAGE TO EARTH SHECKLEY, ROBERT AC
 12 GREAT CLASSICS OF SCIENCE FICTION CONKLIN, GROFF AN
HUMAN MUTANT, THE (FROM "THE LIFE AND ADVENTURES OF
PETER WILKINS") PALTOCK, ROBERT EX
 SCIENCE FICTION THROUGH THE AGES 1 EVANS, I. O. AN
HUMAN OPERATORS, THE ELLISON, HARLAN
    AND VAN VOGT, A. E. NV C FSF 71 01
 BEST SCIENCE FICTION STORIES OF THE YEAR (1971)
      DEL REY, LESTER AN
 PARTNERS IN WONDER ELLISON, HARLAN AC
HUMAN PETS OF MARS, THE STONE, LESLIE F. NV AMZ 36 10
 BEFORE THE GOLDEN AGE ASIMOV, ISAAC AN
HUMAN RACE HAS, MAYBE, THIRTY-FIVE YEARS LEFT, THE
      LYLE, DAVID AR ESQ 67 09
 SCIENCE FICTION: THE FUTURE ALLEN, DICK AN
HUMAN SIDE OF THE VILLAGE MONSTER, THE
      BRYANT, EDWARD SS UNI 71 01
 AMONG THE DEAD BRYANT, EDWARD AC
 UNIVERSE 1 CARR, TERRY OA
HUMAN ZERO, THE GARDNER, EARL S. NV ARG 31 12
 HUMAN ZERO, THE MOSKOWITZ & ELWOOD AN
HUMANITY ON VENUS (FROM "LAST AND FIRST MEN")
      STAPLEDON, OLAF EX MTH 30
 MASTERPIECES OF SCIENCE FICTION MOSKOWITZ, SAM AN
HUMANS, GO HOME! VAN VOGT, A. E. NV GAL 69 09
 MORE THAN SUPERHUMAN VAN VOGT, A. E. AC
HUMMINGBIRD THAT LIVED THROUGH WINTER, THE
      SAROYAN, WILLIAM SS 44
 ECO-FICTION STADLER, JOHN AN
HUMORS, THE (JOIN NOW) SHECKLEY, ROBERT NA GAL 58 12
 STORE OF INFINITY SHECKLEY, ROBERT AC
HUMPTY DUMPTY PADGETT, LEWIS NV ASF 53 09
 MUTANT PADGETT, LEWIS AC
HUMPTY DUMPTY HAD A GREAT FALL LONG, FRANK BELKNAP SS STS 48 11
 *BEYOND TIME AND SPACE DERLETH, AUGUST AN
 RIM OF THE UNKNOWN LONG, FRANK BELKNAP AC
 STRANGE GIFTS SILVERBERG, ROBERT AN
HUNCH, THE ANVIL, CHRISTOPHER SS ASF 61 07
 ANALOG 1 CAMPBELL, JOHN W. JR AN
HUNG LIKE AN ELEPHANT PUMILIA, JOSEPH F.
    AND UTLEY, STEVEN SS C ALT 74
 ALTERNATIES GERROLD, DAVID OA
HUNGARIAN CINCH, THE PRONZINI, BILL NV NEW 76 AN
 ARENA: SPORTS SF FERMAN & MALZBERG AN
HUNGARIAN RHAPSODY (AS WILSON KANE)
      BLOCH, ROBERT SS FAN 58 06
 NIGHTMARES BLOCH, ROBERT AC

 PLEASANT DREAMS BLOCH, ROBERT AC
HUNGER (THE HUNGRY GHOST) PETAJA, EMIL SS WRT 50 03
 STARDRIFT AND OTHER FANTASTIC FLOTSAM PETAJA, EMIL AC
HUNGER OVER SWEET WATERS KAPP, COLIN NV NWR 65 04
 NEW WRITINGS IN SF. 4 CARNELL, JOHN OA
HUNGER PANGS NUETZEL, CHARLES SS
 IMAGES OF TOMORROW NUETZEL, CHARLES AC
HUNGER, THE BEAUMONT, CHARLES SS PBY 55 04
 HUNGER AND OTHER STORIES, THE BEAUMONT, CHARLES AC
 MAGIC MAN AND OTHER SCIENCE-FANTASY STORIES
      BEAUMONT, CHARLES AC
HUNGRY EYE, THE BLOCH, ROBERT NV FAN 59 05
 FEAR TODAY, GONE TOMORROW BLOCH, ROBERT AC
 TIME UNTAMED HOWARD, IVAN AN
HUNGRY GHOST, THE (SEE HUNGER) PETAJA, EMIL TC
HUNGRY GUINEA PIG, THE BREUER, MILES J. MD. SS AMZ 30 01
 *SCIENCE FICTION ADVENTURES IN MUTATION CONKLIN, GROFF AN
HUNGRY HERCYNIAN, THE DE CAMP, L. SPRAGUE NV USF 53 12
 SPELL OF SEVEN, THE DE CAMP, L. SPRAGUE AN
HUNGRY HOUSE, THE BLOCH, ROBERT NV IMG 51 04
 NIGHTMARES BLOCH, ROBERT AC
 PLEASANT DREAMS BLOCH, ROBERT AC
HUNT THE HUNTER NEVILLE, KRIS SS GAL 51 06
 MISSION: MANSTOP NEVILLE, KRIS AC
HUNT THE SPACE-WITCH! SILVERBERG, ROBERT SN SFA 58 01
 GREAT SCIENCE FICTION ADVENTURES SHAW, LARRY T. AN
HUNT, THE LEM, STANISLAW NV 73
 MORTAL ENGINES LEM, STANISLAW AC
HUNTED ONES, THE REYNOLDS, MACK NV SPS 59 11
 WEIRD ONES, THE HOWARD, IVAN AN
HUNTED, THE MACDONALD, JOHN D. SS SSS 49 07
 BEYOND THE END OF TIME POHL, FREDERIK AN
HUNTER AT HIS EASE, THE ALDISS, BRIAN W. SS SAG 70
 BEST SF: 1971 HARRISON & ALDISS AN
 SCIENCE AGAINST MAN CHEETHAM, ANTHONY OA
HUNTER, COME HOME MCKENNA, RICHARD M. NV FSF 63 03
 BEST FROM FANTASY AND SCIENCE FICTION: 13
      DAVIDSON, AVRAM AN
 CASEY AGONISTES, AND OTHER S.F. & FANTASY STORIES
      MCKENNA, RICHARD M. AC
 CENTURY OF GREAT SHORT SCIENCE FICTION NOVELS, A
      KNIGHT, DAMON AN
HUNTER, THE FAST, HOWARD NV
 TIME AND THE RIDDLE FAST, HOWARD AC
HUNTERS, THE SHELDON, WALT SS STS 52 03
 FIFTY SHORT SCIENCE FICTION TALES ASIMOV & CONKLIN AN
HUNTING LODGE, THE GARRETT, RANDALL NV ASF 54 07
 MEN AND MACHINES SILVERBERG, ROBERT AN
HUNTING MACHINE, THE EMSHWILLER, CAROL SS SFS 57 05
 BEST SCIENCE FICTION STORIES AND NOVELS: 9TH SERIES
      DIKTY, T. E. AN
 SCIENCE FICTION INVENTIONS KNIGHT, DAMON AN
HUNTING PROBLEM SHECKLEY, ROBERT SS GAL 55 09
 CITIZEN IN SPACE SHECKLEY, ROBERT AC
 ROBERT SHECKLEY OMNIBUS, THE SHECKLEY, ROBERT AC
 STORIES FROM SCIENCE FICTION DOHERTY, G. D. AN
HUNTING SEASON, THE ROBINSON, FRANK M. SN ASF 51 11
 YEAR'S BEST SCIENCE FICTION NOVELS: 1952 BLEILER & DIKTY AN
HUNTING, THE BEETEM, DORIS SS
 STAR TREK: THE NEW VOYAGES MARSHAK, S&CULBREATH OA
HURKLE IS A HAPPY BEAST, THE STURGEON, THEODORE SS FSF 49 FL
 BEST SCIENCE-FICTION STORIES: 1950, THE BLEILER & DIKTY AN
 FIRST CONTACT KNIGHT, DAMON AN
 SCIENCE FICTION BESTIARY, THE SILVERBERG, ROBERT AN
 SCIENCE FICTION GALAXY, THE CONKLIN, GROFF AN
 SCIENCE FICTION ROLL OF HONOR, THE POHL, FREDERIK AN
 THUNDER AND ROSES STURGEON, THEODORE AC
 *WAY HOME, A STURGEON, THEODORE AC
 ZOO 2000 YOLEN, JANE AN
HURRICANE TRIO STURGEON, THEODORE NV GAL 55 04
 *WAY HOME, A STURGEON, THEODORE AC
HUSBAND FOR MY WIFE, A STUART, WILLIAM W. SS GAL 60 08
 SIXTH GALAXY READER, THE GOLD, H. L. AN
HUSBAND'S SHARE, A BUNCH, DAVID R. SS FAN 60 10
 MODERAN BUNCH, DAVID R. AC
HUSH! HENDERSON, ZENNA SS BEY 53 11
 ANYTHING BOX, THE HENDERSON, ZENNA AC
HYANNIS PORT STORY, THE VONNEGUT, KURT JR. SS NEW 68 AC
 WELCOME TO THE MONKEY HOUSE VONNEGUT, KURT JR. AC
HYBORIAN AGE, THE HOWARD, ROBERT E. AR PHT 36
 COMING OF CONAN, THE HOWARD, ROBERT E. AC
HYBORIAN AGE, THE (PART 1) HOWARD, ROBERT E. AR PHT 36
 CONAN HOWARD, R./DE CAMP/& AC
HYBORIAN AGE, THE (PART 2) HOWARD, ROBERT E. AR PHT 36
 CONAN THE AVENGER HOWARD, R./NYBERG/& AC
HYBRID LAUMER, KEITH SS FSF 61 11
 BEST OF KEITH LAUMER, THE LAUMER, KEITH AC
 DECADE THE 1960S ALDISS & HARRISON AN
 NINE BY LAUMER LAUMER, KEITH AC
HYBRID HYPERBOREAN ANT, THE MCCARDELL, ROY L. SS HAM 10 12
 SCIENCE FICTION BY GASLIGHT MOSKOWITZ, SAM AN
HYPERPELOSITY DE CAMP, L. SPRAGUE SS ASF 38 04
 OMNIBUS OF SCIENCE FICTION CONKLIN, GROFF AN
 SCIENCE FICTION OF THE 30'S KNIGHT, DAMON AN
 WHEELS OF IF, THE DE CAMP, L. SPRAGUE AC
HYPERSPACE ALLEN, DICK PM EDG 73
 FASTER THAN LIGHT DANN & ZEBROWSKI OA
HYPERSPHERICAL BASKETBALL, THE NEARING, H. JR. SS FSF 51 12
 BEST FROM FANTASY AND SCIENCE FICTION: 2
      BOUCHER & MCCOMAS AN
 SINISTER RESEARCHES OF C. P. RANSOM, THE NEARING, H. JR. AC
HYPNOGLYPH, THE ANTHONY, JOHN SS FSF 53 07
 DECADE OF FANTASY AND SCIENCE FICTION, A MILLS, ROBERT P. AN
 PORTALS OF TOMORROW DERLETH, AUGUST AN
I ALWAYS DO WHAT TEDDY SAYS HARRISON, HARRY SS EQM 65 06
 *BEST OF HARRY HARRISON, THE HARRISON, HARRY AC

I ALWAYS DO WHAT TEDDY SAYS   I, DREAMER

    DAYS AFTER TOMORROW, THE   SANTESSON, HANS S.   AN
    NEW IMPROVED SUN, THE   DISCH, THOMAS M.   AN
    SCIENCE FACT/FICTION   FARRELL/GAGE/&   AN
    TWO TALES AND EIGHT TOMORROWS   HARRISON, HARRY   AC
I AM A   MARSHALL, LENORE   PM   69
    SCIENCE FICTION   BRODKIN & PEARSON   AN
I AM A GHOST   COOPER, EDMUND   SS
    VOICES IN THE DARK   COOPER, EDMUND   AC
I AM A NUCLEUS   BARR, STEPHEN   NV   GAL 57 02
    FOURTH GALAXY READER, THE   GOLD, H. L.   AN
I AM ALEPPO   SOHL, JERRY   NV   NMD 73
    FRONTIERS 2; THE NEW MIND   ELWOOD, ROGER   OA
I AM CRYING ALL INSIDE   SIMAK, CLIFFORD D. SS GAL 69 08
    SOULS IN METAL   ASHLEY, MICHAEL   AN
I AM NOTHING   RUSSELL, ERIC FRANK SS ASF 52 07
    BEST SCIENCE-FICTION STORIES: 1953, THE BLEILER & DIKTY AN
    FRONTIERS IN SPACE   BLEILER & DIKTY   AN
    SOMEWHERE A VOICE   RUSSELL, ERIC FRANK   AC
I AM RETURNING   RUSSELL, RAY   SS   61
    SARDONICUS AND OTHER STORIES   RUSSELL, RAY   AC
    SEA OF SPACE, A   NOLAN, WILLIAM F.   AN
I AM TOMORROW   DEL REY, LESTER   NV   DSF 52 12
    NOVELETS OF SCIENCE FICTION   HOWARD, IVAN   AN
I AM WAITING   ISHERWOOD, C.   SS   NYM 39 10
    TIMELESS STORIES FOR TODAY AND TOMORROW BRADBURY, RAY AN
I CHING, WHO YOU?   ALDISS, BRIAN W. SS   NWR 73 22
    NEW WRITINGS IN SF. 22   BULMER, KENNETH   OA
I CURSE THE LESSON AND BLESS THE KNOWLEDGE
                         ELLISON, HARLAN   SS   75
    LOVE AIN'T NOTHING BUT SEX MISSPELLED (REVISED)
                                     ELLISON, HARLAN   AC
I DO NOT HEAR YOU, SIR   DAVIDSON, AVRAM   SS   FSF 58 02
    ABC OF SCIENCE FICTION, AN   BOARDMAN, TOM JR.   AN
    OR ALL THE SEAS WITH OYSTERS   DAVIDSON, AVRAM   AC
    TRANSFORMATIONS II   ROSELLE, DANIEL   AN
I DO NOT LIKE THEE, DR. FELDMAN
                         SLESAR, HENRY   SS   PBY 59 06
    WEIRD SHOW   PLAYBOY, EDITORS OF   AN
I DO NOT LOVE THEE, DOCTOR FELL
                         BLOCH, ROBERT   SS   FSF 55 03
    BEST SCIENCE FICTION STORIES AND NOVELS: 1956
                                     DIKTY, T. E.   AN
    *BLOOD RUNS COLD   BLOCH, ROBERT   AC
    6 FROM WORLDS BEYOND   DIKTY, T. E.   AN
I DON'T MIND   SMITH, RON   SS   FSF 56 10
    BEST FROM FANTASY AND SCIENCE FICTION: 6
                                     BOUCHER, ANTHONY   AN
I GAVE HER SACK AND SHERRY (ALSO AS I THOUGHT SHE WAS AFEARED
    TILL SHE STROKED MY BEARD) RUSS, JOANNA NV ORB 67 02
    BEST FROM ORBIT, THE   KNIGHT, DAMON   AN
    ORBIT 2   KNIGHT, DAMON   OA
I HAVE HEARD THE MERMAIDS TUTTLE, LISA   SS
    SURVIVAL FROM INFINITY   ELWOOD, ROGER   OA
I HAVE MY VIGIL   HARRISON, HARRY   SS   FSF 68 02
    BEST FROM FANTASY AND SCIENCE FICTION: 18
                                     FERMAN, EDWARD L.   AN
    *BEST OF HARRY HARRISON, THE   HARRISON, HARRY   AC
    WONDERMAKERS 2   HOSKINS, ROBERT   AN
I HAVE NO MOUTH, AND I MUST SCREAM
                         ELLISON, HARLAN   SS   IFS 67 03
    ALONE AGAINST TOMORROW   ELLISON, HARLAN   AC
    HUGO WINNERS, THE (VOLUME 2)   ASIMOV, ISAAC   AN
    I HAVE NO MOUTH, AND I MUST SCREAM ELLISON, HARLAN   AC
    MIRROR OF INFINITY, THE   SILVERBERG, ROBERT   AN
    POCKETFUL OF STARS, A   KNIGHT, DAMON   AN
    SURVIVAL PRINTOUT   TOTAL EFFECT   AN
    WORLD'S BEST SCIENCE FICTION: 1968 WOLLHEIM & CARR   AN
I HEAR YOU CALLING   RUSSELL, ERIC FRANK SS SCF 54 12
    DARK TIDES   RUSSELL, ERIC FRANK   AC
I JUST MAKE THEM UP, SEE ASIMOV, ISAAC   PM   FSF 58 02
    NINE TOMORROWS   ASIMOV, ISAAC   AC
I KILL MYSELF   KAWALEC, JULIAN   SS   62
    TRANSFORMATIONS   ROSELLE, DANIEL   AN
    VINTAGE ANTHOLOGY OF SCIENCE FANTASY, THE
                                     CERF, CHRISTOPHER   AN
I KILLER HITLER   FARLEY, RALPH MILNE SS WRT 41 07
    OMNIBUS OF TIME, THE   FARLEY, RALPH MILNE   AC
I KISS YOUR SHADOW   BLOCH, ROBERT   SS   FSF 56 04
    NIGHTMARES   BLOCH, ROBERT   AC
    PLEASANT DREAMS   BLOCH, ROBERT   AC
I LIKE BLONDES   BLOCH, ROBERT   SS   PBY 56 01
    *BLOOD RUNS COLD   BLOCH, ROBERT   AC
    FIEND, THE   PLAYBOY, EDITORS OF   AN
I LIKE MARTIAN MUSIC   FRITCH, CHARLES E. SS FUN 57 09
    CRAZY MIXED-UP PLANET   FRITCH, CHARLES E.   AC
I LOSE MEDEA   BEVAN, ALISTAIR   SS   NWQ 72 03
    NEW WORLDS QUARTERLY NO. 3   MOORCOCK, MICHAEL   OA
I LOSE MEDEA (AS ALISTAIR BEVAN)
                         ROBERTS, KEITH   SS   NWQ 72 03
    GRAIN KINGS, THE   ROBERTS, KEITH   AC
    PASSING OF THE DRAGONS, THE   ROBERTS, KEITH   AC
"I LOVE GALESBURG IN THE SPRINGTIME"
                         FINNEY, JACK   NV   MCC 60 04
    I LOVE GALESBURG IN THE SPRINGTIME FINNEY, JACK   AC
I LOVE YOU   EMSHWILLER, CAROL SS   EPO
    JOY IN OUR CAUSE   EMSHWILLER, CAROL   AC
I MADE YOU   MILLER, WALTER M. JR SS ASF 54 03
    EARTH IN TRANSIT   SCHWARTZ, SHEILA   AN
    INTRODUCING SCIENCE FICTION   ALDISS, BRIAN W.   AN
    METAL SMILE, THE   KNIGHT, DAMON   AN
    YET MORE PENGUIN SCIENCE FICTION ALDISS, BRIAN W.   AN
I NEVER AST NO FAVORS   KORNBLUTH, C. M. SS   FSF 54 04
    BEST FROM FANTASY AND SCIENCE FICTION: 4
                                     BOUCHER, ANTHONY   AN
    BEST SCIENCE FICTION STORIES OF C. M. KORNBLUTH
                                     KORNBLUTH, C. M.   AC

    MARCHING MORONS AND OTHER SCIENCE FICTION
                                     KORNBLUTH, C. M.   AC
I OF NEWTON   HALDEMAN, JOE W. SS
    COSMIC LAUGHTER   HALDEMAN, JOE W.   AN
I PLINGLOT, WHO YOU?   POHL, FREDERIK   NV   GAL 59 02
    FREDERIK POHL OMNIBUS, THE   POHL, FREDERIK   AC
    INFINITE JESTS   SILVERBERG, ROBERT   AN
    TURN LEFT AT THURSDAY   POHL, FREDERIK   AC
I REMEMBER A WINTER   POHL, FREDERIK   SS   ORB 72 1
    IN THE PROBLEM PIT   POHL, FREDERIK   AC
    ORBIT 11   KNIGHT, DAMON   OA
I REMEMBER BABYLON   CLARKE, ARTHUR C. SS   PBY 60 0
    FIEND, THE   PLAYBOY, EDITORS OF   AN
    NINE BILLION NAMES OF GOD, THE   CLARKE, ARTHUR C.   AC
    PLAYBOY BOOK OF SCIENCE FICTION AND FANTASY, THE
                                     PLAYBOY, EDITORS OF   AN
    TALES OF TEN WORLDS   CLARKE, ARTHUR C.   AC
    6TH ANNUAL OF THE YEAR'S BEST S-F, THE MERRIL, JUDITH AN
I REMEMBER, ANITA   JONES, LANGDON   SS   NWS 64 1
    BEST OF NEW WORLDS, THE   MOORCOCK, MICHAEL   AN
I SAY BEGONE! APOTROPAIC NARCOSIS, I'M GOING TO READ THE
    DAMNED THING, HA HA   CLUTE, JOHN   BR   NWB 75 00
    NEW WORLDS EIGHT   BAILEY, HILARY   OA
I SEE A MAN SITTING IN A CHAIR, AND THE CHAIR IS BITING HIS LEG
                         ELLISON, HARLAN
                         AND SHECKLEY, ROBERT NV C FSF 68 01
    PARTNERS IN WONDER   ELLISON, HARLAN   AC
I SEE YOU   KNIGHT, DAMON   SS   FSF 76 11
    BEST SCIENCE FICTION OF THE YEAR, THE NO. 6
                                     CARR, TERRY   AN
    1977 ANNUAL WORLD'S BEST SF, THE WOLLHEIM, DONALD A.   AN
I SEE YOU (ROBOT JUSTICE, FUN 59 07)
                         HARRISON, HARRY   SS   NWS 59 05
    BEST OF NEW WORLDS, THE   MOORCOCK, MICHAEL   AN
    WAR WITH THE ROBOTS   HARRISON, HARRY   AC
I SEE YOU NEVER   BRADBURY, RAY   SS   NYM 47 11
    *GOLDEN APPLES OF THE SUN   BRADBURY, RAY   AC
I SING THE BODY ELECTRIC (BEAUTIFUL ONE IS HERE)
                         BRADBURY, RAY   NV   MCC 69 08
    I SING THE BODY ELECTRIC   BRADBURY, RAY   AC
I TELL YOU, AL   O'NEILL, SCOTT   SS
    MARTIAN SEXPOT   O'NEILL, SCOTT   AC
I TELL YOU, IT'S TRUE   ANDERSON, POUL   NV   NOV 72 02
    EARTH IN TRANSIT   SCHWARTZ, SHEILA   AN
    NOVA 2   HARRISON, HARRY   OA
I THOUGHT SHE WAS AFEARED TILL SHE STROKED MY BEARD (I GAVE
    HER SACK AND SHERRY) RUSS, JOANNA NV ORB 67 02
    ALYX   RUSS, JOANNA   AC
I WANT MY NAME IN THE TITLE MCCLINTIC, WINONA PM FSF 56 07
    BEST FROM FANTASY AND SCIENCE FICTION: 6
                                     BOUCHER, ANTHONY   AN
I WONDER WHAT HE WANTED BERTIN, EDDY C.   SS   70
    YEAR'S BEST HORROR STORIES, THE DAVIS, RICHARD   AN
I'D GIVE A DOLLAR   MARKS, WINSTON K. SS   BEY 54 05
    BEYOND   ANONYMOUS   AN
I'LL BE WAITING FOR YOU WHEN THE SWIMMING POOL IS EMPTY
                         TIPTREE, JAMES JR. SS PRT 71
    BEST SCIENCE FICTION STORIES OF THE YEAR (1971)
                                     DEL REY, LESTER   AN
    PROTOSTARS   GERROLD & GOLDIN   OA
    TEN THOUSAND LIGHT-YEARS FROM HOME TIPTREE, JAMES JR. AC
I'LL BUILD YOUR DREAM CASTLE VANCE, JACK   SS   ASF 47 09
    GREAT STORIES OF SPACE TRAVEL   CONKLIN, GROFF   AN
I'LL DO ANYTHING (SEE A POINT OF HONOR)
                         BEAUMONT, CHARLES TC
I'LL NOT LOOK FOR WINE (SEE YLLA)
                         BRADBURY, RAY   TC
I'M A STRANGER HERE MYSELF REYNOLDS, MACK SS AMZ 60 12
    14 GREAT TALES OF ESP   STONE, IDELLA P.   AN
I'M A STRANGER HERE MYSELF RUSSELL, ERIC FRANK SS OWS 52 03
    DARK TIDES   RUSSELL, ERIC FRANK   AC
I'M GOING TO GET YOU   BUSBY, F. M.   SS   FAN 74 03
    SPACE ODYSSEYS   ALDISS, BRIAN W.   AN
I'M IN MARSPORT WITHOUT HILDA ASIMOV, ISAAC SS VSF 57 11
    ASIMOV'S MYSTERIES   ASIMOV, ISAAC   AC
    NINE TOMORROWS   ASIMOV, ISAAC   AC
I'M LOOKING FOR "JEFF"   LEIBER, FRITZ   SS   FAN 52 FI
    BEST FROM FANTASTIC, THE   WHITE, TED   AN
    NIGHT MONSTERS   LEIBER, FRITZ   DC
    TIME UNTAMED   HOWARD, IVAN   AN
I'M LOOKING FOR KADAK   ELLISON, HARLAN   NV   NEW 74 AN
    APPROACHING OBLIVION   ELLISON, HARLAN   AC
    WANDERING STARS   DANN, JACK M.   AN
I'M SCARED   FINNEY, JACK   SS   COL 51 09
    THIRD LEVEL, THE   FINNEY, JACK   AC
    TOMORROW, THE STARS   HEINLEIN, ROBERT A.   AN
I'M TOO BIG BUT I LOVE TO PLAY TIPTREE, JAMES JR. NV AMZ 70 12
    TEN THOUSAND LIGHT-YEARS FROM HOME TIPTREE, JAMES JR. AC
I'M WITH YOU IN ROCKLAND DANN, JACK M.   SS   NEW 72 AN
    HUMAN-MACHINES   SCORTIA & ZEBROWSKI   AN
    STRANGE BED FELLOWS   SCORTIA, THOMAS N.   AN
I'M YOURS   SCHAFHAUSER, CHARLES SS PBY 54 12
    PLAYBOY BOOK OF HORROR AND THE SUPERNATURAL, THE
                                     PLAYBOY, EDITORS OF   AN
    WEIRD SHOW   PLAYBOY, EDITORS OF   AN
I.O.U.   WELLEN, EDWARD   NV   IFS 61 03
    6 FINGERS OF TIME AND 5 OTHER SCIENCE FICTION NOVELETS, THE
                                     ANONYMOUS   AN
I-C-A-BEM (SEE THE AUGMENTED AGENT)
                         VANCE, JACK   TC
I, BEM   RICHMOND, LEIGH
                         AND RICHMOND, WALT SS C ASF 64 06
    POSITIVE CHARGE   RICHMOND, W. & L.   DC
I, DREAMER   MILLER, WALTER M. JR SS AMZ 53 07
    MAN AGAINST TOMORROW   NOLAN, WILLIAM F.   AN
    VIEW FROM THE STARS, THE   MILLER, WALTER M. JR AC

, MARS   IMAGINARY, THE

, MARS   BRADBURY, RAY   SS   SSS 49 04   IF THE COURT PLEASES   LOOMIS, NOEL   NV   DSF 53 06
TALES OF TERROR FROM OUTER SPACE CHETWYND-HAYES, R.   AN   ESCAPE TO EARTH   HOWARD, IVAN   AN
WILDERNESS OF STARS, A   NOLAN, WILLIAM F.   AN   IF THE RED SLAYER   SHECKLEY, ROBERT   SS   AMZ 59 07
, ROBOT   BINDER, EANDO   SS   AMZ 39 01   STORE OF INFINITY   SHECKLEY, ROBERT   AN
ADAM LINK- ROBOT   BINDER, EANDO   AC   IF THE SABOT FITS...   RICHMOND, LEIGH
COMING OF THE ROBOTS, THE   MOSKOWITZ, SAM   AN   AND RICHMOND, WALT SS C ASF 68 02
EDITOR'S CHOICE IN SCIENCE FICTION MOSKOWITZ, SAM   AN   POSITIVE CHARGE   RICHMOND, W. & L.   DC
, ROCKET   BRADBURY, RAY   SS   AMZ 44 05   IF THE STARS ARE GODS   BENFORD, GREGORY
HUMAN ZERO, THE   MOSKOWITZ & ELWOOD   AN   AND EKLUND, GORDON NV C UNI 74 04
TOMORROW MIDNIGHT   BRADBURY, RAY   AC   BEST SCIENCE FICTION OF THE YEAR, THE NO. 4
, THE UNSPEAKABLE   SHELDON, WALT   NV   GAL 51 04   CARR, TERRY   AN
*GALAXY READER OF SCIENCE FICTION GOLD, H. L.   AN   NEBULA AWARD STORIES 10   GUNN, JAMES E.   AN
BID   EFFINGER, GEO. ALEC SS   UNI 77 07   UNIVERSE 4   CARR, TERRY   OA
UNIVERSE 7   CARR, TERRY   OA   IF THERE WERE NO BENNY CEMOLI DICK, PHILIP K.   SS   GAL 63 12
BM   GERNSBERG, MORT   CT   DUD 63   BEST OF PHILIP K. DICK, THE   DICK, PHILIP K.   AC
9TH ANNUAL OF THE YEAR'S BEST S-F, THE MERRIL, JUDITH SS NEW 73 AN   EIGHTH GALAXY READER, THE   POHL, FREDERIK   AN
CARUS   DE CAMP, CATHERINE C SS   PRESERVING MACHINE, THE   DICK, PHILIP K.   AC
TALES BEYOND TIME   DE CAMP, L. S.&C.   AN   IF THIS GOES ON-   HEINLEIN, ROBERT A. SN   ASF 40 02
CARUS AND DAEDALUS   ALTOV, HENRIK   SS   68   PAST THROUGH TOMORROW, THE   HEINLEIN, ROBERT A.   AC
ULTIMATE THRESHOLD, THE   GINSBURG, MIRRA   AN   REVOLT IN 2100   HEINLEIN, ROBERT A.   AC
CARUS MONTGOLFIER WRIGHT   BRADBURY, RAY   SS   FSF 56 05   IF THIS IS WINNETKA, YOU MUST BE JUDY
BEST FROM FANTASY AND SCIENCE FICTION: 6   BUSBY, F. M.   NV   UNI 74 05
                            BOUCHER, ANTHONY   AN   BEST SCIENCE FICTION STORIES OF THE YEAR (1974)
DAY IT RAINED FOREVER, THE BRADBURY, RAY   AC   DEL REY, LESTER   AN
MEDICINE FOR MELANCHOLY, A BRADBURY, RAY   AC   UNIVERSE 5   CARR, TERRY   OA
S IS FOR SPACE   BRADBURY, RAY   AC   IF YOU WAS A MOKLIN   LEINSTER, MURRAY   NV   GAL 51 09
ICEBOX BLONDE, THE   SCORTIA, THOMAS N.   SS   ROG 59 06   BEST OF MURRAY LEINSTER, THE   LEINSTER, MURRAY   AC
CAUTION! INFLAMMABLE!   SCORTIA, THOMAS N.   AC   *GALAXY READER OF SCIENCE FICTION   GOLD, H. L.   AN
MARRIAGE AND THE FAMILY THROUGH SCIENCE FICTION   MONSTERS AND SUCH   LEINSTER, MURRAY   AC
                            CLEAR/WARRICK/&   AN   IF YOU WERE THE ONLY-   WILSON, RICHARD   SS   GAL 53 06
STRANGE BED FELLOWS   SCORTIA, THOMAS N.   AN   TENTH GALAXY READER, THE   POHL, FREDERIK   AN
CON OF THE IMAGINATION   LEIBER, FRITZ   IN   IF YOU'RE SO SMART   COREY, PAUL   SS   NWR 69 14
BEST SCIENCE-FICTION STORIES: 1954, THE BLEILER & DIKTY   NEW WRITINGS IN SF. 9   CARNELL, JOHN   AN
                                                 AN   NEW WRITINGS IN SF. 14   CARNELL, JOHN   OA
IDEA OF ENTROPY AT MAENPORTH BEACH, THE   IFTH OF OOFTH, THE   TEVIS, WALTER S. JR. SS GAL 57 04
                            REDGROVE, PETER   PM   67   SCIENCE FACT/FICTION   FARRELL/GAGE/&   AN
ENGLAND SWINGS SF   MERRIL, JUDITH   AN   SIXTH GALAXY READER, THE   GOLD, H. L.   AN
SPACE-TIME JOURNAL, THE   MERRIL, JUDITH   AN   IGNATZ   GOULART, RON   SS   IFS 60 03
IDEA, THE   O'DONNELL, K. M.   SS   NEW 71 DC   CHAMELEON CORPS & OTHER SHAPE CHANGERS, THE
IN THE POCKET AND OTHER S-F STORIES O'DONNELL, K. M.   DC   GOULART, RON   AC
IDEAL CAPTAIN, THE   WHITE, JAMES   NV   NWS 58 08 ILL MET IN LANKHMAR   LEIBER, FRITZ   SS   FSF 70 04
DEADLY LITTER   WHITE, JAMES   NO   NEBULA AWARD STORIES NO. 6   SIMAK, CLIFFORD D.   AN
IDEAL CITY, AN   VERNE, JULES   SS   ILLUMINATED MAN, THE   BALLARD, J. G.   NV   FSF 64 05
YESTERDAY AND TOMORROW   VERNE, JULES   AC   BEST FROM FANTASY AND SCIENCE FICTION: 14
IDEAL POLICE STATE, THE   BAXTER, CHARLES   PM   LMG 71   DAVIDSON, AVRAM   AN
BEST SF: 1971   HARRISON & ALDISS   AN   TERMINAL BEACH (BRITISH VERSION)   BALLARD, J. G.   AC
IDEAL, THE   WEINBAUM, STANLEY G. NV   WOS 35 09 ILLUMINATION   BRADBURY, RAY   SS   REP 57 05
BEST OF STANLEY G. WEINBAUM, THE WEINBAUM, STANLEY G. AC   DANDELION WINE   BRADBURY, RAY   NO
MARTIAN ODYSSEY AND OTHER SCIENCE FICTION TALES, A   VINTAGE BRADBURY, THE   BRADBURY, RAY   AC
                            WEINBAUM, STANLEY G. AC   ILLUSIONARIES, THE   RUSSELL, ERIC FRANK SS PLS 51 11
MARTIAN ODYSSEY AND OTHERS, A WEINBAUM, STANLEY G. AC   SPACE PIONEERS   NORTON, ANDRE   AN
IDEAL, THE (SELECTION FROM) WEINBAUM, STANLEY G. EX   WOS 35 09 ILLUSIONIST, THE   GORDON, GILES   SS   NWB 75 09
CENTURY OF SCIENCE FICTION, A KNIGHT, DAMON   AN   NEW WORLDS NINE   BAILEY, HILARY   OA
IDEALIST   DEL REY, LESTER   SS   STR 53 01 ILLUSIONISTS, THE (SPACE FEAR) SCHMITZ, JAMES H. NV ASF 51 03
STAR SCIENCE FICTION STORIES POHL, FREDERIK   OA   AGENT OF VEGA   SCHMITZ, JAMES H.   AC
IDEALIST, THE   CAMPBELL, JOHN W. JR NV   NTL 54   ILLUSTRATED MAN, THE   BRADBURY, RAY   SS   NEW 51 AC
9 TALES OF SPACE AND TIME   HEALY, RAYMOND J.   OA   VINTAGE BRADBURY, THE   BRADBURY, RAY   AC
IDEAS DIE HARD   ASIMOV, ISAAC   NV   GAL 57 10 ILLUSTRATED WOMAN, THE   BRADBURY, RAY   SS   PBY 61 03
FIRST FLIGHTS TO THE MOON   CLEMENT, HAL   AN   LAST TRAIN TO LIMBO   PLAYBOY, EDITORS OF   AN
THIRD GALAXY READER, THE   GOLD, H. L.   AN   MACHINERIES OF JOY, THE   BRADBURY, RAY   AC
IDENTITY (SEE EPILOGUE: IDENTITY)   ILLUSTRATIONS   ARISS, BRUCE   IL
                            SMITH, GEORGE O.   TC   THROUGH TIME AND SPACE WITH FERDINAND FEGHOOT
IDIO   PISERCHIA, DORIS   SS   ORB 74 13   BRIARTON, GRENDEL   AC
ORBIT 13   KNIGHT, DAMON   OA   ILLUSTRATIONS   BURROUGHS, JOHN C. IL
IDIOT SOLVANT   DICKSON, GORDON R.   SS   ASF 62 01   ESCAPE ON VENUS   BURROUGHS, EDGAR R.   NO
MUTANTS   DICKSON, GORDON R.   AC   LLANA OF GATHOL   BURROUGHS, EDGAR R.   NO
13 ABOVE THE NIGHT   CONKLIN, GEOFF   AN   ILLUSTRATIONS   DU BOIS, WILLIAM P. IL
IDIOT STICK   KNIGHT, DAMON   SS   STR 58 04   POISON BELT, THE   DOYLE, ARTHUR CONAN   AC
BEYOND TOMORROW   HARDING, LEE   AN   ILLUSTRATIONS   FISHER, LEONARD E. IL
FAR OUT   KNIGHT, DAMON   AC   WEIGHER OF SOULS AND THE EARTH DWELLERS, THE
STAR SCIENCE FICTION STORIES NO. 4 POHL, FREDERIK OA   MAUROIS, ANDRE   AC
IDIOT'S CRUSADE   SIMAK, CLIFFORD D.   SS   GAL 54 10 ILLUSTRATIONS   KIRK, TIM   IL
ALIENS FOR NEIGHBOURS   SIMAK, CLIFFORD D.   AC   COMPLETE FEGHOOT, THE   BRIARTON, GRENDEL   AC
OTHER WORLDS OF CLIFFORD SIMAK SIMAK, CLIFFORD D. AC   ILLUSTRATIONS   KRENKEL, R.   IL
*WORLDS OF CLIFFORD SIMAK, THE SIMAK, CLIFFORD D. AC   TALES OF THREE PLANETS   BURROUGHS, EDGAR R.   AC
IDIOT'S DELIGHT   WYNDHAM, JOHN   NV   NWS 58 06 ILLUSTRATIONS   LEVIN, SOL   IL
*OUTWARD URGE, THE   WYNDHAM & PARKES   AC   VENUS EQUILATERAL   SMITH, GEORGE O.   AC
IDOL OF THE FLIES, THE   RICE, JANE   SS   UNK 42 06 ILLUSTRATIONS   MAYAN, EARL E.   IL
CHILDREN OF WONDER   TENN, WILLIAM   AN   *ROD SERLING'S THE TWILIGHT ZONE   SERLING, ROD   OC
IDRIS' PIG (THE SACRED MARTIAN PIG)   ILLUSTRATIONS   ST. JOHN, J. ALLEN IL
                            ST. CLAIR, MARGARET NV   STS 49 07   LAND THAT TIME FORGOT, THE   BURROUGHS, EDGAR R.   NO
THREE WORLDS OF FUTURITY   ST. CLAIR, MARGARET DC   MOON MAID, THE   BURROUGHS, EDGAR R.   NO
IF "HAIR" WERE REVIVED IN 2016 AUERBACH, ARNOLD M. FA NYT 71   SAVAGE PELLUCIDAR   BURROUGHS, EDGAR R.   NO
BEST SF: 1971   HARRISON & ALDISS   AN   THREE MARTIAN NOVELS   BURROUGHS, EDGAR R.   AC
IF (PRAISEWORTHY SAUR)   HARRISON, HARRY   SS   IFS 69 02   THREE SCIENCE FICTION NOVELS   BURROUGHS, EDGAR R.   AC
*BEST OF HARRY HARRISON, THE HARRISON, HARRY   AC   ILLUSTRATIONS TO "THE SCARLET PLAGUE"
PRIME NUMBER   HARRISON, HARRY   AC   GRANT, GORDON   IL
WORLDS OF WONDER   HARRISON, HARRY   AC   SCIENCE FICTION OF JACK LONDON, THE LONDON, JACK   AC
IF ALL MEN WERE BROTHERS, WOULD YOU LET ONE MARRY YOUR SISTER? IMAGE OF DESTRUCTION   RANKINE, JOHN   NV   NWR 67 10
                            STURGEON, THEODORE   NA   DVS 67 01   NEW WRITINGS IN SF. 10   CARNELL, JOHN   OA
CASE AND THE DREAMER   STURGEON, THEODORE   AC   IMAGE OF THE GODS, THE   NOURSE, ALAN E.   SS   OSF 54 09
DANGEROUS VISIONS   ELLISON, HARLAN   OA   COUNTERFEIT MAN, THE   NOURSE, ALAN E.   AC
IF AT FIRST-   FRITCH, CHARLES E.   SS   PLANET OF DOOM AND OTHER STORIES   ANONYMOUS   AN
CRAZY MIXED-UP PLANET   FRITCH, CHARLES E.   AC   IMAGES OF MAN   NUETZEL, CHARLES   SS
IF EVER I SHOULD LEAVE YOU (REVISED)   IMAGES OF TOMORROW   NUETZEL, CHARLES   AC
                            SARGENT, PAMELA   SS   IFS 74 02 IMAGINARY HEIR, THE (SEE THE SHADY LIFE OF ANNIBAL)
STARSHADOWS   SARGENT, PAMELA   AC   KERSH, GERALD   TC
IF I FORGET THEE, OH EARTH... CLARKE, ARTHUR C. SS   FUT 51 09 IMAGINARY JOURNEY TO THE MOON, AN
ACROSS THE SEA OF STARS   CLARKE, ARTHUR C.   AC   SABAH, VICTOR   SS   NEW 72 AN
EVIL EARTHS   ALDISS, BRIAN W.   AN   BEST SF: 1972   HARRISON & ALDISS   AN
EXPEDITION TO EARTH   CLARKE, ARTHUR C.   AC   IMAGINARY NUMBERS IN A REAL GARDEN
NINE BILLION NAMES OF GOD, THE CLARKE, ARTHUR C. AC   JONAS, GERALD   PM   FSF 65 04
OF TIME AND STARS   CLARKE, ARTHUR C.   AC   BEST FROM FANTASY AND SCIENCE FICTION: 16
SPECTRUM OF WORLDS, A   CLARESON, THOMAS D. AN   FERMAN, EDWARD L.   AN
IF SOMETHING BEGINS   MOORE, RAYLYN   SS   IMAGINARY, THE   ASIMOV, ISAAC   SS   SSS 42 11
WORLDS FAR AND NEAR   CARR, TERRY   AN   EARLY ASIMOV, THE   ASIMOV, ISAAC   AC

IMAGINARY, THE   IN LONELY LAND

HUMAN ZERO, THE   MOSKOWITZ & ELWOOD   AN
IMAGINATION OF DISASTER, THE   SONTAG, SUSAN   AR   65
SCIENCE FICTION: THE FUTURE   ALLEN, DICK   AN
IMAGINATION TRAP, THE   KAPP, COLIN   NV   NWR 67 10
NEW WRITINGS IN SF. 8   CARNELL, JOHN   AN
NEW WRITINGS IN SF. 10   CARNELL, JOHN   AN
IMAGINE, A PROEM   BROWN, FREDRIC   PM   FSF 55 05
BEST FROM FANTASY AND SCIENCE FICTION: 5   BOUCHER, ANTHONY   AN
BEST OF FREDRIC BROWN, THE   BROWN, FREDRIC   AC
HONEYMOON IN HELL   BROWN, FREDRIC   AC
IMMEASURABLE HORROR, THE   SMITH, CLARK ASHTON SS   WRT 31 09
OTHER DIMENSIONS   SMITH, CLARK ASHTON AC
IMMEDIATELY YOURS   HALE, ROBERT BEVERLY SS   MAD 61 11
7TH ANNUAL OF THE YEAR'S BEST S-F, THE   MERRIL, JUDITH   AN
IMMIGRANT   SIMAK, CLIFFORD D.   SN   ASF 54 03
BEST SCIENCE FICTION STORIES OF CLIFFORD D. SIMAK
                                   SIMAK, CLIFFORD D.   AC
GALACTIC EMPIRES VOLUME ONE   ALDISS, BRIAN W.   AC
*STRANGERS IN THE UNIVERSE   SIMAK, CLIFFORD D.   AC
IMMOBILITY CREW, THE   ALDISS, BRIAN W.   SS   FST 74
FINAL STAGE   FERMAN & MALZBERG   OA
IMMORTAL (THE IMMORTALS)   GUNN, JAMES E.   NV   STR 58 04
IMMORTALS, THE   GUNN, JAMES E.   NO
IMMORTAL BARD, THE   ASIMOV, ISAAC   SS   USF 54 05
EARTH IS ROOM ENOUGH   ASIMOV, ISAAC   AC
INTRODUCING SCIENCE FICTION   ALDISS, BRIAN W.   AN
IMMORTAL FISH, THE   BORGESE, ELISABETH M SS   57
PAST, PRESENT, AND FUTURE PERFECT   WOLFE, J&FITZ GERALD AN
IMMORTAL GAME, THE   ANDERSON, POUL   SS   FSF 54 02
BEST FROM FANTASY AND SCIENCE FICTION: 4
                                   BOUCHER, ANTHONY   AN
RUN TO STARLIGHT, SPORTS THROUGH SCIENCE FICTION
                                   GREENBERG/OLANDER/& AN
IMMORTAL, THE   BORGES, JORGE LUIS   SS   62
NEW WORLDS OF FANTASY   CARR, TERRY   AN
IMMORTAL, THE   DICKSON, GORDON R.   NV   FSF 65 08
MUTANTS   DICKSON, GORDON R.   AC
IMMORTAL, THE   GUNN, JAMES E.   NV   STR 58 04
END OF THE DREAMS, THE   GUNN, JAMES E.   AC
IMMORTAL, THE   ROCKLYNNE, ROSS   SS   CMT 41 03
TOMORROW'S UNIVERSE   CAMPBELL, H. J.   AN
IMMORTAL, THE   RUHEN, OLAF   SS
SECOND PACIFIC BOOK OF SCIENCE FICTION, THE
                                   BAXTER, JOHN   AN
IMMORTALITY (GREAT LOST DISCOVERIES III)
                                   BROWN, FREDRIC   SS   NEW 61 AC
VINTAGE ANTHOLOGY OF SCIENCE FANTASY, THE
                                   CERF, CHRISTOPHER   AN
IMMORTALITY INC. (TIME KILLER) SHECKLEY, ROBERT NO   GAL 58 10
ROBERT SHECKLEY OMNIBUS, THE   SHECKLEY, ROBERT   AC
IMMORTALITY OF ALAN WHIDDEN, THE
                                   FARLEY, RALPH MILNE SS   AMZ 42 02
OMNIBUS OF TIME, THE   FARLEY, RALPH MILNE AC
IMMORTALITY SEEKERS, THE   CAMPBELL, JOHN W. JR NV   TWS 37 10
PLANETEERS, THE   CAMPBELL, JOHN W. JR DC
IMMORTALITY...FOR SOME   MCINTOSH, J. T.   NV   ASF 60 03
12 GREAT CLASSICS OF SCIENCE FICTION   CONKLIN, GROFF   AN
IMMORTALS OF MERCURY, THE SMITH, CLARK ASHTON NV   32
TALES OF SCIENCE AND SORCERY   SMITH, CLARK ASHTON AC
IMMORTALS, THE (ALSO AS IMMORTAL)
                                   GUNN, JAMES E.   NV   STR 58 04
BIO-FUTURES   SARGENT, PAMELA   AN
STAR SCIENCE FICTION STORIES NO. 4   POHL, FREDERIK   OA
IMMUNITY SYNDROME, THE (ROBERT SABAROFF)
                                   BLISH, JAMES   SA   STK 73 09
STAR TREK 9   BLISH, JAMES   OC
IMPACT WITH THE DEVIL   COGSWELL, THEODORE R SS   FSF 56 11
DEALS WITH THE DEVIL   DAVENPORT, BASIL   AN
THIRD EYE, THE   COGSWELL, THEODORE R AC
IMPACTED MAN, THE   SHECKLEY, ROBERT   SS   ASF 52 12
*UNTOUCHED BY HUMAN HANDS   SHECKLEY, ROBERT   AC
IMPEDIMENT   CLEMENT, HAL   NV   ASF 42 08
NATIVES OF SPACE   CLEMENT, HAL   AC
IMPERIAL STARS, THE   SMITH, EDWARD E. PHD SN   IFS 64 05
BEST OF E. E. 'DOC' SMITH, THE   SMITH, EDWARD E. PHD AC
IMPERSONATORS, THE   MACAPP, C. C.   SS   IFS 67 01
OUT OF THIS WORLD 7   WILLIAMS-ELLIS& OWEN AN
IMPLODE AND PEDDLE   FYFE, H. B.   NV   ASF 51 11
SPACE SERVICE   NORTON, ANDRE   AN
IMPOSSIBILITY, A STUDY OF REASON AND SCIENCE
                                   SULLIVAN, JAMES F.   SS   00
ANCESTRAL VOICES   MENVILLE & REGINALD AN
IMPOSSIBLE (SEE THE MARTIAN)   BRADBURY, RAY   TC
IMPOSSIBLE HIGHWAY, THE   FRIEND, OSCAR J.   SS   TWS 40 08
GREAT STORIES OF SCIENCE FICTION   LEINSTER, MURRAY   AN
MOLECULE MONSTERS, THE   ANONYMOUS   AN
SAINT'S CHOICE OF IMPOSSIBLE CRIME, THE   CHARTERIS, LESLIE   AN
IMPOSSIBLE MAN, THE   BALLARD, J. G.   SS   NEW 66 AC
DISASTER AREA, THE   BALLARD, J. G.   AC
IMPOSSIBLE MAN, THE   BALLARD, J. G.   AC
IMPOSSIBLE PLANET, THE   DICK, PHILIP K.   SS   IFS 53 10
HANDFUL OF DARKNESS, A   DICK, PHILIP K.   AC
SPACE ODYSSEYS   ALDISS, BRIAN W.   AN
IMPOSSIBLE STAR, THE   ALDISS, BRIAN W.   NV   WOT 63 08
BEST SCIENCE FICTION FROM WORLDS OF TOMORROW, THE
                                   POHL, FREDERIK   AN
*BEST SCIENCE FICTION STORIES OF BRIAN W. ALDISS
                                   ALDISS, BRIAN W.   AC
BRIAN ALDISS OMNIBUS, A   ALDISS, BRIAN W.   AC
IMPOSSIBLE VOYAGE HOME, THE   WALLACE, F. L.   NV   GAL 54 08
*SCIENCE FICTION ADVENTURES IN MUTATION   CONKLIN, GROFF   AN
IMPOSTOR   DICK, PHILIP K.   SS   ASF 53 06
ASTOUNDING-ANALOG READER, THE VOLUME TWO   HARRISON & ALDISS   AN
BEST OF PHILIP K. DICK, THE   DICK, PHILIP K.   AC
BEST SF 2   CRISPIN, EDMUND   AN

DARK STARS   SILVERBERG, ROBERT   AN
END OF THE WORLD, THE   WOLLHEIM, DONALD A. AN
HANDFUL OF DARKNESS, A   DICK, PHILIP K.   AN
METAL SMILE, THE   KNIGHT, DAMON   AN
SCIENCE FICTION TERROR TALES   CONKLIN, GROFF   AN
SOULS IN METAL   ASHLEY, MICHAEL   AN
UNTRAVELLED WORLDS   BARTER & WILSON   AN
IMPRACTICAL JOKE   DE CAMP, L. SPRAGUE SS   FUT 56 2
GUN FOR DINOSAUR AND OTHER IMAGINATIVE TALES
                                   DE CAMP, L. SPRAGUE A
WEIRD ONES, THE   HOWARD, IVAN   A
IMPRACTICAL JOKER (THE DEADLY JOKER)
                                   BLOCH, ROBERT   SS   SMM 65 C
CHAMBER OF HORRORS   BLOCH, ROBERT   A
IMPRINT OF CHAOS   BRUNNER, JOHN   NV   SCF 60 C
NOW THEN   BRUNNER, JOHN   A
TRAVELER IN BLACK, THE   BRUNNER, JOHN   A
IMPROPER AUTHORITIES, THE LEIBER, FRITZ   SS   FAN 59 1
WORLDS OF FRITZ LEIBER, THE   LEIBER, FRITZ   A
IMPULSE   RUSSELL, ERIC FRANK SS   ASF 38 0
*INVADERS OF EARTH   CONKLIN, GROFF   A
*TWISTED   CONKLIN, GROFF   A
IMT   SARGENT, PAMELA   SS   TVW 73
STARSHADOWS   SARGENT, PAMELA   A
TWO VIEWS OF WONDER   SCORTIA & YARBRO   A
IN A CROOKED YEAR   DOZOIS, GARDNER R.   NV   TTM 73
TEN TOMORROWS   ELWOOD, ROGER   O
IN A GOOD CAUSE-   ASIMOV, ISAAC   NV   NTS 51
NEW TALES OF SPACE AND TIME   HEALY, RAYMOND J.   O
NIGHTFALL AND OTHER STORIES   ASIMOV, ISAAC   A
IN A LAND OF CLEAR COLORS SHECKLEY, ROBERT   NV
NEW CONSTELLATIONS   DISCH & NAYLOR   C
IN A QUART OF WATER   TELFAIR, DAVID   SS   ANA 70
ALCHEMY AND ACADEME   MCCAFFREY, ANNE   O
IN A ROOM WITHOUT WALLS   KERSH, GERALD   SS   ESQ
MEN WITHOUT BONES   KERSH, GERALD   A
IN A SEASON OF CALM WEATHER BRADBURY, RAY   SS   PBY 57 0
BEST FANTASY STORIES   ALDISS, BRIAN W.   A
DAY IT RAINED FOREVER, THE   BRADBURY, RAY   A
MEDICINE FOR MELANCHOLY, A   BRADBURY, RAY   A
IN A SKY OF DAEMONS   YEP, LAURENCE   NV   PRT 71
PROTOSTARS   GERROLD & GOLDIN   A
IN BEHALF OF THE PRODUCT   REED, KIT   SS   BMR 73
BAD MOON RISING   DISCH, THOMAS M.   A
MARRIAGE AND THE FAMILY THROUGH SCIENCE FICTION
                                   CLEAR/WARRICK/&   A
IN BETWEEN THEN AND NOW   COVER, ARTHUR BYRON SS   INY 73 0
INFINITY 5   HOSKINS, ROBERT   O
IN BONDAGE TO A CENTRAL AUTHORITY (FROM "BRAVE NEW WORLD")
                                   HUXLEY, ALDOUS   EX   WND 32
ARMCHAIR SCIENCE READER, THE   GORDON, I. & SORKIN A
IN CHINISTREX FORTRONZA THE PEOPLE ARE MACHINES
                                   BISHOP, MICHAEL   SS
NEW CONSTELLATIONS   DISCH & NAYLOR   O
IN DARK PLACES   HENSLEY, JOE L.   SS   FUC 73
CITY: 2000 A.D., THE   CLEM/GREENBERG/&   A
FUTURE CITY   ELWOOD, ROGER   A
IN DONOVAN'S TIME   GRANT, C. L.   SS   ORB 75 0
ORBIT 16   KNIGHT, DAMON   A
IN ENTROPY'S JAWS   SILVERBERG, ROBERT   NV   INY 71 0
BEST SCIENCE FICTION OF THE YEAR, THE   CARR, TERRY   A
INFINITY 2   HOSKINS, ROBERT   A
MODERN SCIENCE FICTION   SPINRAD, NORMAN   A
REALITY TRIP, THE   SILVERBERG, ROBERT   A
UNFAMILIAR TERRITORY   SILVERBERG, ROBERT   A
IN EXORCISING TEXAS: AN INTRODUCTION   ELLISON, HARLAN   IN
LONE STAR UNIVERSE   PROCTOR & UTLEY   A
IN HIDING   SHIRAS, WILMAR H.   NV   ASF 48 1
ARMCHAIR SCIENCE READER, THE   GORDON, I. & SORKIN A
BEST SCIENCE-FICTION STORIES: 1949, THE   BLEILER & DIKTY   A
CHILDREN OF THE ATOM   SHIRAS, WILMAR H.   A
CHILDREN OF WONDER   TENN, WILLIAM   A
GREAT SCIENCE FICTION STORIES SMITH, CORDELIA T.   A
GREAT STORIES OF SCIENCE FICTION   LEINSTER, MURRAY   A
SCIENCE FICTION FOR PEOPLE WHO HATE SCIENCE FICTION
                                   CARR, TERRY   A
SCIENCE FICTION HALL OF FAME VOLUME 2B   BOVA, BEN   A
*STORIES FOR TOMORROW   SLOANE, WILLIAM   A
TOWARD INFINITY   KNIGHT, DAMON   A
IN HIS IMAGE   CHILSON, ROBERT   NV   ASF 69 0
ANALOG 8   CAMPBELL, JOHN W. JR AN
IN HIS IMAGE (IN MAN'S IMAGE) CARR, TERRY   SS   AMZ 71 1
ALPHA 4   SILVERBERG, ROBERT   A
LIGHT AT THE END OF THE UNIVERSE, THE   CARR, TERRY   A
IN HIS IMAGE (THE MAN WHO MADE HIMSELF)
                                   BEAUMONT, CHARLES NV   IMG 57 0
YONDER   BEAUMONT, CHARLES   A
IN HIS OWN IMAGE   BIGGLE, LLOYD JR.   SS   FSF 68 0
BEST FROM FANTASY AND SCIENCE FICTION: 18
                                   FERMAN, EDWARD L.   A
METALLIC MUSE, THE   BIGGLE, LLOYD JR.   A
IN HIS OWN IMAGE   PAYES, RACHEL C.   SS   STG 74
STRANGE GODS   ELWOOD, ROGER   A
IN HOKA SIGNO VINCES   ANDERSON, POUL
                           AND DICKSON, GORDON R. NV C OWS 53 0
EARTHMAN'S BURDEN   ANDERSON, P.&DICKSON A
IN HOT PURSUIT OF HAPPINESS LEM, STANISLAW   NV
VIEW FROM ANOTHER SHORE   ROTTENSTEINER, FRANZ A
IN HUMAN HANDS   BUDRYS, ALGIS   NV   SFS 54 0
RARE SCIENCE FICTION   HOWARD, IVAN   A
IN LONELY LANDS   ELLISON, HARLAN   SS   FUN 59 0
ALONE AGAINST TOMORROW   ELLISON, HARLAN   A
ELLISON WONDERLAND   ELLISON, HARLAN   A
FANTASTIC UNIVERSE OMNIBUS, THE   SANTESSON, HANS S.   A
MARS, WE LOVE YOU   HIPOLITO & MCNELLY   A

IN LOVING MEMORY   WHITE, JAMES   SS   NEB 56 01
  MONSTERS AND MEDICS   WHITE, JAMES   AC
IN MAN'S IMAGE (SEE IN HIS IMAGE)
                                CARR, TERRY   TC
IN MAN'S OWN IMAGE   VARSHAVSKY, ILYA   SS
  RUSSIAN SCIENCE FICTION, 1968   MAGIDOFF, ROBERT   AN
IN MEMORIAM: DAVID HENRY KELLER
                                SPENCER, PAUL   MS
  FOLSOM FLINT AND OTHER CURIOUS TALES, THE
                                      KELLER, DAVID H. MD. AC
IN MEMORIAM: FLETCHER PRATT   BLISH, JAMES   PM   FSF 57 01
  BEST FROM FANTASY AND SCIENCE FICTION: 7
                                      BOUCHER, ANTHONY   AN
IN MEMORIAM: HENRY KUTTNER   ANDERSON, KAREN   PM   FSF 58 05
  BEST FROM FANTASY AND SCIENCE FICTION: 8
                                      BOUCHER, ANTHONY   AN
IN MEMORIAM- A. A. WYN   WOLLHEIM, DONALD A. MS
  NEBULA AWARD STORIES NO. 4   ANDERSON, POUL   AN
IN MEMORIAM- ANNA KAVAN   ALDISS, BRIAN W.   MS
  NEBULA AWARD STORIES NO. 4   ANDERSON, POUL   AN
IN MEMORIAM- ANTHONY BOUCHER   MCCOMAS, J. FRANCIS MS
  NEBULA AWARD STORIES NO. 4   ANDERSON, POUL   AN
IN MEMORIAM- ARTHUR SELLINGS   CARNELL, TED   MS
  NEBULA AWARD STORIES NO. 4   ANDERSON, POUL   AN
IN MEMORIAM- BERNARD I. KAHN   CAMPBELL, JOHN W. JR MS
  NEBULA AWARD STORIES NO. 4   ANDERSON, POUL   AN
IN MEMORIAM- EDISON MARSHALL   ROGERS, ALVA   MS
  NEBULA AWARD STORIES NO. 4   ANDERSON, POUL   AN
IN MEMORIAM- FRANK OWEN   PETAJA, EMIL   MS
  NEBULA AWARD STORIES NO. 4   ANDERSON, POUL   AN
IN MEMORIAM- GERALD KERSH   ELLISON, HARLAN   MS
  NEBULA AWARD STORIES NO. 4   ANDERSON, POUL   AN
IN MEMORIAM- GROFF CONKLIN   ASIMOV, ISAAC   MS
  NEBULA AWARD STORIES NO. 4   ANDERSON, POUL   AN
IN MEMORIAM- HARL VINCENT   ACKERMAN, FORREST J. MS
  NEBULA AWARD STORIES NO. 4   ANDERSON, POUL   AN
IN MEMORIAM- MERVYN PEAKE   MOORCOCK, MICHAEL   MS
  NEBULA AWARD STORIES NO. 4   ANDERSON, POUL   AN
IN MEMORIAM- ROSEL GEORGE BROWN
                                GALOUYE, DANIEL F. MS
  NEBULA AWARD STORIES NO. 4   ANDERSON, POUL   AN
IN MEMORIAM- STUART PALMER   ANDERSON, KAREN   MS
  NEBULA AWARD STORIES NO. 4   ANDERSON, POUL   AN
IN MEMORIAM, JEANNIE   SAXTON, JOSEPHINE   SS
  STOPWATCH   HAY, GEORGE   OA
IN OUR BLOCK   LAFFERTY, R. A.   SS   IFS 65 07
  NINE HUNDRED GRANDMOTHERS   LAFFERTY, R. A.   AC
  WORLD'S BEST SCIENCE FICTION: 1966 WOLLHEIM & CARR   AN
IN OUTRAGED STONE   LAFFERTY, R. A.   SS   TAL 73
  FRONTIERS 1; TOMORROW'S ALTERNATIVES ELWOOD, ROGER   OA
IN PASSAGE OF THE SUN   COLLYN, GEORGE   SS   NWS 66 07
  BEST SF FROM NEW WORLDS 3   MOORCOCK, MICHAEL   AN
IN PIERSON'S ORCHESTRA   ROBINSON, KIM S.   SS   ORB 76 18
  ORBIT 18   KNIGHT, DAMON   OA
IN PRAISE OF HIS SPIRITS NOBLE AND OTHERWISE
                                ZELAZNY, ROGER   IN
  FROM THE LAND OF FEAR   ELLISON, HARLAN   AC
IN PRAISE OF NEW YORK   DISCH, THOMAS M.   PM   FUC 73
  FUTURE CITY   ELWOOD, ROGER   OA
IN RE GLOVER   TUSHNET, LEONARD   SS   DVS 72 02
  AGAIN, DANGEROUS VISIONS   ELLISON, HARLAN   OA
  BIO-FUTURES   SARGENT, PAMELA   AN
IN RE SPRAGUE   ASIMOV, ISAAC   MS
  CONTINENT MAKERS AND OTHER TALES OF THE VIAGENS
                                      DE CAMP, L. SPRAGUE AC
IN RE STATE VS. FORBES   EARLE, WARREN   SS   BLC 07 06
  SCIENCE FICTION BY GASLIGHT   MOSKOWITZ, SAM   AN
IN REASON'S EAR   BAILEY, HILARY   SS   SCF 65 06
  BEST SF STORIES FROM NEW WORLDS 6   MOORCOCK, MICHAEL   AN
IN SATURN'S REALM   GRIFFITH, GEORGE   SS   PRS 00 05
  WORLDS APART   LOCKE, GEORGE   AN
IN SEARCH OF THE UNKNOWN (EXCERPT)
                                CHAMBERS, ROBERT W. EX   04
  SPACE MAGICIANS, THE   NORTON & MOSKOWITZ   AN
IN SECLUSION   JACOBS, HARVEY   SS   NWS 68 02
  BEST SF STORIES FROM NEW WORLDS 4   MOORCOCK, MICHAEL   AN
  EGG OF THE GLAK, AND OTHER STORIES, THE JACOBS, HARVEY   AC
  SF12   MERRIL, JUDITH   AN
IN SHEEP'S CLOTHING   NOURSE, ALAN E.   SS   FSM 52 11
  RX FOR TOMORROW   NOURSE, ALAN E.   AC
IN SOBIESKI'S SHIELD   MORGAN, EDWIN   PM   68
  HOLDING YOUR EIGHT HANDS   LUCIE-SMITH, EDWARD   AN
IN SPACE WITH RUNYON JONES   CORWIN, NORMAN   SS   52
  SEA OF SPACE, A   NOLAN, WILLIAM F.   AN
IN THE ABYSS   WELLS, H. G.   SS   PRS 96 08
  BEST SCIENCE FICTION STORIES OF H. G. WELLS
                                      WELLS, H. G.   AC
  FIRST CONTACT   KNIGHT, DAMON   AN
  PLATTNER STORY AND OTHERS, THE   WELLS, H. G.   AC
  POCKET BOOK OF SCIENCE-FICTION, THE WOLLHEIM, DONALD A.   AN
  SHORT STORIES OF H. G. WELLS, THE   WELLS, H. G.   AC
  THIRTY STRANGE STORIES   WELLS, H. G.   AC
  TWENTY-EIGHT SCIENCE FICTION STORIES WELLS, H. G.   AC
  WAR OF THE WORLDS, THE TIME MACHINE AND SELECTED SHORT STORIES
                                      WELLS, H. G.   AC
IN THE ANTARCTIC REGIONS OF MARS
                                LACH-SZYRMA, D. S. SS   CSL 87 04
  WORLDS APART   LOCKE, GEORGE   AN
IN THE ARENA   ALDISS, BRIAN W.   SS   IFS 63 07
  BEST SCIENCE FICTION FROM IF, THE   POHL, FREDERIK   AN
  BOOK OF BRIAN ALDISS, THE   ALDISS, BRIAN W.   AC
  SECOND IF READER OF SCIENCE FICTION, THE POHL, FREDERIK   AN
IN THE AVU OBSERVATORY   WELLS, H. G.   SS   PMB 94 08
  BEST SCIENCE FICTION STORIES OF H. G. WELLS
                                      WELLS, H. G.   AC
  BEWARE THE BEASTS   GHIDALIA, V. & ELWOOD AN

COUNTRY OF THE BLIND, THE   WELLS, H. G.   AC
  SHORT STORIES OF H. G. WELLS, THE   WELLS, H. G.   AC
  STOLEN BACILLUS AND OTHER INCIDENTS, THE WELLS, H. G.   AC
  THIRTY STRANGE STORIES   WELLS, H. G.   AC
  TWENTY-EIGHT SCIENCE FICTION STORIES WELLS, H. G.   AC
  WAR OF THE WORLDS, THE TIME MACHINE AND SELECTED SHORT STORIES
                                      WELLS, H. G.   AC
IN THE BAG   JANIFER, LAURENCE M. SS   FSF 64 02
  ABC OF SCIENCE FICTION, AN   BOARDMAN, TOM JR.   AN
  IMPOSSIBLE?   JANIFER, LAURENCE M.   AC
IN THE BARN   ANTHONY, PIERS   NV   DVS 72 02
  AGAIN, DANGEROUS VISIONS   ELLISON, HARLAN   OA
IN THE BEGINNING   KLASS, MORTON   SS   ASF 54 07
  APEMAN, SPACEMAN   STOVER & HARRISON   AN
IN THE BEGINNING   KNIGHT, DAMON   NV   FUT 53 01
  THINGS   HOWARD, IVAN   AN
IN THE BEGINNING   SILVERBERG, ROBERT SS   SAG 70
  SCIENCE AGAINST MAN   CHEETHAM, ANTHONY   OA
IN THE BONE   DICKSON, GORDON R. NV   IFS 66 10
  ANCIENT, MY ENEMY   DICKSON, GORDON R.   AC
IN THE BOWL   VARLEY, JOHN   NV   FSF 75 12
  BEST SCIENCE FICTION OF THE YEAR, THE NO. 5
                                      CARR, TERRY   AN
IN THE CARDS   BLOCH, ROBERT   SS   WOF 70 WI
  COLD CHILLS   BLOCH, ROBERT   AC
IN THE COMA CONDITION   PARTINGTON, CHARLES SS   NWR 76 29
  NEW WRITINGS IN SF. 29   BULMER, KENNETH   OA
IN THE CROWDED PART OF HEAVEN BORSKI, ROBERT   SS   SFZ 74 01
  SCIENCE FICTION EMPHASIS NO. 1   GERROLD, DAVID   OA
IN THE CUP   MALZBERG, BARRY N. SS   SAW 72
  MANY WORLDS OF BARRY MALZBERG, THE MALZBERG, BARRY N.   AC
  SIGNS AND WONDERS   ELWOOD, ROGER   OA
IN THE DAYS OF OUR FATHERS   MCCLINTIC, WINONA   SS   FSF 49 FL
  BEST FROM FANTASY AND SCIENCE FICTION BOUCHER & MCCOMAS   AN
IN THE DAYS OF THE COMET   WELLS, H. G.   NO   DCH 05
  SEVEN FAMOUS NOVELS BY H. G. WELLS WELLS, H. G.   AC
IN THE DEADLANDS   GERROLD, DAVID   NV   NEW 72 AC
  WITH A FINGER IN MY I   GERROLD, DAVID   AC
IN THE DEEP OF TIME   LATHROP, GEORGE P. NV   EIM 97 03
  WORLDS APART   LOCKE, GEORGE   AN
IN THE EGG (TRANSLATED BY MICHAEL HAMBURGER)
                                GRASS, GUNTER   PM   66
  SF12   MERRIL, JUDITH   AN
IN THE EYE OF THE STORM (EYE OF THE STORM)
                                SPINRAD, NORMAN   SS   IFS 74 02
  NO DIRECTION HOME   SPINRAD, NORMAN   AC
IN THE FOOTSTEPS OF THE ABOMINABLE SNOWMAN
                                NESVADBA, JOSEF   NV   64
  LOST FACE, THE   NESVADBA, JOSEF   AC
IN THE FUTURE   LUCIE-SMITH, EDWARD PM   68
  HOLDING YOUR EIGHT HANDS   LUCIE-SMITH, EDWARD   AN
IN THE GARDEN   LAFFERTY, R. A.   SS   IFS 61 03
  DOES ANYONE ELSE HAVE SOMETHING FURTHER TO ADD?
                                      LAFFERTY, R. A.   AC
IN THE GOOD OLD SUMMERTIME   MILLER, P. SCHUYLER SS   ASF 40 03
  TITAN, THE   MILLER, P. SCHUYLER   AC
IN THE GREENHOUSE   NIELSEN, LIN   SS   CLR 72 02
  CLARION II   WILSON, ROBIN SCOTT   OA
IN THE GROUP   SILVERBERG, ROBERT SS   EIO 73
  EROS IN ORBIT   ELDER, JOSEPH   OA
  UNFAMILIAR TERRITORY   SILVERBERG, ROBERT   AC
IN THE HOUR OF NOT QUITE RAIN BORSKI, ROBERT   SS   SFM 74 07
  BEST OF SCIENCE FICTION MONTHLY, THE SACKS, JANET   AN
IN THE HOUSE OF DOUBLE MINDS   SILVERBERG, ROBERT SS   VTX 74 06
  FEAST OF ST. DIONYSUS, THE   SILVERBERG, ROBERT   AC
IN THE HOUSE OF THE WORM   MARTIN, GEORGE R. R. SS
  IDES OF TOMORROW, THE   CARR, TERRY   OA
IN THE HOUSE, ANOTHER   WHITEHILL, JOSEPH   SS   FSF 60 04
  6TH ANNUAL OF THE YEAR'S BEST S-F, THE MERRIL, JUDITH   AN
IN THE IMAGICON   SMITH, GEORGE HENRY SS   GAL 66 02
  NEBULA AWARD STORIES NO. 2   ALDISS & HARRISON   AN
IN THE INNERMOST ROOM OF AUTHORITY
                                BUNCH, DAVID R.   SS
  MODERAN   BUNCH, DAVID R.   AC
IN THE LAND OF SCIENCE FICTION BRANDIS, YEVGENY
                                AND DMITRVSKY, VLADMIR SS C
  RUSSIAN SCIENCE FICTION, 1969   MAGIDOFF, ROBERT   AN
IN THE LAND OF UNBLIND   MERRIL, JUDITH   SS   FSF 74 10
  BEST OF JUDITH MERRIL, THE   MERRIL, JUDITH   AC
IN THE LEFT WING   DERLETH, AUGUST
                                AND SCHORER, MARK   SS C WRT 32 06
  WIZARDS AND WARLOCKS   GHIDALIA, VIC   AN
IN THE LILLIPUTIAN ASYLUM: A STORY IN 8 POEMS AND AN
  INTRODUCTION   BISHOP, MICHAEL   PM   ORB 74 15
  ORBIT 15   KNIGHT, DAMON   OA
IN THE MATTER OF THE ASSASSIN MEREFIRS
                                PURDY, KEN W.   SS   ASF 72 11
  BEST SF: 1972   HARRISON & ALDISS   AN
IN THE METEORIC CLOUD   JONES, NEIL R.   NV   NEW 68 AC
  DOOMSDAY ON AJIAT   JONES, NEIL R.   AC
IN THE MIDST OF DEATH   HECHT, BEN   SS   45
  ALONE BY NIGHT   CONGDON, MICHAEL&DON AN
IN THE MODERN VEIN: AN UNSYMPATHETIC LOVE STORY (A BARDLET'S
  ROMANCE)   WELLS, H. G.   SS   TTH 94 03
  PLATTNER STORY AND OTHERS, THE   WELLS, H. G.   AC
  SHORT STORIES OF H. G. WELLS, THE   WELLS, H. G.   AC
  THIRTY STRANGE STORIES   WELLS, H. G.   AC
IN THE PENAL COLONY   KAFKA, FRANZ   SS   48
  TIMELESS STORIES FOR TODAY AND TOMORROW BRADBURY, RAY   AN
IN THE POCKET   O'DONNELL, K. M.   SS   NOV 70 01
  IN THE POCKET AND OTHER S-F STORIES O'DONNELL, K. M.   DC
  *NOVA 1   HARRISON, HARRY   OA
IN THE PROBLEM PIT   POHL, FREDERIK   NA   FSF 73 09
  IN THE PROBLEM PIT   POHL, FREDERIK   AC
IN THE QUEUE   LAUMER, KEITH   SS   ORB 70 07
  BIG SHOW, THE   LAUMER, KEITH   AC

IN THE QUEUE

NEBULA AWARD STORIES   NO. 6   SIMAK, CLIFFORD D.   AN
ORBIT   7   KNIGHT, DAMON   OA
IN THE RUINS   DAHL, ROALD   SS   64
 11TH ANNUAL OF THE YEAR'S BEST S-F, THE MERRIL, JUDITH   AN
IN THE SCARLET STAR   WILLIAMSON, JACK   SS AMZ 33 03
 EVERY BOY'S BOOK OF SCIENCE FICTION WOLLHEIM, DONALD A. AN
IN THE SHADOW (AS MICHAEL KARAGEORGE)
                        ANDERSON, POUL   NV ASF 67 03
 QUEEN OF AIR AND DARKNESS AND OTHER STORIES, THE
                        ANDERSON, POUL   AC
IN THE STEPS OF THE ANCIENT MINERS
                        YEFREMOV, IVAN   SS
 MEETING OVER TUSCARORA AND OTHER ADVENTURE TALES, A
                        YEFREMOV, IVAN   AC
IN THE STOCKS   MALZBERG, BARRY N.   SS NDM 77 07
 NEW DIMENSIONS 7   SILVERBERG, ROBERT   OA
IN THE STRAW   HOCH, EDWARD D.   SS   72
 BEWARE MORE BEASTS   GHIDALIA, V.& ELWOOD AN
IN THE TEMPLE OF MARS SABERHAGEN, FRED   NV IFS 66 04
 BERSERKER   SABERHAGEN, FRED   AC
IN THE TWENTY NINTH CENTURY (ARS 49 SU)
                        VERNE, JULES   SS FRM 89 02
 YESTERDAY AND TOMORROW   VERNE, JULES   AC
IN THE VAULT   LOVECRAFT, H. P.   SS WRT 32 04
 OTHER WORLDS, THE   STONG, PHILIP D.   AN
IN THE WIND   COOK, GLEN   NV
 TOMORROW TODAY   ZEBROWSKI, GEORGE   OA
IN THE WORLD'S DUSK   HAMILTON, EDMOND   SS WRT 36 03
 BEST OF EDMOND HAMILTON, THE   HAMILTON, EDMOND   AC
 END OF THE WORLD, THE   WOLLHEIM, DONALD A. AN
IN THE YEAR TEN THOUSAND (1892)
                        HARBEN, WILLIAM   SS ARN 92
 FUTURE PERFECT   FRANKLIN, H. BRUCE   AN
IN THE YEAR 2889 (ARS 49 SU) VERNE, JULES SS FRM 89 02
 *BIG BOOK OF SCIENCE FICTION   CONKLIN, GROFF   AN
IN THIS CORNER   GOLD, H. L.   IN
 FOURTH GALAXY READER, THE   GOLD, H. L.   AN
IN THIS IMAGE   BRENNERT, ALAN   NV FOS 74
 FELLOWSHIP OF THE STARS   CARR, TERRY   OA
IN THIS SIGN (ALSO AS THE FIRE BALLOONS)
                        BRADBURY, RAY   SS IMG 51 04
 CHRONICLES OF A COMER AND OTHER RELIGIOUS SCIENCE FICTION
  STORIES   ELWOOD, ROGER   AN
 LOOKING FORWARD   LESSER, MILTON   AN
IN TOMORROW'S LITTLE BLACK BAG BLISH, JAMES   AR
 7TH ANNUAL OF THE YEAR'S BEST S-F, THE MERRIL, JUDITH   AN
IN VALUE DECEIVED   FYFE, H. B.   SS ASF 50 11
 FIRST CONTACT   KNIGHT, DAMON   AN
 *POSSIBLE WORLDS OF SCIENCE FICTION CONKLIN, GROFF   AN
 *STORIES FOR TOMORROW   SLOANE, WILLIAM   AN
 STORIES OF SCIENTIFIC IMAGINATION   GALLANT, JOSEPH   AN
IN-BETWEENS, THE (SEE THE UBIQUITOUS YOU)
                        WILSON, RICHARD   TC
IN-GROUP   DE CAMP, L. SPRAGUE SS MAR 52 05
 GUN FOR DINOSAUR AND OTHER IMAGINATIVE TALES
                        DE-CAMP, L. SPRAGUE   AC
INALIENABLE RITE   BENFORD, GREGORY   SS QRK 70 01
 QUARK/1   DELANY & HACKER   OA
INANIMATE OBJECTION   ELLIOTT, H. CHANDLER NV GAL 54 02
 *SPECTRUM   AMIS & CONQUEST   AN
INCASED IN ANCIENT RIND LAFFERTY, R. A.   NV QRK 71 03
 STRANGE DOINGS   LAFFERTY, R. A.   AC
INCENTIVE   ALDISS, BRIAN W.   SS NWS 58 12
 CANOPY OF TIME, THE   ALDISS, BRIAN W.   AC
 GALAXIES LIKE GRAINS OF SAND   ALDISS, BRIAN W.   AC
INCEPTION OF THE EPOCH OF MRS. BEDONEBYASYOUDID, THE
                        BRUNNER, JOHN   SS QRK 71 02
 BEYOND THIS HORIZON   CARRELL, CHRISTOPHER OA
 FROM THIS DAY FORWARD   BRUNNER, JOHN   AC
 QUARK/2   DELANY & HACKER   OA
INCIDENT AFTER   HENDERSON, ZENNA   SS NEW 71 AC
 HOLDING WONDER   HENDERSON, ZENNA   AC
INCIDENT AT OWL CREEK (AN OCCURENCE AT OWL CREEK BRIDGE)
                        BIERCE, AMBROSE   SS   91
 GHOULS, THE   HAINING, PETER   AN
INCIDENT AT THE GALLOPING HORSE
                        JACOBI, CARL   SS WRT 48 11
 PORTRAITS IN MOONLIGHT   JACOBI, CARL   AC
INCIDENT IN MODERAN   BUNCH, DAVID R.   SS DVS 67 01
 DANGEROUS VISIONS   ELLISON, HARLAN   OA
 MODERAN   BUNCH, DAVID R.   AC
INCIDENT IN SPACE   VERNON, ROGER LEE   SS
 SPACE FRONTIERS, THE   VERNON, ROGER LEE   AC
INCIDENT IN THE IND   HARRISON, HARRY   SS FSF 64 03
 PRIME NUMBER   HARRISON, HARRY   AC
INCIDENT IN THE STREETS OF THE CITY(SEE A PEDESTRIAN ACCIDENT)
                        COOVER, ROBERT   TC
INCIDENT ON A LAKE   COLLIER, JOHN   SS
 BEST FANTASY STORIES   ALDISS, BRIAN W.   AN
INCIDENT ON CALYPSO   LEINSTER, MURRAY   SS STS 45 FL
 INVASION FROM MARS   WELLES, ORSON   AN
INCIDENT ON ROUTE 12, AN SCHMITZ, JAMES H. SS IFS 62 01
 BEST SCIENCE FICTION FROM IF, THE   POHL, FREDERICK   AN
INCOMMUNICADO   MACLEAN, KATHERINE   NV ASF 50 06
 DIPLOIDS AND OTHER FLIGHTS OF FANCY, THE MACLEAN, KATHERINE AC
 SIX GREAT SHORT SCIENCE FICTION NOVELS CONKLIN, GROFF   AN
INCOMMUNICADO   RUSSELL, RAY   SS FSF 57 11
 SARDONICUS AND OTHER STORIES   RUSSELL, RAY   AC
INCONSTANT MOON   NIVEN, LARRY   NV NEW 71 AC
 ALL THE MYRIAD WAYS   NIVEN, LARRY   AC
 BEST SCIENCE FICTION FOR 1972   POHL, FREDERICK   AN
INCORRIGIBLE, THE   DE CAMP, L. SPRAGUE SS ASF 39 01
 FUTURES TO INFINITY   MOSKOWITZ, SAM   AN
INCREDIBLE PLANET, THE CAMPBELL, JOHN W. JR NV
 INCREDIBLE PLANET, THE   CAMPBELL, JOHN W. JR NO

INCUBATION   MACDONALD, JOHN D.   SS   NEW 52 AN
 *FUTURE TENSE   CROSSEN, KENDELL F. AN
INCUBI OF PARALLEL X, THE STURGEON, THEODORE NA PLS 51 09
 STURGEON IN ORBIT   STURGEON, THEODORE   AC
INDEFATIGABLE FROG, THE DICK, PHILIP K.   SS FSM 53 07
 HANDFUL OF DARKNESS, A   DICK, PHILIP K.   AC
INDELIBLE KIND, THE   HENDERSON, ZENNA   NV FSF 68 12
 HOLDING WONDER   HENDERSON, ZENNA   AC
INDEX   MISC. MATERIAL   MS
 INSIDE INFORMATION   MOWSHOWITZ, ABBE   AN
 NEW AWARENESS, THE   WARRICK & GREENBERG AN
INDEX OF AUTHORS   MISC. MATERIAL   MS
 PLAYBOY BOOK OF HORROR AND THE SUPERNATURAL, THE
                        PLAYBOY, EDITORS OF AN
 PLAYBOY BOOK OF SCIENCE FICTION AND FANTASY, THE
                        PLAYBOY, EDITORS OF AN
INDEX OF AUTHORS AND TITLES MISC. MATERIAL MS
 SCIENCE FACT/FICTION   FARRELL/GAGE/&   AN
INDEX TO VOLUMES 1-10 MISC. MATERIAL   MS
 ORBIT 10   KNIGHT, DAMON   OA
INDEX, THE BEST SCIENCE-FICTION STORIES: 1949-1954
                        MISC. MATERIAL   MS
 BEST SCIENCE-FICTION STORIES: 1954, THE BLEILER & DIKTY AN
INDIAN SPIRIT GUIDE, THE BLOCH, ROBERT   SS WRT 48 11
 LIVING DEMONS, THE   BLOCH, ROBERT   AC
INDUSTRIAL REVOLUTION SANDERS, WINSTON P. SN ASF 63 09
 ANALOG 3   CAMPBELL, JOHN W. JR AN
INDUSTRIAL REVOLUTION (SEE THE ROGUE)
                        ANDERSON, POUL   TC
INEXPERIENCED GHOST, THE(THE STORY OF THE INEXPERIENCED GHOST)
                        WELLS, H. G.   SS SND 02 03
 INEXPERIENCED GHOST AND NINE OTHER STORIES, THE
                        WELLS, H. G.   AC
 SHORT STORIES OF H. G. WELLS, THE   WELLS, H. G.   AC
 TWELVE STORIES AND A DREAM   WELLS, H. G.   AC
INFERNAL BOUILLABAISSE, THE BEAUMONT, CHARLES SS NEW 57 AC
 HUNGER AND OTHER STORIES, THE   BEAUMONT, CHARLES   AC
INFINITE ATOM, THE   CAMPBELL, JOHN W. JR NV
 INCREDIBLE PLANET, THE   CAMPBELL, JOHN W. JR NO
INFINITE SUMMER, AN   PRIEST, CHRISTOPHER NV
 ANDROMEDA I   WESTON, PETER   OA
 BEST SCIENCE FICTION OF THE YEAR, THE NO. 6
                        CARR, TERRY   AN
INFINITE VULCAN, THE (WALTER KOENIG)
                        FOSTER, ALAN DEAN   SA SLG 74 02
 STAR TREK LOG TWO   FOSTER, ALAN DEAN   OC
INFINITY   EDDINGTON, ARTHUR   PM   35
 FANTASIA MATHEMATICA   FADIMAN, CLIFTON   AN
INFINITY   REEVES, ROSSER   PM FSF 60 12
 BEST FROM FANTASY AND SCIENCE FICTION: 10
                        MILLS, ROBERT P.   AN
INFINITY BOX, THE   WILHELM, KATE   NA ORB 71 09
 INFINITY BOX, THE   WILHELM, KATE   AC
 ORBIT 9   KNIGHT, DAMON   OA
INFINITY OF GUESTS, A GAMOW, GEORGE   PM   47
 FANTASIA MATHEMATICA   FADIMAN, CLIFTON   AN
INFINITY OF LOVING, AN GERROLD, DAVID   SS TTM 73
 TEN TOMORROWS   ELWOOD, ROGER   OA
INFINITY ZERO   WANDREI, DONALD   SS ASF 36 10
 FAR BOUNDARIES   DERLETH, AUGUST   AN
 STRANGE HARVEST   WANDREI, DONALD   AC
INFLEXIBLE LOGIC   MALONEY, RUSSELL   SS NYM 40 02
 FANTASIA MATHEMATICA   FADIMAN, CLIFTON   AN
 FANTASY: THE LITERATURE OF THE MARVELOUS KELLEY, LEO P. AN
 TIMELESS STORIES FOR TODAY AND TOMORROW BRADBURY, RAY   AN
INFORMAL BIOGRAPHY OF CONAN THE CIMMERIAN, AN
                        CLARK, JOHN D.
                        AND MILLER, P. SCHUYLER AR C
 COMING OF CONAN, THE   HOWARD, ROBERT E.   AC
INFRA DRACONIS   GUREVICH, G.   NV
 SOVIET SCIENCE FICTION   ANONYMOUS   AN
 WORLDS APART   WILLIAMS-ELLIS& OWEN AN
INFRA-MEDIANS, THE   WRIGHT, SEWELL P.   SS ASF 31 12
 EVERY BOY'S BOOK OF SCIENCE FICTION WOLLHEIM, DONALD A. AN
INGENIOUS PATRIOT, THE BIERCE, AMBROSE   SS
 ONE HUNDRED YEARS OF SCIENCE FICTION KNIGHT, DAMON   AN
 PAST, PRESENT, AND FUTURE PERFECT   WOLFE, J&FITZ GERALD AN
INGMAR BERGMAN: FANTASY NOVELIST
                        LEIBER, FRITZ   BR FAN 74 03
 SECOND BOOK OF FRITZ LEIBER, THE   LEIBER, FRITZ
INHABITANT OF CARCOSA, AN BIERCE, AMBROSE SS AFR 48 08
 EDGE OF NEVER, THE   HOSKINS, ROBERT   AN
INHABITED, THE   WILSON, RICHARD   NV GAL 53 01
 THOSE IDIOTS FROM EARTH   WILSON, RICHARD   AC
INHERITANCE (NWS 47 03) CLARKE, ARTHUR C. SS ASF 48 09
 ACROSS THE SEA OF STARS   CLARKE, ARTHUR C.   AC
 EXPEDITION TO EARTH   CLARKE, ARTHUR C.   AC
INHERITANCE, THE   LEIBER, FRITZ   SS WRT 42 01
 NIGHT'S BLACK AGENTS   LEIBER, FRITZ   AC
INHERITORS, THE   LOWNDES, ROBERT W.
                        AND MICHAEL, JOHN   SS C FFS 42 10
 MORE TERROR IN THE MODERN VEIN   WOLLHEIM, DONALD A. AN
 *TERROR IN THE MODERN VEIN   WOLLHEIM, DONALD A. AN
INHUMAN ERROR (SEE WHAT DO YOU WANT ME TO DO TO PROVE
 IM HUMAN STOP)   SABERHAGEN, FRED   TC
INITIATION   MALZBERG, BARRY N.   SS NEW 75 AC
 MANY WORLDS OF BARRY MALZBERG, THE   MALZBERG, BARRY N.   AC
INN OUTSIDE THE WORLD, THE HAMILTON, EDMOND SS WRT 45 07
 *MY BEST SCIENCE FICTION STORY   MARGULIES & FRIEND   AN
 SCIENCE FACT/FICTION   FARRELL/GAGE/&   AN
 WHAT'S IT LIKE OUT THERE? AND OTHER STORIES
                        HAMILTON, EDMOND   AC
INNER CIRCLES, THE (ALSO AS THE WINTER FLIES)
                        LEIBER, FRITZ   SS FSF 67 10
 BEST FROM FANTASY AND SCIENCE FICTION: 17
                        FERMAN, EDWARD L.   AN

INNER CIRCLES, THE (ALSO AS THE WINTER FLIES)   INTO THE SHOP

   NEW WORLDS OF FANTASY NO. 3   CARR, TERRY   AN
INNER WHEEL, THE   ROBERTS, KEITH   NV   NWR 65 06
   NEW WRITINGS IN SF. 6   CARNELL, JOHN   OA
INNER WORLDS, THE   MORRISON, WILLIAM NV   FSF 54 04
   BEST SCIENCE FICTION STORIES AND NOVELS: 1955
                                     DIKTY, T. E.   AN
INNOCENCE OF FATHER BANGS, THE GOULART, RON   SS   PNT 72
   NUTZENBOLTS   GOULART, RON   AC
INNOCENT ARRIVAL, THE (INNOCENT AT LARGE)
                                     ANDERSON, KAREN
                             AND ANDERSON, POUL   NV C GAL 58 07
   SPACE, TIME & CRIME   DEFORD, MIRIAM ALLEN AN
INNOCENT AT LARGE (SEE THE INNOCENT ARRIVAL)
                                     ANDERSON, KAREN
                             AND ANDERSON, POUL   TC C
INNOCENT EYE, THE   KUTTNER, HENRY   IN
   REVOLT IN 2100   HEINLEIN, ROBERT A. AC
INQUIRY CONCERNING THE CURVATURE OF THE EARTH'S SURFACE
                                     PRICE, ROGER   SS   MON 59 WI
   5TH ANNUAL OF THE YEAR'S BEST S-F, THE MERRIL, JUDITH AN
INSANE ONES, THE   BALLARD, J. G.   SS   AMZ 62 01
   BEST OF J. G. BALLARD, THE   BALLARD, J. G.   AC
   BILLENIUM   BALLARD, J. G.   AC
   DAY OF FOREVER, THE   BALLARD, J. G.   AC
   8TH MEN OF THE YEAR'S BEST S-F, THE MERRIL, JUDITH   AN
INSECT MEN OF BOSTON   SALLIS, JAMES   SS   NWQ 74 06
   NEW WORLDS NO. 6   PLATT & BAILEY   OA
INSECTS, THE   FAST, HOWARD   SS
   GENERAL ZAPPED AN ANGEL, THE   FAST, HOWARD   OC
INSERT KNOB A IN HOLE B   ASIMOV, ISAAC   SS   FSF 57 12
   NIGHTFALL AND OTHER STORIES   ASIMOV, ISAAC   AC
INSIDE   CARR, CAROL   SS   ORB 70 08
   INTO THE UNKNOWN   CARR, TERRY   OA
   ORBIT 8   KNIGHT, DAMON   OA
   OTHER DIMENSIONS   SILVERBERG, ROBERT   AN
INSIDE EARTH   ANDERSON, POUL   NV   GAL 51 04
   *GALAXY READER OF SCIENCE FICTION GOLD, H. L.   AN
INSIDE JOHN BARTH   STUART, WILLIAM W. NV GAL 60 06
   FIFTH GALAXY READER, THE   GOLD, H. L.   AN
INSIDE MOTHER   DEGRAW, PAT   SS   INY 70 01
   INFINITY 1   HOSKINS, ROBERT   OA
INSIDE OF THE EARTH, THE   MITCHELL, EDWARD P. SS SUN 76 03
   CRYSTAL MAN, THE   MITCHELL, EDWARD P.   AC
INSIDE STRAIGHT   ANDERSON, POUL   SS   FSF 55 08
   7 CONQUESTS   ANDERSON, POUL   AC
INSIDE THE COMET (ALSO AS INTO THE COMET)
                                     CLARKE, ARTHUR C. SS   FSF 60 10
   OUT OF THIS WORLD 4   WILLIAMS-ELLIS& OWEN AN
INSIDEKICK   BONE, J. F.   NV   GAL 59 02
   ANOTHER PART OF THE GALAXY   CONKLIN, GROFF   AN
   SIXTH GALAXY READER, THE   GOLD, H. L.   AN
INSPECTOR'S TEETH, THE   DE CAMP, L. SPRAGUE SS ASF 50 04
   CONTINENT MAKERS AND OTHER TALES OF THE VIAGENS
                                     DE CAMP, L. SPRAGUE   AC
INSPECTOR, THE   LIEF, EVELYN   SS   CLR 71 01
   CLARION   WILSON, ROBIN SCOTT OA
INSPECTOR, THE   MCKIMMEY, JAMES SS   FRS 68
   FARTHEST REACHES, THE   ELDER, JOSEPH   OA
INSPIRED CHICKEN MOTEL, THE   BRADBURY, RAY   SS   LAT 69 11
   I SING THE BODY ELECTRIC   BRADBURY, RAY   AC
INSTALLMENT PLAN   SIMAK, CLIFFORD D. NA GAL 59 02
   *ALL THE TRAPS OF EARTH AND OTHER STORIES SIMAK, CLIFFORD D. AC
   NIGHT OF THE PUUDLY, THE   SIMAK, CLIFFORD D.   AC
INSTANT MAIDS OF MARS, THE   O'NEILL, SCOTT   SS
   MARTIAN SEXPOT   O'NEILL, SCOTT   AC
INSTEAD OF THE CROSS, THE LOLLIPOP (FROM "WALDEN 2")
                                     SKINNER, B. F.   EX   48
   NEW IMPROVED SUN, THE   DISCH, THOMAS M.   AN
INSTINCT   DEL REY, LESTER SS   ASF 52 01
   INSIDE INFORMATION   MOWSHOWITZ, ABBE   AN
   INTRODUCTORY PSYCHOLOGY THROUGH SCIENCE FICTION
                                     KATZ/WARRICK/&   AN
   MEN AND MACHINES   SILVERBERG, ROBERT   AN
   MORTALS AND MONSTERS   DEL REY, LESTER   AC
   OMNIBUS OF SCIENCE FICTION   CONKLIN, GROFF   AN
   SCIENCE FICTION OMNIBUS   CONKLIN, GROFF   AN
INSTITUTE, THE   EMSHWILLER, CAROL SS   ANA 70
   ALCHEMY AND ACADEME   MCCAFFREY, ANNE   OA
INSTITUTIONS   MALZBERG, BARRY N. SS
   SURVIVAL FROM INFINITY   ELWOOD, ROGER   OA
INSTRUCTOR   THELWELL   CT   PUN 61 01
   6TH ANNUAL OF THE YEAR'S BEST S-F, THE MERRIL, JUDITH   AN
INTANGIBLES, INC.   ALDISS, BRIAN W. NV   SCF 59 02
   BEST FANTASY STORIES   ALDISS, BRIAN W.   AN
   INTANGIBLES INC. AND OTHER STORIES ALDISS, BRIAN W.   AC
   NEANDERTHAL PLANET   ALDISS, BRIAN W.   AC
INTEGRATION MODULE   JAMES, DANIEL B. NV   ASF 73 01
   SOCIOLOGY THROUGH SCIENCE FICTION MILSTEAD/GREENBERG/& AN
INTEGRITY   WOODS, P. F.   SS   NWS 64 10
   BEST SF STORIES FROM NEW WORLDS 3 MOORCOCK, MICHAEL   AN
INTELLIGENCE TEST   WALTON, HARRY   SS   SFP 53 05
   CONTACT   KEYES, NOEL   AN
INTELLIGENT LIFE IN THE UNIVERSE
                                     SAGAN, CARL   AR   66
   ALL ABOUT VENUS   ALDISS, BRIAN W.   AN
   FAREWELL FANTASTIC VENUS   ALDISS & HARRISON   AN
INTENT TO DECEIVE (THE DECEIVERS)
                                     NIVEN, LARRY   SS   GAL 68 04
   TALES OF KNOWN SPACE: THE UNIVERSE OF LARRY NIVEN
                                     NIVEN, LARRY   AC
INTER ALIA   MALZBERG, BARRY N. SS INY 72 03
   INFINITY 3   HOSKINS, ROBERT   OA
   OUT FROM GANYMEDE   MALZBERG, BARRY N.   AC
INTERBALANCE   MACLEAN, KATHERINE SS FSF 60 10
   BEST FROM FANTASY AND SCIENCE FICTION: 10
                                     MILLS, ROBERT P.   AN

INTERCEPTOR, THE   MALZBERG, BARRY N. SS MSM 72
   OUT FROM GANYMEDE   MALZBERG, BARRY N.   AC
INTERFACE   ATTANASIO, A. A. NA   EPC 75
   EPOCH   ELWOOD & SILVERBERG   OA
INTERFERENCE   LEINSTER, MURRAY SS   ASF 45 10
   BEST OF MURRAY LEINSTER, THE   LEINSTER, MURRAY   AC
INTERIM   BRADBURY, RAY   SS   WRT 47 07
   *DARK CARNIVAL   BRADBURY, RAY   AC
   MARTIAN CHRONICLES, THE   BRADBURY, RAY   AC
INTERLOPER   ANDERSON, POUL   SS   FSF 51 04
   *OUTER REACHES, THE   DERLETH, AUGUST   AC
INTERLOPERS, THE   DEE, ROGER   SS   ASF 54 09
   GALACTIC EMPIRES VOLUME TWO   ALDISS, BRIAN W.   AN
INTERLUDE   DICKSON, GORDON R. MS
   THREE TO DORSAI¡   DICKSON, GORDON R.   AC
   THREE TO DORSAI¡   DICKSON, GORDON R.   AC
INTERLUDE (ALSO AS THE EXTERNAL TRIANGLE)
                                     SMITH, GEORGE O. NV   AMA 73
   ASTOUNDING   HARRISON, HARRY   OA
INTERLUDE IN THE DESERT   FAIRMAN, PAUL W. SS
   FORGETFUL ROBOT, THE   FAIRMAN, PAUL W.   OC
INTERMISSION TIME   JONES, RAYMOND F. NV SFQ 53 05
   NON-STATISTICAL MAN, THE   JONES, RAYMOND F.   AC
INTERNAL AFFAIR (RETIEF, INSIDER)
                                     LAUMER, KEITH   NV   INF 71 03
   RETIEF OF THE CDT   LAUMER, KEITH   AC
INTERNAL COMBUSTION   DE CAMP, L. SPRAGUE SS INF 56 02
   GUN FOR DINOSAUR AND OTHER IMAGINATIVE TALES
                                     DE CAMP, L. SPRAGUE   AC
   SOULS IN METAL   ASHLEY, MICHAEL   AN
INTERNATIONAL SMILE, THE   ALDISS, BRIAN W. SS   NEW 63 03
   AIRS OF EARTH, THE   ALDISS, BRIAN W.   AC
INTERPLANETARY COPYRIGHT (THE SHAPE OF COPYRIGHT TO COME)
                                     REINES, DONALD F. AR   FSF 53 04
   COMING ATTRACTIONS   GREENBERG, MARTIN   NF
INTERPLANETARY WARFARE (FROM "A TRUE HISTORY")
                                     LUCIAN OF SAMOSATA EX
   SCIENCE FICTION THROUGH THE AGES 1 EVANS, I. O.   AN
INTERPOSE   ZEBROWSKI, GEORGE SS INY 73 05
   INFINITY 5   HOSKINS, ROBERT   OA
   MONADIC UNIVERSE, THE   ZEBROWSKI, GEORGE   AC
INTERPRETATION OF A DREAM   COLLIER, JOHN   SS   NYM 51 05
   BEYOND THE BARRIERS OF SPACE AND TIME MERRIL, JUDITH   AN
   PERCHANCE TO DREAM   KNIGHT, DAMON   AN
INTERPRETER, THE   ALDISS, BRIAN W. SS
   BRIAN ALDISS OMNIBUS, A   ALDISS, BRIAN W.   AC
INTERROGATOR, THE   PRIEST, CHRISTOPHER NV NWR 69 15
   NEW WRITINGS IN SF. 15   CARNELL, JOHN   OA
INTERRUPTION IN CARNAGE   BUNCH, DAVID R. SS
   MODERAN   BUNCH, DAVID R.   AC
INTERSECTION POINT   COULSON, JUANITA NV
   STAR TREK: THE NEW VOYAGES   MARSHAK, S&CULBREATH OA
INTERSTATE, THE   SLADEK, JOHN T. SS   QRK 71 02
   QUARK/2   DELANY & HACKER   OA
INTERSTELLAR SEARCH, THE   CAMPBELL, JOHN W. JR SS
   INCREDIBLE PLANET, THE   CAMPBELL, JOHN W. JR NO
INTERSTELLAR ZOO, THE   KYLE, DAVID A.   AR
   TRAVELLERS OF SPACE   GREENBERG, MARTIN   AN
INTERURBAN QUEEN   LAFFERTY, R. A. SS   ORB 70 08
   LOOKING AHEAD   ALLEN, D. & L.   AN
   ORBIT 8   KNIGHT, DAMON   OA
   SURVIVAL PRINTOUT   TOTAL EFFECT   AN
INTERVAL IN SUNLIGHT   BRADBURY, RAY   NV   ESQ 54 03
   LONG AFTER MIDNIGHT   BRADBURY, RAY   AC
INTERVAL, THE   FAST, HOWARD   SS
   GENERAL ZAPPED AN ANGEL, THE   FAST, HOWARD   OC
INTERVIEW   FERGUSON, BIRD   PM   FSF 55 12
   BEST FROM FANTASY AND SCIENCE FICTION: 6
                                     BOUCHER, ANTHONY   AN
INTERVIEW   JAVOR, FRANK A. SS   ASF 63 11
   9TH ANNUAL OF THE YEAR'S BEST S-F, THE MERRIL, JUDITH   AN
INTERVIEW WITH A LEMMING   THURBER, JAMES   43
   BEST SF: 1967   HARRISON & ALDISS   AN
   SHOT IN THE DARK   MERRIL, JUDITH   AN
   ZOO 2000   YOLEN, JANE   AN
INTERVIEW WITH A TRAFFIC POLICEMAN
                                     DNIEPROV, ANATOLY SS
   OTHER WORLDS, OTHER SEAS   SUVIN, DARKO   AN
INTO MY OWN   YARBRO, CHELSEA Q. SS
   TOMORROW TODAY   ZEBROWSKI, GEORGE   OA
INTO SPACE   VERNE, JULES   NV
   GREAT SCIENCE FICTION STORIES   SMITH, CORDELIA T.   AN
INTO THE COMET (INSIDE THE COMET)
                                     CLARKE, ARTHUR C. SS   FSF 60 10
   BEST OF ARTHUR C. CLARKE: 1937-1971, THE CLARKE, ARTHUR C. AC
   OF TIME AND STARS   CLARKE, ARTHUR C.   AC
   TALES OF TEN WORLDS   CLARKE, ARTHUR C.   AC
INTO THE DARKNESS   ROCKLYNNE, ROSS NV   AST 40 06
   FUTURES UNLIMITED   NORTON, ALDEN H.   AN
   SUN DESTROYERS, THE   ROCKLYNNE, ROSS   DC
INTO THE FOURTH DIMENSION   CUMMINGS, RAY   NO   SAI 26 09
   INTO THE FOURTH DIMENSION   CUMMINGS, RAY   AC
INTO THE HYDROSPHERE   JONES, NEIL R.   SS   AMZ 33 10
   SUNLESS WORLD, THE   JONES, NEIL R.   AC
INTO THE LION'S DEN   NOLAN, WILLIAM F. SS   56
   IMPACT-20   NOLAN, WILLIAM F.   AC
INTO THE METEORITE ORBIT   KELLY, FRANK K. SS   AMZ 33 12
   SCIENCE FICTION OF THE 30'S   KNIGHT, DAMON   AN
INTO THE SHOP   GOULART, RON   SS   FSF 64 04
   BEST FROM FANTASY AND SCIENCE FICTION: 14
                                     DAVIDSON, AVRAM   AN
                                     AMIS & CONQUEST   AN
   SPECTRUM 4
   WHAT'S BECOME OF SCREWLOOSE? AND OTHER INQUIRIES
                                     GOULART, RON   AC
   YOU AND SCIENCE FICTION   HOLLISTER, BERNARD C AN

INTO THE UNKNOWN (FROM "20,000 LEAGUES UNDER THE SEA")
                          VERNE, JULES   EX   GMS 73
    SCIENCE FICTION THROUGH THE AGES 1   EVANS, I. O.   AN
INTO THY HANDS   DEL REY, LESTER   SS   ASF 45 08
    INVASION OF THE ROBOTS   ELWOOD, ROGER   AN
    LOOKING FORWARD   LESSER, MILTON   AN
    ROBOT AND THE MAN, THE   GREENBERG, MARTIN   AN
    ROBOTS AND CHANGELINGS   DEL REY, LESTER   AC
INTO YOUR TENT I'LL CREEP RUSSELL, ERIC FRANK SS ASF 57 09
    BEST SCIENCE FICTION STORIES AND NOVELS: 9TH SERIES
                          DIKTY, T. E.   AN
    LIKE NOTHING ON EARTH   RUSSELL, ERIC FRANK   AC
    SIX WORLDS YONDER   RUSSELL, ERIC FRANK   DC
INTRACOM   LE GUIN, URSULA K.   PL
    STOPWATCH   HAY, GEORGE   OA
INTREPID AERONAUT, THE (AN OLD TUNE)
                          FINNEY, JACK   NV   MCC 61 10
    I LOVE GALESBURG IN THE SPRINGTIME FINNEY, JACK   AC
INTRODUCTION   ACKERMAN, FORREST J. IN
    BEST SCIENCE FICTION FOR 1973   ACKERMAN, FORREST J. AN
    IF THIS GOES ON   NUETZEL, CHARLES   AN
    IMAGES OF TOMORROW   NUETZEL, CHARLES   AC
    SCIENCE FICTION WORLDS OF FORREST J. ACKERMAN & FRIENDS
                          ACKERMAN, FORREST J.   AC
    STARDRIFT AND OTHER FANTASTIC FLOTSAM PETAJA, EMIL   AC
INTRODUCTION   ALDISS, BRIAN W.   IN
    AIRS OF EARTH, THE   ALDISS, BRIAN W.   AC
    BEST FANTASY STORIES   ALDISS, BRIAN W.   AN
    *BEST SCIENCE FICTION STORIES OF BRIAN W. ALDISS
                          ALDISS, BRIAN W.   AC
    BOOK OF BRIAN ALDISS, THE   ALDISS, BRIAN W.   AC
    DECADE THE 1940S   ALDISS & HARRISON   AN
    EVIL EARTHS   ALDISS, BRIAN W.   AN
    GALACTIC EMPIRES VOLUME ONE   ALDISS, BRIAN W.   AN
    GALACTIC EMPIRES VOLUME TWO   ALDISS, BRIAN W.   AN
    GOLLANCZ - SUNDAY TIMES BEST SF STORIES ANONYMOUS   OA
    INTRODUCING SCIENCE FICTION   ALDISS, BRIAN W.   AN
    MORE PENGUIN SCIENCE FICTION   ALDISS, BRIAN W.   AN
    PENGUIN SCIENCE FICTION   ALDISS, BRIAN W.   AN
    PENGUIN SCIENCE FICTION OMNIBUS, THE ALDISS, BRIAN W. AN
    SPACE ODYSSEYS   ALDISS, BRIAN W.   AN
    SPACE OPERA   ALDISS, BRIAN W.   AN
    TWO TALES AND EIGHT TOMORROWS   HARRISON, HARRY   AC
    YET MORE PENGUIN SCIENCE FICTION ALDISS, BRIAN W.   AN
INTRODUCTION   ALDISS, BRIAN W.   IN C
    ASTOUNDING-ANALOG READER, THE VOLUME ONE HARRISON & ALDISS AN
    ASTOUNDING-ANALOG READER, THE VOLUME TWO HARRISON & ALDISS AN
    DECADE THE 1960S   ALDISS & HARRISON   AN
    NEBULA AWARD STORIES NO. 2   ALDISS & HARRISON   AN
INTRODUCTION   ALLEN, DICK   IN
    SCIENCE FICTION: THE FUTURE   ALLEN, DICK   AN
INTRODUCTION   AMIS, KINGSLEY   IN C
    *SPECTRUM   AMIS & CONQUEST   AN
    SPECTRUM   2   AMIS & CONQUEST   AN
    SPECTRUM   3   AMIS & CONQUEST   AN
    SPECTRUM   5   AMIS & CONQUEST   AN
INTRODUCTION   ANDERSON, POUL   IN
    BEST OF POUL ANDERSON, THE   ANDERSON, POUL   AC
    COMPLETE PEGHOOT, THE   BRIARTON, GRENDEL   AC
    FIRST STEP OUTWARD   HOSKINS, ROBERT   AN
    HOMEWARD AND BEYOND   ANDERSON, POUL   AC
    NEBULA AWARD STORIES NO. 4   ANDERSON, POUL   AN
INTRODUCTION   ASIMOV, ISAAC   IN
    ASIMOV'S MYSTERIES   ASIMOV, ISAAC   AC
    BEST OF ISAAC ASIMOV, THE   ASIMOV, ISAAC   AC
    FIRST FLIGHTS TO THE MOON   CLEMENT, HAL   AN
    HUGO WINNERS, THE (VOLUME 1)   ASIMOV, ISAAC   AC
    I, ROBOT   ASIMOV, ISAAC   AC
    MORE SOVIET SCIENCE FICTION   ANONYMOUS   AN
    OPUS 100   ASIMOV, ISAAC   AC
    *REST OF THE ROBOTS, THE   ASIMOV, ISAAC   AC
    SOVIET SCIENCE FICTION   ANONYMOUS   AN
    TOMORROW'S CHILDREN   ASIMOV, ISAAC   AN
    WHERE DO WE GO FROM HERE?   ASIMOV, ISAAC   AN
INTRODUCTION   BAILEY, HILARY   IN
    NEW WORLDS EIGHT   BAILEY, HILARY   OA
INTRODUCTION   BALCHIN, NIGEL   IN
    AD 2500   WILSON, ANGUS   AN
INTRODUCTION   BALLARD, J. G.   IN
    BEST OF J. G. BALLARD, THE   BALLARD, J. G.   AC
INTRODUCTION   BATTEAU, DWIGHT W. IN
    COMING ATTRACTIONS   GREENBERG, MARTIN   NF
INTRODUCTION   BAXTER, JOHN   IN
    PACIFIC BOOK OF AUSTRALIAN SCIENCE FICTION
                          BAXTER, JOHN   AN
    SECOND PACIFIC BOOK OF SCIENCE FICTION, THE
                          BAXTER, JOHN   AN
INTRODUCTION   BEAUMONT, CHARLES IN
    FIEND IN YOU, THE   BEAUMONT, CHARLES   AN
INTRODUCTION   BENSEN, D. R.   IN
    UNKNOWN 5, THE   BENSEN, D. R.   AN
    UNKNOWN, THE   BENSEN, D. R.   AN
INTRODUCTION   BIGGLE, LLOYD JR. IN
    GALAXY OF STRANGERS, A   BIGGLE, LLOYD JR.   AC
    NEBULA AWARD STORIES NO. 7   BIGGLE, LLOYD JR.   AN
    RULE OF THE DOOR AND OTHER FANCIFUL REGULATIONS
                          BIGGLE, LLOYD JR.   AC
INTRODUCTION   BLEILER, EVERETT F. IN C
    *IMAGINATION UNLIMITED   BLEILER & DIKTY   AN
    YEAR'S BEST SCIENCE FICTION NOVELS: 1953 BLEILER & DIKTY AN
    YEAR'S BEST SCIENCE FICTION NOVELS: 1954 BLEILER & DIKTY AN
INTRODUCTION   BLISH, JAMES   IN
    BEST OF JOHN W. CAMPBELL, THE (BRITISH) CAMPBELL, JOHN W. JR AC
    NEBULA AWARD STORIES NO. 5   BLISH, JAMES   AN
INTRODUCTION   BLOCH, ROBERT   IN
    BEST OF FREDRIC BROWN, THE   BROWN, FREDRIC   AC

    COLD CHILLS   BLOCH, ROBERT   AC
    HOUSE OF THE HATCHET, THE   BLOCH, ROBERT   AC
    KING OF TERRORS, THE   BLOCH, ROBERT   AC
    LIVING DEMONS, THE   BLOCH, ROBERT   AC
    *OPENER OF THE WAY, THE   BLOCH, ROBERT   AC
    YOURS TRULY, JACK THE RIPPER   BLOCH, ROBERT   AC
INTRODUCTION   BOARDMAN, TOM JR. IN
    ABC OF SCIENCE FICTION, AN   BOARDMAN, TOM JR.   AN
    CONNOISSEUR'S S. F.   BOARDMAN, TOM JR.   AN
    UNFRIENDLY FUTURE, THE   BOARDMAN, TOM JR.   AN
INTRODUCTION   BOUCHER, ANTHONY   IN
    BEST FROM FANTASY AND SCIENCE FICTION: 4
                          BOUCHER, ANTHONY   AN
    BEST FROM FANTASY AND SCIENCE FICTION: 6
                          BOUCHER, ANTHONY   AN
    BEST FROM FANTASY AND SCIENCE FICTION: 7
                          BOUCHER, ANTHONY   AN
    BEST FROM FANTASY AND SCIENCE FICTION: 8
                          BOUCHER, ANTHONY   AN
    FAR OUT   KNIGHT, DAMON   AC
INTRODUCTION   BOUCHER, ANTHONY   IN C
    BEST FROM FANTASY AND SCIENCE FICTION BOUCHER & MCCOMAS AN
    BEST FROM FANTASY AND SCIENCE FICTION: 2
                          BOUCHER & MCCOMAS   AN
    BEST FROM FANTASY AND SCIENCE FICTION: 3
                          BOUCHER & MCCOMAS   AN
INTRODUCTION   BOVA, BEN   IN
    ANALOG 9   BOVA, BEN   AN
    FORWARD IN TIME   BOVA, BEN   AC
    MANY WORLDS OF SCIENCE FICTION, THE BOVA, BEN   OA
    NEW VOICES IN SCIENCE FICTION   MARTIN, GEORGE R. R. OA
    SCIENCE FICTION HALL OF FAME VOLUME 2A BOVA, BEN   AN
    SCIENCE FICTION HALL OF FAME VOLUME 2B BOVA, BEN   AN
INTRODUCTION   BRADBURY, RAY   IN
    CIRCUS OF DR. LAO AND OTHER IMPROBABLE STORIES
                          BRADBURY, RAY   AN
    PILLAR OF FIRE AND OTHER PLAYS   BRADBURY, RAY   AC
    R IS FOR ROCKET   BRADBURY, RAY   AC
    S IS FOR SPACE   BRADBURY, RAY   AC
    TIMELESS STORIES FOR TODAY AND TOMORROW BRADBURY, RAY AC
    WITHOUT SORCERY   STURGEON, THEODORE   AC
INTRODUCTION   BRADLEY, MARION Z. IN
    DARK INTRUDER & OTHER STORIES, THE BRADLEY, MARION Z. DC
INTRODUCTION   BROWN, ELIZABETH   IN
    PARADOX LOST, AND 12 OTHER GREAT S.F. STORIES
                          BROWN, FREDRIC   AC
INTRODUCTION   BROWN, FREDRIC   IN
    ANGELS AND SPACESHIPS   BROWN, FREDRIC   AC
    HUMAN?   MERRIL, JUDITH   AN
    *SCIENCE-FICTION CARNIVAL   BROWN, F. & REYNOLDS AN
    SPACE ON MY HANDS   BROWN, FREDRIC   AC
INTRODUCTION   BRUNNER, JOHN   IN
    TIME-JUMP   BRUNNER, JOHN   AC
INTRODUCTION   BUDRYS, ALGIS   IN
    BUDRYS' INFERNO   BUDRYS, ALGIS   AC
INTRODUCTION   BUNCH, DAVID R.   IN
    MODERAN   BUNCH, DAVID R.   AC
INTRODUCTION   BURTON, S. H.   IN
    SCIENCE FICTION   BURTON, S. H.   AN
INTRODUCTION   CAMPBELL, JOHN W. JR IN
    ANALOG 1   CAMPBELL, JOHN W. JR AN
    ANALOG 3   CAMPBELL, JOHN W. JR AN
    ANALOG 6   CAMPBELL, JOHN W. JR AN
    *ASTOUNDING SCIENCE FICTION ANTHOLOGY, THE
                          CAMPBELL, JOHN W. JR   AC
    BLACK STAR PASSES, THE   CAMPBELL, JOHN W. JR AC
    CLOAK OF AESIR   CAMPBELL, JOHN W. JR AC
    *MAN WHO SOLD THE MOON, THE   HEINLEIN, ROBERT A.   AC
    PROLOGUE TO ANALOG   CAMPBELL, JOHN W. JR AC
    VENUS EQUILATERAL   SMITH, GEORGE O.   AC
    14 GREAT TALES OF ESP   STONE, IDELLA P.   AC
INTRODUCTION   CARLFI, CHESTER H. IN
    CRAZY MIXED-UP PLANET   FRITCH, CHARLES E.   AC
INTRODUCTION   CARNELL, JOHN   IN
    WEIRD SHADOWS FROM BEYOND   CARNELL, JOHN   AN
INTRODUCTION   CARR, TERRY   IN
    BEST SCIENCE FICTION OF THE YEAR, THE   CARR, TERRY   AN
    BEST SCIENCE FICTION OF THE YEAR, THE NO. 2
                          CARR, TERRY   AN
    BEST SCIENCE FICTION OF THE YEAR, THE NO. 3
                          CARR, TERRY   AN
    BEST SCIENCE FICTION OF THE YEAR, THE NO. 4
                          CARR, TERRY   AN
    BEST SCIENCE FICTION OF THE YEAR, THE NO. 5
                          CARR, TERRY   AN
    CREATURES FROM BEYOND   CARR, TERRY   AN
    EXALTATION OF STARS, AN   CARR, TERRY   OA
    FELLOWSHIP OF THE STARS   CARR, TERRY   OA
    INFINITE ARENA, THE   CARR, TERRY   AN
    INTO THE UNKNOWN   CARR, TERRY   AN
    NEW WORLDS OF FANTASY   CARR, TERRY   AN
    NEW WORLDS OF FANTASY NO. 2   CARR, TERRY   AN
    NEW WORLDS OF FANTASY NO. 3   CARR, TERRY   AN
    ON OUR WAY TO THE FUTURE   CARR, TERRY   AN
    SCIENCE FICTION FOR PEOPLE WHO HATE SCIENCE FICTION
                          CARR, TERRY   AN
    STARSHADOWS   SARGENT, PAMELA   AC
    THIS SIDE OF INFINITY   CARR, TERRY   AN
    UNIVERSE 1   CARR, TERRY   OA
    UNIVERSE 3   CARR, TERRY   OA
    WORLDS FAR AND NEAR   CARR, TERRY   AN
INTRODUCTION   CARR, TERRY   IN C
    WORLD'S BEST SCIENCE FICTION: 1965 WOLLHEIM & CARR   AN
    WORLD'S BEST SCIENCE FICTION: 1966 WOLLHEIM & CARR   AN
    WORLD'S BEST SCIENCE FICTION: 1967 WOLLHEIM & CARR   AN
    WORLD'S BEST SCIENCE FICTION: 1968 WOLLHEIM & CARR   AN

INTRODUCTION

WORLD'S BEST SCIENCE FICTION: 1969   WOLLHEIM & CARR   AN
WORLD'S BEST SCIENCE FICTION: 1970   WOLLHEIM & CARR   AN
WORLD'S BEST SCIENCE FICTION: 1971   WOLLHEIM & CARR   AN
INTRODUCTION   CERF, CHRISTOPHER   IN
VINTAGE ANTHOLOGY OF SCIENCE FANTASY, THE
                          CERF, CHRISTOPHER   AN
INTRODUCTION   CHEETHAM, ANTHONY   IN
BUG-EYED MONSTERS   CHEETHAM, ANTHONY   AN
SCIENCE AGAINST MAN   CHEETHAM, ANTHONY   OA
INTRODUCTION   CHETWYND-HAYES, R.   IN
TALES OF TERROR FROM OUTER SPACE   CHETWYND-HAYES, R.   AN
INTRODUCTION   CLARK, JOHN D.   IN
PETRIFIED PLANET, THE   CLARK, JOHN D.   OA
INTRODUCTION   CLARKE, ARTHUR C.   IN
COMPLETE VENUS EQUILATERAL, THE   SMITH, GEORGE O.   AC
FROM THE OCEAN, FROM THE STARS   CLARKE, ARTHUR C.   AC
NINE BILLION NAMES OF GOD, THE   CLARKE, ARTHUR C.   AC
INTRODUCTION   CLEAR, VAL   IN C
MARRIAGE AND THE FAMILY THROUGH SCIENCE FICTION
                          CLEAR/WARRICK/&   AN
INTRODUCTION   CONEY, MICHAEL G.   IN
MONITOR FOUND IN ORBIT   CONEY, MICHAEL G.   AC
INTRODUCTION   CONKLIN, GROFF   IN
ADVENTURES IN DIMENSION   CONKLIN, GROFF   AN
*BEST OF SCIENCE FICTION   CONKLIN, GROFF   AN
*BIG BOOK OF SCIENCE FICTION   CONKLIN, GROFF   AN
BR-R-R-!   CONKLIN, GROFF   AN
ELSEWHERE AND ELSEWHEN   CONKLIN, GROFF   AN
FIVE-ODD   CONKLIN, GROFF   AN
GRAVEYARD READER, THE   CONKLIN, GROFF   AN
GREAT STORIES OF SPACE TRAVEL   CONKLIN, GROFF   AN
*INVADERS OF EARTH   CONKLIN, GROFF   AN
OMNIBUS OF SCIENCE FICTION   CONKLIN, GROFF   AN
OPERATION FUTURE   CONKLIN, GROFF   AN
*POSSIBLE WORLDS OF SCIENCE FICTION   CONKLIN, GROFF   AN
*SCIENCE FICTION ADVENTURES IN DIMENSION CONKLIN, GROFF   AN
*SCIENCE FICTION ADVENTURES IN MUTATION CONKLIN, GROFF   AN
SCIENCE FICTION GALAXY, THE   CONKLIN, GROFF   AN
SCIENCE FICTION ODDITIES   CONKLIN, GROFF   AN
SCIENCE FICTION TERROR TALES   CONKLIN, GROFF   AN
*SCIENCE FICTION THINKING MACHINES   CONKLIN, GROFF   AN
SEVEN TRIPS THROUGH TIME AND SPACE   CONKLIN, GROFF   AN
SIX GREAT SHORT SCIENCE FICTION NOVELS CONKLIN, GROFF   AN
STRANGE ADVENTURES IN SCIENCE FICTION CONKLIN, GROFF   AN
STRANGE TRAVELS IN SCIENCE FICTION   CONKLIN, GROFF   AN
SUPERNATURAL READER, THE   CONKLIN, G&L.   AN
THUNDER AND ROSES   STURGEON, THEODORE   AC
*TREASURY OF SCIENCE FICTION, A   CONKLIN, GROFF   AN
*TWISTED   CONKLIN, GROFF   AN
*WAY HOME, A   STURGEON, THEODORE   AC
12 GREAT CLASSICS OF SCIENCE FICTION CONKLIN, GROFF   AN
13 ABOVE THE NIGHT   CONKLIN, GROFF   AN
13 GREAT STORIES OF SCIENCE FICTION   CONKLIN, GROFF   AN
17 X INFINITY   CONKLIN, GROFF   AN
6 GREAT SHORT NOVELS OF SCIENCE FICTION CONKLIN, GROFF   AN
INTRODUCTION   CONKLIN, GROFF   IN C
GREAT SCIENCE FICTION ABOUT DOCTORS   CONKLIN, G&FABRICANT   AN
INTRODUCTION   CONQUEST, ROBERT   IN
ROBERT SHECKLEY OMNIBUS, THE   SHECKLEY, ROBERT   AC
INTRODUCTION   CONQUEST, ROBERT   IN C
*SPECTRUM   AMIS & CONQUEST   AN
SPECTRUM   2   AMIS & CONQUEST   AN
SPECTRUM   3   AMIS & CONQUEST   AN
SPECTRUM   5   AMIS & CONQUEST   AN
INTRODUCTION   COOPER, EDMUND   IN
UNBORN TOMORROW   COOPER, EDMUND   AC
INTRODUCTION   CRISPIN, EDMUND   IN
BEST SCIENCE FICTION STORIES OF C. M. KORNBLUTH
                          KORNBLUTH, C. M.   AC
BEST SF   CRISPIN, EDMUND   AN
BEST SF   2   CRISPIN, EDMUND   AN
BEST SF   3   CRISPIN, EDMUND   AN
BEST SF   4   CRISPIN, EDMUND   AN
BEST SF   5   CRISPIN, EDMUND   AN
INTRODUCTION   CURREY, L. W.   IN C
BATTLE OF THE MONSTERS AND OTHER STORIES, THE
                          HARTWELL & CURREY   AN
INTRODUCTION   DALY, MARSHA   IN
AND WALK NOW GENTLY THROUGH THE FIRE... ELWOOD, ROGER   OA
INTRODUCTION   DANN, JACK M.   IN   SCS 73
SHOWCASE   ELWOOD, ROGER   OA
INTRODUCTION   DANN, JACK M.   IN C
FUTURE POWER   DANN & DOZOIS   OA
INTRODUCTION   DAVENPORT, BASIL   IN
DEALS WITH THE DEVIL   DAVENPORT, BASIL   AN
INTRODUCTION   DAVIDSON, AVRAM   IN
BEST FROM FANTASY AND SCIENCE FICTION: 12
                          DAVIDSON, AVRAM   AN
BEST FROM FANTASY AND SCIENCE FICTION: 13
                          DAVIDSON, AVRAM   AN
BEST FROM FANTASY AND SCIENCE FICTION: 14
                          DAVIDSON, AVRAM   AN
STRANGE SEAS AND SHORES   DAVIDSON, AVRAM   AC
WHAT STRANGE STARS AND SKIES   DAVIDSON, AVRAM   AC
WORLDS OF ROBERT F. YOUNG, THE   YOUNG, ROBERT F.   AC
INTRODUCTION   DAVIS, BRIAN   IN
BEST OF MURRAY LEINSTER, THE   LEINSTER, MURRAY   AC
INTRODUCTION   DAVIS, RICHARD   IN
YEAR'S BEST HORROR STORIES: SERIES III, THE
                          DAVIS, RICHARD   AN
INTRODUCTION   DE CAMP, L. SPRAGUE   IN
COMING OF CONAN, THE   HOWARD, ROBERT E.   AC
CONAN   HOWARD, R./DE CAMP/&   AC
CONAN THE ADVENTURER   HOWARD, R. & DE CAMP   AC
CONAN THE AVENGER   HOWARD, R./NYBERG/&   AC
CONAN THE FREEBOOTER   HOWARD, R. & DE CAMP   AC

CONAN THE USURPER   HOWARD, R. & DE CAMP   AC
CONAN THE WANDERER   HOWARD, R./DE CAMP/&   AC
CONAN THE WARRIOR   HOWARD, R. & DE CAMP   AC
KING CONAN   HOWARD, ROBERT E.   AC
INTRODUCTION   DE LA REE, GERRY   IN
HORROR ON THE ASTEROID AND OTHER TALES OF PLANETARY HORROR
                          HAMILTON, EDMOND   AC
INTRODUCTION   DEFORD, MIRIAM ALLEN   IN
SPACE, TIME & CRIME   DEFORD, MIRIAM ALLEN   AN
INTRODUCTION   DEL REY, LESTER   IN
FANTASTIC UNIVERSE OMNIBUS, THE   SANTESSON, HANS S.   AN
INTRODUCTION   DELANY, SAMUEL R.   IN
ALYX   RUSS, JOANNA   AC
INTRODUCTION   DELANY, SAMUEL R.   IN C
QUARK/2   DELANY & HACKER   OA
INTRODUCTION   DERLETH, AUGUST   IN
*BEACHHEADS IN SPACE   DERLETH, AUGUST   AN
*BEYOND TIME AND SPACE   DERLETH, AUGUST   AN
FROM OTHER WORLDS   DERLETH, AUGUST   AN
HAUNTER OF THE DARK, THE   LOVECRAFT, H. P.   AC
MR. GEORGE AND OTHER ODD PERSONS   DERLETH, AUGUST   AC
PORTALS OF TOMORROW   DERLETH, AUGUST   AN
*STRANGE PORTS OF CALL   DERLETH, AUGUST   AN
*WORLDS OF TOMORROW   DERLETH, AUGUST   AN
INTRODUCTION   DICKSON, GORDON R.   IN
FUTURELOVE   ELWOOD, ROGER   OA
MUTANTS   DICKSON, GORDON R.   AC
THREE TO DORSAI!   DICKSON, GORDON R.   AC
INTRODUCTION   DIKTY, T. E.   IN C
*IMAGINATION UNLIMITED   BLEILER & DIKTY   AN
YEAR'S BEST SCIENCE FICTION NOVELS: 1953 BLEILER & DIKTY   AN
YEAR'S BEST SCIENCE FICTION NOVELS: 1954 BLEILER & DIKTY   AN
INTRODUCTION   DILLON, JOHN   IN C
LATE GREAT FUTURE, THE   FITZ GERALD & DILLON   AN
INTRODUCTION   DISCH, THOMAS M.   IN
*ONE HUNDRED AND TWO H-BOMBS   DISCH, THOMAS M.   AC
INTRODUCTION   DOHERTY, G. D.   IN
SECOND ORBIT   DOHERTY, G. D.   AN
STORIES FROM SCIENCE FICTION   DOHERTY, G. D.   AN
INTRODUCTION   DONALDY, ERNESTINE   IN C
GATES TO TOMORROW   NORTON, AN.&DONALDY   AN
INTRODUCTION   DOZOIS, GARDNER R.   IN
ANOTHER WORLD   DOZOIS, GARDNER R.   AN
DAY IN THE LIFE, A   DOZOIS, GARDNER R.   AN
INTRODUCTION   DOZOIS, GARDNER R.   IN C
FUTURE POWER   DANN & DOZOIS   OA
INTRODUCTION   EISENBERG, LARRY   IN
BEST LAID SCHEMES, THE   EISENBERG, LARRY   AC
INTRODUCTION   ELLISON, HARLAN   IN
TOUCH OF INFINITY, A   ELLISON, HARLAN   DC
INTRODUCTION   ELWOOD, ROGER   IN
BERSERKERS, THE   ELWOOD, ROGER   OA
CONTINUUM 1   ELWOOD, ROGER   OA
CONTINUUM 2   ELWOOD, ROGER   OA
CONTINUUM 3   ELWOOD, ROGER   OA
CRISIS   ELWOOD, ROGER   OA
DEMON KIND   ELWOOD, ROGER   OA
DYSTOPIAN VISIONS   ELWOOD, ROGER   OA
FUTURE KIN   ELWOOD, ROGER   OA
INVASION OF THE ROBOTS   ELWOOD, ROGER   AN
LEARNING MAZE AND OTHER STORIES, THE ELWOOD, ROGER   OA
OTHER SIDE OF TOMORROW, THE   ELWOOD, ROGER   OA
SCIENCE FICTION ADVENTURES FROM WAY OUT ELWOOD, ROGER   OA
SIGNS AND WONDERS   ELWOOD, ROGER   OA
SIX SCIENCE FICTION PLAYS   ELWOOD, ROGER   AN
INTRODUCTION   ELWOOD, ROGER   IN C
EPOCH   ELWOOD & SILVERBERG   OA
INTRODUCTION   EVANS, I. O.   IN
JULES VERNE- MASTER OF SCIENCE FICTION VERNE, JULES   AC
SCIENCE FICTION THROUGH THE AGES 1   EVANS, I. O.   AN
SCIENCE FICTION THROUGH THE AGES 2   EVANS, I. O.   AN
YESTERDAY AND TOMORROW   VERNE, JULES   AC
INTRODUCTION   FABRICANT, NOAH D.   IN C
GREAT SCIENCE FICTION ABOUT DOCTORS   CONKLIN, G&FABRICANT   AN
INTRODUCTION   FADIMAN, CLIFTON   IN
ACROSS THE SEA OF STARS   CLARKE, ARTHUR C.   AC
FANTASIA MATHEMATICA   FADIMAN, CLIFTON   AN
GREAT STORIES OF SCIENCE FICTION   LEINSTER, MURRAY   AN
MATHEMATICAL MAGPIE, THE   FADIMAN, CLIFTON   AN
INTRODUCTION   FAST, HOWARD   IN
TIME AND THE RIDDLE   FAST, HOWARD   AC
INTRODUCTION   FERMAN, EDWARD L.   IN
BEST FROM FANTASY AND SCIENCE FICTION: 15
                          FERMAN, EDWARD L.   AN
BEST FROM FANTASY AND SCIENCE FICTION: 16
                          FERMAN, EDWARD L.   AN
BEST FROM FANTASY AND SCIENCE FICTION: 17
                          FERMAN, EDWARD L.   AN
BEST FROM FANTASY AND SCIENCE FICTION, 25TH ANNIV.
                          FERMAN, EDWARD L.   AN
INTRODUCTION   FERMAN, EDWARD L.   IN C
FINAL STAGE   FERMAN & MALZBERG   OA
INTRODUCTION   FIEDLER, LESLIE A.   IN
IN DREAMS AWAKE   FIEDLER, LESLIE A.   AN
INTRODUCTION   FITZ GERALD, GREGORY   IN C
LATE GREAT FUTURE, THE   FITZ GERALD & DILLON   AN
PAST, PRESENT, AND FUTURE PERFECT   WOLFE, J&FITZ GERALD   AN
INTRODUCTION   FLOOD, LESLIE   IN
BEST OF JOHN WYNDHAM, THE   WYNDHAM, JOHN   AC
INTRODUCTION   FRANKLIN, H. BRUCE   IN
FUTURE PERFECT   FRANKLIN, H. BRUCE   AN
INTRODUCTION   FREMAN, EDWARD L.   IN
ARENA: SPORTS SF   FERMAN & MALZBERG   AN
INTRODUCTION   FRIEND, OSCAR J.   IN C
*MY BEST SCIENCE FICTION STORY   MARGULIES & FRIEND   AN

INTRODUCTION

Title	Author	Code
INTRODUCTION	GARNETT, RICHARD,LLD	IN
TALES AND STORIES	SHELLEY, MARY W.	AC
INTRODUCTION	GERROLD, DAVID	IN
ALTERNATIES	GERROLD, DAVID	OA
GENERATION	GERROLD, DAVID	OA
SCIENCE FICTION EMPHASIS NO. 1	GERROLD, DAVID	OA
INTRODUCTION	GHIDALIA, VIC	IN
DEVIL'S GENERATION, THE	GHIDALIA, VIC	AN
INTRODUCTION	GINSBURG, MIRRA	IN
LAST DOOR TO AIYA	GINSBURG, MIRRA	AN
INTRODUCTION	GOLDIN, STEPHEN	IN
ALIEN CONDITION, THE	GOLDIN, STEPHEN	OA
INTRODUCTION	GREENBERG, MARTIN H.	IN C
BEST OF JOHN JAKES, THE	JAKES, JOHN W.	AC
MARRIAGE AND THE FAMILY THROUGH SCIENCE FICTION	CLEAR/WARRICK/&	AN
NEW AWARENESS, THE	WARRICK & GREENBERG	AN
POLITICAL SCIENCE FICTION	GREENBERG& WARRICK	AN
RUN TO STARLIGHT, SPORTS THROUGH SCIENCE FICTION	GREENBERG/OLANDER/&	AN
SCHOOL AND SOCIETY THROUGH SCIENCE FICTION	OLANDER/GREENBERG/&	AN
SOCIAL PROBLEMS THROUGH SCIENCE FICTION	GREENBERG/MILSTEAD/&	AN
SOCIOLOGY THROUGH SCIENCE FICTION	MILSTEAD/GREENBERG/&	AN
TOMORROW, INC.	GREENBERG& OLANDER	AN
INTRODUCTION	GUNN, JAMES E.	IN
BREAKING POINT	GUNN, JAMES E.	AC
END OF THE DREAMS, THE	GUNN, JAMES E.	AC
NEBULA AWARD STORIES 10	GUNN, JAMES E.	AN
SOME DREAMS ARE NIGHTMARES	GUNN, JAMES E.	AC
INTRODUCTION	HACKER, MARILYN	IN C
QUARK/2	DELANY & HACKER	OA
INTRODUCTION	HAINING, PETER	IN
FANTASTIC PULPS, THE	HAINING, PETER	AN
FUTURE MAKERS, THE	HAINING, PETER	AN
INTRODUCTION	HALDEMAN, JOE W.	IN
COSMIC LAUGHTER	HALDEMAN, JOE W.	AN
INTRODUCTION	HARRISON, HARRY	IN
BEST SF: 1967	HARRISON & ALDISS	AN
BEST SF: 1968	HARRISON & ALDISS	AN
BEST SF: 1969	HARRISON & ALDISS	AN
BEST SF: 1971	HARRISON & ALDISS	AN
BEST SF: 1972	HARRISON & ALDISS	AN
BEST SF: 1973	HARRISON & ALDISS	AN
BEST SF: 75, THE NINTH ANNUAL	HARRISON & ALDISS	AN
DECADE THE 1950S	ALDISS & HARRISON	AN
FOUR FOR THE FUTURE	HARRISON, HARRY	AN
*NOVA 1	HARRISON, HARRY	OA
NOVA 2	HARRISON, HARRY	OA
SF: AUTHORS' CHOICE	HARRISON, HARRY	AN
SF: AUTHORS' CHOICE 2	HARRISON, HARRY	AN
SF: AUTHORS' CHOICE 3	HARRISON, HARRY	AN
TEN THOUSAND LIGHT-YEARS FROM HOME	TIPTREE, JAMES JR.	AC
WORLDS OF WONDER	HARRISON, HARRY	AN
INTRODUCTION	HARRISON, HARRY	IN C
APEMAN, SPACEMAN	STOVER & HARRISON	AN
ASTOUNDING-ANALOG READER, THE VOLUME ONE	HARRISON & ALDISS	AN
ASTOUNDING-ANALOG READER, THE VOLUME TWO	HARRISON & ALDISS	AN
DECADE THE 1960S	ALDISS & HARRISON	AN
NEBULA AWARD STORIES NO. 2	ALDISS & HARRISON	AN
INTRODUCTION	HARTWELL, DAVID G.	IN C
BATTLE OF THE MONSTERS AND OTHER STORIES, THE	HARTWELL & CURREY	AN
INTRODUCTION	HAY, GEORGE	IN
STOPWATCH	HAY, GEORGE	OA
INTRODUCTION	HEALY, RAYMOND J.	IN
NEW TALES OF SPACE AND TIME	HEALY, RAYMOND J.	OA
INTRODUCTION	HEINLEIN, ROBERT A.	IN
BEST FROM STARTLING STORIES, THE	MINES, SAMUEL	AN
BEST OF ROBERT HEINLEIN, THE	HEINLEIN, ROBERT A.	AC
TOMORROW, THE STARS	HEINLEIN, ROBERT A.	AN
INTRODUCTION	HERBERT, FRANK	IN
BEST OF FRANK HERBERT, THE	HERBERT, FRANK	AC
SAVING WORLDS	ELWOOD & KIDD	OA
INTRODUCTION	HIGHET, GILBERT	IN
VINTAGE BRADBURY, THE	BRADBURY, RAY	AC
INTRODUCTION	HILL, DOUGLAS	IN
DEVIL HIS DUE, THE	HILL, DOUGLAS	AN
INTRODUCTION	HOLLISTER, BERNARD C	IN
ANOTHER TOMORROW	HOLLISTER, BERNARD C	AN
YOU AND SCIENCE FICTION	HOLLISTER, BERNARD C	AN
INTRODUCTION	HOSKINS, ROBERT	IN
FAR-OUT PEOPLE, THE	HOSKINS, ROBERT	AN
FUTURE NOW, THE	HOSKINS, ROBERT	AN
LIBERATED FUTURE: VOYAGES INTO TOMORROW, THE	HOSKINS, ROBERT	AN
STARS AROUND US, THE	HOSKINS, ROBERT	AN
STRANGE TOMORROWS	HOSKINS, ROBERT	AN
TOMORROW 1	HOSKINS, ROBERT	AN
INTRODUCTION	JONES, LANGDON	IN
EYE OF THE LENS, THE	JONES, LANGDON	AC
INTRODUCTION	KANDEL, MICHAEL	IN
MORTAL ENGINES	LEM, STANISLAW	AC
INTRODUCTION	KEYES, NOEL	IN
CONTACT	KEYES, NOEL	AN
INTRODUCTION	KIDD, VIRGINIA	IN
BEST OF JUDITH MERRIL, THE	MERRIL, JUDITH	AC
INTRODUCTION	KNIGHT, DAMON	IN
BEST OF DAMON KNIGHT, THE	KNIGHT, DAMON	AC
BEYOND TOMORROW	KNIGHT, DAMON	AN
CASEY AGONISTES, AND OTHER S.F. & FANTASY STORIES	MCKENNA, RICHARD M.	AC
CENTURY OF SCIENCE FICTION, A	KNIGHT, DAMON	AN
CITIES OF WONDER	KNIGHT, DAMON	AN
DARK SIDE, THE	KNIGHT, DAMON	AN
FIRST CONTACT	KNIGHT, DAMON	AN
FIRST FLIGHT	KNIGHT, DAMON	AN
GOLDEN ROAD, THE	KNIGHT, DAMON	AN
NEBULA AWARD STORIES	KNIGHT, DAMON	AN
ONE HUNDRED YEARS OF SCIENCE FICTION	KNIGHT, DAMON	AN
ORBIT 1	KNIGHT, DAMON	OA
PAST THROUGH TOMORROW, THE	HEINLEIN, ROBERT A.	AC
PERCHANCE TO DREAM	KNIGHT, DAMON	AN
POCKETFUL OF STARS, A	KNIGHT, DAMON	AN
SCIENCE FICTION ARGOSY, A	KNIGHT, DAMON	AN
SCIENCE FICTION INVENTIONS	KNIGHT, DAMON	AN
SHAPE OF THINGS, THE	KNIGHT, DAMON	AN
TOMORROW X 4	KNIGHT, DAMON	AN
TOWARD INFINITY	KNIGHT, DAMON	AN
WORLDS TO COME	KNIGHT, DAMON	AN
13 FRENCH SCIENCE-FICTION STORIES	KNIGHT, DAMON	AN
INTRODUCTION	KOONTZ, DEAN R.	IN
SOFT COME THE DRAGONS	KOONTZ, DEAN R.	DC
INTRODUCTION	KUEBLER, HAROLD W.	IN
TREASURY OF SCIENCE FICTION CLASSICS, THE	KUEBLER, HAROLD W.	AN
INTRODUCTION	LE GUIN, URSULA K.	IN
NEBULA AWARD STORIES 11	LE GUIN, URSULA K.	AN
INTRODUCTION	LEAVITT, HART DAY	IN
INEXPERIENCED GHOST AND NINE OTHER STORIES, THE	WELLS, H. G.	AC
INTRODUCTION	LEIBER, FRITZ	IN
GLASS OF STARS, A	YOUNG, ROBERT F.	AC
SECRET SONGS, THE	LEIBER, FRITZ	AC
WORLDS OF FRITZ LEIBER, THE	LEIBER, FRITZ	AC
INTRODUCTION	LEY, WILLY	IN
*MEN AGAINST THE STARS	GREENBERG, MARTIN	AN
TRAVELLERS OF SPACE	GREENBERG, MARTIN	AN
INTRODUCTION	LOCKE, GEORGE	IN
WORLDS APART	LOCKE, GEORGE	AN
INTRODUCTION	LONG, FRANK BELKNAP	IN
EARLY LONG, THE	LONG, FRANK BELKNAP	AC
INTRODUCTION	LOWENKOPF, SHELLY	IN
WILDERNESS OF STARS, A	NOLAN, WILLIAM F.	AN
INTRODUCTION	LUCIE-SMITH, EDWARD	IN
HOLDING YOUR EIGHT HANDS	LUCIE-SMITH, EDWARD	AN
INTRODUCTION	MAGIDOFF, ROBERT	IN
RUSSIAN SCIENCE FICTION	MAGIDOFF, ROBERT	AN
RUSSIAN SCIENCE FICTION, 1968	MAGIDOFF, ROBERT	AN
INTRODUCTION	MALZBERG, BARRY N.	IN
BEST OF BARRY N. MALZBERG, THE	MALZBERG, BARRY N.	AC
BEST OF KEITH LAUMER, THE	LAUMER, KEITH	AC
MANY WORLDS OF BARRY MALZBERG, THE	MALZBERG, BARRY N.	AC
OUT FROM GANYMEDE	MALZBERG, BARRY N.	AC
INTRODUCTION	MALZBERG, BARRY N.	IN C
FINAL STAGE	FERMAN & MALZBERG	OA
INTRODUCTION	MANSFIELD, ROGER	IN
STARLIT CORRIDOR, THE	MANSFIELD, ROGER	AN
INTRODUCTION	MARGULIES, LEO	IN
GHOUL KEEPERS, THE	MARGULIES, LEO	AN
UNEXPECTED, THE	MARGULIES, LEO	AN
WEIRD TALES	MARGULIES, LEO	AN
3 IN 1	MARGULIES, LEO	AN
INTRODUCTION	MARGULIES, LEO	IN C
*MY BEST SCIENCE FICTION STORY	MARGULIES & FRIEND	AN
INTRODUCTION	MARTIN, GEORGE R. R.	IN
SONGS OF STARS AND SHADOWS	MARTIN, GEORGE R. R.	AC
INTRODUCTION	MAUROIS, ANDRE	IN
WEIGHER OF SOULS AND THE EARTH DWELLERS, THE	MAUROIS, ANDRE	AC
INTRODUCTION	MCCAFFREY, ANNE	IN
GET OFF THE UNICORN	MCCAFFREY, ANNE	AC
INTRODUCTION	MCCOMAS, J. FRANCIS	IN
SPECIAL WONDER	MCCOMAS, J. FRANCIS	AN
INTRODUCTION	MCCOMAS, J. FRANCIS	IN C
BEST FROM FANTASY AND SCIENCE FICTION	BOUCHER & MCCOMAS	AN
BEST FROM FANTASY AND SCIENCE FICTION: 2	BOUCHER & MCCOMAS	AN
BEST FROM FANTASY AND SCIENCE FICTION: 3	BOUCHER & MCCOMAS	AN
INTRODUCTION	MCHARGUE, GEORGESS	IN
HOT & COLD RUNNING CITIES	MCHARGUE, GEORGESS	AN
INTRODUCTION	MCNELLY, WILLIS E.	IN C
ABOVE THE HUMAN LANDSCAPE	MCNELLY & STOVER	AN
INTRODUCTION	MERRIL, JUDITH	IN
ENGLAND SWINGS SF	MERRIL, JUDITH	AN
ONCE AND FUTURE TALES FROM THE MAGAZINE OF FANTASY AND SCIENCE FICTION	FERMAN, EDWARD L.	AN
PATH INTO THE UNKNOWN	ANONYMOUS	AN
SF: THE BEST OF THE BEST	MERRIL, JUDITH	AN
SF:58, THE YEAR'S GREATEST SCIENCE FICTION AND FANTASY	MERRIL, JUDITH	AN
SF:59, THE YEAR'S GREATEST SCIENCE FICTION AND FANTASY	MERRIL, JUDITH	AN
11TH ANNUAL OF THE YEAR'S BEST S-F, THE	MERRIL, JUDITH	AN
5TH ANNUAL OF THE YEAR'S BEST S-F, THE	MERRIL, JUDITH	AN
6TH ANNUAL OF THE YEAR'S BEST S-F, THE	MERRIL, JUDITH	AN
INTRODUCTION	MILLER, P. SCHUYLER	IN
TALES OF CONAN	HOWARD, R. & DE CAMP	AC
INTRODUCTION	MILLS, ROBERT P.	IN
DECADE OF FANTASY AND SCIENCE FICTION, A	MILLS, ROBERT P.	AN
WORLDS OF SCIENCE FICTION, THE	MILLS, ROBERT P.	AN
INTRODUCTION	MILSTEAD, JOHN W.	IN C
SOCIAL PROBLEMS THROUGH SCIENCE FICTION	GREENBERG/MILSTEAD/&	AN
SOCIOLOGY THROUGH SCIENCE FICTION	MILSTEAD/GREENBERG/&	AN
INTRODUCTION	MOORCOCK, MICHAEL	IN
BEFORE ARMAGEDDON	MOORCOCK, MICHAEL	AN
BEST SF STORIES FROM NEW WORLDS NO. 1, THE	MOORCOCK, MICHAEL	AN
BEST SF STORIES FROM NEW WORLDS NO. 2, THE	MOORCOCK, MICHAEL	AN
BEST SF STORIES FROM NEW WORLDS 3	MOORCOCK, MICHAEL	AN

INTRODUCTION

BEST SF STORIES FROM NEW WORLDS 4   MOORCOCK, MICHAEL   AN
BEST SF STORIES FROM NEW WORLDS 5   MOORCOCK, MICHAEL   AN
BEST SF STORIES FROM NEW WORLDS 6   MOORCOCK, MICHAEL   AN
BEST SF STORIES FROM NEW WORLDS 7   MOORCOCK, MICHAEL   AN
MOORCOCK'S BOOK OF MARTYRS   MOORCOCK, MICHAEL   AC
NEW WORLDS QUARTERLY NO. 1   MOORCOCK, MICHAEL   OA
NEW WORLDS QUARTERLY NO. 3   MOORCOCK, MICHAEL   OA
NEW WORLDS QUARTERLY NO. 5   MOORCOCK, MICHAEL   OA
TRAPS OF TIME, THE   MOORCOCK, MICHAEL   AN
INTRODUCTION   MOSKOWITZ, SAM   IN
COMING OF THE ROBOTS, THE   MOSKOWITZ, SAM   AN
DOORWAY INTO TIME   MOSKOWITZ, SAM   AN
EXPLORING OTHER WORLDS   MOSKOWITZ, SAM   AN
LIFE EVERLASTING AND OTHER TALES OF SCIENCE, FANTASY
AND HORROR   KELLER, DAVID H. MD.   AC
MODERN MASTERPIECES OF SCIENCE FICTION   MOSKOWITZ, SAM   AN
INTRODUCTION   MOSKOWITZ, SAM   IN C
SPACE MAGICIANS, THE   NORTON & MOSKOWITZ   AN
INTRODUCTION   NOLAN, WILLIAM F.   IN
FUTURE IS NOW, THE   NOLAN, WILLIAM F.   OA
MAN AGAINST TOMORROW   NOLAN, WILLIAM F.   AN
INTRODUCTION   NORTON, ALDEN H.   IN
HORROR TIMES TEN   NORTON, ALDEN H.   AN
INTRODUCTION   NORTON, ALDEN H.   IN C
SPACE MAGICIANS, THE   NORTON & MOSKOWITZ   AN
INTRODUCTION   NORTON, ANDRE   IN
BULLARD OF THE SPACE PATROL   JAMESON, MALCOLM   AC
SPACE POLICE   NORTON, ANDRE   AN
SPACE SERVICE   NORTON, ANDRE   AN
INTRODUCTION   NORTON, ANDRE   IN C
GATES TO TOMORROW   NORTON, AN.&DONALDY   AN
INTRODUCTION   O'DONNELL, K. M.   IN
FINAL WAR AND OTHER FANTASIES   O'DONNELL, K. M.   DC
INTRODUCTION   OLANDER, JOSEPH D.   IN C
BEST OF JOHN JAKES, THE   JAKES, JOHN W.   AC
MARRIAGE AND THE FAMILY THROUGH SCIENCE FICTION
    CLEAR/WARRICK/&   AN
RUN TO STARLIGHT, SPORTS THROUGH SCIENCE FICTION
    GREENBERG/OLANDER/&   AN
SCHOOL AND SOCIETY THROUGH SCIENCE FICTION
    OLANDER/GREENBERG/&   AN
SOCIAL PROBLEMS THROUGH SCIENCE FICTION   GREENBERG/MILSTEAD/& AN
SOCIOLOGY THROUGH SCIENCE FICTION   MILSTEAD/GREENBERG/& AN
TOMORROW, INC.   GREENBERG& OLANDER   AN
INTRODUCTION   PAGE, GERALD W.   IN
YEAR'S BEST HORROR STORIES: SERIES IV, THE
    PAGE, GERALD W.   AN
INTRODUCTION   PARRY, MICHEL   IN
ROOTS OF EVIL, THE   PARRY, MICHEL   AN
STRANGE ECSTASIES   PARRY, MICHEL   AN
INTRODUCTION   PLATT, CHARLES   IN
NEW WORLDS NO. 5   MOORCOCK & PLATT   OA
NEW WORLDS NO. 6   PLATT & BAILEY   OA
INTRODUCTION   POHL, CAROL   IN C
SCIENCE FICTION: THE GREAT YEARS, VOL. II
    POHL, C. & F.   AN
INTRODUCTION   POHL, FREDERIK   IN
ASSIGNMENT IN TOMORROW   POHL, FREDERIK   AN
BEST SCIENCE FICTION FOR 1972   POHL, FREDERIK   AN
BEYOND THE END OF TIME   POHL, FREDERIK   AN
BEYOND TIME   LEY, SANDRA   OA
BODYGUARD AND 4 OTHER SHORT SF NOVELS FROM GALAXY
    GOLD, H. L.   AN
DAY MILLION   POHL, FREDERIK   AC
DIGITS AND DASTARDS   POHL, FREDERIK   AC
EARLY POHL, THE   POHL, FREDERIK   AC
ELEVENTH GALAXY READER, THE   POHL, FREDERIK   AN
EXPERT DREAMERS, THE   POHL, FREDERIK   AN
FRONTIERS 2; THE NEW MIND   ELWOOD, ROGER   OA
IF READER OF SCIENCE FICTION, THE   POHL, FREDERIK   AN
NIGHTMARE AGE   POHL, FREDERIK   AN
NINTH GALAXY READER, THE   POHL, FREDERIK   AN
SCIENCE FICTION ROLL OF HONOR, THE   POHL, FREDERIK   AN
SECOND IF READER OF SCIENCE FICTION, THE POHL, FREDERIK   AN
SEVENTH GALAXY READER, THE   POHL, FREDERIK   AN
SHADOW OF TOMORROW   POHL, FREDERIK   AN
STAR OF STARS   POHL, FREDERIK   AN
STAR SHORT NOVELS   POHL, FREDERIK   OA
WONDER EFFECT, THE   POHL, F. & KORNBLUTH AC
INTRODUCTION   POHL, FREDERIK   IN C
SCIENCE FICTION: THE GREAT YEARS, VOL. II
    POHL, C. & F.   AN
INTRODUCTION   POWERS, RICHARD GID IN
SCIENCE FICTION OF FRANK R. STOCKTON, THE
    STOCKTON, FRANK R.   AC
SCIENCE FICTION OF JACK LONDON, THE   LONDON, JACK   AC
INTRODUCTION   PRATT, FLETCHER   IN
*BEYOND HUMAN KEN   MERRIL, JUDITH   AN
JOURNEY TO INFINITY   GREENBERG, MARTIN   AN
INTRODUCTION   PRICE, VINCENT   IN
GHOULS, THE   HAINING, PETER   AN
INTRODUCTION   PRIEST, CHRISTOPHER IN
REAL-TIME WORLD   PRIEST, CHRISTOPHER AC
INTRODUCTION   PRIESTLEY, J. B.   IN
OF TIME AND STARS   CLARKE, ARTHUR C.   AC
INTRODUCTION   ROBERSON, RICK   IN
UNIVERSE AHEAD   ENGDAHL & ROBERSON   AN
INTRODUCTION   ROSELLE, DANIEL   IN
TRANSFORMATIONS II   ROSELLE, DANIEL   AN
INTRODUCTION   ROTTENSTEINER, FRANZ IN
VIEW FROM ANOTHER SHORE   ROTTENSTEINER, FRANZ AN
INTRODUCTION   RUSS, JOANNA   IN
TALES AND STORIES   SHELLEY, MARY W.   AC
INTRODUCTION   RUSSELL, ERIC FRANK IN
DARK TIDES   RUSSELL, ERIC FRANK AC

INTRODUCTION   SACKS, JANET   IN
BEST OF SCIENCE FICTION MONTHLY, THE   SACKS, JANET   AN
INTRODUCTION   SALLIS, JAMES   IN
CLARION II   WILSON, ROBIN SCOTT OA
INTRODUCTION   SANDERS, THOMAS E.   IN
SPECULATIONS   SANDERS, THOMAS E.   AN
INTRODUCTION   SANDERSON, IVAN T.   IN
ENCOUNTERS WITH ALIENS   EARLEY, GEORGE W.   AN
INTRODUCTION   SANTESSON, HANS S.   IN
CRIME PREVENTION IN THE 30TH CENTURY   SANTESSON, HANS S.   AN
FLYING SAUCERS IN FACT AND FICTION   SANTESSON, HANS S.   AN
GENTLE INVADERS   SANTESSON, HANS S.   AN
GODS FOR TOMORROW   SANTESSON, HANS S.   AN
RULERS OF MEN   SANTESSON, HANS S.   AN
INTRODUCTION   SARGENT, PAMELA   IN
BIO-FUTURES   SARGENT, PAMELA   AN
MORE WOMEN OF WONDER   SARGENT, PAMELA   AN
INTRODUCTION   SCHMITZ, JAMES H.   IN
PRIDE OF MONSTERS, A   SCHMITZ, JAMES H.   AC
INTRODUCTION   SCHWARTZ, SHEILA   IN
EARTH IN TRANSIT   SCHWARTZ, SHEILA   AN
INTRODUCTION   SERLING, ROD   IN
ROD SERLING'S TRIPLE W: WITCHES, WARLOCKS AND WEREWOLVES
    SERLING, ROD   AN
INTRODUCTION   SILVERBERG, ROBERT   IN
ALIENS, THE   SILVERBERG, ROBERT   AN
ALPHA 1   SILVERBERG, ROBERT   AN
ALPHA 2   SILVERBERG, ROBERT   AN
ALPHA 3   SILVERBERG, ROBERT   AN
ALPHA 4   SILVERBERG, ROBERT   AN
ALPHA 5   SILVERBERG, ROBERT   AN
ALPHA 6   SILVERBERG, ROBERT   AN
ALPHA 7   SILVERBERG, ROBERT   AN
BEYOND CONTROL   SILVERBERG, ROBERT   AN
CHAINS OF THE SEA   SILVERBERG, ROBERT   OA
CRYSTAL SHIP, THE   SILVERBERG, ROBERT   OA
CUBE ROOT OF UNCERTAINTY, THE   SILVERBERG, ROBERT   AC
DARK STARS   SILVERBERG, ROBERT   OA
DAY THE SUN STOOD STILL, THE   SILVERBERG, ROBERT   OA
DEEP SPACE   SILVERBERG, ROBERT   AN
EARTH IS THE STRANGEST PLANET   SILVERBERG, ROBERT   AN
EARTHMEN AND STRANGERS   SILVERBERG, ROBERT   AN
ENDS OF TIME, THE   SILVERBERG, ROBERT   AN
EXPLORERS OF SPACE   SILVERBERG, ROBERT   AN
GREAT SHORT NOVELS OF SCIENCE FICTION   SILVERBERG, ROBERT   AN
INFINITE JESTS   SILVERBERG, ROBERT   AN
INVADERS FROM SPACE   SILVERBERG, ROBERT   AN
IRRATIONAL NUMBERS   EFFINGER, GEO. ALEC AC
MEN AND MACHINES   SILVERBERG, ROBERT   AN
MIND TO MIND   SILVERBERG, ROBERT   AN
MIRROR OF INFINITY, THE   SILVERBERG, ROBERT   AN
MUTANTS   SILVERBERG, ROBERT   AN
NEW ATLANTIS AND OTHER NOVELLAS OF S.F., THE
    SILVERBERG, ROBERT   OA
NEW DIMENSIONS 1   SILVERBERG, ROBERT   OA
NEW DIMENSIONS 2   SILVERBERG, ROBERT   OA
NEW DIMENSIONS 3   SILVERBERG, ROBERT   OA
NEW DIMENSIONS 7   SILVERBERG, ROBERT   OA
OTHER DIMENSIONS   SILVERBERG, ROBERT   AN
SCIENCE FICTION BESTIARY, THE   SILVERBERG, ROBERT   AN
SCIENCE FICTION HALL OF FAME VOLUME 1   SILVERBERG, ROBERT   AN
STRANGE GIFTS   SILVERBERG, ROBERT   AN
THREADS OF TIME   SILVERBERG, ROBERT   OA
THREE TRIPS IN TIME AND SPACE   SILVERBERG, ROBERT   OA
TO THE STARS   SILVERBERG, ROBERT   AN
TOMORROW'S WORLDS   SILVERBERG, ROBERT   AN
VALLEY BEYOND TIME   SILVERBERG, ROBERT   AC
VOYAGERS IN TIME   SILVERBERG, ROBERT   AN
WINDOWS INTO TOMORROW   SILVERBERG, ROBERT   AN
WORLDS OF MAYBE   SILVERBERG, ROBERT   AN
INTRODUCTION   SILVERBERG, ROBERT   IN C
EPOCH   ELWOOD & SILVERBERG OA
INTRODUCTION   SIMAK, CLIFFORD D.   IN
NEBULA AWARD STORIES NO. 6   SIMAK, CLIFFORD D.   AN
INTRODUCTION   SLOANE, WILLIAM   IN
SPACE, SPACE, SPACE   SLOANE, WILLIAM   AN
INTRODUCTION   SMITH, CORDELIA T.   IN
GREAT SCIENCE FICTION STORIES   SMITH, CORDELIA T.   AN
INTRODUCTION   STERN, PHILIP VAN D. IN
MOONLIGHT TRAVELER, THE   STERN, PHILIP VAN D. AN
OTHER SIDE OF THE CLOCK, THE   STERN, PHILIP VAN D. AN
STRANGE BEASTS AND UNNATURAL MONSTERS   STERN, PHILIP VAN D. AN
INTRODUCTION   STONE, IDELLA P.   IN
NEVER IN THIS WORLD   STONE, IDELLA P.   AN
INTRODUCTION   STOVER, LEON E.   IN C
ABOVE THE HUMAN LANDSCAPE   MCNELLY & STOVER   AN
APEMAN, SPACEMAN   STOVER & HARRISON   AN
INTRODUCTION   STRICK, PHILIP   IN
ANTIGRAV: COSMIC COMEDIES   STRICK, PHILIP   AN
INTRODUCTION   STURGEON, THEODORE   IN
BEYOND THE BARRIERS OF SPACE AND TIME   MERRIL, JUDITH   AN
CAUTION! INFLAMMABLE!   SCORTIA, THOMAS N.   AC
FOUR FOR TOMORROW   ZELAZNY, ROGER   AC
OUT OF BOUNDS   MERRIL, JUDITH   AC
STURGEON IN ORBIT   STURGEON, THEODORE   AC
YOUNG DEMONS   ELWOOD & GHIDALIA   AN
INTRODUCTION   SULLIVAN, CHARLES W. IN
AS TOMORROW BECOMES TODAY   SULLIVAN, CHARLES W. AN
INTRODUCTION   TENN, WILLIAM   IN
CHILDREN OF WONDER   TENN, WILLIAM   AN
INTRODUCTION   THEALL, DONALD F.   IN
SURVIVAL SHIP AND OTHER STORIES   MERRIL, JUDITH   AC
INTRODUCTION   TUCKER, WILSON   IN
SCIENCE FICTION SUBTREASURY, THE   TUCKER, WILSON   AC
INTRODUCTION   VAN VOGT, A. E.   IN
BEST OF A. E. VAN VOGT, THE (BRITISH)   VAN VOGT, A. E.   AC

PSEUDO PEOPLE, THE   NOLAN, WILLIAM F.   AN
INTRODUCTION   WARRICK, PATRICIA S. IN C
MARRIAGE AND THE FAMILY THROUGH SCIENCE FICTION
                                           CLEAR/WARRICK/&   AN
NEW AWARENESS, THE   WARRICK & GREENBERG   AN
POLITICAL SCIENCE FICTION   GREENBERG& WARRICK   AN
RUN TO STARLIGHT, SPORTS THROUGH SCIENCE FICTION
                                           GREENBERG/OLANDER/&   AN
SCHOOL AND SOCIETY THROUGH SCIENCE FICTION
                                           OLANDER/GREENBERG/&   AN
SOCIAL PROBLEMS THROUGH SCIENCE FICTION   GREENBERG/MILSTEAD/& AN
SOCIOLOGY THROUGH SCIENCE FICTION   MILSTEAD/GREENBERG/& AN
INTRODUCTION   WELLES, ORSON   IN
SF: THE YEAR'S GREATEST SCIENCE FICTION AND FANTASY
                                           MERRIL, JUDITH   AN
INTRODUCTION   WESTON, PETER   IN
ANDROMEDA I   WESTON, PETER   OA
INTRODUCTION   WILHELM, KATE   IN
CLARION SF   WILHELM, KATE   OA
DOWNSTAIRS ROOM AND OTHER SPECULATIVE FICTION, THE
                                           WILHELM, KATE   AC
INFINITY BOX, THE   WILHELM, KATE   AC
NEBULA AWARD STORIES 9   WILHELM, KATE   AN
INTRODUCTION   WILLIAMSON, JACK   IN
EARLY WILLIAMSON, THE   WILLIAMSON, JACK   AC
INTRODUCTION   WILSON, ROBIN SCOTT IN
CLARION   WILSON, ROBIN SCOTT   OA
CLARION III   WILSON, ROBIN SCOTT   OA
INTRODUCTION   WOLFE, JACK C.   IN C
PAST, PRESENT, AND FUTURE PERFECT   WOLFE, J&FITZ GERALD AN
INTRODUCTION   WOLLHEIM, DONALD A.   IN
ACE SCIENCE FICTION READER   WOLLHEIM, DONALD A.   AN
BEST FROM THE REST OF THE WORLD, THE   WOLLHEIM, DONALD A.   AN
DAW SCIENCE FICTION READER, THE   WOLLHEIM, DONALD A.   OA
HIDDEN PLANET, THE   WOLLHEIM, DONALD A.   AN
MANY WORLDS OF ANDRE NORTON, THE   NORTON, ANDRE   AC
MEN ON THE MOON   WOLLHEIM, DONALD A.   DA
MORE ADVENTURES ON OTHER PLANETS   WOLLHEIM, DONALD A.   AN
POCKET BOOK OF SCIENCE-FICTION, THE   WOLLHEIM, DONALD A.   AN
PORTABLE NOVELS OF SCIENCE   WOLLHEIM, DONALD A.   AN
PRIZE SCIENCE FICTION   WOLLHEIM, DONALD A.   AN
TWO DOZEN DRAGON EGGS   WOLLHEIM, DONALD A.   AC
1972 ANNUAL WORLD'S BEST SF, THE   WOLLHEIM, DONALD A.   AN
1973 ANNUAL WORLD'S BEST SF, THE   WOLLHEIM, DONALD A.   AN
1974 ANNUAL WORLD'S BEST SF, THE   WOLLHEIM, DONALD A.   AN
1975 ANNUAL WORLD'S BEST SF, THE   WOLLHEIM, DONALD A.   AN
1976 ANNUAL WORLD'S BEST SF, THE   WOLLHEIM, DONALD A.   AR
1977 ANNUAL WORLD'S BEST SF, THE   WOLLHEIM, DONALD A.   AN
INTRODUCTION   WOLLHEIM, DONALD A. IN C
WORLD'S BEST SCIENCE FICTION: 1965   WOLLHEIM & CARR   AN
WORLD'S BEST SCIENCE FICTION: 1966   WOLLHEIM & CARR   AN
WORLD'S BEST SCIENCE FICTION: 1967   WOLLHEIM & CARR   AN
WORLD'S BEST SCIENCE FICTION: 1968   WOLLHEIM & CARR   AN
WORLD'S BEST SCIENCE FICTION: 1969   WOLLHEIM & CARR   AN
WORLD'S BEST SCIENCE FICTION: 1970   WOLLHEIM & CARR   AN
WORLD'S BEST SCIENCE FICTION: 1971   WOLLHEIM & CARR   AN
INTRODUCTION   WYNDHAM, JOHN   IN
BEST FROM NEW WORLDS SCIENCE FICTION, THE
                                           CARNELL, JOHN   AN
INTRODUCTION   YOLEN, JANE   IN
ZOO 2000   YOLEN, JANE   AN
INTRODUCTION   ZELAZNY, ROGER   IN
NEBULA AWARD STORIES NO. 3   ZELAZNY, ROGER   AN
INTRODUCTION (A DIALOGUE)   POHL, CAROL   IN C
SCIENCE FICTION DISCOVERIES   POHL, C. & F.   OA
INTRODUCTION (A DIALOGUE)   POHL, FREDERIK   IN C
SCIENCE FICTION DISCOVERIES   POHL, C. & F.   OA
INTRODUCTION NO. 1   ASIMOV, ISAAC   IN
FIFTY SHORT SCIENCE FICTION TALES   ASIMOV & CONKLIN   AN
INTRODUCTION NO. 2   CONKLIN, GROFF   IN
FIFTY SHORT SCIENCE FICTION TALES   ASIMOV & CONKLIN   AN
INTRODUCTION PART 1: 1920 TO 1930
                               ASIMOV, ISAAC   IN
BEFORE THE GOLDEN AGE   ASIMOV, ISAAC   AN
INTRODUCTION THE FIRST   POHL, FREDERIK   IN
SCIENCE FICTION: THE GREAT YEARS   POHL, C. & F.   AN
INTRODUCTION THE SECOND   POHL, CAROL   IN
SCIENCE FICTION: THE GREAT YEARS   POHL, C. & F.   AN
INTRODUCTION TO "SUNDANCE"   SILVERBERG, ROBERT   AR
THOSE WHO CAN: A SCIENCE FICTION READER WILSON, ROBIN SCOTT AN
INTRODUCTION TO INTERSECTION POINT
                               DOOHAN, JAMES   IN
STAR TREK: THE NEW VOYAGES   MARSHAK, S&CULBREATH OA
INTRODUCTION TO MIND-SIFTER   SHATNER, WILLIAM   IN
STAR TREK: THE NEW VOYAGES   MARSHAK, S&CULBREATH OA
INTRODUCTION TO NI VAR   NIMOY, LEONARD   IN
STAR TREK: THE NEW VOYAGES   MARSHAK, S&CULBREATH OA
INTRODUCTION TO NIGHTMARES, AN BLOCH, ROBERT   IN
NIGHTMARES   BLOCH, ROBERT   AC
INTRODUCTION TO THE CITY ON THE EDGE OF FOREVER
                               ELLISON, HARLAN   AI
SIX SCIENCE FICTION PLAYS   ELWOOD, ROGER   AN
INTRODUCTION TO THE DOVER EDITION
                               BLEILER, EVERETT F. IN
3 PROPHETIC SCIENCE FICTION NOVELS OF H. G. WELLS
                                           WELLS, H. G.   AC
INTRODUCTION TO THE ENCHANTED POOL
                               NICHOLS, NICHELLE   IN
STAR TREK: THE NEW VOYAGES   MARSHAK, S&CULBREATH OA
INTRODUCTION TO THE FACE ON THE BARROOM FLOOR
                               TAKEI, GEORGE   IN
STAR TREK: THE NEW VOYAGES   MARSHAK, S&CULBREATH OA
INTRODUCTION TO THE FIRST EDITION
                               ELLISON, HARLAN   IN
LOVE AIN'T NOTHING BUT SEX MISSPELLED (REVISED)
                                           ELLISON, HARLAN   AC

INTRODUCTION TO THE HUNTING   CULBREATH, MYRNA   IN C
STAR TREK: THE NEW VOYAGES   MARSHAK, S&CULBREATH OA
INTRODUCTION TO THE HUNTING   MARSHAK, SONDRA   IN C
STAR TREK: THE NEW VOYAGES   MARSHAK, S&CULBREATH OA
INTRODUCTION TO THE POCKET BOOK EDITION
                               FRIEND, OSCAR J.   IN C
MY BEST SCIENCE FICTION STORY (12 OF 25) MARGULIES & FRIEND   AN
INTRODUCTION TO THE POCKET BOOK EDITION
                               MARGULIES, LEO   IN C
MY BEST SCIENCE FICTION STORY (12 OF 25) MARGULIES & FRIEND   AN
INTRODUCTION TO THE SECOND EDITION
                               MALZBERG, BARRY N.   SS   NOV 73 03
BEST OF BARRY N. MALZBERG, THE   MALZBERG, BARRY N.   AC
NOVA 3   HARRISON, HARRY   OA
INTRODUCTION TO THE WINGED DREAMERS
                               KELLEY, DEFOREST   IN
STAR TREK: THE NEW VOYAGES   MARSHAK, S&CULBREATH OA
INTRODUCTION TO VISIT TO A WEIRD PLANET REVISITED
                               RODDENBERRY, MAJEL B IN
STAR TREK: THE NEW VOYAGES   MARSHAK, S&CULBREATH OA
INTRODUCTION: "UNHOLY MARRIAGE": THE CYBORG IN SCIENCE FICTION
                               SCORTIA, THOMAS N.   IN
HUMAN-MACHINES   SCORTIA & ZEBROWSKI   AN
INTRODUCTION: "UNHOLY MARRIAGE": THE CYBORG IN SCIENCE FICTION
                               ZEBROWSKI, GEORGE   IN
HUMAN-MACHINES   SCORTIA & ZEBROWSKI   AN
INTRODUCTION: A HISTORY OF SCIENCE FICTION IN THE POPULAR
MAGAZINES, 1891-1911   MOSKOWITZ, SAM   IN
SCIENCE FICTION BY GASLIGHT   MOSKOWITZ, SAM   AN
INTRODUCTION: A NEW WAY OF EXPRESSION
                               WESTON, PETER   IN
BEYOND THIS HORIZON   CARRELL, CHRISTOPHER OA
INTRODUCTION: A SHORT ONE FOR THE BOYS IN THE BACK ROOM
                               MALZBERG, BARRY N.   IN
DOWN HERE IN THE DREAM QUARTER   MALZBERG, BARRY N.   AC
INTRODUCTION: A SPECTRUM OF WORLDS
                               CLARESON, THOMAS D.   IN
SPECTRUM OF WORLDS, A   CLARESON, THOMAS D.   AN
INTRODUCTION: ALL THE EFFINGERS AT ONCE
                               STURGEON, THEODORE   IN
MIXED FEELINGS   EFFINGER, GEO. ALEC   AC
INTRODUCTION: AN ABC OF BRITISH SCIENCE FICTION- APOCALYPSE,
BLEAKNESS, CATASTROPHE   NICHOLLS, PETER   IN
BEYOND THIS HORIZON   CARRELL, CHRISTOPHER OA
INTRODUCTION: AN AMAZING EXPERIMENT
                               ASHLEY, MICHAEL   AR
HISTORY OF THE SCIENCE FICTION MAGAZINE, THE PART 1 1926-1935
                                           ASHLEY, MICHAEL   AN
INTRODUCTION: AN ENDANGERED SPECIES
                               DEL REY, JUDY-LYNN   IN
STELLAR SHORT NOVELS   DEL REY, JUDY-LYNN   OA
INTRODUCTION: ASTRONOMY TODAY AND TOMORROW
                               MOORE, PATRICK   IN
BEYOND THIS HORIZON   CARRELL, CHRISTOPHER OA
INTRODUCTION: BUCK ROGERS IN THE NEW JERUSALEM
                               DISCH, THOMAS M.   IN
NEW IMPROVED SUN, THE   DISCH, THOMAS M.   AN
INTRODUCTION: DREAMING AGAIN   DANN, JACK M.   IN C
FASTER THAN LIGHT   DANN & ZEBROWSKI   OA
INTRODUCTION: DREAMING AGAIN   ZEBROWSKI, GEORGE   IN C
FASTER THAN LIGHT   DANN & ZEBROWSKI   OA
INTRODUCTION: FLASHFORWARD TO 2076
                               ALTERMAN, PETER S.   AR
2076: THE AMERICAN TRICENTENNIAL   BRYANT, EDWARD   OA
INTRODUCTION: FROM BOMB TO BOOM
                               ASHLEY, MICHAEL   IN
HISTORY OF THE SCIENCE FICTION MAGAZINE, THE PART 3 1946-1955
                                           ASHLEY, MICHAEL   AN
INTRODUCTION: HUGO, JOHN AND THE MAGAZINES
                               BOVA, BEN   IN
ANALOG ANNUAL   BOVA, BEN   OA
INTRODUCTION: LOCI   BRYANT, EDWARD   IN
AMONG THE DEAD   BRYANT, EDWARD   AC
INTRODUCTION: MY UNIVERSE AND WELCOME TO IT|
                               NIVEN, LARRY   IN
TALES OF KNOWN SPACE: THE UNIVERSE OF LARRY NIVEN
                                           NIVEN, LARRY   AC
INTRODUCTION: MYTHOLOGY AND SCIENCE FICTION
                               DISCH, THOMAS M.   IN
NEW CONSTELLATIONS   DISCH & NAYLOR   OA
INTRODUCTION: OBLATIONS AT ALIEN ALTARS
                               ELLISON, HARLAN   IN
DEATHBIRD STORIES   ELLISON, HARLAN   AC
INTRODUCTION: ON THE ROAD TO 1984
                               DISCH, THOMAS M.   IN
BAD MOON RISING   DISCH, THOMAS M.   OA
INTRODUCTION: POETRY AND SCIENCE FICTION
                               LUCIE-SMITH, EDWARD   IN
BEYOND THIS HORIZON   CARRELL, CHRISTOPHER OA
INTRODUCTION: REALITY IN SCIENCE FICTION
                               WHITE, JAMES   IN
MONSTERS AND MEDICS   WHITE, JAMES   AC
INTRODUCTION: RELIGIOUS SCIENCE FICTION
                               LOVIN, ROGER   IN
FLAME TREE PLANET   ELWOOD, ROGER   OA
INTRODUCTION: SCIENCE FICTION - SCIENCE FACT
                               HAY, GEORGE   IN
BEYOND THIS HORIZON   CARRELL, CHRISTOPHER OA
INTRODUCTION: SCIENCE-FICTION GAMES
                               POHL, FREDERIK   IN
IN THE PROBLEM PIT   POHL, FREDERIK   AC
INTRODUCTION: SF BANDWAGON   ASHLEY, MICHAEL   AR
HISTORY OF THE SCIENCE FICTION MAGAZINE, THE   PART 2 1936-1945
                                           ASHLEY, MICHAEL   AN

INTRODUCTION: SPIDER ROBINSON: THE SF WRITER AS EMPATH

INTRODUCTION: SPIDER ROBINSON: THE SF WRITER AS EMPATH
                              BOVA, BEN   IN
  CALLAHAN'S CROSSTIME SALOON   ROBINSON, SPIDER   AC
INTRODUCTION: STARTING IN THE MIDDLE
                              MALZBERG, BARRY N.   IN
  MORE SCIENCE FICTION TALES   ELWOOD, ROGER   OA
INTRODUCTION: THE FUN IN FUTURE FUN
                              ASIMOV, ISAAC   IN   67
  INFINITY 1   HOSKINS, ROBERT   OA
INTRODUCTION: THE ONCE AND FUTURE VOYAGES
                              CULBREATH, MYRNA   IN C
  STAR TREK: THE NEW VOYAGES   MARSHAK, S&CULBREATH OA
INTRODUCTION: THE ONCE AND FUTURE VOYAGES
                              MARSHAK, SONDRA   IN C
  STAR TREK: THE NEW VOYAGES   MARSHAK, S&CULBREATH OA
INTRODUCTION: THE REALITY OF PHILIP K. DICK
                              BRUNNER, JOHN   IN
  BEST OF PHILIP K. DICK, THE   DICK, PHILIP K.   AC
INTRODUCTION: THE THREE CAREERS OF JOHN W. CAMPBELL
                              DEL REY, LESTER   IN
  *BEST OF JOHN W. CAMPBELL, THE   CAMPBELL, JOHN W. JR AC
INTRODUCTION: THE WONDER-FULL AGE
                              STURGEON, THEODORE   IN
  SCIENCE FICTION TALES   ELWOOD, ROGER   OA
INTRODUCTION: TO THE READER   WILSON, ROBIN SCOTT IN
  THOSE WHO CAN: A SCIENCE FICTION READER WILSON, ROBIN SCOTT AN
INTRODUCTION: TODAY'S TOMORROWS
                              MCHALE, JOHN   IN
  TOMORROW TODAY   ZEBROWSKI, GEORGE   OA
INTRODUCTION: WHY THE CITY   CLEM, RALPH   IN C
  CITY: 2000 A.D., THE   CLEM/GREENBERG/&   AN
INTRODUCTION: WHY THE CITY   GREENBERG, MARTIN H. IN C
  CITY: 2000 A.D., THE   CLEM/GREENBERG/&   AN
INTRODUCTION: WHY THE CITY   OLANDER, JOSEPH D.   IN C
  CITY: 2000 A.D., THE   CLEM/GREENBERG/&   AN
INTRODUCTION: YESTERDAY, TOMORROW, AND MAYBY
                              DE CAMP, CATHERINE C IN C
  TALES BEYOND TIME   DE CAMP, L. S.&C.   AN
INTRODUCTION: YESTERDAY, TOMORROW, AND MAYBY
                              DE CAMP, L. SPRAGUE IN C
  TALES BEYOND TIME   DE CAMP, L. S.&C.   AN
INTRODUCTION- BEYOND THE WORLD WE KNOW
                              DE CAMP, CATHERINE C IN C
  3000 YEARS OF FANTASY AND SCIENCE FICTION
                              DE CAMP, L. S.&C.   AN
INTRODUCTION- BEYOND THE WORLD WE KNOW
                              DE CAMP, L. SPRAGUE IN C
  3000 YEARS OF FANTASY AND SCIENCE FICTION
                              DE CAMP, L. S.&C.   AN
INTRODUCTION- MODERN SCIENCE FICTION
                              SPINRAD, NORMAN   IN
  MODERN SCIENCE FICTION   SPINRAD, NORMAN   AN
INTRODUCTION- THE FUNCTION OF SCIENCE FICTION
                              BLISH, JAMES   IN
  LIGHT FANTASTIC, THE   HARRISON, HARRY   AN
INTRODUCTION, WITH NOTES ON STAGING
                              BRADBURY, RAY   IN
  WONDERFUL ICE CREAM SUIT AND OTHER PLAYS, THE
                              BRADBURY, RAY   AC
INTRODUCTORY NOTE   CONKLIN, GROFF   IN
  WORLDS OF WHEN   CONKLIN, GROFF   AN
INTRUDER   DOLAN, MIKE   SS
  SANTANA MORNING AND OTHER STORIES   DOLAN, MIKE   OC
INTRUDER ON THE RIM (SEE OPERATION ZERO)
                              LESSER, MILTON   TC
INTRUDER, THE   THOMAS, THEODORE L. SS   FSF 61 02
  POCKETFUL OF STARS, A   KNIGHT, DAMON   AN
INTRUDERS (INTRUDERS ON THE MOON)
                              COOPER, EDMUND   NV   FUN 57 04
  FIRST FLIGHTS TO THE MOON   CLEMENT, HAL   AN
  NEWS FROM ELSEWHERE   COOPER, EDMUND   AC
  TOMORROW'S GIFT   COOPER, EDMUND   AC
  UNBORN TOMORROW   COOPER, EDMUND   AC
INVADED BY LOVE   DISCH, THOMAS M.   SS   NWS 66 09
  *ONE HUNDRED AND TWO H-BOMBS DISCH, THOMAS M.   AC
  WHITE FANG GOES DINGO AND OTHER FUNNY S.F. STORIES
                              DISCH, THOMAS M.   AC
INVADER   WHITE, JAMES   NV   NWR 66 07
  MAJOR OPERATION   WHITE, JAMES   NO
  NEW WRITINGS IN SF. 7   CARNELL, JOHN   OA
INVADERS FROM THE INFINITE   CAMPBELL, JOHN W. JR NO   FPS 61
  JOHN W. CAMPBELL ANTHOLOGY: THREE NOVELS CAMPBELL, JOHN W. JR AC
INVADERS FROM THE MICROCOSM (INVASION FROM THE MICROCOSM)
                              DERLETH, AUGUST   SS   OSF 53 01
  HARRIGAN'S FILE   DERLETH, AUGUST   AC
INVADERS OF SPACE   LEINSTER, MURRAY   NO   BRK 64
  MURRAY LEINSTER OMNIBUS, A   LEINSTER, MURRAY   AC
INVADERS, THE   CAMPBELL, JOHN W. JR NV   ASF 35 06
  *BEST OF JOHN W. CAMPBELL, THE   CAMPBELL, JOHN W. JR AC
  CLOAK OF AESIR   CAMPBELL, JOHN W. JR AC
INVADERS, THE   JOHNSON, RONALD   PM   69
  HOLDING YOUR EIGHT HANDS   LUCIE-SMITH, EDWARD AN
INVADERS, THE   TALL, STEPHEN   NV   IFS 73 08
  STARDUST VOYAGES, THE   TALL, STEPHEN   AC
INVADERS, THE (ALSO AS BEHIND THE BLACK NEBULA)
                              HUBBARD, L. RON   NV   ASF 42 01
  KINGSLAYER, THE   HUBBARD, L. RON   AC
INVARIANT   PIERCE, JOHN R.   SS   ASF 44 04
  *ASTOUNDING SCIENCE FICTION ANTHOLOGY, THE
                              CAMPBELL, JOHN W. JR AN
  *FIRST ASTOUNDING SCIENCE FICTION ANTHOLOGY, THE
                              CAMPBELL, JOHN W. JR AN
  SCIENCE FICTION INVENTIONS   KNIGHT, DAMON   AN
INVASION   LONG, FRANK BELKNAP SS   STS 50 07
  FAR BOUNDARIES   DERLETH, AUGUST   AN

INVASION   PODOLNY, ROMAN   SS   66
  ULTIMATE THRESHOLD, THE   GINSBURG, MIRRA   AN
INVASION FROM INNER SPACE   KOCH, HOWARD   NV   STR 59 06
  STAR SCIENCE FICTION STORIES NO. 6   POHL, FREDERIK AN
INVASION FROM MARS   KOCH, HOWARD   PL   CBS 38 10
  ARMCHAIR SCIENCE READER, THE   GORDON, I. & SORKIN AN
  BUG-EYED MONSTERS   CHEETHAM, ANTHONY   AN
  CONTACT   KEYES, NOEL   AN
  *INVADERS OF EARTH   CONKLIN, GROFF   AN
  INVASION FROM MARS   WELLES, ORSON   AN
  SPECULATIONS   SANDERS, THOMAS E.   AN
  TREASURY OF SCIENCE FICTION CLASSICS, THE
                              KUEBLER, HAROLD W.   AN
INVASION FROM THE MICROCOSM (SEE INVADERS FROM THE MICROCOSM)
                              DERLETH, AUGUST   TC
INVASION OF DALLAS, THE   SALLIS, JAMES   SS
  LONE STAR UNIVERSE   PROCTOR & UTLEY   OA
INVASION OF PRIVACY   SHAW, BOB   NV   AMZ 70 07
  TALES OF TERROR FROM OUTER SPACE   CHETWYND-HAYES, R. AN
  TOMORROW LIES IN AMBUSH   SHAW, BOB   AC
  WORLD'S BEST SCIENCE FICTION: 1971 WOLLHEIM & CARR AN
INVASION OF THE GIANT STUPID DINOSAURS, THE
                              DISCH, THOMAS M.   SS   AMZ 69 03
  *GETTING INTO DEATH   DISCH, THOMAS M.   AC
  WHITE FANG GOES DINGO AND OTHER FUNNY S.F. STORIES
                              DISCH, THOMAS M.   AC
INVASION OF THE PLANET OF LOVE ELLIOTT, GEORGE P. SS   FSF 59 01
  BEST FROM FANTASY AND SCIENCE FICTION: 9
                              MILLS, ROBERT P.   AN
INVASION REPORT   COGSWELL, THEODORE R SS   GAL 54 08
  WALL AROUND THE WORLD, THE   COGSWELL, THEODORE R AC
INVASION!   SAMBROT, WILLIAM   SS   SEP 56 07
  ISLAND OF FEAR AND OTHER SCIENCE FICTION SAMBROT, WILLIAM AC
INVASION, THE   DAVIDSON, AVRAM   SS   PBY 65 07
  TRANSIT OF EARTH   PLAYBOY, EDITORS OF   AN
INVASION, THE   WILLEY, ROBERT   NV   SSS 40 09
  BEYOND BELIEF   HURLEY, RICHARD J.   AN
  EXPERT DREAMERS, THE   POHL, FREDERIK   AN
INVENTER OF HIS OWN UNDOING   NESVADBA, JOSEF   NV   64
  LOST FACE, THE   NESVADBA, JOSEF   AC
INVERTED WORLD, THE   PRIEST, CHRISTOPHER EX   FAB 74
  BEYOND THIS HORIZON   CARRELL, CHRISTOPHER OA
INVERTED WORLD, THE   PRIEST, CHRISTOPHER NV   NWR 73 22
  NEW WRITINGS IN SF. 22   BULMER, KENNETH   OA
INVESTIGATING THE BIDWELL ENDEAVORS
                              BUNCH, DAVID R.   SS   65
  11TH ANNUAL OF THE YEAR'S BEST S-F, THE MERRIL, JUDITH AN
INVESTIGATING THE CURIOSITY DRIVE
                              HERZOG, TOM   SS   FSF 68 11
  SCHOOL AND SOCIETY THROUGH SCIENCE FICTION
                              OLANDER/GREENBERG/&   AN
INVESTOR, THE   FRIEDMAN, BRUCE JAY SS   PBY 62 02
  PLAYBOY'S STORIES OF THE SINISTER & STRANGE
                              PLAYBOY, EDITORS OF   AN
INVISIBILITY COMPETITION   ARATOVSKY, Y.   CT   PRI
  BEST SF: 1972   HARRISON & ALDISS   AN
INVISIBILITY GAMBIT, THE (ABDICATION)
                              VAN VOGT, A. E.   SS   ASF 43 04
  PROXY INTELLIGENCE AND OTHER MIND BENDERS
                              VAN VOGT, A. E.   AC
INVISIBLE BOMBER, THE   FARLEY, RALPH MILNE SS   AMZ 38 06
  OMNIBUS OF TIME, THE   FARLEY, RALPH MILNE   AC
INVISIBLE BOY   BRADBURY, RAY   SS   MAD 45 11
  *GOLDEN APPLES OF THE SUN   BRADBURY, RAY   AC
  INVISIBLE MEN   DAVENPORT, BASIL   AN
  S IS FOR SPACE   BRADBURY, RAY   AC
  VINTAGE BRADBURY, THE   BRADBURY, RAY   AC
INVISIBLE BOY (SEE BRAIN CHILD)
                              COOPER, EDMUND   TC
INVISIBLE CITY, THE   SMITH, CLARK ASHTON SS   WOS 32 06
  OTHER DIMENSIONS   SMITH, CLARK ASHTON   AC
INVISIBLE DOVE DANCER OF STRATHPEEN ISLAND, THE
                              COLLIER, JOHN   SS   41
  INVISIBLE MEN   DAVENPORT, BASIL   AN
INVISIBLE GIRL, THE   SARGENT, PAMELA   SS
  KILLER PLANTS AND OTHER STORIES, THE ELWOOD, ROGER OA
INVISIBLE GIRL, THE   SHELLEY, MARY W.   SS   KPS 33
  TALES AND STORIES   SHELLEY, MARY W.   AC
INVISIBLE IDIOT, THE   BRUNNER, JOHN   SS   SAG 70
  SCIENCE AGAINST MAN   CHEETHAM, ANTHONY   OA
INVISIBLE JANITOR   INOUYE, JON   SS
  NIGHT TIDE, A   INOUYE, JON   OC
INVISIBLE LIGHT   BELAYEV, ALEXANDER   SS
  RUSSIAN SCIENCE FICTION   MAGIDOFF, ROBERT   AN
INVISIBLE MAN MURDER CASE, THE SLESAR, HENRY   SS   FAN 58 05
  INVISIBLE MEN   DAVENPORT, BASIL   AN
INVISIBLE MAN, THE   WELLS, H. G.   SN   PRS 97 06
  BEST SCIENCE FICTION STORIES OF H. G. WELLS
                              WELLS, H. G.   AC
  CENTURY OF GREAT SHORT SCIENCE FICTION NOVELS, A
                              KNIGHT, DAMON   AN
  SEVEN FAMOUS NOVELS BY H. G. WELLS WELLS, H. G.   AC
INVISIBLE MEN OF MARS   BURROUGHS, EDGAR R. NV   AMZ 41 10
  LLANA OF GATHOL   BURROUGHS, EDGAR R.   NO
INVISIBLE MEN, THE   PRIEST, CHRISTOPHER SS
  STOPWATCH   HAY, GEORGE   OA
INVISIBLE PRISONER, THE   LEBLANC, MAURICE   SS
  INVISIBLE MEN   DAVENPORT, BASIL   AN
IONIAN CIRCLE, THE   TENN, WILLIAM   SS   TWS 49 08
  TRAVELLERS OF SPACE   GREENBERG, MARTIN   AN
IQ SOUP (SEE DUCKWORTH'S IQ SOUP)
                              EISENBERG, LARRY   TC
IRON CHANCELLOR, THE   SILVERBERG, ROBERT   NV   GAL 58 05
  BEYOND CONTROL   SILVERBERG, ROBERT   AN
  CUBE ROOT OF UNCERTAINTY, THE SILVERBERG, ROBERT AC

```
NEEDLE IN A TIMESTACK                SILVERBERG, ROBERT         AC
IRON JACKASS, THE           BRUNNER, JOHN         SS   ASF 62 03
  NO FUTURE IN IT                    BRUNNER, JOHN             AC
IRON MAN                    BINDER, EANDO         SS   FUT 55 28
  WEIRD ONES, THE                    HOWARD, IVAN              AN
IRON MASK                   BLOCH, ROBERT         NV   WRT 44 05
  FANTASTIC PULPS, THE               HAINING, PETER            AN
IRON MOON, THE              ELAM, RICHARD M. JR.  NV   BLF 51
  TEEN-AGE SCIENCE FICTION STORIES   ELAM, RICHARD M. JR.      AC
IRON ONE, THE               HAMILTON, EDMOND      SS   SAW 72
  SIGNS AND WONDERS                  ELWOOD, ROGER             OA
IRON STANDARD, THE          KUTTNER, HENRY        SS   ASF 43 12
  BEST OF HENRY KUTTNER 2, THE       KUTTNER, HENRY            AC
  BEST OF HENRY KUTTNER, THE         KUTTNER, HENRY            AC
IRON STANDARD, THE          PADGETT, LEWIS        SS   ASF 43 12
  *MEN AGAINST THE STARS             GREENBERG, MARTIN         AN
IRRESISTIBLE PARTY CHAIRMAN, THE
                            EISENBERG, LARRY      SS   NEW 71 AC
  BEST LAID SCHEMES, THE             EISENBERG, LARRY          AC
IS BETSY BLAKE STILL ALIVE? (BETSY BLAKE WILL LIVE FOREVER)
                            BLOCH, ROBERT         SS   EQM 58 04
  *BLOOD RUNS COLD                   BLOCH, ROBERT             AC
IS EVERYTHING AN ILLUSION?  ALDISS, BRIAN W.      SI
  SPACE OPERA                        ALDISS, BRIAN W.          AN
IS GENDER NECESSARY?        LE GUIN, URSULA K.    AR
  AURORA: BEYOND EQUALITY            MCINTYRE & ANDERSON       OA
IS IT THE END OF THE WORLD? SHORE, WILMA          SS   FSF 72 03
  BEST FROM FANTASY AND SCIENCE FICTION: 20
                            FERMAN, EDWARD L.         AN
IS THERE HOPE FOR THE FUTURE? ASIMOV, ISAAC       AR   GAL 74 07
  BEST FROM GALAXY, THE   VOLUME III  BAEN, JAMES              AN
IS THERE LIFE IN INNER SPACE? EISENBERG, LARRY    SS   NEW 71 AC
  BEST LAID SCHEMES, THE             EISENBERG, LARRY          AC
IS THERE LIFE ON THE MOON?  WILKINS, PERCY H.     AR   CYE 53 01
  SCIENCE FICTION AND READER'S GUIDE  BARROWS, MARJORIE        AN
IS THERE NO TRUTH IN BEAUTY? (JEAN LISETTE AROESTE)
                            BLISH, JAMES          SA   STK 74 10
  STAR TREK  10                      BLISH, JAMES              OC
IS YOUR CHILD USING DRUGS?  POLLACK, RACHEL       SS   NDM 76 06
  NEW DIMENSIONS 6                   SILVERBERG, ROBERT        OA
ISAAC ASIMOV                BESTER, ALFRED        AR   PBW 73
  STAR LIGHT, STAR BRIGHT            BESTER, ALFRED            AC
ISAAC ASIMOV (YOU CAN'T BEAT BRAINS)
                            DE CAMP, L. SPRAGUE   AR   FSF 66 10
  BEST FROM FANTASY AND SCIENCE FICTION, 25TH ANNIV.
                            FERMAN, EDWARD L.         AN
ISAAC UNDER PRESSURE        EDELSTEIN, SCOTT      SS   INY 73 05
  INFINITY 5                         HOSKINS, ROBERT           OA
ISAIAH                      MALZBERG, BARRY N.    SS   FAN 73 09
  DOWN HERE IN THE DREAM QUARTER     MALZBERG, BARRY N.        AC
ISHMAEL IN LOVE             SILVERBERG, ROBERT    SS   FSF 70 07
  EARTH'S OTHER SHADOW               SILVERBERG, ROBERT        AC
  PARSECS AND PARABLES               SILVERBERG, ROBERT        AC
  WORLD'S BEST SCIENCE FICTION: 1971  WOLLHEIM & CARR          AN
ISHMAEL INTO THE BARRENS     LAFFERTY, R. A.      NV   FFU 71
  FOUR FUTURES                       SILVERBERG, ROBERT        OA
ISLAND IN THE SKY           WELLMAN, MANLY WADE   NV   TWS 41 10
  GIANT ANTHOLOGY OF SCIENCE FICTION  MARGULIES & FRIEND       AN
ISLAND OF DOCTOR DEATH AND OTHER STORIES, THE
                            WOLFE, GENE           SS   ORB 70 07
  BEST FROM ORBIT, THE               KNIGHT, DAMON             AN
  NEBULA AWARD STORIES  NO. 6        SIMAK, CLIFFORD D.        AN
  ORBIT  7                           KNIGHT, DAMON             OA
ISLAND OF DR. MOREAU, THE   WELLS, H. G.          NO   SRV 95 01
  SEVEN FAMOUS NOVELS BY H. G. WELLS  WELLS, H. G.             AC
ISLAND OF FEAR              SAMBROT, WILLIAM      SS   SEP 58 01
  ISLAND OF FEAR AND OTHER SCIENCE FICTION SAMBROT, WILLIAM    AC
  POST READER OF FANTASY AND SCIENCE FICTION
                            SATURDAY EVE. POST        AN
ISLAND OF THE CRABS, THE    DNIEPROV, ANATOLY     SS   ISF 68 06
  OTHER WORLDS, OTHER SEAS           SUVIN, DARKO              AN
ISLAND OF THE ENDANGERED, THE FERGUSON, DALE      SS   NEW 72 AN
  ZOO 2000                           YOLEN, JANE               AN
ISLAND OF THE FIVE COLORS, THE GARDNER, MARTIN    SS   NEW 52 AN
  FANTASIA MATHEMATICA               FADIMAN, CLIFTON          AN
  *FUTURE TENSE                      CROSSEN, KENDELL F.       AN
ISLAND OF THE HANDS, THE    ST. CLAIR, MARGARET   SS   WRT 52 09
  THREE WORLDS OF FUTURITY           ST. CLAIR, MARGARET       DC
ISLAND OF UNREASON, THE     HAMILTON, EDMOND      SS   WOS 33 05
  BEST OF EDMOND HAMILTON, THE       HAMILTON, EDMOND          AN
  HISTORY OF THE SCIENCE FICTION MAGAZINE, THE  PART 1 1926-1935
                            ASHLEY, MICHAEL           AN
ISLAND, THE                 JONES, ROGER          SS   SCF 65 02
  ENGLAND SWINGS SF                  MERRIL, JUDITH            AN
  SPACE-TIME JOURNAL, THE            MERRIL, JUDITH            AN
ISLANDS                     MOORCOCK, MICHAEL     NV   NWS 63
  MOORCOCK'S BOOK OF MARTYRS         MOORCOCK, MICHAEL         AC
ISLANDS OF SPACE            CAMPBELL, JOHN W. JR  NO   FPS 56
  JOHN W. CAMPBELL ANTHOLOGY: THREE NOVELS  CAMPBELL, JOHN W. JR  AC
ISLE OF THE SLEEPER, THE    HAMILTON, EDMOND      SS   WRT 51 05
  GHOUL KEEPERS, THE                 MARGULIES, LEO            AN
  WHAT'S IT LIKE OUT THERE? AND OTHER STORIES
                            HAMILTON, EDMOND          AC
ISOLATIONIST                REYNOLDS, MACK        SS   FAD 50 04
  *BIG BOOK OF SCIENCE FICTION       CONKLIN, GROFF            AN
ISOLATIONISTS, THE          SILVERBERG, ROBERT    SS   SFS 58 11
  SHORES OF TOMORROW, THE            SILVERBERG, ROBERT        AC
ISOLINGUALS, THE            DE CAMP, L. SPRAGUE   SS   ASF 37 09
  FIRST FLIGHT                       KNIGHT, DAMON             AN
IT                          STURGEON, THEODORE    NV   UNK 40 08
  BR-R-R!                            CONKLIN, GROFF            AN
  CREATURES FROM BEYOND              CARR, TERRY               AN
  DARK SIDE, THE                     KNIGHT, DAMON             AN
  NOT WITHOUT SORCERY                STURGEON, THEODORE        AC
  WITHOUT SORCERY                    STURGEON, THEODORE        AC

IT BECOMES NECESSARY (THE COLD PEACE)
                            MOORE, WARD           SS   GNT 61
  7TH ANNUAL OF THE YEAR'S BEST S-F, THE  MERRIL, JUDITH       AN
IT COULD BE ANYTHING (SEE A TRIP TO THE CITY)
                            LAUMER, KEITH         TC
IT COULD BE YOU             ROBERTS, FRANK        SS   SSI 64
  PACIFIC BOOK OF AUSTRALIAN SCIENCE FICTION
                            BAXTER, JOHN              AN
  10TH ANNUAL OF THE YEAR'S BEST S-F, THE  MERRIL, JUDITH      AN
IT DIDN'T HAPPEN            BROWN, FREDRIC        SS   PBY 63 10
  BEST OF FREDRIC BROWN, THE         BROWN, FREDRIC            AC
  PARADOX LOST, AND 12 OTHER GREAT S.F. STORIES
                            BROWN, FREDRIC            AC
  TRANSIT OF EARTH                   PLAYBOY, EDITORS OF   AN
"IT DOES NOT PAY A PROPHET TO BE TOO SPECIFIC"
                            HEINLEIN, ROBERT A.   IN
  *MAN WHO SOLD THE MOON, THE        HEINLEIN, ROBERT A.   AC
IT DOESN'T REALLY MATTER    MALZBERG, BARRY N.    SS
  GRADUATED ROBOT AND OTHER STORIES, THE  ELWOOD, ROGER    OA
IT ENDS WITH A FLICKER (OF ALL POSSIBLE WORLDS)
                            TENN, WILLIAM         SS   GAL 56 12
  WOODEN STAR, THE                   TENN, WILLIAM             AC
IT HAPPENED TOMORROW        BLOCH, ROBERT         NV   SSS 51 06
  FUTURES UNLIMITED                  NORTON, ALDEN H.          AN
IT OPENS THE SKY            STURGEON, THEODORE    NV   VSF 57 11
  *TOUCH OF STRANGE, A                STURGEON, THEODORE       AC
IT PAYS TO ADVERTISE        NEVILLE, KRIS         SS   FSF 53 06
  TOMORROW'S UNIVERSE                CAMPBELL, H. J.           AN
IT WAS BLACK CAT WEATHER    BUNCH, DAVID R.       SS   FAN 63 02
  MODERAN                            BUNCH, DAVID R.           AC
IT WAS NOTHING- REALLY!     STURGEON, THEODORE    SS       69
  ANTIGRAV: COSMIC COMEDIES          STRICK, PHILIP            AN
  STURGEON IS ALIVE AND WELL...      STURGEON, THEODORE        AN
IT WASN'T MY FAULT          O'DONNELL, K. M.      SS
  MISSING WORLD AND OTHER STORIES, THE   ELWOOD, ROGER         OA
IT WASN'T SYZYGY (THE DEADLY RATIO)
                            STURGEON, THEODORE    NV   WRT 48 01
  E PLURIBUS UNICORN                 STURGEON, THEODORE        AC
IT WILL COME TO YOU         LONG, FRANK BELKNAP   SS   UNK 42 12
  ALONE BY NIGHT                     CONGDON, MICHAEL&DON  AN
  DARK BEASTS, THE                   LONG, FRANK BELKNAP       AC
  EARLY LONG, THE                    LONG, FRANK BELKNAP       AC
  *HOUNDS OF TINDALOS, THE           LONG, FRANK BELKNAP       AC
IT WILL GROW ON YOU         WANDREI, DONALD       SS
  EYE AND THE FINGER                 WANDREI, DONALD           AC
IT'S A BIRD, IT'S A PLANE!  SPINRAD, NORMAN       SS   GNT 67
  COSMIC LAUGHTER                    HALDEMAN, JOE W.          AN
  LAST HURRAH OF THE GOLDEN HORDE, THE   SPINRAD, NORMAN       AC
IT'S A GOOD LIFE            BIXBY, JEROME         SS   STR 53 02
  BEST SF  4                         CRISPIN, EDMUND           AN
  IN DREAMS AWAKE                    FIEDLER, LESLIE A.        AN
  INTRODUCING SCIENCE FICTION        ALDISS, BRIAN W.          AN
  MASTERS' CHOICE                    JANIFER, LAURENCE M.      AN
  MUTANTS                            SILVERBERG, ROBERT        AN
  SCIENCE FICTION HALL OF FAME VOLUME 1  SILVERBERG, ROBERT    AN
  SPECULATIONS                       SANDERS, THOMAS E.        AN
  STAR OF STARS                      POHL, FREDERIK            AN
  STAR SCIENCE FICTION STORIES NO. 2 POHL, FREDERIK            OA
  TOMORROW'S CHILDREN                ASIMOV, ISAAC             AN
IT'S A GREAT BIG WONDERFUL UNIVERSE
                            AANDAHL, VANCE        SS   FSF 60 11
  BEST FROM FANTASY AND SCIENCE FICTION: 10
                            MILLS, ROBERT P.          AN
IT'S A YOUNG WORLD          POHL, FREDERIK        NV   AST 41 04
  DAY MILLION                        POHL, FREDERIK            AC
  EARLY POHL, THE                    POHL, FREDERIK            AC
IT'S ALL HOW YOU LOOK AT IT (SEE THE THUNDER-THIEVES)
                            ASIMOV, ISAAC         TC
IT'S COLD OUTSIDE           WILSON, RICHARD       NV   IFS 56 12
  THOSE IDIOTS FROM EARTH            WILSON, RICHARD           AC
IT'S GOING TO BE TRUE!      FRANTHWAY, BURKE      SS
  ADVENTURES TO COME                 ESENWEIN, J. BERG         OA
IT'S GREAT TO BE BACK!      HEINLEIN, ROBERT A.   SS   SEP 47 07
  CITIES OF WONDER                   KNIGHT, DAMON             AN
  GREEN HILLS OF EARTH, THE          HEINLEIN, ROBERT A.       AC
  PAST THROUGH TOMORROW, THE         HEINLEIN, ROBERT A.       AC
  *TREASURY OF SCIENCE FICTION, A    CONKLIN, GROFF            AN
IT'S SMART TO HAVE AN ENGLISH ADDRESS
                            COMPTON, D. G.        SS   IMP 67 02
  WORLD'S BEST SCIENCE FICTION: 1968 WOLLHEIM & CARR           AN
IT'S SO WONDERFUL HERE      PRONZINI, BILL        SS
  SCIENCE FICTION ADVENTURES FROM WAY OUT  ELWOOD, ROGER       AN
IT'S SUCH A BEAUTIFUL DAY   ASIMOV, ISAAC         NV   STR 54 03
  BEYOND BELIEF                      HURLEY, RICHARD J.        AN
  ECO-FICTION                        STADLER, JOHN             AN
  NIGHTFALL AND OTHER STORIES        ASIMOV, ISAAC             AC
  STAR SCIENCE FICTION STORIES NO. 3 POHL, FREDERIK            OA
  THROUGH A GLASS, CLEARLY           ASIMOV, ISAAC             AC
  TRANSFORMATIONS                    ROSELLE, DANIEL           AN
  UNIVERSE AHEAD                     ENGDAHL & ROBERSON        AN
  YOU AND SCIENCE FICTION            HOLLISTER, BERNARD C  AN
IT'S VERY CLEAN             WOLFE, GENE           SS   GEN 72
  GENERATION                         GERROLD, DAVID            AN
IT'S YOU!                   STURGEON, THEODORE    SS   KNT 69
  STURGEON IS ALIVE AND WELL...      STURGEON, THEODORE        AN
ITSELF                      BACON, EDGAR MAYHEW   SS   BLC 07 05
  SCIENCE FICTION BY GASLIGHT        MOSKOWITZ, SAM            AN
ITSELF!                     VAN VOGT, A. E.       SS   GAM 63 01
  FAR-OUT WORLDS OF A. E. VAN VOGT, THE  VAN VOGT, A. E.       AN
  HUMAN ZERO, THE                    MOSKOWITZ & ELWOOD        AN
  WORLDS OF A. E. VAN VOGT, THE      VAN VOGT, A. E.           AN
IVY WAR, THE                KELLER, DAVID H. MD.  SS   AMZ 30 05
  *BEST OF SCIENCE FICTION           CONKLIN, GROFF            AN
  ROOTS OF EVIL, THE                 PARRY, MICHEL             AN
  TALES FROM UNDERWOOD               KELLER, DAVID H. MD.      AC
```

IZZARD AND THE MEMBRANE   MILLER, WALTER M. JR NV   ASF 51 05
  YEAR'S BEST SCIENCE FICTION NOVELS: 1952 BLEILER & DIKTY   AN
J IS FOR JEANNE   TUBB, E. C.   SS   NWS 65 12
  11TH ANNUAL OF THE YEAR'S BEST S-F, THE MERRIL, JUDITH   AN
J.G. (FROM "J.G. THE UPRIGHT APE")
                               PRICE, ROGER   EX   60
  6TH ANNUAL OF THE YEAR'S BEST S-F, THE   MERRIL, JUDITH   AN
J-LINE TO NOWHERE   HENDERSON, ZENNA   NV   FSF 69 09
  HOLDING WONDER   HENDERSON, ZENNA   AC
  VENUS FACTOR, THE   GHIDALIA, V.& ELWOOD   AN
JACHID AND JACHIDAH   SINGER, ISAAC B.   SS   64
  SCIENCE FICTION: THE FUTURE   ALLEN, DICK   AN
JACHID AND JECHIDAH   SINGER, ISAAC B.   SS   64
  WANDERING STARS   DANN, JACK M.   AN
JACK AND BETTY   THURSTON, ROBERT   SS   ORB 75 16
  ORBIT 16   KNIGHT, DAMON   OA
JACK FELL DOWN   BRUNNER, JOHN   NV   SPA 63 03
  CRIME PREVENTION IN THE 30TH CENTURY SANTESSON, HANS S.   AN
JACK-IN-THE-BOX   BRADBURY, RAY   SS   NEW 47 AC
  *DARK CARNIVAL   BRADBURY, RAY   AC
  *OCTOBER COUNTRY, THE   BRADBURY, RAY   AC
  SMALL ASSASSIN, THE   BRADBURY, RAY   AC
JACKAL'S MEAL   DICKSON, GORDON R. SS   ASF 69 06
  STAR ROAD, THE   DICKSON, GORDON R.   AC
JACKDAW   ROCKLYNNE, ROSS   NV   ASF 42 08
  *BEST OF SCIENCE FICTION   CONKLIN, GROFF   AN
JACKIE SEES A STAR   BRADLEY, MARION Z. SS   FUN 54 09
  DARK INTRUDER & OTHER STORIES, THE BRADLEY, MARION Z.   DC
JACKPOT   SIMAK, CLIFFORD D. NV   GAL 56 10
  ALIENS FOR NEIGHBOURS   SIMAK, CLIFFORD D.   AC
  *WORLDS OF CLIFFORD SIMAK, THE SIMAK, CLIFFORD D.   AC
JACKSON'S WRONG STORY   BOLSOVER, JOHN   SS
  AD 2500   WILSON, ANGUS   AN
JACOB WRESTLES WITH THE ANGEL CONRAD, EARL   SS
  DA VINCI MACHINE, THE   CONRAD, EARL   OC
JACOB'S BUG   POSNER, RICHARD   SS   TAL 73
  FRONTIERS 1: TOMORROW'S ALTERNATIVES ELWOOD, ROGER   OA
JADE BLUE   BRYANT, EDWARD   SS   UNI 71 01
  UNIVERSE 1   CARR, TERRY   OA
JAKE'S JOURNAL   WILLEFORD, CHARLES NV
  MACHINE IN WARD ELEVEN, THE   WILLEFORD, CHARLES   NO
JAKE'S PICTURES   LITTLE, MARGARET   SS   ADS 75 01
  ARMADA SCI-FI ONE   DAVIS, RICHARD   OA
JAM, THE   SLESAR, HENRY   SS   PBY 58 11
  FROM THE "S" FILE   PLAYBOY, EDITORS OF   AN
  PLAYBOY BOOK OF HORROR AND THE SUPERNATURAL, THE
                               PLAYBOY, EDITORS OF   AN
JAMBOREE   WILLIAMSON, JACK   SS   GAL 69 12
  PEOPLE MACHINES   WILLIAMSON, JACK   AC
  THOSE WHO CAN: A SCIENCE FICTION READER WILSON, ROBIN SCOTT AN
  YOUNG DEMONS   ELWOOD & GHIDALIA   AN
JAMES   DICKSON, GORDON R. SS   FSF 55 05
  DANGER- HUMAN   DICKSON, GORDON R.   AC
JAMES BLISH   LOWNDES, ROBERT W. AR   FSF 72 04
  BEST FROM FANTASY AND SCIENCE FICTION, 25TH ANNIV.
                               FERMAN, EDWARD L.   AN
JAMESON SATELLITE, THE   JONES, NEIL R.   SS   AMZ 31 07
  BEFORE THE GOLDEN AGE   ASIMOV, ISAAC   AN
  PLANET OF THE DOUBLE SUN   JONES, NEIL R.   AC
JAMEY'S VISITOR   LYTLE, B. J.   SS
  GRADUATED ROBOT AND OTHER STORIES, THE ELWOOD, ROGER   OA
JAMIE'S SMILE   BRENNERT, ALAN   SS
  IDES OF TOMORROW, THE   CARR, TERRY   OA
JANE CRYING   SALLIS, JAMES   SS   70
  FEW LAST WORDS, A   SALLIS, JAMES   AC
JANUARY, 1975   MALZBERG, BARRY N. SS   ASF 75 01
  DOWN HERE IN THE DREAM QUARTER MALZBERG, BARRY N.   AC
JAR OF LATAKIA, THE   COOPER, EDMUND   SS   AUT 54 09
  TOMORROW'S GIFT   COOPER, EDMUND   AC
JAR, THE   BRADBURY, RAY   SS   WRT 44 11
  *DARK CARNIVAL   BRADBURY, RAY   AC
  *OCTOBER COUNTRY, THE   BRADBURY, RAY   AC
JAY SCORE   RUSSELL, ERIC FRANK SS ASF 41 05
  MEN, MARTIANS AND MACHINES   RUSSELL, ERIC FRANK   AN
  TOMORROW, THE STARS   HEINLEIN, ROBERT A.   AN
JAYCEE   BROWN, FREDRIC   SS   FSF 55
  BEST OF FREDRIC BROWN, THE   BROWN, FREDRIC   AC
  NIGHTMARES AND GEEZENSTACKS   BROWN, FREDRIC   AC
JAYWALKER   ROCKLYNNE, ROSS   SS   GAL 50 12
  FIRST STEP OUTWARD   HOSKINS, ROBERT   AN
  *GALAXY READER OF SCIENCE FICTION GOLD, H. L.   AN
JAZZ MACHINE, THE   MATHESON, RICHARD PM   FSF 63 02
  SHOCK III   MATHESON, RICHARD   AC
  9TH ANNUAL OF THE YEAR'S BEST S-F, THE MERRIL, JUDITH   AN
JEAN DUPRES   DICKSON, GORDON R. NV   NOV 70 01
  *NOVA 1   HARRISON, HARRY   OA
JEBABURBA   GALOUYE, DANIEL F. SS   GAL 54 10
  LAST LEAP AND OTHER STORIES OF THE SUPER-MIND, THE
                               GALOUYE, DANIEL F.   AC
JELLY FISH, THE   KELLER, DAVID H. MD. SS WRT 29 01
  TALES FROM UNDERWOOD   KELLER, DAVID H. MD.   AC
JENNY AMONG THE ZEEBS   ANMAR, FRANK   SS   FIN 70
  FUTURE IS NOW, THE   NOLAN, WILLIAM F.   OA
JENNY AMONG THE ZEEBS (AS FRANK ANMAR)
                               NOLAN, WILLIAM F. SS   FIN 70
  ALIEN HORIZONS   NOLAN, WILLIAM F.   AC
JENNY WITH WINGS   WILHELM, KATE   SS   NEW 63 AC
  GOLDEN ROAD, THE   KNIGHT, DAMON   AN
  MILE-LONG SPACESHIP, THE   WILHELM, KATE   AC
JEREMIAD   SALLIS, JAMES   SS   NWS 69 02
  FEW LAST WORDS, A   SALLIS, JAMES   AC
JEREMY IN THE WIND   KNEALE, NIGEL   SS   50
  TIMELESS STORIES FOR TODAY AND TOMORROW BRADBURY, RAY   AN
JERRY WAS A MAN (JERRY IS A MAN)
                               HEINLEIN, ROBERT A. SS TWS 47 10
  ASSIGNMENT IN ETERNITY   HEINLEIN, ROBERT A.   AC

JESSICA, RAYMOND, AND JACK   DISCH, THOMAS M.   SS
  *GETTING INTO DEATH   DISCH, THOMAS M.   AC
JESTER, THE   TENN, WILLIAM   SS   TWS 51 08
  *SCIENCE FICTION THINKING MACHINES CONKLIN, GROFF   AN
  SQUARE ROOT OF MAN, THE   TENN, WILLIAM   AC
JESTING PILOT   KUTTNER, HENRY   SS   ASF 47 05
  CITIES OF WONDER   KNIGHT, DAMON   AN
  CITY: 2000 A.D., THE   CLEM/GREENBERG/&   AN
JESTING PILOT   PADGETT, LEWIS   SS   ASF 47 05
  GNOME THERE WAS, A   PADGETT, LEWIS   AC
JESUS SHOES   BOSWORTH, ALAN R. SS   UNK 42 04
  FROM UNKNOWN WORLDS   CAMPBELL, JOHN W. JR AN
JET-PROPELLED COUCH, THE   LINDNER, ROBERT   AR   FSF 56 01
  BEST FANTASY STORIES   ALDISS, BRIAN W.   AN
JETSAM   CHANDLER, A. BERTRAM SS NWS 53 03
  BEST FROM NEW WORLDS SCIENCE FICTION, THE
                               CARNELL, JOHN   AN
  FIRST FLIGHTS TO THE MOON   CLEMENT, HAL   AN
  FIRST STEP OUTWARD   HOSKINS, ROBERT   AN
  MEN ON THE MOON   WOLLHEIM, DONALD A.   DA
JEWBIRD, THE   MALAMUD, BERNARD   SS   REP 63 04
  WANDERING STARS   DANN, JACK M.   AN
  9TH ANNUAL OF THE YEAR'S BEST S-F, THE MERRIL, JUDITH   AN
JEWEL OF BAS, THE   BRACKETT, LEIGH   NV   PLS 44 SP
  BEST OF LEIGH BRACKETT, THE   BRACKETT, LEIGH   AC
JEWEL THIEF, THE   CROSS, RONALD A.   SS   NWQ 74 06
  NEW WORLDS NO. 6   PLATT & BAILEY   OA
JEWELS OF GWAHLUR   HOWARD, ROBERT E. SS   WRT 35 03
  CONAN THE WARRIOR   HOWARD, R. & DE CAMP   AC
  KING CONAN   HOWARD, ROBERT E.   AC
JEZEBEL   LEINSTER, MURRAY   SS   STS 53 10
  PORTALS OF TOMORROW   DERLETH, AUGUST   AN
JIGSAW MAN, THE   NIVEN, LARRY   SS   DVS 67 01
  ALL THE MYRIAD WAYS   NIVEN, LARRY   AC
  DANGEROUS VISIONS   ELLISON, HARLAN   OA
  TALES OF KNOWN SPACE: THE UNIVERSE OF LARRY NIVEN
                               NIVEN, LARRY   AC
JIHAD (STEPHEN KANDEL)   FOSTER, ALAN DEAN SA   SLG 75 05
  STAR TREK LOG FIVE   FOSTER, ALAN DEAN   OC
JILTING OF JANE, THE   WELLS, H. G.   SS   97
  COUNTRY OF THE BLIND, THE   WELLS, H. G.   AC
  PLATTNER STORY AND OTHERS, THE WELLS, H. G.   AC
  SHORT STORIES OF H. G. WELLS, THE WELLS, H. G.   AC
  THIRTY STRANGE STORIES   WELLS, H. G.   AC
JIM AND MARY G   SALLIS, JAMES   SS   ORB 70 07
  BEST FROM ORBIT, THE   KNIGHT, DAMON   AN
  FEW LAST WORDS, A   SALLIS, JAMES   AC
  ORBIT 7   KNIGHT, DAMON   OA
JIMMY GOGGLES THE GOD   WELLS, H. G.   SS   GRP 98 12
  COUNTRY OF THE BLIND, THE   WELLS, H. G.   AC
  SHORT STORIES OF H. G. WELLS, THE WELLS, H. G.   AC
  TWELVE STORIES AND A DREAM   WELLS, H. G.   AC
JINN   GREEN, JOSEPH   SS   GAL 68 12
  AFFAIR WITH GENIUS, AN   GREEN, JOSEPH   AC
  ELEVENTH GALAXY READER, THE   POHL, FREDERIK   AN
JINX JET   HARVEY, FRANK   SS   CAV 57
  AIR FORCE!   HARVEY, FRANK   AC
JIREL MEETS MAGIC   MOORE, C. L.   NV   WRT 35 07
  JIREL OF JOIRY   MOORE, C. L.   AC
  MORE WOMEN OF WONDER   SARGENT, PAMELA   AN
  *SHAMBLEAU AND OTHERS   MOORE, C. L.   AC
JIZZLE (REVISED FROM COL 49 01)
                               WYNDHAM, JOHN   SS   FSF 52 02
  BEST FROM FANTASY AND SCIENCE FICTION: 2
                               BOUCHER & MCCOMAS   AN
  JIZZLE   WYNDHAM, JOHN   AC
  TALES OF GOOSEFLESH AND LAUGHTER WYNDHAM, JOHN   AC
JOB IS ENDED, THE   TUCKER, WILSON   SS   OWS 50 11
  SCIENCE FICTION SUBTREASURY, THE TUCKER, WILSON   AC
JODY AFTER THE WAR   BRYANT, EDWARD   SS   ORB 72 10
  AMONG THE DEAD   BRYANT, EDWARD   AC
  ORBIT 10   KNIGHT, DAMON   OA
JOE GRIFFIN'S GREAT JUMP   HENDERSON, WILLIAM J SS
  BATTLE FOR THE PACIFIC AND OTHER ADVENTURES AT SEA, THE
                               ANONYMOUS   AN
JOHN CARTER AND THE GIANTS OF MARS
                               BURROUGHS, EDGAR R. NV AMZ 41 01
  JOHN CARTER OF MARS   BURROUGHS, EDGAR R.   AC
JOHN D. MACDONALD   NOLAN, WILLIAM F. AR
  HUMAN EQUATION, THE   NOLAN, WILLIAM F.   AN
JOHN GRANT'S LITTLE ANGEL   GROVE, WALT   SS   PBY 64 07
  PLAYBOY BOOK OF SCIENCE FICTION AND FANTASY, THE
                               PLAYBOY, EDITORS OF   AN
JOHN JAKES BIBLIOGRAPHY, A   MISC. MATERIAL   MS
  BEST OF JOHN JAKES, THE   JAKES, JOHN W.   AC
JOHN JONES' DOLLAR   KEELER, HARRY S.   SS   BLC 15 08
  FANTASIA MATHEMATICA   FADIMAN, CLIFTON   AN
  *STRANGE PORTS OF CALL   DERLETH, AUGUST   AN
JOHN OF THE APOCALYPSE   BENFORD, GREGORY
                               AND BENFORD, JAMES SS C
  TOMORROW TODAY   ZEBROWSKI, GEORGE   OA
JOHN OVINGTON RETURNS   BRAND, MAX   SS   ASW 18 06
  FANTASTIC PULPS, THE   HAINING, PETER   AN
JOHN ROBERTS AND THE DRAGON'S EGG
                               SCORTIA, THOMAS N. SS   FUN 57 08
  CAUTION! INFLAMMABLE!   SCORTIA, THOMAS N.   AC
JOHN SZE'S FUTURE   PIERCE, JOHN R.   SS   NEW 62 AN
  GREAT SCIENCE FICTION BY SCIENTISTS CONKLIN, GROFF   AN
JOHN THE REVELATOR   LA FARGE, OLIVER   SS   FSF 51 02
  BEST FROM FANTASY AND SCIENCE FICTION BOUCHER & MCCOMAS   AN
JOHN THOMAS'S CUBE   LEIMERT, JOHN   SS   ATL 45 08
  ARMCHAIR SCIENCE READER, THE GORDON, I. & SORKIN   AN
  OMNIBUS OF SCIENCE FICTION   CONKLIN, GROFF   AN
  STRANGE TRAVELS IN SCIENCE FICTION CONKLIN, GROFF   AN

```
JOHN W. CAMPBELL, JR. AWARDS 1973 - 1975, THE
                                  MISC. MATERIAL    MS
  NEW VOICES IN SCIENCE FICTION   MARTIN, GEORGE R. R. OA
JOHN'S OTHER LIFE       HALDEMAN, JOE W.   SS   SCS 73
  SHOWCASE                        ELWOOD, ROGER       OA
JOHN'S OTHER PRACTICE   MARKS, WINSTON K.  SS   IMG 54 07
  BEST SCIENCE FICTION STORIES AND NOVELS: 1955
                                  DIKTY, T. E.        AN
JOHNNY CARTWRIGHT'S CAMERA (CARTWRIGHT'S CAMERA)
             BOND, NELSON S.     SS   UNK 40 11
  MR. MERGENTHWIRKER'S LOBBIES AND OTHER FANTASTIC TALES
                                  BOND, NELSON S.     AC
JOIN NOW (SEE THE HUMORS)   SHECKLEY, ROBERT    TC
JOIN OUR GANG?         LANIER, STERLING E.  SS   ASF 61 05
  ANALOG 1                        CAMPBELL, JOHN W. JR AN
JOKE, THE              BROWN, FREDRIC    SS
  NIGHTMARES AND GEEZENSTACKS     BROWN, FREDRIC      AC
JOKER FOR HIRE (ANYTHING FOR LAUGHS)
                       GOULART, RON      NV   FAN 63 05
  BROKE DOWN ENGINE AND OTHER TROUBLES WITH MACHINES
                                  GOULART, RON        AC
JOKSTER                ASIMOV, ISAAC     SS   INF 56 12
  EARTH IS ROOM ENOUGH            ASIMOV, ISAAC       AC
  MORE PENGUIN SCIENCE FICTION    ALDISS, BRIAN W.    AN
JON'S WORLD            DICK, PHILIP K.    NV
  *TIME TO COME                   DERLETH, AUGUST     OA
JORDAN                 HENDERSON, ZENNA  SS   FSF 59 03
  DECADE OF FANTASY AND SCIENCE FICTION, A MILLS, ROBERT P. AN
  PILGRIMAGE: THE BOOK OF THE PEOPLE  HENDERSON, ZENNA  AC
JORRY'S GAP            STURGEON, THEODORE  SS   KNT 69
  STURGEON IS ALIVE AND WELL...   STURGEON, THEODORE  AC
JOURNAL FROM ELLIPSIA (EXCERPT)
             CALISHER, HORTENSE   EX   LBR 65
  SF12                            MERRIL, JUDITH      AN
JOURNAL OF BODLEY CLIVE, THE   PARIS, MATTHEW   SS   NWB 75 09
  NEW WORLDS NINE                 BAILEY, HILARY      OA
JOURNEY ACROSS A CRATER   BALLARD, J. G.   SS   NWS 70 02
  NEW WORLDS QUARTERLY NO. 1      MOORCOCK, MICHAEL   OA
JOURNEY ACROSS THREE WORLDS    ABRAMOV, ALEXANDER
                 AND ABRAMOV, SERGEI  SS  C
  JOURNEY ACROSS THREE WORLDS     ANONYMOUS           AN
JOURNEY BY HELIODROME   DOLAN, MIKE      SS
  SANTANA MORNING AND OTHER STORIES   DOLAN, MIKE     OC
JOURNEY INTO THE FUTURE   GRANIN, DANIIL   SS
  RUSSIAN SCIENCE FICTION, 1969   MAGIDOFF, ROBERT    AN
JOURNEY OF TEN THOUSAND MILES  MOHLER, WILL  SS   FSF 63 03
  ONCE AND FUTURE TALES FROM THE MAGAZINE OF FANTASY AND
  SCIENCE FICTION                 FERMAN, EDWARD L.   AN
JOURNEY OF THE SOUL    SHAPIRO, NEIL     NV
  TOMORROW: NEW WORLDS OF SCIENCE FICTION ELWOOD, ROGER OA
JOURNEY TO ANOTHER STAR   ZEBROWSKI, GEORGE   SS
  JOURNEY TO ANOTHER STAR AND OTHER STORIES
                                  ELWOOD, ROGER       OA
JOURNEY TO BABEL (D. C. FONTANA)
             BLISH, JAMES         SA   STK 71 04
  STAR TREK  4                    BLISH, JAMES        OC
JOURNEY TO THE CENTER OF THE EARTH, A (1864)
             VERNE, JULES         EX   AMZ 26 05
  FROM FRANKENSTEIN TO ANDROMEDA  BROWN, JAMES GOLDIE AN
  JULES VERNE- MASTER OF SCIENCE FICTION  VERNE, JULES  AC
JOURNEY TO THE CENTER OF THE EARTH, A (1864)
             VERNE, JULES         NO   AMZ 26 05
  JOURNEYS IN SCIENCE FICTION     LOUGHLIN, RICHARD L. AN
JOURNEY TO THE HEARTLAND   ALDISS, BRIAN W.   NV   UNI 76 06
UNIVERSE 6                        CARR, TERRY         OA
JOURNEY TO THE INTERIOR (SEE GENE-HIVE)
             ALDISS, BRIAN W.     TC
JOURNEY TO THE MOON, A (ABRIDGED)
             DE BERGERAC, CYRANO  NV
  3000 YEARS OF FANTASY AND SCIENCE FICTION
                                  DE CAMP, L. S.&C.   AN
JOURNEY WORK           DRYFOOS, DAVE     SS   IFS 55 01
  FIRST WORLD OF IF, THE          QUINN & WULFF       AN
JOURNEY'S END (THE SEED OF EARTH)
             SILVERBERG, ROBERT   SS   SUP 58 04
  DIMENSION THIRTEEN              SILVERBERG, ROBERT  AC
JOURNEY, THE           LEINSTER, MURRAY  SS   STR 53 01
  STAR SCIENCE FICTION STORIES    POHL, FREDERIK      OA
JOURNEYS END           ANDERSON, POUL    SS   FSF 57 02
  BEST FROM FANTASY AND SCIENCE FICTION: 7
                                  BOUCHER, ANTHONY    AN
  DARK STARS                      SILVERBERG, ROBERT  AN
  EDGE OF NEVER, THE              HOSKINS, ROBERT     AN
  MANY WORLDS OF POUL ANDERSON, THE  ANDERSON, POUL   AC
  MIND TO MIND                    SILVERBERG, ROBERT  AN
  SCIENCE FICTION ARGOSY, A       KNIGHT, DAMON       AN
  SPECIAL WONDER                  MCCOMAS, J. FRANCIS AN
JOY IN MUDVILLE        ANDERSON, POUL
                 AND DICKSON, GORDON R.  NV C FSF 55 11
  INFINITE ARENA, THE             CARR, TERRY         AN
JOY IN OUR CAUSE       EMSHWILLER, CAROL  SS
  JOY IN OUR CAUSE                EMSHWILLER, CAROL   AC
JOY OF LIVING, THE     NOLAN, WILLIAM F. SS   IFS 54 08
  ALIEN HORIZONS                  NOLAN, WILLIAM F.   AC
  IMPACT-20                       NOLAN, WILLIAM F.   AC
  PSEUDO PEOPLE, THE              NOLAN, WILLIAM F.   AN
JOY RIDE, THE (THE NAKED SKY) GUNN, JAMES E.  NA  STS 55 FL
  END OF THE DREAMS, THE          GUNN, JAMES E.      AC
JOYCELIN SHRAGER STORY, THE   DISCH, THOMAS M.   NV
  GETTING INTO DEATH AND OTHER STORIES  DISCH, THOMAS M. AC
JUDAS                  BRUNNER, JOHN     SS   DVS 67 01
  DANGEROUS VISIONS               ELLISON, HARLAN     OA
  FROM THIS DAY FORWARD           BRUNNER, JOHN       AC
  OTHER WORLDS, OTHER GODS        MOHS, MAYO          AN
  PAST, PRESENT, AND FUTURE PERFECT  WOLFE, J&FITZ GERALD AN

JUDAS BOMB             REED, KIT         SS   FSF 61 04
  BEST SF 6                       CRISPIN, EDMUND     AN
  7TH ANNUAL OF THE YEAR'S BEST S-F, THE  MERRIL, JUDITH  AN
JUDAS DANCED (JUDAS DANCING)  ALDISS, BRIAN W.  SS  SMG 58 0?
  ALPHA 4                         SILVERBERG, ROBERT  AN
  BEST SCIENCE FICTION STORIES OF BRIAN W. ALDISS (REVISED)
                                  ALDISS, BRIAN W.    AC
  CANOPY OF TIME, THE             ALDISS, BRIAN W.    AC
  NO TIME LIKE TOMORROW           ALDISS, BRIAN W.    AC
  SF: AUTHORS' CHOICE             HARRISON, HARRY     AN
JUDAS DANCING (SEE JUDAS DANCED)
             ALDISS, BRIAN W.     TC
JUDAS FISH             SCORTIA, THOMAS N. SS   YRT 70
  CAUTION| INFLAMMABLE|           SCORTIA, THOMAS N.  AC
  YEAR 2000, THE                  HARRISON, HARRY     OA
JUDAS RAM              MERWIN, SAM E.    SS   GAL 50 12
  *GALAXY READER OF SCIENCE FICTION  GOLD, H. L.      AN
JUDAS STORY            STABLEFORD, BRIAN M. SS  NEW 75 AN
  YEAR'S BEST HORROR STORIES: SERIES III, THE
                                  DAVIS, RICHARD      AN
JUDGE'S HOUSE, THE     STOKER, BRAM      SS
  STRANGE BEASTS AND UNNATURAL MONSTERS  STERN, PHILIP VAN D. AN
JUDGEMENT DAY          BIGGLE, LLOYD JR. SS   FUN 58 04
  RULE OF THE DOOR AND OTHER FANCIFUL REGULATIONS
                                  BIGGLE, LLOYD JR.   AC
JUDGEMENT DAY          COOPER, EDMUND    SS
  NEWS FROM ELSEWHERE             COOPER, EDMUND      AC
  TOMORROW CAME                   COOPER, EDMUND      AC
JUDGEMENT NIGHT        MOORE, C. L.      NA   ASF 43 08
  JUDGEMENT NIGHT                 MOORE, C. L.        AC
JUDGMENT DAY           DE CAMP, L. SPRAGUE SS  ASF 55 08
  BEST SCIENCE FICTION STORIES AND NOVELS: 1956
                                  DIKTY, T. E.        AN
  GREAT SCIENCE-FICTION           LICATA, TONY        AN
  GUN FOR DINOSAUR AND OTHER IMAGINATIVE TALES
                                  DE CAMP, L. SPRAGUE AC
  SCIENCE FICTION ARGOSY, A       KNIGHT, DAMON       AN
JUDGMENT NIGHT         SERLING, ROD      SA
  *ROD SERLING'S THE TWILIGHT ZONE  SERLING, ROD      OC
JUDGMENT OF APHRODITE, THE  HOYLE, FRED   SS
  ELEMENT 79                      HOYLE, FRED         AC
JUDGMENT, THE          NUETZEL, CHARLES  SS
  IMAGES OF TOMORROW              NUETZEL, CHARLES    AC
JUGGERNAUT             VAN VOGT, A. E.   SS   ASF 44 08
  BEST OF A. E. VAN VOGT, THE (BRITISH)  VAN VOGT, A. E.  AC
  *TREASURY OF SCIENCE FICTION, A  CONKLIN, GROFF     AN
JUHLI                  MOORE, C. L.      SS   WRT 35 03
  NORTHWEST OF EARTH              MOORE, C. L.        AC
JUICE                  DE CAMP, L. SPRAGUE SS  SSS 40 05
  SPRAGUE DE CAMP'S NEW ANTHOLOGY  DE CAMP, L. SPRAGUE AC
JUKE DOLL (DOLL-FRIEND) YOUNG, ROBERT F. SS   AMZ 59 07
  PSEUDO PEOPLE, THE              NOLAN, WILLIAM F.   AN
JUKE-BOX               KUTTNER, HENRY    SS   TWS 47 02
  BEST OF HENRY KUTTNER 1, THE    KUTTNER, HENRY      AC
  RETURN TO OTHERNESS             KUTTNER, HENRY      AC
JUKEBOX                SELLINGS, ARTHUR  SS   FUN 55 12
  *TIME TRANSFER                  SELLINGS, ARTHUR    AC
JULIETTE               CHEINISSE, CLAUDE F. SS  59
  13 FRENCH SCIENCE-FICTION STORIES  KNIGHT, DAMON    AN
JULIO 204              SARGENT, PAMELA   SS   NWQ 72 03
  NEW WORLDS QUARTERLY NO. 3      MOORCOCK, MICHAEL   OA
  STARSHADOWS                     SARGENT, PAMELA     AC
JULY 24, 1970          O'DONNELL, K. M.  SS   VSF 69 05
  IN THE POCKET AND OTHER S-F STORIES  O'DONNELL, K. M.  DC
JUMP                   EARLS, WILLIAM    SS   ASF 69 10
  ANALOG 8                        CAMPBELL, JOHN W. JR AN
JUNE 6, 2016           ENGLAND, GEORGE A. NV   COL 16 04
  WHEN WOMEN RULE                 MOSKOWITZ, SAM      AN
JUNGLE DOCTOR          YOUNG, ROBERT F.  NV   STS 55 FL
  BEST SCIENCE FICTION STORIES AND NOVELS: 1956
                                  DIKTY, T. E.        AN
  6 FROM WORLDS BEYOND            DIKTY, T. E.        AN
JUNGLE JOURNEY (THE PARADISE CRATER)
             WYLIE, PHILIP        SS   BBM 45 10
  MASTERPIECES OF SCIENCE FICTION  MOSKOWITZ, SAM     AN
JUNGLE ROT KID ON THE NOD, THE  FARMER, PHILIP JOSE  SS  NWS 70 04
  NEW TOMORROWS, THE              SPINRAD, NORMAN     AN
JUNGLE SUBSTITUTE      ALDISS, BRIAN W.  NV   GAL 64 08
  NINTH GALAXY READER, THE        POHL, FREDERIK      AN
JUNGLE, THE            BEAUMONT, CHARLES NV   IFS 54 12
  SECOND WORLD OF IF, THE         QUINN & WULFF       AN
  YONDER                          BEAUMONT, CHARLES   AC
JUNIOR                 ABERNATHY, ROBERT SS   GAL 56 01
  SF: THE BEST OF THE BEST        MERRIL, JUDITH      AN
  SF: THE YEAR'S GREATEST SCIENCE FICTION AND FANTASY
                                  MERRIL, JUDITH      AN
JUNIOR ACHIEVEMENT     LEE, WILLIAM M.   SS   ASF 62 07
  ANALOG 2                        CAMPBELL, JOHN W. JR AN
  TOMORROW'S CHILDREN             ASIMOV, ISAAC       AN
JUNIOR PARTNER         GOULART, RON      SS   FAN 62 09
  WHAT'S BECOME OF SCREWLOOSE? AND OTHER INQUIRIES
                                  GOULART, RON        AC
JUNKMAKERS, THE        TEICHNER, ALBERT  NV   IFS 61 07
  6 FINGERS OF TIME AND 5 OTHER SCIENCE FICTION NOVELETS, THE
                                  ANONYMOUS           AN
JUNKYARD               SIMAK, CLIFFORD D. NV   GAL 53 05
  GALAXY SCIENCE FICTION OMNIBUS  GOLD, H. L.         AN
  SECOND GALAXY READER OF SCIENCE FICTION GOLD, H. L.  AN
JUPITER (SATELLITE FIVE) BARNES, ARTHUR K. NV   TWS 38 10
  INTERPLANETARY HUNTER           BARNES, ARTHUR K.   AC
JUPITER AT LAST        POHL, CAROL       IN C
  JUPITER                         POHL, C. & F.       AN
JUPITER AT LAST        POHL, FREDERIK    IN C
  JUPITER                         POHL, C. & F.       AN
JUPITER FIVE           CLARKE, ARTHUR C. NV   IFS 53 05
  ACROSS THE SEA OF STARS         CLARKE, ARTHUR C.   AC
```

JUPITER FIVE

```
EXPLORERS OF SPACE                          SILVERBERG, ROBERT      AN
REACH FOR TOMORROW                          CLARKE, ARTHUR C.       AC
JUPITER LAUGHS                  COOPER, EDMUND          SS
BEYOND TIME                                 LEY, SANDRA             OA
JUPITER THE GIANT               ASIMOV, ISAAC           IN
JUPITER                                     POHL, C. & F.           AN
JUPITER TRAP                    ROCKLYNNE, ROSS         SS   ASF 37 08
MEN AND THE MIRROR, THE                     ROCKLYNNE, ROSS         AC
JURGEN PROVES IT BY MATHEMATICS
                                CABELL, JAMES BRANCH EX     MBR 19
FANTASIA MATHEMATICA                        FADIMAN, CLIFTON        AN
JURY OF FIVE, A                 HOYLE, FRED             SS
ELEMENT 79                                  HOYLE, FRED             AC
JURY-RIG                        DAVIDSON, AVRAM         SS   VSF 57 11
WHAT STRANGE STARS AND SKIES                DAVIDSON, AVRAM         AC
JUST A MATTER OF TIME           PERRIN, JEFFERY         SS   GAL 73 07
BEST FROM GALAXY, THE  VOLUME II  GALAXY, EDITORS OF             AN
"JUST A SONG AT TWILIGHT"       DERLETH, AUGUST         SS   WRT 30 08
NOT LONG FOR THIS WORLD                     DERLETH, AUGUST         AC
JUST A SUGGESTION               BROWN, ROSEL GEORGE     SS   FSF 60 08
HANDFUL OF TIME, A                          BROWN, ROSEL GEORGE     AC
JUST CALL ME IRISH              WILSON, RICHARD         SS   FUT 58 06
TIME OUT FOR TOMORROW                       WILSON, RICHARD         AC
JUST CURIOUS                    SCHMITZ, JAMES H.       SS        68
SF: AUTHORS' CHOICE 2                        HARRISON, HARRY         AN
JUST DEAD ENOUGH (THE PRICE)    BELCHER, C. DAVIS       NV   ORB 69 05
CLARION                                     WILSON, ROBIN SCOTT     OA
JUST DESSERT                    ROBINSON, SPIDER        SS
CALLAHAN'S CROSSTIME SALOON                 ROBINSON, SPIDER        AC
"JUST LIKE ON TELEVISION-"      WILLEFORD, CHARLES      SS
MACHINE IN WARD ELEVEN, THE                 WILLEFORD, CHARLES      NO
JUSTICE                         WRIGHT, S. FOWLER       SS
NEW GODS LEAD, THE                          WRIGHT, S. FOWLER       AC
JUSTICE OF THE ELEPHANT, THE    SMITH, CLARK ASHTON     SS   ORI 31 08
OTHER DIMENSIONS                            SMITH, CLARK ASHTON     AC
K-FACTOR, THE                   HARRISON, HARRY         NV   ASF 60 12
RULERS OF MEN                               SANTESSON, HANS S.      AN
KALDAR, WORLD OF ANTARES        HAMILTON, EDMOND        NV   MGC 33 04
SWORDSMEN IN THE SKY                        WOLLHEIM, DONALD A.     AN
KALEIDOSCOPE                    BRADBURY, RAY           PL   DMX 51 09
PILLAR OF FIRE AND OTHER PLAYS              BRADBURY, RAY           AC
KALEIDOSCOPE                    BRADBURY, RAY           SS   TWS 49 10
BEST SF 6                                   CRISPIN, EDMUND         AN
GREAT STORIES OF SPACE TRAVEL               CONKLIN, GROFF          AN
HISTORY OF THE SCIENCE FICTION MAGAZINE, THE  PART 3 1946-1955
                                            ASHLEY, MICHAEL         AN
*ILLUSTRATED MAN, THE                       BRADBURY, RAY           AN
OMNIBUS OF SCIENCE FICTION                  CONKLIN, GROFF          AN
SCIENCE FICTION OMNIBUS                     CONKLIN, GROFF          AN
STRANGE TRAVELS IN SCIENCE FICTION          CONKLIN, GROFF          AN
VINTAGE BRADBURY, THE                       BRADBURY, RAY           AC
KANGAROO COURT                  GALOUYE, DANIEL F.      SN   IFS 60 09
LAST LEAP AND OTHER STORIES OF THE SUPER-MIND, THE
                                            GALOUYE, DANIEL F.      AC
KANGAROO COURT (ALSO AS FLOWERING SEASON)
                                KIDD, VIRGINIA          NV   ORB 66 01
ORBIT  1                                    KNIGHT, DAMON           OA
KAPPA NU NEXUS, THE             DAVIDSON, AVRAM
                                AND KLASS, MORTON       SS C FSF 61 08
13 ABOVE THE NIGHT                          CONKLIN, GROFF          AN
KARMESIN AFFAIR, THE (SEE BONE FOR DEBUNKERS)
                                KERSH, GERALD           TC
KATY DIALOGUES, THE             GOULART, RON            SS   FSF 58 07
BROKE DOWN ENGINE AND OTHER TROUBLES WITH MACHINES
                                            GOULART, RON            AC
KAZAM COLLECTS                  KORNBLUTH, C. M.        SS   STI 41 06
*MILE BEYOND THE MOON, A                    KORNBLUTH, C. M.        AN
WORLDS FAR AND NEAR                         CARR, TERRY             AN
KAZOO                           SALLIS, JAMES           SS   NWS 67 08
BEST SF STORIES FROM NEW WORLDS 3           MOORCOCK, MICHAEL       AN
FEW LAST WORDS, A                           SALLIS, JAMES           AC
KEARNY'S LAST CASE              GOULART, RON            SS   FSF 65 09
GHOST BREAKER                               GOULART, RON            DC
KEEP OUT                        BROWN, FREDRIC          SS   AMZ 54 03
HONEYMOON IN HELL                           BROWN, FREDRIC          AC
*SCIENCE FICTION ADVENTURES IN MUTATION  CONKLIN, GROFF         AN
KEEP THEM HAPPY                 ROHRER, ROBERT          SS   FSF 65 04
BEST FROM FANTASY AND SCIENCE FICTION: 15
                                            FERMAN, EDWARD L.       AN
KEEP YOUR SHAPE (SEE SHAPE)     SHECKLEY, ROBERT        TC
KEEPER OF THE DREAM             BEAUMONT, CHARLES       SS        54
*TIME TO COME                               DERLETH, AUGUST         OA
KEEPERS OF THE HOUSE            DEL REY, LESTER         SS   FUN 56 01
DARK STARS                                  SILVERBERG, ROBERT      AN
ROBOTS AND CHANGELINGS                      DEL REY, LESTER         AC
KEEPING AN EYE ON JANEY         GOULART, RON            SS   INY 70 01
INFINITY 1                                  HOSKINS, ROBERT         OA
WHAT'S BECOME OF SCREWLOOSE? AND OTHER INQUIRIES
                                            GOULART, RON            AC
KEEPING PERSPECTIVE             MOORCOCK, MICHAEL       MS
NEW WORLDS QUARTERLY NO. 2                   MOORCOCK, MICHAEL       OA
KELLEY'S EYE, THE               HOSKINS, ROBERT         SS
TOMORROW: NEW WORLDS OF SCIENCE FICTION  ELWOOD, ROGER         OA
KELLY, FREDRIC MICHAEL: 1928-1987
                                NOLAN, WILLIAM F.       SS   INY 73 05
ALIEN HORIZONS                              NOLAN, WILLIAM F.       AC
INFINITY 5                                  HOSKINS, ROBERT         OA
KELPIE, THE                     WELLMAN, MANLY WADE     SS   WRT 36 07
AVON FANTASY READER, THE                    WOLLHEIM &ERNSBERGER    AN
KERSH, THE DEMON PRINCE         ELLISON, HARLAN         IN
NIGHTSHADE & DAMNATIONS                     KERSH, GERALD           AC
KETTLE OF STARS                 SALLIS, JAMES           SS
FEW LAST WORDS, A                           SALLIS, JAMES           AC
KEY ITEM                        ASIMOV, ISAAC           SS   FSF 68 07
BUY JUPITER AND OTHER STORIES               ASIMOV, ISAAC           AC
```

```
KEY OF THE DOOR, THE            SELLINGS, ARTHUR        SS   NWS 67 03
NEW WORLDS QUARTERLY NO. 2                   MOORCOCK, MICHAEL       OA
KEY TO CHAOS                    MACKIN, EDWARD          NV   NWR 64 01
NEW WRITINGS IN SF. 1                        CARNELL, JOHN           AN
KEY TO OUT, THE                 CURTIS, BETSY           SS   ANA 70
ALCHEMY AND ACADEME                         MCCAFFREY, ANNE         OA
KEY, THE                        ASIMOV, ISAAC           NV   FSF 66 10
ASIMOV'S MYSTERIES                          ASIMOV, ISAAC           AC
BEST FROM FANTASY AND SCIENCE FICTION: 16
                                            FERMAN, EDWARD L.       AN
BEST FROM FANTASY AND SCIENCE FICTION, 25TH ANNIV.
                                            FERMAN, EDWARD L.       AN
KEY, THE                        CHANDLER, A. BERTRAM    NV   FAN 59 07
BEYOND THE GALACTIC RIM                     CHANDLER, A. BERTRAM    DC
KEYHOLE                         LEINSTER, MURRAY        SS   TWS 51 12
BEYOND BELIEF                               HURLEY, RICHARD J.      AN
CHILDREN OF WONDER                          TENN, WILLIAM           AN
MEN ON THE MOON                             WOLLHEIM, DONALD A.     DA
SATAN'S PETS                                GHIDALIA, VIC           AN
TOMORROW, AND TOMORROW, AND TOMORROW...  HEINTZ/HERBERT/JOOS/  AN
TOMORROW, THE STARS                         HEINLEIN, ROBERT A.     AN
WORLDS OF WONDER                            HARRISON, HARRY         AN
KEYS TO DECEMBER, THE           ZELAZNY, ROGER          SS   NWS 66 08
BEST SF STORIES FROM NEW WORLDS NO. 1, THE
                                            MOORCOCK, MICHAEL       AN
DOORS OF HIS FACE, THE LAMPS OF HIS MOUTH, THE
                                            ZELAZNY, ROGER          AC
TO THE STARS                                SILVERBERG, ROBERT      AN
WORLD'S BEST SCIENCE FICTION: 1967          WOLLHEIM & CARR         AN
KHARTOUM: A PROSE LIMERICK      BOUCHER, ANTHONY        SS   STF 55 08
STRANGE BED FELLOWS                         SCORTIA, THOMAS N.      AN
KID ANDERSON                    RICHARDSON, R. S.       SS   SPM 57 SP
GREAT SCIENCE FICTION BY SCIENTISTS         CONKLIN, GROFF          AN
KID NOBODY COULD HANDLE, THE    VONNEGUT, KURT JR.      SS   SEP 55 09
WELCOME TO THE MONKEY HOUSE                 VONNEGUT, KURT JR.      AC
KID STUFF                       ASIMOV, ISAAC           SS   BEY 53 09
EARTH IS ROOM ENOUGH                        ASIMOV, ISAAC           AC
KIDDY-LIB                       STOPA, JON              NV   EIO 73
EROS IN ORBIT                               ELDER, JOSEPH           OA
KILEMANJARO DEVICE, THE (THE KILIMANJARO MACHINE)
                                BRADBURY, RAY           SS   LIF 65 01
I SING THE BODY ELECTRIC                    BRADBURY, RAY           AC
KILIMANJARO MACHINE, THE (SEE THE KILIMANJARO DEVICE)
                                BRADBURY, RAY           TC
KILL ME WITH KINDNESS           WILSON, RICHARD         SS   GAL 58 01
FOURTH GALAXY READER, THE                   GOLD, H. L.             AN
KILL, THE                       FLEMING, PETER          SS        42
STRANGE BEASTS AND UNNATURAL MONSTERS  STERN, PHILIP VAN D.  AN
KILLASHANDRA - CRYSTAL SINGER  MCCAFFREY, ANNE         NV   CTM 74 02
CONTINUUM 2                                 ELWOOD, ROGER           OA
KILLASHANDRA- CODA AND FINALE  MCCAFFREY, ANNE         NV   CTM 75 04
CONTINUUM 4                                 ELWOOD, ROGER           OA
KILLDOZER!                      STURGEON, THEODORE      SN   ASF 44 11
ALIENS 4                                    STURGEON, THEODORE      AC
*BEST OF SCIENCE FICTION                    CONKLIN, GROFF          AN
SPECTRUM  3                                 AMIS & CONQUEST         AN
WONDERMAKERS                                HOSKINS, ROBERT         AN
KILLER IN THE TV SET, THE       FRIEDMAN, BRUCE JAY     SS   PBY 61 08
FULLY AUTOMATED LOVE LIFE OF HENRY KEANRIGAN
                                            PLAYBOY, EDITORS OF     AN
PLAYBOY BOOK OF SCIENCE FICTION AND FANTASY
                                            PLAYBOY, EDITORS OF     AN
KILLER PLANTS, THE              GILES, GORDON A.        SS
KILLER PLANTS AND OTHER STORIES, THE  ELWOOD, ROGER           OA
KILLERBOT! (SEE A SEASON FOR FREEDOM)
                                KOONTZ, DEAN R.         TC
KILLING GROUND, THE             BALLARD, J. G.          SS   NWS 69 03
BEST SF STORIES FROM NEW WORLDS 6           MOORCOCK, MICHAEL       AN
BEST SF: 1969                               HARRISON & ALDISS       AN
KIN (SHOW YOUR MIGHT)           WILSON, RICHARD         SS   FUN 56 05
TIME OUT FOR TOMORROW                       WILSON, RICHARD         AC
KIND OF ARTISTRY, A             ALDISS, BRIAN W.        SS   FSF 62 10
AIRS OF EARTH, THE                          ALDISS, BRIAN W.        AC
BEST FROM FANTASY AND SCIENCE FICTION: 12
                                            DAVIDSON, AVRAM         AN
*BEST SCIENCE FICTION STORIES OF BRIAN W. ALDISS
                                            ALDISS, BRIAN W.        AC
STARSWARM                                   ALDISS, BRIAN W.        AC
KIND OF MURDER, A               NIVEN, LARRY            SS   ASF 74 04
HOLE IN SPACE, A                            NIVEN, LARRY            AC
KINDERGARTEN                    LEIBER, FRITZ           SS   FSF 63 04
BOOK OF FRITZ LEIBER, THE                   LEIBER, FRITZ           AC
KINDERGARTEN                    SIMAK, CLIFFORD D.      NV   GAL 53 07
PORTALS OF TOMORROW                         DERLETH, AUGUST         AN
*STRANGERS IN THE UNIVERSE                  SIMAK, CLIFFORD D.      AC
KINDLY ONES, THE                SLADEK, JOHN T.         SS   NWQ 74 06
NEW WORLDS NO. 6                            PLATT & BAILEY          OA
KINDNESS                        DEL REY, LESTER         SS   ASF 44 10
MODERN MASTERPIECES OF SCIENCE FICTION  MOSKOWITZ, SAM         AN
ROBOTS AND CHANGELINGS                      DEL REY, LESTER         AC
VORTEX BLASTERS, THE                        MOSKOWITZ, SAM          AN
YEAR AFTER TOMORROW, THE                    DEL REY, L/MATSCHAT/    AN
KING AND THE DOLLMAKER, THE     JESCHKE, WOLFGANG       NA        70
BEST FROM THE REST OF THE WORLD, THE  WOLLHEIM, DONALD A.    AN
KING AND THE OAK, THE           HOWARD, ROBERT E.       PM
COMING OF CONAN, THE                        HOWARD, ROBERT E.       AC
KING GLOBARES AND THE SAGES     LEM, STANISLAW          SS        72
MORTAL ENGINES                              LEM, STANISLAW          AC
KING HARVEST                    DOZOIS, GARDNER R.      NV   NDM 72 02
NEW DIMENSIONS 2                            SILVERBERG, ROBERT      OA
KING LEAR                       LEIBER, FRITZ           AR        34
BOOK OF FRITZ LEIBER, THE                   LEIBER, FRITZ           AC
KING OF SHADOWS, THE            HAMILTON, EDMOND        NV   WRT 47 01
WHAT'S IT LIKE OUT THERE? AND OTHER STORIES
                                            HAMILTON, EDMOND        AC
```

KING OF THE BEASTS, THE   FARMER, PHILIP JOSE SS   GAL 64 06
  ABC OF SCIENCE FICTION, AN   BOARDMAN, TOM JR.   AN
  NINTH GALAXY READER, THE   POHL, FREDERIK   AN
  SCIENCE FACT/FICTION   FARRELL/GAGE/&   AN
  ZOO 2000   YOLEN, JANE   AN
KING OF THE CATS, THE   BENET, STEPHEN V.   SS   HRP 29 02
  GOLDEN ROAD, THE   KNIGHT, DAMON   AN
  OUT OF THIS WORLD   FAST, JULIUS   AN
KING OF THE CITY, THE   LAUMER, KEITH   NV   GAL 61 08
  GREYLORN   LAUMER, KEITH   AC
  SEVENTH GALAXY READER, THE   POHL, FREDERIK   AN
KING OF THE GOLDEN RIVER, THE   SILVERBERG, ROBERT SS   GAL 67 12
  DIMENSION THIRTEEN   SILVERBERG, ROBERT   AC
KING OF THE GRAY SPACES (ALSO AS R IS FOR ROCKET)
                                 BRADBURY, RAY   SS   FFM 43 12
  EVERY BOY'S BOOK OF SCIENCE FICTION WOLLHEIM, DONALD A. AN
  SCIENCE FICTION GALAXY, THE   CONKLIN, GROFF   AN
  TOMORROW MIDNIGHT   BRADBURY, RAY   AC
KING OF THE HILL   BLISH, JAMES   SS   INF 55 11
  *GALACTIC CLUSTER   BLISH, JAMES   AC
KING OF THE HILL   OLIVER, CHAD   SS   DVS 72 02
  AGAIN, DANGEROUS VISIONS   ELLISON, HARLAN   OA
KING OF THIEVES, THE   VANCE, JACK   NV   STS 49 11
  LOOKING FORWARD   LESSER, MILTON   AN
  MANY WORLDS OF MAGNUS RIDOLPH, THE VANCE, JACK   DC
  WORLDS OF JACK VANCE, THE   VANCE, JACK   AC
KING PEST   POE, EDGAR ALLEN   SS   SLM 35 09
  ANDROIDS, TIME MACHINES AND BLUE GIRAFFES
                                 ELWOOD & GHIDALIA   AN
KING SOLOMON'S RING   ZELAZNY, ROGER   SS   FAN 63 10
  ON OUR WAY TO THE FUTURE   CARR, TERRY   AN
KING WHO COLLECTED CLOCKS, THE (ROYAL IMPOSTOR)
                                 KERSH, GERALD   NV   SEP 47 05
  NIGHTSHADE & DAMNATIONS   KERSH, GERALD   AC
KING'S EVIL   DAVIDSON, AVRAM   SS   FSF 56 10
  BEST FROM FANTASY AND SCIENCE FICTION: 6
                                 BOUCHER, ANTHONY   AN
  OR ALL THE SEAS WITH OYSTERS   DAVIDSON, AVRAM   AC
  SPECIAL WONDER   MCCOMAS, J. FRANCIS   AN
KING'S EYE, THE   POHL, FREDERIK   SS   AST 41 02
  EARLY POHL, THE   POHL, FREDERIK   AC
KING'S SHADOW HAS NO LIMITS, THE
                                 DAVIDSON, AVRAM   SS   WHS 75 04
  ENQUIRIES OF DOCTOR ESZTERHAZY, THE DAVIDSON, AVRAM   NO
KING'S WISHES, THE   SHECKLEY, ROBERT   SS   FSF 53 07
  *UNTOUCHED BY HUMAN HANDS   SHECKLEY, ROBERT   AC
KINGDOM BY THE SEA, A   DOZOIS, GARDNER R. NV   ORB 72 10
  ORBIT 10   KNIGHT, DAMON   OA
KINGDOM OF THE WORM, THE (SEE A TALE OF SIR JOHN MAUNDEVILLE)
                                 SMITH, CLARK ASHTON TC
KINGDOMS OF THE STARS   HAMILTON, EDMOND   NV   AMZ 64 09
  PLANETS OF WONDER   CARR, TERRY   AN
KINGMAKERS   THURSTON, ROBERT   SS
  NEW VOICES IN SCIENCE FICTION   MARTIN, GEORGE R. R.   OA
KINGS IN DARKNESS   MOORCOCK, MICHAEL   NV   SCF 62 08
  SPELL OF SEVEN, THE   DE-CAMP, L. SPRAGUE   AN
KINGS WHO DIE   ANDERSON, POUL   NV   IFS 62 03
  SCIENCE FICTION ROLL OF HONOR, THE POHL, FREDERIK   AN
  7 CONQUESTS   ANDERSON, POUL   AC
  8TH ANNUAL OF THE YEAR'S BEST S-F, THE MERRIL, JUDITH   AN
KINGSLAYER, THE   HUBBARD, L. RON   AC   FPB 49
  FROM DEATH TO THE STARS   HUBBARD, L. RON   AC
KINGSLAYER, THE   HUBBARD, L. RON   NO   FPB 49
KINGSLAYER, THE   HUBBARD, L. RON   AC
KINGSOLVING'S PLANET IRREGULARS (SEE HALL OF FAME)
                                 CHANDLER, A. BERTRAM TC
KISS GOODBYE, A   DISCH, THOMAS M.   SS
  *GETTING INTO DEATH   DISCH, THOMAS M.   AC
KISS OF FIRE   ELLISON, HARLAN   SS   TVW 73
  APPROACHING OBLIVION   ELLISON, HARLAN   AC
  TWO VIEWS OF WONDER   SCORTIA & YARBRO   OA
KISS OF ZORAIDA, THE   SMITH, CLARK ASHTON SS   MGC 33 07
  OTHER DIMENSIONS   SMITH, CLARK ASHTON   AC
KISS PRECISE (GENERALIZED), THE
                                 GOSSETT, THOROLD   PM   NTR 37 01
  MATHEMATICAL MAGPIE, THE   FADIMAN, CLIFTON   AN
KISS PRECISE, THE   SODDY, FREDERICK   SS   NTR 36 06
  MATHEMATICAL MAGPIE, THE   FADIMAN, CLIFTON   AN
'KJWALLL'KJE'K'KOOTHAILLL'KJE'K
                                 ZELAZNY, ROGER   NA   73
  EXALTATION OF STARS, AN   CARR, TERRY   OA
  MY NAME IS LEGION   ZELAZNY, ROGER   AC
KLEON OF THE GOLDEN SUN   REPP, ED EARL   SS   FBK 50 07
  SCIENCE AND SORCERY   FORD, GARRET   AN
KNIFE AND THE SHEATH, THE   ANVIL, CHRISTOPHER SS
  FUTURE KIN   ELWOOD, ROGER   OA
KNIFE THAT KILLED PO HANCY, THE
                                 STOCKTON, FRANK R. NV   93
  SCIENCE FICTION OF FRANK R. STOCKTON, THE
                                 STOCKTON, FRANK R.   AC
KNIGHT FOR MISS MERKINS, A   WELLS, BASIL   SS   FBK 51 07
  PLANETS OF ADVENTURE   WELLS, BASIL   AC
KNIGHT TO MOVE (KNIGHT'S MOVE)   LEIBER, FRITZ   SS   BRD 65 12
  BOOK OF FRITZ LEIBER, THE   LEIBER, FRITZ   AC
KNIGHTS OF ARTHUR, THE   POHL, FREDERIK   NA   GAL 58 01
  FREDERIK POHL OMNIBUS, THE   POHL, FREDERIK   AC
  TOMORROW TIMES SEVEN   POHL, FREDERIK   AC
KNIGHTS OF THE PAPER SPACESHIP: A RETROSPECTIVE GLANCE AT
  SCIENCE FICTION   ALDISS, BRIAN W.   MS
  BEST SF: 1967   HARRISON & ALDISS   AN
KNITTING, THE   WOOD, MARGARET   SS
  AD 2500   WILSON, ANGUS   AN
KNOCK   BROWN, FREDRIC   SS   TWS 48 12
  BEST OF FREDRIC BROWN, THE   BROWN, FREDRIC   AC
  BEST SCIENCE-FICTION STORIES: 1949, THE BLEILER & DIKTY AN
  CONTACT   KEYES, NOEL   AN

PARADOX LOST, AND 12 OTHER GREAT S.F. STORIES
                                 BROWN, FREDRIC   AC
  SHOT IN THE DARK   MERRIL, JUDITH   AN
  SPACE ON MY HANDS   BROWN, FREDRIC   OA
KNOCKER AT THE PORTICO, THE   COPPER, BASIL   SS
  YEAR'S BEST HORROR STORIES: SERIES II, THE
                                 DAVIS, RICHARD   AN
KNOWING HER   BENFORD, GREGORY   SS   NDM 77 07
  NEW DIMENSIONS 7   SILVERBERG, ROBERT   OA
KNOWLEDGE IS POWER   FYFE, H. B.   NV   DSF 52 12
  WAY OUT   HOWARD, IVAN   AN
KNOX   ELLISON, HARLAN   SS   CRW 74 03
  APPROACHING OBLIVION   ELLISON, HARLAN   AC
KOKOD WARRIORS, THE   VANCE, JACK   NV   TWS 52 10
  MANY WORLDS OF MAGNUS RIDOLPH, THE VANCE, JACK   DC
  WORLDS OF JACK VANCE, THE   VANCE, JACK   AC
KON-TIKI MYTH, THE   SUGGS, ROBERT C.   AR   60
  APEMAN, SPACEMAN   STOVER & HARRISON   AN
KONG PAPERS, THE   ELLISON, HARLAN
                                 AND ROTSLER, WILLIAM SS C KNT 73 04
  PARTNERS IN WONDER   ELLISON, HARLAN   AC
KRAKEN WAKES, THE (THE THINGS FROM THE DEEP)
                                 WYNDHAM, JOHN   NO   EVB 53
  JOHN WYNDHAM OMNIBUS, THE   WYNDHAM, JOHN   AC
KYRIE   ANDERSON, POUL   SS   FRS 68
  BEST OF POUL ANDERSON, THE   ANDERSON, POUL   AC
  EXPLORERS OF SPACE   SILVERBERG, ROBERT   AN
  FARTHEST REACHES, THE   ELDER, JOSEPH   OA
  UNIVERSE AHEAD   ENGDAHL & ROBERSON   AN
  WORLD'S BEST SCIENCE FICTION: 1969 WOLLHEIM & CARR   AN
L'ARC DE JEANNE   YOUNG, ROBERT F.   NV   FSF 66 01
  GLASS OF STARS, A   YOUNG, ROBERT F.   AC
L'HOMME   DISCH, THOMAS M.   SS
  *GETTING INTO DEATH   DISCH, THOMAS M.   AC
LA BEFANA   WOLFE, GENE   SS   GAL 73 01
  BEST FROM GALAXY, THE VOLUME II GALAXY, EDITORS OF   AN
  BEST SF: 1973   HARRISON & ALDISS   AN
LA PRELLO PAPER, THE   JACOBI, CARL   SS   WRT 48 03
  PORTRAITS IN MOONLIGHT   JACOBI, CARL   AC
LABORATORY   BIXBY, JEROME   NV   IFS 55 11
  FIRST WORLD OF IF, THE   QUINN & WULFF   AN
  SPACE BY THE TAIL   BIXBY, JEROME   AC
LABYRINTH   JONES, NEIL R.   NV   AMZ 36 04
  SPACE WAR   JONES, NEIL R.   AC
LADIES AND GENTLEMEN, THIS IS YOUR CRISIS
                                 WILHELM, KATE   SS   ORB 76 18
  BEST SCIENCE FICTION STORIES OF THE YEAR (1976)
                                 DOZOIS, GARDNER R.   AN
  ORBIT 18   KNIGHT, DAMON   OA
LADIES OR CLOTHES   KERSH, GERALD   SS   ESQ
  MEN WITHOUT BONES   KERSH, GERALD   AC
LADY ANNE, THE (SEE THE LADY MARGARET)
                                 ROBERTS, KEITH   TC
LADY BOUNTIFUL   KIMBERLY, GAIL   SS
  LEARNING MAZE AND OTHER STORIES, THE ELWOOD, ROGER   AN
LADY IN GRAY, THE   WANDREI, DONALD   SS   WRT 33 12
  EYE AND THE FINGER   WANDREI, DONALD   AC
LADY IN THE TOWER   MCCAFFREY, ANNE   SS   FSF 59 04
  GET OFF THE UNICORN   MCCAFFREY, ANNE   AC
LADY MARGARET, THE (THE LADY ANNE)
                                 ROBERTS, KEITH   NV   IMP 66 04
  DAY IN THE LIFE, A   DOZOIS, GARDNER R.   AN
  PAVANE   ROBERTS, KEITH   NO
LADY OF SPACE   DEL REY, LESTER   NV   VSF 58 07
  MORTALS AND MONSTERS   DEL REY, LESTER   AC
LADY SUNSHINE AND THE MAGOON OF BEATUS
                                 PANSHIN, ALEXEI
                                 AND PANSHIN, CORY   NA C EPC 75
  EPOCH   ELWOOD & SILVERBERG OA
LADY TAKES A POWDER, THE   ACKERMAN, FORREST J.
                                 AND TIGRINA   SS C INS 53
  SCIENCE FICTION WORLDS OF FORREST J. ACKERMAN & FRIENDS
                                 ACKERMAN, FORREST J. AC
LADY WAS A TRAMP, THE   MERRIL, JUDITH   SS   VSF 57 03
  BEST OF JUDITH MERRIL, THE   MERRIL, JUDITH   AC
  OUT OF BOUNDS   MERRIL, JUDITH   AC
  SURVIVAL SHIP AND OTHER STORIES MERRIL, JUDITH   AC
  VENUS FACTOR, THE   GHIDALIA, V.& ELWOOD   AN
LADY WAS FOR KROINKING, THE   BUNCH, DAVID R.   SS   GEN 72
  FUTURE PASTIMES   EDELSTEIN, SCOTT   OA
  GENERATION   GERROLD, DAVID   AN
LADY WHO SAILED THE SOUL, THE   SMITH, CORDWAINER   NV   GAL 60 04
  BEST OF CORDWAINER SMITH, THE   SMITH, CORDWAINER   AC
  MIND PARTNER AND 8 OTHER NOVELETS FROM GALAXY
                                 GOLD, H. L.   AN
  YOU WILL NEVER BE THE SAME   SMITH, CORDWAINER   AC
LAGGING PROFESSION, THE   LOCKHARD, LEONARD   SF   ASF 61 01
  6TH ANNUAL OF THE YEAR'S BEST S-F, THE MERRIL, JUDITH   AN
LAKE OF THE GONE FOREVER, THE   BRACKETT, LEIGH   NV   TWS 49 10
  HALFLING AND OTHER STORIES, THE BRACKETT, LEIGH   AC
  MORE WOMEN OF WONDER   SARGENT, PAMELA   AN
  SPACE ODYSSEYS   ALDISS, BRIAN W.   AC
LAKE OF THE MOUNTAIN SPIRITS, THE
                                 YEFREMOV, IVAN   SS
  MEETING OVER TUSCARORA AND OTHER ADVENTURE TALES, A
                                 YEFREMOV, IVAN   AC
  STORIES   YEFREMOV, IVAN   AC
LAKE OF TUONELA, THE   ROBERTS, KEITH   NV   NWR 74 23
  GRAIN KINGS, THE   ROBERTS, KEITH   AC
  NEW WRITINGS IN SF. 23   BULMER, KENNETH   OA
  PASSING OF THE DRAGONS, THE   ROBERTS, KEITH   AC
LAKE TEMPEST   KEY, EUGENE GEORGE SS
  MARS MOUNTAIN   KEY, EUGENE GEORGE   AC
LAKE, THE   BRADBURY, RAY   SS   WRT 44 05
  AUTUMN PEOPLE, THE   BRADBURY, RAY   AC
  *DARK CARNIVAL   BRADBURY, RAY   AC

GHOUL KEEPERS, THE   MARGULIES, LEO   AN
*OCTOBER COUNTRY, THE   BRADBURY, RAY   AC
SMALL ASSASSIN, THE   BRADBURY, RAY   AC
LAKEWOOD CEMETERY   BERMAN, RUTH   SS   NWQ 74 06
NEW WORLDS NO. 6   PLATT & BAILEY   OA
LAMBDA I   KAPP, COLIN   NV   NWS 62 12
LAMBDA I AND OTHER STORIES   CARNELL, JOHN   AN
LAMBETH BLOSSOM   ALDISS, BRIAN W.   SS   KNT 66 09
STRANGE BED FELLOWS   SCORTIA, THOMAS N.   AN
LAMENT BY A MAKER   DE CAMP, L. SPRAGUE PM   FSF 55 01
BEST FROM FANTASY AND SCIENCE FICTION: 5
                                      BOUCHER, ANTHONY   AN
LAMENT OF THE KEEKU BIRD SKY, KATHLEEN   SS   ALC 73
ALIEN CONDITION, THE   GOLDIN, STEPHEN   OA
LAMIA AND LORD CROMIS, THE HARRISON, M. JOHN NV NWQ 71 01
MACHINE IN SHAFT TEN AND OTHER STORIES, THE
                                      HARRISON, M. JOHN   AC
NEW WORLDS QUARTERLY NO. 1   MOORCOCK, MICHAEL   OA
LAMIA MUTABLE (ALSO AS THE BRINGER WITH THE WINDOW)
                                      HARRISON, M. JOHN SS DVS 72 02
AGAIN, DANGEROUS VISIONS   ELLISON, HARLAN   OA
LAMP OF ALHAZRED, THE   DERLETH, AUGUST
AND LOVECRAFT, H. P.   SS C
SURVIVOR AND OTHER STORIES, THE   LOVECRAFT & DERLETH   AC
LAMPS   MACBETH, GEORGE   PM
BEYOND THIS HORIZON   CARRELL, CHRISTOPHER   OA
LANCELOT BIGGS COOKS A PIRATE BOND, NELSON S. SS FAD 40 02
LANCELOT BIGGS: SPACEMAN   BOND, NELSON S.   AC
LANCELOT BIGGS ON THE SATURN (FROM L.B.: SPACEMAN)
                       BOND, NELSON S.   EX   DBL 50
SCIENCE FICTION AND READER'S GUIDE   BARROWS, MARJORIE   AN
LANCELOT BIGGS, MASTER NAVIGATOR
                       BOND, NELSON S.   SS   FAD 40 05
LANCELOT BIGGS: SPACEMAN   BOND, NELSON S.   AC
LAND IRONCLADS, THE   WELLS, H. G.   NV   SND 03 12
BEST STORIES OF H. G. WELLS   WELLS, H. G.   AC
FUTURE TENSE   CURTIS, RICHARD   AN
SCIENCE FICTION BY GASLIGHT   MOSKOWITZ, SAM   AN
SHORT STORIES OF H. G. WELLS, THE   WELLS, H. G.   AC
*TIME MACHINE AND OTHER STORIES, THE WELLS, H. G.   AC
TWENTY-EIGHT SCIENCE FICTION STORIES WELLS, H. G.   AC
VISIONS OF TOMORROW   ELWOOD, ROGER   AN
WONDERMAKERS   HOSKINS, ROBERT   AN
LAND OF NO SHADOW, THE CLAUDY, CARL H.   NV   AMB 31 02
YEAR AFTER TOMORROW, THE   DEL REY, L/MATSCHAT/   AN
LAND OF THE GREAT HORSES LAFFERTY, R. A. SS   DVS 67 01
DANGEROUS VISIONS   ELLISON, HARLAN   OA
NINE HUNDRED GRANDMOTHERS   LAFFERTY, R. A.   AC
LAND THAT TIME FORGOT, THE BURROUGHS, EDGAR R. NO BBM 18 08
LAND THAT TIME FORGOT AND THE MOON MAID, THE
                                      BURROUGHS, EDGAR R.   AC
LAND THAT TIME FORGOT, THE   BURROUGHS, EDGAR R.   NO
LANDLORD, THE   LESLIE, DELIA   SS   SFM 74 09
BEST OF SCIENCE FICTION MONTHLY, THE SACKS, JANET   AN
LANDMARK   MALEC, ALEXANDER B. SS
EXTRAPOLASIS   MALEC, ALEXANDER B.   AC
LANDRAGON   WOLLHEIM, DONALD A. SS
TWO DOZEN DRAGON EGGS   WOLLHEIM, DONALD A.   AC
LANDSCAPE FOR INSURRECTION HACKER, MARILYN PM QRK 71 02
QUARK/2   DELANY & HACKER   OA
LANDSCAPE OF SHALLOWS, A FINCH, CHRISTOPHER SS NWS 68 07
BEST SF STORIES FROM NEW WORLDS 5   MOORCOCK, MICHAEL   AN
LANDSCAPE WITH ALIENS MARTIN, LARRY W.   SS
CLARION SF   WILHELM, KATE   OA
LANDSCAPE WITH SPHINXES ANDERSON, KAREN   SS   FSF 62 11
BEST FROM FANTASY AND SCIENCE FICTION: 12
                                      DAVIDSON, AVRAM   AN
LANDSCAPES IN SPACE   HARDY, DAVID A.   AR
BEYOND THIS HORIZON   CARRELL, CHRISTOPHER   OA
LANDSLIDE, THE   KELLER, DAVID H. MD. SS
FOLSOM FLINT AND OTHER CURIOUS TALES, THE
                                      KELLER, DAVID H. MD.   AC
LANGUAGE FOR TIME TRAVELERS DE CAMP, L. SPRAGUE AR ASF 38 07
COMING ATTRACTIONS   GREENBERG , MARTIN   NF
LANGUAGE OF LOVE, THE SHECKLEY, ROBERT   SS   GAL 57 05
NOTIONS: UNLIMITED   SHECKLEY, ROBERT   AC
LANSON SCREEN, THE   ZAGAT, ARTHUR LEO   NV   TWS 36 12
*BEST OF SCIENCE FICTION   CONKLIN, GROFF   AN
LAOCOON COMPLEX, THE   FURNAS, J. C.   SS   ESQ 37 04
BEYOND THE BARRIERS OF SPACE AND TIME MERRIL, JUDITH   AN
TIMELESS STORIES FOR TODAY AND TOMORROW BRADBURY, RAY   AN
LAP OF THE PRIMITIVE, THE NOLAN, WILLIAM F. SS FUN 58 10
IMPACT-20   NOLAN, WILLIAM F.   AC
SEA OF SPACE, A   NOLAN, WILLIAM F.   AN
LAPIDA MENACE, THE   CAMPTON, DAVID   NV   ADS 75 02
ARMADA SCI-FI TWO   DAVIS, RICHARD   OA
LAPUTA (FROM "GULLIVER'S TRAVELS", 1726)
                       SWIFT, JONATHAN   EX
*BEYOND TIME AND SPACE   DERLETH, AUGUST   AN
LAPUTAN PROJECTS (FROM "GULLIVER'S TRAVELS")
                       SWIFT, JONATHAN   EX
ARMCHAIR SCIENCE READER, THE   GORDON, I. & SORKIN   AN
LARGE ANT, THE (THE BIG ANT) FAST, HOWARD SS FUN 60 02
CONTACT   KEYES, NOEL   AN
DECADE THE 1950S   ALDISS & HARRISON   AN
EDGE OF TOMORROW, THE   FAST, HOWARD   AC
SPECTRUM 4   AMIS & CONQUEST   AN
6TH ANNUAL OF THE YEAR'S BEST S-F, THE MERRIL, JUDITH   AN
LARGE PAINTING WHICH IS A LANDSCAPE, A
                       TANGUY, YVES   IL
SCIENCE FICTION   BRODKIN & PEARSON   AN
LARGO   STURGEON, THEODORE SS   FAD 47 07
BEYOND   STURGEON, THEODORE   AC
LAST   LEIBER, FRITZ   SS   FSF 57 03
ENDS OF TIME, THE   SILVERBERG, ROBERT   AN
WORLDS OF FRITZ LEIBER, THE   LEIBER, FRITZ   AC

LAST ACT, THE   COOPER, EDMUND   SS
VOICES IN THE DARK   COOPER, EDMUND   AC
LAST AMERICAN, THE   MITCHELL, J. A.   SS   SCR 89 06
FAR BOUNDARIES   DERLETH, AUGUST   AN
LAST AND FIRST MEN   STAPLEDON, OLAF   EX   MTH 30
ALL ABOUT VENUS   ALDISS, BRIAN W.   AN
FAREWELL FANTASTIC VENUS   ALDISS & HARRISON   AN
WORLDS APART   WILLIAMS-ELLIS& OWEN   AN
LAST AND FIRST MEN   STAPLEDON, OLAF   NO   MTH 30
TO THE END OF TIME   STAPLEDON, OLAF   AC
LAST BLAST   RUSSELL, ERIC FRANK NV   ASF 52 11
DEEP SPACE   RUSSELL, ERIC FRANK   AC
LAST BOUNCE, THE   TENN, WILLIAM   NV   FAD 50 09
SQUARE ROOT OF MAN, THE   TENN, WILLIAM   AC
LAST CANTICLE, THE   MILLER, WALTER M. JR NV FSF 57 02
CANTICLE FOR LEIBOWITZ, A   MILLER, WALTER M. JR   NO
LAST CAPER, THE   BEAUMONT, CHARLES   SS   FSF 54 03
EDGE, THE   BEAUMONT, CHARLES   AC
MAGIC MAN AND OTHER SCIENCE-FANTASY STORIES
                                      BEAUMONT, CHARLES   AC
YONDER   BEAUMONT, CHARLES   AC
LAST CASTLE, THE   VANCE, JACK   NV   GAL 66 04
ACE SCIENCE FICTION READER   WOLLHEIM, DONALD A.   AN
BEST OF JACK VANCE, THE   VANCE, JACK   AC
HUGO WINNERS, THE (VOLUME 2)   ASIMOV, ISAAC   AN
NEBULA AWARD STORIES NO. 2   ALDISS & HARRISON   AN
LAST COMMAND, THE   CLARKE, ARTHUR C.   SS   BIZ 65 11
WIND FROM THE SUN, THE   CLARKE, ARTHUR C.   AC
LAST COMMAND, THE   LAUMER, KEITH   SS   ASF 67 01
ANALOG 7   CAMPBELL, JOHN W. JR   AN
BEST SF: 1967   HARRISON & ALDISS   AN
BOLO   LAUMER, KEITH   AC
COMBAT SF   DICKSON, GORDON R.   AN
ONCE THERE WAS A GIANT   LAUMER, KEITH   AC
POCKETFUL OF STARS, A   KNIGHT, DAMON   AN
TALES OF TIME AND SPACE   OLNEY, ROSS R.   AN
THEMES IN SCIENCE FICTION   KELLEY, LEO P.   AN
LAST CONGREGATION, THE GOLDSMITH, HOWARD SS   FCR 75
FUTURE CORRUPTION   ELWOOD, ROGER   OA
VISIONS OF TOMORROW   ELWOOD, ROGER   AN
LAST CRUISE OF THE JUDAS ISCARIOT, THE
                       MITCHELL, EDWARD P. SS   SUN 82 04
CRYSTAL MAN, THE   MITCHELL, EDWARD P.   AC
LAST CRUSADE, THE   SMITH, GEORGE HUDSON SS IFS 55 02
FIRST WORLD OF IF, THE   QUINN & WULFF   AN
THIS SIDE OF INFINITY   CARR, TERRY   AN
LAST DAY OF JULY, THE DOZOIS, GARDNER R. NV   NDM 73 03
NEW DIMENSIONS 3   SILVERBERG, ROBERT   OA
LAST DAY OF SUMMER, THE TUBB, E. C.   SS   SCF 55 02
SF: THE YEAR'S GREATEST SCIENCE FICTION AND FANTASY
                                      MERRIL, JUDITH   AN
TEN FROM TOMORROW   TUBB, E. C.   AC
LAST DAY, THE   MATHESON, RICHARD   SS   AMZ 53 05
BEST SCIENCE-FICTION STORIES: 1954, THE BLEILER & DIKTY   AN
DECADE THE 1950S   ALDISS & HARRISON   AN
HISTORY OF THE SCIENCE FICTION MAGAZINE, THE PART 3 1946-1955
                                      ASHLEY, MICHAEL   AN
SHORES OF SPACE, THE   MATHESON, RICHARD   AC
LAST DAY, THE (SEE THE VERY LAST DAY OF A GOOD WOMAN)
                                      ELLISON, HARLAN   TC
LAST DAYS OF SHANDAKOR, THE BRACKETT, LEIGH NV STS 52 04
BEST OF LEIGH BRACKETT, THE   BRACKETT, LEIGH   AC
COMING OF THE TERRANS, THE   BRACKETT, LEIGH   NO
PRIZE SCIENCE FICTION   WOLLHEIM, DONALD A.   AN
LAST DAYS OF THE CAPTAIN, THE WILHELM, KATE SS AMZ 62 11
MILE-LONG SPACESHIP, THE   WILHELM, KATE   AC
LAST DAYS OF THE PERMANENT FLOATING RIOT CLUB, THE
                       NIVEN, LARRY   SS   NEW 74 AC
HOLE IN SPACE, A   NIVEN, LARRY   AC
LAST DESPERATE HOUR, THE THURSTON, ROBERT SS CLR 71 01
CLARION   WILSON, ROBIN SCOTT   OA
LAST DOOR TO AIYA   PARNOV, YEREMEY
AND YEMTSEV, MIKHAIL   SS C ISF 68 06
LAST DOOR TO AIYA   GINSBURG, MIRRA   AN
LAST DREAMER   CHANDLER, A. BERTRAM NV IFS 68 08
RIM GODS, THE   CHANDLER, A. BERTRAM   DC
LAST ENEMY   PIPER, H. BEAM   NV   ASF 50 08
*ASTOUNDING SCIENCE FICTION ANTHOLOGY, THE
                                      CAMPBELL, JOHN W. JR   AN
LAST EVOLUTION, THE   CAMPBELL, JOHN W. JR SS AMZ 32 08
AWARD SCIENCE FICTION READER   NORTON, ALDEN H.   AN
*BEST OF JOHN W. CAMPBELL, THE   CAMPBELL, JOHN W. JR   AC
LAST FLIGHT OF DR. AIN, THE TIPTREE, JAMES JR. SS GAL 69 03
SF: AUTHORS' CHOICE 4   HARRISON, HARRY   AN
WARM WORLDS AND OTHERWISE   TIPTREE, JAMES JR.   AC
LAST GENERATION, THE   DEFORD, MIRIAM ALLEN SS FSF 50 12
XENOGENESIS   DEFORD, MIRIAM ALLEN   AC
LAST GHOST, THE   GOLDIN, STEPHEN   SS   PRT 71
NEBULA AWARD STORIES NO. 7   BIGGLE, LLOYD JR.   AN
PROTOSTARS   GERROLD & GOLDIN   OA
LAST GUNFIGHT, THE (LEE CRONIN)
                       BLISH, JAMES   SA   STK 69 03
STAR TREK 3   BLISH, JAMES   OC
LAST HEIROGLYPH, THE   SMITH, CLARK ASHTON SS WRT 35 04
OUT OF SPACE AND TIME   SMITH, CLARK ASHTON   AC
LAST HOUSE CALL, THE   NOURSE, ALAN E.   SS   NEW 71 AC
RX FOR TOMORROW   NOURSE, ALAN E.   AC
LAST HURRAH OF THE GOLDEN HORDE, THE
                       SPINRAD, NORMAN   SS   NWS 69 07
BEST SF STORIES FROM NEW WORLDS 5   MOORCOCK, MICHAEL   AN
DECADE THE 1960S   ALDISS & HARRISON   AN
LAST HURRAH OF THE GOLDEN HORDE, THE SPINRAD, NORMAN   AC
NEW TOMORROWS, THE   SPINRAD, NORMAN   AN
SF: AUTHORS' CHOICE 3   HARRISON, HARRY   AN
LAST INN ON THE ROAD, THE PLACHTA, DANNIE
AND ZELAZNY, ROGER   SS C NWS 67 10

LAST INN ON THE ROAD, THE
  BEST SF STORIES FROM NEW WORLDS 5   MOORCOCK, MICHAEL   AN
LAST INNING   BOND, NELSON S.   SS   BBM 48 05
  NIGHTMARES AND DAYDREAMS   BOND, NELSON S.   AC
LAST LAUGH (SEE SPECIAL APTITUDE)
                             STURGEON, THEODORE   TC
LAST LEAF, THE   MACFARLANE, WALLACE SS   ORB 71 09
  ORBIT 9   KNIGHT, DAMON   OA
LAST LEAP, THE   GALOUYE, DANIEL F.   NV   IFS 60 01
  LAST LEAP AND OTHER STORIES OF THE SUPER-MIND, THE
                             GALOUYE, DANIEL F.   AC
LAST LETTER, THE   LEIBER, FRITZ   SS   GAL 58 06
  FIFTH GALAXY READER, THE   GOLD, H. L.   AN
  PAIL OF AIR, A   LEIBER, FRITZ   AC
  WORLDS OF FRITZ LEIBER, THE   LEIBER, FRITZ   AC
LAST LONELY MAN, THE   BRUNNER, JOHN   SS   NWS 64 06
  BEST OF NEW WORLDS, THE   MOORCOCK, MICHAEL AN
  BEST SF STORIES FROM NEW WORLDS 8 MOORCOCK, MICHAEL AN
  MARRIAGE AND THE FAMILY THROUGH SCIENCE FICTION
                             CLEAR/WARRICK/&   AN
 *OUT OF MY MIND   BRUNNER, JOHN   AC
  WORLD'S BEST SCIENCE FICTION: 1965 WOLLHEIM & CARR   AN
  10TH ANNUAL OF THE YEAR'S BEST S-F, THE MERRIL, JUDITH AN
LAST LUNARIANS, THE   WYNDHAM, JOHN   SS   TOW 38 SU
  WANDERERS OF TIME   WYNDHAM, JOHN   AC
LAST MAGICIAN, THE   ELLIOTT, BRUCE   SS   FSF 53 01
  FANTASIA MATHEMATICA   FADIMAN, CLIFTON AN
LAST MAN   INOUYE, JON   SS
  NIGHT TIDE, A   INOUYE, JON   OC
LAST MAN LEFT IN THE BAR, THE KORNBLUTH, C. M.   SS   INF 57 10
  ALPHA 1   SILVERBERG, ROBERT AN
  BEST OF C. M. KORNBLUTH, THE   KORNBLUTH, C. M. AC
 *MILE BEYOND THE MOON, A   KORNBLUTH, C. M. AC
LAST MAN, THE   WEST, WALLACE   NV   AMZ 29 02
  POCKET BOOK OF SCIENCE-FICTION, THE WOLLHEIM, DONALD A. AN
  WHEN WOMEN RULE   MOSKOWITZ, SAM   AN
LAST MAN, THE (NOAH)   BECKMAN, CHARLES JR. SS   OSF 54 11
  SPACE STATION 42 AND OTHER STORIES ANONYMOUS   AN
LAST MAN, THE (1826)   SHELLEY, MARY W.   EX
  SPECULATIONS   SANDERS, THOMAS E. AN
  STRANGE SIGNPOSTS   ELWOOD & MOSKOWITZ AN
  VISIONS OF TOMORROW   ELWOOD, ROGER   AN
LAST MARTIAN, THE   BROWN, FREDRIC   SS   GAL 50 10
  BEST SCIENCE-FICTION STORIES: 1951, THE BLEILER & DIKTY AN
 *GALAXY READER OF SCIENCE FICTION   GOLD, H. L.   AN
  HONEYMOON IN HELL   BROWN, FREDRIC   AC
  MINDWORM, THE   ANONYMOUS   AN
LAST MARTIAN, THE   WEINBAUM, STANLEY G. PM
  MARTIAN ODYSSEY AND OTHER SCIENCE FICTION TALES, A
                             WEINBAUM, STANLEY G. AC
LAST MEN, THE   LONG, FRANK BELKNAP SS   ASF 34 08
  RIM OF THE UNKNOWN   LONG, FRANK BELKNAP AC
  SCIENCE FICTION OF THE 30'S   KNIGHT, DAMON   AN
LAST MONSTER, THE (TERMINAL QUEST)
                             ANDERSON, POUL   SS   SSS 51 08
  ALIEN WORLDS   ELWOOD, ROGER   AN
  LOOKING FORWARD   LESSER, MILTON   AN
LAST NIGHT IN THE RAIN (SIN TOWER)
                             BEAUMONT, CHARLES   SS   NUG 56
  HUNGER AND OTHER STORIES, THE   BEAUMONT, CHARLES AC
LAST NIGHT OF SUMMER, THE   COPPEL, ALFRED   SS   OSF 54 09
  END OF THE WORLD, THE   WOLLHEIM, DONALD A. AN
  PLANET OF DOOM AND OTHER STORIES   ANONYMOUS   AN
LAST NIGHT OF THE WORLD, THE BRADBURY, RAY   SS   ESQ 51 02
 *ILLUSTRATED MAN, THE   BRADBURY, RAY   AC
LAST OBJECTIVE, THE   CARTER, PAUL A.   NV   ASF 46 08
  DECADE THE 1940S   ALDISS & HARRISON AN
 *TREASURY OF SCIENCE FICTION, A   CONKLIN, GROFF   AN
LAST OF THE DELIVERERS, THE ANDERSON, POUL   SS   FSF 58 02
  BEST OF POUL ANDERSON, THE   ANDERSON, POUL   AN
  POLITICAL SCIENCE FICTION   GREENBERG& WARRICK AN
  SF: AUTHORS' CHOICE   HARRISON, HARRY   AN
LAST OF THE MASTERS, THE   DICK, PHILIP K.   SS   OSF 54 11
  SPACE STATION 42 AND OTHER STORIES ANONYMOUS   AN
LAST OF THE MORTICIANS   TUBB, E. C.   SS   GAL 59 10
  TEN FROM TOMORROW   TUBB, E. C.   AC
LAST OF THE ROMANY, THE   SPINRAD, NORMAN   SS   ASF 63 05
  LAST HURRAH OF THE GOLDEN HORDE, THE SPINRAD, NORMAN AC
  THEMES IN SCIENCE FICTION   KELLEY, LEO P.   AN
  WINDOWS INTO TOMORROW   SILVERBERG, ROBERT AN
LAST OF THE SPODE, THE   SMITH, EVELYN E.   SS   FSF 53 06
  17 X INFINITY   CONKLIN, GROFF   AN
LAST OUTPOST, THE   BOND, NELSON S.   NV
  NO TIME LIKE THE FUTURE   BOND, NELSON S.   AC
LAST POET AND THE ROBOTS, THE MERRITT, A.   SS   FMG 34 04
  FOX WOMAN & OTHER STORIES, THE   MERRITT, A.   AC
LAST PRESENT, THE   STANTON, WILL   SS   FSF 56 08
  BEST FROM FANTASY AND SCIENCE FICTION: 6
                             BOUCHER, ANTHONY   AN
LAST PROPHET, THE   CLINGERMAN, MILDRED SS   FSF 55 08
  BEST FROM FANTASY AND SCIENCE FICTION: 5
                             BOUCHER, ANTHONY   AN
  CUPFUL OF SPACE, A   CLINGERMAN, MILDRED AC
LAST QUESTION, THE   ASIMOV, ISAAC   SS   SFQ 56 11
  BEST OF ISAAC ASIMOV, THE   ASIMOV, ISAAC   AC
  NINE TOMORROWS   ASIMOV, ISAAC   AC
  OPUS 100   ASIMOV, ISAAC   AC
  SCIENCE FICTION ROLL OF HONOR, THE POHL, FREDERIK   AN
  SPACE OPERA   ALDISS, BRIAN W. AN
  3000 YEARS OF FANTASY AND SCIENCE FICTION
                             DE CAMP, L. S.&C.   AN
LAST RITES   BEAUMONT, CHARLES   SS   IFS 55 10
  FIRST WORLD OF IF, THE   QUINN & WULFF   AN
  MAGIC MAN AND OTHER SCIENCE-FANTASY STORIES
                             BEAUMONT, CHARLES   AC
  PSEUDO PEOPLE, THE   NOLAN, WILLIAM F. AN
  YONDER   BEAUMONT, CHARLES AC

LAST SALAMANDER, THE   RACKHAM, JOHN   SS   NWS 63 07
  LAMBDA I AND OTHER STORIES   CARNELL, JOHN   AN
LAST SEANCE, THE (1926)   CHRISTIE, AGATHA   SS   EQM 71 11
  BEYOND THE BARRIERS OF SPACE AND TIME MERRIL, JUDITH AN
  VENUS FACTOR, THE   GHIDALIA, V.& ELWOOD AN
LAST SECRET WEAPON OF THE THIRD REICH, THE
                             NESVADBA, JOSEF   SS   64
  10TH ANNUAL OF THE YEAR'S BEST S-F, THE MERRIL, JUDITH AN
LAST SHALL BE FIRST, THE   MILLS, ROBERT P.   SS   FSF 58 08
  DECADE OF FANTASY AND SCIENCE FICTION, A MILLS, ROBERT P. AN
LAST STAND OF A SPACE GRENADIER
                             WOLLHEIM, DONALD A. SS   SFQ 54 08
  TWO DOZEN DRAGON EGGS   WOLLHEIM, DONALD A. AC
LAST STEP, THE   HENDERSON, ZENNA   SS   FSF 58 02
  ANYTHING BOX, THE   HENDERSON, ZENNA AC
LAST SUPER BOWL GAME, THE   MARTIN, GEORGE R. R. NV   GLR 75 02
  RUN TO STARLIGHT, SPORTS THROUGH SCIENCE FICTION
                             GREENBERG/OLANDER/& AN
LAST SUPPER, THE   FITZGERALD, RUSSELL SS   QRK 71 02
  QUARK/2   DELANY & HACKER   OA
LAST TERRESTRIALS, THE (FROM "LAST AND FIRST MEN")
                             STAPLEDON, OLAF   EX   MTH 30
  TREASURY OF SCIENCE FICTION CLASSICS, THE
                             KUEBLER, HAROLD W.   AN
LAST THREE MONTHS, THE   NOLAN, WILLIAM F.   SS   RAT 63
  ALIEN HORIZONS   NOLAN, WILLIAM F. AC
LAST TIME AROUND, THE   SELLINGS, ARTHUR   NV   NWR 68 12
  NEW WRITINGS IN SF. 9   CARNELL, JOHN   AN
  NEW WRITINGS IN SF. 12   CARNELL, JOHN   OA
  WORLD'S BEST SCIENCE FICTION: 1971 WOLLHEIM & CARR   AN
LAST TRAIN TO KANKAKEE   SCOTT, ROBIN S.   SS   DVS 72 02
  AGAIN, DANGEROUS VISIONS   ELLISON, HARLAN   AN
LAST TRAIN TO LIMBO   BABER, ASA   SS   PBY 70 07
  LAST TRAIN TO LIMBO   PLAYBOY, EDITORS OF AN
LAST TRAIN, THE   BROWN, FREDRIC   SS   WRT 50 01
  PARADOX LOST, AND 12 OTHER GREAT S.F. STORIES
                             BROWN, FREDRIC   AC
LAST TRUE GOD, THE   DEL REY, LESTER   SS   IFS 69 09
  BEST FROM IF, THE VOLUME I   IF, EDITORS OF   AN
  LOOKING AHEAD   ALLEN, D. & L.   AN
LAST TRUMP, THE   ASIMOV, ISAAC   SS   FUN 55 06
  EARTH IS ROOM ENOUGH   ASIMOV, ISAAC   AC
LAST VICTORY, THE   GODWIN, TOM   SS   IFS 57 08
  BEST SCIENCE FICTION STORIES AND NOVELS: 9TH SERIES
                             DIKTY, T. E.   AN
LAST WAR, THE   SCORTIA, THOMAS N.   SS   NEW 75 AC
  CAUTION INFLAMMABLE   SCORTIA, THOMAS N. AC
LAST WAR, THE (THE BUTTERFLY KISS)
                             SAVAGE, ARTHUR D.   SS   OSF 54 02
  PLANET OF DOOM AND OTHER STORIES   ANONYMOUS   AN
LAST WEAPON, THE   SHECKLEY, ROBERT   SS   STR 53 05
  PEOPLE TRAP AND OTHER PITFALLS, THE SHECKLEY, ROBERT AC
  STAR SCIENCE FICTION STORIES   POHL, FREDERIK   OA
LAST WILL AND TESTAMENT   RUSSELL, RAY   SS   55
  SARDONICUS AND OTHER STORIES   RUSSELL, RAY   AC
LAST WOMAN, THE   GARDNER, THOMAS S.   SS   WOS 32 04
  FROM OFF THIS WORLD   MARGULIES & FRIEND AN
  WHEN WOMEN RULE   MOSKOWITZ, SAM   AN
LAST WORD, THE   GUNN, JAMES E.   SS   NEW 64 AC
  FUTURE IMPERFECT   GUNN, JAMES E.   AC
LAST WORD, THE   KNIGHT, DAMON   SS   SAT 57 02
  BEST OF DAMON KNIGHT, THE   KNIGHT, DAMON   AC
  FAR OUT   KNIGHT, DAMON   AC
LAST WORD, THE   BEAUMONT, CHARLES
                    AND OLIVER, CHAD   SS C FSF 55 04
  BEST FROM FANTASY AND SCIENCE FICTION: 5
                             BOUCHER, ANTHONY   AN
  EVIL EARTHS   ALDISS, BRIAN W. AN
LAST WORLD OF MR. GODDARD, THE BALLARD, J. G.   SS   SCF 60 10
  DAY OF FOREVER, THE   BALLARD, J. G.   AC
  TERMINAL BEACH (AMERICAN VERSION) BALLARD, J. G.   AC
LAST YEAR'S GRAVE UNDUG   DAVIS, CHAN   SS   NEW 62 04
  GREAT SCIENCE FICTION BY SCIENTISTS CONKLIN, GROFF   AN
LAST, THE VERY LAST, THE   BRADBURY, RAY   SS   REP 55 06
  DANDELION WINE   BRADBURY, RAY   NO
LASTBORN (SEE THE UGLY LITTLE BOY)
                             ASIMOV, ISAAC   TC
LATE   CHANDLER, A. BERTRAM SS   SCF 55 04
  BEYOND TOMORROW   HARDING, LEE   AN
  SF: AUTHORS' CHOICE 2   HARRISON, HARRY   AN
LATE NIGHT FINAL   RUSSELL, ERIC FRANK NV   ASF 48 12
 *ASTOUNDING SCIENCE FICTION ANTHOLOGY, THE
                             CAMPBELL, JOHN W. JR AN
  ASTOUNDING TALES OF SPACE AND TIME CAMPBELL, JOHN W. JR AN
 *SECOND ASTOUNDING SCIENCE FICTION ANTHOLOGY, THE
                             CAMPBELL, JOHN W. JR AN
LATER THAN YOU THINK   LEIBER, FRITZ   SS   GAL 50 10
  BEST SF 5   CRISPIN, EDMUND   AN
  EVIL EARTHS   ALDISS, BRIAN W. AN
  FAR BOUNDARIES   DERLETH, AUGUST   AN
LATEST FROM SIGMA CORVI, THE WELLEN, EDWARD   SS   ALC 73
  ALIEN CONDITION, THE   GOLDIN, STEPHEN   OA
LAUGH, CLONE, LAUGH   ACKERMAN, FORREST J.
                    AND VAN VOGT, A. E.   SS C NEW 69 AC
  MORE THAN SUPERHUMAN   VAN VOGT, A. E.   AC
  SCIENCE FICTION WORLDS OF FORREST J. ACKERMAN & FRIENDS
                             ACKERMAN, FORREST J. AC
LAUGHING LION, THE   JONES, RAYMOND F.   SS   SPT 73
  SCIENCE FICTION TALES   ELWOOD, ROGER   OA
LAURA   SAKI   SS   14
  BEWARE MORE BEASTS   GHIDALIA, V.& ELWOOD AN
  OUT OF THIS WORLD   FAST, JULIUS   AN
LAW OF CONSERVATION OF PAIN, THE
                             ROBINSON, SPIDER   NV   VTX 74 12
  CALLAHAN'S CROSSTIME SALOON   ROBINSON, SPIDER AC

LAW-TWISTER SHORTY, THE   DICKSON, GORDON R.   NV   MWS 71
  MANY WORLDS OF SCIENCE FICTION, THE   BOVA, BEN   OA
LAW, THE   COATES, ROBERT M.   SS   NYM 47 11
  ECO-FICTION   STADLER, JOHN   AN
  MATHEMATICAL MAGPIE, THE   FADIMAN, CLIFTON   AN
LAWBREAKER (VIOLATION)   NOLAN, WILLIAM F.   SS   FUC 73
  ALIEN HORIZONS   NOLAN, WILLIAM F.   AC
LAWGIVER, THE   LAUMER, KEITH   SS   YRT 70
  BEST OF KEITH LAUMER, THE LAUMER, KEITH   AC
  ONCE THERE WAS A GIANT   LAUMER, KEITH   AC
  TOMORROW, AND TOMORROW, AND TOMORROW... HEINTZ/HERBERT/JOOS/ AN
  YEAR 2000, THE   HARRISON, HARRY   OA
LAWNS OF SUMMER, THE   BRADBURY, RAY   SS   NBS 52 02
  DANDELION WINE   BRADBURY, RAY   NO
LAXIAN KEY, THE   SHECKLEY, ROBERT   SS   GAL 54 11
  PEOPLE TRAP AND OTHER PITFALLS, THE   SHECKLEY, ROBERT   AC
LAZARUS   ANDREYEV, LEONID   SS   WRT 27 03
  NEW WORLDS OF FANTASY NO. 2   CARR, TERRY   AN
LAZARUS   ST. CLAIR, MARGARET SS   STS 55 FL
  CHANGE THE SKY AND OTHER STORIES   ST. CLAIR, MARGARET AC
LAZARUS   TUBB, E. C.   SS
  BEYOND THIS HORIZON   CARRELL, CHRISTOPHER OA
LAZARUS COME FORTH| SILVERBERG, ROBERT   NV   GAL 66 04
  TO OPEN THE SKY   SILVERBERG, ROBERT   NO
LAZARUS II   DEFORD, MIRIAM ALLEN SS   NDM 72 02
  NEW DIMENSIONS 2   SILVERBERG, ROBERT   OA
LAZARUS II   MATHESON, RICHARD   SS   FSM 53 07
  SHOCK II   MATHESON, RICHARD   AC
LEADER OF THE CLUB, THE   ZICREE, MARC SCOTT   SS
  CLARION SF   WILHELM, KATE   OA
LEADER OF THE REVOLUTION   DISCH, THOMAS M.   SS   BIZ 65 10
  *ONE HUNDRED AND TWO H-BOMBS   DISCH, THOMAS M.   AC
LEADER, THE   LEINSTER, MURRAY   SS   ASF 60 02
  14 GREAT TALES OF ESP   STONE, IDELLA P.   AN
LEADING MAN   BIGGLE, LLOYD JR.   SS   GAL 57 06
  METALLIC MUSE, THE   BIGGLE, LLOYD JR.   AC
LEADINGTON INCIDENT, THE   PRIESTLEY, J. B.   SS
  OTHER PLACE, THE   PRIESTLEY, J. B.   AC
LEARNING MAZE, THE   BLOCH, ROBERT   SS
  COLD CHILLS   BLOCH, ROBERT   AC
  LEARNING MAZE AND OTHER STORIES, THE   ELWOOD, ROGER OA
LEARNING THEORY   MCCONNELL, JAMES   SS   IFS 57 12
  GREAT SCIENCE FICTION BY SCIENTISTS   CONKLIN, GROFF   AN
  INTRODUCTORY PSYCHOLOGY THROUGH SCIENCE FICTION
                             KATZ/WARRICK/&   AN
LECTURE DEMONSTRATION   CLEMENT, HAL   SS   AMA 73
  ASTOUNDING   HARRISON, HARRY   OA
LECTURES ON PARAPSYCHOLOGY   VARSHAVSKY, ILYA   SS
  OTHER WORLDS, OTHER SEAS   SUVIN, DARKO   AN
LEECH, THE   SHECKLEY, ROBERT   SS   GAL 52 12
  NOTIONS: UNLIMITED   SHECKLEY, ROBERT   AC
  SCIENCE FICTION TERROR TALES   CONKLIN, GROFF   AN
LEFT-HAND WAY, THE   CHANDLER, A. BERTRAM SS   AUS 67
  BEST SF: 1967   HARRISON & ALDISS   AN
LEFT-HANDED BOY, THE   PIERIK, ROBERT   NV
  ANYWHERE, ANYWHEN   ENGDAHL, SYLVIA   OA
LEFTY FEEP GETS HENPECKED   BLOCH, ROBERT   NV   FAD 45 04
  SATAN'S PETS   GHIDALIA, VIC   AN
LEG. FORST.   SIMAK, CLIFFORD D.   NV   INF 58 04
  SO BRIGHT THE VISION   SIMAK, CLIFFORD D.   DC
LEGACY OF TERROR   SLESAR, HENRY   SS   AMZ 58 11
  SATAN'S PETS   GHIDALIA, VIC   AN
LEGAL RITES   ASIMOV, ISAAC
  AND POHL, FREDERIK   NV C WRT 50 09
  BR-R-R-| CONKLIN, GROFF   AN
  EARLY ASIMOV, THE   ASIMOV, ISAAC   AC
  EDGE OF NEVER, THE   HOSKINS, ROBERT   AN
  UNEXPECTED, THE   MARGULIES, LEO   AN
LEGEND OF COUGAR LOU LANDIS, THE
                             BRYANT, EDWARD   SS   UNI 73 03
  UNIVERSE 3   CARR, TERRY   OA
LEGEND OF FIN M'COUL, THE   CARLETON, WILLIAM   SS
  FANTASY: THE LITERATURE OF THE MARVELOUS KELLEY, LEO P.   AN
LEGEND OF HOMBAS, THE   PANGBORN, EDGAR   NV   CTM 74 02
  CONTINUUM 2   ELWOOD, ROGER   OA
LEGEND OF JOE LEE, THE   MACDONALD, JOHN D.   SS   CMP 64
  10TH ANNUAL OF THE YEAR'S BEST S-F, THE   MERRIL, JUDITH   AN
LEGEND OF LONNIE AND THE SEVEN TEN SPLIT, THE
                             BLAKE, E. MICHAEL   NV   ALT 74
  ALTERNATES   GERROLD, DAVID   OA
LEGEND OF MONT ST. MICHEL, THE DE MAUPASSANT, GUY SS
  DEALS WITH THE DEVIL   DAVENPORT, BASIL   AN
LEGEND OF POLDEVIA   AYME, MARCEL   SS
  WALKER THROUGH WALLS, THE AYME, MARCEL   AC
LEGENDARY SHIP, THE   MITCHELL, EDWARD P. SS   SUN 85 05
  CRYSTAL MAN, THE   MITCHELL, EDWARD P.   AC
LEGENDS FROM "THE CHESHIRE CAT" (TRANSLATED BY ISABEL READE)
                             IMBERT, ENRIQUE A.   SS
  NEW CONSTELLATIONS   DISCH & NAYLOR   OA
LEGENDS OF SMITH'S BURST   ALDISS, BRIAN W.   SS   NEB 59 06
  SALIVA TREE AND OTHER STRANGE GROWTHS, THE
                             ALDISS, BRIAN W.   AC
  STARSWARM   ALDISS, BRIAN W.   AC
LEGION   BATES, RUSSELL L.   SS   INY 71 02
  INFINITY 2   HOSKINS, ROBERT   OA
LEGION OF PLOTTERS   MATHESON, RICHARD   SS   53
  SHOCK| MATHESON, RICHARD   AC
LEGWORK   RUSSELL, ERIC FRANK NV   ASF 56 04
  FAR STARS   RUSSELL, ERIC FRANK   AC
  5 UNEARTHLY VISIONS   CONKLIN, GROFF   AN
LEIBER BIBLIOGRAPHY   LEWIS, AL   MS   FSF 69 07
  BEST FROM FANTASY AND SCIENCE FICTION, 25TH ANNIV.
                             FERMAN, EDWARD L.   AN
LEIGH BRACKETT & RAY BRADBURY NOLAN, WILLIAM F.   AR
  HUMAN EQUATION, THE   NOLAN, WILLIAM F.   AN

LEINBACH'S PROOF   SCHNITZLER, ARTHUR   PM   31
  FANTASIA MATHEMATICA   FADIMAN, CLIFTON   AN
LEMMINGS   MATHESON, RICHARD   SS   FSF 58 01
  SHOCK| MATHESON, RICHARD   AC
LEMON-GREEN SPAGHETTI-LOUD DYNAMITE-DRIBBLE DAY(DID YOUR COFFE
  TASTE FUNNY THIS MORNING?) TENN, WILLIAM   SS   CAV 67 01
  SQUARE ROOT OF MAN, THE   TENN, WILLIAM   AC
LENNY   ASIMOV, ISAAC   SS   INF 58 01
  ANDROIDS, TIME MACHINES AND BLUE GIRAFFES
                             ELWOOD & GHIDALIA   AN
  EXPERT DREAMERS, THE   POHL, FREDERIK   AN
  *REST OF THE ROBOTS, THE   ASIMOV, ISAAC   AC
  VISIONS OF TOMORROW   ELWOOD, ROGER   AN
LEPRECHAUN   SAMBROT, WILLIAM   SS   ESC 62
  8TH ANNUAL OF THE YEAR'S BEST S-F, THE   MERRIL, JUDITH   AN
LESANDRO'S FAMILIAR   DERLETH, AUGUST   SS   WRT 36 05
  NOT LONG FOR THIS WORLD   DERLETH, AUGUST   AC
LESSON IN SURVIVAL   LONG, FRANK BELKNAP SS   TWS 52 12
  RIM OF THE UNKNOWN   LONG, FRANK BELKNAP   AC
LET FREEDOM RING (SEE THE WOLF PACK)
                             LEIBER, FRITZ   TC
LET IT RING   OSSIAN, JOHN   SS   INY 72 03
  INFINITY 3   HOSKINS, ROBERT   OA
LET ME HEAR YOU WHISPER   ZINDEL, PAUL   PL   SVM 70
  SIX SCIENCE FICTION PLAYS ELWOOD, ROGER   AN
LET ME LIVE IN A HOUSE (ALSO AS A FRIEND TO MAN)
                             OLIVER, CHAD   NV   USF 54 03
  SCIENCE FICTION TERROR TALES   CONKLIN, GROFF   AN
LET MY PEOPLE GO| GREEN, JOSEPH   SS
  OTHER SIDE OF TOMORROW, THE   ELWOOD, ROGER   OA
LET NOTHING YOU DISMAY   SLOANE, WILLIAM   SS   NEW 55 AN
  *STORIES FOR TOMORROW   SLOANE, WILLIAM   AN
LET THAT BE YOUR LAST BATTLEFIELD (CRAWFORD & CRONIN)
                             BLISH, JAMES   SA   STK 72 05
  STAR TREK 5   BLISH, JAMES   OC
LET THE ANTS TRY   MACCREIGH, JAMES   SS   PLS 49 WI
  BEYOND THE END OF TIME   POHL, FREDERIK   AN
LET THE ANTS TRY   POHL, FREDERIK   SS   PLS 49 WI
  ALTERNATING CURRENTS   POHL, FREDERIK   AC
  IN THE PROBLEM PIT   POHL, FREDERIK   AC
  MUTANTS   SILVERBERG, ROBERT   AN
LET THE TREES   BOOTH, PHILIP   PM   PNW 69 FL
  SPECULATIONS   SANDERS, THOMAS E.   AN
LET THERE BE LIGHT   CLARKE, ARTHUR C.   SS   PBY 58 02
  TALES OF TEN WORLDS   CLARKE, ARTHUR C.   AC
  TRANSIT OF EARTH   PLAYBOY, EDITORS OF   AN
LET THERE BE LIGHT   FYFE, H. B.   SS   IFS 52 11
  CROSSROADS IN TIME   CONKLIN, GROFF   AN
  FIRST WORLD OF IF, THE   QUINN & WULFF   AN
LET THERE BE LIGHT   HEINLEIN, ROBERT A. SS   SSS 40 05
  *MAN WHO SOLD THE MOON, THE   HEINLEIN, ROBERT A.   AC
LET THERE BE NIGHT| HERSHMAN, MORRIS   NV   FAN 63 10
  CRIME PREVENTION IN THE 30TH CENTURY   SANTESSON, HANS S.   AN
LET US QUICKLY HASTEN TO THE GATE OF IVORY
                             DISCH, THOMAS M.   SS   QRK 70 01
  *GETTING INTO DEATH   DISCH, THOMAS M.   AC
  QUARK/1   DELANY & HACKER   OA
LET'S BE FRANK   ALDISS, BRIAN W.   SS   SCP 57 06
  ABC OF SCIENCE FICTION, AN BOARDMAN, TOM JR.   AN
  SF: THE BEST OF THE BEST   MERRIL, JUDITH   AN
  SF:58, THE YEAR'S GREATEST SCIENCE FICTION AND FANTASY
                             MERRIL, JUDITH   AN
LET'S CALL IT A HOBBY   LEINSTER, MURRAY   IN
  GREAT STORIES OF SCIENCE FICTION   LEINSTER, MURRAY   AN
LET'S GET TOGETHER   ASIMOV, ISAAC   SS   INF 57 02
  *REST OF THE ROBOTS, THE   ASIMOV, ISAAC   AC
  SF:58, THE YEAR'S GREATEST SCIENCE FICTION AND FANTASY
                             MERRIL, JUDITH   AN
LET'S GO TO GOLGOTHA| KILWORTH, GARRY   SS
  GOLLANCZ - SUNDAY TIMES BEST SF STORIES ANONYMOUS   OA
LET'S HAVE FUN   DE CAMP, L. SPRAGUE SS   SFQ 57 05
  GUN FOR DINOSAUR AND OTHER IMAGINATIVE TALES
                             DE CAMP, L. SPRAGUE   AC
  RARE SCIENCE FICTION   HOWARD, IVAN   AN
LET'S NOT   ASIMOV, ISAAC   SS   BUG 54 12
  ALL ABOUT THE FUTURE   GREENBERG , MARTIN   AN
  BUY JUPITER AND OTHER STORIES   ASIMOV, ISAAC   AC
LET'S PLAY POISON   BRADBURY, RAY   SS   WRT 46 11
  AUTUMN PEOPLE, THE   BRADBURY, RAY   AC
  *DARK CARNIVAL   BRADBURY, RAY   AC
  LITTLE MONSTERS, THE   ELWOOD & GHIDALIA   AN
  SMALL ASSASSIN, THE   BRADBURY, RAY   AC
LETRON   INOUYE, JON   SS
  NIGHT TIDE, A   INOUYE, JON   OC
LETTER   SWISHER, ROBERT D.   MS   ASF 38 11
  MEN AND THE MIRROR, THE   ROCKLYNNE, ROSS   AC
LETTER FROM A HIGHER CRITIC ROBB, STEWART   SS   ASF 66 11
  ANALOG 6   CAMPBELL, JOHN W. JR AN
LETTER FROM AMERICA   PERCY, H. R.   SS
  BEYOND TIME   LEY, SANDRA   OA
LETTER FROM TENNYSON, A   ANONYMOUS   PM   MAG
  FANTASIA MATHEMATICA   FADIMAN, CLIFTON   AN
LETTER FROM THE STARS   VAN VOGT, A. E.   SS   OTW 50 07
  BEYOND THE END OF TIME   POHL, FREDERIK   AN
  EARTH IN PERIL, THE   WOLLHEIM, DONALD A.   DA
LETTER OF THE LAW   NOURSE, ALAN E.   SS   IFS 54 01
  TIGER BY THE TAIL   NOURSE, ALAN E.   AC
LETTER TO A PHOENIX   BROWN, FREDRIC   SS   ASF 49 08
  ANGELS AND SPACESHIPS   BROWN, FREDRIC   AC
  BEST OF FREDRIC BROWN, THE BROWN, FREDRIC   AC
  BEST SF 6   CRISPIN, EDMUND   AN
  JOURNEY TO INFINITY   GREENBERG , MARTIN   AN
LETTER TO A TYRANT KING   BUTLER, BILL   PM   FSF 66 08
  BEST FROM FANTASY AND SCIENCE FICTION: 16
                             FERMAN, EDWARD L.   AN

LETTER TO A YOUNG POET   SALLIS, JAMES   SS   ORB 68 03
  FEW LAST WORDS, A   SALLIS, JAMES   AC
  ORBIT 3   KNIGHT, DAMON   OA
LETTER TO A.A. (ALMOST ANYBODY), A
                                WILLEFORD, CHARLES   SS
  MACHINE IN WARD ELEVEN, THE   WILLEFORD, CHARLES   NO
LETTER TO AN ANGEL   ACKERMAN, FORREST J. SS
  SCIENCE FICTION WORLDS OF FORREST J. ACKERMAN & FRIENDS
                                ACKERMAN, FORREST J.   AC
LETTER TO DONALD WOLLHEIM LOVECRAFT, H. P.   MS
  COMING OF CONAN, THE   HOWARD, ROBERT E.   AC
LETTER TO ELLEN   DAVIS, CHAN   SS   ASF 47 06
  *SCIENCE FICTION THINKING MACHINES CONKLIN, GROFF   AN
LETTER TO P. SCHUYLER MILLER HOWARD, ROBERT E.   MS
  COMING OF CONAN, THE   HOWARD, ROBERT E.   AC
  CONAN   HOWARD, R./DE CAMP/&   AC
LETTER TO THE MARTIANS, A (CALLING ALL MARTIANS)
                                LEY, WILLY   AR   TWS 40 11
  COMING ATTRACTIONS   GREENBERG, MARTIN   NF
LETTER TO THOSE WHO SEE NO THREAT, A
                                POPE, CARL   AR
  VOYAGES: SCENARIOS FOR A SHIP CALLED EARTH
                                SAUER, ROB   AN
LETTERS FROM LAURA   CLINGERMAN, MILDRED SS   FSF 54 10
  CUPFUL OF SPACE, A   CLINGERMAN, MILDRED   AC
  TREASURY OF GREAT SCIENCE FICTION, A VOL.2
                                BOUCHER, ANTHONY   AN
LETTERS FROM THE PLANETS LACH-SZYRMA, D. S.   GR
  WORLDS APART   LOCKE, GEORGE   AN
LETTERS TO THE EDITOR (PMG 50 10)
                                GOULART, RON   SS   FSF 52 04
  BEST FROM FANTASY AND SCIENCE FICTION: 2
                                BOUCHER & MCCOMAS   AN
LETTING IT ALL HANG OUT (HANGING)
                                MALZBERG, BARRY N. SS   FAN 74 09
  BEST OF BARRY N. MALZBERG, THE   MALZBERG, BARRY N.   AC
LEVIATHAN!   NIVEN, LARRY   SS   PBY 70 08
  FLIGHT OF THE HORSE, THE   NIVEN, LARRY   AC
  LAST TRAIN TO LIMBO   PLAYBOY, EDITORS OF   AN
LEVITICUS: IN THE ARK MALZBERG, BARRY N.   SS   EPC 75
  DOWN HERE IN THE DREAM QUARTER   MALZBERG, BARRY N.   AC
  EPOCH   ELWOOD & SILVERBERG   OA
LEX   HAGGERT, W. T.   NV   GAL 59 08
  SIXTH GALAXY READER, THE   GOLD, H. L.   AN
LIAISON SERVICE   BOUNDS, SYDNEY J.   NV   NWS 51 WI
  LAURIE'S SPACE ANNUAL   ANONYMOUS   AN
LIANE THE WAYFARER   VANCE, JACK   NV   50
  DYING EARTH, THE   VANCE, JACK   OC
LIAR!   ASIMOV, ISAAC   SS   ASF 41 05
  DOORWAY INTO TIME   MOSKOWITZ, SAM   AN
  HUMAN?   MERRIL, JUDITH   AN
  I, ROBOT   ASIMOV, ISAAC   AC
  IN DREAMS AWAKE   FIEDLER, LESLIE A.   AN
  MIND TO MIND   SILVERBERG, ROBERT   AN
  MODERN MASTERPIECES OF SCIENCE FICTION MOSKOWITZ, SAM   AN
LIB   EMSHWILLER, CAROL   SS   NWS 68 03
  BEST SF STORIES FROM NEW WORLDS 6 MOORCOCK, MICHAEL   AN
  JOY IN OUR CAUSE   EMSHWILLER, CAROL   AC
LIBERATION   SPALTEN, RONA   SS   NWQ 74 06
  NEW WORLDS NO. 6   PLATT & BAILEY   OA
LIBERATION OF EARTH, THE TENN, WILLIAM   SS   FUT 53 05
  INVADERS FROM SPACE   SILVERBERG, ROBERT   AN
LIBERATED FUTURE: VOYAGES INTO TOMORROW, THE
                                HOSKINS, ROBERT   AN
  MORE PENGUIN SCIENCE FICTION   ALDISS, BRIAN W.   AN
  OF ALL POSSIBLE WORLDS   TENN, WILLIAM   AC
  SCIENCE FICTION: THE GREAT YEARS POHL, C. & F.   AN
  STARLIT CORRIDOR, THE   MANSFIELD, ROGER   AN
  TOMORROW AND TOMORROW   KNIGHT, DAMON   AN
LIBERATORS, THE   HARDING, LEE   SS   NWR 65 05
  NEW WRITINGS IN SF. 5   CARNELL, JOHN   OA
LIBRARY OF BABEL, THE BORGES, JORGE LUIS   SS   62
  MIRROR OF INFINITY, THE   SILVERBERG, ROBERT   AN
  NEW WORLDS OF FANTASY NO. 2   CARR, TERRY   AN
LICENSE   ANDERSON, POUL   NV   FSF 57 04
  7 CONQUESTS   ANDERSON, POUL   AC
LICENSE TO STEAL   NEWMAN, LOUIS   FA   GAL 59 08
  SIXTH GALAXY READER, THE   GOLD, H. L.   AN
LIE, THE   VONNEGUT, KURT JR.   SS   SEP 62 02
  WELCOME TO THE MONKEY HOUSE   VONNEGUT, KURT JR.   AC
LIFE AMONG THE ASTEROIDS POURNELLE, JERRY AR   GAL 75 07
  BEST FROM GALAXY, THE VOLUME IV BAEN, JAMES   AN
LIFE AND A HALF, A   POHL, FREDERIK   SS   IFS 59 07
  ABOMINABLE EARTHMAN, THE   POHL, FREDERIK   AC
  BEST SF 6   CRISPIN, EDMUND   AN
LIFE AND DEATH OF GOD, THE BALLARD, J. G. SS
  LOW-FLYING AIRCRAFT AND OTHER STORIES BALLARD, J. G.   AC
LIFE AND DEATH OF PLUNKY GOO, THE
                                COOPER, EDMUND   SS
  TOMORROW CAME   COOPER, EDMUND   AC
  UNBORN TOMORROW   COOPER, EDMUND   AC
LIFE AND TIMES OF MULTIVAC, THE
                                ASIMOV, ISAAC   SS   NYT 75 01
  BICENTENNIAL MAN AND OTHER STORIES, THE ASIMOV, ISAAC   AC
LIFE BY TELEVISION, A ARNOLD, JACK   SS
  ADVENTURES TO COME   ESENWEIN, J. BERG   OA
LIFE CURRENT   WANDREI, DONALD   SS   ASF 35 04
  STRANGE HARVEST   WANDREI, DONALD   AC
LIFE CYCLE   ANDERSON, POUL   SS   FSF 57 07
  EARTHMEN AND STRANGERS   SILVERBERG, ROBERT   AN
LIFE CYCLE   HAWKINS, PETER   SS   NWS 51 SP
  GATEWAY TO TOMORROW   CARNELL, JOHN   AN
LIFE ETERNAL   BINDER, EANDO   NV   TWS 38 02
  ANTON YORK, IMMORTAL   BINDER, EANDO   AC
LIFE EVERLASTING   KELLER, DAVID H. MD. NA   AMZ 34 07

LIFE EVERLASTING AND OTHER TALES OF SCIENCE, FANTASY
  AND HORROR   KELLER, DAVID H. MD.   AC
LIFE FOR THE STARS, A BLISH, JAMES   NO   ASF 62 09
  CITIES IN FLIGHT   BLISH, JAMES   AC
LIFE GAME, THE   OLIVER, CHAD   NV   TWS 53 06
  PSEUDO PEOPLE, THE   NOLAN, WILLIAM F.   AN
LIFE GOES ON   BOND, NELSON S.   SS
  NO TIME LIKE THE FUTURE   BOND, NELSON S.   AC
LIFE HATER, THE (ALSO AS THE PEACEMAKER)
                                SABERHAGEN, FRED SS   IFS 64 08
  IF READER OF SCIENCE FICTION, THE POHL, FREDERIK   AN
LIFE HUTCH   ELLISON, HARLAN   SS   IFS 56 04
  ALONE AGAINST TOMORROW   ELLISON, HARLAN   AC
  DEEP SPACE   SILVERBERG, ROBERT   AN
  FROM THE LAND OF FEAR   ELLISON, HARLAN   AC
  TOUCH OF INFINITY, A   ELLISON, HARLAN   DC
LIFE IN OUR NEW CENTURY WINTLE, W. J.   SS   HRM 01 01
  BEFORE ARMAGEDDON   MOORCOCK, MICHAEL   AN
LIFE IN OUR TIME   BLOCH, ROBERT   SS   EQM 66 10
  LIVING DEMONS, THE   BLOCH, ROBERT   AC
LIFE IN THE DAY OF, A ROBINSON, FRANK M.   SS   PBY 69 06
  WEIRD SHOW   PLAYBOY, EDITORS OF   AN
LIFE IN THE TWENTIETH CENTURY (1883)
                                ROBIDA, ALBERT   IL
  BEYOND THIS HORIZON   CARRELL, CHRISTOPHER   OA
LIFE INSIDE A WALL   VINCENT, HARL   SS   SFQ 40 SU
  MOON CONQUERORS, THE   ANONYMOUS   AN
LIFE IS SO DULL FOR LITTLE GIRLS
                                BULYCHEV, KIRILL SS
  RUSSIAN SCIENCE FICTION, 1968   MAGIDOFF, ROBERT   AN
LIFE ON OTHER WORLDS   CARTIER, EDD   IL
  TRAVELLERS OF SPACE   GREENBERG, MARTIN   AN
LIFE ON THE MOON   SAMALMAN, ALEXANDER SS   TWS 46 12
  SHOT IN THE DARK   MERRIL, JUDITH   AN
LIFE PRESERVERS, THE (AS HANK DEMPSEY)
                                HARRISON, HARRY   NV   ASF 70 04
  ONE STEP FROM EARTH   HARRISON, HARRY   AC
LIFE WATCH   DEL REY, LESTER   NV   FUN 54 09
  GODS AND GOLEMS   DEL REY, LESTER   AC
LIFE WORK OF JUAN DIAZ, THE BRADBURY, RAY   SS   PBY 63 09
  MACHINERIES OF JOY, THE   BRADBURY, RAY   AC
  PLAYBOY BOOK OF HORROR AND THE SUPERNATURAL, THE
                                PLAYBOY, EDITORS OF   AN
LIFE-FORCE   GREEN, JOSEPH   SS   NWS 62 11
  AFFAIR WITH GENIUS, AN   GREEN, JOSEPH   AC
LIFE-LINE   HEINLEIN, ROBERT A. SS   ASF 39 08
  BEST OF ROBERT HEINLEIN, THE   HEINLEIN, ROBERT A.   AC
  FIRST FLIGHT   KNIGHT, DAMON   AN
  *MAN WHO SOLD THE MOON, THE   HEINLEIN, ROBERT A.   AC
  PAST THROUGH TOMORROW, THE   HEINLEIN, ROBERT A.   AC
  TALES OF SCIENCE FICTION   BALL, BRIAN N.   AN
  WORLDS OF ROBERT A. HEINLEIN, THE HEINLEIN, ROBERT A.   AC
LIFE-WORK OF PROFESSOR MUNTZ, THE
                                LEINSTER, MURRAY SS   TWS 49 06
  BEST SCIENCE-FICTION STORIES: 1950, THE BLEILER & DIKTY AN
  SCIENCE FICTION GALAXY, THE   CONKLIN, GROFF   AN
LIFEBOAT MUTINY, THE   SHECKLEY, ROBERT   SS   GAL 55 04
  PILGRIMAGE TO EARTH   SHECKLEY, ROBERT   AC
LIFEGUARD   COVER, ARTHUR BYRON SS   75
  YEAR'S BEST HORROR STORIES: SERIES IV, THE
                                PAGE, GERALD W.   AN
LIGHT FANTASTIC, THE   BESTER, ALFRED   AC   BKP 76
  STARLIGHT   BESTER, ALFRED   AN
LIGHT FROM BEYOND, THE (GOD OF LIGHT)
                                ESHBACH, LLOYD A. SS   TWS 44 SU
  TYRANT OF TIME, THE   ESHBACH, LLOYD A.   AC
LIGHT OF DARKNESS, THE CLARKE, ARTHUR C.   SS
  WIND FROM THE SUN, THE   CLARKE, ARTHUR C.   AC
LIGHT OF OTHER DAYS   SHAW, BOB   SS   ASF 66 08
  ABOVE THE HUMAN LANDSCAPE   MCNELLY & STOVER   AN
  ALPHA 6   SILVERBERG, ROBERT   AN
  ANALOG 6   CAMPBELL, JOHN W. JR   AN
  NEBULA AWARD STORIES NO. 2   ALDISS & HARRISON   AN
  OTHER DAYS, OTHER EYES   SHAW, BOB   NO
  SCIENCE FICTION ARGOSY, A   KNIGHT, DAMON   AN
  SCIENCE FICTION: THE FUTURE   ALLEN, DICK   AN
  SF12   MERRIL, JUDITH   AN
  WORLD'S BEST SCIENCE FICTION: 1967 WOLLHEIM & CARR   AN
LIGHT VERSE   ASIMOV, ISAAC   SS   SEP 73 09
  BUY JUPITER AND OTHER STORIES   ASIMOV, ISAAC   AC
LIGHT YEARS, THE   CALVINO, ITALO   SS
  COSMICOMICS   CALVINO, ITALO   AC
LIGHT-HOUSE, THE   BLOCH, ROBERT   SS   FAN 53 02
  NIGHTMARES   BLOCH, ROBERT   AC
  PLEASANT DREAMS   BLOCH, ROBERT   AC
LIGHT, THE   ANDERSON, POUL   NV   GAL 57 03
  SCIENCE FICTION THROUGH THE AGES 2 EVANS, I. O.   AN
  13 GREAT STORIES OF SCIENCE FICTION CONKLIN, GROFF   AN
LIGHTS   FISHER, PHILIP M. JR SS   AAS 22 07
  SUPERNATURAL READER, THE   CONKLIN, G&L.   AN
LIGHTS OF MARS, THE   JONES, RAYMOND F.   NV
  SCIENCE FICTION ADVENTURES FROM WAY OUT ELWOOD, ROGER   OA
LIGHTS OF ZETAR, THE (JEREMY TARCHER& SHARI LEWIS)
                                BLISH, JAMES   SA   STK 72 06
  STAR TREK 6   BLISH, JAMES   OC
LIGHTS OUT   EFFINGER, GEO. ALEC NV   FSF 73 10
  MIXED FEELINGS   EFFINGER, GEO. ALEC   AC
LIGHTS OUTSIDE THE WINDOWS, THE
                                WHITE, JAMES   NV   NWS 57 02
  DEADLY LITTER   WHITE, JAMES   NO
LIKE A BIRD, LIKE A FISH HICKEY, H. B.   SS   WBY 51 02
  *WORLDS OF TOMORROW   DERLETH, AUGUST   AN
LIKE A DIAMOND IN THE SKY MCKINLEY, MARY C. SS
  LONG NIGHT OF WAITING AND OTHER STORIES ELWOOD, ROGER   OA
LIKE ALARM BELLS RINGING WILLIAMS, ROBERT M. SS AMZ 47 01
  TO THE END OF TIME AND OTHER STORIES WILLIAMS, ROBERT M. DC

LIKE BANQUO'S GHOST   NIVEN, LARRY   SS   IFS 68 09
  SHAPE OF SPACE, THE   NIVEN, LARRY   AC
LIKE FATHER   HARTRIDGE, JON   SS   NWS 69 08
  BEST SF: 1969   HARRISON & ALDISS   AN
LIKE GODS THEY CAME   COX, IRVING E. JR. SS   AUS 53 01
  SPACE, SPACE, SPACE   SLOANE, WILLIAM   AN
LIKE NOTHING ON EARTH   ARNOLD, DOUGLAS   AR   KDK 73 02
  BEYOND THIS HORIZON   CARRELL, CHRISTOPHER   OA
LIKE SNOW-HUMPED FIELDS AFRAID OF RAIN
                             WATKINS, WILLIAM JON PM
  2076: THE AMERICAN TRICENTENNIAL   BRYANT, EDWARD   OA
LIKE TWO WHITE SPIDERS   BERTIN, EDDY C.   SS
  YEAR'S BEST HORROR STORIES: SERIES II, THE
                                       DAVIS, RICHARD   AN
LIKE YOUNG   STURGEON, THEODORE SS   FSF 60 03
  BEYOND   STURGEON, THEODORE   AC
LIKELY STORY, A   KNIGHT, DAMON   SS   INF 56 02
  BEST OF DAMON KNIGHT, THE   KNIGHT, DAMON   AC
  TURNING ON   KNIGHT, DAMON   AC
LIKENESS OF APOLLO, THE   ARNOLD, DOUGLAS   AR   PTJ 73 03
  BEYOND THIS HORIZON   CARRELL, CHRISTOPHER   OA
LIKENESS OF JULIE, THE   SWANSON, LOGAN   SS   NEW 62 AN
  ALONE BY NIGHT   CONGDON, MICHAEL&DON   AN
LIKENESS OF JULIE, THE (AS LOGAN SWANSON)
                             MATHESON, RICHARD   SS   NEW 62 AN
  SHOCK II   MATHESON, RICHARD   AC
LILAC BUSH, THE   DERLETH, AUGUST   SS   WRT 30 02
  NOT LONG FOR THIS WORLD   DERLETH, AUGUST   AC
LILIES OF LIFE (ALSO AS PLANET OF DOOM)
                             JAMESON, MALCOLM   SS   ASF 45 02
  *POSSIBLE WORLDS OF SCIENCE FICTION CONKLIN, GROFF   AN
LIMERICK NO. 1   BRUNNER, JOHN   PM   ARA
  BOOK OF JOHN BRUNNER, THE   BRUNNER, JOHN   AC
LIMERICK NO. 2   BRUNNER, JOHN   PM   ARA
  BOOK OF JOHN BRUNNER, THE   BRUNNER, JOHN   AC
LIMERICK NO. 3   BRUNNER, JOHN   PM   VCT
  BOOK OF JOHN BRUNNER, THE   BRUNNER, JOHN   AC
LIMERICK NO. 4   BRUNNER, JOHN   PM   NEW 76 AC
  BOOK OF JOHN BRUNNER, THE   BRUNNER, JOHN   AC
LIMERICK NO. 5   BRUNNER, JOHN   PM   NEW 76 AC
  BOOK OF JOHN BRUNNER, THE   BRUNNER, JOHN   AC
LIMERICKS   ANDERSON, POUL   PM
  HOMEBREW   ANDERSON, POUL   AC
LIMITED ACCOMMODATIONS   PISERCHIA, DORIS   SS
  CRISIS   ELWOOD, ROGER   OA
LIMITING FACTOR   COGSWELL, THEODORE R SS GAL 54 04
  *SCIENCE FICTION ADVENTURES IN MUTATION CONKLIN, GROFF   AN
  THIRD EYE, THE   COGSWELL, THEODORE R   AC
  THIRD GALAXY READER, THE   GOLD, H. L.   AN
LIMITING FACTOR   SIMAK, CLIFFORD D. SS   STS 49 11
  BEYOND THE STARS AND OTHER STORIES   ANONYMOUS   AN
  CONTACT   KEYES, NOEL   AN
  *POSSIBLE WORLDS OF SCIENCE FICTION CONKLIN, GROFF   AN
  *SPECTRUM   AMIS & CONQUEST   AN
LIMITING VELOCITY OF ORTHODOXY, THE
                             LAUMER, KEITH   AR   GAL 70 12
  FASTER THAN LIGHT   DANN & ZEBROWSKI   OA
LIMITS OF WALTER HORTON, THE SHARNIK, JOHN S.   SS   CHM 54
  CIRCUS OF DR. LAO AND OTHER IMPROBABLE STORIES
                                       BRADBURY, RAY   AN
LINDA AND DANIEL AND SPIKE   DISCH, THOMAS M.   SS   NWS 67 12
  BEST SF STORIES FROM NEW WORLDS 4   MOORCOCK, MICHAEL   AN
  FUN WITH YOUR NEW HEAD   DISCH, THOMAS M.   AC
LINDEMANN'S CATCH   SERLING, ROD   SA
  NIGHT GALLERY 2   SERLING, ROD   OC
LINE TO TOMORROW   KUTTNER, HENRY   SS   ASF 45 11
  BEST OF HENRY KUTTNER 2, THE   KUTTNER, HENRY   AC
LINE TO TOMORROW   PADGETT, LEWIS   SS   ASF 45 11
  LINE TO TOMORROW AND OTHER STORIES OF FANTASY AND SCIENCE
    FICTION   PADGETT, LEWIS   AC
  NEW WORLDS FOR OLD   DERLETH, AUGUST   AN
  *WORLDS OF TOMORROW   DERLETH, AUGUST   AN
LINEAMENTS OF GRATIFIED DESIRE, THE
                             DAVIDSON, AVRAM   SS
  WHAT STRANGE STARS AND SKIES   DAVIDSON, AVRAM   AC
LINEMAN, THE   MILLER, WALTER M. JR SN FSF 57 08
  WILDERNESS OF STARS, A   NOLAN, WILLIAM F.   AN
LINGUIST, THE (AS TAK HALLUS) ROBINETT, STEPHEN SS   GAL 75 02
  BEST SF: 75, THE NINTH ANNUAL   HARRISON & ALDISS   AN
LINGUISTIC RELATIVITY IN MIDDLE HIGH MARTIAN
                             MCNELLY, WILLIS E.   AR   68
  MARS, WE LOVE YOU   HIPOLITO & MCNELLY   AN
LINK, THE   CARTMILL, CLEVE   SS   ASF 42 08
  *ADVENTURES IN TIME AND SPACE   HEALY & MCCOMAS   AN
  MORE ADVENTURES IN TIME AND SPACE   HEALY & MCCOMAS   AN
  POLITICAL SCIENCE FICTION   GREENBERG& WARRICK   AN
LINK, THE   NOURSE, ALAN E.   SS   IFS 54 06
  COUNTERFEIT MAN, THE   NOURSE, ALAN E.   AC
LINKAGE   MALZBERG, BARRY N. SS   DEM 73
  BEST OF BARRY N. MALZBERG, THE   MALZBERG, BARRY N.   AC
  DEMON KIND   ELWOOD, ROGER   OA
  OUT FROM GANYMEDE   MALZBERG, BARRY N.   AC
LION AND THE LAMB, THE   LEIBER, FRITZ   NV   ASF 50 09
  SECOND BOOK OF FRITZ LEIBER, THE   LEIBER, FRITZ   AC
LION AND THE UNICORN, THE   PADGETT, LEWIS   NV   ASF 45 07
  MUTANT   PADGETT, LEWIS   AC
LION LOOSE   SCHMITZ, JAMES H.   SN   ASF 61 10
  PRIDE OF MONSTERS, A   SCHMITZ, JAMES H.   AC
LION OF COMARRE   CLARKE, ARTHUR C.   NV   TWS 49 08
  LION OF COMARRE AND AGAINST THE FALL OF NIGHT
                                       CLARKE, ARTHUR C.   AC
LION'S MOUTH   MARLOWE, STEPHEN   SS   FAD 52 06
  LOOKING FORWARD   LESSER, MILTON   AN
LION'S SHARE, THE   JACOBS, HARVEY   SS   PBY 61 09
  EGG OF THE GLAK, AND OTHER STORIES, THE JACOBS, HARVEY   AC

LIONS AND THE HARP, THE   COOPER, EDMUND   SS
  VOICES IN THE DARK   COOPER, EDMUND   AC
LIONS OF ROME, THE   JONES, RAYMOND F.   SS   PTP 73
  FLAME TREE PLANET   ELWOOD, ROGER   OA
LIQUID LIFE   FARLEY, RALPH MILNE NV   TWS 36 10
  *BEST OF SCIENCE FICTION   CONKLIN, GROFF   AN
  GREAT STORIES OF SCIENCE FICTION   LEINSTER, MURRAY   AN
  MUTANTS   SILVERBERG, ROBERT   AN
LISBON CUBED   TENN, WILLIAM   NV   GAL 58 10
  WOODEN STAR, THE   TENN, WILLIAM   AC
LISTEN   DICKSON, GORDON R. SS   FSF 52 08
  MUTANTS   DICKSON, GORDON R.   AC
  PRIZE SCIENCE FICTION   WOLLHEIM, DONALD A.   AN
LISTEN WITH BIG BROTHER   ALDISS, BRIAN W.   SS
  BEST SF: 1974   HARRISON & ALDISS   AN
LISTEN, CHILDREN, LISTEN   WEST, WALLACE   SS   FUN 53 10
  GRAVEYARD READER, THE   CONKLIN, GROFF   AN
  ZACHERLEY'S MIDNIGHT SNACKS   ZACHERLEY   AN
LISTEN, LOVE   DANN, JACK M.
                             AND ZEBROWSKI, GEORGE SS C NWQ 71 02
  NEW WORLDS QUARTERLY NO. 2   MOORCOCK, MICHAEL   OA
LISTENERS, THE   DE LA MARE, WALTER PM
  LOOKING AHEAD   ALLEN, D. & L.   AN
LISTENERS, THE (ALSO AS ROBERT MACDONALD- 2025)
                             GUNN, JAMES E.   NV   GAL 68 09
  BREAKING POINT   GUNN, JAMES E.   AC
  NEBULA AWARD STORIES NO. 4   ANDERSON, POUL   AN
  STARS AROUND US, THE   HOSKINS, ROBERT   AN
  THOSE WHO CAN: A SCIENCE FICTION READER WILSON, ROBIN SCOTT   AN
LISTENING CHILD, THE   SEABRIGHT, IDRIS   SS   FSF 50 12
  BEST FROM FANTASY AND SCIENCE FICTION BOUCHER & MCCOMAS   AN
LITERARY CORKSCREW, THE   KELLER, DAVID H. MD. SS WOS 34 03
  FROM OFF THIS WORLD   MARGULIES & FRIEND   AN
  TALES FROM UNDERWOOD   KELLER, DAVID H. MD.   AC
LITTERBUG   MORPHETT, TONY   NV   FSF 69 07
  BEST FROM FANTASY AND SCIENCE FICTION: 19
                                       FERMAN, EDWARD L.   AN
  BEYOND TOMORROW   HARDING, LEE   AN
  SCIENCE FICTION   BRODKIN & PEARSON   AN
LITTLE ANTON   BRETNOR, REGINALD   NV   NTS 51
  NEVER IN THIS WORLD   STONE, IDELLA P.   AN
  NEW TALES OF SPACE AND TIME   HEALY, RAYMOND J.   OA
LITTLE BLACK BAG, THE   KORNBLUTH, C. M.   NV   ASF 50 07
  ASTOUNDING-ANALOG READER, THE VOLUME TWO HARRISON & ALDISS   AN
  BEST OF C. M. KORNBLUTH, THE   KORNBLUTH, C. M.   AC
  BEST SCIENCE FICTION STORIES OF C. M. KORNBLUTH
                                       KORNBLUTH, C. M.   AC
  BEYOND THE END OF TIME   POHL, FREDERIK   AN
  GREAT SCIENCE FICTION ABOUT DOCTORS CONKLIN, G&FABRICANT   AN
  LIBERATED FUTURE: VOYAGES INTO TOMORROW, THE
                                       HOSKINS, ROBERT   AN
  *MILE BEYOND THE MOON, A   KORNBLUTH, C. M.   AC
  MINDWORM AND OTHER STORIES, THE   KORNBLUTH, C. M.   AC
  SCIENCE FICTION HALL OF FAME VOLUME 1 SILVERBERG, ROBERT   AN
  SCIENCE FICTION: THE GREAT YEARS   POHL, C. & F.   AN
  TIME PROBE: THE SCIENCES IN SF.   CLARKE, ARTHUR C.   AN
LITTLE BLACK TRAIN, THE   WELLMAN, MANLY WADE SS FSF 54 08
  BEST FROM FANTASY AND SCIENCE FICTION: 4
                                       BOUCHER, ANTHONY   AN
  WHO FEARS THE DEVIL?   WELLMAN, MANLY WADE   AC
LITTLE CREEPS, THE   MILLER, WALTER M. JR NV AMZ 51 12
  LOOKING FORWARD   LESSER, MILTON   AN
LITTLE DOG GONE   YOUNG, ROBERT F.   NV   WOT 64 02
  BEST SCIENCE FICTION FROM WORLDS OF TOMORROW, THE
                                       POHL, FREDERIK   AN
  GLASS OF STARS, A   YOUNG, ROBERT F.   AC
LITTLE GIRL LOST   MATHESON, RICHARD   SS   AMZ 53 11
  SHORES OF SPACE, THE   MATHESON, RICHARD   AC
LITTLE GIRL LOST   TUBB, E. C.   SS   NWS 55 10
  SCATTER OF STARDUST, A   TUBB, E. C.   DC
LITTLE GIRL'S XMAS IN MODERAN, A
                             BUNCH, DAVID R.   SS   FSF 60 01
  MODERAN   BUNCH, DAVID R.   AC
LITTLE GREEN MAN   LOOMIS, NOEL   SS   DSF 53 03
  THINGS   HOWARD, IVAN   AN
LITTLE GREEN MEN   NICHOLSON, JOHN   AR   FUN 58 05
  FLYING SAUCERS IN FACT AND FICTION   SANTESSON, HANS S.   AN
LITTLE HUMAN CONTACT, A   BROWN, ROSEL GEORGE SS   FSF 60 04
  HANDFUL OF TIME, A   BROWN, ROSEL GEORGE   AC
LITTLE JIMMY   DEL REY, LESTER   SS   FSF 57 04
  MORE LITTLE MONSTERS   ELWOOD & GHIDALIA   AN
  ROBOTS AND CHANGELINGS   DEL REY, LESTER   AC
LITTLE JOE   CARTMILL, CLEVE   NV   TWS 50 04
  SPACE SCAVENGERS, THE   CARTMILL, CLEVE   NO
LITTLE JOURNEY, A   BRADBURY, RAY   SS   GAL 51 08
  *GALAXY READER OF SCIENCE FICTION   GOLD, H. L.   AN
LITTLE KNOWLEDGE, A   ANDERSON, POUL   NV   ASF 71 08
  BEST SCIENCE FICTION STORIES OF THE YEAR (1971)
                                       DEL REY, LESTER   AN
  1972 ANNUAL WORLD'S BEST SF, THE   WOLLHEIM, DONALD A.   AN
LITTLE KNOWLEDGE, A   DERLETH, AUGUST   SS
  NOT LONG FOR THIS WORLD   DERLETH, AUGUST   AC
LITTLE LAMB, THE   BROWN, FREDRIC   SS
  NIGHTMARES AND GEEZENSTACKS   BROWN, FREDRIC   AC
LITTLE LOST ROBOT   ASIMOV, ISAAC   SS   ASF 47 03
  BEST SF 2   CRISPIN, EDMUND   AC
  I, ROBOT   ASIMOV, ISAAC   AC
  STARS AND UNDER, THE   CRISPIN, EDMUND   AC
LITTLE MAN ON THE SUBWAY, THE ASIMOV, ISAAC
                             AND MACCREIGH, JAMES SS C FBK 50 06
  EARLY ASIMOV, THE   ASIMOV, ISAAC   AC
  SCIENCE AND SORCERY   FORD, GARRET   AN
LITTLE MAN WHO WASN'T QUITE, THE
                             STUART, WILLIAM W. NV   GAL 61 12
  *TWISTED   CONKLIN, GROFF   AN

LITTLE MEN   WEST, JESSAMYN   SN   SSN 54
  STAR SHORT NOVELS   POHL, FREDERIK   OA
LITTLE MEN OF SPACE   LONG, FRANK BELKNAP SS   FUN 53 06
  RIM OF THE UNKNOWN   LONG, FRANK BELKNAP   AC
LITTLE MICE, THE (THE MICE)   BRADBURY, RAY   SS   ESC 55 10
  DAY IT RAINED FOREVER, THE   BRADBURY, RAY   AC
  MEDICINE FOR MELANCHOLY, A   BRADBURY, RAY   AC
  VINTAGE BRADBURY, THE   BRADBURY, RAY   AC
LITTLE MONSTER, THE   ANDERSON, POUL   NV
  SCIENCE FICTION ADVENTURES FROM WAY OUT ELWOOD, ROGER   OA
LITTLE MORE CAVIAR?, A   VEILLOT, CLAUDE   SS   63
  13 FRENCH SCIENCE-FICTION STORIES   KNIGHT, DAMON   AN
LITTLE MORE THAN TWELVE MINUTES, A
                                    JESCHKE, WOLFGANG   NV   NWR 75 25
  NEW WRITINGS IN SF. 25   BULMER, KENNETH   OA
LITTLE MOTHER UP THE MORDERBEN, THE
                                    WELLS, H. G.   SS   SND 10 04
  SHORT STORIES OF H. G. WELLS, THE   WELLS, H. G.   AC
LITTLE MOVEMENT, THE   DICK, PHILIP K.   SS   FSF 52 11
  HANDFUL OF DARKNESS, A   DICK, PHILIP K.   AC
LITTLE NIGHT FLYING, A (DARK ICARUS)
                                    SHAW, BOB   NV   IFS 74 08
  BEST FROM IF, THE   VOLUME III   BAEN, JAMES   AN
  COSMIC KALEIDOSCOPE   SHAW, BOB   AC
LITTLE OIL, A   RUSSELL, ERIC FRANK NV   GAL 52 10
  DEEP SPACE   RUSSELL, ERIC FRANK   AC
  SCIENCE FICTION THROUGH THE AGES 2   EVANS, I. O.   AN
LITTLE OLD LADY   CUMMINGS, M. A.   SS
  EXILE AND OTHER TALES OF FANTASY   CUMMINGS, M. A.   OC
LITTLE OLD MISS MACBETH   LEIBER, FRITZ   SS   FSF 58 12
  BEST OF FRITZ LEIBER, THE   LEIBER, FRITZ   AC
LITTLE ORPHAN ANDROID   GUNN, JAMES E.   NV   GAL 55 09
  FUTURE IMPERFECT   GUNN, JAMES E.   AC
LITTLE RED SCHOOLHOUSE   YOUNG, ROBERT F.   SS   GAL 56 03
  WORLDS OF ROBERT F. YOUNG, THE   YOUNG, ROBERT F.   AC
LITTLE SOMETHING FOR US TEMPUNAUTS, A
                                    DICK, PHILIP K.   NV   FST 74
  BEST OF PHILIP K. DICK, THE   DICK, PHILIP K.   AC
  BEST SCIENCE FICTION OF THE YEAR, THE NO. 4
                                    CARR, TERRY   AN
  FINAL STAGE   FERMAN & MALZBERG   OA
LITTLE TERROR, THE   JENKINS, WILL F.   SS   SEP 53 08
  MARRIAGE AND THE FAMILY THROUGH SCIENCE FICTION
                                         CLEAR/WARRICK/&   AN
  POST READER OF FANTASY AND SCIENCE FICTION
                                         SATURDAY EVE. POST   AN
  TOMORROW'S CHILDREN   ASIMOV, ISAAC   AN
LITTLE THINGS, THE   KUTTNER, HENRY   SS   TWS 46 FL
  BYPASS TO OTHERNESS   KUTTNER, HENRY   AC
LITTLE WITCH OF ELM STREET, THE
                                    CLINGERMAN, MILDRED SS   WHC 56
  CUPFUL OF SPACE, A   CLINGERMAN, MILDRED   AC
  MORE LITTLE MONSTERS   ELWOOD & GHIDALIA   AN
LITTLEST PEOPLE, THE   BANKS, RAYMOND E.   NV   GAL 54 03
  BEST SCIENCE FICTION STORIES AND NOVELS: 1955
                                         DIKTY, T. E.   AN
LIVE COWARD, THE   ANDERSON, POUL   SS   ASF 56 06
  ANOTHER PART OF THE GALAXY   CONKLIN, GROFF   AN
  UN-MAN AND OTHER NOVELLAS   ANDERSON, POUL   DC
LIVE? OUR COMPUTERS WILL DO THAT FOR US
                                    ALDISS, BRIAN W.   SS   ORB 74 15
  ORBIT 15   KNIGHT, DAMON   OA
LIVE, FROM BERCHTESGADEN   EFFINGER, GEO. ALEC SS   ORB 72 10
  ALPHA 5   SILVERBERG, ROBERT   AN
  BEST FROM ORBIT, THE   KNIGHT, DAMON   AN
  ORBIT 10   KNIGHT, DAMON   OA
LIVES OF ALFRED KRAMER, THE   WANDREI, DONALD   SS   WRT 32 12
  EYE AND THE FINGER   WANDREI, DONALD   AC
LIVING DEAD, THE   BLOCH, ROBERT   SS   EQM 67 04
  KING OF TERRORS, THE   BLOCH, ROBERT   AC
LIVING DEAD, THE   BURROUGHS, EDGAR R. NV   FAD 41 11
  ESCAPE ON VENUS   BURROUGHS, EDGAR R.   NO
LIVING DOLL, A   WALLACE, ROBERT   SS   H&P 64 01
  10TH ANNUAL OF THE YEAR'S BEST S-F, THE MERRIL, JUDITH   AN
LIVING END, THE   BLOCH, ROBERT   SS   SMM 63 05
  CHAMBER OF HORRORS   BLOCH, ROBERT   AC
LIVING END, THE   DORMAN, SONYA   SS   ORB 70 07
  ORBIT 7   KNIGHT, DAMON   OA
LIVING FOSSIL   DE CAMP, L. SPRAGUE SS   ASF 39 02
  GATES TO TOMORROW   NORTON, AN.&DONALDY   AN
  *TREASURY OF SCIENCE FICTION, A   CONKLIN, GROFF   AN
LIVING FOSSIL   STOUT, TIM   SS   SPC 74 02
  SPACE 2   DAVIS, RICHARD   OA
LIVING GALAXY, THE   MANNING, LAURENCE   SS   WOS 34 09
  SCIENCE FICTION GALAXY, THE   CONKLIN, GROFF   AN
LIVING MACHINE   KELLER, DAVID H. MD. SS WOS 35 05
  EVERY BOY'S BOOK OF SCIENCE FICTION   WOLLHEIM, DONALD A.   AN
LIVING MIST, THE (SEE WE, THE MIST)
                                    FARLEY, RALPH MILNE TC
LIVING SPACE   ASIMOV, ISAAC   SS   SFS 56 05
  EARTH IS ROOM ENOUGH   ASIMOV, ISAAC   AC
  OUT OF THIS WORLD 3   WILLIAMS-ELLIS& OWEN   AN
  WONDERMAKERS 2   HOSKINS, ROBERT   AN
  WORLDS OF MAYBE   SILVERBERG, ROBERT   AN
LIZARD OF WOZ, THE   COOPER, EDMUND   SS   FUN 58 08
  NEWS FROM ELSEWHERE   COOPER, EDMUND   AC
  TOMORROW CAME   COOPER, EDMUND   AC
  UNBORN TOMORROW   COOPER, EDMUND   AC
LIZARD, THE   HYNE, C.J. CUTCLIFFE SS   04
  ANCESTRAL VOICES   MENVILLE & REGINALD   AN
"LIZZIE BORDEN TOOK AN AXE..."   BLOCH, ROBERT   SS   WRT 46 11
  SKULL OF THE MARQUIS DE SADE, THE   BLOCH, ROBERT   AC
LOAD OF TROUBLE   WOOD, EDWARD W.   SS   BLF
  BOYS' LIFE BOOK OF OUTER SPACE STORIES, THE
                                         BOY'S LIFE, ED. OF   AN

LOBBY   SIMAK, CLIFFORD D. SS   ASF 44 04
  *BEST OF SCIENCE FICTION   CONKLIN, GROFF   AN
LOCAL ALLOSAURUS, THE   UTLEY, STEVEN   PM   NDM 75 05
  NEW DIMENSIONS 5   SILVERBERG, ROBERT   OA
LOCATOR, THE   LORY, ROBERT   SS   FSF 68 02
  HARVEST OF HOODWINKS, A   LORY, ROBERT   DC
LOCKED OUT   FYFE, H. B.   SS   ASF 40 02
  *MEN AGAINST THE STARS   GREENBERG , MARTIN   AN
LOCKED ROOM, THE   SLADEK, JOHN T.   SS   NWQ 72 04
  NEW WORLDS QUARTERLY NO. 4   MOORCOCK, MICHAEL   OA
LOCO PARENTIS   WOLFE, GENE   SS   DVS 72 02
  AGAIN, DANGEROUS VISIONS   ELLISON, HARLAN   OA
LOCUS FOCUS, THE   WILSON, RICHARD   SS   SFQ 57 08
  TIME OUT FOR TOMORROW   WILSON, RICHARD   AC
LOCUSTS, THE   BRADBURY, RAY   SS   NEW 51 AC
  MARTIAN CHRONICLES, THE   BRADBURY, RAY   AC
LODANA   JACOBI, CARL   SS
  PORTRAITS IN MOONLIGHT   JACOBI, CARL   AC
LODESTAR   ANDERSON, POUL   NV   AMA 73
  ASTOUNDING   HARRISON, HARRY   OA
LOFTHOUSE (A MAN'S HOME IS HIS CASTLE)
                                    GOULART, RON   SS   PBY 69 03
  BROKE DOWN ENGINE AND OTHER TROUBLES WITH MACHINES
                                         GOULART, RON   AC
LOGIC (SEE CHAIN OF LOGIC)   ANDERSON, POUL   TC
LOGIC NAMED JOE, A   LEINSTER, MURRAY   SS   ASF 46 03
  DOORWAY INTO TIME   MOSKOWITZ, SAM   AN
  MODERN MASTERPIECES OF SCIENCE FICTION MOSKOWITZ, SAM   AN
  *SCIENCE-FICTION CARNIVAL   BROWN, F. & REYNOLDS   AN
  SIDEWISE IN TIME   LEINSTER, MURRAY   AC
  SOULS IN METAL   ASHLEY, MICHAEL   AC
LOGIC OF EMPIRE   HEINLEIN, ROBERT A. NV   ASF 41 03
  GREEN HILLS OF EARTH, THE   HEINLEIN, ROBERT A.   AC
  PAST THROUGH TOMORROW, THE   HEINLEIN, ROBERT A.   AC
LOGICAL LIFE, THE   CLEMENT, HAL   SS   STL 74 01
  STELLAR 1   DEL REY, JUDY-LYNN   OA
LOGODA'S HEADS   DERLETH, AUGUST   SS   SRS 39 04
  NOT LONG FOR THIS WORLD   DERLETH, AUGUST   AC
LOINT OF PAW, A   ASIMOV, ISAAC   SS   FSF 57 08
  ASIMOV'S MYSTERIES   ASIMOV, ISAAC   AC
  BEST FROM FANTASY AND SCIENCE FICTION: 7
                                         BOUCHER, ANTHONY   AN
LONDON BRIDGE   NORTON, ANDRE   SS   FSF 73 05
  MANY WORLDS OF ANDRE NORTON, THE   NORTON, ANDRE   AC
LONDON CALLING   RUSSELL, RAY   SS   61
  SARDONICUS AND OTHER STORIES   RUSSELL, RAY   AC
LONDON MELANCHOLY   HARRISON, M. JOHN   SS   FSF 69 05
  MACHINE IN SHAFT TEN AND OTHER STORIES, THE
                                         HARRISON, M. JOHN   AC
LONE WARRIOR   DEFORD, MIRIAM ALLEN SS TVW 73
  TWO VIEWS OF WONDER   SCORTIA & YARBRO   OA
LONE WOLF, THE (THE CREATURE FROM CLEVELAND DEPTHS)
                                    LEIBER, FRITZ   NA   GAL 62 12
  NIGHT OF THE WOLF, THE   LEIBER, FRITZ   AC
LONE ZONE   PLATT, CHARLES   SS   NWS 65 07
  BEST SF STORIES FROM NEW WORLDS 7   MOORCOCK, MICHAEL   OA
LONELY HABIT, THE   ALDISS, BRIAN W.   SS   EQM 66 06
  SALIVA TREE AND OTHER STRANGE GROWTHS, THE
                                         ALDISS, BRIAN W.   AC
LONELY MAN, THE   THOMAS, THEODORE L. NV   GAL 63 04
  EIGHTH GALAXY READER, THE   POHL, FREDERIK   AN
LONELY ONE, THE   SILVERBERG, ROBERT SS   FSF 56 07
  GODLING, GO HOME!   SILVERBERG, ROBERT   AC
LONELY PLANET, THE   LEINSTER, MURRAY   NV   TWS 49 12
  BEYOND THE END OF TIME   POHL, FREDERIK   AN
  MONSTERS AND SUCH   LEINSTER, MURRAY   AC
LONELY ROAD   WILSON, RICHARD   SS   FSF 56 09
  THOSE IDIOTS FROM EARTH   WILSON, RICHARD   AC
LONELY ROBOT, THE   LITTLE, MARGARET   SS   ADS 75 01
  ARMADA SCI-FI ONE   DAVIS, RICHARD   OA
LONELY SONGS OF LAREN DORR, THE
                                    MARTIN, GEORGE R. R. SS FAN 76 05
  SONGS OF STARS AND SHADOWS   MARTIN, GEORGE R. R.   AC
LONELY, THE   MERRIL, JUDITH   SS   WOT 63 10
  BEST OF JUDITH MERRIL, THE   MERRIL, JUDITH   AC
  SURVIVAL SHIP AND OTHER STORIES   MERRIL, JUDITH   AC
LONELY, THE   SERLING, ROD   SA
  FROM THE TWILIGHT ZONE   SERLING, ROD   AC
  MORE STORIES FROM THE TWILIGHT ZONE   SERLING, ROD   OC
LONELYACHE   ELLISON, HARLAN   SS   KNT 64 07
  ALONE AGAINST TOMORROW   ELLISON, HARLAN   AC
  I HAVE NO MOUTH, AND I MUST SCREAM   ELLISON, HARLAN   AC
  *LOVE AIN'T NOTHING BUT SEX MISSPELLED ELLISON, HARLAN   AC
LONESOME PLACE, THE   DERLETH, AUGUST   SS   FFM 48 10
  HORROR TIMES TEN   NORTON, ALDEN H.   AN
LONG AFTER MIDNIGHT   BRADBURY, RAY   SS
  LONG AFTER MIDNIGHT   BRADBURY, RAY   AC
LONG DAWN, THE   LOOMIS, NOEL   SS   SSS 50 01
  *BIG BOOK OF SCIENCE FICTION   CONKLIN, GROFF   AN
LONG DAY IN COURT   BRAND, JONATHAN   SS   IFS 63 11
  IF READER OF SCIENCE FICTION, THE   POHL, FREDERIK   AN
LONG DISTANCE CALL (SORRY, RIGHT NUMBER)
                                    MATHESON, RICHARD   SS   BEY 53 11
  SHOCK!   MATHESON, RICHARD   AC
LONG ECHO, THE   DEFORD, MIRIAM ALLEN SS STR 58 04
  STAR SCIENCE FICTION STORIES NO. 4   POHL, FREDERIK   OA
LONG EUREKA, THE   SELLINGS, ARTHUR   SS   SCF 59 08
  LONG EUREKA, THE   SELLINGS, ARTHUR   AC
LONG HOP   FAIRMAN, PAUL W.   SS
  FORGETFUL ROBOT, THE   FAIRMAN, PAUL W.   OC
LONG LIVE LORD KOR!   NORTON, ANDRE   SN   WOF 70 02
  MANY WORLDS OF ANDRE NORTON, THE   NORTON, ANDRE   AC
LONG MEMORY, THE   SPENCER, WILLIAM   SS   NWR 66 09
  NEW WRITINGS IN SF. 7   CARNELL, JOHN   AN
  NEW WRITINGS IN SF. 9   CARNELL, JOHN   OA

LONG NIGHT OF WAITING, THE   NORTON, ANDRE   SS   73
  LONG NIGHT OF WAITING AND OTHER STORIES ELWOOD, ROGER   OA
  MANY WORLDS OF ANDRE NORTON, THE   NORTON, ANDRE   AC
LONG NIGHT, THE (SEE CONVERGENT SERIES)
                                    NIVEN, LARRY   TC
LONG NIGHT, THE (THE EXPLOITS OF ARGO)
                                    RUSSELL, RAY   SS   ROG 61 04
  7TH ANNUAL OF THE YEAR'S BEST S-F, THE   MERRIL, JUDITH   AN
LONG RAIN, THE (DEATH-BY-RAIN) BRADBURY, RAY   SS   PLS 50 SU
  *ILLUSTRATED MAN, THE   BRADBURY, RAY   AC
  R IS FOR ROCKET   BRADBURY, RAY   AC
LONG REMEMBERED THUNDER, THE LAUMER, KEITH   NV   WOT 63 04
  BEST SCIENCE FICTION FROM WORLDS OF TOMORROW, THE
                                           POHL, FREDERIK   AN
  NINE BY LAUMER   LAUMER, KEITH   AC
LONG REMEMBERING, THE   ANDERSON, POUL   SS   FSF 57 11
  HOMEWARD AND BEYOND   ANDERSON, POUL   AC
  SCIENCE FICTION SHOWCASE   KORNBLUTH, MARY   AN
LONG SHOT   VINGE, VERNOR   SS   ASF 72 08
  BEST SCIENCE FICTION STORIES OF THE YEAR (1972)
                                           DEL REY, LESTER   AN
  1973 ANNUAL WORLD'S BEST SF, THE   WOLLHEIM, DONALD A.   AN
LONG SILENCE, THE   NOAKES, DONALD   SS   ASF 72 03
  BEST SCIENCE FICTION STORIES OF THE YEAR (1972)
                                           DEL REY, LESTER   AN
LONG SPOON, A   WYNDHAM, JOHN   SS   60
  CONSIDER HER WAYS AND OTHERS   WYNDHAM, JOHN   AC
  DEVIL HIS DUE, THE   HILL, DOUGLAS   AN
LONG TIME AGO, NOT FORGOTTEN VAN LAERHOVEN, BOB   SS   NWR 75 27
  NEW WRITINGS IN SF. 27   BULMER, KENNETH   OA
LONG VIEW, THE   PRATT, FLETCHER   NA   STS 52 12
  PETRIFIED PLANET, THE   CLARK, JOHN D.   OA
LONG VOYAGE, THE   JACOBI, CARL   SS   FUN 55 09
  PORTRAITS IN MOONLIGHT   JACOBI, CARL   AC
LONG WALK TO FOREVER   VONNEGUT, KURT JR.   SS   LHJ 60 08
  WELCOME TO THE MONKEY HOUSE   VONNEGUT, KURT JR.   AC
LONG WATCH, THE   HEINLEIN, ROBERT A.   SS   ALM 49 12
  BEST OF ROBERT HEINLEIN, THE   HEINLEIN, ROBERT A.   AC
  *BEYOND TIME AND SPACE   DERLETH, AUGUST   AN
  GREEN HILLS OF EARTH, THE   HEINLEIN, ROBERT A.   AC
  PAST THROUGH TOMORROW, THE   HEINLEIN, ROBERT A.   AC
  SCIENCE FICTION ROLL OF HONOR, THE   POHL, FREDERIK   AN
LONG WAY HOME, THE   SABERHAGEN, FRED   SS   GAL 61 06
  BOOK OF SABERHAGEN, THE   SABERHAGEN, FRED   AC
LONG WAY, THE   SMITH, GEORGE O.   NV   ASF 44 04
  COMPLETE VENUS EQUILATERAL, THE   SMITH, GEORGE O.   AC
  VENUS EQUILATERAL   SMITH, GEORGE O.   AC
LONG YEARS, THE (ALSO AS DWELLERS IN SILENCE)
                                    BRADBURY, RAY   SS   MCL 48 09
  MARTIAN CHRONICLES, THE   BRADBURY, RAY   AC
  TOMORROW MIDNIGHT   BRADBURY, RAY   AC
LONG-TERM RESIDENTS, THE   PEDLER, KIT   SS
  YEAR'S BEST HORROR STORIES: SERIES II, THE
                                           DAVIS, RICHARD   AN
LONGER STORIES TOO GOOD TO BE MISSED
                                    MISC. MATERIAL   MS
  TALES BEYOND TIME   DE CAMP, L. S.&C.   AN
LONGEST SCIENCE-FICTION STORY EVER TOLD, THE
                                    CLARKE, ARTHUR C.   SS
  WIND FROM THE SUN, THE   CLARKE, ARTHUR C.   AC
LONGEST VOYAGE, THE   ANDERSON, POUL   NV   ASF 60 12
  BEST OF POUL ANDERSON, THE   ANDERSON, POUL   AC
  HUGO WINNERS, THE (VOLUME 1)   ASIMOV, ISAAC   AN
  MANY WORLDS OF POUL ANDERSON, THE   ANDERSON, POUL   AC
LONGFORD CUP, THE   MOORCOCK, MICHAEL   SS   PNT 73
  LIVES AND TIMES OF JERRY CORNELIUS, THE MOORCOCK, MICHAEL   AC
LONGLINE   CLEMENT, HAL   NV   76
  FASTER THAN LIGHT   DANN & ZEBROWSKI   OA
LONGTOOTH   PANGBORN, EDGAR   NV   FSF 70 01
  BEST FROM FANTASY AND SCIENCE FICTION: 19
                                           FERMAN, EDWARD L.   AN
  GOOD NEIGHBORS AND OTHER STRANGERS   PANGBORN, EDGAR   AC
  NEW WORLDS OF FANTASY NO. 3   CARR, TERRY   AN
LOO REE   HENDERSON, ZENNA   SS   FSF 53 02
  HOLDING WONDER   HENDERSON, ZENNA   AC
LOOK AFTER THE STRANGE GIRL (THE STRANGE GIRL)
                                    PRIESTLEY, J. B.   SS   FSF 54 01
  OTHER PLACE, THE   PRIESTLEY, J. B.   AC
  OTHER SIDE OF THE CLOCK, THE   STERN, PHILIP VAN D.   AN
LOOK HOW THE FISH LIVE   POWERS, J. F.   SS   REP 57 10
  ECO-FICTION   STADLER, JOHN   AN
LOOK NATURAL, PLEASE!   WYNDHAM, JOHN   SS
  JIZZLE   WYNDHAM, JOHN   AC
LOOK OUT! DUCK!   GARRETT, RANDALL   NV   ASF 57 09
  NEVER IN THIS WORLD   STONE, IDELLA P.   AN
LOOK, YOU THINK YOU'VE GOT TROUBLES
                                    CARR, CAROL   SS   ORB 69 05
  ALIENS, THE   SILVERBERG, ROBERT   AN
  ANTIGRAV: COSMIC COMEDIES   STRICK, PHILIP   AN
  BEST FROM ORBIT, THE   KNIGHT, DAMON   AN
  MARRIAGE AND THE FAMILY THROUGH SCIENCE FICTION
                                           CLEAR/WARRICK/&   AN
  ORBIT 5   KNIGHT, DAMON   OA
  POCKETFUL OF STARS, A   KNIGHT, DAMON   AN
  THEMES IN SCIENCE FICTION   KELLEY, LEO P.   AN
  WANDERING STARS   DANN, JACK M.   AN
LOOKING BACK   TURNER, STEPHEN C.   SS
  QUEST   BISCHOFF, DAVID   OA
LOOKING BACKWARD   FEIFFER, JULES   CT   HAS 61 12
  7TH ANNUAL OF THE YEAR'S BEST S-F, THE   MERRIL, JUDITH   AN
LOOKING FOR SOMETHING?   HERBERT, FRANK   SS   STS 52 04
  BEST OF FRANK HERBERT, THE   HERBERT, FRANK   AC
  BOOK OF FRANK HERBERT, THE   HERBERT, FRANK   AC
LOOKING INTO IT   GOULART, RON   SS   NEW 72 AC
  CHAMELEON CORPS & OTHER SHAPE CHANGERS, THE
                                           GOULART, RON   AC

LOOKING ON THE SUNNY SIDE OF AN ECLIPSE
                                    ALDISS, BRIAN W.   SS   NWR 74 24
  NEW WRITINGS IN SF. 24   BULMER, KENNETH   AN
LOOKING-GLASS SEA   YEP, LAURENCE   SS   NEW 72 AN
  STRANGE BED FELLOWS   SCORTIA, THOMAS N.   AN
LOOLIES ARE HERE, THE   RICE, ALLISON   SS   ORB 66 01
  BEST FROM ORBIT, THE   KNIGHT, DAMON   AN
  ORBIT 1   KNIGHT, DAMON   OA
LOOPHOLE   CLARKE, ARTHUR C.   SS   ASF 46 04
  EXPEDITION TO EARTH   CLARKE, ARTHUR C.   AC
  FIRST FLIGHT   KNIGHT, DAMON   AN
  MARS, WE LOVE YOU   HIPOLITO & MCNELLY   AN
  *TREASURY OF SCIENCE FICTION, A   CONKLIN, GROFF   AN
LOOT OF TIME, THE   SIMAK, CLIFFORD D.   NV   TWS 38 12
  ALIEN EARTH AND OTHER STORIES   ELWOOD & MOSKOWITZ   AN
LOP-EARED CAT THAT DEVOURED PHILADELPHIA, THE
                                    PHILLIPS, LOUIS   SS
  BEST SF: 75, THE NINTH ANNUAL   HARRISON & ALDISS   AN
LORD BEDEN'S MOTOR   HARRIS-BURLAND, J. B.   SS   SND 01 12
  SCIENCE FICTION BY GASLIGHT   MOSKOWITZ, SAM   AN
LORD MOUNTDRAGO (DOCTOR AND PATIENT)
                            MAUGHAM, W. SOMERSET SS   ITM 39 02
  MOONLIGHT TRAVELER, THE   STERN, PHILIP VAN D.   AN
  PERCHANCE TO DREAM   KNIGHT, DAMON   AN
LORD OF A THOUSAND SUNS   ANDERSON, POUL   NV   PLS 51 09
  GALACTIC EMPIRES VOLUME TWO   ALDISS, BRIAN W.   AN
  TALES OF OUTER SPACE   WOLLHEIM, DONALD A.   DA
LORD OF EVIL (SEE THE SECOND PRINT)
                                    DERLETH, AUGUST   TC
LORD OF THE DESERT PLANET   WELLS, BASIL   SS
  DOORWAYS TO SPACE   WELLS, BASIL   AC
LORD OF THE DYNAMOS, THE   WELLS, H. G.   SS   PMB 94 09
  BEST SCIENCE FICTION STORIES OF H. G. WELLS
                                           WELLS, H. G.   AC
  BEST STORIES OF H. G. WELLS   WELLS, H. G.   AC
  COUNTRY OF THE BLIND, THE   WELLS, H. G.   AC
  DOOR IN THE WALL, THE   WELLS, H. G.   AC
  SHORT STORIES OF H. G. WELLS, THE   WELLS, H. G.   AC
  STOLEN BACILLUS AND OTHER INCIDENTS, THE WELLS, H. G.   AC
  STORIES FROM SCIENCE FICTION   DOHERTY, G. D.   AN
  THIRTY STRANGE STORIES   WELLS, H. G.   AC
LORD RANDY, MY SON   HENSLEY, JOE L.   SS   DVS 67 01
  DANGEROUS VISIONS   ELLISON, HARLAN   OA
  FANTASY: THE LITERATURE OF THE MARVELOUS KELLEY, LEO P.   AN
LORD TEDRIC   SMITH, EDWARD E. PHD   NV   USF 54 03
  BEST OF E. E. 'DOC' SMITH, THE   SMITH, EDWARD E. PHD   AC
LORDS AND LADIES   ROBERTS, KEITH   NV   IMP 66 06
  PAVANE   ROBERTS, KEITH   NO
LORELEI OF THE RED MIST   BRACKETT, LEIGH
                        AND BRADBURY, RAY   NV C PLS 46 SU
  BEST OF PLANET STORIES NO. 1, THE   BRACKETT, LEIGH   AN
  HUMAN EQUATION, THE   NOLAN, WILLIAM F.   AN
  THREE TIMES INFINITY   MARGULIES, LEO   AN
LORELEI SIGNAL, THE (MARGARET ARMEN)
                                    FOSTER, ALAN DEAN   SA   SLG 74 02
  STAR TREK LOG TWO   FOSTER, ALAN DEAN   OC
LORENZO WATCH, THE   JACOBI, CARL   SS   WRT 48 01
  PORTRAITS IN MOONLIGHT   JACOBI, CARL   AC
LOS AMIGOS FIASCO, THE   DOYLE, ARTHUR CONAN   SS   IDL 92 12
  MASTERPIECES OF SCIENCE FICTION   MOSKOWITZ, SAM   AN
LOST AND FOUND   BAUM, THOMAS   SS
  BEST SF: 1974   HARRISON & ALDISS   AN
LOST ART   SMITH, GEORGE O.   NV   ASF 43 12
  COMPLETE VENUS EQUILATERAL, THE   SMITH, GEORGE O.   AC
  MARS, WE LOVE YOU   HIPOLITO & MCNELLY   AN
  TREASURY OF GREAT SCIENCE FICTION, A VOL.2
                                           BOUCHER, ANTHONY   AN
LOST CAVERN, THE   HEARD, H. F.   NV
LOST CAVERN AND OTHER TALES OF THE FANTASTIC, THE
                                           HEARD, H. F.   AC
LOST CHORD, THE   MOSKOWITZ, SAM   SS   NEW 53 AN
  SCIENCE AND SORCERY   FORD, GARRET   AN
LOST CITY OF MARS, THE   BRADBURY, RAY   NV   PBY 67 01
  I SING THE BODY ELECTRIC   BRADBURY, RAY   AC
  LAST TRAIN TO LIMBO   PLAYBOY, EDITORS OF   AN
  MARS, WE LOVE YOU   HIPOLITO & MCNELLY   AN
  3 TO THE HIGHEST POWER   NOLAN, WILLIAM F.   AN
LOST CONTINENT, THE   HOUSEHOLD, GEOFFREY   SS   SEP 60 09
  ANCIENT MYSTERIES READER, THE   HAINING, PETER   AN
  POST READER OF FANTASY AND SCIENCE FICTION
                                           SATURDAY EVE. POST   AN
LOST CONTINENT, THE   SPINRAD, NORMAN   NV   SAG 70
  ALPHA 6   SILVERBERG, ROBERT   AN
  NO DIRECTION HOME   SPINRAD, NORMAN   AC
  SCIENCE AGAINST MAN   CHEETHAM, ANTHONY   AN
LOST DAY, THE   DERLETH, AUGUST   SS   WRT 45 05
  NOT LONG FOR THIS WORLD   DERLETH, AUGUST   AC
LOST FACE, THE   NESVADBA, JOSEF   NV   64
  BEST SF: 1970   HARRISON & ALDISS   AN
  LOST FACE, THE   NESVADBA, JOSEF   AC
LOST GIANT OF AMERICAN SCIENCE FICTION- A BIOGRAPHICAL
  PERSPECTIVE   MOSKOWITZ, SAM   AR
  CRYSTAL MAN, THE   MITCHELL, EDWARD P.   AC
LOST GROUND   MASSON, DAVID I.   SS   NWS 66 12
  BEST SF: 1968   HARRISON & ALDISS   AN
  CALTRAPS OF TIME, THE   MASSON, DAVID I.   AC
LOST HEARTS   JAMES, M. R.   SS   31
  EDGE OF NEVER, THE   HOSKINS, ROBERT   AN
  SUPERNATURAL READER, THE   CONKLIN, G&L.   AN
LOST IN A COMET'S TAIL, OR, FRANK READE JR'S STRANGE ADVENTURE
  IN HIS NEW AIRSHIP   SENARENS, LOUIS P.   SS   FRL 95 12
  MASTERPIECES OF SCIENCE FICTION   MOSKOWITZ, SAM   AN
LOST IN A JUNKYARD   FAIRMAN, PAUL W.   SS
  FORGETFUL ROBOT, THE   FAIRMAN, PAUL W.   OC
LOST IN THE MARIGOLDS   HOFFMAN, LEE
                        AND TOOMEY, ROBERT E. JR NV C ORB 71 09

```
ORBIT  9                               KNIGHT, DAMON              OA
LOST IN TRANSLATION         BROWN, ROSEL GEORGE  SS    FSF 59  05
  HANDFUL OF TIME, A                   BROWN, ROSEL GEORGE       AC
LOST IN TRANSLATION         JANIFER, LAURENCE M. SS    ASF 61  08
  IMPOSSIBLE?                          JANIFER, LAURENCE M.      AC
LOST INHERITANCE, THE       WELLS, H. G.         SS        97
  PLATTNER STORY AND OTHERS, THE       WELLS, H. G.             AC
  SHORT STORIES OF H. G. WELLS, THE    WELLS, H. G.             AC
  THIRTY STRANGE STORIES               WELLS, H. G.             AC
LOST LANGUAGE, THE          KELLER, DAVID H. MD. SS    AMZ 34  01
  SCIENCE FICTION OF THE 30'S          KNIGHT, DAMON            AN
LOST LEGACY (LOST LEGION)   HEINLEIN, ROBERT A.  NV    SSS 41  11
  ASSIGNMENT IN ETERNITY               HEINLEIN, ROBERT A.      AC
LOST LEGION (SEE LOST LEGACY) HEINLEIN, ROBERT A.  TC
LOST LEONARDO, THE          BALLARD, J. G.       SS    FSF 64  03
  NEW WORLDS OF FANTASY                CARR, TERRY              AN
  TERMINAL BEACH (BRITISH VERSION)     BALLARD, J. G.           AC
LOST MACHINE, THE           HARRIS, JOHN BEYNON  SS    AMZ 32  04
  BEST OF AMAZING, THE                 ROSS, JOSEPH             AN
LOST MACHINE, THE           WYNDHAM, JOHN        SS    AMZ 32  04
  BEST OF JOHN WYNDHAM, THE            WYNDHAM, JOHN            AC
  COMING OF THE ROBOTS, THE            MOSKOWITZ, SAM           AN
  MAN FROM BEYOND AND OTHER STORIES, THE  WYNDHAM, JOHN         AC
LOST MEMORY                 PHILLIPS, PETER      SS    GAL 52  05
  COMING OF THE ROBOTS, THE            MOSKOWITZ, SAM           AN
  CONTACT                              KEYES, NOEL              AN
  GALAXY SCIENCE FICTION OMNIBUS       GOLD, H. L.              AN
  GATEWAY TO TOMORROW                  CARNELL, JOHN            AN
  SCIENCE FICTION TERROR TALES         CONKLIN, GROFF           AN
  SECOND GALAXY READER OF SCIENCE FICTION  GOLD, H. L.          AN
  THEMES IN SCIENCE FICTION            KELLEY, LEO P.           AN
LOST NEWTON                 SCHMIDT, STANLEY     NV    ASF 70  09
  ANTHROPOLOGY THROUGH SCIENCE FICTION MASON, C/GREENBERG/&     AN
  SOCIOLOGY THROUGH SCIENCE FICTION    MILSTEAD/GREENBERG/&     AN
LOST ON VENUS               BURROUGHS, EDGAR R.  NO    ARG 33  03
  PIRATES OF VENUS AND LOST ON VENUS, THE  BURROUGHS, EDGAR R.  AC
LOST PARADISE               MOORE, C. L.         SS    WRT 36  07
  NORTHWEST OF EARTH                   MOORE, C. L.             AC
LOST RACE, THE              LEINSTER, MURRAY     NV    TWS 49  04
  *MY BEST SCIENCE FICTION STORY       MARGULIES & FRIEND       AN
LOST ROOM, THE              O'BRIEN, FITZ-JAMES  SS    WRT 29  10
  SUPERNATURAL READER, THE             CONKLIN, G&L.            AN
LOST SECRETS REVEALED       ANDERSON, POUL       AR        72
  HOMEBREW                             ANDERSON, POUL           AC
LOST STREET, THE (THE STREET THAT WASN'T THERE)
                            JACOBI, CARL
              AND SIMAK, CLIFFORD D.   SS C CMT 41  07
  *STRANGE PORTS OF CALL               DERLETH, AUGUST          AN
LOST VOICE, THE             SPEARMAN, F. H.      SS
  BATTLE FOR THE PACIFIC AND OTHER ADVENTURES AT SEA, THE
                                       ANONYMOUS                AN
LOST WORLD, THE             DOYLE, ARTHUR CONAN  EX    HDS 12
  FROM FRANKENSTEIN TO ANDROMEDA       BROWN, JAMES GOLDIE      AN
LOST YEARS, THE             LEWIS, OSCAR         EX    KNP 51
  TREASURY OF GREAT SCIENCE FICTION, A VOL.2
                                       BOUCHER, ANTHONY         AN
LOST: FIFTY SUNS            VAN VOGT, A. E.      NV    NEW 52  NO
  BOOK OF VAN VOGT, THE                VAN VOGT, A. E.          AC
  MIXED MEN, THE                       VAN VOGT, A. E.          NO
LOSTLING                    BRUNNER, JOHN        SS
  FAR SIDE OF TIME, THE                ELWOOD, ROGER            OA
LOT                         MOORE, WARD          NV    FSF 53  05
  BEST FROM FANTASY AND SCIENCE FICTION: 3
                                       BOUCHER & MCCOMAS        AN
  BEST SCIENCE-FICTION STORIES: 1954, THE  BLEILER & DIKTY      AN
  EARTH IN TRANSIT                     SCHWARTZ, SHEILA         AN
  PENGUIN SCIENCE FICTION              ALDISS, BRIAN W.         AN
LOT'S DAUGHTER              MOORE, WARD          NV    FSF 54  10
  DECADE OF FANTASY AND SCIENCE FICTION, A MILLS, ROBERT P.     AN
LOTTERY IN BABYLON, THE     BORGES, JORGE LUIS   SS        62
  INTO THE UNKNOWN                     CARR, TERRY              AN
LOTUS EATERS               LEIBER, FRITZ        SS    FSF 72  10
  WORLDS OF FRITZ LEIBER, THE          LEIBER, FRITZ            AC
LOTUS EATERS, THE           WEINBAUM, STANLEY G. NV    ASF 35  04
  BEST OF STANLEY G. WEINBAUM, THE     WEINBAUM, STANLEY G.     AC
  *BEYOND TIME AND SPACE               DERLETH, AUGUST          AN
  DAWN OF FLAME                        WEINBAUM, STANLEY G.     AC
  HIDDEN PLANET, THE                   WOLLHEIM, DONALD A.      AN
  MARTIAN ODYSSEY AND OTHER SCIENCE FICTION TALES, A
                                       WEINBAUM, STANLEY G.     AC
  MARTIAN ODYSSEY AND OTHERS, A        WEINBAUM, STANLEY G.     AC
  MARTIAN ODYSSEY, A                   WEINBAUM, STANLEY G.     AC
  MASTERPIECES OF SCIENCE FICTION      MOSKOWITZ, SAM           AN
  UBERWINDUNG VON RAUM UND ZEIT        GUNTHER, GOTTHARD        AN
LOTUS-ENGINE, THE           GALLUN, RAYMOND Z.   SS    SSS 40  03
  JUPITER                              POHL, C. & F.            AN
LOVE                        WILSON, RICHARD      SS    FSF 52  06
  HUMAN AND OTHER BEINGS               DEGRAEFF, ALLEN          AN
  SHADOW OF TOMORROW                   POHL, FREDERIK           AN
  THOSE IDIOTS FROM EARTH              WILSON, RICHARD          AC
LOVE AMONG THE CABBAGES     BIRD, CHRISTOPHER
              AND TOMPKINS, PETER      AR C HRP 72  11
  SCIENCE FACT/FICTION                 FARRELL/GAGE/&           AN
LOVE AND GRAVITY            BOULLE, PIERRE       SS
  TIME OUT OF MIND                     BOULLE, PIERRE           OC
LOVE AND NAPALM: EXPORT U.S.A. BALLARD, J. G.    SS    RUN 68  SU
  LOVE & NAPALM: EXPORT U.S.A.         BALLARD, J. G.           AC
LOVE AND THE TRIANGLE       WATERLOO, STANLEY    SS        99
  ANCESTRAL VOICES                     MENVILLE & REGINALD      AN
LOVE AT LOST SIGHT          MEADLEY, ROBERT      SS    NWB 75  08
  NEW WORLDS EIGHT                     BAILEY, HILARY           OA
LOVE CALLED THIS THING      DAVIDSON, AVRAM
              AND GOFORTH, LAURA       SS C GAL 59  04
  SCIENCE FICTION FOR PEOPLE WHO HATE SCIENCE FICTION
                                       CARR, TERRY              AN
  SIXTH GALAXY READER, THE             GOLD, H. L.              AN
WHAT STRANGE STARS AND SKIES           DAVIDSON, AVRAM          AC
LOVE ETHEREAL (SEE LOVE IN THE DARK)
                            GOLD, H. L.               TC
LOVE EVERY THIRD STIR       HENDERSON, ZENNA     SS    NEW 71  05
  HOLDING WONDER                       HENDERSON, ZENNA         AC
LOVE IN THE DARK (LOVE ETHEREAL)
                            GOLD, H. L.          SS    SUS 51  FL
  BEYOND THE END OF TIME               POHL, FREDERIK           AN
  INVISIBLE MEN                        DAVENPORT, BASIL         AN
  OLD DIE RICH AND OTHER SCIENCE FICTION, THE
                                       GOLD, H. L.              AC
  SF: AUTHORS' CHOICE 2                HARRISON, HARRY          AC
LOVE IS A PUNCH IN THE NOSE JAKES, JOHN W.       SS    BIZ 66  01
  BEST OF JOHN JAKES, THE              JAKES, JOHN W.           AC
LOVE IS AN IMAGINARY NUMBER ZELAZNY, ROGER       SS    NWS 66  01
  DOORS OF HIS FACE, THE LAMPS OF HIS MOUTH, THE
                                       ZELAZNY, ROGER           AC
LOVE IS THE PLAN THE PLAN IS DEATH
                            TIPTREE, JAMES JR.   SS    ALC 73
  ALIEN CONDITION, THE                 GOLDIN, STEPHEN          OA
  NEBULA AWARD STORIES  9              WILHELM, KATE            AN
  WARM WORLDS AND OTHERWISE            TIPTREE, JAMES JR.       AC
LOVE LETTER                 FINNEY, JACK         SS    SEP 59  08
  I LOVE GALESBURG IN THE SPRINGTIME   FINNEY, JACK             AC
LOVE LETTERS FROM MARS      CIARDI, JOHN         PM    FSF 65  01
  BEST FROM FANTASY AND SCIENCE FICTION: 15
                                       FERMAN, EDWARD L.        AN
LOVE ME TRUE                DICKSON, GORDON R.   SS    ASF 61  10
  ANCIENT, MY ENEMY                    DICKSON, GORDON R.       AC
LOVE NEST                   SLADEK, JOHN T.      PM        69
  HOLDING YOUR EIGHT HANDS             LUCIE-SMITH, EDWARD      AN
LOVE OF HEAVEN, THE         STURGEON, THEODORE   SS    ASF 48  11
  *SCIENCE FICTION ADVENTURES IN MUTATION  CONKLIN, GROFF      AN
LOVE ROGO                   CARVER, JEFFREY A.        NA
  FUTURELOVE                           ELWOOD, ROGER            OA
LOVE SONG OF HERSELF        BRYANT, EDWARD       SS    NDM 71  01
  AMONG THE DEAD                       BRYANT, EDWARD           AC
  NEW DIMENSIONS 1                     SILVERBERG, ROBERT       OA
LOVE SONG OF LANCELOT BIGGS, THE
                            BOND, NELSON S.      SS    AMZ 42  03
  LANCELOT BIGGS: SPACEMAN             BOND, NELSON S.          AC
LOVE STORY                  JANIFER, LAURENCE M. SS    FAN 63  05
  IMPOSSIBLE?                          JANIFER, LAURENCE M.     AC
LOVE STORY                  MONIG, CHRISTOPHER   SS    NEW 52  AN
  *FUTURE TENSE                        CROSSEN, KENDELL F.      AN
LOVE STORY                  RUSSELL, ERIC FRANK  SS    ASF 57  08
  ABC OF SCIENCE FICTION, AN           BOARDMAN, TOM JR.        AN
LOVE STORY IN THREE ACTS    GERROLD, DAVID       SS    NOV 70  01
  *NOVA 1                              HARRISON, HARRY          OA
  WITH A FINGER IN MY I                GERROLD, DAVID           AC
LOVE THAT UNIVERSE          CLARKE, ARTHUR C.    SS
  WIND FROM THE SUN, THE               CLARKE, ARTHUR C.        AC
LOVE THY VIMP               NOURSE, ALAN E.      SS    FSF 52  04
  TIGER BY THE TAIL                    NOURSE, ALAN E.          AC
LOVE-MASTER, THE            BEAUMONT, CHARLES    SS    ROG 56
  EDGE, THE                            BEAUMONT, CHARLES        AC
  MAGIC MAN AND OTHER SCIENCE-FANTASY STORIES
                                       BEAUMONT, CHARLES        AC
  NIGHT RIDE AND OTHER JOURNEYS        BEAUMONT, CHARLES        AC
LOVE-NEST, THE              DE CAMP, L. SPRAGUE
              AND PRATT, FLETCHER      SS C NEW 53  11
  TALES FROM GAVAGAN'S BAR             DE CAMP, L. S.&PRATT     AC
LOVE, INCORPORATED (ALSO AS PILGRIMAGE TO EARTH)
                            SHECKLEY, ROBERT     SS    PBY 56  09
  FIEND, THE                           PLAYBOY, EDITORS OF      AN
  INTRODUCTORY PSYCHOLOGY THROUGH SCIENCE FICTION
                                       KATZ/WARRICK/&           AN
  MARRIAGE AND THE FAMILY THROUGH SCIENCE FICTION
                                       CLEAR/WARRICK/&          AN
  PLAYBOY BOOK OF SCIENCE FICTION AND FANTASY, THE
                                       PLAYBOY, EDITORS OF      AN
LOVE, YOUR MAGIC SPELL IS EVERYWHERE (THE MAN WITH THE MAGIC
  GLASSES)                  FINNEY, JACK         NV    MCC 62  03
  I LOVE GALESBURG IN THE SPRINGTIME   FINNEY, JACK             AC
LOVEBEAST, THE              COLVIN, JAMES        SS
  DEEP FIX, THE                        COLVIN, JAMES            AC
LOVECRAFT CONTROVERSY- WHY?, THE
                            PRICE, E. HOFFMANN   AR    NEW 76  AN
  YEAR'S BEST HORROR STORIES: SERIES IV, THE
                                       PAGE, GERALD W.          AN
LOVEMAKER                   EKLUND, GORDON       SS    EIO 73
  EROS IN ORBIT                        ELDER, JOSEPH            OA
LOVEMAKING (ALSO AS MAKING LOVE)
                            POHL, FREDERIK       SS    PBY 66  12
  FIEND, THE                           PLAYBOY, EDITORS OF      AN
LOVER BOY                   COGSWELL, THEODORE R SS    BEY 54  03
  THIRD EYE, THE                       COGSWELL, THEODORE R     AC
LOVER, WHEN YOU'RE NEAR ME  MATHESON, RICHARD    NV    GAL 52  05
  BEST SCIENCE-FICTION STORIES: 1953, THE  BLEILER & DIKTY     AN
  BORN OF MAN AND WOMAN                MATHESON, RICHARD        AC
  SECOND GALAXY READER OF SCIENCE FICTION  GOLD, H. L.         AN
  THIRD FROM THE SUN                   MATHESON, RICHARD        AC
LOVES OF THE TRIANGLES, THE CANNING, GEORGE
              AND FRERE, JOHN H.       PM C
  MATHEMATICAL MAGPIE, THE             FADIMAN, CLIFTON         AN
LOW-FLYING AIRCRAFT         BALLARD, J. G.       SS    BNA 75  SU
  LOW-FLYING AIRCRAFT AND OTHER STORIES BALLARD, J. G.         AC
LOWER THAN ANGELS           BUDRYS, ALGIS        SN    INF 56  10
  BUDRYS' INFERNO                      BUDRYS, ALGIS            AC
  EARTHMEN AND STRANGERS               SILVERBERG, ROBERT       AN
  UNIVERSE AHEAD                       ENGDAHL & ROBERSON       AN
LUANA                       THOMAS, GILBERT      SS    FSF 66  09
  BEST FROM FANTASY AND SCIENCE FICTION: 16
                                       FERMAN, EDWARD L.        AN
  SF12                                 MERRIL, JUDITH           AN
```

LUCIFER   MADE IN U.S.A.

LUCIFER   ZELAZNY, ROGER   SS   WOT 64 06
  DOORS OF HIS FACE, THE LAMPS OF HIS MOUTH, THE
                              ZELAZNY, ROGER   AC
LUCIFER| TUBB, E. C.   SS   VOT 69 11
  YEAR'S BEST HORROR STORIES, THE   DAVIS, RICHARD   AN
LUCK OF IGNATZ, THE   DEL REY, LESTER   NV   ASF 39 08
  *AND SOME WERE HUMAN   DEL REY, LESTER   AC
  HIDDEN PLANET, THE   WOLLHEIM, DONALD A.   AN
  YEAR AFTER TOMORROW, THE   DEL REY, L/MATSCHAT/   AN
LUCK, INC.   HARMON, JIM   SS   SFS 59 11
  RARE SCIENCE FICTION   HOWARD, IVAN   AN
LUCKIEST MAN IN DENV, THE   EISNER, SIMON   SS   GAL 52 06
  SHADOW OF TOMORROW   POHL, FREDERIK   AN
LUCKIEST MAN IN DENV, THE (AS SIMON EISNER)
                              KORNBLUTH, C. M.   SS   GAL 52 06
  ALPHA 7   SILVERBERG, ROBERT   AN
  BEST OF C. M. KORNBLUTH, THE KORNBLUTH, C. M.   AC
  CITIES OF WONDER   KNIGHT, DAMON   AN
  HOT & COLD RUNNING CITIES   MCHARGUE, GEORGESS   AN
  MARCHING MORONS AND OTHER SCIENCE FICTION
                              KORNBLUTH, C. M.   AC
  MINDWORM AND OTHER STORIES, THE KORNBLUTH, C. M.   AC
  NIGHTMARE AGE   POHL, FREDERIK   AN
LUCKIEST MAN IN THE WORLD, THE (FORTUNATE PERSON)
                              SHECKLEY, ROBERT   SS   FUN 55 02
  CITIZEN IN SPACE   SHECKLEY, ROBERT   AC
LUCKY DAY FOR THE BOAR, A   KERSH, GERALD   SS   PBY 62 10
  NIGHTSHADE & DAMNATIONS   KERSH, GERALD   AC
LUCY COMES TO STAY   BLOCH, ROBERT   SS   WRT 52 01
  FIEND IN YOU, THE   BEAUMONT, CHARLES   AN
  LIVING DEMONS, THE   BLOCH, ROBERT   AC
LUGER IS A 9MM AUTOMATIC HANDGUN WITH A PARABELLUM ACTION, THE
                              MUNDIS, JERROLD J. SS   NWS 69 03
  BEST SF STORIES FROM NEW WORLDS 6   MOORCOCK, MICHAEL AN
LUGGAGE STORE, THE   BRADBURY, RAY   SS   NEW 51 11
  MARTIAN CHRONICLES, THE   BRADBURY, RAY   AC
LUKUNDOO   WHITE, EDWARD LUCAS SS   WRT 25 11
  SHOCKING THING, A   KNIGHT, DAMON   AN
"LULLABY FOR THE MAD SCIENTIST'S DAUGHTER"
                              BRUNNER, JOHN   SG   NEW 76 AC
  BOOK OF JOHN BRUNNER, THE   BRUNNER, JOHN   AC
LULU   SIMAK, CLIFFORD D. NV   GAL 57 06
  BEST SCIENCE FICTION STORIES OF CLIFFORD D. SIMAK
                              SIMAK, CLIFFORD D.   AC
  *WORLDS OF CLIFFORD SIMAK, THE SIMAK, CLIFFORD D.   AC
LULUNGOMEENA   DICKSON, GORDON R. NV   GAL 54 01
  DANGER- HUMAN   DICKSON, GORDON R.   AC
  DEEP SPACE   SILVERBERG, ROBERT   AN
  LOOKING FORWARD   LESSER, MILTON   AN
LUNAR ESCAPADE   FYFE, H. B.   SS   OSF 54 02
  PLANET OF DOOM AND OTHER STORIES   ANONYMOUS   AN
LUNAR LANDING   DEL REY, LESTER   NV   ASF 42 10
  EARLY DEL REY   DEL REY, LESTER   AC
LUNAR TRAP   ELAM, RICHARD M. JR. NV   BLF 49
  TEEN-AGE SCIENCE FICTION STORIES   ELAM, RICHARD M. JR. AC
LUNATIC ASSIGNMENT   DORMAN, SONYA   SS   FSF 68 01
  BEST FROM FANTASY AND SCIENCE FICTION: 18
                              FERMAN, EDWARD L.   AN
LUNATIC PLANET, THE   SILVERBERG, ROBERT SS   AMZ 57 11
  ODDBALLS, THE   GHIDALIA, VIC   AN
LUNATICS, THE (THE SYSTEM OF DOCTOR TARR & PROFESSOR FEATHER)
                              POE, EDGAR ALLEN   SS   GLG 45 11
  GHOULS, THE   HAINING, PETER   AN
LUNGFISH (RENDEZVOUS WITH DESTINY, FUN 58 03)
                              BRUNNER, JOHN   NV   SCF 57 12
  ENTRY TO ELSEWHEN (STORIES REVISED)   BRUNNER, JOHN   AC
LUNIANS, THE   BOULLE, PIERRE   NV
  TIME OUT OF MIND   BOULLE, PIERRE   OC
LURANI   LAVOND, PAUL DENNIS PM   UNK 40 02
  FROM UNKNOWN WORLDS   CAMPBELL, JOHN W. JR   AN
LURE AND LORE OF "THE BLIND SPOT", THE
                              ACKERMAN, FORREST J. AR   51
  SCIENCE FICTION WORLDS OF FORREST J. ACKERMAN & FRIENDS
                              ACKERMAN, FORREST J.   AC
LURE OF POLARIS, THE   WEST, WALLACE   SS   TWS 49 10
  BIRD OF TIME, THE   WEST, WALLACE   NO
LURKERS OF BURM, THE   WELLS, BASIL   SS
  DOORWAYS TO SPACE   WELLS, BASIL   AC
LYDECTES: ON THE NATURE OF SPORT
                              EFFINGER, GEO. ALEC NV   FAN 75 12
  IRRATIONAL NUMBERS   EFFINGER, GEO. ALEC   AC
LYRIC FOR ATOM SPLITTERS   BUCK, DORIS PITKIN PM   FSF 57 05
  BEST FROM FANTASY AND SCIENCE FICTION: 7
                              BOUCHER, ANTHONY   AN
LYSENKO MAZE, THE   GRINNELL, DAVID   SS   FSF 54 07
  FUTURE TENSE   CURTIS, RICHARD   AN
  *SCIENCE FICTION ADVENTURES IN MUTATION CONKLIN, GROFF AN
LYSENKO MAZE, THE   WOLLHEIM, DONALD A. SS   FSF 54 07
  INTRODUCTORY PSYCHOLOGY THROUGH SCIENCE FICTION
                              KATZ/WARRICK/&   AN
  TWO DOZEN DRAGON EGGS   WOLLHEIM, DONALD A.   AC
M IS FOR THE MANY   RUSS, J. J.   SS   UNI 74 05
  UNIVERSE 5   CARR, TERRY   OA
M 33 IN ANDROMEDA   VAN VOGT, A. E.   SS   ASF 43 08
  M 33 IN ANDROMEDA   VAN VOGT, A. E.   AC
  TOMORROW'S UNIVERSE   CAMPBELL, H. J.   AN
M'LORD IS THE SHEPHERD   RICHMOND, LEIGH
                              AND RICHMOND, WALT SS C IFS 65 09
  POSITIVE CHARGE   RICHMOND, W. & L.   DC
M&M SEEN AS A LOW-YIELD THERMONUCLEAR DEVICE, THE
                              VARLEY, JOHN   SS   ORB 76 18
  ORBIT 18   KNIGHT, DAMON   OA
M-1   WILSON, GAHAN   SS   FSF 70 02
  TWENTY YEARS OF FANTASY & SCIENCE FICTION
                              FERMAN & MILLS   AN

MACAULEY CIRCUIT, THE   SILVERBERG, ROBERT SS   FUN 56 08
MEN AND MACHINES   SILVERBERG, ROBERT   AN
  SUNRISE ON MERCURY AND OTHER SCIENCE FICTION STORIES
                              SILVERBERG, ROBERT   OA
MACBETH EXPIATION, THE   HARRISON, M. JOHN   SS   NWR 68 13
  NEW WRITINGS IN SF. 9   CARNELL, JOHN   AN
  NEW WRITINGS IN SF. 13   CARNELL, JOHN   AN
MACDONOUGH'S SONG   KIPLING, RUDYARD   PM   MPM 12 03
  17 X INFINITY   CONKLIN, GROFF   AN
MACHINE   JAKES, JOHN W.   SS   FSF 52 04
  BEST OF JOHN JAKES, THE   JAKES, JOHN W.   AC
  BEST SCIENCE-FICTION STORIES: 1953, THE BLEILER & DIKTY AN
  FRONTIERS IN SPACE   BLEILER & DIKTY   AN
MACHINE IN SHAFT TEN, THE   CHURCHILL, JOYCE   SS   NWQ 72 03
  NEW WORLDS QUARTERLY NO. 3   MOORCOCK, MICHAEL   OA
MACHINE IN SHAFT TEN, THE (AS JOYCE CHURCHILL)
                              HARRISON, M. JOHN   SS   NWQ 72 03
  MACHINE IN SHAFT TEN AND OTHER STORIES, THE
                              HARRISON, M. JOHN   AC
MACHINE IN WARD ELEVEN, THE   WILLEFORD, CHARLES NV   PBY 61 03
  MACHINE IN WARD ELEVEN, THE WILLEFORD, CHARLES   NO
  PLAYBOY BOOK OF HORROR AND THE SUPERNATURAL, THE
                              PLAYBOY, EDITORS OF   AN
  WEIRD SHOW   PLAYBOY, EDITORS OF   AN
MACHINE MADE   MCINTOSH, J. T.   SS   NWS 51 SU
  GIANTS UNLEASHED   CONKLIN, GROFF   AN
  *NO PLACE LIKE EARTH   CARNELL, JOHN   AN
  OUT OF THIS WORLD 2   WILLIAMS-ELLIS& OWEN   AN
MACHINE MAN OF ARDATHIA, THE FLAGG, FRANCIS   SS   AMZ 27 11
  ESCALES DANS L'INFINI   GALLET, GEORGES H.   AN
  HISTORY OF THE SCIENCE FICTION MAGAZINE, THE PART 1 1926-1935
                              ASHLEY, MICHAEL   AN
MACHINE RECORD   COGSWELL, THEODORE R SS   SFA 61 05
  THIRD EYE, THE   COGSWELL, THEODORE R   AC
MACHINE STOPS, THE   FORSTER, E. M.   NV   28
  ARMCHAIR SCIENCE READER, THE GORDON, I. & SORKIN   AN
  CITIES OF WONDER   KNIGHT, DAMON   AN
  LIGHT FANTASTIC, THE   HARRISON, HARRY   AN
  SCIENCE FICTION GALAXY, THE CONKLIN, GROFF   AN
  SCIENCE FICTION HALL OF FAME VOLUME 2B BOVA, BEN   AN
  SCIENCE FICTION: THE FUTURE ALLEN, DICK   AN
  TREASURY OF SCIENCE FICTION CLASSICS, THE
                              KUEBLER, HAROLD W.   AN
  WONDERMAKERS   HOSKINS, ROBERT   AN
  17 X INFINITY   CONKLIN, GROFF   AN
MACHINE THAT WAS LONELY, THE WELLS, ROBERT   SS
  AD 2500   WILSON, ANGUS   AN
MACHINE THAT WON THE WAR, THE ASIMOV, ISAAC   SS   FSF 61 10
  *BEST FROM FANTASY AND SCIENCE FICTION: 11
                              MILLS, ROBERT P.   AN
  BEST SF 7   CRISPIN, EDMUND   AN
  NIGHTFALL AND OTHER STORIES ASIMOV, ISAAC   AC
MACHINE-GOD LAUGHS, THE   PRAGNELL, FESTUS   NV   FBK 47 02
  MACHINE-GOD LAUGHS, THE   ANONYMOUS   AN
MACHINE, THE   CAMPBELL, JOHN W. JR SS   ASF 35 02
  ANDROIDS, TIME MACHINES AND BLUE GIRAFFES
                              ELWOOD & GHIDALIA   AN
  *BEST OF JOHN W. CAMPBELL, THE CAMPBELL, JOHN W. JR   AC
  *BEST OF SCIENCE FICTION   CONKLIN, GROFF   AN
  CLOAK OF AESIR   CAMPBELL, JOHN W. JR   AC
MACHINE, THE   GEHMAN, RICHARD   SS   COL 46 12
  13 GREAT STORIES OF SCIENCE FICTION CONKLIN, GROFF   AN
MACHINERIES OF JOY, THE   BRADBURY, RAY   SS   PBY 62 12
  MACHINERIES OF JOY, THE   BRADBURY, RAY   AC
  TRANSIT OF EARTH   PLAYBOY, EDITORS OF   AN
MACHINES DO OUR WORK (FROM "LOOKING BACKWARD")
                              BELLAMY, EDWARD   EX   TIC 88
  ARMCHAIR SCIENCE READER, THE GORDON, I. & SORKIN   AN
MACHINES OF LOVING GRACE   DOZOIS, GARDNER R. SS   ORB 72 11
  INSIDE INFORMATION   MOWSHOWITZ, ABBE   AN
  ORBIT 11   KNIGHT, DAMON   OA
MACHMEN, THE   SCHMITZ, JAMES H.   SS   ASF 64 09
  NICE DAY FOR SCREAMING, AND OTHER TALES OF THE HUB
                              SCHMITZ, JAMES H.   AC
MAD HOLIDAY   SMITH, GEORGE O.   NV   NEW 47 AC
  COMPLETE VENUS EQUILATERAL, THE SMITH, GEORGE O.   AC
  VENUS EQUILATERAL   SMITH, GEORGE O.   AC
MAD HOUSE   MATHESON, RICHARD   NV   FAN 53 02
  BORN OF MAN AND WOMAN   MATHESON, RICHARD   AC
  THIRD FROM THE SUN   MATHESON, RICHARD   AC
MAD MACHINES, THE (CITY OF MACHINES)
                              ARNOLD, FRANK EDWARD NV   TOW 39 SU
  WINGS ACROSS TIME   ARNOLD, FRANK EDWARD   AC
MAD MAN   LAFFERTY, R. A.   SS   IFS 64 10
  DOES ANYONE ELSE HAVE SOMETHING FURTHER TO ADD?
                              LAFFERTY, R. A.   AC
MAD MOON, THE   WEINBAUM, STANLEY G. NV   ASF 35 12
  BEST OF STANLEY G. WEINBAUM, THE WEINBAUM, STANLEY G. AC
  DAWN OF FLAME   WEINBAUM, STANLEY G.   AC
  EXPLORING OTHER WORLDS   MOSKOWITZ, SAM   AN
  JUPITER   POHL, C. & F.   AN
  MARTIAN ODYSSEY AND OTHER SCIENCE FICTION TALES, A
                              WEINBAUM, STANLEY G. AC
  MARTIAN ODYSSEY AND OTHERS, A WEINBAUM, STANLEY G.   AC
  SCIENCE FICTION OF THE 30'S KNIGHT, DAMON   AN
MAD PLANET, THE   LEINSTER, MURRAY   NA   ARG 20 06
  FORGOTTEN PLANET, THE   LEINSTER, MURRAY   AC
  UNDER THE MOONS OF MARS   MOSKOWITZ, SAM   AN
MAD WIZARDS OF MARS, THE (SEE THE EXILES)
                              BRADBURY, RAY   TC
MADE HE A RIB   CONRAD, EARL   SS
  DA VINCI MACHINE, THE   CONRAD, EARL   OC
MADE IN TANGANYIKA   JACOBI, CARL   SS   FUN 54 05
  PORTRAITS IN MOONLIGHT   JACOBI, CARL   AC
MADE IN U.S.A.   MCINTOSH, J. T.   NV   GAL 53 04
  CONNOISSEUR'S S. F.   BOARDMAN, TOM JR.   AC

MADE IN U.S.A.

```
CROSSROADS IN TIME               CONKLIN, GROFF         AN
  HUMAN AND OTHER BEINGS         DEGRAEFF, ALLEN        AN
MADE TO BE BROKEN        TUBB, E. C.      SS   NWR 74  23
  NEW WRITINGS IN SF. 23         BULMER, KENNETH        OA
MADE TO MEASURE        GAULT, WILLIAM C.  SS   GAL 51  01
  *GALAXY READER OF SCIENCE FICTION   GOLD, H. L.        AN
MADEN, THE             BRADBURY, RAY      SS   NEW 47  AC
  *DARK CARNIVAL                 BRADBURY, RAY          AC
MADMAN'S MURDER MELODY  CUMMINGS, RAY     SS   HOS 40  12
  FANTASTIC PULPS, THE           HAINING, PETER         AN
MADMEN FROM EARTH, THE (SEE POLICY)
                       LAUMER, KEITH      TC
MADNESS FROM MARS       SIMAK, CLIFFORD D. SS   TWS 39  04
  ALIEN WORLDS                   ELWOOD, ROGER          AN
MADNESS OF LANCELOT BIGGS, THE BOND, NELSON S.  SS  FAD 40  04
  LANCELOT BIGGS: SPACEMAN       BOND, NELSON S.        AC
MADWOMAN, THE          KERSH, GERALD      SS
  MEN WITHOUT BONES              KERSH, GERALD          AC
MAELSTROM II           CLARKE, ARTHUR C.  SS   PBY 65  04
  DEAD ASTRONAUT, 10 STORIES OF SPACE FLIGHT, THE
                       PLAYBOY, EDITORS OF  AN
  THEMES IN SCIENCE FICTION      KELLEY, LEO P.         AN
  WIND FROM THE SUN, THE         CLARKE, ARTHUR C.      AC
  11TH ANNUAL OF THE YEAR'S BEST S-F, THE MERRIL, JUDITH  AN
MAESTRO                GORDON, GILES      SS   NWB 75  09
  NEW WORLDS NINE                BAILEY, HILARY         OA
MAGIC BOX, THE         BAKER, W. R.       SS   HRP 28  04
  MATHEMATICAL MAGPIE, THE       FADIMAN, CLIFTON       AN
MAGIC CHILD, THE       GRANT, C. L.       SS   NMD 73
  FRONTIERS 2: THE NEW MIND      ELWOOD, ROGER          OA
MAGIC CITY             BOND, NELSON S.    NV   ASF 41  02
  TREASURY OF GREAT SCIENCE FICTION, A VOL.2
                       BOUCHER, ANTHONY       AN
MAGIC MAN, THE         BEAUMONT, CHARLES  SS   NEW 60  AC
  EDGE, THE                      BEAUMONT, CHARLES      AC
MAGIC MAN AND OTHER SCIENCE-FANTASY STORIES
                       BEAUMONT, CHARLES      AC
  NIGHT RIDE AND OTHER JOURNEYS  BEAUMONT, CHARLES      AC
MAGIC PASSES           HERBST, STEVE      SS   CLR 72  02
  CLARION II                     WILSON, ROBIN SCOTT    OA
MAGIC SHOES, THE       SAPARIN, VICTOR    SS
  RUSSIAN SCIENCE FICTION        MAGIDOFF, ROBERT       AN
MAGIC SHOP, THE        WELLS, H. G.       SS   SND 03  06
  BEST STORIES OF H. G. WELLS    WELLS, H. G.           AC
  COUNTRY OF THE BLIND, THE      WELLS, H. G.           AC
  INEXPERIENCED GHOST AND NINE OTHER STORIES, THE
                       WELLS, H. G.           AC
  SHORT STORIES OF H. G. WELLS, THE  WELLS, H. G.       AC
  TWELVE STORIES AND A DREAM     WELLS, H. G.           AC
  TWENTY-EIGHT SCIENCE FICTION STORIES  WELLS, H. G.    AC
MAGIC STAIR-CASE, THE   BOND, NELSON S.    SS
  MR. MERGENTHWIRKER'S LOBBIES AND OTHER FANTASTIC TALES
                       BOND, NELSON S.        AC
MAGIC TRICK            WATKINS, JOAN N.    SS   YNW
  SCIENCE FICTION STORIES        BRADLEY, JOHANNA       AN
MAGIC TYPEWRITER, THE   BIXBY, JEROME      SS         63
  SPACE BY THE TAIL              BIXBY, JEROME          AC
MAGIC WHITE SUIT, THE (SEE THE WONDERFUL ICE CREAM SUIT)
                       BRADBURY, RAY      TC
MAGIC, INC. (THE DEVIL MAKES THE LAW)
                       HEINLEIN, ROBERT A. SN  UNK 40  09
  GOLDEN ROAD, THE               KNIGHT, DAMON          AN
  THREE BY HEINLEIN              HEINLEIN, ROBERT A.    AC
MAGICIAN'S SONG, THE    MCALISTER, PATRICIA SS
  MISSING WORLD AND OTHER STORIES, THE  ELWOOD, ROGER   OA
MAGICIAN, THE          MAUGHAM, W. SOMERSET EX  HEI 08
  GHOULS, THE                    HAINING, PETER         AN
MAGICIANS, THE (SINE OF THE MAGUS)
                       GUNN, JAMES E.     NA   BEY 54  05
  WITCHING HOUR, THE             GUNN, JAMES E.         AC
MAGICKS OF MEGAS-TU, THE (LARRY BRODY)
                       FOSTER, ALAN DEAN  SA   SLG 75  03
  STAR TREK LOG THREE            FOSTER, ALAN DEAN      OC
MAGNETIC MARVIN        HULL, PAUL E.      SS   YNW
  SCIENCE FICTION STORIES        BRADLEY, JOHANNA       AN
MAGNETOSPHERE, THE      HOYLE, FRED        SS
  ELEMENT 79                     HOYLE, FRED            AC
MAGNIFICENT POSESSION, THE ASIMOV, ISAAC   SS   FUT 40  07
  EARLY ASIMOV, THE              ASIMOV, ISAAC          AC
MAGUS, A               CIARDI, JOHN       PM   SRV 65  12
  HOLDING YOUR EIGHT HANDS       LUCIE-SMITH, EDWARD    AN
  11TH ANNUAL OF THE YEAR'S BEST S-F, THE  MERRIL, JUDITH AN
MAHOUT, THE            SMITH, CLARK ASHTON SS  BLC 11  08
  OTHER DIMENSIONS               SMITH, CLARK ASHTON    AC
MAID TO MEASURE        KNIGHT, DAMON      SS   FSF 64  10
  ABC OF SCIENCE FICTION, AN     BOARDMAN, TOM JR.      AN
  TURNING ON                     KNIGHT, DAMON          AC
MAIDEN VOYAGE          RANKINE, JOHN      NV   NWR 64  02
  NEW WRITINGS IN SF. 2          CARNELL, JOHN          OA
MAIL SUPREMACY         PEIRCE, HAYFORD    SS   ASF 75  03
  BEST SCIENCE FICTION STORIES OF THE YEAR (1975)
                       DEL REY, LESTER        AN
MAILMAN COMETH, THE     RAPHAEL, RICK      NV   ASF 65  02
  THIRST QUENCHERS, THE          RAPHAEL, RICK          AC
MAINCHANCE            TATE, PETER        NV   ANA 70
  ALCHEMY AND ACADEME            MCCAFFREY, ANNE        OA
  ANDROIDS, TIME MACHINES AND BLUE GIRAFFES
                       ELWOOD & GHIDALIA      AN
  SEAGULLS UNDER GLASS AND OTHER STORIES  TATE, PETER   AC
MAJOR INCITEMENT TO RIOT, THE O'DONNELL, K. M.  SS  FAN 69  02
  FINAL WAR AND OTHER FANTASIES  O'DONNELL, K. M.       DC
MAJOR OPERATION        WHITE, JAMES       NV   NWR 71  18
  MAJOR OPERATION                WHITE, JAMES           NO
  NEW WRITINGS IN SF. 18         CARNELL, JOHN          OA
```

```
MAJORITY OF PEOPLE NOW BELIEVE IN FLYING SAUCERS, THE
                       DUTTA, REX         AR
  BEYOND THIS HORIZON            CARRELL, CHRISTOPHER   OA
MAKE A PRISON          BLOCK, LAWRENCE    SS   SFS 59  01
  5TH ANNUAL OF THE YEAR'S BEST S-F, THE  MERRIL, JUDITH  AN
MAKE ME LAUGH          SERLING, ROD       SA
  NIGHT GALLERY                  SERLING, ROD           OC
MAKE MINE HOMOGENIZED   RAPHAEL, RICK      NV   ASF 60  04
  NEVER IN THIS WORLD            STONE, IDELLA P.       AC
MAKE MINE MARS          KORNBLUTH, C. M.   NV   SPA 52  11
  *MILE BEYOND THE MOON, A       KORNBLUTH, C. M.       AC
MAKE ROOM FOR ME        STURGEON, THEODORE NV   FAD 51  05
  STURGEON IN ORBIT              STURGEON, THEODORE     AC
MAKE ROOM! MAKE ROOM!   HARRISON, HARRY    NO   IMP 66  08
  SCIENCE FICTION OMNIBUS ON POLLUTION, A  ANONYMOUS    AN
MAKER OF GARGOYLES, THE SMITH, CLARK ASHTON SS  WRT 32  08
  TALES OF SCIENCE AND SORCERY   SMITH, CLARK ASHTON    AC
MAKING IT ALL THE WAY INTO THE FUTURE ON GAXTON FALLS OF THE
  RED PLANET           MALZBERG, BARRY N. SS   NOV 74  04
  NOVA 4                         HARRISON, HARRY        OA
MAKING IT THROUGH       MALZBERG, BARRY N. SS   WLK 73
  AND WALK NOW GENTLY THROUGH THE FIRE...  ELWOOD, ROGER OA
  BEST OF BARRY N. MALZBERG, THE  MALZBERG, BARRY N.    AC
MAKING IT TO GAXTON FALLS ON THE RED PLANET IN THE YEAR
  OF OUR LORD          MALZBERG, BARRY N. SS   NOV 74  04
  DOWN HERE IN THE DREAM QUARTER  MALZBERG, BARRY N.    AC
MAKING LOVE (LOVEMAKING) POHL, FREDERIK    SS   PBY 66  12
  DAY MILLION                    POHL, FREDERIK         AC
MAKING THE CONNECTIONS  MALZBERG, BARRY N. SS   CTM 75  04
  CONTINUUM 4                    ELWOOD, ROGER          OA
  DOWN HERE IN THE DREAM QUARTER  MALZBERG, BARRY N.    AC
MAKING TITAN           O'DONNELL, K. M.   SS   FSF 70  07
  UNIVERSE DAY                   O'DONNELL, K. M.       NO
MAL DEAN               MOORCOCK, MICHAEL  AR   NWB 75  08
  NEW WORLDS EIGHT               BAILEY, HILARY         OA
MALADJUSTED CLASSROOM, THE  NEARING, H. JR. SS  FSF 53  06
  BEST FROM FANTASY AND SCIENCE FICTION: 3
                       BOUCHER & MCCOMAS      AN
MALADJUSTMENT          BAYLEY, BARRINGTON J SS  NWQ 74  06
  NEW WORLDS NO. 6               PLATT & BAILEY         OA
MALATESTA COLLECTION, THE  ZELAZNY, ROGER  SS   FAN 63  04
  BEST FROM FANTASTIC, THE       WHITE, TED             AC
MALAY KRISE, THE        SMITH, CLARK ASHTON  OVL 10  10
  OTHER DIMENSIONS               SMITH, CLARK ASHTON    AC
MALE FIGURE            GROSSMAN, NANCY    IL
  SCIENCE FICTION                BRODKIN & PEARSON      AN
MALE RESPONSE, THE      ALDISS, BRIAN W.   NO   BCN 61
  BRIAN ALDISS OMNIBUS 2         ALDISS, BRIAN W.       AC
MALE STRIKEBREAKER (SEE STRIKEBREAKER)
                       ASIMOV, ISAAC      TC
MALF                   ING, DEAN          NV
  ANALOG ANNUAL                  BOVA, BEN              OA
MALICE AFORETHOUGHT     GRINNELL, DAVID    SS   FSF 52  11
  BEYOND THE BARRIERS OF SPACE AND TIME  MERRIL, JUDITH  AN
MALICE AFORETHOUGHT     WOLLHEIM, DONALD A. SS  FSF 52  11
  TWO DOZEN DRAGON EGGS          WOLLHEIM, DONALD A.    AC
MALIGNANT MARAUDER (DEAD CITY) LEINSTER, MURRAY NV TWS 46 SU
  ULTIMATE INVADER, AND OTHER SCIENCE FICTION, THE
                       WOLLHEIM, DONALD A.    DA
MALIGNANT ORGAN, THE    NEARING, H. JR.    SS   FSF 53  03
  SINISTER RESEARCHES OF C. P. RANSOM, THE NEARING, H. JR. AC
MALLEY SYSTEM, THE      DEFORD, MIRIAM ALLEN SS DVS 67  01
  DANGEROUS VISIONS              ELLISON, HARLAN        OA
MALTED MILK MONSTER, THE  TENN, WILLIAM    NV   GAL 59  08
  SEVEN SEXES, THE               TENN, WILLIAM          AC
MAM SOLA'S HOUSE        PANGBORN, EDGAR    NV   CTM 75  04
  CONTINUUM 4                    ELWOOD, ROGER          OA
MAMA, PAPA IS WOUNDED!  TANGUY, YVES       IL
  SCIENCE FICTION                BRODKIN & PEARSON      AN
MAMMA COME HOME (THE MOTHER SHIP)
                       TIPTREE, JAMES JR. NV   IFS 68  06
  TEN THOUSAND LIGHT-YEARS FROM HOME  TIPTREE, JAMES JR. AC
MAMMOTH HUNTERS, THE    REDD, DAVID        SS   NWB 73  05
  NEW WORLDS QUARTERLY NO. 5     MOORCOCK, MICHAEL      OA
MAN BORN BLIND, THE     LEWIS, C. S.       SS   NEW 77  AC
  DARK TOWER AND OTHER STORIES, THE  LEWIS, C. S.       AC
MAN DOORS SAID HELLO TO, THE  TIPTREE, JAMES JR.  SS  WOF 70  WI
  TEN THOUSAND LIGHT-YEARS FROM HOME  TIPTREE, JAMES JR. AC
MAN DOWN               WILLIAMSON, JACK   NV   ASF 52  03
  TRIAL OF TERRA, THE            WILLIAMSON, JACK       NO
MAN FALLING FORWARD     GENOVES, JUAN      IL
  SCIENCE FICTION                BRODKIN & PEARSON      AN
MAN FOR THE MOON, A     WEBB, LELAND       SS   PBY 60  08
  DEAD ASTRONAUT, 10 STORIES OF SPACE FLIGHT, THE
                       PLAYBOY, EDITORS OF    AN
  PLAYBOY BOOK OF SCIENCE FICTION AND FANTASY, THE
                       PLAYBOY, EDITORS OF    AN
MAN FROM BEYOND, THE    WYNDHAM, JOHN      NV   WOS 34  09
  ALIEN WORLDS                   ELWOOD, ROGER          AN
  BEST OF JOHN WYNDHAM, THE      WYNDHAM, JOHN          AC
  MAN FROM BEYOND AND OTHER STORIES, THE  WYNDHAM, JOHN  AC
MAN FROM EARTH, THE     DICKSON, GORDON R. SS   GAL 64  06
  DANGER- HUMAN                  DICKSON, GORDON R.     AC
MAN FROM MARS, THE      MILLER, P. SCHUYLER NV  WSQ 31  SU
  FROM OFF THIS WORLD            MARGULIES & FRIEND     AN
MAN FROM NOT-YET, THE   SLADEK, JOHN T.    SS   PBY 68  06
  FROM THE "S" FILE              PLAYBOY, EDITORS OF    AN
MAN FROM OCCAM, THE     ANONYMOUS          SS
  STRANGE WORLD OF SCIENCE FICTION  ANONYMOUS           OA
MAN FROM OUTSIDE, THE   WILLIAMSON, JACK   SS   ASF 51  03
  *BEACHHEADS IN SPACE           DERLETH, AUGUST        AN
  FROM OTHER WORLDS              DERLETH, AUGUST        AN
  LOOKING FORWARD                LESSER, MILTON         AN
  PEOPLE MACHINES                WILLIAMSON, JACK       AC
  TRIAL OF TERRA, THE            WILLIAMSON, JACK       NO
```

MAN FROM THE BIG DARK, THE

MAN FROM THE BIG DARK, THE   BRUNNER, JOHN   SN   SPA 58 06
  GREAT SCIENCE FICTION ADVENTURES   SHAW, LARRY T.   AN
  INTERSTELLAR EMPIRE   BRUNNER, JOHN   AC
  NO OTHER GODS BUT ME   BRUNNER, JOHN   AC
MAN FROM THE SOUTH   DAHL, ROALD   SS   53
  SHOCKING THING, A   KNIGHT, DAMON   AN
MAN FROM TIME, THE   LONG, FRANK BELKNAP   SS   FUN 54 03
  RIM OF THE UNKNOWN   LONG, FRANK BELKNAP   AC
MAN FROM VENUS, THE   PAUL, FRANK R.   SS
  FAREWELL FANTASTIC VENUS   ALDISS & HARRISON   AN
MAN FROM WHEN, THE   PLACHTA, DANNIE   SS   IFS 66 07
  WORLD'S BEST SCIENCE FICTION: 1967 WOLLHEIM & CARR   AN
MAN IN A QUANDARY   STECHER, L. J. JR.   SS   GAL 58 07
  FOURTH GALAXY READER, THE   GOLD, H. L.   AN
MAN IN ASBESTOS: AN ALLEGORY OF THE FUTURE, THE
                          LEACOCK, STEPHEN   SS   41
  ASPECTS OF SCIENCE FICTION   DOHERTY, G. D.   AN
MAN IN CUBE   STEINBERG, SAUL   CT   NYM 60 09
  MATHEMATICAL MAGPIE, THE   FADIMAN, CLIFTON   AN
MAN IN HIS TIME   ALDISS, BRIAN W.   SS   SCF 65 04
  *BEST SCIENCE FICTION STORIES OF BRIAN W. ALDISS
                          ALDISS, BRIAN W.   AC
  BRIAN ALDISS OMNIBUS, A   ALDISS, BRIAN W.   AC
  NEBULA AWARD STORIES NO. 2   ALDISS & HARRISON   AN
  SCIENCE FICTION ARGOSY, A   KNIGHT, DAMON   AN
  TRAPS OF TIME, THE   MOORCOCK, MICHAEL   AN
MAN IN SPACE   LANG, DANIEL   AR   NYM 58 11
  SF:59, THE YEAR'S GREATEST SCIENCE FICTION AND FANTASY
                          MERRIL, JUDITH   AN
MAN IN THE BLACK HAT, THE FESSIER, MICHAEL   SS   ESQ 34 02
  OTHER WORLDS, THE   STONG, PHILIP D.   AN
MAN IN THE BOTTLE, THE   SERLING, ROD   SA
  ROD SERLING'S TWILIGHT ZONE REVISITED SERLING, ROD   OC
MAN IN THE JAR   KNIGHT, DAMON   SS   GAL 57 04
  ANOTHER WORLD   DOZOIS, GARDNER R.   AN
  BEST OF DAMON KNIGHT, THE   KNIGHT, DAMON   AC
  THIRD GALAXY READER, THE   GOLD, H. L.   AN
  TURNING ON   KNIGHT, DAMON   AC
MAN IN THE MAZE, THE   SILVERBERG, ROBERT   NO   IFS 68 04
  SCIENCE FICTION SPECIAL 4   ANONYMOUS   AN
MAN IN THE MOON COMES DOWN, A COPEMAN, BERGER SS
  ADVENTURES TO COME   ESENWEIN, J. BERG   OA
MAN IN THE MOON, THE   NORTON, HENRY   SS   ASF 43 02
  ENEMIES IN SPACE   CONKLIN, GROFF   AN
  *INVADERS OF EARTH   CONKLIN, GROFF   AN
MAN IN THE MOON, THE   REYNOLDS, MACK   SS   AMZ 50 07
  LOOKING FORWARD   LESSER, MILTON   AN
MAN IN THE POCKET, THE (THE MEN INSIDE)
                          MALZBERG, BARRY N.   NV   NDM 72 02
  BEST OF BARRY N. MALZBERG, THE   MALZBERG, BARRY N.   AC
MAN IN THE RORSCHACH SHIRT, THE
                          BRADBURY, RAY   SS   PBY 66 10
  I SING THE BODY ELECTRIC   BRADBURY, RAY   AC
  INTRODUCTORY PSYCHOLOGY THROUGH SCIENCE FICTION
                          KATZ/WARRICK/&   AN
  TRANSIT OF EARTH   PLAYBOY, EDITORS OF   AN
MAN IN THE SKY   BUDRYS, ALGIS   SS   ASF 56 03
  EVERY BOY'S BOOK OF OUTER SPACE STORIES DIKTY, T. E.   AN
MAN IN THE UNDERPASS, THE CAMPBELL, J. RAMSEY SS   NEW 75 AN
  YEAR'S BEST HORROR STORIES: SERIES III, THE
                          DAVIS, RICHARD   AN
MAN IN TRANSIT   AUMBRY, ALAN   SS   NWQ 72 04
  NEW WORLDS QUARTERLY NO. 4   MOORCOCK, MICHAEL   OA
MAN INSIDE, THE   MCALLISTER, BRUCE   SS   GAL 69 05
  BEST SF: 1969   HARRISON & ALDISS   AN
MAN MANIFOLD   YOUNG, PETER   SS
  AD 2500   WILSON, ANGUS   AN
MAN MUST DIE, A   CLUTE, JOHN   SS   NWS 66 11
  ALPHA 5   SILVERBERG, ROBERT   AN
  BEST SF STORIES FROM NEW WORLDS 6 MOORCOCK, MICHAEL   AN
MAN OF DESTINY   CHRISTOPHER, JOHN   SS   GAL 51 05
  *GALAXY READER OF SCIENCE FICTION GOLD, H. L.   AN
  LOOKING FORWARD   LESSER, MILTON   AN
MAN OF DISTINCTION   BROWN, FREDRIC   SS   TWS 51 02
  HONEYMOON IN HELL   BROWN, FREDRIC   AC
MAN OF DISTINCTION   LONG, FRANK BELKNAP SS   FUN 54 11
  RIM OF THE UNKNOWN   LONG, FRANK BELKNAP   AC
MAN OF DISTINCTION   SHAARA, MICHAEL   SS   GAL 56 10
  FOURTH GALAXY READER, THE   GOLD, H. L.   AN
MAN OF FAMILY, A   TENN, WILLIAM   SS
  HUMAN ANGLE, THE   TENN, WILLIAM   AC
MAN OF LETTERS   WILHELM, KATE   SS   NEW 75 AC
  INFINITY BOX, THE   WILHELM, KATE   AC
MAN OF LETTERS, A   OBTULOWICZ, MAREK   SS   QRK 71 04
  QUARK/4   DELANY & HACKER   OA
MAN OF PARTS   GOLD, H. L.   SS   NTL 54
  ALPHA 6   SILVERBERG, ROBERT   AN
  OLD DIE RICH AND OTHER SCIENCE FICTION, THE
                          GOLD, H. L.   AC
  9 TALES OF SPACE AND TIME   HEALY, RAYMOND J.   OA
MAN OF SLOW FEELINGS, THE WILDING, MICHAEL   SS
  SECOND PACIFIC BOOK OF SCIENCE FICTION, THE
                          BAXTER, JOHN   AN
MAN OF STEEL- WOMAN OF KLEENEX NIVEN, LARRY   AR   NEW 71 04
  ALL THE MYRIAD WAYS   NIVEN, LARRY   AC
MAN OF TALENT, A (MAN WITH TALENT)
                          SILVERBERG, ROBERT   NV   FUT 56 WI
  MOONFERNS & STARSONGS   SILVERBERG, ROBERT   AC
  NEW DREAMS THIS MORNING   BLISH, JAMES   AN
MAN OF THE RENAISSANCE, A GUIN, WYMAN   SS   GAL 64 12
  ALPHA 2   SILVERBERG, ROBERT   AN
  LIVING WAY OUT   GUIN, WYMAN   AC
MAN OF THE STARS   MOSKOWITZ, SAM   SS   PLS 41 WI
  EXPLORING OTHER WORLDS   MOSKOWITZ, SAM   AN
MAN OF THE YEAR MILLION, THE WELLS, H. G.   SS   PMB 93
  APEMAN, SPACEMAN   STOVER & HARRISON   AN

MAN ON B-17, THE   DERLETH, AUGUST   SS   WRT 50 05
  MR. GEORGE AND OTHER ODD PERSONS   DERLETH, AUGUST   AN
MAN ON BRIDGE   ALDISS, BRIAN W.   SS   NWR 64 01
  BEST FROM NEW WRITINGS IN S-F FIRST SELECTION, THE
                          CARNELL, JOHN   AN
  *BEST SCIENCE FICTION STORIES OF BRIAN W. ALDISS
                          ALDISS, BRIAN W.   AC
  NEW WRITINGS IN SF. 1   CARNELL, JOHN   OA
MAN ON THE HILL, THE   PAYETTE, MICHAEL   SS   INY 70 01
  INFINITY 1   HOSKINS, ROBERT   OA
MAN ON THE JUICE WAGON, THE (AS CORDWAINER BIRD)
                          ELLISON, HARLAN   SS   ABR 63 14
  NO DOORS, NO WINDOWS (STORIES REWRITTEN) ELLISON, HARLAN AC
MAN ON THE MOONE, THE (1638) GODWIN, FRANCIS   EX
  *BEYOND TIME AND SPACE   DERLETH, AUGUST   AN
MAN ON THE 99TH FLOOR, THE BALLARD, J. G.   SS   NWS 62 07
  DAY OF FOREVER, THE   BALLARD, J. G.   AC
  PASSPORT TO ETERNITY   BALLARD, J. G.   AC
MAN ON TOP, THE (SCH 51 10) BRETNOR, REGINALD SS   FSF 60 09
  TRANSFORMATIONS   ROSELLE, DANIEL   AN
  14 GREAT TALES OF ESP   STONE, IDELLA P.   AN
  6TH ANNUAL OF THE YEAR'S BEST S-F, THE MERRIL, JUDITH   AN
MAN OVERBOARD   COLLIER, JOHN   NV   FSF 60 03
  BEST FROM FANTASY AND SCIENCE FICTION: 10
                          MILLS, ROBERT P.   AN
MAN SAID TO THE UNIVERSE, A CRANE, STEPHEN   PM
  SPECULATIONS   SANDERS, THOMAS E.   AN
MAN SPEKITH, A   WILSON, RICHARD   NV   GAL 69 05
  WORLD'S BEST SCIENCE FICTION: 1970 WOLLHEIM & CARR   AN
MAN TO MY WOUNDING, A (STATE OF ASSASSINATION)
                          ANDERSON, POUL   SS   EQM 59 12
  HORN OF TIME, THE   ANDERSON, POUL   AC
MAN TRAP, THE (SEE THE UNREAL MCCOY)
MAN UNDERNEATH, THE   BLISH, JAMES   TC
                          LAFFERTY, R. A.   SS   IFS 71 01
  BEST SCIENCE FICTION STORIES OF THE YEAR (1971)
                          DEL REY, LESTER   AN
  DOES ANYONE ELSE HAVE SOMETHING FURTHER TO ADD?
                          LAFFERTY, R. A.   AC
MAN UPSTAIRS, THE   BRADBURY, RAY   SS   HRP 47 03
  *DARK CARNIVAL   BRADBURY, RAY   AC
  *OCTOBER COUNTRY, THE   BRADBURY, RAY   AC
  SMALL ASSASSIN, THE   BRADBURY, RAY   AC
MAN WHO ALWAYS KNEW, THE   BUDRYS, ALGIS   SS   ASF 56 04
  BEST SCIENCE FICTION STORIES AND NOVELS: 1956
                          DIKTY, T. E.   AN
  TOMORROW AND TOMORROW   KNIGHT, DAMON   AN
MAN WHO ATE THE WORLD, THE POHL, FREDERIK   NV   GAL 56 11
  FREDERIK POHL OMNIBUS, THE   POHL, FREDERIK   AC
  IN THE PROBLEM PIT   POHL, FREDERIK   AC
  MAN WHO ATE THE WORLD, THE   POHL, FREDERIK   AC
  SCIENCE FICTION SHOWCASE   KORNBLUTH, MARY   AN
MAN WHO AWOKE, THE   MANNING, LAURENCE   NV   WOS 33 03
  BEFORE THE GOLDEN AGE   ASIMOV, ISAAC   AN
MAN WHO CAME BACK, THE   SILVERBERG, ROBERT   SS   GAL 74 12
  BEST SCIENCE FICTION STORIES OF THE YEAR (1974)
                          DEL REY, LESTER   AN
MAN WHO CAME EARLY, THE   ANDERSON, POUL   NV   FSF 56 06
  ALPHA 1   SILVERBERG, ROBERT   AN
  BEST FROM FANTASY AND SCIENCE FICTION: 6
                          BOUCHER, ANTHONY   AN
  BEYOND TOMORROW   HARDING, LEE   AN
  COMBAT SF   DICKSON, GORDON R.   AN
  HORN OF TIME, THE   ANDERSON, POUL   AC
  ONE HUNDRED YEARS OF SCIENCE FICTION KNIGHT, DAMON   AN
  THEMES IN SCIENCE FICTION   KELLEY, LEO P.   AN
MAN WHO COLLECTED POE, THE BLOCH, ROBERT   SS   FFM 51 10
  BOGEY MEN   BLOCH, ROBERT   AC
MAN WHO COLLECTED THE FIRST OF SEPTEMBER 1973, THE
                          BRINGSVAERD, TOR AGE SS   73
  BEST SF: 1973   HARRISON & ALDISS   AN
MAN WHO COULD NOT SEE DEVILS, THE
                          RUSS, JOANNA   SS   ANA 70
  ALCHEMY AND ACADEME   MCCAFFREY, ANNE   OA
  THOSE WHO CAN: A SCIENCE FICTION READER WILSON, ROBIN SCOTT AN
MAN WHO COULD NOT STOP, THE CHANDLER, A. BERTRAM NV FSF 59 05
  BEYOND THE GALACTIC RIM   CHANDLER, A. BERTRAM   DC
MAN WHO COULD TURN BACK THE CLOCK, THE
                          FARLEY, RALPH MILNE   SS
  OMNIBUS OF TIME, THE   FARLEY, RALPH MILNE   AC
MAN WHO COULD WORK MIRACLES, THE
                          WELLS, H. G.   SS   ILN 98 07
  BEST SCIENCE FICTION STORIES OF H. G. WELLS
                          WELLS, H. G.   AC
  BEST STORIES OF H. G. WELLS   WELLS, H. G.   AC
  COUNTRY OF THE BLIND, THE   WELLS, H. G.   AC
  INEXPERIENCED GHOST AND NINE OTHER STORIES, THE
                          WELLS, H. G.   AC
  MOONLIGHT TRAVELER, THE   STERN, PHILIP VAN D.   AN
  ODDBALLS, THE   GHIDALIA, VIC   AN
  SCIENCE FACT/FICTION   FARRELL/GAGE/&   AN
  SHORT STORIES OF H. G. WELLS, THE WELLS, H. G.   AC
  TALES OF SPACE AND TIME   WELLS, H. G.   AC
  TIME MACHINE AND OTHER STORIES, THE (PB) WELLS, H. G.   AC
  TWENTY-EIGHT SCIENCE FICTION STORIES WELLS, H. G.   AC
MAN WHO CRIED WOLF!, THE   BLOCH, ROBERT   SS   WRT 45 05
  BLOCH AND BRADBURY   BRADBURY & BLOCH   AC
MAN WHO DEVOURED BOOKS, THE SLADEK, JOHN T.   SS   IFS 71 01
  INTRODUCTORY PSYCHOLOGY THROUGH SCIENCE FICTION
                          KATZ/WARRICK/&   AN
MAN WHO DID NOT FIT, THE   BUDRYS, ALGIS   SS   ASF 59 03
  FALLING TORCH   BUDRYS, ALGIS   NO
MAN WHO DIDN'T DOUBT IT, THE DISCH, THOMAS M.   SS
  *GETTING INTO DEATH   DISCH, THOMAS M.   AC
MAN WHO DROPPED BY, THE   SERLING, ROD   SA
  ROD SERLING'S TWILIGHT ZONE REVISITED SERLING, ROD   OC

MAN WHO EVOLVED, THE

MAN WHO EVOLVED, THE   HAMILTON, EDMOND   SS   WOS 31 04
  BEFORE THE GOLDEN AGE   ASIMOV, ISAAC   AN
  BEST OF EDMOND HAMILTON, THE   HAMILTON, EDMOND   AC
  FROM OFF THIS WORLD   MARGULIES & FRIEND   AN
  HORROR ON THE ASTEROID AND OTHER TALES OF PLANETARY HORROR
                                 HAMILTON, EDMOND   AC
MAN WHO FOUND PROTEUS, THE   ROHRER, ROBERT   SS   FAN 64 11
  10TH ANNUAL OF THE YEAR'S BEST S-F, THE MERRIL, JUDITH   AN
MAN WHO HATED MACHINES, THE   BOULLE, PIERRE   NV
  TIME OUT OF MIND   BOULLE, PIERRE   OC
MAN WHO HATED WAR, THE (SEE PEACEMONGER)
                              PETAJA, EMIL   TC
MAN WHO KNEW ALL THE ANSWERS, THE
                              BERN, DONALD   SS   AMZ 40 08
  OTHER WORLDS, THE   STONG, PHILIP D.   AN
MAN WHO KNEW GRODNIK, THE   COGSWELL, THEODORE R SS SCF 62 06
  THIRD EYE, THE   COGSWELL, THEODORE R AC
MAN WHO KNEW WOMEN, THE   BLOCH, ROBERT   SS   SMM 59 07
  KING OF TERRORS, THE   BLOCH, ROBERT   AC
  SKULL OF THE MARQUIS DE SADE, THE BLOCH, ROBERT   AC
MAN WHO KNEW, THE   SAMBROT, WILLIAM   SS   TIG 57
  ISLAND OF FEAR AND OTHER SCIENCE FICTION SAMBROT, WILLIAM AC
MAN WHO LEARNED LOVING, THE   STURGEON, THEODORE SS   FSF 69 10
  BEST FROM FANTASY AND SCIENCE FICTION: 19
                               FERMAN, EDWARD L.   AN
  NEBULA AWARD STORIES NO. 5 BLISH, JAMES   AN
  NEW AWARENESS, THE   WARRICK & GREENBERG   AN
MAN WHO LIKED LIONS, THE   DALEY, JOHN BERNARD SS INF 56 10
  SF:57, THE YEAR'S GREATEST SCIENCE FICTION AND FANTASY
                               MERRIL, JUDITH   AN
MAN WHO LIKED, THE   HOSKINS, ROBERT   SS   WOF 68 01
  EDGE OF NEVER, THE   HOSKINS, ROBERT   AN
MAN WHO LIVED BACKWARDS, THE FARLEY, RALPH MILNE SS
  OMNIBUS OF TIME, THE   FARLEY, RALPH MILNE   AC
MAN WHO LOST THE SEA, THE   STURGEON, THEODORE SS   FSF 59 10
  BEST FROM FANTASY AND SCIENCE FICTION: 9
                               MILLS, ROBERT P.   AN
  BEYOND BELIEF   HURLEY, RICHARD J.   AN
  FIRST STEP OUTWARD   HOSKINS, ROBERT   AN
  TOWARD INFINITY   KNIGHT, DAMON   AN
  5TH ANNUAL OF THE YEAR'S BEST S-F, THE MERRIL, JUDITH   AN
MAN WHO LOVED THE FAIOLI, THE ZELAZNY, ROGER   SS   GAL 67 06
  DOORS OF HIS FACE, THE LAMPS OF HIS MOUTH, THE
                               ZELAZNY, ROGER   AC
  SF: AUTHORS' CHOICE 4   HARRISON, HARRY   AN
  WORLD'S BEST SCIENCE FICTION: 1968 WOLLHEIM & CARR AN
MAN WHO MADE A BABY, THE   JACOBS, HARVEY   SS   NWQ 74 06
  NEW WORLDS NO. 6   PLATT & BAILEY   OA
MAN WHO MADE FRIENDS WITH ELECTRICITY, THE
                              LEIBER, FRITZ   SS   FSF 62 03
  BEST OF FRITZ LEIBER, THE   LEIBER, FRITZ   AC
  SECRET SONGS, THE   LEIBER, FRITZ   AC
  SHADOWS WITH EYES   LEIBER, FRITZ   AC
  8TH ANNUAL OF THE YEAR'S BEST S-F, THE MERRIL, JUDITH   AN
MAN WHO MADE HIMSELF, THE (SEE IN HIS IMAGE)
                              BEAUMONT, CHARLES   TC
MAN WHO MADE THE WORLD, THE   MATHESON, RICHARD   SS   IMG 54 02
  SHOCK II   MATHESON, RICHARD   AC
MAN WHO MET HIMSELF, THE   FARLEY, RALPH MILNE SS
  OMNIBUS OF TIME, THE   FARLEY, RALPH MILNE   AC
MAN WHO MISSED THE BUS, THE   BENSON, STELLA   SS   36
  MOONLIGHT TRAVELER, THE   STERN, PHILIP VAN D. AN
MAN WHO MISSED THE FERRY, THE MASON, DOUGLAS R.   SS   NWR 66 07
  NEW WRITINGS IN SF. 7   CARNELL, JOHN   AN
  NEW WRITINGS IN SF. 7   CARNELL, JOHN   OA
MAN WHO MURDERED TOMORROW, THE BLOCH, ROBERT   SS   AMZ 60 03
  BOGEY MEN   BLOCH, ROBERT   AC
MAN WHO NEVER FORGOT, THE   SILVERBERG, ROBERT SS   FSF 58 02
  MUTANTS   SILVERBERG, ROBERT   AN
  PARSECS AND PARABLES   SILVERBERG, ROBERT   AC
MAN WHO NEVER GREW YOUNG, THE LEIBER, FRITZ   SS   APR 49 09
  BEST OF FRITZ LEIBER, THE   LEIBER, FRITZ   AC
  DARK SIDE, THE   KNIGHT, DAMON   AN
  NIGHT'S BLACK AGENTS   LEIBER, FRITZ   AC
MAN WHO NEVER LIVED, THE   WANDREI, DONALD   SS   ASF 34 03
  STRANGE HARVEST   WANDREI, DONALD   AC
MAN WHO NEVER WAS, THE   LAFFERTY, R. A.   SS   MOH 67 SU
  WORLD'S BEST SCIENCE FICTION: 1968 WOLLHEIM & CARR AN
MAN WHO OWNED TOMORROW, THE   GUNN, JAMES E.   SS   ARG 53 07
  BREAKING POINT   GUNN, JAMES E.   AC
MAN WHO PICKED UP PINS, THE   BOULLE, PIERRE   SS
  TIME OUT OF MIND   BOULLE, PIERRE   OC
MAN WHO PLAYED THE BLUES   BRUNNER, JOHN   SS   SCF 56 02
  OUT OF MY MIND (BRITISH)   BRUNNER, JOHN   AC
MAN WHO PLAYED TO LOSE, THE   JANIFER, LAURENCE M. SS ASF 61 10
  IMPOSSIBLE?   JANIFER, LAURENCE M. AC
MAN WHO PLOUGHED THE SEA, THE CLARKE, ARTHUR C.   SS   SAT 57 06
  HUMAN ZERO, THE   MOSKOWITZ & ELWOOD   AN
  PRELUDE TO MARS   CLARKE, ARTHUR C.   AC
  TALES FROM THE WHITE HART   CLARKE, ARTHUR C.   AC
MAN WHO RETURNED, THE   HAMILTON, EDMOND   SS   WRT 34 02
  BEST OF EDMOND HAMILTON, THE HAMILTON, EDMOND   AC
  WEIRD TALES   MARGULIES, LEO   AN
MAN WHO RODE THE SAUCER, THE DERLETH, AUGUST   SS   NEW 52 AN
  HARRIGAN'S FILE   DERLETH, AUGUST   AN
MAN WHO RODE THE SAUCER, THE HOLMES, KENYON   SS   NEW 52 AN
  FAR BOUNDARIES   DERLETH, AUGUST   AN
MAN WHO RODE THE TRAINS, THE CARTER, PAUL A.   SS
  TRAVELLERS BY NIGHT   DERLETH, AUGUST   OA
MAN WHO SAILED THE SKY, THE   CHANDLER, A. BERTRAM NV
  ALTERNATE ORBITS   CHANDLER, A. BERTRAM DC
MAN WHO SAVED THE EARTH, THE HALL, AUSTIN   SS   ASW 19 12
  *BEST OF SCIENCE FICTION   CONKLIN, GROFF   AN
MAN WHO SAW EVERYTHING, THE   HAMILTON, EDMOND   SS   AMZ 30 10
  HORROR ON THE ASTEROID AND OTHER TALES OF PLANETARY HORROR
                               HAMILTON, EDMOND   AC

MAN WHO SAW GUNGA DIN THIRTY TIMES, THE
                              BOVA, BEN   SS   SCS 73
  SHOWCASE   ELWOOD, ROGER   OA
MAN WHO SAW THE FUTURE, THE   HAMILTON, EDMOND   SS   AMZ 30 10
  FANTASTIC PULPS, THE   HAINING, PETER   AN
  OTHER WORLDS, OTHER TIMES   MOSKOWITZ & ELWOOD   AN
  STRANGE SIGNPOSTS   ELWOOD & MOSKOWITZ   AN
MAN WHO SOLD ROPE TO THE GNOLES, THE
                              SEABRIGHT, IDRIS   SS   FSF 51 10
  *BEYOND HUMAN KEN   MERRIL, JUDITH   AN
MAN WHO SOLD THE MOON, THE   HEINLEIN, ROBERT A. AC   SHS 50
  ROBERT HEINLEIN OMNIBUS, A   HEINLEIN, ROBERT A.   AC
MAN WHO SOLD THE MOON, THE   HEINLEIN, ROBERT A. NV   NEW 50 AC
  BEST OF ROBERT HEINLEIN, THE HEINLEIN, ROBERT A.   AC
  DIMENSION X   KNIGHT, DAMON   AN
  *MAN WHO SOLD THE MOON, THE HEINLEIN, ROBERT A.   AC
  PAST THROUGH TOMORROW, THE   HEINLEIN, ROBERT A.   AC
  TREASURY OF GREAT SCIENCE FICTION, A VOL.2
                               BOUCHER, ANTHONY   AN
MAN WHO TASTED ASHES, THE   BUDRYS, ALGIS   SS   IFS 59 02
  BUDRYS' INFERNO   BUDRYS, ALGIS   AC
  STORIES FROM SCIENCE FICTION DOHERTY, G. D.   AN
MAN WHO TRAVELED IN ELEPHANTS, THE (THE ELEPHANT CIRCUIT)
                              HEINLEIN, ROBERT A. SS   STN 57 10
  UNPLEASANT PROFESSION OF JONATHAN HOAG, THE
                               HEINLEIN, ROBERT A.   AC
MAN WHO UNDERSTOOD THE DIFFERENCE BETWEEN SALMON AND
ORANGE CHIFFON, THE   DISCH, THOMAS M.   SS
  *GETTING INTO DEATH   DISCH, THOMAS M.   AC
MAN WHO VANISHED, THE   COATES, ROBERT M.   SS   NYM 55 10
  CIRCUS OF DR. LAO AND OTHER IMPROBABLE STORIES
                               BRADBURY, RAY   AN
MAN WHO WALKED HOME, THE   TIPTREE, JAMES JR. NV   AMZ 72 05
  BEST SCIENCE FICTION STORIES OF THE YEAR (1972)
                               DEL REY, LESTER   AN
  LOOKING AHEAD   ALLEN, D. & L.   AN
  TEN THOUSAND LIGHT-YEARS FROM HOME TIPTREE, JAMES JR. AC
  1973 ANNUAL WORLD'S BEST SF, THE WOLLHEIM, DONALD A. AN
MAN WHO WALKED THROUGH GLASS, THE
                              BOND, NELSON S.   SS   ESQ 38 11
  ODDBALLS, THE   GHIDALIA, VIC   AN
  31ST OF FEBRUARY, THE   BOND, NELSON S.   AC
MAN WHO WAS THIRSTY, THE   ACKERMAN, FORREST J. SS
  SCIENCE FICTION WORLDS OF FORREST J. ACKERMAN & FRIENDS
                               ACKERMAN, FORREST J. AC
MAN WHO WASN'T HOME, THE (SEE ORPHAN OF THE VOID)
                              BIGGLE, LLOYD JR.   TC
MAN WHO WAVED HELLO, THE   DOZOIS, GARDNER R. SS   UNI 72 02
  UNIVERSE 2   CARR, TERRY   OA
MAN WHO WENT TO THE MOON- TWICE, THE
                              RODMAN, HOWARD   SS   DVS 67 01
  DANGEROUS VISIONS   ELLISON, HARLAN   OA
MAN WHO WOULD NOT BE, THE (SEE THE POWER AND THE GLORY)
                              GUNN, JAMES E.   TC
MAN WHO, THE   GARNETT, DAVID S.   SS   NWR 75 26
  NEW WRITINGS IN SF. 26   BULMER, KENNETH   AN
MAN WITH A PAST   BROWN, T. K. III   SS   PBY 63 05
  LAST TRAIN TO LIMBO   PLAYBOY, EDITORS OF   AN
MAN WITH A THOUSAND LEGS, THE LONG, FRANK BELKNAP SS   WRT 27 08
  RIM OF THE UNKNOWN   LONG, FRANK BELKNAP   AC
MAN WITH ENGLISH, THE   GOLD, H. L.   SS   STR 53 01
  OLD DIE RICH AND OTHER SCIENCE FICTION, THE
                               GOLD, H. L.   AC
  SCIENCE FICTION FOR PEOPLE WHO HATE SCIENCE FICTION
                               CARR, TERRY   AN
  STAR OF STARS   POHL, FREDERIK   AN
  STAR SCIENCE FICTION STORIES POHL, FREDERIK   OA
  STRANGE GIFTS   SILVERBERG, ROBERT   AN
MAN WITH TALENT, THE   SILVERBERG, ROBERT SS   FUT 56 WI
  GODLING, GO HOME¡   SILVERBERG, ROBERT   AC
MAN WITH THE AURA, THE   LAFFERTY, R. A.   SS   WTS 74 10
  YEAR'S BEST HORROR STORIES: SERIES IV, THE
                               PAGE, GERALD W.   AN
MAN WITH THE GLASS HEART, THE ENGLAND, GEORGE A. SS   CVL 11 05
  FANTASTIC PULPS, THE   HAINING, PETER   AN
MAN WITH THE GOLDEN RETICULATES, THE
                              GOTSCHALK, FELIX C. SS   ORB 75 17
  ORBIT 17   KNIGHT, DAMON   OA
MAN WITH THE GREEN NOSE, THE (SEE SURVIVOR NO. 1)
                              ELLISON, HARLAN
                              AND SLESAR, HENRY   TC C
MAN WITH THE HOUR GLASS, THE ESHBACH, LLOYD A.   SS   MVT 34 04
  GARDEN OF FEAR AND OTHER STORIES, THE CRAWFORD, WILLIAM L. AN
MAN WITH THE MAGIC GLASSES, THE (SEE LOVE, YOUR MAGIC
SPELL IS EVERYWHERE)   FINNEY, JACK   TC
MAN WITH THE SPECKLED EYES, THE
                              LAFFERTY, R. A.   SS   FSF 64 12
  STRANGE DOINGS   LAFFERTY, R. A.   AC
MAN WITH THE STRANGE HEAD, THE BREUER, MILES R. MD. SS AMZ 27 01
  *BIG BOOK OF SCIENCE FICTION CONKLIN, GROFF   AN
MAN WITHOUT A BODY, THE   MITCHELL, EDWARD P. SS   SUN 77 03
  CRYSTAL MAN, THE   MITCHELL, EDWARD P.   AC
MAN WITHOUT A PLANET, THE   WILHELM, KATE   SS   FSF 62 02
  BEST FROM FANTASY AND SCIENCE FICTION: 12
                               DAVIDSON, AVRAM   AN
                               WILHELM, KATE   AC
MAN WITHOUT AN APPETITE   BREUER, MILES R. MD. SS   16
  GREAT SCIENCE FICTION ABOUT DOCTORS CONKLIN, G&FABRICANT AN
MAN WORKING   WILSON, RICHARD   SS   STR 58 04
  STAR SCIENCE FICTION STORIES NO. 4 POHL, FREDERIK   OA
MAN'S ESTATE   ABLEMAN, PAUL   SS   SAG 70
  SCIENCE AGAINST MAN   CHEETHAM, ANTHONY   OA
MAN'S EXPANDING VIEW OF SPACE RONAN, COLIN   AR
  BEYOND THIS HORIZON   CARRELL, CHRISTOPHER OA

MAN'S HOME IS HIS CASTLE, A (ALSO AS LOFTHOUSE)
                              GOULART, RON   SS   PBY 69 03
  FULLY AUTOMATED LOVE LIFE OF HENRY KEANRIDGE
                              PLAYBOY, EDITORS OF   AN
MAN-EATER, THE   BURROUGHS, EDGAR R.   NO   NYW 15 11
  BEYOND THIRTY & THE MAN-EATER BURROUGHS, EDGAR R. AC
MAN-MADE SELF   STERLING, BRUCE   SS
  LONE STAR UNIVERSE   PROCTOR & UTLEY   OA
MAN, THE   BRADBURY, RAY   SS   TWS 49 02
  BEST SCIENCE-FICTION STORIES: 1950, THE BLEILER & DIKTY   AN
  BOYS' LIFE BOOK OF OUTER SPACE STORIES, THE
                              BOY'S LIFE, ED. OF   AN
  *ILLUSTRATED MAN, THE   BRADBURY, RAY   AC
  S IS FOR SPACE   BRADBURY, RAY   AC
MANACLED   CRANE, STEPHEN   SS   ARG 00 08
  FANTASTIC PULPS, THE   HAINING, PETER   AN
MANAGEMENT   MALZBERG, BARRY N.   SS   NEW 75 04
  MANY WORLDS OF BARRY MALZBERG, THE MALZBERG, BARRY N. AC
MANALIVE   BRUNNER, JOHN   EX   REA 64 04
  BOOK OF JOHN BRUNNER, THE   BRUNNER, JOHN   AC
MANDARIN'S CANARIES, THE   BLOCH, ROBERT   SS   WRT 38 09
  HORROR-7   BLOCH, ROBERT   AC
  HOUSE OF THE HATCHET, THE   BLOCH, ROBERT   AC
  *OPENER OF THE WAY, THE   BLOCH, ROBERT   AC
MANDRAKES, THE   SMITH, CLARK ASHTON   SS   WRT 33 02
  OTHER DIMENSIONS   SMITH, CLARK ASHTON   AC
MANGANON   STALL, MICHAEL   NV   NWR 76 28
  NEW WRITINGS IN SF. 28   BULMER, KENNETH   OA
MANHOLE 69   BALLARD, J. G.   SS   NWS 57 11
  BEST OF J. G. BALLARD, THE BALLARD, J. G.   AC
  CHRONOPOLIS AND OTHER STORIES BALLARD, J. G.   AC
  DISASTER AREA, THE   BALLARD, J. G.   AC
  VOICES OF TIME AND OTHER STORIES, THE BALLARD, J. G. AC
MANIPULATION   KINGSTON, JOHN   NV   NWR 65 03
  NEW WRITINGS IN SF. 3   CARNELL, JOHN   OA
MANIPULATION   ROBERTS, KEITH   NV   NWR 65 03
  MACHINES AND MEN   ROBERTS, KEITH   AC
MANLESS WORLDS, THE   LEINSTER, MURRAY   NV   TWS 47 02
  LAST SPACESHIP, THE   LEINSTER, MURRAY   NO
MANNA   PHILLIPS, PETER   NV   ASF 49 02
  *BIG BOOK OF SCIENCE FICTION CONKLIN, GROFF   AN
  SCIENCE FICTION ARGOSY, A   KNIGHT, DAMON   AN
MANNED MISSILES, THE   VONNEGUT, KURT JR.   SS   CMP 58 07
  CANARY IN A CAT HOUSE   VONNEGUT, KURT JR.   AC
  WELCOME TO THE MONKEY HOUSE VONNEGUT, KURT JR.   AC
MANNERS OF THE AGE   FYFE, H. B.   SS   GAL 52 03
  OMNIBUS OF SCIENCE FICTION CONKLIN, GROFF   AN
  STRANGE TRAVELS IN SCIENCE FICTION CONKLIN, GROFF AN
MANNICHON SOLUTION, THE   SHAW, IRWIN   NV   PBY 67 12
  PLAYBOY'S STORIES OF THE SINISTER & STRANGE
                              PLAYBOY, EDITORS OF   AN
MANNIKIN, THE (ALSO AS MANNIKINS OF HORROR)
                              BLOCH, ROBERT   SS   WRT 37 04
  *OPENER OF THE WAY, THE   BLOCH, ROBERT   AC
  YOURS TRULY, JACK THE RIPPER BLOCH, ROBERT   AC
MANNIKINS OF HORROR (THE MANNIKIN)
                              BLOCH, ROBERT   SS   WRT 37 04
  BLOCH AND BRADBURY   BRADBURY & BLOCH   AC
MANOR OF ROSES, THE   SWANN, THOMAS B.   SN   FSF 66 11
  ONCE AND FUTURE TALES FROM THE MAGAZINE OF FANTASY AND
  SCIENCE FICTION   FERMAN, EDWARD L.   AN
MANSCARER   ROBERTS, KEITH   NV   NWR 66 07
  DECADE THE 1960S   ALDISS & HARRISON   AN
  ENGLAND SWINGS SF   MERRIL, JUDITH   AN
  MACHINES AND MEN   ROBERTS, KEITH   AC
  NEW WRITINGS IN SF. 7   CARNELL, JOHN   OA
  PASSING OF THE DRAGONS, THE ROBERTS, KEITH   AC
  SPACE-TIME JOURNAL, THE   MERRIL, JUDITH   AN
MANSION OF FORGETFULNESS, THE LEMON, DON MARK   SS   BLC 07 04
  SCIENCE FICTION BY GASLIGHT MOSKOWITZ, SAM   AN
MANTAGE   MATHESON, RICHARD   NV   NEW 59 AN
  SCIENCE FICTION SHOWCASE   KORNBLUTH, MARY   AN
  SHOCK!   MATHESON, RICHARD   AC
MANUSCRIPT FOUND IN A VACUUM (PUN 52 12)
                              HUBBARD, P. M.   SS   FSF 53 08
  BEST FROM FANTASY AND SCIENCE FICTION: 3
                              BOUCHER & MCCOMAS   AN
MANUSCRIPT OF DR. ARNESS, THE WILSON, GAHAN   SS   PBY 66 08
  FANTASY: THE LITERATURE OF THE MARVELOUS KELLEY, LEO P. AN
  PLAYBOY BOOK OF HORROR AND THE SUPERNATURAL, THE
                              PLAYBOY, EDITORS OF   AN
MANY DOOMS, THE (SEE UNTO MY MANIFOLD DOOMS)
                              HARRISON, HARRY   TC
MANY DREAMS OF EARTH (SEE SPACE STATION 42)
                              FRITCH, CHARLES E.   TC
MANY MANSIONS   KIMBERLY, GAIL   SS   FTP 73
  FLAME TREE PLANET   ELWOOD, ROGER   OA
MANY MANSIONS   SILVERBERG, ROBERT   NV   UNI 73 03
  UNFAMILIAR TERRITORY   SILVERBERG, ROBERT   AC
  UNIVERSE 3   CARR, TERRY   OA
MANY RUBICONS   ORGILL, MICHAEL   NV
  BEYOND TIME   LEY, SANDRA   OA
MANY-SIDED CONAN DOYLE, THE   CARR, JOHN D.   IN
  POISON BELT, THE   DOYLE, ARTHUR CONAN   AC
MANYA, THE   CONEY, MICHAEL G.   SS   FSF 73 03
  MONITOR FOUND IN ORBIT   CONEY, MICHAEL G.   AC
MAP   HOWES, MARGARET   MS
  BEST OF LEIGH BRACKETT, THE BRACKETT, LEIGH   AC
MAP OF ENGLAND AND THE ABSOLUTE, THE
                              SANTAYANA, GEORGE   SS   20
MATHEMATICAL MAGPIE, THE   FADIMAN, CLIFTON   AN
MAPMAKERS, THE   POHL, FREDERIK   NV   GAL 55 07
  ALTERNATING CURRENTS   POHL, FREDERIK   AC
MAR-TI-AN   LORY, ROBERT   SS   FSF 64 05
  HARVEST OF HOODWINKS, A   LORY, ROBERT   DC

MARA   DERLETH, AUGUST   SS   ARS 48 WI
  MR. GEORGE AND OTHER ODD PERSONS DERLETH, AUGUST AC
MARACOT DEEP, THE   DOYLE, ARTHUR CONAN   NO   SEP 27 10
  MARACOT DEEP AND OTHER STORIES, THE DOYLE, ARTHUR CONAN AC
  TREASURY OF SCIENCE FICTION CLASSICS, THE
                              KUEBLER, HAROLD W.   AN
MARATHON PHOTOGRAPH, THE   SIMAK, CLIFFORD D.   NA   TOT 74
  THREADS OF TIME   SILVERBERG, ROBERT   OA
MARCH HARE MISSION   MCCORMACK, FORD   NV   WBY 51 01
  TOWARD INFINITY   KNIGHT, DAMON   AN
MARCHING IN   ASIMOV, ISAAC   SS   HFI 76 04
  BICENTENNIAL MAN AND OTHER STORIES, THE ASIMOV, ISAAC AC
MARCHING MORONS, THE   KORNBLUTH, C. M.   NV   GAL 51 04
  BEST OF C. M. KORNBLUTH, THE KORNBLUTH, C. M.   AC
  BEST SCIENCE FICTION STORIES OF C. M. KORNBLUTH
                              KORNBLUTH, C. M.   AC
  BEST SCIENCE-FICTION STORIES: 1952, THE BLEILER & DIKTY   AN
  DIMENSION X   KNIGHT, DAMON   AN
  LOOKING AHEAD   ALLEN, D. & L.   AN
  MARCHING MORONS AND OTHER SCIENCE FICTION
                              KORNBLUTH, C. M.   AC
  MINDWORM AND OTHER STORIES, THE KORNBLUTH, C. M. AC
  MODERN SCIENCE FICTION   SPINRAD, NORMAN   AN
  NIGHTMARE AGE   POHL, FREDERIK   AN
  SCIENCE FICTION HALL OF FAME VOLUME 2A BOVA, BEN AN
  SHADOW OF TOMORROW   POHL, FREDERIK   AN
  SPECTRUM 4   AMIS & CONQUEST   AN
MARGENES, THE   DEFORD, MIRIAM ALLEN SS   IFS 56 02
  ELSEWHERE, ELSEWHEN, ELSEHOW DEFORD, MIRIAM ALLEN AC
  FIRST WORLD OF IF, THE   QUINN & WULFF   AN
MARGIN FOR ERROR   PADGETT, LEWIS   NV   ASF 47 11
  *BIG BOOK OF SCIENCE FICTION CONKLIN, GROFF   AN
MARGIN OF PROFIT   ANDERSON, POUL   SS   ASF 56 09
  UN-MAN AND OTHER NOVELLAS   ANDERSON, POUL   DC
MARGINAL ERROR   NEVILLE, KRIS   SS   TWS 53 06
  MISSION: MANSTOP   NEVILLE, KRIS   AC
MARGINAL MAN, THE (GUARDIAN SPIRIT)
                              OLIVER, CHAD   NV   FSF 58 04
  3 TO THE HIGHEST POWER   NOLAN, WILLIAM F.   AN
MARI TERRIBLE   WELLS, H. G.   SS   97
  THIRTY STRANGE STORIES   WELLS, H. G.   AC
MARIANA   LEIBER, FRITZ   SS   FAN 60 02
  BEST OF FRITZ LEIBER, THE   LEIBER, FRITZ   AC
  SCIENCE FACT/FICTION   FARRELL/GAGE/&   AN
  SECRET SONGS, THE   LEIBER, FRITZ   AC
  SF: THE BEST OF THE BEST   MERRIL, JUDITH   AN
  5TH ANNUAL OF THE YEAR'S BEST S-F, THE MERRIL, JUDITH AN
MARIONETTES, INC.   BRADBURY, RAY   SS   STS 49 03
  *ILLUSTRATED MAN, THE   BRADBURY, RAY   AC
MARIUS   ANDERSON, POUL   SS   ASF 57 03
  HORN OF TIME, THE   ANDERSON, POUL   AC
MARK ELF   SMITH, CORDWAINER   SS   STN 57 05
  YOU WILL NEVER BE THE SAME SMITH, CORDWAINER   AC
MARK GABLE FOUNDATION, THE   SZILARD, LEO   SS   61
  EXPERT DREAMERS, THE   POHL, FREDERIK   AN
  LIGHT FANTASTIC, THE   HARRISON, HARRY   AN
  VOICE OF THE DOLPHINS, AND OTHER STORIES, THE
                              SZILARD, LEO   AC
MARK OF GIDEON, THE (G. F. SLAVIN & S. ADAMS)
                              BLISH, JAMES   SA   STK 72 06
  STAR TREK 6   BLISH, JAMES   OC
MARK OF THE BEAST, THE   KIPLING, RUDYARD   SS   PIO 90 07
  BEWARE THE BEASTS   GHIDALIA, V.& ELWOOD AN
  ROD SERLING'S TRIPLE W: WITCHES, WARLOCKS AND WEREWOLVES
                              SERLING, ROD   AN
  WORLD OF WONDER   PRATT, FLETCHER   AN
MARK VII (THE THINKER AND THE THOUGHT)
                              DERLETH, AUGUST   SS   OSF 54 09
  HARRIGAN'S FILE   DERLETH, AUGUST   AC
MARKET IN ALIENS, THE   O'DONNELL, K. M.   SS   GAL 68 11
  FINAL WAR AND OTHER FANTASIES O'DONNELL, K. M.   DC
  FIRST STEP OUTWARD   HOSKINS, ROBERT   AN
MARKS OF PAINTED TEETH, THE   DANN, JACK M.   SS   DEM 73
  DEMON KIND   ELWOOD, ROGER   OA
MAROONED   CAMPBELL, JOHN W. JR SN
  SPACE BEYOND, THE   CAMPBELL, JOHN W. JR OC
MAROONED IN ANDROMEDA   SMITH, CLARK ASHTON   NV   WOS 30 10
  OTHER DIMENSIONS   SMITH, CLARK ASHTON   AC
MAROONED OFF VESTA   ASIMOV, ISAAC   SS   AMZ 39 03
  ASIMOV'S MYSTERIES   ASIMOV, ISAAC   AC
  BEST OF AMAZING, THE   ROSS, JOSEPH   AN
  BEST OF ISAAC ASIMOV, THE   ASIMOV, ISAAC   AC
MARQUE AND REPRISAL   ANDERSON, POUL   SN   FSF 65 02
  STAR FOX, THE   ANDERSON, POUL   AC
MARRIAGE MANUAL   ST. CLAIR, MARGARET   SS   STS 54 FL
  CHANGE THE SKY AND OTHER STORIES ST. CLAIR, MARGARET AC
MARRIAGE MENDER, THE   BRADBURY, RAY   SS   COL 54 01
  DAY IT RAINED FOREVER, THE BRADBURY, RAY   AC
  MEDICINE FOR MELANCHOLY, A BRADBURY, RAY   AC
MARS & MISS PICKERELL (FROM MISS P. GOES TO MARS)
                              MACGREGOR, ELLEN   EX   51
  SCIENCE FICTION AND READER'S GUIDE BARROWS, MARJORIE AN
MARS AS THE ABODE OF LIFE   LOWELL, PERCIVAL   AR
  MARS, WE LOVE YOU   HIPOLITO & MCNELLY   AN
MARS BY MOONLIGHT   POHL, FREDERIK   NA   GAL 58 06
  FREDERIK POHL OMNIBUS, THE POHL, FREDERIK   AC
  TURN LEFT AT THURSDAY   POHL, FREDERIK   AC
MARS COLONIZERS   BREUER, MILES J. MD. SS   MVT 35 SU
  GARDEN OF FEAR AND OTHER STORIES, THE CRAWFORD, WILLIAM L. AN
MARS IS HEAVEN!   BRADBURY, RAY   SS   PLS 48 FL
  BEST SCIENCE-FICTION STORIES: 1949, THE BLEILER & DIKTY   AN
  SCIENCE FICTION HALL OF FAME VOLUME 1 SILVERBERG, ROBERT AN
  SHOT IN THE DARK   MERRIL, JUDITH   AN
  TOMORROW MIDNIGHT   BRADBURY, RAY   AC
  WORLDS TO COME   KNIGHT, DAMON   AN

MARS IS OURS| BUCHWALD, ART   SS   65
    POLITICAL SCIENCE FICTION   GREENBERG& WARRICK   AN
    11TH ANNUAL OF THE YEAR'S BEST S-F, THE MERRIL, JUDITH   AN
MARS JAR, THE   LIGHTNER, A. M.   SS   66
    TEEN-AGE SPACE ADVENTURES   FURMAN, A. L.   AN
MARS MINUS BISHA   BRACKETT, LEIGH   SS PLS 54 01
    COMING OF THE TERRANS, THE   BRACKETT, LEIGH   NO
MARS MOUNTAIN   KEY, EUGENE GEORGE   NV
    MARS MOUNTAIN   KEY, EUGENE GEORGE   AC
MARS ON THE ETHER   DUNSANY, LORD   SS CRT 37 09
    *STRANGE PORTS OF CALL   DERLETH, AUGUST   AN
MARS PASTORALE   TATE, PETER   SS NWS 67 08
    BEST SF STORIES FROM NEW WORLDS 5   MOORCOCK, MICHAEL   AN
    SEAGULLS UNDER GLASS AND OTHER STORIES TATE, PETER   AC
MARS-STATION   KEVLES, BETTYANN   SS
    TEEN-AGE SPACE ADVENTURES   FURMAN, A. L.   AN
MARS-TUBE   KORNBLUTH, C. M.
                             AND POHL, FREDERIK   SS C AST 41 09
    WONDER EFFECT, THE   POHL, F. & KORNBLUTH AC
MARTIAN ADVENTURE, A (AT THE PERIHELION)
                                 LEY, WILLY   SN ASF 37 02
    GREAT SCIENCE FICTION BY SCIENTISTS   CONKLIN, GROFF   AN
MARTIAN AND THE MAGICIAN, THE   SMITH, EVELYN E.   SS FSF 52 11
    FIFTY SHORT SCIENCE FICTION TALES   ASIMOV & CONKLIN   AN
MARTIAN AND THE MOBON, THE   STURGEON, THEODORE   NV WRT 49 03
    GHOUL KEEPERS, THE   MARGULIES, LEO   AN
    NEW WORLDS FOR OLD   DERLETH, AUGUST   AN
    *WORLDS OF TOMORROW   DERLETH, AUGUST   AN
MARTIAN ARTIFACT, THE   DERLETH, AUGUST   SS STN 57 07
    HARRIGAN'S FILE   DERLETH, AUGUST   AC
MARTIAN CALENDAR, THE   JACOBI, CARL   SS SPM 57 SP
    PORTRAITS IN MOONLIGHT   JACOBI, CARL   AC
MARTIAN CROWN JEWELS, THE   ANDERSON, POUL   SS EQM 58 02
    GREAT SCIENCE FICTION STORIES   SMITH, CORDELIA T.   AN
    SCIENCE-FICTIONAL SHERLOCK HOLMES, THE COUNCIL OF FOUR   AN
    TALES OF TIME AND SPACE   OLNEY, ROSS R.   AN
    TREASURY OF GREAT SCIENCE FICTION, A VOL.1
                                 BOUCHER, ANTHONY   AN
MARTIAN EL DORADO OF PARKER WINTLEY, THE
                                 CARTER, LIN   SS
    DAW SCIENCE FICTION READER, THE   WOLLHEIM, DONALD A.   OA
MARTIAN IN THE ATTIC, THE   POHL, FREDERIK   SS
    BEST OF FREDERIK POHL, THE   POHL, FREDERIK   AC
    TURN LEFT AT THURSDAY   POHL, FREDERIK   AC
MARTIAN ODDITY, A (BEHIND THE ATE BALL)
                                 ACKERMAN, FORREST J. SS MAR 50 11
    SCIENCE FICTION WORLDS OF FORREST J. ACKERMAN & FRIENDS
                                 ACKERMAN, FORREST J. AC
MARTIAN ODYSSEY, A   WEINBAUM, STANLEY G. NV WOS 34 07
    ANTHROPOLOGY THROUGH SCIENCE FICTION   MASON, C/GREENBERG/& AN
    BEST OF STANLEY G. WEINBAUM, THE   WEINBAUM, STANLEY G. AC
    DAWN OF FLAME   WEINBAUM, STANLEY G. AC
    ESCALES DANS L'INFINI   GALLET, GEORGES H.   AN
    FROM OFF THIS WORLD   MARGULIES & FRIEND   AN
    MARS, WE LOVE YOU   HIPOLITO & MCNELLY   AN
    MARTIAN ODYSSEY AND OTHER SCIENCE FICTION TALES, A
                                 WEINBAUM, STANLEY G. AC
    MARTIAN ODYSSEY AND OTHERS, A   WEINBAUM, STANLEY G. AC
    MARTIAN ODYSSEY, A   WEINBAUM, STANLEY G. AC
    POCKET BOOK OF SCIENCE-FICTION, THE   WOLLHEIM, DONALD A.   AN
    SCIENCE FICTION BESTIARY, THE   SILVERBERG, ROBERT   AN
    SCIENCE FICTION HALL OF FAME VOLUME 1 SILVERBERG, ROBERT   AN
    WHERE DO WE GO FROM HERE?   ASIMOV, ISAAC   AN
    3000 YEARS OF FANTASY AND SCIENCE FICTION
                                 DE CAMP, L. S.&C.   AN
MARTIAN SHOP, THE   FAST, HOWARD   SS FSF 59 11
    DECADE OF FANTASY AND SCIENCE FICTION, A MILLS, ROBERT P.   AN
    EDGE OF TOMORROW, THE   FAST, HOWARD   AC
MARTIAN STAR-GAZERS, THE   POHL, FREDERIK   FA GAL 62 02
    ABOMINABLE EARTHMAN, THE   POHL, FREDERIK   AC
    8TH ANNUAL OF THE YEAR'S BEST S-F, THE MERRIL, JUDITH   AN
MARTIAN WAY, THE   ASIMOV, ISAAC   NA GAL 52 11
    BEST OF ISAAC ASIMOV, THE   ASIMOV, ISAAC   AC
    MARTIAN WAY AND OTHER STORIES, THE   ASIMOV, ISAAC   AC
    SCIENCE FICTION HALL OF FAME VOLUME 2B BOVA, BEN   AN
    WORLDS TO COME   KNIGHT, DAMON   AN
MARTIAN, THE   KAZANTSEV, ALEXANDER SS
    SOVIET SCIENCE FICTION   ANONYMOUS   AN
MARTIAN, THE (IMPOSSIBLE)   BRADBURY, RAY   SS SSS 49 11
    MARTIAN CHRONICLES, THE   BRADBURY, RAY   AC
MARTIANS AND THE COYS, THE   REYNOLDS, MACK   SS IMG 51 06
    GENTLE INVADERS   SANTESSON, HANS S.   AN
    *SCIENCE-FICTION CARNIVAL   BROWN, F. & REYNOLDS AN
MARTIANS AND THE LEADFOOT, THE   NOLAN, WILLIAM F.   SS SCJ 57
    IMPACT-20   NOLAN, WILLIAM F.   AC
MARTIANS, THE   HOYLE, FRED   SS
    ELEMENT 79   HOYLE, FRED   AC
MARTIANS, THE (FROM "LAST AND FIRST MEN")
                                 STAPLEDON, OLAF   EX MTH 30
    TREASURY OF SCIENCE FICTION CLASSICS, THE
                                 KUEBLER, HAROLD W.   AN
MARTIN THE NOVELIST   AYME, MARCEL   SS
    WALKER THROUGH WALLS, THE   AYME, MARCEL   AC
MARTYR FROM MARS   WELLS, BASIL   SS
    DOORWAYS TO SPACE   WELLS, BASIL   AC
MARTYR, THE   ANDERSON, POUL   NV FSF 60 03
    BEST FROM FANTASY AND SCIENCE FICTION: 10
                                 MILLS, ROBERT P.   AN
    BEST SF 5   CRISPIN, EDMUND   AN
MARTYR, THE   NOURSE, ALAN E.   NV FUN 57 01
    PSI-HIGH AND OTHERS   NOURSE, ALAN E.   AC
MARVELOUS BRASS CHESSPLAYING AUTOMATON, THE
                                 WOLFE, GENE   NV UNI 77 07
    UNIVERSE 7   CARR, TERRY   OA

MARVELOUS MARSHAL, THE (THE FASTEST DRAW)
                                 EISENBERG, LARRY   SS AMZ 63 10
    BEST LAID SCHEMES, THE   EISENBERG, LARRY   AC
MARVELOUS POWDER OF LIFE, THE (FROM THE LAND OF OZ)
                                 BAUM, L. FRANK   EX REL 04
    TALES BEYOND TIME   DE CAMP, L. S.&C.   AN
MARY (AN ANCIENT MADNESS)   KNIGHT, DAMON   NV GAL 64 06
    BEST OF DAMON KNIGHT, THE   KNIGHT, DAMON   AC
    DAY IN THE LIFE, A   DOZOIS, GARDNER R.   AN
    TURNING ON   KNIGHT, DAMON   AC
MARY AND JOE   MITCHISON, NAOMI   SS NOV 70 01
    BEST SF: 1970   HARRISON & ALDISS   AN
    *NOVA 1   HARRISON, HARRY   OA
MARY ANONYMOUS   WALTON, BRYCE   SS PLS 54 SU
    EARTH IN PERIL, THE   WOLLHEIM, DONALD A.   DA
MARY CELESTE MOVE, THE   HERBERT, FRANK   SS ANA 64 10
    ANALOG 4   CAMPBELL, JOHN W. JR AN
    BEST OF FRANK HERBERT, THE   HERBERT, FRANK   AC
    ECO-FICTION   STADLER, JOHN   AN
MARY MARGARET ROAD-GRADER   WALDROP, HOWARD   SS ORB 76 18
    BEST SCIENCE FICTION STORIES OF THE YEAR (1976)
                                 DOZOIS, GARDNER R.   AN
    ORBIT 18   KNIGHT, DAMON   OA
MASCULINIST REVOLT, THE   TENN, WILLIAM   NV FSF 65 08
    ONCE AND FUTURE TALES FROM THE MAGAZINE OF FANTASY AND
        SCIENCE FICTION   FERMAN, EDWARD L.   AN
    WOODEN STAR, THE   TENN, WILLIAM   AC
MASK   JEFFERS, DONNAN CALL SS NDM 76 06
    NEW DIMENSIONS 6   SILVERBERG, ROBERT   OA
MASK OF DEMETER   CORWIN, CECIL
                             AND PEARSON, MARTIN   SS C FSF 53 01
    PRIZE SCIENCE FICTION   WOLLHEIM, DONALD A.   AN
MASK OF MEDUSA, THE   BOND, NELSON S.   SS
    31ST OF FEBRUARY, THE   BOND, NELSON S.   AC
MASK OF NIGHT ON HIS FACE, THE LEIGH, STEPHEN   SS
    FUTURE PASTIMES   EDELSTEIN, SCOTT   OA
MASK, THE   LEM, STANISLAW   SS
    MORTAL ENGINES   LEM, STANISLAW   AC
MASKED WORLD, THE   WILLIAMSON, JACK   SS WOT 63 10
    BEST SCIENCE FICTION FROM WORLDS OF TOMORROW
                                 POHL, FREDERIK   AN
    PEOPLE MACHINES   WILLIAMSON, JACK   AC
MASKS   KNIGHT, DAMON   SS PBY 68 07
    AS TOMORROW BECOMES TODAY   SULLIVAN, CHARLES W. AN
    BEST OF DAMON KNIGHT, THE   KNIGHT, DAMON   AC
    DARK STARS   SILVERBERG, ROBERT   AN
    HUMAN-MACHINES   SCORTIA & ZEBROWSKI   AN
    MASKS   PLAYBOY, EDITORS OF   AN
    NEW TOMORROWS, THE   SPINRAD, NORMAN   AN
    OFF CENTRE   KNIGHT, DAMON   AC
    POCKETFUL OF STARS, A   KNIGHT, DAMON   AN
    WORLD'S BEST SCIENCE FICTION: 1969   WOLLHEIM & CARR   AN
MASKS, THE   BLISH, JAMES   SS FSF 59 11
    SO CLOSE TO HOME   BLISH, JAMES   AC
MASON'S LIFE   AMIS, KINGSLEY   SS SDT 72
    BEST SF: 1973   HARRISON & ALDISS   AN
MASQUE   DRACO, S.   SS
    WORLDS AT WAR   RAYER, FRANCIS G.   AN
MASQUE OF THE RED SHIFT   SABERHAGEN, FRED   NV IFS 65 11
    BERSERKER   SABERHAGEN, FRED   AC
    SECOND IF READER OF SCIENCE FICTION, THE POHL, FREDERIK   AN
    WORLD'S BEST SCIENCE FICTION: 1966   WOLLHEIM & CARR   AN
MASQUERADE   KUTTNER, HENRY   SS WRT 42 05
    BEST OF HENRY KUTTNER 2, THE   KUTTNER, HENRY   AC
MASQUERADE (SEE OPERATION MERCURY)
                                 SIMAK, CLIFFORD D.   TC
MASS FOR MIXED VOICES   BEAUMONT, CHARLES   SS SFQ 54 05
    MAN AGAINST TOMORROW   NOLAN, WILLIAM F.   AN
MASTER BUILDER, THE   ALTOV, HENRIK   SS
    OTHER WORLDS, OTHER SEAS   SUVIN, DARKO   AN
MASTER COPY, THE   DOBINSON, FRANK   SS PBY 66 05
    FIEND, THE   PLAYBOY, EDITORS OF   AN
MASTER KEY, THE   ANDERSON, POUL   NV ASF 64 07
    TRADER TO THE STARS   ANDERSON, POUL   AC
MASTER MINDS OF MARS, THE   BURROUGHS, EDGAR R. NO ASA 27
    THREE MARTIAN NOVELS   BURROUGHS, EDGAR R.   AC
MASTER OF CHAOS   MOORCOCK, MICHAEL   SS FAN 64 05
    WEIRD SHADOWS FROM BEYOND   CARNELL, JOHN   AN
MASTER OF COTSWOLD, THE   BOND, NELSON S.   SS WRT 44 01
    MR. MERGENTHWIRKER'S LOBBIES AND OTHER FANTASTIC TALES
                                 BOND, NELSON S.   AC
MASTER OF THE ASTEROID   SMITH, CLARK ASHTON SS WOS 32 10
    *STRANGE PORTS OF CALL   DERLETH, AUGUST   AN
    TALES OF SCIENCE AND SORCERY   SMITH, CLARK ASHTON   AC
MASTER OF THE MILFORD ALTARPIECE, THE
                                 DISCH, THOMAS M.   SS PRV 68
    *GETTING INTO DEATH   DISCH, THOMAS M.   AC
MASTER RACE   ASHBY, RICHARD   SS IMG 51 09
    SPACE, SPACE, SPACE   SLOANE, WILLIAM   AN
    TEEN-AGE SPACE ADVENTURES   FURMAN, A. L.   AN
MASTERMIND OF ZARK   FAIRMAN, PAUL W.   SS
    FORGETFUL ROBOT, THE   FAIRMAN, PAUL W.   OC
MASTERPIECE   GOULART, RON   SS FSF 72 05
    CHAMELEON CORPS & OTHER SHAPE CHANGERS, THE
                                 GOULART, RON   AC
MASTERPIECE, THE   BLOCH, ROBERT   SS ROG 60 06
    *BLOOD RUNS COLD   BLOCH, ROBERT   AC
MASTERS OF MACE AND MAGIC   LEIBER, FRITZ   AR
    BOOK OF FRITZ LEIBER, THE   LEIBER, FRITZ   AC
MASTERS OF TIME (RECRUITING STATION)
                                 VAN VOGT, A. E.   NV ASF 42 03
    MASTERS OF TIME   VAN VOGT, A. E.   AC
MASTERS, THE   COGSWELL, THEODORE R SS TWS 54 SU
    WALL AROUND THE WORLD, THE   COGSWELL, THEODORE R AC
MASTERS, THE   LE GUIN, URSULA K.   SS FAN 63 02
    WINDS TWELVE QUARTERS, THE   LE GUIN, URSULA K.   AC

MASTERSON AND THE CLERKS   MEDDLER, THE

MASTERSON AND THE CLERKS   SLADEK, JOHN T.   SS   NWS 67 09
  BEST SF STORIES FROM NEW WORLDS 4   MOORCOCK, MICHAEL   AN
  SHORES BENEATH, THE   SALLIS, JAMES   AN
MATARAY, TOO   INOUYE, JON   SS
  NIGHT TIDE, A   INOUYE, JON   OC
MATAYAMA   MALEC, ALEXANDER B.   SS   COQ 66 SU
  EXTRAPOLASIS   MALEC, ALEXANDER B.   AC
MATE IN TWO MOVES   MARKS, WINSTON K.   NV   GAL 54 05
  GREAT SCIENCE FICTION ABOUT DOCTORS   CONKLIN, G&FABRICANT AN
MATHEMATICAL LOVE   MARVELL, ANDREW   PM   50
  FANTASIA MATHEMATICA   FADIMAN, CLIFTON   AN
MATHEMATICAL VOODOO, THE   NEARING, H. JR. SS   FSF 51 04
  BEST FROM FANTASY AND SCIENCE FICTION BOUCHER & MCCOMAS AN
  FANTASIA MATHEMATICA   FADIMAN, CLIFTON   AN
  SINISTER RESEARCHES OF C. P. RANSOM, THE NEARING, H. JR. AC
MATHEMATICIAN CONFIDED, A   ANONYMOUS   PM
  MATHEMATICAL MAGPIE, THE   FADIMAN, CLIFTON   AN
MATHEMATICIAN IN LOVE, THE (1874)
                        RANKINE, W. J. M.   PM
  MATHEMATICAL MAGPIE, THE   FADIMAN, CLIFTON   AN
MATHEMATICIAN NAMED KLEIN, A   ANONYMOUS   PM
  MATHEMATICAL MAGPIE, THE   FADIMAN, CLIFTON   AN
MATHEMATICIAN'S NIGHTMARE: THE VISION OF PROFESSOR SQUAREPUNT
                        RUSSELL, BERTRAND   SS   55
  MATHEMATICAL MAGPIE, THE   FADIMAN, CLIFTON   AN
MATHEMATICIANS, THE   FELDMAN, ARTHUR   SS   AMZ 53 11
  FIFTY SHORT SCIENCE FICTION TALES   ASIMOV & CONKLIN   AN
MATHEMATICS CHEZ MADAME MARIETTE
                        PAUL, ELLIOT   MS   42
  MATHEMATICAL MAGPIE, THE   FADIMAN, CLIFTON   AN
MATHEMATICS FOR GOLFERS LEACOCK, STEPHEN   AR   22
  MATHEMATICAL MAGPIE, THE   FADIMAN, CLIFTON   AN
MATHENAUTS, THE   KAGAN, NORMAN   NV   IFS 64 07
  10TH ANNUAL OF THE YEAR'S BEST S-F, THE MERRIL, JUDITH   AN
MATING CALL   HERBERT, FRANK   SS   GAL 61 10
  WORLDS OF FRANK HERBERT, THE HERBERT, FRANK   AC
  13 ABOVE THE NIGHT   CONKLIN, GROFF   AN
MATING OF THE MOONS, THE O'HARA, KENNETH   SS   OSF 54 02
  PLANET OF DOOM AND OTHER STORIES ANONYMOUS   AN
MATING OF THIRDBURT, THE NOLAN, WILLIAM F.   SS   NEW 74 AC
  ALIEN HORIZONS   NOLAN, WILLIAM F.   AC
MATOG   BASCH, JOAN PATRICIA SS   FSF 66 08
  BEST FROM FANTASY AND SCIENCE FICTION: 16
                        FERMAN, EDWARD L.   AN
MATRIX (SEE DANGER: RELIGION!) ALDISS, BRIAN W.
MATTER OF CHOICE, A   LYTLE, B. J.   SS
  SCIENCE FICTION ADVENTURES FROM WAY OUT ELWOOD, ROGER   OA
MATTER OF ENERGY, A (WITH MALICE TO COME)
                        BLISH, JAMES   SS   FSF 55 05
  BEST FROM FANTASY AND SCIENCE FICTION: 5
                        BOUCHER, ANTHONY   AN
MATTER OF ETHICS, A   SHANGO, J. R.   SS   FSF 54 11
  GREAT SCIENCE FICTION ABOUT DOCTORS   CONKLIN, G&FABRICANT AN
MATTER OF FORM, A   GOLD, H. L.   SN   ASF 38 12
  ASSIGNMENT IN TOMORROW   POHL, FREDERIK   AN
  *BIG BOOK OF SCIENCE FICTION CONKLIN, GROFF   AN
  SCIENCE FICTION: THE GREAT YEARS POHL, C. & F.   AN
MATTER OF FREEDOMS, A   O'BRIEN, CLANCY SS   FTP 73
  FLAME TREE PLANET   ELWOOD, ROGER   OA
MATTER OF HONOR, A   HODGELL, PAT   SS
  CLARION SF   WILHELM, KATE   OA
MATTER OF INSTINCT, A   RUSSELL, ERIC FRANK SS
  DARK TIDES   RUSSELL, ERIC FRANK   AC
MATTER OF LIFE, A   BLOCH, ROBERT   SS   KHM 60 06
  BOGEY MEN   BLOCH, ROBERT   AC
MATTER OF OVERTIME, A   ANONYMOUS   AR   TIM 69 03
  SCIENCE FACT/FICTION   FARRELL/GAGE/&   AN
MATTER OF RECORDINGS, A EISENBERG, LARRY SS IFS 70 02
  BEST LAID SCHEMES, THE   EISENBERG, LARRY   AC
MATTER OF SALVAGE, A   BOUNDS, SYDNEY J. SS NWS 52 01
  LAURIE'S SPACE ANNUAL   ANONYMOUS   AN
MATTER OF SIGHT, A   DERLETH, AUGUST SS   WRT 30 01
  NOT LONG FOR THIS WORLD   DERLETH, AUGUST   AC
MATTER OF SIZE, A   BATES, HARRY   NV   ASF 34 04
  *ADVENTURES IN TIME AND SPACE HEALY & MCCOMAS   AN
MATTER OF SIZE, A   FAST, HOWARD   SS
  TOUCH OF INFINITY, A   FAST, HOWARD   OC
MATTER OF SOVEREIGNTY, A POURNELLE, JERRY NV ASF 72 01
  HIGH JUSTICE   POURNELLE, JERRY   AC
MATTER OF TIME AND PLACE, A EISENBERG, LARRY SS FSF 70 01
  BEST LAID SCHEMES, THE   EISENBERG, LARRY   AC
MATTER TRANSMITTER, THE HARRISON, HARRY   IN
  ONE STEP FROM EARTH   HARRISON, HARRY   AC
MATTHEW   SARGENT, PAMELA   SS   TTM 73
  TEN TOMORROWS   ELWOOD, ROGER   OA
MATTHEW SOUTH AND COMPANY JACOBI, CARL   SS   WRT 49 05
  PORTRAITS IN MOONLIGHT   JACOBI, CARL   AC
MATTHEW XVIII, 6   BRUNNER, JOHN   PM   WKS 71 15
  BOOK OF JOHN BRUNNER, THE   BRUNNER, JOHN   AC
MATURATION OF THE ABORIGINES CONRAD, EARL   SS
  DA VINCI MACHINE, THE   CONRAD, EARL   OC
MATURITY   STURGEON, THEODORE   NV   ASF 47 02
  WITHOUT SORCERY   STURGEON, THEODORE   AC
  WORLDS OF THEODORE STURGEON, THE STURGEON, THEODORE AC
  6 GREAT SHORT NOVELS OF SCIENCE FICTION CONKLIN, GROFF AN
MATURITY NIGHT   LONG, FRANK BELKNAP SS   49
  GIRL WITH THE HUNGRY EYES, AND OTHER STORIES, THE
                        WOLLHEIM, DONALD A.   OA
MAUGHAM OBSESSION, THE   DERLETH, AUGUST SS   FUN 53 06
  HARRIGAN'S FILE   DERLETH, AUGUST   AC
MAVERICK (WALKER BETWEEN THE PLANES)
                        DICKSON, GORDON R. NV WOF 70 02
  FIVE FATES   LAUMER, KEITH   AN
MAXWELL EQUATIONS, THE   DNIEPROV, ANATOLY SS
  DESTINATION: AMALTHEIA   DIXON, RICHARD   AN
  RUSSIAN SCIENCE FICTION   MAGIDOFF, ROBERT   AN

MAXWELL'S MONKEY   PANGBORN, EDGAR   SS   GAL 64 10
  GOOD NEIGHBORS AND OTHER STRANGERS   PANGBORN, EDGAR   AC
MAY THE BEST MAN WIN   SCHMIDT, STANLEY SS ASF 71 03
  AMERICAN GOVERNMENT THROUGH SCIENCE FICTION
                        OLANDER/GREENBERG/&   AN
MAYBE ANOTHER LONG MARCH ACROSS CHINA 80,000 STRONG
                        EMSHWILLER, CAROL   SS
  JOY IN OUR CAUSE   EMSHWILLER, CAROL   AC
MAYBE JEAN-BAPTISTE PIERRE ANTOINE DE MONET, CHEVALIER DE LAM-
  ARCK, WAS A LITTLE BIT RIGHT SCOTT, ROBIN S.   SS ORB 70 06
  ORBIT 6   KNIGHT, DAMON   OA
MAYBE JONES AND THE CITY LAFFERTY, R. A. SS
  DOES ANYONE ELSE HAVE SOMETHING FURTHER TO ADD?
                        LAFFERTY, R. A.   AC
MAYBE JUST A LITTLE ONE (HRP 47 08)
                        BRETNOR, REGINALD   SS   FSF 53 02
  BEST FROM FANTASY AND SCIENCE FICTION: 3
                        BOUCHER & MCCOMAS   AN
MAYFLOWER ONE   TAVES, ERNEST   NV   GAL 72 11
  BEST FROM GALAXY, THE VOLUME II   GALAXY, EDITORS OF   AN
MAZE, THE   DYBEK, STUART   SS   ORB 75 17
  ORBIT 17   KNIGHT, DAMON   OA
MAZES   LE GUIN, URSULA K.   SS   EPC 75
  EPOCH   ELWOOD & SILVERBERG   OA
MAZIRIAN THE MAGICIAN   VANCE, JACK   SS   OC
  DYING EARTH, THE   VANCE, JACK   OC
  SPELL OF SEVEN, THE   DE CAMP, L. SPRAGUE   AN
MCGILLAHEE'S BRAT (WAB 70 FL) BRADBURY, RAY   SS FSF 72 01
  INTO THE UNKNOWN   CARR, TERRY   AN
MCILVAINE'S STAR   DERLETH, AUGUST SS   IFS 52 07
  HARRIGAN'S FILE   DERLETH, AUGUST   AC
  PRIZE SCIENCE FICTION   WOLLHEIM, DONALD A.   AN
  *WORLDS OF TOMORROW   DERLETH, AUGUST   AN
MCMLV   TUCKER, WILSON   SS   USF 54 11
  SCIENCE FICTION SUBTREASURY, THE TUCKER, WILSON   AC
MCNAMARA'S FISH   GOULART, RON   SS   FSF 63 07
  BEST FROM FANTASY AND SCIENCE FICTION: 13
                        DAVIDSON, AVRAM   AN
  GHOST BREAKER   GOULART, RON   DC
ME   SCHENCK, HILBERT JR. PM FSF 59 08
  BEST FROM FANTASY AND SCIENCE FICTION: 9
                        MILLS, ROBERT P.   AN
  MATHEMATICAL MAGPIE, THE   FADIMAN, CLIFTON   AN
  5TH ANNUAL OF THE YEAR'S BEST S-F, THE MERRIL, JUDITH AN
ME AND FLAPJACK AND THE MARTIANS
                        BROWN, FREDRIC
                        AND REYNOLDS, MACK   SS C ASF 52 12
  NIGHTMARES AND GEEZENSTACKS BROWN, FREDRIC   AC
ME AND MY ANTRONOSCOPE   BAYLEY, BARRINGTON J NV NWB 73 05
  NEW WORLDS QUARTERLY NO. 5   MOORCOCK, MICHAEL   OA
ME AND MY SHADOW   RUSSELL, ERIC FRANK SS SRS 40 02
  DARK TIDES   RUSSELL, ERIC FRANK   AC
ME, MYSELF, AND I   TENN, WILLIAM   SS   PLS 47 WI
  OF ALL POSSIBLE WORLDS   TENN, WILLIAM   AC
MEADOW, THE   BRADBURY, RAY   PL   BPL 48
  *GOLDEN APPLES OF THE SUN   BRADBURY, RAY   AC
MEALTIME (A CASE OF PTOMAINE) ELLISON, HARLAN SS STM 58 09
  ELLISON WONDERLAND   ELLISON, HARLAN   AC
MEANING OF THE WORD "IMPOSSIBLE", THE
                        LEY, WILLY   AR
  SCIENCE FICTION ROLL OF HONOR, THE POHL, FREDERIK   AN
MEANWHILE, WE ELIMINATE OFFUTT, ANDREW J. SS FUC 73
  FUTURE CITY   ELWOOD, ROGER   OA
MEASURELESS TO MAN (SEE THE DARK INTRUDER)
                        BRADLEY, MARION Z.   TC
MEATBALL   WHITE, JAMES   NV   NWR 69 16
  MAJOR OPERATION   WHITE, JAMES   NO
  NEW WRITINGS IN SF. 16   CARNELL, JOHN   OA
MEATHOUSE MAN   MARTIN, GEORGE R. R. SS ORB 76 18
  BEST SCIENCE FICTION OF THE YEAR, THE NO. 6
                        CARR, TERRY   AN
  ORBIT 18   KNIGHT, DAMON   OA
MECHANIC, THE   CLEMENT, HAL   NV   ASF 66 09
  SMALL CHANGES   CLEMENT, HAL   AC
MECHANICAL ADVANTAGE (RETIEF, THE LONG-AWAITED MASTER)
                        LAUMER, KEITH   NV   IFS 69 04
  RETIEF OF THE CDT   LAUMER, KEITH   AC
MECHANICAL ANSWER   MACDONALD, JOHN D. SS ASF 48 05
  ROBOT AND THE MAN, THE   GREENBERG, MARTIN   AN
MECHANICAL BRIDE, THE   LEIBER, FRITZ   PL   NEW 54 AN
  *SCIENCE FICTION THINKING MACHINES   CONKLIN, GROFF   AN
  SECOND BOOK OF FRITZ LEIBER, THE   LEIBER, FRITZ   AC
  SIX SCIENCE FICTION PLAYS   ELWOOD, ROGER   AN
MECHANICAL HEAD   HAUSMANN, RAOUL IL
  SCIENCE FICTION   BRODKIN & PEARSON   AN
MECHANICAL HOUSE, THE (THE UNGRATEFUL HOUSE)
                        DERLETH, AUGUST SS   OSF 54 03
  HARRIGAN'S FILE   DERLETH, AUGUST   AC
MECHANICAL MICE   HUGI, MAURICE G. NV ASF 41 01
  *ADVENTURES IN TIME AND SPACE HEALY & MCCOMAS   AN
MECHANICAL MICE, THE (AS MAURICE G. HUGI)
                        RUSSELL, ERIC FRANK NV ASF 41 01
  LIKE NOTHING ON EARTH   RUSSELL, ERIC FRANK   AC
MECHANICAL SWEETHEART, THE ALPER, GERALD ARTHUR SS NEW 72 AN
  STRANGE BED FELLOWS   SCORTIA, THOMAS N.   AN
MECHANISTRIA   RUSSELL, ERIC FRANK NV ASF 42 01
  MEN, MARTIANS AND MACHINES   RUSSELL, ERIC FRANK   AC
MED SERVICE   LEINSTER, MURRAY SN ASF 57 08
  SCIENCE FICTION SHOWCASE   KORNBLUTH, MARY   AN
MED SHIP MAN   LEINSTER, MURRAY NV GAL 63 10
  DOCTOR TO THE STARS   LEINSTER, MURRAY   AC
MEDAL FOR HORATIUS, A   HALL, WILLIAM C. SS ARM 55 01
  APEMAN, SPACEMAN   STOVER & HARRISON   AN
MEDDLER, THE   NIVEN, LARRY   NV   FSF 68 10
  SHAPE OF SPACE, THE   NIVEN, LARRY   AC

MEDDLERS, THE

MEDDLERS, THE   KORNBLUTH, C. M.   SS   SFA 53 09
*MILE BEYOND THE MOON, A   KORNBLUTH, C. M.   AC
MEDIC (NOT SO GREAT AN ENEMY) GUNN, JAMES E.   NV   VSF 57 07
  IMMORTALS, THE   GUNN, JAMES E.   NO
  SOME DREAMS ARE NIGHTMARES   GUNN, JAMES E.   AC
MEDIC (O'MARA'S ORPHAN)   WHITE, JAMES   NV   NWS 60 01
  HOSPITAL STATION   WHITE, JAMES   AC
MEDICAL CHART OF STEPHEN PAYNE CONRAD, EARL   SS
  DA VINCI MACHINE, THE   CONRAD, EARL   OC
MEDICINE DANCER   BROWN, BILL   SS   FNF 53 11
  BEYOND THE BARRIERS OF SPACE AND TIME MERRIL, JUDITH   AN
MEDICINE FOR MELANCHOLY, A   BRADBURY, RAY   AC   DBL 58
  TWICE 22   BRADBURY, RAY   AC
MEDICINE FOR MELANCHOLY, A   BRADBURY, RAY   SS   NEW 59 AC
  MEDICINE FOR MELANCHOLY, A   BRADBURY, RAY   AC
  VINTAGE BRADBURY, THE   BRADBURY, RAY   AC
MEDUSA   STURGEON, THEODORE SS   ASF 42 02
  CAVIAR   STURGEON, THEODORE   AC
MEEK, THE   WOODROW, WILLIAM   SS   NWQ 71 02
  NEW WORLDS QUARTERLY NO. 2   MOORCOCK, MICHAEL   OA
MEETING MY BROTHER   KRAPIVIV, VLADISLAV SS
  PATH INTO THE UNKNOWN   ANONYMOUS   AN
MEETING OF MINDS, A   MCCAFFREY, ANNE   NV   FSF 69 01
  GET OFF THE UNICORN   MCCAFFREY, ANNE   AC
  LIBERATED FUTURE: VOYAGES INTO TOMORROW, THE
                                        HOSKINS, ROBERT   AN
MEETING OF RELATIONS (YRV 41 12)
                              COLLIER, JOHN   SS   FSF 59 01
  DECADE OF FANTASY AND SCIENCE FICTION, A MILLS, ROBERT P.   AN
MEETING OF THE BOARD   NOURSE, ALAN E.   SS   IFS 55 10
  COUNTERFEIT MAN, THE   NOURSE, ALAN E.   AC
MEETING OF THE MINDS   SHECKLEY, ROBERT   NA   GAL 60 02
  OUT OF THIS WORLD 7   WILLIAMS-ELLIS& OWEN   AN
  SHARDS OF SPACE   SHECKLEY, ROBERT   AC
MEETING OVER THE TUSCARORA   YEFREMOV, IVAN   SS
  STORIES   YEFREMOV, IVAN   AC
MEETING OVER TUSCARORA, A   YEFREMOV, IVAN   SS
  MEETING OVER TUSCARORA AND OTHER ADVENTURE TALES, A
                                        YEFREMOV, IVAN   AC
MEETING THE ALIENS ON ALGOL IV SCHAEFFER, ROBIN SS
  SURVIVAL FROM INFINITY   ELWOOD, ROGER   OA
MEETING WITH MEDUSA, A   CLARKE, ARTHUR C. NA   PBY 71 12
  BEST OF ARTHUR C. CLARKE: 1937-1971, THE CLARKE, ARTHUR C.   AC
  BEST SCIENCE FICTION OF THE YEAR, THE CARR, TERRY   AN
  BEST SF: 1971   HARRISON & ALDISS   AN
  JUPITER   POHL, C. & F.   AN
  NEBULA AWARD STORIES 8   ASIMOV, ISAAC   AN
  WIND FROM THE SUN, THE   CLARKE, ARTHUR C.   AC
MEETING, THE   KORNBLUTH, C. M.
  AND POHL, FREDERIK   SS C FSF 72 11
  BEST SCIENCE FICTION OF THE YEAR, THE NO. 2
                                        CARR, TERRY   AN
  BEST SCIENCE FICTION STORIES OF THE YEAR (1972)
                                        DEL REY, LESTER   AN
MEGAN'S WORLD   RANDALL, MARTA   NA
  CRYSTAL SHIP, THE   SILVERBERG, ROBERT   OA
MEGATON   INOUYE, JON   SS
  NIGHT TIDE, A   INOUYE, JON   OC
MEIHEM IN CE KLASRUM   EDWARDS, DOLTON   AR   ASF 46 09
  *ASTOUNDING SCIENCE FICTION ANTHOLOGY, THE
                                        CAMPBELL, JOHN W. JR AN
  *SECOND ASTOUNDING SCIENCE FICTION ANTHOLOGY, THE
                                        CAMPBELL, JOHN W. JR AN
MELANCHOLY AND MYSTERY OF A STREET, THE
                              DE CHIRICO, GIORGIO IL
                                        BRODKIN & PEARSON   AN
  SCIENCE FICTION
MELLONTA TAUTA   POE, EDGAR ALLEN   SS   GDY 49 02
  FUTURE PERFECT   FRANKLIN, H. BRUCE   AN
  SPECULATIONS   SANDERS, THOMAS E.   AN
  STRANGE SIGNPOSTS   ELWOOD & MOSKOWITZ   AN
MELODRAMINE   SLESAR, HENRY   SS   PBY 65 08
  FROM THE "S" FILE   PLAYBOY, EDITORS OF AN
MELTING   WOLFE, GENE   SS   ORB 74 15
  ORBIT 15   KNIGHT, DAMON   OA
MEMO TO A MOVIE-MAKER   BLOCH, ROBERT   SS   DUD 61 01
  BOGEY MEN   BLOCH, ROBERT   AC
MEMO TO SECRETARY   DEGRAW, PAT   PM   FSF 66 06
  BEST FROM FANTASY AND SCIENCE FICTION: 16
                                        FERMAN, EDWARD L.   AN
MEMORIAL (SEE ALSO ATOMIC MEMORIAL)
                              STURGEON, THEODORE SS   ASF 46 04
  HISTORY OF THE SCIENCE FICTION MAGAZINE, THE PART 3 1946-1955
                                        ASHLEY, MICHAEL   AN
  *OTHER SIDE OF THE MOON, THE   DERLETH, AUGUST   AN
  SCIENCE FICTION TERROR TALES   CONKLIN, GROFF   AN
  WITHOUT SORCERY   STURGEON, THEODORE   AC
  WORLDS OF THEODORE STURGEON, THE   STURGEON, THEODORE   AC
MEMORY   DOLAN, MIKE   SS
  SANTANA MORNING AND OTHER STORIES   DOLAN, MIKE   OC
MEMORY   STURGEON, THEODORE NV   TWS 48 08
  ADVENTURES IN TOMORROW   CROSSEN, KENDELL F.   AN
MEMORY (A WORLD CALLED MAANEREK)
                              ANDERSON, POUL   NV   GAL 57 07
  BEYOND THE BEYOND   ANDERSON, POUL   AC
MEMORY MACHINE, THE   MISC. MATERIAL   MS
  ORBIT 14   KNIGHT, DAMON   OA
  ORBIT 15   KNIGHT, DAMON   OA
  ORBIT 16   KNIGHT, DAMON   OA
  ORBIT 17   KNIGHT, DAMON   OA
  ORBIT 18   KNIGHT, DAMON   OA
MEMORY OF GOLDEN SUNSHINE, A BULMER, KENNETH   SS   NWR 71 19
  NEW WRITINGS IN SF. 19   CARNELL, JOHN   OA
MEN AGAINST THE STARS   WELLMAN, MANLY WADE NV ASF 38 06
  EVERY BOY'S BOOK OF OUTER SPACE STORIES DIKTY, T. E.   AN
  *MEN AGAINST THE STARS   GREENBERG , MARTIN   AN

MEN AND THE MIRROR, THE   ROCKLYNNE, ROSS   NV   ASF 38 07
  BEFORE THE GOLDEN AGE   ASIMOV, ISAAC   AN
  MEN AND THE MIRROR, THE   ROCKLYNNE, ROSS   AN
MEN ARE COMING BACK!, THE   COLE, BARRY   PM   NWS 67 10
  HOLDING YOUR EIGHT HANDS   LUCIE-SMITH, EDWARD   AN
MEN ARE DIFFERENT   BLOCH, ALAN   SS   NEW 54 AN
  FIFTY SHORT SCIENCE FICTION TALES   ASIMOV & CONKLIN   AN
  *SCIENCE FICTION THINKING MACHINES   CONKLIN, GROFF   AN
MEN IN SPACE   LASSWELL, HAROLD D. AR
  APEMAN, SPACEMAN   STOVER & HARRISON   AN
MEN INSIDE, THE (ALSO AS THE MAN IN THE POCKET)
                              MALZBERG, BARRY N. NV   NDM 72 02
  NEW DIMENSIONS 2   SILVERBERG, ROBERT   OA
MEN LIKE GODS   WELLS, H. G.   NO   HRS 22 11
  TWENTY-EIGHT SCIENCE FICTION STORIES WELLS, H. G.   AC
MEN OF GOOD VALUE   PRIEST, CHRISTOPHER SS NWR 75 26
  NEW WRITINGS IN SF. 26   BULMER, KENNETH   OA
MEN OF GOOD WILL   BOVA, BEN
  AND LEWIS, MYRON R.   SS C GAL 64 06
  COMBAT SF   DICKSON, GORDON R.   AN
  FORWARD IN TIME   BOVA, BEN   AC
  NOTES TO A SCIENCE FICTION WRITER   BOVA, BEN   AC
  WORLD'S BEST SCIENCE FICTION: 1965   WOLLHEIM & CARR   AN
MEN OF GREYWATER STATION   MARTIN, GEORGE R. R. SS AMZ 76 03
  SONGS OF STARS AND SHADOWS   MARTIN, GEORGE R. R.   AC
MEN OF IRON (1940)   ENDORE, GUY   SS   FSF 49 PL
  DECADE OF FANTASY AND SCIENCE FICTION, A MILLS, ROBERT P.   AN
  HUMAN-MACHINES   SCORTIA & ZEBROWSKI   AN
MEN OF THE BRONZE AGE   BURROUGHS, EDGAR R. NV AMZ 42 03
  SAVAGE PELLUCIDAR   BURROUGHS, EDGAR R.   NO
MEN OF THE TEN BOOKS   VANCE, JACK   SS   STS 51 03
  BEST SCIENCE-FICTION STORIES: 1952, THE BLEILER & DIKTY   AN
  OUT OF THIS WORLD 1   WILLIAMS-ELLIS& OWEN   AN
MEN ONLY   TUBB, E. C.   SS   NWS 52 07
  ALIEN DUST   TUBB, E. C.   NO
MEN RETURN, THE   VANCE, JACK   SS   INF 57 07
  ALPHA 2   SILVERBERG, ROBERT   AN
  EIGHT FANTASMS AND MAGICS   VANCE, JACK   AC
  EVIL EARTHS   ALDISS, BRIAN W.   AN
  WORLD BETWEEN AND OTHER STORIES, THE VANCE, JACK   DC
  WORLDS OF JACK VANCE, THE   VANCE, JACK   AC
MEN WHO MURDERED MOHAMMED, THE BESTER, ALFRED   SS   FSF 58 10
  AS TOMORROW BECOMES TODAY   SULLIVAN, CHARLES W. AN
  BEST FROM FANTASY AND SCIENCE FICTION: 8
                                        BOUCHER, ANTHONY   AN
  COSMIC LAUGHTER   HALDEMAN, JOE W.   AN
  DARK SIDE OF THE EARTH, THE   BESTER, ALFRED   AC
  LIGHT FANTASTIC, THE   BESTER, ALFRED   AC
  VINTAGE ANTHOLOGY OF SCIENCE FANTASY, THE
                                        CERF, CHRISTOPHER   AN
  VOYAGERS IN TIME   SILVERBERG, ROBERT   AN
MEN WITHOUT BONES   KERSH, GERALD   SS   ESQ
  ANCIENT MYSTERIES READER, THE   HAINING, PETER   AN
  MEN WITHOUT BONES   KERSH, GERALD   AC
  NIGHTSHADE & DAMNATIONS   KERSH, GERALD   AC
MENACE FROM EARTH, THE   HEINLEIN, ROBERT A. SS FSF 57 08
  HOT & COLD RUNNING CITIES   MCHARGUE, GEORGESS   AN
  MENACE FROM EARTH, THE   HEINLEIN, ROBERT A.   AC
  PAST THROUGH TOMORROW, THE   HEINLEIN, ROBERT A.   AC
  TOMORROW'S CHILDREN   ASIMOV, ISAAC   AN
MENACE OF MARS, THE   HARRIS, CLARE WINGER SS AMZ 28 10
  AWAY FROM THE HERE AND NOW   HARRIS, CLARE WINGER   AC
MENACE OF THE MACHINE, THE (FROM "EREWHON")
                              BUTLER, SAMUEL   EX
  SCIENCE FICTION THROUGH THE AGES 1   EVANS, I. O.   AN
MENAGERIE (GENE RODDENBERRY) BLISH, JAMES   SA   STK 71 04
  STAR TREK 4   BLISH, JAMES   OC
MENHIR, THE   COOPER, EDMUND   SS
  NEWS FROM ELSEWHERE   COOPER, EDMUND   AC
MENSURATION   SALLIS, JAMES   PM   QRK 71 02
  QUARK/2   DELANY & HACKER   OA
MEPHISTO & THE ION EXPLORER   KAPP, COLIN   NV   IFS 74 10
  BEST FROM IF, THE   VOLUME III   BAEN, JAMES   AN
MERCENARY   POURNELLE, JERRY   NV   ASF 72 07
  MERCENARY, THE   POURNELLE, JERRY   NO
MERCHANTS OF VENUS, THE   POHL, FREDERIK   NA   IFS 72 08
  BEST SCIENCE FICTION FOR 1973   ACKERMAN, FORREST J. AN
  FUTURE NOW, THE   HOSKINS, ROBERT   AN
  GOLD AT STARBOW'S END, THE   POHL, FREDERIK   AC
MERCURIAN, THE   LONG, FRANK BELKNAP SS PLS 41 WI
  FLIGHT INTO SPACE   WOLLHEIM, DONALD A.   AN
MERCURY   LACH-SZYRMA, D. S. CSL 87 10
  WORLDS APART   LOCKE, GEORGE   AN
MERCY FLIGHT TO LUNA   ELAM, RICHARD M. JR. SS
  TEEN-AGE SUPER SCIENCE STORIES   ELAM, RICHARD M. JR.   AC
MERCYSHIP, THE   PAGE, GERALD W.   SS   SPC 73 01
  SPACE 1   DAVIS, RICHARD   OA
MERLIN STREET   MACFARLANE, WALLACE NV INY 72 04
  INFINITY 4   HOSKINS, ROBERT   OA
MERMAN, THE   DE CAMP, L. SPRAGUE SS ASF 38 12
  SCIENCE FICTION OF THE 30'S   KNIGHT, DAMON   AC
  WHEELS OF IF, THE   DE CAMP, L. SPRAGUE   AC
MESMERICA   RUSSELL, ERIC FRANK NV NEW 56 AC
  MEN, MARTIANS AND MACHINES   RUSSELL, ERIC FRANK   AC
MESS OF PORRIDGE, A   DORMAN, SONYA   SS   ANA 70
  ALCHEMY AND ACADEME   MCCAFFREY, ANNE   AN
MESSAGE FROM CHARITY, A   LEE, WILLIAM M.   SS   FSF 67 11
  NEW WORLDS OF FANTASY NO. 3   CARR, TERRY   AN
  THEMES IN SCIENCE FICTION   KELLEY, LEO P.   AN
MESSAGE FROM THE MOON, A   ENGLAND, GEORGE A. SS PRS 07 04
  WORLDS APART   LOCKE, GEORGE   AN
MESSAGE FROM THE STARS   COPPER, BASIL   SS   SPC 74 04
  SPACE 2   DAVIS, RICHARD   OA
MESSAGE IN SECRET, A   ANDERSON, POUL   NA   FAN 57 12
  FLANDRY OF TERRA   ANDERSON, POUL   AC

MESSAGE OF JOY   COVER, ARTHUR BYRON   SS   ALT 74
  ALTERNATES   GERROLD, DAVID   OA
MESSAGE TO AN ALIEN   LAUMER, KEITH   SS   ASF 70 06
  BIG SHOW, THE   LAUMER, KEITH   AC
MESSAGE, THE   ASIMOV, ISAAC   SS   FSF 56 02
  EARTH IS ROOM ENOUGH   ASIMOV, ISAAC   AC
MESSAGE, THE   ANTHONY, PIERS
                                   AND HALL, FRANCES   NV C ASF 66 07
  ANALOG 6   CAMPBELL, JOHN W. JR   AN
MESSAGE, THE (SEE WILLIAM MITCHELL- 2028)
                                   GUNN, JAMES E.   TC
MESSENGERS, THE   WANDREI, DONALD   SS
  EYE AND THE FINGER   WANDREI, DONALD   AC
MESSIAH ON MOTT STREET, THE   SERLING, ROD   SA
  NIGHT GALLERY 2   SERLING, ROD   OC
MESSIAH, THE   BRADBURY, RAY   SS   WAB 71 SP
  LONG AFTER MIDNIGHT   BRADBURY, RAY   AC
METAL MAN, THE   WILLIAMSON, JACK   SS   AMZ 28 12
  ANDROIDS, TIME MACHINES AND BLUE GIRAFFES
                                   ELWOOD & GHIDALIA   AN
  BEST OF AMAZING, THE   ROSS, JOSEPH   AN
  EARLY WILLIAMSON, THE   WILLIAMSON, JACK   AC
  PANDORA EFFECT, THE   WILLIAMSON, JACK   AC
  SPECTRUM OF WORLDS, A   CLARESON, THOMAS D.   AN
METAL MOON, THE   JONES, NEIL R.   NV   SSS 49 09
  DOOMSDAY ON AJIAT   JONES, NEIL R.   AC
METAMORPHOSIS   KAFKA, FRANZ   NV   37
  WORLD OF WONDER   PRATT, FLETCHER   AN
METAMORPHOSIS   HARRISON, LIZ
                                   MARSHALL, CHRIS
                                   AND STEPHENS, KEVIN   IL C
  BEYOND THIS HORIZON   CARRELL, CHRISTOPHER OA
METAMORPHOSIS (GENE L. COON)   BLISH, JAMES   SA   STK 72 07
  STAR TREK 7   BLISH, JAMES   OC
METAMORPHOSIS OF EARTH, THE   SMITH, CLARK ASHTON   NV   WRT 51 09
  *BEACHHEADS IN SPACE   DERLETH, AUGUST   AN
  FROM OTHER WORLDS   DERLETH, AUGUST   AN
  OTHER DIMENSIONS   SMITH, CLARK ASHTON   AC
METAMORPHOSITE   RUSSELL, ERIC FRANK   NV   ASF 46 12
  *BEACHHEADS IN SPACE   DERLETH, AUGUST   AN
  JOURNEY TO INFINITY   GREENBERG , MARTIN   AN
METEOR   POWERS, WILLIAM T.   SS   ASF 50 09
  *ASTOUNDING SCIENCE FICTION ANTHOLOGY, THE
                                   CAMPBELL, JOHN W. JR   AN
METEOR (PHONEY METEOR)   HARRIS, JOHN BEYNON   SS   AMZ 41 03
  *BEACHHEADS IN SPACE   DERLETH, AUGUST   AN
  FROM OTHER WORLDS   DERLETH, AUGUST   AN
METEOR (PHONEY METEOR)   WYNDHAM, JOHN   SS   AMZ 41 03
  SEEDS OF TIME, THE   WYNDHAM, JOHN   AC
  TALES OF SCIENCE FICTION   BALL, BRIAN N.   AN
  UNTRAVELLED WORLDS   BARTER & WILSON   AN
METEOR GIRL, THE   WILLIAMSON, JACK   SS   ASF 31 03
  EARLY WILLIAMSON, THE   WILLIAMSON, JACK   AC
METEOR MINERS, THE   ESHBACH, LLOYD A.   SS   AMZ 35 12
  TYRANT OF TIME, THE   ESHBACH, LLOYD A.   AC
METHAPYRILENE HYDROCHLORIDE SOMETIMES HELPS
                                   EMSHWILLER, CAROL   SS   NWS 68 07
  JOY IN OUR CAUSE   EMSHWILLER, CAROL   AC
METHOD BIT IN "B", A   WOLFE, GENE   SS   ORB 70 08
  ORBIT 8   KNIGHT, DAMON   OA
METHOD FOR MURDER   BLOCH, ROBERT   SS   FUR 62 07
  CHAMBER OF HORRORS   BLOCH, ROBERT   AC
  KING OF TERRORS, THE   BLOCH, ROBERT   AC
METHUSELAH'S CHILDREN   HEINLEIN, ROBERT A.   NO   ASF 41 07
  PAST THROUGH TOMORROW, THE   HEINLEIN, ROBERT A.   AC
METRONOME, THE   DERLETH, AUGUST   SS   WRT 35 02
  LITTLE MONSTERS, THE   ELWOOD & GHIDALIA   AN
METROPOLIS UEBER ALLES   ACKERMAN, FORREST J. AR   63
  SCIENCE FICTION WORLDS OF FORREST J. ACKERMAN & FRIENDS
                                   ACKERMAN, FORREST J. AC
METROPOLITAN NIGHTMARE   BENET, STEPHEN V.   PM   27
  HOT & COLD RUNNING CITIES   MCHARGUE, GEORGESS   AN
  WONDERMAKERS   HOSKINS, ROBERT   AN
METZENGERSTEIN   POE, EDGAR ALLEN   SS   SLM 36 02
  BEWARE THE BEASTS   GHIDALIA, V.& ELWOOD   AN
MEWHU'S JET   STURGEON, THEODORE   NV   ASF 46 11
  *BIG BOOK OF SCIENCE FICTION   CONKLIN, GROFF   AN
  SCIENCE FICTION: THE GREAT YEARS, VOL. II
                                   POHL, C. & F.   AN
  THUNDER AND ROSES   STURGEON, THEODORE   AC
  *WAY HOME, A   STURGEON, THEODORE   AC
MEX   HARRIS, LARRY M.   SS   FUN 57 01
  FANTASTIC UNIVERSE OMNIBUS, THE   SANTESSON, HANS S.   AN
MEZZEROW LOVES COMPANY   WALLACE, F. L.   NV   GAL 56 06
  WORLD THAT COULDN'T BE AND 8 OTHER SF NOVELETS
                                   GOLD, H. L.   AN
MICE, THE (SEE THE LITTLE MICE)
                                   BRADBURY, RAY   TC
MICKEY FINN   BUCK, DORIS PITKIN   PM   FSF 66 03
  BEST FROM FANTASY AND SCIENCE FICTION: 16
                                   FERMAN, EDWARD L.   AN
MICRO MAN   ACKERMAN, FORREST J. SS   NWS 46 02
  SCIENCE FICTION WORLDS OF FORREST J. ACKERMAN & FRIENDS
                                   ACKERMAN, FORREST J. AC
MICROCOSM   HOLDSTOCK, ROBERT P. SS   NWR 72 20
  NEW WRITINGS IN SF. 20   CARNELL, JOHN   OA
MICROCOSMIC GOD   STURGEON, THEODORE   NV   ASF 41 04
  CAVIAR   STURGEON, THEODORE   AC
  GIANTS UNLEASHED   CONKLIN, GROFF   AN
  MICROCOSMIC GOD   MOSKOWITZ, SAM   AN
  MODERN MASTERPIECES OF SCIENCE FICTION MOSKOWITZ, SAM   AN
  POCKET BOOK OF SCIENCE-FICTION, THE WOLLHEIM, DONALD A.   AN
  SCIENCE FICTION HALL OF FAME VOLUME 1 SILVERBERG, ROBERT   AN
  WITHOUT SORCERY   STURGEON, THEODORE   AC
MICROMEGAS   VOLTAIRE   NV
  PAST, PRESENT, AND FUTURE PERFECT WOLFE, J&FITZ GERALD AN

MICROSCOPIC GIANTS, THE   ERNST, PAUL   SS   TWS 36 10
  FROM OFF THIS WORLD   MARGULIES & FRIEND   AN
  SCIENCE FICTION TERROR TALES   CONKLIN, GROFF   AN
MIDAS PLAGUE, THE   POHL, FREDERIK   NA   GAL 54 04
  ALL ABOUT THE FUTURE   GREENBERG, MARTIN   AN
  BEST OF FREDERIK POHL, THE   POHL, FREDERIK   AC
  CASE AGAINST TOMORROW, THE   POHL, FREDERIK   AC
  NIGHTMARE AGE   POHL, FREDERIK   AN
  SCIENCE FICTION HALL OF FAME VOLUME 2B BOVA, BEN   AN
  *SPECTRUM   AMIS & CONQUEST   AN
MIDDLE MAN, THE   OLIVER, CHAD   NV   CTM 74 03
  CONTINUUM 3   ELWOOD, ROGER   OA
MIDDLE OF NOWHERE, THE   POHL, FREDERIK   SS   GAL 55 05
  FREDERIK POHL OMNIBUS, THE   POHL, FREDERIK   AC
  TOMORROW TIMES SEVEN   POHL, FREDERIK   AC
MIDDLE OF THE WEEK AFTER NEXT, THE
                                   LEINSTER, MURRAY   SS   TWS 52 08
  BEST SCIENCE-FICTION STORIES: 1953, THE BLEILER & DIKTY   AN
  OUT OF THIS WORLD 1   WILLIAMS-ELLIS& OWEN   AN
  *SCIENCE FICTION ADVENTURES IN DIMENSION CONKLIN, GROFF   AN
MIDDLE PERIOD, THE   KNIGHT, DAMON   SI
  SCIENCE FICTION OF THE 30'S   KNIGHT, DAMON   AN
MIDNIGHT BY THE MORPHY WATCH   LEIBER, FRITZ   NV   IFS 74 08
  BEST FROM IF, THE VOLUME III   BAEN, JAMES   AN
MIDNIGHT IN THE MIRROR WORLD   LEIBER, FRITZ   SS   FAN 64 10
  MIND SPIDER AND OTHER STORIES, THE (ACE 76)
                                   LEIBER, FRITZ   AC
  NIGHT MONSTERS   LEIBER, FRITZ   DC
MIDNIGHT SUN, THE   SERLING, ROD   SA
  FROM THE TWILIGHT ZONE   SERLING, ROD   AC
  NEW STORIES FROM THE TWILIGHT ZONE SERLING, ROD   OC
MIDSUMMER CENTURY   BLISH, JAMES   NO   DBL 72
  MIDSUMMER CENTURY   BLISH, JAMES   AC
MIDSUMMER CENTURY   BLISH, JAMES   SN   FSF 72 04
  BEST FROM FANTASY AND SCIENCE FICTION, 25TH ANNIV.
                                   FERMAN, EDWARD L.   AN
MIGHTIEST QORN (SEE ULTIMATUM) LAUMER, KEITH   TC
MIGHTY CASEY, THE   SERLING, ROD   SA
  FROM THE TWILIGHT ZONE   SERLING, ROD   AC
  STORIES FROM THE TWILIGHT ZONE   SERLING, ROD   OC
MIGHTY MATTERHORN, THE   EISENBERG, LARRY   SS   NEW 71 03
  BEST LAID SCHEMES, THE   EISENBERG, LARRY   AC
MIGHTY TIDES, THE (WHAT MAKES THE MIGHTY TIDES)
                                   LEIBER, FRITZ   AR   SDG 61 04
  SECOND BOOK OF FRITZ LEIBER, THE   LEIBER, FRITZ   AC
MIGRATION, THE   PROCTOR, GEORGE W.   SS
  LONE STAR UNIVERSE   PROCTOR & UTLEY   OA
MILD ATTACK OF LOCUSTS, A   LESSING, DORIS   SS   51
  VOYAGES: SCENARIOS FOR A SHIP CALLED EARTH
                                   SAUER, ROB   AN
MILE-LONG SPACESHIP, THE   WILHELM, KATE   SS   ASF 57 04
  BEST SCIENCE FICTION STORIES AND NOVELS: 9TH SERIES
                                   DIKTY, T. E.   AN
  BEYOND TOMORROW   KNIGHT, DAMON   AN
  MILE-LONG SPACESHIP, THE   WILHELM, KATE   AC
MILKEY MOUNTAIN   MCCAFFREY, ANNE   NV   CTM 74 03
  CONTINUUM 3   ELWOOD, ROGER   OA
MILESTONES . NOVELS WORTH READING
                                   MISC. MATERIAL   MS
  3000 YEARS OF FANTASY AND SCIENCE FICTION
                                   DE CAMP, L. S.&C.   AN
MILK OF PARADISE, THE   TIPTREE, JAMES JR.   SS   DVS 72 02
  AGAIN, DANGEROUS VISIONS   ELLISON, HARLAN   OA
  WARM WORLDS AND OTHERWISE   TIPTREE, JAMES JR.   AC
MILK RUN   SHECKLEY, ROBERT   SS   GAL 54 09
  PILGRIMAGE TO EARTH   SHECKLEY, ROBERT   AC
MILL OF THE GODS, THE   ANDERSON, POUL   NV   NEW 61 AC
  ORBIT UNLIMITED   ANDERSON, POUL   NO
MILLENNIUM   BROWN, FREDRIC   SS   FSF 55 03
  HONEYMOON IN HELL   BROWN, FREDRIC   AC
MILLER'S DAUGHTER   COOPER, EDMUND   SS
  VOICES IN THE DARK   COOPER, EDMUND   AC
MILLION-MILE HUNT (SEE MOON FEVER)
                                   PETAJA, EMIL   TC
MILLION-YEAR PICNIC, THE   BRADBURY, RAY   SS   PLS 46 SU
  BEYOND TOMORROW   KNIGHT, DAMON   AN
  INVASION FROM MARS   WELLES, ORSON   AN
  MARTIAN CHRONICLES, THE   BRADBURY, RAY   AC
  S IS FOR SPACE   BRADBURY, RAY   AC
  *STRANGE PORTS OF CALL   DERLETH, AUGUST   AN
  WORLD OF WONDER   PRATT, FLETCHER   AN
MILLIONTH MURDER, THE (SEE AND THE ROCK CRIED OUT)
                                   BRADBURY, RAY   TC
MILLIONTH YEAR, THE   PEARSON, MARTIN   SS   SFS 43 04
  ADVENTURES IN THE FAR FUTURE   WOLLHEIM, DONALD A.   DA
MILO AND THE MATHEMAGICIAN   JUSTER, NORTON   SS   61
  MATHEMATICAL MAGPIE, THE   FADIMAN, CLIFTON   AN
MILORD SIR SMIHT, THE ENGLISH WIZARD
                                   DAVIDSON, AVRAM   NV
  ENQUIRIES OF DOCTOR ESZTERHAZY, THE DAVIDSON, AVRAM   NO
MIMI SMITH   DISCH, THOMAS M.   SS
  *GETTING INTO DEATH   DISCH, THOMAS M.   AC
MIMIC   WOLLHEIM, DONALD A.   SS   AST 42 12
  CREATURES FROM BEYOND   CARR, TERRY   AN
  MORE TERROR IN THE MODERN VEIN   WOLLHEIM, DONALD A.   AN
  *TERROR IN THE MODERN VEIN   WOLLHEIM, DONALD A.   AN
  TWO DOZEN DRAGON EGGS   WOLLHEIM, DONALD A.   AC
MIMSY WERE THE BOROGOVES   KUTTNER, HENRY   NV   ASF 43 02
  BEST OF HENRY KUTTNER 2, THE   KUTTNER, HENRY   AC
  BEST OF HENRY KUTTNER, THE   KUTTNER, HENRY   AC
  LITTLE MONSTERS, THE   ELWOOD & GHIDALIA   AN
MIMSY WERE THE BOROGOVES   PADGETT, LEWIS   NV   ASF 43 02
  GNOME THERE WAS, A   PADGETT, LEWIS   AC
  SCIENCE FICTION HALL OF FAME VOLUME 1 SILVERBERG, ROBERT   AN
  *TREASURY OF SCIENCE FICTION, A   CONKLIN, GROFF   AN
  UBERWINDUNG VON RAUM UND ZEIT   GUNTHER, GOTTHARD   AN

MIND ALONE   MCINTOSH, J. T.   NA   GAL 53 08
  5 GALAXY SHORT NOVELS   GOLD, H. L.   AN
MIND ANGEL, THE   ORGILL, MICHAEL   SS
  MIND ANGEL AND OTHER STORIES, THE   ELWOOD, ROGER   OA
MIND BOMB, THE (ALSO AS THE BEING MACHINE)
                               HERBERT, FRANK   NV   IFS 69 10
  BEST FROM IF, THE   VOLUME I   IF, EDITORS OF   AN
MIND FOR BUSINESS   SILVERBERG, ROBERT SS   ASF 56 09
  TO WORLDS BEYOND   SILVERBERG, ROBERT   AC
MIND MASTERS OF MARS, THE   CLAUDY, CARL H.   NV   AMB 31 09
  YEAR AFTER TOMORROW, THE   DEL REY, L/MATSCHAT/ AN
MIND OF GOD, THE   FAST, HOWARD   SS
  TOUCH OF INFINITY, A   FAST, HOWARD   OC
MIND OF TOMORROW (ALSO AS CONDITIONED REFLEX)
                               DEL REY, LESTER   SS   FUT 51 05
  THINGS   HOWARD, IVAN   AN
MIND OUT OF TIME, THE   LAUMER, KEITH   SS   FRS 68
  FARTHEST REACHES, THE   ELDER, JOSEPH   OA
  ONCE THERE WAS A GIANT   LAUMER, KEITH   AC
  TIMETRACKS   LAUMER, KEITH   AC
MIND PARTNER   ANVIL, CHRISTOPHER NV   GAL 60 08
  MIND PARTNER AND 8 OTHER NOVELETS FROM GALAXY
                               GOLD, H. L.   AN
MIND PRISON, THE   CONEY, MICHAEL G.   SS   NWR 71 19
  MONITOR FOUND IN ORBIT   CONEY, MICHAEL G.   AC
  NEW WRITINGS IN SF. 19   CARNELL, JOHN   OA
MIND SPIDER, THE   LEIBER, FRITZ   SS   FAN 59 11
 *MIND SPIDER AND OTHER STORIES, THE   LEIBER, FRITZ   DC
MIND-SIFTER   MAIEWSKI, SHIRLEY S. NA
  STAR TREK: THE NEW VOYAGES   MARSHAK, S&CULBREATH OA
MINDSHIP   CONWAY, GERARD F.   SS   UNI 71 01
  UNIVERSE 1   CARR, TERRY   OA
MINDSHIP   INOUYE, JON   SS
  NIGHT TIDE, A   INOUYE, JON   OC
MINDSPOT   INOUYE, JON   SS
  NIGHT TIDE, A   INOUYE, JON   OC
MINDWORM, THE   KORNBLUTH, C. M.   SS   WBY 50 12
  BEST OF C. M. KORNBLUTH, THE   KORNBLUTH, C. M.   AC
  BEST SCIENCE FICTION STORIES OF C. M. KORNBLUTH
                               KORNBLUTH, C. M.   AC
  BEST SCIENCE-FICTION STORIES: 1951, THE BLEILER & DIKTY AN
  EXPLORERS, THE   KORNBLUTH, C. M.   AC
  MIND TO MIND   SILVERBERG, ROBERT   AN
  MINDWORM AND OTHER STORIES, THE   KORNBLUTH, C. M.   AC
  MINDWORM, THE   ANONYMOUS   AN
  ONE HUNDRED YEARS OF SCIENCE FICTION KNIGHT, DAMON   AN
MINE EYES HAVE SEEN THE GLORY (REDEMPTION)
                               YOUNG, ROBERT F.   NV   AMZ 63 07
  GLASS OF STARS, A   YOUNG, ROBERT F.   AC
MINE OWN WAYS   MCKENNA, RICHARD M. SS   FSF 60 02
  BEST FROM FANTASY AND SCIENCE FICTION: 10
                               MILLS, ROBERT P.   AN
  CASEY AGONISTES, AND OTHER S.F. & FANTASY STORIES
                               MCKENNA, RICHARD M.   AC
  6TH ANNUAL OF THE YEAR'S BEST S-F, THE   MERRIL, JUDITH   AN
MINEFIELD, THE   FAIRMAN, PAUL W.   SS
  FORGETFUL ROBOT, THE   FAIRMAN, PAUL W.   OC
MING VASE, THE   TUBB, E. C.   SS   ASF 63 05
  TEN FROM TOMORROW   TUBB, E. C.   AC
  9TH ANNUAL OF THE YEAR'S BEST S-F, THE   MERRIL, JUDITH   AN
MINIATURE, THE   MACDONALD, JOHN D. SS   SSS 49 09
 *BIG BOOK OF SCIENCE FICTION CONKLIN, GROFF   AN
MINIMUM MAN, THE   SHECKLEY, ROBERT   NV   GAL 58 06
  FOURTH GALAXY READER, THE   GOLD, H. L.   AN
  STORE OF INFINITY   SHECKLEY, ROBERT   AC
MINIMUM SENTENCE   COGSWELL, THEODORE R SS GAL 53 08
  GALAXY SCIENCE FICTION OMNIBUS   GOLD, H. L.   AN
  SECOND GALAXY READER OF SCIENCE FICTION GOLD, H. L. AN
  THIRD EYE, THE   COGSWELL, THEODORE R   AC
MINIONS OF MIDAS, THE   LONDON, JACK   SS   PRS 01 05
  SCIENCE FICTION OF JACK LONDON, THE   LONDON, JACK   AC
MINISTER WITHOUT PORTFOLIO   CLINGERMAN, MILDRED SS   FSF 52 02
  CUPFUL OF SPACE, A   CLINGERMAN, MILDRED   AC
  ENCOUNTERS WITH ALIENS   EARLEY, GEORGE W.   AN
 *INVADERS OF EARTH   CONKLIN, GROFF   AN
 *STORIES FOR TOMORROW   SLOANE, WILLIAM   AN
MINISTERING ANGELS (SRV MAY 28, 1955)
                               LEWIS, C. S.   SS   FSF 58 01
  BEST FROM FANTASY AND SCIENCE FICTION: 8
                               BOUCHER, ANTHONY   AN
  DARK TOWER AND OTHER STORIES, THE   LEWIS, C. S.   AC
MINISTRY OF CHILDREN, THE   ROBERTS, KEITH   NV   NWB 75 09
  NEW WORLDS NINE   BAILEY, HILARY   OA
MINISTRY OF DISTURBANCE   PIPER, H. BEAM   NV   ASF 58 12
  SEVEN TRIPS THROUGH TIME AND SPACE CONKLIN, GROFF   AN
MINIVER PROBLEM, THE   STRUTHER, JAN   AR   40
  MATHEMATICAL MAGPIE, THE   FADIMAN, CLIFTON   AN
MINIVER PROBLEM, THE (SOLUTION)
                               GRAHAM, L. A.   AR   59
  MATHEMATICAL MAGPIE, THE   FADIMAN, CLIFTON   AN
MINNA IN THE NIGHT SKY   KIMBERLY, GAIL   SS
  FAR SIDE OF TIME, THE   ELWOOD, ROGER   OA
MINOR INGREDIENT   RUSSELL, ERIC FRANK SS   ASF 56 03
  PROLOGUE TO ANALOG   CAMPBELL, JOHN W. JR   AN
MINORITY REPORT   STURGEON, THEODORE SS   ASF 49 06
 *BEYOND TIME AND SPACE   DERLETH, AUGUST   AN
  THUNDER AND ROSES   STURGEON, THEODORE   AC
 *WAY HOME, A   STURGEON, THEODORE   AC
MINORITY REPORT, THE   DICK, PHILIP K.   SS   FUN 56 01
  VARIABLE MAN, THE   DICK, PHILIP K.   AC
MINOTAUR, THE   GOR, GENNADY   SS
  RUSSIAN SCIENCE FICTION, 1969   MAGIDOFF, ROBERT   AN
MINUKE   KNEALE, NIGEL   SS   HRP 50 09
  SUPERNATURAL READER, THE   CONKLIN, G&L.   AN
MINUS ONE   BALLARD, J. G.   SS   SCF 63 06
  DISASTER AREA, THE   BALLARD, J. G.   AC

  TERMINAL BEACH (AMERICAN VERSION)   BALLARD, J. G.   AC
MINUS PLANET   CLARK, JOHN D.   NV   ASF 37 04
  BEFORE THE GOLDEN AGE   ASIMOV, ISAAC   AN
MINUS SIGN   STEWART, WILL   SN   ASF 42 11
  SEETEE SHIP   STEWART, WILL   AC
MIRACLE OF RARE DEVICE, A   BRADBURY, RAY   SS   PBY 62 01
  FANTASY: THE LITERATURE OF THE MARVELOUS KELLEY, LEO P.   AN
  FULLY AUTOMATED LOVE LIFE OF HENRY KEANRIDGE
                               PLAYBOY, EDITORS OF AN
  MACHINERIES OF JOY, THE   BRADBURY, RAY   AC
  WORLDS OF SCIENCE FICTION, THE   MILLS, ROBERT P.   AN
  8TH ANNUAL OF THE YEAR'S BEST S-F, THE   MERRIL, JUDITH   AN
MIRACLE OF SMALL FISHES, A   FOSTER, ALAN DEAN   NV   STL 74 01
  STELLAR 1   DEL REY, JUDY-LYNN   OA
MIRACLE OF THE BROOM CLOSET, THE
                               NORBERT, W.   SS   TEN 52 04
  EXPERT DREAMERS, THE   POHL, FREDERIK   AN
MIRACLE OF THE FLOWERS, THE   BUNCH, DAVID R.   SS
  MODERAN   BUNCH, DAVID R.   AC
MIRACLE OF THE LILY, THE   HARRIS, CLARE WINGER SS AMZ 28 04
  AWAY FROM THE HERE AND NOW   HARRIS, CLARE WINGER   AC
MIRACLE TOO MANY, A   NOURSE, ALAN E.
                               AND SMITH, PHILIP H. SS C FSF 64 09
  10TH ANNUAL OF THE YEAR'S BEST S-F, THE MERRIL, JUDITH   AN
MIRACLE-WORKERS, THE   VANCE, JACK   SN   ASF 58 07
  EIGHT FANTASMS AND MAGICS   VANCE, JACK   AC
MIRACLE, THE   BOULLE, PIERRE   SS
  TIME OUT OF MIND   BOULLE, PIERRE   OC
MIRACLES OF JAMIE, THE   BRADBURY, RAY   SS   CHM 46 04
  LONG AFTER MIDNIGHT   BRADBURY, RAY   AC
MIRAGE   SIMAK, CLIFFORD D. NV
 *STRANGERS IN THE UNIVERSE   SIMAK, CLIFFORD D.   AC
MIRI (ADRIAN SPIES)   BLISH, JAMES   SA   STK 67 01
  STAR TREK   BLISH, JAMES   OC
MIRIAM   CAPOTE, TRUMAN   SS   45
  CHILDREN OF WONDER   TENN, WILLIAM   AN
MIRROR AT SUNSET, THE   LAMONT, GIL   SS   NDM 75 05
  NEW DIMENSIONS 5   SILVERBERG, ROBERT   OA
MIRROR IMAGE   ASIMOV, ISAAC   SS   ASF 72 05
  BEST OF ISAAC ASIMOV, THE   ASIMOV, ISAAC   AC
MIRROR IMAGE (SEE TIME TO CHANGE)
                               ACKERMAN, FORREST J.
                               AND SOUTO, MARCIAL TC C
MIRROR IMAGE, THE   SERLING, ROD   SA
  ROD SERLING'S TWILIGHT ZONE REVISITED SERLING, ROD   OC
MIRROR OF ICE   WRIGHT, GARY   SS   GAL 67 06
  ARENA: SPORTS SF   FERMAN & MALZBERG   AN
  BEST SF: 1967   HARRISON & ALDISS   AN
  NEBULA AWARD STORIES NO. 3 ZELAZNY, ROGER   AN
  WORLDS OF WONDER   HARRISON, HARRY   AN
MIRROR, MIRROR (JEROME BIXBY) BLISH, JAMES   SA   STK 69 03
  STAR TREK 3   BLISH, JAMES   OC
MIRROR, MIRROR (THE MIRROR)   NOURSE, ALAN E.   NV   FAN 60 06
  PSI-HIGH AND OTHERS   NOURSE, ALAN E.   AC
MIRROR, THE   DOLAN, MIKE   SS
  SANTANA MORNING AND OTHER STORIES DOLAN, MIKE   OC
MIRRORS OF TUZUN THUNE, THE   HOWARD, ROBERT E.   SS   WRT 29 09
  COMING OF CONAN, THE   HOWARD, ROBERT E.   AC
MISADVENTURE   DUNSANY, LORD   SS   FSF 54 10
  BEST FROM FANTASY AND SCIENCE FICTION: 4
                               BOUCHER, ANTHONY   AN
MISBEGOTTEN MISSIONARY (ALSO AS GREEN PATCHES)
                               ASIMOV, ISAAC   SS   GAL 50 11
  FIRST STEP OUTWARD   HOSKINS, ROBERT   AN
  GIANTS UNLEASHED   CONKLIN, GROFF   AN
  SCIENCE FACT/FICTION   FARRELL/GAGE/&   AN
  SPECULATIONS   SANDERS, THOMAS E.   AN
  TOMORROW, THE STARS   HEINLEIN, ROBERT A.   AN
MISCOUNT   GLOECKNER, CAROLYN SS   ASF 72 11
  BEST SCIENCE FICTION STORIES OF THE YEAR (1972)
                               DEL REY, LESTER   AN
MISFIT   FISCHER, MICHAEL   SS   SPP 53 12
  COMING OF THE ROBOTS, THE   MOSKOWITZ, SAM   AN
MISFIT   HEINLEIN, ROBERT A. SS   ASF 39 11
  GIANTS UNLEASHED   CONKLIN, GROFF   AN
  PAST THROUGH TOMORROW, THE   HEINLEIN, ROBERT A.   AC
  REVOLT IN 2100   HEINLEIN, ROBERT A.   AC
MISFIT   SILVERBERG, ROBERT SS   SUP 57 12
  TO WORLDS BEYOND   SILVERBERG, ROBERT   AC
MISFIT, THE   AMMONS, A. R.   PM   65
  SPECULATIONS   SANDERS, THOMAS E.   AN
MISFIT, THE   EDMONDSON, G. C.   SS   FSF 59 02
  STRANGER THAN YOU THINK   EDMONDSON, G. C.   DC
MISFIT, THE   ZELAZNY, ROGER   NV   AMZ 63 10
  BEST FROM AMAZING, THE   WHITE, TED   AN
MISGUIDED HALO, THE   KUTTNER, HENRY   SS   UNK 39 08
  BEST OF HENRY KUTTNER, THE   KUTTNER, HENRY   AC
  UNKNOWN, THE   BENSEN, D. R.   AN
MISINFORMATION   MYERS, HOWARD L.   SS   ASF 72 04
  SOCIOLOGY THROUGH SCIENCE FICTION MILSTEAD/GREENBERG/& AN
MISOGYNIST, THE   GUNN, JAMES E.   SS   GAL 52 11
  FUTURE IMPERFECT   GUNN, JAMES E.   AN
  GALAXY SCIENCE FICTION OMNIBUS   GOLD, H. L.   AN
  SECOND GALAXY READER OF SCIENCE FICTION GOLD, H. L. AN
  SF: AUTHORS' CHOICE 4   HARRISON, HARRY   AN
  SHADOW OF TOMORROW   POHL, FREDERIK   AN
MISS BUTTERMOUTH   DAVIDSON, AVRAM   SS   FSF 62 05
  WHAT STRANGE STARS AND SKIES   DAVIDSON, AVRAM   AC
MISS ESPERSON   DERLETH, AUGUST   SS   62
  MR. GEORGE AND OTHER ODD PERSONS   DERLETH, AUGUST   AC
MISS GENTILBELLE   BEAUMONT, CHARLES   SS   NEW 57 AC
  HUNGER AND OTHER STORIES, THE   BEAUMONT, CHARLES   AC
  MAGIC MAN AND OTHER SCIENCE-FANTASY STORIES
                               BEAUMONT, CHARLES   AC
MISS INMAN AND THE KLOOTS   WILLIAMS-ELLIS, A. NV   NEW 73 AN
  TALES FROM THE GALAXIES   WILLIAMS-ELLIS& P.   AN

ISS OMEGA RAVEN   MONSTER, THE

ISS OMEGA RAVEN   MITCHISON, NAOMI   SS   NOV 72 02
  BEST SCIENCE FICTION OF THE YEAR, THE NO. 2
                       CARR, TERRY   AN
  NOVA 2   HARRISON, HARRY   OA
ISS PRINKS   DICKSON, GORDON R. SS   FSF 54 06
  MUTANTS   DICKSON, GORDON R.   AC
ISS STARDUST   MATHESON, RICHARD   SS   STS 55 SP
  SHOCK III   MATHESON, RICHARD   AC
ISS SUBWAYS   CRAVENS, GWYNETH   SS   NWQ 74 06
  NEW WORLDS NO. 6   PLATT & BAILEY   OA
ISS TEMPTATION   VONNEGUT, KURT JR. SS   SEP 56 04
  WELCOME TO THE MONKEY HOUSE
                       VONNEGUT, KURT JR.   AC
ISS WINCHELSEA'S HEART WELLS, H. G.   SS   QUN 98 10
  COUNTRY OF THE BLIND, THE
                       WELLS, H. G.   AC
  SHORT STORIES OF H. G. WELLS, THE
                       WELLS, H. G.   AC
  TWELVE STORIES AND A DREAM
                       WELLS, H. G.   AC
ISS WINTERS AND THE WIND GOVAN, CHRISTINE N. SS TOM 46 05
  TIMELESS STORIES FOR TODAY AND TOMORROW BRADBURY, RAY AN
MISSING LINK   HERBERT, FRANK   SS   ASF 59 02
  SF: AUTHORS' CHOICE HARRISON, HARRY   AN
MISSING MAN, THE   MACLEAN, KATHERINE NV   ASF 71 03
  ANALOG 9   BOVA, BEN   AN
  MISSING MAN, THE   MACLEAN, KATHERINE   NO
  NEBULA AWARD STORIES NO. 7
                       BIGGLE, LLOYD JR.   AN
ISSING ONE'S COACH: AN ANACHRONISM
                       ANONYMOUS   SS   DLM 38
  FAR BOUNDARIES   DERLETH, AUGUST   AN
ISSING SYMBOL, THE   FAIRMAN, PAUL W.   SS   FAN 52 12
  FIRST FLIGHTS TO THE MOON CLEMENT, HAL   AN
ISSING WORLD, THE   BINDER, EANDO   SS
  MISSING WORLD AND OTHER STORIES, THE ELWOOD, ROGER OA
ISSION "RED CLASH"   POYER, JOE   SS   ASF 65 10
  ANALOG 5   CAMPBELL, JOHN W. JR AN
ISSION: MANSTOP (MISSION) NEVILLE, KRIS   NV   FSF 53 04
  MISSION: MANSTOP   NEVILLE, KRIS   AC
MISSION, THE   NISSENSON, HUGH   SS   PBY 64 12
  FIEND, THE   PLAYBOY, EDITORS OF   AN
  PLAYBOY BOOK OF SCIENCE FICTION AND FANTASY, THE
                       PLAYBOY, EDITORS OF   AN
ISSION, THE   SELLINGS, ARTHUR   SS
  AD 2500   WILSON, ANGUS   AN
ISSIONARY   THOMAS, D. M.   PM   PMP 68 11
  HOLDING YOUR EIGHT HANDS LUCIE-SMITH, EDWARD   AN
IST, THE   CARTUR, PETER   SS   FSF 52 09
  ADVENTURES IN DIMENSION CONKLIN, GROFF   AN
  FIFTY SHORT SCIENCE FICTION TALES ASIMOV & CONKLIN AN
  *SCIENCE FICTION ADVENTURES IN DIMENSION CONKLIN, GROFF AN
ISTAKE   NIVEN, LARRY   SS   STL 76 02
  STELLAR 2   DEL REY, JUDY-LYNN   OA
ISTAKE INSIDE   BLISH, JAMES   NV   STS 48 03
  DARK SIDE, THE   KNIGHT, DAMON   AN
  WORLD OF WONDER   PRATT, FLETCHER   AN
ISTAKEN IDENTITY   TUBB, E. C.   SS   SPC 73 01
  SPACE   DAVIS, RICHARD   OA
ISTRESS OF PORCOSITO (SEE THE QUEEN OF PIG ISLAND)
                       KERSH, GERALD   TC
ISTRESS OF THE MIND   HARDING, LEE   NV   NWR 71 18
  NEW WRITINGS IN SF. 18 CARNELL, JOHN   OA
ISTRESS SARY   TENN, WILLIAM   SS   WRT 47 05
  SEVEN SEXES, THE   TENN, WILLIAM   AC
ITR, THE   VANCE, JACK   SS   53
  SPACE OPERA   ALDISS, BRIAN W.   AN
IX-UP   COLLYN, GEORGE   SS   NWS 64 12
  BEST SF STORIES FROM NEW WORLDS 7 MOORCOCK, MICHAEL AN
IXED MEN, THE   VAN VOGT, A. E.   NV   ASF 45 01
  MIXED MEN, THE   VAN VOGT, A. E.   NO
NARRA MOBILIS   VAN SCYOC, SYDNEY J. NV IFS 73 06
  BEST FROM IF, THE   VOLUME II IF, EDITORS OF   AN
NNEMONE, THE   SHECKLEY, ROBERT   SS   NEW 71 AC
  CAN YOU FEEL ANYTHING WHEN I DO THIS?, AND OTHER STORIES
                       SHECKLEY, ROBERT   AC
OBILE (ALSO AS VENUS SMILES) BALLARD, J. G. SS SCF 57 06
  BILLENIUM   BALLARD, J. G.   AC
OBY, TOO   EKLUND, GORDON   SS   AMZ 73 12
  1974 ANNUAL WORLD'S BEST SF, THE WOLLHEIM, DONALD A. AN
ODEL OF A JUDGE, THE   MORRISON, WILLIAM   SS   GAL 53 10
  BEST SCIENCE-FICTION STORIES: 1954, THE BLEILER & DIKTY AN
  THIRD GALAXY READER, THE GOLD, H. L.   AN
ODEL SHOP, THE   JONES, RAYMOND F.   SS   ASF 47 06
  TOYMAKER, THE   JONES, RAYMOND F.   AC
ODEL WIFE, THE   BLOCH, ROBERT   SS   SWK 61 11
  BOGEY MEN   BLOCH, ROBERT   AC
ODEL, THE   BLOCH, ROBERT   SS   GLR 75 11
  COLD CHILLS   BLOCH, ROBERT   AC
ODERN HIAWATHA, THE   ANONYMOUS   PM
  MATHEMATICAL MAGPIE, THE FADIMAN, CLIFTON   AN
ODERN PENITENTIARY, THE HOWARD, HAYDEN   NV   GAL 66 12
  ESKIMO INVASION   HOWARD, HAYDEN   NO
ODERN VIEW OF SCIENCE FICTION, A
                       SHIPPEY, TOM   AR
  BEYOND THIS HORIZON CARRELL, CHRISTOPHER   OA
ODEST GENIUS, A   SHEFNER, VADIM   SS
  RUSSIAN SCIENCE FICTION, 1969 MAGIDOFF, ROBERT   AN
  VIEW FROM ANOTHER SHORE ROTTENSTEINER, FRANZ   AN
  1974 ANNUAL WORLD'S BEST SF, THE WOLLHEIM, DONALD A. AN
ODEST PROPOSAL, A   BATES, RUSSELL L.   SS   CLR 72 02
  CLARION II   WILSON, ROBIN SCOTT   OA
ODEST PROPOSAL, A   MARTENSSON, BERTIL SS   NWQ 74 06
  NEW WORLDS NO. 6   PLATT & BAILEY   OA
ODULAR STORY, A   MOORE, RAYLYN   SS   ORB 76 18
  ORBIT 18   KNIGHT, DAMON   OA
ODUS VIVENDI   BUPP, WALTER   NV   ASF 61 09
  EARTH IN TRANSIT   SCHWARTZ, SHEILA   AN
  14 GREAT TALES OF ESP STONE, IDELLA P.   AN
OHAWK, THE   FAST, HOWARD   SS
  GENERAL ZAPPED AN ANGEL, THE FAST, HOWARD   OC

MOLD OF YANCY, THE   DICK, PHILIP K.   NV   IFS 55 08
  SECOND WORLD OF IF, THE QUINN & WULFF   AN
MOLE PIRATE, THE   LEINSTER, MURRAY   SN   ASF 34 11
  THREE STORIES   MOSKOWITZ, SAM   AN
MOLECULE MONSTERS, THE FRIEND, OSCAR J.   SS
  MOLECULE MONSTERS, THE ANONYMOUS   AN
MOLTEN CORE   STERN, DONNEL   SS   CLR 73 03
  CLARION III   WILSON, ROBIN SCOTT   OA
MOM'S DIFFERENTIALS   EFFINGER, GEO. ALEC SS
  NEW VOICES IN SCIENCE FICTION MARTIN, GEORGE R. R. OA
MOMENT OF ECLIPSE, THE ALDISS, BRIAN W.   SS   NWS 69 05
  BEST SCIENCE FICTION STORIES OF BRIAN W. ALDISS (REVISED)
                       ALDISS, BRIAN W.   AC
  MOMENT OF ECLIPSE, THE ALDISS, BRIAN W.   AC
MOMENT WITHOUT TIME   ROGERS, JOEL T.   NV   TWS 52 04
  BEST FROM STARTLING STORIES, THE MINES, SAMUEL   AN
MOMENTARY TASTE OF BEING, A TIPTREE, JAMES JR. NA NAL 75
  NEW ATLANTIS AND OTHER NOVELLAS OF S.F., THE
                       SILVERBERG, ROBERT   OA
MOMENTO HOMO (DEATH OF A SPACEMAN)
                       MILLER, WALTER M. JR SS AMZ 54 03
  BEST SCIENCE FICTION STORIES AND NOVELS: 1955
                       DIKTY, T. E.   AN
  MASTERS' CHOICE   JANIFER, LAURENCE M.   AN
  WORLDS OF SCIENCE FICTION, THE MILLS, ROBERT P.   AN
MOMMIES AND DADDIES   BRACKETT, LEIGH   SS
  CRISIS   ELWOOD, ROGER   OA
MOMMY LOVES YA   CHARNEY, DAVID H.   SS   TAL 73
  FRONTIERS 1; TOMORROW'S ALTERNATIVES ELWOOD, ROGER OA
MONA AT HER WINDOWS   ELLISON, HARLAN   SS   ROG 62 06
  *LOVE AIN'T NOTHING BUT SEX MISSPELLED ELLISON, HARLAN AC
MONADIC UNIVERSE, THE ZEBROWSKI, GEORGE   NV   INY 72 03
  MONADIC UNIVERSE, THE ZEBROWSKI, GEORGE   AC
  MONADIC UNIVERSE, THE HULL, GERALD
                       AND ZEBROWSKI, GEORGE NV C INY 72 03
  INFINITY 3   HOSKINS, ROBERT   OA
MONARCH OF DREAMS, THE (1886) HIGGINSON, THOMAS W. SS 86
  FUTURE PERFECT   FRANKLIN, H. BRUCE   AN
MONITOR   BOUNDS, SYDNEY J.   SS   NWR 73 22
  NEW WRITINGS IN SF. 22 BULMER, KENNETH   OA
MONITOR FOUND IN ORBIT CONEY, MICHAEL G. SS   NWQ 71 02
  MONITOR FOUND IN ORBIT CONEY, MICHAEL G.   AC
  NEW WORLDS QUARTERLY NO. 2 MOORCOCK, MICHAEL   OA
MONKEY AND PRU AND SAL ROBERTS, KEITH   SS   NWQ 71 02
  NEW WORLDS QUARTERLY NO. 2 MOORCOCK, MICHAEL   OA
MONKEY WRENCH, THE   DICKSON, GORDON R. SS   ASF 51 08
  ANCIENT, MY ENEMY   DICKSON, GORDON R.   AC
  METAL SMILE, THE   KNIGHT, DAMON   AN
  MORE PENGUIN SCIENCE FICTION ALDISS, BRIAN W.   AN
MONKEY'S FINGER, THE   ASIMOV, ISAAC   SS   STS 53 02
  BUY JUPITER AND OTHER STORIES ASIMOV, ISAAC   AC
  HAVE YOU SEEN THESE? ASIMOV, ISAAC   AC
MONOLOGUE   FARMER, PHILIP JOSE SS   DEM 73
  DEMON KIND   ELWOOD, ROGER   OA
MONSIGNOR PRIMO MACINNO MALEC, ALEXANDER B. SS
  EXTRAPOLASIS   MALEC, ALEXANDER B.   AC
MONSTER   CHRISTOPHER, JOHN   SS   SCF 50 SU
  TWENTY-SECOND CENTURY, THE CHRISTOPHER, JOHN   AC
MONSTER AND THE MAIDEN, THE ZELAZNY, ROGER SS GAL 64 12
  DOORS OF HIS FACE, THE LAMPS OF HIS MOUTH, THE
                       ZELAZNY, ROGER   AC
  NINTH GALAXY READER, THE POHL, FREDERIK   AN
  WONDERMAKERS 2   HOSKINS, ROBERT   AN
MONSTER FROM NOWHERE, THE BOND, NELSON S. SS FAD 39 07
  AS TOMORROW BECOMES TODAY SULLIVAN, CHARLES W.   AN
  *BEST OF SCIENCE FICTION CONKLIN, GROFF   AN
  31ST OF FEBRUARY, THE BOND, NELSON S.   AC
MONSTER FROM NOWHERE, THE WANDREI, DONALD SS ARG 35 11
  EYE AND THE FINGER   WANDREI, DONALD   AC
MONSTER IN ART, THE   LUCIE-SMITH, EDWARD IN
  BEYOND THIS HORIZON CARRELL, CHRISTOPHER   OA
MONSTER IN THE CLEARING, THE FAYETTE, MICHAEL SS INY 71 02
  INFINITY 2   HOSKINS, ROBERT   OA
MONSTER MAKER, THE   MORROW, W. C.   NV
  BATTLE OF THE MONSTERS AND OTHER STORIES, THE
                       HARTWELL & CURREY   AN
MONSTER MAN, SIRE OF SLAN, THE ACKERMAN, FORREST J. IN
  MONSTERS   VAN VOGT, A. E.   AC
MONSTER NAMED SMITH, A GUNN, JAMES E.   NV   IFS 54 07
  BREAKING POINT   GUNN, JAMES E.   AC
  SECOND WORLD OF IF, THE QUINN & WULFF   AN
MONSTER OF LAKE LAMETRIE, THE CURTIS, WARDON ALLEN SS PRS 99 09
  SCIENCE FICTION BY GASLIGHT MOSKOWITZ, SAM   AN
MONSTER OF TERROR (THE COLOUR OUT OF SPACE)
                       LOVECRAFT, H. P.   SS   AMZ 27 09
  GHOULS, THE   HAINING, PETER   AN
MONSTER OF THE PROPHECY, THE SMITH, CLARK ASHTON NV WRT 32 01
  OUT OF SPACE AND TIME SMITH, CLARK ASHTON   AC
MONSTER SHOW, THE   BEAUMONT, CHARLES   SS   PBY 56 05
  LAST TRAIN TO LIMBO PLAYBOY, EDITORS OF   AN
  MAGIC MAN AND OTHER SCIENCE-FANTASY STORIES
                       BEAUMONT, CHARLES   AC
  YONDER   BEAUMONT, CHARLES   AC
MONSTER-GOD OF MAMURTH, THE HAMILTON, EDMOND SS WRT 26 08
  BEST OF EDMOND HAMILTON, THE HAMILTON, EDMOND   AC
  HORROR ON THE ASTEROID AND OTHER TALES OF PLANETARY HORROR
                       HAMILTON, EDMOND   AC
MONSTER, THE   DEFORD, MIRIAM ALLEN SS FSF 60 03
  ELSEWHERE, ELSEWHEN, ELSEHOW DEFORD, MIRIAM ALLEN AC
MONSTER, THE   DEL REY, LESTER   SS   ARG 51 06
  ROBOTS AND CHANGELINGS DEL REY, LESTER   AC
  SCIENCE FICTION ROLL OF HONOR, THE POHL, FREDERIK AN
  TOMORROW, THE STARS HEINLEIN, ROBERT A.   AN
MONSTER, THE   KLEIN, GERARD   SS   58
  13 FRENCH SCIENCE-FICTION STORIES KNIGHT, DAMON   AN

MONSTER, THE (ALSO AS RESURRECTION)   MOTH, THE (A MOTH- GENUS NOVO)

MONSTER, THE (ALSO AS RESURRECTION)   MOON, THE   PARKES, LUCAS   SS
                          VAN VOGT, A. E.   SS   ASF 48 08   OUT OF THIS WORLD 7   WILLIAMS-ELLIS& OWEN A
  BEST OF A. E. VAN VOGT, THE (BRITISH) VAN VOGT, A. E.   AC MOONCHILD   PURDOM, TOM   NV   FUQ 73
  DESTINATION: UNIVERSE| VAN VOGT, A. E.   AC   FUTURE QUEST   ELWOOD, ROGER   O
MONSTER, THE (ALSO AS THE BRIGHTON MONSTER)   MOONCUP, THE   MURPHY, SHIRLEY R.   NV
                          KERSH, GERALD   SS   SEP 48 02   ANYWHERE, ANYWHEN   ENGDAHL, SYLVIA   O
  *OTHER SIDE OF THE MOON, THE   DERLETH, AUGUST   AN   MOONDOG (SEE DOG STAR)   CLARKE, ARTHUR C.   TC
MONSTERS   ANTROBUS, ROSIE   IL   MOONDUST, THE SMELL OF HAY, AND DIALECTICAL MATERIALISM
  BEYOND THIS HORIZON   CARRELL, CHRISTOPHER OA   DISCH, THOMAS M.   SS   FSF 67 0
MONSTERS   BAKER, JULES   IL   FIRST FLIGHTS TO THE MOON   CLEMENT, HAL   A
  BEYOND THIS HORIZON   CARRELL, CHRISTOPHER OA   FUN WITH YOUR NEW HEAD   DISCH, THOMAS M.   AC
MONSTERS AND MONSTER LOVERS LEIBER, FRITZ   AR   FAN 65 03 MOONLIGHT FABLE, THE (ALSO AS THE BEAUTIFUL SUIT)
  BOOK OF FRITZ LEIBER, THE   LEIBER, FRITZ   AC   WELLS, H. G.   SS   COL 09 0
MONSTERS ARE DUE ON MAPLE STREET, THE   DOOR IN THE WALL, THE   WELLS, H. G.   A
                          SERLING, ROD   SA   MOONLIT ROAD, THE   BIERCE, AMBROSE   SS   93
  FROM THE TWILIGHT ZONE   SERLING, ROD   AC   SUPERNATURAL READER, THE   CONKLIN, G&L.   A
  STORIES FROM THE TWILIGHT ZONE SERLING, ROD   OC   MOONRAKERS, THE   ANDERSON, POUL   NV   IFS 66 0
MONSTERS IN THE NIGHT (A PROPHECY OF MONSTERS)   BEYOND THE BEYOND   ANDERSON, POUL   A
                          SMITH, CLARK ASHTON SS   FSF 54 10 MOONSHOT SONNET   SOLT, MARY ELLEN   IL
  OTHER DIMENSIONS   SMITH, CLARK ASHTON AC   SCIENCE FICTION   BRODKIN & PEARSON   A
MONSTERS OF INGRATITUDE IV, THE   MOONWALK   FYFE, H. B.   NA   SSF 52 1
                          ALDISS, BRIAN W.   SS   NOV 74 04   MEN ON THE MOON   WOLLHEIM, DONALD A.   D
  NOVA 4   HARRISON, HARRY   OA   SPACE PIONEERS   NORTON, ANDRE   A
MONSTERS, THE   SHECKLEY, ROBERT   SS   FSF 53 03   WORLDS TO COME   KNIGHT, DAMON   A
  ANTHROPOLOGY THROUGH SCIENCE FICTION MASON, C/GREENBERG/& AN MOP-UP   PORGES, ARTHUR   SS   FSF 53 0
  BEST SF 5   CRISPIN, EDMUND   AN   GALAXY OF GHOULS   MERRIL, JUDITH   A
  STARLIT CORRIDOR, THE   MANSFIELD, ROGER   AN   MORALITY   SCORTIA, THOMAS N.   SS   FAN 69 1
  *UNTOUCHED BY HUMAN HANDS   SHECKLEY, ROBERT   AC   CAUTION| INFLAMMABLE| SCORTIA, THOMAS N.   A
MONTAGE   RUSSELL, RAY   SS   PBY 58 10 MORALITY   STURGEON, THEODORE   NV   NEW 53 N
  SARDONICUS AND OTHER STORIES   RUSSELL, RAY   AC   MORE THAN HUMAN   STURGEON, THEODORE   N
MONTAVARDE CAMERA, THE   DAVIDSON, AVRAM   SS   FSF 59 05 MORE FACTS ABOUT ROBOTS (SOME FACTS ABOUT ROBOTS II)
  OR ALL THE SEAS WITH OYSTERS   DAVIDSON, AVRAM   AC   WOLF, LEONARD   PM   FSF 54 0
MONTE CRISTO COMPLEX   GOULART, RON   SS   BEST FROM FANTASY AND SCIENCE FICTION: 4
  WHAT'S BECOME OF SCREWLOOSE? AND OTHER INQUIRIES   BOUCHER, ANTHONY   A
                          GOULART, RON   AC   MORE GOOD READING IN SCIENCE FICTION
MONTH A MINUTE, A   FARLEY, RALPH MILNE SS   TWS 37 12   MISC. MATERIAL   MS
  OMNIBUS OF TIME, THE   FARLEY, RALPH MILNE AC   BEYOND TOMORROW   KNIGHT, DAMON   A
MONUMENT   BIGGLE, LLOYD JR.   NV   ASF 61 06 MORE GOOD READING IN SCIENCE FICTION
  ANALOG 1   CAMPBELL, JOHN W. JR AN   KNIGHT, DAMON   MS
MOON ARTIST, THE   KELLER, DAVID H. MD. SS   STI 41 06   WORLDS TO COME   KNIGHT, DAMON   A
  TALES FROM UNDERWOOD   KELLER, DAVID H. MD. AC   MORE I CANNOT WISH YOU   SULLIVAN, JEAN   SS   CLR 73 03
MOON CONQUERORS, THE   ROMANS, R. H.   NO   SFQ 40 SU   CLARION III   WILSON, ROBIN SCOTT   O
  MOON CONQUERORS, THE   ANONYMOUS   AN   MORE LIGHT   BLISH, JAMES   SS   ANA 70
MOON CRAZY   SHELTON, WILLIAM ROY SS   SEP   ALCHEMY AND ACADEME   MCCAFFREY, ANNE   A
  POST READER OF FANTASY AND SCIENCE FICTION   MORE PENGUIN SCIENCE FICTION ALDISS, BRIAN W.   AN   PEN 63
                          SATURDAY EVE. POST   AN   PENGUIN SCIENCE FICTION OMNIBUS, THE ALDISS, BRIAN W. A
MOON DANCE   WEST, WALLACE   NV   SFQ 54 11 MORE SPINNED AGAINST   WYNDHAM, JOHN   SS   FNF 53 0
  OUTPOSTS IN SPACE   WEST, WALLACE   AC   JIZZLE   WYNDHAM, JOHN   A
MOON DOWN   CUMMINGS, M. A.   SS   TALES OF GOOSEFLESH AND LAUGHTER WYNDHAM, JOHN   A
  EXILE AND OTHER TALES OF FANTASY CUMMINGS, M. A. OC   MORE STATELY MANSIONS   VONNEGUT, KURT JR.   SS   COL 51 1
MOON DUEL   LEIBER, FRITZ   SS   IFS 65 09   CANARY IN A CAT HOUSE   VONNEGUT, KURT JR.   A
  11TH ANNUAL OF THE YEAR'S BEST S-F, THE MERRIL, JUDITH AN   WELCOME TO THE MONKEY HOUSE VONNEGUT, KURT JR.   A
MOON ERA, THE   WILLIAMSON, JACK   NV   WOS 32 02 MORE THAN HUMAN   STURGEON, THEODORE   NO   FSY 52
  BEFORE THE GOLDEN AGE   ASIMOV, ISAAC   AN   SCIENCE FICTION ARGOSY, A   KNIGHT, DAMON   A
  THREE STORIES   MOSKOWITZ, SAM   AN   MORE THAN SKIN DEEP   DE CAMP, L. SPRAGUE
MOON FEVER (MILLION-MILE HUNT) PETAJA, EMIL   SS   IFS 65 03   AND PRATT, FLETCHER SS C FSF 51 0
  STARDRIFT AND OTHER FANTASTIC FLOTSAM PETAJA, EMIL AC   TALES FROM GAVAGAN'S BAR   DE CAMP, L. S.&PRATT AC
MOON GOLD   HARMON, SETH   SS   58   MORE THINGS IN HEAVEN AND EARTH
  TEEN-AGE OUTER SPACE STORIES   FURMAN, A. L.   AN   HARGREAVES, H. A.   NV   NWR 70 1
MOON IS DEATH, THE   JONES, RAYMOND F.   SS   FUT 53 03   NEW WRITINGS IN SF. 17   CARNELL, JOHN   A
  NON-STATISTICAL MAN, THE   JONES, RAYMOND F. AC   MORE TRIBBLES, MORE TROUBLES (DAVID GERROLD)
MOON IS GREEN, THE   LEIBER, FRITZ   SS   GAL 52 05   FOSTER, ALAN DEAN   SA   SLG 75 0
  BEST SCIENCE-FICTION STORIES: 1953, THE BLEILER & DIKTY AN   STAR TREK LOG FOUR   FOSTER, ALAN DEAN   0
  FRONTIERS IN SPACE   BLEILER & DIKTY   AN   MORNING AFTER   SHECKLEY, ROBERT   NV   GAL 57 1
  SECRET SONGS, THE   LEIBER, FRITZ   AC   NOTIONS: UNLIMITED   SHECKLEY, ROBERT   AC
MOON LANDING   AUDEN, W. H.   PM   NYM 69   MORNING OF THE DAY THEY DID IT, THE
  SPECULATIONS   SANDERS, THOMAS E. AN   WHITE, E. B.   SS   NYM 50 0
MOON MADNESS   WEST, WALLACE   SS   WRT 31 08   ARMCHAIR SCIENCE READER, THE GORDON, I. & SORKIN A
  OUTPOSTS IN SPACE   WEST, WALLACE   AC   PAST, PRESENT, AND FUTURE PERFECT WOLFE, J&FITZ GERALD A
MOON MAID, THE   BURROUGHS, EDGAR R. NO   AAS 23 05 TREASURY OF GREAT SCIENCE FICTION, A VOL.2
  LAND THAT TIME FORGOT AND THE MOON MAID, THE   BOUCHER, ANTHONY   A
                          BURROUGHS, EDGAR R. AC   MORNING RUSH OR HAPPY BIRTHDAY, DEAR LEAH, THE
  MOON MAID, THE   BURROUGHS, EDGAR R. NO   SAYE, LEE   SS   TAL 73
MOON MEN, THE   BURROUGHS, EDGAR R. NV   AAS 25 02   FRONTIERS 1: TOMORROW'S ALTERNATIVES ELWOOD, ROGER O
  MOON MAID, THE   BURROUGHS, EDGAR R. NO   MORNING STAR   CARR, ROBERT S.   NV   SEP 47 12
MOON MOTH, THE   VANCE, JACK   NA   GAL 61 08   BEYOND INFINITY   CARR, ROBERT S.   AC
  ALPHA 1   SILVERBERG, ROBERT AN   MORNING-GLORY   WOLFE, GENE   SS   ANA 70
  BEST OF JACK VANCE, THE   VANCE, JACK   AC   ALCHEMY AND ACADEME   MCCAFFREY, ANNE   O
  SCIENCE FICTION HALL OF FAME VOLUME 2B BOVA, BEN   AN   MORTAL AND THE MONSTER, THE DICKSON, GORDON R.   NA
  WORLD BETWEEN AND OTHER STORIES, THE VANCE, JACK   DC   STELLAR SHORT NOVELS   DEL REY, JUDY-LYNN   AC
  WORLDS OF JACK VANCE, THE   VANCE, JACK   AC   MORTAL IMMORTAL, THE (1834) SHELLEY, MARY W.   SS   KPS 34
MOON MOUNTAIN   YEFREMOV, IVAN   SS   MASTERPIECES OF SCIENCE FICTION MOSKOWITZ, SAM   AN
  STORIES   YEFREMOV, IVAN   AC   TALES AND STORIES   SHELLEY, MARY W.   AC
MOON OF DELIGHT (SEE O MOON OF MY DELIGHT|)   MORTHYLLA   SMITH, CLARK ASHTON SS   WRT 53 05
                          ALDISS, BRIAN W.   TC   TALES OF SCIENCE AND SORCERY SMITH, CLARK ASHTON AC
MOON OF DELIRIUM   JAMES, DANIEL LEWIS SS   ASF 40 01 MOST BEAUTIFUL MUSIC, THE MACKENROTH, NANCY   SS
  *POSSIBLE WORLDS OF SCIENCE FICTION CONKLIN, GROFF   AN   LEARNING MAZE AND OTHER STORIES, THE ELWOOD, ROGER O
MOON POOL, THE   MERRITT, A.   NA   ASW 18 06 MOST BEAUTIFUL WOMAN IN THE WORLD, THE
  ANCIENT MYSTERIES READER, THE HAINING, PETER   AN   WILHELM, KATE   SS   NEW 68 AC
  UNDER THE MOONS OF MARS   MOSKOWITZ, SAM   AN   DOWNSTAIRS ROOM AND OTHER SPECULATIVE FICTION, THE
MOON PROSPECTOR   ELLERN, WILLIAM B.   NV   ASF 66 04   WILHELM, KATE   SS
  GREAT SCIENCE FICTION STORIES ABOUT THE MOON   MOST DANGEROUS GAME, THE CONNELL, RICHARD   NV   24
                          DIKTY, T. E.   AN   GHOULS, THE   HAINING, PETER   AN
MOON SHOT   HARVEY, FRANK   SS   SEP 58 05   NIGHT IN FUNLAND   BRONDFIELD, JEROME   AN
  AIR FORCE| HARVEY, FRANK   AC   MOST FORGETABLE STORY IN THE WORLD, THE
MOON TERROR, THE   BIRCH, A. G.   NA   WRT 23 05   LAFFERTY, R. A.   SS
  MOON TERROR, THE   BIRCH, A. G.   AN   LONG NIGHT OF WAITING AND OTHER STORIES ELWOOD, ROGER A
MOON THAT VANISHED, THE   BRACKETT, LEIGH   NV   TWS 48 10 MOST MADDENING STORY IN THE WORLD
  BEST OF LEIGH BRACKETT, THE   BRACKETT, LEIGH   AC   STRAUS, RALPH   SS   37
  SWORDSMEN IN THE SKY   WOLLHEIM, DONALD A. AN   MOONLIGHT TRAVELER, THE   STERN, PHILIP VAN D. AN
MOON-FISHERS   HENNEBERG, CHARLES   NV   59   MOST PRIMITIVE, THE   RUSSELL, RAY   SS   FUC 73
  13 FRENCH SCIENCE-FICTION STORIES KNIGHT, DAMON   AN   FUTURE CITY   ELWOOD, ROGER   O
MOON-VOYAGE, THE (FROM "SOMNIUM")   MOTH RACE   HILL, RICHARD   SS   DVS 72 0
                          KEPLER, JOHANNES   EX   AGAIN, DANGEROUS VISIONS   ELLISON, HARLAN   A
  SCIENCE FICTION THROUGH THE AGES 1 EVANS, I. O.   AN   MOTH, THE (A MOTH- GENUS NOVO) WELLS, H. G.   SS   PGZ 95 0
                                                              COUNTRY OF THE BLIND, THE   WELLS, H. G.   A

SHORT STORIES OF H. G. WELLS, THE   WELLS, H. G.   AC
STOLEN BACILLUS AND OTHER INCIDENTS, THE   WELLS, H. G.   AC
THIRTY STRANGE STORIES   WELLS, H. G.   AC
MOTHBALLED SPACESHIP, THE   HARRISON, HARRY   SS   AMA 73
   ASTOUNDING   HARRISON, HARRY   OA
   *BEST OF HARRY HARRISON, THE   HARRISON, HARRY   AC
MOTHER   FARMER, PHILIP JOSE   NV   TWS 53 04
   ALPHA 4   SILVERBERG, ROBERT   AN
   ASSIGNMENT IN TOMORROW   POHL, FREDERIK   AN
   BUG-EYED MONSTERS   CHEETHAM, ANTHONY   AN
   IN DREAMS AWAKE   FIEDLER, LESLIE A.   AN
   INTRODUCTORY PSYCHOLOGY THROUGH SCIENCE FICTION
                                            KATZ/WARRICK/&   AN
   MICROCOSMIC GOD   MOSKOWITZ, SAM   AN
   MODERN MASTERPIECES OF SCIENCE FICTION   MOSKOWITZ, SAM   AN
   STRANGE BED FELLOWS   SCORTIA, THOMAS N.   AN
   STRANGE RELATIONS   FARMER, PHILIP JOSE   AC
MOTHER AND CHILD   VINGE, JOAN D.   NA   ORB 75 16
   ORBIT 16   KNIGHT, DAMON   OA
MOTHER AND THE DECIMAL POINT   LLEWELLYN, RICHARD   SS   40
   FANTASIA MATHEMATICA   FADIMAN, CLIFTON   AN
MOTHER BY PROTEST (ALSO AS TRESPASS)
                                 MATHESON, RICHARD   NV   FAN 53 10
   DEVIL'S GENERATION, THE   GHIDALIA, VIC   AN
MOTHER EARTH   ASIMOV, ISAAC   NV   ASF 49 05
   EARLY ASIMOV, THE   ASIMOV, ISAAC   AC
   JOURNEY TO INFINITY   GREENBERG, MARTIN   AN
   3 FROM OUT THERE   MARGULIES, LEO   AN
MOTHER EARTH WANTS YOU   FARMER, PHILIP JOSE   SS   WLK 73
   AND WALK NOW GENTLY THROUGH THE FIRE... ELWOOD, ROGER   OA
MOTHER HITTON'S LITTUL KITTONS   SMITH, CORDWAINER   NV   GAL 61 06
   BEST OF CORDWAINER SMITH, THE   SMITH, CORDWAINER   AC
   BEYOND TOMORROW   HARDING, LEE   AN
   SPACE LORDS   SMITH, CORDWAINER   AC
MOTHER IN THE SKY WITH DIAMONDS
                                 TIPTREE, JAMES JR.   NV   GAL 71 03
   BEST SCIENCE FICTION FOR 1972   POHL, FREDERIK   AN
   TEN THOUSAND LIGHT-YEARS FROM HOME   TIPTREE, JAMES JR.   AC
MOTHER OF INVENTION   GODWIN, TOM   SN   ASF 53 12
   SPECTRUM 5   AMIS & CONQUEST   AN
MOTHER OF NECESSITY, THE   OLIVER, CHAD   SS   NEW 55 AC
   ABOVE THE HUMAN LANDSCAPE   MCNELLY & STOVER   AN
   ANOTHER KIND   OLIVER, CHAD   AC
   GREAT SCIENCE FICTION BY SCIENTISTS   CONKLIN, GROFF   AN
MOTHER OF SERPENTS   BLOCH, ROBERT   SS   WRT 36 12
   HOUSE OF THE HATCHET, THE   BLOCH, ROBERT   AC
   MORE NIGHTMARES   BLOCH, ROBERT   AC
   *OPENER OF THE WAY, THE   BLOCH, ROBERT   AC
MOTHER OF TOADS   SMITH, CLARK ASHTON   SS   WRT 38 07
   TALES OF SCIENCE AND SORCERY   SMITH, CLARK ASHTON   AC
   WORLDS OF WEIRD   MARGULIES, LEO   AN
MOTHER SHIP, THE (SEE MAMMA COME HOME)
                                 TIPTREE, JAMES JR.   TC
MOTHER SUPERIOR   MACBETH, GEORGE   PM   63
   HOLDING YOUR EIGHT HANDS   LUCIE-SMITH, EDWARD   AN
MOTHER TO THE WORLD   WILSON, RICHARD   NV   ORB 68 03
   BEST FROM ORBIT, THE   KNIGHT, DAMON   AN
   NEBULA AWARD STORIES   NO. 4   ANDERSON, POUL   AN
   ORBIT   3   KNIGHT, DAMON   OA
MOTHER'S DAY   BEAUMONT, CHARLES   SS   NEW 58 AC
   EDGE, THE   BEAUMONT, CHARLES   AC
   YONDER   BEAUMONT, CHARLES   AC
MOTHER'S TALE, A   AGEE, JAMES   NV   52
   ECO-FICTION   STADLER, JOHN   AN
MOTHERHOOD, APPLE PIE AND THE AMERICAN WAY
                                 ELLISON, HARLAN   IN
   *LOVE AIN'T NOTHING BUT SEX MISSPELLED   ELLISON, HARLAN   AC
MOTHERS' MARCH ON ECSTACY, THE EFFINGER, GEO. ALEC SS   NDM 75 05
   NEW DIMENSIONS 5   SILVERBERG, ROBERT   OA
MOTHERS, THE MOTHERS, HOW EERILY IT SOUNDS, THE
                                 SKAL, DAVE   SS
   AURORA: BEYOND EQUALITY   MCINTYRE & ANDERSON   OA
MOTIVATION CHART   PLATT, CHARLES   SS   NWB 73 05
   NEW WORLDS QUARTERLY NO. 5   MOORCOCK, MICHAEL   OA
MOUND BUILDERS, THE   HEARN, LAFCADIO   AR
   ANCIENT MYSTERIES READER, THE   HAINING, PETER   AN
MOUNT CHARITY   PANGBORN, EDGAR   NV   UNI 71 01
   NEBULA AWARD STORIES NO. 7   BIGGLE, LLOYD JR.   AN
   UNIVERSE 1   CARR, TERRY   OA
MOUNTAIN JUSTICE (SEE THE MOUNTAINEER)
                                 TUCKER, WILSON   TC
MOUNTAIN MOVERS, THE   CHANDLER, A. BERTRAM NV   GAL 71 03
   HARD WAY UP, THE   CHANDLER, A. BERTRAM   DC
MOUNTAIN WITHOUT A NAME, THE   SHECKLEY, ROBERT   NV   NEW 55 AC
   CITIZEN IN SPACE   SHECKLEY, ROBERT   AC
MOUNTAIN, THE   COLVIN, JAMES   SS   NWS 65 02
   BEST OF NEW WORLDS, THE   MOORCOCK, MICHAEL   AN
   BEST SF STORIES FROM NEW WORLDS 3   MOORCOCK, MICHAEL   AN
MOUNTAIN, THE   HOSKINS, ROBERT   SS   75
   FUTURE NOW, THE   HOSKINS, ROBERT   AN
MOUNTAIN, THE   MOORCOCK, MICHAEL   SS   NWS 65 02
   ENGLAND SWINGS SF   MERRIL, JUDITH   AN
   TIME DWELLER, THE   MOORCOCK, MICHAEL   AC
MOUNTAINEER, THE (MOUNTAIN JUSTICE)
                                 TUCKER, WILSON   SS   FND 53 12
   SCIENCE FICTION SUBTREASURY, THE   TUCKER, WILSON   AC
MOUNTAINS OF SUNSET, THE MOUNTAINS OF DAWN, THE
                                 MCINTYRE, VONDA N.   SS   FSF 74 02
   BEST SCIENCE FICTION STORIES OF THE YEAR (1974)
                                            DEL REY, LESTER   AN
MOURNER, THE   SHELLEY, MARY W.   NV   KPS 30
   TALES AND STORIES   SHELLEY, MARY W.   AC
MOURNERS FOR HIRE (SEE WE MOURN FOR ANYONE...)
                                 ELLISON, HARLAN   TC
MOURNING SONG   BEAUMONT, CHARLES   SS   GAM 63 01
   9TH ANNUAL OF THE YEAR'S BEST S-F, THE   MERRIL, JUDITH   AN

MOUSE   BROWN, FREDRIC   SS   TWS 49 06
   BEST SCIENCE-FICTION STORIES: 1950, THE BLEILER & DIKTY   AN
   GREAT SCIENCE-FICTION   LICATA, TONY   AN
   HONEYMOON IN HELL   BROWN, FREDRIC   AC
MOUSE IN THE WALLS OF THE GLOBAL VILLAGE, A
                                 KOONTZ, DEAN R.   SS   DVS 72 02
   AGAIN, DANGEROUS VISIONS   ELLISON, HARLAN   OA
MOUSE THAT ROARED, THE   COOPER, EDMUND   SS
   TOMORROW CAME   COOPER, EDMUND   AC
   VOICES IN THE DARK   COOPER, EDMUND   AC
MOUSE, THE   FAST, HOWARD   SS   FSF 69 11
   GENERAL ZAPPED AN ANGEL, THE   FAST, HOWARD   OC
   ZOO 2000   YOLEN, JANE   AN
MOUSETRAP   NORTON, ANDRE   SS   FSF 54 06
   BEST SCIENCE FICTION STORIES AND NOVELS: 1955
                                            DIKTY, T. E.   AN
   MANY WORLDS OF ANDRE NORTON, THE   NORTON, ANDRE   AC
MOUSETRAP, THE   DICKSON, GORDON R.   SS   GAL 52 09
   STAR ROAD, THE   DICKSON, GORDON R.   AC
MOUTH IS FOR EATING, THE   ORR, WILLIAM F.   SS   ORB 74 13
   ORBIT 13   KNIGHT, DAMON   OA
MOUTH OF HELL   MASSON, DAVID I.   SS   NWS 66 01
   CALTRAPS OF TIME, THE   MASSON, DAVID I.   AC
MOVER, THE SHAKER, THE   STURGEON, THEODORE   IN
   I HAVE NO MOUTH, AND I MUST SCREAM   ELLISON, HARLAN   AC
MOVIE HOUSE, THE   FAST, HOWARD   NV
   GENERAL ZAPPED AN ANGEL, THE   FAST, HOWARD   OC
MOVIE PEOPLE, THE   BLOCH, ROBERT   SS   FSF 69 10
   COLD CHILLS   BLOCH, ROBERT   AC
   NEW WORLDS OF FANTASY NO. 2   CARR, TERRY   AN
MOVING SPIRIT   CLARKE, ARTHUR C.   SS
   PRELUDE TO MARS   CLARKE, ARTHUR C.   AC
   TALES FROM THE WHITE HART   CLARKE, ARTHUR C.   AC
MOXON'S MASTER   BIERCE, AMBROSE   SS   93
   ANDROIDS, TIME MACHINES AND BLUE GIRAFFES
                                            ELWOOD & GHIDALIA   AN
   CENTURY OF SCIENCE FICTION, A   KNIGHT, DAMON   AN
   FROM FRANKENSTEIN TO ANDROMEDA   BROWN, JAMES GOLDIE   AN
   INSIDE INFORMATION   MOWSHOWITZ, ABBE   AN
   JOURNEYS IN SCIENCE FICTION   LOUGHLIN, RICHARD L.   AN
   POCKET BOOK OF SCIENCE-FICTION, THE   WOLLHEIM, DONALD A.   AN
   *SCIENCE FICTION THINKING MACHINES   CONKLIN, GROFF   AN
   WONDERMAKERS   HOSKINS, ROBERT   AN
MR. ARCULARIS   AIKEN, CONRAD   SS   22
   MOONLIGHT TRAVELER, THE   STERN, PHILIP VAN D.   AN
   PERCHANCE TO DREAM   KNIGHT, DAMON   AN
MR. BAUER AND THE ATOMS   LEIBER, FRITZ   SS   WRT 46 01
   *STRANGE PORTS OF CALL   DERLETH, AUGUST   AN
MR. BERBECK HAD A DREAM   DERLETH, AUGUST   SS   WRT 35 11
   NOT LONG FOR THIS WORLD   DERLETH, AUGUST   AC
MR. BIGGS GOES TO TOWN   BOND, NELSON S.   SS   AMZ 42 10
   LANCELOT BIGGS: SPACEMAN   BOND, NELSON S.   AC
MR. BRISHER'S TREASURE   WELLS, H. G.   SS   SND 99 04
   SHORT STORIES OF H. G. WELLS, THE   WELLS, H. G.   AC
   TWELVE STORIES AND A DREAM   WELLS, H. G.   AC
MR. CAXTON DRAWS A MARTIAN BIRD
                                 LONG, FRANK BELKNAP   SS   FUN 54 07
   RIM OF THE UNKNOWN   LONG, FRANK BELKNAP   AC
MR. COSTELLO, HERO   STURGEON, THEODORE   NV   GAL 53 12
   ABOVE THE HUMAN LANDSCAPE   MCNELLY & STOVER   AN
   ASSIGNMENT IN TOMORROW   POHL, FREDERIK   AN
   CONNOISSEUR'S S. F.   BOARDMAN, TOM JR.   AN
   *TOUCH OF STRANGE, A   STURGEON, THEODORE   AC
MR. DEATH AND THE REDHEADED WOMAN
                                 EUSTIS, HELEN   SS   SEP 50 02
   TIMELESS STORIES FOR TODAY AND TOMORROW BRADBURY, RAY   AN
MR. DINGLE, THE STRONG   SERLING, ROD   SA
   FROM THE TWILIGHT ZONE   SERLING, ROD   AC
   MORE STORIES FROM THE TWILIGHT ZONE   SERLING, ROD   OC
MR. F IS MR. F   BALLARD, J. G.   SS   SCF 61 08
   DISASTER AREA, THE   BALLARD, J. G.   AC
   TRAPS OF TIME, THE   MOORCOCK, MICHAEL   AN
MR. GEORGE   DERLETH, AUGUST   NV   WRT 47 03
   MR. GEORGE AND OTHER ODD PERSONS   DERLETH, AUGUST   AC
MR. GEORGE   GRENDON, STEPHEN   NV   WRT 47 03
   MORE LITTLE MONSTERS   ELWOOD & GHIDALIA   AN
MR. HAMADRYAD   LAFFERTY, R. A.   NV   STL 74 01
   STELLAR 1   DEL REY, JUDY-LYNN   OA
MR. HOSKIN'S HEEL   COGSWELL, THEODORE R SS   FUN 54 11
   THIRD EYE, THE   COGSWELL, THEODORE R   AC
MR. JESTER   SABERHAGEN, FRED   SS   IFS 66 01
   BERSERKER   SABERHAGEN, FRED   AC
MR. JINX   ARTHUR, ROBERT   SS   UNK 41 08
   UNKNOWN, THE   BENSEN, D. R.   AN
MR. KINKAID'S PASTS   COUPLING, J. J.   SS   FSF 53 08
   BEYOND THE BARRIERS OF SPACE AND TIME   MERRIL, JUDITH   AN
MR. KOWTSHOOK   CHRISTOPHER, JOHN   SS   ASR 53 01
   TALES OF SCIENCE FICTION   BALL, BRIAN N.   AN
   TWENTY-SECOND CENTURY, THE   CHRISTOPHER, JOHN   AC
MR. LEDBETTER'S VACATION   WELLS, H. G.   SS   SND 98 10
   SHORT STORIES OF H. G. WELLS, THE   WELLS, H. G.   AC
   TWELVE STORIES AND A DREAM   WELLS, H. G.   AC
MR. LUPESCU   BOUCHER, ANTHONY   SS   WRT 45 09
   COMPLEAT WEREWOLF, THE   BOUCHER, ANTHONY   AC
   DEVIL'S GENERATION, THE   GHIDALIA, VIC   AN
   SHOT IN THE DARK   MERRIL, JUDITH   AN
MR. MEEK PLAYS POLO   SIMAK, CLIFFORD D.   SS   PLS 44 FL
   INFINITE ARENA, THE   CARR, TERRY   AN
MR. MERGENTHWIRKER'S LOBBIES   BOND, NELSON S.   SS   SCR 37 11
   MR. MERGENTHWIRKER'S LOBBIES AND OTHER FANTASTIC TALES
                                            BOND, NELSON S.   AC
   OUT OF THIS WORLD   FAST, JULIUS   AN
MR. MURPHY OF NEW YORK   MCMORROW, THOMAS   SS   SEP 30 03
   *BIG BOOK OF SCIENCE FICTION   CONKLIN, GROFF   AN
   ONE HUNDRED YEARS OF SCIENCE FICTION   KNIGHT, DAMON   AN

MR. NOBODY

MR. NOBODY   TIMPERLEY, ROSEMARY SS   ADS 75 01
ARMADA SCI-FI ONE   DAVIS, RICHARD   OA
MR. PACKER GOES TO HELL (SEE THIRTEEN O'CLOCK & MR. PACKER
  GOES TO HELL)   KORNBLUTH, C. M.   TC   STI 41 06
MR. RAY SHARP AND MISS ME FLAT (1893)
                             VERNE, JULES   SS
  YESTERDAY AND TOMORROW   VERNE, JULES   AC
MR. SAKRIS'S HALT   CLINGERMAN, MILDRED SS   FSF 56 01
  BEST FROM FANTASY AND SCIENCE FICTION: 6
                                          BOUCHER, ANTHONY   AN
  CUPFUL OF SPACE, A   CLINGERMAN, MILDRED   AC
MR. SKELMERSDALE IN FAIRYLAND WELLS, H. G.   SS   SND 01
  BEST STORIES OF H. G. WELLS   WELLS, H. G.   AC
  SHORT STORIES OF H. G. WELLS, THE   WELLS, H. G.   AC
  TWELVE STORIES AND A DREAM   WELLS, H. G.   AC
MR. STEINWAY   BLOCH, ROBERT   SS   FAN 54 04
  NIGHTMARES   BLOCH, ROBERT   AC
  PLEASANT DREAMS   BLOCH, ROBERT   AC
MR. STILWELL'S STAGE   DAVIDSON, AVRAM   SS   FSF 57 09
  BEST FROM FANTASY AND SCIENCE FICTION: 7
                                          BOUCHER, ANTHONY   AN
  WHAT STRANGE STARS AND SKIES   DAVIDSON, AVRAM   AC
MR. STRENBERRY'S TALE   PRIESTLEY, J. B.   SS   34
  OTHER PLACE, THE   PRIESTLEY, J. B.   AC
  TRAVELERS IN TIME   STERN, PHILIP VAN D. AN
  TREASURY OF SCIENCE FICTION CLASSICS, THE
                                          KUEBLER, HAROLD W.   AN
MR. SWIFT AND HIS REMARKABLE THING
                             MCMAHON, JEREMIAH   SS   PBY
  FULLY AUTOMATED LOVE LIFE OF HENRY KEANRIDGE
                                          PLAYBOY, EDITORS OF AN
MR. WATERMAN   REDGROVE, PETER   SS   PRV 63 29
  HOLDING YOUR EIGHT HANDS   LUCIE-SMITH, EDWARD   AN
  9TH ANNUAL OF THE YEAR'S BEST S-F, THE   MERRIL, JUDITH   AN
MRS. AMWORTH (1922)   BENSON, E. F.   SS   FFM 50 06
  STRANGE BEASTS AND UNNATURAL MONSTERS STERN, PHILIP VAN D. AN
MRS. BENTLEY'S DAUGHTER   DERLETH, AUGUST   SS   WRT 30 10
  NOT LONG FOR THIS WORLD   DERLETH, AUGUST   AC
MRS. ELTING DOES HER PART   DERLETH, AUGUST   SS   SRS 39 08
  NOT LONG FOR THIS WORLD   DERLETH, AUGUST   AC
MRS. GALLAGHER'S PSYCHOANALYSIS
                             DISCH, THOMAS M.   SS
*GETTING INTO DEATH   DISCH, THOMAS M.   AC
MRS. HAWK   ST. CLAIR, MARGARET SS   WRT 50 07
  UNEXPECTED, THE   MARGULIES, LEO   AN
MRS. HINCK   DEFORD, MIRIAM ALLEN SS   FSF 54 03
  ELSEWHERE, ELSEWHEN, ELSEHOW   DEFORD, MIRIAM ALLEN AC
MRS. LANNISFREE   DERLETH, AUGUST   SS   WRT 45 11
  NOT LONG FOR THIS WORLD   DERLETH, AUGUST   AC
MRS. MANIFOLD   DERLETH, AUGUST   SS   49
  MR. GEORGE AND OTHER ODD PERSONS   DERLETH, AUGUST   AC
MRS. MANIFOLD   GRENDON, STEPHEN   SS   49
  GIRL WITH THE HUNGRY EYES, AND OTHER STORIES, THE
                                          WOLLHEIM, DONALD A. OA
  SUPERNATURAL READER, THE   CONKLIN, G&L.   AN
*TWISTED   CONKLIN, GROFF   AN
MRS. PIGAFETTA SWIMS WELL   BRETNOR, REGINALD   SS   FSF 63 05
  9TH ANNUAL OF THE YEAR'S BEST S-F, THE MERRIL, JUDITH   AN
MRS. POPPLEDORE'S ID   BRETNOR, REGINALD   SS   FSF 52 02
  SCIENCE FICTION ODDITIES   CONKLIN, GROFF   AN
MS FND IN A LBRY   DRAPER, HAL   SS   FSF 61 12
  INSIDE INFORMATION   MOWSHOWITZ, ABBE   AN
  17 X INFINITY   CONKLIN, GROFF   AN
MS FOUND IN A BOTTLE   POE, EDGAR ALLEN   SS   BSV 33 10
  ANCIENT MYSTERIES READER, THE   HAINING, PETER   AN
MS. FOUND IN A BUS   BAKER, RUSSELL   SS   NYT 62
  8TH ANNUAL OF THE YEAR'S BEST S-F, THE   MERRIL, JUDITH   AN
MS. FOUND IN A CHAMPAGNE BOTTLE
                             BESTER, ALFRED   SS   STA 68
  LIGHT FANTASTIC, THE   BESTER, ALFRED   AC
MS. FOUND IN A CHINESE FORTUNE COOKIE
                             KORNBLUTH, C. M.   SS   FSF 57 07
  BEST FROM FANTASY AND SCIENCE FICTION: 7
                                          BOUCHER, ANTHONY   AN
  MARCHING MORONS AND OTHER SCIENCE FICTION
                                          KORNBLUTH, C. M.   AC
  THIRTEEN O'CLOCK AND OTHER ZERO HOURS   KORNBLUTH, C. M.   AC
  YET MORE PENGUIN SCIENCE FICTION   ALDISS, BRIAN W.   AN
MS. FOUND IN AN ABANDONED TIME MACHINE
                             SILVERBERG, ROBERT   SS   TTM 73
  CAPRICORN GAMES   SILVERBERG, ROBERT   AC
  TEN TOMORROWS   ELWOOD, ROGER   OA
  VISIONS OF TOMORROW   ELWOOD, ROGER   AN
MUCH ADO ABOUT PENDING   BOND, NELSON S.   SS   BBM 47 04
  NIGHTMARES AND DAYDREAMS   BOND, NELSON S.   AC
MUD VIOLET   LAFFERTY, R. A.   SS   DEM 73
  DEMON KIND   ELWOOD, ROGER   OA
MUDD'S PASSION (STEPHEN KANDEL)
                             FOSTER, ALAN DEAN   SA   SLG 75 03
  STAR TREK LOG THREE   FOSTER, ALAN DEAN   OC
MUDDLE OF THE WOAD, THE   GARRETT, RANDALL   NV   ASF 65 06
  SPECIAL WONDER   MCCOMAS, J. FRANCIS   AN
MUGWUMP FOUR   SILVERBERG, ROBERT   NV   GAL 59 08
  CALLIBRATED ALLIGATOR AND OTHER SCIENCE FICTION STORIES, THE
                                          SILVERBERG, ROBERT   AC
  CUBE ROOT OF UNCERTAINTY, THE   SILVERBERG, ROBERT   AC
  OTHER DIMENSIONS   SILVERBERG, ROBERT   AN
MULE, THE   ASIMOV, ISAAC   SN   ASF 45 11
  FOUNDATION AND EMPIRE   ASIMOV, ISAAC   NO
MULTI-VALUE MOTORWAY   ALDISS, BRIAN W.   NV   NWS 67 08
  BEST SF STORIES FROM NEW WORLDS 3   MOORCOCK, MICHAEL   AN
MULTUM IN PARVO   SHARKEY, JACK   SS   GNT 59 12
  5TH ANNUAL OF THE YEAR'S BEST S-F, THE MERRIL, JUDITH   AN
MUMMY TO THE RESCUE   WILSON, ANGUS   SS
  BEST FANTASY STORIES   ALDISS, BRIAN W.   AN

MURDER IN TEN EASY LESSONS   BROWN, FREDRIC   SS
  NIGHTMARES AND GEEZENSTACKS   BROWN, FREDRIC   AC
MURDER IN THE FOURTH DIMENSION SMITH, CLARK ASHTON SS AMD 30 10
  TALES OF SCIENCE AND SORCERY   SMITH, CLARK ASHTON   AC
MURDER MADNESS   LEINSTER, MURRAY   NO   ASF 30 05
  QUADRATIC   CRAWFORD, WILLIAM L. AN
MURDER WILL IN   HERBERT, FRANK   NV   FSF 70 05
  FIVE FATES   LAUMER, KEITH   AN
MURDERER'S CHAIN   BROWN, WENZELL   SS   FUN 60 03
  RULERS OF MEN   SANTESSON, HANS S.   AN
MURDERER'S EYE, THE (SEE THE EYE)
                             KERSH, GERALD   TC
MURDERER, THE   BRADBURY, RAY   SS   ARG 53 06
*GOLDEN APPLES OF THE SUN   BRADBURY, RAY   AC
MURDERERS, THE   BEAUMONT, CHARLES   SS   ESQ 55
  HUNGER AND OTHER STORIES, THE   BEAUMONT, CHARLES   AC
  MAGIC MAN AND OTHER SCIENCE-FANTASY STORIES
                                          BEAUMONT, CHARLES   AC
MURDERS   CAMPBELL, J. RAMSEY SS   NWR 75 26
  NEW WRITINGS IN SF. 26   BULMER, KENNETH   AN
MURKLE FOR JESSE, A   JENNINGS, GARY   SS   FSF 65 07
  BEST FROM FANTASY AND SCIENCE FICTION: 15
                                          FERMAN, EDWARD L.   AN
MURKY GLASS, THE (SEE THE GABEL WINDOW)
                             DERLETH, AUGUST
                         AND LOVECRAFT, H. P.   TC C
MURPHY'S HALL   ANDERSON, KAREN
                         AND ANDERSON, POUL   NV C INY 71 02
  HOMEWARD AND BEYOND   ANDERSON, POUL   AC
  INFINITY 2   HOSKINS, ROBERT   OA
MURRAY LEINSTER OMNIBUS, A   LEINSTER, MURRAY   AC   SID 68
  SCIENCE FICTION SPECIAL 7   ANONYMOUS   AN
MURRAY'S LIGHT   WANDREI, DONALD   SS   ASF 35 06
  STRANGE HARVEST   WANDREI, DONALD   AC
MUSCADINE   GOULART, RON   SS   FSF 68 04
  BEST FROM FANTASY AND SCIENCE FICTION: 18
                                          FERMAN, EDWARD L.   AN
  BROKE DOWN ENGINE AND OTHER TROUBLES WITH MACHINES
                                          GOULART, RON   AC
MUSE   KOONTZ, DEAN R.   SS   FSF 69 09
  THEMES IN SCIENCE FICTION   KELLEY, LEO P.   AN
MUSE, THE   BURGESS, ANTHONY   HUD 68
  BEST SF: 1969   HARRISON & ALDISS   AN
  IN DREAMS AWAKE   FIEDLER, LESLIE A.   AN
  LIGHT FANTASTIC, THE   HARRISON, HARRY   AN
MUSEUM PIECE   CARLSON, ESTHER   SS   47
  WORLD OF WONDER   PRATT, FLETCHER   AN
MUSEUM PIECE   CHRISTOPHER, JOHN   SS   NWS 54 04
  TWENTY-SECOND CENTURY, THE   CHRISTOPHER, JOHN   AC
MUSEUM PIECE   FANCETT, ELIZABETH   SS   SPC 73 01
  SPACE 1   DAVIS, RICHARD   OA
MUSEUM PIECE   MENDELSON, DREW   SS   NDM 75 05
  NEW DIMENSIONS 5   SILVERBERG, ROBERT   OA
MUSHROOM WORLD   TALL, STEPHEN   NA   FSF 74 11
  STARDUST VOYAGES, THE   TALL, STEPHEN   AC
MUSHROOMS   EVANS, MIKE   PM   69
  HOLDING YOUR EIGHT HANDS   LUCIE-SMITH, EDWARD   AN
  SCIENCE FICTION   BRODKIN & PEARSON   AN
MUSHROOMS   PLATH, SYLVIA   PM   60
  SCIENCE FICTION   BRODKIN & PEARSON   AN
MUSIC MAKERS, THE   JONES, LANGDON   SS   NWS 65 11
  BEST SF STORIES FROM NEW WORLDS NO. 1, THE
                                          MOORCOCK, MICHAEL   AN
MUSIC MASTER OF BABYLON, THE PANGBORN, EDGAR   NV   GAL 54 11
  BEST SF 7   CRISPIN, EDMUND   AN
  NEW DREAMS THIS MORNING   BLISH, JAMES   AN
  WORLD THAT COULDN'T BE AND 8 OTHER SF NOVELETS
                                          GOLD, H. L.   AN
MUSIC MONSTERS, THE   JONES, NEIL R.   NV   AMZ 38 04
  TWIN WORLDS   JONES, NEIL R.   AC
MUSIC OF ERICH ZANN, THE   LOVECRAFT, H. P.   SS   WRT 25 05
  HAUNTER OF THE DARK, THE   LOVECRAFT, H. P.   AC
MUSIC OF MINOX, THE   GOLDSMITH, HOWARD   SS
  MORE SCIENCE FICTION TALES   ELWOOD, ROGER   OA
MUSIC OF THE YELLOW BRASS, THE BEAUMONT, CHARLES SS   PBY 59 01
  EDGE, THE   BEAUMONT, CHARLES   AC
  NIGHT RIDE AND OTHER JOURNEYS   BEAUMONT, CHARLES   AC
MUSIC ON THE HILL, THE   SAKI   SS   12
  MOONLIGHT TRAVELER, THE   STERN, PHILIP VAN D. AN
MUSIC, THE   STURGEON, THEODORE   SS   NEW 53 AC
  E PLURIBUS UNICORN   STURGEON, THEODORE   AC
MUSICAL EDUCATION, A   JACOBS, HARVEY   SS
  EGG OF THE GLAK, AND OTHER STORIES, THE JACOBS, HARVEY   AC
MUSICIANS, THE   BRADBURY, RAY   SS   NEW 51 AC
  MARTIAN CHRONICLES, THE   BRADBURY, RAY   AC
MUSIEUM PIECE, A   ZELAZNY, ROGER   SS   FAN 63 06
  DOORS OF HIS FACE, THE LAMPS OF HIS MOUTH, THE
                                          ZELAZNY, ROGER   AC
  NEW WORLDS OF FANTASY NO. 2   CARR, TERRY   AN
MUSSPELSHEIM   LUPOFF, RICHARD A.   NV   STG 74
  STRANGE GODS   ELWOOD, ROGER   AN
MUTANT WEAPON, THE   SILVERBERG, ROBERT   SS   NEW 73 AC
  ANDROIDS, TIME MACHINES AND BLUE GIRAFFES
                                          ELWOOD & GHIDALIA   AN
  UNFAMILIAR TERRITORY   SILVERBERG, ROBERT   AC
MUTANT'S BROTHER, THE   LEIBER, FRITZ   SS   ASF 43 08
  CROSSROADS IN TIME   CONKLIN, GROFF   AN
MUTATION   CARR, ROBERT S.   NV   NEW 51 AC
  BEYOND INFINITY   CARR, ROBERT S.   AC
MUTATION PLANET   BAYLEY, BARRINGTON J NV   TAL 73
  FRONTIERS 1; TOMORROW'S ALTERNATIVES   ELWOOD, ROGER   AN
MUTE   MATHESON, RICHARD   NV   NEW 62 AC
  FIEND IN YOU, THE   BEAUMONT, CHARLES   AN
  SHOCK II   MATHESON, RICHARD   AC
MUTE INGLORIOUS TAM   KORNBLUTH, C. M.
                         AND POHL, FREDERIK   SS C FSF 74 10

UTE INGLORIOUS TAM
                                                        NAMELESS SOMETHING, THE

BEST SCIENCE FICTION STORIES OF THE YEAR (1974)
                              DEL REY, LESTER   AN
MUTE MILTON   HARRISON, HARRY   SS AMZ 66 02
  ABC OF SCIENCE FICTION, AN
                              BOARDMAN, TOM JR.   AN
  *BEST OF HARRY HARRISON, THE
                              HARRISON, HARRY   AC
  PRIME NUMBER   HARRISON, HARRY   AC
MUTE QUESTION, THE   ACKERMAN, FORREST J. SS OWS 50 09
  ADVENTURES IN TOMORROW   CROSSEN, KENDELL F.   AN
  IF THIS GOES ON   NUETZEL, CHARLES   AN
  MUTANTS   SILVERBERG, ROBERT   AN
MUTED HORN, THE   DAVIS, DOROTHY S.   SS FUN 57 05
  FANTASTIC UNIVERSE OMNIBUS, THE
                              SANTESSON, HANS S.   AN
MUTEN   RUSSELL, ERIC FRANK SS ASF 48 10
  *SCIENCE-FICTION CARNIVAL
                              BROWN, F. & REYNOLDS   AN
MUTINY   BAKHNOV, VLADLEN
  RUSSIAN SCIENCE FICTION, 1968   MAGIDOFF, ROBERT   AN
MUTINY ON THE SWALLOW, THE HENDERSON, WILLIAM J SS
  BATTLE FOR THE PACIFIC AND OTHER ADVENTURES AT SEA, THE
                              ANONYMOUS   AN
MY AFFAIR WITH SCIENCE FICTION BESTER, ALFRED   AR NOV 74 04
  NOVA 4   HARRISON, HARRY   OA
  STAR LIGHT, STAR BRIGHT   BESTER, ALFRED   AC
MY BOAT   RUSS, JOANNA   SS FSF 76 01
  1977 ANNUAL WORLD'S BEST SF, THE WOLLHEIM, DONALD A. AN
MY BORROWED TORPEDO-BOAT RALPH, JULIAN   SS
  BATTLE FOR THE PACIFIC AND OTHER ADVENTURES AT SEA, THE
                              ANONYMOUS   AN
MY BOYFRIEND'S NAME IS JELLO DAVIDSON, AVRAM SS FSF 54 07
  BEST FROM FANTASY AND SCIENCE FICTION: 4
                              BOUCHER, ANTHONY   AN
  OR ALL THE SEAS WITH OYSTERS DAVIDSON, AVRAM   AC
MY BROTHER LEOPOLD   PANGBORN, EDGAR   NV   73
  EXALTATION OF STARS, AN   CARR, TERRY   OA
MY BROTHER PAULIE   ELLISON, HARLAN   SS SAT 58 12
  FROM THE LAND OF FEAR   ELLISON, HARLAN   AC
MY BROTHER'S KEEPER DE CAMP, L. SPRAGUE
  AND PRATT, FLETCHER   SS C NEW 53 AC
  TALES FROM GAVAGAN'S BAR   DE CAMP, L. S.&PRATT   AC
MY BROTHER'S WIFE   TUCKER, WILSON   SS FSF 51 02
  SCIENCE FICTION SUBTREASURY, THE TUCKER, WILSON   AC
MY COLLEAGUE   GRIGORIEV, VLADIMIR SS
  LAST DOOR TO AIYA   GINSBURG, MIRRA   AN
MY COUNTRY, RIGHT OR WRONG OFFUTT, ANDREW J. SS PRT 71
  PROTOSTARS   GERROLD & GOLDIN   OA
MY DARLING HECATE   GUIN, WYMAN   NV BEY 53 11
  LIVING WAY OUT   GUIN, WYMAN   AC
MY DEAR EMILY   RUSS, JOANNA   NV FSF 62 07
  BEST FROM FANTASY AND SCIENCE FICTION: 12
                              DAVIDSON, AVRAM   AN
MY DREAM OF FLYING TO WAKE ISLAND
                     BALLARD, J. G.   SS ABT 74 WI
  LOW-FLYING AIRCRAFT AND OTHER STORIES BALLARD, J. G. AC
MY EIGHT DAYS IN THE AUTOMOTIVE INDUSTRY
                     ARNOLD, CHARLES   SS NWQ 73 05
  NEW WORLDS NO. 5   MOORCOCK & PLATT   OA
MY EYES, THEY BURN   BERTIN, EDDY C.   NV   75
  BEST FROM THE REST OF THE WORLD, THE WOLLHEIM, DONALD A. AN
MY FATHER THE CAT   SLESAR, HENRY   SS FUN 57 12
  FANTASTIC UNIVERSE OMNIBUS, THE SANTESSON, HANS S. AN
MY FATHER'S GUEST   BERNOTT, JOAN   SS QRK 70 01
  QUARK/1   DELANY & HACKER   AN
MY FIRST AEROPLANE   WELLS, H. G.   SS SND 10 01
  SHORT STORIES OF H. G. WELLS, THE WELLS, H. G.   AC
MY FRIEND BOBBY   NOURSE, ALAN E.   SS OSF 54 03
  COUNTERFEIT MAN, THE   NOURSE, ALAN E.   AC
MY FRIEND KLATU   YEP, LAURENCE   NV SAW 72
  SIGNS AND WONDERS   ELWOOD, ROGER   OA
  VISIONS OF TOMORROW   ELWOOD, ROGER   AN
MY FRIEND MERTON   FAST, JULIUS   SS NEW 44 AN
  OUT OF THIS WORLD   FAST, JULIUS   AN
MY FRIEND ZARATHUSTRA SALLIS, JAMES   SS ORB 74 13
  ORBIT 13   KNIGHT, DAMON   OA
MY HEAD'S IN A DIFFERENT PLACE, NOW
                     DAVIS, GRANIA   NV UNI 72 02
  UNIVERSE 2   CARR, TERRY   OA
MY LADY GREEN SLEEVES POHL, FREDERIK   NA GAL 57 02
  CASE AGAINST TOMORROW, THE POHL, FREDERIK   AC
                              DEGRAEFF, ALLEN   AN
  HUMAN AND OTHER BEINGS
MY LADY OF PSYCHIATRIC SORROWS ALDISS, BRIAN W. SS UNI 77 07
  UNIVERSE 7   CARR, TERRY   OA
MY MISTRESS   TAFOYA, ALFONSO   PM NWQ 74 06
  NEW WORLDS NO. 6   PLATT & BAILEY   OA
MY MOTHER WAS A WITCH TENN, WILLIAM   66
  SQUARE ROOT OF MAN, THE   TENN, WILLIAM   AC
MY NAME IS EVERYONE (SEE WHO AM I THIS TIME?)
                     VONNEGUT, KURT JR. TC
MY NAME IS LEGION   DEL REY, LESTER   NV ASF 42 06
  EARLY DEL REY   DEL REY, LESTER   AC
MY NEPHEW NORVELL   BOND, NELSON S.   SS
  31ST OF FEBRUARY, THE   BOND, NELSON S.   AC
MY OBJECT ALL SUBLIME ANDERSON, POUL   SS GAL 61 06
  BEST OF POUL ANDERSON, THE ANDERSON, POUL   AC
  12 GREAT CLASSICS OF SCIENCE FICTION CONKLIN, GROFF AN
MY OWN, MY NATIVE LAND ANDERSON, POUL   NV CTM 74 04
  CONTINUUM 1   ELWOOD, ROGER   OA
MY PERFECT MURDER (SEE THE UTTERLY PERFECT MURDER)
                     BRADBURY, RAY   TC
MY PRIVATE WORLD OF SCIENCE FICTION
                     BESTER, ALFRED   MS
  WORLDS OF SCIENCE FICTION, THE MILLS, ROBERT P.   AN
MY SISTER'S BROTHER (OPEN TO ME, MY SISTER)
                     FARMER, PHILIP JOSE NV FSF 60 05
  BOOK OF PHILIP JOSE FARMER, THE FARMER, PHILIP JOSE AC
  STRANGE RELATIONS   FARMER, PHILIP JOSE   AC
MY SON, THE PHYSICIST ASIMOV, ISAAC   SS SAM 62 02
  NIGHTFALL AND OTHER STORIES ASIMOV, ISAAC   AC

SCIENCE FICTION HORIZONS NO. 1   BOARDMAN, TOM JR.   AN
MY SPECIES   BLACK, D. M.   PM   67
  HOLDING YOUR EIGHT HANDS   LUCIE-SMITH, EDWARD   AN
MY SWEET LADY JO   WALDROP, HOWARD   SS UNI 74 04
  UNIVERSE 4   CARR, TERRY   OA
MY TERMINAL MORAINE STOCKTON, FRANK R. NV OAW 92 04
  SCIENCE FICTION OF FRANK R. STOCKTON, THE
                              STOCKTON, FRANK R.   AC
MY TRANSLATOPHONE   STOCKTON, FRANK R. NV HBZ 00 10
  SCIENCE FICTION OF FRANK R. STOCKTON, THE
                              STOCKTON, FRANK R.   AC
MY TRIAL AS A WAR CRIMINAL SZILARD, LEO SS UCL 49 FL
  VOICE OF THE DOLPHINS, AND OTHER STORIES, THE
                              SZILARD, LEO   AC
  7TH ANNUAL OF THE YEAR'S BEST S-F, THE MERRIL, JUDITH AN
MY WORD   GOLD, H. L.   IN
  WEIRD ONES, THE   HOWARD, IVAN   AN
MY WRECK   KING, MAC   PM NWQ 74 06
  NEW WORLDS NO. 6   PLATT & BAILEY   OA
MYSTERIOUS DISAPPEARANCES (1893)
                     BIERCE, AMBROSE   AR   93
  FUTURE PERFECT   FRANKLIN, H. BRUCE   AN
MYSTERIOUS DOINGS IN THE METROPOLITAN MUSEUM
                     LEIBER, FRITZ   SS UNI 74 05
  UNIVERSE 5   CARR, TERRY   OA
  WORLDS OF FRITZ LEIBER, THE LEIBER, FRITZ   AC
MYSTERIOUS FOOTPRINTS, THE ANONYMOUS   SS
  STRANGE WORLD OF SCIENCE FICTION ANONYMOUS   OA
MYSTERIOUS GEM, THE STREET, CLAIRE EDWIN SS SFT 73
  SCIENCE FICTION TALES   ELWOOD, ROGER   OA
MYSTERIOUS MONA LISA SMILE, THE (SEE THE APE AND THE MYSTERY)
                     KERSH, GERALD   TC
MYSTERY DIET OF THE GODS: A REVELATION
                     DISCH, THOMAS M.
                     AND SLADEK, JOHN T. SS C SWK 76 10
  NEW CONSTELLATIONS   DISCH & NAYLOR   OA
MYSTERY EYES OVER EARTH ELAM, RICHARD M. JR. SS
  TEEN-AGE SUPER SCIENCE STORIES ELAM, RICHARD M. JR. AC
MYSTERY OF GREEN CROSSING PARNOV, YEREMEY
                     AND YEMTSEV, MIKHAIL SS C
  RUSSIAN SCIENCE FICTION, 1968 MAGIDOFF, ROBERT   AN
MYSTERY OF THE BOTTLE, THE (SEE THE OXOXOCO BOTTLE)
                     KERSH, GERALD   TC
MYSTERY OF THE LAST GUEST, THE FLANDERS, JOHN SS WRT 35 10
  OTHER WORLDS, THE   STONG, PHILIP D.   AN
MYTH CHILD   INOUYE, JON   SS
  NIGHT TIDE, A   INOUYE, JON   OC
MYTHS MY GREAT-GRANDDAUGHTER TAUGHT ME
                     LEIBER, FRITZ   SS FSF 63 01
  SF: AUTHORS' CHOICE   HARRISON, HARRY   AN
  WORLDS OF FRITZ LEIBER, THE LEIBER, FRITZ   AC
M81: URSA MAJOR (THE END OF THE JOURNEY)
                     COOPER, EDMUND   SS FUN 56 02
  NEWS FROM ELSEWHERE   COOPER, EDMUND   AC
  TOMORROW'S GIFT   COOPER, EDMUND   AC
  UNBORN TOMORROW   COOPER, EDMUND   AC
N DAY   LATHAM, PHILIP   SS ASF 46 01
  *TREASURY OF SCIENCE FICTION, A CONKLIN, GROFF   AN
NACKLES   CLARK, CURT   SS FSF 64 01
  NEW WORLDS OF FANTASY   CARR, TERRY   AN
NADA   DISCH, THOMAS M.   SS FSF 64 08
  BEST FROM FANTASY AND SCIENCE FICTION: 14
                              DAVIDSON, AVRAM   AN
  FUN WITH YOUR NEW HEAD   DISCH, THOMAS M.   AC
  SCHOOL AND SOCIETY THROUGH SCIENCE FICTION
                              OLANDER/GREENBERG/&   AN
NAIL AND THE ORACLE, THE STURGEON, THEODORE NV PBY 65 10
  FROM THE "S" FILE   PLAYBOY, EDITORS OF   AN
  PLAYBOY BOOK OF SCIENCE FICTION AND FANTASY, THE
                              PLAYBOY, EDITORS OF   AN
NAIL IN THE MIDDLE OF THE HAND, THE
                     BRUNNER, JOHN   SS SMM 65 07
  *OUT OF MY MIND   BRUNNER, JOHN   AC
NAKED AND AFRAID I GO PISERCHIA, DORIS   SS ORB 74 13
  ORBIT 13   KNIGHT, DAMON   OA
NAKED AND THE UNASHAMED, THE MARGROFF, ROBERT E. SS PRT 71
  PROTOSTARS   GERROLD & GOLDIN   OA
NAKED IN XANADU   RUSSELL, RAY   NV PBY 64 11
  SAGITTARIUS   RUSSELL, RAY   AC
NAKED LADY   LORD, MINDRET   SS WRT 34 09
  OTHER WORLDS, THE   STONG, PHILIP D.   AN
NAKED SKY, THE (ALSO AS THE JOY RIDE)
                     GUNN, JAMES E.   NA STS 55 FL
  JOY MAKERS, THE   GUNN, JAMES E.   NO
NAKED SUN, THE   ASIMOV, ISAAC   NO ASF 56 10
  *REST OF THE ROBOTS, THE   ASIMOV, ISAAC   AC
NAKED TIME, THE (JOHN D. F. BLACK)
                     BLISH, JAMES   SA STK 67 01
  STAR TREK   BLISH, JAMES   OC
NAKED TO THE INVISIBLE EYE EFFINGER, GEO. ALEC NV ASF 73 05
  MIXED FEELINGS   EFFINGER, GEO. ALEC   AC
  RUN TO STARLIGHT, SPORTS THROUGH SCIENCE FICTION
                              GREENBERG/OLANDER/&   AN
NAME (PLEASE PRINT): SLADEK, JOHN T.   SS NWB 73 05
  NEW WORLDS QUARTERLY NO. 5 MOORCOCK, MICHAEL   OA
NAME OF THE SNAKE   LAFFERTY, R. A.   SS WOT 64 04
  NINE HUNDRED GRANDMOTHERS LAFFERTY, R. A.   AC
NAME YOUR PLEASURE (ALSO AS THE HEDONIST)
                     GUNN, JAMES E.   NA TWS 55 WI
  JOY MAKERS, THE   GUNN, JAMES E.   NO
NAME YOUR SYMPTOM   HARMON, JIM   SS GAL 56 05
  FOURTH GALAXY READER, THE GOLD, H. L.   AN
NAME YOUR TIGER   LESSER, MILTON   NV SFQ 57 05
  WEIRD ONES, THE   HOWARD, IVAN   AN
NAMELESS SOMETHING, THE LEINSTER, MURRAY NV TWS 47 06
  OUT OF THIS WORLD   LEINSTER, MURRAY   NO

NAMING OF NAMES, THE

NAMING OF NAMES, THE   MUDGETT, HERMAN W.   PM   FSF 53 10
  BEST FROM FANTASY AND SCIENCE FICTION: 3
                                          BOUCHER & MCCOMAS   AN
NAMING OF NAMES, THE (ALSO AS DARK THEY WERE, AND GOLDEN-EYED)
                              BRADBURY, RAY   SS   TWS 49 08
  BEST FROM STARTLING STORIES, THE   MINES, SAMUEL   AN
  GATES TO TOMORROW   NORTON, AN.&DONALD Y   AN
  MARTIAN CHRONICLES, THE   BRADBURY, RAY   AC
  SCIENCE AND SORCERY   FORD, GARRET   AN
NANNY   DICK, PHILIP K.   SS   STS 55 SP
  BOOK OF PHILIP K. DICK, THE   DICK, PHILIP K.   AC
NAPIER COURT   CAMPBELL, J. RAMSEY SS
  YEAR'S BEST HORROR STORIES: SERIES II, THE
                                          DAVIS, RICHARD   AN
NAPOLEONIC WARS, THE   GOTSCHALK, FELIX C. SS
  BEYOND TIME   LEY, SANDRA   OA
NARAPOIA (THE ORIGIN OF NARAPOIA, WDG 48 04)
                              NELSON, ALAN   SS   FSF 51 04
  BEST FROM FANTASY AND SCIENCE FICTION BOUCHER & MCCOMAS   AN
  FIFTY SHORT SCIENCE FICTION TALES   ASIMOV & CONKLIN   AN
NARCISSUS   DISCH, THOMAS M.   PM   69
  HOLDING YOUR EIGHT HANDS   LUCIE-SMITH, EDWARD   AN
NARRATIVE OF MASKS   PARTINGTON, CHARLES SS   NWB 75 09
  NEW WORLDS NINE   BAILEY, HILARY   OA
NARROW VALLEY   LAFFERTY, R. A.   SS   FSF 66 09
  EARTH IS THE STRANGEST PLANET SILVERBERG, ROBERT   AN
  NEW WORLDS OF FANTASY   CARR, TERRY   AN
  NINE HUNDRED GRANDMOTHERS   LAFFERTY, R. A.   AC
  OTHER DIMENSIONS   SILVERBERG, ROBERT   AN
  SF12   MERRIL, JUDITH   AN
NASTY   BROWN, FREDRIC   SS   PBY 59 04
  NIGHTMARES AND GEEZENSTACKS   BROWN, FREDRIC   AC
  PLAYBOY BOOK OF HORROR AND THE SUPERNATURAL, THE
                                          PLAYBOY, EDITORS OF   AN
  WEIRD SHOW   PLAYBOY, EDITORS OF   AN
NATIONAL PASTIME, THE   SPINRAD, NORMAN   NV   NOV 73 03
  BEST SCIENCE FICTION STORIES OF THE YEAR (1973)
                                          DEL REY, LESTER   AN
  FUTURE PASTIMES   EDELSTEIN, SCOTT   OA
  NO DIRECTION HOME   SPINRAD, NORMAN   AC
  NOVA 3   HARRISON, HARRY   OA
  RUN TO STARLIGHT, SPORTS THROUGH SCIENCE FICTION
                                      GREENBERG/OLANDER/&   AN
NATIVE INTELLIGENCE (THE GOVERNOR OF GLAVE)
                              LAUMER, KEITH   NV   IFS 63 11
  GALACTIC DIPLOMAT   LAUMER, KEITH   AC
NATIVE PROBLEM, THE   SHECKLEY, ROBERT   NV   GAL 56 12
  NOTIONS: UNLIMITED   SHECKLEY, ROBERT   AC
NATIVE SOIL, THE   NOURSE, ALAN E.   SS   FUN 57 07
  TIGER BY THE TAIL   NOURSE, ALAN E.   AC
NATIVE SON   HAMM, THELMA D.   SS   IMG 53 07
  TALES BEYOND TIME   DE CAMP, L. S.&C.   AN
NATURAL ADVANTAGE   DEL REY, LESTER   SS   AMZ 76 06
  1977 ANNUAL WORLD'S BEST SF, THE   WOLLHEIM, DONALD A. AN
NATURAL HISTORY   MALZBERG, BARRY N.   SS
  LONG NIGHT OF WAITING AND OTHER STORIES ELWOOD, ROGER   OA
NATURAL STATE   KNIGHT, DAMON   NA   GAL 54 01
  ALL ABOUT THE FUTURE   GREENBERG, MARTIN   AN
  HOT & COLD RUNNING CITIES   MCHARGUE, GEORGESS   AN
  THREE NOVELS   KNIGHT, DAMON   AC
  TIME WAITS FOR WINTHROP, AND FOUR OTHER SHORT NOVELS
                                      POHL, FREDERIK   AN
NATURALLY (DOUBLE WHAMMY)   BROWN, FREDRIC   SS   BEY 54 09
  BEYOND   ANONYMOUS   AN
  HONEYMOON IN HELL   BROWN, FREDRIC   AC
NATURE BOY   SAXTON, JOSEPHINE   SS   QRK 71 03
  QUARK/3   DELANY & HACKER   OA
NATURE OF IMAGINATIVE LITERATURE, THE
                              PRATT, FLETCHER   IN
  WORLD OF WONDER   PRATT, FLETCHER   AN
NATURE OF THE CATASTROPHE, THE MOORCOCK, MICHAEL SS   NWS 70 01
  DECADE THE 1960S   ALDISS & HARRISON   AN
  LIVES AND TIMES OF JERRY CORNELIUS, THE MOORCOCK, MICHAEL AC
NATURE OF THE EVIDENCE, THE   SINCLAIR, MAY   SS   FOR 23 05
  STRANGE BEASTS AND UNNATURAL MONSTERS STERN, PHILIP VAN D. AN
  SUPERNATURAL READER, THE   CONKLIN, G&L.   AN
NAUTILUS REACHES THE POLE, THE (FROM "20,000 LEAGUES
UNDER THE SEA")   VERNE, JULES   EX   GMS 73
  ARMCHAIR SCIENCE READER, THE GORDON, I. & SORKIN AN
NE DEJA VU PAS   SAXTON, JOSEPHINE   SS   67
  ENGLAND SWINGS SF   MERRIL, JUDITH   AN
  SPACE-TIME JOURNAL, THE   MERRIL, JUDITH   AN
NEANDERTHAL   ALLEN, MARIJANE   PM   NYT 56
  APEMAN, SPACEMAN   STOVER & HARRISON   AN
NEANDERTHAL PLANET (A TOUCH OF NEANDERTHAL)
                              ALDISS, BRIAN W.   NV   SFA 60 09
  INTANGIBLES INC. AND OTHER STORIES ALDISS, BRIAN W.   AC
  NEANDERTHAL PLANET   ALDISS, BRIAN W.   AC
NEAR MISS   KUTTNER, HENRY   SS   NEW 58 04
  SF:58, THE YEAR'S GREATEST SCIENCE FICTION AND FANTASY
                                      MERRIL, JUDITH   AN
NEBULA AWARD S. F., 1965-1970, THE FICTION
                              STURGEON, THEODORE   MS
  NEBULA AWARD STORIES NO. 7   BIGGLE, LLOYD JR.   AN
NEBULA AWARD S. F., 1965-1970, THE SCIENCE
                              ANDERSON, POUL   MS
  NEBULA AWARD STORIES NO. 7   BIGGLE, LLOYD JR.   AN
NEBULA AWARDS   MISC. MATERIAL   MS
  NEBULA AWARD STORIES 8   ASIMOV, ISAAC   AN
NEBULA AWARDS, 1975: WIN, PLACE, AND SHOW
                              MISC. MATERIAL   MS
  NEBULA AWARD STORIES 11   LE GUIN, URSULA K.   AN
NEBULA WINNERS, 1965-1973, THE MISC. MATERIAL   MS
  NEBULA AWARD STORIES 9   WILHELM, KATE   AN
NECESSARY AND SUFFICIENT   STURGEON, THEODORE   SS   GAL 71 04
  BEST FROM GALAXY, THE VOLUME I   GALAXY, EDITORS OF   AN

NEW ACCELERATOR, THI

NECESSARY THING, THE   SHECKLEY, ROBERT   SS   GAL 55 06
  PEOPLE TRAP AND OTHER PITFALLS, THE SHECKLEY, ROBERT   AC
NECROMANCER   DICKSON, GORDON R.   NO   DBL 62
  THREE TO DORSAI!   DICKSON, GORDON R.   AC
NECROMANTIC TALE, THE   SMITH, CLARK ASHTON SS   WRT 31 01
  OTHER DIMENSIONS   SMITH, CLARK ASHTON   AC
  WIZARDS AND WARLOCKS   GHIDALIA, VIC   AN
NEDRA AT F:5.6 (THE HUNGRY ONE)
                              ELLISON, HARLAN   SS   GNT 57 03
  NO DOORS, NO WINDOWS (STORIES REWRITTEN) ELLISON, HARLAN AC
NEED   STURGEON, THEODORE   NV   NEW 60 AC
  BEYOND   STURGEON, THEODORE   AC
NEEDED: FEMININE MATH   CUMMINGS, PARKE   AR   61
  MATHEMATICAL MAGPIE, THE   FADIMAN, CLIFTON   AN
NEGOTIATORS, THE   LAUMER, KEITH   SS   ASF 75 02
  RETIEF: EMISSARY TO THE STARS LAUMER, KEITH   AC
NEGRA SUM   DAVIDSON, AVRAM   SS   FSF 57 11
  OR ALL THE SEAS WITH OYSTERS DAVIDSON, AVRAM   AC
NEIGHBOR   SILVERBERG, ROBERT   SS   GAL 64 08
  CUBE ROOT OF UNCERTAINTY, THE SILVERBERG, ROBERT   AC
  SUNDANCE AND OTHER SCIENCE FICTION STORIES
                                          SILVERBERG, ROBERT   AC
NEIGHBOR   SIMAK, CLIFFORD D.   NV   ASF 54 06
  ALIENS FOR NEIGHBOURS   SIMAK, CLIFFORD D.   AC
  BEST SCIENCE FICTION STORIES OF CLIFFORD D. SIMAK
                                          SIMAK, CLIFFORD D.   AC
  SPACE 1   DAVIS, RICHARD   OA
  *WORLDS OF CLIFFORD SIMAK, THE   SIMAK, CLIFFORD D.   AC
NEIGHBORS, THE   BEAUMONT, CHARLES   SS   NEW 60 AC
  EDGE, THE   BEAUMONT, CHARLES   AC
  NIGHT RIDE AND OTHER JOURNEYS BEAUMONT, CHARLES   AC
NEITHER DO THEY REAP   YOUNG, ROBERT F.   NV
  GLASS OF STARS, A   YOUNG, ROBERT F.   AC
NEITHER SNOW NOR RAIN (NOT SNOW NOR RAIN)
                              DEFORD, MIRIAM ALLEN SS   IFS 59 11
  FLYING SAUCERS IN FACT AND FICTION SANTESSON, HANS S. AN
NEITHER YOUR JENNY NOR MINE   ELLISON, HARLAN   SS   KNT 64 04
  *LOVE AIN'T NOTHING BUT SEX MISSPELLED ELLISON, HARLAN AC
NELLIE FOSTER   DERLETH, AUGUST   SS   WRT 33 06
  NOT LONG FOR THIS WORLD   DERLETH, AUGUST   AC
NELLTHU   BOUCHER, ANTHONY   SS   FSF 55 08
  BEST FROM FANTASY AND SCIENCE FICTION: 5
                                          BOUCHER, ANTHONY   AN
  DARK SIDE, THE   KNIGHT, DAMON   AN
  DEALS WITH THE DEVIL   DAVENPORT, BASIL   AN
NEON   ELLISON, HARLAN   SS   HOH 73 08
  DEATHBIRD STORIES   ELLISON, HARLAN   AC
NEOSHO'S CHOICEST (SEE THE GIRLS WHO WERE REALLY BUILT)
                              GUNN, JAMES E.   TC
NEPTUNE (SIREN SATELLITE)   BARNES, ARTHUR K.   NV   TWS 48 WI
  INTERPLANETARY HUNTER   BARNES, ARTHUR K.   AC
NERVELESS MAN, THE   WANDREI, DONALD   SS   ASF 34 07
  EYE AND THE FINGER   WANDREI, DONALD   AC
NERVES   DEL REY, LESTER   NV   ASF 42 09
  *ADVENTURES IN TIME AND SPACE HEALY & MCCOMAS   AN
  *AND SOME WERE HUMAN   DEL REY, LESTER   AC
  SCIENCE FICTION HALL OF FAME VOLUME 2A BOVA, BEN   AN
NETWORK   MALZBERG, BARRY N.   SS   FAN 74 01
  BEST OF BARRY N. MALZBERG, THE MALZBERG, BARRY N.   AC
NEURO-GENERATION, THE   INOUYE, JON   SS
  NIGHT TIDE, A   INOUYE, JON   OC
NEUTRAL GROUND   SPINRAD, NORMAN   SS   FSF 66 11
  LAST HURRAH OF THE GOLDEN HORDE, THE SPINRAD, NORMAN   AC
NEUTRAL PLANET   SILVERBERG, ROBERT   SS   SFS 57 07
  GODLING, GO HOME!   SILVERBERG, ROBERT   AC
  SUNDANCE AND OTHER SCIENCE FICTION STORIES
                                          SILVERBERG, ROBERT   AC
NEUTRINO BOMB, THE   COOPER, RALPH S.   SS   LAS 61 07
  GREAT SCIENCE FICTION BY SCIENTISTS CONKLIN, GROFF   AN
NEUTRON STAR   NIVEN, LARRY   NV   IFS 66 10
  HUGO WINNERS, THE (VOLUME 2) ASIMOV, ISAAC   AN
  NEUTRON STAR   NIVEN, LARRY   AC
  SPECULATIONS   SANDERS, THOMAS E.   AN
  WHERE DO WE GO FROM HERE?   ASIMOV, ISAAC   AN
NEUTRON TIDE, THE   CLARKE, ARTHUR C.   SS   GAL 70 05
  WIND FROM THE SUN, THE   CLARKE, ARTHUR C.   AC
NEVER ENDING PENNY, THE   WOLFE, BERNARD   SS   PBY 60 09
  PLAYBOY BOOK OF SCIENCE FICTION AND FANTASY, THE
                                          PLAYBOY, EDITORS OF AN
  6TH ANNUAL OF THE YEAR'S BEST S-F, THE MERRIL, JUDITH AN
NEVER MEET AGAIN   BUDRYS, ALGIS   SS   INF 58 03
  UNEXPECTED DIMENSION, THE   BUDRYS, ALGIS   AC
NEVER ON MARS   WYNDHAM, JOHN   SS   FUN 54 01
  GATEWAY TO THE STARS   CARNELL, JOHN   AN
NEVER UNDERESTIMATE...   STURGEON, THEODORE   SS   IFS 52 03
  OMNIBUS OF SCIENCE FICTION   CONKLIN, GROFF   AN
  STRANGE ADVENTURES IN SCIENCE FICTION CONKLIN, GROFF   AN
  17 X INFINITY   CONKLIN, GROFF   AN
NEVER-ENDING WESTERN MOVIE, THE
                              SHECKLEY, ROBERT   SS
  SCIENCE FICTION DISCOVERIES POHL, C. & F.   AN
NEW ACCELERATOR, THE   WELLS, H. G.   SS   SND 01 12
  BEST SCIENCE FICTION STORIES OF H. G. WELLS
                                          WELLS, H. G.   AC
  BEST STORIES OF H. G. WELLS WELLS, H. G.   AC
  *BEYOND TIME AND SPACE   DERLETH, AUGUST   AC
  COUNTRY OF THE BLIND, THE   WELLS, H. G.   AC
  INVISIBLE MEN   DAVENPORT, BASIL   AN
  MASTERS' CHOICE   JANIFER, LAURENCE M.   AN
  SHORT STORIES OF H. G. WELLS, THE WELLS, H. G.   AC
  STRANGE ECSTASIES   PARRY, MICHEL   AN
  TWELVE STORIES AND A DREAM   WELLS, H. G.   AC
  TWENTY-EIGHT SCIENCE FICTION STORIES WELLS, H. G.   AC
  3000 YEARS OF FANTASY AND SCIENCE FICTION
                                          DE CAMP, L. S.&C.   AN

```
NEW AGE, A
NEW AGE, A                     ALLEN, DICK          PM   SFD 72
  LOOKING AHEAD                ALLEN, D. & L.            AN
NEW APPLES IN THE GARDEN       NEVILLE, KRIS        NV   ASF 63 07
  NIGHTMARE AGE                POHL, FREDERIK            AN
  ONE HUNDRED YEARS OF SCIENCE FICTION  KNIGHT, DAMON    AN
NEW ARCADIA                    DE CAMP, L. SPRAGUE  NV   FUT 56 30
  GUN FOR DINOSAUR AND OTHER IMAGINATIVE TALES
                               DE CAMP, L. SPRAGUE       AC
NEW ATLANTIS, THE              LE GUIN, URSULA K.   NA   NAL 75
  BEST SCIENCE FICTION OF THE YEAR, THE NO. 5
                               CARR, TERRY               AN
  NEW ATLANTIS AND OTHER NOVELLAS OF S.F., THE
                               SILVERBERG, ROBERT        OA
NEW ATLANTIS, THE (1624)       BACON, FRANCIS       EX
  *BEYOND TIME AND SPACE       DERLETH, AUGUST           AN
NEW BALLAD OF SIR PATRICK SPENS, A
                               QUILLER-COUCH, A. T. PM
  FANTASIA MATHEMATICA         FADIMAN, CLIFTON          AN
NEW BLOOD                      GUNN, JAMES E.       NV   ASF 55 10
  IMMORTALS, THE               GUNN, JAMES E.            NO
  SOME DREAMS ARE NIGHTMARES   GUNN, JAMES E.            AC
NEW CANUTE                     RICKETTS, MARTIN I.  SS   NWR 74 24
  NEW WRITINGS IN SF. 24       BULMER, KENNETH           OA
NEW DICTIONARY (THE RANDOM HOUSE DICTIONARY)
                               VONNEGUT, KURT JR.   BR   NYT 66 10
  WELCOME TO THE MONKEY HOUSE  VONNEGUT, KURT JR.        AC
NEW DIRECTIONS                 FIEDLER, LESLIE A.   SI
  IN DREAMS AWAKE              FIEDLER, LESLIE A.        AN
NEW ENCYCLOPAEDIST, THE        BECKER, STEPHEN      SS   FSF 64 05
  10TH ANNUAL OF THE YEAR'S BEST S-F, THE  MERRIL, JUDITH   AN
NEW EXPERIENCE                 TUBB, E. C.          SS   NWS 64 10
  BEST OF NEW WORLDS, THE      MOORCOCK, MICHAEL         AN
NEW FATHER CHRISTMAS, THE      ALDISS, BRIAN W.     SS   FSF 58 01
  *BEST SCIENCE FICTION STORIES OF BRIAN W. ALDISS
                               ALDISS, BRIAN W.          AC
  METAL SMILE, THE             KNIGHT, DAMON             AN
  NO TIME LIKE TOMORROW        ALDISS, BRIAN W.          AC
NEW FOLKS' HOME                SIMAK, CLIFFORD D.   SS   ASF 63 07
  ANALOG 3                     CAMPBELL, JOHN W. JR      AN
  BEST SCIENCE FICTION STORIES OF CLIFFORD D. SIMAK
                               SIMAK, CLIFFORD D.        AC
  PAST, PRESENT, AND FUTURE PERFECT  WOLFE, J&FITZ GERALD  AN
NEW FOUNDATIONS                SHIRAS, WILMAR H.    NV   ASF 50 03
  CHILDREN OF THE ATOM         SHIRAS, WILMAR H.         AC
NEW GAME, A                    LIGHTNER, A. M.      SS   BLF 59
  BOYS' LIFE BOOK OF OUTER SPACE STORIES, THE
                               BOY'S LIFE, ED. OF        AN
  TEEN-AGE OUTER SPACE STORIES FURMAN, A. L.             AN
NEW GOD WAS BORN, A            TRAVERN, B.          AR
  ANCIENT MYSTERIES READER, THE   HAINING, PETER         AN
NEW GODS LEAD, THE             WRIGHT, S. FOWLER    AC   JAR 32
  THRONE OF SATURN, THE        WRIGHT, S. FOWLER         AC
NEW GODS LEAD, THE (SEE THE OLD ORDER)
                               DEL REY, LESTER      TC
NEW INTRODUCTION: HAVING AN AFFAIR WITH A TROLL
                               ELLISON, HARLAN      IN
  LOVE AIN'T NOTHING BUT SEX MISSPELLED (REVISED)
                               ELLISON, HARLAN           AC
NEW INTRODUCTION: YOUR BASIC CROWN OF THORNS
                               ELLISON, HARLAN      IN
  PAINGOD AND OTHER DELUSIONS (THIRD EDITION ADDS:)
                               ELLISON, HARLAN           AC
NEW KINGS ARE NOT FOR LAUGHING BUNCH, DAVID R.      SS
  MODERAN                      BUNCH, DAVID R.           AC
NEW LOI, A                     GOULART, RON         SS   FSF 58 01
  BEST FROM FANTASY AND SCIENCE FICTION: 8
                               BOUCHER, ANTHONY          AN
NEW MEN FOR MARS               SILVERBERG, ROBERT   NV   SUP 57 06
  TO WORLDS BEYOND             SILVERBERG, ROBERT        AC
NEW NEW YORK NEW ORLEANS       EFFINGER, GEO. ALEC  SS   NMD 73
  FRONTIERS 2: THE NEW MIND    ELWOOD, ROGER             OA
NEW ONE, THE                   BROWN, FREDRIC       SS   UNK 42 10
  PARADOX LOST, AND 12 OTHER GREAT S.F. STORIES
                               BROWN, FREDRIC            AC
NEW PEOPLE, THE                BEAUMONT, CHARLES    SS   ROG 58
  EDGE, THE                    BEAUMONT, CHARLES         AC
  MAGIC MAN AND OTHER SCIENCE-FANTASY STORIES
                               BEAUMONT, CHARLES         AC
  NIGHT RIDE AND OTHER JOURNEYS   BEAUMONT, CHARLES      AC
NEW PRIME, THE                 VANCE, JACK          NV
  EIGHT FANTASMS AND MAGICS    VANCE, JACK               AC
NEW RAPPACINI, THE             O'DONNELL, K. M.     SS   FAN 70 12
  IN THE POCKET AND OTHER S-F STORIES   O'DONNELL, K. M.  DC
NEW REALITY, THE               HARNESS, CHARLES L.  NV   TWS 50 12
  AS TOMORROW BECOMES TODAY    SULLIVAN, WALTER H.       AN
  BEST SCIENCE-FICTION STORIES: 1951, THE  BLEILER & DIKTY   AN
  ROSE, THE                    HARNESS, CHARLES L.       AC
  SHAPE OF THINGS, THE         KNIGHT, DAMON             AN
NEW RITUAL                     SEABRIGHT, IDRIS     SS   FSF 53 01
  BEST FROM FANTASY AND SCIENCE FICTION: 3
                               BOUCHER & MCCOMAS         AN
NEW SCIENCE FICTION, THE       BALLARD, J. G.
  AND MACBETH, GEORGE          AR C
  NEW S.F., THE                JONES, LANGDON            OA
NEW SIGNAL STATION, THE        GANSOVSKY, SEVER     SS
  LAST DOOR TO AIYA            GINSBURG, MIRRA           AN
NEW SOUND, THE                 BEAUMONT, CHARLES    SS   FSF 55 06
  ABOVE THE HUMAN LANDSCAPE    MCNELLY & STOVER          AN
  EDGE, THE                    BEAUMONT, CHARLES         AC
  YONDER                       BEAUMONT, CHARLES         AC
NEW THING, THE                 BRUNNER, JOHN        SS   IFS 69 12
  BOOK OF JOHN BRUNNER, THE    BRUNNER, JOHN             AC
NEW TOMORROWS, THE             SPINRAD, NORMAN      IN
  NEW TOMORROWS, THE           SPINRAD, NORMAN           AN
NEW WINE, THE                  CHRISTOPHER, JOHN    SS   FSM 54 SU
  BEST SF                      CRISPIN, EDMUND           AN

  SCIENCE FICTION              BURTON, S. H.             AN
  TWENTY-SECOND CENTURY, THE   CHRISTOPHER, JOHN         AC
NEW WORLDS                     GARDNER, EARL S.     NV   ARG 32 12
  OTHER WORLDS, OTHER TIMES    MOSKOWITZ & ELWOOD        AN
NEW YEAR'S FAIRY TALE, A       DUDINTSEV, VLADIMIR  SS
  RUSSIAN SCIENCE FICTION      MAGIDOFF, ROBERT          AN
NEW YORK A.D. 2660 (RALPH 124C 41+)
                               GERNSBACK, HUGO      EX   MEL 11 04
  CITY: 2000 A.D., THE         CLEM/GREENBERG/&          AN
  FUTURE TENSE                 CURTIS, RICHARD           AN
NEW YORK TIMES                 PLATT, CHARLES       SS   ORB 72 11
  ORBIT 11                     KNIGHT, DAMON             OA
NEW YOU, THE                   REED, KIT            SS   FSF 62 09
  MARRIAGE AND THE FAMILY THROUGH SCIENCE FICTION
                               CLEAR/WARRICK/&           AN
NEW-METAL                      BUNCH, DAVID R.      SS
  MODERAN                      BUNCH, DAVID R.           AC
NEW-METAL MISTRESS TIME        BUNCH, DAVID R.      SS
  MODERAN                      BUNCH, DAVID R.           AC
NEWSOCRATS: CONFESSIONS OF A EUNICH DREAMER, THE
                               WYAL, PG             SS
  FUTURE PASTIMES              EDELSTEIN, SCOTT          OA
NEXT DOOR                      VONNEGUT, KURT JR.   SS   CMP 55 04
  WELCOME TO THE MONKEY HOUSE  VONNEGUT, KURT JR.        AC
NEXT IN LINE, THE              BRADBURY, RAY        NV   NEW 47 AC
  *DARK CARNIVAL               BRADBURY, RAY             AC
  *OCTOBER COUNTRY, THE        BRADBURY, RAY             AC
  SMALL ASSASSIN, THE          BRADBURY, RAY             AC
NEXT LOGICAL STEP, THE         BOVA, BEN            SS   ASF 62 05
  FORWARD IN TIME              BOVA, BEN                 AC
NEXT STOP: THE STARS (SEE THE END OF THE BEGINNING)
                               BRADBURY, RAY        TC
NEXT TENANTS, THE              CLARKE, ARTHUR C.    SS   SAT 57 02
  ACROSS THE SEA OF STARS      CLARKE, ARTHUR C.         AC
  TALES FROM THE WHITE HART    CLARKE, ARTHUR C.         AC
NI VAR                         GABRIEL, CLAIRE      NV
  STAR TREK: THE NEW VOYAGES   MARSHAK, S&CULBREATH      OA
NICE DAY FOR SCREAMING, A      SCHMITZ, JAMES H.    SS   ASF 65 01
  NICE DAY FOR SCREAMING, AND OTHER TALES OF THE HUB
                               SCHMITZ, JAMES H.         AC
NICE GIRL WITH FIVE HUSBANDS   LEIBER, FRITZ        SS   GAL 51 04
  PAIL OF AIR, A               LEIBER, FRITZ             AC
  TIME CURVE, THE              MOSKOWITZ & ELWOOD        AN
  WORLDS OF FRITZ LEIBER, THE  LEIBER, FRITZ             AC
  13 ABOVE THE NIGHT           CONKLIN, GROFF            AN
NICE GUYS FINISH SOMEWHERE IN THE MIDDLE
                               ELLISON, HARLAN      IN
  LIGHT AT THE END OF THE UNIVERSE, THE   CARR, TERRY    AC
NICHE IN TIME, A               TEMPLE, WILLIAM F.   SS   ASF 64 05
  WORLD'S BEST SCIENCE FICTION: 1965   WOLLHEIM & CARR   AN
NIGGER OF THE NARCISSUS        CONRAD, JOSEPH       EX
  VOYAGES: SCENARIOS FOR A SHIP CALLED EARTH
                               SAUER, ROB                AN
NIGHT                          CAMPBELL, JOHN W. JR NV   ASF 35 10
  EVIL EARTHS                  ALDISS, BRIAN W.          AN
  MICROCOSMIC GOD              MOSKOWITZ, SAM            AN
  MODERN MASTERPIECES OF SCIENCE FICTION   MOSKOWITZ, SAM   AN
  WHERE DO WE GO FROM HERE?    ASIMOV, ISAAC             AN
  WHO GOES THERE?              CAMPBELL, JOHN W. JR      AC
  WHO GOES THERE? AND OTHER STORIES   CAMPBELL, JOHN W. JR   AC
NIGHT                          OLIVER, CHAD         SS   IFS 55 03
  ANOTHER KIND                 OLIVER, CHAD              AC
NIGHT AND MORNING OF THE IDIOT CHILD
                               KIDD, VIRGINIA       PM   BER 74
  BERSERKERS, THE              ELWOOD, ROGER             OA
NIGHT AND THE LOVES OF JOE DICOSTANZO
                               DELANY, SAMUEL R.    SS   ANA 70
  ALCHEMY AND ACADEME          MCCAFFREY, ANNE           OA
  DRIFTGLASS                   DELANY, SAMUEL R.         AC
NIGHT AT THE FAIR, A           RAMSAY, KATHRYN      SS
  FUTURE PASTIMES              EDELSTEIN, SCOTT          OA
NIGHT BEFORE CHRISTMAS, THE    COE, NANCY FORSYTHE  PM        59
  FLYING SAUCERS IN FACT AND FICTION   SANTESSON, HANS S.   AN
NIGHT BOXING ENDED, THE        FRIEDMAN, BRUCE JAY  SS   GMQ 66
  ARENA: SPORTS SF             FERMAN & MALZBERG         AN
NIGHT CALL, COLLECT            BRADBURY, RAY        SS   NEW 69 AC
  I SING THE BODY ELECTRIC     BRADBURY, RAY             AC
NIGHT COURT                    COUNSELMAN, MARY E.  NV   WRT 53 03
  GRAVEYARD READER, THE        CONKLIN, GROFF            AN
NIGHT DRIVE                    JENKINS, WILL F.     SS   TDW 60
  *TWISTED                     CONKLIN, GROFF            AN
NIGHT FLIGHT                   JOHNSON, JOSEPHINE   SS   HRP 44 02
  TIMELESS STORIES FOR TODAY AND TOMORROW   BRADBURY, RAY   AN
NIGHT HE CRIED, THE            LEIBER, FRITZ        SS   STR 53 01
  BEST OF FRITZ LEIBER, THE    LEIBER, FRITZ             AC
  GALAXY OF GHOULS             MERRIL, JUDITH            AN
  GENTLE INVADERS              SANTESSON, HANS S.        AN
  STAR SCIENCE FICTION STORIES POHL, FREDERIK            OA
NIGHT IN ELF HILL, A           SPINRAD, NORMAN      SS   FRS 68
  FARTHEST REACHES             ELDER, JOSEPH             OA
  LAST HURRAH OF THE GOLDEN HORDE, THE   SPINRAD, NORMAN   AC
NIGHT IN FUNLAND               PENDEN, WILLIAM      SS        60
  NIGHT IN FUNLAND             BRONDFIELD, JEROME        AN
NIGHT IN MALNEANT, A           SMITH, CLARK ASHTON  SS   WRT 39 09
  EDGE OF NEVER, THE           HOSKINS, ROBERT           AN
  OUT OF SPACE AND TIME        SMITH, CLARK ASHTON       AC
NIGHT IN THE BYZANTINE PALACE, A
                               RUSSELL, RAY         SS   PBY
  SAGITTARIUS                  RUSSELL, RAY              AC
NIGHT IS COLD, THE STARS ARE FAR AWAY, THE
                               BROXON, MILDRED D.   SS   UNI 74 05
  BEST SCIENCE FICTION STORIES OF THE YEAR (1974)
                               DEL REY, LESTER           AN
  UNIVERSE 5                   CARR, TERRY               OA
NIGHT MEETING                  BRADBURY, RAY        SS   NEW 51 AC
  ADVENTURES IN DIMENSION      CONKLIN, GROFF            AN
```

MARTIAN CHRONICLES, THE	BRADBURY, RAY			AC	
*SCIENCE FICTION ADVENTURES IN DIMENSION	CONKLIN, GROFF			AN	
VINTAGE BRADBURY, THE	BRADBURY, RAY			AC	
NIGHT OF DELICATE TERRORS, THE	ELLISON, HARLAN	SS	PPR 61	04	
*LOVE AIN'T NOTHING BUT SEX MISSPELLED	ELLISON, HARLAN			AN	
NIGHT OF HOGGY DARN, THE	MCKENNA, RICHARD	NV	IFS 58	12	
ALPHA 7	SILVERBERG, ROBERT			AN	
NIGHT OF HOGGY DARN, THE	MCKENNA, RICHARD M.	NV	IFS 58	12	
TOMORROW X 4	KNIGHT, DAMON			AN	
NIGHT OF LIES, THE	KNIGHT, DAMON	SS	FSF 58	10	
TURNING ON	KNIGHT, DAMON			AC	
NIGHT OF THE GRAN BAILE MASCARA, THE (1935)					
	BURNETT, WHIT	SS	EQM 65	07	
FIEND IN YOU, THE	BEAUMONT, CHARLES			AN	
NIGHT OF THE LEOPARD	SAMBROT, WILLIAM	NV	67		
NEW AWARENESS, THE	WARRICK & GREENBERG			AN	
SOCIAL PROBLEMS THROUGH SCIENCE FICTION	GREENBERG/MILSTEAD/&			AN	
NIGHT OF THE LONG KNIVES, THE (SEE THE WOLF PAIR)					
	LEIBER, FRITZ	TC			
NIGHT OF THE MEEK	SERLING, ROD	SA			
NEW STORIES FROM THE TWILIGHT ZONE	SERLING, ROD			OC	
NIGHT OF THE MILLENNIUM	HOCH, EDWARD D.	SS			
OTHER SIDE OF TOMORROW, THE	ELWOOD, ROGER			OA	
NIGHT OF THE NICKEL BEER, THE	NEVILLE, KRIS	SS	ESC 67		
NEW WORLDS OF FANTASY NO. 2	CARR, TERRY			AN	
NIGHT OF THE PUUDLY, THE (GOOD NIGHT, MR. JAMES)					
	SIMAK, CLIFFORD D.	NV	GAL 51	03	
NIGHT OF THE PUUDLY, THE	SIMAK, CLIFFORD D.			AC	
NIGHT OF THE SEVENTH FINGER, THE					
	PRESSLIE, ROBERT	SS	NWR 66	07	
NEW WRITINGS IN SF. 7	CARNELL, JOHN			AN	
NEW WRITINGS IN SF. 7	CARNELL, JOHN			OA	
TALES OF TERROR FROM OUTER SPACE	CHETWYND-HAYES, R.			AN	
NIGHT OF THE SPHINX	EXTER, MAUREEN	SS			
NIGHT OF THE SPHINX AND OTHER STORIES	ELWOOD, ROGER			OA	
NIGHT OF THE STORM, THE	KOONTZ, DEAN R.	NV	CTM 74	01	
CONTINUUM 1	ELWOOD, ROGER			OA	
NIGHT OF THE TROLLS, THE	LAUMER, KEITH	SN	WOT 63	10	
BOLO	LAUMER, KEITH			AC	
GREYLORN	LAUMER, KEITH			AC	
UNDEFEATED, THE	LAUMER, KEITH			AC	
NIGHT OF THE VAMPYRES, THE	MARTIN, GEORGE R. R.	NV	AMZ 75	05	
SONGS OF STARS AND SHADOWS	MARTIN, GEORGE R. R.			AC	
NIGHT PASSAGE	LEIBER, FRITZ	NV	75		
WORLDS OF FRITZ LEIBER, THE	LEIBER, FRITZ			AC	
NIGHT PIECE	ANDERSON, POUL	SS	FSF 61	07	
WORLDS OF SCIENCE FICTION, THE	MILLS, ROBERT P.			AN	
NIGHT RIDE	BEAUMONT, CHARLES	SS	PBY 57	03	
EDGE, THE	BEAUMONT, CHARLES			AC	
NIGHT RIDE AND OTHER JOURNEYS	BEAUMONT, CHARLES			AC	
NIGHT SCHOOL	BLOCH, ROBERT	SS	ROG 59	08	
TALES IN A JUGULAR VEIN	BLOCH, ROBERT			AC	
NIGHT SEARCH	FRANKLIN, DONALD	SS			
STRANGE ENCOUNTERS	BISCHOFF, DAVID			OA	
NIGHT SEQUENCE	PRIESTLEY, J. B.	SS	FSF 56	03	
OTHER PLACE, THE	PRIESTLEY, J. B.			AC	
NIGHT SETS, THE	BRADBURY, RAY	SS	NEW 47	AC	
*DARK CARNIVAL	BRADBURY, RAY			AC	
NIGHT SHIFT	MARTIN, GEORGE R. R.	SS	AMZ 73	01	
SONGS OF STARS AND SHADOWS	MARTIN, GEORGE R. R.			AC	
NIGHT TALK	FRITCH, CHARLES E.	SS	STS 52	09	
CRAZY MIXED-UP PLANET	FRITCH, CHARLES E.			AC	
NIGHT THAT ALL TIME BROKE OUT, THE					
	ALDISS, BRIAN W.	SS	DVS 67	01	
DANGEROUS VISIONS	ELLISON, HARLAN			OA	
EARTH IS THE STRANGEST PLANET	SILVERBERG, ROBERT			AN	
NIGHT TIDE, A	INOUYE, JON	SS			
NIGHT TIDE, A	INOUYE, JON			OC	
NIGHT TRAIN TO LOST VALLEY, THE					
	DERLETH, AUGUST	SS	WRT 48	01	
MR. GEORGE AND OTHER ODD PERSONS	DERLETH, AUGUST			AC	
NIGHT VIGIL (YELLOW STREAK HERO)					
	ELLISON, HARLAN	SS	AMZ 57	05	
ALONE AGAINST TOMORROW	ELLISON, HARLAN			AC	
OVER THE EDGE	ELLISON, HARLAN			AC	
NIGHT WATCH	INGLIS, JAMES	SS	NWR 65	03	
BEST FROM NEW WRITINGS IN S-F FIRST SELECTION, THE					
	CARNELL, JOHN			AN	
NEW WRITINGS IN SF. 3	CARNELL, JOHN			OA	
SPACE ODYSSEYS	ALDISS, BRIAN W.			AN	
NIGHT WIND, THE	PANGBORN, EDGAR	SS	UNI 74	05	
UNIVERSE 5	CARR, TERRY			OA	
NIGHT-FEAR	LONG, FRANK BELKNAP	SS	DSF 53	10	
NOVELETS OF SCIENCE FICTION	HOWARD, IVAN			AN	
NIGHT-FLAME, THE	KAPP, COLIN	SS	NWR 64	02	
BEST FROM NEW WRITINGS IN S-F FIRST SELECTION, THE					
	CARNELL, JOHN			AN	
NEW WRITINGS IN SF. 2	CARNELL, JOHN			OA	
NIGHT-MARRIAGE	THOMAS, D. M.	PM	NWQ 73	05	
NEW WORLDS NO. 5	MOORCOCK & PLATT			OA	
NIGHT, THE	BRADBURY, RAY	SS	WRT 46	07	
DANDELION WINE	BRADBURY, RAY			NO	
*DARK CARNIVAL	BRADBURY, RAY			AC	
SMALL ASSASSIN, THE	BRADBURY, RAY			AC	
NIGHTBEAT	BARRETT, NEAL JR.	SS	EPC 75		
EPOCH	ELWOOD & SILVERBERG			AN	
NIGHTBLOOMING SAURIAN, THE	TIPTREE, JAMES JR.	SS	IFS 70	05	
BEST FROM IF, THE VOLUME I	IF, EDITORS OF			AN	
WARM WORLDS AND OTHERWISE	TIPTREE, JAMES JR.			AC	
NIGHTFALL	ASIMOV, ISAAC	NV	ASF 41	09	
*ADVENTURES IN TIME AND SPACE	HEALY & MCCOMAS			AN	
ANTHROPOLOGY THROUGH SCIENCE FICTION	MASON, C/GREENBERG/&			AN	
*ASTOUNDING SCIENCE FICTION ANTHOLOGY, THE					
	CAMPBELL, JOHN W. JR			AN	
ASTOUNDING-ANALOG READER, THE VOLUME ONE	HARRISON & ALDISS			AN	
BEST OF ISAAC ASIMOV, THE	ASIMOV, ISAAC			AC	
BEYOND TOMORROW	KNIGHT, DAMON			AN	
GREAT SCIENCE FICTION STORIES	SMITH, CORDELIA T.			AN	
MIRROR OF INFINITY, THE	SILVERBERG, ROBERT			AN	
MODERN SCIENCE FICTION	SPINRAD, NORMAN			AN	
MORE ADVENTURES IN TIME AND SPACE	HEALY & MCCOMAS			AN	
NIGHTFALL AND OTHER STORIES	ASIMOV, ISAAC			AC	
OTHER DIMENSION, THE	ROSNER, SARA			AN	
PENGUIN SCIENCE FICTION	ALDISS, BRIAN W.			AN	
SCIENCE FICTION	BURTON, S. H.			AN	
SCIENCE FICTION HALL OF FAME VOLUME 1	SILVERBERG, ROBERT			AN	
SECOND ASTOUNDING SCIENCE FICTION ANTHOLOGY, THE (PB)					
	CAMPBELL, JOHN W. JR			AN	
TOMORROW, AND TOMORROW, AND TOMORROW...	HEINTZ/HERBERT/JOOS/			AN	
UBERWINDUNG VON RAUM UND ZEIT	GUNTHER, GOTTHARD			AN	
NIGHTMARE	DOLAN, MIKE	SS			
SANTANA MORNING AND OTHER STORIES	DOLAN, MIKE			OC	
NIGHTMARE	WANDREI, DONALD	SS			
STRANGE HARVEST	WANDREI, DONALD			AC	
NIGHTMARE AT 20,000 FEET	MATHESON, RICHARD	SS	NEW 62	AN	
ALONE BY NIGHT	CONGDON, MICHAEL&DON			AN	
SHOCK III	MATHESON, RICHARD			AC	
NIGHTMARE BLUES (OPERATION SYNDROME)					
	HERBERT, FRANK	NV	ASF 54	06	
BEST OF FRANK HERBERT, THE	HERBERT, FRANK			AC	
BEST SCIENCE FICTION STORIES AND NOVELS: 1955					
	DIKTY, T. E.			AN	
NIGHTMARE BROTHER	NOURSE, ALAN E.	NV	ASF 53	02	
SCIENCE FICTION TERROR TALES	CONKLIN, GROFF			AN	
SPACE, SPACE, SPACE	SLOANE, WILLIAM			AN	
TIGER BY THE TAIL	NOURSE, ALAN E.			AC	
UNIVERSE AHEAD	ENGDAHL & ROBERSON			AN	
NIGHTMARE FOR FUTURE REFERENCE	BENET, STEPHEN V.	PM	SCH 38	09	
CHILDREN OF WONDER	TENN, WILLIAM			AN	
VOICE OF THE DOLPHINS, AND OTHER STORIES, THE					
	SZILARD, LEO			AC	
NIGHTMARE GANG	KOONTZ, DEAN R.	SS	INY 70	01	
EDGE OF NEVER, THE	HOSKINS, ROBERT			AN	
INFINITY 1	HOSKINS, ROBERT			OA	
NIGHTMARE IN BLUE	BROWN, FREDRIC	SS			
NIGHTMARES AND GEEZENSTACKS	BROWN, FREDRIC			AC	
NIGHTMARE IN GRAY	BROWN, FREDRIC	SS			
NIGHTMARES AND GEEZENSTACKS	BROWN, FREDRIC			AC	
NIGHTMARE IN GREEN	BROWN, FREDRIC	SS			
NIGHTMARES AND GEEZENSTACKS	BROWN, FREDRIC			AC	
NIGHTMARE IN RED	BROWN, FREDRIC	SS			
NIGHTMARES AND GEEZENSTACKS	BROWN, FREDRIC			AC	
NIGHTMARE IN TIME	BROWN, FREDRIC	SS	DUD 61		
7TH ANNUAL OF THE YEAR'S BEST S-F, THE	MERRIL, JUDITH			AN	
NIGHTMARE IN WHITE	BROWN, FREDRIC	SS			
NIGHTMARES AND GEEZENSTACKS	BROWN, FREDRIC			AC	
NIGHTMARE IN YELLOW	BROWN, FREDRIC	SS	DUD 61	05	
BEST OF FREDRIC BROWN, THE	BROWN, FREDRIC			AC	
NIGHTMARES AND GEEZENSTACKS	BROWN, FREDRIC			AC	
NIGHTMARE ISLAND	STURGEON, THEODORE	NV	UNK 41	06	
BEYOND	STURGEON, THEODORE			AC	
NIGHTMARE NUMBER FOUR	BLOCH, ROBERT	PM	NEW 59	AN	
SCIENCE FICTION SHOWCASE	KORNBLUTH, MARY			AN	
NIGHTMARE NUMBER THREE	BENET, STEPHEN V.	PM	35		
METAL SMILE, THE	KNIGHT, DAMON			AN	
SHOT IN THE DARK	MERRIL, JUDITH			AN	
SPECULATIONS	SANDERS, THOMAS E.			AN	
WONDERMAKERS	HOSKINS, ROBERT			AN	
NIGHTMARE PLANET	LEINSTER, MURRAY	SN	SFP 53	06	
FORGOTTEN PLANET, THE	LEINSTER, MURRAY			AC	
NIGHTMARE WITH ZEPPELINS	KORNBLUTH, C. M.				
	AND POHL, FREDERIK	NV C	GAL 58	12	
FIFTH GALAXY READER, THE	GOLD, H. L.			AN	
WONDER EFFECT, THE	POHL, F. & KORNBLUTH			AN	
NIGHTMARE, THE	DAVIS, CHAN	NV	ASF 46	05	
*TREASURY OF SCIENCE FICTION, A	CONKLIN, GROFF			AN	
NIGHTSONG	HACKER, MARILYN	PM	QRK 71	04	
QUARK/4	DELANY & HACKER			OA	
NIGHTSOUND (THE ATTIC VOICE)	BUDRYS, ALGIS	SS	SAT 57	02	
BEST SCIENCE FICTION STORIES AND NOVELS: 9TH SERIES					
	DIKTY, T. E.			AN	
NIGHTSPAWN	INOUYE, JON	SS			
NIGHT TIDE, A	INOUYE, JON			OC	
NIGHTWINGS	SILVERBERG, ROBERT	NV	GAL 68	09	
BEST OF ROBERT SILVERBERG, THE	SILVERBERG, ROBERT			AC	
ELEVENTH GALAXY READER, THE	POHL, FREDERIK			AN	
HUGO WINNERS, THE (VOLUME 2)	ASIMOV, ISAAC			AN	
INVADERS FROM SPACE	SILVERBERG, ROBERT			AN	
MOONFERNS & STARSONGS	SILVERBERG, ROBERT			AC	
NIKITA EISENHOWER JONES	YOUNG, ROBERT F.	NV	FSF 60	08	
BEST FROM FANTASY AND SCIENCE FICTION: 10					
	MILLS, ROBERT P.			AN	
NINA SOL	MARTI-IBANEZ, FELIX	SS	FSF 63	05	
BEST FROM FANTASY AND SCIENCE FICTION: 13					
	DAVIDSON, AVRAM			AN	
NINE BILLION NAMES OF GOD, THE	CLARKE, ARTHUR C.	SS	STR 53	01	
APEMAN, SPACEMAN	STOVER & HARRISON			AN	
ASPECTS OF SCIENCE FICTION	DOHERTY, G. D.			AN	
BEST SF 2	CRISPIN, EDMUND			AN	
IN DREAMS AWAKE	FIEDLER, LESLIE A.			AN	
INSIDE INFORMATION	MOWSHOWITZ, ABBE			AN	
MATHEMATICAL MAGPIE, THE	FADIMAN, CLIFTON			AN	
NEW AWARENESS, THE	WARRICK & GREENBERG			AN	
NINE BILLION NAMES OF GOD, THE	CLARKE, ARTHUR C.			AC	
OF TIME AND STARS	CLARKE, ARTHUR C.			AC	
ONE HUNDRED YEARS OF SCIENCE FICTION	KNIGHT, DAMON			AN	
OTHER SIDE OF THE SKY, THE	CLARKE, ARTHUR C.			AC	
OTHER WORLDS, OTHER GODS	MOHS, MAYO			AN	
OUT OF THIS WORLD 6	WILLIAMS-ELLIS& OWEN			AN	
SCIENCE FICTION HALL OF FAME VOLUME 1	SILVERBERG, ROBERT			AN	
STAR SCIENCE FICTION STORIES	POHL, FREDERIK			OA	
*STORIES FOR TOMORROW	SLOANE, WILLIAM			AN	

NINE DAYS TO DIE (STORY OF AN ATOMIC-AGE ORDEAL)
                                  SAMBROT, WILLIAM   SS   SEP 60 07
  ISLAND OF FEAR AND OTHER SCIENCE FICTION SAMBROT, WILLIAM   AC
NINE HUNDRED GRANDMOTHERS   LAFFERTY, R. A.   SS   IFS 66 02
  ALPHA 3   SILVERBERG, ROBERT   AN
  NINE HUNDRED GRANDMOTHERS   LAFFERTY, R. A.   AC
  WORLD'S BEST SCIENCE FICTION: 1967 WOLLHEIM & CARR   AN
NINE LIVES   LE GUIN, URSULA K.   NV   PBY 69 11
  AS TOMORROW BECOMES TODAY   SULLIVAN, CHARLES W.   AN
  BEST SF: 1969   HARRISON & ALDISS   AN
  BEYOND TOMORROW   HARDING, LEE   AN
  BIO-FUTURES   SARGENT, PAMELA   AN
  DEAD ASTRONAUT, 10 STORIES OF SPACE FLIGHT,
                                  PLAYBOY, EDITORS OF   AN
  IN DREAMS AWAKE   FIEDLER, LESLIE A.   AN
  INTRODUCTORY PSYCHOLOGY THROUGH SCIENCE FICTION
                                  KATZ/WARRICK/&   AN
  MODERN SCIENCE FICTION   SPINRAD, NORMAN   AN
  NEBULA AWARD STORIES NO. 5   BLISH, JAMES   AN
  THOSE WHO CAN: A SCIENCE FICTION READER WILSON, ROBIN SCOTT AN
  WINDS TWELVE QUARTERS, THE   LE GUIN, URSULA K.   AC
  WORLD'S BEST SCIENCE FICTION: 1970 WOLLHEIM & CARR   AN
NINE YARDS OF OTHER CLOTH   WELLMAN, MANLY WADE SS   FSF 58 07
  WHO FEARS THE DEVIL?   WELLMAN, MANLY WADE   AC
NINE-FINGER JACK   BOUCHER, ANTHONY   SS   ESQ 51 05
  BEST SCIENCE-FICTION STORIES: 1952, THE BLEILER & DIKTY   AN
  FRONTIERS IN SPACE   BLEILER & DIKTY   AN
NINETEEN NINETY-FOUR   COOPER, EDMUND   SS
  TOMORROW CAME   COOPER, EDMUND   AC
  VOICES IN THE DARK   COOPER, EDMUND   AC
NINTH SYMPHONY OF LUDWIG VAN BEETHOVEN AND OTHER LOST SONGS
                                  SCHOLZ, CARTER   NV   UNI 77 07
  UNIVERSE 7   CARR, TERRY   OA
NIRVANA, GOTTERDAMMERUNG, AND THE SHOT PUT
                                  HARRISON, WILLIAM   SS   72
  ROLLERBALL   HARRISON, WILLIAM   AC
NIZE KITTY   NOURSE, ALAN E.   SS
NO BIZ LIKE SHOW BIZ   BIGGLE, LLOYD JR.   SS   ASF 74 05
  GALAXY OF STRANGERS, A   BIGGLE, LLOYD JR.   AC
NO CERTAIN ARMOUR   KIPPAX, JOHN   NV   NWR 74 24
  NEW WRITINGS IN SF. 24   BULMER, KENNETH   OA
NO CHARGE FOR ALTERATIONS GOLD, H. L.   NV   AMZ 53 05
  BEST FROM AMAZING, THE   WHITE, TED   AN
  OLD DIE RICH AND OTHER SCIENCE FICTION, THE
                                  GOLD, H. L.   AC
NO CONNECTION   ASIMOV, ISAAC   SS   ASF 48 06
  BEST SCIENCE-FICTION STORIES: 1949, THE BLEILER & DIKTY   AN
  EARLY ASIMOV, THE   ASIMOV, ISAAC   AC
NO CRACKS OR SAGGINGS   BUNCH, DAVID R.   SS
  MODERAN   BUNCH, DAVID R.   AC
NO DIFFERENT FLESH   HENDERSON, ZENNA   NV   FSF 65 05
  BEST FROM FANTASY AND SCIENCE FICTION: 15
                                  FERMAN, EDWARD L.   AN
  PEOPLE: NO DIFFERENT FLESH, THE HENDERSON, ZENNA   AC
NO DIRECTION HOME   SPINRAD, NORMAN   SS   NWQ 71 02
  BEST SCIENCE FICTION OF THE YEAR, THE CARR, TERRY   AN
  BEST SF: 1971   HARRISON & ALDISS   AN
  MODERN SCIENCE FICTION   SPINRAD, NORMAN   AN
  NEW WORLDS QUARTERLY NO. 2   MOORCOCK, MICHAEL   OA
  NO DIRECTION HOME   SPINRAD, NORMAN   AC
  SOCIAL PROBLEMS THROUGH SCIENCE FICTION GREENBERG/MILSTEAD/& AN
NO FIRE BURNS   DAVIDSON, AVRAM   SS   PBY 59 07
  5TH ANNUAL OF THE YEAR'S BEST S-F, THE MERRIL, JUDITH   AN
NO FORWARDING ADDRESS   DE CAMP, L. SPRAGUE
                           AND PRATT, FLETCHER SS C NEW 53 AC
  TALES FROM GAVAGAN'S BAR   DE CAMP, L. S.&PRATT   AC
NO FUTURE IN IT   BRUNNER, JOHN   SS   SCF 55 09
  NO FUTURE IN IT   BRUNNER, JOHN   AC
NO GREAT MAGIC   LEIBER, FRITZ   SN   GAL 63 12
  SECRET SONGS, THE   LEIBER, FRITZ   AC
NO GUN TO THE VICTOR (ALSO AS CONSUMER'S REPORT)
                           COGSWELL, THEODORE R SS   IMG 55 10
  THIRD EYE, THE   COGSWELL, THEODORE R   AC
NO HIDING PLACE   CARTMILL, CLEVE   NA   TWS 50 06
  SPACE SCAVENGERS, THE   CARTMILL, CLEVE   NO
NO JOKES ON MARS   BLISH, JAMES   SS   FSF 65 10
  ANYWHEN   BLISH, JAMES   AC
  SPACE   1   DAVIS, RICHARD   OA
NO LAND OF NOD   SPRINGER, SHERWOOD   SS   TWS 52 12
  BEST FROM STARTLING STORIES, THE MINES, SAMUEL   AN
  IF THIS GOES ON   NUETZEL, CHARLES   AN
  MARRIAGE AND THE FAMILY THROUGH SCIENCE FICTION
                                  CLEAR/WARRICK/&   AN
NO LIFE OF THEIR OWN   SIMAK, CLIFFORD D.   NA   GAL 59 08
  *ALL THE TRAPS OF EARTH AND OTHER STORIES SIMAK, CLIFFORD D. AC
  TOMORROW'S CHILDREN   ASIMOV, ISAAC   AN
NO LIGHT IN THE WINDOW   WILHELM, KATE   SS   NEW 63 AC
  MILE-LONG SPACESHIP, THE   WILHELM, KATE   AC
NO MAN PURSUETH   MOORE, WARD   NV   FSF 56 04
  BEST FROM FANTASY AND SCIENCE FICTION: 6
                                  BOUCHER, ANTHONY   AN
NO MATTER WHERE YOU GO   ROGERS, JOEL T.   NV   FSF 59 02
  BEST FROM FANTASY AND SCIENCE FICTION: 9
                                  MILLS, ROBERT P.   AN
NO MOON FOR ME   MILLER, WALTER M. JR SS   ASF 52 09
  ABC OF SCIENCE FICTION, AN   BOARDMAN, TOM JR.   AN
  SPACE, SPACE, SPACE   SLOANE, WILLIAM   AN
NO MORE FOR MARY   BIRKIN, CHARLES   SS   66
  TALES OF TERROR FROM OUTER SPACE CHETWYND-HAYES, R.   AN
NO MORE THE STARS   COX, IRVING E. JR.   SS   OSF 54 09
  SANDS OF MARS AND OTHER STORIES, THE ANONYMOUS   AN
NO MORE TOMORROWS   KELLER, DAVID H. MD. SS   AMZ 32 12
  LIFE EVERLASTING AND OTHER TALES OF SCIENCE, FANTASY
    AND HORROR   KELLER, DAVID H. MD.   AC

NO MORNING AFTER   CLARKE, ARTHUR C.   SS   FSF 56 07
  NINE BILLION NAMES OF GOD, THE CLARKE, ARTHUR C.   AC
  OF TIME AND STARS   CLARKE, ARTHUR C.   AC
  OTHER SIDE OF THE SKY, THE   CLARKE, ARTHUR C.   AC
  TALES OF TERROR FROM OUTER SPACE CHETWYND-HAYES, R.   AC
  *TIME TO COME   DERLETH, AUGUST   OA
NO ONE BELIEVED ME   THOMPSON, WILL   SS   SEP 48 04
  BEYOND THE BARRIERS OF SPACE AND TIME MERRIL, JUDITH   AN
NO OTHER GODS BUT ME (BASED ON A TIME TO REND)
                           BRUNNER, JOHN   NV   SCF 56 12
  ENTRY TO ELSEWHEN (STORIES REVISED) BRUNNER, JOHN   AC
  NO OTHER GODS BUT ME   BRUNNER, JOHN   AC
NO PARTICULAR NIGHT OR MORNING BRADBURY, RAY   SS   NEW 51 AC
  *ILLUSTRATED MAN, THE   BRADBURY, RAY   AC
NO PLACE LIKE EARTH (SEE TIME TO REST)
NO PLACE LIKE EARTH   BEYNON, JOHN   TC   NWS 51 SP
NO PLACE LIKE EARTH (TYRANT AND SLAVE-GIRL ON VENUS)
                           WYNDHAM, JOHN   NV   NWS 51 SP
  OUT OF THIS WORLD 1   WILLIAMS-ELLIS& OWEN   AN
NO PLACE LIKE HOME   DEL REY, LESTER   SS   ASF 52 08
  MORTALS AND MONSTERS   DEL REY, LESTER   AC
NO POWER ON EARTH   WHEWELL, DR. WILLIAM PM
  FANTASIA MATHEMATICA   FADIMAN, CLIFTON   AN
NO RETURN FROM ELBA   REYNOLDS, MACK   SS   FAN 53 10
  BEST OF MACK REYNOLDS, THE   REYNOLDS, MACK   AC
NO ROOM FOR THE WANDERER   SAYE, LEE   SS   ALT 74
  ALTERNATIES   GERROLD, DAVID   OA
NO SALE   WILLIAMS, JOHN   SS
  SECOND PACIFIC BOOK OF SCIENCE FICTION, THE
                                  BAXTER, JOHN   AN
NO SHIPS PASS   SMITH, LADY ELEANOR NV   CSL 32 04
  OTHER SIDE OF THE CLOCK, THE   STERN, PHILIP VAN D.   AN
  TRAVELERS IN TIME   STERN, PHILIP VAN D.   AN
NO SPECIFIC TIME MENTIONED METZGER, LOIS   SS
  CLARION SF   WILHELM, KATE   OA
NO STRINGS ATTACHED   DEL REY, LESTER   SS   IFS 54 06
  ROBOTS AND CHANGELINGS   DEL REY, LESTER   AC
NO SUCH THING AS A VAMPIRE MATHESON, RICHARD   SS   PBY 59 10
  PLAYBOY BOOK OF HORROR AND THE SUPERNATURAL, THE
                                  PLAYBOY, EDITORS OF   AN
  SHOCK II   MATHESON, RICHARD   AC
NO TRUCE WITH KINGS   ANDERSON, POUL   NV   FSF 63 06
  HUGO WINNERS, THE (VOLUME 2)   ASIMOV, ISAAC   AN
  TIME AND STARS   ANDERSON, POUL   AC
NO WAR TOMORROW   WEST, WALLACE   NO   SFQ 51 05
  OUTPOSTS IN SPACE   WEST, WALLACE   AC
NO WAR, OR BATTLE'S SOUND HARRISON, HARRY   NV   68
  COMBAT SF   DICKSON, GORDON R.   AN
  ONE STEP FROM EARTH   HARRISON, HARRY   AC
NO WAY HOME   LUMLEY, BRIAN   SS   FSF 75 09
  YEAR'S BEST HORROR STORIES: SERIES IV, THE
                                  PAGE, GERALD W.   AN
NO WAY OUT, NO WAY BACK   TIME MAGAZINE   AR   TIM 69
  SCIENCE FICTION: THE FUTURE   ALLEN, DICK   AN
NO WOMAN BORN   MOORE, C. L.   NV   ASF 44 12
  BEST OF C. L. MOORE, THE   MOORE, C. L.   AC
  BEST SF   CRISPIN, EDMUND   AN
  GREAT STORIES OF SCIENCE FICTION LEINSTER, MURRAY   AN
  HUMAN-MACHINES   SCORTIA & ZEBROWSKI   AN
  TOMORROW X 4   KNIGHT, DAMON   AN
  *TREASURY OF SCIENCE FICTION, A CONKLIN, GROFF   AN
NO WORLD FOR THE TIMID   FRITCH, CHARLES E.   SS   AMZ 57 05
  CRAZY MIXED-UP PLANET   FRITCH, CHARLES E.   AC
NO. 2 PLAIN TANK AUXILIARY FILL STRUCTURAL LIMIT 17,605 LBS.
  FUEL-PWA SPEC. 522 REVISED BRYANT, EDWARD   SS   NDM 72 02
  AMONG THE DEAD   BRYANT, EDWARD   AC
  NEW DIMENSIONS 2   SILVERBERG, ROBERT   AN
NO-SIDED PROFESSOR (ESQ 47 01) GARDNER, MARTIN SS   FSF 51 02
  AS TOMORROW BECOMES TODAY   SULLIVAN, CHARLES W.   AN
  BEST FROM FANTASY AND SCIENCE FICTION BOUCHER & MCCOMAS   AN
  FANTASIA MATHEMATICA   FADIMAN, CLIFTON   AN
  VINTAGE ANTHOLOGY OF SCIENCE FANTASY, THE
                                  CERF, CHRISTOPHER   AN
NO-WIND SPOTTED TIGER PLANET, THE
                           MACFARLANE, WALLACE SS   GAL 71 05
  BEST FROM GALAXY, THE   VOLUME 1 GALAXY, EDITORS OF   AN
NO, NO, NOT ROGOV!   SMITH, CORDWAINER   SS   IFS 59 02
  SCIENCE FICTION INVENTIONS   KNIGHT, DAMON   AN
  SF: THE BEST OF THE BEST   MERRIL, JUDITH   AN
  YOU WILL NEVER BE THE SAME   SMITH, CORDWAINER   AC
  5TH ANNUAL OF THE YEAR'S BEST S-F, THE MERRIL, JUDITH   AN
NOAH (SEE THE LAST MAN)   BECKMAN, CHARLES JR. TC
NOBEL PRIZE WINNERS   GORDON, W. J. J.   SS   ATL 63 11
  9TH ANNUAL OF THE YEAR'S BEST S-F, THE MERRIL, JUDITH   AN
NOBODY AXED YOU   BRUNNER, JOHN   NV   NWS 65 05
  BEST SF STORIES FROM NEW WORLDS NO. 1, THE
                                  MOORCOCK, MICHAEL   AN
  TIME-JUMP   BRUNNER, JOHN   AC
NOBODY BOTHERS GUS (AS PAUL JANVIER)
                           BUDRYS, ALGIS   SS   ASF 55 11
  ARENA: SPORTS SF   FERMAN & MALZBERG   AN
  ODDBALLS, THE   GHIDALIA, VIC   AN
  ONE HUNDRED YEARS OF SCIENCE FICTION KNIGHT, DAMON   AN
  SF: THE BEST OF THE BEST   MERRIL, JUDITH   AN
  SF: THE YEAR'S GREATEST SCIENCE FICTION AND FANTASY
                                  MERRIL, JUDITH   AN
NOBODY HERE BUT US SHADOWS LUNDWALL, SAM J.   SS   GAL 75 08
  BEST FROM THE REST OF THE WORLD, THE WOLLHEIM, DONALD A.   AN
NOBODY HERE BUT-   ASIMOV, ISAAC   SS   STR 53 01
  NIGHTFALL AND OTHER STORIES   ASIMOV, ISAAC   AC
  STAR SCIENCE FICTION STORIES   POHL, FREDERIK   OA
NOBODY LIVES ON BURTON STREET BENFORD, GREGORY SS   AMZ 70 05
  INSIDE INFORMATION   MOWSHOWITZ, ABBE   AN
  SOCIOLOGY THROUGH SCIENCE FICTION MILSTEAD/GREENBERG/&   AN
  WORLD'S BEST SCIENCE FICTION: 1971 WOLLHEIM & CARR   AN

NOBODY SAW THE SHIP

NOBODY SAW THE SHIP   LEINSTER, MURRAY   SS   FUS 50 05
*BIG BOOK OF SCIENCE FICTION   CONKLIN, GROFF   AN
  INVADERS FROM SPACE   SILVERBERG, ROBERT   AN
  MONSTERS AND SUCH   LEINSTER, MURRAY   AC
NOBODY SPOKE OR WAVED GOODBYE ALDISS, BRIAN W.   SS   NWR 74 23
  NEW WRITINGS IN SF. 23   BULMER, KENNETH   OA
NOBODY STARVES   GOULART, RON   SS   FSF 64 02
  BROKE DOWN ENGINE AND OTHER TROUBLES WITH MACHINES
                                   GOULART, RON   AC
  MAN AGAINST TOMORROW   NOLAN, WILLIAM F.   AN
NOBODY'S HOME   RUSS, JOANNA   SS   NDM 72 02
  BEST SCIENCE FICTION OF THE YEAR, THE NO. 2
                                   CARR, TERRY   AN
  NEW DIMENSIONS 2   SILVERBERG, ROBERT   OA
  WOMEN OF WONDER   SARGENT, PAMELA   AN
NOBODY, THAT'S WHO   NOLAN, WILLIAM F.   SS   NEW 63 AC
  IMPACT-20   NOLAN, WILLIAM F.   AC
NOISE   VANCE, JACK   SS   STS 52 08
  BEST FROM STARTLING STORIES, THE MINES, SAMUEL   AN
  DEEP SPACE   SILVERBERG, ROBERT   AN
  EIGHT FANTASMS AND MAGICS   VANCE, JACK   AC
NOISE LEVEL   JONES, RAYMOND F.   NV   ASF 52 12
  ASTOUNDING-ANALOG READER, THE VOLUME TWO HARRISON & ALDISS AN
  BEST SF 5   CRISPIN, EDMUND   AN
  SPECTRUM 5   AMIS & CONQUEST   AN
*STORIES FOR TOMORROW   SLOANE, WILLIAM   AN
NOISE, THE   PURDY, KEN W.   SS   PBY 59 03
  INTRODUCTORY PSYCHOLOGY THROUGH SCIENCE FICTION
                                   KATZ/WARRICK/&   AN
  PLAYBOY BOOK OF SCIENCE FICTION AND FANTASY, THE
                                   PLAYBOY, EDITORS OF   AN
NOMANSLAND   ALDISS, BRIAN W.   NV   FSF 61 04
  LONG AFTERNOON OF EARTH, THE   ALDISS, BRIAN W.   NO
NON-HUMANS, THE   HENNEBERG, CHARLES SS   58
  13 FRENCH SCIENCE-FICTION STORIES KNIGHT, DAMON   AN
NON-LIMITATION OF INTELLIGENCE, THE
                                   CONKLIN, GROFF   IN
  GIANTS UNLEASHED   CONKLIN, GROFF   AN
NON-STATISTICAL MAN, THE   JONES, RAYMOND F.   NA   SFS 56 05
  NON-STATISTICAL MAN, THE   JONES, RAYMOND F.   AC
NON-STOP   ALDISS, BRIAN W.   NO   FAB 58
  BRIAN ALDISS OMNIBUS 2   ALDISS, BRIAN W.   AC
NON-STOP TO MARS   WILLIAMSON, JACK   NV   ARG 39 02
  GREAT SCIENCE FICTION STORIES ABOUT MARS DIKTY, T. E.   AN
  PEOPLE MACHINES   WILLIAMSON, JACK   AC
NONE BEFORE ME   CARROLL, SIDNEY   SS   CMP 49 07
  TIMELESS STORIES FOR TODAY AND TOMORROW BRADBURY, RAY   AN
NONE SO BLIND (WHO'S IN CHARGE HERE?)
                                   BLISH, JAMES   SS   FSF 62 05
  ANYWHEN   BLISH, JAMES   AC
NONEATRINS, THE   VARSHAVSKY, ILYA   SS
  OTHER WORLDS, OTHER SEAS   SUVIN, DARKO   AN
NOONDAY DEVIL   O'NEIL, DENNIS   SS   SVW 73
  SAVING WORLDS   ELWOOD & KIDD   OA
NOR DUST CORRUPT   MCCONNELL, JAMES   SS   IFS 57 02
  BEST SCIENCE FICTION STORIES AND NOVELS: 9TH SERIES
                                   DIKTY, T. E.   AN
NOR IRON BARS (INCLUDES "DETOUR TO THE STARS" INF 56 12)
                                   BLISH, JAMES   SS   INF 57 11
*GALACTIC CLUSTER   BLISH, JAMES   AC
NOR IRON BARS A CAGE   GOLDIN, STEPHEN
                               AND HENSEL, C. F.   SS C ALC 73
  ALIEN CONDITION, THE   GOLDIN, STEPHEN   OA
NOR LIMESTONE ISLANDS   LAFFERTY, R. A.   SS   UNI 71 01
  DOES ANYONE ELSE HAVE SOMETHING FURTHER TO ADD?
                                   LAFFERTY, R. A.   AC
  UNIVERSE 1   CARR, TERRY   OA
NOR THE MANY-COLORED FIRES OF A STAR RING
                                   MARTIN, GEORGE R. R. NV 76
  FASTER THAN LIGHT   DANN & ZEBROWSKI   OA
NORMAN VS. AMERICA   PLATT, CHARLES   CT   QRK 71 04
  QUARK/4   DELANY & HACKER   OA
NORMAN: FRIENDS AND OTHER STRANGERS
                                   STEVENSON, LYNNDA   SS   CLR 71 01
  CLARION   WILSON, ROBIN SCOTT   OA
NORTH WIND   OLIVER, CHAD   SS   FSF 56 03
  FAR-OUT PEOPLE, THE   HOSKINS, ROBERT   AN
  WILDERNESS OF STARS, A   NOLAN, WILLIAM F.   AN
NORTON BIBLIOGRAPHY   NORTON, ANDRE   MS
  MANY WORLDS OF ANDRE NORTON, THE NORTON, ANDRE   AC
NOSTALGIA GENE, THE   HUTCHINS, ROY   SS   GAL 54 11
  BEST SF 6   CRISPIN, EDMUND   AN
NOSTALGIA TRIPPING   BRENNERT, ALAN   SS   INY 73 05
  INFINITY 5   HOSKINS, ROBERT   OA
NOT A CREATURE WAS STIRRING   EVANS, DEAN   SS   GAL 51 12
  SHADOW OF TOMORROW   POHL, FREDERIK   AN
NOT A PETAL FALLS   BIRELEY, RICHARD   SS   NOV 74 04
  NOVA 4   HARRISON, HARRY   OA
NOT A PRISON MAKE   MARTINO, JOSEPH P. NV   ASF 66 09
  ANALOG 6   CAMPBELL, JOHN W. JR AN
  POLITICAL SCIENCE FICTION   GREENBERG& WARRICK   AN
NOT BORN TO GREATNESS   FAIRMAN, PAUL W.   SS
  FORGETFUL ROBOT, THE   FAIRMAN, PAUL W.   OC
NOT FINAL!   ASIMOV, ISAAC   SS   ASF 41 10
  ASLEEP IN ARMAGEDDON   SISSONS, MICHAEL   AN
  EARLY ASIMOV, THE   ASIMOV, ISAAC   AC
  FIRST CONTACT   KNIGHT, DAMON   AN
*POSSIBLE WORLDS OF SCIENCE FICTION CONKLIN, GROFF   AN
  TIME PROBE: THE SCIENCES IN SF. CLARKE, ARTHUR C.   AN
  TOWARD INFINITY   KNIGHT, DAMON   AN
NOT FIT FOR CHILDREN   SMITH, EVELYN E.   SS   GAL 53 05
  GALAXY SCIENCE FICTION OMNIBUS   GOLD, H. L.   AN
  SECOND GALAXY READER OF SCIENCE FICTION GOLD, H. L.   AN
NOT FOR AN AGE   ALDISS, BRIAN W.   SS   LOB 55 01
  AD 2500   WILSON, ANGUS   AN

NOTES TOWARD A MENTAL BREAKDOWN (THE DEATH MODULE)

*BEST SCIENCE FICTION STORIES OF BRIAN W. ALDISS
                                   ALDISS, BRIAN W.   AC
  NO TIME LIKE TOMORROW   ALDISS, BRIAN W.   AC
  SPACE, TIME AND NATHANIEL   ALDISS, BRIAN W.   AC
NOT IN THE LITERATURE   ANVIL, CHRISTOPHER SS   ASF 63 03
  ANALOG 3   CAMPBELL, JOHN W. JR AN
NOT LONG BEFORE THE END   NIVEN, LARRY   SS   FSF 69 04
  ALL THE MYRIAD WAYS   NIVEN, LARRY   AC
  GOLDEN ROAD, THE   KNIGHT, DAMON   AN
  NEBULA AWARD STORIES NO. 5   BLISH, JAMES   AN
NOT ME, NOT AMOS CABOT!   HARRISON, HARRY   SS   SCF 65 01
*BEST OF HARRY HARRISON, THE   HARRISON, HARRY   AC
  PRIME NUMBER   HARRISON, HARRY   AC
  SCIENCE FICTION HORIZONS NO. 1   BOARDMAN, TOM JR.   AN
NOT ONLY DEAD MEN   VAN VOGT, A. E.   SS   ASF 42 11
  BUG-EYED MONSTERS   CHEETHAM, ANTHONY   AN
*INVADERS OF EARTH   CONKLIN, GROFF   AN
  MONSTERS   VAN VOGT, A. E.   AC
NOT SNOW NOR RAIN (ALSO AS NEITHER SNOW NOR RAIN)
                                   DEFORD, MIRIAM ALLEN SS IFS 59 11
  ELSEWHERE, ELSEWHEN, ELSEHOW   DEFORD, MIRIAM ALLEN   AC
NOT SO CERTAIN   MASSON, DAVID I.   SS   NWS 67 07
  CALTRAPS OF TIME, THE   MASSON, DAVID I.   AC
NOT SO GREAT AN ENEMY (SEE MEDIC)
                                   GUNN, JAMES E.   TC
NOT THAT SHAGGY   GOULART, RON   SS   INY 72 04
  INFINITY 4   HOSKINS, ROBERT   OA
NOT THE FIRST   VAN VOGT, A. E.   SS   ASF 41 04
  FAR-OUT WORLDS OF A. E. VAN VOGT, THE VAN VOGT, A. E.   AC
  WORLDS OF A. E. VAN VOGT, THE   VAN VOGT, A. E.   AC
NOT THERE   METCALF, JOHN   SS
  TRAVELLERS BY NIGHT   DERLETH, AUGUST   OA
NOT TO BE OPENED-   YOUNG, ROBERT F.   NV   ASF 50 01
  BEST SCIENCE-FICTION STORIES: 1951, THE BLEILER & DIKTY AN
  MINDWORM, THE   ANONYMOUS   AN
NOT WITH A BANG   FAST, HOWARD   SS
  TOUCH OF INFINITY, A   FAST, HOWARD   OC
NOT WITH A BANG   KNIGHT, DAMON   SS   FSF 50 WS
  BEST OF DAMON KNIGHT, THE   KNIGHT, DAMON   AC
*BIG BOOK OF SCIENCE FICTION   CONKLIN, GROFF   AN
  FAR OUT   KNIGHT, DAMON   AC
  FIFTY SHORT SCIENCE FICTION TALES ASIMOV & CONKLIN   AN
  SCIENCE FICTION FOR PEOPLE WHO HATE SCIENCE FICTION
                                   CARR, TERRY   AN
NOT YET THE END   BROWN, FREDRIC   SS   CFU 41 WI
  BEST OF FREDRIC BROWN, THE   BROWN, FREDRIC   AC
  GALACTIC EMPIRES VOLUME TWO   ALDISS, BRIAN W.   AN
  NIGHTMARES AND GEEZENSTACKS   BROWN, FREDRIC   AC
NOTARY AND THE CONSPIRACY, THE DAMONTI, HENRI   SS   62
  13 FRENCH SCIENCE-FICTION STORIES KNIGHT, DAMON   AN
NOTE FOR THE MILKMAN, A   CARROLL, SIDNEY   SS   TDW 50 04
  TIMELESS STORIES FOR TODAY AND TOMORROW BRADBURY, RAY   AN
NOTE ON DANGER B   KERSH, GERALD   SS   SEP 47 04
  SATURDAY EVENING POST FANTASY STORIES, THE
                                   FLES, BARTHOLD   AN
NOTE ON THE DARK TOWER, A   HOOPER, WALTER   MS
  DARK TOWER AND OTHER STORIES, THE LEWIS, C. S.   AC
NOTE ON THE EINSTEIN THEORY, A BEERBOHM, MAX   SS   46
  MATHEMATICAL MAGPIE, THE   FADIMAN, CLIFTON   AN
NOTE ON THETA, PHI, AND PSI   ROBERTS, MICHAEL   PM   NSM 35 03
  MATHEMATICAL MAGPIE, THE   FADIMAN, CLIFTON   AN
NOTE TO TEACHERS AND PARENTS:, A
                                   TYRE, RICHARD H.   IN
  CITIZEN IN SPACE   SHECKLEY, ROBERT   AC
NOTES FOR A NOVEL ABOUT THE FIRST SHIP EVER TO VENUS
                                   MALZBERG, BARRY N. SS   UNI 71 01
  OUT FROM GANYMEDE   MALZBERG, BARRY N.   AC
  UNIVERSE 1   CARR, TERRY   OA
NOTES FROM INFINITY   MISC. MATERIAL   MS
  INFINITY 2   HOSKINS, ROBERT   OA
  INFINITY 3   HOSKINS, ROBERT   OA
  INFINITY 4   HOSKINS, ROBERT   OA
NOTES JUST PRIOR TO THE FALL MALZBERG, BARRY N.   SS FSF 70 10
  BEST FROM FANTASY AND SCIENCE FICTION: 19
                                   FERMAN, EDWARD L.   AN
NOTES JUST PRIOR TO THE FALL O'DONNELL, K. M.   SS FSF 70 10
  IN THE POCKET AND OTHER S-F STORIES O'DONNELL, K. M.   DC
NOTES LEADING DOWN TO THE CONQUEST (ALSO AS A RECKONING)
                                   MALZBERG, BARRY N. SS   NDM 73 03
  NEW DIMENSIONS 3   SILVERBERG, ROBERT   OA
NOTES LEADING DOWN TO THE EVENTS AT BEDLAM
                                   MALZBERG, BARRY N. SS   72
  DOWN HERE IN THE DREAM QUARTER   MALZBERG, BARRY N.   AC
NOTES ON A RESTLESS URGE   WISSNER, ROBERT   SS   CLR 72 02
  CLARION II   WILSON, ROBIN SCOTT   OA
NOTES ON SOME OF THE AUTHORS   MISC. MATERIAL   MS
  RUSSIAN SCIENCE FICTION, 1969   MAGIDOFF, ROBERT   AN
NOTES ON THE AUTHORS   MISC. MATERIAL   MS
  AIR OF MARS AND OTHER STORIES, THE GINSBURG, MIRRA   AN
  VIEW FROM ANOTHER SHORE   ROTTENSTEINER, FRANZ AN
NOTES ON THE CONTRIBUTORS   MISC. MATERIAL   MS
  NEW CONSTELLATIONS   DISCH & NAYLOR   OA
NOTES ON THE PERCEPTION OF IMAGINARY DIFFERENCES
                                   SHECKLEY, ROBERT   SS   NEW 71 01
  CAN YOU FEEL ANYTHING WHEN I DO THIS?, AND OTHER STORIES
                                   SHECKLEY, ROBERT   AC
NOTES TO AFTER TEN YEARS   FOWLER, ALASTAIR   MS
  DARK TOWER AND OTHER STORIES, THE LEWIS, C. S.   AC
NOTES TO AFTER TEN YEARS   GREEN, ROGER L.   MS
  DARK TOWER AND OTHER STORIES, THE LEWIS, C. S.   AC
NOTES TOWARD A DEFINITION OF SCIENCE FICTION
                                   ANDERSON, POUL   AR   SFR 71 43
  HOMEBREW   ANDERSON, POUL   AC
NOTES TOWARD A MENTAL BREAKDOWN (THE DEATH MODULE)
                                   BALLARD, J. G.   SS   NWS 67 07
  LOVE & NAPALM: EXPORT U.S.A.   BALLARD, J. G.   AC

NOTES TOWARD A SUPREME SCIENCE FICTION
    THOMAS, D. M.   PM
  BEYOND THIS HORIZON CARRELL, CHRISTOPHER OA
NOTHING BUT GINGERBREAD LEFT KUTTNER, HENRY SS ASF 43 01
  BEST OF HENRY KUTTNER, THE KUTTNER, HENRY AC
  BYPASS TO OTHERNESS KUTTNER, HENRY AC
NOTHING FOR MY NOON MEAL ELLISON, HARLAN SS NEB 58 05
  ALONE AGAINST TOMORROW ELLISON, HARLAN AC
  ELLISON WONDERLAND ELLISON, HARLAN AC
NOTHING HAPPENS ON THE MOON ERNST, PAUL SS ASF 39 02
  OMNIBUS OF SCIENCE FICTION CONKLIN, GROFF AN
  STRANGE TRAVELS IN SCIENCE FICTION CONKLIN, GROFF AN
  TALES OF SCIENCE FICTION BALL, BRIAN N. AN
NOTHING IN THE RULES DE CAMP, L. SPRAGUE NV UNK 39 07
  FROM UNKNOWN WORLDS CAMPBELL, JOHN W. JR AN
NOTHING NEW RUSSELL, ERIC FRANK SS ASF 55 01
  LIKE NOTHING ON EARTH RUSSELL, ERIC FRANK AC
  SIX WORLDS YONDER RUSSELL, ERIC FRANK DC
NOTHING SIRIUS BROWN, FREDRIC SS CFU 44 SP
  BEST OF FREDRIC BROWN, THE BROWN, FREDRIC AC
  *MY BEST SCIENCE FICTION STORY MARGULIES & FRIEND AN
  PARADOX LOST, AND 12 OTHER GREAT S.F. STORIES
    BROWN, FREDRIC AC
  SPACE ON MY HANDS BROWN, FREDRIC AC
NOTHING SUCCEEDS LIKE FAILURE ANDERSON, POUL SS NEW 70 04
  TALES OF THE FLYING MOUNTAINS ANDERSON, POUL AC
NOTHING, THE HERBERT, FRANK SS FUN 56 01
  BOOK OF FRANK HERBERT, THE HERBERT, FRANK AC
  TOMORROW, AND TOMORROW, AND TOMORROW... HEINTZ/HERBERT/JOOS/ AN
NOTHINK INOUYE, JON SS
  NIGHT TIDE, A INOUYE, JON OC
NOVA INCIDENT, THE NUETZEL, CHARLES SS
  IMAGES OF TOMORROW NUETZEL, CHARLES AC
NOVA MORNING BRYANT, EDWARD
  AND HARPER, JODY SS C GEN 72
  GENERATION GERROLD, DAVID OA
NOVELIST WITH WOODEN CHARACTER, THE
  DISCH, THOMAS M. SS
  *GETTING INTO DEATH DISCH, THOMAS M. AC
NOVELTY ACT DICK, PHILIP K. NV FAN 64 02
  HUMAN EQUATION, THE NOLAN, WILLIAM F. AN
NOVEMBER 22, 1963 MALZBERG, BARRY N. SS NEW 74 AC
  OUT FROM GANYMEDE MALZBERG, BARRY N. AC
NOVICE SCHMITZ, JAMES H. NV ASF 62 06
  ANALOG 2 CAMPBELL, JOHN W. JR AN
  MIND TO MIND SILVERBERG, ROBERT AN
  TOMORROW'S CHILDREN ASIMOV, ISAAC AN
NOW COMES TOMORROW WILLIAMS, ROBERT M. NO 71
  SCIENCE FICTION SPECIAL 6 ANONYMOUS AN
NOW HEAR THE WORD GARNETT, DAVID S. NV NWR 74 24
  NEW WRITINGS IN SF. 24 BULMER, KENNETH OA
NOW HEAR THE WORD OF THE LORD BUDRYS, ALGIS SS GAL 69 02
  BEST SF: 1969 HARRISON & ALDISS AN
NOW I'M WATCHING ROGER PANSHIN, ALEXEI SS ORB 72 10
  FAREWELL TO YESTERDAY'S TOMORROW PANSHIN, ALEXEI AC
  ORBIT 10 KNIGHT, DAMON OA
NOW INHALE RUSSELL, ERIC FRANK NV ASF 59 04
  13 ABOVE THE NIGHT CONKLIN, GROFF AN
NOW IS FOREVER ALLEN, EDWARD SS
  STOPWATCH HAY, GEORGE OA
NOW IS FOREVER DISCH, THOMAS M. SS AMZ 64 03
  FUN WITH YOUR NEW HEAD DISCH, THOMAS M. AC
  TRAPS OF TIME, THE MOORCOCK, MICHAEL AN
  WORLD'S BEST SCIENCE FICTION: 1965 WOLLHEIM & CARR AN
NOW LET US SLEEP DAVIDSON, AVRAM SS VSF 57 09
  NO LIMITS FERMAN, JOSEPH W. AN
  OR ALL THE SEAS WITH OYSTERS DAVIDSON, AVRAM AC
  SF:58, THE YEAR'S GREATEST SCIENCE FICTION AND FANTASY
    MERRIL, JUDITH AN
  WORLDS OF SCIENCE FICTION, THE MILLS, ROBERT P. AN
  YOU AND SCIENCE FICTION HOLLISTER, BERNARD C AN
NOW MEET THE NONTERRESTRIAL SANDERSON, IVAN T. AR FUN 59 01
  FLYING SAUCERS IN FACT AND FICTION SANTESSON, HANS S. AN
NOW WAKES THE SEA BALLARD, J. G. SS FSF 63 05
  BEST FROM FANTASY AND SCIENCE FICTION: 13
    DAVIDSON, AVRAM AN
  CHRONOPOLIS AND OTHER STORIES BALLARD, J. G. AC
  DISASTER AREA, THE BALLARD, J. G. AC
  TERMINAL BEACH (AMERICAN VERSION) BALLARD, J. G. AC
NOW YOU SEE IT... ASIMOV, ISAAC NV ASF 48 01
  SECOND FOUNDATION ASIMOV, ISAAC NO
(NOW+N), (NOW-N) SILVERBERG, ROBERT NV NOV 72 02
  INFINITE JESTS SILVERBERG, ROBERT AN
  NOVA 2 HARRISON, HARRY OA
  UNFAMILIAR TERRITORY SILVERBERG, ROBERT AC
NOW: ZERO BALLARD, J. G. SS SCF 59 12
  BILLENIUM BALLARD, J. G. AC
  OVERLOADED MAN, THE BALLARD, J. G. AC
NRACP, THE ELLIOTT, GEORGE P. NV HUD 49 FL
  HUMAN AND OTHER BEINGS DEGRAEFF, ALLEN AN
  SOCIAL PROBLEMS THROUGH SCIENCE FICTION GREENBERG/MILSTEAD/& AN
NUCLEAR GENESIS DOLAN, MIKE SS
  SANTANA MORNING AND OTHER STORIES DOLAN, MIKE OC
NUISANCE VALUE WHITE, JAMES SS ASF 75 10
  MONSTERS AND MEDICS WHITE, JAMES AC
NULL-P TENN, WILLIAM SS WBY 51 01
  *SPECTRUM AMIS & CONQUEST AN
  STARS AND UNDER, THE CRISPIN, EDMUND AN
  WOODEN STAR, THE TENN, WILLIAM AC
  *WORLDS OF TOMORROW DERLETH, AUGUST AN
NUMBER EIGHT MCGIVERN, PATRICK SS PBY 70 06
  FULLY AUTOMATED LOVE LIFE OF HENRY KEANRIDGE
    PLAYBOY, EDITORS OF AN
NUMBER NINE CARTMILL, CLEVE SS ASF 50 02
  GREAT STORIES OF SCIENCE FICTION LEINSTER, MURRAY AN

NUMBER OF THE BEAST, THE LEIBER, FRITZ NV GAL 58 12
  *MIND SPIDER AND OTHER STORIES, THE LEIBER, FRITZ DC
  SIXTH GALAXY READER, THE GOLD, H. L. AN
NUMBER TEN Q STREET MCCLOY, HELEN SS EQM 63 09
  WORLDS APART WILLIAMS-ELLIS& OWEN AN
NUMBER YOU HAVE REACHED, THE DISCH, THOMAS M. IMP 67 02
  FUN WITH YOUR NEW HEAD DISCH, THOMAS M. AC
  SOCIAL PROBLEMS THROUGH SCIENCE FICTION GREENBERG/MILSTEAD/& AN
  WORLD'S BEST SCIENCE FICTION: 1968 WOLLHEIM & CARR AN
NUB-I-DESHT OBSERVATORY, THE YEFREMOV, IVAN SS
  STORIES YEFREMOV, IVAN AC
NURSEMAID TO NIGHTMARES BLOCH, ROBERT NV WRT 42 11
  DRAGONS AND NIGHTMARES BLOCH, ROBERT AC
NURSERY RHYME BEAUMONT, CHARLES SS NEW 57 AC
  BR-R-R-| CONKLIN, GROFF AN
  HUNGER AND OTHER STORIES, THE BEAUMONT, CHARLES AC
NUSE MAN, THE ST. CLAIR, MARGARET SS GAL 60 02
  SIXTH GALAXY READER, THE GOLD, H. L. AN
NUTZENBOLTS GOULART, RON SS
  NUTZENBOLTS GOULART, RON AC
NYARLATHOTEP (1943) LOVECRAFT, H. P. PM MOH 68 11
  HOLDING YOUR EIGHT HANDS LUCIE-SMITH, EDWARD AN
O BRAVE OLD WORLD| DAVIDSON, AVRAM NV
  BEYOND TIME LEY, SANDRA OA
O ISHRAEL| ALDISS, BRIAN W. SS NWS 57 04
  CANOPY OF TIME, THE ALDISS, BRIAN W. AC
  GALAXIES LIKE GRAINS OF SAND ALDISS, BRIAN W. AC
O MOON OF MY DELIGHT| (MOON OF DELIGHT)
  ALDISS, BRIAN W. NV NWS 61 03
  AIRS OF EARTH, THE ALDISS, BRIAN W. AC
  STARSWARM ALDISS, BRIAN W. AC
O UGLY BIRD| WELLMAN, MANLY WADE SS FSF 51 12
  EDGE OF NEVER, THE HOSKINS, ROBERT AN
  GALAXY OF GHOULS MERRIL, JUDITH AN
  WHO FEARS THE DEVIL? WELLMAN, MANLY WADE AC
O YE OF LITTLE FAITH ELLISON, HARLAN SS KNT 68 09
  ALONE AGAINST TOMORROW ELLISON, HARLAN AC
  DEATHBIRD STORIES ELLISON, HARLAN AC
  *LOVE AIN'T NOTHING BUT SEX MISSPELLED ELLISON, HARLAN AC
  SF: AUTHORS' CHOICE 3 HARRISON, HARRY AN
O'BRIEN'S TABLE SYNGE, J. L. SS 51
  MATHEMATICAL MAGPIE, THE FADIMAN, CLIFTON AN
O'GRADY'S GIRL KELLEY, LEO P. SS FSF 65 12
  FANTASY: THE LITERATURE OF THE MARVELOUS KELLEY, LEO P. AN
O'MARA'S ORPHAN (ALSO AS MEDIC)
  WHITE, JAMES NV NWS 60 01
  WORLDS APART WILLIAMS-ELLIS& OWEN AN
OASIS SARGENT, PAMELA SS PRT 71
  PROTOSTARS GERROLD & GOLDIN OA
OATEN O'DONNELL, K. M. SS FAN 68 10
  FINAL WAR AND OTHER FANTASIES O'DONNELL, K. M. DC
OATH, THE BLISH, JAMES SS FSF 60 10
  *BEST SCIENCE FICTION STORIES OF JAMES BLISH
    BLISH, JAMES AC
  BEYOND TOMORROW HARDING, LEE AN
  SO CLOSE TO HOME BLISH, JAMES AC
OBEDIENCE (THE UNDYING ONES) BROWN, FREDRIC SS SSS 50 09
  PARADOX LOST, AND 12 OTHER GREAT S.F. STORIES
    BROWN, FREDRIC AC
OBEY THAT IMPULSE| JANIFER, LAURENCE M. SS FUT 59 06
  IMPOSSIBLE? JANIFER, LAURENCE M. AC
OBITUARIES: MAL DEAN, MAC KING MISC. MATERIAL MS
  NEW WORLDS NO. 6 PLATT & BAILEY OA
OBITUARY ASIMOV, ISAAC SS FSF 59 08
  ASIMOV'S MYSTERIES ASIMOV, ISAAC AC
OBLIGATION, THE DEE, ROGER NV STS 52 09
  ADVENTURES ON OTHER PLANETS WOLLHEIM, DONALD A. AN
OBLITERATED MAN, THE WELLS, H. G. SS
  COUNTRY OF THE BLIND, THE WELLS, H. G. AC
OBLONG BOX, THE POE, EDGAR ALLEN SS GDY 44 09
  GHOULS, THE HAINING, PETER AN
OBSCURE LIFE AND HARD TIMES OF KILGORE TROUT, THE
  FARMER, PHILIP JOSE SS MOB 71 12
  BOOK OF PHILIP JOSE FARMER, THE FARMER, PHILIP JOSE AC
OBSERVATION OF QUADRAGNES ANDREVON,JEAN-PIERRE SS
  VIEW FROM ANOTHER SHORE ROTTENSTEINER, FRANZ AN
OBSERVER, THE CHARNOCK, GRAHAM SS NWR 75 27
  NEW WRITINGS IN SF. 27 BULMER, KENNETH OA
OBSESSION (ART WALLACE) BLISH, JAMES SA STK 73 09
  STAR TREK 9 BLISH, JAMES OC
OBSOLESCENCE OF MAN, THE CLARKE, ARTHUR C. AR PBY 61
  LOOKING AHEAD ALLEN, D. & L. AN
OBVIOUS| FFOLKES, MICHAEL CT PUN 56 10
  6TH ANNUAL OF THE YEAR'S BEST S-F, THE MERRIL, JUDITH AN
OBVIOUSLY SUICIDE WRIGHT, S. FOWLER SS SUS 51 SP
  BEYOND THE END OF TIME POHL, FREDERIK AN
  FIFTY SHORT SCIENCE FICTION TALES ASIMOV & CONKLIN AN
OCCAM'S SCALPEL STURGEON, THEODORE NV IFS 71 08
  BEST FROM IF, THE VOLUME I IF, EDITORS OF AN
  BEST SCIENCE FICTION OF THE YEAR, THE CARR, TERRY AN
  BEST SCIENCE FICTION STORIES OF THE YEAR (1971)
    DEL REY, LESTER AN
  1972 ANNUAL WORLD'S BEST SF, THE WOLLHEIM, DONALD A. AN
OCCASIONS SALLIS, JAMES SS 70
  FEW LAST WORDS, A SALLIS, JAMES AC
OCCUPATION FORCE HERBERT, FRANK SS FAN 55 08
  BOOK OF FRANK HERBERT, THE HERBERT, FRANK AC
OCCUPATION: WARRIOR WHITE, JAMES SN SFA 59 03
  ALIENS AMONG US, THE WHITE, JAMES AC
OCCUPATIONAL RISK CHRISTOPHER, JOHN SS SFS 57 01
  TWENTY-SECOND CENTURY, THE CHRISTOPHER, JOHN AC
OCCURANCE AT OWL CREEK BRIDGE, AN (ALSO AS INCIDENT AT
  OWL CREEK) BIERCE, AMBROSE SS 91
  PERCHANCE TO DREAM KNIGHT, DAMON AN

OCCURRENCE AT THE OWL CREEK REST HOME, AN
    COX, ARTHUR JEAN   NV
  SCIENCE FICTION DISCOVERIES   POHL, C. & F.   OA
OCEAN LEECH, THE   LONG, FRANK BELKNAP SS   WRT 25 01
  DARK BEASTS, THE   LONG, FRANK BELKNAP   AC
  EARLY LONG, THE   LONG, FRANK BELKNAP   AC
  *HOUNDS OF TINDALOS, THE   LONG, FRANK BELKNAP   AC
OCEANS ARE WIDE, THE   ROBINSON, FRANK M. SN SST 54 04
  YEAR'S BEST SCIENCE FICTION NOVELS: 1954 BLEILER & DIKTY   AN
OCEANS AWAY   WEINSTEIN, RICHARD S NA
  STELLAR SHORT NOVELS   DEL REY, JUDY-LYNN   OA
OCTOBER GAME, THE   BRADBURY, RAY SS WRT 48 03
  LONG AFTER MIDNIGHT   BRADBURY, RAY   AC
OD   DANN, JACK M.
    AND ZEBROWSKI, GEORGE   SS C OMG 73
  OMEGA   ELWOOD, ROGER   OA
ODD   WYNDHAM, JOHN SS
  CONSIDER HER WAYS AND OTHERS   WYNDHAM, JOHN   AC
  INFINITE MOMENT, THE   WYNDHAM, JOHN   AC
ODD BOY OUT   ETCHISON, DENNIS SS ESC 61
  NEW WRITINGS IN SF. 2   CARNELL, JOHN   OA
ODD JOB NO. 101   GOULART, RON SS FSF 74
  ODD JOB NO. 101   GOULART, RON   AC
ODD JOHN   STAPLEDON, OLAF NO MTH 35
  PORTABLE NOVELS OF SCIENCE   WOLLHEIM, DONALD A.   AN
  TO THE END OF TIME   STAPLEDON, OLAF   AC
ODD JOHN (SELECTION FROM)   STAPLEDON, OLAF EX MTH 35
  CENTURY OF SCIENCE FICTION, A   KNIGHT, DAMON   AN
ODD MAN IN   RAPHAEL, RICK NV
  THIRST QUENCHERS, THE   RAPHAEL, RICK   AC
ODD ONES, THE   DICKSON, GORDON R. NV IFS 55 02
  ANCIENT, MY ENEMY   DICKSON, GORDON R.   AC
  SECOND WORLD OF IF, THE   QUINN & WULFF   AN
ODDS AGAINST YOU, THE (AGAINST THE ODDS)
    BRUNNER, JOHN SS IFS 65 08
  NO OTHER GODS BUT ME   BRUNNER, JOHN   AC
ODDY AND ID (THE DEVIL'S INVENTION)
    BESTER, ALFRED SS ASF 50 08
  BEST SCIENCE-FICTION STORIES: 1951, THE BLEILER & DIKTY   AN
  FRONTIERS IN SPACE   BLEILER & DIKTY   AN
  STAR LIGHT, STAR BRIGHT   BESTER, ALFRED   AC
  STARBURST   BESTER, ALFRED   AC
  STRANGE GIFTS   SILVERBERG, ROBERT   AN
ODE ON THE SOURCE OF THE CLITUMNUS
    DISCH, THOMAS M. PM SVW 73
  SAVING WORLDS   ELWOOD & KIDD   OA
ODE TO A TIME FLOWER   CALVERT, ROBERT PM NWB 73 05
  NEW WORLDS QUARTERLY NO. 5   MOORCOCK, MICHAEL   OA
ODOR OF THOUGHT, THE   SHECKLEY, ROBERT SS STR 53 02
  PEOPLE TRAP AND OTHER PITFALLS, THE SHECKLEY, ROBERT   AC
  STAR SCIENCE FICTION STORIES NO. 2 POHL, FREDERIK   OA
  TALES FROM THE GALAXIES   WILLIAMS-ELLIS& P.   AN
ODYSSEY OF FLIGHT 33, THE   SERLING, ROD SA
  FROM THE TWILIGHT ZONE   SERLING, ROD   AC
  MORE STORIES FROM THE TWILIGHT ZONE SERLING, ROD   OC
ODYSSEY, THE (EXCERPT)   HOMER EX
  3000 YEARS OF FANTASY AND SCIENCE FICTION
    DE CAMP, L. S.&C.   AN
OF A YELLOW SUMMER   DOLAN, MIKE SS
  SANTANA MORNING AND OTHER STORIES DOLAN, MIKE   OC
OF ALL POSSIBLE WORLDS   BROWN, ROSEL GEORGE SS FSF 61 02
  HANDFUL OF TIME, A   BROWN, ROSEL GEORGE   AC
OF ALL POSSIBLE WORLDS (SEE IT ENDS WITH A FLICKER)
OF COURSE   TENN, WILLIAM TC
    OLIVER, CHAD SS ASF 54 05
  APEMAN, SPACEMAN   STOVER & HARRISON   AN
  BEST SCIENCE FICTION STORIES AND NOVELS: 1955
    DIKTY, T. E.   AN
  SOCIOLOGY THROUGH SCIENCE FICTION MILSTEAD/GREENBERG/& A AN
OF DEATH WHAT DREAMS   LAUMER, KEITH NV WOT 70 24
  FIVE FATES   LAUMER, KEITH   AN
OF DESTINY AND WONDER   DEL REY, LESTER IN
  JOHN W. CAMPBELL ANTHOLOGY: THREE NOVELS CAMPBELL, JOHN W. JR AC
OF HAMMERS AND MEN   BUNCH, DAVID R. SS
  MODERAN   BUNCH, DAVID R.   AC
OF JOVIAN BUILD   FRIEND, OSCAR J. SS TWS 38 10
  *TREASURY OF SCIENCE FICTION, A CONKLIN, GROFF   AN
OF MISSING PERSONS   FINNEY, JACK SS GHK 55 03
  FANTASY: THE LITERATURE OF THE MARVELOUS KELLEY, LEO P.   AN
  SCIENCE FICTION   BRODKIN & PEARSON   AN
  SF: THE YEAR'S GREATEST SCIENCE FICTION AND FANTASY
    MERRIL, JUDITH   AN
  TALES OF TIME AND SPACE   OLNEY, ROSS R.   AN
  THIRD LEVEL, THE   FINNEY, JACK   AC
OF MIST, AND GRASS, AND SAND MCINTYRE, VONDA N. SS ASF 73 10
  BEST SCIENCE FICTION OF THE YEAR, THE NO. 3
    CARR, TERRY   AN
  LOOKING AHEAD   ALLEN, D. & L.   AN
  NEBULA AWARD STORIES 9   WILHELM, KATE   AN
  WOMEN OF WONDER   SARGENT, PAMELA   AN
OF THE PEOPLE   DICKSON, GORDON R. SS FSF 55 12
  MUTANTS   DICKSON, GORDON R.   AC
OF THOSE WHO CAME   LONGDON, GEORGE SS FUN 53 06
  GATEWAY TO TOMORROW   CARNELL, JOHN   AN
  SPACE POLICE   NORTON, ANDRE   AN
OF TIME AND CATS   FAST, HOWARD SS FSF 59 03
  EDGE OF TOMORROW, THE   FAST, HOWARD   AC
OF TIME AND TEXAS   NOLAN, WILLIAM F. SS FUN 56 11
  IMPACT-20   NOLAN, WILLIAM F.   AC
OF TIME AND THIRD AVENUE BESTER, ALFRED SS FSF 51 10
  BEST SCIENCE-FICTION STORIES: 1952, THE BLEILER & DIKTY   AN
  CENTURY OF SCIENCE FICTION, A   KNIGHT, DAMON   AN
  STAR LIGHT, STAR BRIGHT   BESTER, ALFRED   AC
  STARBURST   BESTER, ALFRED   AC
OFF COURSE   MORGAN, EDWIN PM 67
  SCIENCE FICTION   BRODKIN & PEARSON   AN

OFF FOR THE MOON (FROM "ZERO TO EIGHTY")
    NORTHRUP, EDWIN F. EX   37
  SCIENCE IN FICTION   BAYLISS, A.E. & J.C. AN
OFF SEASON, THE   BRADBURY, RAY SS TWS 48 12
  MARTIAN CHRONICLES, THE   BRADBURY, RAY   AC
OFF THE BEAM   SMITH, GEORGE O. NV ASF 44 02
  COMPLETE VENUS EQUILATERAL, THE SMITH, GEORGE O.   AC
  VENUS EQUILATERAL   SMITH, GEORGE O.   AC
OFFERING TO THE MOON, AN SMITH, CLARK ASHTON SS WRT 53 09
  ANCIENT MYSTERIES READER, THE HAINING, PETER   AN
  OTHER DIMENSIONS   SMITH, CLARK ASHTON   AC
OFFICE CALL   FRITCH, CHARLES E. SS FUN 54 10
  CRAZY MIXED-UP PLANET   FRITCH, CHARLES E.   AC
OFFICE MEETING, AN   GORDON, GILES SS NWQ 73 05
  NEW WORLDS NO. 5   MOORCOCK & PLATT   OA
OFFICIAL RECORD   PRATT, FLETCHER NV SSF 52 09
  ASSIGNMENT IN TOMORROW   POHL, FREDERIK   AN
OGRE   SIMAK, CLIFFORD D. NV ASF 44 01
  ADVENTURES ON OTHER PLANETS WOLLHEIM, DONALD A. AN
OGRE IN THE VLY   DAVIDSON, AVRAM SS IFS 59 07
  STRANGE SEAS AND SHORES   DAVIDSON, AVRAM   AC
OGRE!   JESBY, EDWARD NV FSF 68 09
  BEST FROM FANTASY AND SCIENCE FICTION: 18
    FERMAN, EDWARD L.   AN
OGRE, THE   DAVIDSON, AVRAM SS IFS 59 07
  WHAT STRANGE STARS AND SKIES DAVIDSON, AVRAM   AC
OGRESS, THE   YOUNG, ROBERT F. SS FIN 70
  FUTURE IS NOW, THE   NOLAN, WILLIAM F.   OA
OH FATHER OF MINE (SEE FATHER, DEAR FATHER)
    BEAUMONT, CHARLES TC
OH IN JOSE, THE   ALDISS, BRIAN W. SS IMP 66 07
  BEYOND TOMORROW   HARDING, LEE   AN
OH, TO BE A BLOBEL!   DICK, PHILIP K. SS GAL 64 02
  BEST OF PHILIP K. DICK, THE DICK, PHILIP K.   AC
  INFINITE JESTS   SILVERBERG, ROBERT   AC
  PRESERVING MACHINE, THE   DICK, PHILIP K.   AC
  WORLD'S BEST SCIENCE FICTION: 1965 WOLLHEIM & CARR   AN
OH, VALINDA!   CONEY, MICHAEL G. NV NWR 72 20
  NEW WRITINGS IN SF. 20   CARNELL, JOHN   OA
  1973 ANNUAL WORLD'S BEST SF, THE WOLLHEIM, DONALD A. AN
OH, WHERE, NOW, IS PEGGY MACRAFFERTY?
    WYNDHAM, JOHN SS
  CONSIDER HER WAYS AND OTHERS WYNDHAM, JOHN   AC
OIL OF DOG   BIERCE, AMBROSE SS
  SHOCKING THING, A   KNIGHT, DAMON   AN
OIL-MAD BUG-EYED MONSTERS HOWARD, HAYDEN SS GAL 70 06
  BEST SF: 1970   HARRISON & ALDISS   AN
OKIE   BLISH, JAMES NV ASF 50 04
  CITIES OF WONDER   KNIGHT, DAMON   AN
  EARTHMAN, COME HOME   BLISH, JAMES   NO
  *STORIES FOR TOMORROW   SLOANE, WILLIAM   AN
OLD BUNCH AND DUSTY STIGGINS, THE
    DEFORD, MIRIAM ALLEN SS FSF 70 10
  ELSEWHERE, ELSEWHEN, ELSEHOW DEFORD, MIRIAM ALLEN AC
OLD CLOTHES   BLACKWOOD, ALGERNON NV   17
  LITTLE MONSTERS, THE   ELWOOD & GHIDALIA   AN
OLD COLLEGE TRY, THE   BLOCH, ROBERT SS GAM 63 08
  FEAR TODAY, GONE TOMORROW BLOCH, ROBERT   AC
  SEA OF SPACE, A   NOLAN, WILLIAM F.   AN
OLD DEVILNS WAS A-WAITING WELLMAN, MANLY WADE SS FSF 57 02
  WHO FEARS THE DEVIL?   WELLMAN, MANLY WADE AC
OLD DIE RICH, THE   GOLD, H. L. NA GAL 53 03
  OLD DIE RICH AND OTHER SCIENCE FICTION, THE
    GOLD, H. L.   AC
OLD DOCTOR RUTHERFORD   HANNIGAN, D. F. SS LUD 91 09
  SCIENCE FICTION BY GASLIGHT MOSKOWITZ, SAM   AN
OLD FAITHFUL   GALLUN, RAYMOND Z. NV ASF 34 12
  BEFORE THE GOLDEN AGE   ASIMOV, ISAAC   AN
  *IMAGINATION UNLIMITED   BLEILER & DIKTY   AN
  SCIENCE FICTION: THE GREAT YEARS POHL, C. & F.   AN
OLD FASHIONED GIRL, AN   RUSS, JOANNA SS FST 74
  FINAL STAGE   FERMAN & MALZBERG   OA
OLD FLEEING AND FLEETING IMAGES, THE
    ALDISS, BRIAN W. SS NWR 74 24
  NEW WRITINGS IN SF. 24   BULMER, KENNETH   OA
OLD FOLKS, THE   GUNN, JAMES E. SS NOV 72 02
  BEST SF: 1972   HARRISON & ALDISS   AN
  INTO THE UNKNOWN   CARR, TERRY   AN
  NOVA 2   HARRISON, HARRY   OA
OLD FOOT FORGOT   LAFFERTY, R. A. SS ORB 70 07
  ORBIT 7   KNIGHT, DAMON   OA
OLD GROWLER SPACE SHIP NO. 2213
    DEEGAN, JON J. CT AUT 51 04
  AUTHENTIC BOOK OF SPACE   CAMPBELL, H. J.   AN
OLD HORNS, THE   CAMPBELL, J. RAMSEY SS
  YEAR'S BEST HORROR STORIES: SERIES II, THE
    DAVIS, RICHARD   AN
OLD HUNDREDTH   ALDISS, BRIAN W. SS NWS 60 11
  AIRS OF EARTH, THE   ALDISS, BRIAN W.   AC
  ANOTHER WORLD   DOZOIS, GARDNER R.   AN
  *BEST SCIENCE FICTION STORIES OF BRIAN W. ALDISS
    ALDISS, BRIAN W.   AC
  BEST SF 6   CRISPIN, EDMUND   AN
  SF: AUTHORS' CHOICE 4   HARRISON, HARRY   AN
  STARSWARM   ALDISS, BRIAN W.   AC
  6TH ANNUAL OF THE YEAR'S BEST S-F, THE MERRIL, JUDITH   AN
OLD MAN HENDERSON   NEVILLE, KRIS SS FSF 51 06
  BEST FROM FANTASY AND SCIENCE FICTION BOUCHER & MCCOMAS AN
  SPECIAL WONDER   MCCOMAS, J. FRANCIS   AN
  UNIVERSE AHEAD   ENGDAHL & ROBERSON   AN
OLD MAN IN A NEW WORLD   STAPLEDON, OLAF NO ALN 44
  WORLDS OF WONDER   STAPLEDON, OLAF   AC
OLD MAN MORGAN'S GRAVE DEFORD, MIRIAM ALLEN SS FSF 52 10
  ELSEWHERE, ELSEWHEN, ELSEHOW DEFORD, MIRIAM ALLEN AC
OLD MAN MULLIGAN   MILLER, P. SCHUYLER NV ASF 40 12
  TITAN, THE   MILLER, P. SCHUYLER AC

OLD MAN OF THE MOUNTAINS, THE   CARR, TERRY   SS   FSF 63 04
  LIGHT AT THE END OF THE UNIVERSE, THE   CARR, TERRY   AC
  NEW WORLDS OF FANTASY NO. 2   CARR, TERRY   AN
OLD MAN OF THE STARS, THE   BURKE, JONATHAN F.   SN   AUT 53 10
  ALIEN LANDSCAPES   BURKE, JONATHAN F.   AC
OLD MAN, THE   HORN, HOLLOWAY   SS   32
  OTHER SIDE OF THE CLOCK, THE   STERN, PHILIP VAN D.   AN
  TRAVELERS IN TIME   STERN, PHILIP VAN D.   AC
OLD MAN, THE   SILVERBERG, ROBERT   SS   IMG 57 04
  TO WORLDS BEYOND   SILVERBERG, ROBERT   AC
OLD MAX   LYTLE, B. J.   SS
  LONG NIGHT OF WAITING AND OTHER STORIES   ELWOOD, ROGER   OA
OLD ONES, THE   BRADBURY, RAY   SS   NEW 51 AC
  MARTIAN CHRONICLES, THE   BRADBURY, RAY   AC
OLD ORDER, THE (THE NEW GODS LEAD)   DEL REY, LESTER   SS   MSS 51 02
  SHADOW OF TOMORROW   POHL, FREDERIK   AN
OLD RAMBLING HOUSE   HERBERT, FRANK   SS   GAL 58 04
  WORLDS OF FRANK HERBERT, THE   HERBERT, FRANK   AC
OLD SOUL   HERBST, STEVE   SS   ORB 72 11
  ORBIT 11   KNIGHT, DAMON   OA
OLD SQUIDS AND LITTLE SPELLER   MITCHELL, EDWARD P.   SS   SUN 85 07
  CRYSTAL MAN, THE   MITCHELL, EDWARD P.   AC
OLD TESTAMENT   BIXBY, JEROME   SS   IFS 64 07
  IF READER OF SCIENCE FICTION, THE   POHL, FREDERIK   AN
OLD TUNE, AN (SEE THE INTREPID AERONAUT)   FINNEY, JACK   TC
OLD WOMAN WHO LIVED WITH A BEAR, THE   DAVIDSON, AVRAM   NV
  ENQUIRIES OF DOCTOR ESZTERHAZY, THE   DAVIDSON, AVRAM   NO
OLD WOMAN, THE   DEFORD, MIRIAM ALLEN   SS   FUN 57 10
  ELSEWHERE, ELSEWHEN, ELSEHOW   DEFORD, MIRIAM ALLEN   AC
OLD-FASHIONED   ASIMOV, ISAAC   SS   BTM 76 02
  BICENTENNIAL MAN AND OTHER STORIES, THE   ASIMOV, ISAAC   AC
OLD-FASHIONED BIRD CHRISTMAS, AN   ST. CLAIR, MARGARET   NV   GAL 61 12
  CHANGE THE SKY AND OTHER STORIES   ST. CLAIR, MARGARET   AC
  SEVENTH GALAXY READER, THE   POHL, FREDERIK   AN
OLD, OLD DEATH IN NEW, NEW VENICE   SCORTIA, THOMAS N.   SS   NEW 75 AC
  CAUTION! INFLAMMABLE!   SCORTIA, THOMAS N.   AC
OLDEST GLASS, THE   BRUNNER, JOHN   PM   72
  FROM THIS DAY FORWARD   BRUNNER, JOHN   AC
OLDEST SOLDIER, THE   LEIBER, FRITZ   NV   FSF 60 05
  ANOTHER WORLD   DOZOIS, GARDNER R.   AN
  *MIND SPIDER AND OTHER STORIES, THE   LEIBER, FRITZ   DC
OLE DOC METHUSELAH   HUBBARD, L. RON   NV   ASF 47 10
  OLE DOC METHUSELAH   HUBBARD, L. RON   AC
OLE MOTHER METHUSELAH   HUBBARD, L. RON   NV   ASF 50 01
  OLE DOC METHUSELAH   HUBBARD, L. RON   AC
OLGOI-KHORKHOI   YEFREMOV, IVAN   SS
  STORIES   YEFREMOV, IVAN   AC
OLIVIA   DAMONTI, HENRI   SS   60
  13 FRENCH SCIENCE-FICTION STORIES   KNIGHT, DAMON   AN
OLLIE'S HANDS   KOONTZ, DEAN R.   SS   INY 72 04
  INFINITY 4   HOSKINS, ROBERT   OA
OLSEN AND THE GULL   ST. CLAIR, ERIC   SS   FSF 64 09
  BEST FROM FANTASY AND SCIENCE FICTION: 14   DAVIDSON, AVRAM   AN
OMEGA   LONG, AMELIA R.   SS   AMZ 32 07
  END OF THE WORLD, THE   WOLLHEIM, DONALD A.   AN
OMEGA GLORY, THE (GENE RODDENBERRY)   BLISH, JAMES   SA   STK 74 10
  STAR TREK 10   BLISH, JAMES   OC
OMEN, THE   JACKSON, SHIRLEY   SS   FSF 58 03
  BEST FROM FANTASY AND SCIENCE FICTION: 8   BOUCHER, ANTHONY   AN
OMNIA TRISTE   NORWOOD, RICK   SS   CLR 72 02
  CLARION II   WILSON, ROBIN SCOTT   OA
OMNILINGUAL   PIPER, H. BEAM   NV   ASF 57 02
  APEMAN, SPACEMAN   STOVER & HARRISON   AN
  DAYS AFTER TOMORROW, THE   SANTESSON, HANS S.   AN
  GREAT SCIENCE FICTION STORIES ABOUT MARS   DIKTY, T. E.   AN
  MARS, WE LOVE YOU   HIPOLITO & MCNELLY   AN
  PROLOGUE TO ANALOG   CAMPBELL, JOHN W. JR   AN
  SCIENCE FICTION NOVELLAS   HARRISON & MCNELLY   AN
  TOMORROW, AND TOMORROW, AND TOMORROW...   HEINTZ/HERBERT/JOOS/   AN
  WHERE DO WE GO FROM HERE?   ASIMOV, ISAAC   AN
ON BINARY DIGITS AND HUMAN HABITS   POHL, FREDERIK   AR   FSF 62 12
  DIGITS AND DASTARDS   POHL, FREDERIK   AC
ON CAMERA   NOVOTNY, JOHN   SS   FSF 56 04
  SCIENCE FICTION ODDITIES   CONKLIN, GROFF   AN
ON HANDLING THE DATA   HIRSHFIELD, HENRY I.
    AND MATEYKO, G. M.   SS C ASF 59 09
  BEST SF 5   CRISPIN, EDMUND   AN
ON ICE   MALZBERG, BARRY N.   SS   AMZ 73 01
  BEST OF BARRY N. MALZBERG, THE   MALZBERG, BARRY N.   AC
ON LETHAL CLOUDS   SHAPLEY, HARLOW   AR
  POISON BELT, THE   DOYLE, ARTHUR CONAN   AC
ON LOCATION   BAUM, THOMAS   SS   PBY 70 07
  LAST TRAIN TO LIMBO   PLAYBOY, EDITORS OF   AN
ON MESSENGER MOUNTAIN   DICKSON, GORDON R.   NV   WOT 64 06
  STAR ROAD, THE   DICKSON, GORDON R.   AC
ON PAIN OF DEATH   WILLIAMS, ROBERT M.   NV   ASF 42 06
  WHEN TWO WORLDS MEET   WILLIAMS, ROBERT M.   AC
ON POINT OF VIEW   WILHELM, KATE   AR
  THOSE WHO CAN: A SCIENCE FICTION READER   WILSON, ROBIN SCOTT   AN
ON PREDICTION   ASIMOV, ISAAC   IN   68
  FUTURE TENSE   CURTIS, RICHARD   AN
  OPUS 100   ASIMOV, ISAAC   AC
ON SAVING THE WORLD   DISCH, THOMAS M.   IN
  RUINS OF EARTH, THE   DISCH, THOMAS M.   AN
ON SCIENCE FICTION BY SCIENTISTS   CONKLIN, GROFF   IN
  GREAT SCIENCE FICTION BY SCIENTISTS   CONKLIN, GROFF   AN

ON SETTING   RUSS, JOANNA   AR
  THOSE WHO CAN: A SCIENCE FICTION READER   WILSON, ROBIN SCOTT   AN
ON SHOOTING PARTICLES BEYOND THE WORLD   EBERHART, RICHARD   PM   60
  LOOKING AHEAD   ALLEN, D. & L.   AN
ON SPECULATIVE FICTION   DELANY, SAMUEL R.   IN C
  QUARK/4   DELANY & HACKER   OA
ON SPECULATIVE FICTION   HACKER, MARILYN   IN C
  QUARK/4   DELANY & HACKER   OA
ON STYLE   GUNN, JAMES E.   AR
  THOSE WHO CAN: A SCIENCE FICTION READER   WILSON, ROBIN SCOTT   AN
ON THE AIR   MALZBERG, BARRY N.   SS   NDM 76 06
  NEW DIMENSIONS 6   SILVERBERG, ROBERT   OA
ON THE CAMPAIGN TRAIL   MALZBERG, BARRY N.   SS   FCR 75
  DOWN HERE IN THE DREAM QUARTER   MALZBERG, BARRY N.   AC
  FUTURE CORRUPTION   ELWOOD, ROGER   AN
ON THE DOTTED LINE   BIGGLE, LLOYD JR.   NV   IFS 57 06
  RULE OF THE DOOR AND OTHER FANCIFUL REGULATIONS   BIGGLE, LLOYD JR.   AC
ON THE DOWNHILL SIDE   ELLISON, HARLAN   SS   UNI 72 02
  DEATHBIRD STORIES   ELLISON, HARLAN   AC
  NEBULA AWARD STORIES 8   ASIMOV, ISAAC   AN
  UNIVERSE 2   CARR, TERRY   OA
ON THE FEASIBILITY OF COAL-DRIVEN POWER STATIONS   FRISCH, O. R.   SS   SAM 56 03
  EXPERT DREAMERS, THE   POHL, FREDERIK   AN
ON THE FICTION IN SCIENCE FICTION   TENN, WILLIAM   IN   SFA 54 03
  OF ALL POSSIBLE WORLDS   TENN, WILLIAM   AC
ON THE FOURTH PLANET   BONE, J. F.   SS   GAL 63 04
  12 GREAT CLASSICS OF SCIENCE FICTION   CONKLIN, GROFF   AN
  9TH ANNUAL OF THE YEAR'S BEST S-F, THE   MERRIL, JUDITH   AN
ON THE GEM PLANET   SMITH, CORDWAINER   NV   GAL 63 10
  ANOTHER WORLD   DOZOIS, GARDNER R.   AN
  QUEST OF THE THREE WORLDS   SMITH, CORDWAINER   NO
  SEVENTH GALAXY READER, THE   POHL, FREDERIK   AN
ON THE HILLS AND EVERYWHERE   WELLMAN, MANLY WADE   SS   FSF 56 01
  WHO FEARS THE DEVIL?   WELLMAN, MANLY WADE   AC
ON THE INSIDE   HOLDSTOCK, ROBERT P.   NV   NWR 76 28
  NEW WRITINGS IN SF. 28   BULMER, KENNETH   OA
ON THE LAST AFTERNOON   TIPTREE, JAMES JR.   NA   AMZ 72 11
  WARM WORLDS AND OTHERWISE   TIPTREE, JAMES JR.   AC
ON THE MOON   TSIOLKOVSKY, K.   SS
  RUSSIAN SCIENCE FICTION   MAGIDOFF, ROBERT   AN
ON THE PLANET FRAGMENT   JONES, NEIL R.   NV   AMZ 37 10
  TWIN WORLDS   JONES, NEIL R.   AC
ON THE RELATIVITY OF TIME   PAULI, WOLFGANG   AR   49
  SCIENCE FACT/FICTION   FARRELL/GAGE/&   AN
ON THE RIVER   YOUNG, ROBERT F.   SS   FAN 65 01
  GLASS OF STARS, A   YOUNG, ROBERT F.   AC
ON THE ROAD TO HONEYVILLE   WILHELM, KATE   SS   ORB 72 11
  ORBIT 11   KNIGHT, DAMON   OA
ON THE SAND PLANET   SMITH, CORDWAINER   NV   AMZ 65 12
  QUEST OF THE THREE WORLDS   SMITH, CORDWAINER   NO
ON THE STAIRCASE   GEROULD, KATHARINE F   SS   SCR 13 12
  TRAVELERS IN TIME   STERN, PHILIP VAN D.   AN
ON THE STORM PLANET   SMITH, CORDWAINER   SN   GAL 65 02
  DAY IN THE LIFE, A   DOZOIS, GARDNER R.   AN
  QUEST OF THE THREE WORLDS   SMITH, CORDWAINER   NO
ON THE STREET OF SERPENTS,OR THE ASSASSINATION OF CHAIRMAN MAO
  AS EFFECTED BY THE AUTHOR   BISHOP, MICHAEL   NV   SFE 74 01
  SCIENCE FICTION EMPHASIS NO. 1   GERROLD, DAVID   OA
ON THE THRESHOLD OF ETERNITY   WANDREI, DONALD   SS
  EYE AND THE FINGER   WANDREI, DONALD   AC
ON THE THRESHOLD OF FREEDOM   MAGRITTE, RENE   IL
  SCIENCE FICTION   BRODKIN & PEARSON   AN
ON THE WALL OF THE LODGE   BLISH, JAMES
    AND KIDD, VIRGINIA   NV C GAL 62 04
  DARK STARS   SILVERBERG, ROBERT   AN
ON THE WHEEL   KNIGHT, DAMON   SS   NOV 72 02
  NOVA 2   HARRISON, HARRY   OA
  SCIENCE FACT/FICTION   FARRELL/GAGE/&   AN
ON THEME   LE GUIN, URSULA K.   AR
  THOSE WHO CAN: A SCIENCE FICTION READER   WILSON, ROBIN SCOTT   AN
ON VELOCITY EXERCISES   POHL, FREDERIK   AR
  THOSE WHO CAN: A SCIENCE FICTION READER   WILSON, ROBIN SCOTT   AN
ON VENUS, HAVE WE GOT A RABBI   TENN, WILLIAM   NV   NEW 74 AN
  BEST SCIENCE FICTION OF THE YEAR, THE NO. 4   CARR, TERRY   AN
  WANDERING STARS   DANN, JACK M.   AN
ON WRITING FANTASY   NORTON, ANDRE   AR   DIP 71 11
  MANY WORLDS OF ANDRE NORTON, THE   NORTON, ANDRE   AC
ONCE A GREECH   SMITH, EVELYN E.   NV   GAL 57 04
  WORLD THAT COULDN'T BE AND 8 OTHER SF NOVELETS   GOLD, H. L.   AN
ONCE AROUND ARCTURUS   GREEN, JOSEPH   NV   IFS 62 09
  AFFAIR WITH GENIUS, AN   GREEN, JOSEPH   AC
ONCE AROUND THE MOON   PHILLIPS, VIC   NV   ASF 37 06
  FIRST FLIGHTS TO THE MOON   CLEMENT, HAL   AN
ONCE MORE, THE DREAM   ATTANASIO, A. A.   SS   NWQ 74 06
  NEW WORLDS NO. 6   PLATT & BAILEY   OA
ONCE MORE, WITH FEELING   SPINRAD, NORMAN   SS   KNT 69
  LAST HURRAH OF THE GOLDEN HORDE, THE   SPINRAD, NORMAN   AC
ONCE ON ARANEA   LAFFERTY, R. A.   SS   NEW 72 AC
  STRANGE DOINGS   LAFFERTY, R. A.   AC
ONCE THERE WAS A GIANT   LAUMER, KEITH   SN   FSF 68 11
  ONCE THERE WAS A GIANT   LAUMER, KEITH   AC
ONCE UPON A PLANET (LEN JANSON & CHUCK MENVILLE)   FOSTER, ALAN DEAN   SA   SLG 75 03
  STAR TREK LOG THREE   FOSTER, ALAN DEAN   OC
ONCE UPON A TIME   BURKE, JONATHAN F.   SS   SCF 54 05
  ALIEN LANDSCAPES   BURKE, JONATHAN F.   AC
ONCE WAS   MALEC, ALEXANDER B.   NV
  EXTRAPOLASIS   MALEC, ALEXANDER B.   AC
ONE ACROSS   SELLINGS, ARTHUR   SS   GAL 56 05
  LONG EUREKA, THE   SELLINGS, ARTHUR   AC

ONE AFTERNOON IN BUSTERVILLE   GRASTY, WILLIAM K.   SS   STG 74
    STRANGE GODS   ELWOOD, ROGER   OA
ONE AT A TIME   LAFFERTY, R. A.   SS   ORB 68 04
    NINE HUNDRED GRANDMOTHERS   LAFFERTY, R. A.   AC
    ORBIT   4   KNIGHT, DAMON   OA
    WORLDS FAR AND NEAR   CARR, TERRY   AN
ONE DAY IN THE WAR   POSNER, RICHARD   SS   INY 72 03
    INFINITY 3   HOSKINS, ROBERT   OA
ONE FACE   NIVEN, LARRY   NV   GAL 65 06
    SHAPE OF SPACE, THE   NIVEN, LARRY   AC
ONE FALSE STEP   BUNCH, DAVID R.   SS
    MODERAN   BUNCH, DAVID R.   AC
ONE FOOT AND THE GRAVE   STURGEON, THEODORE NV   WRT 49 09
    3 TO THE HIGHEST POWER   NOLAN, WILLIAM F.   AN
ONE FOR THE BOOKS   MATHESON, RICHARD NV   GAL 55 09
    SHOCK!   MATHESON, RICHARD   AC
    UNTRAVELLED WORLDS   BARTER & WILSON   AN
    WORLD THAT COULDN'T BE AND 8 OTHER SF NOVELETS
                                        GOLD, H. L.   AN
ONE FOR THE ROAD   WILHELM, KATE   SS   FUN 59 07
    MILE-LONG SPACESHIP, THE   WILHELM, KATE   AC
ONE FROM CAMELOT MODERAN, THE BUNCH, DAVID R.   SS
    MODERAN   BUNCH, DAVID R.   AC
ONE IN A THOUSAND   MCINTOSH, J. T.   SS   FSF 54 01
    ONE IN THREE HUNDRED   MCINTOSH, J. T.   AC
ONE IN THREE HUNDRED   MCINTOSH, J. T.   NV   FSF 53 02
    BEST SCIENCE-FICTION STORIES: 1954, THE BLEILER & DIKTY   AN
    ONE IN THREE HUNDRED   MCINTOSH, J. T.   AC
ONE LEG TOO MANY   ALEXANDER, W.   SS   AMZ 29 10
    *BIG BOOK OF SCIENCE FICTION   CONKLIN, GROFF   AN
ONE LESS   ROSOKHOVATSKY, IGOR SS   66
    ULTIMATE THRESHOLD, THE   GINSBURG, MIRRA   AN
ONE LIFE, FURNISHED IN EARLY POVERTY
                               ELLISON, HARLAN   SS   ORB 70 08
    APPROACHING OBLIVION   ELLISON, HARLAN   AC
    BEST FROM ORBIT, THE   KNIGHT, DAMON   AN
    ORBIT   8   KNIGHT, DAMON   OA
    1972 ANNUAL WORLD'S BEST SF, THE   WOLLHEIM, DONALD A.   AN
ONE LOVE HAVE I   YOUNG, ROBERT F.   SS   IFS 55 04
    SEA OF SPACE, A   NOLAN, WILLIAM F.   AN
    THEMES IN SCIENCE FICTION   KELLEY, LEO P.   AN
ONE MAN'S POISON (SEE UNTOUCHED BY HUMAN HANDS)
                               SHECKLEY, ROBERT   TC
ONE NIGHT STAND   SIMMONS, HERBERT A. SS   GAM 63 01
    SEA OF SPACE, A   NOLAN, WILLIAM F.   AN
ONE OF OUR PLANETS IS MISSING (MARC DANIELS)
                               FOSTER, ALAN DEAN SA   SLG 74 01
    STAR TREK LOG ONE   FOSTER, ALAN DEAN   OC
ONE OF THEM   HENDERSON, ZENNA   SS   NEW 71 AC
    HOLDING WONDER   HENDERSON, ZENNA   AC
ONE OF THOSE DAYS   NOLAN, WILLIAM F.   SS   FSF 62 05
    FIEND IN YOU, THE   BEAUMONT, CHARLES   AN
    IMPACT-20   NOLAN, WILLIAM F.   AC
    8TH ANNUAL OF THE YEAR'S BEST S-F, THE MERRIL, JUDITH   AN
ONE ORDINARY DAY, WITH BOX   SKY, KATHLEEN   SS   GEN 72
    GENERATION   GERROLD, DAVID   OA
ONE ORDINARY DAY, WITH PEANUTS JACKSON, SHIRLEY SS   FSF 55 01
    BEST FROM FANTASY AND SCIENCE FICTION: 5
                                        BOUCHER, ANTHONY   AN
    NIGHT IN FUNLAND   BRONDFIELD, JEROME   AN
    SCIENCE FICTION ARGOSY, A   KNIGHT, DAMON   AN
    SF: THE BEST OF THE BEST   MERRIL, JUDITH   AN
    SF: THE YEAR'S GREATEST SCIENCE FICTION AND FANTASY
                                        MERRIL, JUDITH   AN
ONE OTHER   WELLMAN, MANLY WADE SS   FSF 53 08
    WHO FEARS THE DEVIL?   WELLMAN, MANLY WADE   AC
ONE PREHISTORIC NIGHT   BARSHOFSKY, PHILIP SS   WOS 34 11
    HISTORY OF THE SCIENCE FICTION MAGAZINE, THE PART 1 1926-1935
                                        ASHLEY, MICHAEL   AN
ONE RACE SHOW   JAKES, JOHN W.   NV   GAL 62 08
    BEST OF JOHN JAKES, THE   JAKES, JOHN W.   AC
ONE ROAD TO DAMASCUS   LUNDE, DAVID
                               AND SALLIS, JAMES   SS C
    2076: THE AMERICAN TRICENTENNIAL   BRYANT, EDWARD   OA
ONE ROLE WITH RELISH   ALDISS, BRIAN W.   SS   NEW 66 AC
    SALIVA TREE AND OTHER STRANGE GROWTHS, THE
                                        ALDISS, BRIAN W.   AC
ONE STATION OF THE WAY   LEIBER, FRITZ   SS   GAL 68 12
    BEST SF: 1968   HARRISON & ALDISS   AN
    ELEVENTH GALAXY READER, THE   POHL, FREDERIK   AN
ONE STEP FROM EARTH (AS HANK DEMPSEY)
                               HARRISON, HARRY   SS   ASF 70 03
    MARS, WE LOVE YOU   HIPOLITO & MCNELLY   AN
    ONE STEP FROM EARTH   HARRISON, HARRY   AC
ONE SUNDAY IN NEPTUNE   PANSHIN, ALEXEI   SS   NEW 69 AN
    FAREWELL TO YESTERDAY'S TOMORROW   PANSHIN, ALEXEI   AC
    TOMORROW'S WORLDS   SILVERBERG, ROBERT   AN
    WORLD'S BEST SCIENCE FICTION: 1970 WOLLHEIM & CARR   AN
ONE THOUSAND MILES UP   ROBINSON, FRANK M. SS   SST 54 04
    BEST SCIENCE FICTION STORIES AND NOVELS: 1955
                                        DIKTY, T. E.   AN
ONE TIME, A RED CARPET...   BUNCH, DAVID R.   SS
    MODERAN   BUNCH, DAVID R.   AC
ONE TIMELESS SPRING   BRADBURY, RAY   SS   COL 46 04
    LONG AFTER MIDNIGHT   BRADBURY, RAY   AC
ONE TO A CUSTOMER   COGSWELL, THEODORE R SS   SUP 58 06
    THIRD EYE, THE   COGSWELL, THEODORE R   AC
ONE TOO MANY   MCINTOSH, J. T.   SS   FSF 54 09
    ONE IN THREE HUNDRED   MCINTOSH, J. T.   AC
ONE WAY STREET   BIXBY, JEROME   SS   AMZ 54 01
    BEST SCIENCE FICTION STORIES AND NOVELS: 1955
                                        DIKTY, T. E.   AN
    SPACE BY THE TAIL   BIXBY, JEROME   AC
ONE WAY TO MARS   BLOCH, ROBERT   SS   WRT 45 07
    HOUSE OF THE HATCHET, THE   BLOCH, ROBERT   AC
    MORE NIGHTMARES   BLOCH, ROBERT   AC

*OPENER OF THE WAY, THE   BLOCH, ROBERT   AC
    STRANGE SIGNPOSTS   ELWOOD & MOSKOWITZ   AN
ONE WHO RETURNS, THE   BERRY, JOHN   SS   FSF 61 03
    *BEST FROM FANTASY AND SCIENCE FICTION: 11
                                        MILLS, ROBERT P.   AN
ONE WHO WAITS, THE   BRADBURY, RAY   SS   FSF 51 02
    FAR BOUNDARIES   DERLETH, AUGUST   AN
    MACHINERIES OF JOY, THE   BRADBURY, RAY   AC
    TOMORROW MIDNIGHT   BRADBURY, RAY   AC
ONE-EYED MAN, THE   DEL REY, LESTER   SS   ASF 45 05
    EARLY DEL REY   DEL REY, LESTER   AC
ONE-SHOT   BLISH, JAMES   SS   ASF 55 08
    SO CLOSE TO HOME   BLISH, JAMES   AC
ONE-WAY JOURNEY   SILVERBERG, ROBERT NV   INF 57 11
    PARSECS AND PARABLES   SILVERBERG, ROBERT   AC
ONE-WAY JOURNEY (ONE WAY)   DEFORD, MIRIAM ALLEN SS GAL 55 03
    XENOGENESIS   DEFORD, MIRIAM ALLEN   AC
ONEIROMACHIA   AIKEN, CONRAD   PM   ATL 61 10
    7TH ANNUAL OF THE YEAR'S BEST S-F, THE MERRIL, JUDITH   AN
ONES WHO WALK AWAY FROM OMELAS, THE
                               LE GUIN, URSULA K. SS   NDM 73 03
    BEST SCIENCE FICTION OF THE YEAR, THE NO. 3
                                        CARR, TERRY   AN
    NEW DIMENSIONS 3   SILVERBERG, ROBERT   OA
    WINDS TWELVE QUARTERS, THE   LE GUIN, URSULA K.   AC
ONLY A GOD   LORY, ROBERT   SS
    HARVEST OF HOODWINKS, A   LORY, ROBERT   DC
ONLY AN ECHO   BARCLAY, ALAN   SS   NWS 54 04
    GATEWAY TO THE STARS   CARNELL, JOHN   AN
ONLY AT NIGHT   MCINTYRE, VONDA N. SS   CLR 71 01
    CLARION   WILSON, ROBIN SCOTT   AN
ONLY GAME IN TOWN, THE   ANDERSON, POUL   NV   FSF 60 01
    GUARDIANS OF TIME   ANDERSON, POUL   AC
ONLY GONE BEFORE   PETAJA, EMIL   SS   MOH 68 03
    STARDRIFT AND OTHER FANTASTIC FLOTSAM PETAJA, EMIL   AC
ONLY MAN ON EARTH, THE   JAMES, LAURENCE   SS   NWB 73 05
    NEW WORLDS QUARTERLY NO. 5   MOORCOCK, MICHAEL   AN
ONLY THE WORDS ARE DIFERENT   SALLIS, JAMES   SS   ORB 71 09
    ORBIT   9   KNIGHT, DAMON   AN
ONLY THING WE LEARN, THE   KORNBLUTH, C. M.   SS   STS 49 07
    BEST OF C. M. KORNBLUTH, THE   KORNBLUTH, C. M.   AC
    BEST SCIENCE FICTION STORIES OF C. M. KORNBLUTH
                                        KORNBLUTH, C. M.   AC
    *BIG BOOK OF SCIENCE FICTION   CONKLIN, GROFF   AN
    MARCHING MORONS AND OTHER SCIENCE FICTION
                                        KORNBLUTH, C. M.   AC
    SHAPE OF THINGS, THE   KNIGHT, DAMON   AN
ONLY WHO CAN MAKE A TREE?   FARMER, PHILIP JOSE SS   FSF 71 11
    BOOK OF PHILIP JOSE FARMER, THE   FARMER, PHILIP JOSE   AC
OOGENESIS OF BIRD CITY, THE   FARMER, PHILIP JOSE SS   AMZ 70 09
    AMERICAN GOVERNMENT THROUGH SCIENCE FICTION
                                        OLANDER/GREENBERG/&   AN
OOK OOK OOK   CONRAD, EARL   SS
    DA VINCI MACHINE, THE   CONRAD, EARL   OC
OOZE   RUD, A. M.   NV   WRT 23 03
    MOON TERROR, THE   BIRCH, A. G.   AN
OPAXTL   MALEC, ALEXANDER B. NV
    EXTRAPOLASIS   MALEC, ALEXANDER B.   AC
OPEN HOUSE   BEAUMONT, CHARLES SS   NEW 57 AC
    HUNGER AND OTHER STORIES, THE   BEAUMONT, CHARLES   AC
    MAGIC MAN AND OTHER SCIENCE-FANTASY STORIES
                                        BEAUMONT, CHARLES   AC
OPEN QUESTION, THE   ALDISS, BRIAN W.   SI
    ALL ABOUT VENUS   ALDISS, BRIAN W.   AN
OPEN SECRET   PADGETT, LEWIS   SS   ASF 43 04
    GREAT STORIES OF SCIENCE FICTION   LEINSTER, MURRAY   AN
OPEN SECRETS, THE   EISENBERG, LARRY   SS   GAL 69 05
    BEST LAID SCHEMES, THE   EISENBERG, LARRY   AC
OPEN THE SKY (SEE TO OPEN THE SKY)
                               SILVERBERG, ROBERT TC
OPEN TO ME, MY SISTER (ALSO AS MY SISTER'S BROTHER)
                               FARMER, PHILIP JOSE NV   FSF 60 05
    ONCE AND FUTURE TALES FROM THE MAGAZINE OF FANTASY AND
    SCIENCE FICTION   FERMAN, EDWARD L.   AC
OPEN WARFARE   GUNN, JAMES E.   NV   GAL 54 05
    ARENA: SPORTS SF   FERMAN & MALZBERG   AN
OPEN WINDOW, THE   SAKI   SS   14
    CHILDREN OF WONDER   TENN, WILLIAM   AN
OPEN, SESAME!   GRENDON, STEPHEN   SS   ARS 49 WI
    FAR BOUNDARIES   DERLETH, AUGUST   AN
OPENER OF THE WAY, THE   BLOCH, ROBERT   SS   WRT 36 10
    HORROR-7   BLOCH, ROBERT   AC
    *OPENER OF THE WAY, THE   BLOCH, ROBERT   AC
OPENING DOORS   SHIRAS, WILMAR H. NV   ASF 49 03
    BEST SCIENCE-FICTION STORIES: 1950, THE BLEILER & DIKTY   AN
    CHILDREN OF THE ATOM   SHIRAS, WILMAR H.   AC
OPENING FIRE   MALZBERG, BARRY N. SS   NMD 73
    BEST OF BARRY N. MALZBERG, THE   MALZBERG, BARRY N.   AC
    FRONTIERS 2: THE NEW MIND   ELWOOD, ROGER   OA
OPENING OF THE TERRAN BALLET, THE
                               SALLIS, JAMES   SS   70
    FEW LAST WORDS, A   SALLIS, JAMES   AC
OPENING PROBLEM   LAWRENCE, J. A.   NV   GAL 74 07
    BEST FROM GALAXY, THE   VOLUME III BAEN, JAMES   AN
OPENING THE DOOR   FARMER, PHILIP JOSE SS   COI 73
    CHILDREN OF INFINITY   ELWOOD, ROGER   OA
OPENING THE DOOR   MACHEN, ARTHUR   SS   31
    TRAVELERS IN TIME   STERN, PHILIP VAN D.   AN
OPERATING INSTRUCTIONS   SHECKLEY, ROBERT   SS   ASF 53 05
    BEYOND THE BARRIERS OF SPACE AND TIME MERRIL, JUDITH   AN
OPERATION AFREET   ANDERSON, POUL   SS   FSF 56 09
    OPERATION CHAOS   ANDERSON, POUL   NO
OPERATION CASSANDRA   DEFORD, MIRIAM ALLEN NV FUN 58 11
    XENOGENESIS   DEFORD, MIRIAM ALLEN   AC
OPERATION CHANGELING   ANDERSON, POUL   NA   FSF 69 05
    OPERATION CHAOS   ANDERSON, POUL   NO

```
OPERATION EXODUS          WRIGHT, LAN         SS   NWS 52 01
  GATEWAY TO THE STARS            CARNELL, JOHN        AN
OPERATION INCUBUS         ANDERSON, POUL      SS   FSF 59 10
  OPERATION CHAOS                 ANDERSON, POUL       NO
OPERATION MARS            TUBB, E. C.         NO   NEB 54 12
  ALIEN DUST                      TUBB, E. C.          NO
OPERATION MERCURY (MASQUERADE) SIMAK, CLIFFORD D.  NV ASF 41 03
  TALES OF OUTER SPACE            WOLLHEIM, DONALD A.  DA
OPERATION P-BUTTON        DICKSON, GORDON R.  SS   INY 70 01
  INFINITY 1                      HOSKINS, ROBERT      OA
OPERATION PEEP (ALSO AS PAWLEY'S PEEPHOLES)
                          WYNDHAM, JOHN       SS   SUS 51 SU
  BEYOND THE END OF TIME          POHL, FREDERIK       AN
  TIME CURVE, THE                 MOSKOWITZ & ELWOOD   AN
OPERATION PUMICE          GALLUN, RAYMOND Z.  SS   TWS 49 04
  MEN ON THE MOON                 WOLLHEIM, DONALD A.  DA
  *POSSIBLE WORLDS OF SCIENCE FICTION  CONKLIN, GROFF  AN
OPERATION RSVP            PIPER, H. BEAM      SS   AMZ 51 01
  WORLD OF WONDER                 PRATT, FLETCHER      AN
OPERATION SALAMANDER      ANDERSON, POUL      NV   FSF 57 01
  OPERATION CHAOS                 ANDERSON, POUL       NO
OPERATION STINKY          SIMAK, CLIFFORD D.  NV   GAL 57 04
  ALIENS FOR NEIGHBOURS           SIMAK, CLIFFORD D.   AC
  *WORLDS OF CLIFFORD SIMAK, THE  SIMAK, CLIFFORD D.   AC
OPERATION SYNDROME (ALSO AS NIGHTMARE BLUES)
                          HERBERT, FRANK      NV   ASF 54 06
  BOOK OF FRANK HERBERT, THE      HERBERT, FRANK       AC
OPERATION TERROR          LEINSTER, MURRAY    NO   BRK 62
  MURRAY LEINSTER OMNIBUS, A      LEINSTER, MURRAY     AC
OPERATION ZERO (INTRUDER ON THE RIM)
                          LESSER, MILTON      SS   OSF 54 09
  SANDS OF MARS AND OTHER STORIES, THE  ANONYMOUS      AN
OPERATION: GRAVITY        WILLIAMSON, JACK    SS   SFP 53 10
  PEOPLE MACHINES                 WILLIAMSON, JACK     AC
OPERATION- ANNIHILATE! (S. W. CARABATSOS)
                          BLISH, JAMES        SA   STK 68 02
  STAR TREK  2                    BLISH, JAMES         OC
OPERATION, THE            HOYLE, FRED         SS
  ELEMENT 79                      HOYLE, FRED          AC
OPIUM EATER, THE          KELLER, DAVID H. MD. SS
  TALES FROM UNDERWOOD            KELLER, DAVID H. MD. AC
OPPOSITE NUMBERS          WYNDHAM, JOHN       SS   NWS 54 04
  SEEDS OF TIME, THE              WYNDHAM, JOHN        AC
  TALES OF GOOSEFLESH AND LAUGHTER  WYNDHAM, JOHN      AC
OPPOSITES ATTRACT (MAD BOMBER) ELLISON, HARLAN  SS  CPR 57 11
  NO DOORS, NO WINDOWS (STORIES REWRITTEN) ELLISON, HARLAN AC
OPPOSITES- REACT!         STEWART, WILL       SN   ASF 43 01
  SEETEE SHIP                     STEWART, WILL        AC
OR ALL THE SEAS WITH OYSTERS  DAVIDSON, AVRAM  SS   GAL 58 05
  EARTH IS THE STRANGEST PLANET   SILVERBERG, ROBERT   AN
  FANTASY: THE LITERATURE OF THE MARVELOUS KELLEY, LEO P. AN
  FOURTH GALAXY READER, THE       GOLD, H. L.          AN
  HUGO WINNERS, THE (VOLUME 1)    ASIMOV, ISAAC        AN
  OR ALL THE SEAS WITH OYSTERS    DAVIDSON, AVRAM      AC
  SF:59, THE YEAR'S GREATEST SCIENCE FICTION AND FANTASY
                                  MERRIL, JUDITH       AN
  VINTAGE ANTHOLOGY OF SCIENCE FANTASY, THE
                                  CERF, CHRISTOPHER    AN
OR ELSE                   KUTTNER, HENRY      SS   AMZ 53 09
  AHEAD OF TIME                   KUTTNER, HENRY       AC
  BEST OF HENRY KUTTNER 1, THE    KUTTNER, HENRY       AC
  BEST OF HENRY KUTTNER, THE      KUTTNER, HENRY       AC
  BEST SF                         CRISPIN, EDMUND      AN
OR ELSE                   KUTTNER, HENRY
                          AND MOORE, C. L.    SS C AMZ 53 09
  NEVER IN THIS WORLD             STONE, IDELLA P.     AN
OR LITTLE DUCKS EACH DAY  LAFFERTY, R. A.     NV   DYS 75
  DYSTOPIAN VISIONS               ELWOOD, ROGER        OA
OR THE GRASSES GROW       DAVIDSON, AVRAM     SS   FSF 58 11
  OR ALL THE SEAS WITH OYSTERS    DAVIDSON, AVRAM      AC
  SCIENCE FICTION SHOWCASE        KORNBLUTH, MARY      AN
ORACLE FOR A WHITE RABBIT GERROLD, DAVID      NV   GAL 69 12
  WHEN HARLIE WAS ONE             GERROLD, DAVID       NO
  WITH A FINGER IN MY I           GERROLD, DAVID       AC
ORACLE, THE               BLOCH, ROBERT       SS   PNT 71 05
  COLD CHILLS                     BLOCH, ROBERT        AC
ORBIT FLIGHT              HARVEY, FRANK       SS   SEP 58 10
  AIR FORCE!                      HARVEY, FRANK        AC
ORBITER 5 SHOWS HOW EARTH LOOKS FROM THE MOON
                          SWENSON, MAY        PM   SOU 69
  SCIENCE FACT/FICTION            FARRELL/GAGE/&       AN
  SCIENCE FICTION                 BRODKIN & PEARSON    AN
ORDEAL IN SPACE           HEINLEIN, ROBERT A. SS   TAC 48 05
  GREEN HILLS OF EARTH, THE       HEINLEIN, ROBERT A.  AC
  OUT OF THIS WORLD  7            WILLIAMS-ELLIS& OWEN AN
  PAST THROUGH TOMORROW, THE      HEINLEIN, ROBERT A.  AC
  WORLDS TO COME                  KNIGHT, DAMON        AN
ORDEAL OF LANCELOT BIGGS, THE BOND, NELSON S.  SS   AMZ 43 05
  LANCELOT BIGGS: SPACEMAN        BOND, NELSON S.      AC
ORDEAL OF PROFESSOR KLEIN, THE DE CAMP, L. SPRAGUE   SFA 52 11
  *BEACHHEADS IN SPACE            DERLETH, AUGUST      AN
ORDERS                    JAMESON, MALCOLM    SS   ASF 45 12
  BULLARD OF THE SPACE PATROL     JAMESON, MALCOLM     AC
ORGANLEGGERS, THE (SEE DEATH BY ECSTACY)
                          NIVEN, LARRY        TC
ORGASM BAND, THE          HARRISON, M. JOHN   SS   TRV
  MACHINE IN SHAFT TEN AND OTHER STORIES, THE
                                  HARRISON, M. JOHN    AC
ORGY OF THE LIVING AND THE DYING
                          ALDISS, BRIAN W.    NV   YRT 70
  MOMENT OF ECLIPSE, THE          ALDISS, BRIAN W.     AC
  YEAR 2000, THE                  HARRISON, HARRY      OA
ORIGIN OF EVERYTHING, THE CALVINO, ITALO      SS   PBY 68 03
  LAST TRAIN TO LIMBO             PLAYBOY, EDITORS OF  AN

ORIGIN OF NARAPOIA, THE (SEE NARAPOIA)
                          NELSON, ALAN        TC
ORIGIN OF THE SPECIES     ANDERSON, KAREN     PM   FSF 58 06
  BEST FROM FANTASY AND SCIENCE FICTION:  8
                                  BOUCHER, ANTHONY     AN
ORIGIN OF THE SPECIES, THE MACLEAN, KATHERINE SS   NEW 53 AN
  CHILDREN OF WONDER              TENN, WILLIAM        AN
ORIGINAL SIN              WRIGHT, S. FOWLER   SS   AFR 50 13
  *OTHER SIDE OF THE MOON, THE    DERLETH, AUGUST      AN
  THRONE OF SATURN, THE           WRIGHT, S. FOWLER    AC
  WITCHFINDER, THE                WRIGHT, S. FOWLER    AC
ORIGINS OF GALACTIC ETIQUETTE WELLEN, EDWARD  FA   GAL 53 10
  ALL ABOUT THE FUTURE            GREENBERG, MARTIN    AN
ORIGINS OF GALACTIC LAW   WELLEN, EDWARD      FA   GAL 53 04
  ALL ABOUT THE FUTURE            GREENBERG, MARTIN    AN
ORIGINS OF GALACTIC MEDICINE WELLEN, EDWARD   FA   GAL 53 12
  ALL ABOUT THE FUTURE            GREENBERG, MARTIN    AN
ORIGINS OF GALACTIC SLANG WELLEN, EDWARD      FA   GAL 52 07
  ALL ABOUT THE FUTURE            GREENBERG, MARTIN    AN
ORIGINS OF PILL AND HAMMER CONRAD, EARL       SS
  DA VINCI MACHINE, THE           CONRAD, EARL         OC
ORIGINS OF THE UNIVERSE   CRAVENS, GWYNETH    SS   NWQ 73 05
  NEW WORLDS NO. 5                MOORCOCK & PLATT     OA
ORION                     STANLEY, GEORGE     SS   QRK 70 01
  QUARK/1                         DELANY & HACKER      OA
ORMOND ALWAYS PAYS HIS BILLS ELLISON, HARLAN  SS   PSD 57 07
  NO DOORS, NO WINDOWS (STORIES REWRITTEN) ELLISON, HARLAN AC
ORNAMENT TO HIS PROFESSION, AN HARNESS, CHARLES L. NV ASF 66 02
  SCIENCE FICTION ARGOSY, A       KNIGHT, DAMON        AN
  SF12                            MERRIL, JUDITH       AN
ORNITHANTHROPUS           BURHOE, B. ALAN     SS   IFS 71 12
  BEST SCIENCE FICTION STORIES OF THE YEAR (1971)
                                  DEL REY, LESTER      AN
  BEST SF: 1971                   HARRISON & ALDISS    AN
ORPHAN OF THE VOID (THE MAN WHO WASN'T HOME)
                          BIGGLE, LLOYD JR.   NV   FAN 60 09
  METALLIC MUSE, THE              BIGGLE, LLOYD JR.    AC
ORPHANS OF THE VOID       SHAARA, MICHAEL     NV   GAL 52 06
  ALPHA 7                         SILVERBERG, ROBERT   AN
  SHADOW OF TOMORROW              POHL, FREDERIK       AN
ORPHEUS'S BROTHER         BRUNNER, JOHN       SS   MHS 65 04
  *OUT OF MY MIND                 BRUNNER, JOHN        AC
OSCAR                     CARTMILL, CLEVE     SS   UNK 41 02
  FIFTY SHORT SCIENCE FICTION TALES  ASIMOV & CONKLIN  AN
OSIRIS ON CRUTCHES        FARMER, PHILIP JOSE
                          AND TINCROWDER, LEO Q. SS C NDM 76 06
  NEW DIMENSIONS 6                SILVERBERG, ROBERT   OA
OTHER CELIA, THE          STURGEON, THEODORE  NV   GAL 57 03
  ONE HUNDRED YEARS OF SCIENCE FICTION KNIGHT, DAMON   AN
  *TOUCH OF STRANGE, A            STURGEON, THEODORE   AC
OTHER CHEEK, THE          COGSWELL, THEODORE R NA  SFA 53 05
  THIRD EYE, THE                  COGSWELL, THEODORE R AC
OTHER DAYS, OTHER EYES    SHAW, BOB           NA   AMZ 72 05
  OTHER DAYS, OTHER EYES          SHAW, BOB            NO
OTHER EYES WATCHING       CAMPBELL, JOHN W. JR AR  ASF 37 02
  BEFORE THE GOLDEN AGE           ASIMOV, ISAAC        AN
OTHER FOOT, THE           BRADBURY, RAY       SS   NST 51 03
  HUMAN AND OTHER BEINGS          DEGRAEFF, ALLEN      AN
  *ILLUSTRATED MAN, THE           BRADBURY, RAY        AC
  SOCIAL PROBLEMS THROUGH SCIENCE FICTION GREENBERG/MILSTEAD/& AN
  TOMORROW, AND TOMORROW, AND TOMORROW... HEINTZ/HERBERT/JOOS/ AN
OTHER HAND, THE           LANGELAAN, GEORGE   SS   FSF 61 10
  *TWISTED                        CONKLIN, GROFF       AN
OTHER INAUGURATION, THE   BOUCHER, ANTHONY    SS   FSF 53 03
  FAR AND AWAY                    BOUCHER, ANTHONY     AC
  SCIENCE FICTION TERROR TALES    CONKLIN, GROFF       AN
OTHER KIDS, THE           YOUNG, ROBERT F.    SS   FUN 56 03
  ENCOUNTERS WITH ALIENS          EARLEY, GEORGE W.    AN
OTHER LIKENESS, THE       SCHMITZ, JAMES H.   SS   ASF 62 07
  NICE DAY FOR SCREAMING, AND OTHER TALES OF THE HUB
                                  SCHMITZ, JAMES H.    AC
OTHER MAN, THE            STURGEON, THEODORE  NA   GAL 56 09
  SF:57, THE YEAR'S GREATEST SCIENCE FICTION AND FANTASY
                                  MERRIL, JUDITH       AN
  WORLDS OF THEODORE STURGEON, THE STURGEON, THEODORE  AC
OTHER NOW, THE            LEINSTER, MURRAY    SS   GAL 51 03
  *GALAXY READER OF SCIENCE FICTION GOLD, H. L.        AN
  ONE HUNDRED YEARS OF SCIENCE FICTION KNIGHT, DAMON   AN
  TWISTS IN TIME                  LEINSTER, MURRAY     AC
OTHER PEOPLE, THE (THE QUEER ONES)
                          BRACKETT, LEIGH     NV   VSF 57 03
  BEST SCIENCE FICTION STORIES AND NOVELS: 9TH SERIES
                                  DIKTY, T. E.         AN
OTHER PERCEIVER, THE      SARGENT, PAMELA     SS   UNI 72 02
  STARSHADOWS                     SARGENT, PAMELA      AC
  UNIVERSE 2                      CARR, TERRY          OA
OTHER PLACE, THE          PRIESTLEY, J. B.    SS
  OTHER PLACE, THE                PRIESTLEY, J. B.     AC
OTHER SIDE OF THE CURTAIN- A REFLECTION OF THE FUTURE, THE
                          ELWOOD, ROGER       IN C
  STRANGE SIGNPOSTS               ELWOOD & MOSKOWITZ   AN
OTHER SIDE OF THE CURTAIN- A REFLECTION OF THE FUTURE, THE
                          MOSKOWITZ, SAM      IN C
  STRANGE SIGNPOSTS               ELWOOD & MOSKOWITZ   AN
OTHER SIDE OF THE SKY, THE CLARKE, ARTHUR C.  GR   INF 57 09
  FROM THE OCEAN, FROM THE STARS  CLARKE, ARTHUR C.    AC
  TREASURY OF GREAT SCIENCE FICTION, A VOL.2
                                  BOUCHER, ANTHONY     AN
OTHER SIDE OF THE WALL, THE DERLETH, AUGUST   SS   TSF 51 SP
  HARRIGAN'S FILE                 DERLETH, AUGUST      AC
OTHER SIDE, THE (ETERNAL EARTHLING)
                          KUBILIUS, WALTER    SS   SSS 51 04
  BEST SCIENCE-FICTION STORIES: 1952, THE BLEILER & DIKTY AN
OTHER SKY, THE (THE FURTHER SKY)
                          LAUMER, KEITH       SN   AMZ 64 12
  GREYLORN                        LAUMER, KEITH        AC
```

OTHER SKY, THE (THE FURTHER SKY)
  TIMETRACKS   LAUMER, KEITH   AC
OTHER TIGER, THE   CLARKE, ARTHUR C. SS FUN 53 06
  PORTALS OF TOMORROW   DERLETH, AUGUST   AN
OTHER TRACKS   SELL, WILLIAM   NV ASF 38 10
  *SCIENCE FICTION ADVENTURES IN DIMENSION CONKLIN, GROFF   AN
OTHER TRADITION, THE   ADLARD, MARK   AR
  BEYOND THIS HORIZON   CARRELL, CHRISTOPHER OA
OTHER WAY AROUND, THE   MYERS, HOWARD L.   NV INY 71 02
  INFINITY 2   HOSKINS, ROBERT   OA
OTHER WIFE, THE (ALSO AS THE COIN COLLECTOR)
                          FINNEY, JACK   SS SEP 60 01
  5TH ANNUAL OF THE YEAR'S BEST S-F, MERRIL, JUDITH   AN
OTHER WING, THE   BLACKWOOD, ALGERNON SS APR 48 08
  DEVIL'S GENERATION, THE   GHIDALIA, VIC   AN
OTHER WORKS OF INTEREST   MISC. MATERIAL   MS
  AURORA: BEYOND EQUALITY   MCINTYRE & ANDERSON AN
OTHER WORLD, THE   LEINSTER, MURRAY   NA STS 49 11
  6 GREAT SHORT NOVELS OF SCIENCE FICTION CONKLIN, GROFF AN
OTHER, THE   GRAHAM, HOWARD W. SS ASF 34 12
  SCIENCE FICTION OF THE 30'S   KNIGHT, DAMON   AN
OTHER, THE   MACLEAN, KATHERINE SS NWS 66 07
  NEW WORLDS OF FANTASY   CARR, TERRY   AN
  SF12   MERRIL, JUDITH   AN
  VOYAGES: SCENARIOS FOR A SHIP CALLED EARTH
                          SAUER, ROB   AN
OTHERS, THE   HOLLY, J. HUNTER   NV
OTHER SIDE OF TOMORROW, THE ELWOOD, ROGER   OA
OTTMAR BALLEAU X 2   BAMBER, GEORGE   SS ROG 61 03
  7TH ANNUAL OF THE YEAR'S BEST S-F, THE MERRIL, JUDITH   AN
OUNCE OF CURE, AN   NOURSE, ALAN E.   SS IMT 55 11
  COUNTERFEIT MAN, THE   NOURSE, ALAN E.   AC
OUNCE OF DISSENSION, AN   LORAN, MARTIN   SS ASF 66 07
  OUT OF THIS WORLD 7   WILLIAMS-ELLIS& OWEN AN
  PACIFIC BOOK OF AUSTRALIAN SCIENCE FICTION
                          BAXTER, JOHN   AN
OUNCE OF PREVENTION   RUSSELL, RAY   SS PBY 60 09
  SAGITTARIUS   RUSSELL, RAY   AC
  SARDONICUS AND OTHER STORIES   RUSSELL, RAY   AC
OUNCE OF PREVENTION, AN   CARTER, PAUL A.   SS FSF 50 SU
  FAR BOUNDARIES   DERLETH, AUGUST   AN
OUR DISTANT COUSINS   DUNSANY, LORD   SS   31
  ARMCHAIR SCIENCE READER, THE GORDON, I. & SORKIN AN
  MOONLIGHT TRAVELER, THE   STERN, PHILIP VAN D. AN
OUR FAIR CITY   HEINLEIN, ROBERT A. SS WRT 49 01
  *BEYOND HUMAN KEN   MERRIL, JUDITH   AN
  UNPLEASANT PROFESSION OF JONATHAN HOAG, THE
                          HEINLEIN, ROBERT A. AC
OUR FIRST DEATH   DICKSON, GORDON R. SS FSF 55 08
  ANCIENT, MY ENEMY   DICKSON, GORDON R.   AC
OUR FRIENDS THE ALIENS   BULMER, KENNETH   SS
  AUTHENTIC BOOK OF SPACE   CAMPBELL, H. J.   AN
OUR KIND OF KNOWLEDGE   ALDISS, BRIAN W.   SS NWS 55 06
  NO TIME LIKE TOMORROW   ALDISS, BRIAN W.   AC
  SPACE, TIME AND NATHANIEL   ALDISS, BRIAN W.   AC
OUR LADY OF THE ENDLESS SKY DUNTEMANN, JEFF   NV NOV 74 04
  NOVA 4   HARRISON, HARRY   OA
OUR MAN IN PEKING   HOWARD, HAYDEN   NV GAL 67 02
  ESKIMO INVASION   HOWARD, HAYDEN   NO
OUR SAUCER VACATION   LEIBER, FRITZ   AR FUN 59 12
  FLYING SAUCERS IN FACT AND FICTION SANTESSON, HANS S. AN
  WORLDS OF FRITZ LEIBER, THE   LEIBER, FRITZ   AC
OUR SECOND VOYAGE TO MARS LACH-SZYRMA, D. S. SS CSL 89 02
  WORLDS APART   LOCKE, GEORGE   AN
OUR TIMES   PRONZINI, BILL   SS SWK 72 04
  FUTURE NOW, THE   HOSKINS, ROBERT   AN
OUR WAR WITH MONACO   MITCHELL, EDWARD P. SS SUN 80 03
  CRYSTAL MAN, THE   MITCHELL, EDWARD P.   AC
OUT AROUND RIGEL   WILSON, ROBERT H. SS ASF 31 12
  SCIENCE FICTION OF THE 30'S   KNIGHT, DAMON   AN
OUT FROM GANYMEDE   MALZBERG, BARRY N. SS NDM 72 02
  NEW DIMENSIONS 2   SILVERBERG, ROBERT   OA
  OUT FROM GANYMEDE   MALZBERG, BARRY N.   AC
OUT IN SPACE   VARSHAVSKY, ILYA   SS
  LAST DOOR TO AIYA   GINSBURG, MIRRA   AN
OUT IN THE GARDEN   DICK, PHILIP K.   SS FNF 53 08
  SATAN'S PETS   GHIDALIA, VIC   AN
OUT OF MINDSHOT   BRUNNER, JOHN   SS GAL 70 06
  BEST FROM GALAXY, THE VOLUME I GALAXY, EDITORS OF AN
OUT OF NIGHT   CAMPBELL, JOHN W. JR NV ASF 37 10
  *BEST OF JOHN W. CAMPBELL, THE CAMPBELL, JOHN W. JR AC
  CLOAK OF AESIR   CAMPBELL, JOHN W. JR AC
  WHO GOES THERE? AND OTHER STORIES CAMPBELL, JOHN W. JR AC
OUT OF ORDER   BRUNNER, JOHN   SS NWS 57 04
  NO FUTURE IN IT   BRUNNER, JOHN   AC
OUT OF PHASE   HALDEMAN, JOE W. SS GAL 69 09
  BEST FROM GALAXY, THE VOLUME I GALAXY, EDITORS OF AN
OUT OF REACH   ALDISS, BRIAN W.   SS AUT 57 08
  GALAXIES LIKE GRAINS OF SAND ALDISS, BRIAN W.   AC
OUT OF THE CRADLE, ENDLESSLY ORBITING
                          CLARKE, ARTHUR C. SS DUD 59 03
  GREAT SCIENCE FICTION ABOUT DOCTORS CONKLIN, G&FABRICANT AN
  TALES OF TEN WORLDS   CLARKE, ARTHUR C.   AC
OUT OF THE FLICKER PATH   KARL, JEAN E.   SS
  TURNING PLACE, THE   KARL, JEAN E.   OC
OUT OF THE JAR   TANNER, CHARLES R. SS STI 41 02
  ZACHERLEY'S VULTURE STEW   ZACHERLEY   AN
OUT OF THE SUB-UNIVERSE   STARZL, R. F.   SS ASQ 28 SU
  HISTORY OF THE SCIENCE FICTION MAGAZINE, THE PART 1 1926-1935
                          ASHLEY, MICHAEL   AN
OUT OF THE SUN   CLARKE, ARTHUR C. SS IFS 58 02
  EARTHMEN AND STRANGERS   SILVERBERG, ROBERT   AN
  NINE BILLION NAMES OF GOD, THE CLARKE, ARTHUR C.   AC
  OTHER SIDE OF THE SKY, THE   CLARKE, ARTHUR C.   AC
OUT OF THE WATERS   MITCHISON, NAOMI   SS NOV 74 04
  NOVA 4   HARRISON, HARRY   OA

OWING TO CIRCUMSTANCES BEYOND OUR CONTROL 1984 HAS BEEN
OUT OF THIS WORLD   BESTER, ALFRED   SS
  DARK SIDE OF THE EARTH, THE   BESTER, ALFRED   AC
OUT OF TIME'S ABYSS   BURROUGHS, EDGAR R. NV BBM 18 12
  LAND THAT TIME FORGOT, THE   BURROUGHS, EDGAR R. NC
OUT OF TIME, OUT OF PLACE COLLYN, GEORGE   SS FSF 67 05
  BEST FROM FANTASY AND SCIENCE FICTION: 17
                          FERMAN, EDWARD L.   AN
OUT-PATIENT   WHITE, JAMES   NV NWS 60 06
  HOSPITAL STATION   WHITE, JAMES   AC
OUZ, WIT   MYERS, HOWARD L. SS ASF 72 06
  ANALOG 9   BOVA, BEN   AN
  BEST SF: 1972   HARRISON & ALDISS   AN
OUTBREEDERS, THE   SILVERBERG, ROBERT SS FUN 59 05
  PARSECS AND PARABLES   SILVERBERG, ROBERT   AC
  SUNDANCE AND OTHER SCIENCE FICTION STORIES
                          SILVERBERG, ROBERT   AC
OUTCASTS OF THE STARS (ALSO AS THE ROCKET)
                          BRADBURY, RAY   SS SSS 50 03
  TOMORROW MIDNIGHT   BRADBURY, RAY   AC
OUTCASTS, THE   SMITH, GEORGE HUDSON SS SFS 58 09
  NOW & BEYOND   HOWARD, IVAN   AN
OUTER BECOMING INNER, THE BRONK, WILLIAM   PM SAR 49
  SPECULATIONS   SANDERS, THOMAS E.   AN
OUTER CONCENTRIC   GOTSCHALK, FELIX C. SS NDM 74 04
  NEW DIMENSIONS 4   SILVERBERG, ROBERT   OA
OUTER LIMIT, THE   DOAR, GRAHAM   SS SEP 49 1.
  *BIG BOOK OF SCIENCE FICTION   CONKLIN, GROFF   AN
OUTER LIMITS OF SPACE, THE EDELSON, EDWARD AR SRV 73 10
  LOOKING AHEAD   ALLEN, D. & L.   AN
OUTLAW   WEST, WALLACE   SS
  OUTPOSTS IN SPACE   WEST, WALLACE   AC
OUTLINE OF HISTORY, AN   BRALY, MALCOLM   SS BMR 73
  BAD MOON RISING   DISCH, THOMAS M.   OA
OUTSIDE   ALDISS, BRIAN W.   SS NWS 55 0
  *BEST SCIENCE FICTION STORIES OF BRIAN W. ALDISS
                          ALDISS, BRIAN W.   AC
  BEST SF 2   CRISPIN, EDMUND   AN
  NO TIME LIKE TOMORROW   ALDISS, BRIAN W.   AC
  SECOND ORBIT   DOHERTY, G. D.   AN
  SPACE, TIME AND NATHANIEL   ALDISS, BRIAN W.   AC
OUTSIDER, THE   LOVECRAFT, H. P. SS WRT 26 04
  GRAVEYARD READER, THE   CONKLIN, GROFF   AN
  HAUNTER OF THE DARK, THE   LOVECRAFT, H. P.   AC
  SPECULATIONS   SANDERS, THOMAS E.   AN
OUTSTRETCHED HAND, THE   SELLINGS, ARTHUR   SS NWS 59 05
  BEST OF NEW WORLDS, THE   MOORCOCK, MICHAEL   AN
OUTWARD BOUND   SPINRAD, NORMAN   NV ASF 64 03
  LAST HURRAH OF THE GOLDEN HORDE, THE SPINRAD, NORMAN   AC
OVER THE ABYSS   BELAYEV, ALEXANDER SS
  DESTINATION: AMALTHEIA   DIXON, RICHARD   AN
OVER THE HILL   KARL, JEAN E.   SS
  TURNING PLACE, THE   KARL, JEAN E.   OC
OVER THE LINE   MALZBERG, BARRY N. SS   74
  BEST OF BARRY N. MALZBERG, THE MALZBERG, BARRY N.   AC
  FUTURE KIN   ELWOOD, ROGER   OA
OVER THE RIVER AND THROUGH THE WOODS
                          SIMAK, CLIFFORD D. SS AMZ 65 05
  TIME CURVE, THE   MOSKOWITZ & ELWOOD AN
  WORLD'S BEST SCIENCE FICTION: 1966 WOLLHEIM & CARR   AN
OVER THE TOP   DEL REY, LESTER   SS ASF 49 11
  *ASTOUNDING SCIENCE FICTION ANTHOLOGY, THE
                          CAMPBELL, JOHN W. JR AN
  EARLY DEL REY   DEL REY, LESTER   AC
  SECOND ASTOUNDING SCIENCE FICTION ANTHOLOGY, THE (PB)
                          CAMPBELL, JOHN W. JR AN
OVERDOSE   ROBINSON, SPIDER SS GAL 75 0
  BEST FROM GALAXY, THE VOLUME IV BAEN, JAMES   AN
OVERDRAWN AT THE MEMORY BANK VARLEY, JOHN   NV GAL 76 0
  1977 ANNUAL WORLD'S BEST SF, THE WOLLHEIM, DONALD A. AN
OVERDRIVE   LEINSTER, MURRAY   NV STS 53 01
  ADVENTURES IN THE FAR FUTURE WOLLHEIM, DONALD A. DA
OVERLOAD, AN   BAYLEY, BARRINGTON J SS NWQ 73 05
  NEW WORLDS NO. 5   MOORCOCK & PLATT   OA
OVERLOADED MAN, THE   BALLARD, J. G.   SS NWS 61 07
  BEST OF J. G. BALLARD, THE   BALLARD, J. G.   AC
  FOUR-DIMENSIONAL NIGHTMARE, THE (REVISED)
                          BALLARD, J. G.   AC
  OVERLOADED MAN, THE   BALLARD, J. G.   AC
  VOICES OF TIME AND OTHER STORIES, THE BALLARD, J. G.   AC
OVERLOOKING   MALZBERG, BARRY N. SS AMZ 74 06
  BEST OF BARRY N. MALZBERG, THE MALZBERG, BARRY N.   AC
OVERLORD'S THUMB, THE   SILVERBERG, ROBERT NV INF 58 0
  SUNDANCE AND OTHER SCIENCE FICTION STORIES
                          SILVERBERG, ROBERT   AC
  TO WORLDS BEYOND   SILVERBERG, ROBERT   AC
OVERMIND   WADSWORTH, PHYLLIS M NO SID 67
  SCIENCE FICTION SPECIAL 3   ANONYMOUS   AN
OVERPROOF   MACKENZIE, J. B. NV ASF 65 10
  ANALOG 5   CAMPBELL, JOHN W. JR AN
  SEVEN TRIPS THROUGH TIME AND SPACE CONKLIN, GROFF   AN
OVERRIDE   MARTIN, GEORGE R. NV ASF 73 09
  SONG FOR LYA, A   MARTIN, GEORGE R. R.   AC
OVERSIGHT   O'DONNELL, K. M. SS STG 74
  STRANGE GODS   ELWOOD, ROGER   AN
OVERSIGHT, AN   MALZBERG, BARRY N. SS STG 74
  BEST OF BARRY N. MALZBERG, THE MALZBERG, BARRY N.   AC
OVERTHROW   CARTMILL, CLEVE   SN ASF 42 1
  JOURNEY TO INFINITY   GREENBERG, MARTIN   AN
OVERTURE   NEVILLE, KRIS   SS NTL 54
  9 TALES OF SPACE AND TIME   HEALY, RAYMOND J.   AN
OWE ME   PHILLIFENT, JOHN T. SS ASF 75
  TOMORROW, INC.   GREENBERG& OLANDER   AN
OWING TO CIRCUMSTANCES BEYOND OUR CONTROL 1984 HAS BEEN
UNAVOIDABLY DETAINED   COREN, ALAN   SS PUN
  BEST SF: 1974   HARRISON & ALDISS   AN

OWL AND THE APE, THE   DE CAMP, L. SPRAGUE SS   IMG 51 11
  TRITONIAN RING, THE   DE CAMP, L. SPRAGUE   AC
OXOXOCO BOTTLE, THE (THE MYSTERY OF THE BOTTLE)
                              KERSH, GERALD   NV   SEP 57 12
  MEN WITHOUT BONES   KERSH, GERALD   AC
OZYMANDIAS   CARR, TERRY   SS   DVS 72 02
  AGAIN, DANGEROUS VISIONS   ELLISON, HARLAN   OA
  LIGHT AT THE END OF THE UNIVERSE, THE CARR, TERRY   AC
  MUTANTS   SILVERBERG, ROBERT   AN
OZYMANDIAS   SILVERBERG, ROBERT   SS   INF 58 11
  REALITY TRIP, THE   SILVERBERG, ROBERT   AC
  TO THE STARS   SILVERBERG, ROBERT   AN
  TO WORLDS BEYOND   SILVERBERG, ROBERT   AC
P.N. 40   WRIGHT, S. FOWLER   SS
  NEW GODS LEAD, THE   WRIGHT, S. FOWLER   AC
P.S.   RUSSELL, ERIC FRANK SS   NEB 58 05
  FAR STARS   RUSSELL, ERIC FRANK   AC
P.T.A. MEETS CHE GUEVARA, THE MALZBERG, BARRY N.   SS   ALT 74
  ALTERNATES   GERROLD, DAVID   OA
PACE THAT KILLS, THE   ROBERTS, KEITH   NV   IMP 66 05
  MACHINES AND MEN   ROBERTS, KEITH   AC
PACEM EST   O'DONNELL, K. M.   SS   INY 70 01
  UNIVERSE DAY   O'DONNELL, K. M.   NO
PACEM EST   NEVILLE, KRIS
                              AND O'DONNELL, K. M. SS C INY 70 01
  BEST SF: 1970   HARRISON & ALDISS   AN
  IN THE POCKET AND OTHER S-F STORIES O'DONNELL, K. M. DC
  INFINITY 1   HOSKINS, ROBERT   OA
PACER   JONES, RAYMOND F.   NV
  FUTURE KIN   ELLWOOD, ROGER   OA
PACIFIST   REYNOLDS, MACK   SS   FSF 64 01
  BEST OF MACK REYNOLDS, THE   REYNOLDS, MACK   AC
  POLITICAL SCIENCE FICTION   GREENBERG& WARRICK   AN
  10TH ANNUAL OF THE YEAR'S BEST S-F, THE MERRIL, JUDITH AN
PACIFIST, THE   CLARKE, ARTHUR C.   SS   FUN 56 10
  ACROSS THE SEA OF STARS   CLARKE, ARTHUR C.   AC
  FANTASTIC UNIVERSE OMNIBUS, THE SANTESSON, HANS S.   AN
  MATHEMATICAL MAGPIE, THE   FADIMAN, CLIFTON   AN
  TALES FROM THE WHITE HART   CLARKE, ARTHUR C.   AC
PACIFISTS, THE   FRITCH, CHARLES E.   SS   IFS 55 05
  HORSES' ASTEROID   FRITCH, CHARLES E.   AC
PACKAGE OF POWER   COOKE, DAVID C.   SS   SFQ 40 SU
  MOON CONQUERORS, THE   ANONYMOUS   AN
PACKERHAUS METHOD, THE   WOLFE, GENE   SS   INY 70 01
  INFINITY 1   HOSKINS, ROBERT   OA
PACT   SANDERS, WINSTON P. SS   FSF 59 08
  BEST FROM FANTASY AND SCIENCE FICTION: 9
                              MILLS, ROBERT P.   AN
PAD, THE   HARRISON, HARRY   SS   NEW 70 AC
  PRIME NUMBER   HARRISON, HARRY   AC
PAGAN RABBI, THE   OZICK, CYNTHIA   NV   66
  BEST SF: 1971   HARRISON & ALDISS   AN
PAGE AND PLAYER   BIXBY, JEROME   NV   STS 52 08
  SPACE PIONEERS   NORTON, ANDRE   AN
PAGE FOR OCTOBER HAS BEEN TORN OFF, THE
                              DISCH, THOMAS M.   SS
  *GETTING INTO DEATH   DISCH, THOMAS M.   AC
PAIL OF AIR, A   LEIBER, FRITZ   SS   GAL 51 12
  BEST OF FRITZ LEIBER, THE   LEIBER, FRITZ   AC
  GALAXY SCIENCE FICTION OMNIBUS GOLD, H. L.   AN
  GATES TO TOMORROW   NORTON, AN.&DONALDY   AN
  PAIL OF AIR, A   LEIBER, FRITZ   AC
  SECOND GALAXY READER OF SCIENCE FICTION GOLD, H. L. AN
  SECRET SONGS, THE   LEIBER, FRITZ   AC
  SPACE PIONEERS   NORTON, ANDRE   AN
  SPECULATIONS   SANDERS, THOMAS E.   AN
  TOMORROW'S CHILDREN   ASIMOV, ISAAC   AN
  WINDOWS INTO TOMORROW   SILVERBERG, ROBERT   AN
  WORLDS OF WONDER   HARRISON, HARRY   AN
PAIN EPICURES, THE   MITCHELL, EDWARD P. SS   SUN 78 08
  CRYSTAL MAN, THE   MITCHELL, EDWARD P.   AC
PAIN PEDDLERS, THE   SILVERBERG, ROBERT   SS   GAL 63 08
  NEEDLE IN A TIMESTACK   SILVERBERG, ROBERT   AC
  SUNDANCE AND OTHER SCIENCE FICTION STORIES
                              SILVERBERG, ROBERT   AC
  WINDOWS INTO TOMORROW   SILVERBERG, ROBERT   AN
PAINGOD   ELLISON, HARLAN   SS   FAN 64 06
  BEST FROM FANTASTIC, THE   WHITE, TED   AC
  DEATHBIRD STORIES   ELLISON, HARLAN   AC
  *PAINGOD AND OTHER DELUSIONS ELLISON, HARLAN   AC
PAINTED MIRROR, THE   WANDREI, DONALD   SS   AFR 49 09
  EYE AND THE FINGER   WANDREI, DONALD   AC
  SECOND AVON FANTASY READER, THE WOLLHEIM &ERNSBERGER AN
PAINWISE   TIPTREE, JAMES JR.   NV   FSF 72 02
  ALPHA 6   SILVERBERG, ROBERT   AN
  BEST SCIENCE FICTION OF THE YEAR, THE NO. 2
                              CARR, TERRY   AN
  TEN THOUSAND LIGHT-YEARS FROM HOME TIPTREE, JAMES JR. AC
PAIR, THE   HENSLEY, JOE L.   SS   FUN 58 07
  COMBAT SF   DICKSON, GORDON R.   AN
PAIRPUPPETS   VAN LOGGEM, MANUEL   SS   74
  BEST FROM THE REST OF THE WORLD, THE WOLLHEIM, DONALD A. AN
PALACE REVOLUTION (GAMBLER'S WORLD)
                              LAUMER, KEITH   NV   IFS 61 11
  ENVOY TO NEW WORLDS   LAUMER, KEITH   AC
PALE HANDS   PISERCHIA, DORIS   SS   ORB 74 05
  ORBIT 15   KNIGHT, DAMON   OA
PALE ROSES   MOORCOCK, MICHAEL   NV   NWQ 74 06
  BEST SCIENCE FICTION OF THE YEAR, THE NO. 4
                              CARR, TERRY   AN
  LEGENDS FROM THE END OF TIME MOORCOCK, MICHAEL   AC
  NEW WORLDS NO. 6   PLATT & BAILEY   OA
PALEONTOLOGY: AN EXPERIMENTAL SCIENCE
                              OLSEN, ROBERT R.   SS   ASF 74 08
  BEST SF: 1974   HARRISON & ALDISS   AN

PALIMPSEST OF ST. AUGUSTINE, THE
                              DE CAMP, L. SPRAGUE
                              AND PRATT, FLETCHER SS C NEW 53 AC
  TALES FROM GAVAGAN'S BAR   DE CAMP, L. S.&PRATT   AC
PALOS OF THE DOG STAR PACK   GIESY, J. U.   NV   ASW 18 07
  UNDER THE MOONS OF MARS   MOSKOWITZ, SAM   AN
PAMELA'S VOICE   SERLING, ROD   SA
  NIGHT GALLERY   SERLING, ROD   OC
PANDORA'S BOX (WHERE TO?)   HEINLEIN, ROBERT A. IN   GAL 52 02
  WORLDS OF ROBERT A. HEINLEIN, THE HEINLEIN, ROBERT A. AC
PANDORA'S BUST   POLLACK, RICHARD A. SS   NWQ 71 02
  NEW WORLDS QUARTERLY NO. 2   MOORCOCK, MICHAEL   OA
PANDORA'S MILLIONS   SMITH, GEORGE O.   NV   ASF 45 06
  COMPLETE VENUS EQUILATERAL, THE SMITH, GEORGE O.   AC
  VENUS EQUILATERAL   SMITH, GEORGE O.   AC
PANDORA'S PLANET   ANVIL, CHRISTOPHER   NV   ASF 56 09
  PROLOGUE TO ANALOG   CAMPBELL, JOHN W. JR AN
PANEL GAME   ALDISS, BRIAN W.   SS   NWS 55 12
  ASPECTS OF SCIENCE FICTION   DOHERTY, G. D.   AN
  SPACE, TIME AND NATHANIEL   ALDISS, BRIAN W.   AC
PANELLED ROOM, THE   DERLETH, AUGUST   SS   WMR 33 09
  OTHER WORLDS, THE   STONG, PHILIP D.   AN
PANIC BUTTON   RUSSELL, ERIC FRANK SS   ASF 59 11
  SEVEN COME INFINITY   CONKLIN, GROFF   AN
PANIC ON RUNWAY 6   HARVEY, FRANK   SS   SEP 56 07
  AIR FORCE!   HARVEY, FRANK   AC
PAPA SCHIMMELHORN AND THE S.O.D.O.M. SERUM
                              BRETNOR, REGINALD   NV   TVW 73
  TWO VIEWS OF WONDER   SCORTIA & YARBRO   OA
PAPA'S PLANET   NOLAN, WILLIAM F.   SS   PBY 68 04
  ALIEN HORIZONS   NOLAN, WILLIAM F.   AC
  FAR-OUT PEOPLE, THE   HOSKINS, ROBERT   AN
  LAST TRAIN TO LIMBO   PLAYBOY, EDITORS OF   AN
PARADISE   SIMAK, CLIFFORD D.   SS   ASF 46 06
  CITY   SIMAK, CLIFFORD D.   NO
PARADISE BEACH   COWPER, RICHARD   NV
  CUSTODIANS AND OTHER STORIES, THE COWPER, RICHARD   AC
PARADISE CRATER, THE (SEE JUNGLE JOURNEY)
                              WYLIE, PHILIP   TC
PARADISE II   SHECKLEY, ROBERT   SS   NWS 55 07
  NOTIONS: UNLIMITED   SHECKLEY, ROBERT   AC
  *TIME TO COME   DERLETH, AUGUST   OA
PARADISE LAST   EFFINGER, GEO. ALEC NV   NEW 74 AN
  WANDERING STARS   DANN, JACK M.   AN
PARADISE LOST AT CAMBRIDGE   HOGG, THOMAS J.   MS
  MATHEMATICAL MAGPIE, THE   FADIMAN, CLIFTON   AN
PARADISE REGAINED   COGSWELL, THOMAS   SS   SVW 73
  BEST SCIENCE FICTION STORIES OF THE YEAR (1973)
                              DEL REY, LESTER   AN
  SAVING WORLDS   ELWOOD & KIDD   OA
PARADISE STREET   MOORE, C. L.   NV   ASF 50 09
  JUDGEMENT NIGHT   MOORE, C. L.   AC
PARADISE SYNDROME, THE (MARGARET ARMEN)
                              BLISH, JAMES   SA   STK 72 07
  STAR TREK   7   BLISH, JAMES   OC
PARADISE 3000   FRANKE, HERBERT W.   SS   75
  BEST FROM THE REST OF THE WORLD, THE WOLLHEIM, DONALD A. AN
PARADOX LOST   BROWN, FREDRIC   SS   ASF 43 10
  PARADOX LOST, AND 12 OTHER GREAT S.F. STORIES
                              BROWN, FREDRIC   AC
  *SCIENCE-FICTION CARNIVAL   BROWN, F. & REYNOLDS AN
PARADOX MEN, THE   HARNESS, CHARLES L. NV   49
  SPACE OPERA   ALDISS, BRIAN W.   AN
PARALLEL DEVELOPMENT, THE   WEINER, GUY   SS
  STRANGE WORLD OF SCIENCE FICTION ANONYMOUS   OA
PARAMOUNT ULJ   DAVIDSON, AVRAM   SS   GAL 58 10
  STRANGE SEAS AND SHORES   DAVIDSON, AVRAM   AC
PARAMUTUEL PLANET (SEE FAITHFUL TO THEE, TERRA,IN OUR FASHION)
                              TIPTREE, JAMES JR.   TC
PARASITE PLANET   WEINBAUM, STANLEY G. NV   ASF 35 02
  BEFORE THE GOLDEN AGE   ASIMOV, ISAAC   AN
  BEST OF STANLEY G. WEINBAUM, THE WEINBAUM, STANLEY G. AC
  FLIGHT INTO SPACE   WOLLHEIM, DONALD A. AN
  MARTIAN ODYSSEY AND OTHER SCIENCE FICTION TALES, A
                              WEINBAUM, STANLEY G. AC
  MARTIAN ODYSSEY AND OTHERS, A WEINBAUM, STANLEY G. AC
PARASITE, THE   CLARKE, ARTHUR C.   SS   AVS 53 04
  PRELUDE TO MARS   CLARKE, ARTHUR C.   AC
  REACH FOR TOMORROW   CLARKE, ARTHUR C.   AC
PARDON MY MISTAKE   PRATT, FLETCHER   SS   TWS 46 12
  *OUTER REACHES, THE   DERLETH, AUGUST   AN
PARIAH PLANET (SEE THE PERFECT PUNISHMENT)
                              BIGGLE, LLOYD JR.   TC
PARKING PROBLEM   MORGAN, DAN   SS   NWR 65 04
  NEW WRITINGS IN SF. 4   CARNELL, JOHN   AN
PARKS OF REST AND CULTURE   ZEBROWSKI, GEORGE   SS   SVW 73
  MONADIC UNIVERSE, THE   ZEBROWSKI, GEORGE   AC
  SAVING WORLDS   ELWOOD & KIDD   OA
PARKY   ROME, DAVID   SS   SCF 61 08
  7TH ANNUAL OF THE YEAR'S BEST S-F, THE MERRIL, JUDITH AN
PARRINGTON'S POOL   DERLETH, AUGUST   SS   WRT 47 07
  MR. GEORGE AND OTHER ODD PERSONS DERLETH, AUGUST   AC
PARROT WHO MET PAPA, THE   BRADBURY, RAY   SS   PBY 72 01
  LONG AFTER MIDNIGHT   BRADBURY, RAY   AC
PARTHEN   LAFFERTY, R. A.   SS   GAL 73 05
  BEST SCIENCE FICTION STORIES OF THE YEAR (1973)
                              DEL REY, LESTER   AN
  BEST SF: 1973   HARRISON & ALDISS   AN
  1974 ANNUAL WORLD'S BEST SF, THE WOLLHEIM, DONALD A. AN
PARTNERED SHIP, THE   MCCAFFREY, ANNE   SS   NEW 69 AN
  SHIP WHO SANG, THE   MCCAFFREY, ANNE   AC
PARTRIDGE PROJECT, THE   LUPOFF, RICHARD A.   NA
  NO MIND OF MAN   SILVERBERG, ROBERT   OA
PARTY LINE   KLEIN, GERARD   NV   73
  BEST FROM THE REST OF THE WORLD, THE WOLLHEIM, DONALD A. AN

PARTY OF THE TWO PARTS   TENN, WILLIAM   NV   GAL 54 08
  CRIME PREVENTION IN THE 30TH CENTURY   SANTESSON, HANS S.   AN
  GENTLE INVADERS   SANTESSON, HANS S.   AN
  HUMAN ANGLE, THE   TENN, WILLIAM   AC
PARTY, THE   NOLAN, WILLIAM F.   SS   PBY 67 04
  ALIEN HORIZONS   NOLAN, WILLIAM F.   AC
  PLAYBOY BOOK OF HORROR AND THE SUPERNATURAL, THE
                                          PLAYBOY, EDITORS OF   AN
  WEIRD SHOW   PLAYBOY, EDITORS OF   AN
PARVENUE, THE   SHELLEY, MARY W.   SS   KPS 37
  TALES AND STORIES   SHELLEY, MARY W.   AC
PAS DE TROIS OF THE CHEF AND THE WAITER AND THE CUSTOMER
  (THREE SINNERS IN THE...)   SHECKLEY, ROBERT   SS   PBY 71 08
  CAN YOU FEEL ANYTHING WHEN I DO THIS?, AND OTHER STORIES
                                          SHECKLEY, ROBERT   AC
PASSAGE FOR PIANO   HERBERT, FRANK   NV   NEW 73 AC
  BOOK OF FRANK HERBERT, THE   HERBERT, FRANK   AC
PASSAGE FROM THE STARS, A   HURLBUT, KAATJE   SS   SEP 61 05
  7TH ANNUAL OF THE YEAR'S BEST S-F, THE   MERRIL, JUDITH   AN
PASSAGE TO MURDSTONE   GOULART, RON   SS   FSF 71 10
  ODD JOB NO. 101   GOULART, RON   AC
PASSAGES   RUSS, JOANNA   AR   GAL 74 01
  BEST FROM GALAXY, THE   VOLUME III   BAEN, JAMES   AN
PASSENGERS   SILVERBERG, ROBERT   SS   ORB 68 04
  BEST FROM ORBIT, THE   KNIGHT, DAMON   AN
  BEST OF ROBERT SILVERBERG, THE   SILVERBERG, ROBERT   AC
  CUBE ROOT OF UNCERTAINTY, THE   SILVERBERG, ROBERT   AC
  MOONFERNS & STARSONGS   SILVERBERG, ROBERT   AC
  NEBULA AWARD STORIES NO. 5   BLISH, JAMES   AN
  ORBIT 4   KNIGHT, DAMON   OA
PASSER-BY (THE OTHER SIDE OF THE SKY)
                     CLARKE, ARTHUR C.   SS   INF 57 10
  OTHER SIDE OF THE SKY, THE   CLARKE, ARTHUR C.   AC
PASSERBY   NIVEN, LARRY   SS   GAL 69 09
  ALL THE MYRIAD WAYS   NIVEN, LARRY   AC
PASSING OF KU SUI, THE   GILMORE, ANTHONY   NV   ASF 32 11
  SPACE HAWK   GILMORE, ANTHONY   AC
PASSING OF THE DRAGONS, THE   ROBERTS, KEITH   NV   NWR 73 21
  GRAIN KINGS, THE   ROBERTS, KEITH   AC
  NEW WRITINGS IN SF. 21   CARNELL, JOHN   OA
  PASSING OF THE DRAGONS, THE   ROBERTS, KEITH   AC
PASSING OF THE THIRD FLOOR BACK
                     JEROME, JEROME K.   NV
  ODDBALLS, THE   GHIDALIA, VIC   AN
PASSING THE LOVE OF WOMEN   ANDERSON, POUL   NV   CTM 74 02
  CONTINUUM 2   ELWOOD, ROGER   OA
PASSION PILLS   KORNBLUTH, C. M.   SS   NEW 58 04
  *MILE BEYOND THE MOON, A   KORNBLUTH, C. M.   AC
PASSION PLAY   REAVES, J. MICHAEL   SS   UNI 74 05
  UNIVERSE 5   CARR, TERRY   OA
PASSPORT TO ETERNITY   BALLARD, J. G.   SS   AMZ 62 06
  BEST OF J. G. BALLARD, THE   BALLARD, J. G.   AC
  OVERLOADED MAN, THE   BALLARD, J. G.   AC
  PASSPORT TO ETERNITY   BALLARD, J. G.   AC
PASSPORT TO SIRIUS   SILVERBERG, ROBERT   SS   IFS 58 04
  NEEDLE IN A TIMESTACK   SILVERBERG, ROBERT   AC
  SUNDANCE AND OTHER SCIENCE FICTION STORIES
                                          SILVERBERG, ROBERT   AC
PAST AND IT'S DEAD PEOPLE, THE   BRETNOR, REGINALD   SS   FSF 56 09
  SPACE, TIME & CRIME   DEFORD, MIRIAM ALLEN AN
PAST MASTER, THE   BLOCH, ROBERT   NV   BBM 55 01
  ALIEN EARTH AND OTHER STORIES   ELWOOD & MOSKOWITZ   AN
  TALES IN A JUGULAR VEIN   BLOCH, ROBERT   AC
PAST, PRESENT AND FUTURE   SCHACHNER, NAT   SN   ASF 37 09
  BEFORE THE GOLDEN AGE   ASIMOV, ISAAC   AN
PASTORAL AFFAIR   STEARNS, CHARLES A.   SS   GAL 59 02
  FIFTH GALAXY READER, THE   GOLD, H. L.   AN
PASTORAL, A   TAFOYA, ALFONSO   PM   NWQ 74 06
  NEW WORLDS NO. 6   PLATT & BAILEY   OA
PATAGONIA'S DELICIOUS FILLING STATION
                     ALDISS, BRIAN W.   GR   NWB 75 09
  NEW WORLDS NINE   BAILEY, HILARY   OA
PATE DE FOIE GRAS   ASIMOV, ISAAC   SF   ASF 56 09
  ASIMOV'S MYSTERIES   ASIMOV, ISAAC   AC
  WHERE DO WE GO FROM HERE?   ASIMOV, ISAAC   AN
PATENT MEDICINE MAN, THE   CASTELL, DAPHNE   SS   BER 74
  BERSERKERS, THE   ELWOOD, ROGER   OA
PATENT PENDING   CLARKE, ARTHUR C.   SS   54
  NINE BILLION NAMES OF GOD, THE   CLARKE, ARTHUR C.   AC
  TALES FROM THE WHITE HART   CLARKE, ARTHUR C.   AC
  TOMORROW, INC.   GREENBERG& OLANDER   AN
  VINTAGE ANTHOLOGY OF SCIENCE FANTASY, THE
                                          CERF, CHRISTOPHER   AN
PATER FAMILIAS   MALZBERG, BARRY N.
                      AND NEVILLE, KRIS   SS C FSF 72 03
  BEST OF BARRY N. MALZBERG, THE   MALZBERG, BARRY N.   AC
  OUT FROM GANYMEDE   MALZBERG, BARRY N.   AC
PATERNAL CARE   ALDISS, BRIAN W.   SS   NEW 66 AC
  SALIVA TREE AND OTHER STRANGE GROWTHS, THE
                                          ALDISS, BRIAN W.   AC
PATH OF DARKNESS   PEASE, M. C.   SS   SFS 55 03
  MASTERS OF SCIENCE FICTION   HOWARD, IVAN   AN
PATH THROUGH THE DARKNESS, A   ELLISON, HARLAN   NV   FLN 63 01
  *LOVE AIN'T NOTHING BUT SEX MISSPELLED   ELLISON, HARLAN   AC
PATIENT, THE   HULL, E. MAYNE   SS   UNK 43 10
  OUT OF THE UNKNOWN   VAN VOGT & HULL   AC
  *SCIENCE FICTION ADVENTURES IN MUTATION   CONKLIN, GROFF   AN
PATRICK HENRY, JUPITER, AND THE LITTLE RED BRICK SPACESHIP
                     MARTIN, GEORGE R. R.   AMZ 76 12
  SONGS OF STARS AND SHADOWS   MARTIN, GEORGE R. R. AC
PATROL, THE   LEM, STANISLAW   SS   AMZ
  OTHER WORLDS, OTHER SEAS   SUVIN, DARKO   AN
PATRON OF THE ARTS   ROTSLER, WILLIAM   NV   UNI 72 02
  BEST SCIENCE FICTION OF THE YEAR, THE NO. 2
                                          CARR, TERRY   AN

BEST SCIENCE FICTION STORIES OF THE YEAR (1972)
                                          DEL REY, LESTER   AN
  NEBULA AWARD STORIES 8   ASIMOV, ISAAC   AN
  UNIVERSE 2   CARR, TERRY   OA
PATRON OF THE ARTS   SABERHAGEN, FRED   SS   IFS 65 08
  BERSERKER   SABERHAGEN, FRED   AC
  COMBAT SF   DICKSON, GORDON R.   AN
PATTERN   BROWN, FREDRIC   SS   NEW 54 AC
  ABC OF SCIENCE FICTION, AN   BOARDMAN, TOM JR.   AN
  ANGELS AND SPACESHIPS   BROWN, FREDRIC   AC
  BEST OF FREDRIC BROWN, THE   BROWN, FREDRIC   AC
  VOYAGES: SCENARIOS FOR A SHIP CALLED EARTH
                                          SAUER, ROB   AN
PATTERN FOR PENELOPE, A   YOUNG, ROBERT F.   SS   IFS 54 10
  FIRST WORLD OF IF, THE   QUINN & WULFF   AN
PATTERN FOR PLUNDER   PETAJA, EMIL   NV
  STARDRIFT AND OTHER FANTASTIC FLOTSAM   PETAJA, EMIL   AC
PATTERN FOR SURVIVAL   MATHESON, RICHARD   SS   FSF 55 05
  BEST FROM FANTASY AND SCIENCE FICTION: 5
                                          BOUCHER, ANTHONY   AN
  SHORES OF SPACE, THE   MATHESON, RICHARD   AC
PATTERNS OF DORNE, THE   STURGEON, THEODORE   SS   70
  STURGEON IS ALIVE AND WELL...   STURGEON, THEODORE   AC
PAUL BUNYAN VERSUS THE CONVEYOR BELT
                     UPSON, WILLIAM H.   SS   FTM 49
  MATHEMATICAL MAGPIE, THE   FADIMAN, CLIFTON   AN
PAUL'S TREEHOUSE   WOLFE, GENE   SS   ORB 69 05
  ORBIT 5   KNIGHT, DAMON   OA
PAULIE CHARMED THE SLEEPING WOMAN
                     ELLISON, HARLAN   SS   FSF 62 08
  APPROACHING OBLIVION   ELLISON, HARLAN   AC
PAUSE, THE   ASIMOV, ISAAC   SS
  BUY JUPITER AND OTHER STORIES   ASIMOV, ISAAC   AC
  HAVE YOU SEEN THESE?   ASIMOV, ISAAC   AC
  *TIME TO COME   DERLETH, AUGUST   OA
PAUSODYNE (1884)   ALLEN, GRANT   SS   84
  *BEYOND TIME AND SPACE   DERLETH, AUGUST   AN
PAVILION, THE   NESBIT, EDITH   SS   23
  SUPERNATURAL READER, THE   CONKLIN, G&L.   AN
PAWLEY'S PEEPHOLES (OPERATION PEEP)
                     WYNDHAM, JOHN   SS   SCF 51 WI
  BEST OF JOHN WYNDHAM, THE   WYNDHAM, JOHN   AC
  ESCALES DANS L'INFINI   GALLET, GEORGES H.   AN
  MAN FROM BEYOND AND OTHER STORIES, THE   WYNDHAM, JOHN   AC
  SEEDS OF TIME, THE   WYNDHAM, JOHN   AC
  STARLIT CORRIDOR, THE   MANSFIELD, ROGER   AN
PAWOB DIVISION, THE (SEE THE PITLL PAWOB DIVISION)
                     ELLISON, HARLAN   TC
PAX GALACTICA   WILLIAMS, RALPH   SS   ASF 52 11
  SPACE POLICE   NORTON, ANDRE   AN
PAXTON'S WORLD   PRONZINI, BILL   SS   FCR 75
  FUTURE CORRUPTION   ELWOOD, ROGER   AN
PAY FOR THE PRINTER   DICK, PHILIP K.   SS   SAT 56 10
  PRESERVING MACHINE, THE   DICK, PHILIP K.   AC
PAYCHECK   DICK, PHILIP K.   NV   IMG 53 06
  BEST OF PHILIP K. DICK, THE   DICK, PHILIP K.   AC
PAYMENT IN FULL   BRADBURY, RAY   SS   TWS 50 02
  MAN AGAINST TOMORROW   NOLAN, WILLIAM F.   AN
PEABODY HERITAGE, THE   DERLETH, AUGUST
                      AND LOVECRAFT, H. P.   NV C
  SURVIVOR AND OTHER STORIES, THE   LOVECRAFT & DERLETH   AC
PEACE ON EARTH   COLVIN, JAMES   SS   NWS 59 12
  DEEP FIX, THE   COLVIN, JAMES   AC
PEACE ON EARTH   COX, IRVING E. JR.   NV   FUT 54 06
  6 AND THE SILENT SCREAM   HOWARD, IVAN   AN
PEACE WITH HONOR   POURNELLE, JERRY   NV   ASF 71 05
  MERCENARY, THE   POURNELLE, JERRY   NO
PEACE, LOVE, AND FOOD FOR THE HUNGRY
                     KIMBERLY, GAIL   NV
  OTHER SIDE OF TOMORROW, THE   ELWOOD, ROGER   OA
PEACEBRINGER (SWORD OF PEACE)   MOORE, WARD   SS   AMZ 50 03
  *BIG BOOK OF SCIENCE FICTION   CONKLIN, GROFF   AN
PEACEFUL MARTIAN, THE   OLIVER, J. T.   SS   FBK 51 08
  SCIENCE AND SORCERY   FORD, GARRET   AN
PEACEFULNESS OF VIVYAN, THE   TIPTREE, JAMES JR.   SS   AMZ 71 07
  TEN THOUSAND LIGHT-YEARS FROM HOME   TIPTREE, JAMES JR.   AC
PEACEMAKER   COPPEL, ALFRED   SS   IFS 53 01
  PRIZE SCIENCE FICTION   WOLLHEIM, DONALD A.   AN
PEACEMAKER, THE (THE LIFE HATER)
                     SABERHAGEN, FRED   SS   IFS 64 08
  BERSERKER   SABERHAGEN, FRED   AC
PEACEMONGER (THE MAN WHO HATED WAR)
                     PETAJA, EMIL   SS   AMZ 44 12
  STARDRIFT AND OTHER FANTASTIC FLOTSAM   PETAJA, EMIL   AC
PEAK LORDS, THE   DEFORD, MIRIAM ALLEN   SS   IFS 66 02
  ELSEWHERE, ELSEWHEN, ELSEHOW   DEFORD, MIRIAM ALLEN AC
PEANUTS   SCHULTZ, CHARLES M.   CT   64
  APEMAN, SPACEMAN   STOVER & HARRISON   AN
PEARL NECKLACE, THE   DISCH, THOMAS M.   SS
  *GETTING INTO DEATH   DISCH, THOMAS M.   AC
PEARL OF LOVE, THE   WELLS, H. G.   SS   24
  SHORT STORIES OF H. G. WELLS, THE   WELLS, H. G.   AC
  *TIME MACHINE AND OTHER STORIES, THE   WELLS, H. G.   AC
PEASANT GIRL, THE   BUDRYS, ALGIS   SS   ASF 56 06
  BUDRYS' INFERNO   BUDRYS, ALGIS   AC
PEAT BOG, THE   ANDERSON, POUL   SS
  HOMEWARD AND BEYOND   ANDERSON, POUL   AC
PEBBLE IN THE SKY   ASIMOV, ISAAC   NO   DBL 50
  TRIANGLE   ASIMOV, ISAAC   AC
PECULIAR PEOPLE, A   CURTIS, BETSY   SS   FSF 51 08
  BEST SCIENCE-FICTION STORIES: 1952, THE   BLEILER & DIKTY   AN
PEDDLER'S APPRENTICE, THE   VINGE, JOAN D.
                      AND VINGE, VERNOR   NV C ASF 75 08
  BEST SCIENCE FICTION STORIES OF THE YEAR (1975)
                                          DEL REY, LESTER   AN
  1976 ANNUAL WORLD'S BEST SF, THE   WOLLHEIM, DONALD A.   AN

```
PEDDLER'S NOSE, THE              WILLIAMSON, JACK   SS  ASF 51 04
  ASSIGNMENT IN TOMORROW         POHL, FREDERICK         AN
  PEOPLE MACHINES                WILLIAMSON, JACK        AC
  STARS AROUND US, THE           HOSKINS, ROBERT         AN
PEDESTRIAN ACCIDENT, A (INCIDENT IN THE STREETS OF THE CITY)
                                 COOVER, ROBERT    SS  PBY 69 01
  BEST SF: 1970                  HARRISON & ALDISS       AN
PEDESTRIAN, THE (REP 51 08)      BRADBURY, RAY     SS  FSF 52 02
  BEST SCIENCE-FICTION STORIES: 1952, THE  BLEILER & DIKTY  AN
  DECADE THE 1950S               ALDISS & HARRISON       AN
  *GOLDEN APPLES OF THE SUN      BRADBURY, RAY           AC
  LATE GREAT FUTURE, THE         FITZ GERALD & DILLON    AN
  S IS FOR SPACE                 BRADBURY, RAY           AC
  SOCIOLOGY THROUGH SCIENCE FICTION  MILSTEAD/GREENBERG/& AN
  TIMELESS STORIES FOR TODAY AND TOMORROW  BRADBURY, RAY  AN
PEEK| I SEE YOU|                 ANDERSON, POUL    NV  ASF 68 02
  HOMEWARD AND BEYOND            ANDERSON, POUL          AC
PEEPER, THE                      LONG, FRANK BELKNAP  SS  WRT 44 03
  EARLY LONG, THE                LONG, FRANK BELKNAP     AC
  *HOUNDS OF TINDALOS, THE       LONG, FRANK BELKNAP     AC
PEEPING TOM                      MERRIL, JUDITH    NV  STS 54 SP
  OUT OF BOUNDS                  MERRIL, JUDITH          AC
  SURVIVAL SHIP AND OTHER STORIES  MERRIL, JUDITH        AC
PEGGY AND PETER GO TO THE MOON WHITE, DON        SS  FSF 63 02
  BEST FROM FANTASY AND SCIENCE FICTION: 13
                                 DAVIDSON, AVRAM         AN
PEKING JUNCTION, THE             MOORCOCK, MICHAEL  SS
  LIVES AND TIMES OF JERRY CORNELIUS, THE  MOORCOCK, MICHAEL  AC
  NEW S.F., THE                  JONES, LANGDON          OA
PELLUCIDAR                       BURROUGHS, EDGAR R.  NO  ASC 15 05
  THREE SCIENCE FICTION NOVELS   BURROUGHS, EDGAR R.     AC
PELT                             EMSHWILLER, CAROL  SS  FSF 58 11
  POCKETFUL OF STARS, A          KNIGHT, DAMON           AN
  SF: THE BEST OF THE BEST       MERRIL, JUDITH          AN
  SF:59, THE YEAR'S GREATEST SCIENCE FICTION AND FANTASY
                                 MERRIL, JUDITH          AN
PEMBERLY'S START-AFRESH CALLIOPE OR, THE NEW PROTEUS
                                 SLADEK, JOHN T.   SS  NWQ 71 01
  NEW WORLDS QUARTERLY NO. 1     MOORCOCK, MICHAEL       OA
PEN AND THE DARK, THE            KAPP, COLIN       NV  NWR 66 08
  NEW WRITINGS IN SF.  7         CARNELL, JOHN           AN
  NEW WRITINGS IN SF.  8         CARNELL, JOHN           OA
PEN PAL                          LESSER, MILTON    SS  GAL 51 07
  *INVADERS OF EARTH             CONKLIN, GROFF          AN
PENANCE DAY IN MODERAN           BUNCH, DAVID R.   SS  AMZ 60 07
  MODERAN                        BUNCH, DAVID R.         AC
PENELOPE                         STARRETT, VINCENT  NV  WRT 23 05
  MOON TERROR, THE               BIRCH, A. G.            AN
PENFIELD MISADVENTURE, THE       DERLETH, AUGUST   SS  OSF 54 11
  HARRIGAN'S FILE                DERLETH, AUGUST         AC
PENGUIN SCIENCE FICTION          ALDISS, BRIAN W.   AN  PEN 61
  PENGUIN SCIENCE FICTION OMNIBUS, THE  ALDISS, BRIAN W.  AN
PENINSULA                        EMSHWILLER, CAROL  SS  RRV
  JOY IN OUR CAUSE               EMSHWILLER, CAROL       AC
PENNIES, OFF A DEAD MAN'S EYES ELLISON, HARLAN   SS  GAL 69 11
  ALONE AGAINST TOMORROW         ELLISON, HARLAN         AC
  BEST FROM GALAXY, THE   VOLUME I  GALAXY, EDITORS OF   AN
  NEW TOMORROWS, THE             SPINRAD, NORMAN         AN
  OVER THE EDGE                  ELLISON, HARLAN         AC
PENT HOUSE, THE                  KELLER, DAVID H. MD. SS  AMZ 32 02
  FOLSOM FLINT AND OTHER CURIOUS TALES, THE
                                 KELLER, DAVID H. MD.    AC
PENTAGRAM                        SELLINGS, ARTHUR  SS  SAT 58 10
  *TIME TRANSFER                 SELLINGS, ARTHUR        AC
PENULTIMATE TRIP, THE            TRAVERS, ANDREW   SS  SAG 70
  SCIENCE AGAINST MAN            CHEETHAM, ANTHONY       OA
PEOPLE OF PRASHAD, THE           KEILTY, JAMES     NV  QRK 71 02
  NEW IMPROVED SUN, THE          DISCH, THOMAS M.        AN
  QUARK/2                        DELANY & HACKER         OA
PEOPLE OF THE BLACK CIRCLE, THE
                                 HOWARD, ROBERT E.  NA  WRT 34 09
  CONAN THE ADVENTURER           HOWARD, R. & DE CAMP    AC
  SWORD OF CONAN, THE            HOWARD, ROBERT E.       AC
PEOPLE OF THE CRATER, THE        NORTON, ANDRE     NV  FBK 47 01
  ALIEN EARTH AND OTHER STORIES  ELWOOD & MOSKOWITZ      AN
  SWORDSMEN IN THE SKY           WOLLHEIM, DONALD A.     AN
PEOPLE OF THE PIT, THE           MERRITT, A.       NV  ASM 18 01
  FANTASTIC PULPS, THE           HAINING, PETER          AN
  FOX WOMAN & OTHER STORIES, THE  MERRITT, A.            AC
  MASTERPIECES OF SCIENCE FICTION  MOSKOWITZ, SAM        AN
PEOPLE REVIEWS                   CHILSON, ROBERT   SS  UNI 77 07
  UNIVERSE 7                     CARR, TERRY             OA
PEOPLE SOUP                      ARKIN, ALAN       SS  GAL 58 11
  SCIENCE FICTION ODDITIES       CONKLIN, GROFF          AN
PEOPLE THAT TIME FORGOT, THE  BURROUGHS, EDGAR R.  NV  BBM 18 10
  LAND THAT TIME FORGOT, THE     BURROUGHS, EDGAR R.     NO
PEOPLE TRAP, THE                 SHECKLEY, ROBERT  SS  FSF 68 06
  BEST FROM FANTASY AND SCIENCE FICTION: 18
                                 FERMAN, EDWARD L.       AN
  PEOPLE TRAP AND OTHER PITFALLS, THE  SHECKLEY, ROBERT  AC
  SOCIAL PROBLEMS THROUGH SCIENCE FICTION  GREENBERG/MILSTEAD/& AN
PERCHANCE TO DREAM               BEAUMONT, CHARLES  SS  PBY 58 10
  FIEND IN YOU, THE              BEAUMONT, CHARLES       AN
  MAGIC MAN AND OTHER SCIENCE-FANTASY STORIES
                                 BEAUMONT, CHARLES       AC
  MASKS                          PLAYBOY, EDITORS OF     AN
  NIGHT RIDE AND OTHER JOURNEYS  BEAUMONT, CHARLES       AC
PERCHANCE TO DREAM               MACLEAN, KATHERINE  SS  NEW 70 SN
  NEW WORLDS OF FANTASY NO. 2    CARR, TERRY             AN
PERCHANCE TO DREAM               WILHELM, KATE     SS  NEW 68 AC
  DOWNSTAIRS ROOM AND OTHER SPECULATIVE FICTION, THE
                                 WILHELM, KATE           AC
PERCHANCE TO DREAM (ASLEEP IN ARMAGEDDON)
                                 BRADBURY, RAY     SS  PLS 48 WI
  DAY IT RAINED FOREVER, THE     BRADBURY, RAY           AC
```

```
PERFECT ANSWER                   STECHER, L. J. JR.  SS  GAL 58 06
  FIFTH GALAXY READER, THE       GOLD, H. L.             AN
PERFECT CREATURE, THE (ALSO AS UNA, FSF 53 01)
                                 WYNDHAM, JOHN     NV  TOW 37 01
  BEST OF JOHN WYNDHAM, THE      WYNDHAM, JOHN           AC
  MAN FROM BEYOND AND OTHER STORIES, THE  WYNDHAM, JOHN  AC
  SHADOW OF TOMORROW             POHL, FREDERICK         AN
PERFECT GENTLEMAN, THE           MCGREGOR, R. J.   SS  STS 52 09
  BEST FROM STARTLING STORIES, THE  MINES, SAMUEL        AN
PERFECT HOST, THE                STURGEON, THEODORE  NV  WRT 48 11
  *BEYOND HUMAN KEN              MERRIL, JUDITH          AN
  TO HERE AND THE EASEL          STURGEON, THEODORE      AC
  WORLDS OF THEODORE STURGEON, THE  STURGEON, THEODORE   AC
PERFECT MURDER                   GOLD, H. L.       SS  TWS 40 03
  *SCIENCE FICTION ADVENTURES IN DIMENSION  CONKLIN, GROFF  AN
PERFECT PUNISHMENT, THE (PARIAH PLANET)
                                 BIGGLE, LLOYD JR.  NV  WOT 65 03
  RULE OF THE DOOR AND OTHER FANCIFUL REGULATIONS
                                 BIGGLE, LLOYD JR.       AC
PERFECT ROBOT, THE               BOULLE, PIERRE    SS
  TIME OUT OF MIND               BOULLE, PIERRE          OC
PERFECT WARRIOR, THE (THE DUELING MACHINE)
                                 BOVA, BEN
                             AND LEWIS, MYRON R.  SN C ASF 63 05
  FORWARD IN TIME                BOVA, BEN               AC
PERFECT WOMAN, THE               SHECKLEY, ROBERT  SS  AMZ 54 01
  FIFTY SHORT SCIENCE FICTION TALES  ASIMOV & CONKLIN    AN
  TOMORROW, AND TOMORROW, AND TOMORROW...  HEINTZ/HERBERT/JOOS/ AN
PERFORCE TO DREAM                JOYCE, MICHAEL    SS
  BEST FANTASY STORIES           ALDISS, BRIAN W.        AN
PERFORCE TO DREAM                WYNDHAM, JOHN     SS  BEY 54 01
  BEYOND THE BARRIERS OF SPACE AND TIME  MERRIL, JUDITH  AN
  JIZZLE                         WYNDHAM, JOHN           AC
PERFUMED GARDEN, THE             KELLER, DAVID H. MD. SS
  TALES FROM UNDERWOOD           KELLER, DAVID H. MD.    AC
PERHAPS WE ARE GOING AWAY        BRADBURY, RAY     SS  TOP 62 01
  MACHINERIES OF JOY, THE        BRADBURY, RAY           AC
PERHAPS WHERE HE IS ONLY LOVING ROCKETS CAN LAND
                                 PATTEN, BRIAN     PM   69
  HOLDING YOUR EIGHT HANDS       LUCIE-SMITH, EDWARD     AN
PERIHELION MAN, THE              PRIEST, CHRISTOPHER  NV  NWR 69 16
  NEW WRITINGS IN SF. 16         CARNELL, JOHN           OA
  REAL-TIME WORLD                PRIEST, CHRISTOPHER     AC
PERIHESPERON                     BEAR, GREG        SS
  TOMORROW: NEW WORLDS OF SCIENCE FICTION  ELWOOD, ROGER  OA
PERIL FROM OUTER SPACE, THE      ELAM, RICHARD M. JR.  NV
  TEEN-AGE SUPER SCIENCE STORIES  ELAM, RICHARD M. JR.   AC
PERIL OF THE BLUE WORLD          ABERNATHY, ROBERT  SS  PLS 42 WI
  FLIGHT INTO SPACE              WOLLHEIM, DONALD A.     AN
  STORIES OF SCIENTIFIC IMAGINATION  GALLANT, JOSEPH     AN
PERIOD OF GESTATION              KEYES, THOM       SS  SCF 64 10
  BEST SF STORIES FROM NEW WORLDS 4  MOORCOCK, MICHAEL   AN
  SCIENCE FICTION HORIZONS NO. 1  BOARDMAN, TOM JR.      AN
PERIOD PIECE                     COUPLING, J. J.   SS  ASF 48 11
  BEST SCIENCE-FICTION STORIES: 1949, THE  BLEILER & DIKTY  AN
  HUMAN-MACHINES                 SCORTIA & ZEBROWSKI     AN
PERITONITIS                      WOLFE, GENE       SS  TAL 73
  FRONTIERS 1; TOMORROW'S ALTERNATIVES  ELWOOD, ROGER    OA
PERLANDRA (SELECTION)            LEWIS, C. S.      EX  LNE 43
  ALL ABOUT VENUS                ALDISS, BRIAN W.        AN
  FAREWELL FANTASTIC VENUS       ALDISS & HARRISON       AN
PERMANENT IMPLOSION, THE         MCLAUGHLIN, DEAN  NV  ASF 64 02
  ANALOG 4                       CAMPBELL, JOHN W. JR    AN
  HAWK AMONG THE SPARROWS        MCLAUGHLIN, DEAN        AC
PERPETUAL MOTION (WIDE-OPEN PLANET)
                                 DE CAMP, L. SPRAGUE  NV  FUT 50 09
  CONTINENT MAKERS AND OTHER TALES OF THE VIAGENS
                                 DE CAMP, L. SPRAGUE     AC
PERSISTENCE OF DESIRE, THE       DISCH, THOMAS M.  SS
  *GETTING INTO DEATH            DISCH, THOMAS M.        AC
PERSON FROM PORLOCK, THE         JONES, RAYMOND F.  NV  ASF 47 08
  *TREASURY OF SCIENCE FICTION, A  CONKLIN, GROFF        AN
PERSON THROWING A STONE AT A BIRD
                                 MIRO, JOAN        IL
  SCIENCE FICTION                BRODKIN & PEARSON       AN
PERSONAGE OF ROYAL BLOOD, A      ROBERTS, WILLO DAVIS  SS  TVW 73
  TWO VIEWS OF WONDER            SCORTIA & YARBRO        OA
PERSONAL                         KUPFERBERG, TULI  SS  ESR 66
  AS TOMORROW BECOMES TODAY      SULLIVAN, CHARLES W.    AN
  SF12                           MERRIL, JUDITH          AN
PERSONNEL PROBLEM                GOLD, H. L.       SS  GAL 58 09
  SIXTH GALAXY READER, THE       GOLD, H. L.             AN
PERUVIAN MUMMY MASK              MISC. MATERIAL    IL
  SCIENCE FICTION                BRODKIN & PEARSON       AN
PET                              JONES, RAYMOND F.  NV  FUQ 73
  FUTURE QUEST                   ELWOOD, ROGER           OA
PET SHOP, THE                    BOND, NELSON S.   SS  BBM 50 03
  NIGHTMARES AND DAYDREAMS       BOND, NELSON S.         AC
PETE CAN FIX IT                  JONES, RAYMOND F.  SS  ASF 47 02
  ADVENTURES IN DIMENSION        CONKLIN, GROFF          AN
  *SCIENCE FICTION ADVENTURES IN DIMENSION  CONKLIN, GROFF  AN
PETER LEARNS ARITHMETIC          WELLS, H. G.      SS  18
  FANTASIA MATHEMATICA           FADIMAN, CLIFTON        AN
PETERSEN'S EYE                   BOND, NELSON S.   SS  BBM 49 03
  NIGHTMARES AND DAYDREAMS       BOND, NELSON S.         AC
PETRIFIED WORLD, THE             SHECKLEY, ROBERT  SS  IFS 68 02
  CAN YOU FEEL ANYTHING WHEN I DO THIS?, AND OTHER STORIES
                                 SHECKLEY, ROBERT        AC
  NEW WORLDS OF FANTASY NO. 2    CARR, TERRY             AN
PETTY LARCENY                    BIGGLE, LLOYD JR.  SS  SAT 58 08
  RULE OF THE DOOR AND OTHER FANCIFUL REGULATIONS
                                 BIGGLE, LLOYD JR.       AC
PHALANSTERY OF THELEME, THE (1534)
                                 RABELAIS, FRANCIS  EX
  *BEYOND TIME AND SPACE         DERLETH, AUGUST         AN
```

PHANTAS   ONIONS, OLIVER   SS   11
  GOLDEN ROAD, THE   KNIGHT, DAMON   AN
  MOONLIGHT TRAVELER, THE   STERN, PHILIP VAN D. AN
  TRAVELERS IN TIME   STERN, PHILIP VAN D. AN
PHANTOM OF KANSAS, THE   VARLEY, JOHN   NV GAL 76 02
  BEST SCIENCE FICTION OF THE YEAR, THE NO. 6
                                      CARR, TERRY   AN
PHANTOM OF TERROR, THE   REPP, ED EARL   SS AMZ 33 04
  RADIUM POOL, THE   REPP, ED EARL   AC
PHANTOM OF THE OPERA   LEROUX, GASTON   NA   11
  GHOULS, THE   HAINING, PETER   AN
PHANTOM SETTER, THE   MURPHY, ROBERT   SS SEP 61 06
  OTHER SIDE OF THE CLOCK, THE   STERN, PHILIP VAN D. AN
  POST READER OF FANTASY AND SCIENCE FICTION
                                      SATURDAY EVE. POST   AN
PHANTOMS OF ZARK   FAIRMAN, PAUL W.   SS
  FORGETFUL ROBOT, THE   FAIRMAN, PAUL W.   OC
PHASE THREE   MOORCOCK, MICHAEL   SS NWS 66 03
  FINAL PROGRAMME, THE   MOORCOCK, MICHAEL   NO
PHASES OF THE NIGHT, THE   ERNST, MAX   IL
  SCIENCE FICTION   BRODKIN & PEARSON   AN
PHILIP K. DICK   NOLAN, WILLIAM F.   AR
  HUMAN EQUATION, THE   NOLAN, WILLIAM F.   AN
PHILIP K. DICK OMNIBUS, A DICK, PHILIP K.   AC SID 70
  SCIENCE FICTION SPECIAL 7   ANONYMOUS   AN
PHILOSOPHER'S STONE   ANVIL, CHRISTOPHER   SS ASF 63 01
  ANALOG 2   CAMPBELL, JOHN W. JR AN
PHILOSOPHERS STONE   WENSKES, HELMUT   IL
  BEYOND THIS HORIZON   CARRELL, CHRISTOPHER OA
PHILOSOPHICAL CORPS   COLE, EVERETT B.   NV ASF 51 03
  PHILOSOPHICAL CORPS, THE   COLE, EVERETT B.   NO
PHILOSOPHICAL DIALOGUE, A ANDERSON, POUL   AR OUT 71 08
  HOMEBREW   ANDERSON, POUL   AC
PHILTRE TIP   BLOCH, ROBERT   SS ROG 61 03
  LIVING DEMONS, THE   BLOCH, ROBERT   AC
PHOBOS TRANSCRIPTS, THE   WILDER, CHERRY   SS NWR 75 26
  NEW WRITINGS IN SF. 26   BULMER, KENNETH   OA
PHOENIX   SMITH, CLARK ASHTON   SS
  BEYOND BELIEF   HURLEY, RICHARD J.   AN
  OTHER DIMENSIONS   SMITH, CLARK ASHTON   AC
  *TIME TO COME   DERLETH, AUGUST   OA
PHOENIX   BRADLEY, MARION Z.
                           AND WHITE, TED   SS C AMZ 63 02
  BEST FROM AMAZING, THE   WHITE, TED   AN
PHOENIX (PHOENIX LAND)   ELLISON, HARLAN   SS IFS 69 03
  BEAST THAT SHOUTED LOVE AT THE HEART OF THE WORLD, THE
                                      ELLISON, HARLAN   AC
PHOENIX HOUSE   MILLER, JESSIE   SS ORB 75 16
  ORBIT 16   KNIGHT, DAMON   OA
PHOENIX ON THE SWORD, THE HOWARD, ROBERT E.   SS WRT 32 12
  CONAN THE USURPER   HOWARD, R. & DE CAMP AC
  KING CONAN   HOWARD, ROBERT E.   AC
PHOENIX WITHOUT ASHES   ELLISON, HARLAN   PL   76
  FASTER THAN LIGHT   DANN & ZEBROWSKI   OA
PHOENIX WITHOUT ASHES   KIRK, TIM   IL   76
  FASTER THAN LIGHT   DANN & ZEBROWSKI   OA
PHOG   ANTHONY, PIERS   SS FAN 65 06
  SF: AUTHORS' CHOICE 3   HARRISON, HARRY   AN
PHOTOGRAPHIC EVIDENCE   GENOVES, JUAN   IL
  SCIENCE FICTION   BRODKIN & PEARSON   AN
PHOTOGRAPHY   HAYCOCK, CHRISTINE   IL
  SCIENCE FICTION BY GASLIGHT   MOSKOWITZ, SAM   AN
PI AND THE ACTUARY   BALL, W. W. R.   MS
  MATHEMATICAL MAGPIE, THE   FADIMAN, CLIFTON   AN
PI IN THE SKY   BROWN, FREDRIC   SS TWS 45 WI
  BEST OF FREDRIC BROWN, THE   BROWN, FREDRIC   AC
  DAYMARES   BROWN, FREDRIC   AC
  SPACE ON MY HANDS   BROWN, FREDRIC   AC
PI MAN, THE   BESTER, ALFRED   SS FSF 59 10
  ALPHA 1   SILVERBERG, ROBERT   AN
  BEST FROM FANTASY AND SCIENCE FICTION: 9
                                      MILLS, ROBERT P.   AN
  DARK SIDE OF THE EARTH, THE   BESTER, ALFRED   AC
  STAR LIGHT, STAR BRIGHT   BESTER, ALFRED   AC
PICCADILLY INTERVAL   COOPER, EDMUND   SS
  TOMORROW CAME   COOPER, EDMUND   AC
PICKMAN'S MODEL   LOVECRAFT, H. P.   SS WRT 27 10
  HAUNTER OF THE DARK, THE   LOVECRAFT, H. P.   AC
PICKUP   VAN ALM, AIDAN   SS FUN 60 01
  FLYING SAUCERS IN FACT AND FICTION SANTESSON, HANS S.   AN
PICKUP FOR OLYMPUS   PANGBORN, EDGAR   SS NEW 53 AN
  GOOD NEIGHBORS AND OTHER STRANGERS PANGBORN, EDGAR   AC
  SUPERNATURAL READER, THE   CONKLIN, G&L.   AN
PICNIC ON PARADISE   RUSS, JOANNA   NO ACE 68
  ALYX   RUSS, JOANNA   AC
PICTURE BY KLEE, A   SAIL, LAWRENCE   PM
  BEST SF: 1974   HARRISON & ALDISS   AN
PICTURE-WELL, THE   AYME, MARCEL   SS
  WALKER THROUGH WALLS, THE   AYME, MARCEL   AC
PICTURES DON'T LIE   MACLEAN, KATHERINE   SS GAL 51 08
  ASPECTS OF SCIENCE FICTION   DOHERTY, G. D.   AN
  BEST SF   CRISPIN, EDMUND   AN
  DIPLOIDS AND OTHER FLIGHTS OF FANCY, THE MACLEAN, KATHERINE AC
  ENEMIES IN SPACE   CONKLIN, GROFF   AN
  INVADERS FROM SPACE   SILVERBERG, ROBERT   AN
  *INVADERS OF EARTH   CONKLIN, GROFF   AN
  SPECULATIONS   SANDERS, THOMAS E.   AN
PIE IN THE SKY   GRAVES, JOCELYN   SS ADS 75 04
  ARMADA SCI-FI TWO   DAVIS, RICHARD   OA
PIE IN THE SKY   STYRON, WILLIAM   SS NEW 66 AN
  VINTAGE ANTHOLOGY OF SCIENCE FANTASY, THE
                                      CERF, CHRISTOPHER   AN
PIEBALD HIPPOGRIFF, THE   ANDERSON, KAREN   SS FAN 62 05
  8TH ANNUAL OF THE YEAR'S BEST S-F, THE MERRIL, JUDITH   AN
PIEBALD HORSE   TUBB, E. C.   SS ASF 60 11
  TEN FROM TOMORROW   TUBB, E. C.   AC

PIECE OF LINOLEUM, A (AS AMY WORTH)
                           KELLER, DAVID H. MD. SS TST 33 12
  FOLSOM FLINT AND OTHER CURIOUS TALES, THE
                                      KELLER, DAVID H. MD. AC
  LIFE EVERLASTING AND OTHER TALES OF SCIENCE, FANTASY
    AND HORROR   KELLER, DAVID H. MD. AC
  TALES FROM UNDERWOOD   KELLER, DAVID H. MD. AC
PIECE OF THE ACTION, A (D. P. HARMON & G. L. COON)
                           BLISH, JAMES   SA STK 71 04
  STAR TREK 4   BLISH, JAMES   OC
PIECE OF WOOD, A   BRADBURY, RAY   SS ESQ 52 06
  LONG AFTER MIDNIGHT   BRADBURY, RAY   AC
PIECEMAKERS, THE   LAUMER, KEITH   NV IFS 70 05
  RETIEF OF THE CDT   LAUMER, KEITH   AC
PIEGE   TELEMAQUE, HERVE   IL
  SCIENCE FICTION   BRODKIN & PEARSON   AN
PIFFINGCAP   COPPARD, A. E.   SS   21
  SUPERNATURAL READER, THE   CONKLIN, G&L.   AN
PIG IN A POKEY   LAFFERTY, R. A.   SS
  DOES ANYONE ELSE HAVE SOMETHING FURTHER TO ADD?
                                      LAFFERTY, R. A.   AC
PIGEON   NOLAN, WILLIAM F.   SS   57
  IMPACT-20   NOLAN, WILLIAM F.   AC
PIGEON CITY   MILLER, JESSIE   NV ASF 72 11
  SOCIOLOGY THROUGH SCIENCE FICTION   MILSTEAD/GREENBERG/& AN
PIGEONS FROM HELL   HOWARD, ROBERT E.   NV WRT 38 05
  WEIRD TALES   MARGULIES, LEO   AN
PIGGY BANK   KUTTNER, HENRY   NV ASF 42 12
  INVASION OF THE ROBOTS   ELWOOD, ROGER   AN
  TREASURY OF GREAT SCIENCE FICTION, A VOL.2
                                      BOUCHER, ANTHONY   AN
PILE OF TROUBLE   KUTTNER, HENRY   SS TWS 48 04
  AHEAD OF TIME   KUTTNER, HENRY   AC
  ZACHERLEY'S MIDNIGHT SNACKS   ZACHERLEY   AN
PILGRIMAGE   OLIVER, CHAD   SS FSF 58 02
  SPECIAL WONDER   MCCOMAS, J. FRANCIS AN
PILGRIMAGE (THE PRIESTESS WHO REBELLED)
                           BOND, NELSON S.   SS AMZ 39 10
  BEST OF AMAZING, THE   ROSS, JOSEPH   AN
  MARRIAGE AND THE FAMILY THROUGH SCIENCE FICTION
                                      CLEAR/WARRICK/&   AN
  31ST OF FEBRUARY, THE   BOND, NELSON S.   AC
PILGRIMAGE TO EARTH (LOVE, INCORPORATED)
                           SHECKLEY, ROBERT   SS PBY 56 09
  PILGRIMAGE TO EARTH   SHECKLEY, ROBERT   AC
  ROBERT SHECKLEY OMNIBUS, THE   SHECKLEY, ROBERT   AC
  *SPECTRUM   AMIS & CONQUEST   AN
PILGRIMS, THE   SHELLEY, MARY W.   NV KPS 38
  TALES AND STORIES   SHELLEY, MARY W.   AC
PILL, THE   NADLER, MAGGIE   SS FAN 72 04
  YOU AND SCIENCE FICTION   HOLLISTER, BERNARD C AN
PILLAR OF FIRE   BRADBURY, RAY   NV PLS 48 SU
  *OTHER SIDE OF THE MOON, THE   DERLETH, AUGUST   AN
  S IS FOR SPACE   BRADBURY, RAY   AC
  TREASURY OF GREAT SCIENCE FICTION, A VOL.1
                                      BOUCHER, ANTHONY   AN
PILLAR OF FIRE   BRADBURY, RAY   PL PLS 48 SU
  PILLAR OF FIRE AND OTHER PLAYS   BRADBURY, RAY   AC
PILLAR TO POST   WYNDHAM, JOHN   NV GAL 51 12
  GALAXY SCIENCE FICTION OMNIBUS   GOLD, H. L.   AN
  SECOND GALAXY READER OF SCIENCE FICTION GOLD, H. L.   AN
  SEEDS OF TIME, THE   WYNDHAM, JOHN   AC
PILLOWS, THE   ST. CLAIR, MARGARET   SS TWS 50 06
  *POSSIBLE WORLDS OF SCIENCE FICTION CONKLIN, GROFF   AN
  SANDS OF MARS AND OTHER STORIES, THE ANONYMOUS   AN
PILOT AND THE BUSHMAN, THE JACOBS, SYLVIA   NV GAL 51 08
  *GALAXY READER OF SCIENCE FICTION   GOLD, H. L.   AN
PILOT LIGHTS OF THE APOCALYPSE RIDENOUR, DR. LOUIS N. SS FOR 46 10
  GREAT SCIENCE FICTION BY SCIENTISTS CONKLIN, GROFF   AN
PILOT PLANT   SHAW, BOB   NV NWS 66 05
  TOMORROW LIES IN AMBUSH   SHAW, BOB   AC
PIME DOESN'T CRAY   LAUMER, KEITH   NV IFS 71 01
  RETIEF OF THE CDT   LAUMER, KEITH   AC
PIN-UP GIRL   BLOCH, ROBERT   SS SHK 60 07
  TALES IN A JUGULAR VEIN   BLOCH, ROBERT   AC
PIN, THE   BLOCH, ROBERT   SS AMZ 54 01
  *BLOOD RUNS COLD   BLOCH, ROBERT   AC
PINBALL MACHINES, THE   HARRISON, WILLIAM   SS SEP 67 04
  ROLLERBALL   HARRISON, WILLIAM   AC
PINCH OF STARDUST, A   POHL, FREDERIK   IN
  STAR SCIENCE FICTION STORIES NO. 4 POHL, FREDERIK   OA
PINK CATERPILLAR, THE   BOUCHER, ANTHONY   SS ADV 45 02
  COMPLEAT WEREWOLF, THE   BOUCHER, ANTHONY   AC
PINUP   BRYANT, EDWARD   SS ORB 73 12
  AMONG THE DEAD   BRYANT, EDWARD   AC
  ORBIT 12   KNIGHT, DAMON   OA
PIPE DREAM   LEIBER, FRITZ   SS IFS 59 02
  PAIL OF AIR, A   LEIBER, FRITZ   AC
  WORLDS OF FRITZ LEIBER, THE   LEIBER, FRITZ   AC
PIPE DREAM   MILLER, CHRIS   SS NLP 72 06
  STRANGE ECSTASIES   PARRY, MICHEL   AN
PIPELINE TO PLUTO   LEINSTER, MURRAY   SS ASF 45 08
  BEST OF MURRAY LEINSTER, THE   LEINSTER, MURRAY   AC
  SCIENCE FICTION TERROR TALES   CONKLIN, GROFF   AN
PIPER AT THE GATES OF DAWN COWPER, RICHARD   NA
  CUSTODIANS AND OTHER STORIES, THE   COWPER, RICHARD   AC
PIPER IN THE WOODS   DICK, PHILIP K.   SS IMG 53 02
  OTHER WORLDS, OTHER TIMES   MOSKOWITZ & ELWOOD   AN
PIPER OF DIS, THE   BLISH, JAMES
                           AND KNIGHT, NORMAN L. NV C GAL 66 08
  TORRENT OF FACES, A   BLISH & KNIGHT, N.   AC
PIPER'S SON, THE   KUTTNER, HENRY   NV ASF 45 02
  BEST OF HENRY KUTTNER 1, THE   KUTTNER, HENRY   AC
  BYPASS TO OTHERNESS   KUTTNER, HENRY   AC
PIPER'S SON, THE   PADGETT, LEWIS   NV ASF 45 02
  *BEST OF SCIENCE FICTION   CONKLIN, GROFF   AN

PIPER'S SON, THE   PLANTS MUST GROW

CHILDREN OF WONDER   TENN, WILLIAM   AN
MUTANT   PADGETT, LEWIS   AC
PIPER, THE   BRADBURY, RAY   SS   TWS 43 02
FUTURE MAKERS, THE   HAINING, PETER   AN
FUTURES TO INFINITY   MOSKOWITZ, SAM   AN
PIPES OF PAN, THE   DEL REY, LESTER   SS   UNK 40 05
OTHER WORLDS, THE   STONG, PHILIP D.   AN
ROBOTS AND CHANGELINGS   DEL REY, LESTER   AC
PIPING DEATH, THE   WILLIAMS, ROBERT M. SS UNK 39 05
ZACHERLEY'S MIDNIGHT SNACKS   ZACHERLEY   AN
PIRACY PREFERRED   CAMPBELL, JOHN W. JR NV AMZ 30 06
BLACK STAR PASSES, THE   CAMPBELL, JOHN W. JR   AC
PIRATE OF THE AIR   BRADFORD, JAMES S. SS
ADVENTURES TO COME   ESENWEIN, J. BERG   OA
PIRATE, THE   ANDERSON, POUL   NV   ASF 68 10
HOMEWARD AND BEYOND   ANDERSON, POUL   AC
PIRATES OF ORION, THE (HOWARD WEINSTEIN)
                          FOSTER, ALAN DEAN SA   SLG 75 05
STAR TREK LOG FIVE   FOSTER, ALAN DEAN   OC
PIRATES OF SPACE (FROM TRIPLANETARY)
                          SMITH, EDWARD E. PHD EX AMZ 34 01
BEST OF E. E. 'DOC' SMITH, THE   SMITH, EDWARD E. PHD   AC
PIRATES OF VENUS (SELECTION) BURROUGHS, EDGAR R. EX ARG 32 09
ALL ABOUT VENUS   ALDISS, BRIAN W.   AN
FAREWELL FANTASTIC VENUS   ALDISS & HARRISON   AN
PIRATES OF VENUS, THE   BURROUGHS, EDGAR R. NO   ARG 32 09
PIRATES OF VENUS AND LOST ON VENUS, THE BURROUGHS, EDGAR R.   AC
PIROKIN EFFECT, THE   EISENBERG, LARRY   SS   AMZ 64 06
BEST LAID SCHEMES, THE   EISENBERG, LARRY   AC
10TH ANNUAL OF THE YEAR'S BEST S-F, THE MERRIL, JUDITH   AN
PISTOL POINT   TUBB, E. C.   SS   NWS 53 06
ALIEN DUST   TUBB, E. C.   NO
PIT MY PARISH, THE   ALDISS, BRIAN W.   SS   NWS 58 01
BEST OF NEW WORLDS, THE   MOORCOCK, MICHAEL   AN
PIT, THE   FAIRMAN, PAUL W.   SS
FORGETFUL ROBOT, THE   FAIRMAN, PAUL W.   OC
PIT, THE   WEST, D.   NA
GOLLANCZ - SUNDAY TIMES BEST SF STORIES ANONYMOUS   OA
PITHECANTHROPUS REJECTUS WELLMAN, MANLY WADE SS   ASF 38 01
SCIENCE FICTION OF THE 30'S   KNIGHT, DAMON   AN
PITLL PAWOB DIVISION, THE (THE PAWOB DIVISION)
                          ELLISON, HARLAN   SS   IFS 68 12
BEAST THAT SHOUTED LOVE AT THE HEART OF THE WORLD, THE
                                      ELLISON, HARLAN   AC
PITY THE POOR OUTDATED MAN SHOFNER, PHILIP   NV   NOV 73 03
NOVA 3   HARRISON, HARRY   OA
PITY THIS BUSY MONSTER, MANUNKIND
                          CUMMINGS, E. E.   PM   44
SPECULATIONS   SANDERS, THOMAS E.   AN
PLACE AND TIME TO DIE, A BALLARD, J. G.   SS   NWS 69 10
LOW-FLYING AIRCRAFT AND OTHER STORIES BALLARD, J. G.   AC
NEW WORLDS QUARTERLY NO. 1   MOORCOCK, MICHAEL   OA
PLACE IN THE WOODS, THE   DERLETH, AUGUST   SS   WRT 54 05
DEVIL'S GENERATION, THE   GHIDALIA, VIC   AN
PLACE OF MEETING   BEAUMONT, CHARLES SS   OSF 54 02
PLANET OF DOOM AND OTHER STORIES   ANONYMOUS   AN
YONDER   BEAUMONT, CHARLES   AC
PLACE OF ORCHIDS, THE (THE GOD THAT SCIENCE MADE)
                          ESHBACH, LLOYD A. SS   SFS 39 08
TYRANT OF TIME, THE   ESHBACH, LLOYD A.   AC
PLACE OF PAIN, THE   SHIEL, M. P.   SS   AFR 51 16
MASTERPIECES OF SCIENCE FICTION   MOSKOWITZ, SAM   AN
PLACE OF THE GODS, THE   BENET, STEPHEN V. SS   SEP 37 07
POST READER OF FANTASY AND SCIENCE FICTION
                                      SATURDAY EVE. POST   AN
TOMORROW'S CHILDREN   ASIMOV, ISAAC   AN
PLACE OF THE TIGRESS, THE MAYNE, ISOBEL   SS
AD 2500   WILSON, ANGUS   AN
PLACE WHERE CHICAGO WAS, THE HARMON, JIM   NV   GAL 62 02
HOT & COLD RUNNING CITIES   MCHARGUE, GEORGESS   AN
TENTH GALAXY READER, THE   POHL, FREDERIK   AN
PLACE WITH NO NAME, THE   ELLISON, HARLAN   SS   FSF 69 07
BEAST THAT SHOUTED LOVE AT THE HEART OF THE WORLD, THE
                                      ELLISON, HARLAN   AC
DEATHBIRD STORIES   ELLISON, HARLAN   AC
PLACEMENT TEST   LAUMER, KEITH   NV   AMZ 64 07
BEST FROM AMAZING, THE   WHITE, TED   AN
NINE BY LAUMER   LAUMER, KEITH   AC
PLACET IS A CRAZY PLACE   BROWN, FREDRIC   SS   ASF 46 05
ANGELS AND SPACESHIPS   BROWN, FREDRIC   AN
ASTOUNDING-ANALOG READER, THE VOLUME ONE HARRISON & ALDISS   AN
BEST SF 2   CRISPIN, EDMUND   AN
OUT OF THIS WORLD 1   WILLIAMS-ELLIS& OWEN   AN
SCIENCE FICTION: THE GREAT YEARS   POHL, C. & F.   AN
TRAVELLERS OF SPACE   GREENBERG, MARTIN   AN
PLAGAIRIST   PHILLIPS, PETER   NV   NWS 50 SU
*FUTURE TENSE   CROSSEN, KENDELL F.   AN
PLAGUE   HUBBARD, L. RON   NV   ASF 49 04
OLE DOC METHUSELAH   HUBBARD, L. RON   AC
PLAGUE   LEINSTER, MURRAY   NV   ASF 44 02
OMNIBUS OF SCIENCE FICTION   CONKLIN, GROFF   AN
SCIENCE FICTION OMNIBUS   CONKLIN, GROFF   AN
STRANGE ADVENTURES IN SCIENCE FICTION CONKLIN, GROFF   AN
PLAGUE CIRCUIT   SHECKLEY, ROBERT   SS   NEW 71 AC
CAN YOU FEEL ANYTHING WHEN I DO THIS?, AND OTHER STORIES
                                      SHECKLEY, ROBERT   AC
PLAGUE OF CARS, A   TUSHNET, LEONARD   SS   NDM 71 01
NEW DIMENSIONS 1   SILVERBERG, ROBERT   OA
PLAGUE OF MASTERS, A   ANDERSON, POUL   NA   FAN 60 12
FLANDRY OF TERRA   ANDERSON, POUL   AC
PLAGUE ON KRYDER II   LEINSTER, MURRAY   NV   ASF 64 12
S.O.S. FROM THREE WORLDS   LEINSTER, MURRAY   AC
PLAGUE-SHIP "TUPISA", THE GRIFFITH, GEORGE   SS
GAMBLES WITH DESTINY   GRIFFITH, GEORGE   AC
PLAGUE!   NOURSE, ALAN E.   SS   NEW 71 AC
RX FOR TOMORROW   NOURSE, ALAN E.   AC

PLAGUE, THE   KELLER, TEDDY   SS   ASF 61 02
ANALOG 1   CAMPBELL, JOHN W. JR   AN
PLAGUE, THE   LAUMER, KEITH   NV   ASF 70 11
ANALOG 9   BOVA, BEN   AN
BIG SHOW, THE   LAUMER, KEITH   AC
GATES TO TOMORROW   NORTON, AN.&DONALDY   AN
PLAN FOR THE ASSASSINATION OF JACQUELINE KENNEDY
                          BALLARD, J. G.   SS   AMB 66 WI
ENGLAND SWINGS SF   MERRIL, JUDITH   AN
IN DREAMS AWAKE   FIEDLER, LESLIE A.   AN
LOVE & NAPALM: EXPORT U.S.A.   BALLARD, J. G.   AC
PLANE GEOMETRY   ROUNDS, EMMA   PM   25
FANTASIA MATHEMATICA   FADIMAN, CLIFTON   AN
PLANET ARCADIA, THE (ET IN ARCADIA EGO)
                          DISCH, THOMAS M.   SS   QRK 71 02
*GETTING INTO DEATH   DISCH, THOMAS M.   AC
PLANET CALLED CERVANTES, A KEITH, JOHN   SS   NWR 75 26
NEW WRITINGS IN SF. 26   BULMER, KENNETH   OA
PLANET ENTITY, THE (SEE SEEDLING OF MARS)
                          SMITH, CLARK ASHTON TC
PLANET FOR PLUNDER (SEE PLANETFALL)
                          CLEMENT, HAL   TC
PLANET FOR PLUNDERING, A WILLIAMSON, JACK   NA   GAL 62 04
TRIAL OF TERRA, THE   WILLIAMSON, JACK   NO
PLANET FOR SALE   NIELSEN, NIELS E. SS   64
BEST FROM THE REST OF THE WORLD, THE WOLLHEIM, DONALD A.   AN
PLANET FOR TRANSIENTS   DICK, PHILIP K.   SS   FUN 53 10
HANDFUL OF DARKNESS, A   DICK, PHILIP K.   AC
PLANET NAMED SHAYOL, A   SMITH, CORDWAINER NA   GAL 61 10
BEST OF CORDWAINER SMITH, THE   SMITH, CORDWAINER   AC
SPACE LORDS   SMITH, CORDWAINER   AC
SPECTRUM 4   AMIS & CONQUEST   AN
7TH ANNUAL OF THE YEAR'S BEST S-F, THE MERRIL, JUDITH   AN
PLANET OF DOOM (LILIES OF LIFE)
                          JAMESON, MALCOLM   SS   ASF 45 02
PLANET OF DOOM AND OTHER STORIES   ANONYMOUS   AN
PLANET OF DOUBT, THE   WEINBAUM, STANLEY G. NV ASF 35 10
MARTIAN ODYSSEY AND OTHER SCIENCE FICTION TALES, A
                                      WEINBAUM, STANLEY G.   AC
MARTIAN ODYSSEY AND OTHERS, A   WEINBAUM, STANLEY G.   AC
MORE ADVENTURES ON OTHER PLANETS   WOLLHEIM, DONALD A.   AN
TOMORROW'S WORLDS   SILVERBERG, ROBERT   AN
PLANET OF FORGETTING   SCHMITZ, JAMES H. NV   GAL 65 07
WORLD'S BEST SCIENCE FICTION: 1966   WOLLHEIM & CARR   AN
PLANET OF NEW MEN   WELLS, BASIL   SS
PLANETS OF ADVENTURE   WELLS, BASIL   AC
PLANET OF NO RETURN (QUESTION AND ANSWER)
                          ANDERSON, POUL   NO   ASF 54 06
WORLDS OF POUL ANDERSON, THE   ANDERSON, POUL   AC
PLANET OF SAND   LEINSTER, MURRAY   NV   FFM 48 02
GET OFF MY WORLD!   LEINSTER, MURRAY   AC
PLANET OF THE DOUBLE SUN JONES, NEIL R.   SS   AMZ 32 02
PLANET OF THE DOUBLE SUN   JONES, NEIL R.   AC
PLANET OF THE LOVE FEAST NUETZEL, CHARLES   SS
IMAGES OF TOMORROW   NUETZEL, CHARLES   AC
PLANET OF THE MIST   WELLS, BASIL   SS
DOORWAYS TO SPACE   WELLS, BASIL   AC
PLANET PASSAGE   WOLLHEIM, DONALD A. SS   FUT 42 10
FLIGHT INTO SPACE   WOLLHEIM, DONALD A.   AN
STORIES OF SCIENTIFIC IMAGINATION   GALLANT, JOSEPH   AN
PLANET STORY   WILHELM, KATE   SS   EPC 75
EPOCH   ELWOOD & SILVERBERG   OA
PLANET WRECKERS, THE   LAUMER, KEITH   NV   WOT 67 02
BEST OF KEITH LAUMER, THE   LAUMER, KEITH   AC
IT'S A MAD, MAD, MAD GALAXY   LAUMER, KEITH   AC
PLANETARY EFFULGENCE   RUSSELL, BERTRAND SS   61
8TH ANNUAL OF THE YEAR'S BEST S-F, THE MERRIL, JUDITH   AN
PLANETARY EXCHANGE   JONES, LEROI   PM   69
SPECULATIONS   SANDERS, THOMAS E.   AN
PLANETARY SURFACES AND INTERIORS
                          TOZER, D. C.   AR
BEYOND THIS HORIZON   CARRELL, CHRISTOPHER   OA
PLANETEER   SABERHAGEN, FRED   NV   GAL 61 04
BOOK OF SABERHAGEN, THE   SABERHAGEN, FRED   AC
PLANETFALL   BRUNNER, JOHN   SS   ASF 65 05
FROM THIS DAY FORWARD   BRUNNER, JOHN   AC
PLANETFALL (PLANET FOR PLUNDER)
                          CLEMENT, HAL   SN   SAT 57 02
STRANGE TOMORROWS   HOSKINS, ROBERT   AN
PLANETOID IDIOT   GOTLEIB, PHYLLIS   NV   FSF 67 05
TO THE STARS   SILVERBERG, ROBERT   AN
PLANETOID OF DOOM, THE   COLLADAY, MORRISON SS   WOS 32 12
*BIG BOOK OF SCIENCE FICTION   CONKLIN, GROFF   AN
PLANETS FOR SALE   HULL, E. MAYNE
                          AND VAN VOGT, A. E.   AC C FEL 54
VAN VOGT OMNIBUS, A   VAN VOGT, A. E.   AC
PLANNERS, THE   WILHELM, KATE   SS   ORB 68 03
BEST FROM ORBIT, THE   KNIGHT, DAMON   AN
BIO-FUTURES   SARGENT, PAMELA   AN
DOWNSTAIRS ROOM AND OTHER SPECULATIVE FICTION, THE
                                      WILHELM, KATE   AC
NEBULA AWARD STORIES NO. 4   ANDERSON, POUL   AN
ORBIT   3   KNIGHT, DAMON   OA
THOSE WHO CAN: A SCIENCE FICTION READER WILSON, ROBIN SCOTT   AN
PLANT REVOLT, THE   HAMILTON, EDMOND   SS   WRT 30 10
EARTH IN PERIL, THE   WOLLHEIM, DONALD A.   DA
PLANT WORLD, THE   VERNON, ROGER LEE SS
SPACE FRONTIERS, THE   VERNON, ROGER LEE   AC
PLANT-THING, THE   MACREADY, R. G.   SS   WRT 25 07
NIGHTMARE GARDEN   GHIDALIA, VIC   AN
PLANTING TIME   ADAMS, PETE
                          AND NIGHTINGALE, CHARLES SS C NEW 76 AN
ANTIGRAV: COSMIC COMEDIES   STRICK, PHILIP   AN
GALACTIC EMPIRES VOLUME ONE   ALDISS, BRIAN W.   AN
PLANTS MUST GROW   LONG, FRANK BELKNAP NV   TWS 41 10
JOHN CARSTAIRS: SPACE DETECTIVE   LONG, FRANK BELKNAP   AC

PLANTS MUST SLAY   LONG, FRANK BELKNAP SS   TWS 42 04
  JOHN CARSTAIRS: SPACE DETECTIVE LONG, FRANK BELKNAP   AC
  SAINT'S CHOICE OF IMPOSSIBLE CRIME, THE CHARTERIS, LESLIE   AN
PLANTS, THE   LEINSTER, MURRAY   SS   ASF 46 01
  *MEN AGAINST THE STARS   GREENBERG, MARTIN   AN
PLASTIC AGE, THE   GOLDSMITH, HOWARD   SS
  ADRIFT IN SPACE AND OTHER STORIES ELWOOD, ROGER   OA
PLATO'S STEPCHILDREN (MEYER DOLINSKY)
                          BLISH, JAMES   SA   STK 75 11
  STAR TREK 11   BLISH, JAMES   OC
PLATTNER STORY, THE   WELLS, H. G.   SS   NRV 96 04
  BEST SCIENCE FICTION STORIES OF H. G. WELLS
                          WELLS, H. G.   AC
  BEST STORIES OF H. G. WELLS WELLS, H. G.   AC
  COUNTRY OF THE BLIND, THE WELLS, H. G.   AC
  PLATTNER STORY AND OTHERS, THE WELLS, H. G.   AC
  SHORT STORIES OF H. G. WELLS, THE WELLS, H. G.   AC
  THIRTY STRANGE STORIES   WELLS, H. G.   AC
  TWENTY-EIGHT SCIENCE FICTION STORIES WELLS, H. G.   AC
PLATYPUS OF DOOM, THE   COVER, ARTHUR BYRON NV
  PLATYPUS OF DOOM AND OTHER NIHILISTS, THE
                          COVER, ARTHUR BYRON OC
PLAUSIBLE IMPROBABLE, THE WILHELM, KATE   SS   NEW 68 AC
  DOWNSTAIRS ROOM AND OTHER SPECULATIVE FICTION, THE
                          WILHELM, KATE   AC
PLAY IT AGAIN, SAM   BUSBY, F. M.   SS   CLR 73 03
  CLARION III   WILSON, ROBIN SCOTT OA
PLAY'S THE THING, A   HOYLE, FRED   SS
  ELEMENT 79   HOYLE, FRED   AC
PLAY'S THE THING, THE   BLOCH, ROBERT   SS   AHM 71 05
  COLD CHILLS   BLOCH, ROBERT   AC
PLAYBACK   CLARKE, ARTHUR C.   SS   PBY 66 12
  WIND FROM THE SUN, THE   CLARKE, ARTHUR C.   AC
PLAYBOY AND THE SLIME GOD, THE (SEE WHAT IS THIS THING
  CALLED LOVE?)   ASIMOV, ISAAC   TC
PLAYERS, THE   COLE, EVERETT B.   NV   ASF 55 04
  PHILOSOPHICAL CORPS, THE COLE, EVERETT B.   NO
PLAYFELLOW, THE   ASQUITH, CYNTHIA   NV   47
  LITTLE MONSTERS, THE   ELWOOD & GHIDALIA   AN
PLAYGROUND, THE   BRADBURY, RAY   SS   ESQ 53 10
  FAHRENHEIT 451   BRADBURY, RAY   AC
  ILLUSTRATED MAN, THE (BRITISH) BRADBURY, RAY   AC
  INTRODUCTORY PSYCHOLOGY THROUGH SCIENCE FICTION
                          KATZ/WARRICK/&   AN
  PORTALS OF TOMORROW   DERLETH, AUGUST   AN
  *TWISTED   CONKLIN, GROFF   AN
PLAYMATE   BUNCH, DAVID R.   SS   FAN 65 05
  MODERAN   BUNCH, DAVID R.   AC
PLAYMATE   CROUTCH, LESLIE A.   SS   IMG 51 11
  AUTHENTIC BOOK OF SPACE   CAMPBELL, H. J.   AN
  TALES BEYOND TIME   DE CAMP, L. S.&C.   AN
PLAYTHING   NIVEN, LARRY   SS   IFS 74 08
  BEST FROM IF, THE   VOLUME III BAEN, JAMES   AN
PLEASANT DREAMS   ROBIN, RALPH   SS   GAL 51 10
  OMNIBUS OF SCIENCE FICTION CONKLIN, GROFF   AN
  STRANGE TRAVELS IN SCIENCE FICTION CONKLIN, GROFF   AN
PLEASE GO 'WAY AND LET ME SLEEP
                          KASSON, HELEN W.   SS   WRT 45 03
  GHOUL KEEPERS, THE   MARGULIES, LEO   AN
PLEASE STAND BY   GOULART, RON   NV   FSF 62 01
  BEST FROM FANTASY AND SCIENCE FICTION: 12
                          DAVIDSON, AVRAM   AN
  CHAMELEON CORPS & OTHER SHAPE CHANGERS, THE
                          GOULART, RON   AC
  GHOST BREAKER   GOULART, RON   DC
PLEASURE GARDEN OF FELIPE SAGITTARIUS, THE
                          COLVIN, JAMES   SS   NWS 65 09
  BEST SF STORIES FROM NEW WORLDS NO. 2, THE
                          MOORCOCK, MICHAEL   AN
  DEEP FIX, THE   COLVIN, JAMES   AC
PLEASURE GARDEN OF FELIPE SAGITTARIUS, THE
                          MOORCOCK, MICHAEL   SS   NWS 65 09
  MODERN SCIENCE FICTION   SPINRAD, NORMAN   AN
  NEW TOMORROWS, THE   SPINRAD, NORMAN   AN
  TIME DWELLER, THE   MOORCOCK, MICHAEL   AC
PLEASURE OF OUR COMPANY, THE (ALSO AS THE PLEASURE OF
  THEIR COMPANY)   SILVERBERG, ROBERT   NV   INY 70 01
  INFINITY 1   HOSKINS, ROBERT   OA
PLEASURE OF THEIR COMPANY, THE (THE PLEASURE OF OUR COMPANY)
                          SILVERBERG, ROBERT   NV   INY 70 01
  MOONFERNS & STARSONGS   SILVERBERG, ROBERT   AC
PLEASURE SHARED, A   ALDISS, BRIAN W.   SS   SCF 65 06
  SALIVA TREE AND OTHER STRANGE GROWTHS, THE
                          ALDISS, BRIAN W.   AC
PLEASURE WAS OURS, THE   RUSSELL, RAY   SS   IMG 55 05
  SARDONICUS AND OTHER STORIES RUSSELL, RAY   AC
PLENITUDE   WORTHINGTON, WILL   SS   FSF 59 11
  AS TOMORROW BECOMES TODAY SULLIVAN, CHARLES W. AN
  HOT & COLD RUNNING CITIES MCHARGUE, GEORGESS   AN
  SF: THE BEST OF THE BEST MERRIL, JUDITH   AN
  5TH ANNUAL OF THE YEAR'S BEST S-F, THE MERRIL, JUDITH AN
PLIABLE ANIMAL, THE   HARRISON, HARRY   NV   SDM 62 09
  TWO TALES AND EIGHT TOMORROWS HARRISON, HARRY   AC
PLOT IS THE THING, THE   BLOCH, ROBERT   SS   FSF 66 07
  LIVING DEMONS, THE   BLOCH, ROBERT   AC
  NEW WORLDS OF FANTASY NO. 3 CARR, TERRY   AN
PLOT TO SAVE THE WORLD, THE BROWNSTEIN, MICHAEL SS PRV 70 48
  RUINS OF EARTH, THE   DISCH, THOMAS M.   AN
PLOT: THE TANGLED WEB   WILSON, ROBIN SCOTT SI
  THOSE WHO CAN: A SCIENCE FICTION READER WILSON, ROBIN SCOTT AN
PLOT, THE   HERZOG, TOM   SS   ROG 65
  INTRODUCTORY PSYCHOLOGY THROUGH SCIENCE FICTION
                          KATZ/WARRICK/&   AN
  11TH ANNUAL OF THE YEAR'S BEST S-F, THE MERRIL, JUDITH   AN
PLOTTING "JAMBOREE"   WILLIAMSON, JACK   AR
  THOSE WHO CAN: A SCIENCE FICTION READER WILSON, ROBIN SCOTT AN

PLUM DUFF   VAN DRESSER, PETER   SS   AMB 35 12
YEAR AFTER TOMORROW, THE DEL REY, L/MATSCHAT/ AN
PLUMROSE   GOULART, RON   SS   FAN 63 06
  ODD JOB NO. 101   GOULART, RON   AC
PLUS X   RUSSELL, ERIC FRANK NV   ASF 56 06
  FOUR FOR THE FUTURE   CONKLIN, GROFF   AN
PLUTONIAN DRUG, THE   SMITH, CLARK ASHTON SS   AMZ 34 09
  *OUTER REACHES, THE   DERLETH, AUGUST   AN
  STRANGE ECSTASIES   PARRY, MICHEL   AN
PLUTONIAN TERROR, THE   WILLIAMSON, JACK   SS   WRT 33 10
  EARLY WILLIAMSON, THE   WILLIAMSON, JACK   AC
POCKET FROM BROOKS BROTHERS, THE
                          DISCH, THOMAS M.   SS
  *GETTING INTO DEATH   DISCH, THOMAS M.   AC
POD AND THE BARRIER, THE STURGEON, THEODORE   NA   GAL 57 09
  STARSHINE   STURGEON, THEODORE   AC
  *TOUCH OF STRANGE, A   STURGEON, THEODORE   AC
POEM   NUTTALL, JEFF   PM   69
  HOLDING YOUR EIGHT HANDS LUCIE-SMITH, EDWARD AN
POEM AT A LUNAR ECLIPSE   HARDY, THOMAS   PM
  MOMENT OF ECLIPSE, THE   ALDISS, BRIAN W.   AC
POEM ROCKET   GINSBERG, ALLEN   PM   61
  SCIENCE FICTION: THE FUTURE ALLEN, DICK   AN
  SPECULATIONS   SANDERS, THOMAS E.   AN
POET IN THE HOLOGRAM IN THE MIDDLE OF PRIME TIME, THE
                          BRYANT, EDWARD   SS   NOV 72 02
  AMONG THE DEAD   BRYANT, EDWARD   AC
  FUTURE PASTIMES   EDELSTEIN, SCOTT   OA
  NOVA 2   HARRISON, HARRY   OA
POETESS AND THE 21 GRAY-HAIRED CADAVERS, THE
                          WOLLHEIM, DONALD A. SS
  TWO DOZEN DRAGON EGGS   WOLLHEIM, DONALD A. AC
POETRY   SANDERS, THOMAS E.   SI
  SPECULATIONS   SANDERS, THOMAS E.   AN
POETRY MACHINE, THE   NEARING, H. JR.   SS   FSF 50 FL
  SINISTER RESEARCHES OF C. P. RANSOM, THE NEARING, H. JR.   AC
POETS OF MILLGROVE IOWA, THE SLADEK, JOHN T.   SS   NWS 66 11
  BEST SF STORIES FROM NEW WORLDS NO. 2, THE
                          MOORCOCK, MICHAEL   AN
POGSMITH   ALDISS, BRIAN W.   SS   AUT 55 05
  SPACE, TIME AND NATHANIEL ALDISS, BRIAN W.   AC
POINT OF FOCUS   SILVERBERG, ROBERT   SS   ASF 58 08
  CALLIBRATED ALLIGATOR AND OTHER SCIENCE FICTION STORIES, THE
                          SILVERBERG, ROBERT   AC
  OUT OF THIS WORLD 7   WILLIAMS-ELLIS& OWEN AN
POINT OF HONOR, A (I'LL DO ANYTHING)
                          BEAUMONT, CHARLES   SS   MHT 55
  HUNGER AND OTHER STORIES, THE BEAUMONT, CHARLES   AC
POINT OF VIEW: THE QUICK-CHANGE ARTIST IN THE TYPE
                          WILSON, ROBIN SCOTT AR
  THOSE WHO CAN: A SCIENCE FICTION READER WILSON, ROBIN SCOTT AN
POINT OF VIEW: WHO'S MINDING THE STORE
                          WILSON, ROBIN SCOTT SI
  THOSE WHO CAN: A SCIENCE FICTION READER WILSON, ROBIN SCOTT AN
POINT OF VIEW, THE   WEINBAUM, STANLEY G. SS   WOS 36 01
  MARTIAN ODYSSEY AND OTHER SCIENCE FICTION TALES, A
                          WEINBAUM, STANLEY G. AC
  MARTIAN ODYSSEY AND OTHERS, A WEINBAUM, STANLEY G. AC
POISON BELT, THE   DOYLE, ARTHUR CONAN NO   HDS 13
  POISON BELT, THE   DOYLE, ARTHUR CONAN AC
POKER FACE   STURGEON, THEODORE   SS   ASF 41 03
  NOT WITHOUT SORCERY   STURGEON, THEODORE   AC
  WITHOUT SORCERY   STURGEON, THEODORE   AC
POLAR DOOM   COLERIDGE, JOHN   SS   SFQ 40 SU
  MOON CONQUERORS, THE   ANONYMOUS   AN
POLARIS OF THE SNOWS   STILSON, CHARLES B. NV   ASW 15 12
  UNDER THE MOONS OF MARS   MOSKOWITZ, SAM   AN
POLE, THE   SHELLEY, MARY W.   NV   CMG 32 08
  TALES AND STORIES   SHELLEY, MARY W.   AC
POLICE OPERATION   PIPER, H. BEAM   NV   ASF 48 07
  SPACE POLICE   NORTON, ANDRE   AN
POLICY (THE MADMAN FROM EARTH) LAUMER, KEITH   NV   IFS 62 03
  ENVOY TO NEW WORLDS   LAUMER, KEITH   AC
POLICY AND CUSTOM OF THE CAMIROI
                          LAFFERTY, R. A.   SS   GAL 67 06
  AMERICAN GOVERNMENT THROUGH SCIENCE FICTION
                          OLANDER/GREENBERG/& AN
  DARK STARS   SILVERBERG, ROBERT   AN
  NINE HUNDRED GRANDMOTHERS LAFFERTY, R. A.   AC
POLITENESS (TRIPLICATE TWISTEROO)
                          BROWN, FREDRIC   SS   PBY 57 03
  ANGELS AND SPACESHIPS   BROWN, FREDRIC   AC
POLITICAL MACHINE   JAKES, JOHN W.   SS   AMZ 61 03
  BEST OF JOHN JAKES, THE   JAKES, JOHN W.   AC
POLITICS   LEINSTER, MURRAY   NV   AMZ 32 06
  FUTURE TENSE   CURTIS, RICHARD   AN
  MASTERS' CHOICE   JANIFER, LAURENCE M. AN
POLITICS OF DARKNESS, THE DISCH, THOMAS M.   PM   SVW 73
  SAVING WORLDS   ELWOOD & KIDD   OA
POLLOCK AND THE PORROH MAN WELLS, H. G.   SS   NBG 95 05
  INEXPERIENCED GHOST AND NINE OTHER STORIES, THE
                          WELLS, H. G.   AC
  PLATTNER STORY AND OTHERS, THE WELLS, H. G.   AC
  SHORT STORIES OF H. G. WELLS, THE WELLS, H. G.   AC
  THIRTY STRANGE STORIES   WELLS, H. G.   AC
POLLY CHARMS, THE SLEEPING WOMAN
                          DAVIDSON, AVRAM   NV   FSF 75 02
  ENQUIRIES OF DOCTOR ESZTERHAZY, THE DAVIDSON, AVRAM   NO
POLONAISE   FOSTER, ALAN DEAN   SS
  BEYOND TIME   LEY, SANDRA   OA
POLYFILLA   MORGAN, EDWIN   PM
  BEYOND THIS HORIZON   CARRELL, CHRISTOPHER OA
POLYTROPICAL PARAMYTHS   FARMER, PHILIP JOSE AI
  BOOK OF PHILIP JOSE FARMER, THE FARMER, PHILIP JOSE AC
POND WATER   BRUNNER, JOHN   SS   FRS 68
  FARTHEST REACHES, THE   ELDER, JOSEPH   OA

POND, THE   KNEALE, NIGEL   SS   50
  CIRCUS OF DR. LAO AND OTHER IMPROBABLE STORIES
                                BRADBURY, RAY   AN
PONDERER, THE   RUSSELL, ERIC FRANK SS WRT 48 11
  DARK TIDES   RUSSELL, ERIC FRANK   AC
PONSONBY CASE, THE   PANGBORN, EDGAR   SS
  GOOD NEIGHBORS AND OTHER STRANGERS PANGBORN, EDGAR   AC
POOL OF THE BLACK ONE, THE   HOWARD, ROBERT E.   SS WRT 33 10
  CONAN THE ADVENTURER   HOWARD, R. & DE CAMP   AC
  SWORD OF CONAN, THE   HOWARD, ROBERT E.   AC
POOL, THE   SHARKEY, JACK   SS PBY 64 11
  FROM THE "S" FILE   PLAYBOY, EDITORS OF   AN
POOR LITTLE WARRIOR!   ALDISS, BRIAN W.   SS FSF 58 04
  ALPHA 1   SILVERBERG, ROBERT   AN
  BEST FROM FANTASY AND SCIENCE FICTION: 8
                                BOUCHER, ANTHONY   AN
  *BEST SCIENCE FICTION STORIES OF BRIAN W. ALDISS
                                ALDISS, BRIAN W.   AC
  NO TIME LIKE TOMORROW   ALDISS, BRIAN W.   AC
  PENGUIN SCIENCE FICTION   ALDISS, BRIAN W.   AN
  RUN TO STARLIGHT, SPORTS THROUGH SCIENCE FICTION
                                GREENBERG/OLANDER/&   AN
  SHOCKING THING, A   KNIGHT, DAMON   AN
POOR MAN, BEGGER MAN   RUSS, JOANNA   NV UNI 71 01
  NEBULA AWARD STORIES NO. 7   BIGGLE, LLOYD JR.   AN
  UNIVERSE 1   CARR, TERRY   OA
POOR PLANET   MCINTOSH, J. T.   NV FSF 64 08
  SEVEN TRIPS THROUGH TIME AND SPACE CONKLIN, GROFF   AN
POOR SUPERMAN (APPOINTMENT IN TOMORROW)
                                LEIBER, FRITZ   NV GAL 51 07
  BEST OF FRITZ LEIBER, THE   LEIBER, FRITZ   AC
  TOMORROW, THE STARS   HEINLEIN, ROBERT A.   AN
POP GOES THE WEASEL   HOSKINS, ROBERT   SS FSF 75 04
  BEST SCIENCE FICTION STORIES OF THE YEAR (1975)
                                DEL REY, LESTER   AN
POPPA NEEDS SHORTS   RICHMOND, LEIGH
                                AND RICHMOND, WALT SS C ASF 64 01
  ABOVE THE HUMAN LANDSCAPE   MCNELLY & STOVER   AN
  9TH ANNUAL OF THE YEAR'S BEST S-F, THE MERRIL, JUDITH   AN
POPPIN' FRESH   WEST, MICHAEL   SS
  CLARION SF   WILHELM, KATE   OA
POPULATION CONTROL, 1986   PAREDES, HORACIO V. SS ATS 70 04
  VOYAGES: SCENARIOS FOR A SHIP CALLED EARTH
                                SAUER, ROB   AN
POPULATION CRISIS: 2550   VERNON, ROGER LEE   SS
  SPACE FRONTIERS, THE   VERNON, ROGER LEE   AC
POPULATION IMPLOSION   OFFUTT, ANDREW J.   NV IFS 67 07
  AS TOMORROW BECOMES TODAY   SULLIVAN, CHARLES W.   AN
  WORLD'S BEST SCIENCE FICTION: 1968 WOLLHEIM & CARR   AN
POPULATION IMPLOSION, THE (PROBABILITY ZERO!)
                                COGSWELL, THEODORE R SS AMA 73
  BEST SCIENCE FICTION STORIES OF THE YEAR (1973)
                                DEL REY, LESTER   AN
PORK CHOP TREE, THE   SCHMITZ, JAMES H.   SS ASF 65 02
  PRIDE OF MONSTERS, A   SCHMITZ, JAMES H.   AC
PORTABLE PHONOGRAPH, THE   CLARK, WALTER VAN T. SS   41
  ADVENTURES IN TOMORROW   CROSSEN, KENDELL F.   AN
  ANOTHER TOMORROW   HOLLISTER, BERNARD C   AN
  ARMCHAIR SCIENCE READER, THE GORDON, I. & SORKIN   AN
  SPECULATIONS   SANDERS, THOMAS E.   AN
  TIMELESS STORIES FOR TODAY AND TOMORROW BRADBURY, RAY   AN
  TOMORROW AND TOMORROW   KNIGHT, DAMON   AN
  TRANSFORMATIONS II   ROSELLE, DANIEL   AN
PORTALS OF THE KING OF DAY, THE
                                LACH-SZYRMA, D. S.   SS CSL 88 01
  WORLDS APART   LOCKE, GEORGE   AN
PORTER OF HELL-GATE, THE   PUMILIA, JOSEPH F.   SS GEN 72
  GENERATION   GERROLD, DAVID   OA
PORTOBELLO ROAD, THE   SPARK, MURIEL   NV CMP 58
  7TH ANNUAL OF THE YEAR'S BEST S-F, THE MERRIL, JUDITH   AN
PORTRAIT IN MOONLIGHT   JACOBI, CARL   SS WRT 47 11
  PORTRAITS IN MOONLIGHT   JACOBI, CARL   AC
PORTRAIT OF THE ARTIST   HARRISON, HARRY   SS FSF 64 11
  *BEST OF HARRY HARRISON, THE HARRISON, HARRY   AC
  NEW DREAMS THIS MORNING   BLISH, JAMES   AN
  TWO TALES AND EIGHT TOMORROWS HARRISON, HARRY   AC
POSEIDON PROJECT   RACKHAM, JOHN   NA NWR 66 09
  NEW WRITINGS IN SF. 9   CARNELL, JOHN   OA
POSITIVE FEEDBACK   ANVIL, CHRISTOPHER   SS ASF 65 08
  ABOVE THE HUMAN LANDSCAPE   MCNELLY & STOVER   AN
  SOCIOLOGY THROUGH SCIENCE FICTION MILSTEAD/GREENBERG/& AN
POSSESSED, THE   BOUNDS, SYDNEY J.   SS NWR 73 21
  NEW WRITINGS IN SF. 21   CARNELL, JOHN   OA
POSSESSED, THE   CLARKE, ARTHUR C.   SS DSF 53 03
  GALACTIC EMPIRES VOLUME ONE   ALDISS, BRIAN W.   AN
  NINE BILLION NAMES OF GOD, THE CLARKE, ARTHUR C.   AC
  NOVELETS OF SCIENCE FICTION   HOWARD, IVAN   AN
  PRELUDE TO MARS   CLARKE, ARTHUR C.   AC
  REACH FOR TOMORROW   CLARKE, ARTHUR C.   AC
POSSIBLE CANDIDATE FOR THE PRESIDENCY, A (TIGER TAMER)
                                FINNEY, JACK   SS COL 52 05
  I LOVE GALESBURG IN THE SPRINGTIME FINNEY, JACK   AC
POSSIBLE EPISODE IN THE PICARESQUE ADVENTURES OF MR. J.H.B.
  MONSTROSEE, A   EMSHWILLER, CAROL   SS QRK 71 02
  QUARK/2   DELANY & HACKER   OA
POSSIBLE, THAT'S ALL!   CLARKE, ARTHUR C.   SS FSF 68 10
  FASTER THAN LIGHT   DANN & ZEBROWSKI   OA
POST-MORTEM PEOPLE, THE (ALSO AS BEYOND THE WEEDS)
                                TATE, PETER   SS NWS 66 03
  BEST SF STORIES FROM NEW WORLDS 3 MOORCOCK, MICHAEL   AN
  SEAGULLS UNDER GLASS AND OTHER STORIES TATE, PETER   AC
  THEMES IN SCIENCE FICTION   KELLEY, LEO P.   AN
POSTATOMIC   BUTTERWORTH, MICHAEL SS
  NEW S.F., THE   JONES, LANGDON   OA

POSTPAID TO PARADISE (POSTMARKED FOR PARADISE, IN FSF 50 WS)
                                ARTHUR, ROBERT   SS ARG 40 06
  BEST FROM FANTASY AND SCIENCE FICTION BOUCHER & MCCOMAS   AN
  GOLDEN ROAD, THE   KNIGHT, DAMON   AN
POSTPONED CURE, THE   NODVIK, STAN   SS VTX 74 06
  BEST SCIENCE FICTION STORIES OF THE YEAR (1974)
                                DEL REY, LESTER   AN
POSTSCRIPT TO "THE UNIVERSAL LIBRARY"
                                LEY, WILLY   AR
  FANTASIA MATHEMATICA   FADIMAN, CLIFTON   AN
POSTWAR AWAKENING, THE   SPINRAD, NORMAN   SI
  MODERN SCIENCE FICTION   SPINRAD, NORMAN   AN
POTENTIAL   MALCOLM, DONALD   NV NWR 65 05
  NEW WRITINGS IN SF. 5   CARNELL, JOHN   OA
POTENTIAL   SHECKLEY, ROBERT   SS ASF 53 11
  ASTOUNDING-ANALOG READER, THE VOLUME TWO HARRISON & ALDISS AN
  PORTALS OF TOMORROW   DERLETH, AUGUST   AN
  SHARDS OF SPACE   SHECKLEY, ROBERT   AC
POTENTIAL AND ACTUALITY IN SCIENCE FICTION
                                MCINTYRE, VONDA N.   AR
  NEBULA AWARD STORIES 11   LE GUIN, URSULA K.   AN
POTENTIAL ENEMY   REYNOLDS, MACK   SS OSF 54 02
  BEYOND THE STARS AND OTHER STORIES ANONYMOUS   AN
POTTAGE   HENDERSON, ZENNA   NV FSF 55 09
  BEST FROM FANTASY AND SCIENCE FICTION: 5
                                BOUCHER, ANTHONY   AN
  GREAT SCIENCE FICTION STORIES SMITH, CORDELIA T.   AN
  PILGRIMAGE: THE BOOK OF THE PEOPLE HENDERSON, ZENNA   AC
  SCHOOL AND SOCIETY THROUGH SCIENCE FICTION
                                OLANDER/GREENBERG/&   AN
  SF: THE YEAR'S GREATEST SCIENCE FICTION AND FANTASY
                                MERRIL, JUDITH   AN
POTTERS OF FIRSK, THE   VANCE, JACK   SS ASF 50 05
  TIME PROBE: THE SCIENCES IN SF. CLARKE, ARTHUR C.   AN
POUL ANDERSON   DICKSON, GORDON R.   AR FSF 71 04
  BEST FROM FANTASY AND SCIENCE FICTION, 25TH ANNIV.
                                FERMAN, EDWARD L.   AN
POUND OF CURE, A   DEL REY, LESTER   SS STR 53 02
  STAR SCIENCE FICTION STORIES NO. 2 POHL, FREDERIK   OA
POVERELLO   MOORE, RAYLYN   SS FTP 73
  FLAME TREE PLANET   ELWOOD, ROGER   OA
POWDER KEG   GUNN, JAMES E.   NV IFS 58 04
  STATION IN SPACE   GUNN, JAMES E.   AC
POWER AND THE GLORY, THE   DIFFIN, CHARLES W.   SS ASF 30 07
  HISTORY OF THE SCIENCE FICTION MAGAZINE, THE PART 1 1926-1935
                                ASHLEY, MICHAEL   AN
POWER AND THE GLORY, THE (THE MAN WHO WOULD NOT)
                                GUNN, JAMES E.   SS IFS 69 12
  BREAKING POINT   GUNN, JAMES E.   AC
POWER FOR THE DARN   WELLS, BASIL   SS FBK 50 06
  PLANETS OF ADVENTURE   WELLS, BASIL   AC
POWER OF EVERY ROOT, THE   DAVIDSON, AVRAM   NV FSF 67 10
  SF: AUTHORS' CHOICE 3   HARRISON, HARRY   AN
  STRANGE SEAS AND SHORES   DAVIDSON, AVRAM   AC
POWER OF POSITIVE THINKING, THE
                                WHITE, M. E.   SS NDR 64 18
  10TH ANNUAL OF THE YEAR'S BEST S-F, THE MERRIL, JUDITH   AN
POWER OF THE HYPERBOREA, THE (SEE THE THEFT OF THE
  THIRTY-NINE GIRDLES)   SMITH, CLARK ASHTON TC
POWER OF THE NAIL, THE   DELANY, SAMUEL R.
                                AND ELLISON, HARLAN SS C AMZ 68 11
  PARTNERS IN WONDER   ELLISON, HARLAN   AC
POWER OF THE PUPPETS, THE   LEIBER, FRITZ   SS TMY 41 FL
  SHADOWS WITH EYES   LEIBER, FRITZ   AC
POWER OF THE SENTENCE, THE   LOCKE, DAVID M.   SS FSF 71 04
  BEST SCIENCE FICTION STORIES OF THE YEAR (1971)
                                DEL REY, LESTER   AN
POWER OF TIME, THE   SAXTON, JOSEPHINE   NV NDM 71 01
  MORE WOMEN OF WONDER   SARGENT, PAMELA   AN
  NEW DIMENSIONS 1   SILVERBERG, ROBERT   OA
POWER PLANT   GREGOR, LEE   SS SFQ 41 WI
  INTO THE FOURTH DIMENSION   CUMMINGS, RAY   AN
POWER TO THE PEOPLE   POURNELLE, JERRY   SS ASF 72 08
  HIGH JUSTICE   POURNELLE, JERRY   AC
POWER, THE   LEINSTER, MURRAY   SS ASF 45 09
  HISTORY OF THE SCIENCE FICTION MAGAZINE, THE PART 2 1936-1945
                                ASHLEY, MICHAEL   AN
  LOOKING FORWARD   LESSER, MILTON   AN
  *OUTER REACHES, THE   DERLETH, AUGUST   AN
  SIDEWISE IN TIME   LEINSTER, MURRAY   AC
POWERHOUSE   BRADBURY, RAY   SS CHM 48 03
  *GOLDEN APPLES OF THE SUN   BRADBURY, RAY   AC
POWERS OF OBSERVATION, THE   HARRISON, HARRY   SS ASF 68 09
  ANALOG 8   CAMPBELL, JOHN W. JR   AN
  PRIME NUMBER   HARRISON, HARRY   AC
PRACTICAL JOKER, THE (CHUCK MENVILLE)
                                FOSTER, ALAN DEAN   SA SLG 76 06
  STAR TREK LOG SIX   FOSTER, ALAN DEAN   OC
PRAGMATIC SEED, THE   FAST, HOWARD   SS
  TOUCH OF INFINITY, A   FAST, HOWARD   OC
PRAISEWORTHY SAUR (SEE IF)   HARRISON, HARRY   TC
PRAYER FOR ONE'S ENEMY, A   ELLISON, HARLAN   NV CAD 66 03
  *LOVE AIN'T NOTHING BUT SEX MISSPELLED ELLISON, HARLAN   AC
PRECEDENT   SILVERBERG, ROBERT   NV ASF 57 12
  CALIBRATED ALLIGATOR AND OTHER SCIENCE FICTION STORIES, THE
                                SILVERBERG, ROBERT   AC
"PRECIPICES OF LIGHT THAT WENT FOREVER UP..."
                                ALDISS, BRIAN W.   SI
  SPACE OPERA   ALDISS, BRIAN W.   AN
PREDATORS   UTLEY, STEVEN   SS
  IDES OF TOMORROW, THE   CARR, TERRY   OA
PREFACE   MISC. MATERIAL   MS
  ABOVE THE HUMAN LANDSCAPE   MCNELLY & STOVER   AN
PREFACE   ALLEN, DICK   IN
  SCIENCE FICTION: THE FUTURE   ALLEN, DICK   AN

```
PREFACE                        ALLEN, DICK        IN C
  LOOKING AHEAD                           ALLEN, D. & L.       AN
PREFACE                        ALLEN, LORI        IN C
  LOOKING AHEAD                           ALLEN, D. & L.       AN
PREFACE                        AMIS, KINGSLEY     IN C
  SPECTRUM  4                             AMIS & CONQUEST      AN
PREFACE                        ASHLEY, MICHAEL    IN
  HISTORY OF THE SCIENCE FICTION MAGAZINE, THE  PART 1 1926-1935
                                          ASHLEY, MICHAEL      AN
  HISTORY OF THE SCIENCE FICTION MAGAZINE, THE  PART 2 1936-1945
                                          ASHLEY, MICHAEL      AN
  HISTORY OF THE SCIENCE FICTION MAGAZINE, THE  PART 3 1946-1955
                                          ASHLEY, MICHAEL      AN
  SOULS IN METAL                          ASHLEY, MICHAEL      AN
PREFACE                        BLISH, JAMES       IN
  ANYWHEN                                 BLISH, JAMES         AC
  BEST SCIENCE FICTION STORIES OF JAMES BLISH (REVISED)
                                          BLISH, JAMES         AC
  NEW DREAMS THIS MORNING                 BLISH, JAMES         AN
  STAR TREK   4                           BLISH, JAMES         OC
  STAR TREK   5                           BLISH, JAMES         OC
  STAR TREK   6                           BLISH, JAMES         OC
  STAR TREK   9                           BLISH, JAMES         OC
  STAR TREK  10                           BLISH, JAMES         OC
  STAR TREK  11                           BLISH, JAMES         OC
  THIRTEEN O'CLOCK AND OTHER ZERO HOURS   KORNBLUTH, C. M.     AC
PREFACE                        BRUNNER, JOHN      IN
  NOW THEN                                BRUNNER, JOHN        AC
PREFACE                        BURROUGHS, WILLIAM IN
  LOVE & NAPALM: EXPORT U.S.A.            BALLARD, J. G.       AC
PREFACE                        CAMPBELL, JOHN W. JR IN
  ANALOG 2                                CAMPBELL, JOHN W. JR AN
PREFACE                        CLARKE, ARTHUR C.  IN
  REACH FOR TOMORROW                      CLARKE, ARTHUR C.    AC
  TALES FROM THE WHITE HART               CLARKE, ARTHUR C.    AC
  WIND FROM THE SUN, THE                  CLARKE, ARTHUR C.    AC
PREFACE                        CONKLIN, GROFF     IN
  SEVEN COME INFINITY                     CONKLIN, GROFF       AN
PREFACE                        CONQUEST, ROBERT   IN C
  SPECTRUM  4                             AMIS & CONQUEST      AN
PREFACE                        DAVIDSON, AVRAM    IN
  STRANGE SEAS AND SHORES                 DAVIDSON, AVRAM      AC
PREFACE                        DEGRAEFF, ALLEN    IN
  HUMAN AND OTHER BEINGS                  DEGRAEFF, ALLEN      AN
PREFACE                        ELDER, JOSEPH      IN
  EROS IN ORBIT                           ELDER, JOSEPH        OA
PREFACE                        ELWOOD, ROGER      IN
  ANDROIDS, TIME MACHINES AND BLUE GIRAFFES
                                          ELWOOD & GHIDALIA    AN
  FRONTIERS 1: TOMORROW'S ALTERNATIVES    ELWOOD, ROGER        OA
  FRONTIERS 2: THE NEW MIND               ELWOOD, ROGER        OA
  FUTURE CITY                             ELWOOD, ROGER        OA
  MANY WORLDS OF BARRY MALZBERG, THE      MALZBERG, BARRY N.   AC
  TOMORROW: NEW WORLDS OF SCIENCE FICTION ELWOOD, ROGER        OA
PREFACE                        ENGDAHL, SYLVIA    IN
  UNIVERSE AHEAD                          ENGDAHL & ROBERSON   AN
PREFACE                        FARMER, PHILIP JOSE IN
  CURIOUS FRAGMENTS                       LONDON, JACK         AC
PREFACE                        FITZ GERALD, GREGORY IN C
  PAST, PRESENT, AND FUTURE PERFECT       WOLFE, J&FITZ GERALD AN
PREFACE                        GALLANT, JOSEPH    IN
  STORIES OF SCIENTIFIC IMAGINATION       GALLANT, JOSEPH      AN
PREFACE                        GINSBURG, MIRRA    IN
  ULTIMATE THRESHOLD, THE                 GINSBURG, MIRRA      AN
PREFACE                        GREENBERG , MARTIN IN
  COMING ATTRACTIONS                      GREENBERG , MARTIN   NF
PREFACE                        GREENBERG, MARTIN H. IN C
  AMERICAN GOVERNMENT THROUGH SCIENCE FICTION
                                          OLANDER/GREENBERG/&  AN
  ANTHROPOLOGY THROUGH SCIENCE FICTION    MASON, C/GREENBERG/& AN
  INTRODUCTORY PSYCHOLOGY THROUGH SCIENCE FICTION
                                          KATZ/WARRICK/&       AN
  NEW AWARENESS, THE                      WARRICK & GREENBERG  AN
  POLITICAL SCIENCE FICTION               GREENBERG& WARRICK   AN
PREFACE                        HARBOTTLE, PHILIP  IN
  BEST OF E. E. 'DOC' SMITH, THE          SMITH, EDWARD E. PHD AC
PREFACE                        HARRISON, WILLIAM  IN
  ROLLERBALL                              HARRISON, WILLIAM    AC
PREFACE                        HEINTZ, BONNIE L.  IN C
  TOMORROW, AND TOMORROW, AND TOMORROW... HEINTZ/HERBERT/JOOS/ AN
PREFACE                        HERBERT, FRANK     IN C
  TOMORROW, AND TOMORROW, AND TOMORROW... HEINTZ/HERBERT/JOOS/ AN
PREFACE                        HOOPER, WALTER     IN
  DARK TOWER AND OTHER STORIES, THE       LEWIS, C. S.         AC
PREFACE                        HUBBARD, L. RON    IN
  KINGSLAYER, THE                         HUBBARD, L. RON      AC
PREFACE                        JANIFER, LAURENCE M. IN
  MASTERS' CHOICE                         JANIFER, LAURENCE M. AN
PREFACE                        JOOS, DONALD A.    IN C
  TOMORROW, AND TOMORROW, AND TOMORROW... HEINTZ/HERBERT/JOOS/ AN
PREFACE                        KATZ, HARVEY A.    IN C
  INTRODUCTORY PSYCHOLOGY THROUGH SCIENCE FICTION
                                          KATZ/WARRICK/&       AN
PREFACE                        KELLEY, LEO P.     IN
  FANTASY: THE LITERATURE OF THE MARVELOUS KELLEY, LEO P.      AN
PREFACE                        MAGIDOFF, ROBERT   IN
  RUSSIAN SCIENCE FICTION, 1969           MAGIDOFF, ROBERT     AN
PREFACE                        MASON, CAROL       IN C
  ANTHROPOLOGY THROUGH SCIENCE FICTION    MASON, C/GREENBERG/& AN
PREFACE                        MCGEE, JANE AGORN  IN C
  TOMORROW, AND TOMORROW, AND TOMORROW... HEINTZ/HERBERT/JOOS/ AN
PREFACE                        MERRIL, JUDITH     IN
  *BEYOND HUMAN KEN                       MERRIL, JUDITH       AN
  SF: THE YEAR'S GREATEST SCIENCE FICTION AND FANTASY
                                          MERRIL, JUDITH       AN

PREFACE                        MOORCOCK, MICHAEL  IN
  NEW S.F., THE                           JONES, LANGDON       OA
PREFACE                        MOSKOWITZ, SAM     IN
  SCIENCE FICTION BY GASLIGHT             MOSKOWITZ, SAM       AN
  UNDER THE MOONS OF MARS                 MOSKOWITZ, SAM       AN
PREFACE                        MOWSHOWITZ, ABBE   IN
  INSIDE INFORMATION                      MOWSHOWITZ, ABBE     AN
PREFACE                        NORTON, ANDRE      IN
  SPACE PIONEERS                          NORTON, ANDRE        AN
PREFACE                        NUETZEL, CHARLES   IN
  IF THIS GOES ON                         NUETZEL, CHARLES     AN
PREFACE                        OLANDER, JOSEPH D. IN C
  AMERICAN GOVERNMENT THROUGH SCIENCE FICTION
                                          OLANDER/GREENBERG/&  AN
PREFACE                        PANSHIN, ALEXEI    IN
  FAREWELL TO YESTERDAY'S TOMORROW        PANSHIN, ALEXEI      AC
PREFACE                        PEARSON, MICHAEL   IN C
  TALES FROM THE GALAXIES                 WILLIAMS-ELLIS& P.   AN
PREFACE                        PLAYBOY, EDITORS OF IN
  DEAD ASTRONAUT, 10 STORIES OF SPACE FLIGHT, THE
                                          PLAYBOY, EDITORS OF  AN
  FIEND, THE                              PLAYBOY, EDITORS OF  AN
  FROM THE "S" FILE                       PLAYBOY, EDITORS OF  AN
  FULLY AUTOMATED LOVE LIFE OF HENRY KEANRIDGE
                                          PLAYBOY, EDITORS OF  AN
  LAST TRAIN TO LIMBO                     PLAYBOY, EDITORS OF  AN
  MASKS                                   PLAYBOY, EDITORS OF  AN
  PLAYBOY BOOK OF HORROR AND THE SUPERNATURAL, THE
                                          PLAYBOY, EDITORS OF  A
  PLAYBOY BOOK OF SCIENCE FICTION AND FANTASY, THE
                                          PLAYBOY, EDITORS OF  AN
  PLAYBOY'S STORIES OF THE SINISTER & STRANGE
                                          PLAYBOY, EDITORS OF  AN
  SAGITTARIUS                             RUSSELL, RAY         AC
  WEIRD SHOW                              PLAYBOY, EDITORS OF  AN
PREFACE                        POURNELLE, JERRY   IN
  2020 VISION                             POURNELLE, JERRY     AN
PREFACE                        REYNOLDS, MACK     IN
  SCIENCE-FICTION CARNIVAL (11 OF 13)     BROWN, F. & REYNOLDS AN
PREFACE                        SANDERS, THOMAS E. IN
  SPECULATIONS                            SANDERS, THOMAS E.   AN
PREFACE                        STADLER, JOHN      IN
  ECO-FICTION                             STADLER, JOHN        AN
PREFACE                        STURGEON, THEODORE IN
  NOT WITHOUT SORCERY                     STURGEON, THEODORE   AC
PREFACE                        SULLIVAN, CHARLES W. IN
  AS TOMORROW BECOMES TODAY               SULLIVAN, CHARLES W. AN
PREFACE                        SUVIN, DARKO       IN
  OTHER WORLDS, OTHER SEAS                SUVIN, DARKO         AN
PREFACE                        VONNEGUT, KURT JR. IN
  WELCOME TO THE MONKEY HOUSE             VONNEGUT, KURT JR.   AC
PREFACE                        WARRICK, PATRICIA S. IN C
  AMERICAN GOVERNMENT THROUGH SCIENCE FICTION
                                          OLANDER/GREENBERG/&  AN
  ANTHROPOLOGY THROUGH SCIENCE FICTION    MASON, C/GREENBERG/& AN
  INTRODUCTORY PSYCHOLOGY THROUGH SCIENCE FICTION
                                          KATZ/WARRICK/&       AN
  NEW AWARENESS, THE                      WARRICK & GREENBERG  AN
  POLITICAL SCIENCE FICTION               GREENBERG& WARRICK   AN
PREFACE                        WILLIAMS-ELLIS, A. IN C
  TALES FROM THE GALAXIES                 WILLIAMS-ELLIS& P.   AN
PREFACE                        WILSON, ROBIN SCOTT IN
  CLARION II                              WILSON, ROBIN SCOTT  OA
PREFACE                        WOLFE, JACK C.     IN C
  PAST, PRESENT, AND FUTURE PERFECT       WOLFE, J&FITZ GERALD AN
PREFACE TO THE COLLECTION      VANCE, JACK        IN
  BEST OF JACK VANCE, THE                 VANCE, JACK          AC
PREFACE: SOME AWARDS FOR STAR TREK- AND AN OPEN LETTER
                                          BLISH, JAMES         IN
  STAR TREK   3                           BLISH, JAMES         OC
PREHISTORIC PRODUCER, THE (SEE TYRANNOSAURUS REX)
                                          BRADBURY, RAY        TC
PRELIMINARY DATA               MOORCOCK, MICHAEL  SS  NWS 65 08
  FINAL PROGRAMME, THE                    MOORCOCK, MICHAEL    NO
PRELIMINARY INVESTIGATION OF AN EARLY MAN SITE IN THE DELAWARE
RIVER VALLEY                   O'LEARY, TIMOTHY J.
                               AND WARD, CHARLES W.  FA C
  APEMAN, SPACEMAN                        STOVER & HARRISON    AN
PRELIMINARY RESEARCH           VARSHAVSKY, ILYA   SS      65
  ULTIMATE THRESHOLD, THE                 GINSBURG, MIRRA      AN
PRELUDE TO A CRYSTAL SONG      MCCAFFREY, ANNE    NV  CTM 74 01
  CONTINUUM 1                             ELWOOD, ROGER        OA
PRELUDE TO A SYMPHONY OF UNBORN SHOUTS
                               GOLDIN, STEPHEN    SS  FCR 75
  FUTURE CORRUPTION                       ELWOOD, ROGER        OA
PRELUDE TO SPACE               CLARKE, ARTHUR C.  EX  GAN 51 03
  SCIENCE IN FICTION                      BAYLISS, A.E. & J.C. AN
PRELUDE TO SPACE               CLARKE, ARTHUR C.  NO  GAN 51 03
  ARTHUR C. CLARKE OMNIBUS, AN            CLARKE, ARTHUR C.    AC
  PRELUDE TO MARS                         CLARKE, ARTHUR C.    AC
PREMIER'S LADY, THE            SCORTIA, THOMAS N. SS  NEW 75 AC
  CAUTION! INFLAMMABLE!                   SCORTIA, THOMAS N.   AC
PREMUMBLE                      BRUNNER, JOHN      MS
  BOOK OF JOHN BRUNNER, THE               BRUNNER, JOHN        AC
PREPOSTEROUS                   BROWN, FREDRIC     SS  NEW 54 AC
  ANGELS AND SPACESHIPS                   BROWN, FREDRIC       AC
  IF THIS GOES ON                         NUETZEL, CHARLES     AN
  14 GREAT TALES OF ESP                   STONE, IDELLA P.     AN
PREROGATIVE                    BRUNNER, JOHN      SS  NWS 60 11
  NOT BEFORE TIME                         BRUNNER, JOHN        AC
  *OUT OF MY MIND                         BRUNNER, JOHN        AC
PRESCIENCE                     BOND, NELSON S.    SS  UNK 41 10
  UNKNOWN, THE                            BENSEN, D. R.        AN
PRESENT FOR PAT, A             DICK, PHILIP K.    SS  STS 54 01
  BOOK OF PHILIP K. DICK, THE             DICK, PHILIP K.      AC
```

PRESENT FROM BRUNSWICK, A (BARGAIN FROM BRUNSWICK)
                                WYNDHAM, JOHN   SS   FSF 51 06
  JIZZLE   WYNDHAM, JOHN   AC
  TALES OF GOOSEFLESH AND LAUGHTER WYNDHAM, JOHN   AC
PRESENT FROM JOE, A   RUSSELL, ERIC FRANK   SS   ASF 49 02
  BEST SF   CRISPIN, EDMUND   AN
  SCIENCE FICTION   BURTON, S. H.   AC
PRESERVING MACHINE, THE   DICK, PHILIP K.   SS   FSF 53 06
  HANDFUL OF DARKNESS, A   DICK, PHILIP K.   AC
  PRESERVING MACHINE, THE   DICK, PHILIP K.   AC
  SCIENCE FICTION BESTIARY, THE SILVERBERG, ROBERT   AN
PRESS CONFERENCE   DEFORD, MIRIAM ALLEN SS   STR 59 06
  STAR SCIENCE FICTION STORIES NO. 6   POHL, FREDERIK   OA
PRESS CONFERENCE (VISITOR FROM THE VOID)
                                WILSON, RICHARD   SS   AMZ 53 11
  FLYING SAUCERS IN FACT AND FICTION   SANTESSON, HANS S. AN
  THOSE IDIOTS FROM EARTH   WILSON, RICHARD   AC
PRESSURE   HARRISON, HARRY   SS   ASF 69 08
  ONE STEP FROM EARTH   HARRISON, HARRY   AC
  TOMORROW'S WORLDS   SILVERBERG, ROBERT   AN
PRESSURE   ROCKLYNNE, ROSS   SS   ASF 39 06
  *IMAGINATION UNLIMITED   BLEILER & DIKTY   AN
PRESSURE (BERSERKER'S PREY)   SABERHAGEN, FRED   SS   IFS 67 06
  BOOK OF SABERHAGEN, THE   SABERHAGEN, FRED   AC
PRESSURE OF TIME, THE   DISCH, THOMAS M.   NV   ORB 70 07
  ORBIT 7   KNIGHT, DAMON   OA
PRETTY MAGGIE MONEYEYES   ELLISON, HARLAN   NV   KNT 67 05
  BEST SF: 1967   HARRISON & ALDISS   AN
  DEATHBIRD STORIES   ELLISON, HARLAN   AC
  I HAVE NO MOUTH, AND I MUST SCREAM   ELLISON, HARLAN   AC
  *LOVE AIN'T NOTHING BUT SEX MISSPELLED   ELLISON, HARLAN AN
  NEBULA AWARD STORIES NO. 3   ZELAZNY, ROGER   AN
  SPECIAL WONDER   MCCOMAS, J. FRANCIS   AN
  THOSE WHO CAN: A SCIENCE FICTION READER   WILSON, ROBIN SCOTT AN
PREVIEW   LONG, FRANK BELKNAP SS   FUN 56 01
  RIM OF THE UNKNOWN   LONG, FRANK BELKNAP   AC
PREY   MATHESON, RICHARD   SS   PBY 69 04
  SHOCK WAVES   MATHESON, RICHARD   AC
  YEAR'S BEST HORROR STORIES, THE   DAVIS, RICHARD   AN
PREZ   GOULART, RON   SS   IFS 70 02
  BEST FROM IF, THE VOLUME I   IF, EDITORS OF   AN
  WHAT'S BECOME OF SCREWLOOSE? AND OTHER INQUIRIES
                                GOULART, RON   AC
PRICE OF A DEMON, THE   BRANDNER, GARY   SS   WTS 72 07
  YEAR'S BEST HORROR STORIES: SERIES II, THE
                                DAVIS, RICHARD   AN
PRICE OF A DRINK, A   BLISH, JAMES   SS   BER 74
  BERSERKERS, THE   ELWOOD, ROGER   OA
PRICE OF SIMERYL, THE   NEVILLE, KRIS   NV   ASF 66 12
  FAR-OUT PEOPLE, THE   HOSKINS, ROBERT   AN
PRICE, THE   FAST, HOWARD
  TOUCH OF INFINITY, A   FAST, HOWARD   OC
PRICE, THE (ALSO AS JUST DEAD ENOUGH)
                                BELCHER, C. DAVIS   NV   ORB 69 05
  ORBIT 5   KNIGHT, DAMON   OA
PRIDE   JAMESON, MALCOLM   SS   ASF 42 09
  *BEYOND HUMAN KEN   MERRIL, JUDITH   AN
PRIDE GOES-   BLOCH, ROBERT   SS   SMM 68 08
  CHAMBER OF HORRORS   BLOCH, ROBERT   AC
PRIDE IN THE PROFESSION   ELLISON, HARLAN   SS   ADM 66 08
  NO DOORS, NO WINDOWS (STORIES REWRITTEN) ELLISON, HARLAN AC
PRIDE OF CARROTS, A   NATHAN, ROBERT   NV   FSF 59 12
  SCIENCE FICTION ODDITIES   CONKLIN, GROFF   AN
PRIDE OF ISLANDS, A   MACAPP, C. C.   NV   IFS 60 05
  6 FINGERS OF TIME AND 5 OTHER SCIENCE FICTION NOVELETS, THE
                                ANONYMOUS   AN
PRIESTESS WHO REBELLED, THE (ALSO AS PILGRIMAGE)
                                BOND, NELSON S.   SS   AMZ 39 10
  WHEN WOMEN RULE   MOSKOWITZ, SAM   AN
PRIMA BELLADONNA   BALLARD, J. G.   SS   SCF 56 12
  BILLENIUM   BALLARD, J. G.   AC
  *FOUR-DIMENSIONAL NIGHTMARE, THE   BALLARD, J. G.   AC
  SF: THE BEST OF THE BEST   MERRIL, JUDITH   AN
  SF:57, THE YEAR'S GREATEST SCIENCE FICTION AND FANTASY
                                MERRIL, JUDITH   AN
  *VERMILLION SANDS   BALLARD, J. G.   AC
PRIMAL URGE, THE   ALDISS, BRIAN W.   SS
  BRIAN ALDISS OMNIBUS, A   ALDISS, BRIAN W.   AC
PRIMARY EDUCATION OF THE CAMIROI
                                LAFFERTY, R. A.   SS   GAL 66 12
  AS TOMORROW BECOMES TODAY   SULLIVAN, CHARLES W.   AN
  NINE HUNDRED GRANDMOTHERS   LAFFERTY, R. A.   AC
  SCHOOL AND SOCIETY THROUGH SCIENCE FICTION
                                OLANDER/GREENBERG/&   AN
  SF12   MERRIL, JUDITH   AN
  SOCIOLOGY THROUGH SCIENCE FICTION   MILSTEAD/GREENBERG/& AN
PRIMITIVES, THE   HERBERT, FRANK   NV   GAL 66 04
  BEST OF FRANK HERBERT, THE   HERBERT, FRANK   AC
  TENTH PLANET READER, THE   POHL, FREDERIK   AN
PRIME COMMANDMENT   SILVERBERG, ROBERT SS   SFS 58 01
  DIMENSION THIRTEEN   SILVERBERG, ROBERT   AC
PRIME OF LIFE, THE   ASIMOV, ISAAC   PM   FSF 66 10
  BICENTENNIAL MAN AND OTHER STORIES, THE ASIMOV, ISAAC   AC
PRIME-TIME TEASER   MCALLISTER, BRUCE SS   FSF 68 12
  TWENTY YEARS OF FANTASY & SCIENCE FICTION
                                FERMAN & MILLS   AN
PRINCE AND THE PIRATE, THE   LAUMER, KEITH   NV   IFS 64 08
  GALACTIC DIPLOMAT   LAUMER, KEITH   AC
PRINCE BORGIA'S MASS   DERLETH, AUGUST   SS   WRT 31 08
  NOT LONG FOR THIS WORLD   DERLETH, AUGUST   AC
PRINCE FERRIX AND PRINCESS CRYSTAL
                                LEM, STANISLAW   SS
  CYBERIAD, THE   LEM, STANISLAW   OC
PRINCESS IN THE TOWER 250,000 MILES HIGH, THE
                                LEIBER, FRITZ   SS   NDM 77 07
  NEW DIMENSIONS 7   SILVERBERG, ROBERT   OA

PRINCESS NO. 22   GOULART, RON   SS   FSF 62 05
  BROKE DOWN ENGINE AND OTHER TROUBLES WITH MACHINES
                                GOULART, RON   AC
PRINCESS OF MARS, A (EXCERPT FROM "UNDER THE MOONS OF MARS")
                                BURROUGHS, EDGAR R. EX   ASM 12 02
  MARS, WE LOVE YOU   HIPOLITO & MCNELLY   AN
PRINCESS OF MARS, A (UNDER THE MOONS OF MARS)
                                BURROUGHS, EDGAR R. NO   ASM 12 02
  PRINCESS OF MARS AND A FIGHTING MAN OF MARS, A
                                BURROUGHS, EDGAR R.   AC
PRINCESS' CARILLON, THE (THE ENCHANTED PRINCE)
                                DISCH, THOMAS M.   SS   FAN 63 08
  *ONE HUNDRED AND TWO H-BOMBS   DISCH, THOMAS M.   AC
  WHITE FANG GOES DINGO AND OTHER FUNNY S.F. STORIES
                                DISCH, THOMAS M.   AC
PRINTOUT   TOTAL EFFECT   IN
  SURVIVAL PRINTOUT   TOTAL EFFECT   AN
PRISON BREAK   DEFORD, MIRIAM ALLEN SS   FUN 59 07
  ELSEWHERE, ELSEWHEN, ELSEHOW   DEFORD, MIRIAM ALLEN   AC
  RULERS OF MEN   SANTESSON, HANS S.   AN
PRISON LEGEND (SEVEN DAYS TO LIVE)
                                FINNEY, JACK   NV   SEP 59 10
  I LOVE GALESBURG IN THE SPRINGTIME   FINNEY, JACK   AC
PRISON OF CLAY, PRISON OF STEEL
                                PLANCHAT, HENRY-LUC SS   ORB 75 16
  ORBIT 16   KNIGHT, DAMON   OA
PRISON RATS (AS GENE ELLERMAN) WELLS, BASIL   SS   FBK 48 04
  PLANETS OF ADVENTURE   WELLS, BASIL   AC
PRISON TRAP   RAYER, FRANCIS G.   SS   NWS 51 SU
  LAURIE'S SPACE ANNUAL   ANONYMOUS   AN
PRISONER OF LOVE   COGSWELL, THEODORE R SS   NEW 62 02
  WALL AROUND THE WORLD, THE   COGSWELL, THEODORE R AC
PRISONER OF THE CORAL DEEP (ABG 64 03)
                                BALLARD, J. G.   SS   NWS 65 05
  DAY OF FOREVER, THE   BALLARD, J. G.   AC
PRISONER, THE   ANVIL, CHRISTOPHER SS   ASF 56 02
  BEST SF 5   CRISPIN, EDMUND   AN
PRISONERS OF PARADISE   REDD, DAVID   SS   NWS 66 10
  NEW WORLDS QUARTERLY NO. 1   MOORCOCK, MICHAEL   OA
  SCIENCE FICTION   BRODKIN & PEARSON   AN
PRIVATE EYE   KUTTNER, HENRY   NV   ASF 49 01
  BEST SCIENCE-FICTION STORIES: 1950, THE BLEILER & DIKTY AN
  LIBERATED FUTURE: VOYAGES INTO TOMORROW, THE
                                HOSKINS, ROBERT   AN
PRIVATE EYE   PADGETT, LEWIS   NV   ASF 49 01
  LINE TO TOMORROW AND OTHER STORIES OF FANTASY AND SCIENCE
  FICTION   PADGETT, LEWIS   AC
  MIRROR OF INFINITY, THE   SILVERBERG, ROBERT   AN
  TOMORROW, AND TOMORROW, AND TOMORROW... HEINTZ/HERBERT/JOOS/ AN
PRIVATE EYE   KUTTNER, HENRY
                                AND MOORE, C. L.   NV C ASF 49 01
  SCIENCE FICTION INVENTIONS   KNIGHT, DAMON   AN
PRIVATE LITTLE WAR, A (D. INGALLS & G. RODDENBERRY)
                                BLISH, JAMES   SA   STK 74 10
  STAR TREK 10   BLISH, JAMES   OC
PRIVATE OR PRIVATEER?   WALSH, GEORGE E.   SS
  BATTLE FOR THE PACIFIC AND OTHER ADVENTURES AT SEA, THE
                                ANONYMOUS   AN
PRIVATE WAR OF PVT. JACOB, THE HALDEMAN, JOE W.   SS   GAL 74 06
  BEST FROM GALAXY, THE VOLUME III   BAEN, JAMES   AN
PRIVATE- KEEP OUT| MACDONALD, PHILIP   SS   FSF 49 FL
  TWENTY YEARS OF FANTASY & SCIENCE FICTION
                                FERMAN & MILLS   AN
  WORLD OF WONDER   PRATT, FLETCHER   AN
PRIZE FOR EDIE, A   BONE, J. F.   SS   ASF 61 04
  NEVER IN THIS WORLD   STONE, IDELLA P.   AN
  7TH ANNUAL OF THE YEAR'S BEST S-F, THE   MERRIL, JUDITH AN
PRIZE OF PERIL, THE   SHECKLEY, ROBERT   SS   FSF 58 05
  ROBERT SHECKLEY OMNIBUS, THE   SHECKLEY, ROBERT   AC
  SECOND ORBIT   DOHERTY, G. D.   AN
  SF: THE BEST OF THE BEST   MERRIL, JUDITH   AN
  SF:59, THE YEAR'S GREATEST SCIENCE FICTION AND FANTASY
                                MERRIL, JUDITH   AN
  SOCIAL PROBLEMS THROUGH SCIENCE FICTION   GREENBERG/MILSTEAD/& AN
  STORE OF INFINITY   SHECKLEY, ROBERT   AC
PRIZE OF WONDER, THE   HOSKINS, ROBERT   IN
  WONDERMAKERS   HOSKINS, ROBERT   AN
PRO, THE   HAMILTON, EDMOND   SS   FSF 64 10
  BEST OF EDMOND HAMILTON, THE   HAMILTON, EDMOND   AC
  GREAT SCIENCE FICTION STORIES ABOUT THE MOON
                                DIKTY, T. E.   AN
PROBABILITY STORM   REID, JULIA   NV   UNI 77 07
  UNIVERSE 7   CARR, TERRY   OA
PROBABILITY ZERO| THE POPULATION IMPLOSION
                                COGSWELL, THEODORE R SS   AMA 73
  ASTOUNDING   HARRISON, HARRY   OA
PROBABLE CAUSE   HARNESS, CHARLES L. NA   ORB 68 04
  ORBIT 4   KNIGHT, DAMON   OA
PROBABLE MAN, THE   BESTER, ALFRED   NV   ASF 41 07
  FUTURES TO INFINITY   MOSKOWITZ, SAM   AN
PROBLEM   NOURSE, ALAN E.   SS   GAL 56 10
  TIGER BY THE TAIL   NOURSE, ALAN E.   AC
PROBLEM CHILD   OLDALE, PETER   SS   VOT 70 06
  YEAR'S BEST HORROR STORIES, THE   DAVIS, RICHARD   AN
PROBLEM CHILD   PORGES, ARTHUR   SS   ASF 64 04
  10TH ANNUAL OF THE YEAR'S BEST S-F, THE MERRIL, JUDITH AN
PROBLEM FOR BIOGRAPHERS, A   LORD, MINDRET   SS   NEW 41 AN
  OTHER WORLDS, THE   STONG, PHILIP D.   AN
PROBLEM FOR EMMY   TOWNES, ROBERT S. SS   STS 52 06
  *SCIENCE FICTION THINKING MACHINES   CONKLIN, GROFF   AN
PROBLEM IN BIONICS, A   BARBET, PIERRE   SS   74
  BEST FROM THE REST OF THE WORLD, THE   WOLLHEIM, DONALD A. AN
PROBLEM IN MURDER   GOLD, H. L.   NV   ASF 39 03
  OLD DIE RICH AND OTHER SCIENCE FICTION, THE
                                GOLD, H. L.   AC

```
PROBLEM MAKERS, THE           HOSKINS, ROBERT      NV   GAL 63 08
  FAR-OUT PEOPLE, THE         HOSKINS, ROBERT                  AN
PROBLEM OF PAIN, THE          ANDERSON, POUL       NV   FSF 73 02
  BEST FROM FANTASY AND SCIENCE FICTION: 20
                              FERMAN, EDWARD L.                AN
  BEST SCIENCE FICTION STORIES OF THE YEAR (1973)
                              DEL REY, LESTER                  AN
  CHRONICLES OF A COMER AND OTHER RELIGIOUS SCIENCE FICTION
  STORIES                     ELWOOD, ROGER                    AN
PROBLEM OF SYMPATHY, THE      HARRISON, M. JOHN    BR   NWQ 72 04
  NEW WORLDS QUARTERLY NO. 4  MOORCOCK, MICHAEL                OA
PROBLEM ON BALAK              DEE, ROGER           SS   GAL 53 09
  GALAXY SCIENCE FICTION OMNIBUS   GOLD, H. L.                 AN
  SECOND GALAXY READER OF SCIENCE FICTION GOLD, H. L.          AN
PROBLEM PROFESSOR, THE (PROJECT SPACESHIP)
                              VAN VOGT, A. E.      SS   TWS 49 08
  PROXY INTELLIGENCE AND OTHER MIND BENDERS
                              VAN VOGT, A. E.                  AC
PROBLEM, A                    ANONYMOUS            PM   NYM 57 03
  FANTASIA MATHEMATICA        FADIMAN, CLIFTON                 AN
PROBLEM, THE                  BUNCH, DAVID R.      SS
  MODERAN                     BUNCH, DAVID R.                  AC
PROBLEMS                      SHIRAS, WILMAR H.    NV   NEW 53 AC
  CHILDREN OF THE ATOM        SHIRAS, WILMAR H.                AC
PROBLEMS OF CREATIVENESS      DISCH, THOMAS M.     SS   FSF 67 04
  BEST FROM FANTASY AND SCIENCE FICTION: 17
                              FERMAN, EDWARD L.                AN
PROCESS                       VAN VOGT, A. E.      SS   FSF 50 12
  BEST SCIENCE-FICTION STORIES: 1951, THE BLEILER & DIKTY     AN
  FAR-OUT WORLDS OF A. E. VAN VOGT, THE  VAN VOGT, A. E.      AC
  FRONTIERS IN SPACE          BLEILER & DIKTY                  AN
  MINDWORM, THE               ANONYMOUS                        AN
  WORLDS OF A. E. VAN VOGT, THE    VAN VOGT, A. E.             AC
PRODIGY                       STURGEON, THEODORE   SS   ASF 49 04
  CAVIAR                      STURGEON, THEODORE               AC
PRODUCT OF THE MASSES, THE    BRUNNER, JOHN        NV   IFS 68 04
  TIME-JUMP                   BRUNNER, JOHN                    AC
PRODUCTION PROBLEM            YOUNG, ROBERT F.     SS   FSF 59 06
  WORLDS OF ROBERT F. YOUNG, THE   YOUNG, ROBERT F.           AC
PRODUCTION TEST               JONES, RAYMOND F.    NV   ASF 49 10
  LOOKING FORWARD             LESSER, MILTON                   AN
PROFESSION                    ASIMOV, ISAAC        SN   ASF 57 07
  NINE TOMORROWS              ASIMOV, ISAAC                    AC
  SCHOOL AND SOCIETY THROUGH SCIENCE FICTION
                              OLANDER/GREENBERG/&              AN
PROFESSION (EDITED)           ASIMOV, ISAAC        SS   ASF 57 07
  YOU AND SCIENCE FICTION     HOLLISTER, BERNARD C             AN
PROFESSOR BERN'S AWAKENING    SAVCHENKO, VLADIMIR  SS
  SOVIET SCIENCE FICTION      ANONYMOUS                        AN
PROFESSOR HYDE                BERGER, THOMAS       SS   PBY 61 12
  FULLY AUTOMATED LOVE LIFE OF HENRY KEANRIDGE
                              PLAYBOY, EDITORS OF  AN
PROFESSOR JONKIN'S CANNIBAL PLANT
                              GARIS, HOWARD R.     SS   ARG 05 08
  SCIENCE FICTION BY GASLIGHT MOSKOWITZ, SAM                  AN
PROFESSOR PLAYS IT SQUARE, THE BLOCH, ROBERT       SS   ARG 57 09
  ATOMS AND EVIL              BLOCH, ROBERT                    AC
PROFESSOR WAS A THIEF, THE    HUBBARD, L. RON      NV   ASF 40 02
  *MY BEST SCIENCE FICTION STORY   MARGULIES & FRIEND         AN
PROFESSOR'S EXPERIMENT, THE   MITCHELL, EDWARD P.  SS   SUN 80 02
  CRYSTAL MAN, THE            MITCHELL, EDWARD P.              AC
PROFESSOR'S TEDDY-BEAR, THE   STURGEON, THEODORE   SS   WRT 48 03
  E PLURIBUS UNICORN          STURGEON, THEODORE               AC
  UNEXPECTED, THE             MARGULIES, LEO                   AC
PROFIT OF DOOM, THE           DIRAC, HUGH          NO        70
  SCIENCE FICTION SPECIAL 8   ANONYMOUS                        AN
PROGENY                       DICK, PHILIP K.      SS   IFS 54 11
  HANDFUL OF DARKNESS, A      DICK, PHILIP K.                  AC
  MARRIAGE AND THE FAMILY THROUGH SCIENCE FICTION
                              CLEAR/WARRICK/&                  AN
  SCHOOL AND SOCIETY THROUGH SCIENCE FICTION
                              OLANDER/GREENBERG/&              AN
PROGNOSIS: TERMINAL           MCDANIEL, DAVE       NV   NEW 74 AN
  2020 VISION                 POURNELLE, JERRY                 AN
PROGRAM NOTES                 GOLD, H. L.          IN
  THIRD GALAXY READER, THE    GOLD, H. L.                      AN
PROGRAMMED LOVE STORY         WATSON, IAN          SS   TRV 74
  BEST SF: 1974               HARRISON & ALDISS                AN
PROGRESS                      ANDERSON, POUL       NV   FSF 62 01
  HORN OF TIME, THE           ANDERSON, POUL                   AC
PROGRESSION OF THE SPECIES    ALDISS, BRIAN W.     PM   PRP 67 SP
  BEST SF: 1969               HARRISON & ALDISS                AN
  HOLDING YOUR EIGHT HANDS    LUCIE-SMITH, EDWARD              AN
PROJECT                       PADGETT, LEWIS       SS   ASF 47 04
  OPERATION FUTURE            CONKLIN, GROFF                   AN
PROJECT AMNION                EISENBERG, LARRY     NV   VSF 69 08
  BEST LAID SCHEMES, THE      EISENBERG, LARRY                 AC
PROJECT BARRIER               GALOUYE, DANIEL F.   SS   FUN 58 01
  PROJECT BARRIER             GALOUYE, DANIEL F.               AC
PROJECT D                     STEPHENS, FRANCES    SS   SPC 74 02
  SPACE  2                    DAVIS, RICHARD                   OA
PROJECT EXCELSIOR (ASYLUM SATELLITE)
                              PRATT, FLETCHER      NO   TWS 51 10
  DOUBLE IN SPACE             PRATT, FLETCHER                  AC
PROJECT HUSH                  TENN, WILLIAM        SS   GAL 54 02
  ABC OF SCIENCE FICTION, AN  BOARDMAN, TOM JR.                AN
  FIFTY SHORT SCIENCE FICTION TALES   ASIMOV & CONKLIN        AN
  HUMAN ANGLE, THE            TENN, WILLIAM                    AC
PROJECT INHUMANE              MALEC, ALEXANDER B.  SS   COQ 64 02
  EXTRAPOLASIS                MALEC, ALEXANDER B.              AC
  11TH ANNUAL OF THE YEAR'S BEST S-F, THE  MERRIL, JUDITH     AN
PROJECT MASTODON              SIMAK, CLIFFORD D.   NV   GAL 55 03
  *ALL THE TRAPS OF EARTH AND OTHER STORIES SIMAK, CLIFFORD D. AC
  NIGHT OF THE PUUDLY, THE    SIMAK, CLIFFORD D.               AC
PROJECT NIGHTMARE             HEINLEIN, ROBERT A.  NV   AMZ 53 05
  MENACE FROM EARTH, THE      HEINLEIN, ROBERT A.              AC

  14 GREAT TALES OF ESP       STONE, IDELLA P.                 AN
PROJECT NURSEMAID             MERRIL, JUDITH       SN   FSF 55 10
  DAUGHTERS OF EARTH          MERRIL, JUDITH                   AC
  SIX GREAT SHORT SCIENCE FICTION NOVELS  CONKLIN, GROFF      AN
PROJECT OCEAN FLOOR           ELAM, RICHARD M. JR. SS
  TEEN-AGE SCIENCE FICTION STORIES   ELAM, RICHARD M. JR.     AC
PROJECT- SPACESHIP (ALSO AS THE PROBLEM PROFESSOR)
                              VAN VOGT, A. E.      NV   TWS 49 08
  *MY BEST SCIENCE FICTION STORY   MARGULIES & FRIEND         AN
PROJECTION, A                 WHITTEMORE, REED     PM        67
  SCIENCE FICTION             BRODKIN & PEARSON                AN
PROLOG                        MCKNIGHT, JOHN P.    SS   FSF 51 08
  FIFTY SHORT SCIENCE FICTION TALES   ASIMOV & CONKLIN        AN
PROLOGUE                      ANDERSON, POUL       IN
  TALES OF THE FLYING MOUNTAINS    ANDERSON, POUL             AC
PROLOGUE                      DICKSON, GORDON R.   MS
  THREE TO DORSAI!            DICKSON, GORDON R.               AC
PROLOGUE                      HOSKINS, ROBERT      MS
  FIRST STEP OUTWARD          HOSKINS, ROBERT                  AN
PROLOGUE                      INOUYE, JON          IN
  NIGHT TIDE, A               INOUYE, JON                      OC
PROLOGUE                      MERRIL, JUDITH       IN
  SURVIVAL SHIP AND OTHER STORIES   MERRIL, JUDITH            AC
PROLOGUE                      SMITH, CORDWAINER    MS
  SPACE LORDS                 SMITH, CORDWAINER                AC
PROLOGUE TO "THE SILKIE"      VAN VOGT, A. E.      EX   IFS 64 07
  BEST OF A. E. VAN VOGT, THE VAN VOGT, A. E.                 AC
PROLOGUE TO ANALOG            CAMPBELL, JOHN W. JR AN  DBL 62
  ANALOG ANTHOLOGY            CAMPBELL, JOHN W. JR AN
PROLOGUE TO...AN ANALOGUE     RICHMOND, LEIGH      NV   ASF 61 06
  ANALOG 1                    CAMPBELL, JOHN W. JR AN
PROLOGUE TO...AN ANALOGUE     RICHMOND, LEIGH
                          AND RICHMOND, WALT       NV C ASF 61 06
  POSITIVE CHARGE             RICHMOND, W. & L.                DC
PROLOGUE: THE ILLUSTRATED MAN BRADBURY, RAY        SS   NEW 51 AC
  *ILLUSTRATED MAN, THE       BRADBURY, RAY                    AC
PROMETHEUS                    FARMER, PHILIP JOSE  NV   FSF 61 03
  DOWN IN THE BLACK GANG AND OTHER STORIES FARMER, PHILIP JOSE AC
  OTHER WORLDS, OTHER GODS    MOHS, MAYO                       AN
  SPECIAL WONDER              MCCOMAS, J. FRANCIS              AN
PROMETHEUS REBOUND            GALOUYE, DANIEL F.   NV   YRT 70
  YEAR 2000, THE              HARRISON, HARRY                  AN
PROMINANT AUTHOR              DICK, PHILIP K.      SS   IFS 54 05
  HANDFUL OF DARKNESS, A      DICK, PHILIP K.                  AC
PROMISED LAND                 MOORE, C. L.         NV   ASF 50 02
  JUDGEMENT NIGHT             MOORE, C. L.                     AC
PROMISED LAND, THE            RANDALL, ROBERT      NV   ASF 56 08
  SHROUDED PLANET, THE        RANDALL, ROBERT                  AC
PROMISED PLANET               YOUNG, ROBERT F.     SS   IFS 55 12
  WORLDS OF ROBERT F. YOUNG, THE   YOUNG, ROBERT F.           AC
PROMISES OF LAUGHTER          ELLISON, HARLAN      SS   ADM 69 11
  NO DOORS, NO WINDOWS (STORIES REWRITTEN) ELLISON, HARLAN    AC
PROMISES TO KEEP: A SCIENCE FICTION DRAMA
                              NOLAN, WILLIAM F.    SS   NEW 74 AC
  ALIEN HORIZONS              NOLAN, WILLIAM F.                AC
PRONE                         REYNOLDS, MACK       SS   FSF 54 09
  BEST OF MACK REYNOLDS, THE  REYNOLDS, MACK                   AC
  WORLDS OF WONDER            HARRISON, HARRY                  AN
  13 ABOVE THE NIGHT          CONKLIN, GROFF                   AN
PRONUNCIATION KEY             MISC. MATERIAL       MS
  SCIENCE FACT/FICTION        FARRELL/GAGE/&                   AN
PROOF                         CLEMENT, HAL         SS   ASF 42 06
  *POSSIBLE WORLDS OF SCIENCE FICTION   CONKLIN, GROFF        AN
  SF: AUTHORS' CHOICE 2       HARRISON, HARRY                  AN
  WHERE DO WE GO FROM HERE?   ASIMOV, ISAAC                    AN
PROOF                         WRIGHT, S. FOWLER    SS
  NEW GODS LEAD, THE          WRIGHT, S. FOWLER                AC
PROOF OF THE PUDDING          SHECKLEY, ROBERT     SS   GAL 52 08
  GALAXY OF GHOULS            MERRIL, JUDITH                   AN
  PEOPLE TRAP AND OTHER PITFALLS, THE   SHECKLEY, ROBERT      AC
PROOF POSITIVE                MALEC, ALEXANDER B.  SS
  EXTRAPOLASIS                MALEC, ALEXANDER B.              AC
PROOF POSITIVE (HRP 47 10)    GREENE, GRAHAM       SS   FSF 52 08
  DECADE OF FANTASY AND SCIENCE FICTION, A MILLS, ROBERT P.   AN
PROOF WAS IN DRINKWATER'S PUDDING, THE
                              CONRAD, EARL         SS
  DA VINCI MACHINE, THE       CONRAD, EARL                     OC
PROPAGANDIST                  LEINSTER, MURRAY     SS   ASF 47 08
  GREAT STORIES OF SPACE TRAVEL   CONKLIN, GROFF              AN
  *POSSIBLE WORLDS OF SCIENCE FICTION   CONKLIN, GROFF        AN
  STORIES OF SCIENTIFIC IMAGINATION   GALLANT, JOSEPH         AN
PROPER SANTA CLAUS, A         MCCAFFREY, ANNE      SS   DEM 73
  DEMON KIND                  ELWOOD, ROGER                    OA
  GET OFF THE UNICORN         MCCAFFREY, ANNE                  AC
PROPER SPIRIT, THE            BLOCH, ROBERT        SS   FSF 57 03
  NIGHTMARES                  BLOCH, ROBERT                    AC
  PLEASANT DREAMS             BLOCH, ROBERT                    AC
PROPER STUDY, THE             ASIMOV, ISAAC        SS   BLF 68 09
  BUY JUPITER AND OTHER STORIES   ASIMOV, ISAAC               AC
PROPER STUDY, THE             HOLLY, JOAN C.       SS
  LONG NIGHT OF WAITING AND OTHER STORIES ELWOOD, ROGER       OA
PROPERTY OF VENUS (SEE GRATITUDE)
                              DE CAMP, L. SPRAGUE  TC
PROPHECY OF MONSTERS, A (SEE MONSTERS IN THE NIGHT)
                              SMITH, CLARK ASHTON  TC
PROPHET OF ZORAYNE, THE       DIXON, TERRY         SS   STG 74
  STRANGE GODS                ELWOOD, ROGER                    AN
PROPHET WITHOUT HONOR         KERSH, GERALD        SS
  ON AN ODD NOTE              KERSH, GERALD                    AC
PROPHET, THE                  CHRISTOPHER, JOHN    SS   NWS 53 03
  TWENTY-SECOND CENTURY, THE  CHRISTOPHER, JOHN                AC
PROPHETS OF DOOM              GERNSBACK, HUGO      AR
  SCIENCE FICTION ROLL OF HONOR, THE   POHL, FREDERICK        AN
PROPOSAL                      DE CAMP, L. SPRAGUE  SS   STS 52 11
  SF: AUTHORS' CHOICE         HARRISON, HARRY                  AN
  SPRAGUE DE CAMP'S NEW ANTHOLOGY   DE CAMP, L. SPRAGUE       AC
```

PROSPECTOR'S SPECIAL   PURPLE PILEUS, THE

PROSPECTOR'S SPECIAL   SHECKLEY, ROBERT   NV   GAL 59 12
  SHARDS OF SPACE   SHECKLEY, ROBERT   AC
PROSPECTS FOR GENETIC ENGINEERING IN MAN
                              SIMNETT, JOHN   AR
  BEYOND THIS HORIZON   CARRELL, CHRISTOPHER OA
PROTECT ME FROM MY FRIENDS   BRUNNER, JOHN   SS   FSF 62 11
  BEST SF 7   CRISPIN, EDMUND   AN
  NO FUTURE IN IT   BRUNNER, JOHN   AC
PROTECTED SPECIES   FYFE, H. B.   SS   ASF 51 03
  *ASTOUNDING SCIENCE FICTION ANTHOLOGY, THE
                              CAMPBELL, JOHN W. JR AN
  ASTOUNDING TALES OF SPACE AND TIME CAMPBELL, JOHN W. JR AN
  GALACTIC EMPIRES VOLUME ONE   ALDISS, BRIAN W.   AN
  SCIENCE FICTION   BURTON, S. H.   AN
  *SECOND ASTOUNDING SCIENCE FICTION ANTHOLOGY, THE
                              CAMPBELL, JOHN W. JR AN
  YET MORE PENGUIN SCIENCE FICTION ALDISS, BRIAN W.   AN
PROTECTION   SHECKLEY, ROBERT   SS   GAL 56 04
  PILGRIMAGE TO EARTH   SHECKLEY, ROBERT   AC
  THIRD GALAXY READER, THE   GOLD, H. L.   AN
PROTECTIVE CAMOUFLAGE   DEVET, CHARLES V.   NV   SFS 55 05
  RARE SCIENCE FICTION   HOWARD, IVAN   AN
PROTECTIVE MIMICRY (SEE THE FRIGHTENED TREE)
                              BUDRYS, ALGIS   TC
PROTECTIVE TEMPORAL STRIKE   GIANNATTASIO, GERARD SS   NOV 74 04
  NOVA 4   HARRISON, HARRY   OA
PROTEST (SEE CRUMBLING HOLLYWOOD MANSION, CRUMBLING
  HOLLYWOOD MAN)   TATE, PETER   TC
PROTEST NOTE (THE DESERT AND THE STARS)
                              LAUMER, KEITH   NV   IFS 62 11
  GALACTIC DIPLOMAT   LAUMER, KEITH   AC
PROTEUS ISLAND   WEINBAUM, STANLEY G. SN   ASF 36 08
  BEST OF STANLEY G. WEINBAUM, THE WEINBAUM, STANLEY G.   AC
  MARTIAN ODYSSEY AND OTHER SCIENCE FICTION TALES, A
                              WEINBAUM, STANLEY G.   AC
  MARTIAN ODYSSEY, A   WEINBAUM, STANLEY G.   AC
  RED PERI, THE   WEINBAUM, STANLEY G.   AC
PROTOCOL (THE YLLIAN WAY)   LAUMER, KEITH   NV   IFS 62 01
  ENVOY TO NEW WORLDS   LAUMER, KEITH   AC
PROTOCOLS OF THE ELDERS OF BRITAIN, THE
                              BRUNNER, JOHN   SS
  STOPWATCH   HAY, GEORGE   OA
  1976 ANNUAL WORLD'S BEST SF, THE WOLLHEIM, DONALD A.   AN
PROTOPLASMA   DERLETH, AUGUST   SS
  HARRIGAN'S FILE   DERLETH, AUGUST   AC
PROTOTAPH   LAUMER, KEITH   SS   ASF 66 03
  ANALOG 6   CAMPBELL, JOHN W. JR AN
  ONCE THERE WAS A GIANT   LAUMER, KEITH   AC
PROTT   ST. CLAIR, MARGARET   SS   GAL 53 01
  BEST SF   CRISPIN, EDMUND   AN
  SCIENCE FICTION TERROR TALES   CONKLIN, GROFF   AN
PROUD ROBOT, THE   KUTTNER, HENRY   NV   ASF 43 10
  BEST OF HENRY KUTTNER 1, THE   KUTTNER, HENRY   AC
  BEST OF HENRY KUTTNER, THE   KUTTNER, HENRY   AC
  RETURN TO OTHERNESS   KUTTNER, HENRY   AC
PROUD ROBOT, THE   PADGETT, LEWIS   NV   ASF 43 10
  *ADVENTURES IN TIME AND SPACE   HEALY & MCCOMAS   AN
  MORE ADVENTURES IN TIME AND SPACE HEALY & MCCOMAS   AN
  ROBOTS HAVE NO TAILS   PADGETT, LEWIS   AC
PROUST SYNDROME, THE   GOLDSMITH, HOWARD   SS
  CRISIS   ELWOOD, ROGER   OA
PROVING GROUND, THE   GANSOVSKY, SEVER   SS
  VIEW FROM ANOTHER SHORE   ROTTENSTEINER, FRANZ AN
PROWLER IN THE CITY AT THE EDGE OF THE WORLD, THE
                              ELLISON, HARLAN   NV   DVS 67 01
  DANGEROUS VISIONS   ELLISON, HARLAN   OA
  OVER THE EDGE   ELLISON, HARLAN   AC
  PARTNERS IN WONDER   ELLISON, HARLAN   AC
PROWLER OF THE WASTELANDS   VINCENT, HARL   SS   ASF 35 04
  STRANGE SIGNPOSTS   ELWOOD & MOSKOWITZ   AN
PROXIES, THE   SELLINGS, ARTHUR   SS   IFS 55 10
  *TIME TRANSFER   SELLINGS, ARTHUR   AC
PROXIMA CENTAURI   LEINSTER, MURRAY   SN   ASF 35 03
  BEFORE THE GOLDEN AGE   ASIMOV, ISAAC   AN
  MONSTERS AND SUCH   LEINSTER, MURRAY   AC
  SIDEWISE IN TIME   LEINSTER, MURRAY   AC
PROXY HEAD, THE   BLOCH, ROBERT   SS   SFP 53 05
  HUMAN ZERO, THE   MOSKOWITZ & ELWOOD   AN
PROXY INTELLIGENCE, THE   VAN VOGT, A. E.   SN   IFS 68 10
  BEST OF A. E. VAN VOGT, THE   VAN VOGT, A. E.   AC
  BEST OF A. E. VAN VOGT, THE (BRITISH) VAN VOGT, A. E.   AC
  PROXY INTELLIGENCE AND OTHER MIND BENDERS
                              VAN VOGT, A. E.   AC
PSALM   DEL REY, LESTER   PM   FUN 60 02
  6TH ANNUAL OF THE YEAR'S BEST S-F, THE MERRIL, JUDITH   AN
PSI CLONE   HOLLY, J. HUNTER   NA
  FUTURELOVE   ELWOOD, ROGER   OA
PSI-HIGH   NOURSE, ALAN E.   NV
  PSI-HIGH AND OTHERS   NOURSE, ALAN E.   AC
PSI-MAN (PSI-MAN HEAL MY CHILD)
                              DICK, PHILIP K.   NV   IMT 55 11
  BOOK OF PHILIP K. DICK, THE   DICK, PHILIP K.   AC
PSY FY PSYCHOLOGY AND SCIENCE FICTION
                              KIRBY, RICHARD
                              AND RADFORD, JOHN   AR C
  BEYOND THIS HORIZON   CARRELL, CHRISTOPHER OA
PSYCHEDELIC CHILDREN, THE   KOONTZ, DEAN R.   SS   FSF 68 07
  SOFT COME THE DRAGONS   KOONTZ, DEAN R.   DC
PSYCHEDELIC FLIGHT   RAY, ROBERT   SS   GEN 72
  GENERATION   GERROLD, DAVID   OA
"PSYCHO"-LOGICAL BLOCH   MOSKOWITZ, SAM   AR   AMZ 62 12
  BOGEY MEN   BLOCH, ROBERT   AC
PSYCHOLOGICAL SHIPWRECK, A (1893)
                              BIERCE, AMBROSE   SS   93
  FUTURE PERFECT   FRANKLIN, H. BRUCE   AN

PSYCHOLOGIST WHO WOULDN'T DO AWFUL THINGS TO RATS, THE
                              TIPTREE, JAMES JR.   NV   NDM 76 06
  BEST SCIENCE FICTION OF THE YEAR, THE NO. 6
                              CARR, TERRY   AN
  NEW DIMENSIONS 6   SILVERBERG, ROBERT   OA
PSYCHOMORPH   GROSSER, E. A.   SS   UNK 40 02
  FROM UNKNOWN WORLDS   CAMPBELL, JOHN W. JR AN
PSYCHOPHONIC NURSE, THE   KELLER, DAVID H. MD. SS   AMZ 28 11
  GREAT SCIENCE FICTION ABOUT DOCTORS CONKLIN, G&FABRICANT AN
  TALES FROM UNDERWOOD   KELLER, DAVID H. MD.   AC
PSYCHOSMOSIS   MASSON, DAVID I.   SS   NWS 66 03
  CALTRAPS OF TIME, THE   MASSON, DAVID I.   AC
  DARK STARS   SILVERBERG, ROBERT   AN
  ENGLAND SWINGS SF   MERRIL, JUDITH   AN
  SPACE-TIME JOURNAL, THE   MERRIL, JUDITH   AN
PSYCHOSOMATICA   EKLUND, GORDON   NV
  CRISIS   ELWOOD, ROGER   OA
PSYCLOPS   ALDISS, BRIAN W.   SS   NWS 56 07
  *BEST SCIENCE FICTION STORIES OF BRIAN W. ALDISS
                              ALDISS, BRIAN W.   AC
  BEST SF 4   CRISPIN, EDMUND   AN
  MIND TO MIND   SILVERBERG, ROBERT   AN
  NO TIME LIKE TOMORROW   ALDISS, BRIAN W.   AC
  SPACE, TIME AND NATHANIEL   ALDISS, BRIAN W.   AC
PUBLIC EYE   BOUCHER, ANTHONY   SS   TWS 52 04
  SPACE, TIME & CRIME   DEFORD, MIRIAM ALLEN AN
PUBLIC HATING, THE   ALLEN, STEVE   SS   BBM 55 01
  SF: THE BEST OF THE BEST   MERRIL, JUDITH   AN
  SF: THE YEAR'S GREATEST SCIENCE FICTION AND FANTASY
                              MERRIL, JUDITH   AN
  SOCIAL PROBLEMS THROUGH SCIENCE FICTION GREENBERG/MILSTEAD/& AN
PUBLIC LOVES A JOHNNY, THE   NOLAN, WILLIAM F.   SS   NEW 63 AC
  IMPACT-20   NOLAN, WILLIAM F.   AC
PUBLIC SERVICE   BOUNDS, SYDNEY J.   SS   NWR 68 13
  NEW WRITINGS IN SF. 13   CARNELL, JOHN   OA
PUBLICITY CAMPAIGN   CLARKE, ARTHUR C.   SS   SAT 56 10
  OTHER SIDE OF THE SKY, THE   CLARKE, ARTHUR C.   AC
PUBLISH AND PERISH   THOMAS, JOHN B.   SS   IFS 68 06
  SCHOOL AND SOCIETY THROUGH SCIENCE FICTION
                              OLANDER/GREENBERG/& AN
PUDDLE   ESCHER, M. C.   IL
  SCIENCE FICTION   BRODKIN & PEARSON   AN
PUDDLE ON THE FLOOR   LAFFERTY, R. A.   SS
  NEW CONSTELLATIONS   DISCH & NAYLOR   OA
PUFF-BALL MENACE, THE   WYNDHAM, JOHN   NV   TOW 38 SU
  WANDERERS OF TIME   WYNDHAM, JOHN   AC
PUGILIST, THE   ANDERSON, POUL   NV   FSF 73 11
  2020 VISION   POURNELLE, JERRY   AN
PULP ARTISTS, THE   MISC. MATERIAL   IL
  FANTASTIC PULPS, THE   HAINING, PETER   AN
PUMPERNICKEL, THE   BRADBURY, RAY   SS   COL 51 05
  LONG AFTER MIDNIGHT   BRADBURY, RAY   AC
PUN IN ORBIT   SCHENCK, HILBERT JR. PM   NEW 62 AN
  MATHEMATICAL MAGPIE, THE   FADIMAN, CLIFTON   AN
PUNCH   POHL, FREDERIK   SS   PBY 62 06
  ABOMINABLE EARTHMAN, THE   POHL, FREDERIK   AC
  BEST OF FREDERIK POHL, THE   POHL, FREDERIK   AC
  FULLY AUTOMATED LOVE LIFE OF HENRY KEANRIDGE
                              PLAYBOY, EDITORS OF AN
  PLAYBOY BOOK OF SCIENCE FICTION AND FANTASY, THE
                              PLAYBOY, EDITORS OF AN
  SCIENCE FICTION ODDITIES   CONKLIN, GROFF   AN
PUNCHLINE (STOP ME BEFORE I TELL MORE)
                              THURSTON, ROBERT   SS   ORB 71 09
  CLARION II   WILSON, ROBIN SCOTT OA
PUNISHMENT TO FIT THE CRIMES, A
                              GORDON, RICHARD M.   SS   62
  FIEND IN YOU, THE   BEAUMONT, CHARLES   AN
PUNISHMENT WITHOUT CRIME   BRADBURY, RAY   SS   OWS 50 03
  LONG AFTER MIDNIGHT   BRADBURY, RAY   AC
  SCIENCE FICTION TERROR TALES   CONKLIN, GROFF   AN
  TOMORROW MIDNIGHT   BRADBURY, RAY   AC
PUNKY AND THE YALE MAN   ELLISON, HARLAN   NV   KNT 66 01
  *LOVE AIN'T NOTHING BUT SEX MISSPELLED ELLISON, HARLAN   AC
PUPA KNOWS BEST (SEE HELP)   TIPTREE, JAMES JR.   TC
PUPPET MASTERS, THE   HEINLEIN, ROBERT A.   NO   GAL 51 09
  THREE BY HEINLEIN   HEINLEIN, ROBERT A.   AC
PUPPET SHOW   BROWN, FREDRIC   SS   PBY 62 11
  BEST OF FREDRIC BROWN, THE   BROWN, FREDRIC   AC
  LAST TRAIN TO LIMBO   PLAYBOY, EDITORS OF AN
  PARADOX LOST, AND 12 OTHER GREAT S.F. STORIES
                              BROWN, FREDRIC   AC
  PLAYBOY BOOK OF SCIENCE FICTION AND FANTASY, THE
                              PLAYBOY, EDITORS OF AN
  SCIENCE FACT/FICTION   FARRELL/GAGE/&   AN
  SPECIAL WONDER   MCCOMAS, J. FRANCIS   AN
  TALES OF TIME AND SPACE   OLNEY, ROSS R.   AN
  THEMES IN SCIENCE FICTION   KELLEY, LEO P.   AN
  8TH ANNUAL OF THE YEAR'S BEST S-F, THE MERRIL, JUDITH   AN
PURITAN PASSIONS (FEATHERTOP)   HAWTHORNE, NATHANIEL SS ITM 52 02
  GHOULS   HAINING, PETER   AN
PURLOINED BUTTER, THE   SLADEK, JOHN T.   SS   NWQ 72 03
  NEW WORLDS QUARTERLY NO. 3   MOORCOCK, MICHAEL   OA
PURPLE CHILD, THE   BELAVAL, EMILIO S.   SS   66
  VOYAGES: SCENARIOS FOR A SHIP CALLED EARTH
                              SAUER, ROB   AN
PURPLE FIELDS, THE   CRANE, ROBERT   SS   STR 53 02
  STAR SCIENCE FICTION STORIES NO. 2 POHL, FREDERIK   OA
PURPLE MUMMY, THE   DNIEPROV, ANATOLY   SS
  PATH INTO THE UNKNOWN   ANONYMOUS   AN
PURPLE PILEUS, THE   WELLS, H. G.   SS   BAW 96 12
  BEST SCIENCE FICTION STORIES OF H. G. WELLS
                              WELLS, H. G.   AC
  COUNTRY OF THE BLIND, THE   WELLS, H. G.   AC
  INEXPERIENCED GHOST AND NINE OTHER STORIES, THE
                              WELLS, H. G.   AC

PLATTNER STORY AND OTHERS, THE   WELLS, H. G.   AC
  SHORT STORIES OF H. G. WELLS, THE   WELLS, H. G.   AC
  THIRTY STRANGE STORIES   WELLS, H. G.   AC
PURPLE PRIESTESS OF THE MAD MOON
                                        BRACKETT, LEIGH   SS FSF 64 10
  COMING OF THE TERRANS, THE   BRACKETT, LEIGH   NO
PURPLE SAPPHIRE, THE   TAINE, JOHN   NO DUT 24
  THREE SCIENCE FICTION NOVELS   TAINE, JOHN   AC
PURPLE TERROR, THE   WHITE, FRED M.   SS SND 99 09
  SCIENCE FICTION BY GASLIGHT   MOSKOWITZ, SAM   AN
PURPLE TESTAMENT, THE   SERLING, ROD   SA
  ROD SERLING'S TWILIGHT ZONE REVISITED SERLING, ROD   OC
PURPOSE (SEE THE CITY)   BRADBURY, RAY   TC
PURPOSE OF LIFE, THE   HOWARD, HAYDEN   NV GAL 67 04
  ESKIMO INVASION   HOWARD, HAYDEN   NO
PURPOSE, THE   VAN VOGT, A. E.   NV ASF 45 05
  FAR-OUT WORLDS OF A. E. VAN VOGT, THE VAN VOGT, A. E.   AC
  WORLDS OF A. E. VAN VOGT, THE   VAN VOGT, A. E.   AC
PURSE OF FORTUNATUS, THE   CARROLL, LEWIS   SS   89
  MATHEMATICAL MAGPIE, THE   FADIMAN, CLIFTON   AN
PURSUERS, THE   WANDREI, DONALD   SS
  EYE AND THE FINGER   WANDREI, DONALD   AC
PURSUIT   DEL REY, LESTER   NA SSF 52 05
  GODS AND GOLEMS   DEL REY, LESTER   AC
PUSH NO MORE   SILVERBERG, ROBERT NV NEW 72 AN
  STRANGE BED FELLOWS   SCORTIA, THOMAS N.   AN
  UNFAMILIAR TERRITORY   SILVERBERG, ROBERT   AN
PUSH OF A FINGER, THE   BESTER, ALFRED   NV ASF 42 05
  ASTOUNDING-ANALOG READER, THE VOLUME ONE HARRISON & ALDISS   AN
PUSH-BUTTON PASSION (CARELESS LOVE)
                                        FRIBORG, ALBERT C. SS FSF 54 07
  5 TALES FROM TOMORROW   DIKTY, T. E.   AN
PUSHBUTTON WAR   MARTINO, JOSEPH P. SS ASF 60 08
  PROLOGUE TO ANALOG   CAMPBELL, JOHN W. JR   AN
PUSHOVER PLANET   PEDERSEN, CON   SS FSF 63 06
  OUT OF THIS WORLD 5   WILLIAMS-ELLIS & OWEN   AN
PUT THEM ALL TOGETHER, THEY SPELL MONSTER
                                        RUSSELL, RAY   SS PBY 56 10
  FULLY AUTOMATED LOVE LIFE OF HENRY KEANRIDGE
                                        PLAYBOY, EDITORS OF AN
  SF:57, THE YEAR'S GREATEST SCIENCE FICTION AND FANTASY
                                        MERRIL, JUDITH   AN
PUTZI   BEMELMANS, LUDWIG   SS   39
  TIMELESS STORIES FOR TODAY AND TOMORROW BRADBURY, RAY   AN
PUZZLE FOR SPACEMEN   BRUNNER, JOHN   SS NWS 55 12
  NO FUTURE IN IT   BRUNNER, JOHN   AC
  SPECIAL WONDER   MCCOMAS, J. FRANCIS   AN
PYGMALION'S SPECTACLES   WEINBAUM, STANLEY G. SS WOS 35 06
  BEST OF STANLEY G. WEINBAUM, THE   WEINBAUM, STANLEY G.   AC
  MARTIAN ODYSSEY AND OTHER SCIENCE FICTION TALES, A
                                        WEINBAUM, STANLEY G.   AC
  MARTIAN ODYSSEY AND OTHERS, A   WEINBAUM, STANLEY G.   AC
PYM MAKES HIS POINT   HOYLE, FRED   SS
  ELEMENT 79   HOYLE, FRED   AC
PYRAMID   ABERNATHY, ROBERT   NV ASF 54 07
  ANTHROPOLOGY THROUGH SCIENCE FICTION MASON, C/GREENBERG/&   AN
  ASTOUNDING-ANALOG READER, THE VOLUME TWO HARRISON & ALDISS   AN
  MORE PENGUIN SCIENCE FICTION   ALDISS, BRIAN W.   AN
PYRAMID IN THE DESERT, THE (AND BE MERRY)
                                        MACLEAN, KATHERINE SS ASF 50 02
  DIPLOIDS AND OTHER FLIGHTS OF FANCY, THE MACLEAN, KATHERINE AC
PYRAMID PROJECT, THE (THE SPHINX)
                                        YOUNG, ROBERT F.   NV AMZ 64 06
  GLASS OF STARS, A   YOUNG, ROBERT F.   AC
PYRAMIDS FOR MINNESOTA: A SERIOUS PROPOSAL
                                        DISCH, THOMAS M.   FA HRP 74 01
  NEW IMPROVED SUN, THE   DISCH, THOMAS M.   AN
PYTHAGORAS AND THE PSYCHOANALYST
                                        KOESTLER, ARTHUR   SS   43
  FANTASIA MATHEMATICA   FADIMAN, CLIFTON   AN
PYTHIAS   POHL, FREDERIK   SS GAL 55 02
  ALTERNATING CURRENTS   POHL, FREDERIK   AC
Q.U.R.   BOUCHER, ANTHONY   SS ASF 43 03
  *ADVENTURES IN TIME AND SPACE   HEALY & MCCOMAS   AN
  COMPLEAT WEREWOLF, THE   BOUCHER, ANTHONY   AC
QRM   WILSON, RICHARD   SS FSF 57 04
  TIME OUT FOR TOMORROW   WILSON, RICHARD   AC
QRM—INTERPLANETARY   SMITH, GEORGE O.   NV ASF 42 10
  COMPLETE VENUS EQUILATERAL, THE   SMITH, GEORGE O.   AC
  FUTURE TENSE   CURTIS, RICHARD   AN
  VENUS EQUILATERAL   SMITH, GEORGE O.   AC
QUADRIOPTICON, THE   BEAUMONT, CHARLES   SS FSF 54 08
  YONDER   BEAUMONT, CHARLES   AC
QUADS FROM MARS   GREER, WILLIAM W.   SS BLF
  BOYS' LIFE BOOK OF OUTER SPACE STORIES, THE
                                        BOY'S LIFE, ED. OF AN
QUAKE, QUAKE, QUAKE (EXCERPT) DEHN, PAUL   PM   61
  7TH ANNUAL OF THE YEAR'S BEST S-F, THE MERRIL, JUDITH   AN
QUAKE, QUAKE, QUAKE (EXCERPT) GOREY, EDWARD   IL   61
  7TH ANNUAL OF THE YEAR'S BEST S-F, THE MERRIL, JUDITH   AN
QUAKER CANNON, THE   KORNBLUTH, C. M.
                                        AND POHL, FREDERIK NV C ASF 61 08
  WONDER EFFECT, THE   POHL, F. & KORNBLUTH AC
  7TH ANNUAL OF THE YEAR'S BEST S-F, THE MERRIL, JUDITH   AN
QUALITY OF MERCY, THE   ASHE, TAMSIN   SS TVW 73
  TWO VIEWS OF WONDER   SCORTIA & YARBRO   OA
QUALITY OF MERCY, THE   KEYES, DANIEL   NV IFS 60 11
  FROZEN PLANET AND 4 OTHER SF NOVELLAS, THE
                                        ANONYMOUS   AN
QUALITY OF THE PRODUCT, THE   NEVILLE, KRIS
                                        AND NEVILLE, LIL   SS C SVW 73
  SAVING WORLDS   ELWOOD & KIDD   OA
QUARANTINE   PISERCHIA, DORIS   SS GAL 73 09
  BEST FROM GALAXY, THE VOLUME II   GALAXY, EDITORS OF   AN
QUARANTINE WORLD   LEINSTER, MURRAY   SN ASF 66 11
  S.O.S. FROM THREE WORLDS   LEINSTER, MURRAY   AC

QUARRY, THE   DICKSON, GORDON R. SS ASF 58 09
  DANGER— HUMAN   DICKSON, GORDON R.   AC
QUE DONN'REZ VOUS? (WHAT'LL YOU GIVE?)
                                        ANDERSON, POUL   NV ASF 63 04
  TALES OF THE FLYING MOUNTAINS   ANDERSON, POUL   AC
QUEEN LIES DYING, THE   HOUSTON, LIBBY   PM NWB 75 08
  NEW WORLDS EIGHT   BAILEY, HILARY   OA
QUEEN OF AIR AND DARKNESS, THE ANDERSON, POUL   SN FSF 71 04
  BEST FROM FANTASY AND SCIENCE FICTION, 25TH ANNIV.
                                        FERMAN, EDWARD L.   AN
  BEST SCIENCE FICTION OF THE YEAR, THE CARR, TERRY   AN
  MANY WORLDS OF POUL ANDERSON, THE   ANDERSON, POUL   AC
  NEBULA AWARD STORIES NO. 7   BIGGLE, LLOYD JR.   AN
QUEEN OF AIR AND DARKNESS AND OTHER STORIES, THE
                                        ANDERSON, POUL   AC
QUEEN OF BEAUTY, OR THE PLANET OF LOVE, THE
                                        LACH-SZYRMA, D. S. SS CSL 87 08
  WORLDS APART   LOCKE, GEORGE   AN
QUEEN OF CALIFORNIA, THE (1510, TRANSLATION AND NOTES BY
  EDWARD EVERETT HALE)   MONTALVO, GARCIA O. NV
  WHEN WOMEN RULE   MOSKOWITZ, SAM   AN
QUEEN OF PIG ISLAND, THE (MISTRESS OF PORCOSITO)
                                        KERSH, GERALD   SS PBY 57 07
  NIGHTSHADE & DAMNATIONS   KERSH, GERALD   AC
  ON AN ODD NOTE   KERSH, GERALD   AC
QUEEN OF SLEEP, THE   EMSHWILLER, CAROL   SS NDR
  JOY IN OUR CAUSE   EMSHWILLER, CAROL   AC
QUEEN OF THE BLACK COAST   HOWARD, ROBERT E.   SS WRT 34 05
  COMING OF CONAN, THE   HOWARD, ROBERT E.   AC
QUEEN'S ASTROLOGER, THE   LEINSTER, MURRAY   SS TWS 49 10
  CROSSROADS IN TIME   CONKLIN, GROFF   AN
QUEEN'S MESSENGER, THE   MCGUIRE, JOHN J.   SS ASF 57 05
  BEST SCIENCE FICTION STORIES AND NOVELS: 9TH SERIES
                                        DIKTY, T. E.   AN
QUEEN'S OWN EVADERS, THE (SEE THE ANTHEM SPRINTERS)
                                        BRADBURY, RAY   TC
QUEER ONES, THE (ALSO AS THE OTHER PEOPLE)
                                        BRACKETT, LEIGH   NV VSF 57 03
  BEST OF LEIGH BRACKETT, THE   BRACKETT, LEIGH   AC
  GENTLE INVADERS   SANTESSON, HANS S.   AN
QUEST   HARDING, LEE   SS NWS 63 04
  LAMBDA I AND OTHER STORIES   CARNELL, JOHN   AN
QUEST FOR SAINT AQUIN, THE   BOUCHER, ANTHONY   SS NTS 51
  BEST SF 5   CRISPIN, EDMUND   AN
  NEW TALES OF SPACE AND TIME   HEALY, RAYMOND J.   OA
  ONE HUNDRED YEARS OF SCIENCE FICTION KNIGHT, DAMON   AN
  OTHER WORLDS, OTHER GODS   MOHS, MAYO   AN
  SCIENCE FICTION HALL OF FAME VOLUME 1 SILVERBERG, ROBERT   AN
  WORLDS OF SCIENCE FICTION, THE   MILLS, ROBERT P.   AN
QUEST FOR THE FUTURE   VAN VOGT, A. E.   NO ACE 70
  SCIENCE FICTION SPECIAL 8   ANONYMOUS   AN
QUEST OF THE IMMORTAL, THE (BUCCANEER OF THE STAR SEAS)
                                        REPP, ED EARL   SS PLS 40 FL
  STELLAR MISSILES, THE   REPP, ED EARL   AC
QUEST OF THE VEIL   DEWEESE, EUGENE   NV
  SHANADU   BRINEY, ROBERT E.   OA
QUEST OF THIG   WELLS, BASIL   SS PLS 42 FL
  BEST OF PLANET STORIES NO. 1, THE   BRACKETT, LEIGH   AN
  PLANETS OF ADVENTURE   WELLS, BASIL   AC
QUESTION AND ANSWER (SEE PLANET OF NO RETURN)
                                        ANDERSON, POUL   TC
QUESTION MARK ON A SEESAW   STEINBERG, SAUL   CT NYM 60 07
  MATHEMATICAL MAGPIE, THE   FADIMAN, CLIFTON   AN
QUESTION OF E.D.D., A   WRIGHT, S. FOWLER   SS
  WITCHFINDER, THE   WRIGHT, S. FOWLER   AC
QUESTION OF ETIQUETTE, A   BLOCH, ROBERT   SS WRT 42 09
  BLOCH AND BRADBURY   BRADBURY & BLOCH   AC
  WEIRD TALES   MARGULIES, LEO   AN
QUESTION OF GUILT, A   CLEMENT, HAL   NV NEW 76 AN
  YEAR'S BEST HORROR STORIES: SERIES IV, THE
                                        PAGE, GERALD W.   AN
QUESTION OF RE-ENTRY, A   BALLARD, J. G.   NV FAN 63 03
  BEST OF J. G. BALLARD, THE   BALLARD, J. G.   AC
  PASSPORT TO ETERNITY   BALLARD, J. G.   AC
  TERMINAL BEACH (BRITISH VERSION)   BALLARD, J. G.   AC
QUESTION OF RESIDENCE, A (VENTURE TO THE MOON)
                                        CLARKE, ARTHUR C.   SS FSF 57 02
  OTHER SIDE OF THE SKY, THE   CLARKE, ARTHUR C.   AC
QUESTION OF SLANT, A   O'DONNELL, K. M.   SS
  IN THE POCKET AND OTHER S-F STORIES   O'DONNELL, K. M.   DC
QUESTION OF TIME, A   COOPER, EDMUND   NV FUN 56 05
  TOMORROW'S GIFT   COOPER, EDMUND   AC
QUESTION, THE   KELLER, DAVID H. MD. SS
  FOLSOM FLINT AND OTHER CURIOUS TALES, THE
                                        KELLER, DAVID H. MD. AC
QUESTION, THE   JANIFER, LAURENCE M.
                                        AND WESTLAKE, DONALD E. SS C FSF 63 03
  IMPOSSIBLE?   JANIFER, LAURENCE M.   AN
QUICK FREEZE   SILVERBERG, ROBERT SS SFQ 57 05
  RARE SCIENCE FICTION   HOWARD, IVAN   AN
  SHORES OF TOMORROW, THE   SILVERBERG, ROBERT   AN
QUICK TO HASTE   DEFORD, MIRIAM ALLEN SS NEW 69 AC
  XENOGENESIS   DEFORD, MIRIAM ALLEN   AC
QUICKENING   MACFARLANE, WALLACE SS GAL 73 09
  BEST FROM GALAXY, THE VOLUME II   GALAXY, EDITORS OF   AN
QUIET AND A WHITE BUSH   KARL, JEAN E.   SS
  TURNING PLACE, THE   KARL, JEAN E.   OC
QUIET FUNERAL, A   BLOCH, ROBERT   SS
  SKULL OF THE MARQUIS DE SADE, THE   BLOCH, ROBERT   AC
QUIET GAME, A   FREMLIN, CELIA   SS ARG 70
  YEAR'S BEST HORROR STORIES, THE   DAVIS, RICHARD   AN
QUIET KIND OF MADNESS, A   REDD, DAVID   NV FSF 68 05
  NEW WORLDS OF FANTASY NO. 2   CARR, TERRY   AN
QUIETUS   ROCKLYNNE, ROSS   SS ASF 40 09
  *ADVENTURES IN TIME AND SPACE   HEALY & MCCOMAS   AN

QUINCUNX   RATS, THE

QUINCUNX   DISCH, THOMAS M.   SS   RAINMAKER   REESE, JOHN   SS   SEP 49 02
  *GETTING INTO DEATH   DISCH, THOMAS M.   AC   TOMORROW, THE STARS   HEINLEIN, ROBERT A.   AN
  NEW S.F., THE   JONES, LANGDON   OA   RAINS OF ALPHA ALEPH, THE BIRLEY, JULIA   SS   ADS 75 01
QUIS CUSTODIET...   ST. CLAIR, MARGARET SS STS 48 07   ARMADA SCI-FI ONE   DAVIS, RICHARD   OA
  SCIENCE FICTION GALAXY, THE CONKLIN, GROFF   AN   RAINY DAY REVOLUTION NO. 39 COZZI, LUIGI   SS   ISF 67 11
QUIT ZOOMIN' THOSE HANDS THROUGH THE AIR   BEST FROM THE REST OF THE WORLD, THE WOLLHEIM, DONALD A. AN
                          FINNEY, JACK   SS FSF 52 12   RAISE   KING, MAC   PM   NWQ 74 06
  CONNOISSEUR'S S. F.   BOARDMAN, TOM JR.   AN   NEW WORLDS NO. 6   PLATT & BAILEY   OA
  JOURNEYS IN SCIENCE FICTION LOUGHLIN, RICHARD L. AN   RAJA AND THE TIGER, THE   SMITH, CLARK ASHTON SS   BLC 12 02
  OPERATION FUTURE   CONKLIN, GROFF   AN   OTHER DIMENSIONS   SMITH, CLARK ASHTON   AC
  THIRD LEVEL, THE   FINNEY, JACK   AC   RAJAH'S TREASURE, THE   WELLS, H. G.   SS   PRS 96 07
QUITE LATE ONE SPRING NIGHT CURLOVICH, JOHN M. SS ORB 75 17   THIRTY STRANGE STORIES   WELLS, H. G.   AC
  ORBIT 17   KNIGHT, DAMON   OA   RAKE   GOULART, RON   SS   FSF 65 06
QUIXOTE AND THE WINDMILL   ANDERSON, POUL   SS ASF 50 11   BEST FROM FANTASY AND SCIENCE FICTION: 15
  METAL SMILE, THE   KNIGHT, DAMON   AN   FERMAN, EDWARD L.   AN
  STRANGERS FROM EARTH   ANDERSON, POUL   AC   CHAMELEON CORPS & OTHER SHAPE CHANGERS, THE
QUIZ GAME   ROBINSON, FRANK M.   SS ASF 53 06   GOULART, RON   AC
  GENTLE INVADERS   SANTESSON, HANS S.   AN   RALPH WOLLSTONECRAFT HEDGE: A MEMOIR
R IS FOR ROCKET (KING OF THE GRAY SPACES)   GOULART, RON   SS   FSF 59 05
                          BRADBURY, RAY   SS FFM 43 12   BEST FROM FANTASY AND SCIENCE FICTION: 9
  R IS FOR ROCKET   BRADBURY, RAY   AC   MILLS, ROBERT P.   AN
R.U.R.   CAPEK, KAREL   PL   21   RAMBLE WITH A GAMBLIN' MAN ANDERSON, POUL   NV   NEW 70 AC
  SCIENCE FACT/FICTION   FARRELL/GAGE/&   AN   TALES OF THE FLYING MOUNTAINS ANDERSON, POUL   AC
  *SCIENCE FICTION THINKING MACHINES CONKLIN, GROFF AN   RAMMER   NIVEN, LARRY   NV   GAL 71 11
  TREASURY OF SCIENCE FICTION CLASSICS, THE   BEST FROM GALAXY, THE VOLUME I GALAXY, EDITORS OF AN
                          KUEBLER, HAROLD W.   AN   BEST SCIENCE FICTION STORIES OF THE YEAR (1971)
RABBEL-DOWSER   MCCAFFREY, ANNE   SS OMG 73   DEL REY, LESTER   AN
  OMEGA   ELWOOD, ROGER   OA   HOLE IN SPACE, A   NIVEN, LARRY   AC
RABBITS TO THE MOON   BANKS, RAYMOND E.   SS FSF 59 07   WORLD OUT OF TIME, A   NIVEN, LARRY   NO
  DECADE OF FANTASY AND SCIENCE FICTION, A MILLS, ROBERT P. AN RAMONA, COME SOFTLY   EKLUND, GORDON   NV   QRK 70 01
RACE AROUND THE SUN   ELAM, RICHARD M. JR. SS   QUARK/1   DELANY & HACKER   OA
  TEEN-AGE SUPER SCIENCE STORIES ELAM, RICHARD M. JR. AC   RAMPARTS, THE   BAILEY, HILARY   NV   UNI 74 05
RACE WITH A DINOSAUR, A (FROM "THE LOST WORLD")   UNIVERSE 5   CARR, TERRY   OA
                          DOYLE, ARTHUR CONAN EX HDS 12   RANDOM QUEST   WYNDHAM, JOHN   NV   NEW 61 AC
  SCIENCE IN FICTION   BAYLISS, A.E. & J.C. AN   AS TOMORROW BECOMES TODAY   SULLIVAN, CHARLES W. AN
RACER, THE   MELCHIOR, IB   SS   56   CONSIDER HER WAYS AND OTHERS WYNDHAM, JOHN   AC
  IF THIS GOES ON   NUETZEL, CHARLES   AN   INFINITE MOMENT, THE   WYNDHAM, JOHN   AC
RADCLYFFE EFFECT, THE   ACKERMAN, FORREST J. SS   VINTAGE ANTHOLOGY OF SCIENCE FANTASY, THE
  SCIENCE FICTION WORLDS OF FORREST J. ACKERMAN & FRIENDS   CERF, CHRISTOPHER   AN
                          ACKERMAN, FORREST J. AC   RANDOM SAMPLE   CARAVAN, T. P.   SS   FSF 53 04
RADIANT ENEMIES, THE   STARZL, R. F.   SS ARG 34 02   FIFTY SHORT SCIENCE FICTION TALES ASIMOV & CONKLIN AN
  EXPLORING OTHER WORLDS   MOSKOWITZ, SAM   AN   SCIENCE FACT/FICTION   FARRELL/GAGE/&   AN
RADIATION BLUES   COGSWELL, THEODORE R SG   60   RANDOM SAMPLE   TUBB, E. C.   SS   NWR 76 29
  6TH ANNUAL OF THE YEAR'S BEST S-F, THE MERRIL, JUDITH   AN   NEW WRITINGS IN SF. 29   BULMER, KENNETH   OA
RADICAL CENTER   REYNOLDS, MACK   NV ASF 67 03   RANDOMHOUSE DICTIONARY, THE (SEE NEW DICTIONARY)
  AMERICAN GOVERNMENT THROUGH SCIENCE FICTION   VONNEGUT, KURT JR.   TC
                          OLANDER/GREENBERG/& AN   RANDY'S SYNDROME   ALDISS, BRIAN W.   NV   FSF 67 04
RADIO MAN, THE   FARLEY, RALPH MILNE NO AAS 24 06   BEST FROM FANTASY AND SCIENCE FICTION: 17
  STRANGE WORLDS   FARLEY, RALPH MILNE AC   FERMAN, EDWARD L.   AN
RADIO WAR, THE (MISSING FIRST CHAPTER OF)   INTANGIBLES INC. AND OTHER STORIES ALDISS, BRIAN W. AC
                          FARLEY, RALPH MILNE EX ARG 32 07   RANDY-TANDY MAN   ROCKLYNNE, ROSS   SS   UNI 73 03
  OMNIBUS OF TIME, THE   FARLEY, RALPH MILNE AC   UNIVERSE 3   CARR, TERRY   OA
RADIUM POOL, THE   REPP, ED EARL   AC FPB 49   RANGING   JAKES, JOHN W.   SS   PRS 68
  SCIENCE-FANTASY QUINTETTE   CRAWFORD, WILLIAM L. AN   FARTHEST REACHES, THE   ELDER, JOSEPH   OA
RADIUM POOL, THE   REPP, ED EARL   NV SWS 29 08   UNIVERSE AHEAD   ENGDAHL & ROBERSON   AN
  RADIUM POOL, THE   REPP, ED EARL   AC   RANSOM   FYFE, H. B.   SS   FSF 52 02
RADIUS RIDERS, THE   BAYLEY, BARRINGTON J SS SFB 62 07   BEST FROM FANTASY AND SCIENCE FICTION: 2
  BEST SF STORIES FROM NEW WORLDS 8   BOUCHER & MCCOMAS
                          MOORCOCK, MICHAEL   AN   SPECIAL WONDER   MCCOMAS, J. FRANCIS   AN
RAFFERTY'S REASONS   POHL, FREDERIK   SS FUN 55 10   RAPE OF OOOOOOO, THE   KEARNS, WINN   SS
  ALTERNATING CURRENTS   POHL, FREDERIK   AC   NEW CONSTELLATIONS   DISCH & NAYLOR   OA
  IN THE PROBLEM PIT   POHL, FREDERIK   AC   RAPE OF THE LOCK, THE   DE CAMP, L. SPRAGUE
RAG THING, THE   GRINNELL, DAVID   SS FSF 51 10   AND PRATT, FLETCHER SS C FSF 52 02
  FIFTY SHORT SCIENCE FICTION TALES ASIMOV & CONKLIN AN   TALES FROM GAVAGAN'S BAR   DE CAMP, L. S.&PRATT AC
  OMNIBUS OF SCIENCE FICTION   CONKLIN, GROFF   AN   RAPE OF THE SOLAR SYSTEM, THE STONE, LESLIE F. SS   AMZ 34 12
  *TERROR IN THE MODERN VEIN   WOLLHEIM, DONALD A. AN   FLIGHT INTO SPACE   WOLLHEIM, DONALD A.   AN
RAG THING, THE   WOLLHEIM, DONALD A. SS FSF 51 10   RAPPACCINI'S DAUGHTER (1844) HAWTHORNE, NATHANIEL NV DMR 44 12
  TWO DOZEN DRAGON EGGS   WOLLHEIM, DONALD A. AC   FUTURE PERFECT   FRANKLIN, H. BRUCE   AN
RAGE, PAIN, ALIENATION AND OTHER ASPECTS OF THE WRITING   GREAT SCIENCE FICTION ABOUT DOCTORS CONKLIN, G&FABRICANT AN
  OF SCIENCE FICTION   MALZBERG, BARRY N.   AR FSF 76 04   NIGHTMARE GARDEN   GHIDALIA, VIC   AN
  DOWN HERE IN THE DREAM QUARTER MALZBERG, BARRY N. AC   OTHER DIMENSION, THE   ROSNER, SARA   AN
RAGES, THE (RATIONS OF TANTALUS)   ROOTS OF EVIL, THE   PARRY, MICHEL   AN
                          ST. CLAIR, MARGARET NV FUN 54 07   STRANGE SIGNPOSTS   ELWOOD & MOSKOWITZ   AN
  THREE WORLDS OF FUTURITY   ST. CLAIR, MARGARET DC   RASTIGNAC THE DEVIL   FARMER, PHILIP JOSE SS   FUN 54 05
RAID OF LE VENGEUR, THE   GRIFFITH, GEORGE   SS PRS 01 02   CELESTIAL BLUEPRINT, THE   FARMER, PHILIP JOSE   DC
  BEFORE ARMAGEDDON   MOORCOCK, MICHAEL   AN   RAT AND THE SNAKE, THE   VAN VOGT, A. E.   SS   WTS 71 01
RAID TAKES PLACE AT MIDNIGHT, A   BOOK OF VAN VOGT, THE   VAN VOGT, A. E.   AC
                          VARSHAVSKY, ILYA   SS   RAT RACE   HERBERT, FRANK   NV   ASF 55 07
  RUSSIAN SCIENCE FICTION, 1969 MAGIDOFF, ROBERT   AN   BOOK OF FRANK HERBERT, THE   HERBERT, FRANK   AC
RAILWAYS UP ON CANNIS, THE KAPP, COLIN   SS NWS 59 10   RAT RACE   JONES, RAYMOND F.   SS   ASF 66 04
  BEST OF NEW WORLDS, THE   MOORCOCK, MICHAEL   AN   ABOVE THE HUMAN LANDSCAPE   MCNELLY & STOVER   AN
  OUT OF THIS WORLD 2   WILLIAMS-ELLIS& OWEN AN   YOU AND SCIENCE FICTION   HOLLISTER, BERNARD C AN
RAIN CHECK   MERRIL, JUDITH   NV SFA 54 06   RAT RACE   DE COURCY, DOROTHY
  CRIME PREVENTION IN THE 30TH CENTURY SANTESSON, HANS S. AN   AND DE COURCY, JOHN SS C STS 48 09
RAIN CHECK   PADGETT, LEWIS   SS ASF 46 07   *BIG BOOK OF SCIENCE FICTION CONKLIN, GROFF   AN
  GNOME THERE WAS, A   PADGETT, LEWIS   AC   RAT RACKET, THE   KELLER, DAVID H. MD. SS   AMZ 31 11
RAIN MAGIC   GARDNER, EARL S.   NV AAS 28 10   SATAN'S PETS   GHIDALIA, VIC   AN
  ALIEN EARTH AND OTHER STORIES ELWOOD & MOSKOWITZ AN   RAT THAT COULD SPEAK, THE (ALSO AS THE DEVIL AND MR. CHIPS)
RAIN, RAIN, GO AWAY   ASIMOV, ISAAC   SS FUN 59 09   DICKENS, CHARLES   SS   FSF 51 08
  BUY JUPITER AND OTHER STORIES ASIMOV, ISAAC   AC   BEST FROM FANTASY AND SCIENCE FICTION BOUCHER & MCCOMAS AN
  HAVE YOU SEEN THESE?   ASIMOV, ISAAC   AC   EDGE OF NEVER, THE   HOSKINS, ROBERT   AN
RAIN, RAIN, GO AWAY   ELLISON, HARLAN   SS SCF 56 12   RAT, THE   WRIGHT, S. FOWLER   SS   WRT 29 03
  ELLISON WONDERLAND   ELLISON, HARLAN   AC   NEW GODS LEAD, THE   WRIGHT, S. FOWLER   AC
RAINBIRD   LAFFERTY, R. A.   SS GAL 61 12   TREASURY OF SCIENCE FICTION CLASSICS, THE
  BEYOND TOMORROW   HARDING, LEE   AN   KUEBLER, HAROLD W.   AN
  SEVENTH GALAXY READER, THE   POHL, FREDERIK   AN   RATHER IMPROBABLE HISTORY OF HILIARY KIFFER, THE
  STRANGE DOINGS   LAFFERTY, R. A.   AC   CHRISTOPHER, JOHN   SS   AVS 53 04
RAINBOW   GARNETT, DAVID S.   SS NWR 74 23   TWENTY-SECOND CENTURY, THE   CHRISTOPHER, JOHN   AC
  NEW WRITINGS IN SF. 23   BULMER, KENNETH   OA   RATIONS OF TANTALUS (ALSO AS THE RAGES)
RAINBOW GOLD, THE   RICE, JANE   SS FSF 59 12   ST. CLAIR, MARGARET NV   FUN 54 07
  BEST FROM FANTASY AND SCIENCE FICTION: 10   WORLDS OF WHEN   CONKLIN, GROFF   AN
                          MILLS, ROBERT P.   AN   RATS IN THE WALLS, THE   LOVECRAFT, H. P.   SS   WRT 24 03
RAINBOW'S END (AFTERNOON OF A FAHN)   HAUNTER OF THE DARK, THE   LOVECRAFT, H. P.   AC
                          RUSSELL, ERIC FRANK SS IMG 51 04   RATS, THE   PORGES, ARTHUR   SS   MSW 51 02
  DEEP SPACE   RUSSELL, ERIC FRANK AC   BEST SCIENCE-FICTION STORIES: 1952, THE BLEILER & DIKTY AN
RAINDROP   CLEMENT, HAL   NV IFS 65 05   FRONTIERS IN SPACE   BLEILER & DIKTY   AN
  SMALL CHANGES   CLEMENT, HAL   AC

RAY BRADBURY   NOLAN, WILLIAM F.   AR
  3 TO THE HIGHEST POWER   NOLAN, WILLIAM F.   AN
RAY BRADBURY   NOLAN, WILLIAM F.   AR   FSF 63 05
  BEST FROM FANTASY AND SCIENCE FICTION, 25TH ANNIV.
                                    FERMAN, EDWARD L.   AN
RAY BRADBURY SF/FANTASY INDEX, A
                            MISC. MATERIAL   MS
  3 TO THE HIGHEST POWER   NOLAN, WILLIAM F.   AN
RAY OF DISPLACEMENT, THE   SPOFFORD, HARRIET P. SS   MPM 03 10
  SCIENCE FICTION BY GASLIGHT   MOSKOWITZ, SAM   AN
RE-BIRTH (ALSO AS THE CHRYSALIDS)
                            WYNDHAM, JOHN   NO   BAL 55
  TREASURY OF GREAT SCIENCE FICTION, A VOL.1
                                    BOUCHER, ANTHONY   AN
RE-CREATION, THE   TOOMEY, ROBERT E. JR SS   GEN 72
  GENERATION   GERROLD, DAVID   OA
REACHING OUT OF TOMORROW   HOSKINS, ROBERT   IN
  WONDERMAKERS 2   HOSKINS, ROBERT   AN
READER'S GUIDE TO SF   MISC. MATERIAL   MS
  ANOTHER WORLD   DOZOIS, GARDNER R. AN
READING BETWEEN THE WORDS   DELANY, SAMUEL R.   AR   CLR 71 01
  CLARION   WILSON, ROBIN SCOTT OA
READING ROOM   DEL REY, LESTER   BR   IFS 74 12
  BEST FROM IF, THE   VOLUME III   BAEN, JAMES   AN
REAL BAD FRIEND, THE   BLOCH, ROBERT   NV   MSM 57 02
  KING OF TERRORS, THE   BLOCH, ROBERT   AC
REAL LIFE OF MR. NEWMAN, THE COLVIN, JAMES   SS
                                    COLVIN, JAMES   AC
REAL PEOPLE, THE   BUDRYS, ALGIS   NA   BEY 53 11
  BEYOND   ANONYMOUS   AN
REAL-TIME WORLD   PRIEST, CHRISTOPHER NV   NWR 71 19
  NEW WRITINGS IN SF. 19   CARNELL, JOHN   OA
  REAL-TIME WORLD   PRIEST, CHRISTOPHER AC
  1972 ANNUAL WORLD'S BEST SF, THE WOLLHEIM, DONALD A. AN
REALITY TRIP, THE   SILVERBERG, ROBERT   NV   IFS 70 05
  BEST FROM IF, THE   VOLUME I   IF, EDITORS OF   AN
  REALITY TRIP, THE   SILVERBERG, ROBERT AC
  THIS SIDE OF INFINITY   CARR, TERRY   AN
REAP THE DARK TIDE (SEE SHARK SHIP)
                            KORNBLUTH, C. M.   TC
REAPING THE WHIRLWIND   ELLISON, HARLAN   IN
  APPROACHING OBLIVION   ELLISON, HARLAN   AC
REASON   ASIMOV, ISAAC   SS   ASF 41 04
  CENTURY OF SCIENCE FICTION, A   KNIGHT, DAMON   AN
  DECADE THE 1940S   ALDISS & HARRISON   AN
  I, ROBOT   ASIMOV, ISAAC   AC
  SPACE ODYSSEYS   ALDISS, BRIAN W.   AC
REASONABLE PEOPLE   RUSS, JOANNA   SS   ORB 74 14
  ORBIT 14   KNIGHT, DAMON   OA
REASONS OF HEALTH   JACOBS, HARVEY   SS
  EGG OF THE GLAK, AND OTHER STORIES, THE JACOBS, HARVEY AC
REAVERS OF SKAITH   BRACKETT, LEIGH   NO   BAL 76 08
  BOOK OF SKAITH, THE   BRACKETT, LEIGH   AC
REBEL   MOORE, WARD   SS   FSF 62 02
  NEVER IN THIS WORLD   STONE, IDELLA P.   AN
REBEL OF THE DARKNESS (REVOLT OF THE DEVIL STAR)
                            ROCKLYNNE, ROSS   NV   IMG 51 02
  SUN DESTROYERS, THE   ROCKLYNNE, ROSS   DC
REBEL OF VALKYR, THE   COPPEL, ALFRED   NV   PLS 50 FL
  GALACTIC EMPIRES VOLUME ONE   ALDISS, BRIAN W.   AN
REBELLION   CAMPBELL, JOHN W. JR NV   ASF 35 08
  *BEST OF JOHN W. CAMPBELL, THE   CAMPBELL, JOHN W. JR AC
  CLOAK OF AESIR   CAMPBELL, JOHN W. JR AC
  FUTURES UNLIMITED   NORTON, ALDEN H.   AN
REBELLION ON VENUS   WELLS, BASIL   SS
  DOORWAYS TO SPACE   WELLS, BASIL   AC
REBIRTH: EARTH (THE FLIGHT THAT FAILED)
                            VAN VOGT, A. E.   SS   ASF 42 12
  PROXY INTELLIGENCE AND OTHER MIND BENDERS
                                    VAN VOGT, A. E.   AC
REBOUND   BROWN, FREDRIC   SS   NEW 61 AC
  BEST OF FREDRIC BROWN, THE   BROWN, FREDRIC   AC
  NIGHTMARES AND GEEZENSTACKS   BROWN, FREDRIC   AC
RECALCITRANT ROBOT, THE (FROM "FRANKENSTEIN")
                            SHELLEY, MARY W.   EX
  SCIENCE FICTION THROUGH THE AGES 1 EVANS, I. O.   AN
RECEDING BROW, THAT   BRAND, MAX   NV   ASW 19 02
  HORROR TIMES TEN   NORTON, ALDEN H.   AN
RECENT SEMIFINALS, THE   LORY, ROBERT   SS
  LONE STAR UNIVERSE   PROCTOR & UTLEY   OA
RECEPTIVE BOSOM, THE   SHANKS, EDWARD   PM
  FANTASIA MATHEMATICA   FADIMAN, CLIFTON   AN
RECESSIONAL   BROWN, FREDRIC   SS   DUD 60 03
  BEST OF FREDRIC BROWN, THE   BROWN, FREDRIC   AC
  NIGHTMARES AND GEEZENSTACKS   BROWN, FREDRIC   AC
RECESSIONAL (FORGIVE US OUR DEBTS)
                            DEL REY, LESTER   SS   FUT 52 05
  MORTALS AND MONSTERS   DEL REY, LESTER   AC
RECIDIVISM PREFERRED   JAKES, JOHN W.   SS   AMZ 62 02
  BEST OF JOHN JAKES, THE   JAKES, JOHN W.   AC
RECKONING, A (NOTES LEADING DOWN TO THE CONQUEST)
                            MALZBERG, BARRY N.   SS   NDM 73 03
  BEST OF BARRY N. MALZBERG, THE   MALZBERG, BARRY N. AC
RECLUSE AND HIS GUEST, A   WILLIAMS, TENNESSEE SS   PBY 70 01
  WEIRD SHOW   PLAYBOY, EDITORS OF AN
RECOGNITION, THE   BALLARD, J. G.   SS   DVS 67 01
  DANGEROUS VISIONS   ELLISON, HARLAN   OA
RECOIL   SMITH, GEORGE O.   NV   ASF 43 11
  COMPLETE VENUS EQUILATERAL, THE   SMITH, GEORGE O.   AC
  VENUS EQUILATERAL   SMITH, GEORGE O.   AC
RECOLLECTING ANDERSON   MALZBERG, BARRY N.   IN
  BEST OF POUL ANDERSON, THE   ANDERSON, POUL   AC
RECOMMENDED OTHER STORIES   MISC. MATERIAL   MS
  GREAT STORIES OF SCIENCE FICTION LEINSTER, MURRAY   AN
RECOMMENDED READING   MISC. MATERIAL   MS
  HUMAN-MACHINES   SCORTIA & ZEBROWSKI AN

  INTRODUCING SCIENCE FICTION   ALDISS, BRIAN W.   AN
RECOMMENDED READING- 1975   CARR, TERRY   MS
  BEST SCIENCE FICTION OF THE YEAR, THE NO. 5
                                    CARR, TERRY   AN
RECONCILIATION   BROWN, FREDRIC   SS   NEW 54 AC
  ANGELS AND SPACESHIPS   BROWN, FREDRIC   AC
  BEST OF FREDRIC BROWN, THE   BROWN, FREDRIC   AC
RECONCILIATION, THE (THE BULLA)
                            WELLS, H. G.   SS   WSL 95 12
  SHORT STORIES OF H. G. WELLS, THE WELLS, H. G.   AC
  THIRTY STRANGE STORIES   WELLS, H. G.   AC
RECONSTITUTION   MALZBERG, BARRY N.   SS   NEW 75 AC
  MANY WORLDS OF BARRY MALZBERG, THE MALZBERG, BARRY N. AC
RECORD, THE   ACKERMAN, FORREST J.
                            AND BRADBURY, RAY   SS C   40
  SCIENCE FICTION WORLDS OF FORREST J. ACKERMAN & FRIENDS
                                    ACKERMAN, FORREST J. AC
RECOURSE, INC.   MCINTYRE, VONDA N.   SS   ALT 74
  ALTERNATES   GERROLD, DAVID   OA
RECOVERY AREA   GALOUYE, DANIEL F.   NA   AMZ 63 02
  PROJECT BARRIER   GALOUYE, DANIEL F. AC
RECRUDESCENCE OF GEOFFREY MARVELL, THE
                            GABBARD, G. N.   SS   NEW 76 AN
  YEAR'S BEST HORROR STORIES: SERIES IV, THE
                                    PAGE, GERALD W.   AN
RECRUITING NATION   ANDERSON, POUL   NV   NEW 70 AC
  TALES OF THE FLYING MOUNTAINS   ANDERSON, POUL   AC
RECRUITING STATION (ALSO AS MASTERS OF TIME)
                            VAN VOGT, A. E.   NV   ASF 42 03
  OMNIBUS OF SCIENCE FICTION   CONKLIN, GROFF   AN
  STRANGE ADVENTURES IN SCIENCE FICTION CONKLIN, GROFF AN
RED ALERT   WHITE, JAMES   NV   NWS 56 01
  ALIENS AMONG US, THE   WHITE, JAMES   AC
RED BRAIN, THE   WANDREI, DONALD   SS   WRT 27 10
  EYE AND THE FINGER   WANDREI, DONALD   AC
RED CANARY, THE   WILHELM, KATE   SS   ORB 73 12
  INFINITY BOX, THE   WILHELM, KATE   AC
  ORBIT 12   KNIGHT, DAMON   OA
RED DEATH OF MARS, THE   WILLIAMS, ROBERT M.   NV   ASF 40 07
  *MEN AGAINST THE STARS   GREENBERG , MARTIN AN
  MORE ADVENTURES ON OTHER PLANETS WOLLHEIM, DONALD A. AN
  YEAR AFTER TOMORROW, THE   DEL REY, L/MATSCHAT/ AN
RED DEATH, THE   KELLER, DAVID H. MD. NV   COS 41 07
  FOLSOM FLINT AND OTHER CURIOUS TALES, THE
                                    KELLER, DAVID H. MD. AC
RED DIMENSION, THE   REPP, ED EARL   SS   SWS 30 01
  RADIUM POOL, THE   REPP, ED EARL   AC
RED DUST, THE   LEINSTER, MURRAY   NV   AAS 21 04
  FORGOTTEN PLANET, THE   LEINSTER, MURRAY   AC
RED EGG, A (TRANSLATED BY TERRY BROCH FONTSERE)
                            GIRONELLA, JOSE MARIA SS   64
  10TH ANNUAL OF THE YEAR'S BEST S-F, THE MERRIL, JUDITH AN
RED HAWK, THE   BURROUGHS, EDGAR R.   NV   AAS 25 09
  MOON MAID, THE   BURROUGHS, EDGAR R. NO
RED HEART AND BLUE ROSES, A CLINGERMAN, MILDRED SS   NEW 61 AC
  CUPFUL OF SPACE, A   CLINGERMAN, MILDRED AC
  NEW WORLDS OF FANTASY   CARR, TERRY   AN
RED HILLS OF SUMMER, THE   PANGBORN, EDGAR   NV   FSF 59 09
  ANOTHER PART OF THE GALAXY   CONKLIN, GROFF   AN
RED NAILS   HOWARD, ROBERT E.   NA   WRT 36 07
  CONAN THE WARRIOR   HOWARD, R. E. & DE CAMP AC
  SWORD OF CONAN, THE   HOWARD, ROBERT E.   AC
RED ONE, THE   LONDON, JACK   NV   CMP 18 10
  ANCESTRAL VOICES   MENVILLE & REGINALD AN
  CURIOUS FRAGMENTS   LONDON, JACK   AC
  SCIENCE FICTION OF JACK LONDON, THE LONDON, JACK   AC
  SPECTRUM OF WORLDS, A   CLARESON, THOMAS D. AN
RED PERI, THE   WEINBAUM, STANLEY G. SN   ASF 35 11
  DAWN OF FLAME   WEINBAUM, STANLEY G. AC
  MARTIAN ODYSSEY AND OTHER SCIENCE FICTION TALES, A
                                    WEINBAUM, STANLEY G. AC
  RED PERI, THE   WEINBAUM, STANLEY G. AC
RED PLANET, THE   DIKTY, T. E.   IN
  GREAT SCIENCE FICTION STORIES ABOUT MARS DIKTY, T. E. AN
RED QUEEN'S RACE, THE   ASIMOV, ISAAC   NV   ASF 49 01
  EARLY ASIMOV, THE   ASIMOV, ISAAC   AC
  SCIENCE FICTION ARGOSY, A   KNIGHT, DAMON   AN
  WORLD OF WONDER   PRATT, FLETCHER   AN
RED ROOM, THE   WELLS, H. G.   SS   IDL 96 03
  COUNTRY OF THE BLIND, THE   WELLS, H. G.   AC
  PLATTNER STORY AND OTHERS, THE   WELLS, H. G.   AC
  SHORT STORIES OF H. G. WELLS, THE WELLS, H. G.   AC
  THIRTY STRANGE STORIES   WELLS, H. G.   AC
  WAR OF THE WORLDS, THE TIME MACHINE AND SELECTED SHORT STORIES
                                    WELLS, H. G.   AC
RED SANDS   ELAM, RICHARD M. JR. SS
  TEEN-AGE SCIENCE FICTION STORIES ELAM, RICHARD M. JR. AC
RED SKY AT NIGHT   CHARLOTTE, JEAN   SS   NWQ 74 06
  NEW WORLDS NO. 6   PLATT & BAILEY   OA
RED STORM ON JUPITER   LONG, FRANK BELKNAP SS   ASF 36 05
  FLIGHT INTO SPACE   WOLLHEIM, DONALD A. AN
RED STUFF, THE   WYNDHAM, JOHN   NV   MSS 51 02
  BEST OF JOHN WYNDHAM, THE   WYNDHAM, JOHN   AC
  MAN FROM BEYOND AND OTHER STORIES, THE WYNDHAM, JOHN AC
  TALES FROM THE GALAXIES   WILLIAMS-ELLIS& P. AN
RED WHITE AND BLUE RUM COLLINS, THE
                            BRUST, JOHN C. M.   SS   HLP
  VINTAGE ANTHOLOGY OF SCIENCE FANTASY, THE
                                    CERF, CHRISTOPHER   AN
RED, WHITE AND BLUE FOURTH OF JULY, A
                            HANSEN, KARL   NV
  2076: THE AMERICAN TRICENTENNIAL BRYANT, EDWARD   OA
REDEMPTION (SEE MINE EYES HAVE SEEN THE GLORY)
                            YOUNG, ROBERT F.   TC
REDEMPTION CAIRN   WEINBAUM, STANLEY G. NV   ASF 36 03
  BEST OF STANLEY G. WEINBAUM, THE WEINBAUM, STANLEY G. AC

MARTIAN ODYSSEY AND OTHER SCIENCE FICTION TALES, A
                                    WEINBAUM, STANLEY G. AC
RED PERI, THE   WEINBAUM, STANLEY G. AC
REDFERN'S LABYRINTH SHECKLEY, ROBERT SS NEW 68 AC
  PEOPLE TRAP AND OTHER PITFALLS, THE SHECKLEY, ROBERT   AC
REDUNDANCY   MALZBERG, BARRY N. SS SWK 76 03
  DOWN HERE IN THE DREAM QUARTER   MALZBERG, BARRY N.   AC
REFERENT (AS BRETT STERLING) BRADBURY, RAY SS TWS 48 10
  DAY IT RAINED FOREVER, THE   BRADBURY, RAY   AC
  *IMAGINATION UNLIMITED   BLEILER & DIKTY   AN
REFLECTED MEN, THE   VAN VOGT, A. E. NV GAL 71 02
  MORE THAN SUPERHUMAN   VAN VOGT, A. E.   AC
  WORLDS OF A. E. VAN VOGT, THE   VAN VOGT, A. E.   AC
REFLECTIONS FROM A STAR JONES, RAYMOND F. SS
  SURVIVAL FROM INFINITY   ELWOOD, ROGER   OA
REFLECTIONS IN A TABLESPOON KERSH, GERALD SS
  ON AN ODD NOTE   KERSH, GERALD   AC
REFUGE FOR TONIGHT   WILLIAMS, ROBERT M. NV BBM 49 03
  BEST SCIENCE-FICTION STORIES: 1950, THE BLEILER & DIKTY AN
  VOID BEYOND, AND OTHER STORIES, THE WILLIAMS, ROBERT M. DC
REFUGEE (CONTEST STORY, ORIGINAL TITLE THIS EARTH OF MAJESTY)
                                    CLARKE, ARTHUR C. SS FSF 55 07
  BEST OF ARTHUR C. CLARKE: 1937-1971, THE CLARKE, ARTHUR C. AC
  OTHER SIDE OF THE SKY, THE   CLARKE, ARTHUR C.   AC
  SCIENCE FICTION THROUGH THE AGES 2 EVANS, I. O.   AC
REFUGEE, THE   RICE, JANE SS UNK 43 10
  FROM UNKNOWN WORLDS   CAMPBELL, JOHN W. JR   AN
  HELL HATH FURY   HAY, GEORGE   AN
REFUGEES, THE   FANCETT, ELIZABETH NV SPC 74 02
  SPACE   2   DAVIS, RICHARD   OA
REFUGEES, THE   LONG, FRANK BELKNAP SS UNK 42 02
  DARK BEASTS, THE   LONG, FRANK BELKNAP   AC
  EARLY LONG, THE   LONG, FRANK BELKNAP   AC
  *HOUNDS OF TINDALOS, THE   LONG, FRANK BELKNAP   AC
REGARDING PATIENT 724 GOULART, RON SS ASF 73 11
  ODD JOB NO. 101   GOULART, RON   AC
REGION BETWEEN, THE   ELLISON, HARLAN NA GAL 70 03
  FIVE FATES   LAUMER, KEITH   AN
REHABILITATED   DICKSON, GORDON R. SS FSF 61 01
  MUTANTS   DICKSON, GORDON R.   AC
REIGN OF THE ROBOTS, THE HAMILTON, EDMOND SS WOS 31 12
  STRANGE LOVE STORIES   ANONYMOUS   AN
REIGN OF THE TELEPUPPETS GALOUYE, DANIEL F. NA AMZ 63 08
  PROJECT BARRIER   GALOUYE, DANIEL F.   AC
REINCARNATE   DEL REY, LESTER NV ASF 40 04
  EARLY DEL REY   DEL REY, LESTER   AC
REJECTED PLANET, THE WILSON, JOHN FLEMING SS PRS 12 06
  WORLDS APART   LOCKE, GEORGE   AC
REJECTION SLIPS   ASIMOV, ISAAC PM NEW 59 AC
  NINE TOMORROWS   ASIMOV, ISAAC   AC
REJOICE, REJOICE, WE HAVE NO CHOICE
                                    CARR, TERRY SS
  ALPHA 7   SILVERBERG, ROBERT   AN
  FUTURE KIN   ELWOOD, ROGER   OA
  LIGHT AT THE END OF THE UNIVERSE, THE CARR, TERRY   AC
REJUVENATION OF MAJOR RATHBONE, THE
                                    LONDON, JACK SS CHJ 99 11
  CURIOUS FRAGMENTS   LONDON, JACK   AC
RELATIVES   EFFINGER, GEO. ALEC SS BMR 73
  BAD MOON RISING   DISCH, THOMAS M.   OA
RELATIVITY   ANONYMOUS PM
  FANTASIA MATHEMATICA   FADIMAN, CLIFTON   AN
RELATIVITY WINS AGAIN ANONYMOUS AR SDG 72 01
  SCIENCE FACT/FICTION   FARRELL/GAGE/&   AN
RELIC OF EMPIRE, A   NIVEN, LARRY NV IFS 66 12
  NEUTRON STAR   NIVEN, LARRY   AC
RELIC OF THE PLIOCENE, A LONDON, JACK SS COL 01 01
  CURIOUS FRAGMENTS   LONDON, JACK   AC
  SCIENCE FICTION OF JACK LONDON, THE LONDON, JACK   AC
RELIC OF WAR, A   LAUMER, KEITH SS ASF 69 10
  BEST OF KEITH LAUMER, THE   LAUMER, KEITH   AC
  BIG SHOW, THE   LAUMER, KEITH   AC
  BOLO   LAUMER, KEITH   AC
RELUCTANT HEROES, THE ROBINSON, FRANK M. NV GAL 51 01
  EVERY BOY'S BOOK OF OUTER SPACE STORIES DIKTY, T. E. AN
  *GALAXY READER OF SCIENCE FICTION GOLD, H. L.   AN
  GREAT SCIENCE FICTION STORIES ABOUT THE MOON
                                    DIKTY, T. E.   AN
  MEN ON THE MOON   WOLLHEIM, DONALD A.   DA
RELUCTANT ORCHID, THE CLARKE, ARTHUR C. SS SAT 56 12
  ACROSS THE SEA OF STARS   CLARKE, ARTHUR C.   AC
  NINE BILLION NAMES OF GOD, THE CLARKE, ARTHUR C.   AC
  OF TIME AND STARS   CLARKE, ARTHUR C.   AC
  SCIENCE FACT/FICTION   FARRELL/GAGE/&   AN
  TALES FROM THE WHITE HART   CLARKE, ARTHUR C.   AC
RELUCTANT WITCH, THE (WHEREVER YOU MAY BE)
                                    GUNN, JAMES E. NA GAL 53 05
  WITCHING HOUR, THE   GUNN, JAMES E.   AC
REMARKABLE CASE OF DAVIDSON'S EYES, THE
                                    WELLS, H. G. SS PMB 95 03
  *BEST OF SCIENCE FICTION   CONKLIN, GROFF   AN
  COUNTRY OF THE BLIND, THE   WELLS, H. G.   AC
  SHORT STORIES OF H. G. WELLS, THE WELLS, H. G.   AC
  STOLEN BACILLUS AND OTHER INCIDENTS, THE WELLS, H. G. AC
  TWENTY-EIGHT SCIENCE FICTION STORIES WELLS, H. G.   AC
REMARKABLE DINGDONG, THE DERLETH, AUGUST SS SWY 54 04
  HARRIGAN'S FILE   DERLETH, AUGUST   AC
REMARKABLE FLIRGLEFLIP, THE (SEE FLIRGLEFLIP)
                                    TENN, WILLIAM TC
REMARKABLE TALENT OF EGBERT HAW, THE
                                    BOND, NELSON S. SS 41
  MR. MERGENTHWIRKER'S LOBBIES AND OTHER FANTASTIC TALES
                                    BOND, NELSON S.   AC
  SATAN'S PETS   GHIDALIA, VIC   AN
REMEMBER THE ALAMO!   FEHRENBACH, T. R. SS ASF 61 12
  ANALOG 1   CAMPBELL, JOHN W. JR   AN

  POLITICAL SCIENCE FICTION   GREENBERG& WARRICK   AN
  TRANSFORMATIONS II   ROSELLE, DANIEL   AN
REMEMBERING   BUNCH, DAVID R. SS AMZ 60 04
  MODERAN   BUNCH, DAVID R.   AC
REMEMBRANCE TO COME   WOLFE, GENE SS ORB 70 06
  ORBIT   6   KNIGHT, DAMON   AN
REMORSEFUL, THE   KORNBLUTH, C. M. SS STR 53 02
  BEST OF C. M. KORNBLUTH, THE   KORNBLUTH, C. M.   AC
  MARCHING MORONS AND OTHER SCIENCE FICTION
                                    KORNBLUTH, C. M.   AC
  STAR SCIENCE FICTION STORIES NO. 2 POHL, FREDERIK   OA
REMOTE INCIDENT   MALEC, ALEXANDER B. SS
  EXTRAPOLASIS   MALEC, ALEXANDER B.   AC
RENAISSANCE MAN   KLEIN, T. E. D. SS SPC 74 02
  SPACE   2   DAVIS, RICHARD   OA
RENDEZVOUS   CHRISTOPHER, JOHN SS PBY 66 09
  PLAYBOY BOOK OF HORROR AND THE SUPERNATURAL, THE
                                    PLAYBOY, EDITORS OF   AN
RENDEZVOUS IN AVEROIGNE, A SMITH, CLARK ASHTON SS WRT 31 04
  OUT OF SPACE AND TIME   SMITH, CLARK ASHTON   AC
RENDEZVOUS WITH DESTINY (SEE LUNGFISH)
                                    BRUNNER, JOHN TC FUN 58 03
RENDEZVOUS WITH RAMA (CHAPTER 1)
                                    CLARKE, ARTHUR C. EX NWR 73 22
  NEW WRITINGS IN SF. 22   BULMER, KENNETH   OA
RENEGADE, THE   DEL REY, LESTER SS ASF 43 07
  *AND SOME WERE HUMAN   DEL REY, LESTER   AC
  APEMAN, SPACEMAN   STOVER & HARRISON   AN
REPAIRER OF REPUTATIONS, THE (1895)
                                    CHAMBERS, ROBERT W. NV 95
  BATTLE OF THE MONSTERS AND OTHER STORIES, THE
                                    HARTWELL & CURREY   AN
REPAIRING THE OFFICE   NAYLOR, CHARLES NV NEW 75 AN
  NEW IMPROVED SUN, THE   DISCH, THOMAS M.   AN
REPAIRMAN, THE   HARRISON, HARRY SS GAL 58 02
  WAR WITH THE ROBOTS   HARRISON, HARRY   AC
REPEAT PERFORMANCE   COOPER, EDMUND SS
  TOMORROW'S GIFT   COOPER, EDMUND   AC
REPEAT PERFORMANCE   SHAW, BOB SS FSF 71 02
  TOMORROW LIES IN AMBUSH   SHAW, BOB   AC
"REPENT, HARLEQUIN!" SAID THE TICKTOCKMAN
                                    ELLISON, HARLAN SS GAL 65 12
  ABOVE THE HUMAN LANDSCAPE   MCNELLY & STOVER   AN
  ALONE AGAINST TOMORROW   ELLISON, HARLAN   AC
  ANOTHER TOMORROW   HOLLISTER, BERNARD C   AN
  AS TOMORROW BECOMES TODAY   SULLIVAN, CHARLES W.   AN
  FANTASY: THE LITERATURE OF THE MARVELOUS KELLEY, LEO P. AN
  HUGO WINNERS, THE (VOLUME 2)   ASIMOV, ISAAC   AN
  IN DREAMS AWAKE   FIEDLER, LESLIE A.   AN
  NEBULA AWARD STORIES   KNIGHT, DAMON   AN
  *PAINGOD AND OTHER DELUSIONS   ELLISON, HARLAN   AC
  POLITICAL SCIENCE FICTION   GREENBERG& WARRICK   AN
  SCIENCE FICTION: THE FUTURE   ALLEN, DICK   AN
  SPECULATIONS   SANDERS, THOMAS E.   AN
  TENTH GALAXY READER, THE   POHL, FREDERIK   AN
  TOMORROW, AND TOMORROW, AND TOMORROW... HEINTZ/HERBERT/JOOS/ AN
  TRANSFORMATIONS   ROSELLE, DANIEL   AN
  WORLD'S BEST SCIENCE FICTION: 1966 WOLLHEIM & CARR   AN
REPETITION (ALSO AS THE GRYB) VAN VOGT, A. E. NV ASF 40 04
  *BEACHHEADS IN SPACE   DERLETH, AUGUST   AN
  WAR AGAINST THE RULL, THE   VAN VOGT, A. E.   NO
REPLACE THE HORSE   JANIFER, LAURENCE M. SS FAN 59 01
  IMPOSSIBLE?   JANIFER, LAURENCE M.   AC
REPLACEMENT, THE   MURRAY, ROBERT SS FSF 60 02
  BEST FROM FANTASY AND SCIENCE FICTION: 10
                                    MILLS, ROBERT P.   AN
REPLICATORS, THE   VAN VOGT, A. E. NV IFS 65 02
  FAR-OUT WORLDS OF A. E. VAN VOGT, THE VAN VOGT, A. E. AC
  WORLDS OF A. E. VAN VOGT, THE VAN VOGT, A. E.   AC
REPLY, THE (SEE THE COMPUTER- 2118)
                                    GUNN, JAMES E. TC
REPORT   AMIS, KINGSLEY PM NSM 71
  BEST SF: 1971   HARRISON & ALDISS   AN
REPORT   BARTHELME, DONALD SS NYM 66
  INSIDE INFORMATION   MOWSHOWITZ, ABBE   AN
REPORT BACK   COTTON, JOHN PM 69
  BEST SF: 1969   HARRISON & ALDISS   AN
  HOLDING YOUR EIGHT HANDS   LUCIE-SMITH, EDWARD   AN
REPORT FROM LINELOS   KING, VINCENT NV NWR 69 15
  NEW WRITINGS IN SF. 15   CARNELL, JOHN   OA
REPORT FROM THE PLANET PROTEUS SAIL, LAWRENCE PM CND 72
  BEST SF: 1972   HARRISON & ALDISS   AN
REPORT OF THE DEFENSE   MALZBERG, BARRY N. SS ETN 72
  OUT FROM GANYMEDE   MALZBERG, BARRY N.   AC
REPORT ON "GRAND CENTRAL TERMINAL"
                                    SZILARD, LEO SS UCM 52 06
  VOICE OF THE DOLPHINS, AND OTHER STORIES, THE
                                    SZILARD, LEO   AC
REPORT ON A SUPERMARKET HAMBURGER, MICHAEL PM
  ENGLAND SWINGS SF   MERRIL, JUDITH   AN
  SPACE-TIME JOURNAL, THE   MERRIL, JUDITH   AN
REPORT ON CANALI   SCHIAPARELLI, G. V. AR
  MARS, WE LOVE YOU   HIPOLITO & MCNELLY   AN
REPORT ON SOL III   BLOCH, ROBERT SS AMZ 58 07
  FEAR TODAY, GONE TOMORROW   BLOCH, ROBERT   AC
REPORT ON THE BARNHOUSE EFFECT VONNEGUT, KURT JR. SS COL 50 02
  CANARY IN A CAT HOUSE   VONNEGUT, KURT JR.   AC
  JOURNEYS IN SCIENCE FICTION   LOUGHLIN, RICHARD L.   AN
  SPECULATIONS   SANDERS, THOMAS E.   AN
  TOMORROW, THE STARS   HEINLEIN, ROBERT A.   AN
  WELCOME TO THE MONKEY HOUSE   VONNEGUT, KURT JR.   AC
REPORT ON THE CONDITION OF POETRY CIRCA A.D. 2022
                                    CONRAD, EARL SS
  DA VINCI MACHINE, THE   CONRAD, EARL   OC

```
REPORT ON THE NATURE OF THE LUNAR SURFACE
                         BRUNNER, JOHN        SS   ASF 60 08
  FIRST FLIGHTS TO THE MOON          CLEMENT, HAL              AN
  FROM FRANKENSTEIN TO ANDROMEDA     BROWN, JAMES GOLDIE       AN
  NO FUTURE IN IT                    BRUNNER, JOHN            AC
  WONDERMAKERS 2                     HOSKINS, ROBERT          AN
  6TH ANNUAL OF THE YEAR'S BEST S-F, THE  MERRIL, JUDITH      AN
REPORT ON THE SEXUAL BEHAVIOR OF THE EXTRA-SENSORY PERCEPTOR
                         MUDGETT, HERMAN W.   PM   FSF 54 08
  BEST FROM FANTASY AND SCIENCE FICTION: 4
                         BOUCHER, ANTHONY         AN
REPORT TO HEADQUARTERS   MALZBERG, BARRY N.   SS   NDM 75 05
  DOWN HERE IN THE DREAM QUARTER     MALZBERG, BARRY N.       AC
  NEW DIMENSIONS 5                   SILVERBERG, ROBERT       OA
REPORT TO THE PEOPLE     SAMBROT, WILLIAM     SS   BBM 33
  ISLAND OF FEAR AND OTHER SCIENCE FICTION SAMBROT, WILLIAM    AC
REPORT, A                FAINLIGHT, RUTH      PM   69
  HOLDING YOUR EIGHT HANDS           LUCIE-SMITH, EDWARD      AN
REPRESENTATIVE           ROME, DAVID          SS   NWR 68 13
  NEW WRITINGS IN SF. 13             CARNELL, JOHN            OA
REPRISAL                 LAURANCE, ALICE      SS   GEN 72
  GENERATION                         GERROLD, DAVID           OA
REPTILE ENCLOSURE, THE (THE SHERRINGTON THEORY)
                         BALLARD, J. G.       SS   AMZ 63 03
  IMPOSSIBLE MAN, THE                BALLARD, J. G.           AC
  TERMINAL BEACH (BRITISH VERSION)   BALLARD, J. G.           AC
REPUBLIC OF THE SOUTHERN CROSS, THE
                         BRUSSOV, VALERY      SS   19
  MORE TERROR IN THE MODERN VEIN     WOLLHEIM, DONALD A.      AN
  *TERROR IN THE MODERN VEIN         WOLLHEIM, DONALD A.      AN
REQUEST FOR PROPOSAL     LEWIS, ANTHONY R.    SS   ASF 72 11
  AMERICAN GOVERNMENT THROUGH SCIENCE FICTION
                         OLANDER/GREENBERG/&      AN
REQUIEM                  HAMILTON, EDMOND     SS   AMZ 62 04
  BEST OF EDMOND HAMILTON, THE       HAMILTON, EDMOND         AC
  LEARNING MAZE AND OTHER STORIES, THE  ELWOOD, ROGER         OA
  MODERN MASTERPIECES OF SCIENCE FICTION MOSKOWITZ, SAM       AN
  VORTEX BLASTERS, THE               MOSKOWITZ, SAM           AN
REQUIEM                  HEINLEIN, ROBERT A.  SS   ASF 40 01
  *ADVENTURES IN TIME AND SPACE      HEALY & MCCOMAS          AN
  *MAN WHO SOLD THE MOON, THE        HEINLEIN, ROBERT A.      AC
  MASTERS' CHOICE                    JANIFER, LAURENCE M.     AN
  PAST THROUGH TOMORROW, THE         HEINLEIN, ROBERT A.      AC
  SCIENCE FICTION                    BURTON, S. H.            AN
REQUIEM FOR METHUSELAH (JEROME BIXBY)
                         BLISH, JAMES         SA   STK 72 05
  STAR TREK  5                       BLISH, JAMES             OC
REQUIEM ON THE MOON      DUNCAN, DAVID        SS   PBY 64 10
  DEAD ASTRONAUT, 10 STORIES OF SPACE FLIGHT, THE
                         PLAYBOY, EDITORS OF      AN
RESCUE                   EDMONDSON, G. C.     SS   FSF 57 06
  BEST FROM FANTASY AND SCIENCE FICTION: 7
                         BOUCHER, ANTHONY         AN
RESCUE INTO THE PAST     FARLEY, RALPH MILNE  SS   AMZ 40 10
  OMNIBUS OF TIME, THE               FARLEY, RALPH MILNE      AC
RESCUE OPERATION         HARRISON, HARRY      SS   ASF 64 12
  ABOVE THE HUMAN LANDSCAPE          MCNELLY & STOVER         AN
  ASTOUNDING-ANALOG READER, THE VOLUME TWO HARRISON & ALDISS  AN
  *BEST OF HARRY HARRISON, THE       HARRISON, HARRY          AC
  STORIES FROM SCIENCE FICTION       DOHERTY, G. D.           AN
  TWO TALES AND EIGHT TOMORROWS      HARRISON, HARRY          AC
  UNFRIENDLY FUTURE, THE             BOARDMAN, TOM JR.        AN
RESCUE PARTY             CLARKE, ARTHUR C.    NV   ASF 46 05
  ACROSS THE SEA OF STARS            CLARKE, ARTHUR C.        AC
  ALPHA 3                            SILVERBERG, ROBERT       AN
  BEYOND THE END OF TIME             POHL, FREDERIK           AN
  END OF THE WORLD, THE              WOLLHEIM, DONALD A.      AN
  NINE BILLION NAMES OF GOD, THE     CLARKE, ARTHUR C.        AC
  REACH FOR TOMORROW                 CLARKE, ARTHUR C.        AC
  TOMORROW, AND TOMORROW, AND TOMORROW... HEINTZ/HERBERT/JOOS/ AN
  *TREASURY OF SCIENCE FICTION, A    CONKLIN, GROFF           AN
RESCUE SQUAD FOR AHMED   MACLEAN, KATHERINE   NV   ASF 70 10
  MISSING MAN, THE                   MACLEAN, KATHERINE       NO
RESCUED GIRLS OF REFUGEE, THE MCCAFFREY, ANNE SS   TTM 73
  TEN TOMORROWS                      ELWOOD, ROGER            OA
  VISIONS OF TOMORROW                ELWOOD, ROGER            AN
RESCUER, THE             PORGES, ARTHUR       SS   ASF 62 07
  ASTOUNDING-ANALOG READER, THE VOLUME TWO HARRISON & ALDISS  AN
  YET MORE PENGUIN SCIENCE FICTION   ALDISS, BRIAN W.         AN
RESEARCH ALPHA           SCHMITZ, JAMES H.
                         AND VAN VOGT, A. E.  SN C IFS 65 07
  MORE THAN SUPERHUMAN               VAN VOGT, A. E.          AC
RESERVATION DEFERRED     WYNDHAM, JOHN        SS   FAN 53 06
  JIZZLE                             WYNDHAM, JOHN            AC
RESIDENT PHYSICIAN       WHITE, JAMES         NV   NWS 61 09
  GALACTIC EMPIRES VOLUME ONE        ALDISS, BRIAN W.         AN
RESIDENT WITCH           SCHMITZ, JAMES H.    NV   ASF 70 05
  TELZEY TOY, THE                    SCHMITZ, JAMES H.        NO
  THIS SIDE OF INFINITY              CARR, TERRY              AN
REST IS SILENCE, THE     GRANT, C. L.         SS   FSF 74 09
  NEBULA AWARD STORIES 10            GUNN, JAMES E.           AN
RESTING GROUND           INOUYE, JON          PM
  NIGHT TIDE, A                      INOUYE, JON              OC
RESTING PLACE, THE       LA FARGE, OLIVER     SS   NYM 54 10
  CIRCUS OF DR. LAO AND OTHER IMPROBABLE STORIES
                         BRADBURY, RAY            AN
RESTRICTED AREA          SHECKLEY, ROBERT     SS   AMZ 53
  PEOPLE TRAP AND OTHER PITFALLS, THE SHECKLEY, ROBERT        AC
  SEA OF SPACE, A                    NOLAN, WILLIAM F.        AN
RESTRICTED CLIENTELE     CROSSEN, KENDELL F.  SS   TWS 51 02
  ADVENTURES IN TOMORROW             CROSSEN, KENDELL F.      AC
  AMERICAN GOVERNMENT THROUGH SCIENCE FICTION
                         OLANDER/GREENBERG/&      AN
RESURGENCE OF MISS ANKLE-STRAP WEDGIE, THE
                         ELLISON, HARLAN      SS   NEW 68 AC
  *LOVE AIN'T NOTHING BUT SEX MISSPELLED ELLISON, HARLAN      AC

RESURRECTION (THE MONSTER)  VAN VOGT, A. E.   SS   ASF 48 08
  IN DREAMS AWAKE                    FIEDLER, LESLIE A.       AN
  INVADERS FROM SPACE                SILVERBERG, ROBERT       AN
  MONSTERS                           VAN VOGT, A. E.          AC
  *OTHER SIDE OF THE MOON, THE       DERLETH, AUGUST          AN
  SPECTRUM  2                        AMIS & CONQUEST          AN
  TOWARD INFINITY                    KNIGHT, DAMON            AN
  UBERWINDUNG VON RAUM UND ZEIT      GUNTHER, GOTTHARD        AN
RESURRECTION OF JIMBER-JAW, THE
                         BURROUGHS, EDGAR R.  NV   ARG 37 02
  FANTASTIC PULPS, THE               HAINING, PETER           AN
  MASTERPIECES OF SCIENCE FICTION    MOSKOWITZ, SAM           AN
  TALES OF THREE PLANETS             BURROUGHS, EDGAR R.      AC
RESURRECTION OF THE RATTLESNAKE, THE
                         SMITH, CLARK ASHTON  SS   WRT 31 10
  OTHER DIMENSIONS                   SMITH, CLARK ASHTON      AC
RETALIATION (TIME OF WAR) REYNOLDS, MACK      SS   IFS 65 11
  SF: AUTHORS' CHOICE                HARRISON, HARRY          AN
RETIEF OF THE RED-TAPE MOUNTAIN (SEE SEALED ORDERS)
                         LAUMER, KEITH        TC
RETIEF, GOD SPEAKER (SEE THE BRASS GOD)
                         LAUMER, KEITH        TC
RETIEF, INSIDER (SEE INTERNAL AFFAIR)
                         LAUMER, KEITH        TC
RETIEF, THE LONG-AWAITED MASTER (SEE MECHANICAL ADVANTAGE)
                         LAUMER, KEITH        TC
RETIEF, WAR CRIMINAL (SEE THE FORBIDDEN CITY)
                         LAUMER, KEITH        TC
RETREAT FROM EARTH       CLARKE, ARTHUR C.    SS   AMS 38 03
  BEST OF ARTHUR C. CLARKE: 1937-1971, THE CLARKE, ARTHUR C.  AC
RETREAT FROM RIGEL (TONY AND THE BEETLES)
                         DICK, PHILIP K.      SS   OSF 54 02
  PLANET OF DOOM AND OTHER STORIES   ANONYMOUS                AN
RETREAT SYNDROME         DICK, PHILIP K.      SS   WOT 65 01
  PRESERVING MACHINE, THE            DICK, PHILIP K.          AC
RETREAT TO MARS, THE     WHITE, CECIL B.      SS   AMZ 27 08
  *BEST OF SCIENCE FICTION           CONKLIN, GROFF           AN
RETREAT TO THE STARS     BRACKETT, LEIGH      SS   AST 41 11
  ADVENTURES IN TOMORROW             CROSSEN, KENDELL F.      AN
RETRO MAN, THE           EKLUND, GORDON       NV   NDM 77 07
  NEW DIMENSIONS 7                   SILVERBERG, ROBERT       OA
RETROACTIVE              SHAW, BOB            NV   UNI 72 02
  UNIVERSE 2                         CARR, TERRY              OA
RETROGRADE EVOLUTION     SIMAK, CLIFFORD D.   NV   SFP 53 04
  *STRANGERS IN THE UNIVERSE         SIMAK, CLIFFORD D.       AC
RETROGRADE SUMMER        VARLEY, JOHN         NV   FSF 75 02
  BEST SCIENCE FICTION OF THE YEAR, THE NO. 5
                         CARR, TERRY              AN
RETURN                   HENDERSON, ZENNA     NV   FSF 61 03
  PEOPLE: NO DIFFERENT FLESH, THE    HENDERSON, ZENNA         AC
RETURN                   MATHESON, RICHARD    SS   TWS 51 10
  BORN OF MAN AND WOMAN              MATHESON, RICHARD        AC
  SHOCK III                          MATHESON, RICHARD        AC
RETURN ENGAGEMENT        DEL REY, LESTER      SS   GAL 61 08
  MORTALS AND MONSTERS               DEL REY, LESTER          AC
  SEVENTH GALAXY READER, THE         POHL, FREDERIK           AN
RETURN FROM OBLIVION     SERLING, ROD         SA
  *ROD SERLING'S THE TWILIGHT ZONE   SERLING, ROD             OC
RETURN OF A LEGEND       GALLUN, RAYMOND Z.   SS   PLS 52 03
  BEST OF PLANET STORIES NO. 1, THE  BRACKETT, LEIGH          AN
  SPACE SERVICE                      NORTON, ANDRE            AN
RETURN OF ANDREW BENTLEY, THE DERLETH, AUGUST
                         AND SCHORER, MARK    SS C WRT 33 09
  OTHER WORLDS, THE                  STONG, PHILIP D.         AN
RETURN OF CONAN, THE (EXPANDED FROM "CONAN THE VICTORIOUS",
PUBLISHED BY GNOME, 1957)  DE CAMP, L. SPRAGUE
                         AND NYBERG, BJORN    NO C FUN 57 09
  CONAN THE AVENGER                  HOWARD, R./NYBERG/&      AC
RETURN OF HAWK CARSE, THE (HARRY BATES)
                         GILMORE, ANTHONY     NA   AMZ 42 07
  SPACE HAWK                         GILMORE, ANTHONY         AC
RETURN OF LANCELOT BIGGS, THE BOND, NELSON S. SS   AMZ 42 05
  LANCELOT BIGGS: SPACEMAN           BOND, NELSON S.          AC
RETURN OF SARAH PURCELL, THE DERLETH, AUGUST  SS   WRT 36 07
  NOT LONG FOR THIS WORLD            DERLETH, AUGUST          AC
RETURN OF THE ARCHONS, THE (BORIS SOBELMAN)
                         BLISH, JAMES         SA   STK 73 09
  STAR TREK  9                       BLISH, JAMES             OC
RETURN OF THE MANDARIN, THE GELLMAN, RICK     SS   NWQ 74 04
  NEW WORLDS NO. 6                   PLATT & BAILEY           OA
RETURN OF THE MEDUSAE, THE DISCH, THOMAS M.   SS   FAN 63 08
  *ONE HUNDRED AND TWO H-BOMBS       DISCH, THOMAS M.         AC
  WHITE FANG GOES DINGO AND OTHER FUNNY S.F. STORIES
                         DISCH, THOMAS M.         AC
RETURN OF THE MOON MAN (ALSO AS WHEN GRANDFATHER FLEW
TO THE MOON)             MALPASS, E. L.       SS   LOB 55 01
  AD 2500                            WILSON, ANGUS            AN
  STARLIT CORRIDOR, THE              MANSFIELD, ROGER         AN
  TALES OF SCIENCE FICTION           BALL, BRIAN N.           AN
RETURN OF THE SORCERER, THE SMITH, CLARK ASHTON NV  STT 31 09
  OUT OF SPACE AND TIME              SMITH, CLARK ASHTON      AC
RETURN OF THE TRIPEDS, THE JONES, NEIL R.     SS   AMZ 32 05
  PLANET OF THE DOUBLE SUN           JONES, NEIL R.           AC
RETURN TO A HOSTILE PLANET THOMAS, JOHN D.    SS   STG 74
  STRANGE GODS                       ELWOOD, ROGER            AN
RETURN TO PELLUCIDAR, THE BURROUGHS, EDGAR R. NV   AMZ 42 02
  SAVAGE PELLUCIDAR                  BURROUGHS, EDGAR R.      NO
RETURN TO THE SABBATH    BLOCH, ROBERT        SS   WRT 38 07
  HORROR-7                           BLOCH, ROBERT            AC
  HOUSE OF THE HATCHET, THE          BLOCH, ROBERT            AC
  *OPENER OF THE WAY, THE            BLOCH, ROBERT            AC
RETURN TO TOMORROW (G. RODDENBERRY & J. T. DOUGAN)
                         BLISH, JAMES         SA   STK 73 09
  STAR TREK  9                       BLISH, JAMES             OC
RETURN VISIT             TUBB, E. C.          SS   SCF 58 04
  DEVIL HIS DUE, THE                 HILL, DOUGLAS            AN
```

SCATTER OF STARDUST, A   TUBB, E. C.   DC
RETURN, THE   MCGUIRE, JOHN J.
                        AND PIPER, H. BEAM   NV C ASF 54 01
  SCIENCE-FICTIONAL SHERLOCK HOLMES, THE   COUNCIL OF FOUR   AN
REUNION   BRADBURY, RAY   SS   WRT 44 03
  *DARK CARNIVAL   BRADBURY, RAY   AC
REUNION   BUNCH, DAVID R. SS   AMZ 65 02
  MODERAN   BUNCH, DAVID R.   AC
REUNION   CLARKE, ARTHUR C. SS   INY 71 02
  INFINITY 2   HOSKINS, ROBERT   OA
  WIND FROM THE SUN, THE   CLARKE, ARTHUR C.   AC
REVENGE OF THE GREAT WHITE LODGE, THE
                        FARLEY, RALPH MILNE SS
  OMNIBUS OF TIME, THE   FARLEY, RALPH MILNE AC
REVERSE PHYLOGENY   LONG, AMELIA R. SS   ASF 37 06
  ADVENTURES IN DIMENSION   CONKLIN, GROFF   AN
  *SCIENCE FICTION ADVENTURES IN DIMENSION CONKLIN, GROFF   AN
REVERSED MAN, THE (SEE TECHNICAL ERROR)
                        CLARKE, ARTHUR C. TC   TWS 50 06
REVERSIBLE REVOLUTIONS, THE   KORNBLUTH, C. M. SS   COS 41 03
  THIRTEEN O'CLOCK AND OTHER ZERO HOURS KORNBLUTH, C. M.   AC
REVIEW COPY   BOUCHER, ANTHONY SS   FSF 49 FL
  FAR AND AWAY   BOUCHER, ANTHONY   AC
REVOLT OF THE DEVIL STAR (SEE REBEL OF THE DARKNESS)
                        ROCKLYNNE, ROSS TC
REVOLT OF THE PEDESTRIANS, THE KELLER, DAVID H. MD. SS AMZ 28 02
  *BEYOND TIME AND SPACE   DERLETH, AUGUST   AN
  TALES FROM UNDERWOOD   KELLER, DAVID H. MD. AC
REVOLT OF THE POTATO-PICKER   LEHRMAN, HERB   SS   FSF 66 07
  SOCIAL PROBLEMS THROUGH SCIENCE FICTION GREENBERG/MILSTEAD/&   AN
REVOLT OF THE TRIFFIDS (SEE THE DAY OF THE TRIFFIDS)
                        WYNDHAM, JOHN   TC
REVOLT OF THE..., THE   BARR, ROBERT   SS   IDL 94 05
  MARRIAGE AND THE FAMILY THROUGH SCIENCE FICTION
                        CLEAR/WARRICK/&   AN
  WHEN WOMEN RULE   MOSKOWITZ, SAM   AN
REVOLUTION   REYNOLDS, MACK   NV   ASF 60 05
  BEST OF MACK REYNOLDS, THE   REYNOLDS, MACK   AC
REVOLUTION   SCHAEFFER, ROBIN SS   FUC 73
  FUTURE CITY   ELWOOD, ROGER   OA
REVOLUTION (AS ROBIN SCHAEFFER)
                        MALZBERG, BARRY N. SS   FUC 73
  BEST OF BARRY N. MALZBERG, THE   MALZBERG, BARRY N.   AC
REVOLUTION OF 1950   WEINBAUM, STANLEY G. NA AMZ 38 10
  MARTIAN ODYSSEY AND OTHER SCIENCE FICTION TALES, A
                        WEINBAUM, STANLEY G. AC
  RED PERI, THE   WEINBAUM, STANLEY G. AC
REX   VINCENT, HARL   SS   ASF 34 06
  COMING OF THE ROBOTS, THE   MOSKOWITZ, SAM   AN
RHYME NEVER PAYS (CRIME IN RHYME)
                        BLOCH, ROBERT   SS   EQM 57 09
  TALES IN A JUGULAR VEIN   BLOCH, ROBERT   AC
RHYMES FOR A MODERN NURSERY (FROM "QUAKE, QUAKE, QUAKE")
                        DEHN, PAUL   PM   61
  SPECULATIONS   SANDERS, THOMAS E.   AN
RHYTHM OF THE RATS   RUSSELL, ERIC FRANK SS   WRT 50 07
  DARK TIDES   RUSSELL, ERIC FRANK   AC
RIBBON IN THE SKY   LEINSTER, MURRAY NV   ASF 57 06
  GREAT SCIENCE FICTION ABOUT DOCTORS   CONKLIN, G&FABRICANT   AN
  S.O.S. FROM THREE WORLDS   LEINSTER, MURRAY   AC
RICE BRANDY   STALL, MICHAEL   NV   NWR 75 25
  NEW WRITINGS IN SF. 25   BULMER, KENNETH   OA
RICH AND STRANGE   CHRISTOPHER, JOHN SS
  TWENTY-SECOND CENTURY, THE   CHRISTOPHER, JOHN   AC
RICHEST MAN IN LEVITTOWN, THE (THE BITTEREST PILL)
                        POHL, FREDERIK   SS   GAL 59 04
  BEST OF FREDERIK POHL, THE   POHL, FREDERIK   AC
  TURN LEFT AT THURSDAY   POHL, FREDERIK   AC
RICOCHET ON MIZA   DICKSON, GORDON R. SS   PLS 52 03
  COMBAT SF   DICKSON, GORDON R.   AN
RIDDLE   ANONYMOUS   PM   51
  MATHEMATICAL MAGPIE, THE   FADIMAN, CLIFTON   AN
RIDDLE OF THE CRYPT, THE   SERLING, ROD   SA
  *ROD SERLING'S THE TWILIGHT ZONE   SERLING, ROD   OC
RIDDLE OF THE DEADLY PARADISE LONG, FRANK BELKNAP NV   SFS 58 11
  6 AND THE SILENT SCREAM   HOWARD, IVAN   AN
RIDE A TIN CAN   LAFFERTY, R. A. SS   IFS 70 04
  STRANGE DOINGS   LAFFERTY, R. A.   AC
  THIS SIDE OF INFINITY   CARR, TERRY   AN
RIDERS OF THE PURPLE WAGE   FARMER, PHILIP JOSE NA   DVS 67 01
  DANGEROUS VISIONS   ELLISON, HARLAN   OA
  HUGO WINNERS, THE (VOLUME 2)   ASIMOV, ISAAC   AN
RIDING   RUSH, NORMAN   SS   BMR 73
  BAD MOON RISING   DISCH, THOMAS M.   OA
RIDING THE DARK TRAIN OUT   ELLISON, HARLAN SS   ROG 61 05
  *LOVE AIN'T NOTHING BUT SEX MISSPELLED ELLISON, HARLAN   AC
RIDING THE TORCH   SPINRAD, NORMAN NA   TOT 74
  THREADS OF TIME   SILVERBERG, ROBERT   OA
RIGHT MAN FOR THE RIGHT JOB, THE
                        THOMPSON, J. C. SS   62
  SHOCKING THING, A   KNIGHT, DAMON   AN
RIGHT OFF THE MAP   WINN, PIP   SS   ORB 70 08
  ORBIT 8   KNIGHT, DAMON   OA
RIGHT THING, THE   ANDREW, WILLIAM SS
  AD 2500   WILSON, ANGUS   AN
RIGHT TO RESIST, THE   LAUMER, KEITH   SS   IFS 71 06
  AMERICAN GOVERNMENT THROUGH SCIENCE FICTION
                        OLANDER/GREENBERG/&   AN
  BEST FROM IF, THE VOLUME I   IF, EDITORS OF   AN
RIGHT TO REVOLT, THE   LAUMER, KEITH   SS   IFS 71 06
  AMERICAN GOVERNMENT THROUGH SCIENCE FICTION
                        OLANDER/GREENBERG/&   AN
  BEST FROM IF, THE VOLUME I   IF, EDITORS OF   AN
RIM GODS, THE   CHANDLER, A. BERTRAM NV IFS 68 04
  RIM GODS, THE   CHANDLER, A. BERTRAM   DC

RIM OF THE DEEP   SIMAK, CLIFFORD D. NV   ASF 40 05
  FUTURES TO INFINITY   MOSKOWITZ, SAM   AN
RIME OF THE ANCIENT SF AUTHOR,OF CONVENTIONS AND RECOLLECTIONS
                        PIERCE, JOHN R. PM   68
  BEST SF: 1968   HARRISON & ALDISS   AN
RING AROUND THE REDHEAD   MACDONALD, JOHN D. SS   STS 48 11
  ADVENTURES IN DIMENSION   CONKLIN, GROFF   AN
  *SCIENCE FICTION ADVENTURES IN DIMENSION CONKLIN, GROFF   AN
RING AROUND THE SUN   ASIMOV, ISAAC   SS   FUT 40 03
  EARLY ASIMOV, THE   ASIMOV, ISAAC   AC
RING OF HANS CARVEL, THE   BROWN, FREDRIC   SS
  NIGHTMARES AND GEEZENSTACKS   BROWN, FREDRIC   AC
RING OF PAIN   HARRISON, M. JOHN SS   QRK 71 03
  MACHINE IN SHAFT TEN AND OTHER STORIES, THE
                        HARRISON, M. JOHN   AC
  QUARK/3   DELANY & HACKER   OA
RING, THE   BOND, NELSON S. SS
  31ST OF FEBRUARY, THE   BOND, NELSON S.   AC
RINGER   EDMONDSON, G. C. SS   FSF 60 04
  ENCOUNTERS WITH ALIENS   EARLEY, GEORGE W.   AN
RINGING THE CHANGES   SILVERBERG, ROBERT SS   ANA 70
  ALCHEMY AND ACADEME   MCCAFFREY, ANNE   OA
  REALITY TRIP, THE   SILVERBERG, ROBERT   AC
RIP VAN WINKLE CAPER, THE   SERLING, ROD   SA
  FROM THE TWILIGHT ZONE   SERLING, ROD   AC
  NEW STORIES FROM THE TWILIGHT ZONE   SERLING, ROD   OC
RIPENESS   PEASE, M. C.   NV   SFS 55 01
  RARE SCIENCE FICTION   HOWARD, IVAN   AN
RIPPLES   RUSSELL, RAY   SS   PBY 67 10
  PLAYBOY'S STORIES OF THE SINISTER & STRANGE
                        PLAYBOY, EDITORS OF   AN
  SAGITTARIUS   RUSSELL, RAY   AC
RISE OF AIRSTRIP ONE, THE   JAMES, CLIVE   SS
  BEST SF: 1974   HARRISON & ALDISS   AN
RISING OF THE SUN, THE   EKLUND, GORDON   SS
  BEYOND TIME   LEY, SANDRA   OA
RISK   ASIMOV, ISAAC   NV   ASF 55 05
  *REST OF THE ROBOTS, THE   ASIMOV, ISAAC   AC
RITE OF PASSAGE   OLIVER, CHAD   NV   ASF 54 04
  ANOTHER KIND   OLIVER, CHAD   AC
  SEVEN COME INFINITY   CONKLIN, GROFF   AN
RITE OF PASSAGE   PANSHIN, ALEXEI NO   ACE 68
  SCIENCE FICTION SPECIAL 5   ANONYMOUS   AN
RITE OF SPRING   DAVIDSON, AVRAM SS   ORB 70 08
  BEST FROM ORBIT, THE   KNIGHT, DAMON   AN
  ORBIT 8   KNIGHT, DAMON   OA
RITE OF SPRING, A   LEIBER, FRITZ   NV   UNI 77 07
  UNIVERSE 7   CARR, TERRY   OA
RITUAL (STRANGE RITUAL)   SHECKLEY, ROBERT SS   CLM 53
  *UNTOUCHED BY HUMAN HANDS   SHECKLEY, ROBERT   AC
RIVER OF RICHES   KERSH, GERALD   SS   SEP 58 03
  SF:59, THE YEAR'S GREATEST SCIENCE FICTION AND FANTASY
                        MERRIL, JUDITH   AN
RIVERS OF DAMASCUS   LAFFERTY, R. A. NV   GAL 74 02
  BEST FROM GALAXY, THE VOLUME III   BAEN, JAMES   AN
RIVERWORLD   FARMER, PHILIP JOSE NV   WOT 66 01
  DOWN IN THE BLACK GANG AND OTHER STORIES FARMER, PHILIP JOSE AC
RIYA'S FOUNDLING   BUDRYS, ALGIS   SS   SFS 53 01
  HUMAN?   MERRIL, JUDITH   AN
  MIND TO MIND   SILVERBERG, ROBERT   AN
ROACHES, THE   DISCH, THOMAS M. SS   ESC 65 10
  FUN WITH YOUR NEW HEAD   DISCH, THOMAS M.   AC
  11TH ANNUAL OF THE YEAR'S BEST S-F, THE MERRIL, JUDITH   AN
ROAD BACK, THE   REED, CLIFFORD C. SN   SFB 60 02
  MARTIAN ENTERPRISE   REED, CLIFFORD C.   AC
ROAD MAP   BUSBY, F. M.   SS   CLR 73 03
  CLARION III   WILSON, ROBIN SCOTT OA
ROAD OF THE EAGLES, THE (CONAN, MAN OF DESTINY)
                        DE CAMP, L. SPRAGUE
                        AND HOWARD, ROBERT E.   NV C FUN 55 12
  CONAN THE FREEBOOTER   HOWARD, R. & DE CAMP AC
  TALES OF CONAN   HOWARD, R. & DE CAMP AC
ROAD TO CINNABAR, THE   BRYANT, EDWARD   SS   INY 71 02
  INFINITY 2   HOSKINS, ROBERT   OA
ROAD TO NIGHTFALL   SILVERBERG, ROBERT NV   FUN 58 07
  BEST OF ROBERT SILVERBERG, THE   SILVERBERG, ROBERT   AC
  DARK STARS   SILVERBERG, ROBERT   AN
  FANTASTIC UNIVERSE OMNIBUS, THE   SANTESSON, HANS S.   AN
  PARSECS AND PARABLES   SILVERBERG, ROBERT   AC
ROAD TO ROME   WOLLHEIM, DONALD A. SS   FUT 53 07
  TWO DOZEN DRAGON EGGS   WOLLHEIM, DONALD A.   AC
ROAD TO SINHARAT, THE   BRACKETT, LEIGH NV   AMZ 63 05
  COMING OF THE TERRANS, THE   BRACKETT, LEIGH   AC
ROAD TO THE SEA, THE (SEEKER OF THE SPHINX)
                        CLARKE, ARTHUR C. NV   TCS 51 SP
  TALES OF TEN WORLDS   CLARKE, ARTHUR C.   AC
ROAD, THE   DOLAN, MIKE   SS
  SANTANA MORNING AND OTHER STORIES   DOLAN, MIKE   OC
ROADS   QUINN, SEABURY   SS   WRT 38 01
  WORLDS OF WEIRD   MARGULIES, LEO   AN
ROADS MUST ROLL, THE   HEINLEIN, ROBERT A. NV   ASF 40 06
  *ADVENTURES IN TIME AND SPACE   HEALY & MCCOMAS   AN
  BEST OF ROBERT HEINLEIN, THE   HEINLEIN, ROBERT A.   AC
  GREAT SCIENCE FICTION STORIES   SMITH, CORDELIA T.   AN
  JOURNEYS IN SCIENCE FICTION   LOUGHLIN, RICHARD L.   AN
  *MAN WHO SOLD THE MOON, THE   HEINLEIN, ROBERT A.   AC
  MORE ADVENTURES IN TIME AND SPACE   HEALY & MCCOMAS   AN
  PAST THROUGH TOMORROW, THE   HEINLEIN, ROBERT A.   AC
  SCIENCE FICTION HALL OF FAME VOLUME 1 SILVERBERG, ROBERT   AN
  TOMORROW X 4   KNIGHT, DAMON   AN
ROADS OF DESTINY   HENRY, O.   NV   09
  FANTASY: THE LITERATURE OF THE MARVELOUS KELLEY, LEO P.   AN
  MOONLIGHT TRAVELER, THE   STERN, PHILIP VAN D. AN
  WORLD OF WONDER   PRATT, FLETCHER   AN

ROADS, THE ROADS, THE BEAUTIFUL ROADS, THE
                                    DAVIDSON, AVRAM   SS   ORB 69 05
   ORBIT 5   KNIGHT, DAMON   OA
ROBBIE   VARSHAVSKY, ILYA   SS
   PATH INTO THE UNKNOWN   ANONYMOUS   AN
ROBBIE (STRANGE PLAYFELLOW)   ASIMOV, ISAAC   SS SSS 40 09
   I, ROBOT   ASIMOV, ISAAC   AC
   *SCIENCE FICTION THINKING MACHINES CONKLIN, GROFF   AN
   TALES BEYOND TIME   DE CAMP, L. S.&C.   AN
ROBBIE AND DAVID AND LITTLE DAHL
                                    MACFARLANE, WALLACE SS GAL 72 05
   MORE LITTLE MONSTERS   ELWOOD & GHIDALIA   AN
ROBERT BLAKE'S UNIVERSE (SEE THE UNIVERSE OF ROBERT BLAKE)
                                    ELLISON, HARLAN   TC
ROBERT MACDONALD- 2025 (THE LISTENERS)
                                    GUNN, JAMES E.   NV GAL 68 09
   LISTENERS, THE   GUNN, JAMES E.   NO
ROBERT MACDONALD- 2058   GUNN, JAMES E.   NV
   LISTENERS, THE   GUNN, JAMES E.   NO
ROBERTA   ST. CLAIR, MARGARET SS GAL 62 10
   THREE WORLDS OF FUTURITY   ST. CLAIR, MARGARET   DC
ROBIN HOOD'S BARN   ANDERSON, POUL   NV ASF 59 01
   ORBIT UNLIMITED   ANDERSON, POUL   NO
ROBIN HOOD, F.R.S. (VENTURE TO THE MOON)
                                    CLARKE, ARTHUR C.   SS FSF 56 12
   OF TIME AND STARS   CLARKE, ARTHUR C.   AC
   OTHER SIDE OF THE SKY, THE   CLARKE, ARTHUR C.   AC
ROBINC   BOUCHER, ANTHONY   SS ASF 43 09
   COMPLEAT WEREWOLF, THE   BOUCHER, ANTHONY   AC
ROBINC   HOLMES, H. H.   SS ASF 43 09
   ROBOT AND THE MAN, THE   GREENBERG, MARTIN   AN
ROBINSON   ROME, DAVID   SS
   SECOND PACIFIC BOOK OF SCIENCE FICTION, THE
                                    BAXTER, JOHN   AN
ROBOT AL-76 GOES ASTRAY   ASIMOV, ISAAC   SS AMZ 42 02
   *MY BEST SCIENCE FICTION STORY   MARGULIES & FRIEND   AN
   *REST OF THE ROBOTS, THE   ASIMOV, ISAAC   AC
ROBOT HUMOR   MUSLIN, E.
                                    AND ZUBKOV, E.   SS C
   RUSSIAN SCIENCE FICTION, 1969   MAGIDOFF, ROBERT   AN
ROBOT JUSTICE (SEE I SEE YOU)   HARRISON, HARRY   TC
ROBOT NEMESIS (WHAT A COURSE!, PART 13 OF COSMOS, FMG 34)
                                    SMITH, EDWARD E. PHD SS TWS 39 06
   BEST OF E. E. 'DOC' SMITH, THE   SMITH, EDWARD E. PHD   AC
ROBOT SLEEP   INOUYE, JON   SS
   NIGHT TIDE, A   INOUYE, JON   OC
ROBOT SON   YOUNG, ROBERT F.   NV FUN 59 09
   GODS FOR TOMORROW   SANTESSON, HANS S.   AN
ROBOT WHO WANTED TO KNOW, THE   BOYD, FELIX   SS FUN 58 03
   FANTASTIC UNIVERSE OMNIBUS, THE SANTESSON, HANS S.   AN
ROBOT WHO WANTED TO KNOW, THE   HARRISON, HARRY   SS FUN 58 03
   WAR WITH THE ROBOTS   HARRISON, HARRY   AC
ROBOT WIFE, THE   BURKE, JONATHAN F.   SS
   EXODUS FROM ELYSIUM   BURKE, JONATHAN F.   AC
ROBOT'S DOZEN   LACK, G. L.   SS NWR 67 10
   NEW WRITINGS IN SF. 8   CARNELL, JOHN   AN
   NEW WRITINGS IN SF. 10   CARNELL, JOHN   OA
ROBOT'S STORY   WOLFE, GENE   SS DVS 72 02
   AGAIN, DANGEROUS VISIONS   ELLISON, HARLAN   OA
ROBOTNIKS, THE   BAKHNOV, VLADLEN   SS
   RUSSIAN SCIENCE FICTION, 1968   MAGIDOFF, ROBERT   AN
ROBOTS ARE HERE, THE   CARR, TERRY   NV IFS 67 05
   COSMIC LAUGHTER   HALDEMAN, JOE W.   AN
   LIGHT AT THE END OF THE UNIVERSE, THE CARR, TERRY   AC
ROBOTS DON'T BLEED   GROVES, J. W.   SS NWS 50 WI
   BEST FROM NEW WORLDS SCIENCE FICTION, THE
                                    CARNELL, JOHN   AN
   *NO PLACE LIKE EARTH   CARNELL, JOHN   AN
ROBOTS RETURN   WILLIAMS, ROBERT M. SS ASF 38 09
   *ADVENTURES IN TIME AND SPACE   HEALY & MCCOMAS   AN
   ANTHROPOLOGY THROUGH SCIENCE FICTION MASON, C/GREENBERG/& AN
   ROBOT AND THE MAN, THE   GREENBERG, MARTIN   AN
ROBOTS SHOULD STICK TOGETHER   FAIRMAN, PAUL W.   SS
   FORGETFUL ROBOT, THE   FAIRMAN, PAUL W.   OC
ROCK DIVER   HARRISON, HARRY   SS WBY 51 02
   BEYOND THE END OF TIME   POHL, FREDERIK   AN
   EARTH IS THE STRANGEST PLANET   SILVERBERG, ROBERT   AN
   SCIENCE FICTION INVENTIONS   KNIGHT, DAMON   AN
ROCK GOD   ELLISON, HARLAN   SS COV 69 11
   DEATHBIRD STORIES   ELLISON, HARLAN   AC
   OVER THE EDGE   ELLISON, HARLAN   AC
ROCK-A-BYE   CHRISTOPHER, JOHN   SS
   TWENTY-SECOND CENTURY, THE   CHRISTOPHER, JOHN   AC
ROCKET MAN, THE   BRADBURY, RAY   SS MCL 51 05
   *ILLUSTRATED MAN, THE   BRADBURY, RAY   AC
   R IS FOR ROCKET   BRADBURY, RAY   AC
ROCKET MAN, THE   LUDWIG, EDWARD W.   SS OWS 51 05
   TALES BEYOND TIME   DE CAMP, L. S.&C.   AN
ROCKET OF 1955, THE   KORNBLUTH, C. M.   SS STI 41 04
   BEST OF C. M. KORNBLUTH, THE   KORNBLUTH, C. M.   AC
   EXPLORERS, THE   KORNBLUTH, C. M.   AC
   MINDWORM AND OTHER STORIES, THE KORNBLUTH, C. M.   AC
   THIRTEEN O'CLOCK AND OTHER ZERO HOURS KORNBLUTH, C. M.   AC
   VINTAGE ANTHOLOGY OF SCIENCE FANTASY, THE
                                    CERF, CHRISTOPHER   AN
ROCKET RIDER   COOMBS, CHARLES   BLF 59
   TEEN-AGE OUTER SPACE STORIES   FURMAN, A. L.   AN
ROCKET SUMMER   BRADBURY, RAY   SS PLS 47 SP
   MARTIAN CHRONICLES, THE   BRADBURY, RAY   AC
ROCKET TO THE SUN   VAN DRESSER, PETER   SS AMB 39 07
   YEAR AFTER TOMORROW, THE   DEL REY, L/MATSCHAT/ AN
ROCKET, THE (OUTCAST OF THE STARS)
                                    BRADBURY, RAY   SS SSS 50 03
   *ILLUSTRATED MAN, THE   BRADBURY, RAY   AC
   R IS FOR ROCKET   BRADBURY, RAY   AC

ROCKETEERS HAVE SHAGGY EARS, THE
                                    BENNETT, KEITH   NV PLS 50 S
   BEST OF PLANET STORIES NO. 1, THE BRACKETT, LEIGH   A
   TRAVELLERS OF SPACE   GREENBERG, MARTIN   A
ROCKETS AREN'T HUMAN   TUBB, E. C.   SS NWS 53 0
   BEST FROM NEW WORLDS SCIENCE FICTION, THE
                                    CARNELL, JOHN   A
ROCKETS TO WHERE?   MERRIL, JUDITH   AR NEW 59 A
   SF:59, THE YEAR'S GREATEST SCIENCE FICTION AND FANTASY
                                    MERRIL, JUDITH   A
ROCKING-HORSE WINNER, THE   LAWRENCE, D. H.   SS   33
   CHILDREN OF WONDER   TENN, WILLIAM   A
   OTHER DIMENSION, THE   ROSNER, SARA   A
   TRAVELERS IN TIME   STERN, PHILIP VAN D. A
RODENT LABORATORY, THE   PLATT, CHARLES   SS NWS 66 0
   BEST SF STORIES FROM NEW WORLDS 5 MOORCOCK, MICHAEL   A
RODNEY PARISH FOR HIRE   ELLISON, HARLAN
                                    AND HENSLEY, JOE L. SS C SWK 62 0
   PARTNERS IN WONDER   ELLISON, HARLAN   A
ROGER BACON FORMULA, THE   PRATT, FLETCHER   SS AMZ 29 0
   *BIG BOOK OF SCIENCE FICTION   CONKLIN, GROFF   A
ROGUE LEONARDO   LACK, G. L.   SS NWR 64 0
   NEW WRITINGS IN SF. 2   CARNELL, JOHN   A
ROGUE MOON   BUDRYS, ALGIS   SN FSF 60 1
   SCIENCE FICTION HALL OF FAME VOLUME 2B BOVA, BEN   A
ROGUE PSI   SCHMITZ, JAMES H.   NV AMZ 62 0
   BEST FROM AMAZING, THE   WHITE, TED   A
ROGUE SHIP (ALSO AS THE TWISTED MEN)
                                    VAN VOGT, A. E.   NV SSS 50 0
   GIANT ANTHOLOGY OF SCIENCE FICTION MARGULIES & FRIEND   A
   ROGUE SHIP   VAN VOGT, A. E.   N
   TOMORROW AND TOMORROW   KNIGHT, DAMON   A
ROGUE STAR   LEINSTER, MURRAY   NV NEW 60 A
   TWISTS IN TIME   LEINSTER, MURRAY   A
ROGUE TOMATO   BISHOP, MICHAEL   SS NDM 75 0
   NEW DIMENSIONS 5   SILVERBERG, ROBERT   O
ROGUE, THE (INDUSTRIAL REVOLUTION)
                                    ANDERSON, POUL   SN ASF 63 0
   TALES OF THE FLYING MOUNTAINS   ANDERSON, POUL   A
ROGUES IN THE HOUSE   HOWARD, ROBERT E.   SS WRT 34 0
   COMING OF CONAN, THE   HOWARD, ROBERT E.   A
   CONAN   HOWARD, R./DE CAMP/&   A
ROLL OF DAUGHTERS, A   AYME, MARCEL   SS
   WALKER THROUGH WALLS, THE   AYME, MARCEL   A
ROLLER BALL MURDERS   HARRISON, WILLIAM   SS ESQ 73 0
   BEST SF: 1973   HARRISON & ALDISS   A
   ROLLERBALL   HARRISON, WILLIAM   A
ROLLER COASTER, THE   BESTER, ALFRED   SS FAN 53 0
   BEST FROM FANTASTIC, THE   WHITE, TED   A
   STARBURST   BESTER, ALFRED   A
ROLLING ROBERT   LORY, ROBERT   SS
   HARVEST OF HOODWINKS, A   LORY, ROBERT   D
ROMANCE IN A 21ST CENTURY USED CAR LOT
                                    YOUNG, ROBERT F.   SS FSF 60 1
   WORLDS OF ROBERT F. YOUNG, THE   YOUNG, ROBERT F.   A
ROMANCE OF DR. TANNER, THE   GOULART, RON   SS UNI 71 0
   UNIVERSE 1   CARR, TERRY   O
ROMANCE OF MARS, THE   ASIMOV, ISAAC   IN
   MARS, WE LOVE YOU   HIPOLITO & MCNELLY   A
ROMANCE OF THE BOY AND THE GIRL, THE
                                    DISCH, THOMAS M.   SS
   *GETTING INTO DEATH   DISCH, THOMAS M.   A
ROMANCE OF THE FIRST RADICAL, THE
                                    LANG, ANDREW   SS   87
   ANCESTRAL VOICES   MENVILLE & REGINALD   A
ROOFS OF SILVER   DICKSON, GORDON R.   NV FSF 62 1
   MUTANTS   DICKSON, GORDON R.   A
ROOG   DICK, PHILIP K.   SS FSF 53 0
   BEST OF PHILIP K. DICK, THE   DICK, PHILIP K.   A
   INVADERS FROM SPACE   SILVERBERG, ROBERT   A
   OTHERS, THE   CARR, TERRY   A
   PRESERVING MACHINE, THE   DICK, PHILIP K.   A
ROOM WITH A VIEW   CARLSON, ESTHER   SS FAN 53 0
   FIEND IN YOU, THE   BEAUMONT, CHARLES   A
ROOM 312   TASSONE, G. L.   SS PBY 67 0
   PLAYBOY'S STORIES OF THE SINISTER & STRANGE
                                    PLAYBOY, EDITORS OF   A
ROOM, THE   RUSSELL, RAY   SS PBY 61 0
   MAN AGAINST TOMORROW   NOLAN, WILLIAM F.   A
   PLAYBOY BOOK OF SCIENCE FICTION AND FANTASY, THE
                                    PLAYBOY, EDITORS OF   A
   SAGITTARIUS   RUSSELL, RAY   A
   SARDONICUS AND OTHER STORIES   RUSSELL, RAY   A
ROOMMATES (BASIS FOR NOVEL "MAKE ROOM! MAKE ROOM!")
                                    HARRISON, HARRY   NV NEW 71 A
   ABOVE THE HUMAN LANDSCAPE   MCNELLY & STOVER   A
   *BEST OF HARRY HARRISON, THE   HARRISON, HARRY   A
   EARTH IN TRANSIT   SCHWARTZ, SHEILA   A
   RUINS OF EARTH, THE   DISCH, THOMAS M.   A
ROOT AND THE RING, THE   GUIN, WYMAN   NV BEY 54 0
   BEYOND   ANONYMOUS   A
   LIVING WAY OUT   GUIN, WYMAN   A
ROOT OF AMPOI, THE   SMITH, CLARK ASHTON SS ARS 49 0
   TALES OF SCIENCE AND SORCERY   SMITH, CLARK ASHTON   A
ROPE ENOUGH   COLLIER, JOHN   SS NYM 39 1
   HUMAN?   MERRIL, JUDITH   A
ROPE OF GLASS   ZEBROWSKI, GEORGE   SS TVW 73
   MONADIC UNIVERSE, THE   ZEBROWSKI, GEORGE   A
   TWO VIEWS OF WONDER   SCORTIA & YARBRO   A
ROPE TRICK   BROWN, FREDRIC   SS
   NIGHTMARES AND GEEZENSTACKS   BROWN, FREDRIC   A
RORQUAL MARU   BASS, T. J.   NV GAL 72 0
   1973 ANNUAL WORLD'S BEST SF, THE WOLLHEIM, DONALD A.   A
ROSE BY OTHER NAME, A   ANVIL, CHRISTOPHER   SS ASF 60 0
   6TH ANNUAL OF THE YEAR'S BEST S-F, THE MERRIL, JUDITH

OSE FOR ECCLESIASTES, A

OSE FOR ECCLESIASTES, A   ZELAZNY, ROGER   NV   FSF 63 11
   BEST FROM FANTASY AND SCIENCE FICTION: 14
                                  DAVIDSON, AVRAM   AN
   DOORS OF HIS FACE, THE LAMPS OF HIS MOUTH, THE
                                  ZELAZNY, ROGER   AC
   FOUR FOR TOMORROW   ZELAZNY, ROGER   AC
   NEW AWARENESS, THE   WARRICK & GREENBERG   AN
   SCIENCE FICTION HALL OF FAME VOLUME 1 SILVERBERG, ROBERT AN
   SCIENCE FICTION: THE FUTURE   ALLEN, DICK   AN
   10TH ANNUAL OF THE YEAR'S BEST S-F, THE MERRIL, JUDITH   AN
OSE-BOWL PLUTO HYPOTHESIS, THE
                                  LATHAM, PHILIP   SS   ORB 69 05
   ORBIT 5   KNIGHT, DAMON   OA
OSE, THE   HARNESS, CHARLES L. NO AUT 53 03
   ROSE, THE   HARNESS, CHARLES L.   AC
   SCIENCE FICTION SPECIAL 4   ANONYMOUS   AN
OSEBUD, THE   RUSSELL, RAY   SS   FSF 59 08
   SARDONICUS AND OTHER STORIES RUSSELL, RAY   AC
OSY FUTURE FOR RODERICK, A   BOND, NELSON S.   SS   BBM 52 08
   MORE LITTLE MONSTERS   ELWOOD & GHIDALIA   AN
   NIGHTMARES AND DAYDREAMS   BOND, NELSON S.   AC
OTIFERS, THE   ABERNATHY, ROBERT   SS   IFS 53 03
   EARTH IS THE STRANGEST PLANET SILVERBERG, ROBERT   AN
   FIRST WORLD OF IF, THE   QUINN & WULFF   AN
OUND AND ROUND AND ROUND AGAIN
                                  SANTOS, DOMINGO   NV   70
   BEST FROM THE REST OF THE WORLD, THE WOLLHEIM, DONALD A. AN
OUND BILLIARD TABLE, A   HALL, STEVE   SS   NWR 64 02
   NEW WRITINGS IN SF. 2   CARNELL, JOHN   OA
OUND THE MOON (1870)   VERNE, JULES   EX
   JULES VERNE- MASTER OF SCIENCE FICTION VERNE, JULES   AC
OUND THE MOON (1870)   VERNE, JULES   NO
   TREASURY OF SCIENCE FICTION CLASSICS, THE
                                  KUEBLER, HAROLD W.   AN
OUND TRIP   BRUNNER, JOHN   SS   FUN 59 09
   NOT BEFORE TIME   BRUNNER, JOHN   AC
   *OUT OF MY MIND   BRUNNER, JOHN   AC
OUND TRIP TO ESIDARAP (ESIDARAP OT PIRT DNUOR)
                                  BIGGLE, LLOYD JR.   SS   IFS 60 11
   GALAXY OF STRANGERS, A   BIGGLE, LLOYD JR.   AC
   OUT OF THIS WORLD 3   WILLIAMS-ELLIS& OWEN   AN
OUSING OF MR. BRADEGAR, THE   HEARD, H. F.   SS   44
   GREAT FOG AND OTHER WEIRD TALES, THE HEARD, H. F.   OC
   TRAVELERS IN TIME   STERN, PHILIP VAN D.   AN
OUTINE EXERCISE   HIGH, PHILIP E.   SS   NWS 61 02
   LAMBDA I AND OTHER STORIES   CARNELL, JOHN   AN
OUTINE PATROL ACTIVITY   PICKENS, THOMAS   SS   ALC 73
   ALIEN CONDITION, THE   GOLDIN, STEPHEN   OA
OVER I WILL BE, A   COURTNEY, ROBERT
                                  AND ROBINSON, FRANK M. SS C
   EVERY BOY'S BOOK OF OUTER SPACE STORIES DIKTY, T. E.   AN
OYAL IMPOSTOR (SEE THE KING WHO COLLECTED CLOCKS)
                                  KERSH, GERALD   TC
OYAL LESSON   NUETZEL, CHARLES   SS
   IMAGES OF TOMORROW   NUETZEL, CHARLES   AC
OYAL LICORICE   LAFFERTY, R. A.   SS   ORB 74 14
   ORBIT 14   KNIGHT, DAMON   OA
UB-A-DUB   GALOUYE, DANIEL F. SS
   PROJECT BARRIER   GALOUYE, DANIEL F.   AC
UB, THE   CHANDLER, A. BERTRAM NV GAL 70 04
   ALTERNATE ORBITS   CHANDLER, A. BERTRAM   DC
UBAIYAT OF AMBROSE BAGLEY, THE
                                  MACFARLANE, WALLACE SS   SFE 74 01
   SCIENCE FICTION EMPHASIS NO. 1 GERROLD, DAVID   OA
UBBER BEND, THE   WOLFE, GENE   NV   UNI 74 05
   UNIVERSE 5   CARR, TERRY   OA
UE D'EVANGILE   AYME, MARCEL   SS
   WALKER THROUGH WALLS, THE   AYME, MARCEL   AC
UINED CITY IN THE MOON, A   LACH-SZYRMA, D. S. SS   CSL 87 01
   WORLDS APART   LOCKE, GEORGE   AN
UINS, THE (AS JAMES COLVIN)   MOORCOCK, MICHAEL   SS   NWS 66 04
   TIME DWELLER, THE   MOORCOCK, MICHAEL   AC
ULE GOLDEN   KNIGHT, DAMON   NV   SPA 54 06
   SIX GREAT SHORT SCIENCE FICTION NOVELS CONKLIN, GROFF AN
   THREE NOVELS   KNIGHT, DAMON   AC
ULE OF NAMES, THE   LE GUIN, URSULA K. SS   FAN 64 04
   WINDS TWELVE QUARTERS, THE   LE GUIN, URSULA K.   AC
ULE OF THE DOOR, THE   BIGGLE, LLOYD JR.   NV   GAL 58 02
   RULE OF THE DOOR AND OTHER FANCIFUL REGULATIONS
                                  BIGGLE, LLOYD JR.   AC
ULE OF THREE   STURGEON, THEODORE NV   GAL 51 01
   *GALAXY READER OF SCIENCE FICTION GOLD, H. L.   AN
ULE, THE   WRIGHT, S. FOWLER   SS
   NEW GODS LEAD, THE   WRIGHT, S. FOWLER   AC
ULERS, THE   VAN VOGT, A. E.   SS   ASF 44 03
   DESTINATION: UNIVERSE!   VAN VOGT, A. E.   AC
ULES OF MOOPSBALL   COHN, GARY   AR   ORB 76 18
   ORBIT 18   KNIGHT, DAMON   OA
ULES OF THE GAME, THE   WOLLHEIM, DONALD A. SS   NWR 73 22
   NEW WRITINGS IN SF. 22   BULMER, KENNETH   OA
ULES OF THE ROAD, THE   SPINRAD, NORMAN   SS   GAL 64 12
   FIRST STEP OUTWARD   HOSKINS, ROBERT   AN
   LAST HURRAH OF THE GOLDEN HORDE, THE SPINRAD, NORMAN AC
ULL, THE   VAN VOGT, A. E.   NV   ASF 48 05
   ADVENTURES ON OTHER PLANETS   WOLLHEIM, DONALD A.   AN
   BEST OF A. E. VAN VOGT, THE   VAN VOGT, A. E.   AC
   SCIENCE FICTION: THE GREAT YEARS, VOL. II
                                  POHL, C. & F.   AN
   TRAVELLERS OF SPACE   GREENBERG, MARTIN   AN
   WAR AGAINST THE RULL, THE   VAN VOGT, A. E.   NO
UMFUDDLE   VANCE, JACK   NA   TTT 73
   BEST OF JACK VANCE, THE   VANCE, JACK   AC
   BEST SCIENCE FICTION OF THE YEAR, THE NO. 3
                                  CARR, TERRY   AN
   THREE TRIPS IN TIME AND SPACE SILVERBERG, ROBERT   OA

SAD STORY OF A DRAMATIC CRITIC, THE

RUMP-TITTY-TITTY-TUM-TAH-TEE   LEIBER, FRITZ   SS   FSF 58 05
   BEST OF FRITZ LEIBER, THE   LEIBER, FRITZ   AC
   PAIL OF AIR, A   LEIBER, FRITZ   AC
   SCIENCE FICTION ARGOSY, A   KNIGHT, DAMON   AN
   SCIENCE FICTION ODDITIES   CONKLIN, GROFF   AN
   SECRET SONGS, THE   LEIBER, FRITZ   AC
RUN FOR THE STARS   ELLISON, HARLAN   NV   SPA 57 06
   BEAST THAT SHOUTED LOVE AT THE HEART OF THE WORLD, THE
                                  ELLISON, HARLAN   AC
   TOUCH OF INFINITY, A   ELLISON, HARLAN   DC
RUN FROM HOME, THE   HENSLEY, JOE L.   SS   FSF 70 12
   LIBERATED FUTURE: VOYAGES INTO TOMORROW, THE
                                  HOSKINS, ROBERT   AN
RUN FROM THE FIRE   HARRISON, HARRY   NV   EPC 75
   EPOCH   ELWOOD & SILVERBERG   OA
RUN TO STARLIGHT   MARTIN, GEORGE R. R. NV AMZ 74 12
   INFINITE ARENA, THE   CARR, TERRY   AN
RUN TO STARLIGHT, SPORTS THROUGH SCIENCE FICTION
                                  GREENBERG/OLANDER/&   AN
   SONG FOR LYA, A   MARTIN, GEORGE R. R.   AC
RUN, THE   PRIEST, CHRISTOPHER SS   IMP 66 05
   ENGLAND SWINGS SF   MERRIL, JUDITH   AN
   REAL-TIME WORLD   PRIEST, CHRISTOPHER   AC
   SPACE-TIME JOURNAL, THE   MERRIL, JUDITH   AN
RUNAROUND   ASIMOV, ISAAC   SS   ASF 42 03
   AS TOMORROW BECOMES TODAY   SULLIVAN, CHARLES W.   AN
   COMING OF THE ROBOTS, THE   MOSKOWITZ, SAM   AN
   I, ROBOT   ASIMOV, ISAAC   AC
RUNAROUND   BROWN, FREDRIC   SS
   NIGHTMARES AND GEEZENSTACKS   BROWN, FREDRIC   AC
RUNAWAY PROP   HARVEY, FRANK   SS   SEP 59 05
   AIR FORCE!   HARVEY, FRANK   AC
RUNAWAY SKYSCRAPER, THE   LEINSTER, MURRAY   NV   ARG 19 02
   BEST OF AMAZING, THE   ROSS, JOSEPH   AN
RUNAWAY WORLD, A   HARRIS, CLARE WINGER SS WRT 26 07
   AWAY FROM THE HERE AND NOW   HARRIS, CLARE WINGER   AC
RUNDOWN   LORY, ROBERT   SS   IFS 63 05
   SCIENCE FICTION ODDITIES   CONKLIN, GROFF   AN
RUNESMITH   ELLISON, HARLAN
                                  AND STURGEON, THEODORE SS C FSF 70 05
   PARTNERS IN WONDER   ELLISON, HARLAN   AC
RUNNERS, THE   MARTIN, GEORGE R. R. SS FSF 75 09
   SONGS OF STARS AND SHADOWS   MARTIN, GEORGE R. R.   AC
RUNNING AROUND   MALZBERG, BARRY N. SS   OMG 73
   BEST OF BARRY N. MALZBERG, THE MALZBERG, BARRY N.   AC
   OMEGA   ELWOOD, ROGER   OA
RUNNING DOWN   HARRISON, M. JOHN   NV   NWB 75 08
   MACHINE IN SHAFT TEN AND OTHER STORIES, THE
                                  HARRISON, M. JOHN   AC
   NEW WORLDS EIGHT   BAILEY, HILARY   OA
RUNNING, THE   POSNER, RICHARD   SS   NEW 73 AN
   ANDROIDS, TIME MACHINES AND BLUE GIRAFFES
                                  ELWOOD & GHIDALIA   AN
   VISIONS OF TOMORROW   ELWOOD, ROGER   AN
RUSSKIES GO HOME!   REYNOLDS, MACK   SS   FSF 60 11
   UNFRIENDLY FUTURE, THE   BOARDMAN, TOM JR.   AN
RUST   KELLEAM, JOSEPH E. SS   ASF 39 10
   GATES TO TOMORROW   NORTON, AN.&DONALDY   AN
   ROBOT AND THE MAN, THE   GREENBERG, MARTIN   AN
RUSTLE OF WINGS   BROWN, FREDRIC   SS   FSF 53 08
   HONEYMOON IN HELL   BROWN, FREDRIC   AC
   PORTALS OF TOMORROW   DERLETH, AUGUST   AN
RUUM, THE   PORGES, ARTHUR   SS   FSF 53 10
   BEST SF   CRISPIN, EDMUND   AN
   FROM FRANKENSTEIN TO ANDROMEDA BROWN, JAMES GOLDIE   AN
   GREAT SCIENCE-FICTION   LICATA, TONY   AN
   OUT OF THIS WORLD 1   WILLIAMS-ELLIS& OWEN   AN
   STARS AND UNDER, THE   CRISPIN, EDMUND   AN
   TALES OF TERROR FROM OUTER SPACE CHETWYND-HAYES, R.   AN
RX   NOURSE, ALAN E.   SS   IFS 57 10
   RX FOR TOMORROW   NOURSE, ALAN E.   AC
R26/5/PSY AND I   CONEY, MICHAEL G.   NV   NWR 69 16
   MONITOR FOUND IN ORBIT   CONEY, MICHAEL G.   AC
   NEW WRITINGS IN SF. 16   CARNELL, JOHN   OA
S AS IN ZEBATINSKY (SEE SPELL MY NAME WITH AN S)
                                  ASIMOV, ISAAC   TC
S*T*A*P*L*E FARM, THE   DNIEPROV, ANATOLY   SS
   OTHER WORLDS, OTHER SEAS   SUVIN, DARKO   AN
S.F.   KLEIN, T. E. D.   SS   NEW 75 AN
   YEAR'S BEST HORROR STORIES: SERIES III, THE
                                  DAVIS, RICHARD   AN
S-F BOOKS- 1960   BOUCHER, ANTHONY   MS
   6TH ANNUAL OF THE YEAR'S BEST S-F, THE MERRIL, JUDITH AN
SABBATICAL   BLOCH, ROBERT   SS   GAL 59 12
   TALES IN A JUGULAR VEIN   BLOCH, ROBERT   AC
SACHEVERELL   DAVIDSON, AVRAM   SS   FSF 64 C3
   BEST FROM FANTASY AND SCIENCE FICTION: 14
                                  DAVIDSON, AVRAM   AN
   STRANGE SEAS AND SHORES   DAVIDSON, AVRAM   AC
SACK, THE   MORRISON, WILLIAM   SS   ASF 50 09
   SCIENCE FACT/FICTION   FARRELL/GAGE/&   AN
   SCIENCE FICTION: THE GREAT YEARS, VOL. II
                                  POHL, C. & F.   AN
   TOMORROW, THE STARS   HEINLEIN, ROBERT A.   AN
SACRED CITY OF CATS, THE (FROM TIME CAT)
                                  ALEXANDER, LLOYD   EX   HRW 63
   TALES BEYOND TIME   DE CAMP, L. S.&C.   AN
SACRED MARTIAN PIG, THE (SEE IDRIS' PIG)
                                  ST. CLAIR, MARGARET   TC
SAD SOLARIAN SCREENWRITER SAM   POHL, FREDERIK   SS   FSF 72 06
   GOLD AT STARBOW'S END, THE   POHL, FREDERIK   AC
SAD STORY OF A DRAMATIC CRITIC, THE
                                  WELLS, H. G.   SS   BON 15
   PLATTNER STORY AND OTHERS, THE WELLS, H. G.   AC
   SHORT STORIES OF H. G. WELLS, THE WELLS, H. G.   AC
   THIRTY STRANGE STORIES   WELLS, H. G.   AC

```
SADASTOR              SMITH, CLARK ASHTON  SS   WRT 30 07
  OUT OF SPACE AND TIME          SMITH, CLARK ASHTON  AC
SAFE AT ANY SPEED     NIVEN, LARRY       SS   FSF 67 05
  SHAPE OF SPACE, THE            NIVEN, LARRY       AC
  TALES OF KNOWN SPACE: THE UNIVERSE OF LARRY NIVEN
                                 NIVEN, LARRY       AC
SAFETY ENGINEER, THE  BOULT, S. KYE      NV   ALC 73
  ALIEN CONDITION, THE           GOLDIN, STEPHEN    OA
SAGA OF DMM, THE      EISENBERG, LARRY   SS   FSF 67 12
  BEST LAID SCHEMES, THE         EISENBERG, LARRY   AC
SAGITTARIUS           RUSSELL, RAY       NA   PBY 62 03
  SAGITTARIUS                    RUSSELL, RAY       AC
SAIL ON! SAIL ON!     FARMER, PHILIP JOSE  SS  STS 52 12
  CENTURY OF SCIENCE FICTION, A  KNIGHT, DAMON      AN
  DECADE THE 1950S               ALDISS & HARRISON  AN
  SF: AUTHORS' CHOICE            HARRISON, HARRY    AN
  WORLDS OF MAYBE                SILVERBERG, ROBERT AN
SAIL THE TIDE OF MOURNING  LUPOFF, RICHARD A.  SS  NDM 75 05
  BEST SCIENCE FICTION OF THE YEAR, THE NO. 5
                                 CARR, TERRY        AN
  NEW DIMENSIONS 5               SILVERBERG, ROBERT OA
SAIL 25 (GATEWAY TO STRANGENESS)
                      VANCE, JACK        NV   AMZ 62 08
  BEST OF JACK VANCE, THE        VANCE, JACK        AC
  FUTURE TENSE                   VANCE, JACK        AC
SAINT KATY THE VIRGIN STEINBECK, JOHN    SS   38
  TIMELESS STORIES FOR TODAY AND TOMORROW  BRADBURY, RAY  AN
SAINT MULLIGAN        BOND, NELSON S.    SS   FAD 43 05
  31ST OF FEBRUARY, THE          BOND, NELSON S.    AC
SAINT 505             CLARKE, JOHN       SS   NWS 67 01
  ENGLAND SWINGS SF              MERRIL, JUDITH     AN
  SPACE-TIME JOURNAL, THE        MERRIL, JUDITH     AN
SALES OF A DEATHMAN   BLOCH, ROBERT      SS   GAL 68 02
  FEAR TODAY, GONE TOMORROW      BLOCH, ROBERT      AC
SALINE SOLUTION       LAUMER, KEITH      NV   IFS 63 03
  GALACTIC DIPLOMAT              LAUMER, KEITH      AC
SALIVA TREE, THE      ALDISS, BRIAN W.   SN   FSF 65 09
  BRIAN ALDISS OMNIBUS, A        ALDISS, BRIAN W.   AC
  DIMENSION X                    KNIGHT, DAMON      AN
  NEBULA AWARD STORIES           KNIGHT, DAMON      AN
  SALIVA TREE AND OTHER STRANGE GROWTHS, THE
                                 ALDISS, BRIAN W.   AC
SALLY                 ASIMOV, ISAAC      SS   FAN 53 05
  BEST FROM FANTASTIC, THE       WHITE, TED         AN
  NIGHTFALL AND OTHER STORIES    ASIMOV, ISAAC      AC
  TIME UNTAMED                   HOWARD, IVAN       AN
SALTZMAN'S MADNESS    LUPOFF, RICHARD A. NV   FCR 75
  FUTURE CORRUPTION              ELWOOD, ROGER      OA
SALVADOR DALI         BALLARD, J. G.     AR   NWS 69 02
  BEST SF STORIES FROM NEW WORLDS 8  MOORCOCK, MICHAEL  AN
SALVAGE               CARTMILL, CLEVE    NV   TWS 49 08
  SPACE SCAVENGERS, THE          CARTMILL, CLEVE    NO
SALVAGE IN SPACE      WILLIAMSON, JACK   SS   ASF 33 03
  EARLY WILLIAMSON, THE          WILLIAMSON, JACK   AC
SAM HALL              ANDERSON, POUL     NV   ASF 53 08
  BEST OF POUL ANDERSON, THE     ANDERSON, POUL     AC
  LIBERATED FUTURE: VOYAGES INTO TOMORROW, THE
                                 HOSKINS, ROBERT    AN
  *SCIENCE FICTION THINKING MACHINES  CONKLIN, GROFF  AN
SAM SMALL'S BETTER HALF  KNIGHT, ERIC    SS   42
  MOONLIGHT TRAVELER, THE        STERN, PHILIP VAN D.  AN
SAM SMALL'S TYKE      KNIGHT, ERIC       SS   42
  OUT OF THIS WORLD              FAST, JULIUS       AN
SAM, THIS IS YOU      LEINSTER, MURRAY   NV   GAL 55 05
  BEST OF MURRAY LEINSTER, THE   LEINSTER, MURRAY   AC
  TWISTS IN TIME                 LEINSTER, MURRAY   AC
SAMARITAN, THE        HARPER, RICHARD    SS   BLF
  BOYS' LIFE BOOK OF OUTER SPACE STORIES, THE
                                 BOY'S LIFE, ED. OF AN
  UNIVERSE AHEAD                 ENGDAHL & ROBERSON AN
SAME AUTUMN IN A DIFFERENT PARK
                      TATE, PETER        SS   FAN 67 09
  ENGLAND SWINGS SF              MERRIL, JUDITH     AN
  SEAGULLS UNDER GLASS AND OTHER STORIES  TATE, PETER  AC
  SPACE-TIME JOURNAL, THE        MERRIL, JUDITH     AN
SAME TIME, SAME PLACE PEAKE, MERVYN      SS   SCF 63 08
  WEIRD SHADOWS FROM BEYOND      CARNELL, JOHN      AN
SAME TO YOU DOUBLED, THE  SHECKLEY, ROBERT  SS  PBY 70 03
  CAN YOU FEEL ANYTHING WHEN I DO THIS?, AND OTHER STORIES
                                 SHECKLEY, ROBERT   AC
  FROM THE "S" FILE              PLAYBOY, EDITORS OF AN
SAMUEL F. MAYNARD AND ANTHROPOLOGIC DEMONOGRAPHY
                      WOOD, RAMSEY       SS   NEW 67 AN
  DEVIL HIS DUE, THE             HILL, DOUGLAS      AN
SAMURAI AND THE WILLOWS, THE  BISHOP, MICHAEL  NV  FSF 76 02
  BEST SCIENCE FICTION STORIES OF THE YEAR (1976)
                                 DOZOIS, GARDNER R. AN
SAN DIEGO LIGHTFOOT SUE  REAMY, TOM      NV   FSF 75 08
  NEBULA AWARD STORIES 11        LE GUIN, URSULA K. AN
SANATORIUM OF DR. VLIPERDIUS, THE
                      LEM, STANISLAW     SS   71
  MORTAL ENGINES                 LEM, STANISLAW     AC
SANCTUARY             GALOUYE, DANIEL F. NV   FSF 54 02
  BEST FROM FANTASY AND SCIENCE FICTION: 4
                                 BOUCHER, ANTHONY   AN
  LAST LEAP AND OTHER STORIES OF THE SUPER-MIND, THE
                                 GALOUYE, DANIEL F. AC
SANCTUARY             TENN, WILLIAM      SS   GAL 57 12
  SEVEN SEXES, THE               TENN, WILLIAM      AC
SAND AND STONES       EFFINGER, GEO. ALEC  SS  CLR 72 02
  CLARION II                     WILSON, ROBIN SCOTT  OA
SAND CASTLES          HALDEMAN, JACK C. II  SS  ALT 74
  ALTERNATES                     GERROLD, DAVID     OA
SAND DOOM             LEINSTER, MURRAY   NV   ASF 55 12
  COLONIAL SURVEY                LEINSTER, MURRAY   NO

SANDIAL               FEDER, MOSHE       SS   ORB 75 1
  ORBIT 16                       KNIGHT, DAMON      O.
SANDRA                ELLIOTT, GEORGE P. SS   FSF 57 1
  TREASURY OF GREAT SCIENCE FICTION, A VOL.1
                                 BOUCHER, ANTHONY   A
SANDS OF MARS, THE    CLARKE, ARTHUR C.  NO   SID 51
  ARTHUR C. CLARKE SECOND OMNIBUS, AN  CLARKE, ARTHUR C.  A
  PRELUDE TO MARS                CLARKE, ARTHUR C.  A
SANDS OF MARS, THE (ENCHANTED VILLAGE)
                      VAN VOGT, A. E.    SS   OWS 50 0
  SANDS OF MARS AND OTHER STORIES, THE  ANONYMOUS  A
SANDS OF TIME, THE    MILLER, P. SCHUYLER  SN  ASF 37 0
  *ADVENTURES IN TIME AND SPACE  HEALY & MCCOMAS    A
  GREAT SCIENCE FICTION STORIES  SMITH, CORDELIA T. A
  VOYAGERS IN TIME               SILVERBERG, ROBERT A
SANDS OUR ABODE       RAYER, FRANCIS G.  SS   NWS 59 0
  OUT OF THIS WORLD 3            WILLIAMS-ELLIS & OWEN  A
SANITY (ALSO AS CRAZY WOLF)  LEIBER, FRITZ  SS   ASF 44 0
  BEST OF FRITZ LEIBER, THE      LEIBER, FRITZ      A
  *BIG BOOK OF SCIENCE FICTION   CONKLIN, GROFF     A
  ONE HUNDRED YEARS OF SCIENCE FICTION  KNIGHT, DAMON  A
  SCIENCE FICTION ROLL OF HONOR, THE  POHL, FREDERIK  A
SANTA CLAUS COMPROMISE, THE  DISCH, THOMAS M.  SS  CRW 74 1
  BEST SF: 75, THE NINTH ANNUAL  HARRISON & ALDISS  A
SANTA CLAUS PLANET, THE  ROBINSON, FRANK M.  SS  NEW 51 A
  BEST SCIENCE-FICTION STORIES: 1951, THE  BLEILER & DIKTY
  MINDWORM, THE                  ANONYMOUS          A
SANTA CLAUS VS. S.P.I.D.E.R.  ELLISON, HARLAN  NV  FSF 69 0
  BEAST THAT SHOUTED LOVE AT THE HEART OF THE WORLD, THE
                                 ELLISON, HARLAN    A
SANTA RIDES A SAUCER  WOLLHEIM, DONALD A.  SS
  TWO DOZEN DRAGON EGGS          WOLLHEIM, DONALD A. A
SANTANA MORNING       DOLAN, MIKE        SS
  SANTANA MORNING AND OTHER STORIES  DOLAN, MIKE   O
SAPPHIRE GODDESS, THE DYALHIS, NICTZIN   NV   WRT 34 0
  WORLDS OF WEIRD                MARGULIES, LEO     A
SAPPHIRE SIREN, THE   DYALHIS, NICTZIN   NV   WRT 34 0
  AVON FANTASY READER, THE       WOLLHEIM & ERNSBERGER  A
SARAH                 KELLER, DAVID H. MD. SS  52
  FOLSOM FLINT AND OTHER CURIOUS TALES, THE
                                 KELLER, DAVID H. MD.  AC
SARDONIC STAR OF TOM DOODY, THE
                      HAMMETT, DASHIELL  SS   BLM 24
  FANTASTIC PULPS, THE           HAINING, PETER     A
SARDONICUS            RUSSELL, RAY       NA   PBY 61 0
  PLAYBOY BOOK OF HORROR AND THE SUPERNATURAL, THE
                                 PLAYBOY, EDITORS OF A
  SAGITTARIUS                    RUSSELL, RAY       A
  SARDONICUS AND OTHER STORIES   RUSSELL, RAY       A
SARGASSO OF LOST CITIES  BLISH, JAMES    SN   TCS 53 S
  EARTHMAN, COME HOME            BLISH, JAMES       N
SATAN AND SAM SHAY    ARTHUR, ROBERT     SS   ELK 42 0
  DEALS WITH THE DEVIL           DAVENPORT, BASIL   A
  OUT OF THIS WORLD              FAST, JULIUS       A
SATANESQUE            WEISS, ALAN        SS   LMF 74
  YEAR'S BEST HORROR STORIES: SERIES III, THE
                                 DAVIS, RICHARD     A
SATELLITE FIVE (SEE JUPITER)  BARNES, ARTHUR K.  TC
SATELLITE OF PERIL    LONG, FRANK BELKNAP  NV  TWS 42 0
  JOHN CARSTAIRS: SPACE DETECTIVE  LONG, FRANK BELKNAP  A
SATELLITE PASSAGE     THOMAS, THEODORE L.  SS  IFS 58 1
  SF: THE BEST OF THE BEST       MERRIL, JUDITH     A
  SF:59, THE YEAR'S GREATEST SCIENCE FICTION AND FANTASY
                                 MERRIL, JUDITH     A
SATIRICAL SCIENCE FICTION (FROM "GULLIVER'S TRAVELS")
                      SWIFT, JONATHAN    EX
  SCIENCE FICTION THROUGH THE AGES 1  EVANS, I. O.  A
SATISFACTION (SEE SEMPER FI)  KNIGHT, DAMON    TC
SATISFACTION GUARANTEED  ASIMOV, ISAAC   SS   AMZ 51 0
  EARTH IS ROOM ENOUGH           ASIMOV, ISAAC      A
  INVASION OF THE ROBOTS         ELWOOD, ROGER      A
  *REST OF THE ROBOTS, THE       ASIMOV, ISAAC      A
SATURN (TROUBLE ON TITAN)  BARNES, ARTHUR K.  NV  TWS 41 0
  INTERPLANETARY HUNTER          BARNES, ARTHUR K.  A
SATURN FACTS          MISC. MATERIAL     MS
  LAURIE'S SPACE ANNUAL          ANONYMOUS          A
SATURN RISING         CLARKE, ARTHUR C.  SS   FSF 61 0
  TALES OF TEN WORLDS            CLARKE, ARTHUR C.  A
SATURNIA CELIA (1903) WALPOLE, HORACE    SS   FSF 57 0
  DECADE OF FANTASY AND SCIENCE FICTION, A  MILLS, ROBERT P.  A
SAUCER OF LONELINESS  STURGEON, THEODORE SS   GAL 53 0
  E PLURIBUS UNICORN             STURGEON, THEODORE A
  FLYING SAUCERS IN FACT AND FICTION  SANTESSON, HANS S.  A
  GALAXY SCIENCE FICTION OMNIBUS GOLD, H. L.        A
  SECOND GALAXY READER OF SCIENCE FICTION  GOLD, H. L.  A
  WORLDS OF SCIENCE FICTION, THE MILLS, ROBERT P.   A
SAUNDER'S LITTLE FRIEND  DERLETH, AUGUST SS   WRT 48 0
  NOT LONG FOR THIS WORLD        DERLETH, AUGUST    A
SAVAGE CURTAIN, THE (G. RODDENBERRY & A. HEINEMANN)
                                 BLISH, JAMES       SS   STK 72 0
  STAR TREK 6                    BLISH, JAMES       A
SAVAGE PELLUCIDAR     BURROUGHS, EDGAR R.  NV  AMZ 63 1
  SAVAGE PELLUCIDAR              BURROUGHS, EDGAR R.  A
SAVAGE WIND (SEE THE WIND FROM BEYOND THE MOUNTAINS)
                                 ELLISON, HARLAN    TC
SAVE YOUR CONFEDERATE MONEY, BOYS
                      BROWN, ROSEL GEORGE  SS  FUN 59 1
  HANDFUL OF TIME, A             BROWN, ROSEL GEORGE  A
SAVING THE WORLD      CARR, TERRY        SS   SVW 73
  SAVING WORLDS                  ELWOOD & KIDD      A
SAVIOR SOLE           FAYETTE, MICHAEL   SS   71
  FAR-OUT PEOPLE, THE            HOSKINS, ROBERT    A
SAXON PRETENDER, THE  DE CAMP, L. SPRAGUE  SS
  SPRAGUE DE CAMP'S NEW ANTHOLOGY  DE CAMP, L. SPRAGUE  A
SAY GOODBYE TO THE WIND  BALLARD, J. G.  SS   FAN 70 0
  NEW WORLDS OF FANTASY NO. 3    CARR, TERRY        AN
```

```
*VERMILLION SANDS                         BALLARD, J. G.          AC
AY GOODBYE TO THE WORLD'S LAST BROTHEL
                                          WISSNER, ROBERT    SS   CLR 73 03
  CLARION III                             WILSON, ROBIN SCOTT     OA
AY IT WITH FLOWERS                        ANDERSON, POUL     SS   ASF 65 09
  TALES OF THE FLYING MOUNTAINS           ANDERSON, POUL          AC
AY IT WITH FLOWERS                        SANDERS, WINSTON P. SS  ASF 65 09
  ANALOG 5                                CAMPBELL, JOHN W. JR    AN
CANNERS LIVE IN VAIN                      SMITH, CORDWAINER  NA   FBK 50 06
  BEST OF CORDWAINER SMITH, THE           SMITH, CORDWAINER       AC
  BEYOND THE END OF TIME                  POHL, FREDERIK          AN
  DECADE THE 1950S                        ALDISS & HARRISON       AN
  SCIENCE AND SORCERY                     FORD, GARRET            AN
  SCIENCE FICTION HALL OF FAME VOLUME 1   SILVERBERG, ROBERT      AN
  SURVIVAL PRINTOUT                       TOTAL EFFECT            AN
  YOU WILL NEVER BE THE SAME              SMITH, CORDWAINER       AC
CAPE-GOAT OF LA JUSTICIA, THE MARTIN, HAROLD  SS
  BATTLE FOR THE PACIFIC AND OTHER ADVENTURES AT SEA, THE
                                          ANONYMOUS               AN
CAPEGOAT                                  HANNAH, E.         SS
  WORLDS AT WAR                           RAYER, FRANCIS G.       AN
CAR, THE                                  CAMPBELL, J. RAMSEY SS  SMS 69 SU
  YEAR'S BEST HORROR STORIES, THE         DAVIS, RICHARD          AN
CARAB IN THE CITY OF TIME, A RANDALL, MARTA  SS   NDM 75 05
  NEW DIMENSIONS 5                        SILVERBERG, ROBERT      OA
CARAB, THE                                GALLUN, RAYMOND Z. SS   ASF 36 08
  *SCIENCE FICTION THINKING MACHINES      CONKLIN, GROFF          AN
CARFE'S WORLD                             ALDISS, BRIAN W.   NV   WOT 65 03
  11TH ANNUAL OF THE YEAR'S BEST S-F, THE MERRIL, JUDITH          AN
CARLET CITADEL, THE                       HOWARD, ROBERT E.  SS   WRT 33 01
  CONAN THE USURPER                       HOWARD, R. & DE CAMP    AC
  KING CONAN                              HOWARD, ROBERT E.       AC
CARLET DREAM                              MOORE, C. L.       NV   WRT 34 05
  *FUTURE TENSE                           CROSSEN, KENDELL F.     AN
  *SHAMBLEAU AND OTHERS                   MOORE, C. L.            AC
CARLET LADY, THE                          ROBERTS, KEITH     NV   IMP 66 08
  NEW WORLDS OF FANTASY NO. 2             CARR, TERRY             AN
CARLET LUNES, THE                         COBLENTZ, STANTON A. SS FBK 50 06
  SCIENCE AND SORCERY                     FORD, GARRET            AN
CARLET PLAGUE, THE                        LONDON, JACK       NA   LOM 12 06
  ASLEEP IN ARMAGEDDON                    SISSONS, MICHAEL        AN
  CURIOUS FRAGMENTS                       LONDON, JACK            AC
  OMNIBUS OF SCIENCE FICTION              CONKLIN, GROFF          AN
  OUT OF THIS WORLD                       FAST, JULIUS            AN
  SCIENCE FICTION OF JACK LONDON, THE     LONDON, JACK            AC
  STRANGE TRAVELS IN SCIENCE FICTION      CONKLIN, GROFF          AN
CARS                                      STURGEON, THEODORE SS   ZGW 49 05
  E PLURIBUS UNICORN                      STURGEON, THEODORE      AC
CAVENGERS, THE                            WHITE, JAMES       SS   ASF 53 10
  ALIENS AMONG US, THE                    WHITE, JAMES            AC
CENE FOR SATAN                            LANGLEY, NOEL      SS   SEP 47 01
  SATURDAY EVENING POST FANTASY STORIES, THE
                                          FLES, BARTHOLD          AN
CENE SHIFTER, THE                         SELLINGS, ARTHUR   SS   STR 59 05
  LONG EUREKA, THE                        SELLINGS, ARTHUR        AC
  STAR SCIENCE FICTION STORIES NO. 5      POHL, FREDERIK          OA
CENT OF SARSAPARILLA, A BRADBURY, RAY  SS   STR 53 01
  DAY IT RAINED FOREVER, THE              BRADBURY, RAY           AC
  MEDICINE FOR MELANCHOLY, A              BRADBURY, RAY           AC
  STAR SCIENCE FICTION STORIES            POHL, FREDERIK          OA
  *STORIES FOR TOMORROW                   SLOANE, WILLIAM         AN
  TRANSFORMATIONS II                      ROSELLE, DANIEL         AN
CENTS OF IT, THE                          BONE, J. F.        NV   INY 71 02
  INFINITY 2                              HOSKINS, ROBERT         OA
CHEDULE                                   WALTON, HARRY      SS   ASF 45 06
  *MEN AGAINST THE STARS                  GREENBERG, MARTIN       AN
CHEMATIC MAN, THE                         POHL, FREDERIK     SS   PBY 69 01
  BEST SF: 1969                           HARRISON & ALDISS       AN
  DAY MILLION                             POHL, FREDERIK          AC
  IN THE PROBLEM PIT                      POHL, FREDERIK          AC
CHERZO FOR SCHIZOIDS: NOTES ON A COLLABORATION
                                          ELLISON, HARLAN    MS   KNT 65 11
  PARTNERS IN WONDER                      ELLISON, HARLAN         AC
CHIZO JIMMIE                              LEIBER, FRITZ      SS   SMM 60 02
  SHADOWS WITH EYES                       LEIBER, FRITZ           AC
CHIZOID CREATOR                           SMITH, CLARK ASHTON SS  FNF 53 11
  TALES OF SCIENCE AND SORCERY            SMITH, CLARK ASHTON     AC
CHOLIA, SEASONED WITH CRABS, BLISH IS
                                          CLUTE, JOHN        AR   NWQ 73 05
  NEW WORLDS NO. 5                        MOORCOCK & PLATT        OA
CHOOL FOR THE UNSPEAKABLE                 WELLMAN, MANLY WADE SS  WRT 37 09
  OTHER WORLDS, THE                       STONG, PHILIP D.        AN
CHRODINGER'S CAT                          LE GUIN, URSULA K. SS   UNI 74 05
  UNIVERSE 5                              CARR, TERRY             OA
CHWARTZ BETWEEN THE GALAXIES SILVERBERG, ROBERT SS STL 74 01
  FEAST OF ST. DIONYSUS, THE              SILVERBERG, ROBERT      AC
  STELLAR 1                               DEL REY, JUDY-LYNN      OA
CIENCE                                    JEFFERS, ROBINSON  PM   25
  SPECULATIONS                            SANDERS, THOMAS E.      AN
CIENCE AND SCIENCE FICTION CLARKE, ARTHUR C.  IN
  TIME PROBE: THE SCIENCES IN SF.         CLARKE, ARTHUR C.       AN
CIENCE FAIR, THE                          VINGE, VERNOR      SS   ORB 71 09
  ORBIT 9                                 KNIGHT, DAMON           OA
CIENCE FICTION                            AMIS, KINGSLEY     PM   ENC 60 05
  SPECULATIONS                            SANDERS, THOMAS E.      AN
  STARLIT CORRIDOR, THE                   MANSFIELD, ROGER        AN
CIENCE FICTION AND FREEDOM ANDERSON, POUL  AR   SFR 69 30
  HOMEBREW                                ANDERSON, POUL          AC
CIENCE FICTION AND IDEAS CONKLIN, GROFF  IN
  HUMAN AND OTHER BEINGS                  DEGRAEFF, ALLEN         AN
CIENCE FICTION AND LITERARY TRADITION
                                          CLARESON, THOMAS D. MS
  NEBULA AWARD STORIES NO. 6              SIMAK, CLIFFORD D.      AN
CIENCE FICTION AND THE WORLD OF RELIGION
                                          MOHS, MAYO         IN
  OTHER WORLDS, OTHER GODS                MOHS, MAYO              AN

SCIENCE FICTION AND YOU                   HERBERT, FRANK     IN
  TOMORROW, AND TOMORROW, AND TOMORROW... HEINTZ/HERBERT/JOOS/ AN
SCIENCE FICTION AS CULTURE CRITICISM
                                          MCNELLY, WILLIS E.
                                 AND STOVER, LEON E.        AR C
  ABOVE THE HUMAN LANDSCAPE               MCNELLY & STOVER        AN
SCIENCE FICTION COMES OF AGE LESSER, MILTON  IN
  LOOKING FORWARD                         LESSER, MILTON          AN
SCIENCE FICTION COVER ILLUSTRATIONS
                                          JONES, EDDIE       IL
  BEYOND THIS HORIZON                     CARRELL, CHRISTOPHER OA
SCIENCE FICTION COVER ILLUSTRATIONS
                                          KIRBY, JOSH        IL
  BEYOND THIS HORIZON                     CARRELL, CHRISTOPHER OA
SCIENCE FICTION COVER ILLUSTRATIONS
                                          THOLE, KAREL       IL
  BEYOND THIS HORIZON                     CARRELL, CHRISTOPHER OA
SCIENCE FICTION DICTIONARY    MISC. MATERIAL  MS
  TRAVELLERS OF SPACE                     GREENBERG, MARTIN       AN
SCIENCE FICTION HALL OF FAME, THE
                                          SILVERBERG, ROBERT SS   INY 73 05
  CAPRICORN GAMES                         SILVERBERG, ROBERT      AC
  INFINITY 5                              HOSKINS, ROBERT         OA
SCIENCE FICTION HORROR MOVIE POCKET COMPUTER, THE
                                          WILSON, GAHAN      MS   NLP 71 11
  BEST SF: 1971                           HARRISON & ALDISS       AN
SCIENCE FICTION NOVEL IN 1968, THE
                                          MCNELLY, WILLIS E. IN
  NEBULA AWARD STORIES  NO. 4             ANDERSON, POUL          AN
SCIENCE FICTION STILL LEADS SCIENCE FACT
                                          BOUCHER, ANTHONY   AR   NYT 57 12
  SF:58, THE YEAR'S GREATEST SCIENCE FICTION AND FANTASY
                                          MERRIL, JUDITH          AN
SCIENCE FICTION STORY                     ACKERSON, DUANE    PM   EDG 74
  BEST SF: 1974                           HARRISON & ALDISS       AN
SCIENCE FICTION STORY FOR JONI MITCHELL, A
                                          JAKUBOWSKI, MAXIM  NV
  NEW S.F., THE                           JONES, LANGDON          OA
SCIENCE FICTION YEAR, THE                 BROWN, CHARLES N.  MS
  BEST SCIENCE FICTION OF THE YEAR, THE NO. 4
                                          CARR, TERRY             AN
  BEST SCIENCE FICTION OF THE YEAR, THE NO. 5
                                          CARR, TERRY             AN
SCIENCE FICTION YEARBOOK, THE DEL REY, LESTER  MS
  BEST SCIENCE FICTION STORIES OF THE YEAR (1971)
                                          DEL REY, LESTER         AN
  BEST SCIENCE FICTION STORIES OF THE YEAR (1972)
                                          DEL REY, LESTER         AN
  BEST SCIENCE FICTION STORIES OF THE YEAR (1973)
                                          DEL REY, LESTER         AN
  BEST SCIENCE FICTION STORIES OF THE YEAR (1974)
                                          DEL REY, LESTER         AN
  BEST SCIENCE FICTION STORIES OF THE YEAR (1975)
                                          DEL REY, LESTER         AN
SCIENCE FICTION: BEFORE CHRIST AND AFTER 2001
                                          BRADBURY, RAY      IN
  SCIENCE FACT/FICTION                    FARRELL/GAGE/&          AN
SCIENCE FICTION, ARCHETYPES, AND THE FUTURE
                                          WRIGHT, R. GLENN   AR   CLR 73 03
  CLARION III                             WILSON, ROBIN SCOTT OA
SCIENCE FICTION, MORALS, AND RELIGION
                                          HEARD, GERALD      AR   NEW 53 NF
  SCIENCE FICTION: THE FUTURE             ALLEN, DICK             AN
SCIENCE OF FICTION? A SURVEY OF ATTITUDES
                                          SUDBERY, TONY      AR
  BEYOND THIS HORIZON                     CARRELL, CHRISTOPHER OA
SCIENCE STEALS A MARCH                    RICHARDS, NELSON   SS
  ADVENTURES TO COME                      ESENWEIN, J. BERG       OA
SCIENCE WONDER STORIES COVER PAUL, FRANK R.  IL
  BEYOND THIS HORIZON                     CARRELL, CHRISTOPHER OA
SCIENCE-FICTION AWARDS        MISC. MATERIAL  MS
  SCIENCE FACT/FICTION                    FARRELL/GAGE/&          AN
SCIENCE-FICTION BOOK INDEX, THE
                                          KEMP, EARL         MS
  BEST SCIENCE FICTION STORIES AND NOVELS: 1955
                                          DIKTY, T. E.            AN
  BEST SCIENCE FICTION STORIES AND NOVELS: 1956
                                          DIKTY, T. E.            AN
  BEST SCIENCE FICTION STORIES AND NOVELS: 9TH SERIES
                                          DIKTY, T. E.            AN
SCIENCE-FICTION YEAR, THE     DIKTY, T. E.  MS
  BEST SCIENCE FICTION STORIES AND NOVELS: 1955
                                          DIKTY, T. E.            AN
  BEST SCIENCE FICTION STORIES AND NOVELS: 1956
                                          DIKTY, T. E.            AN
  BEST SCIENCE FICTION STORIES AND NOVELS: 9TH SERIES
                                          DIKTY, T. E.            AN
SCIENTIFIC CRACKSMAN, THE                 REEVE, ARTHUR B.   SS   AMD 30 08
  SILENT BULLET, THE                      REEVE, ARTHUR B.        AC
SCIENTIFIC METHOD (HANDS ACROSS SPACE)
                                          OLIVER, CHAD       SS   SFP 53 08
  ANOTHER KIND                            OLIVER, CHAD            AC
SCIENTIFIC PIONEER RETURNS, THE
                                          BOND, NELSON S.    SS   AMZ 40 11
  LANCELOT BIGGS: SPACEMAN                BOND, NELSON S.         AC
SCIENTIST DIVIDES, A                      WANDREI, DONALD    SS   ASF 34 09
  *BEST OF SCIENCE FICTION                CONKLIN, GROFF          AN
  EYE AND THE FINGER                      WANDREI, DONALD         AC
SCIENTIST SAYS ICECAP ON VENUS WOULD MAKE LIFE POSSIBLE
                                          CLARK, EVERT       AR   NYT 68 03
  FAREWELL FANTASTIC VENUS                ALDISS & HARRISON       AN
  "SCIENTISTS ARE STUPID!"                CAMPBELL, JOHN W. JR IN
  ANALOG 5                                CAMPBELL, JOHN W. JR AN
SCOPE                                     INOUYE, JON        SS
  NIGHT TIDE, A                           INOUYE, JON             OC
```

SCORNER'S SEAT   LAFFERTY, R. A.   NV   SVW 73
  SAVING WORLDS   ELWOOD & KIDD   OA
SCRAMBLED WORLD   WELLS, BASIL   SS   PLS 47 SP
  PLANETS OF ADVENTURE   WELLS, BASIL   AC
SCRAPING AT THE BONES, A   BUDRYS, ALGIS   SS   ASF 75 05
  BEST SF: 75, THE NINTH ANNUAL   HARRISON & ALDISS   AN
SCRAWNY ONE, THE   BOUCHER, ANTHONY SS   WRT 49 05
  UNEXPECTED, THE   MARGULIES, LEO   AN
SCREAM   GORDON, GILES   SS   NWS 68 07
  BEST SF STORIES FROM NEW WORLDS 5   MOORCOCK, MICHAEL AN
SCREAM WOLF   LEIBER, FRITZ   SS   MSM 61 02
  SECOND BOOK OF FRITZ LEIBER, THE   LEIBER, FRITZ   AC
SCREAM, THE   WILHELM, KATE   NV   ORB 74 13
  BEST SF: 1974   HARRISON & ALDISS   AN
  ORBIT 13   KNIGHT, DAMON   OA
SCREAMING PEOPLE, THE   BLOCH, ROBERT   NV   FAN 59 01
  CHAMBER OF HORRORS   BLOCH, ROBERT   AC
SCREAMING WOMAN, THE   BRADBURY, RAY   SS   TDY 51 05
  AUTUMN PEOPLE, THE   BRADBURY, RAY   AC
  GRAVEYARD READER, THE   CONKLIN, GROFF   AN
  S IS FOR SPACE   BRADBURY, RAY   AC
SCREEN GAME, THE   BALLARD, J. G.   NV   FAN 63 10
  IMPOSSIBLE MAN, THE   BALLARD, J. G.   AC
  *VERMILLION SANDS   BALLARD, J. G.   AC
SCREWTOP   MCINTYRE, VONDA N. NA
  CRYSTAL SHIP, THE   SILVERBERG, ROBERT   OA
SCRIMSHAW   LEINSTER, MURRAY SS   ASF 55 09
  BEST OF MURRAY LEINSTER, THE   LEINSTER, MURRAY   AC
SCULPTORS OF LIFE   WEST, WALLACE   SS   ASF 39 12
  *SCIENCE FICTION THINKING MACHINES   CONKLIN, GROFF   AN
SCYTHE, THE   BRADBURY, RAY   SS   WRT 43 07
  *DARK CARNIVAL   BRADBURY, RAY   AC
  *OCTOBER COUNTRY, THE   BRADBURY, RAY   AC
SCYTHE, THE   SANDRELLI, SANDRO SS   63
  BEST FROM THE REST OF THE WORLD, THE   WOLLHEIM, DONALD A.   AN
SEA BRIGHT   MOORE, HAL R.   SS   FSF 65 09
  BEST FROM FANTASY AND SCIENCE FICTION: 15
                                   FERMAN, EDWARD L.   AN
SEA CHANGE   CHANDLER, A. BERTRAM NV YRT 70
  YEAR 2000, THE   HARRISON, HARRY   OA
SEA CHANGE (ALSO AS THE SHORES OF NIGHT)
                           SCORTIA, THOMAS N. SS ASF 56 06
  CAUTION! INFLAMMABLE!   SCORTIA, THOMAS N.   AC
  HUMAN-MACHINES   SCORTIA & ZEBROWSKI   AN
  SPACE OPERA   ALDISS, BRIAN W.   AN
SEA CHANGE, THE   COX, ARTHUR JEAN SS   FSF 67 03
  BEST FROM FANTASY AND SCIENCE FICTION: 17
                                   FERMAN, EDWARD L.   AN
SEA GULLS, THE   VENEZIS, ELIAS   SS   55
  NIGHT IN FUNLAND   BRONDFIELD, JEROME   AN
SEA HOME   LEE, WILLIAM M.   NV   FSF 68 06
  BEST FROM FANTASY AND SCIENCE FICTION: 18
                                   FERMAN, EDWARD L.   AN
SEA OF FACES, A   SILVERBERG, ROBERT SS UNI 74 04
  CAPRICORN GAMES   SILVERBERG, ROBERT   AC
  UNIVERSE 4   CARR, TERRY   OA
SEA SHELLS, THE   BRADBURY, RAY   SS   WRT 44 01
  FANTASTIC PULPS, THE   HAINING, PETER   AN
SEA THING, THE   VAN VOGT, A. E.   NV   UNK 40 01
  MONSTERS   VAN VOGT, A. E.   AC
  OUT OF THE UNKNOWN   VAN VOGT & HULL   AC
SEA WAS WET AS WET COULD BE, THE
                           WILSON, GAHAN   SS   PBY 67 05
  FANTASY: THE LITERATURE OF THE MARVELOUS KELLEY, LEO P.   AN
  PLAYBOY BOOK OF HORROR AND THE SUPERNATURAL, THE
                                   PLAYBOY, EDITORS OF   AN
SEA WITCH, THE   DYALHIS, NICTZIN NV   WRT 37 12
  WEIRD TALES   MARGULIES, LEO   AN
SEA WOLVES   MOORCOCK, MICHAEL SS   SAG 70
  LIVES AND TIMES OF JERRY CORNELIUS, THE MOORCOCK, MICHAEL AC
  SCIENCE AGAINST MAN   CHEETHAM, ANTHONY   OA
SEA WRACK   JESBY, EDWARD   NV   FSF 64 05
  SCIENCE FICTION ARGOSY, A   KNIGHT, DAMON   AN
  WORLD'S BEST SCIENCE FICTION: 1965   WOLLHEIM & CARR   AN
SEA'S FURTHEST END, THE   BRODERICK, DAMIEN NV NWR 64 01
  NEW WRITINGS IN SF. 1   CARNELL, JOHN   OA
SEA-KINGS OF MARS (SEE THE SWORD OF RHIANNON)
                           BRACKETT, LEIGH   TC
SEA-RAIDERS, THE   WELLS, H. G.   SS   WSL 96 12
  ASPECTS OF SCIENCE FICTION   DOHERTY, G. D.   AN
  BEST SCIENCE FICTION STORIES OF H. G. WELLS
                                   WELLS, H. G.   AC
  BEST STORIES OF H. G. WELLS   WELLS, H. G.   AC
  COUNTRY OF THE BLIND, THE   WELLS, H. G.   AC
  PLATTNER STORY AND OTHERS, THE   WELLS, H. G.   AC
  SHORT STORIES OF H. G. WELLS, THE   WELLS, H. G.   AC
  SPECTRUM OF WORLDS, A   CLARESON, THOMAS D.   AN
  THIRTY STRANGE STORIES   WELLS, H. G.   AC
  TWENTY-EIGHT SCIENCE FICTION STORIES   WELLS, H. G.   AC
SEA, THE   ERNST, MAX   IL
  SCIENCE FICTION   BRODKIN & PEARSON   AN
SEAFARER, THE   PENMAN, THOMAS
                           AND SMITH, RITCHIE SS C NWR 75 26
  NEW WRITINGS IN SF. 26   BULMER, KENNETH   OA
SEAGULLS UNDER GLASS   TATE, PETER   SS
  SEAGULLS UNDER GLASS AND OTHER STORIES TATE, PETER   AC
SEAL OF THE SATYR, THE   BLOCH, ROBERT   SS   SRS 39 06
  MORE NIGHTMARES   BLOCH, ROBERT   AC
  *OPENER OF THE WAY, THE   BLOCH, ROBERT   AC
SEALED ORDERS (RETIEF OF THE RED-TAPE MOUNTAIN)
                           LAUMER, KEITH   NV   IFS 62 05
  ENVOY TO NEW WORLDS   LAUMER, KEITH   AC
SEALMAN, THE (1913)   MASEFIELD, JOHN   SS   FSF 55 07
  DECADE OF FANTASY AND SCIENCE FICTION, A MILLS, ROBERT P.   AN
  EDGE OF NEVER, THE   HOSKINS, ROBERT   AN

SEARCH   BROWN, FREDRIC   SS
  ANGELS AND SPACESHIPS   BROWN, FREDRIC   AC
SEARCH FOR MAN, THE   MOUDY, WALTER F. NA
  IN THE WAKE OF MAN   ELWOOD, ROGER   OA
SEARCH, THE   SIMONDS, BRUCE   PM   FSF 64 06
  10TH ANNUAL OF THE YEAR'S BEST S-F, THE MERRIL, JUDITH   AN
SEARCH, THE   VAN VOGT, A. E.   NV   ASF 43 01
  *BEST OF SCIENCE FICTION   CONKLIN, GROFF   AN
  DESTINATION: UNIVERSE!   VAN VOGT, A. E.   AC
  QUEST FOR THE FUTURE   VAN VOGT, A. E.   NC
SEARCHER, THE   SCHMITZ, JAMES H. SN ASF 66 02
  PRIDE OF MONSTERS, A   SCHMITZ, JAMES H.   AC
SEARCHLIGHT   HEINLEIN, ROBERT A. SS SAM 62 08
  PAST THROUGH TOMORROW, THE   HEINLEIN, ROBERT A.   AC
  WORLDS OF ROBERT A. HEINLEIN, THE HEINLEIN, ROBERT A. AC
SEASCAPE   BENFORD, GREGORY NV   76
  FASTER THAN LIGHT   DANN & ZEBROWSKI   OA
SEASE FIRE   HERBERT, FRANK   SS   ASF 58 01
  BEST OF FRANK HERBERT, THE   HERBERT, FRANK   AC
SEASON FOR FREEDOM, A (KILLERBOT!)
                           KOONTZ, DEAN R.   SS   GAL 69 05
  FUTURE NOW, THE   HOSKINS, ROBERT   AN
  SOFT COME THE DRAGONS   KOONTZ, DEAN R.   DC
SEASON OF DISBELIEF   BRADBURY, RAY   SS   COL 50 11
  DANDELION WINE   BRADBURY, RAY   NC
SEASON OF SITTING, THE   BRADBURY, RAY   AR   CHM 51 08
  DANDELION WINE   BRADBURY, RAY   NC
SEASON OF THE BABIES, THE DEFORD, MIRIAM ALLEN SS FUN 59 12
  XENOGENESIS   DEFORD, MIRIAM ALLEN AC
SEAT OF JUDGMENT, THE   DEL REY, LESTER   SS   VSF 57 02
  MORTALS AND MONSTERS   DEL REY, LESTER   AC
  NO LIMITS   FERMAN, JOSEPH W.   AN
SEAT OF OBLIVION   RUSSELL, ERIC FRANK SS ASF 41 11
  SOMEWHERE A VOICE   RUSSELL, ERIC FRANK   AC
SECOND ADVENT   REYNOLDS, MACK   SS   IFS 74 06
  BEST OF MACK REYNOLDS, THE   REYNOLDS, MACK   AC
SECOND CHALLENGE, THE   KANTOR, MACKINLAY SS RDT 29
  FANTASTIC PULPS, THE   HAINING, PETER   AN
SECOND CHANCE   BROWN, FREDRIC   SS
  NIGHTMARES AND GEEZENSTACKS   BROWN, FREDRIC   AC
SECOND CHANCE   COOPER, EDMUND   SS
  UNBORN TOMORROW   COOPER, EDMUND   AC
SECOND CHANCE   FINNEY, JACK   SS
  THIRD LEVEL, THE   FINNEY, JACK   AC
SECOND CHANCE   KUBILIUS, WALTER
                           AND PRATT, FLETCHER SS C FSM 52 FB
  SPACE, SPACE, SPACE   SLOANE, WILLIAM   AN
SECOND CHILDHOOD   SIMAK, CLIFFORD D. SS GAL 51 02
  *GALAXY READER OF SCIENCE FICTION   GOLD, H. L.   AN
  *STORIES FOR TOMORROW   SLOANE, WILLIAM   AN
SECOND DAWN   CLARKE, ARTHUR C. NV SFQ 51 08
  BEST OF ARTHUR C. CLARKE: 1937-1971, THE CLARKE, ARTHUR C.   AC
  EXPEDITION TO EARTH   CLARKE, ARTHUR C.   AC
  PRELUDE TO MARS   CLARKE, ARTHUR C.   AC
SECOND ENDING   WHITE, JAMES   NA   FAN 61 06
  MONSTERS AND MEDICS   WHITE, JAMES   AC
SECOND EXPERIMENT, THE   SAMBROT, WILLIAM SS
  ISLAND OF FEAR AND OTHER SCIENCE FICTION SAMBROT, WILLIAM AC
SECOND FOUNDATION   ASIMOV, ISAAC   NO   GNM 53
  FOUNDATION TRILOGY, THE   ASIMOV, ISAAC   AC
SECOND GAME   DEVET, CHARLES V.
                           AND MACLEAN, KATHERINE NV C ASF 58 03
  GREAT SHORT NOVELS OF SCIENCE FICTION SILVERBERG, ROBERT AN
SECOND GENESIS   RUSSELL, ERIC FRANK SS   51
  DEEP SPACE   RUSSELL, ERIC FRANK   AC
  NEW WRITINGS IN SF. 9   CARNELL, JOHN   OA
SECOND INQUISITION, THE   RUSS, JOANNA   NV   ORB 70 06
  ALYX   RUSS, JOANNA   AC
  IN DREAMS AWAKE   FIEDLER, LESLIE A.   AN
  MORE WOMEN OF WONDER   SARGENT, PAMELA   AN
  NEBULA AWARD STORIES NO. 6   SIMAK, CLIFFORD D.   AN
  ORBIT 6   KNIGHT, DAMON   OA
SECOND INTERMENT, THE   SMITH, CLARK ASHTON SS STT 33 01
  OUT OF SPACE AND TIME   SMITH, CLARK ASHTON   AC
SECOND KIND OF LONELINESS, THE MARTIN, GEORGE R. R. SS ASF 72 12
  INTRODUCTORY PSYCHOLOGY THROUGH SCIENCE FICTION
                                   KATZ/WARRICK/&   AN
  SONG FOR LYA, A   MARTIN, GEORGE R. R. AC
SECOND LANDING   LEINSTER, MURRAY NA   TWS 54 WI
  GET OFF MY WORLD!   LEINSTER, MURRAY   AC
SECOND MISSILE, THE   REPP, ED EARL   NV   AMZ 30 12
  STELLAR MISSILES, THE   REPP, ED EARL   AC
SECOND NATURE   OLIVER, CHAD   NV   FUQ 73
  FUTURE QUEST   ELWOOD, ROGER   OA
  GIFTS OF ASTI AND OTHER STORIES OF SCIENCE FICTION, THE
                                   ELWOOD, ROGER   AN
SECOND NIGHT OF SUMMER   SCHMITZ, JAMES H. SS GAL 50 12
  AGENT OF VEGA   SCHMITZ, JAMES H.   AC
  *POSSIBLE WORLDS OF SCIENCE FICTION   CONKLIN, GROFF   AN
SECOND NIGHT OUT   LONG, FRANK BELKNAP SS WRT 33 10
  EARLY LONG, THE   LONG, FRANK BELKNAP   AC
  *HOUNDS OF TINDALOS, THE   LONG, FRANK BELKNAP   AC
SECOND NOVA, THE   ASIMOV, ISAAC   IN
  BEST OF STANLEY G. WEINBAUM, THE   WEINBAUM, STANLEY G. AC
SECOND PRINT, THE (LORD OF EVIL)
                           DERLETH, AUGUST   SS   SRS 39 04
  NOT LONG FOR THIS WORLD   DERLETH, AUGUST   AC
SECOND SALLY, OR THE OFFER OF KING KROOL, THE
                           LEM, STANISLAW   NV
  CYBERIAD, THE   LEM, STANISLAW   OC
SECOND SHORT SHORTEST FANTASY STORY EVER PUBLISHED
                           MALZBERG, BARRY N. SS FSF 73 03
  MANY WORLDS OF BARRY MALZBERG, THE MALZBERG, BARRY N. AC
SECOND SIGHT   NOURSE, ALAN E.   SS   FUN 56 04
  COUNTERFEIT MAN, THE   NOURSE, ALAN E.   AC

SECOND SOLUTION, THE   SENDING THE VERY BEST

SECOND SOLUTION, THE   VAN VOGT, A. E.   SS ASF 42 10
  *AWAY AND BEYOND   VAN VOGT, A. E.   AC
  WAR AGAINST THE RULL, THE   VAN VOGT, A. E.   NO
SECOND TRIP TO MARS, THE (ALSO AS DOMINIONS BEYOND)
                            MOORE, WARD   SS SEP 54 08
  POST READER OF FANTASY AND SCIENCE FICTION
                            SATURDAY EVE. POST   AN
SECOND VARIETY   DICK, PHILIP K.   NV SSF 53 05
  BEST OF PHILIP K. DICK, THE   DICK, PHILIP K.   AC
  SPECTRUM 2   AMIS & CONQUEST   AN
  VARIABLE MAN, THE   DICK, PHILIP K.   AC
  YEAR'S BEST SCIENCE FICTION NOVELS: 1954 BLEILER & DIKTY AN
SECOND-CLASS CITIZEN, THE   KNIGHT, DAMON   SS IFS 63 11
  APEMAN, SPACEMAN   STOVER & HARRISON   AN
  *OFF CENTER   KNIGHT, DAMON   DC
SECRET   CAHN, LEE   SS ASF 53 01
  CROSSROADS IN TIME   CONKLIN, GROFF   AN
SECRET OF A MIGHTY CITY (HAVE YOUR HATREDS READY)
                            ALDISS, BRIAN W. SS FSF 58 05
  CANOPY OF TIME, THE   ALDISS, BRIAN W.   AC
  GALAXIES LIKE GRAINS OF SAND   ALDISS, BRIAN W.   AC
SECRET OF ANTON YORK, THE   BINDER, EANDO   NV TWS 40 08
  ANTON YORK, IMMORTAL   BINDER, EANDO   AC
SECRET OF APOLLONIUS SEPTRIO, THE
                            KIP, LEONARD   NV
  BATTLE OF THE MONSTERS AND OTHER STORIES, THE
                            HARTWELL & CURREY   AN
SECRET OF HOLMAN HUNT AND THE CRUDE DEATH RATE,THE
                            ALDISS, BRIAN W. FA NWS 70 01
  NEW WORLDS NO. 6   PLATT & BAILEY   OA
SECRET OF SEBEK, THE   BLOCH, ROBERT   SS WRT 37 11
  HORROR-7   BLOCH, ROBERT   AC
  HOUSE OF THE HATCHET, THE   BLOCH, ROBERT   AC
  *OPENER OF THE WAY, THE   BLOCH, ROBERT   AC
  WIZARDS AND WARLOCKS   GHIDALIA, VIC   AN
SECRET OF STONEHENGE, THE   HARRISON, HARRY   SS FSF 68 06
  ANCIENT MYSTERIES READER, THE   HAINING, PETER   AN
  PRIME NUMBER   HARRISON, HARRY   AC
SECRET OF THE HOUSE   BOUCHER, ANTHONY SS GAL 53 03
  FAR AND AWAY   BOUCHER, ANTHONY   AC
SECRET OF THE ISLAND, THE (THE MYSTERIOUS ISLAND, 1875)
                            VERNE, JULES   EX
  JULES VERNE- MASTER OF SCIENCE FICTION VERNE, JULES   AC
SECRET OF THE OLD CUSTARD, THE (THE BABE IN THE OVEN)
                            SLADEK, JOHN T.   SS IFS 66 11
  ALPHA 6   SILVERBERG, ROBERT   AN
SECRET OF THE TERRIBLE TITANS, THE (FOOTBALL MAJORS AT
PACIFIC U.)   SAMBROT, WILLIAM SS CMP 59 10
  ISLAND OF FEAR AND OTHER SCIENCE FICTION SAMBROT, WILLIAM AC
SECRET PLACE, THE   MCKENNA, RICHARD M. SS ORB 66 01
  BEST FROM ORBIT, THE   KNIGHT, DAMON   AN
  CASEY AGONISTES, AND OTHER S.F. & FANTASY STORIES
                            MCKENNA, RICHARD M. AC
  NEBULA AWARD STORIES NO. 2   ALDISS & HARRISON   AN
  ORBIT 1   KNIGHT, DAMON   OA
SECRET RIDER   RANDALL, MARTA   NV NDM 76 06
  NEW DIMENSIONS 6   SILVERBERG, ROBERT   OA
SECRET SENSE, THE   ASIMOV, ISAAC   SS COS 41 03
  EARLY ASIMOV, THE   ASIMOV, ISAAC   AC
  FUTURES TO INFINITY   MOSKOWITZ, SAM   AN
SECRET SONGS, THE   LEIBER, FRITZ   SS FSF 62 08
  PERCHANCE TO DREAM   KNIGHT, DAMON   AN
  SECRET SONGS, THE   LEIBER, FRITZ   AC
  SPECTRUM 4   AMIS & CONQUEST   AN
  STRANGE ECSTASIES   PARRY, MICHEL   AN
  SURVIVAL PRINTOUT   TOTAL EFFECT   AN
SECRET UNATTAINABLE   VAN VOGT, A. E.   NV ASF 42 07
  *AWAY AND BEYOND   VAN VOGT, A. E.   AC
SECRET WEAPON (BRIDLE SHOWER) BIGGLE, LLOYD JR. NV GAL 58 05
  RULE OF THE DOOR AND OTHER FANCIFUL REGULATIONS
                            BIGGLE, LLOYD JR.   AC
SECRET WEAPON (FROM "COUNT ROBERT OF PARIS")
                            SCOTT, WALTER   EX
  SCIENCE FICTION THROUGH THE AGES 1 EVANS, I. O.   AN
SECRET, THE   CLARKE, ARTHUR C. SS
  WIND FROM THE SUN, THE   CLARKE, ARTHUR C.   AC
SECRET, THE   NADLER, MAGGIE   SS CLR 71 01
  CLARION   WILSON, ROBIN SCOTT OA
SECTOR GENERAL   WHITE, JAMES   NV NWS 57 11
  HOSPITAL STATION   WHITE, JAMES   AC
SECURITY CHECK   CLARKE, ARTHUR C. SS FSF 57 06
  FUTURE TENSE   CURTIS, RICHARD   AN
  OF TIME AND STARS   CLARKE, ARTHUR C.   AC
  OTHER SIDE OF THE SKY, THE   CLARKE, ARTHUR C.   AC
SEDAN DEVILLE   MALZBERG, BARRY N. SS FSF 74 12
  DOWN HERE IN THE DREAM QUARTER   MALZBERG, BARRY N.   AC
SEE HOW THEY RUN   BLOCH, ROBERT   SS EQM 73 04
  COLD CHILLS   BLOCH, ROBERT   AC
SEE ME NOT   WILSON, RICHARD   NV IMP 67 02
  WORLD'S BEST SCIENCE FICTION: 1968 WOLLHEIM & CARR   AN
SEE NO EVIL   PIERCE, JOHN R.   SS NEW 66 AN
  SCIENCE FICTION ODDITIES   CONKLIN, GROFF   AN
SEE WHAT I MEAN¡   BRUNNER, JOHN   SS ASF 64 01
  *OUT OF MY MIND   BRUNNER, JOHN   AC
SEE YOU LATER   KUTTNER, HENRY   SS TWS 49 06
  BEST OF HENRY KUTTNER 1, THE   KUTTNER, HENRY   AC
  RETURN TO OTHERNESS   KUTTNER, HENRY   AC
SEE YOU LATER   PADGETT, LEWIS   SS TWS 49 06
  GNOME THERE WAS, A   PADGETT, LEWIS   AC
SEE?   ROBLES, EDWARD G. SS GAL 54 06
  FIFTY SHORT SCIENCE FICTION TALES ASIMOV & CONKLIN   AN
SEED FROM THE SEPULCHRE, THE SMITH, CLARK ASHTON SS WRT 33 10
  ROOTS OF EVIL, THE   PARRY, MICHEL   AN
  TALES OF SCIENCE AND SORCERY   SMITH, CLARK ASHTON AC
SEED OF DESTRUCTION   KERSH, GERALD   SS ESQ
  ON AN ODD NOTE   KERSH, GERALD   AC

SEED OF EARTH, THE (SEE JOURNEY'S END)
                            SILVERBERG, ROBERT TC
SEED OF EVIL, THE   BAYLEY, BARRINGTON J NV NWR 74 23
  NEW WRITINGS IN SF. 23   BULMER, KENNETH   OA
SEED OF VIOLENCE, THE   WILLIAMS, JAY   SN FUN 58 11
  UNFRIENDLY FUTURE, THE   BOARDMAN, TOM JR.   AN
SEED STOCK   HERBERT, FRANK   SS ASF 70 04
  BEST OF FRANK HERBERT, THE   HERBERT, FRANK   AC
  BOOK OF FRANK HERBERT, THE   HERBERT, FRANK   AC
  NIGHTMARE GARDEN   GHIDALIA, VIC   AN
SEEDING PROGRAMME (A TIME TO SURVIVE)
                            BLISH, JAMES   SS FSF 56 02
  SEEDLING STARS, THE   BLISH, JAMES   NO
SEEDLING OF MARS (THE PLANET ENTITY)
                            SMITH, CLARK ASHTON NV WSQ 31 FL
  TALES OF SCIENCE AND SORCERY   SMITH, CLARK ASHTON AC
SEEDS FROM OUTSIDE, THE   HAMILTON, EDMOND SS WRT 37 03
  BEST OF EDMOND HAMILTON, THE   HAMILTON, EDMOND   AC
SEEDS OF THE DUSK   GALLUN, RAYMOND Z. NV ASF 38 06
  *ADVENTURES IN TIME AND SPACE   HEALY & MCCOMAS   AN
  ASTOUNDING-ANALOG READER, THE VOLUME ONE HARRISON & ALDISS AN
  TOMORROW'S WORLDS   SILVERBERG, ROBERT   AN
  TOMORROW, AND TOMORROW, AND TOMORROW... HEINTZ/HERBERT/JOOS/ AN
SEEING   ELLISON, HARLAN   SS
  ANDROMEDA I   WESTON, PETER   OA
  BEST SCIENCE FICTION OF THE YEAR, THE NO. 6
                            CARR, TERRY   AN
  IDES OF TOMORROW, THE   CARR, TERRY   OA
SEEING-EYE DOG   GALOUYE, DANIEL F. SS GAL 56 09
  LAST LEAP AND OTHER STORIES OF THE SUPER-MIND, THE
                            GALOUYE, DANIEL F.   AC
SEEKER OF THE SPHINX (ALSO AS THE ROAD TO THE SEA)
                            CLARKE, ARTHUR C. NV TCS 51 SP
  YEAR'S BEST SCIENCE FICTION NOVELS: 1952 BLEILER & DIKTY AN
SEEKER OF TOMORROW   JOHNSON, LESLIE T.
                            AND RUSSELL, ERIC FRANK SN C ASF 37 07
  HISTORY OF THE SCIENCE FICTION MAGAZINE, THE PART 2 1936-1945
                            ASHLEY, MICHAEL   AN
  SCIENCE FICTION OF THE 30'S   KNIGHT, DAMON   AN
SEEKERS, THE   TUBB, E. C.   SS NWR 65 06
  NEW WRITINGS IN SF. 6   CARNELL, JOHN   AN
SEEKERS, THE   WILLIAMS, ROBERT M. SS STS 48 05
  FLIGHT INTO SPACE   WOLLHEIM, DONALD A. AN
SEEKING A SUITABLE DONOR   THOMAS, D. M.   SS
  NEW S.F., THE   JONES, LANGDON   OA
SEEKING ASSISTANCE   MALZBERG, BARRY N. SS FSF 76 04
  DOWN HERE IN THE DREAM QUARTER   MALZBERG, BARRY N.   AC
SEESAW, THE   VAN VOGT, A. E.   SS ASF 41 07
  *BEYOND TIME AND SPACE   DERLETH, AUGUST   AN
  BEYOND TOMORROW   KNIGHT, DAMON   AN
  WEAPON SHOPS OF ISHER, THE   VAN VOGT, A. E.   NO
SEETEE SHIP   WILLIAMSON, JACK NO SAS 50
  SEETEE SHIP/SEETEE SHOCK   WILLIAMSON, JACK   AC
SEETEE SHOCK   WILLIAMSON, JACK NO ASF 49 02
  SEETEE SHIP/SEETEE SHOCK   WILLIAMSON, JACK   AC
SEGREGATION (SEE THE GAME OF GOD)
                            ALDISS, BRIAN W. TC
SEGREGATIONIST   ASIMOV, ISAAC   SS ABB 67 04
  BEST SF: 1968   HARRISON & ALDISS   AN
  NIGHTFALL AND OTHER STORIES   ASIMOV, ISAAC   AC
SEISMOGRAPH ADVENTURE, THE REEVE, ARTHUR B. SS SCD 30 03
  SILENT BULLET, THE   REEVE, ARTHUR B.   AC
SELCHEY KIDS, THE   YEP, LAURENCE   NV IFS 68 02
  WORLD'S BEST SCIENCE FICTION: 1969 WOLLHEIM & CARR   AN
SELECTED BIBLIOGRAPHY   MISC. MATERIAL   MS
  AMERICAN GOVERNMENT THROUGH SCIENCE FICTION
                            OLANDER/GREENBERG/& AN
  SCHOOL AND SOCIETY THROUGH SCIENCE FICTION
                            OLANDER/GREENBERG/& AN
SELECTED BIBLIOGRAPHY: INTERSTELLAR TRAVEL, A
                            MISC. MATERIAL   MS
  FASTER THAN LIGHT   DANN & ZEBROWSKI   OA
SELECTED INCIDENTS (THE SIN OF INTEGRITY)
                            WILLEFORD, CHARLES SS GNT
  MACHINE IN WARD ELEVEN, THE   WILLEFORD, CHARLES   NO
SELECTRA SIX-TEN   DAVIDSON, AVRAM   SS FSF 70 10
  BEST FROM FANTASY AND SCIENCE FICTION: 19
                            FERMAN, EDWARD L.   AN
SELF PORTRAIT   WOLFE, BERNARD   NV GAL 51 11
  ROBOT AND THE MAN, THE   GREENBERG , MARTIN   AN
  SECOND GALAXY READER OF SCIENCE FICTION GOLD, H. L.   AN
  TOMORROW AND TOMORROW   KNIGHT, DAMON   AN
SELLERS OF THE DREAM, THE   JAKES, JOHN W.   NA GAL 63 06
  BEST OF JOHN JAKES, THE   JAKES, JOHN W.   AC
  FAR-OUT PEOPLE, THE   HOSKINS, ROBERT   AN
  SPECTRUM 4   AMIS & CONQUEST   AN
  TOMORROW, INC.   GREENBERG& OLANDER   AN
SEMANTICS OF TWENTY-FIRST CENTURY SCIENCE, THE
                            VAN VOGT, A. E.   AR
  BEST OF A. E. VAN VOGT, THE   VAN VOGT, A. E.   AC
SEMLEY'S NECKLACE (DOWRY OF THE ANGYAR)
                            LE GUIN, URSULA K. SS AMZ 64 09
  WINDS TWELVE QUARTERS, THE   LE GUIN, URSULA K.   AC
SEMPER FI (SATISFACTION)   KNIGHT, DAMON   SS ASF 64 08
  BEST OF DAMON KNIGHT, THE   KNIGHT, DAMON   AC
  TURNING ON   KNIGHT, DAMON   AC
SENATOR'S DAUGHTER, THE   MITCHELL, EDWARD P. SS SUN 79 07
  CRYSTAL MAN, THE   MITCHELL, EDWARD P. AC
SEND HER VICTORIOUS   ALDISS, BRIAN W. NV AMZ 68 04
  BOOK OF BRIAN ALDISS, THE   ALDISS, BRIAN W.   AC
  INTANGIBLES INC. AND OTHER STORIES ALDISS, BRIAN W.   AC
SENDING THE VERY BEST   BRYANT, EDWARD   SS NWS 70 01
  AMONG THE DEAD   BRYANT, EDWARD   AC
  CLARION   WILSON, ROBIN SCOTT OA
  NEW TOMORROWS, THE   SPINRAD, NORMAN   AN

SENHOR ZUMBEIRA'S LEG   MARTI-IBANEZ, FELIX   NV   FSF 62 12
   NEVER IN THIS WORLD   STONE, IDELLA P.   AN
SENIOR CITIZEN   SIMAK, CLIFFORD D.   SS   FSF 75 10
   BEST SCIENCE FICTION STORIES OF THE YEAR (1975)
                                    DEL REY, LESTER   AN
SENSE FROM THOUGHT DIVIDE   CLIFTON, MARK   NV   ASF 55 03
   SF: THE BEST OF THE BEST   MERRIL, JUDITH   AN
   SF: THE YEAR'S GREATEST SCIENCE FICTION AND FANTASY
                                    MERRIL, JUDITH   AN
   SPECTRUM 2   AMIS & CONQUEST   AN
SENSE OF BEAUTY, A   TAYLOR, ROBERT   SS   FSF 68 08
   SF: AUTHORS' CHOICE 4   HARRISON, HARRY   AN
SENSE OF DIFFERENCE, A   SARGENT, PAMELA   SS   WLK 73
   AND WALK NOW GENTLY THROUGH THE FIRE... ELWOOD, ROGER   OA
   CLONED LIVES   SARGENT, PAMELA   NO
SENSE OF DIRECTION, A   PANSHIN, ALEXEI   SS   AMZ 69 11
   DAYS AFTER TOMORROW, THE   SANTESSON, HANS S.   AN
   FAREWELL TO YESTERDAY'S TOMORROW PANSHIN, ALEXEI   AC
SENSE OF PROPORTION   TUBB, E. C.   NV   NEB 58 07
   DIMENSION 4   CONKLIN, GROFF   AN
   TEN FROM TOMORROW   TUBB, E. C.   AC
   WINDOW ON THE FUTURE   HILL, DOUGLAS   AN
SENSE OF THE FIRE, THE   MALZBERG, BARRY N.   NV   ESC 67
   OUT FROM GANYMEDE   MALZBERG, BARRY N.   AC
SENSE OF THYME, A   HENSEL, C. F.   SS   GEN 72
   GENERATION   GERROLD, DAVID   OA
SENSE OF WONDER   CHANDLER, A. BERTRAM SS   FUN 58 02
   FLYING SAUCERS IN FACT AND FICTION SANTESSON, HANS S.   AN
SENSE OF WONDER, THE   ASIMOV, ISAAC   IN
   JOHN W. CAMPBELL ANTHOLOGY: THREE NOVELS CAMPBELL, JOHN W. JR AC
SENSE OF WONDER, THE   MOSKOWITZ, SAM   IN
   THREE STORIES   MOSKOWITZ, SAM   AN
SENSIBLE MAN, THE   DAVIDSON, AVRAM   SS   PBY 59 02
   DEAD ASTRONAUT, 10 STORIES OF SPACE FLIGHT, THE
                                    PLAYBOY, EDITORS OF AN
   PLAYBOY BOOK OF SCIENCE FICTION AND FANTASY, THE
                                    PLAYBOY, EDITORS OF AN
SENSITIVE MAN, THE   ANDERSON, POUL   NV   FUN 54 01
   BEYOND THE BEYOND   ANDERSON, POUL   AC
SENTENCE (TRIPLICATE TWISTEROO)
                                    BROWN, FREDRIC   SS   PBY 57 03
   ANGELS AND SPACESHIPS   BROWN, FREDRIC   AC
SENTENCE IN BINARY CODE   PRIEST, CHRISTOPHER   SS   FAN 71 08
   REAL-TIME WORLD   PRIEST, CHRISTOPHER   AC
SENTENCE OF DEATH (DEATH SENTENCE)
                                    CHRISTOPHER, JOHN   SS   IMG 53 06
   TWENTY-SECOND CENTURY, THE   CHRISTOPHER, JOHN   AC
SENTENCED TO A SCHEHERAZADEAN DEATH
                                    WALTERS, DAVID H.   SS   NWR 76 29
   NEW WRITINGS IN SF. 29   BULMER, KENNETH   OA
SENTIMENT, INC.   ANDERSON, POUL   NV   SFS 53 01
   WEIRD ONES, THE   HOWARD, IVAN   AN
SENTIMENTAL JOURNEY   COOPER, EDMUND   SS
   VOICES IN THE DARK   COOPER, EDMUND   AC
SENTIMENTALISTS, THE   LEINSTER, MURRAY   NV   GAL 53 04
   YEAR'S BEST SCIENCE FICTION NOVELS: 1954 BLEILER & DIKTY   AN
SENTINEL OF ETERNITY (SEE THE SENTINEL)
                                    CLARKE, ARTHUR C.   TC
SENTINEL, THE (SENTINEL OF ETERNITY)
                                    CLARKE, ARTHUR C.   SS   TSF 51 SP
   ACROSS THE SEA OF STARS   CLARKE, ARTHUR C.   AC
   AS TOMORROW BECOMES TODAY   SULLIVAN, CHARLES W.   AN
   BEST OF ARTHUR C. CLARKE: 1937-1971, THE CLARKE, ARTHUR C. AC
   EXPEDITION TO EARTH   CLARKE, ARTHUR C.   AC
   MIRROR OF INFINITY, THE   SILVERBERG, ROBERT   AN
   NINE BILLION NAMES OF GOD, THE   CLARKE, ARTHUR C.   AC
   OF TIME AND STARS   CLARKE, ARTHUR C.   AC
   PAST, PRESENT, AND FUTURE PERFECT WOLFE, J&FITZ GERALD   AN
   SCIENCE FICTION   BRODKIN & PEARSON   AN
   SPACE ODYSSEYS   ALDISS, BRIAN W.   AN
   SPECTRUM 3   AMIS & CONQUEST   AN
   TOMORROW, AND TOMORROW, AND TOMORROW... HEINTZ/HERBERT/JOOS/ AN
   WORLDS TO COME   KNIGHT, DAMON   AN
SENTRY (TWO TIMER)   BROWN, FREDRIC   SS   GAL 54 02
   HONEYMOON IN HELL   BROWN, FREDRIC   AC
SERIOUS SEARCH FOR WEIRD WORLDS, A
                                    BRADBURY, RAY   AR   LIF 60 10
   6TH ANNUAL OF THE YEAR'S BEST S-F, THE MERRIL, JUDITH   AN
SERPENT BURNING ON AN ALTAR ALDISS, BRIAN W.   SS   ORB 73 12
   BEST SF: 1973   HARRISON & ALDISS   AN
   ORBIT 12   KNIGHT, DAMON   OA
SERPENT IN EDEN, THE   ANDERSON, POUL   NV   OMG 73
   OMEGA   ELWOOD, ROGER   OA
   VISIONS OF TOMORROW   ELWOOD, ROGER   AN
   WORLD NAMED CLEOPATRA, A   ANDERSON, POUL   AC
SERPENT OF KUNDALINI, THE   ALDISS, BRIAN W.   SS   NWS 68 02
   BEST SF STORIES FROM NEW WORLDS 5 MOORCOCK, MICHAEL   AN
   BEST SF: 1968   HARRISON & ALDISS   AN
SERPENT PRINCESS   HAMILTON, EDMOND   NV   WRT 48 01
   WHAT'S IT LIKE OUT THERE? AND OTHER STORIES
                                    HAMILTON, EDMOND   AC
SERPENTINE   SCHAUB, MARY H.   NV
   SURVIVAL FROM INFINITY   ELWOOD, ROGER   OA
SERVANT PROBLEM, THE   TENN, WILLIAM   NV   GAL 55 04
   HUMAN ANGLE, THE   TENN, WILLIAM   AC
   SEVEN COME INFINITY   CONKLIN, GROFF   AN
SERVANTS   WISE, DAVID   SS   CLR 73 03
   CLARION III   WILSON, ROBIN SCOTT   OA
SERVICE CALL   DICK, PHILIP K.   SS   SFS 55 07
   BEST OF PHILIP K. DICK, THE   DICK, PHILIP K.   AC
   MASTERS OF SCIENCE FICTION   HOWARD, IVAN   AN
SERVICE FIRST   KELLER, DAVID H. MD. SS   AMQ 31 WI
   *OUTER REACHES, THE   DERLETH, AUGUST   AN
SERVO   DEMMON, CALVIN   SS
   FUTURE PASTIMES   EDELSTEIN, SCOTT   OA

SETTING: A LOCAL HABITATION AND A NAME
                                    WILSON, ROBIN SCOTT   SI
   THOSE WHO CAN: A SCIENCE FICTION READER WILSON, ROBIN SCOTT AN
SETTLERS, THE   BRADBURY, RAY   SS   NEW 51 AC
   MARTIAN CHRONICLES, THE   BRADBURY, RAY   AC
SETTLING THE WORLD   HARRISON, M. JOHN   NV   NEW 75 AC
   BEST SF: 75, THE NINTH ANNUAL   HARRISON & ALDISS   AN
   NEW IMPROVED SUN, THE   DISCH, THOMAS M.   AN
SEVEN DAYS TO LIVE (SEE PRISON LEGEND)
                                    FINNEY, JACK   TC
SEVEN DEADLY VIRTUES, THE   POHL, FREDERIK   NV   GAL 58 08
   FREDERIK POHL OMNIBUS, THE   POHL, FREDERIK   AC
   TURN LEFT AT THURSDAY   POHL, FREDERIK   AC
SEVEN DOORS TO EDUCATION   SABERHAGEN, FRED   NV   IFS 61 05
   BOOK OF SABERHAGEN, THE   SABERHAGEN, FRED   AC
SEVEN SLEEPERS, THE (SEE ALMUSSEN'S COMET)
                                    BARNES, ARTHUR K.   TC
SEVEN STORY DREAM   LAFFERTY, R. A.   SS
   DOES ANYONE ELSE HAVE SOMETHING FURTHER TO ADD?
                                    LAFFERTY, R. A.   AC
SEVEN WONDERS OF THE UNIVERSE, THE
                                    MALLETTE, MOSE   SS   FSF 66 08
   BEST FROM FANTASY AND SCIENCE FICTION: 16
                                    FERMAN, EDWARD L.   AN
SEVEN-DAY TERROR   LAFFERTY, R. A.   SS   IFS 62 03
   MASTERS' CHOICE   JANIFER, LAURENCE M.   AN
   NINE HUNDRED GRANDMOTHERS   LAFFERTY, R. A.   AC
   8TH ANNUAL OF THE YEAR'S BEST S-F, THE MERRIL, JUDITH   AN
SEVEN-LEAGUE BOOTS, THE   AYME, MARCEL   SS
   WALKER THROUGH WALLS, THE   AYME, MARCEL   AC
SEVENTH FLOOR, THE   LVOV, ARKADY   NA
   JOURNEY ACROSS THREE WORLDS   ANONYMOUS   AN
SEVENTH SALLY, OR HOW TRURL'S OWN PERFECTION LED TO
   NO GOOD, THE   LEM, STANISLAW   SS
   CYBERIAD, THE   LEM, STANISLAW   OC
SEVENTH VICTIM   SHECKLEY, ROBERT   SS   GAL 53 04
   ABOVE THE HUMAN LANDSCAPE   MCNELLY & STOVER   AN
   INTRODUCTORY PSYCHOLOGY THROUGH SCIENCE FICTION
                                    KATZ/WARRICK/&   AN
   MAN AGAINST TOMORROW   NOLAN, WILLIAM F.   AN
   *UNTOUCHED BY HUMAN HANDS   SHECKLEY, ROBERT   AC
SEVENTY YEARS OF DECPOP   FARMER, PHILIP JOSE   NA   GAL 72 07
   BEST SCIENCE FICTION FOR 1973   ACKERMAN, FORREST J.   AN
SEVERAL WAYS, AND THE SUN   PLANCHAT, HENRY-LUC   NV   NDM 77 07
   NEW DIMENSIONS 7   SILVERBERG, ROBERT   OA
SEX AND/OR MR. MORRISON   EMSHWILLER, CAROL   SS   DVS 67 01
   DANGEROUS VISIONS   ELLISON, HARLAN   OA
   JOY IN OUR CAUSE   EMSHWILLER, CAROL   AC
   WOMEN OF WONDER   SARGENT, PAMELA   AN
SEX OPPOSITE, THE   STURGEON, THEODORE   SS   FAN 52 FL
   E PLURIBUS UNICORN   STURGEON, THEODORE   AC
SEXUAL IMPLICATIONS OF THE CHARGE OF THE LIGHT BRIGADE
                                    FARMER, PHILIP JOSE   SS   DVS 67 01
   BOOK OF PHILIP JOSE FARMER, THE FARMER, PHILIP JOSE   AC
SEXUAL SONG, A   VEITCH, TOM   SS   QRK 71 03
   QUARK/3   DELANY & HACKER   OA
SF NOVEL IN 1969, THE   SUVIN, DARKO   AR
   NEBULA AWARD STORIES NO. 5   BLISH, JAMES   AN
SF: THE GAME-PLAYING LITERATURE
                                    POHL, FREDERIK   AR   CLR 71 01
   IN THE PROBLEM PIT   POHL, FREDERIK   AC
SF, THE SPIRIT OF YOUTH   PAUL, FRANK R.   AR   39
   SCIENCE FICTION ROLL OF HONOR, THE POHL, FREDERIK   AN
SHADES   BOUCHER, SANDY   SS   QRK 70 01
   QUARK/1   DELANY & HACKER   OA
SHADOW AND THE FLASH, THE   LONDON, JACK   SS   BOK 03 06
   CURIOUS FRAGMENTS   LONDON, JACK   AC
   INVISIBLE MEN   DAVENPORT, BASIL   AN
   SCIENCE FICTION OF JACK LONDON, THE LONDON, JACK   AC
   SHOT IN THE DARK   MERRIL, JUDITH   AN
SHADOW FROM THE STEEPLE, THE BLOCH, ROBERT   NV   WRT 50 08
   BLOCH AND BRADBURY   BRADBURY & BLOCH   AC
SHADOW GUIDE (SEE DESERT ROMANCE)
                                    PRICE, E. HOFFMANN   TC
SHADOW KINGDOM, THE   HOWARD, ROBERT E.   SS   WRT 29 08
   COMING OF CONAN, THE   HOWARD, ROBERT E.   AC
SHADOW OF SPACE, THE   FARMER, PHILIP JOSE   NV   IFS 67 11
   ALPHA 3   SILVERBERG, ROBERT   AN
   DOWN IN THE BLACK GANG AND OTHER STORIES FARMER, PHILIP JOSE AC
SHADOW OF WINGS, THE   SILVERBERG, ROBERT   SS   IFS 63 07
   CUBE ROOT OF UNCERTAINTY, THE   SILVERBERG, ROBERT   AC
   NEEDLE IN A TIMESTACK   SILVERBERG, ROBERT   AC
SHADOW ON THE FANCHER TWINS, THE
                                    MITCHELL, EDWARD P.   SS   SUN 86 01
   CRYSTAL MAN, THE   MITCHELL, EDWARD P.   AC
SHADOW ON THE MOON   HENDERSON, ZENNA   SS   FSF 62 03
   PEOPLE: NO DIFFERENT FLESH, THE HENDERSON, ZENNA   AC
SHADOW ON THE SAND   MACDONALD, JOHN D.   SN   TWS 50 10
   STRANGE TOMORROWS   HOSKINS, ROBERT   AN
SHADOW ON THE SKY, THE   DERLETH, AUGUST   SS   STT 32 01
   NOT LONG FOR THIS WORLD   DERLETH, AUGUST   AC
SHADOW OUT OF SPACE, THE   DERLETH, AUGUST
                             AND LOVECRAFT, H. P. NV C
   SURVIVOR AND OTHER STORIES, THE LOVECRAFT & DERLETH   AC
SHADOW OUT OF TIME, THE   LOVECRAFT, H. P.   SN   ASF 36 06
   PORTABLE NOVELS OF SCIENCE   WOLLHEIM, DONALD A.   AN
SHADOW PLAY   FITZPATRICK, E. D.   SS
   AD 2500   WILSON, ANGUS   AN
SHADOW SHOW   SIMAK, CLIFFORD D.   NV   FSF 53 11
   *STRANGERS IN THE UNIVERSE   SIMAK, CLIFFORD D.   AC
   VINTAGE ANTHOLOGY OF SCIENCE FANTASY, THE
                                    CERF, CHRISTOPHER   AN
SHADOW WORLD   SIMAK, CLIFFORD D.   NV   GAL 57 09
   5 UNEARTHLY VISIONS   CONKLIN, GROFF   AN
SHADOW, SHADOW, ON THE WALL STURGEON, THEODORE   SS   IMG 51 02
   CAVIAR   STURGEON, THEODORE   AC

SHADOW, SHADOW, ON THE WALL

OTHER WORLDS, OTHER TIMES   MOSKOWITZ & ELWOOD   AN
SHADOWS   SARGENT, PAMELA   NV FOS 74
  FELLOWSHIP OF THE STARS   CARR, TERRY   OA
  STARSHADOWS   SARGENT, PAMELA   AC
SHADOWS IN THE MOONLIGHT   HOWARD, ROBERT E.   SS WRT 34 04
  CONAN THE BARBARIAN   HOWARD, ROBERT E.   AC
  CONAN THE FREEBOOTER   HOWARD, R. & DE CAMP   AC
SHADOWS IN ZAMBOULA   HOWARD, ROBERT E.   NV WRT 35 11
  CONAN THE BARBARIAN   HOWARD, ROBERT E.   AC
  CONAN THE WANDERER   HOWARD, R./DE CAMP/&   AC
  SPELL OF SEVEN, THE   DE CAMP, L. SPRAGUE   AN
SHADOWS OF EMPIRE   DEL REY, LESTER   SS FUT 50 07
  EARLY DEL REY   DEL REY, LESTER   AC
SHADOWS OF THE PAST   YEFREMOV, IVAN   SS
  RUSSIAN SCIENCE FICTION   MAGIDOFF, ROBERT   AN
  STORIES   YEFREMOV, IVAN   AN
SHADOWS, THE   BRACKETT, LEIGH   SS STS 52 02
  HALFLING AND OTHER STORIES, THE   BRACKETT, LEIGH   AC
SHADOWS, THE   SMITH, CLARK ASHTON SS   22
  OUT OF SPACE AND TIME   SMITH, CLARK ASHTON   AC
SHADOWY THIRD, THE   GLASGOW, ELLEN   NV
  MORE LITTLE MONSTERS   ELWOOD & GHIDALIA   AN
SHADY LIFE OF ANNIBAL, THE (THE IMAGINARY HEIR)
                                     KERSH, GERALD   SS SEP 59 04
  MEN WITHOUT BONES   KERSH, GERALD   AC
SHAFFERY AMONG THE IMMORTALS POHL, FREDERIK SS FSF 72 07
  BEST FROM FANTASY AND SCIENCE FICTION: 20
                                     FERMAN, EDWARD L.   AN
  GOLD AT STARBOW'S END, THE   POHL, FREDERIK   AC
  NEBULA AWARD STORIES 8   ASIMOV, ISAAC   AN
SHAGGY DOG   FRITCH, CHARLES E. SS STN 58 03
  HORSES' ASTEROID   FRITCH, CHARLES E.   AC
SHAH GUIDO G.   ASIMOV, ISAAC   SS MAR 51 11
  BUY JUPITER AND OTHER STORIES   ASIMOV, ISAAC   AC
  HAVE YOU SEEN THESE?   ASIMOV, ISAAC   AC
SHAKA!   OLIVER, CHAD   NV CTM 74 01
  CONTINUUM 1   ELWOOD, ROGER   OA
SHAKE HANDS WITH THE MAN IN THE MOON
                                     LEYSON, CAPT. BURR W SS BLF 59
  TEEN-AGE OUTER SPACE STORIES   FURMAN, A. L.   AN
SHAKER REVIVAL, THE   JONAS, GERALD   NV GAL 70 02
  ALPHA 2   SILVERBERG, ROBERT   AN
  RUINS OF EARTH, THE   DISCH, THOMAS M.   AN
  SOCIOLOGY THROUGH SCIENCE FICTION MILSTEAD/GREENBERG/&   AN
  WORLD'S BEST SCIENCE FICTION: 1971 WOLLHEIM & CARR   AN
SHALL THE DUST PRAISE THEE? KNIGHT, DAMON SS DVS 67 01
  DANGEROUS VISIONS   ELLISON, HARLAN   OA
  OTHER WORLDS, OTHER GODS   MOHS, MAYO   AN
SHALL WE HAVE A LITTLE TALK? SHECKLEY, ROBERT NV GAL 65 10
  PEOPLE TRAP AND OTHER PITFALLS, THE SHECKLEY, ROBERT   AC
SHAMAR'S WAR   NEVILLE, KRIS   NV GAL 64 02
  SEVEN TRIPS THROUGH TIME AND SPACE CONKLIN, GROFF   AN
SHAMBLEAU   MOORE, C. L.   NV WRT 33 11
  ADVENTURES IN TOMORROW   CROSSEN, KENDELL F.   AN
  BEST OF C. L. MOORE, THE   MOORE, C. L.   AC
  ESCALES DANS L'INFINI   GALLET, GEORGES H.   AN
  SECOND AVON FANTASY READER, THE   WOLLHEIM &ERNSBERGER   AN
  *SHAMBLEAU AND OTHERS   MOORE, C. L.   AC
SHAMBLER FROM THE STARS, THE BLOCH, ROBERT SS WRT 35 09
  HORROR-7   BLOCH, ROBERT   AC
  HOUSE OF THE HATCHET, THE   BLOCH, ROBERT   AC
  *OPENER OF THE WAY, THE   BLOCH, ROBERT   AC
SHAMBLERS OF MISERY, THE GREEN, JOSEPH NV FSF 69 08
  CONSCIENCE INTERPLANETARY   GREEN, JOSEPH   NO
SHANDY   GOULART, RON   SS IFS 58 10
  CHAMELEON CORPS & OTHER SHAPE CHANGERS, THE
                                     GOULART, RON   AC
SHANNACH- THE LAST   BRACKETT, LEIGH   NO PLS 52 11
  BEST OF LEIGH BRACKETT, THE   BRACKETT, LEIGH   AC
SHAPE (KEEP YOUR SHAPE)   SHECKLEY, ROBERT   NV GAL 53 11
  ALPHA 7   SILVERBERG, ROBERT   AN
  GATES TO TOMORROW   NORTON, AN.&DONALDY   AN
  *UNTOUCHED BY HUMAN HANDS   SHECKLEY, ROBERT   AC
SHAPE IN TIME, A   BOUCHER, ANTHONY   SS FIN 70
  FUTURE IS NOW, THE   NOLAN, WILLIAM F.   OA
SHAPE OF COPYRIGHT TO COME, THE (SEE INTERPLANETARY COPYRIGHT)
                                     REINES, DONALD F.   TC
SHAPE OF SCIENCE FICTION TO COME, THE
                                     POHL, FREDERIK   AR   73
  BEST SCIENCE FICTION FOR 1973   ACKERMAN, FORREST J. AN
SHAPE OF THINGS THAT CAME, THE DEMING, RICHARD SS FSF 51 10
  SPECIAL WONDER   MCCOMAS, J. FRANCIS   AN
  TREASURY OF GREAT SCIENCE FICTION, A VOL.1
                                     BOUCHER, ANTHONY   AN
SHAPE OF THINGS, THE   BRADBURY, RAY   SS TWS 48 02
  SHAPE OF THINGS, THE   KNIGHT, DAMON   AN
  TRAVELLERS OF SPACE   GREENBERG , MARTIN   AN
SHAPES, THE   ROSNY, J. H. (AINE) SS
  ONE HUNDRED YEARS OF SCIENCE FICTION KNIGHT, DAMON   AN
SHARDS   ALDISS, BRIAN W.   SS FSF 62 04
  BEST SCIENCE FICTION STORIES OF BRIAN W. ALDISS (REVISED)
                                     ALDISS, BRIAN W.   AC
  STARSWARM   ALDISS, BRIAN W.   AC
SHARDS OF DIVINITY   TOMAN, MICHAEL D. SS SFE 74 01
  SCIENCE FICTION EMPHASIS NO. 1   GERROLD, DAVID   OA
SHARE ALIKE   BIXBY, JEROME
                                     AND DEAN, JOE E. SS C BEY 53 07
  GALAXY OF GHOULS   MERRIL, JUDITH   AN
  ZACHERLEY'S MIDNIGHT SNACKS   ZACHERLEY   AN
SHARING OF FLESH, THE   ANDERSON, POUL   NV GAL 68 12
  ANTHROPOLOGY THROUGH SCIENCE FICTION MASON, C/GREENBERG/& AN
  ELEVENTH GALAXY READER, THE   POHL, FREDERIK   AN
  HUGO WINNERS, THE (VOLUME 2)   ASIMOV, ISAAC   AN
SHARING TIME   HENDERSON, ZENNA SS NEW 71 AC
  HOLDING WONDER   HENDERSON, ZENNA   AC

SHIP WHO DISAPPEARED, THE (ALSO AS THE SHIP WHO DISSEMBLED)

SHARK   BRYANT, EDWARD   NV ORB 73 12
  AMONG THE DEAD   BRYANT, EDWARD   AC
  FUTURE NOW, THE   HOSKINS, ROBERT   AN
  NEBULA AWARD STORIES 9   WILHELM, KATE   AN
  ORBIT 12   KNIGHT, DAMON   OA
SHARK SHIP (REAP THE DARK TIDE)
                                     KORNBLUTH, C. M.   NV VAN 58 06
  BEST OF C. M. KORNBLUTH, THE   KORNBLUTH, C. M.   AC
  DARK STARS   SILVERBERG, ROBERT   AN
  *MILE BEYOND THE MOON, A   KORNBLUTH, C. M.   AC
  SCIENCE FICTION OMNIBUS ON POLLUTION, A ANONYMOUS   AN
  VOYAGES: SCENARIOS FOR A SHIP CALLED EARTH
                                     SAUER, ROB   AN
SHARKS OF PENTREATH, THE   CONEY, MICHAEL G. SS GAL 71 02
  BEST FROM GALAXY, THE VOLUME I   GALAXY, EDITORS OF   AN
  1972 ANNUAL WORLD'S BEST SF, THE   WOLLHEIM, DONALD A.   AN
SHATTERDAY   ELLISON, HARLAN   SS GLR 75 09
  NEBULA AWARD STORIES 11   LE GUIN, URSULA K.   AN
SHATTERED LIKE A GLASS GOBLIN ELLISON, HARLAN SS ORB 68 04
  ABOVE THE HUMAN LANDSCAPE   MCNELLY & STOVER   AN
  BEAST THAT SHOUTED LOVE AT THE HEART OF THE WORLD, THE
                                     ELLISON, HARLAN   AC
  BEST FROM ORBIT, THE   KNIGHT, DAMON   AN
  DEATHBIRD STORIES   ELLISON, HARLAN   OA
  ORBIT 4   KNIGHT, DAMON   OA
SHE ONLY GOES OUT AT NIGHT   TENN, WILLIAM   SS FUN 56 10
  FANTASTIC UNIVERSE OMNIBUS, THE   SANTESSON, HANS S.   AN
  SQUARE ROOT OF MAN, THE   TENN, WILLIAM   AC
SHE WAITS FOR ALL MEN BORN   TIPTREE, JAMES JR. SS   76
  FUTURE POWER   DANN & DOZOIS   OA
SHE WAS ASKING FOR YOU   ALLINGHAM, MARGAREY SS 46
  SHOT IN THE DARK   MERRIL, JUDITH   AN
SHE WHO LAUGHS...   PHILLIPS, PETER   SS GAL 52 04
  ASSIGNMENT IN TOMORROW   POHL, FREDERIK   AN
SHE/HER   THURSTON, ROBERT   SS INY 73 05
  INFINITY 5   HOSKINS, ROBERT   OA
SHED, THE   EVANS, E. EVERETT SS ASR 53 01
  *STORIES FOR TOMORROW   SLOANE, WILLIAM   AN
  TALES BEYOND TIME   DE CAMP, L. S.&C.   AN
  ZACHERLEY'S VULTURE STEW   ZACHERLEY   AN
SHELL GAME   DICK, PHILIP K.   SS GAL 54 09
  BOOK OF PHILIP K. DICK, THE   DICK, PHILIP K.   AC
SHELTER, THE   SERLING, ROD   SA
  FROM THE TWILIGHT ZONE   SERLING, ROD   AC
  NEW STORIES FROM THE TWILIGHT ZONE SERLING, ROD   OC
SHELTERING DREAM   PISERCHIA, DORIS   SS IFS 72 02
  BEST SCIENCE FICTION FOR 1972   POHL, FREDERIK   AN
SHEPHERD'S BOY   MIDDLETON, RICHARD SS FSF 53 03
  BEST FROM FANTASY AND SCIENCE FICTION: 3
                                     BOUCHER & MCCOMAS   AN
SHERIFF OF CANYON GULCH, THE (HEROES ARE MADE)
                                     ANDERSON, POUL
                                     AND DICKSON, GORDON R. NV C OWS 51 05
  EARTHMAN'S BURDEN   ANDERSON, P.&DICKSON AN
  GATES TO TOMORROW   NORTON, AN.&DONALDY   AN
  MANY WORLDS OF POUL ANDERSON, THE ANDERSON, POUL   AC
  SCIENCE FICTION BESTIARY, THE   SILVERBERG, ROBERT   AN
SHERLOCK HOLMES AND SCIENCE FICTION
                                     BOUCHER, ANTHONY   IN
  SCIENCE-FICTIONAL SHERLOCK HOLMES, THE COUNCIL OF FOUR   AN
SHERRINGTON THEORY, THE (SEE THE REPTILE ENCLOSURE)
                                     BALLARD, J. G.   TC
SHIFTING PARAMETERS IN DISAPPEARANCE AND MEMORY
                                     HAAS, CHARLIE   NV UNI 76 06
  UNIVERSE 6   CARR, TERRY   OA
SHIFTING SEAS   WEINBAUM, STANLEY G. NV AMZ 37 04
  BEST OF STANLEY G. WEINBAUM, THE   WEINBAUM, STANLEY G. AC
  MARTIAN ODYSSEY AND OTHER SCIENCE FICTION TALES, A
                                     WEINBAUM, STANLEY G. AC
  RED PERI, THE   WEINBAUM, STANLEY G. AC
SHINING ONE, THE   SCHACHNER, NAT   SS ASF 37 05
  VISIONS OF TOMORROW   ELWOOD, ROGER   AN
SHINING ONES, THE   CLARKE, ARTHUR C. SS PBY 64 08
  WIND FROM THE SUN, THE   CLARKE, ARTHUR C.   AC
  10TH ANNUAL OF THE YEAR'S BEST S-F, THE MERRIL, JUDITH   AN
SHINING ONES, THE (FULL VERSION)
                                     BOVA, BEN   NV BLF 74 02
  NOTES TO A SCIENCE FICTION WRITER BOVA, BEN   AC
SHINING PYRAMID, THE   MACHEN, ARTHUR   SS UKW 95 05
  ANCIENT MYSTERIES READER, THE   HAINING, PETER   AN
SHIP FROM THE STARS   HAWKINS, PETER   SS NWS 54 07
  BEST FROM NEW WORLDS SCIENCE FICTION, THE
                                     CARNELL, JOHN   AN
SHIP OF DARKNESS   VAN VOGT, A. E.   SS FBK 47 02
  AWARD SCIENCE FICTION READER   NORTON, ALDEN H.   AN
  FAR-OUT WORLDS OF A. E. VAN VOGT, THE VAN VOGT, A. E.   AC
  WORLDS OF A. E. VAN VOGT, THE   VAN VOGT, A. E.   AC
SHIP OF DISASTER, THE   BAYLEY, BARRINGTON J SS NWS 65 06
  BEST SF STORIES FROM NEW WORLDS 4 MOORCOCK, MICHAEL   AN
  NEW WORLDS OF FANTASY NO. 2   CARR, TERRY   AN
SHIP OF SHADOWS   LEIBER, FRITZ   SN FSF 69 07
  BEST FROM FANTASY AND SCIENCE FICTION, 25TH ANNIV.
                                     FERMAN, EDWARD L.   AN
  WORLD'S BEST SCIENCE FICTION: 1970 WOLLHEIM & CARR   AN
SHIP SAILS AT MIDNIGHT, THE   LEIBER, FRITZ   NV FAD 50 09
  BEST OF FRITZ LEIBER, THE   LEIBER, FRITZ   AC
  *OUTER REACHES, THE   DERLETH, AUGUST   AN
  SHIPS TO THE STARS   LEIBER, FRITZ   DC
SHIP THAT SAILED THE OCEAN OF SPACE, THE
                                     BAYLEY, BARRINGTON J SS NWS
  BEST SF STORIES FROM NEW WORLDS 8 MOORCOCK, MICHAEL   AN
SHIP THAT TURNED ASIDE, THE   PEYTON, GREEN   SS AMZ 30 03
  *BIG BOOK OF SCIENCE FICTION   CONKLIN, GROFF   AN
SHIP WHO DISAPPEARED, THE (ALSO AS THE SHIP WHO DISSEMBLED)
                                     MCCAFFREY, ANNE   NV IFS 69 03
  VENUS FACTOR, THE   GHIDALIA, V.& ELWOOD AN

SHIP WHO DISSEMBLED, THE (THE SHIP WHO DISAPPEARED)
                                    MCCAFFREY, ANNE   NV   IFS 69 03
   SHIP WHO SANG, THE   MCCAFFREY, ANNE   AC
SHIP WHO KILLED, THE   MCCAFFREY, ANNE   NV   GAL 66 10
   SHIP WHO SANG, THE   MCCAFFREY, ANNE   AC
SHIP WHO MOURNED, THE   MCCAFFREY, ANNE   SS   ASF 66 03
   SHIP WHO SANG, THE   MCCAFFREY, ANNE   AC
SHIP WHO SANG, THE   MCCAFFREY, ANNE   SS   FSF 61 04
   LOOKING AHEAD   ALLEN, D. & L.   AN
   SHIP WHO SANG, THE   MCCAFFREY, ANNE   AC
   WOMEN OF WONDER   SARGENT, PAMELA   AN
   7TH ANNUAL OF THE YEAR'S BEST S-F, THE   MERRIL, JUDITH   AN
SHIP-SISTER, STAR-SISTER   SILVERBERG, ROBERT   NV   TAL 73
   CAPRICORN GAMES   SILVERBERG, ROBERT   AC
   FRONTIERS 1: TOMORROW'S ALTERNATIVES   ELWOOD, ROGER   OA
SHIPPING CLERK   MORRISON, WILLIAM   SS   GAL 52 06
   13 GREAT STORIES OF SCIENCE FICTION   CONKLIN, GROFF   AN
SHIPSHAPE HOME   MATHESON, RICHARD   SS   GAL 52 07
   BORN OF MAN AND WOMAN   MATHESON, RICHARD   AC
   MORE TERROR IN THE MODERN VEIN   WOLLHEIM, DONALD A.   AN
   OMNIBUS OF SCIENCE FICTION   CONKLIN, GROFF   AN
   OTHERS, THE   CARR, TERRY   AN
   STRANGE TRAVELS IN SCIENCE FICTION   CONKLIN, GROFF   AN
   *TERROR IN THE MODERN VEIN   WOLLHEIM, DONALD A.   AN
   THIRD FROM THE SUN   MATHESON, RICHARD   AC
SHIPSHAPE MIRACLE, THE   SIMAK, CLIFFORD D.   NV   IFS 63 01
   BEST SCIENCE FICTION FROM IF, THE   POHL, FREDERIK   AN
SHIPWRECK   CHETWYND-HAYES, R.   SS   NEW 75 AN
   TALES OF TERROR FROM OUTER SPACE   CHETWYND-HAYES, R.   AN
SHIPWRECKED HOTEL, THE   BLISH, JAMES
                                    AND KNIGHT, NORMAN L. NV C GAL 65 08
   SCIENCE FICTION HORIZONS NO. 1   BOARDMAN, TOM JR.   AN
   TORRENT OF FACES, A   BLISH & KNIGHT, N.   NO
SHIVER IN THE PINES   WELLMAN, MANLY WADE SS   FSF 55 02
   WHO FEARS THE DEVIL?   WELLMAN, MANLY WADE   AC
SHOCK   KUTTNER, HENRY   SS   ASF 43 03
   AHEAD OF TIME   KUTTNER, HENRY   AC
   BEST OF HENRY KUTTNER 1, THE   KUTTNER, HENRY   AC
   *OUTER REACHES, THE   DERLETH, AUGUST   -AN
SHOCK TREATMENT   FRITCH, CHARLES E.   SS   FUN 55 02
   HORSES' ASTEROID   FRITCH, CHARLES E.   AC
SHOCK TREATMENT   HARDING, LEE   SS   NWR 68 11
   NEW WRITINGS IN SF. 8   CARNELL, JOHN   AN
   NEW WRITINGS IN SF. 11   CARNELL, JOHN   OA
SHOCK TREATMENT   MCCOMAS, J. FRANCIS NV   FSF 56 04
   DECADE OF FANTASY AND SCIENCE FICTION, A   MILLS, ROBERT P.   AN
   9 TALES OF SPACE AND TIME   HEALY, RAYMOND J.   OA
SHOCK TROOP   BOLTON, RICHARD   SS   IFS 56 10
   FIRST WORLD OF IF, THE   QUINN & WULFF   AN
SHOCK WAVE (CRESCENDO)   MATHESON, RICHARD   SS   GAM 63 01
   SHOCK III   MATHESON, RICHARD   AC
SHODDY LANDS, THE   LEWIS, C. S.   SS   FSF 56 02
   BEST FROM FANTASY AND SCIENCE FICTION: 6
                                    BOUCHER, ANTHONY   AN
   DARK TOWER AND OTHER STORIES, THE   LEWIS, C. S.   AC
   LATE GREAT FUTURE, THE   FITZ GERALD & DILLON   AN
   LIGHT FANTASTIC, THE   HARRISON, HARRY   AN
SHOES, THE   BLOCH, ROBERT   SS   UNK 42 02
   BOGEY MEN   BLOCH, ROBERT   AC
SHOO, FLY!   WOLLHEIM, DONALD A. SS
   TWO DOZEN DRAGON EGGS   WOLLHEIM, DONALD A.   AC
SHOPDROPPER, THE   NELSON, ALAN   SS   FSF 55 01
   GREAT SCIENCE FICTION ABOUT DOCTORS   CONKLIN, G&FABRICANT AN
SHOPPING FOR DEATH (SEE TOUCHED WITH FIRE)
                                    BRADBURY, RAY   TC
   ST. CLAIR, MARGARET SS
   CHANGE THE SKY AND OTHER STORIES   ST. CLAIR, MARGARET   AC
SHORE LEAVE
SHORE OF TOMORROW, THE   OLIVER, CHAD   NV   STS 53 03
   TOMORROW'S UNIVERSE   CAMPBELL, H. J.   AN
SHORE, THE   BRADBURY, RAY   SS   NEW 51 AC
   MARTIAN CHRONICLES, THE   BRADBURY, RAY   AC
SHORELINE AT SUNSET, THE (ALSO AS THE SUNSET HARP)
                                    BRADBURY, RAY   SS   FSF 59 03
   MEDICINE FOR MELANCHOLY, A   BRADBURY, RAY   AC
   5TH ANNUAL OF THE YEAR'S BEST S-F, THE   MERRIL, JUDITH   AN
SHORES OF NIGHT, THE (EXPANDED FROM "SEA CHANGE")
                                    SCORTIA, THOMAS N.   SS   ASF 56 06
   BEST SCIENCE FICTION STORIES AND NOVELS: 1956
                                    DIKTY, T. E.   AN
   6 FROM WORLDS BEYOND   DIKTY, T. E.   AN
SHORT COUNT, THE   COGSWELL, THEODORE R SS   AVS 53 01
   THIRD EYE, THE   COGSWELL, THEODORE R   AC
SHORT CUTS TO SUCCESS   KNOX, R. A.   SS   SLP 17 11
   MATHEMATICAL MAGPIE, THE   FADIMAN, CLIFTON   AN
SHORT HAPPY LIVES OF EUSTACE WEAVER I, THE
                                    BROWN, FREDRIC   SS   EQM 61 06
   BEST OF FREDRIC BROWN, THE   BROWN, FREDRIC   AC
   NIGHTMARES AND GEEZENSTACKS   BROWN, FREDRIC   AC
SHORT HAPPY LIVES OF EUSTACE WEAVER II, THE
                                    BROWN, FREDRIC   SS   EQM 61 06
   BEST OF FREDRIC BROWN, THE   BROWN, FREDRIC   AC
   NIGHTMARES AND GEEZENSTACKS   BROWN, FREDRIC   AC
SHORT HAPPY LIVES OF EUSTACE WEAVER III, THE
                                    BROWN, FREDRIC   SS   EQM 61 06
   BEST OF FREDRIC BROWN, THE   BROWN, FREDRIC   AC
   NIGHTMARES AND GEEZENSTACKS   BROWN, FREDRIC   AC
SHORT HISTORY OF THE BOLO FIGHTING MACHINES, A
                                    LAUMER, KEITH   AR
   BOLO   LAUMER, KEITH   AC
SHORT IN THE CHEST   SEABRIGHT, IDRIS   SS   FUN 54 07
   ALPHA 6   SILVERBERG, ROBERT   AN
   METAL SMILE, THE   KNIGHT, DAMON   AN
   OPERATION FUTURE   CONKLIN, GROFF   AN
   17 X INFINITY   CONKLIN, GROFF   AN
SHORT LIFE, THE   DONOVAN, FRANCIS   SN   ASF 55 10
   BEST SF 4   CRISPIN, EDMUND   AN

SHORT ONES, THE   BANKS, RAYMOND E.   NV   FSF 55 03
   BEST FROM FANTASY AND SCIENCE FICTION: 5
                                    BOUCHER, ANTHONY   AN
   POLITICAL SCIENCE FICTION   GREENBERG& WARRICK   AN
SHORT RELIGIOUS NOVEL, A   MALZBERG, BARRY N.   SS   FSF 72 09
   OUT FROM GANYMEDE   MALZBERG, BARRY N.   AC
SHORT SF IN 1968   PANSHIN, ALEXEI   AR
   NEBULA AWARD STORIES NO. 5   BLISH, JAMES   AN
SHORT-CIRCUITED PROBABILITY   KNIGHT, NORMAN L.   SS   ASF 41 09
   *BEST OF SCIENCE FICTION   CONKLIN, GROFF   AN
SHORT-SHORT STORY OF MANKIND, THE
                                    STEINBECK, JOHN   SS   PBY 58 04
   PENGUIN SCIENCE FICTION   ALDISS, BRIAN W.   AN
   SF:59, THE YEAR'S GREATEST SCIENCE FICTION AND FANTASY
                                    MERRIL, JUDITH   AN
SHORT, HAPPY WIFE OF MANSARD ELIOT, THE
                                    SLADEK, JOHN T.   SS   NWQ 71 01
   NEW WORLDS QUARTERLY NO. 1   MOORCOCK, MICHAEL   OA
SHORTEST SCIENCE FICTION STORY EVER TOLD, THE
                                    ACKERMAN, FORREST J. SS   VTX 73 06
   TOMORROW, AND TOMORROW, AND TOMORROW...   HEINTZ/HERBERT/JOOS/ AN
SHORTEST SCIENCE-FICTION STORY EVER TOLD, THE
                                    DEELEY, ROGER   SS   GEN 72
   GENERATION   GERROLD, DAVID   OA
SHORTS WING   RICHMOND, LEIGH
                                    AND RICHMOND, WALT   SS C NEW 70 DC
   POSITIVE CHARGE   RICHMOND, W. & L.   DC
SHORTSIGHTED   HOYLE, FRED   SS
   ELEMENT 79   HOYLE, FRED   AC
SHORTSITE   RICHMOND, LEIGH
                                    AND RICHMOND, WALT   SS C ASF 64 04
   POSITIVE CHARGE   RICHMOND, W. & L.   DC
SHORTSTACK   RICHMOND, LEIGH
                                    AND RICHMOND, WALT   SS C ASF 64 12
   ELSEWHERE AND ELSEWHEN   CONKLIN, GROFF   AN
   POSITIVE CHARGE   RICHMOND, W. & L.   DC
   THEMES IN SCIENCE FICTION   KELLEY, LEO P.   AN
SHOTGUN CURE   SIMAK, CLIFFORD D.   SS   FSF 61 01
   *BEST FROM FANTASY AND SCIENCE FICTION: 11
                                    MILLS, ROBERT P.   AN
SHOTTLE BOP   STURGEON, THEODORE   SS   UNK 41 02
   EDGE OF NEVER, THE   HOSKINS, ROBERT   AN
   INVISIBLE MEN   DAVENPORT, BASIL   AN
   SUPERNATURAL READER, THE   CONKLIN, G&L.   AN
   TO HERE AND THE EASEL   STURGEON, THEODORE   AC
   WITHOUT SORCERY   STURGEON, THEODORE   AC
   WORLDS OF THEODORE STURGEON, THE STURGEON, THEODORE   AC
SHOUT, THE (1929)   GRAVES, ROBERT   SS   FSF 52 04
   BEST FROM FANTASY AND SCIENCE FICTION: 2
                                    BOUCHER & MCCOMAS   AN
   LIGHT FANTASTIC, THE   HARRISON, HARRY   AN
SHOW BIZ   BLOCH, ROBERT   SS   EQM 59 05
   *BLOOD RUNS COLD   BLOCH, ROBERT   AC
SHOW CAUSE   FAST, HOWARD   SS
   TOUCH OF INFINITY, A   FAST, HOWARD   OC
SHOW MUST GO ON, THE   BLOCH, ROBERT   SS   MSM 60 01
   *BLOOD RUNS COLD   BLOCH, ROBERT   AC
SHOW MUST GO ON, THE (SO LOVELY, SO LOST)
                                    CAUSEY, JAMES   SS   OSF 54 11
   PSEUDO PEOPLE, THE   NOLAN, WILLIAM F.   AN
SHOW YOU MIGHT (SEE KIN)   WILSON, RICHARD   TC
SHOWDOWN WITH RANCE MCGREW   SERLING, ROD   SA
   NEW STORIES FROM THE TWILIGHT ZONE   SERLING, ROD   OC
SHOWING OFF REYNOLDS   MALZBERG, BARRY N.   IN
   BEST OF MACK REYNOLDS, THE   REYNOLDS, MACK   AC
SHRINE OF SEBASTIAN, THE   EKLUND, GORDON   NA   CHN 73
   CHAINS OF THE SEA   SILVERBERG, ROBERT   OA
SHRINE OF TEMPTATION, THE   MERRIL, JUDITH   SS   FAN 62 04
   BEST OF JUDITH MERRIL, THE   MERRIL, JUDITH   AC
   DEVIL HIS DUE, THE   HILL, DOUGLAS   AN
   GODS FOR TOMORROW   SANTESSON, HANS S.   AN
   SURVIVAL SHIP AND OTHER STORIES   MERRIL, JUDITH   AC
SHRINE, THE (AS ALAN GUTHRIE)   TUBB, E. C.   SS   NWS 60 02
   SCATTER OF STARDUST, A   TUBB, E. C.   DC
SHRINES OF EARTH, THE   SILVERBERG, ROBERT   SS   ASF 57 11
   REALITY TRIP, THE   SILVERBERG, ROBERT   AC
SHROUD OF SECRECY, THE   JONES, RAYMOND F.   NV   TWS 49 12
   THIS ISLAND EARTH   JONES, RAYMOND F.   NO
SHUBSHUB RACE, THE   ALDISS, BRIAN W.   SS   NEW 57 AC
   SPACE, TIME AND NATHANIEL   ALDISS, BRIAN W.   AC
SHUCKSMA   CLUTE, JOHN   SS   NWB 73 05
   NEW WORLDS QUARTERLY NO. 5   MOORCOCK, MICHAEL   OA
SHUFFLE BOARD   GALOUYE, DANIEL F.   SS   IFS 57 06
   PROJECT BARRIER   GALOUYE, DANIEL F.   AC
SHUNNED HOUSE, THE   LOVECRAFT, H. P.   NV   WRT 37 10
   *TWISTED   CONKLIN, GROFF   AN
SHUT THE LAST DOOR   HENSLEY, JOE L.   SS   ANA 70
   ALCHEMY AND ACADEME   MCCAFFREY, ANNE   OA
   YOUNG DEMONS   ELWOOD & GHIDALIA   AN
SIC TRANSIT...?, A SHAGGY HAIRLESS-DOG STORY
                                    UTLEY, STEVEN
                                    AND WALDROP, HOWARD SS C STL 76 02
   STELLAR 2   DEL REY, JUDY-LYNN   OA
SICKNESS, THE   TENN, WILLIAM   NV   INF 55 11
   OUT OF THIS WORLD 6   WILLIAMS-ELLIS& OWEN   AN
   TIME IN ADVANCE   TENN, WILLIAM   AC
   TOMORROW 1   HOSKINS, ROBERT   AN
SIDE BY SIDE   TOMERLIN, JOHN   SS   PBY 64 09
   PLAYBOY BOOK OF HORROR AND THE SUPERNATURAL, THE
                                    PLAYBOY, EDITORS OF   AN
SIDE EFFECT   WYAL, PG   NV   PRT 71
   PROTOSTARS   GERROLD & GOLDIN   OA
SIDE VIEW OF A CIRCLE   ADDOBATI, MICHAEL   SS   NOV 74 04
   NOVA 4   HARRISON, HARRY   OA
SIDEWISE IN TIME   LEINSTER, MURRAY   SN   ASF 34 06
   BEFORE THE GOLDEN AGE   ASIMOV, ISAAC   AN

SIDEWISE IN TIME   SIR EDMUND ORME

SIDEWISE IN TIME   LEINSTER, MURRAY   AC
  WORLDS OF MAYBE   SILVERBERG, ROBERT   AN
SIEGE OF THE UNSEEN (THE CHRONICLER)
                               VAN VOGT, A. E.   NA ASF 46 10
  M 33 IN ANDROMEDA   VAN VOGT, A. E.   AC
SIEMA   DNIEPROV, ANATOLY   NV
  MORE SOVIET SCIENCE FICTION   ANONYMOUS   AN
SIERRA SAM   DIGHTON, RALPH   AR NYT 60 01
  5TH ANNUAL OF THE YEAR'S BEST S-F, THE MERRIL, JUDITH   AN
SIEZURE (CHILDREN IN HIDING)   BRUNNER, JOHN   SS GAL 66 12
  NOT BEFORE TIME   BRUNNER, JOHN   AC
SIGH FOR CYBERNETICS, A   LAMPORT, FELICIA   PM HRP 61 01
  INSIDE INFORMATION   MOWSHOWITZ, ABBE   AN
  6TH ANNUAL OF THE YEAR'S BEST S-F, THE MERRIL, JUDITH   AN
SIGHT GAG   JANIFER, LAURENCE M. SS ASF 62 05
  IMPOSSIBLE?   JANIFER, LAURENCE M.   AC
SIGHT OF EDEN, THE   FAST, HOWARD   SS FSF 60 10
  EDGE OF TOMORROW, THE   FAST, HOWARD   AC
SIGHTSEERS, THE   BOVA, BEN   SS FUC 73
  FUTURE CITY   ELWOOD, ROGER   OA
SIGHTSEERS, THE   DISCH, THOMAS M. SS WOT 65 11
  *ONE HUNDRED AND TWO H-BOMBS   DISCH, THOMAS M.   AC
SIGN AMONG THE STARS   PRIESTLEY, LEE   SS   58
  TEEN-AGE OUTER SPACE STORIES   FURMAN, A. L.   AN
SIGN AT THE END OF THE UNIVERSE
                               ACKERSON, DUANE   SS ALT 74
  ALTERNATIES   GERROLD, DAVID   OA
SIGN IN SPACE, A   CALVINO, ITALO   SS   68
  COSMICOMICS   CALVINO, ITALO   OC
  TOMORROW AND TOMORROW   KNIGHT, DAMON   AN
SIGN OF THE GOOSE, THE   EDMONDSON, G. C. SS FSF 60 08
  STRANGER THAN YOU THINK   EDMONDSON, G. C.   DC
SIGN OF THE WOLF   SABERHAGEN, FRED SS IFS 65 05
  BERSERKER   SABERHAGEN, FRED   AC
SIGNALLER, THE   ROBERTS, KEITH   NV IMP 66 03
  ANOTHER WORLD   DOZOIS, GARDNER R.   AN
  PAVANE   ROBERTS, KEITH   NO
SIGNALS   CALDER, JOHN   SS NWS 66 09
  ENGLAND SWINGS SF   MERRIL, JUDITH   AN
  SPACE-TIME JOURNAL, THE   MERRIL, JUDITH   AN
SIGNIFICANT EVENTS IN LUNAR EXPLORATION
                               MISC. MATERIAL   MS
  GREAT SCIENCE FICTION STORIES ABOUT THE MOON
                               DIKTY, T. E.   AN
SIGNS OF THE TIMES   BROWN, ROSEL GEORGE SS AMZ 59 12
  HANDFUL OF TIME, A   BROWN, ROSEL GEORGE   AC
SILENCE (SEE ELECTED SILENCE) BRUNNER, JOHN   TC
SILENCE, PLEASE   CLARKE, ARTHUR C. SS SCF 50 WI
  ACROSS THE SEA OF STARS   CLARKE, ARTHUR C.   AC
  TALES FROM THE WHITE HART   CLARKE, ARTHUR C.   AC
  13 GREAT STORIES OF SCIENCE FICTION CONKLIN, GROFF   AN
SILENCE, THE   MCLAUGHLIN, BERNARD SS STI 41 06
  GOLDEN ROAD, THE   KNIGHT, DAMON   AN
  MORE TERROR IN THE MODERN VEIN WOLLHEIM, DONALD A.   AN
  *TERROR IN THE MODERN VEIN   WOLLHEIM, DONALD A.   AN
SILENT BROTHER   BUDRYS, ALGIS   SS ASF 56 02
  BUDRYS' INFERNO   BUDRYS, ALGIS   AC
  SF:57, THE YEAR'S GREATEST SCIENCE FICTION AND FANTASY
                               MERRIL, JUDITH   AN
SILENT BULLET, THE   REEVE, ARTHUR B. SS
  SILENT BULLET, THE   REEVE, ARTHUR B.   AC
SILENT COLONY, THE   SILVERBERG, ROBERT SS FUT 54 10
  CREATURES FROM BEYOND   CARR, TERRY   AN
  GODLING, GO HOME!   SILVERBERG, ROBERT   AC
  SHORES OF TOMORROW, THE   SILVERBERG, ROBERT   AC
SILENT EYES OF TIME, THE   BUDRYS, ALGIS   NA FSF 75 11
  BEST SCIENCE FICTION OF THE YEAR, THE NO. 5
                               CARR, TERRY   AN
SILENT HANDS   CONWAY, GERARD F. SS CLR 71 01
  CLARION   WILSON, ROBIN SCOTT   OA
SILENT IN GEHENNA   ELLISON, HARLAN   SS MWS 71
  APPROACHING OBLIVION   ELLISON, HARLAN   AC
  BEST SCIENCE FICTION FOR 1972 POHL, FREDERIK   AN
  FUTURE NOW, THE   HOSKINS, ROBERT   AN
  MANY WORLDS OF SCIENCE FICTION, THE BOVA, BEN   OA
  2020 VISION   POURNELLE, JERRY   AN
SILENT LEGES   POURNELLE, JERRY SS
  NEW VOICES IN SCIENCE FICTION MARTIN, GEORGE R. R.   OA
SILENT PARTNERS, THE   SHAW, BOB   SS NEB 59 06
  COSMIC KALEIDOSCOPE   SHAW, BOB   AC
SILENT PLANET, THE   BOND, NELSON S.   SS
  NO TIME LIKE THE FUTURE   BOND, NELSON S.   AC
SILENT TOWNS, THE   BRADBURY, RAY   SS CHM 49 03
  MARTIAN CHRONICLES, THE   BRADBURY, RAY   AC
SILENT VICTORY (SEE THE WAR OF TWO WORLDS)
                               ANDERSON, POUL   TC
SILENT, UPON TWO PEAKS   MUDGETT, HERMAN W. PM FSF 55 07
  BEST FROM FANTASY AND SCIENCE FICTION: 5
                               BOUCHER, ANTHONY   AN
SILENZIA   NELSON, ALAN   SS FSF 53 09
  17 X INFINITY   CONKLIN, GROFF   AN
SILHOUETTE   WOLFE, GENE   NA NAL 75
  NEW ATLANTIS AND OTHER NOVELLAS OF S.F., THE
                               SILVERBERG, ROBERT   OA
SILK AND THE SONG, THE   FONTENAY, CHARLES L. NV FSF 56 07
  BEST FROM FANTASY AND SCIENCE FICTION: 6
                               BOUCHER, ANTHONY   AN
  THEMES IN SCIENCE FICTION   KELLEY, LEO P.   AN
SILKEN-SWIFT, THE   STURGEON, THEODORE SS FSF 53 11
  E PLURIBUS UNICORN   STURGEON, THEODORE   AC
SILKIE, THE   VAN VOGT, A. E.   NV IFS 64 07
  IF READER OF SCIENCE FICTION, THE POHL, FREDERIK   AN
  SILKIE, THE   VAN VOGT, A. E.   NO
SILKIES IN SPACE, THE   VAN VOGT, A. E.   NV IFS 66 05
  BEST OF A. E. VAN VOGT, THE (BRITISH) VAN VOGT, A. E. AC
  SILKIE, THE   VAN VOGT, A. E.   NO

SILLY ASSES   ASIMOV, ISAAC   SS FUT 58 02
  BUY JUPITER AND OTHER STORIES ASIMOV, ISAAC   AC
  HAVE YOU SEEN THESE?   ASIMOV, ISAAC   AC
SILLY SEASON, THE   KORNBLUTH, C. M. SS FSF 50 FL
  BEST OF C. M. KORNBLUTH, THE   KORNBLUTH, C. M.   AC
  BEST SCIENCE FICTION STORIES OF C. M. KORNBLUTH
                               KORNBLUTH, C. M.   AC
  EARTH IN PERIL, THE   WOLLHEIM, DONALD A.   DA
  FIRST CONTACT   KNIGHT, DAMON   AN
  INVADERS FROM SPACE   SILVERBERG, ROBERT   AN
  MARCHING MORONS AND OTHER SCIENCE FICTION
                               KORNBLUTH, C. M.   AC
  MINDWORM AND OTHER STORIES, THE KORNBLUTH, C. M.   AC
  TOMORROW, THE STARS   HEINLEIN, ROBERT A.   AN
  TWENTY YEARS OF FANTASY & SCIENCE FICTION
                               FERMAN & MILLS   AN
SILVER CORRIDOR, THE   ELLISON, HARLAN   NV INF 56 10
  ALONE AGAINST TOMORROW   ELLISON, HARLAN   AC
  ELLISON WONDERLAND   ELLISON, HARLAN   AC
SILVER HIGHWAY, THE   LAWLOR, HAROLD   SS WRT 46 05
  SUPERNATURAL READER, THE   CONKLIN, G&L.   AN
SILVER MIRROR, THE   DOYLE, ARTHUR CONAN SS   25
  TRAVELERS IN TIME   STERN, PHILIP VAN D.   AN
SILVER NEEDLE, THE   MACBETH, GEORGE   PM NWS 67 01
  ENGLAND SWINGS SF   MERRIL, JUDITH   AN
  SPACE-TIME JOURNAL, THE   MERRIL, JUDITH   AN
SIMIAN PROBLEM, THE   ALPERT, HOLLIS   SS FSF 60 07
  17 X INFINITY   CONKLIN, GROFF   AN
SIMON   WOODROW, WILLIAM SS NWQ 72 04
  NEW WORLDS QUARTERLY NO. 4   MOORCOCK, MICHAEL   OA
SIMPLE WAY   SIMAK, CLIFFORD D. SS
  CITY   SIMAK, CLIFFORD D.   NO
SIMULATED TRAINER (TRAINEE FOR MARS)
                               HARRISON, HARRY   SS FUN 58 06
  WAR WITH THE ROBOTS   HARRISON, HARRY   AC
SIMWORTHY'S CIRCUS   SHAW, LARRY T.   SS WBY 50 12
  *SCIENCE-FICTION CARNIVAL   BROWN, F. & REYNOLDS   AN
SIN OF HYACINTH PEUCH, THE   RUSSELL, ERIC FRANK NV FAN 52 FL
  DARK TIDES   RUSSELL, ERIC FRANK   AC
  OTHER WORLDS, OTHER TIMES   MOSKOWITZ & ELWOOD   AN
SIN OF INTEGRITY, THE (SEE SELECTED INCIDENTS)
                               WILLEFORD, CHARLES TC
SIN TOWER (SEE LAST NIGHT IN THE RAIN)
                               BEAUMONT, CHARLES   TC
SINCE THE ASSASSINATION   ALDISS, BRIAN W. NV NEW 69 AC
  INTANGIBLES INC. AND OTHER STORIES ALDISS, BRIAN W.   AC
  NEANDERTHAL PLANET   ALDISS, BRIAN W.   AC
SINE OF THE MAGUS (SEE THE MAGICIANS)
                               GUNN, JAMES E.   TC
SINGER, THE   WELLS, BASIL   SS
  DOORWAYS TO SPACE   WELLS, BASIL   AC
SINGERS, THE   WALTER, W. GREY   SS   56
  EXPERT DREAMERS, THE   POHL, FREDERIK   AN
SINGING BELL, THE   ASIMOV, ISAAC   SS FSF 55 01
  ASIMOV'S MYSTERIES   ASIMOV, ISAAC   AC
  BEST FROM FANTASY AND SCIENCE FICTION: 5
                               BOUCHER, ANTHONY   AN
  TOMORROW, AND TOMORROW, AND TOMORROW... HEINTZ/HERBERT/JOOS/ AN
SINGING BLADES   ESHBACH, LLOYD A. SS SRS 40 02
  TYRANT OF TIME, THE   ESHBACH, LLOYD A.   AC
SINGING CITADEL, THE   MOORCOCK, MICHAEL NV   63
  DEVIL HIS DUE, THE   HILL, DOUGLAS   AN
SINGING CLIFFS OF FAUNUS, THE BUNCH, MIRIAM   SS
  LONG NIGHT OF WAITING AND OTHER STORIES ELWOOD, ROGER OA
SINGING STATUES, THE   BALLARD, J. G.   SS FAN 62 07
  VERMILLION SANDS (BRITISH)   BALLARD, J. G.   AC
SINGLE COMBAT   ABERNATHY, ROBERT SS FSF 55 01
  CITIES OF WONDER   KNIGHT, DAMON   AN
  SOCIOLOGY THROUGH SCIENCE FICTION MILSTEAD/GREENBERG/& AN
SINGLE COMBAT   GREEN, JOSEPH   SS NWS 64 08
  AFFAIR WITH GENIUS, AN   GREEN, JOSEPH   AC
  COMBAT SF   DICKSON, GORDON R.   AN
SINGLEMINDED   BRUNNER, JOHN   NV IFS 63 05
  ALIEN WORLDS   ELWOOD, ROGER   AN
  NOT BEFORE TIME   BRUNNER, JOHN   AC
  *OUT OF MY MIND   BRUNNER, JOHN   AC
SINGULAR   GARNETT, BILL   SS NOV 74 04
  NOVA 4   HARRISON, HARRY   OA
SINGULAR CASE OF EXTREME ELECTROLYTE BALANCE ASSOCIATED WITH
  FOLIE A DEUX   TSCHIRGI, ROBERT D. PA   65
  11TH ANNUAL OF THE YEAR'S BEST S-F, THE MERRIL, JUDITH   AN
SINGULAR EVENTS WHICH OCCURRED IN THE HOVEL ON THE ALLEY OFF
  OF EYE STREET, THE   DAVIDSON, AVRAM   SS FSF 62 02
  BEST FROM FANTASY AND SCIENCE FICTION: 12
                               DAVIDSON, AVRAM   AN
  WHAT STRANGE STARS AND SKIES   DAVIDSON, AVRAM   AC
SINGULAR QUEST OF MARTIN BORG, THE
                               COLLYN, GEORGE   SS NWS 65 02
  BEST SF STORIES FROM NEW WORLDS NO. 2, THE
                               MOORCOCK, MICHAEL   AN
  ENGLAND SWINGS SF   MERRIL, JUDITH   AN
  SPACE-TIME JOURNAL, THE   MERRIL, JUDITH   AN
SINGULARITIES MAKE ME NERVOUS NIVEN, LARRY   SS STL 74 01
  STELLAR 1   DEL REY, JUDY-LYNN   OA
SINISTER JOURNEY   RICHTER, CONRAD   SS SEP 53 09
  POST READER OF FANTASY AND SCIENCE FICTION
                               SATURDAY EVE. POST   AN
SINISTER METAMORPHOSIS, A   BAKER, RUSSELL   SS NYT 65
  10TH ANNUAL OF THE YEAR'S BEST S-F, THE MERRIL, JUDITH   AN
SINLESS CHILD, THE   KOONTZ, DEAN R.   SS FTP 73
  FLAME TREE PLANET   ELWOOD, ROGER   OA
SIR DOMINICK'S BARGAIN   LE FANU, J. SHERIDAN SS
  DEALS WITH THE DEVIL   DAVENPORT, BASIL   AN
SIR EDMUND ORME   JAMES, HENRY   NV
  OTHER DIMENSION, THE   ROSNER, SARA   AN

SIR MALLORY'S MAGNITUDE   GOTTESMAN, S. D.   SS   SFQ 41 WI
  INTO THE FOURTH DIMENSION   CUMMINGS, RAY   AN
SIREN SATELLITE (SEE NEPTUNE)   BARNES, ARTHUR K.   TC
SIREN SINGERS   TRACEY, ROBYN   SS
  SECOND PACIFIC BOOK OF SCIENCE FICTION, THE
                               BAXTER, JOHN   AN
SIRIUS   STAPLEDON, OLAF   NO   SKW 44
  TO THE END OF TIME   STAPLEDON, OLAF   AC
SIRLOIN AND WHITE WINE   WILHELM, KATE   SS   NEW 68 AC
  DOWNSTAIRS ROOM AND OTHER SPECULATIVE FICTION, THE
                               WILHELM, KATE   AC
SISOHPROMATEM   REED, KIT   SS   NWS 67 01
  BEST SF STORIES FROM NEW WORLDS NO. 2, THE
                               MOORCOCK, MICHAEL   AN
SISTER CITY, THE   LUMLEY, BRIAN   SS   70
  YEAR'S BEST HORROR STORIES, THE DAVIS, RICHARD   AN
SISTER FRANCETTA AND PIG BABY BERNARD, KENNETH SS   ARV 73 16
  BEST SF: 1973   HARRISON & ALDISS   AN
SISTER PLANET   ANDERSON, POUL   SN   SAT 59 05
  ALL ABOUT VENUS   ALDISS, BRIAN W.   AN
  FAREWELL FANTASTIC VENUS   ALDISS & HARRISON   AN
  GET OUT OF MY SKY   MARGULIES, LEO   AN
SISTER SHIPS, THE   CHANDLER, A. BERTRAM NV GAL 71 09
  ALTERNATE ORBITS   CHANDLER, A. BERTRAM   DC
SISYPHUS, THE SON OF AEOLUS IVANOV, VSEVOLOD   SS
  VIEW FROM ANOTHER SHORE   ROTTENSTEINER, FRANZ   AN
SIT BY THE FIRE   BENEDICT, MYRLE   SS   FUN 58 05
  FANTASTIC UNIVERSE OMNIBUS, THE SANTESSON, HANS S.   AN
  GENTLE INVADERS   SANTESSON, HANS S.   AN
SITTERS, THE   SIMAK, CLIFFORD D. NV   GAL 58 04
  *ALL THE TRAPS OF EARTH AND OTHER STORIES SIMAK, CLIFFORD D. AC
SITTING DUCK   GALOUYE, DANIEL F. SS   IFS 59 07
  6 FINGERS OF TIME AND 5 OTHER SCIENCE FICTION NOVELETS, THE
                               ANONYMOUS   AN
SITTING DUCK   SAARI, OLIVER E.   SS   ASF 52 01
  EVERY BOY'S BOOK OF OUTER SPACE STORIES DIKTY, T. E. AN
SITTING ON A STARWOOD STOOL WATSON, IAN   SS   SFM 74 10
  BEST OF SCIENCE FICTION MONTHLY, THE SACKS, JANET   AN
SIX CARTOONS   WILSON, GAHAN   CT   FSF 66
  BEST FROM FANTASY AND SCIENCE FICTION: 16
                               FERMAN, EDWARD L.   AN
SIX CARTOONS   WILSON, GAHAN   CT   FSF 70
  BEST FROM FANTASY AND SCIENCE FICTION: 19
                               FERMAN, EDWARD L.   AN
SIX CUBED PLUS 1   RANKINE, JOHN   NV   NWR 66 07
  NEW WRITINGS IN SF. 7   CARNELL, JOHN   AN
  NEW WRITINGS IN SF. 7   CARNELL, JOHN   OA
SIX DRAWINGS   GILDEN, STEPHEN   IL   QRK 70 01
  QUARK/1   DELANY & HACKER   OA
SIX DRAWINGS   LAVIGNE, ROBERT   IL   QRK 71 03
  QUARK/3   DELANY & HACKER   OA
SIX DRAWINGS   PENNEY, ROGER   IL   QRK 71 02
  QUARK/2   DELANY & HACKER   OA
SIX EGGS FOR MAFEKING   COOPER, EDMUND   SS
  VOICES IN THE DARK   COOPER, EDMUND   AC
SIX FINGERS OF TIME, THE   LAFFERTY, R. A.   NV   IFS 60 09
  NINE HUNDRED GRANDMOTHERS   LAFFERTY, R. A.   AC
  OTHERS, THE   CARR, TERRY   AN
  6 FINGERS OF TIME AND 5 OTHER SCIENCE FICTION NOVELETS, THE
                               ANONYMOUS   AN
SIX HAIKU   ANDERSON, KAREN   PM   FSF 62 07
  FIFTY SHORT SCIENCE FICTION TALES ASIMOV & CONKLIN   AN
  SPECULATIONS   SANDERS, THOMAS E.   AN
SIX HUNDRED FATHOMS   LESLIE, NORMAN   SS
  ADVENTURES TO COME   ESENWEIN, J. BERG   OA
SIX MATCHES   STRUGATSKY, ARKADY
                             AND STRUGATSKY, BORIS SS C
  MORE SOVIET SCIENCE FICTION   ANONYMOUS   AN
SIX MORE DRAWINGS   LAVIGNE, ROBERT   IL   QRK 71 03
  QUARK/3   DELANY & HACKER   OA
SIX-FINGERED JACKS   JAMES, E. R.   SS   NWS 62 06
  OUT OF THIS WORLD 4   WILLIAMS-ELLIS & OWEN AN
SIXTEEN STORIES (TRANSLATED BY PATRICK BOWLES)
                             BECKETT, SAMUEL   SS   55
  MATHEMATICAL MAGPIE, THE   FADIMAN, CLIFTON   AN
SIXTH PALACE, THE   SILVERBERG, ROBERT SS   GAL 65 02
  BEST OF ROBERT SILVERBERG, THE SILVERBERG, ROBERT   AC
  CUBE ROOT OF UNCERTAINTY, THE SILVERBERG, ROBERT   AC
  DEEP SPACE   SILVERBERG, ROBERT   AN
  NEEDLE IN A TIMESTACK   SILVERBERG, ROBERT   AC
SIXTH SALLY, OR HOW TRURL AND KLAPAUCIUS CREATED A DEMON OF
  THE SECOND KIND..., THE   LEM, STANISLAW   NV
  CYBERIAD, THE   LEM, STANISLAW   OC
SIXTH SEASON, THE   DAVIDSON, AVRAM   SS   FSF 60 06
  OR ALL THE SEAS WITH OYSTERS   DAVIDSON, AVRAM   AC
SIXTH SENSE   CONEY, MICHAEL G.   SS   VOT 69 08
  WORLD'S BEST SCIENCE FICTION: 1970 WOLLHEIM & CARR   AN
SIXTY-THIRD STREET STATION, THE
                             DAVIDSON, AVRAM   SS   FSF 62 03
  STRANGE SEAS AND SHORES   DAVIDSON, AVRAM   AC
SIXTY-YEAR EXTENSION (SEE FREE AGENT)
                             NOURSE, ALAN E.   TC
SKAG WITH THE QUEER HEAD   LEINSTER, MURRAY   SS   MAR 51 08
  *SCIENCE FICTION ADVENTURES IN MUTATION CONKLIN, GROFF AN
SKELETON   BRADBURY, RAY   SS   WRT 45 09
  *DARK CARNIVAL   BRADBURY, RAY   AC
  *OCTOBER COUNTRY, THE   BRADBURY, RAY   AC
  STRANGE BEASTS AND UNNATURAL MONSTERS STERN, PHILIP VAN D. AN
  VINTAGE BRADBURY, THE   BRADBURY, RAY   AC
SKELETON IN THE CLOSET, THE BLOCH, ROBERT   SS   FAD 43 06
  HORROR TIMES TEN   NORTON, ALDEN H.   AN
SKELETON MEN OF JUPITER   BURROUGHS, EDGAR R. NV   AMZ 43 02
  JOHN CARTER OF MARS   BURROUGHS, EDGAR R.   AC
  STRANGE SIGNPOSTS   ELWOOD & MOSKOWITZ   AN

SKETCHES AMONG THE RUINS OF MY MIND
                             FARMER, PHILIP JOSE NV   NOV 73 03
  BEST SCIENCE FICTION OF THE YEAR, THE NO. 3
                               CARR, TERRY   AN
  NOVA 3   HARRISON, HARRY   OA
SKILLS OF XANADU, THE   STURGEON, THEODORE NV   GAL 56 07
  ALPHA 5   SILVERBERG, ROBERT   AN
  TO HERE AND THE EASEL   STURGEON, THEODORE   AC
  WORLDS OF THEODORE STURGEON, THE STURGEON, THEODORE AC
  13 GREAT STORIES OF SCIENCE FICTION CONKLIN, GROFF   AN
SKIN   DAHL, ROALD   SS   NYM 52 05
  GRAVEYARD READER, THE   CONKLIN, GROFF   AN
SKIN GAME   FRITCH, CHARLES E. SS   IFS 54 05
  CRAZY MIXED-UP PLANET   FRITCH, CHARLES E.   AC
SKIN GAME   GUNN, JAMES E.   SS   VSF 58 01
  FUTURE IMPERFECT   GUNN, JAMES E.   AC
SKIN-DEEP   RENCELAW, BRIAN   SS   PBY 63 06
  DEAD ASTRONAUT, 10 STORIES OF SPACE FLIGHT, THE
                               PLAYBOY, EDITORS OF AN
SKINBURN   FARMER, PHILIP JOSE SS   FSF 72 05
  BOOK OF PHILIP JOSE FARMER, THE FARMER, PHILIP JOSE AC
SKINFLOWERS   GERROLD, DAVID   SS   BER 74
  BERSERKERS, THE   ELWOOD, ROGER   OA
SKINNY PEOPLE OF LEPTOPHLEBO STREET, THE
                             LAFFERTY, R. A.   SS   ORB 75 16
  ORBIT 16   KNIGHT, DAMON   OA
SKIRMISH (BATHE YOUR BEARINGS IN BLOOD)
                             SIMAK, CLIFFORD D. SS   AMZ 50 12
  PENGUIN SCIENCE FICTION   ALDISS, BRIAN W.   AN
  *SCIENCE FICTION THINKING MACHINES CONKLIN, GROFF   AN
  *STRANGERS IN THE UNIVERSE   SIMAK, CLIFFORD D.   AC
SKIRMISH ON A SUMMER MORNING SHAW, BOB   NA   76
  COSMIC KALEIDOSCOPE   SHAW, BOB   OA
SKIRMISHER, THE   BUDRYS, ALGIS   SS   INF 57 11
  BUDRYS' INFERNO   BUDRYS, ALGIS   AC
SKIT-TREE PLANET   LEINSTER, MURRAY   SS   TWS 47 04
  ALIENS, THE   LEINSTER, MURRAY   AC
SKULKING PERMIT   SHECKLEY, ROBERT   NV   GAL 54 05
  CITIZEN IN SPACE   SHECKLEY, ROBERT   AC
SKULL OF THE MARQUIS DE SADE, THE
                             BLOCH, ROBERT   SS   WRT 45 09
  BOGEY MEN   BLOCH, ROBERT   AC
  SKULL OF THE MARQUIS DE SADE, THE BLOCH, ROBERT   AC
SKULL, THE (THE SKULL OF THE MARQUIS DE SADE)
                             BLOCH, ROBERT   SS   WRT 45 09
  GHOULS, THE   HAINING, PETER   AN
SKY   LAFFERTY, R. A.   SS   NDM 71 01
  NEBULA AWARD STORIES NO. 7   BIGGLE, LLOYD JR.   AN
  NEW DIMENSIONS 1   SILVERBERG, ROBERT   OA
SKY BLUE   PANSHIN, ALEXEI
                             AND PANSHIN, CORY   SS C AMZ 72 03
  BEST SCIENCE FICTION OF THE YEAR, THE NO. 2
                               CARR, TERRY   AN
  FAREWELL TO YESTERDAY'S TOMORROW PANSHIN, ALEXEI   AC
SKY IS BURNING, THE   ELLISON, HARLAN   SS   IFS 58 08
  ELLISON WONDERLAND   ELLISON, HARLAN   AC
  FROM THE LAND OF FEAR   ELLISON, HARLAN   AC
  TOUCH OF INFINITY, A   ELLISON, HARLAN   AC
SKY IS FALLING, THE   KUTTNER, HENRY   SS   PLS 50 FL
  RETURN TO OTHERNESS   KUTTNER, HENRY   AC
SKY LIFT   HEINLEIN, ROBERT A. SS   IMG 53 11
  CENTURY OF SCIENCE FICTION, A KNIGHT, DAMON   AN
  MENACE FROM EARTH, THE   HEINLEIN, ROBERT A.   AC
SKY PEOPLE, THE   ANDERSON, POUL   NV   FSF 59 03
  BEST OF POUL ANDERSON, THE   ANDERSON, POUL   AC
  DECADE OF FANTASY AND SCIENCE FICTION, A MILLS, ROBERT P. AN
SKY WAS FULL OF SHIPS, THE   STURGEON, THEODORE SS   TWS 47 04
  SHAPE OF THINGS, THE   KNIGHT, DAMON   AN
  SHOT IN THE DARK   MERRIL, JUDITH   AN
  WORLDS OF THEODORE STURGEON, THE STURGEON, THEODORE AC
SKYDRIFT (SEE STARDRIFT)   PETAJA, EMIL   TC
SKYGHOSTS AND DUSK-DEVILS   BRENNERT, ALAN   SS
  FUTURE PASTIMES   EDELSTEIN, SCOTT   OA
SKYHAMMER   TATE, PETER   SS
  SEAGULLS UNDER GLASS AND OTHER STORIES TATE, PETER   AC
SKYHOOK   GLOECKNER, CAROLYN SS
  NIGHT OF THE SPHINX AND OTHER STORIES ELWOOD, ROGER   OA
SKYSIGN   BLISH, JAMES   NV   ASF 68 05
  ANYWHEN (ENGLISH EDITION ADDS:) BLISH, JAMES   AC
  FOUR FOR THE FUTURE   HARRISON, HARRY   AC
  MIDSUMMER CENTURY   BLISH, JAMES   AC
SLACKER'S PARADISE (SEE BLOCKADE RUNNER)
                             JAMESON, MALCOLM   TC
SLAN   VAN VOGT, A. E.   NO   ASF 40 09
  TRIAD   VAN VOGT, A. E.   AC
SLAUGHTER HOUSE   MATHESON, RICHARD   NV   WRT 53 07
  SHOCK III   MATHESON, RICHARD   AC
SLAVE OF THE FLAMES   BLOCH, ROBERT   SS   WRT 38 06
  HOUSE OF THE HATCHET, THE   BLOCH, ROBERT   AC
  MORE NIGHTMARES   BLOCH, ROBERT   AC
  *OPENER OF THE WAY, THE   BLOCH, ROBERT   AC
SLAVE, THE   KORNBLUTH, C. M.   NV   SFA 57 09
  *MILE BEYOND THE MOON, A   KORNBLUTH, C. M.   AC
SLAVES   DISCH, THOMAS M.   SS   TRV 67
  *GETTING INTO DEATH   DISCH, THOMAS M.   AC
SLAVES OF THE FISH MEN   BURROUGHS, EDGAR R. NV   FAD 41 03
  ESCAPE ON VENUS   BURROUGHS, EDGAR R.   NO
SLAVES OF THE STAR GIANTS   SILVERBERG, ROBERT NA   SFA 57 02
  NEXT STOP THE STARS   SILVERBERG, ROBERT   DC
SLAVES OF TIME   SHECKLEY, ROBERT   NV   NOV 74 04
  NOVA 4   HARRISON, HARRY   OA
SLEEPER WITH STILL HANDS, THE (SEE ASLEEP: WITH STILL HANDS)
                             ELLISON, HARLAN   TC
SLEEPING BEAUTY   CARR, TERRY   SS   FSF 67 05
  LIGHT AT THE END OF THE UNIVERSE, THE CARR, TERRY   AC
  NEW WORLDS OF FANTASY NO. 3   CARR, TERRY   AN

```
SLEEPING BEAUTY (THE CASE OF THE SNORING HEIR)
                        CLARKE, ARTHUR C.    SS    INF 57 04
  TALES FROM THE WHITE HART         CLARKE, ARTHUR C.      AC
SLEEPING BEAUTY, THE      CHANDLER, A. BERTRAM NV    GAL 70 02
  HARD WAY UP, THE             CHANDLER, A. BERTRAM  DC
SLEEPING BEAUTY, THE (THE SLEEPING REDHEADS)
                        BLOCH, ROBERT        SS    SWK 58 03
  NIGHTMARES                  BLOCH, ROBERT         AC
  PLEASANT DREAMS              BLOCH, ROBERT         AC
SLEEPING DOGS       ELLISON, HARLAN       SS    ASF 74 10
  BEST SCIENCE FICTION STORIES OF THE YEAR (1974)
                        DEL REY, LESTER       AN
  PAINGOD AND OTHER DELUSIONS (THIRD EDITION ADDS:)
                        ELLISON, HARLAN       AC
SLEEPING REDHEADS, THE (SEE THE SLEEPING BEAUTY)
                        BLOCH, ROBERT        TC
SLICE OF THE UNIVERSE     SALLIS, JAMES     SS    FAN 69 02
  FEW LAST WORDS, A            SALLIS, JAMES         AC
SLICED-CROSSWISE ONLY-ON-TUESDAY WORLD, THE
                        FARMER, PHILIP JOSE SS    NDM 71 01
  BEST SCIENCE FICTION OF THE YEAR, THE    CARR, TERRY      AN
  BEST SCIENCE FICTION STORIES OF THE YEAR (1971)
                        DEL REY, LESTER       AN
  NEW DIMENSIONS 1             SILVERBERG, ROBERT    OA
  SOCIAL PROBLEMS THROUGH SCIENCE FICTION  GREENBERG/MILSTEAD/& AN
SLIDE SHOW          MARTIN, GEORGE R. R.  SS    OMG 73
  OMEGA                     ELWOOD, ROGER         OA
  SONG FOR LYA, A              MARTIN, GEORGE R. R.  AC
SLIGHT CASE OF LIMBO, A   BIGGLE, LLOYD JR.  SS    ASF 63 04
  RULE OF THE DOOR AND OTHER FANCIFUL REGULATIONS
                        BIGGLE, LLOYD JR.     AC
  9TH ANNUAL OF THE YEAR'S BEST S-F, THE   MERRIL, JUDITH    AN
SLIGHT CASE OF SUNSTROKE, A (STROKE OF THE SUN)
                        CLARKE, ARTHUR C.   SS    GAL 58 09
  TALES OF TEN WORLDS          CLARKE, ARTHUR C.     AC
SLIGHT MISCALCULATION, A  BOVA, BEN        SS    FSF 71 08
  COSMIC LAUGHTER             HALDEMAN, JOE W.      AN
  FORWARD IN TIME             BOVA, BEN             AC
SLIGHT OF WIT       DICKSON, GORDON R.   SS    ASF 61 12
  ANALOG 1                  CAMPBELL, JOHN W. JR  AN
SLIME               BRENNAN, JOSEPH P.   NV    WRT 53 03
  STRANGE BEASTS AND UNNATURAL MONSTERS  STERN, PHILIP VAN D. AN
SLIME DWELLERS, THE       EDELSTEIN, SCOTT  SS    VTX 75 06
  CITY: 2000 A.D., THE         CLEM/GREENBERG/&      AN
SLIP UNDER THE KNIFE (ALSO AS UNDER THE KNIFE)
                        WELLS, H. G.        SS    NRV 96 01
  THIRTY STRANGE STORIES         WELLS, H. G.        AC
SLIP UNDER THE MICROSCOPE, A  WELLS, H. G.    SS    YBK 96 01
  COUNTRY OF THE BLIND, THE       WELLS, H. G.        AC
  INEXPERIENCED GHOST AND NINE OTHER STORIES, THE
                        WELLS, H. G.        AC
  PLATTNER STORY AND OTHERS, THE    WELLS, H. G.        AC
  SHORT STORIES OF H. G. WELLS, THE   WELLS, H. G.       AC
  THIRTY STRANGE STORIES         WELLS, H. G.        AC
SLIPS TAKE OVER     DEFORD, MIRIAM ALLEN SS    FSF 64 09
  WORLDS OF MAYBE             SILVERBERG, ROBERT    AN
SLITHERING SHADOW, THE    HOWARD, ROBERT E.   SS    WRT 33 09
  CONAN THE ADVENTURER         HOWARD, R. & DE CAMP AC
  SWORD OF CONAN, THE          HOWARD, ROBERT E.     AC
SLOW DRAG           DEAN, MAL           SS    NWB 75 08
  NEW WORLDS EIGHT            BAILEY, HILARY        OA
SLOW SCULPTURE      STURGEON, THEODORE  NV    GAL 70 02
  NEBULA AWARD STORIES  NO. 6     SIMAK, CLIFFORD D.    AN
  SPECULATIONS               SANDERS, THOMAS E.    AN
  STURGEON IS ALIVE AND WELL...    STURGEON, THEODORE    AC
  WORLD'S BEST SCIENCE FICTION: 1971  WOLLHEIM & CARR    AN
SLOW SEASON, THE    SHECKLEY, ROBERT    SS    FSF 54 10
  SHARDS OF SPACE             SHECKLEY, ROBERT      AC
SLOW TUESDAY NIGHT  LAFFERTY, R. A.     SS    GAL 65 04
  ABOVE THE HUMAN LANDSCAPE       MCNELLY & STOVER     AN
  BIO-FUTURES                SARGENT, PAMELA      AN
  DAY IN THE LIFE, A           DOZOIS, GARDNER R.    AN
  INFINITE JESTS             SILVERBERG, ROBERT    AN
  NINE HUNDRED GRANDMOTHERS       LAFFERTY, R. A.      AC
  NINTH GALAXY READER, THE        POHL, FREDERIK      AN
  SOCIOLOGY THROUGH SCIENCE FICTION   MILSTEAD/GREENBERG/& AN
  11TH ANNUAL OF THE YEAR'S BEST S-F, THE  MERRIL, JUDITH    AN
SLUGGING IT OUT     HALDEMAN, JACK C. II SS
  FAR SIDE OF TIME, THE         ELWOOD, ROGER        OA
SLUM                FRANKE, HERBERT W.   SS
  VIEW FROM ANOTHER SHORE        ROTTENSTEINER, FRANZ AN
SLY BUNGERHOP, THE  MORRISON, WILLIAM   NV    GAL 57 09
  MIND PARTNER AND 8 OTHER NOVELETS FROM GALAXY
                        GOLD, H. L.         AN
SMACK RUN           BERGSTRESSER, MARTA  SS    NWB 73 05
  NEW WORLDS QUARTERLY NO. 5      MOORCOCK, MICHAEL    OA
SMALL ASSASSIN, THE       BRADBURY, RAY    SS    DMN 46 11
  AUTUMN PEOPLE, THE          BRADBURY, RAY        AC
  CHILDREN OF WONDER          TENN, WILLIAM        AN
  *DARK CARNIVAL             BRADBURY, RAY        AC
  *OCTOBER COUNTRY, THE         BRADBURY, RAY        AC
  SMALL ASSASSIN, THE          BRADBURY, RAY        AC
  VINTAGE BRADBURY, THE         BRADBURY, RAY        AC
  YOUNG DEMONS              ELWOOD & GHIDALIA    AN
SMALL BETRAYING DETAIL, THE   ALDISS, BRIAN W.    SS    NWS 65 05
  BEST SF STORIES FROM NEW WORLDS NO. 1, THE
                        MOORCOCK, MICHAEL    AN
SMALL DRAGON, A     PATTEN, BRIAN       PM      69
  HOLDING YOUR EIGHT HANDS       LUCIE-SMITH, EDWARD  AN
SMALL LORDS         POHL, FREDERIK      NV    SFQ 57 02
  DAY MILLION              POHL, FREDERIK      AC
  WEIRD ONES, THE            HOWARD, IVAN        AN
SMALL MIRACLE OF FISHHOOKS AND STRAIGHT PINS, A
                        BUNCH, DAVID R.   NV    FAN 61 06
  7TH ANNUAL OF THE YEAR'S BEST S-F, THE  MERRIL, JUDITH    AN

SMALL MOUTH, BAD TASTE    ANTHONY, PIERS    SS    SAG 70
  SCIENCE AGAINST MAN         CHEETHAM, ANTHONY     OA
SMALL WAR           BIXBY, JEROME       SS    SFQ 54 05
  SPACE BY THE TAIL           BIXBY, JEROME        AC
SMALL WAR           MACLEAN, KATHERINE  SS    SVW 73
  SAVING WORLDS             ELWOOD & KIDD        OA
SMALL WORLD         KURLAND, MICHAEL J.  NV    TVW 73
  TWO VIEWS OF WONDER          SCORTIA & YARBRO     OA
SMALL WORLD OF LEWIS STILLMAN, THE (SMALL WORLD)
                        NOLAN, WILLIAM F.   SS    FUN 57 08
  IMPACT-20               NOLAN, WILLIAM F.     AC
SMALL WORLD OF M-75, THE    CLINTON, ED M. JR.  SS    IFS 54 07
  FIRST WORLD OF IF, THE         QUINN & WULFF       AN
  *SCIENCE FICTION ADVENTURES IN MUTATION  CONKLIN, GROFF    AN
SMALLEST DRAGONBOY, THE    MCCAFFREY, ANNE    SS    SFT 73
  GET OFF THE UNICORN          MCCAFFREY, ANNE      AC
  SCIENCE FICTION TALES         ELWOOD, ROGER       AN
SMALLEST GOD, THE   DEL REY, LESTER     NV    ASF 40 01
  EARLY DEL REY             DEL REY, LESTER      AC
SMALLEST MOON, THE  WILCOX, DON         SS    BLF
  BOYS' LIFE BOOK OF OUTER SPACE STORIES, THE
                        BOY'S LIFE, ED. OF    AN
SMALLEST STARSHIP, THE    ORGILL, MICHAEL    SS
  TUNNEL AND OTHER STORIES, THE     ELWOOD, ROGER       OA
SMELL OF PULPS, THE       INOUYE, JON      SS
  NIGHT TIDE, A             INOUYE, JON        OC
SMILE OF THE SPHINX, THE    TEMPLE, WILLIAM F.  SS    TOW 38 FL
  ESCALES DANS L'INFINI         GALLET, GEORGES H.    AN
SMILE, THE          BRADBURY, RAY       SS    FAN 52 SU
  DAY IT RAINED FOREVER, THE       BRADBURY, RAY       AC
  MEDICINE FOR MELANCHOLY, A       BRADBURY, RAY       AC
  NEW WORLDS FOR OLD          DERLETH, AUGUST      AN
  S IS FOR SPACE            BRADBURY, RAY       AC
  TRANSFORMATIONS            ROSELLE, DANIEL      AN
  *WORLDS OF TOMORROW          DERLETH, AUGUST      AN
  YOU AND SCIENCE FICTION        HOLLISTER, BERNARD C AN
SMILING FUTURE, THE       DEFORD, MIRIAM ALLEN SS    IFS 65 10
  XENOGENESIS              DEFORD, MIRIAM ALLEN AC
SMILING PEOPLE, THE       BRADBURY, RAY    SS    WRT 46 05
  *DARK CARNIVAL            BRADBURY, RAY       AC
  SMALL ASSASSIN, THE          BRADBURY, RAY       AC
SMITH'S REVENGE     BROWN, ROSEL GEORGE SS    NEW 63 AC
  HANDFUL OF TIME, A          BROWN, ROSEL GEORGE   AC
SMOE AND THE IMPLICIT CLAY    LAFFERTY, R. A.   NV      76
  FUTURE POWER             DANN & DOZOIS       OA
SMOKE GHOST         LEIBER, FRITZ       SS    UNK 41 10
  HUMAN?                 MERRIL, JUDITH      AN
  NIGHT'S BLACK AGENTS         LEIBER, FRITZ       AC
  SECRET SONGS, THE           LEIBER, FRITZ       AC
SMOKEY THE BEAR SUTRA, THE    SNYDER, GARY    SS    SVW 73
  SAVING WORLDS             ELWOOD & KIDD       OA
SMOTHERED SEAS      WEINBAUM, STANLEY G. NV    ASF 36 01
  MARTIAN ODYSSEY AND OTHER SCIENCE FICTION TALES, A
                        WEINBAUM, STANLEY G. AC
  RED PERI, THE             WEINBAUM, STANLEY G. AC
SNAIL'S PACE        BUDRYS, ALGIS       SS    DSF 53 10
  WAY OUT                HOWARD, IVAN       AN
SNAIL-WATCHER, THE  HIGHSMITH, PATRICIA  SS    GAM 64 03
  SHOCKING THING, A           KNIGHT, DAMON       AN
SNAKE GODDESS (SEE EVE WAS A SNAKE)
                        PRICE, E. HOFFMANN  TC
SNAPDRAGON          LONG, FRANK BELKNAP  NV    TWS 41 12
  JOHN CARSTAIRS: SPACE DETECTIVE   LONG, FRANK BELKNAP   AC
SNIP SNIP           SCHENCK, HILBERT JR. PM    FSF 59 09
  MATHEMATICAL MAGPIE, THE        FADIMAN, CLIFTON     AN
SNOWBALL EFFECT, THE      MACLEAN, KATHERINE  SS    GAL 52 09
  DECADE THE 1950S           ALDISS & HARRISON    AN
  DIPLOIDS AND OTHER FLIGHTS OF FANCY, THE MACLEAN, KATHERINE  AC
  GALAXY SCIENCE FICTION OMNIBUS    GOLD, H. L.        AN
  PENGUIN SCIENCE FICTION        ALDISS, BRIAN W.     AN
  SCIENCE FICTION INVENTIONS      KNIGHT, DAMON       AN
  SECOND GALAXY READER OF SCIENCE FICTION GOLD, H. L.      AN
SNOWBALL, THE       PARNOV, YEREMEY
                    AND YEMTSEV, MIKHAIL  SS C
  JOURNEY ACROSS THREE WORLDS      ANONYMOUS         AN
SNOWBANK ORBIT, THE       LEIBER, FRITZ    NV    IFS 62 09
  BEST SCIENCE FICTION FROM IF, THE   POHL, FREDERIK     AN
  SHIPS TO THE STARS          LEIBER, FRITZ       DC
SNOWBIRD AND THE SEVEN WARFS   LORY, ROBERT    SS
  HARVEST OF HOODWINKS, A        LORY, ROBERT       DC
SNOWMEN, THE        POHL, FREDERIK      SS    GAL 59 12
  BEST OF FREDERIK POHL, THE       POHL, FREDERIK      AC
  FREDERIK POHL OMNIBUS, THE       POHL, FREDERIK      AC
  MAN WHO ATE THE WORLD, THE       POHL, FREDERIK      AC
SNOWS ARE MELTED, THE SNOWS ARE GONE, THE
                        TIPTREE, JAMES JR.  SS    VSF 69 11
  BEST SF: 1969             HARRISON & ALDISS    AN
  TEN THOUSAND LIGHT-YEARS FROM HOME  TIPTREE, JAMES JR.   AC
SNUFFLES            LAFFERTY, R. A.     NV    GAL 60 12
  BEST SF 7               CRISPIN, EDMUND      AN
  MIND PARTNER AND 8 OTHER NOVELETS FROM GALAXY
                        GOLD, H. L.         AN
  NINE HUNDRED GRANDMOTHERS       LAFFERTY, R. A.      AC
SNULBUG (FIRST IN UNKNOWN, DEC. 1941)
                        BOUCHER, ANTHONY   SS    FSF 53 05
  BEST FROM FANTASY AND SCIENCE FICTION: 3
                        BOUCHER & MCCOMAS    AN
  COMPLEAT WEREWOLF, THE         BOUCHER, ANTHONY     AC
  FAR AND AWAY             BOUCHER, ANTHONY     AC
  UNKNOWN, THE             BENSEN, D. R.       AN
SO BRIGHT THE VISION      SIMAK, CLIFFORD D.  NV    FUN 56 08
  SO BRIGHT THE VISION          SIMAK, CLIFFORD D.    DC
SO FAR FROM PRAGUE  ALDISS, BRIAN W.    SS
  NEW S.F., THE             JONES, LANGDON      OA
SO I NEVER LEFT HOME      COOPER, EDMUND    SS
  VOICES IN THE DARK          COOPER, EDMUND      AC
```

SO LOVELY, SO LOST (SEE THE SHOW MUST GO ON)
                              CAUSEY, JAMES   TC
SO PROUDLY WE CLING   MORGAN, CHRIS   SS
  GOLLANCZ - SUNDAY TIMES BEST SF STORIES ANONYMOUS   OA
SO PROUDLY WE HAIL   MERRIL, JUDITH   SS   STR 53 01
  STAR SCIENCE FICTION STORIES   POHL, FREDERIK   OA
  SURVIVAL SHIP AND OTHER STORIES   MERRIL, JUDITH   AC
SO SWEET AS MAGIC...   ELLIOTT, BRUCE   NV   FNF 53 08
  WIZARDS AND WARLOCKS   GHIDALIA, VIC   AN
SO WHY AREN'T WE RICH?   ASIMOV, ISAAC   IN
  NEBULA AWARD STORIES 8   ASIMOV, ISAAC   AN
SOAP OPERA   NELSON, ALAN   SS   FSF 53 04
  13 GREAT STORIES OF SCIENCE FICTION CONKLIN, GROFF   AN
SOARING STATUE, THE   DE CAMP, L. SPRAGUE SS   NEW 54 AN
  TOMORROW'S UNIVERSE   CAMPBELL, H. J.
SOBER NOISES OF MORNING IN A MARGINAL LAND
                              ALDISS, BRIAN W.   NV   LOM 72 06
  BEST SCIENCE FICTION STORIES OF BRIAN W. ALDISS (REVISED)
                                     ALDISS, BRIAN W.   AC
  SF: AUTHORS' CHOICE 3   HARRISON, HARRY   AN
SOCIAL CONSEQUENCES OF COMMUNICATIONS SATELLITES, THE
                              CLARKE, ARTHUR C.   AR   65
  SURVIVAL PRINTOUT   TOTAL EFFECT   AN
SOCIAL SCIENCE FICTION   ASIMOV, ISAAC   AR   NEW 53 NF
  SCIENCE FICTION: THE FUTURE   ALLEN, DICK   AN
SOCIETY FOR THE PREVENTION   GOULART, RON   SS   GAM 64 03
  SEA OF SPACE, A   NOLAN, WILLIAM F.   AN
SOCK FINISH   BLOCH, ROBERT   SS   EQM 57 10
  *BLOOD RUNS COLD   BLOCH, ROBERT   AC
SOCRATES   CHRISTOPHER, JOHN   SS   GAL 51 03
  *BEYOND HUMAN KEN   MERRIL, JUDITH   AN
  INTRODUCTORY PSYCHOLOGY THROUGH SCIENCE FICTION
                                     KATZ/WARRICK/&   AN
  *STORIES FOR TOMORROW   SLOANE, WILLIAM   AN
SOCRATES AND THE SLAVE   PLATO   SS
  FANTASIA MATHEMATICA   FADIMAN, CLIFTON   AN
SOCRATES OF THE SOUTH FORTY   BOND, NELSON S.   SS
  MR. MERGENTHWIRKER'S LOBBIES AND OTHER FANTASTIC TALES
                                     BOND, NELSON S.   AC
SODOM AND GOMORRAH, TEXAS   LAFFERTY, R. A.   SS   GAL 62 12
  STRANGE DOINGS   LAFFERTY, R. A.   AC
SOFT BLUE BUNNY RABBIT STORY, THE
                              BRYANT, EDWARD   SS   CLR 71 01
  AMONG THE DEAD   BRYANT, EDWARD   AC
  CLARION   WILSON, ROBIN SCOTT   OA
SOFT COME THE DRAGONS   KOONTZ, DEAN R.   SS   FSF 67 08
  LIBERATED FUTURE: VOYAGES INTO TOMORROW, THE
                                     HOSKINS, ROBERT   AN
  SOFT COME THE DRAGONS   KOONTZ, DEAN R.   DC
SOFT LANDING   FOX, WILLIAM   PM
  MARS, WE LOVE YOU   HIPOLITO & MCNELLY   AN
SOFT PREDICAMENT, THE   ALDISS, BRIAN W.   NV   FSF 69 10
  BOOK OF BRIAN ALDISS, THE   ALDISS, BRIAN W.   AC
SOFT WEAPON, THE   NIVEN, LARRY   NV   IFS 67 02
  NEUTRON STAR   NIVEN, LARRY   AC
SOFT WORLD SEQUENCE, THE   MACBETH, GEORGE   PM   NWS 67 07
  BEST SF STORIES FROM NEW WORLDS 3 MOORCOCK, MICHAEL   AN
SOFTLY WALKS THE BEETLE   COLLIER, JOHN   SS   PBY 60 01
  PLAYBOY BOOK OF HORROR AND THE SUPERNATURAL, THE
                                     PLAYBOY, EDITORS OF   AN
  WEIRD SHOW   PLAYBOY, EDITORS OF   AN
SOFTLY WHILE YOU'RE SLEEPING SMITH, EVELYN E.   SS   FSF 61 04
  *BEST FROM FANTASY AND SCIENCE FICTION: 11
                                     MILLS, ROBERT P.   AN
SOJOURNER   INOUYE, JON   SS
  NIGHT TIDE, A   INOUYE, JON   OC
SOL'S LITTLE BROTHER   ELAM, RICHARD M. JR. SS
  TEEN-AGE SCIENCE FICTION STORIES   ELAM, RICHARD M. JR.   AC
SOLAR CONSTANT (CRITICAL DIFFERENCE)
                              LEINSTER, MURRAY   NV   ASF 56 07
  COLONIAL SURVEY   LEINSTER, MURRAY   NO
SOLAR PLEXUS   BLISH, JAMES   SS   AST 41 09
  *BEYOND HUMAN KEN   MERRIL, JUDITH   AN
  HUMAN-MACHINES   SCORTIA & ZEBROWSKI   AN
  MEN AND MACHINES   SILVERBERG, ROBERT   AN
SOLAR SYSTEMS...   B., E. D.   PM   FSF 53 02
  BEST FROM FANTASY AND SCIENCE FICTION: 3
                                     BOUCHER & MCCOMAS   AN
SOLARITE   CAMPBELL, JOHN W. JR NV   AMZ 30 11
  BLACK STAR PASSES, THE   CAMPBELL, JOHN W. JR   AC
SOLD TO SATAN   TWAIN, MARK   SS
  LIGHT FANTASTIC, THE   HARRISON, HARRY   AN
SOLDIER (SOLDIER FROM TOMORROW)
                              ELLISON, HARLAN   SS   FUN 57 10
  FROM THE LAND OF FEAR   ELLISON, HARLAN   AC
  THEMES IN SCIENCE FICTION   KELLEY, LEO P.   AN
SOLDIER (TELEVISION SCRIPT VERSION)
                              ELLISON, HARLAN   PL   ABC 64 09
  FROM THE LAND OF FEAR   ELLISON, HARLAN   AC
SOLDIER BOY   SHAARA, MICHAEL   NV   GAL 53 07
  *SCIENCE FICTION THINKING MACHINES CONKLIN, GROFF   AN
SOLDIER, ASK NOT   DICKSON, GORDON R.   SN   GAL 64 10
  HUGO WINNERS, THE (VOLUME 2)   ASIMOV, ISAAC   AN
SOLDIERS RUNNING (SEE HEARTS AND ENGINES, HOW TO BE A SOLDIER)
                              ALDISS, BRIAN W.   TC
SOLE SOLUTION   RUSSELL, ERIC FRANK SS   FUN 56 04
  DARK TIDES   RUSSELL, ERIC FRANK   AC
  PENGUIN SCIENCE FICTION   ALDISS, BRIAN W.   AN
SOLE SURVIVOR, THE   SERLING, ROD   SA
  NIGHT GALLERY   SERLING, ROD   OC
SOLFY DRINK, A SAFFEL FRAGRANCE, A
                              GILBERT, DOROTHY   SS   NDM 75 05
  NEW DIMENSIONS 5   SILVERBERG, ROBERT   OA
SOLILOQUY   SELLINGS, ARTHUR   SS
  *TIME TRANSFER   SELLINGS, ARTHUR   AC

SOLILOQUY IN THE LAST ACT, THE DISCH, THOMAS M.   SS
  *GETTING INTO DEATH   DISCH, THOMAS M.   AC
SOLIPSIST   BROWN, FREDRIC   SS
  ANGELS AND SPACESHIPS   BROWN, FREDRIC   AC
SOLITARY   SILVERBERG, ROBERT   SS   FUT 57 SP
  DIMENSION THIRTEEN   SILVERBERG, ROBERT   AC
  GODLING, GO HOME!   SILVERBERG, ROBERT   AC
SOLITARY CONFINEMENT (SEE HUB) MACDONALD, PHILIP   TC
SOLUTION (TO SERVE THE SHIP) NOLAN, WILLIAM F.   SS   GAM 63 01
  ALIEN HORIZONS   NOLAN, WILLIAM F.   AC
SOLUTION TO CROSSWORD   BRUNNER, JOHN   MS
  BOOK OF JOHN BRUNNER, THE   BRUNNER, JOHN   AC
SOLUTION UNSATISFACTORY   HEINLEIN, ROBERT A. NV   ASF 41 05
  FUTURE TENSE   CURTIS, RICHARD   AN
  WORLDS OF ROBERT A. HEINLEIN, THE HEINLEIN, ROBERT A.   AC
SOLUTION UNSATISFACTORY   MACDONALD, ANSON   NV   ASF 41 05
  *BEST OF SCIENCE FICTION   CONKLIN, GROFF   AN
SOME ARE BORN CATS   CARR, CAROL
                              AND CARR, TERRY   SS C SFT 73
  CREATURES FROM BEYOND   CARR, TERRY   OA
  SCIENCE FICTION TALES   ELWOOD, ROGER   OA
SOME DAY WE'LL FIND YOU   CARTMILL, CLEVE   NV   ASF 42 12
  DIMENSION 4   CONKLIN, GROFF   AN
SOME DREAMS COME IN PACKAGES KYLE, DAVID A.   NV   NWR 71 18
  NEW WRITINGS IN SF. 18   CARNELL, JOHN   OA
SOME FACTS ABOUT ROBOTS   WOLF, LEONARD   PM   FSF 54 07
  BEST FROM FANTASY AND SCIENCE FICTION: 4
                                     BOUCHER, ANTHONY   AN
SOME FACTS ABOUT ROBOTS I   WOLF, LEONARD   PM   FSF 53 11
  BEST FROM FANTASY AND SCIENCE FICTION: 3
                                     BOUCHER & MCCOMAS   AN
SOME FACTS ABOUT ROBOTS II (SEE MORE FACTS ABOUT ROBOTS)
                              SPRINGER, SHERWOOD   TC
SOME JOYS UNDER THE STARS (THE STAR)
                              POHL, FREDERIK   SS   GAL 73 11
  IN THE PROBLEM PIT   POHL, FREDERIK   AC
SOME LAPSE OF TIME   BRUNNER, JOHN   NV   SCF 63 02
  NOW THEN   BRUNNER, JOHN   AC
SOME LIVE LIKE LAZARUS (VERY LATE IN THE EVENING)
                              BRADBURY, RAY   SS   PBY 60 12
  MACHINERIES OF JOY, THE   BRADBURY, RAY   AC
SOME MYSTERIES OF VENUS RESOLVED
                              LOVELL, BERNARD   AR   TMS 67
  ALL ABOUT VENUS   ALDISS, BRIAN W.   AN
  FAREWELL FANTASTIC VENUS   ALDISS & HARRISON   AN
SOME NOTES ON SOURCES   KARL, JEAN E.   MS
  TURNING PLACE, THE   KARL, JEAN E.   OC
SOME NOTES ON THE PREDYNASTIC EPOCH
                              SILVERBERG, ROBERT   SS   BMR 73
  BAD MOON RISING   DISCH, THOMAS M.   OA
  UNFAMILIAR TERRITORY   SILVERBERG, ROBERT   AC
SOME NOTES TOWARD A USEABLE PAST
                              MALZBERG, BARRY N.   SS   NOV 72 02
  OUT FROM GANYMEDE   MALZBERG, BARRY N.   AC
SOME ROOMS   KESSLER, MERLE   SS   NWB 73 03
  NEW WORLDS QUARTERLY NO. 5   MOORCOCK, MICHAEL   OA
SOMEBODY TO PLAY WITH   WILLIAMS, JAY   SS   FSF 61 05
  *BEST FROM FANTASY AND SCIENCE FICTION: 11
                                     MILLS, ROBERT P.   AN
SOMEDAY   ASIMOV, ISAAC   SS   INF 56 08
  EARTH IS ROOM ENOUGH   ASIMOV, ISAAC   AC
  METAL SMILE, THE   KNIGHT, DAMON   AN
  WORLDS OF WONDER   HARRISON, HARRY   AN
SOMERSET DREAMS   WILHELM, KATE   NV   ORB 69 05
  ORBIT 5   KNIGHT, DAMON   OA
  SCIENCE FICTION ARGOSY, A   KNIGHT, DAMON   AN
SOMETHING   DRURY, ALLEN   SS   FSF 60 10
  BEST FROM FANTASY AND SCIENCE FICTION: 10
                                     MILLS, ROBERT P.   AN
SOMETHING BRIGHT   HENDERSON, ZENNA   SS   GAL 60 02
  ANYTHING BOX, THE   HENDERSON, ZENNA   AC
  SEVENTH GALAXY READER, THE   POHL, FREDERIK   AC
  TALES BEYOND TIME   DE CAMP, L. S.&C.   AN
  6TH ANNUAL OF THE YEAR'S BEST S-F, THE MERRIL, JUDITH   AN
SOMETHING ELSE   TILLEY, ROBERT J.   SS   FSF 65 10
  BEST FROM FANTASY AND SCIENCE FICTION: 15
                                     FERMAN, EDWARD L.   AN
  TWENTY YEARS OF FANTASY & SCIENCE FICTION
                                     FERMAN & MILLS   AN
  11TH ANNUAL OF THE YEAR'S BEST S-F, THE MERRIL, JUDITH   AN
SOMETHING FOR NOTHING   SHECKLEY, ROBERT   SS   GAL 54 06
  CITIZEN IN SPACE   SHECKLEY, ROBERT   AC
  ROBERT SHECKLEY OMNIBUS, THE   SHECKLEY, ROBERT   AC
  TOMORROW, INC.   GREENBERG& OLANDER   AN
  VINTAGE ANTHOLOGY OF SCIENCE FANTASY, THE
                                     CERF, CHRISTOPHER   AN
SOMETHING FROM ABOVE   WANDREI, DONALD   NV   WRT 30 12
  *OTHER SIDE OF THE MOON, THE   DERLETH, AUGUST   AN
  STRANGE HARVEST   WANDREI, DONALD   AN
SOMETHING GREEN   BROWN, FREDRIC   SS   NEW 51 AC
  EXPLORING OTHER WORLDS   MOSKOWITZ, SAM   AN
  PARADOX LOST, AND 12 OTHER GREAT S.F. STORIES
                                     BROWN, FREDRIC   AC
  SPACE ON MY HANDS   BROWN, FREDRIC   AC
SOMETHING HAD TO BE DONE   DRAKE, DAVID   SS   FSF 75 02
  YEAR'S BEST HORROR STORIES: SERIES IV, THE
                                     PAGE, GERALD W.   AN
SOMETHING HAPPENS   WILHELM, KATE   AR   CLR 71 01
  CLARION   WILSON, ROBIN SCOTT   AN
SOMETHING IN A CLOUD   FINNEY, JACK   SS
  THIRD LEVEL, THE   FINNEY, JACK   AC
SOMETHING IN THE SKY   CORREY, LEE   SS   ASF 57 05
  ENCOUNTERS WITH ALIENS   EARLEY, GEORGE W.   AN
SOMETHING IN WOOD   DERLETH, AUGUST   SS   WRT 48 03
  FANTASY: THE LITERATURE OF THE MARVELOUS KELLEY, LEO P.   AN

OMETHING INVENTED ME   PHELAN, R. C.   SS   REP 60 10
  6TH ANNUAL OF THE YEAR'S BEST S-F, THE   MERRIL, JUDITH   AN
OMETHING NEW   SMITH, CLARK ASHTON SS   TST 24 08
  OTHER DIMENSIONS   SMITH, CLARK ASHTON   AC
OMETHING NEW UNDER THE SUN   WILSON, ROBIN SCOTT IN
  WONDERMAKERS   HOSKINS, ROBERT   AN
OMETHING STRANGE   AMIS, KINGSLEY   NV   FSF 61 07
  FIVE-ODD   CONKLIN, GROFF   AN
  LIGHT FANTASTIC, THE   HARRISON, HARRY   AN
OMETHING THAT WORKS   KNIGHT, DAMON   AR
  CLARION SF   WILHELM, KATE   OA
OMETHING TO SAY   BERRYMAN, JOHN   NV   ASF 66 08
  ANALOG 6   CAMPBELL, JOHN W. JR   AN
OMETHING UP THERE LIKES ME   BESTER, ALFRED   NV   AMA 73
  ASTOUNDING   HARRISON, HARRY   OA
  BEST SCIENCE FICTION OF THE YEAR, THE NO. 3
                                     CARR, TERRY   AN
  BEST SCIENCE FICTION STORIES OF THE YEAR (1973)
                                     DEL REY, LESTER   AN
  STAR LIGHT, STAR BRIGHT   BESTER, ALFRED   AC
OMETHING WILD IS LOOSE   SILVERBERG, ROBERT   NV   MWS 71
  EARTH'S OTHER SHADOW   SILVERBERG, ROBERT   AC
  MANY WORLDS OF SCIENCE FICTION, THE BOVA, BEN   OA
  MIND TO MIND   SILVERBERG, ROBERT   AN
  SUNDANCE AND OTHER SCIENCE FICTION STORIES
                                     SILVERBERG, ROBERT   AC
OMETIMES I GET SO HAPPY   BUNCH, DAVID R.   SS   FAN 63 08
  MODERAN   BUNCH, DAVID R.   AC
OMEWHERE A VOICE   RUSSELL, ERIC FRANK NV   OWS 53 01
  SOMEWHERE A VOICE   RUSSELL, ERIC FRANK   AC
OMEWHERE NOT FAR FROM HERE   KERSH, GERALD   SS   PBY 65 03
  PLAYBOY'S STORIES OF THE SINISTER & STRANGE
                                     PLAYBOY, EDITORS OF   AN
  11TH ANNUAL OF THE YEAR'S BEST S-F, THE MERRIL, JUDITH   AN
OMNIUM (1634)   KEPLER, JOHANNES   EX
  *BEYOND TIME AND SPACE   DERLETH, AUGUST   AN
OMP   VARSHAVSKY, ILYA   SS
  OTHER WORLDS, OTHER SEAS   SUVIN, DARKO   AN
ON (QUEEN OF THE DEEP)   FARMER, PHILIP JOSE SS   ARG 54 03
  STRANGE RELATIONS   FARMER, PHILIP JOSE   AC
ON IS BORN, A   VAN VOGT, A. E.   SS   ASF 46 05
  EMPIRE OF THE ATOM   VAN VOGT, A. E.   NO
ON OF EVE, A   SAMBROT, WILLIAM   SS   MRM 59
  ISLAND OF FEAR AND OTHER SCIENCE FICTION SAMBROT, WILLIAM   AC
ON OF THE STARS   BINDER, EANDO   SS   FFM 40 02
  ANDROIDS, TIME MACHINES AND BLUE GIRAFFES
                                     ELWOOD & GHIDALIA   AN
ON OF TWO WORLDS   HAMILTON, EDMOND   NA   TWS 41 08
  3 FROM OUT THERE   MARGULIES, LEO   AN
ONG AGAINST CIRCLES, A   LISTER, R. P.   PM   NYM 61 05
  MATHEMATICAL MAGPIE, THE   FADIMAN, CLIFTON   AN
ONG BEFORE SUNSET, A   GRIGG, DAVID   SS
  BEYOND TOMORROW   HARDING, LEE   AN
ONG FOR A LADY   BEAUMONT, CHARLES   SS   NEW 60 AC
  EDGE, THE   BEAUMONT, CHARLES   AC
  NIGHT RIDE AND OTHER JOURNEYS   BEAUMONT, CHARLES   AC
ONG FOR LYA, A   MARTIN, GEORGE R. R. NV   ASF 74 06
  SONG FOR LYA, A   MARTIN, GEORGE R. R.   AC
  1975 ANNUAL WORLD'S BEST SF, THE   WOLLHEIM, DONALD A.   AN
ONG FROM A FORGOTTEN HILL   COOK, GLEN   SS   WOT 71
  CLARION   WILSON, ROBIN SCOTT   OA
ONG OF INFINITY, THE   SANTOS, DOMINGO   SS   NWR 69 14
  NEW WRITINGS IN SF. 14   CARNELL, JOHN   OA
ONG OF MARYA, THE (VENGEANCE FOR NIKOLAI)
                              MILLER, WALTER M. JR SS   VSF 57 03
  *TWISTED   CONKLIN, GROFF   AN
ONG OF PASSING, THE   CACCHIONI, MARCO   PM   QRK 71 04
  QUARK/4   DELANY & HACKER   OA
ONG OF THE PEWEE, THE   GRENDON, STEPHEN   SS   ARS 49 FL
  FAR BOUNDARIES   DERLETH, AUGUST   AN
ONG OF THE SCREW   ANONYMOUS   PM
  MATHEMATICAL MAGPIE, THE   FADIMAN, CLIFTON   AN
ONG OF THE SLAVES, THE   WELLMAN, MANLY WADE SS   WRT 40 03
  OTHER WORLDS, THE   STONG, PHILIP D.   AN
ONG OF THE SOUL, THE   ELLISON, HARLAN   IN
  ALONE AGAINST TOMORROW   ELLISON, HARLAN   AC
ONG THE ZOMBIE SANG, THE   ELLISON, HARLAN
                              AND SILVERBERG, ROBERT SS C CMP 70 12
  EARTH'S OTHER SHADOW   SILVERBERG, ROBERT   AC
  PARTNERS IN WONDER   ELLISON, HARLAN   AC
ONG, THE   BOND, NELSON S.   SS   BBM 49 04
  NIGHTMARES AND DAYDREAMS   BOND, NELSON S.   AC
ONGS OF DISTANT EARTH, THE   CLARKE, ARTHUR C.   NV   IFS 58 06
  OTHER SIDE OF THE SKY, THE   CLARKE, ARTHUR C.   AC
ONGS OF DYING SWANS   HALDEMAN, JACK C. II SS   STL 76 01
  STELLAR 2   DEL REY, JUDY-LYNN   OA
ONGS OF SUMMER, THE   SILVERBERG, ROBERT   SS   SFM 56 09
  MOONFERNS & STARSONGS   SILVERBERG, ROBERT   AC
  NEXT STOP THE STARS   SILVERBERG, ROBERT   DC
ONGS OF WAR   REED, KIT   NV   NOV 74 04
  BEST SF: 1974   HARRISON & ALDISS   AN
  NOVA 4   HARRISON, HARRY   OA
ONNET FROM THE VULCAN: OMICRON CETI THREE
                              MEECH, SHIRLEY   PM
  STAR TREK: THE NEW VOYAGES   MARSHAK, S&CULBREATH   OA
ONNET: TO SCIENCE (1829)   POE, EDGAR ALLEN   PM   29
  SPECULATIONS   SANDERS, THOMAS E.   AN
ONNY   RAPHAEL, RICK   SS   ASF 63 04
  ANALOG 3   CAMPBELL, JOHN W. JR   AN
  10TH ANNUAL OF THE YEAR'S BEST S-F, THE MERRIL, JUDITH   AN
ONORAN POEMS   THOMAS, D. M.   SS   NWB 73 05
  NEW WORLDS QUARTERLY NO. 5   MOORCOCK, MICHAEL   OA
ONS OF JANUS   ELLISON, HARLAN   IN
  PARTNERS IN WONDER   ELLISON, HARLAN   AC
ONS OF PROMETHEUS, THE   PANSHIN, ALEXEI   NV   ASF 66 10
  FAREWELL TO YESTERDAY'S TOMORROW   PANSHIN, ALEXEI   AC

SONYA, CRANE WESSLEMAN, AND KITTEE
                              WOLFE, GENE   SS   ORB 70 08
  ORBIT 8   KNIGHT, DAMON   AN
SOONER OR LATER OR NEVER NEVER JENNINGS, GARY   NV   FSF 72 05
  BEST FROM FANTASY AND SCIENCE FICTION: 20
                                     FERMAN, EDWARD L.   AN
SOOTHSAYER, THE   BENNETT, KEM   SS   FSF 52 08
  BEST FROM FANTASY AND SCIENCE FICTION: 2
                                     BOUCHER & MCCOMAS   AN
SORCERER'S APPRENTICE, THE   BLOCH, ROBERT   SS   WRT 49 01
  GHOUL KEEPERS, THE   MARGULIES, LEO   AN
  NIGHTMARES   BLOCH, ROBERT   AC
  PLEASANT DREAMS   BLOCH, ROBERT   AC
SORCERER'S APPRENTICE, THE   JAMESON, MALCOLM   SS   ASF 41 12
  OPERATION FUTURE   CONKLIN, GROFF   AN
SORCERER'S MOON   BEAUMONT, CHARLES   SS   PBY 59 07
  PLAYBOY BOOK OF HORROR AND THE SUPERNATURAL, THE
                                     PLAYBOY, EDITORS OF   AN
SORCERERS, THE   DE CAMP, L. SPRAGUE PM   ANA 70
  ALCHEMY AND ACADEME   MCCAFFREY, ANNE   OA
SORRY, RIGHT NUMBER (ALSO AS LONG DISTANCE CALL)
                              MATHESON, RICHARD   SS   BEY 53 11
  ZACHERLEY'S MIDNIGHT SNACKS   ZACHERLEY   AN
SORT OF INTRODUCTION, A   GERROLD, DAVID   IN
  PROTOSTARS   GERROLD & GOLDIN   OA
SORT OF INTRODUCTION, A   KNIGHT, DAMON   IN
  BEST FROM ORBIT, THE   KNIGHT, DAMON   AN
SORT OF INTRODUCTION, A   STARRETT, VINCENT   IN
  BEST SCIENCE-FICTION STORIES: 1950, THE BLEILER & DIKTY   AN
SOS   ANDERSON, POUL   NV   IFS 70 03
  BEST FROM IF, THE VOLUME I   IF, EDITORS OF   AN
SOUL CAGES, THE   CROKER, T. CROFTON   SS
  FANTASY: THE LITERATURE OF THE MARVELOUS KELLEY, LEO P.
                                                             AN
SOUL MACHINE, THE   CHANDLER, A. BERTRAM SS   GAL 69 10
  BEST FROM GALAXY, THE VOLUME I   GALAXY, EDITORS OF   AN
SOUL MATE   SUTTON, LEE   SS   FSF 59 06
  BEST FROM FANTASY AND SCIENCE FICTION: 9
                                     MILLS, ROBERT P.   AN
  OTHER WORLDS, OTHER GODS   MOHS, MAYO   AN
SOUL OF A SERVANT, THE   RUSS, JOANNA   SS   SCS 73
  SHOWCASE   ELWOOD, ROGER   OA
SOUL OF COLONEL 607, THE   KILWORTH, GARRY   SS
  GOLLANCZ - SUNDAY TIMES BEST SF STORIES ANONYMOUS   OA
SOUL SPECTROSCOPE, THE   MITCHELL, EDWARD P. SS   SUN 75 12
  CRYSTAL MAN, THE   MITCHELL, EDWARD P.   AC
SOUL SURVIVORS   HARDING, LEE   NV   NWR 70 17
  NEW WRITINGS IN SF. 17   CARNELL, JOHN   OA
SOULSONG TO THE SAD, SILLY, SOARING SIXTIES, A
                              O'DONNELL, K. M.   SS   FAN 71 02
  IN THE POCKET AND OTHER S-F STORIES O'DONNELL, K. M.   DC
SOUND DECISION   GARRETT, RANDALL
                              AND SILVERBERG, ROBERT NV C ASF 56 10
  DAYS AFTER TOMORROW, THE   SANTESSON, HANS S.   AN
  PROLOGUE TO ANALOG   CAMPBELL, JOHN W. JR   AN
  SHORES OF TOMORROW, THE   SILVERBERG, ROBERT   AC
SOUND INVESTMENT, A   HUBBARD, L. RON   NV   ASF 49 06
  OLE DOC METHUSELAH   HUBBARD, L. RON   AC
SOUND MACHINE, THE   DAHL, ROALD   SS   NYM 49 09
  BR-R-R-| CONKLIN, GROFF   AN
  SCIENCE FACT/FICTION   FARRELL/GAGE/&   AN
  TIMELESS STORIES FOR TODAY AND TOMORROW BRADBURY, RAY   AN
SOUND OF BUGLES, THE   WILLIAMS, ROBERT M. SS   STS 49 03
  ADVENTURES ON OTHER PLANETS   WOLLHEIM, DONALD A.   AN
  GREAT SCIENCE FICTION STORIES ABOUT MARS DIKTY, T. E.   AN
  WHEN TWO WORLDS MEET   WILLIAMS, ROBERT M.   AC
SOUND OF MUZAK, THE   DOZOIS, GARDNER R.   NV   QRK 70 01
  QUARK/1   DELANY & HACKER   OA
SOUND OF SUMMER RUNNING, THE (SUMMER IN THE AIR)
                              BRADBURY, RAY   SS   SEP 56 02
  R IS FOR ROCKET   BRADBURY, RAY   AC
SOUND OF THUNDER, A   BRADBURY, RAY   SS   COL 52 06
  ASPECTS OF SCIENCE FICTION   DOHERTY, G. D.   AN
  ECO-FICTION   STADLER, JOHN   AN
  *GOLDEN APPLES OF THE SUN   BRADBURY, RAY   AC
  R IS FOR ROCKET   BRADBURY, RAY   AC
  SCIENCE FACT/FICTION   FARRELL/GAGE/&   AN
  SCIENCE FICTION   BRODKIN & PEARSON   AN
  SCIENCE FICTION FOR PEOPLE WHO HATE SCIENCE FICTION
                                     CARR, TERRY   AN
  SCIENCE FICTION THROUGH THE AGES 2 EVANS, I. O.   AN
  STARS AND UNDER, THE   CRISPIN, EDMUND   AN
  TRANSFORMATIONS   ROSELLE, DANIEL   AN
SOUND OF WILD LAUGHTER, THE   VAN VOGT, A. E.   NV   NEW 72 AC
  BOOK OF VAN VOGT, THE   VAN VOGT, A. E.   AC
SOUND-SWEEP, THE   BALLARD, J. G.   NV   SCF 60 02
  BEST OF J. G. BALLARD, THE   BALLARD, J. G.   AC
  CHRONOPOLIS AND OTHER STORIES   BALLARD, J. G.   AC
  *FOUR-DIMENSIONAL NIGHTMARE, THE   BALLARD, J. G.   AC
  SF: THE BEST OF THE BEST   MERRIL, JUDITH   AN
  TOMORROW AND TOMORROW   KNIGHT, DAMON   AN
  VOICES OF TIME AND OTHER STORIES, THE BALLARD, J. G.   AC
  5TH ANNUAL OF THE YEAR'S BEST S-F, THE MERRIL, JUDITH   AN
SOUND, THE   VAN VOGT, A. E.   NV   ASF 50 02
  DESTINATION: UNIVERSE| VAN VOGT, A. E.   AC
  WAR AGAINST THE RULL, THE   VAN VOGT, A. E.   NO
SOUNDLESS EVENING   HOFFMAN, LEE   SS   DVS 72 02
  AGAIN, DANGEROUS VISIONS   ELLISON, HARLAN   OA
  EARTH IN TRANSIT   SCHWARTZ, SHEILA   AN
SOURCE, THE   ALDISS, BRIAN W.   SS   NWS 65 08
  BEST SF STORIES FROM NEW WORLDS 4 MOORCOCK, MICHAEL   AN
  SALIVA TREE AND OTHER STRANGE GROWTHS, THE
                                     ALDISS, BRIAN W.   AC
SOURCE, THE   WILHELM, KATE   AR   CLR 73 03
  CLARION III   WILSON, ROBIN SCOTT   OA
SOURCES OF THE NILE, THE   DAVIDSON, AVRAM   NV   FSF 61 01

```
*BEST FROM FANTASY AND SCIENCE FICTION: 11          SPACE: THE THIRD MILLENNIUM   PETHEBRIDGE, DENIS   PM
                       MILLS, ROBERT P.       AN       STARLIT CORRIDOR, THE        MANSFIELD, ROGER     A
  POCKETFUL OF STARS, A       KNIGHT, DAMON   AN     SPACE-BORN          BLOCH, ROBERT    NV   COI 73
  STRANGE SEAS AND SHORES     DAVIDSON, AVRAM AC       CHILDREN OF INFINITY         ELWOOD, ROGER        O
  TOMORROW X 4                KNIGHT, DAMON   AN       COLD CHILLS                  BLOCH, ROBERT        A
SOUTH GATE SEA      PARR, CHRISTIE  SS  ADS 75 02    SPACE-CRIME CONTINUUM   ELLIS, H. F.   SS   FSF 54 0
  ARMADA SCI-FI TWO           DAVIS, RICHARD  OA       SCIENCE FICTION ODDITIES     CONKLIN, GROFF       A
SOUTHBOUND ON THE FREEWAY  SWENSON, MAY  PM  NYM 63 02  SPACE-EATERS, THE   LONG, FRANK BELKNAP  NV  WRT 28 0
  ANOTHER TOMORROW         HOLLISTER, BERNARD C AN      EARLY LONG, THE              LONG, FRANK BELKNAP  A
SOUVENIR (ALSO AS THE DROWNED GIANT)                   *HOUNDS OF TINDALOS, THE     LONG, FRANK BELKNAP  A
                    BALLARD, J. G.  SS  PBY 65 05    SPACE-SHIP DERBY    KALETSKY, MILTON  SS  SFQ 40 S
  PLAYBOY BOOK OF SCIENCE FICTION AND FANTASY, THE      MOON CONQUERORS, THE         ANONYMOUS            A
                    PLAYBOY, EDITORS OF  AN          SPACE-SHUTTLE TRIP, A  ROBISON, NANCY L.  SS  YNW
  TRANSIT OF EARTH          PLAYBOY, EDITORS OF  AN     SCIENCE FICTION STORIES      BRADLEY, JOHANNA     A
SOWER DOES NOT REAP, THE (SEE CRUCIFIXUS ETIAM)      SPACE-TIME FOR SPRINGERS  LEIBER, FRITZ  SS  STR 58 0
                    MILLER, WALTER M. JR TC            BEST OF FRITZ LEIBER, THE    LEIBER, FRITZ        A
SOY LA LIBERTAD     COULSON, ROBERT  SS               SF: THE BEST OF THE BEST     MERRIL, JUDITH       A
  BEYOND TIME                LEY, SANDRA     OA        SF:59, THE YEAR'S GREATEST SCIENCE FICTION AND FANTASY
SPA OF THE STARS, THE  VANCE, JACK  NV  STS 50 07                                 MERRIL, JUDITH       A
  MANY WORLDS OF MAGNUS RIDOLPH, THE  VANCE, JACK  DC   STAR OF STARS                POHL, FREDERIK       A
SPACE               BUCHAN, JOHN    SS  LVA 11 06       STAR SCIENCE FICTION STORIES NO. 4  POHL, FREDERIK O
  *BEYOND TIME AND SPACE     DERLETH, AUGUST AN       SPACE, TIME AND NATHANIEL  ALDISS, BRIAN W.  AC  FAB 57
SPACE ANNIHILATOR, THE  CUMMINS, HARLE OREN SS    02    BRIAN ALDISS OMNIBUS 2       ALDISS, BRIAN W.     A
  ANCESTRAL VOICES         MENVILLE & REGINALD  AN    SPACEBIRD           WHITE, JAMES    SS   NWR 73 2
SPACE BEYOND, THE   CAMPBELL, JOHN W. JR SN            NEW WRITINGS IN SF. 22       BULMER, KENNETH      O
  SPACE BEYOND, THE         CAMPBELL, JOHN W. JR OC   SPACEMAN COMETH, THE  FELSEN, HENRY GREGOR  SS  FSF 56 0
SPACE BURIAL        ALDISS, BRIAN W.  PM  FSF 59 07     17 X INFINITY                CONKLIN, GROFF       A
  BEST FROM FANTASY AND SCIENCE FICTION: 9           SPACEMAN ON A SPREE  REYNOLDS, MACK  NV  WOT 63 0
                    MILLS, ROBERT P.      AN            BEST OF MACK REYNOLDS, THE   REYNOLDS, MACK       A
SPACE CLAUSE, THE   DE CAMP, L. SPRAGUE SS  IFS 52 09  SPACEMAN'S VAN GOGH, THE  SIMAK, CLIFFORD D.  SS  SFS 56 0
  SPRAGUE DE CAMP'S NEW ANTHOLOGY  DE CAMP, L. SPRAGUE AC  WORLDS WITHOUT END         SIMAK, CLIFFORD D.   A
SPACE FEAR (SEE THE ILLUSIONISTS)                    SPACEMASTER         SCHMITZ, JAMES H.  NV  NWR 65 0
                    SCHMITZ, JAMES H.  TC               NEW WRITINGS IN SF.  3       CARNELL, JOHN        O
SPACE FIX           RICHARDSON, R. S.  AR  ASF 43 03  SPACEMEN LIVE FOREVER  PAGE, GERALD W.  SS  NWR 66 0
  COMING ATTRACTIONS       GREENBERG, MARTIN  NF        NEW WRITINGS IN SF.  8       CARNELL, JOHN        O
SPACE FOR INDUSTRY  CAMPBELL, JOHN W. JR AR  ASF 60 04  SPACEMEN THROUGHOUT HISTORY  DRAKE, W. RAYMOND  AR
  *BEST OF JOHN W. CAMPBELL, THE  CAMPBELL, JOHN W. JR AC  BEYOND THIS HORIZON        CARRELL, CHRISTOPHER O
SPACE FOR REFLECTION, A  ALDISS, BRIAN W.  SS  NWR 76 29  SPACEROGUE (AS WEBBER MARTIN)  SILVERBERG, ROBERT  SN  INF 58
  NEW WRITINGS IN SF. 29    BULMER, KENNETH   OA        VALLEY BEYOND TIME           SILVERBERG, ROBERT   A
SPACE IS A LONELY PLACE  GUNN, JAMES E.  NV  VSF 57 05  SPACERS' DANCE, THE  EXTER, MAUREEN  NV
  END OF THE DREAMS, THE    GUNN, JAMES E.   AC         CRISIS                       ELWOOD, ROGER        O
  STATION IN SPACE          GUNN, JAMES E.   AC       SPACESHIP EARTH     FULLER, BUCKMINSTER AR      69
SPACE IS A PROVINCE OF BRAZIL  WYNDHAM, JOHN  NV  NWS 58 09  SCIENCE FACT/FICTION     FARRELL/GAGE/&       A
  *OUTWARD URGE, THE        WYNDHAM & PARKES  AC      SPACESHIP, THE      DE WEESE, GENE    SS
SPACE JOCKEY        HEINLEIN, ROBERT A. SS  SEP 47 04   STRANGE ENCOUNTERS           BISCHOFF, DAVID      A
  GREEN HILLS OF EARTH, THE HEINLEIN, ROBERT A. AC    SPACEWAYS INCIDENT  ESHBACH, LLOYD A.  SS
  PAST THROUGH TOMORROW, THE HEINLEIN, ROBERT A. AC    TYRANT OF TIME, THE          ESHBACH, LLOYD A.    A
SPACE LANE CADET    HALSTEAD, WILLIAM F. SS  BLF      "SPACEWRECK OF THE OLD 97, THE"
  BOYS' LIFE BOOK OF OUTER SPACE STORIES, THE                             BRUNNER, JOHN    SG   NEW 76 A
                    BOY'S LIFE, ED. OF  AN              BOOK OF JOHN BRUNNER, THE    BRUNNER, JOHN        A
SPACE MAN           DEUTSCH, BABETTE  PM    69        SPANISH CAMERA, THE  JACOBI, CARL    SS   WRT 50 A
  SCIENCE FICTION          BRODKIN & PEARSON  AN        PORTRAITS IN MOONLIGHT       JACOBI, CARL         A
SPACE MUSEUM, THE   FAIRMAN, PAUL W.  SS             SPARE THE ROD       BIGGLE, LLOYD JR. NV  GAL 58 0
  FORGETFUL ROBOT, THE      FAIRMAN, PAUL W.  OC        METALLIC MUSE, THE           BIGGLE, LLOYD JR.    A
SPACE OPERA         RUSSELL, RAY      SS  PBY 61 12   SPARKIE'S FALL      HYDE, GAVIN      SS   STR 59 0
  FULLY AUTOMATED LOVE LIFE OF HENRY KEANRIDGE          STAR OF STARS                POHL, FREDERIK       A
                    PLAYBOY, EDITORS OF  AN             STAR SCIENCE FICTION STORIES NO. 5  POHL, FREDERIK O
SPACE PEDLAR, THE   MARSH, JOYCE      SS             SPARTANS' EPITAPH AT THERMOPYLAE (FROM GREEK ANTH)
  STRANGE WORLD OF SCIENCE FICTION  ANONYMOUS  OA                         BRUNNER, JOHN    MS   NEW 76 A
SPACE PILOT, THE    BLACKIE, J.       PM               BOOK OF JOHN BRUNNER, THE    BRUNNER, JOHN        A
  STARLIT CORRIDOR, THE     MANSFIELD, ROGER  AN     SPAWN               MILLER, P. SCHUYLER SS  WRT 39 0
SPACE POEM          KLINE, T. F.      PM  BUL          TITAN, THE                   MILLER, P. SCHUYLER  A
  SECOND PACIFIC BOOK OF SCIENCE FICTION, THE        SPAWN OF DAGON      KUTTNER, HENRY   NV   WRT 38 0
                    BAXTER, JOHN      AN               GHOUL KEEPERS, THE           MARGULIES, LEO       A
SPACE PROBE TO VENUS  FITZGIBBON, C.  PM             SPAWN OF THE SEA    WANDREI, DONALD  NV   WRT 33 0
  STARLIT CORRIDOR, THE     MANSFIELD, ROGER  AN       STRANGE HARVEST              WANDREI, DONALD      A
SPACE RATING (ALSO AS BEYOND THE STARS)              SPAWN OF THE STARS  DIFFIN, CHARLES W. NV  ASF 30 0
                    BERRYMAN, JOHN    SS  ASF 39 10    *BEST OF SCIENCE FICTION      CONKLIN, GROFF       A
  *POSSIBLE WORLDS OF SCIENCE FICTION  CONKLIN, GROFF AN  SPAWNING GROUND   DEL REY, LESTER  SS  IFS 61 0
SPACE RATS OF THE C.C.C.  HARRISON, HARRY  NV  FST 74  BEST SCIENCE FICTION FROM IF, THE  POHL, FREDERIK   A
  ANTIGRAV: COSMIC COMEDIES STRICK, PHILIP    AN       MORTALS AND MONSTERS         DEL REY, LESTER      A
  *BEST OF HARRY HARRISON, THE  HARRISON, HARRY  AC  SPEAKING OF DEMONOLOGY  BAKHNOV, VLADLEN  SS
  FINAL STAGE               FERMAN & MALZBERG OA       RUSSIAN SCIENCE FICTION, 1969  MAGIDOFF, ROBERT   A
SPACE SECRET        PEARL, CLINTON    SS    58       SPEAKING OF GANYMEDE  O'NEILL, SCOTT  SS
  TEEN-AGE OUTER SPACE STORIES  FURMAN, A. L.  AN      MARTIAN SEXPOT               O'NEILL, SCOTT       A
SPACE SECRET        SAMBROT, WILLIAM  SS  SEP 59 02  SPECIAL APTITUDE (LAST LAUGH)  STURGEON, THEODORE  SS  OWS 51 0
  ISLAND OF FEAR AND OTHER SCIENCE FICTION SAMBROT, WILLIAM  AC  *WAY HOME, A         STURGEON, THEODORE   A
  POST READER OF FANTASY AND SCIENCE FICTION         SPECIAL CONDITION IN SUMMIT CITY, A
                    SATURDAY EVE. POST  AN                             LAFFERTY, R. A.  SS   UNI 72 0
SPACE SEED (C. WILBER & GENE L. COON)                  UNIVERSE 2                   CARR, TERRY          A
                    BLISH, JAMES      SA  STK 68 02  SPECIAL CONSENT     HUBBARD, P. M.   SS   FSF 63 1
  STAR TREK  2              BLISH, JAMES      OC        MARRIAGE AND THE FAMILY THROUGH SCIENCE FICTION
SPACE SONNET        MORGAN, EDWIN     PM                                 CLEAR/WARRICK/&      A
  BEYOND THIS HORIZON       CARRELL, CHRISTOPHER OA  SPECIAL DELIVERY    COLLIER, JOHN    NV      41
SPACE STATION NO. 1  WELLMAN, MANLY WADE  AR  ARG 36 10  GRAVEYARD READER, THE      CONKLIN, GROFF       A
  ESCALES DANS L'INFINI     GALLET, GEORGES H.  AN   SPECIAL DELIVERY    KNIGHT, DAMON    NV   GAL 54 0
  *MY BEST SCIENCE FICTION STORY  MARGULIES & FRIEND AN  BEST OF DAMON KNIGHT, THE   KNIGHT, DAMON        A
SPACE STATION 42 (MANY DREAMS OF EARTH)                FAR OUT                      KNIGHT, DAMON        A
                    FRITCH, CHARLES E. SS  OSF 54 11   OPERATION FUTURE             CONKLIN, GROFF       A
  SPACE STATION 42 AND OTHER STORIES  ANONYMOUS  AN  SPECIAL DELIVERY    NEVILLE, KRIS    NO   IMG 52 0
SPACE STEWARD       ELAM, RICHARD M. JR. NV           MAN AGAINST TOMORROW         NOLAN, WILLIAM F.    A
  TEEN-AGE SUPER SCIENCE STORIES  ELAM, RICHARD M. JR. AC  SPECIAL DELIVERY  SMITH, GEORGE O.  NV  ASF 45 0
SPACE SWIMMERS      DICKSON, GORDON R. NO  BKM 67       COMPLETE VENUS EQUILATERAL, THE  SMITH, GEORGE O. A
  SCIENCE FICTION SPECIAL 1  ANONYMOUS       AN        VENUS EQUILATERAL            SMITH, GEORGE O.     A
SPACE TO MOVE       GREEN, JOSEPH     SS  NMD 73      SPECIAL DELIVERY (THE OTHER SIDE OF THE SKY)
  FRONTIERS 2: THE NEW MIND ELWOOD, ROGER    OA                           CLARKE, ARTHUR C. SS  INF 57 0
SPACE WAR           JONES, NEIL R.    NV  AMZ 35 07     OTHER SIDE OF THE SKY, THE   CLARKE, ARTHUR C.    A
  SPACE WAR                 JONES, NEIL R.    AC      SPECIAL EXHIBIT, THE  SHECKLEY, ROBERT  SS  ESQ 53 1
SPACE WAR           LEY, WILLY        AR  ASF 39 08     SHARDS OF SPACE              SHECKLEY, ROBERT     A
  COMING ATTRACTIONS       GREENBERG, MARTIN  NF     SPECIAL FEATURE     DEVET, CHARLES V. NV  ASF 58 0
SPACE WAR TACTICS   JAMESON, MALCOLM  AR  ASF 39 11     SEVEN COME INFINITY          CONKLIN, GROFF       A
  COMING ATTRACTIONS       GREENBERG, MARTIN  NF     SPECIAL FLIGHT      BERRYMAN, JOHN   NV   ASF 39 0
SPACE WOMAN         WELLS, BASIL      SS               *SPECTRUM                     AMIS & CONQUEST      AN
  DOORWAYS TO SPACE        WELLS, BASIL       AC      SPECIAL KIND OF MORNING, A  DOZOIS, GARDNER R.  NV  NDM 71 0
SPACE: FOR MARTIN GREEN  KENNEDY, X. J.  PM            ALPHA 5                      SILVERBERG, ROBERT   A
  SPECULATIONS             SANDERS, THOMAS E.  AN       NEW DIMENSIONS 1             SILVERBERG, ROBERT   O
```

SPECIALIST
SPECIALIST   SHECKLEY, ROBERT   SS   GAL 53 05
  AS TOMORROW BECOMES TODAY   SULLIVAN, CHARLES W. AN
  CONTACT   KEYES, NOEL   AN
  MIRROR OF INFINITY, THE   SILVERBERG, ROBERT AN
  ROBERT SHECKLEY OMNIBUS, THE   SHECKLEY, ROBERT   AC
  SECOND GALAXY READER OF SCIENCE FICTION GOLD, H. L.   AN
  TALES OF TERROR FROM OUTER SPACE   CHETWYND-HAYES, R. AN
  TOMORROW, AND TOMORROW, AND TOMORROW... HEINTZ/HERBERT/JOOS/ AN
  *UNTOUCHED BY HUMAN HANDS   SHECKLEY, ROBERT   AC
*SPECIMEN   CUMMINGS, M. A.   SS
  EXILE AND OTHER TALES OF FANTASY   CUMMINGS, M. A.   OC
SPECIMEN, THE   ANONYMOUS   SS
  STRANGE WORLD OF SCIENCE FICTION   ANONYMOUS   OA
SPECTACLES, THE   LONG, FRANK BELKNAP SS   FUN 56 04
  RIM OF THE UNKNOWN   LONG, FRANK BELKNAP AC
SPECTATOR SPORT   MACDONALD, JOHN D. SS   TWS 50 02
  FIFTY SHORT SCIENCE FICTION TALES ASIMOV & CONKLIN   AN
  OMNIBUS OF SCIENCE FICTION   CONKLIN, GROFF   AN
  SCIENCE FICTION OMNIBUS   CONKLIN, GROFF   AN
  STRANGE ADVENTURES IN SCIENCE FICTION CONKLIN, GROFF   AN
SPECTER GENERAL, THE   COGSWELL, THEODORE R NV ASF 52 06
  SCIENCE FICTION HALL OF FAME VOLUME 2B BOVA, BEN   AN
  SPACE SERVICE   NORTON, ANDRE   AN
  WALL AROUND THE WORLD, THE   COGSWELL, THEODORE R AC
SPECTRA   MCINTYRE, VONDA N. SS   ORB 72 11
  ORBIT 11   KNIGHT, DAMON   OA
SPECTRUM, THE   THOMAS, D. M.   PM   NWS 69 02
  BEST SF STORIES FROM NEW WORLDS 5 MOORCOCK, MICHAEL   AN
SPEECH IS SILVER   BRUNNER, JOHN   SS   AMZ 65 04
  TIME-JUMP   BRUNNER, JOHN   AC
SPEED   MILES, JOSEPHINE   PM   60
  SCIENCE FACT/FICTION   FARRELL/GAGE/&   AN
SPEED TRAP   POHL, FREDERIK   SS   PBY 67 11
  BEST OF FREDERIK POHL, THE   POHL, FREDERIK   AC
  DAY MILLION   POHL, FREDERIK   AC
  TRANSIT OF EARTH   PLAYBOY, EDITORS OF AN
SPEEDERS, THE   TOFTE, ARTHUR   SS
  OTHER SIDE OF TOMORROW, THE   ELWOOD, ROGER   OA
SPELL MY NAME WITH AN S (S AS IN ZEBATINSKY)
                                     ASIMOV, ISAAC   SS   SMG 58 01
  NINE TOMORROWS   ASIMOV, ISAAC   AC
SPERO MELIORA   ELLISON, HARLAN   IN
  *PAINGOD AND OTHER DELUSIONS   ELLISON, HARLAN   AC
SPHERE   INOUYE, JON   SS
  NIGHT TIDE, A   INOUYE, JON   OC
SPHEROID OF ZANZOL   INOUYE, JON   SS
  NIGHT TIDE, A   INOUYE, JON   OC
SPHINX, THE (SEE THE PYRAMID PROJECT)
                                     YOUNG, ROBERT F.   TC
SPIDER MANSION   LEIBER, FRITZ   SS   WRT 42 09
  WEIRD TALES   MARGULIES, LEO   AN
SPIDER, THE   LEIBER, FRITZ   SS   ROG 63 01
  BOOK OF FRITZ LEIBER, THE   LEIBER, FRITZ   AC
SPINSTERS, THE   BOND, NELSON S.   SS   BBM 50 01
  NIGHTMARES AND DAYDREAMS   BOND, NELSON S.   AC
SPIRAL INTELLIGENCE, THE   LONG, FRANK BELKNAP SS   SFP 53 06
  RIM OF THE UNKNOWN   LONG, FRANK BELKNAP AC
SPIRAL, THE   CALVINO, ITALO   SS
  COSMICOMICS   CALVINO, ITALO   OC
SPIRO (VENTURER OF THE MARTIAN MIMICS)
                                     RUSSELL, ERIC FRANK NV   WRT 47 03
  *OTHER SIDE OF THE MOON, THE   DERLETH, AUGUST   AN
SPLENDID FREEDOM, THE   DARNAY, ARSEN   NV   GAL 74 09
  BEST FROM GALAXY, THE   VOLUME III BAEN, JAMES   AN
SPLENDID SOURCE, THE   MATHESON, RICHARD   SS   PBY 56 05
  LAST TRAIN TO LIMBO   PLAYBOY, EDITORS OF AN
  SHOCK!   MATHESON, RICHARD   AC
SPLICE OF LIFE   DORMAN, SONYA   SS   ORB 66 01
  ONE HUNDRED YEARS OF SCIENCE FICTION KNIGHT, DAMON   AN
  ORBIT 1   KNIGHT, DAMON   OA
SPLIT CHERRY TREE   STUART, JESSE   SS
  ARMCHAIR SCIENCE READER, THE   GORDON, I. & SORKIN AN
SPOCK'S BRAIN (LEE CRONIN)   BLISH, JAMES   SA   STK 72 08
  STAR TREK 8   BLISH, JAMES   OC
SPODEGUE'S DROOPER   DOYLE, ARTHUR CONAN SS
  MARACOT DEEP AND OTHER STORIES, THE DOYLE, ARTHUR CONAN AC
SPOIL OF YESTERDAY   BRUNNER, JOHN   NV   SFA 62 03
  TIMES WITHOUT NUMBER   BRUNNER, JOHN   NO
SPOKESMAN FOR TERRA   RAYMOND, HUGH   SS   STI 41 06
  SHOT IN THE DARK   MERRIL, JUDITH   AN
SPONGE DIVE   BLISH, JAMES   SS   INF 56 06
  SO CLOSE TO HOME   BLISH, JAMES   AC
"SPONTANEOUS COMBUSTION"   REEVE, ARTHUR B.   SS
  SILENT BULLET, THE   REEVE, ARTHUR B.   AC
SPONTANEOUS REFLEX   STRUGATSKY, ARKADY
                                     AND STRUGATSKY, BORIS SS AMZ 59 05
  SOVIET SCIENCE FICTION   ANONYMOUS   AN
SPOOKY   REYNOLDS, MACK   SS
  KILLER PLANTS AND OTHER STORIES, THE ELWOOD, ROGER   OA
SPORT   UTLEY, STEVEN   PM   CND 73
  BEST SF: 1973   HARRISON & ALDISS   AN
SPORTING ON APTERYX   PARTINGTON, CHARLES SS   NWR 74 23
  NEW WRITINGS IN SF. 23   BULMER, KENNETH   OA
SPORTSMAN'S DIFFICULTY   BUCK, DORIS PITKIN PM   FSF 59 03
  BEST FROM FANTASY AND SCIENCE FICTION: 9
                                     MILLS, ROBERT P.   AN
SPORTSMAN, THE   BOND, NELSON S.   SS
  31ST OF FEBRUARY, THE   BOND, NELSON S.   AC
SPRING CAME TO BLUE RIDGE EARLY THIS YEAR
                                     ARNOLD, CHARLES   SS   ORB 74 13
  ORBIT 13   KNIGHT, DAMON   OA
SPRING NIGHT, THE (SEE THE SUMMER NIGHT)
                                     BRADBURY, RAY   TC
SPUD AND COCHISE   LA FARGE, OLIVER   NV   FSF 57 12
  DECADE OF FANTASY AND SCIENCE FICTION, A MILLS, ROBERT P. AN

SPUD FAILURE DEFINITE   PEART, NOEL   SS
  AD 2500   WILSON, ANGUS   AN
SPUDGET FOR THWILBERT, A   COGSWELL, THEODORE R SS FUN 58 04
  THIRD EYE, THE   COGSWELL, THEODORE R AC
SPURS (SEE FREAKS)   ROBBINS, TOD   TC
SPUTNIK: ONE REASON WHY WE LOST
                                     STINE, G. HARRY   AR   FSF 58 01
  SF:58, THE YEAR'S GREATEST SCIENCE FICTION AND FANTASY
                                     MERRIL, JUDITH   AN
SPY STORY (ALSO AS CITIZEN IN SPACE)
                                     SHECKLEY, ROBERT   SS   PBY 55 09
  DEAD ASTRONAUT, 10 STORIES OF SPACE FLIGHT, THE
                                     PLAYBOY, EDITORS OF AN
  PLAYBOY BOOK OF SCIENCE FICTION AND FANTASY
                                     PLAYBOY, EDITORS OF AN
SQUARE CUBE LAW, THE   PRATT, FLETCHER   NV   TWS 52 06
  DOUBLE JEOPARDY   PRATT, FLETCHER   AC
SQUARE OF THE HYPOTENUSE, THE (LYRICS)
                                     MERCER, JOHNNY
  MATHEMATICAL MAGPIE, THE   FADIMAN, CLIFTON   AN
SQUARE OF THE HYPOTENUSE, THE (MUSIC)
                                     CHAPLIN, SAUL
  MATHEMATICAL MAGPIE, THE   FADIMAN, CLIFTON   AN
SQUARE ROOT OF BRAIN, THE   LEIBER, FRITZ   SS   NWS 68 02
  BEST SF STORIES FROM NEW WORLDS 4 MOORCOCK, MICHAEL   AN
  WORLD'S BEST SCIENCE FICTION: 1969 WOLLHEIM & CARR   AN
SQUARE ROOT OF MC, THE   JAMES, LAURENCE   SS   NWR 73 22
  NEW WRITINGS IN SF. 22   BULMER, KENNETH   OA
SQUAW, THE   STOKER, BRAM   SS   93
  BEWARE THE BEASTS   GHIDALIA, V.& ELWOOD AN
SQUIRE OF GOTHOS, THE (PAUL SCHNEIDER)
                                     BLISH, JAMES   SA   STK 75 11
  STAR TREK 11   BLISH, JAMES   OC
SQUIRREL CAGE, THE   DISCH, THOMAS M.   SS   NWS 66 10
  BEST SF STORIES FROM NEW WORLDS NO. 1, THE
                                     MOORCOCK, MICHAEL   AN
  ENGLAND SWINGS SF   MERRIL, JUDITH   AN
  FUN WITH YOUR NEW HEAD   DISCH, THOMAS M.   AC
  NEW WORLDS OF FANTASY   CARR, TERRY   AN
SREDNI VASHTAR   SAKI   SS
  SPECULATIONS   SANDERS, THOMAS E. AN
  YOUNG DEMONS   ELWOOD & GHIDALIA   AN
SRIBERDEGIBIT   BOUCHER, ANTHONY   NV   UNK 43 06
  FAR AND AWAY   BOUCHER, ANTHONY   AC
SRL AD   MATHESON, RICHARD   SS   FSF 52 04
  BORN OF MAN AND WOMAN   MATHESON, RICHARD   AC
  *SCIENCE-FICTION CARNIVAL   BROWN, F. & REYNOLDS AN
  THIRD FROM THE SUN   MATHESON, RICHARD   AC
STABILITY   DEL REY, LESTER   SS   VOR 53 01
  ROBOTS AND CHANGELINGS   DEL REY, LESTER   AC
STAGE SET   WENSKES, HELMUT   IL
  BEYOND THIS HORIZON   CARRELL, CHRISTOPHER OA
STAINLESS STEEL LEECH, THE   ZELAZNY, ROGER   SS   AMZ 63 04
  NEW WORLDS OF FANTASY NO. 3   CARR, TERRY   AN
STAIR TRICK   CLINGERMAN, MILDRED SS   FSF 52 08
  BEST FROM FANTASY AND SCIENCE FICTION: 2
                                     BOUCHER & MCCOMAS   AN
  CUPFUL OF SPACE, A   CLINGERMAN, MILDRED AC
  FIFTY SHORT SCIENCE FICTION TALES ASIMOV & CONKLIN   AN
STALIN IN THE SOUL, THE   LE GUIN, URSULA K. AR   73
  FUTURE NOW, THE   HOSKINS, ROBERT   AN
STALKING THE SUN   EKLUND, GORDON   NV   UNI 72 02
  UNIVERSE 2   CARR, TERRY   OA
STAMPED CAUTION   GALLUN, RAYMOND Z. NV   GAL 53 08
  5 UNEARTHLY VISIONS   CONKLIN, GROFF   AN
STANCE OF SPLENDOUR   ZEBROWSKI, GEORGE   SS   NWQ 73 05
  MONADIC UNIVERSE, THE   ZEBROWSKI, GEORGE   AC
  NEW WORLDS NO. 5   MOORCOCK & PLATT   OA
STAND-BY (SEE TOP STAND-BY JOB)
                                     DICK, PHILIP K.   TC
STAND-IN   BURKE, JONATHAN F. SS   AUT 54 03
  ALIEN LANDSCAPES   BURKE, JONATHAN F. AC
STANLEY G. WEINBAUM: A PERSONAL RECOLLECTION
                                     BLOCH, ROBERT   AR
  BEST OF STANLEY G. WEINBAUM, THE   WEINBAUM, STANLEY G. AC
STANLEY TOOTHBRUSH (AS CARL BRANDON)
                                     CARR, TERRY   SS   FSF 62 07
  LIGHT AT THE END OF THE UNIVERSE, THE CARR, TERRY   AC
  NEW WORLDS OF FANTASY   CARR, TERRY   AN
  OTHER DIMENSIONS   SILVERBERG, ROBERT AN
STAR ABOVE IT, A   OLIVER, CHAD   SS   NEW 55 AC
  ANOTHER KIND   OLIVER, CHAD   AC
STAR BEAST, THE   ANDERSON, POUL   NV   SSS 50 09
  AWARD SCIENCE FICTION READER   NORTON, ALDEN H.   AN
  STRANGERS FROM EARTH   ANDERSON, POUL   AN
STAR BEGOTTEN   WELLS, H. G.   NO   VIK 37
  TWENTY-EIGHT SCIENCE FICTION STORIES WELLS, H. G.   AC
STAR BRIDE   BOUCHER, ANTHONY   SS   TWS 51 12
  FAR AND AWAY   BOUCHER, ANTHONY   AC
  *STORIES FOR TOMORROW   SLOANE, WILLIAM   AN
STAR BRIGHT   WILLIAMSON, JACK   NV   ARG 39 11
  *MY BEST SCIENCE FICTION STORY   MARGULIES & FRIEND AN
  PEOPLE MACHINES   WILLIAMSON, JACK   AC
  STRANGE LOVE STORIES   ANONYMOUS   AN
STAR CALLED CYRENE, A (70 LIGHT-YEARS FROM SOL)
                                     TALL, STEPHEN   NV   WOT 66 11
  STARDUST VOYAGES, THE   TALL, STEPHEN   AC
STAR DESCENDING   BUDRYS, ALGIS   SS   STR 59 05
  STAR SCIENCE FICTION STORIES NO. 5 POHL, FREDERIK   OA
STAR DUCKS, THE   BROWN, BILL   SS   FSF 50 FL
  BEST SCIENCE-FICTION STORIES: 1951, THE BLEILER & DIKTY AN
  BEST SF 6   CRISPIN, EDMUND   AN
  FRONTIERS IN SPACE   BLEILER & DIKTY   AN
  SCIENCE FICTION AND READER'S GUIDE BARROWS, MARJORIE   AN
  STARS AND UNDER, THE   CRISPIN, EDMUND   AN

STAR DUMMY, THE   BOUCHER, ANTHONY   SS   FAN 52 FL
   OMNIBUS OF SCIENCE FICTION   CONKLIN, GROFF   AN
   SCIENCE FICTION OMNIBUS   CONKLIN, GROFF   AN
   STRANGE TRAVELS IN SCIENCE FICTION   CONKLIN, GROFF   AN
STAR GYPSIES, THE   GRESHAM, WILLIAM L. SS   FSF 53 07
   BEST FROM FANTASY AND SCIENCE FICTION: 3
                                        BOUCHER & MCCOMAS   AN
STAR HYACINTHS, THE (SEE THE TANGLED WEB)
                             SCHMITZ, JAMES H.   TC
STAR LIGHT   ASIMOV, ISAAC   SS   SAM 62 10
   ASIMOV'S MYSTERIES   ASIMOV, ISAAC   AC
   BEST FROM NEW WRITINGS IN S-F FIRST SELECTION, THE
                                        CARNELL, JOHN   AN
   NEW WRITINGS IN SF. 4   CARNELL, JOHN   OA
STAR LIGHT, STAR BRIGHT   BESTER, ALFRED   AC   BKP 76
   STARLIGHT   BESTER, ALFRED   AC
STAR LIGHT, STAR BRIGHT   BESTER, ALFRED   SS   FSF 53 07
   BEST FROM FANTASY AND SCIENCE FICTION: 3
                                        BOUCHER & MCCOMAS   AN
   STAR LIGHT, STAR BRIGHT   BESTER, ALFRED   AC
   STARBURST   BESTER, ALFRED   AC
STAR MAKER, THE   STAPLEDON, OLAF   NO   MTH 37
   TO THE END OF TIME   STAPLEDON, OLAF   AC
STAR MOTHER   YOUNG, ROBERT F.   SS   AMZ 59 01
   GLASS OF STARS, A   YOUNG, ROBERT F.   AC
STAR MOUSE, THE   BROWN, FREDRIC   SS   PLS 42 02
   *ADVENTURES IN TIME AND SPACE   HEALY & MCCOMAS   AN
   BEST OF FREDRIC BROWN, THE   BROWN, FREDRIC   AC
   BEST OF PLANET STORIES NO. 1, THE   BRACKETT, LEIGH   AN
   DAYMARES   BROWN, FREDRIC   AC
   INVASION FROM MARS   WELLES, ORSON   AN
   SPACE ON MY HANDS   BROWN, FREDRIC   AC
STAR OF LIFE, THE   HAMILTON, EDMOND   EX   STS 47 01
   SPACE OPERA   ALDISS, BRIAN W.   AN
STAR OF THE UNDEAD (ROBERT A. W. LOWNDES)
                             LAVOND, PAUL DENNIS SS   FBK 47 02
   MACHINE-GOD LAUGHS, THE   ANONYMOUS   AN
STAR OF WONDER   MAY, JULIAN C.   SS   TWS 53 02
   EVERY BOY'S BOOK OF OUTER SPACE STORIES DIKTY, T. E.   AN
STAR PARTY, THE   LORY, ROBERT   SS   FSF 64 09
   HARVEST OF HOODWINKS, A   LORY, ROBERT   DC
   WORLD'S BEST SCIENCE FICTION: 1965   WOLLHEIM & CARR   AN
STAR PIT, THE   DELANY, SAMUEL R.   NV   WOT 67 02
   ALPHA 5   SILVERBERG, ROBERT   AN
   DRIFTGLASS   DELANY, SAMUEL R.   AC
   SF12   MERRIL, JUDITH   AN
STAR PLUNDERER, THE   ANDERSON, POUL   NV   PLS 52 09
   GALACTIC EMPIRES VOLUME ONE   ALDISS, BRIAN W.   AN
STAR SHIP   ANDERSON, POUL   NV   PLS 50 FL
   SPACE ODYSSEYS   ALDISS, BRIAN W.   AN
STAR STEALERS, THE   HAMILTON, EDMOND   NV   WRT 29 02
   CRASHING SUNS   HAMILTON, EDMOND   AC
STAR THROWER, THE   EISELEY, SIMON   AR   69
   SURVIVAL PRINTOUT   TOTAL EFFECT   AN
STAR TREK   BLISH, JAMES   OC   BAN 67
   STAR TREK READER II, THE   BLISH, JAMES   AC
STAR TREK 2   BLISH, JAMES   OC   BAN 68
   STAR TREK READER, THE   BLISH, JAMES   AC
STAR TREK 3   BLISH, JAMES   OC   BAN 69 04
   STAR TREK READER, THE   BLISH, JAMES   AC
STAR TREK 4   BLISH, JAMES   OC   BAN 71 07
   STAR TREK READER II, THE   BLISH, JAMES   AC
STAR TREK 8   BLISH, JAMES   OC   BAN 72 11
   STAR TREK READER, THE   BLISH, JAMES   AC
STAR TREK 9   BLISH, JAMES   OC   BAN 73 08
   STAR TREK READER II, THE   BLISH, JAMES   AC
STAR-BOY   FANCETT, ELIZABETH   NV   ADS 75 02
   ARMADA SCI-FI TWO   DAVIS, RICHARD   OA
STAR-CROSSED LOVER   STUART, WILLIAM W.   NV   GAL 62 04
   12 GREAT CLASSICS OF SCIENCE FICTION CONKLIN, GROFF   AN
STAR-GAZE POEM   LYNE, STANDFORD   PM   69
   SPECULATIONS   SANDERS, THOMAS E.   AN
STAR-LINKED   FYFE, H. B.   SS   ASF 52 02
   SPACE SERVICE   NORTON, ANDRE   AN
STAR-SAINT, THE   VAN VOGT, A. E.   NV   PLS 51 03
   PROXY INTELLIGENCE AND OTHER MIND BENDERS
                                        VAN VOGT, A. E.   AC
   TWISTED MEN, THE   VAN VOGT, A. E.   DC
STAR-SENT KNAVES, THE (ALSO AS THE TIME THIEVES)
                             LAUMER, KEITH   NV   WOT 63 06
   IT'S A MAD, MAD, MAD GALAXY   LAUMER, KEITH   AC
STAR-SPLITTER, THE   FROST, ROBERT   PM   23
   LOOKING AHEAD   ALLEN, D. & L.   AN
STAR, BRIGHT   CLIFTON, MARK   NV   GAL 52 07
   GALAXY SCIENCE FICTION OMNIBUS   GOLD, H. L.   AN
   MATHEMATICAL MAGPIE, THE   FADIMAN, CLIFTON   AN
   PRIZE SCIENCE FICTION   WOLLHEIM, DONALD A.   AN
   SECOND GALAXY READER OF SCIENCE FICTION GOLD, H. L.   AN
   SPECULATIONS   SANDERS, THOMAS E.   AN
   TOMORROW'S CHILDREN   ASIMOV, ISAAC   AN
STAR, THE   CLARKE, ARTHUR C.   SS   INF 55 11
   BEST OF ARTHUR C. CLARKE: 1937-1971, THE CLARKE, ARTHUR C. AC
   BEST SF 5   CRISPIN, EDMUND   AN
   CENTURY OF SCIENCE FICTION, A   KNIGHT, DAMON   AN
   DECADE THE 1950S   ALDISS & HARRISON   AN
   HUGO WINNERS, THE (VOLUME 1)   ASIMOV, ISAAC   AN
   INFINITY 1   HOSKINS, ROBERT   OA
   MODERN SCIENCE FICTION   SPINRAD, NORMAN   AN
   NINE BILLION NAMES OF GOD, THE   CLARKE, ARTHUR C.   AC
   OTHER SIDE OF THE SKY, THE   CLARKE, ARTHUR C.   AC
   SCIENCE FICTION   BURTON, S. H.   AN
   SCIENCE FICTION FOR PEOPLE WHO HATE SCIENCE FICTION
                                        CARR, TERRY   AN
   SECOND ORBIT   DOHERTY, G. D.   AN
   SPECULATIONS   SANDERS, THOMAS E.   AN

STAR, THE   KELLER, DAVID H. MD. SS
   *BEACHHEADS IN SPACE   DERLETH, AUGUST   AN
STAR, THE   WELLS, H. G.   SS   GRP 97 12
   BEST SCIENCE FICTION STORIES OF H. G. WELLS
                                        WELLS, H. G.   AC
   BEST STORIES OF H. G. WELLS   WELLS, H. G.   AC
   COUNTRY OF THE BLIND, THE   WELLS, H. G.   AC
   DOOR IN THE WALL, THE   WELLS, H. G.   AC
   EARTH IN PERIL, THE   WOLLHEIM, DONALD A.   DA
   FROM FRANKENSTEIN TO ANDROMEDA   BROWN, JAMES GOLDIE   AN
   GREAT SCIENCE FICTION STORIES   SMITH, CORDELIA T.   AN
   MIRROR OF INFINITY, THE   SILVERBERG, ROBERT   AN
   *OTHER SIDE OF THE MOON, THE   DERLETH, AUGUST   AN
   PAST, PRESENT, AND FUTURE PERFECT   WOLFE, J&FITZ GERALD   AN
   SCIENCE IN FICTION   BAYLISS, A.E. & J.C.   AN
   SECOND ORBIT   DOHERTY, G. D.   AN
   SHORT STORIES OF H. G. WELLS, THE   WELLS, H. G.   AC
   SHOT IN THE DARK   MERRIL, JUDITH   AN
   TALES OF SPACE AND TIME   WELLS, H. G.   AC
   TOMORROW, AND TOMORROW, AND TOMORROW... HEINTZ/HERBERT/JOOS/ AN
   TREASURY OF SCIENCE FICTION CLASSICS, THE
                                        KUEBLER, HAROLD W.   AN
   TWENTY-EIGHT SCIENCE FICTION STORIES WELLS, H. G.   AC
STAR, THE (SEE SOME JOYS UNDER THE STARS)
                             POHL, FREDERIK   TC
STARAS FLONDERANS   WILHELM, KATE   SS   ORB 66 01
   ORBIT 1   KNIGHT, DAMON   OA
STARBIRTH (ENVOI: STARBIRTH) GOLDBARTH, ALBERT   SS   LMG 75
   NEW CONSTELLATIONS   DISCH & NAYLOR   OA
STARBLOOD   NOLAN, WILLIAM F.   SS   INY 72 04
   ALIEN HORIZONS   NOLAN, WILLIAM F.   AC
   INFINITY 4   HOSKINS, ROBERT   OA
STARCOMBER, THE (5,271,009) BESTER, ALFRED   NV   FSF 54 03
   STARBURST   BESTER, ALFRED   AC
STARCOMBERS, THE   HAMILTON, EDMOND   SN   SFA 56 12
   GREAT SCIENCE FICTION ADVENTURES   SHAW, LARRY T.   AN
STARCROSSED   ZEBROWSKI, GEORGE   SS   EIO 73
   EROS IN ORBIT   ELDER, JOSEPH   OA
   HUMAN-MACHINES   SCORTIA & ZEBROWSKI   AN
   MONADIC UNIVERSE, THE   ZEBROWSKI, GEORGE   AC
STARDRIFT (SKYDRIFT)   PETAJA, EMIL   SS   WRT 49 11
   STARDRIFT AND OTHER FANTASTIC FLOTSAM PETAJA, EMIL   AC
STARDUST (ALSO AS FIRST TO THE STARS)
                             OLIVER, CHAD   NV   ASF 52 07
   ADVENTURES IN THE FAR FUTURE   WOLLHEIM, DONALD A.   DA
STARFISH   PRICE, D. M.   PM   SVW 73
   SAVING WORLDS   ELWOOD & KIDD   AN
STARFOG   ANDERSON, POUL   SN   ASF 67 08
   BEYOND THE BEYOND   ANDERSON, POUL   AC
STARLADY   MARTIN, GEORGE R. R. NV
   SCIENCE FICTION DISCOVERIES   POHL, C. & F.   OA
STARPORT   BOUNDS, SYDNEY J.   SS   SFM 74 03
   BEST OF SCIENCE FICTION MONTHLY, THE SACKS, JANET   AN
STARS AND DARKNESS   CHANG, GLENN   NV   UNI 76 06
   UNIVERSE 6   CARR, TERRY   OA
STARS ARE CALLING, MR. KEATS, THE
                             YOUNG, ROBERT F.   SS   AMZ 59 06
   WORLDS OF ROBERT F. YOUNG, THE   YOUNG, ROBERT F.   AC
STARS ARE THE STYX, THE   STURGEON, THEODORE   NV   GAL 50 10
   *GALAXY READER OF SCIENCE FICTION   GOLD, H. L.   AN
STARS ARE WAITING, THE   BRADLEY, MARION Z.   SS   STN 58 03
   DARK INTRUDER & OTHER STORIES, THE   BRADLEY, MARION Z.   DC
STARS BELOW, THE   LE GUIN, URSULA K.   SS   ORB 74 14
   ANOTHER WORLD   DOZOIS, GARDNER R.   AN
   ORBIT 14   KNIGHT, DAMON   OA
   WINDS TWELVE QUARTERS, THE   LE GUIN, URSULA K.   AC
STARS IN MY POCKET LIKE GRAINS OF SAND
                             DELANY, SAMUEL R.   EX
   BEYOND THIS HORIZON   CARRELL, CHRISTOPHER   OA
STARS LIKE DUST, THE   ASIMOV, ISAAC   NO   GAL 51 01
   TRIANGLE   ASIMOV, ISAAC   AC
STARS LOOK DOWN, THE   DEL REY, LESTER   NV   ASF 40 08
   *AND SOME WERE HUMAN   DEL REY, LESTER   AC
   EARLY DEL REY   DEL REY, LESTER   AC
STARS MY DESTINATION, THE (ALSO AS TIGER! TIGER!)
                             BESTER, ALFRED   NO   GAL 56 10
   TREASURY OF GREAT SCIENCE FICTION, A VOL.2
                                        BOUCHER, ANTHONY   AN
STARS, MY BROTHERS, THE   HAMILTON, EDMOND   NV   AMZ 62 05
   ALIEN WORLDS   ELWOOD, ROGER   AN
   WHAT'S IT LIKE OUT THERE? AND OTHER STORIES
                                        HAMILTON, EDMOND   AC
STARS, WON'T YOU HIDE ME?   BOVA, BEN   SS   WOT 66 01
   FORWARD IN TIME   BOVA, BEN   AC
   NOTES TO A SCIENCE FICTION WRITER   BOVA, BEN   AC
STARSCAPE WITH FRIEZE OF DREAMS
                             YOUNG, ROBERT F.   SS   ORB 70 08
   ORBIT 8   KNIGHT, DAMON   OA
STARSONG   SABERHAGEN, FRED   SS   IFS 68 01
   BOOK OF SABERHAGEN, THE   SABERHAGEN, FRED   AC
   WORLD'S BEST SCIENCE FICTION: 1969   WOLLHEIM & CARR   AN
START IN LIFE, A   SELLINGS, ARTHUR   SS   GAL 54 09
   INTRODUCING SCIENCE FICTION   ALDISS, BRIAN W.   AN
   *TIME TRANSFER   SELLINGS, ARTHUR   AC
STARTHINKER 9   CONEY, MICHAEL G.   SS
   ANDROMEDA I   WESTON, PETER   AN
STARTING FROM SCRATCH   SHECKLEY, ROBERT   SS   FSF 70 01
   BEST FROM FANTASY AND SCIENCE FICTION: 19
                                        FERMAN, EDWARD L.   AN
   CAN YOU FEEL ANYTHING WHEN I DO THIS?, AND OTHER STORIES
                                        SHECKLEY, ROBERT   AC
STARTING LINE, THE (VENTURE TO THE MOON)
                             CLARKE, ARTHUR C.   SS   FSF 56 12
   OTHER SIDE OF THE SKY, THE   CLARKE, ARTHUR C.   AC
STARTING POINTS   AMIS, KINGSLEY   AR   60
   SCIENCE FICTION: THE FUTURE   ALLEN, DICK   AN

STATE OF ASSASSINATION (SEE A MAN TO MY WOUNDING)

STATE OF ASSASSINATION (SEE A MAN TO MY WOUNDING)
    ANDERSON, POUL   TC
STATE OF GRACE, THE   AYME, MARCEL   SS   FSF 59 12
    WALKER THROUGH WALLS, THE   AYME, MARCEL   AC
STATE OF THE ART   MALZBERG, BARRY N.   SS   NDM 74 04
    DOWN HERE IN THE DREAM QUARTER   MALZBERG, BARRY N.   AC
    NEW DIMENSIONS 4   SILVERBERG, ROBERT   OA
STATE OF THE ART ON ALYSSUM, THE
    RANDALL, MARTA   SS   NDM 77 07
    NEW DIMENSIONS 7   SILVERBERG, ROBERT   OA
STATION HR972   BULMER, KENNETH   SS   WOT 67 02
    NIGHTMARE AGE   POHL, FREDERIK   AN
STATIONS OF THE NIGHTMARE- PART 1   FARMER, PHILIP JOSE   NV   CTM 74 01
    CONTINUUM 1   ELWOOD, ROGER   OA
STATIONS OF THE NIGHTMARE- PART 2: THE STARTOUCHED
    FARMER, PHILIP JOSE   NV   CTM 74 02
    CONTINUUM 2   ELWOOD, ROGER   OA
STATIONS OF THE NIGHTMARE- PART 3: THE EVOLUTION OF PAUL EYRE
    FARMER, PHILIP JOSE   NV   CTM 74 03
    CONTINUUM 3   ELWOOD, ROGER   OA
STATIONS OF THE NIGHTMARE- PART 4: PASSING ON
    FARMER, PHILIP JOSE   NV   CTM 75 04
    CONTINUUM 4   ELWOOD, ROGER   OA
STATISTICIAN'S DAY   BLISH, JAMES   SS   SAG 70
    BEST SF: 1971   HARRISON & ALDISS   AN
    SCIENCE AGAINST MAN   CHEETHAM, ANTHONY   OA
STATUE FOR FATHER, A   ASIMOV, ISAAC   SS   SAT 59 02
    BUY JUPITER AND OTHER STORIES   ASIMOV, ISAAC   AC
STATUES   BRADBURY, RAY   SS   NEW 57 NO
    DANDELION WINE   BRADBURY, RAY   NO
    VINTAGE BRADBURY, THE   BRADBURY, RAY   AC
STATUES, THE   PRIESTLEY, J. B.   SS
    OTHER PLACE, THE   PRIESTLEY, J. B.   AC
STATUS   WRIGHT, S. FOWLER   SS
    WITCHFINDER, THE   WRIGHT, S. FOWLER   AC
STATUS QUO AT TROYDEN'S   ELLISON, HARLAN   SS   SMM 58 11
    NO DOORS, NO WINDOWS (STORIES REWRITTEN) ELLISON, HARLAN   AC
STATUS QUONDAM   MILLER, P. SCHUYLER   NV   NTS 51
    NEW TALES OF SPACE AND TIME   HEALY, RAYMOND J.   OA
STAWDUST   ST. CLAIR, MARGARET   SS   FSF 56 09
    CHANGE THE SKY AND OTHER STORIES   ST. CLAIR, MARGARET   AC
STAY AT THE OCEAN, A   WILSON, ROBLEY JR.   SS   69
    ECO-FICTION   STADLER, JOHN   AN
STEAM HOUSE, THE (1880)   VERNE, JULES   EX   SCB 81
    JULES VERNE- MASTER OF SCIENCE FICTION   VERNE, JULES   AC
STEAM-DRIVEN BOY, THE   SLADEK, JOHN T.   SS   NOV 72 02
    NOVA 2   HARRISON, HARRY   OA
STEEL   MATHESON, RICHARD   SS   FSF 56 05
    PSEUDO PEOPLE, THE   NOLAN, WILLIAM F.   AN
    RUN TO STARLIGHT, SPORTS THROUGH SCIENCE FICTION
    GREENBERG/OLANDER/&   AN
    SHORES OF SPACE, THE   MATHESON, RICHARD   AC
STEEL BROTHER   DICKSON, GORDON R.   NV   ASF 52 02
    DANGER- HUMAN   DICKSON, GORDON R.   AC
    SPACE SERVICE   NORTON, ANDRE   AN
STEEL DOOR, THE   REEVE, ARTHUR B.   SS
    SILENT BULLET, THE   REEVE, ARTHUR B.   AC
STEEL SONNETS, THE   DUNTEMANN, JEFF   SS   ORB 75 17
    ORBIT 17   KNIGHT, DAMON   OA
STELLA   WHITE, TED   SS   WLK 73
    AND WALK NOW GENTLY THROUGH THE FIRE... ELWOOD, ROGER   OA
    GIFTS OF ASTI AND OTHER STORIES OF SCIENCE FICTION, THE
    ELWOOD, ROGER   AN
STELLAR MISSILE, THE   REPP, ED EARL   SS   SWS 29 11
    STELLAR MISSILES, THE   REPP, ED EARL   AC
STELLAR SHIPS   YEFREMOV, IVAN   SS
    STORIES   YEFREMOV, IVAN   AC
STENTORII LUGGAGE, THE   BARRETT, NEAL JR.   NV   GAL 60 10
    MIND PARTNER AND 8 OTHER NOVELETS FROM GALAXY
    GOLD, H. L.   AN
STEP INTO MY GARDEN   LONG, FRANK BELKNAP   SS   UNK 42 08
    DARK BEASTS, THE   LONG, FRANK BELKNAP   AC
    EARLY LONG, THE   LONG, FRANK BELKNAP   AC
    *HOUNDS OF TINDALOS, THE   LONG, FRANK BELKNAP   AC
    NIGHTMARE GARDEN   GHIDALIA, VIC   AN
STEP IV   BROWN, ROSEL GEORGE   SS   AMZ 60 06
    HANDFUL OF TIME, A   BROWN, ROSEL GEORGE   AC
STEPSON OF SPACE   GALLUN, RAYMOND Z.   SS   AST 40 10
    BEYOND THE END OF TIME   POHL, FREDERIK   AN
STEVE WEINRAUB AND THE SECRET EMPIRE
    EFFINGER, GEO. ALEC SS
    MIXED FEELINGS   EFFINGER, GEO. ALEC   AC
STEVIE AND THE DARK (THE DARK CAME OUT TO PLAY)
    HENDERSON, ZENNA   SS   IMG 52 05
    ANYTHING BOX, THE   HENDERSON, ZENNA   AC
STICK FOR HARRY EDDINGTON, A   OLIVER, CHAD   SS   FSF 65 08
    SF: AUTHORS' CHOICE 2   HARRISON, HARRY   AN
STICKENEY AND THE CRITIC   CLINGERMAN, MILDRED   SS   FSF 53 02
    CUPFUL OF SPACE, A   CLINGERMAN, MILDRED   AC
    PORTALS OF TOMORROW   DERLETH, AUGUST   AN
STILL LIFE (STUDY IN STILL LIFE)
    RUSSELL, ERIC FRANK   SS   ASF 59 01
    ANOTHER PART OF THE GALAXY   CONKLIN, GROFF   AN
STILL TRAJECTORIES   ALDISS, BRIAN W.   SS   NWS 67 09
    BEST SCIENCE FICTION STORIES OF BRIAN W. ALDISS (REVISED)
    ALDISS, BRIAN W.   AC
    ENGLAND SWINGS SF   MERRIL, JUDITH   AN
    SPACE-TIME JOURNAL, THE   MERRIL, JUDITH   AN
    SPECTRUM OF WORLDS, A   CLARESON, THOMAS D.   AN
STILL WATERS, THE   DEL REY, LESTER   SS   FAN 55 04
    OUT OF THIS WORLD 2   WILLIAMS-ELLIS& OWEN   AN
    ROBOTS AND CHANGELINGS   DEL REY, LESTER   AC
STILL-LIFE   O'DONNELL, K. M.   SS   DVS 72 02
    AGAIN, DANGEROUS VISIONS   ELLISON, HARLAN   OA

STILL-LIFE (AS K. M. O'DONNELL)
    MALZBERG, BARRY N.   SS   DVS 72 02
    OUT FROM GANYMEDE   MALZBERG, BARRY N.   AC
STILLED PATTER, THE   GUNN, JAMES E.   SS   INF 56 06
    FUTURE IMPERFECT   GUNN, JAMES E.   AC
STIMULUS   BRUNNER, JOHN   SS   NWS 62 03
    NO FUTURE IN IT   BRUNNER, JOHN   AC
    OUT OF THIS WORLD 6   WILLIAMS-ELLIS& OWEN   AN
STIMULUS-REWARD SITUATION   FISHER, GENE   SS   ASF 73 08
    SCHOOL AND SOCIETY THROUGH SCIENCE FICTION
    OLANDER/GREENBERG/&   AN
STING!   REAMY, TOM   PL   75
    SIX SCIENCE FICTION PLAYS   ELWOOD, ROGER   AN
STITCH IN TIME   MCINTOSH, J. T.   SS   SCF 52 FL
    GATEWAY TO THE STARS   CARNELL, JOHN   AN
STITCH IN TIME, A   LONG, FRANK BELKNAP   SS   SSS 40 03
    DARK BEASTS, THE   LONG, FRANK BELKNAP   AC
    *HOUNDS OF TINDALOS, THE   LONG, FRANK BELKNAP   AC
STITCH IN TIME, A   WYNDHAM, JOHN   SS   FSF 61 03
    CONSIDER HER WAYS AND OTHERS   WYNDHAM, JOHN   AC
    INFINITE MOMENT, THE   WYNDHAM, JOHN   AC
STOCKYARD BLUES   GOULART, RON   SS
    NUTZENBOLTS   GOULART, RON   AC
STOLEN BACILLUS, THE   WELLS, H. G.   SS   PMB 94 06
    COUNTRY OF THE BLIND, THE   WELLS, H. G.   AC
    GREAT SCIENCE FICTION STORIES   SMITH, CORDELIA T.   AN
    SHORT STORIES OF H. G. WELLS, THE   WELLS, H. G.   AC
    STOLEN BACILLUS AND OTHER INCIDENTS, THE WELLS, H. G.   AC
    THIRTY STRANGE STORIES   WELLS, H. G.   AC
    TWENTY-EIGHT SCIENCE FICTION STORIES   WELLS, H. G.   AC
STOLEN BODY, THE   WELLS, H. G.   SS   SND 98 11
    INEXPERIENCED GHOST AND NINE OTHER STORIES, THE
    WELLS, H. G.   AC
    SHORT STORIES OF H. G. WELLS, THE   WELLS, H. G.   AC
    TWELVE STORIES AND A DREAM   WELLS, H. G.   AC
    TWENTY-EIGHT SCIENCE FICTION STORIES   WELLS, H. G.   AC
STOLEN CENTURIES   KLINE, OTIS ADELBERT SS   TWS 39 06
    EDITOR'S CHOICE IN SCIENCE FICTION   MOSKOWITZ, SAM   AN
STONE AND A SPEAR, A   JONES, RAYMOND F.   NV   GAL 50 12
    OMNIBUS OF SCIENCE FICTION   CONKLIN, GROFF   AN
    STRANGE TRAVELS IN SCIENCE FICTION   CONKLIN, GROFF   AN
STONE CITY, THE   MARTIN, GEORGE R. R. SS
    NEW VOICES IN SCIENCE FICTION   MARTIN, GEORGE R. R. OA
STONE FROM THE STARS   ZHURAVLEVA, VALENTINA SS
    MORE SOVIET SCIENCE FICTION   ANONYMOUS   AN
STONE OF THE SAGES, THE   DE CAMP, L. SPRAGUE
    AND PRATT, FLETCHER   SS C NEW 53 AC
    TALES FROM GAVAGAN'S BAR   DE CAMP, L. S.&PRATT AC
STONE PLACE   SABERHAGEN, FRED   NV   IFS 65 03
    BERSERKER   SABERHAGEN, FRED   AC
STONED COUNSEL   HOLLIS, H. H.   SS   DVS 72 02
    AGAIN, DANGEROUS VISIONS   ELLISON, HARLAN   OA
STONES HAVE NAMES, THE   BROXON, MILDRED D.   SS   FOS 74
    FELLOWSHIP OF THE STARS   CARR, TERRY   AN
STOOP TO CONQUER   RACKHAM, JOHN   SS   NWR 71 19
    NEW WRITINGS IN SF. 19   CARNELL, JOHN   OA
STOP AT WILLOUGHBY, A   SERLING, ROD   SA
    MORE STORIES FROM THE TWILIGHT ZONE   SERLING, ROD   OC
STOP ME BEFORE I TELL MORE (ALSO AS PUNCHLINE)
    THURSTON, ROBERT   SS   ORB 71 09
    ORBIT 9   KNIGHT, DAMON   OA
STOP WATCH, THE   VERNON, ROGER LEE   SS
    SPACE FRONTIERS, THE   VERNON, ROGER LEE   AC
STORE OF THE WORLDS, THE (THE WORLD OF HEART'S DESIRE)
    SHECKLEY, ROBERT   SS   PBY 59 09
    MORE PENGUIN SCIENCE FICTION   ALDISS, BRIAN W.   AN
    ROBERT SHECKLEY OMNIBUS, THE   SHECKLEY, ROBERT   AC
    STORE OF INFINITY   SHECKLEY, ROBERT   AC
STORIES OF OTHER WORLDS   GRIFFITH, GEORGE   GR
    WORLDS APART   LOCKE, GEORGE   AN
STORM   ZHURAVLEVA,VALENTINA SS
    RUSSIAN SCIENCE FICTION, 1968   MAGIDOFF, ROBERT   AN
STORM WARNING   WOLLHEIM, DONALD A.   SS   FUT 42 10
    INVADERS FROM SPACE   SILVERBERG, ROBERT   AN
    *INVADERS OF EARTH   CONKLIN, GROFF   AN
    TWO DOZEN DRAGON EGGS   WOLLHEIM, DONALD A.   AC
STORM-BIRD, STORM-DREAMER   BALLARD, J. G.   SS   NWS 66 11
    CHRONOPOLIS AND OTHER STORIES   BALLARD, J. G.   AC
    DISASTER AREA, THE   BALLARD, J. G.   AC
    IMPOSSIBLE MAN, THE   BALLARD, J. G.   AC
STORM-WIND (SEE THE WIND FROM NOWHERE)
    BALLARD, J. G.   TC
STORM, THE   DOZOIS, GARDNER R.   NV   FCR 75
    FUTURE CORRUPTION   ELWOOD, ROGER   OA
    VISIONS OF TOMORROW   ELWOOD, ROGER   AN
STORM, THE   VAN VOGT, A. E.   NV   ASF 43 10
    ASTOUNDING-ANALOG READER, THE VOLUME ONE HARRISON & ALDISS   AN
    BEST OF A. E. VAN VOGT, THE (BRITISH)   VAN VOGT, A. E.   AC
    MIXED MEN, THE   VAN VOGT, A. E.   NO
    SPACE OPERA   ALDISS, BRIAN W.   AN
    WORLDS OF A. E. VAN VOGT, THE   VAN VOGT, A. E.   AC
STORMFALL   JOHNSON, BILL   SS
    CLARION SF   WILHELM, KATE   OA
STORMS OF WINDHAVEN, THE   MARTIN, GEORGE R. R.
    AND TUTTLE, LISA   NV C ASF 75 05
    BEST SCIENCE FICTION OF THE YEAR, THE NO. 5
    CARR, TERRY   AN
    1976 ANNUAL WORLD'S BEST SF, THE   WOLLHEIM, DONALD A.   AN
STORMSEEKER   SHAW, BOB   SS   GAL 72 01
    TOMORROW LIES IN AMBUSH   SHAW, BOB   AC
STORMY WEATHER   MERRIL, JUDITH   SS   STS 54 SU
    BEST OF JUDITH MERRIL, THE   MERRIL, JUDITH   AC
STORY OF A PANIC, THE   FORSTER, E. M.   SS   47
    CHILDREN OF WONDER   TENN, WILLIAM   AN
STORY OF A STRANGE RELATIVE   HOLDEN, LARRY   SS
    LONE STAR UNIVERSE   PROCTOR & UTLEY   OA

STORY OF AN ATOMIC-AGE ORDEAL (SEE NINE DAYS TO DIE)
                              SAMBROT, WILLIAM   TC
STORY OF DAVIDSON'S EYES, THE WELLS, H. G.   SS PMB 95 03
  BEST SCIENCE FICTION STORIES OF H. G. WELLS
                              WELLS, H. G.   AC
  THIRTY STRANGE STORIES   WELLS, H. G.   AC
STORY OF LOVE, A   BRADBURY, RAY   SS
  LONG AFTER MIDNIGHT   BRADBURY, RAY   AC
STORY OF REJECTION, THE   INOUYE, JON   SS
  NIGHT TIDE, A   INOUYE, JON   OC
STORY OF SIDI NORMAN, THE   ANONYMOUS   SS
  ROD SERLING'S TRIPLE W: WITCHES, WARLOCKS AND WEREWOLVES
                              SERLING, ROD   AN
STORY OF THE DAYS TO COME, A WELLS, H. G.   NA PGZ 97
  BEST STORIES OF H. G. WELLS   WELLS, H. G.   AC
  SHORT STORIES OF H. G. WELLS, THE   WELLS, H. G.   AC
  TALES OF SPACE AND TIME   WELLS, H. G.   AC
  TWENTY-EIGHT SCIENCE FICTION STORIES WELLS, H. G. AC
  3 PROPHETIC SCIENCE FICTION NOVELS OF H. G. WELLS
                              WELLS, H. G.   AC
STORY OF THE DELUGE, THE MITCHELL, EDWARD P. SS SUN 75 04
  CRYSTAL MAN, THE   MITCHELL, EDWARD P.   AC
STORY OF THE HEAVENS (1883) BALL, SIR ROBERT   AR   83
  FAREWELL FANTASTIC VENUS   ALDISS & HARRISON   AN
STORY OF THE INEXPERIENCED GHOST, THE (SEE THE INEXPERIENCED
  GHOST)   WELLS, H. G.   TC
STORY OF THE LAST TRUMP, THE WELLS, H. G.   SS BON 15
  SHORT STORIES OF H. G. WELLS, THE   WELLS, H. G.   AC
STORY OF THE LATE MR. ELVESHAM, THE
                              WELLS, H. G.   SS IDL 96 05
  BEST STORIES OF H. G. WELLS   WELLS, H. G.   AC
  COUNTRY OF THE BLIND, THE   WELLS, H. G.   AC
  DARK SIDE, THE   KNIGHT, DAMON   AN
  OTHER SIDE OF THE CLOCK, THE   STERN, PHILIP VAN D. AN
  PLATTNER STORY AND OTHERS, THE WELLS, H. G.   AC
  SHORT STORIES OF H. G. WELLS, THE   WELLS, H. G.   AC
  THIRTY STRANGE STORIES   WELLS, H. G.   AC
  TWENTY-EIGHT SCIENCE FICTION STORIES WELLS, H. G. AC
  WAR OF THE WORLDS, THE TIME MACHINE AND SELECTED SHORT STORIES
                              WELLS, H. G.   AC
STORY OF THE STONE AGE, A WELLS, H. G.   NA IDL 97 05
  SHORT STORIES OF H. G. WELLS, THE   WELLS, H. G.   AC
  TALES OF SPACE AND TIME   WELLS, H. G.   AC
  TWENTY-EIGHT SCIENCE FICTION STORIES WELLS, H. G. AC
STORY OF THREE CITIES, THE CROSS, RONALD A. SS NWQ 73 05
  NEW WORLDS NO. 5   MOORCOCK & PLATT   OA
STORY TIME   JANIFER, LAURENCE M. SS
  JOURNEY TO ANOTHER STAR AND OTHER STORIES
                              ELWOOD, ROGER   OA
STORY-TELLER OF MANY WORLDS HAMILTON, EDMOND   IN
  BEST OF LEIGH BRACKETT, THE   BRACKETT, LEIGH   AC
STORY-TELLER, THE   SAKI   SS
  BEST FANTASY STORIES   ALDISS, BRIAN W.   AN
"STORY, A" BY JOHN V. MARSCH WOLFE, GENE   NV
  FIFTH HEAD OF CERBERUS, THE   WOLFE, GENE   AC
STRANDED IN TIME   FARLEY, RALPH MILNE SS
  OMNIBUS OF TIME, THE   FARLEY, RALPH MILNE   AC
STRANGE AND TERRIBLE SEA, A MALCOLM, DONALD   SS NWR 74 24
  NEW WRITINGS IN SF. 24   BULMER, KENNETH   OA
STRANGE BEDFELLOWS (TO BUILD A WORLD)
                              ANDERSON, POUL   SN GAL 64 06
  7 CONQUESTS   ANDERSON, POUL   AC
STRANGE CASE OF ALAN MORAINE, THE
                              ATKEY, BERTRAM   SS GND 12 09
  WORLDS APART   LOCKE, GEORGE   AN
STRANGE CASE OF DR. JEKYLL AND MR. HYDE
                              STEVENSON, ROBERT L. SN   85
  CENTURY OF GREAT SHORT SCIENCE FICTION NOVELS, A
                              KNIGHT, DAMON   AN
STRANGE CASE OF JOHN KINGMAN, THE
                              LEINSTER, MURRAY SS ASF 48 05
  BEST SCIENCE-FICTION STORIES: 1949, THE BLEILER & DIKTY AN
  GREAT STORIES OF SCIENCE FICTION   LEINSTER, MURRAY AN
STRANGE CASE OF LEMUEL JENKINS, THE
                              FISHER, PHILIP M. JR SS ASW 19 07
 *TERROR IN THE MODERN VEIN   WOLLHEIM, DONALD A.   AN
STRANGE CHILDREN, THE HOLDING, ELIZABETH S SS FSF 55 08
  ALONE BY NIGHT   CONGDON, MICHAEL&DON   AN
STRANGE COMPULSION (SEE THE CAPTAIN'S DAUGHTER)
                              FARMER, PHILIP JOSE   TC
STRANGE DRUG OF DR. CABER, THE DUNSANY, LORD   SS   48
 *OTHER SIDE OF THE MOON, THE   DERLETH, AUGUST   AN
STRANGE EXODUS   ABERNATHY, ROBERT   SS PLS 50 FL
  SPACE ODYSSEYS   ALDISS, BRIAN W.   AN
STRANGE FLIGHT OF RICHARD CLAYTON, THE
                              BLOCH, ROBERT   SS AMZ 39 03
  HORROR-7   BLOCH, ROBERT   AC
  MODERN MASTERPIECES OF SCIENCE FICTION MOSKOWITZ, SAM AN
 *OPENER OF THE WAY, THE   BLOCH, ROBERT   AC
STRANGE GIRL, THE   VAN DOREN, MARK   SS   62
  WORLDS OF SCIENCE FICTION, THE MILLS, ROBERT P. AN
STRANGE GIRL, THE (SEE LOOK AFTER THE STRANGE GIRL)
                              PRIESTLEY, J. B.   TC
STRANGE HARVEST   WANDREI, DONALD   NV WRT 53 05
  NIGHTMARE GARDEN   GHIDALIA, VIC   AN
  STRANGE HARVEST   WANDREI, DONALD   AC
 *WORLDS OF TOMORROW   DERLETH, AUGUST   AN
STRANGE HIGH HOUSE IN THE MIST, THE
                              LOVECRAFT, H. P. SS WRT 31 10
  WEIRD TALES   MARGULIES, LEO   AN
STRANGE IN A FAMILIAR WAY ALDISS, BRIAN W.   SS
  BEYOND THIS HORIZON   CARRELL, CHRISTOPHER   OA
STRANGE ISLAND OF DR. NORK, THE
                              BLOCH, ROBERT   SS WRT 49 03
  UNEXPECTED, THE   MARGULIES, LEO.   AN

STRANGE MEN, THE   ELAM, RICHARD M. JR. SS
  TEEN-AGE SCIENCE FICTION STORIES ELAM, RICHARD M. JR. AC
STRANGE ORCHID, THE (THE FLOWERING OF THE STRANGE ORCHID)
                              WELLS, H. G.   SS PMB 94 08
  BEST SCIENCE FICTION STORIES OF H. G. WELLS
                              WELLS, H. G.   AC
  THIRTY STRANGE STORIES   WELLS, H. G.   AC
STRANGE PLAYFELLOW (ALSO AS ROBBIE)
                              ASIMOV, ISAAC   SS SSS 40 09
  SHOT IN THE DARK   MERRIL, JUDITH   AN
STRANGE RITUAL (SEE RITUAL) SHECKLEY, ROBERT   TC
STRANGE SHAPE IN THE STRONGHOLD
                              BUNCH, DAVID R.   SS FAN 60 03
  MODERAN   BUNCH, DAVID R.   AC
STRANGER FROM SPACE   LEES, GENE   SS SCF 54 03
  GATEWAY TO THE STARS   CARNELL, JOHN   AN
STRANGER IN PARADISE   ASIMOV, ISAAC   NV IFS 74 06
  BEST FROM IF, THE VOLUME II   IF, EDITORS OF   AN
  BICENTENNIAL MAN AND OTHER STORIES, THE ASIMOV, ISAAC AC
  1975 ANNUAL WORLD'S BEST SF, THE WOLLHEIM, DONALD A. AN
STRANGER IN THE HOUSE   TUTTLE, LISA   SS CLR 72 02
  CLARION II   WILSON, ROBIN SCOTT   OA
STRANGER STATION   KNIGHT, DAMON   NV FSF 56 12
  BUG-EYED MONSTERS   CHEETHAM, ANTHONY   AN
  EARTHMEN AND STRANGERS   SILVERBERG, ROBERT   AN
  IN DEEP   KNIGHT, DAMON   AC
  LOOKING AHEAD   ALLEN, D. & L.   AN
  MODERN SCIENCE FICTION   SPINRAD, NORMAN   AN
  SF: THE BEST OF THE BEST   MERRIL, JUDITH   AN
  SF:57, THE YEAR'S GREATEST SCIENCE FICTION AND FANTASY
                              MERRIL, JUDITH   AN
  SPECTRUM 4   AMIS & CONQUEST   AN
STRANGER WITH ROSES   JAKES, JOHN W.   PL INY 72 04
  INFINITY 4   HOSKINS, ROBERT   OA
  SIX SCIENCE FICTION PLAYS ELWOOD, ROGER   OA
STRANGER, THE   HUGHES, RICHARD   SS   31
  SUPERNATURAL READER, THE   CONKLIN, G&L.   AN
STRANGERS   DOZOIS, GARDNER R. NA NDM 74 04
  NEW DIMENSIONS 4   SILVERBERG, ROBERT   OA
STRANGERS   EMSHWILLER, CAROL   SS BMR 73
  BAD MOON RISING   DISCH, THOMAS M.   AN
  JOY IN OUR CAUSE   EMSHWILLER, CAROL   AC
STRANGLEHOLD   ANVIL, CHRISTOPHER SS ASF 66 05
  ANALOG 6   CAMPBELL, JOHN W. JR   AN
STRAW   WOLFE, GENE   SS GAL 75 01
  ANOTHER WORLD   DOZOIS, GARDNER R.   AN
STRAWBERRY WINDOW, THE BRADBURY, RAY   SS STR 54 03
  DAY IT RAINED FOREVER, THE   BRADBURY, RAY   AC
  MEDICINE FOR MELANCHOLY, A   BRADBURY, RAY   AC
  R IS FOR ROCKET   BRADBURY, RAY   AC
  STAR SCIENCE FICTION STORIES NO. 3   POHL, FREDERIK OA
STRAWHOUSE PAVILION, THE GOULART, RON   SS COV 70 01
  GHOST BREAKER   GOULART, RON   DC
STRAY FROM CATHAY, A (SEE CHINESE PUZZLE)
                              WYNDHAM, JOHN   TC
STREAKING   MALZBERG, BARRY N. SS FCR 75
  DOWN HERE IN THE DREAM QUARTER   MALZBERG, BARRY N. AC
STREAKING   O'DONNELL, K. M.   SS FCR 75
  FUTURE CORRUPTION   ELWOOD, ROGER   OA
STREET OF DREAMS, FEET OF CLAY SHECKLEY, ROBERT NV GAL 68 02
  CITY: 2000 A.D., THE   CLEM/GREENBERG/&   AN
  LIBERATED FUTURE: VOYAGES INTO TOMORROW, THE
                              HOSKINS, ROBERT   AN
  SPECULATIONS   SANDERS, THOMAS E.   AN
  TOMORROW, AND TOMORROW, AND TOMORROW... HEINTZ/HERBERT/JOOS/ AN
  WANDERING STARS   DANN, JACK M.   AN
  WORLD'S BEST SCIENCE FICTION: 1969   WOLLHEIM & CARR AN
STREET SCENE (DUNDERBIRD) ELLISON, HARLAN
                          AND LAUMER, KEITH NV C GAL 69 01
  PARTNERS IN WONDER   ELLISON, HARLAN   AC
STREET THAT WASN'T THERE, THE (ALSO AS THE LOST STREET)
                              JACOBI, CARL
                          AND SIMAK, CLIFFORD D. SS C CMT 41 07
  CREATURES FROM BEYOND   CARR, TERRY   AN
STREET WALKER, THE   TUCKER, WILSON   SS
  SCIENCE FICTION SUBTREASURY, THE   TUCKER, WILSON AC
STREETS OF ASHKELON, THE (ALSO AS AN ALIEN AGONY)
                              HARRISON, HARRY   SS NWS 62 09
 *BEST OF HARRY HARRISON, THE   HARRISON, HARRY   AC
  DARK STARS   SILVERBERG, ROBERT   AN
  GODS FOR TOMORROW   SANTESSON, HANS S.   AN
  NEW AWARENESS, THE   WARRICK & GREENBERG   AN
  SCIENCE FICTION NOVELLAS   HARRISON & MCNELLY   AN
  TWO TALES AND EIGHT TOMORROWS HARRISON, HARRY   AC
STRENGTH OF THE STRONG, THE LONDON, JACK   SS HAM 11 03
  CURIOUS FRAGMENTS   LONDON, JACK   AC
  SCIENCE FICTION OF JACK LONDON, THE LONDON, JACK AC
STRESS PATTERN   SILVERBERG, ROBERT   NV ASF 60 01
  SHORES OF TOMORROW, THE   SILVERBERG, ROBERT   AC
STRIKEBREAKER (MALE STRIKEBREAKER)
                              ASIMOV, ISAAC   SS SFS 57 01
  ANTHROPOLOGY THROUGH SCIENCE FICTION   MASON, C/GREENBERG/& AN
  NIGHTFALL AND OTHER STORIES   ASIMOV, ISAAC   AC
  17 X INFINITY   CONKLIN, GROFF   AN
STRING OF PEARLS   BLOCH, ROBERT   SS SMM 56 08
  KING OF TERRORS, THE   BLOCH, ROBERT   AC
STROKE OF THE SUN (SEE A SLIGHT CASE OF SUNSTROKE)
                              CLARKE, ARTHUR C.   TC
STRONG ATTRACTION   SMITH, RON   SS NEW 68 AN
  PACIFIC BOOK OF AUSTRALIAN SCIENCE FICTION
                              BAXTER, JOHN   AN
STRONGER SPELL, THE   DE CAMP, L. SPRAGUE SS FNF 53 11
  TRITONIAN RING, THE   DE CAMP, L. SPRAGUE   AC
STRONGHOLD, THE   BUNCH, DAVID R.   SS
  MODERAN   BUNCH, DAVID R.   AC

STRUGGLE IN THE WOMB (BATTLE OF THE UNBORN)   SUNBURST

STRUGGLE IN THE WOMB (BATTLE OF THE UNBORN)
                              BLISH, JAMES   SS   FUT 50 05
  SO CLOSE TO HOME   BLISH, JAMES   AC
STUBBORN   GOLDIN, STEPHEN   SS   GEN 72
  GENERATION   GERROLD, DAVID   OA
STUBBORN MEN, THE   WILLIAMS, ROBERT M. SS SSS 48 11
  VOID BEYOND, AND OTHER STORIES, THE WILLIAMS, ROBERT M. DC
STUCK WITH IT   CLEMENT, HAL   NV   STL 76 02
  STELLAR 2   DEL REY, JUDY-LYNN   OA
STUDENT BODY   WALLACE, F. L.   NV   GAL 53 03
  CROSSROADS IN TIME   CONKLIN, GEOFF   AN
  GALAXY SCIENCE FICTION OMNIBUS GOLD, H. L.   AN
  SECOND GALAXY READER OF SCIENCE FICTION GOLD, H. L. AN
  SPECTRUM 5   AMIS & CONQUEST   AN
  VOYAGES: SCENARIOS FOR A SHIP CALLED EARTH
                             SAUER, ROB   AN
STUDIO 5, THE STARS   BALLARD, J. G.   NV   SCF 61 02
  BILLENIUM   BALLARD, J. G.   AC
  *FOUR-DIMENSIONAL NIGHTMARE, THE BALLARD, J. G.   AC
  *VERMILLION SANDS   BALLARD, J. G.   AC
STUDY IN STILL LIFE (SEE STILL LIFE)
                             RUSSELL, ERIC FRANK TC
STUNGUN SLIM   GOULART, RON   SS   UNI 74 04
  UNIVERSE 4   CARR, TERRY   OA
STURGEON BIBLIOGRAPHY MOSKOWITZ, SAM   MS   FSF 62 09
  BEST FROM FANTASY AND SCIENCE FICTION, 25TH ANNIV.
                             FERMAN, EDWARD L.   AN
STUTTERER, THE   MERLISS, R. R.   NV   ASF 55 04
  SF: THE YEAR'S GREATEST SCIENCE FICTION AND FANTASY
                             MERRIL, JUDITH   AN
STYLE IN TREASON, A (A HERO'S LIFE)
                             BLISH, JAMES   NV   IMP 66 03
  ANYWHEN   BLISH, JAMES   AC
  MIDSUMMER CENTURY   BLISH, JAMES   AC
STYLE: THE DRESS OF THOUGHT WILSON, ROBIN SCOTT SI
  THOSE WHO CAN: A SCIENCE FICTION READER WILSON, ROBIN SCOTT AN
SUB-LIM   ROBERTS, KEITH   NV   NWR 65 04
  MACHINES AND MEN   ROBERTS, KEITH   AC
  NEW WRITINGS IN SF. 4   CARNELL, JOHN   OA
SUB-STANDARD SARDINES VANCE, JACK   SS   STS 49 01
  SPACE POLICE   NORTON, ANDRE   OA
SUBCOMMITTEE   HENDERSON, ZENNA NV   FSF 62 07
  ANYTHING BOX, THE   HENDERSON, ZENNA   AC
  GENTLE INVADERS   SANTESSON, HANS S.   AN
  8TH ANNUAL OF THE YEAR'S BEST S-F, THE MERRIL, JUDITH AN
SUBJECT TO CHANGE   GOULART, RON   SS   GAL 60 12
  CHAMELEON CORPS & OTHER SHAPE CHANGERS, THE
                             GOULART, RON   AC
SUBJECTIVITY   SPINRAD, NORMAN   SS   ASF 64 01
  ANALOG 4   CAMPBELL, JOHN W. JR AN
  LAST HURRAH OF THE GOLDEN HORDE, THE SPINRAD, NORMAN AC
  STRANGE ECSTASIES   PARRY, MICHEL   OA
SUBLIME VIGIL, THE   CUTHBERT, CHESTER D. SS WOS 34 02
  EDITOR'S CHOICE IN SCIENCE FICTION MOSKOWITZ, SAM   AN
SUBLIMINAL MAN, THE   BALLARD, J. G.   SS   NWS 63 01
  BEST OF J. G. BALLARD, THE BALLARD, J. G.   AC
  DISASTER AREA, THE   BALLARD, J. G.   AC
  EARTH IN TRANSIT   SCHWARTZ, SHEILA   AN
  ECO-FICTION   STADLER, JOHN   AN
  INTRODUCTORY PSYCHOLOGY THROUGH SCIENCE FICTION
                             KATZ/WARRICK/&   AN
  MIRROR OF INFINITY, THE   SILVERBERG, ROBERT   AN
  STORIES FROM SCIENCE FICTION DOHERTY, G. D.   AN
  TERMINAL BEACH (AMERICAN VERSION) BALLARD, J. G.   AC
  TOMORROW, AND TOMORROW, AND TOMORROW... HEINTZ/HERBERT/JOOS/ AN
  TOMORROW, INC.   GREENBERG& OLANDER   AN
  WINDOW ON THE FUTURE   HILL, DOUGLAS   AN
  YOU AND SCIENCE FICTION   HOLLISTER, BERNARD C AN
SUBMARINED   WOOD, WALTER   SS   PRS 05 02
  SCIENCE FICTION BY GASLIGHT MOSKOWITZ, SAM   AN
SUBMICROSCOPIC   MEEK, CAPTAIN S. P. SS AMZ 31 08
  BEFORE THE GOLDEN AGE   ASIMOV, ISAAC   AN
SUBSISTENCE LEVEL   SHECKLEY, ROBERT SS   GAL 54 08
  SHARDS OF SPACE   SHECKLEY, ROBERT   AC
SUBSPACE SURVIVORS   SMITH, EDWARD E. PHD NV ASF 60 07
  BEST OF E. E. 'DOC' SMITH, THE SMITH, EDWARD E. PHD AC
SUBSTITUTE GOD (SEE BY THE NAME OF MAN)
                             BRUNNER, JOHN   TC   FUN 58 08
SUBSTITUTE, THE   HENDERSON, ZENNA SS   IMG 53 08
  ANYTHING BOX, THE   HENDERSON, ZENNA   AC
SUBTERFUGE   BRADBURY, RAY   SS   AST 43 04
  ASSIGNMENT IN TOMORROW   POHL, FREDERIK   AN
SUBTRACTER, THE   CHANDLER, A. BERTRAM SS
  HARD WAY UP, THE   CHANDLER, A. BERTRAM DC
SUBURBAN FRONTIERS   YOUNG, ROBERT F. SS   ASF 50 02
  *SCIENCE FICTION ADVENTURES IN DIMENSION CONKLIN, GEOFF AN
SUBVERSIVE   REYNOLDS, MACK   SS   ASF 62 12
  BEST OF MACK REYNOLDS, THE REYNOLDS, MACK   AC
  DECADE THE 1960S   ALDISS & HARRISON   AN
  SCIENCE FICTION HORIZONS NO. 1 BOARDMAN, TOM JR.   AN
SUBVERSIVES, THE (SEE WIN THE WORLD)
                             OLIVER, CHAD   TC
SUBWAY NAMED MOBIUS, A DEUTSCH, A. J.   SS   ASF 50 12
  BEST SF 4   CRISPIN, EDMUND   AN
  FANTASIA MATHEMATICA   FADIMAN, CLIFTON   AN
  OMNIBUS OF SCIENCE FICTION CONKLIN, GEOFF   AN
  ONE HUNDRED YEARS OF SCIENCE FICTION KNIGHT, DAMON   AN
  SCIENCE FICTION OMNIBUS   CONKLIN, GEOFF   AN
  STRANGE TRAVELS IN SCIENCE FICTION CONKLIN, GEOFF   AN
  WHERE DO WE GO FROM HERE? ASIMOV, ISAAC   AN
SUBWAYS OF TAZOO, THE KAPP, COLIN   NV   NWR 65 03
  BEST FROM NEW WRITINGS IN S-F FIRST SELECTION, THE
                             CARNELL, JOHN   AN
  NEW WRITINGS IN SF. 3   CARNELL, JOHN   AN
SUCCESS STORY   GOODALE, EARL   NV   GAL 60 04
  SIXTH GALAXY READER, THE   GOLD, H. L.   AN

SUCCESS STORY (SEE 88 BEATS 266)
                             WILSON, RICHARD   TC
SUCH INTERESTING NEIGHBORS FINNEY, JACK SS   COL 51 01
  BEYOND THE END OF TIME   POHL, FREDERIK   AN
  OTHER SIDE OF THE CLOCK, THE STERN, PHILIP VAN D. AN
  THIRD LEVEL, THE   FINNEY, JACK   AC
SUCH STUFF   BRUNNER, JOHN   SS   FSF 62 06
  INTRODUCTORY PSYCHOLOGY THROUGH SCIENCE FICTION
                             KATZ/WARRICK/&   AN
  *OUT OF MY MIND   BRUNNER, JOHN   AC
  SPECTRUM 4   AMIS & CONQUEST   AN
  8TH ANNUAL OF THE YEAR'S BEST S-F, THE MERRIL, JUDITH AN
SUCKER BAIT   ASIMOV, ISAAC   SN   ASF 54 02
  MARTIAN WAY AND OTHER STORIES, THE ASIMOV, ISAAC   AC
SUDDEN AFTERNOON, THE BALLARD, J. G.   SS   FAN 63 09
  DAY OF FOREVER, THE   BALLARD, J. G.   AC
  TERMINAL BEACH (AMERICAN VERSION) BALLARD, J. G.   AC
SUDDEN FOREST, THE   WELLS, BASIL   SS
  DOORWAYS TO SPACE   WELLS, BASIL   AC
SUGGESTED READING   MISC. MATERIAL   MS
  CENTURY OF SCIENCE FICTION, A KNIGHT, DAMON   AN
SUGGESTION   SERLING, ROD   SA
  NIGHT GALLERY 2   SERLING, ROD   OC
SUGGESTIONS FOR FURTHER READING
                             MISC. MATERIAL   MS
  SCIENCE FICTION NOVELLAS   HARRISON & MCNELLY   AN
  SCIENCE FICTION THROUGH THE AGES 2 EVANS, I. O.   AN
  SCIENCE FICTION: THE FUTURE ALLEN, DICK   AN
SUGGESTIONS FOR FURTHER READING AND VIEWING
                             MISC. MATERIAL   MS
  LOOKING AHEAD   ALLEN, D. & L.   AN
SUICIDE   STURGEON, THEODORE SS   KNT 70
  STURGEON IS ALIVE AND WELL... STURGEON, THEODORE   AC
SUICIDE CHAPEL   QUINN, SEABURY   NV   WBT 38 06
  FANTASTIC PULPS, THE   HAINING, PETER   AN
SULWEN'S PLANET   VANCE, JACK   SS   FRS 68
  FARTHEST REACHES, THE   ELDER, JOSEPH   OA
SUMERIAN OATH, THE   FARMER, PHILIP JOSE SN NOV 72 02
  BOOK OF PHILIP JOSE FARMER, THE FARMER, PHILIP JOSE AC
  NOVA 2   HARRISON, HARRY   OA
SUMMARY OF EVENTS LEADING UP TO BEDLAM, A
                             MALZBERG, BARRY N. SS   72
  BEWARE MORE BEASTS   GHIDALIA, V.& ELWOOD AN
SUMMATION   MERRIL, JUDITH   MS
  10TH ANNUAL OF THE YEAR'S BEST S-F, THE MERRIL, JUDITH AN
  11TH ANNUAL OF THE YEAR'S BEST S-F, THE MERRIL, JUDITH AN
SUMMATION: S-F, 1961   MERRIL, JUDITH   MS
  7TH ANNUAL OF THE YEAR'S BEST S-F, THE MERRIL, JUDITH AN
SUMMATION: S-F, 1962   MERRIL, JUDITH   MS
  8TH ANNUAL OF THE YEAR'S BEST S-F, THE MERRIL, JUDITH AN
SUMMATION: S-F, 1963   MERRIL, JUDITH   MS
  9TH ANNUAL OF THE YEAR'S BEST S-F, THE MERRIL, JUDITH AN
SUMMER CANNIBALS, THE BALLARD, J. G.   SS   NWS 69 01
  LOVE & NAPALM: EXPORT U.S.A. BALLARD, J. G.   AC
SUMMER IN THE AIR (ALSO AS THE SOUND OF SUMMER RUNNING)
                             BRADBURY, RAY   SS   SEP 56 02
  DANDELION WINE   BRADBURY, RAY   NO
SUMMER NIGHT, THE (THE SPRING NIGHT)
                             BRADBURY, RAY   SS   ARS 48 WI
  MARTIAN CHRONICLES, THE   BRADBURY, RAY   AC
SUMMER OF THE IRISH SEA, THE GRANT, C. L.   SS   ORB 72 11
  FUTURE PASTIMES   EDELSTEIN, SCOTT   OA
  ORBIT 11   KNIGHT, DAMON   OA
SUMMER PEOPLE, THE   JACKSON, SHIRLEY SS   CHM 50
  CIRCUS OF DR. LAO AND OTHER IMPROBABLE STORIES
                             BRADBURY, RAY   AN
SUMMER WEAR   DE CAMP, L. SPRAGUE SS STS 50 05
  BEST SCIENCE-FICTION STORIES: 1951, THE BLEILER & DIKTY AN
  CONTINENT MAKERS AND OTHER TALES OF THE VIAGENS
                             DE CAMP, L. SPRAGUE AC
SUMMERLAND   DAVIDSON, AVRAM   SS   FSF 57 07
  OR ALL THE SEAS WITH OYSTERS DAVIDSON, AVRAM   AC
SUMMERTIME ON ICARUS (THE HOTTEST PIECE OF REAL ESTATE IN THE
  SOLAR SYSTEM)   CLARKE, ARTHUR C. SS VOG 60 06
  BEST OF ARTHUR C. CLARKE: 1937-1971, THE CLARKE, ARTHUR C. AC
  GREAT SCIENCE FICTION BY SCIENTISTS CONKLIN, GEOFF   AN
  NINE BILLION NAMES OF GOD, THE CLARKE, ARTHUR C.   AC
  SCIENCE FICTION   BRODKIN & PEARSON   AN
  TALES OF TEN WORLDS   CLARKE, ARTHUR C.   AC
  UNTRAVELLED WORLDS   BARTER & WILSON   AN
SUMMONS, THE   EVANS, DON   SS   UNK 39 06
  FROM UNKNOWN WORLDS   CAMPBELL, JOHN W. JR AN
SUN   FILER, BURT K.   SS   NEW 71 AN
  POCKETFUL OF STARS, A   KNIGHT, DAMON   AN
SUN AND FOREST   ERNST, MAX   IL
  SCIENCE FICTION   BRODKIN & PEARSON   AN
SUN AND SHADOW   BRADBURY, RAY   SS   REP 53 03
  *GOLDEN APPLES OF THE SUN BRADBURY, RAY   AC
  VINTAGE BRADBURY, THE   BRADBURY, RAY   AC
SUN INVISIBLE, A   ANDERSON, POUL   NV   ASF 66 04
  TROUBLE TWISTERS, THE   ANDERSON, POUL   AC
SUN MAKER, THE   WILLIAMSON, JACK NV   TWS 40 06
  GIANT ANTHOLOGY OF SCIENCE FICTION MARGULIES & FRIEND AN
  RACE TO THE STARS   MARGULIES & FRIEND   AN
SUN PUSH   HALL, GRAHAM M.   SS   NWS 67 01
  ENGLAND SWINGS SF   MERRIL, JUDITH   AN
  SPACE-TIME JOURNAL, THE   MERRIL, JUDITH   AN
SUN SPOT   CLEMENT, HAL   SS   ASF 60 11
  SMALL CHANGES   CLEMENT, HAL   AC
SUN UP   JACKSON, A. A., IV SS   C
  AND WALDROP, HOWARD   76
  FASTER THAN LIGHT   DANN & ZEBROWSKI   OA
SUN'S TEARS, THE   STABLEFORD, BRIAN M. SS AMZ 74 10
  1975 ANNUAL WORLD'S BEST SF, THE WOLLHEIM, DONALD A. AN
SUNBURST   THORP, RODERICK   SS   ORB 70 06
  ORBIT 6   KNIGHT, DAMON   OA

SUNDANCE   SILVERBERG, ROBERT   SS   FSF 69 06
  ALIENS, THE   SILVERBERG, ROBERT   AN
  BEST FROM FANTASY AND SCIENCE FICTION: 19
                                FERMAN, EDWARD L.   AN
  BEST OF ROBERT SILVERBERG, THE SILVERBERG, ROBERT   AC
  BEYOND TOMORROW   HARDING, LEE   AN
  CUBE ROOT OF UNCERTAINTY, THE SILVERBERG, ROBERT   AC
  ON OUR WAY TO THE FUTURE   CARR, TERRY   AN
  SPECTRUM OF WORLDS, A   CLARESON, THOMAS D.   AN
  SPECULATIONS   SANDERS, THOMAS E.   AN
  SUNDANCE AND OTHER SCIENCE FICTION STORIES
                                SILVERBERG, ROBERT   AC
  THOSE WHO CAN: A SCIENCE FICTION READER WILSON, ROBIN SCOTT AN
  TOMORROW, AND TOMORROW, AND TOMORROW... HEINTZ/HERBERT/JOOS/ AN
SUNDOWN   REDD, DAVID   NV   FSF 67 12
  BEST FROM FANTASY AND SCIENCE FICTION: 18
                                FERMAN, EDWARD L.   AN
  THIS SIDE OF INFINITY   CARR, TERRY   AN
SUNFIRE¡   HAMILTON, EDMOND   SS   AMZ 62 09
  BEST OF AMAZING, THE   ROSS, JOSEPH   AN
  WHAT'S IT LIKE OUT THERE? AND OTHER STORIES
                                HAMILTON, EDMOND   AC
SUNFLOWER   GOULART, RON   NV   FSF 70 12
  CHAMELEON CORPS & OTHER SHAPE CHANGERS, THE
                                GOULART, RON   AC
SUNJAMMER   ANDERSON, POUL   NV   ASF 64 04
  ANALOG 4   CAMPBELL, JOHN W. JR   AN
  TALES OF THE FLYING MOUNTAINS ANDERSON, POUL   AC
SUNJAMMER (ALSO AS THE WIND FROM THE SUN)
                             CLARKE, ARTHUR C.   SS   BLF 64
  ANDROIDS, TIME MACHINES AND BLUE GIRAFFES
                                ELWOOD & GHIDALIA   AN
  BEST OF ARTHUR C. CLARKE: 1937-1971, THE CLARKE, ARTHUR C. AC
  INFINITE ARENA, THE   CARR, TERRY   AN
  STORIES FROM SCIENCE FICTION DOHERTY, G. D.   AN
  VISIONS OF TOMORROW   ELWOOD, ROGER   AN
  WILDERNESS OF STARS, A   NOLAN, WILLIAM F.   AN
  WORLD'S BEST SCIENCE FICTION: 1966 WOLLHEIM & CARR   AN
  WORLDS OF WONDER   HARRISON, HARRY   AN
SUNKEN LAND, THE   LEIBER, FRITZ   SS   UNK 42 02
  NIGHT'S BLACK AGENTS   LEIBER, FRITZ   AC
SUNKEN UNIVERSE (AS ARTHUR MERLYN, SEE ALSO SURFACE TENSION)
                             BLISH, JAMES   NV   SSS 42 05
  WORLDS TO COME   KNIGHT, DAMON   AN
SUNLESS WORLD, THE   JONES, NEIL R.   NV   AMZ 34 12
  SUNLESS WORLD, THE   JONES, NEIL R.   AC
SUNOUT   WILLIAMS, ERIC C.   NV   NWR 65 05
  NEW WRITINGS IN SF. 5   CARNELL, JOHN   OA
SUNRISE ON MERCURY   SILVERBERG, ROBERT   SS   SFS 57 05
  FIRST STEP OUTWARD   HOSKINS, ROBERT   AN
  MORE ADVENTURES ON OTHER PLANETS WOLLHEIM, DONALD A. AN
  PARSECS AND PARABLES   SILVERBERG, ROBERT   AC
  SUNRISE ON MERCURY AND OTHER SCIENCE FICTION STORIES
                                SILVERBERG, ROBERT   OA
  TOMORROW'S WORLDS   SILVERBERG, ROBERT   AN
  TOMORROW, AND TOMORROW, AND TOMORROW... HEINTZ/HERBERT/JOOS/ AN
SUNSET HARP, THE (THE SHORELINE AT SUNSET)
                             BRADBURY, RAY   SS   FSF 59 03
  DAY IT RAINED FOREVER, THE   BRADBURY, RAY   AC
SUNSET PERSPECTIVE, THE   MOORCOCK, MICHAEL   SS   71
  LIVES AND TIMES OF JERRY CORNELIUS, THE MOORCOCK, MICHAEL AC
SUNSET, 2217 AD, THE (TRANSLATED BY TETSU YANO AND
  JUDITH MERRIL)   MITSUSE, RYU   NV
  BEST SCIENCE FICTION FOR 1972 POHL, FREDERIK   AN
SUNWARD   COBLENTZ, STANTON A. SS TWS 40 04
  FLIGHT INTO SPACE   WOLLHEIM, DONALD A.   AN
SUPER-NEUTRON   ASIMOV, ISAAC   SS   AST 41 09
  EARLY ASIMOV, THE   ASIMOV, ISAAC   AC
SUPER-TOYS LAST ALL SUMMER LONG
                             ALDISS, BRIAN W.   SS   HBZ 69 12
  MOMENT OF ECLIPSE, THE   ALDISS, BRIAN W.   AC
SUPERCITY   ALDISS, BRIAN W.   SS   NWS 65 07
  SPACE, TIME AND NATHANIEL   ALDISS, BRIAN W.   AC
SUPERIOR SEX, THE   DEFORD, MIRIAM ALLEN SS FSF 68 04
  XENOGENESIS   DEFORD, MIRIAM ALLEN AC
SUPERIORITY   CLARKE, ARTHUR C.   SS   FSF 51 08
  ACROSS THE SEA OF STARS   CLARKE, ARTHUR C.   AC
  EXPEDITION TO EARTH   CLARKE, ARTHUR C.   AC
  FANTASIA MATHEMATICA   FADIMAN, CLIFTON   AN
  NINE BILLION NAMES OF GOD, THE CLARKE, ARTHUR C.   AC
  POLITICAL SCIENCE FICTION   GREENBERG& WARRICK   AN
  *WORLDS OF TOMORROW   DERLETH, AUGUST   AN
SUPERLATIVE DEGREE, THE   CALKINS, ERNEST ELMO PM SRV 59 05
  MATHEMATICAL MAGPIE, THE   FADIMAN, CLIFTON   AN
SUPERNOVA (SEE DAY OF BURNING) ANDERSON, POUL   TC
SUPERNUMERARY CORPSE, THE   SMITH, CLARK ASHTON   SS   WRT 32 11
  OTHER DIMENSIONS   SMITH, CLARK ASHTON   AC
SUPERSTITION   DEL REY, LESTER   NV   ASF 54 08
  GODS AND GOLEMS   DEL REY, LESTER   AC
SUPPLIANT IN SPACE, A   SHECKLEY, ROBERT   NV   GAL 73 11
  BEST FROM GALAXY, THE VOLUME II GALAXY, EDITORS OF   AN
  1974 ANNUAL WORLD'S BEST SF, THE WOLLHEIM, DONALD A. AN
SUPREMACY OF URUGUAY, THE   WHITE, E. B.   SS   NYM 33 11
  ECO-FICTION   STADLER, JOHN   AN
  TIMELESS STORIES FOR TODAY AND TOMORROW BRADBURY, RAY AN
SURFACE IF YOU CAN   CHAMPAGNE, TERRY   SS   NWS 69 07
  NEW TOMORROWS, THE   SPINRAD, NORMAN   AN
SURFACE TENSION   BLISH, JAMES   NA   GAL 52 08
  *BEST SCIENCE FICTION STORIES OF JAMES BLISH
                                BLISH, JAMES   AC
  BUG-EYED MONSTERS   CHEETHAM, ANTHONY   AN
  SCIENCE FICTION HALL OF FAME VOLUME 1 SILVERBERG, ROBERT AN
  SECOND GALAXY READER OF SCIENCE FICTION GOLD, H. L.   AN
  WHERE DO WE GO FROM HERE?   ASIMOV, ISAAC   AN
  WONDERMAKERS   HOSKINS, ROBERT   AN
  YEAR'S BEST SCIENCE FICTION NOVELS: 1953 BLEILER & DIKTY AN

6 GREAT SHORT NOVELS OF SCIENCE FICTION CONKLIN, GROFF   AN
SURFACE TENSION (COMBINED WITH "SUNKEN UNIVERSE", SSS 42.05)
                             BLISH, JAMES   NA   GAL 52 08
  SEEDLING STARS, THE   BLISH, JAMES   NO
SURPRISE¡   BRADFORD, RONALD   SS   62
  FIEND IN YOU, THE   BEAUMONT, CHARLES   AN
SURVIVAL   COFFIN, CARLYN   PM   FSF 55 06
  BEST FROM FANTASY AND SCIENCE FICTION: 5
                                BOUCHER, ANTHONY   AN
SURVIVAL   WYNDHAM, JOHN   NV   TWS 52 02
  BEST SCIENCE-FICTION STORIES: 1953, THE BLEILER & DIKTY AN
  FRONTIERS IN SPACE   BLEILER & DIKTY   AN
  *NO PLACE LIKE EARTH   CARNELL, JOHN   AN
  SEEDS OF TIME, THE   WYNDHAM, JOHN   AC
SURVIVAL DEMANDS   TUBB, E. C.   SS   NWS 60 02
  SCATTER OF STARDUST, A   TUBB, E. C.   DC
SURVIVAL KIT   POHL, FREDERIK   NV   GAL 57 05
  FREDERIK POHL OMNIBUS, THE   POHL, FREDERIK   AC
  TOMORROW TIMES SEVEN   POHL, FREDERIK   AC
SURVIVAL OF THE FITTEST   TAYLOR, JOHN   PL
  BEYOND THIS HORIZON   CARRELL, CHRISTOPHER OA
SURVIVAL ON A PRIMATIVE PLANET TOFTE, ARTHUR   NV
  SURVIVAL FROM INFINITY   ELWOOD, ROGER   OA
SURVIVAL PACKAGES   BUNCH, DAVID R.   SS   FAN 63 04
  MODERAN   BUNCH, DAVID R.   AC
SURVIVAL PLANET   HARRISON, HARRY   SS   FSF 61 08
  WAR WITH THE ROBOTS   HARRISON, HARRY   AC
SURVIVAL POLICY (AS EDWIN JAMES)
                             GUNN, JAMES E.   NV   ASF 52 10
  FUTURE IMPERFECT   GUNN, JAMES E.   AC
SURVIVAL PROBLEMS   NEVILLE, KRIS   SS   UNI 74 05
  UNIVERSE 5   CARR, TERRY   OA
SURVIVAL SHIP   MERRIL, JUDITH   SS   WBY 51 01
  ANTHROPOLOGY THROUGH SCIENCE FICTION MASON, C/GREENBERG/& AN
  SURVIVAL SHIP AND OTHER STORIES MERRIL, JUDITH   AC
  TOMORROW, THE STARS   HEINLEIN, ROBERT A.   AN
  TRANSFORMATIONS   ROSELLE, DANIEL   AN
  YOU AND SCIENCE FICTION   HOLLISTER, BERNARD C AN
SURVIVAL U: PROSPECTUS FOR A REALLY RELEVANT UNIVERSITY
                             FISCHER, JOHN   AR   HRP 69 09
  LOOKING AHEAD   ALLEN, D. & L.   AN
SURVIVAL, A.D. 2000   REYNOLDS, MACK   SS
  SURVIVAL FROM INFINITY   ELWOOD, ROGER   OA
SURVIVOR   REYNOLDS, MACK   SS   ASF 66 07
  BEST OF MACK REYNOLDS, THE   REYNOLDS, MACK   AC
SURVIVOR NO. 1 (THE MAN WITH THE GREEN NOSE)
                             ELLISON, HARLAN
  AND SLESAR, HENRY   SS C KNV 59 09
  PARTNERS IN WONDER   ELLISON, HARLAN   AC
SURVIVOR, THE   MOUDY, WALTER F.   NV   AMZ 65 05
  POLITICAL SCIENCE FICTION   GREENBERG& WARRICK   AN
  THEMES IN SCIENCE FICTION   KELLEY, LEO P.   AN
  11TH ANNUAL OF THE YEAR'S BEST S-F, THE MERRIL, JUDITH AN
SURVIVOR, THE   DERLETH, AUGUST
  AND LOVECRAFT, H. P.   NV C WRT 54 07
  SURVIVOR AND OTHER STORIES, THE LOVECRAFT & DERLETH AC
SURVIVOR, THE (JAMES SCHERMER) FOSTER, ALAN DEAN   SA   SLG 74 02
  STAR TREK LOG TWO   FOSTER, ALAN DEAN   OC
SUSAN   BEVAN, ALISTAIR   SS   SCF 65 04
  11TH ANNUAL OF THE YEAR'S BEST S-F, THE MERRIL, JUDITH AN
SUSCEPTIBILITY   MACDONALD, JOHN D.   SS   GAL 51 01
  *GALAXY READER OF SCIENCE FICTION GOLD, H. L.   AN
SUSIE'S REALITY   STICKGOLD, BOB   NV   IFS 73 06
  BEST FROM IF, THE VOLUME II IF, EDITORS OF   AN
  INTRODUCTORY PSYCHOLOGY THROUGH SCIENCE FICTION
                                KATZ/WARRICK/&   AN
SWAMP WAS UPSIDE DOWN, THE   LEINSTER, MURRAY   NV   ASF 56 05
  COLONIAL SURVEY   LEINSTER, MURRAY   NO
SWAN, THE   BRADBURY, RAY   SS   CMP 54 09
  DANDELION WINE   BRADBURY, RAY   NO
SWAP   GOULART, RON   SS   IFS 70 04
  NUTZENBOLTS   GOULART, RON   AC
SWAP, THE   HEARD, H. F.   SS   44
  GREAT FOG AND OTHER WEIRD TALES, THE HEARD, H. F.   OC
  SUPERNATURAL READER, THE   CONKLIN, G&L.   AN
SWASTIKA SET-UP, THE   MOORCOCK, MICHAEL   NV   72
  LIVES AND TIMES OF JERRY CORNELIUS, THE MOORCOCK, MICHAEL AC
SWASTIKA¡   ALDISS, BRIAN W.   SS   NOV 70 01
  BEST SCIENCE FICTION STORIES OF BRIAN W. ALDISS (REVISED)
                                ALDISS, BRIAN W.   AC
  MOMENT OF ECLIPSE, THE   ALDISS, BRIAN W.   AC
  *NOVA 1   HARRISON, HARRY   OA
SWEEPER OF LORAY, THE   SHECKLEY, ROBERT   SS   GAL 59 04
  SHARDS OF SPACE   SHECKLEY, ROBERT   AC
SWEET DREAMS, MELISSA   GOLDIN, STEPHEN   SS   GAL 68 12
  BEST SF: 1968   HARRISON & ALDISS   AN
  ELEVENTH GALAXY READER, THE POHL, FREDERIK   AN
SWEET HELEN   RUNYON, CHARLES W.   SS   FSF 69 09
  TWENTY YEARS OF FANTASY & SCIENCE FICTION
                                FERMAN & MILLS   AN
SWEET SISTER, GREEN BROTHER VAN SCYOC, SYDNEY J. NA GAL 73 12
  BEST FROM GALAXY, THE VOLUME III BAEN, JAMES   AN
SWEET SIXTEEN   BLOCH, ROBERT   SS
  NIGHTMARES   BLOCH, ROBERT   AC
  PLEASANT DREAMS   BLOCH, ROBERT   AC
SWEETHEART PRIMEVAL   BURROUGHS, EDGAR R.   NO   ASC 15 01
  ETERNAL LOVER, THE   BURROUGHS, EDGAR R.   AC
SWEETS TO THE SWEET   BLOCH, ROBERT   SS   WRT 47 03
  ALONE BY NIGHT   CONGDON, MICHAEL&DON AN
  MORE LITTLE MONSTERS   ELWOOD & GHIDALIA   AN
  PLEASANT DREAMS   BLOCH, ROBERT   AC
  YOURS TRULY, JACK THE RIPPER BLOCH, ROBERT   AC
SWEETWATER FACTOR, THE   KEAMY, TOM   SS
  LONE STAR UNIVERSE   PROCTOR & UTLEY   OA
SWENSON, DISPATCHER   MILLER, R. DEWITT   NV   GAL 56 04

BEST SCIENCE FICTION STORIES AND NOVELS: 1956
                                  DIKTY, T. E.   AN
SWEPT AND GARNISHED   HENDERSON, ZENNA   SS   NEW 71 AC
HOLDING WONDER   HENDERSON, ZENNA   AC
SWIFT PEOPLE, THE   WELLS, BASIL   SS   FUT 43 02
PLANETS OF ADVENTURE   WELLS, BASIL   AC
SWISS PEASANT, THE   SHELLEY, MARY W.   NV   KPS 31
TALES AND STORIES   SHELLEY, MARY W.   AC
SWORD AND SCEPTRE   POURNELLE, JERRY   NA   ASF 73 05
MERCENARY, THE   POURNELLE, JERRY   NO
SWORD GAME   HOLLIS, H. H.   SS   GAL 68 04
NEBULA AWARD STORIES NO. 4   ANDERSON, POUL   AN
TOMORROW, AND TOMORROW, AND TOMORROW... HEINTZ/HERBERT/JOOS/ AN
WORLD'S BEST SCIENCE FICTION: 1969 WOLLHEIM & CARR   AN
SWORD OF FLOWERS   JANIFER, LAURENCE M. SS   FAN 62 08
IMPOSSIBLE?   JANIFER, LAURENCE M. AC
SWORD OF LAERTES, THE   RUSSELL, RAY   SS   59
SARDONICUS AND OTHER STORIES   RUSSELL, RAY   AC
SWORD OF PEACE (SEE PEACEBRINGER)
MOORE, WARD   TC
SWORD OF RHIANNON, THE (SEA-KINGS OF MARS)
                        BRACKETT, LEIGH   EX   TWS 49 06
SPACE OPERA   ALDISS, BRIAN W.   AN
SWORD OF TOMORROW   KUTTNER, HENRY   NV   TWS 45 FL
GIANT ANTHOLOGY OF SCIENCE FICTION MARGULIES & FRIEND   AN
SWORD SWALLOWER, THE   GOULART, RON   NV   FSF 67 11
WORLD'S BEST SCIENCE FICTION: 1968 WOLLHEIM & CARR   AN
SWORDS OF IFTHAN   SUTHERLAND, JAMES   SS   OMG 73
OMEGA   ELWOOD, ROGER   OA
SWORDSMAN OF LOST TERRA ANDERSON, POUL   NA   PLS 51 11
SWORDSMEN IN THE SKY   WOLLHEIM, DONALD A. AN
SWORDSMAN OF VARNIS, THE JACKSON, CLIVE   SS   OWS 50 09
*SCIENCE-FICTION CARNIVAL BROWN, F. & REYNOLDS AN
SYMBIOSIS   JENKINS, WILL F.   SS   COL 47 06
GREAT STORIES OF SCIENCE FICTION LEINSTER, MURRAY   AN
*OTHER SIDE OF THE MOON, THE   DERLETH, AUGUST   AN
STORIES OF SCIENTIFIC IMAGINATION GALLANT, JOSEPH   AN
SYMBIOSIS   LEINSTER, MURRAY   SS   COL 47 06
BEST OF MURRAY LEINSTER, THE   LEINSTER, MURRAY   AC
SYMBIOTE   CONEY, MICHAEL G.   NV   NWR 69 15
NEW WRITINGS IN SF. 9   CARNELL, JOHN   AN
NEW WRITINGS IN SF. 15   CARNELL, JOHN   OA
SYMBIOTICA   RUSSELL, ERIC FRANK NV   ASF 43 10
*ADVENTURES IN TIME AND SPACE   HEALY & MCCOMAS   AN
MEN, MARTIANS AND MACHINES   RUSSELL, ERIC FRANK AC
SYMBOLIC LOGIC OF MURDER, THE REESE, JOHN   SS   EQM 60 10
MATHEMATICAL MAGPIE, THE   FADIMAN, CLIFTON   AN
SYMPATHETIC SOUSE, THE   KERSH, GERALD   SS
ON AN ODD NOTE   KERSH, GERALD   AC
SYMPHONY NO. 6 IN C MINOR "THE TRAGIC"- BY LUDWIG VAN
BEETHOVEN II   JONES, LANGDON   FA   NWS 68 10
EYE OF THE LENS, THE   JONES, LANGDON   AC
SYMPOSIUM   LAFFERTY, R. A.   SS   OMG 73
OMEGA   ELWOOD, ROGER   OA
SYMPOSIUM OF THE GORGON SMITH, CLARK ASHTON SS   FUN 58 10
TALES OF SCIENCE AND SORCERY   SMITH, CLARK ASHTON AC
SYMPTOMATICUS MEDICUS   NOURSE, ALAN E.   SS   USF 54 09
RX FOR TOMORROW   NOURSE, ALAN E.   AC
SYN   STEVENS, JAMES   SS
TOMORROW TODAY   ZEBROWSKI, GEORGE   OA
SYNCHROMOCRACY   CAWOOD, HAP   SS   MOT 64
10TH ANNUAL OF THE YEAR'S BEST S-F, THE MERRIL, JUDITH   AN
SYNDROME JOHNNY   DYE, CHARLES   SS   GAL 51 07
*GALAXY READER OF SCIENCE FICTION GOLD, H. L.   AN
SYNDROME JOHNNY   MACLEAN, KATHERINE   SS   GAL 51 07
SF: AUTHORS' CHOICE   HARRISON, HARRY   AN
SYNTH   ROBERTS, KEITH   SS   NWR 66 08
MACHINES AND MEN   ROBERTS, KEITH   AC
NEW WRITINGS IN SF. 8   CARNELL, JOHN   OA
PASSING OF THE DRAGONS, THE   ROBERTS, KEITH   AC
SYSTEM   CAPEK, JOSEF
                        AND CAPEK, KAREL   SS   C   08
MASTERPIECES OF SCIENCE FICTION   MOSKOWITZ, SAM   AN
SYSTEM OF DOCTOR TARR & PROFESSOR FEATHER, THE (SEE THE
LUNATICS)   POE, EDGAR ALLEN   TC
T   ALDISS, BRIAN W.   SS   NEB 56 11
FIRST FLIGHT   KNIGHT, DAMON   AN
NO TIME LIKE TOMORROW   ALDISS, BRIAN W.   AC
SPACE, TIME AND NATHANIEL   ALDISS, BRIAN W.   AC
T'SAIS   VANCE, JACK   NV   50
DYING EARTH, THE   VANCE, JACK   OC
TA TA, THE (JINGLES)   SIME, SIDNEY H.
MATHEMATICAL MAGPIE, THE   FADIMAN, CLIFTON   AN
TA TA, THE (MUSIC)   HOLBROOKE, JOSEPH C.
MATHEMATICAL MAGPIE, THE   FADIMAN, CLIFTON   AN
TABLE OF COMPARISONS: EARTH AND MOON
                        MISC. MATERIAL   MS
GREAT SCIENCE FICTION STORIES ABOUT THE MOON
                        DIKTY, T. E.   AN
TABLEAU   WHITE, JAMES   NV   NWS 58 05
ALIENS AMONG US, THE   WHITE, JAMES   AC
BEST OF NEW WORLDS, THE   MOORCOCK, MICHAEL   AN
TABLETS OF STONE   HUFFORD, LIZ   SS   ORB 70 08
ORBIT 8   KNIGHT, DAMON   OA
TABOO   LEIBER, FRITZ   SS   ASF 44 02
JOURNEY TO INFINITY   GREENBERG, MARTIN   AN
TACAN FOR THE CHILDREN OF EARTH, A
                        BULYCHEV, KIRILL   SS   72
AIR OF MARS AND OTHER STORIES, THE GINSBURG, MIRRA   AN
TACHYPOMP, THE   MITCHELL, EDWARD P. SS   SCR 74 03
CRYSTAL MAN, THE   MITCHELL, EDWARD P. AC
FANTASIA MATHEMATICA   FADIMAN, CLIFTON   AN
TACTFUL SABOTEUR, THE   HERBERT, FRANK   NV   GAL 64 10
SEVEN TRIPS THROUGH TIME AND SPACE CONKLIN, GROFF   AN
WORLDS OF FRANK HERBERT, THE   HERBERT, FRANK   AC

TACTICS   BRYANT, EDWARD   SS   NEW 73 AC
AMONG THE DEAD   BRYANT, EDWARD   AC
TACTICS OF MISTAKE   DICKSON, GORDON R. NO   ASF 70 10
THREE TO DORSAI   DICKSON, GORDON R. AC
TAIL-TIED KINGS, THE   DAVIDSON, AVRAM   SS   GAL 62 04
SEVENTH GALAXY READER, THE   POHL, FREDERIK   AN
STRANGE SEAS AND SHORES   DAVIDSON, AVRAM   AC
TAILPIPE TO DISASTER   SHECKLEY, ROBERT   SS   FSF
"CAN YOU FEEL ANYTHING WHEN I DO THIS?, AND OTHER STORIES
                                  SHECKLEY, ROBERT   AC
TAIPAN, THE   MAUGHAM, W. SOMERSET SS   PRS 22 10
TRAVELERS IN TIME   STERN, PHILIP VAN D. AN
TAKE A DEEP BREATH   RUSSELL, RAY   SS   TIG 56
SARDONICUS AND OTHER STORIES   RUSSELL, RAY   AC
TAKE A DEEP BREATH   THORNE, ROGER   SS   TIG 56
SF:57, THE YEAR'S GREATEST SCIENCE FICTION AND FANTASY
                        MERRIL, JUDITH   AN
TAKE A DEEP BREATH (THE OTHER SIDE OF THE SKY)
                        CLARKE, ARTHUR C.   SS   INF 57 09
OTHER SIDE OF THE SKY, THE   CLARKE, ARTHUR C.   AC
TIME PROBE: THE SCIENCES IN SF.   CLARKE, ARTHUR C.   AN
TAKE A MATCH   ASIMOV, ISAAC   SS   NDM 72 02
BUY JUPITER AND OTHER STORIES   ASIMOV, ISAAC   AC
NEW DIMENSIONS 2   SILVERBERG, ROBERT   OA
TAKE A SEAT   RUSSELL, ERIC FRANK SS   STS 52 05
HUMAN?   MERRIL, JUDITH   AN
TAKE CARE OF JOEY   STURGEON, THEODORE SS   70
STURGEON IS ALIVE AND WELL...   STURGEON, THEODORE AC
TAKE IT OR LEAVE IT   MASSON, DAVID I.   SS   YRT 70
YEAR 2000, THE   HARRISON, HARRY   AN
TAKE MY DRUM TO ENGLAND- BOND, NELSON S.   SS   UNK 41 08
31ST OF FEBRUARY, THE   BOND, NELSON S.   AC
TAKE TWO QUIGGIES   NEVILLE, KRIS   NV   FSF 50 12
MISSION: MANSTOP   NEVILLE, KRIS   AC
TAKE WOODEN INDIANS   DAVIDSON, AVRAM   NV   GAL 59 06
FIFTH GALAXY READER, THE   GOLD, H. L.   AN
STRANGE SEAS AND SHORES   DAVIDSON, AVRAM   AC
TAKEOVER BID   BAXTER, JOHN   NV   NWR 65 05
BEYOND TOMORROW   HARDING, LEE   AN
NEW WRITINGS IN SF. 5   CARNELL, JOHN   OA
TALE OF A CHEMIST (1843) ANONYMOUS   SS
FAR BOUNDARIES   DERLETH, AUGUST   AN
TALE OF KING GNUFF, THE LEM, STANISLAW   SS   72
MORTAL ENGINES   LEM, STANISLAW   AC
TALE OF NEGATIVE GRAVITY, A STOCKTON, FRANK R. NV   CNY 84 11
*BEYOND TIME AND SPACE   DERLETH, AUGUST   AN
JOURNEYS IN SCIENCE FICTION   LOUGHLIN, RICHARD L. AN
SCIENCE FICTION OF FRANK R. STOCKTON, THE
                        STOCKTON, FRANK R.   AC
TALE OF SIR JOHN MAUNDEVILLE, A (THE KINGDOM OF THE WORM)
                        SMITH, CLARK ASHTON SS   FFN 33 10
OTHER DIMENSIONS   SMITH, CLARK ASHTON AC
TALE OF THE COMPUTER THAT FOUGHT A DRAGON
                        LEM, STANISLAW   SS   72
MORTAL ENGINES   LEM, STANISLAW   AC
TALE OF THE ENDING, A (AS HANK DEMPSEY)
                        HARRISON, HARRY   SS   ASF 70 06
ONE STEP FROM EARTH   HARRISON, HARRY   AC
TALE OF THE PASSIONS: OR, THE DEATH OF DESPINA, A
                        SHELLEY, MARY W.   NV   LIB 22 01
TALES AND STORIES   SHELLEY, MARY W.   AC
TALE OF THE RAGGED MOUNTAINS, A POE, EDGAR ALLEN   SS   GDY 44 04
*BEST OF SCIENCE FICTION   CONKLIN, GROFF   AN
FUTURE PERFECT   FRANKLIN, H. BRUCE   AN
TALE OF THE THIRTEENTH FLOOR, A
                        NASH, OGDEN   PM   FSF 55 07
DECADE OF FANTASY AND SCIENCE FICTION, A MILLS, ROBERT P. AN
TALE OF THE THREE STORYTELLING MACHINES OF KING GENIUS
                        LEM, STANISLAW   NA
CYBERIAD, THE   LEM, STANISLAW   OC
TALENT   BLOCH, ROBERT   SS   IFS 60 07
ATOMS AND EVIL   BLOCH, ROBERT   AC
BEST SCIENCE FICTION FROM IF, THE POHL, FREDERIK   AN
ODDBALLS, THE   GHIDALIA, VIC   AN
TALENT   STURGEON, THEODORE   SS   BEY 53 09
BEYOND   ANONYMOUS   AN
FIFTY SHORT SCIENCE FICTION TALES ASIMOV & CONKLIN   AN
ZACHERLEY'S MIDNIGHT SNACKS   ZACHERLEY   AN
TALENT OF HARVEY, THE   FAST, HOWARD   NV
TOUCH OF INFINITY, A   FAST, HOWARD   OC
TALENT SPOTTER   BOUNDS, SYDNEY J.   SS   NWR 75 25
NEW WRITINGS IN SF. 25   BULMER, KENNETH   OA
TALES OF THE DISTANT PAST PODOLNY, ROMAN   SS
RUSSIAN SCIENCE FICTION, 1968   MAGIDOFF, ROBERT   AN
TALKAROUND, THE   KARL, JEAN E.   SS
TURNING PLACE, THE   KARL, JEAN E.   OC
TALKING STONE, THE   ASIMOV, ISAAC   SS   FSF 55 10
ASIMOV'S MYSTERIES   ASIMOV, ISAAC   AC
SPACE, TIME & CRIME   DEFORD, MIRIAM ALLEN AN
TALKING, THE   BARRETT, NEAL JR.   SS
LONE STAR UNIVERSE   PROCTOR & UTLEY   OA
TALLIEN THREE (THE HATE DISEASE)
                        LEINSTER, MURRAY   NV   ASF 63 08
DOCTOR TO THE STARS   LEINSTER, MURRAY   AC
TANAR OF PELLUCIDAR   BURROUGHS, EDGAR R. NO   BBM 29 03
THREE SCIENCE FICTION NOVELS   BURROUGHS, EDGAR R. AC
TANGLE HOLD   WALLACE, F. L.   NA   GAL 53 06
5 GALAXY SHORT NOVELS   GOLD, H. L.   AN
TANGLED WEB   HARGREAVES, H. A.   NV   NWR 73 21
NEW WRITINGS IN SF. 21   CARNELL, JOHN   OA
TANGLED WEB, THE (THE STAR HYACINTHS)
                        SCHMITZ, JAMES H.   SS   AMZ 61 12
NICE DAY FOR SCREAMING, AND OTHER TALES OF THE HUB
                        SCHMITZ, JAMES H.   AC

TANK TRAPEZE, THE   MOORCOCK, MICHAEL   SS   NWS 69 01
  BEST SF STORIES FROM NEW WORLDS 7   MOORCOCK, MICHAEL   AN
  LIVES AND TIMES OF JERRY CORNELIUS, THE MOORCOCK, MICHAEL   AC
  SF: AUTHORS' CHOICE 3   HARRISON, HARRY   AN
TAPPING OUT   MALZBERG, BARRY N.   SS   FUQ 73
  BEST OF BARRY N. MALZBERG, THE   MALZBERG, BARRY N.   AC
  FUTURE QUEST   ELWOOD, ROGER   OA
TARFU'S LAST SHOW   BOSTON, BRUCE   SS
  FUTURE PASTIMES   EDELSTEIN, SCOTT   OA
TARGET GENERATION   SIMAK, CLIFFORD D.   NV
  *STRANGERS IN THE UNIVERSE   SIMAK, CLIFFORD D.   AC
TARGET ONE   POHL, FREDERIK   SS   GAL 55 04
  ALTERNATING CURRENTS   POHL, FREDERIK   AC
TARGET: BERLIN| EFFINGER, GEO. ALEC   NV   NDM 76 06
  NEW DIMENSIONS 6   SILVERBERG, ROBERT   OA
TARRYING   SCORTIA, THOMAS N.   SS   FTP 73
  FLAME TREE PLANET   ELWOOD, ROGER   OA
TARTARUS OF MAIDS, THE   MELVILLE, HERMAN   SS
  IN DREAMS AWAKE   FIEDLER, LESLIE A.   AN
  SPECULATIONS   SANDERS, THOMAS E.   AN
TARZAN AND THE GOLDEN LOIN ACKERMAN, FORREST J. SS   48
  SCIENCE FICTION WORLDS OF FORREST J. ACKERMAN & FRIENDS
                                      ACKERMAN, FORREST J.   AC
TARZAN LIVES (SEE AN EXCLUSIVE INTERVIEW WITH LORD GREYSTOKE)
                            FARMER, PHILIP JOSE   TC
TASTE FOR DOSTOEVSKY, A   ALDISS, BRIAN W.   SS   NWR 67 10
  NEW WRITINGS IN SF. 10   CARNELL, JOHN   OA
  ON OUR WAY TO THE FUTURE   CARR, TERRY   AN
TASTE OF ARMAGEDDON, A (R. HAMNER & G. L. COON)
                            BLISH, JAMES   SA   STK 68 02
  STAR TREK   2   BLISH, JAMES   OC
TASTE OF AUNT SOPHRONIA, THE HENDERSON, ZENNA   SS   NEW 71 AC
  HOLDING WONDER   HENDERSON, ZENNA   AC
TASTE OF FEAR, THE   FOSTER, HUGH G.   SS   PBY 59 09
  PLAYBOY BOOK OF HORROR AND THE SUPERNATURAL, THE
                                      PLAYBOY, EDITORS OF   AN
  WEIRD SHOW   PLAYBOY, EDITORS OF   AN
TASTE OF YOUR LOVE, THE   BERTIN, EDDY C.   SS   71
  YEAR'S BEST HORROR STORIES: SERIES III, THE
                                      DAVIS, RICHARD   AN
TAXPAYER, THE   BRADBURY, RAY   SS   NEW 51 AC
  MARTIAN CHRONICLES, THE   BRADBURY, RAY   AC
TEA IN A SPACE-SHIP   KIRKUP, JAMES   PM
  STARLIT CORRIDOR, THE   MANSFIELD, ROGER   AN
TEA TRAY IN THE SKY   SMITH, EVELYN E.   SS   GAL 52 09
  GALAXY SCIENCE FICTION OMNIBUS   GOLD, H. L.   AN
  SECOND GALAXY READER OF SCIENCE FICTION GOLD, H. L.   AN
TEACHER FROM MARS, THE   BINDER, EANDO   SS   TWS 41 02
  *MY BEST SCIENCE FICTION STORY   MARGULIES & FRIEND   AN
TEACHER, THE   SIDNEY, KATHLEEN M.   SS   ORB 76 18
  ORBIT 18   KNIGHT, DAMON   OA
TEACHING PRIME   KELLEY, LEO P.   SS   INY 72 03
  INFINITY 3   HOSKINS, ROBERT   OA
  SCHOOL AND SOCIETY THROUGH SCIENCE FICTION
                                      OLANDER/GREENBERG/&   AN
TEAMWORK   YORE, MARY JANE   SS
  ADRIFT IN SPACE AND OTHER STORIES   ELWOOD, ROGER   OA
TEARDROP, THE   OLMSTEAD, DVORA   SS   CLR 73 03
  CLARION III   WILSON, ROBIN SCOTT   OA
TEARS OF THE MADONNA   BEAUMONT, CHARLES   SS   NEW 57 AC
  HUNGER AND OTHER STORIES, THE   BEAUMONT, CHARLES   AC
TECHNICAL ADVISOR   OLIVER, CHAD   SS   FSF 53 02
  CROSSROADS IN TIME   CONKLIN, GROFF   AN
TECHNICAL ERROR   CLEMENT, HAL   NV   ASF 44 01
  NATIVES OF SPACE   CLEMENT, HAL   AC
TECHNICAL ERROR (THE REVERSED MAN)
                            CLARKE, ARTHUR C.   SS   FSB 46 12
  ACROSS THE SEA OF STARS   CLARKE, ARTHUR C.   AC
  REACH FOR TOMORROW   CLARKE, ARTHUR C.   AC
TECHNICAL SLIP (ARS 49 WI) BEYNON, JOHN   SS   IMG 50 12
  OPERATION FUTURE   CONKLIN, GROFF   AN
TECHNICAL SLIP (ARS 49 WI) WYNDHAM, JOHN   SS   IMG 50 12
  INTO THE UNKNOWN   CARR, TERRY   AN
  JIZZLE   WYNDHAM, JOHN   AC
TECHNICALITY   SPINRAD, NORMAN   SS   ASF 66 08
  LAST HURRAH OF THE GOLDEN HORDE, THE SPINRAD, NORMAN   AC
TECHNOLOGICAL FOLK HERO: HAS HE A FUTURE?, THE
                            BRUNNER, JOHN   AR   FLK 72 05
  BOOK OF JOHN BRUNNER, THE   BRUNNER, JOHN   AC
TECHNOLOGICAL RETREAT   EDMONDSON, G. C.   SS   FSF 56 05
  13 GREAT STORIES OF SCIENCE FICTION CONKLIN, GROFF   AN
TECHNOLOGICAL REVOLUTION, THE GUNN, JAMES E.   SS   INY 71 02
  INFINITY 2   HOSKINS, ROBERT   OA
TEDDI   NORTON, ANDRE   NV
  SCIENCE FICTION ADVENTURES FROM WAY OUT ELWOOD, ROGER   OA
TEDDY BEAR   GUNN, JAMES E.   SS   WOF 70 02
  BREAKING POINT   GUNN, JAMES E.   AC
TEDDY|CRAZY||SHOW|||, |||THE|| ELLISON, HARLAN   NV   ADM 68 10
  OVER THE EDGE   ELLISON, HARLAN   AC
TEDDYSAURS, THE   HAMILTON-PATTERSON,J SS   SPC 73 01
  SPACE   1   DAVIS, RICHARD   OA
TEDRIC   SMITH, EDWARD E. PHD SS   OWS 53 03
  BEST OF E. E. 'DOC' SMITH, THE   SMITH, EDWARD E. PHD   AC
TEETH   ROONEY, GRACE   SS   ORB 74 13
  ORBIT 13   KNIGHT, DAMON   OA
TEETH OF DESPAIR, THE   DAVIDSON, AVRAM
                            AND KLEIN, SIDNEY   SS C FSF 61 05
  SCIENCE FICTION ODDITIES   CONKLIN, GROFF   AN
  WHAT STRANGE STARS AND SKIES   DAVIDSON, AVRAM   AC
TEETHING RING   CAUSEY, JAMES   SS   GAL 53 01
  FIFTY SHORT SCIENCE FICTION TALES   ASIMOV & CONKLIN   AN
  SECOND GALAXY READER OF SCIENCE FICTION GOLD, H. L.   AN
TELEIDOSCOPE   BRYANT, EDWARD   SS   NEW 73 AC
  AMONG THE DEAD   BRYANT, EDWARD   AC
TELEK   VANCE, JACK   SN   ASF 52 01
  EIGHT FANTASMS AND MAGICS   VANCE, JACK   AC

GREAT SHORT NOVELS OF SCIENCE FICTION   SILVERBERG, ROBERT   AN
TELEMART THREE   SHAW, BOB   SS   IFS 70 03
  TOMORROW LIES IN AMBUSH   SHAW, BOB   AC
TELEPATHOS   CAIN, RONALD   NV   SFE 74 01
  SCIENCE FICTION EMPHASIS NO. 1   GERROLD, DAVID   OA
TELEPROBE   EISENSTEIN, PHYLLIS   SS
  LONG NIGHT OF WAITING AND OTHER STORIES ELWOOD, ROGER   OA
TELESTASSIS   PEASE, M. C.   SS   SFS 55 05
  NOW & BEYOND   HOWARD, IVAN   AN
TELL ME ALL ABOUT YOURSELF BUSBY, F. M.   SS   NDM 73 03
  BEST SCIENCE FICTION OF THE YEAR, THE NO. 3
                                      CARR, TERRY   AN
  NEW DIMENSIONS 3   SILVERBERG, ROBERT   OA
TELL THE TRUTH   TUBB, E. C.   SS   ASF 59 12
  TEN FROM TOMORROW   TUBB, E. C.   AC
TELL YOUR FORTUNE   BLOCH, ROBERT   SS   WRT 50 05
  LIVING DEMONS, THE   BLOCH, ROBERT   AC
TELL-TALE HEART, THE   POE, EDGAR ALLEN   SS   POI 43 01
  *TWISTED   CONKLIN, GROFF   AN
TELZEY TOY, THE   SCHMITZ, JAMES H.   NV   ASF 71 01
  TELZEY TOY, THE   SCHMITZ, JAMES H.   NO
TEMIRA   LARIONOVA, OLGA   NV   71
  AIR OF MARS AND OTHER STORIES, THE GINSBURG, MIRRA   AN
TEMPERATURE OF GEHENNA SUE, THE
                            WRIGHT, S. FOWLER   SS
  THRONE OF SATURN, THE   WRIGHT, S. FOWLER   AC
  WITCHFINDER, THE   WRIGHT, S. FOWLER   AC
TEMPLE OF DESPAIR   PEASE, M. C.   NV   DSF 53 10
  ESCAPE TO EARTH   HOWARD, IVAN   AN
TEMPOLLUTERS, THE   EDMONDSON, G. C.   SS   INY 72 04
  INFINITY 4   HOSKINS, ROBERT   OA
TEMPORAL TRANSGRESSOR, THE (BRIDGEHEAD)
                            LONG, FRANK BELKNAP   NV   ASF 44 08
  ULTIMATE INVADER, AND OTHER SCIENCE FICTION, THE
                                      WOLLHEIM, DONALD A.   DA
TEMPTATION OF HARRINGAY, THE WELLS, H. G.   SS   SJG 95 02
  HUMAN?   MERRIL, JUDITH   AN
  SHORT STORIES OF H. G. WELLS, THE   WELLS, H. G.   AC
  STOLEN BACILLUS AND OTHER INCIDENTS, THE WELLS, H. G.   AC
TEN HOURS HUNTING   VERNE, JULES   SS
  YESTERDAY AND TOMORROW   VERNE, JULES   AC
TEN PERCENTER   BROWN, FREDRIC   SS
  PARADOX LOST, AND 12 OTHER GREAT S.F. STORIES
                                      BROWN, FREDRIC   AC
TEN YEARS AGO...   BEERBOHM, MAX   SS   72
  BEST SF: 1973   HARRISON & ALDISS   AN
TEN YEARS OF NEBULA AWARDS DICKSON, GORDON R.   AR   NEW 75 AN
  NEBULA AWARD STORIES 10   GUNN, JAMES E.   AN
TEN-STORY JIGSAW   ALDISS, BRIAN W.   SS   NEB 58 01
  SF:59, THE YEAR'S GREATEST SCIENCE FICTION AND FANTASY
                                      MERRIL, JUDITH   AN
TENANT, THE   DERLETH, AUGUST   SS   WRT 28 03
  NOT LONG FOR THIS WORLD   DERLETH, AUGUST   AC
TENANTS, THE   TENN, WILLIAM   SS   FSF 54 04
  OF ALL POSSIBLE WORLDS   TENN, WILLIAM   AC
TENDING TO INFINITY   SYNGE, J. L.   PM   57
  MATHEMATICAL MAGPIE, THE   FADIMAN, CLIFTON   AN
TENNYSON EFFECT, THE   HALL, GRAHAM M.   SS   NWS 66 11
  BEST SF STORIES FROM NEW WORLDS 5   MOORCOCK, MICHAEL   AN
TENTH WORLD, THE   CAMPBELL, JOHN W. JR SS   TWS 37 12
  PLANETEERS, THE   CAMPBELL, JOHN W. JR   DC
TEPONDICON   JACOBI, CARL   SS   PLS 46 WI
  FAR BOUNDARIES   DERLETH, AUGUST   AN
  PORTRAITS IN MOONLIGHT   JACOBI, CARL   AC
TERATOHIPPUS   DAVIS, ROBERT L.   NV   IFS 72 12
  BEST SCIENCE FICTION STORIES OF THE YEAR (1972)
                                      DEL REY, LESTER   AN
TERCENTENARY INCIDENT, THE ASIMOV, ISAAC   SS   EQM 76 08
  BICENTENNIAL MAN AND OTHER STORIES, THE ASIMOV, ISAAC   AC
TERMINAL   GOULART, RON   SS   FAN 65 05
  BROKE DOWN ENGINE AND OTHER TROUBLES WITH MACHINES
                                      GOULART, RON   AC
  11TH ANNUAL OF THE YEAR'S BEST S-F, THE MERRIL, JUDITH   AN
TERMINAL BEACH, THE   BALLARD, J. G.   SS   NWS 64 03
  ALPHA 1   SILVERBERG, ROBERT   AN
  BEST OF J. G. BALLARD, THE   BALLARD, J. G.   AC
  BEST OF NEW WORLDS, THE   MOORCOCK, MICHAEL   AC
  CHRONOPOLIS AND OTHER STORIES   BALLARD, J. G.   AC
  SURVIVAL PRINTOUT   TOTAL EFFECT   AN
  TERMINAL BEACH (AMERICAN VERSION)   BALLARD, J. G.   AC
  TERMINAL BEACH (BRITISH VERSION)   BALLARD, J. G.   AC
  10TH ANNUAL OF THE YEAR'S BEST S-F, THE MERRIL, JUDITH   AN
TERMINAL QUEST (ALSO AS THE LAST MONSTER)
                            ANDERSON, POUL   SS   SSS 51 08
  CHILDREN OF WONDER   TENN, WILLIAM   AN
TERMINUS EST   MALZBERG, BARRY N.   SS   NOV 70 01
  *NOVA 1   HARRISON, HARRY   OA
TERMINUS EST   O'DONNELL, K. M.   SS   NOV 70 01
  UNIVERSE DAY   O'DONNELL, K. M.   NO
TERRA PHOBIA   KOONTZ, DEAN R.   SS   NEW 73 AN
  ANDROIDS, TIME MACHINES AND BLUE GIRAFFES
                                      ELWOOD & GHIDALIA   AN
TERRA-VENUSIAN WAR OF 1979, THE
                            NEYROUD, GERALD E.   SS   FSF 59 12
  SCIENCE FICTION ODDITIES   CONKLIN, GROFF   AN
TERRAFIED   TOFTE, ARTHUR   NV   COI 73
  CHILDREN OF INFINITY   ELWOOD, ROGER   OA
TERRATIN INCIDENT, THE (PAUL SCHNEIDER)
                            FOSTER, ALAN DEAN   SA   SLG 75 04
  STAR TREK LOG FOUR   FOSTER, ALAN DEAN   OC
TERRIBLE ANSWER, THE   GALLICO, PAUL   SS   SEP 50 01
  SATURDAY EVENING POST FANTASY STORIES, THE
                                      FLES, BARTHOLD   AN
TERRIBLE CONFLAGRATION UP AT THE PLACE
                            BRADBURY, RAY   SS   NEW 69 AC
  I SING THE BODY ELECTRIC   BRADBURY, RAY   AC

TERRIBLE INTRUDERS, THE   HINRICHS, JAMES V.   SS   BLF
  BOYS' LIFE BOOK OF OUTER SPACE STORIES, THE
                                BOY'S LIFE, ED. OF   AN
TERRIBLE QUICK SWORD   PETAJA, EMIL   SS   SAW 72
  SIGNS AND WONDERS   ELWOOD, ROGER   OA
TERRIBLE RIDE OF COLONEL TESSIER, THE
                        KERSH, GERALD   NV   SEP 52 10
  MEN WITHOUT BONES   KERSH, GERALD   AC
TERRIBLE SENSE, THE   PEREGOY, CALVIN   SS   ASF 38 08
  *BEST OF SCIENCE FICTION   CONKLIN, GROFF   AN
TERRIBLE VOYAGE OF THE TOAD, THE
                        MITCHELL, EDWARD P.   SS   SUN 78 10
  CRYSTAL MAN, THE   MITCHELL, EDWARD P.   AC
TERRIFIC PLAY OF FORCES NATURAL AND HUMAN, THE
                        WILSON, ROBIN SCOTT   AR   CLR 71 01
  CLARION   WILSON, ROBIN SCOTT   OA
TERRITORY   ANDERSON, POUL   SN   ASF 63 06
  TOMORROW 1   HOSKINS, ROBERT   AN
  TRADER TO THE STARS   ANDERSON, POUL   AC
TERROR IN THE AIR   REEVE, ARTHUR B.   SS   SCD 30 04
  SILENT BULLET, THE   REEVE, ARTHUR B.   AC
TERROR IN THE NIGHT   BLOCH, ROBERT   SS   MHT 56 02
  KING OF TERRORS, THE   BLOCH, ROBERT   AC
TERROR OF ANERLY HOUSE SCHOOL, THE
                        LAWRENCE, MARGERY   SS
  TRAVELLERS BY NIGHT   DERLETH, AUGUST   OA
TERROR OF BLUE JOHN GAP, THE   DOYLE, ARTHUR CONAN   SS   10
  ANCIENT MYSTERIES READER, THE   HAINING, PETER   AN
  STRANGE BEASTS AND UNNATURAL MONSTERS   STERN, PHILIP VAN D.   AN
TERROR OF WILLIAM STICKERS, THE
                        WRIGHT, S. FOWLER   SS
  WITCHFINDER, THE   WRIGHT, S. FOWLER   AC
TERROR OUT OF SPACE   BRACKETT, LEIGH   SS   PLS 44 SU
  HIDDEN PLANET, THE   WOLLHEIM, DONALD A.   AN
TERROR OUT OF TIME   WILLIAMSON, JACK   SS   ASF 33 12
  TIME CURVE, THE   MOSKOWITZ & ELWOOD   AN
TERROR OVER HOLLYWOOD   BLOCH, ROBERT   SS   FUN 57 06
  TALES IN A JUGULAR VEIN   BLOCH, ROBERT   AC
TERTIARY JUSTIFICATION, THE   CONEY, MICHAEL G.   NV   NWR 73 21
  NEW WRITINGS IN SF. 21   CARNELL, JOHN   OA
TEST   THOMAS, THEODORE L.   SS   FSF 62 04
  BEST FROM FANTASY AND SCIENCE FICTION: 12
                                DAVIDSON, AVRAM   AN
TEST AREA   COGSWELL, THEODORE R   SS   FUN 55 02
  WALL AROUND THE WORLD, THE   COGSWELL, THEODORE R   AC
TEST IN ORBIT   BOVA, BEN   SS   ASF 65 09
  FORWARD IN TIME   BOVA, BEN   AC
TEST JUMP   HARVEY, FRANK   SS   SEP 56 06
  AIR FORCE| HARVEY, FRANK   AC
TEST PIECE   RUSSELL, ERIC FRANK   SS   OWS 51 03
  HUMAN AND OTHER BEINGS   DEGRAEFF, ALLEN   AN
  OMNIBUS OF SCIENCE FICTION   CONKLIN, GROFF   AN
  SCIENCE FICTION OMNIBUS   CONKLIN, GROFF   AN
TEST STAND, THE   CORREY, LEE   SS   ASF 55 03
  EXPERT DREAMERS, THE   POHL, FREDERIK   AN
TEST TO DESTRUCTION   LAUMER, KEITH   NV   DVS 67 01
  BIG SHOW, THE   LAUMER, KEITH   AC
  DANGEROUS VISIONS   ELLISON, HARLAN   OA
TEST-TUBE CREATURE, AFTERWARD, THE
                        BERNOTT, JOAN   SS   DVS 72 02
  AGAIN, DANGEROUS VISIONS   ELLISON, HARLAN   OA
TEST-TUBE TERROR   STANDISH, ROBERT   SS   SEP 58 09
  POST READER OF FANTASY AND SCIENCE FICTION
                                SATURDAY EVE. POST   AN
TEST, THE   MATHESON, RICHARD   SS   FSF 54 11
  BEST FROM FANTASY AND SCIENCE FICTION: 4
                                BOUCHER, ANTHONY   AN
  FANTASY: THE LITERATURE OF THE MARVELOUS   KELLEY, LEO P.   AN
  IF THIS GOES ON   NUETZEL, CHARLES   AN
  SHORES OF SPACE, THE   MATHESON, RICHARD   AC
TESTAMENT   BAXTER, JOHN   SS   NWR 65 03
  BEST FROM NEW WRITINGS IN S-F FIRST SELECTION, THE
                                CARNELL, JOHN   AN
  NEW WRITINGS IN SF. 3   CARNELL, JOHN   OA
TESTAMENT   KING, VINCENT   SS   NWR 68 13
  NEW WRITINGS IN SF. 9   CARNELL, JOHN   AN
  NEW WRITINGS IN SF. 13   CARNELL, JOHN   OA
TESTAMENT OF ANDROS   BLISH, JAMES   NV   FUT 53 01
  ALPHA 1   SILVERBERG, ROBERT   AN
  *BEST SCIENCE FICTION STORIES OF JAMES BLISH
                                BLISH, JAMES   AC
  NOVELETS OF SCIENCE FICTION   HOWARD, IVAN   AN
  PORTALS OF TOMORROW   DERLETH, AUGUST   AN
  SO CLOSE TO HOME   BLISH, JAMES   AC
TESTAMENT OF ATHAMMAUS, THE   SMITH, CLARK ASHTON   NV   WRT 32 10
  OUT OF SPACE AND TIME   SMITH, CLARK ASHTON   AC
TESTING...ONE, TWO, THREE, FOUR
                        CHAPMAN, STEVE   SS   ASF 69 12
  ANALOG 8   CAMPBELL, JOHN W. JR   AN
  BEST OF SCIENCE FICTION MONTHLY, THE   SACKS, JANET   AN
TETRAHEDRA OF SPACE   MILLER, P. SCHUYLER   NV   WOS 31 11
  BEFORE THE GOLDEN AGE   ASIMOV, ISAAC   AN
TEXAS WEEK   HERNHUNTER, ALBERT   SS   FUN 54 01
  FIFTY SHORT SCIENCE FICTION TALES   ASIMOV & CONKLIN   AN
  TOMORROW, AND TOMORROW, AND TOMORROW...   HEINTZ/HERBERT/JOOS/   AN
THAG   WOLFE, GENE   SS   CTM 75 04
  CONTINUUM 4   ELWOOD, ROGER   OA
THALIDOMIDE KID, THE   GILCHRIST, JEREMY   SS   NWQ 74 06
  NEW WORLDS NO. 6   PLATT & BAILEY   OA
THAMES VALLEY CATASTROPHY, THE   ALLEN, GRANT   SS   SND 97 12
  SCIENCE FICTION BY GASLIGHT   MOSKOWITZ, SAM   AN
THANATOS   MCINTYRE, VONDA N.   SS   76
  FUTURE POWER   DANN & DOZOIS   OA
THANG   GARDNER, MARTIN   SS   COM 48 FL
  BEST SCIENCE-FICTION STORIES: 1949, THE   BLEILER & DIKTY   AN

THANKS FOR THE FEAST, NOTES ON PHILIP JOSE FARMER
                        FIEDLER, LESLIE A.   MS
  BOOK OF PHILIP JOSE FARMER, THE   FARMER, PHILIP JOSE   AC
THANKS FROM THE WHOLE BOUQUET   JACOBS, HARVEY   SS   NUG 65 09
  SATAN'S PETS   GHIDALIA, VIC   AN
THAT EVENING SUN GO DOWN   SELLINGS, ARTHUR   SS   NWS 66 09
  GODS FOR TOMOROW   SANTESSON, HANS S.   AN
THAT HELL-BOUND TRAIN   BLOCH, ROBERT   SS   FSF 58 09
  HUGO WINNERS, THE (VOLUME 1)   ASIMOV, ISAAC   AN
  MORE NIGHTMARES   BLOCH, ROBERT   AC
  PLEASANT DREAMS   BLOCH, ROBERT   AC
  TWENTY YEARS OF FANTASY & SCIENCE FICTION
                                FERMAN & MILLS   AN
THAT HIGH-UP BLUE DAY THAT SAW THE BLACK SKY-TRAIN COME
SPINNING   BUNCH, DAVID R.   SS   FSF 68 03
  BEST FROM FANTASY AND SCIENCE FICTION: 18
                                FERMAN, EDWARD L.   AN
THAT LOW   STURGEON, THEODORE   SS   FFM 48 10
  SCIENCE FICTION SHOWCASE   KORNBLUTH, MARY   AN
THAT MASON-DIXON LINE   NEWCOMB, SIMON   MS
  MATHEMATICAL MAGPIE, THE   FADIMAN, CLIFTON   AN
THAT ONLY A MOTHER   MERRIL, JUDITH   SS   ASF 48 06
  BEST OF JUDITH MERRIL, THE   MERRIL, JUDITH   AC
  CHILDREN OF WONDER   TENN, WILLIAM   AN
  FIRST FLIGHT   KNIGHT, DAMON   AN
  INTRODUCTORY PSYCHOLOGY THROUGH SCIENCE FICTION
                                KATZ/WARRICK/&   AN
  OUT OF BOUNDS   MERRIL, JUDITH   AC
  SCIENCE FICTION HALL OF FAME VOLUME 1   SILVERBERG, ROBERT   AN
  SPECULATIONS   SANDERS, THOMAS E.   AN
  TRANSFORMATIONS   ROSELLE, DANIEL   AN
  WOMEN OF WONDER   SARGENT, PAMELA   AN
  WORLD OF WONDER   PRATT, FLETCHER   AN
THAT SHARE OF GLORY   KORNBLUTH, C. M.   NV   ASF 52 01
  ALPHA 2   SILVERBERG, ROBERT   AN
  BEST SCIENCE FICTION STORIES OF C. M. KORNBLUTH
                                KORNBLUTH, C. M.   AC
  EVERY BOY'S BOOK OF OUTER SPACE STORIES   DIKTY, T. E.   AN
  EXPLORERS, THE   KORNBLUTH, C. M.   AC
  MINDWORM AND OTHER STORIES, THE   KORNBLUTH, C. M.   AC
  SPACE SERVICE   NORTON, ANDRE   AN
  WORLDS TO COME   KNIGHT, DAMON   AN
THAT THOU ART MINDFUL OF HIM| ASIMOV, ISAAC   NV   FSF 74 05
  BICENTENNIAL MAN AND OTHER STORIES, THE   ASIMOV, ISAAC   AC
  FINAL STAGE   FERMAN & MALZBERG   OA
  SOULS IN METAL   ASHLEY, MICHAEL   AN
THAT UNCOMFORTABLE PAUSE BETWEEN LIFE AND ART
                        ALDISS, BRIAN W.   SS   QUN 69 07
  MOMENT OF ECLIPSE, THE   ALDISS, BRIAN W.   AC
THAT WHICH SURVIVES (J. M. LUCAS & D. C. FONTANA)
                        BLISH, JAMES   SA   STK 73 09
  STAR TREK 9   BLISH, JAMES   OC
THAUMATURGE   MOORE, RAYLYN   SS   BER 74
  BERSERKERS, THE   ELWOOD, ROGER   OA
THAW AND SERVE   LANG, ALLEN KIM   SS   FSF 64 01
  BEST FROM FANTASY AND SCIENCE FICTION: 14
                                DAVIDSON, AVRAM   AN
THAW PLAN, THE   HEARD, H. F.   NV
  LOST CAVERN AND OTHER TALES OF THE FANTASTIC, THE
                                HEARD, H. F.   AC
THEFT OF THE THIRTY-NINE GIRDLES, THE (THE POWER OF THE
HYPERBOREA)   SMITH, CLARK ASHTON   SS   STN 53 03
  TALES OF SCIENCE AND SORCERY   SMITH, CLARK ASHTON   AC
THEIR THOUSANDTH SEASON   BRYANT, EDWARD   SS   CLR 72 02
  AMONG THE DEAD   BRYANT, EDWARD   AC
  BEST SCIENCE FICTION OF THE YEAR, THE NO. 2
                                CARR, TERRY   AN
  CLARION II   WILSON, ROBIN SCOTT   OA
THEM AS CAN, DOES   BRUNNER, JOHN   AR   NWS 66 01
  BOOK OF JOHN BRUNNER, THE   BRUNNER, JOHN   AC
THEMATIC CONTENTS   MISC. MATERIAL   MS
  SPECULATIONS   SANDERS, THOMAS E.   AN
THEME: TO MEAN INTENSELY   WILSON, ROBIN SCOTT   SI
  THOSE WHO CAN: A SCIENCE FICTION READER   WILSON, ROBIN SCOTT   AN
THEN FLY OUR GREETINGS   ST. CLAIR, MARGARET   SS   STS 51 03
  CHANGE THE SKY AND OTHER STORIES   ST. CLAIR, MARGARET   AC
THEN YOU CAN DO WHAT YOU WANT   BILKER, AUDREY L.
                        AND BILKER, HARVEY L.   SS C
  LEARNING MAZE AND OTHER STORIES, THE   ELWOOD, ROGER   OA
THEODORA AND THEODORA   THURSTON, ROBERT   SS   NDM 75 05
  NEW DIMENSIONS 5   SILVERBERG, ROBERT   OA
THEODORE STURGEON   MERRIL, JUDITH   AR   FSF 62 09
  BEST FROM FANTASY AND SCIENCE FICTION, 25TH ANNIV.
                                FERMAN, EDWARD L.   AN
THEODORE STURGEON   NOLAN, WILLIAM F.   AR
  3 TO THE HIGHEST POWER   NOLAN, WILLIAM F.   AN
THEODORE STURGEON SF/FANTASY INDEX, A
                        MISC. MATERIAL   MS
  3 TO THE HIGHEST POWER   NOLAN, WILLIAM F.   AN
THEOPHILUS   ADLARD, MARK   SS
  BEYOND THIS HORIZON   CARRELL, CHRISTOPHER   OA
THEORIES   ALLEN, DICK   SI
  SCIENCE FICTION: THE FUTURE   ALLEN, DICK   AN
THEORY AND PRACTICE OF TIME TRAVEL, THE
                        NIVEN, LARRY   AR   NEW 71 AC
  ALL THE MYRIAD WAYS   NIVEN, LARRY   AC
  LOOKING AHEAD   ALLEN, D. & L.   AN
THEORY OF ROCKETRY   KORNBLUTH, C. M.   SS   FSF 58 07
  BEST FROM FANTASY AND SCIENCE FICTION: 8
                                BOUCHER, ANTHONY   AN
  BEST SCIENCE FICTION STORIES OF C. M. KORNBLUTH
                                KORNBLUTH, C. M.   AC
  MASTERS' CHOICE   JANIFER, LAURENCE M.   AN
THERAPY   WOLF, GARY K.   SS   ORB 74 13
  ORBIT 13   KNIGHT, DAMON   OA

THERAPY 2000   ROBERTS, KEITH   SS   NWR 69 15
  MACHINES AND MEN   ROBERTS, KEITH   AC
  NEW WRITINGS IN SF. 15   CARNELL, JOHN   OA
  PASSING OF THE DRAGONS, THE   ROBERTS, KEITH   AC
  WORLD'S BEST SCIENCE FICTION: 1970 WOLLHEIM & CARR   AN
THERE ARE NO BANISTERS   DANN, JACK M.   SS   NWB 73 05
  NEW WORLDS QUARTERLY NO. 5   MOORCOCK, MICHAEL   OA
THERE IS A CROOKED MAN   WODHAMS, JACK   SN   ASF 67 02
  ANALOG 7   CAMPBELL, JOHN W. JR   AN
  PACIFIC BOOK OF AUSTRALIAN SCIENCE FICTION
                                      BAXTER, JOHN   AN
THERE IS A TIDE   ALDISS, BRIAN W.   SS   NWS 56 02
  SPACE, TIME AND NATHANIEL   ALDISS, BRIAN W.   AC
  SPECTRUM 2   AMIS & CONQUEST   AN
THERE IS A TIDE   FINNEY, JACK   SS   FSF 54 09
  THIRD LEVEL, THE   FINNEY, JACK   AC
THERE IS A TIDE   NIVEN, LARRY   NV   GAL 68 07
  HOLE IN SPACE, A   NIVEN, LARRY   AC
  TALES OF KNOWN SPACE: THE UNIVERSE OF LARRY NIVEN
                                      NIVEN, LARRY   AC
THERE IS NO DEFENSE   STURGEON, THEODORE   NV   ASF 48 02
  TO HERE AND THE EASEL   STURGEON, THEODORE   AC
  WORLDS OF THEODORE STURGEON, THE   STURGEON, THEODORE   AC
  3 IN 1   MARGULIES, LEO   AN
THERE IS NO MORE AWAY   CLINE, STEVE   SS   NWQ 73 05
  NEW WORLDS NO. 5   MOORCOCK & PLATT   OA
THERE ONCE WAS A BREATHY BABOON
                          EDDINGTON, ARTHUR   PM
  FANTASIA MATHEMATICA   FADIMAN, CLIFTON   AN
THERE SHALL BE DARKNESS   MOORE, C. L.   NV   ASF 42 02
  JOURNEY TO INFINITY   GREENBERG, MARTIN   AN
THERE SHALL BE NO DARKNESS BLISH, JAMES   SS   TWS 50 04
  *BEST SCIENCE FICTION STORIES OF JAMES BLISH
                                      BLISH, JAMES   AC
  WITCHES THREE   PRATT, FLETCHER   AN
  ZACHERLEY'S VULTURE STEW   ZACHERLEY   AN
THERE WAS A YOUNG FELLOW NAMED FISK
                          ANONYMOUS   PM
  FANTASIA MATHEMATICA   FADIMAN, CLIFTON   AN
THERE WAS A YOUNG LADY NAMED BRIGHT
                          BULLER, E. REGINALD   PM
  FASTER THAN LIGHT   DANN & ZEBROWSKI   OA
  MATHEMATICAL MAGPIE, THE   FADIMAN, CLIFTON   AN
THERE WAS A YOUNG MAN FROM TRINITY
                          ANONYMOUS   PM
  FANTASIA MATHEMATICA   FADIMAN, CLIFTON   AN
THERE WAS AN OLD MAN WHO SAID, "DO"
                          ANONYMOUS   PM
  FANTASIA MATHEMATICA   FADIMAN, CLIFTON   AN
  MATHEMATICAL MAGPIE, THE   FADIMAN, CLIFTON   AN
THERE WAS AN OLD WOMAN   BRADBURY, RAY   SS   WRT 44 07
  AUTUMN PEOPLE, THE   BRADBURY, RAY   AC
  *DARK CARNIVAL   BRADBURY, RAY   AC
  *OCTOBER COUNTRY, THE   BRADBURY, RAY   AC
THERE WAS AN OLD WOMAN—   SILVERBERG, ROBERT   SS   INF 58 11
  NEEDLE IN A TIMESTACK   SILVERBERG, ROBERT   AC
  SUNRISE ON MERCURY AND OTHER SCIENCE FICTION STORIES
                                      SILVERBERG, ROBERT   OA
THERE WAS THIS FELLA...   MASON, DOUGLAS R.   SS   NWR 68 11
  NEW WRITINGS IN SF. 11   CARNELL, JOHN   AN
THERE WILL COME SOFT RAINS BRADBURY, RAY   SS   COL 50 05
  ADVENTURES IN TOMORROW   CROSSEN, KENDELL F.   AN
  BEYOND THE END OF TIME   POHL, FREDERIK   AN
  FROM FRANKENSTEIN TO ANDROMEDA   BROWN, JAMES GOLDIE   AN
  MARTIAN CHRONICLES, THE   BRADBURY, RAY   AC
  SCIENCE FACT/FICTION   FARRELL/GAGE/&   AN
  TOMORROW MIDNIGHT   BRADBURY, RAY   AC
  VINTAGE ANTHOLOGY OF SCIENCE FANTASY, THE
                                      CERF, CHRISTOPHER   AN
  VINTAGE BRADBURY, THE   BRADBURY, RAY   AC
THERE'S A STARMAN IN WARD 7 ROME, DAVID   SS   NWS 65 01
  11TH ANNUAL OF THE YEAR'S BEST S-F, THE MERRIL, JUDITH   AN
THERE'S A WOLF IN MY TIME MACHINE
                          NIVEN, LARRY   SS   FSF 71 06
  FLIGHT OF THE HORSE, THE   NIVEN, LARRY   AC
  ZOO 2000   YOLEN, JANE   AN
THERE'S NO PLACE LIKE SPACE SILVERBERG, ROBERT NV   SFS 59 05
  GODLING, GO HOME!   SILVERBERG, ROBERT   AC
THERE'S NO VINISM LOKE CHAUVINISM
                          JAKES, JOHN W.   NV   AMZ 65 04
  BEST OF JOHN JAKES, THE   JAKES, JOHN W.   AC
THERESE   MATHESON, RICHARD   SS   68
  SHOCK WAVES   MATHESON, RICHARD   AC
THERMIDOR   CONRAD, EARL   SS
  DA VINCI MACHINE, THE   CONRAD, EARL   OC
THESE ARE THE ARTS   SCHMITZ, JAMES H.   SS   FSF 62 09
  14 GREAT TALES OF ESP   STONE, IDELLA P.   AN
THESE OUR ACTORS   WELLEN, EDWARD   SS   INY 70 01
  INFINITY 1   HOSKINS, ROBERT   OA
THESE STORIES MAY UPSET YOU CAMPBELL, JOHN W. JR AN
  ANALOG 4   CAMPBELL, JOHN W. JR   AN
THESIS ON SOCIAL FORMS AND SOCIAL CONTROLS IN THE U.S.A.
                          DISCH, THOMAS M.   SS   FAN 64 01
  FUN WITH YOUR NEW HEAD   DISCH, THOMAS M.   AC
THEY   HEINLEIN, ROBERT A.   SS   UNK 41 04
  ABOVE THE HUMAN LANDSCAPE   MCNELLY & STOVER   AN
  DARK SIDE, THE   KNIGHT, DAMON   AN
  OTHERS, THE   CARR, TERRY   AN
  SCIENCE FICTION TERROR TALES   CONKLIN, GROFF   AN
  SCIENCE FICTION: THE FUTURE   ALLEN, DICK   AN
  *TERROR IN THE MODERN VEIN   WOLLHEIM, DONALD A.   AN
  UNPLEASANT PROFESSION OF JONATHAN HOAG, THE
                                      HEINLEIN, ROBERT A.   AC
  WORLD OF WONDER   PRATT, FLETCHER   AN
THEY   KIPLING, RUDYARD   NV   SCR 04
  LITTLE MONSTERS, THE   ELWOOD & GHIDALIA   AN

THEY BITE   BOUCHER, ANTHONY   SS   UNK 43 08
  COMPLEAT WEREWOLF, THE   BOUCHER, ANTHONY   AC
  FAR AND AWAY   BOUCHER, ANTHONY   AC
  ZACHERLEY'S VULTURE STEW   ZACHERLEY   AC
THEY COPE   SKAL, DAVE   SS   ORB 72 11
  ORBIT 11   KNIGHT, DAMON   OA
THEY DO NOT ALWAYS REMEMBER BURROUGHS, WILLIAM SS ESQ 66 09
  SF12   MERRIL, JUDITH   AN
THEY DON'T MAKE LIFE LIKE THEY USED TO
                          BESTER, ALFRED   NV   FSF 63 10
  BEST FROM FANTASY AND SCIENCE FICTION: 13
                                      DAVIDSON, AVRAM   AN
  DARK SIDE OF THE EARTH, THE   BESTER, ALFRED   AC
  STAR LIGHT, STAR BRIGHT   BESTER, ALFRED   AC
  9TH ANNUAL OF THE YEAR'S BEST S-F, THE MERRIL, JUDITH   AN
THEY FLY SO HIGH   ROCKLYNNE, ROSS   SS   AMZ 52 06
  HISTORY OF THE SCIENCE FICTION MAGAZINE, THE PART 3 1946-1955
                                      ASHLEY, MICHAEL   AN
  MEN AND THE MIRROR, THE   ROCKLYNNE, ROSS   AC
THEY LIVE ON LEVELS   CARR, TERRY   SS   NDM 73 03
  LIGHT AT THE END OF THE UNIVERSE, THE CARR, TERRY   AC
  NEW DIMENSIONS 3   SILVERBERG, ROBERT   OA
  WORLDS FAR AND NEAR   CARR, TERRY   AN
THEY LOVED ME IN UTICA   DAVIDSON, AVRAM   SS   NEW 70 AN
  NEW WORLDS OF FANTASY NO. 2   CARR, TERRY   AN
THEY SAY   KNIGHT, DAMON   MS
  ORBIT 14   KNIGHT, DAMON   OA
  ORBIT 15   KNIGHT, DAMON   OA
  ORBIT 16   KNIGHT, DAMON   OA
  ORBIT 17   KNIGHT, DAMON   OA
  ORBIT 18   KNIGHT, DAMON   OA
THEY SHALL HAVE STARS (IN U.S. AS "YEAR 2018!")
                          BLISH, JAMES   NO   FAB 56
  CITIES IN FLIGHT   BLISH, JAMES   AC
THEY SHALL INHERIT   ALDISS, BRIAN W.   SS   NEB 58 07
  CANOPY OF TIME, THE   ALDISS, BRIAN W.   AC
THEY SHALL REAP   ROME, DAVID   NV   NWR 68 12
  NEW WRITINGS IN SF. 8   CARNELL, JOHN   AN
  NEW WRITINGS IN SF. 12   CARNELL, JOHN   OA
THEY TWINKLED LIKE JEWELS FARMER, PHILIP JOSE SS   FUN 54 01
  CELESTIAL BLUEPRINT, THE   FARMER, PHILIP JOSE   DC
THEY'RE TEARING DOWN TIM RILEY'S BAR
                          SERLING, ROD   SA
  NIGHT GALLERY   SERLING, ROD   OC
THICKENING THE PLOT   DELANY, SAMUEL R.   AR
  THOSE WHO CAN: A SCIENCE FICTION READER WILSON, ROBIN SCOTT AN
THICKER THAN BLOOD   ELLISON, HARLAN   SS   MSM 58 02
  NO DOORS, NO WINDOWS (STORIES REWRITTEN) ELLISON, HARLAN AC
THICKER THAN WATER   CARTMILL, CLEVE   NV   TWS 49 12
  SPACE SCAVENGERS, THE   CARTMILL, CLEVE   NC
THICKER THAN WATER   KERSH, GERALD   NV
  MEN WITHOUT BONES   KERSH, GERALD   AC
THIEF IN TIME, A   SHECKLEY, ROBERT   NV   GAL 54 07
  CITIZEN IN SPACE   SHECKLEY, ROBERT   AC
  TIMES 4 (ABRIDGED STORIES)   ALLEN, VIRGINIA R   AN
THIMGS   COGSWELL, THEODORE R SS   FSF 58 05
  WALL AROUND THE WORLD, THE   COGSWELL, THEODORE R   AC
THIN EDGE   MACKENZIE, J. B.   SS   ASF 63 12
  ANALOG 3   CAMPBELL, JOHN W. JR   AN
THIN GNAT-VOICES, THE   WYNDHAM, JOHN   NV   NWS 58 07
  *OUTWARD URGE, THE   WYNDHAM & PARKES   AC
THINE ALABASTER CITIES GLEAM JANIFER, LAURENCE M. SS FUC 73
  FUTURE CITY   ELWOOD, ROGER   OA
THING   JANVIER, IVAN   SS   FUN 55 03
  BEST SCIENCE FICTION STORIES AND NOVELS: 1956
                                      DIKTY, T. E.   AN
THING ABOUT MACHINES, A   SERLING, ROD   SA
  MORE STORIES FROM THE TWILIGHT ZONE SERLING, ROD   OC
THING FROM ENNIS ROCK, THE MONTELEONE, THOMAS F SS
  MORE SCIENCE FICTION TALES   ELWOOD, ROGER   OA
THING FROM OUTSIDE, THE (AMZ 26 04)
                          ENGLAND, GEORGE A.   SS   SAI 23 04
  *STRANGE PORTS OF CALL   DERLETH, AUGUST   AN
THING FROM THE SKY   LEINSTER, MURRAY   SS   NEW 60 AC
  ALIENS, THE   LEINSTER, MURRAY   AC
THING IN THE ATTIC, THE   BLISH, JAMES   NV   IFS 54 07
  SECOND WORLD OF IF, THE   QUINN & WULFF   AN
  SEEDLING STARS, THE   BLISH, JAMES   NO
THING IN THE CELLAR, THE KELLER, DAVID H. MD. SS   WRT 32 04
  FOLSOM FLINT AND OTHER CURIOUS TALES, THE
                                      KELLER, DAVID H. MD.   AC
  LIFE EVERLASTING AND OTHER TALES OF SCIENCE, FANTASY
   AND HORROR   KELLER, DAVID H. MD.   AC
  SUPERNATURAL READER, THE   CONKLIN, G&L.   AN
  TALES FROM UNDERWOOD   KELLER, DAVID H. MD.   AC
  *TWISTED   CONKLIN, GROFF   AN
  WORLDS OF WEIRD   MARGULIES, LEO   AN
THING IN THE CRYPT, THE   HOWARD, ROBERT E.   SS
  CONAN   HOWARD, R./DE CAMP/&   AC
THING IN THE POND, THE   ERNST, PAUL   SS   ASF 34 06
  *MY BEST SCIENCE FICTION STORY   MARGULIES & FRIEND   AN
THING IN THE STONE, THE   SIMAK, CLIFFORD D.   NV   IFS 70 03
  WORLD'S BEST SCIENCE FICTION: 1971 WOLLHEIM & CARR   AN
THING IN THE WOODS, THE   PRATT, FLETCHER
                          AND RUBY, B. F.   SS C AMZ 35 02
  OMNIBUS OF SCIENCE FICTION   CONKLIN, GROFF   AN
THING ITSELF, THE   ROBINSON, KIM S.   SS
  CLARION SF   WILHELM, KATE   OA
THING OF BEAUTY   KNIGHT, DAMON   NV   GAL 58 09
  BEST OF DAMON KNIGHT, THE   KNIGHT, DAMON   AC
  FAR OUT   KNIGHT, DAMON   AC
  SIXTH GALAXY READER, THE   GOLD, H. L.   AC
THING OF BEAUTY, A   SPINRAD, NORMAN   SS   ASF 73 01
  BEST SCIENCE FICTION FOR 1973   ACKERMAN, FORREST J. AN
  BEST SCIENCE FICTION STORIES OF THE YEAR (1973)
                                      DEL REY, LESTER   AN

HING OF BEAUTY, A

NEBULA AWARD STORIES 9   WILHELM, KATE   AN
NO DIRECTION HOME   SPINRAD, NORMAN   AC
2020 VISION   POURNELLE, JERRY   AN
HING OF CUSTOM, A   DE CAMP, L. SPRAGUE SS FUN 57 01
FANTASTIC UNIVERSE OMNIBUS, THE   SANTESSON, HANS S.   AN
GUN FOR DINOSAUR AND OTHER IMAGINATIVE TALES
                                   DE CAMP, L. SPRAGUE   AC
LATE GREAT FUTURE, THE   FITZ GERALD & DILLON   AN
RULERS OF MEN   SANTESSON, HANS S.   AN
HING ON OUTER SHOAL, THE MILLER, P. SCHUYLER SS ASF 47 09
*OTHER SIDE OF THE MOON, THE   DERLETH, AUGUST   AN
HING ON THE DOORSTEP, THE LOVECRAFT, H. P.   NV WRT 37 01
HAUNTER OF THE DARK, THE   LOVECRAFT, H. P.   AC
HING UNDER THE GLACIER, THE ALDISS, BRIAN W. SS SPC 74 02
SPACE 2   DAVIS, RICHARD   OA
HING-THING   MALEC, ALEXANDER B. SS
EXTRAPOLASIS   MALEC, ALEXANDER B.   AC
HING, THE   MATHESON, RICHARD SS MSS 51 05
SHOCK WAVES   MATHESON, RICHARD   AC
HINGS   HENDERSON, ZENNA SS FSF 60 07
ANYTHING BOX, THE   HENDERSON, ZENNA   AC
12 GREAT CLASSICS OF SCIENCE FICTION CONKLIN, GROFF   AN
HINGS (THE END)   LE GUIN, URSULA K. SS ORB 70 06
WINDS TWELVE QUARTERS, THE   LE GUIN, URSULA K.   AC
HINGS FROM THE DEEP, THE (SEE THE KRAKEN WAKES)
                                   WYNDHAM, JOHN   TC
HINGS GO BETTER   EFFINGER, GEO. ALEC SS ORB 72 11
MIXED FEELINGS   EFFINGER, GEO. ALEC   OA
ORBIT 11   KNIGHT, DAMON   OA
HINGS LOST   DISCH, THOMAS M. NV DVS 72 02
AGAIN, DANGEROUS VISIONS   ELLISON, HARLAN   OA
HINGS OF DISTINCTION CROSSEN, KENDELL F. NV STS 52 03
*FUTURE TENSE   CROSSEN, KENDELL F.   AN
HINGS PASS BY   LEINSTER, MURRAY NV TWS 45 SU
EARTH IN PERIL, THE   WOLLHEIM, DONALD A.   DA
GIANT ANTHOLOGY OF SCIENCE FICTION MARGULIES & FRIEND   AN
HINGS TO COME   HARRISON, HARRY   IN C
SCIENCE FICTION NOVELLAS   HARRISON & MCNELLY   AN
HINGS TO COME   MCNELLY, WILLIS E. IN C
SCIENCE FICTION NOVELLAS   HARRISON & MCNELLY   AN
HINGS WHICH ARE CAESAR'S DICKSON, GORDON R. NA
DAY THE SUN STOOD STILL, THE   SILVERBERG, ROBERT   OA
HINK BLUE, COUNT TWO   SMITH, CORDWAINER NA GAL 63 02
ELSEWHERE AND ELSEWHEN   CONKLIN, GROFF   AN
STARDREAMER   SMITH, CORDWAINER   AC
HINK ONLY THIS OF ME   KURLAND, MICHAEL J. NV GAL 73 11
BEST SCIENCE FICTION STORIES OF THE YEAR (1973)
                                   DEL REY, LESTER   AN
HINKER AND THE THOUGHT, THE (SEE MARK VII AND THINKER)
                                   DERLETH, AUGUST   TC
HINKER, MARK VII (THE THINKER AND THE THOUGHT)
                                   DERLETH, AUGUST SS OSF 54 09
SANDS OF MARS AND OTHER STORIES, THE ANONYMOUS   AN
HINKERS, THE   KELLY, WALT   CT HAS 61 01
6TH ANNUAL OF THE YEAR'S BEST S-F, THE MERRIL, JUDITH   AN
HINKING ABOUT SILVERBERG MALZBERG, BARRY N. IN
BEST OF ROBERT SILVERBERG, THE   SILVERBERG, ROBERT   AC
HINKING BACK (OUR GOD IS A HELPFUL GOD|)
                                   BUNCH, DAVID R.   SS
MODERAN   BUNCH, DAVID R.   AC
HINKING CAP, THE   BLOCH, ROBERT   NV OWS 53 06
BOGEY MEN   BLOCH, ROBERT   AC
HINKING MACHINE, THE   ASIMOV, ISAAC AR SDG 67 12
SCIENCE FACT/FICTION   FARRELL/GAGE/&   AN
HIOTIMOLINE AND THE SPACE AGE ASIMOV, ISAAC SF ASF 60 10
OPUS 100   ASIMOV, ISAAC   AC
6TH ANNUAL OF THE YEAR'S BEST S-F, THE MERRIL, JUDITH   AN
*HIOTIMOLINE TO THE STARS ASIMOV, ISAAC SS AMA 73
ASTOUNDING   HARRISON, HARRY   OA
BUY JUPITER AND OTHER STORIES   ASIMOV, ISAAC   AC
HIRD BUBBLE, THE   EDMONDSON, G. C. SS FSF 64 06
STRANGER THAN YOU THINK   EDMONDSON, G. C.   DC
HIRD EXPEDITION, THE   BRADBURY, RAY SS PLS 48 FL
MARTIAN CHRONICLES, THE   BRADBURY, RAY   AC
HIRD EYE, THE   CHAMBERS, ROBERT W. SS   15
ANCESTRAL VOICES   MENVILLE & REGINALD   AN
HIRD FROM THE SUN   MATHESON, RICHARD SS GAL 50 10
BEYOND BELIEF   HURLEY, RICHARD J.   AN
BORN OF MAN AND WOMAN   MATHESON, RICHARD   AC
*GALAXY READER OF SCIENCE FICTION GOLD, H. L.   AN
THIRD FROM THE SUN   MATHESON, RICHARD   AC
HIRD HAND, A   KOONTZ, DEAN R.   NV FSF 70 01
SOFT COME THE DRAGONS   KOONTZ, DEAN R.   DC
HIRD LEVEL, THE (COL 50 10) FINNEY, JACK SS FSF 52 10
BEST FROM FANTASY AND SCIENCE FICTION: 2
                                   BOUCHER & MCCOMAS   AN
FIFTY SHORT SCIENCE FICTION TALES ASIMOV & CONKLIN   AN
SCIENCE FACT/FICTION   FARRELL/GAGE/&   AN
SCIENCE FICTION ARGOSY, A   KNIGHT, DAMON   AN
THIRD LEVEL, THE   FINNEY, JACK   AC
*HIRD OFFENSE (AS CHARLES SATTERFIELD)
                                   POHL, FREDERIK SS GAL 58 08
SPACE, TIME & CRIME   DEFORD, MIRIAM ALLEN   AN
TURN LEFT AT THURSDAY   POHL, FREDERIK   AC
*HIRD SALLY, OR THE DRAGONS OF PROBABILITY, THE
                                   LEM, STANISLAW   SS
CYBERIAD, THE   LEM, STANISLAW   OC
*HIRD STAGE   ANDERSON, POUL   SS AMZ 62 02
FIRST STEP OUTWARD   HOSKINS, ROBERT   AN
HIRST FOR BLOOD, A   TOFTE, ARTHUR   NV
MORE SCIENCE FICTION TALES   ELWOOD, ROGER   OA
HIRST QUENCHERS, THE   RAPHAEL, RICK NV ASF 63 09
THIRST QUENCHERS, THE   RAPHAEL, RICK   AC
HIRSTY GOD   ST. CLAIR, MARGARET SS FSF 53 03
CHANGE THE SKY AND OTHER STORIES   ST. CLAIR, MARGARET   AN
CROSSROADS IN TIME   CONKLIN, GROFF   AN

THIS WRITING "GAME"

THIRTEEN AT TABLE   DUNSANY, LORD   SS   16
SUPERNATURAL READER, THE   CONKLIN, G&L.   AN
THIRTEEN O'CLOCK   KORNBLUTH, C. M. NV STI 41 02
EXPLORERS, THE   KORNBLUTH, C. M.   AC
THIRTEEN O'CLOCK & MR. PACKER GOES TO HELL
                                   KORNBLUTH, C. M. NV STI 41 02
THIRTEEN O'CLOCK AND OTHER ZERO HOURS KORNBLUTH, C. M.   AC
THIRTEEN PHANTASMS   SMITH, CLARK ASHTON SS FFN 36 03
OTHER DIMENSIONS   SMITH, CLARK ASHTON   AC
THIRTEEN TO CENTAURUS   BALLARD, J. G.   NV AMZ 62 04
BEST OF J. G. BALLARD, THE   BALLARD, J. G.   AC
FOUR-DIMENSIONAL NIGHTMARE, THE (REVISED)
                                   BALLARD, J. G.   AC
LEARNING MAZE AND OTHER STORIES, THE ELWOOD, ROGER   OA
OVERLOADED MAN, THE   BALLARD, J. G.   AC
PASSPORT TO ETERNITY   BALLARD, J. G.   AC
SPECTRUM OF WORLDS, A   CLARESON, THOMAS D.   AN
THIRTEENTH JOURNEY OF ION TICHY, THE
                                   LEM, STANISLAW   NV
OTHER WORLDS, OTHER SEAS   SUVIN, DARKO   AN
THIRTEENTH STEP, THE   LEIBER, FRITZ   SS NEW 62 AN
FIEND IN YOU, THE   BEAUMONT, CHARLES   AN
THIRTEENTH STORY, THE   SERLING, ROD   SA
*ROD SERLING'S THE TWILIGHT ZONE   SERLING, ROD   OC
THIRTY AND ONE, THE   KELLER, DAVID H. MD. SS MAR 38 11
LIFE EVERLASTING AND OTHER TALES OF SCIENCE, FANTASY
AND HORROR   KELLER, DAVID H. MD.   AC
THIRTY DAYS HAD SEPTEMBER YOUNG, ROBERT F. SS FSF 57 10
ABC OF SCIENCE FICTION, AN   BOARDMAN, TOM JR.   AN
GLASS OF STARS, A   YOUNG, ROBERT F.   AC
12 GREAT CLASSICS OF SCIENCE FICTION CONKLIN, GROFF   AN
THIRTY SECONDS- THIRTY DAYS (ALSO AS BREAKING STRAIN)
                                   CLARKE, ARTHUR C. NV TWS 49 12
BEST FROM STARTLING STORIES, THE   MINES, SAMUEL   AN
THIRTY-SEVEN NORTHWEST MALZBERG, BARRY N. SS NEW 76 AC
DOWN HERE IN THE DREAM QUARTER   MALZBERG, BARRY N.   AC
THIRTY-THREE AND ONE-THIRD DANN, JACK M.
                    AND ZEBROWSKI, GEORGE   SS C
LONG NIGHT OF WAITING AND OTHER STORIES ELWOOD, ROGER   OA
THIRTY-TWO SOOTHSAYERS ELLISON, HARLAN IN DVS 67 01
DANGEROUS VISIONS   ELLISON, HARLAN   OA
THIS BEST OF ALL POSSIBLE WORLDS
                                   HALDEMAN, JOE W. SS ASF 74 11
FOREVER WAR, THE   HALDEMAN, JOE W.   NO
THIS CORRUPTIBLE   TRANSUE, JACOB   NV ORB 68 04
ORBIT 4   KNIGHT, DAMON   OA
THIS EARTH OF HOURS   BLISH, JAMES SS FSF 59 06
*GALACTIC CLUSTER   BLISH, JAMES   AC
THIS EARTH OF MAJESTY (CONTEST STORY WINNING TITLE REFUGEE)
                                   CLARKE, ARTHUR C. SS FSF 55 07
BEST FROM FANTASY AND SCIENCE FICTION: 5
                                   BOUCHER, ANTHONY   AN
RULERS OF MEN   SANTESSON, HANS S.   AN
THIS GRAND CARCASS   LAFFERTY, R. A. SS AMZ 68 11
DOES ANYONE ELSE HAVE SOMETHING FURTHER TO ADD?
                                   LAFFERTY, R. A.   AC
TOMORROW, AND TOMORROW, AND TOMORROW... HEINTZ/HERBERT/JOOS/ AN
WORLD'S BEST SCIENCE FICTION: 1969 WOLLHEIM & CARR   AN
THIS IS THE HOUSE   KUTTNER, HENRY   SS ASF 46 02
RETURN TO OTHERNESS   KUTTNER, HENRY   AC
THIS IS THE HOUSE   PADGETT, LEWIS   SS ASF 46 02
GNOME THERE WAS, A   PADGETT, LEWIS   AC
THIS IS THE LAND   BOND, NELSON S.   SS BBM 51 04
NO TIME LIKE THE FUTURE   BOND, NELSON S.   AC
*OUTER REACHES, THE   DERLETH, AUGUST   AN
THIS IS THE ROAD   SILVERBERG, ROBERT NA
FEAST OF ST. DIONYSUS, THE   SILVERBERG, ROBERT   AC
NO MIND OF MAN   SILVERBERG, ROBERT   OA
THIS IS: AN INTRODUCTION SCORTIA, THOMAS N. IN
MONADIC UNIVERSE, THE   ZEBROWSKI, GEORGE   AC
THIS JOE (SEE THE FIRST MARTIAN)
                                   VAN VOGT, A. E.   TC
THIS MOMENT OF THE STORM ZELAZNY, ROGER NV FSF 66 06
BEST FROM FANTASY AND SCIENCE FICTION: 16
                                   FERMAN, EDWARD L.   AN
DAY IN THE LIFE, A   DOZOIS, GARDNER R.   AN
DOORS OF HIS FACE, THE LAMPS OF HIS MOUTH, THE
                                   ZELAZNY, ROGER   AC
THIS MORTAL MOUNTAIN   ZELAZNY, ROGER   NV IFS 67 03
DOORS OF HIS FACE, THE LAMPS OF HIS MOUTH, THE
                                   ZELAZNY, ROGER   AC
THIS SIDE OF INFINITY   CARR, TERRY   AN
THIS NIGHT   WRIGHT, S. FOWLER   SS
NEW GODS LEAD, THE   WRIGHT, S. FOWLER   AC
THIS NIGHT, AT MY FIRE RUSS, JOANNA SS EPO 66 WI
POCKETFUL OF STARS, A   KNIGHT, DAMON   AN
THIS ONE'S ON ME   RUSSELL, ERIC FRANK SS NEB 53 FL
DARK TIDES   RUSSELL, ERIC FRANK   AC
*SCIENCE FICTION ADVENTURES IN MUTATION CONKLIN, GROFF   AN
THIS SIDE OF PARADISE (N. BUTLER & D. C. FONTANA)
                                   BLISH, JAMES SA STK 72 05
STAR TREK 5   BLISH, JAMES   OC
THIS SIDE UP   BANKS, RAYMOND E. SS GAL 54 07
FIFTH GALAXY READER, THE   GOLD, H. L.   AN
THIS STAR SHALL BE FREE LEINSTER, MURRAY NV SSS 49 11
ASLEEP IN ARMAGEDDON   SISSONS, MICHAEL   AN
*INVADERS OF EARTH   CONKLIN, GROFF   AN
SPECULATIONS   SANDERS, THOMAS E.   AN
THIS TOWER OF ASHES   MARTIN, GEORGE R. R. SS
ANALOG ANNUAL   BOVA, BEN   OA
SONGS OF STARS AND SHADOWS   MARTIN, GEORGE R. R.   AC
THIS WAY TO THE REGRESS (SEE BACKWARD, O TIME)
                                   KNIGHT, DAMON   TC
THIS WRITING "GAME"   EFFINGER, GEO. ALEC SS
MIXED FEELINGS   EFFINGER, GEO. ALEC   AC

THOLIAN WEB, THE (JUDY BURNS & CHET RICHARDS)
                    BLISH, JAMES   SA STK 72 05
  STAR TREK 5   BLISH, JAMES   OC
THOMAS THE PROCLAIMER   SILVERBERG, ROBERT   NA
  BORN WITH THE DEAD   SILVERBERG, ROBERT   AC
  DAY THE SUN STOOD STILL, THE   SILVERBERG, ROBERT   OA
THORNS OF BAREVI, THE   MCCAFFREY, ANNE   SS   70
  GET OFF THE UNICORN   MCCAFFREY, ANNE   AC
THOSE ABOUT TO DIE (FROM "ON THE BEACH")
                    SHUTE, NEVIL   EX
  SCIENCE FICTION THROUGH THE AGES 2 EVANS, I. O.   AN
THOSE AMONG US (ANDROID, AS C. H. LIDDELL)
                    KUTTNER, HENRY   NV FSF 51 06
  PSEUDO PEOPLE, THE   NOLAN, WILLIAM F.   AN
THOSE GOOD OLD DAYS OF LIQUID FUEL
                    CONEY, MICHAEL G. SS FSF 76 01
  1977 ANNUAL WORLD'S BEST SF, THE WOLLHEIM, DONALD A. AN
THOSE IDIOTS FROM EARTH   WILSON, RICHARD SS NEW 57 AC
  THOSE IDIOTS FROM EARTH   WILSON, RICHARD   AC
THOSE MEN FROM MARS (EASTER EGGS)
                    CARR, ROBERT S.   NV SEP 49 09
  BEYOND INFINITY   CARR, ROBERT S.   AC
THOSE REMARKABLE RAVENCRAFTS FAIRMAN, PAUL W.   SS
  FORGETFUL ROBOT, THE   FAIRMAN, PAUL W.   OC
THOSE WERE GIANTS   CUMMINGS, M. A.   SS
  EXILE AND OTHER TALES OF FANTASY CUMMINGS, M. A.   OC
THOSE WHO CAN, DO   KUROSAKA, BOB   SS FSF 65 01
  11TH ANNUAL OF THE YEAR'S BEST S-F, THE MERRIL, JUDITH   AN
THOSE WHO SEEK   DERLETH, AUGUST   SS WRT 32 01
  NOT LONG FOR THIS WORLD   DERLETH, AUGUST   AC
THOSE WILD ALIEN WORDS: I   LEIBER, FRITZ   AR NEW 74 AC
  BOOK OF FRITZ LEIBER, THE   LEIBER, FRITZ   AC
THOSE WILD ALIEN WORDS: II LEIBER, FRITZ   AR NEW 75 AC
  SECOND BOOK OF FRITZ LEIBER, THE LEIBER, FRITZ   AC
THOSE WONDERFUL YEARS   MALZBERG, BARRY N. SS TAL 73
  BEST OF BARRY N. MALZBERG, THE   MALZBERG, BARRY N.   AC
  FRONTIERS 1; TOMORROW'S ALTERNATIVES ELWOOD, ROGER   OA
THOU GOOD AND FAITHFUL   BRUNNER, K. HOUSTON NV ASF 53 03
  SPACE PIONEERS   NORTON, ANDRE   AN
THOU GOOD AND FAITHFUL   SCORTIA, THOMAS N. NV TVW 73
  BEST SCIENCE FICTION STORIES OF THE YEAR (1973)
                    DEL REY, LESTER   AN
  TWO VIEWS OF WONDER   SCORTIA & YARBRO   OA
THOU GOOD AND FAITHFUL (AS JOHN LOXMITH)
                    BRUNNER, JOHN   NV ASF 53 03
  NOW THEN   BRUNNER, JOHN   AC
THOUGH A SPARROW FALL   SCORTIA, THOMAS N. SS ASF 65 07
  CAUTION! INFLAMMABLE!   SCORTIA, THOMAS N.   AC
THOUGH DREAMERS DIE   DEL REY, LESTER   SS ASF 44 02
  EARLY DEL REY   DEL REY, LESTER   AC
  ROBOT AND THE MAN, THE   GREENBERG, MARTIN   AN
THOUGH POPPIES GROW   DEL REY, LESTER   NV UNK 42 08
  EARLY DEL REY   DEL REY, LESTER   AC
THOUSAND DEATHS, A   LONDON, JACK   SS BLC 99 05
  BATTLE OF THE MONSTERS AND OTHER STORIES, THE
                    HARTWELL & CURREY   AN
  CURIOUS FRAGMENTS   LONDON, JACK   AC
  FANTASTIC PULPS, THE   HAINING, PETER   AN
THOUSAND DREAMS OF STELLAVISTA, THE
                    BALLARD, J. G.   SS AMZ 62 03
  PASSPORT TO ETERNITY   BALLARD, J. G.   AC
  *VERMILLION SANDS   BALLARD, J. G.   AC
THOUSAND-AND-SECOND TALE OF SCHEHERAZADE, THE
                    POE, EDGAR ALLEN SS GDY 45 02
  *BEYOND TIME AND SPACE   DERLETH, AUGUST   AN
THRANGS AND OTHER WONDERS ISAACS, LEONARD PM CLR 73 03
  CLARION III   WILSON, ROBIN SCOTT OA
THREAD OF LIFE   SAFRONOV, Y.   SS
  RUSSIAN SCIENCE FICTION, 1968 MAGIDOFF, ROBERT   AN
THREADS OF TIME   BENFORD, GREGORY NA TOT 74
  THREADS OF TIME   SILVERBERG, ROBERT   OA
THREE BLIND MICE   LAUMER, KEITH   NV MWS 71
  MANY WORLDS OF SCIENCE FICTION, THE BOVA, BEN   OA
THREE BLIND MICE   PADGETT, LEWIS   NV ASF 45 06
  MUTANT   PADGETT, LEWIS   AC
THREE BROTHERS, THE   RUSSELL, WILLIAM M. SS LOB 54 12
  AD 2500   WILSON, ANGUS   AN
THREE COMEDIANS   EKLUND, GORDON   NV NDM 73 03
  NEW DIMENSIONS 3   SILVERBERG, ROBERT   OA
THREE DRUGS, THE   NESBIT, EDITH   SS   10
  BEFORE ARMAGEDDON   MOORCOCK, MICHAEL   AN
THREE ELECTROKNIGHTS, THE LEM, STANISLAW   SS   72
  MORTAL ENGINES   LEM, STANISLAW   AC
THREE ENIGMAS: I   ALDISS, BRIAN W. GR NWR 73 22
  NEW WRITINGS IN SF. 22   BULMER, KENNETH   OA
THREE ENIGMAS: II   ALDISS, BRIAN W. GR NWR 74 23
  NEW WRITINGS IN SF. 23   BULMER, KENNETH   OA
THREE ENIGMAS: III   ALDISS, BRIAN W. GR NWR 74 24
  NEW WRITINGS IN SF. 24   BULMER, KENNETH   OA
THREE ETERNALS, THE   BINDER, EANDO   NV TWS 39 12
  ANTON YORK, IMMORTAL   BINDER, EANDO   AC
THREE EXCERPTS   JANIFER, LAURENCE M. SS
  IMPOSSIBLE?   JANIFER, LAURENCE M. AC
THREE FINGERS   WOLFE, THOMAS   SS
  NEW CONSTELLATIONS   DISCH & NAYLOR   OA
THREE FOR CARNIVAL   SHEPLEY, JOHN   SS FSF 66 05
  BEST FROM FANTASY AND SCIENCE FICTION: 16
                    FERMAN, EDWARD L.   AN
THREE FOR THE STARS   DICKINSON, JOSEPH SS FSF 62 04
  BEST FROM FANTASY AND SCIENCE FICTION: 12
                    DAVIDSON, AVRAM   AN
THREE GREEN BLADES OF GRASS ALDISS, BRIAN W.   SI
  EVIL EARTHS   ALDISS, BRIAN W.   AN
THREE JOHNS, THE (ONLY IN REPRINT, LAN 72)
                    ASIMOV, ISAAC   AR
  CLOAK OF AESIR   CAMPBELL, JOHN W. JR AC

THREE LIMERICKS   XERXES, B. T. H.   PM
  ABC OF SCIENCE FICTION, AN   BOARDMAN, TOM JR.   A
THREE LINES OF OLD FRENCH MERRITT, A.   SS ASW 19 0
  ESCALES DANS L'INFINI   GALLET, GEORGES H.   A
  FUTURES UNLIMITED   NORTON, ALDEN H.   A
THREE LITTLE OWLS   BROWN, FREDRIC   SS
  NIGHTMARES AND GEEZENSTACKS   BROWN, FREDRIC   A
THREE MATHEMATICAL DIVERSIONS QUENEAU, RAYMOND   AR   58
  MATHEMATICAL MAGPIE, THE   FADIMAN, CLIFTON   A
THREE MILLION SQUARE MILES WOLFE, GENE   SS NEW 71 A
  RUINS OF EARTH, THE   DISCH, THOMAS M.   A
THREE POINTS ON THE DEMOGRAPHIC CURVE
                    DISCH, THOMAS M. SS IMP 66 1.
  ONE HUNDRED AND TWO H-BOMBS (U.S.) DISCH, THOMAS M.   A
THREE PORTRAITS AND A PRAYER POHL, FREDERIK SS GAL 62 0
  ABOMINABLE EARTHMAN, THE   POHL, FREDERIK   A
  BEST OF FREDERIK POHL, THE   POHL, FREDERIK   A
  LATE GREAT FUTURE, THE   FITZ GERALD & DILLON A
  SEVENTH GALAXY READER, THE   POHL, FREDERIK   A
THREE PROLOGUES AND AN EPILOGUE
                    DOS PASSOS, JOHN PM ADT 61 S
  7TH ANNUAL OF THE YEAR'S BEST S-F, THE MERRIL, JUDITH   A
THREE THOUSAND YEARS AMONG THE MICROBES
                    TWAIN, MARK   SS
  IN DREAMS AWAKE   FIEDLER, LESLIE A.   A
THREE TO A GIVEN STAR   SMITH, CORDWAINER NV GAL 65 10
  QUEST OF THE THREE WORLDS   SMITH, CORDWAINER   N
THREE VERSES   GRAHAM, L. A.   PM   59
  MATHEMATICAL MAGPIE, THE   FADIMAN, CLIFTON   A
THREE VERSES   WINSOR, FREDERICK PM   58
  MATHEMATICAL MAGPIE, THE   FADIMAN, CLIFTON   A
THREE WISHES, THE   RANDOLPH, V.   SS
  DEALS WITH THE DEVIL   DAVENPORT, BASIL   A
THREE'S A CLOUD (THE UNBEATEN TRACK)
                    ALDISS, BRIAN W. SS NWS 59 0
  CANOPY OF TIME, THE   ALDISS, BRIAN W.   A
THREE-CORNERED AND SECURE HENDERSON, ZENNA SS NEW 71 AC
  HOLDING WONDER   HENDERSON, ZENNA   AC
THREE-CORNERED WHEEL, THE ANDERSON, POUL NV ASF 63 1
  TROUBLE TWISTERS, THE   ANDERSON, POUL   AC
THREE-PART PUZZLE   DICKSON, GORDON R. SS ASF 62 0
  STAR ROAD, THE   DICKSON, GORDON R.   AC
THREE, THE   DICKSON, GORDON R. SS STS 53 05
  SPECIAL WONDER   MCCOMAS, J. FRANCIS A
THREEPENNY-PIECE, THE (1913) STEPHENS, JAMES SS FSF 51 0
  BEST FROM FANTASY AND SCIENCE FICTION BOUCHER & MCCOMAS A
THREES (TO BE SUNG BY NIELS BOHR)
                    ATHERTON, JOHN   PM NYM 57 0
  FANTASIA MATHEMATICA   FADIMAN, CLIFTON   A
THREESIE   COGSWELL, THEODORE R SS FSF 56 0
  DEALS WITH THE DEVIL   DAVENPORT, BASIL   A
THRESHOLD   KUTTNER, HENRY   SS UNK 40 12
  CIRCUS OF DR. LAO AND OTHER IMPROBABLE STORIES
                    BRADBURY, RAY   A
  DEALS WITH THE DEVIL   DAVENPORT, BASIL   A
THROUGH A GLASS-DARKLY HENDERSON, ZENNA NV FSF 70 10
  HOLDING WONDER   HENDERSON, ZENNA   A
  NEW WORLDS OF FANTASY NO. 3   CARR, TERRY   A
THROUGH A LASS DARKLY   TIPTREE, JAMES JR. SS GEN 72
  GENERATION   GERROLD, DAVID   OA
  WARM WORLDS AND OTHERWISE   TIPTREE, JAMES JR.   AC
THROUGH A WINDOW (AT A WINDOW) WELLS, H. G.   SS BAW 94 0
  SHORT STORIES OF H. G. WELLS, THE WELLS, H. G.   AC
  STOLEN BACILLUS AND OTHER INCIDENTS, THE WELLS, H. G.   AC
THROUGH CHANNELS   MATHESON, RICHARD SS FSF 51 0
  BORN OF MAN AND WOMAN   MATHESON, RICHARD   AC
  SCIENCE FICTION TERROR TALES CONKLIN, GROFF   A
THROUGH HYPERSPACE WITH BROWN JENKIN
                    LEIBER, FRITZ   AR   66
  SECOND BOOK OF FRITZ LEIBER, THE LEIBER, FRITZ   AC
THROUGH OTHER EYES   LAFFERTY, R. A. SS FUT 60 02
  MIND TO MIND   SILVERBERG, ROBERT   A
  NINE HUNDRED GRANDMOTHERS   LAFFERTY, R. A.   AC
THROUGH THE DRAGON GLASS MERRITT, A.   SS ASW 17 1
  FOX WOMAN & OTHER STORIES, THE MERRITT, A.   AC
THROUGH THE PURPLE CLOUD WILLIAMSON, JACK SS WOS 31 05
  EARLY WILLIAMSON, THE   WILLIAMSON, JACK   AC
  FROM OFF THIS WORLD   MARGULIES & FRIEND   A
THROUGH TIME AND SPACE WITH FERDINAND FEGHOOT
                    BRIARTON, GRENDEL AC PDX 62
  COMPLETE FEGHOOT, THE   BRIARTON, GRENDEL   AC
THROUGH TIME AND SPACE WITH FERDINAND FEGHOOT
                    BRIARTON, GRENDEL SS BSJ 67
  SPECIAL WONDER   MCCOMAS, J. FRANCIS A
THROUGH TIME AND SPACE WITH FERDINAND FEGHOOT: VII
                    BRIARTON, GRENDEL SS FSF 58 0.
  BEST FROM FANTASY AND SCIENCE FICTION: 8
                    BOUCHER, ANTHONY   A
THROUGH TIME AND SPACE WITH FERDINAND FEGHOOT: VIII
                    BRIARTON, GRENDEL SS FSF 58 0.
  BEST FROM FANTASY AND SCIENCE FICTION: 8
                    BOUCHER, ANTHONY   A
THROUGH TIME AND SPACE WITH FERDINAND FEGHOOT: X
                    BRIARTON, GRENDEL SS FSF 59 0
  BEST FROM FANTASY AND SCIENCE FICTION: 9
                    MILLS, ROBERT P.
THROUGH TIME AND SPACE WITH FERDINAND FEGHOOT: XI
                    BRIARTON, GRENDEL SS FSF 59 02
  BEST FROM FANTASY AND SCIENCE FICTION: 9
                    MILLS, ROBERT P.
THROUGH TIME AND SPACE WITH FERDINAND FEGHOOT: XII
                    BRIARTON, GRENDEL SS FSF 59 0.
  BEST FROM FANTASY AND SCIENCE FICTION: 9
                    MILLS, ROBERT P.   A
  NEVER IN THIS WORLD   STONE, IDELLA P.   A

HROUGH TIME AND SPACE WITH FERDINAND FEGHOOT: XIII
                          BRIARTON, GRENDEL   SS   FSF 59 04
  BEST FROM FANTASY AND SCIENCE FICTION: 9
                          MILLS, ROBERT P.   AN
HROUGH TIME AND SPACE WITH FERDINAND FEGHOOT: XIV
                          BRIARTON, GRENDEL   SS   FSF 59 05
  BEST FROM FANTASY AND SCIENCE FICTION: 9
                          MILLS, ROBERT P.   AN
HROUGH TIME AND SPACE WITH FERDINAND FEGHOOT: XV
                          BRIARTON, GRENDEL   SS   FSF 59 06
  BEST FROM FANTASY AND SCIENCE FICTION: 9
                          MILLS, ROBERT P.   AN
HROWBACK   BOUNDS, SYDNEY J.   SS   NWR 69 16
  NEW WRITINGS IN SF. 16 CARNELL, JOHN   OA
HROWBACK   DE CAMP, L. SPRAGUE SS   ASF 49 03
  APEMAN, SPACEMAN   STOVER & HARRISON   AN
  GUN FOR DINOSAUR AND OTHER IMAGINATIVE TALES
                          DE CAMP, L. SPRAGUE   AC
HROWBACK   DEFORD, MIRIAM ALLEN SS   STS 52 10
  *FUTURE TENSE   CROSSEN, KENDELL F.   AN
  XENOGENESIS   DEFORD, MIRIAM ALLEN   AC
HROWBACK   ELWOOD, ROGER   SS   STG 74
  STRANGE GODS   ELWOOD, ROGER   OA
HROWBACKS, THE   SILVERBERG, ROBERT   NV   GAL 70 07
  WORLD INSIDE, THE   SILVERBERG, ROBERT   NO
HUNDER AND ROSES   STURGEON, THEODORE   SS   ASF 47 11
  *ASTOUNDING SCIENCE FICTION ANTHOLOGY, THE
                          CAMPBELL, JOHN W. JR AN
  ASTOUNDING TALES OF SPACE AND TIME CAMPBELL, JOHN W. JR AN
  ASTOUNDING-ANALOG READER, THE VOLUME TWO HARRISON & ALDISS AN
  *FIRST ASTOUNDING SCIENCE FICTION ANTHOLOGY, THE
                          CAMPBELL, JOHN W. JR AN
  *MY BEST SCIENCE FICTION STORY MARGULIES & FRIEND AN
  *STRANGE PORTS OF CALL DERLETH, AUGUST   AN
  THUNDER AND ROSES   STURGEON, THEODORE   AC
  *WAY HOME, A   STURGEON, THEODORE   AC
HUNDER-THIEVES, THE (IT'S ALL HOW YOU LOOK AT IT)
                          ASIMOV, ISAAC   PM   FUT 58 10
  SF:59, THE YEAR'S GREATEST SCIENCE FICTION AND FANTASY
                          MERRIL, JUDITH   AN
HUNDERHEAD   LAUMER, KEITH   NV   GAL 67 04
  BEST OF KEITH LAUMER, THE LAUMER, KEITH   AC
  DAY BEFORE FOREVER AND THUNDER HEAD, THE LAUMER, KEITH AC
  UNDEFEATED, THE   LAUMER, KEITH   AC
HUNDERING WORLDS   HAMILTON, EDMOND   NV   WRT 34 03
  BEST OF EDMOND HAMILTON, THE HAMILTON, EDMOND   AC
HUS I REFUTE BEELZY   COLLIER, JOHN   SS   43
  OUT OF THIS WORLD   FAST, JULIUS   AN
HUS LOVE BETRAYS US   MACLENNAN, PHYLLIS   SS   FSF 72 09
  BEST FROM FANTASY AND SCIENCE FICTION: 20
                          FERMAN, EDWARD L.   AN
  BEST SCIENCE FICTION STORIES OF THE YEAR (1972)
                          DEL REY, LESTER   AN
  1973 ANNUAL WORLD'S BEST SF, THE WOLLHEIM, DONALD A. AN
HUS WE FRUSTRATE CHARLEMAGNE LAFFERTY, R. A. SS   GAL 67 02
  ALPHA 1   SILVERBERG, ROBERT   AN
  AS TOMORROW BECOMES TODAY SULLIVAN, CHARLES W.   AN
  NINE HUNDRED GRANDMOTHERS LAFFERTY, R. A.   AC
  TRANSFORMATIONS   ROSELLE, DANIEL   AN
  WORLD'S BEST SCIENCE FICTION: 1968 WOLLHEIM & CARR AN
HUVIA, MAID OF MARS   BURROUGHS, EDGAR R. NO   ASW 16 04
  THREE MARTIAN NOVELS   BURROUGHS, EDGAR R.   AC
HY BLOOD LIKE MILK   WATSON, IAN   NV   NWQ 73 05
  NEW WORLDS NO. 5   MOORCOCK & PLATT   OA
IC, THE   DISCH, THOMAS M.   SS
  *GETTING INTO DEATH   DISCH, THOMAS M.   AC
ICKET TO ANYWHERE   KNIGHT, DAMON   NV   GAL 52 04
  DEEP SPACE   SILVERBERG, ROBERT   AN
  IN DEEP   KNIGHT, DAMON   AC
  SCIENCE FICTION SHOWCASE KORNBLUTH, MARY   AN
ICKET TO CHILDHOOD, A   KOLUPAYEV, VICTOR   SS   69
  AIR OF MARS AND OTHER STORIES, THE GINSBURG, MIRRA AN
ICKET TO TRANAI, A   SHECKLEY, ROBERT   NA   GAL 55 10
  CITIZEN IN SPACE   SHECKLEY, ROBERT   AC
  ROBERT SHECKLEY OMNIBUS, THE SHECKLEY, ROBERT   AC
ICKING HIS LIFE AWAY   HAMM, THELMA D.   SS   NEW 54 AN
  TOMORROW'S UNIVERSE   CAMPBELL, H. J.   AN
IDDLYWINK WARRIORS, THE   ANDERSON, POUL
                          AND DICKSON, GORDON R.   NV C FSF 55 08
  EARTHMAN'S BURDEN   ANDERSON, P.&DICKSON   AC
IE THAT BINDS, THE   WHITLEY, GEORGE   SS   FUN 58 06
  ENCOUNTERS WITH ALIENS EARLEY, GEORGE W.   AN
IELINE   RUSSELL, ERIC FRANK SS   ASF 55 07
  SIX WORLDS YONDER   RUSSELL, ERIC FRANK   DC
  SOMEWHERE A VOICE   RUSSELL, ERIC FRANK   AC
IES THAT BIND, THE   MILLER, WALTER M. JR NV   IFS 54 05
  SEA OF SPACE, A   NOLAN, WILLIAM F.   AN
IGER BOY   PANGBORN, EDGAR   NV   UNI 72 02
  UNIVERSE 2   CARR, TERRY   OA
IGER BY THE TAIL   ANDERSON, POUL   NV   PLS 51 01
  AGENT OF THE TERRAN EMPIRE ANDERSON, POUL   AC
  MORE ADVENTURES ON OTHER PLANETS WOLLHEIM, DONALD A. AN
IGER BY THE TAIL   HENDERSON, GENE L.   SS   BLF
  BOYS' LIFE BOOK OF OUTER SPACE STORIES, THE
                          BOY'S LIFE, ED. OF   AN
IGER BY THE TAIL   NOURSE, ALAN E.   SS   GAL 51 11
  ADVENTURES IN DIMENSION CONKLIN, GROFF   AN
  FIFTY SHORT SCIENCE FICTION TALES ASIMOV & CONKLIN AN
  *SCIENCE FICTION ADVENTURES IN DIMENSION CONKLIN, GROFF AN
  SECOND GALAXY READER OF SCIENCE FICTION GOLD, H. L. AN
  TIGER BY THE TAIL   NOURSE, ALAN E.   AC
IGER CAT   KELLER, DAVID H. MD. SS   WRT 37 11
  TALES FROM UNDERWOOD   KELLER, DAVID H. MD.   AC
IGER GIRL   BURROUGHS, EDGAR R. NV   AMZ 42 04
  SAVAGE PELLUCIDAR   BURROUGHS, EDGAR R.   NO

TIGER GOD, THE   SERLING, ROD   SA
  *ROD SERLING'S THE TWILIGHT ZONE SERLING, ROD   OC
TIGER GREEN   DICKSON, GORDON R.   NV   IFS 65 11
  ANCIENT, MY ENEMY   DICKSON, GORDON R.   AC
TIGER RIDE   BLISH, JAMES
                          AND KNIGHT, DAMON   SS C ASF 48 10
  SF: AUTHORS' CHOICE   HARRISON, HARRY   AN
TIGER TAMER (SEE A POSSIBLE CANDIDATE FOR THE PRESIDENCY)
                          FINNEY, JACK   TC
TIGER| TIGER| (THE STARS MY DESTINATION)
                          BESTER, ALFRED   NO   GAL 56 10
  ALFRED BESTER OMNIBUS, AN BESTER, ALFRED   AC
TIGER, THE   DEFORD, MIRIAM ALLEN SS   INY 70 01
  INFINITY 1   HOSKINS, ROBERT   OA
TILL HUMAN VOICES WAKE US... TUTTLE, LISA   SS   CLR 73 03
  CLARION III   WILSON, ROBIN SCOTT   OA
TILT ANGLE   MACKELWORTH, R. W.   SS   NWR 69 14
  NEW WRITINGS IN SF. 9 CARNELL, JOHN   AN
  NEW WRITINGS IN SF. 14 CARNELL, JOHN   OA
TILTING ISLAND, THE   BENNETT, G. J.
                          AND VIVIAN, THOMAS J. SS C EVB 09 09
  SCIENCE FICTION BY GASLIGHT MOSKOWITZ, SAM   AN
TIMAIOS (EXCERPT)   PLATO   EX
  3000 YEARS OF FANTASY AND SCIENCE FICTION
                          DE CAMP, L. S.&C.   AN
TIMBERLINE   ALDISS, BRIAN W.   NV   FSF 61 09
  LONG AFTERNOON OF EARTH, THE ALDISS, BRIAN W.   NO
TIME AND TIME AGAIN   PIPER, H. BEAM   SS   ASF 47 04
  *TREASURY OF SCIENCE FICTION, A CONKLIN, GROFF   AN
  UBERWINDUNG VON RAUM UND ZEIT GUNTHER, GOTTHARD AN
TIME BEND   DORMAN, SONYA   SS   ORB 74 13
  ORBIT 13   KNIGHT, DAMON   OA
TIME BROTHER   JONES, RAYMOND F.   NV   COI 73
  CHILDREN OF INFINITY   ELWOOD, ROGER   OA
TIME BUM   KORNBLUTH, C. M.   SS   FAN 53 02
  *MILE BEYOND THE MOON, A KORNBLUTH, C. M.   AC
TIME CONQUEROR, THE (SEE THE TYRANT OF TIME)
                          ESHBACH, LLOYD A.   TC
TIME CONSIDERED AS A HELIX OF SEMI-PRECIOUS STONES
                          DELANY, SAMUEL R.   SS   NWS 68 12
  BEST SF STORIES FROM NEW WORLDS 7 MOORCOCK, MICHAEL AN
  DRIFTGLASS   DELANY, SAMUEL R.   AC
  HUGO WINNERS, THE (VOLUME 2) ASIMOV, ISAAC   AN
  IN DREAMS AWAKE   FIEDLER, LESLIE A.   AN
  NEBULA AWARD STORIES NO. 5 BLISH, JAMES   AN
  SHORES BENEATH, THE   SALLIS, JAMES   AN
  WORLD'S BEST SCIENCE FICTION: 1969 WOLLHEIM & CARR AN
TIME DECELERATOR, THE   MACFADYEN, A. JR.   SS   ASF 36 07
  CROSSROADS IN TIME   CONKLIN, GROFF   AN
  SCIENCE FICTION OF THE 30'S KNIGHT, DAMON   AN
TIME DEER   STRETE, CRAIG   SS   IFS 74 12
  BEST FROM IF, THE VOLUME III BAEN, JAMES   AN
  BEST SF: 1974   HARRISON & ALDISS   AN
  NEBULA AWARD STORIES 11 LE GUIN, URSULA K.   AN
TIME DWELLER, THE   MOORCOCK, MICHAEL   SS   NWS 64 02
  BEST OF NEW WORLDS, THE MOORCOCK, MICHAEL   AN
  TIME DWELLER, THE   MOORCOCK, MICHAEL   AC
TIME ENOUGH (ENOUGH TIME) KNIGHT, DAMON   SS   AMZ 60 07
  BEST OF DAMON KNIGHT, THE KNIGHT, DAMON   AC
  FAR OUT   KNIGHT, DAMON   AC
TIME EXPOSURES   TUCKER, WILSON   NV   UNI 71 01
  UNIVERSE 1   CARR, TERRY   OA
TIME FIGHTER   LEIBER, FRITZ   SS   FUN 57 03
  PAIL OF AIR, A   LEIBER, FRITZ   AC
TIME FOR SALE   FARLEY, RALPH MILNE SS   AMZ 38 08
  ANDROIDS, TIME MACHINES AND BLUE GIRAFFES
                          ELWOOD & GHIDALIA   AN
  OMNIBUS OF TIME, THE   FARLEY, RALPH MILNE   AC
TIME FUZE   GARRETT, RANDALL   SS   IFS 54 03
  SPACE OPERA   ALDISS, BRIAN W.   AN
TIME GATE, THE (BY HIS BOOTSTRAPS)
                          HEINLEIN, ROBERT A. NV   ASF 41 10
  RACE TO THE STARS   MARGULIES & FRIEND   AN
TIME HAS NO BOUNDARIES (SEE THE FACE IN THE PHOTO)
                          FINNEY, JACK   TC
TIME HEALS   ANDERSON, POUL   SS   ASF 49 10
  VOYAGERS IN TIME   SILVERBERG, ROBERT   AN
TIME IN ADVANCE   TENN, WILLIAM   NV   GAL 56 08
  INTRODUCING SCIENCE FICTION ALDISS, BRIAN W.   AN
  TIME IN ADVANCE   TENN, WILLIAM   AC
TIME IN THE ROUND   LEIBER, FRITZ   NV   GAL 57 05
  THIRD GALAXY READER, THE GOLD, H. L.   AN
TIME IN THY FLIGHT   BRADBURY, RAY   SS   FUN 53 06
  S IS FOR SPACE   BRADBURY, RAY   AC
TIME IS THE TRAITOR   BESTER, ALFRED   NV   FSF 53 09
  BEST SCIENCE-FICTION STORIES: 1954, THE BLEILER & DIKTY AN
  DARK SIDE OF THE EARTH, THE BESTER, ALFRED   AC
  SCIENCE FICTION: THE GREAT YEARS, VOL. II
                          POHL, C. & F.   AN
  SPACE ODYSSEYS   ALDISS, BRIAN W.   AN
  STAR LIGHT, STAR BRIGHT BESTER, ALFRED   AC
TIME LAG   ANDERSON, POUL   NV   FSF 61 01
  *BEST FROM FANTASY AND SCIENCE FICTION: 11
                          MILLS, ROBERT P.   AN
  QUEEN OF AIR AND DARKNESS AND OTHER STORIES, THE
                          ANDERSON, POUL   AC
TIME LOCKER   PADGETT, LEWIS   SS   ASF 43 01
  *ADVENTURES IN TIME AND SPACE HEALY & MCCOMAS   AN
  ROBOTS HAVE NO TAILS   PADGETT, LEWIS   AC
TIME MACHINE, THE   JONES, LANGDON   NV   ORB 69 05
  BEST FROM ORBIT, THE   KNIGHT, DAMON   AN
  EYE OF THE LENS, THE   JONES, LANGDON   AC
  ORBIT 5   KNIGHT, DAMON   OA
TIME MACHINE, THE   WELLS, H. G.   NA   NRV 95 01
  SCIENCE FICTION HALL OF FAME VOLUME 2A BOVA, BEN AN
  SEVEN FAMOUS NOVELS BY H. G. WELLS WELLS, H. G.   AC

TIME MACHINE, THE

SHORT STORIES OF H. G. WELLS, THE   WELLS, H. G.   AC
*TIME MACHINE AND OTHER STORIES, THE   WELLS, H. G.   AC
TIMES 4 (ABRIDGED STORIES)   ALLEN, VIRGINIA F.   AN
TRAVELERS IN TIME   STERN, PHILIP VAN D.   AN
TREASURY OF SCIENCE FICTION CLASSICS, THE
                                           KUEBLER, HAROLD W.   AN
WAR OF THE WORLDS, THE TIME MACHINE AND SELECTED SHORT STORIES
                                           WELLS, H. G.   AC
3 PROPHETIC SCIENCE FICTION NOVELS OF H. G. WELLS
                                           WELLS, H. G.   AC
TIME MACHINE, THE (CHAPTER XI, XII-PART)
                                           WELLS, H. G.   EX NRV 95 01
VOYAGERS IN TIME   SILVERBERG, ROBERT   AN
TIME MACHINE, THE (SELECTION FROM)
                                           WELLS, H. G.   EX NRV 95 01
CENTURY OF SCIENCE FICTION, A   KNIGHT, DAMON   AN
TIME MACHINE, THE (THE HAPPINESS MACHINE)
                                           BRADBURY, RAY   SS SEP 57 09
R IS FOR ROCKET   BRADBURY, RAY   AC
TIME OF CHANGES, A   HOSKINS, ROBERT IN INY 72 03
INFINITY 3   HOSKINS, ROBERT   OA
TIME OF GOING AWAY, THE   BRADBURY, RAY   SS REP 56 11
DAY IT RAINED FOREVER, THE   BRADBURY, RAY   AC
MEDICINE FOR MELANCHOLY, A   BRADBURY, RAY   AC
TIME OF HIS LIFE, THE   EISENBERG, LARRY SS FSF 68 04
ALPHA 1   SILVERBERG, ROBERT   AN
BEST LAID SCHEMES, THE   EISENBERG, LARRY   AC
TIME OF MIND, A   WELLS, KEITH   SS NWR 75 27
NEW WRITINGS IN SF. 27   BULMER, KENNETH   OA
TIME OF PASSAGE   BALLARD, J. G.   SS SCF 64 02
IMPOSSIBLE MAN, THE   BALLARD, J. G.   AC
OVERLOADED MAN, THE   BALLARD, J. G.   AC
TIME OF PEACE, A   CHRISTOPHER, JOHN SS STN 57 10
TWENTY-SECOND CENTURY, THE   CHRISTOPHER, JOHN   AC
TIME OF THE BIG SLEEP, THE   ANDREVON,JEAN-PIERRE NV 71
SHOCKING THING, A   KNIGHT, DAMON   AN
TIME OF THE EYE, THE   ELLISON, HARLAN SS SMM 59 05
ALONE AGAINST TOMORROW   ELLISON, HARLAN   AC
FROM THE LAND OF FEAR   ELLISON, HARLAN   AC
TIME OF THE FOURTH HORSEMAN, A YARBRO, CHELSEA Q. NV INY 72 03
INFINITY 3   HOSKINS, ROBERT   OA
TIME ON OUR HANDS: AN INTRODUCTION
                                           EDELSTEIN, SCOTT   IN
FUTURE PASTIMES   EDELSTEIN, SCOTT   OA
TIME OUT   WYNDHAM, JOHN   NV
INFINITE MOMENT, THE   WYNDHAM, JOHN   AC
TIME OUT FOR TOMORROW   WILSON, RICHARD SS SCF 57 12
TIME OUT FOR TOMORROW   WILSON, RICHARD   AC
TIME OUT OF MIND   BOULLE, PIERRE   NV
TIME OUT OF MIND   BOULLE, PIERRE   OC
TIME PATROL   ANDERSON, POUL   NV FSF 55 05
GUARDIANS OF TIME   ANDERSON, POUL   AC
TIME PAWN (SEE DR. FUTURITY)   DICK, PHILIP K. TC TWS 54 SU
TIME PIECE   HALDEMAN, JOE W. SS IFS 70 07
COMBAT SF   DICKSON, GORDON R.   AN
TIME PIECE, THE   WILHELM, KATE   NV NEW 75 AC
INFINITY BOX, THE   WILHELM, KATE   AC
TIME PUSSY   ASIMOV, ISAAC   SS ASF 42 04
EARLY ASIMOV, THE   ASIMOV, ISAAC   AC
THREE SCIENCE FICTION NOVELS   TAINE, JOHN   AC
TIME STREAM, THE   TAINE, JOHN   NO WOS 31 12
TIME THIEVES, THE (THE STAR-SENT KNAVES)
                                           LAUMER, KEITH   NV WOT 63 06
TIMETRACKS   LAUMER, KEITH   AC
TIME TO CHANGE (MIRROR IMAGE) ACKERMAN, FORREST J.
                                           AND SOUTO, MARCIAL SS C 68
SCIENCE FICTION WORLDS OF FORREST J. ACKERMAN & FRIENDS
                                           ACKERMAN, FORREST J. AC
TIME TO DIE   LEINSTER, MURRAY SS ASF 47 01
BEST OF MURRAY LEINSTER, THE   LEINSTER, MURRAY   AC
TIME TO KEEP, A   WILHELM, KATE   SS FSF 62 01
DOWNSTAIRS ROOM AND OTHER SPECULATIVE FICTION, THE
                                           WILHELM, KATE   AC
TIME TO REND, A (SEE NO OTHER GODS BUT ME)
                                           BRUNNER, JOHN   TC
TIME TO REST   HARRIS, JOHN BEYNON SS ARS 49 WI
FAR BOUNDARIES   DERLETH, AUGUST   AN
TIME TO REST   WYNDHAM, JOHN   SS ARS 49 WI
SEEDS OF TIME, THE   WYNDHAM, JOHN   AC
TIME TO REST (COMBINED WITH "NO PLACE LIKE EARTH", NWS 51 SP)
                                           BEYNON, JOHN   NV ARS 49 WI
*NO PLACE LIKE EARTH   CARNELL, JOHN   AN
TIME TO SURVIVE, A (SEE SEEDING PROGRAMME)
                                           BLISH, JAMES   TC
TIME TRANSFER   SELLINGS, ARTHUR   SS
*TIME TRANSFER   SELLINGS, ARTHUR   AC
TIME TRAP   HARNESS, CHARLES L. NV ASF 48 08
ALPHA 1   SILVERBERG, ROBERT   AN
TRAPS OF TIME, THE   MOORCOCK, MICHAEL   AN
TIME TRAP (JOYCE PERRY)   FOSTER, ALAN DEAN SA SLG 75 04
STAR TREK LOG FOUR   FOSTER, ALAN DEAN   OC
TIME TRAP, THE   KUTTNER, HENRY   NO MSS 38 11
EVIL EARTHS   ALDISS, BRIAN W.   AN
TIME TRAVEL AND THE LAW   KORNBLUTH, C. M.   AR
COMING ATTRACTIONS   GREENBERG, MARTIN   NF
TIME TRAVEL FOR PEDESTRIANS   NELSON, RAY   SS DVS 72 02
AGAIN, DANGEROUS VISIONS   ELLISON, HARLAN   OA
TIME TRAVELLER, THE   FARLEY, RALPH MILNE SS WRT 31 08
OMNIBUS OF TIME, THE   FARLEY, RALPH MILNE   AC
TIME TRAWLERS, THE   FILER, BURT K.   SS GAL 68 08
ELEVENTH GALAXY READER, THE   POHL, FREDERIK   AN
TIME WAGER, THE   KIPPAX, JOHN   SS NWR 73 22
NEW WRITINGS IN SF. 22   BULMER, KENNETH   OA
TIME WAITS FOR WINTHROP (ALSO AS WINTHROP WAS STUBBORN)
                                           TENN, WILLIAM   NA GAL 57 08

TO ARKHAM AND THE STARS

TIME WAITS FOR WINTHROP, AND FOUR OTHER SHORT NOVELS
                                           POHL, FREDERIK   AN
TIME WANTS A SKELETON   ROCKLYNNE, ROSS NV ASF 41 06
ASTOUNDING-ANALOG READER, THE VOLUME ONE HARRISON & ALDISS AN
TIME WOUNDS ALL HEELS   BLOCH, ROBERT   SS FAD 42 04
TIME CURVE, THE   MOSKOWITZ & ELWOOD AN
TIME'S ARROW   CLARKE, ARTHUR C. SS SCF 50 SU
ACROSS THE SEA OF STARS   CLARKE, ARTHUR C.   AC
REACH FOR TOMORROW   CLARKE, ARTHUR C.   AC
TIME'S MAUSOLEUM   JONES, NEIL R.   SS AMZ 33 12
SUNLESS WORLD, THE   JONES, NEIL R.   AC
TIME-HOPPERS, THE   SILVERBERG, ROBERT NO DBL 67
SCIENCE FICTION SPECIAL 3   ANONYMOUS   AN
TIME-TOMBS, THE   BALLARD, J. G.   NV IFS 63 03
OVERLOADED MAN, THE   BALLARD, J. G.   AC
SECOND IF READER OF SCIENCE FICTION, THE POHL, FREDERIK   AN
TERMINAL BEACH (AMERICAN VERSION)   BALLARD, J. G.   AC
TIME-TRAVEL HAPPENS!   PHILLIPS, A. M. AR UNK 39 12
*ADVENTURES IN TIME AND SPACE   HEALY & MCCOMAS   AN
TIME-TRAVELER, THE   ROBINSON, SPIDER NV ASF 74 04
CALLAHAN'S CROSSTIME SALOON   ROBINSON, SPIDER   AC
TIME-WISE GUY, THE   FARLEY, RALPH MILNE SS AMZ 40 05
OMNIBUS OF TIME, THE   FARLEY, RALPH MILNE   AC
TIMED CLOCK, THE   VAN VOGT, A. E. SS NEW 72 05
BOOK OF VAN VOGT, THE   VAN VOGT, A. E.   AC
TIMELESS ONES, THE   RUSSELL, ERIC FRANK NV SFQ 52 11
FAR STARS   RUSSELL, ERIC FRANK   AC
PRIZE SCIENCE FICTION   WOLLHEIM, DONALD A.   AN
TIMELINE FOR KNOWN SPACE   NIVEN, LARRY   MS
TALES OF KNOWN SPACE: THE UNIVERSE OF LARRY NIVEN
                                           NIVEN, LARRY   AC
TIMELINE FROM THE INSTRUMENTALITY OF MANKIND
                                           PIERCE, J. J.   MS
BEST OF CORDWAINER SMITH, THE   SMITH, CORDWAINER   AC
TIMESCAPE   BUTLER, MILDRED
                                           AND ENGDAHL, SYLVIA NV C
ANYWHERE, ANYWHEN   ENGDAHL, SYLVIA   OA
TIMESCOOP   BRUNNER, JOHN   NO 69
SCIENCE FICTION SPECIAL 8   ANONYMOUS   AN
TIMESPRAWL   WARDEN, ANTHON   SS INY 71 02
INFINITY 2   HOSKINS, ROBERT   OA
TIMESTORM   BERTIN, EDDY C. SS 71
1972 ANNUAL WORLD'S BEST SF, THE   WOLLHEIM, DONALD A.   AN
TIMESWEEPERS, THE   LAUMER, KEITH   NV ASF 69 08
TIMETRACKS   LAUMER, KEITH   AC
TIMETIPPING   DANN, JACK M.   SS EPC 75
EPOCH   ELWOOD & SILVERBERG   OA
TIMID TIGER, THE   RUSSELL, ERIC FRANK SS ASF 47 02
DEEP SPACE   RUSSELL, ERIC FRANK   AC
TIMOTHY   ROBERTS, KEITH   IN IMP 66 09
NEW WORLDS OF FANTASY   CARR, TERRY   AN
TIN FISHES, THE   CHANDLER, A. BERTRAM NV IFS 68 1.
RIM GODS, THE   CHANDLER, A. BERTRAM DC
TIN LIZZIE   GARRETT, RANDALL NV AMZ 64 06
GREAT SCIENCE FICTION STORIES ABOUT MARS DIKTY, T. E.   AN
TIN MESSIAH, THE   CHANDLER, A. BERTRAM SS
HARD WAY UP, THE   CHANDLER, A. BERTRAM DC
TIN SOLDIER   VINGE, JOAN D.   NA ORB 74 14
MORE WOMEN OF WONDER   SARGENT, PAMELA   AN
ORBIT 14   KNIGHT, DAMON   AC
TIN YOU LOVE TO TOUCH, THE   BLOCH, ROBERT   SS OWS 51 07
OTHER WORLDS, OTHER TIMES   MOSKOWITZ & ELWOOD   AN
TINDAR-B   CONNER, PATRICK G. NV STL 76 02
STELLAR 2   DEL REY, JUDY-LYNN   OA
TINKER   POURNELLE, JERRY NA GAL 75 04
BEST FROM GALAXY, THE   VOLUME IV   BAEN, JAMES   AN
HIGH JUSTICE   POURNELLE, JERRY   AC
TINKER OF TAMLACHT, THE   MACMANUS, S.   SS
DEALS WITH THE DEVIL   DAVENPORT, BASIL   AN
TINKLER, THE   ANDERSON, POUL   SS WBY 51 02
*WORLDS OF TOMORROW   DERLETH, AUGUST   AN
TINY ALLY   ELLISON, HARLAN SS STN 57 10
OVER THE EDGE   ELLISON, HARLAN   AC
TINY AND THE MONSTER   STURGEON, THEODORE NV ASF 47 05
*INVADERS OF EARTH   CONKLIN, GROFF   AN
THUNDER AND ROSES   STURGEON, THEODORE   AC
*WAY HOME, A   STURGEON, THEODORE   AC
TIRED OLD MAN   ELLISON, HARLAN SS MSM 76 01
NO DOORS, NO WINDOWS (STORIES REWRITTEN) ELLISON, HARLAN   AC
'TIS THE SEASON TO BE JELLY   MATHESON, RICHARD SS FSF 63 06
SHOCK III   MATHESON, RICHARD   AC
TISSUE-CULTURE KING, THE   HUXLEY, JULIAN   SS AMZ 27 08
*BEST OF SCIENCE FICTION   CONKLIN, GROFF   AN
GREAT SCIENCE FICTION BY SCIENTISTS   CONKLIN, GROFF   AN
TIME PROBE: THE SCIENCES IN SF.   CLARKE, ARTHUR C.   AN
TITAN, THE   MILLER, P. SCHUYLER NV MVT 34 WI
TITAN, THE   MILLER, P. SCHUYLER   AC
TITHONUS   THOMAS, D. M.   PM PMP 68 1.
HOLDING YOUR EIGHT HANDS   LUCIE-SMITH, EDWARD   AN
SCIENCE FICTION: THE FUTURE   ALLEN, DICK   AN
TITLE   WELLEN, EDWARD   SS ORB 74 15
ORBIT 15   KNIGHT, DAMON   OA
TITLE FIGHT   GAULT, WILLIAM C. SS FUN 56 12
FANTASTIC UNIVERSE OMNIBUS, THE   SANTESSON, HANS S.   AN
RUN TO STARLIGHT, SPORTS THROUGH SCIENCE FICTION
                                           GREENBERG/OLANDER/& AN
TO A MISSING MEMBER OF A FAMILY GROUP OF TERMS IN AN
ALGEBRAIC FORMULA   MORLEY, CHRISTOPHER PM   50
MATHEMATICAL MAGPIE, THE   FADIMAN, CLIFTON   AN
TO A RIPE OLD AGE   TUCKER, WILSON   SS FSF 52 12
SHADOW OF TOMORROW   POHL, FREDERIK   AN
TO AN ASTRONAUT DYING YOUNG KUMIN, MAXINE W. PM ATL 61 12
7TH ANNUAL OF THE YEAR'S BEST S-F, THE MERRIL, JUDITH   AN
TO ARKHAM AND THE STARS   LEIBER, FRITZ   AR 66
BOOK OF FRITZ LEIBER, THE   LEIBER, FRITZ   AC

TO AVENGE MAN (ALSO AS VENGEANCE IS MINE)
                              DEL REY, LESTER   NV   GAL 64 12
  NINTH GALAXY READER, THE   POHL, FREDERIK   AN
TO BE A MAN   COUPLING, J. J.   SS   YRT 70
  YEAR 2000, THE   HARRISON, HARRY   OA
TO BE CONTINUED   KNIGHT, DAMON   SS   FSF 59 10
  OFF CENTRE   KNIGHT, DAMON   AC
TO BE CONTINUED   SILVERBERG, ROBERT   SS   ASF 56 05
  MOONFERNS & STARSONGS   SILVERBERG, ROBERT   AC
  STRANGE GIFTS   SILVERBERG, ROBERT   AN
TO BEHOLD THE SUN   KOONTZ, DEAN R.   SS   FSF 67 12
  SOFT COME THE DRAGONS   KOONTZ, DEAN R.   DC
TO BUILD A WORLD (SEE STRANGE BEDFELLOWS)
                              ANDERSON, POUL   TC
TO CATCH AN ALIEN   MCGUIRE, JOHN J.   SS   STR 59 06
  STAR SCIENCE FICTION STORIES NO. 6 POHL, FREDERIK   OA
TO CEREMARK   BERMAN, RUTH   SS
  NEW VOICES IN SCIENCE FICTION MARTIN, GEORGE R. R. OA
TO CHANGE THE PAST   CUMMINGS, M. A.   SS
  EXILE AND OTHER TALES OF FANTASY CUMMINGS, M. A.   OC
TO CHANGE THEIR WAYS   MARTINO, JOSEPH P.   NV   ASF 67 04
  OUT OF THIS WORLD 7   WILLIAMS-ELLIS& OWEN   AN
TO CIVILIZE   BUDRYS, ALGIS   SS   FUT 54 01
  GALACTIC EMPIRES VOLUME TWO ALDISS, BRIAN W.   AN
TO EACH HIS OWN   SHARKEY, JACK   SS   IFS 60 01
  6 FINGERS OF TIME AND 5 OTHER SCIENCE FICTION NOVELETS, THE
                              ANONYMOUS   AN
TO EACH HIS STAR   WALTON, BRYCE   SS   SSF 52 05
  SPACE ODYSSEYS   ALDISS, BRIAN W.   AN
TO EXPLAIN MRS. THOMPSON   LATHAM, PHILIP   SS   ASF 51 11
  EXPERT DREAMERS, THE   POHL, FREDERIK   AN
TO FACE ETERNITY   BUNCH, DAVID R.   SS
  MODERAN   BUNCH, DAVID R.   AC
TO FELL A TREE   YOUNG, ROBERT F.   NV   FSF 59 07
  DECADE OF FANTASY AND SCIENCE FICTION, A MILLS, ROBERT P. AN
  GLASS OF STARS, A   YOUNG, ROBERT F.   AC
TO FIT THE CRIME   MATHESON, RICHARD   SS   FAN 52 12
  BORN OF MAN AND WOMAN   MATHESON, RICHARD   AC
  THIRD FROM THE SUN   MATHESON, RICHARD   AC
TO FOLLOW KNOWLEDGE   LONG, FRANK BELKNAP SS   ASF 42 12
  ADVENTURES IN DIMENSION   CONKLIN, GROFF   AN
  *SCIENCE FICTION ADVENTURES IN DIMENSION CONKLIN, GROFF AN
TO GIVE THEM BEAUTY FOR ASHES MCCLINTIC, WINONA   PM   FSF 59 09
  BEST FROM FANTASY AND SCIENCE FICTION: 9
                              MILLS, ROBERT P.   AN
TO HELL WITH THE ODDS   FISH, ROBERT L.   SS   FSF 58 02
  RUN TO STARLIGHT, SPORTS THROUGH SCIENCE FICTION
                              GREENBERG/OLANDER/&   AN
TO HERE AND THE EASEL   STURGEON, THEODORE   SN   SSN 54
  STAR SHORT NOVELS   POHL, FREDERIK   OA
  STURGEON IS ALIVE AND WELL... STURGEON, THEODORE   AC
  TO HERE AND THE EASEL   STURGEON, THEODORE   AC
TO KILL OR CURE   WHITE, JAMES   SS   NWS 57 04
  ALIENS AMONG US, THE   WHITE, JAMES   AC
TO LOVE ANOTHER   BLISH, JAMES
                              AND KNIGHT, NORMAN L. NV C ASF 67 04
  TORRENT OF FACES, A   BLISH & KNIGHT, N.   NO
TO MAKE A NEW NEANDERTHAL   MACFARLANE, WALLACE SS   ASF 71 09
  BEST SCIENCE FICTION STORIES OF THE YEAR (1971)
                              DEL REY, LESTER   AN
TO MARK THE YEAR ON AZLAROC   SABERHAGEN, FRED   SS
  SCIENCE FICTION DISCOVERIES POHL, C. & F.   OA
TO MARRY MEDUSA   STURGEON, THEODORE   NA   GAL 58 08
  JOYOUS INVASION, THE   STURGEON, THEODORE   AC
  TIME WAITS FOR WINTHROP, AND FOUR OTHER SHORT NOVELS
                              POHL, FREDERIK   AN
TO MYSELF ON THE OCCASION OF MY TWENTY-FIRST CENTURY
                              BRUNNER, JOHN   PM   69
  HOLDING YOUR EIGHT HANDS   LUCIE-SMITH, EDWARD   AN
TO OPEN THE SKY (OPEN THE SKY) SILVERBERG, ROBERT NV   GAL 66 06
  TO OPEN THE SKY   SILVERBERG, ROBERT   NO
TO PAY THE PIPER   BLISH, JAMES   SS   IFS 56 02
  *GALACTIC CLUSTER   BLISH, JAMES   AC
TO PEOPLE A NEW WORLD   BOND, NELSON S.   SS   BBM 50 11
  *BEACHHEADS IN SPACE   DERLETH, AUGUST   AN
  NIGHTMARES AND DAYDREAMS   BOND, NELSON S.   AC
TO PLANT A SEED   DAVIS, HANK   SS   ORB 72 11
  ORBIT 11   KNIGHT, DAMON   OA
TO PROMOTE THE GENERAL WELFARE ANDERSON, POUL   NV   CTM 75 04
  CONTINUUM 4   ELWOOD, ROGER   OA
TO RELIEVE THE SANITY   MALEC, ALEXANDER B. SS
  EXTRAPOLASIS   MALEC, ALEXANDER B.   AC
TO RIDE PEGASUS   MCCAFFREY, ANNE   NV   NEW 73 02
  TO RIDE PEGASUS   MCCAFFREY, ANNE   AC
TO SEE ANOTHER MOUNTAIN   POHL, FREDERIK   SS   FSF 59 04
  IN THE PROBLEM PIT   POHL, FREDERIK   AC
  TOMORROW TIMES SEVEN   POHL, FREDERIK   AC
TO SEE THE INVISIBLE MAN   SILVERBERG, ROBERT   SS   WOT 63 04
  ANOTHER TOMORROW   HOLLISTER, BERNARD C   AN
  BEST OF ROBERT SILVERBERG, THE SILVERBERG, ROBERT   AC
  EARTH IN TRANSIT   SCHWARTZ, SHEILA   AN
  EARTH'S OTHER SHADOW   SILVERBERG, ROBERT   AC
  NEEDLE IN A TIMESTACK   SILVERBERG, ROBERT   AC
  SF: AUTHORS' CHOICE 2   HARRISON, HARRY   AN
TO SEE THE RABBIT   BROWNJOHN, ALAN   PM
  STARLIT CORRIDOR, THE   MANSFIELD, ROGER   AN
TO SERVE MAN   KNIGHT, DAMON   SS   GAL 50 11
  BEST OF DAMON KNIGHT, THE   KNIGHT, DAMON   AC
  BEST SCIENCE-FICTION STORIES: 1951, THE BLEILER & DIKTY AN
  COSMIC LAUGHTER   HALDEMAN, JOE W.   AN
  FAR OUT   KNIGHT, DAMON   AC
  FRONTIERS IN SPACE   BLEILER & DIKTY   AN
  HISTORY OF THE SCIENCE FICTION MAGAZINE, THE PART 3 1946-1955
                              ASHLEY, MICHAEL   AN
  MINDWORM, THE   ANONYMOUS   AN

TO SERVE THE SHIP (ALSO AS SOLUTION)
                              NOLAN, WILLIAM F.   SS   GAM 63 01
  IMPACT-20   NOLAN, WILLIAM F.   AC
TO SLEEP, PERCHANCE TO DREAM MACKENROTH, NANCY   SS   74
  FAR SIDE OF TIME, THE   ELWOOD, ROGER   OA
  GIFTS OF ASTI AND OTHER STORIES OF SCIENCE FICTION
                              ELWOOD, ROGER   AN
TO SPORT WITH AMARYLLIS   HILL, RICHARD   SS   ORB 70 07
  ORBIT 7   KNIGHT, DAMON   OA
TO START A CONTROVERSY   PORTER, PETER   PM   64
  HOLDING YOUR EIGHT HANDS   LUCIE-SMITH, EDWARD   AN
TO THE ASSOCIATION   EMSHWILLER, CAROL   SS
  JOY IN OUR CAUSE   EMSHWILLER, CAROL   AC
TO THE CHICAGO ABYSS   BRADBURY, RAY   PL   FSF 63 05
  WONDERFUL ICE CREAM SUIT AND OTHER PLAYS, THE
                              BRADBURY, RAY   AC
TO THE CHICAGO ABYSS   BRADBURY, RAY   SS   FSF 63 05
  BEST FROM FANTASY AND SCIENCE FICTION, 25TH ANNIV.
                              FERMAN, EDWARD L.   AN
  MACHINERIES OF JOY, THE   BRADBURY, RAY   AC
  SCIENCE FICTION: THE FUTURE ALLEN, DICK   AN
TO THE CHILD WHOSE BIRTH WILL CHANGE THE WAY THE UNIVERSE
  WORKS   STANLEY, GEORGE   PM   QRK 71 03
  QUARK/3   DELANY & HACKER   OA
TO THE DARK STAR   SILVERBERG, ROBERT   SS   FRS 68
  BEST SF: 1968   HARRISON & ALDISS   AN
  CUBE ROOT OF UNCERTAINTY, THE SILVERBERG, ROBERT   AC
  EARTH'S OTHER SHADOW   SILVERBERG, ROBERT   AC
  FARTHEST REACHES, THE   ELDER, JOSEPH   OA
TO THE END OF TIME   WILLIAMS, ROBERT M. SS   SSS 50 07
  TO THE END OF TIME AND OTHER STORIES WILLIAMS, ROBERT M. DC
TO THE FAR REACHES OF SPACE (FROM THE SKYLARK OF SPACE)
                              SMITH, EDWARD E. PHD EX   AMZ 28 08
  BEST OF E. E. 'DOC' SMITH, THE SMITH, EDWARD E. PHD   AC
TO THE FUTURE (SEE THE FOX AND THE FOREST)
                              BRADBURY, RAY   TC
TO THE HILLS;   GOLD, H. L.   ED   GAL 53 10
  SECOND GALAXY READER OF SCIENCE FICTION GOLD, H. L.   AN
TO THE MOON, 1969   DEUTSCH, BABETTE   PM
  SPECULATIONS   SANDERS, THOMAS E.   AN
TO THE MOUNTAINS   HANEY, LAURA   SS   CLR 72 02
  CLARION II   WILSON, ROBIN SCOTT   OA
TO THE PUMP ROOM WITH JANE   WATSON, IAN   SS   NWR 75 26
  NEW WRITINGS IN SF. 26   BULMER, KENNETH   OA
TO THE PURE   KNIGHT, DAMON   SS   NWS 66 10
  TURNING ON   KNIGHT, DAMON   AC
TO THE RESCUE   GOULART, RON   SS   FSF 66 01
  BROKE DOWN ENGINE AND OTHER TROUBLES WITH MACHINES
                              GOULART, RON   AC
TO THE STARS AND BEYOND ON THE FABULOUS ANTI-SYNTAX DRIVE
                              HARRISON, M. JOHN   SS   NWB 73 05
  NEW WORLDS QUARTERLY NO. 5 MOORCOCK, MICHAEL   OA
TO THE WORLD OF ZZZD   STREET, CLAIRE EDWIN SS
  TUNNEL AND OTHER STORIES, THE ELWOOD, ROGER   OA
TO THINK THAT TWO AND TWO ARE FOUR
                              HOUSEMAN, A. E.   PM   40
  FANTASIA MATHEMATICA   FADIMAN, CLIFTON   AN
TO WALK A CITY'S STREET   SIMAK, CLIFFORD D.   SS   INY 72 02
  INFINITY 3   HOSKINS, ROBERT   OA
  1973 ANNUAL WORLD'S BEST SF, THE WOLLHEIM, DONALD A.   AN
TO WALK THE NIGHT   SLOANE, WILLIAM   NO   FSY 37
  RIM OF MORNING, THE   SLOANE, WILLIAM   AC
TO WHOM THIS MAY COME (1888) BELLAMY, EDWARD   SS   HRP 88
  FUTURE PERFECT   FRANKLIN, H. BRUCE   AN
TOADS OF GRIMMERDALE, THE   NORTON, ANDRE   NV   FLS 73 02
  MANY WORLDS OF ANDRE NORTON, THE NORTON, ANDRE   AC
TOBERMORY   SAKI   SS
  JOURNEYS IN SCIENCE FICTION LOUGHLIN, RICHARD L.   AN
TODAY'S TOMORROWS   GOLD, H. L.   IN
  5 GALAXY SHORT NOVELS   GOLD, H. L.   AN
TOE THE LINE   ELLISON, HARLAN   SS   SMM 57 06
  NO DOORS, NO WINDOWS (STORIES REWRITTEN) ELLISON, HARLAN AC
TOE TO TIP, TIP TO TOE, PIP-POP AS YOU GO
                              NOLAN, WILLIAM F.   SS   FIN 70
  ALIEN HORIZONS   NOLAN, WILLIAM F.   AC
  FUTURE IS NOW, THE   NOLAN, WILLIAM F.   OA
TOLD IN THE DESERT   SMITH, CLARK ASHTON SS   64
  OTHER DIMENSIONS   SMITH, CLARK ASHTON   AC
TOLERANCES OF THE HUMAN FACE BALLARD, J. G.   SS   ENC 69 09
  LOVE & NAPALM: EXPORT U.S.A. BALLARD, J. G.   AC
TOLLIVER'S TRAVELS   FENTON, FRANK
                              AND PETRACCA, JOSEPH NV C NTS 51
  NEW TALES OF SPACE AND TIME HEALY, RAYMOND J.   OA
TOM EDISON'S SHAGGY DOG   VONNEGUT, KURT JR.   SS   COL 53 03
  CANARY IN A CAT HOUSE   VONNEGUT, KURT JR.   AC
  WELCOME TO THE MONKEY HOUSE VONNEGUT, KURT JR.   AC
TOMB TAPPER   BLISH, JAMES   SS   ASF 56 07
  *BEST SCIENCE FICTION STORIES OF JAMES BLISH
                              BLISH, JAMES   AC
  *GALACTIC CLUSTER   BLISH, JAMES   AC
TOMB-SPAWN, THE   SMITH, CLARK ASHTON SS   WRT 34 05
  TALES OF SCIENCE AND SORCERY SMITH, CLARK ASHTON   AC
TOMBLING DAY, THE   BRADBURY, RAY   SS   SHN 52 FL
  I SING THE BODY ELECTRIC   BRADBURY, RAY   AC
  SUPERNATURAL READER, THE   CONKLIN, G&L.   AN
TOMBS OF ATUAN, THE   LE GUIN, URSULA K.   NO   WOF 70 WI
  EARTHSEA   LE GUIN, URSULA K.   AC
TOMBSTONE, THE   BRADBURY, RAY   SS   WRT 45 03
  *DARK CARNIVAL   BRADBURY, RAY   AC
  SMALL ASSASSIN, THE   BRADBURY, RAY   AC
TOMORROW AND TOMORROW   BRADBURY, RAY   SS   FAN 65 11
  TIME UNTAMED   HOWARD, IVAN   AN
TOMORROW AND TOMORROW   PADGETT, LEWIS   SN   ASF 47 01
  TOMORROW AND TOMORROW AND THE FAIRY CHESSMEN
                              PADGETT, LEWIS   AC

TOMORROW AND TOMORROW AND TOMORROW (THE BIG TRIP UP YONDER)
                         VONNEGUT, KURT JR.   SS   GAL 54 01
   CANARY IN A CAT HOUSE   VONNEGUT, KURT JR.   AC
   CONNOISSEUR'S S. F.   BOARDMAN, TOM JR.   AN
   ECO-FICTION   STADLER, JOHN   AN
   LOOKING AHEAD   ALLEN, D. & L.   AN
   WELCOME TO THE MONKEY HOUSE VONNEGUT, KURT JR.   AC
TOMORROW IS A MILLION YEARS BALLARD, J. G. SS ARG 66 10
   DAY OF FOREVER, THE   BALLARD, J. G.   AC
   FARTHEST REACHES, THE   ELDER, JOSEPH   OA
TOMORROW IS HERE TO STAY   CROSSEN, KENDELL F. IN
   *FUTURE TENSE   CROSSEN, KENDELL F.   AN
TOMORROW IS YESTERDAY (D. C. FONTANA)
                             BLISH, JAMES   SA   STK 68 02
   STAR TREK 2   BLISH, JAMES   OC
TOMORROW'S ALTERNATIVES?   HERBERT, FRANK   IN   TAL 73
   FRONTIERS 1: TOMORROW'S ALTERNATIVES ELWOOD, ROGER OA
TOMORROW'S CHILD   BRADBURY, RAY   SS   NEW 69 AC
   I SING THE BODY ELECTRIC   BRADBURY, RAY   AC
   SPACE 2   DAVIS, RICHARD   OA
TOMORROW'S CHILDREN   ANDERSON, POUL   NV   ASF 47 03
   FIRST FLIGHT   KNIGHT, DAMON   AN
   MANY WORLDS OF POUL ANDERSON, THE ANDERSON, POUL AC
   TWILIGHT WORLD   ANDERSON, POUL   NO
TOMORROW'S CHILDREN   ANDERSON, POUL
                        AND WALDROP, F. N. NV C ASF 47 03
   MUTANTS   SILVERBERG, ROBERT   AN
   *TREASURY OF SCIENCE FICTION, A CONKLIN, GROFF   AN
TOMORROW'S GIFT   COOPER, EDMUND   SS   STR 58 04
   STAR SCIENCE FICTION STORIES NO. 4 POHL, FREDERIK OA
   TOMORROW'S GIFT   COOPER, EDMUND   AC
TOMORROW'S WALL STREET JOURNAL FAST, HOWARD   SS
   GENERAL ZAPPED AN ANGEL, THE FAST, HOWARD   OC
TONGUE OF BEAST   CLAUDY, CARL H. SS AMB 39 05
   YEAR AFTER TOMORROW, THE   DEL REY, L/MATSCHAT/ AN
TONIGHT THE SKY WILL FALL| GALOUYE, DANIEL F. SN IMG 52 05
   SPACE OPERA   ALDISS, BRIAN W.   AN
TONIGHT THE STARS REVOLT| FOX, GARDNER F. NA PLS 52 03
   GALACTIC EMPIRES VOLUME TWO ALDISS, BRIAN W.   AN
TONY AND THE BEETLES (SEE RETREAT FROM RIGEL)
                             DICK, PHILIP K. TC
TOO EARLY SPRING   BENET, STEPHEN V. SS   33
   NIGHT IN FUNLAND   BRONDFIELD, JEROME   AN
TOO FAR   BROWN, FREDRIC   SS FSF 55 09
   BEST FROM FANTASY AND SCIENCE FICTION: 5
                                BOUCHER, ANTHONY   AN
   HONEYMOON IN HELL   BROWN, FREDRIC   AC
TOO LATE FOR ETERNITY   WALTON, BRYCE   NO STS 55 SP
   DR. CYCLOPS   KUTTNER, HENRY   AN
TOO LONG AT THE FAIR   WELLEN, EDWARD   SS NOV 74 04
   NOVA 4   HARRISON, HARRY   OA
TOO MANY COOKS   EISENBERG, LARRY SS NEW 71 AC
   BEST LAID SCHEMES, THE   EISENBERG, LARRY   AC
TOO MANY ESKS   HOWARD, HAYDEN   NV GAL 66 10
   ESKIMO INVASION   HOWARD, HAYDEN   NO
TOO MANY PEOPLE   HOLLIS, H. H.   NV GAL 71 01
   BEST SCIENCE FICTION FOR 1972 POHL, FREDERIK   AN
TOOLS   SIMAK, CLIFFORD D. NV ASF 42 07
   *TREASURY OF SCIENCE FICTION, A CONKLIN, GROFF   AN
TOOLS OF THE TRADE   JONES, RAYMOND F. NV ASF 50 11
   SPACE, SPACE, SPACE   SLOANE, WILLIAM   AN
TOOTH FAIRY, THE   JACOBS, HARVEY   SS NEW 73 AN
   MORE LITTLE MONSTERS   ELWOOD & GHIDALIA   AN
TOOTH, THE   DEWEY, G. GORDON SS FSF 52 08
   BEST FROM FANTASY AND SCIENCE FICTION: 2
                                BOUCHER & MCCOMAS   AN
TOP SECRET   GRINNELL, DAVID SS FSF 50 FL
   *INVADERS OF EARTH   CONKLIN, GROFF   AN
TOP SECRET   RUSSELL, ERIC FRANK SS ASF 56 08
   SIX WORLDS YONDER   RUSSELL, ERIC FRANK   DC
TOP SECRET   WOLLHEIM, DONALD A. SS FSF 50 FL
   TWO DOZEN DRAGON EGGS   WOLLHEIM, DONALD A.   AC
TOP STAND-BY JOB (STAND-BY) DICK, PHILIP K. SS AMZ 63 10
   INSIDE INFORMATION   MOWSHOWITZ, ABBE   AN
   PRESERVING MACHINE, THE   DICK, PHILIP K.   AC
TOP, THE   ALBEE, GEORGE SUMNER SS FSF 62 08
   12 GREAT CLASSICS OF SCIENCE FICTION CONKLIN, GROFF AN
TOPICS FOR SHORTER AND LONGER PAPERS
                             MISC. MATERIAL   MS
   LOOKING AHEAD   ALLEN, D. & L.   AN
TOPICS OF WRITING AND RESEARCH MISC. MATERIAL   MS
   SCIENCE FICTION: THE FUTURE ALLEN, DICK   AN
TORRID SACRIFICE (SEE EN LA NOCHE)
                             BRADBURY, RAY   TC
TORTOISE-SHELL CAT, THE   LA SPINA, GREYE SS WRT 24 11
   BEWARE THE BEASTS   GHIDALIA, V.& ELWOOD AN
TOTAL ENVIRONMENT   ALDISS, BRIAN W. NV GAL 68 02
   ALPHA 3   SILVERBERG, ROBERT   AN
   CITY: 2000 A.D., THE   CLEM/GREENBERG/&   AN
   SOCIOLOGY THROUGH SCIENCE FICTION MILSTEAD/GREENBERG/& AN
   WORLD'S BEST SCIENCE FICTION: 1969 WOLLHEIM & CARR AN
TOTAL EXPERIENCE KICK, THE PLATT, CHARLES   SS NWS 66 12
   BEST SF STORIES FROM NEW WORLDS NO. 2, THE
                                MOORCOCK, MICHAEL   AN
   ENGLAND SWINGS SF   MERRIL, JUDITH   AN
   THEMES IN SCIENCE FICTION   KELLEY, LEO P.   AN
TOTAL RECALL   STERNIG, LARRY   SS PLS 46 FL
   TEEN-AGE SPACE ADVENTURES   FURMAN, A. L.   AN
TOTALLY RICH, THE   BRUNNER, JOHN   NV WOT 63 06
   DARK STARS   SILVERBERG, ROBERT   AN
   LATE GREAT FUTURE, THE   FITZ GERALD & DILLON AN
   *OUT OF MY MIND   BRUNNER, JOHN   AC
TOTEM AND TABOO   FARMER, PHILIP JOSE SS FSF 54 12
   BOOK OF PHILIP JOSE FARMER, THE FARMER, PHILIP JOSE AC
   CELESTIAL BLUEPRINT, THE   FARMER, PHILIP JOSE   DC

TOTENBUCH   PARRA (Y FIGUEREDO) SS DVS 72 02
   AGAIN, DANGEROUS VISIONS   ELLISON, HARLAN   OA
TOTO, I HAVE A FEELING WE'RE NOT IN KANSAS ANYMORE
                             MILLAR, JEFF   SS ORB 75 17
   ORBIT 17   KNIGHT, DAMON   OA
TOUCH AND GO (ALSO AS THE FRUIT AT THE BOTTOM OF THE BOWL)
                             BRADBURY, RAY   SS DBM 48 11
   AUTUMN PEOPLE, THE   BRADBURY, RAY   AC
TOUCH OF GRAPEFRUIT, A (ALSO AS THE CREEPING TERROR)
                             MATHESON, RICHARD SS STR 59 05
   STAR SCIENCE FICTION STORIES NO. 5 POHL, FREDERIK OA
TOUCH OF IMMORTALITY, A   MACKELWORTH, R. W. SS NWR 66 07
   NEW WRITINGS IN SF. 7   CARNELL, JOHN.   OA
TOUCH OF INFINITY, A   FAST, HOWARD   OC MOR 73
   TIME AND THE RIDDLE   FAST, HOWARD   AC
TOUCH OF NEANDERTHAL, A (SEE NEANDERTHAL PLANET)
                             ALDISS, BRIAN W. TC
TOUCH OF NUTMEG MAKES IT, THE COLLIER, JOHN SS   43
   SHOCKING THING, A   KNIGHT, DAMON   AN
TOUCH OF STRANGE, A   STURGEON, THEODORE SS FSF 58 01
   *TOUCH OF STRANGE, A   STURGEON, THEODORE   AC
   TWENTY YEARS OF FANTASY & SCIENCE FICTION
                                FERMAN & MILLS   AN
TOUCH OF YOUR HAND, THE   STURGEON, THEODORE NA GAL 53 09
   *TOUCH OF STRANGE, A   STURGEON, THEODORE   AC
TOUCHED WITH FIRE (SHOPPING FOR DEATH)
                             BRADBURY, RAY   SS MCL 54 06
   *OCTOBER COUNTRY, THE   BRADBURY, RAY   AC
TOUCHSTONE   CARR, TERRY   SS FSF 64 05
   BEST FROM FANTASY AND SCIENCE FICTION: 14
                                DAVIDSON, AVRAM   AN
   INTO THE UNKNOWN   CARR, TERRY   AN
   LIGHT AT THE END OF THE UNIVERSE, THE CARR, TERRY AN
TOUCHSTONE   MCLAUGHLIN, DEAN SS INY 72 03
   INFINITY 3   HOSKINS, ROBERT   OA
TOUGH OLD MAN   HUBBARD, L. RON SS STS 50 11
   SPACE POLICE   NORTON, ANDRE   AN
TOURING THE WORKSHOP   MCLAUGHLIN, DEAN IN
   HAWK AMONG THE SPARROWS   MCLAUGHLIN, DEAN   AC
TOURIST TRADE, THE   TUCKER, BOB   SS WBY 51 01
   TOMORROW, THE STARS   HEINLEIN, ROBERT A.   AN
TOURIST TRADE, THE   TUCKER, WILSON   SS WBY 51 01
   BEST SCIENCE-FICTION STORIES: 1952, THE BLEILER & DIKTY AN
TOWARD THE SPACE AGE   STAFFORD, WILLIAM PM   70
   SCIENCE FACT/FICTION   FARRELL/GAGE/&   AN
TOWARDS THE BELOVED CITY   FARMER, PHILIP JOSE NV SAW 72
   BOOK OF PHILIP JOSE FARMER, THE FARMER, PHILIP JOSE AC
   CHRONICLES OF A COMER AND OTHER RELIGIOUS SCIENCE FICTION
    STORIES   ELWOOD, ROGER   AN
   SIGNS AND WONDERS   ELWOOD, ROGER   OA
   VISIONS OF TOMORROW   ELWOOD, ROGER   AN
TOWARDS THE FALL OF NIGHT   ALDISS, BRIAN W. SI
   EVIL EARTHS   ALDISS, BRIAN W.   AN
TOWER OF THE ELEPHANT, THE HOWARD, ROBERT E. SS WRT 33 03
   COMING OF CONAN, THE   HOWARD, ROBERT E.   AC
   CONAN   HOWARD, R./DE CAMP/& AC
TOWER, THE   SCORTIA, THOMAS N. SS COI 73
   CHILDREN OF INFINITY   ELWOOD, ROGER   AN
TOWN WHERE NO ONE GOT OFF, THE BRADBURY, RAY SS EQM 58 10
   DAY IT RAINED FOREVER, THE   BRADBURY, RAY   AC
   MEDICINE FOR MELANCHOLY, A   BRADBURY, RAY   AC
TOY FOR JULIETTE, A   BLOCH, ROBERT   SS DVS 67 01
   DANGEROUS VISIONS   ELLISON, HARLAN   OA
   FEAR TODAY, GONE TOMORROW   BLOCH, ROBERT   AC
   PARTNERS IN WONDER   ELLISON, HARLAN   AC
TOY SHOP   HARRISON, HARRY SS ASF 62 04
   PRIME NUMBER   HARRISON, HARRY   AC
   8TH ANNUAL OF THE YEAR'S BEST S-F, THE MERRIL, JUDITH AN
TOY THEATER, THE   WOLFE, GENE   SS ORB 71 09
   ORBIT 9   KNIGHT, DAMON   OA
TOY, THE   JACOBS, HARVEY   SS
   EGG OF THE GLAK, AND OTHER STORIES, THE JACOBS, HARVEY AC
TOY, THE   NEVILLE, KRIS   SS IMG 52 12
   MISSION: MANSTOP   NEVILLE, KRIS   AC
TOYMAKER, THE   JONES, RAYMOND F. NV ASF 46 09
   TOYMAKER, THE   JONES, RAYMOND F.   AC
TOYS   PURDOM, TOM   SS ASF 67 10
   CRIME PREVENTION IN THE 30TH CENTURY SANTESSON, HANS S. AN
   THIS SIDE OF INFINITY   CARR, TERRY   AN
TOYS FOR DEBBIE   KYLE, DAVID A.   SS IFS 65 12
   SECOND IF READER OF SCIENCE FICTION, THE POHL, FREDERIK AN
TOYS OF PEACE, THE   SAKI   SS
   ECO-FICTION   STADLER, JOHN   AN
TRACE   BIXBY, JEROME   SS   61
   SPACE BY THE TAIL   BIXBY, JEROME   AC
TRACK TWO   MALZBERG, BARRY N. SS FAN 74 07
   BEST OF BARRY N. MALZBERG, THE MALZBERG, BARRY N. AC
TRACK 12   BALLARD, J. G.   SS NWS 58 04
   OVERLOADED MAN, THE   BALLARD, J. G.   AC
   PASSPORT TO ETERNITY   BALLARD, J. G.   AC
   PENGUIN SCIENCE FICTION   ALDISS, BRIAN W.   AC
TRACKING SONG   WOLFE, GENE   NA
   IN THE WAKE OF MAN   ELWOOD, ROGER   OA
TRADE-IN   SELLINGS, ARTHUR SS
   LONG EUREKA, THE   SELLINGS, ARTHUR   AC
TRADE-IN   SHARKEY, JACK   SS FSF 64 06
   BEST FROM FANTASY AND SCIENCE FICTION: 14
                                DAVIDSON, AVRAM   AN
TRADER TEAM (SEE THE TROUBLE TWISTERS)
                             ANDERSON, POUL   TC
TRADERS, THE   SIDNEY, KATHLEEN M. NV
   CLARION SF   WILHELM, KATE   AN
TRAFFIC PROBLEM   EARLS, WILLIAM   SS GAL 70 10
   BEST FROM GALAXY, THE VOLUME I GALAXY, EDITORS OF AN
   BEST SF: 1970   HARRISON & ALDISS   AN
   CITY: 2000 A.D., THE   CLEM/GREENBERG/&   AN

TRAIL BLAZER

TRAIL BLAZER   GALLUN, RAYMOND Z.   SS   FSM 51 FL
  SPACE PIONEERS   NORTON, ANDRE   AN
TRAIL TO THE STARS   LEYSON, CAPT. BURR W SS   BLF 50 02
  SCIENCE FICTION AND READER'S GUIDE BARROWS, MARJORIE   AN
TRAIN, THE   BEAUMONT, CHARLES   SS   NEW 57 AC
  HUNGER AND OTHER STORIES, THE   BEAUMONT, CHARLES   AC
TRAINEE FOR MARS (ALSO AS SIMULATED TRAINER)
                                 HARRISON, HARRY   SS   FUN 58 06
  SECOND ORBIT   DOHERTY, G. D.   AN
TRAINING DEVICE   COGSWELL, THEODORE R SS   IMG 55 03
  THIRD EYE, THE   COGSWELL, THEODORE R   AC
TRAINING TALK   BUNCH, DAVID R.   SS   FAN 64 03
  10TH ANNUAL OF THE YEAR'S BEST S-F, THE   MERRIL, JUDITH   AN
TRAITOR, THE   HART, JAMES S.   SS   FSF 50 FL
  SUPERNATURAL READER, THE   CONKLIN, G&L.   AN
TRAMMEL, THE   DEFORD, MIRIAM ALLEN SS
  DEALS WITH THE DEVIL   DAVENPORT, BASIL   AN
TRANQUILITY, OR ELSE! (SEE THE HAUNTED FUTURE)
                                 LEIBER, FRITZ   TC
TRANS-HUMAN, THE   LEINSTER, MURRAY   SS   SFP 53 12
  MONSTERS AND SUCH   LEINSTER, MURRAY   AC
TRANSCENDENT TIGERS, THE   LAFFERTY, R. A.   SS   WOT 64 02
  STRANGE DOINGS   LAFFERTY, R. A.   AC
  YOUNG DEMONS   ELWOOD & GHIDALIA   AN
TRANSCIENCE   CLARKE, ARTHUR C.   SS   STS 49 07
  LOOKING FORWARD   LESSER, MILTON   AN
  NINE BILLION NAMES OF GOD, THE   CLARKE, ARTHUR C.   AC
  OTHER SIDE OF THE SKY, THE   CLARKE, ARTHUR C.   AC
TRANSFER   MALZBERG, BARRY N.   SS   FAN 75 08
  DOWN HERE IN THE DREAM QUARTER   MALZBERG, BARRY N.   AC
TRANSFER POINT   BOUCHER, ANTHONY   SS   GAL 50 11
  ADVENTURES IN TOMORROW   CROSSEN, KENDELL F.   AN
  ALPHA 7   SILVERBERG, ROBERT   AN
  SHADOW OF TOMORROW   POHL, FREDERIK   AN
TRANSFER, THE   BLACKWOOD, ALGERNON SS   12
  MORE LITTLE MONSTERS   ELWOOD & GHIDALIA   AN
TRANSFER, THE   SELLINGS, ARTHUR   SS
  *TIME TRANSFER   SELLINGS, ARTHUR   AC
TRANSFINITE CHOICE, THE   MASSON, DAVID I.   SS   NWS 66 08
  BEST SF STORIES FROM NEW WORLDS NO. 2, THE
                                 MOORCOCK, MICHAEL   AN
  CALTRAPS OF TIME, THE   MASSON, DAVID I.   AC
  SCIENCE FICTION HORIZONS NO. 1   BOARDMAN, TOM JR.   AN
  SF: AUTHORS' CHOICE 3   HARRISON, HARRY   AN
TRANSFORMATION   SHELLEY, MARY W.   NV   KPS 31
  TALES AND STORIES   SHELLEY, MARY W.   AC
TRANSFORMER   OLIVER, CHAD   SS   FSF 54 11
  ANOTHER KIND   OLIVER, CHAD   AC
  MAN AGAINST TOMORROW   NOLAN, WILLIAM F.   AN
TRANSFUSION   OLIVER, CHAD   NV   ASF 59 06
  EDGE OF FOREVER, THE   OLIVER, CHAD   AC
  WORLDS OF WHEN   CONKLIN, GROFF   AN
TRANSIENT   JONES, LANGDON   SS   NWS 65 12
  BEST SF STORIES FROM NEW WORLDS 4   MOORCOCK, MICHAEL   AN
TRANSIT OF EARTH   CLARKE, ARTHUR C.   SS   PBY 71 01
  TRANSIT OF EARTH   PLAYBOY, EDITORS OF   AN
  WIND FROM THE SUN, THE   CLARKE, ARTHUR C.   AC
  1972 ANNUAL WORLD'S BEST SF, THE   WOLLHEIM, DONALD A.   AN
TRANSIT OF VENUS, THE   DEFORD, MIRIAM ALLEN SS   FSF 62 06
  XENOGENESIS   DEFORD, MIRIAM ALLEN   AC
TRANSITION TROLLEY, THE   HOWELL, JOSEPH   SS   SCS 73
  SHOWCASE   ELWOOD, ROGER   OA
TRANSITION- FROM FANTASY TO SCIENCE
                                 CLARKE, ARTHUR C.   AR   57
  SF:58, THE YEAR'S GREATEST SCIENCE FICTION AND FANTASY
                                 MERRIL, JUDITH   AN
TRANSLATION   EVANS, GLADYS   MS
  JOURNEY ACROSS THREE WORLDS   ANONYMOUS   AN
TRANSLATION   JACOBSON, HELEN   MS
  RUSSIAN SCIENCE FICTION, 1968   MAGIDOFF, ROBERT   AN
TRANSLATION   JOHNSON, DORIS   MS
  RUSSIAN SCIENCE FICTION   MAGIDOFF, ROBERT   AN
TRANSLATION   KOLESNIKOV, LEONID   MS
  DESTINATION: AMALTHEIA   DIXON, RICHARD   AN
TRANSLATION   MILES, HAMIS   MS
  WEIGHER OF SOULS AND THE EARTH DWELLERS, THE
                                 MAUROIS, ANDRE   AC
TRANSLATION   URWIN, IRIS   MS
  LOST FACE, THE   NESVADBA, JOSEF   AC
TRANSLATION ERROR   SILVERBERG, ROBERT   SS   ASF 59 03
  CUBE ROOT OF UNCERTAINTY, THE   SILVERBERG, ROBERT   AC
  TRANSFORMATIONS II   ROSELLE, DANIEL   AN
  WORLDS OF MAYBE   SILVERBERG, ROBERT   AN
TRANSLATIONS   GUNN, JAMES E.   MS
  BREAKING POINT   GUNN, JAMES E.   AC
TRANSLATOR, THE   BLAKE, E. MICHAEL   SS
  MIND ANGEL AND OTHER STORIES, THE   ELWOOD, ROGER   OA
TRANSPLANT   JONES, LANGDON   PM   NWS 69 10
  BEST SF STORIES FROM NEW WORLDS 7   MOORCOCK, MICHAEL   AN
TRANSPLANT   PRIEST, CHRISTOPHER SS   IFS 74 02
  REAL-TIME WORLD   PRIEST, CHRISTOPHER   AC
TRANSURANIC   HAMILTON, EDMOND   SS   TWS 48 02
  WHAT'S IT LIKE OUT THERE? AND OTHER STORIES
                                 HAMILTON, EDMOND   AC
TRAP   SHECKLEY, ROBERT   SS   GAL 56 02
  PILGRIMAGE TO EARTH   SHECKLEY, ROBERT   AC
TRAP, THE   BENNETT, KEM   SS   SEP 56 01
  POST READER OF FANTASY AND SCIENCE FICTION
                                 SATURDAY EVE. POST   AN
TRAP, THE   FAST, HOWARD   NA
  TIME AND THE RIDDLE   FAST, HOWARD   AC
TRAP, THE   LONG, FRANK BELKNAP SS   ASF 45 05
  RIM OF THE UNKNOWN   LONG, FRANK BELKNAP   AC
TRAPPED IN THE SEA OF STARS   LEIBER, FRITZ   SS   NEW 75 AC
  SECOND BOOK OF FRITZ LEIBER, THE   LEIBER, FRITZ   AC

TRIAL OF ADAM LINK, THE

TRAPS OF TIME, THE   BAXTER, JOHN   SS   NWS 64 03
  BEST OF NEW WORLDS, THE   MOORCOCK, MICHAEL   AN
TRASHING   MALZBERG, BARRY N.   SS   INY 73 05
  DOWN HERE IN THE DREAM QUARTER   MALZBERG, BARRY N.   AC
  INFINITY 5   HOSKINS, ROBERT   OA
TRAUMEREI   BEAUMONT, CHARLES   SS   INF 56 02
  YONDER   BEAUMONT, CHARLES   AC
TRAVEL BY WIRE   CLARKE, ARTHUR C.   SS   AMS 37 12
  BEST OF ARTHUR C. CLARKE: 1937-1971, THE CLARKE, ARTHUR C.   AC
TRAVEL DIARY   BESTER, ALFRED   SS   NEW 58 AC
  STARBURST   BESTER, ALFRED   AC
TRAVELER'S REST   MASSON, DAVID I.   SS   NWS 65 09
  CALTRAPS OF TIME, THE   MASSON, DAVID I.   AC
  TRAPS OF TIME, THE   MOORCOCK, MICHAEL   AN
  VOYAGERS IN TIME   SILVERBERG, ROBERT   AN
  WORLD'S BEST SCIENCE FICTION: 1966 WOLLHEIM & CARR   AN
  11TH ANNUAL OF THE YEAR'S BEST S-F, THE   MERRIL, JUDITH   AN
TRAVELER, THE   MATHESON, RICHARD   SS   FSF 62 02
  BORN OF MAN AND WOMAN   MATHESON, RICHARD   AC
  THIRD FROM THE SUN   MATHESON, RICHARD   AC
TRAVELIN' MAN, THE   KELLEY, LEO P.   SS   FSF 70 09
  THEMES IN SCIENCE FICTION   KELLEY, LEO P.   AN
TRAVELING COMPANION WANTED (SEE THE TUNNEL UNDER THE WORLD)
                                 WILSON, RICHARD   TC
TRAVELING CRAG, THE   STURGEON, THEODORE   NV   FAD 51 07
  AWARD SCIENCE FICTION READER   NORTON, ALDEN H.   AN
TRAVELING SALESMAN, THE   BLOCH, ROBERT   SS   PBY 57 02
  PLAYBOY BOOK OF HORROR AND THE SUPERNATURAL, THE
                                 PLAYBOY, EDITORS OF AN
TRAVELLER IN TIME, A (ALSO AS CENTURY JUMPER)
                                 DERLETH, AUGUST   SS   OSF 54 02
  HARRIGAN'S FILE   DERLETH, AUGUST   AC
TRAVELLER, THE   BRADBURY, RAY   SS   WRT 46 03
  *DARK CARNIVAL   BRADBURY, RAY   AC
TRAVELLERS   HOLDSTOCK, ROBERT P. NV
  ANDROMEDA I   WESTON, PETER   OA
TREASON IS A TWO-EDGED SWORD (TREASON)
                                 BRUNNER, JOHN   NV   NEB 57 05
  NOT BEFORE TIME   BRUNNER, JOHN   AC
TREASURE HUNT   GREEN, JOSEPH   SS   NWR 65 05
  NEW WRITINGS IN SF. 5   CARNELL, JOHN   OA
TREASURE IN THE FOREST, THE   WELLS, H. G.   SS   PMB 94
  COUNTRY OF THE BLIND, THE   WELLS, H. G.   AC
  SHORT STORIES OF H. G. WELLS, THE   WELLS, H. G.   AC
  STOLEN BACILLUS AND OTHER INCIDENTS, THE WELLS, H. G.   AC
  THIRTY STRANGE STORIES   WELLS, H. G.   AC
TREASURE OF THE HAUNTED RAMBLER, THE
                                 SLADEK, JOHN T.   PM   69
  HOLDING YOUR EIGHT HANDS   LUCIE-SMITH, EDWARD   AN
TREASURE OF TRANICOS, THE (THE BLACK STRANGER)
                                 DE CAMP, L. SPRAGUE
                                 AND HOWARD, ROBERT E. NA C FMG 53 03
  CONAN THE USURPER   HOWARD, R. & DE CAMP   AC
  KING CONAN   HOWARD, ROBERT E.   AC
TREAT   KERR, WALTER H.   PM   FSF 64 11
  BEST FROM FANTASY AND SCIENCE FICTION: 15
                                 FERMAN, EDWARD L.   AN
TREATY IN TARTESSOS   ANDERSON, KAREN   SS   FSF 63 05
  BEST FROM FANTASY AND SCIENCE FICTION: 13
                                 DAVIDSON, AVRAM   AN
TREE IN THE FOREST, THE   GREENHOUGH, TERRY   SS   SFM 74 02
  BEST OF SCIENCE FICTION MONTHLY, THE SACKS, JANET   AN
TREE MEN OF M'BWA, THE   WANDREI, DONALD   SS   WRT 32 10
  EYE AND THE FINGER   WANDREI, DONALD   AC
TREE MEN OF POTU, THE (1741)   HOLBERG, LUDWIG   EX
  *BEYOND TIME AND SPACE   DERLETH, AUGUST   AN
TREE OF LIFE   EISENSTEIN, PHYLLIS SS   GAL 75 03
  BEST SCIENCE FICTION STORIES OF THE YEAR (1975)
                                 DEL REY, LESTER   AN
TREE OF LIFE, THE   MOORE, C. L.   NV   WRT 36 10
  FANTASTIC PULPS, THE   HAINING, PETER   AN
  *SHAMBLEAU AND OTHERS   MOORE, C. L.   AC
TREE TRUNKS   GALLAGHER, JOHN   CT   SEP 63
  9TH ANNUAL OF THE YEAR'S BEST S-F, THE MERRIL, JUDITH   AN
TREE'S WIFE, THE   COUNSELMAN, MARY E. SS   WRT 50 03
  ROOTS OF EVIL, THE   PARRY, MICHEL   AN
  SUPERNATURAL READER, THE   CONKLIN, G&L.   AN
TREE, THE   CHRISTOPHER, JOHN   SS   NWS 51 FL
  TWENTY-SECOND CENTURY, THE   CHRISTOPHER, JOHN   AC
TREMATODE, A CRITIQUE OF MODERN SCIENCE-FICTION
                                 BESTER, ALFRED   BR
  BEST SCIENCE-FICTION STORIES: 1953, THE BLEILER & DIKTY   AN
TRENDS   ASIMOV, ISAAC   SS   ASF 39 07
  EARLY ASIMOV, THE   ASIMOV, ISAAC   AC
  FIRST FLIGHTS TO THE MOON   CLEMENT, HAL   AN
  GREAT SCIENCE FICTION STORIES ABOUT THE MOON
                                 DIKTY, T. E.   AN
  *MEN AGAINST THE STARS   GREENBERG, MARTIN   AN
  SPECTRUM OF WORLDS, A   CLARESON, THOMAS D.   AN
TRENDS IN MODERN SCIENCE-FICTION
                                 KORSHAK, MELVIN   IN
  BEST SCIENCE-FICTION STORIES: 1949, THE BLEILER & DIKTY   AN
TRESPASS (MOTHER BY PROTEST)   MATHESON, RICHARD   NV   FAN 53 10
  SHORES OF SPACE, THE   MATHESON, RICHARD   AC
TRESPASS!   ANDERSON, POUL
                                 AND DICKSON, GORDON R. SS C FSQ 50 SP
  BEST SCIENCE-FICTION STORIES: 1951, THE BLEILER & DIKTY   AN
  MINDWORM, THE   ANONYMOUS   AN
TRIAL BY FIRE   GUNN, JAMES E.   SN   IFS 69 02
  BURNING, THE   GUNN, JAMES E.   NO
TRIAL NOBODY EVER HEARD OF, THE
                                 NESVADBA, JOSEF   SS
  LOST FACE, THE   NESVADBA, JOSEF   AC
TRIAL OF ADAM LINK, THE   BINDER, EANDO   SS   AMZ 39 07
  ADAM LINK- ROBOT   BINDER, EANDO   AC

TRIAL OF TANTALUS, THE   SAPARIN, VICTOR   NV
  MORE SOVIET SCIENCE FICTION   ANONYMOUS   AN
TRIAL OF THE BLOOD   MALZBERG, BARRY N.   SS   BER 74
  BEST OF BARRY N. MALZBERG, THE   MALZBERG, BARRY N.   AC
TRIAL OF THE BLOOD   O'DONNELL, K. M.   SS   BER 74
  BERSERKERS, THE   ELWOOD, ROGER   OA
TRIAL, THE   SELLINGS, ARTHUR   NV   NWR 69 15
  NEW WRITINGS IN SF. 15   CARNELL, JOHN   OA
TRIBULATIONS OF TECHNOLOGY, THE
    CLARKE, I. F.   AR   PTS 71 06
  BEYOND THIS HORIZON   CARRELL, CHRISTOPHER OA
TRICK OR TREAT   FRITCH, CHARLES E.   SS   AMZ 57 07
  HORSES' ASTEROID   FRITCH, CHARLES E.   AC
TRICK OR TREATY   LAUMER, KEITH   NV   IFS 65 08
  IF READER OF SCIENCE FICTION, THE   POHL, FREDERIK   AN
  RETIEF: AMBASSADOR TO SPACE   LAUMER, KEITH   AC
TRICK OR TWO, A   NOVOTNY, JOHN   SS   FSF 57 07
  DECADE OF FANTASY AND SCIENCE FICTION, A MILLS, ROBERT P.   AN
TRICKY TONNAGE   JAMESON, MALCOLM   SS   ASF 44 12
  *BEST OF SCIENCE FICTION   CONKLIN, GROFF   AN
  WORLDS OF WONDER   HARRISON, HARRY   AN
TRIFFID, THE (FROM "THE DAY OF THE TRIFFIDS")
    WYNDHAM, JOHN   EX   COL 51 01
  SCIENCE IN FICTION   BAYLISS, A.E. & J.C. AN
TRIFLIN' MAN (ALSO AS YOU TRIFLIN' SKUNK!)
    MILLER, WALTER M. JR SS   FUN 55 01
  GALAXY OF GHOULS   MERRIL, JUDITH   AN
TRIGGER TIDE   GUIN, WYMAN   SS   ASF 50 10
  LIVING WAY OUT   GUIN, WYMAN   AC
  OMNIBUS OF SCIENCE FICTION   CONKLIN, GROFF   AN
TRIGGER, THE   BEAUMONT, CHARLES   SS   MDM 58
  NIGHT RIDE AND OTHER JOURNEYS   BEAUMONT, CHARLES   AC
TRIGGERMAN   BONE, J. F.   SS   ASF 58 12
  JOURNEYS IN SCIENCE FICTION   LOUGHLIN, RICHARD L. AN
  POLITICAL SCIENCE FICTION   GREENBERG& WARRICK   AN
  PROLOGUE TO ANALOG   CAMPBELL, JOHN W. JR AN
  SF:59, THE YEAR'S GREATEST SCIENCE FICTION AND FANTASY
    MERRIL, JUDITH   AN
TRIGGERMAN   FISHER, LOU   SS   GAL 73 09
  BEST FROM GALAXY, THE   VOLUME II   GALAXY, EDITORS OF   AN
TRIGONONOMY   MOORE, RAYLYN   NV   SCS 73
  SHOWCASE   ELWOOD, ROGER   OA
TRIP ONE   GRENDON, EDWARD   SS   ASF 49 07
  GIANTS UNLEASHED   CONKLIN, GROFF   AN
  SPACE, SPACE, SPACE   SLOANE, WILLIAM   AN
TRIP TO INFINITY, A   WANDREI, DONALD   NV
  STRANGE HARVEST   WANDREI, DONALD   AC
TRIP TO JUPITER'S MOONLET, A   LACH-SZYRMA, D. S.   SS   CSL 91 12
  WORLDS APART   LOCKE, GEORGE   AN
TRIP TO THE CITY, A (IT COULD BE ANYTHING)
    LAUMER, KEITH   NV   AMZ 63 01
  BEST FROM FANTASTIC, THE   WHITE, TED   AN
  NINE BY LAUMER   LAUMER, KEITH   AC
TRIP TO THE HEAD, A   LE GUIN, URSULA K.   SS   QRK 70 01
  LIBERATED FUTURE: VOYAGES INTO TOMORROW, THE
    HOSKINS, ROBERT   AN
  QUARK/1   DELANY & HACKER   OA
  WINDS TWELVE QUARTERS, THE   LE GUIN, URSULA K.   AC
TRIP TO VENUS, A (1897)   MUNRO, JOHN   SS   97
  FAREWELL FANTASTIC VENUS   ALDISS & HARRISON   AN
TRIP, TRAP   WOLFE, GENE   NV   ORB 67 02
  ORBIT   2   KNIGHT, DAMON   OA
TRIPLE MOONS OF DENEB II, THE CHARNEY, DAVID H.   SS   SFT 73
  SCIENCE FICTION TALES   ELWOOD, ROGER   OA
TRIPLICATE TWISTEROO (SEE DASIES, POLITENESS AND SENTENCE)
    BROWN, FREDRIC   TC
TRIPLICATION   SHECKLEY, ROBERT   SS   PBY 59 05
  FROM THE "S" FILE   PLAYBOY, EDITORS OF   AN
  STORE OF INFINITY   SHECKLEY, ROBERT   AC
TRIPOUT   SHECKLEY, ROBERT   SS   BOA
  CAN YOU FEEL ANYTHING WHEN I DO THIS?, AND OTHER STORIES
    SHECKLEY, ROBERT   AC
TRIPPERS, THE   SCHAEFFER, ROBIN   SS
  LONG NIGHT OF WAITING AND OTHER STORIES ELWOOD, ROGER   OA
TRIPS   SILVERBERG, ROBERT   NV   FST 74
  FEAST OF ST. DIONYSUS, THE   SILVERBERG, ROBERT   AC
  FINAL STAGE   FERMAN & MALZBERG   OA
TRIPTYCH, A   MALZBERG, BARRY N.   SS   FSF 69 07
  ALPHA 1   SILVERBERG, ROBERT   AN
TRIPTYCH, A   O'DONNELL, K. M.   SS   FSF 69 07
  FINAL WAR AND OTHER FANTASIES   O'DONNELL, K. M.   DC
  UNIVERSE DAY   O'DONNELL, K. M.   NO
TRITON (THE UNDIGESTIBLE TRITON)
    HUBBARD, L. RON   NO   UNK 40 04
  SCIENCE-FANTASY QUINTETTE   CRAWFORD, WILLIAM L. AN
TRITONIAN RING, THE   DE CAMP, L. SPRAGUE NO   TCS 51 WI
  TRITONIAN RING, THE   DE CAMP, L. SPRAGUE AC
TRIUMPH OF TIME, THE (IN ENGLAND AS "A CLASH OF CYMBOLS")
    BLISH, JAMES   NO   AVN 58
  CITIES IN FLIGHT   BLISH, JAMES   AC
TRIUMPHANT HEAD, THE   SAXTON, JOSEPHINE   SS   ANA 70
  ALCHEMY AND ACADEME   MCCAFFREY, ANNE   OA
TRIUMPHS OF A TAXIDERMIST, THE WELLS, H. G.   SS   PGZ 94
  SHORT STORIES OF H. G. WELLS, THE   WELLS, H. G.   AC
  STOLEN BACILLUS AND OTHER INCIDENTS, THE WELLS, H. G.   AC
  THIRTY STRANGE STORIES   WELLS, H. G.   AC
TRODES, THE   COPPER, BASIL   SS   ADS 75 01
  ARMADA SCI-FI ONE   DAVIS, RICHARD   OA
TROIKA   CHAPMAN, STEVE   SS   ORB 74 01
  ORBIT   13   KNIGHT, DAMON   OA
TROJAK   OBTULOWICZ, MAREK   SS   QRK 71 02
  QUARK/2   DELANY & HACKER   OA
TROJAN BEAM, THE   WYNDHAM, JOHN   NV   FSB 39 02
  BEST OF JOHN WYNDHAM, THE   WYNDHAM, JOHN   AC
  MAN FROM BEYOND AND OTHER STORIES, THE   WYNDHAM, JOHN   AC

TROJAN FALL   CLEMENT, HAL   SS   ASF 44 0?
  SMALL CHANGES   CLEMENT, HAL   AC
TROJAN HORSE LAUGH   MACDONALD, JOHN D.   NV   ASF 49 08
  DIMENSION 4   CONKLIN, GROFF   A?
  TOMORROW 1   HOSKINS, ROBERT   AN
TROLLEY, THE   BRADBURY, RAY   SS   GHK 55 0?
  DANDELION WINE   BRADBURY, RAY   NO
  S IS FOR SPACE   BRADBURY, RAY   AC
TROLLS   BORSKI, ROBERT   SS   FSF 74 0?
  ANTIGRAV: COSMIC COMEDIES   STRICK, PHILIP   A?
TROPHY   KUTTNER, HENRY   SS   TWS 44 W?
  SAINT'S CHOICE OF IMPOSSIBLE CRIME, THE CHARTERIS, LESLIE   A?
TROUBLE FOLLOWS   EFFINGER, GEO. ALEC SS   CLR 71 0?
  CLARION   WILSON, ROBIN SCOTT OA
TROUBLE I SEE, THE   BRUNNER, JOHN   SS   NWS 59 0?
  FROM THIS DAY FORWARD   BRUNNER, JOHN   AC
TROUBLE IN TIME   KORNBLUTH, C. M.
    AND POHL, FREDERIK   SS C AST 40 1?
  WONDER EFFECT, THE   POHL, F. & KORNBLUTH AC
TROUBLE ON TANTALUS   MILLER, P. SCHUYLER NV   ASF 41 0?
  ASTOUNDING-ANALOG READER, THE VOLUME ONE HARRISON & ALDISS   A?
  TRAVELLERS OF SPACE   GREENBERG, MARTIN   AN
TROUBLE ON TITAN (SEE SATURN) BARNES, ARTHUR K.   TC
TROUBLE TIDE   SCHMITZ, JAMES H.   NV   ASF 65 0?
  ELSEWHERE AND ELSEWHEN   CONKLIN, GROFF   AN
TROUBLE TWISTERS, THE (TRADER TEAM)
    ANDERSON, POUL   NA   ASF 65 07
  TROUBLE TWISTERS, THE   ANDERSON, POUL   AC
TROUBLE WITH EMILY, THE   WHITE, JAMES   NV   NWS 58 1?
  HOSPITAL STATION   WHITE, JAMES   AC
  OUT OF THIS WORLD 2   WILLIAMS-ELLIS& OWEN AN
TROUBLE WITH G.O.D., THE   GERROLD, DAVID   NV   GAL 72 05
  WHEN HARLIE WAS ONE   GERROLD, DAVID   NO
TROUBLE WITH H.A.R.R.I., THE   MACKIN, EDWARD   SS   AUT 57 0?
  SCIENCE FICTION ODDITIES   CONKLIN, GROFF   AN
TROUBLE WITH MACHINES, THE   GOULART, RON   SS   PBY 68 08
  BROKE DOWN ENGINE AND OTHER TROUBLES WITH MACHINES
    GOULART, RON   AC
  FULLY AUTOMATED LOVE LIFE OF HENRY KEANRIDGE
    PLAYBOY, EDITORS OF   AN
TROUBLE WITH TELSTAR, THE   BERRYMAN, JOHN   NV   ASF 63 0?
  ANALOG 3   CAMPBELL, JOHN W. JR AN
TROUBLE WITH THE NATIVES (CAPTAIN WYXTPTHLL'S FLYING SAUCER)
    CLARKE, ARTHUR C.   SS   MAR 51 0?
  OF TIME AND STARS   CLARKE, ARTHUR C.   AC
  PRELUDE TO MARS   CLARKE, ARTHUR C.   AC
  REACH FOR TOMORROW   CLARKE, ARTHUR C.   AC
TROUBLE WITH THE PAST, THE   EISENSTEIN, ALEX
    AND EISENSTEIN, PHYLLIS SS C NDM 71 0?
  NEW DIMENSIONS 1   SILVERBERG, ROBERT   OA
TROUBLE WITH TIME (CRIME ON MARS, EQM 60 07)
    CLARKE, ARTHUR C.   SS   FSF 61 0?
  INTRODUCING SCIENCE FICTION   ALDISS, BRIAN W.   AN
  NINE BILLION NAMES OF GOD, THE   CLARKE, ARTHUR C.   AC
  TALES OF TEN WORLDS   CLARKE, ARTHUR C.   AC
TROUBLE WITH TREATIES   CONDIT, TOM
    AND MACLEAN, KATHERINE NV C STR 59 05
  STAR SCIENCE FICTION STORIES NO. 5   POHL, FREDERIK   OA
TROUBLE WITH TRIBBLES, THE (DAVID GERROLD)
    BLISH, JAMES   SA   STK 69 03
  STAR TREK   3   BLISH, JAMES   OC
TROUBLE WITH TRUTH, THE   GROW, JULIAN F.   NV   WOT 63 12
  BEST SCIENCE FICTION FROM WORLDS OF TOMORROW, THE
    POHL, FREDERIK   AN
TROUBLE WITH TYCHO, THE   SIMAK, CLIFFORD D.   NA   AMZ 60 10
  ACE SCIENCE FICTION READER   WOLLHEIM, DONALD A.   AC
TROUBLE WITH WATER   GOLD, H. L.   SS   UNK 39 03
  DARK SIDE, THE   KNIGHT, DAMON   AN
  FROM UNKNOWN WORLDS   CAMPBELL, JOHN W. JR AN
  OLD DIE RICH AND OTHER SCIENCE FICTION, THE
    GOLD, H. L.   AC
  UNKNOWN, THE   BENSEN, D. R.   AN
  WANDERING STARS   DANN, JACK M.   AN
TROUBLE WITH YOU EARTH PEOPLE, THE
    MACLEAN, KATHERINE   NV   AMZ 68 02
  LIBERATED FUTURE: VOYAGES INTO TOMORROW, THE
    HOSKINS, ROBERT   AN
TROUBLESHOOTER   CONEY, MICHAEL G.   SS   IFS 70 05
  BEST FROM IF, THE   VOLUME I   IF, EDITORS OF   AN
TROUBLESHOOTER, THE   LAUMER, KEITH   NV   NEW 75 AC
  RETIEF: EMISSARY TO THE STARS   LAUMER, KEITH   AC
TROUBLING OF THE WATER   HENDERSON, ZENNA   NV   FSF 66 0?
  PEOPLE: NO DIFFERENT FLESH, THE   HENDERSON, ZENNA   AC
TRUANTS, THE   BRACKETT, LEIGH   SS   STS 50 0?
  HALFLING AND OTHER STORIES, THE   BRACKETT, LEIGH   AC
TRUCE OR CONSEQUENCES   LAUMER, KEITH   NV   IFS 66 1?
  RETIEF: AMBASSADOR TO SPACE   LAUMER, KEITH   AC
TRUCE, THE   LEE, TANITH   SS
  DAW SCIENCE FICTION READER, THE   WOLLHEIM, DONALD A.   OA
TRUE BILL, A   BLISH, JAMES   NV   TTM 73
  TEN TOMORROWS   ELWOOD, ROGER   OA
TRUE CONFESSION   TREMAINE, F. ORLIN   SS   TWS 40 02
  COMING OF THE ROBOTS, THE   MOSKOWITZ, SAM   AN
TRUE HISTORY, A (165 A.D.)   LUCIAN OF SAMOSATA   EX
  *BEYOND TIME AND SPACE   DERLETH, AUGUST   AN
TRUE REASON FOR THE DREADFUL DEATH OF MR. REX ARUNDEL, THE
    ADAM, HELEN   NV   QRK 71 04
  QUARK/4   DELANY & HACKER   OA
TRUE SELF   BORGESE, ELISABETH M SS   GAL 59 10
  SIXTH GALAXY READER, THE   GOLD, H. L.   AC
TRUE WORTH OF RUTH VILLIERS, THE
    CONEY, MICHAEL G.   SS   NWR 70 17
  MONITOR FOUND IN ORBIT   CONEY, MICHAEL G.   AC
  NEW WRITINGS IN SF. 17   CARNELL, JOHN   OA
TRUNK LADY, THE   BRADBURY, RAY   SS   DMM 48 0?
  HORROR TIMES TEN   NORTON, ALDEN H.   AN

Title	Author	Type	Source	Yr	Mo
TRURL'S MACHINE	LEM, STANISLAW	SS			
CYBERIAD, THE	LEM, STANISLAW	OC			
TRUSTIE TREE, THE	ROBERTS, KEITH	SS	NWB	73	05
GRAIN KINGS, THE	ROBERTS, KEITH	AC			
NEW WORLDS QUARTERLY NO. 5	MOORCOCK, MICHAEL	OA			
TRUTH ABOUT CUSHGAR, THE	SCHMITZ, JAMES H.	NV	ASF	50	11
AGENT OF VEGA	SCHMITZ, JAMES H.	AC			
TRUTH ABOUT PYECRAFT, THE	WELLS, H. G.	SS	SND	03	04
BEST STORIES OF H. G. WELLS	WELLS, H. G.	AC			
COUNTRY OF THE BLIND, THE	WELLS, H. G.	AC			
GOLDEN ROAD, THE	KNIGHT, DAMON	AN			
SCIENCE FICTION AND READER'S GUIDE	BARROWS, MARJORIE	AN			
SHORT STORIES OF H. G. WELLS, THE	WELLS, H. G.	AC			
TWELVE STORIES AND A DREAM	WELLS, H. G.	AC			
TWENTY-EIGHT SCIENCE FICTION STORIES	WELLS, H. G.	AC			
WAR OF THE WORLDS, THE TIME MACHINE AND SELECTED SHORT STORIES	WELLS, H. G.	AC			
TRUTH IS A PLAGUE	O'BRIEN, D. W.	SS	AMZ	40	02
OTHER WORLDS, THE	STONG, PHILIP D.	AN			
TRUTH OF IT, THE	MALZBERG, BARRY N.	SS			
SCIENCE FICTION ADVENTURES FROM WAY OUT	ELWOOD, ROGER	OA			
TRUTH TEST	JARVIS, BOB	PM			
BEYOND THIS HORIZON	CARRELL, CHRISTOPHER	OA			
TRY A DULL KNIFE	ELLISON, HARLAN	SS	FSF	68	10
ALONE AGAINST TOMORROW	ELLISON, HARLAN	AC			
BEAST THAT SHOUTED LOVE AT THE HEART OF THE WORLD, THE	ELLISON, HARLAN	AC			
TRY AGAIN	MALZBERG, BARRY N.	SS	STG	74	
BEST OF BARRY N. MALZBERG, THE	MALZBERG, BARRY N.	AC			
STRANGE GODS	ELWOOD, ROGER	OA			
TRY AND CHANGE THE PAST	LEIBER, FRITZ	SS	ASF	58	03
BEST OF FRITZ LEIBER, THE	LEIBER, FRITZ	AC			
*MIND SPIDER AND OTHER STORIES, THE	LEIBER, FRITZ	DC			
TRY THIS FOR PSIS	BLOCH, ROBERT	SS	FSF	56	10
ATOMS AND EVIL	BLOCH, ROBERT	AC			
TRY TO REMEMBER	HERBERT, FRANK	NV	AMZ	61	10
BEST OF AMAZING, THE	ROSS, JOSEPH	AN			
TRYST	BAXTER, JOHN	SS	NWR	66	08
NEW WRITINGS IN SF. 8	CARNELL, JOHN	OA			
TRYST IN TIME	MOORE, C. L.	NV	ASF	36	12
BEST OF C. L. MOORE, THE	MOORE, C. L.	AC			
TSANTSA IN THE PARLOR	DERLETH, AUGUST	SS	WRT	48	07
MR. GEORGE AND OTHER ODD PERSONS	DERLETH, AUGUST	AC			
TSYLANA	GUNN, JAMES E.	NV	GAL	56	03
FUTURE IMPERFECT	GUNN, JAMES E.	AC			
TUBS OF SLAW	POLLACK, RACHEL	SS	NWQ	73	05
NEW WORLDS NO. 5	MOORCOCK & PLATT	OA			
TULPA	DANN, JACK M.	SS	NWQ	73	05
NEW WORLDS NO. 5	MOORCOCK & PLATT	OA			
TUMITHAK IN SHAWM	TANNER, CHARLES R.	NV	AMZ	33	06
BEFORE THE GOLDEN AGE	ASIMOV, ISAAC	AN			
TUMITHAK OF THE CORRIDORS	TANNER, CHARLES R.	NV	AMZ	32	01
BEFORE THE GOLDEN AGE	ASIMOV, ISAAC	AN			
TUNESMITH, THE	BIGGLE, LLOYD JR.	NV	IFS	57	08
BEST SCIENCE FICTION STORIES AND NOVELS: 9TH SERIES	DIKTY, T. E.	AN			
METALLIC MUSE, THE	BIGGLE, LLOYD JR.	AC			
TUNNEL AHEAD, THE	GLASER, ALICE	SS	FSF	61	11
AS TOMORROW BECOMES TODAY	SULLIVAN, CHARLES W.	AN			
VOYAGES: SCENARIOS FOR A SHIP CALLED EARTH	SAUER, ROB	AN			
7TH ANNUAL OF THE YEAR'S BEST S-F, THE	MERRIL, JUDITH	AN			
TUNNEL OF LOVE	GREEN, JOSEPH	SS	NWS	65	01
AFFAIR WITH GENIUS, AN	GREEN, JOSEPH	AC			
TUNNEL UNDER THE WORLD, THE	POHL, FREDERIK	NV	GAL	55	01
ALTERNATING CURRENTS	POHL, FREDERIK	AC			
BEST OF FREDERIK POHL, THE	POHL, FREDERIK	AC			
MORE PENGUIN SCIENCE FICTION	ALDISS, BRIAN W.	AN			
TENTH GALAXY READER, THE	POHL, FREDERIK	AN			
TOMORROW, INC.	GREENBERG& OLANDER	AN			
TUNNEL UNDER THE WORLD, THE (TRAVELING COMPANION WANTED)	WILSON, RICHARD	SS	GAL	59	06
TIME OUT FOR TOMORROW	WILSON, RICHARD	AC			
TUNNEL, THE	LYTLE, B. J.	SS			
TUNNEL AND OTHER STORIES, THE	ELWOOD, ROGER	OA			
TURJAN OF MIIR	VANCE, JACK	NV		50	
DYING EARTH, THE	VANCE, JACK	OC			
TURN OF A CENTURY	BLISH, JAMES	SS	DSF	53	03
THINGS	HOWARD, IVAN	AN			
TURN THE PAGE	HENDERSON, ZENNA	SS	FSF	57	05
ANYTHING BOX, THE	HENDERSON, ZENNA	AC			
TURNABOUT INTRUDER (G. RODDENBERRY & A. H. SINGER)	BLISH, JAMES	SA	STK	72	05
STAR TREK 5	BLISH, JAMES	OC			
TURNING PLACE, THE	KARL, JEAN E.	NV			
TURNING PLACE, THE	KARL, JEAN E.	OC			
TURNING POINT	ANDERSON, POUL	NV	IFS	63	05
ELSEWHERE AND ELSEWHEN	CONKLIN, GROFF	AN			
TIME AND STARS	ANDERSON, POUL	AC			
TURNING WHEEL, THE	DICK, PHILIP K.	SS	SFS	54	02
BOOK OF PHILIP K. DICK, THE	DICK, PHILIP K.	AC			
HANDFUL OF DARKNESS, A	DICK, PHILIP K.	AC			
NOW & BEYOND	HOWARD, IVAN	AN			
TURNTABLE	INOUYE, JON	SS			
NIGHT TIDE, A	INOUYE, JON	OC			
TURTLE, THE (FROM "THE GRAPES OF WRATH")	STEINBECK, JOHN	EX		39	
ECO-FICTION	STADLER, JOHN	AN			
TWEENER, THE	BRACKETT, LEIGH	SS	FSF	55	02
BEST OF LEIGH BRACKETT, THE	BRACKETT, LEIGH	AC			
TWELTH BED, THE	KOONTZ, DEAN R.	SS	FSF	68	08
SOFT COME THE DRAGONS	KOONTZ, DEAN R.	DC			
WONDERMAKERS 2	HOSKINS, ROBERT	AN			
TWELVE ANCILLARY APPROXIMATIONS FOR THE QUARK/ COVER CALLED APPOMATTOX	FITZGERALD, RUSSELL	IL	QRK	70	01
QUARK/1	DELANY & HACKER	OA			
TWELVE DRAWINGS	OLIVIER, OLIVIER	IL	QRK	71	04
QUARK/4	DELANY & HACKER	OA			
TWELVE HOLIDAYS	BAKHNOV, VLADLEN	SS		69	
AIR OF MARS AND OTHER STORIES, THE	GINSBURG, MIRRA	AN			
TWELVE HOURS TO LIVE|	WILLIAMSON, JACK	SS	WOS	31	08
EARLY WILLIAMSON, THE	WILLIAMSON, JACK	AC			
TWELVE POINT THREE SIX NINE	ASIMOV, ISAAC	AR	FSF	67	07
OPUS 100	ASIMOV, ISAAC	AC			
TWELVE STATIONS FROM GEMINI	FAIRFAX, JOHN	PM			
BEYOND THIS HORIZON	CARRELL, CHRISTOPHER	OA			
TWELVEMONTH, A	REDGROVE, PETER	SS	NYT		
BEST SF: 75, THE NINTH ANNUAL	HARRISON & ALDISS	AN			
TWENTIETH CENTURY HOMUNCULUS, A	KELLER, DAVID H. MD.	NV	AMZ	30	02
FANTASTIC PULPS, THE	HAINING, PETER	AN			
TWENTY SIXTY-ONE	MALZBERG, BARRY N.	SS	FSF	74	07
BEST OF BARRY N. MALZBERG, THE	MALZBERG, BARRY N.	AC			
TWENTY THOUSAND LEAGUES UNDER THE SEA (1873)	VERNE, JULES	EX	GMS	73	
CENTURY OF SCIENCE FICTION, A	KNIGHT, DAMON	AN			
JULES VERNE- MASTER OF SCIENCE FICTION	VERNE, JULES	AC			
TWENTY THOUSAND LEAGUES UNDER THE SEA (1873)	VERNE, JULES	NO	GMS	73	
NOVELS	VERNE, JULES	AC			
OMNIBUS, THE	VERNE, JULES	AC			
TWENTY-EIGHTH DAY, THE	PAULSEN, KATHRYN	SS			
NEW CONSTELLATIONS	DISCH & NAYLOR	OA			
TWENTY-FIRST CENTURY MOTHER	MARCUSE, KATHERINE	SS	AUT	54	01
MARRIAGE AND THE FAMILY THROUGH SCIENCE FICTION	CLEAR/WARRICK/&	AN			
TWENTY-FIVE MILES ALOFT	WATSON, RAYMOND	SS			
ADVENTURES TO COME	ESENWEIN, J. BERG	OA			
TWENTY-FOUR LETTERS FROM UNDER THE EARTH	BAILEY, HILARY	SS	QRK	71	03
QUARK/3	DELANY & HACKER	OA			
TWENTY-FOURTH JOURNEY OF ION TICHY, THE	LEM, STANISLAW	SS			
OTHER WORLDS, OTHER SEAS	SUVIN, DARKO	AN			
TWENTY-THIRD PSALM- MODERN STYLE, THE	SIMPSON, ALAN	PM	WUM	61	
INSIDE INFORMATION	MOWSHOWITZ, ABBE	AN			
TWERLIK, THE	SHARKEY, JACK	SS	WOT	64	06
10TH ANNUAL OF THE YEAR'S BEST S-F, THE	MERRIL, JUDITH	AN			
TWICE BITTEN	MALCOLM, DONALD	SS	NWS	63	02
OUT OF THIS WORLD 4	WILLIAMS-ELLIS& OWEN	AN			
TWIG	DICKSON, GORDON R.	NV	STL	74	01
STELLAR 1	DEL REY, JUDY-LYNN	OA			
1975 ANNUAL WORLD'S BEST SF, THE	WOLLHEIM, DONALD A.	AN			
TWILIGHT	CAMPBELL, JOHN W. JR	SS	ASF	34	11
*BEST OF JOHN W. CAMPBELL, THE	CAMPBELL, JOHN W. JR	AC			
ENDS OF TIME, THE	SILVERBERG, ROBERT	AN			
MIRROR OF INFINITY, THE	SILVERBERG, ROBERT	AN			
MODERN SCIENCE FICTION	SPINRAD, NORMAN	AN			
SCIENCE FICTION HALL OF FAME VOLUME 1	SILVERBERG, ROBERT	AN			
WHO GOES THERE?	CAMPBELL, JOHN W. JR	AC			
WHO GOES THERE? AND OTHER STORIES	CAMPBELL, JOHN W. JR	AC			
TWILIGHT	STUART, DON A.	SS	ASF	34	11
BEYOND TOMORROW	KNIGHT, DAMON	AN			
POCKET BOOK OF SCIENCE-FICTION, THE	WOLLHEIM, DONALD A.	AN			
TWILIGHT OF A TYRANNY	MORGAN, EDWIN	PM			
BEYOND THIS HORIZON	CARRELL, CHRISTOPHER	OA			
TWILIGHT OF THE GODS	HAMILTON, EDMOND	NV	WRT	48	07
WHAT'S IT LIKE OUT THERE? AND OTHER STORIES	HAMILTON, EDMOND	AC			
TWILIGHT PEOPLE, THE	ARNOLD, FRANK EDWARD	NV	CBT	41	01
WINGS ACROSS TIME	ARNOLD, FRANK EDWARD	AC			
TWILIGHT PLAY	DERLETH, AUGUST	SS	WRT	49	11
MORE LITTLE MONSTERS	ELWOOD & GHIDALIA	AN			
TWILIGHT YEARS, THE	DRUSSAI, GAREN AND DRUSSAI, KIRK	NV C	IFS	55	06
FIRST WORLD OF IF, THE	QUINN & WULFF	AN			
TWILLA	REAMY, TOM	NV	FSF	74	09
NEBULA AWARD STORIES 10	GUNN, JAMES E.	AN			
TWIN WORLDS	JONES, NEIL R.	NV	AMZ	37	04
TWIN WORLDS	JONES, NEIL R.	AC			
TWIN'S WAIL	BORGESE, ELISABETH M	NV	STR	59	06
STAR OF STARS	POHL, FREDERIK	AN			
STAR SCIENCE FICTION STORIES NO. 6	POHL, FREDERIK	OA			
TWINK	STURGEON, THEODORE	SS	GAL	55	08
CAVIAR	STURGEON, THEODORE	AC			
TWINKLE, TWINKLE, LITTLE BAT	LAWRENCE, J. A.	SS	NDM	77	07
NEW DIMENSIONS 7	SILVERBERG, ROBERT	OA			
TWINKLE, TWINKLE, LITTLE STAR	BARTON, RALPH	PM		24	
FANTASIA MATHEMATICA	FADIMAN, CLIFTON	AN			
TWINS, THE	KELLER, DAVID H. MD.	SS			
FOLSOM FLINT AND OTHER CURIOUS TALES, THE	KELLER, DAVID H. MD.	AC			
TWISTED MEN, THE	WELLS, BASIL	SS			
PLANETS OF ADVENTURE	WELLS, BASIL	AC			
TWISTED MEN, THE (ROGUE SHIP)	VAN VOGT, A. E.	NV	SSS	50	03
TWISTED MEN, THE	VAN VOGT, A. E.	DC			
TWO BY FOURS, THE	CONRAD, EARL	SS			
DA VINCI MACHINE, THE	CONRAD, EARL	OC			
TWO BY TWO (SEE THE WINDOWS OF HEAVEN)	BRUNNER, JOHN	TC			
TWO DANCERS	HANIWA	IL			
SCIENCE FICTION	BRODKIN & PEARSON	AN			
TWO DAYS RUNNING AND THEN SKIP A DAY	GOULART, RON	SS	AMZ	67	02
NUTZENBOLTS	GOULART, RON	AC			
TWO DOOMS	KORNBLUTH, C. M.	NV	VSF	58	07
BEST OF C. M. KORNBLUTH, THE	KORNBLUTH, C. M.	AC			
GREAT SHORT NOVELS OF SCIENCE FICTION	SILVERBERG, ROBERT	AN			
*MILE BEYOND THE MOON, A	KORNBLUTH, C. M.	AC			
TWO EXTRACTS	TWAIN, MARK	EX			
MATHEMATICAL MAGPIE, THE	FADIMAN, CLIFTON	AN			

TWO FACE

UNCHARTED ISLE, TH

```
TWO FACE                         LONG, FRANK BELKNAP   SS    WRT 50 03
  BEST SCIENCE-FICTION STORIES: 1951, THE  BLEILER & DIKTY        AN
  MINDWORM, THE                         ANONYMOUS                 AN
TWO HEADS ARE BETTER THAN ONE  ROBINSON, SPIDER   SS    ASF 75 05
  CALLAHAN'S CROSSTIME SALOON           ROBINSON, SPIDER          AC
TWO INCHES IN TOMORROW'S COLUMN (AS ELLIS HART)
                                 ELLISON, HARLAN      SS    ABR 65 21
  NO DOORS, NO WINDOWS (STORIES REWRITTEN) ELLISON, HARLAN        AC
TWO LIVE GHOSTS                  SERLING, ROD         SA
  ROD SERLING'S TWILIGHT ZONE REVISITED   SERLING, ROD            OC
TWO LIVES OF BEN COULTER, THE  EISENBERG, LARRY   SS    FSF 67 04
  BEST LAID SCHEMES, THE                EISENBERG, LARRY          AC
TWO MONSTERS                     LEM, STANISLAW       SS          72
  MORTAL ENGINES                        LEM, STANISLAW            AC
TWO ODYSSEYS INTO THE CENTER   MALZBERG, BARRY N.  SS    NOV 72 02
  NOVA 2                                HARRISON, HARRY           OA
TWO ODYSSEYS INTO THE CENTER   O'DONNELL, K. M.    SS    NOV 72 02
  UNIVERSE DAY                          O'DONNELL, K. M.          NO
TWO OF A KIND                    BLOCH, ROBERT        SS          61
  CHAMBER OF HORRORS                    BLOCH, ROBERT             AC
TWO PEOPLE WITHIN THE DESIGN   WEBB, VIC            SS
  CLARION SF                            WILHELM, KATE             OA
TWO PERCENT INSPIRATION        STURGEON, THEODORE  SS    ASF 41 10
  NOT WITHOUT SORCERY                   STURGEON, THEODORE        AC
  WITHOUT SORCERY                       STURGEON, THEODORE        AC
TWO POEMS                        WATKINS, WILLIAM JON PM  CND 73
  BEST SF: 1973                         HARRISON & ALDISS         AN
TWO POEMS AFTER STORIES BY BRIAN ALDISS
                                 COUZYN, JENI         GR
  BEYOND THIS HORIZON                   CARRELL, CHRISTOPHER      OA
TWO RIVERS                       MACKELWORTH, R. W.  NV    NWR 70 17
  NEW WRITINGS IN SF. 17                CARNELL, JOHN             OA
TWO SADNESSES                    EFFINGER, GEO. ALEC  SS   BMR 73
  BAD MOON RISING                       DISCH, THOMAS M.          OA
  MIXED FEELINGS                        EFFINGER, GEO. ALEC       AC
TWO SHADOWS, THE                 TEMPLE, WILLIAM F.  NV    STS 51 03
  BEST SCIENCE-FICTION STORIES: 1952, THE  BLEILER & DIKTY        AN
  *NO PLACE LIKE EARTH                  CARNELL, JOHN             AN
TWO SONGS                        ANDERSON, POUL       SG
  HOMEBREW                              ANDERSON, POUL            AC
TWO TELEPATHIC LETTERS TO LORD KELVIN
                                 JARRY, ALFRED        SS          65
  11TH ANNUAL OF THE YEAR'S BEST S-F, THE  MERRIL, JUDITH         AN
TWO TIMER (SEE EXPERIMENT AND SENTRY)
                                 BROWN, FREDRIC       TC
TWO VOICES                       MCCLINTIC, WINONA   PM    FSF 53 06
  BEST FROM FANTASY AND SCIENCE FICTION: 3
                                        BOUCHER & MCCOMAS         AN
TWO WEEKS IN AUGUST              ROBINSON, FRANK M.  SS    GAL 51 02
  FIFTY SHORT SCIENCE FICTION TALES     ASIMOV & CONKLIN          AN
TWO YEARS TO GAEA                BOLES, NICK          SS    SFT 73
  SCIENCE FICTION TALES                 ELWOOD, ROGER             OA
TWO'S A CROWD                    GILIEN, SASHA       SS    FSF 62 07
  BEST FROM FANTASY AND SCIENCE FICTION: 12
                                        DAVIDSON, AVRAM           AN
TWO'S COMPANY                    RANKINE, JOHN       SS    NWR 64 01
  NEW WRITINGS IN SF. 1                 CARNELL, JOHN             OA
  SOCIOLOGY THROUGH SCIENCE FICTION     MILSTEAD/GREENBERG/&      AN
TWO-HANDED ENGINE                KUTTNER, HENRY      SS    FSF 55 08
  BEST OF HENRY KUTTNER 2, THE          KUTTNER, HENRY            AC
  BEST OF HENRY KUTTNER, THE            KUTTNER, HENRY            AC
  DECADE THE 1950S                      ALDISS & HARRISON         AN
  NO BOUNDARIES                         KUTTNER & MOORE           AC
TWO-HANDED ENGINE                KUTTNER, HENRY
                                 AND MOORE, C. L.   SS C  FSF 55 08
  METAL SMILE, THE                      KNIGHT, DAMON             AN
TWO-HEADED LION OF CRIS BENEDETTI, THE
                                 LAFFERTY, R. A.     SS    NMD 73
  FRONTIERS 2: THE NEW MIND             ELWOOD, ROGER             OA
TWO-TIMER, A                     MASSON, DAVID I.    NV    NWS 66 02
  BEST SF STORIES FROM NEW WORLDS NO. 1, THE
                                        MOORCOCK, MICHAEL         AN
  CALTRAPS OF TIME, THE                 MASSON, DAVID I.          AC
TWO, THE                         GANSOVSKY, SEVER    NV
  JOURNEY ACROSS THREE WORLDS           ANONYMOUS                 AN
TWONKY, THE                      KUTTNER, HENRY      SS    ASF 42 09
  BEST OF HENRY KUTTNER 2, THE          KUTTNER, HENRY            AC
  BEST OF HENRY KUTTNER, THE            KUTTNER, HENRY            AC
  SOULS IN METAL                        ASHLEY, MICHAEL           AN
TWONKY, THE                      PADGETT, LEWIS      SS    ASF 42 09
  *ADVENTURES IN TIME AND SPACE         HEALY & MCCOMAS           AN
  GNOME THERE WAS, A                    PADGETT, LEWIS            AC
  LINE TO TOMORROW AND OTHER STORIES OF FANTASY AND SCIENCE
  FICTION                               PADGETT, LEWIS            AC
  MEN AND MACHINES                      SILVERBERG, ROBERT        AN
TYPICAL DAY, A                   PISERCHIA, DORIS    SS    GAL 74 03
  BEST SF: 1974                         HARRISON & ALDISS         AN
TYRANNOSAURUS REX (THE PREHISTORIC PRODUCER)
                                 BRADBURY, RAY       SS    SEP 62 06
  MACHINERIES OF JOY, THE               BRADBURY, RAY             AC
TYRANT AND SLAVE-GIRL ON VENUS (SEE NO PLACE LIKE EARTH)
                                 WYNDHAM, JOHN       TC
TYRANT OF TIME, THE (THE TIME CONQUEROR)
                                 ESHBACH, LLOYD A.   SS    WOS 32 07
  TYRANT OF TIME, THE                   ESHBACH, LLOYD A.         AC
U-GENIE SX-1--HUMAN ENTREPRENEUR: NATURALLY RAPACIOUS YANKEE
                                 GAT, DIMITRI V.     SS
  BEYOND TIME                           LEY, SANDRA               OA
U-TURN                           RUSSELL, ERIC FRANK SS    ASF 50 04
  SOMEWHERE A VOICE                     RUSSELL, ERIC FRANK       AC
UBBO-SATHLA                      SMITH, CLARK ASHTON SS    WRT 33 07
  OUT OF SPACE AND TIME                 SMITH, CLARK ASHTON       AC
  SECOND AVON FANTASY READER, THE       WOLLHEIM &ERNSBERGER      AN
UBIQUITOUS YOU, THE (THE IN-BETWEENS)
                                 WILSON, RICHARD     SS    FUT 57 SP
  TIME OUT FOR TOMORROW                 WILSON, RICHARD           AC

UFO                              FAST, HOWARD        SS
  TOUCH OF INFINITY, A                  FAST, HOWARD              C
UFO DETECTIVE SOLVES 'EM ALL- WELL ALMOST
                                 HILTS, PHILIP J.    AR    WPS 73
  SCIENCE FACT/FICTION                  FARRELL/GAGE/&            A
UFO SPOTTED                      INOUYE, JON         SS
  NIGHT TIDE, A                         INOUYE, JON               O
UGLY JAPANESE, THE               INOUYE, JON         SS
  NIGHT TIDE, A                         INOUYE, JON               O
UGLY LITTLE BOY, THE (LASTBORN)
                                 ASIMOV, ISAAC       NA    GAL 58 0
  DIMENSION X                           KNIGHT, DAMON             A
  NINE TOMORROWS                        ASIMOV, ISAAC             A
  TOMORROW'S CHILDREN                   ASIMOV, ISAAC             A
  WORLDS OF SCIENCE FICTION, THE        MILLS, ROBERT P.          A
UGLY SEA, THE                    LAFFERTY, R. A.     SS    LRV 60 F
  NEW WORLDS OF FANTASY NO. 2           CARR, TERRY               A
  STRANGE DOINGS                        LAFFERTY, R. A.           A
UGLY SISTER (LMR 35 12)          STRUTHER, JAN       SS    FSF 52 0
  BEST FROM FANTASY AND SCIENCE FICTION: 2
                                        BOUCHER & MCCOMAS         A
UGUPU BIRD, THE                  MROZEK, SLAWOMIR    SS          68
  BEST SF: 1970                         HARRISON & ALDISS         A
ULAN DHOR ENDS A DREAM           VANCE, JACK         NV          50
  DYING EARTH, THE                      VANCE, JACK               A
ULLR UPRISING                    PIPER, H. BEAM      NA    SSF 53 0
  PETRIFIED PLANET, THE                 CLARK, JOHN D.            O
ULLWARD'S RETREAT                VANCE, JACK         NV    GAL 58 1
  BEST OF JACK VANCE, THE               VANCE, JACK               A
  FUTURE TENSE                          VANCE, JACK               A
  SF: AUTHORS' CHOICE 4                 HARRISON, HARRY           A
ULTIMA THULE                     RUSSELL, ERIC FRANK SS    ASF 51 1
  BEST SF 7                             CRISPIN, EDMUND           A
  LIKE NOTHING ON EARTH                 RUSSELL, ERIC FRANK       A
  LOOKING FORWARD                       LESSER, MILTON            A
ULTIMATE BRUNETTE, THE           BUDRYS, ALGIS       SS    PBY 65 0
  FIEND, THE                            PLAYBOY, EDITORS OF       A
ULTIMATE CATALYST, THE           BELL, ERIC TEMPLE   NV    TWS 39 0
  GREAT SCIENCE FICTION BY SCIENTISTS   CONKLIN, GROFF            A
ULTIMATE CATALYST, THE           TAINE, JOHN         NV    TWS 39 0
  *BEST OF SCIENCE FICTION              CONKLIN, GROFF            A
  *MY BEST SCIENCE FICTION STORY        MARGULIES & FRIEND        A
ULTIMATE CITY, THE               BALLARD, J. G.      NA
  LOW-FLYING AIRCRAFT AND OTHER STORIES BALLARD, J. G.            A
ULTIMATE COMPUTER, THE (D. C. FONTANA & L. WOLFE)
                                 BLISH, JAMES        SA    STK 73 0
  STAR TREK 9                           BLISH, JAMES              A
ULTIMATE CONSTRUCTION            SHACKLETON, C. C.   SS    TBT 67
  BEST SF: 1967                         HARRISON & ALDISS         A
ULTIMATE CREATURE, THE           LAFFERTY, R. A.     SS    MOH 67 1
  DOES ANYONE ELSE HAVE SOMETHING FURTHER TO ADD?
                                        LAFFERTY, R. A.           A
ULTIMATE EGOIST, THE             STURGEON, THEODORE  NV    UNK 41 0
  HUMAN?                                MERRIL, JUDITH            A
  WITHOUT SORCERY                       STURGEON, THEODORE        A
ULTIMATE END, THE                GLASS, DICK         SS    NOV 73 0
  NOVA 3                                HARRISON, HARRY           O
ULTIMATE HORROR, THE             THOMPSON, R. W.     M.
  LOOKING AHEAD                         ALLEN, D. & L.            A
ULTIMATE INVADER, THE (DESIGN FOR GREAT-DAY)
                                 RUSSELL, ERIC FRANK NO    PLS 53 0
  ULTIMATE INVADER, AND OTHER SCIENCE FICTION, THE
                                        WOLLHEIM, DONALD A.       A
ULTIMATE MELODY, THE             CLARKE, ARTHUR C.   SS    IFS 57 0
  ALIEN EARTH AND OTHER STORIES         ELWOOD & MOSKOWITZ        A
  PRELUDE TO MARS                       CLARKE, ARTHUR C.         A
  TALES FROM THE WHITE HART             CLARKE, ARTHUR C.         A
ULTIMATE METAL, THE              SCHACHNER, NAT      NV    ASF 35 0
  *BEST OF SCIENCE FICTION              CONKLIN, GROFF            A
ULTIMATE SPEED LIMIT, THE        ASIMOV, ISAAC       AR    SRV 72
  FASTER THAN LIGHT                     DANN & ZEBROWSKI          A
ULTIMATE THRESHOLD, THE          MAXIMOV, HERMAN     SS          65
  ULTIMATE THRESHOLD, THE               GINSBURG, MIRRA           A
ULTIMATE WISH, THE               HULL, E. MAYNE      SS    UNK 43 0
  OUT OF THE UNKNOWN                    VAN VOGT & HULL           A
ULTIMATUM (MIGHTIEST QORN)       LAUMER, KEITH       NV    IFS 63 0
  GALACTIC DIPLOMAT                     LAUMER, KEITH             A
  GATES TO TOMORROW                     NORTON, AN.&DONALDY       A
ULTRA MAN, THE                   VAN VOGT, A. E.     NV    WOT 66 0
  FAR-OUT WORLDS OF A. E. VAN VOGT, THE VAN VOGT, A. E.           A
  WORLDS OF A. E. VAN VOGT, THE         VAN VOGT, A. E.           A
ULTRASONIC GOD (ALSO AS THE GALTON WHISTLE)
                                 DE CAMP, L. SPRAGUE NV    FUT 51 0
  NOVELETS OF SCIENCE FICTION           HOWARD, IVAN              A
UN BEL DI                        YARBRO, CHELSEA Q.  NV    TVW 73
  TWO VIEWS OF WONDER                   SCORTIA & YARBRO          A
UN-MAN                           ANDERSON, POUL      SN    ASF 53 0
  ALL ABOUT THE FUTURE                  GREENBERG, MARTIN         A
  UN-MAN AND OTHER NOVELLAS             ANDERSON, POUL            D
UNA (THE PERFECT CREATURE, TOW 37 01)
                                 WYNDHAM, JOHN       NV    FSF 53 0
  BEST SF 2                             CRISPIN, EDMUND           A
  JIZZLE                                WYNDHAM, JOHN             A
  TALES OF GOOSEFLESH AND LAUGHTER      WYNDHAM, JOHN             A
UNBEARABLENESS OF OTHER LIVES, THE
                                 ALDISS, BRIAN W.    SS    NWR 74 2
  NEW WRITINGS IN SF. 24                BULMER, KENNETH           A
UNBEATEN TRACK, THE (SEE THREE'S A CLOUD)
                                 ALDISS, BRIAN W.    TC
UNBIRTHDAY PARTY                 WILHELM, KATE       SS    NEW 68 A
  DOWNSTAIRS ROOM AND OTHER SPECULATIVE FICTION, THE
                                        WILHELM, KATE             A
UNCALCULATED RISK                ANVIL, CHRISTOPHER  SS    ASF 62 0
  NIGHTMARE AGE                         POHL, FREDERIK            A
UNCHARTED ISLE, THE              SMITH, CLARK ASHTON SS    WRT 30 1
  *MY BEST SCIENCE FICTION STORY        MARGULIES & FRIEND        A
```

CHARTED ISLE, THE

OUT OF SPACE AND TIME | SMITH, CLARK ASHTON | AC
CLE ARLY | GOULART, RON | SS | FSF 62 07
GHOST BREAKER | GOULART, RON | DC
CLE EINAR | BRADBURY, RAY | SS | NEW 47 AC
*DARK CARNIVAL | BRADBURY, RAY | AC
*OCTOBER COUNTRY, THE | BRADBURY, RAY | AC
R IS FOR ROCKET | BRADBURY, RAY | AC
CLE FREMMIS | STURGEON, THEODORE | SS | KNT 70
STURGEON IS ALIVE AND WELL... | STURGEON, THEODORE | AC
CLE PHIL ON TV | PRIESTLEY, J. B. | SS | FSF 55 10
OTHER PLACE, THE | PRIESTLEY, J. B. | AC
CLE SAM'S CHILDREN (CHILD'S PLAY)
EISENBERG, LARRY | SS | IFS 70 01
BEST LAID SCHEMES, THE | EISENBERG, LARRY | AC
CLE VLAD | SINCLAIR, CLIVE | SS | TRV 73
YEAR'S BEST HORROR STORIES: SERIES III, THE
DAVIS, RICHARD | AN
CLEAR CALL FOR LEE | MCKENNA, RICHARD M. | SS | NEW 71 AN
POCKETFUL OF STARS, A | KNIGHT, DAMON | AN
CLEAVISH TRUETHINKING | ANDERSON, POUL | AR | 60
HOMEBREW | ANDERSON, POUL | AC
CCOLLECTED WORKS | CARTER, LIN | SS | FSF 65 03
WORLD'S BEST SCIENCE FICTION: 1966 | WOLLHEIM & CARR | AN
COMIC BOOK HORROR STORY, AN | SHAW, BOB | SS | SFM 75 10
COSMIC KALEIDOSCOPE | SHAW, BOB | AC
COMMON CASTAWAY | BOND, NELSON S. | SS | APR 49 11
NO TIME LIKE THE FUTURE | BOND, NELSON S. | AC
COMMON SENSE | CLEMENT, HAL | SS | ASF 45 09
SMALL CHANGES | CLEMENT, HAL | AC
COMMON SORT OF SPECTRE, AN | MITCHELL, EDWARD P. | SS | SUN 79 03
CRYSTAL MAN, THE | MITCHELL, EDWARD P. | AC
COMPROMISING VIEW, AN | ASIMOV, ISAAC | BR | PHY 69 02
OPUS 100 | ASIMOV, ISAAC | AC
COUPLING | MALZBERG, BARRY N. | SS | DYS 75
BEST OF BARRY N. MALZBERG, THE | MALZBERG, BARRY N. | AC
DYSTOPIAN VISIONS | ELWOOD, ROGER | OA
NDECIDED, THE | RUSSELL, ERIC FRANK | NV | ASF 49 04
DEEP SPACE | RUSSELL, ERIC FRANK | AC
NDER OLD EARTH | SMITH, CORDWAINER | NV | GAL 66 02
ALPHA 3 | SILVERBERG, ROBERT | AN
BEST OF CORDWAINER SMITH, THE | SMITH, CORDWAINER | AC
STARDREAMER | SMITH, CORDWAINER | AC
NDER PRESSURE (SEE DRAGON IN THE SEA)
HERBERT, FRANK | TC
NDER THE DRAGON'S TAIL | LATHAM, PHILIP | SS | ASF 66 12
ON OUR WAY TO THE FUTURE | CARR, TERRY | AN
NDER THE GENERATOR | SHIRLEY, JOHN | SS | UNI 76 06
UNIVERSE 6 | CARR, TERRY | OA
NDER THE HOLLYWOOD SIGN | REAMY, TOM | SS | ORB 75 17
ORBIT 17 | KNIGHT, DAMON | OA
NDER THE HORNS | BLOCH, ROBERT | SS | 62
KING OF TERRORS, THE | BLOCH, ROBERT | AC
NDER THE HOUSE | HARRISON, WILLIAM | SS | 72
ROLLERBALL | HARRISON, WILLIAM | AC
NDER THE KNIFE (SLIP UNDER THE KNIFE)
WELLS, H. G. | SS | NRV 96 01
COUNTRY OF THE BLIND, THE | WELLS, H. G. | AC
PERCHANCE TO DREAM | KNIGHT, DAMON | AN
PLATTNER STORY AND OTHERS, THE | WELLS, H. G. | AC
SHORT STORIES OF H. G. WELLS, THE | WELLS, H. G. | AC
TWENTY-EIGHT SCIENCE FICTION STORIES | WELLS, H. G. | AC
NDER THE MOONS OF MARS (ALSO AS A PRINCESS OF MARS)
BURROUGHS, EDGAR R. | NV | ASM 12 02
UNDER THE MOONS OF MARS | MOSKOWITZ, SAM | AN
NDER THE SAND-SEAS | SAARI, OLIVER E. | SS | SSS 41 01
GREAT SCIENCE FICTION STORIES ABOUT MARS DIKTY, T. E. | AN
NDER TWO MOONS | POHL, FREDERIK | NV | IFS 65 09
DAY MILLION | POHL, FREDERIK | AC
SECOND IF READER OF SCIENCE FICTION, THE POHL, FREDERIK | AN
NDERBELLY | EKLUND, GORDON | SS | IFS 72 10
BEST SCIENCE FICTION STORIES OF THE YEAR (1972)
DEL REY, LESTER | AN
NDERCITY, THE | KOONTZ, DEAN R. | SS | FUC 73
CITY: 2000 A.D., THE | CLEM/GREENBERG/& | AN
FUTURE CITY | ELWOOD, ROGER | OA
NDERDWELLER, THE (SMALL WORLD)
NOLAN, WILLIAM F. | SS | FUN 57 08
ALIEN HORIZONS | NOLAN, WILLIAM F. | AC
NDERFOLLOW | JAKES, JOHN W. | SS | FSF 63 05
STARS AROUND US, THE | HOSKINS, ROBERT | AN
NDERGROUND | BLOCH, ROBERT | SS | 67
LIVING DEMONS, THE | BLOCH, ROBERT | AC
NDERGROUND MOVEMENT | NEVILLE, KRIS | SS | FSF 52 06
*BEYOND HUMAN KEN | MERRIL, JUDITH | AN
MISSION: MANSTOP | NEVILLE, KRIS | AC
NDERGROWTH | ALDISS, BRIAN W. | NV | FSF 61 07
LONG AFTERNOON OF EARTH, THE | ALDISS, BRIAN W. | NO
NDERPRIVILEGED, THE | ALDISS, BRIAN W. | SS | NWS 63 05
BOOK OF BRIAN ALDISS, THE | ALDISS, BRIAN W. | AC
CITIES OF WONDER | KNIGHT, DAMON | AN
STARSWARM | ALDISS, BRIAN W. | AC
NDIGESTIBLE TRITON, THE (SEE TRITON)
HUBBARD, L. RON | TC
NDISCOVERED COUNTRY, THE | TEMPLE, WILLIAM F. | SS | NEB 58 10
SEA OF SPACE, A | NOLAN, WILLIAM F. | AN
NDYING ONES, THE (SEE OBEDIENCE)
BROWN, FREDRIC | TC
NEASY CHRYSALIDS, OUR MEMORIES
SHIRLEY, JOHN | SS | EPC 75
EPOCH | ELWOOD & SILVERBERG | OA
NEASY LIE THE DROWNED | WANDREI, DONALD | NV | WRT 37 12
STRANGE HARVEST | WANDREI, DONALD | AC
NEASY LIES THE HEAD | DEL REY, LESTER | SS | TSF 51 SP
ROBOTS AND CHANGELINGS | DEL REY, LESTER | AC
NEVEN EVENING, AN | HERBST, STEVE | SS | CLR 71 01
BEST SF: 1971 | HARRISON & ALDISS | AN

UNPLEASANT PROFESSION OF JONATHAN HOAG, THE

CLARION | WILSON, ROBIN SCOTT | OA
FUTURE PASTIMES | EDELSTEIN, SCOTT | SS | OA
UNFINISHED STORY NO. 1 | NIVEN, LARRY | SS | FSF 70 12
ALL THE MYRIAD WAYS | NIVEN, LARRY | AC
UNFINISHED STORY NO. 2 | NIVEN, LARRY | SS | NEW 71 AC
ALL THE MYRIAD WAYS | NIVEN, LARRY | AC
UNFINISHED, THE | LONG, FRANK BELKNAP | SS | SSS 51 04
SPACE ODYSSEYS | ALDISS, BRIAN W. | AN
UNFORTUNATE MR. MORKY, THE | AANDAHL, VANCE | SS | FSF 62 10
8TH ANNUAL OF THE YEAR'S BEST S-F, THE | MERRIL, JUDITH | AN
UNFORTUNATE PURCHASE | TUBB, E. C. | SS | SCF 54 03
GATEWAY TO THE STARS | CARNELL, JOHN | AN
UNFORTUNATE TOPOLOGIST, THE | KORNBLUTH, C. M. | PM | FSF 57 07
BEST SCIENCE FICTION STORIES OF C. M. KORNBLUTH
KORNBLUTH, C. M. | AC
FANTASIA MATHEMATICA | FADIMAN, CLIFTON | AN
UNFORTUNATELY | BROWN, FREDRIC | SS | FSF 58 10
NIGHTMARES AND GEEZENSTACKS | BROWN, FREDRIC | AC
UNGODLY MICE OF DOCTOR DRAKOS, THE
LAFFERTY, R. A. | SS | NMD 73
FRONTIERS 2; THE NEW MIND | ELWOOD, ROGER | OA
UNGRATEFUL HOUSE, THE (SEE THE MECHANICAL HOUSE)
DERLETH, AUGUST | TC
UNHAPPY MAN, THE | GUNN, JAMES E. | NV | FUN 55 02
JOY MAKERS, THE | GUNN, JAMES E. | NO
UNHUMAN SACRIFICE | MACLEAN, KATHERINE | NV | ASF 58 11
ANTHROPOLOGY THROUGH SCIENCE FICTION | MASON, C/GREENBERG/& | AN
CENTURY OF SCIENCE FICTION, A | KNIGHT, DAMON | AN
GODS FOR TOMORROW | SANTESSON, HANS S. | AN
*SPECTRUM | AMIS & CONQUEST | AN
UNICORN, THE | COOPER, EDMUND | SS
VOICES IN THE DARK | COOPER, EDMUND | AC
UNIDENTIFIED AMAZON, THE | NEARING, H. JR. | SS | FSF 52 12
SINISTER RESEARCHES OF C. P. RANSOM, THE NEARING, H. JR. | AC
UNIFICATION DAY | COLLYN, GEORGE | SS | NWS 66 05
TRAPS OF TIME, THE | MOORCOCK, MICHAEL | AN
UNINVITED GUEST, THE | ANVIL, CHRISTOPHER | SS | ASF 67 03
ENCOUNTERS WITH ALIENS | EARLEY, GEORGE W. | AN
UNION FOREVER, THE | MALZBERG, BARRY N. | SS | SCS 73
MANY WORLDS OF BARRY MALZBERG, THE | MALZBERG, BARRY N. | AC
OUT FROM GANYMEDE | MALZBERG, BARRY N. | AC
SHOWCASE | ELWOOD, ROGER | OA
UNION IN GEHENNA | BOND, NELSON S. | NV | FAD 42 11
MR. MERGENTHWIRKER'S LOBBIES AND OTHER FANTASTIC TALES
BOND, NELSON S. | AC
UNIQUE | BAKHNOV, VLADLEN | SS
RUSSIAN SCIENCE FICTION, 1969 | MAGIDOFF, ROBERT | AN
UNIT | MCINTOSH, J. T. | NV | NWS 57 02
FIVE-ODD | CONKLIN, GROFF | AN
UNITE AND CONQUER | STURGEON, THEODORE | NV | ASF 48 10
JOURNEY TO INFINITY | GREENBERG, MARTIN | AN
*WAY HOME, A | STURGEON, THEODORE | AC
UNIVAC TO UNIVAC | SALOMON, LOUIS B. | PM | HRP 58 03
ANOTHER TOMORROW | HOLLISTER, BERNARD C | AN
INSIDE INFORMATION | MOWSHOWITZ, ABBE | AN
UNIVAC: 2200 | SIMAK, CLIFFORD D. | SS | TAL 73
FRONTIERS 1; TOMORROW'S ALTERNATIVES | ELWOOD, ROGER | OA
UNIVERSAL LIBRARY, THE | LASSWITZ, KURD | SS | 01
FANTASIA MATHEMATICA | FADIMAN, CLIFTON | AN
UNIVERSAL PANCEA, THE (SEE BUILT UP LOGICALLY)
SCHOENFELD, HOWARD | TC
UNIVERSE | HEINLEIN, ROBERT A. | NV | ASF 41 05
*BEST OF SCIENCE FICTION | CONKLIN, GROFF | AN
ORPHANS OF THE SKY | HEINLEIN, ROBERT A. | NO
SCIENCE FICTION HALL OF FAME VOLUME 2A | BOVA, BEN | AN
UNIVERSE ACCORDING TO LAUMER, THE
ELLISON, HARLAN | IN
NINE BY LAUMER | LAUMER, KEITH | AC
UNIVERSE OF ROBERT BLAKE, THE (ROBERT BLAKE'S UNIVERSE)
ELLISON, HARLAN | SS | ROG 62 06
*LOVE AIN'T NOTHING BUT SEX MISSPELLED | ELLISON, HARLAN | AC
UNIVERSES | HENRI, ADRIAN | PM | 68
HOLDING YOUR EIGHT HANDS | LUCIE-SMITH, EDWARD | AN
UNIVERSITY | PHILLIPS, PETER | NV | GAL 53 04
SECOND GALAXY READER OF SCIENCE FICTION GOLD, H. L. | AN
UNIVERSITY OF DEATH, THE | BALLARD, J. G. | SS | TRV 68 SU
LOVE & NAPALM: EXPORT U.S.A. | BALLARD, J. G. | AC
UNKNOWN CITIZEN, THE | AUDEN, W. H. | PM | 40
SPECULATIONS | SANDERS, THOMAS E. | AN
UNKNOWN LAW, THE | DAVIDSON, AVRAM | NV | FSF 64 06
WHAT STRANGE STARS AND SKIES | DAVIDSON, AVRAM | AC
UNKNOWN QUANTITY | PHILLIPS, PETER | SS | NWS 49 05
BEST FROM NEW WORLDS SCIENCE FICTION, THE
CARNELL, JOHN | AN
*NO PLACE LIKE EARTH | CARNELL, JOHN | AN
UNNATURAL ACT | HOCH, EDWARD D. | SS | NEW 69 AN
GENTLE INVADERS | SANTESSON, HANS S. | AN
UNNATURAL CAUSES | ROBINSON, SPIDER | NV | ASF 75 10
CALLAHAN'S CROSSTIME SALOON | ROBINSON, SPIDER | AC
UNPARALLELED INVASION, THE | LONDON, JACK | SS | MCS 10 07
CURIOUS FRAGMENTS | LONDON, JACK | AC
SCIENCE FICTION OF JACK LONDON, THE | LONDON, JACK | AC
WONDERMAKERS | HOSKINS, ROBERT | AN
UNPARDONABLE CRIME, THE | BLOCH, ROBERT | SS | SWK 61 09
CHAMBER OF HORRORS | BLOCH, ROBERT | AC
KING OF TERRORS, THE | BLOCH, ROBERT | AC
UNPICKER, THE | TEMPLE, WILLIAM F. | SS | NEW 73 AN
ANDROIDS, TIME MACHINES AND BLUE GIRAFFES
ELWOOD & GHIDALIA | AN
UNPLEASANT END, AN | EDELSTEIN, SCOTT | SS | NWQ 73 05
NEW WORLDS NO. 5 | MOORCOCK & PLATT | OA
UNPLEASANT PROFESSION OF JONATHAN HOAG, THE
HEINLEIN, ROBERT A. | SN | UNK 42 10
BEST OF ROBERT HEINLEIN, THE | HEINLEIN, ROBERT A. | AC
UNPLEASANT PROFESSION OF JONATHAN HOAG, THE
HEINLEIN, ROBERT A. | AC

UNPLEASANTNESS AT CARVER HOUSE, THE
                          JACOBI, CARL   SS
   TRAVELLERS BY NIGHT   DERLETH, AUGUST   OA
UNPROFESSIONAL   KIPLING, RUDYARD   SS   SRV 30 10
   IN DREAMS AWAKE   FIEDLER, LESLIE A.   AN
UNQUIET GRAVE, THE   MCCLINTIC, WINONA   PM   FSF 53 08
   BEST FROM FANTASY AND SCIENCE FICTION: 3
                          BOUCHER & MCCOMAS   AN
UNREADY TO WEAR   VONNEGUT, KURT JR. SS   GAL 53 04
   CANARY IN A CAT HOUSE   VONNEGUT, KURT JR.   AC
   SECOND GALAXY READER OF SCIENCE FICTION GOLD, H. L. AN
   WELCOME TO THE MONKEY HOUSE VONNEGUT, KURT JR.   AC
UNREAL ESTATES   ALDISS, BRIAN W.   MS C SFH 64 01
   SPECTRUM 4   AMIS & CONQUEST   AN
UNREAL ESTATES   AMIS, KINGSLEY   MS C SFH 64 01
   SPECTRUM 4   AMIS & CONQUEST   AN
UNREAL ESTATES   LEWIS, C. S.   MS C SFH 64 01
   SPECTRUM 4   AMIS & CONQUEST   AN
UNREAL MCCOY, THE (THE MAN TRAP, GEORGE C. JOHNSON)
                          BLISH, JAMES   SA   STK 67 01
   STAR TREK   BLISH, JAMES   OC
UNREASONABLE FACSIMILE DEL REY, LESTER   SS   FUT 52 07
   EARLY DEL REY   DEL REY, LESTER   AC
   NOW & BEYOND   HOWARD, IVAN   AN
UNREASONABLE FACSIMILE SHAW, BOB   SS
   COSMIC KALEIDOSCOPE   SHAW, BOB   AC
   LONG NIGHT OF WAITING AND OTHER STORIES ELWOOD, ROGER OA
UNREMEMBERED, THE   MACKIN, EDWARD   SS   NWS 64 03
   WORLD'S BEST SCIENCE FICTION: 1965 WOLLHEIM & CARR AN
UNSAFE DEPOSIT BOX, THE KERSH, GERALD   SS   SEP 62 04
   LIGHT FANTASTIC, THE   HARRISON, HARRY   AN
   POST READER OF FANTASY AND SCIENCE FICTION
                          SATURDAY EVE. POST   AN
   8TH ANNUAL OF THE YEAR'S BEST S-F, THE MERRIL, JUDITH AN
UNSAVORY EPISODE OF MRS. HECTOR POWELL-CHALLENGER, THE
                          CONEY, MICHAEL G.   SS
   MONITOR FOUND IN ORBIT   CONEY, MICHAEL G.   AC
UNSCHEDULED FLIGHT   COULSON, JUANITA   SS
   BEYOND TIME   LEY, SANDRA   OA
UNSILENT SPRING   SIMAK, CLIFFORD D.
                      AND SIMAK, RICHARD D. NV C STL 76 02
   STELLAR 2   DEL REY, JUDY-LYNN   OA
UNSLEEPING BEAUTY AND THE BEAST
                          WALDROP, HOWARD   SS
   LONE STAR UNIVERSE   PROCTOR & UTLEY   OA
UNSPEAKABLE BETROTHAL, THE BLOCH, ROBERT   SS   AFR 49 09
   LIVING DEMONS, THE   BLOCH, ROBERT   AC
UNSPEAKABLE MCINCH, THE VANCE, JACK   NV   STS 48 11
   MANY WORLDS OF MAGNUS RIDOLPH, THE VANCE, JACK   DC
UNSPOKEN WISH, THE   DISCH, THOMAS M.   SS
   *GETTING INTO DEATH   DISCH, THOMAS M.   AC
UNTELEPORTED MAN, THE DICK, PHILIP K.   SN   FAN 64 12
   PHILIP K. DICK OMNIBUS, A DICK, PHILIP K.   AC
UNTIMELY TOPPER, THE   DE CAMP, L. SPRAGUE
                      AND PRATT, FLETCHER   SS C FSF 53 07
   BEST FROM FANTASY AND SCIENCE FICTION: 3
                          BOUCHER & MCCOMAS   AN
UNTITLED   KING, MAC   PM   NWQ 74 06
   NEW WORLDS NO. 6   PLATT & BAILEY   OA
UNTITLED   PURDY, KEN W.   SS   PBY 66 10
   MASKS   PLAYBOY, EDITORS OF   AN
UNTITLED BOX NO. 3   SAMARIS, LUCAS   IL
   SCIENCE FICTION   BRODKIN & PEARSON   AN
(UNTITLED) (FROM CANCERQUEEN) LANDOLFI, TOMMASO EX
   BEST SF: 1971   HARRISON & ALDISS   AN
UNTO HIM THAT HATH   DEL REY, LESTER   NV   SSF 52 11
   TIME CURVE, THE   MOSKOWITZ & ELWOOD   AN
UNTO MY MANIFOLD DOOMS (THE MANY DOOMS)
                          HARRISON, HARRY   SS   GAL 64 06
   TWO TALES AND EIGHT TOMORROWS HARRISON, HARRY   AC
UNTO THE FOURTH GENERATION ASIMOV, ISAAC   SS   FSF 59 04
   DECADE OF FANTASY AND SCIENCE FICTION, A MILLS, ROBERT P. AN
   NIGHTFALL AND OTHER STORIES ASIMOV, ISAAC   AC
   WANDERING STARS   DANN, JACK M.   AN
UNTO US A CHILD IS BORN KELLER, DAVID H. MD. SS   AMZ 33 07
   FOLSOM FLINT AND OTHER CURIOUS TALES, THE
                          KELLER, DAVID H. MD.   AC
   LIFE EVERLASTING AND OTHER TALES OF SCIENCE, FANTASY
   AND HORROR   KELLER, DAVID H. MD.   AC
UNTOUCHABLE   BLOCH, ROBERT   SS   SMM 62 03
   CHAMBER OF HORRORS   BLOCH, ROBERT   AC
   KING OF TERRORS, THE   BLOCH, ROBERT   AC
UNTOUCHED BY HUMAN HANDS (ONE MAN'S POISON)
                          SHECKLEY, ROBERT   SS   GAL 53 12
   GATES TO TOMORROW   NORTON, AN.&DONALDY   AN
   *UNTOUCHED BY HUMAN HANDS SHECKLEY, ROBERT   AC
UNTOWARD OCCURENCE AT EMBASSY POETRY READING
                          HACKER, MARILYN   PM   BMR 73
   BAD MOON RISING   DISCH, THOMAS M.   OA
UNVEILING THE MYSTERY PLANET LEY, WILLY   AR
   FAREWELL FANTASTIC VENUS   ALDISS & HARRISON   AN
UNWANTED, THE   COUNSELMAN, MARY E. SS   WRT 51 01
   UNEXPECTED, THE   MARGULIES, LEO   AN
UNWELCOME TENANT   DEE, ROGER   SS   PLS 50 SU
   *BEYOND HUMAN KEN   MERRIL, JUDITH   AN
   FIFTY SHORT SCIENCE FICTION TALES ASIMOV & CONKLIN AN
UP AGAINST THE WALL   THURSTON, ROBERT   SS   AMZ 73 08
   SCHOOL AND SOCIETY THROUGH SCIENCE FICTION
                          OLANDER/GREENBERG/&   AN
UP AND DOWN   ESCHER, M. C.   IL
   SCIENCE FICTION   BRODKIN & PEARSON   AN
UP CHRISTOPHER TO MADNESS DAVIDSON, AVRAM
                      AND ELLISON, HARLAN   SS C KNT 65 11
   PARTNERS IN WONDER   ELLISON, HARLAN   AC
UP SCHIST CRICK   ANTHONY, PIERS   SS   GEN 72
   GENERATION   GERROLD, DAVID   OA

UP THE CLOSE AND DOWN THE STAIR
                          DAVIDSON, AVRAM   SS   FSF 58 0
   OR ALL THE SEAS WITH OYSTERS DAVIDSON, AVRAM
UP THERE   WOLLHEIM, DONALD A. SS   SFQ 42 S
   HISTORY OF THE SCIENCE FICTION MAGAZINE, THE PART 2 1936-1945
                          ASHLEY, MICHAEL
UP-TO-DATE SORCERER, THE ASIMOV, ISAAC   SS   FSF 58 0
   BEST FROM FANTASY AND SCIENCE FICTION: 8
                          BOUCHER, ANTHONY   A
   NIGHTFALL AND OTHER STORIES ASIMOV, ISAAC
UPON THE DULL EARTH   DICK, PHILIP K.   NV   BEY 54 0
   HANDFUL OF DARKNESS, A   DICK, PHILIP K.
   PRESERVING MACHINE, THE   DICK, PHILIP K.   A
UPON THE OCCASION OF BEING ASKED TO ARGUE THAT LOVE AND
   MARRIAGE ARE INCOMPATIBLE ANDERSON, POUL   PM   DRC 73 0
   HOMEBREW   ANDERSON, POUL
UPPER LEVEL ROAD, THE VAN LORNE, WARNER   SS   ASF 35 0
   *BEST OF SCIENCE FICTION   CONKLIN, GROFF   A
UPS AND DOWNS   MALZBERG, BARRY N.   SS   EIO 73
   BEST OF BARRY N. MALZBERG, THE MALZBERG, BARRY N.
   EROS IN ORBIT   ELDER, JOSEPH   O
UPSHAW'S UPSET   CONRAD, EARL   SS
   DA VINCI MACHINE, THE   CONRAD, EARL   O
UPTURNED FACE, THE   CRANE, STEPHEN   SS
   *TWISTED   CONKLIN, GROFF   A
URANIUM EARPIECES   LEM, STANISLAW   SS   72
   MORTAL ENGINES   LEM, STANISLAW   A
URSULA MAJOR CONSTRUCT: OR, A FAR GREATER HORROR LOOMED, THE
                          LE GUIN, URSULA K. SS   CLR 73 0
   CLARION III   WILSON, ROBIN SCOTT   O
USEFUL PHRASES FOR THE TOURIST RUSS, JOANNA   SS   UNI 72 0
   FUTURE PASTIMES   EDELSTEIN, SCOTT   O.
   INFINITE JESTS   SILVERBERG, ROBERT   A
   UNIVERSE 2   CARR, TERRY   O.
USELESS PLANET, THE   LARIONOVA, OLGA   NV   67
   ULTIMATE THRESHOLD, THE   GINSBURG, MIRRA
USES OF MATHEMATICS, THE (1863)
                          BUTLER, SAMUEL   PM
   FANTASIA MATHEMATICA   FADIMAN, CLIFTON   A
USHER II (CARNIVAL OF MADNESS) BRADBURY, RAY   SS   TWS 50 0
   ILLUSTRATED MAN, THE (BRITISH) BRADBURY, RAY   A
   MARTIAN CHRONICLES, THE   BRADBURY, RAY   A
UTILITY   JONES, RAYMOND F.   SS   ASF 44 0
   TOYMAKER, THE   JONES, RAYMOND F.   A
UTOPIA   LUNDWALL, SAM J.   AR   71
   LOOKING AHEAD   ALLEN, D. & L.   A
UTOPIA (1516)   MORE, SIR THOMAS   EX
   *BEYOND TIME AND SPACE   DERLETH, AUGUST   A
UTOPIA? NEVER!   DISCH, THOMAS M.   AS   AMZ 63 0
   *ONE HUNDRED AND TWO H-BOMBS DISCH, THOMAS M.   A
   WHITE FANG GOES DINGO AND OTHER FUNNY S.F. STORIES
                          DISCH, THOMAS M.   A
UTOPIAN   REYNOLDS, MACK   SS   YRT 70
   BEST OF MACK REYNOLDS, THE REYNOLDS, MACK   A
   TOMORROW, AND TOMORROW, AND TOMORROW... HEINTZ/HERBERT/JOOS/ A
   YEAR 2000, THE   HARRISON, HARRY   O
UTOPIAN SCIENCE FICTION (FROM "THE NEW ATLANTIS")
                          BACON, FRANCIS   EX
   SCIENCE FICTION THROUGH THE AGES 1 EVANS, I. O.   A
UTTERLY PERFECT MURDER, THE (MY PERFECT MURDER)
                          BRADBURY, RAY   SS   PBY 71 0
   LONG AFTER MIDNIGHT   BRADBURY, RAY   A
V.R.T.   WOLFE, GENE   NV
   FIFTH HEAD OF CERBERUS, THE WOLFE, GENE
V-2: ROCKET CARGO SHIP LEY, WILLY   AR   ASF 45 0
   *ADVENTURES IN TIME AND SPACE HEALY & MCCOMAS   A
VACATION   POSNER, RICHARD   NV   NMD 73
   FRONTIERS 2: THE NEW MIND ELWOOD, ROGER
VACATION   STERNBERG, JACQUES SS
   FUTURE WITHOUT FUTURE   STERNBERG, JACQUES   O
VACATION ON EARTH, A DISCH, THOMAS M.   PM   66
   HOLDING YOUR EIGHT HANDS   LUCIE-SMITH, EDWARD   A
   SF12   MERRIL, JUDITH   A
VACATION, THE   BRADBURY, RAY   SS   PBY 63 1
   MACHINERIES OF JOY, THE   BRADBURY, RAY   AC
   PLAYBOY BOOK OF SCIENCE FICTION AND FANTASY, THE
                          PLAYBOY, EDITORS OF   A
VALE, POLLINI!   JOHNSTON, GEORGE   SS
   SECOND PACIFIC BOOK OF SCIENCE FICTION, THE
                          BAXTER, JOHN   AN
VALERIE   ELLISON, HARLAN   SS   LAF 72 1
   LOVE AIN'T NOTHING BUT SEX MISSPELLED (REVISED)
                          ELLISON, HARLAN   AC
VALISE MACABRE   MCCLINTIC, WINONA   PM   FSF 57 0
   BEST FROM FANTASY AND SCIENCE FICTION: 8
                          BOUCHER, ANTHONY   AN
VALLEY BEYOND TIME   SILVERBERG, ROBERT SN   SFA 57 1
   VALLEY BEYOND TIME   SILVERBERG, ROBERT   AC
VALLEY OF DREAMS   WEINBAUM, STANLEY G. NV WOS 34 1
   BEST OF STANLEY G. WEINBAUM, THE WEINBAUM, STANLEY G. A
   FROM OFF THIS WORLD   MARGULIES & FRIEND   AN
   MARTIAN ODYSSEY AND OTHER SCIENCE FICTION TALES, A
                          WEINBAUM, STANLEY G.
   MARTIAN ODYSSEY AND OTHERS, A WEINBAUM, STANLEY G. AC
VALLEY OF ECHOES, THE KLEIN, GERARD   SS
   VIEW FROM ANOTHER SHORE   ROTTENSTEINER, FRANZ A
VALLEY OF SPIDERS, THE WELLS, H. G.   SS   PRS 03 0
   BEST STORIES OF H. G. WELLS WELLS, H. G.
   COUNTRY OF THE BLIND, THE WELLS, H. G.   AC
   SHORT STORIES OF H. G. WELLS, THE WELLS, H. G.   AC
   TWELVE STORIES AND A DREAM WELLS, H. G.   AC
   TWENTY-EIGHT SCIENCE FICTION STORIES WELLS, H. G. AC
   WAR OF THE WORLDS, THE TIME MACHINE AND SELECTED SHORT STORIES
                          WELLS, H. G.   AC
VALLEY OF THE BUSHES MITCHISON, NAOMI   SS
   ANDROMEDA I   WESTON, PETER   OA

VALLEY OF THE FOUR CROSSES, THE   VIA ASTEROID

VALLEY OF THE FOUR CROSSES, THE
                         ZABELIN, IGOR   SS
  DESTINATION: AMALTHEIA DIXON, RICHARD   AN
VALLEY OF THE SORCERESS, THE ROHMER, SAX   SS
  ANCIENT MYSTERIES READER, THE HAINING, PETER   AN
VALLEY OF THE WORM, THE HOWARD, ROBERT E.   SS WRT 34 02
  WOLFSHEAD   HOWARD, ROBERT E.   AC
  WORLDS OF WEIRD   MARGULIES, LEO   AN
VALLEY WAS STILL, THE WELLMAN, MANLY WADE SS WRT 39 08
  UNEXPECTED, THE   MARGULIES, LEO   AN
VALLEY, THE STOCKHAM, RICHARD SS   IFS 54 06
  EVIL EARTHS   ALDISS, BRIAN W.   AN
VALVE TRANSCRIPT, THE ZOSS, JOEL   SS   NWS 68 04
  BEST SF STORIES FROM NEW WORLDS 4 MOORCOCK, MICHAEL AN
VAMP, THE DISCH, THOMAS M.   SS   FAN 65 02
  *ONE HUNDRED AND TWO H-BOMBS DISCH, THOMAS M.   AC
  WHITE FANG GOES DINGO AND OTHER FUNNY S.F. STORIES
                         DISCH, THOMAS M.   AC
VAMPIRE'S SAGA, A BELKIN, NORMAN   PM   FSF 59 05
  BEST FROM FANTASY AND SCIENCE FICTION: 9
                         MILLS, ROBERT P.   AN
VAMPIRES LTD. NESVADBA, JOSEF   SS   64
  OTHER WORLDS, OTHER SEAS SUVIN, DARKO   AN
  WORLD'S BEST SCIENCE FICTION: 1965 WOLLHEIM & CARR AN
VANA, THE DOREMIEUX, ALAIN   SS   59
  13 FRENCH SCIENCE-FICTION STORIES KNIGHT, DAMON   AN
VANDY, VANDY WELLMAN, MANLY WADE SS   FSF 53 03
  BEST FROM FANTASY AND SCIENCE FICTION: 3
                         BOUCHER & MCCOMAS   AN
  WHO FEARS THE DEVIL? WELLMAN, MANLY WADE   AC
VANISHED CIVILIZATION, THE (FROM "TIMAIOS" AND "CRITIAS")
                         PLATO   EX
  SCIENCE FICTION THROUGH THE AGES 1 EVANS, I. O.   AN
VANISHING AMERICAN, THE BEAUMONT, CHARLES SS   FSF 55 08
  BEST FROM FANTASY AND SCIENCE FICTION: 5
                         BOUCHER, ANTHONY   AN
  CITY: 2000 A.D., THE CLEM/GREENBERG/&   AN
  HUNGER AND OTHER STORIES, THE BEAUMONT, CHARLES   AC
  INVISIBLE MEN DAVENPORT, BASIL   AN
  MAGIC MAN AND OTHER SCIENCE-FANTASY STORIES
                         BEAUMONT, CHARLES   AC
  SOCIAL PROBLEMS THROUGH SCIENCE FICTION GREENBERG/MILSTEAD/& AN
VANISHING BOROUGH, THE EISENBERG, LARRY   SS   NEW 71 AC
  BEST LAID SCHEMES, THE EISENBERG, LARRY   AC
VANISHING MAN, THE HUGHES, RICHARD   SS   26
  MATHEMATICAL MAGPIE, THE FADIMAN, CLIFTON   AN
VANISHING POINT BRAND, JONATHAN   NV   IFS 65 01
  WORLD'S BEST SCIENCE FICTION: 1966 WOLLHEIM & CARR AN
VANISHING POINTS DORMAN, SONYA   PM   QRK 71 03
  QUARK/3 DELANY & HACKER   OA
VANISHING VENUSIANS, THE BRACKETT, LEIGH SS   PLS 45 SP
  BEST OF LEIGH BRACKETT, THE BRACKETT, LEIGH   AC
VANYA GRIGORIEV, VLADIMIR SS
  LAST DOOR TO AIYA GINSBURG, MIRRA   AN
VAPORS DISCH, THOMAS M.   SS
  *GETTING INTO DEATH DISCH, THOMAS M.   AC
VARIABLE MAN, THE DICK, PHILIP K.   NA   SSF 53 09
  VARIABLE MAN, THE DICK, PHILIP K.   AC
VARIETIES OF RELIGIOUS EXPERIENCE
                         GOULART, RON   SS   FSF 73 06
  ODD JOB NO. 101 GOULART, RON   AC
VARIETIES OF THE SCIENCE-FICTION EXPERIENCE, THE
                         POHL, FREDERIK   IN
  EIGHTH GALAXY READER, THE POHL, FREDERIK   AN
VARIETY OF EXCELLENCE, A DEL REY, LESTER   IN
  BEST OF FREDERIK POHL, THE POHL, FREDERIK   AC
VASTER THAN EMPIRES AND MORE SLOW
                         LE GUIN, URSULA K. NV   NDM 71 01
  BEST SCIENCE FICTION OF THE YEAR, THE CARR, TERRY   AN
  EXPLORERS OF SPACE SILVERBERG, ROBERT   AN
  NEW DIMENSIONS 1 SILVERBERG, ROBERT   OA
  WINDS TWELVE QUARTERS, THE LE GUIN, URSULA K.   AC
  WOMEN OF WONDER SARGENT, PAMELA   AN
  WONDERMAKERS 2 HOSKINS, ROBERT   AN
VAT, THE DAVIDSON, AVRAM   SS   FSF 61 10
  STRANGE SEAS AND SHORES DAVIDSON, AVRAM   AC
VAULT OF THE BEAST VAN VOGT, A. E.   NV   ASF 40 08
  *ASTOUNDING SCIENCE FICTION ANTHOLOGY, THE
                         CAMPBELL, JOHN W. JR AN
  *AWAY AND BEYOND VAN VOGT, A. E.   AC
  BEST OF A. E. VAN VOGT, THE (BRITISH) VAN VOGT, A. E. AC
  FIRST ASTOUNDING SCIENCE FICTION ANTHOLOGY, THE (PB)
                         CAMPBELL, JOHN W. JR AN
  MONSTERS VAN VOGT, A. E.   AC
  *OTHER SIDE OF THE MOON, THE DERLETH, AUGUST   AN
  *SECOND ASTOUNDING SCIENCE FICTION ANTHOLOGY, THE
                         CAMPBELL, JOHN W. JR AN
VAULTS OF YOH-VOMBIS, THE SMITH, CLARK ASHTON NV WRT 32 05
  OUT OF SPACE AND TIME SMITH, CLARK ASHTON   AC
VEIL OF ASTELLAR, THE BRACKETT, LEIGH SS   TWS 44 SP
  BEST OF LEIGH BRACKETT, THE BRACKETT, LEIGH   AC
  PLANETS OF WONDER CARR, TERRY   AN
VEILED FEMINISTS OF ATLANTIS, THE
                         TARKINGTON, BOOTH SS   PRM 26 03
  WHEN WOMEN RULE MOSKOWITZ, SAM   AN
VEILED ISLAND MCDOWELL, EMMETT   NV   ASF 46 01
  *SCIENCE FICTION ADVENTURES IN MUTATION CONKLIN, GROFF AN
VELDT, THE BRADBURY, RAY   PL   SEP 50 09
  WONDERFUL ICE CREAM SUIT AND OTHER PLAYS, THE
                         BRADBURY, RAY   AC
VELDT, THE (THE WORLD THE CHILDREN MADE)
                         BRADBURY, RAY   SS   SEP 50 09
  BEYOND THE BARRIERS OF SPACE AND TIME MERRIL, JUDITH AN
  *ILLUSTRATED MAN, THE BRADBURY, RAY   AC
  MASTERS' CHOICE JANIFER, LAURENCE M. AN
  PAST, PRESENT, AND FUTURE PERFECT WOLFE, J&FITZ GERALD AN

  SECOND ORBIT DOHERTY, G. D.   AN
  TOMORROW, AND TOMORROW, AND TOMORROW... HEINTZ/HERBERT/JOOS/ AN
  UNTRAVELLED WORLDS BARTER & WILSON   AN
  VINTAGE BRADBURY, THE BRADBURY, RAY   AC
VELVET GLOVE, THE HARRISON, HARRY   NV   FUN 56 11
  CRIME PREVENTION IN THE 30TH CENTURY SANTESSON, HANS S. AN
  FANTASTIC UNIVERSE OMNIBUS, THE SANTESSON, HANS S.   AN
  SOULS IN METAL ASHLEY, MICHAEL   AN
  WAR WITH THE ROBOTS HARRISON, HARRY   AC
VENGEANCE BY PROXY WYNDHAM, JOHN   SS   STE 40 02
  BEST OF JOHN WYNDHAM, THE WYNDHAM, JOHN   AC
  MAN FROM BEYOND AND OTHER STORIES, THE WYNDHAM, JOHN AC
VENGEANCE FLEET (VENGEANCE, UNLIMITED)
                         BROWN, FREDRIC   SS   SSS 50 07
  NIGHTMARES AND GEEZENSTACKS BROWN, FREDRIC   AC
VENGEANCE FOR NIKOLAI (ALSO AS THE SONG OF MARYA)
                         MILLER, WALTER M. JR SS VSF 57 03
  NO LIMITS FERMAN, JOSEPH W.   AN
VENGEANCE IS MINE (TO AVENGE MAN)
                         DEL REY, LESTER   NV   GAL 64 12
  GODS AND GOLEMS DEL REY, LESTER   AC
VENGEANCE OF THE SPACE ARMADAS KNOX, CALVIN M. SN SFA 58 03
  LEST WE FORGET THEE, EARTH KNOX, CALVIN M.   DN
VENGEANCE, UNLIMITED (SEE VENGEANCE FLEET)
                         BROWN, FREDRIC   TC
VENTURE TO THE MOON CLARKE, ARTHUR C.   GR   FSF 56 12
  BEST FROM FANTASY AND SCIENCE FICTION: 7
                         BOUCHER, ANTHONY   AN
  BEST OF ARTHUR C. CLARKE: 1937-1971, THE CLARKE, ARTHUR C. AC
  FIRST FLIGHTS TO THE MOON CLEMENT, HAL   AN
VENTURER OF THE MARTIAN MIMICS (SEE SPIRO)
                         RUSSELL, ERIC FRANK TC   TOW 40 FL
VENUS (HOTHOUSE PLANET) BARNES, ARTHUR K. NV   TWS 37 10
  INTERPLANETARY HUNTER BARNES, ARTHUR K.   AC
VENUS ADVENTURE, THE WYNDHAM, JOHN   SS   WOS 32 05
  SPACE MAGICIANS, THE NORTON & MOSKOWITZ   AN
VENUS AND THE RABBIT FITZPATRICK, E. M.   SS
  AD 2500 WILSON, ANGUS   AN
VENUS AND THE SEVEN SEXES TENN, WILLIAM   NV   49
  GIRL WITH THE HUNGRY EYES, AND OTHER STORIES, THE
                         WOLLHEIM, DONALD A. OA
  INFINITE JESTS SILVERBERG, ROBERT   AN
  *SCIENCE-FICTION CARNIVAL BROWN, F. & REYNOLDS   AN
  SEVEN SEXES, THE TENN, WILLIAM   AC
VENUS HUNTERS, THE (THE ENCOUNTER)
                         BALLARD, J. G.   NV   AMZ 63 06
  OVERLOADED MAN, THE BALLARD, J. G.   AC
  TERMINAL BEACH (AMERICAN VERSION) BALLARD, J. G.   AC
VENUS IS A MAN'S WORLD TENN, WILLIAM   NV   GAL 51 07
  *GALAXY READER OF SCIENCE FICTION GOLD, H. L.   AN
  GIANTS UNLEASHED CONKLIN, GROFF   AN
  SQUARE ROOT OF MAN, THE TENN, WILLIAM   AC
"VENUS IS HELL!" ALDISS, BRIAN W.   SI
  ALL ABOUT VENUS ALDISS, BRIAN W.   AC
VENUS MISSION MCINTOSH, J. T.   NV   PLS 51 07
  HIDDEN PLANET, THE WOLLHEIM, DONALD A.   AN
VENUS MYSTERY FOR SCIENTISTS DAVY, JOHN   AR   OBS 67 10
  ALL ABOUT VENUS ALDISS, BRIAN W.   AN
  FAREWELL FANTASTIC VENUS ALDISS & HARRISON   AN
VENUS OF AZOMBEII, THE SMITH, CLARK ASHTON NV WRT 31 06
  OTHER DIMENSIONS SMITH, CLARK ASHTON   AC
VENUS PAPERS, THE WILSON, RICHARD   SS   FSF 58 03
  ENCOUNTERS WITH ALIENS EARLEY, GEORGE W.   AN
VENUS PLUS THREE FRITCH, CHARLES E.   NV   GAM 63 01
  HORSES' ASTEROID FRITCH, CHARLES E.   AC
VENUS SMILES (MOBILE) BALLARD, J. G.   NV   IFS 67 09
  *VERMILLION SANDS BALLARD, J. G.   AC
VENUS TRAP SILVERBERG, ROBERT   SS   FUT 56 30
  NOW & BEYOND HOWARD, IVAN   AN
VENUSIAN INVADER STERNIG, LARRY   SS   PLS 45 WI
  TEEN-AGE SPACE ADVENTURES FURMAN, A. L.   AN
VENUSWAY ELAM, RICHARD M. JR. SS   BLF 51
  TEEN-AGE SCIENCE FICTION STORIES ELAM, RICHARD M. JR. AC
VERBAL AGREEMENT SELLINGS, ARTHUR   NV   GAL 56 09
  LONG EUREKA, THE SELLINGS, ARTHUR   AC
VERSE ANONYMOUS   PM   51
  MATHEMATICAL MAGPIE, THE FADIMAN, CLIFTON   AN
VERSE BARR, STEPHEN
  MATHEMATICAL MAGPIE, THE FADIMAN, CLIFTON   AN
VERSE WHEWELL, DR. WILLIAM
  MATHEMATICAL MAGPIE, THE FADIMAN, CLIFTON   AN
VERSE WINSOR, FREDERICK   PM   58
  MATHEMATICAL MAGPIE, THE FADIMAN, CLIFTON   AN
VERTICAL HOLD COOPER, EDMUND   SS
  TOMORROW CAME COOPER, EDMUND   AC
VERTICAL LADDER, THE SANSOM, WILLIAM   SS   60
  NIGHT IN FUNLAND BRONDFIELD, JEROME   AN
VERTIGO WHITE, JAMES   NV   NWR 68 12
  MAJOR OPERATION WHITE, JAMES   NO
  NEW WRITINGS IN SF. 12 CARNELL, JOHN   OA
VERY CULTURED TASTE, A FREDERIC, GEORGE   SS   60
  IF THIS GOES ON NUETZEL, CHARLES   AN
VERY CULTURED TASTE, A (AS GEORGE FREDERIC)
                         NUETZEL, CHARLES   SS   60
  IMAGES OF TOMORROW NUETZEL, CHARLES   AC
VERY LAST DAY OF A GOOD WOMAN, THE (THE LAST DAY)
                         ELLISON, HARLAN   SS   ROG 58 11
  ALONE AGAINST TOMORROW ELLISON, HARLAN   AC
  ELLISON WONDERLAND ELLISON, HARLAN   AC
VERY LATE IN THE EVENING (SEE SOME LIVE LIKE LAZARUS)
                         BRADBURY, RAY   TC
VERY SINCERELY YOURS STERNBERG, JACQUES   NV
  FUTURE WITHOUT FUTURE STERNBERG, JACQUES   OC
VIA ASTEROID BINDER, EANDO   SS   TWS 38 02
  EXPLORING OTHER WORLDS MOSKOWITZ, SAM   AN

VIA DEATH   BINDER, EANDO   SS   TWS 38 08
  GREAT SCIENCE FICTION STORIES ABOUT THE MOON
                             DIKTY, T. E.   AN
VIA ETHERLINE   BINDER, EANDO   SS   TWS 37 10
  GREAT SCIENCE FICTION STORIES ABOUT MARS DIKTY, T. E.   AN
VICIOUS CIRCLE   HARLEY, ALAN   SS   SFM 74 02
  BEST OF SCIENCE FICTION MONTHLY, THE   SACKS, JANET   AN
VICTIM FROM SPACE, THE   SHECKLEY, ROBERT   NV   GAL 57 04
  PEOPLE TRAP AND OTHER PITFALLS, THE   SHECKLEY, ROBERT   AC
VICTIM OF HIGHER SPACE, A (1917)
                             BLACKWOOD, ALGERNON NV   AFR 52 18
  AVON FANTASY READER, THE   WOLLHEIM &ERNSBERGER   AN
VICTORY PARADE   SLESAR, HENRY   SS   PBY 57 04
  FROM THE "S" FILE   PLAYBOY, EDITORS OF   AN
  SCIENCE FICTION   BRODKIN & PEARSON   AN
VICTORY UNINTENTIONAL   ASIMOV, ISAAC   SS   SSS 42 08
  DAYS AFTER TOMORROW, THE   SANTESSON, HANS S.   AN
  INVASION FROM MARS   WELLES, ORSON   AN
  JUPITER   POHL, C. & F.   AN
  LOOKING FORWARD   LESSER, MILTON   AN
  *REST OF THE ROBOTS, THE   ASIMOV, ISAAC   AC
VIDEO   INOUYE, JON   PM
  NIGHT TIDE, A   INOUYE, JON   OC
VIDI VICI VENI   MALZBERG, BARRY N. SS   GEN 72
  GENERATION   GERROLD, DAVID   OA
VIEW FROM A HILL, A   JAMES, M. R.   SS   26
  TRAVELERS IN TIME   STERN, PHILIP VAN D. AN
VIEW FROM THE WINDOW, THE   RUSS, JOANNA   NV   QRK 70 01
  QUARK/1   DELANY & HACKER   OA
VIGIL   TUBB, E. C.   SS   GAL 56 11
  TEN FROM TOMORROW   TUBB, E. C.   AC
VILBAR PARTY, THE   SMITH, EVELYN E.   SS   GAL 55 01
  HUMAN AND OTHER BEINGS   DEGRAEFF, ALLEN   AN
  THIRD GALAXY READER, THE   GOLD, H. L.   AN
VILLAGE DANCE MASK FROM CEYLON MISC. MATERIAL IL
  SCIENCE FICTION   BRODKIN & PEARSON   AN
VILLAGE SWINDLER, THE   ALDISS, BRIAN W.   SS   INT 68 10
  DECADE THE 1960S   ALDISS & HARRISON   AN
  MOMENT OF ECLIPSE, THE   ALDISS, BRIAN W.   AC
VILLAGE, THE   STONEY, LELAND   PM   QRK 71 02
  QUARK/2   DELANY & HACKER   OA
VILLAGE, THE   WILHELM, KATE   SS   BMR 73
  BAD MOON RISING   DISCH, THOMAS M.   OA
  INFINITY BOX, THE   WILHELM, KATE   AC
VINDICAE FLAMMAE   HEARD, H. F.   SS
  GREAT FOG AND OTHER WEIRD TALES, THE   HEARD, H. F.   OC
VINE, THE   REED, KIT   SS   FSF 67 11
  ANTHROPOLOGY THROUGH SCIENCE FICTION   MASON, C/GREENBERG/& AN
  BEST SF: 1967   HARRISON & ALDISS   AN
  MARRIAGE AND THE FAMILY THROUGH SCIENCE FICTION
                                       CLEAR/WARRICK/&   AN
  NIGHTMARE GARDEN   GHIDALIA, VIC   AN
VINTAGE SEASON   KUTTNER, HENRY   NV   ASF 46 09
  NO BOUNDARIES   KUTTNER & MOORE   AC
  SPECTRUM 2   AMIS & CONQUEST   AN
VINTAGE SEASON   MOORE, C. L.   NV   ASF 46 09
  BEST OF C. L. MOORE, THE   MOORE, C. L.   AC
VINTAGE SEASON   O'DONNELL, LAWRENCE NV   ASF 46 09
  ASTOUNDING-ANALOG READER, THE VOLUME ONE HARRISON & ALDISS AN
  *TREASURY OF SCIENCE FICTION, A   CONKLIN, GROFF   AN
VINTAGE SEASON   KUTTNER, HENRY
                             AND MOORE, C. L.   NV C ASF 46 09
  SCIENCE FICTION HALL OF FAME VOLUME 2A BOVA, BEN   AN
VIOLATION (ALSO AS LAWBREAKER) NOLAN, WILLIAM F. SS   FUC 73
  FUTURE CITY   ELWOOD, ROGER   OA
VIOLENT MAN, THE   VAN VOGT, A. E.   AR   65
  BEST OF A. E. VAN VOGT, THE   VAN VOGT, A. E.   AC
VIRGINIA   KORNBLUTH, C. M.   SS   VSF 58 03
  *MILE BEYOND THE MOON, A   KORNBLUTH, C. M.   AC
VIRGINIA   TOMKINS, CALVIN   SS   PBY 67 03
  PLAYBOY BOOK OF HORROR AND THE SUPERNATURAL, THE
                                       PLAYBOY, EDITORS OF   AN
VIRTUOSO   GOLDSTONE, HERBERT SS   FSF 53 02
  *SCIENCE FICTION THINKING MACHINES   CONKLIN, GROFF   AN
VISION OF JUDGEMENT, A   WELLS, H. G.   SS   BUT 99 09
  COUNTRY OF THE BLIND, THE   WELLS, H. G.   AC
  LOOKING AHEAD   ALLEN, D. & L.   AN
  OUT OF THIS WORLD   FAST, JULIUS   AN
  SHORT STORIES OF H. G. WELLS, THE   WELLS, H. G.   AC
  *TIME MACHINE AND OTHER STORIES, THE WELLS, H. G.   AC
VISION OF MILTY BOIL, THE   FAST, HOWARD   SS
  GENERAL ZAPPED AN ANGEL, THE   FAST, HOWARD   OC
VISION OF OLAF STAPLEDON, THE DAVENPORT, BASIL AR
  TO THE END OF TIME   STAPLEDON, OLAF   AC
VISION OF VENUS, A   KLINE, OTIS ADELBERT SS AMZ 33 12
  SWORDSMEN IN THE SKY   WOLLHEIM, DONALD A.   AN
VISIONS OF HELL   BALLARD, J. G.   BR   NWS 66 03
  NEW WORLDS QUARTERLY NO. 2   MOORCOCK, MICHAEL   OA
VISIONS OF MONAD   HARRISON, M. JOHN SS   NWB 68 12
  MACHINE IN SHAFT TEN AND OTHER STORIES, THE
                                       HARRISON, M. JOHN   AC
  NEW WRITINGS IN SF. 8   CARNELL, JOHN   AN
  NEW WRITINGS IN SF. 12   CARNELL, JOHN   OA
VISIT TO A SMALL PLANET   VIDAL, GORE   PL   55
  JOURNEYS IN SCIENCE FICTION   LOUGHLIN, RICHARD L. AN
VISIT TO A WEIRD PLANET REVISITED
                             BERMAN, RUTH   SS
  STAR TREK: THE NEW VOYAGES   MARSHAK, S&CULBREATH OA
VISIT TO CLEVELAND GENERAL, A VAN SCYOC, SYDNEY J. SS   GAL 68 10
  SOCIAL PROBLEMS THROUGH SCIENCE FICTION GREENBERG/MILSTEAD/& AN
  WORLD'S BEST SCIENCE FICTION: 1969   WOLLHEIM & CARR   AN
VISIT TO SANTA CLAUS, A   MATHESON, RICHARD SS   NEW 70 AC
  SHOCK WAVES   MATHESON, RICHARD   AC
VISIT TO THE MOON, A   GRIFFITH, GEORGE   SS   PBS 00 01
  WORLDS APART   LOCKE, GEORGE   AN

VISITING AMOEBA (WHAT TRIUMPHS?)
                             ALDISS, BRIAN W.   NV   AUT 57 07
  CANOPY OF TIME, THE   ALDISS, BRIAN W.   AC
  GALAXIES LIKE GRAINS OF SAND   ALDISS, BRIAN W.   AC
VISITING PROFESSOR   BROWN, ROSEL GEORGE SS   FAN 61 02
  HANDFUL OF TIME, A   BROWN, ROSEL GEORGE   AC
VISITING YOKEL   CARTMILL, CLEVE   SS   TWS 43 08
  *MY BEST SCIENCE FICTION STORY   MARGULIES & FRIEND   AN
VISITOR   REYNOLDS, MACK   NV
  TOMORROW TODAY   ZEBROWSKI, GEORGE   OA
VISITOR AT LARGE   WHITE, JAMES   NV   NWS 59 06
  HOSPITAL STATION   WHITE, JAMES   AC
VISITOR FROM EGYPT, A   LONG, FRANK BELKNAP SS   WRT 30 09
  EARLY LONG, THE   LONG, FRANK BELKNAP   AC
  *HOUNDS OF TINDALOS, THE   LONG, FRANK BELKNAP   AC
VISITOR FROM OUTER SPACE, A KAZANTSEV, ALEXANDER SS
  SOVIET SCIENCE FICTION   ANONYMOUS   AN
VISITOR FROM SPACE   GUPPY, PAULINE D. SS   YNW
  SCIENCE FICTION STORIES   BRADLEY, JOHANNA   AN
VISITOR FROM THE VOID (SEE PRESS CONFERENCE)
                             WILSON, RICHARD   TC
VISITOR, THE   ANDERSON, POUL   SS   FSF 74 05
  HOMEWARD AND BEYOND   ANDERSON, POUL   AC
VISITOR, THE   BRADBURY, RAY   SS   STS 48 11
  *ILLUSTRATED MAN, THE   BRADBURY, RAY   AC
VISITORS FROM OUTER SPACE (FROM "MICROMEGAS")
                             VOLTAIRE   EX
  SCIENCE FICTION THROUGH THE AGES 1   EVANS, I. O.   AN
VISITORS, THE (SEE DE PROFUNDIS)
                             KUTTNER, HENRY   TC
VITAL FACTOR   BOND, NELSON S.   SS   51
  GREAT SCIENCE FICTION STORIES   SMITH, CORDELIA T.   AN
  NO TIME LIKE THE FUTURE   BOND, NELSON S.   AC
VITANULS, THE   BRUNNER, JOHN   SS   FSF 67 07
  FROM THIS DAY FORWARD   BRUNNER, JOHN   AC
  OTHER WORLDS, OTHER GODS   MOHS, MAYO   AN
"VIVE LAQUELLE DIFFERENCE?" SCORTIA, THOMAS N. IN C
  TWO VIEWS OF WONDER   SCORTIA & YARBRO   OA
"VIVE LAQUELLE DIFFERENCE?" YARBRO, CHELSEA Q. IN C
  TWO VIEWS OF WONDER   SCORTIA & YARBRO   OA
VOCATION   SMITH, GEORGE O.   SS   ASF 45 04
  CROSSROADS IN TIME   CONKLIN, GROFF   AN
VOICE AND BITTER WEEPING, A SAUNDERS, BUDDY
                             AND WALDROP, HOWARD SS C GAL 73 07
  BEST FROM GALAXY, THE VOLUME II   GALAXY, EDITORS OF   AN
VOICE FROM THE CURIOUS CUBE, THE
                             BOND, NELSON S.   SS
  NO TIME LIKE THE FUTURE   BOND, NELSON S.   AC
VOICE FROM THE ETHER, THE   ESHBACH, LLOYD A. SS   AMZ 31 05
  HISTORY OF THE SCIENCE FICTION MAGAZINE, THE PART 1 1926-1935
                             ASHLEY, MICHAEL   AN
VOICE FROM THE GALLERY   BROWNLOW, CATHERINE SS
  AD 2500   WILSON, ANGUS   AN
VOICE IN THE EARPHONES, THE SCHRAMM, WILBUR   SS   SEP 47 05
  POST READER OF FANTASY AND SCIENCE FICTION
                             SATURDAY EVE. POST   AN
  SATURDAY EVENING POST FANTASY STORIES, THE
                             FLES, BARTHOLD   AN
VOICE IN THE GARDEN, THE   ELLISON, HARLAN   SS   LGH 67 06
  FROM THE LAND OF FEAR   ELLISON, HARLAN   AC
VOICE IN THE NIGHT, THE   HODGSON, WILLIAM H. SS   BBM 07 11
  AVON FANTASY READER, THE   WOLLHEIM &ERNSBERGER AN
  *BEYOND TIME AND SPACE   DERLETH, AUGUST   AN
  SCIENCE FICTION BY GASLIGHT   MOSKOWITZ, SAM   AN
"VOICE IS HEARD IN RAMAH..., A"
                             ROBINSON, SPIDER   SS   ASF 75 11
  CALLAHAN'S CROSSTIME SALOON   ROBINSON, SPIDER   AC
VOICE OF THE DIAPHRAGM, THE WILSON, RICHARD   SS   GAL 58 05
  TIME OUT FOR TOMORROW   WILSON, RICHARD   AC
VOICE OF THE DOLPHINS, THE   SZILARD, LEO   SS
  VOICE OF THE DOLPHINS, AND OTHER STORIES, THE
                             SZILARD, LEO   AC
VOICE OF THE LOBSTER, THE   KUTTNER, HENRY   NV   TWS 50 02
  ADVENTURES IN TOMORROW   CROSSEN, KENDELL F.   AN
  BEST OF HENRY KUTTNER 2, THE   KUTTNER, HENRY   AC
  BEST OF HENRY KUTTNER, THE   KUTTNER, HENRY   AC
VOICE OF THE SONAR IN MY VERMIFORM APPENDIX, THE
                             FARMER, PHILIP JOSE SS   QRK 71 02
  BOOK OF PHILIP JOSE FARMER, THE   FARMER, PHILIP JOSE   AC
  QUARK/2   DELANY & HACKER   OA
VOICES FROM THE CLIFF   LEAHY, JOHN M.   SS   WRT 25 05
  SCIENCE AND SORCERY   FORD, GARRET   AN
VOICES IN THE DUST OF ANNAN KERSH, GERALD   SS   SEP 47 09
  NIGHTSHADE & DAMNATIONS   KERSH, GERALD   AC
  SHOT IN THE DARK   MERRIL, JUDITH   AN
VOICES OF TIME, THE   BALLARD, J. G.   SS   NWS 60 10
  ALPHA 2   SILVERBERG, ROBERT   AN
  BEST OF J. G. BALLARD, THE   BALLARD, J. G.   AC
  CHRONOPOLIS AND OTHER STORIES   BALLARD, J. G.   AC
  *FOUR-DIMENSIONAL NIGHTMARE, THE   BALLARD, J. G.   AC
  INNER LANDSCAPE, THE   MOORCOCK, MICHAEL   AN
  MODERN SCIENCE FICTION   SPINRAD, NORMAN   AN
  ONE HUNDRED YEARS OF SCIENCE FICTION KNIGHT, DAMON   AN
  SPECTRUM 3   AMIS & CONQUEST   AN
  VOICES OF TIME AND OTHER STORIES, THE BALLARD, J. G.   AC
VOICES, THE (SEE GEORGE THOMAS- 2027)
                             GUNN, JAMES E.   TC
VOID BEYOND, THE   WILLIAMS, ROBERT M. NV   TWS 51 04
  VOID BEYOND, AND OTHER STORIES, THE WILLIAMS, ROBERT M.   DC
VOLCANO DANCES, THE   BALLARD, J. G.   SS   NEW 64 AC
  TERMINAL BEACH (BRITISH VERSION)   BALLARD, J. G.   AC
  11TH ANNUAL OF THE YEAR'S BEST S-F, THE MERRIL, JUDITH   AN
VOLPLA   GUIN, WYMAN   NV   GAL 56 05
  LIVING WAY OUT   GUIN, WYMAN   AC
  THIRD GALAXY READER, THE   GOLD, H. L.   AN
  13 GREAT STORIES OF SCIENCE FICTION CONKLIN, GROFF   AN

VOLUME PAA-PYX

VOLUME PAA-PYX   SABERHAGEN, FRED   SS   GAL 61 02
  BOOK OF SABERHAGEN, THE   SABERHAGEN, FRED   AC
VON GOOM'S GAMBIT   CONTOSKI, VICTOR   SS   FSF 66 12
  BEST FROM FANTASY AND SCIENCE FICTION: 17
                                             FERMAN, EDWARD L.   AN
  NEW WORLDS OF FANTASY NO. 3   CARR, TERRY   AN
VONNEGUT'S SLAUGHTERHOUSE-FIVE: SCIENCE FICTION AS
  OBJECTIVE CORRELATIVE   MCNELLY, WILLIS E.   AR
  ABOVE THE HUMAN LANDSCAPE   MCNELLY & STOVER   AN
VOODOO (DOUBLE WHAMMY)   BROWN, FREDRIC   SS   BEY 54 09
  BEYOND   ANONYMOUS   AN
  HONEYMOON IN HELL   BROWN, FREDRIC   AC
VOOREMP: SPY   DEFORD, MIRIAM ALLEN SS   INY 72 03
  INFINITY 3   HOSKINS, ROBERT   AN
VOORTREKKER   MOORCOCK, MICHAEL   NV   QRK 71 04
  LIVES AND TIMES OF JERRY CORNELIUS, THE   MOORCOCK, MICHAEL   AC
  QUARK/4   DELANY & HACKER   OA
VOORTREKKERS, THE   ANDERSON, POUL   NV   FST 74
  FINAL STAGE   FERMAN & MALZBERG   AN
VORTEX BLASTER, THE   SMITH, EDWARD E. PHD SS   CMT 41 07
  BEST OF E. E. 'DOC' SMITH, THE   SMITH, EDWARD E. PHD   AC
  MODERN MASTERPIECES OF SCIENCE FICTION   MOSKOWITZ, SAM   AN
  VORTEX BLASTERS, THE   MOSKOWITZ, SAM   AC
VOX POPULI   MALZBERG, BARRY N. SS   EDG 73
  DOWN HERE IN THE DREAM QUARTER   MALZBERG, BARRY N.   AC
VOYAGE OF THE "DEBORAH PRATT", THE
                          DEFORD, MIRIAM ALLEN SS   FSF 63 04
  ELSEWHERE, ELSEWHEN, ELSEHOW   DEFORD, MIRIAM ALLEN AC
VOYAGE OF THE MORNING STAR, THE
                          SMYTH, ROBIN   SS
  STRANGE WORLD OF SCIENCE FICTION   ANONYMOUS   OA
VOYAGE OF THE PEANUT, THE   JACOBS, HARVEY   SS   PBY 59 06
  EGG OF THE GLAK, AND OTHER STORIES, THE JACOBS, HARVEY   AC
VOYAGE OF THE SPACE BEAGLE, THE
                          VAN VOGT, A. E.   NO   SAS 50
  TRIAD   VAN VOGT, A. E.   AC
VOYAGE THAT LASTED SIX HUNDRED YEARS, THE
                          WILCOX, DON   NV   AMZ 40 10
  LOOKING FORWARD   LESSER, MILTON   AN
VOYAGE TO SFANOMOE, A   SMITH, CLARK ASHTON SS   WRT 31 08
  *BEYOND TIME AND SPACE   DERLETH, AUGUST   AN
VOYAGE TO THE MOON   DICKEY, WILLIAM   PM   TXQ 64 03
  SCIENCE FICTION   BRODKIN & PEARSON   AN
VOYAGE TO THE MOON (CONDENSED) DE BERGERAC, CYRANO SS
  MASTERPIECES OF SCIENCE FICTION   MOSKOWITZ, SAM   AN
VULCAN'S HAMMER   DICK, PHILIP K.   NV   FUT 56 29
  6 AND THE SILENT SCREAM   HOWARD, IVAN   AN
W-A-V-E-R   KUPFERBERG, TULI PM   ESR 66
  SF12   MERRIL, JUDITH   AN
WABBLER, THE   LEINSTER, MURRAY SS   ASF 42 10
  BEST SF 3   CRISPIN, EDMUND   AN
  *BEYOND HUMAN KEN   MERRIL, JUDITH   AN
  TIME PROBE: THE SCIENCES IN SF.   CLARKE, ARTHUR C.   AN
WAGER LOST BY WINNING, THE   BRUNNER, JOHN   NV   FAN 70 04
  TRAVELER IN BLACK, THE   BRUNNER, JOHN   AC
WAGER, THE   TUBB, E. C.   NV   SCF 55 11
  HISTORY OF THE SCIENCE FICTION MAGAZINE, THE PART 3 1946-1955
                                             ASHLEY, MICHAEL   AN
WAGES OF DEATH, THE   SILVERBERG, ROBERT NV   IFS 58 08
  VALLEY BEYOND TIME   SILVERBERG, ROBERT   AC
WAGES OF SYNERGY, THE   STURGEON, THEODORE NV   STS 53 08
  BEST FROM STARTLING STORIES, THE   MINES, SAMUEL   AN
  STURGEON IN ORBIT   STURGEON, THEODORE   AC
WAGING OF THE PEACE, THE   POHL, FREDERIK   NV   GAL 59 08
  FREDERIK POHL OMNIBUS, THE   POHL, FREDERIK   AC
  MAN WHO ATE THE WORLD, THE   POHL, FREDERIK   AC
WAGTAIL IN THE MORNING   LEMAN, GRAHAME   SS   NWR 74 23
  NEW WRITINGS IN SF. 23   BULMER, KENNETH   OA
WAIF   LEIBER, FRITZ   NV   74
  FAR SIDE OF TIME, THE   ELWOOD, ROGER   OA
  WORLDS OF FRITZ LEIBER, THE   LEIBER, FRITZ   AC
WAIT IT OUT   NIVEN, LARRY   SS   FUP 68
  ALL THE MYRIAD WAYS   NIVEN, LARRY   AC
  TALES OF KNOWN SPACE: THE UNIVERSE OF LARRY NIVEN
                                             NIVEN, LARRY   AC
  TOMORROW'S WORLDS   SILVERBERG, ROBERT   AN
WAIT, THE   PARK, CHRISTIE   NV   ADS 75 01
  ARMADA SCI-FI ONE   DAVIS, RICHARD   OA
WAIT, THE   REED, KIT   SS   FSF 58 04
  APEMAN, SPACEMAN   STOVER & HARRISON   AN
  BEST FROM FANTASY AND SCIENCE FICTION: 8
                                             BOUCHER, ANTHONY   AN
WAITABITS, THE   RUSSELL, ERIC FRANK NV   ASF 55 07
  ASTOUNDING-ANALOG READER, THE VOLUME TWO HARRISON & ALDISS   AN
  BEST SF 6   CRISPIN, EDMUND   AN
  FAR STARS   RUSSELL, ERIC FRANK   AC
  SIX WORLDS YONDER   RUSSELL, ERIC FRANK   DC
WAITING FOR THE END OF TIME... MOORCOCK, MICHAEL SS   VOT 70
  MOORCOCK'S BOOK OF MARTYRS   MOORCOCK, MICHAEL   AC
WAITING FOR THE UNIVERSE TO BEGIN
                          ALDISS, BRIAN W. SS   EPC 75
  EPOCH   ELWOOD & SILVERBERG OA
WAITING GROUNDS, THE   BALLARD, J. G.   NV   NWS 59 11
  BEST OF J. G. BALLARD, THE   BALLARD, J. G.   AC
  DAY OF FOREVER, THE   BALLARD, J. G.   AC
  VOICES OF TIME AND OTHER STORIES, THE   BALLARD, J. G.   AC
WAITING PLACE   HARRISON, HARRY   SS   GAL 68 06
  *BEST OF HARRY HARRISON, THE   HARRISON, HARRY   AC
  ONE STEP FROM EARTH   HARRISON, HARRY   AC
WAITING WORLD, THE   GREEN, JOSEPH   SS
  FUTURE KIN   ELWOOD, ROGER   OA
WAKE FOR THE LIVING (ALSO AS THE COFFIN)
                          BRADBURY, RAY   SS   DMN 47 09
  MICROCOSMIC GOD   MOSKOWITZ, SAM   AN
  MODERN MASTERPIECES OF SCIENCE FICTION   MOSKOWITZ, SAM   AN

WAKE UP DEAD   STOUT, TIM   SS   NEW 75 AN
  YEAR'S BEST HORROR STORIES: SERIES III, THE
                          DAVIS, RICHARD   AN
WAKE UP TO THUNDER   KOONTZ, DEAN R.   NV   COI 73
  CHILDREN OF INFINITY   ELWOOD, ROGER   OA
WAKER DREAMS, THE (ALSO AS WHEN THE WAKER SLEEPS)
                          MATHESON, RICHARD SS   GAL 50 12
  *GALAXY READER OF SCIENCE FICTION   GOLD, H. L.   AN
WALDO   HEINLEIN, ROBERT A. SN   ASF 42 08
  THREE BY HEINLEIN   HEINLEIN, ROBERT A.   AC
  TREASURY OF GREAT SCIENCE FICTION, A VOL.1
                          BOUCHER, ANTHONY   AN
WALK IN THE DARK, A   CLARKE, ARTHUR C. SS   TWS 50 08
  GREAT STORIES OF SPACE TRAVEL   CONKLIN, GROFF   AN
  NINE BILLION NAMES OF GOD, THE   CLARKE, ARTHUR C.   AC
  *POSSIBLE WORLDS OF SCIENCE FICTION   CONKLIN, GROFF   AN
  PRELUDE TO MARS   CLARKE, ARTHUR C.   AC
  REACH FOR TOMORROW   CLARKE, ARTHUR C.   AC
  TO THE STARS   SILVERBERG, ROBERT   AN
WALK LIKE A MOUNTAIN   WELLMAN, MANLY WADE SS   FSF 55 06
  DECADE OF FANTASY AND SCIENCE FICTION, A MILLS, ROBERT P.   AN
  WHO FEARS THE DEVIL?   WELLMAN, MANLY WADE AC
WALK TO THE WORLD   BUDRYS, ALGIS   SS   SSP 52 11
  FIRST FLIGHT   KNIGHT, DAMON   AN
WALKABOUT   EARL, STEPHEN   SS
  AD 2500   WILSON, ANGUS   AN
WALKER BETWEEN THE PLANES (SEE MAVERICK)
                          DICKSON, GORDON R. TC
WALKER-THROUGH-WALLS, THE   AYME, MARCEL   SS   FSF 59 08
  WALKER THROUGH WALLS, THE   AYME, MARCEL   AC
WALKING AUNT DAID   HENDERSON, ZENNA SS   FSF 55 07
  ANYTHING BOX, THE   HENDERSON, ZENNA   AC
WALKING BACKWARDS   LOPATE, PHILLIP   SS   NWB 73 05
  NEW WORLDS QUARTERLY NO. 5   MOORCOCK, MICHAEL   OA
WALKING DISTANCE   SERLING, ROD   SA
  FROM THE TWILIGHT ZONE   SERLING, ROD   AC
  STORIES FROM THE TWILIGHT ZONE   SERLING, ROD   OC
WALKING, TALKING I-DON'T-CARE MAN, THE
                          BUNCH, DAVID R.   SS   AMZ 65 06
  MODERAN   BUNCH, DAVID R.   AC
WALL AROUND THE WORLD, THE COGSWELL, THEODORE R NV   BEY 53 09
  BEYOND THE BARRIERS OF SPACE AND TIME   MERRIL, JUDITH   AN
  WALL AROUND THE WORLD, THE   COGSWELL, THEODORE R AC
  WORLDS OF WONDER   HARRISON, HARRY   AN
  YET MORE PENGUIN SCIENCE FICTION   ALDISS, BRIAN W.   AN
WALL OF CRYSTAL, EYE OF NIGHT BUDRYS, ALGIS   NV   GAL 61 12
  ALPHA 2   SILVERBERG, ROBERT   AN
  TENTH GALAXY READER, THE   POHL, FREDERIK   AN
WALL OF DARKNESS   WELLS, BASIL   SS   FBK 48 04
  PLANETS OF ADVENTURE   WELLS, BASIL   AC
WALL OF DARKNESS, THE   CLARKE, ARTHUR C. SS   SSS 49 07
  EDITOR'S CHOICE IN SCIENCE FICTION   MOSKOWITZ, SAM   AN
  NINE BILLION NAMES OF GOD, THE   CLARKE, ARTHUR C.   AC
  OTHER DIMENSIONS   SILVERBERG, ROBERT   AN
  OTHER SIDE OF THE SKY, THE   CLARKE, ARTHUR C.   AC
WALL OF FIRE, THE   KIRKLAND, JACK   SS   BBM 32 07
  EDITOR'S CHOICE IN SCIENCE FICTION   MOSKOWITZ, SAM   AN
WALL TO END THE WORLD, THE KING, VINCENT   NV   NWR 68 11
  NEW WRITINGS IN SF. 8   CARNELL, JOHN   AN
  NEW WRITINGS IN SF. 11   CARNELL, JOHN   AN
WALL, THE   GRAHAM, HOWARD W. SS   ASF 34 05
  SCIENCE FICTION OF THE 30'S   KNIGHT, DAMON   AN
WALL, THE   SAXTON, JOSEPHINE SS   SCF 65 11
  BEST SF STORIES FROM NEW WORLDS 7   MOORCOCK, MICHAEL   AN
  FANTASY: THE LITERATURE OF THE MARVELOUS KELLEY, LEO P.   AN
  11TH ANNUAL OF THE YEAR'S BEST S-F, THE MERRIL, JUDITH   AN
WALLS   KINSOLVING, MAY R. NV
  SURVIVAL FROM INFINITY   ELWOOD, ROGER   OA
WALLS, THE   HENDERSON, ZENNA SS   NEW 71 AC
  HOLDING WONDER   HENDERSON, ZENNA   AC
WALLS, THE   LAUMER, KEITH   SS   AMZ 63 03
  NINE BY LAUMER   LAUMER, KEITH   AC
WALTER PERKINS IS HERE!   BANKS, RAYMOND E. SS   FIN 70
  FUTURE IS NOW, THE   NOLAN, WILLIAM F.   OA
  INSIDE INFORMATION   MOWSHOWITZ, ABBE   AN
WALTZ OF THE BODYSNATCHERS SHAW, BOB   NV
  ANDROMEDA I   WESTON, PETER   OA
  COSMIC KALEIDOSCOPE   SHAW, BOB   AC
WANDERER OF TIME   FEARN, JOHN RUSSELL SS   STS 44 SU
  HISTORY OF THE SCIENCE FICTION MAGAZINE, THE PART 2 1936-1945
                                             ASHLEY, MICHAEL   AN
  *MY BEST SCIENCE FICTION STORY   MARGULIES & FRIEND   AN
WANDERER'S RETURN, THE   PRATT, FLETCHER   NO   TWS 51 12
  DOUBLE IN SPACE   PRATT, FLETCHER   AC
WANDERERS AND TRAVELERS   STRUGATSKY, ARKADY SS   ISF 67 11
  PATH INTO THE UNKNOWN   ANONYMOUS   AN
WANDERERS OF TIME   WYNDHAM, JOHN   NV   TOW 41 WI
  WANDERERS OF TIME   WYNDHAM, JOHN   AC
WANDERING BOUY, THE   CHANDLER, A. BERTRAM SS   ASF 70 09
  HARD WAY UP, THE   CHANDLER, A. BERTRAM DC
WANTED IN SURGERY   ELLISON, HARLAN   NV   IFS 57 08
  *PAINGOD AND OTHER DELUSIONS   ELLISON, HARLAN   AC
WANTED-AN ENEMY   LEIBER, FRITZ   SS   ASF 45 02
  BEST OF FRITZ LEIBER, THE   LEIBER, FRITZ   AC
  *BEYOND TIME AND SPACE   DERLETH, AUGUST   AN
WANTON OF ARGUS   BRUNNER, JOHN   NO   TCS 53 SU
  INTERSTELLAR EMPIRE   BRUNNER, JOHN   AC
WAPSHOT'S DEMON   POHL, FREDERIK   SS   SFS 56 07
  CASE AGAINST TOMORROW, THE   POHL, FREDERIK   AC
  NOW & BEYOND   HOWARD, IVAN   AN
WAR   LONDON, JACK   SS   NAT 11 07
  CURIOUS FRAGMENTS   LONDON, JACK   AC
WAR AGAINST THE MOON, THE (1928)
                          MAUROIS, ANDRE   SS   FSF 50 SU
  OMNIBUS OF SCIENCE FICTION   CONKLIN, GROFF   AN

WAR GAME   DICK, PHILIP K.   SS GAL 59 12
  PRESERVING MACHINE, THE   DICK, PHILIP K.   AC
WAR IN THE AIR, THE   CASSILL, R. V.   SS FSF 56 09
  WORLDS OF SCIENCE FICTION, THE   MILLS, ROBERT P.   AN
WAR IS OVER, THE   BUDRYS, ALGIS   SS ASF 57 02
  13 GREAT STORIES OF SCIENCE FICTION CONKLIN, GROFF   AN
WAR OF NERVES   VAN VOGT, A. E.   SS OWS 50 05
  BEST OF A. E. VAN VOGT, THE   VAN VOGT, A. E.   AC
  BEST OF A. E. VAN VOGT, THE (BRITISH) VAN VOGT, A. E.   AC
  MONSTERS   VAN VOGT, A. E.   AC
  VOYAGE OF THE SPACE BEAGLE, THE   VAN VOGT, A. E.   NO
WAR OF PASSION, A   PURDOM, TOM   SS FIN 70
  FUTURE IS NOW, THE   NOLAN, WILLIAM F.   OA
WAR OF THE WORLDS, THE   WELLS, H. G.   EX PRS 97 04
  FROM FRANKENSTEIN TO ANDROMEDA   BROWN, JAMES GOLDIE   AN
WAR OF THE WORLDS, THE   WELLS, H. G.   NA PRS 97 04
  MARS, WE LOVE YOU   HIPOLITO & MCNELLY   AN
  SEVEN FAMOUS NOVELS BY H. G. WELLS WELLS, H. G.   AC
  WAR OF THE WORLDS, THE, THE TIME MACHINE AND SELECTED SHORT STORIES
                                      WELLS, H. G.   AC
WAR OF TWO WORLDS, THE (SILENT VICTORY)
                              ANDERSON, POUL   NO TCS 53 WI
  WORLDS OF POUL ANDERSON, THE   ANDERSON, POUL   AC
WAR ON VENUS   BURROUGHS, EDGAR R. NV FAD 42 03
  ESCAPE ON VENUS   BURROUGHS, EDGAR R.   NO
WAR VETERAN   DICK, PHILIP K.   NV IFS 55 03
  PRESERVING MACHINE, THE   DICK, PHILIP K.   AC
WAR WITH THE ROBOTS   HARRISON, HARRY   SS SFE 62 07
  WAR WITH THE ROBOTS   HARRISON, HARRY   AC
WAR WITH THE YUKKS, THE (WAR AGAINST THE YUKKS)
                              LAUMER, KEITH   NV GAL 65 04
  IT'S A MAD, MAD, MAD GALAXY   LAUMER, KEITH   AC
WARLORD OF SATURN'S MOONS, THE ARNASON, ELEANOR   SS NWQ 74 06
  NEW WORLDS NO. 6   PLATT & BAILEY   OA
WARM   SHECKLEY, ROBERT   SS GAL 53 06
  GALAXY SCIENCE FICTION OMNIBUS   GOLD, H. L.   AN
  SECOND GALAXY READER OF SCIENCE FICTION GOLD, H. L.   AN
  *UNTOUCHED BY HUMAN HANDS   SHECKLEY, ROBERT   AC
WARM CORNER IN SOOLOO, A   HALL, OWEN   SS
  BATTLE FOR THE PACIFIC AND OTHER ADVENTURES AT SEA, THE
                                      ANONYMOUS   AN
WARM MAN   SILVERBERG, ROBERT   SS FSF 57 05
  BEST OF ROBERT SILVERBERG, THE   SILVERBERG, ROBERT   AC
  DIMENSION THIRTEEN   SILVERBERG, ROBERT   AC
  NEXT STOP THE STARS   SILVERBERG, ROBERT   DC
  SPECIAL WONDER   MCCOMAS, J. FRANCIS   AN
WARM, DARK PLACES   GOLD, H. L.   SS UNK 40 10
  BR-R-R!   CONKLIN, GROFF   AN
WARNING, THE   BUNCH, DAVID R.   SS AMZ 60 11
  MODERAN   BUNCH, DAVID R.   AC
WARNING, THE   PHILLIPS, PETER   SS FSF 53 09
  BEYOND THE BARRIERS OF SPACE AND TIME MERRIL, JUDITH   AN
WARP   NORTON, RALPH   SS MAY 68
  YEAR'S BEST HORROR STORIES, THE   DAVIS, RICHARD   AN
WARP AND THE WOOF-WOOF, THE   BRUNNER, JOHN   SS SCF 66 02
  NOT BEFORE TIME   BRUNNER, JOHN   AC
  TIME-JUMP   BRUNNER, JOHN   AC
WARRIOR   DICKSON, GORDON R.   SS ASF 65 12
  DAW SCIENCE FICTION READER, THE   WOLLHEIM, DONALD A.   OA
  MUTANTS   DICKSON, GORDON R.   AC
  SF: AUTHORS' CHOICE 4   HARRISON, HARRY   AN
  11TH ANNUAL OF THE YEAR'S BEST S-F, THE MERRIL, JUDITH   AN
WARRIOR RACE, THE   DE CAMP, L. SPRAGUE SS ASF 40 10
  WHEELS OF IF, THE   DE CAMP, L. SPRAGUE   AC
WARRIOR, THE   HARRISON, WILLIAM   IN ESQ 71 11
  ROLLERBALL   HARRISON, WILLIAM   AC
WARRIORS FROM NOWHERE (THE AMBASSADORS OF FLESH)
                              ANDERSON, POUL   SS PLS 54 SU
  AGENT OF THE TERRAN EMPIRE   ANDERSON, POUL   AC
WARRIORS OF LIGHT, THE   SILVERBERG, ROBERT   NV GAL 65 12
  TO OPEN THE SKY   SILVERBERG, ROBERT   NO
WARRIORS, THE   NIVEN, LARRY   SS IFS 66 02
  SHAPE OF SPACE, THE   NIVEN, LARRY   AC
  TALES OF KNOWN SPACE: THE UNIVERSE OF LARRY NIVEN
                                      NIVEN, LARRY   AC
WAS HE DEAD? (1870)   MITCHELL, SILAS W.   NV ATL 70 01
  FUTURE PERFECT   FRANKLIN, H. BRUCE   AN
WAS SHE HORRID?   BUNCH, DAVID R.   SS FAN 59 12
  MODERAN   BUNCH, DAVID R.   AC
WASP (THE WASP)   WILSON, RICHARD   SS FAN 54 06
  TIME OUT FOR TOMORROW   WILSON, RICHARD   AC
WASTE NOT, WANT NOT   ATHERTON, JOHN   SS PBY 59 06
  PLAYBOY BOOK OF SCIENCE FICTION AND FANTASY, THE
                                      PLAYBOY, EDITORS OF   AN
  TRANSIT OF EARTH   PLAYBOY, EDITORS OF   AN
WASTED ON THE YOUNG   BRUNNER, JOHN   SS GAL 65 04
  FROM THIS DAY FORWARD   BRUNNER, JOHN   AC
  NINTH GALAXY READER, THE   POHL, FREDERIK   AN
  WINDOW ON THE FUTURE   HILL, DOUGLAS   AN
WATCH THIS SPACE (VENTURE TO THE MOON)
                              CLARKE, ARTHUR C.   SS FSF 57 02
  OTHER SIDE OF THE SKY, THE   CLARKE, ARTHUR C.   AC
WATCH-TOWERS, THE   BALLARD, J. G.   NV SCF 62 06
  CHRONOPOLIS AND OTHER STORIES   BALLARD, J. G.   AC
  *FOUR-DIMENSIONAL NIGHTMARE, THE   BALLARD, J. G.   AC
  PASSPORT TO ETERNITY   BALLARD, J. G.   AC
WATCHBIRD   SHECKLEY, ROBERT   NV GAL 53 02
  NOTIONS: UNLIMITED   SHECKLEY, ROBERT   AC
  SHADOW OF TOMORROW   POHL, FREDERIK   AN
  UNTOUCHED BY HUMAN HANDS (BRITISH) SHECKLEY, ROBERT   AC
WATCHDØG   HALDEMAN, JACK C. II SS AMZ 72 05
  BEST SCIENCE FICTION STORIES OF THE YEAR (1972)
                                      DEL REY, LESTER   AN
WATCHER OF THE AGES, THE   HAMILTON, EDMOND   SS WRT 48 09
  WHAT'S IT LIKE OUT THERE? AND OTHER STORIES
                                      HAMILTON, EDMOND   AC

WATCHER, THE   FRITCH, CHARLES E.   SS STS 52 06
  CRAZY MIXED-UP PLANET   FRITCH, CHARLES E.   AC
WATCHERS IN THE GLADE, THE   WILSON, RICHARD   NV GAL 64 08
  NINTH GALAXY READER, THE   POHL, FREDERIK   AN
WATCHERS, THE   BRADBURY, RAY   SS WRT 45 05
  BLOCH AND BRADBURY   BRADBURY & BLOCH   AC
  MARTIAN CHRONICLES, THE   BRADBURY, RAY   AC
WATCHERS, THE   BRODE, ANTHONY   PM FSF 58 04
  BEST FROM FANTASY AND SCIENCE FICTION: 8
                                      BOUCHER, ANTHONY   AN
WATCHERS, THE   DEUTSCH, R. H.   SS NEW 53 AN
  SCIENCE AND SORCERY   FORD, GARRET   AN
WATCHFUL POKER CHIP OF H. MATISSE, THE
                              BRADBURY, RAY   SS BEY 54 03
  BEYOND   ANONYMOUS   AN
  *OCTOBER COUNTRY, THE   BRADBURY, RAY   AC
  VINTAGE BRADBURY, THE   BRADBURY, RAY   AC
WATER   MARSHAK, DAVID   NV NDM 76 06
  NEW DIMENSIONS 6   SILVERBERG, ROBERT   OA
WATER EATER, THE   MARKS, WINSTON K.   SS GAL 53 06
  SCIENCE FICTION ODDITIES   CONKLIN, GROFF   AN
WATER IS FOR WASHING   HEINLEIN, ROBERT A. SS ARG 47 11
  MENACE FROM EARTH, THE   HEINLEIN, ROBERT A.   AC
WATER SCULPTOR OF STATION 233, THE
                              ZEBROWSKI, GEORGE   SS INY 70 01
  INFINITY 1   HOSKINS, ROBERT   AN
  MONADIC UNIVERSE, THE   ZEBROWSKI, GEORGE   AC
WATER'S EDGE   BLOCH, ROBERT   SS MSM 56 09
  KING OF TERRORS, THE   BLOCH, ROBERT   AC
WATER-DEVIL, THE (1874)   STOCKTON, FRANK R.   NV SCR 74 10
  SCIENCE FICTION OF FRANK R. STOCKTON, THE
                                      STOCKTON, FRANK R.   AC
WATERCLAP   ASIMOV, ISAAC   NV IFS 70 04
  BEST FROM IF, THE VOLUME I   IF, EDITORS OF   AN
  BICENTENNIAL MAN AND OTHER STORIES, THE ASIMOV, ISAAC   AC
  WORLD'S BEST SCIENCE FICTION: 1971 WOLLHEIM & CARR   AN
WATERS OF DEATH   GREENFIELD, IRVING A NO LAN 67
  SCIENCE FICTION SPECIAL 1   ANONYMOUS   AN
WATERSHED   BLISH, JAMES   SS IFS 55 05
  BIO-FUTURES   SARGENT, PAMELA   AN
  FIRST WORLD OF IF, THE   QUINN & WULFF   AN
  MUTANTS   SILVERBERG, ROBERT   AN
  SEEDLING STARS, THE   BLISH, JAMES   NO
WATERY PLACE, THE   ASIMOV, ISAAC   SS SAT 56 10
  EARTH IS ROOM ENOUGH   ASIMOV, ISAAC   AC
WAVERIES, THE   BROWN, FREDRIC   SS ASF 45 01
  ABOVE THE HUMAN LANDSCAPE   MCNELLY & STOVER   AN
  ANGELS AND SPACESHIPS   BROWN, FREDRIC   AN
  CONNOISSEUR'S S. F.   BOARDMAN, TOM JR.   AN
  ENEMIES IN SPACE   CONKLIN, GROFF   AN
  FIRST CONTACT   KNIGHT, DAMON   AN
  *INVADERS OF EARTH   CONKLIN, GROFF   AN
  SPECULATIONS   SANDERS, THOMAS E.   AN
  TOMORROW, AND TOMORROW, AND TOMORROW... HEINTZ/HERBERT/JOOS/
WAVES IN RIO, THE   ELLISON, HARLAN   IN
  BEAST THAT SHOUTED LOVE AT THE HEART OF THE WORLD, THE
                                      ELLISON, HARLAN   AC
WAXWORKS   BLOCH, ROBERT   SS WRT 39 01
  HOUSE OF THE HATCHET, THE   BLOCH, ROBERT   AC
  MORE NIGHTMARES   BLOCH, ROBERT   AC
  *OPENER OF THE WAY, THE   BLOCH, ROBERT   AC
WAY BACK, THE   MOSKOWITZ, SAM   NV CMT 41 01
  FUTURES TO INFINITY   MOSKOWITZ, SAM   AN
WAY ERVING WENT, THE   LEMAN, GRAHAME   SS NWR 76 28
  NEW WRITINGS IN SF. 28   BULMER, KENNETH   OA
WAY HOME, A   STURGEON, THEODORE   SS AMZ 53 05
  THUNDER AND ROSES   STURGEON, THEODORE   AC
  *WAY HOME, A   STURGEON, THEODORE   AC
WAY HOME, THE   BERNOTT, JOAN   SS QRK 71 02
  QUARK/2   DELANY & HACKER   AN
WAY IN THE MIDDLE OF THE AIR BRADBURY, RAY   SS OWS 50 07
  HUMAN AND OTHER BEINGS   DEGRAEFF, ALLEN   AN
  MARTIAN CHRONICLES, THE   BRADBURY, RAY   AC
WAY OF ESCAPE   TEMPLE, WILLIAM F.   SS TWS 48 06
  ADVENTURES IN DIMENSION   CONKLIN, GROFF   AN
  *SCIENCE FICTION ADVENTURES IN DIMENSION CONKLIN, GROFF   AN
WAY OF LIFE, A   BLOCH, ROBERT   SS FUN 56 10
  FANTASTIC UNIVERSE OMNIBUS   SANTESSON, HANS S.   AN
  RULERS OF MEN   SANTESSON, HANS S.   AN
WAY OF LIFE, A   MACHT, NORMAN L.   SS
  GOLLANCZ - SUNDAY TIMES BEST SF STORIES ANONYMOUS   OA
WAY OF THINKING, A   STURGEON, THEODORE   NV AMZ 53 11
  E PLURIBUS UNICORN   STURGEON, THEODORE   AC
  GALAXY OF GHOULS   MERRIL, JUDITH   AN
WAY OUT IN THE CONTINUUM   RICHARDSON, MAURICE SS HOR
  BEST SF 7   CRISPIN, EDMUND   AN
WAY OUT, THE   DEFORD, MIRIAM ALLEN SS ALC 73
  ALIEN CONDITION, THE   GOLDIN, STEPHEN   OA
WAY THINGS DON'T WORK, THE   GOULART, RON   IN
  BROKE DOWN ENGINE AND OTHER TROUBLES WITH MACHINES
                                      GOULART, RON   AC
WAY THINGS WORK, THE   GOULART, RON   SS FSF 71 03
  ODD JOB NO. 101   GOULART, RON   AC
WAY TO EDEN, THE (A. HEINEMANN & M. RICHARDS)
                              BLISH, JAMES   SA STK 72 05
  STAR TREK 5   BLISH, JAMES   OC
WAY UP YONDER   POHL, FREDERIK   NV GAL 59 10
  DAY MILLION   POHL, FREDERIK   AC
WAYFARING STRANGERS, THE   TUCKER, WILSON   SS FWS 52 FL
  SCIENCE FICTION SUBTREASURY, THE   TUCKER, WILSON   AC
WAYGIFT   PAGE, GERALD W.   SS
  FUTURE PASTIMES   EDELSTEIN, SCOTT   OA
WAYSIDE WORLD   ZEBROWSKI, GEORGE   NV
  WORLD NAMED CLEOPATRA, A   ANDERSON, POUL   OA
WAYWARD CRAVAT, THE   FRIEDBERG, GERTRUDE SS   58
  TOMORROW'S CHILDREN   ASIMOV, ISAAC   AC

"WE AIN'T BEGGARS"

"WE AIN'T BEGGARS"   WILLIAMSON, JACK   SS
  EARLY WILLIAMSON, THE   WILLIAMSON, JACK   AC
WE ALL DIE NAKED   BLISH, JAMES   NA   TFT 69
  ALPHA 4   SILVERBERG, ROBERT   AN
  BEST SCIENCE FICTION STORIES OF JAMES BLISH (REVISED)
                                          BLISH, JAMES   AC
  THREE FOR TOMORROW   SILVERBERG, ROBERT   OA
WE ALL HAVE TO GO   LYNN, ELIZABETH A.   SS
  FUTURE PASTIMES   EDELSTEIN, SCOTT   OA
WE ALSO WALK DOGS   HEINLEIN, ROBERT A. SS   ASF 41 07
  GREEN HILLS OF EARTH, THE   HEINLEIN, ROBERT A.   AC
  MODERN MASTERPIECES OF SCIENCE FICTION MOSKOWITZ, SAM   AN
  PAST THROUGH TOMORROW, THE   HEINLEIN, ROBERT A.   AC
  VORTEX BLASTERS, THE   MOSKOWITZ, SAM   AN
WE ARE ALONE   SHECKLEY, ROBERT   SS   FUT 52 11
  ESCAPE TO EARTH   HOWARD, IVAN   AN
WE ARE DAINTY LITTLE PEOPLE NAYLOR, CHARLES   SS   BMR 73
  BAD MOON RISING   DISCH, THOMAS M.   OA
WE ARE NOT ALONE   GANSOVSKY, SEVER   SS   64
  AIR OF MARS AND OTHER STORIES, THE   GINSBURG, MIRRA   AN
WE ARE VERY HAPPY HERE   HALDEMAN, JOE W.   NV   ASF 73 11
  BEST SF: 1973   HARRISON & ALDISS   AN
  FOREVER WAR, THE   HALDEMAN, JOE W.   NO
WE ARE WAITING   DERBY, PAT   SS   YNW
  SCIENCE FICTION STORIES   BRADLEY, JOHANNA   AN
WE ARE WELL ORGANIZED   SILVERBERG, ROBERT   NV   GAL 70 12
  WORLD INSIDE, THE   SILVERBERG, ROBERT   NO
WE ATE THE WHOLE THING   HARRISON, HARRY   SS   VTX 73 04
  BEST OF HARRY HARRISON, THE (BRITISH)   HARRISON, HARRY   AC
WE CAN REMEMBER IT FOR YOU WHOLESALE
                           DICK, PHILIP K.   NV   FSF 66 04
  ALPHA 5   SILVERBERG, ROBERT   AN
  BEST FROM FANTASY AND SCIENCE FICTION: 16
                                          FERMAN, EDWARD L.   AN
  EARTH IN TRANSIT   SCHWARTZ, SHEILA   AN
  NEBULA AWARD STORIES NO. 2   ALDISS & HARRISON   AN
  PRESERVING MACHINE, THE   DICK, PHILIP K.   AC
  TWENTY YEARS OF FANTASY & SCIENCE FICTION
                                          FERMAN & MILLS   AN
  WORLD'S BEST SCIENCE FICTION: 1967   WOLLHEIM & CARR   AN
WE DIDN'T DO ANYTHING WRONG, HARDLY
                           KUYKENDALL, ROGER   SS   ASF 59 05
  PROLOGUE TO ANALOG   CAMPBELL, JOHN W. JR   AN
  WORLDS OF WONDER   HARRISON, HARRY   AN
WE DON'T WANT ANY TROUBLE SCHMITZ, JAMES H.   SS   GAL 53 06
  ASSIGNMENT IN TOMORROW   POHL, FREDERIK   AN
  FIFTY SHORT SCIENCE FICTION TALES   ASIMOV & CONKLIN   AN
WE GUARD THE BLACK PLANET! KUTTNER, HENRY   NV   SSS 42 11
  MODERN MASTERPIECES OF SCIENCE FICTION MOSKOWITZ, SAM   AN
  PLANETS OF WONDER   CARR, TERRY   AN
  VORTEX BLASTERS, THE   MOSKOWITZ, SAM   AN
WE KILL PEOPLE   PADGETT, LEWIS   NV   ASF 46 03
  LOOKING FORWARD   LESSER, MILTON   AN
WE KNOW WHO WE ARE   SILVERBERG, ROBERT   SS   AMZ 70 07
  MOONFERNS & STARSONGS   SILVERBERG, ROBERT   AC
WE MOURN FOR ANYONE... (MOURNERS FOR HIRE)
                           ELLISON, HARLAN   SS   FAN 57 05
  FROM THE LAND OF FEAR   ELLISON, HARLAN   AC
WE NEVER MENTION AUNT NORA FLEHR, PAUL   SS   GAL 58 07
  FIFTH GALAXY READER, THE   GOLD, H. L.   AN
WE NEVER MENTION AUNT NORA (AS PAUL FLEHR)
                           POHL, FREDERIK   SS   GAL 58 07
  ABOMINABLE EARTHMAN, THE   POHL, FREDERIK   AC
  BEST OF FREDERIK POHL, THE   POHL, FREDERIK   AC
  WONDERMAKERS 2   HOSKINS, ROBERT   AN
WE PLAYED UNDER YOUR WINDOW SHCHERBAKOV, VLADIMIR SS   66
  ULTIMATE THRESHOLD, THE   GINSBURG, MIRRA   AN
WE PRINT THE TRUTH   BOUCHER, ANTHONY   NV   ASF 43 12
  COMPLEAT WEREWOLF, THE   BOUCHER, ANTHONY   AC
WE PURCHASE PEOPLE   POHL, FREDERIK   SS   FST 74
  BEST SCIENCE FICTION OF THE YEAR, THE NO. 4
                                          CARR, TERRY   AN
  FINAL STAGE   FERMAN & MALZBERG   OA
WE THE PEOPLE   MOORE, WARD   SS   SFQ 52 05
  *FUTURE TENSE   CROSSEN, KENDELL F.   AN
WE THREE   KOONTZ, DEAN R.   SS   FST 74
  FINAL STAGE   FERMAN & MALZBERG   OA
WE WOULD SEE A SIGN   ROSE, MARK   SS   NEW 64 AN
  SPECTRUM 3   AMIS & CONQUEST   AN
WE'LL ALL BE SPACEMEN BEFORE WE DIE
                           EVANS, MIKE   PM   NWS 68 10
  HOLDING YOUR EIGHT HANDS   LUCIE-SMITH, EDWARD   AN
  SCIENCE FICTION   BRODKIN & PEARSON   AN
WE'LL NEVER CONQUER SPACE CLARKE, ARTHUR C.   AR   SDG 60 06
  SCIENCE FACT/FICTION   FARRELL/GAGE/&   AN
WE'LL WALK AGAIN IN THE MOONLIGHT
                           GODWIN, TOM   SS
  CRISIS   ELWOOD, ROGER   OA
WE'RE CIVILIZED (ALSO AS CIVILIZED)
                           APOSTOLIDES, ALEX
                           AND CLIFTON, MARK   SS C GAL 53 08
  GALACTIC EMPIRES VOLUME ONE   ALDISS, BRIAN W.   AN
WE'RE COMING THROUGH THE WINDOW
                           O'DONNELL, K. M.   SS   GAL 67 08
  FINAL WAR AND OTHER FANTASIES   O'DONNELL, K. M.   DC
WE, IN SOME STRANGE POWER'S EMPLOY, MOVE ON A RIGOROUS LINE
                           DELANY, SAMUEL R.   NV   FSF 68 05
  DRIFTGLASS   DELANY, SAMUEL R.   AC
  THOSE WHO CAN: A SCIENCE FICTION READER WILSON, ROBIN SCOTT   AN
WE, THE MIST (THE LIVING MIST) FARLEY, RALPH MILNE NV AMZ 40 08
  STRANGE WORLDS   FARLEY, RALPH MILNE   AC
WEALTH OF THE SUN, THE   LAMPTON, CHRIS   SS
  STRANGE ENCOUNTERS   BISCHOFF, DAVID   OA
WEAPON   CHRISTOPHER, JOHN   SS   NEW 54 AC
  BEST SF 6   CRISPIN, EDMUND   AN
  TWENTY-SECOND CENTURY, THE   CHRISTOPHER, JOHN   AC

WEAPON SHOP, THE   VAN VOGT, A. E.   NV   ASF 42 12
  *ADVENTURES IN TIME AND SPACE   HEALY & MCCOMAS   AN
  BEST OF A. E. VAN VOGT, THE (BRITISH)   VAN VOGT, A. E.   AC
  M 33 IN ANDROMEDA   VAN VOGT, A. E.   AC
  SCIENCE FICTION HALL OF FAME VOLUME 1   SILVERBERG, ROBERT   AN
  WEAPON SHOPS OF ISHER, THE   VAN VOGT, A. E.   NO
WEAPON SHOPS OF ISHER, THE VAN VOGT, A. E.   NA   TWS 49 02
  WEAPON SHOPS OF ISHER, THE   VAN VOGT, A. E.   NO
WEAPON SHOPS OF ISHER, THE VAN VOGT, A. E.   NO   GBG 51
  TREASURY OF GREAT SCIENCE FICTION, A VOL.1
                                          BOUCHER, ANTHONY   AN
WEAPON TOO DREADFUL TO USE, THE
                           ASIMOV, ISAAC   SS   AMZ 39 05
  EARLY ASIMOV, THE   ASIMOV, ISAAC   AC
  FUTURE MAKERS, THE   HAINING, PETER   AN
WEAPON, THE   BROWN, FREDRIC   SS   ASF 51 04
  ASLEEP IN ARMAGEDDON   SISSONS, MICHAEL   AN
  FIFTY SHORT SCIENCE FICTION TALES   ASIMOV & CONKLIN   AN
  HONEYMOON IN HELL   BROWN, FREDRIC   AC
  OMNIBUS OF SCIENCE FICTION   CONKLIN, GROFF   AN
  SCIENCE FICTION FOR PEOPLE WHO HATE SCIENCE FICTION
                                          CARR, TERRY   AN
  SCIENCE FICTION OMNIBUS   CONKLIN, GROFF   AN
  STRANGE TRAVELS IN SCIENCE FICTION   CONKLIN, GROFF   AN
WEAPON, THE   WILLIAMS, ROBERT M. SS   AMZ 47 07
  VOID BEYOND, AND OTHER STORIES, THE   WILLIAMS, ROBERT M.   DC
WEAPONS   SARGENT, PAMELA
                           AND ZEBROWSKI, GEORGE SS C DYS 75
  DYSTOPIAN VISIONS   ELWOOD, ROGER   OA
WEAPONS OF ISHER II, THE   SHAW, BOB   SS   AMZ 71 05
  TOMORROW LIES IN AMBUSH   SHAW, BOB   AC
WEARIEST RIVER, THE   SCORTIA, THOMAS N.   NV   FUC 73
  BIO-FUTURES   SARGENT, PAMELA   AN
  CAUTION! INFLAMMABLE!   SCORTIA, THOMAS N.   AC
  FUTURE CITY   ELWOOD, ROGER   OA
  VISIONS OF TOMORROW   ELWOOD, ROGER   AN
WEATHER CLOCK   HOUSTON, LIBBY   PM   NWB 75 08
  NEW WORLDS EIGHT   BAILEY, HILARY   OA
WEATHER FORECAST   KILBURN, DAVID   PM   69
  HOLDING YOUR EIGHT HANDS   LUCIE-SMITH, EDWARD   AN
WEATHER IN THE UNDERWORLD, THE FREE, COLIN   SS   SQU 65 06
  PACIFIC BOOK OF AUSTRALIAN SCIENCE FICTION
                                          BAXTER, JOHN   AN
  WORLD'S BEST SCIENCE FICTION: 1965   WOLLHEIM & CARR   AN
WEATHER MAN, THE   THOMAS, THEODORE L. SN   ASF 62 06
  ANALOG 2   CAMPBELL, JOHN W. JR   AN
  ASTOUNDING-ANALOG READER, THE VOLUME TWO HARRISON & ALDISS   AN
  DAYS AFTER TOMORROW, THE   SANTESSON, HANS S.   AN
  TIME PROBE: THE SCIENCES IN SF.   CLARKE, ARTHUR C.   AN
WEATHER ON THE SUN, THE   THOMAS, THEODORE L. NV   ORB 70 08
  ORBIT 8   KNIGHT, DAMON   OA
WEATHER ON WELLADAY   MCCAFFREY, ANNE   NV   GAL 69 03
  GET OFF THE UNICORN   MCCAFFREY, ANNE   AC
WEATHERMAKERS, THE   BOVA, BEN   NV   ASF 66 12
  FORWARD IN TIME   BOVA, BEN   AC
WEATHERMAN: A THEOLOGICAL NARRATIVE
                           HARRISON, WILLIAM   SS   73
  ROLLERBALL   HARRISON, WILLIAM   AC
WEB SIXTY-FOUR   WOLLHEIM, DONALD A. SS
  TWO DOZEN DRAGON EGGS   WOLLHEIM, DONALD A.   AC
WEBSTER   BEAR, GREG   SS   ALT 74
  ALTERNATIES   GERROLD, DAVID   OA
WEDDING, THE   MATHESON, RICHARD   SS   BEY 53 07
  BORN OF MAN AND WOMAN   MATHESON, RICHARD   AC
  THIRD FROM THE SUN   MATHESON, RICHARD   AC
WEDGE, THE   ASIMOV, ISAAC   SS   ASF 44 10
  FOUNDATION   ASIMOV, ISAAC   NO
WEDNESDAY'S CHILD   TENN, WILLIAM   SS   FUN 56 01
  HUMAN ANGLE, THE   TENN, WILLIAM   AC
  WEIRD SHADOWS FROM BEYOND   CARNELL, JOHN   AN
WEDNESDAY, NOVEMBER 15, 1967 EFFINGER, GEO. ALEC SS NEW 71 04
  MIXED FEELINGS   EFFINGER, GEO. ALEC   AC
  RUINS OF EARTH, THE   DISCH, THOMAS M.   AN
WEEBLIES, THE   BUDRYS, ALGIS   SS   FNF 53 06
  GOLDEN ROAD, THE   KNIGHT, DAMON   AN
WEED OF TIME, THE   SPINRAD, NORMAN   SS   ANA 70
  ALCHEMY AND ACADEME   MCCAFFREY, ANNE   OA
  NO DIRECTION HOME   SPINRAD, NORMAN   AC
  1974 ANNUAL WORLD'S BEST SF, THE   WOLLHEIM, DONALD A.   AN
WEEKEND IN A WAR ZONE   MARTIN, GEORGE R. R. SS
  FUTURE PASTIMES   EDELSTEIN, SCOTT   OA
WEEP NO MORE, OLD LADY   GRANT, C. L.   SS   FUQ 73
  FUTURE QUEST   ELWOOD, ROGER   OA
WEIGHER OF SOULS, THE   MAUROIS, ANDRE   NV   FFM 50 10
  FUTURES UNLIMITED   NORTON, ALDEN H.   AN
WEIGHER OF SOULS AND THE EARTH DWELLERS, THE
                                          MAUROIS, ANDRE   AC
WEIHNACHTABEND   ROBERTS, KEITH   NV   NWQ 72 04
  BEST SF: 1972   HARRISON & ALDISS   AN
  NEW WORLDS QUARTERLY NO. 4   MOORCOCK, MICHAEL   OA
WEIHNACHTSABEND (WEIHNACHTABEND)
                           ROBERTS, KEITH   NV   NWQ 72 04
  GRAIN KINGS, THE   ROBERTS, KEITH   AC
  PASSING OF THE DRAGONS, THE   ROBERTS, KEITH   AC
WEIRD OF AVOOSL WUTHOQQUAN, THE
                           SMITH, CLARK ASHTON SS   WRT 32 06
  OUT OF SPACE AND TIME   SMITH, CLARK ASHTON   AC
WEIRD SHOW   GOLD, HERBERT   SS   PBY 58 04
  PLAYBOY BOOK OF HORROR AND THE SUPERNATURAL, THE
                                          PLAYBOY, EDITORS OF   AN
  WEIRD SHOW   PLAYBOY, EDITORS OF   AN
WEIRD TAILOR, THE   BLOCH, ROBERT   SS   WRT 50 07
  SKULL OF THE MARQUIS DE SADE, THE   BLOCH, ROBERT   AC
WEIRD WORLD OF THE KNIGHT (TOPSY-TURVY WORLD OF..)
                           LEIBER, FRITZ   AR   CCR 60 01
  BOOK OF FRITZ LEIBER, THE   LEIBER, FRITZ   AC

WEIRDEST WORLD, THE   LAFFERTY, R. A.   NV   GAL 61 06
   DOES ANYONE ELSE HAVE SOMETHING FURTHER TO ADD?
                           LAFFERTY, R. A.   AC
WEISSENBROCH SPECTACLES, THE   DE CAMP, L. SPRAGUE
   AND PRATT, FLETCHER   SS C FSF 54 11
   INVISIBLE MEN   DAVENPORT, BASIL   AN
WELCOME HOME   COOPER, EDMUND   SS
   NEWS FROM ELSEWHERE   COOPER, EDMUND   AC
   TOMORROW CAME   COOPER, EDMUND   AC
WELCOME TO PROCYON IV   FRITCH, CHARLES E.   65
   CRAZY MIXED-UP PLANET   FRITCH, CHARLES E.   AC
WELCOME TO SLIPPAGE CITY   HOYLE, FRED   SS
   ELEMENT 79   HOYLE, FRED   AC
WELCOME TO THE LAND OF SMILES TATE, PETER   SS
   SEAGULLS UNDER GLASS AND OTHER STORIES TATE, PETER   AC
WELCOME TO THE MONKEY HOUSE VONNEGUT, KURT JR. SS   PBY 68 01
   FIEND, THE   PLAYBOY, EDITORS OF   AN
   PAST, PRESENT, AND FUTURE PERFECT WOLFE, J&FITZ GERALD AN
   PLAYBOY'S STORIES OF THE SINISTER & STRANGE
                           PLAYBOY, EDITORS OF   AN
   WELCOME TO THE MONKEY HOUSE VONNEGUT, KURT JR.   AC
   WORLD'S BEST SCIENCE FICTION: 1969 WOLLHEIM & CARR AN
WELCOME TO THE STANDARD NIGHTMARE
                           SHECKLEY, ROBERT   SS   NOV 73 03
   BEST SF: 1973   HARRISON & ALDISS   AN
   NOVA 3   HARRISON, HARRY   OA
WELCOME TO THE TRICENTENNIAL PRENTICE, PATRICK H. NV
   2076: THE AMERICAN TRICENTENNIAL BRYANT, EDWARD OA
WELCOME, COMRADE   BAGLEY, SIMON   NV   FSF 64 04
   AMERICAN GOVERNMENT THROUGH SCIENCE FICTION
                           OLANDER/GREENBERG/&   AN
WELCOME, STRANGER   BLOCH, ROBERT   SS   SAT 57 04
   FLYING SAUCERS IN FACT AND FICTION SANTESSON, HANS S. AN
WELL OF THE DEEP WISH   BIGGLE, LLOYD JR.   NV   IFS 61 03
   METALLIC MUSE, THE   BIGGLE, LLOYD JR.   AC
WELL TRAINED HEROES, THE   SELLINGS, ARTHUR   NV   GAL 64 06
   LONG EUREKA, THE   SELLINGS, ARTHUR   AC
WELL-OILED MACHINE, THE   FYFE, H. B.   NV   FSF 50 12
   *SCIENCE-FICTION CARNIVAL BROWN, F. & REYNOLDS   AN
WELLWISHER, THE   HULL, E. MAYNE   SS
   OUT OF THE UNKNOWN (ENGLISH EDITION ADDS:)
                           VAN VOGT & HULL   AC
WENDIGO, THE (1910)   BLACKWOOD, ALGERNON NV   FFM 44 06
   BEWARE THE BEASTS   GHIDALIA, V.& ELWOOD   AN
WENTWORTH'S DAY   DERLETH, AUGUST
   AND LOVECRAFT, H. P.   SS C
   SURVIVOR AND OTHER STORIES, THE LOVECRAFT & DERLETH AC
WEREWOLF GIRL   ANDERSSON, VIC   SS
   MORE SCIENCE FICTION TALES ELWOOD, ROGER   OA
WEREWOMAN   MOORE, C. L.   NV   LVS 38 WI
   EDGE OF NEVER, THE   HOSKINS, ROBERT   AN
WEST WIND   LEINSTER, MURRAY   NV   ASF 48 03
   3 IN 1   MARGULIES, LEO   AN
WEST WIND, FALLING   BENFORD, GREGORY
   AND EKLUND, GORDON   NV C UNI 71 01
   UNIVERSE 1   CARR, TERRY   OA
WESTERN SCIENCE IS SO WONDERFUL
                           SMITH, CORDWAINER   SS   IFS 58 12
   STARDREAMER   SMITH, CORDWAINER   AC
WESTFIELD HEIGHTS MALL MONSTER, THE
                           EFFINGER, GEO. ALEC SS   CLR 71 01
   CLARION   WILSON, ROBIN SCOTT   OA
WESTWIND   WOLFE, GENE   SS   IFS 73 08
   BEST FROM IF, THE   VOLUME II IF, EDITORS OF   AN
WET PAINT   CHANDLER, A. BERTRAM NV   AMZ 59 05
   BEYOND THE GALACTIC RIM CHANDLER, A. BERTRAM   DC
WET STRAW   MATHESON, RICHARD   SS   WRT 53 01
   SHOCK WAVES   MATHESON, RICHARD   AC
WEYR SEARCH   MCCAFFREY, ANNE   SN   ASF 67 10
   ANALOG 7   CAMPBELL, JOHN W. JR   AN
   DRAGONFLIGHT   MCCAFFREY, ANNE   NO
   HUGO WINNERS, THE (VOLUME 2) ASIMOV, ISAAC   AN
   NEBULA AWARD STORIES   NO. 3 ZELAZNY, ROGER   AN
WHACKY   CLARKE, ARTHUR C.   FN   FNT 42 07
   BEST OF ARTHUR C. CLARKE: 1937-1971, THE CLARKE, ARTHUR C. AC
WHAT ABOUT US GRILS?   GILDEN, MEL   SS   CLR 71 01
   CLARION   WILSON, ROBIN SCOTT   OA
   STRANGE BED FELLOWS   SCORTIA, THOMAS N.   AN
WHAT ARE LITTLE GIRLS MADE OF? (ROBERT BLOCH)
                           BLISH, JAMES   SA   STK 75 11
   STAR TREK 11   BLISH, JAMES   OC
WHAT CAN YOU SAY ABOUT CHOCOLATE COVERED MANHOLE COVERS?
                           NIVEN, LARRY   SS   NEW 71 AC
   ALL THE MYRIAD WAYS   NIVEN, LARRY   AC
WHAT DEAD MEN TELL   STURGEON, THEODORE   NV   ASF 49 11
   *IMAGINATION UNLIMITED BLEILER & DIKTY   AN
WHAT DID YOU DO LAST YEAR? BENFORD, GREGORY
   AND EKLUND, GORDON   SS C UNI 76 06
   UNIVERSE 6   CARR, TERRY   OA
"WHAT DO YOU MEAN...HUMAN?" CAMPBELL, JOHN W. JR ED ASF 59 09
   5TH ANNUAL OF THE YEAR'S BEST S-F, THE MERRIL, JUDITH AN
WHAT DO YOU WANT ME TO DO TO PROVE IM HUMAN STOP (INHUMAN
ERROR)   SABERHAGEN, FRED   SS   ASF 74 10
   BOOK OF SABERHAGEN, THE SABERHAGEN, FRED   AC
WHAT FRIENDS ARE FOR   BRUNNER, JOHN   SS   FOS 74
   BEST SCIENCE FICTION STORIES OF THE YEAR (1974)
                           DEL REY, LESTER   AN
   FELLOWSHIP OF THE STARS CARR, TERRY   OA
WHAT GOES UP   CLARKE, ARTHUR C.   SS   FSF 56 01
   PRELUDE TO MARS   CLARKE, ARTHUR C.   AC
   TALES FROM THE WHITE HART CLARKE, ARTHUR C.   AC
WHAT GOES UP   COPPEL, ALFRED   SS   FBK 50 06
   SCIENCE AND SORCERY   FORD, GARRET   AN
WHAT GOOD IS A GLASS DAGGER? NIVEN, LARRY   NV   FSF 72 09
   FLIGHT OF THE HORSE, THE NIVEN, LARRY   AC

WHAT HAPPENED TO AUGUSTE CLAROT?
                           EISENBERG, LARRY   SS   DVS 67 01
   BEST LAID SCHEMES, THE EISENBERG, LARRY   AC
   DANGEROUS VISIONS   ELLISON, HARLAN   AN
WHAT HAPPENED TO SERGEANT MASURO?
                           NULISCH, HARRY   NV   64
   WORLD'S BEST SCIENCE FICTION: 1965 WOLLHEIM & CARR AN
WHAT HAPPENED TO TUESDAY? CUMMINGS, M. A.   SS
   EXILE AND OTHER TALES OF FANTASY CUMMINGS, M. A. OC
WHAT HAPPENED TO WILLIAM COOMBES
                           ROGERS, ANGELA   SS   NWR 76 28
   NEW WRITINGS IN SF. 28 BULMER, KENNETH   AC
WHAT HATH GOD WROUGHT!   BIGGLE, LLOYD JR.   NV   STG 74
   GALAXY OF STRANGERS, A BIGGLE, LLOYD JR.   AC
   STRANGE GODS   ELWOOD, ROGER   OA
WHAT HAVE I DONE?   CLIFTON, MARK   SS   ASF 52 05
   ASTOUNDING-ANALOG READER, THE VOLUME TWO HARRISON & ALDISS AN
   *BEYOND HUMAN KEN   MERRIL, JUDITH   AN
WHAT I DID ON MY VACATION THIS SUMMER BY LITTLE BOBBY
HIRSCHHORN, AGE 27   ELLISON, HARLAN   SS   KNT 64 11
   *LOVE AIN'T NOTHING BUT SEX MISSPELLED ELLISON, HARLAN AC
WHAT IF   ASIMOV, ISAAC   SS   FAN 52 SU
   ADVENTURES IN DIMENSION CONKLIN, GROFF   AN
   GREAT SCIENCE FICTION BY SCIENTISTS CONKLIN, GROFF AN
   NIGHTFALL AND OTHER STORIES ASIMOV, ISAAC   AC
   *SCIENCE FICTION ADVENTURES IN DIMENSION CONKLIN, GROFF AN
WHAT IS THIS THING CALLED LOVE?(THE PLAYBOY AND THE SLIME GOD)
                           ASIMOV, ISAAC   SS   AMZ 61 03
   NIGHTFALL AND OTHER STORIES ASIMOV, ISAAC   AC
   SCIENCE FICTION ODDITIES CONKLIN, GROFF   AN
"WHAT IS WRONG? WHAT IS RIGHT? ANYWAY, WE'RE HERE..."
                           ALDISS, BRIAN W.   SI
   EVIL EARTHS   ALDISS, BRIAN W.   AN
WHAT MAKES A CAGE, JAMIE KNOWS BRADFIELD, SCOTT SS   PRT 71
   PROTOSTARS   GERROLD & GOLDIN   OA
WHAT MAKES ROCKETS ROCKET? YATES, R. F.   AR
   LAURIE'S SPACE ANNUAL   ANONYMOUS   AN
WHAT MAKES THE MIGHTY TIDES (SEE THE MIGHTY TIDES)
                           LEIBER, FRITZ   TC
WHAT NOW, LITTLE MAN?   CLIFTON, MARK   NV   FSF 59 11
   5TH ANNUAL OF THE YEAR'S BEST S-F, THE MERRIL, JUDITH AN
WHAT ROUGH BEAST?   KNIGHT, DAMON   NV   FSF 59 02
   BEST FROM FANTASY AND SCIENCE FICTION: 9
                           MILLS, ROBERT P.   AN
   *OFF CENTER   KNIGHT, DAMON   DC
WHAT SCIENCE FICTION IS   CRISPIN, EDMUND   IN
   STARS AND UNDER, THE   CRISPIN, EDMUND   AC
WHAT SO PROUDLY WE HAIL... KEENE, DAY   SS   IMG 50 12
   ADVENTURES IN DIMENSION CONKLIN, GROFF   AN
   *SCIENCE FICTION ADVENTURES IN DIMENSION CONKLIN, GROFF AN
WHAT SORGHUM SAYS   KORNBLUTH, C. M.   SS   COS 41 05
   THIRTEEN O'CLOCK AND OTHER ZERO HOURS KORNBLUTH, C. M. AC
WHAT STRANGE STARS AND SKIES DAVIDSON, AVRAM   SS   FSF 63 12
   BEST FROM FANTASY AND SCIENCE FICTION: 13
                           DAVIDSON, AVRAM   AN
   WHAT STRANGE STARS AND SKIES DAVIDSON, AVRAM   AN
WHAT T AND I DID   SABERHAGEN, FRED   SS   IFS 65 04
   BERSERKER   SABERHAGEN, FRED   AC
WHAT THE AUTHOR HAS TO SAY ABOUT ALL THIS
                           POHL, FREDERIK   MS
   BEST OF FREDERIK POHL, THE POHL, FREDERIK   AC
WHAT THE BOARD SAID   MALZBERG, BARRY N.   SS   NEW 76 AC
   BEST OF BARRY N. MALZBERG, THE MALZBERG, BARRY N. AC
WHAT THE DEAD MEN SAY   DICK, PHILIP K.   SN   WOT 64 06
   PRESERVING MACHINE, THE DICK, PHILIP K.   AC
WHAT THE LEFT HAND WAS DOING LANGART, DARREL T. NV ASF 60 02
   5TH ANNUAL OF THE YEAR'S BEST S-F, THE MERRIL, JUDITH AN
WHAT THE THUNDER SAID   KAPP, COLIN   SS   NWR 73 21
   NEW WRITINGS IN SF. 21 CARNELL, JOHN   OA
WHAT THEY DO WITH MOTHERS-IN-LAW IN TIERRA DEL FUEGO
                           DISCH, THOMAS M.   SS
   *GETTING INTO DEATH   DISCH, THOMAS M.   AC
WHAT THIN PARTITIONS   APOSTOLIDES, ALEX
   AND CLIFTON, MARK   NV C ASF 53 09
   BEST SCIENCE-FICTION STORIES: 1954, THE BLEILER & DIKTY AN
   EDITOR'S CHOICE IN SCIENCE FICTION MOSKOWITZ, SAM AN
   14 GREAT TALES OF ESP   STONE, IDELLA P.   AN
WHAT TIME DO YOU CALL THIS? SHAW, BOB   SS   AMZ 71 09
   TOMORROW LIES IN AMBUSH SHAW, BOB   AC
WHAT TIME IS IT?   ELAM, RICHARD M. JR. NV
   SCIENCE FICTION AND READER'S GUIDE BARROWS, MARJORIE AN
   TEEN-AGE SCIENCE FICTION STORIES ELAM, RICHARD M. JR. AC
WHAT TIME WAS THAT?   O'DONNELL, K. M.   SS   IFS 69 12
   IN THE POCKET AND OTHER S-F STORIES O'DONNELL, K. M. DC
WHAT TO DO TILL THE ANALYST COMES (EVERYBODY'S HAPPY BUT ME!)
                           POHL, FREDERIK   SS   IMG 56 02
   ALTERNATING CURRENTS   POHL, FREDERIK   AC
   IN THE PROBLEM PIT   POHL, FREDERIK   AC
   SPECULATIONS   SANDERS, THOMAS E.   AN
   STRANGE ECSTASIES   PARRY, MICHEL   AN
   YOU AND SCIENCE FICTION HOLLISTER, BERNARD C   AN
   17 X INFINITY   CONKLIN, GROFF   AN
WHAT TRIUMPHS? (SEE VISITING AMOEBA)
                           ALDISS, BRIAN W.   TC
WHAT WAS IN THE BOX (SEE BIG SUPRISE)
                           MATHESON, RICHARD   TC
WHAT WAS IT? (1859)   O'BRIEN, FITZ-JAMES SS   HRP 59 03
   CENTURY OF SCIENCE FICTION, A KNIGHT, DAMON   AN
   INVISIBLE MEN   DAVENPORT, BASIL   AN
WHAT WE HAVE HERE   BRUNNER, JOHN   PM   70
   BOOK OF JOHN BRUNNER, THE BRUNNER, JOHN   AC
WHAT WE HAVE HERE IS TOO MUCH COMMUNICATION
                           STOVER, LEON E.   SS   ORB 71 09
   ABOVE THE HUMAN LANDSCAPE MCNELLY & STOVER   AN
   ORBIT   9   KNIGHT, DAMON   AN

WHAT WE LEARNED FROM THIS MORNING'S NEWSPAPER
                                   SILVERBERG, ROBERT   SS   INY 72 04
   BEST SCIENCE FICTION FOR 1973   ACKERMAN, FORREST J. AN
   INFINITY 4   HOSKINS, ROBERT   OA
   UNFAMILIAR TERRITORY   SILVERBERG, ROBERT   AC
WHAT YOU GET FOR YOUR DOLLAR (FROM "THE SHAPE OF FURTHER
   THINGS")   ALDISS, BRIAN W.   EX   75
   NEW IMPROVED SUN, THE   DISCH, THOMAS M.   AN
WHAT YOU KNOW   CHANDLER, A. BERTRAM NV   GAL 71 01
   HARD WAY UP, THE   CHANDLER, A. BERTRAM   DC
WHAT YOU NEED   KUTTNER, HENRY   SS   ASF 45 10
   BEST OF HENRY KUTTNER 2, THE   KUTTNER, HENRY   AC
   BEST OF HENRY KUTTNER, THE   KUTTNER, HENRY   AC
WHAT YOU NEED   PADGETT, LEWIS   SS   ASF 45 10
   GNOME THERE WAS, A   PADGETT, LEWIS   AC
   LINE TO TOMORROW AND OTHER STORIES OF FANTASY AND SCIENCE
      FICTION   PADGETT, LEWIS   AC
   OMNIBUS OF SCIENCE FICTION   CONKLIN, GROFF   AN
WHAT'LL YOU GIVE? (SEE QUE DONN'REZ VOUS?)
                                   ANDERSON, POUL   TC
WHAT'S BECOME OF SCREWLOOSE?   GOULART, RON   SS   IFS 70 07
   WHAT'S BECOME OF SCREWLOOSE? AND OTHER INQUIRIES
                                   GOULART, RON   AC
WHAT'S HE DOING IN THERE?   LEIBER, FRITZ   SS   GAL 57 12
   CONTACT   KEYES, NOEL   AN
   FOURTH GALAXY READER, THE   GOLD, H. L.   AN
   WORLDS OF FRITZ LEIBER, THE   LEIBER, FRITZ   AC
WHAT'S IN A NAME   ASIMOV, ISAAC   SS   SDM 56 05
   ASIMOV'S MYSTERIES   ASIMOV, ISAAC   AC
WHAT'S IT LIKE OUT THERE?   HAMILTON, EDMOND NV   TWS 52 12
   BEST FROM STARTLING STORIES, THE MINES, SAMUEL   AN
   BEST OF EDMOND HAMILTON, THE   HAMILTON, EDMOND   AC
   CENTURY OF SCIENCE FICTION, A   KNIGHT, DAMON   AN
   EXPLORERS OF SPACE   SILVERBERG, ROBERT   AN
   SCIENCE FICTION FOR PEOPLE WHO HATE SCIENCE FICTION
                                   CARR, TERRY   AN
   WHAT'S IT LIKE OUT THERE? AND OTHER STORIES
                                   HAMILTON, EDMOND   AC
WHAT'S THE MATTER WITH HERBIE? GILDEN, MEL NV   ORB 73 12
   ORBIT 12   KNIGHT, DAMON   OA
WHAT'S THE NAME OF THAT TOWN? LAFFERTY, R. A. SS   GAL 64 10
   INSIDE INFORMATION   MOWSHOWITZ, ABBE   AN
   NINE HUNDRED GRANDMOTHERS   LAFFERTY, R. A.   AC
   SCIENCE FICTION ODDITIES   CONKLIN, GROFF   AN
WHAT'S YOUR EXCUSE? PANSHIN, ALEXEI   SS   FAN 69 08
   FAREWELL TO YESTERDAY'S TOMORROW PANSHIN, ALEXEI   AC
WHATEVER BECAME OF THE MCGOWANS?
                                   CONEY, MICHAEL G.   NV   GAL 70 05
   WORLD'S BEST SCIENCE FICTION: 1971 WOLLHEIM & CARR   AN
WHATEVER COUNTS   POHL, FREDERICK   NA   GAL 59 06
   ABOMINABLE EARTHMAN, THE   POHL, FREDERICK   AC
   BODYGUARD AND 4 OTHER SHORT SF NOVELS FROM GALAXY
                                   GOLD, H. L.   AN
WHATEVER GODS THERE BE DICKSON, GORDON R. SS   AMZ 61 07
   STAR ROAD, THE   DICKSON, GORDON R.   AC
WHATEVER GODS THERE BE: SPACE-TIME AND DEITY IN SF
                                   ZEBROWSKI, GEORGE   IN   STG 74
   STRANGE GODS   ELWOOD, ROGER   OA
WHATEVER HAPPENED TO CORPORAL CUCKOO? (1953)
                                   KERSH, GERALD   NV   STR 54 03
   NIGHTSHADE & DAMNATIONS   KERSH, GERALD   AC
   ONE HUNDRED YEARS OF SCIENCE FICTION KNIGHT, DAMON   AN
   STAR OF STARS   POHL, FREDERICK   AN
   STAR SCIENCE FICTION STORIES NO. 3 POHL, FREDERICK   OA
WHATEVER HAPPENED TO SUDEROV? KALDOR, STEVE   SS
   SECOND PACIFIC BOOK OF SCIENCE FICTION, THE
                                   BAXTER, JOHN   AN
WHATEVER HAPPENED TO THE OLMECS?
                                   WILHELM, KATE   SS   FSF 73 10
   BEST SCIENCE FICTION STORIES OF THE YEAR (1973)
                                   DEL REY, LESTER   AN
WHEEL AND DEAL   BLOCH, ROBERT   SS   NEW 62 AC
   ATOMS AND EVIL   BLOCH, ROBERT   AC
WHEEL OF TIME, THE ARTHUR, ROBERT   SS   SSS 50 03
   *SCIENCE-FICTION CARNIVAL   BROWN, F. & REYNOLDS   AN
WHEEL, THE   WYNDHAM, JOHN   SS   STS 52 01
   JIZZLE   WYNDHAM, JOHN   AC
   TALES OF GOOSEFLESH AND LAUGHTER WYNDHAM, JOHN   AC
WHEELBARROW BOY, THE PARKER, RICHARD   SS   FSF 53 03
   GALAXY OF GHOULS   MERRIL, JUDITH   AN
WHEELS   THURSTON, ROBERT   SS   CLR 71 01
   CLARION   WILSON, ROBIN SCOTT   OA
WHEELS OF DR. GINOCHIO GYVES, THE
                                   DOUGLASS, ELLSWORTH
                   AND PALLANDER, EDWIN SS C CSL 99 09
   WORLDS APART   LOCKE, GEORGE   AN
WHEELS OF IF, THE DE CAMP, L. SPRAGUE   SN   UNK 40 10
   WHEELS OF IF, THE   DE CAMP, L. SPRAGUE   AC
WHEN ALL THE LANDS POUR OUT AGAIN
                                   LAFFERTY, R. A.   SS   ORB 71 09
   ORBIT 9   KNIGHT, DAMON   OA
WHEN ARISTOTLE FAILS, TRY SCIENCE FICTION
                                   ASIMOV, ISAAC   AR   ITL 71
   SPECULATIONS   SANDERS, THOMAS E.   AN
WHEN DAY IS DUN   MATHESON, RICHARD   SS   FUN 54 05
   SHORES OF SPACE, THE   MATHESON, RICHARD   AC
WHEN DREAMS BECOME NIGHTMARES: SOME CAUTIONARY NOTES ON THE
   CLARION EXPERIENCE ELLISON, HARLAN   AR   CLR 73 03
   CLARION III   WILSON, ROBIN SCOTT   OA
WHEN FRIGHTHOOD WAS IN FLOWER ACKERMAN, FORREST J. SS
   SCIENCE FICTION WORLDS OF FORREST J. ACKERMAN & FRIENDS
                                   ACKERMAN, FORREST J.   AC
WHEN GABRIEL...   BRUNNER, JOHN   SS   SCF 56 08
   BOOK OF JOHN BRUNNER, THE   BRUNNER, JOHN   AC
   OUT OF MY MIND (BRITISH)   BRUNNER, JOHN   AC

WHEN GRANDFATHER FLEW TO THE MOON (RETURN OF THE MOON MAN)
                                   MALPASS, E. L.   SS   LOB 55 01
   SF:57, THE YEAR'S GREATEST SCIENCE FICTION AND FANTASY
                                   MERRIL, JUDITH   AN
WHEN I FIRST READ... ALLEN, DICK   PM   ATR 66
   SF12   MERRIL, JUDITH   AN
WHEN I HAVE PASSED AWAY GREEN, JOSEPH   NV   NWR 69 15
   NEW WRITINGS IN SF. 9   CARNELL, JOHN   AN
   NEW WRITINGS IN SF. 15   CARNELL, JOHN   OA
WHEN I HEARD THE LEARN'D ASTRONOMER
                                   WHITMAN, WALT   PM
   SPECULATIONS   SANDERS, THOMAS E.   AN
WHEN I WAS A HIRED GUN ELLISON, HARLAN   SS   LAF 73 06
   LOVE AIN'T NOTHING BUT SEX MISSPELLED (REVISED)
                                   ELLISON, HARLAN   AC
WHEN I WAS MING THE MERCILESS WOLFE, GENE   SS
   IDES OF TOMORROW, THE   CARR, TERRY   OA
WHEN I WAS MISS DOW DORMAN, SONYA   SS   GAL 66 06
   NEBULA AWARD STORIES NO. 2   ALDISS & HARRISON   AN
   SF12   MERRIL, JUDITH   AN
   WOMEN OF WONDER   SARGENT, PAMELA   AN
WHEN I WAS VERY JUNG ALDISS, BRIAN W.   SS   GAL 68 09
   ELEVENTH GALAXY READER, THE   POHL, FREDERIK   AN
WHEN IT CHANGED   RUSS, JOANNA   SS   DVS 72 02
   AGAIN, DANGEROUS VISIONS   ELLISON, HARLAN   OA
   MARRIAGE AND THE FAMILY THROUGH SCIENCE FICTION
                                   CLEAR/WARRICK/&   AN
   NEBULA AWARD STORIES 8   ASIMOV, ISAAC   AN
WHEN IT WAS MOONLIGHT WELLMAN, MANLY WADE SS UNK 40 02
   UNKNOWN, THE   BENSEN, D. R.   AN
WHEN LILACS LAST IN THE DOORYARD BLOOMED
                                   AANDAHL, VANCE   NV   FSF 62 05
   BEST FROM FANTASY AND SCIENCE FICTION: 12
                                   DAVIDSON, AVRAM   AN
WHEN MORNING COMES FANCETT, ELIZABETH   SS   69
   YEAR'S BEST HORROR STORIES, THE DAVIS, RICHARD   AN
WHEN OLD GODS WAKE MERRITT, A.   SS   ARG 48 07
   FOX WOMAN & OTHER STORIES, THE MERRITT, A.   AC
WHEN PAPPY ISN'T THERE NIELSEN, LIN   SS   CLR 73 03
   CLARION III   WILSON, ROBIN SCOTT   OA
WHEN PETALS FALL   VAN SCYOC, SYDNEY J. NV   TVW 73
   BEST SF: 1974   HARRISON & ALDISS   AN
   TWO VIEWS OF WONDER   SCORTIA & YARBRO   OA
WHEN QUESTIONS ARE ASKED DNIEPROV, ANATOLY SS   63
   ULTIMATE THRESHOLD, THE   GINSBURG, MIRRA   AN
WHEN SHADOWS FALL   HUBBARD, L. RON   SS   STS 48 07
   *MEN AGAINST THE STARS   GREENBERG , MARTIN   AN
WHEN THE BOUGH BREAKS KUTTNER, HENRY   NV   ASF 44 11
   BEST OF HENRY KUTTNER 2, THE   KUTTNER, HENRY   AC
WHEN THE BOUGH BREAKS PADGETT, LEWIS   NV   ASF 44 11
   *ASTOUNDING SCIENCE FICTION ANTHOLOGY, THE
                                   CAMPBELL, JOHN W. JR   AN
   *BEYOND TIME AND SPACE   DERLETH, AUGUST   AN
   LINE TO TOMORROW AND OTHER STORIES OF FANTASY AND SCIENCE
      FICTION   PADGETT, LEWIS   AC
   TOMORROW'S CHILDREN   ASIMOV, ISAAC   AN
WHEN THE CHANGE-WINDS BLOW LEIBER, FRITZ SS   FSF 64 08
   WORLD'S BEST SCIENCE FICTION: 1965 WOLLHEIM & CARR   AN
   WORLDS OF FRITZ LEIBER, THE   LEIBER, FRITZ   AC
WHEN THE COLD CAME TOFTE, ARTHUR   SS
   NIGHT OF THE SPHINX AND OTHER STORIES ELWOOD, ROGER   OA
WHEN THE EARTH LIVED KUTTNER, HENRY   SS   TWS 37 10
   FROM OFF THIS WORLD   MARGULIES & FRIEND   AN
WHEN THE ENGINES HAD TO STOP JONES, ELIS GWYN SS NEW 64 AN
   OUT OF THIS WORLD 4   WILLIAMS-ELLIS& OWEN   AN
WHEN THE FIVE MOONS RISE VANCE, JACK   NV   CSM 54 03
   EIGHT FANTASMS AND MAGICS   VANCE, JACK   AC
WHEN THE GREEN STAR WANED DYALHIS, NICTZIN SS WRT 25 04
   *BEYOND TIME AND SPACE   DERLETH, AUGUST   AN
WHEN THE LAST GODS DIE LEIBER, FRITZ   SS   FSF 51 12
   BOOK OF FRITZ LEIBER, THE   LEIBER, FRITZ   AC
   ENDS OF TIME, THE   SILVERBERG, ROBERT   AN
WHEN THE MOON WAS RED WILHELM, KATE   SS   AMZ 60 09
   DOWNSTAIRS ROOM AND OTHER SPECULATIVE FICTION, THE
                                   WILHELM, KATE   AC
WHEN THE MUSIC'S OVER DARLINGTON, ANDREW SS
   STOPWATCH   HAY, GEORGE   OA
WHEN THE NIGHT WIND HOWLS DE CAMP, L. SPRAGUE
                   AND PRATT, FLETCHER SS C WRT 51 11
   GHOUL KEEPERS, THE   MARGULIES, LEO   AN
   TALES FROM GAVAGAN'S BAR   DE CAMP, L. S.&PRATT   AC
WHEN THE PEOPLE FELL SMITH, CORDWAINER   SS   GAL 59 04
   FIFTH GALAXY READER, THE   GOLD, H. L.   AN
   STARDREAMER   SMITH, CORDWAINER   AC
WHEN THE SAUCERS CAME COOPER, EDMUND   SS
   TOMORROW CAME   COOPER, EDMUND   AC
   UNBORN TOMORROW   COOPER, EDMUND   AC
   VOICES IN THE DARK   COOPER, EDMUND   AC
WHEN THE SHOE FITS (SEE CINDERELLA STORY)
                                   GUNN, JAMES E.   TC
WHEN THE SLEEPER WAKES WELLS, H. G.   NO   HPR 99
   3 PROPHETIC SCIENCE FICTION NOVELS OF H. G. WELLS
                                   WELLS, H. G.   AC
WHEN THE SPOILERS CAME WILLIAMS, ROBERT M. NV PLS 52 05
   TO THE END OF TIME AND OTHER STORIES WILLIAMS, ROBERT M. DC
   WHEN TWO WORLDS MEET   WILLIAMS, ROBERT M.   AC
WHEN THE STARS ANSWER BROWN, T. K. III SS   WOT 64 02
   BEST SCIENCE FICTION FROM WORLDS OF TOMORROW, THE
                                   POHL, FREDERICK   AN
WHEN THE VERTICAL WORLD BECOMES HORIZONTAL
                                   PANSHIN, ALEXEI   SS   UNI 74 04
   FAREWELL TO YESTERDAY'S TOMORROW PANSHIN, ALEXEI   AC
   UNIVERSE 4   CARR, TERRY   OA
WHEN THE WAKER SLEEPS (THE WAKER DREAMS)
                                   MATHESON, RICHARD   SS   GAL 50 12
   SHOCK III   MATHESON, RICHARD   AC

WHEN THE WORLD SCREAMED   DOYLE, ARTHUR CONAN SS   29
  MARACOT DEEP AND OTHER STORIES, THE   DOYLE, ARTHUR CONAN AC
  POISON BELT, THE   DOYLE, ARTHUR CONAN AC
WHEN THE WORLD WAS YOUNG   LONDON, JACK   SS   SEP 10 09
  CURIOUS FRAGMENTS   LONDON, JACK   AC
  SCIENCE FICTION OF JACK LONDON, THE   LONDON, JACK   AC
WHEN TIME WAS NEW   YOUNG, ROBERT F.   NV   IFS 64 12
  IF READER OF SCIENCE FICTION, THE   POHL, FREDERIK   AN
WHEN TIME WENT MAD   KUMMER, FREDERICK A.
                         AND WYLIE, DIRK   NA C TWS 50 02
  SCIENCE FICTION: THE GREAT YEARS, VOL. II
                                 POHL, C. & F.   AN
WHEN TWO WORLDS MEET   WILLIAMS, ROBERT M. NV   AMZ 50 04
  WHEN TWO WORLDS MEET   WILLIAMS, ROBERT M.   AC
WHEN WE WENT TO SEE THE END OF THE WORLD
                         SILVERBERG, ROBERT SS   UNI 72 02
  BEST SCIENCE FICTION OF THE YEAR, THE NO. 2
                                 CARR, TERRY   AN
  BEST SCIENCE FICTION STORIES OF THE YEAR (1972)
                                 DEL REY, LESTER   AN
  EARTH IS THE STRANGEST PLANET   SILVERBERG, ROBERT   AN
  FUTURE PASTIMES   EDELSTEIN, SCOTT   OA
  LATE GREAT FUTURE, THE   FITZ GERALD & DILLON AN
  NEBULA AWARD STORIES 8   ASIMOV, ISAAC   AN
  UNFAMILIAR TERRITORY   SILVERBERG, ROBERT   AC
  UNIVERSE 2   CARR, TERRY   OA
WHEN WE WERE GOOD   SKAL, DAVE   SS   ORB 75 17
  ORBIT 17   KNIGHT, DAMON   OA
WHEN WOMEN RULE   MOSKOWITZ, SAM   AR   IFS 67 08
  WHEN WOMEN RULE   MOSKOWITZ, SAM   AN
WHEN YOU CARE, WHEN YOU LOVE STURGEON, THEODORE NV   FSF 62 09
  BEST FROM FANTASY AND SCIENCE FICTION, 25TH ANNIV.
                                 FERMAN, EDWARD L. AN
  CASE AND THE DREAMER   STURGEON, THEODORE   AC
  ONCE AND FUTURE TALES FROM THE MAGAZINE OF FANTASY AND
    SCIENCE FICTION   FERMAN, EDWARD L. AN
WHEN YOU HEAR THE TONE   SCORTIA, THOMAS N. SS   GAL 71 01
  BEST SCIENCE FICTION STORIES OF THE YEAR (1971)
                                 DEL REY, LESTER   AN
  CAUTION! INFLAMMABLE!   SCORTIA, THOMAS N.   AC
WHEN YOU RETURN   ROSOKHOVATSKY, IGOR NV   67
  ULTIMATE THRESHOLD, THE   GINSBURG, MIRRA   AN
WHEN YOU'RE SMILING   STURGEON, THEODORE NV   GAL 55 01
  BEST SF 2.   CRISPIN, EDMUND   AC
WHERE ARE YOU, MR. BIGGS? BOND, NELSON S.   SS   WRT 41 09
  LANCELOT BIGGS: SPACEMAN   BOND, NELSON S.   AC
WHERE DO WE GO FROM HERE? LEY, WILLY   AR   NEW 58 AN
  SF:58, THE YEAR'S GREATEST SCIENCE FICTION AND FANTASY
                                 MERRIL, JUDITH   AN
WHERE DO YOU LIVE, QUEEN ESTHER?
                         DAVIDSON, AVRAM   SS   FSF 64 11
  WHAT STRANGE STARS AND SKIES DAVIDSON, AVRAM   AC
"WHERE HAVE ALL THE DEFLOWERERS GONE?"
                         SCORTIA, THOMAS N. IN
  STRANGE BED FELLOWS   SCORTIA, THOMAS N.   AN
WHERE HAVE ALL THE FOLLOWERS GONE?
                         MOORE, RAYLYN   SS   BMR 73
  BAD MOON RISING   DISCH, THOMAS M.   OA
WHERE HAVE YOU BEEN, BILLY BOY, BILLY BOY?
                         WILHELM, KATE   SS   QRK 71 03
  INFINITY BOX, THE   WILHELM, KATE   AC
  QUARK/3   DELANY & HACKER   OA
WHERE I LIVE (YOU'VE NEVER BEEN TO BARNSTABLE?)
                         VONNEGUT, KURT JR. AR   VTR 64 10
  WELCOME TO THE MONKEY HOUSE   VONNEGUT, KURT JR.   AC
WHERE IS EVERYBODY?   BOVA, BEN   AR   AMZ 63 05
  9TH ANNUAL OF THE YEAR'S BEST S-F, THE MERRIL, JUDITH   AN
WHERE IS EVERYBODY?   SERLING, ROD   SA
  FROM THE TWILIGHT ZONE   SERLING, ROD   AC
  STORIES FROM THE TWILIGHT ZONE SERLING, ROD   OC
WHERE IS THY STING   PETAJA, EMIL   SS   FSF 67 05
  STARDRIFT AND OTHER FANTASTIC FLOTSAM PETAJA, EMIL   AC
WHERE LATE THE SWEET BIRDS SANG
                         WILHELM, KATE   NA   ORB 74 15
  ORBIT 15   KNIGHT, DAMON   OA
WHERE NO MAN HAS GONE BEFORE (SAMUEL A. PEEPLES)
                         BLISH, JAMES   SA   STK 72 08
  STAR TREK   8   BLISH, JAMES   OC
WHERE NO SUN SHINES   DOZOIS, GARDNER R. SS   ORB 70 06
  ORBIT 6   KNIGHT, DAMON   OA
WHERE SUMMER SONG RINGS HOLLOW KIMBERLY, GAIL   SS   DYS 75
  DYSTOPIAN VISIONS   ELWOOD, ROGER   OA
WHERE TALL TOWERS GLEAM   WILLIAMS, ROBERT M. SS   FAD 50 08
  TO THE END OF TIME AND OTHER STORIES   WILLIAMS, ROBERT M. DC
WHERE THE AIR QUIVERED   EUSTACE, ROBERT
                         AND MEADE, L. T.   SS C SND 98 12
  SCIENCE FICTION BY GASLIGHT   MOSKOWITZ, SAM   AN
WHERE THE BUFFALO ROAM   BLOCH, ROBERT   SS   OWS 55 07
  *BLOOD RUNS COLD   BLOCH, ROBERT   AC
WHERE THE CHANGED ONES GO SILVERBERG, ROBERT NV   GAL 66 02
  TO OPEN THE SKY   SILVERBERG, ROBERT   NO
WHERE THE CLUETTS ARE   FINNEY, JACK   NV   MCC 62 01
  I LOVE GALESBURG IN THE SPRINGTIME FINNEY, JACK   AC
WHERE THE STRAY DREAMS GO ELLISON, HARLAN   IN
  FROM THE LAND OF FEAR   ELLISON, HARLAN   AC
WHERE THE TIME WENT   SCHMITZ, JAMES H. SS   IFS 68 11
  ANDROIDS, TIME MACHINES AND BLUE GIRAFFES
                                 ELWOOD & GHIDALIA AN
WHERE TO? (ALSO AS PANDORA'S BOX)
                         HEINLEIN, ROBERT A. IN   GAL 52 02
  ALL ABOUT THE FUTURE   GREENBERG , MARTIN AN
WHERE TO, PLEASE?   DE CAMP, L. SPRAGUE
                         AND PRATT, FLETCHER SS C WRT 52 09
  TALES FROM GAVAGAN'S BAR   DE CAMP, L. S.&PRATT AC
WHEREVER YOU MAY BE (ALSO AS THE RELUCTANT WITCH)

                                 GUNN, JAMES E.   NA   GAL 53 05
  5 GALAXY SHORT NOVELS   GOLD, H. L.   AN
WHICH IN THE WOOD DECAYS MCEVOY, SETH   SS   ORB 75 17
  ORBIT 17   KNIGHT, DAMON   OA
WHICH WAY DO I GO FOR JERICHO? KAPP, COLIN   NV   NWR 72 20
  NEW WRITINGS IN SF. 20   CARNELL, JOHN   OA
WHIMPER OF WHIPPED DOGS, THE   ELLISON, HARLAN NV   BMR 73
  BAD MOON RISING   DISCH, THOMAS M.   OA
  DEATHBIRD STORIES   ELLISON, HARLAN   AC
  NO DOORS, NO WINDOWS (STORIES REWRITTEN) ELLISON, HARLAN AC
  YEAR'S BEST HORROR STORIES: SERIES III, THE
                                 DAVIS, RICHARD   AN
WHIRL CAGE   DANN, JACK M.   SS   ORB 72 10
  ORBIT 10   KNIGHT, DAMON   OA
WHIRLIGIG OF TIME, THE   VINGE, VERNOR   SS   STL 74 01
  STELLAR 1   DEL REY, JUDY-LYNN OA
WHIRLIGIG!   BRUNNER, JOHN   SS   BYI 67 11
  OUT OF MY MIND (BRITISH)   BRUNNER, JOHN   AC
  TIME-JUMP   BRUNNER, JOHN   AC
WHISPER, THE (SEE THE EXTRAORDINARILY HORRIBLE DUMMY)
                         KERSH, GERALD   TC
WHISPERER IN DARKNESS, THE LOVECRAFT, H. P. NV   WRT 31 08
  HAUNTER OF THE DARK, THE   LOVECRAFT, H. P.   AC
  STRANGE SIGNPOSTS   ELWOOD & MOSKOWITZ AN
WHISPERER RE-EXAMINED, THE LEIBER, FRITZ   AR
  BOOK OF FRITZ LEIBER, THE   LEIBER, FRITZ   AC
WHISPERING GALLERY, THE   TEMPLE, WILLIAM F. SS   FUN 53 10
  ZACHERLEY'S MIDNIGHT SNACKS   ZACHERLEY   AC
WHISPERS IN BEDLAM   SHAW, IRWIN   NA   PBY 69 02
  ARENA: SPORTS SF   FERMAN & MALZBERG   AN
WHISTLER   GOULART, RON   SS   EIO 73
  EROS IN ORBIT   ELDER, JOSEPH   OA
  NUTZENBOLTS   GOULART, RON   AC
WHITE APE, THE   LOVECRAFT, H. P. SS   WRT 24 07
  ANDROIDS, TIME MACHINES AND BLUE GIRAFFES
                                 ELWOOD & GHIDALIA AN
WHITE ARMY, THE   DRESSLER, DR. DANIEL SS   AMZ 29 09
  EVERY BOY'S BOOK OF SCIENCE FICTION WOLLHEIM, DONALD A. AN
  STORIES OF SCIENTIFIC IMAGINATION GALLANT, JOSEPH   AN
WHITE BOAT, THE   ROBERTS, KEITH   SS   NWS 66 12
  GRAIN KINGS, THE   ROBERTS, KEITH   AC
  PASSING OF THE DRAGONS, THE   ROBERTS, KEITH   AC
  PAVANE   ROBERTS, KEITH   NO
WHITE CITY, THE   KELLER, DAVID H. MD. SS   AMZ 35 05
  FOLSOM FLINT AND OTHER CURIOUS TALES, THE
                                 KELLER, DAVID H. MD. AC
WHITE CONE OF THE ALAID, THE   STRUGATSKY, ARKADY
                         AND STRUGATSKY, BORIS SS C
  LAST DOOR TO AIYA   GINSBURG, MIRRA   AN
WHITE CREATURES   BENFORD, GREGORY   SS   NDM 75 05
  NEW DIMENSIONS 5   SILVERBERG, ROBERT   OA
WHITE DEATH, THE   LEM, STANISLAW   SS   72
  MORTAL ENGINES   LEM, STANISLAW   AC
WHITE FANG GOES DINGO   DISCH, THOMAS M. NV   IFS 65 04
  *ONE HUNDRED AND TWO H-BOMBS DISCH, THOMAS M.   AC
  WHITE FANG GOES DINGO AND OTHER FUNNY S.F. STORIES
                                 DISCH, THOMAS M.   AC
WHITE GODDESS   SEABRIGHT, IDRIS SS   FSF 56 07
  BR-R-R!   CONKLIN, GROFF   AN
WHITE HERON, A   JEWETT, SARAH ORNE SS
  ECO-FICTION   STADLER, JOHN   AC
WHITE HORN   YEFREMOV, IVAN   SS
  STORIES   YEFREMOV, IVAN   AC
WHITE MOTH, THE   DERLETH, AUGUST   SS   WRT 33 04
  NOT LONG FOR THIS WORLD   DERLETH, AUGUST   AC
WHITE MUTINY   JAMESON, MALCOLM SS   ASF 40 10
  BULLARD OF THE SPACE PATROL   JAMESON, MALCOLM   AC
WHITE ON WHITE   ELLISON, HARLAN   SS   KNT 68 11
  BEAST THAT SHOUTED LOVE AT THE HEART OF THE WORLD, THE
                                 ELLISON, HARLAN   AC
WHITE PEOPLE, THE   MACHEN, ARTHUR   NV   HLK 04 01
  GOLDEN ROAD, THE   KNIGHT, DAMON   AN
WHITE PILOT, THE   PARNOV, YEREMEY
                         AND YEMTSEV, MIKHAIL NV C   69
  AIR OF MARS AND OTHER STORIES, THE   GINSBURG, MIRRA   AN
WHITE PINNACLE, THE   JACOBI, CARL   SS
  *TIME TO COME   DERLETH, AUGUST   OA
WHITE POWDER, THE   MACHEN, ARTHUR   NV   FFM 44 09
  STRANGE ECSTASIES   PARRY, MICHEL   AN
WHITE ROAD, THE   MERRITT, A.   SS   49
  FOX WOMAN & OTHER STORIES, THE   MERRITT, A.   AC
WHITE SPOT   LEINSTER, MURRAY NV   STS 55 FL
  GET OFF MY WORLD!   LEINSTER, MURRAY   AC
WHITE STARS   MOORCOCK, MICHAEL NV   NWB 75 08
  LEGENDS FROM THE END OF TIME MOORCOCK, MICHAEL   AC
  NEW WORLDS EIGHT   BAILEY, HILARY   OA
WHITE SUMMER IN MEMPHIS   EKLUND, GORDON   NV   NDM 72 02
  NEW DIMENSIONS 2   SILVERBERG, ROBERT   OA
WHITE TRASH DON'T EXIST (MURDER BAIT)
                         ELLISON, HARLAN   SS   MTP 56 10
  NO DOORS, NO WINDOWS (STORIES REWRITTEN) ELLISON, HARLAN AC
WHITE WOLF CALLING   GRANT, C. L.   SS   FSF 75 04
  YEAR'S BEST HORROR STORIES: SERIES IV, THE
                                 PAGE, GERALD W.   AN
WHITER SHADE OF PALE, A   BING, JON   SS   74
  BEST FROM THE REST OF THE WORLD, THE   WOLLHEIM, DONALD A. AN
WHO AM I THIS TIME? (MY NAME IS EVERYONE)
                         VONNEGUT, KURT JR. SS   SEP 61 12
  WELCOME TO THE MONKEY HOUSE   VONNEGUT, KURT JR.   AC
  YOU AND SCIENCE FICTION   HOLLISTER, BERNARD C AN
WHO BELIEVES IN GHOSTS!   LONDON, JACK   SS   HSA 95 10
  CURIOUS FRAGMENTS   LONDON, JACK   AC
WHO CAN REPLACE A MAN? (BUT WHO CAN REPLACE A MAN)
                         ALDISS, BRIAN W. SS   INF 58 06
  ABOVE THE HUMAN LANDSCAPE   MCNELLY & STOVER   AN

WHO CAN REPLACE A MAN? (BUT WHO CAN REPLACE A MAN)

*BEST SCIENCE FICTION STORIES OF BRIAN W. ALDISS
                            ALDISS, BRIAN W.   AC
  BEST SF 5   CRISPIN, EDMUND   AN
  CANOPY OF TIME, THE   ALDISS, BRIAN W.   AC
  CENTURY OF SCIENCE FICTION, A   KNIGHT, DAMON   AN
  GALAXIES LIKE GRAINS OF SAND   ALDISS, BRIAN W.   AC
  SOULS IN METAL   ASHLEY, MICHAEL   AN
  STORIES FROM SCIENCE FICTION   DOHERTY, G. D.   AN
  WORLDS OF WONDER   HARRISON, HARRY   AN
WHO DREAMS OF IVY   WORTHINGTON, WILL   SS   FSF 60 11
  BEST FROM FANTASY AND SCIENCE FICTION: 10
                            MILLS, ROBERT P.   AN
WHO ELSE BUT SHE?   WRIGHT, S. FOWLER   SS
  WITCHFINDER, THE   WRIGHT, S. FOWLER   AC
WHO GOES THERE?   CAMPBELL, JOHN W. JR NV   ASF 38 08
  *BEST OF JOHN W. CAMPBELL, THE   CAMPBELL, JOHN W. JR AC
  SCIENCE FICTION HALL OF FAME VOLUME 2A   BOVA, BEN   AN
  SCIENCE FICTION ROLL OF HONOR, THE   POHL, FREDERIK   AN
  UBERWINDUNG VON RAUM UND ZEIT   GUNTHER, GOTTHARD   AN
  WHO GOES THERE?   CAMPBELL, JOHN W. JR AC
  WHO GOES THERE? AND OTHER STORIES   CAMPBELL, JOHN W. JR AC
WHO GOES THERE?   STUART, DON A.   NV   ASF 38 08
  *ADVENTURES IN TIME AND SPACE   HEALY & MCCOMAS   AN
  TOWARD INFINITY   KNIGHT, DAMON   AN
WHO IS CHARLES AVISON?   MARSHALL, EDISON T. SS   ARG 16 04
  SHOT IN THE DARK   MERRIL, JUDITH   NV
WHO IS CINDY?   FANCETT, ELIZABETH   SS   ADS 75 01
  ARMADA SCI-FI ONE   DAVIS, RICHARD   OA
WHO IS HUMAN?   HOWARD, HAYDEN   NV   GAL 66 08
  ESKIMO INVASION   HOWARD, HAYDEN   NO
WHO IS TIPTREE, WHAT IS HE?   SILVERBERG, ROBERT   IN
  WARM WORLDS AND OTHERWISE   TIPTREE, JAMES JR.   AC
WHO KNOWS HIS BROTHER   DOAR, GRAHAM   SS   STS 52 02
  HUMAN?   MERRIL, JUDITH   AN
WHO MOURNS FOR ADONAIS? (G. RALSTON & G. COON)
                            BLISH, JAMES   SA   STK 72 07
  STAR TREK 7   BLISH, JAMES   OC
WHO NEEDS INSURANCE?   SCOTT, ROBIN S.   NV   ASF 66 04
  NEBULA AWARD STORIES NO. 2   ALDISS & HARRISON   AN
WHO SHALL DWELL...   NEAL, H. C.   SS   PBY 62 07
  LAST TRAIN TO LIMBO   PLAYBOY, EDITORS OF AN
  PLAYBOY BOOK OF SCIENCE FICTION AND FANTASY, THE
                            PLAYBOY, EDITORS OF AN
  THEMES IN SCIENCE FICTION   KELLEY, LEO P.   AN
"WHO SHALL I SAY IS CALLING?"   DERLETH, AUGUST   SS   FSF 52 08
  HUMAN?   MERRIL, JUDITH   AN
WHO STEALS MY PURSE   BRUNNER, JOHN   NV   ASF 73 03
  BOOK OF JOHN BRUNNER, THE   BRUNNER, JOHN   AC
WHO WAS THE FIRST OSCAR TO WIN A NEGRO?
                            STRETE, CRAIG   SS   ORB 76 18
  ORBIT 18   KNIGHT, DAMON   OA
WHO'S CRIBBING?   LEWIS, JACK   SS   STS 53 01
  BEST FROM STARTLING STORIES, THE   MINES, SAMUEL   AN
  FIFTY SHORT SCIENCE FICTION TALES   ASIMOV & CONKLIN   AN
  SCIENCE FACT/FICTION   FARRELL/GAGE/&   AN
WHO'S IN CHARGE HERE? (ALSO AS NONE SO BLIND)
                            BLISH, JAMES   SS   FSF 62 05
  BEST FROM FANTASY AND SCIENCE FICTION: 12
                            DAVIDSON, AVRAM   AN
WHO'S IN THERE WITH ME?   CASTELL, DAPHNE   SS   NEW 68 AN
  ENGLAND SWINGS SF   MERRIL, JUDITH   AN
  SPACE-TIME JOURNAL, THE   MERRIL, JUDITH   AN
WHO'S ON FIRST?   BIGGLE, LLOYD JR.   NV   IFS 58 08
  GALAXY OF STRANGERS, A   BIGGLE, LLOYD JR.   AC
WHO'S THERE? (ALSO AS THE HAUNTED SPACESUIT)
                            CLARKE, ARTHUR C.   SS   NWS 58 11
  NINE BILLION NAMES OF GOD, THE   CLARKE, ARTHUR C.   AC
  OF TIME AND STARS   CLARKE, ARTHUR C.   AC
  OUT OF THIS WORLD 3   WILLIAMS-ELLIS & OWEN   AN
  SCIENCE FACT/FICTION   FARRELL/GAGE/&   AN
  TALES OF TEN WORLDS   CLARKE, ARTHUR C.   AC
WHOEVER YOU ARE   MERRIL, JUDITH   NV   STS 52 12
  BEST OF JUDITH MERRIL, THE   MERRIL, JUDITH   AC
  OUT OF BOUNDS   MERRIL, JUDITH   AC
  SURVIVAL SHIP AND OTHER STORIES   MERRIL, JUDITH   AC
WHOLE CITY, THE   ERNST, MAX   IL
  SCIENCE FICTION   BRODKIN & PEARSON   AN
WHOLE MAN, THE   BRUNNER, JOHN   SN   SCF 59 04
  WHOLE MAN, THE   BRUNNER, JOHN   NO
WHOLE ROUND WORLD, THE   GOULART, RON   NV   FIN 70
  FUTURE IS NOW, THE   NOLAN, WILLIAM F.   OA
WHOLE TOWN'S SLEEPING, THE   BRADBURY, RAY   SS   MCC 50 09
  DANDELION WINE   BRADBURY, RAY   NO
WHOLE TRUTH, THE   ANTHONY, PIERS   SS   NOV 70 01
  *NOVA 1   HARRISON, HARRY   OA
WHOLE TRUTH, THE   SERLING, ROD   SA
  FROM THE TWILIGHT ZONE   SERLING, ROD   AC
  NEW STORIES FROM THE TWILIGHT ZONE   SERLING, ROD   OC
WHOM GODS DESTROY (LEE ERWIN & JERRY SOHL)
                            BLISH, JAMES   SA   STK 72 05
  STAR TREK 5   BLISH, JAMES   OC
WHOM THE GODS LOVE   DEL REY, LESTER   SS   ASF 43 06
  EARLY DEL REY   DEL REY, LESTER   AC
WHORE WITH A HEART OF IRON PYRITES: OR, WHERE DOES A WRITER GO
TO FIND A MAGGIE?   ELLISON, HARLAN   AR
  THOSE WHO CAN: A SCIENCE FICTION READER   WILSON, ROBIN SCOTT   AN
WHY ANTHOLOGIZE?   DEL REY, JUDY-LYNN   IN
  STELLAR 1   DEL REY, JUDY-LYNN   OA
WHY ATLANTIS SANK   DONEV, ANTON   SS
  OTHER WORLDS, OTHER SEAS   SUVIN, DARKO   AN
WHY HAS THE VIRGIN MARY NEVER ENTERED THE WIGWAM OF
STANDING BEAR?   STRETE, CRAIG   SS
  AURORA: BEYOND EQUALITY   MCINTYRE & ANDERSON   OA
WHY I SELECTED ALMOST HUMAN   BLOCH, ROBERT   AI
  *MY BEST SCIENCE FICTION STORY   MARGULIES & FRIEND   AN

WHY I SELECTED BLINDNESS   CAMPBELL, JOHN W. JR AI
  *MY BEST SCIENCE FICTION STORY   MARGULIES & FRIEND   AN
WHY I SELECTED DOCTOR GRIMSHAW'S SANITARIUM
                            PRATT, FLETCHER   AI
  *MY BEST SCIENCE FICTION STORY   MARGULIES & FRIEND   AN
WHY I SELECTED DON'T LOOK NOW   KUTTNER, HENRY   AI
  *MY BEST SCIENCE FICTION STORY   MARGULIES & FRIEND   AN
WHY I SELECTED GRIEF OF BAGDAD   BARNES, ARTHUR K.   AI
  *MY BEST SCIENCE FICTION STORY   MARGULIES & FRIEND   AN
WHY I SELECTED NOTHING SIRIUS   BROWN, FREDRIC   AI
  *MY BEST SCIENCE FICTION STORY   MARGULIES & FRIEND   AN
WHY I SELECTED PROJECT- SPACESHIP
                            VAN VOGT, A. E.   AI
  *MY BEST SCIENCE FICTION STORY   MARGULIES & FRIEND   AN
WHY I SELECTED ROBOT AL-76 GOES ASTRAY
                            ASIMOV, ISAAC   AI
  *MY BEST SCIENCE FICTION STORY   MARGULIES & FRIEND   AN
WHY I SELECTED SPACE STATION NO. 1
                            WELLMAN, MANLY WADE AI
  *MY BEST SCIENCE FICTION STORY   MARGULIES & FRIEND   AN
WHY I SELECTED STAR BRIGHT   WILLIAMSON, JACK   AI
  *MY BEST SCIENCE FICTION STORY   MARGULIES & FRIEND   AN
WHY I SELECTED THE CARRIERS   MERWIN, SAM JR.   AI
  *MY BEST SCIENCE FICTION STORY   MARGULIES & FRIEND   AN
WHY I SELECTED THE GREEN HILLS OF EARTH
                            HEINLEIN, ROBERT A.   AI
  *MY BEST SCIENCE FICTION STORY   MARGULIES & FRIEND   AN
WHY I SELECTED THE HIBITED MAN   DE CAMP, L. SPRAGUE AI
  *MY BEST SCIENCE FICTION STORY   MARGULIES & FRIEND   AN
WHY I SELECTED THE HOUSE OF RISING WINDS
                            LONG, FRANK BELKNAP AI
  *MY BEST SCIENCE FICTION STORY   MARGULIES & FRIEND   AN
WHY I SELECTED THE INN OUTSIDE THE WORLD
                            HAMILTON, EDMOND   AI
  *MY BEST SCIENCE FICTION STORY   MARGULIES & FRIEND   AN
WHY I SELECTED THE LOST RACE   LEINSTER, MURRAY   AI
  *MY BEST SCIENCE FICTION STORY   MARGULIES & FRIEND   AN
WHY I SELECTED THE PROFESSOR WAS A THIEF
                            HUBBARD, L. RON   AI
  *MY BEST SCIENCE FICTION STORY   MARGULIES & FRIEND   AN
WHY I SELECTED THE TEACHER FROM MARS
                            BINDER, EANDO   AI
  *MY BEST SCIENCE FICTION STORY   MARGULIES & FRIEND   AN
WHY I SELECTED THE THING IN THE POND
                            ERNST, PAUL   AI
  *MY BEST SCIENCE FICTION STORY   MARGULIES & FRIEND   AN
WHY I SELECTED THE ULTIMATE CATALYST
                            TAINE, JOHN   AI
  *MY BEST SCIENCE FICTION STORY   MARGULIES & FRIEND   AN
WHY I SELECTED THUNDER AND ROSES
                            STURGEON, THEODORE   AI
  *MY BEST SCIENCE FICTION STORY   MARGULIES & FRIEND   AN
WHY I SELECTED UNCHARTED ISLE   SMITH, CLARK ASHTON AI
  *MY BEST SCIENCE FICTION STORY   MARGULIES & FRIEND   AN
WHY I SELECTED VISITING YOKEL   CARTMILL, CLEVE   AI
  *MY BEST SCIENCE FICTION STORY   MARGULIES & FRIEND   AN
WHY I SELECTED WANDERER OF TIME
                            FEARN, JOHN RUSSELL AI
  *MY BEST SCIENCE FICTION STORY   MARGULIES & FRIEND   AN
WHY I SELECTED ZERO HOUR   BRADBURY, RAY   AI
  *MY BEST SCIENCE FICTION STORY   MARGULIES & FRIEND   AN
WHY I WANT TO FUCK RONALD REAGAN
                            BALLARD, J. G.   SS   MOP 68 SU
  LOVE & NAPALM: EXPORT U.S.A.   BALLARD, J. G.   AC
WHY IS IT SO HARD?   WILHELM, KATE   AR   CLR 72 02
  CLARION II   WILSON, ROBIN SCOTT   OA
WHY ME?   ASIMOV, ISAAC   IN
  WANDERING STARS   DANN, JACK M.   AN
WHY THEY MOBBED THE WHITE HOUSE
                            BUCK, DORIS PITKIN   SS   ORB 68 03
  ORBIT 3   KNIGHT, DAMON   OA
WHY?   SILVERBERG, ROBERT   SS   SFS 57 11
  CALLIBRATED ALLIGATOR AND OTHER SCIENCE FICTION STORIES, THE
                            SILVERBERG, ROBERT   AC
  GODLING, GO HOME| SILVERBERG, ROBERT   AC
WHY?   STURGEON, THEODORE   AR   CLR 73 03
  CLARION III   WILSON, ROBIN SCOTT   OA
WICKED FLEE, THE   HARRISON, HARRY   SS   NDM 71 01
  BEST OF HARRY HARRISON, THE (BRITISH)   HARRISON, HARRY   AC
  BEST SCIENCE FICTION STORIES OF THE YEAR (1971)
                            DEL REY, LESTER   AN
  NEW DIMENSIONS 1   SILVERBERG, ROBERT   OA
WICKER WONDERLAND (THE CITY THAT GREW IN THE SEA)
                            LAUMER, KEITH   NV   IFS 64 03
  GALACTIC DIPLOMAT   LAUMER, KEITH   AC
WIDE-OPEN PLANET (SEE PERPETUAL MOTION)
                            DE CAMP, L. SPRAGUE TC
WIDENING CIRCLE, THE   MCCLOUD, RICHARD   SS   NEW 72 AN
  STRANGE BED FELLOWS   SCORTIA, THOMAS N.   AN
(WIDGET), THE (WADGET), AND BOFF, THE
                            STURGEON, THEODORE   SN   FSF 55 11
  ALIENS 4   STURGEON, THEODORE   AC
  JOYOUS INVASION, THE   STURGEON, THEODORE   AC
  TREASURY OF GREAT SCIENCE FICTION, A VOL.1
                            BOUCHER, ANTHONY   AC
WIFE TO THE LORD   HARRISON, HARRY   SS   FSF 70 06
  ONE STEP FROM EARTH   HARRISON, HARRY   AC
WILBUR   GREENHOUGH, TERRY   SS   SFM 74 04
  BEST OF SCIENCE FICTION MONTHLY, THE   SACKS, JANET   AN
WILD FLOWER   WYNDHAM, JOHN   SS   FUN 55 11
  SEEDS OF TIME, THE   WYNDHAM, JOHN   AC
  TALES OF GOOSEFLESH AND LAUGHTER   WYNDHAM, JOHN   AC
WILD GRAPES   DERLETH, AUGUST   SS   WRT 34 07
  NOT LONG FOR THIS WORLD   DERLETH, AUGUST   AC
WILD MAN OF THE SEA, THE   HODGSON, WILLIAM H. SS
  TRAVELLERS BY NIGHT   DERLETH, AUGUST   OA

WILD MAN OF THE SEA, THE

WILD SURMISE, A   KUTTNER, HENRY   SS   STR 53 01
  BEST OF HENRY KUTTNER 2, THE   KUTTNER, HENRY   AC
WILD SURMISE, A   KUTTNER, HENRY
                            AND MOORE, C. L.   SS C STR 53 01
  STAR SCIENCE FICTION STORIES   POHL, FREDERIK   OA
WILD WOOD, THE   CLINGERMAN, MILDRED SS FSF 57 01
  BEST FROM FANTASY AND SCIENCE FICTION: 7
                            BOUCHER, ANTHONY   AN
  CUPFUL OF SPACE, A   CLINGERMAN, MILDRED   AC
  SPECIAL WONDER   MCCOMAS, J. FRANCIS   AN
WILDCAT   ANDERSON, POUL   NV FSF 58 11
  7 CONQUESTS   ANDERSON, POUL   AC
WILDERNESS   HENDERSON, ZENNA   SS FSF 57 01
  PILGRIMAGE: THE BOOK OF THE PEOPLE HENDERSON, ZENNA   AC
  SF:58, THE YEAR'S GREATEST SCIENCE FICTION AND FANTASY
                            MERRIL, JUDITH   AN
WILDERNESS, THE   BRADBURY, RAY   SS FSF 52 11
  *GOLDEN APPLES OF THE SUN   BRADBURY, RAY   AC
  MARTIAN CHRONICLES, THE (BRITISH SFBC, ADDS:)
                            BRADBURY, RAY   AC
  *STORIES FOR TOMORROW   SLOANE, WILLIAM   AN
  UNIVERSE AHEAD   ENGDAHL & ROBERSON   AN
WILL YOU WAIT?   BESTER, ALFRED   SS FSF 59 03
  DARK SIDE OF THE EARTH, THE   BESTER, ALFRED   AC
  DECADE OF FANTASY AND SCIENCE FICTION, A MILLS, ROBERT P.   AN
  GOLDEN ROAD, THE   KNIGHT, DAMON   AN
WILL YOU WALK A LITTLE FASTER? TENN, WILLIAM   SS MAR 51 11
  *INVADERS OF EARTH   CONKLIN, GROFF   AN
  WOODEN STAR, THE   TENN, WILLIAM   AC
WILL-HUNG AND WAITING   BUNCH, DAVID R.   SS
  MODERAN   BUNCH, DAVID R.   AC
WILL, THE   MILLER, WALTER M. JR SS FAN 54 02
  BEST SCIENCE FICTION STORIES AND NOVELS: 1955
                            DIKTY, T. E.   AN
  VIEW FROM THE STARS, THE   MILLER, WALTER M. JR   AC
WILLIAM AND MARY   DAHL, ROALD   NV   59
  LATE GREAT FUTURE, THE   FITZ GERALD & DILLON   AN
WILLIAM MITCHELL- 2028 (THE MESSAGE)
                            GUNN, JAMES E.   NV GAL 71 05
  LISTENERS, THE   GUNN, JAMES E.   NO
WILLIAM WILSON (1839)   POE, EDGAR ALLEN   NV GFT 39 09
  MOONLIGHT TRAVELER, THE   STERN, PHILIP VAN D.   AN
  OTHER DIMENSION, THE   ROSNER, SARA   AN
"WILLIE'S BLUES"   TILLEY, ROBERT J.   NV FSF 72 05
  1973 ANNUAL WORLD'S BEST SF, THE   WOLLHEIM, DONALD A.   AN
WILLOW TREE, THE   RICE, JANE   SS FSF 59 02
  BEST FROM FANTASY AND SCIENCE FICTION: 9
                            MILLS, ROBERT P.   AN
WILLOWISP   PUMILIA, JOSEPH F.   SS SPE 74 01
  SCIENCE FICTION EMPHASIS NO. 1   GERROLD, DAVID   OA
WIN THE WORLD (THE SUBVERSIVES)
                            OLIVER, CHAD   SS STS 52 02
  LOOKING FORWARD   LESSER, MILTON   AN
WIND AND THE RAIN, THE   SILVERBERG, ROBERT   SS SVW 73
  BEST SF: 1973   HARRISON & ALDISS   AN
  FUTURE NOW, THE   HOSKINS, ROBERT   AN
  SAVING WORLDS   ELWOOD & KIDD   OA
  UNFAMILIAR TERRITORY   SILVERBERG, ROBERT   AC
WIND BETWEEN THE WORLDS, THE DEL REY, LESTER   NV GAL 51 03
  ADVENTURES IN THE FAR FUTURE   WOLLHEIM, DONALD A.   DA
  EARLY DEL REY   DEL REY, LESTER   AC
WIND BLOWS FREE, THE   OLIVER, CHAD   NV FSF 57 07
  SEA OF SPACE, A   NOLAN, WILLIAM F.   AN
WIND FROM BEYOND THE MOUNTAINS, THE (SAVAGE WIND)
                            ELLISON, HARLAN   SS AMZ 57 01
  ELLISON WONDERLAND   ELLISON, HARLAN   AC
WIND FROM NOWHERE, THE (ENLARGED FROM STORM-WIND)
                            BALLARD, J. G.   NO NWS 61 09
  DROWNED WORLD AND THE WIND FROM NOWHERE, THE
                            BALLARD, J. G.   AC
WIND FROM THE SUN, THE (THE SUNJAMMER)
                            CLARKE, ARTHUR C.   SS BLF 64
  WIND FROM THE SUN, THE   CLARKE, ARTHUR C.   AC
WIND IN THE LILACS, THE   DERLETH, AUGUST   SS ARS 48 SP
  MR. GEORGE AND OTHER ODD PERSONS DERLETH, AUGUST   AC
WIND IS RISING, A   O'DONNEVAN, FINN   SS GAL 57 07
  THIRD GALAXY READER, THE   GOLD, H. L.   AN
WIND IS RISING, A   SHECKLEY, ROBERT   SS GAL 57 07
  NOTIONS: UNLIMITED   SHECKLEY, ROBERT   AC
WIND PEOPLE, THE   BRADLEY, MARION Z.   SS IFS 59 02
  CENTURY OF SCIENCE FICTION, A   KNIGHT, DAMON   AN
  WOMEN OF WONDER   SARGENT, PAMELA   AN
WIND-DREAM   KING, MAC   PM NWQ 74 06
  NEW WORLDS NO. 6   PLATT & BAILEY   OA
WIND, THE   BRADBURY, RAY   SS WRT 43 03
  *DARK CARNIVAL   BRADBURY, RAY   AC
  GREAT SCIENCE-FICTION   LICATA, TONY   AN
  *OCTOBER COUNTRY, THE   BRADBURY, RAY   AC
WINDMILL   ANDERSON, POUL   NV SVW 73
  SAVING WORLDS   ELWOOD & KIDD   OA
WINDOW DRESSING   RUSS, JOANNA   SS NEW 70 AN
  NEW WORLDS OF FANTASY NO. 2   CARR, TERRY   AN
WINDOW, THE   BRADBURY, RAY   SS COL 50 08
  DANDELION WINE   BRADBURY, RAY   NO
WINDOWS   DANN, JACK M.   SS NWQ 72 03
  NEW WORLDS QUARTERLY NO. 3   MOORCOCK, MICHAEL   OA
WINDOWS IN DANTE'S HELL, THE BISHOP, MICHAEL   SS ORB 73 12
  BEST SF: 1973   HARRISON & ALDISS   AN
  ORBIT 12   KNIGHT, DAMON   OA
WINDOWS OF HEAVEN, THE   ANONYMOUS   SS
  UNTRAVELLED WORLDS   BARTER & WILSON   AN
WINDOWS OF HEAVEN, THE (TWO BY TWO)
                            BRUNNER, JOHN   SS NWS 56 05
  NO FUTURE IN IT   BRUNNER, JOHN   AC
  SCIENCE FICTION   BURTON, S. H.   AN
  YET MORE PENGUIN SCIENCE FICTION ALDISS, BRIAN W.   AN

WINDS AT STARMONT, THE   CARR, TERRY   NA
  LIGHT AT THE END OF THE UNIVERSE, THE CARR, TERRY   A
  NO MIND OF MAN   SILVERBERG, ROBERT   A
WINDS OF TIME, THE   SCHMITZ, JAMES H.   NV ASF 62 0
  NICE DAY FOR SCREAMING, AND OTHER TALES OF THE HUB
                            SCHMITZ, JAMES H.   A
  PRIDE OF MONSTERS, A   SCHMITZ, JAMES H.   A
WINDSONG   WILHELM, KATE   NV ORB 68 0
  DOWNSTAIRS ROOM AND OTHER SPECULATIVE FICTION, THE
                            WILHELM, KATE   A
  ORBIT 4   KNIGHT, DAMON   O
  POCKETFUL OF STARS, A   KNIGHT, DAMON   A
WINE HAS BEEN LEFT OPEN TOO LONG AND THE MEMORY HAS
  GONE FLAT, THE   ELLISON, HARLAN   SS UNI 76 0
  UNIVERSE 6   CARR, TERRY   A
WINE OF PARIS, THE   AYME, MARCEL   SS
  WALKER THROUGH WALLS, THE   AYME, MARCEL   A
WINES OF EARTH, THE   SEABRIGHT, IDRIS   SS FSF 57 0
  BEST FROM FANTASY AND SCIENCE FICTION: 7
                            BOUCHER, ANTHONY   A
WINES OF EARTH, THE   ST. CLAIR, MARGARET SS FSF 57 0
  CHANGE THE SKY AND OTHER STORIES   ST. CLAIR, MARGARET   A
WINGED DREAMERS, THE   GUTTRIDGE, JENNIFER NV
  STAR TREK: THE NEW VOYAGES   MARSHAK, S&CULBREATH   O
WINGED MAN, THE   HULL, E. MAYNE
                            AND VAN VOGT, A. E. NO C ASF 44 0
  SCIENCE FICTION SPECIAL 4   ANONYMOUS   A
WINGLESS ON AVALON   ANDERSON, POUL   SS COI 73
  CHILDREN OF INFINITY   ELWOOD, ROGER   O
WINGLESS VICTORY   HEARD, H. F.   SS   44
  *BEYOND TIME AND SPACE   DERLETH, AUGUST   A
  GREAT FOG AND OTHER WEIRD TALES, THE HEARD, H. F.   A
WINGS   MCINTYRE, VONDA N.   SS ALC 73
  ALIEN CONDITION, THE   GOLDIN, STEPHEN   A
WINGS ACROSS THE COSMOS   CROSS, POLTON   SS TWS 38 0
  *TREASURY OF SCIENCE FICTION, A   CONKLIN, GROFF   A
WINGS ACROSS TIME   ARNOLD, FRANK EDWARD NV SFQ 42 W
  WINGS ACROSS TIME   ARNOLD, FRANK EDWARD   A
WINGS OF A BAT, THE   ASH, PAUL   NV ASF 66 0
  WORLD'S BEST SCIENCE FICTION: 1967 WOLLHEIM & CARR   A
WINGS OF NIGHT, THE   DEL REY, LESTER   SS ASF 42 0
  *AND SOME WERE HUMAN   DEL REY, LESTER   A
  *BIG BOOK OF SCIENCE FICTION   CONKLIN, GROFF   A
  GREAT STORIES OF SPACE TRAVEL   CONKLIN, GROFF   A
WINGS OF SONG   BIGGLE, LLOYD JR.   SS FSF 63 1
  RULE OF THE DOOR AND OTHER FANCIFUL REGULATIONS
                            BIGGLE, LLOYD JR.   A
WINGS OF THE LIGHTNING LAND MACCREIGH, JAMES   NV AST 41 1
  SCIENCE FICTION: THE GREAT YEARS   POHL, C. & F.   A
WINGS OF VICTORY   ANDERSON, POUL   SS ASF 72 0
  HOMEWARD AND BEYOND   ANDERSON, POUL   A
WINGS OUT OF SHADOW   SABERHAGEN, FRED   NV IFS 74 0
  BEST FROM IF, THE   VOLUME II   IF, EDITORS OF   A
WINK OF AN EYE (ARTHUR HEINEMANN & LEE CRONIN)
                            BLISH, JAMES   SA STK 75 1
  STAR TREK 11   BLISH, JAMES   A
WINKIN, BLINKIN AND PI R SQUARE
                            FITZPATRICK, R. C.   SS ASF 68 0
  ANALOG 8   CAMPBELL, JOHN W. JR A
WINNER LOSE ALL   VANCE, JACK   SS GAL 51 1
  OMNIBUS OF SCIENCE FICTION   CONKLIN, GROFF   A
WINNER TAKE ALL   ROCKLYNNE, ROSS   NV
  *TIME TO COME   DERLETH, AUGUST   A
WINNER, THE   WESTLAKE, DONALD E. SS NOV 70 0
  ANOTHER TOMORROW   HOLLISTER, BERNARD C A
  EARTH IN TRANSIT   SCHWARTZ, SHEILA   A
  *NOVA 1   HARRISON, HARRY   A
  SCIENCE FICTION   BRODKIN & PEARSON   A
  TOMORROW, AND TOMORROW, AND TOMORROW... HEINTZ/HERBERT/JOOS/ A
WINNING OF THE GREAT AMERICAN GREENING REVOLUTION
                            YACO, MURRAY F.   SS ORB 74 1
  ORBIT 14   KNIGHT, DAMON   A
WINNING RECIPE   CLINGERMAN, MILDRED SS FSF 52 1
  CUPFUL OF SPACE, A   CLINGERMAN, MILDRED   A
WINNOWING, THE   ASIMOV, ISAAC   SS ASF 76 0
  BICENTENNIAL MAN AND OTHER STORIES, THE ASIMOV, ISAAC   A
WINSTON   REED, KIT   SS ORB 69 0
  ORBIT 5   KNIGHT, DAMON   A
WINTER   REED, KIT   SS ARG 70
  YEAR'S BEST HORROR STORIES, THE   DAVIS, RICHARD   A
WINTER ARRIVAL   INOUYE, JON   SS
  NIGHT TIDE, A   INOUYE, JON   A
WINTER FLIES, THE (THE INNER CIRCLES)
                            LEIBER, FRITZ   SS FSF 67 1
  POCKETFUL OF STARS, A   KNIGHT, DAMON   A
  SECRET SONGS, THE   LEIBER, FRITZ   A
  SF12   MERRIL, JUDITH   A
WINTER HOUSECLEANING   DANIEL, MOLLY   SS CLR 72 0
  CLARION II   WILSON, ROBIN SCOTT   A
WINTER IN THIS LATITUDE   RUBIN, RICK   NV PBY 62 1
  MASKS   PLAYBOY, EDITORS OF   A
WINTER'S KING   LE GUIN, URSULA K.   NV ORB 69 0
  ORBIT 5   KNIGHT, DAMON   A
  WINDS TWELVE QUARTERS, THE   LE GUIN, URSULA K.   A
WINTER'S TALE, A   LECHTLINER, RUTH   PM   69
  HOLDING YOUR EIGHT HANDS   LUCIE-SMITH, EDWARD   A
WINTHROP WAS STUBBORN (TIME WAITS FOR WINTHROP)
                            TENN, WILLIAM   NA GAL 57 0
  OUT OF THIS WORLD 5   WILLIAMS-ELLIS& OWEN A
  TIME IN ADVANCE   TENN, WILLIAM   A
WIRELESS   KIPLING, RUDYARD   SS SCR 02 0
  JOURNEYS IN SCIENCE FICTION   LOUGHLIN, RICHARD L. A
  MOONLIGHT TRAVELER, THE   STERN, PHILIP VAN D. A
WISE CHILD   RACKHAM, JOHN   SS NWR 73 2
  NEW WRITINGS IN SF. 22   BULMER, KENNETH   O

ISE CHILD   WYNDHAM, JOHN   SS   PBY 67 05
  PLAYBOY'S STORIES OF THE SINISTER & STRANGE
                                   PLAYBOY, EDITORS OF   AN
ISEL   RUSSELL, ERIC FRANK   SS
  DARK TIDES   RUSSELL, ERIC FRANK   AC
ISH UPON A STAR   MERRIL, JUDITH   SS   FSF 58 12
  BEST OF JUDITH MERRIL, THE   MERRIL, JUDITH   AC
  SURVIVAL SHIP AND OTHER STORIES MERRIL, JUDITH   AC
ISH UPON A STAR   YOUNG, ROBERT F.   SS   FUN 56 12
  GLASS OF STARS, A   YOUNG, ROBERT F.   AC
ISH, THE   BRADBURY, RAY   SS   WDM 73 12
  LONG AFTER MIDNIGHT   BRADBURY, RAY   AC
ISH, THE   DAHL, ROALD   SS   53
  CIRCUS OF DR. LAO AND OTHER IMPROBABLE STORIES
                                   BRADBURY, RAY   AN
ISHES WE MAKE, THE   HULL, E. MAYNE   SS   UNK 43 06
  OUT OF THE UNKNOWN   VAN VOGT & HULL   AC
ITCH FROM HELL'S KITCHEN, THE HOWARD, ROBERT E.   NV   APR 52 18
  AVON FANTASY READER, THE   WOLLHEIM &ERNSBERGER   AN
ITCH HUNT   GUNN, JAMES E.   NV   GAL 69 04
  BURNING, THE   GUNN, JAMES E.   NO
ITCH IN THE FOG, THE   ALTSHULER, HARRY   SS   WRT 38 09
  GHOUL KEEPERS, THE   MARGULIES, LEO   AN
ITCH SHALL BE BORN, A   HOWARD, ROBERT E.   SS   WRT 34 12
  CONAN THE BARBARIAN   HOWARD, ROBERT E.   AC
  CONAN THE FREEBOOTER   HOWARD, R. & DE CAMP   AC
ITCH TRIALS AND THE LAW (1841)
                                   MACKAY, CHARLES   AR
  ROD SERLING'S TRIPLE W: WITCHES, WARLOCKS AND WEREWOLVES
                                   SERLING, ROD   AN
ITCH WAR   MATHESON, RICHARD   SS   STS 51 07
  BEST SCIENCE-FICTION STORIES: 1952, THE BLEILER & DIKTY AN
  BORN OF MAN AND WOMAN   MATHESON, RICHARD   AC
  SHOCK III   MATHESON, RICHARD   AC
  THEMES IN SCIENCE FICTION   KELLEY, LEO P.   AN
ITCH-MAKERS, THE   WANDREI, DONALD   SS   ARG 36 05
  EYE AND THE FINGER   WANDREI, DONALD   AC
ITCH, THE   VAN VOGT, A. E.   SS   UNK 43 02
  OUT OF THE UNKNOWN   VAN VOGT & HULL   AC
  ZACHERLEY'S VULTURE STEW   ZACHERLEY   AN
ITCHES IN THE CORNFIELD   JACOBI, CARL   SS
  PORTRAITS IN MOONLIGHT   JACOBI, CARL   AC
ITCHES MUST BURN   GUNN, JAMES E.   NV   ASF 56 08
  BURNING, THE   GUNN, JAMES E.   NO
ITCHES OF KARRES, THE   SCHMITZ, JAMES H.   NV   ASF 49 12
  *ASTOUNDING SCIENCE FICTION ANTHOLOGY, THE
                                   CAMPBELL, JOHN W. JR   AN
  *FIRST ASTOUNDING SCIENCE FICTION ANTHOLOGY, THE
                                   CAMPBELL, JOHN W. JR   AN
  SCIENCE FICTION HALL OF FAME VOLUME 2B BOVA, BEN   AN
  SECOND ASTOUNDING SCIENCE FICTION ANTHOLOGY, THE (PB)
                                   CAMPBELL, JOHN W. JR   AN
  TOWARD INFINITY   KNIGHT, DAMON   AN
ITCHES OF NUPAL, THE   PANGBORN, EDGAR   NV   CTM 74 03
  CONTINUUM 3   ELWOOD, ROGER   OA
ITCHFINDER, THE   WRIGHT, S. FOWLER   SS
  WITCHFINDER, THE   WRIGHT, S. FOWLER   AC
ITH A BLUNT INSTRUMENT   RUSSELL, ERIC FRANK   SS   UNK 41 12
  DARK TIDES   RUSSELL, ERIC FRANK   AC
ITH A FINGER IN MY I   GERROLD, DAVID   SS   DVS 72 02
  AGAIN, DANGEROUS VISIONS   ELLISON, HARLAN   OA
  WITH A FINGER IN MY I   GERROLD, DAVID   AC
ITH APOLOGIES TO ROYAL   GAMOW, GEORGE   MS   47
  MATHEMATICAL MAGPIE, THE   FADIMAN, CLIFTON   AN
ITH CROOKED HANDS   CRAIS, ROBERT   SS
  CLARION SF   WILHELM, KATE   OA
ITH FLAMING SWORDS   CARTMILL, CLEVE   NV   ASF 42 09
  *TREASURY OF SCIENCE FICTION, A CONKLIN, GROFF   AN
ITH FOLDED HANDS...   WILLIAMSON, JACK   NV   ASF 47 07
  DOORWAY INTO TIME   MOSKOWITZ, SAM   AN
  INVASION OF THE ROBOTS   ELWOOD, ROGER   AN
  MEN AND MACHINES   SILVERBERG, ROBERT   AN
  MODERN MASTERPIECES OF SCIENCE FICTION MOSKOWITZ, SAM AN
  PANDORA EFFECT, THE   WILLIAMSON, JACK   AC
  SCIENCE FICTION HALL OF FAME VOLUME 2A BOVA, BEN   AN
  *TREASURY OF SCIENCE FICTION, A CONKLIN, GROFF   AN
ITH FRIENDS LIKE THESE...   FOSTER, ALAN DEAN   SS   ASF 71 06
  1972 ANNUAL WORLD'S BEST SF, THE WOLLHEIM, DONALD A.   AN
ITH GOOD INTENTIONS   CHANDLER, A. BERTRAM   SS
  HARD WAY UP, THE   CHANDLER, A. BERTRAM   DC
ITH MALACE TO COME (SEE A MATTER OF ENERGY)
                                   BLISH, JAMES   TC
ITH MORNING COMES MISTFALL   MARTIN, GEORGE R. R.   SS   ASF 73 05
  BEST SCIENCE FICTION STORIES OF THE YEAR (1973)
                                   DEL REY, LESTER   AN
  NEBULA AWARD STORIES 9   WILHELM, KATE   AN
  SONG FOR LYA, A   MARTIN, GEORGE R. R.   AC
ITH REDFERN ON CAPELLA XII   SATTERFIELD, CHARLES NV GAL 55 11
  MIND PARTNER AND 8 OTHER NOVELETS FROM GALAXY
                                   GOLD, H. L.   AN
ITH REDFERN ON CAPELLA XII (AS CHAS. SATTERFIELD)
                                   POHL, FREDERIK   NV   GAL 55 11
  DIGITS AND DASTARDS   POHL, FREDERIK   AC
  STARS AROUND US, THE   HOSKINS, ROBERT   AN
ITH THE BENTFIN BOOMER BOYS ON LITTLE OLD NEW ALABAMA
                                   LUPOFF, RICHARD A.   NA   DVS 72 02
  AGAIN, DANGEROUS VISIONS   ELLISON, HARLAN   OA
ITH THE NIGHT MAIL   KIPLING, RUDYARD   NV   MCS 05 11
  ONE HUNDRED YEARS OF SCIENCE FICTION KNIGHT, DAMON   AN
  VISIONS OF TOMORROW   ELWOOD, ROGER   AN
  WONDERMAKERS   HOSKINS, ROBERT   AN
ITH THESE HANDS   KORNBLUTH, C. M.   NV   GAL 51 12
  ALPHA 6   SILVERBERG, ROBERT   AN
  BEST OF C. M. KORNBLUTH, THE   KORNBLUTH, C. M.   AC
  BEST SCIENCE FICTION STORIES OF C. M. KORNBLUTH
                                   KORNBLUTH, C. M.   AC

  EXPLORERS, THE   KORNBLUTH, C. M.   AC
  FUTURE TENSE   CURTIS, RICHARD   AN
  MINDWORM AND OTHER STORIES, THE KORNBLUTH, C. M.   AC
  NEW DREAMS THIS MORNING   BLISH, JAMES   AN
  SECOND ORBIT   DOHERTY, G. D.   AN
WITHIN THE NEBULA   HAMILTON, EDMOND   NV   WRT 28 05
  CRASHING SUNS   HAMILTON, EDMOND   AC
WITHIN THE PYRAMID   MILLER, R. DEWITT   SS   ASF 37 03
  *ADVENTURES IN TIME AND SPACE   HEALY & MCCOMAS   AN
  MORE ADVENTURES IN TIME AND SPACE HEALY & MCCOMAS   AN
WITHOUT A THOUGHT (FORTRESS SHIP)
                                   SABERHAGEN, FRED   SS   IFS 63 01
  BERSERKER   SABERHAGEN, FRED   AC
  MEN AND MACHINES   SILVERBERG, ROBERT   AN
WITHOUT BUGLES   TUBB, E. C.   SS   NWS 52 01
  ALIEN DUST   TUBB, E. C.   NO
WITHOUT COLORS   CALVINO, ITALO   SS
  COSMICOMICS   CALVINO, ITALO   OC
WITNESS, THE   RUSSELL, ERIC FRANK   SS   OWS 51 09
  DEEP SPACE   RUSSELL, ERIC FRANK   AC
  MODERN MASTERPIECES OF SCIENCE FICTION MOSKOWITZ, SAM AN
  VORTEX BLASTERS, THE   MOSKOWITZ, SAM   AN
WITNESSES, THE   SANSOM, WILLIAM   SS   44
  TIMELESS STORIES FOR TODAY AND TOMORROW BRADBURY, RAY AN
WIZARD   JANIFER, LAURENCE M.   SS   ASF 60 05
  IMPOSSIBLE?   JANIFER, LAURENCE M.   AC
WIZARD OF EARTHSEA, A   LE GUIN, URSULA K.   NO
  EARTHSEA   LE GUIN, URSULA K.   AC
WIZARD OF NEHWON-, THE   ANDERSON, POUL   IN
  BEST OF FRITZ LEIBER, THE   LEIBER, FRITZ   AC
WIZARD OF SCORPIO   AKERS, ALAN BURT   NV
  DAW SCIENCE FICTION READER, THE WOLLHEIM, DONALD A.   OA
WIZARD OF VENUS, THE   BURROUGHS, EDGAR R.   NV   NEW 64 05
  TALES OF THREE PLANETS   BURROUGHS, EDGAR R.   AC
WIZARD'S NEW MEETING, THE   REDGROVE, PETER   PM   69
  HOLDING YOUR EIGHT HANDS   LUCIE-SMITH, EDWARD   AN
WIZARDS AND WARRIORS   DE CAMP, L. SPRAGUE   IN
  SPELL OF SEVEN, THE   DE CAMP, L. SPRAGUE   AN
WIZARDS OF PUNG'S CORNERS, THE POHL, FREDERIK   NV   GAL 58 10
  AS TOMORROW BECOMES TODAY   SULLIVAN, CHARLES W.   AN
  CONNOISSEUR'S S. F.   BOARDMAN, TOM JR.   AN
  FREDERIK POHL OMNIBUS, THE   POHL, FREDERIK   AC
  MAN WHO ATE THE WORLD, THE   POHL, FREDERIK   AC
WOBBLIES IN THE MOON   LONG, FRANK BELKNAP NV TWS 43 06
  JOHN CARSTAIRS: SPACE DETECTIVE LONG, FRANK BELKNAP   AC
WOCKYJABBER   SCHENCK, HILBERT JR. PM FSF 60 05
  MATHEMATICAL MAGPIE, THE   FADIMAN, CLIFTON   AN
WOGGLEBEAST   PANGBORN, EDGAR   SS   FSF 65 01
  GOOD NEIGHBORS AND OTHER STRANGERS PANGBORN, EDGAR   AC
WOLF   MOORCOCK, MICHAEL   SS   66
  TIME DWELLER, THE   MOORCOCK, MICHAEL   AC
WOLF IN THE FOLD (ROBERT BLOCH)
                                   BLISH, JAMES   SA   STK 72 08
  STAR TREK 8   BLISH, JAMES   OC
WOLF PACK   MILLER, WALTER M. JR NV FAN 53 11
  BEYOND THE BARRIERS OF SPACE AND TIME MERRIL, JUDITH   AN
WOLF PACK, THE (LET FREEDOM RING)
                                   LEIBER, FRITZ   SN   AMZ 50 04
  NIGHT OF THE WOLF, THE   LEIBER, FRITZ   AC
WOLF PAIR, THE (THE NIGHT OF THE LONG KNIVES)
                                   LEIBER, FRITZ   NA   AMZ 60 01
  NIGHT OF THE WOLF, THE   LEIBER, FRITZ   AC
WOLF THAT FOLLOWS, THE   HARRISON, M. JOHN   NV   NWQ 74 01
  NEW WORLDS NO. 6   PLATT & BAILEY   OA
WOLF WOMAN, THE   BEDFORD-JONES, HENRY S. BBM 34
  FANTASTIC PULPS, THE   HAINING, PETER   AN
WOLFIE   COGSWELL, THEODORE R SS BEY 54 01
  WALL AROUND THE WORLD, THE   COGSWELL, THEODORE R   AC
WOLFRAM   ANDERSON, POUL   SS
  HOMEWARD AND BEYOND   ANDERSON, POUL   AC
WOLFRAM HUNTERS, THE   HOCH, EDWARD D.   SS   SMM 64 03
  CHRONICLES OF A COMER AND OTHER RELIGIOUS SCIENCE FICTION
  STORIES   ELWOOD, ROGER   AN
  GODS FOR TOMORROW   SANTESSON, HANS S.   AN
  RULERS OF MEN   SANTESSON, HANS S.   AN
WOLFSHEAD   HOWARD, ROBERT E.   SS   WRT 26 04
  WOLFSHEAD   HOWARD, ROBERT E.   AC
WOLLY WORLD OF BARNABY SHEEN, THE
                                   LAFFERTY, R. A.   SS   NMD 73
  FRONTIERS 2: THE NEW MIND   ELWOOD, ROGER   OA
WOLVES BEYOND THE BORDER   DE CAMP, L. SPRAGUE
                                   AND HOWARD, ROBERT E. SS C
  CONAN THE USURPER   HOWARD, R. & DE CAMP   AC
WOLVES DON'T CRY   ELLIOTT, BRUCE   SS   FSF 54 04
  GALAXY OF GHOULS   MERRIL, JUDITH   AN
  ROD SERLING'S TRIPLE W: WITCHES, WARLOCKS AND WEREWOLVES
                                   SERLING, ROD   AN
WOLVES OF DARKNESS   WILLIAMSON, JACK   NA   STT 32 01
  BEWARE MORE BEASTS   GHIDALIA, V.& ELWOOD   AN
WOMAN AT THE WINDOW   WANDREI, DONALD   SS
  EYE AND THE FINGER   WANDREI, DONALD   AC
WOMAN FROM ALTAIR, THE   BRACKETT, LEIGH   NV   STS 51 07
  BEST OF LEIGH BRACKETT, THE   BRACKETT, LEIGH   AC
WOMAN IN GRAY, THE   EVERETT, WALKER G.   SS   WRT 35 06
  OTHER WORLDS, THE   STONG, PHILIP D.   AN
WOMAN IN SUNLIGHT WITH MANDOLIN
                                   ALDISS, BRIAN W.   SS   ORB 73 12
  ORBIT 12   KNIGHT, DAMON   OA
WOMAN NAKED, A   PRIEST, CHRISTOPHER   SS   SFM 74 01
  BEST OF SCIENCE FICTION MONTHLY, THE SACKS, JANET   AN
  REAL-TIME WORLD   PRIEST, CHRISTOPHER   AC
WOMAN ON THE EDGE OF TIME   PIERCY, MARGE   NV
  AURORA: BEYOND EQUALITY   MCINTYRE & ANDERSON   OA
WOMAN WAITING   EMSHWILLER, CAROL   SS   ORB 70 07
  ORBIT 7   KNIGHT, DAMON   OA

WOMAN WAITING   TUTTLE, LISA   NV
  LONE STAR UNIVERSE   PROCTOR & UTLEY   OA
WOMAN WHO THOUGHT SHE COULD READ, THE
                                 DAVIDSON, AVRAM   SS   FSF 59 01
  OR ALL THE SEAS WITH OYSTERS   DAVIDSON, AVRAM   AC
WOMAN'S PLACE, A   CLIFTON, MARK   NV   GAL 55 05
  WORLD THAT COULDN'T BE AND 8 OTHER SF NOVELETS
                                 GOLD, H. L.   AN
WOMAN'S RIB   SCORTIA, THOMAS N. SS   GAL 72 07
  BEST SCIENCE FICTION STORIES OF THE YEAR (1972)
                                 DEL REY, LESTER   AN
  CAUTION! INFLAMMABLE!   SCORTIA, THOMAS N.   AC
  MARRIAGE AND THE FAMILY THROUGH SCIENCE FICTION
                                 CLEAR/WARRICK/&   AN
WOMANLY TALENT, A   MCCAFFREY, ANNE   SN   ASF 69 02
  TO RIDE PEGASUS   MCCAFFREY, ANNE   AC
WOMB TO TOMB   WESLEY, JOSEPH   SS   ASF 69 08
  ANALOG 8   CAMPBELL, JOHN W. JR   AN
  BEST SF: 1969   HARRISON & ALDISS   AN
WOMB, WITH A VIEW   UTLEY, STEVEN   SS   ALT 74
  ALTERNATES   GERROLD, DAVID   OA
WOMEN IN SCIENCE FICTION   SARGENT, PAMELA   IN
  WOMEN OF WONDER   SARGENT, PAMELA   AN
WOMEN MEN DON'T SEE, THE   TIPTREE, JAMES JR. NV   FSF 73 12
  BEST SCIENCE FICTION OF THE YEAR, THE NO. 3
                                 CARR, TERRY   AN
  BEST SF: 1974   HARRISON & ALDISS   AN
  WARM WORLDS AND OTHERWISE   TIPTREE, JAMES JR.   AC
WOMEN OF THE WOOD, THE   MERRITT, A.   SS   WRT 26 08
  FOX WOMAN & OTHER STORIES, THE MERRITT, A.   AC
WOMEN, THE   BRADBURY, RAY   SS   FFM 48 10
  FIEND IN YOU, THE   BEAUMONT, CHARLES   AN
  I SING THE BODY ELECTRIC   BRADBURY, RAY   AC
WON'T YOU WALK?   STURGEON, THEODORE NV   ASF 56 01
  DIMENSION 4   CONKLIN, GROFF   AN
WONDER AS I WANDER   WELLMAN, MANLY WADE SS FSF 62 03
  WHO FEARS THE DEVIL?   WELLMAN, MANLY WADE   AC
WONDER CHILD   SHALLIT, JOSEPH   NV   FAN 53 01
  BEST SCIENCE-FICTION STORIES: 1954, THE BLEILER & DIKTY AN
WONDER HORSE, THE   BYRAM, GEORGE   SS   ATL 57 08
  SF: THE BEST OF THE BEST   MERRIL, JUDITH   AN
  SF:58, THE YEAR'S GREATEST SCIENCE FICTION AND FANTASY
                                 MERRIL, JUDITH   AN
WONDERBIRD   BUDRYS, ALGIS
                             AND ELLISON, HARLAN   SS C INF 57 09
  PARTNERS IN WONDER   ELLISON, HARLAN   AC
WONDERFUL CONSPIRACY, THE   ROBINSON, SPIDER   SS
  CALLAHAN'S CROSSTIME SALOON   ROBINSON, SPIDER   AC
WONDERFUL COROT, THE   MITCHELL, EDWARD P. SS SUN 81 12
  CRYSTAL MAN, THE   MITCHELL, EDWARD P.   AC
WONDERFUL DEATH OF DUDLEY STONE, THE
                                 BRADBURY, RAY   SS   CHM 54 07
  *OCTOBER COUNTRY, THE   BRADBURY, RAY   AC
WONDERFUL DOG SUIT, THE   HALL, DONALD   SS
  10TH ANNUAL OF THE YEAR'S BEST S-F, THE MERRIL, JUDITH AN
WONDERFUL ICE CREAM SUIT, THE   BRADBURY, RAY   PL   SEP 58 10
  WONDERFUL ICE CREAM SUIT AND OTHER PLAYS, THE
                                 BRADBURY, RAY   AC
WONDERFUL ICE CREAM SUIT, THE (THE MAGIC WHITE SUIT)
                                 BRADBURY, RAY   SS   SEP 58 10
  DAY IT RAINED FOREVER, THE   BRADBURY, RAY   AC
  MEDICINE FOR MELANCHOLY, A   BRADBURY, RAY   AC
  VINTAGE BRADBURY, THE   BRADBURY, RAY   AC
WONDERFUL MAN, THE (THE CHANGELING)
                                 VAN VOGT, A. E.   SN   ASF 44 04
  BEAST, THE   VAN VOGT, A. E.   NO
WONDERFUL WORLD OF FIGURES, THE
                                 FORD, COREY   AR   61
  MATHEMATICAL MAGPIE, THE   FADIMAN, CLIFTON   AN
WONDERFUL WORLD OF GRISWALD TRACTORS, THE
                                 DISCH, THOMAS M.   SS   NWQ 72 03
  NEW WORLDS QUARTERLY NO. 3   MOORCOCK, MICHAEL   OA
  WHITE FANG GOES DINGO AND OTHER FUNNY S.F. STORIES
                                 DISCH, THOMAS M.   AC
WONDERFUL, ALL-PURPOSE TRANSMOGRIFIER, THE
                                 MALZBERG, BARRY N. SS   FST 74
  FINAL STAGE   FERMAN & MALZBERG   OA
WONDERS OF WEINBAUM, THE   MOSKOWITZ, SAM   IN
  MARTIAN ODYSSEY, A   WEINBAUM, STANLEY G.   AC
WOODS GROW DARKER, THE   DRAKE, LEAH BODINE PM   FSF 55 11
  BEST FROM FANTASY AND SCIENCE FICTION: 6
                                 BOUCHER, ANTHONY   AN
WORD "RANDOM", DELIBERATELY REPEATED, THE
                                 SHIRLEY, JOHN   SS   CLR 73 03
  CLARION III   WILSON, ROBIN SCOTT   OA
WORD FOR WORLD IS FOREST, THE   LE GUIN, URSULA K. NV   DVS 72 02
  AGAIN, DANGEROUS VISIONS   ELLISON, HARLAN   OA
WORD FROM OUR SPONSOR, A   BROWN, FREDRIC   SS   OWS 51 09
  HONEYMOON IN HELL   BROWN, FREDRIC   AC
WORD FROM THE (HUMAN) EDITOR..., A
                                 HARRISON, HARRY   IN
  WAR WITH THE ROBOTS   HARRISON, HARRY   AC
WORD FROM THE EDITOR, A   FAST, JULIUS   IN
  OUT OF THIS WORLD   FAST, JULIUS   AN
WORD FROM THE EDITOR, A   HOSKINS, ROBERT   IN   INY 70 01
  INFINITY 1   HOSKINS, ROBERT   OA
WORD IN ADVANCE, A   DEFORD, MIRIAM ALLEN IN
  ELSEWHERE, ELSEWHEN, ELSEHOW   DEFORD, MIRIAM ALLEN   AC
WORD NOT WRITTEN, THE   BRUNNER, JOHN   NV   SFA 62 06
  TIMES WITHOUT NUMBER   BRUNNER, JOHN   NO
WORD OF HONOR   BLOCH, ROBERT   SS   PBY 58 08
  *BLOOD RUNS COLD   BLOCH, ROBERT   AC
  LAST TRAIN TO LIMBO   PLAYBOY, EDITORS OF   AN

PLAYBOY BOOK OF SCIENCE FICTION AND FANTASY, THE
                                 PLAYBOY, EDITORS OF   AN
WORD OF UNBINDING, THE   LE GUIN, URSULA K. SS   FAN 64 01
  GOLDEN ROAD, THE   KNIGHT, DAMON   AN
  WINDS TWELVE QUARTERS, THE   LE GUIN, URSULA K.   AC
WORD TO SPACE, THE   SANDERS, WINSTON P. SS FSF 60 09
  OTHER WORLDS, OTHER GODS   MOHS, MAYO   AN
WORD TO THE READER, A   HURLEY, RICHARD J. IN
  TIME MACHINE AND OTHER STORIES, THE (PB) WELLS, H. G. AC
WORD TO THE WISE   NUETZEL, CHARLES   SS
  IMAGES OF TOMORROW   NUETZEL, CHARLES   AC
WORD, THE   CLINGERMAN, MILDRED SS FSF 53 11
  CUPFUL OF SPACE, A   CLINGERMAN, MILDRED   AC
  PORTALS OF TOMORROW   DERLETH, AUGUST   AN
WORDLESS ONES, THE   SELLINGS, ARTHUR   SS
  *TIME TRANSFER   SELLINGS, ARTHUR   AC
WORDS OF GURU, THE   KORNBLUTH, C. M.   SS   STI 41 06
  BEST OF C. M. KORNBLUTH, THE   KORNBLUTH, C. M.   AC
  CHILDREN OF WONDER   TENN, WILLIAM   AN
  GOLDEN ROAD, THE   KNIGHT, DAMON   AN
  *MILE BEYOND THE MOON, A   KORNBLUTH, C. M.   AC
WORDS OF WARNING   HAMILTON, ALEX   SS   72
  BEST SF: 1972   HARRISON & ALDISS   AN
WORDSMITH   FORTEY, BRYN   SS   NWR 76 28
  NEW WRITINGS IN SF. 28   BULMER, KENNETH   OA
WORK OF ART, A (ART-WORK)   BLISH, JAMES   SS   SFS 56 07
  *BEST SCIENCE FICTION STORIES OF JAMES BLISH
                                 BLISH, JAMES   AC
  BEST SF 6   CRISPIN, EDMUND   AN
  *GALACTIC CLUSTER   BLISH, JAMES   AC
  NEW DREAMS THIS MORNING   BLISH, JAMES   AN
  SCIENCE FICTION SHOWCASE   KORNBLUTH, MARY   AN
  STARS AROUND US, THE   HOSKINS, ROBERT   AN
  WORLDS OF SCIENCE FICTION, THE MILLS, ROBERT P.   AN
WORK POEM, THE   INOUYE, JON   PM
  NIGHT TIDE, A   INOUYE, JON   OC
WORKING IN THE SPACESHIP YARDS   ALDISS, BRIAN W.   SS   PUN 69 04
  BEST SF: 1969   HARRISON & ALDISS   AN
  MOMENT OF ECLIPSE, THE   ALDISS, BRIAN W.   AC
WORLD ABOUNDING   LAFFERTY, R. A.   NV   FSF 71 02
  STRANGE DOINGS   LAFFERTY, R. A.   AC
WORLD AS WILL AND WALLPAPER, THE
                                 LAFFERTY, R. A.   SS   FUC 73
  BEST SCIENCE FICTION OF THE YEAR, THE NO. 3
                                 CARR, TERRY   AN
  FUTURE CITY   ELWOOD, ROGER   OA
WORLD BETWEEN, THE   VANCE, JACK   NV
  WORLD BETWEEN AND OTHER STORIES, THE VANCE, JACK   DC
  WORLDS OF JACK VANCE, THE   VANCE, JACK   AC
WORLD BEYOND, THE   HOSKINS, ROBERT   IN
  EDGE OF NEVER, THE   HOSKINS, ROBERT   AC
WORLD BY THE TALE, A   MCKETTRIG, SEATON SS   ASF 63 10
  ANALOG 3   CAMPBELL, JOHN W. JR   AN
WORLD CALLED MAANEREK, A (SEE MEMORY)
                                 ANDERSON, POUL   TC
WORLD HE LEFT BEHIND, THE   SILVERBERG, ROBERT SS   NEB 59 02
  GODLING, GO HOME!   SILVERBERG, ROBERT   AC
WORLD IN A BOTTLE   LANG, ALLEN KIM   NV   GAL 60 10
  ELSEWHERE AND ELSEWHEN   CONKLIN, GROFF   AN
WORLD IN WHICH I DISAPPEARED, THE
                                 DNIEPROV, ANATOLY SS   ISF 68 06
  LAST DOOR TO AIYA   GINSBURG, MIRRA   AN
WORLD IS A SPHERE, THE   PANGBORN, EDGAR   NV   UNI 73 03
  UNIVERSE 3   CARR, TERRY   OA
WORLD IS MINE, THE   PADGETT, LEWIS   NV   ASF 43 06
  ROBOTS HAVE NO TAILS   PADGETT, LEWIS   AC
WORLD MUST NEVER KNOW, THE   EDMONDSON, G. C.   SS   FSF 63 04
  STRANGER THAN YOU THINK   EDMONDSON, G. C.   DC
WORLD NAMED CLEOPATRA, A   ANDERSON, POUL   FA   NEW 74 01
  MANY WORLDS OF POUL ANDERSON, THE ANDERSON, POUL   AC
  WORLD NAMED CLEOPATRA, A   ANDERSON, POUL   AC
WORLD OF A THOUSAND COLORS   SILVERBERG, ROBERT SS   SUP 57 06
  DIMENSION THIRTEEN   SILVERBERG, ROBERT   AC
WORLD OF CRYSTAL CITIES, THE   GRIFFITH, GEORGE   SS   PRS 00 04
  WORLDS APART   LOCKE, GEORGE   AN
WORLD OF DIFFERENTS, A   BEAUMONT, CHARLES SS   NEW 58
  YONDER   BEAUMONT, CHARLES   AC
WORLD OF GRAY   SPINRAD, NORMAN   SS   DEM 73
  DEMON KIND   ELWOOD, ROGER   OA
WORLD OF HEART'S DESIRE, THE (ALSO AS THE STORE OF THE WORLDS)
                                 SHECKLEY, ROBERT   SS   PBY 59
  FROM THE "S" FILE   PLAYBOY, EDITORS OF   AN
WORLD OF MISTERS (AS GENE ELLERMAN)
                                 WELLS, BASIL   SS   FBK 50 06
  PLANETS OF ADVENTURE   WELLS, BASIL   AC
WORLD OF MYRION FLOWERS, THE   KORNBLUTH, C. M.
                             AND POHL, FREDERIK   SS C FSF 61 10
  HUMAN AND OTHER BEINGS   DEGRAEFF, ALLEN   AN
  THEMES IN SCIENCE FICTION   KELLEY, LEO P.   AN
  WONDER EFFECT, THE   POHL, F. & KORNBLUTH   AC
WORLD OF NULL-A, THE   VAN VOGT, A. E.   NO   ASF 45 08
  TRIAD   VAN VOGT, A. E.   AC
WORLD OF SOUND, A   STAPLEDON, OLAF   SS   SFM 74 11
  BEST OF SCIENCE FICTION MONTHLY, THE SACKS, JANET   AN
WORLD OF TALENT, A   DICK, PHILIP K.   NV   GAL 54 10
  VARIABLE MAN, THE   DICK, PHILIP K.   AC
WORLD OF THE MYTH   ELLISON, HARLAN   NV   KNT 64 06
  I HAVE NO MOUTH, AND I MUST SCREAM ELLISON, HARLAN   AC
WORLD OF THE RED SUN, THE   SIMAK, CLIFFORD D. SS   WOS 31 12
  BEFORE THE GOLDEN AGE   ASIMOV, ISAAC   AN
WORLD OF THE WAR GOD, THE   GRIFFITH, GEORGE   SS   PRS 00 02
  WORLDS APART   LOCKE, GEORGE   AN
WORLD OF THE WARS   MCALLISTER, BRUCE SS   NEW 71 04
  MARS, WE LOVE YOU   HIPOLITO & MCNELLY   AN
WORLD OF WILLIAM GRESHAM, THE   BOND, NELSON S.   NV
  NO TIME LIKE THE FUTURE   BOND, NELSON S.   AC

WORLD OF WULKINS, THE   YELLOW PILL, THE

WORLD OF WULKINS, THE   LONG, FRANK BELKNAP SS   TWS 48 04
*OTHER SIDE OF THE MOON, THE   DERLETH, AUGUST   AN
  RIM OF THE UNKNOWN   LONG, FRANK BELKNAP   AC
WORLD OTALMI MADE, THE   HARRISON, HARRY   SN   SFA 58 06
  GREAT SCIENCE FICTION ADVENTURES SHAW, LARRY T.   AN
WORLD OUTSIDE, THE   SILVERBERG, ROBERT NA   GAL 70 10
  WORLD INSIDE, THE   SILVERBERG, ROBERT   NO
WORLD THAT COULDN'T BE, THE   SIMAK, CLIFFORD D. NV   GAL 58 01
  WORLD THAT COULDN'T BE AND 8 OTHER SF NOVELETS
                             GOLD, H. L.   AN
WORLD THAT JONES MADE, THE   DICK, PHILIP K.   NO   ACE 56
  SCIENCE FICTION SPECIAL 1 ANONYMOUS   AN
WORLD THAT WOMB MADE, THE   NUETZEL, CHARLES   SS
  IMAGES OF TOMORROW   NUETZEL, CHARLES   AC
WORLD THE CHILDREN MADE, THE (SEE THE VELDT)
                             BRADBURY, RAY   TC
WORLD WAR TWO   EFFINGER, GEO. ALEC SS   VTX 73 10
  ALPHA 7   SILVERBERG, ROBERT   AN
  MIXED FEELINGS   EFFINGER, GEO. ALEC   AC
WORLD WELL LOST, THE   STURGEON, THEODORE SS   USF 53 06
  E PLURIBUS UNICORN   STURGEON, THEODORE   AC
  SOCIAL PROBLEMS THROUGH SCIENCE FICTION GREENBERG/MILSTEAD/& AN
  STARSHINE   STURGEON, THEODORE   AC
  STRANGE BED FELLOWS   SCORTIA, THOMAS N.   AN
  *TWISTED   CONKLIN, GROFF   AN
WORLD WHERE WISHES WORKED, THE GOLDIN, STEPHEN SS   PRT 71
  PROTOSTARS   GERROLD & GOLDIN   OA
WORLD WITHOUT CHILDREN   KNIGHT, DAMON   NA   GAL 51 12
  5 GALAXY SHORT NOVELS   GOLD, H. L.   AN
WORLD WITHOUT STARS (THE ANCIENT GODS)
                             ANDERSON, POUL   NO   ASF 66 06
  WORLDS OF POUL ANDERSON, THE ANDERSON, POUL   AC
WORLD WITHOUT, THE   HERBERT, BENSON   SS   WOS 31 02
  FROM OFF THIS WORLD   MARGULIES & FRIEND   AN
WORLD'S GREATEST SALESMAN, THE O'NEILL, SCOTT   SS
  MARTIAN SEXPOT   O'NEILL, SCOTT   AC
WORLD-TIMER, THE   BLOCH, ROBERT   SS   FAN 60 08
  FEAR TODAY, GONE TOMORROW   BLOCH, ROBERT   AC
WORLDMASTER   LAUMER, KEITH   NV   WOT 65 11
  ONCE THERE WAS A GIANT   LAUMER, KEITH   AC
  UNDEFEATED, THE   LAUMER, KEITH   AC
WORLDS ENOUGH   THOMPSON, DON   SS
  BEYOND TIME   LEY, SANDRA   OA
WORLDS OF CHAD OLIVER: A BIOGRAPHICAL INTRODUCTION
                             NOLAN, WILLIAM F.   IN
  EDGE OF FOREVER, THE   OLIVER, CHAD   AC
WORLDS OF IF, THE   WEINBAUM, STANLEY G. SS   WOS 35 08
  BEST OF STANLEY G. WEINBAUM, THE WEINBAUM, STANLEY G. AC
  DAWN OF FLAME   WEINBAUM, STANLEY G.   AC
  MARTIAN ODYSSEY AND OTHER SCIENCE FICTION TALES, A
                             WEINBAUM, STANLEY G. AC
  MARTIAN ODYSSEY AND OTHERS, A WEINBAUM, STANLEY G. AC
  OTHER DIMENSIONS   SILVERBERG, ROBERT   AN
WORLDS OF MONTY WILLSON, THE NOLAN, WILLIAM F. SS   AMZ 71 07
  ALIEN HORIZONS   NOLAN, WILLIAM F.   AC
WORLDS OF THE IMPERIUM (SELECTION FROM)
                             LAUMER, KEITH   EX   FAN 61 02
  CENTURY OF SCIENCE FICTION, A KNIGHT, DAMON   AN
WORLDS OF WONDER   STAPLEDON, OLAF   AC   FPB 49
  QUADRATIC   CRAWFORD, WILLIAM L.   AN
WORLDS TO KILL   ELLISON, HARLAN   NV   IFS 68 03
  BEAST THAT SHOUTED LOVE AT THE HEART OF THE WORLD, THE
                             ELLISON, HARLAN   AC
WORLDS WITHOUT END   SIMAK, CLIFFORD D. NA   FUT 56 WI
  WORLDS WITHOUT END   SIMAK, CLIFFORD D.   AC
WORM IN THE BUD   RANKINE, JOHN   SS   NWR 68 12
  NEW WRITINGS IN SF. 12   CARNELL, JOHN   OA
WORM IN THE ROSE, THE   SCORTIA, THOMAS N. SS   SWK 72 05
  CAUTION¡ INFLAMMABLE¡   SCORTIA, THOMAS N.   AC
WORM IN THE WOODWORK   TUBB, E. C.   NV   ASF 62 01
  TEN FROM TOMORROW   TUBB, E. C.   AC
WORM THAT FLIES, THE   ALDISS, BRIAN W.   SS   FRS 68
  FARTHEST REACHES, THE   ELDER, JOSEPH   OA
  MOMENT OF ECLIPSE, THE   ALDISS, BRIAN W.   AC
  WORLD'S BEST SCIENCE FICTION: 1969 WOLLHEIM & CARR   AN
WORM, THE   KELLER, DAVID H. MD. SS   AMZ 29 03
  BEST OF AMAZING, THE   ROSS, JOSEPH   AN
  BR-R-R-¡   CONKLIN, GROFF   AN
  CREATURES FROM BEYOND   CARR, TERRY   AN
  *STRANGE PORTS OF CALL   DERLETH, AUGUST   AN
  TALES FROM UNDERWOOD   KELLER, DAVID H. MD.   AC
WORM, THE   SCORTIA, THOMAS N. NV
  BEWARE MORE BEASTS   GHIDALIA, V.& ELWOOD   AN
WORRYWORT   SIMAK, CLIFFORD D. SS   GAL 53 09
  BEST SF 2   CRISPIN, EDMUND   AN
  OPERATION FUTURE   CONKLIN, GROFF   AN
WORSHIP NIGHT   NEVILLE, KRIS   SS   FSF 53 11
  SEA OF SPACE, A   NOLAN, WILLIAM F.   AN
WOULDN'T YOU AFTER A JAUNT OF 964,000,000,000,000 MILLION
  MILES?   PATCHEN, KENNETH   PM   NDR 49
  HOLDING YOUR EIGHT HANDS   LUCIE-SMITH, EDWARD   AN
WOUND, THE   FAST, HOWARD   SS   70
  EVIL EARTHS   ALDISS, BRIAN W.   AN
  GENERAL ZAPPED AN ANGEL, THE FAST, HOWARD   OC
  SCIENCE FACT/FICTION   FARRELL/GAGE/&   AN
WRECK OF THE SHIP JOHN B., THE ROBINSON, FRANK M. NV   PBY 67 06
  BEST SF: 1967   HARRISON & ALDISS   AN
  DEAD ASTRONAUT, 10 STORIES OF SPACE FLIGHT, THE
                             PLAYBOY, EDITORS OF AN
WRENS IN GRAMPA'S WHISKERS, THE
                             PANGBORN, EDGAR   SS   FSF 60 04
  GOOD NEIGHBORS AND OTHER STRANGERS PANGBORN, EDGAR   AC
WRITE SCIENCE FICTION? RIGHT HOLLISTER, BERNARD C AR   74
  ANOTHER TOMORROW   HOLLISTER, BERNARD C AN
WRITER AS TEACHER, THE   SALLIS, JAMES   AR   CLR 72 02
  CLARION II   WILSON, ROBIN SCOTT OA

WRITING OF THE RAT, THE   BLISH, JAMES   SS   GAL 56 06
  ANYWHEN   BLISH, JAMES   AC
WRITTEN IN THE STARS   YOUNG, ROBERT F.   SS   VSF 57 09
  WORLDS OF ROBERT F. YOUNG, THE YOUNG, ROBERT F.   AC
WRONG WORLD, THE   MCINTOSH, J. T.   NV   GAL 60 12
  ELSEWHERE AND ELSEWHEN   CONKLIN, GROFF   AN
WRONG-WAY STREET   NIVEN, LARRY   SS   GAL 65 04
  FIRST FLIGHTS TO THE MOON   CLEMENT, HAL   AN
  NINTH GALAXY READER, THE   POHL, FREDERICK   AN
  VOYAGERS IN TIME   SILVERBERG, ROBERT   AN
X MARKS THE PEDWALK   LEIBER, FRITZ   SS   WOT 63 04
  ABC OF SCIENCE FICTION, AN BOARDMAN, TOM JR.   AN
  BEST SCIENCE FICTION FROM WORLDS OF TOMORROW, THE
                             POHL, FREDERICK   AN
  NIGHTMARE AGE   POHL, FREDERICK   AN
  THEMES IN SCIENCE FICTION   KELLEY, LEO P.   AN
[X] YES   DISCH, THOMAS M.   SS   FAN 69 12
  *GETTING INTO DEATH   DISCH, THOMAS M.   AC
X+1   POE, EDGAR ALLEN   PM
  FANTASIA MATHEMATICA   FADIMAN, CLIFTON   AN
  "X" FOR "EXPENDABLE"   BAILEY, WILLIAM C. NV   DSF 52 12
  WAY OUT   HOWARD, IVAN   AN
X-2076   DILLINGHAM, PETER PM
  2076: THE AMERICAN TRICENTENNIAL BRYANT, EDWARD   OA
XENOFREAK/XENOPHOBE   BRYANT, EDWARD   SS   DYS 75
  DYSTOPIAN VISIONS   ELWOOD, ROGER   OA
XENOPHOBIA   VERNON, ROGER LEE NV
  SPACE FRONTIERS, THE   VERNON, ROGER LEE   AC
XI EFFECT, THE   LATHAM, PHILIP   SS   ASF 50 01
  BEST SF   CRISPIN, EDMUND   AN
  DECADE THE 1940S   ALDISS & HARRISON   AN
  *IMAGINATION UNLIMITED   BLEILER & DIKTY   AN
XONG OF XUXAN   RUSSELL, RAY   SS   PBY 70 10
  CRISIS   ELWOOD, ROGER   OA
  WEIRD SHOW   PLAYBOY, EDITORS OF AN
  WONDERMAKERS 2   HOSKINS, ROBERT   AN
YACHID AND YECHIDA   SINGER, ISAAC B.   SS   64
  10TH ANNUAL OF THE YEAR'S BEST S-F, THE MERRIL, JUDITH AN
YAHRZEIT   MALZBERG, BARRY N. SS   TTM 73
  TEN TOMORROWS   ELWOOD, ROGER   OA
YANKEE EXODUS   GOLDSMITH, RUTH M. SS   FSF 53 07
  BEST SCIENCE-FICTION STORIES: 1954, THE BLEILER & DIKTY AN
YARST¡   GERROLD, DAVID   SS   NEW 72 AC
  WITH A FINGER IN MY I   GERROLD, DAVID   AC
YE PHANTASIE WRITER AND HIS CATTE
                             MCCLINTIC, WINONA PM   FSF 58 03
  BEST FROM FANTASY AND SCIENCE FICTION: 8
                             BOUCHER, ANTHONY   AN
YEAR BY YEAR THE EVIL GAINS   ALDISS, BRIAN W.   NV   NWR 75 27
  NEW WRITINGS IN SF. 27   BULMER, KENNETH   OA
YEAR DAY   KUTTNER, HENRY   SS   NEW 53 AC
  AHEAD OF TIME   KUTTNER, HENRY   AC
  BEST OF HENRY KUTTNER 1, THE KUTTNER, HENRY   AC
YEAR IN S-F, THE   MERRIL, JUDITH   MS
  6TH ANNUAL OF THE YEAR'S BEST S-F, THE MERRIL, JUDITH AN
YEAR NINE   CONNOLLY, CYRIL   SS   46
  PAST, PRESENT, AND FUTURE PERFECT WOLFE, J&FITZ GERALD AN
YEAR OF THE JACKPOT, THE   HEINLEIN, ROBERT A. NV   GAL 52 03
  END OF THE WORLD, THE   WOLLHEIM, DONALD A.   AN
  LOOKING AHEAD   ALLEN, D. & L.   AN
  MENACE FROM EARTH, THE   HEINLEIN, ROBERT A.   AC
  NIGHTMARE AGE   POHL, FREDERICK   AN
  SCIENCE FICTION FOR PEOPLE WHO HATE SCIENCE FICTION
                             CARR, TERRY   AN
  SECOND GALAXY READER OF SCIENCE FICTION GOLD, H. L.   AN
  SHADOW OF TOMORROW   POHL, FREDERICK   AN
  SHOCKING THING, A   KNIGHT, DAMON   AN
  WINDOWS INTO TOMORROW   SILVERBERG, ROBERT   AN
YEAR OF THE QUIET COMPUTER, THE
                             ALDISS, BRIAN W.   SS   NWR 75 26
  NEW WRITINGS IN SF. 26   BULMER, KENNETH   OA
YEAR 2018¡ (SEE THEY SHALL HAVE STARS)
                             BLISH, JAMES   TC
YEAR'S S-F, THE, SUMMATION AND HONORABLE MENTIONS
                             MERRIL, JUDITH   MS
  SF: THE YEAR'S GREATEST SCIENCE FICTION AND FANTASY
                             MERRIL, JUDITH   AN
  SF:57, THE YEAR'S GREATEST SCIENCE FICTION AND FANTASY
                             MERRIL, JUDITH   AN
  SF:58, THE YEAR'S GREATEST SCIENCE FICTION AND FANTASY
                             MERRIL, JUDITH   AN
  SF:59, THE YEAR'S GREATEST SCIENCE FICTION AND FANTASY
                             MERRIL, JUDITH   AN
  5TH ANNUAL OF THE YEAR'S BEST S-F, THE MERRIL, JUDITH AN
YEARBOOK, THE   MALZBERG, BARRY N. SS   FSF 71 05
  OUT FROM GANYMEDE   MALZBERG, BARRY N.   AC
  "YEARS DRAW NIGH, THE"   DEL REY, LESTER   SS   ASF 51 10
  *BEACHHEADS IN SPACE   DERLETH, AUGUST   AN
  MORTALS AND MONSTERS   DEL REY, LESTER   AC
YEARS, THE   YOUNG, ROBERT F.   SS   GAL 72 09
  BEST SF: 1972   HARRISON & ALDISS   AN
YEAST MEN, THE   KELLER, DAVID H. MD. SS   AMZ 28 04
  TALES FROM UNDERWOOD   KELLER, DAVID H. MD.   AC
YEHUDI PRINCIPLE, THE   BROWN, FREDRIC   SS   ASF 44 05
  ANGELS AND SPACESHIPS   BROWN, FREDRIC   AC
  BEST OF FREDRIC BROWN, THE BROWN, FREDRIC   AC
YELLOW MEN OF MARS   BURROUGHS, EDGAR R. NV   AMZ 41 08
  LLANA OF GATHOL   BURROUGHS, EDGAR R.   NO
YELLOW PILL, THE   PHILLIPS, ROG   SS   ASF 58 10
  ASTOUNDING-ANALOG READER, THE VOLUME TWO HARRISON & ALDISS AN
  BEST SF 4   CRISPIN, EDMUND   AN
  INTRODUCTORY PSYCHOLOGY THROUGH SCIENCE FICTION
                             KATZ/WARRICK/&   AN
  SCIENCE FICTION   BRODKIN & PEARSON   AN
  SF:59, THE YEAR'S GREATEST SCIENCE FICTION AND FANTASY
                             MERRIL, JUDITH   AN

YELLOW ROOM, THE   CHEEVER, JOHN   NV   PBY 68 01
  MASKS   PLAYBOY, EDITORS OF AN
YELLOW SIGN, THE (1895)   CHAMBERS, ROBERT W.   NV   FFM 43 09
  EDGE OF NEVER, THE   HOSKINS, ROBERT   AN
YELLOW STREAK HERO (SEE NIGHT VIGIL)
                          ELLISON, HARLAN   TC
YELLOWHEAD   DANN, JACK M.
  AND ZEBROWSKI, GEORGE   SS C
  NEW CONSTELLATIONS   DISCH & NAYLOR   OA
YES-MEN OF VENUS, THE   GOULART, RON   SS   AMZ 63 07
  WHAT'S BECOME OF SCREWLOOSE? AND OTHER INQUIRIES
                          GOULART, RON   AC
YES, BUT...   BRODE, ANTHONY   PM   FSF 57 09
  BEST FROM FANTASY AND SCIENCE FICTION: 7
                          BOUCHER, ANTHONY   AN
YES, VIRGINIA   EMSHWILLER, CAROL   SS   TRV
  JOY IN OUR CAUSE   EMSHWILLER, CAROL   AC
YES, WE HAVE NO RICHARD   FRIEDMAN, BRUCE JAY SS   FSF 60 11
  TWENTY YEARS OF FANTASY & SCIENCE FICTION
                          FERMAN & MILLS   AN
YES, WE'LL GATHER AT THE RIVER BRADBURY, RAY   SS   NEW 69 04
  I SING THE BODY ELECTRIC   BRADBURY, RAY   AC
YESTERDAY HOUSE   LEIBER, FRITZ   NV   GAL 52 08
  ALPHA 5   SILVERBERG, ROBERT   AN
  BOOK OF FRITZ LEIBER, THE   LEIBER, FRITZ   AC
YESTERDAY WAS MONDAY   STURGEON, THEODORE   SS   UNK 41 06
  FROM UNKNOWN WORLDS   CAMPBELL, JOHN W. JR   AN
  *SCIENCE FICTION ADVENTURES IN DIMENSION CONKLIN, GROFF AN
  UNKNOWN, THE   BENSEN, D. R.   AN
YESTERDAY'S FANTASY, TODAY'S FACT- AN INTRODUCTION
                          OLNEY, ROSS R.   IN
  TALES OF TIME AND SPACE   OLNEY, ROSS R.   AN
YESTERDAY, TOMORROW, AND THE DESERT
                          ALDISS, BRIAN W.   SI
  EVIL EARTHS   ALDISS, BRIAN W.   AN
YESTERDAYS' GARDENS   BYRNE, JOHNNY   SS   SCF 65 11
  11TH ANNUAL OF THE YEAR'S BEST S-F, THE MERRIL, JUDITH AN
YESTERYEAR (D. C. FONTANA) FOSTER, ALAN DEAN   SA   SLG 74 01
  STAR TREK LOG ONE   FOSTER, ALAN DEAN   OC
YET MORE PENGUIN SCIENCE FICTION
                          ALDISS, BRIAN W.   AN   PEN 64
  PENGUIN SCIENCE FICTION OMNIBUS, THE ALDISS, BRIAN W.   AN
YET WHAT ARE ALL...   CARROLL, LEWIS   PM
  FANTASIA MATHEMATICA   FADIMAN, CLIFTON   AN
YHREE LINES OF OLD FRENCH MERRITT, A.   SS   ASW 19 08
  FOX WOMAN & OTHER STORIES, THE MERRITT, A.   AC
YLLA (I'LL NOT LOOK FOR WINE) BRADBURY, RAY   SS   MCL 50 01
  MARTIAN CHRONICLES, THE   BRADBURY, RAY   AC
  *OUTER REACHES, THE   DERLETH, AUGUST   AN
  VINTAGE BRADBURY, THE   BRADBURY, RAY   AC
YLLIAN WAY, THE (SEE PROTOCOL) LAUMER, KEITH   TC
YO HO HOKA¡   ANDERSON, POUL
  AND DICKSON, GORDON R.   NV C FSF 55 03
  EARTHMAN'S BURDEN   ANDERSON, P.&DICKSON AC
YO-HO, AND UP   DAVIDSON, AVRAM   SS   FSF 60 12
  STRANGE SEAS AND SHORES   DAVIDSON, AVRAM   AC
YOU AND ME AND THE CONTINUUM BALLARD, J. G.   SS   IMP 66 03
  ENGLAND SWINGS SF   MERRIL, JUDITH   AN
  LOVE & NAPALM: EXPORT U.S.A. BALLARD, J. G.   AC
  SPACE-TIME JOURNAL, THE   MERRIL, JUDITH   AN
YOU ARE HERE   EISENSTEIN, ALEX
  AND EISENSTEIN, PHYLLIS   NV C NDM 77 07
  NEW DIMENSIONS 7   SILVERBERG, ROBERT   OA
YOU ARE WHAT YOU WRITE   ELLISON, HARLAN   AR   CLR 72 02
  CLARION II   WILSON, ROBIN SCOTT   OA
YOU ARE WITH IT¡   STANTON, WILL   SS   FSF 61 12
  CENTURY OF SCIENCE FICTION, A KNIGHT, DAMON   AN
YOU CAN'T BEAT BRAINS (SEE ISAAC ASIMOV)
                          DE CAMP, L. SPRAGUE   TC
YOU CAN'T HAVE THEM ALL   BEAUMONT, CHARLES   SS   PBY 56 08
  BEST FANTASY STORIES   ALDISS, BRIAN W.   AN
  FIEND, THE   PLAYBOY, EDITORS OF AN
  YONDER   BEAUMONT, CHARLES   AC
YOU CAN'T SAY THAT   CARTMILL, CLEVE   NV   NTS 51
  NEW TALES OF SPACE AND TIME HEALY, RAYMOND J.   OA
YOU COULD BE WRONG   BLOCH, ROBERT   SS   AMZ 55 03
  ATOMS AND EVIL   BLOCH, ROBERT   AC
YOU CREATED US   GODWIN, TOM   SS   FUN 55 10
  BEST SCIENCE FICTION STORIES AND NOVELS: 1956
                          DIKTY, T. E.   AN
  6 FROM WORLDS BEYOND   DIKTY, T. E.   AN
YOU GET LOTS OF YESTERDAYS, LOTS OF TOMORROWS, AND ONLY
  ONE TODAY   JAMES, LAURENCE   SS   NWR 75 26
  NEW WRITINGS IN SF. 26   BULMER, KENNETH   OA
YOU GOT TO HAVE BRAINS   BLOCH, ROBERT   SS   FUN 56 01
  ATOMS AND EVIL   BLOCH, ROBERT   AC
YOU KNOW WHAT, TEACHER?   HENDERSON, ZENNA   SS   EQM 54 09
  HOLDING WONDER   HENDERSON, ZENNA   AC
YOU KNOW WILLIE   COGSWELL, THEODORE R SS   FSF 57 05
  SF: THE BEST OF THE BEST   MERRIL, JUDITH   AN
  SF:58, THE YEAR'S GREATEST SCIENCE FICTION AND FANTASY
                          MERRIL, JUDITH   AN
YOU MEN OF VIOLENCE   HARRISON, HARRY   SS   GAL 67 04
  PRIME NUMBER   HARRISON, HARRY   AC
YOU TRIFLIN' SKUNK¡ (TRIFLIN' MAN)
                          MILLER, WALTER M. JR SS   FUN 55 01
  VIEW FROM THE STARS, THE   MILLER, WALTER M. JR   AC
YOU WERE RIGHT, JOE   MCINTOSH, J. T.   SS   GAL 57 11
  FOURTH GALAXY READER, THE   GOLD, H. L.   AN
YOU: COMA: MARILYN MONROE BALLARD, J. G.   SS   NWS 66 06
  BEST SF STORIES FROM NEW WORLDS NO. 2, THE
                          MOORCOCK, MICHAEL   AN
  LOVE & NAPALM: EXPORT U.S.A. BALLARD, J. G.   AC
  SF12   MERRIL, JUDITH   AN

YOU'LL NEVER GO HOME AGAIN (ALSO AS BEACHHEAD)
                          SIMAK, CLIFFORD D.   SS   FAD 51 07
  AWARD SCIENCE FICTION READER NORTON, ALDEN H.   AN
  TIME UNTAMED   HOWARD, IVAN   AN
YOU'LL TAKE THE HIGH ROAD BRUNNER, JOHN   NA   TTT 73
  THREE TRIPS IN TIME AND SPACE SILVERBERG, ROBERT   OA
YOU'RE ALL ALONE   LEIBER, FRITZ   NO   FAD 50 07
  YOU'RE ALL ALONE   LEIBER, FRITZ   AC
YOU'RE ANOTHER   KNIGHT, DAMON   NV   FSF 55 06
  BEST FROM FANTASY AND SCIENCE FICTION: 5
                          BOUCHER, ANTHONY   AN
  FAR OUT   KNIGHT, DAMON   AC
  SPECIAL WONDER   MCCOMAS, J. FRANCIS AN
YOU'VE NEVER BEEN TO BARNSTABLE? (SEE WHERE I LIVE)
                          VONNEGUT, KURT JR.   TC
YOUNG ARCHIMEDES   HUXLEY, ALDOUS   SS   24
  FANTASIA MATHEMATICA   FADIMAN, CLIFTON   AN
YOUNG GIRL AT AN OPEN HALF-DOOR
                          SABERHAGEN, FRED   SS   FSF 68 11
  BOOK OF SABERHAGEN, THE   SABERHAGEN, FRED   AC
  THEMES IN SCIENCE FICTION   KELLEY, LEO P.   AN
YOUNG GOODMAN BROWN (1835) HAWTHORNE, NATHANIEL SS   NEM 35 04
  ROD SERLING'S TRIPLE W: WITCHES, WARLOCKS AND WEREWOLVES
                          SERLING, ROD   AN
  WIZARDS AND WARLOCKS   GHIDALIA, VIC   AN
YOUNG LOVE   DAVIS, GRANIA   NV   ORB 74 13
  ORBIT 13   KNIGHT, DAMON   OA
YOUNG MAN OF SID SUSSEX, THE HILTON, A. C.   PM   45
  MATHEMATICAL MAGPIE, THE   FADIMAN, CLIFTON   AN
YOUNG ONE, THE   BIXBY, JEROME   NV   FAN 54 05
  SPACE BY THE TAIL   BIXBY, JEROME   AC
YOUNG SOLDIER'S HOROSCOPE, THE ALDISS, BRIAN W. SS   ORB 73 12
  ORBIT 12   KNIGHT, DAMON   OA
YOUNG TOM   MORGAN, DAN   SS   NWR 76 29
  NEW WRITINGS IN SF. 29   BULMER, KENNETH   OA
YOUR ATTENTION PLEASE   PORTER, PETER   PM   PMP 62 09
  HOLDING YOUR EIGHT HANDS   LUCIE-SMITH, EDWARD AN
YOUR FACES, O MY SISTERS¡ YOUR FACES FILLED OF LIGHT¡
                          SHELDON, RACCOONA   SS
  AURORA: BEYOND EQUALITY   MCINTYRE & ANDERSON OA
YOUR GHOST WILL WALK...   YOUNG, ROBERT F.   SS   FSF 57 07
  WORLDS OF ROBERT F. YOUNG, THE YOUNG, ROBERT F.   AC
YOUR HAPLOID HEART   TIPTREE, JAMES JR.   NV   ASF 69 09
  WORLD'S BEST SCIENCE FICTION: 1970 WOLLHEIM & CARR   AN
YOUR LIFE IN 1977   LEY, WILLY   AR
  IF THIS GOES ON   NUETZEL, CHARLES   AN
YOUR NAME SHALL BE...DARKNESS (SEE THE ERSATZ EGO)
                          SPINRAD, NORMAN   TC
YOUR SOUL COMES C.O.D.   REYNOLDS, MACK   SS   FAD 52 03
  BEST OF MACK REYNOLDS, THE   REYNOLDS, MACK   AC
YOURS TRULY, JACK THE RIPPER BLOCH, ROBERT   SS   WRT 43 07
  *OPENER OF THE WAY, THE   BLOCH, ROBERT   AC
  YOURS TRULY, JACK THE RIPPER BLOCH, ROBERT   AC
YOUTH   ASIMOV, ISAAC   NV   SSF 52 05
  MARTIAN WAY AND OTHER STORIES, THE ASIMOV, ISAAC   AC
  SCIENCE FICTION   BURTON, S. H.   AN
YSOLDE   HENNEBERG, CHARLES   SS   ISF 68 06
  BEST FROM THE REST OF THE WORLD, THE WOLLHEIM, DONALD A. AN
YVALA   MOORE, C. L.   SS   WRT 36 02
  NORTHWEST OF EARTH   MOORE, C. L.   AC
Z   FONTENAY, CHARLES L. NV   IFS 56 06
  SECOND WORLD OF IF, THE   QUINN & WULFF   AN
Z FACTOR, THE   HILL, ERNEST   NV   NWR 76 01
  NEW WRITINGS IN SF. 29   BULMER, KENNETH   OA
ZANZIBAR CAT, THE   RUSS, JOANNA   SS   QRK 71 03
  QUARK/3   DELANY & HACKER   OA
ZARGON MENACE, THE   ANONYMOUS   SS
  STRANGE WORLD OF SCIENCE FICTION ANONYMOUS   OA
ZEEPSDAY   DICKSON, GORDON R.   SS   FSF 56 11
  DANGER- HUMAN   DICKSON, GORDON R.   AC
ZEN   BIXBY, JEROME   SS   GAL 52 10
  CROSSROADS IN TIME   CONKLIN, GROFF   AN
ZEN ARCHER, THE   GREENBLATT, JONATHAN SS   NEW 75 04
  NEW IMPROVED SUN, THE   DISCH, THOMAS M.   AN
ZERITSKY'S LAW   GRIFFITH, ANN WARREN SS   GAL 51 11
  OMNIBUS OF SCIENCE FICTION   CONKLIN, GROFF   AN
ZERO GEE   BOVA, BEN   NV   DVS 72 02
  AGAIN, DANGEROUS VISIONS   ELLISON, HARLAN   OA
  BEST SCIENCE FICTION OF THE YEAR, THE NO. 2
                          CARR, TERRY   AN
  FORWARD IN TIME   BOVA, BEN   AN
ZERO HOUR   BRADBURY, RAY   SS   PLS 47 FL
  ASPECTS OF SCIENCE FICTION   DOHERTY, G. D.   AN
  BEST SF 2   CRISPIN, EDMUND   AN
  *ILLUSTRATED MAN, THE   BRADBURY, RAY   AC
  INVASION FROM MARS   WELLES, ORSON   AN
  *MY BEST SCIENCE FICTION STORY MARGULIES & FRIEND   AN
  S IS FOR SPACE   BRADBURY, RAY   AC
  SCIENCE FICTION   BRODKIN & PEARSON   AN
ZERO POPULATION GROWTH: A STATEMENT
                          MISC. MATERIAL   MS
  VOYAGES: SCENARIOS FOR A SHIP CALLED EARTH
                          SAUER, ROB   AN
ZIRN LEFT UNGUARDED, THE JENGHIK PALACE IN FLAMES,
  JOHN WESTERLY DEAD   SHECKLEY, ROBERT   SS   NOV 72 02
  NOVA 2   HARRISON, HARRY   OA
  SPACE OPERA   ALDISS, BRIAN W.   AN
ZONE   LINNETT, PETER   SS   NWR 75 27
  NEW WRITINGS IN SF. 27   BULMER, KENNETH   OA
ZONE OF TERROR   BALLARD, J. G.   SS   NWS 60 03
  CHRONOPOLIS AND OTHER STORIES BALLARD, J. G.   AC
  DISASTER AREA, THE   BALLARD, J. G.   AC
  VOICES OF TIME AND OTHER STORIES, THE BALLARD, J. G.   AC
ZOO 2000   CURTIS, RICHARD   SS   NEW 72 AN
  ZOO 2000   YOLEN, JANE   AN

ZOOMEN   HOYLE, FRED   SS   FSF 67 03
  ELEMENT 79   HOYLE, FRED   AC
ZORA OF THE ZOROMES   JONES, NEIL R.   NV   AMZ 35 03
  SPACE WAR   JONES, NEIL R.   AC
$1.98   PORGES, ARTHUR   SS   FSF 54 05
  BEST FROM FANTASY AND SCIENCE FICTION: 4
                                  BOUCHER, ANTHONY   AN
1-A   DISCH, THOMAS M.   SS   NWS 68 04
  FUN WITH YOUR NEW HEAD   DISCH, THOMAS M.   AC
$1,000 A PLATE   MCKENTY, JACK   SS   GAL 54 10
  FIFTH GALAXY READER, THE   GOLD, H. L.   AN
1,000,000 A.D.   ANONYMOUS   PM   PUN 93
  APEMAN, SPACEMAN   STOVER & HARRISON   AN
10:00 REPORT IS BROUGHT TO YOU BY..., THE
                                  BRYANT, EDWARD   SS   DVS 72 02
  AGAIN, DANGEROUS VISIONS   ELLISON, HARLAN   OA
10:01 A.M.   MALEC, ALEXANDER B. SS   ASF 66 03
  ANALOG 6   CAMPBELL, JOHN W. JR AN
  EXTRAPOLASIS   MALEC, ALEXANDER B.   AC
100 MILES UP   HARVEY, FRANK   SS   ARG 58
  AIR FORCE| HARVEY, FRANK   AC
102 H-BOMBS   DISCH, THOMAS M.   NV   FAN 65 03
  *ONE HUNDRED AND TWO H-BOMBS   DISCH, THOMAS M.   AC
  WHITE FANG GOES DINGO AND OTHER FUNNY S.F. STORIES
                                  DISCH, THOMAS M.   AC
$16,940.00   NIVEN, LARRY   SS   AHM 74
  HOLE IN SPACE, A   NIVEN, LARRY   AC
1933: A SCIENCE FICTION ODYSSEY
                                  CLARKE, ARTHUR C.   IN
  BEST OF ARTHUR C. CLARKE: 1937-1971, THE CLARKE, ARTHUR C.   AC
1937 A.D.| SLADEK, JOHN T.   SS   NWS 67 07
  BEST SF: 1967   HARRISON & ALDISS   AN
1971: THE YEAR IN SCIENCE FICTION
                                  KNIGHT, DAMON   AR
  NEBULA AWARD STORIES NO. 7   BIGGLE, LLOYD JR.   AN
1973: THE YEAR IN SCIENCE FICTION
                                  KNIGHT, DAMON   AR
  NEBULA AWARD STORIES 9   WILHELM, KATE   AN
1975: THE YEAR IN SCIENCE FICTION, OR LET'S HEAR IT FOR THE
  DECLINE AND FALL OF THE...   NICHOLLS, PETER   AR
  NEBULA AWARD STORIES 11   LE GUIN, URSULA K.   AN
198-, A TALE OF "TOMORROW"   SLADEK, JOHN T.   SS   NWS 70 01
  NEW TOMORROWS, THE   SPINRAD, NORMAN   AN
1980 OVERTURES   MCCLINTIC, WINONA PM   FSF 55 04
  BEST FROM FANTASY AND SCIENCE FICTION: 5
                                  BOUCHER, ANTHONY   AN
1980 PRESIDENT, THE   DEFORD, MIRIAM ALLEN SS GAL 64 10
  AMERICAN GOVERNMENT THROUGH SCIENCE FICTION
                                  OLANDER/GREENBERG/&   AN
  ELSEWHERE, ELSEWHEN, ELSEHOW   DEFORD, MIRIAM ALLEN AC
2 B R 0 2 B   VONNEGUT, KURT JR. SS   IFS 62 01
  BEST SCIENCE FICTION FROM IF, THE   POHL, FREDERIK   AN
2.46593   BRYANT, EDWARD   SS   EIO 73
  EROS IN ORBIT   ELDER, JOSEPH   OA
2001: A SPACE ODYSSEY- REVIEW 1
                                  DEL REY, LESTER   MR   GAL 68 07
  BEST SF: 1968   HARRISON & ALDISS   AN
2001: A SPACE ODYSSEY- REVIEW 2
                                  DELANY, SAMUEL R. MR FSF 68 08
  BEST SF: 1968   HARRISON & ALDISS   AN
2001: A SPACE ODYSSEY- REVIEW 3

                                  EMSHWILLER, ED   MR   FSF 68 08
  BEST SF: 1968   HARRISON & ALDISS   AN
2001: A SPACE ODYSSEY- REVIEW 4
                                  STOVER, LEON E.   MR   AMZ 69 03
  BEST SF: 1968   HARRISON & ALDISS   AN
2064, OR THEREABOUTS   BUNCH, DAVID R.   SS   FAN 64 09
  MODERAN   BUNCH, DAVID R.   AC
2066: ELECTION DAY   SHAARA, MICHAEL   SS   ASF 56 12
  BEST SCIENCE FICTION STORIES AND NOVELS: 9TH SERIES
                                  DIKTY, T. E.   AN
  POLITICAL SCIENCE FICTION   GREENBERG& WARRICK   AN
2076   INOUYE, JON   SS
  NIGHT TIDE, A   INOUYE, JON   OC
237 TALKING STATUES, ETC.   LEIBER, FRITZ   SS   FSF 63 09
  TWENTY YEARS OF FANTASY & SCIENCE FICTION
                                  FERMAN & MILLS   AN
  WORLDS OF FRITZ LEIBER, THE   LEIBER, FRITZ   AC
  9TH ANNUAL OF THE YEAR'S BEST S-F, THE   MERRIL, JUDITH   AN
2430 A.D.   ASIMOV, ISAAC   SS   IBM 70 10
  BUY JUPITER AND OTHER STORIES   ASIMOV, ISAAC   AC
25 CRUNCH SPLIT RIGHT ON TWO EFFINGER, GEO. ALEC NV   FSF 75 04
  IRRATIONAL NUMBERS   EFFINGER, GEO. ALEC   AC
3 FACES OF FEAR: AN ESSAY   ELLISON, HARLAN   MS
  OVER THE EDGE   ELLISON, HARLAN   AC
32ND OF MAY, THE   ERNST, PAUL   SS   ASF 35 04
  *BEST OF SCIENCE FICTION   CONKLIN, GROFF   AN
334   DISCH, THOMAS M.   NA   NWQ 72 04
  NEW WORLDS QUARTERLY NO. 4   MOORCOCK, MICHAEL   OA
334   DISCH, THOMAS M.   NO
4 O'CLOCK   DAY, PRICE   SS   58
  NIGHT IN FUNLAND   BRONDFIELD, JEROME   AN
4-SIDED TRIANGLE, THE   TEMPLE, WILLIAM F. NV   AMZ 39 11
  HISTORY OF THE SCIENCE FICTION MAGAZINE, THE   PART 2 1936-1945
                                  ASHLEY, MICHAEL   AN
5 EGGS   DISCH, THOMAS M.   SS   ORB 66 01
  ONE HUNDRED AND TWO H-BOMBS (U.S.)   DISCH, THOMAS M.   OA
  ORBIT 1   KNIGHT, DAMON   OA
5,000,000 A.D.   DEFORD, MIRIAM ALLEN SS FUC 73
  FUTURE CITY   ELWOOD, ROGER   OA
5,271,009 (ALSO AS THE STARCOMBER)
                                  BESTER, ALFRED   NV   FSF 54 03
  ALPHA 4   SILVERBERG, ROBERT   AN
  ASSIGNMENT IN TOMORROW   POHL, FREDERIK   AN
  LIGHT FANTASTIC, THE   BESTER, ALFRED   AC
  MODERN SCIENCE FICTION   SPINRAD, NORMAN   AN
  TWENTY YEARS OF FANTASY & SCIENCE FICTION
                                  FERMAN & MILLS   AN
50 FEGHOOT PUNS, 45 FROM F&SF AND 5 ORIGINAL
                                  BRIARTON, GRENDEL   MS
  THROUGH TIME AND SPACE WITH FERDINAND FEGHOOT
                                  BRIARTON, GRENDEL   AC
53RD AMERICAN DREAM   SALLIS, JAMES   SS   DVS 72 02
  AGAIN, DANGEROUS VISIONS   ELLISON, HARLAN   OA
$64 QUESTION, THE   CHRISTOPHER, JOHN SS   NEW 54 04
  TWENTY-SECOND CENTURY, THE   CHRISTOPHER, JOHN   AC
64-SQUARE MADHOUSE, THE   LEIBER, FRITZ   NA   IFS 62 05
  IF READER OF SCIENCE FICTION, THE   POHL, FREDERIK   AN
  PAIL OF AIR, A   LEIBER, FRITZ   AC
70 LIGHT-YEARS FROM SOL (SEE A STAR CALLED CYRENE)
                                  TALL, STEPHEN   TC
88 BEATS 266 (SUCCESS STORY) WILSON, RICHARD   SS   FUN 57 02
  THOSE IDIOTS FROM EARTH   WILSON, RICHARD   AC

Book Contents

ABC OF SCIENCE FICTION, AN   ADVENTURES IN TIME AND SPACE

ABC OF SCIENCE FICTION, AN   BOARDMAN, TOM JR.   AN   AVN 68 12
  INTRODUCTION   BOARDMAN, TOM JR.   IN
  LET'S BE FRANK   ALDISS, BRIAN W.   SS   SCF 57 06
  PATTERN   BROWN, FREDRIC   SS   NEW 54 AC
  AWAKENING, THE   CLARKE, ARTHUR C.   SS   ZEN 42 02
  I DO NOT HEAR YOU, SIR   DAVIDSON, AVRAM   SS   FSF 58 02
  DAY AT THE BEACH   EMSHWILLER, CAROL   SS   FSF 59 08
  KING OF THE BEASTS, THE   FARMER, PHILIP JOSE   SS   GAL 64 06
  HOMEY ATMOSPHERE   GALOUYE, DANIEL F.   SS   GAL 61 04
  MUTE MILTON   HARRISON, HARRY   SS   AMZ 66 02
  CONQUEST OF THE MOON, THE IRVING, WASHINGTON   SS
  IN THE BAG   JANIFER, LAURENCE M. SS   FSF 64 02
  MAID TO MEASURE   KNIGHT, DAMON   SS   FSF 64 10
  X MARKS THE PEDWALK   LEIBER, FRITZ   SS   WOT 63 04
  NO MOON FOR ME   MILLER, WALTER M. JR SS   ASF 52 09
  FAMILY RESEMBLANCE   NOURSE, ALAN E.   SS   ASF 53 04
  FINAL EXAM   OLIVER, CHAD   SS   FAN 52 11
  BITTEREST PILL, THE (ALSO AS THE RICHEST MAN IN LEVITTOWN)
                             POHL, FREDERIK   SS   GAL 59 04
  HE HAD A BIG HEART   QUATTROCCHI, FRANK   SS   FSF 55 03
  LOVE STORY   RUSSELL, ERIC FRANK   SS   ASF 57 08
  FENCE, THE   SIMAK, CLIFFORD D.   SS   SSF 52 09
  PROJECT HUSH   TENN, WILLIAM   SS   GAL 54 02
  FINER BREED, THE   URBAN, HELEN M.   SS   FSF 56 03
  HARRISON BERGERON   VONNEGUT, KURT JR.   SS   FSF 61 10
  CLOSE BEHIND HIM   WYNDHAM, JOHN   SS   FAN 53 02
  THREE LIMERICKS   XERXES, B. T. H.   PM
  THIRTY DAYS HAD SEPTEMBER YOUNG, ROBERT F.   SS   FSF 57 10
  GREAT SLOW KINGS, THE   ZELAZNY, ROGER   SS   WOT 63 12

ABOMINABLE EARTHMAN, THE   POHL, FREDERIK   AC   BAL 63
  ABOMINABLE EARTHMAN, THE   POHL, FREDERIK   NV   GAL 61 10
  WE NEVER MENTION AUNT NORA (AS PAUL FLEHR)
                             POHL, FREDERIK   SS   GAL 58 07
  LIFE AND A HALF, A   POHL, FREDERIK   SS   IFS 59 07
  PUNCH   POHL, FREDERIK   SS   PBY 62 06
  MARTIAN STAR-GAZERS, THE   POHL, FREDERIK   FA   GAL 62 02
  WHATEVER COUNTS   POHL, FREDERIK   NA   GAL 59 06
  THREE PORTRAITS AND A PRAYER POHL, FREDERIK   SS   GAL 62 08

ABOVE THE HUMAN LANDSCAPE   MCNELLY & STOVER   AN H GYR 72
  A SOCIAL SCIENCE FICTION ANTHOLOGY
  INTRODUCTION   MCNELLY, WILLIS E.
                             AND STOVER, LEON E.   IN C
  HIGHWAY, THE (AS LEONARD SPALDING)
                             BRADBURY, RAY   SS   CPY 50 SP
  WAVERIES, THE   BROWN, FREDRIC   SS   ASF 45 01
  MOTHER OF NECESSITY, THE   OLIVER, CHAD   SS   NEW 55 AC
  BLACK IS BEAUTIFUL   SILVERBERG, ROBERT   SS   YRT 70
  GOLDEN ACRES   REED, KIT   NV   68
  ADRIFT ON THE POLICY LEVEL DAVIS, CHAN   SS   STR 59 05
  "REPENT, HARLEQUIN!" SAID THE TICKTOCKMAN
                             ELLISON, HARLAN   SS   GAL 65 12
  BALANCED ECOLOGY   SCHMITZ, JAMES H.   SS   ASF 65 03
  POSITIVE FEEDBACK   ANVIL, CHRISTOPHER   SS   ASF 65 08
  POPPA NEEDS SHORTS   RICHMOND, WALT
                             AND RICHMOND, LEIGH   SS C ASF 64 01
  GREAT RADIO PERIL, THE   RUSSELL, ERIC FRANK   SS   ASF 37 04
  RESCUE OPERATION   HARRISON, HARRY   SS   ASF 64 12
  SLOW TUESDAY NIGHT   LAFFERTY, R. A.   SS   GAL 65 04
  LIGHT OF OTHER DAYS   SHAW, BOB   SS   ASF 66 08
  WHO CAN REPLACE A MAN? (BUT WHO CAN REPLACE A MAN)
                             ALDISS, BRIAN W.   SS   INF 58 06
  WHAT WE HAVE HERE IS TOO MUCH COMMUNICATION
                             STOVER, LEON E.   SS   ORB 71 09
  HANDLER, THE   KNIGHT, DAMON   SS   ROG 60 08
  THEY   HEINLEIN, ROBERT A.   SS   UNK 41 04
  CARCINOMA ANGELS   SPINRAD, NORMAN   SS   DVS 67 01
  SHATTERED LIKE A GLASS GOBLIN
                             ELLISON, HARLAN   SS   ORB 68 04
  NEW SOUND, THE   BEAUMONT, CHARLES   SS   FSF 55 06
  RAT RACE   JONES, RAYMOND F.   SS   ASF 66 04
  COMING-OF-AGE DAY   JORGENSSON, A. K.   SS   SCF 65 09
  ECCE FEMINA!   MCALLISTER, BRUCE   NV   FSF 72 02
  SEVENTH VICTIM   SHECKLEY, ROBERT   SS   GAL 53 04
  ROOMMATES (BASIS FOR NOVEL "MAKE ROOM! MAKE ROOM!")
                             HARRISON, HARRY   NV   NEW 71 AN
  MR. COSTELLO, HERO   STURGEON, THEODORE   NV   GAL 53 12
  SCIENCE FICTION AS CULTURE CRITICISM
                             MCNELLY, WILLIS E.
                             AND STOVER, LEON E.   AR C
  PREFACE   MISC. MATERIAL   MS
  APEMAN, SPACEMAN- OR 2001'S ANSWER TO THE WORLD RIDDLE
                             STOVER, LEON E.   AR
  VONNEGUT'S SLAUGHTERHOUSE-FIVE: SCIENCE FICTION AS
    OBJECTIVE CORRELATIVE   MCNELLY, WILLIS E.   AR

ACE SCIENCE FICTION READER WOLLHEIM, DONALD A.   AN   ACE 71
  IN ENGLAND AS "TRILOGY OF THE FUTURE"
  INTRODUCTION   WOLLHEIM, DONALD A.   IN
  TROUBLE WITH TYCHO, THE   SIMAK, CLIFFORD D.   NA   AMZ 60 10
  LAST CASTLE, THE   VANCE, JACK   NV   GAL 66 04
  EMPIRE STAR   DELANY, SAMUEL R.   NO   ACE 66

ACROSS PARIS AND OTHER STORIES
                             AYME, MARCEL   AC H BDL 57
  SEE "THE WALKER THROUGH WALLS"

ACROSS THE SEA OF STARS   CLARKE, ARTHUR C.   AC H HBW 59
  INTRODUCTION   FADIMAN, CLIFTON   IN
  SENTINEL, THE (SENTINEL OF ETERNITY)
                             CLARKE, ARTHUR C.   SS   TSF 51 SP
  INHERITANCE (NWS 47 03)   CLARKE, ARTHUR C.   SS   ASF 48 09
  ENCOUNTER AT DAWN (ENCOUNTER IN THE DAWN)
                             CLARKE, ARTHUR C.   SS   AMZ 53 07
  SUPERIORITY   CLARKE, ARTHUR C.   SS   FSF 51 08

  HIDE AND SEEK   CLARKE, ARTHUR C.   SS   ASF 49 09
  HISTORY LESSON   CLARKE, ARTHUR C.   SS   STS 49 05
  IF I FORGET THEE, OH EARTH...
                             CLARKE, ARTHUR C.   SS   FUT 51 09
  BREAKING STRAIN (THIRTY SECONDS - THIRTY DAYS)
                             CLARKE, ARTHUR C.   NV   TWS 49 12
  SILENCE, PLEASE   CLARKE, ARTHUR C.   SS   SCF 50 WI
  ARMAMENTS RACE   CLARKE, ARTHUR C.   SS   ADV 54 04
  PACIFIST, THE   CLARKE, ARTHUR C.   SS   FUN 56 10
  NEXT TENANTS, THE   CLARKE, ARTHUR C.   SS   SAT 57 02
  RELUCTANT ORCHID, THE   CLARKE, ARTHUR C.   SS   SAT 56 12
  RESCUE PARTY   CLARKE, ARTHUR C.   NV   ASF 46 05
  TECHNICAL ERROR (THE REVERSED MAN)
                             CLARKE, ARTHUR C.   SS   FSB 46 12
  FIRES WITHIN, THE   CLARKE, ARTHUR C.   SS   FSB 47 08
  TIME'S ARROW   CLARKE, ARTHUR C.   SS   SCF 50 SU
  JUPITER FIVE   CLARKE, ARTHUR C.   NV   IFS 53 05
  CHILDHOOD'S END (EXPANDED FROM "GUARDIAN ANGEL")
                             CLARKE, ARTHUR C.   NO   NWS 50 WI
  EARTHLIGHT   CLARKE, ARTHUR C.   NO   TWS 51 08

AD 2500   WILSON, ANGUS   AN H HEI 55
  THE OBSERVER PRIZE STORIES 1954
  INTRODUCTION   BALCHIN, NIGEL   IN
  RETURN OF THE MOON MAN (ALSO AS WHEN GRANDFATHER FLEW
    TO THE MOON)   MALPASS, E. L.   SS   LOB 55 01
  NOT FOR AN AGE   ALDISS, BRIAN W.   SS   LOB 55 01
  RIGHT THING, THE   ANDREW, WILLIAM   SS
  JACKSON'S WRONG STORY   BOLSOVER, JOHN   SS
  VOICE FROM THE GALLERY   BROWNLOW, CATHERINE   SS
  WALKABOUT   EARL, STEPHEN   SS
  SHADOW PLAY   FITZPATRICK, E. D.   SS
  VENUS AND THE RABBIT   FITZPATRICK, E. M.   SS
  PLACE OF THE TIGRESS, THE MAYNE, ISOBEL   SS
  ANOTHER ANTIGONE   MORRISON, D. A. C.   SS
  SPUD FAILURE DEFINITE   PEART, NOEL   SS
  THREE BROTHERS, THE   RUSSELL, WILLIAM M.   SS   LOB 54 12
  ATAVISTS, THE   RYMER, G. A.   SS
  MISSION, THE   SELLINGS, ARTHUR   SS
  ALPHA IN OMEGA   STONES, JONATHAN   SS
  BLOND KID, THE   SUTHERLAND, HERB   SS
  CASE OF OMEGA SMITH, THE   WALSH, BUTHRAM   SS
  MACHINE THAT WAS LONELY, THE WELLS, ROBERT   SS
  HITCH HIKE TO PARADISE   WHYBROW, GEOFFREY   SS
  KNITTING, THE   WOOD, MARGARET   SS
  MAN MANIFOLD   YOUNG, PETER   SS

ADAM LINK- ROBOT   BINDER, EANDO   AC   PBK 65 09
  I, ROBOT   BINDER, EANDO   SS   AMZ 39 01
  TRIAL OF ADAM LINK, THE   BINDER, EANDO   SS   AMZ 39 07
  ADAM LINK IN BUSINESS   BINDER, EANDO   SS   AMZ 40 01
  ADAM LINK'S VENGEANCE   BINDER, EANDO   NV   AMZ 40 02
  ADAM LINK, ROBOT DETECTIVE BINDER, EANDO   SS   AMZ 40 05
  ADAM LINK, CHAMPION ATHLETE BINDER, EANDO   SS   AMZ 40 07
  ADAM LINK SAVES THE WORLD BINDER, EANDO   SS   AMZ 42 04

ADRIFT IN SPACE AND OTHER STORIES
                             ELWOOD, ROGER   OA H LER 74
  FOREWORD   ASIMOV, ISAAC   IN
  ADRIFT IN SPACE   ZEBROWSKI, GEORGE   SS
  PLASTIC AGE, THE   GOLDSMITH, HOWARD   SS
  TEAMWORK   YORE, MARY JANE   SS

ADVENTURES IN DIMENSION   CONKLIN, GROFF   AN H GRY 55
  SELECTIONS FROM "SCIENCE FICTION ADVENTURES IN DIMENSION"
  INTRODUCTION   CONKLIN, GROFF   IN
  REVERSE PHYLOGENY   LONG, AMELIA R.   SS   ASF 37 06
  WHAT SO PROUDLY WE HAIL... KEENE, DAY   SS   IMG 50 12
  NIGHT MEETING   BRADBURY, RAY   SS   NEW 51 AC
  FLIGHT THAT FAILED, THE   HULL, E. MAYNE   SS   ASF 42 12
  ENDOWMENT POLICY   PADGETT, LEWIS   SS   ASF 43 08
  PETE CAN FIX IT   JONES, RAYMOND F.   SS   ASF 47 02
  MIST, THE   CARTUR, PETER   SS   FSF 52 09
  GOSTAK AND THE DOSHES, THE BREUER, MILES J. MD. SS   AMZ 30 03
  WHAT IF   ASIMOV, ISAAC   SS   FAN 52 SU
  RING AROUND THE REDHEAD   MACDONALD, JOHN D.   SS   STS 48 11
  TIGER BY THE TAIL   NOURSE, ALAN E.   SS   GAL 51 11
  WAY OF ESCAPE   TEMPLE, WILLIAM F.   SS   TWS 48 06
  TO FOLLOW KNOWLEDGE   LONG, FRANK BELKNAP   SS   ASF 42 12

ADVENTURES IN THE FAR FUTURE WOLLHEIM, DONALD A.   DA   ACE 54
  WIND BETWEEN THE WORLDS, THE DEL REY, LESTER   NV   GAL 51 03
  STARDUST (ALSO AS FIRST TO THE STARS)
                             OLIVER, CHAD   NV   ASF 52 07
  OVERDRIVE   LEINSTER, MURRAY   NV   STS 53 04
  MILLIONTH YEAR, THE   PEARSON, MARTIN   SS   SFS 43 04
  CHAPTER ENDS, THE   ANDERSON, POUL   NV   DSF 54 01

ADVENTURES IN TIME AND SPACE HEALY & MCCOMAS   AN H RDM 46 08
  SECOND EDITION, 1953, OMITS LAST FIVE STORIES,
    ALSO AS "FAMOUS SCIENCE-FICTION STORIES"
    DERIVATIVE ANTHOLOGY "MORE ADVENTURES IN TIME AND SPACE"
  REQUIEM   HEINLEIN, ROBERT A.   SS   ASF 40 01
  FORGETFULNESS   STUART, DON A.   SN   ASF 37 06
  NERVES   DEL REY, LESTER   NV   ASF 42 09
  SANDS OF TIME, THE   MILLER, P. SCHUYLER   SN   ASF 37 04
  PROUD ROBOT, THE   PADGETT, LEWIS   NV   ASF 43 10
  BLACK DESTROYER   VAN VOGT, A. E.   NV   ASF 39 07
  SYMBIOTICA   RUSSELL, ERIC FRANK   NV   ASF 43 10
  SEEDS OF THE DUSK   GALLUN, RAYMOND Z.   NV   ASF 38 06
  HEAVY PLANET   GREGOR, LEE   SS   ASF 39 08
  TIME LOCKER   PADGETT, LEWIS   SS   ASF 43 01
  LINK, THE   CARTMILL, CLEVE   SS   ASF 42 08
  MECHANICAL MICE   HUGI, MAURICE G.   NV   ASF 41 01
  V-2: ROCKET CARGO SHIP   LEY, WILLY   AR   ASF 45 05
  ADAM AND NO EVE   BESTER, ALFRED   SS   ASF 41 09

Title	Author	Type	Source
ADVENTURES IN TIME AND SPACE			
NIGHTFALL	ASIMOV, ISAAC	NV	ASF 41 09
MATTER OF SIZE, A	BATES, HARRY	NV	ASF 34 04
AS NEVER WAS	MILLER, P. SCHUYLER	SS	ASF 44 01
Q.U.R.	BOUCHER, ANTHONY	SS	ASF 43 03
WHO GOES THERE?	STUART, DON A.	NV	ASF 38 08
ROADS MUST ROLL, THE	HEINLEIN, ROBERT A.	NV	ASF 40 06
ASYLUM	VAN VOGT, A. E.	NV	ASF 42 05
QUIETUS	ROCKLYNNE, ROSS	SS	ASF 40 09
TWONKY, THE	PADGETT, LEWIS	SS	ASF 42 09
TIME-TRAVEL HAPPENS!	PHILLIPS, A. M.	AR	UNK 39 12
ROBOTS RETURN	WILLIAMS, ROBERT M.	SS	ASF 38 09
BLUE GIRAFFE, THE	DE CAMP, L. SPRAGUE	NV	ASF 39 08
FLIGHT INTO DARKNESS	MARLOWE, WEBB	SS	ASF 43 02
WEAPON SHOP, THE	VAN VOGT, A. E.	NV	ASF 42 12
FAREWELL TO THE MASTER	BATES, HARRY	NV	ASF 40 10
WITHIN THE PYRAMID	MILLER, R. DEWITT	SS	ASF 37 03
HE WHO SHRANK	HASSE, HENRY	NV	AMZ 36 08
BY HIS BOOTSTRAPS (ALSO AS THE TIME GATE)	MACDONALD, ANSON	NV	ASF 41 10
STAR MOUSE, THE	BROWN, FREDRIC	SS	PLS 42 02
CORRESPONDENCE COURSE	JONES, RAYMOND F.	SS	ASF 45 04
BRAIN	WRIGHT, S. FOWLER	SS	32
ADVENTURES IN TIME AND SPACE (BRITISH)	HEALY & MCCOMAS	AN H	GRY 52
SANDS OF TIME, THE	MILLER, P. SCHUYLER	SN	ASF 37 04
SEEDS OF THE DUSK	GALLUN, RAYMOND Z.	NV	ASF 38 06
TIME LOCKER	PADGETT, LEWIS	SS	ASF 43 01
LINK, THE	CARTMILL, CLEVE	SS	ASF 42 08
MECHANICAL MICE	HUGI, MAURICE G.	NV	ASF 41 01
ADAM AND NO EVE	BESTER, ALFRED	SS	ASF 41 09
NIGHTFALL	ASIMOV, ISAAC	NV	ASF 41 09
MATTER OF SIZE, A	BATES, HARRY	NV	ASF 34 04
ROADS MUST ROLL, THE	HEINLEIN, ROBERT A.	NV	ASF 40 06
TWONKY, THE	PADGETT, LEWIS	SS	ASF 42 09
FLIGHT INTO DARKNESS	MARLOWE, WEBB	SS	ASF 43 02
ADVENTURES IN TIME AND SPACE (SELECTIONS FROM)	HEALY & MCCOMAS	AN	BAN 54
REQUIEM	HEINLEIN, ROBERT A.	SS	ASF 40 01
BLACK DESTROYER	VAN VOGT, A. E.	NV	ASF 39 07
TIME LOCKER	PADGETT, LEWIS	SS	ASF 43 01
MECHANICAL MICE	HUGI, MAURICE G.	NV	ASF 41 01
AS NEVER WAS	MILLER, P. SCHUYLER	SS	ASF 44 01
QUIETUS	ROCKLYNNE, ROSS	SS	ASF 40 09
ROBOTS RETURN	WILLIAMS, ROBERT M.	SS	ASF 38 09
FAREWELL TO THE MASTER	BATES, HARRY	NV	ASF 40 10
ADVENTURES IN TOMORROW	CROSSEN, KENDELL F.	AN H	GBG 51
EDITOR'S NOTE	CROSSEN, KENDELL F.	IN	
FLYING DUTCHMAN	MOORE, WARD	SS	FSF 56 09
THERE WILL COME SOFT RAINS	BRADBURY, RAY	SS	COL 50 05
MUTE QUESTION, THE	ACKERMAN, FORREST J.	SS	OWS 50 09
PORTABLE PHONOGRAPH, THE	CLARK, WALTER VAN T.	SS	41
AUTOMATON	VAN VOGT, A. E.	SS	OWS 50 09
RESTRICTED CLIENTELE	CROSSEN, KENDELL F.	SS	TWS 51 02
SHAMBLEAU	MOORE, C. L.	NV	WRT 33 11
CHRISTMAS ON GANYMEDE	ASIMOV, ISAAC	SS	STS 42 01
MEMORY	STURGEON, THEODORE	NV	TWS 48 08
EXILED FROM EARTH	MERWIN, SAM JR.	SS	TWS 40 12
RETREAT TO THE STARS	BRACKETT, LEIGH	SS	AST 41 11
VOICE OF THE LOBSTER, THE	KUTTNER, HENRY	NV	TWS 50 02
EVOLUTION'S END	ARTHUR, ROBERT	SS	TWS 41 04
TRANSFER POINT	BOUCHER, ANTHONY	SS	GAL 50 11
DEVIL WAS SICK, THE	ELLIOTT, BRUCE	SS	FSF 51 04
ADVENTURES ON OTHER PLANETS	WOLLHEIM, DONALD A.	AN	ACE 55
OBLIGATION, THE	DEE, ROGER	NV	STS 52 09
SOUND OF BUGLES, THE	WILLIAMS, ROBERT M.	SS	STS 49 03
OGRE	SIMAK, CLIFFORD D.	NV	ASF 44 01
ASSIGNMENT ON PASIK	LEINSTER, MURRAY	SS	TWS 49 02
RULL, THE	VAN VOGT, A. E.	NV	ASF 48 05
ADVENTURES TO COME	ESENWEIN, J. BERG	OA H	MLB 37
MAN IN THE MOON COMES DOWN, A	COPEMAN, BERGER	SS	
LIFE BY TELEVISION, A	ARNOLD, JACK	SS	
CRUISE OF THE S-900, THE	KENT, RUSSELL	SS	
TWENTY-FIVE MILES ALOFT	WATSON, RAYMOND	SS	
SCIENCE STEALS A MARCH	RICHARDS, NELSON	SS	
DAWN ATTACK	COPEMAN, BERGER	SS	
PIRATE OF THE AIR	BRADFORD, JAMES S.	SS	
SIX HUNDRED FATHOMS	LESLIE, NORMAN	SS	
IT'S GOING TO BE TRUE!	FRANTHWAY, BURKE	SS	
AFFAIR WITH GENIUS, AN	GREEN, JOSEPH	AC H	GOL 69
JINN	GREEN, JOSEPH	SS	GAL 68 12
DECISION MAKERS, THE	GREEN, JOSEPH	NV	GAL 65 04
ONCE AROUND ARCTURUS	GREEN, JOSEPH	NV	IFS 62 09
ENGINEER, THE	GREEN, JOSEPH	SS	NWS 62 02
SINGLE COMBAT	GREEN, JOSEPH	SS	NWS 64 08
LIFE-FORCE	GREEN, JOSEPH	SS	NWS 62 11
AFFAIR WITH GENIUS, AN	GREEN, JOSEPH	SS	FSF 69 03
TUNNEL OF LOVE	GREEN, JOSEPH	SS	NWS 65 01
DANCE OF THE CATS	GREEN, JOSEPH	SS	NWS 65 12
AGAIN, DANGEROUS VISIONS	ELLISON, HARLAN	OA H	DBL 72
ASSAULT ON NEW DREAMERS, AN	ELLISON, HARLAN	IN	DVS 72 02
COUNTERPOINT OF VIEW, THE	HEIDENRY, JOHN	MS	DVS 72 02
CHING WITCH!	ROCKLYNNE, ROSS	SS	DVS 72 02
WORD FOR WORLD IS FOREST, THE	LE GUIN, URSULA K.	NV	DVS 72 02
FOR VALUE RECEIVED	OFFUTT, ANDREW J.	SS	DVS 72 02
ROBOT'S STORY	WOLFE, GENE	SS	DVS 72 02
AGAINST THE LAFAYETTE ESCADRILLE	WOLFE, GENE	SS	DVS 72 02
LOCO PARENTIS	WOLFE, GENE	SS	DVS 72 02
TIME TRAVEL FOR PEDESTRIANS	NELSON, RAY	SS	DVS 72 02
CHRIST, OLD STUDENT IN A NEW SCHOOL	BRADBURY, RAY	PM	DVS 72 02
KING OF THE HILL	OLIVER, CHAD	SS	DVS 72 02
10:00 REPORT IS BROUGHT TO YOU BY..., THE	BRYANT, EDWARD	SS	DVS 72 02
FUNERAL, THE	WILHELM, KATE	NV	DVS 72 02
HARRY THE HARE	HEMESATH, JAMES B.	SS	DVS 72 02
WHEN IT CHANGED	RUSS, JOANNA	SS	DVS 72 02
BIG SPACE FUCK, THE	VONNEGUT, KURT JR.	SS	DVS 72 02
BOUNTY	SHERRED, T. L.	SS	DVS 72 02
STILL-LIFE	O'DONNELL, K. M.	SS	DVS 72 02
STONED COUNSEL	HOLLIS, H. H.	SS	DVS 72 02
BISQUIT POSITION, THE	WOLFE, BERNARD	NV	DVS 72 02
GIRL WITH RAPID EYE MOVEMENTS, THE	WOLFE, BERNARD	NV	DVS 72 02
WITH A FINGER IN MY I	GERROLD, DAVID	SS	DVS 72 02
IN THE BARN	ANTHONY, PIERS	NV	DVS 72 02
SOUNDLESS EVENING	HOFFMAN, LEE	SS	DVS 72 02
*	WILSON, GAHAN	SS	DVS 72 02
TEST-TUBE CREATURE, AFTERWARD, THE	BERNOTT, JOAN	SS	DVS 72 02
AND THE SEA LIKE MIRRORS	BENFORD, GREGORY	SS	DVS 72 02
BED SHEETS ARE WHITE	LIEF, EVELYN	SS	DVS 72 02
AT THE FITTING SHOP	SALLIS, JAMES	SS	DVS 72 02
53RD AMERICAN DREAM	SALLIS, JAMES	SS	DVS 72 02
ELOUISE AND THE DOCTORS OF THE PLANET PERGAMON	SAXTON, JOSEPHINE	SS	DVS 72 02
CHUCK BERRY, WON'T YOU PLEASE COME HOME?	MCCULLOUGH, KEN	SS	DVS 72 02
EPIPHANY FOR ALIENS	KERR, DAVID	SS	DVS 72 02
EYE OF THE BEHOLDER	FILER, BURT K.	SS	DVS 72 02
MOTH RACE	HILL, RICHARD	SS	DVS 72 02
IN RE GLOVER	TUSHNET, LEONARD	SS	DVS 72 02
ZERO GEE	BOVA, BEN	NV	DVS 72 02
MOUSE IN THE WALLS OF THE GLOBAL VILLAGE, A	KOONTZ, DEAN R.	SS	DVS 72 02
GETTING ALONG	BLISH, JAMES AND LAWRENCE, JUDITH ANN	NV C	DVS 72 02
TOTENBUCH	PARRA (Y FIGUEREDO)	SS	DVS 72 02
THINGS LOST	DISCH, THOMAS M.	NV	DVS 72 02
WITH THE BENTFIN BOOMER BOYS ON LITTLE OLD NEW ALABAMA	LUPOFF, RICHARD A.	NA	DVS 72 02
LAMIA MUTABLE (ALSO AS THE BRINGER WITH THE WINDOW)	HARRISON, M. JOHN	SS	DVS 72 02
LAST TRAIN TO KANKAKEE	SCOTT, ROBIN S.	SS	DVS 72 02
EMPIRE OF THE SUN	WEINER, ANDREW	SS	DVS 72 02
OZYMANDIAS	CARR, TERRY	SS	DVS 72 02
MILK OF PARADISE, THE	TIPTREE, JAMES JR.	SS	DVS 72 02
ED EMSHWILLER	MISC. MATERIAL	MS	
AGENT OF THE TERRAN EMPIRE	ANDERSON, POUL	AC H	CHL 65
TIGER BY THE TAIL	ANDERSON, POUL	NV	PLS 51 01
WARRIORS FROM NOWHERE (THE AMBASSADORS OF FLESH)	ANDERSON, POUL	SS	PLS 54 SU
HONORABLE ENEMIES	ANDERSON, POUL	NV	FUT 51 05
HANDFUL OF STARS, A	ANDERSON, POUL	NA	AMZ 59 06
AGENT OF VEGA	SCHMITZ, JAMES H.	AC H	GNM 60
AGENT OF VEGA	SCHMITZ, JAMES H.	NV	ASF 49 07
TRUTH ABOUT CUSHGAR, THE	SCHMITZ, JAMES H.	NV	ASF 50 11
ILLUSIONISTS, THE (SPACE FEAR)	SCHMITZ, JAMES H.	NV	ASF 51 03
SECOND NIGHT OF SUMMER	SCHMITZ, JAMES H.	SS	GAL 50 12
AHEAD OF TIME	KUTTNER, HENRY	AC	BAL 53 07
OR ELSE	KUTTNER, HENRY	SS	AMZ 53 09
HOME IS THE HUNTER	KUTTNER, HENRY	NV	GAL 53 07
BY THESE PRESENTS	KUTTNER, HENRY	SS	FAN 53 03
DE PROFUNDIS (THE VISITORS)	KUTTNER, HENRY	SS	SFQ 53 05
CAMOUFLAGE	KUTTNER, HENRY	NV	ASF 45 09
YEAR DAY	KUTTNER, HENRY	SS	NEW 53 AC
GHOST	KUTTNER, HENRY	SS	ASF 43 05
SHOCK	KUTTNER, HENRY	SS	ASF 43 03
PILE OF TROUBLE	KUTTNER, HENRY	SS	TWS 48 04
DEADLOCK	KUTTNER, HENRY	SS	ASF 42 08
AIR FORCE!	HARVEY, FRANK	AC	BAL 59
ORBIT FLIGHT	HARVEY, FRANK	SS	SEP 58 10
PANIC ON RUNWAY 6	HARVEY, FRANK	SS	SEP 56 07
TEST JUMP	HARVEY, FRANK	SS	SEP 56 06
RUNAWAY PROP	HARVEY, FRANK	SS	SEP 59 05
JINX JET	HARVEY, FRANK	SS	CAV 57
100 MILES UP	HARVEY, FRANK	SS	ARG 58
MOON SHOT	HARVEY, FRANK	SS	SEP 58 05
DESTRUCT BUTTON	HARVEY, FRANK	SS	ARG 59
AIR OF MARS AND OTHER STORIES, THE	GINSBURG, MIRRA	AN H	MAC 76
EDITOR'S NOTE	GINSBURG, MIRRA	IN	
TEMIRA	LARIONOVA, OLGA	NV	71
BRAT, THE	ZHURAVLEVA, VALENTINA	SS	67
TACAN FOR THE CHILDREN OF EARTH, A	BULYCHEV, KIRILL	SS	72
WE ARE NOT ALONE	GANSOVSKY, SEVER	SS	64
TWELVE HOLIDAYS	BAKHNOV, VLADLEN	SS	69
WHITE PILOT, THE	YEMTSEV, MIKHAIL AND PARNOV, YEREMEY	NV C	69
TICKET TO CHILDHOOD, A	KOLUPAYEV, VICTOR	SS	69
GARDEN, THE	GOR, GENNADY	SS	68
AIR OF MARS, THE	BILENKIN, DMITRY	SS	69
NOTES ON THE AUTHORS	MISC. MATERIAL	MS	
AIRS OF EARTH, THE	ALDISS, BRIAN W.	AC H	FAB 63
INTRODUCTION	ALDISS, BRIAN W.	IN	

.IRS OF EARTH, THE   ALL ABOUT VENUS

KIND OF ARTISTRY, A   ALDISS, BRIAN W.   SS   FSF 62 10
HOW TO BE A SOLDIER (SOLDIERS RUNNING)
                                 ALDISS, BRIAN W.   SS   NWS 60 06
BASIS FOR NEGOTIATION   ALDISS, BRIAN W.   NV   NWS 62 01
O MOON OF MY DELIGHT| (MOON OF DELIGHT)
                                 ALDISS, BRIAN W.   NV   NWS 61 03
INTERNATIONAL SMILE, THE   ALDISS, BRIAN W.   SS   NEW 63 AC
GAME OF GOD, THE (SEGREGATION)
                                 ALDISS, BRIAN W.   NV   NWS 58 07
OLD HUNDREDTH   ALDISS, BRIAN W.   SS   NWS 60 11

ALCHEMY AND ACADEME   MCCAFFREY, ANNE   OA H DBL 70
FOREWORD   MCCAFFREY, ANNE   IN
DANCE OF THE SOLIDS, THE   UPDIKE, JOHN   PM   SAM 69 01
MESS OF PORRIDGE, A   DORMAN, SONYA   SS   ANA 70
INSTITUTE, THE   EMSHWILLER, CAROL   SS   ANA 70
CONDILLAC'S STATUE   LAFFERTY, R. A.   SS   ANA 70
SORCERERS, THE   DE CAMP, L. SPRAGUE   PM   ANA 70
WEED OF TIME, THE   SPINRAD, NORMAN   SS   ANA 70
NIGHT AND THE LOVES OF JOE DICOSTANZO
                                 DELANY, SAMUEL R.   SS   ANA 70
COME UP AND SEE ME   CASTELL, DAPHNE   SS   ANA 70
SHUT THE LAST DOOR   HENSLEY, JOE L.   SS   ANA 70
BIG SAM   DAVIDSON, AVRAM   SS   ANA 70
MORE LIGHT   BLISH, JAMES   SS   ANA 70
MAN WHO COULD NOT SEE DEVILS, THE
                                 RUSS, JOANNA   SS   ANA 70
KEY TO OUT, THE   CURTIS, BETSY   SS   ANA 70
RINGING THE CHANGES   SILVERBERG, ROBERT   SS   ANA 70
IN A QUART OF WATER   TELFAIR, DAVID   SS   ANA 70
MORNING-GLORY   WOLFE, GENE   SS   ANA 70
ASCENSION: A WORKDAY ARABESQUE
                                 KIDD, VIRGINIA   PM   ANA 70
DEVIL YOU DON'T, THE   LAUMER, KEITH   NV   ANA 70
TRIUMPHANT HEAD, THE   SAXTON, JOSEPHINE   SS   ANA 70
MAINCHANCE   TATE, PETER   NV   ANA 70

ALFRED BESTER OMNIBUS, AN   BESTER, ALFRED   AC H SID 67
DEMOLISHED MAN, THE   BESTER, ALFRED   NO   GAL 52 01
TIGER| TIGER| (THE STARS MY DESTINATION)
                                 BESTER, ALFRED   NO   GAL 56 10
DARK SIDE OF THE EARTH, THE   BESTER, ALFRED   AC   SIG 64 05

ALIEN CONDITION, THE   GOLDIN, STEPHEN   OA   BAL 73 04
INTRODUCTION   GOLDIN, STEPHEN   IN
LAMENT OF THE KEEKU BIRD   SKY, KATHLEEN   SS   ALC 73
WINGS   MCINTYRE, VONDA N.   SS   ALC 73
EMPIRE OF T'ANG LANG, THE   FOSTER, ALAN DEAN   SS   ALC 73
WAY OUT, A   DEFORD, MIRIAM ALLEN SS   ALC 73
GEE, ISN'T HE THE CUTEST LITTLE THING?
                                 COVER, ARTHUR BYRON   SS   ALC 73
DEAF LISTENER   PAYES, RACHEL C.   SS   ALC 73
NOR IRON BARS A CAGE   HENSEL, C. F.
                                 AND GOLDIN, STEPHEN   SS C ALC 73
ROUTINE PATROL ACTIVITY   PICKENS, THOMAS   SS   ALC 73
CALL FROM KERLYANA   CARLSON, WILLIAM
                                 AND LAURANCE, ALICE   SS C ALC 73
SAFETY ENGINEER, THE   BOULT, S. KYE   NV   ALC 73
LOVE IS THE PLAN THE PLAN IS DEATH
                                 TIPTREE, JAMES JR.   SS   ALC 73
LATEST FROM SIGMA CORVI, THE   WELLEN, EDWARD   SS   ALC 73

ALIEN DUST   TUBB, E. C.   NO H BDM 55
WITHOUT BUGLES   TUBB, E. C.   SS   NWS 52 01
HOME IS THE HERO   TUBB, E. C.   SS   NWS 52 05
MEN ONLY   TUBB, E. C.   SS   NWS 52 07
ALIEN DUST   TUBB, E. C.   SS   NWS 53 01
PISTOL POINT   TUBB, E. C.   SS   NWS 53 06
OPERATION MARS   TUBB, E. C.   NO   NEB 54 12

ALIEN EARTH AND OTHER STORIES
                                 ELWOOD & MOSKOWITZ   AN   MCF 69
ALIEN EARTH   HAMILTON, EDMOND   SS   TWS 49 04
PAST MASTER, THE   BLOCH, ROBERT   NV   BBM 55 01
RAIN MAGIC   GARDNER, EARL S.   NV   AAS 28 10
ULTIMATE MELODY, THE   CLARKE, ARTHUR C.   SS   IFS 57 02
LOOT OF TIME, THE   SIMAK, CLIFFORD D.   NV   TWS 38 12
DOODAD   BRADBURY, RAY   SS   ASF 43 09
AUTOMATON   VAN VOGT, A. E.   SS   OWS 50 09
PEOPLE OF THE CRATER, THE   NORTON, ANDRE   NV   FBK 47 01
FRANCHISE   ASIMOV, ISAAC   SS   IFS 55 08

ALIEN HORIZONS   NOLAN, WILLIAM F.   AC   PKT 74 08
FROM THE OTHER SIDE OF THE MASK
                                 NOLAN, WILLIAM F.   IN
STARBLOOD   NOLAN, WILLIAM F.   SS   INY 72 04
JENNY AMONG THE ZEEBS (AS FRANK ANMAR)
                                 NOLAN, WILLIAM F.   SS   FIN 70
JOY OF LIVING, THE   NOLAN, WILLIAM F.   SS   IFS 54 08
LAST THREE MONTHS, THE   NOLAN, WILLIAM F.   SS   RAT 63
UNDERDWELLER, THE (SMALL WORLD)
                                 NOLAN, WILLIAM F.   SS   FUN 57 08
FULL OF, MOSTLY, BAGELS AND CREAM CHEESE
                                 NOLAN, WILLIAM F.   SS   NEW 74 AC
KELLY, FREDRIC MICHAEL: 1928-1987
                                 NOLAN, WILLIAM F.   SS   INY 73 05
DAY THE GORF TOOK OVER, THE (GORF| GORF| GORF|)
                                 NOLAN, WILLIAM F.   SS   INY 71 02
HAPPILY EVER AFTER   NOLAN, WILLIAM F.   SS   GAM 65 04
FASTERFASTER| (THE FASTERFASTER AFFAIR)
                                 NOLAN, WILLIAM F.   SS   NEW 65 AN
HE KILT IT WITH A STICK   NOLAN, WILLIAM F.   SS   FSF 68 02
TOE TO TIP, TIP TO TOE, PIP-POP AS YOU GO
                                 NOLAN, WILLIAM F.   SS   FIN 70
PARTY, THE   NOLAN, WILLIAM F.   SS   PBY 67 04
PAPA'S PLANET   NOLAN, WILLIAM F.   SS   PBY 68 04

SOLUTION (TO SERVE THE SHIP)   NOLAN, WILLIAM F.   SS   GAM 63 01
LAWBREAKER (VIOLATION)   NOLAN, WILLIAM F.   SS   FUC 73
MATING OF THIRDBURT, THE   NOLAN, WILLIAM F.   SS   NEW 74 AC
WORLDS OF MONTY WILLSON, THE   NOLAN, WILLIAM F.   SS   AMZ 71 07
PROMISES TO KEEP: A SCIENCE FICTION DRAMA
                                 NOLAN, WILLIAM F.   SS   NEW 74 AC

ALIEN LANDSCAPES   BURKE, JONATHAN F.   AC H MUS 55
STAND-IN   BURKE, JONATHAN F.   SS   AUT 54 03
ONCE UPON A TIME   BURKE, JONATHAN F.   SS   SCF 54 05
FOR YOU, THE POSSESSED   BURKE, JONATHAN F.   SS   AUT 53 12
CENSORS, THE   BURKE, JONATHAN F.   SS   AUT 54 01
APPLE FOR THE TEACHER, AN   BURKE, JONATHAN F.   SS   NEB 55 04
OLD MAN OF THE STARS, THE   BURKE, JONATHAN F.   SN   AUT 53 10

ALIEN WORLDS   ELWOOD, ROGER   AN   PBK 64 09
EDITOR'S INTRODUCTION   ELWOOD, ROGER   IN
AFTERNOON OF A FAHN (ALSO AS RAINBOW'S END)
                                 RUSSELL, ERIC FRANK   SS   IMG 51 04
COSMIC POACHERS, THE   DICK, PHILIP K.   SS   IMG 53 07
DAWN INVADER   SHECKLEY, ROBERT   SS   FSF 57 03
LAST MONSTER, THE (TERMINAL QUEST)
                                 ANDERSON, POUL   SS   SSS 51 08
FEAR PLANET, THE   BLOCH, ROBERT   SS   SSS 43 02
SINGLEMINDED   BRUNNER, JOHN   NV   IFS 63 05
STARS, MY BROTHERS, THE   HAMILTON, EDMOND   NV   AMZ 62 05
BRAIN STEALERS OF MARS, THE   CAMPBELL, JOHN W. JR SS   TWS 36 12
MAN FROM BEYOND, THE   WYNDHAM, JOHN   NV   WOS 34 09
MADNESS FROM MARS   SIMAK, CLIFFORD D.   SS   TWS 39 04

ALIENS AMONG US, THE   WHITE, JAMES   AC   BAL 69 03
COUNTERCHARM   WHITE, JAMES   SS   NWS 60 11
TO KILL OR CURE   WHITE, JAMES   SS   NWS 57 04
RED ALERT   WHITE, JAMES   NV   NWS 56 01
TABLEAU   WHITE, JAMES   NV   NWS 58 05
CONSPIRATORS, THE   WHITE, JAMES   NV   NWS 54 06
SCAVENGERS, THE   WHITE, JAMES   SS   ASF 53 10
OCCUPATION: WARRIOR   WHITE, JAMES   SN   SFA 59 03

ALIENS FOR NEIGHBOURS   SIMAK, CLIFFORD D.   AC H FAB 61
9 STORIES FROM "THE WORLDS OF CLIFFORD SIMAK"
DUSTY ZEBRA   SIMAK, CLIFFORD D.   NV   GAL 54 09
HONORABLE OPPONENT   SIMAK, CLIFFORD D.   SS   GAL 56 08
CARBON COPY   SIMAK, CLIFFORD D.   NA   GAL 57 12
IDIOT'S CRUSADE   SIMAK, CLIFFORD D.   SS   GAL 54 10
OPERATION STINKY   SIMAK, CLIFFORD D.   NV   GAL 57 04
JACKPOT   SIMAK, CLIFFORD D.   NV   GAL 56 10
DEATH SCENE   SIMAK, CLIFFORD D.   SS   INF 57 10
GREEN THUMB   SIMAK, CLIFFORD D.   NV   GAL 54 07
NEIGHBOR   SIMAK, CLIFFORD D.   NV   ASF 54 06

ALIENS 4   STURGEON, THEODORE   AC   AVN 59
KILLDOZER| STURGEON, THEODORE   SN   ASF 44 11
CACTUS DANCE   STURGEON, THEODORE   NV   LSW 54 10
COMEDIAN'S CHILDREN, THE   STURGEON, THEODORE   NV   VSF 58 05
(WIDGET), THE (WADGET), AND BOFF, THE
                                 STURGEON, THEODORE   SN   FSF 55 11

ALIENS, THE   LEINSTER, MURRAY   AC   BKM 60 03
ALIENS, THE   LEINSTER, MURRAY   NV   ASF 59 08
FUGITIVE FROM SPACE   LEINSTER, MURRAY   NA   AMZ 54 05
ANTHROPOLOGICAL NOTE   LEINSTER, MURRAY   NV   FSF 57 04
SKIT-TREE PLANET   LEINSTER, MURRAY   SS   TWS 47 04
THING FROM THE SKY   LEINSTER, MURRAY   SS   NEW 60 AC

ALIENS, THE   SILVERBERG, ROBERT   AN H NEL 76
INTRODUCTION   SILVERBERG, ROBERT   IN
EYE FOR A WHAT?, AN   KNIGHT, DAMON   NV   GAL 57 03
HOP-FRIEND   CARR, TERRY   SS   FSF 62 11
FIREWATER   TENN, WILLIAM   SN   ASF 52 02
ARENA   BROWN, FREDRIC   NV   ASF 44 06
COUNTERCHARM   WHITE, JAMES   SS   NWS 60 11
LOOK, YOU THINK YOU'VE GOT TROUBLES
                                 CARR, CAROL   SS   ORB 69 05
SUNDANCE   SILVERBERG, ROBERT   SS   FSF 69 06

ALL ABOUT THE FUTURE   GREENBERG , MARTIN   AN H GNM 55
FOREWORD   GREENBERG , MARTIN   IN
WHERE TO? (ALSO AS PANDORA'S BOX)
                                 HEINLEIN, ROBERT A.   IN   GAL 52 02
LET'S NOT   ASIMOV, ISAAC   SS   BUG 54 12
MIDAS PLAGUE, THE   POHL, FREDERIK   NA   GAL 54 04
UN-MAN   ANDERSON, POUL   SN   ASF 53 01
GRANNY WON'T KNIT   STURGEON, THEODORE   NA   GAL 54 05
NATURAL STATE   KNIGHT, DAMON   NA   GAL 54 01
HOBO GOD   JAMESON, MALCOLM   SS   ASF 44 09
BLOOD BANK   MILLER, WALTER M. JR NV   ASF 52 06
ORIGINS OF GALACTIC ETIQUETTE
                                 WELLEN, EDWARD   FA   GAL 53 10
ORIGINS OF GALACTIC LAW   WELLEN, EDWARD   FA   GAL 53 04
ORIGINS OF GALACTIC SLANG   WELLEN, EDWARD   FA   GAL 52 07
ORIGINS OF GALACTIC MEDICINE   WELLEN, EDWARD   FA   GAL 53 10

ALL ABOUT VENUS   ALDISS, BRIAN W.   AN   DEL 68 12
FOREWORD   ALDISS, BRIAN W.   IN
CLOUDED JUDGEMENTS   ALDISS, BRIAN W.   SI
DESTINIES OF THE STARS   ARRHENIUS, SVANTE   AR   18
LAST AND FIRST MEN   STAPLEDON, OLAF   EX   MTH 30
PIRATES OF VENUS (SELECTION)   BURROUGHS, EDGAR R.   EX   ARG 32 09
PERLANDRA (SELECTION)   LEWIS, C. S.   EX   LNE 43
"VENUS IS HELL|"   ALDISS, BRIAN W.   SI
EXPLORING THE PLANETS   FIRSOFF, V. A.   AR   SID 64
BIG RAIN, THE   ANDERSON, POUL   SN   ASF 54 10
INTELLIGENT LIFE IN THE UNIVERSE
                                 SAGAN, CARL   AR   66
BIG SISTER   ALDISS, BRIAN W.   SI

ALL ABOUT VENUS

```
ESCAPE TO VENUS            LOTT, S. MAKEPEACE    SS        56
SISTER PLANET             ANDERSON, POUL        SN    SAT 59 05
BEFORE EDEN               CLARKE, ARTHUR C.     SS    AMZ 61 06
OPEN QUESTION, THE        ALDISS, BRIAN W.      SI
SOME MYSTERIES OF VENUS RESOLVED
                          LOVELL, BERNARD       AR    TMS 67
DREAM OF DISTANCE         ANONYMOUS             MS        67
VENUS MYSTERY FOR SCIENTISTS DAVY, JOHN         AR    OBS 67 10
BIBLIOGRAPHY OF PRINCIPAL NONFICTION WORKS CONSULTED
                          MISC. MATERIAL        MS

ALL THE MYRIAD WAYS       NIVEN, LARRY          AC    BAL 71 06
ALL THE MYRIAD WAYS       NIVEN, LARRY          SS    GAL 68 10
PASSERBY                  NIVEN, LARRY          SS    GAL 69 09
FOR A FOGGY NIGHT         NIVEN, LARRY          SS    FSF 71 07
WAIT IT OUT               NIVEN, LARRY          SS    FUP 68
JIGSAW MAN, THE           NIVEN, LARRY          SS    DVS 67 01
NOT LONG BEFORE THE END   NIVEN, LARRY          SS    FSF 69 04
UNFINISHED STORY NO. 1    NIVEN, LARRY          SS    FSF 70 12
UNFINISHED STORY NO. 2    NIVEN, LARRY          SS    NEW 71 AC
MAN OF STEEL- WOMAN OF KLEENEX
                          NIVEN, LARRY          AR    NEW 71 AC
EXERCISE IN SPECULATION: THE THEORY AND PRACTICE OF
   TELEPORTATION          NIVEN, LARRY          AR    GAL 69 03
THEORY AND PRACTICE OF TIME TRAVEL, THE
                          NIVEN, LARRY          AR    NEW 71 AC
INCONSTANT MOON           NIVEN, LARRY          NV    NEW 71 AC
WHAT CAN YOU SAY ABOUT CHOCOLATE COVERED MANHOLE COVERS?
                          NIVEN, LARRY          SS    NEW 71 AC
BECALMED IN HELL          NIVEN, LARRY          SS    FSF 65 07

ALL THE SOUNDS OF FEAR    ELLISON, HARLAN       AC    PTH 73
FIRST 9 STORIES FROM "ALONE AGAINST TOMORROW"

ALL THE TRAPS OF EARTH AND OTHER STORIES
                          SIMAK, CLIFFORD D.    AC H DBL 62
IN ENGLAND AS "THE NIGHT OF THE PUUDLY"
ALL THE TRAPS OF EARTH    SIMAK, CLIFFORD D.    SS    FSF 60 03
GOOD NIGHT, MR. JAMES     SIMAK, CLIFFORD D.    NV    GAL 51 03
DROP DEAD                 SIMAK, CLIFFORD D.    NV    GAL 56 07
NO LIFE OF THEIR OWN      SIMAK, CLIFFORD D.    NA    GAL 59 08
SITTERS, THE              SIMAK, CLIFFORD D.    NV    GAL 58 04
CRYING JAG                SIMAK, CLIFFORD D.    SS    GAL 60 02
INSTALLMENT PLAN          SIMAK, CLIFFORD D.    NA    GAL 59 02
CONDITION OF EMPLOYMENT   SIMAK, CLIFFORD D.    SS    GAL 60 04
PROJECT MASTODON          SIMAK, CLIFFORD D.    NV    GAL 55 03

ALL THE TRAPS OF EARTH AND OTHER STORIES (BRITISH PB 2)
                          SIMAK, CLIFFORD D.    AC    FSP 64
ALL THE TRAPS OF EARTH    SIMAK, CLIFFORD D.    SS    FSF 60 03
DROP DEAD                 SIMAK, CLIFFORD D.    NV    GAL 56 07
NO LIFE OF THEIR OWN      SIMAK, CLIFFORD D.    NA    GAL 59 08
SITTERS, THE              SIMAK, CLIFFORD D.    NV    GAL 58 04

ALL THE TRAPS OF EARTH AND OTHER STORIES (6 OF 9)
                          SIMAK, CLIFFORD D.    AC    MCP 63
ALL THE TRAPS OF EARTH    SIMAK, CLIFFORD D.    SS    FSF 60 03
GOOD NIGHT, MR. JAMES     SIMAK, CLIFFORD D.    NV    GAL 51 03
DROP DEAD                 SIMAK, CLIFFORD D.    NV    GAL 56 07
SITTERS, THE              SIMAK, CLIFFORD D.    NV    GAL 58 04
INSTALLMENT PLAN          SIMAK, CLIFFORD D.    NA    GAL 59 02
CONDITION OF EMPLOYMENT   SIMAK, CLIFFORD D.    SS    GAL 60 04

ALLEY GOD, THE            FARMER, PHILIP JOSE   AC    BAL 62
ALLEY MAN, THE            FARMER, PHILIP JOSE   NV    FSF 59 06
CAPTAIN'S DAUGHTER, THE (STRANGE COMPULSION)
                          FARMER, PHILIP JOSE   SN    SPP 53 10
GOD BUSINESS, THE         FARMER, PHILIP JOSE   NA    BEY 54 03

ALMOST HUMAN              NOLAN, WILLIAM F.     AN H SVN 66
SEE "THE PSEUDO-PEOPLE"

ALONE AGAINST TOMORROW    ELLISON, HARLAN       AC H MAC 71
IN ENGLAND AS "ALL THE SOUNDS OF FEAR" AND
   "THE TIME OF THE EYE"
SONG OF THE SOUL, THE     ELLISON, HARLAN       IN
I HAVE NO MOUTH, AND I MUST SCREAM
                          ELLISON, HARLAN       SS    IFS 67 03
DISCARDED, THE (THE ABNORMALS)
                          ELLISON, HARLAN       SS    FAN 59 04
DEEPER THAN DARKNESS      ELLISON, HARLAN       NV    INF 57 04
BLIND LIGHTNING           ELLISON, HARLAN       SS    FUN 56 06
ALL THE SOUNDS OF FEAR    ELLISON, HARLAN       SS    SDM 62 07
SILVER CORRIDOR, THE      ELLISON, HARLAN       NV    INF 56 10
"REPENT, HARLEQUIN!" SAID THE TICKTOCKMAN
                          ELLISON, HARLAN       SS    GAL 65 12
BRIGHT EYES               ELLISON, HARLAN       SS    FAN 65 04
ARE YOU LISTENING?        ELLISON, HARLAN       SS    AMZ 58 12
TRY A DULL KNIFE          ELLISON, HARLAN       SS    FSF 68 10
IN LONELY LANDS           ELLISON, HARLAN       SS    FUN 59 01
EYES OF DUST              ELLISON, HARLAN       SS    ROG 59 12
NOTHING FOR MY NOON MEAL  ELLISON, HARLAN       SS    NEB 58 05
O YE OF LITTLE FAITH      ELLISON, HARLAN       SS    KNT 68 09
TIME OF THE EYE, THE      ELLISON, HARLAN       SS    SMM 59 05
LIFE HUTCH                ELLISON, HARLAN       SS    IFS 56 04
VERY LAST DAY OF A GOOD WOMAN, THE (THE LAST DAY)
                          ELLISON, HARLAN       SS    ROG 58 11
NIGHT VIGIL (YELLOW STREAK HERO)
                          ELLISON, HARLAN       SS    AMZ 57 05
LONELYACHE               ELLISON, HARLAN       SS    KNT 64 07
PENNIES, OFF A DEAD MAN'S EYES
                          ELLISON, HARLAN       SS    GAL 69 11

ALONE BY NIGHT            CONGDON, MICHAEL&DON  AN    BAL 62 01
SWEETS TO THE SWEET       BLOCH, ROBERT         SS    WRT 47 03
STRANGE CHILDREN, THE     HOLDING, ELIZABETH S  SS    FSF 55 08
```

```
LIKENESS OF JULIE, THE    SWANSON, LOGAN        SS    NEW 62 AN
IT WILL COME TO YOU       LONG, FRANK BELKNAP   SS    UNK 42 AN
GNOME THERE WAS, A        KUTTNER, HENRY        NV    UNK 41 10
NIGHTMARE AT 20,000 FEET  MATHESON, RICHARD     SS    NEW 62 AN
IN THE MIDST OF DEATH     HECHT, BEN            SS        45
GABRIEL-ERNEST            SAKI                  SS        30
BAYNTER'S IMP             DERLETH, AUGUST       SS    WRT 43 09
ENOCH                     BLOCH, ROBERT         SS    WRT 46 09
FOR THE BLOOD IS THE LIFE CRAWFORD, F. MARION   SS        11

ALPHA 1                   SILVERBERG, ROBERT    AN    BAL 70 09
INTRODUCTION              SILVERBERG, ROBERT    IN
POOR LITTLE WARRIOR!      ALDISS, BRIAN W.      SS    FSF 58 04
MOON MOTH, THE            VANCE, JACK           NA    GAL 61 08
TESTAMENT OF ANDROS       BLISH, JAMES          NV    FUT 53 01
TRIPTYCH, A               MALZBERG, BARRY N.    SS    FSF 69 07
FOR A BREATH I TARRY      ZELAZNY, ROGER        NV    NWS 66 0
GAME FOR MOTEL ROOM       LEIBER, FRITZ         SS    FSF 63 03
THUS WE FRUSTRATE CHARLEMAGNE
                          LAFFERTY, R. A.       SS    GAL 67 02
MAN WHO CAME EARLY, THE   ANDERSON, POUL        NV    FSF 56 06
TIME OF HIS LIFE, THE     EISENBERG, LARRY      SS    FSF 68 04
DOCTOR, THE               THOMAS, THEODORE L.   SS    ORB 67 0
TIME TRAP                 HARNESS, CHARLES L.   NV    ASF 48 08
PI MAN, THE               BESTER, ALFRED        SS    FSF 59 10
LAST MAN LEFT IN THE BAR, THE
                          KORNBLUTH, C. M.      SS    INF 57 1
TERMINAL BEACH, THE       BALLARD, J. G.        SS    NWS 64 03

ALPHA 2                   SILVERBERG, ROBERT    AN    BAL 71 11
INTRODUCTION              SILVERBERG, ROBERT    IN
CALL ME JOE               ANDERSON, POUL        NV    ASF 57 04
GOODBYE AMANDA JEAN       SHORE, WILMA          SS    GAL 70 0
MAN OF THE RENAISSANCE, A GUIN, WYMAN           SS    GAL 64 12
WALL OF CRYSTAL, EYE OF NIGHT
                          BUDRYS, ALGIS         NV    GAL 61 12
FAITH OF OUR FATHERS      DICK, PHILIP K.       NV    DVS 67 0
THAT SHARE OF GLORY       KORNBLUTH, C. M.      NV    ASF 52 0
MEN RETURN, THE           VANCE, JACK           SS    INF 57 0
VOICES OF TIME, THE       BALLARD, J. G.        NV    NWS 60 1
BURNING OF THE BRAIN, THE SMITH, CORDWAINER     SS    IFS 58 1
SHAKER REVIVAL, THE       JONAS, GERALD         NV    GAL 70 0

ALPHA 3                   SILVERBERG, ROBERT    AN    BAL 72 10
INTRODUCTION              SILVERBERG, ROBERT    IN
GIFT OF GAB, THE          VANCE, JACK           NV    ASF 55 0
BEYOND LIES THE WUB       DICK, PHILIP K.       SS    PLS 52 0
NINE HUNDRED GRANDMOTHERS LAFFERTY, R. A.       SS    IFS 66 0
TOTAL ENVIRONMENT         ALDISS, BRIAN W.      NV    GAL 68 0
DAY MILLION               POHL, FREDERIK        SS    ROG 66 0
ARISTOTLE AND THE GUN     DE CAMP, L. SPRAGUE   NV    ASF 58 0
UNDER OLD EARTH           SMITH, CORDWAINER     NV    GAL 66 0
SHADOW OF SPACE, THE      FARMER, PHILIP JOSE   NV    IFS 67 1
COME TO VENUS MELANCHOLY  DISCH, THOMAS M.      SS    FSF 65 1
RESCUE PARTY              CLARKE, ARTHUR C.     NV    ASF 46 0

ALPHA 4                   SILVERBERG, ROBERT    AN    BAL 73 10
INTRODUCTION              SILVERBERG, ROBERT    IN
CASABLANCA                DISCH, THOMAS M.      NV        67
DIO (ALSO AS THE DYING MAN) KNIGHT, DAMON       SN    INF 57 0
EASTWARD HO!              TENN, WILLIAM         SS    FSF 58 1
JUDAS DANCED (JUDAS DANCING) ALDISS, BRIAN W.   SS    SMG 58 0
ANGEL'S EGG               PANGBORN, EDGAR       NV    GAL 51 0
IN HIS IMAGE (IN MAN'S IMAGE)
                          CARR, TERRY           SS    AMZ 71 0
ALL PIECES OF A RIVER SHORE LAFFERTY, R. A.     SS    ORB 70 0
WE ALL DIE NAKED          BLISH, JAMES          NA    TFT 69
CARCINOMA ANGELS          SPINRAD, NORMAN       SS    DVS 67 0
MOTHER                    FARMER, PHILIP JOSE   NV    TWS 53 0
5,271,009 (ALSO AS THE STARCOMBER)
                          BESTER, ALFRED        NV    FSF 54 0

ALPHA 5                   SILVERBERG, ROBERT    AN    BAL 74 08
INTRODUCTION              SILVERBERG, ROBERT    IN
STAR PIT, THE             DELANY, SAMUEL R.     NV    WOT 67 0
BABY, YOU WERE GREAT      WILHELM, KATE         SS    ORB 67 0
LIVE, FROM BERCHTESGADEN  EFFINGER, GEO. ALEC   SS    ORB 72 1
AS NEVER WAS              MILLER, P. SCHUYLER   SS    ASF 44 0
WE CAN REMEMBER IT FOR YOU WHOLESALE
                          DICK, PHILIP K.       NV    FSF 66 0
YESTERDAY HOUSE           LEIBER, FRITZ         NV    GAL 52 0
MAN MUST DIE, A           CLUTE, JOHN           SS    NWS 66 1
SKILLS OF XANADU, THE     STURGEON, THEODORE    NV    GAL 56 0
SPECIAL KIND OF MORNING, A DOZOIS, GARDNER R.   NV    NDM 71 0

ALPHA 6                   SILVERBERG, ROBERT    AN    BKM 76 04
INTRODUCTION              SILVERBERG, ROBERT    IN
LOST CONTINENT, THE       SPINRAD, NORMAN       NV    SAG 70
LIGHT OF OTHER DAYS       SHAW, BOB             SS    ASF 66 0
SECRET OF THE OLD CUSTARD, THE (THE BABE IN THE OVEN)
                          SLADEK, JOHN T.       SS    IFS 66 1
DOWN AMONG THE DEAD MEN   TENN, WILLIAM         NV    GAL 54 0
WITH THESE HANDS          KORNBLUTH, C. M.      NV    GAL 51 1
SHORT IN THE CHEST        SEABRIGHT, IDRIS      SS    FUN 54 0
BROWN ROBERT              CARR, TERRY           SS    FSF 62 0
FOOD FARM, THE            REED, KIT             SS    ORB 67 0
HONORABLE DEATH, AN       DICKSON, GORDON R.    NV    GAL 61 0
MAN OF PARTS              GOLD, H. L.           SS    NTL 54
PAINWISE                  TIPTREE, JAMES JR.    SS    FSF 72 0

ALPHA 7                   SILVERBERG, ROBERT    AN    BKM 77 07
INTRODUCTION              SILVERBERG, ROBERT    IN
DUNE ROLLER               MAY, JULIAN C.        NV    ASF 51 1
SHAPE (KEEP YOUR SHAPE)   SHECKLEY, ROBERT      NV    GAL 53 1
TRANSFER POINT            BOUCHER, ANTHONY      SS    GAL 50 1
GALAXY CALLED ROME, A     MALZBERG, BARRY N.    NV    FSF 75 0
```

LPHA 7   ANALOG 7

REJOICE, REJOICE, WE HAVE NO CHOICE
                          CARR, TERRY   SS
ORPHANS OF THE VOID   SHAARA, MICHAEL   NV   GAL 52 06
LUCKIEST MAN IN DENV, THE (AS SIMON EISNER)
                          KORNBLUTH, C. M.   SS   GAL 52 06
FOR LOVE   BUDRYS, ALGIS   NV   GAL 62 06
WORLD WAR TWO   EFFINGER, GEO. ALEC   SS   VTX 73 10
NIGHT OF HOGGY DARN, THE MCKENNA, RICHARD   NV   IFS 58 12

LTERNATE ORBITS   CHANDLER, A. BERTRAM   DC   ACE 71
HALL OF FAME (KINGSOLVING'S PLANET IRREGULARS)
                          CHANDLER, A. BERTRAM   NV   GAL 69 07
SISTER SHIPS, THE   CHANDLER, A. BERTRAM   NV   GAL 71 09
MAN WHO SAILED THE SKY, THE CHANDLER, A. BERTRAM NV
RUB, THE   CHANDLER, A. BERTRAM   NV   GAL 70 04

LTERNATIES   GERROLD, DAVID   OA   DEL 74 07
INTRODUCTION   GERROLD, DAVID   IN
SAND CASTLES   HALDEMAN, JACK C. II   SS   ALT 74
P.T.A. MEETS CHE GUEVARA, THE
                         MALZBERG, BARRY N.   SS   ALT 74
LEGEND OF LONNIE AND THE SEVEN TEN SPLIT, THE
                         BLAKE, E. MICHAEL   NV   ALT 74
WEBSTER   BEAR, GREG   SS   ALT 74
FIRST FEW KINDS OF TRUTH, THE
                         SALLIS, JAMES   SS   ALT 74
GROSS LOVE STORY, A   COVER, ARTHUR BYRON   SS   ALT 74
RECOURSE, INC.   MCINTYRE, VONDA N.   SS   ALT 74
SIGN AT THE END OF THE UNIVERSE
                         ACKERSON, DUANE   SS   ALT 74
NO ROOM FOR THE WANDERER SAYE, LEE   SS   ALT 74
HUNG LIKE AN ELEPHANT   PUMILIA, JOSEPH F.
                         AND UTLEY, STEVEN   SS C ALT 74
DELTA FLIGHT 281   SALLIS, JAMES   SS   ALT 74
MESSAGE OF JOY   COVER, ARTHUR BYRON   SS   ALT 74
WOMB, WITH A VIEW   UTLEY, STEVEN   SS   ALT 74
HOW XMAS GHOSTS ARE MADE BUNCH, DAVID R.   SS   ALT 74
COWBOYS, INDIANS   BRYANT, EDWARD   SS   ALT 74

LTERNATING CURRENTS   POHL, FREDERIK   AC   BAL 56
HAPPY BIRTHDAY, DEAR JESUS POHL, FREDERIK   SS   NEW 56 AC
GHOST MAKER, THE   POHL, FREDERIK   SS   BEY 54 01
LET THE ANTS TRY   POHL, FREDERIK   SS   PLS 49 WI
PYTHIAS   POHL, FREDERIK   SS   GAL 55 02
MAPMAKERS, THE   POHL, FREDERIK   NV   GAL 55 07
RAFFERTY'S REASONS   POHL, FREDERIK   SS   FUN 55 10
TARGET ONE   POHL, FREDERIK   SS   GAL 55 04
GRANDY DEVIL   POHL, FREDERIK   SS   GAL 55 06
TUNNEL UNDER THE WORLD, THE POHL, FREDERIK   NV   GAL 55 01
WHAT TO DO TILL THE ANALYST COMES (EVERYBODY'S HAPPY BUT ME|)
                         POHL, FREDERIK   SS   IMG 56 02

LYX   RUSS, JOANNA   AC H GRG 76 06
INTRODUCTION   DELANY, SAMUEL R.   IN
BLUESTOCKING (THE ADVENTURESS)
                         RUSS, JOANNA   NV   ORB 67 02
I THOUGHT SHE WAS AFEARED TILL SHE STROKED MY BEARD (I GAVE
   HER SACK AND SHERRY) RUSS, JOANNA   NV   ORB 67 02
BARBARIAN, THE   RUSS, JOANNA   NV   ORB 68 03
PICNIC ON PARADISE   RUSS, JOANNA   NO   ACE 68
SECOND INQUISITION, THE RUSS, JOANNA   NV   ORB 70 06

MERICAN GOVERNMENT THROUGH SCIENCE FICTION
                         OLANDER/GREENBERG/&   AN L RAN 74
PREFACE   OLANDER, JOSEPH D.
                         GREENBERG, MARTIN H.
                         AND WARRICK, PATRICIA S. IN C
FOREWORD   POHL, FREDERIK   IN
RADICAL CENTER   REYNOLDS, MACK   NV   ASF 67 03
OOGENESIS OF BIRD CITY, THE FARMER, PHILIP JOSE SS   AMZ 70 09
FRANK MERRIWELL IN THE WHITE HOUSE
                         MOORE, WARD   NV   GAL 73 11
HAIL TO THE CHIEF   GARRETT, RANDALL   SS   ASF 62
HAIL TO THE CHIEF   SACKETT, SAM   SN   FUT 54 06
POLICY AND CUSTOM OF THE CAMIROI
                         LAFFERTY, R. A.   SS   GAL 72 06
REQUEST FOR PROPOSAL   LEWIS, ANTHONY R.   SS   ASF 72 11
MAY THE BEST MAN WIN   SCHMIDT, STANLEY   SS   ASF 71 03
1980 PRESIDENT, THE   DEFORD, MIRIAM ALLEN   SS   GAL 64 10
RESTRICTED CLIENTELE   CROSSEN, KENDELL F.   SS   TWS 51 02
WELCOME, COMRADE   BAGLEY, SIMON   NV   FSF 64 04
DELEGATE FROM GUAPANGA, THE GUIN, WYMAN   NV   GAL 64 08
CHAMELEON, THE   EISENBERG, LARRY   SS   FSF 70 03
FREAK, THE   WYAL, PG   SS   FSF 69 04
RIGHT TO RESIST, THE   LAUMER, KEITH   SS   IFS 71 06
RIGHT TO REVOLT, THE   LAUMER, KEITH   SS   IFS 71 06
ASSASSINATION OF JOHN FITZGERALD KENNEDY CONSIDERED AS A
   DOWNHILL MOTOR RACE, THE BALLARD, J. G.   SS   NWS 67 02
SELECTED BIBLIOGRAPHY   MISC. MATERIAL   MS

MONG THE DEAD   BRYANT, EDWARD   AC H MAC 73
INTRODUCTION: LOCI   BRYANT, EDWARD   IN
HANGED MAN, THE   BRYANT, EDWARD   SS   CLR 72 02
SHARK   BRYANT, EDWARD   NV   ORB 73 12
NO. 2 PLAIN TANK AUXILIARY FILL STRUCTURAL LIMIT 17,605 LBS.
   FUEL-PWA SPEC. 522 REVISED BRYANT, EDWARD   NV   NDM 72 02
ADRIFT ON THE FREEWAY   BRYANT, EDWARD   SS   QRK 70 01
JODY AFTER THE WAR   BRYANT, EDWARD   SS   ORB 72 10
TELEIDOSCOPE   BRYANT, EDWARD   SS   NEW 73 AC
POET IN THE HOLOGRAM IN THE MIDDLE OF PRIME TIME, THE
                         BRYANT, EDWARD   SS   NOV 72 02
HUMAN SIDE OF THE VILLAGE MONSTER, THE
                         BRYANT, EDWARD   SS   UNI 71 01
AMONG THE DEAD   BRYANT, EDWARD   SS   QRK 71 02
FILE ON THE PLAGUE   BRYANT, EDWARD   SS   NLP 71 04

SOFT BLUE BUNNY RABBIT STORY, THE
                         BRYANT, EDWARD   SS   CLR 71 01
TACTICS   BRYANT, EDWARD   SS   NEW 73 AC
SENDING THE VERY BEST   BRYANT, EDWARD   SS   NWS 70 01
THEIR THOUSANDTH SEASON BRYANT, EDWARD   SS   CLR 72 02
LOVE SONG OF HERSELF   BRYANT, EDWARD   SS   NDM 71 01
PINUP   BRYANT, EDWARD   SS   ORB 73 12
DUNE'S EDGE   BRYANT, EDWARD   SS   ORB 72 11

ANALOG ANNUAL   BOVA, BEN   OA   PYR 76 04
INTRODUCTION: HUGO, JOHN AND THE MAGAZINES
                         BOVA, BEN   IN
FIGHTING MADNESS   PLAUGER, P. J.   NO
MALF   ING, DEAN   NV
HALF AN OAF   ROBINSON, SPIDER   NV
THIS TOWER OF ASHES   MARTIN, GEORGE R. R.   SS
CLIMATIC THREAT, THE   GRIBBIN, DR. JOHN   AR

ANALOG ANTHOLOGY   CAMPBELL, JOHN W. JR AN   DOB 65
PROLOGUE TO ANALOG   CAMPBELL, JOHN W. JR AN   DBL 62
ANALOG 1   CAMPBELL, JOHN W. JR AN   DBL 63
ANALOG 2   CAMPBELL, JOHN W. JR AN   DBL 64

ANALOG 1   CAMPBELL, JOHN W. JR AN H DBL 63
   IN "ANALOG ANTHOLOGY"
INTRODUCTION   CAMPBELL, JOHN W. JR   IN
MONUMENT   BIGGLE, LLOYD JR.   NV   ASF 61 06
PLAGUE, THE   KELLER, TEDDY   SS   ASF 61 02
REMEMBER THE ALAMO| FEHRENBACH, T. R.   SS   ASF 61 12
HUNCH, THE   ANVIL, CHRISTOPHER   SS   ASF 61 07
BARNACLE BULL   SANDERS, WINSTON P.   SS   ASF 60 09
JOIN OUR GANG?   LANIER, STERLING E.   SS   ASF 61 05
SLIGHT OF WIT   DICKSON, GORDON R.   SS   ASF 61 12
PROLOGUE TO...AN ANALOGUE RICHMOND, LEIGH   NV   ASF 61 06

ANALOG 2   CAMPBELL, JOHN W. JR AN H DBL 64
   IN "ANALOG ANTHOLOGY"
PREFACE   CAMPBELL, JOHN W. JR   IN
WEATHER MAN, THE   THOMAS, THEODORE L.   SN   ASF 62 06
GOOD INDIAN   REYNOLDS, MACK   SS   ASF 62 09
BLIND MAN'S LANTERN   LANG, ALLEN KIM   NV   ASF 62 12
JUNIOR ACHIEVEMENT   LEE, WILLIAM M.   SS   ASF 62 07
NOVICE   SCHMITZ, JAMES H.   NV   ASF 62 06
ETHICAL QUOTIENT   PHILLIFENT, JOHN T.   SN   ASF 62 12
PHILOSOPHER'S STONE   ANVIL, CHRISTOPHER   SS   ASF 63 01
CIRCUIT RIDERS, THE   FITZPATRICK, R. C.   SS   ASF 62 04

ANALOG 3   CAMPBELL, JOHN W. JR AN H DBL 65
   ALSO AS "A WORLD BY THE TALE"
INTRODUCTION   CAMPBELL, JOHN W. JR   IN
HILIFTER   DICKSON, GORDON R.   SS   ASF 63 02
NOT IN THE LITERATURE   ANVIL, CHRISTOPHER   SS   ASF 63 03
SONNY   RAPHAEL, RICK   SS   ASF 63 04
TROUBLE WITH TELSTAR, THE BERRYMAN, JOHN   NV   ASF 63 06
NEW FOLKS' HOME   SIMAK, CLIFFORD D.   SS   ASF 63 07
INDUSTRIAL REVOLUTION   SANDERS, WINSTON P.   SN   ASF 63 09
WORLD BY THE TALE, A   MCKETTRIG, SEATON   SS   ASF 63 10
THIN EDGE   MACKENZIE, J. B.   SS   ASF 63 12

ANALOG 4   CAMPBELL, JOHN W. JR AN H DBL 66
   ALSO AS "THE PERMANENT IMPLOSION"
THESE STORIES MAY UPSET YOU CAMPBELL, JOHN W. JR IN
SUBJECTIVITY   SPINRAD, NORMAN   SS   ASF 64 01
PERMANENT IMPLOSION, THE MCLAUGHLIN, DEAN   NV   ASF 64 02
SUNJAMMER   ANDERSON, POUL   NV   ASF 64 04
DAY IN THE LIFE OF KELVIN THROOP, A
                         PHILLIPS, R. A. J.   SS   ASF 64 07
GENUS TRAITOR   REYNOLDS, MACK   NV   ASF 64 09
CASE OF IDENTITY, A   GARRETT, RANDALL   NV   ASF 64 09
MARY CELESTE MOVE, THE   HERBERT, FRANK   SS   ASF 64 10

ANALOG 5   CAMPBELL, JOHN W. JR AN H DBL 67
   ALSO AS "COUNTERCOMMANDMENT"
"SCIENTISTS ARE STUPID|" CAMPBELL, JOHN W. JR   IN
COINCIDENCE DAY   BRUNNER, JOHN   SS   ASF 65 02
ADVENTURE OF THE EXTRATERRESTRIAL, THE
                         REYNOLDS, MACK   NV   ASF 65 07
FIGHTING DIVISION   GARRETT, RANDALL   SS   ASF 65 08
COMPUTERS DON'T ARGUE   DICKSON, GORDON R.   SS   ASF 65 09
SAY IT WITH FLOWERS   SANDERS, WINSTON P.   SS   ASF 65 09
MISSION "RED CLASH"   POYER, JOE   NV   ASF 65 12
COUNTERCOMMANDMENT   MEADOWS, PATRICK   SS   ASF 65 05
BALANCED ECOLOGY   SCHMITZ, JAMES H.   SS   ASF 65 03
OVERPROOF   MACKENZIE, J. B.   NV   ASF 65 10

ANALOG 6   CAMPBELL, JOHN W. JR AN H DBL 68
INTRODUCTION   CAMPBELL, JOHN W. JR   IN
PROTOTAPH   LAUMER, KEITH   SS   ASF 66 03
BOOKWORM, RUN| VINGE, VERNOR   NV   ASF 66 03
EASY WAY OUT, THE   CORREY, LEE   SS   ASF 66 03
GIANT METEOR IMPACT   ENEVER, J. E.   AR   ASF 66 03
EARLY WARNING   SCOTT, ROBIN S.   SS   ASF 66 06
CALL HIM LORD   DICKSON, GORDON R.   SS   ASF 66 05
CWACC STRIKES AGAIN   DEMPSEY, HANK   NV   ASF 66 06
STRANGLEHOLD   ANVIL, CHRISTOPHER   SS   ASF 66 06
MESSAGE, THE   ANTHONY, PIERS
                         AND HALL, FRANCES   NV C ASF 66 07
LIGHT OF OTHER DAYS   SHAW, BOB   SS   ASF 66 08
SOMETHING TO SAY   BERRYMAN, JOHN   NV   ASF 66 08
LETTER FROM A HIGHER CRITIC ROBB, STEWART   SS   ASF 66 11
NOT A PRISON MAKE   MARTINO, JOSEPH P.   SS   ASF 66 08
10:01 A.M.   MALEC, ALEXANDER B.   SS   ASF 66 03

ANALOG 7   CAMPBELL, JOHN W. JR AN H DBL 70
AIM FOR THE HEEL   PHILLIFENT, JOHN T.   NV   ASF 67 07
FIESTA BRAVA   REYNOLDS, MACK   SN   ASF 67 09

ANALOG 7   ANOTHER PART OF THE GALAXY

FREE VACATION   MACFARLANE, WALLACE SS   ASF 67 10
FEATHERBEDDERS, THE   HERBERT, FRANK   NV   ASF 67 08
WEYR SEARCH   MCCAFFREY, ANNE   SN   ASF 67 10
LAST COMMAND, THE   LAUMER, KEITH   SS   ASF 67 01
DEAD END   HODUS, MIKE   SS   ASF 67 05
THERE IS A CROOKED MAN   WODHAMS, JACK   SN   ASF 67 02
BURDEN OF PROOF   SHAW, BOB   SS   ASF 67 05

ANALOG 8   CAMPBELL, JOHN W. JR AN H DBL 71
GOTTLOS   KAPP, COLIN   NV   ASF 69 11
IN HIS IMAGE   CHILSON, ROBERT   NV   ASF 69 09
HAWK AMONG THE SPARROWS   MCLAUGHLIN, DEAN   SN   ASF 68 07
POWERS OF OBSERVATION, THE   HARRISON, HARRY   SS   ASF 68 09
JUMP   EARLS, WILLIAM   SS   ASF 69 10
WOMB TO TOMB   WESLEY, JOSEPH   SS   ASF 69 08
HIDDEN EARS, THE   PERKINS, LAWRENCE A. SS   ASF 69 01
WINKIN, BLINKIN AND PI R SQUARE
                             FITZPATRICK, R. C.   SS   ASF 68 07
TESTING...ONE, TWO, THREE, FOUR
                             CHAPMAN, STEVE   SS   ASF 69 12

ANALOG 9   BOVA, BEN   AN H DBL 73
INTRODUCTION   BOVA, BEN   IN
ANSWER "AFFIRMATIVE" OR "NEGATIVE"
                             PAUL, BARBARA   SS   ASF 72 04
GOLD AT THE STARBOW'S END, THE
                             POHL, FREDERIK   NV   ASF 72 03
PLAGUE, THE   LAUMER, KEITH   NV   ASF 70 11
MISSING MAN, THE   MACLEAN, KATHERINE   NV   ASF 71 03
OUT, WIT!   MYERS, HOWARD L.   SS   ASF 72 06
HERO   HALDEMAN, JOE W.   NV   ASF 72 06

ANCESTRAL VOICES   MENVILLE & REGINALD AN H ANO 74
GLANCE AHEAD: BEING A CHRISTMAS TALE OF A.D. 3568, A
                             BANGS, JOHN KENDRICK SS   01
THIRD EYE, THE   CHAMBERS, ROBERT W. SS   15
SPACE ANNIHILATOR, THE   CUMMINS, HARLE OREN SS   02
CORNER IN LIGHTNING, A   GRIFFITH, GEORGE   SS   PRS 98 03
LIZARD, THE   HYNE, C.J. CUTCLIFFE SS   04
ROMANCE OF THE FIRST RADICAL, THE
                             LANG, ANDREW   SS   87
RED ONE, THE   LONDON, JACK   NV   CMP 18 10
BEYOND THE SPECTRUM   ROBERTSON, MORGAN   SS   14
IMPOSSIBILITY, A STUDY OF REASON AND SCIENCE
                             SULLIVAN, JAMES F.   SS   00
LOVE AND THE TRIANGLE   WATERLOO, STANLEY   SS   99

ANCIENT MYSTERIES READER, THE
                             HAINING, PETER   AN H DBL 75
GRISLY FOLK, THE   WELLS, H. G.   AR   SRY 21 04
MOUND BUILDERS, THE   HEARN, LAFCADIO   AR
NEW GOD WAS BORN, A   TRAVERN, B.   AR
COMING RACE, THE (EXCERPT)   LYTTON, EDWARD B.   EX
SHINING PYRAMID, THE   MACHEN, ARTHUR   SS   UKW 95 05
TERROR OF BLUE JOHN GAP, THE DOYLE, ARTHUR CONAN SS   10
VALLEY OF THE SORCERESS, THE ROHMER, SAX   SS
MS FOUND IN A BOTTLE   POE, EDGAR ALLEN   SS   BSV 33 10
LOST CONTINENT, THE   HOUSEHOLD, GEOFFREY SS   SEP 60 09
OFFERING TO THE MOON, AN   SMITH, CLARK ASHTON SS   WRT 53 09
MOON POOL, THE   MERRITT, A.   NA   ASW 18 06
CALL OF CTHULHU, THE   LOVECRAFT, H. P.   NV   WRT 28 02
CONVENIENT MONSTER, THE   CHARTERIS, LESLIE   SS
MEN WITHOUT BONES   KERSH, GERALD   SS   ESQ
CREATURE OF THE SNOWS   SAMBROT, WILLIAM   SS   SEP 60 10
SECRET OF STONEHENGE, THE   HARRISON, HARRY   SS   FSF 68 06
BALD-HEADED MIRAGE, THE   BLOCH, ROBERT   SS   AMZ 60 06
CAVE OF HISTORY, THE   STURGEON, THEODORE   SS

ANCIENT, MY ENEMY   DICKSON, GORDON R.   AC H DBL 74
ANCIENT, MY ENEMY   DICKSON, GORDON R.   NV   IFS 69 12
ODD ONES, THE   DICKSON, GORDON R.   SS   IFS 55 02
MONKEY WRENCH, THE   DICKSON, GORDON R.   SS   ASF 51 08
TIGER GREEN   DICKSON, GORDON R.   NV   IFS 65 11
FRIENDLY MAN, THE   DICKSON, GORDON R.   SS   ASF 51 02
LOVE ME TRUE   DICKSON, GORDON R.   SS   ASF 61 10
OUR FIRST DEATH   DICKSON, GORDON R.   SS   FSF 55 08
IN THE BONE   DICKSON, GORDON R.   NV   IFS 66 10
BLEAK AND BARREN LAND, THE   DICKSON, GORDON R.   NV   SPS 53 02

AND SOME WERE HUMAN   DEL REY, LESTER   AC H PRM 48
FOREWORD   DEL REY, LESTER   IN
HEREAFTER, INC.   DEL REY, LESTER   SS   UNK 41 12
DAY IS DONE, THE   DEL REY, LESTER   SS   ASF 39 05
FORSAKING ALL OTHERS   DEL REY, LESTER   SS   UNK 39 08
COPPERSMITH, THE   DEL REY, LESTER   SS   UNK 39 09
LUCK OF IGNATZ, THE   DEL REY, LESTER   NV   ASF 39 08
FAITHFUL, THE   DEL REY, LESTER   SS   ASF 38 04
DARK MISSION   DEL REY, LESTER   SS   ASF 40 07
HELEN O'LOY   DEL REY, LESTER   SS   ASF 38 12
STARS LOOK DOWN, THE   DEL REY, LESTER   NV   ASF 40 08
RENEGADE, THE   DEL REY, LESTER   SS   ASF 43 07
WINGS OF NIGHT, THE   DEL REY, LESTER   SS   ASF 42 03
NERVES   DEL REY, LESTER   NV   ASF 42 09

AND SOME WERE HUMAN (8 OF 12)
                             DEL REY, LESTER   AC   BAL 61
FOREWORD   DEL REY, LESTER   IN
HEREAFTER, INC.   DEL REY, LESTER   SS   UNK 41 12
DAY IS DONE, THE   DEL REY, LESTER   SS   ASF 39 05
FORSAKING ALL OTHERS   DEL REY, LESTER   SS   UNK 39 08
LUCK OF IGNATZ, THE   DEL REY, LESTER   NV   ASF 39 08
DARK MISSION   DEL REY, LESTER   SS   ASF 40 07
HELEN O'LOY   DEL REY, LESTER   SS   ASF 38 12
RENEGADE, THE   DEL REY, LESTER   SS   ASF 43 07
WINGS OF NIGHT, THE   DEL REY, LESTER   SS   ASF 42 03

AND WALK NOW GENTLY THROUGH THE FIRE...
                             ELWOOD, ROGER   OA H CHL 72
INTRODUCTION   DALY, MARSHA   IN
STELLA   WHITE, TED   SS   WLK 73
MAKING IT THROUGH   MALZBERG, BARRY N.   SS   WLK 73
AND WALK NOW GENTLY THROUGH THE FIRE...
                             LAFFERTY, R. A.   NV   WLK 73
GIFT OF NOTHING, THE   HOLLY, JOAN C.   NV   WLK 73
FOREVER AND AMEN   BLOCH, ROBERT   SS   WLK 73
AND THE POWER...   PAYES, RACHEL C.   SS   WLK 73
CAUGHT IN THE ORGAN DRAFT   SILVERBERG, ROBERT   SS   WLK 73
SENSE OF DIFFERENCE, A   SARGENT, PAMELA   SS   WLK 73
MOTHER EARTH WANTS YOU   FARMER, PHILIP JOSE SS   WLK 73
CHRONICLES OF A COMER   O'DONNELL, K. M.   SS   WLK 73

ANDOVER AND THE ANDROID   WILHELM, KATE   AC H DOB 66
     SEE "THE MILE-LONG SPACESHIP"

ANDROIDS, TIME MACHINES AND BLUE GIRAFFES
                             ELWOOD & GHIDALIA   AN H FOL 73
PREFACE   ELWOOD, ROGER   IN
MOXON'S MASTER   BIERCE, AMBROSE   SS   93
METAL MAN, THE   WILLIAMSON, JACK   SS   AMZ 28 12
LENNY   ASIMOV, ISAAC   SS   INF 58 01
GRANDMA WAS NEVER LIKE THIS PAYES, RACHEL C.   SS   NEW 73 AM
HORLA, THE (1886)   DE MAUPASSANT, GUY   SS   WRT 26 08
COUNTER CHARM, THE   ST. CLAIR, MARGARET SS   FFM 49 08
HOUSE IN THE VALLEY, THE   DERLETH, AUGUST   NV   WRT 53 07
UNPICKER, THE   TEMPLE, WILLIAM F.   SS   NEW 73 AM
FRANK READE JUNIOR'S AIR WONDER (1876)
                             SENARENS, LOUIS P.   SS   BNY 76
MACHINE, THE   CAMPBELL, JOHN W. JR SS   ASF 35 02
CALLING DR. CLOCKWORK   GOULART, RON   SS   AMZ 65 03
RUNNING, THE   POSNER, RICHARD   SS   NEW 73 AM
KING PEST   POE, EDGAR ALLEN   SS   SLM 35 09
WHITE APE, THE   LOVECRAFT, H. P.   SS   WRT 24 04
BLUE GIRAFFE, THE   DE CAMP, L. SPRAGUE NV   ASF 39 08
MUTANT WEAPON, THE   SILVERBERG, ROBERT   SS   NEW 73 AM
CHRONIC ARGONAUTS, THE   WELLS, H. G.   NV   SSJ 88 04
TIME FOR SALE   FARLEY, RALPH MILNE SS   AMZ 38 03
WHERE THE TIME WENT   SCHMITZ, JAMES H.   SS   IFS 68 11
FORERUNNER   SUTTON, JEFF   SS   NEW 73 AM
BEGUM'S FORTUNE, THE (1879) VERNE, JULES   EX
SON OF THE STARS   BINDER, EANDO   SS   FFM 40 02
SUNJAMMER (ALSO AS THE WIND FROM THE SUN)
                             CLARKE, ARTHUR C.   SS   BLF 64
TERRA PHOBIA   KOONTZ, DEAN R.   SS   NEW 73 AM
MAINCHANCE   TATE, PETER   NV   ANA 70

ANDROMEDA I   WESTON, PETER   OA   FPL 76
INTRODUCTION   WESTON, PETER   IN
APPEARANCE OF LIFE   ALDISS, BRIAN W.   SS   76
STARTHINKER 9   CONEY, MICHAEL G.   SS
WALTZ OF THE BODYSNATCHERS   SHAW, BOB   NV
TRAVELLERS   HOLDSTOCK, ROBERT P. NV
VALLEY OF THE BUSHES   MITCHISON, NAOMI   SS
INFINITE SUMMER, AN   PRIEST, CHRISTOPHER NV
DOLL   GREENHOUGH, TERRY   SS
BEAST FOR NORN, A   MARTIN, GEORGE R. R. NV
GIANT KILLERS, THE   STEPHENSON, ANDREW M NV
SEEING   ELLISON, HARLAN   SS

ANGELS AND SPACESHIPS   BROWN, FREDRIC   AC H DUT 54 09
   ALSO AS "STAR SHINE"
INTRODUCTION   BROWN, FREDRIC   IN
PATTERN   BROWN, FREDRIC   SS   NEW 54 AC
PLACET IS A CRAZY PLACE   BROWN, FREDRIC   SS   ASF 46 05
ANSWER   BROWN, FREDRIC   SS   NEW 54 AC
ETAOIN SHRDLU   BROWN, FREDRIC   SS   UNK 42 02
PREPOSTEROUS   BROWN, FREDRIC   SS   NEW 54 AC
ARMAGEDDON   BROWN, FREDRIC   SS   UNK 41 08
POLITENESS (TRIPLICATE TWISTEROO)
                             BROWN, FREDRIC   SS   PBY 57 03
WAVERIES, THE   BROWN, FREDRIC   SS   ASF 45 01
RECONCILIATION   BROWN, FREDRIC   SS   NEW 54 AC
HAT TRICK, THE   BROWN, FREDRIC   SS   UNK 43 02
SEARCH   BROWN, FREDRIC   SS
LETTER TO A PHOENIX   BROWN, FREDRIC   SS   ASF 49 08
DAISIES (TRIPLICATE TWISTEROO)
                             BROWN, FREDRIC   SS   PBY 57 03
ANGELIC ANGLEWORM, THE   BROWN, FREDRIC   NV   UNK 43 02
SENTENCE (TRIPLICATE TWISTEROO)
                             BROWN, FREDRIC   SS   PBY 57 03
YEHUDI PRINCIPLE, THE   BROWN, FREDRIC   SS   ASF 44 05
SOLIPSIST   BROWN, FREDRIC   SS

ANOTHER KIND   OLIVER, CHAD   AC H BAL 55
MOTHER OF NECESSITY, THE   OLIVER, CHAD   SS   NEW 55 AC
RITE OF PASSAGE   OLIVER, CHAD   NV   ASF 54 04
SCIENTIFIC METHOD (HANDS ACROSS SPACE)
                             OLIVER, CHAD   SS   SFP 53 08
NIGHT   OLIVER, CHAD   SS   IFS 55 03
TRANSFORMER   OLIVER, CHAD   SS   FSF 54 11
ARTIFACT   OLIVER, CHAD   NV   FSF 55 06
STAR ABOVE IT, A   OLIVER, CHAD   SS   NEW 55 AC

ANOTHER PART OF THE GALAXY   CONKLIN, GROFF   AN   FGM 66
"ACT III. SCENE V. ANOTHER PART OF THE FOREST"
                             CONKLIN, GROFF   IN
RED HILLS OF SUMMER, THE   PANGBORN, EDGAR   NV   FSF 59 09
BIG SWORD   ASH, PAUL   NV   ASF 58 10
FIRST LADY   MCINTOSH, J. T.   NV   GAL 53 09
INSIDEKICK   BONE, J. F.   NV   GAL 59 02
LIVE COWARD, THE   ANDERSON, POUL   SS   ASF 56 06
STILL LIFE (STUDY IN STILL LIFE)
                             RUSSELL, ERIC FRANK SS   ASF 59 01

ANOTHER TOMORROW   HOLLISTER, BERNARD C AN L PFL 74
  INTRODUCTION   HOLLISTER, BERNARD C IN
  HISTORY LESSON   CLARKE, ARTHUR C.   SS   STS 49 05
  SOUTHBOUND ON THE FREEWAY   SWENSON, MAY   PM   NYM 63 02
  GADGET VS. TREND   ANVIL, CHRISTOPHER   SS   ASF 62 10
  WRITE SCIENCE FICTION? RIGHT HOLLISTER, BERNARD C AR   74
  GAS MASK   HOUSTON, JAMES D.   SS   NUG 64
  DEVIL CAR   ZELAZNY, ROGER   SS   GAL 65 06
  UNIVAC TO UNIVAC   SALOMON, LOUIS B.   PM   HRP 58 03
  TO SEE THE INVISIBLE MAN   SILVERBERG, ROBERT   SS   WOT 63 04
  HANDLER, THE   KNIGHT, DAMON   SS   ROG 60 08
  "REPENT, HARLEQUIN!" SAID THE TICKTOCKMAN
                              ELLISON, HARLAN   SS   GAL 65 12
  WINNER, THE   WESTLAKE, DONALD E.   SS   NOV 70 01
  PORTABLE PHONOGRAPH, THE   CLARK, WALTER VAN T. SS   41
  CRAB-APPLE CRISIS, THE   MACBETH, GEORGE   SS   NWS 66 10
  BIBLIOGRAPHY   MISC. MATERIAL   MS

ANOTHER WORLD   DOZOIS, GARDNER R.   AN H FOL 77
  INTRODUCTION   DOZOIS, GARDNER R.   IN
  OLDEST SOLDIER, THE   LEIBER, FRITZ   NV   FSF 60 05
  AFTER THE MYTHS WENT HOME   SILVERBERG, ROBERT   SS   FSF 69 11
  STARS BELOW, THE   LE GUIN, URSULA K.   SS   ORB 74 14
  STRAW   WOLFE, GENE   SS   GAL 75 01
  ON THE GEM PLANET   SMITH, CORDWAINER   NV   GAL 63 04
  BEAM US HOME   TIPTREE, JAMES JR.   SS   GAL 69 04
  BARBARIAN, THE   RUSS, JOANNA   NV   ORB 68 03
  AMONG THE HAIRY EARTHMEN   LAFFERTY, R. A.   SS   GAL 66 08
  MAN IN THE JAR   KNIGHT, DAMON   SS   GAL 57 04
  OLD HUNDREDTH   ALDISS, BRIAN W.   SS   NWS 60 11
  SIGNALLER, THE   ROBERTS, KEITH   NV   IMP 66 03
  READER'S GUIDE TO SF   MISC. MATERIAL   MS

ANTHROPOLOGY THROUGH SCIENCE FICTION
                              MASON, C/GREENBERG/& AN H SMP 74
  PREFACE   MASON, CAROL   IN
                              GREENBERG, MARTIN H.
                              AND WARRICK, PATRICIA S. IN C
  MARTIAN ODYSSEY, A   WEINBAUM, STANLEY G. NV   WOS 34 07
  ARENA   BROWN, FREDRIC   NV   ASF 44 06
  ENCHANTED VILLAGE (ALSO AS THE SANDS OF MARS)
                              VAN VOGT, A. E.   SS   OWS 50 07
  ROBOTS RETURN   WILLIAMS, ROBERT M.   SS   ASF 38 09
  HOUSE THE BLAKENEYS BUILT, THE
                              DAVIDSON, AVRAM   SS   FSF 65 01
  FROG POND   YARBRO, CHELSEA Q.   SS   GAL 71 03
  VINE, THE   REED, KIT   SS   FSF 67 11
  STRIKEBREAKER (MALE STRIKEBREAKER)
                              ASIMOV, ISAAC   SS   SFS 57 01
  SHARING OF FLESH, THE   ANDERSON, POUL   NV   GAL 68 12
  SURVIVAL SHIP   MERRIL, JUDITH   SS   WBY 51 01
  FAR FROM THIS EARTH   OLIVER, CHAD   SS   YRT 70
  CAGE, THE   CHANDLER, A. BERTRAM SS   FSF 57 06
  PYRAMID   ABERNATHY, ROBERT   NV   ASF 54 07
  LOST NEWTON   SCHMIDT, STANLEY   NV   ASF 70 09
  AUNT JENNIE'S TONIC   TUSHNET, LEONARD   SS   FSF 71 12
  NIGHTFALL   ASIMOV, ISAAC   NV   ASF 41 09
  UNHUMAN SACRIFICE   MACLEAN, KATHERINE   NV   ASF 53 11
  MONSTERS, THE   SHECKLEY, ROBERT   SS   FSF 53 03

ANTIGRAV: COSMIC COMEDIES   STRICK, PHILIP   AN H HUT 76 01
  INTRODUCTION   STRICK, PHILIP   IN
  SPACE RATS OF THE C.C.C.   HARRISON, HARRY   NV   FST 74
  HOW THE WORLD WAS SAVED   LEM, STANISLAW   SS
  IT WAS NOTHING- REALLY!   STURGEON, THEODORE   SS   69
  GLITCH, THE   BLISH, JAMES
                              AND STANTON, L. JEROME NV C GAL 74 06
  CONVERSATION ON A STARSHIP IN WARPDRIVE
                              BROSNAN, JOHN   SS   NEW 76 AN
  ALIBI MACHINE, THE   NIVEN, LARRY   SS   VTX 73 06
  EMERGENCY SOCIETY   FRITH, UTA   SS   NEW 76 AN
  LOOK, YOU THINK YOU'VE GOT TROUBLES
                              CARR, CAROL   SS   ORB 69 05
  DELIGHTFUL COMEDIC PREMISE, A
                              MALZBERG, BARRY N.   SS   FSF 74 02
  TROLLS   BORSKI, ROBERT   SS   FSF 74 05
  ELEPHANT WITH WOODEN LEG   SLADEK, JOHN T.   SS   GAL 75 06
  PLANTING TIME   ADAMS, PETE
                              AND NIGHTINGALE, CHARLES SS C NEW 76 AN
  BY THE SEASHORE   LAFFERTY, R. A.   SS   GAL 73 11
  HARDCASTLE   GOULART, RON   SS   NEW 71 AC
  ERGOT SHOW, THE   ALDISS, BRIAN W.   SS   NOV 72 02

ANTON YORK, IMMORTAL   BINDER, EANDO   AC   BEL 65
  CONQUEST OF LIFE   BINDER, EANDO   SS   TWS 37 08
  LIFE ETERNAL   BINDER, EANDO   NV   TWS 38 02
  THREE ETERNALS, THE   BINDER, EANDO   NV   TWS 39 12
  SECRET OF ANTON YORK, THE   BINDER, EANDO   NV   TWS 40 08

ANYTHING BOX, THE   HENDERSON, ZENNA   AC H DBL 65
  ANYTHING BOX   HENDERSON, ZENNA   SS   FSF 56 10
  SUBCOMMITTEE   HENDERSON, ZENNA   NV   FSF 62 07
  SOMETHING BRIGHT   HENDERSON, ZENNA   SS   GAL 60 02
  HUSH!   HENDERSON, ZENNA   SS   BEY 53 11
  FOOD TO ALL FLESH   HENDERSON, ZENNA   SS   FSF 53 11
  COME ON, WAGON!   HENDERSON, ZENNA   SS   FSF 51 12
  WALKING AUNT DAID   HENDERSON, ZENNA   SS   FSF 55 07
  SUBSTITUTE, THE   HENDERSON, ZENNA   SS   IMG 53 08
  GRUNDER, THE   HENDERSON, ZENNA   SS   IMG 53 06
  THINGS   HENDERSON, ZENNA   SS   FSF 60 07
  TURN THE PAGE   HENDERSON, ZENNA   SS   FSF 57 05
  STEVIE AND THE DARK (THE DARK CAME OUT TO PLAY)
                              HENDERSON, ZENNA   SS   IMG 52 05
  AND A LITTLE CHILD-   HENDERSON, ZENNA   SS   FSF 59 10
  LAST STEP, THE   HENDERSON, ZENNA   SS   FSF 58 02

ANYWHEN   BLISH, JAMES   AC H DBL 70
  PREFACE   BLISH, JAMES   IN
  STYLE IN TREASON, A (A HERO'S LIFE)
                              BLISH, JAMES   NV   IMP 66 03
  WRITING OF THE RAT, THE   BLISH, JAMES   SS   GAL 56 06
  AND SOME WERE SAVAGES   BLISH, JAMES   NV   AMZ 60 11
  DUSK OF IDOLS, A   BLISH, JAMES   NV   AMZ 61 03
  NONE SO BLIND (WHO'S IN CHARGE HERE?)
                              BLISH, JAMES   SS   FSF 62 05
  NO JOKES ON MARS   BLISH, JAMES   SS   FSF 65 10
  HOW BEAUTIFUL WITH BANNERS BLISH, JAMES   SS   ORB 66 01

ANYWHEN (ENGLISH EDITION ADDS:)
                              BLISH, JAMES   AC H FAB 71
  SKYSIGN   BLISH, JAMES   NV   ASF 68 05

ANYWHERE, ANYWHEN   ENGDAHL, SYLVIA   OA H ATH 76
  FOREWORD   ENGDAHL, SYLVIA   IN
  LEFT-HANDED BOY, THE   PIERIK, ROBERT   NV
  DILOPS ARE COMING, THE   FARLEY, CAROL   NV
  MOONCUP, THE   MURPHY, SHIRLEY R.   NV
  ASTORIA INCIDENT, THE   ROBERSON, RICK   NV
  TIMESCAPE   ENGDAHL, SYLVIA
                              AND BUTLER, MILDRED   NV C

APEMAN, SPACEMAN   STOVER & HARRISON   AN H DBL 68
  ANTHROPOLOGICAL SCIENCE FICTION
  FOREWORD   COON, CARLETON S.   IN
  INTRODUCTION   STOVER, LEON E.
                              AND HARRISON, HARRY   IN C
  NEANDERTHAL   ALLEN, MARIJANE   PM   NYT 56
  THROWBACK   DE CAMP, L. SPRAGUE   NV   ASF 49 03
  APOLOGY FOR MAN'S PHYSIQUE HOOTON, EARNEST A.   AR
  RENEGADE, THE   DEL REY, LESTER   SS   ASF 43 07
  ELTONIAN PYRAMID   DEXTER, RALPH W.   MS   SCM 52 10
  GOLDFISH BOWL   HEINLEIN, ROBERT A.   NV   ASF 42 03
  SECOND-CLASS CITIZEN, THE   KNIGHT, DAMON   SS   IFS 63 11
  CULTURE   SHELTON, JERRY   NV   ASF 44 09
  MAN OF THE YEAR MILLION, THE WELLS, H. G.   SS   PMB 93
  1,000,000 A.D.   ANONYMOUS   PM   PUN 93
  IN THE BEGINNING   KLASS, MORTON   SS   ASF 54 07
  FUTURE OF THE RACES OF MAN, THE
                              COON, CARLETON S.   AR   65
  EVOLUTION MAN, THE   LEWIS, ROY   SS   60
  KON-TIKI MYTH, THE   SUGGS, ROBERT C.   AR   60
  MEDAL FOR HORATIUS, A   HALL, WILLIAM C.   SS   ARM 55 01
  OMNILINGUAL   PIPER, H. BEAM   NV   ASF 57 02
  FOR THOSE WHO FOLLOW AFTER MCLAUGHLIN, DEAN   SS   ASF 51 07
  PRELIMINARY INVESTIGATION OF AN EARLY MAN SITE IN THE DELAWARE
  RIVER VALLEY   WARD, CHARLES W.
                              AND O'LEARY, TIMOTHY J. FA C
  BODY RITUAL AMONG THE NACIREMA
                              MINOR, HORACE M.   FA   ANT 66 03
  WAIT, THE   REED, KIT   SS   FSF 58 04
  EVERYBODYOVSKYISM IN CAT CITY
                              SHAW, LAO   SS
  NINE BILLION NAMES OF GOD, THE
                              CLARKE, ARTHUR C.   SS   STR 53 01
  PEANUTS   SCHULTZ, CHARLES M.   CT   64
  CAPTIVES, THE   CHAIN, JULIAN   NV   ASF 53 01
  MEN IN SPACE   LASSWELL, HAROLD D.   AR
  OF COURSE   OLIVER, CHAD   SS   ASF 54 05
  AFTERWORD   STOVER, LEON E.   MS

APPROACHING OBLIVION   ELLISON, HARLAN   AC H WKR 74
  APPROACHING ELLISON   CRICHTON, MICHAEL   MS
  REAPING THE WHIRLWIND   ELLISON, HARLAN   IN
  KNOX   ELLISON, HARLAN   SS   CRW 74 03
  COLD FRIEND   ELLISON, HARLAN   SS   GAL 73 10
  KISS OF FIRE   ELLISON, HARLAN   SS   TVW 73
  PAULIE CHARMED THE SLEEPING WOMAN
                              ELLISON, HARLAN   SS   FSF 62 08
  I'M LOOKING FOR KADAK   ELLISON, HARLAN   NV   NEW 74 AN
  SILENT IN GEHENNA   ELLISON, HARLAN   SS   MWS 71
  EROTOPHOBIA   ELLISON, HARLAN   SS   PNT 71 08
  ONE LIFE, FURNISHED IN EARLY POVERTY
                              ELLISON, HARLAN   SS   ORB 70 08
  ECOWARENESS   ELLISON, HARLAN   SS   NEW 74 AC
  CATMAN   ELLISON, HARLAN   NV   FST 74
  HINDSIGHT: 480 SECONDS   ELLISON, HARLAN   SS   FUC 73

ARENA: SPORTS SF   FERMAN & MALZBERG   AN H DBL 76
  INTRODUCTION   FREMAN, EDWARD L.   IN
  WHISPERS IN BEDLAM   SHAW, IRWIN   NA   PBY 69 02
  MIRROR OF ICE   WRIGHT, GARY   SS   GAL 67 06
  DODGER FAN   STANTON, WILL   SS   FSF 57 06
  CLOSED SICILIAN   MALZBERG, BARRY N.   SS   FSF 73 11
  ARENA   BROWN, FREDRIC   NV   ASF 44 06
  NOBODY BOTHERS GUS (AS PAUL JANVIER)
                              BUDRYS, ALGIS   SS   ASF 55 11
  OPEN WARFARE   GUNN, JAMES E.   NV   GAL 54 05
  GLADYS'S GREGORY   WEST, JOHN ANTHONY   SS   FSF 63 02
  NIGHT BOXING ENDED, THE   FRIEDMAN, BRUCE JAY   SS   GMQ 66
  BEYOND THE GAME   AANDAHL, VANCE   SS   FSF 68 05
  HUNGARIAN CINCH, THE   PRONZINI, BILL   NV   NEW 76 AN
  AFTERWORD: ON THE NON-TRANSCENDENCE OF SPORT
                              MALZBERG, BARRY N.   MS

ARMADA SCI-FI ONE   DAVIS, RICHARD   OA   ARM 75 04
  RAINS OF ALPHA ALEPH, THE   BIRLEY, JULIA   SS   ADS 75 01
  "FLAP"   STOUT, TIM   SS   ADS 75 01
  AT THE BOTTOM OF THE GARDEN CAMPTON, DAVID   NV   ADS 75 01
  LONELY ROBOT, THE   LITTLE, MARGARET   SS   ADS 75 01
  MR. NOBODY   TIMPERLEY, ROSEMARY   SS   ADS 75 01
  WHO IS CINDY?   FANCETT, ELIZABETH   SS   ADS 75 01
  TRODES, THE   COPPER, BASIL   SS   ADS 75 01

ARMADA SCI-FI ONE

| JAKE'S PICTURES | LITTLE, MARGARET | SS | ADS 75 01 |
| WAIT, THE | PARR, CHRISTIE | NV | ADS 75 01 |

ARMADA SCI-FI TWO DAVIS, RICHARD OA ARM 75 04

STAR-BOY	FANCETT, ELIZABETH	NV	ADS 75 02
SOUTH GATE SEA	PARR, CHRISTIE	SS	ADS 75 02
DESMOND'S DINOSAUR	CAMPTON, DAVID	SS	ADS 75 02
COMPUTER THAT FELL IN LOVE, THE			
	TIMPERLEY, ROSEMARY	SS	ADS 75 02
ALL IN THE MIND	CLEAVER, PAMELA	SS	ADS 75 02
LAPIDA MENACE, THE	CAMPTON, DAVID	NV	ADS 75 02
"HAPPY LANDINGS, PROFESSOR|"	STOUT, TIM	SS	ADS 75 02
PIE IN THE SKY	GRAVES, JOCELYN	SS	ADS 75 02

ARMCHAIR SCIENCE READER, THE GORDON, I. & SORKIN AN H SAS 59
    ONLY SCIENCE FICTION LISTED

INVASION FROM MARS	KOCH, HOWARD	PL	CBS 38 10
FLIGHT TO MALACANDRA (FROM "OUT OF THE SILENT PLANET")			
	LEWIS, C. S.	EX	LNE 38
OUR DISTANT COUSINS	DUNSANY, LORD	SS	31
NAUTILUS REACHES THE POLE, THE (FROM "20,000 LEAGUES			
UNDER THE SEA")	VERNE, JULES	EX	GMS 73
DESCENT INTO THE MAELSTROM, A			
	POE, EDGAR ALLEN	SS	GLG 41 05
JOHN THOMAS'S CUBE	LEIMERT, JOHN	SS	ATL 45 08
IN HIDING	SHIRAS, WILMAR H.	NV	ASF 48 11
CREATIVE EVOLUTION (FROM PREFACE TO "BACK TO METHUSELAH")			
	SHAW, GEORGE BERNARD	EX	
SPLIT CHERRY TREE	STUART, JESSE	SS	
CABINET DECISION (FROM "WHO IS MY NEIGHBOUR")			
	BALCHIN, NIGEL	EX	
DR. SOUTHPORT VULPES'S NIGHTMARE (FROM "NIGHTMARES OF			
EMINENT PERSONS")	RUSSELL, BERTRAND	EX	
PORTABLE PHONOGRAPH, THE	CLARK, WALTER VAN T.	SS	41
BY THE WATERS OF BABYLON (THE PLACE OF THE GODS)			
	BENET, STEPHEN V.	SS	SEP 37 07
LAPUTAN PROJECTS (FROM "GULLIVER'S TRAVELS")			
	SWIFT, JONATHAN	EX	
MACHINES DO OUR WORK (FROM "LOOKING BACKWARD")			
	BELLAMY, EDWARD	EX	TIC 88
IN BONDAGE TO A CENTRAL AUTHORITY (FROM "BRAVE NEW WORLD")			
	HUXLEY, ALDOUS	EX	WND 32
MACHINE STOPS, THE	FORSTER, E. M.	NV	28
MORNING OF THE DAY THEY DID IT, THE			
	WHITE, E. B.	SS	NYM 50 02

ARTHUR C. CLARKE OMNIBUS, AN CLARKE, ARTHUR C. AC H SID 65

CHILDHOOD'S END (EXPANDED FROM "GUARDIAN ANGEL")			
	CLARKE, ARTHUR C.	NO	NWS 50 WI
PRELUDE TO SPACE	CLARKE, ARTHUR C.	NO	GAN 51 03
EXPEDITION TO EARTH	CLARKE, ARTHUR C.	AC	BAL 53 12

ARTHUR C. CLARKE SECOND OMNIBUS, AN
                                CLARKE, ARTHUR C. AC H SID 68

FALL OF MOONDUST, A	CLARKE, ARTHUR C.	NO	GOL 61
EARTHLIGHT	CLARKE, ARTHUR C.	NO	TWS 51 08
SANDS OF MARS, THE	CLARKE, ARTHUR C.	NO	SID 51

AS TOMORROW BECOMES TODAY SULLIVAN, CHARLES W. AN L PRH 74

PREFACE	SULLIVAN, CHARLES W.	IN	
INTRODUCTION	SULLIVAN, CHARLES W.	IN	
BACKTRACKED	FILER, BURT K.	SS	FSF 68 06
ALL YOU ZOMBIES-	HEINLEIN, ROBERT A.	SS	FSF 59 03
MEN WHO MURDERED MOHAMMED, THE			
	BESTER, ALFRED	SS	FSF 58 10
RANDOM QUEST	WYNDHAM, JOHN	NV	NEW 61 AC
THUS WE FRUSTRATE CHARLEMAGNE			
	LAFFERTY, R. A.	SS	GAL 67 02
MONSTER FROM NOWHERE, THE	BOND, NELSON S.	SS	FAD 39 07
NEW REALITY, THE	HARNESS, CHARLES L.	NV	TWS 50 12
NO-SIDED PROFESSOR (ESQ 47 01)			
	GARDNER, MARTIN	SS	FSF 51 02
AND HE BUILT A CROOKED HOUSE	HEINLEIN, ROBERT A.	SS	ASF 41 02
FUN THEY HAD, THE (NEA 51 12)			
	ASIMOV, ISAAC	SS	FSF 54 02
PRIMARY EDUCATION OF THE CAMIROI			
	LAFFERTY, R. A.	SS	GAL 66 12
HEMEAC	VON WALD, E. G.	SS	GAL 68 08
PERSONAL	KUPFERBERG, TULI	SS	ESR 66
BOY AND HIS DOG, A	ELLISON, HARLAN	NV	NWS 69 04
RUNAROUND	ASIMOV, ISAAC	SS	ASF 42 03
CALLING DR. CLOCKWORK	GOULART, RON	SS	AMZ 65 03
MASKS	KNIGHT, DAMON	SS	PBY 68 07
SPECIALIST	SHECKLEY, ROBERT	SS	GAL 53 05
SENTINEL, THE (SENTINEL OF ETERNITY)			
	CLARKE, ARTHUR C.	SS	TSF 51 SP
GAME OF RAT AND DRAGON, THE	SMITH, CORDWAINER	NV	GAL 55 10
DECISION MAKERS, THE	GREEN, JOSEPH	NV	GAL 65 04
DEATH IN THE HOUSE, A	SIMAK, CLIFFORD D.	NV	GAL 59 10
BUILD-UP (ALSO AS THE CONCENTRATION CITY)			
	BALLARD, J. G.	SS	NWS 57 01
PLENITUDE	WORTHINGTON, WILL	SS	FSF 59 11
WIZARDS OF PUNG'S CORNERS, THE			
	POHL, FREDERIK	NV	GAL 58 10
"REPENT, HARLEQUIN|" SAID THE TICKTOCKMAN			
	ELLISON, HARLAN	SS	GAL 65 12
NINE LIVES	LE GUIN, URSULA K.	NV	PBY 69 11
GOLDEN ACRES	REED, KIT	NV	68
POPULATION IMPLOSION	OFFUTT, ANDREW J.	NV	IFS 67 07
TUNNEL AHEAD, THE	GLASER, ALICE	SS	FSF 61 11
AFTERWORD	SULLIVAN, CHARLES W.	MS	
BIBLIOGRAPHY	MISC. MATERIAL	MS	

ASIMOV'S MYSTERIES ASIMOV, ISAAC AC H DBL 68

| INTRODUCTION | ASIMOV, ISAAC | IN | |
| SINGING BELL, THE | ASIMOV, ISAAC | SS | FSF 55 01 |

TALKING STONE, THE	ASIMOV, ISAAC	SS	FSF 55 10
WHAT'S IN A NAME	ASIMOV, ISAAC	SS	SDM 56 05
DYING NIGHT, THE	ASIMOV, ISAAC	SS	FSF 56 07
PATE DE FOIE GRAS	ASIMOV, ISAAC	SF	ASF 56 09
DUST OF DEATH, THE	ASIMOV, ISAAC	SS	VSF 57 01
LOINT OF PAW, A	ASIMOV, ISAAC	SS	FSF 57 08
I'M IN MARSPORT WITHOUT HILDA			
	ASIMOV, ISAAC	SS	VSF 57 11
MAROONED OFF VESTA	ASIMOV, ISAAC	SS	AMZ 39 03
ANNIVERSARY	ASIMOV, ISAAC	SS	AMZ 59 03
OBITUARY	ASIMOV, ISAAC	SS	FSF 59 08
STAR LIGHT	ASIMOV, ISAAC	SS	SAM 62 10
KEY, THE	ASIMOV, ISAAC	NV	FSF 66 10
BILLIARD BALL, THE	ASIMOV, ISAAC	NV	IFS 67 03

ASLEEP IN ARMAGEDDON SISSONS, MICHAEL AN PTH 62 06

ASLEEP IN ARMAGEDDON (ALSO AS PERCHANCE TO DREAM)			
	BRADBURY, RAY	SS	PLS 48 WI
WEAPON, THE	BROWN, FREDRIC	SS	ASF 51 04
NOT FINAL|	ASIMOV, ISAAC	SS	ASF 41 10
HOME THERE'S NO RETURNING	MOORE, C. L.	NV	NEW 55 AC
THIS STAR SHALL BE FREE	LEINSTER, MURRAY	NV	SSS 49 11
SCARLET PLAGUE, THE	LONDON, JACK	NA	LOM 12 06
ENCHANTED VILLAGE (ALSO AS THE SANDS OF MARS)			
	VAN VOGT, A. E.	SS	OWS 50 07
CRUCIFIXUS ETIAM	MILLER, WALTER M. JR	SS	ASF 53 02
BEING	MATHESON, RICHARD	NV	IFS 57 04
CAMOUFLAGE	KUTTNER, HENRY	NV	ASF 45 09

ASPECTS OF SCIENCE FICTION DOHERTY, G. D. AN H MUR 59

PICTURES DON'T LIE	MACLEAN, KATHERINE	SS	GAL 51 08
COLD EQUATIONS, THE	GODWIN, TOM	NV	ASF 54 08
SOUND OF THUNDER, A	BRADBURY, RAY	SS	COL 52 06
HE WALKED AROUND THE HORSES	PIPER, H. BEAM	NV	ASF 48 04
ZERO HOUR	BRADBURY, RAY	SS	PLS 47 FL
CRYSTAL EGG, THE	WELLS, H. G.	SS	NRV 97 05
DORMANT	VAN VOGT, A. E.	SS	STS 48 11
SEA-RAIDERS, THE	WELLS, H. G.	SS	WSL 96 12
DUMB SHOW	ALDISS, BRIAN W.	SS	NEB 56 12
NINE BILLION NAMES OF GOD, THE			
	CLARKE, ARTHUR C.	SS	STR 53 01
PANEL GAME	ALDISS, BRIAN W.	SS	NWS 55 12
MAN IN ASBESTOS: AN ALLEGORY OF THE FUTURE, THE			
	LEACOCK, STEPHEN	SS	41

ASSIGNMENT IN ETERNITY HEINLEIN, ROBERT A. AC H FPS 53

GULF	HEINLEIN, ROBERT A.	SN	ASF 49 11
ELSEWHEN (ELSEWHERE)	HEINLEIN, ROBERT A.	NV	ASF 41 09
LOST LEGACY (LOST LEGION)	HEINLEIN, ROBERT A.	NV	SSS 41 11
JERRY WAS A MAN (JERRY IS A MAN)			
	HEINLEIN, ROBERT A.	SS	TWS 47 10

ASSIGNMENT IN TOMORROW POHL, FREDERIK AN H HAN 54

INTRODUCTION	POHL, FREDERIK	IN	
MR. COSTELLO, HERO	STURGEON, THEODORE	NV	GAL 53 12
ANGELS IN THE JETS	BIXBY, JEROME	SS	FAN 52 PL
ADVENTURER, THE	KORNBLUTH, C. M.	SS	SSF 53 05
SUBTERFUGE	BRADBURY, RAY	SS	AST 43 04
HELEN O'LOY	DEL REY, LESTER	SS	ASF 38 12
5,271,009 (ALSO AS THE STARCOMBER)			
	BESTER, ALFRED	NV	FSF 54 03
BIG TRIP UP YONDER, THE (ALSO AS TOMORROW AND TOMORROW			
AND TOMORROW)	VONNEGUT, KURT JR.	SS	GAL 54 01
WE DON'T WANT ANY TROUBLE	SCHMITZ, JAMES H.	SS	GAL 53 06
PEDDLER'S NOSE, THE	WILLIAMSON, JACK	SS	ASF 51 04
FRIGHTENED TREE, THE (PROTECTIVE MIMICRY)			
	BUDRYS, ALGIS	SS	GAL 53 02
MATTER OF FORM, A	GOLD, H. L.	SN	ASF 38 12
BACK TO JULIE	WILSON, RICHARD	SS	GAL 54 05
SHE WHO LAUGHS...	PHILLIPS, PETER	SS	GAL 52 04
OFFICIAL RECORD	PRATT, FLETCHER	NV	SSF 52 09
HALL OF MIRRORS	BROWN, FREDRIC	SS	GAL 53 12
MOTHER	FARMER, PHILIP JOSE	NV	TWS 53 04

ASTOUNDING HARRISON, HARRY OA H RDM 73
    JOHN W. CAMPBELL MEMORIAL ANTHOLOGY

FATHER OF SCIENCE FICTION, THE			
	ASIMOV, ISAAC	IN	AMA 73
LODESTAR	ANDERSON, POUL	NV	AMA 73
THIOTIMOLINE TO THE STARS	ASIMOV, ISAAC	SS	AMA 73
SOMETHING UP THERE LIKES ME	BESTER, ALFRED	NV	AMA 73
LECTURE DEMONSTRATION	CLEMENT, HAL	SS	AMA 73
EARLY BIRD	COGSWELL, THEODORE R		
	AND THOMAS, THEODORE L.	SS C	AMA 73
EMPEROR'S FAN, THE	DE CAMP, L. SPRAGUE	NV	AMA 73
BROTHERS	DICKSON, GORDON R.	NV	AMA 73
MOTHBALLED SPACESHIP, THE	HARRISON, HARRY	SS	AMA 73
BLACK SHEEP ASTRAY	REYNOLDS, MACK	NV	AMA 73
EPILOG	SIMAK, CLIFFORD D.	SS	AMA 73
INTERLUDE (ALSO AS THE EXTERNAL TRIANGLE)			
	SMITH, GEORGE O.	NV	AMA 73
HELIX THE CAT	STURGEON, THEODORE	NV	AMA 73
PROBABILITY ZERO| THE POPULATION IMPLOSION			
	COGSWELL, THEODORE R	SS	AMA 73

ASTOUNDING SCIENCE FICTION ANTHOLOGY, THE
                                CAMPBELL, JOHN W. JR AN H SAS 52
    DERIVATIVE ANTHOLOGY "ASTOUNDING TALES OF SPACE AND TIME"
    IN ENGLAND AS "THE FIRST AND SECOND ASTOUNDING SCIENCE
    FICTION ANTHOLOGIES"

INTRODUCTION	CAMPBELL, JOHN W. JR	IN	
BLOWUPS HAPPEN	HEINLEIN, ROBERT A.	NV	ASF 40 09
HINDSIGHT	WILLIAMSON, JACK	SS	ASF 40 05
VAULT OF THE BEAST	VAN VOGT, A. E.	NV	ASF 40 08
EXALTED, THE	DE CAMP, L. SPRAGUE	NV	ASF 40 11
NIGHTFALL	ASIMOV, ISAAC	NV	ASF 41 09

```
WHEN THE BOUGH BREAKS        PADGETT, LEWIS         NV   ASF 44 11
CLASH BY NIGHT               O'DONNELL, LAWRENCE   NV   ASF 43 03
INVARIANT                    PIERCE, JOHN R.        SS   ASF 44 04
FIRST CONTACT                LEINSTER, MURRAY       NV   ASF 45 05
MEIHEM IN CE KLASRUM         EDWARDS, DOLTON        AR   ASF 46 09
HOBBYIST                     RUSSELL, ERIC FRANK    NV   ASF 47 09
E FOR EFFORT                 SHERRED, T. L.         NV   ASF 47 05
CHILD'S PLAY                 TENN, WILLIAM          NV   ASF 47 03
THUNDER AND ROSES            STURGEON, THEODORE     SS   ASF 47 11
LATE NIGHT FINAL             RUSSELL, ERIC FRANK    NV   ASF 48 12
COLD WAR                     NEVILLE, KRIS          SS   ASF 49 10
ETERNITY LOST                SIMAK, CLIFFORD D.     NV   ASF 49 07
WITCHES OF KARRES, THE       SCHMITZ, JAMES H.      NV   ASF 49 12
OVER THE TOP                 DEL REY, LESTER        SS   ASF 49 11
METEOR                       POWERS, WILLIAM T.     SS   ASF 50 09
LAST ENEMY                   PIPER, H. BEAM         NV   ASF 50 08
HISTORICAL NOTE              LEINSTER, MURRAY       SS   ASF 51 02
PROTECTED SPECIES            FYFE, H. B.            SS   ASF 51 03

STOUNDING SCIENCE FICTION ANTHOLOGY, THE (8 OF 22)
                             CAMPBELL, JOHN W. JR AN   BRK 56 12
NIGHTFALL                    ASIMOV, ISAAC          NV   ASF 41 09
FIRST CONTACT                LEINSTER, MURRAY       NV   ASF 45 05
ETERNITY LOST                SIMAK, CLIFFORD D.     NV   ASF 49 07
VAULT OF THE BEAST           VAN VOGT, A. E.        NV   ASF 40 08
INVARIANT                    PIERCE, JOHN R.        SS   ASF 44 04
WHEN THE BOUGH BREAKS        PADGETT, LEWIS         NV   ASF 44 11
COLD WAR                     NEVILLE, KRIS          SS   ASF 49 10
OVER THE TOP                 DEL REY, LESTER        SS   ASF 49 11

STOUNDING TALES OF SPACE AND TIME
                             CAMPBELL, JOHN W. JR AN   BRK 57 02
    STORIES FROM "THE ASTOUNDING SCIENCE FICTION ANTHOLOGY"
HOBBYIST                     RUSSELL, ERIC FRANK    NV   ASF 47 09
HINDSIGHT                    WILLIAMSON, JACK       SS   ASF 40 05
THUNDER AND ROSES            STURGEON, THEODORE     SS   ASF 47 11
E FOR EFFORT                 SHERRED, T. L.         NV   ASF 47 05
LATE NIGHT FINAL             RUSSELL, ERIC FRANK    NV   ASF 48 12
PROTECTED SPECIES            FYFE, H. B.            SS   ASF 51 03
HISTORICAL NOTE              LEINSTER, MURRAY       SS   ASF 51 02

STOUNDING-ANALOG READER, THE VOLUME ONE
                             HARRISON & ALDISS      AN H DBL 72
INTRODUCTION                 HARRISON, HARRY
                             AND ALDISS, BRIAN W.   IN C
FORGETFULNESS                STUART, DON A.         SN   ASF 37 06
SEEDS OF THE DUSK            GALLUN, RAYMOND Z.     NV   ASF 38 06
FAREWELL TO THE MASTER       BATES, HARRY           NV   ASF 40 10
TROUBLE ON TANTALUS          MILLER, P. SCHUYLER    NV   ASF 41 02
TIME WANTS A SKELETON        ROCKLYNNE, ROSS        NV   ASF 41 06
NIGHTFALL                    ASIMOV, ISAAC          NV   ASF 41 09
BY HIS BOOTSTRAPS (ALSO AS THE TIME GATE)
                             MACDONALD, ANSON       NV   ASF 41 10
PUSH OF A FINGER, THE        BESTER, ALFRED         NV   ASF 42 05
CLASH BY NIGHT               O'DONNELL, LAWRENCE   NV   ASF 43 03
STORM, THE                   VAN VOGT, A. E.        NV   ASF 43 10
CITY                         SIMAK, CLIFFORD D.     NV   ASF 44 05
FIRST CONTACT                LEINSTER, MURRAY       NV   ASF 45 05
GIANT KILLER                 CHANDLER, A. BERTRAM NV   ASF 45 10
VINTAGE SEASON               O'DONNELL, LAWRENCE   NV   ASF 46 09
PLACET IS A CRAZY PLACE      BROWN, FREDRIC         SS   ASF 46 05

STOUNDING-ANALOG READER, THE VOLUME TWO
                             HARRISON & ALDISS      AN H DBL 73
INTRODUCTION                 HARRISON, HARRY
                             AND ALDISS, BRIAN W.   IN C
CHILD'S PLAY                 TENN, WILLIAM          NV   ASF 47 03
THUNDER AND ROSES            STURGEON, THEODORE     SS   ASF 47 11
DREAMS ARE SACRED            PHILLIPS, PETER        SS   ASF 48 09
HIDE AND SEEK                CLARKE, ARTHUR C.      SS   ASF 49 09
LITTLE BLACK BAG, THE        KORNBLUTH, C. M.       NV   ASF 50 07
BRIDGE                       BLISH, JAMES           NV   ASF 52 02
WHAT HAVE I DONE?            CLIFTON, MARK          SS   ASF 52 05
NOISE LEVEL                  JONES, RAYMOND F.      NV   ASF 52 12
IMPOSTOR                     DICK, PHILIP K.        SS   ASF 53 06
POTENTIAL                    SHECKLEY, ROBERT       SS   ASF 53 11
PYRAMID                      ABERNATHY, ROBERT      NV   ASF 54 07
COLD EQUATIONS, THE          GODWIN, TOM            NV   ASF 54 08
GRANDPA                      SCHMITZ, JAMES H.      SS   ASF 55 02
WAITABITS, THE               RUSSELL, ERIC FRANK    NV   ASF 55 07
CALL ME JOE                  ANDERSON, POUL         NV   ASF 57 04
YELLOW PILL, THE             PHILLIPS, ROG          SS   ASF 58 10
WEATHER MAN, THE             THOMAS, THEODORE L.   SN   ASF 62 06
RESCUER, THE                 PORGES, ARTHUR         SS   ASF 62 07
AFTER A FEW WORDS            GARRETT, RANDALL       SS   ASF 62 10
RESCUE OPERATION             HARRISON, HARRY        SS   ASF 64 12
COMPUTERS DON'T ARGUE        DICKSON, GORDON R.     SS   ASF 65 09

TOMS AND EVIL                BLOCH, ROBERT          AC   GMB 62 08
TRY THIS FOR PSIS            BLOCH, ROBERT          SS   FSF 56 10
COMFORT ME, MY ROBOT         BLOCH, ROBERT          SS   IMG 55 01
TALENT                       BLOCH, ROBERT          SS   IFS 60 07
PROFESSOR PLAYS IT SQUARE, THE
                             BLOCH, ROBERT          SS   ARG 57 09
BLOCK THAT METAPHOR          BLOCH, ROBERT          SS   GAL 58 10
WHEEL AND DEAL               BLOCH, ROBERT          SS   NEW 62 AC
YOU GOT TO HAVE BRAINS       BLOCH, ROBERT          SS   FUN 56 01
YOU COULD BE WRONG           BLOCH, ROBERT          SS   AMZ 55 03
EGGHEAD                      BLOCH, ROBERT          SS   FUN 58 07
DEAD-END DOCTOR              BLOCH, ROBERT          SS   GAL 56 02
CHANGE OF HEART              BLOCH, ROBERT          SS   ARS 48 FL
EDIFICE COMPLEX              BLOCH, ROBERT          SS   ESC 58 02
CONSTANT READER              BLOCH, ROBERT          SS   USF 53 06

TROCITY EXHIBITION           BALLARD, J. G.         AC H CAP 70
    SEE "LOVE & NAPALM: EXPORT U.S.A."
```

```
AURORA: BEYOND EQUALITY      MCINTYRE & ANDERSON    OA   PGM 76 05
    FEMINISM AND SCIENCE FICTION: BEYOND BEMS AND BOOBS
                             ANDERSON, SUSAN J.     IN
    YOUR FACES, O MY SISTERS! YOUR FACES FILLED OF LIGHT!
                             SHELDON, RACCOONA      SS
    HOUSTON, HOUSTON, DO YOU READ?
                             TIPTREE, JAMES JR.     NA
    MOTHERS, THE MOTHERS, HOW EERILY IT SOUNDS, THE
                             SKAL, DAVE             SS
ANTRIM HILLS, THE            BROXON, MILDRED D.     NV
IS GENDER NECESSARY?         LE GUIN, URSULA K.     AR
CORRUPTION                   RUSS, JOANNA           SS
HERE BE DRAGONS              PLAUGER, P. J.         SS
WHY HAS THE VIRGIN MARY NEVER ENTERED THE WIGWAM OF
    STANDING BEAR?           STRETE, CRAIG          SS
WOMAN ON THE EDGE OF TIME    PIERCY, MARGE          NV
OTHER WORKS OF INTEREST      MISC. MATERIAL         MS
ABOUT THE AUTHORS            MISC. MATERIAL         MS

AUTHENTIC BOOK OF SPACE      CAMPBELL, H. J.        AN H HML 54
FOREWORD                     CLARKE, ARTHUR C.      IN
ARTICLES                     MISC. MATERIAL         AR
EXPLORERS OF MARS            TEMPLE, WILLIAM F.     SS
DEATH RIDES THE SPACEWAYS    ACKERMAN, FORREST J.   SS
BLUE CLOUD, THE              DOGGE, MARY            SS
OLD GROWLER SPACE SHIP NO. 2213
                             DEEGAN, JON J.         CT   AUT 51 04
PLAYMATE                     CROUTCH, LESLIE A.     SS   IMG 51 11
OUR FRIENDS THE ALIENS       BULMER, KENNETH        SS

AUTUMN PEOPLE, THE           BRADBURY, RAY          AC   BAL 65 10
    COMIC BOOK VERSIONS OF STORIES FROM E.C. COMICS
ADAPTATION                   FELDSTEIN, ALBERT B. MS
FOREWORD                     BRADBURY, RAY          IN

AVON FANTASY READER, THE     WOLLHEIM &ERNSBERGER AN   AVN 68
FOREWORD                     ERNSBERGER, GEORGE     IN
WITCH FROM HELL'S KITCHEN, THE
                             HOWARD, ROBERT E.      NV   AFR 52 18
BLACK THIRST                 MOORE, C. L.           NV   WRT 34 04
VICTIM OF HIGHER SPACE, A (1917)
                             BLACKWOOD, ALGERNON    NV   AFR 52 18
SAPPHIRE SIREN, THE          DYALHIS, NICTZIN       NV   WRT 34 02
VOICE IN THE NIGHT, THE      HODGSON, WILLIAM H.    SS   BBM 07 11
CRAWLING HORROR, THE         MCCLUSKY, THORP        NV   WRT 36 11
KELPIE, THE                  WELLMAN, MANLY WADE   SS   WRT 36 07

AWARD SCIENCE FICTION READER NORTON, ALDEN H.      AN   AWD 66
    COLORFUL SCIENCE FICTION WORLDS OF ALDEN H. NORTON
                             MOSKOWITZ, SAM         IN
TRAVELING CRAG, THE          STURGEON, THEODORE     NV   FAD 51 07
EXILE OF THE EONS            CLARKE, ARTHUR C.      SS   SSS 50 03
SHIP OF DARKNESS             VAN VOGT, A. E.        SS   FBK 47 02
YOU'LL NEVER GO HOME AGAIN (ALSO AS BEACHHEAD)
                             SIMAK, CLIFFORD D.     SS   FAD 51 07
DANCING GIRL OF GANYMEDE, THE
                             BRACKETT, LEIGH        SS   TWS 50 02
STAR BEAST, THE              ANDERSON, POUL         SS   SSS 50 09
LAST EVOLUTION, THE          CAMPBELL, JOHN W. JR SS   AMZ 32 08

AWAY AND BEYOND              VAN VOGT, A. E.        AC H PEL 52
GREAT ENGINE, THE            VAN VOGT, A. E.        NV   ASF 43 07
GREAT JUDGE, THE             VAN VOGT, A. E.        SS   FBK 48 03
SECRET UNATTAINABLE          VAN VOGT, A. E.        NV   ASF 42 07
HARMONIZER, THE              VAN VOGT, A. E.        SS   ASF 44 11
SECOND SOLUTION, THE         VAN VOGT, A. E.        SS   ASF 42 10
FILM LIBRARY                 VAN VOGT, A. E.        SS   ASF 46 07
ASYLUM                       VAN VOGT, A. E.        NV   ASF 42 05
HEIR UNAPPARENT (HEIR APPARENT)
                             VAN VOGT, A. E.        SS   ASF 45 06
VAULT OF THE BEAST           VAN VOGT, A. E.        NV   ASF 40 08

AWAY AND BEYOND (7 OF 9)     VAN VOGT, A. E.        AC   BKM 59 02
GREAT ENGINE, THE            VAN VOGT, A. E.        NV   ASF 43 07
GREAT JUDGE, THE             VAN VOGT, A. E.        SS   FBK 48 03
SECRET UNATTAINABLE          VAN VOGT, A. E.        NV   ASF 42 07
HARMONIZER, THE              VAN VOGT, A. E.        SS   ASF 44 11
SECOND SOLUTION, THE         VAN VOGT, A. E.        SS   ASF 42 10
FILM LIBRARY                 VAN VOGT, A. E.        SS   ASF 46 07
ASYLUM                       VAN VOGT, A. E.        NV   ASF 42 05

AWAY FROM THE HERE AND NOW   HARRIS, CLARE WINGER AC H DOR 47
RUNAWAY WORLD, A             HARRIS, CLARE WINGER SS   WRT 26 07
FATE OF THE POSEIDONIA, THE  HARRIS, CLARE WINGER SS   AMZ 27 06
CERTAIN SOLDIER, A           HARRIS, CLARE WINGER SS   WRT 27 11
DIABOLICAL DRUG, THE         HARRIS, CLARE WINGER SS   AMZ 29 05
MIRACLE OF THE LILY, THE     HARRIS, CLARE WINGER SS   AMZ 28 04
BABY ON NEPTUNE, A           HARRIS, CLARE WINGER
                             AND BREUER, MILES J. MD. SS C AMZ 29 12
ARTIFICIAL MAN, THE          HARRIS, CLARE WINGER SS   WSQ 29 FL
MENACE OF MARS, THE          HARRIS, CLARE WINGER SS   AMZ 28 10
EVOLUTIONARY MONSTROSITY, THE
                             HARRIS, CLARE WINGER SS   AMQ 29 WI
FIFTH DIMENSION, THE         HARRIS, CLARE WINGER SS   AMZ 28 12
APE CYCLE, THE               HARRIS, CLARE WINGER SS   WSQ 30 SP

BACKDROP OF STARS            HARRISON, HARRY        AC H DOB 68
    SEE "SF: AUTHORS' CHOICE"

BAD MOON RISING              DISCH, THOMAS M.       OA H HPR 73
    INTRODUCTION: ON THE ROAD TO 1984
                             DISCH, THOMAS M.       IN
HO CHI MINH ELEGY            SCHJELDAHL, PETER      PM   BMR 73
ELEGY FOR JANIS JOPLIN       HACKER, MARILYN        PM   BMR 73
WE ARE DAINTY LITTLE PEOPLE  NAYLOR, CHARLES        SS   BMR 73
STRANGERS                    EMSHWILLER, CAROL      SS   BMR 73
```

BAD MOON RISING

```
RELATIVES                    EFFINGER, GEO. ALEC   SS    BMR 73
RIDING                       RUSH, NORMAN          SS    BMR 73
APOCALYPSE: SOME SCENES FROM EUROPEAN LIFE, AN
                             MOORCOCK, MICHAEL     NV    BMR 73
WHIMPER OF WHIPPED DOGS, THE ELLISON, HARLAN       NV    BMR 73
GREAT WALL OF MEXICO, THE    SLADEK, JOHN T.       NV    BMR 73
VILLAGE, THE                 WILHELM, KATE         SS    BMR 73
IN BEHALF OF THE PRODUCT     REED, KIT             SS    BMR 73
HOUR OF TRUST                WOLFE, GENE           NV    BMR 73
FIGHTING FASCISM             RUSH, NORMAN          SS    BMR 73
COLD TURKEY                  GALLUP, DICK
                             AND PADGETT, RON      SS  C BMR 73
WHERE HAVE ALL THE FOLLOWERS GONE?
                             MOORE, RAYLYN         SS    BMR 73
OUTLINE OF HISTORY, AN       BRALY, MALCOLM        SS    BMR 73
TWO SADNESSES                EFFINGER, GEO. ALEC   SS    BMR 73
EVERYDAY LIFE IN THE LATER ROMAN EMPIRE
                             DISCH, THOMAS M.      NV    BMR 73
UNTOWARD OCCURENCE AT EMBASSY POETRY READING
                             HACKER, MARILYN       PM    BMR 73
FOR APOLLO 11                SCHJELDAHL, PETER     PM    BMR 73
SOME NOTES ON THE PREDYNASTIC EPOCH
                             SILVERBERG, ROBERT    SS    BMR 73

BATTLE FOR THE PACIFIC AND OTHER ADVENTURES AT SEA, THE
                             ANONYMOUS         AN H HPR 08
BATTLE FOR THE PACIFIC, THE  STEVENS, ROWAN        SS
BOMBARDMENT OF THE GOLDEN GATE, THE
                             STIRLING, YATES JR.   SS
FIGHT IN THE FOG, A          STIRLING, YATES JR.   SS
BATTLE OFF THE HOOK, THE     STIRLING, YATES JR.   SS
HARRY BORDEN'S NAVAL MONSTER HENDERSON, WILLIAM J  SS
CRUISE OF A COMMERCE DESTROYER, THE
                             STIRLING, YATES JR.   SS
PRIVATE OR PRIVATEER?        WALSH, GEORGE E.      SS
MUTINY ON THE SWALLOW, THE   HENDERSON, WILLIAM J  SS
SCAPE-GOAT OF LA JUSTICIA, THE
                             MARTIN, HAROLD        SS
CAPTAIN SAMPSON'S QUEER CARGO
                             WALSH, GEORGE E.      SS
WARM CORNER IN SOOLOO, A     HALL, OWEN            SS
"CAP'N IL'S" CLOSEST CALL    MUNRO, KIRK           SS
MY BORROWED TORPEDO-BOAT     RALPH, JULIAN         SS
LOST VOICE, THE              SPEARMAN, F. H.       SS
JOE GRIFFIN'S GREAT JUMP     HENDERSON, WILLIAM J  SS

BATTLE OF THE MONSTERS AND OTHER STORIES, THE
                             HARTWELL & CURREY  AN H GRG 76
INTRODUCTION                 HARTWELL, DAVID G.
                             AND CURREY, L. W.     IN C
SECRET OF APOLLONIUS SEPTRIO, THE
                             KIP, LEONARD          NV
REPAIRER OF REPUTATIONS, THE (1895)
                             CHAMBERS, ROBERT W.   NV         95
MONSTER MAKER, THE           MORROW, W. C.         NV
BATTLE OF THE MONSTERS, THE  ROBERTSON, MORGAN     SS         99
THOUSAND DEATHS, A           LONDON, JACK          SS    BLC 99 05
END OF THE WORLD, THE        NEWCOMB, SIMON        SS
BATTLE FOR THE PACIFIC, THE  STEVENS, ROWAN        SS
HARRY BORDEN'S NAVAL MONSTER HENDERSON, WILLIAM J  SS

BEACHHEADS IN SPACE          DERLETH, AUGUST    AN H PEL 52
ENGLISH DERIVATIVE ANTHOLOGY "FROM OTHER WORLDS"
INTRODUCTION                 DERLETH, AUGUST       IN
STAR, THE                    KELLER, DAVID H. MD.  SS
MAN FROM OUTSIDE, THE        WILLIAMSON, JACK      SS    ASF 51 03
BEACHHEAD (YOU'LL NEVER GO HOME AGAIN)
                             SIMAK, CLIFFORD D.    SS    FAD 51 07
"YEARS DRAW NIGH, THE"       DEL REY, LESTER       SS    ASF 51 10
METAMORPHOSITE               RUSSELL, ERIC FRANK   NV    ASF 46 12
ORDEAL OF PROFESSOR KLEIN, THE
                             DE CAMP, L. SPRAGUE   SS    SFA 52 11
REPETITION (ALSO AS THE GRYB)
                             VAN VOGT, A. E.       NV    ASF 40 04
BREEDS THERE A MAN...?       ASIMOV, ISAAC         NV    ASF 51 06
METEOR (PHONEY METEOR)       HARRIS, JOHN BEYNON   SS    AMZ 41 03
AND THE WALLS CAME TUMBLING DOWN
                             WYNDHAM, JOHN         SS    STS 51 05
BLINDING SHADOWS             WANDREI, DONALD       SS    ASF 34 05
METAMORPHOSIS OF EARTH, THE  SMITH, CLARK ASHTON   NV    WRT 51 09
AMBASSADORS FROM VENUS, THE  CROSSEN, KENDELL F.   NV    PLS 52 03
TO PEOPLE A NEW WORLD        BOND, NELSON S.       SS    BBM 50 11

BEACHHEADS IN SPACE (BRITISH PB)
                             DERLETH, AUGUST   AN     FSP 64
INTRODUCTION                 DERLETH, AUGUST       IN
STAR, THE                    KELLER, DAVID H. MD.  SS
BEACHHEAD (YOU'LL NEVER GO HOME AGAIN)
                             SIMAK, CLIFFORD D.    SS    FAD 51 07
"YEARS DRAW NIGH, THE"       DEL REY, LESTER       3S    ASF 51 10
METAMORPHOSITE               RUSSELL, ERIC FRANK   NV    ASF 46 12
ORDEAL OF PROFESSOR KLEIN, THE
                             DE CAMP, L. SPRAGUE   SS    SFA 52 11
REPETITION (ALSO AS THE GRYB)
                             VAN VOGT, A. E.       NV    ASF 40 04
TO PEOPLE A NEW WORLD        BOND, NELSON S.       SS    BBM 50 11

BEACHHEADS IN SPACE (BRITISH)
                             DERLETH, AUGUST    AN H WEI 54
INTRODUCTION                 DERLETH, AUGUST       IN
BEACHHEAD (YOU'LL NEVER GO HOME AGAIN)
                             SIMAK, CLIFFORD D.    SS    FAD 51 07
"YEARS DRAW NIGH, THE"       DEL REY, LESTER       SS    ASF 51 10
METAMORPHOSITE               RUSSELL, ERIC FRANK   NV    ASF 46 12
BREEDS THERE A MAN...?       ASIMOV, ISAAC         NV    ASF 51 06
```

```
AND THE WALLS CAME TUMBLING DOWN
                             WYNDHAM, JOHN         SS    STS 51 0
BLINDING SHADOWS             WANDREI, DONALD       SS    ASF 34 0
METAMORPHOSIS OF EARTH, THE  SMITH, CLARK ASHTON   NV    WRT 51 0

BEACHHEADS IN SPACE (7 OF 14)
                             DERLETH, AUGUST       AN    BRK 57
"YEARS DRAW NIGH, THE"       DEL REY, LESTER       SS    ASF 51 1
BREEDS THERE A MAN...?       ASIMOV, ISAAC         NV    ASF 51 0
REPETITION (ALSO AS THE GRYB)
                             VAN VOGT, A. E.       NV    ASF 40 0
BLINDING SHADOWS             WANDREI, DONALD       SS    ASF 34 0
METAMORPHOSITE               RUSSELL, ERIC FRANK   NV    ASF 46 1
AND THE WALLS CAME TUMBLING DOWN
                             WYNDHAM, JOHN         SS    STS 51 0
TO PEOPLE A NEW WORLD        BOND, NELSON S.       SS    BBM 50 1

BEAST THAT SHOUTED LOVE AT THE HEART OF THE WORLD, THE
                             ELLISON, HARLAN   AC   AVN 69 07
ENGLISH EDITION (H. MILLINGTON, 1976) OMITS:
"ALONG THE SCENIC ROUTE", "THE PLACE WITH NO NAME"
AND "SHATTERED LIKE A GLASS GOBLIN"
WAVES IN RIO, THE            ELLISON, HARLAN       IN
BEAST THAT SHOUTED LOVE AT THE HEART OF THE WORLD, THE
                             ELLISON, HARLAN       NV    GAL 68 0
ALONG THE SCENIC ROUTE (DOGFIGHT ON 101)
                             ELLISON, HARLAN       SS    AMZ 69 0
PHOENIX (PHOENIX LAND)       ELLISON, HARLAN       SS    IFS 69 0
ASLEEP: WITH STILL HANDS (THE SLEEPER WITH STILL HANDS)
                             ELLISON, HARLAN       NV    IFS 68 0
SANTA CLAUS VS. S.P.I.D.E.R. ELLISON, HARLAN       NV    FSF 69 0
TRY A DULL KNIFE             ELLISON, HARLAN       SS    FSF 68 1
PITLL PAWOB DIVISION, THE (THE PAWOB DIVISION)
                             ELLISON, HARLAN       SS    IFS 68 1
PLACE WITH NO NAME, THE      ELLISON, HARLAN       SS    FSF 69 0
WHITE ON WHITE               ELLISON, HARLAN       SS    KNT 68 1
RUN FOR THE STARS            ELLISON, HARLAN       NV    SFA 57 0
ARE YOU LISTENING?           ELLISON, HARLAN       SS    AMZ 58 1
WORLDS TO KILL               ELLISON, HARLAN       NV    IFS 68 0
SHATTERED LIKE A GLASS GOBLIN
                             ELLISON, HARLAN       SS    ORB 68 0
BOY AND HIS DOG, A           ELLISON, HARLAN       NV    NWS 69 0

BEAST, THE                   VAN VOGT, A. E.       NO H DBL 63
ALSO IN "A VAN VOGT OMNIBUS"
GREAT ENGINE, THE            VAN VOGT, A. E.       NV    ASF 43 0
BEAST, THE                   VAN VOGT, A. E.       NV    ASF 43 1
WONDERFUL MAN, THE (THE CHANGELING)
                             VAN VOGT, A. E.       SN    ASF 44 0

BEFORE ARMAGEDDON            MOORCOCK, MICHAEL  AN H ALL 75
AN ANTHOLOGY OF VICTORIAN AND EDWARDIAN IMAGINATIVE FICTION
PUBLISHED BEFORE 1914
INTRODUCTION                 MOORCOCK, MICHAEL     IN
BATTLE OF DORKING, THE       CHESNEY, G. T.        NA
DR. TRIFULGAS                VERNE, JULES          SS    SND 92 0
RAID OF LE VENGEUR, THE      GRIFFITH, GEORGE      SS    PRS 01 0
GREAT WAR IN ENGLAND IN 1897, THE
                             LE QUEX, WILLIAM      NV
LIFE IN OUR NEW CENTURY      WINTLE, W. J.         SS    HRM 01 0
THREE DRUGS, THE             NESBIT, EDITH         SS         10

BEFORE THE GOLDEN AGE        ASIMOV, ISAAC     AN H DBL 74
INTRODUCTION PART 1: 1920 TO 1930
                             ASIMOV, ISAAC         IN
MAN WHO EVOLVED, THE         HAMILTON, EDMOND      SS    WOS 31 0
JAMESON SATELLITE, THE       JONES, NEIL R.        SS    AMZ 31 0
SUBMICROSCOPIC               MEEK, CAPTAIN S. P.   SS    AMZ 31 0
AWLO OF ULM                  MEEK, CAPTAIN S. P.   NV    AMZ 31 0
TETRAHEDRA OF SPACE          MILLER, P. SCHUYLER   NV    WOS 31 1
WORLD OF THE RED SUN, THE    SIMAK, CLIFFORD D.    SS    WOS 31 1
TUMITHAK OF THE CORRIDORS    TANNER, CHARLES R.    NV    AMZ 32 0
MOON ERA, THE                WILLIAMSON, JACK      NV    WOS 32 0
MAN WHO AWOKE, THE           MANNING, LAURENCE     NV    WOS 33 0
TUMITHAK IN SHAWM            TANNER, CHARLES R.    NV    AMZ 33 0
COLOSSUS                     WANDREI, DONALD       NV    ASF 34 0
BORN OF THE SUN              WILLIAMSON, JACK      NV    ASF 34 0
SIDEWISE IN TIME             LEINSTER, MURRAY      SN    ASF 34 0
OLD FAITHFUL                 GALLUN, RAYMOND Z.    NV    ASF 34 1
PARASITE PLANET              WEINBAUM, STANLEY G.  NV    ASF 35 0
PROXIMA CENTAURI             LEINSTER, MURRAY      SN    ASF 35 0
ACCURSED GALAXY, THE         HAMILTON, EDMOND      SS    ASF 35 0
HE WHO SHRANK                HASSE, HENRY          NV    AMZ 36 0
HUMAN PETS OF MARS, THE      STONE, LESLIE F.      NV    AMZ 36 1
BRAIN STEALERS OF MARS, THE  CAMPBELL, JOHN W. JR  SS    TWS 36 1
DEVOLUTION                   HAMILTON, EDMOND      SS    AMZ 36 1
BIG GAME (WRITTEN 11/18/41)  ASIMOV, ISAAC         SS    NEW 74 A
OTHER EYES WATCHING          CAMPBELL, JOHN W. JR  AR    ASF 37 0
MINUS PLANET                 CLARK, JOHN D.        NV    ASF 37 0
PAST, PRESENT AND FUTURE     SCHACHNER, NAT        SN    ASF 37 0
MEN AND THE MIRROR, THE      ROCKLYNNE, ROSS       NV    ASF 38 0

BERSERKER                    SABERHAGEN, FRED      AC    BAL 67 01
WITHOUT A THOUGHT (FORTRESS SHIP)
                             SABERHAGEN, FRED      SS    IFS 63 0
GOODLIFE                     SABERHAGEN, FRED      NV    WOT 63 1
PATRON OF THE ARTS           SABERHAGEN, FRED      SS    IFS 65 0
PEACEMAKER, THE (THE LIFE HATER)
                             SABERHAGEN, FRED      SS    IFS 65 0
STONE PLACE                  SABERHAGEN, FRED      NV    IFS 65 0
WHAT T AND I DID             SABERHAGEN, FRED      SS    IFS 65 0
MR. JESTER                   SABERHAGEN, FRED      SS    IFS 65 1
MASQUE OF THE RED SHIFT      SABERHAGEN, FRED      NV    IFS 65 1
SIGN OF THE WOLF             SABERHAGEN, FRED      SS    IFS 65 0
IN THE TEMPLE OF MARS        SABERHAGEN, FRED      NV    IFS 66 0
FACE OF THE DEEP, THE        SABERHAGEN, FRED      SS    IFS 66 0
```

ERSERKERS, THE

BERSERKERS, THE   ELWOOD, ROGER   OA H TRI 74
  INTRODUCTION   ELWOOD, ROGER   IN
  BERSERKS, THE   TOFTE, ARTHUR   SS   BER 74
  TRIAL OF THE BLOOD   O'DONNELL, K. M.   SS   BER 74
  HORSEMAN FROM HEL, THE KIMBERLY, GAIL   NV   BER 74
  PRICE OF A DRINK, A   BLISH, JAMES   SS   BER 74
  AS IN A VISION APPREHENDED MALZBERG, BARRY N. SS   BER 74
  AND MAD UNDANCING BEARS LAFFERTY, R. A.   SS   BER 74
  THAUMATURGE   MOORE, RAYLYN   SS   BER 74
  COINCIDENCE   NOLAN, WILLIAM F.   SS   BER 74
  PATENT MEDICINE MAN, THE CASTELL, DAPHNE   SS   BER 74
  FREEWAY FOR DRACULAS, A LUPOFF, RICHARD A.   NV   BER 74
  NIGHT AND MORNING OF THE IDIOT CHILD
                         KIDD, VIRGINIA   PM   BER 74
  SKINFLOWERS   GERROLD, DAVID   SS   BER 74
  FORM IN REMISSION   SCHAEFFER, ROBIN   SS   BER 74
  ECHO   SALLIS, JAMES   SS   BER 74
  GENUINE ARTICLE, THE   COLE, ADRIAN   SS   BER 74

EST FANTASY STORIES   ALDISS, BRIAN W.   AN H FAB 62
  INTRODUCTION   ALDISS, BRIAN W.   IN
  JET-PROPELLED COUCH, THE LINDNER, ROBERT   AR   FSF 56 01
  BARON BAGGE   LERNET-HOLENIA, ALEX SS
  PERFORCE TO DREAM   JOYCE, MICHAEL   SS
  MUMMY TO THE RESCUE   WILSON, ANGUS   SS
  IN A SEASON OF CALM WEATHER BRADBURY, RAY   SS   PBY 57 01
  INCIDENT ON A LAKE   COLLIER, JOHN   SS
  COUSIN LEN'S WONDERFUL ADJECTIVE CELLAR
                         FINNEY, JACK   SS
  YOU CAN'T HAVE THEM ALL BEAUMONT, CHARLES   SS   PBY 56 08
  STORY-TELLER, THE   SAKI   SS
  INTANGIBLES, INC.   ALDISS, BRIAN W.   NV   SCF 59 02

BEST FROM AMAZING, THE   WHITE, TED   AN MAN 73
  NO CHARGE FOR ALTERATIONS GOLD, H. L.   NV   AMZ 53 05
  AUGMENTED AGENT, THE (I-C-A-BEM)
                         VANCE, JACK   NV   AMZ 61 10
  MISFIT, THE   ZELAZNY, ROGER   NV   AMZ 63 10
  DOWRY OF THE ANGYAR, THE (ALSO AS SEMLEY'S NECKLACE)
                         LE GUIN, URSULA K.   SS   AMZ 64 09
  PLACEMENT TEST   LAUMER, KEITH   NV   AMZ 64 07
  HORN OF TIME THE HUNTER, THE (HOMO AQUATICUS)
                         ANDERSON, POUL   SS   AMZ 63 09
  PHOENIX   WHITE, TED
                         AND BRADLEY, MARION Z. SS C AMZ 63 02
  ROGUE PSI   SCHMITZ, JAMES H.   NV   AMZ 62 08

BEST FROM FANTASTIC, THE WHITE, TED   AN MAN 73
  FOREWORD   WHITE, TED   IN
  I'M LOOKING FOR "JEFF" LEIBER, FRITZ   SS   FAN 52 FL
  ANGELS IN THE JETS   BIXBY, JEROME   SS   FAN 52 FL
  PAINGOD   ELLISON, HARLAN   SS   FAN 64 06
  MALATESTA COLLECTION, THE ZELAZNY, ROGER   SS   FAN 63 04
  SALLY   ASIMOV, ISAAC   SS   FAN 53 05
  ROLLER COASTER, THE   BESTER, ALFRED   SS   FAN 53 06
  EVE TIMES FOUR   ANDERSON, POUL   NV   FAN 60 04
  FINAL EXAM   OLIVER, CHAD   SS   FAN 52 11
  APRIL IN PARIS   LE GUIN, URSULA K.   SS   FAN 62 09
  TRIP TO THE CITY, A (IT COULD BE ANYTHING)
                         LAUMER, KEITH   NV   AMZ 63 01

BEST FROM FANTASY AND SCIENCE FICTION
                         BOUCHER & MCCOMAS   AN H LBR 52
  INTRODUCTION   BOUCHER, ANTHONY
                         AND MCCOMAS, J. FRANCIS IN C
  HUGE BEAST   CARTMILL, CLEVE   SS   FSF 50 SU
  JOHN THE REVELATOR   LA FARGE, OLIVER   SS   FSF 51 02
  ELEPHAS FRUMENTI   DE CAMP, L. SPRAGUE
                         AND PRATT, FLETCHER SS C FSF 50 WS
  GIFT OF GOD, THE   DE CAMP, L. SPRAGUE
                         AND PRATT, FLETCHER SS C FSF 50 WS
  FRIENDLY DEMON, THE (1726) DEFOE, DANIEL   SS   FSF 51 02
  OLD MAN HENDERSON   NEVILLE, KRIS   SS   FSF 51 06
  THREEPENNY-PIECE, THE (1913) STEPHENS, JAMES SS   FSF 51 06
  NO-SIDED PROFESSOR (ESQ 47 01)
                         GARDNER, MARTIN   SS   FSF 51 02
  LISTENING CHILD, THE   SEABRIGHT, IDRIS   SS   FSF 50 12
  DRESS OF WHITE SILK   MATHESON, RICHARD   SS   FSF 51 10
  MATHEMATICAL VOODOO, THE NEARING, H. F.   SS   FSF 51 04
  HUB (SOLITARY CONFINEMENT) MACDONALD, PHILIP SS   FSF 51 08
  BUILT UP LOGICALLY (THE UNIVERSAL TANCEA, RET 49 WI)
                         SCHOENFELD, HOWARD   SS   FSF 50 FL
  RAT THAT COULD SPEAK, THE (ALSO AS THE DEVIL AND MR. CHIPS)
                         DICKENS, CHARLES   SS   FSF 51 08
  NARAPOIA (THE ORIGIN OF NARAPOIA, WDG 48 04)
                         NELSON, ALAN   SS   FSF 51 04
  POSTPAID TO PARADISE (POSTMARKED FOR PARADISE, IN FSF 50 WS)
                         ARTHUR, ROBERT   SS   ARG 40 06
  IN THE DAYS OF OUR FATHERS MCCLINTIC, WINONA SS   FSF 49 FL
  BARNEY   STANTON, WILL   SS   FSF 51 02
  COLLECTOR, THE   HEARD, H. F.   SS   FSF 51 08
  FEARSOME FABLE   ELLIOTT, BRUCE   SS   FSF 51 02

BEST FROM FANTASY AND SCIENCE FICTION: 2
                         BOUCHER & MCCOMAS   AN H LBR 53
  INTRODUCTION   BOUCHER, ANTHONY
                         AND MCCOMAS, J. FRANCIS IN C
  BUDDING EXPLORER   ROBIN, RALPH   SS   FSF 52 09
  SHOUT, THE (1929)   GRAVES, ROBERT   SS   FSF 52 04
  TOOTH, THE   DEWEY, G. GORDON   SS   FSF 52 08
  UGLY SISTER (LMR 35 12) STRUTHER, JAN   SS   FSF 52 02
  BLACK BALL, THE   DE CAMP, L. SPRAGUE
                         AND PRATT, FLETCHER SS C FSF 52 10
  HOLE IN THE MOON, THE SEABRIGHT, IDRIS   SS   FSF 52 02
  THIRD LEVEL, THE (COL 50 10) FINNEY, JACK   SS   FSF 52 10
  CHEERY SOUL, THE (1945) BOWEN, ELIZABETH   SS   FSF 52 04

BEST FROM FANTASY AND SCIENCE FICTION: 5

RANSOM   FYFE, H. B.   SS   FSF 52 02
EARLIER SERVICE, THE (1935) IRWIN, MARGARET   SS   FSF 51 12
HYPERSPHERICAL BASKETBALL, THE
                         NEARING, H. JR.   SS   FSF 51 12
DESRICK ON YANDRO, THE   WELLMAN, MANLY WADE SS   FSF 52 06
COME ON, WAGON!   HENDERSON, ZENNA   SS   FSF 51 12
JIZZLE (REVISED FROM COL 49 01)
                         WYNDHAM, JOHN   SS   FSF 52 02
STAIR TRICK   CLINGERMAN, MILDRED SS   FSF 52 08
SOOTHSAYER, THE   BENNETT, KEM   SS   FSF 52 08
HOBSON'S CHOICE   BESTER, ALFRED   SS   FSF 52 08
LETTERS TO THE EDITOR (PMG 50 10)
                         GOULART, RON   SS   FSF 52 04

BEST FROM FANTASY AND SCIENCE FICTION: 3
                         BOUCHER & MCCOMAS   AN H DBL 54
  ACE PB EDITION OMITS ALL POEMS
  INTRODUCTION   BOUCHER, ANTHONY
                         AND MCCOMAS, J. FRANCIS IN C
  ATTITUDES   FARMER, PHILIP JOSE NV   FSF 53 10
  MAYBE JUST A LITTLE ONE (HRP 47 08)
                         BRETNOR, REGINALD   SS   FSF 53 02
  SOLAR SYSTEMS...   B., E. D.   PM   FSF 53 02
  STAR GYPSIES, THE   GRESHAM, WILLIAM L. SS   FSF 53 07
  NAMING OF NAMES, THE   MUDGETT, HERMAN W.   PM   FSF 53 10
  UNTIMELY TOPPER, THE   DE CAMP, L. SPRAGUE
  SOME FACTS ABOUT ROBOTS I WOLF, LEONARD   PM   FSF 53 11
  UNTIMELY TOPPER, THE   PRATT, FLETCHER
  VANDY, VANDY   WELLMAN, MANLY WADE SS   FSF 53 03
  EXPERIMENT   ROGERS, KAY   SS   FSF 53 02
  LOT   MOORE, WARD   NV   FSF 53 05
  MANUSCRIPT FOUND IN A VACUUM (PUN 52 12)
                         HUBBARD, P. M.   SS   FSF 53 08
  ESCAPIST, THE   B., E. D.   PM   FSF 53 02
  MALADJUSTED CLASSROOM, THE NEARING, H. JR. SS   FSF 53 06
  CHILD BY CHRONOS   HARNESS, CHARLES L. SS   FSF 53 06
  ANTIQUARY, THE   MCCLINTIC, WINONA   PM   FSF 53 07
  NEW RITUAL   SEABRIGHT, IDRIS   SS   FSF 53 01
  DEVLIN   READY, W. B.   SS   FSF 53 04
  TWO VOICES   MCCLINTIC, WINONA   PM   FSF 53 06
  CAPTIVE AUDIENCE   GRIFFITH, ANN WARREN SS   FSF 53 08
  SNULBUG (FIRST IN UNKNOWN, DEC. 1941)
                         BOUCHER, ANTHONY   SS   FSF 53 05
  SHEPHERD'S BOY   MIDDLETON, RICHARD   SS   FSF 53 08
  UNQUIET GRAVE, THE   MCCLINTIC, WINONA   PM   FSF 53 08
  STAR LIGHT, STAR BRIGHT BESTER, ALFRED   SS   FSF 53 07
  HIS MASTER'S VOICE   MCCLINTIC, WINONA   PM   FSF 53 06

BEST FROM FANTASY AND SCIENCE FICTION: 4
                         BOUCHER, ANTHONY   AN H DBL 55
  ACE PB EDITION OMITS ALL POEMS EXCEPT ASIMOV'S
  INTRODUCTION   BOUCHER, ANTHONY   IN
  FONDLY FAHRENHEIT   BESTER, ALFRED   SS   FSF 54 08
  I NEVER AST NO FAVORS KORNBLUTH, C. M.   SS   FSF 54 04
  SOME FACTS ABOUT ROBOTS WOLF, LEONARD   PM   FSF 54 07
  HEIRS APPARENT   ABERNATHY, ROBERT   NV   FSF 54 06
  $1.98   PORGES, ARTHUR   SS   FSF 54 05
  IMMORTAL GAME, THE   ANDERSON, POUL   SS   FSF 54 02
  ALL SUMMER IN A DAY   BRADBURY, RAY   SS   FSF 54 03
  ACCOUNTANT, THE   SHECKLEY, ROBERT   SS   FSF 54 07
  EPITAPH NEAR MOONPORT   SPRINGER, SHERWOOD PM   FSF 54 01
  BRAVE NEW WORD   MCCOMAS, J. FRANCIS SS   FSF 54 09
  MY BOYFRIEND'S NAME IS JELLO DAVIDSON, AVRAM SS   FSF 54 07
  TEST, THE   MATHESON, RICHARD   SS   FSF 54 11
  CARELESS LOVE (ALSO AS PUSH-BUTTON PASSION)
                         FRIBORG, ALBERT C.   SS   FSF 54 07
  REPORT ON THE SEXUAL BEHAVIOR OF THE EXTRA-SENSORY PERCEPTOR
                         MUDGETT, HERMAN W.   PM   FSF 54 08
  BULLETIN   JACKSON, SHIRLEY   SS   FSF 54 03
  EPITAPH IN AVALON   SPRINGER, SHERWOOD   PM   FSF 54 07
  SANCTUARY   GALOUYE, DANIEL F.   NV   FSF 54 02
  MISADVENTURE   DUNSANY, LORD   SS   FSF 54 10
  MORE FACTS ABOUT ROBOTS (SOME FACTS ABOUT ROBOTS II)
                         WOLF, LEONARD   PM   FSF 54 01
  LITTLE BLACK TRAIN, THE WELLMAN, MANLY WADE SS   FSF 54 08
  COWBOY LAMENT   JAFFRAY, NORMAN R.   PM   FSF 54 01
  FOUNDATION OF SCIENCE FICTION SUCCESS, THE
                         ASIMOV, ISAAC   PM   FSF 54 10

BEST FROM FANTASY AND SCIENCE FICTION: 5
                         BOUCHER, ANTHONY   AN H DBL 56
  ACE PB EDITION OMITS POEMS "1980 OVERTURES", "SILENT UPON TWO
  PEAKS" AND "THE GLASS OF THE FUTURE"
  IMAGINE, A PROEM   BROWN, FREDRIC   PM   FSF 55 05
  YOU'RE ANOTHER   KNIGHT, DAMON   NV   FSF 55 06
  SURVIVAL   COFFIN, CARLYN   PM   FSF 55 06
  THIS EARTH OF MAJESTY (CONTEST STORY WINNING TITLE REFUGEE)
                         CLARKE, ARTHUR C.   SS   FSF 55 07
  BIRDS CAN'T COUNT   CLINGERMAN, MILDRED SS   FSF 55 02
  GOLEM, THE   DAVIDSON, AVRAM   SS   FSF 55 03
  1980 OVERTURES   MCCLINTIC, WINONA   PM   FSF 55 04
  POTTAGE   HENDERSON, ZENNA   NV   FSF 55 09
  VANISHING AMERICAN, THE BEAUMONT, CHARLES   SS   FSF 55 08
  CREATED HE THEM   JONES, ALICE ELEANOR SS   FSF 55 06
  SILENT, UPON TWO PEAKS MUDGETT, HERMAN W.   PM   FSF 55 07
  TOO FAR   BROWN, FREDRIC   SS   FSF 55 09
  MATTER OF ENERGY, A (WITH MALICE TO COME)
                         BLISH, JAMES   SS   FSF 55 05
  NELLTHU   BOUCHER, ANTHONY   SS   FSF 55 08
  DREAMWORLD   ASIMOV, ISAAC   SS   FSF 55 11
  ONE ORDINARY DAY, WITH PEANUTS
                         JACKSON, SHIRLEY   SS   FSF 55 01
  GLASS OF THE FUTURE, THE MUDGETT, HERMAN W. PM   FSF 55 01
  SHORT ONES, THE   BANKS, RAYMOND E.   NV   FSF 55 03
  LAST PROPHET, THE   CLINGERMAN, MILDRED SS   FSF 55 08
  BOTANY BAY   HUBBARD, P. M.   SS   FSF 55 02

BEST FROM FANTASY AND SCIENCE FICTION: 5

CANTICLE FOR LEIBOWITZ, A   MILLER, WALTER M. JR NV   FSF 55 04
LAMENT BY A MAKER   DE CAMP, L. SPRAGUE   PM   FSF 55 01
DOCTRINE OF ORIGINAL DESIGN, THE
                              MCCLINTIC, WINONA   PM   FSF 55 03
PATTERN FOR SURVIVAL   MATHESON, RICHARD   SS   FSF 55 05
SINGING BELL, THE   ASIMOV, ISAAC   SS   FSF 55 01
LAST WORD, THE   OLIVER, CHAD
                              AND BEAUMONT, CHARLES SS C FSF 55 04

BEST FROM FANTASY AND SCIENCE FICTION: 6
                              BOUCHER, ANTHONY   AN H DBL 57
    ACE PB EDITION OMITS POEMS "FLYING CHAUCER" AND
    "I WANT MY NAME IN THE TITLE"
INTRODUCTION   BOUCHER, ANTHONY   IN
COSMIC EXPENSE ACCOUNT, THE (THE COSMIC CHARGE ACCOUNT)
                              KORNBLUTH, C. M.   NV   FSF 56 01
BLAZE OF GLORY   GARRETT, RANDALL   PM   FSF 55 12
MR. SAKRIS'S HALT   CLINGERMAN, MILDRED   SS   FSF 56 01
WOODS GROW DARKER, THE   DRAKE, LEAH BODINE   PM   FSF 55 11
ASA RULE, THE   WILLIAMS, JAY   SS   FSF 56 06
KING'S EVIL   DAVIDSON, AVRAM   SS   FSF 56 10
INTERVIEW   FERGUSON, BIRD   PM   FSF 55 12
CENSUS TAKERS, THE   POHL, FREDERIK   SS   FSF 56 02
FLYING CHAUCER   BRODE, ANTHONY   PM   FSF 56 03
MAN WHO CAME EARLY, THE   ANDERSON, POUL   NV   FSF 56 06
ANTI-CLIMAX, THE   MCCLINTIC, WINONA   PM   FSF 56 01
FINAL CLEARANCE   MADDUX, RACHEL   SS   FSF 56 02
SILK AND THE SONG, THE   FONTENAY, CHARLES L.   NV   FSF 56 07
SHODDY LANDS, THE   LEWIS, C. S.   SS   FSF 56 02
I WANT MY NAME IN THE TITLE   MCCLINTIC, WINONA   PM   FSF 56 07
LAST PRESENT, THE   STANTON, WILL   SS   FSF 56 08
NO MAN PURSUETH   MOORE, WARD   NV   FSF 56 04
I DON'T MIND   SMITH, RON   SS   FSF 56 10
BARBARIAN, THE   ANDERSON, POUL   SS   FSF 56 05
BRIGHT DESTRUCTION   MCCLINTIC, WINONA   PM   FSF 56 06
AND NOW THE NEWS...   STURGEON, THEODORE   SS   FSF 56 12
ICARUS MONTGOLFIER WRIGHT   BRADBURY, RAY   SS   FSF 56 05
FREE FLIGHT   HUBBARD, P. M.   PM   FSF 56 04

BEST FROM FANTASY AND SCIENCE FICTION: 7
                              BOUCHER, ANTHONY   AN H DBL 58
    ACE PB EDITION OMITS ALL POEMS EXCEPT BUCK'S
INTRODUCTION   BOUCHER, ANTHONY   IN
WINES OF EARTH, THE   SEABRIGHT, IDRIS   SS   FSF 57 09
IN MEMORIAM: FLETCHER PRATT   BLISH, JAMES   PM   FSF 57 01
ADJUSTMENT   MOORE, WARD   NV   FSF 57 05
CAGE, THE   CHANDLER, A. BERTRAM   SS   FSF 57 06
MR. STILWELL'S STAGE   DAVIDSON, AVRAM   SS   FSF 57 09
VENTURE TO THE MOON   CLARKE, ARTHUR C.   GR   FSF 56 12
EXPEDITION   BROWN, FREDRIC   SS   FSF 57 02
LYRIC FOR ATOM SPLITTERS   BUCK, DORIS PITKIN   PM   FSF 57 05
RESCUE   EDMONDSON, G. C.   SS   FSF 57 06
HORROR STORY SHORTER BY ONE LETTER THAN THE SHORTEST HORROR
    STORY EVER WRITTEN, A   SMITH, RON   SS   FSF 57 07
BETWEEN THE THUNDER AND THE SUN
                              OLIVER, CHAD   NV   FSF 57 05
LOINT OF PAW, A   ASIMOV, ISAAC   SS   FSF 57 08
WILD WOOD, THE   CLINGERMAN, MILDRED   SS   FSF 57 01
DODGER FAN   STANTON, WILL   SS   FSF 57 06
GODDESS IN GRANITE   YOUNG, ROBERT F.   NV   FSF 57 09
YES, BUT...   BRODE, ANTHONY   PM   FSF 57 09
MS. FOUND IN A CHINESE FORTUNE COOKIE
                              KORNBLUTH, C. M.   SS   FSF 57 07
JOURNEYS END   ANDERSON, POUL   SS   FSF 57 02
FULL CIRCLE   PINKNEY, DOROTHY C.   PM   FSF 56 12
BIG TREK, THE   LEIBER, FRITZ   SS   FSF 57 10

BEST FROM FANTASY AND SCIENCE FICTION: 8
                              BOUCHER, ANTHONY   AN H DBL 59
    ACE PB EDITION OMITS FEGHOOTS AND POEMS
INTRODUCTION   BOUCHER, ANTHONY   IN
MINISTERING ANGELS (SRV MAY 28, 1955)
                              LEWIS, C. S.   SS   FSF 58 01
THROUGH TIME AND SPACE WITH FERDINAND FEGHOOT: VII
                              BRIARTON, GRENDEL   SS   FSF 58 03
BACKWARDNESS   ANDERSON, POUL   SS   FSF 58 03
WAIT, THE   REED, KIT   SS   FSF 58 04
ORIGIN OF THE SPECIES   ANDERSON, KAREN   PM   FSF 58 06
UP-TO-DATE SORCERER, THE   ASIMOV, ISAAC   SS   FSF 58 07
EPITHALAMIUM   BUCK, DORIS PITKIN   PM   FSF 58 01
DESKFUL OF GIRLS, A   LEIBER, FRITZ   NV   FSF 58 04
WATCHERS, THE   BRODE, ANTHONY   PM   FSF 58 04
ERIPMAV   KNIGHT, DAMON   SS   FSF 58 06
POOR LITTLE WARRIOR!   ALDISS, BRIAN W.   SS   FSF 58 04
BETTER BET, THE   BRODE, ANTHONY   PM   FSF 58 02
OMEN, THE   JACKSON, SHIRLEY   SS   FSF 58 03
YE PHANTASIE WRITER AND HIS CATTE
                              MCCLINTIC, WINONA   PM   FSF 58 03
GIL BRALTAR (1857)   VERNE, JULES   SS   FSF 58 07
IN MEMORIAM: HENRY KUTTNER   ANDERSON, KAREN   PM   FSF 58 05
GRANTHA SIGHTING, THE   DAVIDSON, AVRAM   SS   FSF 58 04
THEORY OF ROCKETRY   KORNBLUTH, C. M.   SS   FSF 58 07
C. M. KORNBLUTH: A MEMORIAL BIBLIOGRAPHY
                              BOUCHER, ANTHONY   MS   FSF 58 07
NEW LO!, A   GOULART, RON   SS   FSF 58 01
GORILLA SUIT   SHEPLEY, JOHN   SS   FSF 58 05
CAPTIVITY   HENDERSON, ZENNA   SS   FSF 58 06
MEN WHO MURDERED MOHAMMED, THE
                              BESTER, ALFRED   SS   FSF 58 10
THROUGH TIME AND SPACE WITH FERDINAND FEGHOOT: VIII
                              BRIARTON, GRENDEL   SS   FSF 58 08
VALISE MACABRE   MCCLINTIC, WINONA   PM   FSF 57 11

BEST FROM FANTASY AND SCIENCE FICTION: 9
                              MILLS, ROBERT P.   AN H DBL 60
    ALSO AS "FLOWERS FOR ALGERNON AND OTHER STORIES"

BEST FROM FANTASY AND SCIENCE FICTION: 1
    BRITISH EDITIONS OMIT FEGHOOTS,
    ACE PB EDITION OMITS FEGHOOTS AND POEMS
FLOWERS FOR ALGERNON   KEYES, DANIEL   SS   FSF 59 04
ME   SCHENCK, HILBERT JR. PM   FSF 59 0
DIFFERENT PURPOSE, A   BENNETT, KEM   SS   FSF 58 1
VAMPIRE'S SAGA, A   BELKIN, NORMAN   PM   FSF 59 0
RALPH WOLLSTONECRAFT HEDGE: A MEMOIR
                              GOULART, RON   SS   FSF 59 0
SPORTSMAN'S DIFFICULTY   BUCK, DORIS PITKIN   PM   FSF 59 0
ALL YOU ZOMBIES-   HEINLEIN, ROBERT A.   SS   FSF 59 0
EXPOSTULATION, AN   LEWIS, C. S.   PM   FSF 59 0
CASEY AGONISTES   MCKENNA, RICHARD M.   SS   FSF 58 0
THROUGH TIME AND SPACE WITH FERDINAND FEGHOOT: XI
                              BRIARTON, GRENDEL   SS   FSF 59 0
EASTWARD HO!   TENN, WILLIAM   SS   FSF 58 1
THROUGH TIME AND SPACE WITH FERDINAND FEGHOOT: XIV
                              BRIARTON, GRENDEL   SS   FSF 59 0
SOUL MATE   SUTTON, LEE   SS   FSF 59 0
CALL ME MISTER   BRODE, ANTHONY   PM   FSF 59 0
WHAT ROUGH BEAST?   KNIGHT, DAMON   NV   FSF 59 0
CLASSICAL QUERY COMPOSED WHILE SHAMPOOING
                              BUCK, DORIS PITKIN   PM   FSF 59 0
FAR FROM HOME   TEVIS, WALTER S. JR. SS   FSF 58 1
SPACE BURIAL   ALDISS, BRIAN W.   PM   FSF 59 0
INVASION OF THE PLANET OF LOVE
                              ELLIOTT, GEORGE P.   SS   FSF 59 0
THROUGH TIME AND SPACE WITH FERDINAND FEGHOOT: X
                              BRIARTON, GRENDEL   SS   FSF 59 0
DAGON   DAVIDSON, AVRAM   SS   FSF 59 1
PACT   SANDERS, WINSTON P.   SS   FSF 59 0
TO GIVE THEM BEAUTY FOR ASHES
                              MCCLINTIC, WINONA   PM   FSF 59 0
NO MATTER WHERE YOU GO   ROGERS, JOEL T.   NV   FSF 59 0
THROUGH TIME AND SPACE WITH FERDINAND FEGHOOT: XII
                              BRIARTON, GRENDEL   SS   FSF 59 0
WILLOW TREE, THE   RICE, JANE   SS   FSF 59 0
THROUGH TIME AND SPACE WITH FERDINAND FEGHOOT: XIII
                              BRIARTON, GRENDEL   SS   FSF 59 0
PI MAN, THE   BESTER, ALFRED   SS   FSF 59 1
MAN WHO LOST THE SEA, THE   STURGEON, THEODORE   SS   FSF 59 1
THROUGH TIME AND SPACE WITH FERDINAND FEGHOOT: XV
                              BRIARTON, GRENDEL   SS   FSF 59 0

BEST FROM FANTASY AND SCIENCE FICTION: 10
                              MILLS, ROBERT P.   AN H DBL 61
NIKITA EISENHOWER JONES   YOUNG, ROBERT F.   NV   FSF 60 08
WHO DREAMS OF IVY   WORTHINGTON, WILL   SS   FSF 60 11
MINE OWN WAYS   MCKENNA, RICHARD M.   SS   FSF 60 02
RAINBOW GOLD, THE   RICE, JANE   SS   FSF 59 12
CRAZY MARO   KEYES, DANIEL   NV   FSF 60 04
SOMETHING   DRURY, ALLEN   SS   FSF 60 10
IT'S A GREAT BIG WONDERFUL UNIVERSE
                              AANDAHL, VANCE   SS   FSF 60 11
MAN OVERBOARD   COLLIER, JOHN   NV   FSF 60 03
BLIND PILOT, THE (TRANSLATED BY DAMON KNIGHT)
                              HENNEBERG, CHARLES   SS   FSF 60 0
DIVVIL WITH THE WOMEN, A   WILDE, NIALL   SS   FSF 60 0
MARTYR, THE   ANDERSON, POUL   NV   FSF 60 0
DOUBLE, DOUBLE, TOIL AND TROUBLE
                              CANTINE, HOLLEY   SS   FSF 60 0
APRES NOUS   DAVIDSON, AVRAM   SS   FSF 60 0
INTERBALANCE   MACLEAN, KATHERINE   SS   FSF 60 10
INFINITY   REEVES, ROSSER   PM   FSF 60 12
REPLACEMENT, THE   MURRAY, ROBERT   SS   FSF 60 02
FELLOW WHO MARRIED THE MAXILL GIRL, THE
                              MOORE, WARD   NV   FSF 60 0

BEST FROM FANTASY AND SCIENCE FICTION: 11
                              MILLS, ROBERT P.   AN H DBL 62
SOURCES OF THE NILE, THE   DAVIDSON, AVRAM   NV   FSF 61 01
SOMEBODY TO PLAY WITH   WILLIAMS, JAY   SS   FSF 61 05
SOFTLY WHILE YOU'RE SLEEPING SMITH, EVELYN E.   SS   FSF 61 04
MACHINE THAT WON THE WAR, THE
                              ASIMOV, ISAAC   SS   FSF 61 10
GO FOR BAROQUE   SCOTT, JODY   SS   FSF 61 06
TIME LAG   ANDERSON, POUL   NV   FSF 61 01
GEORGE   WEST, JOHN ANTHONY   SS   FSF 61 06
SHOTGUN CURE   SIMAK, CLIFFORD D.   SS   FSF 61 0
ONE WHO RETURNS, THE   BERRY, JOHN   SS   FSF 61 03
CAPTIVITY   FINNEY, CHARLES G.   SS   FSF 61 06
ALPHA RALPHA BOULEVARD   SMITH, CORDWAINER   NV   FSF 61 06
EFFIGY   REEVES, ROSSER   PM   FSF 61 09
E=MC2   REEVES, ROSSER   PM   FSF 61 10
HARRISON BERGERON   VONNEGUT, KURT JR.   SS   FSF 61 10
HAUNTED VILLAGE, THE   DICKSON, GORDON R.   NV   FSF 61 08

BEST FROM FANTASY AND SCIENCE FICTION: 11 (BRITISH)
                              MILLS, ROBERT P.   AN   PTH 66
SOURCES OF THE NILE, THE   DAVIDSON, AVRAM   NV   FSF 61 01
SOMEBODY TO PLAY WITH   WILLIAMS, JAY   SS   FSF 61 05
GO FOR BAROQUE   SCOTT, JODY   SS   FSF 61 06
MACHINE THAT WON THE WAR, THE
                              ASIMOV, ISAAC   SS   FSF 61 10
TIME LAG   ANDERSON, POUL   NV   FSF 61 01
SHOTGUN CURE   SIMAK, CLIFFORD D.   SS   FSF 61 01
ONE WHO RETURNS, THE   BERRY, JOHN   SS   FSF 61 03
CAPTIVITY, THE   FINNEY, CHARLES G.   SS   FSF 61 10
ALPHA RALPHA BOULEVARD   SMITH, CORDWAINER   NV   FSF 61 06
HARRISON BERGERON   VONNEGUT, KURT JR.   SS   FSF 61 10
HAUNTED VILLAGE, THE   DICKSON, GORDON R.   NV   FSF 61 08

BEST FROM FANTASY AND SCIENCE FICTION: 12
                              DAVIDSON, AVRAM   AN H DBL 63
INTRODUCTION   DAVIDSON, AVRAM   IN
TEST   THOMAS, THEODORE L.   SS   FSF 62 04
PLEASE STAND BY   GOULART, RON   NV   FSF 62 01

BEST FROM FANTASY AND SCIENCE FICTION: 12

WHO'S IN CHARGE HERE? (ALSO AS NONE SO BLIND)					
	BLISH, JAMES	SS	FSF	62	05
THREE FOR THE STARS	DICKINSON, JOSEPH	SS	FSF	62	04
WHEN LILACS LAST IN THE DOORYARD BLOOMED					
	AANDAHL, VANCE	NV	FSF	62	05
LANDSCAPE WITH SPHINXES	ANDERSON, KAREN	SS	FSF	62	11
MY DEAR EMILY	RUSS, JOANNA	NV	FSF	62	07
GUMDROP KING, THE	STANTON, WILL	SS	FSF	62	08
GOLDEN HORN, THE	PANGBORN, EDGAR	NV	FSF	62	02
SINGULAR EVENTS WHICH OCCURRED IN THE HOVEL ON THE ALLEY OFF					
OF EYE STREET, THE	DAVIDSON, AVRAM	SS	FSF	62	02
KIND OF ARTISTRY, A	ALDISS, BRIAN W.	SS	FSF	62	10
TWO'S A CROWD	GILIEN, SASHA	SS	FSF	62	07
MAN WITHOUT A PLANET, THE	WILHELM, KATE	SS	FSF	62	07
GARDEN OF TIME, THE	BALLARD, J. G.	SS	FSF	62	02
HOP-FRIEND	CARR, TERRY	SS	FSF	62	11

BEST FROM FANTASY AND SCIENCE FICTION: 13

	DAVIDSON, AVRAM	AN H DBL 64			
INTRODUCTION	DAVIDSON, AVRAM	IN			
GOLDEN BRICK, THE	HUBBARD, P. M.	SS	FSF	63	01
PEGGY AND PETER GO TO THE MOON					
	WHITE, DON	SS	FSF	63	02
NOW WAKES THE SEA	BALLARD, J. G.	SS	FSF	63	05
GREEN MAGIC	VANCE, JACK	SS	FSF	63	06
CAPTAIN HONARIO HARPPLAYER, R.N.					
	HARRISON, HARRY	SS	FSF	63	03
TREATY IN TARTESSOS	ANDERSON, KAREN	SS	FSF	63	05
HUNTER, COME HOME	MCKENNA, RICHARD M.	NV	FSF	63	03
MCNAMARA'S FISH	GOULART, RON	SS	FSF	63	07
NINA SOL	MARTI-IBANEZ, FELIX	SS	FSF	63	05
THEY DON'T MAKE LIFE LIKE THEY USED TO					
	BESTER, ALFRED	NV	FSF	63	10
WHAT STRANGE STARS AND SKIES	DAVIDSON, AVRAM	SS	FSF	63	12
EIGHT O'CLOCK IN THE MORNING	NELSON, RAY	SS	FSF	63	11
DELUGE	HENDERSON, ZENNA	NV	FSF	63	10

BEST FROM FANTASY AND SCIENCE FICTION: 14

	DAVIDSON, AVRAM	AN H DBL 65			
INTRODUCTION	DAVIDSON, AVRAM	IN			
SACHEVERELL	DAVIDSON, AVRAM	SS	FSF	64	03
TRADE-IN	SHARKEY, JACK	SS	FSF	64	06
ILLUMINATED MAN, THE	BALLARD, J. G.	NV	FSF	64	05
BULLETIN FROM THE TRUSTEES, A					
	SHORE, WILMA	SS	FSF	64	08
AUTOMATIC TIGER	REED, KIT	SS	FSF	64	03
COURT OF TARTARY, THE	CARAVAN, T. P.	SS	FSF	63	12
TOUCHSTONE	CARR, TERRY	SS	FSF	64	05
THAW AND SERVE	LANG, ALLEN KIM	SS	FSF	64	01
NADA	DISCH, THOMAS M.	SS	FSF	64	08
INTO THE SHOP	GOULART, RON	SS	FSF	64	04
ROSE FOR ECCLESIASTES, A	ZELAZNY, ROGER	NV	FSF	63	11
OLSEN AND THE GULL	ST. CLAIR, ERIC	SS	FSF	64	09
DARK CONCEPTION	ADAMS, LOUIS J. A.	SS	FSF	64	11
COMPLEAT CONSUMATORS, THE	NOURSE, ALAN E.	SS	FSF	64	04
HOUSE BY THE CRAB APPLE TREE, THE					
	JOHNSON, S. S.	NV	FSF	64	02
GIRL WITH THE HUNDRED PROOF EYES, THE					
	WEBB, RON	SS	FSF	64	07
FRED ONE	RANSOM, JAMES	SS	FSF	64	04

BEST FROM FANTASY AND SCIENCE FICTION: 15

	FERMAN, EDWARD L.	AN H DBL 66			
INTRODUCTION	FERMAN, EDWARD L.	IN			
DOORS OF HIS FACE, THE LAMPS OF HIS MOUTH, THE					
	ZELAZNY, ROGER	NV	FSF	65	03
RAKE	GOULART, RON	SS	FSF	65	06
HISTORY OF DOCTOR FROST, THE	HODGINS, RODERIC C.	SS	FSF	65	04
FOUR GHOSTS IN HAMLET	LEIBER, FRITZ	NV	FSF	65	01
KEEP THEM HAPPY	ROHRER, ROBERT	SS	FSF	65	04
MURKLE FOR JESSE, A	JENNINGS, GARY	SS	FSF	65	07
EYES DO MORE THAN SEE	ASIMOV, ISAAC	SS	FSF	65	04
HOUSE THE BLAKENEYS BUILT, THE					
	DAVIDSON, AVRAM	SS	FSF	65	01
EIGHT BILLION, THE	WILSON, RICHARD	SS	FSF	65	07
SOMETHING ELSE	TILLEY, ROBERT J.	SS	FSF	65	10
AUNT MILLICENT AT THE RACES	GUTTRIDGE, LEN	SS	FSF	65	04
SEA BRIGHT	MOORE, HAL R.	SS	FSF	65	09
HOG-BELLY HONEY	LAFFERTY, R. A.	SS	FSF	65	09
NO DIFFERENT FLESH	HENDERSON, ZENNA	NV	FSF	65	05
LOVE LETTERS FROM MARS	CIARDI, JOHN	PM	FSF	65	01
TREAT	KERR, WALTER H.	PM	FSF	64	11
FROM TWO UNIVERSES	BUCK, DORIS PITKIN	PM	FSF	64	12
FIVE CARTOONS	WILSON, GAHAN	CT	FSF	65	

BEST FROM FANTASY AND SCIENCE FICTION: 16

	FERMAN, EDWARD L.	AN H DBL 67			
INTRODUCTION	FERMAN, EDWARD L.	IN			
LUANA	THOMAS, GILBERT	SS	FSF	66	09
AND MADLY TEACH	BIGGLE, LLOYD JR.	NV	FSF	66	05
MATOG	BASCH, JOAN PATRICIA	SS	FSF	66	08
KEY, THE	ASIMOV, ISAAC	NV	FSF	66	10
SEVEN WONDERS OF THE UNIVERSE, THE					
	MALLETTE, MOSE	SS	FSF	66	08
FEW KINDRED SPIRITS, A	CHRISTOPHER, JOHN	SS	FSF	65	11
WE CAN REMEMBER IT FOR YOU WHOLESALE					
	DICK, PHILIP K.	NV	FSF	66	04
THREE FOR CARNIVAL	SHEPLEY, JOHN	SS	FSF	66	05
EXPERIMENT IN AUTOBIOGRAPHY	GOULART, RON	SS	FSF	66	07
ADJUSTED, THE	BULMER, KENNETH	SS	FSF	66	06
AGE OF INVENTION, THE	SPINRAD, NORMAN	SS	FSF	66	07
APOLOGY TO INKY	GREEN, ROBERT M. JR.	NV	FSF	66	01
THIS MOMENT OF THE STORM	ZELAZNY, ROGER	NV	FSF	66	06
MICKEY FINN	BUCK, DORIS PITKIN	PM	FSF	66	03
IMAGINARY NUMBERS IN A REAL GARDEN					
	JONAS, GERALD	PM	FSF	65	04

BEST FROM FANTASY AND SCIENCE FICTION, 25TH ANNIV.

LETTER TO A TYRANT KING	BUTLER, BILL	PM	FSF	66	08
MEMO TO SECRETARY	DEGRAW, PAT	PM	FSF	66	06
SIX CARTOONS	WILSON, GAHAN	CT	FSF	66	

BEST FROM FANTASY AND SCIENCE FICTION: 17

	FERMAN, EDWARD L.	AN H DBL 68			
INTRODUCTION	FERMAN, EDWARD L.	IN			
CYPRIAN'S ROOM	STERBA, MONICA	NV	FSF	67	05
OUT OF TIME, OUT OF PLACE	COLLYN, GEORGE	SS	FSF	67	09
VON GOOM'S GAMBIT	CONTOSKI, VICTOR	SS	FSF	66	12
BUMBERBOOM	DAVIDSON, AVRAM	NV	FSF	66	12
FILL IN THE BLANK	GOULART, RON	SS	FSF	67	05
BALGRUMMO'S HELL	KIRK, RUSSELL	SS	FSF	67	07
CORONA	DELANY, SAMUEL R.	SS	FSF	67	10
INNER CIRCLES, THE (ALSO AS THE WINTER FLIES)					
	LEIBER, FRITZ	SS	FSF	67	10
PROBLEMS OF CREATIVENESS	DISCH, THOMAS M.	SS	FSF	67	04
ENCOUNTER IN THE PAST	NATHAN, ROBERT	SS	FSF	67	07
SEA CHANGE, THE	COX, ARTHUR JEAN	SS	FSF	67	03
DEVIL AND DEMOCRACY, THE	CLEEVE, BRIAN	SS	FSF	66	11
RANDY'S SYNDROME	ALDISS, BRIAN W.	NV	FSF	67	04
FOUR CARTOONS	WILSON, GAHAN	CT	FSF	67	

BEST FROM FANTASY AND SCIENCE FICTION: 18

	FERMAN, EDWARD L.	AN H DBL 69			
CLOUD-SCULPTORS OF CORAL D, THE					
	BALLARD, J. G.	SS	FSF	67	12
PEOPLE TRAP, THE	SHECKLEY, ROBERT	SS	FSF	68	06
IN HIS OWN IMAGE	BIGGLE, LLOYD JR.	SS	FSF	68	01
OGRE!	JESBY, EDWARD	NV	FSF	68	09
LUNATIC ASSIGNMENT	DORMAN, SONYA	SS	FSF	68	01
GIFTS FROM THE UNIVERSE	TUSHNET, LEONARD	SS	FSF	68	05
SUNDOWN	REDD, DAVID	NV	FSF	67	12
BEYOND THE GAME	AANDAHL, VANCE	SS	FSF	68	05
SEA HOME	LEE, WILLIAM M.	NV	FSF	68	06
THAT HIGH-UP BLUE DAY THAT SAW THE BLACK SKY-TRAIN COME					
SPINNING	BUNCH, DAVID R.	SS	FSF	68	03
MUSCADINE	GOULART, RON	SS	FSF	68	04
FINAL WAR	O'DONNELL, K. M.	NV	FSF	68	04
I HAVE MY VIGIL	HARRISON, HARRY	SS	FSF	68	02
EGG OF THE GLAK, THE	JACOBS, HARVEY	NV	FSF	68	03
FIVE CARTOONS	WILSON, GAHAN	CT	FSF	68	

BEST FROM FANTASY AND SCIENCE FICTION: 19

	FERMAN, EDWARD L.	AN H DBL 71			
GONE FISHIN'	WILSON, ROBIN SCOTT	SS	FSF	70	10
SELECTRA SIX-TEN	DAVIDSON, AVRAM	SS	FSF	70	10
LONGTOOTH	PANGBORN, EDGAR	NV	FSF	70	01
SUNDANCE	SILVERBERG, ROBERT	SS	FSF	69	06
BRIEF, SWINGING CAREER OF DAN AND JUDY SMYTHE, THE					
	WILSON, CARTER	SS	FSF	70	04
DREAM PATROL	RUNYON, CHARLES W.	SS	FSF	70	02
CALLIOPE AND GHERKIN AND THE YANKEE DOODLE THING					
	SMITH, EVELYN E.	NV	FSF	69	03
NOTES JUST PRIOR TO THE FALL	MALZBERG, BARRY N.	SS	FSF	70	10
CONFESSIONS	GOULART, RON	NV	FSF	70	08
GET A HORSE! (ALSO AS THE FLIGHT OF THE HORSE)					
	NIVEN, LARRY	SS	FSF	69	10
MAN WHO LEARNED LOVING, THE	STURGEON, THEODORE	SS	FSF	69	10
LITTERBUG	MORPHETT, TONY	NV	FSF	69	07
ADVENTURE IN THE YOLLA BOLLY MIDDLE EEL WILDERNESS, AN					
	AANDAHL, VANCE	NV	FSF	69	08
STARTING FROM SCRATCH	SHECKLEY, ROBERT	SS	FSF	70	11
BENJI'S PENCIL	MCALLISTER, BRUCE	SS	FSF	69	03
SIX CARTOONS	WILSON, GAHAN	CT	FSF	70	

BEST FROM FANTASY AND SCIENCE FICTION: 20

	FERMAN, EDWARD L.	AN H DBL 73			
SHAFFERY AMONG THE IMMORTALS	POHL, FREDERIK	SS	FSF	72	07
DIFFERENT DRUMMER, A	MOORE, RAYLYN	SS	FSF	71	02
DEATHBIRD, THE	ELLISON, HARLAN	NV	FSF	73	03
BORN TO EXILE	EISENSTEIN, PHYLLIS	NV	FSF	71	08
THUS LOVE BETRAYS US	MACLENNAN, PHYLLIS	SS	FSF	72	09
ANIMAL FAIR, THE	BESTER, ALFRED	NV	FSF	72	10
IS IT THE END OF THE WORLD?	SHORE, WILMA	SS	FSF	72	03
BEAR WITH THE KNOT ON HIS TAIL, THE					
	TALL, STEPHEN	NV	FSF	71	05
BIRDLIME	KELLER, B. L.	SS	FSF	71	03
PROBLEM OF PAIN, THE	ANDERSON, POUL	NV	FSF	73	02
SOONER OR LATER OR NEVER NEVER					
	JENNINGS, GARY	NV	FSF	72	05
CARTOONS	WILSON, GAHAN	CT	FSF		

BEST FROM FANTASY AND SCIENCE FICTION, 25TH ANNIV.

	FERMAN, EDWARD L.	AN H DBL 74			
INTRODUCTION	FERMAN, EDWARD L.	IN			
WHEN YOU CARE, WHEN YOU LOVE	STURGEON, THEODORE	NV	FSF	62	09
THEODORE STURGEON	MERRIL, JUDITH	AR	FSF	62	09
STURGEON BIBLIOGRAPHY	MOSKOWITZ, SAM	MS	FSF	62	09
TO THE CHICAGO ABYSS	BRADBURY, RAY	SS	FSF	63	05
RAY BRADBURY	NOLAN, WILLIAM F.	AR	FSF	63	05
BRADBURY BIBLIOGRAPHY	NOLAN, WILLIAM F.	MS	FSF	63	05
KEY, THE	ASIMOV, ISAAC	NV	FSF	66	10
ISAAC ASIMOV (YOU CAN'T BEAT BRAINS)					
	DE CAMP, L. SPRAGUE	AR	FSF	66	10
ASIMOV BIBLIOGRAPHY	MISC. MATERIAL	MS	FSF	66	10
SHIP OF SHADOWS	LEIBER, FRITZ	SN	FSF	69	07
FRITZ LEIBER	MERRIL, JUDITH	AR	FSF	69	07
LEIBER BIBLIOGRAPHY	LEWIS, AL	MS	FSF	69	07
QUEEN OF AIR AND DARKNESS, THE					
	ANDERSON, POUL	SN	FSF	71	04
POUL ANDERSON	DICKSON, GORDON R.	AR	FSF	71	04
ANDERSON BIBLIOGRAPHY	MISC. MATERIAL	MS	FSF	71	04
MIDSUMMER CENTURY	BLISH, JAMES	SN	FSF	72	04
JAMES BLISH	LOWNDES, ROBERT W.	AR	FSF	72	04
BLISH BIBLIOGRAPHY	OWINGS, MARK	MS	FSF	72	04

BEST FROM GALAXY, THE VOLUME I

BEST FROM GALAXY, THE VOLUME I
                                GALAXY, EDITORS OF   AN   AWD 72
NECESSARY AND SUFFICIENT   STURGEON, THEODORE   SS   GAL 71 04
GETTING TOGETHER   ROTHMAN, MILTON A.   SS   GAL 72 03
SOUL MACHINE, THE   CHANDLER, A. BERTRAM SS   GAL 69 10
RAMMER   NIVEN, LARRY   NV   GAL 71 11
SHARKS OF PENTREATH, THE   CONEY, MICHAEL G.   SS   GAL 71 02
OUT OF PHASE   HALDEMAN, JOE W.   SS   GAL 69 09
DARKSIDE CROSSING   BLISH, JAMES   NV   GAL 70 12
TRAFFIC PROBLEM   EARLS, WILLIAM   SS   GAL 70 10
ABOUT A SECRET CROCODILE   LAFFERTY, R. A.   SS   GAL 70 08
OUT OF MINDSHOT   BRUNNER, JOHN   SS   GAL 70 06
NO-WIND SPOTTED TIGER PLANET, THE
                              MACFARLANE, WALLACE   SS   GAL 71 05
ALLISON, CARMICHAEL AND TATTERSALL
                              TALL, STEPHEN   NV   GAL 70 04
PENNIES, OFF A DEAD MAN'S EYES
                              ELLISON, HARLAN   SS   GAL 69 11

BEST FROM GALAXY, THE VOLUME II
                                GALAXY, EDITORS OF   AN   AWD 74
FIELD OF VISION, THE   LE GUIN, URSULA K.   SS   GAL 73 10
QUICKENING   MACFARLANE, WALLACE   SS   GAL 73 09
BY THE SEASHORE   LAFFERTY, R. A.   SS   GAL 73 11
TRIGGERMAN   FISHER, LOU   SS   GAL 73 09
VOICE AND BITTER WEEPING, A   SAUNDERS, BUDDY
                              AND WALDROP, HOWARD   SS C GAL 73 07
COLD FRIEND   ELLISON, HARLAN   SS   GAL 73 10
QUARANTINE   PISERCHIA, DORIS   SS   GAL 73 09
SUPPLIANT IN SPACE, A   SHECKLEY, ROBERT   NV   GAL 73 11
AGNES, ACCENT AND ACCESS   STURGEON, THEODORE   SS   GAL 73 10
MAYFLOWER ONE   TAVES, ERNEST   NV   GAL 72 11
JUST A MATTER OF TIME   PERRIN, JEFFERY   SS   GAL 73 07
LA BEFANA   WOLFE, GENE   SS   GAL 73 01

BEST FROM GALAXY, THE VOLUME III
                                BAEN, JAMES   AN   AWD 75
DAY BEFORE THE REVOLUTION, THE
                              LE GUIN, URSULA K.   SS   GAL 74 08
PRIVATE WAR OF PVT. JACOB, THE
                              HALDEMAN, JOE W.   SS   GAL 74 06
PASSAGES   RUSS, JOANNA   AR   GAL 74 01
SWEET SISTER, GREEN BROTHER   VAN SCYOC, SYDNEY J. NA   GAL 73 12
RIVERS OF DAMASCUS   LAFFERTY, R. A.   NV   GAL 74 02
GLITCH, THE   BLISH, JAMES
                              AND STANTON, L. JEROME NV C GAL 74 06
ANSWER CAME THERE NONE   WHITE, JAMES   SS   GAL 74 01
SPLENDID FREEDOM, THE   DARNAY, ARSEN   NV   GAL 74 09
END CITY   SHECKLEY, ROBERT   SS   GAL 74 05
OPENING PROBLEM   LAWRENCE, J. A.   NV   GAL 74 07
GIFT OF GARIGOLLI, THE   POHL, FREDERIK
                              AND KORNBLUTH, C. M. NV C GAL 74 08
IS THERE HOPE FOR THE FUTURE?
                              ASIMOV, ISAAC   AR   GAL 74 07

BEST FROM GALAXY, THE VOLUME IV
                                BAEN, JAMES   AN   AWD 76
GAME OF BLOOD AND DUST, THE   ZELAZNY, ROGER   SS   GAL 75 04
DOWN AND OUT   NIVEN, LARRY   NV   GAL 76 02
HORSE OF A DIFFERENT TECHNICOLOR, A
                              STRETE, CRAIG   SS   GAL 75 01
ALLEGIANCES   BISHOP, MICHAEL   NA   GAL 75 02
OVERDOSE   ROBINSON, SPIDER   SS   GAL 75 09
ELEPHANT WITH WOODEN LEG   SLADEK, JOHN T.   SS   GAL 75 06
LIFE AMONG THE ASTEROIDS   POURNELLE, JERRY   AR   GAL 75 07
TINKER   POURNELLE, JERRY   NA   GAL 75 07
HELBENT 4   ROBINETT, STEPHEN   NV   GAL 75 10
EXPERIMENTER, THE   RUSS, JOANNA   NV   GAL 75 10

BEST FROM IF, THE VOLUME I   IF, EDITORS OF   AN   AWD 73
HEADNOTES   FRENKEL, JAMES   MS
REALITY TRIP, THE   SILVERBERG, ROBERT   NV   IFS 70 05
TROUBLESHOOTER   CONEY, MICHAEL G.   SS   IFS 70 05
MIND BOMB, THE (ALSO AS THE BEING MACHINE)
                              HERBERT, FRANK   NV   IFS 69 10
LAST TRUE GOD, THE   DEL REY, LESTER   SS   IFS 69 09
BY THE FALLS   HARRISON, HARRY   SS   IFS 70 01
SOS   ANDERSON, POUL   NV   IFS 70 03
RIGHT TO REVOLT, THE   LAUMER, KEITH   SS   IFS 71 06
RIGHT TO RESIST, THE   LAUMER, KEITH   SS   IFS 71 06
WATERCLAP   ASIMOV, ISAAC   NV   IFS 70 04
HABITS OF THE RIGELIAN NIGHTFOX
                              BIANCHI, ED   SS   IFS 71 12
NIGHTBLOOMING SAURIAN, THE   TIPTREE, JAMES JR.   SS   IFS 70 05
PREZ   GOULART, RON   SS   IFS 70 02
OCCAM'S SCALPEL   STURGEON, THEODORE   NV   IFS 71 08

BEST FROM IF, THE VOLUME II IF, EDITORS OF   AN   AWD 74
CONSTRUCTION SHACK   SIMAK, CLIFFORD D.   SS   IFS 73 02
SUSIE'S REALITY   STICKGOLD, BOB   SS   IFS 73 06
MNARRA MOBILIS   VAN SCYOC, SYDNEY J. NV   IFS 73 06
WESTWIND   WOLFE, GENE   SS   IFS 73 08
DEATH AND DESIGNATION AMONG THE ASADI
                              BISHOP, MICHAEL   NA   IFS 73 02
GUEST EDITORIAL   POHL, FREDERIK   ED   IFS 74 06
WINGS OUT OF SHADOW   SABERHAGEN, FRED   NV   IFS 74 04
STRANGER IN PARADISE   ASIMOV, ISAAC   NV   IFS 74 06

BEST FROM IF, THE VOLUME III
                                BAEN, JAMES   AN   AWD 76
MIDNIGHT BY THE MORPHY WATCH LEIBER, FRITZ   NV   IFS 74 08
PLAYTHING   NIVEN, LARRY   SS   IFS 74 08
LITTLE NIGHT FLYING, A (DARK ICARUS)
                              SHAW, BOB   NV   IFS 74 08
HALF-BAKED PUBLISHER'S DELIGHT
                              HUDSON, JEFFREY S.

BEST FROM THE REST OF THE WORLD, THE

                              AND ASIMOV, ISAAC   SS C IFS 74 08
MEPHISTO & THE ION EXPLORER   KAPP, COLIN   NV   IFS 74 10
FOLLOWING YONDER STAR   HOAGLAND, RICHARD C. AR   IFS 74 11
GUT IN PERIL   DARNAY, ARSEN   SS   IFS 74 12
TIME DEER   STRETE, CRAIG   SS   IFS 74 12
ALIEN VIEWPOINT, THE   GEIS, RICHARD E.   AR   IFS 74 10
DESCENT OF MAN, THE   LAWRENCE, J. A.   SS   IFS 74 12
ANGEL FIX   SHELDON, RACCOONA   NV   IFS 74 08
READING ROOM   DEL REY, LESTER   BR   IFS 74 12

BEST FROM NEW WORLDS SCIENCE FICTION, THE
                              CARNELL, JOHN   AN   BDM 55
INTRODUCTION   WYNDHAM, JOHN   IN
FOREWORD   CARNELL, JOHN   IN
HARD WAY, THE   BARCLAY, ALAN   SS   NWS 53 06
CROSSFIRE   WHITE, JAMES   SS   NWS 53 06
JETSAM   CHANDLER, A. BERTRAM SS   NWS 53 03
ROCKETS AREN'T HUMAN   TUBB, E. C.   SS   NWS 53 03
SHIP FROM THE STARS   HAWKINS, PETER   SS   NWS 54 07
ROBOTS DON'T BLEED   GROVES, J. W.   SS   NWS 50 WI
BROKEN RECORD, THE   MCINTOSH, J. T.   SS   NWS 52 09
UNKNOWN QUANTITY   PHILLIPS, PETER   SS   NWS 49 05

BEST FROM NEW WRITINGS IN S-F FIRST SELECTION, THE
                              CARNELL, JOHN   AN H DOB 71
FOREWORD   CARNELL, JOHN   IN
MAN ON BRIDGE   ALDISS, BRIAN W.   SS   NWR 64 01
NIGHT-FLAME, THE   KAPP, COLIN   SS   NWR 64 02
ETERNAL MACHINES, THE   SPENCER, WILLIAM   SS   NWR 64 02
CREATORS, THE   GREEN, JOSEPH   SS   NWR 64 02
TESTAMENT   BAXTER, JOHN   SS   NWR 65 03
FIEND, THE   POHL, FREDERIK   SS   PBY 64 04
SUBWAYS OF TAZOO, THE   KAPP, COLIN   NV   NWR 65 03
NIGHT WATCH   INGLIS, JAMES   SS   NWR 65 03
BERNIE THE FAUST   TENN, WILLIAM   NV   PBY 63 11
STAR LIGHT   ASIMOV, ISAAC   SS   SAM 62 10
HIGH EIGHT   STRINGER, DAVID   NV   NWR 65 04

BEST FROM ORBIT, THE   KNIGHT, DAMON   AN H BRK 75
SORT OF INTRODUCTION, A   KNIGHT, DAMON   IN
SECRET PLACE, THE   MCKENNA, RICHARD M.   SS   ORB 66 01
LOOLIES ARE HERE, THE   RICE, ALLISON   SS   ORB 66 01
DOCTOR, THE   THOMAS, THEODORE L.   SS   ORB 67 02
BABY, YOU WERE GREAT   WILHELM, KATE   SS   ORB 67 02
HOLE ON THE CORNER, THE   LAFFERTY, R. A.   SS   ORB 67 02
I GAVE HER SACK AND SHERRY (ALSO AS I THOUGHT SHE WAS AFEARED
    TILL SHE STROKED MY BEARD) RUSS, JOANNA   NV   ORB 67 02
MOTHER TO THE WORLD   WILSON, RICHARD   NV   ORB 68 03
DON'T WASH THE CARATS   FARMER, PHILIP JOSE   SS   ORB 68 03
PLANNERS, THE   WILHELM, KATE   SS   ORB 68 03
CHANGELING, THE   WOLFE, GENE   SS   ORB 68 03
PASSENGERS   SILVERBERG, ROBERT   SS   ORB 68 04
SHATTERED LIKE A GLASS GOBLIN
                              ELLISON, HARLAN   SS   ORB 68 04
TIME MACHINE, THE   JONES, LANGDON   NV   ORB 69 05
LOOK, YOU THINK YOU'VE GOT TROUBLES
                              CARR, CAROL   SS   ORB 69 05
BIG FLASH, THE   SPINRAD, NORMAN   NV   ORB 69 05
JIM AND MARY G   SALLIS, JAMES   SS   ORB 70 07
END, THE (ALSO AS THINGS)   LE GUIN, URSULA K.   SS   ORB 70 06
CONTINUED ON NEXT ROCK   LAFFERTY, R. A.   NV   ORB 70 07
ISLAND OF DOCTOR DEATH AND OTHER STORIES, THE
                              WOLFE, GENE   SS   ORB 70 08
HORSE OF AIR   DOZOIS, GARDNER R.   SS   ORB 70 08
ONE LIFE, FURNISHED IN EARLY POVERTY
                              ELLISON, HARLAN   SS   ORB 70 08
RITE OF SPRING   DAVIDSON, AVRAM   SS   ORB 70 08
BYSTANDER, THE   WHARTON, THOM LEE   SS   ORB 70 08
ENCOUNTER, THE   WILHELM, KATE   NV   ORB 70 08
GLEEPSITE   RUSS, JOANNA   SS   ORB 71 09
BINARIES   SALLIS, JAMES   SS   ORB 71 09
AL   EMSHWILLER, CAROL   SS   ORB 72 10
LIVE, FROM BERCHTESGADEN   EFFINGER, GEO. ALEC   SS   ORB 72 10

BEST FROM STARTLING STORIES, THE
                              MINES, SAMUEL   AN H HLT 53
    ALSO AS "STARTLING STORIES" AND "MOMENT WITHOUT TIME"
BLUEPRINT FOR TOMORROW   MINES, SAMUEL   IN
INTRODUCTION   HEINLEIN, ROBERT A.   IN
WAGES OF SYNERGY, THE   STURGEON, THEODORE   NV   STS 53 08
PERFECT GENTLEMAN, THE   MCGREGOR, R. J.   SS   STS 52 09
MOMENT WITHOUT TIME   ROGERS, JOEL T.   NV   TWS 52 04
NAMING OF NAMES, THE (ALSO AS DARK THEY WERE, AND GOLDEN-EYED)
                              BRADBURY, RAY   SS   TWS 49 08
NO LAND OF NOD   SPRINGER, SHERWOOD   SS   TWS 52 12
WHO'S CRIBBING?   LEWIS, JACK   SS   STS 53 01
THIRTY SECONDS- THIRTY DAYS (ALSO AS BREAKING STRAIN)
                              CLARKE, ARTHUR C.   NV   TWS 49 12
NOISE   VANCE, JACK   SS   STS 52 08
WHAT'S IT LIKE OUT THERE?   HAMILTON, EDMOND   NV   TWS 52 12
DORMANT   VAN VOGT, A. E.   SS   STS 48 11
DARK NUPTIAL   LOCKE, ROBERT DONALD SS   TWS 53 02

BEST FROM THE REST OF THE WORLD, THE
                              WOLLHEIM, DONALD A.   AN H DBL 76
INTRODUCTION   WOLLHEIM, DONALD A.   IN
PARTY LINE   KLEIN, GERARD   NV   73
PARAPUPPETS   VAN LOGGEM, MANUEL   SS   74
SCYTHE, THE   SANDRELLI, SANDRO   SS   63
WHITER SHADE OF PALE, A   BING, JON   SS   74
PARADISE 3000   FRANKE, HERBERT W.   SS   75
MY EYES, THEY BURN   BERTIN, EDDY C.   NV   75
PROBLEM IN BIONICS, A   BARBET, PIERRE   SS   74
KING AND THE DOLLMAKER, THE   JESCHKE, WOLFGANG   NA   70
CODEMUS   BRINGSVAERD, TOR AGE SS   68
RAINY DAY REVOLUTION NO. 39   COZZI, LUIGI   SS   ISF 67 11

EST FROM THE REST OF THE WORLD, THE

```
NOBODY HERE BUT US SHADOWS    LUNDWALL, SAM J.      SS   GAL 75 08
ROUND AND ROUND AND ROUND AGAIN
                              SANTOS, DOMINGO       NV       70
PLANET FOR SALE               NIELSEN, NIELS E.     SS       64
YSOLDE                        HENNEBERG, CHARLES    SS   ISF 68 06

EST LAID SCHEMES, THE    EISENBERG, LARRY    AC H MAC 71
INTRODUCTION                  EISENBERG, LARRY      IN
SAGA OF DMM, THE              EISENBERG, LARRY      SS   FSF 67 12
OPEN SECRETS, THE             EISENBERG, LARRY      SS   GAL 69 05
TIME OF HIS LIFE, THE         EISENBERG, LARRY      SS   FSF 68 04
HOLD YOUR FIRE                EISENBERG, LARRY      SS   NEW 71 AC
DUCKWORTH'S FOREVER           EISENBERG, LARRY      SS   NEW 71 AC
UNCLE SAM'S CHILDREN (CHILD'S PLAY)
                              EISENBERG, LARRY      SS   IFS 70 01
CHAMELEON, THE                EISENBERG, LARRY      SS   FSF 70 03
IS THERE LIFE IN INNER SPACE? EISENBERG, LARRY      SS   NEW 71 AC
MATTER OF TIME AND PLACE, A   EISENBERG, LARRY      SS   FSF 70 01
DUCKWORTH'S IQ SOUP (IQ SOUP)
                              EISENBERG, LARRY      SS   VSF 69 11
TOO MANY COOKS                EISENBERG, LARRY      SS   NEW 71 AC
IRRESISTIBLE PARTY CHAIRMAN, THE
                              EISENBERG, LARRY      SS   NEW 71 AC
MATTER OF RECORDINGS, A       EISENBERG, LARRY      SS   IFS 70 02
VANISHING BOROUGH, THE        EISENBERG, LARRY      SS   NEW 71 AC
TWO LIVES OF BEN COULTER, THE
                              EISENBERG, LARRY      SS   FSF 67 04
PIROKIN EFFECT, THE           EISENBERG, LARRY      SS   AMZ 64 06
PROJECT AMNION                EISENBERG, LARRY      SS   VSF 69 08
CONQUEROR                     EISENBERG, LARRY      SS   IFS 67 10
MIGHTY MATTERHORN, THE        EISENBERG, LARRY      SS   NEW 71 AC
MARVELOUS MARSHAL, THE (THE FASTEST DRAW)
                              EISENBERG, LARRY      SS   AMZ 63 10
WHAT HAPPENED TO AUGUSTE CLAROT?
                              EISENBERG, LARRY      SS   DVS 67 01

EST OF A. E. VAN VOGT, THE  VAN VOGT, A. E.    AC PKT 76 07
AH, CARELESS, RAPTUROUS VAN VOGT!
                              MALZBERG, BARRY N.    IN
DON'T HOLD YOUR BREATH        VAN VOGT, A. E.       SS   SVW 73
ALL WE HAVE ON THIS PLANET    VAN VOGT, A. E.       SS
WAR OF NERVES                 VAN VOGT, A. E.       SS   OWS 50 05
RULL, THE                     VAN VOGT, A. E.       NV   ASF 48 05
SEMANTICS OF TWENTY-FIRST CENTURY SCIENCE, THE
                              VAN VOGT, A. E.       AR
FUTURE PERFECT                VAN VOGT, A. E.       SS   VTX 73 08
BEING AN EXAMINATION OF THE PONSIAN AND HOLMESIAN SECRET
   DEDUCTIVE SYSTEMS          VAN VOGT, A. E.       AR       71
HOME OF THE GODS              VAN VOGT, A. E.       NV   ASF 47 04
VIOLENT MAN, THE              VAN VOGT, A. E.       AR       65
PROLOGUE TO "THE SILKIE"      VAN VOGT, A. E.       EX   IFS 64 07
PROXY INTELLIGENCE, THE       VAN VOGT, A. E.       SN   IFS 68 10
FINAL COMMENT                 VAN VOGT, A. E.       MS

EST OF A. E. VAN VOGT, THE (BRITISH)
                              VAN VOGT, A. E.    AC H SID 74 05
   EDITED BY ANGUS WELLS
INTRODUCTION                  VAN VOGT, A. E.       IN
VAULT OF THE BEAST            VAN VOGT, A. E.       NV   ASF 40 08
WEAPON SHOP, THE              VAN VOGT, A. E.       NV   ASF 42 12
STORM, THE                    VAN VOGT, A. E.       NV   ASF 43 10
JUGGERNAUT                    VAN VOGT, A. E.       SS   ASF 44 08
HAND OF THE GODS              VAN VOGT, A. E.       NV   ASF 46 12
CATAAAAA, THE                 VAN VOGT, A. E.       SS   FBK 47 01
MONSTER, THE (ALSO AS RESURRECTION)
                              VAN VOGT, A. E.       SS   ASF 48 08
DEAR PEN PAL                  VAN VOGT, A. E.       SS   ARS 49 WI
GREEN FOREST, THE             VAN VOGT, A. E.       NV   ASF 49 06
WAR OF NERVES                 VAN VOGT, A. E.       SS   OWS 50 05
EXPENDABLES, THE              VAN VOGT, A. E.       NV   IFS 63 09
SILKIES IN SPACE              VAN VOGT, A. E.       NV   IFS 66 05
PROXY INTELLIGENCE, THE       VAN VOGT, A. E.       SN   IFS 68 10
BIBLIOGRAPHY                  MISC. MATERIAL        MS

EST OF AMAZING, THE    ROSS, JOSEPH    AN H DBL 67
FOREWORD                      ROSS, JOSEPH          IN
LOST MACHINE, THE             HARRIS, JOHN BEYNON   SS   AMZ 32 04
WORM, THE                     KELLER, DAVID H. MD.  SS   AMZ 29 03
RUNAWAY SKYSCRAPER, THE       LEINSTER, MURRAY      NV   ARG 19 02
MAROONED OFF VESTA            ASIMOV, ISAAC         SS   AMZ 39 03
ANNIVERSARY                   ASIMOV, ISAAC         SS   AMZ 59 03
METAL MAN, THE                WILLIAMSON, JACK      SS   AMZ 28 12
PILGRIMAGE (THE PRIESTESS WHO REBELLED)
                              BOND, NELSON S.       SS   AMZ 39 10
SUNFIRE!                      HAMILTON, EDMOND      SS   AMZ 62 09
TRY TO REMEMBER!              HERBERT, FRANK        NV   AMZ 61 10

EST OF ARTHUR C. CLARKE: 1937-1971, THE
                              CLARKE, ARTHUR C.    AC H SID 73
1933: A SCIENCE FICTION ODYSSEY
                              CLARKE, ARTHUR C.     IN
TRAVEL BY WIRE                CLARKE, ARTHUR C.     SS   AMS 37 12
RETREAT FROM EARTH            CLARKE, ARTHUR C.     SS   AMS 38 03
AWAKENING, THE                CLARKE, ARTHUR C.     SS   ZEN 42 02
WHACKY                        CLARKE, ARTHUR C.     SS   FNT 42 07
CASTAWAY                      CLARKE, ARTHUR C.     SS   FSB 47 04
HISTORY LESSON                CLARKE, ARTHUR C.     SS   STS 49 05
HIDE AND SEEK                 CLARKE, ARTHUR C.     SS   ASF 49 09
SECOND DAWN                   CLARKE, ARTHUR C.     NV   SFQ 51 08
SENTINEL, THE (SENTINEL OF ETERNITY)
                              CLARKE, ARTHUR C.     SS   TSF 51 SP
STAR, THE                     CLARKE, ARTHUR C.     SS   INF 55 11
REFUGEE (CONTEST STORY, ORIGINAL TITLE THIS EARTH OF MAJESTY)
                              CLARKE, ARTHUR C.     SS   FSF 55 07
VENTURE TO THE MOON           CLARKE, ARTHUR C.     GR   FSF 56 12
```

BEST OF C. M. KORNBLUTH, THE

```
INTO THE COMET (INSIDE THE COMET)
                              CLARKE, ARTHUR C.     SS   FSF 60 10
SUMMERTIME ON ICARUS (THE HOTTEST PIECE OF REAL ESTATE IN THE
   SOLAR SYSTEM)              CLARKE, ARTHUR C.     SS   VOG 60 06
DEATH AND THE SENATOR         CLARKE, ARTHUR C.     NV   ASF 61 05
HATE (AT THE END OF THE ORBIT)
                              CLARKE, ARTHUR C.     NV   IFS 61 11
SUNJAMMER (ALSO AS THE WIND FROM THE SUN)
                              CLARKE, ARTHUR C.     SS   BLF 64
MEETING WITH MEDUSA, A        CLARKE, ARTHUR C.     NA   PBY 71 12
BIBLIOGRAPHY                  MISC. MATERIAL        MS

EST OF BARRY N. MALZBERG, THE
                              MALZBERG, BARRY N.    AC PKT 76 01
INTRODUCTION                  MALZBERG, BARRY N.    IN
RECKONING, A (NOTES LEADING DOWN TO THE CONQUEST)
                              MALZBERG, BARRY N.    SS   NDM 73 03
LETTING IT ALL HANG OUT (HANGING)
                              MALZBERG, BARRY N.    SS   FAN 74 09
MAN IN THE POCKET, THE (THE MEN INSIDE)
                              MALZBERG, BARRY N.    NV   NDM 72 02
PATER FAMILIAS                MALZBERG, BARRY N.
                              AND NEVILLE, KRIS     SS C FSF 72 03
GOING DOWN                    MALZBERG, BARRY N.    NV   DYS 75
THOSE WONDERFUL YEARS         MALZBERG, BARRY N.    SS   TAL 73
ON ICE                        MALZBERG, BARRY N.    SS   AMZ 73 01
REVOLUTION (AS ROBIN SCHAEFFER)
                              MALZBERG, BARRY N.    SS   FUC 73
UPS AND DOWNS                 MALZBERG, BARRY N.    SS   EIO 73
BEARING WITNESS               MALZBERG, BARRY N.    SS   FTP 73
AT THE INSTITUTE              MALZBERG, BARRY N.    SS   FAN 74 03
MAKING IT THROUGH             MALZBERG, BARRY N.    SS   WLK 73
TAPPING OUT                   MALZBERG, BARRY N.    SS   FUQ 73
CLOSED SICILIAN               MALZBERG, BARRY N.    SS   FSF 73 11
LINKAGE                       MALZBERG, BARRY N.    SS   DEM 73
INTRODUCTION TO THE SECOND EDITION
                              MALZBERG, BARRY N.    SS   NOV 73 03
TRIAL OF THE BLOOD            MALZBERG, BARRY N.    SS   BER 74
GETTING AROUND                MALZBERG, BARRY N.    SS   TAL 73
TRACK TWO                     MALZBERG, BARRY N.    SS   FAN 74 07
BATTERED-EARTH SYNDROME, THE  MALZBERG, BARRY N.    SS   SVW 73
NETWORK                       MALZBERG, BARRY N.    SS   FAN 74 01
DELIGHTFUL COMEDIC PREMISE, A
                              MALZBERG, BARRY N.    SS   FSF 74 02
GERANIUMS                     MALZBERG, BARRY N.
                              AND KING, VALERIE     SS C OMG 73
CITY LIGHTS, CITY NIGHTS      MALZBERG, BARRY N.    SS   FUC 73
CULTURE LOCK                  MALZBERG, BARRY N.    SS   FUC 73
AS IN A VISION APPREHENDED    MALZBERG, BARRY N.    SS   BER 74
FORM IN REMISSION (AS ROBIN SCHAEFFER)
                              MALZBERG, BARRY N.    SS   NMD 73
OPENING FIRE                  MALZBERG, BARRY N.    SS   NMD 73
RUNNING AROUND                MALZBERG, BARRY N.    SS   OMG 73
OVERLOOKING                   MALZBERG, BARRY N.    SS   AMZ 74 06
TWENTY SIXTY-ONE              MALZBERG, BARRY N.    SS   FSF 74 07
CLOSING THE DEAL              MALZBERG, BARRY N.    SS   ASF 74 03
WHAT THE BOARD SAID           MALZBERG, BARRY N.    SS   NEW 76 AC
UNCOUPLING                    MALZBERG, BARRY N.    SS   DYS 75
OVER THE LINE                 MALZBERG, BARRY N.    SS       74
TRY AGAIN                     MALZBERG, BARRY N.    SS   STG 74
OVERSIGHT, AN                 MALZBERG, BARRY N.    SS   STG 74
AND STILL IN THE DARKNESS     MALZBERG, BARRY N.    SS   NEW 76 AC

BEST OF C. L. MOORE, THE    MOORE, C. L.    AC H NDB 75
   EDITED BY LESTER DEL REY
FORTY YEARS OF C. L. MOORE    DEL REY, LESTER       IN
SHAMBLEAU                     MOORE, C. L.          NV   WRT 33 11
BLACK THIRST                  MOORE, C. L.          NV   WRT 34 04
BRIGHT ILLUSION, THE          MOORE, C. L.          NV   ASF 34 10
BLACK GOD'S KISS              MOORE, C. L.          NV   WRT 34 10
TRYST IN TIME                 MOORE, C. L.          NV   ASF 36 12
GREATER THAN GODS             MOORE, C. L.          NV   ASF 39 07
FRUIT OF KNOWLEDGE            MOORE, C. L.          NV   UNK 40 10
NO WOMAN BORN                 MOORE, C. L.          NV   ASF 44 12
DAEMON                        MOORE, C. L.          NV   FFM 46 10
VINTAGE SEASON                MOORE, C. L.          NV   ASF 46 09
AFTERWORD: FOOTNOTE TO "SHAMBLEAU"... AND OTHERS
                              MOORE, C. L.          MS

BEST OF C. M. KORNBLUTH, THE  KORNBLUTH, C. M.    AC H NDB 76
   EDITED BY FREDERIK POHL
APPRECIATION, AN              POHL, FREDERIK        IN
ROCKET OF 1955, THE           KORNBLUTH, C. M.      SS   STI 41 04
WORDS OF GURU, THE            KORNBLUTH, C. M.      SS   STI 41 06
ONLY THING WE LEARN, THE      KORNBLUTH, C. M.      SS   STS 49 07
ADVENTURER, THE               KORNBLUTH, C. M.      SS   SSF 53 05
LITTLE BLACK BAG, THE         KORNBLUTH, C. M.      NV   ASF 50 07
LUCKIEST MAN IN DENV, THE (AS SIMON EISNER)
                              KORNBLUTH, C. M.      SS   GAL 52 06
SILLY SEASON, THE             KORNBLUTH, C. M.      SS   FSF 50 FL
REMORSEFUL, THE               KORNBLUTH, C. M.      SS   STR 53 02
GOMEZ                         KORNBLUTH, C. M.      NV   NEW 54 AC
ADVENT ON CHANNEL TWELVE, THE
                              KORNBLUTH, C. M.      SS   STR 58 04
MARCHING MORONS, THE          KORNBLUTH, C. M.      NV   GAL 51 04
LAST MAN LEFT IN THE BAR, THE
                              KORNBLUTH, C. M.      SS   INF 57 10
MINDWORM, THE                 KORNBLUTH, C. M.      SS   WBY 50 12
WITH THESE HANDS              KORNBLUTH, C. M.      NV   GAL 51 12
SHARK SHIP (REAP THE DARK TIDE)
                              KORNBLUTH, C. M.      NV   VAN 58 06
FRIEND TO MAN                 KORNBLUTH, C. M.      SS   TSF 51 SP
ALTAR AT MIDNIGHT, THE        KORNBLUTH, C. M.      SS   GAL 52 11
DOMINOES                      KORNBLUTH, C. M.      SS   STR 53 01
TWO DOOMS                     KORNBLUTH, C. M.      NV   VSF 58 07
ABOUT THE AUTHOR              KORNBLUTH, C. M.      MS
```

BEST OF CORDWAINER SMITH, THE
                          SMITH, CORDWAINER   AC   BAL 75
     EDITED BY J. J. PIERCE
TIMELINE FROM THE INSTRUMENTALITY OF MANKIND
                          PIERCE, J. J.   MS
CORDWAINER SMITH: THE SHAPER OF MYTHS
                          PIERCE, J. J.   IN
SCANNERS LIVE IN VAIN   SMITH, CORDWAINER   NA   FBK 50 06
LADY WHO SAILED THE SOUL, THE
                          SMITH, CORDWAINER   NV   GAL 60 04
GAME OF RAT AND DRAGON, THE SMITH, CORDWAINER   NV   GAL 55 10
BURNING OF THE BRAIN, THE SMITH, CORDWAINER   SS   IFS 58 10
CRIME AND THE GLORY OF COMMANDER SUZDAL, THE
                          SMITH, CORDWAINER   SS   AMZ 64 05
GOLDEN THE SHIP WAS- OH! OH! OH!
                          SMITH, CORDWAINER   SS   AMZ 59 04
DEAD LADY OF CLOWN TOWN, THE SMITH, CORDWAINER   SN   GAL 64 08
UNDER OLD EARTH   SMITH, CORDWAINER   NV   GAL 66 02
MOTHER HITTON'S LITTUL KITTONS
                          SMITH, CORDWAINER   NV   GAL 61 06
ALPHA RALPHA BOULEVARD   SMITH, CORDWAINER   NV   FSF 61 06
BALLAD OF LOST C'MELL, THE SMITH, CORDWAINER   NV   GAL 62 10
PLANET NAMED SHAYOL, A   SMITH, CORDWAINER   NA   GAL 61 10

BEST OF DAMON KNIGHT, THE KNIGHT, DAMON   AC H NDB 76
DARK OF KNIGHT   MALZBERG, BARRY N.   IN
INTRODUCTION   KNIGHT, DAMON   IN
NOT WITH A BANG   KNIGHT, DAMON   SS   FSF 50 WS
TO SERVE MAN   KNIGHT, DAMON   SS   GAL 50 11
CABIN BOY   KNIGHT, DAMON   NV   GAL 51 09
ANALOGUES, THE   KNIGHT, DAMON   SS   ASF 52 01
BABEL II   KNIGHT, DAMON   NV   BEY 53 07
SPECIAL DELIVERY   KNIGHT, DAMON   NV   GAL 54 04
THING OF BEAUTY   KNIGHT, DAMON   NV   GAL 58 09
ANACHRON   KNIGHT, DAMON   SS   IFS 54 01
EXTEMPORE (THE BEACH WHERE TIME BEGAN)
                         KNIGHT, DAMON   SS   INF 56 08
BACKWARD, O TIME (THIS WAY TO THE REGRESS)
                         KNIGHT, DAMON   SS   GAL 56 08
LAST WORD, THE   KNIGHT, DAMON   SS   SAT 57 02
MAN IN THE JAR   KNIGHT, DAMON   SS   GAL 57 04
ENEMY, THE   KNIGHT, DAMON   SS   VSF 58 01
ERIPMAV   KNIGHT, DAMON   SS   FSF 58 06
LIKELY STORY, A   KNIGHT, DAMON   SS   INF 56 02
TIME ENOUGH (ENOUGH TIME) KNIGHT, DAMON   SS   AMZ 60 07
MARY (AN ANCIENT MADNESS) KNIGHT, DAMON   NV   GAL 64 06
HANDLER, THE   KNIGHT, DAMON   SS   ROG 60 08
BIG PAT BOOM, THE   KNIGHT, DAMON   SS   GAL 63 12
SEMPER FI (SATISFACTION) KNIGHT, DAMON   SS   ASF 64 08
MASKS   KNIGHT, DAMON   SS   PBY 68 07
DOWN THERE   KNIGHT, DAMON   SS   NDM 73 03

BEST OF E. E. 'DOC' SMITH, THE
                         SMITH, EDWARD E. PHD AC H WEI 75
PREFACE   HARBOTTLE, PHILIP   IN
FOREWORD   GILLINGS, WALTER   IN
TO THE FAR REACHES OF SPACE (FROM THE SKYLARK OF SPACE)
                         SMITH, EDWARD E. PHD EX   AMZ 28 08
ROBOT NEMESIS (WHAT A COURSE!, PART 13 OF COSMOS, FMG 34)
                         SMITH, EDWARD E. PHD SS   TWS 39 06
PIRATES OF SPACE (FROM TRIPLANETARY)
                         SMITH, EDWARD E. PHD EX   AMZ 34 01
VORTEX BLASTER, THE   SMITH, EDWARD E. PHD SS   CMT 41 07
TEDRIC   SMITH, EDWARD E. PHD SS   OWS 53 03
LORD TEDRIC   SMITH, EDWARD E. PHD NV   USF 54 03
SUBSPACE SURVIVORS   SMITH, EDWARD E. PHD NV   ASF 60 07
IMPERIAL STARS, THE   SMITH, EDWARD E. PHD SN   IFS 64 05
AFTERWORD: THE EPIC OF SPACE BY E. E. 'DOC' SMITH
                         MISC. MATERIAL   MS
BIBLIOGRAPHY   MISC. MATERIAL   MS

BEST OF EDMOND HAMILTON, THE HAMILTON, EDMOND   AC H NDB 77
     EDITED BY LEIGH BRACKETT
FIFTY YEARS OF WONDER   BRACKETT, LEIGH   IN
MONSTER-GOD OF MAMURTH, THE HAMILTON, EDMOND   SS   WRT 26 08
MAN WHO EVOLVED, THE   HAMILTON, EDMOND   SS   WOS 31 04
CONQUEST OF TWO WORLDS, A HAMILTON, EDMOND   NV   WOS 32 02
ISLAND OF UNREASON, THE HAMILTON, EDMOND   SS   WOS 33 05
THUNDERING WORLDS   HAMILTON, EDMOND   NV   WRT 34 03
MAN WHO RETURNED, THE   HAMILTON, EDMOND   SS   WRT 34 02
ACCURSED GALAXY, THE   HAMILTON, EDMOND   SS   ASF 35 07
IN THE WORLD'S DUSK   HAMILTON, EDMOND   SS   WRT 36 03
CHILD OF THE WINDS   HAMILTON, EDMOND   SS   WRT 36 05
SEEDS FROM OUTSIDE, THE HAMILTON, EDMOND   SS   WRT 37 03
FESSENDEN'S WORLDS   HAMILTON, EDMOND   SS   WRT 37 04
EASY MONEY   HAMILTON, EDMOND   SS   TWS 38 04
HE THAT HATH WINGS   HAMILTON, EDMOND   SS   WRT 38 07
EXILE   HAMILTON, EDMOND   SS   SSS 43 05
DAY OF JUDGMENT   HAMILTON, EDMOND   SS   WRT 46 09
ALIEN EARTH   HAMILTON, EDMOND   SS   TWS 49 04
WHAT'S IT LIKE OUT THERE? HAMILTON, EDMOND   NV   TWS 52 12
REQUIEM   HAMILTON, EDMOND   SS   AMZ 62 04
AFTER A JUDGMENT DAY   HAMILTON, EDMOND   SS   FSF 63 12
PRO, THE   HAMILTON, EDMOND   SS   FSF 64 10
CASTAWAY   HAMILTON, EDMOND   SS   68
AFTERWORD   HAMILTON, EDMOND   MS

BEST OF FRANK HERBERT, THE HERBERT, FRANK   AC H SID 75
     EDITED BY ANGUS WELLS
INTRODUCTION   HERBERT, FRANK   IN
LOOKING FOR SOMETHING?   HERBERT, FRANK   SS   STS 52 04
NIGHTMARE BLUES (OPERATION SYNDROME)
                         HERBERT, FRANK   NV   ASF 54 06
DRAGON IN THE SEA (UNDER PRESSURE)
                         HERBERT, FRANK   EX   ASF 55 11
SEASE FIRE   HERBERT, FRANK   SS   ASF 58 01

EGG AND ASHES   HERBERT, FRANK   SS   IFS 60 1░
MARY CELESTE MOVE, THE   HERBERT, FRANK   SS   ASF 64 0░
COMMITTEE OF THE WHOLE   HERBERT, FRANK   NV   GAL 65 0░
DUNE   HERBERT, FRANK   EX   CHL 65
BY THE BOOK   HERBERT, FRANK   NV   ASF 66 0░
PRIMATIVES, THE   HERBERT, FRANK   NV   GAL 66 C░
HEAVEN MAKERS, THE   HERBERT, FRANK   EX   AMZ 67 0░
BEING MACHINE, THE (THE MIND BOMB)
                         HERBERT, FRANK   NV   IFS 69 10░
SEED STOCK   HERBERT, FRANK   SS   ASF 70 0░
BIBLIOGRAPHY   MISC. MATERIAL   MS

BEST OF FREDERIK POHL, THE POHL, FREDERIK   AC H NDB 75
     EDITED BY LESTER DEL REY
VARIETY OF EXCELLENCE, A DEL REY, LESTER   IN
TUNNEL UNDER THE WORLD, THE POHL, FREDERIK   NV   GAL 55 0░
PUNCH   POHL, FREDERIK   SS   PBY 62 0░
THREE PORTRAITS AND A PRAYER POHL, FREDERIK   SS   GAL 62 0░
DAY MILLION   POHL, FREDERIK   SS   ROG 66 0░
HAPPY BIRTHDAY, DEAR JESUS POHL, FREDERIK   SS   NEW 56 A░
WE NEVER MENTION AUNT NORA (AS PAUL FLEHR)
                         POHL, FREDERIK   SS   GAL 58 0░
FATHER OF THE STARS   POHL, FREDERIK   SS   IFS 64 1░
DAY THE MARTIANS CAME, THE (THE DAY AFTER THE DAY THE MARTIANS
     CAME)   POHL, FREDERIK   SS   DVS 67 0░
MIDAS PLAGUE, THE   POHL, FREDERIK   NA   GAL 54 0░
SNOWMEN, THE   POHL, FREDERIK   SS   GAL 59 12░
HOW TO COUNT ON YOUR FINGERS POHL, FREDERIK   AR   SFS 56 0░
GRANDY DEVIL   POHL, FREDERIK   SS   GAL 55 0░
SPEED TRAP   POHL, FREDERIK   SS   PBY 67 1░
RICHEST MAN IN LEVITTOWN, THE (THE BITTEREST PILL)
                         POHL, FREDERIK   SS   GAL 59 0░
DAY THE ICICLE WORKS CLOSED, THE
                         POHL, FREDERIK   NV   GAL 60 02░
HATED, THE   POHL, FREDERIK   SS   GAL 58 0░
MARTIAN IN THE ATTIC, THE POHL, FREDERIK   SS   IFS 60 0░
CENSUS TAKERS, THE   POHL, FREDERIK   SS   FSF 56 0░
CHILDREN OF NIGHT, THE   POHL, FREDERIK   NV   GAL 64 10░
WHAT THE AUTHOR HAS TO SAY ABOUT ALL THIS
                         POHL, FREDERIK   MS

BEST OF FREDRIC BROWN, THE BROWN, FREDRIC   AC H NDB 76
     EDITED BY ROBERT BLOCH
INTRODUCTION   BLOCH, ROBERT   IN
ARENA   BROWN, FREDRIC   NV   ASF 44 0░
IMAGINE, A PROEM   BROWN, FREDRIC   PM   FSF 55 0░
IT DIDN'T HAPPEN   BROWN, FREDRIC   SS   PBY 63 1░
RECESSIONAL   BROWN, FREDRIC   SS   DUD 60 0░
EINE KLEINE NACHTMUSIK   BROWN, FREDRIC
                         AND ONSPAUGH, CARL   SS C FSF 65 0░
PUPPET SHOW   BROWN, FREDRIC   SS   PBY 62 1░
NIGHTMARE IN YELLOW   BROWN, FREDRIC   SS   DUD 61 0░
EARTHMEN BEARING GIFTS   BROWN, FREDRIC   SS   GAL 60 0░
JAYCEE   BROWN, FREDRIC   SS   FSF 55
PI IN THE SKY   BROWN, FREDRIC   SS   TWS 45 W░
ANSWER   BROWN, FREDRIC   SS   NEW 54 A░
GEEZENSTACKS, THE   BROWN, FREDRIC   SS   WRT 43 0░
HALL OF MIRRORS   BROWN, FREDRIC   SS   GAL 53 1░
KNOCK   BROWN, FREDRIC   SS   TWS 48 1░
REBOUND   BROWN, FREDRIC   SS   NEW 61 A░
STAR MOUSE, THE   BROWN, FREDRIC   SS   PLS 42 0░
ABOMINABLE   BROWN, FREDRIC   SS   DUD 60 0░
LETTER TO A PHOENIX   BROWN, FREDRIC   SS   ASF 49 0░
NOT YET THE END   BROWN, FREDRIC   SS   CFU 41 W░
ETAOIN SHRDLU   BROWN, FREDRIC   SS   UNK 42 0░
ARMAGEDDON   BROWN, FREDRIC   SS   UNK 41 0░
EXPERIMENT (TWO TIMER)   BROWN, FREDRIC   SS   GAL 54 0░
SHORT HAPPY LIVES OF EUSTACE WEAVER I, THE
                         BROWN, FREDRIC   SS   EQM 61 0░
SHORT HAPPY LIVES OF EUSTACE WEAVER II, THE
                         BROWN, FREDRIC   SS   EQM 61 0░
SHORT HAPPY LIVES OF EUSTACE WEAVER III, THE
                         BROWN, FREDRIC   SS   EQM 61 0░
RECONCILIATION   BROWN, FREDRIC   SS   NEW 54 A░
NOTHING SIRIUS   BROWN, FREDRIC   SS   CFU 44 S░
PATTERN   BROWN, FREDRIC   SS   NEW 54 A░
YEHUDI PRINCIPLE, THE   BROWN, FREDRIC   SS   NEW 54 0░
COME AND GO MAD   BROWN, FREDRIC   NV   WRT 49 0░
END, THE   BROWN, FREDRIC   SS   NEW 61 A░

BEST OF FRITZ LEIBER, THE LEIBER, FRITZ   AC H NDB 74
WIZARD OF NEHWON-, THE   ANDERSON, POUL   IN
GONNA ROLL THE BONES   LEIBER, FRITZ   NV   DVS 67 0░
SANITY (ALSO AS CRAZY WOLF) LEIBER, FRITZ   SS   ASF 44 0░
WANTED- AN ENEMY   LEIBER, FRITZ   SS   ASF 45 0░
MAN WHO NEVER GREW YOUNG, THE
                         LEIBER, FRITZ   SS   APR 49 0░
SHIP SAILS AT MIDNIGHT, THE LEIBER, FRITZ   NV   FAD 50 0░
ENCHANTED FOREST, THE   LEIBER, FRITZ   SS   ASF 50 1░
COMING ATTRACTION   LEIBER, FRITZ   SS   GAL 50 1░
POOR SUPERMAN (APPOINTMENT IN TOMORROW)
                         LEIBER, FRITZ   NV   GAL 51 0░
PAIL OF AIR, A   LEIBER, FRITZ   SS   GAL 51 1░
FOXHOLES OF MARS, THE   LEIBER, FRITZ   SS   TWS 52 0░
BIG HOLIDAY, THE   LEIBER, FRITZ   SS   FSF 53 0░
NIGHT HE CRIED, THE   LEIBER, FRITZ   SS   STR 53 0░
BIG TREK, THE   LEIBER, FRITZ   SS   FSF 57 1░
SPACE-TIME FOR SPRINGERS LEIBER, FRITZ   SS   STR 58 0░
TRY AND CHANGE THE PAST LEIBER, FRITZ   SS   ASF 58 0░
DESKFUL OF GIRLS, A   LEIBER, FRITZ   NV   FSF 58 0░
RUMP-TITTY-TITTY-TUM-TAH-TEE LEIBER, FRITZ   SS   FSF 58 0░
LITTLE OLD MISS MACBETH LEIBER, FRITZ   SS   FSF 58 1░
MARIANA   LEIBER, FRITZ   SS   FAN 60 0░
MAN WHO MADE FRIENDS WITH ELECTRICITY, THE
                         LEIBER, FRITZ   SS   FSF 62 0░
GOOD NEW DAYS, THE   LEIBER, FRITZ   SS   GAL 65 1░

BEST OF FRITZ LEIBER, THE

| AMERICA THE BEAUTIFUL | LEIBER, FRITZ | SS | YRT 70 |
| AFTERWORD | LEIBER, FRITZ | MS | |

BEST OF HARRY HARRISON, THE   HARRISON, HARRY   AC   PKT 76 06

HARRY HARRISON: THE MAN WHO WALKED HOME			
	MALZBERG, BARRY N.	IN	
STREETS OF ASHKELON, THE (ALSO AS AN ALIEN AGONY)			
	HARRISON, HARRY	SS	NWS 62 09
CAPTAIN HONARIO HARPPLAYER, R.N.			
	HARRISON, HARRY	SS	FSF 63 03
RESCUE OPERATION	HARRISON, HARRY	SS	ASF 64 12
AT LAST, THE TRUE STORY OF FRANKENSTEIN			
	HARRISON, HARRY	SS	FSF 63
I ALWAYS DO WHAT TEDDY SAYS	HARRISON, HARRY	SS	EQM 65 06
PORTRAIT OF THE ARTIST	HARRISON, HARRY	SS	FSF 64 11
NOT ME, NOT AMOS CABOT!	HARRISON, HARRY	SS	SCF 65 01
MUTE MILTON	HARRISON, HARRY	SS	AMZ 66 02
CRIMINAL ACT, A	HARRISON, HARRY	SS	ASF 67 01
WAITING PLACE	HARRISON, HARRY	SS	GAL 68 06
IF (PRAISEWORTHY SAUR)	HARRISON, HARRY	SS	IFS 69 02
I HAVE MY VIGIL	HARRISON, HARRY	SS	FSF 68 02
FROM FANATICISM, OR FOR REWARD			
	HARRISON, HARRY	SS	ASF 69 03
BY THE FALLS	HARRISON, HARRY	SS	IFS 70 01
EVER-BRANCHING TREE, THE	HARRISON, HARRY	SS	SAG 70
BRAVE NEWER WORLD	HARRISON, HARRY	NV	FFU 71
ROOMMATES (BASIS FOR NOVEL "MAKE ROOM! MAKE ROOM!")			
	HARRISON, HARRY	NV	NEW 71 AN
MOTHBALLED SPACESHIP, THE	HARRISON, HARRY	SS	AMA 73
HONEST DAY'S WORK, AN	HARRISON, HARRY	NV	NWR 73 22
SPACE RATS OF THE C.C.C.	HARRISON, HARRY	NV	FST 74

BEST OF HARRY HARRISON, THE (BRITISH)

	HARRISON, HARRY	AC H	SID 76 09
HARRY HARRISON: THE MAN WHO WALKED HOME			
	MALZBERG, BARRY N.	IN	
STREETS OF ASHKELON, THE (ALSO AS AN ALIEN AGONY)			
	HARRISON, HARRY	SS	NWS 62 09
CAPTAIN HONARIO HARPPLAYER, R.N.			
	HARRISON, HARRY	SS	FSF 63 03
RESCUE OPERATION	HARRISON, HARRY	SS	ASF 64 12
AT LAST, THE TRUE STORY OF FRANKENSTEIN			
	HARRISON, HARRY	SS	FSF 63
I ALWAYS DO WHAT TEDDY SAYS	HARRISON, HARRY	SS	EQM 65 06
PORTRAIT OF THE ARTIST	HARRISON, HARRY	SS	FSF 64 11
MUTE MILTON	HARRISON, HARRY	SS	AMZ 66 02
CRIMINAL ACT, A	HARRISON, HARRY	SS	ASF 67 01
WAITING PLACE	HARRISON, HARRY	SS	GAL 68 06
IF (PRAISEWORTHY SAUR)	HARRISON, HARRY	SS	IFS 69 02
I HAVE MY VIGIL	HARRISON, HARRY	SS	FSF 68 02
FROM FANATICISM, OR FOR REWARD			
	HARRISON, HARRY	SS	ASF 69 03
BY THE FALLS	HARRISON, HARRY	SS	IFS 70 01
EVER-BRANCHING TREE, THE	HARRISON, HARRY	SS	SAG 70
BRAVE NEWER WORLD	HARRISON, HARRY	NV	FFU 71
WICKED FLEE, THE	HARRISON, HARRY	SS	NDM 71 01
ROOMMATES (BASIS FOR NOVEL "MAKE ROOM! MAKE ROOM!")			
	HARRISON, HARRY	NV	NEW 71 AN
MOTHBALLED SPACESHIP, THE	HARRISON, HARRY	SS	AMA 73
HONEST DAY'S WORK, AN	HARRISON, HARRY	NV	NWR 73 22
WE ATE THE WHOLE THING	HARRISON, HARRY	SS	VTX 73 04
SPACE RATS OF THE C.C.C.	HARRISON, HARRY	NV	FST 74

BEST OF HENRY KUTTNER 1, THE   KUTTNER, HENRY   AC   MFL 65

OR ELSE	KUTTNER, HENRY	SS	AMZ 53 09
YEAR DAY	KUTTNER, HENRY	SS	NEW 53 AC
SHOCK	KUTTNER, HENRY	SS	ASF 43 03
SEE YOU LATER	KUTTNER, HENRY	SS	TWS 49 06
PROUD ROBOT, THE	KUTTNER, HENRY	NV	ASF 43 10
EGO MACHINE, THE	KUTTNER, HENRY	NV	SSF 52 05
JUKE-BOX	KUTTNER, HENRY	SS	TWS 47 02
COLD WAR	KUTTNER, HENRY	SS	TWS 49 10
CALL HIM DEMON	KUTTNER, HENRY	SS	TWS 46 FL
PIPER'S SON, THE	KUTTNER, HENRY	NV	ASF 45 02
ABSALOM	KUTTNER, HENRY	SS	STS 46 FL
HOUSING PROBLEM	KUTTNER, HENRY	SS	CHM 44 10
GNOME THERE WAS, A	KUTTNER, HENRY	NV	UNK 41 10
BIG NIGHT, THE (AS HUDSON HASTINGS)			
	KUTTNER, HENRY	NV	TWS 47 06
DON'T LOOK NOW	KUTTNER, HENRY	SS	STS 48 04

BEST OF HENRY KUTTNER 2, THE   KUTTNER, HENRY   AC   MFL 66

VOICE OF THE LOBSTER, THE	KUTTNER, HENRY	NV	TWS 50 02
MASQUERADE	KUTTNER, HENRY	SS	WRT 42 05
IRON STANDARD, THE	KUTTNER, HENRY	SS	ASF 43 12
ENDOWMENT POLICY	KUTTNER, HENRY	SS	ASF 43 08
WHEN THE BOUGH BREAKS	KUTTNER, HENRY	NV	ASF 44 11
LINE TO TOMORROW	KUTTNER, HENRY	SS	ASF 45 11
CLASH BY NIGHT	KUTTNER, HENRY	NV	ASF 43 03
WILD SURMISE, A	KUTTNER, HENRY	SS	STR 45 01
WHAT YOU NEED	KUTTNER, HENRY	SS	ASF 45 10
TWONKY, THE	KUTTNER, HENRY	SS	ASF 42 09
MIMSY WERE THE BOROGOVES	KUTTNER, HENRY	NV	ASF 43 02
DEVIL WE KNOW, THE	KUTTNER, HENRY	NV	UNK 41 08
EXIT THE PROFESSOR	KUTTNER, HENRY	SS	TWS 47 10
TWO-HANDED ENGINE	KUTTNER, HENRY	SS	FSF 55 08

BEST OF HENRY KUTTNER, THE   KUTTNER, HENRY   AC H   NDB 75

HENRY KUTTNER: A NEGLECTED MASTER			
	BRADBURY, RAY	IN	75
MIMSY WERE THE BOROGOVES	KUTTNER, HENRY	NV	ASF 43 02
TWO-HANDED ENGINE	KUTTNER, HENRY	SS	FSF 55 08
PROUD ROBOT, THE	KUTTNER, HENRY	NV	ASF 43 10
MISGUIDED HALO, THE	KUTTNER, HENRY	SS	UNK 39 08
VOICE OF THE LOBSTER, THE	KUTTNER, HENRY	NV	TWS 50 02
EXIT THE PROFESSOR	KUTTNER, HENRY	SS	TWS 47 10

BEST OF JOHN W. CAMPBELL, THE (BRITISH)

TWONKY, THE	KUTTNER, HENRY	SS	ASF 42 09
GNOME THERE WAS, A	KUTTNER, HENRY	NV	UNK 41 10
BIG NIGHT, THE (AS HUDSON HASTINGS)			
	KUTTNER, HENRY	NV	TWS 47 06
NOTHING BUT GINGERBREAD LEFT	KUTTNER, HENRY	SS	ASF 43 01
IRON STANDARD, THE	KUTTNER, HENRY	SS	ASF 43 12
COLD WAR	KUTTNER, HENRY	SS	TWS 49 10
OR ELSE	KUTTNER, HENRY	SS	AMZ 53 09
ENDOWMENT POLICY	KUTTNER, HENRY	SS	ASF 43 08
HOUSING PROBLEM	KUTTNER, HENRY	SS	CHM 44 10
WHAT YOU NEED	KUTTNER, HENRY	SS	ASF 45 10
ABSALOM	KUTTNER, HENRY	SS	STS 46 FL

BEST OF ISAAC ASIMOV, THE   ASIMOV, ISAAC   AC H   SID 73

EDITED BY ANGUS WELLS, U.S. EDITION OMITS			
BIBLIOGRAPHY AND PART OF INTRODUCTION			
INTRODUCTION	ASIMOV, ISAAC	IN	
MAROONED OFF VESTA	ASIMOV, ISAAC	SS	AMZ 39 03
NIGHTFALL	ASIMOV, ISAAC	NV	ASF 41 09
C-CHUTE, THE	ASIMOV, ISAAC	NV	GAL 51 10
MARTIAN WAY, THE	ASIMOV, ISAAC	NA	GAL 52 11
DEEP, THE	ASIMOV, ISAAC	NV	GAL 52 12
FUN THEY HAD, THE (NEA 51 12)			
	ASIMOV, ISAAC	SS	FSF 54 02
LAST QUESTION, THE	ASIMOV, ISAAC	SS	SFQ 56 11
DEAD PAST, THE	ASIMOV, ISAAC	NV	ASF 56 04
DYING NIGHT, THE	ASIMOV, ISAAC	SS	FSF 56 07
ANNIVERSARY	ASIMOV, ISAAC	SS	AMZ 59 03
BILLIARD BALL, THE	ASIMOV, ISAAC	NV	IFS 67 03
MIRROR IMAGE	ASIMOV, ISAAC	SS	ASF 72 05
BIBLIOGRAPHY	BISHOP, GERALD	MS	

BEST OF J. G. BALLARD, THE   BALLARD, J. G.   AC   FPL 77

INTRODUCTION	BALLARD, J. G.	IN	
CONCENTRATION CITY, THE (BUILD-UP)			
	BALLARD, J. G.	SS	NWS 57 01
MANHOLE 69	BALLARD, J. G.	SS	NWS 57 11
WAITING GROUNDS, THE	BALLARD, J. G.	NV	NWS 59 11
SOUND-SWEEP, THE	BALLARD, J. G.	NV	SCF 60 02
CHRONOPOLIS	BALLARD, J. G.	NV	NWS 60 06
VOICES OF TIME, THE	BALLARD, J. G.	SS	NWS 60 10
OVERLOADED MAN, THE	BALLARD, J. G.	SS	NWS 61 07
BILLENIUM	BALLARD, J. G.	SS	NWS 61 11
INSANE ONES, THE	BALLARD, J. G.	SS	AMZ 62 01
GARDEN OF TIME, THE	BALLARD, J. G.	SS	FSF 62 02
THIRTEEN TO CENTAURUS	BALLARD, J. G.	NV	AMZ 62 04
SUBLIMINAL MAN, THE	BALLARD, J. G.	SS	NWS 63 01
PASSPORT TO ETERNITY	BALLARD, J. G.	SS	AMZ 62 06
CAGE OF SAND, THE	BALLARD, J. G.	SS	NWS 62 06
QUESTION OF RE-ENTRY, A	BALLARD, J. G.	NV	FAN 63 03
TERMINAL BEACH, THE	BALLARD, J. G.	SS	NWS 64 03
DAY OF FOREVER, THE	BALLARD, J. G.	SS	NWS 67 01

BEST OF JACK VANCE, THE   VANCE, JACK   AC   PKT 76 05

PREFACE TO THE COLLECTION	VANCE, JACK	IN	
CAPTURING VANCE	MALZBERG, BARRY N.	IN	
SAIL 25 (GATEWAY TO STRANGENESS)			
	VANCE, JACK	NV	AMZ 62 08
ULLWARD'S RETREAT	VANCE, JACK	NV	GAL 58 12
LAST CASTLE, THE	VANCE, JACK	NV	GAL 66 04
ABERCROMBIE STATION	VANCE, JACK	NA	TWS 52 02
MOON MOTH, THE	VANCE, JACK	NA	GAL 61 08
RUMFUDDLE	VANCE, JACK	NA	TTT 73

BEST OF JOHN JAKES, THE   JAKES, JOHN W.   AC   DAW 77 06

EDITED BY MARTIN HARRY GREENBERG AND JOSEPH D. OLANDER			
INTRODUCTION	GREENBERG, MARTIN H.		
	AND OLANDER, JOSEPH D.	IN C	
MACHINE	JAKES, JOHN W.	SS	FSF 52 04
FROM ON WHEELS	JAKES, JOHN W.	EX	WPB 73
POLITICAL MACHINE	JAKES, JOHN W.	SS	AMZ 61 03
SELLERS OF THE DREAM, THE	JAKES, JOHN W.	NA	GAL 63 06
HIGHEST FORM OF LIFE, THE	JAKES, JOHN W.	SS	AMZ 61 08
ONE RACE SHOW	JAKES, JOHN W.	NV	GAL 62 08
LOVE IS A PUNCH IN THE NOSE	JAKES, JOHN W.	SS	BIZ 66 01
THERE'S NO VINISM LOKE CHAUVINISM			
	JAKES, JOHN W.	NV	AMZ 65 04
RECIDIVISM PREFERRED	JAKES, JOHN W.	SS	AMZ 62 02
HERE IS THY STING	JAKES, JOHN W.	NV	ORB 68 03
JOHN JAKES BIBLIOGRAPHY, A	MISC. MATERIAL	MS	

BEST OF JOHN W. CAMPBELL, THE

	CAMPBELL, JOHN W. JR	AC	BAL 76 05
EDITED BY LESTER DEL REY			
INTRODUCTION: THE THREE CAREERS OF JOHN W. CAMPBELL			
	DEL REY, LESTER	IN	
LAST EVOLUTION, THE	CAMPBELL, JOHN W. JR	SS	AMZ 32 08
TWILIGHT	CAMPBELL, JOHN W. JR	SS	ASF 34 11
MACHINE, THE	CAMPBELL, JOHN W. JR	SS	ASF 35 02
INVADERS, THE	CAMPBELL, JOHN W. JR	SS	ASF 35 06
REBELLION	CAMPBELL, JOHN W. JR	NV	ASF 35 08
BLINDNESS	CAMPBELL, JOHN W. JR	SS	ASF 35 03
ELIMINATION	CAMPBELL, JOHN W. JR	SS	ASF 36 05
FORGETFULNESS	CAMPBELL, JOHN W. JR	SN	ASF 37 06
OUT OF NIGHT	CAMPBELL, JOHN W. JR	NV	ASF 37 10
CLOAK OF AESIR	CAMPBELL, JOHN W. JR	NV	ASF 39 03
WHO GOES THERE?	CAMPBELL, JOHN W. JR	NV	ASF 38 08
SPACE FOR INDUSTRY	CAMPBELL, JOHN W. JR	AR	ASF 60 04
AFTERWORD: POSTSCRIPTUM	CAMPBELL, MRS. JOHN	MS	

BEST OF JOHN W. CAMPBELL, THE (BRITISH)

	CAMPBELL, JOHN W. JR	AC H	SID 73
COMPILED BY GEORGE HAY			
INTRODUCTION	BLISH, JAMES	IN	
DOUBLE MINDS, THE	CAMPBELL, JOHN W. JR	NV	TWS 37 08
FORGETFULNESS	CAMPBELL, JOHN W. JR	SN	ASF 37 06

BEST OF JOHN W. CAMPBELL, THE (BRITISH)

BEST OF SCIENCE FICTION

Title	Author	Type	Source
WHO GOES THERE?	CAMPBELL, JOHN W. JR	NV	ASF 38 08
OUT OF NIGHT	CAMPBELL, JOHN W. JR	NV	ASF 37 10
CLOAK OF AESIR	CAMPBELL, JOHN W. JR	NV	ASF 39 03
BIBLIOGRAPHY	MISC. MATERIAL	MS	
BEST OF JOHN WYNDHAM, THE	WYNDHAM, JOHN	AC	SPH 73
INTRODUCTION	FLOOD, LESLIE	IN	
LOST MACHINE, THE	WYNDHAM, JOHN	SS	AMZ 32 04
MAN FROM BEYOND, THE	WYNDHAM, JOHN	NV	WOS 34 09
PERFECT CREATURE, THE (ALSO AS UNA, FSF 53 01)	WYNDHAM, JOHN	NV	TOW 37 01
TROJAN BEAM, THE	WYNDHAM, JOHN	NV	FSB 39 02
VENGEANCE BY PROXY	WYNDHAM, JOHN	SS	STE 40 02
ADAPTATION	WYNDHAM, JOHN	SS	ASF 49 07
PAWLEY'S PEEPHOLES (OPERATION PEEP)	WYNDHAM, JOHN	SS	SCP 51 WI
RED STUFF, THE	WYNDHAM, JOHN	NV	MSS 51 02
AND THE WALLS CAME TUMBLING DOWN, THE	WYNDHAM, JOHN	SS	STS 51 05
DUMB MARTIAN	WYNDHAM, JOHN	NV	GAL 52 07
CLOSE BEHIND HIM	WYNDHAM, JOHN	SS	FAN 53 02
EMPTYNESS OF SPACE, THE (ALSO AS THE ASTEROIDS, 2194)	WYNDHAM, JOHN	SS	NWS 60 11
BIBLIOGRAPHY	BISHOP, GERALD	MS	
BEST OF JUDITH MERRIL, THE	MERRIL, JUDITH	AC	WBK 76 01
INTRODUCTION	KIDD, VIRGINIA	IN	
THAT ONLY A MOTHER	MERRIL, JUDITH	SS	ASF 48 06
SHRINE OF TEMPTATION, THE	MERRIL, JUDITH	SS	FAN 62 04
WHOEVER YOU ARE	MERRIL, JUDITH	NV	STS 52 12
DAUGHTERS OF EARTH	MERRIL, JUDITH	SN	52
STORMY WEATHER	MERRIL, JUDITH	SS	STS 54 SU
DEAD CENTER	MERRIL, JUDITH	NV	FSF 54 11
LADY WAS A TRAMP, THE	MERRIL, JUDITH	SS	VSF 57 03
WISH UPON A STAR	MERRIL, JUDITH	SS	FSF 58 12
LONELY, THE	MERRIL, JUDITH	SS	WOT 63 10
AUCTION PIT	MERRIL, JUDITH	PM	46
IN THE LAND OF UNBLIND	MERRIL, JUDITH	SS	FSF 74 10
BEST OF KEITH LAUMER, THE	LAUMER, KEITH	AC	PKT 76 03
INTRODUCTION	MALZBERG, BARRY N.	IN	
PLANET WRECKERS, THE	LAUMER, KEITH	NV	WOT 67 02
BODY BUILDERS, THE	LAUMER, KEITH	NV	GAL 66 08
COCOON	LAUMER, KEITH	SS	FAN 62 12
LAWGIVER, THE	LAUMER, KEITH	SS	YRT 70
THUNDERHEAD	LAUMER, KEITH	NV	GAL 67 04
HYBRID	LAUMER, KEITH	SS	FSF 61 11
DEVIL YOU DON'T, THE	LAUMER, KEITH	NV	ANA 70
DOORSTEP	LAUMER, KEITH	SS	GAL 61 02
RELIC OF WAR, A	LAUMER, KEITH	SS	ASF 69 10
BEST OF LEIGH BRACKETT, THE EDITED BY EDMOND HAMILTON	BRACKETT, LEIGH	AC H	NDB 77
STORY-TELLER OF MANY WORLDS	HAMILTON, EDMOND	IN	
JEWEL OF BAS, THE	BRACKETT, LEIGH	NV	PLS 44 SP
VANISHING VENUSIANS, THE	BRACKETT, LEIGH	SS	PLS 45 SP
VEIL OF ASTELLAR, THE	BRACKETT, LEIGH	SS	TWS 44 SP
MOON THAT VANISHED, THE	BRACKETT, LEIGH	NV	TWS 48 10
ENCHANTRESS OF VENUS (ALSO AS CITY OF THE LOST ONES)	BRACKETT, LEIGH	NV	PLS 49 FL
WOMAN FROM ALTAIR, THE	BRACKETT, LEIGH	NV	STS 51 07
LAST DAYS OF SHANDAKOR, THE	BRACKETT, LEIGH	NV	STS 52 04
SHANNACH- THE LAST	BRACKETT, LEIGH	NO	PLS 52 11
TWEENER, THE	BRACKETT, LEIGH	SS	FSF 55 02
QUEER ONES, THE (ALSO AS THE OTHER PEOPLE)	BRACKETT, LEIGH	NV	VSF 57 03
AFTERWORD	BRACKETT, LEIGH	MS	
MAP	HOWES, MARGARET	MS	
BEST OF MACK REYNOLDS, THE	REYNOLDS, MACK	AC	PKT 76 04
SHOWING OFF REYNOLDS	MALZBERG, BARRY N.	IN	
DOWN THE RIVER	REYNOLDS, MACK	SS	STS 50 09
COME IN, SPACEPORT	REYNOLDS, MACK	SS	GOM 74
COMPOUND INTEREST	REYNOLDS, MACK	SS	FSF 56 08
BUSINESS, AS USUAL, THE	REYNOLDS, MACK	SS	FSF 52 06
FREEDOM	REYNOLDS, MACK	NV	ASF 61 02
REVOLUTION	REYNOLDS, MACK	NV	ASF 60 05
BURNT TOAST	REYNOLDS, MACK	SS	PBY 55 11
YOUR SOUL COMES C.O.D.	REYNOLDS, MACK	SS	FAD 52 03
GOOD INDIAN	REYNOLDS, MACK	SS	ASF 62 09
NO RETURN FROM ELBA	REYNOLDS, MACK	SS	FAN 53 10
PACIFIST	REYNOLDS, MACK	SS	FSF 64 01
SUBVERSIVE	REYNOLDS, MACK	SS	ASF 62 12
EARTHLINGS GO HOME	REYNOLDS, MACK	SS	ROG 62 08
ALBATROSS	REYNOLDS, MACK	SS	IMG 55 04
ENEMY WITHIN, THE	REYNOLDS, MACK	SS	ASF 67 04
SURVIVOR	REYNOLDS, MACK	SS	ASF 66 07
FAD	REYNOLDS, MACK	SS	ASF 65 04
SPACEMAN ON A SPREE	REYNOLDS, MACK	NV	WOT 63 06
ADVENTURE OF THE EXTRATERRESTRIAL, THE	REYNOLDS, MACK	NV	ASF 65 07
UTOPIAN	REYNOLDS, MACK	SS	YRT 70
PRONE	REYNOLDS, MACK	SS	FSF 54 09
SECOND ADVENT	REYNOLDS, MACK	SS	IFS 74 06
BEST OF MURRAY LEINSTER, THE EDITED BY BRIAN DAVIS	LEINSTER, MURRAY	AC	COR 76
INTRODUCTION	DAVIS, BRIAN	IN	
TIME TO DIE	LEINSTER, MURRAY	SS	ASF 47 01
ETHICAL EQUATIONS, THE	LEINSTER, MURRAY	SS	ASF 45 06
SYMBIOSIS	LEINSTER, MURRAY	SS	COL 47 06
INTERFERENCE	LEINSTER, MURRAY	SS	ASF 45 10
DE PROFUNDIS	LEINSTER, MURRAY	SS	TWS 45 WI
PIPELINE TO PLUTO	LEINSTER, MURRAY	SS	ASF 45 08
SAM, THIS IS YOU	LEINSTER, MURRAY	NV	GAL 55 05
DEVIL OF EAST LUPTON, THE	LEINSTER, MURRAY	SS	TWS 48 08
SCRIMSHAW	LEINSTER, MURRAY	SS	ASF 55 09
IF YOU WAS A MOKLIN	LEINSTER, MURRAY	NV	GAL 51 09
BEST OF NEW WORLDS, THE	MOORCOCK, MICHAEL	AN	CPT 65
PIT MY PARISH, THE	ALDISS, BRIAN W.	SS	NWS 58 01
TABLEAU	WHITE, JAMES	NV	NWS 58 05
ANOTHER WORD FOR MAN	PRESSLIE, ROBERT	SS	NWS 58 12
I SEE YOU (ROBOT JUSTICE, FUN 59 07)	HARRISON, HARRY	SS	NWS 59 05
OUTSTRETCHED HAND, THE	SELLINGS, ARTHUR	SS	NWS 59 05
RAILWAYS UP ON CANNIS, THE	KAPP, COLIN	SS	NWS 59 10
TERMINAL BEACH, THE	BALLARD, J. G.	SS	NWS 64 03
TIME DWELLER, THE	MOORCOCK, MICHAEL	SS	NWS 64 02
TRAPS OF TIME, THE	BAXTER, JOHN	SS	NWS 64 03
LAST LONELY MAN, THE	BRUNNER, JOHN	SS	NWS 64 06
FALL OF FRENCHY STEINER, THE	BAILEY, HILARY	NV	NWS 64 08
NEW EXPERIENCE	TUBB, E. C.	SS	NWS 64 10
I REMEMBER, ANITA	JONES, LANGDON	SS	NWS 64 10
MOUNTAIN, THE	COLVIN, JAMES	SS	NWS 65 02
ALL THE KING'S MEN	BAYLEY, BARRINGTON J	NV	NWS 65 03
BEST OF PHILIP K. DICK, THE EDITED BY JOHN BRUNNER	DICK, PHILIP K.	AC	BAL 77 03
INTRODUCTION: THE REALITY OF PHILIP K. DICK	BRUNNER, JOHN	IN	
BEYOND LIES THE WUB	DICK, PHILIP K.	SS	PLS 52 07
ROOG	DICK, PHILIP K.	SS	FSF 53 02
SECOND VARIETY	DICK, PHILIP K.	NV	SSF 53 05
PAYCHECK	DICK, PHILIP K.	NV	IMG 53 06
IMPOSTOR	DICK, PHILIP K.	SS	ASF 53 06
COLONY	DICK, PHILIP K.	NV	GAL 53 06
EXPENDABLE	DICK, PHILIP K.	SS	FSF 53 07
DAYS OF PERKY PAT, THE	DICK, PHILIP K.	NV	AMZ 63 12
BREAKFAST AT TWILIGHT	DICK, PHILIP K.	SS	AMZ 54 07
FOSTER, YOU'RE DEAD	DICK, PHILIP K.	NV	STR 54 03
FATHER-THING, THE	DICK, PHILIP K.	SS	FSF 54 12
SERVICE CALL	DICK, PHILIP K.	SS	SFS 55 07
AUTOFAC	DICK, PHILIP K.	NV	GAL 55 11
HUMAN IS	DICK, PHILIP K.	SS	STS 55 WI
IF THERE WERE NO BENNY CEMOLI	DICK, PHILIP K.	SS	GAL 63 12
OH, TO BE A BLOBEL|	DICK, PHILIP K.	SS	GAL 64 02
FAITH OF OUR FATHERS	DICK, PHILIP K.	NV	DVS 67 02
ELECTRIC ANT, THE	DICK, PHILIP K.	NV	FSF 69 07
LITTLE SOMETHING FOR US TEMPUNAUTS, A	DICK, PHILIP K.	NV	FST 74
AFTERTHOUGHTS BY THE AUTHOR	DICK, PHILIP K.	MS	
BEST OF PLANET STORIES NO. 1, THE	BRACKETT, LEIGH	AN	BAL 75 01
BEYOND OUR NARROW SKIES	BRACKETT, LEIGH	IN	
LORELEI OF THE RED MIST	BRACKETT, LEIGH AND BRADBURY, RAY	NV C	PLS 46 SU
STAR MOUSE, THE	BROWN, FREDRIC	SS	PLS 42 02
RETURN OF A LEGEND	GALLUN, RAYMOND Z.	SS	PLS 52 03
QUEST OF THIG	WELLS, BASIL	SS	PLS 42 FL
ROCKETEERS HAVE SHAGGY EARS, THE	BENNETT, KEITH	NV	PLS 50 SP
DIVERSIFAL, THE	ROCKLYNNE, ROSS	SS	PLS 51 03
DUEL ON SYRTIS	ANDERSON, POUL	SS	PLS 51 03
BEST OF POUL ANDERSON, THE	ANDERSON, POUL	AC	PKT 76 08
RECOLLECTING ANDERSON	MALZBERG, BARRY N.	IN	
INTRODUCTION	ANDERSON, POUL	IN	
LONGEST VOYAGE, THE	ANDERSON, POUL	NV	ASF 60 12
BARBARIAN, THE	ANDERSON, POUL	SS	FSF 56 05
LAST OF THE DELIVERERS, THE	ANDERSON, POUL	SS	FSF 58 02
MY OBJECT ALL SUBLIME	ANDERSON, POUL	SS	GAL 61 06
SAM HALL	ANDERSON, POUL	NV	ASF 53 08
KYRIE	ANDERSON, POUL	SS	FRS 68
FATAL FULFILLMENT, THE	ANDERSON, POUL	SN	FSF 70 03
HIDING PLACE	ANDERSON, POUL	NV	ASF 61 03
SKY PEOPLE, THE	ANDERSON, POUL	NV	FSF 59 03
BEST OF ROBERT HEINLEIN, THE	HEINLEIN, ROBERT A.	AC H	SID 73
INTRODUCTION	HEINLEIN, ROBERT A.	IN	
LIFE-LINE	HEINLEIN, ROBERT A.	SS	ASF 39 08
ROADS MUST ROLL, THE	HEINLEIN, ROBERT A.	NV	ASF 40 06
AND HE BUILT A CROOKED HOUSE	HEINLEIN, ROBERT A.	SS	ASF 41 02
UNPLEASANT PROFESSION OF JONATHAN HOAG, THE	HEINLEIN, ROBERT A.	SN	UNK 42 10
GREEN HILLS OF EARTH, THE	HEINLEIN, ROBERT A.	SS	SEP 47 02
LONG WATCH, THE	HEINLEIN, ROBERT A.	SS	ALM 49 11
MAN WHO SOLD THE MOON, THE	HEINLEIN, ROBERT A.	NV	NEW 50 AC
ALL YOU ZOMBIES-	HEINLEIN, ROBERT A.	SS	FSF 59 03
BIBLIOGRAPHY	MISC. MATERIAL	MS	
BEST OF ROBERT SILVERBERG, THE	SILVERBERG, ROBERT	AC	PKT 76 02
THINKING ABOUT SILVERBERG	MALZBERG, BARRY N.	IN	
ROAD TO NIGHTFALL	SILVERBERG, ROBERT	NV	FUN 58 07
WARM MAN	SILVERBERG, ROBERT	SS	FSF 57 05
TO SEE THE INVISIBLE MAN	SILVERBERG, ROBERT	SS	WOT 63 04
SIXTH PALACE, THE	SILVERBERG, ROBERT	SS	GAL 65 02
FLIES	SILVERBERG, ROBERT	SS	DVS 67 01
HAWKSBILL STATION	SILVERBERG, ROBERT	NV	GAL 67 08
PASSENGERS	SILVERBERG, ROBERT	SS	ORB 68 04
NIGHTWINGS	SILVERBERG, ROBERT	NV	GAL 68 09
SUNDANCE	SILVERBERG, ROBERT	SS	FSF 69 06
GOOD NEWS FROM THE VATICAN	SILVERBERG, ROBERT	SS	UNI 71 07
BEST OF SCIENCE FICTION	CONKLIN, GROFF	AN H	CRN 46
CONCERNING SCIENCE FICTION	CAMPBELL, JOHN W. JR	IN	
INTRODUCTION	CONKLIN, GROFF	IN	
SOLUTION UNSATISFACTORY	MACDONALD, ANSON	NV	ASF 41 05

BEST OF SCIENCE FICTION

GREAT WAR SYNDICATE, THE (ABRIDGED)
                              STOCKTON, FRANK R.   NV   OAW 88 12
PIPER'S SON, THE   PADGETT, LEWIS   NV   ASF 45 02
DEADLINE   CARTMILL, CLEVE   NV   ASF 44 03
LOBBY   SIMAK, CLIFFORD D.   SS   ASF 44 04
BLOWUPS HAPPEN   HEINLEIN, ROBERT A.   NV   ASF 40 09
ATOMIC POWER   STUART, DON A.   SS   ASF 34 12
KILLDOZER!   STURGEON, THEODORE   SN   ASF 44 11
DAVEY JONES' AMBASSADOR   GALLUN, RAYMOND Z.   NV   ASF 35 12
GIANT IN THE EARTH   COLLADAY, MORRISON   SS   WOS 33 04
GOLDFISH BOWL   HEINLEIN, ROBERT A.   NV   ASF 42 03
IVY WAR, THE   KELLER, DAVID H. MD.   SS   AMZ 30 05
LIQUID LIFE   FARLEY, RALPH MILNE   NV   TWS 36 10
TALE OF THE RAGGED MOUNTAINS, A
                              POE, EDGAR ALLEN   SS   GDY 44 04
GREAT KEINPLATZ EXPERIMENT, THE
                              DOYLE, ARTHUR CONAN   SS   WRT 36 10
REMARKABLE CASE OF DAVIDSON'S EYES, THE
                              WELLS, H. G.   SS   PMB 95 03
TISSUE-CULTURE KING, THE   HUXLEY, JULIAN   SS   AMZ 27 08
ULTIMATE CATALYST, THE   TAINE, JOHN   NV   TWS 39 06
TERRIBLE SENSE, THE   PEREGOY, CALVIN   SS   ASF 38 08
SCIENTIST DIVIDES, A   WANDREI, DONALD   SS   ASF 34 09
TRICKY TONNAGE   JAMESON, MALCOLM   SS   ASF 44 12
LANSON SCREEN, THE   ZAGAT, ARTHUR LEO   NV   TWS 36 12
ULTIMATE METAL, THE   SCHACHNER, NAT   NV   ASF 35 02
MACHINE, THE   CAMPBELL, JOHN W. JR   SS   ASF 35 02
SHORT-CIRCUITED PROBABILITY   KNIGHT, NORMAN L.   SS   ASF 41 09
SEARCH, THE   VAN VOGT, A. E.   NV   ASF 43 01
UPPER LEVEL ROAD, THE   VAN LORNE, WARNER   SS   ASF 35 08
32ND OF MAY, THE   ERNST, PAUL   SS   ASF 35 04
MONSTER FROM NOWHERE, THE   BOND, NELSON S.   SS   FAD 39 07
FIRST CONTACT   LEINSTER, MURRAY   NV   ASF 45 05
UNIVERSE   HEINLEIN, ROBERT A.   NV   ASF 41 05
BLIND ALLEY   ASIMOV, ISAAC   SS   ASF 45 03
EN ROUTE TO PLUTO   WEST, WALLACE   SS   ASF 36 08
RETREAT TO MARS, THE   WHITE, CECIL B.   SS   AMZ 27 08
MAN WHO SAVED THE EARTH, THE HALL, AUSTIN   SS   ASW 19 12
SPAWN OF THE STARS   DIFFIN, CHARLES W.   NV   ASF 30 02
FLAME MIDGET, THE   LONG, FRANK BELKNAP   SS   ASF 36 12
EXPEDITION   BOUCHER, ANTHONY   SS   TWS 43 08
CONQUEST OF GOLA, THE   STONE, LESLIE F.   SS   WOS 31 04
JACKDAW   ROCKLYNNE, ROSS   NV   ASF 42 08

BEST OF SCIENCE FICTION (22 OF 40)
                              CONKLIN, GROFF   AN L CRB 63
INTRODUCTION   CONKLIN, GROFF   IN
PIPER'S SON, THE   PADGETT, LEWIS   NV   ASF 45 02
DEADLINE   CARTMILL, CLEVE   NV   ASF 44 03
LOBBY   SIMAK, CLIFFORD D.   SS   ASF 44 04
KILLDOZER!   STURGEON, THEODORE   SN   ASF 44 11
DAVEY JONES' AMBASSADOR   GALLUN, RAYMOND Z.   NV   ASF 35 12
GIANT IN THE EARTH   COLLADAY, MORRISON   SS   WOS 33 04
GOLDFISH BOWL   HEINLEIN, ROBERT A.   NV   ASF 42 03
IVY WAR, THE   KELLER, DAVID H. MD.   SS   AMZ 30 05
TERRIBLE SENSE, THE   PEREGOY, CALVIN   SS   ASF 38 08
TRICKY TONNAGE   JAMESON, MALCOLM   SS   ASF 44 12
MACHINE, THE   CAMPBELL, JOHN W. JR   SS   ASF 35 02
SHORT-CIRCUITED PROBABILITY   KNIGHT, NORMAN L.   SS   ASF 41 09
SEARCH, THE   VAN VOGT, A. E.   NV   ASF 43 01
32ND OF MAY, THE   ERNST, PAUL   SS   ASF 35 04
MONSTER FROM NOWHERE, THE   BOND, NELSON S.   SS   FAD 39 07
FIRST CONTACT   LEINSTER, MURRAY   NV   ASF 45 05
UNIVERSE   HEINLEIN, ROBERT A.   NV   ASF 41 05
BLIND ALLEY   ASIMOV, ISAAC   SS   ASF 45 03
EN ROUTE TO PLUTO   WEST, WALLACE   SS   ASF 36 08
FLAME MIDGET, THE   LONG, FRANK BELKNAP   SS   ASF 36 12
EXPEDITION   BOUCHER, ANTHONY   SS   TWS 43 08
JACKDAW   ROCKLYNNE, ROSS   NV   ASF 42 08

BEST OF SCIENCE FICTION MONTHLY, THE
                              SACKS, JANET   AN H NLB 75
INTRODUCTION   SACKS, JANET   IN
WOMAN NAKED, A   PRIEST, CHRISTOPHER   SS   SFM 74 01
STARPORT   BOUNDS, SYDNEY J.   SS   SFM 74 03
TREE IN THE FOREST, THE   GREENHOUGH, TERRY   SS   SFM 74 02
DARK ICARUS (ALSO AS A LITTLE NIGHT FLYING)
                              SHAW, BOB   SS   SFM 74 04
VICIOUS CIRCLE   HARLEY, ALAN   SS   SFM 74 02
IN THE HOUR OF NOT QUITE RAIN
                              BORSKI, ROBERT   SS   SFM 74 07
SITTING ON A STARWOOD STOOL   WATSON, IAN   SS   SFM 74 10
WORLD OF SOUND, A   STAPLEDON, OLAF   SS   SFM 74 11
EXHIBITION, THE   EDELSTEIN, SCOTT   SS   NOV 73 03
TESTING...ONE, TWO, THREE, FOUR
                              CHAPMAN, STEVE   SS   ASF 69 12
WILBUR   GREENHOUGH, TERRY   SS   SFM 74 04
FIRST DAY OF THE REST OF YOUR LIFE, THE
                              MORGAN, DAN   SS   SFM 74 05
LANDLORD, THE   LESLIE, DELIA   SS   SFM 74 09
BLINDNESS   VOM SCHEIDT, JURGEN   SS   SFM 74 09
BLUE THEME AND FUGUE   WELLS, ROBERT   SS   SFM 74 02
DEATH OF MAN, THE   FULTHORPE, DOUGLAS   SS   SFM 74 05

BEST OF SCIENCE FICTION 2, THE
                              MERRIL, JUDITH   AN   MFL 64
    SEE "THE 7TH ANNUAL OF THE YEAR'S BEST S-F, THE"

BEST OF SCIENCE FICTION 4, THE
                              MERRIL, JUDITH   AN   MFL 65
    SEE "THE 8TH ANNUAL OF THE YEAR'S BEST S-F, THE"

BEST OF SCIENCE FICTION 5, THE
                              MERRIL, JUDITH   AN   MFL 66
    SEE "THE 5TH ANNUAL OF THE YEAR'S BEST S-F, THE"

BEST OF SCIENCE FICTION, THE MERRIL, JUDITH   AN   MFL 63
    SEE "THE 6TH ANNUAL OF THE YEAR'S BEST S-F, THE"

BEST OF STANLEY G. WEINBAUM, THE
                              WEINBAUM, STANLEY G. AC   BAL 74
SECOND NOVA, THE   ASIMOV, ISAAC
MARTIAN ODYSSEY, A   WEINBAUM, STANLEY G. NV   WOS 34 07
VALLEY OF DREAMS   WEINBAUM, STANLEY G. NV   WOS 34 11
ADAPTIVE ULTIMATE, THE   WEINBAUM, STANLEY G. NV   ASF 35 11
PARASITE PLANET   WEINBAUM, STANLEY G. NV   ASF 35 02
PYGMALION'S SPECTACLES   WEINBAUM, STANLEY G. SS   WOS 35 06
SHIFTING SEAS   WEINBAUM, STANLEY G. NV   AMZ 37 04
WORLDS OF IF, THE   WEINBAUM, STANLEY G. SS   WOS 35 08
MAD MOON, THE   WEINBAUM, STANLEY G. NV   ASF 35 12
REDEMPTION CAIRN   WEINBAUM, STANLEY G. NV   ASF 36 03
IDEAL, THE   WEINBAUM, STANLEY G. NV   WOS 35 09
LOTUS EATERS, THE   WEINBAUM, STANLEY G. NV   ASF 35 04
PROTEUS ISLAND   WEINBAUM, STANLEY G. SN   ASF 36 08
STANLEY G. WEINBAUM: A PERSONAL RECOLLECTION
                              BLOCH, ROBERT   AR

BEST SCIENCE FICTION FOR 1972
                              POHL, FREDERIK   AN   ACE 72 09
INTRODUCTION   POHL, FREDERIK   IN
INCONSTANT MOON   NIVEN, LARRY   NV   NEW 71 AC
SUNSET, 2217 AD, THE (TRANSLATED BY TETSU YANO AND
    JUDITH MERRIL)   MITSUSE, RYU   NV
MOTHER IN THE SKY WITH DIAMONDS
                              TIPTREE, JAMES JR.   NV   GAL 71 03
CONVERSATIONAL MODE   LEMAN, GRAHAME   SS   NWR 72 20
SHELTERING DREAM   PISERCHIA, DORIS   SS   IFS 72 02
AT THE MOUSE CIRCUS   ELLISON, HARLAN   SS   NDM 71 01
SILENT IN GEHENNA   ELLISON, HARLAN   SS   MWS 71
TOO MANY PEOPLE   HOLLIS, H. H.   NV   GAL 71 01
EASY WAY OUT, THE   BRUNNER, JOHN   NV   IFS 71 06
GOLD AT THE STARBOW'S END, THE
                              POHL, FREDERIK   NV   ASF 72 03

BEST SCIENCE FICTION FOR 1973
                              ACKERMAN, FORREST J. AN   ACE 73
INTRODUCTION   ACKERMAN, FORREST J.   IN
THING OF BEAUTY, A   SPINRAD, NORMAN   SS   ASF 73 01
WHAT WE LEARNED FROM THIS MORNING'S NEWSPAPER
                              SILVERBERG, ROBERT   SS   INY 72 04
SEVENTY YEARS OF DECPOP   FARMER, PHILIP JOSE   NA   GAL 72 07
SHAPE OF SCIENCE FICTION TO COME, THE
                              POHL, FREDERIK   AR   73
GETTING TOGETHER   ROTHMAN, MILTON A.   SS   GAL 72 03
BY THE TIME I GET TO PHOENIX SCORTIA, THOMAS N.   SS   INY 72 04
FOREVER AND AMEN   BLOCH, ROBERT   SS   WLK 73
ERSATZ ETERNAL   VAN VOGT, A. E.   NV   NEW 72 AC
MERCHANTS OF VENUS, THE   POHL, FREDERIK   NA   IFS 72 08
AFTERWORD   ACKERMAN, FORREST J.   MS

BEST SCIENCE FICTION FROM IF, THE
                              POHL, FREDERIK   AN D GPC 64
2 B R 0 2 B   VONNEGUT, KURT JR.   SS   IFS 62 01
FROM GUSTIBLES PLANET   SMITH, CORDWAINER   SS   IFS 62 07
IN THE ARENA   ALDISS, BRIAN W.   SS   IFS 63 07
EGG AND ASHES   HERBERT, FRANK   SS   IFS 60 11
SNOWBANK ORBIT, THE   LEIBER, FRITZ   NV   IFS 62 09
EXPENDABLES, THE   VAN VOGT, A. E.   NV   IFS 63 09
SPAWNING GROUND   DEL REY, LESTER   SS   IFS 61 09
TALENT   BLOCH, ROBERT   SS   IFS 60 07
DIE, SHADOW!   BUDRYS, ALGIS   NV   IFS 63 05
SHIPSHAPE MIRACLE, THE   SIMAK, CLIFFORD D.   NV   IFS 63 01
FIVE HELLS OF ORION, THE   POHL, FREDERIK   NV   IFS 63 01
INCIDENT ON ROUTE 12, AN   SCHMITZ, JAMES H.   SS   IFS 62 01

BEST SCIENCE FICTION FROM WORLDS OF TOMORROW, THE
                              POHL, FREDERIK   AN D GPC 64
LONG REMEMBERED THUNDER, THE LAUMER, KEITH   NV   WOT 63 04
X MARKS THE PEDWALK   LEIBER, FRITZ   SS   WOT 63 04
IMPOSSIBLE STAR, THE   ALDISS, BRIAN W.   SS   WOT 63 08
APPRENTICE GOD, THE   DEFORD, MIRIAM ALLEN   PM   WOT 64 04
GUEST OF GANYMEDE, A   MACAPP, C. C.   NV   WOT 63 06
MASKED WORLD, THE   WILLIAMSON, JACK   SS   WOT 63 10
TROUBLE WITH TRUTH, THE   GROW, JULIAN F.   NV   WOT 63 12
GOOD FRIENDS, THE   SMITH, CORDWAINER   SS   WOT 63 10
WHEN THE STARS ANSWER   BROWN, T. K. III   SS   WOT 64 02
LITTLE DOG GONE   YOUNG, ROBERT F.   NV   WOT 64 02

BEST SCIENCE FICTION OF THE YEAR, THE
                              CARR, TERRY   AN   BAL 72 07
INTRODUCTION   CARR, TERRY   IN
OCCAM'S SCALPEL   STURGEON, THEODORE   NV   IFS 71 08
QUEEN OF AIR AND DARKNESS, THE
                              ANDERSON, POUL   SN   FSF 71 04
IN ENTROPY'S JAWS   SILVERBERG, ROBERT   NV   INY 71 02
SLICED-CROSSWISE ONLY-ON-TUESDAY WORLD, THE
                              FARMER, PHILIP JOSE   SS   NDM 71 01
MEETING WITH MEDUSA, A   CLARKE, ARTHUR C.   NA   PBY 71 12
FRAYED STRING ON THE STRETCHED FOREFINGER OF TIME, THE
                              BIGGLE, LLOYD JR.   SS   FSF 71 05
HOW CAN WE SINK WHEN WE CAN FLY?
                              PANSHIN, ALEXEI   NV   FFU 71
NO DIRECTION HOME   SPINRAD, NORMAN   SS   NWQ 71 02
VASTER THAN EMPIRES AND MORE SLOW
                              LE GUIN, URSULA K.   NV   NDM 71 01
ALL THE LAST WARS AT ONCE   EFFINGER, GEO. ALEC   SS   UNI 71 01
FOURTH PROFESSION, THE   NIVEN, LARRY   NV   QRK 71 04

BEST SCIENCE FICTION OF THE YEAR, THE NO. 2
                              CARR, TERRY   AN   BAL 73 07
INTRODUCTION   CARR, TERRY   IN
MEETING, THE   POHL, FREDERIK

BEST SCIENCE FICTION OF THE YEAR, THE NO. 2

```
                           AND KORNBLUTH, C. M.    SS C FSF 72 11
NOBODY'S HOME              RUSS, JOANNA            SS   NDM 72 02
FORTUNE HUNTER             ANDERSON, POUL          SS   INY 72 04
FIFTH HEAD OF CERBERUS, THE WOLFE, GENE            NV   ORB 72 10
CALIBAN                    SILVERBERG, ROBERT      SS   INY 72 03
CONVERSATIONAL MODE        LEMAN, GRAHAME          SS   NWR 72 20
THEIR THOUSANDTH SEASON    BRYANT, EDWARD          SS   CLR 72 02
EUREMA'S DAM               LAFFERTY, R. A.         SS   NDM 72 02
ZERO GEE                   BOVA, BEN               NV   DVS 72 02
SKY BLUE                   PANSHIN, ALEXEI
                           AND PANSHIN, CORY       SS C AMZ 72 03
MISS OMEGA RAVEN           MITCHISON, NAOMI        SS   NOV 72 02
PATRON OF THE ARTS         ROTSLER, WILLIAM        NV   UNI 72 02
GRASSHOPPER TIME           EKLUND, GORDON          SS   FSF 72 03
HERO                       HALDEMAN, JOE W.        NV   ASF 72 06
WHEN WE WENT TO SEE THE END OF THE WORLD
                           SILVERBERG, ROBERT      SS   UNI 72 02
PAINWISE                   TIPTREE, JAMES JR.      NV   FSF 72 02
HONORABLE MENTIONS         MISC. MATERIAL          MS
```

BEST SCIENCE FICTION OF THE YEAR, THE NO. 3
```
                           CARR, TERRY             AN   BAL 74 07
INTRODUCTION               CARR, TERRY             IN
SOMETHING UP THERE LIKES ME BESTER, ALFRED         NV   AMA 73
WORLD AS WILL AND WALLPAPER, THE
                           LAFFERTY, R. A.         SS   FUC 73
BRECKENRIDGE AND THE CONTINUUM
                           SILVERBERG, ROBERT      NV   SCS 73
RUMFUDDLE                  VANCE, JACK             NA   TTT 73
TELL ME ALL ABOUT YOURSELF BUSBY, F. M.            SS   NDM 73 03
DEATHBIRD, THE             ELLISON, HARLAN         NV   FSF 73 03
OF MIST, AND GRASS, AND SAND MCINTYRE, VONDA N.    SS   ASF 73 10
DEATH OF DOCTOR ISLAND, THE WOLFE, GENE            NV   UNI 73 03
ONES WHO WALK AWAY FROM OMELAS, THE
                           LE GUIN, URSULA K.      SS   NDM 73 03
SKETCHES AMONG THE RUINS OF MY MIND
                           FARMER, PHILIP JOSE     NV   NOV 73 03
WOMEN MEN DON'T SEE, THE   TIPTREE, JAMES JR.      NV   FSF 73 12
HONORABLE MENTIONS         MISC. MATERIAL          MS
```

BEST SCIENCE FICTION OF THE YEAR, THE NO. 4
```
                           CARR, TERRY             AN   BAL 75 07
INTRODUCTION               CARR, TERRY             IN
WE PURCHASE PEOPLE         POHL, FREDERIK          SS   FST 74
PALE ROSES                 MOORCOCK, MICHAEL       NV   NWQ 74 06
HOLE MAN, THE              NIVEN, LARRY            SS   ASF 74 01
BORN WITH THE DEAD         SILVERBERG, ROBERT      NA   FSF 74 04
AUTHOR OF THE ACACIA SEEDS AND OTHER EXTRACTS FROM THE JOURNAL
  OF THE ASSOCIATION OF THERO LE GUIN, URSULA K.   SS   FOS 74
DARK ICARUS (ALSO AS A LITTLE NIGHT FLYING)
                           SHAW, BOB               SS   SFM 74 04
LITTLE SOMETHING FOR US TEMPUNAUTS, A
                           DICK, PHILIP K.         NV   FST 74
ON VENUS, HAVE WE GOT A RABBI
                           TENN, WILLIAM           NV   NEW 74 AN
ENGINE AT HEARTSPRING'S CENTER, THE
                           ZELAZNY, ROGER          SS   ASF 74 07
IF THE STARS ARE GODS      EKLUND, GORDON
                           AND BENFORD, GREGORY    NV C UNI 74 04
HONORABLE MENTIONS- 1974   CARR, TERRY             MS
SCIENCE FICTION YEAR, THE  BROWN, CHARLES N.       MS
```

BEST SCIENCE FICTION OF THE YEAR, THE NO. 5
```
                           CARR, TERRY             AN   BAL 76 07
INTRODUCTION               CARR, TERRY             IN
DOWN TO A SUNLESS SEA      SMITH, CORDWAINER       NV   FSF 75 10
RETROGRADE SUMMER          VARLEY, JOHN            NV   FSF 75 02
HERO AS WERWOLF, THE       WOLFE, GENE             SS   NEW 75 AN
SILENT EYES OF TIME, THE   BUDRYS, ALGIS           NA   FSF 75 11
CROATOAN                   ELLISON, HARLAN         SS   FSF 75 05
DOING LENNON               BENFORD, GREGORY        SS   ASF 75 04
NEW ATLANTIS, THE          LE GUIN, URSULA K.      NA   NAL 75
CLAY SUBURB                YOUNG, ROBERT F.        SS   AMZ 75 11
STORMS OF WINDHAVEN, THE   MARTIN, GEORGE R. R.
                           AND TUTTLE, LISA        NV C ASF 75 05
CHILD OF ALL AGES          PLAUGER, P. J.          SS   ASF 75 03
IN THE BOWL                VARLEY, JOHN            SS   FSF 75 12
SAIL THE TIDE OF MOURNING  LUPOFF, RICHARD A.      SS   NDM 75 05
RECOMMENDED READING- 1975  CARR, TERRY             MS
SCIENCE FICTION YEAR, THE  BROWN, CHARLES N.       MS
```

BEST SCIENCE FICTION OF THE YEAR, THE NO. 6
```
                           CARR, TERRY             AN   HRW 77 07
I SEE YOU                  KNIGHT, DAMON           SS   FSF 76 11
PHANTOM OF KANSAS, THE     VARLEY, JOHN            NV   GAL 76 02
DEATH OF PRINCES, THE      LEIBER, FRITZ           NV   AMZ 76 06
SEEING                     ELLISON, HARLAN         SS
MEATHOUSE MAN              MARTIN, GEORGE R. R. SS  ORB 76 18
CUSTER'S LAST JUMP         UTLEY, STEVEN
                           AND WALDROP, HOWARD     NV C UNI 76 06
EYEFLASH MIRACLES, THE     WOLFE, GENE             NA        76
INFINITE SUMMER, AN        PRIEST, CHRISTOPHER     NV
HIGHEST DIVE, THE          WILLIAMSON, JACK        SS   SFM 76 01
BICENTENNIAL MAN, THE      ASIMOV, ISAAC           NV   STL 76 02
PSYCHOLOGIST WHO WOULDN'T DO AWFUL THINGS TO RATS, THE
                           TIPTREE, JAMES JR.      NV   NDM 76 06
```

BEST SCIENCE FICTION STORIES AND NOVELS: 1955
```
                           DIKTY, T. E.            AN H FEL 55
  DERIVATIVE ANTHOLOGY "5 TALES FROM TOMORROW"
SCIENCE-FICTION YEAR, THE  DIKTY, T. E.            MS
COLD EQUATIONS, THE        GODWIN, TOM             NV   ASF 54 08
OF COURSE                  OLIVER, CHAD            SS   ASF 54 05
DOMINIONS BEYOND (THE SECOND TRIP TO MARS)
                           MOORE, WARD             SS   SEP 54 08
GUILTY AS CHARGED          PORGES, ARTHUR          SS   NEW 55 AN
```

BEST SCIENCE FICTION STORIES OF BRIAN W. ALDISS (REVISED)
```
CARELESS LOVE (ALSO AS PUSH-BUTTON PASSION)
                           FRIBORG, ALBERT C.      SS   FSF 54 07
MOMENTO HOMO (DEATH OF A SPACEMAN)
                           MILLER, WALTER M. JR SS  AMZ 54 03
MOUSETRAP                  NORTON, ANDRE           SS   FSF 54 06
CHRISTMAS TROMBONE         BANKS, RAYMOND E.       SS   FSF 54 10
ONE THOUSAND MILES UP      ROBINSON, FRANK M.      SS   SST 54 04
HOW-2                      SIMAK, CLIFFORD D.      NV   GAL 54 11
HEIRS APPARENT             ABERNATHY, ROBERT       NV   FSF 54 07
JOHN'S OTHER PRACTICE      MARKS, WINSTON K.       SS   IMG 54 07
INNER WORLDS, THE          MORRISON, WILLIAM       NV   FSF 54 04
WILL, THE                  MILLER, WALTER M. JR SS  FAN 54 07
FELONY                     CAUSEY, JAMES           SS   GAL 54 04
LITTLEST PEOPLE, THE       BANKS, RAYMOND E.       NV   GAL 54 03
ONE WAY STREET             BIXBY, JEROME           SS   AMZ 54 04
AXOLOTL (ALSO AS DEEP SPACE) ABERNATHY, ROBERT     SS   FSF 54 01
EXILE                      COLE, EVERETT B.        SN   ASF 54 01
NIGHTMARE BLUES (OPERATION SYNDROME)
                           HERBERT, FRANK          NV   ASF 54 06
SCIENCE-FICTION BOOK INDEX, THE
                           KEMP, EARL              MS
```

BEST SCIENCE FICTION STORIES AND NOVELS: 1956
```
                           DIKTY, T. E.            AN H FEL 56
  DERIVATIVE ANTHOLOGY "6 FROM WORLDS BEYOND"
SCIENCE-FICTION YEAR, THE  DIKTY, T. E.            MS
JUNGLE DOCTOR              YOUNG, ROBERT F.        NV   STS 55 FI
JUDGMENT DAY               DE CAMP, L. SPRAGUE     SS   ASF 55 08
GAME OF RAT AND DRAGON, THE SMITH, CORDWAINER      NV   GAL 55 10
MAN WHO ALWAYS KNEW, THE   BUDRYS, ALGIS           SS   ASF 55 04
DREAM STREET               ROBINSON, FRANK M.      SS   IMT 55 03
YOU CREATED US             GODWIN, TOM             SS   FUN 55 10
SWENSON, DISPATCHER        MILLER, R. DEWITT       NV   GAL 55 04
THING                      JANVIER, IVAN           SS   FUN 55 03
I DO NOT LOVE THEE, DOCTOR FELL
                           BLOCH, ROBERT           SS   FSF 55 03
CLERICAL ERROR             CLIFTON, MARK           NV   ASF 56 02
CANTICLE FOR LEIBOWITZ, A  MILLER, WALTER M. JR NV  FSF 55 04
CYBER AND JUSTICE HOLMES, THE
                           RILEY, FRANK            SS   IFS 55 03
SHORES OF NIGHT, THE (EXPANDED FROM "SEA CHANGE")
                           SCORTIA, THOMAS N.      SS   ASF 56 06
SCIENCE-FICTION BOOK INDEX, THE
                           KEMP, EARL              MS
```

BEST SCIENCE FICTION STORIES AND NOVELS: 9TH SERIES
```
                           DIKTY, T. E.            AN H AVT 58
SCIENCE-FICTION YEAR, THE  DIKTY, T. E.            MS
2066: ELECTION DAY         SHAARA, MICHAEL         SS   ASF 56 12
MILE-LONG SPACESHIP, THE   WILHELM, KATE           SS   ASF 57 04
LAST VICTORY, THE          GODWIN, TOM             SS   IFS 57 08
CALL ME JOE                ANDERSON, POUL          NV   ASF 57 04
DIDN'T HE RAMBLE           OLIVER, CHAD            SS   FSF 57 04
QUEEN'S MESSENGER, THE     MCGUIRE, JOHN J.        SS   ASF 57 05
OTHER PEOPLE, THE (THE QUEER ONES)
                           BRACKETT, LEIGH         NV   VSF 57 03
INTO YOUR TENT I'LL CREEP  RUSSELL, ERIC FRANK     SS   ASF 57 09
NOR DUST CORRUPT           MCCONNELL, JAMES        SS   IFS 57 02
NIGHTSOUND (THE ATTIC VOICE) BUDRYS, ALGIS         SS   SAT 57 02
TUNESMITH, THE             BIGGLE, LLOYD JR.       NV   IFS 57 08
HUNTING MACHINE, THE       EMSHWILLER, CAROL       SS   SFS 57 05
SCIENCE-FICTION BOOK INDEX, THE
                           KEMP, EARL              MS
```

BEST SCIENCE FICTION STORIES OF BRIAN W. ALDISS
```
                           ALDISS, BRIAN W.        AC H FAB 65
  ALSO AS "WHO CAN REPLACE A MAN?"
INTRODUCTION               ALDISS, BRIAN W.        IN
WHO CAN REPLACE A MAN? (BUT WHO CAN REPLACE A MAN)
                           ALDISS, BRIAN W.        SS   INF 58 06
NOT FOR AN AGE             ALDISS, BRIAN W.        SS   LOB 55 01
PSYCLOPS                   ALDISS, BRIAN W.        SS   NWS 56 07
OUTSIDE                    ALDISS, BRIAN W.        SS   NWS 55 01
DUMB SHOW                  ALDISS, BRIAN W.        SS   NEB 56 12
NEW FATHER CHRISTMAS, THE  ALDISS, BRIAN W.        SS   FSF 58 01
AHEAD (THE FAILED MEN)     ALDISS, BRIAN W.        SS   SCF 56 05
POOR LITTLE WARRIOR¡       ALDISS, BRIAN W.        SS   FSF 58 04
MAN ON BRIDGE              ALDISS, BRIAN W.        SS   NWR 64 01
IMPOSSIBLE STAR, THE       ALDISS, BRIAN W.        NV   WOT 63 08
BASIS FOR NEGOTIATION      ALDISS, BRIAN W.        NV   NWS 63 01
OLD HUNDREDTH              ALDISS, BRIAN W.        SS   NWS 60 11
KIND OF ARTISTRY, A        ALDISS, BRIAN W.        SS   FSF 62 10
MAN IN HIS TIME            ALDISS, BRIAN W.        SS   SCF 65 04
```

BEST SCIENCE FICTION STORIES OF BRIAN W. ALDISS (REVISED)
```
                           ALDISS, BRIAN W.        AC H FAB 71
INTRODUCTION               ALDISS, BRIAN W.        IN
WHO CAN REPLACE A MAN? (BUT WHO CAN REPLACE A MAN)
                           ALDISS, BRIAN W.        SS   INF 58 06
NOT FOR AN AGE             ALDISS, BRIAN W.        SS   LOB 55 01
OUTSIDE                    ALDISS, BRIAN W.        SS   NWS 55 01
POOR LITTLE WARRIOR¡       ALDISS, BRIAN W.        SS   FSF 58 04
MAN ON BRIDGE              ALDISS, BRIAN W.        SS   NWR 64 01
IMPOSSIBLE STAR, THE       ALDISS, BRIAN W.        NV   WOT 63 08
OLD HUNDREDTH              ALDISS, BRIAN W.        SS   NWS 60 11
MAN IN HIS TIME            ALDISS, BRIAN W.        SS   SCF 65 04
SHARDS                     ALDISS, BRIAN W.        SS   FSF 62 04
GIRL AND ROBOT WITH FLOWERS ALDISS, BRIAN W.       SS   NWS 65 09
MOMENT OF ECLIPSE, THE     ALDISS, BRIAN W.        SS   NWS 69 05
SWASTIKA¡                  ALDISS, BRIAN W.        SS   NOV 70 01
SOBER NOISES OF MORNING IN A MARGINAL LAND
                           ALDISS, BRIAN W.        NV   LOM 72 06
JUDAS DANCED (JUDAS DANCING) ALDISS, BRIAN W.      SS   SMG 58 01
STILL TRAJECTORIES         ALDISS, BRIAN W.        SS   NWS 67 09
ANOTHER LITTLE BOY         ALDISS, BRIAN W.        SS   NWS 66 09
```

BEST SCIENCE FICTION STORIES OF BRIAN W. ALDISS (REVISED)

BEST SCIENCE FICTION STORIES OF C. M. KORNBLUTH

```
BEST SCIENCE FICTION STORIES OF C. M. KORNBLUTH
                                KORNBLUTH, C. M.     AC H FAB 68
INTRODUCTION                    CRISPIN, EDMUND      IN
UNFORTUNATE TOPOLOGIST, THE     KORNBLUTH, C. M.     PM  FSF 57 07
MARCHING MORONS, THE            KORNBLUTH, C. M.     NV  GAL 51 04
ALTAR AT MIDNIGHT, THE          KORNBLUTH, C. M.     SS  GAL 52 11
LITTLE BLACK BAG, THE           KORNBLUTH, C. M.     NV  ASF 50 07
MINDWORM, THE                   KORNBLUTH, C. M.     SS  WBY 50 12
SILLY SEASON, THE               KORNBLUTH, C. M.     SS  FSF 50 FL
I NEVER AST NO FAVORS           KORNBLUTH, C. M.     SS  FSF 54 04
FRIEND TO MAN                   KORNBLUTH, C. M.     SS  TSF 51 SP
ONLY THING WE LEARN, THE        KORNBLUTH, C. M.     SS  STS 49 07
GOMEZ                           KORNBLUTH, C. M.     NV  NEW 54 AC
WITH THESE HANDS                KORNBLUTH, C. M.     NV  GAL 51 12
THEORY OF ROCKETRY              KORNBLUTH, C. M.     SS  FSF 58 07
THAT SHARE OF GLORY             KORNBLUTH, C. M.     NV  ASF 52 01

BEST SCIENCE FICTION STORIES OF CLIFFORD D. SIMAK
                                SIMAK, CLIFFORD D.   AC H FAB LM
FOUNDING FATHER                 SIMAK, CLIFFORD D.   SS  GAL 57 05
IMMIGRANT                       SIMAK, CLIFFORD D.   SN  ASF 54 03
NEW FOLKS' HOME                 SIMAK, CLIFFORD D.   SS  ASF 63 07
CRYING JAG                      SIMAK, CLIFFORD D.   NV  GAL 60 02
ALL THE TRAPS OF EARTH          SIMAK, CLIFFORD D.   SS  FSF 60 03
LULU                            SIMAK, CLIFFORD D.   NV  GAL 57 06
NEIGHBOR                        SIMAK, CLIFFORD D.   NV  ASF 54 06

BEST SCIENCE FICTION STORIES OF H. G. WELLS
                                WELLS, H. G.         AC L DOV 66
INVISIBLE MAN, THE              WELLS, H. G.         SN  PRS 97 06
CRYSTAL EGG, THE                WELLS, H. G.         SS  NRV 97 05
MAN WHO COULD WORK MIRACLES, THE
                                WELLS, H. G.         SS  ILN 98 07
PLATTNER STORY, THE             WELLS, H. G.         SS  NRV 96 04
STRANGE ORCHID, THE (THE FLOWERING OF THE STRANGE ORCHID)
                                WELLS, H. G.         SS  PMB 94 08
NEW ACCELERATOR, THE            WELLS, H. G.         SS  SND 01 12
DIAMOND MAKER, THE              WELLS, H. G.         SS  PMB 94
APPLE, THE                      WELLS, H. G.         SS  IDL 96 10
PURPLE PILEUS, THE              WELLS, H. G.         SS  BAW 96 12
DREAM OF ARMAGEDDON, A          WELLS, H. G.         NV  BAW 01
AEPYORNIS ISLAND                WELLS, H. G.         SS  PMB 94 12
IN THE ABYSS                    WELLS, H. G.         SS  PRS 96 08
STAR, THE                       WELLS, H. G.         SS  GRP 97 12
LORD OF THE DYNAMOS, THE        WELLS, H. G.         SS  PMB 94 09
STORY OF DAVIDSON'S EYES, THE
                                WELLS, H. G.         SS  PMB 95 03
IN THE AVU OBSERVATORY          WELLS, H. G.         SS  PMB 94 08
SEA-RAIDERS, THE                WELLS, H. G.         SS  WSL 96 12
FILMER                          WELLS, H. G.         SS  GRP 01

BEST SCIENCE FICTION STORIES OF JAMES BLISH
                                BLISH, JAMES         AC H FAB 65
THERE SHALL BE NO DARKNESS      BLISH, JAMES         SS  TWS 50 04
SURFACE TENSION                 BLISH, JAMES         NA  GAL 52 08
TESTAMENT OF ANDROS             BLISH, JAMES         NV  FUT 53 01
COMMON TIME                     BLISH, JAMES         SS  SFQ 53 08
WORK OF ART, A (ART-WORK)       BLISH, JAMES         SS  SFS 56 07
TOMB TAPPER                     BLISH, JAMES         SS  ASF 56 07
OATH, THE                       BLISH, JAMES         SS  FSF 60 10

BEST SCIENCE FICTION STORIES OF JAMES BLISH (REVISED)
                                BLISH, JAMES         AC H FAB 73
PREFACE                         BLISH, JAMES         IN
SURFACE TENSION                 BLISH, JAMES         NA  GAL 52 08
TESTAMENT OF ANDROS             BLISH, JAMES         NV  FUT 53 01
COMMON TIME                     BLISH, JAMES         SS  SFQ 53 08
WORK OF ART, A (ART-WORK)       BLISH, JAMES         SS  SFS 56 07
TOMB TAPPER                     BLISH, JAMES         SS  ASF 56 07
OATH, THE                       BLISH, JAMES         SS  FSF 60 10
HOW BEAUTIFUL WITH BANNERS      BLISH, JAMES         SS  ORB 66 01
WE ALL DIE NAKED                BLISH, JAMES         NA  TFT 69

BEST SCIENCE FICTION STORIES OF THE YEAR (1971)
                                DEL REY, LESTER      AN H DUT 72
FOREWORD: ALTERNATE POSSIBILITIES
                                DEL REY, LESTER      IN
SLICED-CROSSWISE ONLY-ON-TUESDAY WORLD, THE
                                FARMER, PHILIP JOSE  SS  NDM 71 01
GOOD NEWS FROM THE VATICAN      SILVERBERG, ROBERT   SS  UNI 71 01
I'LL BE WAITING FOR YOU WHEN THE SWIMMING POOL IS EMPTY
                                TIPTREE, JAMES JR.   SS  PRT 71
POWER OF THE SENTENCE, THE      LOCKE, DAVID M.      SS  FSF 71 04
WICKED FLEE, THE                HARRISON, HARRY      SS  NDM 71 01
WHEN YOU HEAR THE TONE          SCORTIA, THOMAS N.   SS  GAL 71 01
OCCAM'S SCALPEL                 STURGEON, THEODORE   NV  IFS 71 08
HOT POTATO                      FILER, BURT K.       SS  MWS 71
HUMAN OPERATORS, THE            ELLISON, HARLAN
                                AND VAN VOGT, A. E.  NV C FSF 71 01
AUTUMNTIME                      LENTINI, A.          SS  GAL 71 11
LITTLE KNOWLEDGE, A             ANDERSON, POUL       NV  ASF 71 08
TO MAKE A NEW NEANDERTHAL       MACFARLANE, WALLACE  SS  ASF 71 09
MAN UNDERNEATH, THE             LAFFERTY, R. A.      SS  IFS 71 01
ORNITHANTHROPUS                 BURHOE, B. ALAN      SS  IFS 71 12
RAMMER                          NIVEN, LARRY         NV  GAL 71 11
SCIENCE FICTION YEARBOOK, THE
                                DEL REY, LESTER      MS

BEST SCIENCE FICTION STORIES OF THE YEAR (1972)
                                DEL REY, LESTER      AN H DUT 73
FOREWORD: THE SPICE OF VARIETY
                                DEL REY, LESTER      IN
CLOAK OF ANARCHY                NIVEN, LARRY         NV  ASF 72 03
WHEN WE WENT TO SEE THE END OF THE WORLD
                                SILVERBERG, ROBERT   SS  UNI 72 02
UNDERBELLY                      EKLUND, GORDON       SS  IFS 72 10
```

BEST SCIENCE FICTION STORIES: FIFTH SERIES, THE

```
GREATEST ASSET, THE             ASIMOV, ISAAC        SS  ASF 72 01
MEETING, THE                    POHL, FREDERIK
                                AND KORNBLUTH, C. M. SS C FSF 72 11
EUREMA'S DAM                    LAFFERTY, R. A.      SS  NDM 72 02
TERATOHIPPUS                    DAVIS, ROBERT L.     NV  IFS 72 12
LONG SILENCE, THE               NOAKES, DONALD       SS  ASF 72 03
LONG SHOT                       VINGE, VERNOR        SS  ASF 72 08
MISCOUNT                        GLOECKNER, CAROLYN   SS  ASF 72 11
THUS LOVE BETRAYS US            MACLENNAN, PHYLLIS   SS  FSF 72 09
WOMAN'S RIB                     SCORTIA, THOMAS N.   SS  GAL 72 07
MAN WHO WALKED HOME, THE        TIPTREE, JAMES JR.   NV  AMZ 72 05
WATCHDOG                        HALDEMAN, JACK C. II SS  AMZ 72 05
PATRON OF THE ARTS              ROTSLER, WILLIAM     NV  UNI 72 02
SCIENCE FICTION YEARBOOK, THE
                                DEL REY, LESTER      MS

BEST SCIENCE FICTION STORIES OF THE YEAR (1973)
                                DEL REY, LESTER      AN H DUT 74
FOREWORD: A SPATE OF CHANGES    DEL REY, LESTER      IN
SOMETHING UP THERE LIKES ME     BESTER, ALFRED       NV  AMA 73
THING OF BEAUTY, A              SPINRAD, NORMAN      SS  ASF 73 01
WITH MORNING COMES MISTFALL     MARTIN, GEORGE R. R. SS  ASF 73 05
CONSTRUCTION SHACK              SIMAK, CLIFFORD D.   SS  IFS 73 02
THOU GOOD AND FAITHFUL          SCORTIA, THOMAS N.   NV  TVW 73
ANDROIDS DON'T CRY              WELLEN, EDWARD       SS  FSF 73 05
POPULATION IMPLOSION, THE (PROBABILITY ZERO!)
                                COGSWELL, THEODORE R SS  AMA 73
THINK ONLY THIS OF ME           KURLAND, MICHAEL J.  NV  GAL 73 11
GHOSTS                          YOUNG, ROBERT F.     SS  IFS 73 02
AFTERWORD                       POHL, FREDERIK       MS  FUC 73
PROBLEM OF PAIN, THE            ANDERSON, POUL       NV  FSF 73 02
PARTHEN                         LAFFERTY, R. A.      SS  GAL 73 05
NATIONAL PASTIME, THE           SPINRAD, NORMAN      NV  NOV 73 03
PARADISE REGAINED               COGSWELL, THOMAS     SS  SVW 73
WHATEVER HAPPENED TO THE OLMECS?
                                WILHELM, KATE        SS  FSF 73 10
SCIENCE FICTION YEARBOOK, THE
                                DEL REY, LESTER      MS

BEST SCIENCE FICTION STORIES OF THE YEAR (1974)
                                DEL REY, LESTER      AN H DUT 75
FOREWORD: THE SENSE OF WONDER
                                DEL REY, LESTER      IN
IF THIS IS WINNETKA, YOU MUST BE JUDY
                                BUSBY, F. M.         NV  UNI 74 05
SLEEPING DOGS                   ELLISON, HARLAN      SS  ASF 74 10
MOUNTAINS OF SUNSET, THE MOUNTAINS OF DAWN, THE
                                MCINTYRE, VONDA N.   SS  FSF 74 02
EARTH MOTHER                    GLOECKNER, CAROLYN   SS      74
DREAM DONE GREEN                FOSTER, ALAN DEAN    SS  FOS 74
NIGHT IS COLD, THE STARS ARE FAR AWAY, THE
                                BROXON, MILDRED D.   SS  UNI 74 05
AD ASTRA                        HARRISON, HARRY      SS  VTX 74 08
AND NAME MY NAME                LAFFERTY, R. A.      SS  ORB 74 13
WHAT FRIENDS ARE FOR            BRUNNER, JOHN        SS  FOS 74
MUTE INGLORIOUS TAM             POHL, FREDERIK
                                AND KORNBLUTH, C. M. SS C FSF 74 10
MAN WHO CAME BACK, THE          SILVERBERG, ROBERT   SS  GAL 74 12
DRESS REHEARSAL                 JACOBS, HARVEY       SS  FSF 74 07
ENTER A PILGRIM                 DICKSON, GORDON R.   SS  ASF 74 08
POSTPONED CURE, THE             NODVIK, STAN         SS  VTX 74 06
BIRCH CLUMP CYLINDER, THE       SIMAK, CLIFFORD D.   NV  STL 74 01
SCIENCE FICTION YEARBOOK, THE
                                DEL REY, LESTER      MS

BEST SCIENCE FICTION STORIES OF THE YEAR (1975)
                                DEL REY, LESTER      AN H DUT 76
FOREWORD: FIFTY YEARS OF SCIENCE FICTION
                                DEL REY, LESTER      IN
BITTER BREAD, THE               ANDERSON, POUL       NV  ASF 75 12
MAIL SUPREMACY                  PEIRCE, HAYFORD      SS  ASF 75 03
CHILD OF ALL AGES               PLAUGER, P. J.       SS  ASF 75 03
TREE OF LIFE                    EISENSTEIN, PHYLLIS  SS  GAL 75 03
HELBENT 4                       ROBINETT, STEPHEN    NV  GAL 75 10
POP GOES THE WEASEL             HOSKINS, ROBERT      SS  FSF 75 04
BOOK LEARNERS, THE              HUFFORD, LIZ         SS  FSF 75 04
HIGH YIELD BONDAGE              PEIRCE, HAYFORD      NV  GAL 75 08
SENIOR CITIZEN                  SIMAK, CLIFFORD D.   SS  FSF 75 10
PEDDLER'S APPRENTICE, THE       VINGE, JOAN D.
                                AND VINGE, VERNOR    NV C ASF 75 08
SCIENCE FICTION YEARBOOK, THE
                                DEL REY, LESTER      MS

BEST SCIENCE FICTION STORIES OF THE YEAR (1976)
                                DOZOIS, GARDNER R.   AN H DUT 77 07
DIARY OF THE ROSE, THE          LE GUIN, URSULA K.   NV      76
CUSTER'S LAST JUMP              UTLEY, STEVEN
                                AND WALDROP, HOWARD  NV C UNI 76 06
AIR RAID                        VARLEY, JOHN         SS      76
LADIES AND GENTLEMEN, THIS IS YOUR CRISIS
                                WILHELM, KATE        SS  ORB 76 18
ARMAJA DAS                      HALDEMAN, JOE W.     SS      76
BACK TO THE STONE AGE           SAUNDERS, JAKE       SS
MARY MARGARET ROAD-GRADER       WALDROP, HOWARD      SS  ORB 76 18
SAMURAI AND THE WILLOWS, THE    BISHOP, MICHAEL      NV  FSF 76 02

BEST SCIENCE FICTION STORIES 3, THE
                                SMITH, CORDELIA T.   AN  MFL 64
    SEE "GREAT SCIENCE FICTION STORIES"

BEST SCIENCE FICTION STORIES: FIFTH SERIES, THE
                                BLEILER & DIKTY      AN H GRY 56
    SEE "THE BEST SCIENCE-FICTION STORIES: 1954",
    OMITS STORIES BY LEIBER (2), MCINTOSH AND BESTER,
    "CRUCIFIXUS ETIAM" LISTED AS "THE SOWER DOES NOT REAP"
```

BEST SCIENCE FICTION STORIES: FOURTH SERIES, THE

BEST SF   3

BEST SCIENCE FICTION STORIES: FOURTH SERIES, THE
                          BLEILER & DIKTY   AN H GRY 55
    SEE "THE BEST SCIENCE-FICTION STORIES: 1953", OMITS
"THE FLY" AND "LOVER, WHEN YOU'RE NEAR ME"

BEST SCIENCE FICTION STORIES: SECOND SERIES, THE
                          BLEILER & DIKTY   AN H GRY 52
    SEE "THE BEST SCIENCE-FICTION STORIES: 1951", OMITS STORIES BY
TEMPLE, BESTER, HARNESS AND LEIBER

BEST SCIENCE FICTION STORIES: THIRD SERIES, THE
                          BLEILER & DIKTY   AN H GRY 53
    SEE "THE BEST SCIENCE-FICTION STORIES: 1952", OMITS
"DARK INTERLUDE" AND "THE PEDESTRIAN"

BEST SCIENCE-FICTION STORIES, THE
                          BLEILER & DIKTY   AN H GRY 51
    SEE "THE BEST SCIENCE-FICTION STORIES: 1950", OMITS STORIES BY
STURGEON, KREPPS, BRADBURY (2) AND MACDONALD

BEST SCIENCE-FICTION STORIES: 1949, THE
                          BLEILER & DIKTY   AN H FEL 49 08
    ALSO IN "SCIENCE FICTION OMNIBUS"
TRENDS IN MODERN SCIENCE-FICTION
                          KORSHAK, MELVIN   IN
MARS IS HEAVEN¡   BRADBURY, RAY   SS   PLS 48 FL
EX MACHINA   PADGETT, LEWIS   NV   ASF 48 04
STRANGE CASE OF JOHN KINGMAN, THE
                          LEINSTER, MURRAY   SS   ASF 48 05
DOUGHNUT JOCKEY   FENNEL, ERIC   SS   BBM 48 05
THANG   GARDNER, MARTIN   SS   COM 48 FL
PERIOD PIECE   COUPLING, J. J.   SS   ASF 48 11
KNOCK   BROWN, FREDRIC   SS   TWS 48 12
GENIUS   ANDERSON, POUL   NV   ASF 48 12
AND THE MOON BE STILL AS BRIGHT
                          BRADBURY, RAY   SS   TWS 48 06
NO CONNECTION   ASIMOV, ISAAC   SS   ASF 48 06
IN HIDING   SHIRAS, WILMAR H.   NV   ASF 48 11
HAPPY ENDING   KUTTNER, HENRY   NV   TWS 48 08

BEST SCIENCE-FICTION STORIES: 1950, THE
                          BLEILER & DIKTY   AN H FEL 50 08
    ALSO IN "SCIENCE FICTION OMNIBUS"
    IN ENGLAND AS "THE BEST SCIENCE FICTION STORIES"
SORT OF INTRODUCTION, A   STARRETT, VINCENT   IN
PRIVATE EYE   KUTTNER, HENRY   NV   ASF 49 01
DOOMSDAY DEFERRED   JENKINS, WILL F.   SS   SEP 49 09
HURKLE IS A HAPPY BEAST, THE STURGEON, THEODORE SS   FSF 49 FL
ETERNITY LOST   SIMAK, CLIFFORD D.   NV   ASF 49 07
EASTER EGGS (ALSO AS THOSE MEN FROM MARS)
                          CARR, ROBERT S.   NV   SEP 49 09
OPENING DOORS   SHIRAS, WILMAR H.   NV   ASF 49 03
FIVE YEARS IN THE MARMALADE KREPPS, ROBERT W.   SS   FAD 49 07
DWELLERS IN SILENCE (THE LONG YEARS)
                          BRADBURY, RAY   SS   MCL 48 09
MOUSE   BROWN, FREDRIC   SS   TWS 49 06
REFUGE FOR TONIGHT   WILLIAMS, ROBERT M. NV   BBM 49 03
LIFE-WORK OF PROFESSOR MUNTZ, THE
                          LEINSTER, MURRAY   SS   TWS 49 06
FLAW   MACDONALD, JOHN D.   SS   STS 49 01
MAN, THE   BRADBURY, RAY   SS   TWS 49 02
ABOUT THE AUTHORS   MISC. MATERIAL   MS

BEST SCIENCE-FICTION STORIES: 1951, THE
                          BLEILER & DIKTY   AN H FEL 51
    IN ENGLAND AS
"THE BEST SCIENCE FICTION STORIES: SECOND SERIES"
SANTA CLAUS PLANET, THE ROBINSON, FRANK M.   SS   NEW 51 AN
GNURRS COME FROM THE VOODVORK OUT, THE
                          BRETNOR, REGINALD   SS   FSF 50 WS
MINDWORM, THE   KORNBLUTH, C. M.   SS   WBY 50 12
STAR DUCKS, THE   BROWN, BILL   SS   FSF 50 FL
NOT TO BE OPENED—   YOUNG, ROBERT F.   NV   ASF 50 01
PROCESS   VAN VOGT, A. E.   SS   FSF 50 12
FORGET-ME-NOT   TEMPLE, WILLIAM F.   NV   OWS 50 09
CONTAGION   MACLEAN, KATHERINE   NV   GAL 50 10
TRESPASS¡   ANDERSON, POUL
                      AND DICKSON, GORDON R. SS C FSQ 50 SP
ODDY AND ID (THE DEVIL'S INVENTION)
                          BESTER, ALFRED   SS   ASF 50 08
TO SERVE MAN   KNIGHT, DAMON   SS   GAL 50 11
SUMMER WEAR   DE CAMP, L. SPRAGUE SS   STS 50 05
BORN OF MAN AND WOMAN MATHESON, RICHARD   SS   FSF 50 SU
FOX AND THE FOREST, THE (TO THE FUTURE)
                          BRADBURY, RAY   SS   COL 50 05
LAST MARTIAN, THE   BROWN, FREDRIC   SS   GAL 50 10
NEW REALITY, THE   HARNESS, CHARLES L. NV   TWS 50 12
TWO FACE   LONG, FRANK BELKNAP SS   WRT 50 03
COMING ATTRACTION   LEIBER, FRITZ   SS   GAL 50 11
ABOUT THE AUTHORS   MISC. MATERIAL   MS

BEST SCIENCE-FICTION STORIES: 1952, THE
                          BLEILER & DIKTY   AN H FEL 52
    IN ENGLAND AS "THE BEST SCIENCE FICTION STORIES: THIRD SERIES"
OTHER SIDE, THE (ETERNAL EARTHLING)
                          KUBILIUS, WALTER   SS   SSS 51 04
OF TIME AND THIRD AVENUE BESTER, ALFRED   SS   FSF 51 10
MARCHING MORONS, THE   KORNBLUTH, C. M.   NV   GAL 51 04
PECULIAR PEOPLE, A   CURTIS, BETSY   SS   FSF 51 08
EXTENDING THE HOLDINGS GRINNELL, DAVID   SS   FSF 51 04
TOURIST TRADE, THE   TUCKER, WILSON   SS   WBY 51 01
TWO SHADOWS, THE   TEMPLE, WILLIAM F.   NV   STS 51 03
BALANCE   CHRISTOPHER, JOHN   SS   NWS 51 SP
BRIGHTNESS FALLS FROM THE AIR (CONTEST STORY)
                          SEABRIGHT, IDRIS   SS   FSF 51 04
WITCH WAR   MATHESON, RICHARD   SS   STS 51 07

AT NO EXTRA COST   PHILLIPS, PETER   SS   MSS 51 08
NINE-FINGER JACK   BOUCHER, ANTHONY   SS   ESQ 51 05
APPOINTMENT IN TOMORROW (ALSO AS POOR SUPERMAN)
                          LEIBER, FRITZ   NV   GAL 51 07
RATS, THE   PORGES, ARTHUR   SS   MSW 51 02
MEN OF THE TEN BOOKS   VANCE, JACK   SS   STS 51 03
GENERATION OF NOAH   TENN, WILLIAM   SS   SUS 51 SP
DARK INTERLUDE   BROWN, FREDRIC
                      AND REYNOLDS, MACK   SS C GAL 51 01
PEDESTRIAN, THE (REP 51 08) BRADBURY, RAY   SS   FSF 52 02
ABOUT THE AUTHORS   MISC. MATERIAL   MS

BEST SCIENCE-FICTION STORIES: 1953, THE
                          BLEILER & DIKTY   AN H FEL 53
    IN ENGLAND AS
"THE BEST SCIENCE FICTION STORIES: FOURTH SERIES"
TREMATODE, A CRITIQUE OF MODERN SCIENCE-FICTION
                          BESTER, ALFRED   BR
FLY, THE   PORGES, ARTHUR   SS   FSF 52 09
ARARAT   HENDERSON, ZENNA   SS   FSF 52 10
COUNTER-TRANSFERENCE   TEMPLE, WILLIAM F.   NV   TWS 52 04
CONQUEROR, THE   CLIFTON, MARK   SS   ASF 52 08
MACHINE   JAKES, JOHN W.   SS   FSF 52 04
MIDDLE OF THE WEEK AFTER NEXT, THE
                          LEINSTER, MURRAY   SS   TWS 52 08
DREAMER, THE   COPPEL, ALFRED   SS   FSF 52 04
MOON IS GREEN, THE   LEIBER, FRITZ   SS   GAL 52 05
I AM NOTHING   RUSSELL, ERIC FRANK SS   ASF 52 07
COMMAND PERFORMANCE (ALSO AS ANYBODY ELSE LIKE ME?)
                          MILLER, WALTER M. JR NV   GAL 52 11
SURVIVAL   WYNDHAM, JOHN   NV   TWS 52 02
GAME FOR BLONDES   MACDONALD, JOHN D.   NV   GAL 52 10
GIRLS FROM EARTH, THE   ROBINSON, FRANK M.   NV   GAL 52 01
LOVER, WHEN YOU'RE NEAR ME MATHESON, RICHARD   NV   GAL 52 05
FAST FALLS THE EVENTIDE RUSSELL, ERIC FRANK SS   ASF 52 05
ABOUT THE AUTHORS   MISC. MATERIAL   MS

BEST SCIENCE-FICTION STORIES: 1954, THE
                          BLEILER & DIKTY   AN H FEL 54
    IN ENGLAND AS "THE BEST SCIENCE FICTION STORIES: FIFTH SERIES"
EDITORS' PREFACE   BLEILER, EVERETT F.
                      AND DIKTY, T. E.   IN C
ICON OF THE IMAGINATION LEIBER, FRITZ   IN
DP¡   VANCE, JACK   NV   AVS 53 04
BIG HOLIDAY, THE   LEIBER, FRITZ   SS   FSF 53 01
COLLECTORS, THE   DEWEY, G. GORDON
                      AND DANCEY, MAX   SS C AMZ 53 07
ONE IN THREE HUNDRED   MCINTOSH, J. T.   NV   FSF 53 02
WONDER CHILD   SHALLIT, JOSEPH   NV   FAN 53 01
CRUCIFIXUS ETIAM   MILLER, WALTER M. JR SS   ASF 53 02
MODEL OF A JUDGE, THE   MORRISON, WILLIAM   SS   GAL 53 10
LAST DAY, THE   MATHESON, RICHARD   SS   AMZ 53 08
TIME IS THE TRAITOR   BESTER, ALFRED   NV   FSF 53 09
LOT   MOORE, WARD   NV   FSF 53 05
YANKEE EXODUS   GOLDSMITH, RUTH M.   SS   FSF 53 07
WHAT THIN PARTITIONS   CLIFTON, MARK
                      AND APOSTOLIDES, ALEX NV C ASF 53 09
BAD DAY FOR SALES, A   LEIBER, FRITZ   SS   GAL 53 07
ABOUT THE AUTHORS   MISC. MATERIAL   MS
INDEX, THE BEST SCIENCE-FICTION STORIES: 1949-1954
                          MISC. MATERIAL   MS

BEST SF   CRISPIN, EDMUND   AN H FAB 55
INTRODUCTION   CRISPIN, EDMUND   IN
DORMANT   VAN VOGT, A. E.   SS   STS 48 11
PICTURES DON'T LIE   MACLEAN, KATHERINE   SS   GAL 51 08
DUMB MARTIAN   WYNDHAM, JOHN   NV   GAL 52 07
OR ELSE   KUTTNER, HENRY   SS   AMZ 53 09
NO WOMAN BORN   MOORE, C. L.   NV   ASF 44 12
FIRE BALLOONS, THE (IN THIS SIGN)
                          BRADBURY, RAY   SS   IMG 51 04
NEW WINE, THE   CHRISTOPHER, JOHN   SS   FSM 54 SU
PROTT   ST. CLAIR, MARGARET SS   GAL 53 01
PRESENT FROM JOE, A   RUSSELL, ERIC FRANK SS   ASF 49 02
CEREBRATIVE PSITTACOID, THE NEARING, H. JR.   SS   FSF 53 08
FIRST LADY   MCINTOSH, J. T.   NV   GAL 53 06
RUUM, THE   PORGES, ARTHUR   SS   FSF 53 10
XI EFFECT, THE   LATHAM, PHILIP   SS   ASF 50 01
CASE OF CONSCIENCE, A   BLISH, JAMES   SN   IFS 53 09

BEST SF 2   CRISPIN, EDMUND   AN H FAB 56
INTRODUCTION   CRISPIN, EDMUND   IN
ALTAR AT MIDNIGHT, THE KORNBLUTH, C. M.   SS   GAL 52 11
HOBSON'S CHOICE   BESTER, ALFRED   SS   FSF 52 08
OUTSIDE   ALDISS, BRIAN W.   SS   NWS 55 01
ANGEL'S EGG   PANGBORN, EDGAR   NV   GAL 51 06
PLACET IS A CRAZY PLACE BROWN, FREDRIC   SS   ASF 46 05
LITTLE LOST ROBOT   ASIMOV, ISAAC   SS   ASF 47 03
COPPER DAHLIA, THE   KERSH, GERALD   SS   53
WHEN YOU'RE SMILING   STURGEON, THEODORE   NV   GAL 55 01
ZERO HOUR   BRADBURY, RAY   SS   PLS 47 FL
WORRYWORT   SIMAK, CLIFFORD D.   SS   GAL 53 09
UNA (THE PERFECT CREATURE, TOW 37 01)
                          WYNDHAM, JOHN   NV   FSF 53 07
BLOWUPS HAPPEN   HEINLEIN, ROBERT A. NV   ASF 40 09
IMPOSTOR   DICK, PHILIP K.   SS   ASF 53 06
NINE BILLION NAMES OF GOD, THE
                          CLARKE, ARTHUR C.   SS   STR 53 01

BEST SF 3   CRISPIN, EDMUND   AN H FAB 58
INTRODUCTION   CRISPIN, EDMUND   IN
GRENVILLE'S PLANET   SHAARA, MICHAEL   SS   FSF 52 10
COUNTERSPY   EDWARDS, KELLEY   SS   ASF 53 12
WABBLER, THE   LEINSTER, MURRAY   SS   ASF 42 10
FOOD TO ALL FLESH   HENDERSON, ZENNA   SS   FSF 53 07
HE WALKED AROUND THE HORSES PIPER, H. BEAM   NV   ASF 48 04

BEST SF 3   BEST SF: 1967

AVAILABLE DATA ON THE WORP REACTION, THE   MULTI-VALUE MOTORWAY   ALDISS, BRIAN W.   NV NWS 67 08
                    MILLER, LION   SS FSF 53 09   GREAT CLOCK, THE   JONES, LANGDON   SS NWS 66 03
COLD EQUATIONS, THE GODWIN, TOM   NV ASF 54 08   POST-MORTEM PEOPLE, THE (ALSO AS BEYOND THE WEEDS)
GIFT OF GAB, THE   VANCE, JACK   NV ASF 55 09   TATE, PETER   SS NWS 66 03
FOUR IN ONE   KNIGHT, DAMON   NV GAL 53 02   DISASTER STORY, THE   PLATT, CHARLES   AR NWS 66 03
GAME OF RAT AND DRAGON, THE SMITH, CORDWAINER NV GAL 55 10 HEAT DEATH OF THE UNIVERSE, THE
ANSWER   BROWN, FREDRIC   SS NEW 54 AC   ZOLINE, PAMELA A.   SS NWS 67 07
                                                         CORANDA   ROBERTS, KEITH   SS NWS 67 01
BEST SF 4   CRISPIN, EDMUND   AN H FAB 61   SOFT WORLD SEQUENCE, THE   MACBETH, GEORGE   PM NWS 67 07
INTRODUCTION   CRISPIN, EDMUND   IN   KAZOO   SALLIS, JAMES   SS NWS 67 08
SHORT LIFE, THE   DONOVAN, FRANCIS   SN ASF 55 10   INTEGRITY   WOODS, P. F.   SS NWS 64 10
SUBWAY NAMED MOBIUS, A DEUTSCH, A. J. SS ASF 50 12   MOUNTAIN, THE   COLVIN, JAMES   SS NWS 65 02
IT'S A GOOD LIFE   BIXBY, JEROME   SS STR 53 02
FLOWERS FOR ALGERNON KEYES, DANIEL   SS FSF 59 04   BEST SF STORIES FROM NEW WORLDS 4
BALAAM   BOUCHER, ANTHONY   SS NTL 54   MOORCOCK, MICHAEL   AN BKM 69
YELLOW PILL, THE   PHILLIPS, ROG   SS ASF 58 10   INTRODUCTION   MOORCOCK, MICHAEL   IN
BLISS OF SOLITUDE, THE (HALLUCINATION ORBIT)   SHIP OF DISASTER, THE   BAYLEY, BARRINGTON J SS NWS 65 06
                    MCINTOSH, J. T.   NV GAL 52 01   SQUARE ROOT OF BRAIN, THE LEIBER, FRITZ   SS NWS 68 02
PSYCLOPS   ALDISS, BRIAN W.   SS NWS 56 07   IN SECLUSION   JACOBS, HARVEY   SS NWS 68 02
HOBBYIST   RUSSELL, ERIC FRANK NV ASF 47 09   TRANSIENT   JONES, LANGDON   SS NWS 65 12
BAXBR DAXBR   SMITH, EVELYN E.   SS FSF 56 09   HEAD-RAPE, THE   THOMAS, D. M.   PM NWS 68 03
                                                         SOURCE, THE   ALDISS, BRIAN W.   SS NWS 65 08
BEST SF 5   CRISPIN, EDMUND   AN H FAB 63   PERIOD OF GESTATION   KEYES, THOM   SS SCP 64 10
INTRODUCTION   CRISPIN, EDMUND   IN   DR. GELABIUS   BAILEY, HILARY   SS NWS 68 04
ON HANDLING THE DATA HIRSHFIELD, HENRY I.   VALVE TRANSCRIPT, THE   ZOSS, JOEL   SS NWS 68 04
                    AND MATEYKO, G. M. SS C ASF 59 09   LINDA AND DANIEL AND SPIKE DISCH, THOMAS M.   SS NWS 67 12
NOISE LEVEL   JONES, RAYMOND F.   NV ASF 52 12   MASTERSON AND THE CLERKS   SLADEK, JOHN T.   SS NWS 67 09
GREEN THUMB   SIMAK, CLIFFORD D. NV GAL 54 07
QUEST FOR SAINT AQUIN, THE BOUCHER, ANTHONY SS NTS 51 BEST SF STORIES FROM NEW WORLDS 5
MONSTERS, THE   SHECKLEY, ROBERT   SS FSF 53 03   MOORCOCK, MICHAEL   AN BKM 69
WHO CAN REPLACE A MAN? (BUT WHO CAN REPLACE A MAN)   INTRODUCTION   MOORCOCK, MICHAEL   IN
                    ALDISS, BRIAN W.   SS INF 58 06   LAST HURRAH OF THE GOLDEN HORDE, THE
PRISONER, THE   ANVIL, CHRISTOPHER SS ASF 56 02   SPINRAD, NORMAN   SS NWS 69 07
STAR, THE   CLARKE, ARTHUR C.   SS INF 55 11   DEATH MODULE, THE (ALSO AS NOTES TOWARD A MENTAL BREAKDOWN)
CONSIDER HER WAYS   WYNDHAM, JOHN   NV 56   BALLARD, J. G.   SS NWS 67 07
MARTYR, THE   ANDERSON, POUL   NV FSF 60 03   LAST INN ON THE ROAD, THE ZELAZNY, ROGER
LATER THAN YOU THINK LEIBER, FRITZ   SS GAL 50 10   AND PLACHTA, DANNIE SS C NWS 67 10
                                                         SPECTRUM, THE   THOMAS, D. M.   PM NWS 69 02
BEST SF 6   CRISPIN, EDMUND   AN H FAB 66   TENNYSON EFFECT, THE   HALL, GRAHAM M.   SS NWS 66 11
FOREWORD   CRISPIN, EDMUND   IN   SERPENT OF KUNDALINI, THE ALDISS, BRIAN W.   SS NWS 68 02
JUDAS BOMB   REED, KIT   SS FSF 61 04   MARS PASTORALE   TATE, PETER   SS NWS 67 08
WORK OF ART, A (ART-WORK) BLISH, JAMES SS SFS 56 07   BIOGRAPHICAL NOTE ON LUDWIG VAN BEETHOVEN II
LIFE AND A HALF, A POHL, FREDERIK   SS IFS 59 07   JONES, LANGDON   FA NWS 68 10
STAR DUCKS, THE   BROWN, BILL   SS FSF 50 FL   LANDSCAPE OF SHALLOWS, A   FINCH, CHRISTOPHER SS NWS 68 07
WAITABITS, THE   RUSSELL, ERIC FRANK NV ASF 55 07   SCREAM   GORDON, GILES   SS NWS 68 07
FLY, THE   PORGES, ARTHUR   SS FSF 52 09   RODENT LABORATORY, THE   PLATT, CHARLES   SS NWS 66 08
KALEIDOSCOPE   BRADBURY, RAY   SS TWS 49 10
NOSTALGIA GENE, THE HUTCHINS, ROY   SS GAL 54 11   BEST SF STORIES FROM NEW WORLDS 6
CAMOUFLAGE   KUTTNER, HENRY   NV ASF 45 09   MOORCOCK, MICHAEL   AN BKM 70
LETTER TO A PHOENIX BROWN, FREDRIC   SS ASF 49 08   INTRODUCTION   MOORCOCK, MICHAEL   IN
DEATH MARCH   BUDRYS, ALGIS   NV ASF 56 10   KILLING GROUND, THE   BALLARD, J. G.   SS NWS 69 03
WEAPON   CHRISTOPHER, JOHN   SS NEW 54 AC   GRAVITY   JACOBS, HARVEY   SS NWS 69 08
BILLENIUM   BALLARD, J. G.   SS NWS 61 11   EYE OF THE LENS, THE   JONES, LANGDON   SS NWS 68 03
OLD HUNDREDTH   ALDISS, BRIAN W.   SS NWS 60 11   MAN MUST DIE, A   CLUTE, JOHN   SS NWS 66 11
                                                         IN REASON'S EAR   BAILEY, HILARY   SS SCP 65 06
BEST SF 7   CRISPIN, EDMUND   AN H FAB 70   ERSATZ WINE, THE   PRIEST, CHRISTOPHER SS NWS 67 02
FOREWORD   CRISPIN, EDMUND   IN   LIB   EMSHWILLER, CAROL   SS NWS 68 03
CHILDREN OF NIGHT, THE POHL, FREDERIK NV GAL 64 10   BAA BAA BLOCKSHEEP   HARRISON, M. JOHN   SS NWS 68 11
HARRISON BERGERON   VONNEGUT, KURT JR. SS FSF 61 10   LUGER IS A 9MM AUTOMATIC HANDGUN WITH A PARABELLUM ACTION, THE
WAY OUT IN THE CONTINUUM RICHARDSON, MAURICE SS HOR   MUNDIS, JERROLD J. SS NWS 69 03
MACHINE THAT WON THE WAR, THE   DELHI DIVISION, THE   MOORCOCK, MICHAEL   SS NWS 68 12
                    ASIMOV, ISAAC   SS FSF 61 10
ULTIMA THULE   RUSSELL, ERIC FRANK SS ASF 51 10   BEST SF STORIES FROM NEW WORLDS 7
HERESIES OF THE HUGE GOD ALDISS, BRIAN W. FA GAL 66 08   MOORCOCK, MICHAEL   AN PTH 71
DOORS OF HIS FACE, THE LAMPS OF HIS MOUTH, THE   INTRODUCTION   MOORCOCK, MICHAEL   IN
                    ZELAZNY, ROGER   NV FSF 65 03   ASH CIRCUS, THE   HARRISON, M. JOHN   SS NWS 69 04
SNUFFLES   LAFFERTY, R. A.   NV GAL 60 12   ALL THE KING'S MEN   BAYLEY, BARRINGTON J NV NWS 65 03
COFFIN CURE, THE   NOURSE, ALAN E.   SS GAL 57 04   MIX-UP   COLLYN, GEORGE   SS NWS 64 12
MUSIC MASTER OF BABYLON, THE PANGBORN, EDGAR NV GAL 54 11 TIME CONSIDERED AS A HELIX OF SEMI-PRECIOUS STONES
PROTECT ME FROM MY FRIENDS BRUNNER, JOHN SS FSF 62 11   DELANY, SAMUEL R.   SS NWS 68 12
COME TO VENUS MELANCHOLY DISCH, THOMAS M. SS FSF 65 11 LONE ZONE   PLATT, CHARLES   SS NWS 65 07
                                                         FLOWER-GATHERING   JONES, LANGDON   PM NWS 69 06
BEST SF STORIES FROM NEW WORLDS NO. 1, THE   TRANSPLANT   JONES, LANGDON   PM NWS 69 10
                    MOORCOCK, MICHAEL   AN BKM 67   APOCALYPSE MACHINE, THE   ZORIN, LEO   SS NWS 68 12
INTRODUCTION   MOORCOCK, MICHAEL   IN   BEACH MURDERS, THE (CONFETTI ROYALE, ROG 66 01)
SMALL BETRAYING DETAIL, THE ALDISS, BRIAN W. SS NWS 65 05   BALLARD, J. G.   SS NWS 69 04
KEYS TO DECEMBER, THE ZELAZNY, ROGER   SS NWS 66 08   WALL, THE   SAXTON, JOSEPHINE   SS SCP 65 11
ASSASSINATION WEAPON, THE BALLARD, J. G. SS NWS 66 04 TANK TRAPEZE, THE   MOORCOCK, MICHAEL   SS NWS 69 01
NOBODY AXED YOU   BRUNNER, JOHN   NV NWS 65 05
TWO-TIMER, A   MASSON, DAVID I.   NV NWS 66 02   BEST SF STORIES FROM NEW WORLDS 8
MUSIC MAKERS, THE   JONES, LANGDON   SS NWS 65 11   MOORCOCK, MICHAEL   AN PTH 74
SQUIRREL CAGE, THE DISCH, THOMAS M.   SS NWS 66 10   BOY AND HIS DOG, A   ELLISON, HARLAN   NV NWS 69 04
                                                         FALL OF FRENCHY STEINER, THE BAILEY, HILARY   NV NWS 64 08
BEST SF STORIES FROM NEW WORLDS NO. 2, THE   BAIT PRINCIPLE, THE   HARRISON, M. JOHN   SS NWS 70 02
                    MOORCOCK, MICHAEL   AN BKM 68   SALVADOR DALI   BALLARD, J. G.   AR NWS 69 02
INTRODUCTION   MOORCOCK, MICHAEL   IN   LAST LONELY MAN, THE   BRUNNER, JOHN   SS NWS 64 06
ANOTHER LITTLE BOY ALDISS, BRIAN W.   SS NWS 66 09   RADIUS RIDERS, THE   BAYLEY, BARRINGTON J SS SPB 62 07
POETS OF MILLGROVE IOWA, THE SLADEK, JOHN T. SS NWS 66 11 BIG SOUND, THE   BAYLEY, BARRINGTON J SS SPB 62 02
TRANSFINITE CHOICE, THE MASSON, DAVID I. SS NWS 66 08 SHIP THAT SAILED THE OCEAN OF SPACE, THE
YOU: COMA: MARILYN MONROE BALLARD, J. G. SS NWS 66 06   BAYLEY, BARRINGTON J SS NWS
TOTAL EXPERIENCE KICK, THE PLATT, CHARLES SS NWS 66 12 DOUBLE TIME   BAYLEY, BARRINGTON J SS NWS 62 07
CONTEST, THE   DISCH, THOMAS M.   SS NWS 67 03   EROGENOUS ZONE, THE   CHARNOCK, GRAHAM   SS NWS 69 07
EMPTY ROOM, THE   DISCH, THOMAS M.   SS NWS 67 03
DESCENT OF THE WEST END, THE DISCH, THOMAS M. SS NWS 67 03 BEST SF: 1967   HARRISON & ALDISS   AN BKM 68 03
SINGULAR QUEST OF MARTIN BORG, THE   IN ENGLAND AS "THE YEAR'S BEST SCIENCE FICTION NO. 1"
                    COLLYN, GEORGE   SS NWS 65 02   INTRODUCTION   HARRISON, HARRY   IN
COUNTENANCE, THE   WOODS, P. F.   SS NWS 64 01   CREDO   BLISH, JAMES   IN
PLEASURE GARDEN OF FELIPE SAGITTARIUS, THE   HAWKSBILL STATION   SILVERBERG, ROBERT NV GAL 67 08
                    COLVIN, JAMES   SS NWS 65 09   ULTIMATE CONSTRUCTION   SHACKLETON, C. C.   SS TBT 67
SISOHPROMATEM   REED, KIT   SS NWS 67 01   1937 A.D.!   SLADEK, JOHN T.   SS NWS 67 07
FOR A BREATH I TARRY ZELAZNY, ROGER   NV NWS 66 03   FIFTEEN MILES   BOVA, BEN   SS FSF 67 05
                                                         BLACKMAIL   HOYLE, FRED   SS FSF 67 02
BEST SF STORIES FROM NEW WORLDS 3   VINE, THE   REED, KIT   SS FSF 67 11
                    MOORCOCK, MICHAEL   AN BKM 68   INTERVIEW WITH A LEMMING   THURBER, JAMES   SS   43
INTRODUCTION   MOORCOCK, MICHAEL   IN   WRECK OF THE SHIP JOHN B., THE
IN PASSAGE OF THE SUN COLLYN, GEORGE   SS NWS 66 07   ROBINSON, FRANK M. NV PBY 67 06

BEST SF: 1967

```
LEFT-HAND WAY, THE           CHANDLER, A. BERTRAM SS    AUS 67
FOREST OF ZIL, THE           NEVILLE, KRIS        SS    AMZ 67 12
ASSASSINATION OF JOHN FITZGERALD KENNEDY CONSIDERED AS A
  DOWNHILL MOTOR RACE, THE   BALLARD, J. G.       SS    NWS 67 02
ANSWERING SERVICE            LEIBER, FRITZ        SS    IFS 67 12
LAST COMMAND, THE            LAUMER, KEITH        SS    ASF 67 01
MIRROR OF ICE                WRIGHT, GARY         SS    GAL 67 06
PRETTY MAGGIE MONEYEYES      ELLISON, HARLAN      NV    KNT 67 05
KNIGHTS OF THE PAPER SPACESHIP: A RETROSPECTIVE GLANCE AT
  SCIENCE FICTION            ALDISS, BRIAN W.     MS

BEST SF: 1968            HARRISON & ALDISS   AN H PUT 69
  IN ENGLAND AS "THE YEAR'S BEST SCIENCE FICTION NO. 2"
INTRODUCTION                 HARRISON, HARRY      IN
BUDGET PLANET                SHECKLEY, ROBERT     EX    FSF 68 03
APPOINTMENT ON PRILA         SHAW, BOB            SS    ASF 68 08
LOST GROUND                  MASSON, DAVID I.     SS    NWS 66 12
RIME OF THE ANCIENT SF AUTHOR,OF CONVENTIONS AND RECOLLECTIONS
                             PIERCE, JOHN R.      PM         68
ANNEX, THE                   MACDONALD, JOHN D.   SS    PBY 68 05
SEGREGATIONIST               ASIMOV, ISAAC        SS    ABB 67 04
FINAL WAR                    O'DONNELL, K. M.     NV    FSF 68 04
2001: A SPACE ODYSSEY- REVIEW 1
                             DEL REY, LESTER      MR    GAL 68 07
2001: A SPACE ODYSSEY- REVIEW 2
                             DELANY, SAMUEL R.    MR    FSF 68 08
2001: A SPACE ODYSSEY- REVIEW 3
                             EMSHWILLER, ED       MR    FSF 68 08
2001: A SPACE ODYSSEY- REVIEW 4
                             STOVER, LEON E.      MR    AMZ 69 03
SERPENT OF KUNDALINI, THE    ALDISS, BRIAN W.     SS    NWS 68 02
GOLDEN ACRES                 REED, KIT            NV         68
CRIMINAL IN UTOPIA           REYNOLDS, MACK       NV    GAL 68 10
ONE STATION OF THE WAY       LEIBER, FRITZ        SS    GAL 68 12
SWEET DREAMS, MELISSA        GOLDIN, STEPHEN      SS    GAL 68 12
TO THE DARK STAR             SILVERBERG, ROBERT   SS    PRS 68
HOUSE THAT JULES BUILT, THE  ALDISS, BRIAN W.     MS

BEST SF: 1969            HARRISON & ALDISS   AN H PUT 70
  IN ENGLAND AS "THE YEAR'S BEST SCIENCE FICTION NO. 3"
INTRODUCTION                 HARRISON, HARRY      IN
MUSE, THE                    BURGESS, ANTHONY     SS    HUD 68
WORKING IN THE SPACESHIP YARDS
                             ALDISS, BRIAN W.     SS    PUN 69 04
SCHEMATIC MAN, THE           POHL, FREDERIK       SS    PBY 69 01
SNOWS ARE MELTED, THE SNOWS ARE GONE, THE
                             TIPTREE, JAMES JR.   SS    VSF 69 11
HOSPITAL OF TRANSPLANTED HEARTS
                             THOMAS, D. M.        SS    NWS 69 01
ECO-CATASTROPHE!             EHRLICH, DR. PAUL R. SS    RAM 69 09
CASTLE ON THE CRAG, THE      WYAL, PG             SS    FAN 69 02
NINE LIVES                   LE GUIN, URSULA K.   NV    PBY 69 11
PROGRESSION OF THE SPECIES   ALDISS, BRIAN W.     PM    PRP 67 SP
REPORT BACK                  COTTON, JOHN         PM         69
KILLING GROUND, THE          BALLARD, J. G.       SS    NWS 69 03
DANNOLD CHEQUE, THE          PURDY, KEN W.        SS    PBY 69 09
WOMB TO TOMB                 WESLEY, JOSEPH       SS    ASF 69 08
LIKE FATHER                  HARTRIDGE, JON       SS    NWS 69 08
ELECTRIC ANT, THE            DICK, PHILIP K.      NV    FSF 69 10
MAN INSIDE, THE              MCALLISTER, BRUCE    SS    GAL 69 05
NOW HEAR THE WORD OF THE LORD
                             BUDRYS, ALGIS        SS    GAL 69 02
AWFUL LOT OF COPY, AN        ALDISS, BRIAN W.     MS

BEST SF: 1970            HARRISON & ALDISS   AN H PUT 71
  IN ENGLAND AS "THE YEAR'S BEST SCIENCE FICTION NO. 4"
GONE FISHIN'                 WILSON, ROBIN SCOTT  SS    FSF 70 10
UGUPU BIRD, THE              MROZEK, SLAWOMIR     SS
BLACK IS BEAUTIFUL           SILVERBERG, ROBERT   SS    YRT 70
LOST FACE, THE               NESVADBA, JOSEF      NV         64
MARY AND JOE                 MITCHISON, NAOMI     SS    NOV 70 01
GORMAN                       FARBER, JERRY        SS         69
OIL-MAD BUG-EYED MONSTERS    HOWARD, HAYDEN       SS    GAL 70 06
PEDESTRIAN ACCIDENT, A (INCIDENT IN THE STREETS OF THE CITY)
                             COOVER, ROBERT       SS    PBY 69 01
TRAFFIC PROBLEM              EARLS, WILLIAM       SS    GAL 70 10
ASIAN SHORE, THE             DISCH, THOMAS M.     NV    ORB 70 06
EREM                         ANFILOV, GLEB        SS         63
CAR SINISTER                 WOLFE, GENE          SS    FSF 70 01
"FRANZ KAFKA" BY JORGE LUIS BORGES
                             GREENBERG , ALVIN    SS    NAR 70 08
PACEM EST                    NEVILLE, KRIS
                             AND O'DONNELL, K. M. SS C INY 70 01
DAY EQUALITY BROKE OUT, THE  ALDISS, BRIAN W.     MS

BEST SF: 1971            HARRISON & ALDISS   AN H PUT 72
  IN ENGLAND AS "THE YEAR'S BEST SCIENCE FICTION NO. 5"
INTRODUCTION                 HARRISON, HARRY      IN
DOCTOR ZOMBIE AND HIS FURRY LITTLE FRIENDS
                             SHECKLEY, ROBERT     SS    NEW 71 AC
CONQUEST                     MALZBERG, BARRY N.   SS    NDM 71 01
GEHENNA                      MALZBERG, BARRY N.   SS    GAL 71 03
MEETING WITH MEDUSA, A       CLARKE, ARTHUR C.    NA    PBY 71 12
GENIUS, THE                  BARTHELME, DONALD    SS    NYM 71 02
ANGOULEME                    DISCH, THOMAS M.     SS    NWQ 71 01
IF "HAIR" WERE REVIVED IN 2016
                             AUERBACH, ARNOLD M.  FA    NYT 71
STATISTICIAN'S DAY           BLISH, JAMES         SS    SAG 70
SCIENCE FICTION HORROR MOVIE POCKET COMPUTER, THE
                             WILSON, GAHAN        MS    NLP 71 11
HUNTER AT HIS EASE, THE      ALDISS, BRIAN W.     SS    SAG 70
COHEN DOG EXCLUSION ACT, THE SCHRADER, STEVEN     SS    NEW 71 AN
GANTLET                      PECK, RICHARD E.     SS    ORB 72 10
REPORT                       AMIS, KINGSLEY       PM    NSM 71
FISHERMAN                    SAIL, LAWRENCE       PM    NSM 71
IDEAL POLICE STATE, THE      BAXTER, CHARLES      PM    LMG 71
```

BEST SF: 1974

```
PAGAN RABBI, THE             OZICK, CYNTHIA       NV         66
(UNTITLED) (FROM CANCERQUEEN)
                             LANDOLFI, TOMMASO    EX
UNEVEN EVENING, AN           HERBST, STEVE        SS    CLR 71 01
ORNITHANTHROPUS              BURHOE, B. ALAN      SS    IFS 71 12
NO DIRECTION HOME            SPINRAD, NORMAN      SS    NWQ 71 02
AFTERWORD: A DAY IN THE LIFE-STYLE OF...
                             ALDISS, BRIAN W.     MS

BEST SF: 1972            HARRISON & ALDISS   AN H PUT 73
  IN ENGLAND AS "THE YEAR'S BEST SCIENCE FICTION NO. 6"
INTRODUCTION                 HARRISON, HARRY      IN
IN THE MATTER OF THE ASSASSIN MEREFIRS
                             PURDY, KEN W.        SS    ASF 72 11
AS FOR OUR FATAL CONTINUITY...
                             ALDISS, BRIAN W.     SS    NWQ 72 03
OLD FOLKS, THE               GUNN, JAMES E.       SS    NOV 72 02
FROM SEA TO SHINING SEA      ELA, JONATHAN        FA    SCL 72
WEIHNACHTABEND               ROBERTS, KEITH       NV    NWQ 72 04
INVISIBILITY COMPETITION     ARATOVSKY, Y.        CT    PRI
CARTOON                      TESLER, O.           CT    SME
GRIN AND BEAR IT             LICHTY               CT    PHS 72 06
BEST SF: 1972                ROTSLER, WILLIAM     CT
YEARS, THE                   YOUNG, ROBERT F.     SS    GAL 72 09
DARKNESS (TRANSLATED BY LEO L. BARROW)
                             CARNEIRO, ANDRE      SS    NOV 72 02
CYMBAL PLAYER                SAIL, LAWRENCE       PM    CND 72
REPORT FROM THE PLANET PROTEUS
                             SAIL, LAWRENCE       PM    CND 72
COLUMBUS ON ST. DOMENICA     COTTON, JOHN         PM         72
AFTER DEATH                  BEER, PATRICIA       PM    NSM 72
FAEX DELENDA EST             COGSWELL, THEODORE R PM    CND 72
WORDS OF WARNING             HAMILTON, ALEX       SS         72
OUT, WIT!                    MYERS, HOWARD L.     SS    ASF 72 06
IMAGINARY JOURNEY TO THE MOON, AN
                             SABAH, VICTOR        SS    NEW 72 AN
HEAD AND THE HAND, THE       PRIEST, CHRISTOPHER  SS    NWQ 72 03
HERO                         HALDEMAN, JOE W.     NV    ASF 72 06
AFTERWORD: THE YEAR OF THE BIG SPRING CLEAN
                             ALDISS, BRIAN W.     MS

BEST SF: 1973            HARRISON & ALDISS   AN H PUT 74
  IN ENGLAND AS "THE YEAR'S BEST SCIENCE FICTION NO. 7"
INTRODUCTION                 HARRISON, HARRY      IN
ROLLER BALL MURDERS          HARRISON, WILLIAM    SS    ESQ 73 09
MASON'S LIFE                 AMIS, KINGSLEY       SS    SDT 72
WELCOME TO THE STANDARD NIGHTMARE
                             SHECKLEY, ROBERT     SS    NOV 73 03
SERPENT BURNING ON AN ALTAR  ALDISS, BRIAN W.     SS    ORB 73 12
WE ARE VERY HAPPY HERE       HALDEMAN, JOE W.     NV    ASF 73 11
BIRDS, THE                   DISCH, THOMAS M.     SS         73
WIND AND THE RAIN, THE       SILVERBERG, ROBERT   SS    SVW 73
TEN YEARS AGO...             BEERBOHM, MAX        SS         72
PARTHEN                      LAFFERTY, R. A.      SS    GAL 73 05
MAN WHO COLLECTED THE FIRST OF SEPTEMBER 1973, THE
                             BRINGSVAERD, TOR AGE SS         73
CAPTAIN NEMO'S LAST ADVENTURE
                             NESVADBA, JOSEF      NV         73
LA BEFANA                    WOLFE, GENE          SS    GAL 73 01
CURSE, A                     AUDEN, W. H.         PM    DTM 72
AUTO-APOTHEOSIS              HADEN-GUEST, ANTHONY PM    DTM 72
TWO POEMS                    WATKINS, WILLIAM JON PM    CND 73
SPORT                        UTLEY, STEVEN        PM    CND 73
WINDOWS IN DANTE'S HELL, THE BISHOP, MICHAEL      SS    ORB 73 12
SISTER FRANCETTA AND PIG BABY
                             BERNARD, KENNETH     SS    ARV 73 16
ESCAPE                       VARSHAVSKY, ILYA     SS         73
EARLY BIRD                   THOMAS, THEODORE L.
               AND COGSWELL, THEODORE R SS C AMA 73
AFTERWORD: THE WIZARD AND THE PLUMBER
                             ALDISS, BRIAN W.     MS

BEST SF: 1974            HARRISON & ALDISS   AN H BML 75
  IN ENGLAND AS "THE YEAR'S BEST SCIENCE FICTION NO. 8"
EDITORIAL                    HARRISON, HARRY      ED
AFTER KING KONG FELL         FARMER, PHILIP JOSE  SS    OMG 73
WHEN PETALS FALL             VAN SCYOC, SYDNEY J. NV    TVW 73
PALEONTOLOGY: AN EXPERIMENTAL SCIENCE
                             OLSEN, ROBERT R.     SS    ASF 74 08
WOMEN MEN DON'T SEE, THE     TIPTREE, JAMES JR.   NV    FSF 73 12
LISTEN WITH BIG BROTHER      ALDISS, BRIAN W.     SS
RISE OF AIRSTRIP ONE, THE    JAMES, CLIVE         SS
OWING TO CIRCUMSTANCES BEYOND OUR CONTROL 1984 HAS BEEN
  UNAVOIDABLY DETAINED       COREN, ALAN          SS    PUN
LOST AND FOUND               BAUM, THOMAS         SS
FOUR-HOUR FUGUE, THE         BESTER, ALFRED       SS    ASF 74 06
SCREAM, THE                  WILHELM, KATE        NV    ORB 74 13
GAHAN WILSON HORROR MOVIE POCKET COMPUTER, THE
                             WILSON, GAHAN        MS    NLP 74 05
EXECUTIONER'S BEAUTIFUL DAUGHTER, THE
                             CARTER, ANGELA       SS
AFTER WEIGHTLESSNESS         SAIL, LAWRENCE       PM         74
PICTURE BY KLEE, A           SAIL, LAWRENCE       PM
BACKWARD, INTO BEASTS EVOLVING
                             ALLEN, DICK          PM
SCIENCE FICTION STORY        ACKERSON, DUANE      PM    EDG 74
DNA                          ACKERSON, DUANE      PM
EYES OF A WOMAN- FROM A PORTRAIT BY PICASSO
                             CONESA, LISA         PM
SONGS OF WAR                 REED, KIT            NV    NOV 74 04
TIME DEER                    STRETE, CRAIG        SS    IFS 74 12
TYPICAL DAY, A               PISERCHIA, DORIS     SS    GAL 74 03
PROGRAMMED LOVE STORY        WATSON, IAN          SS    TRV 74
AFTERWORD: THE GALAXY BEGINS AT HOME
                             ALDISS, BRIAN W.     MS
```

BEST SF: 75, THE NINTH ANNUAL
                                  HARRISON & ALDISS   AN H BML 76
     IN ENGLAND AS "THE YEAR'S BEST SCIENCE FICTION NO. 9"
  INTRODUCTION   HARRISON, HARRY   IN
  SCRAPING AT THE BONES, A   BUDRYS, ALGIS   SS   ASF 75 05
  CHANGELINGS   TUTTLE, LISA   SS   GAL 75 03
  SANTA CLAUS COMPROMISE, THE   DISCH, THOMAS M.   SS   CRW 74 12
  GALAXY CALLED ROME, A   MALZBERG, BARRY N.   NV   FSF 75 07
  TWELVEMONTH, A   REDGROVE, PETER   SS   NYT
  CUSTODIANS, THE   COWPER, RICHARD   NV   FSF 75 10
  LINGUIST, THE (AS TAK HALLUS)
                                  ROBINETT, STEPHEN   SS   GAL 75 02
  SETTLING THE WORLD   HARRISON, M. JOHN   NV   NEW 75 AN
  CHASTE PLANET, THE   UPDIKE, JOHN   SS   75
  END GAME   HALDEMAN, JOE W.   NV   ASF 75 01
  LOP-EARED CAT THAT DEVOURED PHILADELPHIA, THE
                                  PHILLIPS, LOUIS   SS
  DEAD SINGER, A   MOORCOCK, MICHAEL   NV   74
  AFTERWORD: SCIENCE FICTION ON THE TITANIC
                                  ALDISS, BRIAN W.   MS

BEST STORIES OF H. G. WELLS WELLS, H. G.   AC   BAL 60 08
  LORD OF THE DYNAMOS, THE   WELLS, H. G.   SS   PMB 94 09
  PLATTNER STORY, THE   WELLS, H. G.   SS   NRV 96 04
  ARGONAUTS OF THE AIR, THE   WELLS, H. G.   SS   PMY 95
  STORY OF THE LATE MR. ELVESHAM, THE
                                  WELLS, H. G.   SS   IDL 96 05
  CRYSTAL EGG, THE   WELLS, H. G.   SS   NRV 97 05
  STAR, THE   WELLS, H. G.   SS   GRP 97 12
  MAN WHO COULD WORK MIRACLES, THE
                                  WELLS, H. G.   SS   ILN 98 07
  SEA-RAIDERS, THE   WELLS, H. G.   SS   WSL 96 12
  MAGIC SHOP, THE   WELLS, H. G.   SS   SND 03 06
  VALLEY OF SPIDERS, THE   WELLS, H. G.   SS   PRS 03 03
  TRUTH ABOUT PYECRAFT, THE   WELLS, H. G.   SS   SND 03 04
  LAND IRONCLADS, THE   WELLS, H. G.   NV   SND 03 12
  MR. SKELMERSDALE IN FAIRYLAND
                                  WELLS, H. G.   SS   SND 01
  NEW ACCELERATOR, THE   WELLS, H. G.   SS   SND 01 12
  DREAM OF ARMAGEDDON, A   WELLS, H. G.   NV   BAW 01
  STORY OF THE DAYS TO COME, A WELLS, H. G.   NA   PGZ 97

BEWARE MORE BEASTS   GHIDALIA, V.& ELWOOD AN   MAN 75
  WOLVES OF DARKNESS   WILLIAMSON, JACK   NA   STT 32 01
  LAURA   SAKI   SS   14
  BEYOND THE THRESHOLD   DERLETH, AUGUST   NV   WRT 41 09
  CREW OF THE LANCING, THE   HODGSON, WILLIAM H. SS
  IN THE STRAW   HOCH, EDWARD D.   SS   72
  SUMMARY OF EVENTS LEADING UP TO BEDLAM, A
                                  MALZBERG, BARRY N.   SS   72
  WORM, THE   SCORTIA, THOMAS N.   NV   72

BEWARE THE BEASTS   GHIDALIA, V.& ELWOOD AN   MBB 70
  IN THE AVU OBSERVATORY   WELLS, H. G.   SS   PMB 94 08
  CATS OF ULTHAR, THE   LOVECRAFT, H. P.   SS   TRY 20 11
  HERE, DAEMOS¡   DERLETH, AUGUST   SS   WRT 42 03
  HOUND, THE   LEIBER, FRITZ   SS   WRT 42 11
  HOUSE OF THE NIGHTMARE, THE   WHITE, EDWARD LUCAS SS   TTB 19 09
  MARK OF THE BEAST, THE   KIPLING, RUDYARD   SS   PIO 90 07
  SQUAW, THE   STOKER, BRAM   SS   93
  METZENGERSTEIN   POE, EDGAR ALLEN   SS   SLM 36 02
  TORTOISE-SHELL CAT, THE   LA SPINA, GREYE   SS   WRT 24 11
  WENDIGO, THE (1910)   BLACKWOOD, ALGERNON NV   PFM 44 06

BEYOND   ANONYMOUS   AN   BKM 63 01
  WATCHFUL POKER CHIP OF H. MATISSE, THE
                                  BRADBURY, RAY   SS   BEY 54 03
  GHOST MAKER, THE   POHL, FREDERIK   SS   BEY 54 01
  CAN SUCH BEAUTY BE?   BIXBY, JEROME   SS   BEY 53 09
  REAL PEOPLE, THE   BUDRYS, ALGIS   NA   BEY 53 11
  BEAUTIFUL BREW, THE   GUNN, JAMES E.   NV   BEY 54 09
  I'D GIVE A DOLLAR   MARKS, WINSTON K.   SS   BEY 54 05
  ROOT AND THE RING, THE   GUIN, WYMAN   NV   BEY 54 09
  NATURALLY (DOUBLE WHAMMY)   BROWN, FREDRIC   SS   BEY 54 09
  VOODOO (DOUBLE WHAMMY)   BROWN, FREDRIC   SS   BEY 54 09
  TALENT   STURGEON, THEODORE   SS   BEY 53 09

BEYOND   STURGEON, THEODORE   AC   AVN 60
  NEED   STURGEON, THEODORE   NV   NEW 60 AC
  ABREACTION   STURGEON, THEODORE   SS   WRT 48 07
  NIGHTMARE ISLAND   STURGEON, THEODORE   NV   UNK 41 06
  LARGO   STURGEON, THEODORE   SS   FAD 47 07
  BONES, THE   STURGEON, THEODORE   SS   UNK 43 08
  LIKE YOUNG   STURGEON, THEODORE   SS   FSF 60 03

BEYOND BELIEF   HURLEY, RICHARD J.   AN   SBS 66 04
  HARDEST BARGAIN, THE   SMITH, EVELYN E.   NV   GAL 57 06
  INVASION, THE   WILLEY, ROBERT   NV   SSS 40 09
  IT'S SUCH A BEAUTIFUL DAY   ASIMOV, ISAAC   NV   STR 54 03
  MAN WHO LOST THE SEA, THE   STURGEON, THEODORE   SS   FSF 59 10
  PHOENIX   SMITH, CLARK ASHTON SS
  THIRD FROM THE SUN   MATHESON, RICHARD   SS   GAL 50 10
  KEYHOLE   LEINSTER, MURRAY   SS   TWS 51 12
  HISTORY LESSON   CLARKE, ARTHUR C.   SS   STS 49 05

BEYOND CONTROL   SILVERBERG, ROBERT   AN H NEL 72
  INTRODUCTION   SILVERBERG, ROBERT   IN
  CHILD'S PLAY   TENN, WILLIAM   NV   ASF 47 03
  AUTOFAC   DICK, PHILIP K.   NV   GAL 55 11
  ADAM AND NO EVE   BESTER, ALFRED   SS   ASF 41 09
  CITY OF YESTERDAY   CARR, TERRY   SS   IFS 67 12
  IRON CHANCELLOR, THE   SILVERBERG, ROBERT   NV   GAL 58 05
  BOX, THE   BLISH, JAMES   SS   TWS 49 04
  DEAD PAST, THE   ASIMOV, ISAAC   NV   ASF 56 04

BEYOND HUMAN KEN   MERRIL, JUDITH   AN H RDM 52
  PREFACE   MERRIL, JUDITH   IN
  INTRODUCTION   PRATT, FLETCHER   IN
  FITTEST, THE   MACLEAN, KATHERINE   SS   WBY 51 01
  HOUSE DUTIFUL, THE   TENN, WILLIAM   SS   ASF 48 04
  PRIDE   JAMESON, MALCOLM   SS   ASF 42 09
  UNWELCOME TENANT   DEE, ROGER   SS   PLS 50 SU
  GLASS EYE, THE   RUSSELL, ERIC FRANK SS   ASF 49 03
  UNDERGROUND MOVEMENT   NEVILLE, KRIS   SS   FSF 52 06
  GNOME THERE WAS, A   PADGETT, LEWIS   NV   UNK 41 10
  SOLAR PLEXUS   BLISH, JAMES   SS   AST 41 09
  OUR FAIR CITY   HEINLEIN, ROBERT A. SS   WRT 49 01
  FLY, THE   PORGES, ARTHUR   SS   FSF 52 09
  AFTERTHOUGHT   FYFE, H. B.   SS   FUS 51 01
  COMPLEAT WEREWOLF, THE   BOUCHER, ANTHONY   NV   UNK 42 04
  WABBLER, THE   LEINSTER, MURRAY   SS   ASF 42 10
  MAN WHO SOLD ROPE TO THE GNOLES, THE
                                  SEABRIGHT, IDRIS   SS   FSF 51 10
  WHAT HAVE I DONE?   CLIFTON, MARK   SS   ASF 52 05
  ANGEL WAS A YANKEE, THE   BENET, STEPHEN V.   SS   MCL 40 10
  HELEN O'LOY   DEL REY, LESTER   SS   ASF 38 12
  SOCRATES   CHRISTOPHER, JOHN   SS   GAL 51 03
  GOOD-BYE, ILHA¡   MANNING, LAURENCE   SS   NEW 52 AN
  FOXHOLES OF MARS, THE   LEIBER, FRITZ   SS   TWS 52 06
  PERFECT HOST, THE   STURGEON, THEODORE   NV   WRT 48 11
  BIBLIOGRAPHY   MISC. MATERIAL   MS

BEYOND HUMAN KEN (BRITISH)   MERRIL, JUDITH   AN H GRY 53
  HOUSE DUTIFUL, THE   TENN, WILLIAM   SS   ASF 48 04
  PRIDE   JAMESON, MALCOLM   SS   ASF 42 09
  UNWELCOME TENANT   DEE, ROGER   SS   PLS 50 SU
  GLASS EYE, THE   RUSSELL, ERIC FRANK SS   ASF 49 03
  SOLAR PLEXUS   BLISH, JAMES   SS   AST 41 09
  OUR FAIR CITY   HEINLEIN, ROBERT A. SS   WRT 49 01
  FLY, THE   PORGES, ARTHUR   SS   FSF 52 09
  WABBLER, THE   LEINSTER, MURRAY   SS   ASF 42 10
  MAN WHO SOLD ROPE TO THE GNOLES, THE
                                  SEABRIGHT, IDRIS   SS   FSF 51 10
  WHAT HAVE I DONE?   CLIFTON, MARK   SS   ASF 52 05
  ANGEL WAS A YANKEE, THE   BENET, STEPHEN V.   SS   MCL 40 10
  HELEN O'LOY   DEL REY, LESTER   SS   ASF 38 12
  SOCRATES   CHRISTOPHER, JOHN   SS   GAL 51 03
  GOOD-BYE, ILHA¡   MANNING, LAURENCE   SS   NEW 52 AN
  PERFECT HOST, THE   STURGEON, THEODORE   NV   WRT 48 11

BEYOND HUMAN KEN (SELECTIONS FROM)
                                  MERRIL, JUDITH   AN   PNN 54 06
  HOUSE DUTIFUL, THE   TENN, WILLIAM   SS   ASF 48 04
  PRIDE   JAMESON, MALCOLM   SS   ASF 42 09
  GLASS EYE, THE   RUSSELL, ERIC FRANK SS   ASF 49 03
  SOLAR PLEXUS   BLISH, JAMES   SS   AST 41 09
  OUR FAIR CITY   HEINLEIN, ROBERT A. SS   WRT 49 01
  COMPLEAT WEREWOLF, THE   BOUCHER, ANTHONY   NV   UNK 42 04
  WABBLER, THE   LEINSTER, MURRAY   SS   ASF 42 10
  MAN WHO SOLD ROPE TO THE GNOLES, THE
                                  SEABRIGHT, IDRIS   SS   FSF 51 10
  WHAT HAVE I DONE?   CLIFTON, MARK   SS   ASF 52 05
  SOCRATES   CHRISTOPHER, JOHN   SS   GAL 51 03
  GOOD-BYE, ILHA¡   MANNING, LAURENCE   SS   NEW 52 AN
  PERFECT HOST, THE   STURGEON, THEODORE   NV   WRT 48 11

BEYOND INFINITY   CARR, ROBERT S.   AC H FPS 51
  MORNING STAR   CARR, ROBERT S.   NV   SEP 47 12
  MUTATION   CARR, ROBERT S.   NV   NEW 51 AC
  THOSE MEN FROM MARS (EASTER EGGS)
                                  CARR, ROBERT S.   NV   SEP 49 09
  BEYOND INFINITY   CARR, ROBERT S.   NV   NEW 51 AC

BEYOND INFINITY   NOURSE, ALAN E.   AC   COR 64
     SEE "TIGER BY THE TAIL"

BEYOND THE BARRIERS OF SPACE AND TIME
                                  MERRIL, JUDITH   AN H RDM 54
  INTRODUCTION   STURGEON, THEODORE   IN
  EDITOR'S PREFACE   MERRIL, JUDITH   IN
  WOLF PACK   MILLER, WALTER M. JR SS   FAN 53 10
  NO ONE BELIEVED ME   THOMPSON, WILL   SS   SEP 48 04
  PERFORCE TO DREAM   WYNDHAM, JOHN   SS   BEY 54 01
  LAOCOON COMPLEX, THE   FURNAS, J. C.   SS   ESQ 37 04
  CRAZY JOEY   CLIFTON, MARK
                              AND APOSTOLIDES, ALEX   SS C ASF 53 08
  GOLDEN MAN, THE   DICK, PHILIP K.   NV   IFS 54 04
  MALICE AFORETHOUGHT   GRINNELL, DAVID   SS   FSF 52 11
  LAST SEANCE, THE (1926)   CHRISTIE, AGATHA   SS   EQM 71 11
  MEDICINE DANCER   BROWN, BILL   SS   FNF 53 11
  BEHOLD IT WAS A DREAM (1873) BROUGHTON, RHODA   SS
  BELIEF   ASIMOV, ISAAC   NV   ASF 53 10
  VELDT, THE (THE WORLD THE CHILDREN MADE)
                                  BRADBURY, RAY   SS   SEP 50 09
  MR. KINKAID'S PASTS   COUPLING, J. J.   SS   FSF 53 08
  WARNING, THE   PHILLIPS, PETER   SS   FSF 53 09
  GHOST OF ME, THE   BOUCHER, ANTHONY   SS   UNK 42 06
  WALL AROUND THE WORLD, THE   COGSWELL, THEODORE R NV   BEY 53 09
  OPERATING INSTRUCTIONS   SHECKLEY, ROBERT   SS   ASF 53 05
  INTERPRETATION OF A DREAM   COLLIER, JOHN   SS   NYM 51 05
  DEFENSE MECHANISM   MACLEAN, KATHERINE   SS   ASF 49 10

BEYOND THE BEYOND   ANDERSON, POUL   AC   SIG 69 08
     ENGLISH EDITION (GOL 70) OMITS STORY "DAY OF BURNING"
  MEMORY (A WORLD CALLED MAANEREK)
                                  ANDERSON, POUL   NV   GAL 57 07
  BRAKE   ANDERSON, POUL   NV   ASF 57 08
  DAY OF BURNING (SUPERNOVA)   ANDERSON, POUL   SN   ASF 67 01
  SENSITIVE MAN, THE   ANDERSON, POUL   NV   FUN 54 01
  MOONRAKERS, THE   ANDERSON, POUL   NV   IFS 66 01
  STARFOG   ANDERSON, POUL   SN   ASF 67 08

BEYOND THE END OF TIME   POHL, FREDERIK   AN H DBL 52
  INTRODUCTION   POHL, FREDERIK   IN
  EMBASSY, THE   PEARSON, MARTIN   SS   SSS 49 07
  HUNTED, THE   MACDONALD, JOHN D.   SS   SSS 49 07
  HEREDITY   ASIMOV, ISAAC   SS   AST 41 04
  LITTLE BLACK BAG, THE   KORNBLUTH, C. M.   NV   AST 50 07
  LONELY PLANET, THE   LEINSTER, MURRAY   NV   TWS 49 12
  OPERATION PEEP (ALSO AS PAWLEY'S PEEPHOLES)
                           WYNDHAM, JOHN   SS   SUS 51 SU
  LET THE ANTS TRY   MACCREIGH, JAMES   SS   PLS 49 WI
  THERE WILL COME SOFT RAINS BRADBURY, RAY   SS   COL 50 05
  SCANNERS LIVE IN VAIN   SMITH, CORDWAINER   NA   FBK 50 06
  SUCH INTERESTING NEIGHBORS FINNEY, JACK   SS   COL 51 01
  BRIDGE CROSSING   DRYFOOS, DAVE   SS   GAL 51 05
  LETTER FROM THE STARS   VAN VOGT, A. E.   SS   OTW 50 07
  LOVE IN THE DARK (LOVE ETHEREAL)
                           GOLD, H. L.   SS   SUS 51 FL
  OBVIOUSLY SUICIDE   WRIGHT, S. FOWLER   SS   SUS 51 SP
  BEYOND DOUBT   HEINLEIN, ROBERT A.
                           AND WENTZ, ELMA   SS C AST 41 04
  DEATH IS THE PENALTY   MERRIL, JUDITH   SS   ASF 49 01
  ROCK DIVER   HARRISON, HARRY   SS   WBY 51 02
  STEPSON OF SPACE   GALLUN, RAYMOND Z.   SS   AST 40 10
  RESCUE PARTY   CLARKE, ARTHUR C.   NV   ASF 46 05

BEYOND THE GALACTIC RIM   CHANDLER, A. BERTRAM DC   ACE 63
  FORBIDDEN PLANET   CHANDLER, A. BERTRAM SS   FUN 59 07
  WET PAINT   CHANDLER, A. BERTRAM SS   AMZ 59 05
  MAN WHO COULD NOT STOP, THE CHANDLER, A. BERTRAM NV FSF 59 05
  KEY, THE   CHANDLER, A. BERTRAM NV   FAN 59 07

BEYOND THE STARS AND OTHER STORIES
                           ANONYMOUS   AN   JBL 58
  BEYOND THE STARS (SPACE RATING)
                           BERRYMAN, JOHN   SS   ASF 39 10
  COLD EQUATIONS, THE   GODWIN, TOM   SS   ASF 54 08
  LIMITING FACTOR   SIMAK, CLIFFORD D.   SS   STS 49 11
  ASLEEP IN ARMAGEDDON (ALSO AS PERCHANCE TO DREAM)
                           BRADBURY, RAY   SS   PLS 48 WI
  EXPLOITERS' END   CAUSEY, JAMES   SS   OSF 54 02
  POTENTIAL ENEMY   REYNOLDS, MACK   SS   OSF 54 02
  CENTURY JUMPER (A TRAVELLER IN TIME)
                           DERLETH, AUGUST   SS   OSF 54 02

BEYOND THIRTY & THE MAN-EATER
                           BURROUGHS, EDGAR R.   AC H SCP 57
  BEYOND THIRTY   BURROUGHS, EDGAR R.   NV   AAM 16 02
  MAN-EATER, THE   BURROUGHS, EDGAR R.   NO   NYW 15 11

BEYOND THIS HORIZON   CARRELL, CHRISTOPHER OA   CEO 73 10
  INTRODUCTION: A NEW WAY OF EXPRESSION
                           WESTON, PETER   IN
  H. G. WELLS: EXPONENT OF EXTRAPOLATION
                           CLARKE, I. F.   AR   FTS 70 06
  EVOLUTION OF SCIENCE FICTION, THE
                           STABLEFORD, BRIAN M. AR
  SCIENCE OF FICTION? A SURVEY OF ATTITUDES
                           SUDBERY, TONY   AR
  MODERN VIEW OF SCIENCE FICTION, A
                           SHIPPEY, TOM   AR
  OTHER TRADITION, THE   ADLARD, MARK   AR
  HISTORY OF BRITISH SCIENCE FICTION MAGAZINES, A
                           HARBOTTLE, PHILIP   AR
  INTRODUCTION: AN ABC OF BRITISH SCIENCE FICTION- APOCALYPSE,
    BLEAKNESS, CATASTROPHE NICHOLLS, PETER   IN
  THEOPHILUS   ADLARD, MARK   SS
  STRANGE IN A FAMILIAR WAY ALDISS, BRIAN W.   SS
  ALTAR EGOES   SHAW, BOB   SS
  INTRODUCTION: ASTRONOMY TODAY AND TOMORROW
                           MOORE, PATRICK   IN
  MAN'S EXPANDING VIEW OF SPACE
                           RONAN, COLIN   AR
  END OF THE UNIVERSE?, THE TAYLOR, JOHN   AR   LIS 71 09
  LANDSCAPES IN SPACE   HARDY, DAVID A.   AR
  LIKENESS OF APOLLO, THE   ARNOLD, DOUGLAS   AR   PTJ 73 03
  PLANETARY SURFACES AND INTERIORS
                           TOZER, D. C.   AR
  ASTRONOMY AND ART: PAINTINGS EARLY, DAVID   IL
  INTRODUCTION: POETRY AND SCIENCE FICTION
                           LUCIE-SMITH, EDWARD   IN
  NOTES TOWARD A SUPREME SCIENCE FICTION
                           THOMAS, D. M.   PM
  TWILIGHT OF A TYRANNY   MORGAN, EDWIN   PM
  SPACE SONNET   MORGAN, EDWIN   PM
  POLYFILLA   MORGAN, EDWIN   PM
  TRUTH TEST   JARVIS, BOB   PM
  TWELVE STATIONS FROM GEMINI FAIRFAX, JOHN   PM
  ALL ADAM AGAIN   FAIRFAX, JOHN   PM
  TWO POEMS AFTER STORIES BY BRIAN ALDISS
                           COUZYN, JENI   GR
  DAY WE EMBARKED FOR CYTHERA, THE
                           COUZYN, JENI   PM
  HERESIES OF THE HUGE GOD COUZYN, JENI   PM
  ASTRONAUT (EXTRACT)   LUCIE-SMITH, EDWARD   PM
  LAMPS   MACBETH, GEORGE   PM
  GALACTIC LOVEPOEM TWO   MISC. MATERIAL   PM
  DISCOVERY   MITCHELL, ADRIAN   PM
  LIFE IN THE TWENTIETH CENTURY (1883)
                           ROBIDA, ALBERT   IL
  INVERTED WORLD, THE   PRIEST, CHRISTOPHER   EX   FAB 74
  STARS IN MY POCKET LIKE GRAINS OF SAND
                           DELANY, SAMUEL R.   EX
  FOWLING, THE   BULMER, KENNETH   EX
  HEIGHT OF THE SCREAM, THE CAMPBELL, J. RAMSEY   EX
  INTRODUCTION: SCIENCE FICTION - SCIENCE FACT
                           HAY, GEORGE   IN

TRIBULATIONS OF TECHNOLOGY, THE
                           CLARKE, I. F.   AR   FTS 71 06
CHATTING WITH COMPUTERS (REVISED)
                           EVANS, CHRISTOPHER   AR   DSP 73 10
PSY FY PSYCHOLOGY AND SCIENCE FICTION
  RADFORD, JOHN
                           AND KIRBY, RICHARD   AR C
PROSPECTS FOR GENETIC ENGINEERING IN MAN
                           SIMNETT, JOHN   AR
CONTACT WITH ANOTHER CIVILISATION
                           LUNAN, DUNCAN   AR
MONSTER IN ART, THE   LUCIE-SMITH, EDWARD   IN
MONSTERS   BAKER, JULES   IL
MONSTERS   ANTROBUS, ROSIE   IL
SCIENCE FICTION COVER ILLUSTRATIONS
                           THOLE, KAREL   IL
SCIENCE FICTION COVER ILLUSTRATIONS
                           KIRBY, JOSH   IL
SCIENCE FICTION COVER ILLUSTRATIONS
                           JONES, EDDIE   IL
PHILOSOPHERS STONE   WENSKES, HELMUT   IL
DALIS ASCENSION   WENSKES, HELMUT   IL
GREED   WENSKES, HELMUT   IL
STAGE SET   WENSKES, HELMUT   IL
BUG-EYED SCREEN, THE   STRICK, PHILIP   AR
SURVIVAL OF THE FITTEST   TAYLOR, JOHN   PL
METAMORPHOSIS   HARRISON, LIZ
                           MARSHALL, CHRIS
                           AND STEPHENS, KEVIN   IL C
FYI   BLISH, JAMES   SS   STR 53 02
INCEPTION OF THE EPOCH OF MRS. BEDONEBYASYOUDID, THE
                           BRUNNER, JOHN   SS   QRK 71 02
LAZARUS   TUBB, E. C.   SS
LIKE NOTHING ON EARTH   ARNOLD, DOUGLAS   AR   KDK 73 02
SPACEMEN THROUGHOUT HISTORY DRAKE, W. RAYMOND   AR
MAJORITY OF PEOPLE NOW BELIEVE IN FLYING SAUCERS, THE
                           DUTTA, REX   AR
FLYING SAUCERS - PEOPLE AND REALITY
                           BEER, LIONEL   AR
SCIENCE WONDER STORIES COVER PAUL, FRANK R.   IL

BEYOND TIME   LEY, SANDRA   OA   PKT 76 10
  EDITOR'S NOTE   LEY, SANDRA   IN
  INTRODUCTION   POHL, FREDERIK   IN
  CLIOMETRICON, THE   ZEBROWSKI, GEORGE   SS   AMZ 75 05
  RISING OF THE SUN, THE   EKLUND, GORDON   SS
  JUPITER LAUGHS   COOPER, EDMUND   SS
  WORLDS ENOUGH   THOMPSON, DON   SS
  ASSAULT ON FAT MOUNTAIN LAFFERTY, R. A.   SS
  O BRAVE OLD WORLD!   DAVIDSON, AVRAM   NV
  HAIL TO THE CHIEF   CORES, LUCY   NV
  SOY LA LIBERTAD   COULSON, ROBERT   SS
  DEVIL AND THE DEEP BLUE SEA, THE
                           CHILSON, ROBERT   SS
  CLASS WITH DR. CHANG, A MOORE, WARD   SS
  UNSCHEDULED FLIGHT   COULSON, JUANITA   SS
  ALTERNATE UNIVERSE I   DISCH, THOMAS M.   PM
  ALTERNATE UNIVERSE II   DISCH, THOMAS M.   PM
  ALTERNATE UNIVERSE III   DISCH, THOMAS M.   PM
  POLONAISE   FOSTER, ALAN DEAN   SS
  U-GENIE SX-1--HUMAN ENTREPRENEUR: NATURALLY RAPACIOUS YANKEE
                           GAT, DIMITRI V.   SS
  LETTER FROM AMERICA   PERCY, H. R.   SS
  NAPOLEONIC WARS, THE   GOTSCHALK, FELIX C.   SS
  CHECKMATE IN SIX MOVES   LEY, OLGA   SS
  MANY RUBICONS   ORGILL, MICHAEL   NV
  FELLINI BEGGAR, THE   YARBRO, CHELSEA Q.   SS
  ALL POSSIBLE WORLDS   JANIFER, LAURENCE M. SS

BEYOND TIME AND SPACE   DERLETH, AUGUST   AN H PEL 50
  INTRODUCTION   DERLETH, AUGUST   IN
  ATLANTIS (370 B.C.)   PLATO   EX
  TRUE HISTORY, A (165 A.D.) LUCIAN OF SAMOSATA EX
  UTOPIA (1516)   MORE, SIR THOMAS   EX
  PHALANSTERY OF THELEME, THE (1534)
                           RABELAIS, FRANCIS   EX
  CITY OF THE SUN, THE (1623) CAMPANELLA, G. D. EX
  MAN ON THE MOONE, THE (1638) GODWIN, FRANCIS   EX
  LAPUTA (FROM "GULLIVER'S TRAVELS", 1726)
                           SWIFT, JONATHAN   EX
  SOMNIUM (1634)   KEPLER, JOHANNES   EX
  NEW ATLANTIS, THE (1624) BACON, FRANCIS   EX
  TREE MEN OF POTU, THE (1741) HOLBERG, LUDWIG   EX
  THOUSAND-AND-SECOND TALE OF SCHEHERAZADE, THE
                           POE, EDGAR ALLEN   SS   GDY 45 02
  DR. OX'S EXPERIMENT (1874) VERNE, JULES   SS   AMZ 26 08
  PAUSODYNE (1884)   ALLEN, GRANT   SS   84
  TALE OF NEGATIVE GRAVITY, A STOCKTON, FRANK R. NV   CNY 84 11
  BLINDMAN'S WORLD, THE (1886) BELLAMY, EDWARD   SS   ATL 86
  BATTLE OF THE MONSTERS, THE ROBERTSON, MORGAN SS   99
  NEW ACCELERATOR, THE   WELLS, H. G.   SS   SND 01 12
  VOICE IN THE NIGHT, THE HODGSON, WILLIAM H.   SS   BBM 07 11
  SPACE   BUCHAN, JOHN   SS   LVA 11 06
  WHEN THE GREEN STAR WANED DYALHIS, NICTZIN   SS   WRT 25 04
  REVOLT OF THE PEDESTRIANS, THE
                           KELLER, DAVID H. MD. SS   AMZ 28 02
  LOTUS EATERS, THE   WEINBAUM, STANLEY G. NV   ASF 35 04
  WINGLESS VICTORY   HEARD, H. F.   SS   44
  WHEN THE BOUGH BREAKS   PADGETT, LEWIS   NV   ASF 44 11
  WANTED- AN ENEMY   LEIBER, FRITZ   SS   ASF 45 02
  EXILES, THE (THE MAD WIZARDS OF MARS, MCL 49 09)
                           BRADBURY, RAY   SS   FSF 50 WS
  LONG WATCH, THE   HEINLEIN, ROBERT A.   SS   ALM 49 12
  MINORITY REPORT   STURGEON, THEODORE   SS   ASF 49 06
  COLOSSUS   WANDREI, DONALD   NV   ASF 34 01
  VOYAGE TO SFANOMOE, A   SMITH, CLARK ASHTON   SS   WRT 31 08

```
SEESAW, THE                        VAN VOGT, A. E.       SS    ASF 41 07
FLYING MEN, THE (FROM "LAST AND FIRST MEN")
                                   STAPLEDON, OLAF       EX    MTH 30
FESSENDEN'S WORLDS                 HAMILTON, EDMOND      SS    WRT 37 04
HUMPTY DUMPTY HAD A GREAT FALL
                                   LONG, FRANK BELKNAP   SS    STS 48 11

BEYOND TIME AND SPACE (8 OF 32)
                                   DERLETH, AUGUST       AN    BRK 58
LONG WATCH, THE                    HEINLEIN, ROBERT A.   SS    ALM 49 12
MINORITY REPORT                    STURGEON, THEODORE    SS    ASF 49 06
COLOSSUS                           WANDREI, DONALD       NV    ASF 34 01
VOYAGE TO SFANOMOE, A              SMITH, CLARK ASHTON   SS    WRT 31 08
SEESAW, THE                        VAN VOGT, A. E.       SS    ASF 41 07
FLYING MEN, THE (FROM "LAST AND FIRST MEN")
                                   STAPLEDON, OLAF       EX    MTH 30
FESSENDEN'S WORLDS                 HAMILTON, EDMOND      SS    WRT 37 04
HUMPTY DUMPTY HAD A GREAT FALL
                                   LONG, FRANK BELKNAP   SS    STS 48 11

BEYOND TOMORROW                    HARDING, LEE        AN H  WRN 76
BAD NEWS AND THE GOOD, THE         ASIMOV, ISAAC         IN
RAINBIRD                           LAFFERTY, R. A.       SS    GAL 61 12
NINE LIVES                         LE GUIN, URSULA K.    NV    PBY 69 11
IDIOT STICK                        KNIGHT, DAMON         SS    STR 58 04
ARK OF JAMES CARLYLE, THE          WILDER, CHERRY        SS    NWR 74 24
COMMUTER, THE                      DICK, PHILIP K.       SS    AMZ 53 09
OATH, THE                          BLISH, JAMES          SS    FSF 60 10
TAKEOVER BID                       BAXTER, JOHN          NV    NWR 65 05
COMES NOW THE POWER                ZELAZNY, ROGER        SS    MOH 66 WI
LITTERBUG                          MORPHETT, TONY        NV    FSF 69 07
LATE                               CHANDLER, A. BERTRAM  SS    SCF 55 04
MOTHER HITTON'S LITTUL KITTONS
                                   SMITH, CORDWAINER     NV    GAL 61 06
SONG BEFORE SUNSET, A              GRIGG, DAVID          SS
SUNDANCE                           SILVERBERG, ROBERT    SS    FSF 69 06
OH IN JOSE, THE                    ALDISS, BRIAN W.      SS    IMP 66 07
MAN WHO CAME EARLY, THE            ANDERSON, POUL        NV    FSF 56 06
CALL HIM LORD                      DICKSON, GORDON R.    SS    ASF 66 05
GARDEN OF TIME, THE                BALLARD, J. G.        SS    FSF 62 02

BEYOND TOMORROW                    KNIGHT, DAMON       AN H  HPR 65
INTRODUCTION                       KNIGHT, DAMON         IN
BRIGHTSIDE CROSSING                NOURSE, ALAN E.       NV    GAL 56 01
DEEP RANGE, THE (ARB 54 04)        CLARKE, ARTHUR C.     NV    STR 54 03
COVENTRY                           HEINLEIN, ROBERT A.   NV    ASF 40 07
MILE-LONG SPACESHIP, THE           WILHELM, KATE         SS    ASF 57 04
SEESAW, THE                        VAN VOGT, A. E.       SS    ASF 41 07
NIGHTFALL                          ASIMOV, ISAAC         NV    ASF 41 09
MILLION-YEAR PICNIC, THE           BRADBURY, RAY         SS    PLS 46 SU
DESERTION                          SIMAK, CLIFFORD D.    SS    ASF 44 11
TWILIGHT                           STUART, DON A.        SS    ASF 34 11
HAPPY ENDING                       KUTTNER, HENRY        NV    TWS 48 08
MORE GOOD READING IN SCIENCE FICTION
                                   MISC. MATERIAL        MS

BICENTENNIAL MAN AND OTHER STORIES, THE
                                   ASIMOV, ISAAC       AC H  DBL 76
PRIME OF LIFE, THE                 ASIMOV, ISAAC         PM    FSF 66 10
FEMININE INTUITION                 ASIMOV, ISAAC         NV    FSF 69 10
WATERCLAP                          ASIMOV, ISAAC         NV    IFS 70 04
THAT THOU ART MINDFUL OF HIM!
                                   ASIMOV, ISAAC         NV    FSF 74 05
STRANGER IN PARADISE               ASIMOV, ISAAC         NV    IFS 74 06
LIFE AND TIMES OF MULTIVAC, THE
                                   ASIMOV, ISAAC         SS    NYT 75 01
WINNOWING, THE                     ASIMOV, ISAAC         SS    ASF 76 02
BICENTENNIAL MAN, THE              ASIMOV, ISAAC         NV    STL 76 02
MARCHING IN                        ASIMOV, ISAAC         SS    HFI 76 04
OLD-FASHIONED                      ASIMOV, ISAAC         SS    BTM 76 02
TERCENTENARY INCIDENT, THE         ASIMOV, ISAAC         SS    EQM 76 08
BIRTH OF A NOTION                  ASIMOV, ISAAC         SS    AMZ 76 06

BIG BOOK OF SCIENCE FICTION  CONKLIN, GROFF       AN H  CRN 50
INTRODUCTION                       CONKLIN, GROFF        IN
MR. MURPHY OF NEW YORK             MCMORROW, THOMAS      SS    SEP 30 03
DIMINISHING DRAFT, THE             KAEMPFFERT, WALDEMAR  SS    ASW 18 02
PEACEBRINGER (SWORD OF PEACE)
                                   MOORE, WARD           SS    AMZ 50 03
MATTER OF FORM, A                  GOLD, H. L.           SN    ASF 38 12
PLANETOID OF DOOM, THE             COLLADAY, MORRISON    SS    WOS 32 12
ONE LEG TOO MANY                   ALEXANDER, W.         SS    AMZ 29 10
MAN WITH THE STRANGE HEAD, THE
                                   BREUER, MILES J. MD.  SS    AMZ 27 01
DEFENSE MECHANISM                  MACLEAN, KATHERINE    SS    ASF 49 10
MARGIN FOR ERROR                   PADGETT, LEWIS        NV    ASF 47 11
ISOLATIONIST                       REYNOLDS, MACK        SS    FAD 50 04
NOBODY SAW THE SHIP                LEINSTER, MURRAY      SS    FUS 50 05
MEWHU'S JET                        STURGEON, THEODORE    NV    ASF 46 11
OUTER LIMIT, THE                   DOAR, GRAHAM          SS    SEP 49 12
RAT RACE                           DE COURCY, DOROTHY
                                   AND DE COURCY, JOHN   SS C  STS 48 09
DEAR DEVIL                         RUSSELL, ERIC FRANK   NV    OWS 50 05
EMERGENCY LANDING                  WILLIAMS, RALPH       SS    ASF 40 07
SHIP THAT TURNED ASIDE, THE        PEYTON, GREEN         SS    AMZ 30 03
MANNA                              PHILLIPS, PETER       NV    ASF 49 02
LONG DAWN, THE                     LOOMIS, NOEL          SS    SSS 50 01
E FOR EFFORT                       SHERRED, T. L.        NV    ASF 47 05
ROGER BACON FORMULA, THE           PRATT, FLETCHER       SS    AMZ 29 01
WINGS OF NIGHT, THE                DEL REY, LESTER       SS    ASF 42 03
DESERTION                          SIMAK, CLIFFORD D.    SS    ASF 44 11
CONTACT, INCORPORATED (ACTION ON AZURA)
                                   OSBORNE, ROBERTSON    NV    PLS 49 FL
ARENA                              BROWN, FREDRIC        NV    ASF 44 06
CULTURE                            SHELTON, JERRY        NV    ASF 44 09
IN THE YEAR 2889 (ARS 49 SU) VERNE, JULES              SS    FRM 89 02
```

```
FOREVER AND THE EARTH              BRADBURY, RAY         SS    PLS 50 SP
MINIATURE, THE                     MACDONALD, JOHN D.    SS    SSS 49 09
SANITY (ALSO AS CRAZY WOLF)        LEIBER, FRITZ         SS    ASF 44 04
ONLY THING WE LEARN, THE           KORNBLUTH, C. M.      SS    STS 49 07
NOT WITH A BANG                    KNIGHT, DAMON         SS    FSF 50 WS

BIG BOOK OF SCIENCE FICTION (10 OF 32)
                                   CONKLIN, GROFF        AN    BRK 57
DESERTION                          SIMAK, CLIFFORD D.    SS    ASF 44 11
MEWHU'S JET                        STURGEON, THEODORE    NV    ASF 46 11
NOBODY SAW THE SHIP                LEINSTER, MURRAY      SS    FUS 50 05
WINGS OF NIGHT, THE                DEL REY, LESTER       SS    ASF 42 03
ARENA                              BROWN, FREDRIC        NV    ASF 44 06
ROGER BACON FORMULA, THE           PRATT, FLETCHER       SS    AMZ 29 01
FOREVER AND THE EARTH              BRADBURY, RAY         SS    PLS 50 SP
MINIATURE, THE                     MACDONALD, JOHN D.    SS    SSS 49 09
SANITY (ALSO AS CRAZY WOLF)        LEIBER, FRITZ         SS    ASF 44 04
ONLY THING WE LEARN, THE           KORNBLUTH, C. M.      SS    STS 49 07

BIG SHOW, THE                      LAUMER, KEITH       AC    ACE 72 10
IN THE QUEUE                       LAUMER, KEITH         SS    ORB 70 07
RELIC OF WAR, A                    LAUMER, KEITH         SS    ASF 69 10
BIG SHOW, THE                      LAUMER, KEITH         NV    GAL 68 02
MESSAGE TO AN ALIEN                LAUMER, KEITH         SS    ASF 70 06
PLAGUE, THE                        LAUMER, KEITH         NV    ASF 70 11
TEST TO DESTRUCTION                LAUMER, KEITH         NV    DVS 67 01

BILLENIUM                          BALLARD, J. G.      AC    BRK 62
BILLENIUM                          BALLARD, J. G.        SS    NWS 61 11
INSANE ONES, THE                   BALLARD, J. G.        SS    AMZ 62 01
STUDIO 5, THE STARS                BALLARD, J. G.        NV    SCF 61 02
GENTLE ASSASSIN, THE               BALLARD, J. G.        SS    NWS 61 12
BUILD-UP (ALSO AS THE CONCENTRATION CITY)
                                   BALLARD, J. G.        SS    NWS 57 01
NOW: ZERO                          BALLARD, J. G.        SS    SCF 59 12
MOBILE (ALSO AS VENUS SMILES)
                                   BALLARD, J. G.        SS    SCF 57 06
CHRONOPOLIS                        BALLARD, J. G.        NV    NWS 60 06
PRIMA BELLADONNA                   BALLARD, J. G.        SS    SCF 56 12
GARDEN OF TIME, THE                BALLARD, J. G.        SS    FSF 62 02

BIO-FUTURES                        SARGENT, PAMELA     AN    VNT 76 06
INTRODUCTION                       SARGENT, PAMELA       IN
PLANNERS, THE                      WILHELM, KATE         SS    ORB 68 03
SLOW TUESDAY NIGHT                 LAFFERTY, R. A.       SS    GAL 65 04
IN RE GLOVER                       TUSHNET, LEONARD      SS    DVS 72 02
EMANCIPATION: A ROMANCE OF THE TIMES TO COME
                                   DISCH, THOMAS M.      NV    NDM 71 01
NINE LIVES                         LE GUIN, URSULA K.    NV    PBY 69 11
CALL ME JOE                        ANDERSON, POUL        NV    ASF 57 04
IMMORTALS, THE (ALSO AS IMMORTAL)
                                   GUNN, JAMES E.        NV    STR 58 04
WEARIEST RIVER, THE                SCORTIA, THOMAS N.    NV    FUC 73
DAY MILLION                        POHL, FREDERIK        SS    ROG 66 02
WATERSHED                          BLISH, JAMES          SS    IFS 55 05
FURTHER READING                    MISC. MATERIAL        MS
ABOUT THE AUTHORS                  MISC. MATERIAL        MS

BIRD OF TIME, THE                  WEST, WALLACE       NO H  GNM 59
EN ROUTE TO PLUTO                  WEST, WALLACE         SS    ASF 36 08
LURE OF POLARIS, THE               WEST, WALLACE         SS    TWS 49 10
BIRD OF TIME, THE                  WEST, WALLACE         NO    TWS 52 08
CAPTIVE AUDIENCE                   WEST, WALLACE         NO    TWS 53 06

BLACK STAR PASSES, THE       CAMPBELL, JOHN W. JR AC H FPS 53
INTRODUCTION                       CAMPBELL, JOHN W. JR  IN
BLACK STAR PASSES, THE             CAMPBELL, JOHN W. JR  NA    AMQ 30 FL
PIRACY PREFERRED                   CAMPBELL, JOHN W. JR  NV    AMZ 30 06
SOLARITE                           CAMPBELL, JOHN W. JR  NV    AMZ 30 11

BLAL, THE                          VAN VOGT, A. E.     AC    ZEB 76 08
SEE "MONSTERS"

BLOCH AND BRADBURY                 BRADBURY & BLOCH    AC    TWR 69
IN ENGLAND AS "FEVER DREAM"
SHADOW FROM THE STEEPLE, THE  BLOCH, ROBERT            NV    WRT 50 08
WATCHERS, THE                      BRADBURY, RAY         SS    WRT 45 05
GRINNING GHOUL, THE                BLOCH, ROBERT         SS    WRT 36 06
MANNIKINS OF HORROR (THE MANNIKIN)
                                   BLOCH, ROBERT         SS    WRT 37 04
FEVER DREAM                        BRADBURY, RAY         SS    WRT 48 09
DRUIDIC DOOM, THE                  BLOCH, ROBERT         SS    WRT 36 04
DEAD MAN, THE                      BRADBURY, RAY         SS    WRT 45 07
QUESTION OF ETIQUETTE, A           BLOCH, ROBERT         SS    WRT 42 09
HANDLER, THE                       BRADBURY, RAY         SS    WRT 47 01
MAN WHO CRIED WOLF!, THE           BLOCH, ROBERT         SS    WRT 45 05

BLOOD RUNS COLD                    BLOCH, ROBERT       AC H  SAS 61
SHOW MUST GO ON, THE               BLOCH, ROBERT         SS    MSM 60 01
CURE, THE                          BLOCH, ROBERT         SS    PBY 57 10
DAYBROKE                           BLOCH, ROBERT         SS    SMG 58 01
SHOW BIZ                           BLOCH, ROBERT         SS    EQM 59 05
MASTERPIECE, THE                   BLOCH, ROBERT         SS    ROG 60 06
I LIKE BLONDES                     BLOCH, ROBERT         SS    PBY 56 01
DIG THAT CRAZY GRAVE!              BLOCH, ROBERT         SS    EQM 57 06
WHERE THE BUFFALO ROAM             BLOCH, ROBERT         SS    OWS 55 07
IS BETSY BLAKE STILL ALIVE? (BETSY BLAKE WILL LIVE FOREVER)
                                   BLOCH, ROBERT         SS    EQM 58 04
WORD OF HONOR                      BLOCH, ROBERT         SS    PBY 58 08
FINAL PERFORMANCE                  BLOCH, ROBERT         NV    SHK 60 09
ALL ON A GOLDEN AFTERNOON          BLOCH, ROBERT         NV    FSF 56 06
GLOATING PLACE, THE                BLOCH, ROBERT         SS    ROG 59 06
PIN, THE                           BLOCH, ROBERT         SS    AMZ 54 01
I DO NOT LOVE THEE, DOCTOR FELL
                                   BLOCH, ROBERT         SS    FSF 55 03
BIG KICK, THE                      BLOCH, ROBERT         SS    ROG 59 07
```

SOCK FINISH	BLOCH, ROBERT	SS	EQM 57	10
BLOOD RUNS COLD (BRITISH)	BLOCH, ROBERT	AC	COR 64	
SHOW MUST GO ON, THE	BLOCH, ROBERT	SS	MSM 60	01
DAYBROKE	BLOCH, ROBERT	SS	SMG 58	01
MASTERPIECE, THE	BLOCH, ROBERT	SS	ROG 60	06
I LIKE BLONDES	BLOCH, ROBERT	SS	PBY 56	01
WHERE THE BUFFALO ROAM	BLOCH, ROBERT	SS	OWS 55	07
IS BETSY BLAKE STILL ALIVE? (BETSY BLAKE WILL LIVE FOREVER)				
	BLOCH, ROBERT	SS	EQM 58	04
WORD OF HONOR	BLOCH, ROBERT	SS	PBY 58	08
FINAL PERFORMANCE	BLOCH, ROBERT	NV	SHK 60	09
GLOATING PLACE, THE	BLOCH, ROBERT	SS	ROG 59	06
PIN, THE	BLOCH, ROBERT	SS	AMZ 54	01
I DO NOT LOVE THEE, DOCTOR FELL				
	BLOCH, ROBERT	SS	FSF 55	03
BIG KICK, THE	BLOCH, ROBERT	SS	ROG 59	07
SOCK FINISH	BLOCH, ROBERT	SS	EQM 57	10
BODYGUARD AND 4 OTHER SHORT SF NOVELS FROM GALAXY				
	GOLD, H. L.	AN H	DBL 60	
INTRODUCTION	POHL, FREDERIK	IN		
BODYGUARD	GRIMM, CHRISTOPHER	NA	GAL 56	02
HOW-2	SIMAK, CLIFFORD D.	NV	GAL 54	11
DELAY IN TRANSIT	WALLACE, F. L.	NA	GAL 52	09
CITY OF FORCE, THE	GALOUYE, DANIEL F.	NA	GAL 59	04
WHATEVER COUNTS	POHL, FREDERIK	NA	GAL 59	06
BOGEY MEN	BLOCH, ROBERT	AC	PYR 63	03
MATTER OF LIFE, A	BLOCH, ROBERT	SS	KHM 60	06
MODEL WIFE, THE	BLOCH, ROBERT	SS	SWK 61	11
BROOMSTICK RIDE	BLOCH, ROBERT	SS	SUP 57	12
SKULL OF THE MARQUIS DE SADE, THE				
	BLOCH, ROBERT	SS	WRT 45	09
MEMO TO A MOVIE-MAKER	BLOCH, ROBERT	SS	DUD 61	01
THINKING CAP, THE	BLOCH, ROBERT	NV	OWS 53	06
SHOES, THE	BLOCH, ROBERT	SS	UNK 42	02
MAN WHO COLLECTED POE, THE	BLOCH, ROBERT	SS	FFM 51	10
GHOST WRITER, THE	BLOCH, ROBERT	SS	WRT 40	05
MAN WHO MURDERED TOMORROW, THE				
	BLOCH, ROBERT	SS	AMZ 60	03
"PSYCHO"-LOGICAL BLOCH	MOSKOWITZ, SAM	AR	AMZ 62	12
BOLO	LAUMER, KEITH	AC H	BKP 76	
SHORT HISTORY OF THE BOLO FIGHTING MACHINES, A				
	LAUMER, KEITH	AR		
NIGHT OF THE TROLLS, THE	LAUMER, KEITH	SN	WOT 63	10
COURIER (THE FROZEN PLANET)	LAUMER, KEITH	NV	IFS 61	09
FIELD TEST	LAUMER, KEITH	SS	ASF 76	03
LAST COMMAND, THE	LAUMER, KEITH	SS	ASF 67	01
RELIC OF WAR, A	LAUMER, KEITH	SS	ASF 69	10
COMBAT UNIT (ALSO AS DINOCHROME)				
	LAUMER, KEITH	SS	FSF 60	11
BOOK OF ANDRE NORTON, THE	NORTON, ANDRE	AC	DAW 75	10
SEE "THE MANY WORLDS OF ANDRE NORTON"				
BOOK OF BRIAN ALDISS, THE	ALDISS, BRIAN W.	AC	DAW 72	
IN ENGLAND AS "THE COMIC INFERNO"				
INTRODUCTION	ALDISS, BRIAN W.	IN		
COMIC INFERNO	ALDISS, BRIAN W.	NA	GAL 63	02
UNDERPRIVILEGED, THE	ALDISS, BRIAN W.	SS	NWS 63	05
CARDIAC ARREST	ALDISS, BRIAN W.	NV	FAN 70	12
IN THE ARENA	ALDISS, BRIAN W.	SS	IFS 63	07
ALL THE WORLD'S TEARS	ALDISS, BRIAN W.	SS	NEB 57	05
AMEN AND OUT	ALDISS, BRIAN W.	SS	NWS 66	08
SOFT PREDICAMENT, THE	ALDISS, BRIAN W.	NV	FSF 69	10
AS FOR OUR FATAL CONTINUITY...				
	ALDISS, BRIAN W.	SS	NWQ 72	03
SEND HER VICTORIOUS	ALDISS, BRIAN W.	NV	AMZ 68	04
BOOK OF FRANK HERBERT, THE	HERBERT, FRANK	AC	DAW 73	01
SEED STOCK	HERBERT, FRANK	SS	ASF 70	04
NOTHING, THE	HERBERT, FRANK	SS	FUN 56	01
RAT RACE	HERBERT, FRANK	NV	ASF 55	07
GAMBLING DEVICE	HERBERT, FRANK	SS	NEW 73	AC
LOOKING FOR SOMETHING?	HERBERT, FRANK	SS	STS 52	04
GONE DOGS, THE	HERBERT, FRANK	SS	AMZ 54	11
PASSAGE FOR PIANO	HERBERT, FRANK	NV	NEW 73	AC
ENCOUNTER IN A LONELY PLACE	HERBERT, FRANK	SS	NEW 73	AC
OPERATION SYNDROME (ALSO AS NIGHTMARE BLUES)				
	HERBERT, FRANK	NV	ASF 54	06
OCCUPATION FORCE	HERBERT, FRANK	SS	FAN 55	08
BOOK OF FRITZ LEIBER, THE	LEIBER, FRITZ	AC	DAW 74	01
FOREWORD	LEIBER, FRITZ	IN		
SPIDER, THE	LEIBER, FRITZ	SS	ROG 63	01
MONSTERS AND MONSTER LOVERS	LEIBER, FRITZ	AR	FAN 65	03
HITCH IN SPACE, A	LEIBER, FRITZ	SS	WOT 63	08
HOTTEST AND COLDEST MOLECULES				
	LEIBER, FRITZ	AR	SDG 52	03
KINDERGARTEN	LEIBER, FRITZ	SS	FSF 63	04
THOSE WILD ALIEN WORDS: I	LEIBER, FRITZ	AR	NEW 74	AC
CRAZY ANNAOJ	LEIBER, FRITZ	SS	GAL 68	02
DEBUNKING THE I MACHINE	LEIBER, FRITZ	AR		49
WHEN THE LAST GODS DIE	LEIBER, FRITZ	SS	FSF 51	12
KING LEAR	LEIBER, FRITZ	AR		34
YESTERDAY HOUSE	LEIBER, FRITZ	NV	GAL 52	08
AFTER SUCH KNOWLEDGE	LEIBER, FRITZ	AR		74
KNIGHT TO MOVE (KNIGHT'S MOVE)				
	LEIBER, FRITZ	SS	BRD 65	12
WEIRD WORLD OF THE KNIGHT (TOPSY-TURVY WORLD OF..)				
	LEIBER, FRITZ	AR	CCR 60	01
TO ARKHAM AND THE STARS	LEIBER, FRITZ	AR		66
WHISPERER RE-EXAMINED, THE	LEIBER, FRITZ	AR		
BEAUTY AND THE BEASTS	LEIBER, FRITZ	SS	NEW 74	AC
MASTERS OF MACE AND MAGIC	LEIBER, FRITZ	AR		
CAT'S CRADLE	LEIBER, FRITZ	SS		
BOOK OF GORDON DICKSON, THE	DICKSON, GORDON R.	AC	DAW 73	05
SEE "DANGER- HUMAN"				
BOOK OF JOHN BRUNNER, THE	BRUNNER, JOHN	AC	DAW 76	01
PREMUMBLE	BRUNNER, JOHN	MS		
CROSSWORD	BRUNNER, JOHN	MS		
LIMERICK NO. 1	BRUNNER, JOHN	PM	ABA	
DIFFERENT KICK, OR HOW TO GET HIGH WITHOUT ACTUALLY GOING				
INTO ORBIT, A	BRUNNER, JOHN	AR	NIE 65	
"LULLABY FOR THE MAD SCIENTIST'S DAUGHTER"				
	BRUNNER, JOHN	SG	NEW 76	AC
BLOODSTREAM	BRUNNER, JOHN	SS	VTX 74	06
DOMESTIC CRISIS 2017	BRUNNER, JOHN	PM	TRB 74	03
HIDE AND SEEK (CACHE-CACHE BY GERARD KLEIN, TRANS)				
	BRUNNER, JOHN	SS		73
LIMERICK NO. 2	BRUNNER, JOHN	PM	ABA	
TECHNOLOGICAL FOLK HERO: HAS HE A FUTURE?, THE				
	BRUNNER, JOHN	AR	FLK 72	05
"BALLAD OF TEDDY HART, THE"	BRUNNER, JOHN	SG	NEW 76	AC
WHO STEALS MY PURSE	BRUNNER, JOHN	NV	ASF 73	03
EXCERPT FROM A SOCIAL HISTORY OF THE 20TH CENTURY				
	BRUNNER, JOHN	SS		70
FEGHOOT I	BRUNNER, JOHN	SS	FSF 62	06
DIE SPANGE (BY STEFAN GEORGE, TRANSLATION)				
	BRUNNER, JOHN	PM	NEW 76	AC
LIMERICK NO. 3	BRUNNER, JOHN	PM	VCT	
THEM AS CAN, DOES	BRUNNER, JOHN	AR	NWS 66	01
"FAITHLESS JACK THE SPACEMAN"				
	BRUNNER, JOHN	SG	NEW 76	AC
WHEN GABRIEL...	BRUNNER, JOHN	SS	SCF 56	08
WHAT WE HAVE HERE	BRUNNER, JOHN	PM		70
FEGHOOT II	BRUNNER, JOHN	SS	NEW 76	AC
SPARTANS' EPITAPH AT THERMOPYLAE (FROM GREEK ANTH)				
	BRUNNER, JOHN	MS	NEW 76	AC
LIMERICK NO. 4	BRUNNER, JOHN	PM	NEW 76	AC
EDUCATIONAL RELEVANCE OF SCIENCE FICTION, THE				
	BRUNNER, JOHN	AR	PHE 71	06
"SPACEWRECK OF THE OLD 97, THE"				
	BRUNNER, JOHN	SG	NEW 76	AC
MANALIVE	BRUNNER, JOHN	EX	REA 64	04
MATTHEW XVIII, 6	BRUNNER, JOHN	PM	WKS 71	15
FEGHOOT III	BRUNNER, JOHN	SS	NEW 76	AC
CORRIDA (BY RAINER MARIA RILKE, TRANSLATION)				
	BRUNNER, JOHN	PM	CHP 73	
LIMERICK NO. 5	BRUNNER, JOHN	PM	NEW 76	AC
EVOLUTION OF A SCIENCE FICTION WRITER, THE				
	BRUNNER, JOHN	AR	FDN 72	01
"H-BOMBS' THUNDER, THE"	BRUNNER, JOHN	SG	SNG 58	10
NEW THING, THE	BRUNNER, JOHN	SS	IFS 69	12
ATOM BOMB IS TWENTY-FIVE THIS YEAR, THE				
	BRUNNER, JOHN	PM	STY 70	
EPIGRAMMATA LXV (BY DECIMUS MAGNUS AUSONIUS, TRANS)				
	BRUNNER, JOHN	PM	NEW 76	AC
SOLUTION TO CROSSWORD	BRUNNER, JOHN	MS		
BOOK OF PHILIP JOSE FARMER, THE				
	FARMER, PHILIP JOSE	AC	DAW 73	07
FOREWORD	FARMER, PHILIP JOSE	IN		
MY SISTER'S BROTHER (OPEN TO ME, MY SISTER)				
	FARMER, PHILIP JOSE	NV	FSF 60	05
SKINBURN	FARMER, PHILIP JOSE	SS	FSF 72	10
ALLEY MAN, THE	FARMER, PHILIP JOSE	NV	FSF 59	06
FATHER'S IN THE BASEMENT	FARMER, PHILIP JOSE	SS	ORB 72	11
TOWARDS THE BELOVED CITY	FARMER, PHILIP JOSE	NV	SAW 72	
POLYTROPICAL PARAMYTHS	FARMER, PHILIP JOSE	AI		
TOTEM AND TABOO	FARMER, PHILIP JOSE	SS	FSF 54	12
DON'T WASH THE CARATS	FARMER, PHILIP JOSE	SS	ORB 68	03
SUMERIAN OATH, THE	FARMER, PHILIP JOSE	SS	NOV 72	02
VOICE OF THE SONAR IN MY VERMIFORM APPENDIX, THE				
	FARMER, PHILIP JOSE	SS	QRK 71	02
BRASS AND GOLD, OR HORSE AND ZEPPELIN IN BEVERLY HILLS				
	FARMER, PHILIP JOSE	SS	QRK 71	04
ONLY WHO CAN MAKE A TREE?	FARMER, PHILIP JOSE	SS	FSF 71	11
EXCLUSIVE INTERVIEW WITH LORD GREYSTOKE, AN (TARZAN LIVES)				
	FARMER, PHILIP JOSE	SS	ESQ 72	04
SEXUAL IMPLICATIONS OF THE CHARGE OF THE LIGHT BRIGADE				
	FARMER, PHILIP JOSE	SS	DVS 67	01
OBSCURE LIFE AND HARD TIMES OF KILGORE TROUT, THE				
	FARMER, PHILIP JOSE	SS	MOB 71	12
THANKS FOR THE FEAST, NOTES ON PHILIP JOSE FARMER				
	FIEDLER, LESLIE A.	MS		
BOOK OF PHILIP K. DICK, THE	DICK, PHILIP K.	AC	DAW 73	02
NANNY	DICK, PHILIP K.	SS	STS 55	SP
TURNING WHEEL, THE	DICK, PHILIP K.	SS	SFS 54	02
DEFENDERS, THE	DICK, PHILIP K.	NV	GAL 53	01
ADJUSTMENT TEAM	DICK, PHILIP K.	NV	OSF 54	09
PSI-MAN (PSI-MAN HEAL MY CHILD)				
	DICK, PHILIP K.	NV	IMT 55	11
COMMUTER, THE	DICK, PHILIP K.	SS	AMZ 53	09
PRESENT FOR PAT, A	DICK, PHILIP K.	SS	STS 54	01
BREAKFAST AT TWILIGHT	DICK, PHILIP K.	SS	AMZ 54	07
SHELL GAME	DICK, PHILIP K.	SS	GAL 54	09
BOOK OF POUL ANDERSON, THE	ANDERSON, POUL	AC	DAW 75	06
SEE "THE MANY WORLDS OF POUL ANDERSON"				
BOOK OF SABERHAGEN, THE	SABERHAGEN, FRED	AC	DAW 75	01
LONG WAY HOME, THE	SABERHAGEN, FRED	SS	GAL 61	06
PLANETEER	SABERHAGEN, FRED	NV	GAL 61	04
VOLUME PAA-PYX	SABERHAGEN, FRED	SS	GAL 61	02
SEVEN DOORS TO EDUCATION	SABERHAGEN, FRED	NV	IFS 61	05
DEEP SPACE	SABERHAGEN, FRED	SS		

BOOK OF SABERHAGEN, THE

PRESSURE (BERSERKER'S PREY) SABERHAGEN, FRED SS IFS 67 06
STARSONG SABERHAGEN, FRED SS IFS 68 01
CALENDARS SABERHAGEN, FRED SS GAL 74 01
YOUNG GIRL AT AN OPEN HALF-DOOR
  SABERHAGEN, FRED SS FSF 68 11
WHAT DO YOU WANT ME TO DO TO PROVE IM HUMAN STOP (INHUMAN
  ERROR) SABERHAGEN, FRED SS ASF 74 10

BOOK OF SKAITH, THE BRACKETT, LEIGH AC H NDB 76
  THE ADVENTURES OF ERIC JOHN STARK
GINGER STAR, THE BRACKETT, LEIGH NO IFS 74 02
HOUNDS OF SKAITH, THE BRACKETT, LEIGH NO BAL 74 10
REAVERS OF SKAITH, THE BRACKETT, LEIGH NO BAL 76 08

BOOK OF VAN VOGT, THE VAN VOGT, A. E. AC DAW 72
TIMED CLOCK, THE VAN VOGT, A. E. SS NEW 72 AC
CONFESSION, THE VAN VOGT, A. E. SS NEW 72 AC
RAT AND THE SNAKE, THE VAN VOGT, A. E. SS WTS 71 01
BARBARIAN, THE VAN VOGT, A. E. NV ASF 47 12
ERSATZ ETERNAL VAN VOGT, A. E. NV NEW 72 AC
SOUND OF WILD LAUGHTER, THE VAN VOGT, A. E. NV NEW 72 AC
LOST: FIFTY SUNS VAN VOGT, A. E. NV NEW 52 NO

BORN OF MAN AND WOMAN MATHESON, RICHARD AC H CHB 54 03
  DERIVATIVE COLLECTION "THIRD FROM THE SUN"
BORN OF MAN AND WOMAN MATHESON, RICHARD SS FSF 50 SU
THIRD FROM THE SUN MATHESON, RICHARD SS GAL 50 10
THROUGH CHANNELS MATHESON, RICHARD SS FSF 51 04
LOVER, WHEN YOU'RE NEAR ME MATHESON, RICHARD NV GAL 52 05
SRL AD MATHESON, RICHARD SS FSF 52 04
MAD HOUSE MATHESON, RICHARD NV FAN 53 02
F--- (THE FOODLEGGER) MATHESON, RICHARD SS TWS 52 04
DEAR DIARY MATHESON, RICHARD SS NEW 54 AN
TO FIT THE CRIME MATHESON, RICHARD SS FAN 52 12
WITCH WAR MATHESON, RICHARD SS STS 51 07
RETURN MATHESON, RICHARD SS TWS 51 10
DRESS OF WHITE SILK MATHESON, RICHARD SS FSF 51 10
FULL CIRCLE MATHESON, RICHARD SS FUN 53 08
DISAPPEARING ACT MATHESON, RICHARD SS FSF 53 03
WEDDING, THE MATHESON, RICHARD SS BEY 53 07
SHIPSHAPE HOME MATHESON, RICHARD SS GAL 52 07
TRAVELER, THE MATHESON, RICHARD SS FSF 62 02

BORN WITH THE DEAD SILVERBERG, ROBERT AC H RDM 74
BORN WITH THE DEAD SILVERBERG, ROBERT NA FSF 74 04
THOMAS THE PROCLAIMER SILVERBERG, ROBERT NA
GOING SILVERBERG, ROBERT NA FFU 71

BOYS' LIFE BOOK OF OUTER SPACE STORIES, THE
  BOY'S LIFE, ED. OF AN H RDM 64
MAN, THE BRADBURY, RAY SS TWS 49 02
NEW GAME, A LIGHTNER, A. M. SS BLF 59
TIGER BY THE TAIL HENDERSON, GENE L. SS BLF
SMALLEST MOON, THE WILCOX, DON SS BLF
SPACE LANE CADET HALSTEAD, WILLIAM F. SS BLF
LOAD OF TROUBLE WOOD, EDWARD W. SS BLF
BEST FRIEND LIGHTNER, A. M. SS BLF 61
TERRIBLE INTRUDERS, THE HINRICHS, JAMES V. SS BLF
SAMARITAN, THE HARPER, RICHARD SS BLF
QUADS FROM MARS GREER, WILLIAM W. SS BLF

BR-R-R-! CONKLIN, GROFF AN AVN 59
INTRODUCTION CONKLIN, GROFF IN
IT STURGEON, THEODORE NV UNK 40 08
NURSERY RHYME BEAUMONT, CHARLES SS NEW 57 AC
DOOMSDAY DEFERRED JENKINS, WILL F. SS SEP 49 09
WARM, DARK PLACES GOLD, H. L. SS UNK 40 10
LEGAL RITES ASIMOV, ISAAC NV C WRT 50 09
  AND POHL, FREDERIK
EGYPTIAN HORNET, AN BLACKWOOD, ALGERNON SS 17
WHITE GODDESS SEABRIGHT, IDRIS SS FSF 56 07
HANDLER, THE BRADBURY, RAY SS WRT 47 01
SOUND MACHINE, THE DAHL, ROALD SS NYM 49 09
WORM, THE KELLER, DAVID H. MD. SS AMZ 29 03

BREAKING POINT GUNN, JAMES E. AC H WKR 72
INTRODUCTION GUNN, JAMES E. IN
BREAKING POINT GUNN, JAMES E. NV SSF 53 03
MONSTER NAMED SMITH, A GUNN, JAMES E. NV IFS 54 07
CINDERELLA STORY (WHEN THE SHOE FITS)
  GUNN, JAMES E. SS VAN 58 06
TEDDY BEAR GUNN, JAMES E. SS WOF 70 02
MAN WHO OWNED TOMORROW, THE GUNN, JAMES E. SS ARG 53 07
GREEN THUMB GUNN, JAMES E. NV IFS 57 04
POWER AND THE GLORY, THE (THE MAN WHO WOULD NOT)
  GUNN, JAMES E. SS IFS 69 12
LISTENERS, THE (ALSO AS ROBERT MACDONALD- 2025)
  GUNN, JAMES E. NV GAL 68 09
TRANSLATIONS GUNN, JAMES E. MS

BRIAN ALDISS OMNIBUS 2 ALDISS, BRIAN W. AC H SID 71
SPACE, TIME AND NATHANIEL ALDISS, BRIAN W. AC FAB 57
NON-STOP ALDISS, BRIAN W. NO FAB 58
MALE RESPONSE, THE ALDISS, BRIAN W. NO BCN 61

BRIAN ALDISS OMNIBUS, A ALDISS, BRIAN W. AC H SID 69
SALIVA TREE, THE ALDISS, BRIAN W. SN FSF 65 09
IMPOSSIBLE STAR, THE ALDISS, BRIAN W. NV WOT 63 08
BASIS FOR NEGOTIATION ALDISS, BRIAN W. NV NWS 62 01
MAN IN HIS TIME ALDISS, BRIAN W. SS SCF 65 04
PRIMAL URGE, THE ALDISS, BRIAN W. SS
INTERPRETER, THE ALDISS, BRIAN W. SS

BROKE DOWN ENGINE AND OTHER TROUBLES WITH MACHINES
  GOULART, RON AC H MAC 71
WAY THINGS DON'T WORK, THE GOULART, RON IN

CALLAHAN'S CROSSTIME SALOON

TROUBLE WITH MACHINES, THE GOULART, RON SS PBY 68 08
BROKE DOWN ENGINE (BROKE AND HUNGRY, NO PLACE TO GO)
  GOULART, RON SS GAL 69 11
LOFTHOUSE (A MAN'S HOME IS HIS CASTLE)
  GOULART, RON SS PBY 69 03
CALLING DR. CLOCKWORK GOULART, RON SS AMZ 65 03
PRINCESS NO. 22 GOULART, RON SS FSF 62 05
ALL FOR LOVE (BY WAY OF MARS)
  GOULART, RON SS WOT 65 03
KATY DIALOGUES, THE GOULART, RON SS FSF 58 07
NOBODY STARVES GOULART, RON SS FSF 64 02
MUSCADINE GOULART, RON SS FSF 68 04
DISPOSAL GOULART, RON SS VSF 70 02
TO THE RESCUE GOULART, RON SS FSF 66 01
JOKER FOR HIRE (ANYTHING FOR LAUGHS)
  GOULART, RON NV FAN 63 05
TERMINAL GOULART, RON SS FAN 65 05

BUDRYS' INFERNO BUDRYS, ALGIS AC BKM 63 07
  IN ENGLAND AS "THE FURIOUS FUTURE"
INTRODUCTION BUDRYS, ALGIS IN
SILENT BROTHER BUDRYS, ALGIS SS ASF 56 02
BETWEEN THE DARK AND THE DAYLIGHT
  BUDRYS, ALGIS SS INF 58 10
AND THEN SHE FOUND HIM... BUDRYS, ALGIS SS VSF 57 07
SKIRMISHER, THE BUDRYS, ALGIS SS INF 57 11
MAN WHO TASTED ASHES, THE BUDRYS, ALGIS SS IFS 59 02
LOWER THAN ANGELS BUDRYS, ALGIS SN INF 56 10
CONTACT BETWEEN EQUALS BUDRYS, ALGIS SS VSF 58 07
DREAM OF VICTORY BUDRYS, ALGIS NV AMZ 53 09
PEASANT GIRL, THE BUDRYS, ALGIS SS ASF 56 06

BUG-EYED MONSTERS CHEETHAM, ANTHONY AN PTH 74
INTRODUCTION CHEETHAM, ANTHONY IN
INVASION FROM MARS KOCH, HOWARD PL CBS 38 10
NOT ONLY DEAD MEN VAN VOGT, A. E. SS ASF 42 11
ARENA BROWN, FREDRIC NV ASF 44 06
SURFACE TENSION BLISH, JAMES NA GAL 52 08
DESERTER, THE TENN, WILLIAM SS STR 53 01
MOTHER FARMER, PHILIP JOSE NV TWS 53 04
STRANGER STATION KNIGHT, DAMON NV FSF 56 12
GREENSLAVES HERBERT, FRANK NV AMZ 65 03
BALANCED ECOLOGY SCHMITZ, JAMES H. SS ASF 65 03
DANCE OF THE CHANGER AND THE THREE, THE
  CARR, TERRY SS FRS 68

BULLARD OF THE SPACE PATROL JAMESON, MALCOLM AC H WOR 51
  EDITED BY ANDRE NORTON, SECOND EDITION OMITS "THE BUREAUCRAT"
INTRODUCTION NORTON, ANDRE IN
ADMIRAL'S INSPECTION JAMESON, MALCOLM NV ASF 40 04
WHITE MUTINY JAMESON, MALCOLM NV ASF 40 10
BLOCKADE RUNNER (SLACKER'S PARADISE)
  JAMESON, MALCOLM SS ASF 41 04
BULLARD REFLECTS JAMESON, MALCOLM SS ASF 41 12
BRIMSTONE BILL JAMESON, MALCOLM SS ASF 42 07
ORDERS JAMESON, MALCOLM SS ASF 45 12
BUREAUCRAT, THE JAMESON, MALCOLM NV ASF 44 04

BURNING, THE GUNN, JAMES E. NO DEL 72 02
WITCHES MUST BURN GUNN, JAMES E. NV ASF 56 08
TRIAL BY FIRE GUNN, JAMES E. SN IFS 69 02
WITCH HUNT GUNN, JAMES E. NV GAL 69 04

BUY JUPITER AND OTHER STORIES
  ASIMOV, ISAAC AC H DBL 75
DARWINIAN POOL ROOM ASIMOV, ISAAC SS GAL 50 10
DAY OF THE HUNTERS ASIMOV, ISAAC SS FUT 50 11
SHAH GUIDO G. ASIMOV, ISAAC SS MAR 51 11
BUTTON, BUTTON ASIMOV, ISAAC SS STS 53 01
MONKEY'S FINGER, THE ASIMOV, ISAAC SS STS 53 02
EVEREST ASIMOV, ISAAC SS USF 53 12
PAUSE, THE ASIMOV, ISAAC SS
LET'S NOT ASIMOV, ISAAC SS BUG 54 12
EACH AN EXPLORER ASIMOV, ISAAC SS FUT 56 30
BLANK! ASIMOV, ISAAC SS INF 57 06
DOES A BEE CARE? ASIMOV, ISAAC SS IFS 57 06
SILLY ASSES ASIMOV, ISAAC SS FUT 58 02
BUY JUPITER! ASIMOV, ISAAC SS VSF 58 05
STATUE FOR FATHER, A ASIMOV, ISAAC SS SAT 59 02
RAIN, RAIN, GO AWAY ASIMOV, ISAAC SS FUN 59 09
FOUNDING FATHER ASIMOV, ISAAC SS GAL 65 10
EXILE TO HELL ASIMOV, ISAAC SS ASF 68 05
KEY ITEM ASIMOV, ISAAC SS FSF 68 07
PROPER STUDY, THE ASIMOV, ISAAC SS BLF 68 09
2430 A.D. ASIMOV, ISAAC SS IBM 70 10
GREATEST ASSET, THE ASIMOV, ISAAC SS ASF 72 01
TAKE A MATCH ASIMOV, ISAAC SS NDM 72 02
THIOTIMOLINE TO THE STARS ASIMOV, ISAAC SS AMA 73
LIGHT VERSE ASIMOV, ISAAC SS SEP 73 09

BYPASS TO OTHERNESS KUTTNER, HENRY AC BAL 61
COLD WAR KUTTNER, HENRY SS TWS 49 10
CALL HIM DEMON KUTTNER, HENRY SS TWS 46 FL
DARK ANGEL, THE KUTTNER, HENRY SS STS 46 03
PIPER'S SON, THE KUTTNER, HENRY NV ASF 45 02
ABSALOM KUTTNER, HENRY SS STS 46 FL
LITTLE THINGS, THE KUTTNER, HENRY SS TWS 46 FL
NOTHING BUT GINGERBREAD LEFT KUTTNER, HENRY SS ASF 43 01
HOUSING PROBLEM KUTTNER, HENRY SS CHM 44 10

CALLAHAN'S CROSSTIME SALOON ROBINSON, SPIDER AC ACE 77 06
  INTRODUCTION: SPIDER ROBINSON: THE SF WRITER AS EMPATH
  BOVA, BEN IN
FOREWORD ROBINSON, SPIDER IN
GUY WITH THE EYES, THE ROBINSON, SPIDER SS ASF 73 02
TIME-TRAVELER, THE ROBINSON, SPIDER NV ASF 74 04

CALLAHAN'S CROSSTIME SALOON

CENTIPEDE'S DILEMMA, THE	ROBINSON, SPIDER	SS	
TWO HEADS ARE BETTER THAN ONE			
	ROBINSON, SPIDER	SS	ASF 75 05
LAW OF CONSERVATION OF PAIN, THE			
	ROBINSON, SPIDER	NV	VTX 74 12
JUST DESSERT	ROBINSON, SPIDER	SS	
"VOICE IS HEARD IN RAMAH..., A"			
	ROBINSON, SPIDER	SS	ASF 75 11
UNNATURAL CAUSES	ROBINSON, SPIDER	NV	ASF 75 10
WONDERFUL CONSPIRACY, THE	ROBINSON, SPIDER	SS	

CALLIBRATED ALLIGATOR AND OTHER SCIENCE FICTION STORIES, THE

	SILVERBERG, ROBERT	AC H	HRW 69
CALIBRATED ALLIGATOR, THE	SILVERBERG, ROBERT	NV	ASF 60 02
BLAZE OF GLORY	SILVERBERG, ROBERT	SS	GAL 57 08
ARTIFACT BUSINESS, THE	SILVERBERG, ROBERT	SS	FUN 57 04
PRECEDENT	SILVERBERG, ROBERT	NV	ASF 57 12
MUGWUMP FOUR	SILVERBERG, ROBERT	NV	GAL 59 08
WHY?	SILVERBERG, ROBERT	SS	SFS 57 11
HIS HEAD IN THE CLOUDS	SILVERBERG, ROBERT	SS	SFS 57 09
POINT OF FOCUS	SILVERBERG, ROBERT	SS	ASF 57 08
DELIVERY GUARANTEED	SILVERBERG, ROBERT	SS	SFS 59 02

CALTRAPS OF TIME, THE

	MASSON, DAVID I.	AC H	FAB 68
LOST GROUND	MASSON, DAVID I.	SS	NWS 66 12
NOT SO CERTAIN	MASSON, DAVID I.	SS	NWS 67 07
MOUTH OF HELL	MASSON, DAVID I.	SS	NWS 66 01
TWO-TIMER, A	MASSON, DAVID I.	NV	NWS 66 02
TRANSFINITE CHOICE, THE	MASSON, DAVID I.	SS	NWS 66 08
PSYCHOSMOSIS	MASSON, DAVID I.	SS	NWS 66 03
TRAVELER'S REST	MASSON, DAVID I.	SS	NWS 65 09

CAN YOU FEEL ANYTHING WHEN I DO THIS?, AND OTHER STORIES

	SHECKLEY, ROBERT	AC H	DBL 71
IN ENGLAND AS "THE SAME TO YOU DOUBLED"			
CAN YOU FEEL ANYTHING WHEN I DO THIS?			
	SHECKLEY, ROBERT	SS	PBY 69 08
CORDLE TO ONION TO CARROT	SHECKLEY, ROBERT	SS	PBY 69 12
PETRIFIED WORLD, THE	SHECKLEY, ROBERT	SS	IFS 68 02
GAME: FIRST SCHEMATIC	SHECKLEY, ROBERT	SS	NEW 71 AC
DOCTOR ZOMBIE AND HIS FURRY LITTLE FRIENDS			
	SHECKLEY, ROBERT	SS	NEW 71 AC
CRUEL EQUATIONS, THE	SHECKLEY, ROBERT	SS	BOA
SAME TO YOU DOUBLED, THE	SHECKLEY, ROBERT	SS	PBY 70 03
STARTING FROM SCRATCH	SHECKLEY, ROBERT	SS	FSF 70 11
MNEMONE, THE	SHECKLEY, ROBERT	SS	NEW 71 AC
TRIPOUT	SHECKLEY, ROBERT	SS	BOA
NOTES ON THE PERCEPTION OF IMAGINARY DIFFERENCES			
	SHECKLEY, ROBERT	SS	NEW 71 AC
DOWN THE DIGESTIVE TRACT AND INTO THE COSMOS WITH MANTRA,			
TANTRA, AND SPECKLEBANG	SHECKLEY, ROBERT	SS	GAL 71 02
PAS DE TROIS OF THE CHEF AND THE WAITER AND THE CUSTOMER			
(THREE SINNERS IN THE...)	SHECKLEY, ROBERT	SS	PBY 71 08
ASPECTS OF LANGRANAK	SHECKLEY, ROBERT	SS	NEW 71 AC
PLAGUE CIRCUIT	SHECKLEY, ROBERT	SS	NEW 71 AC
TAILPIPE TO DISASTER	SHECKLEY, ROBERT	SS	FSF

CANARY IN A CAT HOUSE

	VONNEGUT, KURT JR.	AC	FAW 61 09
REPORT ON THE BARNHOUSE EFFECT			
	VONNEGUT, KURT JR.	SS	COL 50 02
ALL THE KING'S HORSES	VONNEGUT, KURT JR.	SS	COL 51 02
D.P.	VONNEGUT, KURT JR.	SS	LHJ 53 08
MANNED MISSILES, THE	VONNEGUT, KURT JR.	SS	CMP 58 07
EUPHIO QUESTION, THE	VONNEGUT, KURT JR.	SS	COL 51 05
MORE STATELY MANSIONS	VONNEGUT, KURT JR.	SS	COL 51 12
FOSTER PORTFOLIO, THE	VONNEGUT, KURT JR.	SS	COL 51 09
DEER IN THE WORKS	VONNEGUT, KURT JR.	SS	ESQ 55 04
HAL IRWIN'S MAGIC LAMP	VONNEGUT, KURT JR.	SS	CMP 57 06
TOM EDISON'S SHAGGY DOG	VONNEGUT, KURT JR.	SS	COL 53 03
UNREADY TO WEAR	VONNEGUT, KURT JR.	SS	GAL 53 04
TOMORROW AND TOMORROW AND TOMORROW (THE BIG TRIP UP YONDER)			
	VONNEGUT, KURT JR.	SS	GAL 54 01

CANOPY OF TIME, THE

	ALDISS, BRIAN W.	AC H	FAB 59
THREE'S A CLOUD (THE UNBEATEN TRACK)			
	ALDISS, BRIAN W.	SS	NWS 59 01
ALL THE WORLD'S TEARS	ALDISS, BRIAN W.	SS	NEB 57 05
WHO CAN REPLACE A MAN? (BUT WHO CAN REPLACE A MAN)			
	ALDISS, BRIAN W.	SS	INF 58 06
BLIGHTED PROFILE	ALDISS, BRIAN W.	SS	SCF 58 06
JUDAS DANCED (JUDAS DANCING)	ALDISS, BRIAN W.	SS	SMG 58 01
O ISHRAEL!	ALDISS, BRIAN W.	SS	NWS 57 04
INCENTIVE	ALDISS, BRIAN W.	SS	NWS 58 12
GENE-HIVE (JOURNEY TO THE INTERIOR)			
	ALDISS, BRIAN W.	NV	NEB 58 05
SECRET OF A MIGHTY CITY (HAVE YOUR HATREDS READY)			
	ALDISS, BRIAN W.	SS	FSF 58 05
THEY SHALL INHERIT	ALDISS, BRIAN W.	SS	NEB 58 07
VISITING AMOEBA (WHAT TRIUMPHS?)			
	ALDISS, BRIAN W.	NV	AUT 57 07

CANTICLE FOR LEIBOWITZ, A

	MILLER, WALTER M. JR	NO H	LIP 60
CANTICLE FOR LEIBOWITZ, A	MILLER, WALTER M. JR	NV	FSF 55 04
AND THE LIGHT IS RISEN	MILLER, WALTER M. JR	SN	FSF 56 08
LAST CANTICLE, THE	MILLER, WALTER M. JR	SN	FSF 57 02

CAPRICORN GAMES

	SILVERBERG, ROBERT	AC H	RDM 76
CAPRICORN GAMES	SILVERBERG, ROBERT	SS	74
SCIENCE FICTION HALL OF FAME, THE			
	SILVERBERG, ROBERT	SS	INY 73 05
MS. FOUND IN AN ABANDONED TIME MACHINE			
	SILVERBERG, ROBERT	SS	TTM 73
BRECKENRIDGE AND THE CONTINUUM			
	SILVERBERG, ROBERT	NV	SCS 73
SHIP-SISTER, STAR-SISTER	SILVERBERG, ROBERT	NV	TAL 73
SEA OF FACES, A	SILVERBERG, ROBERT	SS	UNI 74 04

CENTURY OF SCIENCE FICTION, A

DYBBUK OF MAZEL TOV IV, THE	SILVERBERG, ROBERT	SS	NEW 74 AN
GETTING ACROSS	SILVERBERG, ROBERT	NV	FUC 73

CASE AGAINST TOMORROW, THE

	POHL, FREDERIK	AC	BAL 57 05
MIDAS PLAGUE, THE	POHL, FREDERIK	NA	GAL 54 04
CENSUS TAKERS, THE	POHL, FREDERIK	SS	FSF 56 02
CANDLE LIGHTER, THE	POHL, FREDERIK	SS	GAL 55 03
CELEBRATED NO-HIT INNING, THE			
	POHL, FREDERIK	SS	FUN 56 09
WAPSHOT'S DEMON	POHL, FREDERIK	SS	SFS 56 07
MY LADY GREEN SLEEVES	POHL, FREDERIK	NA	FSF 57 02

CASE AND THE DREAMER

	STURGEON, THEODORE	AC H	NDB 74
CASE AND THE DREAMER	STURGEON, THEODORE	NV	GAL 73 01
IF ALL MEN WERE BROTHERS, WOULD YOU LET ONE MARRY YOUR SISTER?			
	STURGEON, THEODORE	NA	DVS 67 01
WHEN YOU CARE, WHEN YOU LOVE	STURGEON, THEODORE	NV	FSF 62 09

CASEY AGONISTES, AND OTHER S.F. & FANTASY STORIES

	MCKENNA, RICHARD M.	AC H	HPR 73
INTRODUCTION	KNIGHT, DAMON	IN	
CASEY AGONISTES	MCKENNA, RICHARD M.	SS	FSF 58 09
HUNTER, COME HOME	MCKENNA, RICHARD M.	NV	FSF 63 03
SECRET PLACE, THE	MCKENNA, RICHARD M.	SS	ORB 66 01
MINE OWN WAYS	MCKENNA, RICHARD M.	SS	FSF 60 02
FIDDLER'S GREEN	MCKENNA, RICHARD M.	NV	ORB 67 02

CATEGORY PHOENIX

	BLEILER & DIKTY	AN H	BDL 55
SEE "YEAR'S BEST SCIENCE FICTION NOVELS: 1953"			
OMITS "THE GADGET HAD A GHOST" AND "CONDITIONALLY HUMAN"			

CAUTION! INFLAMMABLE!

	SCORTIA, THOMAS N.	AC H	DBL 75 07
INTRODUCTION	STURGEON, THEODORE	IN	
CAUTION! INFLAMMABLE! (THE END OF THE LINE)			
	SCORTIA, THOMAS N.	SS	FAN 55 02
SEA CHANGE (ALSO AS THE SHORES OF NIGHT)			
	SCORTIA, THOMAS N.	SS	ASF 56 06
THOUGH A SPARROW FALL	SCORTIA, THOMAS N.	SS	ASF 65 07
JOHN ROBERTS AND THE DRAGON'S EGG			
	SCORTIA, THOMAS N.	SS	FUN 57 08
LAST WAR, THE	SCORTIA, THOMAS N.	SS	NEW 75 AC
WHEN YOU HEAR THE TONE	SCORTIA, THOMAS N.	SS	GAL 71 01
WOMAN'S RIB	SCORTIA, THOMAS N.	SS	GAL 72 07
MORALITY	SCORTIA, THOMAS N.	SS	FAN 69 12
WORM IN THE ROSE, THE	SCORTIA, THOMAS N.	SS	SWK 72 05
FLOWERING NARCISSUS	SCORTIA, THOMAS N.	SS	EIO 73
ICEBOX BLONDE, THE	SCORTIA, THOMAS N.	SS	ROG 59 06
BOMB IN THE BATHTUB, THE	SCORTIA, THOMAS N.	SS	GAL 57 02
JUDAS FISH	SCORTIA, THOMAS N.	SS	YRT 70
FALL OUT ONE	SCORTIA, THOMAS N.	SS	MSM 72 03
BY THE TIME I GET TO PHOENIX	SCORTIA, THOMAS N.	SS	INY 72 04
GEE, WURLITZER! IT'S A DAD!	SCORTIA, THOMAS N.	SS	DAP 71 06
OLD, OLD DEATH IN NEW, NEW VENICE			
	SCORTIA, THOMAS N.	SS	NEW 75 AC
PREMIER'S LADY, THE	SCORTIA, THOMAS N.	SS	NEW 75 AC
GODDESS OF THE CATS, THE	SCORTIA, THOMAS N.	SS	72
WEARIEST RIVER, THE	SCORTIA, THOMAS N.	SS	FUC 73

CAVE GIRL, THE

	BURROUGHS, EDGAR R.	AC H	MCG 25
CAVE GIRL, THE	BURROUGHS, EDGAR R.	NO	ASM 13 07
CAVE MAN, THE	BURROUGHS, EDGAR R.	NO	ASW 17 03

CAVIAR

	STURGEON, THEODORE	AC H	BAL 55 11
ALSO IN "SCIENCE FICTION SPECIAL 3"			
BRIGHT SEGMENT	STURGEON, THEODORE	NV	NEW 55 AC
MICROCOSMIC GOD	STURGEON, THEODORE	NV	ASF 41 04
GHOST OF A CHANCE (THE GREEN EYED MONSTER)			
	STURGEON, THEODORE	SS	UNK 43 06
PRODIGY	STURGEON, THEODORE	SS	ASF 49 04
MEDUSA	STURGEON, THEODORE	SS	ASF 42 02
BLABBERMOUTH	STURGEON, THEODORE	SS	AMZ 47 02
SHADOW, SHADOW, ON THE WALL	STURGEON, THEODORE	SS	IMG 51 02
TWINK	STURGEON, THEODORE	SS	GAL 55 08

CELESTIAL BLUEPRINT, THE

	FARMER, PHILIP JOSE	DC	ACE 62
RASTIGNAC THE DEVIL	FARMER, PHILIP JOSE	SS	FUN 54 05
CELESTIAL BLUEPRINT, THE	FARMER, PHILIP JOSE	SS	FUN 54 07
THEY TWINKLED LIKE JEWELS	FARMER, PHILIP JOSE	SS	FUN 54 01
TOTEM AND TABOO	FARMER, PHILIP JOSE	SS	FSF 54 12

CENTURY OF GREAT SHORT SCIENCE FICTION NOVELS, A

	KNIGHT, DAMON	AN H	DCT 64
STRANGE CASE OF DR. JEKYLL AND MR. HYDE			
	STEVENSON, ROBERT L.	SN	85
INVISIBLE MAN, THE	WELLS, H. G.	SN	PKS 97 06
ABSOLUTE AT LARGE, THE	CAPEK, KAREL	SN	MAC 27
GULF	HEINLEIN, ROBERT A.	SN	ASF 49 11
E FOR EFFORT	SHERRED, T. L.	NV	ASF 47 05
HUNTER, COME HOME	MCKENNA, RICHARD M.	NV	FSF 63 03

CENTURY OF SCIENCE FICTION, A

	KNIGHT, DAMON	AN H	SAS 62
INTRODUCTION	KNIGHT, DAMON	IN	
IDEAL, THE (SELECTION FROM)	WEINBAUM, STANLEY G.	EX	WOS 35 09
MOXON'S MASTER	BIERCE, AMBROSE	SS	93
REASON	ASIMOV, ISAAC	SS	ASF 41 04
WHO CAN REPLACE A MAN? (BUT WHO CAN REPLACE A MAN)			
	ALDISS, BRIAN W.	SS	INF 58 06
TIME MACHINE, THE (SELECTION FROM)			
	WELLS, H. G.	EX	NRV 95 01
OF TIME AND THIRD AVENUE	BESTER, ALFRED	SS	FSF 51 10
SAIL ON! SAIL ON!	FARMER, PHILIP JOSE	SS	STS 52 12
WORLDS OF THE IMPERIUM (SELECTION FROM)			
	LAUMER, KEITH	EX	FAN 61 02
BUSINESS, AS USUAL, THE	REYNOLDS, MACK	SS	FSF 52 06
WHAT'S IT LIKE OUT THERE?	HAMILTON, EDMOND	NV	TWS 52 12

CENTURY OF SCIENCE FICTION, A   CITIZEN IN SPACE

SKY LIFT   HEINLEIN, ROBERT A.   SS   IMG 53 11
STAR, THE   CLARKE, ARTHUR C.   SS   INF 55 11
CRYSTAL EGG, THE   WELLS, H. G.   SS   NRV 97 05
WIND PEOPLE, THE   BRADLEY, MARION Z.   SS   IFS 59 02
UNHUMAN SACRIFICE   MACLEAN, KATHERINE   NV   ASF 58 11
WHAT WAS IT? (1859)   O'BRIEN, FITZ-JAMES   SS   HRP 59 03
FIRST DAYS OF MAY, THE (FCT 60 05)
                            VEILLOT, CLAUDE   SS   FSF 61 12
DAY OF SUCCESSION   THOMAS, THEODORE L.   SS   ASF 59 08
ANGEL'S EGG   PANGBORN, EDGAR   NV   GAL 51 06
ANOTHER WORLD (1895)   ROSNY, J. H. (AINE)   NV   RVP 95
ODD JOHN (SELECTION FROM)   STAPLEDON, OLAF   EX   MTH 35
CALL ME JOE   ANDERSON, POUL   NV   ASF 57 04
FROM THE "LONDON TIMES" OF 1904
                            TWAIN, MARK   SS   CNY 98 11
TWENTY THOUSAND LEAGUES UNDER THE SEA (1873)
                            VERNE, JULES   EX   GMS 73
YOU ARE WITH IT!   STANTON, WILL   SS   FSF 61 12
CEASE FIRE   HERBERT, FRANK   SS   ASF 58 01
SUGGESTED READING   MISC. MATERIAL   MS

CHAINS OF THE SEA   SILVERBERG, ROBERT   OA H NDB 73
INTRODUCTION   SILVERBERG, ROBERT   IN
AND US, TOO, I GUESS   EFFINGER, GEO. ALEC   NA   CHN 73
CHAINS OF THE SEA   DOZOIS, GARDNER R.   NA   CHN 73
SHRINE OF SEBASTIAN, THE   EKLUND, GORDON   NA   CHN 73

CHAMBER OF HORRORS   BLOCH, ROBERT   AC   AWD 66
LIVING END, THE   BLOCH, ROBERT   SS   SMM 63 05
HEAD HUNTER, THE (THE HEAD MAN)
                            BLOCH, ROBERT   SS   FIF 50 06
IMPRACTICAL JOKER (THE DEADLY JOKER)
                            BLOCH, ROBERT   SS   SMM 65 08
PRIDE GOES-   BLOCH, ROBERT   SS   SMM 66 08
SCREAMING PEOPLE, THE   BLOCH, ROBERT   NV   PAN 59 01
FAT CHANCE   BLOCH, ROBERT   SS   KHM 60 08
UNPARDONABLE CRIME, THE   BLOCH, ROBERT   SS   SWK 61 09
METHOD FOR MURDER   BLOCH, ROBERT   SS   FUR 62 07
TWO OF A KIND   BLOCH, ROBERT   SS   61
UNTOUCHABLE   BLOCH, ROBERT   SS   SMM 62 03
BEELZEBUB   BLOCH, ROBERT   SS   PBY 63 12
FROZEN FEAR   BLOCH, ROBERT   SS   WRT 46 05

CHAMELEON CORPS & OTHER SHAPE CHANGERS, THE
                            GOULART, RON   AC H MAC 72
FOREWORD: MAN OF A THOUSAND FACES
                            GOULART, RON   IN
CHAMELEON   GOULART, RON   SS   FSF 64 09
RAKE   GOULART, RON   SS   FSF 65 06
COPSTATE   GOULART, RON   SS   FSF 65 05
MASTERPIECE   GOULART, RON   SS   FSF 72 05
SUNFLOWER   GOULART, RON   NV   FSF 70 12
IGNATZ   GOULART, RON   SS   IFS 60 03
SUBJECT TO CHANGE   GOULART, RON   SS   GAL 60 12
PLEASE STAND BY   GOULART, RON   NV   FSF 62 01
SHANDY   GOULART, RON   SS   IFS 58 10
CHANGE OVER   GOULART, RON   SS   NEW 72 AC
LOOKING INTO IT   GOULART, RON   SS   NEW 72 AC

CHANGE THE SKY AND OTHER STORIES
                            ST. CLAIR, MARGARET   AC   ACE 74
CHANGE THE SKY   ST. CLAIR, MARGARET   SS   FSF 55 03
BEAULIEU   ST. CLAIR, MARGARET   SS   FSF 57 07
MARRIAGE MANUAL   ST. CLAIR, MARGARET   SS   STS 54 FL
AGE OF PROPHECY, THE   ST. CLAIR, MARGARET   NA   FUT 51 03
THEN FLY OUR GREETINGS   ST. CLAIR, MARGARET   SS   STS 51 03
OLD-FASHIONED BIRD CHRISTMAS, AN
                            ST. CLAIR, MARGARET   NV   GAL 61 12
STARDUST   ST. CLAIR, MARGARET   SS   FSF 56 09
THIRSTY GOD   ST. CLAIR, MARGARET   SS   FSF 53 03
ALTRUISTS, THE   ST. CLAIR, MARGARET   SS   FSF 53 11
SHORE LEAVE   ST. CLAIR, MARGARET   SS
WINES OF EARTH, THE   ST. CLAIR, MARGARET   SS   FSF 57 09
ASKING   ST. CLAIR, MARGARET   SS   FSF 55 11
GRAVEYARD SHIFT   ST. CLAIR, MARGARET   SS   FSF 59 02
PORT IRON   ST. CLAIR, MARGARET   SS   SFQ 55 11
GODDESS ON THE STREET CORNER, THE
                            ST. CLAIR, MARGARET   SS   BEY 53 09
EGG A MONTH FROM ALL OVER, AN
                            ST. CLAIR, MARGARET   SS   FSF 52 10
DEATH OF EACH DAY, THE   ST. CLAIR, MARGARET   SS   FSF 58 04
LAZARUS   ST. CLAIR, MARGARET   SS   STS 55 FL

CHILDREN OF INFINITY   ELWOOD, ROGER   OA H WAT 73
FOREWORD   ELWOOD, ROGER   IN
GAME OF FUTURES- AN INTRODUCTION, A
                            DEL REY, LESTER   IN
TIME BROTHER   JONES, RAYMOND F.   NV   COI 73
CONVERSATIONS AT LOTHAR'S   MALZBERG, BARRY N.   SS   COI 73
WINGLESS ON AVALON   ANDERSON, POUL   SS   COI 73
SPACE-BORN   BLOCH, ROBERT   NV   COI 73
ALL YOU CAN EAT   BILKER, HARVEY L.
                            AND BILKER, AUDREY L. NV C COI 73
OPENING THE DOOR   FARMER, PHILIP JOSE   SS   COI 73
TERRAFIED   TOFTE, ARTHUR   NV   COI 73
HALF LIFE   PAYES, RACHEL C.   SS   COI 73
TOWER, THE   SCORTIA, THOMAS N.   SS   COI 73
WAKE UP TO THUNDER   KOONTZ, DEAN R.   NV   COI 73

CHILDREN OF THE ATOM   SHIRAS, WILMAR H.   AC H GNM 53
IN HIDING   SHIRAS, WILMAR H.   NV   ASF 48 11
OPENING DOORS   SHIRAS, WILMAR H.   NV   ASF 49 03
NEW FOUNDATIONS   SHIRAS, WILMAR H.   NV   ASF 50 03
PROBLEMS   SHIRAS, WILMAR H.   NV   NEW 53 AC
CHILDREN OF THE ATOM   SHIRAS, WILMAR H.   NV   NEW 53 AC

CHILDREN OF WONDER   TENN, WILLIAM   AN H SAS 53
ALSO AS "OUTSIDERS: CHILDREN OF WONDER"
INTRODUCTION   TENN, WILLIAM   IN
ROCKING-HORSE WINNER, THE   LAWRENCE, D. H.   SS   33
WORDS OF GURU, THE   KORNBLUTH, C. M.   SS   STI 41 06
BABY IS THREE   STURGEON, THEODORE   NA   GAL 52 10
SMALL ASSASSIN, THE   BRADBURY, RAY   SS   DMN 46 11
STORY OF A PANIC, THE   FORSTER, E. M.   SS   47
PIPER'S SON, THE   PADGETT, LEWIS   NV   ASF 45 02
MIRIAM   CAPOTE, TRUMAN   SS   45
ADAM AND EVE AND PINCH ME   COPPARD, A. E.   SS   21
CHILD'S PLAY   SCHNIRRING,ALICEMARY   SS   WRT 42 03
OPEN WINDOW, THE   SAKI   SS   14
END OF THE PARTY, THE (1947) GREENE, GRAHAM   SS   WBY 50 12
IDOL OF THE FLIES, THE   RICE, JANE   SS   UNK 42 05
THAT ONLY A MOTHER   MERRIL, JUDITH   SS   ASF 48 06
BORN OF MAN AND WOMAN   MATHESON, RICHARD   SS   FSF 50 SU
KEYHOLE   LEINSTER, MURRAY   SS   TWS 51 12
TERMINAL QUEST (ALSO AS THE LAST MONSTER)
                            ANDERSON, POUL   SS   SSS 51 08
ORIGIN OF THE SPECIES, THE MACLEAN, KATHERINE   SS   NEW 53 AN
IN HIDING   SHIRAS, WILMAR H.   NV   ASF 48 11
HATCHERY, THE (FROM BRAVE NEW WORLD)
                            HUXLEY, ALDOUS   EX   WND 32
ERRAND BOY   TENN, WILLIAM   SS   ASF 47 06
NIGHTMARE FOR FUTURE REFERENCE
                            BENET, STEPHEN V.   PM   SCH 38 09
ABOUT THE EDITOR   MISC. MATERIAL   MS

CHRONICLES OF A COMER AND OTHER RELIGIOUS SCIENCE FICTION
STORIES   ELWOOD, ROGER   AN L JKP 74
FOREWORD   ELWOOD, ROGER   IN
PROBLEM OF PAIN, THE   ANDERSON, POUL   NV   FSF 73 02
WOLFRAM HUNTERS, THE   HOCH, EDWARD D.   SS   SMM 64 03
GIFT OF NOTHING, THE   HOLLY, JOAN C.   NV   WLK 73
TOWARDS THE BELOVED CITY   FARMER, PHILIP JOSE   NV   SAW 72
CHRONICLES OF A COMER   O'DONNELL, K. M.   SS   WLK 73
IN THIS SIGN (ALSO AS THE FIRE BALLOONS)
                            BRADBURY, RAY   SS   IMG 51 04
CONTRIBUTORS   MISC. MATERIAL   MS

CHRONOPOLIS AND OTHER STORIES
                            BALLARD, J. G.   AC H PUT 71
VOICES OF TIME, THE   BALLARD, J. G.   SS   NWS 60 10
DROWNED GIANT, THE (SOUVENIR)
                            BALLARD, J. G.   SS   PBY 65 05
TERMINAL BEACH, THE   BALLARD, J. G.   SS   NWS 64 03
MANHOLE 69   BALLARD, J. G.   SS   NWS 57 11
STORM-BIRD, STORM-DREAMER   BALLARD, J. G.   SS   NWS 66 11
SOUND-SWEEP, THE   BALLARD, J. G.   NV   SCF 60 02
BILLENIUM   BALLARD, J. G.   SS   NWS 61 11
CHRONOPOLIS   BALLARD, J. G.   NV   NWS 60 06
BUILD-UP (ALSO AS THE CONCENTRATION CITY)
                            BALLARD, J. G.   SS   NWS 57 01
GARDEN OF TIME, THE   BALLARD, J. G.   SS   FSF 62 02
END-GAME   BALLARD, J. G.   SS   NWS 63 06
WATCH-TOWERS, THE   BALLARD, J. G.   NV   SCF 62 06
NOW WAKES THE SEA   BALLARD, J. G.   SS   FSF 63 05
ZONE OF TERROR   BALLARD, J. G.   SS   NWS 60 03
CAGE OF SAND, THE   BALLARD, J. G.   SS   NWS 62 06
DEEP END   BALLARD, J. G.   SS   NWS 61 05

CIRCUS OF DR. LAO AND OTHER IMPROBABLE STORIES
                            BRADBURY, RAY   AN   BAN 56 10
INTRODUCTION   BRADBURY, RAY   IN
CIRCUS OF DR. LAO, THE   FINNEY, CHARLES G.   NA   35
POND, THE   KNEALE, NIGEL   SS   50
HOUR OF LETDOWN, THE   WHITE, E. B.   SS   FSF 52 08
WISH, THE   DAHL, ROALD   SS   53
SUMMER PEOPLE, THE   JACKSON, SHIRLEY   SS   CHM 50
EARTH'S HOLOCAUST   HAWTHORNE, NATHANIEL   SS   GLG 44 05
BUSBY'S PETRIFIED WOMAN   EISELEY, LOREN   SS   HRP 48 11
RESTING PLACE, THE   LA FARGE, OLIVER   SS   NYM 54 10
THRESHOLD   KUTTNER, HENRY   SS   UNK 40 12
GREENFACE   SCHMITZ, JAMES H.   NV   UNK 43 08
LIMITS OF WALTER HORTON, THE SHARNIK, JOHN S.   SS   CHM 54
MAN WHO VANISHED, THE   COATES, ROBERT M.   SS   NYM 55 10

CITIES IN FLIGHT   BLISH, JAMES   AC   AVN 70 02
THEY SHALL HAVE STARS (IN U.S. AS "YEAR 2018!")
                            BLISH, JAMES   NO   FAB 56
LIFE FOR THE STARS, A   BLISH, JAMES   NO   ASF 62 09
EARTHMAN, COME HOME   BLISH, JAMES   NO   PUT 55
TRIUMPH OF TIME, THE (IN ENGLAND AS "A CLASH OF CYMBOLS")
                            BLISH, JAMES   NO   AVN 58
EARTHMANIST CULTURE, THE   MULLEN, RICHARD D.   AR   68

CITIES OF WONDER   KNIGHT, DAMON   AN H DBL 66
INTRODUCTION   KNIGHT, DAMON   IN
SINGLE COMBAT   ABERNATHY, ROBERT   SS   FSF 55 01
DUMB WAITER   MILLER, WALTER M. JR   NV   ASF 52 04
JESTING PILOT   KUTTNER, HENRY   SS   ASF 47 05
IT'S GREAT TO BE BACK!   HEINLEIN, ROBERT A.   SS   SEP 47 07
BILLENIUM   BALLARD, J. G.   SS   NWS 61 11
OKIE   BLISH, JAMES   NV   ASF 50 04
LUCKIEST MAN IN DENV, THE (AS SIMON EISNER)
                            KORNBLUTH, C. M.   SS   GAL 52 06
MACHINE STOPS, THE   FORSTER, E. M.   NV   28
UNDERPRIVILEGED, THE   ALDISS, BRIAN W.   SS   NWS 63 05
BY THE WATERS OF BABYLON (THE PLACE OF THE GODS)
                            BENET, STEPHEN V.   SS   SEP 37 07
FORGETFULNESS   STUART, DON A.   SN   ASF 37 06

CITIZEN IN SPACE   SHECKLEY, ROBERT   AC   BAL 55 12
NOTE TO TEACHERS AND PARENTS:, A
                            TYRE, RICHARD H.   IN

Title	Author	Type	Source
CITIZEN IN SPACE			
MOUNTAIN WITHOUT A NAME, THE	SHECKLEY, ROBERT	SS	NEW 55 AC
ACCOUNTANT, THE	SHECKLEY, ROBERT	SS	FSF 54 07
HUNTING PROBLEM	SHECKLEY, ROBERT	SS	GAL 55 09
THIEF IN TIME, A	SHECKLEY, ROBERT	NV	GAL 54 07
LUCKIEST MAN IN THE WORLD, THE (FORTUNATE PERSON)	SHECKLEY, ROBERT	SS	FUN 55 02
HANDS OFF	SHECKLEY, ROBERT	NV	GAL 54 04
SOMETHING FOR NOTHING	SHECKLEY, ROBERT	SS	GAL 54 06
TICKET TO TRANAI, A	SHECKLEY, ROBERT	NA	GAL 55 10
BATTLE, THE	SHECKLEY, ROBERT	SS	IFS 54 09
SKULKING PERMIT	SHECKLEY, ROBERT	NV	GAL 54 12
CITIZEN IN SPACE (SPY STORY)	SHECKLEY, ROBERT	SS	PBY 55 09
ASK A FOOLISH QUESTION	SHECKLEY, ROBERT	SS	SFS 53 01
CITY	SIMAK, CLIFFORD D.	NO H	GNM 52 05
AESOP	SIMAK, CLIFFORD D.	NV	ASF 47 12
CENSUS	SIMAK, CLIFFORD D.	NV	ASF 44 09
CITY	SIMAK, CLIFFORD D.	NV	ASF 44 05
DESERTION	SIMAK, CLIFFORD D.	SS	ASF 44 11
HOBBIES	SIMAK, CLIFFORD D.	NV	ASF 46 11
HUDDLING PLACE	SIMAK, CLIFFORD D.	SS	ASF 44 07
PARADISE	SIMAK, CLIFFORD D.	SS	ASF 46 06
SIMPLE WAY	SIMAK, CLIFFORD D.	SS	
CITY: 2000 A.D., THE	CLEM:GREENBERG:&	AN	FAW 76 07
INTRODUCTION: WHY THE CITY	CLEM, RALPH GREENBERG, MARTIN H. AND OLANDER, JOSEPH D.	IN C	
NEW YORK A.D. 2660 (RALPH 124C 41+)	GERNSBACK, HUGO	EX	MEL 11 04
JESTING PILOT	KUTTNER, HENRY	SS	ASF 47 05
CHICAGO	MONTELEONE, THOMAS F	SS	FUC 73
STREET OF DREAMS, FEET OF CLAY	SHECKLEY, ROBERT	NV	GAL 68 02
VANISHING AMERICAN, THE	BEAUMONT, CHARLES	SS	FSF 55 08
BILLENIUM	BALLARD, J. G.	SS	NWS 61 11
TOTAL ENVIRONMENT	ALDISS, BRIAN W.	NV	GAL 68 02
BLACK IS BEAUTIFUL	SILVERBERG, ROBERT	SS	YRT 70
IN DARK PLACES	HENSLEY, JOE L.	SS	FUC 73
"EAST WIND, WEST WIND"	ROBINSON, FRANK M.	NV	NOV 72 02
DISPOSAL	GOULART, RON	SS	VSF 70 02
UNDERCITY, THE	KOONTZ, DEAN R.	SS	FUC 73
GAS MASK	HOUSTON, JAMES D.	SS	NUG 64
TRAFFIC PROBLEM	EARLS, WILLIAM	SS	GAL 70 10
GANTLET	PECK, RICHARD E.	SS	ORB 72 10
CITY'S END	REYNOLDS, MACK	NV	FUQ 73
SLIME DWELLERS, THE	EDELSTEIN, SCOTT	SS	VTX 75 06
HAPPY DAY IN 2381, A	SILVERBERG, ROBERT	SS	NOV 70 01
CLARION	WILSON, ROBIN SCOTT	OA	SIG 71 06
INTRODUCTION	WILSON, ROBIN SCOTT	IN	
SOMETHING HAPPENS	WILHELM, KATE	AR	CLR 71 01
WHAT ABOUT US GRILS?	GILDEN, MEL	SS	CLR 71 01
ONLY AT NIGHT	MCINTYRE, VONDA N.	SS	CLR 71 01
SOFT BLUE BUNNY RABBIT STORY, THE	BRYANT, EDWARD	SS	CLR 71 01
DREAMERS ON THE BARRICADES	ELLISON, HARLAN	AR	CLR 71 01
WHEELS	THURSTON, ROBERT	SS	CLR 71 01
TROUBLE FOLLOWS	EFFINGER, GEO. ALEC	SS	CLR 71 01
GAME-PLAYING LITERATURE, THE	POHL, FREDERIK	AR	CLR 71 01
JUST DEAD ENOUGH (THE PRICE)	BELCHER, C. DAVIS	NV	ORB 69 05
SENDING THE VERY BEST	BRYANT, EDWARD	SS	NWS 70 01
CHARTING UTOPIA	KNIGHT, DAMON	AR	CLR 71 01
FREE PASS TO THE CARNIVAL, A	EFFINGER, GEO. ALEC	SS	FSF 71 05
BEHOLDER'S EYE, THE	HUTTON, AMY	SS	CLR 71 01
CHAINS	SKAL, DAVE	SS	CLR 71 01
FANTASY: MANY MANSIONS AND HOVELS	LEIBER, FRITZ	AR	CLR 71 01
ANACONDA	THURSTON, ROBERT	SS	CLR 71 01
CROSSOVER	BUTLER, OCTAVIA E.	SS	CLR 71 01
NORMAN: FRIENDS AND OTHER STRANGERS	STEVENSON, LYNNDA	SS	CLR 71 01
READING BETWEEN THE WORDS	DELANY, SAMUEL R.	AR	CLR 71 01
SILENT HANDS	CONWAY, GERARD F.	SS	CLR 71 01
UNEVEN EVENING, AN	HERBST, STEVE	SS	CLR 71 01
INSPECTOR, THE	LIEF, EVELYN	SS	CLR 71 01
GENRE	RUSS, JOANNA	AR	CLR 71 01
LAST DESPERATE HOUR, THE	THURSTON, ROBERT	SS	CLR 71 01
WESTFIELD HEIGHTS MALL MONSTER, THE	EFFINGER, GEO. ALEC	SS	CLR 71 01
TERRIFIC PLAY OF FORCES NATURAL AND HUMAN, THE	WILSON, ROBIN SCOTT	AR	CLR 71 01
SONG FROM A FORGOTTEN HILL	COOK, GLEN	SS	WOT 71
SECRET, THE	NADLER, MAGGIE	SS	CLR 71 01
BANDEMAR, THE	WEHRLE, JOE JR.	SS	CLR 71 01
CLARION II	WILSON, ROBIN SCOTT	OA	SIG 72 06
PREFACE	WILSON, ROBIN SCOTT	IN	
INTRODUCTION	SALLIS, JAMES	IN	
PUNCHLINE (STOP ME BEFORE I TELL MORE)	THURSTON, ROBERT	SS	ORB 71 09
MAGIC PASSES	HERBST, STEVE	SS	CLR 72 02
FIFTEEN VULTURES, THE STROP, AND THE OLD LADY	LE GUIN, URSULA K.	AR	CLR 72 02
IN THE GREENHOUSE	NIELSEN, LIN	SS	CLR 72 02
EARLY TO BED	EFFINGER, GEO. ALEC	SS	CLR 72 02
GOLDEN AGES GONE AWAY	POHL, FREDERIK	AR	CLR 72 02
GOODBYE, HENRY J. KOSTKOS, GOODBYE	KNIGHT, DAMON	AR	CLR 72 02
HERE, THERE, AND EVERYWHERE	BUSBY, F. M.	SS	CLR 72 02
HANGED MAN, THE	BRYANT, EDWARD	SS	CLR 72 02
WINTER HOUSECLEANING	DANIEL, MOLLY	SS	CLR 72 02
FROZEN ASSETS	WISSNER, ROBERT	SS	CLR 72 02
CRAYOLA	SKAL, DAVE	SS	CLR 72 02
WHY IS IT SO HARD?	WILHELM, KATE	AR	CLR 72 02
TO THE MOUNTAINS	HANEY, LAURA	SS	CLR 72 02
THEIR THOUSANDTH SEASON	BRYANT, EDWARD	SS	CLR 72 02
GET FDR!	THURSTON, ROBERT	SS	CLR 72 02
AT THE SECOND SOLSTICE	SUTHERLAND, JAMES	SS	CLR 72 02
YOU ARE WHAT YOU WRITE	ELLISON, HARLAN	AR	CLR 72 02
NOTES ON A RESTLESS URGE	WISSNER, ROBERT	SS	CLR 72 02
AND DRAGONS IN THE SKY	COOK, GLEN	NV	CLR 72 02
MODEST PROPOSAL, A	BATES, RUSSELL L.	SS	CLR 72 02
HE-MAN ETHOS IN SCIENCE FICTION, THE	RUSS, JOANNA	AR	CLR 72 02
OMNIA TRISTE	NORWOOD, RICK	SS	CLR 72 02
STRANGER IN THE HOUSE	TUTTLE, LISA	SS	CLR 72 02
GOOD LIFE, THE	THURSTON, ROBERT	SS	CLR 72 02
SAND AND STONES	EFFINGER, GEO. ALEC	SS	CLR 72 02
WRITER AS TEACHER, THE	SALLIS, JAMES	AR	CLR 72 02
CLARION III	WILSON, ROBIN SCOTT	OA	SIG 73 10
INTRODUCTION	WILSON, ROBIN SCOTT	IN	
ROAD MAP	BUSBY, F. M.	SS	CLR 73 03
EVERYBODY LOVES: IN A CIRCULAR MOTION	GILDEN, MEL	SS	CLR 73 03
URSULA MAJOR CONSTRUCT: OR, A FAR GREATER HORROR LOOMED, THE	LE GUIN, URSULA K.	SS	CLR 73 03
ASCLEPIUS HAS PAWS	BROXON, MILDRED D.	SS	CLR 73 03
WORD "RANDOM", DELIBERATELY REPEATED, THE	SHIRLEY, JOHN	SS	CLR 73 03
WHY?	STURGEON, THEODORE	AR	CLR 73 03
TEARDROP, THE	OLMSTEAD, DVORA	SS	CLR 73 03
BUS STATION	EARLS, WILLIAM	SS	CLR 73 03
SAY GOODBYE TO THE WORLD'S LAST BROTHEL	WISSNER, ROBERT	SS	CLR 73 03
FLAT HATTER	WISE, DAVID	SS	CLR 73 03
BABY MAKES TWO	CONWAY, GERARD F.	SS	CLR 73 03
THRANGS AND OTHER WONDERS	ISAACS, LEONARD	PM	CLR 73 03
CANTALOUPES AND KANGAROOS	CARO, DENNIS R.	SS	CLR 73 03
BREATH OF DRAGONS, THE	REAVES, J. MICHAEL	SS	CLR 73 03
SOURCE, THE	WILHELM, KATE	AR	CLR 73 03
SERVANTS	WISE, DAVID	SS	CLR 73 03
WHEN PAPPY ISN'T THERE	NIELSEN, LIN	SS	CLR 73 03
MORE I CANNOT WISH YOU	SULLIVAN, JEAN	SS	CLR 73 03
DEEP WELL OF THE UNCONSCIOUS- WELL, WELL..., THE	KNIGHT, DAMON	AR	CLR 73 03
GIVE MY REGARDS TO THE CZAR	WILLIAMS, DAVID N.	SS	CLR 73 03
MOLTEN CORE	STERN, DONNEL	SS	CLR 73 03
SCIENCE FICTION, ARCHETYPES, AND THE FUTURE	WRIGHT, R. GLENN	AR	CLR 73 03
DIGGERS, THE	STERN, DONNEL	SS	CLR 73 03
PLAY IT AGAIN, SAM	BUSBY, F. M.	SS	CLR 73 03
TILL HUMAN VOICES WAKE US...	TUTTLE, LISA	SS	CLR 73 03
WHEN DREAMS BECOME NIGHTMARES: SOME CAUTIONARY NOTES ON THE CLARION EXPERIENCE	ELLISON, HARLAN	AR	CLR 73 03
CLARION SF	WILHELM, KATE	OA	BKM 77 01
INTRODUCTION	WILHELM, KATE	IN	
LANDSCAPE WITH ALIENS	MARTIN, LARRY W.	SS	
MATTER OF HONOR, A	HODGELL, PAT	SS	
CLOSED CIRCUIT	SCHOLZ, CARTER	SS	
LEADER OF THE CLUB, THE	ZICREE, MARC SCOTT	SS	
BELLMAN'S WONDER RING, THE	WOLFE, GENE	AR	
ENEMY YOU KILLED, MY FRIEND, THE	BREADY, RICHARD S.	SS	
STORMFALL	JOHNSON, BILL	SS	
CAN ANYTHING BE TAUGHT?	MCINTYRE, VONDA N.	AR	
THING ITSELF, THE	ROBINSON, KIM S.	SS	
POPPIN' FRESH	WEST, MICHAEL	SS	
WITH CROOKED HANDS	CRAIS, ROBERT	SS	
BRIAN IN THE DREAMING SEAT	BRENNERT, ALAN	SS	
SOMETHING THAT WORKS	KNIGHT, DAMON	AR	
NO SPECIFIC TIME MENTIONED	METZGER, LOIS	SS	
TWO PEOPLE WITHIN THE DESIGN	WEBB, VIC	SS	
TRADERS, THE	SIDNEY, KATHLEEN M.	NV	
CLOAK OF AESIR	CAMPBELL, JOHN W. JR	AC H	SHS 52
THREE JOHNS, THE (ONLY IN REPRINT, LAN 72)	ASIMOV, ISAAC	AR	
INTRODUCTION	CAMPBELL, JOHN W. JR	IN	
FORGETFULNESS	CAMPBELL, JOHN W. JR	SS	ASF 37 06
ESCAPE, THE	CAMPBELL, JOHN W. JR	NV	ASF 35 05
MACHINE, THE	CAMPBELL, JOHN W. JR	SS	ASF 35 02
INVADERS, THE	CAMPBELL, JOHN W. JR	NV	ASF 35 06
REBELLION	CAMPBELL, JOHN W. JR	NV	ASF 35 08
OUT OF NIGHT	CAMPBELL, JOHN W. JR	NV	ASF 37 10
CLOAK OF AESIR	CAMPBELL, JOHN W. JR	NV	ASF 39 03
CLOCK OF TIME, THE	FINNEY, JACK	AC H	EYR 58
SEE "THE THIRD LEVEL"			
CLONED LIVES	SARGENT, PAMELA	NO	FGM 76 06
FATHER	SARGENT, PAMELA	SN	AMZ 74 02
CLONE SISTER	SARGENT, PAMELA	NV	EIO 73
SENSE OF DIFFERENCE, A	SARGENT, PAMELA	SS	WLK 73
COLD CHILLS	BLOCH, ROBERT	AC H	DBL 77
INTRODUCTION	BLOCH, ROBERT	IN	
GODS ARE NOT MOCKED, THE	BLOCH, ROBERT	SS	EQM 68 08
HOW LIKE A GOD	BLOCH, ROBERT	SS	GAL 69 04
MOVIE PEOPLE, THE	BLOCH, ROBERT	SS	FSF 69 10
DOUBLE WHAMMY	BLOCH, ROBERT	SS	FAN 70 02
IN THE CARDS	BLOCH, ROBERT	SS	WOF 70 WI
ANIMAL FAIR, THE	BLOCH, ROBERT	SS	PBY 71 05
ORACLE, THE	BLOCH, ROBERT	SS	PNT 71 05
PLAY'S THE THING, THE	BLOCH, ROBERT	SS	AHM 71 05
EGO TRIP	BLOCH, ROBERT	SS	PNT 72 03
FOREVER AND AMEN	BLOCH, ROBERT	SS	WLK 73
SEE HOW THEY RUN	BLOCH, ROBERT	SS	EQM 73 04
SPACE-BORN	BLOCH, ROBERT	NV	COI 73
LEARNING MAZE, THE	BLOCH, ROBERT	SS	

MODEL, THE   BLOCH, ROBERT   SS   GLR 75 11
COLONIAL SURVEY   LEINSTER, MURRAY   NO H GNM 56
  ALSO AS "THE PLANET EXPLORER"
  SOLAR CONSTANT (CRITICAL DIFFERENCE)
                     LEINSTER, MURRAY   NV   ASF 56 07
  SAND DOOM   LEINSTER, MURRAY   NV   ASF 55 12
  COMBAT TEAM (EXPLORATION TEAM)
                     LEINSTER, MURRAY   NV   ASF 56 03
  SWAMP WAS UPSIDE DOWN, THE   LEINSTER, MURRAY   NV   ASF 56 09
COMBAT SF   DICKSON, GORDON R.   AN H DBL 75
  COMBAT SF: INTRODUCTION   DICKSON, GORDON R.   IN
  LAST COMMAND, THE LAUMER, KEITH   SS   ASF 67 01
  MEN OF GOOD WILL   BOVA, BEN
                     AND LEWIS, MYRON R. SS C GAL 64 06
  PAIR, THE   HENSLEY, JOE L.   SS   FUN 58 07
  BUTCHER'S BILL, THE DRAKE, DAVID   NV   GAL 74 11
  SINGLE COMBAT   GREEN, JOSEPH   SS   NWS 64 08
  MAN WHO CAME EARLY, THE ANDERSON, POUL NV   FSF 56 06
  PATRON OF THE ARTS SABERHAGEN, FRED   SS   IFS 65 08
  TIME PIECE   HALDEMAN, JOE W.   SS   IFS 70 07
  RICOCHET ON MIZA   DICKSON, GORDON R.   SS   PLS 52 03
  NO WAR, OR BATTLE'S SOUND HARRISON, HARRY NV   68
  HIS TRUTH GOES MARCHING ON POURNELLE, JERRY SS NEW 75 AN
  HORARS OF WAR, THE WOLFE, GENE   SS   NOV 70 01
COMIC INFERNO, THE   ALDISS, BRIAN W.   AC   NLB 73 10
  SEE "THE BOOK OF BRIAN ALDISS"
COMING ATTRACTIONS   GREENBERG , MARTIN   NF H GNM 57
  PREFACE   GREENBERG , MARTIN   IN
  INTRODUCTION   BATTEAU, DWIGHT W.   IN
  LETTER TO THE MARTIANS, A (CALLING ALL MARTIANS)
                     LEY, WILLY   AR   TWS 40 11
  HOW TO LEARN MARTIAN HOCKETT, CHARLES F. AR ASF 55 05
  LANGUAGE FOR TIME TRAVELERS DE CAMP, L. SPRAGUE AR ASF 38 07
  GEOGRAPHY FOR TIME TRAVELERS LEY, WILLY AR ASF 39 07
  TIME TRAVEL AND THE LAW KORNBLUTH, C. M. AR
  SPACE FIX   RICHARDSON, R. S.   AR   ASF 43 03
  SPACE WAR   LEY, WILLY   AR   ASF 39 08
  SPACE WAR TACTICS JAMESON, MALCOLM   AR   ASF 39 11
  FUEL FOR THE FUTURE HATCHER, JACK   AR   ASF 40 03
  HOW TO COUNT ON YOUR FINGERS POHL, FREDERIK AR SFS 56 09
  INTERPLANETARY COPYRIGHT (THE SHAPE OF COPYRIGHT TO COME)
                     REINES, DONALD F.   AR   FSF 53 04
COMING OF CONAN, THE HOWARD, ROBERT E.   AC H GNM 53
  INTRODUCTION   DE CAMP, L. SPRAGUE IN
  HYBORIAN AGE, THE HOWARD, ROBERT E.   AR   PHT 36
  LETTER TO P. SCHUYLER MILLER HOWARD, ROBERT E. MS
  LETTER TO DONALD WOLLHEIM LOVECRAFT, H. P. MS
  INFORMAL BIOGRAPHY OF CONAN THE CIMMERIAN, AN
                     CLARK, JOHN D.
                     AND MILLER, P. SCHUYLER AR C
  SHADOW KINGDOM, THE HOWARD, ROBERT E.   SS   WRT 29 08
  MIRRORS OF TUZUN THUNE, THE HOWARD, ROBERT E. SS WRT 29 09
  KING AND THE OAK, THE HOWARD, ROBERT E. PM
  TOWER OF THE ELEPHANT, THE HOWARD, ROBERT E. SS WRT 33 03
  GOD IN THE BOWL, THE HOWARD, ROBERT E. SS SSF 52 09
  ROGUES IN THE HOUSE HOWARD, ROBERT E. SS   WRT 34 01
  FROST-GIANT'S DAUGHTER, THE HOWARD, ROBERT E.
                     AND DE CAMP, L. SPRAGUE SS C FMG 53 08
  QUEEN OF THE BLACK COAST HOWARD, ROBERT E. SS WRT 34 05
COMING OF THE ROBOTS, THE MOSKOWITZ, SAM AN CLB 63
  INTRODUCTION   MOSKOWITZ, SAM   IN
  I, ROBOT   BINDER, EANDO   SS   AMZ 39 01
  HELEN O'LOY   DEL REY, LESTER   SS   ASF 38 12
  LOST MACHINE, THE WYNDHAM, JOHN   SS   AMZ 32 04
  RUNAROUND   ASIMOV, ISAAC   SS   ASF 42 03
  EARTH FOR INSPIRATION SIMAK, CLIFFORD D. SS TWS 41 04
  LOST MEMORY   PHILLIPS, PETER   SS   GAL 52 05
  REX   VINCENT, HARL   SS   ASF 34 06
  TRUE CONFESSION   TREMAINE, F. ORLIN   SS   TWS 40 02
  DERELICT   GALLUN, RAYMOND Z.   SS   ASF 35 10
  MISFIT   FISCHER, MICHAEL   SS   SFP 53 12
COMING OF THE TERRANS, THE BRACKETT, LEIGH NO ACE 67
  BEAST-JEWEL OF MARS, THE BRACKETT, LEIGH SS PLS 55 SP
  MARS MINUS BISHA   BRACKETT, LEIGH   SS   PLS 54 01
  LAST DAYS OF SHANDAKOR, THE BRACKETT, LEIGH NV STS 52 04
  PURPLE PRIESTESS OF THE MAD MOON
                     BRACKETT, LEIGH   SS   FSF 64 10
  ROAD TO SINHARAT, THE BRACKETT, LEIGH NV   AMZ 63 05
COMPLEAT WEREWOLF, THE BOUCHER, ANTHONY AC H SAS 69
  COMPLEAT WEREWOLF, THE BOUCHER, ANTHONY NV UNK 42 04
  PINK CATERPILLAR, THE BOUCHER, ANTHONY SS ADV 45 02
  Q.U.R.   BOUCHER, ANTHONY   SS   ASF 43 03
  ROBINC   BOUCHER, ANTHONY   SS   ASF 43 09
  SNULBUG (FIRST IN UNKNOWN, DEC. 1941)
                     BOUCHER, ANTHONY   SS   FSF 53 05
  MR. LUPESCU   BOUCHER, ANTHONY   SS   WRT 45 09
  THEY BITE   BOUCHER, ANTHONY   SS   UNK 43 08
  EXPEDITION   BOUCHER, ANTHONY   SS   TWS 43 08
  WE PRINT THE TRUTH BOUCHER, ANTHONY   NV   ASF 43 12
  GHOST OF ME, THE   BOUCHER, ANTHONY   SS   UNK 42 06
COMPLETE FEGHOOT, THE BRIARTON, GRENDEL AC MRG 75
  INTRODUCTION   ANDERSON, POUL   IN
  ILLUSTRATIONS   KIRK, TIM   IL
  THROUGH TIME AND SPACE WITH FERDINAND FEGHOOT
                     BRIARTON, GRENDEL   AC   PDX 62
  ADDITIONAL FEGHOOT PUNS (LAST IN BSJ)
                     BRIARTON, GRENDEL   MS

COMPLETE VENUS EQUILATERAL, THE
                     SMITH, GEORGE O.   AC   BAL 76 11
  IN ENGLAND (ORBIT, 1977) AS "VENUS EQUILATERAL"
  INTRODUCTION   CLARKE, ARTHUR C.   IN
  QRM-INTERPLANETARY SMITH, GEORGE O.   NV   ASF 42 10
  CALLING THE EMPRESS SMITH, GEORGE O.   NV   ASF 43 06
  RECOIL   SMITH, GEORGE O.   NV   ASF 43 11
  LOST ART   SMITH, GEORGE O.   NV   ASF 43 12
  OFF THE BEAM   SMITH, GEORGE O.   NV   ASF 44 02
  LONG WAY, THE   SMITH, GEORGE O.   NV   ASF 44 04
  BEAM PIRATE   SMITH, GEORGE O.   NV   ASF 44 10
  FIRING LINE   SMITH, GEORGE O.   NV   ASF 44 12
  SPECIAL DELIVERY   SMITH, GEORGE O.   NV   ASF 45 03
  PANDORA'S MILLIONS SMITH, GEORGE O.   NV   ASF 45 06
  MAD HOLIDAY   SMITH, GEORGE O.   NV   NEW 47 AC
  EXTERNAL TRIANGLE, THE (INTERLUDE)
                     SMITH, GEORGE O.   NV   AMA 73
  EPILOGUE: IDENTITY (IDENTITY)
                     SMITH, GEORGE O.   NV   ASF 45 11
CONAN   HOWARD, R./DE CAMP/& AC LAN 67
  INTRODUCTION   DE CAMP, L. SPRAGUE IN
  LETTER TO P. SCHUYLER MILLER HOWARD, ROBERT E. MS
  HYBORIAN AGE, THE (PART 1) HOWARD, ROBERT E. AR PHT 36
  THING IN THE CRYPT, THE HOWARD, ROBERT E. SS
  TOWER OF THE ELEPHANT, THE HOWARD, ROBERT E. SS WRT 33 03
  HALL OF THE DEAD, THE
                     HOWARD, ROBERT E.
                     AND DE CAMP, L. SPRAGUE NV C FSF 67 02
  GOD IN THE BOWL, THE HOWARD, ROBERT E. SS SSF 52 09
  ROGUES IN THE HOUSE HOWARD, ROBERT E. SS WRT 34 01
  HAND OF NERGAL, THE HOWARD, ROBERT E.
                     AND CARTER, LIN   SS C
  CHAINS OF SHAMBALLAH CARTER, LIN
                     AND DE CAMP, L. SPRAGUE SS C
CONAN THE ADVENTURER HOWARD, R. & DE CAMP AC LAN 66
  INTRODUCTION   DE CAMP, L. SPRAGUE IN
  PEOPLE OF THE BLACK CIRCLE, THE
                     HOWARD, ROBERT E.   NA   WRT 34 09
  SLITHERING SHADOW, THE HOWARD, ROBERT E. SS WRT 33 09
  DRUMS OF TOMBALKU HOWARD, ROBERT E.
                     AND DE CAMP, L. SPRAGUE SS C
  POOL OF THE BLACK ONE, THE HOWARD, ROBERT E. SS WRT 33 10
CONAN THE AVENGER   HOWARD, R./NYBERG/& AC   LAN 68
  INTRODUCTION   DE CAMP, L. SPRAGUE IN
  RETURN OF CONAN, THE (EXPANDED FROM "CONAN THE VICTORIOUS",
    PUBLISHED BY GNOME, 1957) NYBERG, BJORN
                     AND DE CAMP, L. SPRAGUE NO C FUN 57 09
  HYBORIAN AGE, THE (PART 2) HOWARD, ROBERT E. AR PHT 36
CONAN THE BARBARIAN HOWARD, ROBERT E.   AC H GNM 55
  BLACK COLOSSUS   HOWARD, ROBERT E.   SS   WRT 33 06
  SHADOWS IN THE MOONLIGHT HOWARD, ROBERT E. SS WRT 34 04
  WITCH SHALL BE BORN, A HOWARD, ROBERT E. SS WRT 34 12
  SHADOWS IN ZAMBOULA HOWARD, ROBERT E. NV   WRT 35 11
  DEVIL IN IRON, THE HOWARD, ROBERT E.   SS   WRT 34 08
CONAN THE FREEBOOTER HOWARD, R. & DE CAMP AC   LAN 68
  INTRODUCTION   DE CAMP, L. SPRAGUE IN
  HAWKS OVER SHEM (FROM "HAWKS OVER EGYPT" BY REH.)
                     HOWARD, ROBERT E.
                     AND DE CAMP, L. SPRAGUE NV C FUN 55 10
  BLACK COLOSSUS   HOWARD, ROBERT E.   SS   WRT 33 06
  SHADOWS IN THE MOONLIGHT HOWARD, ROBERT E. SS WRT 34 04
  ROAD OF THE EAGLES, THE (CONAN, MAN OF DESTINY)
                     HOWARD, ROBERT E.
                     AND DE CAMP, L. SPRAGUE NV C FUN 55 12
  WITCH SHALL BE BORN, A HOWARD, ROBERT E. SS WRT 34 12
CONAN THE USURPER   HOWARD, R. & DE CAMP AC   LAN 67
  INTRODUCTION   DE CAMP, L. SPRAGUE IN
  TREASURE OF TRANICOS, THE (THE BLACK STRANGER)
                     HOWARD, ROBERT E.
                     AND DE CAMP, L. SPRAGUE NA C FMG 53 03
  WOLVES BEYOND THE BORDER HOWARD, ROBERT E.
                     AND DE CAMP, L. SPRAGUE SS C
  PHOENIX ON THE SWORD, THE HOWARD, ROBERT E. SS WRT 32 12
  SCARLET CITADEL, THE HOWARD, ROBERT E. SS WRT 33 01
CONAN THE WANDERER   HOWARD, R./DE CAMP/& AC   LAN 68
  INTRODUCTION   DE CAMP, L. SPRAGUE IN
  BLACK TEARS   DE CAMP, L. SPRAGUE
                     AND CARTER, LIN   SS C
  SHADOWS IN ZAMBOULA HOWARD, ROBERT E. NV   WRT 35 11
  DEVIL IN IRON, THE HOWARD, ROBERT E.   SS   WRT 34 08
  FLAME KNIFE, THE   HOWARD, ROBERT E.   SS
CONAN THE WARRIOR   HOWARD, R. & DE CAMP AC   LAN 67
  INTRODUCTION   DE CAMP, L. SPRAGUE IN
  RED NAILS   HOWARD, ROBERT E.   NA   WRT 36 07
  JEWELS OF GWAHLUR HOWARD, ROBERT E.   SS   WRT 35 03
  BEYOND THE BLACK RIVER HOWARD, ROBERT E. NA WRT 35 05
CONDITIONALLY HUMAN MILLER, WALTER M. JR AC BAL 62
  CONDITIONALLY HUMAN MILLER, WALTER M. JR NV GAL 52 02
  DARFSTELLER, THE   MILLER, WALTER M. JR SN   ASF 55 01
  DARK BENEDICTION   MILLER, WALTER M. JR SN   FAD 51 09
CONNOISSEUR'S S. F. BOARDMAN, TOM JR.   AN   PEN 64
  INTRODUCTION   BOARDMAN, TOM JR.   IN
  DISAPPEARING ACT   BESTER, ALFRED   SS   STR 53 02
  WIZARDS OF PUNG'S CORNERS, THE
                     POHL, FREDERIK   NV   GAL 58 10
  TOMORROW AND TOMORROW AND TOMORROW (THE BIG TRIP UP YONDER)
                     VONNEGUT, KURT JR.   SS   GAL 54 01

CONNOISSEUR'S S. F.

MR. COSTELLO, HERO	STURGEON, THEODORE	NV	GAL 53 12
QUIT ZOOMIN' THOSE HANDS THROUGH THE AIR	FINNEY, JACK	SS	FSF 52 12
BUILD-UP (ALSO AS THE CONCENTRATION CITY)	BALLARD, J. G.	SS	NWS 57 01
FUN THEY HAD, THE (NEA 51 12)	ASIMOV, ISAAC	SS	FSF 54 02
DIABOLOGIC	RUSSELL, ERIC FRANK	SS	ASF 55 03
MADE IN U.S.A.	MCINTOSH, J. T.	NV	GAL 53 04
WAVERIES, THE	BROWN, FREDRIC	SS	ASF 45 01

CONSCIENCE INTERPLANETARY	GREEN, JOSEPH	NO	DAW 74
DECISION MAKERS, THE	GREEN, JOSEPH	NV	GAL 65 04
SHAMBLERS OF MISERY, THE	GREEN, JOSEPH	NV	FSF 69 08
BUTTERFLYS OF BEAUTY, THE	GREEN, JOSEPH	NV	FSF 71 06
CRYER OF CRYSTAL, THE	GREEN, JOSEPH	SS	ASF 71 10

CONSIDER HER WAYS AND OTHERS	WYNDHAM, JOHN	AC H	JOS 61
CONSIDER HER WAYS	WYNDHAM, JOHN	NV	56
ODD	WYNDHAM, JOHN	SS	
OH, WHERE, NOW, IS PEGGY MACRAFFERTY?	WYNDHAM, JOHN	SS	
STITCH IN TIME, A	WYNDHAM, JOHN	SS	FSF 61 03
RANDOM QUEST	WYNDHAM, JOHN	NV	NEW 61 AC
LONG SPOON, A	WYNDHAM, JOHN	SS	60

CONTACT	KEYES, NOEL	AN	PBK 63 05
INTRODUCTION	KEYES, NOEL	IN	
FIRST CONTACT	LEINSTER, MURRAY	NV	ASF 45 05
INTELLIGENCE TEST	WALTON, HARRY	SS	SFP 53 05
LARGE ANT, THE (THE BIG ANT)	FAST, HOWARD	SS	FUN 60 02
WHAT'S HE DOING IN THERE?	LEIBER, FRITZ	SS	GAL 57 12
CHEMICAL PLANT	WILLIAMSON, IAN	SS	NWS 50 WI
LIMITING FACTOR	SIMAK, CLIFFORD D.	SS	STS 49 11
FIRE BALLOONS, THE (IN THIS SIGN)	BRADBURY, RAY	SS	IMG 51 04
INVASION FROM MARS	KOCH, HOWARD	PL	CBS 38 10
GENTLE VULTURES, THE	ASIMOV, ISAAC	SS	SUP 57 12
KNOCK	BROWN, FREDRIC	SS	TWS 48 12
SPECIALIST	SHECKLEY, ROBERT	SS	GAL 53 05
LOST MEMORY	PHILLIPS, PETER	SS	GAL 52 05

CONTINENT MAKERS AND OTHER TALES OF THE VIAGENS	DE CAMP, L. SPRAGUE	AC H	TWN 53
IN RE SPRAGUE	ASIMOV, ISAAC	MS	
AUTHOR'S NOTE	DE CAMP, L. SPRAGUE	IN	
INSPECTOR'S TEETH, THE	DE CAMP, L. SPRAGUE	SS	ASF 50 04
SUMMER WEAR	DE CAMP, L. SPRAGUE	SS	STS 50 05
FINISHED	DE CAMP, L. SPRAGUE	SS	ASF 49 11
GALTON WHISTLE, THE (ULTRASONIC GOD)	DE CAMP, L. SPRAGUE	NV	FUT 51 07
ANIMAL-CRACKER PLOT, THE	DE CAMP, L. SPRAGUE	SS	ASF 49 07
GIT ALONG|	DE CAMP, L. SPRAGUE	SS	ASF 50 08
PERPETUAL MOTION (WIDE-OPEN PLANET)	DE CAMP, L. SPRAGUE	NV	FUT 50 09
CONTINENT MAKERS, THE	DE CAMP, L. SPRAGUE	NA	TWS 51 04

CONTINUUM 1	ELWOOD, ROGER	OA H	PUT 74
INTRODUCTION	ELWOOD, ROGER	IN	
STATIONS OF THE NIGHTMARE- PART 1	FARMER, PHILIP JOSE	NV	CTM 74 01
MY OWN, MY NATIVE LAND	ANDERSON, POUL	NV	CTM 74 01
SHAKA|	OLIVER, CHAD	NV	CTM 74 01
ARMAGEDDON TAPES, THE- TAPE I	SCORTIA, THOMAS N.	SS	CTM 74 01
PRELUDE TO A CRYSTAL SONG	MCCAFFREY, ANNE	NV	CTM 74 01
DARK OF THE JUNE, THE	WOLFE, GENE	SS	CTM 74 01
CHILDREN'S CRUSADE, THE	PANGBORN, EDGAR	NV	CTM 74 01
NIGHT OF THE STORM, THE	KOONTZ, DEAN R.	NV	CTM 74 01

CONTINUUM 2	ELWOOD, ROGER	OA H	BKP 74
INTRODUCTION	ELWOOD, ROGER	IN	
STATIONS OF THE NIGHTMARE- PART 2: THE STARTOUCHED	FARMER, PHILIP JOSE	NV	CTM 74 02
PASSING THE LOVE OF WOMEN	ANDERSON, POUL	NV	CTM 74 02
CARAVANS UNLIMITED: STABILITY	OLIVER, CHAD	NV	CTM 74 02
ARMAGEDDON TAPES, THE- TAPE II	SCORTIA, THOMAS N.	NV	CTM 74 02
KILLASHANDRA - CRYSTAL SINGER	MCCAFFREY, ANNE	NV	CTM 74 02
DEATH OF HYLE, THE	WOLFE, GENE	SS	CTM 74 02
LEGEND OF HOMBAS, THE	PANGBORN, EDGAR	NV	CTM 74 02
FIRE FOUNTAIN, THE	KIMBERLY, GAIL	NV	CTM 74 02

CONTINUUM 3	ELWOOD, ROGER	OA H	BKP 74
INTRODUCTION	ELWOOD, ROGER	IN	
STATIONS OF THE NIGHTMARE- PART 3: THE EVOLUTION OF PAUL EYRE	FARMER, PHILIP JOSE	NV	CTM 74 03
FAIR EXCHANGE, A	ANDERSON, POUL	NV	CTM 74 03
MIDDLE MAN, THE	OLIVER, CHAD	NV	CTM 74 03
ARMAGEDDON TAPES, THE- TAPE III	SCORTIA, THOMAS N.	NV	CTM 74 03
MILEKEY MOUNTAIN	MCCAFFREY, ANNE	NV	CTM 74 03
FROM THE NOTEBOOK OF DOCTOR STEIN	WOLFE, GENE	SS	CTM 74 03
WITCHES OF NUPAL, THE	PANGBORN, EDGAR	NV	CTM 74 03
DARKNESS OF DAY	SARGENT, PAMELA AND ZEBROWSKI, GEORGE	SS C	CTM 74 03

CONTINUUM 4	ELWOOD, ROGER	OA H	BKP 75
STATIONS OF THE NIGHTMARE- PART 4: PASSING ON	FARMER, PHILIP JOSE	NV	CTM 75 04
TO PROMOTE THE GENERAL WELFARE	ANDERSON, POUL	NV	CTM 75 04
CARAVANS UNLIMITED: MONITOR	OLIVER, CHAD	NV	CTM 75 04

COUNTRY OF THE BLIND, THE

ARMAGEDDON TAPES, THE- TAPE IV	SCORTIA, THOMAS N.	SS	CTM 75 04
KILLASHANDRA- CODA AND FINALE	MCCAFFREY, ANNE	NV	CTM 75 04
THAG	WOLFE, GENE	SS	CTM 75 04
MAM SOLA'S HOUSE	PANGBORN, EDGAR	NV	CTM 75 04
MAKING THE CONNECTIONS	MALZBERG, BARRY N.	SS	CTM 75 04

COSMIC KALEIDOSCOPE	SHAW, BOB	AC H	GOL 76
SKIRMISH ON A SUMMER MORNING	SHAW, BOB	NA	76
UNREASONABLE FACSIMILE	SHAW, BOB	SS	
FULL MEMBER OF THE CLUB, A	SHAW, BOB	NV	GAL 74 0
SILENT PARTNERS, THE	SHAW, BOB	SS	NEB 59 06
GIACONDA CAPER, THE	SHAW, BOB	NV	76
UNCOMIC BOOK HORROR STORY, AN	SHAW, BOB	SS	SFM 75 1
BRINK, THE	SHAW, BOB	SS	FAN 76
WALTZ OF THE BODYSNATCHERS	SHAW, BOB	NV	
LITTLE NIGHT FLYING, A (DARK ICARUS)	SHAW, BOB	NV	IFS 74 08

COSMIC LAUGHTER	HALDEMAN, JOE W.	AN H	HRW 74
INTRODUCTION	HALDEMAN, JOE W.	IN	
SLIGHT MISCALCULATION, A	BOVA, BEN	SS	FSF 71 0
IT'S A BIRD, IT'S A PLANE|	SPINRAD, NORMAN	SS	GNT 67
ROBOTS ARE HERE, THE	CARR, TERRY	NV	IFS 67 05
I OF NEWTON	HALDEMAN, JOE W.	SS	
MEN WHO MURDERED MOHAMMED, THE	BESTER, ALFRED	SS	FSF 58 1
TO SERVE MAN	KNIGHT, DAMON	SS	GAL 50 11
BOMB IN THE BATHTUB, THE	SCORTIA, THOMAS N.	SS	GAL 57 0
BLACK SORCERER OF THE BLACK CASTLE, THE	OFFUTT, ANDREW J.	SS	NEW 74 AN
GALLEGHER PLUS	KUTTNER, HENRY	NV	ASF 43 11

COSMICOMICS	CALVINO, ITALO	OC H	HBW 68
DISTANCE OF THE MOON, THE	CALVINO, ITALO	SS	
AT DAYBREAK	CALVINO, ITALO	SS	
SIGN IN SPACE, A	CALVINO, ITALO	SS	68
ALL AT ONE POINT	CALVINO, ITALO	SS	
WITHOUT COLORS	CALVINO, ITALO	SS	
GAMES WITHOUT END	CALVINO, ITALO	SS	
AQUATIC UNCLE, THE	CALVINO, ITALO	SS	
HOW MUCH SHALL WE BET?	CALVINO, ITALO	SS	
DINOSAURS, THE	CALVINO, ITALO	SS	
FORM OF SPACE, THE	CALVINO, ITALO	SS	
LIGHT YEARS, THE	CALVINO, ITALO	SS	
SPIRAL, THE	CALVINO, ITALO	SS	

COUNTERCOMMANDMENT SEE "ANALOG 5"	CAMPBELL, JOHN W. JR	AN	CUR 67

COUNTERFEIT MAN, THE	NOURSE, ALAN E.	AC H	MCK 63
COUNTERFEIT MAN, THE (COUNTERFEIT)	NOURSE, ALAN E.	NV	TWS 52 08
CANVAS BAG, THE	NOURSE, ALAN E.	SS	FSF 55 04
OUNCE OF CURE, AN	NOURSE, ALAN E.	SS	IMT 55 11
DARK DOOR, THE	NOURSE, ALAN E.	NV	GAL 53 12
MEETING OF THE BOARD	NOURSE, ALAN E.	SS	IFS 55 10
CIRCUS	NOURSE, ALAN E.	SS	
MY FRIEND BOBBY	NOURSE, ALAN E.	SS	OSF 54 03
LINK, THE	NOURSE, ALAN E.	SS	IFS 54 06
IMAGE OF THE GODS, THE	NOURSE, ALAN E.	SS	OSF 54 09
EXPERT TOUCH, THE	NOURSE, ALAN E.	NV	FSF 55 11
SECOND SIGHT	NOURSE, ALAN E.	SS	FUN 56 04

COUNTRY OF THE BLIND, THE	WELLS, H. G.	AC H	NEL 13
JILTING OF JANE, THE	WELLS, H. G.	SS	97
CONE, THE	WELLS, H. G.	SS	UCN 95 05
STOLEN BACILLUS, THE	WELLS, H. G.	SS	PMB 94 06
FLOWERING OF THE STRANGE ORCHID, THE (ALSO AS THE STRANGE ORCHID)	WELLS, H. G.	SS	PMB 94 08
IN THE AVU OBSERVATORY	WELLS, H. G.	SS	PMB 94 08
AEPYORNIS ISLAND	WELLS, H. G.	SS	PMB 94
REMARKABLE CASE OF DAVIDSON'S EYES, THE	WELLS, H. G.	SS	PMB 95 03
LORD OF THE DYNAMOS, THE	WELLS, H. G.	SS	PMB 94 09
MOTH, THE (A MOTH- GENUS NOVO)	WELLS, H. G.	SS	PGZ 95 03
TREASURE IN THE FOREST, THE	WELLS, H. G.	SS	PMB 94
STORY OF THE LATE MR. ELVESHAM, THE	WELLS, H. G.	SS	IDL 96 05
UNDER THE KNIFE (SLIP UNDER THE KNIFE)	WELLS, H. G.	SS	NRV 96 01
SEA-RAIDERS, THE	WELLS, H. G.	SS	WSL 96 12
OBLITERATED MAN, THE	WELLS, H. G.	SS	
PLATTNER STORY, THE	WELLS, H. G.	SS	NRV 96 04
RED ROOM, THE	WELLS, H. G.	SS	IDL 96
PURPLE PILEUS, THE	WELLS, H. G.	SS	BAW 96 12
SLIP UNDER THE MICROSCOPE, A	WELLS, H. G.	SS	YBK 96 01
CRYSTAL EGG, THE	WELLS, H. G.	SS	NRV 97 05
STAR, THE	WELLS, H. G.	SS	GRP 97 12
MAN WHO COULD WORK MIRACLES, THE	WELLS, H. G.	SS	ILN 98 07
VISION OF JUDGEMENT, A	WELLS, H. G.	SS	BUT 99 09
JIMMY GOGGLES THE GOD	WELLS, H. G.	SS	GRP 98 12
MISS WINCHELSEA'S HEART	WELLS, H. G.	SS	QUN 98 10
DREAM OF ARMAGEDDON, A	WELLS, H. G.	NV	BAW 00
VALLEY OF SPIDERS, THE	WELLS, H. G.	SS	PRS 03 03
NEW ACCELERATOR, THE	WELLS, H. G.	SS	SND 01 12
TRUTH ABOUT PYECRAFT, THE	WELLS, H. G.	SS	SND 03 04
MAGIC SHOP, THE	WELLS, H. G.	SS	SND 03 06
EMPIRE OF THE ANTS, THE	WELLS, H. G.	SS	SND 05 12
DOOR IN THE WALL, THE	WELLS, H. G.	SS	DCH 06 07
COUNTRY OF THE BLIND, THE	WELLS, H. G.	SS	SND 04 04

COUNTRY OF THE BLIND, THE

BEAUTIFUL SUIT, THE (A MOONLIGHT FABLE)
    WELLS, H. G.   SS COL 09 04

CRASHING SUNS   HAMILTON, EDMOND AC ACE 65
  CRASHING SUNS   HAMILTON, EDMOND NV WRT 28 08
  STAR STEALERS, THE   HAMILTON, EDMOND NV WRT 29 02
  WITHIN THE NEBULA   HAMILTON, EDMOND NV WRT 28 05
  COMET DRIVERS, THE   HAMILTON, EDMOND NV WRT 30 02
  COSMIC CLOUD, THE   HAMILTON, EDMOND NV WRT 30 11

CRAZY MIXED-UP PLANET   FRITCH, CHARLES E. AC POW 69 11
  INTRODUCTION   CARLFI, CHESTER H. IN
  NO WORLD FOR THE TIMID   FRITCH, CHARLES E. SS AMZ 57 05
  I LIKE MARTIAN MUSIC   FRITCH, CHARLES E. SS FUN 57 09
  WELCOME TO PROCYON IV   FRITCH, CHARLES E. SS 65
  CRAZY, MIXED-UP PLANET   FRITCH, CHARLES E. NV FUN 55 08
  BIRTHDAY PRESENT   FRITCH, CHARLES E. SS SCF 55 09
  NIGHT TALK   FRITCH, CHARLES E. SS STS 52 09
  COME INTO MY PARLOR   FRITCH, CHARLES E. SS SPA 53 02
  WATCHER, THE   FRITCH, CHARLES E. SS STS 52 06
  SKIN GAME   FRITCH, CHARLES E. SS IFS 54 05
  EMISSARY   FRITCH, CHARLES E. SS FNF 53 06
  OFFICE CALL   FRITCH, CHARLES E. SS FUN 54 10
  COG, THE   FRITCH, CHARLES E. SS ASF 53 02
  IF AT FIRST-   FRITCH, CHARLES E. SS
  BIG, WIDE, WONDERFUL WORLD FRITCH, CHARLES E. SS FSF 58 03

CREATURES FROM BEYOND   CARR, TERRY AN H NEL 75
  INTRODUCTION   CARR, TERRY IN
  WORM, THE   KELLER, DAVID H. MD. SS AMZ 29 03
  MIMIC   WOLLHEIM, DONALD A. SS AST 42 12
  IT   STURGEON, THEODORE NV UNK 40 08
  BEAUTY AND THE BEAST   KUTTNER, HENRY SS TWS 40 04
  SOME ARE BORN CATS   CARR, TERRY
    AND CARR, CAROL SS C SPT 73
  FULL SUN   ALDISS, BRIAN W. SS ORB 67 02
  SILENT COLONY, THE   SILVERBERG, ROBERT SS FUT 54 10
  STREET THAT WASN'T THERE, THE (ALSO AS THE LOST STREET)
    SIMAK, CLIFFORD D.
    AND JACOBI, CARL SS C CMT 41 07
  DEAR DEVIL   RUSSELL, ERIC FRANK NV OWS 50 05

CRIME PREVENTION IN THE 30TH CENTURY
    SANTESSON, HANS S. AN H WLK 69
  INTRODUCTION   SANTESSON, HANS S. IN
  JACK FELL DOWN   BRUNNER, JOHN SS SPA 63 03
  EEL, THE   DEFORD, MIRIAM ALLEN SS GAL 58 04
  FUTURE IS OURS, THE   DENTINGER, STEPHEN SS NEW 69 AN
  VELVET GLOVE, THE   HARRISON, HARRY NV FUN 56 11
  LET THERE BE NIGHT| HERSHMAN, MORRIS NV FAN 63 10
  COMPUTER COPS   HOCH, EDWARD D. SS NEW 69 AN
  APPLE   MCCAFFREY, ANNE NV NEW 69 AN
  RAIN CHECK   MERRIL, JUDITH NV SPA 54 06
  TOYS   PURDOM, TOM SS ASF 67 10
  PARTY OF THE TWO PARTS   TENN, WILLIAM NV GAL 54 08

CRISIS   ELWOOD, ROGER OA H NEL 74
  INTRODUCTION   ELWOOD, ROGER IN
  DAY THE FOUNDER DIED, THE SILVERBERG, ROBERT SS
  MOMMIES AND DADDIES   BRACKETT, LEIGH SS
  WE'LL WALK AGAIN IN THE MOONLIGHT
    GODWIN, TOM SS
  PSYCHOSOMATICA   EKLUND, GORDON NV
  LIMITED ACCOMMODATIONS PISERCHIA, DORIS SS
  BOY WHO BROUGHT LOVE, THE HOCH, EDWARD D. SS
  SPACERS' DANCE, THE   EXTER, MAUREEN NV
  GAMESMAN   BONE, J. F. NV
  PROUST SYNDROME, THE   GOLDSMITH, HOWARD SS
  XONG OF XUXAN   RUSSELL, RAY SS PBY 70 10

CROSSROADS IN TIME   CONKLIN, GROFF AN PMA 53
  ASSUMPTION UNJUSTIFIED CLEMENT, HAL NV ASF 46 10
  EAGLES GATHER, THE   KELLEAM, JOSEPH E. SS ASF 42 04
  QUEEN'S ASTROLOGER, THE LEINSTER, MURRAY SS TWS 49 10
  DERM FOOL   STURGEON, THEODORE SS UNK 40 03
  COURTESY   SIMAK, CLIFFORD D. SS ASF 51 08
  SECRET   CAHN, LEE SS ASF 53 01
  THIRSTY GOD   ST. CLAIR, MARGARET SS FSF 53 03
  MUTANT'S BROTHER, THE   LEIBER, FRITZ SS ASF 43 08
  STUDENT BODY   WALLACE, F. L. NV GAL 53 03
  MADE IN U.S.A.   MCINTOSH, J. T. NV GAL 53 04
  TECHNICAL ADVISOR   OLIVER, CHAD SS FSF 53 02
  FEEDBACK   MACLEAN, KATHERINE SS ASF 51 07
  CAVE, THE   MILLER, P. SCHUYLER SS ASF 43 01
  VOCATION   SMITH, GEORGE O. SS ASF 45 04
  TIME DECELERATOR, THE   MACFADYEN, A. JR. SS ASF 36 07
  ZEN   BIXBY, JEROME SS GAL 52 10
  LET THERE BE LIGHT   FYFE, H. B. SS IFS 52 11
  BRAIN, THE   NORBERT, W. SS TEN 52 04

CRUCIBLE OF POWER, THE   GREENBERG , MARTIN AN H BDL 53
  3 SELECTIONS FROM "FIVE SCIENCE FICTION NOVELS"
  BUT WITHOUT HORNS   PAGE, NORVELL W. SN UNK 40 06
  CRISIS IN UTOPIA   KNIGHT, NORMAN L. NO ASF 40 07
  CRUCIBLE OF POWER, THE WILLIAMSON, JACK NV ASF 39 02

CRYSTAL MAN, THE   MITCHELL, EDWARD P. AC H DBL 73
  LOST GIANT OF AMERICAN SCIENCE FICTION- A BIOGRAPHICAL
  PERSPECTIVE   MOSKOWITZ, SAM AR
  CRYSTAL MAN, THE   MITCHELL, EDWARD P. SS SUN 81 01
  BALLOON TREE, THE   MITCHELL, EDWARD P. SS SUN 83 02
  ABLEST MAN IN THE WORLD, THE MITCHELL, EDWARD P. SS SUN 79 05
  TACHYPOMP, THE   MITCHELL, EDWARD P. SS SCR 74 03
  MAN WITHOUT A BODY, THE MITCHELL, EDWARD P. SS SUN 77 03
  CLOCK THAT WENT BACKWARDS, THE
    MITCHELL, EDWARD P. SS SUN 81 01

CYBERIAD, THE

  SENATOR'S DAUGHTER, THE MITCHELL, EDWARD P. SS SUN 79 07
  OLD SQUIDS AND LITTLE SPELLER
    MITCHELL, EDWARD P. SS SUN 85 07
  FACTS IN THE RATCLIFF CASE, THE
    MITCHELL, EDWARD P. SS SUN 79 03
  STORY OF THE DELUGE, THE MITCHELL, EDWARD P. SS SUN 75 04
  PROFESSOR'S EXPERIMENT, THE MITCHELL, EDWARD P. SS SUN 80 02
  SOUL SPECTROSCOPE, THE MITCHELL, EDWARD P. SS SUN 75 12
  INSIDE OF THE EARTH, THE MITCHELL, EDWARD P. SS SUN 76 03
  UNCOMMON SORT OF SPECTRE, AN MITCHELL, EDWARD P. SS SUN 79 03
  CAVE OF THE SPLURGLES, THE MITCHELL, EDWARD P. SS SUN 77 07
  DEVIL'S FUNERAL, THE   MITCHELL, EDWARD P. SS SUN 79 03
  WONDERFUL COROT, THE   MITCHELL, EDWARD P. SS SUN 81 12
  TERRIBLE VOYAGE OF THE TOAD, THE
    MITCHELL, EDWARD P. SS SUN 78 10
  DEVILISH RAT, THE   MITCHELL, EDWARD P. SS SUN 78 01
  EXCHANGING THEIR SOULS MITCHELL, EDWARD P. SS SUN 77 04
  CASE OF THE DOW TWINS, THE MITCHELL, EDWARD P. SS SUN 77 04
  EXTRAORDINARY WEDDING, AN MITCHELL, EDWARD P. SS SUN 78 01
  BACK FROM THAT BOURNE   MITCHELL, EDWARD P. SS SUN 74 12
  LAST CRUISE OF THE JUDAS ISCARIOT, THE
    MITCHELL, EDWARD P. SS SUN 82 04
  FLYING WEATHERCOCK, THE MITCHELL, EDWARD P. SS SUN 84 04
  LEGENDARY SHIP, THE   MITCHELL, EDWARD P. SS SUN 85 05
  SHADOW ON THE FANCHER TWINS, THE
    MITCHELL, EDWARD P. SS SUN 86 01
  PAIN EPICURES, THE   MITCHELL, EDWARD P. SS SUN 78 08
  DAY AMONG THE LIARS, A MITCHELL, EDWARD P. SS SUN 85 08
  OUR WAR WITH MONACO   MITCHELL, EDWARD P. SS SUN 80 03

CRYSTAL SHIP, THE   SILVERBERG, ROBERT OA H NEL 76
  INTRODUCTION   SILVERBERG, ROBERT IN
  CRYSTAL SHIP, THE   VINGE, JOAN D. NA
  MEGAN'S WORLD   RANDALL, MARTA NA
  SCREWTOP   MCINTYRE, VONDA N. NA

CUBE ROOT OF UNCERTAINTY, THE
    SILVERBERG, ROBERT AC H MAC 70
  INTRODUCTION   SILVERBERG, ROBERT IN
  PASSENGERS   SILVERBERG, ROBERT SS ORB 68 04
  DOUBLE DARE   SILVERBERG, ROBERT SS GAL 56 11
  SIXTH PALACE, THE   SILVERBERG, ROBERT SS GAL 65 02
  TRANSLATION ERROR   SILVERBERG, ROBERT SS ASF 59 03
  SHADOW OF WINGS, THE SILVERBERG, ROBERT SS IFS 63 07
  ABSOLUTELY INFLEXIBLE SILVERBERG, ROBERT SS FUN 56 07
  IRON CHANCELLOR, THE SILVERBERG, ROBERT NV GAL 58 05
  MUGWUMP FOUR   SILVERBERG, ROBERT NV GAL 59 08
  TO THE DARK STAR   SILVERBERG, ROBERT SS FRS 68
  NEIGHBOR   SILVERBERG, ROBERT SS GAL 64 08
  HALFWAY HOUSE   SILVERBERG, ROBERT SS IFS 66 11
  SUNDANCE   SILVERBERG, ROBERT SS FSF 69 06

CUPFUL OF SPACE, A   CLINGERMAN, MILDRED AC BAL 61
  FIRST LESSON   CLINGERMAN, MILDRED SS FSF 56 12
  STICKENEY AND THE CRITIC CLINGERMAN, MILDRED SS FSF 53 02
  STAIR TRICK   CLINGERMAN, MILDRED SS FSF 52 08
  MINISTER WITHOUT PORTFOLIO CLINGERMAN, MILDRED SS FSF 52 02
  BIRDS CAN'T COUNT   CLINGERMAN, MILDRED SS FSF 55 02
  WORD, THE   CLINGERMAN, MILDRED SS FSF 53 11
  DAY OF THE GREEN VELVET CLOAK, THE
    CLINGERMAN, MILDRED SS FSF 58 07
  WINNING RECIPE   CLINGERMAN, MILDRED SS FSF 52 11
  LETTERS FROM LAURA   CLINGERMAN, MILDRED SS FSF 54 10
  LAST PROPHET, THE   CLINGERMAN, MILDRED SS FSF 55 08
  MR. SAKRIS'S HALT   CLINGERMAN, MILDRED SS FSF 56 01
  WILD WOOD, THE   CLINGERMAN, MILDRED SS FSF 57 01
  LITTLE WITCH OF ELM STREET, THE
    CLINGERMAN, MILDRED SS WHC 56
  DAY FOR WAVING, A   CLINGERMAN, MILDRED SS FSF 57 08
  GAY DECEIVER, THE   CLINGERMAN, MILDRED SS NEW 61 AC
  RED HEART AND BLUE ROSES, A CLINGERMAN, MILDRED SS NEW 61 AC

CURIOUS FRAGMENTS   LONDON, JACK AC H KNK 75
  EDITED BY DALE L. WALKER
  PREFACE   FARMER, PHILIP JOSE IN
  SCARLET PLAGUE, THE   LONDON, JACK NA LOM 12 06
  WHEN THE WORLD WAS YOUNG LONDON, JACK SS SEP 10 09
  RED ONE, THE   LONDON, JACK NV CMP 18 10
  UNPARALLELED INVASION, THE LONDON, JACK SS MCS 10 07
  GOLIAH   LONDON, JACK NV BOK 10 02
  ENEMY OF ALL THE WORLD, THE LONDON, JACK SS RBM 08 10
  WAR   LONDON, JACK SS NAT 11 07
  WHO BELIEVES IN GHOSTS| LONDON, JACK SS HSA 95 10
  THOUSAND DEATHS, A   LONDON, JACK SS BLC 99 05
  REJUVENATION OF MAJOR RATHBONE, THE
    LONDON, JACK SS CHJ 99 11
  EVEN UNTO DEATH   LONDON, JACK SS EPM 00 07
  RELIC OF THE PLIOCENE, A LONDON, JACK SS COL 01 01
  SHADOW AND THE FLASH, THE LONDON, JACK SS BOK 03 06
  CURIOUS FRAGMENT, A   LONDON, JACK SS TTP 08 12
  STRENGTH OF THE STRONG, THE LONDON, JACK SS HAM 11 03

CUSTODIANS AND OTHER STORIES, THE
    COWPER, RICHARD AC H GOL 76
  CUSTODIANS, THE   COWPER, RICHARD NV FSF 75 10
  PARADISE BEACH   COWPER, RICHARD NV
  PIPER AT THE GATES OF DAWN COWPER, RICHARD NA
  HERTFORD MANUSCRIPT, THE COWPER, RICHARD NV FSF 76 10

CYBERIAD, THE   LEM, STANISLAW OC H SEA 74
  HOW THE WORLD WAS SAVED LEM, STANISLAW SS
  TRURL'S MACHINE   LEM, STANISLAW SS
  GOOD SHELLACKING, A   LEM, STANISLAW SS
  FIRST SALLY, OR THE TRAP OF GARGANTIUS, THE
    LEM, STANISLAW SS

CYBERIAD, THE

FIRST SALLY(A), OR TRURL'S ELECTRONIC BARD, THE
                            LEM, STANISLAW   SS
SECOND SALLY, OR THE OFFER OF KING KROOL, THE
                            LEM, STANISLAW   NV
THIRD SALLY, OR THE DRAGONS OF PROBABILITY, THE
                            LEM, STANISLAW   SS
FOURTH SALLY, OR HOW TRURL BUILT A FEMFATALATRON TO SAVE
  PRINCE PANTAGOON..., THE LEM, STANISLAW   SS
FIFTH SALLY, OR THE MISCHIEF OF KING BALERION, THE
                            LEM, STANISLAW   SS
FIFTH SALLY(A), OR TRURL'S PRESCRIPTION
                            LEM, STANISLAW   SS
SIXTH SALLY, OR HOW TRURL AND KLAPAUCIUS CREATED A DEMON OF
  THE SECOND KIND..., THE   LEM, STANISLAW   NV
SEVENTH SALLY, OR HOW TRURL'S OWN PERFECTION LED TO
  NO GOOD, THE   LEM, STANISLAW   SS
TALE OF THE THREE STORYTELLING MACHINES OF KING GENIUS
                            LEM, STANISLAW   NA
ALTRUIZINE   LEM, STANISLAW   NV
PRINCE FERRIX AND PRINCESS CRYSTAL
                            LEM, STANISLAW   SS

DA VINCI MACHINE, THE   CONRAD, EARL   OC H FPC 68
PROOF WAS IN DRINKWATER'S PUDDING, THE
                            CONRAD, EARL   SS
THERMIDOR   CONRAD, EARL   SS
TWO BY FOURS, THE   CONRAD, EARL   SS
JACOB WRESTLES WITH THE ANGEL
                            CONRAD, EARL   SS
COSMIC MEGILLAH, THE   CONRAD, EARL   SS
HODSON'S CAPER   CONRAD, EARL   SS
ECSTASY MACHINE OR PROFESSOR A'GLEY IN ANTIMATTERLAND, THE
                            CONRAD, EARL   NA
MATURATION OF THE ABORIGINES CONRAD, EARL   SS
UPSHAW'S UPSET   CONRAD, EARL   SS
FEASIBILITY PLAN, THE   CONRAD, EARL   SS
MEDICAL CHART OF STEPHEN PAYNE
                            CONRAD, EARL   SS
DA VINCI MACHINE, THE   CONRAD, EARL   SS
OOK OOK OOK   CONRAD, EARL   SS
REPORT ON THE CONDITION OF POETRY CIRCA A.D. 2022
                            CONRAD, EARL   SS
ORIGINS OF PILL AND HAMMER CONRAD, EARL   SS
MADE HE A RIB   CONRAD, EARL   SS

DANDELION WINE   BRADBURY, RAY   NO H DBL 57
ILLUMINATION   BRADBURY, RAY   SS   REP 57 05
DANDELION WINE   BRADBURY, RAY   SS   GOR 53 06
SUMMER IN THE AIR (ALSO AS THE SOUND OF SUMMER RUNNING)
                            BRADBURY, RAY   SS   SEP 56 02
SEASON OF SITTING, THE   BRADBURY, RAY   AR   CHM 51 08
NIGHT, THE   BRADBURY, RAY   SS   WRT 46 07
LAWNS OF SUMMER, THE   BRADBURY, RAY   SS   NBS 52 02
HAPPINESS MACHINE, THE (ALSO AS THE TIME MACHINE)
                            BRADBURY, RAY   SS   SEP 57 09
SEASON OF DISBELIEF   BRADBURY, RAY   SS   COL 50 11
LAST, THE VERY LAST, THE   BRADBURY, RAY   SS   REP 55 06
GREEN MACHINE, THE   BRADBURY, RAY   SS   ARG 51 03
TROLLEY, THE   BRADBURY, RAY   SS   GHK 55 07
STATUES   BRADBURY, RAY   SS   NEW 57 NO
WINDOW, THE   BRADBURY, RAY   SS   COL 50 08
SWAN, THE   BRADBURY, RAY   SS   CMP 54 09
WHOLE TOWN'S SLEEPING, THE BRADBURY, RAY   SS   MCC 50 09
GOOD-BY, GRANDMA   BRADBURY, RAY   SS   SEP 57 05
DINNER AT DAWN   BRADBURY, RAY   SS   EVW 54 02

DANGER- HUMAN   DICKSON, GORDON R.   AC H DBL 70
  ALSO AS "THE BOOK OF GORDON DICKSON"
DANGER- HUMAN| DICKSON, GORDON R.   SS   ASF 57 12
DOLPHIN'S WAY   DICKSON, GORDON R.   SS   ASF 64 06
AND THEN THERE WAS PEACE   DICKSON, GORDON R.   SS   IFS 62 09
MAN FROM EARTH, THE   DICKSON, GORDON R.   SS   GAL 64 06
BLACK CHARLIE   DICKSON, GORDON R.   SS   GAL 54 04
ZEEPSDAY   DICKSON, GORDON R.   SS   FSF 56 11
LULUNGOMEENA   DICKSON, GORDON R.   NV   GAL 54 01
HONORABLE DEATH, AN   DICKSON, GORDON R.   NV   GAL 61 02
FLAT TIGER   DICKSON, GORDON R.   SS   GAL 56 03
JAMES   DICKSON, GORDON R.   SS   FSF 55 05
QUARRY, THE   DICKSON, GORDON R.   SS   ASF 58 09
CALL HIM LORD   DICKSON, GORDON R.   SS   ASF 66 05
STEEL BROTHER   DICKSON, GORDON R.   NV   ASF 52 02

DANGEROUS VISIONS   ELLISON, HARLAN   OA H DBL 67 10
FOREWORD 1- THE SECOND REVOLUTION
                            ASIMOV, ISAAC   IN   DVS 67 01
FOREWORD 2- HARLAN AND I   ASIMOV, ISAAC   IN   DVS 67 01
THIRTY-TWO SOOTHSAYERS   ELLISON, HARLAN   IN   DVS 67 01
EVENSONG   DEL REY, LESTER   SS   DVS 67 01
FLIES   SILVERBERG, ROBERT SS DVS 67 01
DAY AFTER THE DAY THE MARTIANS CAME, THE (ALSO AS THE DAY
  THE MARTIANS CAME)   POHL, FREDERIK   SS   DVS 67 01
RIDERS OF THE PURPLE WAGE   FARMER, PHILIP JOSE NA DVS 67 01
MALLEY SYSTEM, THE   DEFORD, MIRIAM ALLEN SS DVS 67 01
TOY FOR JULIETTE, A   BLOCH, ROBERT   SS   DVS 67 01
PROWLER IN THE CITY AT THE EDGE OF THE WORLD, THE
                            ELLISON, HARLAN   NV   DVS 67 01
NIGHT THAT ALL TIME BROKE OUT, THE
                            ALDISS, BRIAN W. SS   DVS 67 01
MAN WHO WENT TO THE MOON- TWICE, THE
                            RODMAN, HOWARD   SS   DVS 67 01
FAITH OF OUR FATHERS   DICK, PHILIP K.   NV   DVS 67 01
JIGSAW MAN, THE   NIVEN, LARRY   SS   DVS 67 01
GONNA ROLL THE BONES   LEIBER, FRITZ   NV   DVS 67 01
LORD RANDY, MY SON   HENSLEY, JOE L.   SS   DVS 67 01
EUTOPIA   ANDERSON, POUL   SS   DVS 67 01
INCIDENT IN MODERAN   BUNCH, DAVID R.   SS   DVS 67 01

ESCAPING, THE   BUNCH, DAVID R.   SS   DVS 67 01
DOLL-HOUSE, THE   CROSS, JAMES   SS   DVS 67 01
SEX AND/OR MR. MORRISON   EMSHWILLER, CAROL SS   DVS 67 01
SHALL THE DUST PRAISE THEE? KNIGHT, DAMON   SS   DVS 67 01
IF ALL MEN WERE BROTHERS, WOULD YOU LET ONE MARRY YOUR SISTER?
                            STURGEON, THEODORE NA DVS 67 01
WHAT HAPPENED TO AUGUSTE CLAROT?
                            EISENBERG, LARRY SS   DVS 67 01
GO, GO, GO, SAID THE BIRD   DORMAN, SONYA   SS   DVS 67 01
HAPPY BREED, THE   SLADEK, JOHN T.   SS   DVS 67 01
ENCOUNTER WITH A HICK   BRAND, JONATHAN   SS   DVS 67 01
FROM THE GOVERNMENT PRINTING OFFICE
                            NEVILLE, KRIS   SS   DVS 67 01
LAND OF THE GREAT HORSES   LAFFERTY, R. A.   SS   DVS 67 01
RECOGNITION, THE   BALLARD, J. G.   SS   DVS 67 01
JUDAS   BRUNNER, JOHN   SS   DVS 67 01
TEST TO DESTRUCTION   LAUMER, KEITH   NV   DVS 67 01
CARCINOMA ANGELS   SPINRAD, NORMAN   SS   DVS 67 01
AUTO-DA-FE   ZELAZNY, ROGER   SS   DVS 67 01
AYE, AND GOMORRAH...   DELANY, SAMUEL R. SS   DVS 67 01

DARK BEASTS, THE   LONG, FRANK BELKNAP AC BEL 64 01
DARK BEASTS, THE   LONG, FRANK BELKNAP SS MVT 34 07
STITCH IN TIME, A   LONG, FRANK BELKNAP SS SSS 40 03
DEATH-WATERS   LONG, FRANK BELKNAP SS WRT 24 12
STEP INTO MY GARDEN   LONG, FRANK BELKNAP SS UNK 42 08
FLAME MIDGET, THE   LONG, FRANK BELKNAP SS ASF 36 12
IT WILL COME TO YOU   LONG, FRANK BELKNAP SS UNK 42 12
OCEAN LEECH, THE   LONG, FRANK BELKNAP SS WRT 25 01
CENSUS TAKER, THE   LONG, FRANK BELKNAP SS UNK 42 04
REFUGEES, THE   LONG, FRANK BELKNAP SS UNK 42 02

DARK CARNIVAL   BRADBURY, RAY   AC H ARK 47
HOMECOMING, THE   BRADBURY, RAY   SS   MAD 46 10
SKELETON   BRADBURY, RAY   SS   WRT 45 09
JAR, THE   BRADBURY, RAY   SS   WRT 44 11
LAKE, THE   BRADBURY, RAY   SS   WRT 44 05
MADEN, THE   BRADBURY, RAY   SS   NEW 47 AC
TOMBSTONE, THE   BRADBURY, RAY   SS   WRT 45 03
SMILING PEOPLE, THE   BRADBURY, RAY   SS   WRT 46 05
EMISSARY, THE   BRADBURY, RAY   SS   NEW 47 AC
TRAVELLER, THE   BRADBURY, RAY   SS   WRT 46 03
SMALL ASSASSIN, THE   BRADBURY, RAY   SS   DMN 46 11
CROWD, THE   BRADBURY, RAY   SS   WRT 43 05
REUNION   BRADBURY, RAY   SS   WRT 44 03
HANDLER, THE   BRADBURY, RAY   SS   WRT 47 01
COFFIN, THE (WAKE FOR THE LIVING)
                            BRADBURY, RAY   SS   DMN 47 09
INTERIM   BRADBURY, RAY   SS   WRT 47 07
JACK-IN-THE-BOX   BRADBURY, RAY   SS   NEW 47 AC
SCYTHE, THE   BRADBURY, RAY   SS   WRT 43 07
LET'S PLAY POISON   BRADBURY, RAY   SS   WRT 46 11
UNCLE EINAR   BRADBURY, RAY   SS   NEW 47 AC
WIND, THE   BRADBURY, RAY   SS   WRT 43 03
NIGHT, THE   BRADBURY, RAY   SS   WRT 46 07
THERE WAS AN OLD WOMAN   BRADBURY, RAY   SS   WRT 44 07
DEAD MAN, THE   BRADBURY, RAY   SS   WRT 45 07
MAN UPSTAIRS, THE   BRADBURY, RAY   SS   HRP 47 03
NIGHT SETS, THE   BRADBURY, RAY   SS   NEW 47 AC
CISTERN, THE   BRADBURY, RAY   SS   MAD 47 05
NEXT IN LINE, THE   BRADBURY, RAY   NV   NEW 47 AC

DARK CARNIVAL (BRITISH)   BRADBURY, RAY   AC H HML 48
HOMECOMING, THE   BRADBURY, RAY   SS   MAD 46 10
SKELETON   BRADBURY, RAY   SS   WRT 45 09
JAR, THE   BRADBURY, RAY   SS   WRT 44 11
LAKE, THE   BRADBURY, RAY   SS   WRT 44 05
TOMBSTONE, THE   BRADBURY, RAY   SS   WRT 45 03
SMILING PEOPLE, THE   BRADBURY, RAY   SS   WRT 46 05
EMISSARY, THE   BRADBURY, RAY   SS   NEW 47 AC
TRAVELLER, THE   BRADBURY, RAY   SS   WRT 46 03
SMALL ASSASSIN, THE   BRADBURY, RAY   SS   DMN 46 11
CROWD, THE   BRADBURY, RAY   SS   WRT 43 05
HANDLER, THE   BRADBURY, RAY   SS   WRT 47 01
LET'S PLAY POISON   BRADBURY, RAY   SS   WRT 46 11
UNCLE EINAR   BRADBURY, RAY   SS   NEW 47 AC
WIND, THE   BRADBURY, RAY   SS   WRT 43 03
NIGHT, THE   BRADBURY, RAY   SS   WRT 46 07
THERE WAS AN OLD WOMAN   BRADBURY, RAY   SS   WRT 44 07
DEAD MAN, THE   BRADBURY, RAY   SS   WRT 45 07
MAN UPSTAIRS, THE   BRADBURY, RAY   SS   HRP 47 03
CISTERN, THE   BRADBURY, RAY   SS   MAD 47 05
NEXT IN LINE, THE   BRADBURY, RAY   NV   NEW 47 AC

DARK INTRUDER & OTHER STORIES, THE
                            BRADLEY, MARION Z. DC ACE 64
INTRODUCTION   BRADLEY, MARION Z. IN
DARK INTRUDER, THE (MEASURELESS TO MAN)
                            BRADLEY, MARION Z. NV AMZ 62 12
JACKIE SEES A STAR   BRADLEY, MARION Z. SS FUN 54 09
EXILES OF TOMORROW   BRADLEY, MARION Z. SS FUN 55 05
DEATH BETWEEN THE STARS   BRADLEY, MARION Z. SS FUN 56 03
CRIME THERAPIST, THE   BRADLEY, MARION Z. SS FUT 54 10
STARS ARE WAITING, THE   BRADLEY, MARION Z. SS STN 58 03
BLACK AND WHITE   BRADLEY, MARION Z. SS AMZ 62 11

DARK SIDE OF THE EARTH, THE BESTER, ALFRED   AC   SIG 64 05
TIME IS THE TRAITOR   BESTER, ALFRED   NV   FSF 53 09
MEN WHO MURDERED MOHAMMED, THE
                            BESTER, ALFRED   SS   FSF 58 10
OUT OF THIS WORLD   BESTER, ALFRED   SS
PI MAN, THE   BESTER, ALFRED   SS   FSF 59 10
FLOWERED THUNDERMUG, THE   BESTER, ALFRED   NV
WILL YOU WAIT?   BESTER, ALFRED   SS   FSF 59 03
THEY DON'T MAKE LIFE LIKE THEY USED TO
                            BESTER, ALFRED   NV   FSF 63 10

```
DARK SIDE, THE                KNIGHT, DAMON        AN H DBL 65
  INTRODUCTION                KNIGHT, DAMON        IN
  BLACK FERRIS, THE           BRADBURY, RAY        SS    WRT 48 05
  THEY                        HEINLEIN, ROBERT A.  SS    UNK 41 04
  MISTAKE INSIDE              BLISH, JAMES         NV    STS 48 03
  TROUBLE WITH WATER          GOLD, H. L.          SS    UNK 39 03
  C/O MR. MAKEPEACE           PHILLIPS, PETER      SS    FSF 54 02
  GOLEM, THE                  DAVIDSON, AVRAM      SS    FSF 55 03
  STORY OF THE LATE MR. ELVESHAM, THE
                              WELLS, H. G.         SS    IDL 96 05
  IT                          STURGEON, THEODORE   NV    UNK 40 08
  NELLTHU                     BOUCHER, ANTHONY     SS    FSF 55 08
  CASEY AGONISTES             MCKENNA, RICHARD M.  SS    FSF 58 09
  EYE FOR INIQUITY            SHERRED, T. L.       NV    BEY 53 07
  MAN WHO NEVER GREW YOUNG, THE
                              LEIBER, FRITZ        SS    AFR 49 09

DARK STARS                    SILVERBERG, ROBERT   AN    BAL 69 12
  INTRODUCTION                SILVERBERG, ROBERT   IN
  SHARK SHIP (REAP THE DARK TIDE)
                              KORNBLUTH, C. M.     NV    VAN 58 06
  POLICY AND CUSTOM OF THE CAMIROI
                              LAFFERTY, R. A.      SS    GAL 67 06
  COMING-OF-AGE DAY           JORGENSSON, A. K.    SS    SCF 65 09
  HERESIES OF THE HUGE GOD    ALDISS, BRIAN W.     FA    GAL 66 08
  STREETS OF ASHKELON, THE (ALSO AS AN ALIEN AGONY)
                              HARRISON, HARRY      SS    NWS 62 09
  TOTALLY RICH, THE           BRUNNER, JOHN        NV    WOT 63 06
  IMPOSTOR                    DICK, PHILIP K.      SS    ASF 53 06
  ROAD TO NIGHTFALL           SILVERBERG, ROBERT   NV    FUN 58 07
  BEAST THAT SHOUTED LOVE AT THE HEART OF THE WORLD, THE
                              ELLISON, HARLAN      NV    GAL 68 06
  PSYCHOSMOSIS                MASSON, DAVID I.     SS    NWS 66 03
  CAGE OF SAND, THE           BALLARD, J. G.       SS    NWS 62 06
  DESKFUL OF GIRLS, A         LEIBER, FRITZ        NV    FSF 58 04
  ON THE WALL OF THE LODGE    BLISH, JAMES
                              AND KIDD, VIRGINIA   NV C  GAL 62 04
  MASKS                       KNIGHT, DAMON        SS    PBY 68 07
  KEEPERS OF THE HOUSE        DEL REY, LESTER      SS    FUN 56 01
  JOURNEYS END                ANDERSON, POUL       SS    FSF 57 02

DARK TIDES                    RUSSELL, ERIC FRANK  AC H DOB 62
  INTRODUCTION                RUSSELL, ERIC FRANK  IN
  SIN OF HYACINTH PEUCH, THE  RUSSELL, ERIC FRANK  NV    FAN 52 FL
  WITH A BLUNT INSTRUMENT     RUSSELL, ERIC FRANK  SS    UNK 41 12
  MATTER OF INSTINCT, A       RUSSELL, ERIC FRANK  SS
  I'M A STRANGER HERE MYSELF  RUSSELL, ERIC FRANK  SS    OWS 52 03
  THIS ONE'S ON ME            RUSSELL, ERIC FRANK  SS    NEB 53 FL
  I HEAR YOU CALLING          RUSSELL, ERIC FRANK  SS    SCF 54 12
  WISEL                       RUSSELL, ERIC FRANK  SS
  PONDERER, THE               RUSSELL, ERIC FRANK  SS    WRT 48 11
  SOLE SOLUTION               RUSSELL, ERIC FRANK  SS    FUN 56 04
  RHYTHM OF THE RATS          RUSSELL, ERIC FRANK  SS    WRT 50 07
  ME AND MY SHADOW            RUSSELL, ERIC FRANK  SS    SRS 40 02
  BITTER END                  RUSSELL, ERIC FRANK  SS    SFP 53 12

DARK TOWER AND OTHER STORIES, THE
                              LEWIS, C. S.         AC H HBJ 77
  EDITED BY WALTER HOOPER
  PREFACE                     HOOPER, WALTER       IN
  DARK TOWER, THE (UNFINISHED) LEWIS, C. S.        NA    NEW 77 AC
  NOTE ON THE DARK TOWER, A   HOOPER, WALTER       MS
  MAN BORN BLIND, THE         LEWIS, C. S.         SS    NEW 77 AC
  SHODDY LANDS, THE           LEWIS, C. S.         SS    FSF 56 02
  MINISTERING ANGELS (SRV MAY 28, 1955)
                              LEWIS, C. S.         SS    FSF 58 01
  FORMS OF THINGS UNKNOWN     LEWIS, C. S.         SS    66
  AFTER TEN YEARS             LEWIS, C. S.         NV    66
  NOTES TO AFTER TEN YEARS    GREEN, ROGER L.      MS
  NOTES TO AFTER TEN YEARS    FOWLER, ALASTAIR     MS

DARKNESS AND DAWN             ENGLAND, GEORGE A.   NO H SMY 14
  DARKNESS AND DAWN           ENGLAND, GEORGE A.   NO    CSB 12 01
  BEYOND THE GREAT OBLIVION   ENGLAND, GEORGE A.   NO    CSB 13 01
  AFTERGLOW, THE              ENGLAND, GEORGE A.   NO    CSB 13 06

DAUGHTERS OF EARTH            MERRIL, JUDITH       AC H DBL 68
  PROJECT NURSEMAID           MERRIL, JUDITH       SN    FSF 55 10
  DAUGHTERS OF EARTH          MERRIL, JUDITH       SN    52
  HOMECALLING                 MERRIL, JUDITH       NV    SFS 56 11

DAW SCIENCE FICTION READER, THE
                              WOLLHEIM, DONALD A.  OA H DAW 76 07
  INTRODUCTION                WOLLHEIM, DONALD A.  IN
  AUTHOR'S INTRODUCTION TO THIS EDITION OF FUR MAGIC
                              NORTON, ANDRE        AI
  FUR MAGIC                   NORTON, ANDRE        NO    WOR 68
  WARRIOR                     DICKSON, GORDON R.   SS    ASF 65 12
  TRUCE, THE                  LEE, TANITH          SS
  WIZARD OF SCORPIO           AKERS, ALAN BURT     NV
  MARTIAN EL DORADO OF PARKER WINTLEY, THE
                              CARTER, LIN          SS
  DAY OF THE BUTTERFLIES, THE BRADLEY, MARION Z.   SS
  CAPTAIN FAGAN DIED ALONE    STABLEFORD, BRIAN M. SS

DAWN OF FLAME                 WEINBAUM, STANLEY G. AC H CHR 36
  THE WEINBAUM MEMORIAL VOLUME
  MAD MOON, THE               WEINBAUM, STANLEY G. NV    ASF 35 12
  MARTIAN ODYSSEY, A          WEINBAUM, STANLEY G. NV    WOS 34 07
  LOTUS EATERS, THE           WEINBAUM, STANLEY G. NV    ASF 35 04
  RED PERI, THE               WEINBAUM, STANLEY G. SN    ASF 35 11
  WORLDS OF IF, THE           WEINBAUM, STANLEY G. NV    WOS 35 08
  ADAPTIVE ULTIMATE, THE      WEINBAUM, STANLEY G. NV    ASF 35 11
  DAWN OF FLAME               WEINBAUM, STANLEY G. NV    TWS 39 06

DAY BEFORE FOREVER AND THUNDER HEAD, THE
                              LAUMER, KEITH        AC H DBL 68
  DAY BEFORE FOREVER, THE     LAUMER, KEITH        SN    FSF 67 07
  THUNDERHEAD                 LAUMER, KEITH        NV    GAL 67 04

DAY IN THE LIFE, A            DOZOIS, GARDNER R.   AN H HPR 72
  INTRODUCTION                DOZOIS, GARDNER R.   IN
  SLOW TUESDAY NIGHT          LAFFERTY, R. A.      SS    GAL 65 04
  LADY MARGARET, THE (THE LADY ANNE)
                              ROBERTS, KEITH       NV    IMP 66 04
  MARY (AN ANCIENT MADNESS)   KNIGHT, DAMON        NV    GAL 64 06
  DRIFTGLASS                  DELANY, SAMUEL R.    NV    IFS 67 06
  HAPPY DAY IN 2381, A        SILVERBERG, ROBERT   SS    NOV 70 01
  THIS MOMENT OF THE STORM    ZELAZNY, ROGER       NV    FSF 66 06
  HAUNTED FUTURE, THE (TRANQUILITY, OR ELSE!)
                              LEIBER, FRITZ        NV    FAN 59 11
  ON THE STORM PLANET         SMITH, CORDWAINER    SN    GAL 65 02

DAY IT RAINED FOREVER, THE    BRADBURY, RAY        AC H HDV 60
  BRITISH VERSION OF "A MEDICINE FOR MELANCHOLY"
  DAY IT RAINED FOREVER, THE  BRADBURY, RAY        SS    HRP 57 07
  IN A SEASON OF CALM WEATHER BRADBURY, RAY        SS    PBY 57 01
  DRAGON, THE                 BRADBURY, RAY        SS    FSF 56 03
  END OF THE BEGINNING, THE (NEXT STOP: THE STARS)
                              BRADBURY, RAY        SS    MCL 56 10
  WONDERFUL ICE CREAM SUIT, THE (THE MAGIC WHITE SUIT)
                              BRADBURY, RAY        SS    SEP 58 10
  FEVER DREAM                 BRADBURY, RAY        SS    WRT 48 09
  REFERENT (AS BRETT STERLING) BRADBURY, RAY       SS    TWS 48 10
  MARRIAGE MENDER             BRADBURY, RAY        SS    COL 54 01
  TOWN WHERE NO ONE GOT OFF, THE
                              BRADBURY, RAY        SS    EQM 58 10
  ICARUS MONTGOLFIER WRIGHT   BRADBURY, RAY        SS    FSF 56 05
  ALMOST THE END OF THE WORLD BRADBURY, RAY        SS    REP 57 12
  DARK THEY WERE, AND GOLDEN-EYED (THE NAMING OF NAMES)
                              BRADBURY, RAY        SS    TWS 49 08
  SMILE, THE                  BRADBURY, RAY        SS    FAN 52 SU
  HERE THERE BE TYGERS        BRADBURY, RAY        SS    NTS 51
  HEADPIECE, THE              BRADBURY, RAY        SS    LIL 58 05
  PERCHANCE TO DREAM (ASLEEP IN ARMAGEDDON)
                              BRADBURY, RAY        SS    PLS 48 WI
  TIME OF GOING AWAY, THE     BRADBURY, RAY        SS    REP 56 11
  GIFT, THE                   BRADBURY, RAY        SS    FAN 59 07
  LITTLE MICE, THE (THE MICE) BRADBURY, RAY        SS    ESC 55 10
  SUNSET HARP, THE (THE SHORELINE AT SUNSET)
                              BRADBURY, RAY        SS    FSF 59 03
  SCENT OF SARSAPARILLA, A    BRADBURY, RAY        SS    STR 53 01
  AND THE ROCK CRIED OUT (THE MILLIONTH MURDER)
                              BRADBURY, RAY        SS    MHT 53 09
  STRAWBERRY WINDOW, THE      BRADBURY, RAY        SS    STR 54 03

DAY MILLION                   POHL, FREDERIK       AC    BAL 70 06
  INTRODUCTION                POHL, FREDERIK       IN
  DAY MILLION                 POHL, FREDERIK       SS    ROG 66 02
  DEADLY MISSION OF PHINEAS SNODGRASS, THE
                              POHL, FREDERIK       SS    GAL 62 06
  DAY THE MARTIANS CAME, THE (THE DAY AFTER THE DAY THE MARTIANS
  CAME)                       POHL, FREDERIK       SS    DVS 67 01
  SCHEMATIC MAN, THE          POHL, FREDERIK       SS    PBY 69 01
  SMALL LORDS                 POHL, FREDERIK       NV    SFQ 57 02
  MAKING LOVE (LOVEMAKING)    POHL, FREDERIK       SS    PBY 66 12
  WAY UP YONDER               POHL, FREDERIK       NV    GAL 59 10
  SPEED TRAP                  POHL, FREDERIK       SS    PBY 67 11
  IT'S A YOUNG WORLD          POHL, FREDERIK       NV    AST 41 04
  UNDER TWO MOONS             POHL, FREDERIK       NV    IFS 65 09

DAY OF FOREVER, THE           BALLARD, J. G.       AC    PTH 67 09
  DAY OF FOREVER, THE         BALLARD, J. G.       SS    NWS 67 01
  PRISONER OF THE CORAL DEEP (ARG 64 03)
                              BALLARD, J. G.       SS    NWS 65 05
  TOMORROW IS A MILLION YEARS BALLARD, J. G.       SS    ARG 66 10
  MAN ON THE 99TH FLOOR, THE  BALLARD, J. G.       SS    NWS 62 07
  WAITING GROUNDS, THE        BALLARD, J. G.       NV    NWS 59 11
  LAST WORLD OF MR. GODDARD, THE
                              BALLARD, J. G.       SS    SCF 60 10
  GENTLE ASSASSIN, THE        BALLARD, J. G.       SS    NWS 61 12
  SUDDEN AFTERNOON, THE       BALLARD, J. G.       SS    FAN 63 09
  INSANE ONES, THE            BALLARD, J. G.       SS    AMZ 62 01
  ASSASSINATION OF JOHN FITZGERALD KENNEDY CONSIDERED AS A
  DOWNHILL MOTOR RACE, THE    BALLARD, J. G.       SS    NWS 67 02

DAY THE SUN STOOD STILL, THE  SILVERBERG, ROBERT   OA H NEL 72
  INTRODUCTION                SILVERBERG, ROBERT   IN
  FOREWORD                    DEL REY, LESTER      IN
  CHAPTER OF REVELATION, A    ANDERSON, POUL       NA
  THOMAS THE PROCLAIMER       SILVERBERG, ROBERT   NA
  THINGS WHICH ARE CAESAR'S   DICKSON, GORDON R.   NA

DAYMARES                      BROWN, FREDRIC       AC    LAN 68
  GATEWAY TO DARKNESS         BROWN, FREDRIC       NV    SSS 49 11
  DAYMARE                     BROWN, FREDRIC       NV    TWS 43 FL
  COME AND GO MAD             BROWN, FREDRIC       NV    WRT 49 07
  ANGELIC ANGLEWORM, THE      BROWN, FREDRIC       NV    UNK 43 02
  STAR MOUSE, THE             BROWN, FREDRIC       SS    PLS 42 02
  HONEYMOON IN HELL           BROWN, FREDRIC       NV    GAL 50 11
  PI IN THE SKY               BROWN, FREDRIC       SS    TWS 45 WI

DAYS AFTER TOMORROW, THE      SANTESSON, HANS S.   AN H LBR 71
  SOUND DECISION              GARRETT, RANDALL
                              AND SILVERBERG, ROBERT NV C ASF 56 10
  GREEN FINGERS (VENTURE TO THE MOON)
                              CLARKE, ARTHUR C.    SS    FSF 57 01
  VICTORY UNINTENTIONAL       ASIMOV, ISAAC        SS    SSS 42 08
  WEATHER MAN, THE            THOMAS, THEODORE L.  SN    ASF 62 06
  I ALWAYS DO WHAT TEDDY SAYS HARRISON, HARRY      SS    EQM 65 06
  SENSE OF DIRECTION, A       PANSHIN, ALEXEI      SS    AMZ 69 11
```

OMNILINGUAL	PIPER, H. BEAM	NV	ASF 57 02
DREAM STREET	ROBINSON, FRANK M.	SS	IMT 55 03

DEAD ASTRONAUT, 10 STORIES OF SPACE FLIGHT, THE
	PLAYBOY, EDITORS OF	AN	PBP 71
PREFACE	PLAYBOY, EDITORS OF	IN	
DEAD ASTRONAUT, THE	BALLARD, J. G.	SS	PBY 68 05
HERE COMES JOHN HENRY	RUSSELL, RAY	SS	PBY 68 09
MAN FOR THE MOON, A	WEBB, LELAND	SS	PBY 60 08
NINE LIVES	LE GUIN, URSULA K.	NV	PBY 69 11
REQUIEM ON THE MOON	DUNCAN, DAVID	SS	PBY 64 10
SENSIBLE MAN, THE	DAVIDSON, AVRAM	SS	PBY 59 02
SKIN-DEEP	RENCELAW, BRIAN	SS	PBY 63 06
WRECK OF THE SHIP JOHN B., THE			
	ROBINSON, FRANK M.	NV	PBY 67 06
MAELSTROM II	CLARKE, ARTHUR C.	SS	PBY 65 04
SPY STORY (ALSO AS CITIZEN IN SPACE)			
	SHECKLEY, ROBERT	SS	PBY 55 09

DEADLY LITTER	WHITE, JAMES	NO	BAL 64 10
GRAPELINER	WHITE, JAMES	NV	NWS 59 11
IDEAL CAPTAIN, THE	WHITE, JAMES	NV	NWS 58 08
LIGHTS OUTSIDE THE WINDOWS, THE			
	WHITE, JAMES	NV	NWS 57 02
DEADLY LITTER	WHITE, JAMES	NV	SFB 60 02

DEALS WITH THE DEVIL	DAVENPORT, BASIL	AN H	DOM 58
INTRODUCTION	DAVENPORT, BASIL	IN	
BRAZEN LOCKED ROOM, THE (ALSO AS GIMMICKS THREE)			
	ASIMOV, ISAAC	SS	FSF 56 11
TRAMMEL, THE	DEFORD, MIRIAM ALLEN	SS	
IMPACT WITH THE DEVIL	COGSWELL, THEODORE R	SS	FSF 56 11
DOCTOR FAUSTUS	ANONYMOUS	SS	
DEVIL AND MR. CHIPS, THE (THE RAT THAT COULD SPEAK)			
	DICKENS, CHARLES	SS	FSF 51 08
SIR DOMINICK'S BARGAIN	LE FANU, J. SHERIDAN	SS	
ENOCH SOAMES	BEERBOHM, MAX	NV	CNY 16 05
DEAL WITH THE DEVIL, A	DUNSANY, LORD	SS	48
SATAN AND SAM SHAY	ARTHUR, ROBERT	SS	ELK 42 08
LEGEND OF MONT ST. MICHEL, THE			
	DE MAUPASSANT, GUY	SS	
TINKER OF TAMLACHT, THE	MACMANUS, S.	SS	
DEVIL AND SIMON FLAGG, THE	PORGES, ARTHUR	SS	FSF 54 08
DEVIL AND THE OLD MAN, THE	MASEFIELD, JOHN	SS	13
DEVIL-PUZZLERS	PERKINS, F. B.	SS	
THRESHOLD	KUTTNER, HENRY	SS	UNK 40 12
THREE WISHES, THE	RANDOLPH, V.	SS	
NELLTHU	BOUCHER, ANTHONY	SS	FSF 55 08
THREESIE	COGSWELL, THEODORE R	SS	FSF 56 01
BARGAIN IN BODIES, A	SCHERE, MOSES	SS	UNK 43 06
CAVEAT EMPTOR	DE CAMP, L. SPRAGUE		
	AND PRATT, FLETCHER	SS C	WRT 53 03
HELL-BENT (CONTEST STORY)	MCCORMACK, FORD	SS	FSF 51 06
DEVIL AND DANIEL WEBSTER, THE (ALSO AS ALL THAT MONEY CAN BUY)			
	BENET, STEPHEN V.	NV	SEP 36 10
COUNTESS KATHLEEN O'SHEA	ANONYMOUS	SS	
DEVIL, GEORGE, AND ROSIE, THE			
	COLLIER, JOHN	SS	34
DEVIL WAS SICK, THE	ELLIOTT, BRUCE	SS	FSF 51 04

DEATHBIRD STORIES	ELLISON, HARLAN	AC H	HPR 75
INTRODUCTION: OBLATIONS AT ALIEN ALTARS			
	ELLISON, HARLAN	IN	
WHIMPER OF WHIPPED DOGS, THE	ELLISON, HARLAN	NV	BMR 73
ALONG THE SCENIC ROUTE (DOGFIGHT ON 101)			
	ELLISON, HARLAN	SS	AMZ 69 09
ON THE DOWNHILL SIDE	ELLISON, HARLAN	SS	UNI 72 02
O YE OF LITTLE FAITH	ELLISON, HARLAN	SS	KNT 68 09
NEON	ELLISON, HARLAN	SS	HQH 73 08
BASILISK	ELLISON, HARLAN	SS	FSF 72 08
PRETTY MAGGIE MONEYEYES	ELLISON, HARLAN	NV	KNT 67 05
CORPSE	ELLISON, HARLAN	SS	FSF 72 01
SHATTERED LIKE A GLASS GOBLIN			
	ELLISON, HARLAN	SS	ORB 68 04
DELUSION FOR A DRAGON SLAYER	ELLISON, HARLAN	SS	KNT 66 09
FACE OF HELENE BOURNOUW, THE	ELLISON, HARLAN	SS	CLG 60 10
BLEEDING STONES	ELLISON, HARLAN	SS	VTX 73 04
AT THE MOUSE CIRCUS	ELLISON, HARLAN	SS	NDM 71 01
PLACE WITH NO NAME, THE	ELLISON, HARLAN	SS	FSF 69 07
PAINGOD	ELLISON, HARLAN	SS	FAN 64 06
ERNEST AND THE MACHINE GOD	ELLISON, HARLAN	NV	KNT 68 01
ROCK GOD	ELLISON, HARLAN	SS	COV 69 11
ADRIFT JUST OFF THE ISLETS OF LANGERHANS: LATITUDE 38° 54' N,			
LONGITUDE 77° 00' 13" W	ELLISON, HARLAN	NV	FSF 74 10
DEATHBIRD, THE	ELLISON, HARLAN	NV	FSF 73 03

DEATHWORLD TRILOGY, THE	HARRISON, HARRY	AC H	BKM 75
DEATHWORLD	HARRISON, HARRY	NO	ASF 60 01
DEATHWORLD 2 (THE ETHICAL ENGINEER)			
	HARRISON, HARRY	NO	ASF 63 07
DEATHWORLD 3 (THE HORSE BARBARIANS)			
	HARRISON, HARRY	NO	ASF 68 02

DECADE OF FANTASY AND SCIENCE FICTION, A			
	MILLS, ROBERT P.	AN H	DBL 60
INTRODUCTION	MILLS, ROBERT P.	IN	
MARTIAN SHOP, THE	FAST, HOWARD	SS	FSF 59 11
WALK LIKE A MOUNTAIN	WELLMAN, MANLY WADE	SS	FSF 55 06
MEN OF IRON (1940)	ENDORE, GUY	SS	FSF 49 FL
RABBITS TO THE MOON	BANKS, RAYMOND E.	SS	FSF 59 07
CERTIFICATE, THE	DAVIDSON, AVRAM	SS	FSF 59 03
SEALMAN, THE (1913)	MASEFIELD, JOHN	SS	FSF 55 07
SKY PEOPLE, THE	ANDERSON, POUL	NV	FSF 59 03
CAUSES, THE	SEABRIGHT, IDRIS	SS	FSF 52 06
HYPNOGLYPH, THE	ANTHONY, JOHN	SS	FSF 53 07

TALE OF THE THIRTEENTH FLOOR, A			
	NASH, OGDEN	PM	FSF 55 07
SPUD AND COCHISE	LA FARGE, OLIVER	NV	FSF 59 04
UNTO THE FOURTH GENERATION	ASIMOV, ISAAC	SS	FSF 59 04
JORDAN	HENDERSON, ZENNA	SS	FSF 59 03
WILL YOU WAIT?	BESTER, ALFRED	SS	FSF 59 03
PROOF POSITIVE (HRP 47 10)	GREENE, GRAHAM	SS	FSF 52 08
SHOCK TREATMENT	MCCOMAS, J. FRANCIS	NV	FSF 56 04
GANDOLPHUS	BOUCHER, ANTHONY	SS	FSF 56 12
LAST SHALL BE FIRST, THE	MILLS, ROBERT P.	SS	FSF 58 08
TRICK OR TWO, A	NOVOTNY, JOHN	SS	FSF 57 07
LOT'S DAUGHTER	MOORE, WARD	NV	FSF 54 10
SATURNIA CELIA (1903)	WALPOLE, HORACE	SS	FSF 57 04
FEAR IS A BUSINESS	STURGEON, THEODORE	SS	FSF 56 08
MEETING OF RELATIONS (YRV 41 12)			
	COLLIER, JOHN	SS	FSF 59 01
FIRST LESSON	CLINGERMAN, MILDRED	SS	FSF 56 12
TO FELL A TREE	YOUNG, ROBERT F.	NV	FSF 59 07

DECADE THE 1940S	ALDISS & HARRISON	AN H	MCM 75
INTRODUCTION	ALDISS, BRIAN W.	IN	
CO-OPERATE- OR ELSE¡	VAN VOGT, A. E.	NV	ASF 42 04
REASON	ASIMOV, ISAAC	SS	ASF 41 04
ARENA	BROWN, FREDRIC	NV	ASF 44 06
FIREPROOF	CLEMENT, HAL	SS	ASF 49 03
LAST OBJECTIVE, THE	CARTER, PAUL A.	NV	ASF 46 08
HUDDLING PLACE	SIMAK, CLIFFORD D.	SS	ASF 44 07
HOBBYIST	RUSSELL, ERIC FRANK	NV	ASF 47 09
XI EFFECT, THE	LATHAM, PHILIP	SS	ASF 50 01

DECADE THE 1950S	ALDISS & HARRISON	AN H	MCM 76
INTRODUCTION	HARRISON, HARRY	IN	
GRANDPA	SCHMITZ, JAMES H.	SS	ASF 55 02
SNOWBALL EFFECT, THE	MACLEAN, KATHERINE	SS	GAL 52 09
EDGE OF THE SEA, THE	BUDRYS, ALGIS	SS	VSF 58 03
SCANNERS LIVE IN VAIN	SMITH, CORDWAINER	NA	FBK 50 06
PEDESTRIAN, THE (REP 51 08)	BRADBURY, RAY	SS	FSF 52 02
LAST DAY, THE	MATHESON, RICHARD	SS	AMZ 53 05
HOLES AROUND MARS, THE	BIXBY, JEROME	SS	GAL 54 01
STAR, THE	CLARKE, ARTHUR C.	SS	INF 55 11
TWO-HANDED ENGINE	KUTTNER, HENRY	SS	FSF 55 08
LARGE ANT, THE (THE BIG ANT)	FAST, HOWARD	SS	FUN 60 02
EARLY MODEL	SHECKLEY, ROBERT	NV	GAL 56 08
SAIL ON¡ SAIL ON¡	FARMER, PHILIP JOSE	SS	STS 52 12

DECADE THE 1960S	ALDISS & HARRISON	AN H	MCM 77
INTRODUCTION	ALDISS, BRIAN W.		
	AND HARRISON, HARRY	IN C	
ASSASSINATION OF JOHN FITZGERALD KENNEDY CONSIDERED AS A			
DOWNHILL MOTOR RACE, THE	BALLARD, J. G.	SS	NWS 67 02
GRAVITY	JACOBS, HARVEY	SS	NWS 69 08
HARRISON BERGERON	VONNEGUT, KURT JR.	SS	FSF 61 10
COMPUTERS DON'T ARGUE	DICKSON, GORDON R.	SS	ASF 65 09
FOOD GOES IN THE TOP, THE	WORTHINGTON, WILL	SS	SCF 61 08
SUBVERSIVE	REYNOLDS, MACK	SS	ASF 62 12
DESCENDING	DISCH, THOMAS M.	SS	FAN 64 07
VILLAGE SWINDLER, THE	ALDISS, BRIAN W.	SS	INT 68 10
MANSCARER	ROBERTS, KEITH	NV	NWR 66 07
HYBRID	LAUMER, KEITH	SS	FSF 61 11
HEAT DEATH OF THE UNIVERSE, THE			
	ZOLINE, PAMELA A.	SS	NWS 67 07
DEVIL CAR	ZELAZNY, ROGER	SS	GAL 65 06
NATURE OF THE CATASTROPHE, THE			
	MOORCOCK, MICHAEL	SS	NWS 70 01
HAWKSBILL STATION	SILVERBERG, ROBERT	NV	GAL 67 08
DAY MILLION	POHL, FREDERIK	SS	ROG 66 02
ELECTRIC ANT, THE	DICK, PHILIP K.	NV	FSF 69 10
LAST HURRAH OF THE GOLDEN HORDE, THE			
	SPINRAD, NORMAN	SS	NWS 69 07
HEMINGWAY IN SPACE	AMIS, KINGSLEY	SS	PUN 60 12

DEEP FIX, THE	COLVIN, JAMES	AC	CPT 66
DEEP FIX, THE	COLVIN, JAMES	NV	SCF 64 04
PEACE ON EARTH	COLVIN, JAMES	SS	NWS 59 12
LOVEBEAST, THE	COLVIN, JAMES	SS	
PLEASURE GARDEN OF FELIPE SAGITTARIUS, THE			
	COLVIN, JAMES	SS	NWS 65 09
REAL LIFE OF MR. NEWMAN, THE	COLVIN, JAMES	SS	

DEEP SPACE	RUSSELL, ERIC FRANK	AC H	FPS 54
BANTAM 1955 EDITION OMITS "FIRST PERSON SINGULAR"			
FIRST PERSON SINGULAR	RUSSELL, ERIC FRANK	NV	TWS 50 10
WITNESS, THE	RUSSELL, ERIC FRANK	SS	OWS 51 09
LAST BLAST	RUSSELL, ERIC FRANK	NV	ASF 52 11
HOMO SAPS	RUSSELL, ERIC FRANK	SS	ASF 41 12
TIMID TIGER, THE	RUSSELL, ERIC FRANK	SS	ASF 47 02
LITTLE OIL, A	RUSSELL, ERIC FRANK	NV	GAL 52 10
RAINBOW'S END (AFTERNOON OF A FAHN)			
	RUSSELL, ERIC FRANK	SS	IMG 51 04
UNDECIDED, THE	RUSSELL, ERIC FRANK	NV	ASF 49 04
SECOND GENESIS	RUSSELL, ERIC FRANK	SS	51

DEEP SPACE	SILVERBERG, ROBERT	AN H	NDB 73
INTRODUCTION	SILVERBERG, ROBERT	IN	
BLOOD'S A ROVER	OLIVER, CHAD	NV	ASF 52 05
NOISE	VANCE, JACK	SS	STS 52 08
LIFE HUTCH	ELLISON, HARLAN	SS	IFS 56 04
TICKET TO ANYWHERE	KNIGHT, DAMON	NV	GAL 52 04
SIXTH PALACE, THE	SILVERBERG, ROBERT	SS	GAL 65 02
LULUNGOMEENA	DICKSON, GORDON R.	NV	GAL 54 01
DANCE OF THE CHANGER AND THE THREE, THE			
	CARR, TERRY	SS	FRS 68
FAR CENTAURUS	VAN VOGT, A. E.	SS	ASF 44 01

DEMON KIND	ELWOOD, ROGER	OA	AVN 73 03
INTRODUCTION	ELWOOD, ROGER	IN	

EMON KIND   DOORWAY INTO TIME

LINKAGE   MALZBERG, BARRY N.   SS   DEM 73
MUD VIOLET   LAFFERTY, R. A.   SS   DEM 73
BETTYANN'S CHILDREN   NEVILLE, KRIS   SS   DEM 73
CHILD   HOLLY, JOAN C.   SS   DEM 73
WORLD OF GRAY   SPINRAD, NORMAN   SS   DEM 73
DANDY   WHITE, TED   SS   DEM 73
PROPER SANTA CLAUS, A   MCCAFFREY, ANNE   SS   DEM 73
MARKS OF PAINTED TEETH, THE   DANN, JACK M.   SS   DEM 73
EDDYSTONE LIGHT, THE   YEP, LAURENCE   NV   DEM 73
FROM DARKNESS TO DARKNESS   CARR, TERRY   SS   DEM 73
MONOLOGUE   FARMER, PHILIP JOSE   SS   DEM 73

EPRESSION OR BUST   REYNOLDS, MACK   DN   ACE 74
DEPRESSION...OR BUST   REYNOLDS, MACK   SS   ASF 67 08
EXPEDITER   REYNOLDS, MACK   SS   ASF 63 05
FAD   REYNOLDS, MACK   SS   ASF 65 04

ESTINATION: AMALTHEIA   DIXON, RICHARD   AN   FLP 63
TRANSLATION   KOLESNIKOV, LEONID   MS
ASTRONAUT, THE   ZHURAVLEVA,VALENTINA   SS
OVER THE ABYSS   BELAYEV, ALEXANDER   SS
MAXWELL EQUATIONS, THE   DNIEPROV, ANATOLY   SS
VALLEY OF THE FOUR CROSSES, THE
                              ZABELIN, IGOR   SS
GOLUB-YAVAN, THE   STANYUKOVICH, KIRILL   SS
FLYING FLOWERS   VASILYEV, MIKHAIL   SS
DESTINATION: AMALTHEIA   STRUGATSKY, ARKADY
                              AND STRUGATSKY, BORIS   SS C

ESTINATION: UNIVERSE!   VAN VOGT, A. E.   AC H   PEL 52
FAR CENTAURUS   VAN VOGT, A. E.   SS   ASF 44 01
MONSTER, THE (ALSO AS RESURRECTION)
                              VAN VOGT, A. E.   SS   ASF 48 08
DORMANT   VAN VOGT, A. E.   SS   STS 48 11
ENCHANTED VILLAGE (ALSO AS THE SANDS OF MARS)
                              VAN VOGT, A. E.   SS   OWS 50 07
CAN OF PAINT, A   VAN VOGT, A. E.   SS   ASF 44 09
DEFENSE   VAN VOGT, A. E.   SS   AFR 47 04
RULERS, THE   VAN VOGT, A. E.   SS   ASF 44 03
DEAR PEN PAL   VAN VOGT, A. E.   SS   ARS 49 WI
SOUND, THE   VAN VOGT, A. E.   NV   ASF 50 02
SEARCH, THE   VAN VOGT, A. E.   NV   ASF 43 01

EVIL HIS DUE, THE   HILL, DOUGLAS   AN   AVN 69 03
INTRODUCTION   HILL, DOUGLAS   IN
LONG SPOON, A   WYNDHAM, JOHN   SS   60
SHRINE OF TEMPTATION, THE   MERRIL, JUDITH   SS   FAN 62 04
SAMUEL F. MAYNARD AND ANTHROPOLOGIC DEMONOGRAPHY
                              WOOD, RAMSEY   SS   NEW 67 AN
RETURN VISIT   TUBB, E. C.   SS   SCF 58 04
EASTERN WINDOWS, THE   ROBERTS, KEITH   SS   NEW 67 AN
DEVIL OF A DRUMMER   BAILEY, HILARY   SS   NEW 67 AN
ATHEIST'S BARGAIN, THE   DISCH, THOMAS M.
                              AND SLADEK, JOHN T.   SS C NEW 67 AN
SINGING CITADEL, THE   MOORCOCK, MICHAEL   NV   63

EVIL'S GENERATION, THE   GHIDALIA, VIC   AN   LAN 73
INTRODUCTION   GHIDALIA, VIC   IN
BLACK FERRIS, THE   BRADBURY, RAY   SS   WRT 48 05
CALL HIM DEMON   KUTTNER, HENRY   SS   TWS 46 FL
MOTHER BY PROTEST (ALSO AS TRESPASS)
                              MATHESON, RICHARD   NV   FAN 53 10
FLORAL TRIBUTE   BLOCH, ROBERT   SS   WRT 49 07
PLACE IN THE WOODS, THE   DERLETH, AUGUST   SS   WRT 54 05
HOLE IN THE AIR   SILVERBERG, ROBERT   SS   AMZ 56 01
MR. LUPESCU   BOUCHER, ANTHONY   SS   WRT 45 09
DAY OF TRUCE   SIMAK, CLIFFORD D.   NV   GAL 63 02
OTHER WING, THE   BLACKWOOD, ALGERNON   SS   AFR 48 08

IGITS AND DASTARDS   POHL, FREDERIK   AC   BAL 66 06
INTRODUCTION   POHL, FREDERIK   IN
CHILDREN OF NIGHT, THE   POHL, FREDERIK   NV   GAL 64 10
FIEND, THE   POHL, FREDERIK   SS   PBY 64 04
EARTH EIGHTEEN   POHL, FREDERIK   FA   GAL 64 04
FATHER OF THE STARS   POHL, FREDERIK   SS   IFS 64 11
FIVE HELLS OF ORION, THE   POHL, FREDERIK   NV   IFS 63 01
WITH REDFERN ON CAPELLA XII (AS CHAS. SATTERFIELD)
                              POHL, FREDERIK   NV   GAL 55 11
HOW TO COUNT ON YOUR FINGERS POHL, FREDERIK   AR   SFS 56 09
ON BINARY DIGITS AND HUMAN HABITS
                              POHL, FREDERIK   AR   FSF 62 12

IMENSION THIRTEEN   SILVERBERG, ROBERT   AC   BAL 69 05
EVE AND THE TWENTY-THREE ADAMS
                              SILVERBERG, ROBERT   SS   VSF 58 03
WARM MAN   SILVERBERG, ROBERT   SS   FSF 57 05
BY THE SEAWALL   SILVERBERG, ROBERT   SS   IFS 67 01
DARK COMPANION   SILVERBERG, ROBERT   NV   AMZ 61 01
FOUR, THE   SILVERBERG, ROBERT   SS   SFS 58 08
BRIDE NINETY-ONE   SILVERBERG, ROBERT   SS   IFS 67 09
WORLD OF A THOUSAND COLORS   SILVERBERG, ROBERT   SS   SUP 57 06
EN ROUTE TO EARTH   SILVERBERG, ROBERT   SS   SFQ 57 08
KING OF THE GOLDEN RIVER, THE
                              SILVERBERG, ROBERT   SS   GAL 67 12
PRIME COMMANDMENT   SILVERBERG, ROBERT   SS   SFS 58 01
HALFWAY HOUSE   SILVERBERG, ROBERT   SS   IFS 66 11
JOURNEY'S END (THE SEED OF EARTH)
                              SILVERBERG, ROBERT   SS   SUP 58 04
SOLITARY   SILVERBERG, ROBERT   SS   FUT 57 SP

IMENSION X   KNIGHT, DAMON   AN H   SAS 70
MAN WHO SOLD THE MOON, THE   HEINLEIN, ROBERT A.   NV   NEW 50 AC
MARCHING MORONS, THE   KORNBLUTH, C. M.   NV   GAL 51 04
FIDDLER'S GREEN   MCKENNA, RICHARD M.   NV   ORB 67 02
SALIVA TREE, THE   ALDISS, BRIAN W.   SN   FSF 65 09

UGLY LITTLE BOY, THE (LASTBORN)
                              ASIMOV, ISAAC   NA   GAL 58 09

DIMENSION 4   CONKLIN, GROFF   AN   PYR 64 02
WON'T YOU WALK?   STURGEON, THEODORE   NV   ASF 56 01
SENSE OF PROPORTION   TUBB, E. C.   NV   NEB 58 07
TROJAN HORSE LAUGH   MACDONALD, JOHN D.   NV   ASF 49 08
SOME DAY WE'LL FIND YOU   CARTMILL, CLEVE   NV   ASF 42 12

DIPLOIDS AND OTHER FLIGHTS OF FANCY, THE
                              MACLEAN, KATHERINE   AC   AVN 62
DIPLOIDS, THE   MACLEAN, KATHERINE   NA   TWS 53 04
DEFENSE MECHANISM   MACLEAN, KATHERINE   SS   ASF 49 10
PYRAMID IN THE DESERT, THE (AND BE MERRY)
                              MACLEAN, KATHERINE   SS   ASF 50 02
SNOWBALL EFFECT, THE   MACLEAN, KATHERINE   SS   GAL 52 09
INCOMMUNICADO   MACLEAN, KATHERINE   NV   ASF 50 06
FEEDBACK   MACLEAN, KATHERINE   SS   ASF 51 07
GAMES   MACLEAN, KATHERINE   SS   GAL 53 03
PICTURES DON'T LIE   MACLEAN, KATHERINE   SS   GAL 51 08

DISASTER AREA, THE   BALLARD, J. G.   AC H   CAP 67 10
STORM-BIRD, STORM-DREAMER   BALLARD, J. G.   SS   NWS 66 11
CONCENTRATION CITY, THE (BUILD-UP)
                              BALLARD, J. G.   SS   NWS 57 01
SUBLIMINAL MAN, THE   BALLARD, J. G.   SS   NWS 63 01
NOW WAKES THE SEA   BALLARD, J. G.   SS   FSF 63 05
MINUS ONE   BALLARD, J. G.   SS   SCF 63 06
MR. F IS MR. F   BALLARD, J. G.   SS   SCF 61 08
ZONE OF TERROR   BALLARD, J. G.   SS   NWS 60 03
MANHOLE 69   BALLARD, J. G.   SS   NWS 57 11
IMPOSSIBLE MAN, THE   BALLARD, J. G.   SS   NEW 66 AC

DOCTOR TO THE STARS   LEINSTER, MURRAY   AC   PYR 64 03
GRANDFATHERS' WAR, THE   LEINSTER, MURRAY   SN   ASF 57 10
MED SHIP MAN   LEINSTER, MURRAY   NV   GAL 63 10
TALLIEN THREE (THE HATE DISEASE)
                              LEINSTER, MURRAY   NV   ASF 63 08

DOES ANYONE ELSE HAVE SOMETHING FURTHER TO ADD?
                              LAFFERTY, R. A.   AC H   SCB 74
ABOUT A SECRET CROCODILE   LAFFERTY, R. A.   SS   GAL 70 08
MAD MAN   LAFFERTY, R. A.   SS   IFS 64 10
NOR LIMESTONE ISLANDS   LAFFERTY, R. A.   SS   UNI 71 01
MAN UNDERNEATH, THE   LAFFERTY, R. A.   SS   IFS 71 01
BOOMER FLATS   LAFFERTY, R. A.   SS   IFS 71 08
THIS GRAND CARCASS   LAFFERTY, R. A.   SS   AMZ 68 11
IN THE GARDEN   LAFFERTY, R. A.   SS   IFS 61 03
GROANING HINGES OF THE WORLD LAFFERTY, R. A.   SS   NEW 71 AN
GOLDEN TRABANT   LAFFERTY, R. A.   SS   IFS 66 05
HOW THEY GAVE IT BACK   LAFFERTY, R. A.   SS   GAL 68 02
MAYBE JONES AND THE CITY   LAFFERTY, R. A.   SS
SEVEN STORY DREAM   LAFFERTY, R. A.   SS
ADAM HAD THREE BROTHERS   LAFFERTY, R. A.   SS   NMQ 69
PIG IN A POKEY   LAFFERTY, R. A.   SS
WEIRDEST WORLD, THE   LAFFERTY, R. A.   NV   GAL 61 06
ULTIMATE CREATURE, THE   LAFFERTY, R. A.   SS   MOH 67 11

DOOMSDAY ON AJIAT   JONES, NEIL R.   AC   ACE 68
IN THE METEORIC CLOUD   JONES, NEIL R.   NV   NEW 68 AC
ACCELERATED WORLD, THE   JONES, NEIL R.   NV   NEW 68 AC
METAL MOON, THE   JONES, NEIL R.   NV   SSS 49 09
DOOMSDAY ON AJIAT   JONES, NEIL R.   SS   AST 42 10

DOOR IN THE WALL, THE   WELLS, H. G.   AC H   KEN 11
CONE, THE   WELLS, H. G.   SS   UCN 95 09
COUNTRY OF THE BLIND, THE   WELLS, H. G.   SS   SND 04 04
DIAMOND MAKER, THE   WELLS, H. G.   SS   PMB 94
DOOR IN THE WALL, THE   WELLS, H. G.   SS   DCH 06 07
DREAM OF ARMAGEDDON, A   WELLS, H. G.   NV   BAW 01
LORD OF THE DYNAMOS, THE   WELLS, H. G.   SS   PMB 94 09
MOONLIGHT FABLE, THE (ALSO AS THE BEAUTIFUL SUIT)
                              WELLS, H. G.   SS   COL 09 04
STAR, THE   WELLS, H. G.   SS   GRP 97 12

DOOR TO ANYWHERE   POHL, FREDERIK   AN   CUR 67
SEE "THE TENTH GALAXY READER"

DOORS OF HIS FACE, THE LAMPS OF HIS MOUTH, THE
                              ZELAZNY, ROGER   AC H   DBL 71
DOORS OF HIS FACE, THE LAMPS OF HIS MOUTH, THE
                              ZELAZNY, ROGER   NV   FSF 65 03
KEYS TO DECEMBER, THE   ZELAZNY, ROGER   SS   NWS 66 08
DEVIL CAR   ZELAZNY, ROGER   SS   GAL 65 06
ROSE FOR ECCLESIASTES, A   ZELAZNY, ROGER   NV   FSF 63 11
MONSTER AND THE MAIDEN, THE   ZELAZNY, ROGER   SS   GAL 64 12
COLLECTOR'S FEVER   ZELAZNY, ROGER   SS   GAL 64 06
THIS MORTAL MOUNTAIN   ZELAZNY, ROGER   NV   IFS 67 03
THIS MOMENT OF THE STORM   ZELAZNY, ROGER   NV   FSF 66 06
GREAT SLOW KINGS, THE   ZELAZNY, ROGER   SS   WOT 63 12
MUSEUM PIECE, A   ZELAZNY, ROGER   SS   FAN 63 06
DIVINE MADNESS   ZELAZNY, ROGER   SS   MOH 66 SU
CORRIDA   ZELAZNY, ROGER   SS   68
LOVE IS AN IMAGINARY NUMBER   ZELAZNY, ROGER   SS   NWS 66 01
MAN WHO LOVED THE FAIOLI, THE
                              ZELAZNY, ROGER   SS   GAL 67 06
LUCIFER   ZELAZNY, ROGER   SS   WOT 64 06

DOORWAY INTO TIME   MOSKOWITZ, SAM   AN   MBB 66
AND OTHER STORIES FROM MODERN MASTERPIECES OF SCIENCE FICTION
INTRODUCTION   MOSKOWITZ, SAM   IN
DOORWAY INTO TIME   MOORE, C. L.   SS   FFM 43 09
LOGIC NAMED JOE, A   LEINSTER, MURRAY   SS   ASF 46 03
WITH FOLDED HANDS...   WILLIAMSON, JACK   NV   ASF 47 07
COMMAND, THE   DE CAMP, L. SPRAGUE   SS   ASF 38 10
LIAR!   ASIMOV, ISAAC   SS   ASF 41 05

DOORWAY INTO TIME   EARLY ASIMOV, TH

BEFORE EDEN   CLARKE, ARTHUR C.   SS   AMZ 61 06
DOORWAYS TO SPACE   WELLS, BASIL   AC H FPB 51
  LURKERS OF BURM, THE   WELLS, BASIL   SS
  SINGER, THE   WELLS, BASIL   SS
  BARREN WORLD   WELLS, BASIL   SS
  PLANET OF THE MIST   WELLS, BASIL   SS
  LORD OF THE DESERT PLANET WELLS, BASIL   SS
  REBELLION ON VENUS   WELLS, BASIL   SS
  ALIENS, THE   WELLS, BASIL   SS
  SPACE WOMAN   WELLS, BASIL   SS
  SUDDEN FOREST, THE   WELLS, BASIL   SS
  ELFIN HILLS, THE   WELLS, BASIL   SS
  CONQUEST   WELLS, BASIL   SS
  MARTYR FROM MARS   WELLS, BASIL   SS
  CHRYSALID   WELLS, BASIL   SS
  EXILES OF THE FORBIDDEN PLANET
                           WELLS, BASIL   SS
  CHAIR, THE   WELLS, BASIL   SS
DOUBLE IN SPACE   PRATT, FLETCHER   AC H DBL 51
  PROJECT EXCELSIOR (ASYLUM SATELLITE)
                           PRATT, FLETCHER   NO   TWS 51 10
  WANDERER'S RETURN, THE   PRATT, FLETCHER   NO   TWS 51 12
DOUBLE JEOPARDY   PRATT, FLETCHER   AC H DBL 52
  DOUBLE JEOPARDY   PRATT, FLETCHER   NO   TWS 52 04
  SQUARE CUBE LAW, THE   PRATT, FLETCHER   NV   TWS 52 06
DOWN HERE IN THE DREAM QUARTER
                           MALZBERG, BARRY N. AC H DBL 76
  INTRODUCTION: A SHORT ONE FOR THE BOYS IN THE BACK ROOM
                           MALZBERG, BARRY N. IN
  GALAXY CALLED ROME, A   MALZBERG, BARRY N. NV   FSF 75 07
  THIRTY-SEVEN NORTHWEST   MALZBERG, BARRY N. SS   NEW 76 AC
  SEDAN DEVILLE   MALZBERG, BARRY N. SS   FSF 74 12
  STATE OF THE ART   MALZBERG, BARRY N. SS   NDM 74 04
  ISAIAH   MALZBERG, BARRY N. SS   FAN 73 09
  ON THE CAMPAIGN TRAIL   MALZBERG, BARRY N. SS   FCR 75
  REPORT TO HEADQUARTERS   MALZBERG, BARRY N. SS   NDM 75 05
  STREAKING   MALZBERG, BARRY N. SS   FCR 75
  MAKING IT TO GAXTON FALLS ON THE RED PLANET IN THE YEAR
    OF OUR LORD   MALZBERG, BARRY N. SS   NOV 74 04
  AFTER THE GREAT SPACE WAR MALZBERG, BARRY N. SS   ALT 74
  TRASHING   MALZBERG, BARRY N. SS   INY 73 05
  VOX POPULI   MALZBERG, BARRY N. SS   EDG 73
  FIREDAY: FIRENIGHT   MALZBERG, BARRY N. SS   74
  MAKING THE CONNECTIONS   MALZBERG, BARRY N. SS   CTM 75 04
  JANUARY, 1975   MALZBERG, BARRY N. SS   ASF 75 01
  DESTRUCTION AND EXCULPATION OF EARTH, THE
                            MALZBERG, BARRY N. SS   NOV 73 03
  TRANSFER   MALZBERG, BARRY N. SS   FAN 75 08
  BALLAD OF SLICK SID, THE MALZBERG, BARRY N. SS   INY 72 04
  NOTES LEADING DOWN TO THE EVENTS AT BEDLAM
                            MALZBERG, BARRY N. SS   72
  SEEKING ASSISTANCE   MALZBERG, BARRY N. SS   FSF 76 04
  REDUNDANCY   MALZBERG, BARRY N. SS   SWK 76 03
  LEVITICUS: IN THE ARK   MALZBERG, BARRY N. SS   EPC 75
  RAGE, PAIN, ALIENATION AND OTHER ASPECTS OF THE WRITING
    OF SCIENCE FICTION   MALZBERG, BARRY N. AR   FSF 76 04
  DOWN HERE IN THE DREAM QUARTER
                            MALZBERG, BARRY N. SS   AMZ 76 06

DOWN IN THE BLACK GANG AND OTHER STORIES
                           FARMER, PHILIP JOSE AC H DBL 71
  DOWN IN THE BLACK GANG   FARMER, PHILIP JOSE NV   IFS 69 03
  SHADOW OF SPACE, THE   FARMER, PHILIP JOSE NV   IFS 67 11
  BOWL BIGGER THAN EARTH, A FARMER, PHILIP JOSE NV   IFS 67 09
  RIVERWORLD   FARMER, PHILIP JOSE NV   WOT 66 01
  FEW MILES, A   FARMER, PHILIP JOSE NV   FSF 60 10
  PROMETHEUS   FARMER, PHILIP JOSE NV   FSF 61 03
  BLASPHEMERS, THE   FARMER, PHILIP JOSE NV   GAL 64 04
  HOW DEEP THE GROOVES   FARMER, PHILIP JOSE SS   AMZ 63 02

DOWNSTAIRS ROOM AND OTHER SPECULATIVE FICTION, THE
                           WILHELM, KATE   AC H DBL 68
  INTRODUCTION   WILHELM, KATE   IN
  UNBIRTHDAY PARTY   WILHELM, KATE   SS   NEW 68 AC
  BABY, YOU WERE GREAT   WILHELM, KATE   SS   ORB 67 02
  WHEN THE MOON WAS RED   WILHELM, KATE   SS   AMZ 60 09
  SIRLOIN AND WHITE WINE   WILHELM, KATE   SS   NEW 68 AC
  PERCHANCE TO DREAM   WILHELM, KATE   SS   NEW 68 AC
  HOW MANY MILES TO BABYLON? WILHELM, KATE   SS   NEW 68 AC
  DOWNSTAIRS ROOM, THE   WILHELM, KATE   SS   NEW 68 AC
  COUNTDOWN   WILHELM, KATE   SS   NEW 68 AC
  PLAUSIBLE IMPROBABLE, THE WILHELM, KATE   SS   NEW 68 AC
  FEEL OF DESPERATION, THE (A CASE OF DESPERATION)
                            WILHELM, KATE   SS   AHM 64
  TIME TO KEEP, A   WILHELM, KATE   SS   FSF 62 01
  MOST BEAUTIFUL WOMAN IN THE WORLD, THE
                            WILHELM, KATE   SS   NEW 68 AC
  PLANNERS, THE   WILHELM, KATE   SS   ORB 68 03
  WINDSONG   WILHELM, KATE   NV   ORB 68 04

DR. CYCLOPS   KUTTNER, HENRY   AN   POP 67
  DR. CYCLOPS   KUTTNER, HENRY   SS   TWS 40 06
  TOO LATE FOR ETERNITY   WALTON, BRYCE   NO   STS 55 SP
  HARPERS OF TITAN, THE   HAMILTON, EDMOND   SS   STS 50 09

DRAGONFLIGHT   MCCAFFREY, ANNE   NO H WKR 69
  WEYR SEARCH   MCCAFFREY, ANNE   SN   ASF 67 10
  DRAGONRIDER   MCCAFFREY, ANNE   NA   ASF 67 12

DRAGONS AND NIGHTMARES   BLOCH, ROBERT   AC   BEL 69 11
  GOOD KNIGHT'S WORK, A   BLOCH, ROBERT   NV   UNK 41 10
  EAGER DRAGON, THE   BLOCH, ROBERT   NV   WRT 43 01

  NURSEMAID TO NIGHTMARES BLOCH, ROBERT   NV   WRT 42 1
  BACK WORD   BLOCH, ROBERT   MS

DRIFTGLASS   DELANY, SAMUEL R.   AC   SIG 71 11
  STAR PIT, THE   DELANY, SAMUEL R.   NV   WOT 67 0
  DOG IN A FISHERMAN'S NET DELANY, SAMUEL R.   SS   QRK 71 1
  CORONA   DELANY, SAMUEL R.   SS   FSF 67 1
  AYE, AND GOMORRAH...   DELANY, SAMUEL R.   SS   DVS 67 0
  DRIFTGLASS   DELANY, SAMUEL R.   NV   IFS 67 0
  WE, IN SOME STRANGE POWER'S EMPLOY, MOVE ON A RIGOROUS LINE
                            DELANY, SAMUEL R.   NV   FSF 68 0
  CAGE OF BRASS   DELANY, SAMUEL R.   SS   IFS 68 0
  HIGH WEIR   DELANY, SAMUEL R.   NV   IFS 68 1
  TIME CONSIDERED AS A HELIX OF SEMI-PRECIOUS STONES
                            DELANY, SAMUEL R.   SS   NWS 68 0
  NIGHT AND THE LOVES OF JOE DICOSTANZO
                            DELANY, SAMUEL R.   SS   ANA 70

DROWNED WORLD AND THE WIND FROM NOWHERE, THE
                           BALLARD, J. G.   AC H DBL 65
  DROWNED WORLD, THE (ENLARGED)
                           BALLARD, J. G.   NO   SFB 62 0
  WIND FROM NOWHERE, THE (ENLARGED FROM STORM-WIND)
                           BALLARD, J. G.   NO   NWS 61 0

DYING EARTH, THE   VANCE, JACK   OC H HIL 50
  MAZIRIAN THE MAGICIAN   VANCE, JACK   SS   50
  TURJAN OF MIIR   VANCE, JACK   NV   50
  T'SAIS   VANCE, JACK   NV   50
  LIANE THE WAYFARER   VANCE, JACK   NV   50
  ULAN DHOR ENDS A DREAM   VANCE, JACK   NV   50
  GUYAL OF SFERE   VANCE, JACK   NV   50

DYSTOPIAN VISIONS   ELWOOD, ROGER   OA H PRH 75
  INTRODUCTION   ELWOOD, ROGER   IN
  BREATH'S A WARE THAT WILL NOT KEEP
                           MONTELEONE, THOMAS F SS   DYS 75
  COME TAKE A DIP WITH ME IN THE GENETIC POOL
                           PAYES, RACHEL C.   SS   DYS 75
  UNCOUPLING   MALZBERG, BARRY N. SS   DYS 75
  FACES FORWARD   DANN, JACK M.
                           AND ZEBROWSKI, GEORGE SS C DYS 75
  CIVIS LAPVTVS SVM   WOLFE, GENE   SS   DYS 75
  WEAPONS   SARGENT, PAMELA
                           AND ZEBROWSKI, GEORGE SS C DYS 75
  DEATH IN COVENTRY, A   GREEN, JOSEPH   SS   DYS 75
  OR LITTLE DUCKS EACH DAY LAFFERTY, R. A.   NV   DYS 75
  CIVIS OBIT   JANIFER, LAURENCE M. SS DYS 75
  WHERE SUMMER SONG RINGS HOLLOW
                           KIMBERLY, GAIL   SS   DYS 75
  GOING DOWN   MALZBERG, BARRY N. NV   DYS 75
  GIFT, THE   JANIFER, LAURENCE M. SS DYS 75
  XENOFREAK/XENOPHOBE   BRYANT, EDWARD   SS   DYS 75

E PLURIBUS UNICORN   STURGEON, THEODORE AC H ABE 53
  ESSAY ON STURGEON   CONKLIN, GROFF   IN
  SILKEN-SWIFT, THE   STURGEON, THEODORE SS   FSF 53 1
  PROFESSOR'S TEDDY-BEAR, THE STURGEON, THEODORE SS WRT 48 0
  BIANCA'S HANDS   STURGEON, THEODORE SS   ARB 47 0
  SAUCER OF LONELINESS   STURGEON, THEODORE SS   GAL 53 0
  WORLD WELL LOST, THE   STURGEON, THEODORE SS   USF 53 0
  IT WASN'T SYZYGY (THE DEADLY RATIO)
                           STURGEON, THEODORE NV   WRT 48 0
  MUSIC, THE   STURGEON, THEODORE SS   NEW 53 A
  SCARS   STURGEON, THEODORE SS   ZGW 49 0
  FLUFFY   STURGEON, THEODORE SS   WRT 47 0
  SEX OPPOSITE, THE   STURGEON, THEODORE SS   FAN 52 F
  DIE, MAESTRO, DIE!   STURGEON, THEODORE NV   DDT 49 0
  CELLMATE   STURGEON, THEODORE SS   WRT 47 0
  WAY OF THINKING, A   STURGEON, THEODORE NV   AMZ 53 1

EARLY ASIMOV, THE   ASIMOV, ISAAC   AC H DBL 72
  CALLISTAN MENACE, THE   ASIMOV, ISAAC   SS   AST 40 0
  RING AROUND THE SUN   ASIMOV, ISAAC   SS   FUT 40 0
  MAGNIFICENT POSESSION, THE ASIMOV, ISAAC   SS   FUT 40 0
  TRENDS   ASIMOV, ISAAC   SS   ASF 39 0
  WEAPON TOO DREADFUL TO USE, THE
                           ASIMOV, ISAAC   SS   AMZ 39 0
  BLACK FRIAR OF THE FLAME ASIMOV, ISAAC   NV   PLS 42 0
  HALF-BREED   ASIMOV, ISAAC   SS   AST 40 0
  SECRET SENSE, THE   ASIMOV, ISAAC   SS   COS 41 0
  HOMO SOL   ASIMOV, ISAAC   SS   ASF 40 0
  HALF-BREEDS ON VENUS   ASIMOV, ISAAC   SS   AST 40 1
  IMAGINARY, THE   ASIMOV, ISAAC   SS   SSS 42 1
  HEREDITY   ASIMOV, ISAAC   SS   AST 41 0
  HISTORY   ASIMOV, ISAAC   SS   SSS 41 0
  CHRISTMAS ON GANYMEDE   ASIMOV, ISAAC   SS   STS 42 0
  LITTLE MAN ON THE SUBWAY, THE
                           ASIMOV, ISAAC
                           AND MACCREIGH, JAMES SS C FBK 50 0
  HAZING, THE   ASIMOV, ISAAC   SS   TWS 42 1
  SUPER-NEUTRON   ASIMOV, ISAAC   SS   AST 41 0
  NOT FINAL!   ASIMOV, ISAAC   SS   ASF 41 1
  LEGAL RITES   ASIMOV, ISAAC
                           AND POHL, FREDERIK NV C WRT 50 0
  TIME PUSSY   ASIMOV, ISAAC   SS   ASF 42 0
  AUTHOR! AUTHOR!   ASIMOV, ISAAC   NV   NEW 64 A
  DEATH SENTENCE   ASIMOV, ISAAC   SS   ASF 43 1
  BLIND ALLEY   ASIMOV, ISAAC   SS   ASF 45 0
  NO CONNECTION   ASIMOV, ISAAC   SS   ASF 48 0
  ENDOCHRONIC PROPERTIES OF RESUBLIMATED THIOTIMOLINE, THE
                           ASIMOV, ISAAC   FA   ASF 48 0
  RED QUEEN'S RACE, THE   ASIMOV, ISAAC   NV   ASF 49 0
  MOTHER EARTH   ASIMOV, ISAAC   NV   ASF 49 0

ARLY DEL REY   ECO-FICTION

ARLY DEL REY   DEL REY, LESTER   AC H DBL 75
  FAITHFUL, THE   DEL REY, LESTER   SS   ASF 38 04
  CROSS OF FIRE   DEL REY, LESTER   SS   WRT 39 05
  ANYTHING   DEL REY, LESTER   SS   UNK 39 10
  HABIT   DEL REY, LESTER   SS   ASF 39 11
  SMALLEST GOD, THE   DEL REY, LESTER   NV   ASF 40 01
  STARS LOOK DOWN, THE   DEL REY, LESTER   NV   ASF 40 08
  DOUBLED IN BRASS   DEL REY, LESTER   SS   UNK 40 01
  REINCARNATE   DEL REY, LESTER   NV   ASF 40 04
  CARILLON OF SKULLS   DEL REY, LESTER
                          AND BEARD, JAMES H. SS C UNK 41 02
  DONE WITHOUT EAGLES   DEL REY, LESTER   SS   ASF 40 08
  MY NAME IS LEGION   DEL REY, LESTER   NV   ASF 42 06
  THOUGH POPPIES GROW   DEL REY, LESTER   NV   UNK 42 08
  LUNAR LANDING   DEL REY, LESTER   NV   ASF 42 10
  FIFTH FREEDOM   DEL REY, LESTER   SS   ASF 43 05
  WHOM THE GODS LOVE   DEL REY, LESTER   SS   ASF 43 06
  THOUGH DREAMERS DIE   DEL REY, LESTER   SS   ASF 44 02
  FOOL'S ERRAND   DEL REY, LESTER   SS   SFQ 51 11
  ONE-EYED MAN, THE   DEL REY, LESTER   SS   ASF 45 05
  AND THE DARKNESS (OMEGA AND THE WOLF GIRL)
                          DEL REY, LESTER   SS   OTW 50 07
  SHADOWS OF EMPIRE   DEL REY, LESTER   SS   FUT 50 07
  UNREASONABLE FACSIMILE DEL REY, LESTER   SS   FUT 52 07
  CONDITIONED REFLEX (MIND OF TOMORROW)
                          DEL REY, LESTER   SS   FUT 51 05
  OVER THE TOP   DEL REY, LESTER   SS   ASF 49 11
  WIND BETWEEN THE WORLDS, THE DEL REY, LESTER NV   GAL 51 03
  APPENDIX   MISC. MATERIAL   MS

ARLY LONG, THE   LONG, FRANK BELKNAP AC H DBL 75
  INTRODUCTION   LONG, FRANK BELKNAP IN
  DEATH-WATERS   LONG, FRANK BELKNAP SS   WRT 24 12
  OCEAN LEECH, THE   LONG, FRANK BELKNAP SS   WRT 25 01
  SPACE-EATERS, THE   LONG, FRANK BELKNAP NV   WRT 28 07
  HOUNDS OF TINDALOS, THE LONG, FRANK BELKNAP SS   WRT 29 03
  VISITOR FROM EGYPT, A   LONG, FRANK BELKNAP SS   WRT 30 09
  SECOND NIGHT OUT   LONG, FRANK BELKNAP SS   WRT 33 10
  DARK BEASTS, THE   LONG, FRANK BELKNAP SS   MVT 34 07
  FLAME MIDGET, THE   LONG, FRANK BELKNAP SS   ASF 36 12
  DARK VISION   LONG, FRANK BELKNAP SS   UNK 39 03
  ELEMENTAL, THE   LONG, FRANK BELKNAP SS   UNK 39 07
  FISHERMAN'S LUCK   LONG, FRANK BELKNAP SS   UNK 40 07
  REFUGEES, THE   LONG, FRANK BELKNAP SS   UNK 42 02
  CENSUS TAKER, THE   LONG, FRANK BELKNAP SS   UNK 42 04
  GRAB BAGS ARE DANGEROUS LONG, FRANK BELKNAP SS   UNK 42 06
  STEP INTO MY GARDEN   LONG, FRANK BELKNAP SS   UNK 42 08
  IT WILL COME TO YOU   LONG, FRANK BELKNAP SS   UNK 42 12
  PEEPER, THE   LONG, FRANK BELKNAP SS   WRT 44 03

ARLY POHL, THE   POHL, FREDERIK   AC H DBL 76
  INTRODUCTION   POHL, FREDERIK   IN
  ELEGY TO A DEAD PLANET: LUNA POHL, FREDERIK PM   AMZ 37 10
  DWELLER IN THE ICE, THE POHL, FREDERIK   SS   SSS 41 01
  KING'S EYE, THE   POHL, FREDERIK   SS   AST 41 02
  IT'S A YOUNG WORLD   POHL, FREDERIK   NV   AST 41 04
  DAUGHTERS OF ETERNITY   POHL, FREDERIK   SS   AST 42 03
  EARTH, FAREWELL!   POHL, FREDERIK   SS   AST 43 02
  CONSPIRACY ON CALLISTO POHL, FREDERIK   SS   PLS 43 WI
  HIGHWAYMAN OF THE VOID POHL, FREDERIK   NV   PLS 44 FL
  DOUBLE-CROSS   POHL, FREDERIK   SS   PLS 44 WI

ARLY WILLIAMSON, THE   WILLIAMSON, JACK   AC H DBL 75
  INTRODUCTION   WILLIAMSON, JACK   IN
  METAL MAN, THE   WILLIAMSON, JACK   SS   AMZ 28 12
  GIRL FROM MARS, THE (FIRST OF "SCIENCE FICTION SERIES")
                          WILLIAMSON, JACK   EX   29
  COSMIC EXPRESS, THE   WILLIAMSON, JACK   SS   AMZ 30 11
  METEOR GIRL, THE   WILLIAMSON, JACK   SS   ASF 31 03
  THROUGH THE PURPLE CLOUD WILLIAMSON, JACK   SS   WOS 31 05
  DOOM FROM PLANET 4, THE WILLIAMSON, JACK   SS   ASF 31 07
  TWELVE HOURS TO LIVE!   WILLIAMSON, JACK   SS   WOS 31 08
  PLUTONIAN TERROR, THE   WILLIAMSON, JACK   SS   WRT 33 10
  SALVAGE IN SPACE   WILLIAMSON, JACK   SS   ASF 33 03
  "WE AIN'T BEGGARS"   WILLIAMSON, JACK   SS
  DEAD STAR STATION   WILLIAMSON, JACK   SS   ASF 33 11

ARTH IN PERIL, THE   WOLLHEIM, DONALD A. DA   ACE 57
  THINGS PASS BY   LEINSTER, MURRAY   NV   TWS 45 SU
  LETTER FROM THE STARS   VAN VOGT, A. E.   SS   OTW 50 07
  SILLY SEASON, THE   KORNBLUTH, C. M.   SS   FSF 50 FL
  PLANT REVOLT, THE   HAMILTON, EDMOND   SS   WRT 30 04
  MARY ANONYMOUS   WALTON, BRYCE   SS   PLS 54 SU
  STAR, THE   WELLS, H. G.   SS   GRP 97 12

ARTH IN TRANSIT   SCHWARTZ, SHEILA   AN   LLL 76 11
  INTRODUCTION   SCHWARTZ, SHEILA   IN
  LOT   MOORE, WARD   NV   FSF 53 05
  HISTORY LESSON   CLARKE, ARTHUR C.   SS   STS 49 05
  TO SEE THE INVISIBLE MAN SILVERBERG, ROBERT SS   WOT 63 04
  MODUS VIVENDI   BUPP, WALTER   NV   ASF 61 09
  ROOMMATES (BASIS FOR NOVEL "MAKE ROOM! MAKE ROOM!")
                          HARRISON, HARRY   NV   NEW 71 AN
  HAPPY DAY IN 2381, A   SILVERBERG, ROBERT   SS   NOV 70 01
  BILLENIUM   BALLARD, J. G.   SS   NWS 61 11
  SOUNDLESS EVENING   HOFFMAN, LEE   SS   DVS 72 02
  WINNER, THE   WESTLAKE, DONALD E. SS   NOV 70 01
  I TELL YOU, IT'S TRUE   ANDERSON, POUL   NV   NOV 72 02
  WE CAN REMEMBER IT FOR YOU WHOLESALE
                          DICK, PHILIP K.   NV   FSF 66 04
  SUBLIMINAL MAN, THE   BALLARD, J. G.   SS   NWS 63 01
  I MADE YOU   MILLER, WALTER M. JR SS   ASF 54 03
  CITY OF YESTERDAY   CARR, TERRY   SS   IFS 67 12
  HEMEAC   VON WALD, E. G.   SS   GAL 68 08

EARTH IS ROOM ENOUGH   ASIMOV, ISAAC   AC H DBL 57 10
  DEAD PAST, THE   ASIMOV, ISAAC   NV   ASF 56 04
  FOUNDATION OF SCIENCE FICTION SUCCESS, THE
                          ASIMOV, ISAAC   PM   FSF 54 10
  FRANCHISE   ASIMOV, ISAAC   SS   IFS 55 08
  GIMMICKS THREE (THE BRAZEN LOCKED ROOM)
                          ASIMOV, ISAAC   SS   FSF 56 11
  KID STUFF   ASIMOV, ISAAC   SS   BEY 53 09
  WATERY PLACE, THE   ASIMOV, ISAAC   SS   SAT 56 10
  LIVING SPACE   ASIMOV, ISAAC   SS   SFS 56 05
  MESSAGE, THE   ASIMOV, ISAAC   SS   FSF 56 02
  SATISFACTION GUARANTEED ASIMOV, ISAAC   SS   AMZ 51 04
  HELL-FIRE   ASIMOV, ISAAC   SS   FUN 56 05
  LAST TRUMP, THE   ASIMOV, ISAAC   SS   FUN 55 06
  FUN THEY HAD, THE (NEA 51 12)
                          ASIMOV, ISAAC   SS   FSF 54 02
  JOKSTER   ASIMOV, ISAAC   SS   INF 56 12
  IMMORTAL BARD, THE   ASIMOV, ISAAC   SS   USF 54 05
  SOMEDAY   ASIMOV, ISAAC   SS   INF 56 08
  AUTHOR'S ORDEAL, THE   ASIMOV, ISAAC   PM   SFQ 57 05
  DREAMING IS A PRIVATE THING ASIMOV, ISAAC   SS   FSF 55 12

EARTH IS THE STRANGEST PLANET
                          SILVERBERG, ROBERT   AN H NEL 77
  INTRODUCTION   SILVERBERG, ROBERT   IN
  AND LO! THE BIRD   BOND, NELSON S.   SS   BBM 50 09
  NARROW VALLEY   LAFFERTY, R. A.   SS   FSF 66 09
  EMPIRE OF THE ANTS, THE WELLS, H. G.   SS   SND 05 12
  NIGHT THAT ALL TIME BROKE OUT, THE
                          ALDISS, BRIAN W.   SS   DVS 67 01
  DAVY JONES' AMBASSADOR GALLUN, RAYMOND Z.   NV   ASF 35 12
  ROCK DIVER   HARRISON, HARRY   SS   WBY 51 02
  OR ALL THE SEAS WITH OYSTERS DAVIDSON, AVRAM SS   GAL 58 05
  CHRYSALIS, THE   MILLER, P. SCHUYLER SS   ASF 36 04
  ROTIFERS, THE   ABERNATHY, ROBERT   SS   IFS 53 03
  WHEN WE WENT TO SEE THE END OF THE WORLD
                          SILVERBERG, ROBERT   SS   UNI 72 02

EARTH'S OTHER SHADOW   SILVERBERG, ROBERT   AC   SIG 73 06
  SOMETHING WILD IS LOOSE SILVERBERG, ROBERT   NV   MWS 71
  TO SEE THE INVISIBLE MAN SILVERBERG, ROBERT SS   WOT 63 04
  ISHMAEL IN LOVE   SILVERBERG, ROBERT   SS   FSF 70 07
  HOW IT WAS WHEN THE PAST WENT AWAY
                          SILVERBERG, ROBERT   NA   TFT 69
  TO THE DARK STAR   SILVERBERG, ROBERT   SS   FRS 68
  FANGS OF THE TREES, THE SILVERBERG, ROBERT   NV   FSF 68 10
  HIDDEN TALENT   SILVERBERG, ROBERT   NV   IFS 57 04
  SONG THE ZOMBIE SANG, THE SILVERBERG, ROBERT
                          AND ELLISON, HARLAN SS C CMP 70 12
  FLIES   SILVERBERG, ROBERT   SS   DVS 67 01

EARTHMAN'S BURDEN   ANDERSON, P.&DICKSON AC H GNM 57
  SHERIFF OF CANYON GULCH, THE (HEROES ARE MADE)
                          ANDERSON, POUL
                          AND DICKSON, GORDON R. NV C OWS 51 05
  DON JONES   ANDERSON, POUL
                          AND DICKSON, GORDON R. NV C NEW 57 AC
  IN HOKA SIGNO VINCES   ANDERSON, POUL
                          AND DICKSON, GORDON R. NV C OWS 53 06
  ADVENTURE OF THE MISPLACED HOUND, THE
                          ANDERSON, POUL
                          AND DICKSON, GORDON R. NV C USF 53 12
  YO HO HOKA!   ANDERSON, POUL
                          AND DICKSON, GORDON R. NV C FSF 55 03
  TIDDLYWINK WARRIORS, THE ANDERSON, POUL
                          AND DICKSON, GORDON R. NV C FSF 55 08

EARTHMAN, COME HOME   BLISH, JAMES   NO H PUT 55
  OKIE   BLISH, JAMES   NV   ASF 50 04
  BINDLESTIFF   BLISH, JAMES   NV   ASF 50 12
  SARGASSO OF LOST CITIES BLISH, JAMES   SN   TCS 53 SP
  EARTHMAN, COME HOME   BLISH, JAMES   NV   ASF 53 11

EARTHMAN, GO HOME!   ELLISON, HARLAN   AC   PBK 64 12
  SEE "ELLISON WONDERLAND"

EARTHMEN AND STRANGERS   SILVERBERG, ROBERT   AN H MDT 66
  INTRODUCTION   SILVERBERG, ROBERT   IN
  DEAR DEVIL   RUSSELL, ERIC FRANK NV   OWS 50 05
  BEST POLICY, THE   GARRETT, RANDALL   SS   ASF 57 07
  ALAREE   SILVERBERG, ROBERT   SS   STN 58 03
  LIFE CYCLE   ANDERSON, POUL   SS   FSF 57 07
  GENTLE VULTURES, THE   ASIMOV, ISAAC   SS   SUP 57 12
  STRANGER STATION   KNIGHT, DAMON   NV   FSF 56 12
  LOWER THAN ANGELS   BUDRYS, ALGIS   SN   INF 56 10
  BLIND LIGHTNING   ELLISON, HARLAN   SS   FUN 56 06
  OUT OF THE SUN   CLARKE, ARTHUR C.   SS   IFS 58 02

EARTHSEA   LE GUIN, URSULA K.   AC H GOL 77
  WIZARD OF EARTHSEA, A   LE GUIN, URSULA K.   NO
  TOMBS OF ATUAN, THE   LE GUIN, URSULA K.   NO   WOF 70 WI
  FARTHEST SHORE, THE   LE GUIN, URSULA K.   NO

ECO-FICTION   STADLER, JOHN   AN   WSP 71 04
  PREFACE   STADLER, JOHN   IN
  SOUND OF THUNDER, A   BRADBURY, RAY   SS   COL 52 06
  TURTLE, THE (FROM "THE GRAPES OF WRATH")
                          STEINBECK, JOHN   EX   39
  CONVERSATION OF EIROS AND CHARMION, THE
                          POE, EDGAR ALLEN   SS   BGM 39 12
  FAIR YOUNG WILLOWY TREE, THE COPPARD, A. E. SS
  MOTHER'S TALE, A   AGEE, JAMES   NV   52
  LAW, THE   COATES, ROBERT M.   SS   NYM 47 11
  BIRDS, THE   DU MAURIER, DAPHNE   NV   GHK 52 10
  STAY AT THE OCEAN, A   WILSON, ROBLEY JR.   SS   69
  SUPREMACY OF URUGUAY, THE WHITE, E. B.   SS   NYM 33 11

ECO-FICTION

```
LOOK HOW THE FISH LIVE        POWERS, J. F.        SS   REP 57 10
TOMORROW AND TOMORROW AND TOMORROW (THE BIG TRIP UP YONDER)
                              VONNEGUT, KURT JR.   SS   GAL 54 01
WHITE HERON, A                JEWETT, SARAH ORNE   SS
MARY CELESTE MOVE, THE        HERBERT, FRANK       SS   ASF 64 10
TOYS OF PEACE, THE            SAKI                 SS
SUBLIMINAL MAN, THE           BALLARD, J. G.       SS   NWS 63 01
COHEN DOG EXCLUSION ACT, THE  SCHRADER, STEVEN     SS   NEW 71 AN
IT'S SUCH A BEAUTIFUL DAY     ASIMOV, ISAAC        NV   STR 54 03
HUMMINGBIRD THAT LIVED THROUGH WINTER, THE
                              SAROYAN, WILLIAM     SS   44

EDGE OF FOREVER, THE          OLIVER, CHAD         AC H SHB 71
  WORLDS OF CHAD OLIVER: A BIOGRAPHICAL INTRODUCTION
                              NOLAN, WILLIAM F.    IN
  TRANSFUSION                 OLIVER, CHAD         NV   ASF 59 06
  FRIEND TO MAN, A (LET ME LIVE IN A HOUSE)
                              OLIVER, CHAD         NV   USF 54 03
  FIELD EXPEDIENT             OLIVER, CHAD         NV   ASF 55 01
  ANT AND THE EYE, THE        OLIVER, CHAD         NV   ASF 53 04
  FIRST TO THE STARS (STARDUST)
                              OLIVER, CHAD         NV   ASF 52 07
  DIDN'T HE RAMBLE            OLIVER, CHAD         SS   FSF 57 04
  AFTERTHOUGHTS               OLIVER, CHAD         MS
  CHAD OLIVER'S COLLECTED SCIENCE FICTION: A BASIC CHECKLIST
                              NOLAN, WILLIAM F.    MS

EDGE OF NEVER, THE            HOSKINS, ROBERT      AN   FPR 73 06
  WORLD BEYOND, THE           HOSKINS, ROBERT      IN
  ACCOUNT OF SOME STRANGE DISTURBANCES IN AUNGIER ST
                              LE FANU, J. SHERIDAN NV
  RAT THAT COULD SPEAK, THE (ALSO AS THE DEVIL AND MR. CHIPS)
                              DICKENS, CHARLES     SS   FSF 51 08
  INHABITANT OF CARCOSA, AN   BIERCE, AMBROSE      SS   APR 48 08
  LOST HEARTS                 JAMES, M. R.         SS   31
  YELLOW SIGN, THE (1895)     CHAMBERS, ROBERT W.  NV   FFM 43 09
  SEALMAN, THE (1913)         MASEFIELD, JOHN      SS   FSF 55 07
  NIGHT IN MALNEANT, A        SMITH, CLARK ASHTON  SS   WRT 39 09
  WEREWOMAN                   MOORE, C. L.         NV   LVS 38 WI
  SHOTTLE BOP                 STURGEON, THEODORE   SS   UNK 41 02
  ARMAGEDDON                  BROWN, FREDRIC       SS   UNK 41 08
  CHEATERS, THE               BLOCH, ROBERT        NV   WRT 47 11
  LEGAL RITES                 ASIMOV, ISAAC
                              AND POHL, FREDERIK   NV C WRT 50 09
  O UGLY BIRD!                WELLMAN, MANLY WADE  SS   FSF 51 12
  JOURNEYS END                ANDERSON, POUL       SS   FSF 57 02
  MAN WHO LIKED, THE          HOSKINS, ROBERT      SS   WOF 68 01
  NIGHTMARE GANG              KOONTZ, DEAN R.      SS   INY 70 01
  ELEPHANTS                   MALZBERG, BARRY N.   SS   INY 71 02

EDGE OF TOMORROW, THE         FAST, HOWARD         AC   BAN 61 06
  ALSO IN "TIME AND THE RIDDLE"
  FIRST MEN, THE              FAST, HOWARD         NV   FSF 60 02
  LARGE ANT, THE (THE BIG ANT) FAST, HOWARD        SS   FUN 60 02
  OF TIME AND CATS            FAST, HOWARD         SS   FSF 59 03
  CATO THE MARTIAN            FAST, HOWARD         SS   FSF 60 06
  COLD, COLD BOX, THE         FAST, HOWARD         SS   FSF 59 07
  MARTIAN SHOP, THE           FAST, HOWARD         SS   FSF 59 11
  SIGHT OF EDEN, THE          FAST, HOWARD         SS   FSF 60 10

EDGE, THE                     BEAUMONT, CHARLES    AC   PTH 66
  LAST CAPER, THE             BEAUMONT, CHARLES    SS   FSF 54 03
  MOTHER'S DAY                BEAUMONT, CHARLES    SS   NEW 58 AC
  NEW SOUND, THE              BEAUMONT, CHARLES    SS   FSF 55 06
  MUSIC OF THE YELLOW BRASS, THE
                              BEAUMONT, CHARLES    SS   PBY 59 01
  NEW PEOPLE, THE             BEAUMONT, CHARLES    SS   ROG 58
  MAGIC MAN, THE              BEAUMONT, CHARLES    SS   NEW 60 AC
  SONG FOR A LADY             BEAUMONT, CHARLES    SS   NEW 60 AC
  LOVE-MASTER, THE            BEAUMONT, CHARLES    SS   ROG 56
  NEIGHBORS, THE              BEAUMONT, CHARLES    SS   NEW 60 AC
  HOWLING MAN, THE            BEAUMONT, CHARLES    SS   NEW 60 AC
  NIGHT RIDE                  BEAUMONT, CHARLES    SS   PBY 57 03

EDITOR'S CHOICE IN SCIENCE FICTION
                              MOSKOWITZ, SAM       AN H MBR 54
  WALL OF FIRE, THE           KIRKLAND, JACK       SS   BBM 32 07
  WHAT THIN PARTITIONS        CLIFTON, MARK
                              AND APOSTOLIDES, ALEX NV C ASF 53 09
  I, ROBOT                    BINDER, EANDO        SS   AMZ 39 01
  AND SOMEDAY TO MARS         LONG, FRANK BELKNAP  SS   TWS 52 02
  WALL OF DARKNESS, THE       CLARKE, ARTHUR C.    SS   SSS 49 07
  ALL ROADS                   FARNSWORTH, MONA     SS   UNK 40 08
  EXIT                        TUCKER, WILSON       SS   AST 43 04
  SUBLIME VIGIL, THE          CUTHBERT, CHESTER D. SS   WOS 34 02
  FAR BELOW                   JOHNSON, ROBERT B.   NV   WRT 39 06
  DEATH OF A SENSITIVE        BATES, HARRY         NV   SFP 53 05
  DEMOISELLE D'YS, THE        CHAMBERS, ROBERT W.  SS   WRT 28 08
  STOLEN CENTURIES            KLINE, OTIS ADELBERT SS   TWS 39 06

EGG OF THE GLAK, AND OTHER STORIES, THE
                              JACOBS, HARVEY       AC H HPR 69
  EPILOGUE (EPILOGUE FOR AN OFFICE PICNIC)
                              JACOBS, HARVEY       SS   NWS 69 01
  REASONS OF HEALTH           JACOBS, HARVEY       SS
  GIRL WHO DREW THE GODS, THE JACOBS, HARVEY       NV   MAD 65 05
  IN SECLUSION                JACOBS, HARVEY       SS   NWS 68 02
  MUSICAL EDUCATION, A        JACOBS, HARVEY       SS
  VOYAGE OF THE PEANUT, THE   JACOBS, HARVEY       SS   PBY 59 06
  LION'S SHARE, THE           JACOBS, HARVEY       SS   PBY 61 09
  DISTURBANCE OF THE PEACE, A JACOBS, HARVEY       SS   NWS 68 10
  BREAK IN THE WEATHER, A     JACOBS, HARVEY       SS
  TOY, THE                    JACOBS, HARVEY       SS
  EGG OF THE GLAK, THE        JACOBS, HARVEY       NV   FSF 68 03
```

ELSEWHERE, ELSEWHEN, ELSEHO◄

```
EIGHT FANTASMS AND MAGICS     VANCE, JACK          AC H MAC 69
  FOREWORD                    VANCE, JACK          IN
  MIRACLE-WORKERS, THE        VANCE, JACK          SN   ASF 58 0
  WHEN THE FIVE MOONS RISE    VANCE, JACK          NV   CSM 54 0
  TELEK                       VANCE, JACK          SN   ASF 52 0
  NOISE                       VANCE, JACK          SS   STS 52 0
  NEW PRIME, THE              VANCE, JACK          NV
  CIL (THE EYES OF THE OVERWORLD)
                              VANCE, JACK          NV
  GUYAL OF SFERE              VANCE, JACK          NV   50
  MEN RETURN, THE             VANCE, JACK          SS   INF 57 0

EIGHTH GALAXY READER, THE     POHL, FREDERIK       AN H DBL 65
  ALSO AS "FINAL ENCOUNTER"
  VARIETIES OF THE SCIENCE-FICTION EXPERIENCE, THE
                              POHL, FREDERIK       IN
  COMIC INFERNO               ALDISS, BRIAN W.     NA   GAL 63 0
  BIG ENGINE, THE             LEIBER, FRITZ        SS   GAL 62 0
  DAY ON DEATH HIGHWAY, A     ELLIOTT, H. CHANDLER NV   GAL 63 1
  END OF THE RACE, THE        BERMEL, ALBERT       SS   GAL 64 0
  LONELY MAN, THE             THOMAS, THEODORE L.  NV   GAL 63 0
  BAD DAY FOR VERMIN, A       LAUMER, KEITH        SS   GAL 64 0
  DAWNINGSBURGH               WEST, WALLACE        SS   GAL 62 0
  AND ALL THE EARTH A GRAVE   MACAPP, C. C.        SS   GAL 63 1
  HOT PLANET                  CLEMENT, HAL         NV   GAL 63 0
  FINAL ENCOUNTER             HARRISON, HARRY      NV   GAL 64 0
  IF THERE WERE NO BENNY CEMOLI
                              DICK, PHILIP K.      SS   GAL 63 1
  CRITICAL MASS               POHL, FREDERIK
                              AND KORNBLUTH, C. M. NA C GAL 62 0

ELEMENT 79                    HOYLE, FRED          AC H NAM 67
  ZOOMEN                      HOYLE, FRED          SS   FSF 67 0
  PYM MAKES HIS POINT         HOYLE, FRED          SS
  MAGNETOSPHERE, THE          HOYLE, FRED          SS
  PLAY'S THE THING, A         HOYLE, FRED          SS
  CATTLE TRUCKS               HOYLE, FRED          SS
  WELCOME TO SLIPPAGE CITY    HOYLE, FRED          SS
  AX, THE                     HOYLE, FRED          SS
  AGENT 38                    HOYLE, FRED          SS
  MARTIANS, THE               HOYLE, FRED          SS
  SHORTSIGHTED                HOYLE, FRED          SS
  JURY OF FIVE, A             HOYLE, FRED          SS
  BLACKMAIL                   HOYLE, FRED          SS   FSF 67 0
  ELEMENT 79                  HOYLE, FRED          SS
  JUDGMENT OF APHRODITE, THE  HOYLE, FRED          SS
  OPERATION, THE              HOYLE, FRED          SS

ELEVENTH GALAXY READER, THE   POHL, FREDERIK       AN H DBL 69
  INTRODUCTION                POHL, FREDERIK       IN
  TIME TRAWLERS, THE          FILER, BURT K.       SS   GAL 68 0
  SHARING OF FLESH, THE       ANDERSON, POUL       NV   GAL 68 1
  NIGHTWINGS                  SILVERBERG, ROBERT   NV   GAL 68 0
  AMONG THE BAD BABOONS       REYNOLDS, MACK       NV   GAL 68 0
  BEHIND THE SANDRAT HOAX     ANVIL, CHRISTOPHER   NV   GAL 68 1
  ONE STATION OF THE WAY      LEIBER, FRITZ        SS   GAL 68 0
  SWEET DREAMS, MELISSA       GOLDIN, STEPHEN      SS   GAL 68 1
  WHEN I WAS VERY JUNG        ALDISS, BRIAN W.     SS   GAL 68 1
  JINN                        GREEN, JOSEPH        SS   GAL 68 1
  FIND THE FACE               ROCKLYNNE, ROSS      SS   GAL 68 0

ELLISON WONDERLAND            ELLISON, HARLAN      AC   PBK 62 06
  ALSO AS "EARTHMAN, GO HOME!"
  COMMUTER'S PROBLEM          ELLISON, HARLAN      SS   FUN 57 0
  DO-IT-YOURSELF              ELLISON, HARLAN
                              AND HENSLEY, JOE L.  SS C ROG 61 0
  SILVER CORRIDOR, THE        ELLISON, HARLAN      NV   INF 56 1
  ALL THE SOUNDS OF FEAR      ELLISON, HARLAN      SS   SDM 62 0
  GNOMEBODY                   ELLISON, HARLAN      SS   AMZ 56 1
  SKY IS BURNING, THE         ELLISON, HARLAN      SS   IFS 58 0
  MEALTIME (A CASE OF PTOMAINE)
                              ELLISON, HARLAN      SS   STM 58 0
  VERY LAST DAY OF A GOOD WOMAN, THE (THE LAST DAY)
                              ELLISON, HARLAN      SS   ROG 58 0
  BATTLEFIELD (HIS FIRST DAY AT WAR)
                              ELLISON, HARLAN      SS   STM 58 1
  DEAL FROM THE BOTTOM        ELLISON, HARLAN      SS   ROG 60 0
  WIND FROM BEYOND THE MOUNTAINS, THE (SAVAGE WIND)
                              ELLISON, HARLAN      SS   AMZ 57 0
  BACK TO THE DRAWING BOARDS  ELLISON, HARLAN      SS   FUN 58 0
  NOTHING FOR MY NOON MEAL    ELLISON, HARLAN      SS   NEB 58 0
  HADJ                        ELLISON, HARLAN      SS   SFA 56 1
  RAIN, RAIN, GO AWAY         ELLISON, HARLAN      SS   SCF 56 1
  IN LONELY LANDS             ELLISON, HARLAN      SS   FUN 59 0

ELSEWHERE AND ELSEWHEN        CONKLIN, GROFF       AN   BKM 68 05
  INTRODUCTION                CONKLIN, GROFF       IN
  SHORTSTACK                  RICHMOND, WALT
                              AND RICHMOND, LEIGH  SS C ASF 64 1
  HOW ALLIED                  CLIFTON, MARK        NV   ASF 57 0
  WRONG WORLD, THE            MCINTOSH, J. T.      NV   GAL 60 1
  WORLD IN A BOTTLE           LANG, ALLEN KIM      NV   GAL 60 1
  THINK BLUE, COUNT TWO       SMITH, CORDWAINER    NA   GAL 63 0
  TURNING POINT               ANDERSON, POUL       NV   IFS 63 0
  BOOK, THE                   SHAARA, MICHAEL      NV   GAL 53 1
  TROUBLE TIDE                SCHMITZ, JAMES H.    NV   ASF 65 0
  EARTHMAN'S BURDEN, THE      WESTLAKE, DONALD E.  NA   GAL 63 0

ELSEWHERE, ELSEWHEN, ELSEHOW  DEFORD, MIRIAM ALLEN AC H WLK 71
  STORIES "MARTIE AND I" AND "THE CAGE" ARE LISTED IN THE
  ACKNOWLEDGEMENTS BUT ARE NOT IN THE BOOK
  WORD IN ADVANCE, A          DEFORD, MIRIAM ALLEN IN
  OLD MAN MORGAN'S GRAVE      DEFORD, MIRIAM ALLEN SS   FSF 52 0
  MRS. HINCK                  DEFORD, MIRIAM ALLEN SS   FSF 54 0
  GONE TO THE DOGS (HENRY MARTINDALE, GREAT DANE)
                              DEFORD, MIRIAM ALLEN SS   BEY 54 0
```

ELSEWHERE, ELSEWHEN, ELSEHOW

Title	Author	Type	Source
MARGENES, THE	DEFORD, MIRIAM ALLEN	SS	IFS 56 02
OLD WOMAN, THE	DEFORD, MIRIAM ALLEN	SS	FUN 57 10
APOTHEOSIS OF KI, THE	DEFORD, MIRIAM ALLEN	SS	FSF 56 12
FREAK SHOW	DEFORD, MIRIAM ALLEN	SS	FUN 58 02
EEL, THE	DEFORD, MIRIAM ALLEN	SS	GAL 58 04
FIRST DIG	DEFORD, MIRIAM ALLEN	SS	FSF 59 05
PRISON BREAK	DEFORD, MIRIAM ALLEN	SS	FUN 59 07
NOT SNOW NOR RAIN (ALSO AS NEITHER SNOW NOR RAIN)	DEFORD, MIRIAM ALLEN	SS	IFS 59 11
MONSTER, THE	DEFORD, MIRIAM ALLEN	SS	FSF 60 03
VOYAGE OF THE "DEBORAH PRATT", THE	DEFORD, MIRIAM ALLEN	SS	FSF 63 04
1980 PRESIDENT, THE	DEFORD, MIRIAM ALLEN	SS	GAL 64 10
PEAK LORDS, THE	DEFORD, MIRIAM ALLEN	SS	IFS 66 02
COLONY, THE	DEFORD, MIRIAM ALLEN	SS	FSF 66 05
CRIB CIRCUIT, THE	DEFORD, MIRIAM ALLEN	SS	FSF 69 11
OLD BUNCH AND DUSTY STIGGINS, THE	DEFORD, MIRIAM ALLEN	SS	FSF 70 10
EMPIRE OF THE ATOM	VAN VOGT, A. E.	NO H	SHS 57
SON IS BORN, A	VAN VOGT, A. E.	SS	ASF 46 05
CHILD OF THE GODS	VAN VOGT, A. E.	NV	ASF 46 08
HAND OF THE GODS	VAN VOGT, A. E.	NV	ASF 46 12
HOME OF THE GODS	VAN VOGT, A. E.	NV	ASF 47 04
BARBARIAN, THE	VAN VOGT, A. E.	NV	ASF 47 12
ENCOUNTERS WITH ALIENS	EARLEY, GEORGE W.	AN H	SHB 68
INTRODUCTION	SANDERSON, IVAN T.	IN	
EDITOR'S PREFACE	EARLEY, GEORGE W.	IN	
FOUR-FACED VISITORS OF EZEKIEL, THE	ORTON, ARTHUR W.	SS	ASF 61 03
CAVE OF HISTORY, THE	STURGEON, THEODORE	SS	
UNINVITED GUEST, THE	ANVIL, CHRISTOPHER	SS	ASF 67 03
SOMETHING IN THE SKY	CORREY, LEE	SS	ASF 57 05
ALBATROSS	REYNOLDS, MACK	SS	IMG 55 04
OTHER KIDS, THE	YOUNG, ROBERT F	SS	FUN 56 03
GRANTHA SIGHTING, THE	DAVIDSON, AVRAM	SS	FSF 58 04
TIE THAT BINDS, THE	WHITLEY, GEORGE	SS	FUN 58 06
VENUS PAPERS, THE	WILSON, RICHARD	SS	FSF 58 03
MINISTER WITHOUT PORTFOLIO	CLINGERMAN, MILDRED	SS	FSF 52 02
FEAR IS A BUSINESS	STURGEON, THEODORE	SS	FSF 56 08
RINGER	EDMONDSON, G. C.	SS	FSF 60 04
END OF THE DREAMS, THE	GUNN, JAMES E.	AC H	SCB 75
INTRODUCTION	GUNN, JAMES E.	IN	
SPACE IS A LONELY PLACE	GUNN, JAMES E.	NV	VSF 57 05
JOY RIDE, THE (THE NAKED SKY)	GUNN, JAMES E.	NA	STS 55 FL
IMMORTAL, THE	GUNN, JAMES E.	NV	STR 58 04
END OF THE WORLD, THE	WOLLHEIM, DONALD A.	AN	ACE 56
YEAR OF THE JACKPOT, THE	HEINLEIN, ROBERT A.	NV	GAL 52 03
LAST NIGHT OF SUMMER, THE	COPPEL, ALFRED	SS	OSF 54 09
IMPOSTOR	DICK, PHILIP K.	SS	ASF 53 06
RESCUE PARTY	CLARKE, ARTHUR C.	NV	ASF 46 05
OMEGA	LONG, AMELIA R.	SS	AMZ 32 07
IN THE WORLD'S DUSK	HAMILTON, EDMOND	SS	WRT 36 03
ENDS OF TIME, THE	SILVERBERG, ROBERT	AN H	HAW 70
INTRODUCTION	SILVERBERG, ROBERT	IN	
ALPHA RALPHA BOULEVARD	SMITH, CORDWAINER	NV	FSF 61 06
AWAKENING, THE	CLARKE, ARTHUR C.	SS	ZEN 42 02
TWILIGHT	CAMPBELL, JOHN W. JR	SS	ASF 34 11
GUYAL OF SFERE	VANCE, JACK	NV	50
AT THE END OF DAYS	SILVERBERG, ROBERT	SS	NWS 65 09
EPILOGUE	ANDERSON, POUL	SN	ASF 62 03
WHEN THE LAST GODS DIE	LEIBER, FRITZ	SS	FSF 51 12
LAST	LEIBER, FRITZ	SS	FSF 57 03
ENEMIES IN SPACE	CONKLIN, GROFF	AN	DIG 62
SELECTIONS FROM "INVADERS OF EARTH"			
INVASION FROM MARS	KOCH, HOWARD	PL	CBS 38 10
WAVERIES, THE	BROWN, FREDRIC	SS	ASF 45 01
ANGEL'S EGG	PANGBORN, EDGAR	NV	GAL 51 06
PICTURES DON'T LIE	MACLEAN, KATHERINE	SS	GAL 51 08
GREATEST TERTIAN, THE	BOUCHER, ANTHONY	SS	NEW 52 AN
MAN IN THE MOON, THE	NORTON, HENRY	SS	ASF 43 02
ENGLAND SWINGS SF	MERRIL, JUDITH	AN H	DBL 68
ENGLISH DERIVATIVE ANTHOLOGY "THE SPACE-TIME JOURNAL"			
INTRODUCTION	MERRIL, JUDITH	IN	
ISLAND, THE	JONES, ROGER	SS	SCF 65 02
NE DEJA VU PAS	SAXTON, JOSEPHINE	SS	67
SIGNALS	CALDER, JOHN	SS	NWS 66 09
SAINT 505	CLARKE, JOHN	SS	NWS 67 01
SINGULAR QUEST OF MARTIN BORG, THE	COLLYN, GEORGE	SS	NWS 65 02
FIRST GORILLA ON THE MOON, THE	BUTLER, BILL	PM	NEW 68 AN
BLASTOFF	BONFIGLIOLI, KYRIL	SS	64
YOU AND ME AND THE CONTINUUM	BALLARD, J. G.	SS	IMP 66 03
WHO'S IN THERE WITH ME?	CASTELL, DAPHNE	SS	NEW 68 AN
SQUIRREL CAGE, THE	DISCH, THOMAS M.	SS	NWS 66 10
MANSCARER	ROBERTS, KEITH	NV	NWR 66 07
TOTAL EXPERIENCE KICK, THE	PLATT, CHARLES	SS	NWS 66 12
SILVER NEEDLE, THE	MACBETH, GEORGE	PM	NWS 67 01
BAKED BEAN FACTORY, THE	BUTTERWORTH, MICHAEL	SS	NWS 67 10
HALL OF MACHINES, THE	JONES, LANGDON	SS	NWS 68 03
RUN, THE	PRIEST, CHRISTOPHER	SS	IMP 66 05
ALL THE KING'S MEN	BAYLEY, BARRINGTON J	NV	NWS 65 03
STILL TRAJECTORIES	ALDISS, BRIAN W.	SS	NWS 67 09
SUN PUSH	HALL, GRAHAM M.	SS	NWS 67 01
REPORT ON A SUPERMARKET	HAMBURGER, MICHAEL	PM	
DR. GELABIUS	BAILEY, HILARY	SS	NWS 68 04
HEAT DEATH OF THE UNIVERSE, THE	ZOLINE, PAMELA A.	SS	NWS 67 07

ESCALES DANS L'INFINI

Title	Author	Type	Source
MOUNTAIN, THE	MOORCOCK, MICHAEL	SS	NWS 65 02
PSYCHOSMOSIS	MASSON, DAVID I.	SS	NWS 66 03
IDEA OF ENTROPY AT MAENPORTH BEACH, THE	REDGROVE, PETER	PM	67
SAME AUTUMN IN A DIFFERENT PARK	TATE, PETER	SS	FAN 67 09
ASSASSINATION OF JOHN FITZGERALD KENNEDY CONSIDERED AS A DOWNHILL MOTOR RACE, THE	BALLARD, J. G.	SS	NWS 67 02
PLAN FOR THE ASSASSINATION OF JACQUELINE KENNEDY	BALLARD, J. G.	SS	AMB 66 WI
ENQUIRIES OF DOCTOR ESZTERHAZY, THE	DAVIDSON, AVRAM	NO	WPB 75 12
POLLY CHARMS, THE SLEEPING WOMAN	DAVIDSON, AVRAM	NV	FSF 75 02
CROWN JEWELS OF JERUSALEM, OR, THE TELL-TALE HEAD, THE	DAVIDSON, AVRAM	NV	FSF 75 08
OLD WOMAN WHO LIVED WITH A BEAR, THE	DAVIDSON, AVRAM	NV	
CHURCH OF SAINT SATAN AND PANDAEMONS, THE	DAVIDSON, AVRAM	NV	FAN 75 12
MILORD SIR SMIHT, THE ENGLISH WIZARD	DAVIDSON, AVRAM	NV	
CASE OF THE MOTHER-IN-LAW OF PEARL, THE	DAVIDSON, AVRAM	NV	FAN 75 10
CEASELESS STONES, THE	DAVIDSON, AVRAM	NV	
KING'S SHADOW HAS NO LIMITS, THE	DAVIDSON, AVRAM	SS	WHS 75 04
ENTRY TO ELSEWHEN (STORIES REVISED)	BRUNNER, JOHN	AC	DAW 72 10
HOST AGE	BRUNNER, JOHN	NV	NWS 56 01
LUNGFISH (RENDEZVOUS WITH DESTINY, FUN 58 03)	BRUNNER, JOHN	NV	SCF 57 12
NO OTHER GODS BUT ME (BASED ON A TIME TO REND)	BRUNNER, JOHN	NV	SCF 56 12
ENVOY TO NEW WORLDS	LAUMER, KEITH	AC	ACE 63
PROTOCOL (THE YLLIAN WAY)	LAUMER, KEITH	NV	IFS 62 01
SEALED ORDERS (RETIEF OF THE RED-TAPE MOUNTAIN)	LAUMER, KEITH	NV	IFS 62 05
CULTURAL EXCHANGE	LAUMER, KEITH	NV	IFS 62 09
AIDE MEMOIRE	LAUMER, KEITH	NV	IFS 62 07
POLICY (THE MADMAN FROM EARTH)	LAUMER, KEITH	NV	IFS 62 03
PALACE REVOLUTION (GAMBLER'S WORLD)	LAUMER, KEITH	NV	IFS 61 11
EPOCH	ELWOOD & SILVERBERG	OA H	BRK 75
INTRODUCTION	SILVERBERG, ROBERT AND ELWOOD, ROGER	IN C	
ARM	NIVEN, LARRY	NA	EPC 75
ANGEL OF TRUTH	EKLUND, GORDON	NV	EPC 75
MAZES	LE GUIN, URSULA K.	SS	EPC 75
FOR ALL POOR FOLKS AT PICKETWIRE	LAFFERTY, R. A.	SS	EPC 75
GROWING UP IN EDGE CITY	POHL, FREDERIK	SS	EPC 75
DURANCE	MOORE, WARD	SS	EPC 75
GHOST OF A MODEL T, THE	SIMAK, CLIFFORD D.	NV	EPC 75
PLANET STORY	WILHELM, KATE	SS	EPC 75
GRADUATION DAY	MACFARLANE, WALLACE	SS	EPC 75
TIMETIPPING	DANN, JACK M.	SS	EPC 75
ENCOUNTER WITH A CARNIVORE	GREEN, JOSEPH	SS	EPC 75
LADY SUNSHINE AND THE MAGOON OF BEATUS	PANSHIN, ALEXEI AND PANSHIN, CORY	NA C	EPC 75
"FOR A SINGLE YESTERDAY"	MARTIN, GEORGE R. R.	NV	EPC 75
BLOODSTREAM	FISHER, LOU	SS	EPC 75
EXISTENCE	RUSS, JOANNA	SS	EPC 75
INTERFACE	ATTANASIO, A. A.	NA	EPC 75
BLOODED ON ARACHNE	BISHOP, MICHAEL	NV	EPC 75
LEVITICUS: IN THE ARK	MALZBERG, BARRY N.	SS	EPC 75
CAMBRIDGE: 1:58 A.M.	BENFORD, GREGORY	SS	EPC 75
RUN FROM THE FIRE	HARRISON, HARRY	NV	EPC 75
APERTURE MOMENT, THE	ALDISS, BRIAN W.	GR	EPC 75
WAITING FOR THE UNIVERSE TO BEGIN	ALDISS, BRIAN W.	SS	EPC 75
BUT WITHOUT ORIFICES	ALDISS, BRIAN W.	SS	EPC 75
AIMEZ-VOUS HOLMAN HUNT?	ALDISS, BRIAN W.	SS	EPC 75
NIGHTBEAT	BARRETT, NEAL JR.	SS	EPC 75
UNEASY CHRYSALIDS, OUR MEMORIES	SHIRLEY, JOHN	SS	EPC 75
DOGTOWN TOURIST AGENCY, THE	VANCE, JACK	NO	EPC 75
EROS IN ORBIT	ELDER, JOSEPH	OA H	TRI 73
PREFACE	ELDER, JOSEPH	IN	
2.46593	BRYANT, EDWARD	SS	EIO 73
LOVEMAKER	EKLUND, GORDON	SS	EIO 73
CLONE SISTER	SARGENT, PAMELA	NV	EIO 73
WHISTLER	GOULART, RON	SS	EIO 73
IN THE GROUP	SILVERBERG, ROBERT	SS	EIO 73
FLOWERING NARCISSUS	SCORTIA, THOMAS N.	SS	EIO 73
KIDDY-LIB	STOPA, JON	NV	EIO 73
DON SLOW AND HIS ELECTRIC GIRL GETTER	BRAND, THOMAS	SS	EIO 73
UPS AND DOWNS	MALZBERG, BARRY N.	SS	EIO 73
STARCROSSED	ZEBROWSKI, GEORGE	SS	EIO 73
ESCALES DANS L'INFINI	GALLET, GEORGES H.	AN	LHT 54 04
SCALES OF THE INFINITE, STORIES IN FRENCH			
MARTIAN ODYSSEY, A	WEINBAUM, STANLEY G.	NV	WOS 34 07
PAWLEY'S PEEPHOLES (OPERATION PEEP)	WYNDHAM, JOHN	SS	SCF 51 WI
BLUE GIRAFFE, THE	DE CAMP, L. SPRAGUE	NV	ASF 39 08
SHAMBLEAU	MOORE, C. L.	NV	WRT 33 11
BLIND MAN'S BUFF	GIESY, J. U.	SS	ASW 20 01

ESCALES DANS L'INFINI

MACHINE MAN OF ARDATHIA, THE	FLAGG, FRANCIS	SS	AMZ 27	11
BEAST OF THE VOID, A	GALLUN, RAYMOND Z.	SS	ASF 36	09
THREE LINES OF OLD FRENCH	MERRITT, A.	SS	ASW 19	08
SPACE STATION NO. 1	WELLMAN, MANLY WADE	SS	ARG 36	10
SMILE OF THE SPHINX, THE	TEMPLE, WILLIAM F.	SS	TOW 38	FL

ESCAPE ON VENUS	BURROUGHS, EDGAR R.	NO H	BUR 46	
ILLUSTRATIONS	BURROUGHS, JOHN C.	IL		
SLAVES OF THE FISH MEN	BURROUGHS, EDGAR R.	NV	FAD 41	03
GODDESS OF FIRE	BURROUGHS, EDGAR R.	NV	FAD 41	07
LIVING DEAD, THE	BURROUGHS, EDGAR R.	NV	FAD 41	11
WAR ON VENUS	BURROUGHS, EDGAR R.	NV	FAD 42	03

ESCAPE TO EARTH	HOWARD, IVAN	AN	BEL 63	09
ESCAPE TO EARTH	BANISTER, MANLY	NV	SFQ 57	11
WE ARE ALONE	SHECKLEY, ROBERT	SS	FUT 52	11
DOOMSDAY'S COLOR-PRESS	JONES, RAYMOND F.	NV	FUT 52	11
BIG MAN WITH THE GIRLS, A	MACCREIGH, JAMES AND MERRIL, JUDITH	SS C	FUT 53	03
TEMPLE OF DESPAIR	PEASE, M. C.	NV	DSF 53	10
IF THE COURT PLEASES	LOOMIS, NOEL	NV	DSF 53	06

ESKIMO INVASION	HOWARD, HAYDEN	NO	BAL 67	
DEATH AND BIRTH OF THE ANGAKOK, THE	HOWARD, HAYDEN	NV	GAL 65	04
ESKIMO INVASION, THE	HOWARD, HAYDEN	NV	GAL 66	06
WHO IS HUMAN?	HOWARD, HAYDEN	NV	GAL 66	08
TOO MANY ESKS	HOWARD, HAYDEN	NV	GAL 66	10
MODERN PENITENTIARY, THE	HOWARD, HAYDEN	NV	GAL 66	12
OUR MAN IN PEKING	HOWARD, HAYDEN	NV	GAL 67	02
PURPOSE OF LIFE, THE	HOWARD, HAYDEN	NV	GAL 67	04

ETERNAL LOVER, THE	BURROUGHS, EDGAR R.	AC H	MCG 25	
ETERNAL LOVER, THE	BURROUGHS, EDGAR R.	NV	ASW 14	03
SWEETHEART PRIMEVAL	BURROUGHS, EDGAR R.	NO	ASC 15	01

EVERY BOY'S BOOK OF OUTER SPACE STORIES	DIKTY, T. E.	AN H	FEL 60	
AND A STAR TO STEER HER BY	CORREY, LEE	NV	ASF 53	06
SITTING DUCK	SAARI, OLIVER E.	SS	ASF 52	01
BLIND MAN'S BUFF	JAMESON, MALCOLM	NV	ASF 44	10
GYPSY	ANDERSON, POUL	SS	ASF 50	01
CANAL BUILDERS, THE	ABERNATHY, ROBERT	SS	ASF 45	01
STAR OF WONDER	MAY, JULIAN C.	SS	TWS 53	02
RELUCTANT HEROES, THE	ROBINSON, FRANK M.	NV	GAL 51	01
THAT SHARE OF GLORY	KORNBLUTH, C. M.	NV	ASF 52	01
MEN AGAINST THE STARS	WELLMAN, MANLY WADE	NV	ASF 38	06
MAN IN THE SKY	BUDRYS, ALGIS	SS	ASF 56	03
ROVER I WILL BE, A	COURTNEY, ROBERT AND ROBINSON, FRANK M.	SS C		

EVERY BOY'S BOOK OF SCIENCE FICTION	WOLLHEIM, DONALD A.	AN H	FEL 51	
GRAVITY PROFESSOR	CUMMINGS, RAY	SS	AAS 21	05
FOUR-DIMENSIONAL ROLLER-PRESS, THE	OLSEN, BOB	SS	AMZ 27	06
INFRA-MEDIANS, THE	WRIGHT, SEWELL P.	SS	ASF 31	12
WHITE ARMY, THE	DRESSLER, DR. DANIEL	SS	AMZ 29	09
DR. LU-MIE	KRUSE, CLIFTON B.	SS	ASF 34	07
LIVING MACHINE	KELLER, DAVID H. MD.	SS	WOS 35	05
CONQUEST OF TWO WORLDS, A	HAMILTON, EDMOND	NV	WOS 32	02
ASTEROID OF GOLD, THE	SIMAK, CLIFFORD D.	SS	WOS 32	11
IN THE SCARLET STAR	WILLIAMSON, JACK	SS	AMZ 33	03
KING OF THE GRAY SPACES (ALSO AS R IS FOR ROCKET)	BRADBURY, RAY	SS	FFM 43	12

EVIL EARTHS	ALDISS, BRIAN W.	AN H	WEI 75	
AN ANTHOLOGY OF WAY-BACK-WHEN FUTURES				
INTRODUCTION	ALDISS, BRIAN W.	IN		
"WHAT IS WRONG? WHAT IS RIGHT? ANYWAY, WE'RE HERE..."	ALDISS, BRIAN W.	SI		
LAST WORD, THE	OLIVER, CHAD AND BEAUMONT, CHARLES	SS C	FSF 55	04
FILM OF DEATH	CAMPBELL, J. SCOTT	SS	ASF 48	03
WOUND, THE	FAST, HOWARD	SS		70
THREE GREEN BLADES OF GRASS	ALDISS, BRIAN W.	SI		
GOLDEN MAN, THE	DICK, PHILIP K.	NV	IFS 54	04
GUEST EXPERT	LANG, ALLEN KIM	SS	PLS 51	01
VALLEY, THE	STOCKHAM, RICHARD	SS	IFS 54	06
DARK THEY WERE AND GOLEM-EYED	ALDISS, BRIAN W.	SI		
DOWN AMONG THE DEAD MEN	TENN, WILLIAM	NV	GAL 54	06
AMONG THE HAIRY EARTHMEN	LAFFERTY, R. A.	SS	GAL 66	08
LATER THAN YOU THINK	LEIBER, FRITZ	SS	GAL 50	10
YESTERDAY, TOMORROW, AND THE DESERT	ALDISS, BRIAN W.	SI		
TIME TRAP, THE	KUTTNER, HENRY	NO	MSS 38	11
TOWARDS THE FALL OF NIGHT	ALDISS, BRIAN W.	SI		
MEN RETURN, THE	VANCE, JACK	SS	INF 57	07
HERESIES OF THE HUGE GOD	ALDISS, BRIAN W.	FA	GAL 66	08
IF I FORGET THEE, OH EARTH...	CLARKE, ARTHUR C.	SS	FUT 51	09
NIGHT	CAMPBELL, JOHN W. JR	NV	ASF 35	10

EXALTATION OF STARS, AN	CARR, TERRY	OA H	SAS 73	
INTRODUCTION	CARR, TERRY	IN		
FEAST OF ST. DIONYSUS, THE	SILVERBERG, ROBERT	NV		73
'KJWALLL'KJE'K'KOOTHAILLL'KJE'K	ZELAZNY, ROGER	NA		73
MY BROTHER LEOPOLD	PANGBORN, EDGAR	NV		73

EXILE AND OTHER TALES OF FANTASY	CUMMINGS, M. A.	OC	FLG 68	
EXILE	CUMMINGS, M. A.	SN		
THOSE WERE GIANTS	CUMMINGS, M. A.	SS		
DON'T YOU REMEMBER?	CUMMINGS, M. A.	SS		
BUY ME A WOOFL	CUMMINGS, M. A.	SS		
SPECIMEN	CUMMINGS, M. A.	SS		
WHAT HAPPENED TO TUESDAY?	CUMMINGS, M. A.	SS		
GET RICH QUICK	CUMMINGS, M. A.	SS		
TO CHANGE THE PAST	CUMMINGS, M. A.	SS		
MOON DOWN	CUMMINGS, M. A.	SS		
ALIENS AREN'T WANTED	CUMMINGS, M. A.	SS		
LITTLE OLD LADY	CUMMINGS, M. A.	SS		
GIRL WITH THE GREEN GLASS EYES, THE	CUMMINGS, M. A.	SS		
FULL MOON	CUMMINGS, M. A.	SS		
CAT WHO LIKED THRILLERS, THE	CUMMINGS, M. A.	SS		

EXODUS FROM ELYSIUM	BURKE, JONATHAN F.	AC	HWZ 65	
ROBOT WIFE, THE	BURKE, JONATHAN F.	SS		
ALL MAD, EXCEPT ME	BURKE, JONATHAN F.	SS		
ENTITY STRIKES TWICE, THE	BURKE, JONATHAN F.	SS		
EXODUS FROM ELYSIUM	BURKE, JONATHAN F.	SN		

EXPEDITION TO EARTH	CLARKE, ARTHUR C.	AC	BAL 53	12
ALSO IN "AN ARTHUR C. CLARKE OMNIBUS"				
SECOND DAWN	CLARKE, ARTHUR C.	NV	SFQ 51	08
IF I FORGET THEE, OH EARTH...	CLARKE, ARTHUR C.	SS	FUT 51	09
BREAKING STRAIN (THIRTY SECONDS - THIRTY DAYS)	CLARKE, ARTHUR C.	NV	TWS 49	12
HISTORY LESSON	CLARKE, ARTHUR C.	SS	STS 49	05
SUPERIORITY	CLARKE, ARTHUR C.	SS	FSF 51	08
EXILE OF THE EONS	CLARKE, ARTHUR C.	SS	SSS 50	03
HIDE AND SEEK	CLARKE, ARTHUR C.	SS	ASF 49	09
EXPEDITION TO EARTH (ENCOUNTER IN THE DAWN)	CLARKE, ARTHUR C.	SS	AMZ 53	07
LOOPHOLE	CLARKE, ARTHUR C.	SS	ASF 46	04
INHERITANCE (NWS 47 03)	CLARKE, ARTHUR C.	SS	ASF 48	03
SENTINEL, THE (SENTINEL OF ETERNITY)	CLARKE, ARTHUR C.	SS	TSF 51	SP

EXPERT DREAMERS, THE	POHL, FREDERIK	AN H	DBL 62	
INTRODUCTION	POHL, FREDERIK	IN		
AT THE END OF THE ORBIT	CLARKE, ARTHUR C.	NV	IFS 61	11
ON THE FEASIBILITY OF COAL-DRIVEN POWER STATIONS	FRISCH, O. R.	SS	SAM 56	03
FEAST OF DEMONS, A	MORRISON, WILLIAM	NV	GAL 58	02
HEART ON THE OTHER SIDE, THE	GAMOW, GEORGE	SS		
LENNY	ASIMOV, ISAAC	SS	INF 58	01
SINGERS, THE	WALTER, W. GREY	SS		56
INVASION, THE	WILLEY, ROBERT	NV	SSS 40	09
TO EXPLAIN MRS. THOMPSON	LATHAM, PHILIP	SS	ASF 51	11
ADRIFT ON THE POLICY LEVEL	DAVIS, CHAN	SS	STR 59	05
BLACK CLOUD, THE (EXCERPT)	HOYLE, FRED	EX	HEI 57	
CHAIN REACTION	ELLANBY, BOYD	NV	GAL 56	09
MIRACLE OF THE BROOM CLOSET, THE	NORBERT, W.	SS	TEN 52	04
HEAVY PLANET	GREGOR, LEE	SS	ASF 39	08
TEST STAND, THE	CORREY, LEE	SS	ASF 55	03
AMATEUR IN CHANCERY	SMITH, GEORGE O.	SS	GAL 61	10
MARK GABLE FOUNDATION, THE	SZILARD, LEO	SS		61

EXPLORERS OF SPACE	SILVERBERG, ROBERT	AN H	NEL 75	
INTRODUCTION	SILVERBERG, ROBERT	IN		
EXPLORATION TEAM (ALSO AS COMBAT TEAM)	LEINSTER, MURRAY	NV	ASF 56	03
BEACHHEAD (YOU'LL NEVER GO HOME AGAIN)	SIMAK, CLIFFORD D.	SS	FAD 51	07
KYRIE	ANDERSON, POUL	SS	FRS 68	
JUPITER FIVE	CLARKE, ARTHUR C.	NV	IFS 53	05
COLLECTING TEAM	SILVERBERG, ROBERT	SS	AUT 57	06
EACH AN EXPLORER	ASIMOV, ISAAC	SS	FUT 56	03
VASTER THAN EMPIRES AND MORE SLOW	LE GUIN, URSULA K.	NV	NDM 71	01
WHAT'S IT LIKE OUT THERE?	HAMILTON, EDMOND	NV	TWS 52	12

EXPLORERS, THE	KORNBLUTH, C. M.	AC	BAL 54	08
FOREWORD	POHL, FREDERIK	IN		
GOMEZ	KORNBLUTH, C. M.	NV	NEW 54	AC
MINDWORM, THE	KORNBLUTH, C. M.	SS	WBY 50	12
ROCKET OF 1955, THE	KORNBLUTH, C. M.	SS	STI 41	04
ALTAR AT MIDNIGHT, THE	KORNBLUTH, C. M.	SS	GAL 52	11
GOODLY CREATURES, THE	KORNBLUTH, C. M.	SS	FSF 52	12
FRIEND TO MAN	KORNBLUTH, C. M.	SS	TSF 51	SP
WITH THESE HANDS	KORNBLUTH, C. M.	NV	GAL 51	12
THAT SHARE OF GLORY	KORNBLUTH, C. M.	NV	ASF 52	01
THIRTEEN O'CLOCK	KORNBLUTH, C. M.	NV	STI 41	02

EXPLORING OTHER WORLDS	MOSKOWITZ, SAM	AN	CLB 63	
INTRODUCTION	MOSKOWITZ, SAM	IN		
MAD MOON	WEINBAUM, STANLEY G.	NV	ASF 35	12
GARDEN IN THE VOID	ANDERSON, POUL	NV	GAL 52	05
AT THE CENTER OF GRAVITY	ROCKLYNNE, ROSS	SS	ASF 36	06
SOMETHING GREEN	BROWN, FREDRIC	SS	NEW 54	AC
DEAD PLANET, THE	HAMILTON, EDMOND	SS	STS 46	SP
RADIANT ENEMIES, THE	STARZL, R. F.	SS	ARG 34	02
VIA ASTEROID	BINDER, EANDO	SS	TWS 38	02
MAN OF THE STARS	MOSKOWITZ, SAM	SS	PLS 41	WI

EXTRAPOLASIS	MALEC, ALEXANDER B.	AC H	DBL 67	
OPAXTL	MALEC, ALEXANDER B.	NV		
ONCE WAS	MALEC, ALEXANDER B.	NV		
DIEHL	MALEC, ALEXANDER B.	NV		
10:01 A.M.	MALEC, ALEXANDER B.	SS	ASF 66	03
MONSIGNOR PRIMO MACINNO	MALEC, ALEXANDER B.	SS		
PROJECT INHUMANE	MALEC, ALEXANDER B.	SS	COQ 64	SU
MATAYAMA	MALEC, ALEXANDER B.	SS	COQ 66	SU
PROOF POSITIVE	MALEC, ALEXANDER B.	SS		
LANDMARK	MALEC, ALEXANDER B.	SS		
TO RELIEVE THE SANITY	MALEC, ALEXANDER B.	SS		

XTRAPOLASIS

```
REMOTE INCIDENT                  MALEC, ALEXANDER B.   SS
THING-THING                      MALEC, ALEXANDER B.   SS

EYE AND THE FINGER               WANDREI, DONALD       AC H ARK 44
  LADY IN GRAY, THE              WANDREI, DONALD       SS   WRT 33 12
  EYE AND THE FINGER             WANDREI, DONALD       SS
  PAINTED MIRROR, THE            WANDREI, DONALD       SS   AFR 49 09
  IT WILL GROW ON YOU            WANDREI, DONALD       SS
  TREE MEN OF M'BWA, THE         WANDREI, DONALD       SS   WRT 32 02
  LIVES OF ALFRED KRAMER, THE    WANDREI, DONALD       SS   WRT 32 12
  MONSTER FROM NOWHERE, THE      WANDREI, DONALD       SS   ARG 36 05
  WITCH-MAKERS, THE              WANDREI, DONALD       SS   ARG 35 11
  NERVELESS MAN, THE             WANDREI, DONALD       SS   ASF 34 07
  BLACK FOG                      WANDREI, DONALD       SS   TWS 37 02
  BLINDING SHADOWS               WANDREI, DONALD       SS   ASF 34 05
  SCIENTIST DIVIDES, A           WANDREI, DONALD       SS   ASF 34 09
  EARTH MINUS                    WANDREI, DONALD       NV   ASF 35 09
  FINALITY UNLIMITED             WANDREI, DONALD       SN   ASF 36 09
  CRYSTAL BULLET, THE            WANDREI, DONALD       SS   WRT 41 03
  FRAGMENT OF A DREAM            WANDREI, DONALD       SS
  WOMAN AT THE WINDOW            WANDREI, DONALD       SS
  MESSENGERS, THE                WANDREI, DONALD       SS
  PURSUERS, THE                  WANDREI, DONALD       SS
  RED BRAIN, THE                 WANDREI, DONALD       SS   WRT 27 10
  ON THE THRESHOLD OF ETERNITY   WANDREI, DONALD       SS

EYE OF THE LENS, THE             JONES, LANGDON        AC H MAC 72
  INTRODUCTION                   JONES, LANGDON        IN
  GREAT CLOCK, THE               JONES, LANGDON        SS   NWS 66 03
  HALL OF MACHINES, THE          JONES, LANGDON        SS   NWS 68 03
  COMING OF THE SUN, THE         JONES, LANGDON        SS   NWS 68 03
  EYE OF THE LENS, THE           JONES, LANGDON        SS   NWS 68 03
  TIME MACHINE, THE              JONES, LANGDON        NV   ORB 69 05
  SYMPHONY NO. 6 IN C MINOR "THE TRAGIC"- BY LUDWIG VAN
    BEETHOVEN II                 JONES, LANGDON        FA   NWS 68 10
  GARDEN OF DELIGHTS, THE        JONES, LANGDON        NV   NWS 69 07

FAHRENHEIT 451                   BRADBURY, RAY         AC H BAL 53
  FAHRENHEIT 451 (EXPANSION OF "THE FIREMAN")
                                 BRADBURY, RAY         NO   GAL 51 02
  PLAYGROUND, THE                BRADBURY, RAY         SS   ESQ 53 10
  AND THE ROCK CRIED OUT (THE MILLIONTH MURDER)
                                 BRADBURY, RAY         SS   MHT 53 09

FALLING TORCH, THE               BUDRYS, ALGIS         NO   PYR 59 06
  FALLING TORCH                  BUDRYS, ALGIS         NV   VSF 58 01
  MAN WHO DID NOT FIT, THE       BUDRYS, ALGIS         SS   ASF 59 03
  HOT POTATO                     BUDRYS, ALGIS         SS   ASF 57 07

FAMOUS SCIENCE-FICTION STORIES
                                 HEALY & MCCOMAS       AN H MDL 57
  SEE "ADVENTURES IN TIME AND SPACE"

FANTASIA MATHEMATICA             FADIMAN, CLIFTON      AN H SAS 58
  INTRODUCTION                   FADIMAN, CLIFTON      IN
  YOUNG ARCHIMEDES               HUXLEY, ALDOUS        SS        24
  PYTHAGORAS AND THE PSYCHOANALYST
                                 KOESTLER, ARTHUR      SS        43
  MOTHER AND THE DECIMAL POINT   LLEWELLYN, RICHARD    SS        40
  JURGEN PROVES IT BY MATHEMATICS
                                 CABELL, JAMES BRANCH  EX   MBR 19
  PETER LEARNS ARITHMETIC        WELLS, H. G.          SS        18
  SOCRATES AND THE SLAVE         PLATO                 SS
  DEATH OF ARCHIMEDES, THE       CAPEK, KAREL          SS        49
  DEVIL AND SIMON FLAGG, THE     PORGES, ARTHUR        SS   FSF 54 08
  AND HE BUILT A CROOKED HOUSE   HEINLEIN, ROBERT A.   SS   ASF 41 02
  INFLEXIBLE LOGIC               MALONEY, RUSSELL      SS   NYM 40 02
  NO-SIDED PROFESSOR (ESQ 47 01)
                                 GARDNER, MARTIN       SS   FSF 51 02
  SUPERIORITY                    CLARKE, ARTHUR C.     SS   FSF 51 08
  MATHEMATICAL VOODOO, THE       NEARING, H. JR.       SS   FSF 51 04
  EXPEDITION                     BROWN, FREDRIC        SS   FSF 57 02
  CAPTURED CROSS-SECTION, THE    BREUER, MILES J. MD.  SS   AMZ 29 02
  A. BOTTS AND THE MOEBIUS STRIP
                                 UPSON, WILLIAM H.     SS   SEP 45 12
  GOD AND THE MACHINE            BALCHIN, NIGEL        SS        51
  TACHYPOMP, THE                 MITCHELL, EDWARD P.   SS   SCR 74 03
  ISLAND OF THE FIVE COLORS, THE
                                 GARDNER, MARTIN       SS   NEW 52 AN
  LAST MAGICIAN, THE             ELLIOTT, BRUCE        SS   FSF 53 10
  SUBWAY NAMED MOBIUS, A         DEUTSCH, A. J.        SS   ASF 50 12
  UNIVERSAL LIBRARY, THE         LASSWITZ, KURD        SS        01
  POSTSCRIPT TO "THE UNIVERSAL LIBRARY"
                                 LEY, WILLY            AR
  JOHN JONES' DOLLAR             KEELER, HARRY S.      SS   BLC 15 08
  NEW BALLAD OF SIR PATRICK SPENS, A
                                 QUILLER-COUCH, A. T.  PM
  UNFORTUNATE TOPOLOGIST, THE    KORNBLUTH, C. M.      PM   FSF 57 07
  THERE ONCE WAS A BREATHY BABOON
                                 EDDINGTON, ARTHUR     PM
  YET WHAT ARE ALL...            CARROLL, LEWIS        PM
  TWINKLE, TWINKLE, LITTLE STAR
                                 BARTON, RALPH         PM        24
  MATHEMATICAL LOVE              MARVELL, ANDREW       PM        50
  CIRCLE, THE                    MORLEY, CHRISTOPHER   PM
  CIRCLE AND THE SQUARE, THE     DEKKER, THOMAS        PM
  EUCLID ALONE HAS LOOKED ON BEAUTY BARE
                                 MILLAY, EDNA ST. V.   PM        24
  EUCLID                         LINDSAY, VACHEL       PM        14
  TO THINK THAT TWO AND TWO ARE FOUR
                                 HOUSEMAN, A. E.       PM        40
  USES OF MATHEMATICS, THE (1863)
                                 BUTLER, SAMUEL        PM
  ARITHMETIC                     SANDBURG, CARL        PM        50
  THREES (TO BE SUNG BY NIELS BOHR)
                                 ATHERTON, JOHN        PM   NYM 57 03
```

FANTASY: THE LITERATURE OF THE MARVELOUS

```
  PLANE GEOMETRY                 ROUNDS, EMMA          PM        25
  HE THOUGHT HE SAW ELECTRONS SWIFT
                                 DINGLE, HERBERT       PM
  FEARSOME FABLE                 ELLIOTT, BRUCE        SS   FSF 51 02
  BERTRAND RUSSELL'S DREAM       HARDY, G. H.          PM        48
  FOR ALL PRACTICAL PURPOSES     OGILVY, G. S.         PM
  ETERNITY: A NIGHTMARE          CARROLL, LEWIS        PM        93
  INFINITY OF GUESTS, A          GAMOW, GEORGE         PM        47
  INFINITY                       EDDINGTON, ARTHUR     PM        35
  NO POWER ON EARTH              WHEWELL, DR. WILLIAM  PM
  X+1                            POE, EDGAR ALLEN      PM
  RECEPTIVE BOSOM, THE           SHANKS, EDWARD        PM
  LEINBACH'S PROOF               SCHNITZLER, ARTHUR    PM        31
  PROBLEM, A                     ANONYMOUS             PM   NYM 57 03
  LETTER FROM TENNYSON, A        ANONYMOUS             PM   MAG
  FABLE, A                       ANONYMOUS             PM   MAG 54 38
  THERE WAS A YOUNG MAN FROM TRINITY
                                 ANONYMOUS             PM
  RELATIVITY                     ANONYMOUS             PM
  THERE WAS AN OLD MAN WHO SAID, "DO"
                                 ANONYMOUS             PM
  THERE WAS A YOUNG FELLOW NAMED FISK
                                 ANONYMOUS             PM

FANTASTIC PULPS, THE             HAINING, PETER        AN H SMP 75
  INTRODUCTION                   HAINING, PETER        IN
  MANACLED                       CRANE, STEPHEN        SS   ARG 00 08
  THOUSAND DEATHS, A             LONDON, JACK          SS   BLC 99 05
  AUTHOR'S ADVENTURE             SINCLAIR, UPTON       SS   POM 04
  RESURRECTION OF JIMBER-JAW, THE
                                 BURROUGHS, EDGAR R.   NV   ARG 37 02
  JOHN OVINGTON RETURNS          BRAND, MAX            SS   ASW 18 06
  PEOPLE OF THE PIT, THE         MERRITT, A.           NV   ASM 18 01
  MAN WITH THE GLASS HEART, THE
                                 ENGLAND, GEORGE A.    SS   CVL 11 05
  WOLF WOMAN, THE                BEDFORD-JONES, HENRY  SS   BBM 34
  CRY FROM BEYOND, A             ROUSSEAU, VICTOR      NV   STT 31 09
  MADMAN'S MURDER MELODY         CUMMINGS, RAY         SS   HOS 40 12
  PULP ARTISTS, THE              MISC. MATERIAL        IL
  GHOST PATROL, THE              LEWIS, SINCLAIR       SS   DSM 17
  SARDONIC STAR OF TOM DOODY, THE
                                 HAMMETT, DASHIELL     SS   BLM 24
  SECOND CHALLENGE, THE          KANTOR, MACKINLAY     SS   RDT 29
  BARON MUNCHAUSEN'S SCIENTIFIC ADVENTURES (HOW THE MARTIAN
    CANALS ARE BUILT)            GERNSBACK, HUGO       SS   ELX 16 11
  TWENTIETH CENTURY HOMUNCULUS, A
                                 KELLER, DAVID H. MD.  NV   AMZ 30 02
  MAN WHO SAW THE FUTURE, THE    HAMILTON, EDMOND      SS   AMZ 30 10
  SUICIDE CHAPEL                 QUINN, SEABURY        NV   WRT 38 06
  DIARY OF ALONZO TYPER, THE     LOVECRAFT, H. P.
                                 AND LUMLEY, WILLIAM   NV C WRT 38 02
  TREE OF LIFE, THE              MOORE, C. L.          NV   WRT 36 10
  IRON MASK                      BLOCH, ROBERT         NV   WRT 44 05
  SEA SHELLS, THE                BRADBURY, RAY         SS   WRT 44 01
  APPENDICES                     MISC. MATERIAL        MS
  BIBLIOGRAPHY                   MISC. MATERIAL        MS

FANTASTIC UNIVERSE OMNIBUS, THE
                                 SANTESSON, HANS S.    AN H PRH 60
  INTRODUCTION                   DEL REY, LESTER       IN
  FLOWERS OF VENUS, THE          O'QUINN, VITHALDAS H  MS
  FIRST LAW                      ASIMOV, ISAAC         SS   FUN 56 10
  SHE ONLY GOES OUT AT NIGHT     TENN, WILLIAM         SS   FUN 56 10
  PACIFIST, THE                  CLARKE, ARTHUR C.     SS   FUN 56 10
  BOUNTY HUNTER, THE             DAVIDSON, AVRAM       SS   FUN 58 03
  MUTED HORN, THE                DAVIS, DOROTHY S.     SS   FUN 57 05
  WAY OF LIFE, A                 BLOCH, ROBERT         SS   FUN 56 10
  IN LONELY LANDS                ELLISON, HARLAN       SS   FUN 59 01
  FALL OF KNIGHT                 CHANDLER, A. BERTRAM  SS   FUN 58 06
  SIT BY THE FIRE                BENEDICT, MYRLE       SS   FUN 58 05
  THING OF CUSTOM, A             DE CAMP, L. SPRAGUE   SS   FUN 57 01
  EXILE FROM SPACE               MERRIL, JUDITH        NV   FUN 56 11
  MEX                            HARRIS, LARRY M.      SS   FUN 57 01
  AMAZING MRS. MIMMS, THE        KNIGHT, DAVID C.      SS   FUN 58 08
  MY FATHER THE CAT              SLESAR, HENRY         SS   FUN 57 12
  TITLE FIGHT                    GAULT, WILLIAM C.     SS   FUN 56 12
  GOLDEN PYRAMID, THE            MOSKOWITZ, SAM        SS   FUN 56 11
  ROBOT WHO WANTED TO KNOW, THE
                                 BOYD, FELIX           SS   FUN 58 03
  ROAD TO NIGHTFALL              SILVERBERG, ROBERT    NV   FUN 58 07
  VELVET GLOVE, THE              HARRISON, HARRY       NV   FUN 56 11
  DAY WILL COME..., THE          O'QUINN, VITHALDAS H  MS

FANTASY: THE LITERATURE OF THE MARVELOUS
                                 KELLEY, LEO P.        AN L MGH 74
  PREFACE                        KELLEY, LEO P.        IN
  HICKORY, DICKORY, KEROUAC (AS MARTIN SCOTT)
                                 GEHMAN, RICHARD       SS   PBY 58 03
  INFLEXIBLE LOGIC               MALONEY, RUSSELL      SS   NYM 40 02
  OR ALL THE SEAS WITH OYSTERS   DAVIDSON, AVRAM       SS   GAL 58 05
  FLOWER KID CASHES IN, THE      MALKO, GEORGE         SS   FSF 69 05
  SOUL CAGES, THE                CROKER, T. CROFTON    SS
  DREAMING IS A PRIVATE THING    ASIMOV, ISAAC         SS   FSF 55 12
  ROADS OF DESTINY               HENRY, O.             NV        09
  TEST, THE                      MATHESON, RICHARD     SS   FSF 54 11
  SEA WAS WET AS WET COULD BE, THE
                                 WILSON, GAHAN         SS   PBY 67 05
  EVENING PRIMROSE (1941)        COLLIER, JOHN         SS   AFR 47 03
  MANUSCRIPT OF DR. ARNESS, THE
                                 WILSON, GAHAN         SS   PBY 66 08
  ANCESTOR, THE                  LOVECRAFT, H. P.
                                 AND DERLETH, AUGUST   SS C
  AFTERNOON WITH A DEAD BUS      GERROLD, DAVID        SS   PRT 71
  MIRACLE OF RARE DEVICE, A      BRADBURY, RAY         SS   PBY 62 01
  WALL, THE                      SAXTON, JOSEPHINE     SS   SCF 65 11
```

"REPENT, HARLEQUIN|" SAID THE TICKTOCKMAN
                                ELLISON, HARLAN   SS   GAL 65 12
HOUSING PROBLEM   KUTTNER, HENRY   SS   CHM 44 10
CHEATERS, THE   BLOCH, ROBERT   NV   WRT 47 11
GRAVEYARD READER, THE   STURGEON, THEODORE   SS   SCF 58 10
ACADEMY, THE   ELY, DAVID   SS   PBY 65 06
CARCINOMA ANGELS   SPINRAD, NORMAN   SS   DVS 67 01
SOMETHING IN WOOD   DERLETH, AUGUST   SS   WRT 48 03
O'GRADY'S GIRL   KELLEY, LEO P.   SS   FSF 65 12
LEGEND OF FIN M'COUL, THE   CARLETON, WILLIAM   SS
DAY AT THE BEACH   EMSHWILLER, CAROL   SS   FSF 59 08
DOLL-HOUSE, THE   CROSS, JAMES   SS   DVS 67 01
LORD RANDY, MY SON   HENSLEY, JOE L.   SS   DVS 67 01
AUTO-DA-FE   ZELAZNY, ROGER   SS   DVS 67 01
OF MISSING PERSONS   FINNEY, JACK   SS   GHK 55 03

FAR AND AWAY   BOUCHER, ANTHONY   AC   BAL 55
ANOMALY OF THE EMPTY MAN, THE
                                BOUCHER, ANTHONY   SS   FSF 52 04
FIRST, THE   BOUCHER, ANTHONY   SS   FSF 52 10
BALAAM   BOUCHER, ANTHONY   SS   NTL 54
THEY BITE   BOUCHER, ANTHONY   SS   UNK 43 08
SNULBUG (FIRST IN UNKNOWN, DEC. 1941)
                                BOUCHER, ANTHONY   SS   FSF 53 05
ELSEWHEN   BOUCHER, ANTHONY   NV   ASF 43 01
SECRET OF THE HOUSE   BOUCHER, ANTHONY   SS   GAL 53 03
SRIBERDEGIBIT   BOUCHER, ANTHONY   NV   UNK 43 04
STAR BRIDE   BOUCHER, ANTHONY   SS   TWS 51 12
REVIEW COPY   BOUCHER, ANTHONY   SS   FSF 49 FL
OTHER INAUGURATION, THE   BOUCHER, ANTHONY   SS   FSF 53 03

FAR BOUNDARIES   DERLETH, AUGUST   AN H PEL 52
FROM A PRIVATE MAD-HOUSE (1787)
                                REPTON, HUMPHREY   SS   VAR 87
MISSING ONE'S COACH: AN ANACHRONISM
                                ANONYMOUS   SS   DLM 38
TALE OF A CHEMIST (1843)   ANONYMOUS   SS
LAST AMERICAN, THE   MITCHELL, J. A.   SS   SCR 89 06
INFINITY ZERO   WANDREI, DONALD   SS   ASF 36 10
FRANKENSTEIN UNLIMITED   HIGHSTONE, H. A.   SS   ASF 36 12
OPEN, SESAME| GRENDON, STEPHEN   SS   ARS 49 WI
TEPONDICON   JACOBI, CARL   SS   PLS 46 WI
FEAR PLANET, THE   BLOCH, ROBERT   SS   SSS 43 02
DE PROFUNDIS   LEINSTER, MURRAY   SS   TWS 45 WI
INVASION   LONG, FRANK BELKNAP   SS   STS 50 07
DEAR PEN PAL   VAN VOGT, A. E.   SS   ARS 49 WI
TIME TO REST   HARRIS, JOHN BEYNON   SS   ARS 49 WI
OUNCE OF PREVENTION, AN   CARTER, PAUL A.   SS   FSF 50 SU
SONG OF THE PEWEE, THE   GRENDON, STEPHEN   SS   ARS 49 FL
AND LO| THE BIRD   BOND, NELSON S.   SS   BBM 50 09
ONE WHO WAITS, THE   BRADBURY, RAY   SS   FSF 51 02
HOLIDAY   BRADBURY, RAY   SS   ARS 49 FL
MAN WHO RODE THE SAUCER, THE   HOLMES, KENYON   SS   NEW 52 AN
LATER THAN YOU THINK   LEIBER, FRITZ   SS   GAL 50 10

FAR OUT   KNIGHT, DAMON   AC H SAS 61
INTRODUCTION   BOUCHER, ANTHONY   IN
TO SERVE MAN   KNIGHT, DAMON   SS   GAL 50 11
IDIOT STICK   KNIGHT, DAMON   SS   STR 58 04
THING OF BEAUTY   KNIGHT, DAMON   NV   GAL 58 09
ENEMY, THE   KNIGHT, DAMON   SS   VSF 58 01
NOT WITH A BANG   KNIGHT, DAMON   SS   FSF 50 WS
BABEL II   KNIGHT, DAMON   NV   BEY 53 07
ANACHRON   KNIGHT, DAMON   SS   IFS 54 01
SPECIAL DELIVERY   KNIGHT, DAMON   NV   GAL 54 04
YOU'RE ANOTHER   KNIGHT, DAMON   NV   FSF 55 06
TIME ENOUGH (ENOUGH TIME)   KNIGHT, DAMON   SS   AMZ 60 07
EXTEMPORE (THE BEACH WHERE TIME BEGAN)
                                KNIGHT, DAMON   SS   INF 56 08
CABIN BOY   KNIGHT, DAMON   NV   GAL 51 09
LAST WORD, THE   KNIGHT, DAMON   SS   SAT 57 02

FAR SIDE OF TIME, THE   ELWOOD, ROGER   OA H DOM 74
FOREWORD   ELWOOD, ROGER   IN
CAPRICORN GAMES   SILVERBERG, ROBERT   SS   74
ANNIE MAE: A LOVE STORY   O'NEIL, DENNIS   SS
FIREDAY: FIRENIGHT   MALZBERG, BARRY N.   SS   74
LOSTLING   BRUNNER, JOHN   SS
AMBIGUITIES OF YESTERDAY, THE
                                EKLUND, GORDON   SS
MINNA IN THE NIGHT SKY   KIMBERLY, GAIL   SS
WAIF   LEIBER, FRITZ   NV   74
GREAT SUPERSONIC ZEPPELIN RACE, THE
                                BOVA, BEN   NV
CUES   WOLFE, GENE   SS
SLUGGING IT OUT   HALDEMAN, JACK C. II   SS
FLAUNA   JONES, RAYMOND F.   NV
TO SLEEP, PERCHANCE TO DREAM   MACKENROTH, NANCY   SS   74
EYE FOR AN EYE   BIGGLE, LLOYD JR.   NV

FAR STARS   RUSSELL, ERIC FRANK   AC H DOB 61
WAITABITS, THE   RUSSELL, ERIC FRANK   NV   ASF 55 07
TIMELESS ONES, THE   RUSSELL, ERIC FRANK   SS   SFQ 52 11
ALLAMAGOOSA   RUSSELL, ERIC FRANK   SS   ASF 55 05
DIABOLOGIC   RUSSELL, ERIC FRANK   SS   ASF 55 03
LEGWORK   RUSSELL, ERIC FRANK   NV   ASF 56 04
P.S.   RUSSELL, ERIC FRANK   SS   NEB 58 05

FAR-OUT PEOPLE, THE   HOSKINS, ROBERT   AN   SIG 71 07
INTRODUCTION   HOSKINS, ROBERT   IN
DESTINY OF MILTON GOMRATH, THE
                                PANSHIN, ALEXEI   SS   ASF 67 12
NORTH WIND   OLIVER, CHAD   SS   FSF 56 03
PRICE OF SIMERYL, THE   NEVILLE, KRIS   SS   ASF 66 12
COP-OUT   O'DONNELL, K. M.   SS   ESC 68
PAPA'S PLANET   NOLAN, WILLIAM F.   SS   PBY 68 04

ANGEL, DARK ANGEL   ZELAZNY, ROGER   SS   GAL 67 0▮
PROBLEM MAKERS, THE   HOSKINS, ROBERT   NV   GAL 63 0▮
SAVIOR SOLE   FAYETTE, MICHAEL   SS   71
SELLERS OF THE DREAM, THE   JAKES, JOHN W.   NA   GAL 63 0▮
EXILE TO HELL   ASIMOV, ISAAC   SS   ASF 68 05

FAR-OUT WORLDS OF A. E. VAN VOGT, THE
                                VAN VOGT, A. E.   AC   ACE 68
REPLICATORS, THE   VAN VOGT, A. E.   NV   IFS 65 02
FIRST MARTIAN, THE (THIS JOE)
                                VAN VOGT, A. E.   SS   39
PURPOSE, THE   VAN VOGT, A. E.   NV   ASF 45 0▮
EARTH KILLERS, THE   VAN VOGT, A. E.   NV   SSS 49 04
CATAAAAA, THE   VAN VOGT, A. E.   SS   FBK 47 0▮
AUTOMATON   VAN VOGT, A. E.   SS   OWS 50 09
ITSELF| VAN VOGT, A. E.   SS   GAM 63 0▮
PROCESS   VAN VOGT, A. E.   SS   FSF 50 12
NOT THE FIRST   VAN VOGT, A. E.   SS   ASF 41 04
FULFILLMENT   VAN VOGT, A. E.   NV   NTS 51
SHIP OF DARKNESS   VAN VOGT, A. E.   SS   FBK 47 02
ULTRA MAN, THE   VAN VOGT, A. E.   NV   WOT 66 05

FAREWELL FANTASTIC VENUS   ALDISS & HARRISON   AN H MDN 68
TRIP TO VENUS, A (1897)   MUNRO, JOHN   SS   97
STORY OF THE HEAVENS (1883)   BALL, SIR ROBERT   AR   83
HONEYMOON IN SPACE, A   GRIFFITH, GEORGE   EX   PRS 00 0▮
DESTINIES OF THE STARS   ARRHENIUS, SVANTE   AR   18
LAST AND FIRST MEN   STAPLEDON, OLAF   EX   MTH 30
PIRATES OF VENUS (SELECTION)   BURROUGHS, EDGAR R.   EX   ARG 32 09
PERLANDRA (SELECTION)   LEWIS, C. S.   EX   LNE 43
ALCHEMY   DE COURCY, JOHN
                                AND DE COURCY, DOROTHY SS C OTW 50 12
MAN FROM VENUS, THE   PAUL, FRANK R.   SS
CITY ON VENUS, A   GADE, HENRY   SS
UNVEILING THE MYSTERY PLANET   LEY, WILLY   AR
EXPLORING THE PLANETS   FIRSOFF, V. A.   AR   SID 64
BIG RAIN, THE   ANDERSON, POUL   SN   ASF 54 10
INTELLIGENT LIFE IN THE UNIVERSE
                                SAGAN, CARL   AR   66
ESCAPE TO VENUS   LOTT, S. MAKEPEACE   SS   56
SISTER PLANET   ANDERSON, POUL   SN   SAT 59 05
BEFORE EDEN   CLARKE, ARTHUR C.   SS   AMZ 61 06
SOME MYSTERIES OF VENUS RESOLVED
                                LOVELL, BERNARD   AR   TMS 67
DREAM OF DISTANCE   ANONYMOUS   MS   67
VENUS MYSTERY FOR SCIENTISTS   DAVY, JOHN   AR   OBS 67 10
SCIENTIST SAYS ICECAP ON VENUS WOULD MAKE LIFE POSSIBLE
                                CLARK, EVERT   AR   NYT 68 03

FAREWELL TO YESTERDAY'S TOMORROW
                                PANSHIN, ALEXEI   AC H PUT 75
PREFACE   PANSHIN, ALEXEI   IN
WHAT'S YOUR EXCUSE?   PANSHIN, ALEXEI   SS   FAN 69 08
SONS OF PROMETHEUS, THE   PANSHIN, ALEXEI   NV   ASF 66 10
DESTINY OF MILTON GOMRATH, THE
                                PANSHIN, ALEXEI   SS   ASF 67 12
SENSE OF DIRECTION, A   PANSHIN, ALEXEI   SS   AMZ 69 11
HOW GEORGES DUCHAMPS DISCOVERED A PLOT TO TAKE OVER THE WORLD
                                PANSHIN, ALEXEI   SS   FAN 71 04
ONE SUNDAY IN NEPTUNE   PANSHIN, ALEXEI   SS   NEW 69 AN
NOW I'M WATCHING ROGER   PANSHIN, ALEXEI   SS   ORB 72 10
ARPAD   PANSHIN, ALEXEI   SS   QRK 71 02
HOW CAN WE SINK WHEN WE CAN FLY?
                                PANSHIN, ALEXEI   NV   FFU 71
SKY BLUE   PANSHIN, ALEXEI
                                AND PANSHIN, CORY   SS C AMZ 72 03
WHEN THE VERTICAL WORLD BECOMES HORIZONTAL
                                PANSHIN, ALEXEI   SS   UNI 74 04
FAREWELL TO YESTERDAY'S TOMORROW
                                PANSHIN, ALEXEI
                                AND PANSHIN, CORY   AR C GAL 74 06

FARTHEST REACHES, THE   ELDER, JOSEPH   OA H TRI 68 08
FOREWORD   ELDER, JOSEPH   IN
WORM THAT FLIES, THE   ALDISS, BRIAN W.   SS   FRS 68
KYRIE   ANDERSON, POUL   SS   FRS 68
TOMORROW IS A MILLION YEARS   BALLARD, J. G.   SS   ARG 66 10
POND WATER   BRUNNER, JOHN   SS   FRS 68
DANCE OF THE CHANGER AND THE THREE, THE
                                CARR, TERRY   SS   FRS 68
CRUSADE   CLARKE, ARTHUR C.   SS   FRS 68
RANGING   JAKES, JOHN W.   SS   FRS 68
MIND OUT OF TIME, THE   LAUMER, KEITH   SS   FRS 68
INSPECTOR, THE   MCKIMMEY, JAMES   SS   FRS 68
TO THE DARK STAR   SILVERBERG, ROBERT   SS   FRS 68
NIGHT IN ELF HILL, A   SPINRAD, NORMAN   SS   FRS 68
SULWEN'S PLANET   VANCE, JACK   SS   FRS 68

FASTER THAN LIGHT   DANN & ZEBROWSKI   OA H HPR 76
INTRODUCTION: DREAMING AGAIN   DANN, JACK A.
                                AND ZEBROWSKI, GEORGE IN C
THERE WAS A YOUNG LADY NAMED BRIGHT
                                BULLER, E. REGINALD   PM
EPIGRAPH (FROM "THE SCIENCE IN SCIENCE FICTION")
                                BLISH, JAMES   EX   VCT 75 SU
ULTIMATE SPEED LIMIT, THE   ASIMOV, ISAAC   AR   SRV 72
POSSIBLE, THAT'S ALL| CLARKE, ARTHUR C.   AR   FSF 68 10
LIMITING VELOCITY OF ORTHODOXY, THE
                                LAUMER, KEITH   AR   GAL 70 12
BUT WHAT IF WE TRIED IT?   BOVA, BEN   AR   76
SUN UP   JACKSON, A. A., IV
                                AND WALDROP, HOWARD   SS C   76
DIALOGUE   ANDERSON, POUL   NV   76
LONGLINE   CLEMENT, HAL   NV   76
PHOENIX WITHOUT ASHES   ELLISON, HARLAN   PL   76
PHOENIX WITHOUT ASHES   KIRK, TIM   IL   76

FASTER THAN LIGHT

EVENT HORIZON, THE	WATSON, IAN	NV	76
NOR THE MANY-COLORED FIRES OF A STAR RING			
	MARTIN, GEORGE R. R.	NV	76
DEAD IN IRONS	YARBRO, CHELSEA Q.	NV	76
SEASCAPE	BENFORD, GREGORY	NV	76
FAST-FRIEND	MARTIN, GEORGE R. R.	NV	76
HYPERSPACE	ALLEN, DICK	PM	EDG 73
AFTERWORD: OUR MANY ROADS TO THE STARS			
	ANDERSON, POUL	AR	GAL 75 09
CONTRIBUTORS, THE	MISC. MATERIAL	MS	
SELECTED BIBLIOGRAPHY: INTERSTELLIAR TRAVEL, A			
	MISC. MATERIAL	MS	

FEAR TODAY, GONE TOMORROW	BLOCH, ROBERT	AC	AWD 71 09
HUNGRY EYE, THE	BLOCH, ROBERT	NV	FAN 59 05
OLD COLLEGE TRY, THE	BLOCH, ROBERT	SS	GAM 63 02
WORLD-TIMER, THE	BLOCH, ROBERT	SS	FAN 60 08
F.O.B. VENUS	BLOCH, ROBERT	SS	FAN 58 11
GODS ARE NOT MOCKED, THE	BLOCH, ROBERT	SS	EQM 68 08
GODDESS OF WISDOM, THE	BLOCH, ROBERT	SS	FUN 54 05
SALES OF A DEATHMAN	BLOCH, ROBERT	SS	GAL 68 02
CRIME MACHINE	BLOCH, ROBERT	SS	GAL 61 10
FUNNEL OF GOD, THE	BLOCH, ROBERT	NV	FAN 60 01
TOY FOR JULIETTE, A	BLOCH, ROBERT	SS	DVS 67 01
REPORT ON SOL III	BLOCH, ROBERT	SS	AMZ 58 07
BALD-HEADED MIRAGE, THE	BLOCH, ROBERT	SS	AMZ 60 06

FEAST OF ST. DIONYSUS, THE	SILVERBERG, ROBERT	AC H	SCB 75 03
FEAST OF ST. DIONYSUS, THE	SILVERBERG, ROBERT	NV	73
SCHWARTZ BETWEEN THE GALAXIES			
	SILVERBERG, ROBERT	SS	STL 74 01
TRIPS	SILVERBERG, ROBERT	NV	FST 74
IN THE HOUSE OF DOUBLE MINDS	SILVERBERG, ROBERT	SS	VTX 74 06
THIS IS THE ROAD	SILVERBERG, ROBERT	NA	

FELLOWSHIP OF THE STARS	CARR, TERRY	OA H	SAS 74
INTRODUCTION	CARR, TERRY	IN	
DREAM DONE GREEN	FOSTER, ALAN DEAN	SS	FOS 74
ASHES ALL MY LUST	EFFINGER, GEO. ALEC	NV	FOS 74
ENJOY, ENJOY	POHL, FREDERIK	SS	FOS 74
STONES HAVE NAMES, THE	BROXON, MILDRED D.	SS	FOS 74
DO YOU KNOW DAVE WENZEL?	LEIBER, FRITZ	SS	FOS 74
SHADOWS	SARGENT, PAMELA	NV	FOS 74
IN THIS IMAGE	BRENNERT, ALAN	NV	FOS 74
WHAT FRIENDS ARE FOR	BRUNNER, JOHN	SS	FOS 74
AUTHOR OF THE ACACIA SEEDS AND OTHER EXTRACTS FROM THE JOURNAL			
OF THE ASSOCIATION OF THERO LE GUIN, URSULA K.		SS	FOS 74

FEVER DREAM	BRADBURY & BLOCH	AC	SPH 70
SEE "BLOCH AND BRADBURY"			
THERE WAS AN OLD WOMAN	BRADBURY, RAY	SS	WRT 44 07
SCREAMING WOMAN, THE	BRADBURY, RAY	SS	TDY 51 05
TOUCH AND GO (ALSO AS THE FRUIT AT THE BOTTOM OF THE BOWL)			
	BRADBURY, RAY	SS	DBM 48 11
SMALL ASSASSIN, THE	BRADBURY, RAY	SS	DMN 46 11
HANDLER, THE	BRADBURY, RAY	SS	WRT 47 01
LAKE, THE	BRADBURY, RAY	SS	WRT 44 05
COFFIN, THE (WAKE FOR THE LIVING)			
	BRADBURY, RAY	SS	DMN 47 09
LET'S PLAY POISON	BRADBURY, RAY	SS	WRT 46 11

FEW LAST WORDS, A	SALLIS, JAMES	AC H	MAC 70
JIM AND MARY G	SALLIS, JAMES	SS	ORB 70 07
LETTER TO A YOUNG POET	SALLIS, JAMES	SS	ORB 68 03
FACES & HANDS	SALLIS, JAMES	NV	NOV 70 01
KETTLE OF STARS	SALLIS, JAMES	SS	
FLOORS OF HIS HEART, THE	SALLIS, JAMES	SS	
OPENING OF THE TERRAN BALLET, THE			
	SALLIS, JAMES	SS	70
HISTORY MAKERS, THE	SALLIS, JAMES	SS	ORB 69 05
AND THEN THE DARK-	SALLIS, JAMES	SS	69
FRONT & CENTAUR	SALLIS, JAMES	SS	NWS 70 03
ENCLAVE	SALLIS, JAMES	SS	70
SLICE OF THE UNIVERSE	SALLIS, JAMES	SS	FAN 69 02
ANXIETY IN THE EYES OF THE CRICKET			
	SALLIS, JAMES	SS	
JEREMIAD	SALLIS, JAMES	SS	NWS 69 02
OCCASIONS	SALLIS, JAMES	SS	70
KAZOO	SALLIS, JAMES	SS	NWS 67 08
CREATION OF BENNIE GOOD, THE	SALLIS, JAMES	SS	ORB 70 06
JANE CRYING	SALLIS, JAMES	SS	70
BUBBLES	SALLIS, JAMES	SS	NWS 68 10
FEW LAST WORDS, A	SALLIS, JAMES	SS	ORB 68 04

FIEND IN YOU, THE	BEAUMONT, CHARLES	AN	BAL 62
INTRODUCTION	BEAUMONT, CHARLES	IN	
FINGER PRINTS	MATHESON, RICHARD	SS	NEW 62 AN
FOOL'S MATE	ELLIN, STANLEY	SS	SEM 48
BIG, WIDE, WONDERFUL WORLD	FRITCH, CHARLES E.	SS	FSF 58 03
NIGHT OF THE GRAN BAILE MASCARA, THE (1935)			
	BURNETT, WHIT	SS	EQM 65 07
PUNISHMENT TO FIT THE CRIMES, A			
	GORDON, RICHARD M.	SS	62
HORNET, THE	JOHNSON, GEORGE C.	SS	ROG 62 09
PERCHANCE TO DREAM	BEAUMONT, CHARLES	SS	PBY 58 10
THIRTEENTH STEP, THE	LEIBER, FRITZ	SS	NEW 62 AN
CONSPIRACY, THE	LOWRY, ROBERT	SS	58
ROOM WITH A VIEW	CARLSON, ESTHER	SS	FAN 53 05
CANDIDATE, THE	SLESAR, HENRY	SS	ROG 61
ONE OF THOSE DAYS	NOLAN, WILLIAM F.	SS	FSF 62 05
LUCY COMES TO STAY	BLOCH, ROBERT	SS	WRT 52 01
WOMEN, THE	BRADBURY, RAY	SS	FFM 48 10
SURPRISE|	BRADFORD, RONALD	SS	62
MUTE	MATHESON, RICHARD	NV	NEW 62 AN

FIFTY SHORT SCIENCE FICTION TALES

FIEND, THE	PLAYBOY, EDITORS OF	AN	PBP 71
PREFACE	PLAYBOY, EDITORS OF	IN	
FIEND, THE	POHL, FREDERIK	SS	PBY 64 04
ULTIMATE BRUNETTE, THE	BUDRYS, ALGIS	SS	PBY 65 09
YOU CAN'T HAVE THEM ALL	BEAUMONT, CHARLES	SS	PBY 56 08
DOUBLE STANDARD	BROWN, FREDRIC	SS	PBY 63
CROOKED MAN, THE	BEAUMONT, CHARLES	SS	PBY 55 08
MISSION, THE	NISSENSON, HUGH	SS	PBY 64 12
MASTER COPY, THE	DOBINSON, FRANK	SS	PBY 66 05
BETTER MAN, THE	RUSSELL, RAY	SS	PBY 66 07
WELCOME TO THE MONKEY HOUSE	VONNEGUT, KURT JR.	SS	PBY 68 01
CAN YOU FEEL ANYTHING WHEN I DO THIS?			
	SHECKLEY, ROBERT	SS	PBY 69 08
ADAM FROST	AANDAHL, VANCE	SS	PBY 62 04
I LIKE BLONDES	BLOCH, ROBERT	SS	PBY 56 01
I REMEMBER BABYLON	CLARKE, ARTHUR C.	SS	PBY 60 05
LOVE, INCORPORATED (ALSO AS PILGRIMAGE TO EARTH)			
	SHECKLEY, ROBERT	SS	PBY 56 09
LOVEMAKING (ALSO AS MAKING LOVE)			
	POHL, FREDERIK	SS	PBY 66 12

FIFTH GALAXY READER, THE	GOLD, H. L.	AN H	DBL 61
INSIDE JOHN BARTH	STUART, WILLIAM W.	NV	GAL 60 06
LAST LETTER, THE	LEIBER, FRITZ	SS	GAL 58 06
PERFECT ANSWER	STECHER, L. J. JR.	SS	GAL 58 06
DOUBLE DARE	SILVERBERG, ROBERT	SS	GAL 56 11
PASTORAL AFFAIR	STEARNS, CHARLES A.	SS	GAL 59 02
BLACK CHARLIE	DICKSON, GORDON R.	SS	GAL 54 04
$1,000 A PLATE	MCKENTY, JACK	SS	GAL 54 10
TAKE WOODEN INDIANS	DAVIDSON, AVRAM	NV	GAL 59 06
BITTEREST PILL, THE (ALSO AS THE RICHEST MAN IN LEVITTOWN)			
	POHL, FREDERIK	SS	GAL 59 04
THIS SIDE UP	BANKS, RAYMOND E.	SS	GAL 54 07
EEL, THE	DEFORD, MIRIAM ALLEN	SS	GAL 58 04
FEAST OF DEMONS, A	MORRISON, WILLIAM	NV	GAL 58 03
NIGHTMARE WITH ZEPPELINS	POHL, FREDERIK		
	AND KORNBLUTH, C. M.	NV C	GAL 58 12
WE NEVER MENTION AUNT NORA	FLEHR, PAUL	SS	GAL 58 07
WHEN THE PEOPLE FELL	SMITH, CORDWAINER	SS	GAL 59 04

FIFTH HEAD OF CERBERUS, THE	WOLFE, GENE	AC H	SCB 72
FIFTH HEAD OF CERBERUS, THE	WOLFE, GENE	NV	ORB 72 10
"STORY, A" BY JOHN V. MARSCH	WOLFE, GENE	NV	
V.R.T.	WOLFE, GENE	NV	

FIFTY SHORT SCIENCE FICTION TALES

	ASIMOV & CONKLIN	AN	CLB 63
INTRODUCTION NO. 1	ASIMOV, ISAAC	IN	
INTRODUCTION NO. 2	CONKLIN, GEOFF	IN	
BALLADE OF AN ARTIFICIAL SATELLITE			
	ANDERSON, POUL	PM	FSF 58 10
FUN THEY HAD, THE (NEA 51 12)			
	ASIMOV, ISAAC	SS	FSF 54 02
MEN ARE DIFFERENT	BLOCH, ALAN	SS	NEW 54 AN
AMBASSADORS, THE	BOUCHER, ANTHONY	SS	STS 52 06
WEAPON, THE	BROWN, FREDRIC	SS	ASF 51 04
RANDOM SAMPLE	CARAVAN, T. P.	SS	FSF 53 04
OSCAR	CARTMILL, CLEVE	SS	UNK 41 02
MIST, THE	CARTUR, PETER	SS	FSF 52 09
TEETHING RING	CAUSEY, JAMES	SS	GAL 53 01
HAUNTED SPACESUIT, THE (WHO'S THERE?)			
	CLARKE, ARTHUR C.	SS	NWS 58 11
STAIR TRICK	CLINGERMAN, MILDRED	SS	FSF 52 08
UNWELCOME TENANT	DEE, ROGER	SS	PLS 50 SU
MATHEMATICIANS, THE	FELDMAN, ARTHUR	SS	AMZ 53 11
THIRD LEVEL, THE (COL 50 10)	FINNEY, JACK	SS	FSF 52 10
BEAUTIFUL, BEAUTIFUL, BEAUTIFUL|			
	FRIEDMAN, STUART	SS	FUT 52 03
FIGURE, THE	GRENDON, EDWARD	SS	ASF 47 07
RAG THING, THE	GRINNELL, DAVID	SS	FSF 51 10
GOOD PROVIDER, THE	GROSS, MARION	SS	FSF 52 09
COLUMBUS WAS A DOPE	HEINLEIN, ROBERT A.	SS	STS 47 05
TEXAS WEEK	HERNHUNTER, ALBERT	SS	FUN 54 01
HILDA	HICKEY, H. B.	SS	FSF 52 09
CHOICE, THE	HILTON-YOUNG, WAYLAND	SS	PUN 52 03
NOT WITH A BANG	KNIGHT, DAMON	SS	FSF 50 WS
ALTAR AT MIDNIGHT, THE	KORNBLUTH, C. M.	SS	GAL 52 11
BAD DAY FOR SALES, A	LEIBER, FRITZ	SS	GAL 53 07
WHO'S CRIBBING?	LEWIS, JACK	SS	STS 53 01
SPECTATOR SPORT	MACDONALD, JOHN D.	SS	TWS 50 02
CRICKET BALL, THE	MANHATTAN, AVRO	SS	FSF 55 10
DOUBLE-TAKE (AS KEN WINNEY)	MARKS, WINSTON K.	SS	SFA 53 12
PROLOG	MCKNIGHT, JOHN P.	SS	FSF 51 08
AVAILABLE DATA ON THE WORP REACTION, THE			
	MILLER, LION	SS	FSF 53 09
NARAPOIA (THE ORIGIN OF NARAPOIA, WDG 48 04)			
	NELSON, ALAN	SS	FSF 51 04
TIGER BY THE TAIL	NOURSE, ALAN E.	SS	GAL 51 11
COUNTER CHARM	PHILLIPS, PETER	SS	SLN 51 SP
FLY, THE	PORGES, ARTHUR	SS	FSF 52 09
BUSINESS, AS USUAL, THE	REYNOLDS, MACK	SS	FSF 52 06
TWO WEEKS IN AUGUST	ROBINSON, FRANK M.	SS	GAL 51 02
SEE?	ROBLES, EDWARD G.	SS	GAL 54 06
APPOINTMENT AT NOON	RUSSELL, ERIC FRANK	SS	AMZ 54 03
WE DON'T WANT ANY TROUBLE	SCHMITZ, JAMES H.	SS	GAL 53 06
BUILT DOWN LOGICALLY	SCHOENFELD, HOWARD	SS	FSF 51 12
EGG A MONTH FROM ALL OVER, AN			
	SEABRIGHT, IDRIS	SS	FSF 52 10
PERFECT WOMAN, THE	SHECKLEY, ROBERT	SS	AMZ 54 01
HUNTERS, THE	SHELDON, WALT	SS	STS 52 03
MARTIAN AND THE MAGICIAN, THE			
	SMITH, EVELYN E.	SS	FSF 52 11
BARNEY	STANTON, WILL	SS	FSF 51 02
TALENT	STURGEON, THEODORE	SS	BEY 53 09
PROJECT HUSH	TENN, WILLIAM	SS	GAL 54 02
GREAT JUDGE, THE	VAN VOGT, A. E.	SS	FBK 48 03

FIFTY SHORT SCIENCE FICTION TALES

EMERGENCY LANDING	WILLIAMS, RALPH	SS	ASF 40 07
OBVIOUSLY SUICIDE	WRIGHT, S. FOWLER	SS	SUS 51 SP
SIX HAIKU	ANDERSON, KAREN	PM	FSF 62 07

FINAL ENCOUNTER   POHL, FREDERIK   AN   CUR 65
SEE "THE EIGHTH GALAXY READER"

FINAL PROGRAMME, THE   MOORCOCK, MICHAEL   NO   AVN 68

PRELIMINARY DATA	MOORCOCK, MICHAEL	SS	NWS 65 08
FURTHER INFORMATION	MOORCOCK, MICHAEL	SS	NWS 65 12
PHASE THREE	MOORCOCK, MICHAEL	SS	NWS 66 03

FINAL STAGE   FERMAN & MALZBERG   OA H CHT 74

INTRODUCTION	FERMAN, EDWARD L.	IN	
	AND MALZBERG, BARRY N.	IN C	
WE PURCHASE PEOPLE	POHL, FREDERIK	SS	FST 74
VOORTREKKERS, THE	ANDERSON, POUL	NV	FST 74
GREAT ESCAPE TOURS, INC.	REED, KIT	SS	FST 74
DIAGRAMS FOR THREE ENIGMATIC STORIES	ALDISS, BRIAN W.	GR	FST 74
GIRL IN THE TRU-DREAM, THE	ALDISS, BRIAN W.	SS	FST 74
IMMOBILITY CREW, THE	ALDISS, BRIAN W.	SS	FST 74
CULTURAL SIDE EFFECT, A	ALDISS, BRIAN W.	SS	FST 74
THAT THOU ART MINDFUL OF HIM|	ASIMOV, ISAAC	NV	FSF 74 05
WE THREE	KOONTZ, DEAN R.	SS	FST 74
OLD FASHIONED GIRL, AN	RUSS, JOANNA	SS	FST 74
CATMAN	ELLISON, HARLAN	NV	FST 74
SPACE RATS OF THE C.C.C.	HARRISON, HARRY	NV	FST 74
TRIPS	SILVERBERG, ROBERT	NV	FST 74
WONDERFUL, ALL-PURPOSE TRANSMOGRIFIER, THE	MALZBERG, BARRY N.	SS	FST 74
HER SMOKE ROSE UP FOREVER	TIPTREE, JAMES JR.	NV	FST 74
LITTLE SOMETHING FOR US TEMPUNAUTS, A	DICK, PHILIP K.	NV	FST 74

FINAL WAR AND OTHER FANTASIES   O'DONNELL, K. M.   DC   ACE 69

INTRODUCTION	O'DONNELL, K. M.	IN	
FINAL WAR	O'DONNELL, K. M.	NV	FSF 68 04
DEATH TO THE KEEPER	O'DONNELL, K. M.	NV	FSF 68 08
TRIPTYCH, A	O'DONNELL, K. M.	SS	FSF 69 07
HOW I TAKE THEIR MEASURE	O'DONNELL, K. M.	SS	FSF 69 01
OATEN	O'DONNELL, K. M.	SS	FAN 68 10
ASCENSION, THE	O'DONNELL, K. M.	SS	FAN 69 04
MAJOR INCITEMENT TO RIOT, THE	O'DONNELL, K. M.	SS	FAN 69 02
COP-OUT	O'DONNELL, K. M.	SS	ESC 68
WE'RE COMING THROUGH THE WINDOW	O'DONNELL, K. M.	SS	GAL 67 08
MARKET IN ALIENS, THE	O'DONNELL, K. M.	SS	GAL 68 11
BY RIGHT OF SUCCESSION	O'DONNELL, K. M.	SS	IFS 69 10

FIRST ASTOUNDING SCIENCE FICTION ANTHOLOGY, THE   CAMPBELL, JOHN W. JR AN H GRY 54

BLOWUPS HAPPEN	HEINLEIN, ROBERT A.	NV	ASF 40 09
INVARIANT	PIERCE, JOHN R.	SS	ASF 44 04
FIRST CONTACT	LEINSTER, MURRAY	NV	ASF 45 05
HOBBYIST	RUSSELL, ERIC FRANK	NV	ASF 47 09
CHILD'S PLAY	TENN, WILLIAM	NV	ASF 47 03
THUNDER AND ROSES	STURGEON, THEODORE	NV	ASF 47 11
WITCHES OF KARRES, THE	SCHMITZ, JAMES H.	NV	ASF 49 12

FIRST ASTOUNDING SCIENCE FICTION ANTHOLOGY, THE (PB)   CAMPBELL, JOHN W. JR AN   FSP 64

BLOWUPS HAPPEN	HEINLEIN, ROBERT A.	NV	ASF 40 09
HINDSIGHT	WILLIAMSON, JACK	SS	ASF 40 05
VAULT OF THE BEAST	VAN VOGT, A. E.	NV	ASF 40 08
EXALTED, THE	DE CAMP, L. SPRAGUE	NV	ASF 40 11
WHEN THE BOUGH BREAKS	PADGETT, LEWIS	NV	ASF 44 11
CLASH BY NIGHT	O'DONNELL, LAWRENCE	NV	ASF 43 03
INVARIANT	PIERCE, JOHN R.	SS	ASF 44 04
FIRST CONTACT	LEINSTER, MURRAY	NV	ASF 45 05
MEIHEM IN CE KLASRUM	EDWARDS, DOLTON	AR	ASF 46 09
HOBBYIST	RUSSELL, ERIC FRANK	NV	ASF 47 09
E FOR EFFORT	SHERRED, T. L.	NV	ASF 47 05

FIRST CONTACT   KNIGHT, DAMON   AN   PIN 71 11

INTRODUCTION	KNIGHT, DAMON	IN	
FIRST CONTACT	LEINSTER, MURRAY	NV	ASF 45 05
DOOMSDAY DEFERRED	JENKINS, WILL F.	SS	SEP 49 09
HURKLE IS A HAPPY BEAST, THE	STURGEON, THEODORE	SS	FSF 49 FL
NOT FINAL|	ASIMOV, ISAAC	SS	ASF 41 10
BLIND PILOT, THE (TRANSLATED BY DAMON KNIGHT)	HENNEBERG, CHARLES	SS	FSF 60 01
SILLY SEASON, THE	KORNBLUTH, C. M.	SS	FSF 50 FL
GOLDFISH BOWL	HEINLEIN, ROBERT A.	NV	ASF 42 03
IN VALUE DECEIVED	FYFE, H. B.	SS	ASF 50 11
WAVERIES, THE	BROWN, FREDRIC	SS	ASF 45 01
IN THE ABYSS	WELLS, H. G.	SS	PRS 96 08

FIRST FLIGHT   KNIGHT, DAMON   AN   LAN 63
MAIDEN VOYAGES IN SPACE AND TIME,
ALSO AS "NOW BEGINS TOMORROW"

INTRODUCTION	KNIGHT, DAMON	IN	
ISOLINGUALS, THE	DE CAMP, L. SPRAGUE	SS	ASF 37 09
FAITHFUL, THE	DEL REY, LESTER	SS	ASF 38 04
BLACK DESTROYER	VAN VOGT, A. E.	NV	ASF 39 07
LIFE-LINE	HEINLEIN, ROBERT A.	SS	ASF 39 08
ETHER BREATHER	STURGEON, THEODORE	SS	ASF 39 09
LOOPHOLE	CLARKE, ARTHUR C.	SS	ASF 46 04
TOMORROW'S CHILDREN	ANDERSON, POUL	NV	ASF 47 03
THAT ONLY A MOTHER	MERRIL, JUDITH	SS	ASF 48 06
WALK TO THE WORLD	BUDRYS, ALGIS	SS	SSF 52 11
T	ALDISS, BRIAN W.	SS	NEB 56 11

FIRST FLIGHTS TO THE MOON   CLEMENT, HAL   AN H DBL 70

INTRODUCTION	ASIMOV, ISAAC	IN	
IDEAS DIE HARD	ASIMOV, ISAAC	NV	GAL 57 10
TRENDS	ASIMOV, ISAAC	SS	ASF 39 07
REPORT ON THE NATURE OF THE LUNAR SURFACE	BRUNNER, JOHN	SS	ASF 60 08
CRITICAL ANGLE	CHANDLER, A. BERTRAM	SS	FSF 58 11
JETSAM	CHANDLER, A. BERTRAM	SS	NWS 53 03
VENTURE TO THE MOON	CLARKE, ARTHUR C.	GR	FSF 56 12
INTRUDERS (INTRUDERS ON THE MOON)	COOPER, EDMUND	NV	FUN 57 04
MOONDUST, THE SMELL OF HAY, AND DIALECTICAL MATERIALISM	DISCH, THOMAS M.	SS	FSF 67 08
MISSING SYMBOL, THE	FAIRMAN, PAUL W.	SS	FAN 52 12
EXTENDING THE HOLDINGS	GRINNELL, DAVID	SS	FSF 51 04
WRONG-WAY STREET	NIVEN, LARRY	SS	GAL 65 04
ONCE AROUND THE MOON	PHILLIPS, VIC	NV	ASF 37 06

FIRST PERSON, PECULIAR   SHERRED, T. L.   AC   BAL 72 01

E FOR EFFORT	SHERRED, T. L.	NV	ASF 47 05
CURE, GUARANTEED	SHERRED, T. L.	NV	FUT 54 08
EYE FOR INIQUITY	SHERRED, T. L.	NV	BEY 53 07
CUE FOR QUIET	SHERRED, T. L.	NA	SSF 53 05

FIRST STEP OUTWARD   HOSKINS, ROBERT   AN   DEL 69 08

INTRODUCTION	ANDERSON, POUL	IN	
PROLOGUE	HOSKINS, ROBERT	IN	
COLD WAR	NEVILLE, KRIS	SS	ASF 49 10
THIRD STAGE	ANDERSON, POUL	SS	AMZ 62 02
GENTLEMEN, BE SEATED|	HEINLEIN, ROBERT A.	SS	ARG 48 05
JAYWALKER	ROCKLYNNE, ROSS	SS	GAL 50 12
HATED, THE	POHL, FREDERIK	SS	GAL 58 01
SUNRISE ON MERCURY	SILVERBERG, ROBERT	SS	SFS 57 05
HOP-FRIEND	CARR, TERRY	SS	FSF 62 11
MAN WHO LOST THE SEA, THE	STURGEON, THEODORE	SS	FSF 59 10
FIRST CONTACT	LEINSTER, MURRAY	NV	ASF 45 05
MISBEGOTTEN MISSIONARY (ALSO AS GREEN PATCHES)	ASIMOV, ISAAC	SS	GAL 50 11
MARKET IN ALIENS, THE	O'DONNELL, K. M.	SS	GAL 68 11
RULES OF THE ROAD, THE	SPINRAD, NORMAN	SS	GAL 64 11
JETSAM	CHANDLER, A. BERTRAM	SS	NWS 53 03

FIRST WORLD OF IF, THE   QUINN & WULFF   AN D QUI 57

LET THERE BE LIGHT	FYFE, H. B.	SS	IFS 53 11
ROTIFERS, THE	ABERNATHY, ROBERT	SS	IFS 53 03
BATTLE, THE	SHECKLEY, ROBERT	SS	IFS 54 09
PATTERN FOR PENELOPE, A	YOUNG, ROBERT F.	SS	IFS 54 10
DISQUALIFIED	FONTENAY, CHARLES L.	SS	IFS 54 09
COLD NIGHT FOR CRYING, A	LESSER, MILTON	SS	IFS 54 12
FIRST STAGE: MOON	HETSCHEL, DICK	SS	IFS 54 12
SMALL WORLD OF M-75, THE	CLINTON, ED M. JR.	SS	IFS 54 07
JOURNEY WORK	DRYFOOS, DAVE	SS	IFS 55 01
LAST CRUSADE, THE	SMITH, GEORGE HUDSON	SS	IFS 55 02
CYBER AND JUSTICE HOLMES, THE	RILEY, FRANK	SS	IFS 55 03
CAPTIVE MARKET	DICK, PHILIP K.	SS	IFS 55 04
WATERSHED	BLISH, JAMES	SS	IFS 55 05
TWILIGHT YEARS, THE	DRUSSAI, KIRK AND DRUSSAI, GAREN	NV C	IFS 55 06
FRANCHISE	ASIMOV, ISAAC	SS	IFS 55 08
LAST RITES	BEAUMONT, CHARLES	SS	IFS 55 10
LABORATORY	BIXBY, JEROME	NV	IFS 55 12
MARGENES, THE	DEFORD, MIRIAM ALLEN	SS	IFS 56 02
DRIVERS, THE	LUDWIG, EDWARD W.	SS	IFS 56 03
SHOCK TROOP	BOLTON, RICHARD	SS	IFS 56 10

FIVE FATES   LAUMER, KEITH   AN H DBL 70

FATAL FULFILLMENT, THE	ANDERSON, POUL	SN	FSF 70 03
MURDER WILL IN	HERBERT, FRANK	NV	FSF 70 05
MAVERICK (WALKER BETWEEN THE PLANES)	DICKSON, GORDON R.	NV	WOF 70 02
REGION BETWEEN, THE	ELLISON, HARLAN	NA	GAL 70 03
OF DEATH WHAT DREAMS	LAUMER, KEITH	NV	WOT 70 24

FIVE SCIENCE FICTION NOVELS   GREENBERG , MARTIN   AN H GNM 52
ENGLISH DERIVATIVE ANTHOLOGY "CRUCIBLE OF POWER"

BUT WITHOUT HORNS	PAGE, NORVELL W.	SN	UNK 40 06
DESTINY TIMES THREE	LEIBER, FRITZ	SN	ASF 45 03
CRISIS IN UTOPIA	KNIGHT, NORMAN L.	NO	ASF 40 07
CHRONICLER, THE (ALSO AS SIEGE OF THE UNSEEN)	VAN VOGT, A. E.	NA	ASF 46 10
CRUCIBLE OF POWER, THE	WILLIAMSON, JACK	NV	ASF 39 02

FIVE-ODD   CONKLIN, GROFF   AN   PYR 64 08
IN ENGLAND AS "POSSIBLE TOMORROWS"

INTRODUCTION	CONKLIN, GROFF	IN	
DEAD PAST, THE	ASIMOV, ISAAC	NV	ASF 56 04
SOMETHING STRANGE	AMIS, KINGSLEY	NV	FSF 61 07
UNIT	MCINTOSH, J. T.	NV	NWS 57 02
GONE FISHING	SCHMITZ, JAMES H.	NV	ASF 61 05
BIG ANCESTOR	WALLACE, F. L.	NV	GAL 54 11

FLAME TREE PLANET   ELWOOD, ROGER   OA   CNC 73
INTRODUCTION: RELIGIOUS SCIENCE FICTION

	LOVIN, ROGER	IN	
FLAME TREE PLANET	SMITH, GEORGE HENRY	NV	FTP 73
POVERELLO	MOORE, RAYLYN	SS	FTP 73
SINLESS CHILD, THE	KOONTZ, DEAN R.	SS	FTP 73
APOSTLE	LOVIN, ROGER	SS	FTP 73
MATTER OF FREEDOMS, A	O'BRIEN, CLANCY	SS	FTP 73
HOW BRIGHT THE STARS	BRACKETT, LEIGH	SS	FTP 73
LIONS OF ROME, THE	JONES, RAYMOND F.	SS	FTP 73
MANY MANSIONS	KIMBERLY, GAIL	SS	FTP 73
BEARING WITNESS	MALZBERG, BARRY N.	SS	FTP 73
TARRYING	SCORTIA, THOMAS N.	SS	FTP 73

FLANDRY OF TERRA   ANDERSON, POUL   AC H CHL 65
  GAME OF GLORY, THE   ANDERSON, POUL   NV   VSF 58 03
  MESSAGE IN SECRET, A   ANDERSON, POUL   NA   FAN 57 12
  PLAGUE OF MASTERS, A   ANDERSON, POUL   NA   FAN 60 12

FLIGHT INTO SPACE   WOLLHEIM, DONALD A. AN H FEL 50
  SUNWARD   COBLENTZ, STANTON A. SS TWS 40 04
  MERCURIAN, THE   LONG, FRANK BELKNAP SS   PLS 41 WI
  PARASITE PLANET   WEINBAUM, STANLEY G. NV ASF 35 02
  PERIL OF THE BLUE WORLD   ABERNATHY, ROBERT   SS   PLS 42 WI
  DEATH OF THE MOON, THE   PHILLIPS, A. M.   SS   AMZ 29 02
  SEEKERS, THE   WILLIAMS, ROBERT M. SS   STS 48 05
  AJAX OF AJAX   PEARSON, MARTIN   SS   FUT 42 08
  RED STORM ON JUPITER   LONG, FRANK BELKNAP SS   ASF 36 05
  HERMIT OF SATURN'S RING   JONES, NEIL R.   SS   PLS 40 FL
  PLANET PASSAGE   WOLLHEIM, DONALD A. SS   FUT 42 10
  BABY ON NEPTUNE, A   HARRIS, CLARE WINGER
                           AND BREUER, MILES J. MD. SS C AMZ 29 12
  RAPE OF THE SOLAR SYSTEM, THE
                           STONE, LESLIE F.   SS   AMZ 34 12

FLIGHT OF THE HORSE, THE   NIVEN, LARRY   AC   BAL 73 09
  FLIGHT OF THE HORSE, THE (GET A HORSE!)
                           NIVEN, LARRY   SS   FSF 69 10
  LEVIATHAN!   NIVEN, LARRY   SS   PBY 70 08
  BIRD IN THE HAND   NIVEN, LARRY   SS   FSF 70 10
  THERE'S A WOLF IN MY TIME MACHINE
                           NIVEN, LARRY   SS   FSF 71 06
  DEATH IN A CAGE   NIVEN, LARRY   SS   NEW 73 AC
  FLASH CROWD   NIVEN, LARRY   NA   TTT 73
  WHAT GOOD IS A GLASS DAGGER? NIVEN, LARRY   NV   FSF 72 09
  AFTERWORD   NIVEN, LARRY   MS

FLOWERS FOR ALGERNON AND OTHER STORIES
                           MILLS, ROBERT P.   AN   ACE 60
  SEE "BEST FROM FANTASY AND SCIENCE FICTION: 9"

FLYING SAUCERS IN FACT AND FICTION
                           SANTESSON, HANS S. AN   LAN 68
  INTRODUCTION   SANTESSON, HANS S. IN
  FLYING SAUCER MYTH, THE   DEL REY, LESTER   AR   FUN 57 08
  NOW MEET THE NONTERRESTRIAL SANDERSON, IVAN T. AR FUN 59 01
  WELCOME, STRANGER   BLOCH, ROBERT   SS   SAT 57 04
  OUR SAUCER VACATION   LEIBER, FRITZ   AR   FUN 59 12
  SAUCER OF LONELINESS   STURGEON, THEODORE SS   GAL 53 02
  AMUSED VISITOR   STEPHENS, JOHN   SS   NEW 68 AN
  NIGHT BEFORE CHRISTMAS, THE COE, NANCY FORSYTHE PM   59
  NEITHER SNOW NOR RAIN (NOT SNOW NOR RAIN)
                           DEFORD, MIRIAM ALLEN SS IFS 59 11
  SENSE OF WONDER   CHANDLER, A. BERTRAM SS FUN 58 02
  CASSIDY'S SAUCER   HOCH, EDWARD D.   SS   NEW 68 AN
  PICKUP   VAN ALM, AIDAN   SS   FUN 60 01
  LITTLE GREEN MEN   NICHOLSON, JOHN   AR   FUN 58 05
  EXILE FROM SPACE   MERRIL, JUDITH   NV   FUN 56 11
  PRESS CONFERENCE (VISITOR FROM THE VOID)
                           WILSON, RICHARD   SS   AMZ 53 11

FOLSOM FLINT AND OTHER CURIOUS TALES, THE
                           KELLER, DAVID H. MD. AC H ARK 69
  IN MEMORIAM: DAVID HENRY KELLER
                           SPENCER, PAUL   MS
  UNTO US A CHILD IS BORN   KELLER, DAVID H. MD. SS AMZ 33 07
  GOLDEN KEY, THE   KELLER, DAVID H. MD. SS   53
  QUESTION, THE   KELLER, DAVID H. MD. SS
  RED DEATH, THE   KELLER, DAVID H. MD. NV COS 41 07
  WHITE CITY, THE   KELLER, DAVID H. MD. SS AMZ 35 05
  PENT HOUSE, THE   KELLER, DAVID H. MD. SS AMZ 32 02
  AIR LINES   KELLER, DAVID H. MD. SS AMZ 30 01
  CHASM OF MONSTERS   KELLER, DAVID H. MD. SS   51
  DUST IN THE HOUSE   KELLER, DAVID H. MD. SS WRT 38 07
  LANDSLIDE, THE   KELLER, DAVID H. MD. SS
  FOLSOM FLINT, THE   KELLER, DAVID H. MD. SS   52
  TWINS, THE   KELLER, DAVID H. MD. SS
  SARAH   KELLER, DAVID H. MD. SS   52
  FINGERS IN THE SKY   KELLER, DAVID H. MD. SS   52
  THING IN THE CELLAR, THE KELLER, DAVID H. MD. SS WRT 32 03
  PIECE OF LINOLEUM, A (AS AMY WORTH)
                           KELLER, DAVID H. MD. SS TST 33 12
  DEAD WOMAN, THE (STE 39 04) KELLER, DAVID H. MD. SS FMG 34 04

FOREVER WAR, THE   HALDEMAN, JOE W.   NO H SMP 74
  HERO   HALDEMAN, JOE W.   NV   ASF 72 06
  WE ARE VERY HAPPY HERE   HALDEMAN, JOE W.   NV   ASF 73 11
  THIS BEST OF ALL POSSIBLE WORLDS
                           HALDEMAN, JOE W.   SS   ASF 74 11
  END GAME   HALDEMAN, JOE W.   NV   ASF 75 01

FORGETFUL ROBOT, THE   FAIRMAN, PAUL W.   OC H HRW 68
  LOST IN A JUNKYARD   FAIRMAN, PAUL W.   SS
  THOSE REMARKABLE RAVENCRAFTS FAIRMAN, PAUL W. SS
  SPACE MUSEUM, THE   FAIRMAN, PAUL W.   SS
  GALLANT LADY, THE   FAIRMAN, PAUL W.   SS
  LONG HOP   FAIRMAN, PAUL W.   SS
  BROWN PACKAGE, THE   FAIRMAN, PAUL W.   SS
  PHANTOMS OF ZARK   FAIRMAN, PAUL W.   SS
  MASTERMIND OF ZARK   FAIRMAN, PAUL W.   SS
  MINEFIELD, THE   FAIRMAN, PAUL W.   SS
  PIT, THE   FAIRMAN, PAUL W.   SS
  ROBOTS SHOULD STICK TOGETHER FAIRMAN, PAUL W. SS
  INTERLUDE IN THE DESERT   FAIRMAN, PAUL W.   SS
  DELENDA EST CARTHAGO   FAIRMAN, PAUL W.   SS
  NOT BORN TO GREATNESS   FAIRMAN, PAUL W.   SS
  CULTURE FOR THE PLANETS   FAIRMAN, PAUL W.   SS

FORGOTTEN PLANET, THE   LEINSTER, MURRAY   AC H GNM 54
  MAD PLANET, THE   LEINSTER, MURRAY   NA   ARG 20 06
  RED DUST, THE   LEINSTER, MURRAY   NV   AAS 21 04
  NIGHTMARE PLANET   LEINSTER, MURRAY   SN   SFP 53 06

FORWARD IN TIME   BOVA, BEN   AC H WKR 73
  INTRODUCTION   BOVA, BEN   IN
  NEXT LOGICAL STEP, THE   BOVA, BEN   SS   ASF 62 05
  SLIGHT MISCALCULATION, A BOVA, BEN   SS   FSF 71 08
  BLOOD OF TYRANTS   BOVA, BEN   NV   AMZ 70 05
  ZERO GEE   BOVA, BEN   NV   DVS 72 02
  TEST IN ORBIT   BOVA, BEN   SS   ASF 65 09
  FIFTEEN MILES   BOVA, BEN   SS   FSF 67 05
  WEATHERMAKERS, THE   BOVA, BEN   NV   ASF 66 12
  MEN OF GOOD WILL   BOVA, BEN
                           AND LEWIS, MYRON R. SS C GAL 64 06
  PERFECT WARRIOR, THE (THE DUELING MACHINE)
                           BOVA, BEN
                           AND LEWIS, MYRON R. SN C ASF 63 05
  STARS, WON'T YOU HIDE ME? BOVA, BEN   SS   WOT 66 01

FOUNDATION   ASIMOV, ISAAC   NO H GNM 51
  ALSO IN "THE FOUNDATION TRILOGY" AND AS "THE 1,000 YEAR PLAN"
  FOUNDATION   ASIMOV, ISAAC   NV   ASF 42 05
  BRIDLE AND SADDLE   ASIMOV, ISAAC   NV   ASF 42 06
  BIG AND THE LITTLE, THE   ASIMOV, ISAAC   NV   ASF 44 08
  WEDGE, THE   ASIMOV, ISAAC   SS   ASF 44 10

FOUNDATION AND EMPIRE   ASIMOV, ISAAC   NO H GNM 52
  ALSO IN "THE FOUNDATION TRILOGY" AND AS
  "THE MAN WHO UPSET THE UNIVERSE"
  DEAD HAND   ASIMOV, ISAAC   NV   ASF 45 04
  MULE, THE   ASIMOV, ISAAC   SN   ASF 45 11

FOUNDATION TRILOGY, THE   ASIMOV, ISAAC   AC H DBL 64
  IN ENGLAND AS "AN ISAAC ASIMOV OMNIBUS"
  FOUNDATION   ASIMOV, ISAAC   NO   GNM 51
  FOUNDATION AND EMPIRE   ASIMOV, ISAAC   NO   GNM 52
  SECOND FOUNDATION   ASIMOV, ISAAC   NO   GNM 53

FOUR FOR THE FUTURE   CONKLIN, GROFF   AN   PYR 59 08
  ENOUGH ROPE   ANDERSON, POUL   NV   ASF 53 07
  CLAUSTROPHILE, THE   STURGEON, THEODORE NV   GAL 56 08
  CHILDREN'S HOUR, THE   KUTTNER, HENRY   NV   ASF 44 03
  PLUS X   RUSSELL, ERIC FRANK NV   ASF 56 06

FOUR FOR THE FUTURE   HARRISON, HARRY   AN H MAC 69
  INTRODUCTION   HARRISON, HARRY   IN
  CIRCULATION OF THE BLOOD, THE
                           ALDISS, BRIAN W.   NV   IMP 66 03
  AND THE STAGNATION OF THE HEART
                           ALDISS, BRIAN W.   SS   NWS 68 12
  HIGH TREASON   ANDERSON, POUL   SS   IMP 66 03
  DIPTEROID PHENOMENON, THE ANDERSON, POUL   SS
  HERO'S LIFE, A (ALSO AS A STYLE IN TREASON)
                           BLISH, JAMES   NV   IMP 66 03
  SKYSIGN   BLISH, JAMES   NV   ASF 68 05
  GODS THEMSELVES THROW INCENSE, THE
                           HARRISON, HARRY   SS   IMP 66 03
  GHOUL, THE   HARRISON, HARRY   SS

FOUR FOR TOMORROW   ZELAZNY, ROGER   AC   ACE 67 03
  IN ENGLAND AS "A ROSE FOR ECCLESIASTES"
  INTRODUCTION   STURGEON, THEODORE IN
  FURIES, THE   ZELAZNY, ROGER   NV   AMZ 65 06
  GRAVEYARD HEART, THE   ZELAZNY, ROGER   NV   FAN 64 03
  DOORS OF HIS FACE, THE LAMPS OF HIS MOUTH, THE
                           ZELAZNY, ROGER   NV   FSF 65 03
  ROSE FOR ECCLESIASTES, A ZELAZNY, ROGER   NV   FSF 63 11

FOUR FUTURES   SILVERBERG, ROBERT OA H HAW 71
  FOREWORD: FOUR THEMES FOR FOUR FUTURES
                           ASIMOV, ISAAC   IN   FFU 71
  GOING   SILVERBERG, ROBERT NA   FFU 71
  HOW CAN WE SINK WHEN WE CAN FLY?
                           PANSHIN, ALEXEI   NV   FFU 71
  BRAVE NEWER WORLD   HARRISON, HARRY   NV   FFU 71
  ISHMAEL INTO THE BARRENS LAFFERTY, R. A.   NV   FFU 71

FOUR-DIMENSIONAL NIGHTMARE, THE
                           BALLARD, J. G.   AC H GOL 63 05
  VOICES OF TIME, THE   BALLARD, J. G.   SS   NWS 60 10
  SOUND-SWEEP, THE   BALLARD, J. G.   NV   SCF 60 02
  PRIMA BELLADONNA   BALLARD, J. G.   SS   SCF 56 12
  STUDIO 5, THE STARS   BALLARD, J. G.   NV   SCF 61 02
  GARDEN OF TIME, THE   BALLARD, J. G.   SS   FSF 62 02
  CAGE OF SAND, THE   BALLARD, J. G.   SS   NWS 62 06
  WATCH-TOWERS, THE   BALLARD, J. G.   NV   SCF 62 06
  CHRONOPOLIS   BALLARD, J. G.   NV   NWS 60 06

FOUR-DIMENSIONAL NIGHTMARE, THE (REVISED)
                           BALLARD, J. G.   AC H GOL 74
  VOICES OF TIME, THE   BALLARD, J. G.   SS   NWS 60 10
  SOUND-SWEEP, THE   BALLARD, J. G.   NV   SCF 60 02
  GARDEN OF TIME, THE   BALLARD, J. G.   SS   FSF 62 02
  CAGE OF SAND, THE   BALLARD, J. G.   SS   NWS 62 06
  WATCH-TOWERS, THE   BALLARD, J. G.   NV   SCF 62 06
  CHRONOPOLIS   BALLARD, J. G.   NV   NWS 60 06
  THIRTEEN TO CENTAURUS   BALLARD, J. G.   NV   AMZ 62 04
  OVERLOADED MAN, THE   BALLARD, J. G.   SS   NWS 61 07

FOURTH GALAXY READER, THE   GOLD, H. L.   AN H DBL 59
  IN THIS CORNER   GOLD, H. L.   IN
  I AM A NUCLEUS   BARR, STEPHEN   NV   GAL 57 02
  NAME YOUR SYMPTOM   HARMON, JIM   SS   GAL 56 05
  HORRER HOWCE   ST. CLAIR, MARGARET SS   GAL 56 07
  MAN OF DISTINCTION   SHAARA, MICHAEL   SS   GAL 56 10
  BOMB IN THE BATHTUB, THE SCORTIA, THOMAS N. SS   GAL 57 02

FOURTH GALAXY READER, THE

YOU WERE RIGHT, JOE	MCINTOSH, J. T.	SS	GAL 57	11
WHAT'S HE DOING IN THERE?	LEIBER, FRITZ	SS	GAL 57	12
GENTLEST UNPEOPLE, THE (ALSO AS THE GENTLE VENUSIAN)				
	POHL, FREDERIK	NV	GAL 58	06
HATED, THE	FLEHR, PAUL	SS	GAL 58	01
KILL ME WITH KINDNESS	WILSON, RICHARD	SS	GAL 58	01
OR ALL THE SEAS WITH OYSTERS	DAVIDSON, AVRAM	SS	GAL 58	05
GUN WITHOUT A BANG, THE	O'DONNEVAN, FINN	NV	GAL 58	06
MAN IN A QUANDARY	STECHER, L. J. JR.	SS	GAL 58	07
BLANK FORM	SELLINGS, ARTHUR	SS	GAL 58	07
MINIMUM MAN, THE	SHECKLEY, ROBERT	NV	GAL 58	06

FOX WOMAN & OTHER STORIES, THE

	MERRITT, A.	AC	AVN 49	
FOX WOMAN, THE	MERRITT, A.	NV		46
PEOPLE OF THE PIT, THE	MERRITT, A.	NV	ASM 18	01
THROUGH THE DRAGON GLASS	MERRITT, A.	SS	ASW 17	11
DRONE, THE	MERRITT, A.	SS	FMG 34	09
LAST POET AND THE ROBOTS, THE				
	MERRITT, A.	SS	FMG 34	04
THREE LINES OF OLD FRENCH	MERRITT, A.	SS	ASW 19	08
WHITE ROAD, THE	MERRITT, A.	SS		49
WHEN OLD GODS WAKE	MERRITT, A.	SS	AFR 48	07
WOMEN OF THE WOOD, THE	MERRITT, A.	SS	WRT 26	08

FREDERIK POHL OMNIBUS, THE   POHL, FREDERIK   AC H GOL 66

MAN WHO ATE THE WORLD, THE	POHL, FREDERIK	NV	GAL 56	11
SEVEN DEADLY VIRTUES, THE	POHL, FREDERIK	NV	GAL 58	08
DAY THE ICICLE WORKS CLOSED, THE				
	POHL, FREDERIK	NV	GAL 60	02
KNIGHTS OF ARTHUR, THE	POHL, FREDERIK	NA	GAL 58	01
MARS BY MOONLIGHT	POHL, FREDERIK	NA	GAL 58	06
HAUNTED CORPSE, THE	POHL, FREDERIK	SS	GAL 57	01
MIDDLE OF NOWHERE, THE	POHL, FREDERIK	SS	GAL 55	05
DAY OF THE BOOMER DUKES, THE	POHL, FREDERIK	SS	FUT 56	30
SNOWMEN, THE	POHL, FREDERIK	SS	GAL 59	12
WIZARDS OF PUNG'S CORNERS, THE				
	POHL, FREDERIK	NV	GAL 58	10
WAGING OF THE PEACE, THE	POHL, FREDERIK	NV	GAL 59	08
SURVIVAL KIT	POHL, FREDERIK	NV	GAL 57	05
I PLINGLOT, WHO YOU?	POHL, FREDERIK	NV	GAL 59	02

FROM DEATH TO THE STARS   HUBBARD, L. RON   AC H FPB 53

DEATH'S DEPUTY	HUBBARD, L. RON	NO	UNK 40	02
KINGSLAYER, THE	HUBBARD, L. RON	AC	FPB 49	

FROM FRANKENSTEIN TO ANDROMEDA

	BROWN, JAMES GOLDIE	AN	MCM 66	
MOXON'S MASTER	BIERCE, AMBROSE	SS		93
THERE WILL COME SOFT RAINS	BRADBURY, RAY	SS	COL 50	05
REPORT ON THE NATURE OF THE LUNAR SURFACE				
	BRUNNER, JOHN	SS	ASF 60	08
CURSE, THE	CLARKE, ARTHUR C.	SS	CSM 53	09
DEEP RANGE, THE (ARB 54 04)	CLARKE, ARTHUR C.	NV	STR 54	03
LOST WORLD, THE	DOYLE, ARTHUR CONAN	EX	HDS 12	
A FOR ANDROMEDA	HOYLE, FRED			
	AND ELLIOT, JOHN	EX C	SVN 62	
DANCING PARTNER, THE	JEROME, JEROME K.	SS	FFM 51	03
RUUM, THE	PORGES, ARTHUR	SS	FSF 53	10
ADVENTURES OF BARON MUNCHAUSEN, THE				
	RASPE, RUDOLPH	EX		
FRANKENSTEIN, OR, THE MODERN PROMETHEUS				
	SHELLEY, MARY W.	EX	WRT 32	05
JOURNEY TO THE CENTER OF THE EARTH, A (1864)				
	VERNE, JULES	EX	AMZ 26	05
STAR, THE	WELLS, H. G.	SS	GRP 97	12
WAR OF THE WORLDS, THE	WELLS, H. G.	EX	PRS 97	04
DAY OF THE TRIFFIDS, THE (REVOLT OF THE TRIFFIDS)				
	WYNDHAM, JOHN	EX	COL 51	01

FROM OFF THIS WORLD   MARGULIES & FRIEND   AN H MER 49

LAST WOMAN, THE	GARDNER, THOMAS S.	SS	WOS 32	04
MAN WHO EVOLVED, THE	HAMILTON, EDMOND	SS	WOS 31	04
WORLD WITHOUT, THE	HERBERT, BENSON	SS	WOS 31	02
GREEN TORTURE, THE	HILLIARD, A. ROWLEY	SS	WOS 31	03
LITERARY CORKSCREW, THE	KELLER, DAVID H. MD.	SS	WOS 34	03
MAN FROM MARS, THE	MILLER, P. SCHUYLER	SS	WSQ 31	SU
ANCIENT BRAIN, THE	STANGLAND, A. G.	SS	SWS 29	10
CITY OF THE SINGING FLAME, THE				
	SMITH, CLARK ASHTON	SS	WOS 31	07
BEYOND THE SINGING FLAME, THE	SMITH, CLARK ASHTON	SS	WOS 31	11
ETERNAL MAN, THE	SHARP, D. D.	SS	SWS 29	08
HORNETS OF SPACE	STAERL, R. F.	SS	WOS 31	11
CUBIC CITY, THE	TUCKER, LOUIS	SS	SWS 29	09
MARTIAN ODYSSEY, A	WEINBAUM, STANLEY G.	NV	WOS 34	07
VALLEY OF DREAMS	WEINBAUM, STANLEY G.	NV	WOS 34	11
THROUGH THE PURPLE CLOUD	WILLIAMSON, JACK	SS	WOS 31	05
MICROSCOPIC GIANTS, THE	ERNST, PAUL	SS	TWS 36	10
WHEN THE EARTH LIVED	KUTTNER, HENRY	SS	TWS 37	10
CONQUEST OF LIFE	BINDER, EANDO	SS	TWS 37	08

FROM OTHER WORLDS   DERLETH, AUGUST   AN   FSP 64
    STORIES FROM "BEACHHEADS IN SPACE"

INTRODUCTION	DERLETH, AUGUST	IN		
MAN FROM OUTSIDE, THE	WILLIAMSON, JACK	SS	ASF 51	03
BREEDS THERE A MAN...?	ASIMOV, ISAAC	NV	ASF 51	06
METEOR (PHONEY METEOR)	HARRIS, JOHN BEYNON	SS	AMZ 41	03
AND THE WALLS CAME TUMBLING DOWN				
	WYNDHAM, JOHN	SS	STS 51	05
METAMORPHOSIS OF EARTH, THE	SMITH, CLARK ASHTON	NV	WRT 51	09
AMBASSADORS FROM VENUS, THE	CROSSEN, KENDELL F.	NV	PLS 52	03

FROM THE "S" FILE   PLAYBOY, EDITORS OF   AN   PBP 71

PREFACE	PLAYBOY, EDITORS OF	IN		
NAIL AND THE ORACLE, THE	STURGEON, THEODORE	NV	PBY 65	10

WORLD OF HEART'S DESIRE, THE (ALSO AS THE STORE OF THE WORLDS)				
	SHECKLEY, ROBERT	SS	PBY 59	09
CAN YOU FEEL ANYTHING WHEN I DO THIS?				
	SHECKLEY, ROBERT	SS	PBY 69	08
TRIPLICATION	SHECKLEY, ROBERT	SS	PBY 59	05
SAME TO YOU DOUBLED, THE	SHECKLEY, ROBERT	SS	PBY 70	03
CORDLE TO ONION TO CARROT	SHECKLEY, ROBERT	SS	PBY 69	12
CONTROL SOMNAMBULE	SAMBROT, WILLIAM	SS	PBY 62	05
MAN FROM NOT-YET, THE	SLADEK, JOHN T.	SS	PBY 68	06
MELODRAMINE	SLESAR, HENRY	SS	PBY 65	08
VICTORY PARADE	SLESAR, HENRY	SS	PBY 57	04
EXAMINATION DAY	SLESAR, HENRY	SS	PBY 58	02
JAM, THE	SLESAR, HENRY	SS	PBY 58	11
AFTER	SLESAR, HENRY	SS	PBY 60	06
POOL, THE	SHARKEY, JACK	SS	PBY 64	11
CONVERSATION WITH A BUG	SHARKEY, JACK	SS	PBY 61	10
DEATHWATCH	SPINRAD, NORMAN	SS	PBY 65	11

FROM THE LAND OF FEAR   ELLISON, HARLAN   AC   BEL 67 12
IN PRAISE OF HIS SPIRITS NOBLE AND OTHERWISE

	ZELAZNY, ROGER	IN		
WHERE THE STRAY DREAMS GO	ELLISON, HARLAN	IN		
SKY IS BURNING, THE	ELLISON, HARLAN	SS	IFS 58	08
TIME OF THE EYE, THE	ELLISON, HARLAN	SS	SMM 59	05
BACK TO THE DRAWING BOARDS	ELLISON, HARLAN	SS	FUN 58	08
BATTLE WITHOUT BANNERS	ELLISON, HARLAN	SS	NEW 64	OC
VOICE IN THE GARDEN, THE	ELLISON, HARLAN	SS	LGH 67	06
LIFE HUTCH	ELLISON, HARLAN	SS	IFS 56	04
WE MOURN FOR ANYONE... (MOURNERS FOR HIRE)				
	ELLISON, HARLAN	SS	FAN 57	05
FRIEND TO MAN, A	ELLISON, HARLAN	SS	FUN 59	10
MY BROTHER PAULIE	ELLISON, HARLAN	SS	SAT 58	12
SOLDIER (SOLDIER FROM TOMORROW)				
	ELLISON, HARLAN	SS	FUN 57	10
SOLDIER (TELEVISION SCRIPT VERSION)				
	ELLISON, HARLAN	PL	ABC 64	09

FROM THE OCEAN, FROM THE STARS

	CLARKE, ARTHUR C.	AC H	HBW 61	
INTRODUCTION	CLARKE, ARTHUR C.	IN		
DEEP RANGE, THE (ARB 54 04)	CLARKE, ARTHUR C.	NO	STR 54	03
OTHER SIDE OF THE SKY, THE	CLARKE, ARTHUR C.	GR	INF 57	59
CITY AND THE STARS, THE	CLARKE, ARTHUR C.	NO	HBW 56	

FROM THE TWILIGHT ZONE   SERLING, ROD   AC H NDB 62

MIGHTY CASEY, THE	SERLING, ROD	SA		
ESCAPE CLAUSE	SERLING, ROD	SA		
WHERE IS EVERYBODY?	SERLING, ROD	SA		
MONSTERS ARE DUE ON MAPLE STREET, THE				
	SERLING, ROD	SA		
WALKING DISTANCE	SERLING, ROD	SA		
WHOLE TRUTH, THE	SERLING, ROD	SA		
LONELY, THE	SERLING, ROD	SA		
DUST	SERLING, ROD	SA		
MIDNIGHT SUN, THE	SERLING, ROD	SA		
MR. DINGLE, THE STRONG	SERLING, ROD	SA		
ODYSSEY OF FLIGHT 33, THE	SERLING, ROD	SA		
BIG, TALL WISH, THE	SERLING, ROD	SA		
RIP VAN WINKLE CAPER, THE	SERLING, ROD	SA		
SHELTER, THE	SERLING, ROD	SA		

FROM THIS DAY FORWARD   BRUNNER, JOHN   AC H DBL 72
"FROM THIS DAY FOREWORD", AS IT WERE, A

	BRUNNER, JOHN	IN		
BIGGEST GAME, THE (AS KEITH WOODCOTT)				
	BRUNNER, JOHN	SS	SCF 56	02
TROUBLE I SEE, THE	BRUNNER, JOHN	SS	NWS 59	03
ELIXER FOR THE EMPEROR, THE	BRUNNER, JOHN	SS	FAN 64	11
WASTED ON THE YOUNG	BRUNNER, JOHN	SS	GAL 65	04
EVEN CHANCE	BRUNNER, JOHN	SS	ASF 65	11
PLANETFALL	BRUNNER, JOHN	SS	ASF 65	05
JUDAS	BRUNNER, JOHN	SS	DVS 67	01
VITANULS, THE	BRUNNER, JOHN	SS	FSF 67	07
FACTSHEET SIX	BRUNNER, JOHN	NV	GAL 68	07
FIFTH COMMANDMENT	BRUNNER, JOHN	SS	VOT 70	03
FAIRY TALE	BRUNNER, JOHN	SS	VOT 70	07
INCEPTION OF THE EPOCH OF MRS. BEDONEBYASYOUDID, THE				
	BRUNNER, JOHN	SS	QRK 71	02
OLDEST GLASS, THE	BRUNNER, JOHN	PM		72

FROM UNKNOWN WORLDS   CAMPBELL, JOHN W. JR AN   SMT 53

FOREWORD	CAMPBELL, JOHN W. JR	IN		
ENCHANTED WEEKEND, THE	MACCORMAC, JOHN	NO	UNK 39	07
NOTHING IN THE RULES	DE CAMP, L. SPRAGUE	NV	UNK 39	07
COMPLEAT WEREWOLF, THE	BOUCHER, ANTHONY	NV	UNK 42	04
REFUGEE	RICE, JANE	SS	UNK 43	10
CLOAK, THE	BLOCH, ROBERT	SS	UNK 39	05
YESTERDAY WAS MONDAY	STURGEON, THEODORE	SS	UNK 41	06
TROUBLE WITH WATER	GOLD, H. L.	SS	UNK 39	03
ANYTHING	ST. JOHN, PHILIP	SS	UNK 39	10
DEVIL WE KNOW, THE	KUTTNER, HENRY	NV	UNK 41	08
PSYCHOMORPH	GROSSER, E. A.	SS	UNK 40	02
HEXER, THE	GUERNSEY, H. W.	SS	UNK 39	06
SUMMONS, THE	EVANS, DON	SS	UNK 30	11
JESUS SHOES	BOSWORTH, ALAN R.	SS	UNK 42	04
FICTION	GRANT, ALLAN	PM	UNK 42	10
LURANI	LAVOND, PAUL DENNIS	PM	UNK 40	02
BLACK CATS	HASTINGS, CHRISTEL	PM	UNK 40	12
DAWN OF REASON, THE	BEARD, JAMES H.	PM	UNK 39	10

FRONTIERS IN SPACE   BLEILER & DIKTY   AN   BAN 55 04
    SELECTIONS FROM "THE BEST SCIENCE FICTION STORIES 1951-1953"
ODDY AND ID (THE DEVIL'S INVENTION)

	BESTER, ALFRED	SS	ASF 50	08
PROCESS	VAN VOGT, A. E.	SS	FSF 50	12
STAR DUCKS, THE	BROWN, BILL	SS	FSF 50	FL

FRONTIERS IN SPACE

TO SERVE MAN	KNIGHT, DAMON	SS	GAL 50 11
FOX AND THE FOREST, THE (TO THE FUTURE)			
	BRADBURY, RAY	SS	COL 50 05
NINE-FINGER JACK	BOUCHER, ANTHONY	SS	ESQ 51 05
DARK INTERLUDE	REYNOLDS, MACK		
	AND BROWN, FREDRIC	SS C	GAL 51 01
GENERATION OF NOAH	TENN, WILLIAM	SS	SUS 51 SP
RATS, THE	PORGES, ARTHUR	SS	MSW 51 02
ARARAT	HENDERSON, ZENNA	SS	FSF 52 10
MOON IS GREEN, THE	LEIBER, FRITZ	SS	GAL 52 05
SURVIVAL	WYNDHAM, JOHN	NV	TWS 52 02
MACHINE	JAKES, JOHN W.	SS	FSF 52 04
I AM NOTHING	RUSSELL, ERIC FRANK	SS	ASF 52 07

FRONTIERS 1: TOMORROW'S ALTERNATIVES

	ELWOOD, ROGER	OA H	MAC 73
PREFACE	ELWOOD, ROGER	IN	
TOMORROW'S ALTERNATIVES?	HERBERT, FRANK	IN	TAL 73
THOSE WONDERFUL YEARS	MALZBERG, BARRY N.	SS	TAL 73
UNIVAC: 2200	SIMAK, CLIFFORD D.	SS	TAL 73
MOMMY LOVES YA	CHARNEY, DAVID H.	SS	TAL 73
PERITONITIS	WOLFE, GENE	SS	TAL 73
SHIP-SISTER, STAR-SISTER	SILVERBERG, ROBERT	NV	TAL 73
HARRIET	GOLDIN, STEPHEN		
	AND HENSEL, C. F.	SS C	TAL 73
MUTATION PLANET	BAYLEY, BARRINGTON J	NV	TAL 73
JACOB'S BUG	POSNER, RICHARD	SS	TAL 73
GETTING AROUND	O'DONNELL, K. M.	SS	TAL 73
ANSWER, THE	CARR, TERRY	SS	TAL 73
IN OUTRAGED STONE	LAFFERTY, R. A.	SS	TAL 73
MORNING RUSH OR HAPPY BIRTHDAY, DEAR LEAH, THE			
	SAYE, LEE	SS	TAL 73

FRONTIERS 2: THE NEW MIND   ELWOOD, ROGER   OA H   MAC 73

PREFACE	ELWOOD, ROGER	IN	
INTRODUCTION	POHL, FREDERIK	IN	
MAGIC CHILD, THE	GRANT, C. L.	SS	NMD 73
VACATION	POSNER, RICHARD	NV	NMD 73
FOUR SIDES OF INFINITY	LAFFERTY, R. A.	GR	
UNGODLY MICE OF DOCTOR DRAKOS, THE			
	LAFFERTY, R. A.	SS	NMD 73
TWO-HEADED LION OF CRIS BENEDETTI, THE			
	LAFFERTY, R. A.	SS	NMD 73
HELLACEOUS ROCKET OF HARRY O'DONOVAN, THE			
	LAFFERTY, R. A.	SS	NMD 73
WOLLY WORLD OF BARNABY SHEEN, THE			
	LAFFERTY, R. A.	SS	NMD 73
FROM ALL OF US	BAUER, GERALD M.	SS	NMD 73
NEW NEW YORK NEW ORLEANS	EFFINGER, GEO. ALEC	SS	NMD 73
I AM ALEPPO	SOHL, JERRY	NV	NMD 73
OPENING FIRE	MALZBERG, BARRY N.	SS	NMD 73
SPACE TO MOVE	GREEN, JOSEPH	SS	NMD 73
BRAIN WIPE	MACLEAN, KATHERINE	SS	NMD 73

FROZEN PLANET AND 4 OTHER SF NOVELLAS, THE

	ANONYMOUS	AN	MBB 66
FROZEN PLANET, THE (ALSO AS COURIER)			
	LAUMER, KEITH	NV	IFS 61 09
GROWING SEASON	WALLACE, F. L.	NV	IFS 59 07
CINDERELLA STORY	LANG, ALLEN KIM	SN	IFS 61 05
QUALITY OF MERCY, THE	KEYES, DANIEL	NV	IFS 60 11
GLEANERS	SIMAK, CLIFFORD D.	SN	IFS 60 03

FULLY AUTOMATED LOVE LIFE OF HENRY KEANRIDGE

	PLAYBOY, EDITORS OF	AN	PBP 71
PREFACE	PLAYBOY, EDITORS OF	IN	
FULLY AUTOMATED LOVE LIFE OF HENRY KEANRIDGE, THE			
	DRYER, STAN	NV	PBY 68 07
SPACE OPERA	RUSSELL, RAY	SS	PBY 61 12
TROUBLE WITH MACHINES, THE	GOULART, RON	SS	PBY 68 08
KILLER IN THE TV SET, THE	FRIEDMAN, BRUCE JAY	SS	PBY 61 08
PUNCH	POHL, FREDERIK	SS	PBY 62 06
PROFESSOR HYDE	BERGER, THOMAS	SS	PBY 61 12
CHIMERAS, THE	KOESTLER, ARTHUR	SS	PBY 69 05
NUMBER EIGHT	MCGIVERN, PATRICK	SS	PBY 70 06
MR. SWIFT AND HIS REMARKABLE THING			
	MCMAHON, JEREMIAH	SS	PBY
MIRACLE OF RARE DEVICE, A	BRADBURY, RAY	SS	PBY 62 01
FOOT IN THE DOOR, A	FRIEDMAN, BRUCE JAY	SS	PBY 60 10
MAN'S HOME IS HIS CASTLE, A (ALSO AS LOFTHOUSE)			
	GOULART, RON	SS	PBY 69 03
PUT THEM ALL TOGETHER, THEY SPELL MONSTER			
	RUSSELL, RAY	SS	PBY 56 10

FUN WITH YOUR NEW HEAD   DISCH, THOMAS M.   AC H   DBL 71

IN ENGLAND AS "UNDER COMPULSION"			
ROACHES, THE	DISCH, THOMAS M.	SS	ESC 65 10
COME TO VENUS MELANCHOLY	DISCH, THOMAS M.	SS	FSF 65 11
LINDA AND DANIEL AND SPIKE	DISCH, THOMAS M.	SS	NWS 67 12
FLIGHT USELESS, INEXORABLE THE PURSUIT			
	DISCH, THOMAS M.	SS	
DESCENDING	DISCH, THOMAS M.	SS	FAN 64 07
NADA	DISCH, THOMAS M.	SS	FSF 64 08
NOW IS FOREVER	DISCH, THOMAS M.	SS	AMZ 64 03
CONTEST, THE	DISCH, THOMAS M.	SS	NWS 67 03
EMPTY ROOM, THE	DISCH, THOMAS M.	SS	NWS 67 03
SQUIRREL CAGE, THE	DISCH, THOMAS M.	SS	NWS 66 10
NUMBER YOU HAVE REACHED, THE	DISCH, THOMAS M.	SS	IMP 67 02
1-A	DISCH, THOMAS M.	SS	NWS 68 04
FUN WITH YOUR NEW HEAD (CEPHALOTRON)			
	DISCH, THOMAS M.	SS	PBY 66 12
CITY OF PENETRATING LIGHT, THE			
	DISCH, THOMAS M.	SS	
MOONDUST, THE SMELL OF HAY, AND DIALECTICAL MATERIALISM			
	DISCH, THOMAS M.	SS	FSF 67 08

FUTURE MAKERS, THE

THESIS ON SOCIAL FORMS AND SOCIAL CONTROLS IN THE U.S.A.

	DISCH, THOMAS M.	SS	FAN 64 01
CASABLANCA	DISCH, THOMAS M.	NV	67

FURIOUS FUTURE, THE   BUDRYS, ALGIS   AC H   GOL 64
SEE "BUDRYS' INFERNO"

FUTURE CITY   ELWOOD, ROGER   OA H   TRI 73

PREFACE	ELWOOD, ROGER	IN	
FOREWORD	SIMAK, CLIFFORD D.	IN	
IN PRAISE OF NEW YORK	DISCH, THOMAS M.	PM	FUC 73
SIGHTSEERS, THE	BOVA, BEN	SS	FUC 73
MEANWHILE, WE ELIMINATE	OFFUTT, ANDREW J.	SS	FUC 73
THINE ALABASTER CITIES GLEAM	JANIFER, LAURENCE M.	SS	FUC 73
CULTURE LOCK	MALZBERG, BARRY N.	SS	FUC 73
WORLD AS WILL AND WALLPAPER, THE			
	LAFFERTY, R. A.	SS	FUC 73
VIOLATION (ALSO AS LAWBREAKER)			
	NOLAN, WILLIAM F.	SS	FUC 73
CITY LIGHTS, CITY NIGHTS	O'DONNELL, K. M.	SS	FUC 73
UNDERCITY, THE	KOONTZ, DEAN R.	SS	FUC 73
APARTMENT HUNTING	BILKER, HARVEY L.		
	AND BILKER, AUDREY L.	SS C	FUC 73
AS A DROP	PRICE, D. M.	PM	FUC 73
ABENDLANDES	KIDD, VIRGINIA	PM	FUC 73
WEARIEST RIVER, THE	SCORTIA, THOMAS N.	NV	FUC 73
DEATH OF A CITY	HERBERT, FRANK	SS	FUC 73
ASSASSINS OF AIR	ZEBROWSKI, GEORGE	SS	FUC 73
GETTING ACROSS	SILVERBERG, ROBERT	NV	FUC 73
IN DARK PLACES	HENSLEY, JOE L.	SS	FUC 73
REVOLUTION	SCHAEFFER, ROBIN	SS	FUC 73
CHICAGO	MONTELEONE, THOMAS F	SS	FUC 73
MOST PRIMATIVE, THE	RUSSELL, RAY	SS	FUC 73
HINDSIGHT: 480 SECONDS	ELLISON, HARLAN	SS	FUC 73
5,000,000 A.D.	DEFORD, MIRIAM ALLEN	SS	FUC 73
AFTERWORD	POHL, FREDERIK	MS	FUC 73

FUTURE CORRUPTION   ELWOOD, ROGER   OA   WPB 75 01

EDITOR'S PREFACE	ELWOOD, ROGER	IN	
SALTZMAN'S MADNESS	LUPOFF, RICHARD A.	NV	FCR 75
ANDREW	GLOECKNER, CAROLYN	SS	FCR 75
PRELUDE TO A SYMPHONY OF UNBORN SHOUTS			
	GOLDIN, STEPHEN	SS	FCR 75
HEART GROW FONDER	LAFFERTY, R. A.	NV	FCR 75
AURELIA	RUSS, J. J.	SS	FCR 75
ON THE CAMPAIGN TRAIL	MALZBERG, BARRY N.	SS	FCR 75
PAXTON'S WORLD	PRONZINI, BILL	SS	FCR 75
FEAST	ELWOOD, ROGER	SS	FCR 75
STREAKING	O'DONNELL, K. M.	SS	FCR 75
LAST CONGREGATION, THE	GOLDSMITH, HOWARD	SS	FCR 75
BEFORE A LIVE AUDIENCE	SOHL, JERRY	SS	FCR 75
STORM, THE	DOZOIS, GARDNER R.	NV	FCR 75

FUTURE IMPERFECT   GUNN, JAMES E.   AC   BAN 64 01

MISOGYNIST, THE	GUNN, JAMES E.	SS	GAL 52 11
LAST WORD, THE	GUNN, JAMES E.	SS	NEW 64 AC
LITTLE ORPHAN ANDROID	GUNN, JAMES E.	NV	GAL 55 09
STILLED PATTER, THE	GUNN, JAMES E.	SS	INF 56 06
SKIN GAME	GUNN, JAMES E.	SS	VSF 58 01
EVERY DAY IS CHRISTMAS	GUNN, JAMES E.	NV	SUP 57 02
GIRLS WHO WERE REALLY BUILT, THE (NEOSHO'S CHOICEST)			
	GUNN, JAMES E.	SS	FAN 58 06
SURVIVAL POLICY (AS EDWIN JAMES)			
	GUNN, JAMES E.	NV	ASF 52 10
TSYLANA	GUNN, JAMES E.	NV	GAL 56 03
FEEDING TIME	GUNN, JAMES E.	SS	ASF 55 08

FUTURE IS NOW, THE   NOLAN, WILLIAM F.   OA H   SHB 70

INTRODUCTION	NOLAN, WILLIAM F.	IN	
OGRESS, THE	YOUNG, ROBERT F.	SS	FIN 70
JENNY AMONG THE ZEEBS	ANMAR, FRANK	SS	FIN 70
EARTHCOMING	MEREDITH, RICHARD C.	NV	FIN 70
BELLES LETTRES, 2272	CORWIN, NORMAN	SS	FIN 70
SHAPE IN TIME, A	BOUCHER, ANTHONY	SS	FIN 70
DAMECHILD	ETCHISON, DENNIS	SS	FIN 70
TOE TO TIP, TIP TO TOE, PIP-POP AS YOU GO			
	NOLAN, WILLIAM F.	SS	FIN 70
WAR OF PASSION, A	PURDOM, TOM	SS	FIN 70
HATE IS A SANDPAPER ICE CUBE WITH POLKA DOTS OF LOVE ON IT			
	DIXON, TERRY	SS	FIN 70
WALTER PERKINS IS HERE!	BANKS, RAYMOND E.	SS	FIN 70
DARWIN SAMPLER, THE	RUSSELL, RAY	SS	FIN 70
WHOLE ROUND WORLD, THE	GOULART, RON	NV	FIN 70

FUTURE KIN   ELWOOD, ROGER   OA H   DBL 74

INTRODUCTION	ELWOOD, ROGER	IN	
PACER	JONES, RAYMOND F.	NV	
GIFT, THE	OLIVER, CHAD	NV	
GENERATION GAP	REYNOLDS, MACK	NV	
WAITING WORLD, THE	GREEN, JOSEPH	SS	
KNIFE AND THE SHEATH, THE	ANVIL, CHRISTOPHER	SS	
REJOICE, REJOICE, WE HAVE NO CHOICE			
	CARR, TERRY	SS	
OVER THE LINE	MALZBERG, BARRY N.	SS	74
BLOOD BROTHER	SCORTIA, THOMAS N.	SS	

FUTURE MAKERS, THE   HAINING, PETER   AN   BEL 71 05

ALSO IN "SCIENCE FICTION SPECIAL 5"			
INTRODUCTION	HAINING, PETER	IN	
FOURTH-DIMENSIONAL DEMONSTRATOR, THE			
	LEINSTER, MURRAY	SS	ASF 35 12
WEAPON TOO DREADFUL TO USE, THE			
	ASIMOV, ISAAC	SS	AMZ 39 05
ABREACTION	STURGEON, THEODORE	SS	WRT 48 07
PIPER, THE	BRADBURY, RAY	SS	TWS 43 02
COLUMBUS WAS A DOPE	HEINLEIN, ROBERT A.	SS	STS 47 05

```
CASTAWAY                        CLARKE, ARTHUR C.    SS  FSB 47 04
HOUR OF BATTLE, THE             SHECKLEY, ROBERT     SS  SSF 53 09
EQUATOR                         ALDISS, BRIAN W.     NA  NWS 58 09

FUTURE NOW, THE                 HOSKINS, ROBERT      AN  FCR 77 06
INTRODUCTION                    HOSKINS, ROBERT      IN
STALIN IN THE SOUL, THE         LE GUIN, URSULA K.   AR      73
ALL THE TROUBLES OF THE WORLD
                                ASIMOV, ISAAC        SS  SUP 58 04
HOME (THE DISINHERITED)         ANDERSON, POUL       SS  ORB 66 01
SILENT IN GEHENNA               ELLISON, HARLAN      SS  MWS 71
SHARK                           BRYANT, EDWARD       NV  ORB 73 12
FLOWERING SEASON (KANGAROO COURT)
                                KIDD, VIRGINIA       NV  ORB 66 01
SEASON FOR FREEDOM, A (KILLERBOT!)
                                KOONTZ, DEAN R.      SS  GAL 69 05
FINAL WAR                       MALZBERG, BARRY N.   NV  FSF 68 04
MOUNTAIN, THE                   HOSKINS, ROBERT      SS      75
OUR TIMES                       PRONZINI, BILL       SS  SWK 72 04
WIND AND THE RAIN, THE          SILVERBERG, ROBERT   SS  SVW 73
MERCHANTS OF VENUS, THE         POHL, FREDERIK       NA  IPS 72 08

FUTURE PASTIMES                 EDELSTEIN, SCOTT     OA H AUR 77
TIME ON OUR HANDS: AN INTRODUCTION
                                EDELSTEIN, SCOTT     IN
UNEVEN EVENING, AN              HERBST, STEVE        SS  CLR 71 01
WE ALL HAVE TO GO               LYNN, ELIZABETH A.   SS
NATIONAL PASTIME, THE           SPINRAD, NORMAN      NV  NOV 73 03
AGENT, THE                      HILL, RICHARD        SS
HOTSY-TOTSY MACHINE, THE        WYAL, PG             SS
TARFU'S LAST SHOW               BOSTON, BRUCE        SS
HALCYON IN A MIRROR AT MIDNIGHT
                                BRADFIELD, SCOTT     SS
SUMMER OF THE IRISH SEA, THE    GRANT, C. L.         SS  ORB 72 11
NEWSOCRATS: CONFESSIONS OF A EUNICH DREAMER, THE
                                WYAL, PG             SS
CANIS FAMILIARIS                WALLACE, ROBIN E.
                                AND BRONSON, DONNA   SS C
WEEKEND IN A WAR ZONE           MARTIN, GEORGE R. R. SS
EPIC                            ROTSLER, WILLIAM     NV
LADY WAS FOR KROINKING, THE     BUNCH, DAVID R.      SS  GEN 72
HIGH BANK                       CLINGAN, C. C.       SS
POET IN THE HOLOGRAM IN THE MIDDLE OF PRIME TIME, THE
                                BRYANT, EDWARD       SS  NOV 72 02
HEAVY METAL                     BISCHOFF, DAVE       SS
FUTURE SPORTSMAN'S MANUAL, THE
                                ACKERSON, DUANE      SS
AT THE ACCIDENT                 WISE, DAVID          SS
NIGHT AT THE FAIR, A            RAMSAY, KATHRYN      SS
FRAGMENTARY BLUE                DANN, JACK M.        NV  FAN 75 04
GETTING OFF                     CROSS, RONALD A.     SS
MASK OF NIGHT ON HIS FACE, THE
                                LEIGH, STEPHEN       SS
WHEN WE WENT TO SEE THE END OF THE WORLD
                                SILVERBERG, ROBERT   SS  UNI 72 02
SERVO                           DEMMON, CALVIN       SS
USEFUL PHRASES FOR THE TOURIST
                                RUSS, JOANNA         SS  UNI 72 02
DIRTY WAR, THE                  BUNCH, DAVID R.      SS
SKYGHOSTS AND DUSK-DEVILS       BRENNERT, ALAN       SS
WAYGIFT                         PAGE, GERALD W.      SS

FUTURE PERFECT                  FRANKLIN, H. BRUCE   AN H OXF 66
INTRODUCTION                    FRANKLIN, H. BRUCE   IN
BIRTHMARK, THE (1843)           HAWTHORNE, NATHANIEL SS  PIO 43 03
ARTIST OF THE BEAUTIFUL, THE (1844)
                                HAWTHORNE, NATHANIEL NV  DMR 44 06
RAPPACCINI'S DAUGHTER (1844)    HAWTHORNE, NATHANIEL NV  DMR 44 12
TALE OF THE RAGGED MOUNTAINS, A
                                POE, EDGAR ALLEN     SS  GDY 44 04
FACTS IN THE CASE OF M. VALDEMAR
                                POE, EDGAR ALLEN     SS  AWR 45 12
MELLONTA TAUTA                  POE, EDGAR ALLEN     SS  GDY 49 02
BELL-TOWER, THE (1855)          MELVILLE, HERMAN     SS  PTM 55
DR. MATERIALISMUS               STIMSON, FREDERIC J. SS  SCR 90 08
ATOMS OF CHLADNI, THE (1859)    WHELPLEY, J. D.      SS  HRP 59
WAS HE DEAD? (1870)             MITCHELL, SILAS W.   NV  ATL 70 01
MONARCH OF DREAMS, THE (1886)
                                HIGGINSON, THOMAS W. SS      86
PSYCHOLOGICAL SHIPWRECK, A (1893)
                                BIERCE, AMBROSE      SS      93
TO WHOM THIS MAY COME (1888)    BELLAMY, EDWARD      SS  HRP 88
BLINDMAN'S WORLD, THE (1886)    BELLAMY, EDWARD      SS  ATL 86
DIAMOND LENS, THE (1858)        O'BRIEN, FITZ-JAMES  NV  ATL 58 01
FOUR-DIMENSIONAL SPACE (1885)
                                ANONYMOUS            AR  NTR 85
MYSTERIOUS DISAPPEARANCES (1893)
                                BIERCE, AMBROSE      AR      93
FROM "FOUR-DIMENSIONAL SPACE" (1896)
                                BOSTWICK, ARTHUR E.  AR  NSR 96
CHRISTMAS 200,000 B.C. (1887)
                                WATERLOO, STANLEY    SS      87
FROM THE "LONDON TIMES" OF 1904
                                TWAIN, MARK          SS  CNY 98 11
IN THE YEAR TEN THOUSAND (1892)
                                HARBEN, WILLIAM      SS  ARN 92

FUTURE POWER                    DANN & DOZOIS        OA H RDM 76
INTRODUCTION                    DANN, JACK M.
                                AND DOZOIS, GARDNER R. IN C
DIARY OF THE ROSE, THE          LE GUIN, URSULA K.   NV      76
COUNTRY OF THE KIND, THE        KNIGHT, DAMON        SS  FSF 56 02
SHOE AND THE IMPLICIT CLAY      LAFFERTY, R. A.      NV      76
SHE WAITS FOR ALL MEN BORN      TIPTREE, JAMES JR.   SS      76
DAY OF THE BIG TEST, THE        GOTSCHALK, FELIX C.  NV      76
```

```
CONTENTMENT, SATISFACTION, CHEER, WELL-BEING, GLADNESS, JOY,
  COMFORT, AND NOT HAVING...  EFFINGER, GEO. ALEC  NV      76
COMING-OF-AGE DAY               JORGENSSON, A. K.    SS  SCF 65 09
THANATOS                        MCINTYRE, VONDA N.   SS      76
EYEFLASH MIRACLES, THE          WOLFE, GENE          NA      76

FUTURE QUEST                    ELWOOD, ROGER        OA  AVN 73 09
DULL DRUMS                      MCCAFFREY, ANNE      NV  FUQ 73
SECOND NATURE                   OLIVER, CHAD         NV  FUQ 73
TAPPING OUT                     MALZBERG, BARRY N.   SS  FUQ 73
HOW TO BE ETHNIC IN ONE EASY LESSON
                                ANDERSON, POUL       NV  FUQ 73
WEEP NO MORE, OLD LADY          GRANT, C. L.         SS  FUQ 73
CITY'S END                      REYNOLDS, MACK       NV  FUQ 73
MOONCHILD                       PURDOM, TOM          NV  FUQ 73
PET                             JONES, RAYMOND F.    NV  FUQ 73

FUTURE TENSE                    CURTIS, RICHARD      AN  DEL 68 09
ON PREDICTION                   ASIMOV, ISAAC        IN      68
LAND IRONCLADS, THE             WELLS, H. G.         NV  SND 03 12
NEW YORK A.D. 2660 (RALPH 124C 41+)
                                GERNSBACK, HUGO      EX  MEL 11 04
BILLENIUM                       BALLARD, J. G.       SS  NWS 61 11
LYSENKO MAZE, THE               GRINNELL, DAVID      SS  FSF 54 07
QRM-INTERPLANETARY              SMITH, GEORGE O.     NV  ASF 42 10
WITH THESE HANDS                KORNBLUTH, C. M.     NV  GAL 51 12
POLITICS                        LEINSTER, MURRAY     NV  AMZ 32 06
DAY REMBRANDT WENT PUBLIC, THE
                                AUERBACH, ARNOLD M.  SS  HRP 62 07
SOLUTION UNSATISFACTORY         HEINLEIN, ROBERT A.  NV  ASF 41 05
SECURITY CHECK                  CLARKE, ARTHUR C.    SS  FSF 57 06

FUTURE TENSE                    VANCE, JACK          AC  BAL 64 06
DODKIN'S JOB                    VANCE, JACK          NV  ASF 59 10
ULLWARD'S RETREAT               VANCE, JACK          NV  GAL 58 12
SAIL 25 (GATEWAY TO STRANGENESS)
                                VANCE, JACK          NV  AMZ 62 08
GIFT OF GAB, THE                VANCE, JACK          NV  ASF 55 09

FUTURE TENSE                    CROSSEN, KENDELL F.  AN H GBG 52 03
TOMORROW IS HERE TO STAY        CROSSEN, KENDELL F.  IN
PLAGAIRIST                      PHILLIPS, PETER      NV  NWS 50 SU
AMBASSADORS, THE                BOUCHER, ANTHONY     SS  STS 52 06
DREAM'S END                     KUTTNER, HENRY       SS  STS 47 07
WE THE PEOPLE                   MOORE, WARD          SS  SFQ 52 05
THROWBACK                       DEFORD, MIRIAM ALLEN SS  STS 52 10
THINGS OF DISTINCTION           CROSSEN, KENDELL F.  NV  STS 52 03
SCARLET DREAM                   MOORE, C. L.         NV  WRT 34 05
CYCLOPS                         HEARD, H. F.         SS  NEW 52 AN
BATTLE OF THE S...S, THE        ELLIOTT, BRUCE       SS  NEW 52 AN
ISLAND OF THE FIVE COLORS, THE
                                GARDNER, MARTIN      SS  NEW 52 AN
BABY KILLERS                    ELLIOTT, ROSE B.     SS  NEW 52 AN
BEANSTALK                       BLISH, JAMES         NA  NEW 52 AN
INCUBATION                      MACDONALD, JOHN D.   SS  NEW 52 AN
LOVE STORY                      MONIG, CHRISTOPHER   SS  NEW 52 AN

FUTURE TENSE (BRITISH)          CROSSEN, KENDELL F.  AN H BDL 54
TOMORROW IS HERE TO STAY        CROSSEN, KENDELL F.  IN
PLAGAIRIST                      PHILLIPS, PETER      NV  NWS 50 SU
AMBASSADORS, THE                BOUCHER, ANTHONY     SS  STS 52 06
DREAM'S END                     KUTTNER, HENRY       SS  STS 47 07
THROWBACK                       DEFORD, MIRIAM ALLEN SS  STS 52 10
THINGS OF DISTINCTION           CROSSEN, KENDELL F.  NV  STS 52 03
BEANSTALK                       BLISH, JAMES         NA  NEW 52 AN
INCUBATION                      MACDONALD, JOHN D.   SS  NEW 52 AN

FUTURE WITHOUT FUTURE           STERNBERG, JACQUES   OC H SEA 73
FIN DE SIECLE                   STERNBERG, JACQUES   NO
VERY SINCERELY YOURS            STERNBERG, JACQUES   SS
EPHEMERA, THE                   STERNBERG, JACQUES   SS
VACATION                        STERNBERG, JACQUES   SS
FUTURE WITHOUT FUTURE           STERNBERG, JACQUES   SS

FUTURELOVE                      ELWOOD, ROGER        OA H BML 77
INTRODUCTION                    DICKSON, GORDON R.   IN
GREATEST LOVE, THE              MCCAFFREY, ANNE      NA
PSI CLONE                       HOLLY, J. HUNTER     NA
LOVE ROGO                       CARVER, JEFFREY A.   NA

FUTURES TO INFINITY             MOSKOWITZ, SAM       AN  PYR 70 09
PROBABLE MAN, THE               BESTER, ALFRED       NV  ASF 41 07
RIM OF THE DEEP                 SIMAK, CLIFFORD D.   NV  ASF 40 05
HEIL!                           HEINLEIN, ROBERT A.  SS  FUF 40 04
INCORRIGIBLE, THE               DE CAMP, L. SPRAGUE  SS  ASF 39 01
BEAUTY AND THE BEAST            KUTTNER, HENRY       SS  TWS 40 04
DANGEROUS DIMENSION, THE        HUBBARD, L. RON      SS  ASF 38 07
GREEN FOREST, THE               VAN VOGT, A. E.      NV  ASF 49 06
SECRET SENSE, THE               ASIMOV, ISAAC        SS  COS 41 03
PIPER, THE                      BRADBURY, RAY        SS  TWS 43 02
WAY BACK, THE                   MOSKOWITZ, SAM       NV  CMT 41 01

FUTURES UNLIMITED               NORTON, ALDEN H.     AN  PYR 69 06
THREE LINES OF OLD FRENCH       MERRITT, A.          SS  ASW 19 08
CALLISTAN MENACE, THE           ASIMOV, ISAAC        SS  AST 40 04
HASHISH MAN, THE                DUNSANY, LORD        SS  FFM 45 12
WEIGHER OF SOULS, THE           MAUROIS, ANDRE       NV  FFM 50 10
HORROR OF THE HEIGHTS, THE      DOYLE, ARTHUR CONAN  SS  EVB 13 11
INTO THE DARKNESS               ROCKLYNNE, ROSS      NV  AST 40 06
IT HAPPENED TOMORROW            BLOCH, ROBERT        NV  SSS 51 06
EXILE OF THE EONS               CLARKE, ARTHUR C.    SS  SSS 50 03
REBELLION                       CAMPBELL, JOHN W. JR NV  ASF 35 08

GALACTIC CLUSTER                BLISH, JAMES         AC  SIG 59
TOMB TAPPER                     BLISH, JAMES         SS  ASF 56 07
KING OF THE HILL                BLISH, JAMES         SS  INF 55 11
```

GALACTIC CLUSTER

COMMON TIME	BLISH, JAMES	SS	SFQ 53 08
WORK OF ART, A (ART-WORK)	BLISH, JAMES	SS	SFS 56 07
TO PAY THE PIPER	BLISH, JAMES	SS	IFS 56 02
NOR IRON BARS (INCLUDES "DETOUR TO THE STARS" INF 56 12)			
	BLISH, JAMES	SS	INF 57 11
BEEP	BLISH, JAMES	NV	GAL 54 02
THIS EARTH OF HOURS	BLISH, JAMES	SS	FSF 59 06

GALACTIC CLUSTER (BRITISH PB)

	BLISH, JAMES	AC	FPS 63
COMMON TIME	BLISH, JAMES	SS	SFQ 53 08
WORK OF ART, A (ART-WORK)	BLISH, JAMES	SS	SFS 56 07
TO PAY THE PIPER	BLISH, JAMES	SS	IFS 56 02
NOR IRON BARS (INCLUDES "DETOUR TO THE STARS" INF 56 12)			
	BLISH, JAMES	SS	INF 57 11
BEEP	BLISH, JAMES	NV	GAL 54 02

GALACTIC CLUSTER (BRITISH)   BLISH, JAMES   AC H FAB 60

COMMON TIME	BLISH, JAMES	SS	SFQ 53 08
WORK OF ART, A (ART-WORK)	BLISH, JAMES	SS	SFS 56 07
TO PAY THE PIPER	BLISH, JAMES	SS	IFS 56 02
BEEP	BLISH, JAMES	NV	GAL 54 02
THIS EARTH OF HOURS	BLISH, JAMES	SS	FSF 59 06
BEANSTALK	BLISH, JAMES	NA	NEW 52 AN

GALACTIC DIPLOMAT   LAUMER, KEITH   AC H DBL 65

ULTIMATUM (MIGHTIEST QORN)	LAUMER, KEITH	NV	IFS 63 07
SALINE SOLUTION	LAUMER, KEITH	NV	IFS 63 03
BRASS GOD, THE (RETIEF, GOD SPEAKER)			
	LAUMER, KEITH	NV	IFS 65 01
CASTLE OF LIGHT, THE	LAUMER, KEITH	NV	IFS 64 10
WICKER WONDERLAND (THE CITY THAT GREW IN THE SEA)			
	LAUMER, KEITH	NV	IFS 64 03
NATIVE INTELLIGENCE (THE GOVERNOR OF GLAVE)			
	LAUMER, KEITH	NV	IFS 63 11
PRINCE AND THE PIRATE, THE	LAUMER, KEITH	NV	IFS 64 08
COURIER (THE FROZEN PLANET)	LAUMER, KEITH	NV	IFS 61 09
PROTEST NOTE (THE DESERT AND THE STARS)			
	LAUMER, KEITH	NV	IFS 62 11

GALACTIC EMPIRES VOLUME ONE ALDISS, BRIAN W.   AN H WEI 76
AN ANTHOLOGY OF WAY-BACK-WHEN FUTURES

INTRODUCTION	ALDISS, BRIAN W.	IN	
BEEN A LONG, LONG TIME	LAFFERTY, R. A.	SS	FAN 70 12
POSSESSED, THE	CLARKE, ARTHUR C.	SS	DSF 53 03
PROTECTED SPECIES	FYFE, H. B.	SS	ASF 51 03
ALL THE WAY BACK	SHAARA, MICHAEL	SS	ASF 52 07
STAR PLUNDERER, THE	ANDERSON, POUL	NV	PLS 52 09
FOUNDATION	ASIMOV, ISAAC	NV	ASF 42 05
WE'RE CIVILIZED (ALSO AS CIVILIZED)			
	CLIFTON, MARK		
	AND APOSTOLIDES, ALEX	SS C GAL 53 08
CRIME AND THE GLORY OF COMMANDER SUZDAL, THE			
	SMITH, CORDWAINER	SS	AMZ 64 05
REBEL OF VALKYR, THE	COPPEL, ALFRED	NV	PLS 50 FL
BRIGHTNESS FALLS FROM THE AIR (CONTEST STORY)			
	SEABRIGHT, IDRIS	SS	FSF 51 04
IMMIGRANT	SIMAK, CLIFFORD D.	SN	ASF 54 03
RESIDENT PHYSICIAN	WHITE, JAMES	NV	NWS 61 09
AGE OF RETIREMENT	LYNCH, MAL	SS	ASF 54 04
PLANTING TIME	ADAMS, PETE		
	AND NIGHTINGALE, CHARLES SS C NEW 76 AN

GALACTIC EMPIRES VOLUME TWO ALDISS, BRIAN W.   AN H WEI 76
AN ANTHOLOGY OF WAY-BACK-WHEN FUTURES

INTRODUCTION	ALDISS, BRIAN W.	IN	
ESCAPE TO CHAOS	MACDONALD, JOHN D.	NA	SSS 51 06
CONCEALMENT	VAN VOGT, A. E.	SS	ASF 43 09
TO CIVILIZE	BUDRYS, ALGIS	SS	FUT 54 01
BEEP	BLISH, JAMES	NV	GAL 54 02
DOWN THE RIVER	REYNOLDS, MACK	SS	STS 50 09
BOUNTY HUNTER, THE	DAVIDSON, AVRAM	SS	FUN 58 03
NOT YET THE END	BROWN, FREDRIC	SS	CFU 41 WI
TONIGHT THE STARS REVOLT!	FOX, GARDNER F.	NA	PLS 52 03
FINAL ENCOUNTER	HARRISON, HARRY	NV	GAL 64 04
LORD OF A THOUSAND SUNS	ANDERSON, POUL	NV	PLS 51 09
BIG ANCESTOR	WALLACE, F. L.	NV	GAL 54 11
INTERLOPERS, THE	DEE, ROGER	SS	ASF 54 09
EPILOGUE	ALDISS, BRIAN W.	MS	

GALAXIES LIKE GRAINS OF SAND ALDISS, BRIAN W.   AC   SIG 60 07

OUT OF REACH	ALDISS, BRIAN W.	SS	AUT 57 08
ALL THE WORLD'S TEARS	ALDISS, BRIAN W.	SS	NEB 57 05
WHO CAN REPLACE A MAN? (BUT WHO CAN REPLACE A MAN)			
	ALDISS, BRIAN W.	SS	INF 58 06
O ISHRAEL!	ALDISS, BRIAN W.	SS	NWS 57 04
INCENTIVE	ALDISS, BRIAN W.	SS	NWS 58 12
GENE-HIVE (JOURNEY TO THE INTERIOR)			
	ALDISS, BRIAN W.	NV	NEB 58 05
SECRET OF A MIGHTY CITY (HAVE YOUR HATREDS READY)			
	ALDISS, BRIAN W.	SS	FSF 58 05
VISITING AMOEBA (WHAT TRIUMPHS?)			
	ALDISS, BRIAN W.	NV	AUT 57 07

GALAXY OF GHOULS   MERRIL, JUDITH   AN   LIO 55 05
ALSO AS "OFF THE BEATEN ORBIT"

WOLVES DON'T CRY	ELLIOTT, BRUCE	SS	FSF 54 04
AMBASSADORS, THE	BOUCHER, ANTHONY	SS	STS 52 06
SHARE ALIKE	BIXBY, JEROME		
	AND DEAN, JOE E.	SS C BEY 53 07
BLOOD	BROWN, FREDRIC	SS	FSF 55 02
WAY OF THINKING, A	STURGEON, THEODORE	NV	AMZ 53 11
CHILD'S PLAY	TENN, WILLIAM	NV	ASF 47 03
O UGLY BIRD!	WELLMAN, MANLY WADE	SS	FSF 51 12
WHEELBARROW BOY, THE	PARKER, RICHARD	SS	FSF 53 03
FISH STORY	CHARTERIS, LESLIE	SS	BBM 53 11

DESERTION	SIMAK, CLIFFORD D.	SS	ASF 44 11
TRIFLIN' MAN (ALSO AS YOU TRIFLIN' SKUNK!)			
	MILLER, WALTER M. JR	SS	FUN 55 01
NIGHT HE CRIED, THE	LEIBER, FRITZ	SS	STR 53 01
DEMON KING, THE	PRIESTLEY, J. B.	SS	34
PROOF OF THE PUDDING	SHECKLEY, ROBERT	SS	GAL 52 08
HOMECOMING, THE	BRADBURY, RAY	SS	MAD 46 10
MOP-UP	PORGES, ARTHUR	SS	FSF 53 07

GALAXY OF STRANGERS, A   BIGGLE, LLOYD JR.   AC H DBL 76

INTRODUCTION	BIGGLE, LLOYD JR.	IN	
AND MADLY TEACH	BIGGLE, LLOYD JR.	NV	FSF 66 05
DOUBLE-EDGED ROPE, THE	BIGGLE, LLOYD JR.	SS	ASF 67 06
EYE FOR AN EYE	BIGGLE, LLOYD JR.	NV	
FIRST LOVE	BIGGLE, LLOYD JR.	SS	AMZ 59 09
WHO'S ON FIRST?	BIGGLE, LLOYD JR.	NV	IFS 58 08
ROUND TRIP TO ESIDARAP (ESIDARAP OT PIRT DNUOR)			
	BIGGLE, LLOYD JR.	SS	IFS 60 11
NO BIZ LIKE SHOW BIZ	BIGGLE, LLOYD JR.	SS	ASF 74 05
WHAT HATH GOD WROUGHT!	BIGGLE, LLOYD JR.	NV	STG 74

GALAXY READER OF SCIENCE FICTION   GOLD, H. L.   AN H CRN 52

HONEYMOON IN HELL	BROWN, FREDRIC	NV	GAL 50 11
COMING ATTRACTION	LEIBER, FRITZ	SS	GAL 50 11
RULE OF THREE	STURGEON, THEODORE	NV	GAL 51 01
THIRD FROM THE SUN	MATHESON, RICHARD	SS	GAL 50 10
LAST MARTIAN, THE	BROWN, FREDRIC	SS	GAL 50 10
JAYWALKER	ROCKLYNNE, ROSS	SS	GAL 50 12
RELUCTANT HEROES, THE	ROBINSON, FRANK M.	NV	GAL 51 01
LITTLE JOURNEY, A	BRADBURY, RAY	SS	GAL 51 08
VENUS IS A MAN'S WORLD	TENN, WILLIAM	NV	GAL 51 07
BEYOND BEDLAM	GUIN, WYMAN	NA	GAL 51 08
STARS ARE THE STYX, THE	STURGEON, THEODORE	NV	GAL 50 10
INSIDE EARTH	ANDERSON, POUL	NV	GAL 51 04
I, THE UNSPEAKABLE	SHELDON, WALT	NV	GAL 51 04
PILOT AND THE BUSHMAN, THE	JACOBS, SYLVIA	NV	GAL 51 08
JUDAS RAM	MERWIN, SAM JR.	SS	GAL 50 12
HOSTESS	ASIMOV, ISAAC	NV	GAL 51 05
BETELGEUSE BRIDGE	TENN, WILLIAM	SS	GAL 51 04
CABIN BOY	KNIGHT, DAMON	SS	GAL 51 09
FIELD STUDY	PHILLIPS, PETER	SS	GAL 51 04
GOOD NIGHT, MR. JAMES	SIMAK, CLIFFORD D.	NV	GAL 51 03
SYNDROME JOHNNY	DYE, CHARLES	SS	GAL 51 07
MADE TO MEASURE	GAULT, WILLIAM C.	SS	GAL 51 01
ASK ME ANYTHING	KNIGHT, DAMON	NV	GAL 51 05
IF YOU WAS A MOKLIN	LEINSTER, MURRAY	SS	GAL 51 09
MAN OF DESTINY	CHRISTOPHER, JOHN	SS	GAL 51 05
SUSCEPTIBILITY	MACDONALD, JOHN D.	SS	GAL 51 01
WAKER DREAMS, THE (ALSO AS WHEN THE WAKER SLEEPS)			
	MATHESON, RICHARD	SS	GAL 50 12
COMMON DENOMINATOR	MACDONALD, JOHN D.	SS	GAL 51 07
SECOND CHILDHOOD	SIMAK, CLIFFORD D.	SS	GAL 51 02
DON'T LIVE IN THE PAST	KNIGHT, DAMON	NV	GAL 51 06
BIOGRAPHY PROJECT, THE	DELL, DUDLEY	SS	GAL 51 09
DARK INTERLUDE	REYNOLDS, MACK		
	AND BROWN, FREDRIC	SS C GAL 51 01
OTHER NOW, THE	LEINSTER, MURRAY	SS	GAL 51 03

GALAXY READER OF SCIENCE FICTION (BRITISH)
GOLD, H. L.   AN H GRY 53

THIRD FROM THE SUN	MATHESON, RICHARD	SS	GAL 50 10
STARS ARE THE STYX, THE	STURGEON, THEODORE	NV	GAL 50 10
INSIDE EARTH	ANDERSON, POUL	NV	GAL 51 04
PILOT AND THE BUSHMAN, THE	JACOBS, SYLVIA	NV	GAL 51 08
BETELGEUSE BRIDGE	TENN, WILLIAM	SS	GAL 51 04
FIELD STUDY	PHILLIPS, PETER	SS	GAL 51 04
GOOD NIGHT, MR. JAMES	SIMAK, CLIFFORD D.	NV	GAL 51 03
MADE TO MEASURE	GAULT, WILLIAM C.	SS	GAL 51 01
MAN OF DESTINY	CHRISTOPHER, JOHN	SS	GAL 51 05
SUSCEPTIBILITY	MACDONALD, JOHN D.	SS	GAL 51 01
COMMON DENOMINATOR	MACDONALD, JOHN D.	SS	GAL 51 07
BIOGRAPHY PROJECT, THE	DELL, DUDLEY	SS	GAL 51 09
DARK INTERLUDE	REYNOLDS, MACK		
	AND BROWN, FREDRIC	SS C GAL 51 01

GALAXY SCIENCE FICTION OMNIBUS
GOLD, H. L.   AN H GRY 55
SELECTIONS FROM "SECOND GALAXY READER OF SCIENCE FICTION"

BAD DAY FOR SALES, A	LEIBER, FRITZ	SS	GAL 53 07
MISOGYNIST, THE	GUNN, JAMES E.	SS	GAL 52 11
SAUCER OF LONELINESS	STURGEON, THEODORE	SS	GAL 53 02
GLEEB FOR EARTH, A	SCHAFHAUSER, CHARLES SS	GAL 53 05
HALLUCINATION ORBIT (ALSO AS THE BLISS OF SOLITUDE)			
	MCINTOSH, J. T.	NV	GAL 52 04
C-CHUTE, THE	ASIMOV, ISAAC	NV	GAL 51 10
JUNKYARD	SIMAK, CLIFFORD D.	NV	GAL 53 05
PROBLEM ON BALAK	DEE, ROGER	SS	GAL 53 09
FOUR IN ONE	KNIGHT, DAMON	NV	GAL 53 02
CARETAKER	SCHMITZ, JAMES H.	SS	GAL 53 07
LOST MEMORY	PHILLIPS, PETER	SS	GAL 52 05
NOT FIT FOR CHILDREN	SMITH, EVELYN E.	SS	GAL 53 05
STUDENT BODY	WALLACE, F. L.	NV	GAL 53 03
STAR, BRIGHT	CLIFTON, MARK	NV	GAL 52 07
WARM	SHECKLEY, ROBERT	SS	GAL 53 06
SNOWBALL EFFECT, THE	MACLEAN, KATHERINE	SS	GAL 52 09
PILLAR TO POST	WYNDHAM, JOHN	NV	GAL 51 12
MINIMUM SENTENCE	COGSWELL, THEODORE R SS	GAL 53 08
TEA TRAY IN THE SKY	SMITH, EVELYN E.	SS	GAL 52 09
PAIL OF AIR, A	LEIBER, FRITZ	SS	GAL 51 12

GAMBLES WITH DESTINY   GRIFFITH, GEORGE   AC H FVW 99

HELLVILLE U.S.A.	GRIFFITH, GEORGE	SS	
GREAT CRELLIN COMET, THE	GRIFFITH, GEORGE	SS	
CORNER IN LIGHTNING, A	GRIFFITH, GEORGE	SS	PRS 98 03
GENIUS FOR A YEAR, A	GRIFFITH, GEORGE	SS	

```
PLAGUE-SHIP "TUPISA", THE    GRIFFITH, GEORGE      SS

GARDEN OF FEAR AND OTHER STORIES, THE
                    CRAWFORD, WILLIAM L. AN    CRF 45
  GARDEN OF FEAR, THE       HOWARD, ROBERT E.    SS    MVT 34 07
  MAN WITH THE HOUR GLASS, THE ESHBACH, LLOYD A.  SS    MVT 34 05
  CELEPHAIS                 LOVECRAFT, H. P.     SS    MVT 34 05
  MARS COLONIZERS           BREUER, MILES J. MD. SS    MVT 35 SU
  GOLDEN BOUGH, THE         KELLER, DAVID H. MD. SS    MVT 34 WI

GATES TO TOMORROW          NORTON, AN.&DONALDY  AN H ATH 73
  INTRODUCTION             NORTON, ANDRE
                    AND DONALDY, ERNESTINE    IN C
  SHAPE (KEEP YOUR SHAPE)   SHECKLEY, ROBERT     NV    GAL 53 11
  RUST                      KELLEAM, JOSEPH E.   SS    ASF 39 10
  COMMAND                   KAHN, BERNARD I.     NV    ASF 47 01
  NAMING OF NAMES, THE (ALSO AS DARK THEY WERE, AND GOLDEN-EYED)
                           BRADBURY, RAY        SS    TWS 49 08
  PLAGUE, THE               LAUMER, KEITH        NV    ASF 70 11
  PAIL OF AIR, A            LEIBER, FRITZ        SS    GAL 51 12
  LIVING FOSSIL             DE CAMP, L. SPRAGUE  SS    ASF 39 02
  FLAME MIDGET, THE         LONG, FRANK BELKNAP  SS    ASF 36 12
  EXPEDITION POLYCHROME     WINTER, JOSEPH A. MD NV    ASF 49 01
  UNTOUCHED BY HUMAN HANDS (ONE MAN'S POISON)
                           SHECKLEY, ROBERT     SS    GAL 53 12
  ULTIMATUM (MIGHTIEST QORN)    LAUMER, KEITH    NV    IFS 63 07
  SHERIFF OF CANYON GULCH, THE (HEROES ARE MADE)
                           DICKSON, GORDON R.
                    AND ANDERSON, POUL    NV C OWS 51 05

GATEWAY TO THE STARS       CARNELL, JOHN        AN    MUS 55
  STITCH IN TIME            MCINTOSH, J. T.      SS    SCP 52 FL
  ONLY AN ECHO              BARCLAY, ALAN        SS    NWS 54 04
  CONSPIRACY                CHRISTOPHER, JOHN    SS    AUT 55 01
  STRANGER FROM SPACE       LEES, GENE           SS    SCP 54 03
  NEVER ON MARS             WYNDHAM, JOHN        SS    FUN 54 01
  ASSISTED PASSAGE          WHITE, JAMES         SS    NWS 53 01
  CIRCUS                    HAWKINS, PETER       SS    SCP 52 FL
  UNFORTUNATE PURCHASE      TUBB, E. C.          SS    SCP 54 03
  OPERATION EXODUS          WRIGHT, LAN          SS    NWS 52 01

GATEWAY TO TOMORROW        CARNELL, JOHN        AN    MUS 54
  DUMB MARTIAN             WYNDHAM, JOHN        NV    GAL 52 07
  HIDE AND SEEK            CLARKE, ARTHUR C.    SS    ASF 49 09
  HOME IS THE HERO         TUBB, E. C.          SS    NWS 52 05
  LOST MEMORY              PHILLIPS, PETER      SS    GAL 52 05
  OF THOSE WHO CAME        LONGDON, GEORGE      SS    FUN 53 06
  BLISS OF SOLITUDE, THE (HALLUCINATION ORBIT)
                          MCINTOSH, J. T.      NV    GAL 52 01
  FINISHING TOUCH         CHANDLER, A. BERTRAM SS    NWS 52 07
  DROP, THE               CHRISTOPHER, JOHN    SS    GAL 53 03
  EMERGENCY WORKING        JAMES, E. R.         SS    NWS 52 09
  LIFE CYCLE               HAWKINS, PETER       SS    NWS 51 SP

GENERAL ZAPPED AN ANGEL, THE FAST, HOWARD      OC H MOR 70
  ALSO IN "TIME AND THE RIDDLE"
  GENERAL ZAPPED AN ANGEL, THE FAST, HOWARD      SS
  MOUSE, THE               FAST, HOWARD         SS    FSF 69 11
  VISION OF MILTY BOIL, THE    FAST, HOWARD     SS
  MOHAWK, THE              FAST, HOWARD         SS
  WOUND, THE               FAST, HOWARD         SS    70
  TOMORROW'S WALL STREET JOURNAL
                          FAST, HOWARD         SS
  INTERVAL, THE            FAST, HOWARD         SS
  INSECTS, THE             FAST, HOWARD         SS
  MOVIE HOUSE, THE         FAST, HOWARD         NV

GENERATION                GERROLD, DAVID       OA    DEL 72 07
  INTRODUCTION            GERROLD, DAVID       IN
  EVERY FOURTH HOUSE       LEIF, EVELYN         SS    GEN 72
  UP SCHIST CRICK          ANTHONY, PIERS       SS    GEN 72
  THROUGH A LASS DARKLY    TIPTREE, JAMES JR.   SS    GEN 72
  BIRTHDAY BOY, THE        STEVENS, JAMES       SS    GEN 72
  REPRISAL                 LAURANCE, ALICE      SS    GEN 72
  IT'S VERY CLEAN          WOLFE, GENE          SS    GEN 72
  PSYCHEDELIC FLIGHT       RAY, ROBERT          SS    GEN 72
  STUBBORN                 GOLDIN, STEPHEN      SS    GEN 72
  LADY WAS FOR KROINKING, THE BUNCH, DAVID R.   SS    GEN 72
  AFTER THEY'VE SEEN PAREE O'NEIL, DENNIS       SS    GEN 72
  SHORTEST SCIENCE-FICTION STORY EVER TOLD, THE
                          DEELEY, ROGER        SS    GEN 72
  RE-CREATION, THE         TOOMEY, ROBERT E. JR SS    GEN 72
  VIDI VICI VENI           MALZBERG, BARRY N.   SS    GEN 72
  AMBERJACK                TIPTREE, JAMES JR.   SS    GEN 72
  GALACTIC CLOCK, THE      MCINTYRE, VONDA N.   SS    GEN 72
  CONSTITUTION IN E FLAT   CARTER, PAUL A.      SS    GEN 72
  ONE ORDINARY DAY, WITH BOX SKY, KATHLEEN      SS    GEN 72
  BESIDE STILL WATERS      BRYANT, EDWARD
                    AND SUTHERLAND, JAMES    SS C GEN 72
  NOVA MORNING             BRYANT, EDWARD
                    AND HARPER, JODY    SS C GEN 72
  HERE'S A HEALTH UNTO HIS MAJESTY
                          DEELEY, ROGER        SS    GEN 72
  EVERYTHING THAT BEGINS WITH AN "M"
                          YARBRO, CHELSEA Q.   SS    GEN 72
  CONDITIONED REFLEX       DOZOIS, GARDNER R.   SS    GEN 72
  PORTER OF HELL-GATE, THE PUMILIA, JOSEPH F.   SS    GEN 72
  SENSE OF THYME, A        HENSEL, C. F.        SS    GEN 72
  ALL OF THEM WERE EMPTY   GERROLD, DAVID       SS    NEW 72 AC

GENTLE INVADERS           SANTESSON, HANS S.   AN    BEL 69 05
  INTRODUCTION            SANTESSON, HANS S.   IN
  SIT BY THE FIRE          BENEDICT, MYRLE      SS    FUN 58 05
  QUEER ONES, THE (ALSO AS THE OTHER PEOPLE)
                          BRACKETT, LEIGH      NV    VSF 57 03
  FREAK SHOW               DEFORD, MIRIAM ALLEN SS    FUN 58 02
```

```
SUBCOMMITTEE              HENDERSON, ZENNA     NV    FSF 62 07
UNNATURAL ACT             HOCH, EDWARD D.      SS    NEW 69 05
NIGHT HE CRIED, THE       LEIBER, FRITZ        SS    STR 53 01
MARTIANS AND THE COYS, THE REYNOLDS, MACK      SS    IMG 51 05
QUIZ GAME                 ROBINSON, FRANK M.   SS    ASF 53 06
DEAR DEVIL                RUSSELL, ERIC FRANK  NV    OWS 50 05
PARTY OF THE TWO PARTS    TENN, WILLIAM        NV    GAL 54 08

GET OFF MY WORLD|         LEINSTER, MURRAY     AC    BEL 66 04
  SECOND LANDING           LEINSTER, MURRAY     NA    TWS 54 WI
  WHITE SPOT               LEINSTER, MURRAY     NV    STS 55 FL
  PLANET OF SAND           LEINSTER, MURRAY     NV    FFM 48 02

GET OFF THE UNICORN       MCCAFFREY, ANNE      AC    BAL 77 06
  INTRODUCTION            MCCAFFREY, ANNE      IN
  LADY IN THE TOWER        MCCAFFREY, ANNE      SS    FSF 59 04
  MEETING OF MINDS, A      MCCAFFREY, ANNE      NV    FSF 69 01
  DAUGHTER                 MCCAFFREY, ANNE      NV    MWS 71
  DULL DRUMS               MCCAFFREY, ANNE      NV    FUQ 73
  CHANGELING               MCCAFFREY, ANNE      SS    NEW 77 AC
  WEATHER ON WELLADAY      MCCAFFREY, ANNE      NV    GAL 69 03
  THORNS OF BAREVI, THE    MCCAFFREY, ANNE      SS    70
  HORSE FROM A DIFFERENT SEA MCCAFFREY, ANNE    SS    NEW 77 AC
  GREAT CANINE CHORUS, THE MCCAFFREY, ANNE      SS    INY 70 01
  FINDER'S FEEPER          MCCAFFREY, ANNE      SS    HOH 73 08
  PROPER SANTA CLAUS, A    MCCAFFREY, ANNE      SS    DEM 73
  SMALLEST DRAGONBOY, THE  MCCAFFREY, ANNE      SS    SFT 73
  APPLE                    MCCAFFREY, ANNE      NV    NEW 69 AN
  HONEYMOON                MCCAFFREY, ANNE      NV    NEW 77 AC

GET OUT OF MY SKY         MARGULIES, LEO       AN    CRS 60
  GET OUT OF MY SKY        BLISH, JAMES         SN    ASF 57 01
  SISTER PLANET            ANDERSON, POUL       SN    SAT 59 05
  ALIEN NIGHT              SCORTIA, THOMAS N.   NV    SPA 57 08

GETTING INTO DEATH        DISCH, THOMAS M.     AC H HDV 73
  THE BEST SHORT STORIES OF THOMAS M. DISCH
  SLAVES                   DISCH, THOMAS M.     SS    TRV 67
  HAPPY STORY, THE         DISCH, THOMAS M.     SS
  ASIAN SHORE, THE         DISCH, THOMAS M.     NV    ORB 70 06
  PERSISTENCE OF DESIRE, THE DISCH, THOMAS M.   SS
  QUINCUNX                 DISCH, THOMAS M.     SS
  DISPLAYING THE FLAG      DISCH, THOMAS M.     SS
  BEGINNING OF APRIL OR THE END OF MARCH, THE
                          DISCH, THOMAS M.     SS    FSF 71 02
  PLANET ARCADIA, THE (ET IN ARCADIA EGO)
                          DISCH, THOMAS M.     SS    QRK 71 02
  INVASION OF THE GIANT STUPID DINOSAURS, THE
                          DISCH, THOMAS M.     SS    AMZ 69 03
  KISS GOODBYE, A          DISCH, THOMAS M.     SS
  X YES                    DISCH, THOMAS M.     SS    FAN 69 12
  FEATHERS FROM THE WINGS OF AN ANGEL
                          DISCH, THOMAS M.     SS    NWS 71 03
  LET US QUICKLY HASTEN TO THE GATE OF IVORY
                          DISCH, THOMAS M.     SS    QRK 70 01
  COLORS, THE              DISCH, THOMAS M.     SS    NWS 68 12
  MASTER OF THE MILFORD ALTARPIECE, THE
                          DISCH, THOMAS M.     SS    PRV 68
  COMPLETE SHORT STORIES, THE DISCH, THOMAS M.  GR
  MAN WHO UNDERSTOOD THE DIFFERENCE BETWEEN SALMON AND
  ORANGE CHIFFON, THE      DISCH, THOMAS M.     SS
  EXTENSION CORD, THE      DISCH, THOMAS M.     SS
  MRS. GALLAGHER'S PSYCHOANALYSIS
                          DISCH, THOMAS M.     SS
  NOVELIST WITH WOODEN CHARACTER, THE
                          DISCH, THOMAS M.     SS
  DAWN BREAKS OVER CRAKOW  DISCH, THOMAS M.     SS
  TIC, THE                 DISCH, THOMAS M.     SS
  WHAT THEY DO WITH MOTHERS-IN-LAW IN TIERRA DEL FUEGO
                          DISCH, THOMAS M.     SS
  COTTONWOOD TREE, THE     DISCH, THOMAS M.     SS
  GOLDEN LEMONS, THE       DISCH, THOMAS M.     SS
  PAGE FOR OCTOBER HAS BEEN TORN OFF, THE
                          DISCH, THOMAS M.     SS
  ROMANCE OF THE BOY AND THE GIRL, THE
                          DISCH, THOMAS M.     SS
  MAN WHO DIDN'T DOUBT IT, THE DISCH, THOMAS M. SS
  GRATITUDE, OR, THE SERPENT'S TOOTH
                          DISCH, THOMAS M.     SS
  HAPPY FAMILIES ALL LIKE SCRABBLE
                          DISCH, THOMAS M.     SS
  JESSICA, RAYMOND, AND JACK DISCH, THOMAS M.   SS
  POCKET FROM BROOKS BROTHERS, THE
                          DISCH, THOMAS M.     SS
  VAPORS                   DISCH, THOMAS M.     SS
  DAY IN THE LIFE OF THE ARTIST, A
                          DISCH, THOMAS M.     SS
  FAREWELL TO THE RIVIERA  DISCH, THOMAS M.     SS
  CHOCOLATE EGG, THE       DISCH, THOMAS M.     SS
  UNSPOKEN WISH, THE       DISCH, THOMAS M.     SS
  L'HOMME                  DISCH, THOMAS M.     SS
  MIMI SMITH               DISCH, THOMAS M.     SS
  SOLILOQUY IN THE LAST ACT, THE
                          DISCH, THOMAS M.     SS
  PEARL NECKLACE, THE      DISCH, THOMAS M.     SS
  GETTING INTO DEATH       DISCH, THOMAS M.     NV

GETTING INTO DEATH AND OTHER STORIES
                          DISCH, THOMAS M.     AC H KNP 76
  APOLLO                   DISCH, THOMAS M.     SS
  ASIAN SHORE, THE         DISCH, THOMAS M.     NV    ORB 70 06
  BIRDS, THE               DISCH, THOMAS M.     SS    73
  COLORS, THE              DISCH, THOMAS M.     SS    NWS 68 12
  DEATH AND THE SINGLE GIRL DISCH, THOMAS M.    SS
  DISPLAYING THE FLAG      DISCH, THOMAS M.     SS
```

GETTING INTO DEATH AND OTHER STORIES

FEATHERS FROM THE WINGS OF AN ANGEL				
	DISCH, THOMAS M.	SS	NWS 71 03	
GETTING INTO DEATH	DISCH, THOMAS M.	NV		
JOYCELIN SHRAGER STORY, THE	DISCH, THOMAS M.	NV		
LET US QUICKLY HASTEN TO THE GATE OF IVORY				
	DISCH, THOMAS M.	SS	QRK 70 01	
MASTER OF THE MILFORD ALTARPIECE, THE				
	DISCH, THOMAS M.	SS	PRV 68	
PERSISTENCE OF DESIRE, THE	DISCH, THOMAS M.	SS		
PLANET ARCADIA, THE (ET IN ARCADIA EGO)				
	DISCH, THOMAS M.	SS	QRK 71 02	
QUINCUNX	DISCH, THOMAS M.	SS		
SLAVES	DISCH, THOMAS M.	SS	TRV 67	
[X] YES	DISCH, THOMAS M.	SS	FAN 69 12	

GHOST BREAKER   GOULART, RON   DC   ACE 71

PLEASE STAND BY	GOULART, RON	NV	FSF 62 01
UNCLE ARLY	GOULART, RON	SS	FSF 62 07
HELP STAMP OUT CHESNEY	GOULART, RON	SS	NEW 71 DC
MCNAMARA'S FISH	GOULART, RON	SS	FSF 63 07
KEARNY'S LAST CASE	GOULART, RON	SS	FSF 65 09
BREAKAWAY HOUSE	GOULART, RON	SS	FSF 66 05
GHOST PATROL, THE	GOULART, RON	SS	FSF 68 10
STRAWHOUSE PAVILION, THE	GOULART, RON	SS	COV 70 01
FILL IN THE BLANK	GOULART, RON	SS	FSF 67 05

GHOUL KEEPERS, THE   MARGULIES, LEO   AN   PYR 61

INTRODUCTION	MARGULIES, LEO	IN	
SORCERER'S APPRENTICE, THE	BLOCH, ROBERT	SS	WRT 49 01
MARTIAN AND THE MORON, THE	STURGEON, THEODORE	NV	WRT 49 03
ISLE OF THE SLEEPER, THE	HAMILTON, EDMOND	SS	WRT 51 05
PLEASE GO 'WAY AND LET ME SLEEP			
	KASSON, HELEN W.	SS	WRT 45 03
LAKE, THE	BRADBURY, RAY	SS	WRT 44 05
WITCH IN THE FOG, THE	ALTSHULER, HARRY	SS	WRT 38 09
WHEN THE NIGHT WIND HOWLS	DE CAMP, L. SPRAGUE		
	AND PRATT, FLETCHER	SS C	WRT 51 11
CLAIR DE LUNE	QUINN, SEABURY	NV	WRT 47 11
SPAWN OF DAGON	KUTTNER, HENRY	SS	WRT 38 07

GHOULS, THE   HAINING, PETER   AN H SAD 71 05

EDITOR'S FOREWORD	HAINING, PETER	IN	
INTRODUCTION	PRICE, VINCENT	IN	
DEVIL IN A CONVENT, THE	MANN, FRANCIS OSCAR	SS	
LUNATICS, THE (THE SYSTEM OF DOCTOR TARR & PROFESSOR FEATHER)			
	POE, EDGAR ALLEN	SS	GLG 45 11
PURITAN PASSIONS (FEATHERTOP)			
	HAWTHORNE, NATHANIEL	SS	ITM 52 02
PHANTOM OF THE OPERA	LEROUX, GASTON	NA	11
MAGICIAN, THE	MAUGHAM, W. SOMERSET	EX	HEI 08
FREAKS (SPURS)	ROBBINS, TOD	SS	
MOST DANGEROUS GAME, THE	CONNELL, RICHARD	NV	24
DRACULA'S DAUGHTER (DRACULA'S GUEST)			
	STOKER, BRAM	SS	WRT 27 12
ALL THAT MONEY CAN BUY (THE DEVIL AND DANIEL WEBSTER)			
	BENET, STEPHEN V.	NV	SEP 36 10
BODY SNATCHER, THE	STEVENSON, ROBERT L.	SS	
BEAST WITH FIVE FINGERS, THE	HARVEY, WILLIAM F.	NV	
BEAST FROM 20,000 FATHOMS, THE (ALSO AS THE FOGHORN)			
	BRADBURY, RAY	SS	SEP 51 06
FLY, THE	LANGELAAN, GEORGE	NV	PBY 57 06
BLACK SUNDAY (THE VLY)	GOGOL, NIKOLAI	NV	
INCIDENT AT OWL CREEK (AN OCCURENCE AT OWL CREEK BRIDGE)			
	BIERCE, AMBROSE	SS	91
MONSTER OF TERROR (THE COLOUR OUT OF SPACE)			
	LOVECRAFT, H. P.	SS	AMZ 27 09
SKULL, THE (THE SKULL OF THE MARQUIS DE SADE)			
	BLOCH, ROBERT	SS	WRT 45 09
OBLONG BOX, THE	POE, EDGAR ALLEN	SS	GDY 44 09
AFTERWORD	LEE, CHRISTOPHER	MS	
CAST AND CREDITS	MISC. MATERIAL	MS	

GIANT ANTHOLOGY OF SCIENCE FICTION

MARGULIES & FRIEND   AN H MER 54

DERIVATIVE ANTHOLOGY "RACE TO THE STARS"				
ENCHANTRESS OF VENUS (ALSO AS CITY OF THE LOST ONES)				
	BRACKETT, LEIGH	NV	PLS 49 FL	
GATEWAY TO DARKNESS	BROWN, FREDRIC	NV	SSS 49 11	
GIRL IN THE GOLDEN ATOM, THE	CUMMINGS, RAY	NA	ASW 19 03	
FORGOTTEN WORLD	HAMILTON, EDMOND	NV	TWS 46 WI	
BY HIS BOOTSTRAPS (ALSO AS THE TIME GATE)				
	HEINLEIN, ROBERT A.	NV	ASF 41 10	
SWORD OF TOMORROW	KUTTNER, HENRY	NV	TWS 45 FL	
THINGS PASS BY	LEINSTER, MURRAY	NV	TWS 45 SU	
ROGUE SHIP (ALSO AS THE TWISTED MEN)				
	VAN VOGT, A. E.	NV	SSS 50 03	
ISLAND IN THE SKY	WELLMAN, MANLY WADE	NV	TWS 41 10	
SUN MAKER, THE	WILLIAMSON, JACK	NV	TWS 40 06	

GIANTS UNLEASHED   CONKLIN, GROFF   AN H GRS 65
ALSO AS "MINDS UNLEASHED"

NON-LIMITATION OF INTELLIGENCE, THE			
	CONKLIN, GROFF	IN	
MICROCOSMIC GOD	STURGEON, THEODORE	NV	ASF 41 04
COMMENCEMENT NIGHT	ASHBY, RICHARD	SS	ASF 53 08
DEEP RANGE, THE (ARB 54 04)	CLARKE, ARTHUR C.	NV	STR 54 03
MACHINE MADE	MCINTOSH, J. T.	SS	NWS 51 SU
TRIP ONE	GRENDON, EDWARD	SS	ASF 49 07
VENUS IS A MAN'S WORLD	TENN, WILLIAM	NV	GAL 51 07
GOOD-BYE, ILHA	MANNING, LAURENCE	SS	NEW 52 AN
MISBEGOTTEN MISSIONARY (ALSO AS GREEN PATCHES)			
	ASIMOV, ISAAC	SS	GAL 50 11
ETHICAL EQUATIONS, THE	LEINSTER, MURRAY	SS	ASF 45 06
MISFIT	HEINLEIN, ROBERT A.	SS	ASF 39 11
GENIUS	ANDERSON, POUL	NV	ASF 48 12
BASIC RIGHT	RUSSELL, ERIC FRANK	NV	ASF 58 04

GIFTS OF ASTI AND OTHER STORIES OF SCIENCE FICTION, THE

ELWOOD, ROGER   AN H FOL 75

FIREDAY: FIRENIGHT	MALZBERG, BARRY N.	SS	74
BETTYANN	NEVILLE, KRIS	NV	NTS 51
STELLA	WHITE, TED	SS	WLK 73
FOREVER AND AMEN	BLOCH, ROBERT	SS	WLK 73
SECOND NATURE	OLIVER, CHAD	NV	FUQ 73
HAWKSBILL STATION	SILVERBERG, ROBERT	NV	GAL 67 08
TO SLEEP, PERCHANCE TO DREAM	MACKENROTH, NANCY	SS	74
GIFTS OF ASTI, THE	NORTON, ANDRE	SS	FBK 48 03

GIRL WITH THE HUNGRY EYES, AND OTHER STORIES, THE

WOLLHEIM, DONALD A. OA   AVN 49

GIRL WITH THE HUNGRY EYES, THE			
	LEIBER, FRITZ	SS	49
VENUS AND THE SEVEN SEXES	TENN, WILLIAM	NV	49
MRS. MANIFOLD	GRENDON, STEPHEN	SS	49
DAYDREAM	MILLER, P. SCHUYLER	SS	49
MATURITY NIGHT	LONG, FRANK BELKNAP	SS	49
COME INTO MY PARLOR	WELLMAN, MANLY WADE	SS	49

GLASS OF STARS, A   YOUNG, ROBERT F.   AC H HWF 68

INTRODUCTION	LEIBER, FRITZ	IN	
BOY MEETS DYEVITZA	YOUNG, ROBERT F.	SS	AMZ 62 10
STAR MOTHER	YOUNG, ROBERT F.	SS	AMZ 59 01
L'ARC DE JEANNE	YOUNG, ROBERT F.	NV	FSF 66 01
ON THE RIVER	YOUNG, ROBERT F.	SS	FAN 65 01
NEITHER DO THEY REAP	YOUNG, ROBERT F.	NV	
TO FELL A TREE	YOUNG, ROBERT F.	NV	FSF 59 07
WISH UPON A STAR	YOUNG, ROBERT F.	SS	FUN 56 12
FUGITIVES, THE	YOUNG, ROBERT F.	SS	
PYRAMID PROJECT, THE (THE SPHINX)			
	YOUNG, ROBERT F.	NV	AMZ 64 06
THIRTY DAYS HAD SEPTEMBER	YOUNG, ROBERT F.	SS	FSF 57 10
LITTLE DOG GONE	YOUNG, ROBERT F.	NV	WOT 64 02
GROWN-UP PEOPLE'S FEET, THE	YOUNG, ROBERT F.	SS	FUN 55 06
MINE EYES HAVE SEEN THE GLORY (REDEMPTION)			
	YOUNG, ROBERT F.	NV	AMZ 63 07

GNOME THERE WAS, A   PADGETT, LEWIS   AC H SAS 50

GNOME THERE WAS, A	PADGETT, LEWIS	NV	UNK 41 10
WHAT YOU NEED	PADGETT, LEWIS	SS	ASF 45 10
TWONKY, THE	PADGETT, LEWIS	SS	ASF 42 09
CURE, THE	PADGETT, LEWIS	SS	ASF 46 05
EXIT THE PROFESSOR	PADGETT, LEWIS	SS	TWS 47 11
SEE YOU LATER	PADGETT, LEWIS	SS	TWS 49 06
MIMSY WERE THE BOROGOVES	PADGETT, LEWIS	NV	ASF 43 02
JESTING PILOT	PADGETT, LEWIS	SS	ASF 47 05
THIS IS THE HOUSE	PADGETT, LEWIS	SS	ASF 46 02
RAIN CHECK	PADGETT, LEWIS	SS	ASF 46 07
COMPLIMENTS OF THE AUTHOR	PADGETT, LEWIS	NV	UNK 42 10

GODLING, GO HOME   SILVERBERG, ROBERT   AC   BEL 64 06

GODLING, GO HOME	SILVERBERG, ROBERT	SS	SFS 57 01
WHY?	SILVERBERG, ROBERT	SS	SFS 57 11
SILENT COLONY, THE	SILVERBERG, ROBERT	SS	FUT 54 10
FORCE OF MORTALITY	SILVERBERG, ROBERT	SS	FUT 57 FL
THERE'S NO PLACE LIKE SPACE	SILVERBERG, ROBERT	NV	SFS 59 05
NEUTRAL PLANET	SILVERBERG, ROBERT	SS	SFS 57 07
LONELY ONE, THE	SILVERBERG, ROBERT	SS	FSF 56 07
SOLITARY	SILVERBERG, ROBERT	SS	FUT 57 SP
MAN WITH TALENT, THE	SILVERBERG, ROBERT	SS	FUT 56 WI
DESICCATOR, THE	SILVERBERG, ROBERT	SS	SFS 56 05
WORLD HE LEFT BEHIND, THE	SILVERBERG, ROBERT	SS	NEB 59 02

GODS AND GOLEMS   DEL REY, LESTER   AC   BAL 73 02

VENGEANCE IS MINE (TO AVENGE MAN)			
	DEL REY, LESTER	NV	GAL 64 12
SUPERSTITION	DEL REY, LESTER	NV	ASF 54 08
LIFE WATCH	DEL REY, LESTER	NV	FUN 54 09
FOR I AM A JEALOUS PEOPLE	DEL REY, LESTER	SN	SSN 54
PURSUIT	DEL REY, LESTER	NA	SSF 52 05

GODS FOR TOMORROW   SANTESSON, HANS S.   AN   AWD 67

INTRODUCTION	SANTESSON, HANS S.	IN	
STREETS OF ASHKELON, THE (ALSO AS AN ALIEN AGONY)			
	HARRISON, HARRY	SS	NWS 62 09
BALAAM	BOUCHER, ANTHONY	SS	NTL 54
UNHUMAN SACRIFICE	MACLEAN, KATHERINE	NV	ASF 58 11
SHRINE OF TEMPTATION, THE	MERRIL, JUDITH	SS	FAN 62 04
ARMY COMES TO VENUS, THE	RUSSELL, ERIC FRANK	NV	FUN 59 05
APOSTLE TO ALPHA	BALKE, BETTY T.	SS	EPS 66 01
GOD OF THE PLAYBACK	DENTINGER, STEPHEN	SS	NEW 67 04
ROBOT SON	YOUNG, ROBERT F.	NV	FUN 59 09
THAT EVENING SUN GO DOWN	SELLINGS, ARTHUR	SS	NWS 66 09
WOLFRAM HUNTERS, THE	HOCH, EDWARD D.	SS	SMM 64 03

GOLD AT STARBOW'S END, THE   POHL, FREDERIK   AC   BAL 72 08

GOLD AT THE STARBOW'S END, THE			
	POHL, FREDERIK	NV	ASF 72 03
SAD SOLARIAN SCREENWRITER SAM			
	POHL, FREDERIK	SS	FSF 72 06
CALL ME MILLION	POHL, FREDERIK	SS	WOF 70 02
SHAFFERY AMONG THE IMMORTALS	POHL, FREDERIK	SS	FSF 72 07
MERCHANTS OF VENUS, THE	POHL, FREDERIK	NA	IFS 72 08

GOLDEN APPLES OF THE SUN   BRADBURY, RAY   AC H DBL 53 03
ALSO IN "TWICE 22"
ENGLISH EDITION (HDV 53) OMITS STORIES "THE BIG BLACK AND
WHITE GAME" AND "THE GREAT FIRE"

FOG HORN, THE (THE BEAST FROM 20,000 FATHOMS)			
	BRADBURY, RAY	SS	SEP 51 06
PEDESTRIAN, THE (REP 51 08)	BRADBURY, RAY	SS	FSF 52 02
APRIL WITCH, THE	BRADBURY, RAY	SS	SEP 52 04
WILDERNESS, THE	BRADBURY, RAY	SS	FSF 52 11

GOLDEN APPLES OF THE SUN

FRUIT AT THE BOTTOM OF THE BOWL, THE (TOUCH AND GO)
                              BRADBURY, RAY   SS   DBM 48 11
INVISIBLE BOY   BRADBURY, RAY   SS   MAD 45 11
FLYING MACHINE, THE   BRADBURY, RAY   SS   NEW 53 AC
MURDERER, THE   BRADBURY, RAY   SS   ARG 53 06
GOLDEN KITE, THE SILVER WIND, THE
                              BRADBURY, RAY   SS   EPO 53 WI
I SEE YOU NEVER   BRADBURY, RAY   SS   NYM 47 11
EMBROIDERY   BRADBURY, RAY   SS   MAR 51 11
BIG BLACK AND WHITE GAME, THE
                              BRADBURY, RAY   SS   AMM 45 08
SOUND OF THUNDER, A   BRADBURY, RAY   SS   COL 52 06
GREAT WIDE WORLD OVER THERE, THE (CORA AND THE GREAT WIDE
  WORLD OVER THERE)   BRADBURY, RAY   SS   MCL 52 08
POWERHOUSE   BRADBURY, RAY   SS   CHM 48 03
EN LA NOCHE (TORRID SACRIFICE)
                              BRADBURY, RAY   SS   CAV 52 11
SUN AND SHADOW   BRADBURY, RAY   SS   REP 53 03
MEADOW, THE   BRADBURY, RAY   PL   BPL 48
GARBAGE COLLECTOR, THE   BRADBURY, RAY   SS   NAT 53 10
GREAT FIRE, THE   BRADBURY, RAY   SS   SEV 49 03
HAIL AND FAREWELL   BRADBURY, RAY   SS   TDY 53 03
GOLDEN APPLES OF THE SUN, THE
                              BRADBURY, RAY   SS   PLS 53 11

GOLDEN ROAD, THE   KNIGHT, DAMON   AN H SAS 73
INTRODUCTION   KNIGHT, DAMON   IN
ARE YOU TOO LATE OR WAS I TOO EARLY
                              COLLIER, JOHN   SS   NYM 51 04
ENTIRE AND PERFECT CHRYSOLITE
                              LAFFERTY, R. A.   SS   ORB 70 06
JENNY WITH WINGS   WILHELM, KATE   SS   NEW 63 AC
TRUTH ABOUT PYECRAFT, THE   WELLS, H. G.   SS   SND 03 04
WORDS OF GURU, THE   KORNBLUTH, C. M.   SS   STI 41 06
POSTPAID TO PARADISE (POSTMARKED FOR PARADISE, IN FSF 50 WS)
                              ARTHUR, ROBERT   SS   ARG 40 06
WHITE PEOPLE, THE   MACHEN, ARTHUR   NV   HLK 04 01
EXTRACT FROM CAPTAIN STORMFIELD'S VISIT TO HEAVEN
                              TWAIN, MARK   EX   HRP 07 12
WILL YOU WAIT?   BESTER, ALFRED   SS   FSF 59 03
KING OF THE CATS, THE   BENET, STEPHEN V. SS   HRP 29 02
WORD OF UNBINDING, THE   LE GUIN, URSULA K. SS   FAN 64 01
MAGIC, INC. (THE DEVIL MAKES THE LAW)
                              HEINLEIN, ROBERT A. SN UNK 40 09
ANYTHING BOX   HENDERSON, ZENNA   SS   FSF 56 10
ARTIST UNKNOWN   BROUN, HEYWOOD   SS   41
SILENCE, THE   MCLAUGHLIN, BERNARD SS STI 41 06
DREAM QUEST OF UNKNOWN KADATH, THE
                              LOVECRAFT, H. P.   NA   ARS 48 WI
WEEBLIES, THE   BUDRYS, ALGIS   SS   FNF 53 06
PHANTAS   ONIONS, OLIVER   SS   11
NOT LONG BEFORE THE END   NIVEN, LARRY   SS   FSF 69 04

GOLLANCZ - SUNDAY TIMES BEST SF STORIES
                              ANONYMOUS   OA H GOL 75
INTRODUCTION   ALDISS, BRIAN W.   IN
LET'S GO TO GOLGOTHA!   KILWORTH, GARRY   SS
FROM ALKAID ASCENDING   MORGAN, CHRIS   SS
COLD STORAGE   CASTELL, DAPHNE   SS
HIBBIE, THE   ALEXANDER, JAMES   SS
BLUE DANUBE   MORRIS, VIC   NA
SO PROUDLY WE CLING   MORGAN, CHRIS   SS
SOUL OF COLONEL 607, THE   KILWORTH, GARRY   SS
WAY OF LIFE, A   MACHT, NORMAN L.   SS
ESMERALDA   CASTELL, DAPHNE   SS
PIT, THE   WEST, D.   NA

GOOD NEIGHBORS AND OTHER STRANGERS
                              PANGBORN, EDGAR   AC H MAC 72
GOOD NEIGHBORS   PANGBORN, EDGAR   SS   GAL 60 06
BETTER MOUSEHOLE, A   PANGBORN, EDGAR   SS   GAL 65 10
LONGTOOTH   PANGBORN, EDGAR   NV   FSF 70 01
MAXWELL'S MONKEY   PANGBORN, EDGAR   SS   GAL 64 10
PONSONBY CASE, THE   PANGBORN, EDGAR   SS
PICKUP FOR OLYMPUS   PANGBORN, EDGAR   SS   NEW 53 AN
DARIUS   PANGBORN, EDGAR   SS
WOGGLEBEAST   PANGBORN, EDGAR   SS   FSF 65 01
ANGEL'S EGG   PANGBORN, EDGAR   NV   GAL 51 06
WRENS IN GRAMPA'S WHISKERS, THE
                              PANGBORN, EDGAR   SS   FSF 60 04

GRADUATED ROBOT AND OTHER STORIES, THE
                              ELWOOD, ROGER   OA H LER 74
FOREWORD   ASIMOV, ISAAC   IN
GRADUATED ROBOT, THE   HOLLY, J. HUNTER   SS
IT DOESN'T REALLY MATTER   MALZBERG, BARRY N. SS
JAMEY'S VISITOR   LYTLE, B. J.   SS

GRAIN KINGS, THE   ROBERTS, KEITH   AC H HUT 76
WEIHNACHTSABEND (WEIHNACHTABEND)
                              ROBERTS, KEITH   NV   NWQ 72 04
WHITE BOAT, THE   ROBERTS, KEITH   SS   NWS 66 12
PASSING OF THE DRAGONS, THE   ROBERTS, KEITH   NV   NWR 73 21
TRUSTIE TREE, THE   ROBERTS, KEITH   SS   NWR 73 05
LAKE OF TUONELA, THE   ROBERTS, KEITH   NV   NWR 74 23
GRAIN KINGS, THE   ROBERTS, KEITH   NV   NWQ 72 03
I LOSE MEDEA (AS ALISTAIR BEVAN)
                              ROBERTS, KEITH   SS   NWQ 72 03

GRAVEYARD READER, THE   CONKLIN, GROFF   AN   BAL 58
INTRODUCTION   CONKLIN, GROFF   IN
SCREAMING WOMAN, THE   BRADBURY, RAY   SS   TDY 51 05
BOTTOMLESS GRAVE, A   BIERCE, AMBROSE   SS
CART, THE   HUGHES, RICHARD   SS   34
GRAVEYARD RATS, THE   KUTTNER, HENRY   SS   WRT 36 03
SKIN   DAHL, ROALD   SS   NYM 52 05

GREAT SCIENCE FICTION STORIES ABOUT MARS

NIGHT COURT   COUNSELMAN, MARY E. NV WRT 53 03
FREE DIRT   BEAUMONT, CHARLES SS   FSF 55 05
LISTEN, CHILDREN, LISTEN   WEST, WALLACE   SS   FUN 53 10
SPECIAL DELIVERY   COLLIER, JOHN   NV   41
CHILD THAT LOVED A GRAVE, THE
                              O'BRIEN, FITZ-JAMES SS
OUTSIDER, THE   LOVECRAFT, H. P.   SS   WRT 26 04
GRAVEYARD READER, THE   STURGEON, THEODORE SS   SCF 58 10

GREAT FOG AND OTHER WEIRD TALES, THE
                              HEARD, H. F.   OC H VPR 44
CRAYFISH, THE   HEARD, H. F.   SS
GREAT FOG, THE   HEARD, H. F.   SS   44
WINGLESS VICTORY   HEARD, H. F.   SS   44
VINDICAE FLAMMAE   HEARD, H. F.   SS
ECLIPSE   HEARD, H. F.   SS
SWAP, THE   HEARD, H. F.   SS   44
DROMENON   HEARD, H. F.   SS
CAT "I AM", THE   HEARD, H. F.   SS
ROUSING OF MR. BRADEGAR, THE HEARD, H. F.   SS   44

GREAT SCIENCE FICTION ABOUT DOCTORS
                              CONKLIN, G&FABRICANT AN CLB 63
INTRODUCTION   CONKLIN, GROFF
                              AND FABRICANT, NOAH D. IN C
MAN WITHOUT AN APPETITE   BREUER, MILES J. MD. SS   16
OUT OF THE CRADLE, ENDLESSLY ORBITING
                              CLARKE, ARTHUR C. SS   DUD 59 03
BROTHERS, THE   DANCE, CLIFTON JR. SS   FSF 52 06
GREAT KEINPLATZ EXPERIMENT, THE
                              DOYLE, ARTHUR CONAN SS WRT 36 10
COMPOUND B   FINK, DAVID H. MD. NV   NTL 54
RAPPACCINI'S DAUGHTER (1844) HAWTHORNE, NATHANIEL NV DMR 44 12
PSYCHOPHONIC NURSE, THE   KELLER, DAVID H. MD. SS AMZ 28 11
LITTLE BLACK BAG, THE   KORNBLUTH, C. M.   NV   ASF 50 07
RIBBON IN THE SKY   LEINSTER, MURRAY   NV   ASF 57 06
MATE IN TWO MOVES   MARKS, WINSTON K. NV   GAL 54 05
BEDSIDE MANNOR   MORRISON, WILLIAM NV   GAL 54 05
SHOPDROPPER, THE   NELSON, ALAN   SS   FSF 55 01
FAMILY RESEMBLANCE   NOURSE, ALAN E.   SS   ASF 53 04
FACTS IN THE CASE OF M. VALDEMAR
                              POE, EDGAR ALLEN   SS   AWR 45 12
EMERGENCY OPERATION   PORGES, ARTHUR   SS   FSF 56 05
MATTER OF ETHICS, A   SHANGO, J. R.   SS   FSF 54 11
BOLDEN'S PETS   WALLACE, F. L.   NV   GAL 55 10
EXPEDITION MERCY   WINTER, JOSEPH A. MD NV ASF 48 11

GREAT SCIENCE FICTION ADVENTURES
                              SHAW, LARRY T.   AN   LAN 63
STARCOMBERS, THE   HAMILTON, EDMOND   SN   SFA 56 12
HUNT THE SPACE-WITCH!   SILVERBERG, ROBERT SN   SFA 58 01
MAN FROM THE BIG DARK, THE   BRUNNER, JOHN   SN   SFA 58 06
WORLD OTALMI MADE, THE   HARRISON, HARRY   SN   SFA 58 06

GREAT SCIENCE FICTION BY SCIENTISTS
                              CONKLIN, GROFF   AN   CLB 62
ON SCIENCE FICTION BY SCIENTISTS
                              CONKLIN, GROFF   IN
WHAT IF   ASIMOV, ISAAC   SS   FAN 52 SU
ULTIMATE CATALYST, THE   BELL, ERIC TEMPLE NV   TWS 39 06
GOSTAK AND THE DOSHES, THE   BREUER, MILES J. MD. SS AMZ 30 03
SUMMERTIME ON ICARUS (THE HOTTEST PIECE OF REAL ESTATE IN THE
  SOLAR SYSTEM)   CLARKE, ARTHUR C. SS   VOG 60 06
NEUTRINO BOMB, THE   COOPER, RALPH S.   SS   LAS 61 07
LAST YEAR'S GRAVE UNDUG   DAVIS, CHAN   SS   NEW 62 01
GOLD-MAKERS, THE (1932)   HALDANE, J. B. S. SS   EQM 52 10
TISSUE-CULTURE KING, THE   HUXLEY, JULIAN   SS   AMZ 27 08
MARTIAN ADVENTURE, A (AT THE PERIHELION)
                              LEY, WILLY   SN   ASF 37 02
LEARNING THEORY   MCCONNELL, JAMES   SS   IFS 57 12
MOTHER OF NECESSITY, THE   OLIVER, CHAD   SS   NEW 55 AC
JOHN SZE'S FUTURE   PIERCE, JOHN R.   SS   NEW 62 AN
KID ANDERSON   RICHARDSON, R. S. SS   SPM 57 SP
PILOT LIGHTS OF THE APOCALYPSE
                              RIDENOUR, DR. LOUIS SS FOR 46 10
GRAND CENTRAL TERMINAL   SZILARD, LEO   SS   UCM 52 06
BRAIN, THE   WEINER, NORBERT   SS   TEN 52 04

GREAT SCIENCE FICTION STORIES
                              SMITH, CORDELIA T. AN   DEL 64 02
  IN ENGLAND AS "THE BEST SCIENCE FICTION STORIES 3"
INTRODUCTION   SMITH, CORDELIA T. IN
VITAL FACTOR   BOND, NELSON S.   SS   51
POTTAGE   HENDERSON, ZENNA   NV   FSF 55 09
ROADS MUST ROLL, THE   HEINLEIN, ROBERT A. NV ASF 40 06
STOLEN BACILLUS, THE   WELLS, H. G.   SS   PMB 94 06
STAR, THE   WELLS, H. G.   SS   GRP 97 12
NIGHTFALL   ASIMOV, ISAAC   NV   ASF 41 09
HISTORY LESSON   CLARKE, ARTHUR C. SS   STS 49 05
IN HIDING   SHIRAS, WILMAR H. NV   ASF 48 11
MARTIAN CROWN JEWELS, THE   ANDERSON, POUL   SS   EQM 58 02
SANDS OF TIME, THE   MILLER, P. SCHUYLER SN ASF 37 04
INTO SPACE   VERNE, JULES   NV

GREAT SCIENCE FICTION STORIES ABOUT MARS
                              DIKTY, T. E.   AN H FEL 66
RED PLANET, THE   DIKTY, T. E.   IN
SOUND OF BUGLES, THE   WILLIAMS, ROBERT M. SS STS 49 03
NON-STOP TO MARS   WILLIAMSON, JACK   NV   ARG 39 03
FIRST MARTIAN, THE (THIS JOE)
                              VAN VOGT, A. E.   SS   39
VIA ETHERLINE   BINDER, EANDO   SS   TWS 37 10
TIN LIZZIE   GARRETT, RANDALL   NV   AMZ 64 06
UNDER THE SAND-SEAS   SAARI, OLIVER E.   SS   SSS 41 01
OMNILINGUAL   PIPER, H. BEAM   NV   ASF 57 02

GREAT SCIENCE FICTION STORIES ABOUT THE MOON

GREAT SCIENCE FICTION STORIES ABOUT THE MOON
                            DIKTY, T. E.   AN H FEL 67
EARTH'S NATURAL SATELLITE   DIKTY, T. E.   IN
TABLE OF COMPARISONS: EARTH AND MOON
                            MISC. MATERIAL   MS
SIGNIFICANT EVENTS IN LUNAR EXPLORATION
                            MISC. MATERIAL   MS
MOON PROSPECTOR   ELLERN, WILLIAM B.   NV ASF 66 04
RELUCTANT HEROES, THE   ROBINSON, FRANK M.   NV GAL 51 01
GLIMPSES OF THE MOON   WEST, WALLACE   NV ASF 65 06
PRO, THE   HAMILTON, EDMOND   SS FSF 64 10
HONEYMOON IN HELL   BROWN, FREDRIC   NV GAL 50 11
VIA DEATH   BINDER, EANDO   SS TWS 38 08
TRENDS   ASIMOV, ISAAC   SS ASF 39 07
GLOSSARY   MISC. MATERIAL   MS

GREAT SCIENCE-FICTION   LICATA, TONY   AN   TSB 65
WIND, THE   BRADBURY, RAY   SS WRT 43 03
MOUSE   BROWN, FREDRIC   SS TWS 49 06
GOLEM, THE   DAVIDSON, AVRAM   SS FSF 55 03
JUDGMENT DAY   DE CAMP, L. SPRAGUE SS ASF 55 08
HISTORY LESSON   CLARKE, ARTHUR C.   SS STS 49 05
RUUM, THE   PORGES, ARTHUR   SS FSF 53 10
DARK MISSION   DEL REY, LESTER   SS ASF 40 07
BETTER RAT TRAP, A   STEIGER, BRAD   SS NEW 65 AN

GREAT SHORT NOVELS OF SCIENCE FICTION
                            SILVERBERG, ROBERT   AN   BAL 70 07
INTRODUCTION   SILVERBERG, ROBERT   IN
GIANT KILLER   CHANDLER, A. BERTRAM NV ASF 45 10
TWO DOOMS   KORNBLUTH, C. M.   NV VSF 58 07
TELEK   VANCE, JACK   SN ASF 52 01
SECOND GAME   DEVET, CHARLES V.
                        AND MACLEAN, KATHERINE   NV C ASF 58 03
BEYOND BEDLAM   GUIN, WYMAN   NA GAL 51 08
GRAVEYARD HEART, THE   ZELAZNY, ROGER   NV FAN 64 03

GREAT STORIES OF SCIENCE FICTION
                            LEINSTER, MURRAY   AN H RDM 51
INTRODUCTION   PADIMAN, CLIFTON   IN
LET'S CALL IT A HOBBY   LEINSTER, MURRAY   IN
FASCINATING STRANGER, THE   FESSIER, MICHAEL   NV SEP 48 05
LIQUID LIFE   FARLEY, RALPH MILNE NV TWS 36 10
SYMBIOSIS   JENKINS, WILL F.   SS COL 47 06
NUMBER NINE   CARTMILL, CLEVE   SS ASF 50 02
BLIND ALLEY   JAMESON, MALCOLM   NV UNK 43 06
IN HIDING   SHIRAS, WILMAR H.   NV ASF 48 11
NO WOMAN BORN   MOORE, C. L.   NV ASF 44 12
STRANGE CASE OF JOHN KINGMAN, THE
                            LEINSTER, MURRAY   SS ASF 48 05
IMPOSSIBLE HIGHWAY, THE   FRIEND, OSCAR J.   SS TWS 40 08
OPEN SECRET   PADGETT, LEWIS   SS ASF 43 04
CHRONOKINESIS OF JONATHAN HULL, THE
                            BOUCHER, ANTHONY   SS ASF 46 06
CHROMIUM HELMET, THE   STURGEON, THEODORE   NV ASF 46 06
RECOMMENDED OTHER STORIES   MISC. MATERIAL   MS

GREAT STORIES OF SPACE TRAVEL
                            CONKLIN, GROFF   AN   TMP 63 07
INTRODUCTION   CONKLIN, GROFF   IN
WINGS OF NIGHT, THE   DEL REY, LESTER   SS ASF 42 03
HOLES AROUND MARS, THE   BIXBY, JEROME   SS GAL 54 01
KALEIDOSCOPE   BRADBURY, RAY   SS TWS 49 10
I'LL BUILD YOUR DREAM CASTLE VANCE, JACK   SS ASF 47 09
FAR CENTAURUS   VAN VOGT, A. E.   SS ASF 44 01
PROPAGANDIST   LEINSTER, MURRAY   SS ASF 47 08
CABIN BOY   KNIGHT, DAMON   NV GAL 51 09
WALK IN THE DARK, A   CLARKE, ARTHUR C.   SS TWS 50 08
BLIND ALLEY   ASIMOV, ISAAC   SS ASF 45 03
HELPING HAND, THE   ANDERSON, POUL   NV ASF 50 05
ALLAMAGOOSA   RUSSELL, ERIC FRANK SS ASF 55 05

GREAT TALES OF FANTASY AND IMAGINATION
                            STERN, PHILIP VAN D. AN   PKT 54 11
    SEE "THE MOONLIGHT TRAVELER"

GREEN HILLS OF EARTH, THE   HEINLEIN, ROBERT A. AC H SHS 51
    ALSO IN "A ROBERT HEINLEIN OMNIBUS"
DELILAH AND THE SPACE-RIGGER HEINLEIN, ROBERT A. SS BBM 49 12
SPACE JOCKEY   HEINLEIN, ROBERT A. SS SEP 47 04
LONG WATCH, THE   HEINLEIN, ROBERT A. SS ALM 49 12
GENTLEMEN, BE SEATED!   HEINLEIN, ROBERT A. SS ARG 48 05
BLACK PITS OF LUNA, THE   HEINLEIN, ROBERT A. SS SEP 48 01
IT'S GREAT TO BE BACK!   HEINLEIN, ROBERT A. SS SEP 47 07
WE ALSO WALK DOGS   HEINLEIN, ROBERT A. SS ASF 41 07
ORDEAL IN SPACE   HEINLEIN, ROBERT A. SS TAC 48 05
GREEN HILLS OF EARTH, THE   HEINLEIN, ROBERT A. SS SEP 47 02
LOGIC OF EMPIRE   HEINLEIN, ROBERT A. NV ASF 41 03

GREYLORN   LAUMER, KEITH   AC   BKM 68 02
GREYLORN   LAUMER, KEITH   NA AMZ 59 04
NIGHT OF THE TROLLS, THE   LAUMER, KEITH   SN WOT 63 10
OTHER SKY, THE (THE FURTHER SKY)
                            LAUMER, KEITH   SN AMZ 64 12
KING OF THE CITY, THE   LAUMER, KEITH   NV GAL 61 08

GUARDIANS OF TIME   ANDERSON, POUL   AC   BAL 60 09
TIME PATROL   ANDERSON, POUL   NV FSF 55 05
BRAVE TO BE A KING   ANDERSON, POUL   NV FSF 59 08
ONLY GAME IN TOWN, THE   ANDERSON, POUL   NV FSF 60 01
DELENDA EST   ANDERSON, POUL   NV FSF 55 12

GUN FOR DINOSAUR AND OTHER IMAGINATIVE TALES
                            DE CAMP, L. SPRAGUE AC H DBL 63
GUN FOR DINOSAUR, A   DE CAMP, L. SPRAGUE NV GAL 56 03
ARISTOTLE AND THE GUN   DE CAMP, L. SPRAGUE NV ASF 58 02

GUIDED MAN, THE   DE CAMP, L. SPRAGUE NV STS 52 10
INTERNAL COMBUSTION   DE CAMP, L. SPRAGUE SS INF 56 02
CORNZAN THE MIGHTY   DE CAMP, L. SPRAGUE SS FUT 55 28
THROWBACK   DE CAMP, L. SPRAGUE NV ASF 49 03
JUDGMENT DAY   DE CAMP, L. SPRAGUE SS ASF 55 08
GRATITUDE (PROPERTY OF VENUS)
                            DE CAMP, L. SPRAGUE NV GAL 55 07
THING OF CUSTOM, A   DE CAMP, L. SPRAGUE SS FUN 57 01
EGG, THE   DE CAMP, L. SPRAGUE SS SAT 56 10
LET'S HAVE FUN   DE CAMP, L. SPRAGUE SS SFQ 57 05
IMPRACTICAL JOKE   DE CAMP, L. SPRAGUE SS FUT 56 29
IN-GROUP   DE CAMP, L. SPRAGUE SS MAR 52 05
NEW ARCADIA   DE CAMP, L. SPRAGUE NV FUT 56 30

HALFLING AND OTHER STORIES, THE
                            BRACKETT, LEIGH   AC   ACE 73 09
HALFLING, THE   BRACKETT, LEIGH   SS AST 43 02
DANCING GIRL OF GANYMEDE, THE
                            BRACKETT, LEIGH   SS TWS 50 02
CITADEL OF LOST AGES, THE   BRACKETT, LEIGH   NV TWS 50 12
ALL THE COLORS OF THE RAINBOW
                            BRACKETT, LEIGH   SS VSF 57 11
SHADOWS, THE   BRACKETT, LEIGH   SS STS 52 02
ENCHANTRESS OF VENUS (ALSO AS CITY OF THE LOST ONES)
                            BRACKETT, LEIGH   NV PLS 49 FL
LAKE OF THE GONE FOREVER, THE
                            BRACKETT, LEIGH   NV TWS 49 10
TRUANTS, THE   BRACKETT, LEIGH   SS STS 50 07

HANDFUL OF DARKNESS, A   DICK, PHILIP K.   AC H RCH 55
COLONY   DICK, PHILIP K.   NV GAL 53 06
IMPOSTOR   DICK, PHILIP K.   SS ASF 53 06
EXPENDABLE   DICK, PHILIP K.   SS FSF 53 07
PLANET FOR TRANSIENTS   DICK, PHILIP K.   SS FUN 53 10
PROMINANT AUTHOR   DICK, PHILIP K.   SS IFS 54 05
BUILDER, THE   DICK, PHILIP K.   SS AMZ 54 01
LITTLE MOVEMENT, THE   DICK, PHILIP K.   SS FSF 52 11
PRESERVING MACHINE, THE   DICK, PHILIP K.   SS FSF 53 06
IMPOSSIBLE PLANET, THE   DICK, PHILIP K.   SS IFS 53 10
INDEFATIGABLE FROG, THE   DICK, PHILIP K.   SS FSM 53 07
TURNING WHEEL, THE   DICK, PHILIP K.   SS SFS 54 02
PROGENY   DICK, PHILIP K.   SS IFS 54 11
UPON THE DULL EARTH   DICK, PHILIP K.   NV BEY 54 09
COOKIE LADY, THE   DICK, PHILIP K.   SS FNF 53 06
EXHIBIT PIECE   DICK, PHILIP K.   SS IFS 54 08

HANDFUL OF TIME, A   BROWN, ROSEL GEORGE AC   BAL 63
LOST IN TRANSLATION   BROWN, ROSEL GEORGE SS FSF 59 05
STEP IV   BROWN, ROSEL GEORGE SS AMZ 60 06
LITTLE HUMAN CONTACT, A   BROWN, ROSEL GEORGE SS FSF 60 04
SIGNS OF THE TIMES   BROWN, ROSEL GEORGE SS AMZ 59 12
OF ALL POSSIBLE WORLDS   BROWN, ROSEL GEORGE SS FSF 61 02
JUST A SUGGESTION   BROWN, ROSEL GEORGE SS FSF 60 08
SAVE YOUR CONFEDERATE MONEY, BOYS
                            BROWN, ROSEL GEORGE SS FUN 59 11
VISITING PROFESSOR   BROWN, ROSEL GEORGE SS FAN 61 02
CAR POOL   BROWN, ROSEL GEORGE NV IFS 59 07
FRUITING BODY   BROWN, ROSEL GEORGE NV FSF 62 08
SMITH'S REVENGE   BROWN, ROSEL GEORGE SS NEW 63 AC
DEVALUATION OF THE SYMBOL, THE
                            BROWN, ROSEL GEORGE SS NEW 63 AC

HARD WAY UP, THE   CHANDLER, A. BERTRAM DC   ACE 72
WITH GOOD INTENTIONS   CHANDLER, A. BERTRAM SS
SUBTRACTER, THE   CHANDLER, A. BERTRAM SS
TIN MESSIAH, THE   CHANDLER, A. BERTRAM SS
SLEEPING BEAUTY, THE   CHANDLER, A. BERTRAM NV GAL 70 02
WANDERING BUOY, THE   CHANDLER, A. BERTRAM SS ASF 70 09
MOUNTAIN MOVERS, THE   CHANDLER, A. BERTRAM NV GAL 71 03
WHAT YOU KNOW   CHANDLER, A. BERTRAM NV GAL 71 01

HARRIGAN'S FILE   DERLETH, AUGUST   AC H ARK 75
MCILVAINE'S STAR   DERLETH, AUGUST   SS IFS 52 07
CORNER FOR LUCIA, A   DERLETH, AUGUST   SS WRT 53 05
INVADERS FROM THE MICROCOSM (INVASION FROM THE MICROCOSM)
                            DERLETH, AUGUST   SS OSF 53 01
MARK VII (THE THINKER AND THE THOUGHT)
                            DERLETH, AUGUST   SS OSF 54 09
OTHER SIDE OF THE WALL, THE DERLETH, AUGUST   SS TSF 51 SP
EYE FOR HISTORY, AN   DERLETH, AUGUST   SS
MAUGHAM OBSESSION, THE   DERLETH, AUGUST   SS FUN 53 06
TRAVELLER IN TIME, A (ALSO AS CENTURY JUMPER)
                            DERLETH, AUGUST   SS OSF 54 02
DETECTIVE AND THE SENATOR, THE
                            DERLETH, AUGUST   SS SDM 53 08
PROTOPLASMA   DERLETH, AUGUST   SS
MECHANICAL HOUSE, THE (THE UNGRATEFUL HOUSE)
                            DERLETH, AUGUST   SS OSF 54 03
BY ROCKET TO THE MOON   DERLETH, AUGUST   SS VTA 65
MAN WHO RODE THE SAUCER, THE DERLETH, AUGUST   SS NEW 52 AN
FERGUSON'S CAPSULES   DERLETH, AUGUST   SS
PENFIELD MISADVENTURE, THE DERLETH, AUGUST   SS OSF 54 11
REMARKABLE DINGDONG, THE   DERLETH, AUGUST   SS SWY 54 04
MARTIAN ARTIFACT, THE   DERLETH, AUGUST   SS STN 57 07

HARVEST OF HOODWINKS, A   LORY, ROBERT   DC   ACE 70
FOREWORD   LORY, ROBERT   IN
ARCHIMEDES' LEVER (THE COURTEOUS OF GHOOR)
                            LORY, ROBERT   SS IFS 68 02
MAR-TI-AN   LORY, ROBERT   SS FSF 64 05
STAR PARTY, THE   LORY, ROBERT   SS FSF 64 09
FUTILITY IS ZUCK   LORY, ROBERT   SS
SNOWBIRD AND THE SEVEN WARFS LORY, ROBERT   SS
LOCATOR, THE   LORY, ROBERT   SS FSF 68 02
APPOINTMENT AT TEN O'CLOCK LORY, ROBERT   SS FSF 64 01
ONLY A GOD   LORY, ROBERT   SS

HARVEST OF HOODWINKS, A

Title	Author	Type	Source
FALL OF ALL-FATHER, THE	LORY, ROBERT	SS	
BECAUSE OF PURPLE ELEPHANTS	LORY, ROBERT	SS	
ROLLING ROBERT	LORY, ROBERT	SS	
DEBUT	LORY, ROBERT	SS	66

Title	Author	Type	Source
HAUNTER OF THE DARK, THE	LOVECRAFT, H. P.	AC H GOL 51	
INTRODUCTION	DERLETH, AUGUST	IN	
OUTSIDER, THE	LOVECRAFT, H. P.	SS	WRT 26 04
RATS IN THE WALLS, THE	LOVECRAFT, H. P.	SS	WRT 24 03
PICKMAN'S MODEL	LOVECRAFT, H. P.	SS	WRT 27 10
CALL OF CTHULHU, THE	LOVECRAFT, H. P.	NV	WRT 28 02
DUNWICH HORROR, THE	LOVECRAFT, H. P.	NV	WRT 29 04
WHISPERER IN DARKNESS, THE	LOVECRAFT, H. P.	NV	WRT 31 08
COLOUR OUT OF SPACE, THE (ALSO AS MONSTER OF TERROR)	LOVECRAFT, H. P.	SS	AMZ 27 09
HAUNTER OF THE DARK, THE	LOVECRAFT, H. P.	NV	WRT 36 12
THING ON THE DOORSTEP, THE	LOVECRAFT, H. P.	NV	WRT 37 01
MUSIC OF ERICH ZANN, THE	LOVECRAFT, H. P.	SS	WRT 25 05

Title	Author	Type	Source
HAVE YOU SEEN THESE?	ASIMOV, ISAAC	AC H NES 74	
ALL STORIES ALSO IN "BUY JUPITER"			
DAY OF THE HUNTERS	ASIMOV, ISAAC	SS	FUT 50 11
SHAH GUIDO G.	ASIMOV, ISAAC	SS	MAR 51 11
MONKEY'S FINGER, THE	ASIMOV, ISAAC	SS	STS 53 02
EVEREST	ASIMOV, ISAAC	SS	USF 53 12
PAUSE, THE	ASIMOV, ISAAC	SS	
BLANK!	ASIMOV, ISAAC	SS	INF 57 06
SILLY ASSES	ASIMOV, ISAAC	SS	FUT 58 02
RAIN, RAIN, GO AWAY	ASIMOV, ISAAC	SS	FUN 59 09

Title	Author	Type	Source
HAWK AMONG THE SPARROWS	MCLAUGHLIN, DEAN	AC H SCB 76	
TOURING THE WORKSHOP	MCLAUGHLIN, DEAN	IN	
HAWK AMONG THE SPARROWS	MCLAUGHLIN, DEAN	SN	ASF 68 07
PERMANENT IMPLOSION, THE	MCLAUGHLIN, DEAN	NV	ASF 64 02
BROTHERHOOD OF KEEPERS, THE	MCLAUGHLIN, DEAN	NV	ASF 60 07

Title	Author	Type	Source
HEART OF THE SERPENT, THE	ANONYMOUS	AN H FLP 61	
SEE "MORE SOVIET SCIENCE FICTION"			

Title	Author	Type	Source
HEINLEIN TRIAD, A	HEINLEIN, ROBERT A.	AC H GOL 66	
SEE "THREE BY HEINLEIN"			

Title	Author	Type	Source
HELL HATH FURY	HAY, GEORGE	AN H NSP 63 10	
HELL HATH FURY	CARTMILL, CLEVE	SN	UNK 43 08
BLEAK SHORE, THE	LEIBER, FRITZ	SS	UNK 40 11
FROG, THE	MILLER, P. SCHUYLER	SS	UNK 42 10
REFUGEE, THE	RICE, JANE	SS	UNK 43 10
DEVIL'S RESCUE, THE	HUBBARD, L. RON	SS	UNK 40 10
CLOAK, THE	BLOCH, ROBERT	SS	UNK 39 05
EXTRA BRICKLAYER, THE	PHILLIPS, A. M.	SS	UNK 40 09

Title	Author	Type	Source
HIDDEN PLANET, THE	WOLLHEIM, DONALD A.	AN	ACE 59
INTRODUCTION	WOLLHEIM, DONALD A.	IN	
FIELD EXPEDIENT	OLIVER, CHAD	NV	ASF 55 01
VENUS MISSION	MCINTOSH, J. T.	NV	PLS 51 07
LUCK OF IGNATZ, THE	DEL REY, LESTER	NV	ASF 39 08
LOTUS EATERS, THE	WEINBAUM, STANLEY G.	NV	ASF 35 04
TERROR OUT OF SPACE	BRACKETT, LEIGH	SS	PLS 44 SU

Title	Author	Type	Source
HIGH JUSTICE	POURNELLE, JERRY	AC	PKT 77 05
MATTER OF SOVEREIGNTY, A	POURNELLE, JERRY	NV	ASF 72 01
POWER TO THE PEOPLE	POURNELLE, JERRY	SS	ASF 72 08
ENFORCER	POURNELLE, JERRY	NV	FSF 74 06
HIGH JUSTICE	POURNELLE, JERRY	NV	ASF 74 03
EXTREME PREJUDICE	POURNELLE, JERRY	NV	ASF 74 07
CONSORT	POURNELLE, JERRY	SS	ASF 75 08
TINKER	POURNELLE, JERRY	NA	GAL 75 07

Title	Author	Type	Source
HISTORY OF THE SCIENCE FICTION MAGAZINE, THE PART 1 1926-1935	ASHLEY, MICHAEL	AN H NLB 74	
PREFACE	ASHLEY, MICHAEL	IN	
INTRODUCTION: AN AMAZING EXPERIMENT	ASHLEY, MICHAEL	AR	
COMING OF THE ICE, THE	WERTENBAKER, G. P.	SS	AMZ 26 06
MACHINE MAN OF ARDATHIA, THE	FLAGG, FRANCIS	SS	AMZ 27 11
OUT OF THE SUB-UNIVERSE	STARZL, R. F.	SS	ASQ 28 SU
ETERNAL MAN, THE	SHARP, D. D.	SS	SWS 29 08
POWER AND THE GLORY, THE	DIFFIN, CHARLES W.	SS	ASF 30 07
VOICE FROM THE ETHER, THE	ESHBACH, LLOYD A.	NV	AMZ 31 05
ASTEROID OF GOLD, THE	SIMAK, CLIFFORD D.	SS	WOS 32 11
ISLAND OF UNREASON, THE	HAMILTON, EDMOND	SS	WOS 33 05
ONE PREHISTORIC NIGHT	BARSHOFSKY, PHILIP	SS	WOS 34 11
DAVEY JONES' AMBASSADOR	GALLUN, RAYMOND Z.	NV	ASF 35 12
APPENDICES	MISC. MATERIAL	MS	

Title	Author	Type	Source
HISTORY OF THE SCIENCE FICTION MAGAZINE, THE PART 2 1936-1945	ASHLEY, MICHAEL	AN H NLB 75	
PREFACE	ASHLEY, MICHAEL	IN	
INTRODUCTION: SF BANDWAGON	ASHLEY, MICHAEL	AR	
CIRCLE OF ZERO, THE	WEINBAUM, STANLEY G.	SS	TWS 36 08
SEEKER OF TOMORROW	RUSSELL, ERIC FRANK AND JOHNSON, LESLIE T.	SN C	ASF 37 07
DEAD SPOT, THE	WILLIAMSON, JACK	NV	MAR 38 11
4-SIDED TRIANGLE, THE	TEMPLE, WILLIAM F.	NV	AMZ 39 11
HERMIT OF SATURN'S RING	JONES, NEIL R.	SS	PLS 40 FL
ABYSS, THE	LOWNDES, ROBERT W.	SS	STI 41 02
UP THERE	WOLLHEIM, DONALD A.	SS	SFQ 42 SU
ALMOST HUMAN (AS TARLETON FISKE)	BLOCH, ROBERT	SS	FAD 43 06
WANDERER OF TIME	FEARN, JOHN RUSSELL	SS	STS 44 SU
POWER, THE	LEINSTER, MURRAY	SS	ASF 45 09
APPENDICES	MISC. MATERIAL	MS	
BIBLIOGRAPHY	MISC. MATERIAL	MS	

Title	Author	Type	Source
HISTORY OF THE SCIENCE FICTION MAGAZINE, THE PART 3 1946-1955	ASHLEY, MICHAEL	AN H NLB 76	

Title	Author	Type	Source
PREFACE	ASHLEY, MICHAEL	IN	
INTRODUCTION: FROM BOMB TO BOOM	ASHLEY, MICHAEL	IN	
MEMORIAL (SEE ALSO ATOMIC MEMORIAL)	STURGEON, THEODORE	SS	ASF 46 04
FIRES WITHIN, THE	CLARKE, ARTHUR C.	SS	FSB 47 08
DON'T LOOK NOW	KUTTNER, HENRY	SS	STS 48 03
KALEIDOSCOPE	BRADBURY, RAY	SS	TWS 49 10
TO SERVE MAN	KNIGHT, DAMON	SS	GAL 50 11
EARTHMAN, BEWARE!	ANDERSON, POUL	NV	SSS 51 06
THEY FLY SO HIGH	ROCKLYNNE, ROSS	SS	AMZ 52 06
LAST DAY, THE	MATHESON, RICHARD	SS	AMZ 53 05
HANDS OFF	SHECKLEY, ROBERT	NV	GAL 54 04
WAGER, THE	TUBB, E. C.	NV	SCF 55 07
APPENDICES	MISC. MATERIAL	MS	
BIBLIOGRAPHY	MISC. MATERIAL	MS	

Title	Author	Type	Source
HOLDING WONDER	HENDERSON, ZENNA	AC H DBL 71	
INDELIBLE KIND, THE	HENDERSON, ZENNA	NV	FSF 68 12
J-LINE TO NOWHERE	HENDERSON, ZENNA	NV	FSF 69 09
YOU KNOW WHAT, TEACHER?	HENDERSON, ZENNA	SS	EQM 54 09
EFFECTIVES, THE	HENDERSON, ZENNA	SS	WOT 65 05
LOO REE	HENDERSON, ZENNA	SS	FSF 53 02
CLOSEST SCHOOL, THE	HENDERSON, ZENNA	SS	FAN 60 04
THREE-CORNERED AND SECURE	HENDERSON, ZENNA	SS	NEW 71 AC
TASTE OF AUNT SOPHRONIA, THE	HENDERSON, ZENNA	SS	NEW 71 AC
BELIEVING CHILD, THE	HENDERSON, ZENNA	SS	FSF 70 06
THROUGH A GLASS- DARKLY	HENDERSON, ZENNA	NV	FSF 70 10
AS SIMPLE AS THAT	HENDERSON, ZENNA	SS	NEW 71 AC
SWEPT AND GARNISHED	HENDERSON, ZENNA	SS	NEW 71 AC
ONE OF THEM	HENDERSON, ZENNA	SS	NEW 71 AC
SHARING TIME	HENDERSON, ZENNA	SS	NEW 71 AC
AD ASTRA	HENDERSON, ZENNA	SS	NEW 71 AC
INCIDENT AFTER	HENDERSON, ZENNA	SS	NEW 71 AC
WALLS, THE	HENDERSON, ZENNA	SS	NEW 71 AC
CROWNING GLORY	HENDERSON, ZENNA	SS	NEW 71 AC
BOONA ON SCANCIA	HENDERSON, ZENNA	SS	NEW 71 AC
LOVE EVERY THIRD STIR	HENDERSON, ZENNA	SS	NEW 71 AC

Title	Author	Type	Source
HOLDING YOUR EIGHT HANDS	LUCIE-SMITH, EDWARD	AN H DBL 69	
INTRODUCTION	LUCIE-SMITH, EDWARD	IN	
PROGRESSION OF THE SPECIES	ALDISS, BRIAN W.	PM	PRP 67 SE
BELOVED HEAD, A	BENEDIKT, MICHAEL	PM	69
GARDENERS, THE	BENVENISTE, ASA	PM	68
BASILISK, THE	BLACK, D. M.	PM	69
MY SPECIES	BLACK, D. M.	PM	67
TO MYSELF ON THE OCCASION OF MY TWENTY-FIRST CENTURY	BRUNNER, JOHN	PM	69
CITIZEN BACILLUS	BRUNNER, JOHN	PM	69
MAGUS, A	CIARDI, JOHN	PM	SRV 65 12
END TO COMPLACENCY, AN	COLE, BARRY	PM	69
MEN ARE COMING BACK!, THE	COLE, BARRY	PM	NWS 67 10
FRANKENSTEIN	COLOMBO, JOHN ROBERT	PM	69
FAR OUT	CONQUEST, ROBERT	PM	69
GOLDEN AGE, THE	CONQUEST, ROBERT	PM	69
REPORT BACK	COTTON, JOHN	PM	69
NARCISSUS	DISCH, THOMAS M.	PM	69
VACATION ON EARTH, A	DISCH, THOMAS M.	PM	66
DAY EUTERPE DIED, THE	DISCH, THOMAS M.	PM	69
WE'LL ALL BE SPACEMEN BEFORE WE DIE	EVANS, MIKE	PM	NWS 68 10
MUSHROOMS	EVANS, MIKE	PM	69
REPORT, A	FAINLIGHT, RUTH	PM	69
BEYOND ASTRONAUT	FAIRFAX, JOHN	PM	69
HOW THE CONSOLATIONS OF PHILOSOPHY WORKED OUT IN ACTUAL PRACTICE	HADEN-GUEST, ANTHONY	PM	69
FROM AN ECCLESIASTICAL CHRONICLE	HEATH-STUBBS, JOHN	PM	
GALACTIC LOVEPOEM	HENRI, ADRIAN	PM	68
UNIVERSES	HENRI, ADRIAN	PM	68
GHOST CRABS	HUGHES, TED	PM	66
INVADERS, THE	JOHNSON, RONALD	PM	69
WEATHER FORECAST	KILBURN, DAVID	PM	69
ARTIST, THE	KOCH, KENNETH	PM	62
WINTER'S TALE, A	LECHTLINER, RUTH	PM	69
EXPOSTULATION, AN	LEWIS, C. S.	PM	FSF 59 06
NYARLATHOTEP (1943)	LOVECRAFT, H. P.	PM	MOH 68 10
HARBOR WHISTLES	LOVECRAFT, H. P.	PM	
AFTERWARDS	LUCIE-SMITH, EDWARD	PM	64
IN THE FUTURE	LUCIE-SMITH, EDWARD	PM	68
CRAB-APPLE CRISIS, THE	MACBETH, GEORGE	SS	NWS 66 10
CIRCE UNDERSEA	MACBETH, GEORGE	PM	65
BEDTIME STORY	MACBETH, GEORGE	PM	63
MOTHER SUPERIOR	MACBETH, GEORGE	PM	63
IN SOBIESKI'S SHIELD	MORGAN, EDWIN	PM	68
FROM THE DOMAIN OF ARNHEIM	MORGAN, EDWIN	PM	68
POEM	NUTTALL, JEFF	PM	
WOULDN'T YOU AFTER A JAUNT OF 964,000,000,000,000 MILLION MILES?	PATCHEN, KENNETH	PM	NDR 49
PERHAPS WHERE HE IS ONLY LOVING ROCKETS CAN LAND	PATTEN, BRIAN	PM	69
SMALL DRAGON, A	PATTEN, BRIAN	PM	69
YOUR ATTENTION PLEASE	PORTER, PETER	PM	PMP 62 07
TO START A CONTROVERSY	PORTER, PETER	PM	64
AH THE POETRY OF MISS PARROT'S FEET DEMONSTRATING THE TANGO	RAWORTH, TOM	PM	68
MR. WATERMAN	REDGROVE, PETER	SS	PRV 63 2
WIZARD'S NEW MEETING, THE	REDGROVE, PETER	PM	69
LOVE NEST	SLADEK, JOHN T.	PM	69
TREASURE OF THE HAUNTED RAMBLER, THE	SLADEK, JOHN T.	PM	69
TITHONUS	THOMAS, D. M.	PM	PMP 68 1
MISSIONARY	THOMAS, D. M.	PM	PMP 68 1
HEAD-RAPE, THE	THOMAS, D. M.	PM	NWS 68 0
EVERYBODY'S HOMESICK SOLDIER BOY	WILLIAMS, JONATHAN	PM	62

HOLDING YOUR EIGHT HANDS

```
BIOGRAPHICAL NOTES            MISC. MATERIAL      MS

HOLE IN SPACE, A              NIVEN, LARRY        AC  BAL 74 06
  RAMMER                      NIVEN, LARRY        NV  GAL 71 11
  ALIBI MACHINE, THE          NIVEN, LARRY        SS  VTX 73 06
  LAST DAYS OF THE PERMANENT FLOATING RIOT CLUB, THE
                              NIVEN, LARRY        SS  NEW 74 AC
  KIND OF MURDER, A           NIVEN, LARRY        SS  ASF 74 04
  ALL THE BRIDGES RUSTING     NIVEN, LARRY        NV  VTX 73 08
  THERE IS A TIDE             NIVEN, LARRY        NV  GAL 68 07
  BIGGER THAN WORLDS          NIVEN, LARRY        AR  ASF 74 03
  $16,940.00                  NIVEN, LARRY        SS  AHM 74
  HOLE MAN, THE               NIVEN, LARRY        SS  ASF 74 01
  FOURTH PROFESSION, THE      NIVEN, LARRY        NV  QRK 71 04

HOMEBREW                      ANDERSON, POUL      AC H NES 76
  FOREWARD                    ANDERSON, POUL      IN
  HOUSE RULE                  ANDERSON, POUL      SS  NEW 76 AC
  BALLADE OF AN ARTIFICIAL SATELLITE
                              ANDERSON, POUL      PM  FSF 58 10
  FIRST LOVE, THE             ANDERSON, POUL      PM  ABA 60 12
  UPON THE OCCASION OF BEING ASKED TO ARGUE THAT LOVE AND
    MARRIAGE ARE INCOMPATIBLE ANDERSON, POUL      PM  DRC 73 01
  LIMERICKS                   ANDERSON, POUL      PM
  TWO SONGS                   ANDERSON, POUL      SG
  SCIENCE FICTION AND FREEDOM ANDERSON, POUL      AR  SFR 69 30
  NOTES TOWARD A DEFINITION OF SCIENCE FICTION
                              ANDERSON, POUL      AR  SFR 71 43
  ARCHETYPICAL HOLMES, THE    ANDERSON, POUL      AR  BSJ 68 09
  BLESSEDNESS OF SAINTS, A    ANDERSON, POUL      AR  VPG 62 04
  PHILOSOPHICAL DIALOGUE, A   ANDERSON, POUL      AR  OUT 71 08
  LOST SECRETS REVEALED       ANDERSON, POUL      AR      72
  UNCLEAVISH TRUETHINKING     ANDERSON, POUL      AR      60
  HERRINGS                    ANDERSON, POUL      MS      59

HOMEWARD AND BEYOND           ANDERSON, POUL      AC H DBL 75 06
  INTRODUCTION                ANDERSON, POUL      IN
  WINGS OF VICTORY            ANDERSON, POUL      SS  ASF 72 04
  LONG REMEMBERING, THE       ANDERSON, POUL      SS  FSF 57 11
  PEEK! I SEE YOU!            ANDERSON, POUL      NV  ASF 68 02
  MURPHY'S HALL               ANDERSON, POUL
                          AND ANDERSON, KAREN     NV C INY 71 02
  PIRATE, THE                 ANDERSON, POUL      NV  ASF 68 10
  GOAT SONG                   ANDERSON, POUL      NV  FSF 72 02
  VISITOR, THE                ANDERSON, POUL      SS  FSF 74 10
  WOLFRAM                     ANDERSON, POUL      SS
  PEAT BOG, THE               ANDERSON, POUL      SS

HONEYMOON IN HELL             BROWN, FREDRIC      AC  BAN 58 08
  HONEYMOON IN HELL           BROWN, FREDRIC      NV  GAL 50 11
  TOO FAR                     BROWN, FREDRIC      SS  FSF 55 09
  MAN OF DISTINCTION          BROWN, FREDRIC      SS  TWS 51 02
  MILLENNIUM                  BROWN, FREDRIC      SS  FSF 55 03
  DOME, THE                   BROWN, FREDRIC      SS  TWS 51 08
  BLOOD                       BROWN, FREDRIC      SS  FSF 55 02
  HALL OF MIRRORS             BROWN, FREDRIC      SS  GAL 53 12
  EXPERIMENT (TWO TIMER)      BROWN, FREDRIC      SS  GAL 54 02
  LAST MARTIAN, THE           BROWN, FREDRIC      SS  GAL 50 10
  SENTRY (TWO TIMER)          BROWN, FREDRIC      SS  GAL 54 02
  MOUSE                       BROWN, FREDRIC      SS  TWS 49 06
  NATURALLY (DOUBLE WHAMMY)   BROWN, FREDRIC      SS  BEY 54 09
  VOODOO (DOUBLE WHAMMY)      BROWN, FREDRIC      SS  BEY 54 09
  ARENA                       BROWN, FREDRIC      NV  ASF 44 06
  KEEP OUT                    BROWN, FREDRIC      SS  AMZ 54 03
  FIRST TIME MACHINE          BROWN, FREDRIC      SS  EQM 55 09
  AND THE GODS LAUGHED        BROWN, FREDRIC      SS  TIS 53 FL
  WEAPON, THE                 BROWN, FREDRIC      SS  ASF 51 04
  WORD FROM OUR SPONSOR, A    BROWN, FREDRIC      SS  OWS 51 09
  RUSTLE OF WINGS             BROWN, FREDRIC      SS  FSF 53 08
  IMAGINE, A PROEM            BROWN, FREDRIC      PM  FSF 55 05

HORN OF TIME, THE             ANDERSON, POUL      AC  SIG 68 01
  HORN OF TIME THE HUNTER, THE (HOMO AQUATICUS)
                              ANDERSON, POUL      SS  AMZ 63 09
  MAN TO MY WOUNDING, A (STATE OF ASSASSINATION)
                              ANDERSON, POUL      SS  EQM 59 12
  HIGH ONES, THE              ANDERSON, POUL      NV  INF 58 06
  MAN WHO CAME EARLY, THE     ANDERSON, POUL      NV  FSF 56 06
  MARIUS                      ANDERSON, POUL      SS  ASF 57 03
  PROGRESS                    ANDERSON, POUL      NV  FSF 62 01

HORROR FROM THE HILLS, THE  LONG, FRANK BELKNAP AC  DIG 65
  SEE "ODD SCIENCE FICTION"

HORROR ON THE ASTEROID AND OTHER TALES OF PLANETARY HORROR
                              HAMILTON, EDMOND    AC H GRG 75 06
  REPRINT OF 1936 EDITION PUBLISHED BY P. ALLEN, LONDON
  INTRODUCTION                DE LA REE, GERRY    IN
  HORROR ON THE ASTEROID      HAMILTON, EDMOND    SS  WRT 33 09
  ACCURSED GALAXY, THE        HAMILTON, EDMOND    SS  AMZ 35 07
  MAN WHO SAW EVERYTHING, THE HAMILTON, EDMOND    SS  AMZ 30 10
  EARTH-BRAIN, THE            HAMILTON, EDMOND    SS  WRT 32 04
  MONSTER-GOD OF MAMURTH, THE HAMILTON, EDMOND    SS  WRT 26 08
  MAN WHO EVOLVED, THE        HAMILTON, EDMOND    SS  WOS 31 04

HORROR TIMES TEN              NORTON, ALDEN H.    AN  BKM 67 06
  INTRODUCTION                NORTON, ALDEN H.    IN
  TRUNK LADY, THE             BRADBURY, RAY       SS  DMM 48 01
  COOL AIR                    LOVECRAFT, H. P.    SS  TMM 28 03
  LONESOME PLACE, THE         DERLETH, AUGUST     SS  FFM 48 02
  DEAD REMEMBER, THE          HOWARD, ROBERT E.   SS  ARG 36 08
  CAPTAIN OF THE "POLE STAR", THE
                              DOYLE, ARTHUR CONAN NV      94
  RECEDING BROW, THAT         BRAND, MAX          NV  ASW 19 03
  HIS UNCONQUERABLE ENEMY     MORROW, W. C.       SS      97
  DEAD VALLEY, THE            CRAM, RALPH ADAMS   SS      95
```

HOUSE OF THE HATCHET, THE

```
  GORGON'S HEAD, THE          BAKER, DOROTHY      SS  SND 99 12
  SKELETON IN THE CLOSET, THE BLOCH, ROBERT       SS  FAD 43 06

HORROR-7                      BLOCH, ROBERT       AC  BEL 63 02
  ENOCH                       BLOCH, ROBERT       SS  WRT 46 09
  STRANGE FLIGHT OF RICHARD CLAYTON, THE
                              BLOCH, ROBERT       SS  AMZ 39 03
  OPENER OF THE WAY, THE      BLOCH, ROBERT       SS  WRT 36 10
  RETURN TO THE SABBATH       BLOCH, ROBERT       SS  WRT 38 07
  MANDARIN'S CANARIES, THE    BLOCH, ROBERT       SS  WRT 38 09
  SHAMBLER FROM THE STARS, THE BLOCH, ROBERT      SS  WRT 35 09
  SECRET OF SEBEK, THE        BLOCH, ROBERT       SS  WRT 37 11

HORSES' ASTEROID              FRITCH, CHARLES E.  AC  POW 70
  HORSES' ASTEROID            FRITCH, CHARLES E.  SS      58
  HONEYMOON                   FRITCH, CHARLES E.  SS  VOR 53 05
  BLOODMOBILE                 FRITCH, CHARLES E.  SS
  BIG LEAP, THE               FRITCH, CHARLES E.  SS  IFS 55 02
  TRICK OR TREAT              FRITCH, CHARLES E.  SS  AMZ 57 07
  VENUS PLUS THREE            FRITCH, CHARLES E.  NV  GAM 63 01
  BREATHES THERE A MAN        FRITCH, CHARLES E.  SS  RKS 53 07
  DANGER IN THE VOID          FRITCH, CHARLES E.  SS  INF 54 08
  ESCAPE MECHANISM            FRITCH, CHARLES E.  SS  IFS 55 04
  PACIFISTS, THE              FRITCH, CHARLES E.  SS  IFS 55 05
  SHAGGY DOG                  FRITCH, CHARLES E.  SS  STN 58 03
  SHOCK TREATMENT             FRITCH, CHARLES E.  SS  FUN 55 02
  ATAVIST, THE                FRITCH, CHARLES E.  SS

HOSPITAL STATION              WHITE, JAMES        AC  BAL 62
  MEDIC (O'MARA'S ORPHAN)     WHITE, JAMES        NV  NWS 60 01
  SECTOR GENERAL              WHITE, JAMES        NV  NWS 57 11
  TROUBLE WITH EMILY, THE     WHITE, JAMES        NV  NWS 58 11
  VISITOR AT LARGE            WHITE, JAMES        NV  NWS 59 06
  OUT-PATIENT                 WHITE, JAMES        NV  NWS 60 06

HOT & COLD RUNNING CITIES     MCHARGUE, GEORGESS  AN H HRW 74
  INTRODUCTION                MCHARGUE, GEORGESS  IN
  ENCHANTED VILLAGE (ALSO AS THE SANDS OF MARS)
                              VAN VOGT, A. E.     SS  OWS 50 07
  DEEPS, THE                  ROBERTS, KEITH      SS  ORB 66 01
  MENACE FROM EARTH, THE      HEINLEIN, ROBERT A. SS  FSF 57 08
  METROPOLITAN NIGHTMARE      BENET, STEPHEN V.   PM      27
  LUCKIEST MAN IN DENV, THE (AS SIMON EISNER)
                              KORNBLUTH, C. M.    SS  GAL 52 06
  CITY THAT LOVES YOU, THE    BANKS, RAYMOND E.   SS  GAL 69 03
  PLACE WHERE CHICAGO WAS, THE HARMON, JIM        NV  GAL 62 02
  NATURAL STATE               KNIGHT, DAMON       NA  GAL 54 01
  PLENITUDE                   WORTHINGTON, WILL   SS  FSF 59 11

HOTHOUSE                      ALDISS, BRIAN W.    NO H FAB 62
  SEE "THE LONG AFTERNOON OF EARTH"

HOUNDS OF TINDALOS, THE       LONG, FRANK BELKNAP AC H ARK 46
  VISITOR FROM EGYPT, A       LONG, FRANK BELKNAP SS  WRT 30 09
  REFUGEES, THE               LONG, FRANK BELKNAP SS  UNK 42 02
  FISHERMAN'S LUCK            LONG, FRANK BELKNAP SS  UNK 40 07
  DEATH-WATERS                LONG, FRANK BELKNAP SS  WRT 24 12
  GRAB BAGS ARE DANGEROUS     LONG, FRANK BELKNAP SS  UNK 42 06
  ELEMENTAL, THE              LONG, FRANK BELKNAP SS  UNK 39 07
  PEEPER, THE                 LONG, FRANK BELKNAP SS  WRT 44 03
  BRIDGEHEAD (ALSO AS THE TEMPORAL TRANSGRESSOR)
                              LONG, FRANK BELKNAP NV  ASF 44 08
  SECOND NIGHT OUT            LONG, FRANK BELKNAP SS  WRT 33 10
  DARK BEASTS, THE            LONG, FRANK BELKNAP SS  MVT 34 07
  CENSUS TAKER, THE           LONG, FRANK BELKNAP SS  UNK 42 04
  OCEAN LEECH, THE            LONG, FRANK BELKNAP SS  WRT 25 01
  SPACE-EATERS, THE           LONG, FRANK BELKNAP NV  WRT 28 07
  IT WILL COME TO YOU         LONG, FRANK BELKNAP SS  UNK 42 12
  STITCH IN TIME, A           LONG, FRANK BELKNAP SS  SSS 40 03
  STEP INTO MY GARDEN         LONG, FRANK BELKNAP SS  UNK 42 08
  HOUNDS OF TINDALOS, THE     LONG, FRANK BELKNAP SS  WRT 29 03
  DARK VISION                 LONG, FRANK BELKNAP SS  UNK 39 03
  FLAME MIDGET, THE           LONG, FRANK BELKNAP SS  ASF 36 12
  GOLDEN CHILD                LONG, FRANK BELKNAP NV
  BLACK DRUID, THE            LONG, FRANK BELKNAP SS  WRT 30 07

HOUNDS OF TINDALOS, THE (9 OF 21)
                              LONG, FRANK BELKNAP AC  BEL 63 08
  DARK VISION                 LONG, FRANK BELKNAP SS  UNK 39 03
  BLACK DRUID, THE            LONG, FRANK BELKNAP SS  WRT 30 07
  SPACE-EATERS, THE           LONG, FRANK BELKNAP NV  WRT 28 07
  GRAB BAGS ARE DANGEROUS     LONG, FRANK BELKNAP SS  UNK 42 06
  FISHERMAN'S LUCK            LONG, FRANK BELKNAP SS  UNK 40 07
  ELEMENTAL, THE              LONG, FRANK BELKNAP SS  UNK 39 07
  GOLDEN CHILD                LONG, FRANK BELKNAP NV
  PEEPER, THE                 LONG, FRANK BELKNAP SS  WRT 44 03
  HOUNDS OF TINDALOS, THE     LONG, FRANK BELKNAP SS  WRT 29 03

HOUSE OF THE HATCHET AND OTHER TALES OF HORROR, THE
                              BLOCH, ROBERT       AC  TDM 65
  SEE "YOURS TRULY, JACK THE RIPPER"

HOUSE OF THE HATCHET, THE     BLOCH, ROBERT       AC  PTH 76
  11 STORIES FROM "THE OPENER OF THE WAY"
  INTRODUCTION                BLOCH, ROBERT       IN
  HOUSE OF THE HATCHET, THE   BLOCH, ROBERT       SS  WRT 41 01
  RETURN TO THE SABBATH       BLOCH, ROBERT       SS  WRT 38 07
  MANDARIN'S CANARIES, THE    BLOCH, ROBERT       SS  WRT 38 09
  WAXWORKS                    BLOCH, ROBERT       SS  WRT 39 01
  FEAST IN THE ABBEY, THE     BLOCH, ROBERT       SS  WRT 35 01
  SLAVE OF THE FLAMES         BLOCH, ROBERT       SS  WRT 38 06
  SHAMBLER FROM THE STARS, THE BLOCH, ROBERT      SS  WRT 35 09
  MOTHER OF SERPENTS          BLOCH, ROBERT       SS  WRT 36 12
  SECRET OF SEBEK, THE        BLOCH, ROBERT       SS  WRT 37 11
  EYES OF THE MUMMY, THE      BLOCH, ROBERT       SS  WRT 38 04
  ONE WAY TO MARS             BLOCH, ROBERT       SS  WRT 45 07
```

HUGO WINNERS, THE (VOLUME 1)   I SING THE BODY ELECTRIC

HUGO WINNERS, THE (VOLUME 1) ASIMOV, ISAAC   AN H DBL 62
  INTRODUCTION   ASIMOV, ISAAC   IN
  DARFSTELLER, THE   MILLER, WALTER M. JR SN   ASF 55 01
  ALLAMAGOOSA   RUSSELL, ERIC FRANK   SS   ASF 55 05
  EXPLORATION TEAM (ALSO AS COMBAT TEAM)
                                 LEINSTER, MURRAY   NV   ASF 56 03
  STAR, THE   CLARKE, ARTHUR C.   SS   INF 55 11
  OR ALL THE SEAS WITH OYSTERS   DAVIDSON, AVRAM   SS   GAL 58 05
  BIG FRONT YARD, THE   SIMAK, CLIFFORD D.   NV   ASF 58 10
  THAT HELL-BOUND TRAIN   BLOCH, ROBERT   SS   FSF 58 09
  FLOWERS FOR ALGERNON   KEYES, DANIEL   SS   FSF 59 04
  LONGEST VOYAGE, THE   ANDERSON, POUL   NV   ASF 60 12
  APPENDIX: THE HUGO AWARDS   MISC. MATERIAL   MS

HUGO WINNERS, THE (VOLUME 2) ASIMOV, ISAAC   AN H DBL 71
  DERIVATIVE ANTHOLOGIES "STORIES FROM THE HUGO WINNERS VOL. 2"
    AND "MORE STORIES FROM THE HUGO WINNERS VOL. 2"
  HERE I AM AGAIN   ASIMOV, ISAAC   IN
  DRAGON MASTERS, THE   VANCE, JACK   SN   GAL 62 08
  NO TRUCE WITH KINGS   ANDERSON, POUL   NV   FSF 63 06
  SOLDIER, ASK NOT   DICKSON, GORDON R.   SN   GAL 64 10
  "REPENT, HARLEQUIN!" SAID THE TICKTOCKMAN
                                 ELLISON, HARLAN   SS   GAL 65 12
  LAST CASTLE, THE   VANCE, JACK   NV   GAL 66 04
  NEUTRON STAR   NIVEN, LARRY   NV   IFS 66 10
  WEYR SEARCH   MCCAFFREY, ANNE   SN   ASF 67 10
  RIDERS OF THE PURPLE WAGE   FARMER, PHILIP JOSE   NA   DVS 67 01
  GONNA ROLL THE BONES   LEIBER, FRITZ   NV   DVS 67 01
  I HAVE NO MOUTH, AND I MUST SCREAM
                                 ELLISON, HARLAN   SS   IFS 67 03
  NIGHTWINGS   SILVERBERG, ROBERT   NV   GAL 68 09
  SHARING OF FLESH, THE   ANDERSON, POUL   NV   GAL 68 12
  BEAST THAT SHOUTED LOVE AT THE HEART OF THE WORLD, THE
                                 ELLISON, HARLAN   NV   GAL 68 06
  TIME CONSIDERED AS A HELIX OF SEMI-PRECIOUS STONES
                                 DELANY, SAMUEL R.   SS   NWS 68 12

HUMAN AND OTHER BEINGS   DEGRAEFF, ALLEN   AN   CLB 63
  SCIENCE FICTION AND IDEAS   CONKLIN, GROFF   IN
  PREFACE   DEGRAEFF, ALLEN   IN
  DARK INTERLUDE   BROWN, FREDRIC
                                 AND REYNOLDS, MACK   SS C GAL 51 01
  LOVE   WILSON, RICHARD   SS   FSF 52 06
  HONOR   WILSON, RICHARD   SS   SFQ 56 02
  DOUBLE DOME   BANKS, RAYMOND E.   SS   GAL 57 05
  WAY IN THE MIDDLE OF THE AIR   BRADBURY, RAY   SS   OWS 50 07
  OTHER FOOT, THE   BRADBURY, RAY   SS   NST 51 03
  VILBAR PARTY, THE   SMITH, EVELYN E.   SS   GAL 55 01
  MADE IN U.S.A.   MCINTOSH, J. T.   NV   GAL 53 04
  NRACP, THE   ELLIOTT, GEORGE P.   NV   HUD 49 FL
  BIG STINK, THE   COGSWELL, THEODORE R   SS   IFS 54 07
  DOWN AMONG THE DEAD MEN   TENN, WILLIAM   NV   GAL 54 06
  ALL THE COLORS OF THE RAINBOW
                                 BRACKETT, LEIGH   SS   VSF 57 11
  WORLD OF MYRION FLOWERS, THE   POHL, FREDERIK
                                 AND KORNBLUTH, C. M.   SS C FSF 61 10
  MY LADY GREEN SLEEVES   POHL, FREDERIK   NA   GAL 57 02
  HOLDOUT   SHECKLEY, ROBERT   SS   FSF 57 12
  TEST PIECE   RUSSELL, ERIC FRANK   SS   OWS 51 03

HUMAN ANGLE, THE   TENN, WILLIAM   AC   BAL 56 08
  PROJECT HUSH   TENN, WILLIAM   SS   GAL 54 02
  DISCOVERY OF MORNIEL MATHAWAY, THE
                                 TENN, WILLIAM   SS   GAL 55 10
  WEDNESDAY'S CHILD   TENN, WILLIAM   SS   FUN 56 01
  SERVANT PROBLEM, THE   TENN, WILLIAM   NV   GAL 55 04
  PARTY OF THE TWO PARTS   TENN, WILLIAM   NV   GAL 54 08
  FLAT-EYED MONSTER, THE   TENN, WILLIAM   NV   GAL 55 08
  HUMAN ANGLE, THE   TENN, WILLIAM   SS   FFM 48 10
  MAN OF FAMILY, A   TENN, WILLIAM   SS

HUMAN EQUATION, THE   NOLAN, WILLIAM F.   AN H SHB 71
  EDITOR'S PREFACE   NOLAN, WILLIAM F.   IN
  ALFRED BESTER   NOLAN, WILLIAM F.   AR
  FLOWERED THUNDERMUG, THE   BESTER, ALFRED   NV
  LEIGH BRACKETT & RAY BRADBURY
                                 NOLAN, WILLIAM F.   AR
  LORELEI OF THE RED MIST   BRACKETT, LEIGH
                                 AND BRADBURY, RAY   NV C PLS 46 SU
  JOHN D. MACDONALD   NOLAN, WILLIAM F.   AR
  HALF-PAST ETERNITY   MACDONALD, JOHN D.   NV   SSS 50 07
  PHILIP K. DICK   NOLAN, WILLIAM F.   AR
  NOVELTY ACT   DICK, PHILIP K.   NV   FAN 64 02

HUMAN ZERO, THE   MOSKOWITZ & ELWOOD   AN   TWR 67
  HUMAN ZERO, THE   GARDNER, EARL S.   NV   ARG 31 12
  MAN WHO PLOUGHED THE SEA, THE
                                 CLARKE, ARTHUR C.   SS   SAT 57 06
  PROXY HEAD, THE   BLOCH, ROBERT   SS   SFP 53 05
  HANDS ACROSS SPACE (ALSO AS SCIENTIFIC METHOD)
                                 OLIVER, CHAD   SS   SFP 53 08
  ITSELF   VAN VOGT, A. E.   SS   GAM 53 01
  IMAGINARY, THE   ASIMOV, ISAAC   SS   SSS 42 11
  COSMIC RELIC, THE   RUSSELL, ERIC FRANK   NV   FAN 61 06
  I, ROCKET   BRADBURY, RAY   SS   AMZ 44 05

HUMAN?   MERRIL, JUDITH   AN   LIO 54 04
  INTRODUCTION   BROWN, FREDRIC   IN
  BIG CONTEST, THE   MACDONALD, JOHN D.   SS   WBY 50 12
  BOY NEXT DOOR, THE   OLIVER, CHAD   SS   FSF 51 06
  TAKE A SEAT   RUSSELL, ERIC FRANK   SS   STS 52 05
  EGG A MONTH FROM ALL OVER, AN
                                 SEABRIGHT, IDRIS   SS   FSF 52 10
  RIYA'S FOUNDLING   BUDRYS, ALGIS   SS   SFS 53 01
  GHOSTS (FROM ARCHIE AND MEHITABLE)
                                 MARQUIS, DON   EX   27

  SMOKE GHOST   LEIBER, FRITZ   SS   UNK 41 10
  "WHO SHALL I SAY IS CALLING?"
                                 DERLETH, AUGUST   SS   FSF 52 08
  GNARLY MAN, THE   DE CAMP, L. SPRAGUE   NV   UNK 39 06
  TEMPTATION OF HARRINGAY, THE   WELLS, H. G.   SS   SJG 95 02
  ULTIMATE EGOIST, THE   STURGEON, THEODORE   NV   UNK 41 02
  ROPE ENOUGH   COLLIER, JOHN   SS   NYM 39 11
  LIAR!   ASIMOV, ISAAC   SS   ASF 41 05
  WHO KNOWS HIS BROTHER   DOAR, GRAHAM   SS   STS 52 02
  CRUCIFIXUS ETIAM   MILLER, WALTER M. JR   SS   ASF 53 02

HUMAN-MACHINES   SCORTIA & ZEBROWSKI   AN   VNT 75 11
  INTRODUCTION: "UNHOLY MARRIAGE": THE CYBORG IN SCIENCE FICTION
                                 SCORTIA, THOMAS N.
                                 AND ZEBROWSKI, GEORGE IN C
  MEN OF IRON (1940)   ENDORE, GUY   SS   FSF 49 FL
  I'M WITH YOU IN ROCKLAND   DANN, JACK M.   SS   NEW 72 AN
  MASKS   KNIGHT, DAMON   SS   PBY 68 07
  FORTITUDE   VONNEGUT, KURT JR.   SS   PBY 68 09
  NO WOMAN BORN   MOORE, C. L.   NV   ASF 44 12
  CAMOUFLAGE   KUTTNER, HENRY   NV   ASF 45 09
  CRUCIFIXUS ETIAM   MILLER, WALTER M. JR   SS   ASF 53 02
  PERIOD PIECE   COUPLING, J. J.   SS   ASF 48 11
  SOLAR PLEXUS   BLISH, JAMES   SS   AST 41 09
  SEA CHANGE (ALSO AS THE SHORES OF NIGHT)
                                 SCORTIA, THOMAS N.   SS   ASF 56 06
  STARCROSSED   ZEBROWSKI, GEORGE   SS   EIO 73
  RECOMMENDED READING   MISC. MATERIAL   MS

HUNGER AND OTHER STORIES, THE
                                 BEAUMONT, CHARLES   AC H PUT 58 04
  IN ENGLAND AS "SHADOW PLAY", OMITS STORY "THE HUNGER"
  MISS GENTILBELLE   BEAUMONT, CHARLES   SS   NEW 57 AC
  VANISHING AMERICAN, THE   BEAUMONT, CHARLES   SS   FSF 55 08
  POINT OF HONOR, A (I'LL DO ANYTHING)
                                 BEAUMONT, CHARLES   SS   MHT 55
  FAIR LADY   BEAUMONT, CHARLES   SS   NEW 57 AC
  FREE DIRT   BEAUMONT, CHARLES   SS   FSF 55 05
  OPEN HOUSE   BEAUMONT, CHARLES   SS   NEW 57 AC
  TRAIN, THE   BEAUMONT, CHARLES   SS   NEW 57 AC
  DARK MUSIC, THE   BEAUMONT, CHARLES   SS   PBY 56 12
  CUSTOMERS, THE   BEAUMONT, CHARLES   SS   NEW 57 AC
  LAST NIGHT IN THE RAIN (SIN TOWER)
                                 BEAUMONT, CHARLES   SS   NUG 56
  CROOKED MAN, THE   BEAUMONT, CHARLES   SS   PBY 55 08
  NURSERY RHYME   BEAUMONT, CHARLES   SS   NEW 57 AC
  MURDERERS, THE   BEAUMONT, CHARLES   SS   ESQ 55
  HUNGER, THE   BEAUMONT, CHARLES   SS   PBY 55 04
  TEARS OF THE MADONNA   BEAUMONT, CHARLES   SS   NEW 57 AC
  INFERNAL BOUILLABAISSE, THE   BEAUMONT, CHARLES   SS   NEW 57 AC
  BLACK COUNTRY   BEAUMONT, CHARLES   SS   PBY 54 09

I HAVE NO MOUTH, AND I MUST SCREAM
                                 ELLISON, HARLAN   AC   PYR 67 04
  MOVER, THE SHAKER, THE   STURGEON, THEODORE   IN
  HOW SCIENCE FICTION SAVED ME FROM A LIFE OF CRIME
                                 ELLISON, HARLAN   IN
  I HAVE NO MOUTH, AND I MUST SCREAM
                                 ELLISON, HARLAN   SS   IFS 67 03
  BIG SAM WAS MY FRIEND   ELLISON, HARLAN   SS   SFA 58 03
  EYES OF DUST   ELLISON, HARLAN   SS   ROG 59 12
  WORLD OF THE MYTH   ELLISON, HARLAN   NV   KNT 64 08
  LONELYACHE   ELLISON, HARLAN   SS   KNT 64 07
  DELUSION FOR A DRAGON SLAYER   ELLISON, HARLAN   SS   KNT 66 09
  PRETTY MAGGIE MONEYEYES   ELLISON, HARLAN   NV   KNT 67 05

I LOVE GALESBURG IN THE SPRINGTIME
                                 FINNEY, JACK   AC H SAS 63
  "I LOVE GALESBURG IN THE SPRINGTIME"
                                 FINNEY, JACK   NV   MCC 60 04
  LOVE, YOUR MAGIC SPELL IS EVERYWHERE (THE MAN WITH THE MAGIC
    GLASSES)   FINNEY, JACK   NV   MCC 62 03
  THIRD LEVEL, THE (COL 50 10)   FINNEY, JACK   SS   FSF 52 10
  SUCH INTERESTING NEIGHBORS   FINNEY, JACK   SS   COL 51 01
  WHERE THE CLUETTS ARE   FINNEY, JACK   NV   MCC 62 01
  HEY! LOOK AT ME!   FINNEY, JACK   SS   PBY 62 09
  I'M SCARED   FINNEY, JACK   SS   COL 51 09
  COUSIN LEN'S WONDERFUL ADJECTIVE CELLAR
                                 FINNEY, JACK   SS
  POSSIBLE CANDIDATE FOR THE PRESIDENCY, A (TIGER TAMER)
                                 FINNEY, JACK   SS   COL 52 05
  OF MISSING PERSONS   FINNEY, JACK   SS   GHK 55 03
  PRISON LEGEND (SEVEN DAYS TO LIVE)
                                 FINNEY, JACK   NV   SEP 59 10
  FACE IN THE PHOTO, THE (TIME HAS NO BOUNDARIES)
                                 FINNEY, JACK   SS   SEP 62 10
  SOMETHING IN A CLOUD   FINNEY, JACK   SS
  INTREPID AERONAUT, THE (AN OLD TUNE)
                                 FINNEY, JACK   NV   MCC 61 10
  THERE IS A TIDE   FINNEY, JACK   SS   FSF 54 09
  COIN COLLECTOR, THE (THE OTHER WIFE)
                                 FINNEY, JACK   SS   SEP 60 01
  QUIT ZOOMIN' THOSE HANDS THROUGH THE AIR
                                 FINNEY, JACK   SS   FSF 52 12
  DASH OF SPRING, A   FINNEY, JACK   SS
  LOVE LETTER, THE   FINNEY, JACK   SS   SEP 59 08
  SECOND CHANCE   FINNEY, JACK   SS
  CONTENTS OF THE DEAD MAN'S POCKETS
                                 FINNEY, JACK   NV   NEW 57 AC

I SING THE BODY ELECTRIC   BRADBURY, RAY   AC H KNP 69
  KILIMANJARO DEVICE, THE (THE KILIMANJARO MACHINE)
                                 BRADBURY, RAY   SS   LIF 65 01
  TERRIBLE CONFLAGRATION UP AT THE PLACE
                                 BRADBURY, RAY   SS   NEW 69 AC
  TOMORROW'S CHILD   BRADBURY, RAY   SS   NEW 69 AC

I SING THE BODY ELECTRIC

```
WOMEN, THE                                BRADBURY, RAY     SS   FFM 48 10
INSPIRED CHICKEN MOTEL, THE   BRADBURY, RAY     SS   LAT 69 11
DOWNWIND FROM GETTYSBERG      BRADBURY, RAY     SS   PBY 69 06
YES, WE'LL GATHER AT THE RIVER
                                          BRADBURY, RAY     SS   NEW 69 AC
COLD WIND AND THE WARM, THE   BRADBURY, RAY     SS   HRP 64 07
NIGHT CALL, COLLECT              BRADBURY, RAY     SS   NEW 69 AC
HAUNTING OF THE NEW, THE         BRADBURY, RAY     SS   VOB 69 10
I SING THE BODY ELECTRIC (BEAUTIFUL ONE IS HERE)
                                          BRADBURY, RAY     NV   MCC 69 08
TUMBLING DAY, THE                 BRADBURY, RAY     SS   SHN 52 FL
ANY FRIEND OF NICHOLAS NICKLEBY'S IS A FRIEND OF MINE
  (THE BEST OF TIMES)            BRADBURY, RAY     NV   MCC 66 01
HEAVY-SET                         BRADBURY, RAY     SS   PBY 64 10
MAN IN THE RORSCHACH SHIRT, THE
                                          BRADBURY, RAY     SS   PBY 66 10
HENRY THE NINTH (FINAL SCEPTRE, A LASTING CROWN)
                                          BRADBURY, RAY     SS   FSF 69 10
LOST CITY OF MARS, THE           BRADBURY, RAY     NV   FSF 67 01
CHRISTUS APOLLO                   BRADBURY, RAY     PM   NEW 69 AC

I, ROBOT                          ASIMOV, ISAAC     AC H GNM 50
INTRODUCTION                      ASIMOV, ISAAC     IN
ROBBIE (STRANGE PLAYFELLOW)    ASIMOV, ISAAC     SS   SSS 40 09
RUNAROUND                         ASIMOV, ISAAC     SS   ASF 42 03
REASON                            ASIMOV, ISAAC     SS   ASF 41 04
CATCH THAT RABBIT                 ASIMOV, ISAAC     SS   ASF 44 02
LIAR!                             ASIMOV, ISAAC     SS   ASF 41 05
LITTLE LOST ROBOT                 ASIMOV, ISAAC     SS   ASF 47 03
ESCAPE (PARADOXICAL ESCAPE)    ASIMOV, ISAAC     SS   ASF 45 08
EVIDENCE                          ASIMOV, ISAAC     SS   ASF 46 09
EVITABLE CONFLICT, THE           ASIMOV, ISAAC     NV   ASF 50 06

I, ROBOT (BRITISH PB)            ASIMOV, ISAAC     AC   DIG 58
  OMITS LAST TWO STORIES

IDES OF TOMORROW, THE            CARR, TERRY       OA H LBR 76
SEEING                            ELLISON, HARLAN   SS
DARK SOUL OF THE NIGHT, THE   ALDISS, BRIAN W.  SS
PREDATORS                         UTLEY, STEVEN     SS
IN THE HOUSE OF THE WORM        MARTIN, GEORGE R. R. SS
WHEN I WAS MING THE MERCILESS
                                          WOLFE, GENE       SS
HEAD, THE                         BLOCH, ROBERT     SS
JAMIE'S SMILE                     BRENNERT, ALAN    SS
EERIEST RUINED DAWN WORLD, THE
                                          LEIBER, FRITZ     SS

IF READER OF SCIENCE FICTION, THE
                                          POHL, FREDERIK    AN H DBL 66
INTRODUCTION                      POHL, FREDERIK    IN
WHEN TIME WAS NEW                 YOUNG, ROBERT F.  NV   IFS 64 12
FATHER OF THE STARS              POHL, FREDERIK    SS   IFS 64 11
LIFE HATER, THE (ALSO AS THE PEACEMAKER)
                                          SABERHAGEN, FRED  SS   IFS 64 08
OLD TESTAMENT                     BIXBY, JEROME     SS   IFS 64 07
SILKIE, THE                       VAN VOGT, A. E.   NV   IFS 64 07
BETTER MOUSETRAP, A              BRUNNER, JOHN     NV   IFS 63 11
LONG DAY IN COURT                 BRAND, JONATHAN   SS   IFS 63 11
TRICK OR TREATY                   LAUMER, KEITH     NV   IFS 65 08
64-SQUARE MADHOUSE, THE         LEIBER, FRITZ     NA   IFS 62 05

IF THIS GOES ON                   NUETZEL, CHARLES  AN   BCA 65
  STORY "ALMOST THE END OF THE WORLD" BY RAY BRADBURY LISTED
  IN CONTENTS AND ON COVER BUT NOT IN BOOK
INTRODUCTION                      ACKERMAN, FORREST J. IN
PREFACE                           NUETZEL, CHARLES  IN
TEST, THE                         MATHESON, RICHARD SS   FSF 54 11
EARTH KILLERS, THE              VAN VOGT, A. E.   NV   SSS 49 04
RACER, THE                        MELCHIOR, IB      SS   56
ALL THE TROUBLES OF THE WORLD
                                          ASIMOV, ISAAC     SS   SUP 58 04
FRIENDS AND ENEMIES              LEIBER, FRITZ     SS   INF 57 04
NO LAND OF NOD                    SPRINGER, SHERWOOD SS  TWS 52 12
VERY CULTURED TASTE, A          FREDERIC, GEORGE  SS   60
MUTE QUESTION, THE              ACKERMAN, FORREST J. SS OWS 50 09
HOMO SAP, THE ALSO AS THE GROOVY HOMO SAP)
                                          NUETZEL, CHARLES  SS
AQUELLA                           WOLLHEIM, DONALD A. SS AFR 48 07
CLIMBING WAVE, THE              BRADLEY, MARION Z. SS  FSF 55 02
YOUR LIFE IN 1977                LEY, WILLY        AR
PREPOSTEROUS                      BROWN, FREDRIC    SS   NEW 54 AC

ILLUSTRATED MAN, THE             BRADBURY, RAY     AC H DBL 51 02
PROLOGUE: THE ILLUSTRATED MAN
                                          BRADBURY, RAY     SS   NEW 51 AC
VELDT, THE (THE WORLD THE CHILDREN MADE)
                                          BRADBURY, RAY     SS   SEP 50 09
KALEIDOSCOPE                      BRADBURY, RAY     SS   TWS 49 10
OTHER FOOT, THE                   BRADBURY, RAY     SS   NST 51 03
HIGHWAY, THE (AS LEONARD SPALDING)
                                          BRADBURY, RAY     SS   CPY 50 SP
MAN, THE                          BRADBURY, RAY     SS   TWS 49 02
LONG RAIN, THE (DEATH-BY-RAIN)
                                          BRADBURY, RAY     SS   PLS 50 SU
ROCKET MAN, THE                   BRADBURY, RAY     SS   MCL 51 05
FIRE BALLOONS, THE (IN THIS SIGN)
                                          BRADBURY, RAY     SS   IMG 51 04
LAST NIGHT OF THE WORLD, THE  BRADBURY, RAY     SS   ESQ 51 02
EXILES, THE (THE MAD WIZARDS OF MARS, MCL 49 09)
                                          BRADBURY, RAY     SS   FSF 50 WS
NO PARTICULAR NIGHT OR MORNING
                                          BRADBURY, RAY     SS   NEW 51 AC
FOX AND THE FOREST, THE (TO THE FUTURE)
                                          BRADBURY, RAY     SS   COL 50 05
VISITOR, THE                      BRADBURY, RAY     SS   STS 48 11
```

```
CONCRETE MIXER, THE              BRADBURY, RAY     SS   TWS 49 04
MARIONETTES, INC.                 BRADBURY, RAY     SS   STS 49 03
CITY, THE (PURPOSE)              BRADBURY, RAY     SS   STS 50 07
ZERO HOUR                         BRADBURY, RAY     SS   PLS 47 FL
ROCKET, THE (OUTCAST OF THE STARS)
                                          BRADBURY, RAY     SS   SSS 50 03
EPILOGUE                          BRADBURY, RAY     MS   51

ILLUSTRATED MAN, THE (BRITISH)
                                          BRADBURY, RAY     AC H HDV 52
PROLOGUE: THE ILLUSTRATED MAN
                                          BRADBURY, RAY     SS   NEW 51 AC
VELDT, THE (THE WORLD THE CHILDREN MADE)
                                          BRADBURY, RAY     SS   SEP 50 09
KALEIDOSCOPE                      BRADBURY, RAY     SS   TWS 49 10
OTHER FOOT, THE                   BRADBURY, RAY     SS   NST 51 03
HIGHWAY, THE (AS LEONARD SPALDING)
                                          BRADBURY, RAY     SS   CPY 50 SP
MAN, THE                          BRADBURY, RAY     SS   TWS 49 02
LONG RAIN, THE (DEATH-BY-RAIN)
                                          BRADBURY, RAY     SS   PLS 50 SU
LAST NIGHT OF THE WORLD, THE  BRADBURY, RAY     SS   ESQ 51 02
NO PARTICULAR NIGHT OR MORNING
                                          BRADBURY, RAY     SS   NEW 51 AC
FOX AND THE FOREST, THE (TO THE FUTURE)
                                          BRADBURY, RAY     SS   COL 50 05
VISITOR, THE                      BRADBURY, RAY     SS   STS 48 11
MARIONETTES, INC.                 BRADBURY, RAY     SS   STS 49 03
CITY, THE (PURPOSE)              BRADBURY, RAY     SS   STS 50 07
ZERO HOUR                         BRADBURY, RAY     SS   PLS 47 FL
ROCKET, THE (OUTCAST OF THE STARS)
                                          BRADBURY, RAY     SS   SSS 50 03
USHER II (CARNIVAL OF MADNESS)
                                          BRADBURY, RAY     SS   TWS 50 04
PLAYGROUND, THE                   BRADBURY, RAY     SS   ESQ 53 10
EPILOGUE                          BRADBURY, RAY     MS   51

IMAGES OF TOMORROW               NUETZEL, CHARLES  AC   POW 69 03
INTRODUCTION                      ACKERMAN, FORREST J. IN
IMAGES OF MAN                     NUETZEL, CHARLES  SS
JUDGMENT, THE                     NUETZEL, CHARLES  SS
WORLD THAT WOMB MADE, THE      NUETZEL, CHARLES  SS
GUIDED TOUR                       NUETZEL, CHARLES  SS
PLANET OF THE LOVE FEAST        NUETZEL, CHARLES  SS
GOOD DOCTOR, THE                  NUETZEL, CHARLES  SS
GROOVY HOMO SAP, THE (HOMO SAP)
                                          NUETZEL, CHARLES  SS
HUNGER PANGS                      NUETZEL, CHARLES  SS
NOVA INCIDENT, THE              NUETZEL, CHARLES  SS
WORD TO THE WISE                  NUETZEL, CHARLES  SS
ERSATZ, THE                       NUETZEL, CHARLES  SS
VERY CULTURED TASTE, A (AS GEORGE FREDERIC)
                                          NUETZEL, CHARLES  SS   60
ROYAL LESSON                      NUETZEL, CHARLES  SS

IMAGINATION UNLIMITED           BLEILER & DIKTY   AN H FSY 52
  ALSO AS "MEN OF SPACE AND TIME"
INTRODUCTION                      BLEILER, EVERETT F.
                                  AND DIKTY, T. E.  IN C
WHAT DEAD MEN TELL              STURGEON, THEODORE NV  ASF 49 11
REFERENT (AS BRETT STERLING)   BRADBURY, RAY     SS   TWS 48 10
BLIND MAN'S BUFF                  JAMESON, MALCOLM  NV   ASF 44 10
PRESSURE                          ROCKLYNNE, ROSS   SS   ASF 39 06
XI EFFECT, THE                    LATHAM, PHILIP    SS   ASF 50 01
OLD FAITHFUL                      GALLUN, RAYMOND Z. NV  ASF 34 12
ALAS, ALL THINKING!              BATES, HARRY      SN   ASF 35 06
DUNE ROLLER                       MAY, JULIAN C.    NV   ASF 51 12
EMPLOYMENT (AS LYMAN R. LYON)
                                          DE CAMP, L. SPRAGUE SS ASF 39 05
DREAMS ARE SACRED                PHILLIPS, PETER   SS   ASF 48 09
HOLD BACK TOMORROW               NEVILLE, KRIS     SS   IMG 51 09
BEROM                             BERRYMAN, JOHN    NV   ASF 51 01
FIRE AND THE SWORD, THE         ROBINSON, FRANK M. NV  GAL 51 08

IMAGINATION UNLIMITED (BRITISH)
                                          BLEILER & DIKTY   AN H BDL 53
  FIRST 6 STORIES OF AMERICAN VERSION, REMAINDER IN
  "MEN OF SPACE AND TIME"

IMAGINATION UNLIMITED (7 OF 13)
                                          BLEILER & DIKTY   AN   BRK 59 04
REFERENT (AS BRETT STERLING)   BRADBURY, RAY     SS   TWS 48 10
WHAT DEAD MEN TELL              STURGEON, THEODORE NV  ASF 49 11
DUNE ROLLER                       MAY, JULIAN C.    NV   ASF 51 12
EMPLOYMENT (AS LYMAN R. LYON)
                                          DE CAMP, L. SPRAGUE SS ASF 39 05
DREAMS ARE SACRED                PHILLIPS, PETER   SS   ASF 48 09
BEROM                             BERRYMAN, JOHN    NV   ASF 51 01
FIRE AND THE SWORD, THE         ROBINSON, FRANK M. NV  GAL 51 08

IMMORTALS, THE                    GUNN, JAMES E.    NO   BAN 62 11
NEW BLOOD                         GUNN, JAMES E.    NV   ASF 55 10
DONOR                             GUNN, JAMES E.    NV   FAN 60 11
MEDIC (NOT SO GREAT AN ENEMY)
                                          GUNN, JAMES E.    NV   VSF 57 07
IMMORTAL (THE IMMORTALS)        GUNN, JAMES E.    NV   STR 58 04

IMPACT-20                         NOLAN, WILLIAM F. AC   PBK 63 11
ABOUT BILL NOLAN                  BRADBURY, RAY     IN
SMALL WORLD OF LEWIS STILLMAN, THE (SMALL WORLD)
                                          NOLAN, WILLIAM F. SS   FUN 57 08
BEAUTIFUL DOLL CAPER, THE       NOLAN, WILLIAM F. SS   NUG 56
INTO THE LION'S DEN              NOLAN, WILLIAM F. SS   56
MARTIANS AND THE LEADFOOT, THE
                                          NOLAN, WILLIAM F. SS   SCJ 57
END WITH NO PERHAPS, THE        NOLAN, WILLIAM F. SS   NEW 63 AC
```

```
IMPACT-20                                                          INFINITE MOMENT, THE

AMAZON KICK, THE            NOLAN, WILLIAM F.    SS   ROG 59      AUTHOR'S INTRODUCTION       O'DONNELL, K. M.    IN
FULL QUOTA                 NOLAN, WILLIAM F.    SS   FUN 58 04    IN THE POCKET               O'DONNELL, K. M.    SS   NOV 70 01
AND MILES TO GO BEFORE I SLEEP                                   GEHENNA                     O'DONNELL, K. M.    SS   GAL 71 03
                           NOLAN, WILLIAM F.    SS   INF 58 08    AH, FAIR URANUS             O'DONNELL, K. M.    SS   NEW 71 DC
PUBLIC LOVES A JOHNNY, THE NOLAN, WILLIAM F.    SS   NEW 63 AC    NOTES JUST PRIOR TO THE FALL O'DONNELL, K. M.   SS   FSF 70 10
DUTCH                      NOLAN, WILLIAM F.    SS        58      AS BETWEEN GENERATIONS      O'DONNELL, K. M.    SS   FAN 70 10
OF TIME AND TEXAS          NOLAN, WILLIAM F.    SS   FUN 56 11    FALCON AND THE FALCONEER, THE
DEATH DOUBLE               NOLAN, WILLIAM F.    SS   NEW 63 AC                                O'DONNELL, K. M.    SS   FSF 69 12
DARK ENCOUNTER             NOLAN, WILLIAM F.    SS        59      JULY 24, 1970               O'DONNELL, K. M.    SS   VSP 69 05
LAP OF THE PRIMITIVE, THE  NOLAN, WILLIAM F.    SS   FUN 58 10    PACEM EST                   O'DONNELL, K. M.
NOBODY, THAT'S WHO         NOLAN, WILLIAM F.    SS   NEW 63 AC                                AND NEVILLE, KRIS   SS C INY 70 01
DARENDINGER BUILD-UP, THE  NOLAN, WILLIAM F.    SS   PBY 56 06    NEW RAPPACINI, THE          O'DONNELL, K. M.    SS   FAN 70 12
PIGEON                     NOLAN, WILLIAM F.    SS        57      BAT                         O'DONNELL, K. M.    SS   NEW 71 DC
JOY OF LIVING, THE         NOLAN, WILLIAM F.    SS   IFS 54 08    QUESTION OF SLANT, A        O'DONNELL, K. M.    SS
ONE OF THOSE DAYS          NOLAN, WILLIAM F.    SS   FSF 62 05    WHAT TIME WAS THAT?         O'DONNELL, K. M.    SS   IFS 69 12
TO SERVE THE SHIP (ALSO AS SOLUTION)                             SOULSONG TO THE SAD, SILLY, SOARING SIXTIES, A
                           NOLAN, WILLIAM F.    SS   GAM 63 01                                O'DONNELL, K. M.    SS   FAN 71 12
                                                                 ADDENDUM                    O'DONNELL, K. M.    SS   NEW 71 DC
IMPOSSIBLE MAN, THE        BALLARD, J. G.   AC   BRK 66 04        IDEA, THE                   O'DONNELL, K. M.    SS   NEW 71 DC
DROWNED GIANT, THE (SOUVENIR)
                           BALLARD, J. G.   SS   PBY 65 05        IN THE PROBLEM PIT          POHL, FREDERIK      AC   BAN 76 06
REPTILE ENCLOSURE, THE (THE SHERRINGTON THEORY)                  INTRODUCTION: SCIENCE-FICTION GAMES
                           BALLARD, J. G.   SS   AMZ 63 03                                    POHL, FREDERIK      IN
DELTA AT SUNSET, THE       BALLARD, J. G.   SS   NEW 64 04        IN THE PROBLEM PIT          POHL, FREDERIK      NA   FSF 73 09
STORM-BIRD, STORM-DREAMER  BALLARD, J. G.   SS   NWS 66 11        LET THE ANTS TRY            POHL, FREDERIK      SS   PLS 49 WI
SCREEN GAME, THE           BALLARD, J. G.   NV   FAN 63 10        TO SEE ANOTHER MOUNTAIN     POHL, FREDERIK      SS   FSF 59 04
DAY OF FOREVER, THE        BALLARD, J. G.   SS   NWS 67 01        DEADLY MISSION OF PHINEAS SNODGRASS, THE
TIME OF PASSAGE            BALLARD, J. G.   SS   SCF 64 02                                    POHL, FREDERIK      SS   GAL 62 06
GIOCONDA OF THE TWILIGHT NOON, THE                               GOLDEN AGES GONE AWAY       POHL, FREDERIK      AR   CLR 72 02
                           BALLARD, J. G.   SS   NEW 64 AC        RAFFERTY'S REASONS          POHL, FREDERIK      SS   FUN 55 10
IMPOSSIBLE MAN, THE        BALLARD, J. G.   SS   NEW 66 AC        I REMEMBER A WINTER         POHL, FREDERIK      SS   ORB 72 11
                                                                 SCHEMATIC MAN, THE          POHL, FREDERIK      SS   PBY 69 01
IMPOSSIBLE?               JANIFER, LAURENCE M. AC BEL 68 08       WHAT TO DO TILL THE ANALYST COMES (EVERYBODY'S HAPPY BUT ME|)
BUT FIRST...              JANIFER, LAURENCE M. IN                                             POHL, FREDERIK      SS   IMG 56 07
CHARLEY DE MILO           JANIFER, LAURENCE M. SS ASF 60 06       SOME JOYS UNDER THE STARS (THE STAR)
QUESTION, THE             JANIFER, LAURENCE M.                                               POHL, FREDERIK      SS   GAL 73 05
                          AND WESTLAKE, DONALD E. SS C FSF 63 03  MAN WHO ATE THE WORLD, THE  POHL, FREDERIK      NV   GAL 56 11
MAN WHO PLAYED TO LOSE, THE JANIFER, LAURENCE M. SS ASF 61 10     SF: THE GAME-PLAYING LITERATURE
FIRE SALE                 JANIFER, LAURENCE M. SS FAN 64 09                                   POHL, FREDERIK      AR   CLR 71 01
OBEY THAT IMPULSE|        JANIFER, LAURENCE M. SS FUT 59 06
LOST IN TRANSLATION       JANIFER, LAURENCE M. SS ASF 61 08       IN THE WAKE OF MAN          ELWOOD, ROGER       OA H BML 75
EXPATRIATE                JANIFER, LAURENCE M. NV CSM 53 11        FROM THE THUNDER COLT'S MOUTH
EXCERPTS FROM THE GALACTICK ALMANACK: MUSIC                                                   LAFFERTY, R. A.     NA
                          JANIFER, LAURENCE M. FA GAL 59 06       TRACKING SONG               WOLFE, GENE         NA
WIZARD                    JANIFER, LAURENCE M. SS ASF 60 05       SEARCH FOR MAN, THE         MOUDY, WALTER F.    NA
ELEMENTARY                JANIFER, LAURENCE M.
                          AND KURLAND, MICHAEL J. SS C FSF 64 09  INCREDIBLE PLANET, THE      CAMPBELL, JOHN W. JR NO H FPS 49
SIGHT GAG                 JANIFER, LAURENCE M. SS ASF 62 05       INCREDIBLE PLANET, THE      CAMPBELL, JOHN W. JR NV
SWORD OF FLOWERS          JANIFER, LAURENCE M. SS FAN 62 08       INTERSTELLAR SEARCH, THE    CAMPBELL, JOHN W. JR NV
THREE EXCERPTS            JANIFER, LAURENCE M. SS                 INFINITE ATOM, THE          CAMPBELL, JOHN W. JR NV
REPLACE THE HORSE         JANIFER, LAURENCE M. SS FAN 59 01
IN THE BAG                JANIFER, LAURENCE M. SS FSF 64 02       INEXPERIENCED GHOST AND NINE OTHER STORIES, THE
LOVE STORY                JANIFER, LAURENCE M. SS FAN 63 05                                   WELLS, H. G.    AC   BAN 65 02
                                                                 INTRODUCTION                LEAVITT, HART DAY   IN
IN DEEP                   KNIGHT, DAMON    AC   BKM 63            INEXPERIENCED GHOST, THE (THE STORY OF THE INEXPERIENCED GHOST)
BRITISH EDITIONS OMIT "THE HANDLER"                                                           WELLS, H. G.    SS   SND 02 03
FOUR IN ONE               KNIGHT, DAMON    NV   GAL 53 02         MAGIC SHOP, THE             WELLS, H. G.    SS   SND 03 06
EYE FOR A WHAT?, AN       KNIGHT, DAMON    NV   GAL 57 03         COUNTRY OF THE BLIND, THE   WELLS, H. G.    SS   SND 04 04
HANDLER, THE              KNIGHT, DAMON    SS   ROG 60 08         APPLE, THE                  WELLS, H. G.    SS   IDL 96 10
STRANGER STATION          KNIGHT, DAMON    NV   FSF 56 12         STOLEN BODY, THE            WELLS, H. G.    SS   SND 98 11
ASK ME ANYTHING           KNIGHT, DAMON    NV   GAL 51 05         SLIP UNDER THE MICROSCOPE, A WELLS, H. G.   SS   YBK 96 01
COUNTRY OF THE KIND, THE  KNIGHT, DAMON    SS   FSF 56 02         PURPLE PILEUS, THE          WELLS, H. G.    SS   BAW 96 01
TICKET TO ANYWHERE        KNIGHT, DAMON    NV   GAL 52 04         POLLOCK AND THE PORROH MAN  WELLS, H. G.    SS   NBG 95 05
BEACHCOMBER               KNIGHT, DAMON    SS   IMG 52 12         MAN WHO COULD WORK MIRACLES, THE
                                                                                             WELLS, H. G.    SS   ILN 98 07
IN DREAMS AWAKE           FIEDLER, LESLIE A.   AN   DEL 75 07     FLOWERING OF THE STRANGE ORCHID, THE (ALSO AS THE STRANGE
INTRODUCTION              FIEDLER, LESLIE A.   IN                 ORCHID)                     WELLS, H. G.    SS   PMB 94 08
BEGINNINGS, THE           FIEDLER, LESLIE A.   SI
CRYSTAL EGG, THE          WELLS, H. G.     SS   NRV 97 05         INFINITE ARENA, THE         CARR, TERRY     AN H NEL 77
UNPROFESSIONAL            KIPLING, RUDYARD SS   SRV 30 10         INTRODUCTION                CARR, TERRY     IN
CONVERSATION OF EIROS AND CHARMION, THE                          JOY IN MUDVILLE             ANDERSON, POUL
                          POE, EDGAR ALLEN SS   BGM 39 12                                     AND DICKSON, GORDON R. NV C FSF 55 11
TARTARUS OF MAIDS, THE    MELVILLE, HERMAN SS                    BULLARD REFLECTS            JAMESON, MALCOLM   SS   ASF 41 12
THREE THOUSAND YEARS AMONG THE MICROBES                          BODY BUILDERS, THE          LAUMER, KEITH      NV   GAL 66 08
                          TWAIN, MARK      SS                    GREAT KLADNAR RACE, THE (AS RICHARD GREER)
COLOUR OUT OF SPACE, THE (ALSO AS MONSTER OF TERROR)                                          SILVERBERG, ROBERT
                          LOVECRAFT, H. P. SS   AMZ 27 09                                     AND GARRETT, RANDALL SS C AMZ 56 12
GOLDEN AGE, THE           FIEDLER, LESLIE A.   SI                MR. MEEK PLAYS POLO         SIMAK, CLIFFORD D.  SS   PLS 44 FL
COLD EQUATIONS, THE       GODWIN, TOM      NV   ASF 54 08         SUNJAMMER (ALSO AS THE WIND FROM THE SUN)
HELEN O'LOY               DEL REY, LESTER  SS   ASF 38 12                                     CLARKE, ARTHUR C.  SS   BLF 64
IT'S A GOOD LIFE          BIXBY, JEROME    SS   STR 53 02         RUN TO STARLIGHT            MARTIN, GEORGE R. R. NV  AMZ 74 12
RESURRECTION (THE MONSTER) VAN VOGT, A. E. SS   ASF 48 08
GREEN HILLS OF EARTH, THE HEINLEIN, ROBERT A. SS SEP 47 02       INFINITE JESTS              SILVERBERG, ROBERT  AN H CHL 74
LIAR|                     ASIMOV, ISAAC    SS   ASF 41 05         INTRODUCTION                SILVERBERG, ROBERT  IN
NINE BILLION NAMES OF GOD, THE                                   VENUS AND THE SEVEN SEXES   TENN, WILLIAM      NV        49
                          CLARKE, ARTHUR C. SS  STR 53 01         BABEL II                    KNIGHT, DAMON      NV   BEY 53 07
AUGUST 2026: THERE WILL COME SOFT RAINS                          USEFUL PHRASES FOR THE TOURIST
                          BRADBURY, RAY    SS   COL 50 05                                     RUSS, JOANNA       SS   UNI 72 02
MOTHER                    FARMER, PHILIP JOSE NV TWS 53 04        CONVERSATIONAL MODE         LEMAN, GRAHAME     SS   NWR 72 20
MUSE, THE                 BURGESS, ANTHONY SS   HUD 68            HERESIES OF THE HUGE GOD    ALDISS, BRIAN W.   FA   GAL 66 08
NEW DIRECTIONS            FIEDLER, LESLIE A.   SI                 (NOW+N), (NOW-N)            SILVERBERG, ROBERT  NV   NOV 72 02
NINE LIVES                LE GUIN, URSULA K. NV PBY 69 11         SLOW TUESDAY NIGHT          LAFFERTY, R. A.    SS   GAL 65 04
"REPENT, HARLEQUIN|" SAID THE TICKTOCKMAN                        HELP| I AM DR. MORRIS GOLDPEPPER
                          ELLISON, HARLAN  SS   GAL 65 12                                     DAVIDSON, AVRAM    NV   GAL 57 07
TIME CONSIDERED AS A HELIX OF SEMI-PRECIOUS STONES               OH, TO BE A BLOBEL|         DICK, PHILIP K.    SS   GAL 64 02
                          DELANY, SAMUEL R. SS  NWS 68 12         HOBSON'S CHOICE             BESTER, ALFRED     SS   FSF 52 08
SECOND INQUISITION, THE   RUSS, JOANNA     NV   ORB 70 06         I PLINGLOT, WHO YOU?        POHL, FREDERIK     NV   GAL 59 02
PLAN FOR THE ASSASSINATION OF JACQUELINE KENNEDY
                          BALLARD, J. G.   SS   AMB 66 WI         INFINITE MOMENT, THE        WYNDHAM, JOHN   AC   BAL 61
                                                                 CONSIDER HER WAYS           WYNDHAM, JOHN   NV        56
IN THE FOOTSTEPS OF THE ABOMINABLE SNOWMAN                       ODD                         WYNDHAM, JOHN   SS
                          NESVADBA, JOSEF  AC        70           HOW DO I DO?                WYNDHAM, JOHN   SS   BEY 53 09
    SEE "THE LOST FACE"                                          STITCH IN TIME, A           WYNDHAM, JOHN   SS   FSF 61 03
                                                                 RANDOM QUEST                WYNDHAM, JOHN   NV   NEW 61 AC
IN THE POCKET AND OTHER S-F STORIES                              TIME OUT                    WYNDHAM, JOHN   NV
                          O'DONNELL, K. M. DC   ACE 71
```

INFINITY BOX, THE   WILHELM, KATE   AC H HPR 75
  INTRODUCTION   WILHELM, KATE   IN
  INFINITY BOX, THE   WILHELM, KATE   NA   ORB 71 09
  TIME PIECE, THE   WILHELM, KATE   NV   NEW 75 AC
  RED CANARY, THE   WILHELM, KATE   SS   ORB 73 12
  MAN OF LETTERS   WILHELM, KATE   SS   NEW 75 AC
  APRIL FOOL'S DAY FOREVER   WILHELM, KATE   NV   ORB 70 07
  WHERE HAVE YOU BEEN, BILLY BOY, BILLY BOY?
                               WILHELM, KATE   SS   QRK 71 03
  FUSION BOMB, THE   WILHELM, KATE   NV   ORB 72 10
  VILLAGE, THE   WILHELM, KATE   SS   BMR 73
  FUNERAL, THE   WILHELM, KATE   NV   DVS 72 02

INFINITY 1   HOSKINS, ROBERT   OA   LAN 70
  INTRODUCTION: THE FUN IN FUTURE FUN
                               ASIMOV, ISAAC   IN   67
  WORD FROM THE EDITOR, A   HOSKINS, ROBERT   IN   INY 70 01
  PLEASURE OF OUR COMPANY, THE (ALSO AS THE PLEASURE OF
    THEIR COMPANY)   SILVERBERG, ROBERT NV   INY 70 01
  ABSOLUTE ULTIMATE INVENTION, THE
                               BARR, STEPHEN   SS   INY 70 01
  OPERATION P-BUTTON   DICKSON, GORDON R. SS   INY 70 01
  MAN ON THE HILL, THE   FAYETTE, MICHAEL   SS   INY 70 01
  STAR, THE   CLARKE, ARTHUR C.   SS   INF 55 11
  ECHO   MACLEAN, KATHERINE SS   INY 70 01
  GREAT CANINE CHORUS, THE   MCCAFFREY, ANNE   SS   INY 70 01
  PACEM EST   NEVILLE, KRIS
                               AND O'DONNELL, K. M. SS C INY 70 01
  KEEPING AN EYE ON JANEY   GOULART, RON   SS   INY 70 01
  PACKERHAUS METHOD, THE   WOLFE, GENE   SS   INY 70 01
  WATER SCULPTOR OF STATION 233, THE
                               ZEBROWSKI, GEORGE   SS   INY 70 01
  TIGER, THE   DEFORD, MIRIAM ALLEN SS   INY 70 01
  HANDS OF THE MAN   LAFFERTY, R. A.   SS   INY 70 01
  NIGHTMARE GANG   KOONTZ, DEAN R.   SS   INY 70 01
  THESE OUR ACTORS   WELLEN, EDWARD   SS   INY 70 01
  INSIDE MOTHER   DEGRAW, PAT   SS   INY 70 01
  COMMUNICATORS, THE   ANDERSON, POUL   SN   INY 70 01

INFINITY 2   HOSKINS, ROBERT   OA   LAN 71
  ALIEN AMONG US, THE   HOSKINS, ROBERT   IN   INY 71 02
  MURPHY'S HALL   ANDERSON, POUL
                               AND ANDERSON, KAREN NV C INY 71 02
  MONSTER IN THE CLEARING, THE FAYETTE, MICHAEL   SS   INY 71 02
  SCENTS OF IT, THE   BONE, J. F.   NV   INY 71 02
  ROAD TO CINNABAR, THE   BRYANT, EDWARD   SS   INY 71 02
  TECHNOLOGICAL REVOLUTION, THE
                               GUNN, JAMES E.   SS   INY 71 02
  ELEPHANTS   O'DONNELL, K. M.   SS   INY 71 02
  OTHER WAY AROUND, THE   MYERS, HOWARD L.   NV   INY 71 02
  LEGION   BATES, RUSSELL L.   SS   INY 71 02
  GORF! GORF! GORF! (ALSO AS THE DAY THE GORF TOOK OVER)
                               NOLAN, WILLIAM F.   SS   INY 71 02
  TIMESPRAWL   WARDEN, ANTHON   SS   INY 71 02
  IN ENTROPY'S JAWS   SILVERBERG, ROBERT NV   INY 71 02
  REUNION   CLARKE, ARTHUR C.   SS   INY 71 02
  NOTES FROM INFINITY   MISC. MATERIAL   MS

INFINITY 3   HOSKINS, ROBERT   OA   LAN 72
  TIME OF CHANGES, A   HOSKINS, ROBERT   IN   INY 72 03
  CALIBAN   SILVERBERG, ROBERT SS   INY 72 03
  CYBERNETIC TABERNACLE JOB, THE
                               GOULART, RON   NV   INY 72 03
  INTER ALIA   MALZBERG, BARRY N. SS   INY 72 03
  TO WALK A CITY'S STREET   SIMAK, CLIFFORD D. SS   INY 72 03
  ALTARBOY   KOONTZ, DEAN R.   SS   INY 72 03
  ANTIQUITY   WELLER, ANTHONY   PM   INY 72 03
  BEECH HILL   WOLFE, GENE   SS   INY 72 03
  TIME OF THE FOURTH HORSEMAN, A
                               YARBRO, CHELSEA Q. NV   INY 72 03
  VOOREMP: SPY   DEFORD, MIRIAM ALLEN SS   INY 72 03
  LET IT RING   OSSIAN, JOHN   SS   INY 72 03
  ONE DAY IN THE WAR   POSNER, RICHARD   SS   INY 72 03
  TOUCHSTONE   MCLAUGHLIN, DEAN   SS   INY 72 03
  BARD'S TALE, THE   DIXON, TERRY   SS   INY 72 03
  MONADIC UNIVERSE, THE   ZEBROWSKI, GEORGE
                               AND HULL, GERALD   NV C INY 72 03
  TEACHING PRIME   KELLEY, LEO P.   SS   INY 72 03
  BEYOND THE SAND RIVER RANGE BRYANT, EDWARD   SS   INY 72 03
  NOTES FROM INFINITY   MISC. MATERIAL   MS

INFINITY 4   HOSKINS, ROBERT   OA   LAN 72
  FUTURE OF THE FUTURE, THE   HOSKINS, ROBERT   IN   INY 72 04
  BUMP, THE   LEIBER, FRITZ   SS   INY 72 04
  WHAT WE LEARNED FROM THIS MORNING'S NEWSPAPER
                               SILVERBERG, ROBERT SS   INY 72 04
  STARBLOOD   NOLAN, WILLIAM F.   SS   INY 72 04
  TEMPOLLUTERS, THE   EDMONDSON, G. C.   SS   INY 72 04
  OLLIE'S HANDS   KOONTZ, DEAN R.   SS   INY 72 04
  MERLIN STREET   MACFARLANE, WALLACE NV   INY 72 04
  AUDITION: SOON TO BE A MAJOR PRODUCTION
                               BRYANT, EDWARD   SS   INY 72 04
  DAY DARK, NIGHT BRIGHT   LEIBER, FRITZ   SS   INY 72 04
  BY THE TIME I GET TO PHOENIX SCORTIA, THOMAS N. SS   INY 72 04
  NOT THAT SHAGGY   GOULART, RON   SS   INY 72 04
  BALLAD OF SLICK SID, THE   MALZBERG, BARRY N. SS   INY 72 04
  DING DONG, THE WITCH IS WELL PICKENS, THOMAS   SS   INY 72 04
  FOREIGNER, THE   BLAKE, E. MICHAEL   SS   INY 72 04
  FOUNTAIN OF FORCE   ZEBROWSKI, GEORGE
                               AND CARRINGTON, GRANT SS C INY 72 04
  STRANGER WITH ROSES   JAKES, JOHN W.   PL   INY 72 04
  FORTUNE HUNTER   ANDERSON, POUL   SS   INY 72 04
  ANOTHER CASK OF WINE   LEIBER, FRITZ   SS   INY 72 04
  NOTES FROM INFINITY   MISC. MATERIAL   MS

INFINITY 5   HOSKINS, ROBERT   OA   LAN 73
  HOW TO BUILD TOMORROW   HOSKINS, ROBERT   IN   INY 73 05
  SCIENCE FICTION HALL OF FAME, THE
                               SILVERBERG, ROBERT SS   INY 73 05
  IN BETWEEN THEN AND NOW   COVER, ARTHUR BYRON SS   INY 73 05
  KELLY, FREDRIC MICHAEL: 1928-1987
                               NOLAN, WILLIAM F.   SS   INY 73 05
  NOSTALGIA TRIPPING   BRENNERT, ALAN   SS   INY 73 05
  SHE/HER   THURSTON, ROBERT   SS   INY 73 05
  TRASHING   MALZBERG, BARRY N. SS   INY 73 05
  HELLO, WALLS AND FENCES   BATES, RUSSELL L.   SS   INY 73 05
  FREE AT LAST   GOULART, RON   SS   INY 73 05
  CHANGING OF THE GODS   CARR, TERRY   NV   INY 73 05
  INTERPOSE   ZEBROWSKI, GEORGE   SS   INY 73 05
  GRAYWORLD   KOONTZ, DEAN R.   SN   INY 73 05
  ISAAC UNDER PRESSURE   EDELSTEIN, SCOTT   SS   INY 73 05

INNER LANDSCAPE, THE   MOORCOCK, MICHAEL   AN H ALS 69
  BOY IN DARKNESS   PEAKE, MERVYN   NV   56
  VOICES OF TIME, THE   BALLARD, J. G.   SS   NWS 60 10
  DANGER: RELIGION! (MATRIX)   ALDISS, BRIAN W.   TC   SCF 62 10

INSIDE INFORMATION   MOWSHOWITZ, ABBE   AN L ADW 77
  COMPUTERS IN FICTION
  PREFACE   MOWSHOWITZ, ABBE   IN
  ALL WATCHED OVER BY MACHINES OF LOVING GRACE
                               BRAUTIGAN, RICHARD PM   68
  FROM: THE MOON IS A HARSH MISTRESS
                               HEINLEIN, ROBERT A. EX   IFS 65 12
  FROM: THE JAGGED ORBIT   BRUNNER, JOHN   EX   ACE 69
  FROM: PLAYER PIANO   VONNEGUT, KURT JR. EX   HRW 52
  FROM: JOURNEY BEYOND TOMORROW
                               SHECKLEY, ROBERT   EX   DEL 62
  REPORT   BARTHELME, DONALD   SS   NYM 66
  NINE BILLION NAMES OF GOD, THE
                               CLARKE, ARTHUR C.   SS   STR 53 01
  WHAT'S THE NAME OF THAT TOWN?
                               LAFFERTY, R. A.   SS   GAL 64 10
  FROM: GILES GOAT-BOY   BARTH, JOHN   EX   DBL 66
  ANSWER   BROWN, FREDRIC   SS   NEW 54 AC
  FROM: A MODERN UTOPIA   WELLS, H. G.   EX   05
  EXAMINATION DAY   SLESAR, HENRY   SS   PBY 58 02
  FROM: THIS PERFECT DAY   LEVIN, IRA   EX   RDM 70
  FROM: THE CITY AND THE STARS CLARKE, ARTHUR C.   EX   HBW 56
  WALTER PERKINS IS HERE!   BANKS, RAYMOND E.   SS   PIN 70
  NOBODY LIVES ON BURTON STREET
                               BENFORD, GREGORY   SS   AMZ 70 05
  FROM: THE STEEL CROCODILE   COMPTON, D. G.   EX   ACE 70
  TOP STAND-BY JOB (STAND-BY) DICK, PHILIP K.   SS   AMZ 63 10
  FRANCHISE   ASIMOV, ISAAC   SS   IFS 55 08
  SIGH FOR CYBERNETICS, A   LAMPORT, FELICIA   PM   HRP 61 01
  FORM 5640: REPORT OF A MALFUNCTION
                               KAWIN, BRUCE   SS   DPM 67
  MS FND IN A LBRY   DRAPER, HAL   SS   FSF 61 12
  MOXON'S MASTER   BIERCE, AMBROSE   SS   93
  TWENTY-THIRD PSALM- MODERN STYLE, THE
                               SIMPSON, ALAN   PM   WUM 61
  FROM: THE 480   BURDICK, EUGENE   EX   MGH 64
  MACHINES OF LOVING GRACE   DOZOIS, GARDNER R. SS   ORB 72 11
  FROM: JOURNEY BEYOND TOMORROW
                               SHECKLEY, ROBERT   EX   DEL 62
  FROM: FISTFUL OF DIGITS   HODDER-WILLIAMS, C. EX   HDS 68
  HARDCASTLE   GOULART, RON   SS   NEW 71 AC
  INSTINCT   DEL REY, LESTER   SS   ASF 52 01
  FEELING OF POWER, THE   ASIMOV, ISAAC   SS   IFS 58 02
  UNIVAC TO UNIVAC   SALOMON, LOUIS B.   PM   HRP 58 03
  FROM: NOVA   DELANY, SAMUEL R.   EX   DBL 68
  FROM: THE ADDING MACHINE   RICE, ELMER L.   EX   DBL 22
  FULL SUN   ALDISS, BRIAN W.   SS   ORB 67 02
  FROM: THE TALE OF THE BIG COMPUTER
                               JOHANNESSON, OLOF   EX   GOL 68
  BIBLIOGRAPHY   MISC. MATERIAL   MS
  INDEX   MISC. MATERIAL   MS

INTANGIBLES INC. AND OTHER STORIES
                               ALDISS, BRIAN W.   AC H FAB 69
  NEANDERTHAL PLANET (A TOUCH OF NEANDERTHAL)
                               ALDISS, BRIAN W.   NV   SFA 60 09
  RANDY'S SYNDROME   ALDISS, BRIAN W.   NV   FSF 67 04
  SEND HER VICTORIOUS   ALDISS, BRIAN W.   NV   AMZ 68 04
  INTANGIBLES, INC.   ALDISS, BRIAN W.   NV   SCF 59 02
  SINCE THE ASSASSINATION   ALDISS, BRIAN W.   NV   NEW 69 AC

INTERPLANETARY HUNTER   BARNES, ARTHUR K.   AC H GNM 56
  VENUS (HOTHOUSE PLANET)   BARNES, ARTHUR K.   NV   TWS 37 10
  JUPITER (SATELLITE FIVE)   BARNES, ARTHUR K.   NV   TWS 38 10
  NEPTUNE (SIREN SATELLITE)   BARNES, ARTHUR K.   NV   TWS 48 WI
  ALMUSSEN'S COMET (THE SEVEN SLEEPERS)
                               BARNES, ARTHUR K.   NV   TWS 40 05
  SATURN (TROUBLE ON TITAN)   BARNES, ARTHUR K.   NV   TWS 41 02

INTERSTELLAR EMPIRE   BRUNNER, JOHN   AC   DAW 76 09
  ALTAR OF ASCONEL   BRUNNER, JOHN   NO   IFS 65 04
  MAN FROM THE BIG DARK, THE   BRUNNER, JOHN   SN   SFA 58 06
  WANTON OF ARGUS   BRUNNER, JOHN   NO   TCS 53 SU

INTO THE FOURTH DIMENSION   CUMMINGS, RAY   AN   SWN 41
  INTO THE FOURTH DIMENSION   CUMMINGS, RAY   NO   SAI 26 09
  POWER PLANT   GREGOR, LEE   SS   SFQ 41 WI
  EPHONY'S SPECTACLES   GRANOSKI, CLARENCE SS   SFQ 41 WI
  SIR MALLORY'S MAGNITUDE   GOTTESMAN, S. D.   SS   SFQ 41 WI
  BABY DREAMS   WARLAND, ALAN   SS   SFQ 41 WI
  CARIDI SHALL NOT DIE   KUBILIUS, WALTER   SS   SFQ 41 WI

INTO THE UNKNOWN   CARR, TERRY   AN H NEL 73
  INTRODUCTION   CARR, TERRY   IN

INTO THE UNKNOWN   INVISIBLE MEN

MCGILLAHEE'S BRAT (WAB 70 FL)
                          BRADBURY, RAY   SS   FSF 72 01
AS IS   SILVERBERG, ROBERT   NV   WOF 68 01
TECHNICAL SLIP (ARS 49 WI) WYNDHAM, JOHN   SS   IMG 50 12
BEYOND THE GAME   AANDAHL, VANCE   SS   FSF 68 05
TOUCHSTONE   CARR, TERRY   SS   FSF 64 05
ARE YOU LISTENING?   ELLISON, HARLAN   SS   AMZ 58 12
LOTTERY IN BABYLON, THE   BORGES, JORGE LUIS   SS   62
DOGMAN OF ISLINGTON   BAILEY, HILARY   SS   QRK 70 01
DROWNED GIANT, THE (SOUVENIR)
                          BALLARD, J. G.   SS   PBY 65 05
INSIDE   CARR, CAROL   SS   ORB 70 08
OLD FOLKS, THE   GUNN, JAMES E.   SS   NOV 72 02

INTRODUCING SCIENCE FICTION ALDISS, BRIAN W.   AN H FAB 64
INTRODUCTION   ALDISS, BRIAN W.   IN
EDGE OF THE SEA, THE   BUDRYS, ALGIS   SS   VSF 58 03
TROUBLE WITH TIME (CRIME ON MARS, EQM 60 07)
                          CLARKE, ARTHUR C.   SS   FSF 61 06
TIME IN ADVANCE   TENN, WILLIAM   NV   GAL 56 08
ARENA   BROWN, FREDRIC   NV   ASF 44 06
GESTURE OF FAREWELL   ALDISS, BRIAN W.   SS   NWS 57 07
IMMORTAL BARD, THE   ASIMOV, ISAAC   SS   USF 54 05
CAVE, THE   MILLER, P. SCHUYLER   SS   ASF 43 01
START IN LIFE, A   SELLINGS, ARTHUR   SS   GAL 54 09
HAPPY MAN, THE   PAGE, GERALD W.   NV   ASF 63 03
I MADE YOU   MILLER, WALTER M. JR   SS   ASF 54 03
IT'S A GOOD LIFE   BIXBY, JEROME   SS   STR 53 02
GARDEN OF TIME, THE   BALLARD, J. G.   SS   FSF 62 02
GLOSSARY   MISC. MATERIAL   MS
RECOMMENDED READING   MISC. MATERIAL   MS

INTRODUCTORY PSYCHOLOGY THROUGH SCIENCE FICTION
                          KATZ/WARRICK/&   AN L RAN 74
PREFACE   KATZ, HARVEY A.
                          WARRICK, PATRICIA S.
                          AND GREENBERG, MARTIN H. IN C
SOCRATES   CHRISTOPHER, JOHN   SS   GAL 51 03
LYSENKO MAZE, THE   WOLLHEIM, DONALD A.   SS   FSF 54 07
FLOWERS FOR ALGERNON   KEYES, DANIEL   SS   FSF 59 04
NINE LIVES   LE GUIN, URSULA K.   NV   PBY 69 11
MAN WHO DEVOURED BOOKS, THE SLADEK, JOHN T.   SS   IFS 71 01
LEARNING THEORY   MCCONNELL, JAMES   SS   IFS 57 12
SUSIE'S REALITY   STICKGOLD, BOB   NV   IFS 73 06
MAN IN THE RORSCHACH SHIRT, THE
                          BRADBURY, RAY   SS   PBY 66 10
SUCH STUFF   BRUNNER, JOHN   SS   FSF 62 06
SUBLIMINAL MAN, THE   BALLARD, J. G.   SS   NWS 63 01
AND HE BUILT A CROOKED HOUSE HEINLEIN, ROBERT A. SS   ASF 41 02
ALL THE LAST WARS AT ONCE EFFINGER, GEO. ALEC   SS   UNI 71 01
LOVE, INCORPORATED (ALSO AS PILGRIMAGE TO EARTH)
                          SHECKLEY, ROBERT   SS   PBY 56 09
SEVENTH VICTIM   SHECKLEY, ROBERT   SS   GAL 53 04
ADJUSTMENT   MOORE, WARD   NV   FSF 57 05
THAT ONLY A MOTHER   MERRIL, JUDITH   SS   ASF 48 06
FIRST MEN, THE   FAST, HOWARD   NV   FSF 60 02
PLAYGROUND, THE   BRADBURY, RAY   SS   ESQ 53 10
MOTHER   FARMER, PHILIP JOSE   NV   TWS 53 04
SECOND KIND OF LONELINESS, THE
                          MARTIN, GEORGE R. R.   SS   ASF 72 12
INSTINCT   DEL REY, LESTER   SS   ASF 52 01
ALTER EGO   CORREA, HUGO   SS   FSF 67 07
AND NOW THE NEWS...   STURGEON, THEODORE   SS   FSF 56 12
PLOT, THE   HERZOG, TOM   SS   ROG 65
NOISE, THE   PURDY, KEN W.   SS   PBY 59 03
YELLOW PILL, THE   PHILLIPS, ROG   SS   ASF 58 10
GOING DOWN SMOOTH   SILVERBERG, ROBERT   SS   GAL 68 08
BIBLIOGRAPHY   MISC. MATERIAL   MS

INVADERS FROM SPACE   SILVERBERG, ROBERT   AN H HAW 72
INTRODUCTION   SILVERBERG, ROBERT   IN
LIBERATION OF EARTH, THE TENN, WILLIAM   SS   FUT 53 05
SILLY SEASON, THE   KORNBLUTH, C. M.   SS   FSF 50 FL
ROOG   DICK, PHILIP K.   SS   FSF 53 02
NIGHTWINGS   SILVERBERG, ROBERT   NV   GAL 68 09
NOBODY SAW THE SHIP   LEINSTER, MURRAY   SS   FUS 50 05
STORM WARNING   WOLLHEIM, DONALD A.   SS   FUT 42 10
CATCH THAT MARTIAN   KNIGHT, DAMON   SS   GAL 52 03
RESURRECTION (THE MONSTER) VAN VOGT, A. E.   SS   ASF 48 08
PICTURES DON'T LIE   MACLEAN, KATHERINE   SS   GAL 51 08
HERESIES OF THE HUGE GOD ALDISS, BRIAN W.   FA   GAL 66 08

INVADERS OF EARTH   CONKLIN, GROFF   AN H VPR 52
     ENGLISH DERIVATIVE ANTHOLOGY "ENEMIES IN SPACE"
INTRODUCTION   CONKLIN, GROFF   IN
THIS STAR SHALL BE FREE   LEINSTER, MURRAY   NV   SSS 49 11
CASTAWAY   WILLIAMS, ROBERT M.   SS   ASF 41 02
IMPULSE   RUSSELL, ERIC FRANK   SS   ASF 38 09
TOP SECRET   GRINNELL, DAVID   SS   FSF 50 FL
EEL BY THE TAIL, AN   LANG, ALLEN KIM   SS   IMG 51 04
DATE TO REMEMBER, A   TEMPLE, WILLIAM F.   SS   TWS 49 08
STORM WARNING   WOLLHEIM, DONALD A.   SS   FUT 42 10
CHILD OF VOID   ST. CLAIR, MARGARET   SS   SSS 49 11
TINY AND THE MONSTER   STURGEON, THEODORE   NV   ASF 47 05
DISCORD MAKERS, THE   REYNOLDS, MACK   SS   OTW 50 07
PEN PAL   LESSER, MILTON   SS   GAL 51 07
NOT ONLY DEAD MEN   VAN VOGT, A. E.   SS   ASF 42 11
ENEMIES IN SPACE (TRANSLATED BY WILLY LEY)
                          GRUNERT, KARL   SS   07
INVASION FROM MARS   KOCH, HOWARD   PL   CBS 38 10
MINISTER WITHOUT PORTFOLIO CLINGERMAN, MILDRED   SS   FSF 52 02
WAVERIES, THE   BROWN, FREDRIC   SS   ASF 45 01
CRISIS   GRENDON, EDWARD   SS   ASF 51 06
ANGEL'S EGG   PANGBORN, EDGAR   NV   GAL 51 06
WILL YOU WALK A LITTLE FASTER?
                          TENN, WILLIAM   SS   MAR 51 11

MAN IN THE MOON, THE   NORTON, HENRY   SS   ASF 43 02
PICTURES DON'T LIE   MACLEAN, KATHERINE   SS   GAL 51 08
GREATEST TERTIAN, THE   BOUCHER, ANTHONY   SS   NEW 52 AN

INVADERS OF EARTH (BRITISH PB)
                          CONKLIN, GROFF   AN   DIG 62
INTRODUCTION   CONKLIN, GROFF   IN
THIS STAR SHALL BE FREE   LEINSTER, MURRAY   NV   SSS 49 11
CASTAWAY   WILLIAMS, ROBERT M.   SS   ASF 41 02
IMPULSE   RUSSELL, ERIC FRANK   SS   ASF 38 09
EEL BY THE TAIL, AN   LANG, ALLEN KIM   SS   IMG 51 04
STORM WARNING   WOLLHEIM, DONALD A.   SS   FUT 42 10
CHILD OF VOID   ST. CLAIR, MARGARET   SS   SSS 49 11
NOT ONLY DEAD MEN   VAN VOGT, A. E.   SS   ASF 42 11
ENEMIES IN SPACE (TRANSLATED BY WILLY LEY)
                          GRUNERT, KARL   SS   07

INVADERS OF EARTH (BRITISH) CONKLIN, GROFF   AN H WEI 53
INTRODUCTION   CONKLIN, GROFF   IN
THIS STAR SHALL BE FREE   LEINSTER, MURRAY   NV   SSS 49 11
CASTAWAY   WILLIAMS, ROBERT M.   SS   ASF 41 02
IMPULSE   RUSSELL, ERIC FRANK   SS   ASF 38 09
EEL BY THE TAIL, AN   LANG, ALLEN KIM   SS   IMG 51 04
STORM WARNING   WOLLHEIM, DONALD A.   SS   FUT 42 10
CHILD OF VOID   ST. CLAIR, MARGARET   SS   SSS 49 11
NOT ONLY DEAD MEN   VAN VOGT, A. E.   SS   ASF 42 11
ENEMIES IN SPACE (TRANSLATED BY WILLY LEY)
                          GRUNERT, KARL   SS   07
INVASION FROM MARS   KOCH, HOWARD   PL   CBS 38 10
WAVERIES, THE   BROWN, FREDRIC   SS   ASF 45 01
ANGEL'S EGG   PANGBORN, EDGAR   NV   GAL 51 06
MAN IN THE MOON, THE   NORTON, HENRY   SS   ASF 43 02
PICTURES DON'T LIE   MACLEAN, KATHERINE   SS   GAL 51 08
GREATEST TERTIAN, THE   BOUCHER, ANTHONY   SS   NEW 52 AN

INVADERS OF EARTH (15 OF 22) CONKLIN, GROFF   AN   PKT 55 09
INTRODUCTION   CONKLIN, GROFF   IN
THIS STAR SHALL BE FREE   LEINSTER, MURRAY   NV   SSS 49 11
IMPULSE   RUSSELL, ERIC FRANK   SS   ASF 38 09
TOP SECRET   GRINNELL, DAVID   SS   FSF 50 FL
EEL BY THE TAIL, AN   LANG, ALLEN KIM   SS   IMG 51 04
STORM WARNING   WOLLHEIM, DONALD A.   SS   FUT 42 10
TINY AND THE MONSTER   STURGEON, THEODORE   NV   ASF 47 05
DISCORD MAKERS, THE   REYNOLDS, MACK   SS   OTW 50 07
PEN PAL   LESSER, MILTON   SS   GAL 51 07
INVASION FROM MARS   KOCH, HOWARD   PL   CBS 38 10
MINISTER WITHOUT PORTFOLIO CLINGERMAN, MILDRED   SS   FSF 52 02
CRISIS   GRENDON, EDWARD   SS   ASF 51 06
ANGEL'S EGG   PANGBORN, EDGAR   NV   GAL 51 06
WILL YOU WALK A LITTLE FASTER?
                          TENN, WILLIAM   SS   MAR 51 11
PICTURES DON'T LIE   MACLEAN, KATHERINE   SS   GAL 51 08
GREATEST TERTIAN, THE   BOUCHER, ANTHONY   SS   NEW 52 AN

INVADERS OF EARTH (17 OF 22) CONKLIN, GROFF   AN   TMP 62 09
INTRODUCTION   CONKLIN, GROFF   IN
THIS STAR SHALL BE FREE   LEINSTER, MURRAY   NV   SSS 49 11
CASTAWAY   WILLIAMS, ROBERT M.   SS   ASF 41 02
IMPULSE   RUSSELL, ERIC FRANK   SS   ASF 38 09
TOP SECRET   GRINNELL, DAVID   SS   FSF 50 FL
DATE TO REMEMBER, A   TEMPLE, WILLIAM F.   SS   TWS 49 08
CHILD OF VOID   ST. CLAIR, MARGARET   SS   SSS 49 11
TINY AND THE MONSTER   STURGEON, THEODORE   NV   ASF 47 05
DISCORD MAKERS, THE   REYNOLDS, MACK   SS   OTW 50 07
NOT ONLY DEAD MEN   VAN VOGT, A. E.   SS   ASF 42 11
INVASION FROM MARS   KOCH, HOWARD   PL   CBS 38 10
MINISTER WITHOUT PORTFOLIO CLINGERMAN, MILDRED   SS   FSF 52 02
WAVERIES, THE   BROWN, FREDRIC   SS   ASF 45 01
CRISIS   GRENDON, EDWARD   SS   ASF 51 06
ANGEL'S EGG   PANGBORN, EDGAR   NV   GAL 51 06
WILL YOU WALK A LITTLE FASTER?
                          TENN, WILLIAM   SS   MAR 51 11
PICTURES DON'T LIE   MACLEAN, KATHERINE   SS   GAL 51 08
GREATEST TERTIAN, THE   BOUCHER, ANTHONY   SS   NEW 52 AN

INVASION FROM MARS   WELLES, ORSON   AN   DEL 49
     CAN A MARTIAN HELP IT IF HE'S COLORED GREEN?
                          WELLES, ORSON   IN
INVASION FROM MARS   KOCH, HOWARD   PL   CBS 38 10
GREEN HILLS OF EARTH, THE HEINLEIN, ROBERT A.   SS   SEP 47 02
ZERO HOUR   BRADBURY, RAY   SS   PLS 47 FL
EXPEDITION   BOUCHER, ANTHONY   SS   TWS 43 04
INCIDENT ON CALYPSO   LEINSTER, MURRAY   SS   STS 45 FL
STAR MOUSE, THE   BROWN, FREDRIC   SS   PLS 42 02
CASTAWAY, THE   BOND, NELSON S.   SS   PLS 40 WI
VICTORY UNINTENTIONAL   ASIMOV, ISAAC   SS   SSS 42 08
FAREWELL TO EDEN   STURGEON, THEODORE   SS   NEW 49 AN
MILLION-YEAR PICNIC, THE BRADBURY, RAY   SS   PLS 46 SU

INVASION OF THE ROBOTS   ELWOOD, ROGER   AN   PBK 65 04
INTRODUCTION   ELWOOD, ROGER   IN
SATISFACTION GUARANTEED   ASIMOV, ISAAC   SS   AMZ 51 04
PIGGY BANK   KUTTNER, HENRY   NV   ASF 42 12
WITH FOLDED HANDS...   WILLIAMSON, JACK   NV   ASF 47 07
BROTHER TO THE MACHINE   MATHESON, RICHARD   SS   IFS 52 11
DEFENDERS, THE   DICK, PHILIP K.   NV   GAL 53 01
ALMOST HUMAN (AS TARLETON FISKE)
                          BLOCH, ROBERT   SS   FAD 43 06
INTO THY HANDS   DEL REY, LESTER   SS   ASF 45 08
BOOMERANG (A GREAT DEAL OF POWER)
                          RUSSELL, ERIC FRANK   SS   FUN 53 08

INVISIBLE MEN   DAVENPORT, BASIL   AN   BAL 60
WEISSENBROCH SPECTACLES, THE DE CAMP, L. SPRAGUE
                          AND PRATT, FLETCHER   SS C FSF 54 11
SHADOW AND THE FLASH, THE LONDON, JACK   SS   BOK 03 06

```
INVISIBLE MEN                                                    JOY MAKERS, THE

NEW ACCELERATOR, THE          WELLS, H. G.          SS    SND 01 12
INVISIBLE BOY                 BRADBURY, RAY         SS    MAD 45 11
INVISIBLE PRISONER, THE       LEBLANC, MAURICE      SS
LOVE IN THE DARK (LOVE ETHEREAL)
                              GOLD, H. L.           SS    SUS 51 FL
WHAT WAS IT? (1859)           O'BRIEN, FITZ-JAMES   SS    HRP 59 03
INVISIBLE DOVE DANCER OF STRATHPEEN ISLAND, THE
                              COLLIER, JOHN         SS        41
VANISHING AMERICAN, THE       BEAUMONT, CHARLES     SS    FSF 55 08
SHOTTLE BOP                   STURGEON, THEODORE    SS    UNK 41 02
INVISIBLE MAN MURDER CASE, THE
                              SLESAR, HENRY         SS    FAN 58 05

IRRATIONAL NUMBERS            EFFINGER, GEO. ALEC   AC H  DBL 76
INTRODUCTION                  SILVERBERG, ROBERT    IN
LYDECTES: ON THE NATURE OF SPORT
                              EFFINGER, GEO. ALEC   NV    FAN 75 12
AND US, TOO, I GUESS          EFFINGER, GEO. ALEC   NA    CHN 73
25 CRUNCH SPLIT RIGHT ON TWO  EFFINGER, GEO. ALEC   NV    FSF 75 04
HARD TIMES                    EFFINGER, GEO. ALEC   SS    AMZ 73 03
AT THE BRAN FOUNDRY           EFFINGER, GEO. ALEC   SS    NDM 73 03
CURTAINS                      EFFINGER, GEO. ALEC   SS    FSF 74 08
HOW IT FELT                   EFFINGER, GEO. ALEC   SS    UNI 74 05
BITING DOWN HARD ON TRUTH     EFFINGER, GEO. ALEC   NV    ORB 74 15

ISAAC ASIMOV OMNIBUS, AN      ASIMOV, ISAAC         AC H  SID 65
     SEE "THE FOUNDATION TRILOGY"

ISAAC ASIMOV SECOND OMNIBUS, AN
                              ASIMOV, ISAAC         AC H  SID 69
     SEE "TRIANGLE"

ISLAND OF FEAR AND OTHER SCIENCE FICTION
                              SAMBROT, WILLIAM      AC    PMA 63 03
SPACE SECRET                  SAMBROT, WILLIAM      SS    SEP 59 02
CONTROL SOMNAMBULE            SAMBROT, WILLIAM      SS    PBY 62 05
DISTANT SHRINE, A (CATHEDRAL OF MARS)
                              SAMBROT, WILLIAM      SS    SEP 61 06
ISLAND OF FEAR                SAMBROT, WILLIAM      SS    SEP 58 01
CREATURE OF THE SNOWS         SAMBROT, WILLIAM      SS    SEP 60 10
NINE DAYS TO DIE (STORY OF AN ATOMIC-AGE ORDEAL)
                              SAMBROT, WILLIAM      SS    SEP 60 07
SECRET OF THE TERRIBLE TITANS, THE (FOOTBALL MAJORS AT
PACIFIC U.)                   SAMBROT, WILLIAM      SS    CMP 59 10
INVASION                      SAMBROT, WILLIAM      SS    SEP 56 07
REPORT TO THE PEOPLE          SAMBROT, WILLIAM      SS    BBM 33
DEADLY DECISION               SAMBROT, WILLIAM      SS    EXT 58
MAN WHO KNEW, THE             SAMBROT, WILLIAM      SS    TIG 57
CATHARTIC                     SAMBROT, WILLIAM      SS    SAT 57 08
SECOND EXPERIMENT, THE        SAMBROT, WILLIAM      SS
SON OF EVE, A                 SAMBROT, WILLIAM      SS    MRM 59

IT'S A MAD, MAD, MAD GALAXY   LAUMER, KEITH         AC    BKM 68 12
BODY BUILDERS, THE            LAUMER, KEITH         NV    GAL 66 08
PLANET WRECKERS, THE          LAUMER, KEITH         NV    WOT 67 02
STAR-SENT KNAVES, THE (ALSO AS THE TIME THIEVES)
                              LAUMER, KEITH         NV    WOT 63 06
WAR WITH THE YUKKS, THE (WAR AGAINST THE YUKKS)
                              LAUMER, KEITH         NV    GAL 65 04
GOOBEREALITY                  LAUMER, KEITH         NV    NEW 68 AC

JIREL OF JOIRY                MOORE, C. L.          AC    PBK 69 08
JIREL MEETS MAGIC             MOORE, C. L.          NV    WRT 35 07
BLACK GOD'S KISS              MOORE, C. L.          NV    WRT 34 10
BLACK GOD'S SHADOW            MOORE, C. L.          NV    WRT 34 12
DARK LAND, THE                MOORE, C. L.          NV    WRT 36 01
HELLSGARDE                    MOORE, C. L.          SS    WRT 39 04

JIZZLE                        WYNDHAM, JOHN         AC H  DOB 54
JIZZLE (REVISED FROM COL 49 01)
                              WYNDHAM, JOHN         SS    FSF 52 02
TECHNICAL SLIP (ARS 49 WI)    WYNDHAM, JOHN         SS    IMG 50 12
PRESENT FROM BRUNSWICK, A (BARGAIN FROM BRUNSWICK)
                              WYNDHAM, JOHN         SS    FSF 51 06
CHINESE PUZZLE (A STRAY FROM CATHAY)
                              WYNDHAM, JOHN         NV    FNF 53 08
ESMERALDA                     WYNDHAM, JOHN         SS
HOW DO I DO?                  WYNDHAM, JOHN         SS    BEY 53 09
UNA (THE PERFECT CREATURE, TOW 37 01)
                              WYNDHAM, JOHN         NV    FSF 53 01
AFFAIR OF THE HEART           WYNDHAM, JOHN         SS
CONFIDENCE TRICK              WYNDHAM, JOHN         SS    FAN 53 08
WHEEL, THE                    WYNDHAM, JOHN         SS    STS 52 01
LOOK NATURAL, PLEASE!         WYNDHAM, JOHN         SS
PERFORCE TO DREAM             WYNDHAM, JOHN         SS    BEY 54 01
RESERVATION DEFERRED          WYNDHAM, JOHN         SS    FAN 53 06
HEAVEN SCENT                  WYNDHAM, JOHN         SS
MORE SPINNED AGAINST          WYNDHAM, JOHN         SS    FNF 53 06

JOHN CARSTAIRS: SPACE DETECTIVE
                              LONG, FRANK BELKNAP   AC H  FEL 49
PLANTS MUST GROW              LONG, FRANK BELKNAP   NV    TWS 41 10
SNAPDRAGON                    LONG, FRANK BELKNAP   NV    TWS 41 12
PLANTS MUST SLAY              LONG, FRANK BELKNAP   SS    TWS 42 04
SATELLITE OF PERIL            LONG, FRANK BELKNAP   NV    TWS 42 08
ETHER ROBOTS, THE             LONG, FRANK BELKNAP   NV    TWS 42 12
WOBBLIES IN THE MOON          LONG, FRANK BELKNAP   NV    TWS 43 06

JOHN CARTER OF MARS           BURROUGHS, EDGAR R.   AC H  CAN 64
JOHN CARTER AND THE GIANTS OF MARS
                              BURROUGHS, EDGAR R.   NV    AMZ 41 01
SKELETON MEN OF JUPITER       BURROUGHS, EDGAR R.   NV    AMZ 43 02

JOHN W. CAMPBELL ANTHOLOGY: THREE NOVELS
                              CAMPBELL, JOHN W. JR  AC H  DBL 73
SENSE OF WONDER, THE          ASIMOV, ISAAC         IN

OF DESTINY AND WONDER         DEL REY, LESTER       IN
BLACK STAR PASSES, THE        CAMPBELL, JOHN W. JR  NA    AMQ 30 FL
ISLANDS OF SPACE              CAMPBELL, JOHN W. JR  NO    FPS 56
INVADERS FROM THE INFINITE    CAMPBELL, JOHN W. JR  NO    FPS 61

JOHN WYNDHAM OMNIBUS, THE     WYNDHAM, JOHN         AC H  SAS 65
DAY OF THE TRIFFIDS, THE (REVOLT OF THE TRIFFIDS)
                              WYNDHAM, JOHN         NO    COL 51 01
KRAKEN WAKES, THE (THE THINGS FROM THE DEEP)
                              WYNDHAM, JOHN         NO    EVB 53
CHRYSALIDS, THE (RE-BIRTH)    WYNDHAM, JOHN         NO    BAL 55

JOURNEY ACROSS THREE WORLDS   ANONYMOUS             AN H  MIR 73
TRANSLATION                   EVANS, GLADYS         MS
FOREWORD                      GUREVICH, G.          IN
JOURNEY ACROSS THREE WORLDS   ABRAMOV, ALEXANDER
                              AND ABRAMOV, SERGEI   SS C
GIGANTIC FLUCTUATION, THE     STRUGATSKY, ARKADY
                              AND STRUGATSKY, BORIS NO C
SNOWBALL, THE                 PARNOV, YEREMEY
                              AND YEMTSEV, MIKHAIL  SS C
CADET PLOSHKIN                VARSHAVSKY, ILYA      NV
TWO, THE                      GANSOVSKY, SEVER      NV
GIRL NOTHING HAPPENS TO, THE  BULYCHEV, KIRILL      SS
SEVENTH FLOOR, THE            LVOV, ARKADY          NA

JOURNEY TO ANOTHER STAR AND OTHER STORIES
                              ELWOOD, ROGER         OA H  LER 74
FOREWORD                      ASIMOV, ISAAC         IN
JOURNEY TO ANOTHER STAR       ZEBROWSKI, GEORGE     SS
GUIDANCE                      MALZBERG, BARRY N.    SS
BETTER DUMB THAN DEAD         BINDER, EANDO         SS
GOOD OLD DAYS, THE            DANN, JACK M.         SS
STORY TIME                    JANIFER, LAURENCE M.  SS

JOURNEY TO INFINITY           GREENBERG, MARTIN     AN H  GNM 51
FOREWORD                      GREENBERG, MARTIN     IN
INTRODUCTION                  PRATT, FLETCHER       IN
FALSE DAWN                    CHANDLER, A. BERTRAM  NV    ASF 46 10
ATLANTIS (FROM TRIPLANETARY)  SMITH, EDWARD E. PHD  EX    AMZ 34 01
LETTER TO A PHOENIX           BROWN, FREDRIC        SS    ASF 49 08
UNITE AND CONQUER             STURGEON, THEODORE    NV    ASF 48 10
BREAKDOWN                     WILLIAMSON, JACK      NV    ASF 42 01
DANCE OF A NEW WORLD          MACDONALD, JOHN D.    SS    ASF 48 09
MOTHER EARTH                  ASIMOV, ISAAC         NV    ASF 49 05
THERE SHALL BE DARKNESS       MOORE, C. L.          NV    ASF 42 02
TABOO                         LEIBER, FRITZ         SS    ASF 44 02
OVERTHROW                     CARTMILL, CLEVE       SN    ASF 42 11
BARRIER OF DREAD              MERRIL, JUDITH        SS    FUT 50 07
METAMORPHOSITE                RUSSELL, ERIC FRANK   NV    ASF 46 12

JOURNEYS IN SCIENCE FICTION   LOUGHLIN, RICHARD L.  AN H  GLB 61
DAEDALUS (1855)               BULFINCH, THOMAS      SS
BIRTHMARK, THE (1843)         HAWTHORNE, NATHANIEL  SS    PIO 43 03
DESCENT INTO THE MAELSTROM, A
                              POE, EDGAR ALLEN      SS    GLG 41 05
JOURNEY TO THE CENTER OF THE EARTH, A (1864)
                              VERNE, JULES          NO    AMZ 26 05
MOXON'S MASTER                BIERCE, AMBROSE       SS        93
TALE OF NEGATIVE GRAVITY, A   STOCKTON, FRANK R.    NV    CNY 84 11
DISINTEGRATION MACHINE, THE   DOYLE, ARTHUR CONAN   SS    CMP 28
AEPYORNIS ISLAND              WELLS, H. G.          SS    PMB 94 12
WIRELESS                      KIPLING, RUDYARD      SS    SCR 02 08
TOBERMORY                     SAKI                  SS
ROADS MUST ROLL, THE          HEINLEIN, ROBERT A.   NV    ASF 40 06
VISIT TO A SMALL PLANET       VIDAL, GORE           PL        55
QUIT ZOOMIN' THOSE HANDS THROUGH THE AIR
                              FINNEY, JACK          SS    FSF 52 12
FUN THEY HAD, THE (NEA 51 12)
                              ASIMOV, ISAAC         SS    FSF 54 02
TRIGGERMAN                    BONE, J. F.           SS    ASF 58 12
REPORT ON THE BARNHOUSE EFFECT
                              VONNEGUT, KURT JR.    SS    COL 50 02
BAXBR DAXBR                   SMITH, EVELYN E.      SS    FSF 56 09
CHECK YOUR UNDERSTANDING      MISC. MATERIAL        MS

JOY IN OUR CAUSE              EMSHWILLER, CAROL     AC H  HPR 74
JOY IN OUR CAUSE              EMSHWILLER, CAROL     SS
QUEEN OF SLEEP, THE           EMSHWILLER, CAROL     SS    NDR
STRANGERS                     EMSHWILLER, CAROL     SS    BMR 73
AUTOBIOGRAPHY                 EMSHWILLER, CAROL     SS
LIB                           EMSHWILLER, CAROL     SS    NWS 68 03
EOHIPPUS                      EMSHWILLER, CAROL     SS    TRV
DESTINATIONS, PREMONITIONS AND THE NATURE OF ANXIETY
                              EMSHWILLER, CAROL     SS
TO THE ASSOCIATION            EMSHWILLER, CAROL     SS
BIOGRAPHY OF AN UNCIRCUMCISED MAN (INCLUDING INTERVIEW)
                              EMSHWILLER, CAROL     SS
YES, VIRGINIA                 EMSHWILLER, CAROL     SS    TRV
CHILDHOOD OF THE HUMAN HERO, THE
                              EMSHWILLER, CAROL     SS    SCS 73
ANIMAL                        EMSHWILLER, CAROL     SS    ORB 68 04
SEX AND/OR MR. MORRISON       EMSHWILLER, CAROL     SS    DVS 67 01
DOG IS DEAD                   EMSHWILLER, CAROL     SS
I LOVE YOU                    EMSHWILLER, CAROL     SS    EPO
PENINSULA                     EMSHWILLER, CAROL     SS    RRV
CHICKEN ICARUS (A DREAM OF FLYING)
                              EMSHWILLER, CAROL     SS    CAV 66
AL                            EMSHWILLER, CAROL     SS    ORB 72 10
METHAPYRILENE HYDROCHLORIDE SOMETIMES HELPS
                              EMSHWILLER, CAROL     SS    NWS 68 07
MAYBE ANOTHER LONG MARCH ACROSS CHINA 80,000 STRONG
                              EMSHWILLER, CAROL     SS

JOY MAKERS, THE               GUNN, JAMES E.        NO    BAN 61 03
UNHAPPY MAN, THE              GUNN, JAMES E.        NV    FUN 55 02
```

NAKED SKY, THE (ALSO AS THE JOY RIDE)
                         GUNN, JAMES E.   NA   STS 55 FL
NAME YOUR PLEASURE (ALSO AS THE HEDONIST)
                         GUNN, JAMES E.   NA   TWS 55 WI

JOYOUS INVASION, THE   STURGEON, THEODORE   AC H GOL 65
  TO MARRY MEDUSA   STURGEON, THEODORE   NA   GAL 58 08
  COMEDIAN'S CHILDREN, THE STURGEON, THEODORE   NV   VSF 58 05
  (WIDGET), THE (WADGET), AND BOFF, THE
                         STURGEON, THEODORE   SN   FSF 55 11

JUDGEMENT NIGHT   MOORE, C. L.   AC H GNM 52
  JUDGEMENT NIGHT   MOORE, C. L.   NA   ASF 43 08
  PARADISE STREET   MOORE, C. L.   NV   ASF 50 09
  PROMISED LAND   MOORE, C. L.   NV   ASF 50 02
  CODE, THE   MOORE, C. L.   NV   ASF 45 07
  HEIR APPARENT   MOORE, C. L.   NV   ASF 50 07

JULES VERNE- MASTER OF SCIENCE FICTION
                         VERNE, JULES   AC H SID 56
  EDITED BY I. O. EVANS
  INTRODUCTION   EVANS, I. O.   IN
  JOURNEY TO THE CENTER OF THE EARTH, A (1864)
                         VERNE, JULES   EX   AMZ 26 05
  FROM THE EARTH TO THE MOON (1865)
                         VERNE, JULES   EX
  ROUND THE MOON (1870) VERNE, JULES   EX
  TWENTY THOUSAND LEAGUES UNDER THE SEA (1873)
                         VERNE, JULES   EX   GMS 73
  DROPPED FROM THE CLOUDS (THE MYSTERIOUS ISLAND, 1875)
                         VERNE, JULES   EX
  SECRET OF THE ISLAND, THE (THE MYSTERIOUS ISLAND, 1875)
                         VERNE, JULES   EX
  CHILD OF THE CAVERN, THE (1877)
                         VERNE, JULES   EX
  HECTOR SERVADAC (1877) VERNE, JULES   EX
  BEGUM'S FORTUNE, THE (1879) VERNE, JULES   EX
  STEAM HOUSE, THE (1880) VERNE, JULES   EX   SCB 81
  CLIPPER OF THE CLOUDS, THE VERNE, JULES   EX   86
  FLOATING ISLAND, THE (1895) VERNE, JULES   EX
  FOR THE FLAG (1896)   VERNE, JULES   EX
  ANTARCTIC MYSTERY, AN (THE MYSTERY OF ARTHUR GORDON PYM, 1897)
                         VERNE, JULES   EX   97
  FIVE WEEKS IN A BALLOON (1863)
                         VERNE, JULES   EX
  BIBLIOGRAPHY   MISC. MATERIAL   MS

JUPITER   POHL, C. & F.   AN   BAL 73 12
  JUPITER THE GIANT   ASIMOV, ISAAC   IN
  JUPITER AT LAST   POHL, FREDERICK
                         AND POHL, CAROL   IN C
  BRIDGE   BLISH, JAMES   NV   ASF 52 02
  VICTORY UNINTENTIONAL ASIMOV, ISAAC   SS   SSS 42 08
  DESERTION   SIMAK, CLIFFORD D.   SS   ASF 44 11
  MAD MOON, THE   WEINBAUM, STANLEY G.   NV   ASF 35 12
  HEAVY PLANET   ROTHMAN, MILTON A.   SS   ASF 39 08
  LOTUS-ENGINE, THE   GALLUN, RAYMOND Z.   SS   SSS 40 03
  CALL ME JOE   ANDERSON, POUL   NV   ASF 57 04
  HABIT   DEL REY, LESTER   SS   ASF 39 11
  MEETING WITH MEDUSA, A CLARKE, ARTHUR C.   NA   PBY 71 12

KILLER PLANTS AND OTHER STORIES, THE
                         ELWOOD, ROGER   OA H LER 74
  FOREWORD   ASIMOV, ISAAC   IN
  KILLER PLANTS, THE   GILES, GORDON A.   SS
  INVISIBLE GIRL, THE   SARGENT, PAMELA   SS
  FLOWER THAT MISSED THE MORNING, THE
                         ZEBROWSKI, GEORGE
                         AND DANN, JACK M.   SS C
  SPOOKY   REYNOLDS, MACK   SS

KING CONAN   HOWARD, ROBERT E.   AC H GNM 53
  INTRODUCTION   DE CAMP, L. SPRAGUE   IN
  JEWELS OF GWAHLUR   HOWARD, ROBERT E.   SS   WRT 35 03
  BEYOND THE BLACK RIVER HOWARD, ROBERT E.   NA   WRT 35 05
  TREASURE OF TRANICOS, THE (THE BLACK STRANGER)
                         HOWARD, ROBERT E.
                         AND DE CAMP, L. SPRAGUE NA C FMG 53 03
  PHOENIX ON THE SWORD, THE HOWARD, ROBERT E.   SS   WRT 32 12
  SCARLET CITADEL, THE   HOWARD, ROBERT E.   SS   WRT 33 01

KING OF TERRORS, THE   BLOCH, ROBERT   AC H MYS 77
  TALES OF MADNESS AND DEATH
  INTRODUCTION   BLOCH, ROBERT   IN
  WATER'S EDGE   BLOCH, ROBERT   SS   MSM 56 09
  DEADLIEST ART, THE   BLOCH, ROBERT   SS   BMM 58 11
  FAT CHANCE   BLOCH, ROBERT   SS   KHM 60 08
  GOOD IMAGINATION, A   BLOCH, ROBERT   SS   SUS 56 01
  HOME AWAY FROM HOME, A BLOCH, ROBERT   SS   AHM 61 06
  LIVING DEAD, THE   BLOCH, ROBERT   SS   EQM 67 04
  MAN WHO KNEW WOMEN, THE BLOCH, ROBERT   SS   SMM 59 07
  METHOD FOR MURDER   BLOCH, ROBERT   SS   FUR 62 07
  REAL BAD FRIEND, THE   BLOCH, ROBERT   NV   MSM 57 02
  STRING OF PEARLS   BLOCH, ROBERT   SS   SMM 56 08
  UNDER THE HORNS   BLOCH, ROBERT   SS   62
  UNPARDONABLE CRIME, THE BLOCH, ROBERT   SS   SWK 61 09
  UNTOUCHABLE   BLOCH, ROBERT   SS   SMM 62 03
  TERROR IN THE NIGHT   BLOCH, ROBERT   SS   MHT 56 02

KINGSLAYER, THE   HUBBARD, L. RON   AC H FPB 49
  ALSO IN "FROM DEATH TO THE STARS"
  ALSO AS "SEVEN STEPS TO THE ARBITER"
  PREFACE   HUBBARD, L. RON   IN
  KINGSLAYER, THE   HUBBARD, L. RON   NO   FPB 49
  BEAST, THE   HUBBARD, L. RON   SS   ASF 42 10

  INVADERS, THE (ALSO AS BEHIND THE BLACK NEBULA)
                         HUBBARD, L. RON   NV   ASF 42 01

LAMBDA I AND OTHER STORIES CARNELL, JOHN   AN   BKM 64 02
  FOREWORD   CARNELL, JOHN   IN
  LAMBDA I   KAPP, COLIN   NV   NWS 62 12
  BASIS FOR NEGOTIATION ALDISS, BRIAN W.   NV   NWS 62 01
  QUEST   HARDING, LEE   SS   NWS 63 04
  ALL LACED UP   WHITLEY, GEORGE   SS   NWS 61 11
  ROUTINE EXERCISE   HIGH, PHILIP E.   SS   NWS 61 02
  FLUX   MOORCOCK, MICHAEL   NV   NWS 63 07
  LAST SALAMANDER, THE   RACKHAM, JOHN   SS   NWS 63 07

LANCELOT BIGGS: SPACEMAN BOND, NELSON S.   AC H DBL 50
  F.O.B. VENUS   BOND, NELSON S.   SS   FAD 39 11
  LANCELOT BIGGS COOKS A PIRATE
                         BOND, NELSON S.   SS   FAD 40 02
  MADNESS OF LANCELOT BIGGS, THE
                         BOND, NELSON S.   SS   FAD 40 04
  LANCELOT BIGGS, MASTER NAVIGATOR
                         BOND, NELSON S.   SS   FAD 40 05
  GENIUS OF LANCELOT BIGGS, THE
                         BOND, NELSON S.   SS   FAD 40 06
  HONEYMOON IN BEDLAM   BOND, NELSON S.   SS   WRT 41 01
  WHERE ARE YOU, MR. BIGGS? BOND, NELSON S.   SS   WRT 41 09
  GHOST OF LANCELOT BIGGS, THE BOND, NELSON S. SS   WRT 42 01
  RETURN OF LANCELOT BIGGS, THE
                         BOND, NELSON S.   SS   AMZ 42 05
  LOVE SONG OF LANCELOT BIGGS, THE
                         BOND, NELSON S.   SS   AMZ 42 09
  MR. BIGGS GOES TO TOWN BOND, NELSON S.   SS   AMZ 42 10
  ORDEAL OF LANCELOT BIGGS, THE
                         BOND, NELSON S.   SS   AMZ 43 05
  SCIENTIFIC PIONEER RETURNS, THE
                         BOND, NELSON S.   SS   AMZ 40 11

LAND THAT TIME FORGOT AND THE MOON MAID, THE
                         BURROUGHS, EDGAR R. AC H DOV 63
  LAND THAT TIME FORGOT, THE BURROUGHS, EDGAR R. NO BBM 18 08
  MOON MAID, THE   BURROUGHS, EDGAR R.   NO   AAS 23 05

LAND THAT TIME FORGOT, THE BURROUGHS, EDGAR R. NO H MCG 24
  ILLUSTRATIONS   ST. JOHN, J. ALLEN   IL
  LAND THAT TIME FORGOT, THE BURROUGHS, EDGAR R. NO BBM 18 08
  PEOPLE THAT TIME FORGOT, THE BURROUGHS, EDGAR R. NV BBM 18 10
  OUT OF TIME'S ABYSS   BURROUGHS, EDGAR R.   NV   BBM 18 12

LAST DOOR TO AIYA   GINSBURG, MIRRA   AN H PHI 68
  INTRODUCTION   GINSBURG, MIRRA   IN
  WORLD IN WHICH I DISAPPEARED, THE
                         DNIEPROV, ANATOLY   SS   ISF 68 06
  NEW SIGNAL STATION, THE GANSOVSKY, SEVER   SS
  GOLDEN LOTUS, A LEGEND, THE GRESHNOV, M.   SS
  MY COLLEAGUE   GRIGORIEV, VLADIMIR   SS
  VANYA   GRIGORIEV, VLADIMIR   SS
  LAST DOOR TO AIYA   PARNOV, YEREMEY
                         AND YEMTSEV, MIKHAIL   SS C ISF 68 06
  HOMER'S SECRET   POLESHCHUK, A.   SS
  WHITE CONE OF THE ALAID, THE STRUGATSKY, ARKADY
                         AND STRUGATSKY, BORIS   SS C
  OUT IN SPACE   VARSHAVSKY, ILYA   SS

LAST HURRAH OF THE GOLDEN HORDE, THE
                         SPINRAD, NORMAN   AC H DBL 70
  CARCINOMA ANGELS   SPINRAD, NORMAN   SS   DVS 67 01
  AGE OF INVENTION, THE SPINRAD, NORMAN   SS   FSF 66 07
  OUTWARD BOUND   SPINRAD, NORMAN   NV   ASF 64 03
  CHILD OF MIND, A   SPINRAD, NORMAN   SS   AMZ 65 01
  EQUALIZER, THE   SPINRAD, NORMAN   SS   ASF 64 12
  LAST OF THE ROMANY, THE SPINRAD, NORMAN   SS   ASF 63 05
  TECHNICALITY   SPINRAD, NORMAN   SS   ASF 66 08
  RULES OF THE ROAD, THE SPINRAD, NORMAN   SS   GAL 64 12
  DEAD END   SPINRAD, NORMAN   SS   GAL 69 11
  NIGHT IN ELF HILL, A   SPINRAD, NORMAN   SS   FRS 68
  DEATHWATCH   SPINRAD, NORMAN   SS   PBY 65 01
  ERSATZ EGO, THE (YOUR NAME SHALL BE...DARKNESS)
                         SPINRAD, NORMAN   SS   AMZ 64 11
  NEUTRAL GROUND   SPINRAD, NORMAN   SS   FSF 66 11
  ONCE MORE, WITH FEELING SPINRAD, NORMAN   SS   KNT 69
  IT'S A BIRD, IT'S A PLANE! SPINRAD, NORMAN   SS   GNT 67
  SUBJECTIVITY   SPINRAD, NORMAN   SS   ASF 64 01
  ENTROPIC GANG BANG CAPER, THE
                         SPINRAD, NORMAN   SS   NWS 69 08
  LAST HURRAH OF THE GOLDEN HORDE, THE
                         SPINRAD, NORMAN   SS   NWS 69 07

LAST LEAP AND OTHER STORIES OF THE SUPER-MIND, THE
                         GALOUYE, DANIEL F.   AC   COR 64
  LAST LEAP, THE   GALOUYE, DANIEL F.   NV   IFS 60 01
  KANGAROO COURT   GALOUYE, DANIEL F.   SN   IFS 60 09
  SANCTUARY   GALOUYE, DANIEL F.   NV   FSF 54 07
  DEADLINE SUNDAY   GALOUYE, DANIEL F.   NV   IMG 55 10
  FIGHTING SPIRIT   GALOUYE, DANIEL F.   NV   GAL 60 12
  JEBABURBA   GALOUYE, DANIEL F.   SS   GAL 54 10
  SEEING-EYE DOG   GALOUYE, DANIEL F.   SS   GAL 56 09

LAST SPACESHIP, THE   LEINSTER, MURRAY   NO H FEL 49
  DISCIPLINARY CIRCUIT, THE LEINSTER, MURRAY   NV   TWS 46 WI
  MANLESS WORLDS, THE   LEINSTER, MURRAY   NV   TWS 47 02
  BOOMERANG CIRCUIT, THE LEINSTER, MURRAY   NV   TWS 47 07

LAST TRAIN TO LIMBO   PLAYBOY, EDITORS OF AN   PBP 71
  PREFACE   PLAYBOY, EDITORS OF   IN
  LAST TRAIN TO LIMBO   BABER, ASA   SS   PBY 70 07
  LEVIATHAN!   NIVEN, LARRY   SS   PBY 70 08
  MONSTER SHOW, THE   BEAUMONT, CHARLES   SS   PBY 56 05

AST TRAIN TO LIMBO

ILLUSTRATED WOMAN, THE	BRADBURY, RAY	SS	PBY 61 03
FOOD OF THE GODS, THE	CLARKE, ARTHUR C.	SS	PBY 64 05
SPLENDID SOURCE, THE	MATHESON, RICHARD	SS	PBY 56 05
ORIGIN OF EVERYTHING, THE	CALVINO, ITALO	SS	PBY 68 03
ON LOCATION	BAUM, THOMAS	SS	PBY 70 07
MAN WITH A PAST	BROWN, T. K. III	SS	PBY 63 05
WORD OF HONOR	BLOCH, ROBERT	SS	PBY 58 08
LOST CITY OF MARS, THE	BRADBURY, RAY	NV	PBY 67 01
DECEMBER 28TH	THOMAS, THEODORE L.	SS	PBY 59 12
WHO SHALL DWELL...	NEAL, H. C.	SS	PBY 62 07
PUPPET SHOW	BROWN, FREDRIC	SS	PBY 62 11
PAPA'S PLANET	NOLAN, WILLIAM F.	SS	PBY 68 04
DIAL "F" FOR FRANKENSTEIN	CLARKE, ARTHUR C.	SS	PBY 65 01

ATE GREAT FUTURE, THE — FITZ GERALD & DILLON AN — FCR 76

INTRODUCTION	FITZ GERALD, GREGORY AND DILLON, JOHN	IN C	
WHEN WE WENT TO SEE THE END OF THE WORLD	SILVERBERG, ROBERT	SS	UNI 72 02
THING OF CUSTOM, A	DE CAMP, L. SPRAGUE	SS	FUN 57 01
PEDESTRIAN, THE (REP 51 08)	BRADBURY, RAY	SS	FSF 52 02
WILLIAM AND MARY	DAHL, ROALD	NV	59
FLOWERS FOR ALGERNON	KEYES, DANIEL	SS	FSF 59 04
COUNTRY OF THE KIND, THE	KNIGHT, DAMON	SS	FSF 56 02
COME TO VENUS MELANCHOLY	DISCH, THOMAS M.	SS	FSF 65 11
HOW BEAUTIFUL WITH BANNERS	BLISH, JAMES	SS	ORB 66 01
TOTALLY RICH, THE	BRUNNER, JOHN	NV	WOT 63 06
AMERICA THE BEAUTIFUL	LEIBER, FRITZ	SS	YRT 70
ANNEX, THE	MACDONALD, JOHN D.	SS	PBY 68 05
SHODDY LANDS, THE	LEWIS, C. S.	SS	FSF 56 02
CRUCIFIXUS ETIAM	MILLER, WALTER M. JR	SS	ASF 53 02
THREE PORTRAITS AND A PRAYER	POHL, FREDERIK	SS	GAL 62 08

AURIE'S SPACE ANNUAL — ANONYMOUS — AN H LAU 53

LIAISON SERVICE	BOUNDS, SYDNEY J.	NV	NWS 51 WI
MATTER OF SALVAGE, A	BOUNDS, SYDNEY J.	SS	NWS 52 01
BEST HOLIDAY I EVER HAD, THE	CROSS, JOHN KEIR	SS	
PRISON TRAP	RAYER, FRANCIS G.	SS	NWS 51 SU
WHAT MAKES ROCKETS ROCKET?	YATES, R. F.	AR	
AND SO TO THE MOON	YATES, R. F.	AR	
ADRIFT ON THE SEA OF SPACE	YATES, R. F.	AR	
GRAVITY IS A THING	ANONYMOUS	AR	
DEATH OF A PLANET	ANONYMOUS	CT	
DREADED BLACK PLANET, THE	ANONYMOUS	CT	
SATURN FACTS	MISC. MATERIAL	MS	
BRITISH INTERPLANETARY SOCIETY, THE	MISC. MATERIAL	MS	

LEARNING MAZE AND OTHER STORIES, THE — ELWOOD, ROGER — OA H MES 74

INTRODUCTION	ELWOOD, ROGER	IN	
LEARNING MAZE, THE	BLOCH, ROBERT	SS	
REQUIEM	HAMILTON, EDMOND	SS	AMZ 62 04
THIRTEEN TO CENTAURUS	BALLARD, J. G.	NV	AMZ 62 04
LADY BOUNTIFUL	KIMBERLY, GAIL	SS	
GIFT OF THE GODS, THE	JONES, RAYMOND F.	NV	SFS 55 01
THEN YOU CAN DO WHAT YOU WANT	BILKER, AUDREY L. AND BILKER, HARVEY L.	SS C	
MOST BEAUTIFUL MUSIC, THE	MACKENROTH, NANCY	SS	

LEGENDS FROM THE END OF TIME — MOORCOCK, MICHAEL — AC H HPR 76

PALE ROSES	MOORCOCK, MICHAEL	NV	NWQ 74 06
WHITE STARS	MOORCOCK, MICHAEL	NV	NWB 75 08
ANCIENT SHADOWS	MOORCOCK, MICHAEL	NV	NWB 75 09

LEST WE FORGET THEE, EARTH — KNOX, CALVIN M. — DN ACE 58

CHALICE OF DEATH	KNOX, CALVIN M.	NO	SFA 57 06
EARTH SHALL LIVE AGAIN	KNOX, CALVIN M.	SN	SFA 57 12
VENGEANCE OF THE SPACE ARMADAS	KNOX, CALVIN M.	SN	SFA 58 03

LIBERATED FUTURE: VOYAGES INTO TOMORROW, THE — HOSKINS, ROBERT — AN FAW 74 12

INTRODUCTION	HOSKINS, ROBERT	IN	
SAM HALL	ANDERSON, POUL	NV	ASF 53 08
ENCASED IN ANCIENT RIND	LAFFERTY, R. A.	NV	QRK 71 03
LITTLE BLACK BAG, THE	KORNBLUTH, C. M.	NV	ASF 50 07
TROUBLE WITH YOU EARTH PEOPLE, THE	MACLEAN, KATHERINE	NV	AMZ 68 02
STREET OF DREAMS, FEET OF CLAY	SHECKLEY, ROBERT	NV	GAL 68 02
PRIVATE EYE	KUTTNER, HENRY	NV	ASF 49 01
SOFT COME THE DRAGONS	KOONTZ, DEAN R.	SS	FSF 67 08
RUN FROM HOME, THE	HENSLEY, JOE L.	SS	FSF 70 12
CONVERSATIONS AT LOTHAR'S	MALZBERG, BARRY N.	SS	COI 73
MEETING OF MINDS, A	MCCAFFREY, ANNE	NV	FSF 69 01
LIBERATION OF EARTH, THE	TENN, WILLIAM	SS	FUT 53 05
TRIP TO THE HEAD, A	LE GUIN, URSULA K.	SS	QRK 70 01

LIFE EVERLASTING AND OTHER TALES OF SCIENCE, FANTASY AND HORROR — KELLER, DAVID H. MD. AC H AVL 49

EDITED BY SAM MOSKOWITZ			
INTRODUCTION	MOSKOWITZ, SAM	IN	
LIFE EVERLASTING	KELLER, DAVID H. MD.	NA	AMZ 34 07
BONELESS HORROR, THE	KELLER, DAVID H. MD.	SS	SWS 29 07
UNTO US A CHILD IS BORN	KELLER, DAVID H. MD.	SS	AMZ 33 07
NO MORE TOMORROWS	KELLER, DAVID H. MD.	SS	AMZ 32 12
THING IN THE CELLAR, THE	KELLER, DAVID H. MD.	SS	WRT 32 03
DEAD WOMAN, THE (STE 39 04)	KELLER, DAVID H. MD.	SS	FMG 34 04
HEREDITY	KELLER, DAVID H. MD.	SS	47
FACE IN THE MIRROR, THE	KELLER, DAVID H. MD.	SS	
CEREBRAL LIBRARY, THE	KELLER, DAVID H. MD.	SS	AMZ 31 05
PIECE OF LINOLEUM, A (AS AMY WORTH)	KELLER, DAVID H. MD.	SS	TST 33 12
THIRTY AND ONE, THE	KELLER, DAVID H. MD.	SS	MAR 38 11

LIGHT AT THE END OF THE UNIVERSE, THE	CARR, TERRY	AC	PYR 76 10
NICE GUYS FINISH SOMEWHERE IN THE MIDDLE	ELLISON, HARLAN	IN	
DANCE OF THE CHANGER AND THE THREE, THE	CARR, TERRY	SS	FRS 68
WINDS AT STARMONT, THE	CARR, TERRY	NA	
OZYMANDIAS	CARR, TERRY	SS	DVS 72 02
REJOICE, REJOICE, WE HAVE NO CHOICE	CARR, TERRY	SS	
HOP-FRIEND	CARR, TERRY	SS	FSF 62 11
TOUCHSTONE	CARR, TERRY	SS	FSF 64 05
BROWN ROBERT	CARR, TERRY	SS	FSF 62 07
CHANGING OF THE GODS	CARR, TERRY	NV	INY 73 05
STANLEY TOOTHBRUSH (AS CARL BRANDON)	CARR, TERRY	SS	FSF 62 07
COLORS OF FEAR, THE	CARR, TERRY	SS	NDM 74 04
SLEEPING BEAUTY	CARR, TERRY	SS	FSF 67 05
IN HIS IMAGE (IN MAN'S IMAGE)	CARR, TERRY	SS	AMZ 71 11
OLD MAN OF THE MOUNTAINS, THE	CARR, TERRY	SS	FSF 63 04
ROBOTS ARE HERE, THE	CARR, TERRY	NV	IFS 67 05
THEY LIVE ON LEVELS	CARR, TERRY	SS	NDM 73 03

LIGHT FANTASTIC, THE — BESTER, ALFRED — AC H BKP 76

ALSO IN "STARLIGHT"			
5,271,009 (ALSO AS THE STARCOMBER)	BESTER, ALFRED	NV	FSF 54 03
MS. FOUND IN A CHAMPAGNE BOTTLE	BESTER, ALFRED	SS	STA 68
FONDLY FAHRENHEIT	BESTER, ALFRED	SS	FSF 54 08
COMMENT ON FONDLY FAHRENHEIT	BESTER, ALFRED	AR	
FOUR-HOUR FUGUE, THE	BESTER, ALFRED	SS	ASF 74 06
MEN WHO MURDERED MOHAMMED, THE	BESTER, ALFRED	SS	FSF 58 10
DISAPPEARING ACT	BESTER, ALFRED	SS	STR 53 02
HELL IS FOREVER	BESTER, ALFRED	SN	UNK 42 08

LIGHT FANTASTIC, THE — HARRISON, HARRY — AN H SCB 71

INTRODUCTION- THE FUNCTION OF SCIENCE FICTION	BLISH, JAMES	IN	
MUSE, THE	BURGESS, ANTHONY	SS	HUD 68
UNSAFE DEPOSIT BOX, THE	KERSH, GERALD	SS	SEP 62 04
SOMETHING STRANGE	AMIS, KINGSLEY	NV	FSF 61 07
SOLD TO SATAN	TWAIN, MARK	SS	
END OF THE PARTY, THE (1947)	GREENE, GRAHAM	SS	WBY 50 12
CIRCULAR RUINS, THE (TRANSLATED BY JAMES E. IRBY)	BORGES, JORGE LUIS	SS	62
SHOUT, THE (1929)	GRAVES, ROBERT	SS	FSF 52 04
DOOR, THE	WHITE, E. B.	SS	NYM 39
MACHINE STOPS, THE	FORSTER, E. M.	NV	28
MARK GABLE FOUNDATION, THE	SZILARD, LEO	SS	61
ENORMOUS RADIO, THE	CHEEVER, JOHN	SS	NYM 47 05
FINEST STORY IN THE WORLD, THE	KIPLING, RUDYARD	NV	CRV 91 07
SHODDY LANDS, THE	LEWIS, C. S.	SS	FSF 56 02
AFTERWORD	HARRISON, HARRY	MS	

LIKE NOTHING ON EARTH — RUSSELL, ERIC FRANK — AC H DOB 75

HOBBYIST	RUSSELL, ERIC FRANK	NV	ASF 47 09
MECHANICAL MICE, THE (AS MAURICE G. HUGI)	RUSSELL, ERIC FRANK	NV	ASF 41 01
INTO YOUR TENT I'LL CREEP	RUSSELL, ERIC FRANK	SS	ASF 57 09
NOTHING NEW	RUSSELL, ERIC FRANK	SS	ASF 55 01
EXPOSURE	RUSSELL, ERIC FRANK	SS	ASF 50 07
ULTIMA THULE	RUSSELL, ERIC FRANK	SS	ASF 51 10

LINE TO TOMORROW AND OTHER STORIES OF FANTASY AND SCIENCE FICTION — PADGETT, LEWIS — AC BAN 54 08

LINE TO TOMORROW	PADGETT, LEWIS	SS	ASF 45 11
GNOME THERE WAS, A	PADGETT, LEWIS	NV	UNK 41 10
WHAT YOU NEED	PADGETT, LEWIS	SS	ASF 45 10
PRIVATE EYE	PADGETT, LEWIS	NV	ASF 49 01
TWONKY, THE	PADGETT, LEWIS	SS	ASF 42 09
COMPLIMENTS OF THE AUTHOR	PADGETT, LEWIS	NV	UNK 42 10
WHEN THE BOUGH BREAKS	PADGETT, LEWIS	NV	ASF 44 11

LION OF COMARRE AND AGAINST THE FALL OF NIGHT — CLARKE, ARTHUR C. — AC H HBW 68

LION OF COMARRE	CLARKE, ARTHUR C.	NV	TWS 49 08
AGAINST THE FALL OF NIGHT	CLARKE, ARTHUR C.	NO	STS 48 11

LISTENERS, THE — GUNN, JAMES E. — NO H SCB 72

ROBERT MACDONALD- 2025 (THE LISTENERS)	GUNN, JAMES E.	NV	GAL 68 09
GEORGE THOMAS- 2027 (THE VOICES)	GUNN, JAMES E.	NV	FSF 72 09
WILLIAM MITCHELL- 2028 (THE MESSAGE)	GUNN, JAMES E.	NV	GAL 71 05
ANDREW WHITE- 2028 (THE ANSWER)	GUNN, JAMES E.	NV	GAL 72 01
ROBERT MACDONALD- 2058	GUNN, JAMES E.	NV	
COMPUTER- 2118, THE (THE REPLY)	GUNN, JAMES E.	NV	GAL 72 05

LITTLE MONSTERS, THE — ELWOOD & GHIDALIA — AN MBB 69

METRONOME, THE	DERLETH, AUGUST	SS	WRT 35 02
LET'S PLAY POISON	BRADBURY, RAY	SS	WRT 46 11
PLAYFELLOW, THE	ASQUITH, CYNTHIA	NV	47
MIMSY WERE THE BOROGOVES	KUTTNER, HENRY	NV	ASF 43 02
ANTIMACASSAR, THE	LA SPINA, GREYE	SS	WRT 49 05
OLD CLOTHES	BLACKWOOD, ALGERNON	NV	17
HOW FEAR DEPARTED FROM THE LONG GALLERY	BENSON, E. F.	SS	12
THEY	KIPLING, RUDYARD	NV	SCR 04

LIVES AND TIMES OF JERRY CORNELIUS, THE			
	MOORCOCK, MICHAEL	AC H	ALB 76
PEKING JUNCTION, THE	MOORCOCK, MICHAEL	SS	
DELHI DIVISION, THE	MOORCOCK, MICHAEL	SS	NWS 68 12
TANK TRAPEZE, THE	MOORCOCK, MICHAEL	SS	NWS 69 01
NATURE OF THE CATASTROPHE, THE			
	MOORCOCK, MICHAEL	SS	NWS 70 01
SWASTIKA SET-UP, THE	MOORCOCK, MICHAEL	NV	72
SUNSET PERSPECTIVE, THE	MOORCOCK, MICHAEL	SS	71
SEA WOLVES	MOORCOCK, MICHAEL	SS	SAG 70
VOORTREKKER	MOORCOCK, MICHAEL	NV	QRK 71 04
DEAD SINGERS	MOORCOCK, MICHAEL	SS	INK 71
LONGFORD CUP, THE	MOORCOCK, MICHAEL	SS	PNT 73
ENTROPY CIRCUIT, THE	MOORCOCK, MICHAEL	SS	74

LIVING DEMONS, THE	BLOCH, ROBERT	AC	BEL 67 09
INTRODUCTION	BLOCH, ROBERT	IN	
LIFE IN OUR TIME	BLOCH, ROBERT	SS	EQM 66 10
INDIAN SPIRIT GUIDE, THE	BLOCH, ROBERT	SS	WRT 48 11
LUCY COMES TO STAY	BLOCH, ROBERT	SS	WRT 52 01
PLOT IS THE THING, THE	BLOCH, ROBERT	SS	FSF 66 07
UNDERGROUND	BLOCH, ROBERT	SS	67
BEASTS OF BARSAC, THE	BLOCH, ROBERT	SS	WRT 44 07
PHILTRE TIP	BLOCH, ROBERT	SS	ROG 61 03
UNSPEAKABLE BETROTHAL, THE	BLOCH, ROBERT	SS	APR 49 09
BLACK BARGAIN	BLOCH, ROBERT	SS	WRT 42 05
GIRL FROM MARS, THE	BLOCH, ROBERT	SS	FAD 50 03
BEAUTY'S BEAST	BLOCH, ROBERT	SS	WRT 41 05
TELL YOUR FORTUNE	BLOCH, ROBERT	SS	WRT 50 05

LIVING WAY OUT	GUIN, WYMAN	AC	AVN 67 08
MAN OF THE RENAISSANCE, A	GUIN, WYMAN	SS	GAL 64 12
MY DARLING HECATE	GUIN, WYMAN	NV	BEY 53 11
DELEGATE FROM GUAPANGA, THE	GUIN, WYMAN	NV	GAL 64 08
ROOT AND THE RING, THE	GUIN, WYMAN	NV	BEY 54 09
TRIGGER TIDE	GUIN, WYMAN	SS	ASF 50 10
VOLPLA	GUIN, WYMAN	NV	GAL 56 05
BEYOND BEDLAM	GUIN, WYMAN	NA	GAL 51 08

LLANA OF GATHOL	BURROUGHS, EDGAR R.	NO H	BUR 48
ILLUSTRATIONS	BURROUGHS, JOHN C.	IL	
CITY OF THE MUMMIES, THE	BURROUGHS, EDGAR R.	NV	AMZ 41 03
BLACK PIRATES OF BARSOOM	BURROUGHS, EDGAR R.	NV	AMZ 41 06
YELLOW MEN OF MARS	BURROUGHS, EDGAR R.	NV	AMZ 41 08
INVISIBLE MEN OF MARS	BURROUGHS, EDGAR R.	NV	AMZ 41 10

LONE STAR UNIVERSE	PROCTOR & UTLEY	OA H	HDL 76
SPECULATIVE FICTION & FANTASY FROM TEXAS			
IN EXORCISING TEXAS: AN INTRODUCTION			
	ELLISON, HARLAN	IN	
UNSLEEPING BEAUTY AND THE BEAST			
	WALDROP, HOWARD	SS	
TALKING, THE	BARRETT, NEAL JR.	SS	
SWEETWATER FACTOR, THE	REAMY, TOM	SS	
COMMUNITY STUDY	OLIVER, CHAD	NV	
COMING OF BAST, THE	HOWARD, ROBERT E.	PM	
EVERY DAY IN EVERY WAY	HOLLIS, H. H.	NV	
AND DEATH ONCE DEAD	PUMILIA, JOSEPH F.	SS	
MAN-MADE SELF	STERLING, BRUCE	SS	
MIGRATION, THE	PROCTOR, GEORGE W.	SS	
STORY OF A STRANGE RELATIVE	HOLDEN, LARRY	SS	
INVASION OF DALLAS, THE	SALLIS, JAMES	SS	
FIDDLE ESS	GILLETTE, GLEN L.	NV	
GHOST SEAS	UTLEY, STEVEN	SS	
FROM THE TOWER OF ERIDU	FEHRENBACH, T. R.	SS	
RECENT SEMIFINALS, THE	LORY, ROBERT	SS	
WOMAN WAITING	TUTTLE, LISA	NV	
BACK TO THE STONE AGE	SAUNDERS, JAKE	SS	

LONG AFTER MIDNIGHT	BRADBURY, RAY	AC H	KNP 76
BLUE BOTTLE, THE (DEATH WISH)			
	BRADBURY, RAY	SS	PLS 50 FL
ONE TIMELESS SPRING	BRADBURY, RAY	SS	COL 46 04
PARROT WHO MET PAPA, THE	BRADBURY, RAY	SS	PBY 72 01
BURNING MAN, THE	BRADBURY, RAY	SS	
PIECE OF WOOD, A	BRADBURY, RAY	SS	ESQ 52 06
MESSIAH, THE	BRADBURY, RAY	SS	WAB 71 SP
G.B.S.-MARK V	BRADBURY, RAY	SS	
UTTERLY PERFECT MURDER, THE (MY PERFECT MURDER)			
	BRADBURY, RAY	SS	PBY 71 08
PUNISHMENT WITHOUT CRIME	BRADBURY, RAY	SS	OWS 50 03
GETTING THROUGH SUNDAY SOMEHOW			
	BRADBURY, RAY	SS	
DRINK ENTIRE: AGAINST THE MADNESS OF CROWDS			
	BRADBURY, RAY	SS	GLR
INTERVAL IN SUNLIGHT	BRADBURY, RAY	NV	ESQ 54 03
STORY OF LOVE, A	BRADBURY, RAY	SS	
WISH, THE	BRADBURY, RAY	SS	WDM 73 12
FOREVER AND THE EARTH	BRADBURY, RAY	SS	PLS 50 SP
BETTER PART OF WISDOM, THE	BRADBURY, RAY	SS	
DARLING ADOLPH	BRADBURY, RAY	SS	
MIRACLES OF JAMIE, THE	BRADBURY, RAY	SS	CHM 46 04
OCTOBER GAME, THE	BRADBURY, RAY	SS	WRT 48 03
PUMPERNICKEL, THE	BRADBURY, RAY	SS	COL 51 05
LONG AFTER MIDNIGHT	BRADBURY, RAY	SS	
HAVE I GOT A CHOCOLATE BAR FOR YOU!			
	BRADBURY, RAY	SS	PNT 73 10

LONG AFTERNOON OF EARTH, THE	ALDISS, BRIAN W.	NO	SIG 62 01
IN ENGLAND AS "HOTHOUSE"			
HOTHOUSE	ALDISS, BRIAN W.	NV	FSF 61 02
NOMANSLAND	ALDISS, BRIAN W.	NV	FSF 61 04
UNDERGROWTH	ALDISS, BRIAN W.	NV	FSF 61 07
TIMBERLINE	ALDISS, BRIAN W.	NV	FSF 61 09
EVERGREEN	ALDISS, BRIAN W.	NV	FSF 61 12

LONG ARM OF GIL HAMILTON, THE			
	NIVEN, LARRY	AC	BAL 76 02
DEATH BY ECSTASY (THE ORGANLEGGERS)			
	NIVEN, LARRY	NV	GAL 69 01
DEFENSELESS DEAD, THE	NIVEN, LARRY	NV	TTM 73
ARM	NIVEN, LARRY	NA	EPC 75
AFTERWORD: THE LAST WORD ABOUT SF DETECTIVES			
	NIVEN, LARRY	MS	

LONG EUREKA, THE	SELLINGS, ARTHUR	AC H	DOB 68
BLANK FORM	SELLINGS, ARTHUR	SS	GAL 58 07
SCENE SHIFTER, THE	SELLINGS, ARTHUR	SS	STR 59 05
ONE ACROSS	SELLINGS, ARTHUR	SS	GAL 56 05
WELL TRAINED HEROES, THE	SELLINGS, ARTHUR	NV	GAL 64 06
HOMECOMING	SELLINGS, ARTHUR	SS	
LONG EUREKA, THE	SELLINGS, ARTHUR	SS	SCF 59 08
VERBAL AGREEMENT	SELLINGS, ARTHUR	NV	GAL 56 09
TRADE-IN	SELLINGS, ARTHUR	SS	
BIRTHRIGHT	SELLINGS, ARTHUR	SS	NWS 56 11

LONG NIGHT OF WAITING AND OTHER STORIES			
	ELWOOD, ROGER	OA H	AUR 74
FOREWORD	STURGEON, THEODORE	IN	
LONG NIGHT OF WAITING, THE	NORTON, ANDRE	SS	73
TELEPROBE	EISENSTEIN, PHYLLIS	SS	
LIKE A DIAMOND IN THE SKY	MCKINLEY, MARY C.	SS	
PROPER STUDY, THE	HOLLY, JOAN C.	SS	
NATURAL HISTORY	MALZBERG, BARRY N.	SS	
MOST FORGETABLE STORY IN THE WORLD, THE			
	LAFFERTY, R. A.	SS	
UNREASONABLE FACSIMILE	SHAW, BOB	SS	
SINGING CLIFFS OF FAUNUS, THE			
	BUNCH, MIRIAM	SS	
EARTH MOTHER	GLOECKNER, CAROLYN	SS	74
THIRTY-THREE AND ONE-THIRD	ZEBROWSKI, GEORGE		
	AND DANN, JACK M.	SS C	
OLD MAX	LYTLE, B. J.	SS	
TRIPPERS, THE	SCHAEFFER, ROBIN	SS	
ANY RESEMBLANCE TO MAGIC	BINDER, EANDO	SS	
FIRST MISSION	CARLSON, WILLIAM	NV	
EPILOGUE: THE FUTURE OF SCIENCE FICTION			
	BILKER, AUDREY L.		
	AND BILKER, HARVEY L.	MS C	

LOOKING AHEAD	ALLEN, D. & L.	AN L	HBL 75
THE VISION OF SCIENCE FICTION			
PREFACE	ALLEN, DICK		
	AND ALLEN, LORI	IN C	
LISTENERS, THE	DE LA MARE, WALTER	PM	
FROM "THE FALL OF JAPAN"	CRAIG, WILLIAM	AR	67
ULTIMATE HORROR, THE	THOMPSON, R. W.	AR	
FROM "THE LIMITS TO GROWTH"	MEADOWS, DONELLA H.		
	MEADOWS, DENNIS L.		
	RANDERS, JORGEN		
	AND BEHRENS, WILLIAM W.	AR C	72
FROM "OF A FIRE ON THE MOON"	MAILER, NORMAN	EX	69
SURVIVAL U: PROSPECTUS FOR A REALLY RELEVANT UNIVERSITY			
	FISCHER, JOHN	AR	HRP 69 09
NEW AGE, A	ALLEN, DICK	PM	SFD 72
ARTIST OF THE BEAUTIFUL, THE (1844)			
	HAWTHORNE, NATHANIEL	NV	DMR 44 06
INTERURBAN QUEEN	LAFFERTY, R. A.	SS	ORB 70 08
CORONA	DELANY, SAMUEL R.	SS	FSF 67 10
MARCHING MORONS, THE	KORNBLUTH, C. M.	NV	GAL 51 04
FOREVER PEOPLE, THE	KIRBY, JACK	CT	70
STAR-SPLITTER, THE	FROST, ROBERT	PM	23
ON SHOOTING PARTICLES BEYOND THE WORLD			
	EBERHART, RICHARD	PM	60
FAR LOOK, THE	THOMAS, THEODORE L.	NV	ASF 56 08
OF MIST, AND GRASS, AND SAND	MCINTYRE, VONDA N.	SS	ASF 73 10
STRANGER STATION	KNIGHT, DAMON	NV	FSF 56 12
SHIP WHO SANG, THE	MCCAFFREY, ANNE	SS	FSF 61 04
LAST TRUE GOD, THE	DEL REY, LESTER	SS	IFS 69 09
TOMORROW AND TOMORROW AND TOMORROW (THE BIG TRIP UP YONDER)			
	VONNEGUT, KURT JR.	SS	GAL 54 01
MAN WHO WALKED HOME, THE	TIPTREE, JAMES JR.	NV	AMZ 72 05
YEAR OF THE JACKPOT, THE	HEINLEIN, ROBERT A.	NV	GAL 52 03
VISION OF JUDGEMENT, A	WELLS, H. G.	SS	BUT 99 09
HORSES, THE	MUIR, EDWIN	PM	60
CROSS THE BORDER, CLOSE THE GAP			
	FIEDLER, LESLIE A.	AR	
UTOPIA	LUNDWALL, SAM J.	AR	71
THEORY AND PRACTICE OF TIME TRAVEL, THE			
	NIVEN, LARRY	AR	NEW 71 AC
OBSOLESCENCE OF MAN, THE	CLARKE, ARTHUR C.	AR	PBY 61
OUTER LIMITS OF SPACE, THE	EDELSON, EDWARD	AR	SRV 73 10
TOPICS FOR SHORTER AND LONGER PAPERS			
	MISC. MATERIAL	MS	
CHRONOLOGY OF SCIENCE FICTION, A			
	MISC. MATERIAL	MS	
SUGGESTIONS FOR FURTHER READING AND VIEWING			
	MISC. MATERIAL	MS	

LOOKING FORWARD	LESSER, MILTON	AN H	BCH 53
SCIENCE FICTION COMES OF AGE	LESSER, MILTON	IN	
MAN FROM OUTSIDE, THE	WILLIAMSON, JACK	SS	ASF 51 03
WE KILL PEOPLE	PADGETT, LEWIS	NV	ASF 46 03
WIN THE WORLD (THE SUBVERSIVES)			
	OLIVER, CHAD	SS	STS 52 02
LITTLE CREEPS, THE	MILLER, WALTER M. JR	NV	AMZ 51 12
HIGHWAY	LOWNDES, ROBERT W.	SS	SFQ 42 FL
EXILE	HAMILTON, EDMOND	SS	SSS 43 05
POWER, THE	LEINSTER, MURRAY	SS	ASF 45 09
MAN IN THE MOON, THE	REYNOLDS, MACK	SS	AMZ 50 07
PRODUCTION TEST	JONES, RAYMOND F.	NV	ASF 51 10
LION'S MOUTH	MARLOWE, STEPHEN	SS	FAD 52 06

LOOKING FORWARD

IN THIS SIGN (ALSO AS THE FIRE BALLOONS)
                          BRADBURY, RAY   SS   IMG 51 04
VICTORY UNINTENTIONAL   ASIMOV, ISAAC   SS   SSS 42 08
VOYAGE THAT LASTED SIX HUNDRED YEARS, THE
                          WILCOX, DON   NV   AMZ 40 10
LAST MONSTER, THE (TERMINAL QUEST)
                          ANDERSON, POUL   SS   SSS 51 08
KING OF THIEVES, THE   VANCE, JACK   NV   STS 49 11
MAN OF DESTINY   CHRISTOPHER, JOHN   SS   GAL 51 05
LULUNGOMEENA   DICKSON, GORDON R.   NV   GAL 54 01
ULTIMA THULE   RUSSELL, ERIC FRANK SS   ASF 51 10
INTO THY HANDS   DEL REY, LESTER   SS   ASF 45 08
TRANSCIENCE   CLARKE, ARTHUR C.   SS   STS 49 07

LOST CAVERN AND OTHER TALES OF THE FANTASTIC, THE
                          HEARD, H. F.   AC H VPR 48
CUP, THE   HEARD, H. F.   NV
CHAPEL OF EASE, THE   HEARD, H. F.   NV
LOST CAVERN, THE   HEARD, H. F.   NV
THAW PLAN, THE   HEARD, H. F.   NV

LOST FACE, THE   NESVADBA, JOSEF   AC H TAP 71
    BEST SCIENCE FICTION FROM CZECHOSLOVAKIA
    IN ENGLAND AS "IN THE FOOTSTEPS OF THE ABOMINABLE SNOWMAN"
    ALL BUT FIRST AND THIRD STORIES ARE IN "VAMPIRES LTD."
TRANSLATION   URWIN, IRIS   MS
DEATH OF AN APEMAN, THE   NESVADBA, JOSEF   NV
EXPEDITION IN THE OPPOSITE DIRECTION
                          NESVADBA, JOSEF   NV   64
TRIAL NOBODY EVER HEARD OF, THE
                          NESVADBA, JOSEF   SS
LOST FACE, THE   NESVADBA, JOSEF   NV   64
CHEMICAL FORMULA OF DESTINY, THE
                          NESVADBA, JOSEF   SS   64
INVENTER OF HIS OWN UNDOING NESVADBA, JOSEF   NV   64
DOCTOR MOREAU'S OTHER ISLAND NESVADBA, JOSEF   SS   64
IN THE FOOTSTEPS OF THE ABOMINABLE SNOWMAN
                          NESVADBA, JOSEF   NV   64

LOVE & NAPALM: EXPORT U.S.A. BALLARD, J. G.   AC H GRV 72
    IN ENGLAND AS "ATROCITY EXHIBITION"
PREFACE   BURROUGHS, WILLIAM   IN
ATROCITY EXHIBITION, THE BALLARD, J. G.   SS   NWS 66 09
UNIVERSITY OF DEATH, THE BALLARD, J. G.   SS   TRV 68 SU
ASSASSINATION WEAPON, THE BALLARD, J. G.   SS   NWS 66 04
YOU: COMA: MARILYN MONROE BALLARD, J. G.   SS   NWS 66 06
NOTES TOWARD A MENTAL BREAKDOWN (THE DEATH MODULE)
                          BALLARD, J. G.   SS   NWS 67 07
GREAT AMERICAN NUDE, THE BALLARD, J. G.   SS   AMB 68 SU
SUMMER CANNIBALS, THE   BALLARD, J. G.   SS   NWS 69 01
TOLERANCES OF THE HUMAN FACE BALLARD, J. G.   SS   ENC 69 09
YOU AND ME AND THE CONTINUUM BALLARD, J. G.   SS   IMP 66 03
PLAN FOR THE ASSASSINATION OF JACQUELINE KENNEDY
                          BALLARD, J. G.   SS   AMB 66 WI
LOVE AND NAPALM: EXPORT U.S.A.
                          BALLARD, J. G.   SS   RUN 68 SU
CRASH!   BALLARD, J. G.   SS   ICA 69
GENERATIONS OF AMERICA, THE BALLARD, J. G.   SS   NWS 68 10
WHY I WANT TO FUCK RONALD REAGAN
                          BALLARD, J. G.   SS   MOP 68 SU
ASSASSINATION OF JOHN FITZGERALD KENNEDY CONSIDERED AS A
    DOWNHILL MOTOR RACE, THE BALLARD, J. G.   SS   NWS 67 02

LOVE AIN'T NOTHING BUT SEX MISSPELLED
                          ELLISON, HARLAN   AC H TRI 68
MOTHERHOOD, APPLE PIE AND THE AMERICAN WAY
                          ELLISON, HARLAN   IN
PRETTY MAGGIE MONEYEYES   ELLISON, HARLAN   NV   KNT 67 05
NIGHT OF DELICATE TERRORS, THE
                          ELLISON, HARLAN   SS   PPR 61 04
WHAT I DID ON MY VACATION THIS SUMMER BY LITTLE BOBBY
    HIRSCHHORN, AGE 27   ELLISON, HARLAN   SS   KNT 64 11
NEITHER YOUR JENNY NOR MINE ELLISON, HARLAN   SS   KNT 64 04
FINAL SHTICK   ELLISON, HARLAN   SS   ROG 60 08
O YE OF LITTLE FAITH   ELLISON, HARLAN   SS   KNT 68 09
BLIND BIRD, BLIND BIRD, GO AWAY FROM ME!
                          ELLISON, HARLAN   SS   KNT 63 07
RIDING THE DARK TRAIN OUT ELLISON, HARLAN   SS   ROG 61 05
DELUSION FOR A DRAGON SLAYER ELLISON, HARLAN   SS   KNT 66 09
DANIEL WHITE FOR THE GREATER GOOD
                          ELLISON, HARLAN   SS   ROG 61 03
LONELYACHE   ELLISON, HARLAN   SS   KNT 64 07
UNIVERSE OF ROBERT BLAKE, THE (ROBERT BLAKE'S UNIVERSE)
                          ELLISON, HARLAN   SS   ROG 62 06
MONA AT HER WINDOWS   ELLISON, HARLAN   SS   ROG 62 06
G.B.K.- A MANY FLAVORED BIRD ELLISON, HARLAN   SS   ROG 62 06
FACE OF HELENE BOURNOUW, THE ELLISON, HARLAN   SS   CLG 60 10
RESURGENCE OF MISS ANKLE-STRAP WEDGIE, THE
                          ELLISON, HARLAN   SS   NEW 68 AC
ERNEST AND THE MACHINE GOD ELLISON, HARLAN   NV   KNT 68 01
BATTLE WITHOUT BANNERS   ELLISON, HARLAN   SS   NEW 64 OC
PUNKY AND THE YALE MAN   ELLISON, HARLAN   NV   KNT 66 01
PATH THROUGH THE DARKNESS, A ELLISON, HARLAN   NV   FLN 63 01
PRAYER FOR ONE'S ENEMY, A ELLISON, HARLAN   NV   CAD 66 03
ALL THE SOUNDS OF FEAR   ELLISON, HARLAN   SS   SDM 62 07

LOVE AIN'T NOTHING BUT SEX MISSPELLED (REVISED)
                          ELLISON, HARLAN   AC   PYR 76 02
NEW INTRODUCTION: HAVING AN AFFAIR WITH A TROLL
                          ELLISON, HARLAN   IN
INTRODUCTION TO THE FIRST EDITION
                          ELLISON, HARLAN   IN
NEITHER YOUR JENNY NOR MINE ELLISON, HARLAN   SS   KNT 64 04
UNIVERSE OF ROBERT BLAKE, THE (ROBERT BLAKE'S UNIVERSE)
                          ELLISON, HARLAN   SS   ROG 62 06
G.B.K.- A MANY FLAVORED BIRD ELLISON, HARLAN   SS   ROG 62 06

RIDING THE DARK TRAIN OUT ELLISON, HARLAN   SS   ROG 61 05
VALERIE   ELLISON, HARLAN   SS   LAF 72 11
RESURGENCE OF MISS ANKLE-STRAP WEDGIE, THE
                          ELLISON, HARLAN   SS   NEW 68 AC
DANIEL WHITE FOR THE GREATER GOOD
                          ELLISON, HARLAN   SS   ROG 61 03
BLIND BIRD, BLIND BIRD, GO AWAY FROM ME!
                          ELLISON, HARLAN   SS   KNT 63 07
WHAT I DID ON MY VACATION THIS SUMMER BY LITTLE BOBBY
    HIRSCHHORN, AGE 27   ELLISON, HARLAN   SS   KNT 64 11
MONA AT HER WINDOWS   ELLISON, HARLAN   SS   ROG 62 06
WHEN I WAS A HIRED GUN   ELLISON, HARLAN   SS   LAF 73 06
PATH THROUGH THE DARKNESS, A ELLISON, HARLAN   NV   FLN 63 01
BATTLE WITHOUT BANNERS   ELLISON, HARLAN   SS   NEW 64 OC
PRAYER FOR ONE'S ENEMY, A ELLISON, HARLAN   NV   CAD 66 03
PUNKY AND THE YALE MAN   ELLISON, HARLAN   NV   KNT 66 01
I CURSE THE LESSON AND BLESS THE KNOWLEDGE
                          ELLISON, HARLAN   SS   75

LOW-FLYING AIRCRAFT AND OTHER STORIES
                          BALLARD, J. G.   AC H CAP 76
ULTIMATE CITY, THE   BALLARD, J. G.   NA
LOW-FLYING AIRCRAFT   BALLARD, J. G.   SS   BNA 75 SU
DEAD ASTRONAUT, THE   BALLARD, J. G.   SS   PBY 68 05
MY DREAM OF FLYING TO WAKE ISLAND
                          BALLARD, J. G.   SS   ABT 74 WI
LIFE AND DEATH OF GOD, THE BALLARD, J. G.   SS
GREATEST TELEVISION SHOW ON EARTH, THE
                          BALLARD, J. G.   SS   ABT 72 WI
PLACE AND TIME TO DIE, A BALLARD, J. G.   SS   NWS 69 10
COMSAT ANGELS, THE   BALLARD, J. G.   SS   IFS 68 12
BEACH MURDERS, THE (CONFETTI ROYALE, ROG 66 01)
                          BALLARD, J. G.   SS   NWS 69 04

M 33 IN ANDROMEDA   VAN VOGT, A. E.   AC   PBK 71 04
SIEGE OF THE UNSEEN (THE CHRONICLER)
                          VAN VOGT, A. E.   NA   ASF 46 10
DISCORD IN SCARLET   VAN VOGT, A. E.   NV   ASF 39 12
M 33 IN ANDROMEDA   VAN VOGT, A. E.   SS   ASF 43 08
EXPENDABLES, THE   VAN VOGT, A. E.   NV   IFS 63 09
HEIR UNAPPARENT (HEIR APPARENT)
                          VAN VOGT, A. E.   SS   ASF 45 06
WEAPON SHOP, THE   VAN VOGT, A. E.   NV   ASF 42 12

MACHINE IN SHAFT TEN AND OTHER STORIES, THE
                          HARRISON, M. JOHN   AC   PTH 75
MACHINE IN SHAFT TEN, THE (AS JOYCE CHURCHILL)
                          HARRISON, M. JOHN   SS   NWQ 72 03
LAMIA AND LORD CROMIS, THE HARRISON, M. JOHN   NV   NWQ 71 01
BAIT PRINCIPLE, THE   HARRISON, M. JOHN   SS   NWS 70 02
RUNNING DOWN   HARRISON, M. JOHN   NV   NWB 75 08
ORGASM BAND, THE   HARRISON, M. JOHN   SS   TRV
VISIONS OF MONAD   HARRISON, M. JOHN   SS   NWR 68 12
EVENTS WITNESSED FROM A CITY HARRISON, M. JOHN SS
LONDON MELANCHOLY   HARRISON, M. JOHN   SS   FSF 69 05
RING OF PAIN   HARRISON, M. JOHN   SS   QRK 71 03
CAUSEWAY, THE   HARRISON, M. JOHN   SS   NWQ 71 02
BRINGER WITH THE WINDOW, THE (LAMIA MUTABLE)
                          HARRISON, M. JOHN   SS   DVS 72 02
COMING FROM BEHIND   HARRISON, M. JOHN   SS   NWQ 73 05

MACHINE IN WARD ELEVEN, THE WILLEFORD, CHARLES NO   BEL 63 06
MACHINE IN WARD ELEVEN, THE WILLEFORD, CHARLES NV   PBY 61 03
SELECTED INCIDENTS (THE SIN OF INTEGRITY)
                          WILLEFORD, CHARLES   SS   GNT
LETTER TO A.A. (ALMOST ANYBODY), A
                          WILLEFORD, CHARLES   SS
JAKE'S JOURNAL   WILLEFORD, CHARLES   NV
"JUST LIKE ON TELEVISION-" WILLEFORD, CHARLES SS
ALECTRYOMANCER, THE   WILLEFORD, CHARLES   NV   AHM

MACHINE-GOD LAUGHS, THE   ANONYMOUS   AN H GRI 49
MACHINE-GOD LAUGHS, THE   PRAGNELL, FESTUS   NV   FBK 47 02
STAR OF THE UNDEAD (ROBERT A. W. LOWNDES)
                          LAVOND, PAUL DENNIS SS   FBK 47 02
CRUSADER (AS GENE ELLERMAN) WELLS, BASIL   SS   FBK 49 05

MACHINERIES OF JOY, THE   BRADBURY, RAY   AC H SAS 64 02
    ENGLISH EDITION (HDV 64) OMITS "ALMOST THE END OF THE WORLD"
MACHINERIES OF JOY, THE   BRADBURY, RAY   SS   PBY 62 12
ONE WHO WAITS, THE   BRADBURY, RAY   SS   FSF 51 02
TYRANNOSAURUS REX (THE PREHISTORIC PRODUCER)
                          BRADBURY, RAY   SS   SEP 62 06
VACATION, THE   BRADBURY, RAY   SS   PBY 63 12
DRUMMER BOY OF SHILOH, THE BRADBURY, RAY   SS   SEP 60 04
BOYS, RAISE GIANT MUSHROOMS IN YOUR CELLAR (COME INTO MY
    CELLAR)   BRADBURY, RAY   SS   GAL 62 10
ALMOST THE END OF THE WORLD BRADBURY, RAY   SS   REP 57 12
PERHAPS WE ARE GOING AWAY BRADBURY, RAY   SS   TOP 62 01
AND THE SAILOR, HOME FROM THE SEA (FOREVER VOYAGE)
                          BRADBURY, RAY   SS   SEP 60 01
EL DIA DE MUERTE (THE DAY OF DEATH)
                          BRADBURY, RAY   SS   TCH 47 FL
ILLUSTRATED WOMAN, THE   BRADBURY, RAY   SS   PBY 61 03
SOME LIVE LIKE LAZARUS (VERY LATE IN THE EVENING)
                          BRADBURY, RAY   SS   PBY 60 12
MIRACLE OF RARE DEVICE, A BRADBURY, RAY   SS   PBY 62 01
AND SO DIED RIABOUCHINSKA BRADBURY, RAY   SS   SDM 53 06
BEGGAR ON O'CONNELL BRIDGE, THE (THE BEGGAR ON DUBLIN BRIDGE)
                          BRADBURY, RAY   SS   SEP 61 01
DEATH AND THE MAIDEN   BRADBURY, RAY   SS   FSF 60 03
FLIGHT OF RAVENS, A   BRADBURY, RAY   SS   CFQ 52 WI
BEST OF ALL POSSIBLE WORLDS BRADBURY, RAY   SS   PBY 60 08
LIFE WORK OF JUAN DIAZ, THE BRADBURY, RAY   SS   PBY 63 09
TO THE CHICAGO ABYSS   BRADBURY, RAY   SS   FSF 63 05

MACHINERIES OF JOY, THE

ANTHEM SPRINTERS, THE (THE QUEEN'S OWN EVADERS)				
	BRADBURY, RAY	SS	PBY 63	06

MACHINES AND MEN   ROBERTS, KEITH   AC H HUT 73

MANIPULATION	ROBERTS, KEITH	NV	NWR 65	03
ESCAPISM	ROBERTS, KEITH	SS	SCF 64	10
BOULTER'S CANARIES	ROBERTS, KEITH	NV	NWR 65	03
SUB-LIM	ROBERTS, KEITH	NV	NWR 65	04
BREAKDOWN	ROBERTS, KEITH	SS	IMP 66	10
THERAPY 2000	ROBERTS, KEITH	SS	NWR 69	15
DEEPS, THE	ROBERTS, KEITH	SS	ORB 66	01
MANSCARER	ROBERTS, KEITH	NV	NWR 66	07
SYNTH	ROBERTS, KEITH	SS	NWR 66	08
PACE THAT KILLS, THE	ROBERTS, KEITH	NV	IMP 66	05

MAGIC MAN AND OTHER SCIENCE-FANTASY STORIES

	BEAUMONT, CHARLES	AC	FAW 65	
FOREWORD	BRADBURY, RAY	IN		
MISS GENTILBELLE	BEAUMONT, CHARLES	SS	NEW 57	AC
LAST CAPER, THE	BEAUMONT, CHARLES	SS	FSF 54	03
NEW PEOPLE, THE	BEAUMONT, CHARLES	SS	ROG 58	
VANISHING AMERICAN, THE	BEAUMONT, CHARLES	SS	FSF 55	08
MONSTER SHOW, THE	BEAUMONT, CHARLES	SS	PBY 56	05
MAGIC MAN, THE	BEAUMONT, CHARLES	SS	NEW 60	AC
CLASSIC AFFAIR, A	BEAUMONT, CHARLES	SS	PBY 55	
HUNGER, THE	BEAUMONT, CHARLES	SS	PBY 55	04
BLACK COUNTRY	BEAUMONT, CHARLES	SS	PBY 54	09
LOVE-MASTER, THE	BEAUMONT, CHARLES	SS	ROG 56	
DARK MUSIC, THE	BEAUMONT, CHARLES	SS	PBY 56	12
FAIR LADY	BEAUMONT, CHARLES	SS	NEW 57	AC
PERCHANCE TO DREAM	BEAUMONT, CHARLES	SS	PBY 58	10
CROOKED MAN, THE	BEAUMONT, CHARLES	SS	PBY 55	08
OPEN HOUSE	BEAUMONT, CHARLES	SS	NEW 57	AC
LAST RITES	BEAUMONT, CHARLES	SS	IFS 55	10
MURDERERS, THE	BEAUMONT, CHARLES	SS	ESQ 55	
DEATH IN THE COUNTRY, A (THE DEADLY WILL TO WIN)				
	BEAUMONT, CHARLES	SS	PBY 57	11
AFTERWORD	MATHESON, RICHARD	MS		

MAJOR OPERATION   WHITE, JAMES   NO BAL 71 02

INVADER	WHITE, JAMES	NV	NWR 66	07
VERTIGO	WHITE, JAMES	NV	NWR 68	12
BLOOD BROTHER	WHITE, JAMES	NV	NWR 69	14
MEATBALL	WHITE, JAMES	NV	NWR 69	16
MAJOR OPERATION	WHITE, JAMES	NV	NWR 71	18

MAN AGAINST TOMORROW   NOLAN, WILLIAM F. AN AVN 65 12

INTRODUCTION	NOLAN, WILLIAM F.	IN		
SPECIAL DELIVERY	NEVILLE, KRIS	NO	IMG 52	01
ROOM, THE	RUSSELL, RAY	SS	PBY 61	02
AFTER THE SIRENS	HOOD, HUGH	SS	ESQ 60	
I, DREAMER	MILLER, WALTER M. JR	SS	AMZ 53	07
PAYMENT IN FULL	BRADBURY, RAY	SS	TWS 50	02
SEVENTH VICTIM	SHECKLEY, ROBERT	SS	GAL 53	04
BIRTHDAY PRESENT	FRITCH, CHARLES E.	SS	SCF 55	09
TRANSFORMER	OLIVER, CHAD	SS	FSF 54	11
MASS FOR MIXED VOICES	BEAUMONT, CHARLES	SS	SFQ 54	05
FREEWAY, THE	JOHNSON, GEORGE C.	SS	GAM 63	01
NOBODY STARVES	GOULART, RON	SS	FSF 64	02
AND MILES TO GO BEFORE I SLEEP				
	NOLAN, WILLIAM F.	SS	INF 58	08

MAN FROM BEYOND AND OTHER STORIES, THE

	WYNDHAM, JOHN	AC H	JOS 75	
LOST MACHINE, THE	WYNDHAM, JOHN	SS	AMZ 32	04
MAN FROM BEYOND, THE	WYNDHAM, JOHN	NV	WOS 34	09
PERFECT CREATURE, THE (ALSO AS UNA, FSF 53 01)				
	WYNDHAM, JOHN	NV	TOW 37	01
TROJAN BEAM, THE	WYNDHAM, JOHN	NV	FSB 39	02
VENGEANCE BY PROXY	WYNDHAM, JOHN	SS	STE 40	02
ADAPTATION	WYNDHAM, JOHN	SS	ASF 49	07
PAWLEY'S PEEPHOLES (OPERATION PEEP)				
	WYNDHAM, JOHN	SS	SCP 51	WI
RED STUFF, THE	WYNDHAM, JOHN	NV	MSS 51	02
AND THE WALLS CAME TUMBLING DOWN				
	WYNDHAM, JOHN	SS	STS 51	05
DUMB MARTIAN	WYNDHAM, JOHN	NV	GAL 52	07
CLOSE BEHIND HIM	WYNDHAM, JOHN	SS	FAN 53	02
EMPTYNESS OF SPACE, THE (ALSO AS THE ASTEROIDS, 2194)				
	WYNDHAM, JOHN	SS	NWS 60	11

MAN WHO ATE THE WORLD, THE POHL, FREDERIK   AC BAL 60

MAN WHO ATE THE WORLD, THE	POHL, FREDERIK	NV	GAL 56	11
WIZARDS OF PUNG'S CORNERS, THE				
	POHL, FREDERIK	NV	GAL 58	10
WAGING OF THE PEACE, THE	POHL, FREDERIK	NV	GAL 59	08
SNOWMEN, THE	POHL, FREDERIK	SS	GAL 59	12
DAY THE ICICLE WORKS CLOSED, THE				
	POHL, FREDERIK	NV	GAL 60	02

MAN WHO SOLD THE MOON, THE HEINLEIN, ROBERT A. AC H SHS 50
   ALSO IN "A ROBERT HEINLEIN OMNIBUS"
"IT DOES NOT PAY A PROPHET TO BE TOO SPECIFIC"

	HEINLEIN, ROBERT A.	IN		
INTRODUCTION	CAMPBELL, JOHN W. JR	IN		
LIFE-LINE	HEINLEIN, ROBERT A.	SS	ASF 39	08
LET THERE BE LIGHT	HEINLEIN, ROBERT A.	SS	SSS 40	05
ROADS MUST ROLL, THE	HEINLEIN, ROBERT A.	NV	ASF 40	06
BLOWUPS HAPPEN	HEINLEIN, ROBERT A.	NV	ASF 40	09
MAN WHO SOLD THE MOON, THE	HEINLEIN, ROBERT A.	NV	NEW 50	AC
REQUIEM	HEINLEIN, ROBERT A.	SS	ASF 40	01

MAN WHO SOLD THE MOON, THE (4 OF 6)

	HEINLEIN, ROBERT A.	AC	SIG 51
"IT DOES NOT PAY A PROPHET TO BE TOO SPECIFIC"			
	HEINLEIN, ROBERT A.	IN	

LET THERE BE LIGHT	HEINLEIN, ROBERT A.	SS	SSS 40	05
ROADS MUST ROLL, THE	HEINLEIN, ROBERT A.	NV	ASF 40	06
MAN WHO SOLD THE MOON, THE	HEINLEIN, ROBERT A.	NV	NEW 50	AC
REQUIEM	HEINLEIN, ROBERT A.	SS	ASF 40	01

MAN WHO UPSET THE UNIVERSE, THE

	ASIMOV, ISAAC	DN	ACE 55
SEE "FOUNDATION AND EMPIRE"			

MANY WORLDS OF ANDRE NORTON, THE

	NORTON, ANDRE	AC H	CHL 74	
EDITED BY ROGER ELWOOD, ALSO AS "THE BOOK OF ANDRE NORTON"				
INTRODUCTION	WOLLHEIM, DONALD A.	IN		
TOADS OF GRIMMERDALE, THE	NORTON, ANDRE	NV	FLS 73	02
LONDON BRIDGE	NORTON, ANDRE	SS	FSF 73	10
ON WRITING FANTASY	NORTON, ANDRE	AR	DIP 71	11
MOUSETRAP	NORTON, ANDRE	SS	FSF 54	06
ALL CATS ARE GRAY (AS ANDREW NORTH)				
	NORTON, ANDRE	SS	FUN 53	08
LONG NIGHT OF WAITING, THE	NORTON, ANDRE	SS	73	
GIFTS OF ASTI, THE	NORTON, ANDRE	SS	FBK 48	03
LONG LIVE LORD KOR	NORTON, ANDRE	SN	WOF 70	02
ANDRE NORTON: LOSS OF FAITH	BROOKS, RICK	AR	DIP 71	11
NORTON BIBLIOGRAPHY	NORTON, ANDRE	MS		

MANY WORLDS OF BARRY MALZBERG, THE

	MALZBERG, BARRY N.	AC	POP 75	
PREFACE	ELWOOD, ROGER	IN		
INTRODUCTION	MALZBERG, BARRY N.	IN		
INITIATION	MALZBERG, BARRY N.	SS	NEW 75	AC
MANAGEMENT	MALZBERG, BARRY N.	SS	NEW 75	AC
UNION FOREVER, THE	MALZBERG, BARRY N.	SS	SCS 73	
RECONSTITUTION	MALZBERG, BARRY N.	SS	NEW 75	AC
FINAL WAR	MALZBERG, BARRY N.	NV	FSF 68	04
CLOSED SICILIAN	MALZBERG, BARRY N.	SS	FSF 73	11
AFTER THE UNFORTUNATE ACCIDENT				
	MALZBERG, BARRY N.	SS	NEW 75	AC
SECOND SHORT SHORTEST FANTASY STORY EVER PUBLISHED				
	MALZBERG, BARRY N.	SS	FSF 73	03
IN THE CUP	MALZBERG, BARRY N.	SS	SAW 72	
DEATH TO THE KEEPER	MALZBERG, BARRY N.	NV	FSF 68	08
CHRONICLES OF A COMER	MALZBERG, BARRY N.	SS	WLK 73	

MANY WORLDS OF MAGNUS RIDOLPH, THE

	VANCE, JACK	DC	ACE 66	
KOKOD WARRIORS, THE	VANCE, JACK	NV	TWS 52	10
UNSPEAKABLE MCINCH, THE	VANCE, JACK	NV	STS 48	11
HOWLING BOUNDERS, THE	VANCE, JACK	NV	STS 49	03
KING OF THIEVES, THE	VANCE, JACK	NV	STS 49	11
SPA OF THE STARS, THE	VANCE, JACK	NV	STS 50	07
COUPE DE GRACE	VANCE, JACK	NV		

MANY WORLDS OF POUL ANDERSON, THE

	ANDERSON, POUL	AC H	CHL 74	
EDITED BY ROGER ELWOOD, ALSO AS "THE BOOK OF POUL ANDERSON"				
TOMORROW'S CHILDREN	ANDERSON, POUL	NV	ASF 47	03
QUEEN OF AIR AND DARKNESS, THE				
	ANDERSON, POUL	SN	FSF 71	04
HER STRONG ENCHANTMENTS FAILING				
	MCGUIRE, PATRICK	AR		
EPILOGUE	ANDERSON, POUL	SN	ASF 62	03
LONGEST VOYAGE, THE	ANDERSON, POUL	NV	ASF 60	12
CHALLENGE AND RESPONSE	MIESEL, SANDRA	AR	RVQ 70	
JOURNEYS END	ANDERSON, POUL	SS	FSF 57	02
WORLD NAMED CLEOPATRA, A	ANDERSON, POUL	FA	NEW 74	AC
SHERIFF OF CANYON GULCH, THE (HEROES ARE MADE)				
	ANDERSON, POUL			
	AND DICKSON, GORDON R.	NV C	OWS 51	05
DAY OF BURNING (SUPERNOVA)	ANDERSON, POUL	SN	ASF 67	01

MANY WORLDS OF SCIENCE FICTION, THE

	BOVA, BEN	OA H	DUT 71	
INTRODUCTION	BOVA, BEN	IN		
BLUE MOUSE, THE	WOLFE, GENE	SS	MWS 71	
HOT POTATO	FILER, BURT K.	SS	MWS 71	
ALL CATS ARE GRAY (AS ANDREW NORTH)				
	NORTON, ANDRE	SS	FUN 53	08
LAW-TWISTER SHORTY, THE	DICKSON, GORDON R.	NV	MWS 71	
THREE BLIND MICE	LAUMER, KEITH	NV	MWS 71	
DAUGHTER	MCCAFFREY, ANNE	NV	MWS 71	
SOMETHING WILD IS LOOSE	SILVERBERG, ROBERT	NV	MWS 71	
SILENT IN GEHENNA	ELLISON, HARLAN	SS	MWS 71	

MARACOT DEEP AND OTHER STORIES, THE

	DOYLE, ARTHUR CONAN	AC H	DBL 29	
MARACOT DEEP, THE	DOYLE, ARTHUR CONAN	NO	SEP 27	10
SPODEGUE'S DROOPER	DOYLE, ARTHUR CONAN	SS		
DISINTEGRATION MACHINE, THE	DOYLE, ARTHUR CONAN	SS	CMP 28	
WHEN THE WORLD SCREAMED	DOYLE, ARTHUR CONAN	SS	29	

MARCHING MORONS AND OTHER SCIENCE FICTION

	KORNBLUTH, C. M.	AC	BAL 59	04
MARCHING MORONS, THE	KORNBLUTH, C. M.	NV	GAL 51	04
DOMINOES	KORNBLUTH, C. M.	SS	STR 53	01
LUCKIEST MAN IN DENV, THE (AS SIMON EISNER)				
	KORNBLUTH, C. M.	SS	GAL 52	06
SILLY SEASON, THE	KORNBLUTH, C. M.	SS	FSF 50	FL
MS. FOUND IN A CHINESE FORTUNE COOKIE				
	KORNBLUTH, C. M.	SS	FSF 57	07
ONLY THING WE LEARN, THE	KORNBLUTH, C. M.	SS	STS 49	07
COSMIC CHARGE ACCOUNT, THE (ALSO AS THE COSMIC EXPENSE ACCOUNT)				
	KORNBLUTH, C. M.	NV	FSF 56	01
I NEVER AST NO FAVORS	KORNBLUTH, C. M.	SS	FSF 54	04
REMORSEFUL, THE	KORNBLUTH, C. M.	SS	STR 53	02

MARRIAGE AND THE FAMILY THROUGH SCIENCE FICTION
                              CLEAR/WARRICK/&   AN L SMP 76
    INTRODUCTION   CLEAR, VAL
                              WARRICK, PATRICIA S.
                              GREENBERG, MARTIN H.
                              AND OLANDER, JOSEPH D.   IN C
VINE, THE   REED, KIT   SS   FSF 67 11
TWENTY-FIRST CENTURY MOTHER   MARCUSE, KATHERINE SS   AUT 54 01
PILGRIMAGE (THE PRIESTESS WHO REBELLED)
                              BOND, NELSON S.   SS   AMZ 39 10
SPECIAL CONSENT   HUBBARD, P. M.   SS   FSF 63 10
ADJUSTED, THE   BULMER, KENNETH   SS   FSF 66 06
LOOK, YOU THINK YOU'VE GOT TROUBLES
                              CARR, CAROL   SS   ORB 69 05
NO LAND OF NOD   SPRINGER, SHERWOOD SS   TWS 52 12
IN BEHALF OF THE PRODUCT   REED, KIT   SS   BMR 73
LOVE, INCORPORATED (ALSO AS PILGRIMAGE TO EARTH)
                              SHECKLEY, ROBERT   SS   PBY 56 09
COMPLEAT CONSUMERS, THE   NOURSE, ALAN E.   SS   FSF 64 04
EARTHWOMAN   BRETNOR, REGINALD   SS   FSF 67 08
GIRLS FROM EARTH, THE   ROBINSON, FRANK M. NV   GAL 52 01
EDUCATION OF TIGRESS MACARDLE, THE
                              KORNBLUTH, C. M.   SS   VSF 57 07
PROGENY   DICK, PHILIP K.   SS   IFS 54 11
GIGOLO   GOULART, RON   SS   FSF 72 08
CYNOSURE   REED, KIT   SS   FSF 64 06
DAY MILLION   POHL, FREDERIK   SS   ROG 66 02
ICEBOX BLONDE, THE   SCORTIA, THOMAS N. SS   ROG 59 06
NEW YOU, THE   REED, KIT   SS   FSF 62 09
WOMAN'S RIB   SCORTIA, THOMAS N. SS   GAL 72 07
LAST LONELY MAN, THE   BRUNNER, JOHN   SS   NWS 64 06
LITTLE TERROR, THE   JENKINS, WILL F.   SS   SEP 53 08
FIRST LADY   MCINTOSH, J. T.   NV   GAL 53 06
REVOLT OF THE..., THE   BARR, ROBERT   SS   IDL 94 05
WHEN IT CHANGED   RUSS, JOANNA   SS   DVS 72 02
CLONE SISTER   SARGENT, PAMELA   NV   EIO 73

MARS MOUNTAIN   KEY, EUGENE GEORGE AC H PNP 34
    MARS MOUNTAIN   KEY, EUGENE GEORGE NV
    EARTH SEES MARS   KEY, EUGENE GEORGE NV
    LAKE TEMPEST   KEY, EUGENE GEORGE NV

MARS, WE LOVE YOU   HIPOLITO & MCNELLY AN H DBL 71
    FOREWORD   HIPOLITO, JANE
                              AND MCNELLY, WILLIS E. IN C
ROMANCE OF MARS, THE   ASIMOV, ISAAC   IN
REPORT ON CANALI   SCHIAPARELLI, G. V. AR
MARS AS THE ABODE OF LIFE   LOWELL, PERCIVAL   AR
WAR OF THE WORLDS, THE   WELLS, H. G.   NA   PRS 97 04
PRINCESS OF MARS, A (EXCERPT FROM "UNDER THE MOONS OF MARS")
                              BURROUGHS, EDGAR R. EX   ASM 12 02
MARTIAN ODYSSEY, A   WEINBAUM, STANLEY G. NV WOS 34 07
EMBASSY, THE   WOLLHEIM, DONALD A. SS   ASF 42 03
DARK MISSION   DEL REY, LESTER   SS   ASF 40 07
LOST ART   SMITH, GEORGE O.   NV   ASF 43 12
CAVE, THE   MILLER, P. SCHUYLER SS   ASF 43 01
EXPEDITION   BOUCHER, ANTHONY   SS   TWS 43 08
LOOPHOLE   CLARKE, ARTHUR C.   SS   ASF 46 04
CATCH THAT MARTIAN   KNIGHT, DAMON   SS   GAL 52 03
OMNILINGUAL   PIPER, H. BEAM   NV   ASF 57 02
LOST CITY OF MARS, THE   BRADBURY, RAY   NV   PBY 67 01
ONE STEP FROM EARTH (AS HANK DEMPSEY)
                              HARRISON, HARRY   SS   ASF 70 03
CARTHAGE: REFLECTIONS OF A MARTIAN
                              HERBERT, FRANK   PM   NEW 71 AN
SOFT LANDING   FOX, WILLIAM   PM
EARTHBOUND   JACKSON, IRENE   PM
IN LONELY LANDS   ELLISON, HARLAN   SS   FUN 59 01
WORLD OF THE WARS   MCALLISTER, BRUCE   SS   NEW 71 AN
EXPLORATION   MALZBERG, BARRY N. SS   NEW 71 AN
DOUBLE STAR (EXCERPT)   HEINLEIN, ROBERT A. EX   ASF 56 02
LINGUISTIC RELATIVITY IN MIDDLE HIGH MARTIAN
                              MCNELLY, WILLIS E. AR   68

MARTIAN CHRONICLES, THE   BRADBURY, RAY   AC H DBL 50 05
    IN ENGLAND AS "THE SILVER LOCUSTS"
ROCKET SUMMER   BRADBURY, RAY   SS   PLS 47 SP
YLLA (I'LL NOT LOOK FOR WINE)
                              BRADBURY, RAY   SS   MCL 50 01
SUMMER NIGHT, THE (THE SPRING NIGHT)
                              BRADBURY, RAY   SS   ARS 48 WI
EARTH MEN, THE   BRADBURY, RAY   SS   TWS 48 08
TAXPAYER, THE   BRADBURY, RAY   SS   NEW 51 AC
THIRD EXPEDITION, THE   BRADBURY, RAY   SS   PLS 48 FL
AND THE MOON BE STILL AS BRIGHT
                              BRADBURY, RAY   SS   TWS 48 06
SETTLERS, THE   BRADBURY, RAY   SS   NEW 51 AC
GREEN MORNING, THE   BRADBURY, RAY   SS   NEW 51 AC
LOCUSTS, THE   BRADBURY, RAY   SS   NEW 51 AC
NIGHT MEETING   BRADBURY, RAY   SS   NEW 51 AC
SHORE, THE   BRADBURY, RAY   SS   NEW 51 AC
INTERIM   BRADBURY, RAY   SS   WRT 47 07
MUSICIANS, THE   BRADBURY, RAY   SS   NEW 51 AC
WAY IN THE MIDDLE OF THE AIR BRADBURY, RAY   SS   OWS 50 07
NAMING OF NAMES, THE (ALSO AS DARK THEY WERE, AND GOLDEN-EYED)
                              BRADBURY, RAY   SS   TWS 49 08
USHER II (CARNIVAL OF MADNESS)
                              BRADBURY, RAY   SS   TWS 50 04
OLD ONES, THE   BRADBURY, RAY   SS   NEW 51 AC
MARTIAN, THE (IMPOSSIBLE)   BRADBURY, RAY   SS   SSS 49 11
LUGGAGE STORE, THE   BRADBURY, RAY   SS   NEW 51 AC
OFF SEASON, THE   BRADBURY, RAY   SS   TWS 48 12
WATCHERS, THE   BRADBURY, RAY   SS   WRT 45 05
SILENT TOWNS, THE   BRADBURY, RAY   SS   CHM 49 03
LONG YEARS, THE (ALSO AS DWELLERS IN SILENCE)
                              BRADBURY, RAY   SS   MCL 48 09

THERE WILL COME SOFT RAINS   BRADBURY, RAY   SS   COL 50 05
MILLION-YEAR PICNIC, THE   BRADBURY, RAY   SS   PLS 46 SU

MARTIAN CHRONICLES, THE (BRITISH SFBC, ADDS:)
                              BRADBURY, RAY   AC H SBB 53
    OMITS STORY "USHER II"
WILDERNESS, THE   BRADBURY, RAY   SS   FSF 52 11
FIRE BALLOONS, THE (IN THIS SIGN)
                              BRADBURY, RAY   SS   IMG 51 04

MARTIAN ENTERPRISE   REED, CLIFFORD C.   AC   DIG 62
    CHILDREN OF THE STARS   REED, CLIFFORD C.   SN   SFB 59 07
    FORGOTTEN KNOWLEDGE   REED, CLIFFORD C.   SN   SFB 59 11
    ROAD BACK, THE   REED, CLIFFORD C.   SN   SFB 60 02

MARTIAN ODYSSEY AND OTHER SCIENCE FICTION TALES, A
                              WEINBAUM, STANLEY G. AC H HYP 74
    EDITED BY SAM MOSKOWITZ
DAWN OF FAME: THE CAREER OF STANLEY G. WEINBAUM
                              MOSKOWITZ, SAM   AR   SAT 59 05
AUTOBIOGRAPHICAL SKETCH OF STANLEY G. WEINBAUM, A
                              WEINBAUM, STANLEY G. MS
MARTIAN ODYSSEY, A   WEINBAUM, STANLEY G. NV WOS 34 07
VALLEY OF DREAMS   WEINBAUM, STANLEY G. NV WOS 34 11
ADAPTIVE ULTIMATE, THE   WEINBAUM, STANLEY G. NV ASF 35 11
MAD MOON, THE   WEINBAUM, STANLEY G. NV ASF 35 12
WORLDS OF IF, THE   WEINBAUM, STANLEY G. SS WOS 35 08
IDEAL, THE   WEINBAUM, STANLEY G. SS WOS 35 09
POINT OF VIEW, THE   WEINBAUM, STANLEY G. SS WOS 36 01
PYGMALION'S SPECTACLES   WEINBAUM, STANLEY G. SS WOS 35 06
PARASITE PLANET   WEINBAUM, STANLEY G. NV ASF 35 02
LOTUS EATERS, THE   WEINBAUM, STANLEY G. NV ASF 35 04
PLANET OF DOUBT, THE   WEINBAUM, STANLEY G. SS ASF 35 10
CIRCLE OF ZERO, THE   WEINBAUM, STANLEY G. SS TWS 36 08
RED PERI, THE   WEINBAUM, STANLEY G. SN ASF 35 11
PROTEUS ISLAND   WEINBAUM, STANLEY G. SN ASF 36 08
FLIGHT ON TITAN   WEINBAUM, STANLEY G. NV ASF 35 01
SMOTHERED SEAS   WEINBAUM, STANLEY G. NV ASF 36 01
REDEMPTION CAIRN   WEINBAUM, STANLEY G. NV ASF 36 03
BRINK OF INFINITY, THE   WEINBAUM, STANLEY G. SS TWS 36 12
SHIFTING SEAS   WEINBAUM, STANLEY G. NV AMZ 37 04
REVOLUTION OF 1950   WEINBAUM, STANLEY G. NA AMZ 38 10
GRAPH   WEINBAUM, STANLEY G. SS FMG 36 09
LAST MARTIAN, THE   WEINBAUM, STANLEY G. PM

MARTIAN ODYSSEY AND OTHERS, A
                              WEINBAUM, STANLEY G. AC H FPS 49
MARTIAN ODYSSEY, A   WEINBAUM, STANLEY G. NV WOS 34 07
VALLEY OF DREAMS   WEINBAUM, STANLEY G. NV WOS 34 11
ADAPTIVE ULTIMATE, THE   WEINBAUM, STANLEY G. NV ASF 35 11
MAD MOON, THE   WEINBAUM, STANLEY G. NV ASF 35 12
WORLDS OF IF, THE   WEINBAUM, STANLEY G. SS WOS 35 08
IDEAL, THE   WEINBAUM, STANLEY G. NV WOS 35 09
POINT OF VIEW, THE   WEINBAUM, STANLEY G. SS WOS 36 01
PYGMALION'S SPECTACLES   WEINBAUM, STANLEY G. SS WOS 35 06
PARASITE PLANET   WEINBAUM, STANLEY G. NV ASF 35 02
LOTUS EATERS, THE   WEINBAUM, STANLEY G. NV ASF 35 04
PLANET OF DOUBT, THE   WEINBAUM, STANLEY G. NV ASF 35 10
CIRCLE OF ZERO, THE   WEINBAUM, STANLEY G. SS TWS 36 08

MARTIAN ODYSSEY, A   WEINBAUM, STANLEY G. AC   LAN 62
    AND OTHER CLASSICS OF SCIENCE FICTION, EDITED BY SAM MOSKOWITZ
WONDERS OF WEINBAUM, THE   MOSKOWITZ, SAM   IN
MARTIAN ODYSSEY, A   WEINBAUM, STANLEY G. NV WOS 34 07
PROTEUS ISLAND   WEINBAUM, STANLEY G. SN ASF 36 08
BRINK OF INFINITY, THE   WEINBAUM, STANLEY G. SS TWS 36 12
ADAPTIVE ULTIMATE, THE   WEINBAUM, STANLEY G. NV ASF 35 11
LOTUS EATERS, THE   WEINBAUM, STANLEY G. NV ASF 35 04

MARTIAN SEXPOT   O'NEILL, SCOTT   AC   JAD 63
    INSTANT MAIDS OF MARS, THE O'NEILL, SCOTT   SS
    I TELL YOU, AL   O'NEILL, SCOTT   SS
    WORLD'S GREATEST SALESMAN, THE
                              O'NEILL, SCOTT   SS
    DEAR MAVIS   O'NEILL, SCOTT   SS
    AND THEY'RE ALL EXACTLY TWENTY-SIX YEARS OLD
                              O'NEILL, SCOTT   SS
    SPEAKING OF GANYMEDE   O'NEILL, SCOTT   SS

MARTIAN WAY AND OTHER STORIES, THE
                              ASIMOV, ISAAC   AC H DBL 55
    MARTIAN WAY, THE   ASIMOV, ISAAC   NA   GAL 52 11
    YOUTH   ASIMOV, ISAAC   NV   SSF 52 05
    DEEP, THE   ASIMOV, ISAAC   NV   GAL 52 12
    SUCKER BAIT   ASIMOV, ISAAC   SN   ASF 54 02

MASKS   PLAYBOY, EDITORS OF AN   PBP 71
    PREFACE   PLAYBOY, EDITORS OF IN
    MASKS   KNIGHT, DAMON   SS   PBY 68 07
    PERCHANCE TO DREAM   BEAUMONT, CHARLES   SS   PBY 58 10
    YELLOW ROOM, THE   CHEEVER, JOHN   NV   PBY 68 01
    FORTITUDE   VONNEGUT, KURT JR. SS   PBY 68 09
    WINTER IN THIS LATITUDE   RUBIN, RICK   NV   PBY 62 12
    HAT ACT, THE   COOVER, ROBERT   SS   PBY 68 02
    DEATH'S DOOR   MCNEAR, ROBERT   SS   PBY 69 03
    COLORLESS IN LIMESTONE CAVERNS
                              SEAGER, ALLAN   SS   PBY 69 11
    UNTITLED   PURDY, KEN W.   SS   PBY 66 10
    BREATH OF LUCIFER, A   NARAYAN, R. K.   SS   PBY 69 07

MASTERPIECES OF SCIENCE FICTION
                              MOSKOWITZ, SAM   AN H WOR 66
    VOYAGE TO THE MOON (CONDENSED)
                              DE BERGERAC, CYRANO
    MORTAL IMMORTAL, THE (1834) SHELLEY, MARY W. SS   KPS 34
    HANS PHAALL- A TALE   POE, EDGAR ALLEN   SS   SLM 35 06

```
WONDERSMITH, THE (1859, FSF 50 12)
                              O'BRIEN, FITZ-JAMES     NV   ATL 59 10
ETERNAL ADAM, THE (1905)      VERNE, JULES            NV   STN 57 03
BRICK MOON, THE (1869, INCLUDES SEQUEL "LIFE IN THE
  BRICK MOON" ATL 70 02)      HALE, EDWARD EVERETT    NA   ATL 69 10
LOST IN A COMET'S TAIL, OR, FRANK READE JR'S STRANGE ADVENTURE
  IN HIS NEW AIRSHIP          SENARENS, LOUIS P.      SS   FRL 95 12
COUNTRY OF THE BLIND, THE     WELLS, H. G.            SS   SND 04 04
PLACE OF PAIN, THE            SHIEL, M. P.            SS   AFR 51 16
LOS AMIGOS FIASCO, THE        DOYLE, ARTHUR CONAN     SS   IDL 92 12
RESURRECTION OF JIMBER-JAW, THE
                              BURROUGHS, EDGAR R.     NV   ARG 37 02
PEOPLE OF THE PIT, THE        MERRITT, A.             NV   ASM 18 01
SYSTEM                        CAPEK, JOSEF
                          AND CAPEK, KAREL            SS C    08
EXTRA SENSORY PERFECTION      GERNSBACK, HUGO         SS
COLOUR OUT OF SPACE, THE (ALSO AS MONSTER OF TERROR)
                              LOVECRAFT, H. P.        SS   AMZ 27 09
HUMANITY ON VENUS (FROM "LAST AND FIRST MEN")
                              STAPLEDON, OLAF         EX   MTH 30
JUNGLE JOURNEY (THE PARADISE CRATER)
                              WYLIE, PHILIP           SS   BBM 45 10
LOTUS EATERS, THE             WEINBAUM, STANLEY G.    NV   ASF 35 04

MASTERS OF SCIENCE FICTION    HOWARD, IVAN            AN   BEL 64 10
  SERVICE CALL                DICK, PHILIP K.         SS   SFS 55 07
  PATH OF DARKNESS            PEASE, M. C.            SS   SFS 55 03
  EARLY BIRD                  RUSSELL, ERIC FRANK     NV   SFS 57 11
  FORGIVE US OUR DEBTS (ALSO AS RECESSIONAL)
                              DEL REY, LESTER         SS   FUT 52 05
  GREEN THUMB, THE            ANDERSON, POUL          SS   SFQ 53 02
  DAY OF THE BOOMER DUKES, THE POHL, FREDERIK         SS   FUT 56 30
  FINAL FIGURE, THE           MERWIN, SAM JR.         NV   DSF 54 01

MASTERS OF TIME               VAN VOGT, A. E.         AC H FPS 50
  MASTERS OF TIME (RECRUITING STATION)
                              VAN VOGT, A. E.         NV   ASF 42 03
  CHANGELING, THE (ALSO AS THE WONDERFUL MAN)
                              VAN VOGT, A. E.         NA   ASF 44 04

MASTERS' CHOICE               JANIFER, LAURENCE M.    AN H SAS 66
  ALSO AS "18 GREAT SCIENCE FICTION STORIES"
  PREFACE                     JANIFER, LAURENCE M.    IN
  IT'S A GOOD LIFE            BIXBY, JEROME           SS   STR 53 02
  VELDT, THE (THE WORLD THE CHILDREN MADE)
                              BRADBURY, RAY           SS   SEP 50 09
  GOLEM, THE                  DAVIDSON, AVRAM         SS   FSF 55 03
  HELEN O'LOY                 DEL REY, LESTER         SS   ASF 38 12
  COLD EQUATIONS, THE         GODWIN, TOM             NV   ASF 54 08
  DWINDLING SPHERE, THE       HAWKINS, WILLIAM        SS   ASF 40 03
  REQUIEM                     HEINLEIN, ROBERT A.     SS   ASF 40 01
  THEORY OF ROCKETRY          KORNBLUTH, C. M.        SS   FSF 58 07
  DON'T LOOK NOW              KUTTNER, HENRY          SS   STS 48 03
  SEVEN-DAY TERROR            LAFFERTY, R. A.         SS   IFS 62 03
  COMING ATTRACTION           LEIBER, FRITZ           SS   GAL 50 11
  POLITICS                    LEINSTER, MURRAY        NV   AMZ 32 06
  MOMENTO HOMO (DEATH OF A SPACEMAN)
                              MILLER, WALTER M. JR    SS   AMZ 54 03
  BRIGHT ILLUSION, THE        MOORE, C. L.            NV   ASF 34 10
  AND NOW THE NEWS...         STURGEON, THEODORE      SS   FSF 56 12
  CUSTODIAN, THE              TENN, WILLIAM           NV   IFS 53 11
  NEW ACCELERATOR, THE        WELLS, H. G.            SS   SND 01 12
  HONOR ROLL, THE             MISC. MATERIAL          MS

MATHEMATICAL MAGPIE, THE      FADIMAN, CLIFTON        AN H SAS 62
  CARTOON                     DEAN, ABNER             CT      47
  INTRODUCTION                FADIMAN, CLIFTON        IN
  CARTOON                     DUNN, ALAN              CT   SRV 55 03
  FEELING OF POWER, THE       ASIMOV, ISAAC           SS   IFS 58 02
  LAW, THE                    COATES, ROBERT M.       SS   NYM 47 11
  APPENDIX AND THE SPECTACLES, THE
                              BREUER, MILES J. MD.    SS   AMZ 28 12
  PAUL BUNYAN VERSUS THE CONVEYOR BELT
                              UPSON, WILLIAM H.       SS   FTM 49
  PACIFIST, THE               CLARKE, ARTHUR C.       SS   FUN 56 10
  HERMENEUTICAL DOUGHNUT, THE NEARING, H. JR.         SS   NEW 54 AC
  STAR, BRIGHT                CLIFTON, MARK           NV   GAL 52 07
  F Y I                       BLISH, JAMES            SS   STR 53 02
  VANISHING MAN, THE          HUGHES, RICHARD         SS      26
  NINE BILLION NAMES OF GOD, THE
                              CLARKE, ARTHUR C.       SS   STR 53 01
  THREE MATHEMATICAL DIVERSIONS
                              QUENEAU, RAYMOND        AR      58
  WONDERFUL WORLD OF FIGURES, THE
                              FORD, COREY             AR      61
  A, B AND C- THE HUMAN ELEMENTS IN MATHEMATICS
                              LEACOCK, STEPHEN        AR      12
  B.C.                        HART, JOHNNY            CT   NYH 61 08
  NOTE ON THE EINSTEIN THEORY, A
                              BEERBOHM, MAX           SS      46
  ACHIEVEMENT OF H. T. WENSEL, THE
                              SMITH, H. ALLEN         SS   SRV 60 05
  NEEDED: FEMININE MATH       CUMMINGS, PARKE         AR      61
  CULVER CITY ARITHMATIC EXERCISE PAPER
                              ANONYMOUS               MS   NYM 61 02
  CARTOON                     FRUCH, A.               CT   NYM 58 04
  TWO EXTRACTS                TWAIN, MARK             EX
  MATHEMATICS FOR GOLFERS     LEACOCK, STEPHEN        AR      22
  MATHEMATICIAN'S NIGHTMARE: THE VISION OF PROFESSOR SQUAREPUNT
                              RUSSELL, BERTRAND       SS      55
  MILO AND THE MATHEMAGICIAN  JUSTER, NORTON          SS      61
  ALLIGATOR WALKING LINE      STEINBERG, SAUL         CT      60
  SIXTEEN STORIES (TRANSLATED BY PATRICK BOWLES)
                              BECKETT, SAMUEL         SS      55
  O'BRIEN'S TABLE             SYNGE, J. L.            SS      51
  ABOMINABLE MR. GUNN, THE    GRAVES, ROBERT          SS
```

```
COCONUTS                      WILLIAMS, BEN A.        SS
EUCLID AND THE BRIGHT BOY     SYNGE, J. L.            SS
PURSE OF FORTUNATUS, THE      CARROLL, LEWIS          SS      89
MAN IN CUBE                   STEINBERG, SAUL         CT   NYM 60 09
SYMBOLIC LOGIC OF MURDER, THE
                              REESE, JOHN             SS   EQM 60 10
CARTOON                       FRANKPORT, JAMES        CT   VLG 61 10
SQUARE OF THE HYPOTENUSE, THE (MUSIC)
                              CHAPLIN, SAUL
SQUARE OF THE HYPOTENUSE, THE (LYRICS)
                              MERCER, JOHNNY
TA TA, THE (MUSIC)            HOLBROOKE, JOSEPH C.
TA TA, THE (JINGLES)          SIME, SIDNEY H.
QUESTION MARK ON A SEESAW     STEINBERG, SAUL         CT   NYM 60 07
APOTHEM                       LICHTENBERG, GEORGE     MS      59
APOTHEM                       LEE, STANISLAW G.       MS      62
APOTHEM                       POLYA, G.               MS      45
APOTHEM                       CARROLL, LEWIS          MS      96
APOTHEM                       RENARD, JULES           MS
APOTHEM                       ORWELL, GEORGE          MS      45
APOTHEM                       GOETHE, J. V.           MS
APOTHEM                       CHURCHILL, WINSTON      MS
APOTHEM (1715)                MENCKEN, J. B.          MS
APOTHEM (1872)                DEMORGAN, AUGUSTUS      MS
APOTHEM                       DE CONDILLAC, E. B.     MS
APOTHEM                       MORTLOCK, BILL          MS      59
APOTHEM                       ANONYMOUS               MS
EULER, DIDEROT, ALGEBRA AND GOD (1872)
                              DEMORGAN, AUGUSTUS      MS
PARADISE LOST AT CAMBRIDGE    HOGG, THOMAS J.         MS
WITH APOLOGIES TO BOYAL       GAMOW, GEORGE           MS      47
EXTINCTION BY SUBTRACTION     BALL, W. W. R.          MS
PI AND THE ACTUARY            BALL, W. W. R.          MS
THAT MASON-DIXON LINE         NEWCOMB, SIMON          MS
MATHEMATICS CHEZ MADAME MARIETTE
                              PAUL, ELLIOT            MS      42
DEVIL A MATHEMATICIAN WOULD BE, THE
                              LOHWATER, A. J.         MS
VERSE                         ANONYMOUS               PM      51
VERSE                         WINSOR, FREDERICK       PM      58
RIDDLE                        ANONYMOUS               PM      51
THREE VERSES                  WINSOR, FREDERICK       PM      58
THREE VERSES                  GRAHAM, L. A.           PM      59
TO A MISSING MEMBER OF A FAMILY GROUP OF TERMS IN AN
  ALGEBRAIC FORMULA           MORLEY, CHRISTOPHER     PM      50
FROM "THE DUNCIAD" (1728)     POPE, ALEXANDER         PM   DPS 28 09
GEOMETRY (1805)               WORDSWORTH, WILLIAM     PM
ME                            SCHENCK, HILBERT JR.    PM   FSF 59 08
CARTOON                       DEMARE, LEO             CT   MNS 58
SONG OF THE SCREW             ANONYMOUS               PM
MODERN HIAWATHA, THE          ANONYMOUS               PM
LOVES OF THE TRIANGLES, THE   FRERE, JOHN H.
                          AND CANNING, GEORGE         PM C
MATHEMATICIAN IN LOVE, THE (1874)
                              RANKINE, W. J. M.       PM
E=MC2                         BISHOP, MORRIS          PM   NYM 46
ENGINEER'S YELL               ANONYMOUS               PM
VERSE                         WHEWELL, DR. WILLIAM
VERSE                         BARR, STEPHEN
NOTE ON THETA, PHI, AND PSI   ROBERTS, MICHAEL        PM   NSM 35 03
SONG AGAINST CIRCLES, A       LISTER, R. P.           PM   NYM 61 09
WOCKYJABBER                   SCHENCK, HILBERT JR.    PM   FSF 60 09
EINSTEIN: A PARODY IN THE MANNER OF EDW-N MARKH-M
                              UNTERMEYER, L.          SS      26
TENDING TO INFINITY           SYNGE, J. L.            PM      57
SUPERLATIVE DEGREE, THE       CALKINS, ERNEST ELMO    PM   SRV 59 05
MAGIC BOX, THE                BAKER, W. R.            SS   HRP 28 09
KISS PRECISE, THE             SODDY, FREDERICK        SS   NTR 36 06
KISS PRECISE (GENERALIZED), THE
                              GOSSETT, THOROLD        PM   NTR 37 01
HEXLET, THE                   SODDY, FREDERICK        PM   NTR 36 12
SHORT CUTS TO SUCCESS         KNOX, R. A.             SS   SLP 17 11
THERE WAS A YOUNG LADY NAMED BRIGHT
                              BULLER, E. REGINALD     PM
THERE WAS AN OLD MAN WHO SAID, "DO"
                              ANONYMOUS               PM
SNIP SNIP                     SCHENCK, HILBERT JR.    PM   FSF 59 09
CARTOON                       PORGES, PAUL PETER      CT   ALM 55 07
YOUNG MAN OF SID SUSSEX, THE  HILTON, A. C.           PM      45
PUN IN ORBIT                  SCHENCK, HILBERT JR.    PM   NEW 62 AC
MATHEMATICIAN CONFIDED, A     ANONYMOUS               PM
MATHEMATICIAN NAMED KLEIN, A  ANONYMOUS               PM
MAP OF ENGLAND AND THE ABSOLUTE, THE
                              SANTAYANA, GEORGE       SS      20
CUPID WITH AN ADDING MACHINE  RICE, CHARLES D.        SS   TWK 60 09
MINIVER PROBLEM, THE          STRUTHER, JAN           AR      40
MINIVER PROBLEM, THE (SOLUTION)
                              GRAHAM, L. A.           AR      59

MEDICINE FOR MELANCHOLY, A    BRADBURY, RAY           AC H DBL 58
  ALSO IN "TWICE 22"
  IN ENGLAND WITH SOME CONTENTS CHANGE AS
  "THE DAY IT RAINED FOREVER"
  IN A SEASON OF CALM WEATHER  BRADBURY, RAY          SS   PBY 57 09
  DRAGON, THE                 BRADBURY, RAY           SS   FSF 56 09
  MEDICINE FOR MELANCHOLY, A  BRADBURY, RAY           SS   NEW 59 AC
  END OF THE BEGINNING, THE (NEXT STOP: THE STARS)
                              BRADBURY, RAY           SS   MCL 56 09
  WONDERFUL ICE CREAM SUIT, THE (THE MAGIC WHITE SUIT)
                              BRADBURY, RAY           SS   SEP 58 10
  FEVER DREAM                 BRADBURY, RAY           SS   WRT 48 09
  MARRIAGE MENDER, THE        BRADBURY, RAY           SS   COL 54 09
  TOWN WHERE NO ONE GOT OFF, THE
                              BRADBURY, RAY           SS   EQM 58 10
  SCENT OF SARSAPARILLA, A    BRADBURY, RAY           SS   STR 53 09
  ICARUS MONTGOLFIER WRIGHT   BRADBURY, RAY           SS   FSF 56 09
```

EDICINE FOR MELANCHOLY, A

HEADPIECE, THE	BRADBURY, RAY	SS	LIL	58 05
DARK THEY WERE, AND GOLDEN-EYED (THE NAMING OF NAMES)				
	BRADBURY, RAY	SS	TWS	49 08
SMILE, THE	BRADBURY, RAY	SS	FAN	52 SU
FIRST NIGHT OF LENT, THE	BRADBURY, RAY	SS	PBY	56 03
TIME OF GOING AWAY, THE	BRADBURY, RAY	SS	REP	56 11
ALL SUMMER IN A DAY	BRADBURY, RAY	SS	FSF	54 03
GIFT, THE	BRADBURY, RAY	SS	FAN	59 07
GREAT COLLISION OF MONDAY LAST, THE				
	BRADBURY, RAY	SS	CON	58 01
LITTLE MICE, THE (THE MICE)	BRADBURY, RAY	SS	ESC	55 10
SHORELINE AT SUNSET, THE (ALSO AS THE SUNSET HARP)				
	BRADBURY, RAY	SS	FSF	59 03
STRAWBERRY WINDOW, THE	BRADBURY, RAY	SS	STR	54 03
DAY IT RAINED FOREVER, THE	BRADBURY, RAY	SS	HRP	57 07

EETING OVER TUSCARORA AND OTHER ADVENTURE TALES, A

	YEFREMOV, IVAN	AC H	HUT	46
MEETING OVER TUSCARORA, A	YEFREMOV, IVAN	SS		
LAKE OF THE MOUNTAIN SPIRITS, THE				
	YEFREMOV, IVAN	SS		
IN THE STEPS OF THE ANCIENT MINERS				
	YEFREMOV, IVAN	SS		
ALLERGORKHOY-KHORKHOV (THE MONSTROUS WORM)				
	YEFREMOV, IVAN	SS		
BARE MOUNTAIN BENEATH THE MOON				
	YEFREMOV, IVAN	SS		

EN AGAINST THE STARS

	GREENBERG , MARTIN	AN H	GNM	50
FOREWORD	GREENBERG , MARTIN	IN		
INTRODUCTION	LEY, WILLY	IN		
TRENDS	ASIMOV, ISAAC	SS	ASF	39 07
MEN AGAINST THE STARS	WELLMAN, MANLY WADE	NV	ASF	38 06
RED DEATH OF MARS, THE	WILLIAMS, ROBERT M.	NV	ASF	40 07
LOCKED OUT	FYFE, H. B.	SS	ASF	40 02
IRON STANDARD, THE	PADGETT, LEWIS	SS	ASF	43 12
SCHEDULE	WALTON, HARRY	SS	ASF	45 06
FAR CENTAURUS	VAN VOGT, A. E.	SS	ASF	44 01
COLD FRONT	CLEMENT, HAL	NV	ASF	46 07
PLANTS, THE	LEINSTER, MURRAY	SS	ASF	46 01
COMPETITION	HULL, E. MAYNE	SS	ASF	43 06
BRIDLE AND SADDLE	ASIMOV, ISAAC	NV	ASF	42 06
WHEN SHADOWS FALL	HUBBARD, L. RON	SS	STS	48 07

EN AGAINST THE STARS (BRITISH)

	GREENBERG , MARTIN	AN H	GRY	51
INTRODUCTION	LEY, WILLY	IN		
TRENDS	ASIMOV, ISAAC	SS	ASF	39 07
MEN AGAINST THE STARS	WELLMAN, MANLY WADE	NV	ASF	38 06
RED DEATH OF MARS, THE	WILLIAMS, ROBERT M.	NV	ASF	40 07
IRON STANDARD, THE	PADGETT, LEWIS	SS	ASF	43 12
FAR CENTAURUS	VAN VOGT, A. E.	SS	ASF	44 01
COMPETITION	HULL, E. MAYNE	SS	ASF	43 06
BRIDLE AND SADDLE	ASIMOV, ISAAC	NV	ASF	42 06
WHEN SHADOWS FALL	HUBBARD, L. RON	SS	STS	48 07

EN AGAINST THE STARS (9 OF 12)

	GREENBERG , MARTIN	AN	PYR	56 12
FOREWORD	GREENBERG , MARTIN	IN		
INTRODUCTION	LEY, WILLY	IN		
MEN AGAINST THE STARS	WELLMAN, MANLY WADE	NV	ASF	38 06
RED DEATH OF MARS, THE	WILLIAMS, ROBERT M.	NV	ASF	40 07
IRON STANDARD, THE	PADGETT, LEWIS	SS	ASF	43 12
SCHEDULE	WALTON, HARRY	SS	ASF	45 06
FAR CENTAURUS	VAN VOGT, A. E.	SS	ASF	44 01
COLD FRONT	CLEMENT, HAL	NV	ASF	46 07
PLANTS, THE	LEINSTER, MURRAY	SS	ASF	46 01
COMPETITION	HULL, E. MAYNE	SS	ASF	43 06
WHEN SHADOWS FALL	HUBBARD, L. RON	SS	STS	48 07

EN AND MACHINES

	SILVERBERG, ROBERT	AN H	MDT	68
INTRODUCTION	SILVERBERG, ROBERT	IN		
COUNTER FOIL	SMITH, GEORGE O.	NV	ASF	64 04
BAD DAY FOR SALES, A	LEIBER, FRITZ	SS	GAL	53 07
WITHOUT A THOUGHT (FORTRESS SHIP)				
	SABERHAGEN, FRED	SS	IFS	63 01
SOLAR PLEXUS	BLISH, JAMES	SS	AST	41 09
MACAULEY CIRCUIT, THE	SILVERBERG, ROBERT	SS	FUN	56 08
BUT WHO CAN REPLACE A MAN?	ALDISS, BRIAN W.	SS	INF	58 06
INSTINCT	DEL REY, LESTER	SS	ASF	52 01
TWONKY, THE	PADGETT, LEWIS	SS	ASF	42 09
HUNTING LODGE, THE	GARRETT, RANDALL	NV	ASF	54 07
WITH FOLDED HANDS...	WILLIAMSON, JACK	NV	ASF	47 07

EN AND THE MIRROR, THE

	ROCKLYNNE, ROSS	AC	ACE	73 02
AT THE CENTER OF GRAVITY	ROCKLYNNE, ROSS	SS	ASF	36 06
JUPITER TRAP	ROCKLYNNE, ROSS	SS	ASF	37 08
MEN AND THE MIRROR, THE	ROCKLYNNE, ROSS	NV	ASF	38 07
LETTER	SWISHER, ROBERT D.	MS	ASF	38 11
THEY FLY SO HIGH	ROCKLYNNE, ROSS	SS	AMZ	52 06
BOTTLED MEN, THE	ROCKLYNNE, ROSS	NV	ASF	46 06
AND THEN THERE WAS ONE	ROCKLYNNE, ROSS	SS	ASF	40 02

EN OF SPACE AND TIME

	BLEILER & DIKTY	AN H	LNE	53
LAST SEVEN STORIES FROM "IMAGINATION UNLIMITED"				

EN ON THE MOON

	WOLLHEIM, DONALD A.	DA	ACE	58
INTRODUCTION	WOLLHEIM, DONALD A.	IN		
OPERATION PUMICE	GALLUN, RAYMOND Z.	SS	TWS	49 04
JETSAM	CHANDLER, A. BERTRAM	SS	NWS	53 03
RELUCTANT HEROES, THE	ROBINSON, FRANK M.	SS	GAL	51 01
MOONWALK	FYFE, H. B.	NA	SSF	52 11
KEYHOLE	LEINSTER, MURRAY	SS	TWS	51 12

EN WITHOUT BONES

	KERSH, GERALD	AC	PKB	62 01
MEN WITHOUT BONES	KERSH, GERALD	SS	ESQ	

SHADY LIFE OF ANNIBAL, THE (THE IMAGINARY HEIR)				
	KERSH, GERALD	SS	SEP	59 04
APE AND THE MYSTERY, THE (THE MYSTERIOUS MONA LISA SMILE)				
	KERSH, GERALD	SS	SEP	48 06
OXOXOCO BOTTLE, THE (THE MYSTERY OF THE BOTTLE)				
	KERSH, GERALD	NV	SEP	57 12
THICKER THAN WATER	KERSH, GERALD	NV		
MADWOMAN, THE	KERSH, GERALD	SS		
TERRIBLE RIDE OF COLONEL TESSIER, THE				
	KERSH, GERALD	NV	SEP	52 10
DANCING DOLL, THE	KERSH, GERALD	SS		
HACK, THE	KERSH, GERALD	SS		
LADIES OR CLOTHES	KERSH, GERALD	SS	ESQ	
IN A ROOM WITHOUT WALLS	KERSH, GERALD	SS	ESQ	
CLOCK WITHOUT HANDS	KERSH, GERALD	NV	COL	46 10
EPISTLE OF SIMPLE SIMON, THE	KERSH, GERALD	SS	TOM	47

MEN, MARTIANS AND MACHINES

	RUSSELL, ERIC FRANK	AC H	DOB	55
JAY SCORE	RUSSELL, ERIC FRANK	SS	ASF	41 05
MECHANISTRIA	RUSSELL, ERIC FRANK	NV	ASF	42 01
SYMBIOTICA	RUSSELL, ERIC FRANK	NV	ASF	43 10
MESMERICA	RUSSELL, ERIC FRANK	NV	NEW	56 AC

MENACE FROM EARTH, THE

	HEINLEIN, ROBERT A.	AC H	GNM	59
YEAR OF THE JACKPOT, THE	HEINLEIN, ROBERT A.	NV	GAL	52 03
BY HIS BOOTSTRAPS (ALSO AS THE TIME GATE)				
	HEINLEIN, ROBERT A.	NV	ASF	41 10
COLUMBUS WAS A DOPE	HEINLEIN, ROBERT A.	SS	STS	47 05
MENACE FROM EARTH, THE	HEINLEIN, ROBERT A.	SS	FSF	57 08
SKY LIFT	HEINLEIN, ROBERT A.	SS	IMG	53 11
GOLDFISH BOWL	HEINLEIN, ROBERT A.	NV	ASF	42 03
PROJECT NIGHTMARE	HEINLEIN, ROBERT A.	NV	AMZ	53 05
WATER IS FOR WASHING	HEINLEIN, ROBERT A.	SS	ARG	47 11

MERCENARY, THE

	POURNELLE, JERRY	NO	PKT	77 02
PEACE WITH HONOR	POURNELLE, JERRY	NV	ASF	71 05
MERCENARY	POURNELLE, JERRY	NV	ASF	72 07
SWORD AND SCEPTRE	POURNELLE, JERRY	NA	ASF	73 05

METAL SMILE, THE

	KNIGHT, DAMON	AN	BEL	68
NEW FATHER CHRISTMAS, THE	ALDISS, BRIAN W.	SS	FSF	58 01
ANSWER	BROWN, FREDRIC	SS	NEW	54 AC
FOOL'S MATE	SHECKLEY, ROBERT	SS	ASF	53 03
QUIXOTE AND THE WINDMILL	ANDERSON, POUL	SS	ASF	50 11
TWO-HANDED ENGINE	KUTTNER, HENRY			
	AND MOORE, C. L.	SS C	FSF	55 08
FIRST TO SERVE	BUDRYS, ALGIS	SS	ASF	54 05
I MADE YOU	MILLER, WALTER M. JR	SS	ASF	54 03
MONKEY WRENCH, THE	DICKSON, GORDON R.	SS	ASF	51 08
IMPOSTOR	DICK, PHILIP K.	SS	ASF	53 06
SOMEDAY	ASIMOV, ISAAC	SS	INF	56 08
SHORT IN THE CHEST	SEABRIGHT, IDRIS	SS	FUN	54 07
NIGHTMARE NUMBER THREE	BENET, STEPHEN V.	PM		35

METALLIC MUSE, THE

	BIGGLE, LLOYD JR.	AC H	DBL	72
TUNESMITH, THE	BIGGLE, LLOYD JR.	NV	IFS	57 08
LEADING MAN	BIGGLE, LLOYD JR.	SS	GAL	57 06
SPARE THE ROD	BIGGLE, LLOYD JR.	NV	GAL	58 03
ORPHAN OF THE VOID (THE MAN WHO WASN'T HOME)				
	BIGGLE, LLOYD JR.	NV	FAN	60 09
WELL OF THE DEEP WISH	BIGGLE, LLOYD JR.	NV	IFS	61 03
IN HIS OWN IMAGE	BIGGLE, LLOYD JR.	SS	FSF	68 01
BOTTICELLI HORROR, THE	BIGGLE, LLOYD JR.	NV	FAN	60 03

MICROCOSMIC GOD

	MOSKOWITZ, SAM	AN	MBB	65
AND OTHER STORIES FROM MODERN MASTERPIECES OF SCIENCE FICTION				
MICROCOSMIC GOD	STURGEON, THEODORE	NV	ASF	41 04
NIGHT	CAMPBELL, JOHN W. JR	NV	ASF	35 10
ADAPTATION	WYNDHAM, JOHN	SS	ASF	49 07
ENCHANTED VILLAGE (ALSO AS THE SANDS OF MARS)				
	VAN VOGT, A. E.	SS	OWS	50 07
HUDDLING PLACE	SIMAK, CLIFFORD D.	SS	ASF	44 07
WAKE FOR THE LIVING (ALSO AS THE COFFIN)				
	BRADBURY, RAY	SS	DMN	47 09
MOTHER	FARMER, PHILIP JOSE	NV	TWS	53 04

MIDSUMMER CENTURY

	BLISH, JAMES	AC	DAW	74 02
MIDSUMMER CENTURY	BLISH, JAMES	NO	DBL	72
SKYSIGN	BLISH, JAMES	NV	ASF	68 05
STYLE IN TREASON, A (A HERO'S LIFE)				
	BLISH, JAMES	NV	IMP	66 03

MILE BEYOND THE MOON, A

	KORNBLUTH, C. M.	AC H	DBL	58
MAKE MINE MARS	KORNBLUTH, C. M.	NV	SFA	52 11
MEDDLERS, THE	KORNBLUTH, C. M.	SS	SFA	53 09
EVENTS LEADING DOWN TO THE TRAGEDY, THE				
	KORNBLUTH, C. M.	SS	FSF	58 01
LITTLE BLACK BAG, THE	KORNBLUTH, C. M.	NV	ASF	50 07
EVERYBODY KNOWS JOE	KORNBLUTH, C. M.	SS	FUN	53 10
TIME BUM	KORNBLUTH, C. M.	SS	FAN	53 02
PASSION PILLS	KORNBLUTH, C. M.	SS	NEW	58 AC
VIRGINIA	KORNBLUTH, C. M.	SS	VSF	58 03
SLAVE, THE	KORNBLUTH, C. M.	NV	SFA	57 09
KAZAM COLLECTS	KORNBLUTH, C. M.	SS	STI	41 06
LAST MAN LEFT IN THE BAR, THE				
	KORNBLUTH, C. M.	SS	INF	57 10
ADVENTURER, THE	KORNBLUTH, C. M.	SS	SSF	53 05
WORDS OF GURU, THE	KORNBLUTH, C. M.	SS	STI	41 06
SHARK SHIP (REAP THE DARK TIDE)				
	KORNBLUTH, C. M.	NV	VAN	58 06
TWO DOOMS	KORNBLUTH, C. M.	NV	VSF	58 07

MILE BEYOND THE MOON, A (11 OF 15)

	KORNBLUTH, C. M.	AC	MCF	62
MAKE MINE MARS	KORNBLUTH, C. M.	NV	SFA	52 11

EVENTS LEADING DOWN TO THE TRAGEDY, THE
                              KORNBLUTH, C. M.   SS   FSF 58 01
LITTLE BLACK BAG, THE   KORNBLUTH, C. M.   NV   ASF 50 07
EVERYBODY KNOWS JOE   KORNBLUTH, C. M.   SS   FUN 53 10
TIME BUM   KORNBLUTH, C. M.   SS   FAN 53 02
VIRGINIA   KORNBLUTH, C. M.   SS   VSF 58 03
KAZAM COLLECTS   KORNBLUTH, C. M.   SS   STI 41 06
LAST MAN LEFT IN THE BAR, THE
                              KORNBLUTH, C. M.   SS   INF 57 10
ADVENTURER, THE   KORNBLUTH, C. M.   SS   SSF 53 05
WORDS OF GURU, THE   KORNBLUTH, C. M.   SS   STI 41 06
SHARK SHIP (REAP THE DARK TIDE)
                              KORNBLUTH, C. M.   NV   VAN 58 06

MILE-LONG SPACESHIP, THE   WILHELM, KATE   AC   BKM 63 12
  IN ENGLAND AS "ANDOVER AND THE ANDROID"
MILE-LONG SPACESHIP, THE   WILHELM, KATE   SS   ASF 57 04
FEAR IS A COLD BLACK   WILHELM, KATE   NV   NEW 63 AC
JENNY WITH WINGS   WILHELM, KATE   SS   NEW 63 AC
A IS FOR AUTOMATION   WILHELM, KATE   SS   FUT 59 10
GIFT FROM THE STARS   WILHELM, KATE   SS   FUT 58 12
NO LIGHT IN THE WINDOW   WILHELM, KATE   SS   NEW 63 AC
ONE FOR THE ROAD   WILHELM, KATE   SS   FUN 59 07
ANDOVER AND THE ANDROID   WILHELM, KATE   SS   NEW 63 AC
MAN WITHOUT A PLANET, THE   WILHELM, KATE   SS   FSF 62 07
APOSTOLIC TRAVELERS, THE   WILHELM, KATE   SS   NEW 63 AC
LAST DAYS OF THE CAPTAIN, THE
                              WILHELM, KATE   SS   AMZ 62 11

MIND ANGEL AND OTHER STORIES, THE
                              ELWOOD, ROGER   OA H LER 74
  FOREWORD   ASIMOV, ISAAC   IN
  MIND ANGEL, THE   ORGILL, MICHAEL   SS
  GREEN BOY, THE   LOUDEN, LEO   SS
  TRANSLATOR, THE   BLAKE, E. MICHAEL   SS

MIND PARTNER AND 8 OTHER NOVELETS FROM GALAXY
                              GOLD, H. L.   AN H DBL 61
  MIND PARTNER   ANVIL, CHRISTOPHER   NV   GAL 60 08
  LADY WHO SAILED THE SOUL, THE
                              SMITH, CORDWAINER   NV   GAL 60 04
  STENTORII LUGGAGE, THE   BARRETT, NEAL JR.   NV   GAL 60 10
  SNUFFLES   LAFFERTY, R. A.   NV   GAL 60 12
  SLY BUNGERHOP, THE   MORRISON, WILLIAM   NV   GAL 57 09
  BLACKSWORD   OFFUTT, ANDREW J.   NV   GAL 59 12
  CIVILIZATION GAME, THE   SIMAK, CLIFFORD D.   NV   GAL 58 11
  HARDEST BARGAIN, THE   SMITH, EVELYN E.   NV   GAL 57 06
  WITH REDFERN ON CAPELLA XII SATTERFIELD, CHARLES NV   GAL 55 11

MIND SPIDER AND OTHER STORIES, THE
                              LEIBER, FRITZ   DC   ACE 61
  MIND SPIDER, THE   LEIBER, FRITZ   SS   FAN 59 11
  HAUNTED FUTURE, THE (TRANQUILITY, OR ELSE!)
                              LEIBER, FRITZ   NV   FAN 59 11
  DAMNATION MORNING   LEIBER, FRITZ   SS   FAN 59 08
  OLDEST SOLDIER, THE   LEIBER, FRITZ   NV   FSF 60 05
  TRY AND CHANGE THE PAST   LEIBER, FRITZ   SS   ASF 58 03
  NUMBER OF THE BEAST, THE   LEIBER, FRITZ   NV   GAL 58 12

MIND SPIDER AND OTHER STORIES, THE (ACE 76)
                              LEIBER, FRITZ   AC   ACE 76
  FOREWORD   LEIBER, FRITZ   IN
  HAUNTED FUTURE, THE (TRANQUILITY, OR ELSE!)
                              LEIBER, FRITZ   NV   FAN 59 11
  DAMNATION MORNING   LEIBER, FRITZ   SS   FAN 59 08
  OLDEST SOLDIER, THE   LEIBER, FRITZ   NV   FSF 60 05
  MIDNIGHT IN THE MIRROR WORLD LEIBER, FRITZ   SS   FAN 64 10
  NUMBER OF THE BEAST, THE   LEIBER, FRITZ   NV   GAL 58 12
  MIND SPIDER, THE   LEIBER, FRITZ   SS   FAN 59 11

MIND TO MIND   SILVERBERG, ROBERT   AN H NEL 71
  INTRODUCTION   SILVERBERG, ROBERT   IN
  MINDWORM, THE   KORNBLUTH, C. M.   SS   WBY 50 12
  PSYCLOPS   ALDISS, BRIAN W.   SS   NWS 56 07
  NOVICE   SCHMITZ, JAMES H.   NV   ASF 62 06
  LIAR!   ASIMOV, ISAAC   SS   ASF 41 05
  SOMETHING WILD IS LOOSE   SILVERBERG, ROBERT   NV   MWS 71
  RIYA'S FOUNDLING   BUDRYS, ALGIS   SS   SFS 53 G1
  THROUGH OTHER EYES   LAFFERTY, R. A.   SS   FUT 60 02
  CONSPIRATORS, THE   WHITE, JAMES   NV   NWS 54 06
  JOURNEYS END   ANDERSON, POUL   SS   FSF 57 02

MINDS UNLEASHED   CONKLIN, GROFF   AN   TMP 70 10
  SEE "GIANTS UNLEASHED"

MINDWORM AND OTHER STORIES, THE
                              KORNBLUTH, C. M.   AC H JOS 55
  MINDWORM, THE   KORNBLUTH, C. M.   SS   WBY 50 12
  GOMEZ   KORNBLUTH, C. M.   NV   NEW 54 AC
  ROCKET OF 1955, THE   KORNBLUTH, C. M.   SS   STI 41 04
  ALTAR AT MIDNIGHT, THE   KORNBLUTH, C. M.   SS   GAL 52 11
  LITTLE BLACK BAG, THE   KORNBLUTH, C. M.   NV   ASF 50 07
  GOODLY CREATURES, THE   KORNBLUTH, C. M.   SS   FSF 52 12
  FRIEND TO MAN   KORNBLUTH, C. M.   SS   TSF 51 SP
  WITH THESE HANDS   KORNBLUTH, C. M.   NV   GAL 51 12
  THAT SHARE OF GLORY   KORNBLUTH, C. M.   NV   ASF 52 01
  LUCKIEST MAN IN DENV, THE (AS SIMON EISNER)
                              KORNBLUTH, C. M.   SS   GAL 52 06
  SILLY SEASON, THE   KORNBLUTH, C. M.   SS   FSF 50 FL
  MARCHING MORONS, THE   KORNBLUTH, C. M.   NV   GAL 51 04

MINDWORM, THE   ANONYMOUS   AN   TDM 67
  NOT TO BE OPENED-   YOUNG, ROBERT F.   NV   ASF 50 01
  SANTA CLAUS PLANET, THE   ROBINSON, FRANK M.   SS   NEW 51 AN
  MINDWORM, THE   KORNBLUTH, C. M.   SS   WBY 50 12
  PROCESS   VAN VOGT, A. E.   SS   FSF 50 12

CONTAGION   MACLEAN, KATHERINE   NV   GAL 50 1
TRESPASS!   ANDERSON, POUL
                              AND DICKSON, GORDON R. SS C FSQ 50 S
TO SERVE MAN   KNIGHT, DAMON   SS   GAL 50 1
BORN OF MAN AND WOMAN   MATHESON, RICHARD   SS   FSF 50 S
FOX AND THE FOREST, THE (TO THE FUTURE)
                              BRADBURY, RAY   SS   COL 50 0
LAST MARTIAN, THE   BROWN, FREDRIC   SS   GAL 50 1
TWO FACE   LONG, FRANK BELKNAP SS   WRT 50 0

MIRROR OF INFINITY, THE   SILVERBERG, ROBERT   AN H HPR 70
  INTRODUCTION   SILVERBERG, ROBERT   IN
  FOREWORD TO "THE STAR"   WILLIAMSON, JACK   IN
  STAR, THE   WELLS, H. G.   SS   GRP 97 1.
  FOREWORD TO "TWILIGHT"   BUDRYS, ALGIS   IN
  TWILIGHT   CAMPBELL, JOHN W. JR SS   ASF 34 1
  FOREWORD TO "NIGHTFALL"   HARRISON, HARRY   IN
  NIGHTFALL   ASIMOV, ISAAC   NV   ASF 41 0
  FOREWORD TO "PRIVATE EYE"   BLISH, JAMES   IN
  PRIVATE EYE   PADGETT, LEWIS   NV   ASF 49 0
  FOREWORD TO "THE SENTINEL" CLARESON, THOMAS D. IN
  SENTINEL, THE (SENTINEL OF ETERNITY)
                              CLARKE, ARTHUR C.   SS   TSF 51 S.
  FOREWORD TO "SPECIALIST"   CONQUEST, ROBERT   IN
  SPECIALIST   SHECKLEY, ROBERT   SS   GAL 53 0
  FOREWORD TO "COMMON TIME"   KNIGHT, DAMON   AR   SFF 57
  COMMON TIME   BLISH, JAMES   SS   SFQ 53 0
  FOREWORD TO "THE GAME OF RAT AND DRAGON"
                              AMIS, KINGSLEY   IN
  GAME OF RAT AND DRAGON, THE SMITH, CORDWAINER   NV   GAL 55 1
  FOREWORD TO "ALL YOU ZOMBIES-"
                              PANSHIN, ALEXEI   IN
  ALL YOU ZOMBIES   HEINLEIN, ROBERT A. SS   FSF 59 0
  FOREWORD TO "THE SUBLIMINAL MAN"
                              FRANKLIN, H. BRUCE   AR   70
  SUBLIMINAL MAN, THE   BALLARD, J. G.   SS   NWS 63 0
  FOREWORD TO "I HAVE NO MOUTH, AND I MUST SCREAM"
                              MCNELLY, WILLIS E.   IN
  I HAVE NO MOUTH, AND I MUST SCREAM
                              ELLISON, HARLAN   SS   IFS 67 0
  FOREWORD TO "THE HEAT DEATH OF THE UNIVERSE"
                              ALDISS, BRIAN W.   IN
  HEAT DEATH OF THE UNIVERSE, THE
                              ZOLINE, PAMELA A.   SS   NWS 67 0
  FOREWORD TO "THE LIBRARY OF BABEL"
                              ROGERS, IVIR   IN
  LIBRARY OF BABEL, THE   BORGES, JORGE LUIS   SS   62
  BIBLIOGRAPHY: THE CRITICAL LITERATURE OF S. F., A
                              MISC. MATERIAL   MS

MISSING MAN, THE   MACLEAN, KATHERINE   NO   BKM 75
  FEAR HOUND   MACLEAN, KATHERINE   NV   ASF 68 0
  RESCUE SQUAD FOR AHMED   MACLEAN, KATHERINE   NV   ASF 70 1
  MISSING MAN, THE   MACLEAN, KATHERINE   NV   ASF 71 0

MISSING WORLD AND OTHER STORIES, THE
                              ELWOOD, ROGER   OA H LER 74
  FOREWORD   ASIMOV, ISAAC   IN
  MISSING WORLD, THE   BINDER, EANDO   SS
  IT WASN'T MY FAULT   O'DONNELL, K. M.   SS
  FRIEND FROM THE STARS   SARGENT, PAMELA   SS
  MAGICIAN'S SONG, THE   MCALISTER, PATRICIA SS

MISSION TO THE STARS   VAN VOGT, A. E.   NO   BKM 71 03
  SEE "THE MIXED MEN"

MISSION: INTERPLANETARY   VAN VOGT, A. E.   NO   NAM 52
  SEE "THE VOYAGE OF THE SPACE BEAGLE"

MISSION: MANSTOP   NEVILLE, KRIS   AC   LEI 71 10
  MISSION: MANSTOP (MISSION) NEVILLE, KRIS   NV   FSF 53 0
  HUNT THE HUNTER   NEVILLE, KRIS   SS   GAL 51 0
  TAKE TWO QUIGGIES   NEVILLE, KRIS   NV   FSF 50 1
  UNDERGROUND MOVEMENT   NEVILLE, KRIS   SS   FSF 52 0
  EXPERIMENTAL STATION (THE FIRST)
                              NEVILLE, KRIS   SS   SSS 50 0
  MARGINAL ERROR   NEVILLE, KRIS   SS   TWS 53 0
  TOY, THE   NEVILLE, KRIS   SS   IMG 52 1.

MIXED FEELINGS   EFFINGER, GEO. ALEC AC H HPR 74
  INTRODUCTION: ALL THE EFFINGERS AT ONCE
                              STURGEON, THEODORE   IN
  THIS WRITING "GAME"   EFFINGER, GEO. ALEC SS
  STEVE WEINRAUB AND THE SECRET EMPIRE
                              EFFINGER, GEO. ALEC SS
  TWO SADNESSES   EFFINGER, GEO. ALEC SS   BMR 73
  NAKED TO THE INVISIBLE EYE EFFINGER, GEO. ALEC NV   ASF 73 0
  F(X)=(11/15/67) X=HER, F(X)≠0
                              EFFINGER, GEO. ALEC SS   NDM 72 0
  GHOST WRITER, THE   EFFINGER, GEO. ALEC SS   UNI 73 0
  ALL THE LAST WARS AT ONCE   EFFINGER, GEO. ALEC SS   UNI 71 0
  THINGS GO BETTER   EFFINGER, GEO. ALEC SS   ORB 72 1
  WEDNESDAY, NOVEMBER 15, 1967 EFFINGER, GEO. ALEC SS   NEW 71 A
  WORLD WAR TWO   EFFINGER, GEO. ALEC SS   VTX 73 1
  LIGHTS OUT   EFFINGER, GEO. ALEC NV   FSF 73 1

MIXED MEN, THE   VAN VOGT, A. E.   NO H GNM 52
  ALSO AS "MISSION TO THE STARS"
  CONCEALMENT   VAN VOGT, A. E.   SS   ASF 43 0
  STORM, THE   VAN VOGT, A. E.   NV   ASF 43 1
  MIXED MEN, THE   VAN VOGT, A. E.   NV   ASF 45 0
  LOST: FIFTY SUNS   VAN VOGT, A. E.   NV   NEW 52 N

MODERAN   BUNCH, DAVID R.   AC   AVN 71 05
  INTRODUCTION   BUNCH, DAVID R.   IN

MODERAN   MONSTERS AND SUCH

THINKING BACK (OUR GOD IS A HELPFUL GOD!)
                                BUNCH, DAVID R.   SS
NO CRACKS OR SAGGINGS   BUNCH, DAVID R.   SS
BUTTERFLIES WERE EAGLE-BIG THAT DAY, THE
                                BUNCH, DAVID R.   SS
NEW KINGS ARE NOT FOR LAUGHING
                                BUNCH, DAVID R.   SS
ONE TIME, A RED CARPET...   BUNCH, DAVID R.   SS
BATTLE WON   BUNCH, DAVID R.   SS
HEAD THUMPING THE TROOPS   BUNCH, DAVID R.   SS
NEW-METAL MISTRESS TIME   BUNCH, DAVID R.   SS
AND SO WHITE WITCH VALLEY   BUNCH, DAVID R.   SS
BIRD MAN OF MODERAN, THE   BUNCH, DAVID R.   SS
BUBBLE-DOME HOMES   BUNCH, DAVID R.   SS
ONE FALSE STEP   BUNCH, DAVID R.   SS
SURVIVAL PACKAGES   BUNCH, DAVID R.   SS   FAN 63 04
NEW-METAL   BUNCH, DAVID R.   SS
OF HAMMERS AND MEN   BUNCH, DAVID R.   SS
STRONGHOLD, THE   BUNCH, DAVID R.   SS
2064, OR THEREABOUTS   BUNCH, DAVID R.   SS   FAN 64 09
PENANCE DAY IN MODERAN   BUNCH, DAVID R.   SS   AMZ 60 07
STRANGE SHAPE IN THE STRONGHOLD
                                BUNCH, DAVID R.   SS   FAN 60 03
GETTING REGULAR   BUNCH, DAVID R.   SS   AMZ 60 08
WALKING, TALKING I-DON'T-CARE MAN, THE
                                BUNCH, DAVID R.   SS   AMZ 65 06
TO FACE ETERNITY   BUNCH, DAVID R.   SS
IN THE INNERMOST ROOM OF AUTHORITY
                                BUNCH, DAVID R.   SS
PROBLEM, THE   BUNCH, DAVID R.   SS
PLAYMATE   BUNCH, DAVID R.   SS   FAN 65 05
HUSBAND'S SHARE, A   BUNCH, DAVID R.   SS   FAN 60 10
COMPLETE FATHER, A   BUNCH, DAVID R.   SS   FAN 60 01
WAS SHE HORRID?   BUNCH, DAVID R.   SS   FAN 59 12
GLANCE AT THE PAST, A   BUNCH, DAVID R.   SS   FAN 70 10
EDUCATIONAL   BUNCH, DAVID R.   SS
IT WAS BLACK CAT WEATHER   BUNCH, DAVID R.   SS   FAN 63 02
SOMETIMES I GET SO HAPPY   BUNCH, DAVID R.   SS   FAN 63 08
REMEMBERING   BUNCH, DAVID R.   SS   AMZ 60 04
LITTLE GIRL'S XMAS IN MODERAN, A
                                BUNCH, DAVID R.   SS   FSF 60 01
FLESH-MAN FROM FAR WIDE, THE   BUNCH, DAVID R.   SS   AMZ 59 11
ONE FROM CAMELOT MODERAN, THE
                                BUNCH, DAVID R.   SS
REUNION   BUNCH, DAVID R.   SS   AMZ 65 02
WARNING, THE   BUNCH, DAVID R.   SS   AMZ 60 11
HAS ANYONE SEEN THIS HORSEMAN?
                                BUNCH, DAVID R.   SS
INTERRUPTION IN CARNAGE   BUNCH, DAVID R.   SS
MIRACLE OF THE FLOWERS, THE   BUNCH, DAVID R.   SS
INCIDENT IN MODERAN   BUNCH, DAVID R.   SS   DVS 67 01
FINAL DECISION, THE   BUNCH, DAVID R.   SS   AMZ 61 02
WILL-HUNG AND WAITING   BUNCH, DAVID R.   SS
HOW THEY TOOK CARE OF SOUL IN A LAST DAY FOR A NON-BEGINNING
                                BUNCH, DAVID R.   SS
HOW IT ENDED   BUNCH, DAVID R.   SS   AMZ 69 01

MODERN MASTERPIECES OF SCIENCE FICTION
                                MOSKOWITZ, SAM   AN H WOR 65
 DERIVATIVE ANTHOLOGIES "DOORWAY INTO TIME", "MICROCOSMIC GOD"
 AND "THE VORTEX BLASTERS"
INTRODUCTION   MOSKOWITZ, SAM   IN
VORTEX BLASTER, THE   SMITH, EDWARD E. PHD SS CMT 41 07
NIGHT   CAMPBELL, JOHN W. JR NV ASF 35 10
LOGIC NAMED JOE, A   LEINSTER, MURRAY   SS   ASF 46 03
REQUIEM   HAMILTON, EDMOND   SS   AMZ 62 04
WITH FOLDED HANDS...   WILLIAMSON, JACK   NV   ASF 47 07
ADAPTATION   WYNDHAM, JOHN   SS   ASF 49 07
WITNESS, THE   RUSSELL, ERIC FRANK SS   OWS 51 09
COMMAND, THE   DE CAMP, L. SPRAGUE SS   ASF 38 10
KINDNESS   DEL REY, LESTER   SS   ASF 44 10
WE ALSO WALK DOGS   HEINLEIN, ROBERT A. SS   ASF 41 07
ENCHANTED VILLAGE (ALSO AS THE SANDS OF MARS)
                                VAN VOGT, A. E.   SS   OWS 50 07
LIAR!   ASIMOV, ISAAC   SS   ASF 41 05
MICROCOSMIC GOD   STURGEON, THEODORE NV   ASF 41 04
HUDDLING PLACE   SIMAK, CLIFFORD D. SS   ASF 44 07
COMING ATTRACTION   LEIBER, FRITZ   SS   GAL 50 11
DOORWAY INTO TIME   MOORE, C. L.   SS   FFM 43 09
WE GUARD THE BLACK PLANET   KUTTNER, HENRY   NV   SSS 42 11
STRANGE FLIGHT OF RICHARD CLAYTON, THE
                                BLOCH, ROBERT   SS   AMZ 39 03
WAKE FOR THE LIVING (ALSO AS THE COFFIN)
                                BRADBURY, RAY   SS   DMN 47 09
BEFORE EDEN   CLARKE, ARTHUR C. SS   AMZ 61 06
MOTHER   FARMER, PHILIP JOSE NV   TWS 53 04

MODERN SCIENCE FICTION   SPINRAD, NORMAN   AN   ANC 74
FOREWORD   SPINRAD, NORMAN   IN
INTRODUCTION- MODERN SCIENCE FICTION
                                SPINRAD, NORMAN   IN
GOLDEN AGE, THE   SPINRAD, NORMAN   SI
TWILIGHT   CAMPBELL, JOHN W. JR SS ASF 34 11
ENCHANTED VILLAGE (ALSO AS THE SANDS OF MARS)
                                VAN VOGT, A. E.   SS   OWS 50 07
HELEN O'LOY   DEL REY, LESTER   SS   ASF 38 12
NIGHTFALL   ASIMOV, ISAAC   NV   ASF 41 09
POSTWAR AWAKENING, THE   SPINRAD, NORMAN   SI
STAR, THE   CLARKE, ARTHUR C. SS   INF 55 11
AFFAIR WITH A GREEN MONKEY   STURGEON, THEODORE SS   VSF 57 05
STRANGER STATION   KNIGHT, DAMON   NV   FSF 56 12
COLD EQUATIONS, THE   GODWIN, TOM   NV   ASF 54 08
MARCHING MORONS, THE   KORNBLUTH, C. M.   NV   GAL 51 04
5,271,009 (ALSO AS THE STARCOMBER)
                                BESTER, ALFRED   NV   FSF 54 03
FULL FLOWERING, THE   SPINRAD, NORMAN   SI

VOICES OF TIME, THE   BALLARD, J. G.   SS   NWS 60 10
PLEASURE GARDEN OF FELIPE SAGITTARIUS, THE
                                MOORCOCK, MICHAEL SS   NWS 65 09
NO DIRECTION HOME   SPINRAD, NORMAN   SS   NWQ 71 02
DESCENDING   DISCH, THOMAS M.   SS   FAN 64 07
FOR A BREATH I TARRY   ZELAZNY, ROGER   NV   NWS 66 03
DON'T WASH THE CARATS   FARMER, PHILIP JOSE SS   ORB 68 03
FAITH OF OUR FATHERS   DICK, PHILIP K.   NV   DVS 67 01
AYE, AND GOMORRAH...   DELANY, SAMUEL R. SS   DVS 67 01
AT THE MOUSE CIRCUS   ELLISON, HARLAN   SS   NDM 71 01
IN ENTROPY'S JAWS   SILVERBERG, ROBERT NV   INY 71 02
NINE LIVES   LE GUIN, URSULA K. NV   PBY 69 11
ADDITIONAL SIGNIFICANT WORKS OF SPECULATIVE FICTION
                                MISC. MATERIAL   MS

MOLECULE MONSTERS, THE   ANONYMOUS   AN   WHP 50
MOLECULE MONSTERS, THE   FRIEND, OSCAR J.   SS
GALACTIC HERITAGE   LONG, FRANK BELKNAP SS   TWS 48 10
IMPOSSIBLE HIGHWAY, THE   FRIEND, OSCAR J.   SS   TWS 40 08
CABLES PARTING! (NOT SF)   HAIL, STEVE   SS

MOMENT OF ECLIPSE, THE   ALDISS, BRIAN W.   AC H FAB 70
POEM AT A LUNAR ECLIPSE   HARDY, THOMAS   PM
MOMENT OF ECLIPSE, THE   ALDISS, BRIAN W.   SS   NWS 69 05
DAY WE EMBARKED FOR CYTHERA, THE
                                ALDISS, BRIAN W.   SS   NWQ 71 01
ORGY OF THE LIVING AND THE DYING
                                ALDISS, BRIAN W.   NV   YRT 70
SUPER-TOYS LAST ALL SUMMER LONG
                                ALDISS, BRIAN W.   SS   HBZ 69 12
VILLAGE SWINDLER, THE   ALDISS, BRIAN W.   SS   INT 68 10
DOWN THE UP ESCALATION   ALDISS, BRIAN W.   SS   LOM 67
THAT UNCOMFORTABLE PAUSE BETWEEN LIFE AND ART
                                ALDISS, BRIAN W.   SS   QUN 69 07
CONFLUENCE   ALDISS, BRIAN W.   SS   PUN 67 08
HERESIES OF THE HUGE GOD   ALDISS, BRIAN W.   FA   GAL 66 08
CIRCULATION OF THE BLOOD, THE
                                ALDISS, BRIAN W.   NV   IMP 66 03
AND THE STAGNATION OF THE HEART
                                ALDISS, BRIAN W.   SS   NWS 68 12
WORM THAT FLIES, THE   ALDISS, BRIAN W.   SS   FRS 68
WORKING IN THE SPACESHIP YARDS
                                ALDISS, BRIAN W.   SS   PUN 69 04
SWASTIKA!   ALDISS, BRIAN W.   SS   NOV 70 01

MOMENT WITHOUT TIME   MINES, SAMUEL   AN H SBB 56
 SEE "THE BEST FROM STARTLING STORIES"

MONADIC UNIVERSE, THE   ZEBROWSKI, GEORGE AC   ACE 77 03
THIS IS: AN INTRODUCTION   SCORTIA, THOMAS N. IN
FIRST LOVE, FIRST FEAR   ZEBROWSKI, GEORGE SS   NEW 72 AN
STARCROSSED   ZEBROWSKI, GEORGE SS   EIO 73
ASSASSINS OF AIR   ZEBROWSKI, GEORGE SS   FUC 73
PARKS OF REST AND CULTURE   ZEBROWSKI, GEORGE SS   SVW 73
WATER SCULPTOR OF STATION 233, THE
                                ZEBROWSKI, GEORGE SS   INY 70 01
ROPE OF GLASS   ZEBROWSKI, GEORGE SS   TVW 73
HEATHEN GOD   ZEBROWSKI, GEORGE SS   FSF 71 01
INTERPOSE   ZEBROWSKI, GEORGE SS   INY 73 05
HISTORY MACHINE, THE   ZEBROWSKI, GEORGE SS   NWQ 72 03
CLIOMETRICON, THE   ZEBROWSKI, GEORGE SS   AMZ 75 05
STANCE OF SPLENDOUR   ZEBROWSKI, GEORGE SS   NWQ 73 05
MONADIC UNIVERSE, THE   ZEBROWSKI, GEORGE NV   INY 72 03

MONITOR FOUND IN ORBIT   CONEY, MICHAEL G. AC   DAW 74 09
INTRODUCTION   CONEY, MICHAEL G. IN
TRUE WORTH OF RUTH VILLIERS, THE
                                CONEY, MICHAEL G. SS   NWR 70 17
MANYA, THE   CONEY, MICHAEL G. SS   FSF 73 03
HOLD MY HAND, MY LOVE!   CONEY, MICHAEL G. SS   WOT 71 SP
BENEATH STILL WATERS   CONEY, MICHAEL G. SS   IFS 71 01
UNSAVORY EPISODE OF MRS. HECTOR POWELL-CHALLENGER, THE
                                CONEY, MICHAEL G. SS
MONITOR FOUND IN ORBIT   CONEY, MICHAEL G. SS   NWQ 71 02
MIND PRISON   CONEY, MICHAEL G. SS   NWR 71 19
R26/5/PSY AND I   CONEY, MICHAEL G. NV   NWR 69 16
ESMERALDA   CONEY, MICHAEL G. SS   GAL 72 01

MONSTERS   VAN VOGT, A. E.   AC   PKT 65
 EDITED BY FORREST J. ACKERMAN, ALSO AS "THE BLAL"
MONSTER MAN, SIRE OF SLAN, THE
                                ACKERMAN, FORREST J. IN
NOT ONLY DEAD MEN   VAN VOGT, A. E.   SS   ASF 42 11
FINAL COMMAND   VAN VOGT, A. E.   SS   ASF 49 11
WAR OF NERVES   VAN VOGT, A. E.   SS   OWS 50 05
ENCHANTED VILLAGE (ALSO AS THE SANDS OF MARS)
                                VAN VOGT, A. E.   SS   OWS 50 07
CONCEALMENT   VAN VOGT, A. E.   SS   ASF 43 09
SEA THING, THE   VAN VOGT, A. E.   NV   UNK 40 01
RESURRECTION (THE MONSTER)   VAN VOGT, A. E.   SS   ASF 48 08
VAULT OF THE BEAST   VAN VOGT, A. E.   NV   ASF 40 08

MONSTERS AND MEDICS   WHITE, JAMES   AC   BAL 77 03
INTRODUCTION: REALITY IN SCIENCE FICTION
                                WHITE, JAMES   IN
SECOND ENDING   WHITE, JAMES   NA   FAN 61 06
COUNTER SECURITY   WHITE, JAMES   NV   FSF 63 02
DOGFIGHT   WHITE, JAMES   NV   NWS 59 03
NUISANCE VALUE   WHITE, JAMES   SS   ASF 57 10
IN LOVING MEMORY   WHITE, JAMES   SS   NEB 56 01
APPRENTICE, THE   WHITE, JAMES   NV   NWS 60 10
ANSWER CAME THERE NONE   WHITE, JAMES   SS   GAL 74 01

MONSTERS AND SUCH   LEINSTER, MURRAY   AC   AVN 59
LONELY PLANET, THE   LEINSTER, MURRAY   NV   TWS 49 12
IF YOU WAS A MOKLIN   LEINSTER, MURRAY   NV   GAL 51 09

```
MONSTERS AND SUCH                                              MORE TERROR IN THE MODERN VEIN

CASTAWAY, THE            LEINSTER, MURRAY    NV   USF 53 06
PROXIMA CENTAURI         LEINSTER, MURRAY    SN   ASF 35 03
NOBODY SAW THE SHIP      LEINSTER, MURRAY    SS   FUS 50 05
TRANS-HUMAN, THE         LEINSTER, MURRAY    SS   SFP 53 12
DE PROFUNDIS             LEINSTER, MURRAY    SS   TWS 45 WI

MOON CONQUERORS, THE     ANONYMOUS           AN   SWN 43
  MOON CONQUERORS, THE   ROMANS, R. H.       NO   SFQ 40 SU
  SPACE-SHIP DERBY       KALETSKY, MILTON    SS   SFQ 40 SU
  PACKAGE OF POWER       COOKE, DAVID C.     SS   SFQ 40 SU
  POLAR DOOM             COLERIDGE, JOHN     SS   SFQ 40 SU
  GENTLE BRAIN, THE      ALLPORT, ARTHUR     SS   SFQ 40 SU
  LIFE INSIDE A WALL     VINCENT, HARL       SS   SFQ 40 SU

MOON ERA, THE            MOSKOWITZ, SAM      AN H DBL 67
  SEE "THREE STORIES"

MOON MAID, THE           BURROUGHS, EDGAR R. NO H MCG 26
  ILLUSTRATIONS          ST. JOHN, J. ALLEN  IL
  MOON MAID, THE         BURROUGHS, EDGAR R. NO   AAS 23 05
  MOON MEN, THE          BURROUGHS, EDGAR R. NV   AAS 25 02
  RED HAWK, THE          BURROUGHS, EDGAR R. NV   AAS 25 09

MOON MOTH AND OTHER STORIES, THE
                         VANCE, JACK         AC H DOB 76
  SEE "THE WORLD BETWEEN AND OTHER STORIES"
  WORLD BETWEEN, THE     VANCE, JACK         NV
  MOON MOTH, THE         VANCE, JACK         NA   GAL 61 08
  BRAIN OF THE GALAXY    VANCE, JACK         NV   WBY 51 02
  DEVIL ON SALVATION BLUFF, THE
                         VANCE, JACK         NV   STR 54 03
  MEN RETURN, THE        VANCE, JACK         SS   INF 57 07

MOON TERROR, THE         BIRCH, A. G.        AN H PFP 27
  MOON TERROR, THE       BIRCH, A. G.        NA   WRT 23 05
  OOZE                   RUD, A. M.          NV   WRT 23 03
  PENELOPE               STARRETT, VINCENT   NV   WRT 23 05
  ADVENTURE IN THE FOURTH DIMENSION, AN
                         WRIGHT, FARNSWORTH  NV   WRT 23 10

MOONFERNS & STARSONGS    SILVERBERG, ROBERT  AC   BAL 71 06
  HAPPY DAY IN 2381, A   SILVERBERG, ROBERT  SS   NOV 70 01
  AFTER THE MYTHS WENT HOME  SILVERBERG, ROBERT SS FSF 69 11
  PASSENGERS             SILVERBERG, ROBERT  SS   ORB 68 04
  TO BE CONTINUED        SILVERBERG, ROBERT  SS   ASF 56 05
  NIGHTWINGS             SILVERBERG, ROBERT  NV   GAL 68 09
  WE KNOW WHO WE ARE     SILVERBERG, ROBERT  SS   AMZ 70 07
  PLEASURE OF THEIR COMPANY, THE (THE PLEASURE OF OUR COMPANY)
                         SILVERBERG, ROBERT  NV   INY 70 01
  SONGS OF SUMMER, THE   SILVERBERG, ROBERT  SS   SFS 56 09
  MAN OF TALENT, A (MAN WITH TALENT)
                         SILVERBERG, ROBERT  NV   FUT 56 WI
  COLLECTING TEAM        SILVERBERG, ROBERT  SS   AUT 57 06
  GOING DOWN SMOOTH      SILVERBERG, ROBERT  SS   GAL 68 08

MOONLIGHT TRAVELER, THE  STERN, PHILIP VAN D. AN H DBL 43 05
  ALSO AS "GREAT TALES OF FANTASY AND IMAGINATION"
  INTRODUCTION           STERN, PHILIP VAN D. IN
  CELESTIAL OMNIBUS, THE FORSTER, E. M.      SS        23
  DESIRE                 STEPHENS, JAMES     SS        28
  ENOCH SOAMES           BEERBOHM, MAX       NV   CNY 16 05
  MAN WHO COULD WORK MIRACLES, THE
                         WELLS, H. G.        SS   ILN 98 07
  BOTTLE IMP, THE        STEVENSON, ROBERT L. SS  BAW 91 03
  ADAM AND EVE AND PINCH ME  COPPARD, A. E.  SS        21
  LORD MOUNTDRAGO (DOCTOR AND PATIENT)
                         MAUGHAM, W. SOMERSET SS  ITM 39 02
  ALL HALLOWS            DE LA MARE, WALTER  SS        26
  OUR DISTANT COUSINS    DUNSANY, LORD       SS        31
  COBBLER, COBBLER, MEND MY SHOE
                         STRUTHER, JAN       SS   WRV 29 11
  MAN WHO MISSED THE BUS, THE  BENSON, STELLA SS       36
  SAM SMALL'S BETTER HALF  KNIGHT, ERIC      SS        42
  MR. ARCULARIS          AIKEN, CONRAD       SS        22
  DIAMOND AS BIG AS THE RITZ, THE
                         FITZGERALD, F. SCOTT SS       22
  WILLIAM WILSON (1839)  POE, EDGAR ALLEN    NV   GFT 39 09
  CURFEW TOLLS, THE      BENET, STEPHEN V.   SS   SEP 35 10
  MOST MADDENING STORY IN THE WORLD
                         STRAUS, RALPH       SS        37
  PHANTAS                ONIONS, OLIVER      SS        11
  ROADS OF DESTINY       HENRY, O.           NV        09
  WIRELESS               KIPLING, RUDYARD    SS   SCR 02 08
  MUSIC ON THE HILL, THE SAKI                SS        12

MOORCOCK'S BOOK OF MARTYRS  MOORCOCK, MICHAEL AC  QRT 76
  INTRODUCTION           MOORCOCK, MICHAEL   IN
  DEAD SINGER, A         MOORCOCK, MICHAEL   NV        74
  GREAT CONQUEROR, THE   MOORCOCK, MICHAEL   NV   SCF 63 04
  BEHOLD THE MAN         MOORCOCK, MICHAEL   NV   NWS 66 09
  GOOD-BYE, MIRANDA      MOORCOCK, MICHAEL   SS   NWS 64 08
  FLUX                   MOORCOCK, MICHAEL   NV   NWS 63 07
  ISLANDS                MOORCOCK, MICHAEL   NV   NWS 63
  WAITING FOR THE END OF TIME...
                         MOORCOCK, MICHAEL   SS   VOT 70

MORE ADVENTURES IN TIME AND SPACE
                         HEALY & MCCOMAS     AN   BAN 55 03
  STORIES FROM "ADVENTURES IN TIME AND SPACE"
  PROUD ROBOT, THE       PADGETT, LEWIS      NV   ASF 43 10
  HEAVY PLANET           GREGOR, LEE         SS   ASF 39 08
  LINK, THE              CARTMILL, CLEVE     SS   ASF 42 08
  ADAM AND NO EVE        BESTER, ALFRED      SS   ASF 41 09
  NIGHTFALL              ASIMOV, ISAAC       NV   ASF 41 09
  ROADS MUST ROLL, THE   HEINLEIN, ROBERT A. NV   ASF 40 06
  WITHIN THE PYRAMID     MILLER, R. DEWITT   SS   ASF 37 03

MORE ADVENTURES ON OTHER PLANETS
                         WOLLHEIM, DONALD A. AN   ACE 63
  INTRODUCTION           WOLLHEIM, DONALD A. IN
  CHILD OF THE SUN       BRACKETT, LEIGH     SS   PLS 42 SP
  SUNRISE ON MERCURY     SILVERBERG, ROBERT  SS   SFS 57 05
  BY THE NAME OF MAN (SUBSTITUTE GOD, FUN 58 08)
                         BRUNNER, JOHN       NV   NEB 56 07
  RED DEATH OF MARS, THE WILLIAMS, ROBERT M. NV   ASF 40 07
  PLANET OF DOUBT, THE   WEINBAUM, STANLEY G. NV  ASF 35 10
  TIGER BY THE TAIL      ANDERSON, POUL      NV   PLS 51 01

MORE LITTLE MONSTERS     ELWOOD & GHIDALIA   AN   MAN 73
  SWEETS TO THE SWEET    BLOCH, ROBERT       SS   WRT 47 03
  DOLL THAT DOES EVERYTHING, THE
                         MATHESON, RICHARD   SS   FUN 54 12
  FRIENDS?               GHIDALIA, ROBERTA   SS   NEW 73 AN
  TWILIGHT PLAY          DERLETH, AUGUST     SS   WRT 49 11
  SHADOWY THIRD, THE     GLASGOW, ELLEN      NV
  TRANSFER, THE          BLACKWOOD, ALGERNON SS        12
  ROSY FUTURE FOR RODERICK, A  BOND, NELSON S. SS BBM 52 08
  BRENDA                 ST. CLAIR, MARGARET SS   WRT 54 03
  MR. GEORGE             GRENDON, STEPHEN    NV   WRT 47 03
  LITTLE WITCH OF ELM STREET, THE
                         CLINGERMAN, MILDRED SS   WHC 56
  LITTLE JIMMY           DEL REY, LESTER     SS   FSF 57 04
  TOOTH FAIRY, THE       JACOBS, HARVEY      SS   NEW 73 AN
  ROBBIE AND DAVID AND LITTLE DAHL
                         MACFARLANE, WALLACE SS   GAL 72 05

MORE NIGHTMARES          BLOCH, ROBERT       AC   BEL 62 02
  THAT HELL-BOUND TRAIN  BLOCH, ROBERT       SS   FSF 58 09
  FEAST IN THE ABBEY, THE  BLOCH, ROBERT     SS   WRT 35 01
  SLAVE OF THE FLAMES    BLOCH, ROBERT       SS   WRT 38 06
  ONE WAY TO MARS        BLOCH, ROBERT       SS   WRT 45 07
  CHEATERS, THE          BLOCH, ROBERT       NV   WRT 47 11
  FIDDLER'S FEE, THE     BLOCH, ROBERT       SS   WRT 40 07
  MOTHER OF SERPENTS     BLOCH, ROBERT       SS   WRT 36 12
  WAXWORKS               BLOCH, ROBERT       SS   WRT 39 01
  SEAL OF THE SATYR, THE BLOCH, ROBERT       SS   SRS 39 06
  DARK DEMON, THE        BLOCH, ROBERT       SS   WRT 36 11

MORE PENGUIN SCIENCE FICTION ALDISS, BRIAN W. AN  PEN 63
  ALSO IN "THE PENGUIN SCIENCE FICTION OMNIBUS"
  INTRODUCTION           ALDISS, BRIAN W.    IN
  MONKEY WRENCH, THE     DICKSON, GORDON R.  SS   ASF 51 08
  FIRST MEN, THE         FAST, HOWARD        NV   FSF 60 02
  COUNTERFEIT (ALSO AS THE COUNTERFEIT MAN)
                         NOURSE, ALAN E.     NV   TWS 52 08
  GREATER THING, THE     GODWIN, TOM         NV   ASF 54 02
  BUILT UP LOGICALLY (THE UNIVERSAL TANCEA, RET 49 WI)
                         SCHOENFELD, HOWARD  SS   FSF 50 FL
  LIBERATION OF EARTH, THE  TENN, WILLIAM    SS   FUT 53 05
  ALIEN AGONY, AN (THE STREETS OF ASHKELON)
                         HARRISON, HARRY     SS   NWS 62 09
  TUNNEL UNDER THE WORLD, THE  POHL, FREDERIK NV  GAL 55 01
  STORE OF THE WORLDS, THE (THE WORLD OF HEART'S DESIRE)
                         SHECKLEY, ROBERT    SS   PBY 59 09
  JOKSTER                ASIMOV, ISAAC       SS   INF 56 12
  PYRAMID                ABERNATHY, ROBERT   NV   ASF 54 07
  FORGOTTEN ENEMY, THE   CLARKE, ARTHUR C.   SS   NWS 49 05

MORE SCIENCE FICTION TALES ELWOOD, ROGER     OA H RAN 74
  INTRODUCTION: STARTING IN THE MIDDLE
                         MALZBERG, BARRY N.  IN
  MUSIC OF MINOX, THE    GOLDSMITH, HOWARD   SS
  WEREWOLF GIRL          ANDERSSON, VIC      SS
  HIDE AND SEEK          MARTIN, MARIO JR.   SS
  THIRST FOR BLOOD, A    TOFTE, ARTHUR       NV
  HOLE IN JENNIFER'S ROOM, THE  LO MEDICO, BRIAN T. SS
  THING FROM ENNIS ROCK, THE  MONTELEONE, THOMAS F SS
  BEND OF TIME, THE      DANTON, WILLIAM     SS

MORE SOVIET SCIENCE FICTION ANONYMOUS        AN   CLB 62
  ALSO AS "THE HEART OF THE SERPENT"
  INTRODUCTION           ASIMOV, ISAAC       IN
  HEART OF THE SERPENT, THE  YEFREMOV, IVAN  NV
  SIEMA                  DNIEPROV, ANATOLY   NV
  TRIAL OF TANTALUS, THE SAPARIN, VICTOR     NV
  STONE FROM THE STARS   ZHURAVLEVA, VALENTINA SS
  SIX MATCHES            STRUGATSKY, ARKADY
                         AND STRUGATSKY, BORIS SS C

MORE STORIES FROM THE HUGO WINNERS VOLUME 2
                         ASIMOV, ISAAC       AN   FCR 73 12
  LAST 8 STORIES

MORE STORIES FROM THE TWILIGHT ZONE
                         SERLING, ROD        OC   BAN 61 04
  LONELY, THE            SERLING, ROD        SA
  MR. DINGLE, THE STRONG SERLING, ROD        SA
  THING ABOUT MACHINES, A  SERLING, ROD      SA
  BIG, TALL WISH, THE    SERLING, ROD        SA
  STOP AT WILLOUGHBY, A  SERLING, ROD        SA
  ODYSSEY OF FLIGHT 33, THE  SERLING, ROD    SA
  DUST                   SERLING, ROD        SA

MORE TERROR IN THE MODERN VEIN
                         WOLLHEIM, DONALD A. AN   DIG 61
  7 STORIES FROM "TERROR IN THE MODERN VEIN"
  GONE AWAY              COPPARD, A. E.      SS        46
  SILENCE, THE           MCLAUGHLIN, BERNARD SS   STI 41 06
  MIMIC                  WOLLHEIM, DONALD A. SS   AST 42 11
  SHIPSHAPE HOME         MATHESON, RICHARD   SS   GAL 52 07
  DREAM MAKERS, THE      BLOCH, ROBERT       NV   BEY 53 09
  REPUBLIC OF THE SOUTHERN CROSS, THE
                         BRUSSOV, VALERY     SS        19
```

ORE TERROR IN THE MODERN VEIN

| INHERITORS, THE | LOWNDES, ROBERT W. | | | | |
| | AND MICHAEL, JOHN | SS C FFS 42 10 | | | |

MORE THAN HUMAN   STURGEON, THEODORE   NO H PSY 53
FABULOUS IDIOT, THE	STURGEON, THEODORE	NV		NEW 53 NO
BABY IS THREE	STURGEON, THEODORE	NA		GAL 52 10
MORALITY	STURGEON, THEODORE	NV		NEW 53 NO

MORE THAN SUPERHUMAN   VAN VOGT, A. E.   AC   DEL 71 05
HUMANS, GO HOME!	VAN VOGT, A. E.	NV		GAL 69 09
REFLECTED MEN, THE	VAN VOGT, A. E.	NV		GAL 71 02
ALL THE LOVING ANDROIDS	VAN VOGT, A. E.	NV		NEW 71 AC
LAUGH, CLONE, LAUGH	VAN VOGT, A. E.			
	AND ACKERMAN, FORREST J.	SS C NEW 69 AC		
RESEARCH ALPHA	VAN VOGT, A. E.			
	AND SCHMITZ, JAMES H.	SN C IFS 65 07		
HIM	VAN VOGT, A. E.	SS		SPW 69 01

MORE WOMEN OF WONDER   SARGENT, PAMELA   AN   VNT 76 08
INTRODUCTION	SARGENT, PAMELA	IN		
JIREL MEETS MAGIC	MOORE, C. L.	NV		WRT 35 07
LAKE OF THE GONE FOREVER, THE				
	BRACKETT, LEIGH	NV		TWS 49 10
SECOND INQUISITION, THE	RUSS, JOANNA	NV		ORB 70 06
POWER OF TIME, THE	SAXTON, JOSEPHINE	NV		NDM 71 01
FUNERAL, THE	WILHELM, KATE	NV		DVS 72 02
TIN SOLDIER	VINGE, JOAN D.	NA		ORB 74 14
DAY BEFORE THE REVOLUTION, THE				
	LE GUIN, URSULA K.	SS		GAL 74 08
FURTHER READING	MISC. MATERIAL	MS		
ABOUT THE AUTHORS	MISC. MATERIAL	MS		
ABOUT THE EDITOR	MISC. MATERIAL	MS		

MORTAL ENGINES   LEM, STANISLAW   AC H SEA 77 05
INTRODUCTION	KANDEL, MICHAEL	IN		
THREE ELECTROKNIGHTS, THE	LEM, STANISLAW	SS		72
URANIUM EARPIECES	LEM, STANISLAW	SS		72
HOW ERG THE SELF-INDUCTING SLEW A PALEFACE				
	LEM, STANISLAW	SS		72
TWO MONSTERS	LEM, STANISLAW	SS		72
WHITE DEATH, THE	LEM, STANISLAW	SS		72
HOW MICROX AND GIGANT MADE THE UNIVERSE EXPAND				
	LEM, STANISLAW	SS		72
TALE OF THE COMPUTER THAT FOUGHT A DRAGON				
	LEM, STANISLAW	SS		72
ADVISERS OF KING HYDROPS, THE				
	LEM, STANISLAW	SS		72
AUTOMATTHEW'S FRIEND	LEM, STANISLAW	NV		72
KING GLOBARES AND THE SAGES	LEM, STANISLAW	SS		72
TALE OF KING GNUFF, THE	LEM, STANISLAW	SS		72
SANATORIUM OF DR. VLIPERDIUS, THE				
	LEM, STANISLAW	SS		71
HUNT, THE	LEM, STANISLAW	NV		73
MASK, THE	LEM, STANISLAW	SS		

MORTALS AND MONSTERS   DEL REY, LESTER   AC   BAL 65
AND THE TRUTH (DEAD RINGER)	DEL REY, LESTER	SS		GAL 56 11
"YEARS DRAW NIGH, THE"	DEL REY, LESTER	SS		ASF 51 10
AND IT COMES OUT HERE	DEL REY, LESTER	SS		GAL 51 02
SEAT OF JUDGMENT, THE	DEL REY, LESTER	SS		VSF 57 07
DWINDLING YEARS, THE	DEL REY, LESTER	SS		GAL 56 01
NO PLACE LIKE HOME	DEL REY, LESTER	SS		ASF 52 08
LADY OF SPACE	DEL REY, LESTER	SS		VSF 58 07
INSTINCT	DEL REY, LESTER	SS		ASF 52 01
RETURN ENGAGEMENT	DEL REY, LESTER	SS		GAL 61 08
COURSE OF LOGIC, THE	DEL REY, LESTER	SS		IFS 63 09
SPAWNING GROUND	DEL REY, LESTER	SS		IFS 61 09
RECESSIONAL (FORGIVE US OUR DEBTS)				
	DEL REY, LESTER	SS		FUT 52 05

MR. GEORGE AND OTHER ODD PERSONS
	DERLETH, AUGUST	AC H ARK 63		
INTRODUCTION	DERLETH, AUGUST	IN		
MR. GEORGE	DERLETH, AUGUST	NV		WRT 47 03
PARRINGTON'S POOL	DERLETH, AUGUST	SS		WRT 47 07
GENTLEMAN FROM PRAGUE, A	DERLETH, AUGUST	SS		WRT 44 11
MAN ON B-17, THE	DERLETH, AUGUST	SS		WRT 50 05
BLESSED ARE THE MEEK	DERLETH, AUGUST	SS		WRT 48 11
MARA	DERLETH, AUGUST	SS		ARS 48 WI
BLUE SPECTACLES, THE	DERLETH, AUGUST	SS		WRT 49 07
ALANNAH	DERLETH, AUGUST	SS		WRT 45 03
DEAD MAN'S SHOES	DERLETH, AUGUST	SS		WRT 46 03
TSANTSA IN THE PARLOR, THE	DERLETH, AUGUST	SS		WRT 48 07
BALU	DERLETH, AUGUST	SS		WRT 49 01
EXTRA PASSENGER, THE	DERLETH, AUGUST	SS		WRT 47 01
WIND IN THE LILACS, THE	DERLETH, AUGUST	SS		ARS 48 SP
MISS ESPERSON	DERLETH, AUGUST	SS		62
NIGHT TRAIN TO LOST VALLEY, THE				
	DERLETH, AUGUST	SS		WRT 48 01
BISHOP'S GAMBIT	DERLETH, AUGUST	SS		AFR 47 03
MRS. MANIFOLD	DERLETH, AUGUST	SS		49

MR. MERGENTHWIRKER'S LOBBIES AND OTHER FANTASTIC TALES
	BOND, NELSON S.	AC H CMC 46		
MR. MERGENTHWIRKER'S LOBBIES	BOND, NELSON S.	SS		SCR 37 11
MAGIC STAIR-CASE, THE	BOND, NELSON S.	SS		
REMARKABLE TALENT OF EGBERT HAW, THE				
	BOND, NELSON S.	SS		41
JOHNNY CARTWRIGHT'S CAMERA (CARTWRIGHT'S CAMERA)				
	BOND, NELSON S.	SS		UNK 40 11
MASTER OF COTSWOLD, THE	BOND, NELSON S.	SS		WRT 44 01
EINSTEIN INSHOOT, THE	BOND, NELSON S.	SS		ASF 38 11
FOUNTAIN, THE	BOND, NELSON S.	SN		UNK 41 06
DR. FUDDLE'S FINGERS	BOND, NELSON S.	SS		
CONQUEROR'S ISLE	BOND, NELSON S.	SS		BBM 46 06
SOCRATES OF THE SOUTH FORTY	BOND, NELSON S.	SS		

MY BEST SCIENCE FICTION STORY

BACULAR CLOCK, THE	BOND, NELSON S.	SS		BBM 42 07
UNION IN GEHENNA	BOND, NELSON S.	NV		FAD 42 11
BOOKSHOP, THE	BOND, NELSON S.	SS		

MURRAY LEINSTER OMNIBUS, A   LEINSTER, MURRAY   AC H SID 68
ALSO IN "SCIENCE FICTION SPECIAL 7"				
OPERATION TERROR	LEINSTER, MURRAY	NO		BRK 62
CHECKPOINT LAMBDA (STOPOVER IN SPACE)				
	LEINSTER, MURRAY	NO		AMZ 66 06
INVADERS OF SPACE	LEINSTER, MURRAY	NO		BRK 64

MUTANT   PADGETT, LEWIS   AC H GNM 53
PIPER'S SON, THE	PADGETT, LEWIS	NV		ASF 45 02
THREE BLIND MICE	PADGETT, LEWIS	NV		ASF 45 06
LION AND THE UNICORN, THE	PADGETT, LEWIS	NV		ASF 45 07
BEGGARS IN VELVET	PADGETT, LEWIS	NV		ASF 45 12
HUMPTY DUMPTY	PADGETT, LEWIS	NV		ASF 53 09

MUTANTS   DICKSON, GORDON R.   AC H MAC 70
INTRODUCTION	DICKSON, GORDON R.	IN		
WARRIOR	DICKSON, GORDON R.	SS		ASF 65 12
OF THE PEOPLE	DICKSON, GORDON R.	SS		FSF 55 12
DANGER- HUMAN!	DICKSON, GORDON R.	SS		ASF 57 12
REHABILITATED	DICKSON, GORDON R.	SS		FSF 61 01
LISTEN	DICKSON, GORDON R.	SS		FSF 52 08
ROOFS OF SILVER	DICKSON, GORDON R.	NV		FSF 62 12
BY NEW HEARTH FIRES	DICKSON, GORDON R.	SS		ASF 59 01
IDIOT SOLVANT	DICKSON, GORDON R.	SS		ASF 62 01
IMMORTAL, THE	DICKSON, GORDON R.	NV		FSF 65 08
MISS PRINKS	DICKSON, GORDON R.	SS		FSF 54 06
HOME FROM THE SHORE	DICKSON, GORDON R.	NA		GAL 63 02

MUTANTS   SILVERBERG, ROBERT   AN H NDB 74
INTRODUCTION	SILVERBERG, ROBERT	IN		
TOMORROW'S CHILDREN	ANDERSON, POUL			
	AND WALDROP, F. N.	NV C ASF 47 03		
IT'S A GOOD LIFE	BIXBY, JEROME	SS		STR 53 02
MUTE QUESTION, THE	ACKERMAN, FORREST J.	SS		OWS 50 09
LET THE ANTS TRY	POHL, FREDERIK	SS		PLS 49 WI
CONQUEROR, THE	CLIFTON, MARK	SS		ASF 52 08
LIQUID LIFE	FARLEY, RALPH MILNE	NV		TWS 36 10
HOTHOUSE	ALDISS, BRIAN W.	NV		FSF 61 02
OZYMANDIAS	CARR, TERRY	SS		DVS 72 02
MAN WHO NEVER FORGOT, THE	SILVERBERG, ROBERT	SS		FSF 58 02
GINNY WRAPPED IN THE SUN	LAFFERTY, R. A.	SS		GAL 67 08
WATERSHED	BLISH, JAMES	SS		IFS 55 05

MY BEST SCIENCE FICTION STORY
	MARGULIES & FRIEND	AN H MER 49		
INTRODUCTION	MARGULIES, LEO			
	AND FRIEND, OSCAR J.	IN C		
WHY I SELECTED ROBOT AL-76 GOES ASTRAY				
	ASIMOV, ISAAC	AI		
ROBOT AL-76 GOES ASTRAY	ASIMOV, ISAAC	SS		AMZ 42 02
WHY I SELECTED GRIEF OF BAGDAD				
	BARNES, ARTHUR K.	AI		
GRIEF OF BAGDAD	BARNES, ARTHUR K.	SS		TWS 43 06
WHY I SELECTED THE TEACHER FROM MARS				
	BINDER, EANDO	AI		
TEACHER FROM MARS, THE	BINDER, EANDO	SS		TWS 41 02
WHY I SELECTED ALMOST HUMAN	BLOCH, ROBERT	AI		
ALMOST HUMAN (AS TARLETON FISKE)				
	BLOCH, ROBERT	SS		FAD 43 06
WHY I SELECTED ZERO HOUR	BRADBURY, RAY	AI		
ZERO HOUR	BRADBURY, RAY	SS		PLS 47 FL
WHY I SELECTED NOTHING SIRIUS				
	BROWN, FREDRIC	AI		
NOTHING SIRIUS	BROWN, FREDRIC	SS		CFU 44 SP
WHY I SELECTED BLINDNESS	CAMPBELL, JOHN W. JR	AI		
BLINDNESS	CAMPBELL, JOHN W. JR	SS		ASF 35 03
WHY I SELECTED VISITING YOKEL				
	CARTMILL, CLEVE	AI		
VISITING YOKEL	CARTMILL, CLEVE	SS		TWS 43 08
WHY I SELECTED THE HIBITED MAN				
	DE CAMP, L. SPRAGUE	AI		
HIBITED MAN, THE	DE CAMP, L. SPRAGUE	SS		TWS 49 10
WHY I SELECTED THE THING IN THE POND				
	ERNST, PAUL	AI		
THING IN THE POND, THE	ERNST, PAUL	SS		ASF 34 06
WHY I SELECTED WANDERER OF TIME				
	FEARN, JOHN RUSSELL	AI		
WANDERER OF TIME	FEARN, JOHN RUSSELL	SS		STS 44 SU
WHY I SELECTED THE INN OUTSIDE THE WORLD				
	HAMILTON, EDMOND	AI		
INN OUTSIDE THE WORLD, THE	HAMILTON, EDMOND	SS		WRT 45 07
WHY I SELECTED THE GREEN HILLS OF EARTH				
	HEINLEIN, ROBERT A.	AI		
GREEN HILLS OF EARTH, THE	HEINLEIN, ROBERT A.	SS		SEP 47 02
WHY I SELECTED THE PROFESSOR WAS A THIEF				
	HUBBARD, L. RON	AI		
PROFESSOR WAS A THIEF, THE	HUBBARD, L. RON	NV		ASF 40 02
WHY I SELECTED DON'T LOOK NOW				
	KUTTNER, HENRY	AI		
DON'T LOOK NOW	KUTTNER, HENRY	SS		STS 48 03
WHY I SELECTED THE LOST RACE	LEINSTER, MURRAY	AI		
LOST RACE, THE	LEINSTER, MURRAY	NV		TWS 49 04
WHY I SELECTED THE HOUSE OF RISING WINDS				
	LONG, FRANK BELKNAP	AI		
HOUSE OF RISING WINDS, THE	LONG, FRANK BELKNAP	SS		STS 48 05
WHY I SELECTED THE CARRIERS	MERWIN, SAM JR.	AI		
CARRIERS, THE	MERWIN, SAM JR.	SS		TWS 49 02
WHY I SELECTED DOCTOR GRIMSHAW'S SANITARIUM				
	PRATT, FLETCHER	AI		
DOCTOR GRIMSHAW'S SANITARIUM	PRATT, FLETCHER	SS		AMZ 34 05
WHY I SELECTED UNCHARTED ISLE				
	SMITH, CLARK ASHTON	AI		

MY BEST SCIENCE FICTION STORY

```
UNCHARTED ISLE, THE          SMITH, CLARK ASHTON  SS   WRT 30 11
WHY I SELECTED THUNDER AND ROSES
                             STURGEON, THEODORE   AI
THUNDER AND ROSES            STURGEON, THEODORE   SS   ASF 47 11
WHY I SELECTED THE ULTIMATE CATALYST
                             TAINE, JOHN          AI
ULTIMATE CATALYST, THE       TAINE, JOHN          NV   TWS 39 06
WHY I SELECTED PROJECT- SPACESHIP
                             VAN VOGT, A. E.      AI
PROJECT- SPACESHIP (ALSO AS THE PROBLEM PROFESSOR)
                             VAN VOGT, A. E.      NV   TWS 49 08
WHY I SELECTED SPACE STATION NO. 1
                             WELLMAN, MANLY WADE  AI
SPACE STATION NO. 1          WELLMAN, MANLY WADE  SS   ARG 36 10
WHY I SELECTED STAR BRIGHT   WILLIAMSON, JACK     AI
STAR BRIGHT                  WILLIAMSON, JACK     NV   ARG 39 11

MY BEST SCIENCE FICTION STORY (12 OF 25)
                             MARGULIES & FRIEND   AN   PKT 54 05
INTRODUCTION TO THE POCKET BOOK EDITION
                             MARGULIES, LEO
                             AND FRIEND, OSCAR J. IN C
WHY I SELECTED ROBOT AL-76 GOES ASTRAY
                             ASIMOV, ISAAC        AI
ROBOT AL-76 GOES ASTRAY      ASIMOV, ISAAC        SS   AMZ 42 02
WHY I SELECTED THE TEACHER FROM MARS
                             BINDER, EANDO        AI
TEACHER FROM MARS, THE       BINDER, EANDO        SS   TWS 41 02
WHY I SELECTED ALMOST HUMAN  BLOCH, ROBERT        AI
ALMOST HUMAN (AS TARLETON FISKE)
                             BLOCH, ROBERT        SS   FAD 43 06
WHY I SELECTED BLINDNESS     CAMPBELL, JOHN W. JR AI
BLINDNESS                    CAMPBELL, JOHN W. JR SS   ASF 35 03
WHY I SELECTED THE INN OUTSIDE THE WORLD
                             HAMILTON, EDMOND     AI
INN OUTSIDE THE WORLD, THE   HAMILTON, EDMOND     SS   WRT 45 07
WHY I SELECTED DON'T LOOK NOW
                             KUTTNER, HENRY       AI
DON'T LOOK NOW               KUTTNER, HENRY       SS   STS 48 03
WHY I SELECTED THE LOST RACE LEINSTER, MURRAY     AI
LOST RACE, THE               LEINSTER, MURRAY     NV   TWS 49 04
WHY I SELECTED DOCTOR GRIMSHAW'S SANITARIUM
                             PRATT, FLETCHER      AI
DOCTOR GRIMSHAW'S SANITARIUM PRATT, FLETCHER      SS   AMZ 34 05
WHY I SELECTED THE ULTIMATE CATALYST
                             TAINE, JOHN          AI
ULTIMATE CATALYST, THE       TAINE, JOHN          NV   TWS 39 06
WHY I SELECTED PROJECT- SPACESHIP
                             VAN VOGT, A. E.      AI
PROJECT- SPACESHIP (ALSO AS THE PROBLEM PROFESSOR)
                             VAN VOGT, A. E.      NV   TWS 49 08
WHY I SELECTED SPACE STATION NO. 1
                             WELLMAN, MANLY WADE  AI
SPACE STATION NO. 1          WELLMAN, MANLY WADE  SS   ARG 36 10
WHY I SELECTED STAR BRIGHT   WILLIAMSON, JACK     AI
STAR BRIGHT                  WILLIAMSON, JACK     NV   ARG 39 11

MY NAME IS LEGION            ZELAZNY, ROGER       AC   BAL 76 04
EVE OF RUMOKO, THE           ZELAZNY, ROGER       NA   TFT 69
'KJWALLL'KJE'K'KOOTHAILLL'KJE'K
                             ZELAZNY, ROGER       NA        73
HOME IS THE HANGMAN          ZELAZNY, ROGER       NV   ASF 75 11

NATIVES OF SPACE             CLEMENT, HAL         AC   BAL 65 04
ASSUMPTION UNJUSTIFIED       CLEMENT, HAL         NV   ASF 46 10
TECHNICAL ERROR              CLEMENT, HAL         NV   ASF 44 01
IMPEDIMENT                   CLEMENT, HAL         NV   ASF 42 08

NEANDERTHAL PLANET           ALDISS, BRIAN W.     AC   AVN 70 01
NEANDERTHAL PLANET (A TOUCH OF NEANDERTHAL)
                             ALDISS, BRIAN W.     NV   SFA 60 09
DANGER: RELIGION! (MATRIX)   ALDISS, BRIAN W.     TC   SCF 62 10
INTANGIBLES, THE             ALDISS, BRIAN W.     NV   SCF 59 02
SINCE THE ASSASSINATION      ALDISS, BRIAN W.     NV   NEW 69 AC

NEBULA AWARD STORIES         KNIGHT, DAMON        AN H DBL 66
INTRODUCTION                 KNIGHT, DAMON        IN
DOORS OF HIS FACE, THE LAMPS OF HIS MOUTH, THE
                             ZELAZNY, ROGER       NV   FSF 65 03
BALANCED ECOLOGY             SCHMITZ, JAMES H.    SS   ASF 65 03
"REPENT, HARLEQUIN!" SAID THE TICKTOCKMAN
                             ELLISON, HARLAN      SS   GAL 65 12
HE WHO SHAPES                ZELAZNY, ROGER       NV   AMZ 65 01
COMPUTERS DON'T ARGUE        DICKSON, GORDON R.   SS   ASF 65 09
BECALMED IN HELL             NIVEN, LARRY         SS   FSF 65 07
SALIVA TREE, THE             ALDISS, BRIAN W.     SN   FSF 65 09
DROWNED GIANT, THE (SOUVENIR)
                             BALLARD, J. G.       SS   PBY 65 05

NEBULA AWARD STORIES  NO. 2  ALDISS & HARRISON    AN H DBL 67
INTRODUCTION                 ALDISS, BRIAN W.
                             AND HARRISON, HARRY  IN C
SECRET PLACE, THE            MCKENNA, RICHARD M.  SS   ORB 66 01
LIGHT OF OTHER DAYS          SHAW, BOB            SS   ASF 66 08
WHO NEEDS INSURANCE?         SCOTT, ROBIN S.      NV   ASF 66 04
AMONG THE HAIRY EARTHMEN     LAFFERTY, R. A.      SS   GAL 66 08
LAST CASTLE, THE             VANCE, JACK          NV   GAL 66 04
DAY MILLION                  POHL, FREDERIK       SS   ROG 66 02
WHEN I WAS MISS DOW          DORMAN, SONYA        SS   GAL 66 06
CALL HIM LORD                DICKSON, GORDON R.   SS   ASF 66 05
IN THE IMAGICON              SMITH, GEORGE HENRY  SS   GAL 66 02
WE CAN REMEMBER IT FOR YOU WHOLESALE
                             DICK, PHILIP K.      NV   FSF 66 04
MAN IN HIS TIME              ALDISS, BRIAN W.     SS   SCF 65 04
```

NEBULA AWARD STORIES 9

```
NEBULA AWARD STORIES  NO. 3  ZELAZNY, ROGER       AN H DBL 68 12
INTRODUCTION                 ZELAZNY, ROGER       IN
CLOUD-SCULPTORS OF CORAL D, THE
                             BALLARD, J. G.       SS   FSF 67 12
PRETTY MAGGIE MONEYEYES      ELLISON, HARLAN      NV   KNT 67 05
MIRROR OF ICE                WRIGHT, GARY         SS   GAL 67 06
AYE, AND GOMORRAH...         DELANY, SAMUEL R.    SS   DVS 67 01
GONNA ROLL THE BONES         LEIBER, FRITZ        NV   DVS 67 01
BEHOLD THE MAN               MOORCOCK, MICHAEL    NV   NWS 66 09
WEYR SEARCH                  MCCAFFREY, ANNE      SN   ASF 67 10
AFTERWORD                    ZELAZNY, ROGER       MS

NEBULA AWARD STORIES  NO. 4  ANDERSON, POUL       AN H DBL 69 12
INTRODUCTION                 ANDERSON, POUL       IN
SCIENCE FICTION NOVEL IN 1968, THE
                             MCNELLY, WILLIS E.    IN
MOTHER TO THE WORLD          WILSON, RICHARD      NV   ORB 68 03
DANCE OF THE CHANGER AND THE THREE, THE
                             CARR, TERRY          SS   FRS 68
PLANNERS, THE                WILHELM, KATE        SS   ORB 68 03
SWORD GAME                   HOLLIS, H. H.        SS   GAL 68 04
LISTENERS, THE (ALSO AS ROBERT MACDONALD- 2025)
                             GUNN, JAMES E.       NV   GAL 68 09
DRAGONRIDER                  MCCAFFREY, ANNE      NA   ASF 67 12
IN MEMORIAM- ANTHONY BOUCHER MCCOMAS, J. FRANCIS  MS
IN MEMORIAM- ROSEL GEORGE BROWN
                             GALOUYE, DANIEL F.   MS
IN MEMORIAM- GROFF CONKLIN   ASIMOV, ISAAC        MS
IN MEMORIAM- BERNARD I. KAHN CAMPBELL, JOHN W. JR MS
IN MEMORIAM- ANNA KAVAN      ALDISS, BRIAN W.     MS
IN MEMORIAM- GERALD KERSH    ELLISON, HARLAN      MS
IN MEMORIAM- EDISON MARSHALL ROGERS, ALVA         MS
IN MEMORIAM- FRANK OWEN      PETAJA, EMIL         MS
IN MEMORIAM- STUART PALMER   ANDERSON, KAREN      MS
IN MEMORIAM- MERVYN PEAKE    MOORCOCK, MICHAEL    MS
IN MEMORIAM- ARTHUR SELLINGS CARNELL, TED         MS
IN MEMORIAM- HARL VINCENT    ACKERMAN, FORREST J. MS
IN MEMORIAM- A. A. WYN       WOLLHEIM, DONALD A.  MS

NEBULA AWARD STORIES  NO. 5  BLISH, JAMES         AN H DBL 70 12
INTRODUCTION                 BLISH, JAMES         IN
BOY AND HIS DOG, A           ELLISON, HARLAN      NV   NWS 69 04
NINE LIVES                   LE GUIN, URSULA K.   NV   PBY 69 11
PASSENGERS                   SILVERBERG, ROBERT   SS   ORB 68 04
NOT LONG BEFORE THE END      NIVEN, LARRY         SS   FSF 69 04
TIME CONSIDERED AS A HELIX OF SEMI-PRECIOUS STONES
                             DELANY, SAMUEL R.    SS   NWS 68 12
MAN WHO LEARNED LOVING, THE  STURGEON, THEODORE   SS   FSF 69 10
SF NOVEL IN 1969, THE        SUVIN, DARKO         AR
SHORT SF IN 1968             PANSHIN, ALEXEI      AR

NEBULA AWARD STORIES  NO. 6  SIMAK, CLIFFORD D.   AN H DBL 71 12
INTRODUCTION                 SIMAK, CLIFFORD D.   IN
SCIENCE FICTION AND LITERARY TRADITION
                             CLARESON, THOMAS D.  MS
SLOW SCULPTURE               STURGEON, THEODORE   NV   GAL 70 02
IN THE QUEUE                 LAUMER, KEITH        SS   ORB 70 07
ISLAND OF DOCTOR DEATH AND OTHER STORIES, THE
                             WOLFE, GENE          SS   ORB 70 07
ILL MET IN LANKHMAR          LEIBER, FRITZ        SN   FSF 70 04
CONTINUED ON NEXT ROCK       LAFFERTY, R. A.      NV   ORB 70 07
BY THE FALLS                 HARRISON, HARRY      SS   IFS 70 07
SECOND INQUISITION, THE      RUSS, JOANNA         NV   ORB 70 06

NEBULA AWARD STORIES  NO. 7  BIGGLE, LLOYD JR.    AN H HPR 73
INTRODUCTION                 BIGGLE, LLOYD JR.    IN
1971: THE YEAR IN SCIENCE FICTION
                             KNIGHT, DAMON        AR
QUEEN OF AIR AND DARKNESS, THE
                             ANDERSON, POUL       SN   FSF 71 04
LAST GHOST, THE              GOLDIN, STEPHEN      SS   PRT 71
ENCOUNTER, THE               WILHELM, KATE        NV   ORB 70 08
SKY                          LAFFERTY, R. A.      SS   NDM 71 01
MOUNT CHARITY                PANGBORN, EDGAR      NV   UNI 71 01
GOOD NEWS FROM THE VATICAN   SILVERBERG, ROBERT   SS   UNI 71 01
HORSE OF AIR                 DOZOIS, GARDNER R.   SS   ORB 70 08
HEATHEN GOD                  ZEBROWSKI, GEORGE    SS   FSF 71 01
POOR MAN, BEGGER MAN         RUSS, JOANNA         NV   UNI 71 01
GIBEREL, THE                 BUCK, DORIS PITKIN   SS   NDM 71 01
MISSING MAN, THE             MACLEAN, KATHERINE   NV   ASF 71 03
NEBULA AWARD S. F., 1965-1970, THE SCIENCE
                             ANDERSON, POUL       MS
NEBULA AWARD S. F., 1965-1970, THE FICTION
                             STURGEON, THEODORE   MS

NEBULA AWARD STORIES  8      ASIMOV, ISAAC        AN H HPR 73
SO WHY AREN'T WE RICH?       ASIMOV, ISAAC        IN
MEETING WITH MEDUSA, THE     CLARKE, ARTHUR C.    NA   PBY 71 12
SHAFFERY AMONG THE IMMORTALS POHL, FREDERIK       SS   FSF 72 07
PATRON OF THE ARTS           ROTSLER, WILLIAM     NV   UNI 72 02
WHEN IT CHANGED              RUSS, JOANNA         SS   DVS 72 02
ON THE DOWNHILL SIDE         ELLISON, HARLAN      SS   UNI 72 02
FIFTH HEAD OF CERBERUS, THE  WOLFE, GENE          NV   ORB 72 10
WHEN WE WENT TO SEE THE END OF THE WORLD
                             SILVERBERG, ROBERT   SS   UNI 72 02
GOAT SONG                    ANDERSON, POUL       NV   FSF 72 02
NEBULA AWARDS                MISC. MATERIAL       MS
HUGO AWARDS                  MISC. MATERIAL       MS

NEBULA AWARD STORIES  9      WILHELM, KATE        AN H HPR 74
INTRODUCTION                 WILHELM, KATE        IN
DEATH OF DOCTOR ISLAND, THE  WOLFE, GENE          NV   UNI 73 03
SHARK                        BRYANT, EDWARD       NV   ORB 73 12
WITH MORNING COMES MISTFALL  MARTIN, GEORGE R. R. SS   ASF 73 05
FUTURE OF SCIENCE: PROMETHEUS, APOLLO, ATHENA, THE
                             BOVA, BEN            AR
```

NEBULA AWARD STORIES 9

OF MIST, AND GRASS, AND SAND	MCINTYRE, VONDA N.	SS	ASF	73 10
DEATHBIRD, THE	ELLISON, HARLAN	NV	FSF	73 03
THING OF BEAUTY, A	SPINRAD, NORMAN	SS	ASF	73 01
LOVE IS THE PLAN THE PLAN IS DEATH				
	TIPTREE, JAMES JR.	SS	ALC	73
1973: THE YEAR IN SCIENCE FICTION				
	KNIGHT, DAMON	AR		
CHILDHOOD OF THE HUMAN HERO, THE				
	EMSHWILLER, CAROL	SS	SCS	73
NEBULA WINNERS, 1965-1973, THE				
	MISC. MATERIAL	MS		
AUTHORS, THE	MISC. MATERIAL	MS		

NEBULA AWARD STORIES 10   GUNN, JAMES E.   AN H HPR 75

INTRODUCTION	GUNN, JAMES E.	IN		
ENGINE AT HEARTSPRING'S CENTER, THE				
	ZELAZNY, ROGER	SS	ASF	74 07
IF THE STARS ARE GODS	BENFORD, GREGORY			
	AND EKLUND, GORDON	NV C	UNI	74 04
TWILLA	REAMY, TOM	NV	FSF	74 09
TEN YEARS OF NEBULA AWARDS	DICKSON, GORDON R.	AR	NEW 75	AN
AS THE WALL CRUMBLES	SCHOLES, ROBERT	AR	NEW 75	AN
AFTER KING KONG FELL	FARMER, PHILIP JOSE	SS	OMG	73
DAY BEFORE THE REVOLUTION, THE				
	LE GUIN, URSULA K.	SS	GAL	74 08
REST IS SILENCE, THE	GRANT, C. L.	SS	FSF	74 09
BORN WITH THE DEAD	SILVERBERG, ROBERT	NA	FSF	74 04
AWARD WINNING SCIENCE FICTION, 1965-1974				
	MISC. MATERIAL	MS		

NEBULA AWARD STORIES 11   LE GUIN, URSULA K.   AN H HPR 77

INTRODUCTION	LE GUIN, URSULA K.	IN		
CATCH THAT ZEPPELIN!	LEIBER, FRITZ	SS	FSF	75 03
END GAME	HALDEMAN, JOE W.	NV	ASF	75 01
1975: THE YEAR IN SCIENCE FICTION, OR LET'S HEAR IT FOR THE				
DECLINE AND FALL OF THE...	NICHOLLS, PETER	AR		
HOME IS THE HANGMAN	ZELAZNY, ROGER	NV	ASF	75 11
CHILD OF ALL AGES	PLAUGER, P. J.	SS	ASF	75 03
POTENTIAL AND ACTUALITY IN SCIENCE FICTION				
	MCINTYRE, VONDA N.	AR		
SHATTERDAY	ELLISON, HARLAN	SS	GLR	75 09
SAN DIEGO LIGHTFOOT SUE	REAMY, TOM	NV	FSF	75 08
TIME DEER	STRETE, CRAIG	SS	IFS	74 12
NEBULA AWARDS, 1975: WIN, PLACE, AND SHOW				
	MISC. MATERIAL	MS		

NEEDLE IN A TIMESTACK   SILVERBERG, ROBERT   AC BAL 66 11

PAIN PEDDLERS, THE	SILVERBERG, ROBERT	SS	GAL	63 08
PASSPORT TO SIRIUS	SILVERBERG, ROBERT	SS	IFS	58 04
BIRDS OF A FEATHER	SILVERBERG, ROBERT	NV	GAL	58 11
THERE WAS AN OLD WOMAN-	SILVERBERG, ROBERT	SS	INF	58 11
SHADOW OF WINGS, THE	SILVERBERG, ROBERT	SS	IFS	63 07
ABSOLUTELY INFLEXIBLE	SILVERBERG, ROBERT	SS	FUN	56 07
HIS BROTHER'S WEEPER	SILVERBERG, ROBERT	NV	FUN	59 03
SIXTH PALACE, THE	SILVERBERG, ROBERT	SS	GAL	65 02
TO SEE THE INVISIBLE MAN	SILVERBERG, ROBERT	SS	WOT	63 04
IRON CHANCELLOR, THE	SILVERBERG, ROBERT	NV	GAL	58 05

NEUTRON STAR   NIVEN, LARRY   AC BAL 68 04

NEUTRON STAR	NIVEN, LARRY	NV	IFS	66 10
RELIC OF EMPIRE, A	NIVEN, LARRY	NV	IFS	66 12
AT THE CORE	NIVEN, LARRY	NV	IFS	66 11
SOFT WEAPON, THE	NIVEN, LARRY	NV	IFS	67 02
FLATLANDER	NIVEN, LARRY	NV	IFS	67 03
ETHICS OF MADNESS, THE	NIVEN, LARRY	NV	IFS	67 04
HANDICAPPED, THE (HANDICAP)	NIVEN, LARRY	NV	GAL	67 12
GRENDEL	NIVEN, LARRY	NV	NEW 68	AC

NEVER IN THIS WORLD   STONE, IDELLA P.   AN FGM 71 04

INTRODUCTION	STONE, IDELLA P.	IN		
AMBULANCE MADE TWO TRIPS, THE				
	LEINSTER, MURRAY	SS	ASF	60 04
DODGER FAN	STANTON, WILL	SS	FSF	57 06
LOOK OUT! DUCK!	GARRETT, RANDALL	NV	ASF	57 09
PRIZE FOR EDIE, A	BONE, J. F.	SS	ASF	61 04
LITTLE ANTON	BRETNOR, REGINALD	NV	NTS	51
DREAMWORLD	ASIMOV, ISAAC	SS	FSF	55 11
MAKE MINE HOMOGENIZED	RAPHAEL, RICK	NV	ASF	60 04
THROUGH TIME AND SPACE WITH FERDINAND FEGHOOT: XII				
	BRIARTON, GRENDEL	SS	FSF	59 03
REBEL	MOORE, WARD	SS	FSF	62 02
SENHOR ZUMBEIRA'S LEG	MARTI-IBANEZ, FELIX	NV	FSF	62 12
OR ELSE	KUTTNER, HENRY			
	AND MOORE, C. L.	SS C	AMZ	53 09
CRITIQUE OF IMPURE REASON, THE				
	ANDERSON, POUL	NV	IFS	62 11

NEW ATLANTIS AND OTHER NOVELLAS OF S.F., THE

SILVERBERG, ROBERT   OA H HAW 75

INTRODUCTION	SILVERBERG, ROBERT	IN		
SILHOUETTE	WOLFE, GENE	NA	NAL	75
NEW ATLANTIS, THE	LE GUIN, URSULA K.	NA	NAL	75
MOMENTARY TASTE OF BEING, A	TIPTREE, JAMES JR.	NA	NAL	75

NEW AWARENESS, THE   WARRICK & GREENBERG   AN H DCT 75

PREFACE	WARRICK, PATRICIA S.			
	AND GREENBERG, MARTIN H.	IN C		
INTRODUCTION	WARRICK, PATRICIA S.			
	AND GREENBERG, MARTIN H.	IN C		
NIGHT OF THE LEOPARD	SAMBROT, WILLIAM	NV		67
BEHOLD THE MAN	MOORCOCK, MICHAEL	NV	NWS	66 09
CANTICLE FOR LEIBOWITZ, A	MILLER, WALTER M. JR	NV	FSF	55 04
GOOD NEWS FROM THE VATICAN	SILVERBERG, ROBERT	SS	UNI	71 01
STREETS OF ASHKELON, THE (ALSO AS AN ALIEN AGONY)				
	HARRISON, HARRY	SS	NWS	62 09
ASK AND IT MAY BE GIVEN	DAVIS, WESLEY FORD	SS	FSF	71 10

NEW DIMENSIONS 4

COLD EQUATIONS, THE	GODWIN, TOM	NV	ASF	54 08
DAZED	STURGEON, THEODORE	NV	GAL	71 09
EYES OF ONYX	BRYANT, EDWARD	SS	PRT	71
NINE BILLION NAMES OF GOD, THE				
	CLARKE, ARTHUR C.	SS	STR	53 01
ROSE FOR ECCLESIASTES, A	ZELAZNY, ROGER	NV	FSF	63 11
EVOLUTION'S END	ARTHUR, ROBERT	SS	TWS	41 04
FIRE BALLOONS, THE (IN THIS SIGN)				
	BRADBURY, RAY	SS	IMG	51 04
MAN WHO LEARNED LOVING, THE	STURGEON, THEODORE	SS	FSF	69 10
AND I HAVE COME UPON THIS PLACE BY LOST WAYS				
	TIPTREE, JAMES JR.	NV	NOV	72 02
FURTHER READINGS	MISC. MATERIAL	MS		
INDEX	MISC. MATERIAL	MS		

NEW CONSTELLATIONS   DISCH & NAYLOR   OA H HPR 76

INTRODUCTION: MYTHOLOGY AND SCIENCE FICTION				
	DISCH, THOMAS M.	IN		
FABLES (THE FROG PRINCE & MICKEY MOUSE)				
	DIEFENDORF, DAVID	SS	NYT	75 12
THREE FINGERS	WOLFE, THOMAS	SS		
RAPE OF OOOOOOO, THE	KEARNS, WINN	SS		
EARTHBLOSSOM	FAST, JON	SS		
YELLOWHEAD	DANN, JACK M.			
	AND ZEBROWSKI, GEORGE	SS C		
PUDDLE ON THE FLOOR	LAFFERTY, R. A.	SS		
HADES AND EUCLID (TRANSLATED BY ROBERT BLY)				
	MARTINSON, HARRY	SS		70
CHRISTMAS IN WATSON HOLLOW	MUNDIS, JERROLD J.	SS		
IN A LAND OF CLEAR COLORS	SHECKLEY, ROBERT	NV		
TWENTY-EIGHTH DAY, THE	PAULSEN, KATHRYN	SS		
CALL ME ISHTAR (EXCERPT)	LERMAN, RHODA	EX	DBL	73
HARP THAT CONQUERED HELL, THE				
	THARP, BEEBE	SS		
EXTINCTION OF CONFIDENCE, THE EXERCISE OF HONESTY				
	CONNER, MICHAEL	SS		
MYSTERY DIET OF THE GODS: A REVELATION				
	DISCH, THOMAS M.			
	AND SLADEK, JOHN T.	SS C	SWK	76 10
IN CHINISTREX FORTRONZA THE PEOPLE ARE MACHINES				
	BISHOP, MICHAEL	SS		
LEGENDS FROM "THE CHESHIRE CAT" (TRANSLATED BY ISABEL READE)				
	IMBERT, ENRIQUE A.	SS		
STARBIRTH (ENVOI: STARBIRTH)	GOLDBARTH, ALBERT	SS	LMG	75
NOTES ON THE CONTRIBUTORS	MISC. MATERIAL	MS		

NEW DIMENSIONS 1   SILVERBERG, ROBERT   OA H DBL 71

INTRODUCTION	SILVERBERG, ROBERT	IN		
SPECIAL KIND OF MORNING, A	DOZOIS, GARDNER R.	NV	NDM	71 01
TROUBLE WITH THE PAST, THE	EISENSTEIN, ALEX			
	AND EISENSTEIN, PHYLLIS	SS C	NDM	71 01
POWER OF TIME, THE	SAXTON, JOSEPHINE	NV	NDM	71 01
GIBEREL, THE	BUCK, DORIS PITKIN	SS	NDM	71 01
VASTER THAN EMPIRES AND MORE SLOW				
	LE GUIN, URSULA K.	NV	NDM	71 01
GREAT A, THE	MALSTROM, ROBERT C.	SS	NDM	71 01
AT THE MOUSE CIRCUS	ELLISON, HARLAN	SS	NDM	71 01
PLAGUE OF CARS, A	TUSHNET, LEONARD	SS	NDM	71 01
SKY	LAFFERTY, R. A.	SS	NDM	71 01
LOVE SONG OF HERSELF	BRYANT, EDWARD	SS	NDM	71 01
WICKED FLEE, THE	HARRISON, HARRY	SS	NDM	71 01
SLICED-CROSSWISE ONLY-ON-TUESDAY WORLD, THE				
	FARMER, PHILIP JOSE	SS	NDM	71 01
CONQUEST	MALZBERG, BARRY N.	SS	NDM	71 01
EMANCIPATION: A ROMANCE OF THE TIMES TO COME				
	DISCH, THOMAS M.	NV	NDM	71 01

NEW DIMENSIONS 2   SILVERBERG, ROBERT   OA H DBL 72

INTRODUCTION	SILVERBERG, ROBERT	IN		
NOBODY'S HOME	RUSS, JOANNA	SS	NDM	72 02
FILOMENA & GREG & RIKKI-TIKKI & BARLOW & THE ALIEN (ALSO AS				
ALL THE KINDS OF YES)	TIPTREE, JAMES JR.	NV	NDM	72 02
OUT FROM GANYMEDE	MALZBERG, BARRY N.	SS	NDM	72 02
NO. 2 PLAIN TANK AUXILIARY FILL STRUCTURAL LIMIT 17,605 LBS.				
FUEL-PWA SPEC. 522 REVISED	BRYANT, EDWARD	SS	NDM	72 02
EUREMA'S DAM	LAFFERTY, R. A.	SS	NDM	72 02
KING HARVEST	DOZOIS, GARDNER R.	NV	NDM	72 02
TAKE A MATCH	ASIMOV, ISAAC	SS	NDM	72 02
$F(X)=(11/15/67) \ X=HER, \ F(X) \neq 0$				
WHITE SUMMER IN MEMPHIS	EFFINGER, GEO. ALEC	SS	NDM	72 02
LAZARUS II	EKLUND, GORDON	NV	NDM	72 02
	DEFORD, MIRIAM ALLEN	SS	NDM	72 02
MEN INSIDE, THE (ALSO AS THE MAN IN THE POCKET)				
	MALZBERG, BARRY N.	NV	NDM	72 02

NEW DIMENSIONS 3   SILVERBERG, ROBERT   OA SIG 74 02

INTRODUCTION	SILVERBERG, ROBERT	IN		
ONES WHO WALK AWAY FROM OMELAS, THE				
	LE GUIN, URSULA K.	SS	NDM	73 03
DOWN THERE	KNIGHT, DAMON	SS	NDM	73 03
HOW SHALL WE CONQUER?	MACFARLANE, WALLACE	SS	NDM	73 03
THEY LIVE ON LEVELS	CARR, TERRY	SS	NDM	73 03
GIRL WHO WAS PLUGGED IN, THE	TIPTREE, JAMES JR.	NV	NDM	73 03
DAYS OF GRASS, DAYS OF STRAW	LAFFERTY, R. A.	SS	NDM	73 03
NOTES LEADING DOWN TO THE CONQUEST (ALSO AS A RECKONING)				
	MALZBERG, BARRY N.	SS	NDM	73 03
AT THE BRAN FOUNDRY	EFFINGER, GEO. ALEC	SS	NDM	73 03
TELL ME ALL ABOUT YOURSELF	BUSBY, F. M.	SS	NDM	73 03
THREE COMEDIANS	EKLUND, GORDON	NV	NDM	73 03
LAST DAY OF JULY, THE	DOZOIS, GARDNER R.	NV	NDM	73 03

NEW DIMENSIONS 4   SILVERBERG, ROBERT   OA SIG 74 10

AFTER THE DREAMTIME	LUPOFF, RICHARD A.	NV	NDM	74 04
BIBLE AFTER THE APOCALYPSE, THE				
	JANIFER, LAURENCE M.	SS	NDM	74 04
OUTER CONCENTRIC	GOTSCHALK, FELIX C.	SS	NDM	74 04

```
NEW DIMENSIONS 4                                                      NEW WORLDS EIGH

  EXAMINATION, THE           GOTSCHALK, FELIX C.  SS    NDM 74 04
  COLORS OF FEAR, THE        CARR, TERRY          SS    NDM 74 04
  ARIEL                      ELWOOD, ROGER        SS    NDM 74 04
  STATE OF THE ART           MALZBERG, BARRY N.   SS    NDM 74 04
  AMONG THE METAL-AND-PEOPLE PEOPLE
                             BUNCH, DAVID R.      SS    NDM 74 04
  ANIMAL FAIR                LAFFERTY, R. A.      NV    NDM 74 04
  STRANGERS                  DOZOIS, GARDNER R.   NA    NDM 74 04

NEW DIMENSIONS 5             SILVERBERG, ROBERT   OA H HPR 75
  FIND THE LADY              FISK, NICHOLAS       SS    NDM 75 05
  SOLFY DRINK, A SAFFEL FRAGRANCE, A
                             GILBERT, DOROTHY     SS    NDM 75 05
  SCARAB IN THE CITY OF TIME, A
                             RANDALL, MARTA       SS    NDM 75 05
  THEODORA AND THEODORA      THURSTON, ROBERT     SS    NDM 75 05
  DAY IN THE SOUTH QUAD, A   GOTSCHALK, FELIX C.  SS    NDM 75 05
  ROGUE TOMATO               BISHOP, MICHAEL      SS    NDM 75 05
  MOTHERS' MARCH ON ECSTACY, THE
                             EFFINGER, GEO. ALEC  SS    NDM 75 05
  LOCAL ALLOSAURUS, THE      UTLEY, STEVEN        PM    NDM 75 05
  ACHIEVEMENTS               WISE, DAVID          SS    NDM 75 05
  DYBBUK DOLLS, THE          DANN, JACK M.        SS    NDM 75 05
  MIRROR AT SUNSET, THE      LAMONT, GIL          SS    NDM 75 05
  REPORT TO HEADQUARTERS     MALZBERG, BARRY N.   SS    NDM 75 05
  MUSEUM PIECE               MENDELSON, DREW      SS    NDM 75 05
  WHITE CREATURES            BENFORD, GREGORY     SS    NDM 75 05
  CONTRIBUTORS TO PLENUM FOUR, THE
                             BISHOP, MICHAEL      SS    NDM 75 05
  SAIL THE TIDE OF MOURNING  LUPOFF, RICHARD A.   SS    NDM 75 05

NEW DIMENSIONS 6             SILVERBERG, ROBERT   OA H HPR 76
  TARGET: BERLIN;            EFFINGER, GEO. ALEC  NV    NDM 76 06
  PSYCHOLOGIST WHO WOULDN'T DO AWFUL THINGS TO RATS, THE
                             TIPTREE, JAMES JR.   NV    NDM 76 06
  IS YOUR CHILD USING DRUGS? POLLACK, RACHEL      SS    NDM 76 06
  CHARISMA LEAK              GOTSCHALK, FELIX C.  NV    NDM 76 06
  SECRET RIDER               RANDALL, MARTA       NV    NDM 76 06
  ON THE AIR                 MALZBERG, BARRY N.   SS    NDM 76 06
  DINOSAURS                  REAMY, TOM           NV    NDM 76 06
  MASK                       JEFFERS, DONNAN CALL SS    NDM 76 06
  WATER                      MARSHAK, DAVID       NV    NDM 76 06
  OSIRIS ON CRUTCHES         FARMER, PHILIP JOSE
                       AND TINCROWDER, LEO Q.  SS C NDM 76 06
  CHASE OUR BLUES AWAY       EFFINGER, GEO. ALEC  SS    NDM 76 06
  ALTERNATES, THE            GIRARD, JAMES P.     NV    NDM 76 06

NEW DIMENSIONS 7             SILVERBERG, ROBERT   OA H HPR 77
  INTRODUCTION               SILVERBERG, ROBERT   IN
  RETRO MAN, THE             EKLUND, GORDON       NV    NDM 77 07
  STATE OF THE ART ON ALYSSUM, THE
                             RANDALL, MARTA       SS    NDM 77 07
  BLACK AS THE PIT, FROM POLE TO POLE
                             UTLEY, STEVEN
                       AND WALDROP, HOWARD     NV C NDM 77 07
  YOU ARE HERE               EISENSTEIN, PHYLLIS
                       AND EISENSTEIN, ALEX    NV C NDM 77 07
  TWINKLE, TWINKLE, LITTLE BAT LAWRENCE, J. A.   SS    NDM 77 07
  ALMOST EMPTY ROOMS, THE    SHIRLEY, JOHN        NV    NDM 77 07
  IN THE STOCKS              MALZBERG, BARRY N.   SS    NDM 77 07
  HOME SWEET GERIATRIC DOME  GOTSCHALK, FELIX C.  SS    NDM 77 07
  KNOWING HER                BENFORD, GREGORY     SS    NDM 77 07
  BLOOD'S HORIZON, THE       ATTANASIO, A. A.     NV    NDM 77 07
  SEVERAL WAYS, AND THE SUN  PLANCHAT, HENRY-LUC  NV    NDM 77 07
  PRINCESS IN THE TOWER 250,000 MILES HIGH, THE
                             LEIBER, FRITZ        SS    NDM 77 07

NEW DREAMS THIS MORNING      BLISH, JAMES         AN    BAL 66 10
  PREFACE                    BLISH, JAMES         IN
  DREAMING IS A PRIVATE THING ASIMOV, ISAAC      SS    FSF 55 12
  WORK OF ART, A (ART-WORK)  BLISH, JAMES         SS    SFS 56 07
  DARK NIGHT OF THE SOUL, THE (GENIUS HEAP)
                             BLISH, JAMES         SS    GAL 56 08
  PORTRAIT OF THE ARTIST     HARRISON, HARRY      SS    FSF 64 11
  COUNTRY OF THE KIND, THE   KNIGHT, DAMON        SS    FSF 56 02
  WITH THESE HANDS           KORNBLUTH, C. M.     NV    GAL 51 12
  MUSIC MASTER OF BABYLON, THE PANGBORN, EDGAR    NV    GAL 54 11
  MAN OF TALENT, A (MAN WITH TALENT)
                             SILVERBERG, ROBERT   NV    FUT 56 WI

NEW GODS LEAD, THE           WRIGHT, S. FOWLER   AC H JAR 32
  ALSO IN "THE THRONE OF SATURN"
  JUSTICE                    WRIGHT, S. FOWLER    SS
  THIS NIGHT                 WRIGHT, S. FOWLER    SS
  BRAIN                      WRIGHT, S. FOWLER    SS          32
  APPEAL                     WRIGHT, S. FOWLER    SS
  PROOF                      WRIGHT, S. FOWLER    SS
  P.N. 40                    WRIGHT, S. FOWLER    SS
  AUTOMATA                   WRIGHT, S. FOWLER    NV    WRT 29 09
  RAT, THE                   WRIGHT, S. FOWLER    SS    WRT 29 03
  RULE, THE                  WRIGHT, S. FOWLER    SS
  CHOICE                     WRIGHT, S. FOWLER    SS

NEW IMPROVED SUN, THE        DISCH, THOMAS M.     AN H HPR 75
  INTRODUCTION: BUCK ROGERS IN THE NEW JERUSALEM
                             DISCH, THOMAS M.     IN
  HEAVENS BELOW: FIFTEEN UTOPIAS
                             SLADEK, JOHN T.      SS    NEW 75 AN
  REPAIRING THE OFFICE       NAYLOR, CHARLES      NV    NEW 75 AN
  WHAT YOU GET FOR YOUR DOLLAR (FROM "THE SHAPE OF FURTHER
    THINGS")                 ALDISS, BRIAN W.     EX          75
  PEOPLE OF PRASHAD, THE     KEILTY, JAMES        NV    QRK 71 02
  FEW THINGS I KNOW ABOUT WHILEAWAY, A (FROM "THE FEMALE MAN")
                             RUSS, JOANNA         EX    BAN 75
  DRUMBLE                    NYE, CASSANDRA       SS    NEW 75 AN

  CLEAR DAY IN THE MOTOR CITY, A
                             ARNASON, ELEANOR     SS    NWQ 73 0
  SETTLING THE WORLD         HARRISON, M. JOHN    NV    NEW 75 A
  INSTEAD OF THE CROSS, THE LOLLIPOP (FROM "WALDEN 2")
                             SKINNER, B. F.       EX          48
  I ALWAYS DO WHAT TEDDY SAYS HARRISON, HARRY     SS    EQM 65 0
  PYRAMIDS FOR MINNESOTA: A SERIOUS PROPOSAL
                             DISCH, THOMAS M.     FA    HRP 74 0
  ZEN ARCHER, THE            GREENBLATT, JONATHAN SS   NEW 75 A
  HERO AS WERWOLF, THE       WOLFE, GENE          SS    NEW 75 A
  CHANGE, THE (FROM "IN THE DAYS OF THE COMET")
                             WELLS, H. G.         EX    CMP 05 1

NEW MIND, THE                ELWOOD, ROGER        OA H MAC 73
  SEE "FRONTIERS 2; THE NEW MIND"

NEW S.F., THE                JONES, LANGDON       OA H HUT 69
  PREFACE                    MOORCOCK, MICHAEL    IN
  FOURTEEN STATIONS ON THE NORTHERN LINE
                             GORDON, GILES        SS
  PEKING JUNCTION, THE       MOORCOCK, MICHAEL    SS
  FAST CAR WASH              MACBETH, GEORGE      SS
  ANXIETY IN THE EYES OF THE CRICKET
                             SALLIS, JAMES        SS
  NEW SCIENCE FICTION, THE   BALLARD, J. G.
                       AND MACBETH, GEORGE     AR C
  SO FAR FROM PRAGUE         ALDISS, BRIAN W.     SS
  DIRECTION                  PLATT, CHARLES       SS
  POSTATOMIC                 BUTTERWORTH, MICHAEL SS
  FOR THOMAS TOMPION         MOORCOCK, MICHAEL    SS
  SCIENCE FICTION STORY FOR JONI MITCHELL, A
                             JAKUBOWSKI, MAXIM    NV
  COMMUNICANTS, THE          SLADEK, JOHN T.      NA
  SEEKING A SUITABLE DONOR   THOMAS, D. M.        SS
  HOLLAND OF THE MIND, THE   ZOLINE, PAMELA A.    NV
  QUINCUNX                   DISCH, THOMAS M.     SS

NEW STORIES FROM THE TWILIGHT ZONE
                             SERLING, ROD         OC    BAN 62 05
  WHOLE TRUTH, THE           SERLING, ROD         SA
  SHELTER, THE               SERLING, ROD         SA
  SHOWDOWN WITH RANCE MCGREW SERLING, ROD         SA
  NIGHT OF THE MEEK          SERLING, ROD         SA
  MIDNIGHT SUN, THE          SERLING, ROD         SA
  RIP VAN WINKLE CAPER, THE  SERLING, ROD         SA

NEW TALES OF SPACE AND TIME  HEALY, RAYMOND J.    OA H HLT 51 11
  INTRODUCTION               HEALY, RAYMOND J.    IN
  HERE THERE BE TYGERS       BRADBURY, RAY        SS    NTS 51
  IN A GOOD CAUSE-           ASIMOV, ISAAC        NV    NTS 51
  TOLLIVER'S TRAVELS         FENTON, FRANK
                       AND PETRACCA, JOSEPH    NV C NTS 51
  BETTYANN                   NEVILLE, KRIS        NV    NTS 51
  LITTLE ANTON               BRETNOR, REGINALD    NV    NTS 51
  STATUS QUONDAM             MILLER, P. SCHUYLER  NV    NTS 51
  B + M - PLANET 4           HEARD, GERALD        NV    NTS 51
  YOU CAN'T SAY THAT         CARTMILL, CLEVE      NV    NTS 51
  FULFILLMENT                VAN VOGT, A. E.      NV    NTS 51
  QUEST FOR SAINT AQUIN, THE BOUCHER, ANTHONY     SS    NTS 51

NEW TOMORROWS, THE           SPINRAD, NORMAN      AN    BEL 71
  NEW TOMORROWS, THE         SPINRAD, NORMAN      IN
  PLEASURE GARDEN OF FELIPE SAGITTARIUS, THE
                             MOORCOCK, MICHAEL    SS    NWS 65 09
  DRIFTGLASS                 DELANY, SAMUEL R.    NV    IFS 67 06
  SENDING THE VERY BEST      BRYANT, EDWARD       SS    NWS 70 01
  GOING DOWN SMOOTH          SILVERBERG, ROBERT   SS    GAL 68 08
  GARDEN OF DELIGHTS, THE    JONES, LANGDON       NV    NWS 69 07
  SURFACE IF YOU CAN         CHAMPAGNE, TERRY     SS    NWS 69 07
  MASKS                      KNIGHT, DAMON        SS    PBY 68 07
  PENNIES, OFF A DEAD MAN'S EYES
                             ELLISON, HARLAN      SS    GAL 69 11
  198-, A TALE OF "TOMORROW" SLADEK, JOHN T.      SS    NWS 70 01
  FLIGHT USELESS, INEXORABLE THE PURSUIT
                             DISCH, THOMAS M.     SS
  LAST HURRAH OF THE GOLDEN HORDE, THE
                             SPINRAD, NORMAN      SS    NWS 69 07
  DOWN THE UP ESCALATION     ALDISS, BRIAN W.     SS    LOM 67
  CIRCULARIZATION OF CONDENSED CONVENTIONAL STRAIGHT-LINE
    WORD-IMAGE STRUCTURES    BUTTERWORTH, MICHAEL SS   NWS 69 07
  DEFINITION, THE            MARSDEN, BOB         SS    NWS 68 07
  JUNGLE ROT KID ON THE NOD, THE
                             FARMER, PHILIP JOSE  SS    NWS 70 04

NEW VOICES IN SCIENCE FICTION
                             MARTIN, GEORGE R. R. OA H MAC 77
  INTRODUCTION               BOVA, BEN            IN
  FAMILY MONKEY, THE         TUTTLE, LISA         SS
  KINGMAKERS                 THURSTON, ROBERT     SS
  STONE CITY, THE            MARTIN, GEORGE R. R. SS
  TO CEREMARK                BERMAN, RUTH         SS
  MOM'S DIFFERENTIALS        EFFINGER, GEO. ALEC  SS
  SILENT LEGES               POURNELLE, JERRY     SS
  JOHN W. CAMPBELL, JR. AWARDS 1973 - 1975, THE
                             MISC. MATERIAL       MS

NEW WORLDS EIGHT             BAILEY, HILARY       OA    SPH 75 03
  INTRODUCTION               BAILEY, HILARY       IN
  RUNNING DOWN               HARRISON, M. JOHN    NV    NWB 75 08
  WHITE STARS                MOORCOCK, MICHAEL    NV    NWB 75 08
  BEES OF KNOWLEDGE, THE     BAYLEY, BARRINGTON J NV   NWB 75 08
  BUILDING BLOCKS            JOBLING, PETER       NV    NWB 75 08
  MAL DEAN                   MOORCOCK, MICHAEL    AR    NWB 75 08
  SLOW DRAG                  DEAN, MAL            SS    NWB 75 08
  WEATHER CLOCK              HOUSTON, LIBBY       PM    NWB 75 08
  GHOST BREAD                HOUSTON, LIBBY       PM    NWB 75 08
```

NEW WORLDS EIGHT

QUEEN LIES DYING, THE   HOUSTON, LIBBY   PM   NWB 75 08
CONVERSATIONS AT MA MAIA METRON
                               MEADLEY, ROBERT   SS   NWB 75 08
LOVE AT LOST SIGHT   MEADLEY, ROBERT   SS   NWB 75 08
BROKEN FIELD, THE   FRANCIS, NIGEL   SS   NWB 75 08
BLACK HOLE   FRANCIS, NIGEL   SS   NWB 75 08
I SAY BEGONE! APOTROPAIC NARCOSIS, I'M GOING TO READ THE
  DAMNED THING, HA HA   CLUTE, JOHN   BR   NWB 75 08
COMING TO LIFE   HARRISON, M. JOHN   MS   NWB 75 08

NEW WORLDS FOR OLD   DERLETH, AUGUST   AN   FSP 63
9 STORIES FROM "WORLDS OF TOMORROW"
SMILE, THE   BRADBURY, RAY   SS   FAN 52 SU
FIRES WITHIN, THE   CLARKE, ARTHUR C.   SS   FSB 47 08
GENTLEMAN IS AN EPWA, THE   JACOBI, CARL   NV   NEW 53 AN
ENCHANTED FOREST, THE   LEIBER, FRITZ   SS   ASF 50 10
GREAT COLD, THE   LONG, FRANK BELKNAP   SS   ASF 35 02
FROM BEYOND   LOVECRAFT, H. P.   SS   WRT 38 02
LINE TO TOMORROW   PADGETT, LEWIS   SS   ASF 45 11
BUSINESS, AS USUAL, THE   REYNOLDS, MACK   SS   FSF 52 06
MARTIAN AND THE MORON, THE   STURGEON, THEODORE   NV   WRT 49 03

NEW WORLDS NINE   BAILEY, HILARY   OA   COR 75 11
MINISTRY OF CHILDREN, THE   ROBERTS, KEITH   NV   NWB 75 09
ANCIENT SHADOWS   MOORCOCK, MICHAEL   NV   NWB 75 09
DADDY'S GIRL   RUSS, JOANNA   SS   NWB 75 09
HAMMER OF EVIL, THE   SLADEK, JOHN T.   SS   NWB 75 09
PATAGONIA'S DELICIOUS FILLING STATION
                               ALDISS, BRIAN W.   GR   NWB 75 09
CROWDED CITIES OF PATAGONIA, THE
                               ALDISS, BRIAN W.   PL   NWB 75 09
DELICIOUS CIRCLE, A   ALDISS, BRIAN W.   PL   NWB 75 09
DISHONESTIES OF A LONELY FILLING STATION
                               ALDISS, BRIAN W.   PL   NWB 75 09
MAESTRO   GORDON, GILES   SS   NWB 75 09
ILLUSIONIST, THE   GORDON, GILES   SS   NWB 75 09
NARRATIVE OF MASKS   PARTINGTON, CHARLES   SS   NWB 75 09
JOURNAL OF BODLEY CLIVE, THE   PARIS, MATTHEW   SS   NWB 75 09

NEW WORLDS NO. 5   MOORCOCK & PLATT   OA L EQN 73
INTRODUCTION   PLATT, CHARLES   IN
COMING FROM BEHIND   HARRISON, M. JOHN   SS   NWQ 73 05
OFFICE MEETING, AN   GORDON, GILES   SS   NWQ 73 05
COUNT D'UNADIX   OBTULOWICZ, MAREK   SS   NWQ 73 05
BEHIND THE WALLS   TOKUNAGA, LAURA   SS   NWQ 73 05
AMONG OTHER THINGS   MEADLEY, ROBERT   SS   NWQ 73 05
MY EIGHT DAYS IN THE AUTOMOTIVE INDUSTRY
                               ARNOLD, CHARLES   SS   NWQ 73 05
COLDNESS, THE   PLATT, CHARLES   SS   NWQ 73 05
STORY OF THREE CITIES, THE   CROSS, RONALD A.   SS   NWQ 73 05
TUBS OF SLAW   POLLACK, RACHEL   SS   NWQ 73 05
TULPA   DANN, JACK M.   SS   NWQ 73 05
OVERLOAD, AN   BAYLEY, BARRINGTON J   SS   NWQ 73 05
SCHOLIA, SEASONED WITH CRABS, BLISH IS
                               CLUTE, JOHN   AR   NWQ 73 05
NIGHT-MARRIAGE   THOMAS, D. M.   PM   NWQ 73 05
ACCEPTING FOR WINKELMEYER   JACOBS, HARVEY   SS   NWQ 73 05
BEAUTIFUL ONE, THE   ROBERTS, KEITH   NV   NWQ 73 05
GORGIAS   CARLSSON, PEDER   SS   NWQ 73 05
BELLA GOES TO THE DARK TOWER   BAILEY, HILARY   SS   NWQ 73 05
UNPLEASANT END, AN   EDELSTEIN, SCOTT   SS   NWQ 73 05
CLEAR DAY IN THE MOTOR CITY, A
                               ARNASON, ELEANOR   SS   NWQ 73 05
THERE IS NO MORE AWAY   CLINE, STEVE   SS   NWQ 73 05
ORIGINS OF THE UNIVERSE   CRAVENS, GWYNETH   SS   NWQ 73 05
STANCE OF SPLENDOUR   ZEBROWSKI, GEORGE   SS   NWQ 73 05
THY BLOOD LIKE MILK   WATSON, IAN   NV   NWQ 73 05
AURORA IN ZENITH   ABBOTT, GORDON   SS   NWQ 73 05
DISINTEGRATION   BUTTERWORTH, MICHAEL   SS   NWQ 73 05
FILLING US UP   HARRISON, M. JOHN   SS   NWQ 73 05
AFTERWORD   MOORCOCK, MICHAEL   MS   NWQ 73 05

NEW WORLDS NO. 6   PLATT & BAILEY   OA L EQN 74
INTRODUCTION   PLATT, CHARLES   IN
PALE ROSES   MOORCOCK, MICHAEL   NV   NWQ 74 06
WIND-DREAM   KING, MAC   PM   NWQ 74 06
MY WRECK   KING, MAC   PM   NWQ 74 06
UNTITLED   KING, MAC   PM   NWQ 74 06
FAMILY, THE   KING, MAC   PM   NWQ 74 06
RAISE   KING, MAC   PM   NWQ 74 06
MALADJUSTMENT   BAYLEY, BARRINGTON J   SS   NWQ 74 06
BLACK ROSE AND WHITE ROSE   POLLACK, RACHEL   SS   NWQ 74 06
KINDLY ONES, THE   SLADEK, JOHN T.   SS   NWQ 74 06
RETURN OF THE MANDARIN, THE   GELLMAN, RICK   SS   NWQ 74 06
G. I. SPARROW   GIANNATTASIO, GERARD   SS   NWQ 74 06
MODEST PROPOSAL, A   MARTENSSON, BERTIL   SS   NWQ 74 06
JEWEL THIEF, THE   CROSS, RONALD A.   SS   NWQ 74 06
WARLORD OF SATURN'S MOONS, THE
                               ARNASON, ELEANOR   SS   NWQ 74 06
SECRET OF HOLMAN HUNT AND THE CRUDE DEATH RATE, THE
                               ALDISS, BRIAN W.   FA   NWS 70 01
MISS SUBWAYS   CRAVENS, GWYNETH   SS   NWQ 74 06
LAKEWOOD CEMETERY   BERMAN, RUTH   SS   NWQ 74 06
GHOSTS OF LUNA, THE   WATSON, IAN   SS   NWQ 74 06
WOLF THAT FOLLOWS, THE   HARRISON, M. JOHN   NV   NWQ 74 06
RED SKY AT NIGHT   CHARLOTTE, JEAN   SS   NWQ 74 06
BREAK   BOSTON, BRUCE   SS   NWQ 74 06
LIBERATION   SPALTEN, RONA   SS   NWQ 74 06
ONCE MORE, THE DREAM   ATTANASIO, A. A.   SS   NWQ 74 06
BIRDS OF PREY   TAFOYA, ALFONSO   PM   NWQ 74 06
MY MISTRESS   TAFOYA, ALFONSO   PM   NWQ 74 06
PASTORAL, A   TAFOYA, ALFONSO   PM   NWQ 74 06
INSECT MEN OF BOSTON   SALLIS, JAMES   SS   NWQ 74 06
THALIDOMIDE KID, THE   GILCHRIST, JEREMY   SS   NWQ 74 06
MAN WHO MADE A BABY, THE   JACOBS, HARVEY   SS   NWQ 74 06

NEW WORLDS QUARTERLY NO. 2

BIRDSEED FOR OUR FEATHERED FANS
                               CLUTE, JOHN   BR   NWQ 74 06
ABSORBING THE MIRACULOUS   HARRISON, M. JOHN   BR   NWQ 74 06
OBITUARIES: MAL DEAN, MAC KING
                               MISC. MATERIAL   MS
AUTHORS, THE   MISC. MATERIAL   MS

NEW WORLDS OF FANTASY   CARR, TERRY   AN   ACE 67
IN ENGLAND AS "STEP OUTSIDE YOUR MIND"
INTRODUCTION   CARR, TERRY   IN
DIVINE MADNESS   ZELAZNY, ROGER   SS   MOH 66 SU
BREAK THE DOOR OF HELL   BRUNNER, JOHN   NV   IMP 66 04
IMMORTAL, THE   BORGES, JORGE LUIS   SS   62
NARROW VALLEY   LAFFERTY, R. A.   SS   FSF 66 09
COMET WINE   RUSSELL, RAY   NV   PBY 67 03
OTHER, THE   MACLEAN, KATHERINE   SS   NWS 66 07
RED HEART AND BLUE ROSES, A   CLINGERMAN, MILDRED   SS   NEW 61 AC
STANLEY TOOTHBRUSH (AS CARL BRANDON)
                               CARR, TERRY   SS   FSF 62 07
SQUIRREL CAGE, THE   DISCH, THOMAS M.   SS   NWS 66 10
COME LADY DEATH   BEAGLE, PETER S.   SS   ATL 63 09
NACKLES   CLARK, CURT   SS   FSF 64 01
LOST LEONARDO, THE   BALLARD, J. G.   SS   FSF 64 03
TIMOTHY   ROBERTS, KEITH   SS   IMP 66 09
BASILISK   DAVIDSON, AVRAM   NV   NEW 67 AN
EVIL EYE, THE   GILLESPIE, ALFRED   SS   SEP 66 01

NEW WORLDS OF FANTASY NO. 2   CARR, TERRY   AN   ACE 70
INTRODUCTION   CARR, TERRY   IN
PETRIFIED WORLD, THE   SHECKLEY, ROBERT   SS   IFS 68 02
SCARLET LADY, THE   ROBERTS, KEITH   NV   IMP 66 08
THEY LOVED ME IN UTICA   DAVIDSON, AVRAM   SS   NEW 70 AN
LIBRARY OF BABEL, THE   BORGES, JORGE LUIS   SS   62
SHIP OF DISASTER, THE   BAYLEY, BARRINGTON J   SS   NWS 65 06
WINDOW DRESSING   RUSS, JOANNA   SS   NEW 70 AN
BY THE FALLS   HARRISON, HARRY   SS   IFS 70 01
NIGHT OF THE NICKEL BEER, THE
                               NEVILLE, KRIS   SS   ESC 67
QUIET KIND OF MADNESS, A   REDD, DAVID   NV   FSF 68 05
MUSEUM PIECE, A   ZELAZNY, ROGER   SS   FAN 63 06
OLD MAN OF THE MOUNTAINS, THE
                               CARR, TERRY   SS   FSF 63 04
EN PASSANT   SCHWEITZER, BRITT   SS   HBK 60 12
BACKWARD, TURN BACKWARD   SHIRAS, WILMAR H.   NV   NEW 70 AN
HIS OWN KIND   DISCH, THOMAS M.   SS   NEW 70 AN
PERCHANCE TO DREAM   MACLEAN, KATHERINE   SS   NEW 70 AN
LAZARUS   ANDREYEV, LEONID   SS   WRT 27 03
UGLY SEA, THE   LAFFERTY, R. A.   SS   LRV 60 FL
MOVIE PEOPLE, THE   BLOCH, ROBERT   SS   FSF 69 10

NEW WORLDS OF FANTASY NO. 3   CARR, TERRY   AN   ACE 71
INTRODUCTION   CARR, TERRY   IN
FARRELL AND LILA THE WEREWOLF
                               BEAGLE, PETER S.   SS   GUA 69
ADAM HAD THREE BROTHERS   LAFFERTY, R. A.   SS   NMQ 69
BIG SAM   DAVIDSON, AVRAM   SS   ANA 70
LONGTOOTH   PANGBORN, EDGAR   NV   FSF 70 01
INNER CIRCLES, THE (ALSO AS THE WINTER FLIES)
                               LEIBER, FRITZ   SS   FSF 67 10
VON GOOM'S GAMBIT   CONTOSKI, VICTOR   SS   FSF 66 12
THROUGH A GLASS- DARKLY   HENDERSON, ZENNA   NV   FSF 70 10
STAINLESS STEEL LEECH, THE   ZELAZNY, ROGER   SS   AMZ 63 04
SLEEPING BEAUTY   CARR, TERRY   SS   FSF 67 05
PLOT IS THE THING, THE   BLOCH, ROBERT   SS   FSF 66 07
FUNES THE MEMORIOUS   BORGES, JORGE LUIS   SS   62
SAY GOODBYE TO THE WIND   BALLARD, J. G.   SS   FAN 70 08
MESSAGE FROM CHARITY, A   LEE, WILLIAM M.   SS   FSF 67 11

NEW WORLDS QUARTERLY NO. 1   MOORCOCK, MICHAEL   OA   BKM 71 09
INTRODUCTION   MOORCOCK, MICHAEL   IN
ANGOULEME   DISCH, THOMAS M.   SS   NWQ 71 01
JOURNEY ACROSS A CRATER   BALLARD, J. G.   SS   NWQ 70 01
LAMIA AND LORD CROMIS, THE   HARRISON, M. JOHN   NV   NWQ 71 01
DAY WE EMBARKED FOR CYTHERA, THE
                               ALDISS, BRIAN W.   SS   NWQ 71 01
PEMBERLY'S START-AFRESH CALLIOPE OR, THE NEW PROTEUS
                               SLADEK, JOHN T.   SS   NWQ 71 01
GOD HOUSE, THE   ROBERTS, KEITH   NV   NWQ 71 01
PRISONERS OF PARADISE   REDD, DAVID   SS   NWS 66 10
SHORT, HAPPY WIFE OF MANSARD ELIOT, THE
                               SLADEK, JOHN T.   SS   NWQ 71 01
PLACE AND TIME TO DIE, A   BALLARD, J. G.   SS   NWS 69 10
EXIT FROM CITY 5   BAYLEY, BARRINGTON J   NV   NWQ 71 01
ESSAY: A LITERATURE OF COMFORT
                               HARRISON, M. JOHN   BR   NWQ 71 01
AUTHORS, THE   MISC. MATERIAL   MS

NEW WORLDS QUARTERLY NO. 2   MOORCOCK, MICHAEL   OA   BKM 71 12
KEEPING PERSPECTIVE   MOORCOCK, MICHAEL   MS
MONKEY AND PRU AND SAL   ROBERTS, KEITH   SS   NWQ 71 02
NO DIRECTION HOME   SPINRAD, NORMAN   SS   NWQ 71 02
MEEK, THE   WOODROW, WILLIAM   SS   NWQ 71 02
CAUSEWAY, THE   HARRISON, M. JOHN   SS   NWQ 71 02
VISIONS OF HELL   BALLARD, J. G.   BR   NWQ 66 03
FOUR-COLOR PROBLEM   BAYLEY, BARRINGTON J   NV   NWQ 71 02
FIFTH PERSON SINGULAR   TATE, PETER   SS   NWS 66 05
LISTEN, LOVE   ZEBROWSKI, GEORGE
                               AND DANN, JACK M.   SS C NWQ 71 02
FEATHERS FROM THE WINGS OF AN ANGEL
                               DISCH, THOMAS M.   SS   NWS 71 03
MONITOR FOUND IN ORBIT   CONEY, MICHAEL G.   SS   NWQ 71 02
PANDORA'S BUST   POLLACK, RICHARD A.   SS   NWQ 71 02
KEY OF THE DOOR, THE   SELLINGS, ARTHUR   SS   NWS 67 03
BY TENNYSON OUT OF DISNEY   HARRISON, M. JOHN   SS   NWQ 71 02
AUTHORS, THE   MISC. MATERIAL   MS

NEW WORLDS QUARTERLY NO. 3   NEW WRITINGS IN SF. 11

```
NEW WORLDS QUARTERLY NO. 3    MOORCOCK, MICHAEL        OA    BKM 72 03
  INTRODUCTION                MOORCOCK, MICHAEL        IN
  MACHINE IN SHAFT TEN, THE   CHURCHILL, JOYCE        SS    NWQ 72 03
  I LOSE MEDEA                BEVAN, ALISTAIR         SS    NWQ 72 03
  AS FOR OUR FATAL CONTINUITY...
                              ALDISS, BRIAN W.        SS    NWQ 72 03
  JULIO 204                   SARGENT, PAMELA         SS    NWQ 72 03
  WONDERFUL WORLD OF GRISWALD TRACTORS, THE
                              DISCH, THOMAS M.        SS    NWQ 72 03
  AND DUG THE DOG A TOMB      JAMES, LAURENCE         SS    NWQ 72 03
  GRAIN KINGS, THE            ROBERTS, KEITH          NV    NWQ 72 03
  WINDOWS                     DANN, JACK M.           SS    NWQ 72 03
  CLEANSING OF THE SYSTEM, A  PLATT, CHARLES          SS    NWQ 72 03
  PURLOINED BUTTER, THE       SLADEK, JOHN T.         SS    NWQ 72 03
  HEAD AND THE HAND, THE      PRIEST, CHRISTOPHER     SS    NWQ 72 03
  HISTORY MACHINE, THE        ZEBROWSKI, GEORGE       SS    NWQ 72 03
  CHRONICLE OF BLACKTON, A    BAILEY, HILARY          SS    NWQ 72 03
  BLACK GLAK, THE             HARRISON, M. JOHN       AR    NWQ 72 03
  AUTHORS, THE                MISC. MATERIAL          MS

NEW WORLDS QUARTERLY NO. 4    MOORCOCK, MICHAEL        OA    BKM 72 06
  PROBLEM OF SYMPATHY, THE    HARRISON, M. JOHN       BR    NWQ 72 04
  EXPLORATION OF SPACE, THE   BAYLEY, BARRINGTON J    SS    NWQ 72 04
  SIMON                       WOODROW, WILLIAM        SS    NWQ 72 04
  FIRST OF TWO RAPED PROSPECTS, THE
                              OBTULOWICZ, MAREK       SS    NWQ 72 04
  334                         DISCH, THOMAS M.        NA    NWQ 72 04
  MAN IN TRANSIT              AUMBRY, ALAN            SS    NWQ 72 04
  LOCKED ROOM, THE            SLADEK, JOHN T.         SS    NWQ 72 04
  WEIHNACHTABEND              ROBERTS, KEITH          NV    NWQ 72 04
  ATTACK-ESCAPE, AN INTERVIEW WITH ALFRED BESTER
                              PLATT, CHARLES          AR    NWQ 72 04
  AUTHORS, THE                MISC. MATERIAL          MS

NEW WORLDS QUARTERLY NO. 5    MOORCOCK, MICHAEL        OA    SPH 73
  INTRODUCTION                MOORCOCK, MICHAEL        IN
  CRACK, THE                  TENNANT, EMMA           NV    NWB 73 05
  SOME ROOMS                  KESSLER, MERLE          SS    NWB 73 05
  NAME (PLEASE PRINT):        SLADEK, JOHN T.         SS    NWB 73 05
  SONORAN POEMS               THOMAS, D. M.           SS    NWB 73 05
  MAMMOTH HUNTERS, THE        REDD, DAVID             SS    NWB 73 05
  FUTURE ON A CHIPPED PLATE, THE
                              ALDISS, BRIAN W.        NV    NWB 73 05
  CAKE CHRONICLE, THE         AHERN, MICHAEL          SS    NWB 73 05
  ME AND MY ANTRONOSCOPE      BAYLEY, BARRINGTON J    NV    NWB 73 05
  FAMILY LITERATURE           PLATT, CHARLES          SS    NWB 73 05
  THERE ARE NO BANISTERS      DANN, JACK M.           SS    NWB 73 05
  WALKING BACKWARDS           LOPATE, PHILLIP         SS    NWB 73 05
  DISINHERITING PARTY, THE    CLUTE, JOHN             NV    NWB 73 05
  BILL GETS HEP TO GOD|       SLADEK, JOHN T.         SS    NWB 73 05
  SMACK RUN                   BERGSTRESSER, MARTA     SS    NWB 73 05
  ODE TO A TIME FLOWER        CALVERT, ROBERT         PM    NWB 73 05
  ONLY MAN ON EARTH, THE      JAMES, LAURENCE         SS    NWB 73 05
  TO THE STARS AND BEYOND ON THE FABULOUS ANTI-SYNTAX DRIVE
                              HARRISON, M. JOHN       SS    NWB 73 05
  MOTIVATION CHART            PLATT, CHARLES          SS    NWB 73 05
  TRUSTIE TREE, THE           ROBERTS, KEITH          SS    NWB 73 05
  ASSASSINATION OF THE MAYOR, THE
                              DISCH, THOMAS M.        SS    NWB 73 05
  FLATLAND                    SLADEK, JOHN T.         SS    NWB 73 05
  SHUCKSMA                    CLUTE, JOHN             SS    NWB 73 05
  AUTHORS, THE                MISC. MATERIAL          MS

NEW WRITINGS IN SF. 1         CARNELL, JOHN           OA    BAN 66 04
  FOREWORD                    CARNELL, JOHN           IN
  KEY TO CHAOS                MACKIN, EDWARD          NV    NWR 64 01
  TWO'S COMPANY               RANKINE, JOHN           SS    NWR 64 01
  MAN ON BRIDGE               ALDISS, BRIAN W.        SS    NWR 64 01
  HAGGARD HONEYMOON           GREEN, JOSEPH
                              AND WEBBERT, JAMES      NV  C NWR 64 01
  SEA'S FURTHEST END, THE     BRODERICK, DAMIEN       NV    NWR 64 01

NEW WRITINGS IN SF. 2         CARNELL, JOHN           OA    BAN 66 10
  FOREWORD                    CARNELL, JOHN           IN
  HELL-PLANET                 RACKHAM, JOHN           NV    NWR 64 02
  NIGHT-FLAME, THE            KAPP, COLIN             SS    NWR 64 02
  CREATORS, THE               GREEN, JOSEPH           SS    NWR 64 02
  ROGUE LEONARDO              LACK, G. L.             SS    NWR 64 02
  MAIDEN VOYAGE               RANKINE, JOHN           NV    NWR 64 02
  ODD BOY OUT                 ETCHISON, DENNIS        SS    ESC 61
  ETERNAL MACHINES, THE       SPENCER, WILLIAM        SS    NWR 64 02
  ROUND BILLIARD TABLE, A     HALL, STEVE             SS    NWR 64 02

NEW WRITINGS IN SF. 3         CARNELL, JOHN           OA    BAN 67 02
  FOREWORD                    CARNELL, JOHN           IN
  SUBWAYS OF TAZOO, THE       KAPP, COLIN             NV    NWR 65 03
  FIEND, THE                  POHL, FREDERIK          SS    PBY 64 04
  MANIPULATION                KINGSTON, JOHN          NV    NWR 65 03
  TESTAMENT                   BAXTER, JOHN            SS    NWR 65 03
  NIGHT WATCH                 INGLIS, JAMES           SS    NWR 65 03
  BOULTER'S CANARIES          ROBERTS, KEITH          NV    NWR 65 03
  EMRETH                      MORGAN, DAN             SS    NWR 65 03
  SPACEMASTER                 SCHMITZ, JAMES H.       NV    NWR 65 03

NEW WRITINGS IN SF. 4         CARNELL, JOHN           OA    BAN 68 03
  FOREWORD                    CARNELL, JOHN           IN
  HIGH EIGHT                  STRINGER, DAVID         NV    NWR 65 04
  STAR LIGHT                  ASIMOV, ISAAC           SS    SAM 62 10
  HUNGER OVER SWEET WATERS    KAPP, COLIN             NV    NWR 65 04
  COUNTRY OF THE STRONG, THE  ETCHISON, DENNIS        SS    SEV 62
  PARKING PROBLEM             MORGAN, DAN             SS    NWR 65 04
  SUB-LIM                     ROBERTS, KEITH          NV    NWR 65 04
  BERNIE THE FAUST            TENN, WILLIAM           NV    PBY 63 11

NEW WRITINGS IN SF. 5         CARNELL, JOHN           OA    BAN 70 08
  FOREWORD                    CARNELL, JOHN           IN
```

```
  POTENTIAL                   MALCOLM, DONALD         NV    NWR 65 05
  LIBERATORS, THE             HARDING, LEE            SS    NWR 65 05
  TAKEOVER BID                BAXTER, JOHN            NV    NWR 65 05
  ACCLIMATIZATION             STRINGER, DAVID         NV    NWR 65 05
  EXPANDING MAN, THE          MACKELWORTH, R. W.      SS    NWR 65 05
  TREASURE HUNT               GREEN, JOSEPH           SS    NWR 65 05
  SUNOUT                      WILLIAMS, ERIC C.       NV    NWR 65 05

NEW WRITINGS IN SF. 6         CARNELL, JOHN           OA    BAN 71 03
  FOREWORD                    CARNELL, JOHN           IN
  INNER WHEEL, THE            ROBERTS, KEITH          NV    NWR 65 06
  HORIZONTAL MAN              SPENCER, WILLIAM        SS    NWR 65 06
  DAY BEFORE NEVER, THE       PRESSLIE, ROBERT        NV    NWR 65 06
  HANDS, THE                  BAXTER, JOHN            SS    NWR 65 06
  SEEKERS, THE                TUBB, E. C.             SS    NWR 65 06
  ATROPHY                     HILL, ERNEST            SS    NWR 65 06
  ADVANTAGE                   RACKHAM, JOHN           NV    NWR 65 06

NEW WRITINGS IN SF. 7         CARNELL, JOHN           AN    BAN 71 08
  FOREWORD                    CARNELL, JOHN           IN
  PEN AND THE DARK, THE       KAPP, COLIN             NV    NWR 66 08
  GIFTS OF THE GODS           SELLINGS, ARTHUR        NV    NWR 66 09
  LONG MEMORY, THE            SPENCER, WILLIAM        SS    NWR 66 09
  MAN WHO MISSED THE FERRY, THE
                              MASON, DOUGLAS R.       SS    NWR 66 07
  NIGHT OF THE SEVENTH FINGER, THE
                              PRESSLIE, ROBERT        SS    NWR 66 07
  SIX CUBED PLUS 1            RANKINE, JOHN           NV    NWR 66 07
  DEFENSE MECHANISM           KING, VINCENT           NV    NWR 66 09

NEW WRITINGS IN SF. 7         CARNELL, JOHN           OA H  DOB 66
  FOREWORD                    CARNELL, JOHN           IN
  INVADER                     WHITE, JAMES            NV    NWR 66 07
  MAN WHO MISSED THE FERRY, THE
                              MASON, DOUGLAS R.       SS    NWR 66 07
  NIGHT OF THE SEVENTH FINGER, THE
                              PRESSLIE, ROBERT        SS    NWR 66 07
  SIX CUBED PLUS 1            RANKINE, JOHN           NV    NWR 66 07
  COCO-TALK                   TEMPLE, WILLIAM F.      SS    NWR 66 07
  TOUCH OF IMMORTALITY, A     MACKELWORTH, R. W.      SS    NWR 66 07
  MANSCARER                   ROBERTS, KEITH          NV    NWR 66 07

NEW WRITINGS IN SF. 8         CARNELL, JOHN           AN    BAN 71 12
  FOREWORD                    CARNELL, JOHN           IN
  IMAGINATION TRAP, THE       KAPP, COLIN             NV    NWR 67 10
  APPLE                       BAXTER, JOHN            SS    NWR 67 10
  ROBOT'S DOZEN               LACK, G. L.             SS    NWR 67 10
  BIRTH OF A BUTTERFLY        GREEN, JOSEPH           SS    NWR 67 10
  THEY SHALL REAP             ROME, DAVID             NV    NWR 68 12
  SHOCK TREATMENT             HARDING, LEE            SS    NWR 68 11
  DEAD TO THE WORLD           HARGREAVES, H. A.       SS    NWR 68 11
  VISIONS OF MONAD            HARRISON, M. JOHN       SS    NWR 68 12
  WALL TO END THE WORLD, THE  KING, VINCENT           NV    NWR 68 11

NEW WRITINGS IN SF. 8         CARNELL, JOHN           OA H  DOB 66
  FOREWORD                    CARNELL, JOHN           IN
  PEN AND THE DARK, THE       KAPP, COLIN             NV    NWR 66 08
  SPACEMEN LIVE FOREVER       PAGE, GERALD W.         SS    NWR 66 08
  FINAL SOLUTION              MACKELWORTH, R. W.      SS    NWR 66 08
  COMPUTER'S MATE             RACKHAM, JOHN           SS    NWR 66 08
  TRYST                       BAXTER, JOHN            SS    NWR 66 08
  SYNTH                       ROBERTS, KEITH          SS    NWR 66 08

NEW WRITINGS IN SF. 9         CARNELL, JOHN           AN    BAN 72 05
  FOREWORD                    CARNELL, JOHN           IN
  WHEN I HAVE PASSED AWAY     GREEN, JOSEPH           NV    NWR 69 15
  SYMBIOTE                    CONEY, MICHAEL G.       NV    NWR 69 15
  IF YOU'RE SO SMART          COREY, PAUL             SS    NWR 69 14
  TESTAMENT                   KING, VINCENT           SS    NWR 68 13
  MACBETH EXPIATION, THE      HARRISON, M. JOHN       SS    NWR 68 13
  LAST TIME AROUND, THE       SELLINGS, ARTHUR        NV    NWR 68 12
  TILT ANGLE                  MACKELWORTH, R. W.      SS    NWR 69 14
  CITY, DYING, THE            BERTIN, EDDY C.         SS    NWR 68 13

NEW WRITINGS IN SF. 9         CARNELL, JOHN           OA H  DOB 66
  FOREWORD                    CARNELL, JOHN           IN
  POSEIDON PROJECT            RACKHAM, JOHN           NA    NWR 66 09
  FOLLY TO BE WISE            MASON, DOUGLAS R.       SS    NWR 66 09
  GIFTS OF THE GODS           SELLINGS, ARTHUR        NV    NWR 66 09
  LONG MEMORY, THE            SPENCER, WILLIAM        SS    NWR 66 09
  GUARDIAN ANGEL              PAGE, GERALD W.         SS    NWR 66 09
  SECOND GENESIS              RUSSELL, ERIC FRANK     SS    51
  DEFENSE MECHANISM           KING, VINCENT           NV    NWR 66 09

NEW WRITINGS IN SF. 10        CARNELL, JOHN           OA H  DOB 67
  FOREWORD                    CARNELL, JOHN           IN
  IMAGINATION TRAP, THE       KAPP, COLIN             NV    NWR 67 10
  APPLE                       BAXTER, JOHN            SS    NWR 67 10
  ROBOT'S DOZEN               LACK, G. L.             SS    NWR 67 10
  BIRTH OF A BUTTERFLY        GREEN, JOSEPH           SS    NWR 67 10
  AFFLUENCE OF EDWIN LOLLARD, THE
                              DISCH, THOMAS M.        SS    NWR 67 10
  TASTE FOR DOSTOEVSKY, A     ALDISS, BRIAN W.        SS    NWR 67 10
  IMAGE OF DESTRUCTION        RANKINE, JOHN           NV    NWR 67 10

NEW WRITINGS IN SF. 11        CARNELL, JOHN           OA    COR 68
  FOREWORD                    CARNELL, JOHN           IN
  WALL TO END THE WORLD, THE  KING, VINCENT           NV    NWR 68 11
  CATHARSIS                   RACKHAM, JOHN           SS    NWR 68 11
  SHOCK TREATMENT             HARDING, LEE            SS    NWR 68 11
  BRIGHT ARE THE STARS THAT SHINE, DARK IS THE SKY
                              ETCHISON, DENNIS        SS    NWR 68 11
  THERE WAS THIS FELLA...     MASON, DOUGLAS R.       SS    NWR 68 11
  FOR WHAT PURPOSE?           WEBB, W. T.             SS    NWR 68 11
  FLIGHT OF A PLASTIC BEE     RANKINE, JOHN           SS    NWR 68 11
  DEAD TO THE WORLD           HARGREAVES, H. A.       SS    NWR 68 11
```

EW WRITINGS IN SF. 11

HELMET OF HADES, THE	WODHAMS, JACK	SS	NWR 68 11

EW WRITINGS IN SF. 12   CARNELL, JOHN   OA   COR 68

FOREWORD	CARNELL, JOHN	IN	
VERTIGO	WHITE, JAMES	NV	NWR 68 12
VISIONS OF MONAD	HARRISON, M. JOHN	SS	NWR 68 12
WORM IN THE BUD	RANKINE, JOHN	SS	NWR 68 12
THEY SHALL REAP	ROME, DAVID	NV	NWR 68 12
LAST TIME AROUND, THE	SELLINGS, ARTHUR	NV	NWR 68 12
CLOUDBUILDERS, THE	KAPP, COLIN	NV	NWR 68 12

EW WRITINGS IN SF. 13   CARNELL, JOHN   OA   COR 68

FOREWORD	CARNELL, JOHN	IN	
DIVIDED HOUSE, THE	RACKHAM, JOHN	SS	NWR 68 13
PUBLIC SERVICE	BOUNDS, SYDNEY J.	SS	NWR 68 13
FERRYMAN ON THE RIVER, THE	KYLE, DAVID A.	SS	NWR 68 13
TESTAMENT	KING, VINCENT	SS	NWR 68 13
MACBETH EXPIATION, THE	HARRISON, M. JOHN	SS	NWR 68 13
REPRESENTATIVE	ROME, DAVID	SS	NWR 68 13
BEACH, THE	BAXTER, JOHN	SS	NWR 68 13
CITY, DYING, THE	BERTIN, EDDY C.	SS	NWR 68 13

EW WRITINGS IN SF. 14   CARNELL, JOHN   OA H DOB 69

FOREWORD	CARNELL, JOHN	IN	
BLOOD BROTHER	WHITE, JAMES	NV	NWR 69 14
IF YOU'RE SO SMART	COREY, PAUL	SS	NWR 69 14
BALLAD OF LUNA LIL, THE	BOUNDS, SYDNEY J.	SS	NWR 69 14
ETERNITY GAME, THE	KING, VINCENT	NV	NWR 69 14
TILT ANGLE	MACKELWORTH, R. W.	SS	NWR 69 14
SONG OF INFINITY, THE	SANTOS, DOMINGO	SS	NWR 69 14
GREEN FIVE RENEGADE	HARRISON, M. JOHN	NV	NWR 69 14

EW WRITINGS IN SF. 15   CARNELL, JOHN   OA H DOB 69

FOREWORD	CARNELL, JOHN	IN	
REPORT FROM LINELOS	KING, VINCENT	NV	NWR 69 15
INTERROGATOR, THE	PRIEST, CHRISTOPHER	NV	NWR 69 15
WHEN I HAVE PASSED AWAY	GREEN, JOSEPH	NV	NWR 69 15
SYMBIOTE	CONEY, MICHAEL G.	NV	NWR 69 15
TRIAL, THE	SELLINGS, ARTHUR	NV	NWR 69 15
THERAPY 2000	ROBERTS, KEITH	SS	NWR 69 15

EW WRITINGS IN SF. 16   CARNELL, JOHN   OA H DOB 69

FOREWORD	CARNELL, JOHN	IN	
GETAWAY FROM GETAWEHI	KAPP, COLIN	NA	NWR 69 16
ALL DONE BY MIRRORS	MASON, DOUGLAS R.	SS	NWR 69 16
THROWBACK	BOUNDS, SYDNEY J.	SS	NWR 69 16
PERIHELION MAN, THE	PRIEST, CHRISTOPHER	NV	NWR 69 16
R26/5/PSY AND I	CONEY, MICHAEL G.	NV	NWR 69 16
MEATBALL	WHITE, JAMES	NV	NWR 69 16

EW WRITINGS IN SF. 17   CARNELL, JOHN   OA H DOB 70

FOREWORD	CARNELL, JOHN	IN	
MORE THINGS IN HEAVEN AND EARTH	HARGREAVES, H. A.	NV	NWR 70 17
ASPECT OF ENVIRONMENT	DAVISON, L.	SS	NWR 70 17
SOUL SURVIVORS	HARDING, LEE	NV	NWR 70 17
DEATH AND THE SENSPERIENCE POET	GREEN, JOSEPH	SS	NWR 70 17
TWO RIVERS	MACKELWORTH, R. W.	NV	NWR 70 17
HERO, THE	HILL, ERNEST	SS	NWR 70 17
TRUE WORTH OF RUTH VILLIERS, THE	CONEY, MICHAEL G.	SS	NWR 70 17

NEW WRITINGS IN SF. 18   CARNELL, JOHN   OA H DOB 71

FOREWORD	CARNELL, JOHN	IN	
MISTRESS OF THE MIND	HARDING, LEE	NV	NWR 71 18
FRONTIER INCIDENT	WELLS, ROBERT	SS	NWR 71 18
BIG DAY, THE	MALCOLM, DONALD	SS	NWR 71 18
MAJOR OPERATION	WHITE, JAMES	NV	NWR 71 18
CYCLOPS PATROL, THE	SPENCER, WILLIAM	SS	NWR 71 18
SOME DREAMS COME IN PACKAGES	KYLE, DAVID A.	NV	NWR 71 18
DJANGO MAVERICK: 2051	LEMAN, GRAHAME	SS	NWR 71 18

NEW WRITINGS IN SF. 19   CARNELL, JOHN   OA H DOB 71

FOREWORD	CARNELL, JOHN	IN	
MIND PRISON, THE	CONEY, MICHAEL G.	SS	NWR 71 19
MEMORY OF GOLDEN SUNSHINE, A	BULMER, KENNETH	SS	NWR 71 19
CRITICAL PATH	COLES, DAVID	NV	NWR 71 19
DISCONTENT CONTINGENCY, THE	KING, VINCENT	NV	NWR 71 19
STOOP TO CONQUER	RACKHAM, JOHN	SS	NWR 71 19
FIRST LIGHT ON A DARKLING PLAIN	GREEN, JOSEPH	SS	NWR 71 19
REAL-TIME WORLD	PRIEST, CHRISTOPHER	NV	NWR 71 19

NEW WRITINGS IN SF. 20   CARNELL, JOHN   OA H DOB 72

FOREWORD	CARNELL, JOHN	IN	
CONVERSATIONAL MODE	LEMAN, GRAHAME	SS	NWR 72 20
WHICH WAY DO I GO FOR JERICHO?	KAPP, COLIN	NV	NWR 72 20
MICROCOSM	HOLDSTOCK, ROBERT P.	SS	NWR 72 20
CAIN N	HARGREAVES, H. A.	NV	NWR 72 20
CANARY	MORGAN, DAN	SS	NWR 72 20
OH, VALINDA!	CONEY, MICHAEL G.	NV	NWR 72 20

NEW WRITINGS IN SF. 21   CARNELL, JOHN   OA H SID 73

FOREWORD	LLOYD, DANIEL	IN	
PASSING OF THE DRAGONS, THE	ROBERTS, KEITH	NV	NWR 73 21
ALGORA ONE SIX	MASON, DOUGLAS R.	SS	NWR 73 21
COMMUTER	WHITE, JAMES	SS	NWR 73 21
POSSESSED, THE	BOUNDS, SYDNEY J.	SS	NWR 73 21
WHAT THE THUNDER SAID	KAPP, COLIN	SS	NWR 73 21
TANGLED WEB	HARGREAVES, H. A.	NV	NWR 73 21
TERTIARY JUSTIFICATION, THE	CONEY, MICHAEL G.	NV	NWR 73 21

NEW WRITINGS IN SF. 22   BULMER, KENNETH   OA H SID 73

FOREWORD	BULMER, KENNETH	IN	

NEW WRITINGS IN SF. 28

HONEST DAY'S WORK, AN	HARRISON, HARRY	NV	NWR 73 22
EVANE	TUBB, E. C.	SS	NWR 73 22
RENDEZVOUS WITH RAMA (CHAPTER 1)	CLARKE, ARTHUR C.	EX	NWR 73 22
SPACEBIRD	WHITE, JAMES	SS	NWR 73 22
THREE ENIGMAS: I	ALDISS, BRIAN W.	GR	NWR 73 22
E OF HER VOICE, THE	ALDISS, BRIAN W.	SS	NWR 73 22
I CHING, WHO YOU?	ALDISS, BRIAN W.	SS	NWR 73 22
GREAT CHAIN OF BEING WHAT?, THE	ALDISS, BRIAN W.	SS	NWR 73 22
WISE CHILD	RACKHAM, JOHN	SS	NWR 73 22
RULES OF THE GAME, THE	WOLLHEIM, DONALD A.	SS	NWR 73 22
MONITOR	BOUNDS, SYDNEY J.	SS	NWR 73 22
TIME WAGER, THE	KIPPAX, JOHN	SS	NWR 73 22
SQUARE ROOT OF MC, THE	JAMES, LAURENCE	SS	NWR 73 22
INVERTED WORLD, THE	PRIEST, CHRISTOPHER	NV	NWR 73 22

NEW WRITINGS IN SF. 23   BULMER, KENNETH   OA H SID 74

FOREWORD	BULMER, KENNETH	IN	
LAKE OF TUONELA, THE	ROBERTS, KEITH	NV	NWR 74 23
WAGTAIL IN THE MORNING	LEMAN, GRAHAME	SS	NWR 74 23
MADE TO BE BROKEN	TUBB, E. C.	SS	NWR 74 23
THREE ENIGMAS: II	ALDISS, BRIAN W.	GR	NWR 74 23
ETERNAL THEME OF EXILE, THE	ALDISS, BRIAN W.	SS	NWR 74 23
ALL THOSE ENDURING OLD CHARMS	ALDISS, BRIAN W.	SS	NWR 74 23
NOBODY SPOKE OR WAVED GOODBYE	ALDISS, BRIAN W.		NWR 74 23
FIVE DOORS, THE	STALL, MICHAEL	SS	NWR 74 23
SPORTING ON APTERYX	PARTINGTON, CHARLES	SS	NWR 74 23
RAINBOW	GARNETT, DAVID S.	SS	NWR 74 23
ACCOLADE	GREY, CHARLES	SS	NWR 74 23
SEED OF EVIL, THE	BAYLEY, BARRINGTON J	NV	NWR 74 23

NEW WRITINGS IN SF. 24   BULMER, KENNETH   OA H SID 74

FOREWORD	BULMER, KENNETH	IN	
ARK OF JAMES CARLYLE, THE	WILDER, CHERRY	SS	NWR 74 24
AND WHEN I DIE...	LINNETT, PETER	SS	NWR 74 24
THREE ENIGMAS: III	ALDISS, BRIAN W.	GR	NWR 74 24
UNBEARABLENESS OF OTHER LIVES, THE	ALDISS, BRIAN W.	SS	NWR 74 24
OLD FLEEING AND FLEETING IMAGES, THE	ALDISS, BRIAN W.	SS	NWR 74 24
LOOKING ON THE SUNNY SIDE OF AN ECLIPSE	ALDISS, BRIAN W.	SS	NWR 74 24
STRANGE AND TERRIBLE SEA, A	MALCOLM, DONALD	SS	NWR 74 24
NEW CANUTE	RICKETTS, MARTIN I.	SS	NWR 74 24
NO CERTAIN ARMOUR	KIPPAX, JOHN	NV	NWR 74 24
NOW HEAR THE WORD	GARNETT, DAVID S.	NV	NWR 74 24

NEW WRITINGS IN SF. 25   BULMER, KENNETH   OA H DOB 75

FOREWORD	BULMER, KENNETH	IN	
RICE BRANDY	STALL, MICHAEL	NV	NWR 75 25
CAT AND THE COIN, THE	WELLS, KEITH	NV	NWR 75 25
DEBRIS OF RECENT LIVES, THE	PARTINGTON, CHARLES	SS	NWR 75 25
TALENT SPOTTER	BOUNDS, SYDNEY J.	SS	NWR 75 25
BLACK HOLE OF NEGRAV, THE	KAPP, COLIN	NV	NWR 75 25
LITTLE MORE THAN TWELVE MINUTES, A	JESCHKE, WOLFGANG	NV	NWR 75 25
ENEMY WITHIN, THE	MALCOLM, DONALD	NV	NWR 75 25
HALTED VILLAGE, THE	RACKHAM, JOHN	NV	NWR 75 25
GREEN FUSE, THE	RICKETTS, MARTIN I.	SS	NWR 75 25

NEW WRITINGS IN SF. 26   BULMER, KENNETH   OA H SID 75

FOREWORD	BULMER, KENNETH	IN	
PLANET CALLED CERVANTES, A	KEITH, JOHN	SS	NWR 75 26
MEN OF GOOD VALUE	PRIEST, CHRISTOPHER	SS	NWR 75 26
CAREFULLY OBSERVED WOMEN	ALDISS, BRIAN W.	SS	NWR 75 26
DAFFODIL RETURNS THE SMILE, THE	ALDISS, BRIAN W.	SS	NWR 75 26
YEAR OF THE QUIET COMPUTER, THE	ALDISS, BRIAN W.	SS	NWR 75 26
PHOBOS TRANSCRIPTS, THE	WILDER, CHERRY	SS	NWR 75 26
MAN WHO, THE	GARNETT, DAVID S.	SS	NWR 75 26
YOU GET LOTS OF YESTERDAYS, LOTS OF TOMORROWS, AND ONLY ONE TODAY	JAMES, LAURENCE	SS	NWR 75 26
MURDERS	CAMPBELL, J. RAMSEY	SS	NWR 75 26
TO THE PUMP ROOM WITH JANE	WATSON, IAN	SS	NWR 75 26
SEAFARER, THE	SMITH, RITCHIE AND PENMAN, THOMAS	SS C	NWR 75 26

NEW WRITINGS IN SF. 27   BULMER, KENNETH   OA H SID 75

FOREWORD	BULMER, KENNETH	IN	
BARTHOLOMEW & SON (AND THE FISH-GIRL)	CONEY, MICHAEL G.	NV	NWR 75 27
DAY THEY CUT OFF THE POWER, THE	JOHNSON, VERA	SS	NWR 75 27
TIME OF MIND, A	WELLS, KEITH	SS	NWR 75 27
YEAR BY YEAR THE EVIL GAINS	ALDISS, BRIAN W.	NV	NWR 75 27
LONG TIME AGO, NOT FORGOTTEN	VAN LAERHOVEN, BOB	SS	NWR 75 27
ZONE	LINNETT, PETER	SS	NWR 75 27
HEATWAVE	LANGFORD, DAVID	SS	NWR 75 27
HEAL THYSELF	RACKHAM, JOHN	SS	NWR 75 27
OBSERVER, THE	CHARNOCK, GRAHAM	SS	NWR 75 27
CASSIUS AND THE MIND-JAUNT	KAPP, COLIN	NV	NWR 75 27

NEW WRITINGS IN SF. 28   BULMER, KENNETH   OA H DOB 76

FOREWORD	BULMER, KENNETH	IN	
WHAT HAPPENED TO WILLIAM COOMBES	ROGERS, ANGELA	SS	NWR 76 28
WAY ERVING WENT, THE	LEMAN, GRAHAME	SS	NWR 76 28
BANKS OF THE NILE, THE	SMITH, RITCHIE AND PENMAN, THOMAS	NV C	NWR 76 28
BONES OF BERTRAND RUSSELL, THE	ALDISS, BRIAN W.	SS	NWR 76 28
ON THE INSIDE	HOLDSTOCK, ROBERT P.	NV	NWR 76 28

NEW WRITINGS IN SF. 28

GREAT PLAN, THE	KETTLE, LEROY	SS	NWR 76	28
FACE TO INFINITY	TUBB, E. C.	SS	NWR 76	28
CALL OF THE WILD, THE	VAN LOGGEM, MANUEL	SS	NWR 76	28
WORDSMITH	FORTEY, BRYN	SS	NWR 76	28
MANGANON	STALL, MICHAEL	NV	NWR 76	28

NEW WRITINGS IN SF. 29   BULMER, KENNETH   OA H SID 76

FOREWORD	BULMER, KENNETH	IN		
DOUBLE SUMMER TIME	WILDER, CHERRY	NV	NWR 76	29
Z FACTOR, THE	HILL, ERNEST	NV	NWR 76	29
SPACE FOR REFLECTION, A	ALDISS, BRIAN W.	SS	NWR 76	29
RANDOM SAMPLE	TUBB, E. C.	SS	NWR 76	29
SENTENCED TO A SCHEHRRAZADEAN DEATH				
	WALTERS, DAVID H.	SS	NWR 76	29
BETWEEN THE TIDES	MALCOLM, DONALD	NV	NWR 76	29
YOUNG TOM	MORGAN, DAN	SS	NWR 76	29
IN THE COMA CONDITION	PARTINGTON, CHARLES	SS	NWR 76	29

NEWS FROM ELSEWHERE   COOPER, EDMUND   AC BKM 69 05

MENHIR, THE	COOPER, EDMUND	SS	
M81: URSA MAJOR (THE END OF THE JOURNEY)			
	COOPER, EDMUND	SS	FUN 56 02
ENLIGHTENED ONES, THE	COOPER, EDMUND	NV	FUN 59 01
JUDGEMENT DAY	COOPER, EDMUND	SS	
INTRUDERS (INTRUDERS ON THE MOON)			
	COOPER, EDMUND	NV	FUN 57 04
BUTTERFLIES, THE	COOPER, EDMUND	SS	
LIZARD OF WOZ, THE	COOPER, EDMUND	SS	FUN 58 08
WELCOME HOME	COOPER, EDMUND	SS	

NEXT STOP THE STARS   SILVERBERG, ROBERT   DC ACE 62

SLAVES OF THE STAR GIANTS	SILVERBERG, ROBERT	NA	SPA 57 02
SONGS OF SUMMER, THE	SILVERBERG, ROBERT	SS	SFS 56 09
HOPPER	SILVERBERG, ROBERT	NV	INF 56 10
BLAZE OF GLORY	SILVERBERG, ROBERT	SS	GAL 57 08
WARM MAN	SILVERBERG, ROBERT	SS	FSF 57 05

NICE DAY FOR SCREAMING, AND OTHER TALES OF THE HUB
     SCHMITZ, JAMES H.   AC H CHL 65

NICE DAY FOR SCREAMING, A	SCHMITZ, JAMES H.	SS	ASF 65 01
WINDS OF TIME, THE	SCHMITZ, JAMES H.	NV	ASF 62 09
OTHER LIKENESS, THE	SCHMITZ, JAMES H.	SS	ASF 62 07
TANGLED WEB, THE (THE STAR HYACINTHS)			
	SCHMITZ, JAMES H.	SS	AMZ 61 12
MACHMEN, THE	SCHMITZ, JAMES H.	SS	ASF 64 09
BALANCED ECOLOGY	SCHMITZ, JAMES H.	SS	ASF 65 03

NIGHT GALLERY   SERLING, ROD   OC BAN 71 11

SOLE SURVIVOR, THE	SERLING, ROD	SA
MAKE ME LAUGH	SERLING, ROD	SA
PAMELA'S VOICE	SERLING, ROD	SA
DOES THE NAME GRIMSBY DO ANYTHING TO YOU?		
	SERLING, ROD	SA
CLEAN KILLS AND OTHER TROPHIES		
	SERLING, ROD	SA
THEY'RE TEARING DOWN TIM RILEY'S BAR		
	SERLING, ROD	SA

NIGHT GALLERY 2   SERLING, ROD   OC BAN 72 12

COLLECTOR'S ITEMS	SERLING, ROD	SA
MESSIAH ON MOTT STREET, THE	SERLING, ROD	SA
DIFFERENT ONES, THE	SERLING, ROD	SA
LINDEMANN'S CATCH	SERLING, ROD	SA
SUGGESTION	SERLING, ROD	SA

NIGHT IN FUNLAND   BRONDFIELD, JEROME   AN SBS 68
   AND OTHER STORIES FROM LITERARY CAVALCADE

FOREWORD	BRONDFIELD, JEROME	IN	
NIGHT IN FUNLAND	PENDEN, WILLIAM	SS	60
4 O'CLOCK	DAY, PRICE	SS	58
VERTICAL LADDER, THE	SANSOM, WILLIAM	SS	60
AUGUST HEAT	HARVEY, WILLIAM F.	SS	28
SEA GULLS, THE	VENEZIS, ELIAS	SS	55
ANTAEUS	DEAL, BORDEN	SS	61
EXCHANGE OF MEN	NEMEROV, HOWARD		
	AND JOHNSON, W. R.	SS C STO 63 01	
FLOWERS FOR ALGERNON	KEYES, DANIEL	SS	FSF 59 04
ONE ORDINARY DAY, WITH PEANUTS			
	JACKSON, SHIRLEY	SS	FSF 55 01
MOST DANGEROUS GAME, THE	CONNELL, RICHARD	NV	24
CONTENTS OF THE DEAD MAN'S POCKETS			
	FINNEY, JACK	NV	NEW 57 AC
AS BEST WE CAN	HOUSEHOLD, GEOFFREY	SS	58
TOO EARLY SPRING	BENET, STEPHEN V.	SS	33

NIGHT MONSTERS   LEIBER, FRITZ   DC ACE 69

BLACK GONDOLIER, THE	LEIBER, FRITZ	NV	NEW 64 AN
MIDNIGHT IN THE MIRROR WORLD	LEIBER, FRITZ	SS	FAN 64 10
I'M LOOKING FOR "JEFF"	LEIBER, FRITZ	SS	FAN 52 FL
CASKET-DEMON, THE	LEIBER, FRITZ	SS	FAN 63 04

NIGHT OF THE PUUDLY, THE   SIMAK, CLIFFORD D.   AC FSP 64
   5 STORIES FROM "ALL THE TRAPS OF EARTH"
   NIGHT OF THE PUUDLY, THE (GOOD NIGHT, MR. JAMES)

	SIMAK, CLIFFORD D.	NV	GAL 51 03
CRYING JAG	SIMAK, CLIFFORD D.	NV	GAL 60 02
INSTALLMENT PLAN	SIMAK, CLIFFORD D.	NA	GAL 59 02
CONDITION OF EMPLOYMENT	SIMAK, CLIFFORD D.	SS	GAL 60 04
PROJECT MASTODON	SIMAK, CLIFFORD D.	NV	GAL 55 03

NIGHT OF THE SPHINX AND OTHER STORIES
   ELWOOD, ROGER   OA H LER 74

FOREWORD	ASIMOV, ISAAC	IN
NIGHT OF THE SPHINX	EXTER, MAUREEN	SS
WHEN THE COLD CAME	TOFTE, ARTHUR	SS
SKYHOOK	GLOECKNER, CAROLYN	SS

NIGHTFALL AND OTHER STORIES

AUNT ELVIRA'S ZOO	SARGENT, PAMELA	SS	
NIGHT OF THE WOLF, THE	LEIBER, FRITZ	AC	BAL 66 07
LONE WOLF, THE (THE CREATURE FROM CLEVELAND DEPTHS)			
	LEIBER, FRITZ	NA	GAL 62 12
WOLF PAIR, THE (THE NIGHT OF THE LONG KNIVES)			
	LEIBER, FRITZ	NA	AMZ 60 01
CRAZY WOLF (SANITY)	LEIBER, FRITZ	SS	ASF 44 04
WOLF PACK, THE (LET FREEDOM RING)			
	LEIBER, FRITZ	SN	AMZ 50 04

NIGHT RIDE AND OTHER JOURNEYS
   BEAUMONT, CHARLES   AC BAN 60 03

MUSIC OF THE YELLOW BRASS, THE			
	BEAUMONT, CHARLES	SS	PBY 59 01
CLASSIC AFFAIR, A	BEAUMONT, CHARLES	SS	PBY 55
NEW PEOPLE, THE	BEAUMONT, CHARLES	SS	ROG 58
BUCK FEVER	BEAUMONT, CHARLES	SS	NEW 60 AC
MAGIC MAN, THE	BEAUMONT, CHARLES	SS	NEW 60 AC
FATHER, DEAR FATHER (OH FATHER OF MINE)			
	BEAUMONT, CHARLES	SS	VSF 57 01
PERCHANCE TO DREAM	BEAUMONT, CHARLES	SS	PBY 58 10
SONG FOR A LADY	BEAUMONT, CHARLES	SS	NEW 60 AC
TRIGGER, THE	BEAUMONT, CHARLES	SS	MDM 58
GUESTS OF CHANCE, THE	BEAUMONT, CHARLES		
	AND OLIVER, CHAD	SS C INF 56 06	
LOVE-MASTER, THE	BEAUMONT, CHARLES	SS	ROG 56
DEATH IN THE COUNTRY, A (THE DEADLY WILL TO WIN)			
	BEAUMONT, CHARLES	SS	PBY 57 11
NEIGHBORS, THE	BEAUMONT, CHARLES	SS	NEW 60 AC
HOWLING MAN, THE	BEAUMONT, CHARLES	SS	NEW 60 AC
NIGHT RIDE	BEAUMONT, CHARLES	SS	PBY 57 03

NIGHT TIDE, A   INOUYE, JON   OC RDN 76 12

PROLOGUE	INOUYE, JON	MS
NIGHT TIDE, A	INOUYE, JON	SS
WORK POEM, THE	INOUYE, JON	PM
FINAL DINEB	INOUYE, JON	SS
FROM CRIMSON CAME STARDUST	INOUYE, JON	PM
ARM	INOUYE, JON	SS
ESCAPE ARTIST	INOUYE, JON	SS
UGLY JAPANESE, THE	INOUYE, JON	SS
COMIX	INOUYE, JON	SS
RESTING GROUND	INOUYE, JON	PM
TURNTABLE	INOUYE, JON	SS
UFO SPOTTED	INOUYE, JON	SS
NEURO-GENERATION, THE	INOUYE, JON	SS
VIDEO	INOUYE, JON	PM
HOGARTH	INOUYE, JON	SS
SMELL OF PULPS, THE	INOUYE, JON	SS
LAST MAN	INOUYE, JON	SS
INVISIBLE JANITOR	INOUYE, JON	SS
DOUBLE	INOUYE, JON	PM
2076	INOUYE, JON	SS
NOTHINK	INOUYE, JON	SS
NIGHTSPAWN	INOUYE, JON	SS
MYTH CHILD	INOUYE, JON	SS
MATARAY, TOO	INOUYE, JON	SS
MEGATON	INOUYE, JON	SS
CYB	INOUYE, JON	SS
SOJOURNER	INOUYE, JON	SS
ROBOT SLEEP	INOUYE, JON	SS
MINDSHIP	INOUYE, JON	SS
STORY OF REJECTION, THE	INOUYE, JON	SS
SCOPE	INOUYE, JON	SS
MINDSPOT	INOUYE, JON	SS
SPHERE	INOUYE, JON	SS
WINTER ARRIVAL	INOUYE, JON	SS
FAR PULSAR	INOUYE, JON	SS
LETRON	INOUYE, JON	SS
SPHEROID OF ZANZOL	INOUYE, JON	SS
GUIDELIGHT	INOUYE, JON	SS
FAREWELL DREAM	INOUYE, JON	SS
EPILOGUE	INOUYE, JON	MS

NIGHT'S BLACK AGENTS   LEIBER, FRITZ   AC H ARK 47
   BALLANTINE 1961 EDITION OMITS "ADEPT'S GAMBIT"

SMOKE GHOST	LEIBER, FRITZ	SS	UNK 41 10
AUTOMATIC PISTOL, THE	LEIBER, FRITZ	SS	WRT 40 05
INHERITANCE, THE	LEIBER, FRITZ	SS	WRT 42 01
HILL AND THE HOLE, THE	LEIBER, FRITZ	SS	UNK 42 08
DREAMS OF ALBERT MORELAND, THE			
	LEIBER, FRITZ	NV	APR 48 07
HOUND, THE	LEIBER, FRITZ	SS	WRT 42 11
DIARY IN THE SNOW	LEIBER, FRITZ	NV	NEW 47 AC
MAN WHO NEVER GREW YOUNG, THE			
	LEIBER, FRITZ	SS	APR 49 09
SUNKEN LAND, THE	LEIBER, FRITZ	SS	UNK 42 02
ADEPT'S GAMBIT	LEIBER, FRITZ	SS	NEW 47 AC

NIGHTFALL AND OTHER STORIES   ASIMOV, ISAAC   AC H DBL 69

NIGHTFALL	ASIMOV, ISAAC	NV	ASF 41 09
GREEN PATCHES (MISBEGOTTEN MISSIONARY)			
	ASIMOV, ISAAC	SS	GAL 50 11
HOSTESS	ASIMOV, ISAAC	NV	GAL 51 05
BREEDS THERE A MAN...?	ASIMOV, ISAAC	NV	ASF 51 06
C-CHUTE, THE	ASIMOV, ISAAC	NV	GAL 51 10
IN A GOOD CAUSE—	ASIMOV, ISAAC	NV	NTS 51
WHAT IF	ASIMOV, ISAAC	SS	FAN 52 SU
SALLY	ASIMOV, ISAAC	SS	FAN 53 05
FLIES	ASIMOV, ISAAC	SS	FSF 53 06
NOBODY HERE BUT—	ASIMOV, ISAAC	SS	STR 53 01
IT'S SUCH A BEAUTIFUL DAY	ASIMOV, ISAAC	NV	STR 54 03
STRIKEBREAKER (MALE STRIKEBREAKER)			
	ASIMOV, ISAAC	SS	SFS 57 01
INSERT KNOB A IN HOLE B	ASIMOV, ISAAC	SS	FSF 57 12

NIGHTFALL AND OTHER STORIES   NINE HUNDRED GRANDMOTHERS

UP-TO-DATE SORCERER, THE   ASIMOV, ISAAC   SS FSF 58 07
UNTO THE FOURTH GENERATION   ASIMOV, ISAAC   SS FSF 59 04
WHAT IS THIS THING CALLED LOVE? (THE PLAYBOY AND THE SLIME GOD)
                                ASIMOV, ISAAC   SS AMZ 61 03
MACHINE THAT WON THE WAR, THE
                                ASIMOV, ISAAC   SS FSF 61 10
MY SON, THE PHYSICIST   ASIMOV, ISAAC   SS SAM 62 02
EYES DO MORE THAN SEE   ASIMOV, ISAAC   SS FSF 65 04
SEGREGATIONIST   ASIMOV, ISAAC   SS ABB 67 04

NIGHTMARE AGE   POHL, FREDERIK   AN BAL 70 10
  INTRODUCTION   POHL, FREDERIK   IN
  ECO-CATASTROPHE¡   EHRLICH, DR. PAUL R. SS RAM 69 09
  UNCALCULATED RISK   ANVIL, CHRISTOPHER SS ASF 62 03
  CENSUS TAKERS, THE   POHL, FREDERIK   SS FSF 56 02
  MARCHING MORONS, THE   KORNBLUTH, C. M.   NV GAL 51 04
  BAD DAY FOR SALES, A   LEIBER, FRITZ   SS GAL 53 07
  STATION HR972   BULMER, KENNETH   SS WOT 67 02
  X MARKS THE PEDWALK   LEIBER, FRITZ   SS WOT 63 04
  DAY OF TRUCE   SIMAK, CLIFFORD D. NV GAL 63 02
  AMONG THE BAD BABOONS   REYNOLDS, MACK   NV GAL 68 08
  LUCKIEST MAN IN DENV, THE (AS SIMON EISNER)
                                KORNBLUTH, C. M.   SS GAL 52 06
  MIDAS PLAGUE, THE   POHL, FREDERIK   NA GAL 54 04
  NEW APPLES IN THE GARDEN   NEVILLE, KRIS   SS ASF 63 07
  YEAR OF THE JACKPOT, THE   HEINLEIN, ROBERT A. NV GAL 52 03

NIGHTMARE GARDEN   GHIDALIA, VIC   AN MAN 76
  COME INTO MY CELLAR (ALSO AS BOYS, RAISE GIANT MUSHROOMS
    IN YOUR CELLAR)   BRADBURY, RAY   SS GAL 62 10
  FANGS OF THE TREES, THE   SILVERBERG, ROBERT NV FSF 68 10
  SEED STOCK   HERBERT, FRANK   SS ASF 70 04
  VINE, THE   REED, KIT   SS FSF 67 11
  BLOOD-FLOWER, THE   QUINN, SEABURY   NV WRT 27 03
  STRANGE HARVEST   WANDREI, DONALD   NV WRT 53 05
  STEP INTO MY GARDEN   LONG, FRANK BELKNAP SS UNK 42 08
  FLOWERING OF THE STRANGE ORCHID, THE (ALSO AS THE STRANGE
    ORCHID)   WELLS, H. G.   SS PMB 94 08
  PLANT-THING, THE   MACREADY, R. G.   SS WRT 25 07
  RAPPACCINI'S DAUGHTER (1844) HAWTHORNE, NATHANIEL NV DMR 44 12

NIGHTMARES   BLOCH, ROBERT   AC BEL 61
    TEN WEIRD TALES FROM PLEASANT DREAMS
  INTRODUCTION TO NIGHTMARES, AN
                                BLOCH, ROBERT   IN
  SORCERER'S APPRENTICE, THE   BLOCH, ROBERT   SS WRT 49 01
  I KISS YOUR SHADOW   BLOCH, ROBERT   SS FSF 56 04
  MR. STEINWAY   BLOCH, ROBERT   SS FAN 54 04
  PROPER SPIRIT, THE   BLOCH, ROBERT   SS FSF 57 03
  CATNIP   BLOCH, ROBERT   SS WRT 48 03
  HUNGARIAN RHAPSODY (AS WILSON KANE)
                                BLOCH, ROBERT   SS FAN 58 06
  LIGHT-HOUSE, THE   BLOCH, ROBERT   SS FAN 53 02
  HUNGRY HOUSE, THE   BLOCH, ROBERT   NV IMG 51 04
  SLEEPING BEAUTY, THE (THE SLEEPING REDHEADS)
                                BLOCH, ROBERT   SS SWK 58 03
  SWEET SIXTEEN   BLOCH, ROBERT   SS

NIGHTMARES AND DAYDREAMS   BOND, NELSON S.   AC H ARK 68
  TO PEOPLE A NEW WORLD   BOND, NELSON S.   SS BBM 50 11
  ROSY FUTURE FOR RODERICK, A   BOND, NELSON S.   SS BBM 52 08
  SONG, THE   BOND, NELSON S.   SS BBM 49 04
  PETERSEN'S EYE   BOND, NELSON S.   SS BBM 49 03
  ABDUCTION OF ABNER GREER, THE
                                BOND, NELSON S.   SS BBM 41 06
  BIRD OF PREY   BOND, NELSON S.   SS BBM 49 08
  SPINSTERS, THE   BOND, NELSON S.   SS BBM 50 01
  DEVIL TO PAY, THE   BOND, NELSON S.   SS BBM 51 02
  DOWN WILL COME THE SKY   BOND, NELSON S.   SS USF 53 06
  PET SHOP, THE   BOND, NELSON S.   SS BBM 50 03
  AL HADDON'S LAMP   BOND, NELSON S.   NV UNK 42 06
  LAST INNING   BOND, NELSON S.   SS BBM 48 05
  DARK DOOR, THE   BOND, NELSON S.   SS BBM 52 05
  MUCH ADO ABOUT PENDING   BOND, NELSON S.   SS BBM 47 04
  FINAL REPORT   BOND, NELSON S.   PM FUN 58 01

NIGHTMARES AND GEEZENSTACKS   BROWN, FREDRIC   AC BAN 61 07
  NASTY   BROWN, FREDRIC   SS PBY 59 04
  ABOMINABLE   BROWN, FREDRIC   SS DUD 60 03
  REBOUND   BROWN, FREDRIC   SS NEW 61 AC
  NIGHTMARE IN GRAY   BROWN, FREDRIC   SS
  NIGHTMARE IN GREEN   BROWN, FREDRIC   SS
  NIGHTMARE IN WHITE   BROWN, FREDRIC   SS
  NIGHTMARE IN BLUE   BROWN, FREDRIC   SS
  NIGHTMARE IN YELLOW   BROWN, FREDRIC   SS DUD 61 05
  NIGHTMARE IN RED   BROWN, FREDRIC   SS
  UNFORTUNATELY   BROWN, FREDRIC   SS FSF 58 10
  GRANNY'S BIRTHDAY   BROWN, FREDRIC   SS
  CAT BURGLAR   BROWN, FREDRIC   SS
  HOUSE, THE   BROWN, FREDRIC   SS FAN 60 08
  SECOND CHANCE   BROWN, FREDRIC   SS
  GREAT LOST DISCOVERIES I - INVISIBILITY
                                BROWN, FREDRIC   SS
  GREAT LOST DISCOVERIES II - INVULNERABILITY
                                BROWN, FREDRIC   SS
  GREAT LOST DISCOVERIES III - IMMORTALITY
                                BROWN, FREDRIC   SS NEW 61 AC
  DEAD LETTER   BROWN, FREDRIC   SS
  RECESSIONAL   BROWN, FREDRIC   SS DUD 60 03
  HOBBYIST   BROWN, FREDRIC   SS PBY 61 05
  RING OF HANS CARVEL, THE   BROWN, FREDRIC   SS
  VENGEANCE FLEET (VENGEANCE, UNLIMITED)
                                BROWN, FREDRIC   SS SSS 50 07
  ROPE TRICK   BROWN, FREDRIC   SS
  FATAL ERROR   BROWN, FREDRIC   SS

SHORT HAPPY LIVES OF EUSTACE WEAVER I, THE
                                BROWN, FREDRIC   SS EQM 61 06
SHORT HAPPY LIVES OF EUSTACE WEAVER II, THE
                                BROWN, FREDRIC   SS EQM 61 06
SHORT HAPPY LIVES OF EUSTACE WEAVER III, THE
                                BROWN, FREDRIC   SS EQM 61 06
  EXPEDITION   BROWN, FREDRIC   SS FSF 57 02
  BRIGHT BEARD   BROWN, FREDRIC   SS
  JAYCEE   BROWN, FREDRIC   SS FSF 55
  CONTACT   BROWN, FREDRIC   SS
  HORSE RACE   BROWN, FREDRIC   SS
  DEATH ON THE MOUNTAIN   BROWN, FREDRIC   SS
  BEAR POSSIBILITY   BROWN, FREDRIC   SS
  NOT YET THE END   BROWN, FREDRIC   SS CFU 41 WI
  FISH STORY   BROWN, FREDRIC   SS
  THREE LITTLE OWLS   BROWN, FREDRIC   SS
  RUNAROUND   BROWN, FREDRIC   SS
  MURDER IN TEN EASY LESSONS   BROWN, FREDRIC   SS
  DARK INTERLUDE   BROWN, FREDRIC
                            AND REYNOLDS, MACK   SS C GAL 51 01
  ENTITY TRAP   BROWN, FREDRIC   SS
  LITTLE LAMB, THE   BROWN, FREDRIC   SS
  ME AND FLAPJACK AND THE MARTIANS
                                BROWN, FREDRIC
                            AND REYNOLDS, MACK   SS C ASF 52 12
  JOKE, THE   BROWN, FREDRIC   SS
  CARTOONIST   BROWN, FREDRIC
                            AND REYNOLDS, MACK   SS C
  GEEZENSTACKS, THE   BROWN, FREDRIC   SS WRT 43 09
  END, THE   BROWN, FREDRIC   SS NEW 61 AC

NIGHTSHADE & DAMNATIONS   KERSH, GERALD   AC FGM 68
  KERSH, THE DEMON PRINCE   ELLISON, HARLAN   IN
  QUEEN OF PIG ISLAND, THE (MISTRESS OF PORCOSITO)
                                KERSH, GERALD   SS PBY 57 07
  FROZEN BEAUTY   KERSH, GERALD   SS   58
  BRIGHTON MONSTER, THE (THE MONSTER)
                                KERSH, GERALD   SS SEP 48 02
  MEN WITHOUT BONES   KERSH, GERALD   SS ESQ
  BUSTO IS A GHOST, TOO MEAN TO GIVE US A FRIGHT¡
                                KERSH, GERALD   SS
  APE AND THE MYSTERY, THE (THE MYSTERIOUS MONA LISA SMILE)
                                KERSH, GERALD   SS SEP 48 06
  KING WHO COLLECTED CLOCKS, THE (ROYAL IMPOSTOR)
                                KERSH, GERALD   NV SEP 47 05
  BONE FOR DEBUNKERS (THE KARMESIN AFFAIR)
                                KERSH, GERALD   SS SEP 62 12
  LUCKY DAY FOR THE BOAR, A   KERSH, GERALD   SS PBY 62 10
  VOICES IN THE DUST OF ANNAN   KERSH, GERALD   SS SEP 47 09
  WHATEVER HAPPENED TO CORPORAL CUCKOO? (1953)
                                KERSH, GERALD   NV STR 54 03

NINE BILLION NAMES OF GOD, THE
                                CLARKE, ARTHUR C. AC H HBW 67
  INTRODUCTION   CLARKE, ARTHUR C. IN
  NINE BILLION NAMES OF GOD, THE
                                CLARKE, ARTHUR C. SS STR 53 01
  I REMEMBER BABYLON   CLARKE, ARTHUR C. SS PBY 60 05
  TROUBLE WITH TIME (CRIME ON MARS, EQM 60 07)
                                CLARKE, ARTHUR C. SS FSF 61 06
  RESCUE PARTY   CLARKE, ARTHUR C. NV ASF 46 05
  CURSE, THE   CLARKE, ARTHUR C. SS CSM 53 09
  SUMMERTIME ON ICARUS (THE HOTTEST PIECE OF REAL ESTATE IN THE
    SOLAR SYSTEM)   CLARKE, ARTHUR C. SS VOG 60 06
  DOG STAR (MOONDOG)   CLARKE, ARTHUR C. SS GAL 62 04
  HIDE AND SEEK   CLARKE, ARTHUR C. SS ASF 49 09
  OUT OF THE SUN   CLARKE, ARTHUR C. SS IFS 58 02
  WALL OF DARKNESS, THE   CLARKE, ARTHUR C. SS SSS 49 07
  NO MORNING AFTER   CLARKE, ARTHUR C. SS FSF 56 07
  POSSESSED, THE   CLARKE, ARTHUR C. SS DSP 53 03
  DEATH AND THE SENATOR   CLARKE, ARTHUR C. NV ASF 61 05
  WHO'S THERE? (ALSO AS THE HAUNTED SPACESUIT)
                                CLARKE, ARTHUR C. SS NWS 58 11
  BEFORE EDEN   CLARKE, ARTHUR C. SS AMZ 61 06
  SUPERIORITY   CLARKE, ARTHUR C. SS FSF 51 08
  WALK IN THE DARK, A   CLARKE, ARTHUR C. SS TWS 50 08
  CALL OF THE STARS, THE (THE OTHER SIDE OF THE SKY)
                                CLARKE, ARTHUR C. SS INF 57 10
  RELUCTANT ORCHID, THE   CLARKE, ARTHUR C. SS SAT 56 12
  ENCOUNTER AT DAWN (ENCOUNTER IN THE DAWN)
                                CLARKE, ARTHUR C. SS AMZ 53 07
  IF I FORGET THEE, OH EARTH...
                                CLARKE, ARTHUR C. SS FUT 51 09
  PATENT PENDING   CLARKE, ARTHUR C. SS   54
  SENTINEL, THE (SENTINEL OF ETERNITY)
                                CLARKE, ARTHUR C. SS TSF 51 SP
  TRANSCIENCE   CLARKE, ARTHUR C. SS STS 49 07
  STAR, THE   CLARKE, ARTHUR C. SS INF 55 11

NINE BY LAUMER   LAUMER, KEITH   AC H DBL 67
  UNIVERSE ACCORDING TO LAUMER, THE
                                ELLISON, HARLAN   IN
  HYBRID   LAUMER, KEITH   SS FSF 61 11
  END AS A HERO   LAUMER, KEITH   NA GAL 63 06
  WALLS, THE   LAUMER, KEITH   SS AMZ 63 03
  DINOCHROME (COMBAT UNIT)   LAUMER, KEITH   SS FSF 60 11
  PLACEMENT TEST   LAUMER, KEITH   NV AMZ 64 07
  DOORSTEP   LAUMER, KEITH   SS GAL 61 02
  LONG REMEMBERED THUNDER, THE LAUMER, KEITH   NV WOT 62 12
  COCOON   LAUMER, KEITH   SS FAN 62 12
  TRIP TO THE CITY, A (IT COULD BE ANYTHING)
                                LAUMER, KEITH   NV AMZ 63 01

NINE HUNDRED GRANDMOTHERS   LAFFERTY, R. A.   AC ACE 70
  NINE HUNDRED GRANDMOTHERS   LAFFERTY, R. A.   SS IFS 66 02
  LAND OF THE GREAT HORSES   LAFFERTY, R. A.   SS DVS 67 01

NINE HUNDRED GRANDMOTHERS

GINNY WRAPPED IN THE SUN	LAFFERTY, R. A.	SS	GAL 67 08
SIX FINGERS OF TIME, THE	LAFFERTY, R. A.	NV	IFS 60 09
FROG ON THE MOUNTAIN	LAFFERTY, R. A.	NV	NEW 70 AC
ALL THE PEOPLE	LAFFERTY, R. A.	SS	GAL 61 04
PRIMARY EDUCATION OF THE CAMIROI			
	LAFFERTY, R. A.	SS	GAL 66 12
SLOW TUESDAY NIGHT	LAFFERTY, R. A.	SS	GAL 65 04
SNUFFLES	LAFFERTY, R. A.	NV	GAL 60 12
THUS WE FRUSTRATE CHARLEMAGNE			
	LAFFERTY, R. A.	SS	GAL 67 02
NAME OF THE SNAKE	LAFFERTY, R. A.	SS	WOT 64 04
NARROW VALLEY	LAFFERTY, R. A.	SS	FSF 66 09
POLICY AND CUSTOM OF THE CAMIROI			
	LAFFERTY, R. A.	SS	GAL 67 06
IN OUR BLOCK	LAFFERTY, R. A.	SS	IFS 65 07
HOG-BELLY HONEY	LAFFERTY, R. A.	SS	FSF 65 09
SEVEN-DAY TERROR	LAFFERTY, R. A.	SS	IFS 62 03
HOLE ON THE CORNER, THE	LAFFERTY, R. A.	SS	ORB 67 02
WHAT'S THE NAME OF THAT TOWN?			
	LAFFERTY, R. A.	SS	GAL 64 10
THROUGH OTHER EYES	LAFFERTY, R. A.	SS	FUT 60 02
ONE AT A TIME	LAFFERTY, R. A.	SS	ORB 68 04
GUESTING TIME	LAFFERTY, R. A.	SS	IFS 65 05

NINE TOMORROWS   ASIMOV, ISAAC   AC H DBL 59

I JUST MAKE THEM UP, SEE	ASIMOV, ISAAC	PM	FSF 58 02
REJECTION SLIPS	ASIMOV, ISAAC	PM	NEW 59 AC
PROFESSION	ASIMOV, ISAAC	SN	ASF 57 07
FEELING OF POWER, THE	ASIMOV, ISAAC	SS	IFS 58 02
DYING NIGHT, THE	ASIMOV, ISAAC	SS	FSF 56 07
I'M IN MARSPORT WITHOUT HILDA			
	ASIMOV, ISAAC	SS	VSF 57 11
GENTLE VULTURES, THE	ASIMOV, ISAAC	SS	SUP 57 12
ALL THE TROUBLES OF THE WORLD			
	ASIMOV, ISAAC	SS	SUP 58 04
SPELL MY NAME WITH AN S (S AS IN ZEBATINSKY)			
	ASIMOV, ISAAC	SS	SMG 58 01
LAST QUESTION, THE	ASIMOV, ISAAC	SS	SFQ 56 11
UGLY LITTLE BOY, THE (LASTBORN)			
	ASIMOV, ISAAC	NA	GAL 58 09

NINTH GALAXY READER, THE   POHL, FREDERIK   AN H DBL 66 02

INTRODUCTION	POHL, FREDERIK	IN	
ANCIENT MADNESS, AN (ALSO AS MARY)			
	KNIGHT, DAMON	NV	GAL 64 06
KING OF THE BEASTS, THE	FARMER, PHILIP JOSE	SS	GAL 64 06
WATCHERS IN THE GLADE, THE	WILSON, RICHARD	NV	GAL 64 08
JUNGLE SUBSTITUTE	ALDISS, BRIAN W.	NV	GAL 64 08
HOW THE OLD WORLD DIED	HARRISON, HARRY	SS	GAL 64 10
CHILDREN OF NIGHT, THE	POHL, FREDERIK	NV	GAL 64 10
TO AVENGE MAN (ALSO AS VENGEANCE IS MINE)			
	DEL REY, LESTER	NV	GAL 64 12
MONSTER AND THE MAIDEN, THE	ZELAZNY, ROGER	SS	GAL 64 12
FLASK OF FINE ARCTURAN, A	MACAPP, C. C.	SS	GAL 65 02
WRONG-WAY STREET	NIVEN, LARRY	SS	GAL 65 04
WASTED ON THE YOUNG	BRUNNER, JOHN	SS	GAL 65 04
SLOW TUESDAY NIGHT	LAFFERTY, R. A.	SS	GAL 65 04

NO BOUNDARIES   KUTTNER & MOORE   AC H BAL 55

VINTAGE SEASON	KUTTNER, HENRY	NV	ASF 46 09
DEVIL WE KNOW, THE	KUTTNER, HENRY	NV	UNK 41 08
HOME THERE'S NO RETURNING	KUTTNER, HENRY		
	AND MOORE, C. L.	NV C	NEW 55 AC
EXIT THE PROFESSOR	KUTTNER, HENRY	SS	TWS 47 10
TWO-HANDED ENGINE	KUTTNER, HENRY	SS	FSF 55 08

NO DIRECTION HOME   SPINRAD, NORMAN   AC PKT 75 05

NO DIRECTION HOME	SPINRAD, NORMAN	SS	NWQ 71 02
HEIRLOOM	SPINRAD, NORMAN	SS	LST 72
BIG FLASH, THE	SPINRAD, NORMAN	NV	ORB 69 05
CONSPIRACY, THE	SPINRAD, NORMAN	SS	NWS 69 02
WEED OF TIME, THE	SPINRAD, NORMAN	SS	ANA 70
THING OF BEAUTY, A	SPINRAD, NORMAN	SS	ASF 73 01
LOST CONTINENT, THE	SPINRAD, NORMAN	NV	SAG 70
HEROES DIE BUT ONCE	SPINRAD, NORMAN	SS	IFS 69 12
NATIONAL PASTIME, THE	SPINRAD, NORMAN	NV	NOV 73 03
IN THE EYE OF THE STORM (EYE OF THE STORM)			
	SPINRAD, NORMAN	SS	IFS 74 02
ALL THE SOUNDS OF THE RAINBOW			
	SPINRAD, NORMAN	NV	VTX 73 06

NO DOORS, NO WINDOWS (STORIES REWRITTEN)

	ELLISON, HARLAN	AC	PYR 75 11
BLOOD/THOUGHTS	ELLISON, HARLAN	IN	
WHIMPER OF WHIPPED DOGS, THE	ELLISON, HARLAN	NV	BMR 73
EDDIE, YOU'RE MY FRIEND	ELLISON, HARLAN	SS	KNT 75
STATUS QUO AT TROYDEN'S	ELLISON, HARLAN	SS	SMM 58 11
NEDRA AT F:5.6 (THE HUNGRY ONE)			
	ELLISON, HARLAN	SS	GNT 57 03
OPPOSITES ATTRACT (MAD BOMBER)			
	ELLISON, HARLAN	SS	CPR 57 11
TOE THE LINE	ELLISON, HARLAN	SS	SMM 57 06
DOWN IN THE DARK (AS ELLIS HART)			
	ELLISON, HARLAN	SS	ABR 67 30
PRIDE IN THE PROFESSION	ELLISON, HARLAN	SS	ADM 66 08
CHILDREN'S HOUR, THE (AS WALLACE EDMONDSON)			
	ELLISON, HARLAN	SS	FUN 58 07
WHITE TRASH DON'T EXIST (MURDER BAIT)			
	ELLISON, HARLAN	SS	MTP 56 10
THICKER THAN BLOOD	ELLISON, HARLAN	SS	MSM 58 02
TWO INCHES IN TOMORROW'S COLUMN (AS ELLIS HART)			
	ELLISON, HARLAN	SS	ABR 65 21
PROMISES OF LAUGHTER	ELLISON, HARLAN	SS	ADM 69 11
ORMOND ALWAYS PAYS HIS BILLS	ELLISON, HARLAN	SS	PSD 57 07
MAN ON THE JUICE WAGON, THE (AS CORDWAINER BIRD)			
	ELLISON, HARLAN	SS	ABR 63 14

NON-STATISTICAL MAN, THE

TIRED OLD MAN	ELLISON, HARLAN	SS	MSM 76 01

NO FUTURE IN IT   BRUNNER, JOHN   AC H DBL 64

NO FUTURE IN IT	BRUNNER, JOHN	SS	SCF 55 09
PUZZLE FOR SPACEMEN	BRUNNER, JOHN	SS	NWS 55 12
FAIR (AS KEITH WOODCOTT)	BRUNNER, JOHN	SS	NWS 56 03
WINDOWS OF HEAVEN, THE (TWO BY TWO)			
	BRUNNER, JOHN	SS	NWS 56 05
OUT OF ORDER	BRUNNER, JOHN	SS	NWS 57 04
ELECTED SILENCE (SILENCE)	BRUNNER, JOHN	NV	GAL 59 10
BADMAN	BRUNNER, JOHN	SS	NWS 60 03
REPORT ON THE NATURE OF THE LUNAR SURFACE			
	BRUNNER, JOHN	SS	ASF 60 08
IRON JACKASS, THE	BRUNNER, JOHN	SS	ASF 62 03
PROTECT ME FROM MY FRIENDS	BRUNNER, JOHN	SS	FSF 62 11
STIMULUS	BRUNNER, JOHN	SS	NWS 62 02

NO LIMITS   FERMAN, JOSEPH W. AN BAL 64 08

EDUCATION OF TIGRESS MACARDLE, THE			
	KORNBLUTH, C. M.	SS	VSF 57 07
ALL THE COLORS OF THE RAINBOW			
	BRACKETT, LEIGH	SS	VSF 57 11
NOW LET US SLEEP	DAVIDSON, AVRAM	SS	VSF 57 09
VENGEANCE FOR NIKOLAI (ALSO AS THE SONG OF MARYA)			
	MILLER, WALTER M. JR	SS	VSF 57 03
SEAT OF JUDGMENT, THE	DEL REY, LESTER	SS	VSF 58 05
BUY JUPITER!	ASIMOV, ISAAC	SS	VSF 58 05
AND THEN SHE FOUND HIM...	BUDRYS, ALGIS	SS	VSF 57 07
BEFORE THE TALENT DIES	SLESAR, HENRY	SS	VSF 57 09
COMEDIAN'S CHILDREN, THE	STURGEON, THEODORE	NV	VSF 58 05

NO MIND OF MAN   SILVERBERG, ROBERT OA H HAW 73

FOREWORD	SILVERBERG, ROBERT	IN	
WINDS OF STARMONT, THE	CARR, TERRY	NA	
PARTRIDGE PROJECT, THE	LUPOFF, RICHARD A.	NA	
THIS IS THE ROAD	SILVERBERG, ROBERT	NA	

NO OTHER GODS BUT ME   BRUNNER, JOHN   AC CPT 66

NO OTHER GODS BUT ME (BASED ON A TIME TO REND)			
	BRUNNER, JOHN	NV	SCF 56 12
MAN FROM THE BIG DARK, THE	BRUNNER, JOHN	SN	SFA 58 06
ODDS AGAINST YOU, THE (AGAINST THE ODDS)			
	BRUNNER, JOHN	SS	IFS 65 08

NO PLACE LIKE EARTH   CARNELL, JOHN   AN H BDM 52 10

TIME TO REST (COMBINED WITH "NO PLACE LIKE EARTH", NWS 51 SP)			
	BEYNON, JOHN	NV	ARS 49 WI
BREAKING STRAIN (THIRTY SECONDS - THIRTY DAYS)			
	CLARKE, ARTHUR C.	NV	TWS 49 12
SURVIVAL	WYNDHAM, JOHN	NV	TWS 52 02
TWO SHADOWS, THE	TEMPLE, WILLIAM F.	NV	STS 51 03
UNKNOWN QUANTITY	PHILLIPS, PETER	SS	NWS 49 05
BALANCE	CHRISTOPHER, JOHN	SS	NWS 51 SP
ROBOTS DON'T BLEED	GROVES, J. W.	SS	NWS 50 WI
CASTAWAY	WHITLEY, GEORGE	SS	WRT 47 11
MACHINE MADE	MCINTOSH, J. T.	SS	NWS 51 SU
CHEMICAL PLANT	WILLIAMSON, IAN	SS	NWS 50 WI

NO PLACE LIKE EARTH (7 OF 10)

	CARNELL, JOHN	AN	BDM 54 02
TIME TO REST (COMBINED WITH "NO PLACE LIKE EARTH", NWS 51 SP)			
	BEYNON, JOHN	NV	ARS 49 WI
BREAKING STRAIN (THIRTY SECONDS - THIRTY DAYS)			
	CLARKE, ARTHUR C.	NV	TWS 49 12
SURVIVAL	WYNDHAM, JOHN	NV	TWS 52 02
TWO SHADOWS, THE	TEMPLE, WILLIAM F.	NV	STS 51 03
BALANCE	CHRISTOPHER, JOHN	SS	NWS 51 SP
MACHINE MADE	MCINTOSH, J. T.	SS	NWS 51 SU
CHEMICAL PLANT	WILLIAMSON, IAN	SS	NWS 50 WI

NO TIME LIKE THE FUTURE   BOND, NELSON S.   AC AVN 54

VITAL FACTOR	BOND, NELSON S.	SS	51
VOICE FROM THE CURIOUS CUBE, THE			
	BOND, NELSON S.	SS	
BUTTON, BUTTON	BOND, NELSON S.	SS	
CONQUEROR'S ISLE	BOND, NELSON S.	SS	BBM 46 06
LIFE GOES ON	BOND, NELSON S.	SS	
UNCOMMON CASTAWAY	BOND, NELSON S.	SS	AFR 49 11
CUNNING OF THE BEAST, THE (ANOTHER WORLD BEGINS)			
	BOND, NELSON S.	SS	BBM 42 11
LAST OUTPOST, THE	BOND, NELSON S.	NV	
AND LO! THE BIRD	BOND, NELSON S.	SS	BBM 50 09
THIS IS THE LAND	BOND, NELSON S.	SS	BBM 51 04
WORLD OF WILLIAM GRESHAM, THE			
	BOND, NELSON S.	NV	
SILENT PLANET, THE	BOND, NELSON S.	SS	

NO TIME LIKE TOMORROW   ALDISS, BRIAN W. AC SIG 59 07

T	ALDISS, BRIAN W.	SS	NEB 56 11
NOT FOR AN AGE	ALDISS, BRIAN W.	SS	LOB 55 01
FAILED MEN, THE	ALDISS, BRIAN W.	SS	SCF 56 05
POOR LITTLE WARRIOR!	ALDISS, BRIAN W.	SS	FSF 58 04
CARRION COUNTRY	ALDISS, BRIAN W.	SS	NWS 58 11
JUDAS DANCED (JUDAS DANCING)	ALDISS, BRIAN W.	SS	SMG 54 03
PSYCLOPS	ALDISS, BRIAN W.	SS	NWS 56 07
OUTSIDE	ALDISS, BRIAN W.	SS	NWS 55 01
GESTURE OF FAREWELL	ALDISS, BRIAN W.	SS	NWS 57 07
NEW FATHER CHRISTMAS, THE	ALDISS, BRIAN W.	SS	FSF 58 01
BLIGHTED PROFILE	ALDISS, BRIAN W.	SS	SCF 58 06
OUR KIND OF KNOWLEDGE	ALDISS, BRIAN W.	SS	NWS 55 05

NON-STATISTICAL MAN, THE   JONES, RAYMOND F. AC BEL 64

NON-STATISTICAL MAN, THE	JONES, RAYMOND F.	NA	SFS 56 05
MOON IS DEATH, THE	JONES, RAYMOND F.	SS	FUT 53 03
GARDENER, THE	JONES, RAYMOND F.	SS	SFS 57 07
INTERMISSION TIME	JONES, RAYMOND F.	NV	SFQ 53 05

Title	Author	Type	Source
NORTHWEST OF EARTH	MOORE, C. L.	AC H	GNM 54
COLD GRAY GOD, THE	MOORE, C. L.	SS	WRT 35 10
DARK LAND, THE	MOORE, C. L.	NV	WRT 36 01
DUST OF GODS	MOORE, C. L.	NV	WRT 34 08
HELLSGARDE	MOORE, C. L.	SS	WRT 39 04
JIRELI	MOORE, C. L.	SS	WRT 35 03
LOST PARADISE	MOORE, C. L.	SS	WRT 36 07
YVALA	MOORE, C. L.	SS	WRT 36 02
NOT BEFORE TIME	BRUNNER, JOHN	AC	FSP 68
PREROGATIVE	BRUNNER, JOHN	SS	NWS 60 11
FAIR WARNING	BRUNNER, JOHN	SS	ASF 64 05
WARP AND THE WOOF-WOOF, THE	BRUNNER, JOHN	SS	SCF 66 02
SINGLEMINDED	BRUNNER, JOHN	NV	IFS 63 05
BETTER MOUSETRAP, A	BRUNNER, JOHN	NV	IFS 63 11
COINCIDENCE DAY	BRUNNER, JOHN	SS	ASF 65 02
SIEZURE (CHILDREN IN HIDING)	BRUNNER, JOHN	SS	GAL 66 12
TREASON IS A TWO-EDGED SWORD (TREASON)	BRUNNER, JOHN	NV	NEB 57 05
EYE OF THE BEHOLDER, THE	BRUNNER, JOHN	SS	FUN 57 01
ROUND TRIP	BRUNNER, JOHN	SS	FUN 59 09
NOT LONG FOR THIS WORLD	DERLETH, AUGUST	AC H	ARK 48
FOREWORD	DERLETH, AUGUST	IN	
SHADOW ON THE SKY, THE	DERLETH, AUGUST	SS	STT 32 01
BIRKETT'S TWELFTH CORPSE	DERLETH, AUGUST	SS	SRS 40 08
WHITE MOTH, THE	DERLETH, AUGUST	SS	WRT 33 04
NELLIE FOSTER	DERLETH, AUGUST	SS	WRT 33 06
WILD GRAPES	DERLETH, AUGUST	SS	WRT 34 07
FEIGMAN'S BEARD	DERLETH, AUGUST	SS	WRT 34 11
DRIFTING SNOW, THE	DERLETH, AUGUST	SS	WRT 39 02
RETURN OF SARAH PURCELL, THE	DERLETH, AUGUST	SS	WRT 36 07
LOGODA'S HEADS	DERLETH, AUGUST	SS	SRS 39 04
SECOND PRINT, THE (LORD OF EVIL)	DERLETH, AUGUST	SS	SRS 39 04
MRS. ELTING DOES HER PART	DERLETH, AUGUST	SS	SRS 39 08
LITTLE KNOWLEDGE, A	DERLETH, AUGUST	SS	
MRS. BENTLEY'S DAUGHTER	DERLETH, AUGUST	SS	WRT 30 10
THOSE WHO SEEK	DERLETH, AUGUST	SS	WRT 32 01
MR. BERBECK HAD A DREAM	DERLETH, AUGUST	SS	WRT 35 11
TENANT, THE	DERLETH, AUGUST	SS	WRT 28 03
LILAC BUSH, THE	DERLETH, AUGUST	SS	WRT 30 02
"JUST A SONG AT TWILIGHT"	DERLETH, AUGUST	SS	WRT 30 08
MATTER OF SIGHT, A	DERLETH, AUGUST	SS	WRT 30 01
PRINCE BORGIA'S MASS	DERLETH, AUGUST	SS	WRT 31 08
DINNER AT IMOLA, A	DERLETH, AUGUST	SS	WRT 29 04
LESANDRO'S FAMILIAR	DERLETH, AUGUST	SS	WRT 36 05
BRIDGE OF SIGHS, THE	DERLETH, AUGUST	SS	WRT 31 09
CLOAK FROM MESSER LANDO, A	DERLETH, AUGUST	SS	WRT 34 09
HE SHALL COME	DERLETH, AUGUST	SS	MSP 29 12
MRS. LANNISFREE	DERLETH, AUGUST	SS	WRT 45 11
AFTER YOU, MR. HENDERSON	DERLETH, AUGUST	SS	SRS 40 06
BAYNTER'S IMP	DERLETH, AUGUST	SS	WRT 43 09
LOST DAY, THE	DERLETH, AUGUST	SS	WRT 45 05
COLLECTOR OF STONES, A	DERLETH, AUGUST	SS	WRT 46 11
GOD-BOX, THE	DERLETH, AUGUST	SS	WRT 45 09
SAUNDER'S LITTLE FRIEND	DERLETH, AUGUST	SS	WRT 48 05
NOT WITHOUT SORCERY	STURGEON, THEODORE	AC	BAL 61 06
8 STORIES FROM "WITHOUT SORCERY"			
PREFACE	STURGEON, THEODORE	IN	
IT	STURGEON, THEODORE	NV	UNK 40 08
POKER FACE	STURGEON, THEODORE	SS	ASF 41 03
ARTNAN PROCESS	STURGEON, THEODORE	NV	ASF 41 06
ETHER BREATHER	STURGEON, THEODORE	SS	ASF 39 09
BUTYL AND THE BREATHER	STURGEON, THEODORE	NV	ASF 40 10
BRAT	STURGEON, THEODORE	SS	UNK 41 12
TWO PERCENT INSPIRATION	STURGEON, THEODORE	SS	ASF 41 10
CARGO	STURGEON, THEODORE	NV	UNK 40 11
NOTES TO A SCIENCE FICTION WRITER	BOVA, BEN	AC H	SCB 75
ONLY STORIES USED TO ILLUSTRATE WRITING TECHNIQUES ARE LISTED			
FIFTEEN MILES	BOVA, BEN	SS	FSF 67 05
MEN OF GOOD WILL	BOVA, BEN AND LEWIS, MYRON R.	SS C	GAL 64 06
STARS, WON'T YOU HIDE ME?	BOVA, BEN	SS	WOT 66 01
SHINING ONES, THE (FULL VERSION)	BOVA, BEN	NV	BLF 74 02
NOTIONS: UNLIMITED	SHECKLEY, ROBERT	AC	BAN 60 06
GRAY FLANNEL ARMOR	SHECKLEY, ROBERT	SS	GAL 57 11
LEECH, THE	SHECKLEY, ROBERT	SS	GAL 52 12
WATCHBIRD	SHECKLEY, ROBERT	NV	GAL 53 02
WIND IS RISING, A	SHECKLEY, ROBERT	SS	GAL 57 07
MORNING AFTER	SHECKLEY, ROBERT	NV	GAL 57 11
NATIVE PROBLEM, THE	SHECKLEY, ROBERT	NV	GAL 56 12
FEEDING TIME	SHECKLEY, ROBERT	SS	FNF 53 02
PARADISE II	SHECKLEY, ROBERT	SS	NWS 55 07
DOUBLE INDEMNITY	SHECKLEY, ROBERT	NV	GAL 57 10
HOLDOUT	SHECKLEY, ROBERT	SS	FSF 57 12
DAWN INVADER	SHECKLEY, ROBERT	SS	FSF 57 03
LANGUAGE OF LOVE, THE	SHECKLEY, ROBERT	SS	GAL 57 05
NOVA 1	HARRISON, HARRY	OA H	DCT 70
INTRODUCTION	HARRISON, HARRY	IN	
BIG CONNECTION, THE	SCOTT, ROBIN S.	SS	NOV 70 01
HAPPY DAY IN 2381, A	SILVERBERG, ROBERT	SS	NOV 70 01
TERMINUS EST	MALZBERG, BARRY N.	SS	NOV 70 01
HEXAMINATION	DAVIS, CHAN	SS	NOV 70 01
AND THIS DID DANTE DO	BRADBURY, RAY	SS	NOV 70 01
HIGHER THINGS, THE	PIERCE, JOHN R.	SS	NOV 70 01
SWASTIKA!	ALDISS, BRIAN W.	SS	NOV 70 01
HORARS OF WAR, THE	WOLFE, GENE	SS	NOV 70 01
LOVE STORY IN THREE ACTS	GERROLD, DAVID	SS	NOV 70 01
JEAN DUPRES	DICKSON, GORDON R.	NV	NOV 70 01
IN THE POCKET	O'DONNELL, K. M.	SS	NOV 70 01
MARY AND JOE	MITCHISON, NAOMI	SS	NOV 70 01
FACES & HANDS	SALLIS, JAMES	SS	NOV 70 01
WINNER, THE	WESTLAKE, DONALD E.	SS	NOV 70 01
WHOLE TRUTH, THE	ANTHONY, PIERS	SS	NOV 70 01
NOVA 1 (BRITISH)	HARRISON, HARRY	OA H	HAL 76
INTRODUCTION	HARRISON, HARRY	IN	
HAPPY DAY IN 2381, A	SILVERBERG, ROBERT	SS	NOV 70 01
TERMINUS EST	MALZBERG, BARRY N.	SS	NOV 70 01
HEXAMINATION	DAVIS, CHAN	SS	NOV 70 01
AND THIS DID DANTE DO	BRADBURY, RAY	SS	NOV 70 01
HIGHER THINGS, THE	PIERCE, JOHN R.	SS	NOV 70 01
SWASTIKA!	ALDISS, BRIAN W.	SS	NOV 70 01
HORARS OF WAR, THE	WOLFE, GENE	SS	NOV 70 01
LOVE STORY IN THREE ACTS	GERROLD, DAVID	SS	NOV 70 01
JEAN DUPRES	DICKSON, GORDON R.	NV	NOV 70 01
IN THE POCKET	O'DONNELL, K. M.	SS	NOV 70 01
MARY AND JOE	MITCHISON, NAOMI	SS	NOV 70 01
WINNER, THE	WESTLAKE, DONALD E.	SS	NOV 70 01
NOVA 2	HARRISON, HARRY	OA H	WKR 72
INTRODUCTION	HARRISON, HARRY	IN	
ZIRN LEFT UNGUARDED, THE JENGHIK PALACE IN FLAMES, JOHN WESTERLY DEAD	SHECKLEY, ROBERT	SS	NOV 72 02
"EAST WIND, WEST WIND"	ROBINSON, FRANK M.	NV	NOV 72 02
SUMERIAN OATH, THE	FARMER, PHILIP JOSE	SS	NOV 72 02
(NOW+N), (NOW-N)	SILVERBERG, ROBERT	NV	NOV 72 02
TWO ODYSSEYS INTO THE CENTER	MALZBERG, BARRY N.	SS	NOV 72 02
DARKNESS (TRANSLATED BY LEO L. BARROW)	CARNEIRO, ANDRE	SS	NOV 72 02
ON THE WHEEL	KNIGHT, DAMON	SS	NOV 72 02
MISS OMEGA RAVEN	MITCHISON, NAOMI	SS	NOV 72 02
POET IN THE HOLOGRAM IN THE MIDDLE OF PRIME TIME, THE	BRYANT, EDWARD	SS	NOV 72 02
OLD FOLKS, THE	GUNN, JAMES E.	SS	NOV 72 02
STEAM-DRIVEN BOY, THE	SLADEK, JOHN T.	SS	NOV 72 02
I TELL YOU, IT'S TRUE	ANDERSON, POUL	NV	NOV 72 02
AND I HAVE COME UPON THIS PLACE BY LOST WAYS	TIPTREE, JAMES JR.	NV	NOV 72 02
ERGOT SHOW, THE	ALDISS, BRIAN W.	SS	NOV 72 02
NOVA 3	HARRISON, HARRY	OA H	WKR 73
ALSO AS "THE OUTDATED MAN"			
WELCOME TO THE STANDARD NIGHTMARE	SHECKLEY, ROBERT	SS	NOV 73 03
EXPENSIVE DELICATE SHIP, THE	ALDISS, BRIAN W.	SS	NOV 73 03
DESTRUCTION AND EXCULPATION OF EARTH, THE	MALZBERG, BARRY N.	SS	NOV 73 03
INTRODUCTION TO THE SECOND EDITION	MALZBERG, BARRY N.	SS	NOV 73 03
BREAKOUT IN ECOL 2	BUNCH, DAVID R.	SS	NOV 73 03
COLD WAR...CONTINUED, THE	REYNOLDS, MACK	NV	NOV 73 03
FACTORY, THE	MITCHISON, NAOMI	SS	NOV 73 03
DEFENSIVE BOMBER, THE	DEMPSEY, HANK	SS	NOV 73 03
ENDORSEMENT, PERSONAL	MCLAUGHLIN, DEAN	SS	NOV 73 03
NATIONAL PASTIME, THE	SPINRAD, NORMAN	NV	NOV 73 03
ULTIMATE END, THE	GLASS, DICK	SS	NOV 73 03
PITY THE POOR OUTDATED MAN	SHOFNER, PHILIP	NV	NOV 73 03
EXHIBITION, THE	EDELSTEIN, SCOTT	SS	NOV 73 03
SKETCHES AMONG THE RUINS OF MY MIND	FARMER, PHILIP JOSE	NV	NOV 73 03
NOVA 4	HARRISON, HARRY	OA H	WKR 74
MONSTERS OF INGRATITUDE IV, THE	ALDISS, BRIAN W.	SS	NOV 74 04
SONGS OF WAR	REED, KIT	NV	NOV 74 04
PROTECTIVE TEMPORAL STRIKE	GIANNATTASIO, GERARD	SS	NOV 74 04
MAKING IT ALL THE WAY INTO THE FUTURE ON GAXTON FALLS OF THE RED PLANET	MALZBERG, BARRY N.	SS	NOV 74 04
SLAVES OF TIME	SHECKLEY, ROBERT	NV	NOV 74 04
SINGULAR	GARNETT, BILL	SS	NOV 74 04
TOO LONG AT THE FAIR	WELLEN, EDWARD	SS	NOV 74 04
NOT A PETAL FALLS	BIRELEY, RICHARD	SS	NOV 74 04
MY AFFAIR WITH SCIENCE FICTION	BESTER, ALFRED	AR	NOV 74 04
OUT OF THE WATERS	MITCHISON, NAOMI	SS	NOV 74 04
SIDE VIEW OF A CIRCLE	ADDOBATI, MICHAEL	SS	NOV 74 04
BEYOND THE CLEFT	REAMY, TOM	NV	NOV 74 04
OUR LADY OF THE ENDLESS SKY	DUNTEMANN, JEFF	NV	NOV 74 04
AFTERWORD	HARRISON, HARRY	MS	
NOVELETS OF SCIENCE FICTION	HOWARD, IVAN	AN	BEL 63
ULTRASONIC GOD (ALSO AS THE GALTON WHISTLE)	DE CAMP, L. SPRAGUE	NV	FUT 51 07
CHAPTER ENDS, THE	ANDERSON, POUL	NV	DSF 54 01
"A" AS IN ANDROID	LESSER, MILTON	SS	FUT 51 05
AND THE TRUTH SHALL MAKE YOU FREE (ALSO AS THE ANSWERS)	SIMAK, CLIFFORD D.	SS	FUT 53 03
NIGHT-FEAR	LONG, FRANK BELKNAP	SS	DSF 53 10
I AM TOMORROW	DEL REY, LESTER	NV	DSF 52 12
TESTAMENT OF ANDROS	BLISH, JAMES	NV	FUT 53 01
POSSESSED, THE	CLARKE, ARTHUR C.	SS	DSF 53 03
NOVELS	VERNE, JULES	AC H	GOL 29
EDITED BY H. C. HARWOOD			
TWENTY THOUSAND LEAGUES UNDER THE SEA (1873)	VERNE, JULES	NO	GMS 73
AROUND THE WORLD IN EIGHTY DAYS (1873)	VERNE, JULES	NO	
HECTOR SERVADAC (1877)	VERNE, JULES	NO	
FLOATING ISLAND, THE (1895)	VERNE, JULES	NO	
BLOCKADE RUNNERS, THE	VERNE, JULES	NA	
NOW & BEYOND	HOWARD, IVAN	AN	BEL 65 09
TURNING WHEEL, THE	DICK, PHILIP K.	SS	SFS 54 02

NOW & BEYOND

UNREASONABLE FACSIMILE	DEL REY, LESTER	SS	FUT 52	07
HEAV'N, HEAV'N	RUSSELL, ERIC FRANK	SS	FUT 56	30
VENUS TRAP	SILVERBERG, ROBERT	SS	FUT 56	30
TELESTASSIS	PEASE, M. C.	SS	SFS 55	05
WAPSHOT'S DEMON	POHL, FREDERIK	SS	SFS 56	07
CASE FOR EARTH, THE	RUSSELL, ERIC FRANK	SS	FUT 58	04
OUTCASTS, THE	SMITH, GEORGE HUDSON	SS	SFS 58	09

NOW BEGINS TOMORROW	KNIGHT, DAMON	AN	LAN 69	11
SEE "FIRST FLIGHT"				

NOW THEN	BRUNNER, JOHN	AC	MFL 65	10
PREFACE	BRUNNER, JOHN	IN		
SOME LAPSE OF TIME	BRUNNER, JOHN	NV	SCF 63	02
IMPRINT OF CHAOS	BRUNNER, JOHN	NV	SCF 60	08
THOU GOOD AND FAITHFUL (AS JOHN LOXMITH)				
	BRUNNER, JOHN	NV	ASF 53	03

NUTZENBOLTS	GOULART, RON	AC H	MAC 75	
FOREWORD: POPULAR MECHANICS	GOULART, RON	IN		
GIGOLO	GOULART, RON	SS	FSF 72	08
DOWN AND OUT	GOULART, RON	SS	FSF 73	08
INNOCENCE OF FATHER BANGS, THE				
	GOULART, RON	SS	PNT 72	
NUTZENBOLTS	GOULART, RON	SS		
SWAP	GOULART, RON	SS	IFS 70	04
TWO DAYS RUNNING AND THEN SKIP A DAY				
	GOULART, RON	SS	AMZ 67	02
WHISTLER	GOULART, RON	SS	EIO 73	
BADINAGE	GOULART, RON	SS	NEW 65	AN
STOCKYARD BLUES	GOULART, RON	SS		
FREE AT LAST	GOULART, RON	SS	INY 73	05
DINGBAT	GOULART, RON	NV	IFS 73	12

OCTOBER COUNTRY, THE	BRADBURY, RAY	AC H	BAL 55	
DWARF, THE	BRADBURY, RAY	SS	FAN 54	01
NEXT IN LINE, THE	BRADBURY, RAY	NV	NEW 47	AC
WATCHFUL POKER CHIP OF H. MATISSE, THE				
	BRADBURY, RAY	SS	BEY 54	03
SKELETON	BRADBURY, RAY	SS	WRT 45	09
JAR, THE	BRADBURY, RAY	SS	WRT 44	11
LAKE, THE	BRADBURY, RAY	SS	WRT 44	05
EMISSARY, THE	BRADBURY, RAY	SS	NEW 47	AC
TOUCHED WITH FIRE (SHOPPING FOR DEATH)				
	BRADBURY, RAY	SS	MCL 54	06
SMALL ASSASSIN, THE	BRADBURY, RAY	SS	DMN 46	11
CROWD, THE	BRADBURY, RAY	SS	WRT 43	05
JACK-IN-THE-BOX	BRADBURY, RAY	SS	NEW 47	AC
SCYTHE, THE	BRADBURY, RAY	SS	WRT 43	07
UNCLE EINAR	BRADBURY, RAY	SS	NEW 47	AC
WIND, THE	BRADBURY, RAY	SS	WRT 43	03
MAN UPSTAIRS, THE	BRADBURY, RAY	SS	HRP 47	03
THERE WAS AN OLD WOMAN	BRADBURY, RAY	SS	WRT 44	07
CISTERN, THE	BRADBURY, RAY	SS	MAD 47	05
HOMECOMING, THE	BRADBURY, RAY	SS	MAD 46	10
WONDERFUL DEATH OF DUDLEY STONE, THE				
	BRADBURY, RAY	SS	CHM 54	07

OCTOBER COUNTRY, THE (BRITISH)				
	BRADBURY, RAY	AC H	HDV 56	
DWARF, THE	BRADBURY, RAY	SS	FAN 54	01
WATCHFUL POKER CHIP OF H. MATISSE, THE				
	BRADBURY, RAY	SS	BEY 54	03
SKELETON	BRADBURY, RAY	SS	WRT 45	09
JAR, THE	BRADBURY, RAY	SS	WRT 44	11
EMISSARY, THE	BRADBURY, RAY	SS	NEW 47	AC
TOUCHED WITH FIRE (SHOPPING FOR DEATH)				
	BRADBURY, RAY	SS	MCL 54	06
SCYTHE, THE	BRADBURY, RAY	SS	WRT 43	07
UNCLE EINAR	BRADBURY, RAY	SS	NEW 47	AC
WIND, THE	BRADBURY, RAY	SS	WRT 43	03
THERE WAS AN OLD WOMAN	BRADBURY, RAY	SS	WRT 44	07
HOMECOMING, THE	BRADBURY, RAY	SS	MAD 46	10
WONDERFUL DEATH OF DUDLEY STONE, THE				
	BRADBURY, RAY	SS	CHM 54	07
TRAVELLER, THE	BRADBURY, RAY	SS	WRT 46	03

ODD JOB NO. 101	GOULART, RON	AC H	SCB 75	
PASSAGE TO MURDSTONE	GOULART, RON	SS	FSF 71	10
CYBERNETIC TABERNACLE JOB, THE				
	GOULART, RON	NV	INY 72	03
REGARDING PATIENT 724	GOULART, RON	SS	ASF 73	11
WAY THINGS WORK, THE	GOULART, RON	SS	FSF 71	03
PLUMROSE	GOULART, RON	SS	FAN 63	06
VARIETIES OF RELIGIOUS EXPERIENCE				
	GOULART, RON	SS	FSF 73	06
ODD JOB NO. 101	GOULART, RON	SS	FSF 74	

ODD SCIENCE FICTION	LONG, FRANK BELKNAP	AC	BEL 64	08
IN ENGLAND AS "THE HORROR FROM THE HILLS"				
HORROR FROM THE HILLS, THE	LONG, FRANK BELKNAP	SN	WRT 31	01
FLAME OF LIFE, THE	LONG, FRANK BELKNAP	SS	FUT 59	06
GIANT IN THE FOREST	LONG, FRANK BELKNAP	SS	SFQ 55	02

ODDBALLS, THE	GHIDALIA, VIC	AN	MAN 73	
MAN WHO COULD WORK MIRACLES, THE				
	WELLS, H. G.	SS	ILN 98	07
LUNATIC PLANET, THE	SILVERBERG, ROBERT	SS	AMZ 57	11
NOBODY BOTHERS GUS (AS PAUL JANVIER)				
	BUDRYS, ALGIS	SS	ASF 55	11
DREAMS OF ALBERT MORELAND, THE				
	LEIBER, FRITZ	NV	AFR 48	07
MAN WHO WALKED THROUGH GLASS, THE				
	BOND, NELSON S.	SS	ESQ 38	11
TALENT	BLOCH, ROBERT	SS	IFS 60	07
BARBARIAN, THE	ANDERSON, POUL	SS	FSF 56	05

EACH AN EXPLORER	ASIMOV, ISAAC	SS	FUT 56	30
PASSING OF THE THIRD FLOOR BACK				
	JEROME, JEROME K.	NV		

OF ALL POSSIBLE WORLDS	TENN, WILLIAM	AC	BAL 55	
ON THE FICTION IN SCIENCE FICTION				
	TENN, WILLIAM	IN	SFA 54	03
DOWN AMONG THE DEAD MEN	TENN, WILLIAM	NV	GAL 54	06
ME, MYSELF, AND I	TENN, WILLIAM	SS	PLS 47	WI
LIBERATION OF EARTH, THE	TENN, WILLIAM	SS	FUT 53	05
EVERYBODY LOVES IRVING BOMMER				
	TENN, WILLIAM	SS	FAD 51	08
FLIRGLEFLIP (THE REMARKABLE FLIRGLEFLIP)				
	TENN, WILLIAM	SS	FAD 50	05
TENANTS, THE	TENN, WILLIAM	SS	FSF 54	04
CUSTODIAN, THE	TENN, WILLIAM	NV	IFS 53	11
ABOUT WILLIAM TENN	MISC. MATERIAL	MS		

OF TIME AND STARS	CLARKE, ARTHUR C.	AC H	GOL 72	
INTRODUCTION	PRIESTLEY, J. B.	IN		
FOREWORD	CLARKE, ARTHUR C.	IN		
NINE BILLION NAMES OF GOD, THE				
	CLARKE, ARTHUR C.	SS	STR 53	01
APE ABOUT THE HOUSE, AN	CLARKE, ARTHUR C.	SS	DUD 62	
GREEN FINGERS (VENTURE TO THE MOON)				
	CLARKE, ARTHUR C.	SS	FSF 57	01
TROUBLE WITH THE NATIVES (CAPTAIN WYXTPTHLL'S FLYING SAUCER)				
	CLARKE, ARTHUR C.	SS	MAR 51	05
INTO THE COMET (INSIDE THE COMET)				
	CLARKE, ARTHUR C.	SS	FSF 60	10
NO MORNING AFTER	CLARKE, ARTHUR C.	SS	FSF 56	07
IF I FORGET THEE, OH EARTH...				
	CLARKE, ARTHUR C.	SS	FUT 51	09
WHO'S THERE? (ALSO AS THE HAUNTED SPACESUIT)				
	CLARKE, ARTHUR C.	SS	NWS 58	11
ALL THE TIME IN THE WORLD	CLARKE, ARTHUR C.	SS	STS 52	07
HIDE AND SEEK	CLARKE, ARTHUR C.	SS	ASF 49	09
ROBIN HOOD, F.R.S. (VENTURE TO THE MOON)				
	CLARKE, ARTHUR C.	SS	FSF 56	12
FIRES WITHIN, THE	CLARKE, ARTHUR C.	SS	FSB 47	08
FORGOTTEN ENEMY, THE	CLARKE, ARTHUR C.	SS	NWS 49	05
RELUCTANT ORCHID, THE	CLARKE, ARTHUR C.	SS	SAT 56	12
ENCOUNTER AT DAWN (ENCOUNTER IN THE DAWN)				
	CLARKE, ARTHUR C.	SS	AMZ 53	07
SECURITY CHECK	CLARKE, ARTHUR C.	SS	FSF 57	06
FEATHERED FRIEND (THE OTHER SIDE OF THE SKY)				
	CLARKE, ARTHUR C.	SS	INF 57	09
SENTINEL, THE (SENTINEL OF ETERNITY)				
	CLARKE, ARTHUR C.	SS	TSF 51	SP
BIBLIOGRAPHY: BOOKS BY ARTHUR C. CLARKE				
	MISC. MATERIAL	MS		

OFF CENTER	KNIGHT, DAMON	DC	ACE 65	
WHAT ROUGH BEAST?	KNIGHT, DAMON	NV	FSF 59	02
SECOND-CLASS CITIZEN, THE	KNIGHT, DAMON	SS	IFS 63	11
BE MY GUEST	KNIGHT, DAMON	NV	FUN 58	09
GOD'S NOSE	KNIGHT, DAMON	SS	ROG 64	
CATCH THAT MARTIAN	KNIGHT, DAMON	SS	GAL 52	03

OFF CENTRE	KNIGHT, DAMON	AC H	GOL 69	
WHAT ROUGH BEAST?	KNIGHT, DAMON	NV	FSF 59	02
SECOND-CLASS CITIZEN, THE	KNIGHT, DAMON	SS	IFS 63	11
BE MY GUEST	KNIGHT, DAMON	NV	FUN 58	09
GOD'S NOSE	KNIGHT, DAMON	SS	ROG 64	
CATCH THAT MARTIAN	KNIGHT, DAMON	SS	GAL 52	03
DULCIE AND DECORUM	KNIGHT, DAMON	NV	GAL 55	03
MASKS	KNIGHT, DAMON	SS	PBY 68	07
TO BE CONTINUED	KNIGHT, DAMON	SS	FSF 59	11

OFF THE BEATEN ORBIT	MERRIL, JUDITH	AN	PYR 59	
SEE "GALAXY OF GHOULS"				

OLD DIE RICH AND OTHER SCIENCE FICTION, THE				
	GOLD, H. L.	AC H	CRN 55	
OLD DIE RICH, THE	GOLD, H. L.	NA	GAL 53	03
TROUBLE WITH WATER	GOLD, H. L.	SS	UNK 39	03
NO CHARGE FOR ALTERATIONS	GOLD, H. L.	NV	AMZ 53	05
DON'T TAKE IT TO HEART	GOLD, H. L.	SS	FAN 53	08
MAN OF PARTS	GOLD, H. L.	SS	NTL 54	
LOVE IN THE DARK (LOVE ETHEREAL)				
	GOLD, H. L.	SS	SUS 51	FL
MAN WITH ENGLISH, THE	GOLD, H. L.	SS	STR 53	01
BIOGRAPHY PROJECT, THE	GOLD, H. L.	SS	GAL 51	09
AT THE POST	GOLD, H. L.	NV	GAL 53	10
HERO	GOLD, H. L.	SS	TWS 39	11
AND THREE TO GET READY	GOLD, H. L.	SS	FAN 52	SU
PROBLEM IN MURDER	GOLD, H. L.	NV	ASF 39	03

OLE DOC METHUSELAH	HUBBARD, L. RON	AC	DAW 70	
OLE DOC METHUSELAH	HUBBARD, L. RON	NV	ASF 47	10
HER MAJESTY'S ABERRATION	HUBBARD, L. RON	SS	ASF 48	03
EXPENSIVE SLAVES, THE	HUBBARD, L. RON	SS	ASF 47	11
GREAT AIR MONOPOLY, THE	HUBBARD, L. RON	NV	ASF 48	09
PLAGUE	HUBBARD, L. RON	NV	ASF 49	04
SOUND INVESTMENT, A	HUBBARD, L. RON	SS	ASF 49	06
OLE MOTHER METHUSELAH	HUBBARD, L. RON	NV	ASF 50	01

OMEGA	ELWOOD, ROGER	OA H	WKR 73	
RUNNING AROUND	MALZBERG, BARRY N.	SS	OMG 73	
EMPTY FIELD, THE (TRANSLATED BY TSURUTA & MERRIL)				
	KITA, MORIO	SS	OMG 73	
OD	DANN, JACK M.			
	AND ZEBROWSKI, GEORGE	SS C	OMG 73	
AMFORTAS	JANIFER, LAURENCE M.	SS	OMG 73	
AFTER KING KONG FELL	FARMER, PHILIP JOSE	SS	OMG 73	
SYMPOSIUM	LAFFERTY, R. A.	SS	OMG 73	

OMEGA
SWORDS OF IFTHAN   SUTHERLAND, JAMES   SS   OMG 73
BEAST IN VIEW   DEFORD, MIRIAM ALLEN SS   OMG 73
SLIDE SHOW   MARTIN, GEORGE R. R. SS   OMG 73
RABBEL-DOWSER   MCCAFFREY, ANNE   SS   OMG 73
SERPENT IN EDEN, THE   ANDERSON, POUL   NV   OMG 73
BEACHHEAD IN UTOPIA   BIGGLE, LLOYD JR.   SS   OMG 73
GERANIUMS   MALZBERG, BARRY N.
                             AND KING, VALERIE   SS C OMG 73

OMNIBUS OF SCIENCE FICTION   CONKLIN, GROFF   AN H CRN 52
   DERIVATIVE ANTHOLOGIES ARE "SCIENCE FICTION OMNIBUS",
   "STRANGE TRAVELS IN SCIENCE FICTION" AND
   "STRANGE ADVENTURES IN SCIENCE FICTION"
INTRODUCTION   CONKLIN, GROFF   IN
JOHN THOMAS'S CUBE   LEIMERT, JOHN   SS   ATL 45 08
HYPERPELOSITY   DE CAMP, L. SPRAGUE SS   ASF 38 04
THING IN THE WOODS, THE   PRATT, FLETCHER
                             AND RUBY, B. F.   SS C AMZ 35 02
AND BE MERRY... (ALSO AS THE PYRAMID IN THE DESERT)
                             MACLEAN, KATHERINE   SS   ASF 50 02
BEES FROM BORNEO, THE   GRAY, WILL H.   SS   AMZ 31 02
RAG THING, THE   GRINNELL, DAVID   SS   FSF 51 10
CONQUEROR, THE   CLIFTON, MARK   SS   ASF 52 08
NEVER UNDERESTIMATE...   STURGEON, THEODORE   SS   IFS 52 03
DOORBELL, THE   KELLER, DAVID H. MD. SS   WOS 34 06
SUBWAY NAMED MOBIUS, A   DEUTSCH, A. J.   SS   ASF 50 12
BACKFIRE   ROCKLYNNE, ROSS   SS   ASF 43 01
BOX, THE   BLISH, JAMES   SS   TWS 49 04
ZERITSKY'S LAW   GRIFFITH, ANN WARREN SS   GAL 51 11
FOURTH DYNASTY, THE   WINTERBOTHAM, R. R. SS   ASF 36 12
COLOUR OUT OF SPACE, THE (ALSO AS MONSTER OF TERROR)
                             LOVECRAFT, H. P.   SS   AMZ 27 09
HEAD HUNTERS, THE   WILLIAMS, RALPH   SS   ASF 51 10
STAR DUMMY, THE   BOUCHER, ANTHONY   SS   FAN 52 FL
CATCH THAT MARTIAN   KNIGHT, DAMON   SS   GAL 52 03
SHIPSHAPE HOME   MATHESON, RICHARD   SS   GAL 52 07
HOMO SOL   ASIMOV, ISAAC   SS   ASF 40 09
ALEXANDER THE BAIT   TENN, WILLIAM   SS   ASF 46 05
KALEIDOSCOPE   BRADBURY, RAY   SS   TWS 49 10
NOTHING HAPPENS ON THE MOON ERNST, PAUL   SS   ASF 39 02
TRIGGER TIDE   GUIN, WYMAN   SS   ASF 50 10
PLAGUE   LEINSTER, MURRAY   NV   ASF 44 02
WINNER LOSE ALL   VANCE, JACK   SS   GAL 51 12
TEST PIECE   RUSSELL, ERIC FRANK SS   OWS 51 03
ENVIRONMENT   GEIER, CHESTER S.   SS   ASF 44 05
HIGH THRESHOLD   NOURSE, ALAN E.   SS   ASF 51 03
SPECTATOR SPORT   MACDONALD, JOHN D.   SS   TWS 50 02
RECRUITING STATION (ALSO AS MASTERS OF TIME)
                             VAN VOGT, A. E.   NV   ASF 42 03
STONE AND A SPEAR, A   JONES, RAYMOND F.   NV   GAL 50 12
WHAT YOU NEED   PADGETT, LEWIS   SS   ASF 45 10
CHOICE, THE   HILTON-YOUNG,WAYLAND SS   PUN 52 03
WAR AGAINST THE MOON, THE (1928)
                             MAUROIS, ANDRE   SS   FSF 50 SU
PLEASANT DREAMS   ROBIN, RALPH   SS   GAL 51 10
MANNERS OF THE AGE   FYFE, H. B.   SS   GAL 52 03
WEAPON, THE   BROWN, FREDRIC   SS   ASF 51 04
SCARLET PLAGUE, THE   LONDON, JACK   NA   LOM 12 06
HERITAGE   ABERNATHY, ROBERT   NV   ASF 42 06
HISTORY LESSON   CLARKE, ARTHUR C.   SS   STS 49 05
INSTINCT   DEL REY, LESTER   SS   ASF 52 01
COUNTER CHARM   PHILLIPS, PETER   SS   SLN 51 SP

OMNIBUS OF TIME, THE   FARLEY, RALPH MILNE AC H FPB 50
MAN WHO MET HIMSELF, THE   FARLEY, RALPH MILNE SS
TIME FOR SALE   FARLEY, RALPH MILNE SS   AMZ 38 08
RESCUE INTO THE PAST   FARLEY, RALPH MILNE SS   AMZ 40 10
IMMORTALITY OF ALAN WHIDDEN, THE
                             FARLEY, RALPH MILNE SS   AMZ 42 02
TIME-WISE GUY, THE   FARLEY, RALPH MILNE SS   AMZ 40 05
MONTH A MINUTE, A   FARLEY, RALPH MILNE SS   TWS 37 12
INVISIBLE BOMBER, THE   FARLEY, RALPH MILNE SS   AMZ 38 06
TIME TRAVELLER, THE   FARLEY, RALPH MILNE SS   WRT 31 08
I KILLER HITLER   FARLEY, RALPH MILNE SS   WRT 41 07
RADIO WAR, THE (MISSING FIRST CHAPTER OF)
                             FARLEY, RALPH MILNE EX   ARG 32 07
GOLDEN CITY, THE   FARLEY, RALPH MILNE EX   ARG 33 05
HIDDEN UNIVERSE, THE   FARLEY, RALPH MILNE EX   AMZ 39 11
STRANDED IN TIME   FARLEY, RALPH MILNE SS
MAN WHO LIVED BACKWARDS, THE FARLEY, RALPH MILNE SS
REVENGE OF THE GREAT WHITE LODGE, THE
                             FARLEY, RALPH MILNE SS
MAN WHO COULD TURN BACK THE CLOCK, THE
                             FARLEY, RALPH MILNE SS
END OF THE WORLD, THE   FARLEY, RALPH MILNE SS
AFTER MATH   FARLEY, RALPH MILNE AR

OMNIBUS, THE   VERNE, JULES   AC H LIP 31
TWENTY THOUSAND LEAGUES UNDER THE SEA (1873)
                             VERNE, JULES   NO   GMS 73
AROUND THE WORLD IN EIGHTY DAYS (1873)
                             VERNE, JULES   NO
BLOCKADE RUNNERS, THE   VERNE, JULES   NA
FROM THE EARTH TO THE MOON AND A TRIP AROUND IT (1865)
                             VERNE, JULES   NO

ON AN ODD NOTE   KERSH, GERALD   AC H BAL 58
SEED OF DESTRUCTION   KERSH, GERALD   SS   ESQ
FROZEN BEAUTY   KERSH, GERALD   SS   58
REFLECTIONS IN A TABLESPOON KERSH, GERALD   SS
CREWEL NEEDLE, THE   KERSH, GERALD   SS   ESQ
SYMPATHETIC SOUSE, THE   KERSH, GERALD   SS
QUEEN OF PIG ISLAND, THE (MISTRESS OF PORCOSITO)
                             KERSH, GERALD   SS   PBY 57 07
PROPHET WITHOUT HONOR   KERSH, GERALD   SS
BEGGARS' STONE, THE   KERSH, GERALD   SS   ESQ
BRIGHTON MONSTER, THE (THE MONSTER)
                             KERSH, GERALD   SS   SEP 48 02
EXTRAORDINARILY HORRIBLE DUMMY, THE (THE WHISPER)
                             KERSH, GERALD   SS   CMP 46 04
FANTASY OF A HUNTED MAN   KERSH, GERALD   SS
GENTLEMAN ALL IN BLACK, THE KERSH, GERALD   SS   TDY
EYE, THE (THE MURDERER'S EYE)
                             KERSH, GERALD   NV   SEP 57 03

ON OUR WAY TO THE FUTURE   CARR, TERRY   AN   ACE 70
INTRODUCTION   CARR, TERRY   IN
GREENSLAVES   HERBERT, FRANK   NV   AMZ 65 03
BETTER MOUSEHOLE, A   PANGBORN, EDGAR   SS   GAL 65 10
BALLENGER'S PEOPLE   NEVILLE, KRIS   SS   GAL 67 04
KING SOLOMON'S RING   ZELAZNY, ROGER   SS   FAN 63 10
SUNDANCE   SILVERBERG, ROBERT   SS   FSF 69 06
BE MERRY   BUDRYS, ALGIS   NV   IFS 66 12
UNDER THE DRAGON'S TAIL   LATHAM, PHILIP   SS   ASF 66 12
TASTE FOR DOSTOEVSKY, A   ALDISS, BRIAN W.   SS   NWR 67 10
CYCLOPS   LEIBER, FRITZ   SS   WOT 65 09
GOBLIN NIGHT   SCHMITZ, JAMES H.   NV   ASF 65 04

ONCE AND FUTURE TALES FROM THE MAGAZINE OF FANTASY AND
SCIENCE FICTION   FERMAN, EDWARD L.   AN H HWF 68
INTRODUCTION   MERRIL, JUDITH   IN
MANOR OF ROSES, THE   SWANN, THOMAS B.   SN   FSF 66 11
END OF THE LINE   OLIVER, CHAD   NV   FSF 65 01
FIFTEENTH WIND OF MARCH, THE BLAND, FREDERICK   NV   FSF 62 06
JOURNEY OF TEN THOUSAND MILES
                             MOHLER, WILL   SS   FSF 63 03
FRUITING BODY   BROWN, ROSEL GEORGE NV   FSF 62 08
OPEN TO ME, MY SISTER (ALSO AS MY SISTER'S BROTHER)
                             FARMER, PHILIP JOSE NV   FSF 60 05
CASE OF THE HOMOCIDAL ROBOTS, THE
                             LEINSTER, MURRAY   NV   FSF 61 08
WHEN YOU CARE, WHEN YOU LOVE STURGEON, THEODORE   NV   FSF 62 09
MASCULINIST REVOLT, THE   TENN, WILLIAM   NV   FSF 65 08

ONCE THERE WAS A GIANT   LAUMER, KEITH   AC H DBL 71
PROTOTAPH   LAUMER, KEITH   SS   ASF 66 03
LAST COMMAND, THE   LAUMER, KEITH   SS   ASF 67 01
LAWGIVER, THE   LAUMER, KEITH   SS   YRT 70
FOUNDER'S DAY   LAUMER, KEITH   NV   FSF 66 07
WORLDMASTER   LAUMER, KEITH   NV   WOT 65 11
EXTERMINATOR, THE   LAUMER, KEITH   NV
MIND OUT OF TIME, THE   LAUMER, KEITH   SS   FRS 68
ONCE THERE WAS A GIANT   LAUMER, KEITH   SN   FSF 68 11

ONE HUNDRED YEARS OF SCIENCE FICTION
                             KNIGHT, DAMON   AN H SAS 68
INTRODUCTION   KNIGHT, DAMON   IN
WITH THE NIGHT MAIL   KIPLING, RUDYARD   NV   MCS 05 11
MR. MURPHY OF NEW YORK   MCMORROW, THOMAS   SS   SEP 30 03
NEW APPLES IN THE GARDEN   NEVILLE, KRIS   SS   ASF 63 07
SANITY (ALSO AS CRAZY WOLF) LEIBER, FRITZ   SS   ASF 44 04
SHAPES, THE   ROSNY, J. H. (AINE) SS
OTHER CELIA, THE   STURGEON, THEODORE   SS   GAL 57 03
BLACK CHARLIE   DICKSON, GORDON R.   SS   GAL 54 04
SUBWAY NAMED MOBIUS, A   DEUTSCH, A. J.   SS   ASF 50 12
MAN WHO CAME EARLY, THE   ANDERSON, POUL   NV   FSF 56 06
OTHER NOW, THE   LEINSTER, MURRAY   SS   GAL 51 03
WHATEVER HAPPENED TO CORPORAL CUCKOO? (1953)
                             KERSH, GERALD   NV   STR 54 03
MINDWORM, THE   KORNBLUTH, C. M.   SS   WBY 50 12
NOBODY BOTHERS GUS (AS PAUL JANVIER)
                             BUDRYS, ALGIS   SS   ASF 55 11
INGENIOUS PATRIOT, THE   BIERCE, AMBROSE   SS
EQUALIZER, THE   SPINRAD, NORMAN   SS   ASF 64 12
SPLICE OF LIFE   DORMAN, SONYA   SS   ORB 66 01
BUSINESS AS USUAL, DURING ALTERATIONS
                             WILLIAMS, RALPH   NV   ASF 58 07
QUEST FOR SAINT AQUIN, THE   BOUCHER, ANTHONY   SS   NTS 51
NINE BILLION NAMES OF GOD, THE
                             CLARKE, ARTHUR C.   SS   STR 53 01
VOICES OF TIME, THE   BALLARD, J. G.   SS   NWS 60 10

ONE HUNDRED AND TWO H-BOMBS DISCH, THOMAS M.   AC   CPT 66
INTRODUCTION   DISCH, THOMAS M.   IN
102 H-BOMBS   DISCH, THOMAS M.   NV   FAN 65 03
SIGHTSEERS, THE   DISCH, THOMAS M.   SS   WOT 65 11
FINAL AUDIT   DISCH, THOMAS M.   SS   FAN 63 07
VAMP, THE   DISCH, THOMAS M.   SS   FAN 65 02
UTOPIA? NEVER!   DISCH, THOMAS M.   SS   AMZ 63 08
RETURN OF THE MEDUSAE, THE   DISCH, THOMAS M.   SS   FAN 63 08
PRINCESS' CARILLON, THE (THE ENCHANTED PRINCE)
                             DISCH, THOMAS M.   SS   FAN 63 08
GENETIC CODA   DISCH, THOMAS M.   SS   FAN 64 06
WHITE FANG GOES DINGO   DISCH, THOMAS M.   NV   IFS 65 04
DEMI-URGE, THE   DISCH, THOMAS M.   SS   AMZ 63 06
DANGEROUS FLAGS   DISCH, THOMAS M.   SS   FAN 64 08
INVADED BY LOVE   DISCH, THOMAS M.   SS   NWS 66 09
BONE OF CONTENTION   DISCH, THOMAS M.   SS   AHM 66
LEADER OF THE REVOLUTION   DISCH, THOMAS M.   SS   BIZ 65 10

ONE HUNDRED AND TWO H-BOMBS (U.S.)
                             DISCH, THOMAS M.   AC   BKM 71 08
INTRODUCTION   DISCH, THOMAS M.   IN
102 H-BOMBS   DISCH, THOMAS M.   NV   FAN 65 03
SIGHTSEERS, THE   DISCH, THOMAS M.   SS   WOT 65 11
FINAL AUDIT   DISCH, THOMAS M.   SS   FAN 63 07
VAMP, THE   DISCH, THOMAS M.   SS   FAN 65 02
UTOPIA? NEVER!   DISCH, THOMAS M.   SS   AMZ 63 08
RETURN OF THE MEDUSAE, THE   DISCH, THOMAS M.   SS   FAN 63 08
PRINCESS' CARILLON, THE (THE ENCHANTED PRINCE)
                             DISCH, THOMAS M.   SS   FAN 63 08
GENETIC CODA   DISCH, THOMAS M.   SS   FAN 64 06

ONE HUNDRED AND TWO H-BOMBS (U.S.)   ORBIT

THREE POINTS ON THE DEMOGRAPHIC CURVE
                              DISCH, THOMAS M.   SS   IMP 66 12
DEMI-URGE, THE   DISCH, THOMAS M.   SS   AMZ 63 06
DANGEROUS FLAGS   DISCH, THOMAS M.   SS   FAN 64 08
INVADED BY LOVE   DISCH, THOMAS M.   SS   NWS 66 09
BONE OF CONTENTION   DISCH, THOMAS M.   SS   AHM 66
5 EGGS   DISCH, THOMAS M.   SS   ORB 66 01

ONE IN THREE HUNDRED   MCINTOSH, J. T.   AC H DBL 54
  ONE IN THREE HUNDRED   MCINTOSH, J. T.   NV   FSF 53 02
  ONE IN A THOUSAND   MCINTOSH, J. T.   SS   FSF 54 01
  ONE TOO MANY   MCINTOSH, J. T.   SS   FSF 54 09

ONE STEP FROM EARTH   HARRISON, HARRY   AC H MAC 70
  MATTER TRANSMITTER, THE   HARRISON, HARRY   IN
  ONE STEP FROM EARTH (AS HANK DEMPSEY)
                              HARRISON, HARRY   SS   ASF 70 03
  PRESSURE   HARRISON, HARRY   SS   ASF 69 08
  NO WAR, OR BATTLE'S SOUND   HARRISON, HARRY   NV   68
  WIFE TO THE LORD   HARRISON, HARRY   SS   FSF 70 06
  WAITING PLACE   HARRISON, HARRY   SS   GAL 68 06
  LIFE PRESERVERS, THE (AS HANK DEMPSEY)
                              HARRISON, HARRY   NV   ASF 70 04
  FROM FANATICISM, OR FOR REWARD
                              HARRISON, HARRY   SS   ASF 69 03
  HEAVY DUTY (AS HANK DEMPSEY) HARRISON, HARRY   SS   ASF 70 05
  TALE OF THE ENDING, A (AS HANK DEMPSEY)
                              HARRISON, HARRY   SS   ASF 70 06

OPENER OF THE WAY, THE   BLOCH, ROBERT   AC H ARK 45
  ENGLISH DERIVATIVE ANTHOLOGY "THE HOUSE OF THE HATCHET"
  INTRODUCTION   BLOCH, ROBERT   IN
  CLOAK, THE   BLOCH, ROBERT   SS   UNK 39 05
  BEETLES   BLOCH, ROBERT   SS   WRT 38 12
  FIDDLER'S FEE, THE   BLOCH, ROBERT   SS   WRT 40 07
  MANNIKIN, THE (ALSO AS MANNIKINS OF HORROR)
                              BLOCH, ROBERT   SS   WRT 37 04
  STRANGE FLIGHT OF RICHARD CLAYTON, THE
                              BLOCH, ROBERT   SS   AMZ 39 03
  YOURS TRULY, JACK THE RIPPER BLOCH, ROBERT   SS   WRT 43 07
  SEAL OF THE SATYR, THE   BLOCH, ROBERT   SS   SRS 39 06
  DARK DEMON, THE   BLOCH, ROBERT   SS   WRT 36 11
  FACELESS GOD, THE   BLOCH, ROBERT   SS   WRT 36 05
  HOUSE OF THE HATCHET, THE   BLOCH, ROBERT   SS   WRT 41 01
  OPENER OF THE WAY, THE   BLOCH, ROBERT   SS   WRT 36 10
  RETURN TO THE SABBATH   BLOCH, ROBERT   SS   WRT 38 07
  MANDARIN'S CANARIES, THE   BLOCH, ROBERT   SS   WRT 38 09
  WAXWORKS   BLOCH, ROBERT   SS   WRT 39 01
  FEAST IN THE ABBEY, THE   BLOCH, ROBERT   SS   WRT 35 01
  SLAVE OF THE FLAMES   BLOCH, ROBERT   SS   WRT 38 06
  SHAMBLER FROM THE STARS, THE BLOCH, ROBERT   SS   WRT 35 09
  MOTHER OF SERPENTS   BLOCH, ROBERT   SS   WRT 36 12
  SECRET OF SEBEK, THE   BLOCH, ROBERT   SS   WRT 37 11
  EYES OF THE MUMMY, THE   BLOCH, ROBERT   SS   WRT 38 04
  ONE WAY TO MARS   BLOCH, ROBERT   SS   WRT 45 07

OPENER OF THE WAY, THE (BRITISH PB)
                              BLOCH, ROBERT   AC   PTH 76
  BY WAY OF INTRODUCTION   BLOCH, ROBERT   IN
  OPENER OF THE WAY, THE   BLOCH, ROBERT   SS   WRT 36 10
  CLOAK, THE   BLOCH, ROBERT   SS   UNK 39 05
  BEETLES   BLOCH, ROBERT   SS   WRT 38 12
  FIDDLER'S FEE, THE   BLOCH, ROBERT   SS   WRT 40 07
  MANNIKIN, THE (ALSO AS MANNIKINS OF HORROR)
                              BLOCH, ROBERT   SS   WRT 37 04
  STRANGE FLIGHT OF RICHARD CLAYTON, THE
                              BLOCH, ROBERT   SS   AMZ 39 03
  YOURS TRULY, JACK THE RIPPER BLOCH, ROBERT   SS   WRT 43 07
  SEAL OF THE SATYR, THE   BLOCH, ROBERT   SS   SRS 39 06
  DARK DEMON, THE   BLOCH, ROBERT   SS   WRT 36 11
  FACELESS GOD, THE   BLOCH, ROBERT   SS   WRT 36 05

OPERATION CHAOS   ANDERSON, POUL   NO   LAN 71
  OPERATION AFREET   ANDERSON, POUL   SS   FSF 56 09
  OPERATION SALAMANDER   ANDERSON, POUL   NV   FSF 57 01
  OPERATION INCUBUS   ANDERSON, POUL   SS   FSF 59 10
  OPERATION CHANGELING   ANDERSON, POUL   NA   FSF 69 05

OPERATION FUTURE   CONKLIN, GROFF   AN   PMA 55 05
  INTRODUCTION   CONKLIN, GROFF   IN
  EDUCATION OF DRUSILLA STRANGE, THE
                              STURGEON, THEODORE   NV   GAL 54 03
  C/O MR. MAKEPEACE   PHILLIPS, PETER   SS   FSF 54 02
  TECHNICAL SLIP (ARS 49 WI) BEYNON, JOHN   SS   IMG 50 12
  SHORT IN THE CHEST   SEABRIGHT, IDRIS   SS   FUN 54 07
  CURE FOR A YLITH   LEINSTER, MURRAY   SS   STS 49 11
  EXPOSURE   RUSSELL, ERIC FRANK   SS   ASF 50 07
  WORRYWORT   SIMAK, CLIFFORD D.   SS   GAL 53 09
  DAY IS DONE, THE   DEL REY, LESTER   SS   ASF 39 05
  QUIT ZOOMIN' THOSE HANDS THROUGH THE AIR
                              FINNEY, JACK   SS   FSF 52 12
  HILDA   HICKEY, H. B.   SS   FSF 52 09
  BLOOD'S A ROVER   OLIVER, CHAD   NV   ASF 52 05
  CALL ME ADAM   MARKS, WINSTON K.   SS   FSF 54 02
  SPECIAL DELIVERY   KNIGHT, DAMON   NV   GAL 54 04
  GARDEN IN THE FOREST, THE   YOUNG, ROBERT F.   SS   ASF 53 09
  SORCERER'S APPRENTICE, THE JAMESON, MALCOLM   SS   ASF 41 12
  GAMES   MACLEAN, KATHERINE   SS   GAL 53 03
  HOLES AROUND MARS, THE   BIXBY, JEROME   SS   GAL 54 01
  PROJECT   PADGETT, LEWIS   SS   ASF 47 04
  FUN THEY HAD, THE (NEA 51 12)
                              ASIMOV, ISAAC   SS   FSF 54 02

OPUS 100   ASIMOV, ISAAC   AC H HMF 69
  INTRODUCTION   ASIMOV, ISAAC   IN
  FROM "THE CALLISTAN MENACE" ASIMOV, ISAAC   EX   AST 40 04

FROM "LUCKIE STARR AND THE MOONS OF JUPITER"
                              ASIMOV, ISAAC   EX   DBL 57
FROM "VIEW FROM AMALTHEA"   ASIMOV, ISAAC   AR   FSF 68 12
FROM "LUCKIE STARR AND THE OCEANS OF VENUS"
                              ASIMOV, ISAAC   EX   DBL 54
FROM "THE MARTIAN WAY"   ASIMOV, ISAAC   EX   GAL 52 11
FROM "THE UNIVERSE"   ASIMOV, ISAAC   AR   WKR 66
FROM "GALAXIES"   ASIMOV, ISAAC   AR   FOL 68
FROM "THE PERFECT MACHINE"   ASIMOV, ISAAC   AR   SJR 68 1
FROM "STRANGE PLAYFELLOW"   ASIMOV, ISAAC   EX   SSS 40 09
FROM "LIAR!"   ASIMOV, ISAAC   EX   ASF 41 05
FROM "RUNAROUND"   ASIMOV, ISAAC   EX   ASF 42 0
FROM "I, ROBOT"   ASIMOV, ISAAC   EX   GNM 50
FROM "THE INTELLIGENT MAN'S GUIDE TO SCIENCE"
                              ASIMOV, ISAAC   AR   BAS 60
LAST QUESTION, THE   ASIMOV, ISAAC   SS   SFQ 56 11
FROM "THE REALM OF NUMBERS"   ASIMOV, ISAAC   AR   HMF 59
FROM "QUICK AND EASY MATH"   ASIMOV, ISAAC   AR   HMF 64
FEELING OF POWER, THE   ASIMOV, ISAAC   SS   IFS 58 0
FROM "ASIMOV'S BIOGRAPHICAL ENCYCLOPEDIA OF SCIENCE"
                              ASIMOV, ISAAC   AR   DBL 64
FROM "ONLY A TRILLION"   ASIMOV, ISAAC   AR   ABE 57
FROM "THE NUTRINO"   ASIMOV, ISAAC   AR   DBL 66
FROM "SUPERNUTRON"   ASIMOV, ISAAC   EX   AST 41 09
FROM "THE SOUND OF PANTING"   ASIMOV, ISAAC   AR   ASF 55 0
FROM "BIOCHEMISTRY AND HUMAN METABOLISM"
                              ASIMOV, ISAAC   AR   WMW 52
FROM "THE CHEMICALS OF LIFE" ASIMOV, ISAAC   AR   ABE 54
FROM "THE NOBLE GASSES"   ASIMOV, ISAAC   AR   BAS 66
THIOTIMOLINE AND THE SPACE AGE
                              ASIMOV, ISAAC   SF   ASF 60 10
FROM "THE KINETICS OF THE REACTION INACTIVATION OF TYROSINASE
   DURING ITS CATALYSIS OF.." ASIMOV, ISAAC   AR   48
FROM "THE WELLSPRINGS OF LIFE"
                              ASIMOV, ISAAC   AR   ABE 60
FROM "PHOTOSYNTHESIS"   ASIMOV, ISAAC   AR   BAS 68
FROM "WORDS OF SCIENCE"   ASIMOV, ISAAC   AR   HMF 59
FROM "WORDS ON THE MAP"   ASIMOV, ISAAC   AR   HMF 62
FROM "WORDS FROM HISTORY"   ASIMOV, ISAAC   AR   HMF 68
FROM "THE GREEKS"   ASIMOV, ISAAC   AR   HMF 65
FROM "THE ROMAN REPUBLIC"   ASIMOV, ISAAC   AR   HMF 66
FROM "THE EGYPTIANS"   ASIMOV, ISAAC   AR   HMF 67
FROM "THE NEAR EAST"   ASIMOV, ISAAC   AR   HMF 68
FROM "THERE'S NOTHING LIKE A GOOD FOUNDATION"
                              ASIMOV, ISAAC   AR   67
FROM "THE DEAD HAND"   ASIMOV, ISAAC   EX   ASF 45 04
FROM "ASIMOV'S GUIDE TO THE BIBLE"
                              ASIMOV, ISAAC   AR   DBL 68
TWELVE POINT THREE SIX NINE   ASIMOV, ISAAC   AR   FSF 67 0
FROM "ISAAC ASIMOV EXPLAINS" (FORCE FIELDS)
                              ASIMOV, ISAAC   AR   SDG 68
FROM "ISAAC ASIMOV EXPLAINS" (IRRESISTABLE FORCE)
                              ASIMOV, ISAAC   AR   SDG 68
ON PREDICTION   ASIMOV, ISAAC   IN   68
UNCOMPROMISING VIEW, AN   ASIMOV, ISAAC   BR   PHY 69 02
DREAMWORLD   ASIMOV, ISAAC   SS   FSF 55 1
HOLMES-GINSBOOK DEVICE, THE   ASIMOV, ISAAC   SS   IFS 68 1
APPENDIX: MY HUNDRED BOOKS   ASIMOV, ISAAC   MS

OR ALL THE SEAS WITH OYSTERS DAVIDSON, AVRAM   AC   BKM 52
OR ALL THE SEAS WITH OYSTERS DAVIDSON, AVRAM   SS   GAL 58 0
UP THE CLOSE AND DOWN THE STAIR
                              DAVIDSON, AVRAM   SS   FSF 58 09
NOW LET US SLEEP   DAVIDSON, AVRAM   SS   VSF 57 09
GRANTHA SIGHTING, THE   DAVIDSON, AVRAM   SS   FSF 58 0
HELP! I AM DR. MORRIS GOLDPEPPER
                              DAVIDSON, AVRAM   NV   GAL 57 0
SIXTH SEASON, THE   DAVIDSON, AVRAM   SS   FSF 60 06
NEGRA SUM   DAVIDSON, AVRAM   SS   FSF 57 11
OR THE GRASSES GROW   DAVIDSON, AVRAM   SS   FSF 58 1
MY BOYFRIEND'S NAME IS JELLO DAVIDSON, AVRAM   SS   FSF 54 0
GOLEM, THE   DAVIDSON, AVRAM   SS   FSF 55 0
SUMMERLAND   DAVIDSON, AVRAM   SS   FSF 57 0
KING'S EVIL   DAVIDSON, AVRAM   SS   FSF 56 1
GREAT IS DIANA   DAVIDSON, AVRAM   SS   FSF 58 0
I DO NOT HEAR YOU, SIR   DAVIDSON, AVRAM   SS   FSF 58 0
AUTHOR, AUTHOR   DAVIDSON, AVRAM   SS   FSF 59 0
DAGON   DAVIDSON, AVRAM   SS   FSF 59 1
MONTAVARDE CAMERA, THE   DAVIDSON, AVRAM   SS   FSF 59 0
WOMAN WHO THOUGHT SHE COULD READ, THE
                              DAVIDSON, AVRAM   SS   FSF 59 0

ORBIT   1   KNIGHT, DAMON   OA   BKM 66 10
INTRODUCTION   KNIGHT, DAMON   IN
STARAS FLONDERANS   WILHELM, KATE   SS   ORB 66 0
SECRET PLACE, THE   MCKENNA, RICHARD M.   SS   ORB 66 0
HOW BEAUTIFUL WITH BANNERS   BLISH, JAMES   SS   ORB 66 0
DISINHERITED, THE (ALSO AS HOME)
                              ANDERSON, POUL   SS   ORB 66 0
LOOLIES ARE HERE, THE   RICE, ALLISON   SS   ORB 66 0
KANGAROO COURT (ALSO AS FLOWERING SEASON)
                              KIDD, VIRGINIA   NV   ORB 66 0
SPLICE OF LIFE   DORMAN, SONYA   SS   ORB 66 0
5 EGGS   DISCH, THOMAS M.   SS   ORB 66 0
DEEPS, THE   ROBERTS, KEITH   SS   ORB 66 0

ORBIT   2   KNIGHT, DAMON   OA   BKM 67 09
DOCTOR, THE   THOMAS, THEODORE L.   SS   ORB 67 0
BABY, YOU WERE GREAT   WILHELM, KATE   SS   ORB 67 0
FIDDLER'S GREEN   MCKENNA, RICHARD M.   NV   ORB 67 0
TRIP, TRAP   WOLFE, GENE   NV   ORB 67 0
DIMPLE IN DRACO, THE   LATHAM, PHILIP   SS   ORB 67 0
I GAVE HER SACK AND SHERRY (ALSO AS I THOUGHT SHE WAS AFEARED
   TILL SHE STROKED MY BEARD) RUSS, JOANNA   NV   ORB 67 0
ADVENTURESS, THE (ALSO AS BLUESTOCKING)
                              RUSS, JOANNA   NV   ORB 67 0

RBIT 2

HOLE ON THE CORNER, THE	LAFFERTY, R. A.	SS	ORB 67 02
FOOD FARM, THE	REED, KIT	SS	ORB 67 02
FULL SUN	ALDISS, BRIAN W.	SS	ORB 67 02

RBIT 3   KNIGHT, DAMON   OA H PUT 68

MOTHER TO THE WORLD	WILSON, RICHARD	NV	ORB 68 03
BRAMBLE BUSH	MCKENNA, RICHARD M.	NV	ORB 68 03
BARBARIAN, THE	RUSS, JOANNA	NV	ORB 68 03
CHANGELING, THE	WOLFE, GENE	SS	ORB 68 03
WHY THEY MOBBED THE WHITE HOUSE			
	BUCK, DORIS PITKIN	SS	ORB 68 03
PLANNERS, THE	WILHELM, KATE	SS	ORB 68 03
DON'T WASH THE CARATS	FARMER, PHILIP JOSE	SS	ORB 68 03
LETTER TO A YOUNG POET	SALLIS, JAMES	SS	ORB 68 03
HERE IS THY STING	JAKES, JOHN W.	NV	ORB 68 03

RBIT 4   KNIGHT, DAMON   OA H PUT 68

WINDSONG	WILHELM, KATE	NV	ORB 68 04
PROBABLE CAUSE	HARNESS, CHARLES L.	NA	ORB 68 04
SHATTERED LIKE A GLASS GOBLIN			
	ELLISON, HARLAN	SS	ORB 68 04
THIS CORRUPTIBLE	TRANSUE, JACOB	NV	ORB 68 04
ANIMAL	EMSHWILLER, CAROL	SS	ORB 68 04
ONE AT A TIME	LAFFERTY, R. A.	SS	ORB 68 04
PASSENGERS	SILVERBERG, ROBERT	SS	ORB 68 04
GRIMM'S STORY	VINGE, VERNOR	NA	ORB 68 04
FEW LAST WORDS, A	SALLIS, JAMES	SS	ORB 68 04

RBIT 5   KNIGHT, DAMON   OA H PUT 69

SOMERSET DREAMS	WILHELM, KATE	NV	ORB 69 05
ROADS, THE ROADS, THE BEAUTIFUL ROADS, THE			
	DAVIDSON, AVRAM	SS	ORB 69 05
LOOK, YOU THINK YOU'VE GOT TROUBLES			
	CARR, CAROL	SS	ORB 69 05
WINTER'S KING	LE GUIN, URSULA K.	NV	ORB 69 05
TIME MACHINE, THE	JONES, LANGDON	NV	ORB 69 05
CONFIGURATION OF THE NORTH SHORE			
	LAFFERTY, R. A.	SS	ORB 69 05
PAUL'S TREEHOUSE	WOLFE, GENE	SS	ORB 69 05
PRICE, THE (ALSO AS JUST DEAD ENOUGH)			
	BELCHER, C. DAVIS	NV	ORB 69 05
ROSE-BOWL PLUTO HYPOTHESIS, THE			
	LATHAM, PHILIP	SS	ORB 69 05
WINSTON	REED, KIT	SS	ORB 69 05
HISTORY MAKERS, THE	SALLIS, JAMES	SS	ORB 69 05
BIG FLASH, THE	SPINRAD, NORMAN	NV	ORB 69 05

RBIT 6   KNIGHT, DAMON   OA H PUT 70

SECOND INQUISITION, THE	RUSS, JOANNA	NV	ORB 70 06
REMEMBRANCE TO COME	WOLFE, GENE	SS	ORB 70 06
HOW THE WHIP CAME BACK	WOLFE, GENE	SS	ORB 70 06
GOSLIN DAY	DAVIDSON, AVRAM	SS	ORB 70 06
MAYBE JEAN-BAPTISTE PIERRE ANTOINE DE MONET, CHEVALIER DE LAM-			
ARCK,WAS A LITTLE BIT RIGHT	SCOTT, ROBIN S.	SS	ORB 70 06
CHOSEN, THE	WILHELM, KATE	SS	ORB 70 06
ENTIRE AND PERFECT CHRYSOLITE			
	LAFFERTY, R. A.	SS	ORB 70 06
SUNBURST	THORP, RODERICK	SS	ORB 70 06
CREATION OF BENNIE GOOD, THE	SALLIS, JAMES	SS	ORB 70 06
END, THE (ALSO AS THINGS)	LE GUIN, URSULA K.	SS	ORB 70 06
COLD DARK NIGHT WITH SNOW, A	WILHELM, KATE	SS	ORB 70 06
FAME	COX, ARTHUR JEAN	SS	ORB 70 06
DEBUT	EMSHWILLER, CAROL	SS	ORB 70 06
WHERE NO SUN SHINES	DOZOIS, GARDNER R.	SS	ORB 70 06
ASIAN SHORE, THE	DISCH, THOMAS M.	NV	ORB 70 06

RBIT 7   KNIGHT, DAMON   OA H PUT 70

APRIL FOOL'S DAY FOREVER	WILHELM, KATE	NV	ORB 70 07
EYEBEM	WOLFE, GENE	SS	ORB 70 07
CONTINUED ON NEXT ROCK	LAFFERTY, R. A.	NV	ORB 70 07
TO SPORT WITH AMARYLLIS	HILL, RICHARD	SS	ORB 70 07
IN THE QUEUE	LAUMER, KEITH	SS	ORB 70 07
LIVING END, THE	DORMAN, SONYA	SS	ORB 70 07
DREAM AT NOONDAY, A	DOZOIS, GARDNER R.	SS	ORB 70 07
WOMAN WAITING	EMSHWILLER, CAROL	SS	ORB 70 07
OLD FOOT FORGOT	LAFFERTY, R. A.	SS	ORB 70 07
JIM AND MARY G	SALLIS, JAMES	SS	ORB 70 07
PRESSURE OF TIME, THE	DISCH, THOMAS M.	NV	ORB 70 07
ISLAND OF DOCTOR DEATH AND OTHER STORIES, THE			
	WOLFE, GENE	SS	ORB 70 07

RBIT 8   KNIGHT, DAMON   OA H PUT 70

HORSE OF AIR	DOZOIS, GARDNER R.	SS	ORB 70 08
ONE LIFE, FURNISHED IN EARLY POVERTY			
	ELLISON, HARLAN	SS	ORB 70 08
RITE OF SPRING	DAVIDSON, AVRAM	SS	ORB 70 08
BYSTANDER, THE	WHARTON, THOM LEE	SS	ORB 70 08
ALL PIECES OF A RIVER SHORE	LAFFERTY, R. A.	SS	ORB 70 08
SONYA, CRANE WESSLEMAN, AND KITTEE			
	WOLFE, GENE	SS	ORB 70 08
TABLETS OF STONE	HUFFORD, LIZ	SS	ORB 70 08
STARSCAPE WITH FRIEZE OF DREAMS			
	YOUNG, ROBERT F.	SS	ORB 70 08
BOOK, THE	MARGROFF, ROBERT E.		
	AND OFFUTT, ANDREW J.	SS C	ORB 70 08
INSIDE	CARR, CAROL	SS	ORB 70 08
RIGHT OFF THE MAP	WINN, PIP	SS	ORB 70 08
WEATHER ON THE SUN, THE	THOMAS, THEODORE L.	NV	ORB 70 08
CHINESE BOXES, THE	CHARNOCK, GRAHAM	SS	ORB 70 08
METHOD BIT IN "B", A	WOLFE, GENE	SS	ORB 70 08
INTERURBAN QUEEN	LAFFERTY, R. A.	SS	ORB 70 08
ENCOUNTER, THE	WILHELM, KATE	NV	ORB 70 08

RBIT 9   KNIGHT, DAMON   OA H PUT 71

HEADS AFRICA TAILS AMERICA	SAXTON, JOSEPHINE	SS	ORB 71 09
WHAT WE HAVE HERE IS TOO MUCH COMMUNICATION			
	STOVER, LEON E.	SS	ORB 71 09
DOMINANT SPECIES	NEVILLE, KRIS	SS	ORB 71 09
TOY THEATER, THE	WOLFE, GENE	SS	ORB 71 09
STOP ME BEFORE I TELL MORE (ALSO AS PUNCHLINE)			
	THURSTON, ROBERT	SS	ORB 71 09
GLEEPSITE	RUSS, JOANNA	SS	ORB 71 09
BINARIES	SALLIS, JAMES	SS	ORB 71 09
LOST IN THE MARIGOLDS	HOFFMAN, LEE		
	AND TOOMEY, ROBERT E. JR	NV C	ORB 71 09
ACROSS THE BAR	REED, KIT	SS	ORB 71 09
SCIENCE FAIR, THE	VINGE, VERNOR	SS	ORB 71 09
LAST LEAF, THE	MACFARLANE, WALLACE	SS	ORB 71 09
WHEN ALL THE LANDS POUR OUT AGAIN			
	LAFFERTY, R. A.	SS	ORB 71 09
ONLY THE WORDS ARE DIFERENT	SALLIS, JAMES	SS	ORB 71 09
INFINITY BOX, THE	WILHELM, KATE	NA	ORB 71 09

ORBIT 10   KNIGHT, DAMON   OA H PUT 72

FIFTH HEAD OF CERBERUS, THE	WOLFE, GENE	NV	ORB 72 10
JODY AFTER THE WAR	BRYANT, EDWARD	SS	ORB 72 10
AL	EMSHWILLER, CAROL	SS	ORB 72 10
NOW I'M WATCHING ROGER	PANSHIN, ALEXEI	SS	ORB 72 10
WHIRL CAGE	DANN, JACK M.	SS	ORB 72 10
KINGDOM BY THE SEA, A	DOZOIS, GARDNER R.	NV	ORB 72 10
CHRISTLINGS	TEICHNER, ALBERT	SS	ORB 72 10
LIVE, FROM BERCHTESGADEN	EFFINGER, GEO. ALEC	SS	ORB 72 10
DORG	LAFFERTY, R. A.	SS	ORB 72 10
GANTLET	PECK, RICHARD E.	SS	ORB 72 10
FUSION BOMB, THE	WILHELM, KATE	NV	ORB 72 10
INDEX TO VOLUMES 1-10	MISC. MATERIAL	MS	

ORBIT 11   KNIGHT, DAMON   OA H PUT 73

ALIEN STONES	WOLFE, GENE	NV	ORB 72 11
SPECTRA	MCINTYRE, VONDA N.	SS	ORB 72 11
I REMEMBER A WINTER	POHL, FREDERIK	SS	ORB 72 11
DOUCEMENT, S'IL VOUS PLAIT	SALLIS, JAMES	SS	ORB 72 11
SUMMER OF THE IRISH SEA, THE	GRANT, C. L.	SS	ORB 72 11
GOOD-BYE, SHELLEY, SHIRLEY, CHARLOTTE, CHARLENE			
	THURSTON, ROBERT	SS	ORB 72 11
FATHER'S IN THE BASEMENT	FARMER, PHILIP JOSE	SS	ORB 72 11
DOWN BY THE OLD MAELSTROM	WELLEN, EDWARD	SS	ORB 72 11
THINGS GO BETTER	EFFINGER, GEO. ALEC	SS	ORB 72 11
DISSOLVE	WOLF, GARY K.	SS	ORB 72 11
DUNE'S EDGE	BRYANT, EDWARD	SS	ORB 72 11
DRUM LOLLIPOP, THE	DANN, JACK M.	SS	ORB 72 11
MACHINES OF LOVING GRACE	DOZOIS, GARDNER R.	SS	ORB 72 11
THEY COPE	SKAL, DAVE	SS	ORB 72 11
COUNTERPOINT	HALDEMAN, JOE W.	SS	ORB 72 11
OLD SOUL	HERBST, STEVE	SS	ORB 72 11
NEW YORK TIMES	PLATT, CHARLES	SS	ORB 72 11
CHRYSTALLIZATION OF THE MYTH	BARFOOT, JOHN	SS	ORB 72 11
TO PLANT A SEED	DAVIS, HANK	SS	ORB 72 11
ON THE ROAD TO HONEYVILLE	WILHELM, KATE	SS	ORB 72 11

ORBIT 12   KNIGHT, DAMON   OA H PUT 73

SHARK	BRYANT, EDWARD	NV	ORB 73 12
DIRECTION OF THE ROAD	LE GUIN, URSULA K.	SS	ORB 73 12
WINDOWS IN DANTE'S HELL, THE	BISHOP, MICHAEL	SS	ORB 73 12
SERPENT BURNING ON AN ALTAR	ALDISS, BRIAN W.	SS	ORB 73 12
WOMAN IN SUNLIGHT WITH MANDOLIN			
	ALDISS, BRIAN W.	SS	ORB 73 12
YOUNG SOLDIER'S HOROSCOPE, THE			
	ALDISS, BRIAN W.	SS	ORB 73 12
CASTLE SCENE WITH PENITENTS	ALDISS, BRIAN W.	SS	ORB 73 12
RED CANARY, THE	WILHELM, KATE	SS	ORB 73 12
WHAT'S THE MATTER WITH HERBIE?			
	GILDEN, MEL	NV	ORB 73 12
PINUP	BRYANT, EDWARD	SS	ORB 73 12
GENIUS FREAKS, THE	MCINTYRE, VONDA N.	SS	ORB 73 12
BURGER CREATURE	CHAPMAN, STEVE	SS	ORB 73 12
HALF THE KINGDOM	PISERCHIA, DORIS	SS	ORB 73 12
CONTINUING WESTWARD	WOLFE, GENE	SS	ORB 73 12
ARCS & SECANTS	MISC. MATERIAL	MS	

ORBIT 13   KNIGHT, DAMON   OA H PUT 74

SCREAM, THE	WILHELM, KATE	NV	ORB 74 13
YOUNG LOVE	DAVIS, GRANIA	NV	ORB 74 13
AND NAME MY NAME	LAFFERTY, R. A.	SS	ORB 74 13
GOING WEST	BRYANT, EDWARD	SS	ORB 74 13
MY FRIEND ZARATHUSTRA	SALLIS, JAMES	SS	ORB 74 13
THERAPY	WOLF, GARY K.	SS	ORB 74 13
GARDENING NOTES FROM ALL OVER			
	MACFARLANE, WALLACE	SS	ORB 74 13
IDIO	PISERCHIA, DORIS	SS	ORB 74 13
FANTASY'S PROFESSION	TEICHNER, ALBERT	SS	ORB 74 13
SPRING CAME TO BLUE RIDGE EARLY THIS YEAR			
	ARNOLD, CHARLES	SS	ORB 74 13
CREATION OF A FUTURE WORLD IN THE TRACER			
	HERBST, STEVE	SS	ORB 74 13
COILS	BARFOOT, JOHN	SS	ORB 74 13
TIME BEND	DORMAN, SONYA	SS	ORB 74 13
EVERYBODY A WINNER, THE BARKER CRIED			
	GRANT, C. L.	SS	ORB 74 13
NAKED AND AFRAID I GO	PISERCHIA, DORIS	SS	ORB 74 13
TEETH	ROONEY, GRACE	SS	ORB 74 13
TROIKA	CHAPMAN, STEVE	SS	ORB 74 13
BLACK SUN	ETCHISON, DENNIS	SS	ORB 74 13
MOUTH IS FOR EATING, THE	ORR, WILLIAM F.	SS	ORB 74 13
FLASH POINT	DOZOIS, GARDNER R.	NV	ORB 74 13
ARCS & SECANTS	MISC. MATERIAL	MS	

ORBIT 14   KNIGHT, DAMON   OA H HPR 74

THEY SAY	KNIGHT, DAMON	MS	
TIN SOLDIER	VINGE, JOAN D.	NA	ORB 74 14
REASONABLE PEOPLE	RUSS, JOANNA	SS	ORB 74 14

```
ORBIT  14                                                          OTHER SIDE OF THE MOON, TH:

ROYAL LICORICE          LAFFERTY, R. A.     SS   ORB 74 14    OTHER DAYS, OTHER EYES     SHAW, BOB           NO   ACE 72 07
BOOK REVIEWS            KNIGHT, DAMON       BR   ORB 74 14      LIGHT OF OTHER DAYS       SHAW, BOB           SS   ASF 66 0
STARS BELOW, THE        LE GUIN, URSULA K.  SS   ORB 74 14      BURDEN OF PROOF           SHAW, BOB           SS   ASF 67 0
BROTHER TO DRAGONS, A COMPANION OF OWLS                         DOME OF MANY-COLORED GLASS, A
                        WILHELM, KATE       NV   ORB 74 14                                SHAW, BOB           SS   FAN 72 0
BRIDGE BUILDER, THE     WOLF, GARY K.       SS   ORB 74 14      OTHER DAYS, OTHER EYES    SHAW, BOB           NA   AMZ 72 0
WINNING OF THE GREAT AMERICAN GREENING REVOLUTION
                        YACO, MURRAY F.     SS   ORB 74 14    OTHER DIMENSION, THE       ROSNER, SARA        AN   SBS 72 11
FORLESEN               WOLFE, GENE         NV   ORB 74 14      ROCKING-HORSE WINNER, THE LAWRENCE, D. H.     SS        33
MEMORY MACHINE, THE     MISC. MATERIAL      MS                 DAEMON LOVER, THE         JACKSON, SHIRLEY    NV        48
ARCS & SECANTS          MISC. MATERIAL      MS                 NIGHTFALL                 ASIMOV, ISAAC       NV   ASF 41 0
                                                               SIR EDMUND ORME           JAMES, HENRY        NV
ORBIT  15              KNIGHT, DAMON       OA H HPR 74          DARK THEY WERE, AND GOLDEN-EYED (THE NAMING OF NAMES)
THEY SAY               KNIGHT, DAMON       MS                                            BRADBURY, RAY       SS   TWS 49 08
FLAMING DUCKS AND GIANT BREAD                                  WILLIAM WILSON (1839)     POE, EDGAR ALLEN    NV   GFT 39 0
                        LAFFERTY, R. A.     SS   ORB 74 15      RAPPACCINI'S DAUGHTER (1844) HAWTHORNE, NATHANIEL NV DMR 44 12
PALE HANDS             PISERCHIA, DORIS    SS   ORB 74 15      CANTICLE FOR LEIBOWITZ, A  MILLER, WALTER M. JR  FSF 55 0
TITLE                  WELLEN, EDWARD      SS   ORB 74 15      AFTERWARD                 WHARTON, EDITH      NV   CNY 10 0
"END, THE"             WELLEN, EDWARD      SS   ORB 74 15
WHERE LATE THE SWEET BIRDS SANG                                OTHER DIMENSIONS          SILVERBERG, ROBERT  AN H HAW 73
                        WILHELM, KATE       NA   ORB 74 15      INTRODUCTION             SILVERBERG, ROBERT  IN
MELTING                WOLFE, GENE         SS   ORB 74 15      AND HE BUILT A CROOKED HOUSE HEINLEIN, ROBERT A. SS ASF 41 02
IN THE LILLIPUTIAN ASYLUM: A STORY IN 8 POEMS AND AN           NARROW VALLEY             LAFFERTY, R. A.     SS   FSF 66 0
  INTRODUCTION          BISHOP, MICHAEL     PM   ORB 74 15      WALL OF DARKNESS, THE     CLARKE, ARTHUR C.   SS   SSS 49 0
ERNIE                  SMITH, LOWELL KENT  SS   ORB 74 15      DESTINY OF MILTON GOMRATH, THE
MEMORY MACHINE, THE     MISC. MATERIAL      MS                                           PANSHIN, ALEXEI     SS   ASF 67 12
LIVE? OUR COMPUTERS WILL DO THAT FOR US                        STANLEY TOOTHBRUSH (AS CARL BRANDON)
                        ALDISS, BRIAN W.    SS   ORB 74 15                               CARR, TERRY         SS   FSF 62 0
ACE 167                ARNASON, ELEANOR    SS   ORB 74 15      INSIDE                    CARR, CAROL         SS   ORB 70 0
BITING DOWN HARD ON TRUTH EFFINGER, GEO. ALEC NV ORB 74 15     CAPTURED CROSS-SECTION, THE BREUER, MILES J. MD. SS AMZ 29 0
ARCS & SECANTS          MISC. MATERIAL      MS                 MUGWUMP FOUR              SILVERBERG, ROBERT  NV   GAL 59 0
                                                               WORLDS OF IF, THE         WEINBAUM, STANLEY G. SS  WOS 35 0
ORBIT  16              KNIGHT, DAMON       OA H HPR 75          DISAPPEARING ACT          BESTER, ALFRED      SS   STR 53 0
THEY SAY               KNIGHT, DAMON       MS
MOTHER AND CHILD        VINGE, JOAN D.      NA   ORB 75 16    OTHER DIMENSIONS          SMITH, CLARK ASHTON AC H ARK 70
SKINNY PEOPLE OF LEPTOPHLEBO STREET, THE                       MAROONED IN ANDROMEDA     SMITH, CLARK ASHTON NV   WOS 30 1
                        LAFFERTY, R. A.     SS   ORB 75 16      AMAZING PLANET, THE       SMITH, CLARK ASHTON NV   WSQ 31 S
BRILLIANT CURIOSITY, A  PISERCHIA, DORIS    NV   ORB 75 16      ADVENTURE IN FUTURITY, AN SMITH, CLARK ASHTON NV   WOS 31 04
PHOENIX HOUSE          MILLER, JESSIE      SS   ORB 75 16      IMMEASURABLE HORROR, THE  SMITH, CLARK ASHTON SS   WRT 31 0
JACK AND BETTY          THURSTON, ROBERT    SS   ORB 75 16      INVISIBLE CITY, THE       SMITH, CLARK ASHTON SS   WOS 32 0
PRISON OF CLAY, PRISON OF STEEL                                DIMENSION OF CHANCE, THE  SMITH, CLARK ASHTON NV   WOS 32 1
                        PLANCHAT, HENRY-LUC SS   ORB 75 16      METAMORPHOSIS OF EARTH, THE SMITH, CLARK ASHTON NV WRT 51 0
HEARTLAND              HASFORD, GUSTAV     SS   ORB 75 16      PHOENIX                   SMITH, CLARK ASHTON SS
SANDIAL                FEDER, MOSHE        SS   ORB 75 16      NECROMANTIC TALE, THE     SMITH, CLARK ASHTON SS   WRT 31 0
MEMORY MACHINE, THE     MISC. MATERIAL      MS                 VENUS OF AZOMBEII, THE    SMITH, CLARK ASHTON NV   WRT 31 0
IN DONOVAN'S TIME       GRANT, C. L.        SS   ORB 75 16    RESURRECTION OF THE RATTLESNAKE, THE
AMBIENCE               SKAL, DAVE          SS   ORB 75 16                                SMITH, CLARK ASHTON SS   WRT 31 1
BINARY JUSTICE          BIRELEY, RICHARD    SS   ORB 75 16      SUPERNUMERARY CORPSE, THE SMITH, CLARK ASHTON SS   WRT 32 1
HOUSE BY THE SEA, THE   ARNASON, ELEANOR    SS   ORB 75 16      MANDRAKES, THE            SMITH, CLARK ASHTON SS   WRT 33 0
EUCLID ALONE           ORR, WILLIAM F.     NV   ORB 75 16      THIRTEEN PHANTASMS        SMITH, CLARK ASHTON SS   FFN 36 0
ARCS & SECANTS          MISC. MATERIAL      MS                 OFFERING TO THE MOON, AN  SMITH, CLARK ASHTON SS   WRT 53 09
                                                             MONSTERS IN THE NIGHT (A PROPHECY OF MONSTERS)
ORBIT  17              KNIGHT, DAMON       OA H HPR 75                                   SMITH, CLARK ASHTON SS   FSF 54 1
THEY SAY               KNIGHT, DAMON       MS                 MALAY KRISE, THE          SMITH, CLARK ASHTON SS   OVL 10 1
ANTHROPOLOGIST, THE     SIDNEY, KATHLEEN M. SS   ORB 75 17      GHOST OF MOHAMMED DIN, THE SMITH, CLARK ASHTON SS  OVL 10 1
MAN WITH THE GOLDEN RETICULATES, THE                           MAHOUT, THE               SMITH, CLARK ASHTON SS   BLC 11 0
                        GOTSCHALK, FELIX C. SS   ORB 75 17      RAJA AND THE TIGER, THE   SMITH, CLARK ASHTON SS   BLC 12 0
STEEL SONNETS, THE      DUNTEMANN, JEFF     SS   ORB 75 17      SOMETHING NEW             SMITH, CLARK ASHTON SS   TST 24 0
TOTO, I HAVE A FEELING WE'RE NOT IN KANSAS ANYMORE             JUSTICE OF THE ELEPHANT, THE SMITH, CLARK ASHTON SS ORI 31 0
                        MILLAR, JEFF        SS   ORB 75 17      KISS OF ZORAIDA, THE      SMITH, CLARK ASHTON SS   MGC 33 0
AUTOPSY IN TRANSIT      CHAPMAN, STEVE      SS   ORB 75 17    TALE OF SIR JOHN MAUNDEVILLE, A (THE KINGDOM OF THE WORM)
HOUSE                  BARFOOT, JOHN       SS   ORB 75 17                                SMITH, CLARK ASHTON SS   FFN 33 1
FUN PALACE             MOORE, RAYLYN       SS   ORB 75 17      GHOUL, THE                SMITH, CLARK ASHTON SS   FFN 34 0
WHEN WE WERE GOOD       SKAL, DAVE          SS   ORB 75 17      TOLD IN THE DESERT        SMITH, CLARK ASHTON SS        64
WHICH IN THE WOOD DECAYS MCEVOY, SETH       SS   ORB 75 17
GREAT DAY IN THE MORNING LAFFERTY, R. A.    SS   ORB 75 17    OTHER PLACE, THE          PRIESTLEY, J. B.    AC H HPR 53
MAZE, THE              DYBEK, STUART       SS   ORB 75 17      OTHER PLACE, THE          PRIESTLEY, J. B.    SS
QUITE LATE ONE SPRING NIGHT CURLOVICH, JOHN M. SS ORB 75 17    GRAY ONES, THE            PRIESTLEY, J. B.    SS
UNDER THE HOLLYWOOD SIGN REAMY, TOM         SS   ORB 75 17      UNCLE PHIL ON TV          PRIESTLEY, J. B.    SS   FSF 55 1
MEMORY MACHINE, THE     MISC. MATERIAL      MS                 GUEST OF HONOR            PRIESTLEY, J. B.    SS
ARCS & SECANTS          MISC. MATERIAL      MS               LOOK AFTER THE STRANGE GIRL (THE STRANGE GIRL)
                                                                                         PRIESTLEY, J. B.    SS   FSF 54 0
ORBIT  18              KNIGHT, DAMON       OA H HPR 76          STATUES, THE              PRIESTLEY, J. B.    SS
THEY SAY               KNIGHT, DAMON       MS                 LEADINGTON INCIDENT, THE  PRIESTLEY, J. B.    SS
LADIES AND GENTLEMEN, THIS IS YOUR CRISIS                      MR. STRENBERRY'S TALE     PRIESTLEY, J. B.    SS        34
                        WILHELM, KATE       SS   ORB 76 18      NIGHT SEQUENCE            PRIESTLEY, J. B.    SS   FSF 56 03
HAND WITH ONE HUNDRED FINGERS, THE
                        LAFFERTY, R. A.     SS   ORB 76 18    OTHER SIDE OF THE CLOCK, THE STERN, PHILIP VAN D. AN H VNR 69
MEATHOUSE MAN          MARTIN, GEORGE R. R. SS  ORB 76 18      INTRODUCTION             STERN, PHILIP VAN D. IN
RULES OF MOOPSBALL      COHN, GARY          AR   ORB 76 18      CHRONOCLASM, THE          WYNDHAM, JOHN       NV   STR 53 0
IN PIERSON'S ORCHESTRA  ROBINSON, KIM S.    SS   ORB 76 18    STORY OF THE LATE MR. ELVESHAM, THE
WHO WAS THE FIRST OSCAR TO WIN A NEGRO?                                                  WELLS, H. G.        SS   IDL 96 05
                        STRETE, CRAIG       SS   ORB 76 18      NO SHIPS PASS             SMITH, LADY ELEANOR NV   CSL 32 04
MARY MARGARET ROAD-GRADER WALDROP, HOWARD   SS   ORB 76 18    LOOK AFTER THE STRANGE GIRL (THE STRANGE GIRL)
COMING BACK TO DIXIELAND ROBINSON, KIM S.   SS   ORB 76 18                               PRIESTLEY, J. B.    SS   FSF 54 0
TEACHER, THE           SIDNEY, KATHLEEN M. SS   ORB 76 18      AND HE BUILT A CROOKED HOUSE HEINLEIN, ROBERT A. SS ASF 41 02
FAMILY WINTER OF 1986, THE GOTSCHALK, FELIX C. SS ORB 76 18    SUCH INTERESTING NEIGHBORS FINNEY, JACK        SS   COL 51 0
MODULAR STORY, A        MOORE, RAYLYN       SS   ORB 76 18      AUGUST HEAT               HARVEY, WILLIAM F.  SS        28
M&M SEEN AS A LOW-YIELD THERMONUCLEAR DEVICE, THE              PHANTOM SETTER, THE       MURPHY, ROBERT      SS   SEP 61 06
                        VARLEY, JOHN        SS   ORB 76 18      AND IT COMES OUT HERE     DEL REY, LESTER     SS   GAL 51 0
EVE OF THE LAST APOLLO, THE SCHOLZ, CARTER  SS   ORB 76 18      OLD MAN, THE              HORN, HOLLOWAY      SS        32
MEMORY MACHINE, THE     MISC. MATERIAL      MS                 DIAL "O" FOR OPERATOR     PRESSLIE, ROBERT    SS   SCF 58 0
ARCS & SECANTS          MISC. MATERIAL      MS                 GREATEST GIFT, THE        STERN, PHILIP VAN D. SS        43

ORBIT UNLIMITED        ANDERSON, POUL      NO   PYR 61 05    OTHER SIDE OF THE MOON, THE DERLETH, AUGUST     AN H PEL 49
ROBIN HOOD'S BARN       ANDERSON, POUL      NV   ASF 59 01      APPEARANCE OF MAN, THE    BERESFORD, JOHN D.  PL        21
BURNING BRIDGE, THE     ANDERSON, POUL      NV   ASF 60 01      STAR, THE                 WELLS, H. G.        SS   GRP 97 0
AND YET SO FAR (CONDEMNED TO DEATH)                            THING ON OUTER SHOAL, THE MILLER, P. SCHUYLER SS   ASF 47 09
                        ANDERSON, POUL      SS   FUN 59 10    STRANGE DRUG OF DR. CABER, THE
MILL OF THE GODS, THE   ANDERSON, POUL      NV   NEW 61 AC                               DUNSANY, LORD       SS        48
                                                               WORLD OF WULKINS, THE     LONG, FRANK BELKNAP SS   TWS 48 04
ORPHANS OF THE SKY      HEINLEIN, ROBERT A. NO H GOL 63       CITY OF THE SINGING FLAME, THE
UNIVERSE               HEINLEIN, ROBERT A. NV   ASF 41 05                                SMITH, CLARK ASHTON SS   WOS 31 07
COMMON SENSE           HEINLEIN, ROBERT A. NV   ASF 41 10      BEYOND THE WALL OF SLEEP  LOVECRAFT, H. P.    SS   WRT 38 0
                                                               DEVIL OF EAST LUPTON, THE LEINSTER, MURRAY    SS   TWS 48 08
                                                               CONQUEROR'S ISLE          BOND, NELSON S.     SS   BBM 46 0
```

OTHER SIDE OF THE MOON, THE

SOMETHING FROM ABOVE	WANDREI, DONALD	NV	WRT	30 12
PILLAR OF FIRE	BRADBURY, RAY	NV	PLS	48 SU
MONSTER, THE (ALSO AS THE BRIGHTON MONSTER)				
	KERSH, GERALD	SS	SEP	48 02
SYMBIOSIS	JENKINS, WILL F.	SS	COL	47 06
CURE, THE	PADGETT, LEWIS	SS	ASF	46 05
VAULT OF THE BEAST	VAN VOGT, A. E.	NV	ASF	40 08
EARTH MEN, THE	BRADBURY, RAY	SS	TWS	48 08
ORIGINAL SIN	WRIGHT, S. FOWLER	SS	AFR	50 13
SPIRO (VENTURER OF THE MARTIAN MIMICS)				
	RUSSELL, ERIC FRANK	NV	WRT	47 03
MEMORIAL (SEE ALSO ATOMIC MEMORIAL)				
	STURGEON, THEODORE	SS	ASF	46 04
RESURRECTION (THE MONSTER)	VAN VOGT, A. E.	SS	ASF	48 08

OTHER SIDE OF THE MOON, THE (BRITISH PB 1)

	DERLETH, AUGUST	AN	PTH	63
APPEARANCE OF MAN, THE	BERESFORD, JOHN D.	PL		21
STAR, THE	WELLS, H. G.	SS	GRP	97 12
BEYOND THE WALL OF SLEEP	LOVECRAFT, H. P.	SS	WRT	38 03
DEVIL OF EAST LUPTON, THE	LEINSTER, MURRAY	SS	TWS	48 08
PILLAR OF FIRE	BRADBURY, RAY	NV	PLS	48 SU
MONSTER, THE (ALSO AS THE BRIGHTON MONSTER)				
	KERSH, GERALD	SS	SEP	48 02
CURE, THE	PADGETT, LEWIS	SS	ASF	46 05
VAULT OF THE BEAST	VAN VOGT, A. E.	NV	ASF	40 08
SPIRO (VENTURER OF THE MARTIAN MIMICS)				
	RUSSELL, ERIC FRANK	NV	WRT	47 03
MEMORIAL (SEE ALSO ATOMIC MEMORIAL)				
	STURGEON, THEODORE	SS	ASF	46 04

OTHER SIDE OF THE MOON, THE (BRITISH PB 2)

	DERLETH, AUGUST	AN	MFL	66
THING ON OUTER SHOAL, THE	MILLER, P. SCHUYLER	SS	ASF	47 09
STRANGE DRUG OF DR. CABER, THE				
	DUNSANY, LORD	SS		48
WORLD OF WULKINS, THE	LONG, FRANK BELKNAP	SS	TWS	48 04
CITY OF THE SINGING FLAME, THE				
	SMITH, CLARK ASHTON	SS	WOS	31 07
CONQUEROR'S ISLE	BOND, NELSON S.	SS	BBM	46 06
SOMETHING FROM ABOVE	WANDREI, DONALD	NV	WRT	30 12
SYMBIOSIS	JENKINS, WILL F.	SS	COL	47 06
EARTH MEN, THE	BRADBURY, RAY	SS	TWS	48 08
ORIGINAL SIN	WRIGHT, S. FOWLER	SS	AFR	50 13
RESURRECTION (THE MONSTER)	VAN VOGT, A. E.	SS	ASF	48 08

OTHER SIDE OF THE MOON, THE (BRITISH)

	DERLETH, AUGUST	AN H	GRY	56
APPEARANCE OF MAN, THE	BERESFORD, JOHN D.	PL		21
CITY OF THE SINGING FLAME, THE				
	SMITH, CLARK ASHTON	SS	WOS	31 07
BEYOND THE WALL OF SLEEP	LOVECRAFT, H. P.	SS	WRT	38 03
DEVIL OF EAST LUPTON, THE	LEINSTER, MURRAY	SS	TWS	48 08
SOMETHING FROM ABOVE	WANDREI, DONALD	NV	WRT	30 12
PILLAR OF FIRE	BRADBURY, RAY	NV	PLS	48 SU
SYMBIOSIS	JENKINS, WILL F.	SS	COL	47 06
ORIGINAL SIN	WRIGHT, S. FOWLER	SS	AFR	50 13
SPIRO (VENTURER OF THE MARTIAN MIMICS)				
	RUSSELL, ERIC FRANK	NV	WRT	47 03
MEMORIAL (SEE ALSO ATOMIC MEMORIAL)				
	STURGEON, THEODORE	SS	ASF	46 04
RESURRECTION (THE MONSTER)	VAN VOGT, A. E.	SS	ASF	48 08

OTHER SIDE OF THE MOON, THE (10 OF 20)

	DERLETH, AUGUST	AN	BRK	59
RESURRECTION (THE MONSTER)	VAN VOGT, A. E.	SS	ASF	48 08
ORIGINAL SIN	WRIGHT, S. FOWLER	SS	AFR	50 13
SPIRO (VENTURER OF THE MARTIAN MIMICS)				
	RUSSELL, ERIC FRANK	NV	WRT	47 03
MEMORIAL (SEE ALSO ATOMIC MEMORIAL)				
	STURGEON, THEODORE	SS	ASF	46 04
THING ON OUTER SHOAL, THE	MILLER, P. SCHUYLER	SS	ASF	47 09
DEVIL OF EAST LUPTON, THE	LEINSTER, MURRAY	SS	TWS	48 08
CONQUEROR'S ISLE	BOND, NELSON S.	SS	BBM	46 06
SOMETHING FROM ABOVE	WANDREI, DONALD	NV	WRT	30 12
SYMBIOSIS	JENKINS, WILL F.	SS	COL	47 06
CURE, THE	PADGETT, LEWIS	SS	ASF	46 05

OTHER SIDE OF THE SKY, THE   CLARKE, ARTHUR C.   AC H HBW 58
  ALSO IN "FROM THE OCEAN, FROM THE STARS"

BIBLIOGRAPHICAL NOTE	CLARKE, ARTHUR C.	IN		
NINE BILLION NAMES OF GOD, THE				
	CLARKE, ARTHUR C.	SS	STR	53 01
REFUGEE (CONTEST STORY, ORIGINAL TITLE THIS EARTH OF MAJESTY)				
	CLARKE, ARTHUR C.	SS	FSF	55 07
SPECIAL DELIVERY (THE OTHER SIDE OF THE SKY)				
	CLARKE, ARTHUR C.	SS	INF	57 09
FEATHERED FRIEND (THE OTHER SIDE OF THE SKY)				
	CLARKE, ARTHUR C.	SS	INF	57 09
TAKE A DEEP BREATH (THE OTHER SIDE OF THE SKY)				
	CLARKE, ARTHUR C.	SS	INF	57 09
FREEDOM OF SPACE (THE OTHER SIDE OF THE SKY)				
	CLARKE, ARTHUR C.	SS	INF	57 10
PASSER-BY (THE OTHER SIDE OF THE SKY)				
	CLARKE, ARTHUR C.	SS	INF	57 10
CALL OF THE STARS, THE (THE OTHER SIDE OF THE SKY)				
	CLARKE, ARTHUR C.	SS	INF	57 10
WALL OF DARKNESS, THE	CLARKE, ARTHUR C.	SS	SSS	49 07
SECURITY CHECK	CLARKE, ARTHUR C.	SS	FSF	57 06
NO MORNING AFTER	CLARKE, ARTHUR C.	SS	FSF	56 07
STARTING LINE, THE (VENTURE TO THE MOON)				
	CLARKE, ARTHUR C.	SS	FSF	56 12
ROBIN HOOD, F.R.S. (VENTURE TO THE MOON)				
	CLARKE, ARTHUR C.	SS	FSF	56 12
GREEN FINGERS (VENTURE TO THE MOON)				
	CLARKE, ARTHUR C.	SS	FSF	57 01

OTHER WORLDS, THE

ALL THAT GLITTERS (VENTURE TO THE MOON)				
	CLARKE, ARTHUR C.	SS	FSF	57 01
WATCH THIS SPACE (VENTURE TO THE MOON)				
	CLARKE, ARTHUR C.	SS	FSF	57 02
QUESTION OF RESIDENCE, A (VENTURE TO THE MOON)				
	CLARKE, ARTHUR C.	SS	FSF	57 02
PUBLICITY CAMPAIGN	CLARKE, ARTHUR C.	SS	SAT	56 10
ALL THE TIME IN THE WORLD	CLARKE, ARTHUR C.	SS	STS	52 07
COSMIC CASANOVA	CLARKE, ARTHUR C.	SS	VSF	58 05
STAR, THE	CLARKE, ARTHUR C.	SS	INF	55 11
OUT OF THE SUN	CLARKE, ARTHUR C.	SS	IFS	58 02
TRANSCIENCE	CLARKE, ARTHUR C.	SS	STS	49 07
SONGS OF DISTANT EARTH, THE	CLARKE, ARTHUR C.	NV	IFS	58 06

OTHER SIDE OF TOMORROW, THE   ELWOOD, ROGER   OA H RDM 73

INTRODUCTION	ELWOOD, ROGER	IN		
COME SING THE MOONS OF MORAVENN				
	BRACKETT, LEIGH	NV		
EXAMINATION DAY	EKLUND, GORDON	NV		
SPEEDERS, THE	TOFTE, ARTHUR	SS		
LET MY PEOPLE GO|	GREEN, JOSEPH	SS		
NIGHT OF THE MILLENNIUM	HOCH, EDWARD D.	SS		
BOWL OF BISKIES MAKES A GROWING BOY, A				
	JONES, RAYMOND F.	NV		
FINAL EXAM	SCORTIA, THOMAS N.	SS		
OTHERS, THE	HOLLY, J. HUNTER	NV		
PEACE, LOVE, AND FOOD FOR THE HUNGRY				
	KIMBERLY, GAIL	NV		

OTHER WORLDS OF CLIFFORD SIMAK

	SIMAK, CLIFFORD D.	AC	AVN	62
6 STORIES FROM "THE WORLDS OF CLIFFORD SIMAK"				
DUSTY ZEBRA	SIMAK, CLIFFORD D.	NV	GAL	54 09
CARBON COPY	SIMAK, CLIFFORD D.	NA	GAL	57 12
FOUNDING FATHER	SIMAK, CLIFFORD D.	SS	GAL	57 05
IDIOT'S CRUSADE	SIMAK, CLIFFORD D.	SS	GAL	54 10
DEATH SCENE	SIMAK, CLIFFORD D.	SS	INF	57 10
GREEN THUMB	SIMAK, CLIFFORD D.	NV	GAL	54 07

OTHER WORLDS, OTHER GODS   MOHS, MAYO   AN H DBL 71
  SCIENCE FICTION AND THE WORLD OF RELIGION

	MOHS, MAYO	IN		
CUNNING OF THE BEAST, THE (ANOTHER WORLD BEGINS)				
	BOND, NELSON S.	SS	BBM	42 11
CROSS OF CENTURIES, A	KUTTNER, HENRY	SS	STR	58 04
SOUL MATE	SUTTON, LEE	SS	FSF	59 06
WORD TO SPACE, THE	SANDERS, WINSTON P.	SS	FSF	60 09
PROMETHEUS	FARMER, PHILIP JOSE	NV	FSF	61 03
NINE BILLION NAMES OF GOD, THE				
	CLARKE, ARTHUR C.	SS	STR	53 01
VITANULS, THE	BRUNNER, JOHN	SS	FSF	67 07
JUDAS	BRUNNER, JOHN	SS	DVS	67 01
QUEST FOR SAINT AQUIN, THE	BOUCHER, ANTHONY	SS	NTS	51
BALAAM	BOUCHER, ANTHONY	SS	NTL	54
EVENSONG	DEL REY, LESTER	SS	DVS	67 01
SHALL THE DUST PRAISE THEE?	KNIGHT, DAMON	SS	DVS	67 01
CHRISTUS APOLLO (SELECTION)	BRADBURY, RAY	PM	NEW	69 AC

OTHER WORLDS, OTHER SEAS   SUVIN, DARKO   AN H RDM 70

PREFACE	SUVIN, DARKO	IN		
PATROL, THE	LEM, STANISLAW	NV		
COMPUTER THAT FOUGHT A DRAGON, THE				
	LEM, STANISLAW	SS		
THIRTEENTH JOURNEY OF ION TICHY, THE				
	LEM, STANISLAW	NV		
TWENTY-FOURTH JOURNEY OF ION TICHY, THE				
	LEM, STANISLAW	SS		
CONTACT, THE	COLIN, VLADIMIR	SS		
VAMPIRES LTD.	NESVADBA, JOSEF	SS		64
WHY ATLANTIS SANK	DONEV, ANTON	SS		
MASTER BUILDER, THE	ALTOV, HENRIK	SS		
FOUNDING OF CIVILIZATION, THE				
	YAROV, ROMAIN	SS	ISF	68 06
LECTURES ON PARAPSYCHOLOGY	VARSHAVSKY, ILYA	SS		
BIOCURRENTS, BIOCURRENTS...	VARSHAVSKY, ILYA	SS		
SOMP	VARSHAVSKY, ILYA	SS		
NONEATRINS, THE	VARSHAVSKY, ILYA	SS		
DEBATE ON SF- MOSCOW 1965, A	TOMAN, NIKOLAY	SS		
INTERVIEW WITH A TRAFFIC POLICEMAN				
	DNIEPROV, ANATOLY	SS		
S*T*A*P*L*E FARM, THE	DNIEPROV, ANATOLY	SS		
ISLAND OF THE CRABS, THE	DNIEPROV, ANATOLY	SS	ISF	68 06
ABOUT THE EDITOR	MISC. MATERIAL	MS		

OTHER WORLDS, OTHER TIMES   MOSKOWITZ & ELWOOD   AN   MBB 69

NEW WORLDS	GARDNER, EARL S.	NV	ARG	32 12
HIGHWAY J	MAINE, CHARLES ERIC	NV	PLS	53 11
SIN OF HYACINTH PEUCH, THE	RUSSELL, ERIC FRANK	NV	FAN	52 FL
DOES A BEE CARE?	ASIMOV, ISAAC	SS	IFS	57 06
TIN YOU LOVE TO TOUCH, THE	BLOCH, ROBERT	SS	OWS	51 07
SHADOW, SHADOW, ON THE WALL	STURGEON, THEODORE	SS	IMG	51 02
MAN WHO SAW THE FUTURE, THE	HAMILTON, EDMOND	SS	AMZ	30 10
PIPER IN THE WOODS	DICK, PHILIP K.	SS	IMG	53 02

OTHER WORLDS, THE   STONG, PHILIP D.   AN H FNK 41
  ALSO AS "25 MODERN STORIES OF MYSTERY AND IMAGINATION"

FOREWORD	STONG, PHILIP D.	IN		
CONSIDERATE HOSTS, THE	MCCLUSKY, THORP	SS	WRT	39 12
MAN IN THE BLACK HAT, THE	FESSIER, MICHAEL	SS	ESQ	34 02
NAKED LADY	LORD, MINDRET	SS	WRT	34 09
HOUSE OF ECSTASY, THE	FARLEY, RALPH MILNE	SS	WRT	38 04
ESCAPE	ERNST, PAUL	SS	WRT	38 07
ADAPTIVE ULTIMATE, THE	JESSEL, JOHN	NV	ASF	35 11
WOMAN IN GRAY, THE	EVERETT, WALKER G.	SS	WRT	35 06
PIPES OF PAN, THE	DEL REY, LESTER	SS	UNK	40 05
AUNT CASSIE	SWAN, VIRGINIA	SS	NEW	41 AN

OTHER WORLDS, THE   OUT OF THIS WORLD

GOD IN A GARDEN, A   STURGEON, THEODORE   SS   UNK 39 10
MAN WHO KNEW ALL THE ANSWERS, THE
                            BERN, DONALD   SS   AMZ 40 08
ADAM LINK'S VENGEANCE   BINDER, EANDO   NV   AMZ 40 02
TRUTH IS A PLAGUE   O'BRIEN, D. W.   SS   AMZ 40 02
FOURTH-DIMENSIONAL DEMONSTRATOR, THE
                            LEINSTER, MURRAY   SS   ASF 35 12
ALAS, ALL THINKING| BATES, HARRY   SN   ASF 35 06
COMEDY OF ERAS, THE   KENT, KELVIN   SS   TWS 40 09
PROBLEM FOR BIOGRAPHERS, A LORD, MINDRET   SS   NEW 41 AN
IN THE VAULT   LOVECRAFT, H. P.   SS   WRT 32 04
SCHOOL FOR THE UNSPEAKABLE WELLMAN, MANLY WADE SS   WRT 37 09
HOUSE WHERE TIME STOOD STILL, THE
                            QUINN, SEABURY   SS   WRT 39 03
MYSTERY OF THE LAST GUEST, THE
                            FLANDERS, JOHN   SS   WRT 35 10
SONG OF THE SLAVES, THE   WELLMAN, MANLY WADE SS   WRT 40 03
PANELLED ROOM, THE   DERLETH, AUGUST   SS   WMR 33 09
GRAVEYARD RATS, THE   KUTTNER, HENRY   SS   WRT 36 03
RETURN OF ANDREW BENTLEY, THE
                            DERLETH, AUGUST
                            AND SCHORER, MARK   SS C WRT 33 09

OTHERS, THE   CARR, TERRY   AN   PGM 69
ROOG   DICK, PHILIP K.   SS   FSF 53 02
BLUE LENSES, THE   DU MAURIER, DAPHNE   NV   59
SHIPSHAPE HOME   MATHESON, RICHARD   SS   GAL 52 07
EIGHT O'CLOCK IN THE MORNING NELSON, RAY   SS   FSF 63 11
SIX FINGERS OF TIME, THE   LAFFERTY, R. A.   NV   IFS 60 09
BE MY GUEST   KNIGHT, DAMON   NV   FUN 58 09
THEY   HEINLEIN, ROBERT A. SS   UNK 41 04

OUT FROM GANYMEDE   MALZBERG, BARRY N.   AC   WPB 74 12
INTRODUCTION   MALZBERG, BARRY N.   IN
OUT FROM GANYMEDE   MALZBERG, BARRY N.   SS   NDM 72 02
NOVEMBER 22, 1963   MALZBERG, BARRY N.   SS   NEW 74 AC
STILL-LIFE (AS K. M. O'DONNELL)
                            MALZBERG, BARRY N.   SS   DVS 72 02
CONQUEST OF MARS, THE   MALZBERG, BARRY N.   SS   NOV 72 02
SOME NOTES TOWARD A USEABLE PAST
                            MALZBERG, BARRY N.   SS   NOV 72 02
LINKAGE   MALZBERG, BARRY N.   SS   DEM 73
UNION FOREVER, THE   MALZBERG, BARRY N.   SS   SCS 73
YEARBOOK, THE   MALZBERG, BARRY N.   SS   FSF 71 05
INTER ALIA   MALZBERG, BARRY N.   SS   INY 72 03
ALLOWANCES   MALZBERG, BARRY N.   SS   FAN 72 08
HELMET, THE   MALZBERG, BARRY N.   SS   FSF 73 09
BREAKING IN   MALZBERG, BARRY N.   SS   FAN 72 06
PATER FAMILIAS   MALZBERG, BARRY N.
                            AND NEVILLE, KRIS   SS C FSF 72 03
CAUSATION   MALZBERG, BARRY N.   SS   FSF 71 12
ART OF FICTION, THE   MALZBERG, BARRY N.   SS   MSM 72
SHORT RELIGIOUS NOVEL, A   MALZBERG, BARRY N.   SS   FSF 72 09
REPORT OF THE DEFENSE   MALZBERG, BARRY N.   SS   ETN 72
NOTES FOR A NOVEL ABOUT THE FIRST SHIP EVER TO VENUS
                            MALZBERG, BARRY N.   SS   UNI 71 01
BEYOND SLEEP   MALZBERG, BARRY N.   SS   EQM 70 11
INTERCEPTOR, THE   MALZBERG, BARRY N.   SS   MSM 72
AGONY COLUMN   MALZBERG, BARRY N.   SS   EQM 71 12
SENSE OF THE FIRE, THE   MALZBERG, BARRY N.   NV   ESC 67

OUT OF BOUNDS   MERRIL, JUDITH   AC   PYR 60 04
INTRODUCTION   STURGEON, THEODORE   IN
THAT ONLY A MOTHER   MERRIL, JUDITH   SS   ASF 48 06
PEEPING TOM   MERRIL, JUDITH   NV   STS 54 SP
LADY WAS A TRAMP, THE   MERRIL, JUDITH   SS   VSF 57 03
WHOEVER YOU ARE   MERRIL, JUDITH   NV   STS 52 12
CONNECTION COMPLETED   MERRIL, JUDITH   SS   USF 54 SU
DEAD CENTER   MERRIL, JUDITH   NV   FSF 54 11
DEATH CANNOT WITHER   MERRIL, JUDITH   NV   FSF 59 02

OUT OF MY MIND   BRUNNER, JOHN   AC   BAL 67 02
FAIR WARNING   BRUNNER, JOHN   SS   ASF 64 05
NAIL IN THE MIDDLE OF THE HAND, THE
                            BRUNNER, JOHN   SS   SMM 65 07
ORPHEUS'S BROTHER   BRUNNER, JOHN   SS   MHS 65 04
PREROGATIVE   BRUNNER, JOHN   SS   NWS 60 11
SUCH STUFF   BRUNNER, JOHN   SS   FSF 62 06
TOTALLY RICH, THE   BRUNNER, JOHN   NV   WOT 63 06
SEE WHAT I MEAN| BRUNNER, JOHN   SS   ASF 64 01
FOURTH POWER, THE   BRUNNER, JOHN   NV   NWS 60 04
LAST LONELY MAN, THE   BRUNNER, JOHN   SS   NWS 64 06
SINGLEMINDED   BRUNNER, JOHN   NV   IFS 63 05
BETTER MOUSETRAP, A   BRUNNER, JOHN   NV   IFS 63 11
EYE OF THE BEHOLDER, THE   BRUNNER, JOHN   SS   FUN 57 01
ROUND TRIP   BRUNNER, JOHN   SS   FUN 59 09

OUT OF MY MIND (BRITISH)   BRUNNER, JOHN   AC   FSP 68
FOURTH POWER, THE   BRUNNER, JOHN   NV   NWS 60 04
MAN WHO PLAYED THE BLUES   BRUNNER, JOHN   SS   SCF 56 02
ORPHEUS'S BROTHER   BRUNNER, JOHN   SS   MHS 65 04
SUCH STUFF   BRUNNER, JOHN   SS   FSF 62 06
WHEN GABRIEL...   BRUNNER, JOHN   SS   SCF 56 08
NAIL IN THE MIDDLE OF THE HAND, THE
                            BRUNNER, JOHN   SS   SMM 65 07
LAST LONELY MAN, THE   BRUNNER, JOHN   SS   NWS 64 06
WHIRLIGIG| BRUNNER, JOHN   SS   BYI 67 11
SEE WHAT I MEAN| BRUNNER, JOHN   SS   ASF 64 01
TOTALLY RICH, THE   BRUNNER, JOHN   NV   WOT 63 06

OUT OF SPACE AND TIME   SMITH, CLARK ASHTON AC H NSP 71
CLARK ASHTON SMITH: MASTER OF FANTASY
                            MISC. MATERIAL   IN
END OF THE STORY, THE   SMITH, CLARK ASHTON NV   WRT 30 05
RENDEZVOUS IN AVEROIGNE, A SMITH, CLARK ASHTON SS   WRT 31 04
NIGHT IN MALNEANT, A   SMITH, CLARK ASHTON SS   WRT 39 09

CITY OF THE SINGING FLAME, THE
                            SMITH, CLARK ASHTON SS   WOS 31 0
UNCHARTED ISLE, THE   SMITH, CLARK ASHTON SS   WRT 30 1
SECOND INTERMENT, THE   SMITH, CLARK ASHTON SS   STT 33 0
CHAIN OF AFORGOMON, THE   SMITH, CLARK ASHTON SS   WRT 35 1
DARK EIDOLON, THE   SMITH, CLARK ASHTON NV   WRT 35 0
DOUBLE SHADOW, THE   SMITH, CLARK ASHTON SS   WRT 39 0.
LAST HEIROGLYPH, THE   SMITH, CLARK ASHTON SS   WRT 35 04
SADASTOR   SMITH, CLARK ASHTON SS   WRT 30 0
DEATH OF ILALOTHA, THE   SMITH, CLARK ASHTON SS   WRT 37 09
RETURN OF THE SORCERER, THE SMITH, CLARK ASHTON NV   STT 31 0
TESTAMENT OF ATHAMMAUS, THE SMITH, CLARK ASHTON NV   WRT 32 1
WEIRD OF AVOOSL WUTHOQQUAN, THE
                            SMITH, CLARK ASHTON SS   WRT 32 0
UBBO-SATHLA   SMITH, CLARK ASHTON SS   WRT 33 0
MONSTER OF THE PROPHECY, THE SMITH, CLARK ASHTON NV   WRT 32 0
VAULTS OF YOH-VOMBIS, THE   SMITH, CLARK ASHTON NV   WRT 32 0
FROM THE CRYPTS OF MEMORY   SMITH, CLARK ASHTON SS   22
SHADOWS, THE   SMITH, CLARK ASHTON SS   22

OUT OF THE SILENT SKY   BIGGLE, LLOYD JR.   AC   BET 77
ON COVER AS "THE SILENT SKY", SEE "RULE OF THE DOOR"

OUT OF THE UNKNOWN   VAN VOGT & HULL   AC H FPB 48
IN ENGLAND AS "THE SEA THING AND OTHER STORIES"
SEA THING, THE   VAN VOGT, A. E.   NV   UNK 40 0
WISHES WE MAKE, THE   HULL, E. MAYNE   SS   UNK 43 0
WITCH, THE   VAN VOGT, A. E.   SS   UNK 43 02
PATIENT, THE   HULL, E. MAYNE   SS   UNK 43 1
ULTIMATE WISH, THE   HULL, E. MAYNE   SS   UNK 43 0.
GHOST, THE   VAN VOGT, A. E.   NV   UNK 42 08

OUT OF THE UNKNOWN (ENGLISH EDITION ADDS:)
                            VAN VOGT & HULL   AC H SID 70
WELLWISHER, THE   HULL, E. MAYNE   SS

OUT OF THIS WORLD   FAST, JULIUS   AN   PEN 44 06
WORD FROM THE EDITOR, A   FAST, JULIUS   IN
EVENING PRIMROSE (1941)   COLLIER, JOHN   SS   AFR 47 03
LAURA   SAKI   SS   14
SAM SMALL'S TYKE   KNIGHT, ERIC   SS   42
SATAN AND SAM SHAY   ARTHUR, ROBERT   SS   ELK 42 08
DISPUTED AUTHORSHIP, A (1895)
                            BANGS, JOHN KENDRICK SS
MR. MERGENTHWIRKER'S LOBBIES BOND, NELSON S.   SS   SCR 37 1
VISION OF JUDGEMENT, A   WELLS, H. G.   SS   BUT 99 0
THUS I REFUTE BEELZY   COLLIER, JOHN   SS   43
KING OF THE CATS, THE   BENET, STEPHEN V.   SS   HRP 29 02
CANTERVILLE GHOST, THE   WILDE, OSCAR   SS   CSR 87 03
MY FRIEND MERTON   FAST, JULIUS   SS   NEW 44 AN
AND ADAM BEGOT   OBOLER, ARCH   SS   42
CLUB SECRETARY   DUNSANY, LORD   SS   34
SCARLET PLAGUE, THE   LONDON, JACK   NA   LOM 12 06

OUT OF THIS WORLD   LEINSTER, MURRAY   NO H AVL 58
GREGORY CIRCLE, THE   LEINSTER, MURRAY   NV   TWS 47 04
NAMELESS SOMETHING, THE   LEINSTER, MURRAY   NV   TWS 47 06
DEADLY DUST, THE   LEINSTER, MURRAY   NV   TWS 47 04

OUT OF THIS WORLD 1   WILLIAMS-ELLIS& OWEN AN H BLK 60
BREAKING STRAIN (THIRTY SECONDS - THIRTY DAYS)
                            CLARKE, ARTHUR C.   NV   TWS 49 12
NO PLACE LIKE EARTH (TYRANT AND SLAVE-GIRL ON VENUS)
                            WYNDHAM, JOHN   NV   NWS 51 SP
RUUM, THE   PORGES, ARTHUR   SS   FSF 53 10
FRIDAY   KIPPAX, JOHN   SS   NWS 59 02
MIDDLE OF THE WEEK AFTER NEXT, THE
                            LEINSTER, MURRAY   SS   TWS 52 08
PLACET IS A CRAZY PLACE   BROWN, FREDRIC   SS   ASF 46 05
CHEMICAL PLANT   WILLIAMSON, IAN   SS   NWS 50 WI
MEN OF THE TEN BOOKS   VANCE, JACK   SS   STS 51 03

OUT OF THIS WORLD 2   WILLIAMS-ELLIS& OWEN AN H BLK 61
TROUBLE WITH EMILY, THE   WHITE, JAMES   NV   NWS 58 1
DUSTY DEATH, THE   KIPPAX, JOHN   SS   NWS 58 11
ANOTHER WORD FOR MAN   PRESSLIE, ROBERT   SS   NWS 58 12
RAILWAYS UP ON CANNIS, THE KAPP, COLIN   SS   NWS 59 10
MACHINE MADE   MCINTOSH, J. T.   SS   NWS 51 SU
BUT WHO CAN REPLACE A MAN? ALDISS, BRIAN W.   SS   INF 58 06
GIFT OF GAB, THE   VANCE, JACK   NV   ASF 55 09
STILL WATERS, THE   DEL REY, LESTER   SS   FAN 55 04

OUT OF THIS WORLD 3   WILLIAMS-ELLIS& OWEN AN H BLK 61
SANDS OUR ABODE   RAYER, FRANCIS G.   SS   NWS 59 06
ROUND TRIP TO ESIDARAP (ESIDARAP OT PIRT DNUOR)
                            BIGGLE, LLOYD JR.   SS   IFS 60 11
LIVING SPACE   ASIMOV, ISAAC   SS   SFS 56 05
APPRENTICE, THE   WHITE, JAMES   NV   NWS 60 10
BAXBR DAXBR   SMITH, EVELYN E.   SS   FSF 56 09
DUMB MARTIAN   WYNDHAM, JOHN   NV   GAL 52 07
WHO'S THERE? (ALSO AS THE HAUNTED SPACESUIT)
                            CLARKE, ARTHUR C.   SS   NWS 58 1
ARARAT   HENDERSON, ZENNA   SS   FSF 52 10

OUT OF THIS WORLD 4   WILLIAMS-ELLIS& OWEN AN H BLK 64
INSIDE THE COMET (ALSO AS INTO THE COMET)
                            CLARKE, ARTHUR C.   SS   FSF 60 10
HOTHOUSE   ALDISS, BRIAN W.   NV   FSF 61 02
WHEN THE ENGINES HAD TO STOP JONES, ELIS GWYN   SS   NEW 64 AN
TWICE BITTEN   MALCOLM, DONALD   SS   NWS 63 02
CHANGELING   WILLIAMS-ELLIS, A.   SS   NEW 64 AN
ASTRONAUT, THE   ZHURAVLEVA, VALENTINA SS
BILLENIUM   BALLARD, J. G.   SS   NWS 61 11
SIX-FINGERED JACKS   JAMES, E. R.   SS   NWS 62 06

OUT OF THIS WORLD 5

OUT OF THIS WORLD 5	WILLIAMS-ELLIS& OWEN	AN H BLK 65		
FOUR IN ONE	KNIGHT, DAMON	NV	GAL	53 02
BOTTOMLESS PIT	HIGH, PHILIP E.	SS	NWS	63 03
HOUR OF LETDOWN, THE	WHITE, E. B.	SS	FSF	52 08
COLONIAL	CHRISTOPHER, JOHN	NV	ASF	49 04
BADMAN	BRUNNER, JOHN	SS	NWS	60 03
PUSHOVER PLANET	PEDERSEN, CON	SS	FSF	63 06
FICTION MACHINES, THE	OKHOTNIKOV, VADIM	SS		
WINTHROP WAS STUBBORN (TIME WAITS FOR WINTHROP)				
	TENN, WILLIAM	NA	GAL	57 08

OUT OF THIS WORLD 6

	WILLIAMS-ELLIS& OWEN	AN H BLK 67		
ALL THE TROUBLES OF THE WORLD				
	ASIMOV, ISAAC	SS	SUP	58 04
FAST TRIP	WHITE, JAMES	SS	FSF	63 04
SICKNESS, THE	TENN, WILLIAM	SS	INF	55 11
HEART OF BLACKNESS, THE (THE CRAVING FOR BLACKNESS)				
	RAY, ROBERT	SS	NWS	62 09
ALIENS, THE	LEINSTER, MURRAY	NV	ASF	59 08
NINE BILLION NAMES OF GOD, THE				
	CLARKE, ARTHUR C.	SS	STR	53 01
STIMULUS	BRUNNER, JOHN	SS	NWS	62 03

OUT OF THIS WORLD 7

	WILLIAMS-ELLIS& OWEN	AN H BLK 68		
IMPERSONATORS, THE	MACAPP, C. C.	SS	IFS	67 01
ORDEAL IN SPACE	HEINLEIN, ROBERT A.	SS	TAC	48 05
COLD, COLD BOX, THE	FAST, HOWARD	SS	FSF	59 07
TO CHANGE THEIR WAYS	MARTINO, JOSEPH P.	NV	ASF	67 04
MOON, THE	PARKES, LUCAS	SS		
MEETING OF THE MINDS	SHECKLEY, ROBERT	NA	GAL	60 02
OUNCE OF DISSENSION, AN	LORAN, MARTIN	SS	ASF	66 07
POINT OF FOCUS	SILVERBERG, ROBERT	SS	ASF	58 08

OUTDATED MAN, THE	HARRISON, HARRY	OA	DEL	75 04
SEE "NOVA 3"				

OUTER REACHES, THE	DERLETH, AUGUST	AN H PEL 51		
ENGLISH DERIVATIVE ANTHOLOGY "THE TIME OF INFINITY"				
FOREWORD	DERLETH, AUGUST	IN		
INTERLOPER	ANDERSON, POUL	SS	FSF	51 04
DEATH SENTENCE	ASIMOV, ISAAC	SS	ASF	43 11
THIS IS THE LAND	BOND, NELSON S.	SS	BBM	51 04
YLLA (I'LL NOT LOOK FOR WINE)				
	BRADBURY, RAY	SS	MCL	50 01
GREEN CAT, THE	CARTMILL, CLEVE	SS	WBY	51 01
GIT ALONG!	DE CAMP, L. SPRAGUE	SS	ASF	50 08
SERVICE FIRST	KELLER, DAVID H. MD.	SS	AMQ	31 WI
SHOCK	KUTTNER, HENRY	SS	ASF	43 03
SHIP SAILS AT MIDNIGHT, THE	LEIBER, FRITZ	NV	FAD	50 09
POWER, THE	LEINSTER, MURRAY	SS	ASF	45 09
CRITTERS, THE	LONG, FRANK BELKNAP	SS	ASF	45 11
PARDON MY MISTAKE	PRATT, FLETCHER	SS	TWS	46 12
GOOD NIGHT, MR. JAMES	SIMAK, CLIFFORD D.	NV	GAL	51 03
PLUTONIAN DRUG, THE	SMITH, CLARK ASHTON	SS	AMZ	34 09
FAREWELL TO EDEN	STURGEON, THEODORE	SS	NEW	49 AN
CO-OPERATE- OR ELSE!	VAN VOGT, A. E.	NV	ASF	42 04
FINALITY UNLIMITED	WANDREI, DONALD	SN	ASF	36 09

OUTER REACHES, THE (BRITISH)	DERLETH, AUGUST	AN	CNL 63	
FIRST 8 STORIES OF AMERICAN EDITION, LAST 9 IN				
"THE TIME OF INFINITY"				

OUTER REACHES, THE (10 OF 17)				
	DERLETH, AUGUST	AN	BRK 58	
CO-OPERATE- OR ELSE!	VAN VOGT, A. E.	NV	ASF	42 04
GOOD NIGHT, MR. JAMES	SIMAK, CLIFFORD D.	NV	GAL	51 03
CRITTERS, THE	LONG, FRANK BELKNAP	SS	ASF	45 11
DEATH SENTENCE	ASIMOV, ISAAC	SS	ASF	43 11
THIS IS THE LAND	BOND, NELSON S.	SS	BBM	51 04
YLLA (I'LL NOT LOOK FOR WINE)				
	BRADBURY, RAY	SS	MCL	50 01
GREEN CAT, THE	CARTMILL, CLEVE	SS	WBY	51 01
PARDON MY MISTAKE	PRATT, FLETCHER	SS	TWS	46 12
PLUTONIAN DRUG, THE	SMITH, CLARK ASHTON	SS	AMZ	34 09
FAREWELL TO EDEN	STURGEON, THEODORE	SS	NEW	49 AN

OUTER SPACE STORIES	FURMAN, A. L.	AN	LPB 65 12	
SEE "TEEN-AGE OUTER SPACE STORIES"				

OUTPOSTS IN SPACE	WEST, WALLACE	AC H AVL 62		
MOON MADNESS	WEST, WALLACE	SS	WRT	31 08
MOON DANCE	WEST, WALLACE	NV	SFQ	54 11
OUTLAW	WEST, WALLACE	SS		
NO WAR TOMORROW	WEST, WALLACE	NO	SFQ	51 05
HAUNTED CENTENNIAL	WEST, WALLACE	NV	FUT	58 02

OUTSIDERS: CHILDREN OF WONDER				
	TENN, WILLIAM	AN	PMA 54	
SEE "CHILDREN OF WONDER"				

OUTWARD URGE, THE	WYNDHAM & PARKES	AC	BAL 59	
ONLY LATER EDITIONS CONTAIN "THE EMPTYNESS OF SPACE"				
FOR ALL THE NIGHT	WYNDHAM, JOHN	NV	NWS	58 04
IDIOT'S DELIGHT	WYNDHAM, JOHN	NV	NWS	58 06
THIN GNAT-VOICES, THE	WYNDHAM, JOHN	NV	NWS	58 07
SPACE IS A PROVINCE OF BRAZIL				
	WYNDHAM, JOHN	NV	NWS	58 09
EMPTYNESS OF SPACE, THE (ALSO AS THE ASTEROIDS, 2194)				
	WYNDHAM, JOHN	SS	NWS	60 11

OVER THE EDGE	ELLISON, HARLAN	AC	BEL 70 05	
FRONTIERS OF EDGEVILLE, THE	SPINRAD, NORMAN	IN		
BRINKMANSHIP	ELLISON, HARLAN	IN		
PENNIES, OFF A DEAD MAN'S EYES				
	ELLISON, HARLAN	SS	GAL	69 11
FINAL TROPHY	ELLISON, HARLAN	NV	SUP	57 06

PARADOX LOST, AND 12 OTHER GREAT S.F. STORIES

TEDDY CRAZY SHOW , THE				
	ELLISON, HARLAN	NV	ADM	68 10
ERNEST AND THE MACHINE GOD	ELLISON, HARLAN	NV	KNT	68 01
TINY ALLY	ELLISON, HARLAN	SS	STN	57 10
PROWLER IN THE CITY AT THE EDGE OF THE WORLD, THE				
	ELLISON, HARLAN	NV	DVS	67 01
BLIND LIGHTNING	ELLISON, HARLAN	SS	FUN	56 06
3 FACES OF FEAR: AN ESSAY	ELLISON, HARLAN	MS		
BLANK	ELLISON, HARLAN	SS	INF	57 06
NIGHT VIGIL (YELLOW STREAK HERO)				
	ELLISON, HARLAN	SS	AMZ	57 05
ENTER THE FANATIC, STAGE CENTER				
	ELLISON, HARLAN	SS	ADM	66 07
ROCK GOD	ELLISON, HARLAN	SS	COV	69 11

OVERLOADED MAN, THE	BALLARD, J. G.	AC	PTH 67 11	
NOW: ZERO	BALLARD, J. G.	SS	SCF	59 12
TIME-TOMBS, THE	BALLARD, J. G.	NV	IFS	63 03
THIRTEEN TO CENTAURUS	BALLARD, J. G.	NV	AMZ	62 04
TRACK 12	BALLARD, J. G.	SS	NWS	58 04
PASSPORT TO ETERNITY	BALLARD, J. G.	SS	AMZ	62 06
ESCAPEMENT	BALLARD, J. G.	SS	NWS	56 12
TIME OF PASSAGE	BALLARD, J. G.	SS	SCF	64 02
VENUS HUNTERS, THE (THE ENCOUNTER)				
	BALLARD, J. G.	NV	AMZ	63 06
COMING OF THE UNCONSCIOUS, THE				
	BALLARD, J. G.	BR	NWS	66 07
OVERLOADED MAN, THE	BALLARD, J. G.	SS	NWS	61 07

PACIFIC BOOK OF AUSTRALIAN SCIENCE FICTION				
	BAXTER, JOHN	AN	AAR 68	
INTRODUCTION	BAXTER, JOHN	IN		
BURNING SPEAR	DENTON, KIT	SS	FSF	64 02
IT COULD BE YOU	ROBERTS, FRANK	SS	SSI	64
EVIDENCE, THE	HARDING, LEE	SS	NWS	64 08
OUNCE OF DISSENSION, AN	LORAN, MARTIN	SS	ASF	66 07
WEATHER IN THE UNDERWORLD, THE				
	FREE, COLIN	SS	SQU	65 06
ALL MY YESTERDAYS	BRODERICK, DAMIEN	SS		65
FINAL FLOWER	COOK, STEPHEN	SS	NEW	68 AN
FOR MEN MUST WORK (AUJ 55 08)				
	BRYNING, FRANK B.	SS	FUN	56 02
BEACH, THE	BAXTER, JOHN	SS	NWR	68 13
ALL LACED UP	CHANDLER, A. BERTRAM	SS	NWS	61 11
STRONG ATTRACTION	SMITH, RON	SS	NEW	68 AN
THERE IS A CROOKED MAN	WODHAMS, JACK	SN	ASF	67 02

PAIL OF AIR, A	LEIBER, FRITZ	AC	BAL 64 07	
PAIL OF AIR, A	LEIBER, FRITZ	SS	GAL	51 12
BEAT CLUSTER, THE	LEIBER, FRITZ	SS	GAL	61 10
FOXHOLES OF MARS, THE	LEIBER, FRITZ	SS	TWS	52 06
PIPE DREAM	LEIBER, FRITZ	SS	IFS	59 02
TIME FIGHTER	LEIBER, FRITZ	SS	FUN	57 03
64-SQUARE MADHOUSE, THE	LEIBER, FRITZ	NA	IFS	62 05
BREAD OVERHEAD	LEIBER, FRITZ	NV	GAL	58 02
LAST LETTER, THE	LEIBER, FRITZ	SS	GAL	58 06
RUMP-TITTY-TITTY-TUM-TAH-TEE	LEIBER, FRITZ	SS	FSF	58 05
COMING ATTRACTION	LEIBER, FRITZ	SS	GAL	50 11
NICE GIRL WITH FIVE HUSBANDS	LEIBER, FRITZ	SS	GAL	51 04

PAINGOD AND OTHER DELUSIONS	ELLISON, HARLAN	AC	PYR 65 12	
SPERO MELIORA	ELLISON, HARLAN	IN		
PAINGOD	ELLISON, HARLAN	SS	FAN	64 06
"REPENT, HARLEQUIN!" SAID THE TICKTOCKMAN				
	ELLISON, HARLAN	SS	GAL	65 12
CRACKPOTS, THE	ELLISON, HARLAN	NV	IFS	56 06
BRIGHT EYES	ELLISON, HARLAN	SS	FAN	65 04
DISCARDED, THE (THE ABNORMALS)				
	ELLISON, HARLAN	SS	FAN	59 04
WANTED IN SURGERY	ELLISON, HARLAN	NV	IFS	57 08
DEEPER THAN DARKNESS	ELLISON, HARLAN	NV	INF	57 04

PAINGOD AND OTHER DELUSIONS (THIRD EDITION ADDS:)				
	ELLISON, HARLAN	AC	PYR 75 03	
NEW INTRODUCTION: YOUR BASIC CROWN OF THORNS				
	ELLISON, HARLAN	IN		
SLEEPING DOGS	ELLISON, HARLAN	SS	ASF	74 10

PANDORA EFFECT, THE	WILLIAMSON, JACK	AC	ACE 69	
AUTHOR'S INTRODUCTION	WILLIAMSON, JACK	IN		
HAPPIEST CREATURE, THE	WILLIAMSON, JACK	SS	STR	53 02
COSMIC EXPRESS, THE	WILLIAMSON, JACK	SS	AMZ	30 11
METAL MAN, THE	WILLIAMSON, JACK	SS	AMZ	28 12
COLD GREEN EYE, THE	WILLIAMSON, JACK	SS	FAN	53 03
GUINEVERE FOR EVERYBODY	WILLIAMSON, JACK	SS	STR	54 03
WITH FOLDED HANDS...	WILLIAMSON, JACK	NV	ASF	47 07
EQUALIZER, THE	WILLIAMSON, JACK	NV	ASF	47 03

PARADOX LOST, AND 12 OTHER GREAT S.F. STORIES				
	BROWN, FREDRIC	AC H RDM 73		
INTRODUCTION	BROWN, ELIZABETH	IN		
AELUROPHOBE	BROWN, FREDRIC	SS	DUD	62
DOUBLE STANDARD	BROWN, FREDRIC	SS	PBY	63
EINE KLEINE NACHTMUSIK	BROWN, FREDRIC			
	AND ONSPAUGH, CARL	SS C FSF	65 06	
IT DIDN'T HAPPEN	BROWN, FREDRIC	SS	PBY	63 10
KNOCK	BROWN, FREDRIC	SS	TWS	48 12
LAST TRAIN, THE	BROWN, FREDRIC	SS	WRT	50 01
NEW ONE, THE	BROWN, FREDRIC	SS	UNK	42 10
NOTHING SIRIUS	BROWN, FREDRIC	SS	CPU	44 SP
OBEDIENCE (THE UNDYING ONES)	BROWN, FREDRIC	SS	SSS	50 09
PARADOX LOST	BROWN, FREDRIC	SS	ASF	43 10
PUPPET SHOW	BROWN, FREDRIC	SS	PBY	62 11
SOMETHING GREEN	BROWN, FREDRIC	SS	NEW	51 AC
TEN PERCENTER	BROWN, FREDRIC	SS		

PARSECS AND PARABLES

PARSECS AND PARABLES   SILVERBERG, ROBERT   AC H DBL 70
  MAN WHO NEVER FORGOT, THE   SILVERBERG, ROBERT   SS   FSF 58 02
  ISHMAEL IN LOVE   SILVERBERG, ROBERT   SS   FSF 70 07
  ONE-WAY JOURNEY   SILVERBERG, ROBERT   NV   INF 57 11
  SUNRISE ON MERCURY   SILVERBERG, ROBERT   SS   SFS 57 05
  OUTBREEDERS, THE   SILVERBERG, ROBERT   SS   FUN 59 09
  ROAD TO NIGHTFALL   SILVERBERG, ROBERT   NV   FUN 58 07
  GOING DOWN SMOOTH   SILVERBERG, ROBERT   SS   GAL 68 08
  COUNTERPART   SILVERBERG, ROBERT   NV   FUN 59 10
  FLIES   SILVERBERG, ROBERT   SS   DVS 67 01
  FANGS OF THE TREES, THE   SILVERBERG, ROBERT   NV   FSF 68 10

PARTNERS IN WONDER   ELLISON, HARLAN   AC H WKR 71
  SONS OF JANUS   ELLISON, HARLAN   IN
  I SEE A MAN SITTING IN A CHAIR, AND THE CHAIR IS BITING HIS LEG
                              ELLISON, HARLAN
                              AND SHECKLEY, ROBERT   NV C FSF 68 01
  BRILLO   ELLISON, HARLAN
                              AND SHECKLEY, ROBERT   NV C ASF 70 08
  TOY FOR JULIETTE, A   BLOCH, ROBERT   SS   DVS 67 01
  PROWLER IN THE CITY AT THE EDGE OF THE WORLD, THE
                              ELLISON, HARLAN   NV   DVS 67 01
  SCHERZO FOR SCHIZOIDS: NOTES ON A COLLABORATION
                              ELLISON, HARLAN   MS   KNT 65 11
  UP CHRISTOPHER TO MADNESS   ELLISON, HARLAN
                              AND DAVIDSON, AVRAM   SS C KNT 65 11
  RUNESMITH   ELLISON, HARLAN
                              AND STURGEON, THEODORE SS C FSF 70 05
  RODNEY PARISH FOR HIRE   ELLISON, HARLAN
                              AND HENSLEY, JOE L.   SS C SWK 62 05
  KONG PAPERS, THE   ELLISON, HARLAN
                              AND ROTSLER, WILLIAM   SS C KNT 73 04
  HUMAN OPERATORS, THE   ELLISON, HARLAN
                              AND VAN VOGT, A. E.   NV C FSF 71 01
  SURVIVOR NO. 1 (THE MAN WITH THE GREEN NOSE)
                              ELLISON, HARLAN
                              AND SLESAR, HENRY   SS C KNV 59 09
  POWER OF THE NAIL, THE   ELLISON, HARLAN
                              AND DELANY, SAMUEL R. SS C AMZ 68 11
  WONDERBIRD   ELLISON, HARLAN
                              AND BUDRYS, ALGIS   SS C INF 57 09
  SONG THE ZOMBIE SANG, THE   ELLISON, HARLAN
                              AND SILVERBERG, ROBERT SS C CMP 70 12
  STREET SCENE (DUNDERBIRD)   ELLISON, HARLAN
                              AND LAUMER, KEITH   NV C GAL 69 01
  COME TO ME NOT IN WINTER'S WHITE
                              ELLISON, HARLAN
                              AND ZELAZNY, ROGER   SS C FSF 69 10

PASSING OF THE DRAGONS, THE   ROBERTS, KEITH   AC   BKM 77 04
  DEEPS, THE   ROBERTS, KEITH   SS   ORB 66 01
  THERAPY 2000   ROBERTS, KEITH   SS   NWR 69 15
  BOULTER'S CANARIES   ROBERTS, KEITH   NV   NWR 65 03
  SYNTH   ROBERTS, KEITH   SS   NWR 66 08
  MANSCARER   ROBERTS, KEITH   NV   NWR 66 07
  CORANDA   ROBERTS, KEITH   SS   NWS 67 01
  GRAIN KINGS, THE   ROBERTS, KEITH   NV   NWQ 72 03
  WHITE BOAT, THE   ROBERTS, KEITH   SS   NWS 66 12
  PASSING OF THE DRAGONS, THE ROBERTS, KEITH   NV   NWR 73 21
  LAKE OF TUONELA, THE   ROBERTS, KEITH   NV   NWR 74 23
  I LOSE MEDEA (AS ALISTAIR BEVAN)
                              ROBERTS, KEITH   SS   NWQ 72 03
  WEIHNACHTSABEND (WEIHNACHTABEND)
                              ROBERTS, KEITH   NV   NWQ 72 04

PASSPORT TO ETERNITY   BALLARD, J. G.   AC   BKM 63 09
  MAN ON THE 99TH FLOOR, THE BALLARD, J. G.   SS   NWS 62 Q7
  THIRTEEN TO CENTAURUS   BALLARD, J. G.   NV   AMZ 62 04
  TRACK 12   BALLARD, J. G.   SS   NWS 58 04
  WATCH-TOWERS, THE   BALLARD, J. G.   NV   SCF 62 06
  QUESTION OF RE-ENTRY, A   BALLARD, J. G.   NV   PAN 63 03
  ESCAPEMENT   BALLARD, J. G.   SS   NWS 56 12
  THOUSAND DREAMS OF STELLAVISTA, THE
                              BALLARD, J. G.   SS   AMZ 62 03
  CAGE OF SAND, THE   BALLARD, J. G.   SS   NWS 62 06
  PASSPORT TO ETERNITY   BALLARD, J. G.   SS   AMZ 62 06

PAST THROUGH TOMORROW, THE   HEINLEIN, ROBERT A.   AC H PUT 67
  INTRODUCTION   KNIGHT, DAMON   IN
  LIFE-LINE   HEINLEIN, ROBERT A.   SS   ASF 39 08
  ROADS MUST ROLL, THE   HEINLEIN, ROBERT A.   NV   ASF 40 06
  BLOWUPS HAPPEN   HEINLEIN, ROBERT A.   NV   ASF 40 09
  MAN WHO SOLD THE MOON, THE HEINLEIN, ROBERT A.   NV   NEW 50 AC
  DELILAH AND THE SPACE-RIGGER HEINLEIN, ROBERT A.   SS   BBM 49 12
  SPACE JOCKEY   HEINLEIN, ROBERT A.   SS   SEP 47 04
  REQUIEM   HEINLEIN, ROBERT A.   SS   ASF 40 01
  LONG WATCH, THE   HEINLEIN, ROBERT A.   SS   ALM 49 12
  GENTLEMEN, BE SEATED   HEINLEIN, ROBERT A.   SS   ARG 48 05
  BLACK PITS OF LUNA, THE   HEINLEIN, ROBERT A.   SS   SEP 48 01
  IT'S GREAT TO BE BACK   HEINLEIN, ROBERT A.   SS   SEP 47 07
  WE ALSO WALK DOGS   HEINLEIN, ROBERT A.   SS   ASF 41 07
  SEARCHLIGHT   HEINLEIN, ROBERT A.   SS   SAM 62 08
  ORDEAL IN SPACE   HEINLEIN, ROBERT A.   SS   TAC 48 05
  GREEN HILLS OF EARTH, THE   HEINLEIN, ROBERT A.   SS   SEP 47 02
  LOGIC OF EMPIRE   HEINLEIN, ROBERT A.   NV   ASF 41 03
  MENACE FROM EARTH, THE   HEINLEIN, ROBERT A.   SS   FSF 57 08
  IF THIS GOES ON-   HEINLEIN, ROBERT A.   SN   ASF 40 02
  COVENTRY   HEINLEIN, ROBERT A.   NV   ASF 40 07
  MISFIT   HEINLEIN, ROBERT A.   SS   ASF 39 11
  METHUSELAH'S CHILDREN   HEINLEIN, ROBERT A.   NO   ASF 41 07

PAST, PRESENT, AND FUTURE PERFECT
                              WOLFE, J&FITZ GERALD AN FPR 73 08
  PREFACE   FITZ GERALD, GREGORY
                              AND WOLFE, JACK C.   IN C
  INTRODUCTION   FITZ GERALD, GREGORY

PEOPLE MACHINES

                              AND WOLFE, JACK C.   IN C
  WELCOME TO THE MONKEY HOUSE VONNEGUT, KURT JR.   SS   PBY 68 01
  SENTINEL, THE (SENTINEL OF ETERNITY)
                              CLARKE, ARTHUR C.   SS   TSF 51 SP
  DISCOVERY IN THE WOODS, A   GREENE, GRAHAM   NV   63
  VELDT, THE (THE WORLD THE CHILDREN MADE)
                              BRADBURY, RAY   SS   SEP 50 09
  JUDAS   BRUNNER, JOHN   SS   DVS 67 01
  EUTOPIA   ANDERSON, POUL   SS   DVS 67 01
  MORNING OF THE DAY THEY DID IT, THE
                              WHITE, E. B.   SS   NYM 50 02
  FROM "WALDEN TWO" (CHAPTER 29)
                              SKINNER, B. F.   EX   48
  IMMORTAL FISH, THE   BORGESE, ELISABETH M   SS   57
  YEAR NINE   CONNOLLY, CYRIL   SS   46
  FEELING OF POWER, THE   ASIMOV, ISAAC   SS   IFS 58 02
  NEW FOLKS' HOME   SIMAK, CLIFFORD D.   SS   ASF 63 07
  FROM "THE POISON BELT"   DOYLE, ARTHUR CONAN   EX   SND 13 03
  INGENIOUS PATRIOT, THE   BIERCE, AMBROSE   SS
  STAR, THE   WELLS, H. G.   SS   GRP 97 12
  FROM- A CONNECTICUT YANKEE IN KING ARTHUR'S COURT
                              TWAIN, MARK   EX   HRP 89
  FROM "LOOKING BACKWARD"   BELLAMY, EDWARD   EX   TIC 88
  FROM "TWENTY THOUSAND LEAGUES UNDER THE SEA" (1873)
                              VERNE, JULES   EX
  FROM "EREWHON, OR OVER THE RANGE" (1872)
                              BUTLER, SAMUEL   EX
  BALLOON-HOAX, THE   POE, EDGAR ALLEN   SS   SUN 44 04
  BIRTHMARK, THE (1843)   HAWTHORNE, NATHANIEL   SS   PIO 43 03
  FROM "THE LAST MAN" (1826) SHELLEY, MARY W.   EX
  FROM "FRANKENSTEIN, OR THE MODERN PROMETHEUS" (1818)
                              SHELLEY, MARY W.   EX   WRT 32 05
  FROM "GULLIVER'S TRAVELS"   SWIFT, JONATHAN   EX
  MICROMEGAS   VOLTAIRE   NV
  FROM "A VOYAGE TO THE MOON" (1650)
                              DE BERGERAC, CYRANO   EX
  FROM "NEW ATLANTIS" (1624) BACON, FRANCIS   EX
  FROM "THE CITY OF THE SUN" (1623)
                              CAMPANELLA, G. D.   EX
  FROM "UTOPIA" (1516)   MORE, SIR THOMAS   EX
  FROM "A TRUE HISTORY" (165 A.D.)
                              LUCIAN OF SAMOSATA   EX
  FROM "CRITIAS, OR THE ISLAND OF ATLANTIS" (370 B.C.)
                              PLATO   EX

PATH INTO THE UNKNOWN   ANONYMOUS   AN H DCT 68
  THE BEST OF SOVIET SCIENCE FICTION
  INTRODUCTION   MERRIL, JUDITH   IN
  CONFLICT, THE   VARSHAVSKY, ILYA   SS
  ROBBIE   VARSHAVSKY, ILYA   SS
  MEETING MY BROTHER   KRAPIVIV, VLADISLAV   SS
  DAY OF WRATH, A   GANSOVSKY, SEVER   SS
  EMERGENCY CASE, AN   STRUGATSKY, ARKADY
                              AND STRUGATSKY, BORIS SS C
  WANDERERS AND TRAVELERS   STRUGATSKY, ARKADY   SS   ISF 67 11
  BOY, THE   GOR, GENNADY   SS
  PURPLE MUMMY, THE   DNIEPROV, ANATOLY   SS

PAVANE   ROBERTS, KEITH   NO H DBL 68
  LADY MARGARET, THE (THE LADY ANNE)
                              ROBERTS, KEITH   NV   IMP 66 04
  SIGNALLER, THE   ROBERTS, KEITH   NV   IMP 66 03
  WHITE BOAT, THE   ROBERTS, KEITH   SS   NWS 66 12
  BROTHER JOHN   ROBERTS, KEITH   NV   IMP 66 05
  LORDS AND LADIES   ROBERTS, KEITH   NV   IMP 66 06
  CORFE GATE   ROBERTS, KEITH   NV   IMP 66 07

PENGUIN SCIENCE FICTION   ALDISS, BRIAN W.   AN   PEN 61
  ALSO IN "THE PENGUIN SCIENCE FICTION OMNIBUS"
  INTRODUCTION   ALDISS, BRIAN W.   IN
  SOLE SOLUTION   RUSSELL, ERIC FRANK   SS   FUN 56 04
  LOT   MOORE, WARD   NV   FSF 53 05
  SHORT-SHORT STORY OF MANKIND, THE
                              STEINBECK, JOHN   SS   PBY 58 04
  SKIRMISH (BATHE YOUR BEARINGS IN BLOOD)
                              SIMAK, CLIFFORD D.   SS   AMZ 50 12
  POOR LITTLE WARRIOR   ALDISS, BRIAN W.   SS   FSF 58 04
  GRANDPA   SCHMITZ, JAMES H.   SS   ASF 55 02
  HALF PAIR, THE   CHANDLER, A. BERTRAM   SS   NWS 57 11
  COMMAND PERFORMANCE (ALSO AS ANYBODY ELSE LIKE ME?)
                              MILLER, WALTER M. JR   NV   GAL 52 11
  NIGHTFALL   ASIMOV, ISAAC   NV   ASF 41 09
  SNOWBALL EFFECT, THE   MACLEAN, KATHERINE   SS   GAL 52 09
  END OF SUMMER, THE   BUDRYS, ALGIS   NV   ASF 54 11
  TRACK 12   BALLARD, J. G.   SS   NWS 56 04

PENGUIN SCIENCE FICTION OMNIBUS, THE
                              ALDISS, BRIAN W.   AN   PEN 73
  INTRODUCTION   ALDISS, BRIAN W.   IN
  PENGUIN SCIENCE FICTION   ALDISS, BRIAN W.   AN   PEN 61
  MORE PENGUIN SCIENCE FICTION ALDISS, BRIAN W.   AN   PEN 63
  YET MORE PENGUIN SCIENCE FICTION
                              ALDISS, BRIAN W.   AN   PEN 64

PEOPLE MACHINES   WILLIAMSON, JACK   AC   ACE 71
  AUTHOR'S INTRODUCTION- WITH HINTS FOR DESIGN AND ASSEMBLY
                              WILLIAMSON, JACK   IN
  STAR BRIGHT   WILLIAMSON, JACK   NV   ARG 39 11
  NON-STOP TO MARS   WILLIAMSON, JACK   NV   ARG 39 02
  OPERATION: GRAVITY   WILLIAMSON, JACK   SS   SPP 53 10
  MASKED WORLD, THE   WILLIAMSON, JACK   SS   WOT 63 10
  MAN FROM OUTSIDE, THE   WILLIAMSON, JACK   SS   ASF 51 03
  HINDSIGHT   WILLIAMSON, JACK   SS   ASF 40 05
  JAMBOREE   WILLIAMSON, JACK   SS   GAL 69 12
  PEDDLER'S NOSE, THE   WILLIAMSON, JACK   SS   ASF 51 04
  BREAKDOWN   WILLIAMSON, JACK   NV   ASF 42 01

PEOPLE MACHINES

AFTERWORD ABOUT THEME   WILLIAMSON, JACK   MS

PEOPLE TRAP AND OTHER PITFALLS, THE
                             SHECKLEY, ROBERT   AC   DEL 68 12
  PEOPLE TRAP, THE   SHECKLEY, ROBERT   SS   FSF 68 06
  VICTIM FROM SPACE, THE   SHECKLEY, ROBERT   NV   GAL 57 04
  SHALL WE HAVE A LITTLE TALK? SHECKLEY, ROBERT   NV   GAL 65 10
  RESTRICTED AREA   SHECKLEY, ROBERT   SS   AMZ 53 07
  ODOR OF THOUGHT, THE   SHECKLEY, ROBERT   SS   STR 53 02
  NECESSARY THING, THE   SHECKLEY, ROBERT   SS   GAL 55 06
  REDFERN'S LABYRINTH   SHECKLEY, ROBERT   SS   NEW 68 AC
  PROOF OF THE PUDDING   SHECKLEY, ROBERT   SS   GAL 52 08
  LAXIAN KEY, THE   SHECKLEY, ROBERT   SS   GAL 54 11
  LAST WEAPON, THE   SHECKLEY, ROBERT   SS   STR 53 01
  FISHING SEASON   SHECKLEY, ROBERT   SS   TWS 53 08
  DREAMWORLD   SHECKLEY, ROBERT   SS   NEW 68 AC
  DIPLOMATIC IMMUNITY   SHECKLEY, ROBERT   NV   GAL 53 08
  GHOST V   SHECKLEY, ROBERT   SS   GAL 54 10

PEOPLE: NO DIFFERENT FLESH, THE
                             HENDERSON, ZENNA   AC H DBL 67
  NO DIFFERENT FLESH   HENDERSON, ZENNA   NV   FSF 65 05
  DELUGE   HENDERSON, ZENNA   NV   FSF 63 10
  ANGELS UNAWARES   HENDERSON, ZENNA   NV   FSF 66 03
  TROUBLING OF THE WATER   HENDERSON, ZENNA   NV   FSF 66 09
  RETURN   HENDERSON, ZENNA   NV   FSF 61 03
  SHADOW ON THE MOON   HENDERSON, ZENNA   SS   FSF 62 03

PERCHANCE TO DREAM   KNIGHT, DAMON   AN H DBL 72
  INTRODUCTION   KNIGHT, DAMON   IN
  FRIEND TO ALEXANDER, A   THURBER, JAMES   SS   NYM 42 01
  END OF THE PARTY, THE (1947) GREENE, GRAHAM   SS   WBY 50 12
  DREAM'S END   KUTTNER, HENRY   SS   STS 47 07
  OCCURANCE AT OWL CREEK BRIDGE, AN (ALSO AS INCIDENT AT
  OWL CREEK)   BIERCE, AMBROSE   SS   91
  UNDER THE KNIFE (SLIP UNDER THE KNIFE)
                             WELLS, H. G.   SS   NRV 96 01
  DREAM OF A RIDICULOUS MAN, THE
                             DOSTOEVSKY, FYODOR   SS
  BRUSHWOOD BOY, THE   KIPLING, RUDYARD   SS   CNY 95 12
  LORD MOUNTDRAGO (DOCTOR AND PATIENT)
                             MAUGHAM, W. SOMERSET   SS   ITM 39 02
  MR. ARCULARIS   AIKEN, CONRAD   SS   22
  INTERPRETATION OF A DREAM COLLIER, JOHN   SS   NYM 11 05
  SECRET SONGS, THE   LEIBER, FRITZ   SS   FSF 62 08
  CIRCULAR RUINS, THE (TRANSLATED BY JAMES E. IRBY)
                             BORGES, JORGE LUIS   SS   62

PERMANENT IMPLOSION, THE   CAMPBELL, JOHN W. JR   AN   CUR 66
  SEE "ANALOG 4"

PETRIFIED PLANET, THE   CLARK, JOHN D.   OA H TWN 52
  INTRODUCTION   CLARK, JOHN D.   IN
  LONG VIEW, THE   PRATT, FLETCHER   NA   STS 52 12
  ULLR UPRISING   PIPER, H. BEAM   NA   SSF 53 02
  DAUGHTERS OF EARTH   MERRIL, JUDITH   SN   52

PHILIP K. DICK OMNIBUS, A   DICK, PHILIP K.   AC H SID 70
  CRACK IN SPACE, THE (CANTATA 140, FSF 64 07)
                             DICK, PHILIP K.   NO   ACE 66
  UNTELEPORTED MAN, THE   DICK, PHILIP K.   SN   FAN 64 12
  DR. FUTURITY (TIME PAWN, TWS 54 SU)
                             DICK, PHILIP K.   DN   ACE 60

PHILOSOPHICAL CORPS, THE   COLE, EVERETT B.   NO H GNM 62
  FIGHTING PHILOSOPHER   COLE, EVERETT B.   NV   ASF 54 04
  PHILOSOPHICAL CORPS   COLE, EVERETT B.   NV   ASF 51 03
  PLAYERS, THE   COLE, EVERETT B.   NV   ASF 55 04

PILGRIMAGE TO EARTH   SHECKLEY, ROBERT   AC   BAN 57 10
  PILGRIMAGE TO EARTH (LOVE, INCORPORATED)
                             SHECKLEY, ROBERT   SS   PBY 56 09
  ALL THE THINGS YOU ARE   SHECKLEY, ROBERT   SS   GAL 56 07
  TRAP   SHECKLEY, ROBERT   SS   GAL 56 02
  BODY, THE   SHECKLEY, ROBERT   SS   GAL 56 01
  EARLY MODEL   SHECKLEY, ROBERT   NV   GAL 56 08
  DISPOSAL SERVICE   SHECKLEY, ROBERT   SS   BBM 55
  HUMAN MAN'S BURDEN   SHECKLEY, ROBERT   SS   GAL 56 09
  FEAR IN THE NIGHT   SHECKLEY, ROBERT   SS   TDW 52
  BAD MEDICINE   SHECKLEY, ROBERT   NV   GAL 56 07
  PROTECTION   SHECKLEY, ROBERT   SS   GAL 56 04
  EARTH, AIR, FIRE AND WATER SHECKLEY, ROBERT   SS   ASF 55 07
  DEADHEAD   SHECKLEY, ROBERT   SS   GAL 55 07
  ACADEMY, THE   SHECKLEY, ROBERT   NV   IFS 54 08
  MILK RUN   SHECKLEY, ROBERT   SS   GAL 54 09
  LIFEBOAT MUTINY, THE   SHECKLEY, ROBERT   SS   GAL 55 04

PILGRIMAGE: THE BOOK OF THE PEOPLE
                             HENDERSON, ZENNA   AC H DBL 61
  ARARAT   HENDERSON, ZENNA   SS   FSF 52 10
  GILEAD   HENDERSON, ZENNA   SS   FSF 54 08
  POTTAGE   HENDERSON, ZENNA   NV   FSF 55 09
  WILDERNESS   HENDERSON, ZENNA   SS   FSF 57 01
  CAPTIVITY   HENDERSON, ZENNA   SS   FSF 58 06
  JORDAN   HENDERSON, ZENNA   SS   FSF 59 03

PILLAR OF FIRE AND OTHER PLAYS
                             BRADBURY, RAY   AC   BAN 57 11
  INTRODUCTION   BRADBURY, RAY   IN
  PILLAR OF FIRE   BRADBURY, RAY   PL   PLS 48 SU
  KALEIDOSCOPE   BRADBURY, RAY   PL   DMX 51 09
  FOGHORN, THE   BRADBURY, RAY   PL   SEP 51 06

PIRATES OF VENUS AND LOST ON VENUS, THE
                             BURROUGHS, EDGAR R.   AC H DOV 63
  PIRATES OF VENUS, THE   BURROUGHS, EDGAR R.   NO   ARG 32 09

  LOST ON VENUS   BURROUGHS, EDGAR R.   NO   ARG 33 03

PLANET EXPLORER, THE   LEINSTER, MURRAY   NO   AVN 57
  SEE "COLONIAL SURVEY"

PLANET OF DOOM AND OTHER STORIES
                             ANONYMOUS   AN   JBL 58
  PLANET OF DOOM (LILIES OF LIFE)
                             JAMESON, MALCOLM   SS   ASF 45 02
  LUNAR ESCAPADE   FYFE, H. B.   SS   OSF 54 02
  RETREAT FROM RIGEL (TONY AND THE BEETLES)
                             DICK, PHILIP K.   SS   OSF 54 02
  LAST WAR, THE (THE BUTTERFLY KISS)
                             SAVAGE, ARTHUR D.   SS   OSF 54 02
  MATING OF THE MOONS, THE   O'HARA, KENNETH   SS   OSF 54 02
  IMAGE OF THE GODS, THE   NOURSE, ALAN E.   SS   OSF 54 09
  PLACE OF MEETING   BEAUMONT, CHARLES   SS   OSF 54 02
  LAST NIGHT OF SUMMER, THE COPPEL, ALFRED   SS   OSF 54 09

PLANET OF THE DOUBLE SUN   JONES, NEIL R.   AC   ACE 67
  JAMESON SATELLITE, THE   JONES, NEIL R.   SS   AMZ 31 07
  PLANET OF THE DOUBLE SUN   JONES, NEIL R.   SS   AMZ 32 02
  RETURN OF THE TRIPEDS, THE JONES, NEIL R.   SS   AMZ 32 05

PLANETEERS, THE   CAMPBELL, JOHN W. JR   DC   ACE 66
  BRAIN STEALERS OF MARS, THE CAMPBELL, JOHN W. JR SS   TWS 36 12
  DOUBLE MINDS, THE   CAMPBELL, JOHN W. JR   SS   TWS 37 09
  IMMORTALITY SEEKERS, THE   CAMPBELL, JOHN W. JR   NV   TWS 37 10
  TENTH WORLD, THE   CAMPBELL, JOHN W. JR   SS   TWS 37 12
  BRAIN PIRATES, THE   CAMPBELL, JOHN W. JR   SS   TWS 38 10

PLANETS FOR SALE   HULL, E. MAYNE   AC H FEL 54
  COMPETITION   HULL, E. MAYNE   SS   ASF 43 06
  DEBT, THE   HULL, E. MAYNE   NV   ASF 43 12
  CONTRACT, THE   HULL, E. MAYNE   NV   ASF 44 03
  ENTER THE PROFESSOR   HULL, E. MAYNE   SS   ASF 45 01
  BANKRUPTCY PROCEEDINGS   HULL, E. MAYNE   NV   ASF 46 08

PLANETS OF ADVENTURE   WELLS, BASIL   AC H FPB 49
  EMPIRE OF THE DUST   WELLS, BASIL   SS   FBK 49 05
  TWISTED MEN, THE   WELLS, BASIL   SS
  HAIRY ONES, THE   WELLS, BASIL   SS
  PRISON RATS (AS GENE ELLERMAN)
                             WELLS, BASIL   SS   FBK 48 04
  GATEWAYS   WELLS, BASIL   SS
  QUEST OF THIG   WELLS, BASIL   SS   PLS 42 FL
  POWER FOR THE DARM   WELLS, BASIL   SS   FBK 50 06
  KNIGHT FOR MISS MERKINS, A WELLS, BASIL   SS   FBK 51 07
  CAVERNS OF ITH   WELLS, BASIL   SS   FBK 47 02
  WALL OF DARKNESS   WELLS, BASIL   SS   FBK 48 04
  SWIFT PEOPLE, THE   WELLS, BASIL   SS   FUT 43 02
  WORLD OF MISTERS (AS GENE ELLERMAN)
                             WELLS, BASIL   SS   FBK 50 06
  PLANET OF NEW MEN   WELLS, BASIL   SS
  CRUSADER (AS GENE ELLERMAN) WELLS, BASIL   SS   FBK 49 05
  SCRAMBLED WORLD   WELLS, BASIL   SS   PLS 47 SP

PLANETS OF WONDER   CARR, TERRY   AN H NEL 76
  A TREASURY OF SPACE OPERA
  DUST OF GODS   MOORE, C. L.   NV   WRT 34 08
  WE GUARD THE BLACK PLANET KUTTNER, HENRY   NV   SSS 42 11
  VEIL OF ASTELLAR, THE   BRACKETT, LEIGH   SS   TWS 44 SP
  KINGDOMS OF THE STARS   HAMILTON, EDMOND   NV   AMZ 64 09

PLATTNER STORY AND OTHERS, THE
                             WELLS, H. G.   AC H MTH 97
  PLATTNER STORY, THE   WELLS, H. G.   SS   NRV 96 04
  ARGONAUTS OF THE AIR, THE WELLS, H. G.   SS   PMY 95
  STORY OF THE LATE MR. ELVESHAM, THE
                             WELLS, H. G.   SS   IDL 96 05
  IN THE ABYSS   WELLS, H. G.   SS   PRS 96 08
  APPLE, THE   WELLS, H. G.   SS   IDL 96 10
  UNDER THE KNIFE (SLIP UNDER THE KNIFE)
                             WELLS, H. G.   SS   NRV 96 01
  SEA-RAIDERS, THE   WELLS, H. G.   SS   WSL 96 12
  POLLOCK AND THE PORROH MAN WELLS, H. G.   SS   NBG 95 05
  RED ROOM, THE   WELLS, H. G.   SS   IDL 96 03
  CONE, THE   WELLS, H. G.   SS   UCN 95 09
  PURPLE PILEUS, THE   WELLS, H. G.   SS   BAW 96 12
  JILTING OF JANE, THE   WELLS, H. G.   SS   97
  IN THE MODERN VEIN: AN UNSYMPATHETIC LOVE STORY (A BARDLET'S
  ROMANCE)   WELLS, H. G.   SS   TTH 94 03
  CATASTROPHE, A   WELLS, H. G.   SS   NBG 95 08
  LOST INHERITANCE, THE   WELLS, H. G.   SS   97
  SAD STORY OF A DRAMATIC CRITIC, THE
                             WELLS, H. G.   SS   BON 15
  SLIP UNDER THE MICROSCOPE, A WELLS, H. G.   SS   YBK 96 01

PLATYPUS OF DOOM AND OTHER NIHILISTS, THE
                             COVER, ARTHUR BYRON   OC   WPB 76 06
  PLATYPUS OF DOOM, THE   COVER, ARTHUR BYRON   NV
  ARMADILLO OF DESTRUCTION, THE
                             COVER, ARTHUR BYRON   NV
  AARDVARK OF DESPAIR, THE   COVER, ARTHUR BYRON   NV
  CLAM OF CATASTROPHE, THE   COVER, ARTHUR BYRON   NV

PLAYBOY BOOK OF HORROR AND THE SUPERNATURAL, THE
                             PLAYBOY, EDITORS OF   AN H PBP 67
  PREFACE   PLAYBOY, EDITORS OF   IN
  SOFTLY WALKS THE BEETLE   COLLIER, JOHN   SS   PBY 60 01
  HEAVY-SET   BRADBURY, RAY   SS   PBY 64 10
  NASTY   BROWN, FREDRIC   SS   PBY 59 04
  SARDONICUS   RUSSELL, RAY   NA   PBY 61 01
  SORCERER'S MOON   BEAUMONT, CHARLES   SS   PBY 59 07
  FIRST ANNIVERSARY   MATHESON, RICHARD   SS   PBY 60 07
  JAM, THE   SLESAR, HENRY   SS   PBY 58 11

PLAYBOY BOOK OF HORROR AND THE SUPERNATURAL, THE

BEELZEBUB	BLOCH, ROBERT	SS	PBY	63 12
MACHINE IN WARD ELEVEN, THE	WILLEFORD, CHARLES	NV	PBY	61 03
ACADEMY, THE	ELY, DAVID	SS	PBY	65 06
MANUSCRIPT OF DR. ARNESS, THE				
	WILSON, GAHAN	SS	PBY	66 08
PARTY, THE	NOLAN, WILLIAM F.	SS	PBY	67 04
BURNT TOAST	REYNOLDS, MACK	SS	PBY	55 11
RENDEZVOUS	CHRISTOPHER, JOHN	SS	PBY	66 09
SIDE BY SIDE	TOMERLIN, JOHN	SS	PBY	64 09
SEA WAS WET AS WET COULD BE, THE				
	WILSON, GAHAN	SS	PBY	67 05
HEY! LOOK AT ME!	FINNEY, JACK	SS	PBY	62 09
FOR THE RICH THEY SING- SOMETIMES				
	PURDY, KEN W.	SS	PBY	62 05
I'M YOURS	SCHAPHAUSER, CHARLES	SS	PBY	54 12
DOUBLE EXPOSURE	REESE, JOHN	SS	PBY	65 02
TASTE OF FEAR, THE	FOSTER, HUGH G.	SS	PBY	59 09
NO SUCH THING AS A VAMPIRE	MATHESON, RICHARD	SS	PBY	59 10
VIRGINIA	TOMKINS, CALVIN	SS	PBY	67 03
BLACK COUNTRY	BEAUMONT, CHARLES	SS	PBY	54 09
TRAVELING SALESMAN, THE	BLOCH, ROBERT	SS	PBY	57 02
WEIRD SHOW	GOLD, HERBERT	SS	PBY	58 04
LIFE WORK OF JUAN DIAZ, THE	BRADBURY, RAY	SS	PBY	63 09
COMET WINE	RUSSELL, RAY	NV	PBY	67 03
INDEX OF AUTHORS	MISC. MATERIAL	MS		

PLAYBOY BOOK OF SCIENCE FICTION AND FANTASY, THE

	PLAYBOY, EDITORS OF	AN H	PBP 66	
PREFACE	PLAYBOY, EDITORS OF	IN		
FLY, THE	LANGELAAN, GEORGE	NV	PBY	57 06
BLOOD BROTHER	BEAUMONT, CHARLES	SS	PBY	61 04
LOVE, INCORPORATED (ALSO AS PILGRIMAGE TO EARTH)				
	SHECKLEY, ROBERT	SS	PBY	56 09
FOOT IN THE DOOR, A	FRIEDMAN, BRUCE JAY	SS	PBY	60 10
VACATION, THE	BRADBURY, RAY	SS	PBY	63 12
NEVER ENDING PENNY, THE	WOLFE, BERNARD	SS	PBY	60 09
BERNIE THE FAUST	TENN, WILLIAM	NV	PBY	63 11
MAN FOR THE MOON, A	WEBB, LELAND	SS	PBY	60 08
NOISE, THE	PURDY, KEN W.	SS	PBY	59 03
KILLER IN THE TV SET, THE	FRIEDMAN, BRUCE JAY	SS	PBY	61 08
I REMEMBER BABYLON	CLARKE, ARTHUR C.	SS	PBY	60 05
WORD OF HONOR	BLOCH, ROBERT	SS	PBY	58 08
JOHN GRANT'S LITTLE ANGEL	GROVE, WALT	SS	PBY	64 07
FIEND, THE	POHL, FREDERIK	SS	PBY	64 04
HARD BARGAIN	NOURSE, ALAN E.	SS	PBY	58 05
NAIL AND THE ORACLE, THE	STURGEON, THEODORE	NV	PBY	65 10
AFTER	SLESAR, HENRY	SS	PBY	60 06
DECEMBER 28TH	THOMAS, THEODORE L.	SS	PBY	59 12
SPY STORY (ALSO AS CITIZEN IN SPACE)				
	SHECKLEY, ROBERT	SS	PBY	55 09
PUNCH	POHL, FREDERIK	SS	PBY	62 06
CROOKED MAN, THE	BEAUMONT, CHARLES	SS	PBY	55 08
WHO SHALL DWELL...	NEAL, H. C.	SS	PBY	62 07
DOUBLE TAKE	FINNEY, JACK	SS	PBY	65 04
MISSION, THE	NISSENSON, HUGH	SS	PBY	64 12
WASTE NOT, WANT NOT	ATHERTON, JOHN	SS	PBY	59 06
DOT AND DASH BIRD, THE	WOLFE, BERNARD	SS	PBY	64 12
SENSIBLE MAN, THE	DAVIDSON, AVRAM	SS	PBY	59 02
SOUVENIR (ALSO AS THE DROWNED GIANT)				
	BALLARD, J. G.	SS	PBY	65 05
PUPPET SHOW	BROWN, FREDRIC	SS	PBY	62 11
ROOM, THE	RUSSELL, RAY	SS	PBY	61 02
DIAL "F" FOR FRANKENSTEIN	CLARKE, ARTHUR C.	SS	PBY	65 01
INDEX OF AUTHORS	MISC. MATERIAL	MS		

PLAYBOY'S STORIES OF THE SINISTER & STRANGE

	PLAYBOY, EDITORS OF	AN	PBP 69	
PREFACE	PLAYBOY, EDITORS OF	IN		
HANNICHON SOLUTION, THE	SHAW, IRWIN	NV	PBY	67 12
DARK MUSIC, THE	BEAUMONT, CHARLES	SS	PBY	56 12
SOMEWHERE NOT FAR FROM HERE	KERSH, GERALD	SS	PBY	65 03
INVESTOR, THE	FRIEDMAN, BRUCE JAY	SS	PBY	62 02
RIPPLES	RUSSELL, RAY	SS	PBY	67 10
DISPATCHER, THE	GREEN, GERALD	NV	PBY	67 08
WISE CHILD	WYNDHAM, JOHN	SS	PBY	67 05
WELCOME TO THE MONKEY HOUSE	VONNEGUT, KURT JR.	SS	PBY	68 01
ROOM 312	TASSONE, G. L.	SS	PBY	67 08
GOLDEN FROG, THE	PURDY, KEN W.	NV	PBY	63 11
ANNEX, THE	MACDONALD, JOHN D.	SS	PBY	68 05

PLEASANT DREAMS

	BLOCH, ROBERT	AC H	ARK 60	
SWEETS TO THE SWEET	BLOCH, ROBERT	SS	WRT	47 03
DREAM MAKERS, THE	BLOCH, ROBERT	NV	BEY	53 09
SORCERER'S APPRENTICE, THE	BLOCH, ROBERT	SS	WRT	49 01
I KISS YOUR SHADOW	BLOCH, ROBERT	SS	FSF	56 04
MR. STEINWAY	BLOCH, ROBERT	SS	FAN	54 04
PROPER SPIRIT, THE	BLOCH, ROBERT	SS	FSF	57 09
CATNIP	BLOCH, ROBERT	SS	WRT	48 03
CHEATERS, THE	BLOCH, ROBERT	NV	WRT	47 11
HUNGARIAN RHAPSODY (AS WILSON KANE)				
	BLOCH, ROBERT	SS	FAN	58 06
LIGHT-HOUSE, THE	BLOCH, ROBERT	SS	FAN	53 02
HUNGRY HOUSE, THE	BLOCH, ROBERT	NV	IMG	51 04
SLEEPING BEAUTY, THE (THE SLEEPING REDHEADS)				
	BLOCH, ROBERT	SS	SWK	58 03
SWEET SIXTEEN	BLOCH, ROBERT	SS		
THAT HELL-BOUND TRAIN	BLOCH, ROBERT	SS	FSF	58 09
ENOCH	BLOCH, ROBERT	SS	WRT	46 09

POCKET BOOK OF SCIENCE-FICTION, THE

	WOLLHEIM, DONALD A.	AN	PKT 43 03	
INTRODUCTION	WOLLHEIM, DONALD A.	IN		
BY THE WATERS OF BABYLON (THE PLACE OF THE GODS)				
	BENET, STEPHEN V.	SS	SEP	37 07
MOXON'S MASTER	BIERCE, AMBROSE	SS		93
GREEN THOUGHTS	COLLIER, JOHN	SS		31

IN THE ABYSS	WELLS, H. G.	SS	PRS	96 08
GREEN SPLOTCHES, THE	STRIBLING, T. S.	NV	ADV	20 01
LAST MAN, THE	WEST, WALLACE	NV	AMZ	29 02
MARTIAN ODYSSEY, A	WEINBAUM, STANLEY G.	NV	WOS	34 07
TWILIGHT	STUART, DON A.	SS	ASF	34 11
MICROCOSMIC GOD	STURGEON, THEODORE	NV	ASF	41 04
AND HE BUILT A CROOKED HOUSE	HEINLEIN, ROBERT A.	SS	ASF	41 02

POCKETFUL OF STARS, A

	KNIGHT, DAMON	AN H	DBL 71	
INTRODUCTION	KNIGHT, DAMON	IN		
WINDSONG	WILHELM, KATE	NV	ORB	68 04
INTRUDER, THE	THOMAS, THEODORE L.	SS	FSF	61 02
HONORABLE DEATH, AN	DICKSON, GORDON R.	NV	GAL	61 02
BURNING, THE	COGSWELL, THEODORE R	SS	FSF	60 07
HARRY THE TAILOR	DORMAN, SONYA	SS	CMP	61
FIFTEEN MILES	BOVA, BEN	SS	FSF	67 05
I HAVE NO MOUTH, AND I MUST SCREAM				
	ELLISON, HARLAN	SS	IFS	67 03
WINTER FLIES, THE (THE INNER CIRCLES)				
	LEIBER, FRITZ	SS	FSF	67 10
SUN	FILER, BURT K.	SS	NEW	71 AN
HORARS OF WAR, THE	WOLFE, GENE	SS	NOV	70 01
HOP-FRIEND	CARR, TERRY	SS	FSF	62 11
FEW LAST WORDS, A	SALLIS, JAMES	SS	ORB	68 04
THIS NIGHT, AT MY FIRE	RUSS, JOANNA	SS	EPO	66 WI
LOOK, YOU THINK YOU'VE GOT TROUBLES				
	CARR, CAROL	SS	ORB	69 05
UNCLEAR CALL FOR LEE	MCKENNA, RICHARD M.	SS	NEW	71 AN
LAST COMMAND, THE	LAUMER, KEITH	SS	ASF	67 01
PELT	EMSHWILLER, CAROL	SS	FSF	58 11
MASKS	KNIGHT, DAMON	SS	PBY	68 07
SOURCES OF THE NILE, THE	DAVIDSON, AVRAM	NV	FSF	61 01

POISON BELT, THE

	DOYLE, ARTHUR CONAN	AC H	MCM 64	
ILLUSTRATIONS	DU BOIS, WILLIAM P.	IL		
MANY-SIDED CONAN DOYLE, THE	CARR, JOHN D.	IN		
POISON BELT, THE	DOYLE, ARTHUR CONAN	NO	HDS	13
ON LETHAL CLOUDS	SHAPLEY, HARLOW	AR		
DISINTEGRATION MACHINE, THE	DOYLE, ARTHUR CONAN	SS	ChP	28
WHEN THE WORLD SCREAMED	DOYLE, ARTHUR CONAN	SS		29

POLITICAL SCIENCE FICTION

	GREENBERG& WARRICK	AN L	PRH 74	
PREFACE	GREENBERG, MARTIN H.			
	AND WARRICK, PATRICIA S.	IN C		
INTRODUCTION	GREENBERG, MARTIN H.			
	AND WARRICK, PATRICIA S.	IN C		
FREEDOM	REYNOLDS, MACK	NV	ASF	61 02
REMEMBER THE ALAMO!	FEHRENBACH, T. R.	SS	ASF	61 12
DISAPPEARING ACT	BESTER, ALFRED	SS	STR	53 03
LAST OF THE DELIVERERS, THE	ANDERSON, POUL	SS	FSF	58 02
CALL HIM LORD	DICKSON, GORDON R.	SS	ASF	66 05
SHORT ONES, THE	BANKS, RAYMOND E.	NV	FSF	55 03
ADRIFT ON THE POLICY LEVEL	DAVIS, CHAN	SS	STR	59 05
ETERNITY LOST	SIMAK, CLIFFORD D.	NV	ASF	49 07
DEATH AND THE SENATOR	CLARKE, ARTHUR C.	NV	ASF	61 05
EVIDENCE	ASIMOV, ISAAC	SS	ASF	46 09
FRANCHISE	ASIMOV, ISAAC	SS	IFS	55 08
BEYOND DOUBT	MONROE, LYLE			
	AND WENTZ, ELMA	SS C	AST	41 04
2066: ELECTION DAY	SHAARA, MICHAEL	SS	ASF	56 12
"REPENT, HARLEQUIN!" SAID THE TICKTOCKMAN				
	ELLISON, HARLAN	SS	GAL	65 12
BURNING QUESTION	ALDISS, BRIAN W.	SS	FSF	66 12
NOT A PRISON MAKE	MARTINO, JOSEPH P.	NV	ASF	66 09
GENERAL ZAPPED AN ANGEL, THE	FAST, HOWARD	SS		
CRAB-APPLE CRISIS, THE	MACBETH, GEORGE	SS	NWS	66 10
DP!	VANCE, JACK	NV	AVS	53 04
HELPING HAND, THE	ANDERSON, POUL	NV	ASF	50 05
DAY THEY GOT BOSTON, THE	GOLD, HERBERT	SS	FSF	61 09
TRIGGERMAN	BONE, J. F.	SS	ASF	58 12
SUPERIORITY	CLARKE, ARTHUR C.	SS	FSF	51 08
LINK, THE	CARTMILL, CLEVE	SS	ASF	42 08
SURVIVOR, THE	MOUDY, WALTER F.	NV	AMZ	65 05
PACIFIST	REYNOLDS, MACK	SS	FSF	64 01
MARS IS OURS!	BUCHWALD, ART	SS		65

PORTABLE NOVELS OF SCIENCE

	WOLLHEIM, DONALD A.	AN H	VIK 45	
INTRODUCTION	WOLLHEIM, DONALD A.	IN		
FIRST MEN IN THE MOON, THE	WELLS, H. G.	NO	SND	00 11
BEFORE THE DAWN (ALSO IN FFM 46 02)				
	TAINE, JOHN	NO	WMW	34
SHADOW OUT OF TIME, THE	LOVECRAFT, H. P.	SN	ASF	36 06
ODD JOHN	STAPLEDON, OLAF	NO	MTH	35

PORTALS OF TOMORROW

	DERLETH, AUGUST	AN H	RNH 54	
INTRODUCTION	DERLETH, AUGUST	IN		
HYPNOGLYPH, THE	ANTHONY, JOHN	SS	FSF	53 07
TESTAMENT OF ANDROS	BLISH, JAMES	NV	FUT	53 01
PLAYGROUND	BRADBURY, RAY	SS	ESQ	53 10
GRATITUDE GUARANTEED	BRETNOR, REGINALD			
	AND NEVILLE, KRIS	SS C	FSF	53 08
RUSTLE OF WINGS	BROWN, FREDRIC	SS	FSF	53 08
OTHER TIGER, THE	CLARKE, ARTHUR C.	SS	FUN	53 06
CIVILIZED (WE'RE CIVILIZED)	CLIFTON, MARK			
	AND APOSTOLIDES, ALEX	SS C	GAL	53 08
STICKENEY AND THE CRITIC	CLINGERMAN, MILDRED	SS	FSF	53 02
WORD, THE	CLINGERMAN, MILDRED	SS	FSF	53 11
HERMIT ON BIKINI	LANGDON, JOHN	SS	BBM	53 02
JEZEBEL	LEINSTER, MURRAY	SS	STS	53 10
D. P. FROM TOMORROW	REYNOLDS, MACK	SS	OSF	53 FL
ALTRUISTS, THE	SEABRIGHT, IDRIS	SS	FSF	53 11
POTENTIAL	SHECKLEY, ROBERT	SS	ASF	53 11
EYE FOR INIQUITY	SHERRED, T. L.	NV	BEY	53 07
KINDERGARTEN	SIMAK, CLIFFORD D.	NV	GAL	53 07

PORTRAITS IN MOONLIGHT   JACOBI, CARL   AC H ARK 64
   PORTRAIT IN MOONLIGHT   JACOBI, CARL   SS   WRT 47 11
   WITCHES IN THE CORNFIELD   JACOBI, CARL   SS
   MARTIAN CALENDAR, THE   JACOBI, CARL   SS   SPM 57 SP
   CORBIE DOOR, THE   JACOBI, CARL   SS   WRT 47 05
   TEPONDICON   JACOBI, CARL   SS   PLS 46 WI
   INCIDENT AT THE GALLOPING HORSE
                                JACOBI, CARL   SS   WRT 48 11
   MADE IN TANGANYIKA   JACOBI, CARL   SS   FUN 54 05
   MATTHEW SOUTH AND COMPANY   JACOBI, CARL   SS   WRT 49 05
   LONG VOYAGE, THE   JACOBI, CARL   SS   FUN 55 09
   HISTORIAN, THE   JACOBI, CARL   SS
   LODANA   JACOBI, CARL   SS
   LORENZO WATCH, THE   JACOBI, CARL   SS   WRT 48 01
   LA PRELLO PAPER, THE   JACOBI, CARL   SS   WRT 48 03
   SPANISH CAMERA, THE   JACOBI, CARL   SS   WRT 50 09

POSITIVE CHARGE   RICHMOND, W. & L.   DC   ACE 70
   M'LORD IS THE SHEPHERD   RICHMOND, WALT
                                AND RICHMOND, LEIGH   SS C IFS 65 09
   IF THE SABOT FITS...   RICHMOND, WALT
                                AND RICHMOND, LEIGH   SS C ASF 68 02
   COWS CAN'T EAT GRASS   RICHMOND, WALT
                                AND RICHMOND, LEIGH   SS C ASF 67 08
   SHORTS WING   RICHMOND, WALT
                                AND RICHMOND, LEIGH   SS C NEW 70 DC
   SHORTSTACK   RICHMOND, WALT
                                AND RICHMOND, LEIGH   SS C ASF 64 12
   SHORTSITE   RICHMOND, WALT
                                AND RICHMOND, LEIGH   SS C ASF 64 04
   I, BEM   RICHMOND, WALT
                                AND RICHMOND, LEIGH   SS C ASF 64 06
   PROLOGUE TO...AN ANALOGUE   RICHMOND, WALT
                                AND RICHMOND, LEIGH   NV C ASF 61 06

POSSIBLE TOMORROWS   CONKLIN, GROFF   AN   71
   SEE "FIVE-ODD"

POSSIBLE WORLDS OF SCIENCE FICTION
                                CONKLIN, GROFF   AN H VPR 51
   INTRODUCTION   CONKLIN, GROFF   IN
   OPERATION PUMICE   GALLUN, RAYMOND Z.   SS   TWS 49 04
   BLACK PITS OF LUNA, THE   HEINLEIN, ROBERT A.   SS   SEP 48 01
   ENCHANTED VILLAGE (ALSO AS THE SANDS OF MARS)
                                VAN VOGT, A. E.   SS   OWS 50 07
   LILIES OF LIFE (ALSO AS PLANET OF DOOM)
                                JAMESON, MALCOLM   SS   ASF 45 02
   ASLEEP IN ARMAGEDDON (ALSO AS PERCHANCE TO DREAM)
                                BRADBURY, RAY   SS   PLS 48 WI
   NOT FINAL| ASIMOV, ISAAC   SS   ASF 41 10
   CONES   LONG, FRANK BELKNAP   NV   ASF 36 02
   MOON OF DELIRIUM   JAMES, DANIEL LEWIS   SS   ASF 40 01
   COMPLETELY AUTOMATIC   STURGEON, THEODORE   SS   ASF 41 02
   DAY WE CELEBRATE, THE   BOND, NELSON S.   SS   ASF 41 01
   PILLOWS, THE   ST. CLAIR, MARGARET   SS   TWS 50 06
   PROOF   CLEMENT, HAL   SS   ASF 42 06
   PROPAGANDIST   LEINSTER, MURRAY   SS   ASF 47 08
   IN VALUE DECEIVED   FYFE, H. B.   SS   ASF 50 11
   HARD LUCK DIGGINGS   VANCE, JACK   SS   STS 48 07
   SPACE RATING (ALSO AS BEYOND THE STARS)
                                BERRYMAN, JOHN   SS   ASF 39 10
   CONTAGION   MACLEAN, KATHERINE   NV   GAL 50 10
   LIMITING FACTOR   SIMAK, CLIFFORD D.   SS   STS 49 11
   EXIT LINE   MERWIN, SAM JR.   SS   STS 50 09
   SECOND NIGHT OF SUMMER   SCHMITZ, JAMES H.   SS   GAL 50 12
   WALK IN THE DARK, A   CLARKE, ARTHUR C.   SS   TWS 50 08
   HELPING HAND, THE   ANDERSON, POUL   NV   ASF 50 05

POSSIBLE WORLDS OF SCIENCE FICTION (BRITISH)
                                CONKLIN, GROFF   AN H GRY 51
   INTRODUCTION   CONKLIN, GROFF   IN
   OPERATION PUMICE   GALLUN, RAYMOND Z.   SS   TWS 49 04
   ENCHANTED VILLAGE (ALSO AS THE SANDS OF MARS)
                                VAN VOGT, A. E.   SS   OWS 50 07
   LILIES OF LIFE (ALSO AS PLANET OF DOOM)
                                JAMESON, MALCOLM   SS   ASF 45 02
   ASLEEP IN ARMAGEDDON (ALSO AS PERCHANCE TO DREAM)
                                BRADBURY, RAY   SS   PLS 48 WI
   NOT FINAL| ASIMOV, ISAAC   SS   ASF 41 10
   MOON OF DELIRIUM   JAMES, DANIEL LEWIS   SS   ASF 40 01
   PILLOWS, THE   ST. CLAIR, MARGARET   SS   TWS 50 06
   PROPAGANDIST   LEINSTER, MURRAY   SS   ASF 47 08
   HARD LUCK DIGGINGS   VANCE, JACK   SS   STS 48 07
   SPACE RATING (ALSO AS BEYOND THE STARS)
                                BERRYMAN, JOHN   SS   ASF 39 10
   LIMITING FACTOR   SIMAK, CLIFFORD D.   SS   STS 49 11
   EXIT LINE   MERWIN, SAM JR.   SS   STS 50 09
   HELPING HAND, THE   ANDERSON, POUL   NV   ASF 50 05

POSSIBLE WORLDS OF SCIENCE FICTION (10 OF 22)
                                CONKLIN, GROFF   AN   BRK 55 07
   ENCHANTED VILLAGE (ALSO AS THE SANDS OF MARS)
                                VAN VOGT, A. E.   SS   OWS 50 07
   LILIES OF LIFE (ALSO AS PLANET OF DOOM)
                                JAMESON, MALCOLM   SS   ASF 45 02
   ASLEEP IN ARMAGEDDON (ALSO AS PERCHANCE TO DREAM)
                                BRADBURY, RAY   SS   PLS 48 WI
   NOT FINAL| ASIMOV, ISAAC   SS   ASF 41 10
   PILLOWS, THE   ST. CLAIR, MARGARET   SS   TWS 50 06
   PROPAGANDIST   LEINSTER, MURRAY   SS   ASF 47 08
   IN VALUE DECEIVED   FYFE, H. B.   SS   ASF 50 11
   SPACE RATING (ALSO AS BEYOND THE STARS)
                                BERRYMAN, JOHN   SS   ASF 39 10
   LIMITING FACTOR   SIMAK, CLIFFORD D.   SS   STS 49 11
   HELPING HAND, THE   ANDERSON, POUL   NV   ASF 50 05

POST READER OF FANTASY AND SCIENCE FICTION
                                SATURDAY EVE. POST   AN H DBL 64
   DOCTOR HANRAY'S SECOND CHANCE
                                RICHTER, CONRAD   SS   SEP 50 01
   FALLOUT ISLAND   MURPHY, ROBERT   SS   SEP 62 03
   GREEN HILLS OF EARTH, THE   HEINLEIN, ROBERT A.   SS   SEP 47 02
   DOOMSDAY DEFERRED   JENKINS, WILL F.   SS   SEP 49 09
   TEST-TUBE TERROR   STANDISH, ROBERT   SS   SEP 58 09
   ISLAND OF FEAR   SAMBROT, WILLIAM   SS   SEP 58 01
   SINISTER JOURNEY   RICHTER, CONRAD   SS   SEP 53 09
   PLACE OF THE GODS, THE   BENET, STEPHEN V.   SS   SEP 37 07
   PHANTOM SETTER, THE   MURPHY, ROBERT   SS   SEP 61 06
   BIG WHEEL, THE   MCMORROW, FRED   SS   SEP 61 07
   DEATH DUST, THE   HARVEY, FRANK   SS   SEP 59 08
   LOST CONTINENT, THE   HOUSEHOLD, GEOFFREY   SS   SEP 60 09
   TRAP, THE   BENNETT, KEM   SS   SEP 56 01
   SPACE SECRET   SAMBROT, WILLIAM   SS   SEP 59 02
   UNSAFE DEPOSIT BOX, THE   KERSH, GERALD   SS   SEP 62 04
   SECOND TRIP TO MARS, THE (ALSO AS DOMINIONS BEYOND)
                                MOORE, WARD   SS   SEP 54 08
   VOICE IN THE EARPHONES, THE SCHRAMM, WILBUR   SS   SEP 47 05
   MOON CRAZY   SHELTON, WILLIAM ROY SS   SEP
   LITTLE TERROR, THE   JENKINS, WILL F.   SS   SEP 53 08
   ANSWER, THE   WYLIE, PHILIP   NV   SEP 55 05

PRELUDE TO MARS   CLARKE, ARTHUR C.   AC H HBW 65
   FOREWORD   CLARKE, ARTHUR C.   IN
   PRELUDE TO SPACE   CLARKE, ARTHUR C.   NO   GAN 51 03
   BIG GAME HUNT   CLARKE, ARTHUR C.   SS   54
   CRITICAL MASS (ORIGINAL VERSION IN LILLIPUT MARCH 1949)
                                CLARKE, ARTHUR C.   SS   SPM 57 08
   ULTIMATE MELODY, THE   CLARKE, ARTHUR C.   SS   IFS 57 02
   MOVING SPIRIT   CLARKE, ARTHUR C.   SS
   MAN WHO PLOUGHED THE SEA, THE
                                CLARKE, ARTHUR C.   SS   SAT 57 06
   COLD WAR   CLARKE, ARTHUR C.   SS   SAT 57 04
   WHAT GOES UP   CLARKE, ARTHUR C.   SS   FSF 56 01
   TROUBLE WITH THE NATIVES (CAPTAIN WYXTPTHLL'S FLYING SAUCER)
                                CLARKE, ARTHUR C.   SS   MAR 51 05
   WALK IN THE DARK, A   CLARKE, ARTHUR C.   SS   TWS 50 08
   FORGOTTEN ENEMY, THE   CLARKE, ARTHUR C.   SS   NWS 49 05
   PARASITE, THE   CLARKE, ARTHUR C.   SS   AVS 53 04
   CURSE, THE   CLARKE, ARTHUR C.   SS   CSM 53 09
   POSSESSED, THE   CLARKE, ARTHUR C.   SS   DSF 53 03
   AWAKENING, THE   CLARKE, ARTHUR C.   SS   ZEN 42 02
   EXILE OF THE EONS   CLARKE, ARTHUR C.   SS   SSS 50 03
   SECOND DAWN   CLARKE, ARTHUR C.   NV   SFQ 51 08
   SANDS OF MARS, THE   CLARKE, ARTHUR C.   NO   SID 51

PRESERVING MACHINE, THE   DICK, PHILIP K.   AC H ACE 69
   ENGLISH EDITION (GOL 71) OMITS STORY "WHAT THE DEAD MEN SAY"
   PRESERVING MACHINE, THE   DICK, PHILIP K.   SS   FSF 53 06
   WAR GAME   DICK, PHILIP K.   SS   GAL 59 12
   UPON THE DULL EARTH   DICK, PHILIP K.   NV   BEY 54 09
   ROOG   DICK, PHILIP K.   SS   FSF 53 02
   WAR VETERAN   DICK, PHILIP K.   NV   IFS 55 03
   TOP STAND-BY JOB (STAND-BY) DICK, PHILIP K.   SS   AMZ 63 10
   BEYOND LIES THE WUB   DICK, PHILIP K.   SS   PLS 52 07
   WE CAN REMEMBER IT FOR YOU WHOLESALE
                                DICK, PHILIP K.   NV   FSF 66 04
   CAPTIVE MARKET   DICK, PHILIP K.   SS   IFS 55 04
   IF THERE WERE NO BENNY CEMOLI
                                DICK, PHILIP K.   SS   GAL 63 12
   RETREAT SYNDROME   DICK, PHILIP K.   SS   WOT 65 01
   CRAWLERS, THE   DICK, PHILIP K.   SS   IMG 54 07
   OH, TO BE A BLOBEL| DICK, PHILIP K.   SS   GAL 64 02
   WHAT THE DEAD MEN SAY   DICK, PHILIP K.   SN   WOT 64 06
   PAY FOR THE PRINTER   DICK, PHILIP K.   SS   SAT 56 10

PRIDE OF MONSTERS, A   SCHMITZ, JAMES H.   AC H MAC 70
   INTRODUCTION   SCHMITZ, JAMES H.   IN
   LION LOOSE   SCHMITZ, JAMES H.   SN   ASF 61 10
   SEARCHER, THE   SCHMITZ, JAMES H.   SN   ASF 66 02
   WINDS OF TIME, THE   SCHMITZ, JAMES H.   NV   ASF 62 09
   PORK CHOP TREE, THE   SCHMITZ, JAMES H.   SS   ASF 65 02
   GREENFACE   SCHMITZ, JAMES H.   NV   UNK 43 08

PRIME NUMBER   HARRISON, HARRY   AC   BKM 70 07
   MUTE MILTON   HARRISON, HARRY   SS   AMZ 66 02
   GREATEST CAR IN THE WORLD, THE
                                HARRISON, HARRY   SS   NWS 66 10
   FINAL BATTLE   HARRISON, HARRY   SS   NEW 70 04
   POWERS OF OBSERVATION, THE   HARRISON, HARRY   SS   ASF 68 09
   GHOUL SQUAD, THE   HARRISON, HARRY   SS   ASF 69 06
   TOY SHOP   HARRISON, HARRY   SS   ASF 62 04
   YOU MEN OF VIOLENCE   HARRISON, HARRY   SS   GAL 67 04
   FINEST HUNTER IN THE WORLD, THE
                                HARRISON, HARRY   SS   NEW 70 AC
   DOWN TO EARTH   HARRISON, HARRY   SS   AMZ 63 11
   COMMANDO RAID   HARRISON, HARRY   SS   NEW 70 AC
   NOT ME, NOT AMOS CABOT| HARRISON, HARRY   SS   SCF 65 01
   SECRET OF STONEHENGE, THE   HARRISON, HARRY   SS   FSF 68 06
   INCIDENT IN THE IND   HARRISON, HARRY   SS   FSF 64 03
   IF (PRAISEWORTHY SAUR)   HARRISON, HARRY   SS   IFS 69 02
   CONTACT MAN   HARRISON, HARRY   SS   66
   PAD, THE   HARRISON, HARRY   SS   NEW 70 AC
   CIVIL SERVICE SERVANT, A (THE FAIRLY CIVIL SERVANT)
                                HARRISON, HARRY   SS   GAL 67 12
   CRIMINAL ACT, A   HARRISON, HARRY   SS   ASF 67 01
   FAMOUS FIRST WORDS   HARRISON, HARRY   SS   FSF 65 01

PRINCESS OF MARS AND A FIGHTING MAN OF MARS, A
                                BURROUGHS, EDGAR R.   AC H DOV 64
   PRINCESS OF MARS, A (UNDER THE MOONS OF MARS)
                                BURROUGHS, EDGAR R.   NO   ASM 12 02
   FIGHTING MAN OF MARS, A   BURROUGHS, EDGAR R.   NO   BBM 30 04

PRIZE SCIENCE FICTION   QUARK/4

PRIZE SCIENCE FICTION   WOLLHEIM, DONALD A. AN H MBR 53
    IN ENGLAND AS "PRIZE STORIES OF SPACE AND TIME"
INTRODUCTION   WOLLHEIM, DONALD A.   IN
ALL THE TIME IN THE WORLD   CLARKE, ARTHUR C.   SS   STS 52 07
MCILVAINE'S STAR   DERLETH, AUGUST   SS   IFS 52 07
DEMOTION   LOCKE, ROBERT DONALD SS   ASF 52 09
MASK OF DEMETER   PEARSON, MARTIN
                               AND CORWIN, CECIL   SS C FSF 53 01
BEAUTIFUL WOMAN, THE (THE BEAUTIFUL PEOPLE)
                             BEAUMONT, CHARLES   SS   IFS 52 09
ALTAR AT MIDNIGHT, THE   KORNBLUTH, C. M.   SS   GAL 52 11
LAST DAYS OF SHANDAKOR, THE BRACKETT, LEIGH   NV   STS 52 04
PEACEMAKER, THE   COPPEL, ALFRED   SS   IFS 53 01
LISTEN   DICKSON, GORDON R.   SS   FSF 52 08
STAR, BRIGHT   CLIFTON, MARK   NV   GAL 52 07
TIMELESS ONES, THE   RUSSELL, ERIC FRANK   SS   SFQ 52 11
BIG HUNGER, THE   MILLER, WALTER M. JR SS   ASF 52 10

PRIZE STORIES OF SPACE AND TIME
                             WOLLHEIM, DONALD A. AN H WEI 53
    SEE "PRIZE SCIENCE FICTION"

PROJECT BARRIER   GALOUYE, DANIEL F.   AC H GOL 68
SHUFFLE BOARD   GALOUYE, DANIEL F.   SS   IFS 57 06
RECOVERY AREA   GALOUYE, DANIEL F.   NA   AMZ 63 02
RUB-A-DUB   GALOUYE, DANIEL F.   SS
REIGN OF THE TELEPUPPETS   GALOUYE, DANIEL F.   NA   AMZ 63 08
PROJECT BARRIER   GALOUYE, DANIEL F.   SS   FUN 58 01

PROLOGUE TO ANALOG   CAMPBELL, JOHN W. JR AN H DBL 62
    IN "ANALOG ANTHOLOGY"
INTRODUCTION   CAMPBELL, JOHN W. JR IN
BELIEF   ASIMOV, ISAAC   NV   ASF 53 10
PANDORA'S PLANET   ANVIL, CHRISTOPHER   NV   ASF 56 09
SOUND DECISION   GARRETT, RANDALL
                               AND SILVERBERG, ROBERT NV C ASF 56 10
OMNILINGUAL   PIPER, H. BEAM   NV   ASF 57 02
TRIGGERMAN   BONE, J. F.   SS   ASF 58 12
FILBERT IS A NUT, A   RAPHAEL, RICK   SS   ASF 59 11
BUSINESS AS USUAL, DURING ALTERATIONS
                             WILLIAMS, RALPH   NV   ASF 58 07
PUSHBUTTON WAR   MARTINO, JOSEPH P.   SS   ASF 60 08
WE DIDN'T DO ANYTHING WRONG, HARDLY
                             KUYKENDALL, ROGER   SS   ASF 59 05
MINOR INGREDIENT   RUSSELL, ERIC FRANK   SS   ASF 56 03

PROTOSTARS   GERROLD & GOLDIN   OA   BAL 71 10
SORT OF INTRODUCTION, A   GERROLD, DAVID   IN
WHAT MAKES A CAGE, JAMIE KNOWS
                             BRADFIELD, SCOTT   SS   PRT 71
I'LL BE WAITING FOR YOU WHEN THE SWIMMING POOL IS EMPTY
                             TIPTREE, JAMES JR.   SS   PRT 71
IN A SKY OF DAEMONS   YEP, LAURENCE   NV   PRT 71
LAST GHOST, THE   GOLDIN, STEPHEN   SS   PRT 71
AFTERNOON WITH A DEAD BUS   GERROLD, DAVID   SS   PRT 71
EYES OF ONYX   BRYANT, EDWARD   SS   PRT 71
WORLD WHERE WISHES WORKED, THE
                             GOLDIN, STEPHEN   SS   PRT 71
COLD, THE FIRE OF THE PHOENIX
                             KELLEY, LEO P.   SS   PRT 71
OASIS   SARGENT, PAMELA   SS   PRT 71
HOLDHOLTZER'S BOX   BUNCH, DAVID R.   SS   PRT 71
FIVE-DIMENSIONAL SUGAR CUBE, THE
                             DEELEY, ROGER   SS   PRT 71
AND WATCH THE SMOG ROLL IN...
                             WEISSMAN, BARRY   SS   PRT 71
CHANCES ARE   LAURANCE, ALICE   SS   PRT 71
NAKED AND THE UNASHAMED, THE MARGROFF, ROBERT E. SS   PRT 71
MY COUNTRY, RIGHT OR WRONG   OFFUTT, ANDREW J.   SS   PRT 71
SIDE EFFECT   WYAL, PG   NV   PRT 71

PROXY INTELLIGENCE AND OTHER MIND BENDERS
                             VAN VOGT, A. E.   AC   PBK 71 01
PROXY INTELLIGENCE, THE   VAN VOGT, A. E.   SN   IFS 68 10
PROBLEM PROFESSOR, THE (PROJECT SPACESHIP)
                             VAN VOGT, A. E.   SS   TWS 49 08
REBIRTH: EARTH (THE FLIGHT THAT FAILED)
                             VAN VOGT, A. E.   SS   ASF 42 12
GRYB, THE (REPETITION)   VAN VOGT, A. E.   NV   ASF 40 04
INVISIBILITY GAMBIT, THE (ABDICATION)
                             VAN VOGT, A. E.   SS   ASF 43 04
STAR-SAINT, THE   VAN VOGT, A. E.   NV   PLS 51 03

PSEUDO PEOPLE, THE   NOLAN, WILLIAM F.   AN H SHB 65
    IN ENGLAND AS "ALMOST HUMAN"
EDITOR'S PREFACE: A IS FOR ANDROID
                             NOLAN, WILLIAM F.   IN
INTRODUCTION   VAN VOGT, A. E.   IN
THOSE AMONG US (ANDROID, AS C. H. LIDDELL)
                             KUTTNER, HENRY   NV   FSF 51 06
CHANGELING   BRADBURY, RAY   SS   SSS 49 07
ADDICT, THE   LOWENKOPF, SHELLY   SS   NEW 65 AN
LIFE GAME, THE   OLIVER, CHAD   NV   TWS 53 06
EVIDENCE   ASIMOV, ISAAC   SS   ASF 46 09
SHOW MUST GO ON, THE (SO LOVELY, SO LOST)
                             CAUSEY, JAMES   SS   OSF 54 11
GEEVER'S FLIGHT   FRITCH, CHARLES E.   SS   NEW 65 AN
FIRES OF NIGHT, THE   ETCHISON, DENNIS   SS   NEW 65 AN
STEEL   MATHESON, RICHARD   SS   FSF 56 05
BADINAGE   GOULART, RON   SS   NEW 65 AN
JUKE DOLL (DOLL-FRIEND)   YOUNG, ROBERT F.   SS   AMZ 59 07
LAST RITES   BEAUMONT, CHARLES   SS   IFS 55 10
FASTERFASTER AFFAIR, THE   ANMAR, FRANK   SS   NEW 65 AN
JOY OF LIVING, THE   NOLAN, WILLIAM F.   SS   IFS 54 08
BIBLIOGRAPHY OF ROBOT FICTION, A
                             MISC. MATERIAL   MS

PSI-HIGH AND OTHERS   NOURSE, ALAN E.   AC H MCK 67
MARTYR, THE   NOURSE, ALAN E.   NV   FUN 57 01
PSI-HIGH   NOURSE, ALAN E.   NV
MIRROR, MIRROR (THE MIRROR) NOURSE, ALAN E.   NV   FAN 60 06

QUADRATIC   CRAWFORD, WILLIAM L. AN H FPB 53
WORLDS OF WONDER   STAPLEDON, OLAF   AC   FPB 49
MURDER MADNESS   LEINSTER, MURRAY   NO   ASF 30 05

QUARK/1   DELANY & HACKER   OA   PBK 70 11
FRONTISPIECE   GILDEN, STEPHEN   MS   QRK 70 01
EDITORIAL   DELANY, SAMUEL R.
                               AND HACKER, MARILYN ED C QRK 70 01
CLIFF CLIMBERS, THE   LAFFERTY, R. A.   SS   QRK 70 01
SOUND OF MUZAK, THE   DOZOIS, GARDNER R.   NV   QRK 70 01
TRIP TO THE HEAD, A   LE GUIN, URSULA K.   SS   QRK 70 01
LET US QUICKLY HASTEN TO THE GATE OF IVORY
                             DISCH, THOMAS M.   SS   QRK 70 01
INALIENABLE RITE   BENFORD, GREGORY   SS   QRK 70 01
ORION   STANLEY, GEORGE   SS   QRK 70 01
VIEW FROM THE WINDOW, THE   RUSS, JOANNA   NV   QRK 70 01
GONE ARE THE LUPO   HICKEY, H. B.   SS   QRK 70 01
FIRE STORM   PRIEST, CHRISTOPHER   SS   QRK 70 01
GETTING TO KNOW YOU   LINK   PM   QRK 70 01
DOGMAN OF ISLINGTON   BAILEY, HILARY   SS   QRK 70 01
SHADES   BOUCHER, SANDY   SS   QRK 70 01
TWELVE ANCILLARY APPROXIMATIONS FOR THE QUARK/ COVER CALLED
    APPOMATTOX   FITZGERALD, RUSSELL   IL   QRK 70 01
CARTHING   VAN VOGT, A. E.   SS   QRK 70 01
DAUGHTER OF ROSES   ADAM, HELEN   PM   QRK 70 01
ADRIFT ON THE FREEWAY   BRYANT, EDWARD   SS   QRK 70 01
MY FATHER'S GUEST   BERNOTT, JOAN   SS   QRK 70 01
CRITICAL METHODS: SPECULATIVE FICTION
                             DELANY, SAMUEL R.   AR   QRK 70 01
RAMONA, COME SOFTLY   EKLUND, GORDON   NV   QRK 70 01
SIX DRAWINGS   GILDEN, STEPHEN   IL   QRK 70 01
CONTRIBUTORS' NOTES   MISC. MATERIAL   MS

QUARK/2   DELANY & HACKER   OA   PBK 71 02
INTRODUCTION   DELANY, SAMUEL R.
                               AND HACKER, MARILYN IN C
INTERSTATE, THE   SLADEK, JOHN T.   SS   QRK 71 02
POSSIBLE EPISODE IN THE PICARESQUE ADVENTURES OF MR. J.H.B.
    MONSTROSEE, A   EMSHWILLER, CAROL   SS   QRK 71 02
TROJAK   OBTULOWICZ, MAREK   SS   QRK 71 02
GOLD, BLACK, AND SILVER   LEIBER, FRITZ   SS   QRK 71 02
MENSURATION   SALLIS, JAMES   PM   QRK 71 02
SIX DRAWINGS   PENNEY, ROGER   IL   QRK 71 02
VOICE OF THE SONAR IN MY VERMIFORM APPENDIX, THE
                             FARMER, PHILIP JOSE   SS   QRK 71 02
WAY HOME, THE   BERNOTT, JOAN   SS   QRK 71 02
AMONG THE DEAD   BRYANT, EDWARD   SS   QRK 71 02
LAST SUPPER, THE   FITZGERALD, RUSSELL   SS   QRK 71 02
VILLAGE, THE   STONEY, LELAND   PM   QRK 71 02
ARPAD   PANSHIN, ALEXEI   SS   QRK 71 02
BITCHING IT   DORMAN, SONYA   SS   QRK 71 02
FIVE DRAWINGS   FROST, NEMI   IL   QRK 71 02
ET IN ARCADIA EGO (ALSO AS THE PLANET ARCADIA)
                             DISCH, THOMAS M.   SS   QRK 71 02
LANDSCAPE FOR INSURRECTION   HACKER, MARILYN   PM   QRK 71 02
PEOPLE OF PRASHAD, THE   KEILTY, JAMES   NV   QRK 71 02
INCEPTION OF THE EPOCH OF MRS. BEDONEBYASYOUDID, THE
                             BRUNNER, JOHN   SS   QRK 71 02
ELECTRIC NEON MERMAID, THE   YEP, LAURENCE   NV   QRK 71 02

QUARK/3   DELANY & HACKER   OA   PBK 71 05
FOREWORD   DELANY, SAMUEL R.
                               AND HACKER, MARILYN IN C
CONTINUOUS LANDSCAPE   SIMPSON, DONALD   AR   QRK 71 03
ENCASED IN ANCIENT RIND   LAFFERTY, R. A.   NV   QRK 71 03
HOME AGAIN, HOME AGAIN   EKLUND, GORDON   SS   QRK 71 03
DOG IN A FISHERMAN'S NET   DELANY, SAMUEL R.   SS   QRK 71 03
TO THE CHILD WHOSE BIRTH WILL CHANGE THE WAY THE UNIVERSE
    WORKS   STANLEY, GEORGE   PM   QRK 71 03
SEXUAL SONG, A   VEITCH, TOM   SS   QRK 71 03
TWENTY-FOUR LETTERS FROM UNDER THE EARTH
                             BAILEY, HILARY   SS   QRK 71 03
SIX DRAWINGS   LAVIGNE, ROBERT   IL   QRK 71 03
SIX MORE DRAWINGS   LAVIGNE, ROBERT   IL   QRK 71 03
ZANZIBAR CAT, THE   RUSS, JOANNA   SS   QRK 71 03
CODED SUN GAME, THE   VICKERS, BRIAN   NA   QRK 71 03
FIELD   SALLIS, JAMES   SS   QRK 71 03
VANISHING POINTS   DORMAN, SONYA   PM   QRK 71 03
WHERE HAVE YOU BEEN, BILLY BOY, BILLY BOY?
                             WILHELM, KATE   SS   QRK 71 03
BRAVE SALT   HILL, RICHARD   SS   QRK 71 03
NATURE BOY   SAXTON, JOSEPHINE   SS   QRK 71 03
BALLS: A MEDITATION AT THE GRAVESIDE
                             KIDD, VIRGINIA   SS   QRK 71 03
RING OF PAIN   HARRISON, M. JOHN   SS   QRK 71 03
CONTRIBUTORS' NOTES   MISC. MATERIAL   MS

QUARK/4   DELANY & HACKER   OA   PBK 71 08
ON SPECULATIVE FICTION   DELANY, SAMUEL R.
                               AND HACKER, MARILYN IN C
BASILEIKON: SUMMER   DAVIDSON, AVRAM   SS   QRK 71 04
VOORTREKKER   MOORCOCK, MICHAEL   NV   QRK 71 04
BRASS AND GOLD, OR HORSE AND ZEPPELIN IN BEVERLY HILLS
                             FARMER, PHILIP JOSE   SS   QRK 71 04
SONG OF PASSING, THE   CACCHIONI, MARCO   PM   QRK 71 04
NORMAN VS. AMERICA   PLATT, CHARLES   CT   QRK 71 04
TRUE REASON FOR THE DREADFUL DEATH OF MR. REX ARUNDEL, THE
                             ADAM, HELEN   NV   QRK 71 04
ACID SOAP OPERA   MADONIA, GAIL   SS   QRK 71 04
BODIES   DISCH, THOMAS M.   NV   QRK 71 04
NIGHTSONG   HACKER, MARILYN   PM   QRK 71 04

CAGES	MCINTYRE, VONDA N.	SS	QRK 71 04
MAN OF LETTERS, A	OBTULOWICZ, MAREK	SS	QRK 71 04
FOURTH PROFESSION, THE	NIVEN, LARRY	NV	QRK 71 04
TWELVE DRAWINGS	OLIVIER, OLIVIER	IL	QRK 71 04
FROM "THE DAY"	PERSKY, STAN	EX	QRK 71 04

QUEEN OF AIR AND DARKNESS AND OTHER STORIES, THE
	ANDERSON, POUL	AC	SIG 73 12
FOREWORD	ANDERSON, POUL	IN	
QUEEN OF AIR AND DARKNESS, THE			
	ANDERSON, POUL	SN	FSF 71 04
HOME (THE DISINHERITED)	ANDERSON, POUL	SS	ORB 66 01
ALIEN ENEMY, THE (AS MICHAEL KARAGEORGE)			
	ANDERSON, POUL	SS	ASF 68 11
FAUN, THE	ANDERSON, POUL	SS	BLF 68 09
IN THE SHADOW (AS MICHAEL KARAGEORGE)			
	ANDERSON, POUL	NV	ASF 67 03
TIME LAG	ANDERSON, POUL	NV	FSF 61 01

QUEST
	BISCHOFF, DAVID	OA H	RTR 77
GORGONS, THE	PAYES, RACHEL C.	SS	
LOOKING BACK	TURNER, STEPHEN C.	SS	
COLD TOMORROWS	SIMONS, WALTON	SS	
BECKONING STAR	LAMPTON, CHRIS	SS	
FIRST FLIGHT OF SCAVENGER I, THE			
	LITTKE, LAEL J.	SS	

QUEST FOR THE FUTURE
	VAN VOGT, A. E.	NO	ACE 70
FILM LIBRARY	VAN VOGT, A. E.	SS	ASF 46 07
SEARCH, THE	VAN VOGT, A. E.	NV	ASF 43 01
FAR CENTAURUS	VAN VOGT, A. E.	SS	ASF 44 01

QUEST OF THE THREE WORLDS
	SMITH, CORDWAINER	NO	ACE 66
ON THE GEM PLANET	SMITH, CORDWAINER	NV	GAL 63 10
ON THE STORM PLANET	SMITH, CORDWAINER	SN	GAL 65 02
ON THE SAND PLANET	SMITH, CORDWAINER	NV	AMZ 65 12
THREE TO A GIVEN STAR	SMITH, CORDWAINER	NV	GAL 65 10

R IS FOR ROCKET
	BRADBURY, RAY	AC H	DBL 62 10
INTRODUCTION	BRADBURY, RAY	IN	
R IS FOR ROCKET (KING OF THE GRAY SPACES)			
	BRADBURY, RAY	SS	FFM 43 12
END OF THE BEGINNING, THE (NEXT STOP: THE STARS)			
	BRADBURY, RAY	SS	MCL 56 10
FOG HORN, THE (THE BEAST FROM 20,000 FATHOMS)			
	BRADBURY, RAY	SS	SEP 51 06
ROCKET, THE (OUTCAST OF THE STARS)			
	BRADBURY, RAY	SS	SSS 50 03
ROCKET MAN, THE	BRADBURY, RAY	SS	MCL 51 05
GOLDEN APPLES OF THE SUN, THE			
	BRADBURY, RAY	SS	PLS 53 11
SOUND OF THUNDER, A	BRADBURY, RAY	SS	COL 52 06
LONG RAIN, THE (DEATH-BY-RAIN)			
	BRADBURY, RAY	SS	PLS 50 SU
EXILES, THE (THE MAD WIZARDS OF MARS, MCL 49 09)			
	BRADBURY, RAY	SS	FSF 50 WS
HERE THERE BE TYGERS	BRADBURY, RAY	SS	NTS 51
STRAWBERRY WINDOW, THE	BRADBURY, RAY	SS	STR 54 03
DRAGON, THE	BRADBURY, RAY	SS	FSF 56 03
GIFT, THE	BRADBURY, RAY	SS	FAN 59 07
FROST AND FIRE (THE CREATURES THAT TIME FORGOT)			
	BRADBURY, RAY	NV	PLS 46 FL
UNCLE EINAR	BRADBURY, RAY	SS	NEW 47 AC
TIME MACHINE, THE (THE HAPPINESS MACHINE)			
	BRADBURY, RAY	SS	SEP 57 09
SOUND OF SUMMER RUNNING, THE (SUMMER IN THE AIR)			
	BRADBURY, RAY	SS	SEP 56 02

RACE TO THE STARS
	MARGULIES & FRIEND	AN	CRS 58 10

4 STORIES FROM "GIANT ANTHOLOGY OF SCIENCE FICTION"
CITY OF THE LOST ONES (ENCHANTRESS OF VENUS)			
	BRACKETT, LEIGH	NV	PLS 49 FL
FORGOTTEN WORLD	HAMILTON, EDMOND	NV	TWS 46 WI
TIME GATE, THE (BY HIS BOOTSTRAPS)			
	HEINLEIN, ROBERT A.	NV	ASF 41 10
SUN MAKER, THE	WILLIAMSON, JACK	NV	TWS 40 06

RADIUM POOL, THE
	REPP, ED EARL	AC H	FPB 49
ALSO IN "SCIENCE-FANTASY QUINTETTE"
PHANTOM OF TERROR, THE	REPP, ED EARL	SS	AMZ 33 04
RADIUM POOL, THE	REPP, ED EARL	NV	SWS 29 08
BATTLE OF WIZARDS	REPP, ED EARL	SS	
RED DIMENSION, THE	REPP, ED EARL	SS	SWS 30 01

RARE SCIENCE FICTION
	HOWARD, IVAN	AN	BEL 63 01
LET'S HAVE FUN	DE CAMP, L. SPRAGUE	SS	SFQ 57 05
DO IT YOURSELF	LESSER, MILTON	SS	SFQ 57 11
IN HUMAN HANDS	BUDRYS, ALGIS	NV	SFS 54 12
PROTECTIVE CAMOUFLAGE	DEVET, CHARLES V.	NV	SFS 55 05
ASYLUM	BULLOCK, ALICE	SS	FUT 54 08
QUICK FREEZE	SILVERBERG, ROBERT	SS	SFQ 57 05
LUCK, INC.	HARMON, JIM	SS	SFS 59 11
RIPENESS	PEASE, M. C.	NV	SFS 55 01

REACH FOR TOMORROW
	CLARKE, ARTHUR C.	AC	BAL 56 03
PREFACE	CLARKE, ARTHUR C.	IN	
RESCUE PARTY	CLARKE, ARTHUR C.	NV	ASF 46 05
WALK IN THE DARK, A	CLARKE, ARTHUR C.	SS	TWS 50 08
FORGOTTEN ENEMY, THE	CLARKE, ARTHUR C.	SS	NWS 49 05
TECHNICAL ERROR (THE REVERSED MAN)			
	CLARKE, ARTHUR C.	SS	FSB 46 12
PARASITE, THE	CLARKE, ARTHUR C.	SS	AVS 53 04
FIRES WITHIN, THE	CLARKE, ARTHUR C.	SS	FSB 47 08
AWAKENING, THE	CLARKE, ARTHUR C.	SS	ZEN 42 02
TROUBLE WITH THE NATIVES (CAPTAIN WYXTPTHLL'S FLYING SAUCER)			
	CLARKE, ARTHUR C.	SS	MAR 51 05

CURSE, THE	CLARKE, ARTHUR C.	SS	CSM 53 09
TIME'S ARROW	CLARKE, ARTHUR C.	SS	SCF 50 SU
JUPITER FIVE	CLARKE, ARTHUR C.	NV	IFS 53 05
POSSESSED, THE	CLARKE, ARTHUR C.	SS	DSF 53 03

REAL-TIME WORLD
	PRIEST, CHRISTOPHER	AC H	NLB 74
INTRODUCTION	PRIEST, CHRISTOPHER	IN	
HEAD AND THE HAND, THE	PRIEST, CHRISTOPHER	SS	NWQ 72 03
FIRE STORM	PRIEST, CHRISTOPHER	SS	QRK 70 01
DOUBLE CONSUMMATION	PRIEST, CHRISTOPHER	SS	70
WOMAN NAKED, A	PRIEST, CHRISTOPHER	SS	SFM 74 01
TRANSPLANT	PRIEST, CHRISTOPHER	SS	IFS 74 02
BREEDING GROUND	PRIEST, CHRISTOPHER	SS	VOT 70 01
SENTENCE IN BINARY CODE	PRIEST, CHRISTOPHER	SS	FAN 71 08
PERIHELION MAN, THE	PRIEST, CHRISTOPHER	NV	NWR 69 16
RUN, THE	PRIEST, CHRISTOPHER	SS	IMP 66 05
REAL-TIME WORLD	PRIEST, CHRISTOPHER	NV	NWR 71 19

REALITY TRIP, THE
	SILVERBERG, ROBERT	AC	BAL 72 03
IN ENTROPY'S JAWS	SILVERBERG, ROBERT	NV	INY 71 02
REALITY TRIP, THE	SILVERBERG, ROBERT	NV	IFS 70 05
BLACK IS BEAUTIFUL	SILVERBERG, ROBERT	SS	YRT 70
OZYMANDIAS	SILVERBERG, ROBERT	SS	INF 58 11
CALIBAN	SILVERBERG, ROBERT	SS	INY 72 03
SHRINES OF EARTH, THE	SILVERBERG, ROBERT	SS	ASF 57 11
RINGING THE CHANGES	SILVERBERG, ROBERT	SS	ANA 70
HAWKSBILL STATION	SILVERBERG, ROBERT	NV	GAL 67 08

RED PERI, THE
	WEINBAUM, STANLEY G.	AC H	FPS 52
SMOTHERED SEAS	WEINBAUM, STANLEY G.	NV	ASF 36 01
REVOLUTION OF 1950	WEINBAUM, STANLEY G.	NA	AMZ 38 10
RED PERI, THE	WEINBAUM, STANLEY G.	SN	ASF 35 11
PROTEUS ISLAND	WEINBAUM, STANLEY G.	SS	ASF 36 08
BRINK OF INFINITY, THE	WEINBAUM, STANLEY G.	SS	TWS 36 12
SHIFTING SEAS	WEINBAUM, STANLEY G.	NV	AMZ 37 04
FLIGHT ON TITAN	WEINBAUM, STANLEY G.	NV	ASF 35 01
REDEMPTION CAIRN	WEINBAUM, STANLEY G.	NV	ASF 36 03

REST OF THE ROBOTS, THE
	ASIMOV, ISAAC	AC H	DBL 64
INTRODUCTION	ASIMOV, ISAAC	IN	
ROBOT AL-76 GOES ASTRAY	ASIMOV, ISAAC	SS	AMZ 42 02
VICTORY UNINTENTIONAL	ASIMOV, ISAAC	SS	SSS 42 08
FIRST LAW	ASIMOV, ISAAC	SS	FUN 56 10
LET'S GET TOGETHER	ASIMOV, ISAAC	SS	INF 57 02
SATISFACTION GUARANTEED	ASIMOV, ISAAC	SS	AMZ 51 04
RISK	ASIMOV, ISAAC	NV	ASF 55 05
LENNY	ASIMOV, ISAAC	SS	INF 58 01
GALLEY SLAVE	ASIMOV, ISAAC	NV	GAL 57 12
CAVES OF STEEL, THE	ASIMOV, ISAAC	NO	GAL 53 10
NAKED SUN, THE	ASIMOV, ISAAC	NO	ASF 56 10

REST OF THE ROBOTS, THE (EIGHT STORIES FROM)
	ASIMOV, ISAAC	AC	PYR 66 01
INTRODUCTION	ASIMOV, ISAAC	IN	
ROBOT AL-76 GOES ASTRAY	ASIMOV, ISAAC	SS	AMZ 42 02
VICTORY UNINTENTIONAL	ASIMOV, ISAAC	SS	SSS 42 08
FIRST LAW	ASIMOV, ISAAC	SS	FUN 56 10
LET'S GET TOGETHER	ASIMOV, ISAAC	SS	INF 57 02
SATISFACTION GUARANTEED	ASIMOV, ISAAC	SS	AMZ 51 04
RISK	ASIMOV, ISAAC	NV	ASF 55 05
LENNY	ASIMOV, ISAAC	SS	INF 58 01
GALLEY SLAVE	ASIMOV, ISAAC	NV	GAL 57 12

RETIEF OF THE CDT
	LAUMER, KEITH	AC H	DBL 71
BALLOTS AND BANDITS	LAUMER, KEITH	NV	IFS 70 09
MECHANICAL ADVANTAGE (RETIEF, THE LONG-AWAITED MASTER)			
	LAUMER, KEITH	NV	IFS 69 04
PIME DOESN'T CRAY	LAUMER, KEITH	NV	IFS 71 01
INTERNAL AFFAIR (RETIEF, INSIDER)			
	LAUMER, KEITH	NV	INF 71 03
PIECEMAKERS, THE	LAUMER, KEITH	NV	IFS 70 05

RETIEF: AMBASSADOR TO SPACE
	LAUMER, KEITH	AC H	DBL 69
GIANT KILLER	LAUMER, KEITH	NV	IFS 65 09
FORBIDDEN CITY, THE (RETIEF, WAR CRIMINAL)			
	LAUMER, KEITH	NV	IFS 67 04
GRIME AND PUNISHMENT (CLEAR AS MUD)			
	LAUMER, KEITH	NV	IFS 67 08
DAM NUISANCE	LAUMER, KEITH	NV	IFS 66 03
TRICK OR TREATY	LAUMER, KEITH	NV	IFS 65 08
FOREST IN THE SKY, THE	LAUMER, KEITH	NV	IFS 67 02
TRUCE OR CONSEQUENCES	LAUMER, KEITH	NV	IFS 66 11

RETIEF: EMISSARY TO THE STARS
	LAUMER, KEITH	AC	DEL 75 12
HOOB MELON CRISIS, THE	LAUMER, KEITH	NV	NEW 75 AC
GARBAGE INVASION, THE	LAUMER, KEITH	NV	FSF 72 12
EXCERPT FROM RETIEF & THE WARLORDS			
	LAUMER, KEITH	EX	DBL 68
TROUBLESHOOTER, THE	LAUMER, KEITH	NV	NEW 75 AC
NEGOTIATORS, THE	LAUMER, KEITH	SS	ASF 75 02

RETURN TO OTHERNESS
	KUTTNER, HENRY	AC	BAL 62
SEE YOU LATER	KUTTNER, HENRY	SS	TWS 49 06
THIS IS THE HOUSE	KUTTNER, HENRY	SS	ASF 46 02
PROUD ROBOT, THE	KUTTNER, HENRY	NV	ASF 43 10
GALLEGHER PLUS	KUTTNER, HENRY	NV	ASF 43 11
EGO MACHINE, THE	KUTTNER, HENRY	NV	SSF 52 05
ANDROID (ALSO AS THOSE AMONG US)			
	KUTTNER, HENRY	NV	FSF 51 06
SKY IS FALLING, THE	KUTTNER, HENRY	SS	PLS 50 FL
JUKE-BOX	KUTTNER, HENRY	SS	TWS 47 02

REVOLT IN 2100
	HEINLEIN, ROBERT A.	AC H	SHS 53
INNOCENT EYE, THE	KUTTNER, HENRY	IN	
IF THIS GOES ON-	HEINLEIN, ROBERT A.	SN	ASF 40 02

REVOLT IN 2100   ROSE, THE

COVENTRY   HEINLEIN, ROBERT A.   NV   ASF 40 07
MISFIT   HEINLEIN, ROBERT A.   SS   ASF 39 11
CONCERNING STORIES NEVER WRITTEN: POSTSCRIPT
                                 HEINLEIN, ROBERT A.   MS

RIM GODS, THE   CHANDLER, A. BERTRAM DC   ACE 68
  RIM GODS, THE   CHANDLER, A. BERTRAM NV   IFS 68 04
  BIRD-BRAINED NAVIGATOR, THE   CHANDLER, A. BERTRAM NV   IFS 68 06
  LAST DREAMER   CHANDLER, A. BERTRAM NV   IFS 68 08
  TIN FISHES, THE   CHANDLER, A. BERTRAM NV   IFS 68 12

RIM OF MORNING, THE   SLOANE, WILLIAM   AC H DOM 64
  EDGE OF RUNNING WATER, THE   SLOANE, WILLIAM   NA
  TO WALK THE NIGHT   SLOANE, WILLIAM   NO   FSY 37

RIM OF THE UNKNOWN   LONG, FRANK BELKNAP AC H ARK 72
  SPIRAL INTELLIGENCE, THE   LONG, FRANK BELKNAP SS   SFP 53 06
  WORLD OF WULKINS, THE   LONG, FRANK BELKNAP SS   TWS 48 04
  MAN WITH A THOUSAND LEGS, THE
                                 LONG, FRANK BELKNAP SS   WRT 27 08
  HUMPTY DUMPTY HAD A GREAT FALL
                                 LONG, FRANK BELKNAP SS   STS 48 11
  GUEST IN THE HOUSE   LONG, FRANK BELKNAP SS   ASF 46 03
  TRAP, THE   LONG, FRANK BELKNAP SS   ASF 45 05
  FUZZY HEAD   LONG, FRANK BELKNAP SS   TWS 48 12
  HOUSE OF RISING WINDS, THE   LONG, FRANK BELKNAP SS   STS 48 05
  MR. CAXTON DRAWS A MARTIAN BIRD
                                 LONG, FRANK BELKNAP SS   FUN 54 07
  CRITTERS, THE   LONG, FRANK BELKNAP SS   ASF 45 11
  COTTAGE, THE   LONG, FRANK BELKNAP SS   FUN 54 09
  MAN FROM TIME, THE   LONG, FRANK BELKNAP SS   FUN 54 03
  CONES   LONG, FRANK BELKNAP NV   ASF 36 02
  PREVIEW   LONG, FRANK BELKNAP SS   FUN 56 01
  LESSON IN SURVIVAL   LONG, FRANK BELKNAP SS   TWS 52 12
  GOOD TO BE A MARTIAN   LONG, FRANK BELKNAP SS   FUN 55 02
  FILCH   LONG, FRANK BELKNAP SS   ASF 45 03
  LITTLE MEN OF SPACE   LONG, FRANK BELKNAP SS   FUN 53 06
  SPECTACLES, THE   LONG, FRANK BELKNAP SS   FUN 56 04
  MAN OF DISTINCTION   LONG, FRANK BELKNAP SS   FUN 54 11
  GREAT COLD, THE   LONG, FRANK BELKNAP SS   ASF 35 02
  GREEN GLORY   LONG, FRANK BELKNAP SS   ASF 35 01
  LAST MEN, THE   LONG, FRANK BELKNAP SS   ASF 34 08

ROBERT HEINLEIN OMNIBUS, A   HEINLEIN, ROBERT A. AC H SID 66
  BEYOND THIS HORIZON   HEINLEIN, ROBERT A. NO   ASF 42 04
  MAN WHO SOLD THE MOON, THE   HEINLEIN, ROBERT A. AC   SHS 50
  GREEN HILLS OF EARTH, THE   HEINLEIN, ROBERT A. AC   SHS 51

ROBERT SHECKLEY OMNIBUS, THE SHECKLEY, ROBERT   AC H GOL 73
  EDITED BY ROBERT CONQUEST
  INTRODUCTION   CONQUEST, ROBERT   IN
  IMMORTALITY INC. (TIME KILLER)
                                 SHECKLEY, ROBERT   NO   GAL 58 10
  SPECIALIST   SHECKLEY, ROBERT   SS   GAL 53 05
  BAD MEDICINE   SHECKLEY, ROBERT   NV   GAL 56 07
  PILGRIMAGE TO EARTH (LOVE, INCORPORATED)
                                 SHECKLEY, ROBERT   SS   PBY 56 09
  ASK A FOOLISH QUESTION   SHECKLEY, ROBERT   SS   SFS 53 01
  TICKET TO TRANAI, A   SHECKLEY, ROBERT   NA   GAL 55 10
  BATTLE, THE   SHECKLEY, ROBERT   SS   IFS 54 09
  HANDS OFF   SHECKLEY, ROBERT   NV   GAL 54 04
  PRIZE OF PERIL, THE   SHECKLEY, ROBERT   SS   FSF 58 05
  HUNTING PROBLEM   SHECKLEY, ROBERT   SS   GAL 55 09
  GHOST V   SHECKLEY, ROBERT   SS   GAL 54 10
  SOMETHING FOR NOTHING   SHECKLEY, ROBERT   SS   GAL 54 06
  STORE OF THE WORLDS, THE (THE WORLD OF HEART'S DESIRE)
                                 SHECKLEY, ROBERT   SS   PBY 59 09

ROBOT AND THE MAN, THE   GREENBERG , MARTIN AN H GNM 53
  FOREWORD   GREENBERG , MARTIN   IN
  MECHANICAL ANSWER   MACDONALD, JOHN D.   SS   ASF 48 05
  SELF PORTRAIT   WOLFE, BERNARD   NV   GAL 51 11
  DEADLOCK   PADGETT, LEWIS   SS   ASF 42 08
  ROBINC   HOLMES, H. H.   SS   ASF 43 09
  BURNING BRIGHT   BROWNING, JOHN S.   SS   ASF 48 07
  FINAL COMMAND   VAN VOGT, A. E.   SS   ASF 49 11
  THOUGH DREAMERS DIE   DEL REY, LESTER   SS   ASF 44 02
  RUST   KELLEAM, JOSEPH E.   SS   ASF 39 10
  ROBOTS RETURN   WILLIAMS, ROBERT M. SS   ASF 38 09
  INTO THY HANDS   DEL REY, LESTER   SS   ASF 45 08

ROBOTS AND CHANGELINGS   DEL REY, LESTER   AC   BAL 57
  PIPES OF PAN, THE   DEL REY, LESTER   SS   UNK 40 05
  LITTLE JIMMY   DEL REY, LESTER   SS   FSF 57 04
  COPPERSMITH   DEL REY, LESTER   SS   UNK 39 09
  NO STRINGS ATTACHED   DEL REY, LESTER   SS   IFS 54 06
  STILL WATERS, THE   DEL REY, LESTER   SS   FAN 55 04
  KINDNESS   DEL REY, LESTER   SS   ASF 44 10
  STABILITY   DEL REY, LESTER   SS   VOR 53 01
  KEEPERS OF THE HOUSE   DEL REY, LESTER   SS   FUN 56 01
  UNEASY LIES THE HEAD   DEL REY, LESTER   SS   TSF 51 SP
  MONSTER, THE   DEL REY, LESTER   SS   ARG 51 06
  INTO THY HANDS   DEL REY, LESTER   SS   ASF 45 08

ROBOTS HAVE NO TAILS   PADGETT, LEWIS   AC H GNM 52
  PROUD ROBOT, THE   PADGETT, LEWIS   NV   ASF 43 10
  GALLEGHER PLUS   PADGETT, LEWIS   NV   ASF 43 11
  WORLD IS MINE, THE   PADGETT, LEWIS   NV   ASF 43 06
  EX MACHINA   PADGETT, LEWIS   NV   ASF 48 04
  TIME LOCKER   PADGETT, LEWIS   SS   ASF 43 01

ROD SERLING'S THE TWILIGHT ZONE
                                 SERLING, ROD   OC H GRS 63
  ADAPTATION   GIBSON, WALTER B.   MS
  ILLUSTRATIONS   MAYAN, EARL E.   IL
  AVENGING GHOST, THE   SERLING, ROD   SA

BACK THERE   SERLING, ROD   SA
CURSE OF SEVEN TOWERS, THE   SERLING, ROD   SA
DEAD MAN'S CHEST   SERLING, ROD   SA
DEATH'S MASQUERADE   SERLING, ROD   SA
GHOST OF TICONDEROGA, THE   SERLING, ROD   SA
GHOST-TOWN GHOST, THE   SERLING, ROD   SA
HOUSE ON THE SQUARE, THE   SERLING, ROD   SA
JUDGMENT NIGHT   SERLING, ROD   SA
RETURN FROM OBLIVION   SERLING, ROD   SA
RIDDLE OF THE CRYPT, THE   SERLING, ROD   SA
THIRTEENTH STORY, THE   SERLING, ROD   SA
TIGER GOD, THE   SERLING, ROD   SA

ROD SERLING'S THE TWILIGHT ZONE (CHILLING STORIES FROM)
                                 SERLING, ROD   OC   TMP 65 08
  ADAPTATION   GIBSON, WALTER B.   MS
  FOREWORD   SERLING, ROD   IN
  GHOST OF TICONDEROGA, THE   SERLING, ROD   SA
  BACK THERE   SERLING, ROD   SA
  JUDGMENT NIGHT   SERLING, ROD   SA
  CURSE OF SEVEN TOWERS, THE   SERLING, ROD   SA
  AVENGING GHOST, THE   SERLING, ROD   SA
  RETURN FROM OBLIVION   SERLING, ROD   SA
  HOUSE ON THE SQUARE, THE   SERLING, ROD   SA
  DEATH'S MASQUERADE   SERLING, ROD   SA
  RIDDLE OF THE CRYPT, THE   SERLING, ROD   SA
  DEAD MAN'S CHEST   SERLING, ROD   SA

ROD SERLING'S TRIPLE W: WITCHES, WARLOCKS AND WEREWOLVES
                                 SERLING, ROD   AN   BAN 63 05
  INTRODUCTION   SERLING, ROD   IN
  AMULET, THE   DICKSON, GORDON R.   SS   FSF 59 04
  STORY OF SIDI NORMAN, THE   ANONYMOUS   SS
  FINAL INGREDIENT, THE   SHARKEY, JACK   SS   FSF 60 08
  BLIND ALLEY   JAMESON, MALCOLM   NV   UNK 43 06
  YOUNG GOODMAN BROWN (1835)   HAWTHORNE, NATHANIEL SS   NEM 35 04
  CHESTNUT BEADS, THE   ROBERTS, JANE   NV   FSF 57 10
  HATCHERY OF DREAMS   LEIBER, FRITZ   SS   FAN 61 11
  MARK OF THE BEAST, THE   KIPLING, RUDYARD   SS   PIO 90 07
  AND NOT QUITE HUMAN   HENSLEY, JOE L.   SS   BEY 53 09
  WOLVES DON'T CRY   ELLIOTT, BRUCE   SS   FSF 54 05
  BLACK RETRIEVER, THE   FINNEY, CHARLES G.   SS   FSF 58 10
  WITCH TRIALS AND THE LAW (1841)
                                 MACKAY, CHARLES   AR

ROD SERLING'S TWILIGHT ZONE REVISITED
                                 SERLING, ROD   OC H GRS 64
  ADAPTATION   GIBSON, WALTER B.   MS
  FOREWORD   SERLING, ROD   IN
  TWO LIVE GHOSTS   SERLING, ROD   SA
  GHOST OF THE DIXIE BELLE, THE
                                 SERLING, ROD   SA
  PURPLE TESTAMENT, THE   SERLING, ROD   SA
  GHOST TRAIN, THE   SERLING, ROD   SA
  BEYOND THE RIM   SERLING, ROD   SA
  GHOST OF JOLLY ROGER, THE   SERLING, ROD   SA
  MAN IN THE BOTTLE, THE   SERLING, ROD   SA
  MIRROR IMAGE, THE   SERLING, ROD   SA
  MAN WHO DROPPED BY, THE   SERLING, ROD   SA

ROGUE SHIP   VAN VOGT, A. E.   NO H DBL 65
  CENTAURUS II   VAN VOGT, A. E.   NV   ASF 47 06
  EXPENDABLES, THE   VAN VOGT, A. E.   NV   IFS 63 09
  ROGUE SHIP (ALSO AS THE TWISTED MEN)
                                 VAN VOGT, A. E.   NV   SSS 50 03

ROLLERBALL   HARRISON, WILLIAM   AC   WPB 75 07
  PREFACE   HARRISON, WILLIAM   IN
  WARRIOR, THE   HARRISON, WILLIAM   SS   ESQ 71 11
  HERMIT, THE   HARRISON, WILLIAM   SS   68
  DOWN THE BLUE HOLE   HARRISON, WILLIAM   SS   73
  EATING IT   HARRISON, WILLIAM   SS   70
  PINBALL MACHINES, THE   HARRISON, WILLIAM   SS   SEP 67 04
  ROLLER BALL MURDERS   HARRISON, WILLIAM   SS   ESQ 73 09
  BLURB KING, THE   HARRISON, WILLIAM   SS   71
  COOK'S TALE, A   HARRISON, WILLIAM   NV   66
  ARSONS OF DESIRE, THE   HARRISON, WILLIAM   SS   72
  GOOD SHIP ERASMUS, THE   HARRISON, WILLIAM   SS   71
  UNDER THE HOUSE   HARRISON, WILLIAM   SS   72
  NIRVANA, GOTTERDAMMERUNG, AND THE SHOT PUT
                                 HARRISON, WILLIAM   SS   72
  WEATHERMAN: A THEOLOGICAL NARRATIVE
                                 HARRISON, WILLIAM   SS   73

ROOTS OF EVIL, THE   PARRY, MICHEL   AN H TAP 76
  INTRODUCTION   PARRY, MICHEL   IN
  SEED FROM THE SEPULCHRE, THE SMITH, CLARK ASHTON   SS   WRT 33 10
  FLOWERING OF THE STRANGE ORCHID, THE (ALSO AS THE STRANGE
  ORCHID)   WELLS, H. G.   SS   PMB 94 08
  RAPPACCINI'S DAUGHTER (1844) HAWTHORNE, NATHANIEL   NV   DMR 44 12
  DORNER CORDAIANTHUS   HOLLAND, HESTER   SS   25
  COME INTO MY PARLOR   WELLMAN, MANLY WADE SS   49
  TREE'S WIFE, THE   COUNSELMAN, MARY E. SS   WRT 50 03
  IVY WAR, THE   KELLER, DAVID H. MD. SS   AMZ 30 05
  GREEN THOUGHTS   COLLIER, JOHN   SS   31
  DR. ADAMS' GARDEN OF EVIL   LEIBER, FRITZ   SS   FAN 63 02
  DAISES (TRIPLICATE TWISTEROO)
                                 BROWN, FREDRIC   SS   PBY 57 03
  GARDENER, THE   ST. CLAIR, MARGARET SS   TWS 49 10
  GREEN THUMB   SIMAK, CLIFFORD D.   NV   GAL 54 07

ROSE FOR ECCLESIASTES, A   ZELAZNY, ROGER   AC H HDV 69
  SEE "FOUR FOR TOMORROW"

ROSE, THE   HARNESS, CHARLES L. AC   CPT 66
  ROSE, THE   HARNESS, CHARLES L. NO   AUT 53 03

ROSE, THE

CHESSPLAYERS, THE	HARNESS, CHARLES L.	SS	FSF 53 10
NEW REALITY, THE	HARNESS, CHARLES L.	NV	TWS 50 12

RUINS OF EARTH, THE | DISCH, THOMAS M. | AN H | PUT 71 |
ON SAVING THE WORLD	DISCH, THOMAS M.	IN	
DEER IN THE WORKS	VONNEGUT, KURT JR.	SS	ESQ 55 04
THREE MILLION SQUARE MILES	WOLFE, GENE	SS	NEW 71 AN
CLOSING WITH NATURE	RUSH, NORMAN	SS	MRV 70
PLOT TO SAVE THE WORLD, THE	BROWNSTEIN, MICHAEL	SS	PRV 70 48
AUTOFAC	DICK, PHILIP K.	NV	GAL 55 11
ROOMMATES (BASIS FOR NOVEL "MAKE ROOM! MAKE ROOM!")			
	HARRISON, HARRY	NV	NEW 71 AN
GROANING HINGES OF THE WORLD	LAFFERTY, R. A.	SS	NEW 71 AN
GAS MASK	HOUSTON, JAMES D.	SS	NUG 64
WEDNESDAY, NOVEMBER 15, 1967	EFFINGER, GEO. ALEC	SS	NEW 71 AN
CAGE OF SAND, THE	BALLARD, J. G.	SS	NWS 62 06
ACCIDENT VERTIGO	ELMSLIE, KENWARD	SS	PRV 71 50
BIRDS, THE	DU MAURIER, DAPHNE	NV	GHK 52 10
DO IT FOR MOMMA	MUNDIS, JERROLD J.	SS	NEW 71 AN
DREADFUL HAS ALREADY HAPPENED, THE			
	KAGAN, NORMAN	SS	NEW 71 AN
SHAKER REVIVAL, THE	JONAS, GERALD	NV	GAL 70 02
AMERICA THE BEAUTIFUL	LEIBER, FRITZ	SS	YRT 70

RULE OF THE DOOR AND OTHER FANCIFUL REGULATIONS
	BIGGLE, LLOYD JR.	AC H	DBL 67
ALSO AS "(OUT OF) THE SILENT SKY"			
INTRODUCTION	BIGGLE, LLOYD JR.	IN	
RULE OF THE DOOR, THE	BIGGLE, LLOYD JR.	NV	GAL 58 02
PETTY LARCENY	BIGGLE, LLOYD JR.	SS	SAT 58 08
ON THE DOTTED LINE	BIGGLE, LLOYD JR.	NV	IFS 57 06
JUDGEMENT DAY	BIGGLE, LLOYD JR.	SS	FUN 58 04
SECRET WEAPON (BRIDLE SHOWER)			
	BIGGLE, LLOYD JR.	NV	GAL 58 05
PERFECT PUNISHMENT, THE (PARIAH PLANET)			
	BIGGLE, LLOYD JR.	NV	WOT 65 03
SLIGHT CASE OF LIMBO, A	BIGGLE, LLOYD JR.	SS	ASF 63 04
D.F.C. (CHRONIUS OF THE D.F.C.)			
	BIGGLE, LLOYD JR.	SS	IFS 57 02
WINGS OF SONG	BIGGLE, LLOYD JR.	SS	FSF 63 11

RULERS OF MEN | SANTESSON, HANS S. | AN | PYR 65 |
INTRODUCTION	SANTESSON, HANS S.	IN	
WAY OF LIFE, A	BLOCH, ROBERT	SS	FUN 56 10
BE OF GOOD CHEER	LEIBER, FRITZ	SS	GAL 64 10
THIS EARTH OF MAJESTY (CONTEST STORY WINNING TITLE REFUGEE)			
	CLARKE, ARTHUR C.	SS	FSF 55 07
THING OF CUSTOM, A	DE CAMP, L. SPRAGUE	SS	FUN 57 01
PRISON BREAK	DEFORD, MIRIAM ALLEN	SS	FUN 59 07
EYES HAVE IT, THE	GARRETT, RANDALL	NV	ASF 64 01
MURDERER'S CHAIN	BROWN, WENZELL	SS	FUN 60 03
FALL OF KNIGHT	CHANDLER, A. BERTRAM	SS	FUN 58 06
K-FACTOR, THE	HARRISON, HARRY	NV	ASF 60 12
WOLFRAM HUNTERS, THE	HOCH, EDWARD D.	SS	SMM 64 03

RUN TO STARLIGHT, SPORTS THROUGH SCIENCE FICTION
	GREENBERG/OLANDER/&	AN H	DCT 75
INTRODUCTION	GREENBERG, MARTIN H.		
	OLANDER, JOSEPH D.		
	AND WARRICK, PATRICIA S.	IN C	
LAST SUPER BOWL GAME, THE	MARTIN, GEORGE R. R.	NV	GLR 75 02
NATIONAL PASTIME, THE	SPINRAD, NORMAN	NV	NOV 73 03
RUN TO STARLIGHT	MARTIN, GEORGE R. R.	NV	AMZ 74 12
DODGER FAN	STANTON, WILL	SS	FSF 57 06
CELEBRATED NO-HIT INNING, THE			
	POHL, FREDERIK	SS	FUN 56 09
NAKED TO THE INVISIBLE EYE	EFFINGER, GEO. ALEC	NV	ASF 73 05
GOAL TENDING	BLAKE, E. MICHAEL	NV	75
TO HELL WITH THE ODDS	FISH, ROBERT L.	SS	FSF 58 02
TITLE FIGHT	GAULT, WILLIAM C.	SS	FUN 56 12
STEEL	MATHESON, RICHARD	SS	FSF 56 05
IMMORTAL GAME, THE	ANDERSON, POUL	SS	FSF 54 02
DOORS OF HIS FACE, THE LAMPS OF HIS MOUTH, THE			
	ZELAZNY, ROGER	NV	FSF 65 03
POOR LITTLE WARRIOR!	ALDISS, BRIAN W.	SS	FSF 58 04

RUSSIAN SCIENCE FICTION | MAGIDOFF, ROBERT | AN H | NYU 64 |
TRANSLATION	JOHNSON, DORIS	MS	
INTRODUCTION	MAGIDOFF, ROBERT	IN	
INVISIBLE LIGHT	BELAYEV, ALEXANDER	SS	
MAGIC SHOES, THE	SAPARIN, VICTOR	SS	
DANGEROUS INVENTION, A	ZELIKOVICH, E.	SS	
FICTION MACHINES, THE	OKHOTNIKOV, VADIM	SS	
SHADOWS OF THE PAST	YEFREMOV, IVAN	SS	
COR SERPENTIS	YEFREMOV, IVAN	NV	
FLYING FLOWERS	VASILYEV, MIKHAIL	SS	
MAXWELL EQUATIONS, THE	DNIEPROV, ANATOLY	SS	
ASTRONAUT, THE	ZHURAVLEVA, VALENTINA	SS	
NEW YEAR'S FAIRY TALE, A	DUDINTSEV, VLADIMIR	SS	
ON THE MOON	TSIOLKOVSKY, K.	SS	

RUSSIAN SCIENCE FICTION, 1968
	MAGIDOFF, ROBERT	AN H	NYU 68
TRANSLATION	JACOBSON, HELEN	MS	
INTRODUCTION	MAGIDOFF, ROBERT	IN	
DWELLER IN TWO WORLDS, A	GOR, GENNADY	SS	
DESERT ENCOUNTER	ROSOKHOVATSKY, IGOR	SS	
TALES OF THE DISTANT PAST	PODOLNY, ROMAN	SS	
HEROIC FEAT, THE	DNIEPROV, ANATOLY	SS	
FORMULA FOR THE IMPOSSIBLE	LUKODIANOV, ISAI		
	AND VOISKUNSKY, YEVGENY	SS C	
THREAD OF LIFE	SAFRONOV, Y.	SS	
LIFE IS SO DULL FOR LITTLE GIRLS			
	BULYCHEV, KIRILL	SS	
MYSTERY OF GREEN CROSSING	YEMTSEV, MIKHAIL		
	AND PARNOV, YEREMEY	SS C	

IN MAN'S OWN IMAGE	VARSHAVSKY, ILYA	SS	
STORM	ZHURAVLEVA, VALENTINA	SS	
FOUNDING OF CIVILIZATION, THE			
	YAROV, ROMAIN	SS	ISF 68 06
ROBOTNIKS, THE	BAKHNOV, VLADLEN	SS	
MUTINY	BAKHNOV, VLADLEN	SS	

RUSSIAN SCIENCE FICTION, 1969 | MAGIDOFF, ROBERT | AN H | NYU 69 |
PREFACE	MAGIDOFF, ROBERT	IN	
NOTES ON SOME OF THE AUTHORS	MISC. MATERIAL	MS	
IN THE LAND OF SCIENCE FICTION			
	BRANDIS, YEVGENY		
	AND DMITRVSKY, VLADIMIR	SS C	
JOURNEY INTO THE FUTURE	GRANIN, DANIIL	SS	
UNIQUE	BAKHNOV, VLADLEN	SS	
SPEAKING OF DEMONOLOGY	BAKHNOV, VLADLEN	SS	
CRABS TAKE OVER THE ISLAND	DNIEPROV, ANATOLY	SS	ISF 68 06
GARDEN, THE	GOR, GENNADY	SS	68
HUMAN FRAILTY	XLEBNIKOV, A.	SS	
MODEST GENIUS, A	SHEFNER, VADIM	SS	
RAID TAKES PLACE AT MIDNIGHT, A			
	VARSHAVSKY, ILYA	SS	
FAREWELL ON THE SHORE, A	VOISKUNSKY, YEVGENY		
	AND LUKODIANOV, ISAI	NV C	
ROBOT HUMOR	ZUBKOV, E.		
	AND MUSLIN, E.	SS C	
MINOTAUR, THE	GOR, GENNADY	SS	

RX FOR TOMORROW | NOURSE, ALAN E. | AC H | MCK 71 |
SYMPTOMATICUS MEDICUS	NOURSE, ALAN E.	SS	USF 54 09
RX	NOURSE, ALAN E.	SS	IFS 57 10
CONTAMINATION CREW	NOURSE, ALAN E.	SS	IFS 58 02
IN SHEEP'S CLOTHING	NOURSE, ALAN E.	SS	FSM 52 11
GIFT FOR NUMBERS, A	NOURSE, ALAN E.	SS	SUP 58 08
FREE AGENT (SIXTY-YEAR EXTENSION)			
	NOURSE, ALAN E.	NV	PLS 54 05
LAST HOUSE CALL, THE	NOURSE, ALAN E.	SS	NEW 71 AC
GRAND ROUNDS	NOURSE, ALAN E.	SS	FUN 55 08
BRAMBLE BUSH	NOURSE, ALAN E.	SS	IFS 57 08
HEIR APPARENT	NOURSE, ALAN E.	SS	IMG 53 10
PLAGUE!	NOURSE, ALAN E.	SS	NEW 71 AC

S IS FOR SPACE | BRADBURY, RAY | AC H | DBL 66 08 |
INTRODUCTION	BRADBURY, RAY	IN	
CHRYSALIS	BRADBURY, RAY	SS	AMZ 46 07
PILLAR OF FIRE	BRADBURY, RAY	NV	PLS 48 SU
ZERO HOUR	BRADBURY, RAY	SS	PLS 47 FL
MAN, THE	BRADBURY, RAY	SS	TWS 49 02
TIME IN THY FLIGHT	BRADBURY, RAY	SS	FUN 53 06
PEDESTRIAN, THE (REP 51 08)	BRADBURY, RAY	SS	FSF 52 02
HAIL AND FAREWELL	BRADBURY, RAY	SS	TDY 53 03
INVISIBLE BOY	BRADBURY, RAY	SS	MAD 45 11
COME INTO MY CELLAR (ALSO AS BOYS, RAISE GIANT MUSHROOMS			
IN YOUR CELLAR)	BRADBURY, RAY	SS	GAL 62 10
MILLION-YEAR PICNIC, THE	BRADBURY, RAY	SS	PLS 46 SU
SCREAMING WOMAN, THE	BRADBURY, RAY	SS	TDY 51 05
SMILE, THE	BRADBURY, RAY	SS	FAN 52 SU
DARK THEY WERE, AND GOLDEN-EYED (THE NAMING OF NAMES)			
	BRADBURY, RAY	SS	TWS 49 08
TROLLEY, THE	BRADBURY, RAY	SS	GHK 55 07
FLYING MACHINE, THE	BRADBURY, RAY	SS	NEW 53 AC
ICARUS MONTGOLFIER WRIGHT	BRADBURY, RAY	SS	FSF 56 05

S.O.S. FROM THREE WORLDS | LEINSTER, MURRAY | AC | ACE 66 |
PLAGUE ON KRYDER II	LEINSTER, MURRAY	NV	ASF 64 12
RIBBON IN THE SKY	LEINSTER, MURRAY	NV	ASF 57 06
QUARANTINE WORLD	LEINSTER, MURRAY	SN	ASF 66 11

SAGITTARIUS | RUSSELL, RAY | AC | PBP 71 |
PREFACE	PLAYBOY, EDITORS OF	IN	
SAGITTARIUS	RUSSELL, RAY	NA	PBY 62 03
RIPPLES	RUSSELL, RAY	SS	PBY 67 10
SARDONICUS	RUSSELL, RAY	NA	PBY 61 01
ROOM, THE	RUSSELL, RAY	SS	PBY 61 02
COMET WINE	RUSSELL, RAY	NV	PBY 67 03
OUNCE OF PREVENTION	RUSSELL, RAY	SS	PBY 60 09
NAKED IN XANADU	RUSSELL, RAY	NV	PBY 64 11
NIGHT IN THE BYZANTINE PALACE, A			
	RUSSELL, RAY	SS	PBY

SAINT'S CHOICE OF IMPOSSIBLE CRIME, THE
	CHARTERIS, LESLIE	AN	BNC 45
GOLD STANDARD, THE	CHARTERIS, LESLIE	SS	33
IMPOSSIBLE HIGHWAY, THE	FRIEND, OSCAR J.	SS	TWS 40 08
PLANTS MUST SLAY	LONG, FRANK BELKNAP	SS	TWS 42 04
DAYMARE	BROWN, FREDRIC	NV	TWS 43 FL
TROPHY	KUTTNER, HENRY	SS	TWS 44 WI

SALIVA TREE AND OTHER STRANGE GROWTHS, THE
	ALDISS, BRIAN W.	AC H	FAB 66
SALIVA TREE, THE	ALDISS, BRIAN W.	SN	FSF 65 09
DANGER: RELIGION! (MATRIX)	ALDISS, BRIAN W.	TC	SCF 62 10
SOURCE, THE	ALDISS, BRIAN W.	SS	NWS 65 08
LONELY HABIT, THE	ALDISS, BRIAN W.	SS	EQM 66 06
PLEASURE SHARED, A	ALDISS, BRIAN W.	SS	SCF 65 06
ONE ROLE WITH RELISH	ALDISS, BRIAN W.	SS	NEW 66 AC
LEGENDS OF SMITH'S BURST	ALDISS, BRIAN W.	SS	NEB 59 06
DAY OF THE DOOMED KING	ALDISS, BRIAN W.	SS	SCF 65 04
PATERNAL CARE	ALDISS, BRIAN W.	SS	NEW 66 AC
GIRL AND ROBOT WITH FLOWERS	ALDISS, BRIAN W.	SS	NWS 65 09

SAME TO YOU DOUBLED AND OTHER STORIES, THE
| | SHECKLEY, ROBERT | AC | PAN 74 |
| SEE "CAN YOU FEEL ANYTHING WHEN I DO THIS?" | | | |

SANDS OF MARS AND OTHER STORIES, THE

SANDS OF MARS AND OTHER STORIES, THE
                     ANONYMOUS   AN   JBL 58
  SANDS OF MARS, THE (ENCHANTED VILLAGE)
                     VAN VOGT, A. E.   SS   OWS 50 07
  PILLOWS, THE   ST. CLAIR, MARGARET SS   TWS 50 06
  OPERATION ZERO (INTRUDER ON THE RIM)
                     LESSER, MILTON   SS   OSF 54 09
  ADJUSTMENT TEAM   DICK, PHILIP K.   NV   OSF 54 09
  THINKER, MARK VII (THE THINKER AND THE THOUGHT)
                     DERLETH, AUGUST   SS   OSF 54 09
  NO MORE THE STARS   COX, IRVING E. JR. SS   OSF 54 09

SANTANA MORNING AND OTHER STORIES
                     DOLAN, MIKE   OC   POW 70
  FOREWORD   DOLAN, MIKE   IN
  OF A YELLOW SUMMER   DOLAN, MIKE   SS
  HOLE, THE   DOLAN, MIKE   SS
  NIGHTMARE   DOLAN, MIKE   SS
  MIRROR, THE   DOLAN, MIKE   SS
  ROAD, THE   DOLAN, MIKE   SS
  SANTANA MORNING   DOLAN, MIKE   SS
  FOG, THE   DOLAN, MIKE   SS
  CITY, THE   DOLAN, MIKE   SS
  NUCLEAR GENESIS   DOLAN, MIKE   SS
  JOURNEY BY HELIODROME DOLAN, MIKE   SS
  DYNAMO   DOLAN, MIKE   SS
  HANDS, THE   DOLAN, MIKE   SS
  INTRUDER   DOLAN, MIKE   SS
  GRASS, THE   DOLAN, MIKE   SS
  GOLDEN EFFECT, THE   DOLAN, MIKE   SS
  MEMORY   DOLAN, MIKE   SS

SARDONICUS AND OTHER STORIES RUSSELL, RAY   AC   BAL 61
  SARDONICUS   RUSSELL, RAY   NA   PBY 61 01
  ACTOR, THE   RUSSELL, RAY   SS   PBY 60 03
  CAGE, THE   RUSSELL, RAY   SS   59
  EXPLOITS OF ARGO, THE (ALSO AS THE LONG NIGHT)
                     RUSSELL, RAY   SS   ROG 61 04
  SWORD OF LAERTES, THE RUSSELL, RAY   SS   59
  MONTAGE   RUSSELL, RAY   SS   PBY 58 10
  BOOKED SOLID   RUSSELL, RAY   SS   61
  TAKE A DEEP BREATH   RUSSELL, RAY   SS   TIG 56
  PLEASURE WAS OURS, THE RUSSELL, RAY   SS   IMG 55 05
  ROOM, THE   RUSSELL, RAY   SS   PBY 61 02
  I AM RETURNING   RUSSELL, RAY   SS   61
  INCOMMUNICADO   RUSSELL, RAY   SS   FSF 57 11
  HIS FATHER'S HOUSE   RUSSELL, RAY   SS   IFS 60 03
  LAST WILL AND TESTAMENT RUSSELL, RAY·   SS   55
  ROSEBUD, THE   RUSSELL, RAY   SS   FSF 59 08
  LONDON CALLING   RUSSELL, RAY   SS   61
  OUNCE OF PREVENTION   RUSSELL, RAY   SS   PBY 60 09

SATAN'S PETS   GHIDALIA, VIC   AN   MAN 72
  OUT IN THE GARDEN   DICK, PHILIP K.   SS   FNF 53 08
  LEGACY OF TERROR   SLESAR, HENRY   SS   AMZ 58 11
  DOGS OF DOCTOR DWANN, THE HAMILTON, EDMOND NV   WRT 32 10
  LEFTY FEEP GETS HENPECKED BLOCH, ROBERT   NV   FAD 45 04
  RAT RACKET, THE   KELLER, DAVID H. MD. SS   AMZ 31 11
  KEYHOLE   LEINSTER, MURRAY   SS   TWS 51 12
  THANKS FROM THE WHOLE BOUQUET
                     JACOBS, HARVEY   SS   NUG 65 09
  REMARKABLE TALENT OF EGBERT HAW, THE
                     BOND, NELSON S.   SS   41
  ANIMALS IN THE CASE, THE WAKEFIELD, H.RUSSELL SS   62
  CAT, THE   BENSON, E. F.   SS   12

SATURDAY EVENING POST FANTASY STORIES, THE
                     FLES, BARTHOLD   AN   AVN 51 10
  ENEMY PLANET, THE   GALLERY, D. V.   SS   SEP 50 09
  CHILD WHO BELIEVED, THE AMUNDSON, GRACE   SS   SEP 50 12
  SCENE FOR SATAN   LANGLEY, NOEL   SS   SEP 47 01
  DOOMSDAY DEFERRED   JENKINS, WILL F.   SS   SEP 49 09
  ETERNAL DUFFER, THE   TEMPLE, WILLARD   SS   SEP 46 01
  NOTE ON DANGER B   KERSH, GERALD   SS   SEP 47 04
  TERRIBLE ANSWER, THE   GALLICO, PAUL   SS   SEP 50 01
  VOICE IN THE EARPHONES, THE SCHRAMM, WILBUR SS   SEP 47 05
  DOCTOR HANRAY'S SECOND CHANCE
                     RICHTER, CONRAD   SS   SEP 50 01

SAVAGE PELLUCIDAR   BURROUGHS, EDGAR R. NO H CAN 63
  ILLUSTRATIONS   ST. JOHN, J. ALLEN IL
  RETURN TO PELLUCIDAR, THE BURROUGHS, EDGAR R. NV   AMZ 42 02
  MEN OF THE BRONZE AGE BURROUGHS, EDGAR R. NV   AMZ 42 03
  TIGER GIRL   BURROUGHS, EDGAR R. NV   AMZ 42 04
  SAVAGE PELLUCIDAR   BURROUGHS, EDGAR R. NV   AMZ 63 11

SAVING WORLDS   ELWOOD & KIDD   OA H DBL 73
  ALSO AS "THE WOUNDED PLANET"
  INTRODUCTION   HERBERT, FRANK   IN
  SAVING THE WORLD   CARR, TERRY   SS   SVW 73
  PARKS OF REST AND CULTURE ZEBROWSKI, GEORGE SS   SVW 73
  QUALITY OF THE PRODUCT, THE NEVILLE, KRIS
                     AND NEVILLE, LIL   SS C SVW 73
  ODE ON THE SOURCE OF THE CLITUMNUS
                     DISCH, THOMAS M.   PM   SVW 73
  POLITICS OF DARKNESS, THE DISCH, THOMAS M.   PM   SVW 73
  SMALL WAR   MACLEAN, KATHERINE SS   SVW 73
  DESIRABLE LAKESIDE RESIDENCE NORTON, ANDRE   SS   SVW 73
  SMOKEY THE BEAR SUTRA, THE SNYDER, GARY   SS   SVW 73
  ARTICLE ABOUT HUNTING, AN WOLFE, GENE   SS   SVW 73
  NOONDAY DEVIL   O'NEIL, DENNIS   SS   SVW 73
  SCORNER'S SEAT   LAFFERTY, R. A.   NV   SVW 73
  BATTERED-EARTH SYNDROME, THE MALZBERG, BARRY N. SS   SVW 73
  WINDMILL   ANDERSON, POUL   NV   SVW 73
  PARADISE REGAINED   COGSWELL, THOMAS   SS   SVW 73
  BEAUTYLAND   WOLFE, GENE   SS   SVW 73

  DAY, THE   SAXTON, COLIN   SS   SVW 73
  STARFISH   PRICE, D. M.   PM   SVW 73
  BILLENNIUM: A NOTE TO DEADCAT
                     PRICE, D. M.   PM   SVW 73
  DON'T HOLD YOUR BREATH VAN VOGT, A. E.   SS   SVW 73
  WIND AND THE RAIN, THE SILVERBERG, ROBERT SS   SVW 73

SCATTER OF STARDUST, A   TUBB, E. C.   DC   ACE 72
  BELLS OF ACHERON, THE TUBB, E. C.   SS   SCF 57 04
  ANNE   TUBB, E. C.   SS   NWS 66 01
  RETURN VISIT   TUBB, E. C.   SS   SCF 58 04
  SHRINE, THE (AS ALAN GUTHRIE)
                     TUBB, E. C.   SS   NWS 60 02
  SURVIVAL DEMANDS   TUBB, E. C.   SS   NWS 60 02
  LITTLE GIRL LOST   TUBB, E. C.   SS   NWS 55 10
  EYES OF SILENCE, THE   TUBB, E. C.   SS   INF 57 04
  ENCHANTER'S ENCOUNTER TUBB, E. C.   NV   SCF 59 12

SCHOOL AND SOCIETY THROUGH SCIENCE FICTION
                OLANDER/GREENBERG/& AN L RAN 74
  INTRODUCTION   OLANDER, JOSEPH D.
                     GREENBERG, MARTIN H.
             AND WARRICK, PATRICIA S. IN C
  PROFESSION   ASIMOV, ISAAC   SN   ASF 57 07
  GREAT INTELLECT BOOM, THE ANVIL, CHRISTOPHER SS   ASF 69 07
  EXAMINATION DAY   SLESAR, HENRY   SS   PBY 58 02
  PRIMARY EDUCATION OF THE CAMIROI
                     LAFFERTY, R. A.   SS   GAL 66 12
  BOHASSIAN LEARNS   ROTSLER, WILLIAM   SS   AMZ 71 07
  INVESTIGATING THE CURIOSITY DRIVE
                     HERZOG, TOM   SS   FSP 68 11
  BACKWARDNESS   ANDERSON, POUL   SS   FSP 58 03
  STIMULUS-REWARD SITUATION FISHER, GENE   SS   ASP 73 08
  FIRST MEN, THE   FAST, HOWARD   NV   FSP 60 02
  DIFFERENT DRUMMER, A   MOORE, RAYLYN   SS   FSP 71 02
  FOUR BRANDS OF IMPOSSIBLE KAGAN, NORMAN   NV   FSP 64 09
  DOCS, THE   LEWIS, RICHARD O. SS   FSP 64 12
  POTTAGE   HENDERSON, ZENNA   NV   FSP 55 09
  TEACHING PRIME   KELLEY, LEO P.   SS   INY 72 03
  PROGENY   DICK, PHILIP K.   SS   IFS 54 11
  EVER-BRANCHING TREE, THE HARRISON, HARRY   SS   SAG 70
  BOOKMOBILE   HARNESS, CHARLES L. SS   IFS 68 11
  NADA   DISCH, THOMAS M.   SS   FSP 64 08
  UP AGAINST THE WALL   THURSTON, ROBERT   SS   AMZ 73 08
  PUBLISH AND PERISH   THOMAS, JOHN B.   SS   IFS 68 06
  GORMAN   FARBER, JERRY   SS   69
  SELECTED BIBLIOGRAPHY MISC. MATERIAL   MS

SCIENCE AGAINST MAN   CHEETHAM, ANTHONY OA AVN 70 12
  INTRODUCTION   CHEETHAM, ANTHONY IN
  LOST CONTINENT, THE   SPINRAD, NORMAN   NV   SAG 70
  IN THE BEGINNING   SILVERBERG, ROBERT· SS   SAG 70
  HUNTER AT HIS EASE, THE ALDISS, BRIAN W.   SS   SAG 70
  MAN'S ESTATE   ABLEMAN, PAUL   SS   SAG 70
  HAROLD WILSON AT THE COSMIC COCKTAIL PARTY (ALSO AS THE
    COSMIC COCKTAIL PARTY) SHAW, BOB   SS   SAG 70
  STATISTICIAN'S DAY   BLISH, JAMES   SS   SAG 70
  INVISIBLE IDIOT, THE   BRUNNER, JOHN   SS   SAG 70
  SMALL MOUTH, BAD TASTE ANTHONY, PIERS   SS   SAG 70
  EVER-BRANCHING TREE, THE HARRISON, HARRY   SS   SAG 70
  SEA WOLVES   MOORCOCK, MICHAEL SS   SAG 70
  PENULTIMATE TRIP, THE TRAVERS, ANDREW   SS   SAG 70

SCIENCE AND SORCERY   FORD, GARRET   AN H FPB 53
  SCANNERS LIVE IN VAIN SMITH, CORDWAINER NA   FBK 50 06
  LITTLE MAN ON THE SUBWAY, THE
                     ASIMOV, ISAAC
             AND MACCREIGH, JAMES SS C FBK 50 06
  WHAT GOES UP   COPPEL, ALFRED   SS   FBK 50 06
  KLEON OF THE GOLDEN SUN REPP, ED EARL   SS   FBK 50 07
  HOW HIGH ON THE LADDER? PAIGE, LEO   SS   FBK 50 07
  FOOTPRINTS   GILBERT, ROBERT E. SS   FBK 51 08
  NAMING OF NAMES, THE (ALSO AS DARK THEY WERE, AND GOLDEN-EYED)
                     BRADBURY, RAY   SS   TWS 49 08
  EYES, THE   HASSE, HENRY   SS   FBK 51 08
  SCARLET LUNES, THE   COBLENTZ, STANTON A. SS   FBK 50 06
  DEMOBILIZATION   COWIE, GEORGE R.   SS   VOX 47
  VOICES FROM THE CLIFF LEAHY, JOHN M.   SS   WRT 25 05
  LOST CHORD, THE   MOSKOWITZ, SAM   SS   NEW 53 AN
  WATCHERS, THE   DEUTSCH, R. H.   SS   NEW 53 AN
  PEACEFUL MARTIAN, THE OLIVER, J. T.   SS   FBK 51 08
  ESCAPE TO YESTERDAY   BURKS, ARTHUR J.   SS   NEW 53 AN

SCIENCE FACT/FICTION   FARRELL/GAGE/&   AN L SFC 74
  SCIENCE FICTION: BEFORE CHRIST AND AFTER 2001
                     BRADBURY, RAY   IN
  GUN WITHOUT A BANG, THE SHECKLEY, ROBERT   NV   GAL 58 06
  CRABS TAKE OVER THE ISLAND DNIEPROV, ANATOLY SS   ISF 68 06
  ALL WATCHED OVER BY MACHINES OF LOVING GRACE
                     BRAUTIGAN, RICHARD PM   68
  EPICAC   VONNEGUT, KURT JR. SS   COL 50 11
  R.U.R.   CAPEK, KAREL   PL   21
  HUMAN FACTOR, THE   ELY, DAVID   SS   SEP 63 11
  THINKING MACHINE, THE ASIMOV, ISAAC   AR   SDG 67 07
  MISBEGOTTEN MISSIONARY (ALSO AS GREEN PATCHES)
                     ASIMOV, ISAAC   SS   GAL 50 11
  ELEGY   BEAUMONT, CHARLES SS   IMG 53 02
  AESTHETICS OF THE MOON ANDERSON, JACK   PM
  CONSTANT READER   BLOCH, ROBERT   SS   USF 53 06
  WHO'S THERE? (ALSO AS THE HAUNTED SPACESUIT)
                     CLARKE, ARTHUR C. SS   NWS 58 11
  WE'LL NEVER CONQUER SPACE CLARKE, ARTHUR C. AR   SDG 60 06
  SACK, THE   MORRISON, WILLIAM SS   ASF 50 09
  MARIANA   LEIBER, FRITZ   SS   FAN 60 02
  I ALWAYS DO WHAT TEDDY SAYS HARRISON, HARRY   SS   EQM 65 06

SCIENCE FACT/FICTION

Title	Author	Type	Mag	Yr	Mo
MAN WHO COULD WORK MIRACLES, THE	WELLS, H. G.	SS	ILN	98	07
ECHOES OF THE MIND	KOESTLER, ARTHUR	AR	ESQ	72	08
RELUCTANT ORCHID, THE	CLARKE, ARTHUR C.	SS	SAT	56	12
FOUNDING FATHER	ASIMOV, ISAAC	SS	GAL	65	10
WOUND, THE	FAST, HOWARD	SS		70	
SOUND MACHINE, THE	DAHL, ROALD	SS	NYM	49	09
LOVE AMONG THE CABBAGES	TOMPKINS, PETER AND BIRD, CHRISTOPHER	AR C	HRP	72	11
PUPPET SHOW	BROWN, FREDRIC	SS	PBY	62	11
RANDOM SAMPLE	CARAVAN, T. P.	SS	FSF	53	04
ON THE WHEEL	KNIGHT, DAMON	SS	NOV	72	02
ORBITER 5 SHOWS HOW EARTH LOOKS FROM THE MOON	SWENSON, MAY	PM	SOU	69	
KING OF THE BEASTS, THE	FARMER, PHILIP JOSE	SS	GAL	64	06
UFO DETECTIVE SOLVES 'EM ALL- WELL ALMOST	HILTS, PHILIP J.	AR	WPS	73	
GOOD PROVIDER, THE	GROSS, MARION	SS	FSF	52	09
SOUND OF THUNDER, A	BRADBURY, RAY	SS	COL	52	06
WHO'S CRIBBING?	LEWIS, JACK	SS	STS	53	01
THIRD LEVEL, THE (COL 50 10)	FINNEY, JACK	SS	FSF	52	10
SPEED	MILES, JOSEPHINE	PM		60	
INN OUTSIDE THE WORLD, THE	HAMILTON, EDMOND	SS	WRT	45	07
ON THE RELATIVITY OF TIME	PAULI, WOLFGANG	AR		49	
RELATIVITY WINS AGAIN	ANONYMOUS	AR	SDG	72	01
MATTER OF OVERTIME, A	ANONYMOUS	AR	TIM	69	03
THERE WILL COME SOFT RAINS	BRADBURY, RAY	SS	COL	50	05
FORGOTTEN ENEMY, THE	CLARKE, ARTHUR C.	SS	NWS	49	05
EARTHMEN BEARING GIFTS	BROWN, FREDRIC	SS	GAL	60	06
IFTH OF OOFTH, THE	TEVIS, WALTER S. JR.	SS	GAL	57	04
ELECTRONIC TAPE FOUND IN A BOTTLE	CABRAL, OLGA	PM			
BRACE YOURSELF FOR ANOTHER ICE AGE	COLLIGAN, DOUGLAS	AR	SDG	73	02
CENSUS TAKERS, THE	POHL, FREDERIK	SS	FSF	56	02
DISAPPEARING ACT	BESTER, ALFRED	SS	STR	53	02
BULLETIN	JACKSON, SHIRLEY	SS	FSF	54	03
AUTOFAC	DICK, PHILIP K.	NV	GAL	55	11
TOWARD THE SPACE AGE	STAFFORD, WILLIAM	PM		70	
SPACESHIP EARTH	FULLER, BUCKMINSTER	AR		69	
BIOGRAPHIES OF AUTHORS	MISC. MATERIAL	MS			
SCIENCE-FICTION AWARDS	MISC. MATERIAL	MS			
PRONUNCIATION KEY	MISC. MATERIAL	MS			
DISCUSSION QUESTIONS	MISC. MATERIAL	MS			
INDEX OF AUTHORS AND TITLES	MISC. MATERIAL	MS			

SCIENCE FICTION — BRODKIN & PEARSON — AN L MCD 73

Title	Author	Type	Mag	Yr	Mo
PHOTOGRAPHIC EVIDENCE	GENOVES, JUAN	IL			
OF MISSING PERSONS	FINNEY, JACK	SS	GHK	55	03
PHASES OF THE NIGHT, THE	ERNST, MAX	IL			
UP AND DOWN	ESCHER, M. C.	IL			
AND HE BUILT A CROOKED HOUSE	HEINLEIN, ROBERT A.	SS	ASF	41	02
EQUIVOCATION	CUNNINGHAM, BEN	IL			
PUDDLE	ESCHER, M. C.	IL			
SOUND OF THUNDER, A	BRADBURY, RAY	SS	COL	52	06
BUTTERFLIES	ESCHER, M. C.	IL			
HEAD	BELLING, RUDOLPH	IL			
AND IT WILL SERVE US RIGHT	ASIMOV, ISAAC	AR	PSY	69	04
PIEGE	TELEMAQUE, HERVE	IL			
LITTERBUG	MORPHETT, TONY	NV	FSF	69	07
VILLAGE DANCE MASK FROM CEYLON	MISC. MATERIAL	IL			
MAMA, PAPA IS WOUNDED!	TANGUY, YVES	IL			
ELECTRONIC CONCERT	DEUTSCH, BABETTE	PM		63	
TWO DANCERS	HANIWA	IL			
HEMEAC	VON WALD, E. G.	SS	GAL	68	08
MAN FALLING FORWARD	GENOVES, JUAN	IL			
WINNER, THE	WESTLAKE, DONALD E.	SS	NOV	70	01
MECHANICAL HEAD	HAUSMANN, RAOUL	IL			
HARRISON BERGERON	VONNEGUT, KURT JR.	SS	FSF	61	10
PERUVIAN MUMMY MASK	MISC. MATERIAL	IL			
MALE FIGURE	GROSSMAN, NANCY	IL			
YELLOW PILL, THE	PHILLIPS, ROG	SS	ASF	58	10
ON THE THRESHOLD OF FREEDOM	MAGRITTE, RENE	IL			
VICTORY PARADE	SLESAR, HENRY	SS	PBY	57	04
UNTITLED BOX NO. 3	SAMARIS, LUCAS	IL			
CHIEF	SLESAR, HENRY	SS	PBY	60	06
WHOLE CITY, THE	ERNST, MAX	IL			
BY THE WATERS OF BABYLON (THE PLACE OF THE GODS)	BENET, STEPHEN V.	SS	SEP	37	07
CASTLE OF THE PYRENEES, THE	MAGRITTE, RENE	IL			
SENTINEL, THE (SENTINEL OF ETERNITY)	CLARKE, ARTHUR C.	SS	TSF	51	SP
SEA, THE	ERNST, MAX	IL			
SUMMERTIME ON ICARUS (THE HOTTEST PIECE OF REAL ESTATE IN THE SOLAR SYSTEM)	CLARKE, ARTHUR C.	SS	VOG	60	06
EYEBALL OF THE SUN	CHILDS, BERNARD	IL			
SPACE MAN	DEUTSCH, BABETTE	PM		69	
I AM A	MARSHALL, LENORE	PM		69	
PERSON THROWING A STONE AT A BIRD	MIRO, JOAN	IL			
OFF COURSE	MORGAN, EDWIN	PM		67	
ORBITER 5 SHOWS HOW EARTH LOOKS FROM THE MOON	SWENSON, MAY	PM	SOU	69	
FLIGHT OF APOLLO, THE	KUNITZ, STANLEY	PM		69	
VOYAGE TO THE MOON	DICKEY, WILLIAM	PM	TXQ	64	03
AFTERWARDS	LUCIE-SMITH, EDWARD	PM		64	
PROJECTION, A	WHITTEMORE, REED	PM		67	
WE'LL ALL BE SPACEMEN BEFORE WE DIE	EVANS, MIKE	PM	NWS	68	10
MOONSHOT SONNET	SOLT, MARY ELLEN	IL			
DEAD CHILD, THE	STANCIC, MILJENKO	IL			
ENCHANTED VILLAGE (ALSO AS THE SANDS OF MARS)	VAN VOGT, A. E.	SS	OWS	50	07
LARGE PAINTING WHICH IS A LANDSCAPE, A	TANGUY, YVES	IL			

SCIENCE FICTION ADVENTURES IN MUTATION

Title	Author	Type	Mag	Yr	Mo
ALIENS, THE	PAALEN, WOLFGANG	IL			
PRISONERS OF PARADISE	REDD, DAVID	SS	NWS	66	10
A.D. 2267	NIMS, JOHN FREDERICK	PM		67	
EARTH IS A MAN, THE	ECHAURREN, ROBERTO	IL			
GHOST CRABS	HUGHES, TED	PM		66	
MELANCHOLY AND MYSTERY OF A STREET, THE	DE CHIRICO, GIORGIO	IL			
ZERO HOUR	BRADBURY, RAY	SS	PLS	47	FL
FOOL FROM THE DEPTHS	KLEE, PAUL	IL			
SUN AND FOREST	ERNST, MAX	IL			
GREEN PATCHES (MISBEGOTTEN MISSIONARY)	ASIMOV, ISAAC	SS	GAL	50	11
MUSHROOMS	PLATH, SYLVIA	PM		60	
MUSHROOMS	EVANS, MIKE	PM		69	
EUROPE AFTER THE RAIN	ERNST, MAX	IL			

SCIENCE FICTION — BURTON, S. H. — AN LNG 67

Title	Author	Type	Mag	Yr	Mo
INTRODUCTION	BURTON, S. H.	IN			
REQUIEM	HEINLEIN, ROBERT A.	SS	ASF	40	01
PRESENT FROM JOE, A	RUSSELL, ERIC FRANK	SS	ASF	49	02
DARK THEY WERE, AND GOLDEN-EYED (THE NAMING OF NAMES)	BRADBURY, RAY	SS	TWS	49	08
PROTECTED SPECIES	FYFE, H. B.	SS	ASF	51	03
NEW WINE, THE	CHRISTOPHER, JOHN	SS	FSM	54	SU
NIGHTFALL	ASIMOV, ISAAC	NV	ASF	41	09
WINDOWS OF HEAVEN, THE (TWO BY TWO)	BRUNNER, JOHN	SS	NWS	56	05
YOUTH	ASIMOV, ISAAC	NV	SSF	52	05
STAR, THE	CLARKE, ARTHUR C.	SS	INF	55	11
GLOSSARY	MISC. MATERIAL	MS			
FOR FURTHER READING	MISC. MATERIAL	MS			

SCIENCE FICTION ADVENTURES FROM WAY OUT — ELWOOD, ROGER — OA L WHT 74

Title	Author	Type	Mag	Yr	Mo
INTRODUCTION	ELWOOD, ROGER	IN			
LIGHTS OF MARS, THE	JONES, RAYMOND F.	NV			
FACE OF THE ENEMY, THE	KIMBERLY, GAIL	NV			
BUCK AND THE GENTS FROM SPACE	REYNOLDS, MACK	NV			
MATTER OF CHOICE, A	LYTLE, B. J.	SS			
TEDDI	NORTON, ANDRE	NV			
IT'S SO WONDERFUL HERE	PRONZINI, BILL	SS			
LITTLE MONSTER, THE	ANDERSON, POUL	NV			
TRUTH OF IT, THE	MALZBERG, BARRY N.	SS			

SCIENCE FICTION ADVENTURES IN DIMENSION — CONKLIN, GROFF — AN H VPR 53
IN ENGLAND AS "ADVENTURES IN DIMENSION" (13 OF 23)

Title	Author	Type	Mag	Yr	Mo
INTRODUCTION	CONKLIN, GROFF	IN			
YESTERDAY WAS MONDAY	STURGEON, THEODORE	SS	UNK	41	06
AMBITION	BADE, WILLIAM L.	NV	GAL	51	10
MIDDLE OF THE WEEK AFTER NEXT, THE	LEINSTER, MURRAY	SS	TWS	52	08
AND IT COMES OUT HERE	DEL REY, LESTER	SS	GAL	51	02
CASTAWAY	CHANDLER, A. BERTRAM	SS	WRT	47	11
GOOD PROVIDER, THE	GROSS, MARION	SS	FSF	52	09
REVERSE PHYLOGENY	LONG, AMELIA R.	SS	ASF	37	06
OTHER TRACKS	SELL, WILLIAM	NV	ASF	38	10
WHAT SO PROUDLY WE HAIL...	KEENE, DAY	SS	IMG	50	12
NIGHT MEETING	BRADBURY, RAY	SS	NEW	51	AC
PERFECT MURDER	GOLD, H. L.	SS	TWS	40	03
FLIGHT THAT FAILED, THE	HULL, E. MAYNE	SS	ASF	42	12
ENDOWMENT POLICY	PADGETT, LEWIS	SS	ASF	43	08
PETE CAN FIX IT	JONES, RAYMOND F.	SS	ASF	47	02
MIST, THE	CARTUR, PETER	SS	FSF	52	09
GOSTAK AND THE DOSHES, THE	BREUER, MILES J. MD.	SS	AMZ	30	03
WHAT IF	ASIMOV, ISAAC	SS	FAN	52	SU
RING AROUND THE REDHEAD	MACDONALD, JOHN D.	SS	STS	48	11
TIGER BY THE TAIL	NOURSE, ALAN E.	SS	GAL	51	11
WAY OF ESCAPE	TEMPLE, WILLIAM F.	SS	TWS	48	06
SUBURBAN FRONTIERS	YOUNG, ROBERT F.	SS	ASF	50	02
BUSINESS OF KILLING	LEIBER, FRITZ	SS	ASF	44	09
TO FOLLOW KNOWLEDGE	LONG, FRANK BELKNAP	SS	ASF	42	12

SCIENCE FICTION ADVENTURES IN DIMENSION (12 OF 23) — CONKLIN, GROFF — AN BKM 65 03

Title	Author	Type	Mag	Yr	Mo
YESTERDAY WAS MONDAY	STURGEON, THEODORE	SS	UNK	41	06
AMBITION	BADE, WILLIAM L.	NV	GAL	51	10
MIDDLE OF THE WEEK AFTER NEXT, THE	LEINSTER, MURRAY	SS	TWS	52	08
AND IT COMES OUT HERE	DEL REY, LESTER	SS	GAL	51	02
OTHER TRACKS	SELL, WILLIAM	NV	ASF	38	10
NIGHT MEETING	BRADBURY, RAY	SS	NEW	51	AC
FLIGHT THAT FAILED, THE	HULL, E. MAYNE	SS	ASF	42	12
ENDOWMENT POLICY	PADGETT, LEWIS	SS	ASF	43	08
MIST, THE	CARTUR, PETER	SS	FSF	52	09
WHAT IF	ASIMOV, ISAAC	SS	FAN	52	SU
TIGER BY THE TAIL	NOURSE, ALAN E.	SS	GAL	51	11
BUSINESS OF KILLING	LEIBER, FRITZ	SS	ASF	44	09

SCIENCE FICTION ADVENTURES IN MUTATION — CONKLIN, GROFF — AN H VPR 55

Title	Author	Type	Mag	Yr	Mo
INTRODUCTION	CONKLIN, GROFF	IN			
CHAIN OF COMMAND	ARR, STEPHEN	SS	GAL	54	05
BATTLE OF THE UNBORN (ALSO AS STRUGGLE IN THE WOMB)	BLISH, JAMES	SS	FUT	50	05
HUNGRY GUINEA PIG, THE	BREUER, MILES J. MD.	SS	AMZ	30	01
KEEP OUT	BROWN, FREDRIC	SS	AMZ	54	03
SMALL WORLD OF M-75, THE	CLINTON, ED M. JR.	SS	IFS	54	07
LIMITING FACTOR	COGSWELL, THEODORE R	SS	GAL	54	04
LYSENKO MAZE, THE	GRINNELL, DAVID	SS	FSF	54	07
PATIENT, THE	HULL, E. MAYNE	SS	UNK	43	10
COLD WAR	KUTTNER, HENRY	SS	TWS	49	10
SKAG WITH THE QUEER HEAD	LEINSTER, MURRAY	SS	MAR	51	08
VEILED ISLAND	MCDOWELL, EMMETT	NV	ASF	46	01

SCIENCE FICTION ADVENTURES IN MUTATION

```
EXPERIMENTAL STATION (THE FIRST)
                    NEVILLE, KRIS        SS   SSS 50 09
FAMILY RESEMBLANCE  NOURSE, ALAN E.      SS   ASF 53 04
AND THOU BESIDE ME  REYNOLDS, MACK       SS   FSF 54 04
THIS ONE'S ON ME    RUSSELL, ERIC FRANK  SS   NEB 53 FL
AGE OF PROPHECY, THE  ST. CLAIR, MARGARET  NA   FUT 51 03
LOVE OF HEAVEN, THE   STURGEON, THEODORE  SS   ASF 48 11
IMPOSSIBLE VOYAGE HOME, THE  WALLACE, F. L.  NV  GAL 54 08
CONSPIRATORS, THE   WHITE, JAMES         NV   NWS 54 06
BETTER CHOICE, THE  WRIGHT, S. FOWLER    SS   NEW 55 AN
BIBLIOGRAPHY OF MUTATION STORIES
                    MISC. MATERIAL       MS
```

SCIENCE FICTION ADVENTURES IN MUTATION (14 OF 20)

```
                    CONKLIN, GROFF       AN   BKM 65 06
CHAIN OF COMMAND    ARR, STEPHEN         SS   GAL 54 05
BATTLE OF THE UNBORN (ALSO AS STRUGGLE IN THE WOMB)
                    BLISH, JAMES         SS   FUT 50 05
KEEP OUT            BROWN, FREDRIC       SS   AMZ 54 03
LIMITING FACTOR     COGSWELL, THEODORE R SS   GAL 54 04
LYSENKO MAZE, THE   GRINNELL, DAVID      SS   FSF 54 07
PATIENT, THE        HULL, E. MAYNE       SS   UNK 43 10
COLD WAR            KUTTNER, HENRY       SS   TWS 49 10
SKAG WITH THE QUEER HEAD  LEINSTER, MURRAY  SS  MAR 51 08
FAMILY RESEMBLANCE  NOURSE, ALAN E.      SS   ASF 53 04
AND THOU BESIDE ME  REYNOLDS, MACK       SS   FSF 54 04
THIS ONE'S ON ME    RUSSELL, ERIC FRANK  SS   NEB 53 FL
LOVE OF HEAVEN, THE  STURGEON, THEODORE  SS   ASF 48 11
CONSPIRATORS, THE   WHITE, JAMES         NV   NWS 54 06
BETTER CHOICE, THE  WRIGHT, S. FOWLER    SS   NEW 55 AN
```

SCIENCE FICTION AND READER'S GUIDE

```
                    BARROWS, MARJORIE    AN H SPN 54
    VOLUME 16 OF "THE CHILDREN'S HOUR" SET
WHAT TIME IS IT?    ELAM, RICHARD M. JR. NV
ADVENTURES ON MARS  ELAM, RICHARD M. JR. SS   STP 52 12
MARS & MISS PICKERELL (FROM MISS P. GOES TO MARS)
                    MACGREGOR, ELLEN     EX        51
STAR DUCKS, THE     BROWN, BILL          SS   FSF 50 FL
LANCELOT BIGGS ON THE SATURN (FROM L.B.: SPACEMAN)
                    BOND, NELSON S.      EX   DBL 50
TRUTH ABOUT PYECRAFT, THE  WELLS, H. G.  SS   SND 03 04
BLACK PITS OF LUNA, THE  HEINLEIN, ROBERT A.  SS  SEP 48 01
IS THERE LIFE ON THE MOON?  WILKINS, PERCY H.  AR  CYE 53 01
TRAIL TO THE STARS  LEYSON, CAPT. BURR W SS   BLF 50 02
```

SCIENCE FICTION ARGOSY, A   KNIGHT, DAMON   AN H SAS 72

```
INTRODUCTION        KNIGHT, DAMON        IN
GREEN THOUGHTS      COLLIER, JOHN        SS        31
RED QUEEN'S RACE, THE  ASIMOV, ISAAC     NV   ASF 49 01
CURE, THE           KUTTNER, HENRY
                    AND MOORE, C. L.     SS C ASF 46 05
CONSIDER HER WAYS   WYNDHAM, JOHN        NV        56
ORNAMENT TO HIS PROFESSION, AN
                    HARNESS, CHARLES L.  NV   ASF 66 02
THIRD LEVEL, THE (COL 50 10) FINNEY, JACK  SS  FSF 52 10
ONE ORDINARY DAY, WITH PEANUTS
                    JACKSON, SHIRLEY     SS   FSF 55 01
BERNIE THE FAUST    TENN, WILLIAM        NV   PBY 63 11
LIGHT OF OTHER DAYS SHAW, BOB            SS   ASF 66 08
GAME OF RAT AND DRAGON, THE  SMITH, CORDWAINER  NV  GAL 55 10
BECALMED IN HELL    NIVEN, LARRY         SS   FSF 65 07
APOLOGY TO INKY     GREEN, ROBERT M. JR. NV   FSF 66 01
DEMOLISHED MAN, THE BESTER, ALFRED       NO   GAL 52 01
DAY MILLION         POHL, FREDERIK       SS   ROG 66 02
MANNA               PHILLIPS, PETER      NV   ASF 49 02
CAN YOU FEEL ANYTHING WHEN I DO THIS?
                    SHECKLEY, ROBERT     SS   PBY 69 08
SOMERSET DREAMS     WILHELM, KATE        NV   ORB 69 05
HE WALKED AROUND THE HORSES  PIPER, H. BEAM  NV  ASF 48 04
RUMP-TITTY-TITTY-TUM-TAH-TEE  LEIBER, FRITZ  SS  FSF 58 05
SEA WRACK           JESBY, EDWARD        NV   FSF 64 05
MAN IN HIS TIME     ALDISS, BRIAN W.     SS   SCF 65 04
FOUR BRANDS OF IMPOSSIBLE  KAGAN, NORMAN  NV   FSF 64 09
BUILT UP LOGICALLY (THE UNIVERSAL TANCEA, RET 49 WI)
                    SCHOENFELD, HOWARD   SS   FSF 55 FL
JUDGMENT DAY        DE CAMP, L. SPRAGUE  SS   ASF 55 08
JOURNEYS END        ANDERSON, POUL       SS   FSF 57 02
MORE THAN HUMAN     STURGEON, THEODORE   NO   FSY 52
```

SCIENCE FICTION BESTIARY, THE

```
                    SILVERBERG, ROBERT   AN H NEL 71
INTRODUCTION        SILVERBERG, ROBERT   IN
HURKLE IS A HAPPY BEAST, THE  STURGEON, THEODORE  SS  FSF 49 FL
GRANDPA             SCHMITZ, JAMES H.    SS   ASF 55 02
BLUE GIRAFFE, THE   DE CAMP, L. SPRAGUE  NV   ASF 39 08
PRESERVING MACHINE, THE  DICK, PHILIP K.  SS  FSF 53 06
MARTIAN ODYSSEY, A  WEINBAUM, STANLEY G. NV   WQS 34 07
SHERIFF OF CANYON GULCH, THE (HEROES ARE MADE)
                    ANDERSON, POUL
                    AND DICKSON, GORDON R.  NV C OWS 51 05
DROP DEAD           SIMAK, CLIFFORD D.   NV   GAL 56 07
GNURRS COME FROM THE VOODVORK OUT, THE
                    BRETNOR, REGINALD    SS   FSF 50 WS
COLLECTING TEAM     SILVERBERG, ROBERT   SS   AUT 57 06
```

SCIENCE FICTION BY GASLIGHT MOSKOWITZ, SAM   AN H WOR 68

```
    A HISTORY AND ANTHOLOGY OF SCIENCE FICTION
    IN THE POPULAR MAGAZINES 1891 TO 1911
PHOTOGRAPHY         HAYCOCK, CHRISTINE   IL
PREFACE             MOSKOWITZ, SAM       IN
INTRODUCTION: A HISTORY OF SCIENCE FICTION IN THE POPULAR
    MAGAZINES, 1891-1911  MOSKOWITZ, SAM  IN
THAMES VALLEY CATASTROPHY, THE
                    ALLEN, GRANT         SS   SND 97 12
DOOM OF LONDON, THE BARR, ROBERT         SS   IDL 92 11
```

SCIENCE FICTION HALL OF FAME VOLUME

```
CORNER IN LIGHTNING, A  GRIFFITH, GEORGE  SS   PRS 98 0
TILTING ISLAND, THE VIVIAN, THOMAS J.
                    AND BENNETT, G. J.   SS C EVB 09 09
FINIS               POLLOCK, FRANK L.    SS   ARG 06 06
EXPRESS OF THE FUTURE, AN  VERNE, JULES  SS   SND 95 0
RAY OF DISPLACEMENT, THE  SPOFFORD, HARRIET P. SS MPN 03 10
CONGEALING THE ICE TRUST  BISHOP, H. G.  SS   NBM 07 1
LORD BEDEN'S MOTOR  HARRIS-BURLAND, J.B. SS   SND 01 12
DEATH-TRAP, THE     DAULTON, GEORGE      SS   PRS 08 0
AIR SERPENT, THE    PAGE, WILL A.        SS   RBM 11 04
MONSTER OF LAKE LAMETRIE, THE
                    CURTIS, WARDON ALLEN SS   PRS 99 09
VOICE IN THE NIGHT, THE  HODGSON, WILLIAM H. SS BBM 07 1
LAND IRONCLADS, THE WELLS, H. G.         NV   SND 03 12
DAM, THE            JOHNSON, HUGH S.     SS   EBM 11 04
SUBMARINED          WOOD, WALTER         SS   PRS 05 09
PURPLE TERROR, THE  WHITE, FRED M.       SS   SND 99 09
PROFESSOR JONKIN'S CANNIBAL PLANT
                    GARIS, HOWARD R.     SS   ARG 05 08
EXPERIMENT IN GYRO-HATS, AN  BUTLER, ELLIS PARKER  SS  HAM 10 0
HYBRID HYPERBOREAN ANT, THE  MCCARDELL, ROY L.  SS  HAM 10 12
WHERE THE AIR QUIVERED  MEADE, L. T.
                    AND EUSTACE, ROBERT  SS C SND 98 12
IN RE STATE VS. FORBES  EARLE, WARREN    SS   BLC 07 0
OLD DOCTOR RUTHERFORD  HANNIGAN, D. F.   SS   LUD 91 09
ITSELF              BACON, EDGAR MAYHEW  SS   BLC 07 05
CITIZEN 504         PALMER, CHARLES H.   SS   ARG 96 12
MANSION OF FORGETFULNESS, THE
                    LEMON, DON MARK      SS   BLC 07 04
```

SCIENCE FICTION DISCOVERIES POHL, C. & F.   OA   BAN 76 08

```
INTRODUCTION (A DIALOGUE)  POHL, CAROL
                    AND POHL, FREDERIK   IN C
STARLADY            MARTIN, GEORGE R. R. NV
NEVER-ENDING WESTERN MOVIE, THE
                    SHECKLEY, ROBERT     SS
AGE OF LIBRA, THE   EDELSTEIN, SCOTT     SS
TO MARK THE YEAR ON AZLAROC  SABERHAGEN, FRED  SS
OCCURRENCE AT THE OWL CREEK REST HOME, AN
                    COX, ARTHUR JEAN     NV
FORCE THAT THROUGH THE CIRCUIT DRIVES THE CURRENT, THE
                    ZELAZNY, ROGER       SS
DEATHRIGHTS DEFERRED  PISERCHIA, DORIS   SS
ERROR HURLED        ROSMOND, BABETTE     NO
```

SCIENCE FICTION EMPHASIS NO. 1

```
                    GERROLD, DAVID       OA   BAL 74 05
INTRODUCTION        GERROLD, DAVID       IN
WILLOWISP           PUMILIA, JOSEPH F.   SS   SFE 74 0
BONUS BABY          GOTSCHALK, FELIX C.  SS   SFE 74 0
TELEPATHOS          CAIN, RONALD         NV   SFE 74 0
IN THE CROWDED PART OF HEAVEN
                    BORSKI, ROBERT       SS   SFE 74 0
RUBAIYAT OF AMBROSE BAGLEY, THE
                    MACFARLANE, WALLACE  SS   SFE 74 0
GATO-O              PICARD, DON          NV   SFE 74 0
SHARDS OF DIVINITY  TOMAN, MICHAEL D.    SS   SFE 74 0
ON THE STREET OF SERPENTS,OR THE ASSASSINATION OF CHAIRMAN MAO
    AS EFFECTED BY THE AUTHOR  BISHOP, MICHAEL  NV  SFE 74 0
```

SCIENCE FICTION FOR PEOPLE WHO HATE SCIENCE FICTION

```
                    CARR, TERRY          AN H DBL 66
INTRODUCTION        CARR, TERRY          IN
STAR, THE           CLARKE, ARTHUR C.    SS   INF 55 1
SOUND OF THUNDER, A BRADBURY, RAY        SS   COL 52 0
YEAR OF THE JACKPOT, THE  HEINLEIN, ROBERT A.  NV  GAL 52 0
MAN WITH ENGLISH, THE  GOLD, H. L.       SS   STR 53 0
IN HIDING           SHIRAS, WILMAR H.    NV   ASF 48 1
NOT WITH A BANG     KNIGHT, DAMON        SS   FSF 50 WS
LOVE CALLED THIS THING  DAVIDSON, AVRAM
                    AND GOFORTH, LAURA   SS C GAL 59 0
WEAPON, THE         BROWN, FREDRIC       SS   ASF 51 0
WHAT'S IT LIKE OUT THERE?  HAMILTON, EDMOND  NV  TWS 52 1
```

SCIENCE FICTION GALAXY, THE CONKLIN, GROFF   AN   PMA 50

```
INTRODUCTION        CONKLIN, GROFF       IN
MACHINE STOPS, THE  FORSTER, E. M.       NV        28
AS EASY AS A. B. C. KIPLING, RUDYARD     NV   LOM 12 04
DERELICT, THE (1914)  HODGSON, WILLIAM H.  SS  FFM 43 12
FIRES WITHIN, THE   CLARKE, ARTHUR C.    SS   FSB 47 08
CHILD IS CRYING, A  MACDONALD, JOHN D.   SS   TWS 48 1
QUIS CUSTODIET...   ST. CLAIR, MARGARET  SS   STS 48 0
LIFE-WORK OF PROFESSOR MUNTZ, THE
                    LEINSTER, MURRAY     SS   TWS 49 0
APPENDIX AND THE SPECTACLES, THE
                    BREUER, MILES J. MD. SS   AMZ 28 1
DEATH FROM THE STARS  HILLIARD, A. ROWLEY  NV  WOS 31 1
HURKLE IS A HAPPY BEAST, THE  STURGEON, THEODORE  SS  FSF 49 F
KING OF THE GRAY SPACES (ALSO AS R IS FOR ROCKET)
                    BRADBURY, RAY        SS   FFM 43 1
LIVING GALAXY, THE  MANNING, LAURENCE    SS   WOS 34 09
```

SCIENCE FICTION HALL OF FAME VOLUME 1

```
                    SILVERBERG, ROBERT   AN H DBL 70
INTRODUCTION        SILVERBERG, ROBERT   IN
MARTIAN ODYSSEY, A  WEINBAUM, STANLEY G. NV   WOS 34 07
TWILIGHT            CAMPBELL, JOHN W. JR SS   ASF 34 11
HELEN O'LOY         DEL REY, LESTER      SS   ASF 38 1
ROADS MUST ROLL, THE  HEINLEIN, ROBERT A.  NV  ASF 40 0
MICROCOSMIC GOD     STURGEON, THEODORE   NV   ASF 41 0
NIGHTFALL           ASIMOV, ISAAC        NV   ASF 41 0
WEAPON SHOP, THE    VAN VOGT, A. E.      NV   ASF 42 1
MIMSY WERE THE BOROGOVES  PADGETT, LEWIS  NV  ASF 43 0
HUDDLING PLACE      SIMAK, CLIFFORD D.   SS   ASF 44 0
ARENA               BROWN, FREDRIC       NV   ASF 44 0
FIRST CONTACT       LEINSTER, MURRAY     NV   ASF 45 05
```

SCIENCE FICTION HALL OF FAME VOLUME 1

THAT ONLY A MOTHER	MERRIL, JUDITH	SS	ASF 48 06
SCANNERS LIVE IN VAIN	SMITH, CORDWAINER	NA	FBK 50 06
MARS IS HEAVEN!	BRADBURY, RAY	SS	PLS 48 FL
LITTLE BLACK BAG, THE	KORNBLUTH, C. M.	NV	ASF 50 07
BORN OF MAN AND WOMAN	MATHESON, RICHARD	SS	FSF 50 SU
COMING ATTRACTION	LEIBER, FRITZ	SS	GAL 50 11
QUEST FOR SAINT AQUIN, THE	BOUCHER, ANTHONY	SS	NTS 51
SURFACE TENSION	BLISH, JAMES	NA	GAL 52 08
NINE BILLION NAMES OF GOD, THE			
	CLARKE, ARTHUR C.	SS	STR 53 01
IT'S A GOOD LIFE	BIXBY, JEROME	SS	STR 53 02
COLD EQUATIONS, THE	GODWIN, TOM	NV	ASF 54 08
FONDLY FAHRENHEIT	BESTER, ALFRED	SS	FSF 54 08
COUNTRY OF THE KIND, THE	KNIGHT, DAMON	SS	FSF 56 02
ROSE FOR ECCLESIASTES, A	ZELAZNY, ROGER	NV	FSF 63 11

SCIENCE FICTION HALL OF FAME VOLUME 2A

	BOVA, BEN	AN H DBL 73	
INTRODUCTION	BOVA, BEN	IN	
CALL ME JOE	ANDERSON, POUL	NV	ASF 57 04
WHO GOES THERE?	CAMPBELL, JOHN W. JR	NV	ASF 38 08
NERVES	DEL REY, LESTER	NV	ASF 42 09
UNIVERSE	HEINLEIN, ROBERT A.	NV	ASF 41 05
MARCHING MORONS, THE	KORNBLUTH, C. M.	NV	GAL 51 04
VINTAGE SEASON	KUTTNER, HENRY		
	AND MOORE, C. L.	NV C ASF 46 09	
AND THEN THERE WERE NONE	RUSSELL, ERIC FRANK	NV	ASF 51 06
BALLAD OF LOST C'MELL, THE	SMITH, CORDWAINER	NV	GAL 62 10
BABY IS THREE	STURGEON, THEODORE	NA	GAL 52 10
TIME MACHINE, THE	WELLS, H. G.	NA	NRV 95 01
WITH FOLDED HANDS...	WILLIAMSON, JACK	NV	ASF 47 07

SCIENCE FICTION HALL OF FAME VOLUME 2B

	BOVA, BEN	AN H DBL 73	
INTRODUCTION	BOVA, BEN	IN	
MARTIAN WAY, THE	ASIMOV, ISAAC	NA	GAL 52 11
EARTHMAN, COME HOME	BLISH, JAMES	NV	ASF 53 11
ROGUE MOON	BUDRYS, ALGIS	SN	FSF 60 12
SPECTER GENERAL, THE	COGSWELL, THEODORE R	NV	ASF 52 06
MACHINE STOPS, THE	FORSTER, E. M.	NV	28
MIDAS PLAGUE, THE	POHL, FREDERIK	NA	GAL 54 04
WITCHES OF KARRES, THE	SCHMITZ, JAMES H.	NV	ASF 49 12
E FOR EFFORT	SHERRED, T. L.	NV	ASF 47 05
IN HIDING	SHIRAS, WILMAR H.	NV	ASF 48 11
BIG FRONT YARD, THE	SIMAK, CLIFFORD D.	NV	ASF 58 10
MOON MOTH, THE	VANCE, JACK	NA	GAL 61 08

SCIENCE FICTION HORIZONS NO. 1

	BOARDMAN, TOM JR.	AN H DOB 68	
FOREWORD	BOARDMAN, TOM JR.	IN	
SUBVERSIVE	REYNOLDS, MACK	SS	ASF 62 12
GAME FOR MOTEL ROOM	LEIBER, FRITZ	SS	FSF 63 03
COMIC INFERNO	ALDISS, BRIAN W.	NA	GAL 63 02
AFTER A FEW WORDS	MCKETTRIG, SEATON	SS	ASF 62 10
PERIOD OF GESTATION	KEYES, THOM	SS	SCF 64 10
MY SON, THE PHYSICIST	ASIMOV, ISAAC	SS	SAM 62 02
SHIPWRECKED HOTEL, THE	BLISH, JAMES		
	AND KNIGHT, NORMAN L.	NV C GAL 65 08	
NOT ME, NOT AMOS CABOT!	HARRISON, HARRY	SS	SCF 65 01
TRANSFINITE CHOICE, THE	MASSON, DAVID I.	SS	NWS 66 08
BIG PAT BOOM, THE	KNIGHT, DAMON	SS	GAL 63 12

SCIENCE FICTION INVENTIONS   KNIGHT, DAMON   AN   LAN 67

INTRODUCTION	KNIGHT, DAMON	IN	
NO, NO, NOT ROGOV!	SMITH, CORDWAINER	SS	IFS 59 02
ROCK DIVER	HARRISON, HARRY	SS	WBY 51 02
PRIVATE EYE	KUTTNER, HENRY		
	AND MOORE, C. L.	NV C ASF 49 01	
SNOWBALL EFFECT, THE	MACLEAN, KATHERINE	SS	GAL 52 09
CHROMIUM HELMET, THE	STURGEON, THEODORE	NV	ASF 46 06
EMPLOYMENT (AS LYMAN R. LYON)			
	DE CAMP, L. SPRAGUE	SS	ASF 39 05
DREAMING IS A PRIVATE THING	ASIMOV, ISAAC	SS	FSF 55 12
INVARIANT	PIERCE, JOHN R.	SS	ASF 44 04
HUNTING MACHINE, THE	EMSHWILLER, CAROL	SS	SFS 57 05
COMMITTEE OF THE WHOLE	HERBERT, FRANK	NV	GAL 65 04

SCIENCE FICTION NOVELLAS   HARRISON & MCNELLY   AN L SCB 75

THINGS TO COME	HARRISON, HARRY		
	AND MCNELLY, WILLIS E.	IN C	
BLACK DESTROYER	VAN VOGT, A. E.	NV	ASF 39 07
CALL ME JOE	ANDERSON, POUL	NV	ASF 57 04
FAR LOOK, THE	THOMAS, THEODORE L.	NV	ASF 56 08
"EAST WIND, WEST WIND"	ROBINSON, FRANK M.	NV	NOV 72 02
STREETS OF ASHKELON, THE (ALSO AS AN ALIEN AGONY)			
	HARRISON, HARRY	SS	NWS 62 09
OMNILINGUAL	PIPER, H. BEAM	NV	ASF 57 02
ASIAN SHORE, THE	DISCH, THOMAS M.	NV	ORB 70 06
SUGGESTIONS FOR FURTHER READING			
	MISC. MATERIAL	MS	
CRITICAL WORKS ABOUT SCIENCE FICTION			
	MISC. MATERIAL	MS	

SCIENCE FICTION ODDITIES   CONKLIN, GROFF   AN   BKM 66 11

INTRODUCTION	CONKLIN, GROFF	IN	
PEOPLE SOUP	ARKIN, ALAN	SS	GAL 58 11
WHAT IS THIS THING CALLED LOVE? (THE PLAYBOY AND THE SLIME GOD)			
	ASIMOV, ISAAC	SS	AMZ 61 03
CALLAHAN AND THE WHEELIES	BARR, STEPHEN	NV	FSF 60 08
MRS. POPPLEDORE'S ID	BRETNOR, REGINALD	SS	FSF 52 02
TEETH OF DESPAIR, THE	DAVIDSON, AVRAM		
	AND KLEIN, SIDNEY	SS C FSF 61 05	
GALACTIC CALABASH, THE	EDMONDSON, G. C.	SS	FSF 60 01
SPACE-CRIME CONTINUUM	ELLIS, H. F.	SS	FSF 54 09
CHESSPLAYERS, THE	HARNESS, CHARLES L.	SS	FSF 53 10

SCIENCE FICTION ROLL OF HONOR, THE

WHAT'S THE NAME OF THAT TOWN?			
	LAFFERTY, R. A.	SS	GAL 64 10
RUMP-TITTY-TITTY-TUM-TAH-TEE	LEIBER, FRITZ	SS	FSF 58 05
RUNDOWN	LORY, ROBERT	SS	IFS 63 05
TROUBLE WITH H.A.R.R.I., THE	MACKIN, EDWARD	SS	AUT 57 02
WATER EATER, THE	MARKS, WINSTON K.	SS	GAL 53 06
PRIDE OF CARROTS, A	NATHAN, ROBERT	NV	FSF 59 12
TERRA-VENUSIAN WAR OF 1979, THE			
	NEYROUD, GERALD E.	SS	FSF 59 12
COFFIN CURE, THE	NOURSE, ALAN E.	SS	GAL 57 04
ON CAMERA	NOVOTNY, JOHN	SS	FSF 56 04
SEE NO EVIL	PIERCE, JOHN R.	SS	NEW 66 AN
PUNCH	POHL, FREDERIK	SS	PBY 62 06

SCIENCE FICTION OF FRANK R. STOCKTON, THE

	STOCKTON, FRANK R.	AC H GRG 76 06	
INTRODUCTION	POWERS, RICHARD GID	IN	
WATER-DEVIL, THE (1874)	STOCKTON, FRANK R.	NV	SCR 74 10
TALE OF NEGATIVE GRAVITY, A	STOCKTON, FRANK R.	NV	CNY 84 11
AMOS KILBRIGHT: HIS ADSCITITIOUS EXPERIENCES			
	STOCKTON, FRANK R.	NA	AMR 88 04
KNIFE THAT KILLED PO HANCY, THE			
	STOCKTON, FRANK R.	NV	93
MY TERMINAL MORAINE	STOCKTON, FRANK R.	NV	OAW 92 04
GREAT STONE OF SARDIS, THE	STOCKTON, FRANK R.	NO	HPM 97 11
MY TRANSLATOPHONE	STOCKTON, FRANK R.	NV	HBZ 00 10

SCIENCE FICTION OF JACK LONDON, THE

	LONDON, JACK	AC H GRG 75	
INTRODUCTION	POWERS, RICHARD GID	IN	
RELIC OF THE PLIOCENE, A	LONDON, JACK	SS	COL 01 01
MINIONS OF MIDAS, THE	LONDON, JACK	SS	PHS 01 05
SHADOW AND THE FLASH, THE	LONDON, JACK	SS	BOK 03 06
CURIOUS FRAGMENT, A	LONDON, JACK	SS	TTP 08 12
GOLIAH	LONDON, JACK	NV	BOK 10 02
DREAM OF DEBS, THE	LONDON, JACK	SS	ISR 09 01
UNPARALLELED INVASION, THE	LONDON, JACK	SS	MCS 10 07
WHEN THE WORLD WAS YOUNG	LONDON, JACK	SS	SEP 10 09
STRENGTH OF THE STRONG, THE	LONDON, JACK	SS	HAM 11 03
SCARLET PLAGUE, THE	LONDON, JACK	NA	LON 12 06
ILLUSTRATIONS TO "THE SCARLET PLAGUE"			
	GRANT, GORDON	IL	
RED ONE, THE	LONDON, JACK	NV	CMP 18 10

SCIENCE FICTION OF THE 30'S   KNIGHT, DAMON   AN H BML 75

FOREWORD	KNIGHT, DAMON	IN	
EARLY YEARS, THE	KNIGHT, DAMON	SI	
OUT AROUND RIGEL	WILSON, ROBERT H.	SS	ASF 31 12
FIFTH-DIMENSION CATAPULT, THE			
	LEINSTER, MURRAY	NV	ASF 31 01
INTO THE METEORITE ORBIT	KELLY, FRANK K.	SS	AMZ 33 12
BATTERY OF HATE, THE	CAMPBELL, JOHN W. JR	SS	AMZ 33 11
MIDDLE PERIOD, THE	KNIGHT, DAMON	SI	
WALL, THE	GRAHAM, HOWARD W.	SS	ASF 34 05
LOST LANGUAGE, THE	KELLER, DAVID H. MD.	SS	AMZ 34 01
LAST MEN, THE	LONG, FRANK BELKNAP	SS	ASF 34 08
OTHER, THE	GRAHAM, HOWARD W.	SS	ASF 34 12
MAD MOON, THE	WEINBAUM, STANLEY G.	NV	ASF 35 12
DAVEY JONES' AMBASSADOR	GALLUN, RAYMOND Z.	NV	ASF 35 12
ALAS, ALL THINKING!	BATES, HARRY	SN	ASF 35 06
TIME DECELERATOR, THE	MACFADYEN, A. JR.	SS	ASF 36 07
COUNCIL OF THE DRONES, THE	SONNEMANN, W. K.	NV	AMZ 36 10
END, THE	KNIGHT, DAMON	SI	
SEEKER OF TOMORROW	RUSSELL, ERIC FRANK		
	AND JOHNSON, LESLIE T.	SN C ASF 37 07	
HYPERPELOSITY	DE CAMP, L. SPRAGUE	SS	ASF 38 04
PITHECANTHROPUS REJECTUS	WELLMAN, MANLY WADE	SS	ASF 38 01
MERMAN, THE	DE CAMP, L. SPRAGUE	SS	ASF 38 12
DAY IS DONE, THE	DEL REY, LESTER	SS	ASF 39 05
BIBLIOGRAPHY	MISC. MATERIAL	MS	

SCIENCE FICTION OMNIBUS   BLEILER & DIKTY   AN H GCB 52 01

BEST SCIENCE-FICTION STORIES: 1949, THE			
	BLEILER & DIKTY	AN	FEL 49 08
BEST SCIENCE-FICTION STORIES: 1950, THE			
	BLEILER & DIKTY	AN	FEL 50 08

SCIENCE FICTION OMNIBUS   CONKLIN, GROFF   AN   BRK 56 08

STORIES FROM "OMNIBUS OF SCIENCE FICTION"			
SUBWAY NAMED MOBIUS, A	DEUTSCH, A. J.	SS	ASF 50 12
COLOUR OUT OF SPACE, THE (ALSO AS MONSTER OF TERROR)			
	LOVECRAFT, H. P.	SS	AMZ 27 09
STAR DUMMY, THE	BOUCHER, ANTHONY	SS	FAN 52 FL
HOMO SOL	ASIMOV, ISAAC	SS	ASF 40 09
KALEIDOSCOPE	BRADBURY, RAY	SS	TWS 49 10
PLAGUE	LEINSTER, MURRAY	SS	ASF 44 02
TEST PIECE	RUSSELL, ERIC FRANK	SS	OWS 51 03
SPECTATOR SPORT	MACDONALD, JOHN D.	SS	TWS 50 02
WEAPON, THE	BROWN, FREDRIC	SS	ASF 51 04
HISTORY LESSON	CLARKE, ARTHUR C.	SS	STS 49 05
INSTINCT	DEL REY, LESTER	SS	ASF 52 01

SCIENCE FICTION OMNIBUS ON POLLUTION, A   ANONYMOUS   AN H SID 71

MAKE ROOM! MAKE ROOM!	HARRISON, HARRY	NO	IMP 66 08
SHARK SHIP (REAP THE DARK TIDE)			
	KORNBLUTH, C. M.	NV	VAN 58 06
CITY	SIMAK, CLIFFORD D.	NV	ASF 44 05

SCIENCE FICTION ROLL OF HONOR, THE

	POHL, FREDERIK	AN H RDM 75	
INTRODUCTION	POHL, FREDERIK	IN	
KINGS WHO DIE	ANDERSON, POUL	NV	IFS 62 03
LAST QUESTION, THE	ASIMOV, ISAAC	SS	SFQ 56 11
HOW BEAUTIFUL WITH BANNERS	BLISH, JAMES	SS	ORB 66 01
DAYBROKE	BLOCH, ROBERT	SS	SMG 58 01

SCIENCE FICTION ROLL OF HONOR, THE

SCIENCE FICTION ROLL OF HONOR, THE

WHO GOES THERE?	CAMPBELL, JOHN W. JR NV	ASF 38 08	
DOG STAR (MOONDOG)	CLARKE, ARTHUR C. SS	GAL 62 04	
MONSTER, THE	DEL REY, LESTER SS	ARG 51 06	
DUST	ESHBACH, LLOYD A. SS	MSS 39 08	
PROPHETS OF DOOM, THE	GERNSBACK, HUGO AR		
LONG WATCH, THE	HEINLEIN, ROBERT A. SS	ALM 49 12	
SANITY (ALSO AS CRAZY WOLF)	LEIBER, FRITZ SS	ASF 44 04	
MEANING OF THE WORD "IMPOSSIBLE", THE			
	LEY, WILLY AR		
SF, THE SPIRIT OF YOUTH	PAUL, FRANK R. AR	39	
FROM "THE SKYLARK OF SPACE"	SMITH, EDWARD E. PHD EX	AMZ 28 08	
HURKLE IS A HAPPY BEAST, THE	STURGEON, THEODORE SS	FSF 49 PL	
ABDICATION (ALSO AS THE INVISIBILITY GAMBIT)			
	VAN VOGT, A. E.		
	AND HULL, E. MAYNE SS C	ASF 43 04	

SCIENCE FICTION SHOWCASE   KORNBLUTH, MARY   AN H DBL 59
CURTIS PB EDITION OMITS STORY "MED SERVICE"

FOR C. M. KORNBLUTH	POHL, FREDERIK MS		
TICKET TO ANYWHERE	KNIGHT, DAMON NV	GAL 52 04	
THAT LOW	STURGEON, THEODORE SS	FFM 48 10	
OR THE GRASSES GROW	DAVIDSON, AVRAM SS	FSF 58 11	
MAN WHO ATE THE WORLD, THE	POHL, FREDERIK NV	GAL 56 11	
LONG REMEMBERING, THE	ANDERSON, POUL SS	FSF 57 11	
END OF THE BEGINNING, THE (NEXT STOP: THE STARS)			
	BRADBURY, RAY SS	MCL 56 10	
WORK OF ART, A (ART-WORK)	BLISH, JAMES SS	SFS 56 07	
COLD GREEN EYE, THE	WILLIAMSON, JACK SS	FAN 53 03	
MED SERVICE	LEINSTER, MURRAY SN	ASF 57 08	
EXPENDABLE	DICK, PHILIP K. SS	FSF 53 07	
MANTAGE	MATHESON, RICHARD NV	NEW 59 AN	
NIGHTMARE NUMBER FOUR	BLOCH, ROBERT PM	NEW 59 AN	

SCIENCE FICTION SPECIAL 1 ANONYMOUS   AN H SID 70 08

WORLD THAT JONES MADE, THE	DICK, PHILIP K. NO	ACE 56	
SPACE SWIMMERS	DICKSON, GORDON R. NO	BKM 67	
WATERS OF DEATH	GREENFIELD, IRVING A NO	LAN 67	

SCIENCE FICTION SPECIAL 3 ANONYMOUS   AN H SID 71

OVERMIND	WADSWORTH, PHYLLIS M NO	SID 67	
CAVIAR	STURGEON, THEODORE AC	BAL 55 11	
TIME-HOPPERS, THE	SILVERBERG, ROBERT NO	DBL 67	

SCIENCE FICTION SPECIAL 4 ANONYMOUS   AN H SID 71

WINGED MAN, THE	VAN VOGT, A. E.		
	AND HULL, E. MAYNE NO C	ASF 44 05	
ROSE, THE	HARNESS, CHARLES L. NO	AUT 53 03	
MAN IN THE MAZE, THE	SILVERBERG, ROBERT NO	IFS 68 04	

SCIENCE FICTION SPECIAL 5 ANONYMOUS   AN H SID 71 07

RITE OF PASSAGE	PANSHIN, ALEXEI NO	ACE 68	
CRADLE OF THE SUN	STABLEFORD, BRIAN M. NO		
FUTURE MAKERS, THE	HAINING, PETER AN	BEL 71 05	

SCIENCE FICTION SPECIAL 6 ANONYMOUS   AN H SID 73

CHILDREN OF TOMORROW	VAN VOGT, A. E. NO	70	
NOW COMES TOMORROW	WILLIAMS, ROBERT M. NO	71	

SCIENCE FICTION SPECIAL 7 ANONYMOUS   AN H SID

MURRAY LEINSTER OMNIBUS, A	LEINSTER, MURRAY AC	SID 68	
PHILIP K. DICK OMNIBUS, A	DICK, PHILIP K. AC	SID 70	

SCIENCE FICTION SPECIAL 8 ANONYMOUS   AN H SID 73

TIMESCOOP	BRUNNER, JOHN NO	69	
QUEST FOR THE FUTURE	VAN VOGT, A. E. NO	ACE 70	
PROFIT OF DOOM, THE	DIRAC, HUGH NO	70	

SCIENCE FICTION STORIES   BRADLEY, JOHANNA   AN H YPB 75

FORBIDDEN FRUIT	BERGER, MICHAEL SS	YNW	
VISITOR FROM SPACE	GUPPY, PAULINE D. SS	YNW	
DOLLHOUSE, THE	PRESTON, L. E. SS	YNW	
MAGNETIC MARVIN	HULL, PAUL E. SS	YNW	
SPACE-SHUTTLE TRIP, A	ROBISON, NANCY L. SS	YNW	
GIFT FROM EARTH	PACINI, KATHLEEN SS	YNW	
WE ARE WAITING	DERBY, PAT SS	YNW	
MAGIC TRICK	WATKINS, JOAN N. SS	YNW	

SCIENCE FICTION STORIES   ELAM, RICHARD M. JR. AC   LPB 64 12
SEE "TEEN-AGE SCIENCE FICTION STORIES"

SCIENCE FICTION SUBTREASURY, THE
                        TUCKER, WILSON   AC H RIN 54 09
ALSO AS "TIME: X"

INTRODUCTION	TUCKER, WILSON IN		
STREET WALKER, THE	TUCKER, WILSON SS		
MCMLV	TUCKER, WILSON SS	USF 54 11	
HOME IS WHERE THE WRECK IS	TUCKER, WILSON SS	USF 54 05	
MY BROTHER'S WIFE	TUCKER, WILSON SS	FSF 51 02	
GENTLEMEN- THE QUEEN!	TUCKER, WILSON SS	SFQ 42 FL	
JOB IS ENDED, THE	TUCKER, WILSON SS	OWS 50 11	
EXIT	TUCKER, WILSON SS	AST 43 04	
WAYFARING STRANGERS, THE	TUCKER, WILSON SS	FWS 52 FL	
ABLE TO ZEBRA	TUCKER, WILSON SS	FSF 53 03	
MOUNTAINEER, THE (MOUNTAIN JUSTICE)			
	TUCKER, WILSON SS	FND 53 12	

SCIENCE FICTION TALES   ELWOOD, ROGER   OA H RAN 73
INTRODUCTION: THE WONDER-FULL AGE

	STURGEON, THEODORE IN		
SMALLEST DRAGONBOY, THE	MCCAFFREY, ANNE SS	SFT 73	
ALONE IN SPACE	TOFTE, ARTHUR SS	SFT 73	
MYSTERIOUS GEM, THE	STREET, CLAIRE EDWIN SS	SFT 73	
TRIPLE MOONS OF DENEB II, THE			
	CHARNEY, DAVID H. SS	SFT 73	
LAUGHING LION, THE	JONES, RAYMOND F. SS	SFT 73	
TWO YEARS TO GAEA	BOLES, NICK SS	SFT 73	

SOME ARE BORN CATS	CARR, TERRY		
	AND CARR, CAROL SS C	SFT 73	

SCIENCE FICTION TERROR TALES CONKLIN, GROFF   AN H GNM 55 01

INTRODUCTION	CONKLIN, GROFF IN		
PUNISHMENT WITHOUT CRIME	BRADBURY, RAY SS	OWS 50 03	
ARENA	BROWN, FREDRIC NV	ASF 44 06	
LEECH, THE	SHECKLEY, ROBERT SS	GAL 52 12	
THROUGH CHANNELS	MATHESON, RICHARD SS	FSF 51 04	
LOST MEMORY	PHILLIPS, PETER SS	GAL 52 05	
MEMORIAL (SEE ALSO ATOMIC MEMORIAL)			
	STURGEON, THEODORE SS	ASF 46 04	
PROTT	ST. CLAIR, MARGARET SS	GAL 53 01	
FLIES	ASIMOV, ISAAC SS	FSF 53 06	
MICROSCOPIC GIANTS, THE	ERNST, PAUL SS	TWS 36 10	
OTHER INAUGURATION, THE	BOUCHER, ANTHONY SS	FSF 53 03	
NIGHTMARE BROTHER	NOURSE, ALAN E. NV	ASF 53 02	
PIPELINE TO PLUTO	LEINSTER, MURRAY SS	ASF 45 08	
IMPOSTOR	DICK, PHILIP K. SS	ASF 53 06	
THEY	HEINLEIN, ROBERT A. SS	UNK 41 04	
LET ME LIVE IN A HOUSE (ALSO AS A FRIEND TO MAN)			
	OLIVER, CHAD NV	USF 54 03	

SCIENCE FICTION THINKING MACHINES
                        CONKLIN, GROFF   AN H VPR 54

INTRODUCTION	CONKLIN, GROFF IN		
AUTOMATA: I	WRIGHT, S. FOWLER SS	WRT 29 09	
MOXON'S MASTER	BIERCE, AMBROSE SS	93	
ROBBIE (STRANGE PLAYFELLOW)	ASIMOV, ISAAC SS	SSS 40 09	
SCARAB, THE	GALLUN, RAYMOND Z. SS	ASF 36 08	
MECHANICAL BRIDE, THE	LEIBER, FRITZ PL	NEW 54 AN	
VIRTUOSO	GOLDSTONE, HERBERT SS	FSF 53 02	
AUTOMATA: II	WRIGHT, S. FOWLER SS	WRT 29 09	
BOOMERANG (A GREAT DEAL OF POWER)			
	RUSSELL, ERIC FRANK SS	FUN 53 08	
JESTER, THE	TENN, WILLIAM SS	TWS 51 08	
R.U.R.	CAPEK, KAREL PL	21	
SKIRMISH (BATHE YOUR BEARINGS IN BLOOD)			
	SIMAK, CLIFFORD D. SS	AMZ 50 12	
SOLDIER BOY	SHAARA, MICHAEL NV	GAL 53 07	
AUTOMATA: III	WRIGHT, S. FOWLER SS	WRT 29 09	
MEN ARE DIFFERENT	BLOCH, ALAN SS	NEW 54 AN	
LETTER TO ELLEN	DAVIS, CHAN SS	ASF 47 06	
SCULPTORS OF LIFE	WEST, WALLACE SS	ASF 39 12	
GOLDEN EGG, THE	STURGEON, THEODORE NV	UNK 41 08	
DEAD END	MACFARLANE, WALLACE SS	GAL 52 01	
ANSWER	CLEMENT, HAL SS	ASF 47 04	
SAM HALL	ANDERSON, POUL NV	ASF 53 08	
DUMB WAITER	MILLER, WALTER M. JR SS	ASF 52 04	
PROBLEM FOR EMMY	TOWNES, ROBERT S. SS	STS 52 06	

SCIENCE FICTION THINKING MACHINES (SELECTIONS FROM)
                        CONKLIN, GROFF   AN BAN 55 08

ROBBIE (STRANGE PLAYFELLOW)	ASIMOV, ISAAC SS	SSS 40 09	
VIRTUOSO	GOLDSTONE, HERBERT SS	FSF 53 02	
BOOMERANG (A GREAT DEAL OF POWER)			
	RUSSELL, ERIC FRANK SS	FUN 53 08	
JESTER, THE	TENN, WILLIAM SS	TWS 51 08	
SKIRMISH (BATHE YOUR BEARINGS IN BLOOD)			
	SIMAK, CLIFFORD D. SS	AMZ 50 12	
MEN ARE DIFFERENT	BLOCH, ALAN SS	NEW 54 AN	
LETTER TO ELLEN	DAVIS, CHAN SS	ASF 47 06	
GOLDEN EGG, THE	STURGEON, THEODORE NV	UNK 41 08	
DEAD END	MACFARLANE, WALLACE SS	GAL 52 01	
SAM HALL	ANDERSON, POUL NV	ASF 53 08	
DUMB WAITER	MILLER, WALTER M. JR NV	ASF 52 04	
PROBLEM FOR EMMY	TOWNES, ROBERT S. SS	STS 52 06	

SCIENCE FICTION THROUGH THE AGES 1
                        EVANS, I. O.   AN PTH 66

INTRODUCTION   EVANS, I. O.   IN
SECRET WEAPON (FROM "COUNT ROBERT OF PARIS")
                        SCOTT, WALTER   EX
VANISHED CIVILIZATION, THE (FROM "TIMAIOS" AND "CRITIAS")
                        PLATO   EX
INTERPLANETARY WARFARE (FROM "A TRUE HISTORY")
                        LUCIAN OF SAMOSATA   EX
MOON-VOYAGE, THE (FROM "SOMNIUM")
                        KEPLER, JOHANNES   EX
UTOPIAN SCIENCE FICTION (FROM "THE NEW ATLANTIS")
                        BACON, FRANCIS   EX
SATIRICAL SCIENCE FICTION (FROM "GULLIVER'S TRAVELS")
                        SWIFT, JONATHAN   EX
HUMAN MUTANT, THE (FROM "THE LIFE AND ADVENTURES OF
  PETER WILKINS")   PALTOCK, ROBERT   EX
VISITORS FROM OUTER SPACE (FROM "MICROMEGAS")
                        VOLTAIRE   EX
RECALCITRANT ROBOT, THE (FROM "FRANKENSTEIN")
                        SHELLEY, MARY W.   EX
MENACE OF THE MACHINE, THE (FROM "EREWHON")
                        BUTLER, SAMUEL   EX
CONQUEST OF THE AIR, THE (FROM "THE BALLOON HOAX")
                        POE, EDGAR ALLEN   EX   SUN 44 04
INTO THE UNKNOWN (FROM "20,000 LEAGUES UNDER THE SEA")
                        VERNE, JULES   EX   GMS 73
BIBLIOGRAPHY   MISC. MATERIAL   MS

SCIENCE FICTION THROUGH THE AGES 2
                        EVANS, I. O.   AN PTH 66

INTRODUCTION   EVANS, I. O.   IN
EXPOSTULATION, AN   LEWIS, C. S.   PM   FSF 59 06
ATOMIC BOMB, THE (FROM "THE WORLD SET FREE")
                        WELLS, H. G.   EX
ACTION FROM A DISTANCE (FROM "RALPH 124C 41+")
                        GERNSBACK, HUGO   EX   MEL 11 04

SCIENCE FICTION THROUGH THE AGES 2

REFUGEE (CONTEST STORY, ORIGINAL TITLE THIS EARTH OF MAJESTY)
                                   CLARKE, ARTHUR C.   SS   FSF 55 07
FEELING OF POWER, THE   ASIMOV, ISAAC   SS   IFS 58 02
LITTLE OIL, A   RUSSELL, ERIC FRANK   NV   GAL 52 10
COLD EQUATIONS, THE   GODWIN, TOM   NV   ASF 54 08
FLINTIES, THE   EVANS, I. O.   SS
SOUND OF THUNDER, A   BRADBURY, RAY   SS   COL 52 06
HE WALKED AROUND THE HORSES   PIPER, H. BEAM   NV   ASF 48 04
LIGHT, THE   ANDERSON, POUL   NV   GAL 57 03
THOSE ABOUT TO DIE (FROM "ON THE BEACH")
                                   SHUTE, NEVIL   EX
SUGGESTIONS FOR FURTHER READING
                                   MISC. MATERIAL   MS

SCIENCE FICTION WORLDS OF FORREST J. ACKERMAN & FRIENDS
                                   ACKERMAN, FORREST J. AC   POW 69 04
INTRODUCTION   ACKERMAN, FORREST J. IN
DWELLERS IN THE DUST   ACKERMAN, FORREST J. SS   FBK 48 04
MICRO MAN   ACKERMAN, FORREST J. SS   NWS 46 02
MARTIAN ODDITY, A (BEHIND THE ATE BALL)
                                   ACKERMAN, FORREST J. SS   MAR 50 11
ATOMIC MONUMENT, THE (MEMORIAL)
                                   STURGEON, THEODORE
                           AND ACKERMAN, FORREST J. SS C ASF 46 04
CONFESSIONS OF A SCIENCE FICTION ADDICT
                                   ACKERMAN, FORREST J. AR   AFT 57
BIG SLEEP, THE   ACKERMAN, FORREST J. SS   50
METROPOLIS UEBER ALLES   ACKERMAN, FORREST J. AR   63
BURN WITCH, BURN   ACKERMAN, FORREST J. SS   SEX 58
TIME TO CHANGE (MIRROR IMAGE)
                                   ACKERMAN, FORREST J.
                           AND SOUTO, MARCIAL   SS C   68
LURE AND LORE OF "THE BLIND SPOT", THE
                                   ACKERMAN, FORREST J. AR   51
DHACTWHU¡- REMEMBER?   ACKERMAN, FORREST J.
                           AND LOWNDES, ROBERT W. SS C SSS 49 04
TARZAN AND THE GOLDEN LOIN   ACKERMAN, FORREST J. SS   48
COUNT DOWN TO DOOM   ACKERMAN, FORREST J.
                           AND NUETZEL, CHARLES SS C FMS 66
FAR-OUT PHILOSOPHER OF SCIENCE FICTION, THE
                                   ACKERMAN, FORREST J. AR   49
GIRL WHO WASN'T THERE, THE   ACKERMAN, FORREST J.
                                   TIGRINA
                                   NOLAN, WILLIAM F.
                           AND FRITCH, CHARLES E. SS C GAM 63 01
LADY TAKES A POWDER, THE   TIGRINA
                           AND ACKERMAN, FORREST J. SS C INS 53
LAUGH, CLONE, LAUGH   ACKERMAN, FORREST J.
                           AND VAN VOGT, A. E.   SS C NEW 69 AC
WHEN FRIGHTHOOD WAS IN FLOWER
                                   ACKERMAN, FORREST J. SS
RECORD, THE   ACKERMAN, FORREST J.
                           AND BRADBURY, RAY   SS C   40
MAN WHO WAS THIRSTY, THE   ACKERMAN, FORREST J. SS
HOUSE IN THE TWILIGHT ZONE, THE
                                   ACKERMAN, FORREST J. AR
LETTER TO AN ANGEL   ACKERMAN, FORREST J. SS
RADCLYFFE EFFECT, THE   ACKERMAN, FORREST J. SS

SCIENCE FICTION: THE FUTURE ALLEN, DICK   AN H HBJ 71
PREFACE   ALLEN, DICK   IN
INTRODUCTION   ALLEN, DICK   IN
FIRST PERSPECTIVES   ALLEN, DICK   SI
ADVICE TO A PROPHET   WILBUR, RICHARD   PM   59
NO WAY OUT, NO WAY BACK   TIME MAGAZINE   AR   TIM 69
HUMAN RACE HAS, MAYBE, THIRTY-FIVE YEARS LEFT, THE
                                   LYLE, DAVID   AR   ESQ 67 09
CRAB-APPLE CRISIS, THE   MACBETH, GEORGE   SS   NWS 66 10
EARTH'S HOLOCAUST   HAWTHORNE, NATHANIEL SS   GLG 44 05
ALTERNATIVE FUTURES: THE PRESENT AS FUTURE
                                   ALLEN, DICK   SI
POEM ROCKET   GINSBERG, ALLEN   PM   61
COUNTRY OF THE BLIND, THE   WELLS, H. G.   SS   SND 04 04
JACHID AND JACHIDAH   SINGER, ISAAC B.   SS   64
THEY   HEINLEIN, ROBERT A.   SS   UNK 41 04
ARTIST, THE   KOCH, KENNETH   PM   62
BALLOON, THE   BARTHELME, DONALD   SS   NYM 66 04
FUTURE, THE   ALLEN, DICK   SI
TO THE CHICAGO ABYSS   BRADBURY, RAY   SS   FSF 63 05
LIGHT OF OTHER DAYS   SHAW, BOB   SS   ASF 66 08
HARRISON BERGERON   VONNEGUT, KURT JR.   SS   FSF 61 10
GREEN HILLS OF EARTH, THE   HEINLEIN, ROBERT A.   SS   SEP 47 02
TITHONUS   THOMAS, D. M.   PM   PMP 68 11
MACHINE STOPS, THE   FORSTER, E. M.   NV   28
ROSE FOR ECCLESIASTES, A   ZELAZNY, ROGER   NV   FSF 63 11
"REPENT, HARLEQUIN!" SAID THE TICKTOCKMAN
                                   ELLISON, HARLAN   SS   GAL 65 12
DAY MILLION   POHL, FREDERIK   SS   ROG 66 02
HISTORY LESSON   CLARKE, ARTHUR C.   SS   STS 49 05
FROM "THE TIME MACHINE"   WELLS, H. G.   EX   NRV 95 01
THEORIES   ALLEN, DICK   SI
STARTING POINTS   AMIS, KINGSLEY   AR   60
SOCIAL SCIENCE FICTION   ASIMOV, ISAAC   AR   NEW 53 NF
SCIENCE FICTION, MORALS, AND RELIGION
                                   HEARD, GERALD   AR   NEW 53 NF
BOREDOM OF FANTASY, THE   KOESTLER, ARTHUR   AR   55
IMAGINATION OF DISASTER, THE   SONTAG, SUSAN   AR   65
FUTURE OF PREDICTION, THE   SISK, JOHN P.   AR   CMM 70
TOPICS OF WRITING AND RESEARCH
                                   MISC. MATERIAL   MS
SUGGESTIONS FOR FURTHER READING
                                   MISC. MATERIAL   MS

SCIENCE FICTION: THE GREAT YEARS
                                   POHL, C. & F.   AN   ACE 73 01

SCIENCE-FICTIONAL SHERLOCK HOLMES, THE

INTRODUCTION THE FIRST   POHL, FREDERIK   IN
INTRODUCTION THE SECOND   POHL, CAROL   IN
AND THEN THERE WERE NONE   RUSSELL, ERIC FRANK   NV   ASF 51 06
LIBERATION OF EARTH, THE   TENN, WILLIAM   SS   FUT 53 05
OLD FAITHFUL   GALLUN, RAYMOND Z.   NV   ASF 34 12
PLACET IS A CRAZY PLACE   BROWN, FREDRIC   SS   ASF 46 05
WINGS OF THE LIGHTNING LAND   MACCREIGH, JAMES   NV   AST 41 11
LITTLE BLACK BAG, THE   KORNBLUTH, C. M.   NV   ASF 50 07
MATTER OF FORM, A   GOLD, H. L.   SN   ASF 38 12

SCIENCE FICTION: THE GREAT YEARS, VOL. II
                                   POHL, C. & F.   AN   ACE 76
INTRODUCTION   POHL, CAROL
                           AND POHL, FREDERIK   IN C
RULL, THE   VAN VOGT, A. E.   NV   ASF 48 05
AND BE MERRY... (ALSO AS THE PYRAMID IN THE DESERT)
                                   MACLEAN, KATHERINE   SS   ASF 50 02
SACK, THE   MORRISON, WILLIAM   SS   ASF 50 09
MEWHU'S JET   STURGEON, THEODORE   NV   ASF 46 11
TIME IS THE TRAITOR   BESTER, ALFRED   NV   FSF 53 09
COLUMBUS WAS A DOPE   HEINLEIN, ROBERT A.   SS   STS 47 05
WHEN TIME WENT MAD   WYLIE, DIRK
                           AND KUMMER, FREDERICK A. NA C TWS 50 02

SCIENCE IN FICTION   BAYLISS, A.E. & J.C. AN   UOL 57
PRELUDE TO SPACE   CLARKE, ARTHUR C.   EX   GAN 51 03
STAR, THE   WELLS, H. G.   SS   GRP 97 12
ANCIENT GULLIVER, AN (FROM "A TRUE HISTORY", 165AD)
                                   LUCIAN OF SAMOSATA   EX
FLYING ISLAND, THE (FROM "THE THIRD VOYAGE OF GULLIVER", 1726)
                                   SWIFT, JONATHAN   EX
RACE WITH A DINOSAUR, A (FROM "THE LOST WORLD")
                                   DOYLE, ARTHUR CONAN   EX   HDS 12
EARLY TIME-TRAVELER, AN (FROM "JOURNAL OF THE YEAR 2440",1795)
                                   MERCIER, LOUIS S.   EX
ADVENTURE IN A SPACE SHIP (FROM "OUT OF THE SILENT PLANET")
                                   LEWIS, C. S.   EX   LNE 38
EXPERIMENTAL FARM, THE (FROM "THE FOOD OF THE GODS")
                                   WELLS, H. G.   EX   PRS 03 12
AVENGING RAY, THE   SERMARK   EX   30
CAPTAIN NEMO'S THUNDERBOLT (FROM "20,000 LEAGUES UNDER
THE SEA", 1873)   VERNE, JULES   EX   GMS 73
TRIFFID, THE (FROM "THE DAY OF THE TRIFFIDS")
                                   WYNDHAM, JOHN   EX   COL 51 01
OFF FOR THE MOON (FROM "ZERO TO EIGHTY")
                                   NORTHRUP, EDWIN F.   EX   37

SCIENCE-FANTASY QUINTETTE   CRAWFORD, WILLIAM L. AN H FPB 53
TRITON (THE UNDIGESTIBLE TRITON)
                                   HUBBARD, L. RON   NO   UNK 40 04
RADIUM POOL, THE   REPP, ED EARL   AC   FPB 49

SCIENCE-FICTION CARNIVAL   BROWN, F. & REYNOLDS AN H SHS 53 12
INTRODUCTION   BROWN, FREDRIC   IN
WHEEL OF TIME, THE   ARTHUR, ROBERT   SS   SSS 50 03
SRL AD   MATHESON, RICHARD   SS   FSF 52 04
LOGIC NAMED JOE, A   LEINSTER, MURRAY   SS   ASF 46 03
SIMWORTHY'S CIRCUS   SHAW, LARRY T.   SS   WBY 50 12
WELL-OILED MACHINE, THE   FYFE, H. B.   NV   FSF 50 12
VENUS AND THE SEVEN SEXES   TENN, WILLIAM   NV   49
SWORDSMAN OF VARNIS, THE   JACKSON, CLIVE   SS   OWS 50 09
PARADOX LOST   BROWN, FREDRIC   SS   ASF 43 10
MUTEN   RUSSELL, ERIC FRANK   SS   ASF 48 10
MARTIANS AND THE COYS, THE   REYNOLDS, MACK   SS   IMG 51 06
EGO MACHINE, THE   KUTTNER, HENRY   NV   SSF 52 05
COSMIC JACKPOT, THE   SMITH, GEORGE O.   SS   TWS 48 10
ABDUCTION OF ABNER GREER, THE
                                   BOND, NELSON S.   SS   BBM 41 06

SCIENCE-FICTION CARNIVAL (11 OF 13)
                                   BROWN, F. & REYNOLDS AN   BAN 57 06
INTRODUCTION   BROWN, FREDRIC   IN
PREFACE   REYNOLDS, MACK   IN
WHEEL OF TIME, THE   ARTHUR, ROBERT   SS   SSS 50 03
LOGIC NAMED JOE, A   LEINSTER, MURRAY   SS   ASF 46 03
SIMWORTHY'S CIRCUS   SHAW, LARRY T.   SS   WBY 50 12
WELL-OILED MACHINE, THE   FYFE, H. B.   NV   FSF 50 12
SWORDSMAN OF VARNIS, THE   JACKSON, CLIVE   SS   OWS 50 09
PARADOX LOST   BROWN, FREDRIC   SS   ASF 43 10
MUTEN   RUSSELL, ERIC FRANK   SS   ASF 48 10
MARTIANS AND THE COYS, THE   REYNOLDS, MACK   SS   IMG 51 06
EGO MACHINE, THE   KUTTNER, HENRY   NV   SSF 52 05
COSMIC JACKPOT, THE   SMITH, GEORGE O.   SS   TWS 48 10
ABDUCTION OF ABNER GREER, THE
                                   BOND, NELSON S.   SS   BBM 41 06

SCIENCE-FICTIONAL SHERLOCK HOLMES, THE
                                   COUNCIL OF FOUR   AN   60
SHERLOCK HOLMES AND SCIENCE FICTION
                                   BOUCHER, ANTHONY   IN
MARTIAN CROWN JEWELS, THE   ANDERSON, POUL   SS   EQM 58 02
HALF A HOKA- POUL ANDERSON   DICKSON, GORDON R.   AR   59
ADVENTURE OF THE MISPLACED HOUND, THE
                                   ANDERSON, POUL
                           AND DICKSON, GORDON R. NV C USF 53 12
ANOMALY OF THE EMPTY MAN, THE
                                   BOUCHER, ANTHONY   SS   FSF 52 04
GREATEST TERTIAN, THE   BOUCHER, ANTHONY   SS   NEW 52 AN
ADVENTURE OF THE SNITCH IN TIME, THE
                                   REYNOLDS, MACK
                           AND DERLETH, AUGUST   SS C FSF 53 07
ADVENTURE OF THE BALL OF NOSTRADAMUS, THE
                                   REYNOLDS, MACK
                           AND DERLETH, AUGUST   SS C FSF 55 06

SCIENCE-FICTIONAL SHERLOCK HOLMES, THE   SECRET SONGS, THE

```
    RETURN, THE                  PIPER, H. BEAM
                                 AND MCGUIRE, JOHN J.    NV C ASF 54 01
SEA OF SPACE, A                  NOLAN, WILLIAM F.       AN   BAN 70 05
    EDITOR'S PREFACE             NOLAN, WILLIAM F.       IN
    BLUE BOTTLE, THE (DEATH WISH)
                                 BRADBURY, RAY           SS   PLS 50 FL
    WIND BLOWS FREE, THE         OLIVER, CHAD            NV   FSF 57 07
    SOCIETY FOR THE PREVENTION   GOULART, RON            SS   GAM 64 03
    ONE NIGHT STAND              SIMMONS, HERBERT A.     SS   GAM 63 01
    ELEGY                        BEAUMONT, CHARLES       SS   IMG 53 02
    LAP OF THE PRIMITIVE, THE    NOLAN, WILLIAM F.       SS   FUN 58 10
    OLD COLLEGE TRY, THE         BLOCH, ROBERT           SS   GAM 63 02
    I AM RETURNING               RUSSELL, RAY            SS      61
    UNDISCOVERED COUNTRY, THE    TEMPLE, WILLIAM F.      SS   NEB 58 10
    RESTRICTED AREA              SHECKLEY, ROBERT        SS   AMZ 53 07
    ONE LOVE HAVE I              YOUNG, ROBERT F.        SS   IFS 55 04
    WORSHIP NIGHT                NEVILLE, KRIS           SS   FSF 53 11
    IN SPACE WITH RUNYON JONES   CORWIN, NORMAN          SS      52
    TIES THAT BIND, THE          MILLER, WALTER M. JR NV      IFS 54 05

SEAGULLS UNDER GLASS AND OTHER STORIES
                                 TATE, PETER             AC H DBL 75
    MAINCHANCE                   TATE, PETER             NV   ANA 70
    DAYLENGTH TALKING BLUES      TATE, PETER             SS
    SKYHAMMER                    TATE, PETER             SS
    MARS PASTORALE               TATE, PETER             SS   NWS 67 08
    GLOOM PATTERN, THE           TATE, PETER             SS   NWS 66 06
    WELCOME TO THE LAND OF SMILES
                                 TATE, PETER             SS
    POST-MORTEM PEOPLE, THE (ALSO AS BEYOND THE WEEDS)
                                 TATE, PETER             SS   NWS 66 03
    SEAGULLS UNDER GLASS         TATE, PETER             SS
    DAY THE WIND DIED, THE       TATE, PETER             NV   FSF 69 03
    SAME AUTUMN IN A DIFFERENT PARK
                                 TATE, PETER             SS   FAN 67 09
    DEAR WITCH HAZEL, MY BIRDS WON'T FLY
                                 TATE, PETER             NV
    CRUMBLING HOLLYWOOD MANSION, CRUMBLING HOLLYWOOD MAN (PROTEST)
                                 TATE, PETER             SS   GAL 74 02

SECOND ASTOUNDING SCIENCE FICTION ANTHOLOGY, THE
                                 CAMPBELL, JOHN W. JR AN H GRY 54
    VAULT OF THE BEAST           VAN VOGT, A. E.         NV   ASF 40 08
    CLASH BY NIGHT               O'DONNELL, LAWRENCE     NV   ASF 43 03
    MEIHEM IN CE KLASRUM         EDWARDS, DOLTON         AR   ASF 46 09
    E FOR EFFORT                 SHERRED, T. L.          NV   ASF 47 05
    LATE NIGHT FINAL             RUSSELL, ERIC FRANK     NV   ASF 48 12
    COLD WAR                     NEVILLE, KRIS           SS   ASF 49 10
    HISTORICAL NOTE              LEINSTER, MURRAY        SS   ASF 51 02
    PROTECTED SPECIES            FYFE, H. B.             SS   ASF 51 03

SECOND ASTOUNDING SCIENCE FICTION ANTHOLOGY, THE (PB)
                                 CAMPBELL, JOHN W. JR AN   FSF 65
    NIGHTFALL                    ASIMOV, ISAAC           NV   ASF 41 09
    CHILD'S PLAY                 TENN, WILLIAM           NV   ASF 47 03
    THUNDER AND ROSES            STURGEON, THEODORE      SS   ASF 47 11
    LATE NIGHT FINAL             RUSSELL, ERIC FRANK     NV   ASF 48 12
    COLD WAR                     NEVILLE, KRIS           SS   ASF 49 10
    ETERNITY LOST                SIMAK, CLIFFORD D.      NV   ASF 49 07
    WITCHES OF KARRES, THE       SCHMITZ, JAMES H.       NV   ASF 49 12
    OVER THE TOP                 DEL REY, LESTER         SS   ASF 49 11
    METEOR                       POWERS, WILLIAM T.      SS   ASF 50 09
    LAST ENEMY                   PIPER, H. BEAM          NV   ASF 50 08
    HISTORICAL NOTE              LEINSTER, MURRAY        SS   ASF 51 02
    PROTECTED SPECIES            FYFE, H. B.             SS   ASF 51 03

SECOND AVON FANTASY READER, THE
                                 WOLLHEIM &ERNSBERGER AN   AVN 69
    FOREWORD                     ERNSBERGER, GEORGE      IN
    BLONDE GODDESS OF BAL-SAGOTH, THE
                                 HOWARD, ROBERT E.       NV   WRT 31 10
    SHAMBLEAU                    MOORE, C. L.            NV   WRT 33 11
    CURSE OF YIG, THE            BISHOP, ZEALIA BROWN    SS   WRT 29 11
    UBBO-SATHLA                  SMITH, CLARK ASHTON     SS   WRT 33 07
    PAINTED MIRROR, THE          WANDREI, DONALD         SS   AFR 49 09
    AMINA                        WHITE, EDWARD LUCAS     SS      27
    BLACK KISS, THE              BLOCH, ROBERT           SS   WRT 37 06
    CITY OF THE LIVING DEAD, THE MANNING, LAURENCE
                                 AND PRATT, FLETCHER     NV C SWS 30 05
    CURSE OF A THOUSAND KISSES, THE
                                 ROHMER, SAX             SS   AFR 48 07

SECOND BOOK OF FRITZ LEIBER, THE
                                 LEIBER, FRITZ           AC   DAW 75 09
    FOREWORD                     LEIBER, FRITZ           IN
    LION AND THE LAMB, THE       LEIBER, FRITZ           NV   ASF 50 09
    MIGHTY TIDES, THE (WHAT MAKES THE MIGHTY TIDES)
                                 LEIBER, FRITZ           AR   SDG 61 04
    TRAPPED IN THE SEA OF STARS  LEIBER, FRITZ           SS   NEW 75 AC
    FAFHRD AND ME                LEIBER, FRITZ           AR      63
    BELSEN EXPRESS               LEIBER, FRITZ           SS   NEW 75 AC
    INGMAR BERGMAN: FANTASY NOVELIST
                                 LEIBER, FRITZ           BR   FAN 74 03
    SCREAM WOLF                  LEIBER, FRITZ           SS   MSM 61 02
    THOSE WILD ALIEN WORDS: II   LEIBER, FRITZ           AR   NEW 75 AC
    MECHANICAL BRIDE, THE        LEIBER, FRITZ           PL   NEW 54 AN
    THROUGH HYPERSPACE WITH BROWN JENKIN
                                 LEIBER, FRITZ           AR      66
    DEFENSE OF WEREWOLVES, A (FANTASY ON THE MARCH)
                                 LEIBER, FRITZ           AR   ARS 48 SP

SECOND FOUNDATION             ASIMOV, ISAAC           NO H GNM 53
    ALSO IN "THE FOUNDATION TRILOGY"
    NOW YOU SEE IT...            ASIMOV, ISAAC           NV   ASF 48 01
    AND NOW YOU DON'T            ASIMOV, ISAAC           NO   ASF 49 11
```

SECOND GALAXY READER OF SCIENCE FICTION
```
                                 GOLD, H. L.             AN H CRN 54
    ENGLISH DERIVATIVE ANTHOLOGY "GALAXY SCIENCE FICTION OMNIBUS"
    TO THE HILLS!                GOLD, H. L.             ED   GAL 53 10
    YEAR OF THE JACKPOT, THE     HEINLEIN, ROBERT A.     NV   GAL 52 03
    BAD DAY FOR SALES, A         LEIBER, FRITZ           SS   GAL 53 07
    MISOGYNIST, THE              GUNN, JAMES E.          SS   GAL 52 11
    SAUCER OF LONELINESS         STURGEON, THEODORE      SS   GAL 53 02
    TEETHING RING                CAUSEY, JAMES           SS   GAL 53 01
    GLEEB FOR EARTH, A           SCHAFHAUSER, CHARLES SS      GAL 53 05
    HALLUCINATION ORBIT (ALSO AS THE BLISS OF SOLITUDE)
                                 MCINTOSH, J. T.         NV   GAL 52 01
    C-CHUTE, THE                 ASIMOV, ISAAC           NV   GAL 51 10
    JUNKYARD                     SIMAK, CLIFFORD D.      NV   GAL 53 05
    PROBLEM ON BALAK             DEE, ROGER              SS   GAL 53 09
    SURFACE TENSION              BLISH, JAMES            NA   GAL 52 08
    SPECIALIST                   SHECKLEY, ROBERT        SS   GAL 53 05
    FOUR IN ONE                  KNIGHT, DAMON           NV   GAL 53 07
    CARETAKER                    SCHMITZ, JAMES H.       SS   GAL 53 07
    LOST MEMORY                  PHILLIPS, PETER         SS   GAL 52 05
    NOT FIT FOR CHILDREN         SMITH, EVELYN E.        SS   GAL 53 05
    STUDENT BODY                 WALLACE, F. L.          NV   GAL 53 03
    LOVER, WHEN YOU'RE NEAR ME   MATHESON, RICHARD       NV   GAL 52 05
    COMMAND PERFORMANCE (ALSO AS ANYBODY ELSE LIKE ME?)
                                 MILLER, WALTER M. JR NV      GAL 52 11
    STAR, BRIGHT                 CLIFTON, MARK           NV   GAL 52 07
    WARM                         SHECKLEY, ROBERT        SS   GAL 53 04
    UNREADY TO WEAR              VONNEGUT, KURT JR.      SS   GAL 53 04
    TIGER BY THE TAIL            NOURSE, ALAN E.         SS   GAL 51 11
    SELF PORTRAIT                WOLFE, BERNARD          NV   GAL 51 11
    SNOWBALL EFFECT, THE         MACLEAN, KATHERINE      SS   GAL 52 09
    PILLAR TO POST               WYNDHAM, JOHN           NV   GAL 51 12
    MINIMUM SENTENCE             COGSWELL, THEODORE R SS      GAL 53 08
    GAME FOR BLONDES             MACDONALD, JOHN D.      SS   GAL 52 10
    UNIVERSITY                   PHILLIPS, PETER         NV   GAL 53 04
    TEA TRAY IN THE SKY          SMITH, EVELYN E.        SS   GAL 52 09
    PAIL OF AIR, A               LEIBER, FRITZ           SS   GAL 51 12

SECOND IF READER OF SCIENCE FICTION, THE
                                 POHL, FREDERIK          AN H DBL 68
    INTRODUCTION                 POHL, FREDERIK          IN
    IN THE ARENA                 ALDISS, BRIAN W.        SS   IFS 63 07
    BILLIARD BALL, THE           ASIMOV, ISAAC           NV   IFS 67 03
    TIME-TOMBS, THE              BALLARD, J. G.          NV   IFS 63 03
    DIE, SHADOW!                 BUDRYS, ALGIS           NV   IFS 63 05
    FOUNDLING STARS, THE         CLEMENT, HAL            SS   IFS 66 08
    TOYS FOR DEBBIE              KYLE, DAVID A.          SS   IFS 65 12
    FOREST IN THE SKY, THE       LAUMER, KEITH           NV   IFS 67 02
    AT THE CORE                  NIVEN, LARRY            NV   IFS 66 11
    UNDER TWO MOONS              POHL, FREDERIK          NV   IFS 65 09
    MASQUE OF THE RED SHIFT      SABERHAGEN, FRED        NV   IFS 65 12

SECOND ORBIT                     DOHERTY, G. D.          AN H MUR 65
    INTRODUCTION                 DOHERTY, G. D.          IN
    STAR, THE                    WELLS, H. G.            SS   GRP 97 19
    AND NOW THE NEWS...          STURGEON, THEODORE      SS   FSF 56 12
    PRIZE OF PERIL, THE          SHECKLEY, ROBERT        SS   FSF 58 05
    TRAINEE FOR MARS (ALSO AS SIMULATED TRAINER)
                                 HARRISON, HARRY         SS   FUN 58 06
    WITH THESE HANDS             KORNBLUTH, C. M.        NV   GAL 51 12
    ALLAMAGOOSA                  RUSSELL, ERIC FRANK     SS   ASF 55 05
    OUTSIDE                      ALDISS, BRIAN W.        SS   NWS 55 01
    VELDT, THE (THE WORLD THE CHILDREN MADE)
                                 BRADBURY, RAY           SS   SEP 50 09
    COMMON TIME                  BLISH, JAMES            SS   SFQ 53 08
    STAR, THE                    CLARKE, ARTHUR C.       SS   INF 55 11

SECOND PACIFIC BOOK OF SCIENCE FICTION, THE
                                 BAXTER, JOHN            AN H AAR 71
    INTRODUCTION                 BAXTER, JOHN            IN
    IMMORTAL, THE                RUHEN, OLAF             SS
    SIREN SINGERS                TRACEY, ROBYN           SS
    CASE OF THE PERJURED PLANET, THE
                                 LORAN, MARTIN           NV   ASF 67 11
    SPACE POEM                   KLINE, T. F.            PM   BUL
    ROBINSON                     ROME, DAVID             SS
    NO SALE                      WILLIAMS, JOHN          SS
    MAN OF SLOW FEELINGS, THE    WILDING, MICHAEL        SS
    VALE, POLLINI!               JOHNSTON, GEORGE        SS
    FROM: RUTHERFORD             STEWART, DOUGLAS        PM
    APPLE                        BAXTER, JOHN            SS   NWR 67 10
    HAPPENING, A                 ROBERTS, FRANK          SS
    DANCING GERONTIUS            HARDING, LEE            SS   VOT 69 12
    WHATEVER HAPPENED TO SUDEROV?
                                 KALDOR, STEVE           SS

SECOND WORLD OF IF, THE          QUINN & WULFF           AN D QUI 58
    COLONISTS, THE               JONES, RAYMOND F.       NV   IFS 54 06
    THING IN THE ATTIC, THE      BLISH, JAMES            NV   IFS 54 07
    MONSTER NAMED SMITH, A       GUNN, JAMES E.          NV   IFS 54 07
    JUNGLE, THE                  BEAUMONT, CHARLES       NV   IFS 54 07
    ODD ONES, THE                DICKSON, GORDON R.      NV   IFS 55 02
    MOLD OF YANCY, THE           DICK, PHILIP K.         NV   IFS 55 08
    CHROME PASTURES              YOUNG, ROBERT F.        NV   IFS 56 04
    Z                            FONTENAY, CHARLES L. NV      IFS 56 06
    HAPPY HERD, THE              WALTON, BRYCE           NV   IFS 56 10

SECRET SONGS, THE                LEIBER, FRITZ           AC H HDV 68
    INTRODUCTION                 LEIBER, FRITZ           IN
    WINTER FLIES, THE (THE INNER CIRCLES)
                                 LEIBER, FRITZ           SS   FSF 67 10
    MAN WHO MADE FRIENDS WITH ELECTRICITY, THE
                                 LEIBER, FRITZ           SS   FSF 62 03
    RUMP-TITTY-TITTY-TUM-TAH-TEE LEIBER, FRITZ           SS   FSF 58 05
    MARIANA                      LEIBER, FRITZ           SS   FAN 60 02
    COMING ATTRACTION            LEIBER, FRITZ           SS   GAL 50 11
```

SECRET SONGS, THE

MOON IS GREEN, THE	LEIBER, FRITZ	SS	GAL 52 05
PAIL OF AIR, A	LEIBER, FRITZ	SS	GAL 51 12
SMOKE GHOST	LEIBER, FRITZ	SS	UNK 41 10
GIRL WITH THE HUNGRY EYES, THE			
	LEIBER, FRITZ	SS	49
NO GREAT MAGIC	LEIBER, FRITZ	SN	GAL 63 12
SECRET SONGS, THE	LEIBER, FRITZ	SS	FSF 62 08

SEEDLING STARS, THE   BLISH, JAMES   NO H GNM 56

SEEDING PROGRAMME (A TIME TO SURVIVE)			
	BLISH, JAMES	SS	FSF 56 02
THING IN THE ATTIC, THE	BLISH, JAMES	NV	IFS 54 07
SURFACE TENSION (COMBINED WITH "SUNKEN UNIVERSE", SSS 42 05)			
	BLISH, JAMES	NA	GAL 52 08
WATERSHED	BLISH, JAMES	SS	IFS 55 05

SEEDS OF TIME, THE   WYNDHAM, JOHN   AC H JOS 56

CHRONOCLASM, THE	WYNDHAM, JOHN	NV	STR 53 01
TIME TO REST	WYNDHAM, JOHN	SS	ARS 49 WI
METEOR (PHONEY METEOR)	WYNDHAM, JOHN	SS	AMZ 41 03
SURVIVAL	WYNDHAM, JOHN	NV	TWS 52 02
PAWLEY'S PEEPHOLES (OPERATION PEEP)			
	WYNDHAM, JOHN	SS	SCF 51 WI
OPPOSITE NUMBERS	WYNDHAM, JOHN	SS	NWS 54 04
PILLAR TO POST	WYNDHAM, JOHN	NV	GAL 51 12
DUMB MARTIAN	WYNDHAM, JOHN	NV	GAL 52 07
COMPASSION CIRCUIT	WYNDHAM, JOHN	SS	FUN 54 12
WILD FLOWER	WYNDHAM, JOHN	SS	FUN 55 11

SEETEE SHIP   STEWART, WILL   AC H GNM 51

COLLISION ORBIT	STEWART, WILL	NV	ASF 42 07
MINUS SIGN	STEWART, WILL	SN	ASF 42 11
OPPOSITES- REACT!	STEWART, WILL	SN	ASF 43 01

SEETEE SHIP/SEETEE SHOCK   WILLIAMSON, JACK   AC LAN

SEETEE SHIP	WILLIAMSON, JACK	NO	SAS 50
SEETEE SHOCK	WILLIAMSON, JACK	NO	ASF 49 02

SENSE OF WONDER, A   MOSKOWITZ, SAM   AN H SID 67
    SEE "THREE STORIES"

SEVEN COME INFINITY   CONKLIN, GROFF   AN FGM 66

PREFACE	CONKLIN, GROFF	IN	
GOLDEN BUGS, THE	SIMAK, CLIFFORD D.	NV	FSF 60 06
SPECIAL FEATURE	DEVET, CHARLES V.	NV	ASF 58 05
PANIC BUTTON	RUSSELL, ERIC FRANK	SS	ASF 59 11
DISCONTINUITY	JONES, RAYMOND F.	NV	ASF 50 10
CORIANIS DISASTER, THE	LEINSTER, MURRAY	NV	SFS 60 05
SERVANT PROBLEM, THE	TENN, WILLIAM	NV	GAL 55 04
RITE OF PASSAGE	OLIVER, CHAD	NV	ASF 54 04

SEVEN FAMOUS NOVELS BY H. G. WELLS
    WELLS, H. G.   AC H KNP 34
    ALSO AS "SEVEN SCIENCE FICTION NOVELS"

FIRST MEN IN THE MOON, THE	WELLS, H. G.	NO	SND 00 11
FOOD OF THE GODS, THE	WELLS, H. G.	NO	PRS 03 12
IN THE DAYS OF THE COMET	WELLS, H. G.	NO	DCH 05
INVISIBLE MAN, THE	WELLS, H. G.	SN	PRS 97 06
ISLAND OF DR. MOREAU, THE	WELLS, H. G.	NO	SRV 95 01
TIME MACHINE, THE	WELLS, H. G.	NA	NRV 95 01
WAR OF THE WORLDS, THE	WELLS, H. G.	NA	PRS 97 04

SEVEN SCIENCE FICTION NOVELS WELLS, H. G.   AC H DOV 50
    SEE "SEVEN FAMOUS NOVELS BY H. G. WELLS"

SEVEN SEXES, THE   TENN, WILLIAM   AC BAL 68 06

AUTHOR'S NOTE	TENN, WILLIAM	IN	
CHILD'S PLAY	TENN, WILLIAM	NV	ASF 47 03
MALTED MILK MONSTER, THE	TENN, WILLIAM	NV	GAL 59 08
ERRAND BOY	TENN, WILLIAM	SS	ASF 47 06
HOUSE DUTIFUL, THE	TENN, WILLIAM	SS	ASF 48 04
MISTRESS SARY	TENN, WILLIAM	SS	WRT 47 05
SANCTUARY	TENN, WILLIAM	SS	GAL 57 12
VENUS AND THE SEVEN SEXES	TENN, WILLIAM	NV	49
BERNIE THE FAUST	TENN, WILLIAM	NV	PBY 63 11

SEVEN STEPS TO THE ARBITER   HUBBARD, L. RON   AC MJR 75
    SEE "THE KINGSLAYER"

SEVEN TRIPS THROUGH TIME AND SPACE

	CONKLIN, GROFF	AN	FGM 68
INTRODUCTION	CONKLIN, GROFF	IN	
FLATLANDER	NIVEN, LARRY	NV	IFS 67 03
CRIME AND THE GLORY OF COMMANDER SUZDAL, THE			
	SMITH, CORDWAINER	SS	AMZ 64 05
OVERPROOF	MACKENZIE, J. B.	NV	ASF 65 10
POOR PLANET	MCINTOSH, J. T.	NV	FSF 64 08
SHAMAR'S WAR	NEVILLE, KRIS	NV	GAL 64 02
TACTFUL SABOTEUR, THE	HERBERT, FRANK	NV	GAL 64 10
MINISTRY OF DISTURBANCE	PIPER, H. BEAM	NV	ASF 58 12

SEVENTH GALAXY READER, THE   POHL, FREDERIK   AN H DBL 64

INTRODUCTION	POHL, FREDERIK	IN	
FOR LOVE	BUDRYS, ALGIS	NV	GAL 62 06
COME INTO MY CELLAR (ALSO AS BOYS, RAISE GIANT MUSHROOMS			
IN YOUR CELLAR)	BRADBURY, RAY	SS	GAL 62 10
TAIL-TIED KINGS, THE	DAVIDSON, AVRAM	SS	GAL 62 04
CRIME MACHINE	BLOCH, ROBERT	SS	GAL 61 10
RETURN ENGAGEMENT	DEL REY, LESTER	SS	GAL 61 08
EARTHMEN BEARING GIFTS	BROWN, FREDRIC	SS	GAL 60 06
RAINBIRD	LAFFERTY, R. A.	SS	GAL 61 12
THREE PORTRAITS AND A PRAYER	POHL, FREDERIK	SS	GAL 62 08
SOMETHING BRIGHT	HENDERSON, ZENNA	SS	GAL 60 02
ON THE GEM PLANET	SMITH, CORDWAINER	NV	GAL 63 10
DEEP DOWN DRAGON, THE	MERRIL, JUDITH	SS	GAL 61 08
KING OF THE CITY, THE	LAUMER, KEITH	NV	GAL 61 08

BEAT CLUSTER, THE	LEIBER, FRITZ	SS	GAL 61 10
OLD-FASHIONED BIRD CHRISTMAS, AN			
	ST. CLAIR, MARGARET	NV	GAL 61 12
BIG PAT BOOM, THE	KNIGHT, DAMON	SS	GAL 63 12

SF: AUTHORS' CHOICE   HARRISON, HARRY   AN BKM 68 06
    IN ENGLAND AS "BACKDROP OF STARS"

INTRODUCTION	HARRISON, HARRY	IN	
JUDAS DANCED (JUDAS DANCING)	ALDISS, BRIAN W.	SS	SMG 58 01
LAST OF THE DELIVERERS, THE	ANDERSON, POUL	SS	FSF 58 02
FOUNDING FATHER	ASIMOV, ISAAC	SS	GAL 65 10
END-GAME	BALLARD, J. G.	SS	NWS 63 06
TIGER RIDE	BLISH, JAMES		
	AND KNIGHT, DAMON	SS C	ASF 48 10
CONSUMER'S REPORT (NO GUN TO THE VICTOR)			
	COGSWELL, THEODORE R	SS	IMG 55 10
PROPOSAL	DE CAMP, L. SPRAGUE	SS	STS 52 11
SAIL ON! SAIL ON!	FARMER, PHILIP JOSE	SS	STS 52 12
MISSING LINK	HERBERT, FRANK	SS	ASF 59 02
MYTHS MY GREAT-GRANDDAUGHTER TAUGHT ME			
	LEIBER, FRITZ	SS	FSF 63 01
SYNDROME JOHNNY	MACLEAN, KATHERINE	SS	GAL 51 07
DAY MILLION	POHL, FREDERIK	SS	ROG 66 02
RETALIATION (TIME OF WAR)	REYNOLDS, MACK	SS	IFS 65 11

SF: AUTHORS' CHOICE 2   HARRISON, HARRY   AN BKM 70 05

INTRODUCTION	HARRISON, HARRY	IN	
FONDLY FAHRENHEIT	BESTER, ALFRED	SS	FSF 54 08
CONTACT BETWEEN EQUALS	BUDRYS, ALGIS	SS	VSF 58 07
LATE	CHANDLER, A. BERTRAM	SS	SCF 55 04
PROOF	CLEMENT, HAL	SS	ASF 42 06
DIPLOMATIC COOP	GALOUYE, DANIEL F.	SS	STR 59 05
LOVE IN THE DARK (LOVE ETHEREAL)			
	GOLD, H. L.	SS	SUS 51 FL
EXPERT TOUCH, THE	NOURSE, ALAN E.	NV	FSF 55 11
STICK FOR HARRY EDDINGTON, A	OLIVER, CHAD	SS	FSF 65 08
JUST CURIOUS	SCHMITZ, JAMES H.	SS	68
TO SEE THE INVISIBLE MAN	SILVERBERG, ROBERT	SS	WOT 63 04
HEIR UNAPPARENT (HEIR APPARENT)			
	VAN VOGT, A. E.	SS	ASF 45 06
AUTO-ANCESTRAL FRACTURE	ALDISS, BRIAN W.	NV	NWS 67 12

SF: AUTHORS' CHOICE 3   HARRISON, HARRY   AN H PUT 71

INTRODUCTION	HARRISON, HARRY	IN	
SOBER NOISES OF MORNING IN A MARGINAL LAND			
	ALDISS, BRIAN W.	NV	LOM 72 06
PHOG	ANTHONY, PIERS	SS	FAN 65 06
POWER OF EVERY ROOT, THE	DAVIDSON, AVRAM	NV	FSF 67 10
DEEPEST BLUE IN THE WORLD, THE			
	DORMAN, SONYA	SS	FSF 64 09
O YE OF LITTLE FAITH	ELLISON, HARLAN	SS	KNT 68 09
BY THE FALLS	HARRISON, HARRY	SS	IFS 70 01
COMING OF THE SUN, THE	JONES, LANGDON	SS	NWS 68 03
FALCON AND THE FALCONEER, THE			
	MALZBERG, BARRY N.	SS	FSF 69 12
TRANSFINITE CHOICE, THE	MASSON, DAVID I.	SS	NWS 66 08
TANK TRAPEZE	MOORCOCK, MICHAEL	SS	NWS 69 01
BORDERED IN BLACK	NIVEN, LARRY	SS	FSF 66 04
AT CENTRAL	REED, KIT	SS	67
LAST HURRAH OF THE GOLDEN HORDE, THE			
	SPINRAD, NORMAN	SS	NWS 69 07

SF: AUTHORS' CHOICE 4   HARRISON, HARRY   AN H PUT 74

OLD HUNDREDTH	ALDISS, BRIAN W.	SS	NWS 60 11
FAIR (AS KEITH WOODCOTT)	BRUNNER, JOHN	SS	NWS 56 03
FORGOTTEN ENEMY, THE	CLARKE, ARTHUR C.	SS	NWS 49 05
WARRIOR	DICKSON, GORDON R.	SS	ASF 65 12
ET IN ARCADIA EGO (ALSO AS THE PLANET ARCADIA)			
	DISCH, THOMAS M.	SS	QRK 71 02
BUT SOFT, WHAT LIGHT...	EMSHWILLER, CAROL	SS	FSF 66 04
MISOGYNIST, THE	GUNN, JAMES E.	SS	GAL 52 11
ALL OF US ARE DYING	JOHNSON, GEORGE C.	SS	ROG 61 10
FIRE AND THE SWORD, THE	ROBINSON, FRANK M.	NV	GAL 51 08
BAD MEDICINE	SHECKLEY, ROBERT	NV	GAL 56 07
AUTUMN LAND, THE	SIMAK, CLIFFORD D.	NV	FSF 71 10
SENSE OF BEAUTY, A	TAYLOR, ROBERT	SS	FSF 68 08
LAST FLIGHT OF DR. AIN, THE	TIPTREE, JAMES JR.	SS	GAL 69 03
ULLWARD'S RETREAT	VANCE, JACK	NV	GAL 58 12
MAN WHO LOVED THE FAIOLI, THE			
	ZELAZNY, ROGER	SS	GAL 67 06

SF: THE BEST OF THE BEST   MERRIL, JUDITH   AN H DCT 67

INTRODUCTION	MERRIL, JUDITH	IN	
HOOFER, THE	MILLER, WALTER M. JR	SS	FUN 55 09
BULKHEAD (WHO?)	STURGEON, THEODORE	NV	GAL 55 03
ANYTHING BOX	HENDERSON, ZENNA	SS	FSF 56 10
PRIMA BELLADONNA	BALLARD, J. G.	SS	SCF 56 12
CASEY AGONISTES	MCKENNA, RICHARD M.	SS	FSF 58 09
DEATH IN THE HOUSE, A	SIMAK, CLIFFORD D.	NV	GAL 59 10
SPACE-TIME FOR SPRINGERS	LEIBER, FRITZ	SS	STR 58 04
PELT	EMSHWILLER, CAROL	SS	FSF 58 11
STRANGER STATION	KNIGHT, DAMON	NV	FSF 56 12
SATELLITE PASSAGE	THOMAS, THEODORE L.	SS	IFS 58 12
NO, NO, NOT ROGOV!	SMITH, CORDWAINER	SS	IFS 59 02
COMPOUND INTEREST	REYNOLDS, MACK	SS	FSF 56 08
JUNIOR	ABERNATHY, ROBERT	SS	GAL 56 01
SENSE FROM THOUGHT DIVIDE	CLIFTON, MARK	NV	ASF 55 03
MARIANA	LEIBER, FRITZ	SS	FAN 60 02
PLENITUDE	WORTHINGTON, WILL	SS	FSF 59 11
DAY AT THE BEACH	EMSHWILLER, CAROL	SS	FSF 59 08
LET'S BE FRANK	ALDISS, BRIAN W.	SS	SCF 57 06
WONDER HORSE, THE	BYRAM, GEORGE	SS	ATL 57 08
NOBODY BOTHERS GUS (AS PAUL JANVIER)			
	BUDRYS, ALGIS	SS	ASF 55 11
PRIZE OF PERIL, THE	SHECKLEY, ROBERT	SS	FSF 58 05
HANDLER, THE	KNIGHT, DAMON	SS	ROG 60 09

SF: THE BEST OF THE BEST

```
GOLEM, THE                      DAVIDSON, AVRAM      SS   FSF 55 03
SOUND-SWEEP, THE                BALLARD, J. G.       NV   SCF 60 02
HICKORY, DICKORY, KEROUAC (AS MARTIN SCOTT)
                                GEHMAN, RICHARD      SS   PBY 58 03
DREAMING IS A PRIVATE THING     ASIMOV, ISAAC        SS   FSF 55 12
PUBLIC HATING, THE              ALLEN, STEVE         SS   BBM 55 01
YOU KNOW WILLIE                 COGSWELL, THEODORE R SS   FSF 57 05
ONE ORDINARY DAY, WITH PEANUTS
                                JACKSON, SHIRLEY     SS   FSF 55 01
```

SF: THE YEAR'S GREATEST SCIENCE FICTION AND FANTASY
```
                                MERRIL, JUDITH       AN H GNM 56
INTRODUCTION                    WELLES, ORSON        IN
PREFACE                         MERRIL, JUDITH       IN
STUTTERER, THE                  MERLISS, R. R.       NV   ASF 55 04
GOLEM, THE                      DAVIDSON, AVRAM      SS   FSF 55 03
JUNIOR                          ABERNATHY, ROBERT    SS   GAL 56 01
CAVE OF NIGHT, THE              GUNN, JAMES E.       SS   GAL 55 02
HOOPER, THE                     MILLER, WALTER M. JR SS   FUN 55 09
BULKHEAD (WHO?)                 STURGEON, THEODORE   NV   GAL 55 03
SENSE FROM THOUGHT DIVIDE       CLIFTON, MARK        NV   ASF 55 03
POTTAGE                         HENDERSON, ZENNA     NV   FSF 55 09
NOBODY BOTHERS GUS (AS PAUL JANVIER)
                                BUDRYS, ALGIS        SS   ASF 55 11
LAST DAY OF SUMMER, THE         TUBB, E. C.          SS   SCF 55 02
ONE ORDINARY DAY, WITH PEANUTS
                                JACKSON, SHIRLEY     SS   FSF 55 01
ETHICATORS, THE                 MARSH, WILLARD       SS   IFS 55 08
BIRDS CAN'T COUNT               CLINGERMAN, MILDRED  SS   FSF 55 02
OF MISSING PERSONS              FINNEY, JACK         SS   GHK 55 03
DREAMING IS A PRIVATE THING     ASIMOV, ISAAC        SS   FSF 55 12
COUNTRY OF THE KIND, THE        KNIGHT, DAMON        SS   FSF 56 02
PUBLIC HATING, THE              ALLEN, STEVE         SS   BBM 55 01
HOME THERE'S NO RETURNING       KUTTNER, HENRY
                                AND MOORE, C. L.     NV C NEW 55 AC
YEAR'S S-F, THE, SUMMATION AND HONORABLE MENTIONS
                                MERRIL, JUDITH       MS
```

SF: THE YEAR'S GREATEST SCIENCE-FICTION AND FANTASY, FOURTH
ANNUAL VOLUME   MERRIL, JUDITH   AN   DEL 59 06
    SEE "SF:59"

SF: THE YEAR'S GREATEST SCIENCE-FICTION AND FANTASY, SECOND
ANNUAL VOLUME   MERRIL, JUDITH   AN   DEL 57 06
    SEE "SF:57"

SF: THE YEAR'S GREATEST SCIENCE-FICTION AND FANTASY, THIRD
ANNUAL VOLUME   MERRIL, JUDITH   AN   DEL 58 07
    SEE "SF:58"

SF:57, THE YEAR'S GREATEST SCIENCE FICTION AND FANTASY
```
                                MERRIL, JUDITH       AN H GNM 57
MAN WHO LIKED LIONS, THE        DALEY, JOHN BERNARD  SS   INF 56 10
COSMIC EXPENSE ACCOUNT, THE (THE COSMIC CHARGE ACCOUNT)
                                KORNBLUTH, C. M.     NV   FSF 56 01
FAR LOOK, THE                   THOMAS, THEODORE L.  NV   ASF 56 08
WHEN GRANDFATHER FLEW TO THE MOON (RETURN OF THE MOON MAN)
                                MALPASS, E. L.       SS   LOB 55 01
DOORSTOP, THE                   BRETNOR, REGINALD    SS   ASF 56 11
SILENT BROTHER                  BUDRYS, ALGIS        SS   ASF 56 02
STRANGER STATION                KNIGHT, DAMON        NV   FSF 56 12
EACH AN EXPLORER                ASIMOV, ISAAC        SS   FUT 56 30
ALL ABOUT "THE THING" (PARODIES TOSSED)
                                GARRETT, RANDALL     PM   SFS 56 05
PUT THEM ALL TOGETHER, THEY SPELL MONSTER
                                RUSSELL, RAY         SS   PBY 56 10
DIGGING THE WEANS               NATHAN, ROBERT       FA   HRP 56 11
TAKE A DEEP BREATH              THORNE, ROGER        SS   TIG 56
GRANDMA'S LIE SOAP              ABERNATHY, ROBERT    SS   FUN 56 02
COMPOUND INTEREST               REYNOLDS, MACK       SS   FSF 56 08
PRIMA BELLADONNA                BALLARD, J. G.       SS   SCF 56 12
OTHER MAN, THE                  STURGEON, THEODORE   NA   GAL 56 09
DAMNEDEST THING, THE            KANIN, GARSON        SS   ESQ 56 02
ANYTHING BOX                    HENDERSON, ZENNA     SS   FSF 56 10
YEAR'S S-F, THE, SUMMATION AND HONORABLE MENTIONS
                                MERRIL, JUDITH       MS
```

SF:58, THE YEAR'S GREATEST SCIENCE FICTION AND FANTASY
```
                                MERRIL, JUDITH       AN H GNM 58
INTRODUCTION                    MERRIL, JUDITH       IN
LET'S BE FRANK                  ALDISS, BRIAN W.     SS   SCF 57 06
FLY, THE                        LANGELAAN, GEORGE    NV   PBY 57 06
LET'S GET TOGETHER              ASIMOV, ISAAC        SS   INF 57 02
WONDER HORSE, THE               BYRAM, GEORGE        SS   ATL 57 08
YOU KNOW WILLIE                 COGSWELL, THEODORE R SS   FSF 57 05
NEAR MISS                       KUTTNER, HENRY       SS   NEW 58 AN
GAME PRESERVE                   PHILLIPS, ROG        SS   IFS 57 10
NOW LET US SLEEP                DAVIDSON, AVRAM      SS   VSF 57 09
WILDERNESS                      HENDERSON, ZENNA     SS   FSF 57 01
FLYING HIGH                     IONESCO, EUGENE      SS   MAD 57 10
EDGE OF THE SEA, THE            BUDRYS, ALGIS        SS   VSF 58 03
HOW NEAR IS THE MOON?           MERRIL, JUDITH       AR   NEW 58 AN
TRANSITION- FROM FANTASY TO SCIENCE
                                CLARKE, ARTHUR C.    AR        57
SPUTNIK: ONE REASON WHY WE LOST
                                STINE, G. HARRY      AR   FSF 58 01
GOING UP! (FROM THE ARTICLE "SPACE TRAVEL")
                                DRISCOLL, DENNIS     AR   BLF 57 05
WHERE DO WE GO FROM HERE?       LEY, WILLY           AR   NEW 58 AN
SCIENCE FICTION STILL LEADS SCIENCE FACT
                                BOUCHER, ANTHONY     AR   NYT 57 12
YEAR'S S-F, THE, SUMMATION AND HONORABLE MENTIONS
                                MERRIL, JUDITH       MS
```

SF:59, THE YEAR'S GREATEST SCIENCE FICTION AND FANTASY
                                MERRIL, JUDITH   AN H GNM 59
```
INTRODUCTION                    MERRIL, JUDITH       IN
PELT                            EMSHWILLER, CAROL    SS   FSF 58 11
TRIGGERMAN                      BONE, J. F.          SS   ASF 58 12
PRIZE OF PERIL, THE             SHECKLEY, ROBERT     SS   FSF 58 05
HICKORY, DICKORY, KEROUAC (AS MARTIN SCOTT)
                                GEHMAN, RICHARD      SS   PBY 58 03
YELLOW PILL, THE                PHILLIPS, ROG        SS   ASF 58 10
RIVER OF RICHES                 KERSH, GERALD        SS   SEP 58 03
SATELLITE PASSAGE               THOMAS, THEODORE L.  SS   IFS 58 12
CASEY AGONISTES                 MCKENNA, RICHARD M.  SS   FSF 58 09
SPACE-TIME FOR SPRINGERS        LEIBER, FRITZ        SS   STR 58 04
OR ALL THE SEAS WITH OYSTERS    DAVIDSON, AVRAM      SS   GAL 58 05
TEN-STORY JIGSAW                ALDISS, BRIAN W.     SS   NEB 58 01
FRESH GUY                       TUBB, E. C.          SS   SCF 58 06
BEAUTIFUL THINGS, THE           ZIRUL, ARTHUR        SS   FUN 58 05
COMEDIAN'S CHILDREN, THE        STURGEON, THEODORE   NV   VSF 58 05
SHORT-SHORT STORY OF MANKIND, THE
                                STEINBECK, JOHN      SS   PBY 58 04
FROM SCIENCE FICTION TO SCIENCE FACT: THE UNIVERSE
                                MISC. MATERIAL       MS
MAN IN SPACE                    LANG, DANIEL         AR   NYM 58 11
ROCKETS TO WHERE?               MERRIL, JUDITH       AR   NEW 59 AN
THUNDER-THIEVES, THE (IT'S ALL HOW YOU LOOK AT IT)
                                ASIMOV, ISAAC        PM   FUT 58 10
YEAR'S S-F, THE, SUMMATION AND HONORABLE MENTIONS
                                MERRIL, JUDITH       MS
```

SF12   MERRIL, JUDITH   AN H DCT 68
FISH OUT OF WATER, MAN BESIDE HIMSELF
```
                                MERRIL, JUDITH       IN
CINEMAGICIANS                   KUPFERBERG, TULI     PM   ESR 66
IN SECLUSION                    JACOBS, HARVEY       SS   NWS 68 02
FOOD FARM, THE                  REED, KIT            SS   ORB 67 02
GOGOL'S WIFE                    LANDOLFI, TOMMASO    SS   ENC 63
BALLOON, THE                    BARTHELME, DONALD    SS   NYM 66 04
CLOUD-SCULPTORS OF CORAL D, THE
                                BALLARD, J. G.       SS   FSF 67 12
LUANA                           THOMAS, GILBERT      SS   FSF 66 09
W-A-V-E-R                       KUPFERBERG, TULI     PM   ESR 66
DURING THE JURASSIC             UPDIKE, JOHN         SS   TRV 66 SU
FALL OF FRENCHY STEINER, THE    BAILEY, HILARY       NV   NWS 64 04
LIGHT OF OTHER DAYS             SHAW, BOB            SS   ASF 66 08
BEYOND THE WEEDS (THE POST-MORTEM PEOPLE)
                                TATE, PETER          SS   NWS 66 03
CRAB-APPLE CRISIS, THE          MACBETH, GEORGE      SS   NWS 66 10
PRIMARY EDUCATION OF THE CAMIROI
                                LAFFERTY, R. A.      SS   GAL 66 12
WHEN I WAS MISS DOW             DORMAN, SONYA        SS   GAL 66 06
VACATION ON EARTH, A            DISCH, THOMAS M.     PM        66
CONFLUENCE                      ALDISS, BRIAN W.     SS   FUN 67 08
JOURNAL FROM ELLIPSIA (EXCERPT)
                                CALISHER, HORTENSE   EX   LBR 65
ORNAMENT TO HIS PROFESSION, AN
                                HARNESS, CHARLES L.  NV   ASF 66 02
NARROW VALLEY                   LAFFERTY, R. A.      SS   FSF 66 09
THEY DO NOT ALWAYS REMEMBER     BURROUGHS, WILLIAM   SS   ESQ 66 05
WINTER FLIES, THE (THE INNER CIRCLES)
                                LEIBER, FRITZ        SS   FSF 67 10
WHEN I FIRST READ...            ALLEN, DICK          PM   ATR 66
YOU: COMA: MARILYN MONROE       BALLARD, J. G.       SS   NWS 66 06
AND MORE CHANGES STILL          MICHAUX, HENRI       SS
OTHER, THE                      MACLEAN, KATHERINE   SS   NWS 66 07
CHICKEN ICARUS (A DREAM OF FLYING)
                                EMSHWILLER, CAROL    SS   CAV 66
IN THE EGG (TRANSLATED BY MICHAEL HAMBURGER)
                                GRASS, GUNTER        PM        66
STAR PIT, THE                   DELANY, SAMUEL R.    NV   WOT 67 02
PERSONAL                        KUPFERBERG, TULI     SS   ESR 66
```

SHADOW OF TOMORROW   POHL, FREDERIK   AN H DBL 53
```
INTRODUCTION                    POHL, FREDERIK       IN
YEAR OF THE JACKPOT, THE        HEINLEIN, ROBERT A.  NV   GAL 52 03
BAD DAY FOR SALES, A            LEIBER, FRITZ        SS   GAL 53 07
C-CHUTE, THE                    ASIMOV, ISAAC        NV   GAL 51 10
PERFECT CREATURE, THE (ALSO AS UNA, FSF 53 01)
                                WYNDHAM, JOHN        NV   TOW 37 01
MARCHING MORONS, THE            KORNBLUTH, C. M.     NV   GAL 51 04
TRANSFER POINT                  BOUCHER, ANTHONY     SS   GAL 50 11
WATCHBIRD                       SHECKLEY, ROBERT     NV   GAL 53 02
TO A RIPE OLD AGE               TUCKER, WILSON       SS   FSF 52 12
ORPHANS OF THE VOID             SHAARA, MICHAEL      NV   GAL 52 06
OLD ORDER, THE (THE NEW GODS LEAD)
                                DEL REY, LESTER      SS   MSS 51 01
GENESIS                         PIPER, H. BEAM       NV   FUT 51 09
HALO                            CLEMENT, HAL         NV   GAL 52 10
COMMON TIME                     BLISH, JAMES         SS   SFQ 53 08
LOVE                            WILSON, RICHARD      SS   FSF 52 06
MISOGYNIST, THE                 GUNN, JAMES E.       SS   GAL 52 11
LUCKIEST MAN IN DENV, THE       EISNER, SIMON        SS   GAL 51 12
NOT A CREATURE WAS STIRRING     EVANS, DEAN          SS   GAL 51 12
```

SHADOW PLAY   BEAUMONT, CHARLES   AC   PTH 64
    SEE "THE HUNGER AND OTHER STORIES"

SHADOWS WITH EYES   LEIBER, FRITZ   AC   BAL 62 03
```
BIT OF THE DARK WORLD, A        LEIBER, FRITZ        NV   FAN 62 02
DEAD MAN, THE                   LEIBER, FRITZ        NV   PNM 58 04
POWER OF THE PUPPETS, THE       LEIBER, FRITZ        SS   TMY 41 FL
SCHIZO JIMMIE                   LEIBER, FRITZ        SS   SMM 60 02
MAN WHO MADE FRIENDS WITH ELECTRICITY, THE
                                LEIBER, FRITZ        SS   FSF 62 03
DESKFUL OF GIRLS, A             LEIBER, FRITZ        NV   FSF 58 04
```

SHAMBLEAU AND OTHERS   MOORE, C. L.   AC H GNM 53
    BRITISH CONSUL EDITION OMITS "JIREL MEETS MAGIC"
BLACK GOD'S KISS   MOORE, C. L.   NV   WRT 34 10

SHAMBLEAU AND OTHERS

SHAMBLEAU	MOORE, C. L.	NV	WRT 33 11
BLACK GOD'S SHADOW	MOORE, C. L.	NV	WRT 34 12
BLACK THIRST	MOORE, C. L.	NV	WRT 34 04
TREE OF LIFE, THE	MOORE, C. L.	NV	WRT 36 10
JIREL MEETS MAGIC	MOORE, C. L.	NV	WRT 35 07
SCARLET DREAM	MOORE, C. L.	NV	WRT 34 05

SHAMBLEAU AND OTHERS (3 OF 7)

	MOORE, C. L.	AC	GAN 58 31
SHAMBLEAU	MOORE, C. L.	NV	WRT 33 11
BLACK THIRST	MOORE, C. L.	NV	WRT 34 04
TREE OF LIFE, THE	MOORE, C. L.	NV	WRT 36 10

SHANADU

	BRINEY, ROBERT E.	OA	SSR 53 11
QUEST OF THE VEIL	DEWEESE, EUGENE	NV	
FIRE BORN, THE	DUANE, TOBY	NV	
BLACK TOWER, THE	MCNAUGHTON, BRIAN J. AND DUANE, ANDREW	NV C	

SHAPE OF SPACE, THE

	NIVEN, LARRY	AC	BAL 69 09
WARRIORS, THE	NIVEN, LARRY	SS	IFS 66 02
SAFE AT ANY SPEED	NIVEN, LARRY	SS	FSF 67 05
HOW THE HEROES DIE	NIVEN, LARRY	NV	GAL 66 10
AT THE BOTTOM OF A HOLE	NIVEN, LARRY	NV	GAL 66 12
BORDERED IN BLACK	NIVEN, LARRY	SS	FSF 66 04
LIKE BANQUO'S GHOST	NIVEN, LARRY	SS	IFS 68 09
ONE FACE	NIVEN, LARRY	NV	GAL 65 06
MEDDLER, THE	NIVEN, LARRY	NV	FSF 68 10
DRY RUN	NIVEN, LARRY	SS	FSF 68 05
CONVERGENT SERIES (THE LONG NIGHT)	NIVEN, LARRY	SS	FSF 67 03
DEADLIER WEAPON, THE	NIVEN, LARRY	SS	EQM 68 06
DEATH BY ECSTASY (THE ORGANLEGGERS)	NIVEN, LARRY	NV	GAL 69 01

SHAPE OF THINGS, THE

	KNIGHT, DAMON	AN	POP 67
INTRODUCTION	KNIGHT, DAMON	IN	
DON'T LOOK NOW	KUTTNER, HENRY	SS	STS 48 03
BOX, THE	BLISH, JAMES	SS	TWS 49 04
NEW REALITY, THE	HARNESS, CHARLES L.	NV	TWS 50 12
ETERNAL NOW, THE	LEINSTER, MURRAY	NV	TWS 44 FL
SKY WAS FULL OF SHIPS, THE	STURGEON, THEODORE	SS	TWS 47 06
SHAPE OF THINGS, THE	BRADBURY, RAY	SS	TWS 48 02
ONLY THING WE LEARN, THE	KORNBLUTH, C. M.	SS	STS 49 07
HIBITED MAN, THE	DE CAMP, L. SPRAGUE	SS	TWS 49 10
DORMANT	VAN VOGT, A. E.	SS	STS 48 11
AMBASSADORS, THE	BOUCHER, ANTHONY	SS	STS 52 06
CHILD IS CRYING, A	MACDONALD, JOHN D.	SS	TWS 48 12

SHARDS OF SPACE

	SHECKLEY, ROBERT	AC	BAN 62 07
PROSPECTOR'S SPECIAL	SHECKLEY, ROBERT	NV	GAL 59 12
GIRLS AND NUGENT MILLER, THE	SHECKLEY, ROBERT	SS	FSF 60 03
MEETING OF THE MINDS	SHECKLEY, ROBERT	NA	GAL 60 02
POTENTIAL	SHECKLEY, ROBERT	SS	ASF 53 11
FOOL'S MATE	SHECKLEY, ROBERT	SS	ASF 53 03
SUBSISTENCE LEVEL	SHECKLEY, ROBERT	SS	GAL 54 08
SLOW SEASON, THE	SHECKLEY, ROBERT	SS	FSF 54 10
ALONE AT LAST	SHECKLEY, ROBERT	SS	INF 57 02
FOREVER (AS NED LANG)	SHECKLEY, ROBERT	SS	GAL 59 02
SWEEPER OF LORAY, THE	SHECKLEY, ROBERT	SS	GAL 59 04
SPECIAL EXHIBIT, THE	SHECKLEY, ROBERT	SS	ESQ 53 10

SHIP WHO SANG, THE

	MCCAFFREY, ANNE	AC H	WKR 69
SHIP WHO SANG, THE	MCCAFFREY, ANNE	SS	FSF 61 04
SHIP WHO MOURNED, THE	MCCAFFREY, ANNE	SS	ASF 66 03
SHIP WHO KILLED, THE	MCCAFFREY, ANNE	NV	GAL 66 10
SHIP WHO DISSEMBLED, THE (THE SHIP WHO DISAPPEARED)	MCCAFFREY, ANNE	NV	IFS 69 03
DRAMATIC MISSION	MCCAFFREY, ANNE	SN	ASF 69 06
PARTNERED SHIP, THE	MCCAFFREY, ANNE	SS	NEW 69 AC

SHIPS TO THE STARS

	LEIBER, FRITZ	DC	ACE 64
DR. KOMETEVSKY'S DAY	LEIBER, FRITZ	SS	GAL 52 02
BIG TREK, THE	LEIBER, FRITZ	SS	FSF 57 10
ENCHANTED FOREST, THE	LEIBER, FRITZ	SS	ASF 50 10
DEADLY MOON	LEIBER, FRITZ	NV	FAN 60 11
SNOWBANK ORBIT, THE	LEIBER, FRITZ	NV	IFS 62 09
SHIP SAILS AT MIDNIGHT, THE	LEIBER, FRITZ	NV	FAD 50 09

SHOCK II

	MATHESON, RICHARD	AC	DEL 64 10
FLOURISH OF STRUMPETS, A	MATHESON, RICHARD	SS	PBY 56 11
BROTHER TO THE MACHINE	MATHESON, RICHARD	SS	IFS 52 11
NO SUCH THING AS A VAMPIRE	MATHESON, RICHARD	SS	PBY 59 10
DESCENT	MATHESON, RICHARD	SS	IFS 54 05
DEADLINE	MATHESON, RICHARD	SS	ROG 59
MAN WHO MADE THE WORLD, THE	MATHESON, RICHARD	SS	IMG 54 02
GRAVEYARD SHIFT (THE FACES)	MATHESON, RICHARD	SS	MCB 60
LIKENESS OF JULIE, THE (AS LOGAN SWANSON)	MATHESON, RICHARD	SS	NEW 62 AN
LAZARUS II	MATHESON, RICHARD	SS	FSM 53 07
BIG SUPRISE (WHAT WAS IN THE BOX)	MATHESON, RICHARD	SS	EQM 59 04
CRICKETS	MATHESON, RICHARD	SS	SHK 60 05
MUTE	MATHESON, RICHARD	NV	NEW 62 AN
FROM SHADOWED PLACES	MATHESON, RICHARD	NV	FSF 60 10

SHOCK III

	MATHESON, RICHARD	AC	DEL 66 03
GIRL OF MY DREAMS	MATHESON, RICHARD	SS	FSF 63 10
'TIS THE SEASON TO BE JELLY	MATHESON, RICHARD	SS	FSF 63 06
RETURN	MATHESON, RICHARD	SS	TWS 51 10
JAZZ MACHINE, THE	MATHESON, RICHARD	PM	FSF 63 02
DISINHERITORS, THE	MATHESON, RICHARD	SS	FSM 53 01
SLAUGHTER HOUSE	MATHESON, RICHARD	NV	WRT 53 07
SHOCK WAVE (CRESCENDO)	MATHESON, RICHARD	SS	GAM 63 01
WHEN THE WAKER SLEEPS (THE WAKER DREAMS)	MATHESON, RICHARD	SS	GAL 50 12

SHORT STORIES OF H. G. WELLS, THE

WITCH WAR	MATHESON, RICHARD	SS	STS 51 07
FIRST ANNIVERSARY	MATHESON, RICHARD	SS	PBY 60 07
MISS STARDUST	MATHESON, RICHARD	SS	STS 55 SP
FULL CIRCLE	MATHESON, RICHARD	SS	FUN 53 08
NIGHTMARE AT 20,000 FEET	MATHESON, RICHARD	SS	NEW 62 AN

SHOCK WAVES

	MATHESON, RICHARD	AC	DEL 70 10
VISIT TO SANTA CLAUS, A	MATHESON, RICHARD	SS	NEW 70 AC
FINGER PRINTS	MATHESON, RICHARD	SS	NEW 62 AN
DEUS EX MACHINA	MATHESON, RICHARD	SS	GAM 63 02
THING, THE	MATHESON, RICHARD	SS	MSS 51 05
CONQUEROR, THE	MATHESON, RICHARD	SS	54
DRINK OF WATER, A	MATHESON, RICHARD	SS	SGN 67
DYING ROOM ONLY	MATHESON, RICHARD	SS	53
ADVANCE NOTICE	MATHESON, RICHARD	SS	ROG 59
WET STRAW	MATHESON, RICHARD	SS	WRT 53 01
THERESE	MATHESON, RICHARD	SS	68
DAY OF RECKONING	MATHESON, RICHARD	SS	MCB 60
PREY	MATHESON, RICHARD	SS	PBY 69 04
COME FYGURES, COME SHADOWES	MATHESON, RICHARD	NV	NEW 70 AC
FINISHING TOUCHES, THE	MATHESON, RICHARD	SS	NEW 70 AC

SHOCK!

	MATHESON, RICHARD	AC	DEL 61 06
CHILDREN OF NOAH, THE	MATHESON, RICHARD	SS	57
LEMMINGS	MATHESON, RICHARD	SS	FSF 58 01
SPLENDID SOURCE, THE	MATHESON, RICHARD	SS	PBY 56 05
LONG DISTANCE CALL (SORRY, RIGHT NUMBER)	MATHESON, RICHARD	SS	BEY 53 11
MANTAGE	MATHESON, RICHARD	NV	NEW 59 AN
ONE FOR THE BOOKS	MATHESON, RICHARD	NV	GAL 55 09
HOLIDAY MAN, THE	MATHESON, RICHARD	SS	FSF 57 07
DANCE OF THE DEAD	MATHESON, RICHARD	SS	STR 54 03
LEGION OF PLOTTERS	MATHESON, RICHARD	SS	53
EDGE, THE	MATHESON, RICHARD	SS	FSF 58 08
CREEPING TERROR, THE (A TOUCH OF GRAPEFRUIT)	MATHESON, RICHARD	SS	STR 59 05
DEATH SHIP	MATHESON, RICHARD	NV	FSM 53 03
DISTRIBUTOR, THE	MATHESON, RICHARD	SS	PBY 58 03

SHOCKING THING, A

	KNIGHT, DAMON	AN	PKT 74 11
MAN FROM THE SOUTH	DAHL, ROALD	SS	53
SNAIL-WATCHER, THE	HIGHSMITH, PATRICIA	SS	GAM 64 03
BIANCA'S HANDS	STURGEON, THEODORE	SS	ARB 47 05
POOR LITTLE WARRIOR!	ALDISS, BRIAN W.	SS	FSF 58 04
HOUNDS, THE	WILHELM, KATE	NV	NEW 74 AN
CLONE, THE	THOMAS, THEODORE L.	SS	FAN 59 12
TOUCH OF NUTMEG MAKES IT, THE	COLLIER, JOHN	SS	43
CASEY AGONISTES	MCKENNA, RICHARD M.	SS	FSF 58 09
ABYSS, THE	ANDREYEV, LEONID	SS	43
CASE HISTORY, A	WEST, JOHN ANTHONY	SS	73
FONDLY FAHRENHEIT	BESTER, ALFRED	SS	FSF 54 08
LUKUNDOO	WHITE, EDWARD LUCAS	SS	WRT 25 11
CABBAGE PATCH, THE	COGSWELL, THEODORE R	SS	FSF 57 12
OIL OF DOG	BIERCE, AMBROSE	SS	
TIME OF THE BIG SLEEP, THE	ANDREVON, JEAN-PIERRE	NV	71
RIGHT MAN FOR THE RIGHT JOB, THE	THOMPSON, J. C.	SS	62
YEAR OF THE JACKPOT, THE	HEINLEIN, ROBERT A.	NV	GAL 52 03

SHORES BENEATH, THE

	SALLIS, JAMES	AN	AVN 71 08
TIME CONSIDERED AS A HELIX OF SEMI-PRECIOUS STONES	DELANY, SAMUEL R.	SS	NWS 68 12
GRAVEYARD HEART, THE	ZELAZNY, ROGER	NV	FAN 64 03
MASTERSON AND THE CLERKS	SLADEK, JOHN T.	NV	NWS 67 09
ASIAN SHORE, THE	DISCH, THOMAS M.	NV	ORB 70 06

SHORES OF SPACE, THE

	MATHESON, RICHARD	AC	BAN 57 02
BEING	MATHESON, RICHARD	NV	IFS 54 08
PATTERN FOR SURVIVAL	MATHESON, RICHARD	SS	FSF 55 05
STEEL	MATHESON, RICHARD	SS	FSF 56 05
TEST, THE	MATHESON, RICHARD	SS	FSF 54 11
CLOTHS MAKE THE MAN	MATHESON, RICHARD	SS	WBY 51 02
BLOOD SON (DRINK MY RED BLOOD)	MATHESON, RICHARD	SS	IMG 51 04
TRESPASS (MOTHER BY PROTEST)	MATHESON, RICHARD	NV	FAN 53 10
WHEN DAY IS DUN	MATHESON, RICHARD	SS	FUN 54 05
CURIOUS CHILD, THE	MATHESON, RICHARD	SS	FAN 54 06
FUNERAL, THE	MATHESON, RICHARD	SS	FSF 55 04
LAST DAY, THE	MATHESON, RICHARD	SS	AMZ 53 05
LITTLE GIRL LOST	MATHESON, RICHARD	SS	AMZ 53 11
DOLL THAT DOES EVERYTHING, THE	MATHESON, RICHARD	SS	FUN 54 12

SHORES OF TOMORROW, THE

	SILVERBERG, ROBERT	AC H	NEL 76
SOUND DECISION	SILVERBERG, ROBERT AND GARRETT, RANDALL	NV C	ASF 56 10
DAY THE FOUNDER DIED, THE	SILVERBERG, ROBERT	SS	
QUICK FREEZE	SILVERBERG, ROBERT	SS	SFQ 57 05
STRESS PATTERN	SILVERBERG, ROBERT	NV	ASF 60 01
SILENT COLONY, THE	SILVERBERG, ROBERT	SS	FUT 54 10
ISOLATIONISTS, THE	SILVERBERG, ROBERT	SS	SFS 58 11
DEADLOCK	SILVERBERG, ROBERT AND SILVERBERG, BARBARA	NV C	ASF 59 01
FINAL CHALLENGE, THE	SILVERBERG, ROBERT	SS	INF 56 08

SHORT STORIES OF H. G. WELLS, THE

	WELLS, H. G.	AC H	BEN 27
TIME MACHINE, THE	WELLS, H. G.	NA	NRV 95 01
EMPIRE OF THE ANTS, THE	WELLS, H. G.	SS	SND 05 12
VISION OF JUDGEMENT, A	WELLS, H. G.	SS	BUT 99 09
LAND IRONCLADS, THE	WELLS, H. G.	NV	SND 03 12
BEAUTIFUL SUIT, THE (A MOONLIGHT FABLE)	WELLS, H. G.	SS	COL 09 04
DOOR IN THE WALL, THE	WELLS, H. G.	SS	DCH 06 07
PEARL OF LOVE, THE	WELLS, H. G.	SS	24

SHORT STORIES OF H. G. WELLS, THE

COUNTRY OF THE BLIND, THE   WELLS, H. G.   SS   SND 04 04
STOLEN BACILLUS, THE   WELLS, H. G.   SS   PMB 94 06
FLOWERING OF THE STRANGE ORCHID, THE (ALSO AS THE STRANGE
  ORCHID)   WELLS, H. G.   SS   PMB 94 08
IN THE AVU OBSERVATORY   WELLS, H. G.   SS   PMB 94 08
TRIUMPHS OF A TAXIDERMIST, THE
                                  WELLS, H. G.   SS   PGZ 94
DEAL IN OSTRICHES, A   WELLS, H. G.   SS   PMB 94
THROUGH A WINDOW (AT A WINDOW)
                                  WELLS, H. G.   SS   BAW 94 08
TEMPTATION OF HARRINGAY, THE   WELLS, H. G.   SS   SJG 95 02
FLYING MAN, THE (THE ADVENT OF THE FLYING MAN)
                                  WELLS, H. G.   SS   PGZ 93 12
DIAMOND MAKER, THE   WELLS, H. G.   SS   PMB 94
AEPYORNIS ISLAND   WELLS, H. G.   SS   PMB 94 12
REMARKABLE CASE OF DAVIDSON'S EYES, THE
                                  WELLS, H. G.   SS   PMB 95 03
LORD OF THE DYNAMOS, THE   WELLS, H. G.   SS   PMB 94 09
HAMMERPOUND PARK BURGLARY, THE
                                  WELLS, H. G.   SS   PMB 94
MOTH, THE (A MOTH- GENUS NOVO)
                                  WELLS, H. G.   SS   PGZ 95 03
TREASURE IN THE FOREST, THE   WELLS, H. G.   SS   PMB 94
PLATTNER STORY, THE   WELLS, H. G.   SS   NRV 96 04
ARGONAUTS OF THE AIR, THE   WELLS, H. G.   SS   PMY 95
STORY OF THE LATE MR. ELVESHAM, THE
                                  WELLS, H. G.   SS   IDL 96 05
IN THE ABYSS   WELLS, H. G.   SS   PRS 96 08
APPLE, THE   WELLS, H. G.   SS   IDL 96 10
UNDER THE KNIFE (SLIP UNDER THE KNIFE)
                                  WELLS, H. G.   SS   NRV 96 01
SEA-RAIDERS, THE   WELLS, H. G.   SS   WSL 96 12
POLLOCK AND THE PORROH MAN   WELLS, H. G.   SS   NBG 95 05
RED ROOM, THE   WELLS, H. G.   SS   IDL 96 03
CONE, THE   WELLS, H. G.   SS   UCN 95 09
PURPLE PILEUS, THE   WELLS, H. G.   SS   BAW 96 12
JILTING OF JANE, THE   WELLS, H. G.   SS   97
IN THE MODERN VEIN: AN UNSYMPATHETIC LOVE STORY (A BARDLET'S
  ROMANCE)   WELLS, H. G.   SS   TTH 94 03
CATASTROPHE, A   WELLS, H. G.   SS   NBG 95 08
LOST INHERITANCE, THE   WELLS, H. G.   SS   97
SAD STORY OF A DRAMATIC CRITIC, THE
                                  WELLS, H. G.   SS   BON 15
SLIP UNDER THE MICROSCOPE, A   WELLS, H. G.   SS   YBK 96 01
RECONCILIATION, THE (THE BULLA)
                                  WELLS, H. G.   SS   WSL 95 12
MY FIRST AEROPLANE   WELLS, H. G.   SS   SND 10 01
LITTLE MOTHER UP THE MORDERBEN, THE
                                  WELLS, H. G.   SS   SND 10 04
STORY OF THE LAST TRUMP, THE   WELLS, H. G.   SS   BON 15
GRISLY FOLK, THE   WELLS, H. G.   AR   SRY 21 04
CRYSTAL EGG, THE   WELLS, H. G.   SS   NRV 97 05
STAR, THE   WELLS, H. G.   NA   GRP 97 12
STORY OF THE STONE AGE, A   WELLS, H. G.   NA   IDL 97 05
STORY OF THE DAYS TO COME, A   WELLS, H. G.   NA   PGZ 97
MAN WHO COULD WORK MIRACLES, THE
                                  WELLS, H. G.   SS   ILN 98 07
FILMER   WELLS, H. G.   SS   GRP 01
MAGIC SHOP, THE   WELLS, H. G.   SS   SND 03 06
VALLEY OF SPIDERS, THE   WELLS, H. G.   SS   PRS 03 03
TRUTH ABOUT PYECRAFT, THE   WELLS, H. G.   SS   SND 03 04
MR. SKELMERSDALE IN FAIRYLAND
                                  WELLS, H. G.   SS   SND 01
INEXPERIENCED GHOST, THE (THE STORY OF THE INEXPERIENCED GHOST)
                                  WELLS, H. G.   SS   SND 02 03
JIMMY GOGGLES THE GOD   WELLS, H. G.   SS   GRP 98 12
NEW ACCELERATOR, THE   WELLS, H. G.   SS   SND 01 12
MR. LEDBETTER'S VACATION   WELLS, H. G.   SS   SND 98 10
STOLEN BODY, THE   WELLS, H. G.   SS   SND 98 11
MR. BRISHER'S TREASURE   WELLS, H. G.   SS   SND 99 04
MISS WINCHELSEA'S HEART   WELLS, H. G.   SS   QUN 98 10
DREAM OF ARMAGEDDON, A   WELLS, H. G.   NV   BAW 01

SHOT IN THE DARK   MERRIL, JUDITH   AN   BAN 50
SKY WAS FULL OF SHIPS, THE   STURGEON, THEODORE SS   TWS 47 06
HALFLING, THE   BRACKETT, LEIGH   SS   AST 43 02
KNOCK   BROWN, FREDRIC   SS   TWS 48 12
VOICES IN THE DUST OF ANNAN   KERSH, GERALD   SS   SEP 47 09
HITCH IN TIME, A   MACCREIGH, JAMES   SS   TWS 47 06
GENTLEMEN, BE SEATED   HEINLEIN, ROBERT A. SS   ARG 48 05
NIGHTMARE NUMBER THREE   BENET, STEPHEN V.   PM   35
STAR, THE   WELLS, H. G.   SS   GRP 97 12
DARK ANGEL, THE   PADGETT, LEWIS   SS   STS 46 03
MR. LUPESCU   BOUCHER, ANTHONY   SS   WRT 45 09
DAY OF THE DEEPIES, THE   LEINSTER, MURRAY   SS   FFM 47 10
SHADOW AND THE FLASH, THE   LONDON, JACK   SS   BOK 03 06
SPOKESMAN FOR TERRA   RAYMOND, HUGH   SS   STI 41 06
SHE WAS ASKING FOR YOU   ALLINGHAM, MARGAREY SS   46
STRANGE PLAYFELLOW (ALSO AS ROBBIE)
                                  ASIMOV, ISAAC   SS   SSS 40 09
BROOKLYN PROJECT   TENN, WILLIAM   SS   PLS 48 FL
INTERVIEW WITH A LEMMING   THURBER, JAMES   SS   43
MARS IS HEAVEN!   BRADBURY, RAY   SS   PLS 48 FL
WHO IS CHARLES AVISON?   MARSHALL, EDISON T. SS   ARG 16 04
FACTS IN THE CASE OF M. VALDEMAR
                                  POE, EDGAR ALLEN   SS   AWR 45 12
BRONZE PARROT, THE   FREEMAN, AUSTIN   SS   24
LIFE ON THE MOON   SAMALMAN, ALEXANDER SS   TWS 46 12
BLUNDER   WYLIE, PHILIP   SS   COL 46 01

SHOWCASE   ELWOOD, ROGER   OA H HRP 73
INTRODUCTION   DANN, JACK M.   IN   SCS 73
BRECKENRIDGE AND THE CONTINUUM
                                  SILVERBERG, ROBERT NV   SCS 73
CHILDHOOD OF THE HUMAN HERO, THE
                                  EMSHWILLER, CAROL   SS   SCS 73

JOHN'S OTHER LIFE   HALDEMAN, JOE W.   SS   SCS 73
TRIGONONOMY   MOORE, RAYLYN   NV   SCS 73
BARNABY'S CLOCK   LAFFERTY, R. A.   SS   SCS 73
ARRANGEMENT, THE   MCALLISTER, BRUCE   SS   SCS 73
UNION FOREVER, THE   MALZBERG, BARRY N.   SS   SCS 73
BIRD LOVER, THE   GREEN, JOSEPH   NV   SCS 73
MAN WHO SAW GUNGA DIN THIRTY TIMES, THE
                            BOVA, BEN   SS   SCS 73
TRANSITION TROLLEY, THE   HOWELL, JOSEPH   SS   SCS 73
GOING TO THE BEACH   WOLFE, GENE   SS   SCS 73
SOUL OF A SERVANT, THE   RUSS, JOANNA   SS   SCS 73

SHROUDED PLANET, THE   RANDALL, ROBERT   AC H GNM 58
CHOSEN PEOPLE, THE   RANDALL, ROBERT   NV   ASF 56 04
PROMISED LAND, THE   RANDALL, ROBERT   NV   ASF 56 04
FALSE PROPHET   RANDALL, ROBERT   NV   ASF 56 12

SIDEWISE IN TIME   LEINSTER, MURRAY   AC H SHS 50
SIDEWISE IN TIME   LEINSTER, MURRAY   SN   ASF 34 04
PROXIMA CENTAURI   LEINSTER, MURRAY   SN   ASF 35 04
LOGIC NAMED JOE, A   LEINSTER, MURRAY   SS   ASF 46 03
DE PROFUNDIS   LEINSTER, MURRAY   SS   TWS 45 W.
FOURTH-DIMENSIONAL DEMONSTRATOR, THE
                            LEINSTER, MURRAY   SS   ASF 35 12
POWER, THE   LEINSTER, MURRAY   SS   ASF 45 09

SIGNS AND WONDERS   ELWOOD, ROGER   OA H REV 72
INTRODUCTION   ELWOOD, ROGER   IN
ALL IN GOOD TIME   BINDER, EANDO   SS   SAW 72
GENTLE CAPTIVE, THE   GODWIN, TOM   SS   SAW 72
GLIMPSE OF MARY, A   GYLES, GORDON A.   SS   SAW 72
IN THE CUP   MALZBERG, BARRY N.   SS   SAW 72
IRON ONE, THE   HAMILTON, EDMOND   SS   SAW 72
MY FRIEND KLATU   YEP, LAURENCE   NV   SAW 72
TERRIBLE QUICK SWORD   PETAJA, EMIL   SS   SAW 72
TOWARDS THE BELOVED CITY   FARMER, PHILIP JOSE NV   SAW 72

SILENT BULLET, THE   REEVE, ARTHUR B.   AC H DOM 12
ARTIFICIAL PARADISE   REEVE, ARTHUR B.   SS
AZURE RING, THE   REEVE, ARTHUR B.   SS   SCD 30 09
BACTERIOLOGICAL DETECTIVE, THE
                            REEVE, ARTHUR B.   SS   SCD 30 02
BLACK HAND, THE   REEVE, ARTHUR B.   SS
DEADLY TUBE, THE   REEVE, ARTHUR B.   SS
DIAMOND MAKER, THE   REEVE, ARTHUR B.   SS   AMD 30 06
SCIENTIFIC CRACKSMAN, THE   REEVE, ARTHUR B.   SS   AMD 30 08
SEISMOGRAPH ADVENTURE, THE REEVE, ARTHUR B.   SS   SCD 30 03
SILENT BULLET, THE   REEVE, ARTHUR B.   SS
"SPONTANEOUS COMBUSTION"   REEVE, ARTHUR B.   SS
STEEL DOOR, THE   REEVE, ARTHUR B.   SS
TERROR IN THE AIR   REEVE, ARTHUR B.   SS   SCD 30 04

SILKIE, THE   VAN VOGT, A. E.   NO   ACE 69
SILKIE, THE   VAN VOGT, A. E.   NV   IFS 64 07
SILKIES IN SPACE   VAN VOGT, A. E.   NV   IFS 66 05
ENEMY OF THE SILKIE   VAN VOGT, A. E.   NV   IFS 67 10

SILVER LOCUSTS, THE   BRADBURY, RAY   AC H HDV 51
  SEE "THE MARTIAN CHRONICLES", OMITS STORY "USHER II"
FIRE BALLOONS, THE (IN THIS SIGN)
                            BRADBURY, RAY   SS   IMG 51 04

SINISTER RESEARCHES OF C. P. RANSOM, THE
                            NEARING, H. JR.   AC H DBL 54
DILEMNA, THE (PROLOGUE)   NEARING, H. JR.   MS
POETRY MACHINE, THE   NEARING, H. JR.   SS   FSF 50 FL
MATHEMATICAL VOODOO, THE   NEARING, H. JR.   SS   FSF 51 04
MALIGNANT ORGAN, THE   NEARING, H. JR.   SS   FSF 53 03
ACTINIC GHOST, THE (THE ACTINIC ACTOR)
                            NEARING, H. JR.   SS   FSF 52 04
FACETITIOUS PENTANGLE, THE NEARING, H. JR.   SS   FSF 52 09
AESTHETIC DECAPITATIONS, THE NEARING, H. JR.   SS   NEW 54 AC
HYPERSPHERICAL BASKETBALL, THE
                            NEARING, H. JR.   SS   FSF 51 12
HERMENEUTICAL DOUGHNUT, THE NEARING, H. JR.   SS   NEW 54 AC
UNIDENTIFIED AMAZON, THE   NEARING, H. JR.   SS   FSF 52 12
AWARD, THE (EPILOGUE)   NEARING, H. JR.   MS

SIX GREAT SHORT SCIENCE FICTION NOVELS
                            CONKLIN, GROFF   AN   DEL 60 11
INTRODUCTION   CONKLIN, GROFF   IN
GALLEY SLAVE   ASIMOV, ISAAC   NV   GAL 57 12
PROJECT NURSEMAID   MERRIL, JUDITH   SN   FSF 55 10
FINAL GENTLEMAN   SIMAK, CLIFFORD D.   NV   FSF 60 01
CHAIN REACTION (AS JOHN A. SENTRY)
                            BUDRYS, ALGIS   NV   ASF 57 04
RULE GOLDEN   KNIGHT, DAMON   NV   SPA 54 06
INCOMMUNICADO   MACLEAN, KATHERINE   NV   ASF 50 06

SIX SCIENCE FICTION PLAYS   ELWOOD, ROGER   AN   WSP 76 01
INTRODUCTION   ELWOOD, ROGER   IN
INTRODUCTION TO THE CITY ON THE EDGE OF FOREVER
                            ELLISON, HARLAN   AI
CITY ON THE EDGE OF FOREVER, THE
                            ELLISON, HARLAN   PL   NBC 67 04
STING!   REAMY, TOM   PL   75
CONTACT POINT   COGSWELL, THEODORE R
                        AND COGSWELL, GEORGE RAE PL C   75
STRANGER WITH ROSES   JAKES, JOHN W.   PL   INY 72 04
MECHANICAL BRIDE, THE   LEIBER, FRITZ   PL   NEW 54 AN
LET ME HEAR YOU WHISPER   ZINDEL, PAUL   PL   SVM 70

SIX WORLDS YONDER   RUSSELL, ERIC FRANK DC   ACE 58
WAITABITS, THE   RUSSELL, ERIC FRANK NV   ASF 55 07
TIELINE   RUSSELL, ERIC FRANK SS   ASF 55 07
TOP SECRET   RUSSELL, ERIC FRANK SS   ASF 56 08

NOTHING NEW   RUSSELL, ERIC FRANK   SS   ASF 55 01
INTO YOUR TENT I'LL CREEP   RUSSELL, ERIC FRANK   SS   ASF 57 09
DIABOLOGIC   RUSSELL, ERIC FRANK   SS   ASF 55 03

IXTH GALAXY READER, THE   GOLD, H. L.   AN H   DBL 62
NUSE MAN, THE   ST. CLAIR, MARGARET   SS   GAL 60 02
SUCCESS STORY   GOODALE, EARL   NV   GAL 60 04
HUSBAND FOR MY WIFE, A   STUART, WILLIAM W.   SS   GAL 60 08
INSIDEKICK   BONE, J. F.   NV   GAL 59 02
LOVE CALLED THIS THING   DAVIDSON, AVRAM
                                  AND GOFORTH, LAURA   SS C   GAL 59 04
LEX   HAGGERT, W. T.   NV   GAL 59 08
LICENSE TO STEAL   NEWMAN, LOUIS   FA   GAL 59 08
TRUE SELF   BORGESE, ELISABETH M   SS   GAL 59 10
FLOWER ARRANGEMENT   BROWN, ROSEL GEORGE   SS   GAL 59 12
THING OF BEAUTY   KNIGHT, DAMON   NV   GAL 58 09
PERSONNEL PROBLEM   GOLD, H. L.   SS   GAL 58 08
NUMBER OF THE BEAST, THE   LEIBER, FRITZ   NV   GAL 58 12
IFTH OF OOFTH, THE   TEVIS, WALTER S. JR.   SS   GAL 57 04
GENIUS HEAP, THE (ALSO AS THE DARK NIGHT OF THE SOUL)
                                  BLISH, JAMES   SS   GAL 56 08

KULL OF THE MARQUIS DE SADE, THE
                                  BLOCH, ROBERT   AC   PYR 65 10
SKULL OF THE MARQUIS DE SADE, THE
                                  BLOCH, ROBERT   SS   WRT 45 09
QUIET FUNERAL, A   BLOCH, ROBERT   SS
WEIRD TAILOR, THE   BLOCH, ROBERT   SS   WRT 50 07
MAN WHO KNEW WOMEN, THE   BLOCH, ROBERT   SS   SMM 59 07
"LIZZIE BORDEN TOOK AN AXE..."
                                  BLOCH, ROBERT   SS   WRT 46 11
DEVIL'S TICKET, THE   BLOCH, ROBERT   SS   WRT 44 09
BOGEY MAN WILL GET YOU, THE   BLOCH, ROBERT   SS   WRT 46 03

MALL ASSASSIN, THE   BRADBURY, RAY   AC   ACB 62
SMALL ASSASSIN, THE   BRADBURY, RAY   SS   DMN 46 11
NEXT IN LINE, THE   BRADBURY, RAY   NV   NEW 47 AC
LAKE, THE   BRADBURY, RAY   SS   WRT 44 05
CROWD, THE   BRADBURY, RAY   SS   WRT 43 05
JACK-IN-THE-BOX   BRADBURY, RAY   SS   NEW 47 AC
MAN UPSTAIRS, THE   BRADBURY, RAY   SS   HRP 47 03
CISTERN, THE   BRADBURY, RAY   SS   MAD 47 05
TOMBSTONE, THE   BRADBURY, RAY   SS   WRT 45 03
SMILING PEOPLE, THE   BRADBURY, RAY   SS   WRT 46 05
HANDLER, THE   BRADBURY, RAY   SS   WRT 47 01
LET'S PLAY POISON   BRADBURY, RAY   SS   WRT 46 11
NIGHT, THE   BRADBURY, RAY   SS   WRT 46 07
DEAD MAN, THE   BRADBURY, RAY   SS   WRT 45 07

MALL CHANGES   CLEMENT, HAL   AC H   DBL 69
  ALSO AS "SPACE LASH"
DUST RAG   CLEMENT, HAL   SS   ASF 56 09
SUN SPOT   CLEMENT, HAL   SS   ASF 60 11
UNCOMMON SENSE   CLEMENT, HAL   SS   ASF 45 09
TROJAN FALL   CLEMENT, HAL   SS   ASF 44 06
FIREPROOF   CLEMENT, HAL   SS   ASF 49 03
HALO   CLEMENT, HAL   NV   GAL 52 10
FOUNDLING STARS, THE   CLEMENT, HAL   SS   IFS 66 08
RAINDROP   CLEMENT, HAL   NV   IFS 65 05
MECHANIC, THE   CLEMENT, HAL   NV   ASF 66 09

O BRIGHT THE VISION   SIMAK, CLIFFORD D.   DC   ACE 68
GOLDEN BUGS, THE   SIMAK, CLIFFORD D.   NV   FSF 60 06
LEG. FORST.   SIMAK, CLIFFORD D.   NV   INF 58 04
SO BRIGHT THE VISION   SIMAK, CLIFFORD D.   NV   FUN 56 08
GALACTIC CHEST   SIMAK, CLIFFORD D.   NV   SFS 56 09

O CLOSE TO HOME   BLISH, JAMES   AC   BAL 61 02
STRUGGLE IN THE WOMB (BATTLE OF THE UNBORN)
                                  BLISH, JAMES   SS   FUT 50 05
SPONGE DIVE   BLISH, JAMES   SS   INF 56 06
ONE-SHOT   BLISH, JAMES   SS   ASF 55 08
BOX, THE   BLISH, JAMES   SS   TWS 49 04
FIRST STRIKE   BLISH, JAMES   SS   FSF 53 06
ABATTOIR EFFECT, THE   BLISH, JAMES   SS   NEW 61 AC
OATH, THE   BLISH, JAMES   SS   FSF 60 10
F Y I   BLISH, JAMES   SS   STR 53 02
MASKS, THE   BLISH, JAMES   SS   FSF 59 11
TESTAMENT OF ANDROS   BLISH, JAMES   NV   FUT 53 01

OCIAL PROBLEMS THROUGH SCIENCE FICTION
                                  GREENBERG/MILSTEAD/& AN L SMP 75
INTRODUCTION   GREENBERG, MARTIN H.
                                  MILSTEAD, JOHN W.
                                  OLANDER, JOSEPH D.
                                  AND WARRICK, PATRICIA S. IN C
PEOPLE TRAP, THE   SHECKLEY, ROBERT   SS   FSF 68 06
SLICED-CROSSWISE ONLY-ON-TUESDAY WORLD, THE
                                  FARMER, PHILIP JOSE   SS   NDM 71 01
BILLENIUM   BALLARD, J. G.   SS   NWS 61 11
NRACP, THE   ELLIOTT, GEORGE P.   NV   HUD 49 FL
OTHER FOOT, THE   BRADBURY, RAY   SS   NST 51 03
NUMBER YOU HAVE REACHED, THE   DISCH, THOMAS M.   SS   IMP 67 02
VANISHING AMERICAN, THE   BEAUMONT, CHARLES   SS   FSF 55 08
NO DIRECTION HOME   SPINRAD, NORMAN   SS   NWQ 71 02
WORLD WELL LOST, THE   STURGEON, THEODORE   SS   USF 53 06
FATHER-THING, THE   DICK, PHILIP K.   SS   FSF 54 12
GOLDEN ACRES   REED, KIT   NV   68
GREAT INTELLECT BOOM, THE   ANVIL, CHRISTOPHER   SS   ASF 69 07
REVOLT OF THE POTATO-PICKER   LEHRMAN, HERB   SS   FSF 66 07
NIGHT OF THE LEOPARD   SAMBROT, WILLIAM   NV   67
GOOD NEWS FROM THE VATICAN   SILVERBERG, ROBERT   SS   UNI 71 01
HIPPIE-DIP FILE, THE   THURSTON, ROBERT   SS   FSF 71 03
BIG FLASH, THE   SPINRAD, NORMAN   NV   ORB 69 05
PRIZE OF PERIL, THE   SHECKLEY, ROBERT   SS   FSF 58 05
ABOUT A SECRET CROCODILE   LAFFERTY, R. A.   SS   GAL 70 08

BOUNTY   SHERRED, T. L.   SS   DVS 72 02
PUBLIC HATING, THE   ALLEN, STEVE   SS   BBM 55 01
HOW I TAKE THEIR MEASURE   O'DONNELL, K. M.   SS   FSF 69 01
VISIT TO CLEVELAND GENERAL, A
                                  VAN SCYOC, SYDNEY J. SS   GAL 68 10

SOCIOLOGY THROUGH SCIENCE FICTION
                                  MILSTEAD/GREENBERG/& AN H SMP 74
INTRODUCTION   MILSTEAD, JOHN W.
                                  GREENBERG, MARTIN H.
                                  OLANDER, JOSEPH D.
                                  AND WARRICK, PATRICIA S. IN C
LOST NEWTON   SCHMIDT, STANLEY   NV   ASF 70 09
MISINFORMATION   MYERS, HOWARD L.   SS   ASF 72 04
POSITIVE FEEDBACK   ANVIL, CHRISTOPHER   SS   ASF 65 08
DEEPER THAN THE DARKNESS   BENFORD, GREGORY   NV   FSF 69 04
OF COURSE   OLIVER, CHAD   SS   ASF 54 05
SLOW TUESDAY NIGHT   LAFFERTY, R. A.   SS   GAL 65 04
GADGET VS. TREND   ANVIL, CHRISTOPHER   SS   ASF 62 10
NOBODY LIVES ON BURTON STREET
                                  BENFORD, GREGORY   SS   AMZ 70 05
SHAKER REVIVAL, THE   JONAS, GERALD   NV   GAL 70 02
GUILTY AS CHARGED   PORGES, ARTHUR   SS   NEW 55 AN
INTEGRATION MODULE   JAMES, DANIEL B.   NV   ASF 73 01
DAY IN THE SUBURBS, A   SMITH, EVELYN E.   SS   FSF 60 09
PIGEON CITY   MILLER, JESSIE   NV   ASF 72 11
GENERATION GAPS   O'BRIEN, CLANCY   SS   ASF 72 09
TWO'S COMPANY   RANKINE, JOHN   SS   NWR 64 01
PRIMARY EDUCATION OF THE CAMIROI
                                  LAFFERTY, R. A.   SS   GAL 66 12
BIRTHRIGHT   ANDERSON, POUL   NV   ASF 70 02
PEDESTRIAN, THE (REP 51 08)   BRADBURY, RAY   SS   FSF 52 02
CANTICLE FOR LEIBOWITZ, A   MILLER, WALTER M. JR   NV   FSF 55 04
TOTAL ENVIRONMENT   ALDISS, BRIAN W.   NV   GAL 68 02
SINGLE COMBAT   ABERNATHY, ROBERT   SS   FSF 55 01

SOFT COME THE DRAGONS   KOONTZ, DEAN R.   DC   ACE 70
INTRODUCTION   KOONTZ, DEAN R.   IN
SOFT COME THE DRAGONS   KOONTZ, DEAN R.   SS   FSF 67 08
THIRD HAND, A   KOONTZ, DEAN R.   NV   FSF 70 01
DARKNESS IN MY SOUL, A   KOONTZ, DEAN R.   NV   FAN 68 01
TWELTH BED, THE   KOONTZ, DEAN R.   SS   FSF 68 08
SEASON FOR FREEDOM, A (KILLERBOT!)
                                  KOONTZ, DEAN R.   SS   GAL 69 05
PSYCHEDELIC CHILDREN, THE   KOONTZ, DEAN R.   SS   FSF 67 08
DRAGON IN THE LAND   KOONTZ, DEAN R.   SS   VSF 69 08
TO BEHOLD THE SUN   KOONTZ, DEAN R.   SS   FSF 67 12

SOME DREAMS ARE NIGHTMARES   GUNN, JAMES E.   AC H   SCB 74
INTRODUCTION   GUNN, JAMES E.   IN
CAVE OF NIGHT, THE   GUNN, JAMES E.   SS   GAL 55 02
HEDONIST, THE (NAME YOUR PLEASURE)
                                  GUNN, JAMES E.   NA   TWS 55 WI
NEW BLOOD   GUNN, JAMES E.   NV   ASF 55 10
MEDIC (NOT SO GREAT AN ENEMY)
                                  GUNN, JAMES E.   NV   VSF 57 07

SOMETIME, NEVER   ANONYMOUS   OA   BAL 56
ENVOY EXTRAORDINARY   GOLDING, WILLIAM   NV   56
CONSIDER HER WAYS   WYNDHAM, JOHN   NV   56
BOY IN DARKNESS   PEAKE, MERVYN   NV   56

SOMEWHERE A VOICE   RUSSELL, ERIC FRANK   AC H   DOB 65
SOMEWHERE A VOICE   RUSSELL, ERIC FRANK   NV   OWS 53 01
U-TURN   RUSSELL, ERIC FRANK   SS   ASF 50 04
SEAT OF OBLIVION   RUSSELL, ERIC FRANK   SS   ASF 41 11
TIELINE   RUSSELL, ERIC FRANK   SS   ASF 55 07
DISPLACED PERSON   RUSSELL, ERIC FRANK   SS   WRT 48 09
DEAR DEVIL   RUSSELL, ERIC FRANK   NV   OWS 50 05
I AM NOTHING   RUSSELL, ERIC FRANK   SS   ASF 52 07

SONG FOR LYA, A   MARTIN, GEORGE R. R. AC   AVN 76 02
WITH MORNING COMES MISTFALL MARTIN, GEORGE R. R. SS   ASF 73 05
SECOND KIND OF LONELINESS, THE
                                  MARTIN, GEORGE R. R. SS   ASF 72 12
OVERRIDE   MARTIN, GEORGE R. R. NV   ASF 73 09
DARK, DARK WERE THE TUNNELS MARTIN, GEORGE R. R. SS   VTX 73 12
HERO, THE   MARTIN, GEORGE R. R. SS   GAL 71 02
FTA   MARTIN, GEORGE R. R. SS   ASF 74 05
RUN TO STARLIGHT   MARTIN, GEORGE R. R. NV   AMZ 74 12
EXIT TO SAN BRETA, THE   MARTIN, GEORGE R. R. SS   FAN 72 02
SLIDE SHOW   MARTIN, GEORGE R. R. SS   OMG 73
SONG FOR LYA, A   MARTIN, GEORGE R. R. NV   ASF 74 06

SONGS OF STARS AND SHADOWS   MARTIN, GEORGE R. R. AC   PKT 77 07
INTRODUCTION   MARTIN, GEORGE R. R. IN
THIS TOWER OF ASHES   MARTIN, GEORGE R. R. SS
PATRICK HENRY, JUPITER, AND THE LITTLE RED BRICK SPACESHIP
                                  MARTIN, GEORGE R. R. SS   AMZ 76 12
MEN OF GREYWATER STATION   MARTIN, GEORGE R. R. SS   AMZ 76 03
LONELY SONGS OF LAREN DORR, THE
                                  MARTIN, GEORGE R. R. SS   FAN 76 05
NIGHT OF THE VAMPYRES, THE   MARTIN, GEORGE R. R. NV   AMZ 75 05
RUNNERS, THE   MARTIN, GEORGE R. R. SS   FSF 75 09
NIGHT SHIFT   MARTIN, GEORGE R. R. SS   AMZ 73 01
"FOR A SINGLE YESTERDAY"   MARTIN, GEORGE R. R. NV   EPC 75
AND SEVEN TIMES NEVER KILL MAN
                                  MARTIN, GEORGE R. R. NV   ASF 75 07

SOULS IN METAL   ASHLEY, MICHAEL   AN H   SMP 77
PREFACE   ASHLEY, MICHAEL   IN
HELEN O'LOY   DEL REY, LESTER   SS   ASF 38 12
THAT THOU ART MINDFUL OF HIM
                                  ASIMOV, ISAAC   NV   FSF 74 05
TWONKY, THE   KUTTNER, HENRY   SS   ASF 42 09
LOGIC NAMED JOE, A   LEINSTER, MURRAY   SS   ASF 46 03

SOULS IN METAL

IMPOSTOR	DICK, PHILIP K.	SS	ASF 53	06
WHO CAN REPLACE A MAN? (BUT WHO CAN REPLACE A MAN)				
	ALDISS, BRIAN W.	SS	INF 58	06
VELVET GLOVE, THE	HARRISON, HARRY	NV	FUN 56	11
I AM CRYING ALL INSIDE	SIMAK, CLIFFORD D.	SS	GAL 69	08
INTERNAL COMBUSTION	DE CAMP, L. SPRAGUE	SS	INF 56	02
AFTERWORD	ASHLEY, MICHAEL	MS		

SOVIET SCIENCE FICTION ANONYMOUS AN CLB 62
ALSO AS "A VISITOR FROM OUTER SPACE"

INTRODUCTION	ASIMOV, ISAAC	IN	
HOITY-TOITY	BELAYEV, ALEXANDER	NV	
SPONTANEOUS REFLEX	STRUGATSKY, ARKADY		
	AND STRUGATSKY, BORIS	NV	C
VISITOR FROM OUTER SPACE, A	KAZANTSEV, ALEXANDER	SS	
MARTIAN, THE	KAZANTSEV, ALEXANDER	SS	
INFRA DRACONIS	GUREVICH, G.	NV	
PROFESSOR BERN'S AWAKENING	SAVCHENKO, VLADIMIR	SS	

SPACE 1	DAVIS, RICHARD	OA H	ABS 73	06
TEDDYSAURS, THE	HAMILTON-PATTERSON,J	SS	SPC 73	01
MERCYSHIP, THE	PAGE, GERALD W.	SS	SPC 73	01
MISTAKEN IDENTITY	TUBB, E. C.	SS	SPC 73	01
CHRISTMAS TREASON	WHITE, JAMES	NV	FSF 62	01
ENVIRONMENT PROBLEM	MOORCOCK, MICHAEL	SS	SPC 73	01
MUSEUM PIECE	FANCETT, ELIZABETH	SS	SPC 73	01
NEIGHBOR	SIMAK, CLIFFORD D.	NV	ASF 54	06
NO JOKES ON MARS	BLISH, JAMES	SS	FSF 65	10

SPACE 2	DAVIS, RICHARD	OA H	ABS 74	01
TOMORROW'S CHILD	BRADBURY, RAY	SS	NEW 69	AC
AQUAMAN	BULMER, KENNETH	SS	SPC 74	02
LIVING FOSSIL	STOUT, TIM	SS	SPC 74	02
THING UNDER THE GLACIER, THE	ALDISS, BRIAN W.	SS	SPC 74	02
REFUGEES, THE	FANCETT, ELIZABETH	NV	SPC 74	02
PROJECT D	STEPHENS, FRANCES	SS	SPC 74	02
RENAISSANCE MAN	KLEIN, T. E. D.	SS	SPC 74	02
MESSAGE FROM THE STARS	COPPER, BASIL	SS	SPC 74	02
HARMONY AGGRO, THE	CLEAVER, PAMELA	SS	SPC 74	02

SPACE ADVENTURES FURMAN, A. L. AN LPB 75 01
SEE "TEEN-AGE SPACE ADVENTURES"

SPACE BEYOND, THE	CAMPBELL, JOHN W. JR	OC	PYR 76	06
BIG, BIG, BIG	ASIMOV, ISAAC	IN		
MAROONED	CAMPBELL, JOHN W. JR	SN		
ALL	CAMPBELL, JOHN W. JR	SN		
SPACE BEYOND, THE	CAMPBELL, JOHN W. JR	SN		
AFTERWORD	ZEBROWSKI, GEORGE	MS		

SPACE BY THE TAIL	BIXBY, JEROME	AC	BAL 64	
DRAW, THE	BIXBY, JEROME	SS	AMZ 54	03
YOUNG ONE, THE	BIXBY, JEROME	NV	FAN 54	05
LABORATORY	BIXBY, JEROME	NV	IFS 55	12
GOOD DOG, THE	BIXBY, JEROME	SS	FAN 54	02
ONE WAY STREET	BIXBY, JEROME	SS	AMZ 54	01
SMALL WAR	BIXBY, JEROME	SS	SFQ 54	05
TRACE	BIXBY, JEROME	SS	61	
ANGELS IN THE JETS	BIXBY, JEROME	SS	FAN 52	FL
BATTLE OF THE BELLS, THE	BIXBY, JEROME	SS	IMG 54	09
MAGIC TYPEWRITER, THE	BIXBY, JEROME	SS	63	
BAD LIFE, THE	BIXBY, JEROME	NA	GAL 63	02

SPACE FRONTIERS, THE	VERNON, ROGER LEE	AC	SIG 55 08
BATTLE	VERNON, ROGER LEE	SS	
INCIDENT IN SPACE	VERNON, ROGER LEE	SS	
XENOPHOBIA	VERNON, ROGER LEE	NV	
CITY AND THE SHIP, THE	VERNON, ROGER LEE	NV	
CHESS CIVILIZATION, THE	VERNON, ROGER LEE	SS	
PLANT WORLD, THE	VERNON, ROGER LEE	SS	
STOP WATCH, THE	VERNON, ROGER LEE	SS	
POPULATION CRISIS: 2550	VERNON, ROGER LEE	SS	
DEATH SEEKERS, THE	VERNON, ROGER LEE	NV	

SPACE HAWK	GILMORE, ANTHONY	AC H	GBG 52	
HAWK CARSE	GILMORE, ANTHONY	NV	ASF 31	11
AFFAIR OF THE BRAINS, THE	GILMORE, ANTHONY	NV	ASF 32	03
BLUFF OF THE HAWK, THE	GILMORE, ANTHONY	SS	ASF 32	05
PASSING OF KU SUI, THE	GILMORE, ANTHONY	NV	ASF 32	11
RETURN OF HAWK CARSE, THE (HARRY BATES)				
	GILMORE, ANTHONY	NA	AMZ 42	07

SPACE LASH CLEMENT, HAL AC DEL 69 12
SEE "SMALL CHANGES"

SPACE LORDS	SMITH, CORDWAINER	AC	PYR 65	05
PROLOGUE	SMITH, CORDWAINER	MS		
MOTHER HITTON'S LITTUL KITTONS				
	SMITH, CORDWAINER	NV	GAL 61	06
DEAD LADY OF CLOWN TOWN, THE	SMITH, CORDWAINER	SN	GAL 64	08
DRUNKBOAT	SMITH, CORDWAINER	NV	AMZ 63	10
BALLAD OF LOST C'MELL, THE	SMITH, CORDWAINER	NV	GAL 62	10
PLANET NAMED SHAYOL, A	SMITH, CORDWAINER	NA	GAL 61	10
EPILOGUE	SMITH, CORDWAINER	MS		

SPACE MAGICIANS, THE	NORTON & MOSKOWITZ	AN	PYR 71	01
INTRODUCTION	NORTON, ALDEN H.			
	AND MOSKOWITZ, SAM	IN C		
VENUS ADVENTURE, THE	WYNDHAM, JOHN	SS	WOS 32	05
BLACK SUN RISES, THE	KUTTNER, HENRY	NV	SSS 49	01
HALF-BREED	ASIMOV, ISAAC	SS	AST 40	02
CALL FROM BEYOND, THE	SIMAK, CLIFFORD D.	NV	SSS 50	05
BITTER END	RUSSELL, ERIC FRANK	SS	SFP 53	12
CONSTANT READER	BLOCH, ROBERT	SS	USF 53	06
IN SEARCH OF THE UNKNOWN (EXCERPT)				
	CHAMBERS, ROBERT W.	EX	04	

SPACE STATION 42 AND OTHER STORIES

SPACE ODYSSEYS	ALDISS, BRIAN W.	AN H	WEI 75	
INTRODUCTION	ALDISS, BRIAN W.	IN		
SENTINEL, THE (SENTINEL OF ETERNITY)				
	CLARKE, ARTHUR C.	SS	TSF 51	SP
GALACTIC PATROL	SMITH, EDWARD E. PHD	EX	ASF 37	09
LAKE OF THE GONE FOREVER, THE				
	BRACKETT, LEIGH	NV	TWS 49	10
REASON	ASIMOV, ISAAC	SS	ASF 41	04
TIME IS THE TRAITOR	BESTER, ALFRED	NV	FSF 53	09
IMPOSSIBLE PLANET, THE	DICK, PHILIP K.	SS	IFS 53	10
UNFINISHED, THE	LONG, FRANK BELKNAP	SS	SSS 51	04
AND I AWOKE AND FOUND ME HERE ON THE COLD HILL'S SIDE				
	TIPTREE, JAMES JR.	SS	FSF 72	03
EMPRESS OF MARS, THE	ROCKLYNNE, ROSS	NV	FAD 39	05
I'M GOING TO GET YOU	BUSBY, F. M.	SS	FAN 74	03
STRANGE EXODUS	ABERNATHY, ROBERT	SS	PLS 50	FL
STAR SHIP	ANDERSON, POUL	NV	PLS 50	FL
TO EACH HIS STAR	WALTON, BRYCE	SS	SSF 52	05
BIG HUNGER, THE	MILLER, WALTER M. JR	SS	ASF 52	10
NIGHT WATCH	INGLIS, JAMES	SS	NWB 65	03

SPACE ON MY HANDS	BROWN, FREDRIC	AC H	SHS 51	07
INTRODUCTION	BROWN, FREDRIC	IN		
SOMETHING GREEN	BROWN, FREDRIC	SS	NEW 51	AC
CRISIS, 1999	BROWN, FREDRIC	SS	EQM 49	08
PI IN THE SKY	BROWN, FREDRIC	SS	TWS 45	WI
KNOCK	BROWN, FREDRIC	SS	TWS 48	12
ALL GOOD BEMS	BROWN, FREDRIC	SS	TWS 49	04
DAYMARE	BROWN, FREDRIC	NV	TWS 43	FL
NOTHING SIRIUS	BROWN, FREDRIC	SS	CFU 44	SP
STAR MOUSE, THE	BROWN, FREDRIC	SS	PLS 42	02
COME AND GO MAD	BROWN, FREDRIC	NV	WRT 49	07

SPACE OPERA	ALDISS, BRIAN W.	AN H	WEI 74	
INTRODUCTION	ALDISS, BRIAN W.	IN		
IS EVERYTHING AN ILLUSION?	ALDISS, BRIAN W.	SI		
ZIRN LEFT UNGUARDED, THE JENGHIK PALACE IN FLAMES,				
JOHN WESTERLY DEAD	SHECKLEY, ROBERT	SS	NOV 72	02
HONEYMOON IN SPACE, A	GRIFFITH, GEORGE	EX	PRS 00	01
TONIGHT THE SKY WILL FALL	GALOUYE, DANIEL F.	SN	IMG 53	03
"PRECIPICES OF LIGHT THAT WENT FOREVER UP..."				
	ALDISS, BRIAN W.	SI		
STAR OF LIFE, THE	HAMILTON, EDMOND	EX	STS 47	01
AFTER IXMAL	SUTTON, JEFF	SS	AMZ 62	10
SEA CHANGE (ALSO AS THE SHORES OF NIGHT)				
	SCORTIA, THOMAS N.	SS	ASF 56	06
EXILE IS OUR LOT	ALDISS, BRIAN W.	SI		
COLONY	DICK, PHILIP K.	NV	GAL 53	06
SWORD OF RHIANNON, THE (SEA-KINGS OF MARS)				
	BRACKETT, LEIGH	EX	TWS 49	06
ALL SUMMER IN A DAY	BRADBURY, RAY	SS	FSF 54	03
MITR, THE	VANCE, JACK	SS	53	
GODLIKE MACHINES, THE	ALDISS, BRIAN W.	SI		
STORM, THE	VAN VOGT, A. E.	NV	ASF 43	10
PARADOX MEN, THE	HARNESS, CHARLES L.	NV	49	
TIME FUZE	GARRETT, RANDALL	SS	IFS 54	03
LAST QUESTION, THE	ASIMOV, ISAAC	SS	SFQ 56	11
ENVOI	ALDISS, BRIAN W.	MS		

SPACE PIONEERS	NORTON, ANDRE	AN H	WOR 54	
PREFACE	NORTON, ANDRE	IN		
ILLUSIONARIES, THE	RUSSELL, ERIC FRANK	SS	PLS 51	11
MOONWALK	FYFE, H. B.	NA	SSF 52	11
TRAIL BLAZER	GALLUN, RAYMOND Z.	SS	FSM 51	FL
THOU GOOD AND FAITHFUL	BRUNNER, K. HOUSTON	NV	ASF 53	03
END OF THE LINE, THE	SCHMITZ, JAMES H.	NV	ASF 51	07
PAIL OF AIR, A	LEIBER, FRITZ	SS	GAL 51	12
FARTHEST HORIZON, THE	JONES, RAYMOND F.	SS	ASF 52	04
ASTEROID OF FEAR	GALLUN, RAYMOND Z.	NV	PLS 51	03
PAGE AND PLAYER	BIXBY, JEROME	NV	STS 52	08

SPACE POLICE	NORTON, ANDRE	AN H	WOR 56	
INTRODUCTION	NORTON, ANDRE	IN		
BAIT	CLOUGH, ROY L.	SS	ASF 51	06
CLOSED DOOR, THE	CROSSEN, KENDELL F.	SS	AMZ 53	09
BEEP	BLISH, JAMES	NV	GAL 54	02
OF THOSE WHO CAME	LONGDON, GEORGE	SS	FUN 53	06
POLICE OPERATION	PIPER, H. BEAM	NV	ASF 48	07
PAX GALACTICA	WILLIAMS, RALPH	SS	ASF 52	11
TOUGH OLD MAN	HUBBARD, L. RON	SS	STS 50	11
AGENT OF VEGA	SCHMITZ, JAMES H.	NV	ASF 49	07
SUB-STANDARD SARDINES	VANCE, JACK	SS	STS 49	07

SPACE SCAVENGERS, THE	CARTMILL, CLEVE	NO	MAJ 75	
SALVAGE	CARTMILL, CLEVE	NV	TWS 49	08
HIGH JACK AND DAME	CARTMILL, CLEVE	NV	TWS 49	10
THICKER THAN WATER	CARTMILL, CLEVE	NV	TWS 49	12
DEAD RUN	CARTMILL, CLEVE	NV	TWS 50	02
LITTLE JOE	CARTMILL, CLEVE	NV	TWS 50	04
NO HIDING PLACE	CARTMILL, CLEVE	NA	TWS 50	06

SPACE SERVICE	NORTON, ANDRE	AN H	WOR 53	
INTRODUCTION	NORTON, ANDRE	IN		
COMMAND	KAHN, BERNARD I.	NV	ASF 47	01
STAR-LINKED	FYFE, H. B.	SS	ASF 52	02
CHORE FOR A SPACEMAN	SHELDON, WALT	SS	TWS 50	12
SPECTER GENERAL, THE	COGSWELL, THEODORE R	NV	ASF 52	06
IMPLODE AND PEDDLE	FYFE, H. B.	NV	ASF 51	11
STEEL BROTHER	DICKSON, GORDON R.	NV	ASF 52	02
FOR THE PUBLIC	KAHN, BERNARD I.	NV	ASF 46	12
EXPEDITION POLYCHROME	WINTER, JOSEPH A. MD	NV	ASF 49	01
RETURN OF A LEGEND	GALLUN, RAYMOND Z.	SS	PLS 52	03
THAT SHARE OF GLORY	KORNBLUTH, C. M.	NV	ASF 52	01

SPACE STATION 42 AND OTHER STORIES			
	ANONYMOUS	AN	JBL 58

SPACE STATION 42 AND OTHER STORIES   SPECTRUM 5

  SPACE STATION 42 (MANY DREAMS OF EARTH)
                              FRITCH, CHARLES E.   SS   OSF 54 11
  CONTROLLED EXPERIMENT   OLIVER, CHAD   SS   OSF 54 11
  LAST OF THE MASTERS, THE   DICK, PHILIP K.   SS   OSF 54 11
  LAST MAN, THE (NOAH)   BECKMAN, CHARLES JR. SS   OSF 54 11
  BETWEEN TWO WORLDS (AUNT ELSIE'S STAIRWAY)
                              RIKER, ANTHONY   SS   OSF 54 11
  DREAMER, THE (THE ENCHANTED PRINCESS)
                              VANCE, JACK   SS   OSF 54 11

SPACE WAR   JONES, NEIL R.   AC   ACE 67
  ZORA OF THE ZOROMES   JONES, NEIL R.   NV   AMZ 35 03
  SPACE WAR   JONES, NEIL R.   NV   AMZ 35 07
  LABYRINTH   JONES, NEIL R.   NV   AMZ 36 04

SPACE-TIME JOURNAL, THE   MERRIL, JUDITH   AN   PTH 72
  21 STORIES FROM "ENGLAND SWINGS SF"
  ISLAND, THE   JONES, ROGER   SS   SCF 65 02
  NE DEJA VU PAS   SAXTON, JOSEPHINE   SS   67
  SIGNALS   CALDER, JOHN   SS   NWS 66 09
  SAINT 505   CLARKE, JOHN   SS   NWS 67 01
  SINGULAR QUEST OF MARTIN BORG, THE
                              COLLYN, GEORGE   SS   NWS 65 02
  FIRST GORILLA ON THE MOON, THE
                              BUTLER, BILL   PM   NEW 68 AN
  BLASTOFF   BONFIGLIOLI, KYRIL   SS   64
  YOU AND ME AND THE CONTINUUM BALLARD, J. G.   SS   IMP 66 03
  WHO'S IN THERE WITH ME?   CASTELL, DAPHNE   SS   NEW 68 AN
  MANSCARER   ROBERTS, KEITH   NV   NWR 66 07
  SILVER NEEDLE, THE   MACBETH, GEORGE   PM   NWS 67 01
  BAKED BEAN FACTORY, THE   BUTTERWORTH, MICHAEL SS   NWS 67 10
  HALL OF MACHINES, THE   JONES, LANGDON   SS   NWS 68 03
  RUN, THE   PRIEST, CHRISTOPHER   SS   IMP 66 05
  STILL TRAJECTORIES   ALDISS, BRIAN W.   SS   NWS 67 09
  SUN PUSH   HALL, GRAHAM M.   SS   NWS 67 01
  REPORT ON A SUPERMARKET   HAMBURGER, MICHAEL   PM
  DR. GELABIUS   BAILEY, HILARY   SS   NWS 68 04
  PSYCHOSMOSIS   MASSON, DAVID I.   SS   NWS 66 03
  IDEA OF ENTROPY AT MAENPORTH BEACH, THE
                              REDGROVE, PETER   PM   67
  SAME AUTUMN IN A DIFFERENT PARK
                              TATE, PETER   SS   FAN 67 09

SPACE, SPACE, SPACE   SLOANE, WILLIAM   AN H WAT 53
  INTRODUCTION   SLOANE, WILLIAM   IN
  NO MOON FOR ME   MILLER, WALTER M. JR SS   ASF 52 09
  TRIP ONE   GRENDON, EDWARD   SS   ASF 49 07
  TOOLS OF THE TRADE   JONES, RAYMOND F.   NV   ASF 50 11
  HIDE AND SEEK   CLARKE, ARTHUR C.   SS   ASF 49 09
  MASTER RACE   ASHBY, RICHARD   SS   IMG 51 09
  DEAR DEVIL   RUSSELL, ERIC FRANK   NV   OWS 50 05
  COURTESY   SIMAK, CLIFFORD D.   SS   ASF 51 08
  NIGHTMARE BROTHER   NOURSE, ALAN E.   NV   ASF 53 02
  SECOND CHANCE   KUBILIUS, WALTER
                              AND PRATT, FLETCHER   SS C FSM 52 FL
  LIKE GODS THEY CAME   COX, IRVING E. JR.   SS   AUS 53 01

SPACE, TIME & CRIME   DEFORD, MIRIAM ALLEN AN   PBK 64 11
  INTRODUCTION   DEFORD, MIRIAM ALLEN IN
  CRISIS, 1999   BROWN, FREDRIC   SS   EQM 49 08
  CRIMINAL NEGLIGENCE   MCCOMAS, J. FRANCIS   SS   ASF 55 06
  TALKING STONE, THE   ASIMOV, ISAAC   SS   F9F 55 10
  PAST AND IT'S DEAD PEOPLE, THE
                              BRETNOR, REGINALD   SS   FSF 56 09
  ADVENTURE OF THE SNITCH IN TIME, THE
                              REYNOLDS, MACK
                              AND DERLETH, AUGUST   SS C FSF 53 07
  EYES HAVE IT, THE   MCKIMMEY, JAMES   SS   IFS 53 11
  PUBLIC EYE   BOUCHER, ANTHONY   SS   TWS 52 04
  INNOCENT ARRIVAL, THE (INNOCENT AT LARGE)
                              ANDERSON, POUL
                              AND ANDERSON, KAREN   NV C GAL 58 07
  THIRD OFFENSE (AS CHARLES SATTERFIELD)
                              POHL, FREDERIK   SS   GAL 58 08

SPACE, TIME AND NATHANIEL   ALDISS, BRIAN W.   AC H FAB 57
  ALSO IN "BRIAN ALDISS OMNIBUS II"
  T   ALDISS, BRIAN W.   SS   NEB 56 11
  OUR KIND OF KNOWLEDGE   ALDISS, BRIAN W.   SS   NWS 55 06
  PSYCLOPS   ALDISS, BRIAN W.   SS   NWS 56 07
  CONVICTION   ALDISS, BRIAN W.   SS   NWS 56 09
  NOT FOR AN AGE   ALDISS, BRIAN W.   SS   LOB 55 01
  SHUBSHUB RACE, THE   ALDISS, BRIAN W.   SS   NEW 57 AC
  CRIMINAL RECORD   ALDISS, BRIAN W.   SS   SCF 54 07
  FAILED MEN, THE   ALDISS, BRIAN W.   SS   SCF 56 05
  SUPERCITY   ALDISS, BRIAN W.   SS   NWS 65 07
  THERE IS A TIDE   ALDISS, BRIAN W.   SS   NWS 56 02
  POGSMITH   ALDISS, BRIAN W.   SS   AUT 55 05
  OUTSIDE   ALDISS, BRIAN W.   SS   NWS 55 01
  PANEL GAME   ALDISS, BRIAN W.   SS   NWS 55 12
  DUMB SHOW   ALDISS, BRIAN W.   SS   NEB 56 12

SPECIAL WONDER   MCCOMAS, J. FRANCIS   AN H RDM 70
  THE ANTHONY BOUCHER MEMORIAL ANTHOLOGY OF FANTASY AND
  SCIENCE FICTION
  INTRODUCTION   MCCOMAS, J. FRANCIS   IN
  JOURNEYS END   ANDERSON, POUL   SS   FSF 57 02
  BRAZEN LOCKED ROOM, THE (ALSO AS GIMMICKS THREE)
                              ASIMOV, ISAAC   SS   FSF 56 11
  FIRE BALLOONS, THE (IN THIS SIGN)
                              BRADBURY, RAY   SS   IMG 51 04
  GNURRS COME FROM THE VOODVORK OUT, THE
                              BRETNOR, REGINALD   SS   FSF 50 WS
  THROUGH TIME AND SPACE WITH FERDINAND FEGHOOT
                              BRIARTON, GRENDEL   SS   BSJ 67
  PUPPET SHOW   BROWN, FREDRIC   SS   PBY 62 11

PUZZLE FOR SPACEMEN   BRUNNER, JOHN   SS   NWS 55 12
AUNT AGATHA   BUCK, DORIS PITKIN   SS   FSF 52 10
WILD WOOD, THE   CLINGERMAN, MILDRED   SS   FSF 57 01
KING'S EVIL   DAVIDSON, AVRAM   SS   FSF 56 10
CRUELTY   DE CLES, JON   SS   NEW 71 AN
APOTHEOSIS OF KI, THE   DEFORD, MIRIAM ALLEN SS   FSF 56 12
SHAPE OF THINGS THAT CAME, THE
                              DEMING, RICHARD   SS   FSF 51 10
THREE, THE   DICKSON, GORDON R.   SS   STS 53 05
PRETTY MAGGIE MONEYEYES   ELLISON, HARLAN   NV   KNT 67 05
PROMETHEUS   FARMER, PHILIP JOSE   NV   FSF 61 03
RANSOM   FYFE, H. B.   SS   FSF 52 02
MUDDLE OF THE WOAD, THE   GARRETT, RANDALL   NV   ASF 65 06
YOU'RE ANOTHER   KNIGHT, DAMON   NV   FSF 55 06
OLD MAN HENDERSON   NEVILLE, KRIS   SS   FSF 51 06
HE KILT 'IT WITH A STICK   NOLAN, WILLIAM F.   SS   FSF 68 02
CANVAS BAG, THE   NOURSE, ALAN E.   SS   FSF 55 04
PILGRIMAGE   OLIVER, CHAD   SS   FSF 58 02
GUN FOR HIRE   REYNOLDS, MACK   SS   ASF 60 12
BRIGHTNESS FALLS FROM THE AIR (CONTEST STORY)
                              ST. CLAIR, MARGARET   SS   FSF 51 04
BUILT UP LOGICALLY (THE UNIVERSAL TANCEA, RET 49 WI)
                              SCHOENFELD, HOWARD   SS   FSF 50 FL
WARM MAN   SILVERBERG, ROBERT   SS   FSF 57 05
GREEN MAGIC   VANCE, JACK   SS   FSF 63 06
DENY THE SLAKE   WILSON, RICHARD   SS   INF 57 04

SPECTRUM   AMIS & CONQUEST   AN H HBW 62
  INTRODUCTION   AMIS, KINGSLEY
                              AND CONQUEST, ROBERT IN C
  MIDAS PLAGUE, THE   POHL, FREDERIK   NA   GAL 54 04
  LIMITING FACTOR   SIMAK, CLIFFORD D.   SS   STS 49 11
  EXECUTIONER, THE   BUDRYS, ALGIS   NV   ASF 56 01
  NULL-P   TENN, WILLIAM   SS   WBY 51 01
  HOMING INSTINCT OF JOE VARGO, THE
                              BARR, STEPHEN   SS   FSF 59 12
  SPECIAL FLIGHT   BERRYMAN, JOHN   NV   ASF 39 05
  INANIMATE OBJECTION   ELLIOTT, H. CHANDLER NV   GAL 54 02
  PILGRIMAGE TO EARTH (LOVE, INCORPORATED)
                              SHECKLEY, ROBERT   SS   PBY 56 09
  UNHUMAN SACRIFICE   MACLEAN, KATHERINE   NV   ASF 58 11
  BY HIS BOOTSTRAPS (ALSO AS THE TIME GATE)
                              HEINLEIN, ROBERT A.   NV   ASF 41 10

SPECTRUM (7 OF 10)   AMIS & CONQUEST   AN   BKM 63 03
  INTRODUCTION   AMIS, KINGSLEY
                              AND CONQUEST, ROBERT IN C
  MIDAS PLAGUE, THE   POHL, FREDERIK   NA   GAL 54 04
  LIMITING FACTOR   SIMAK, CLIFFORD D.   SS   STS 49 11
  EXECUTIONER, THE   BUDRYS, ALGIS   NV   ASF 56 01
  NULL-P   TENN, WILLIAM   SS   WBY 51 01
  INANIMATE OBJECTION   ELLIOTT, H. CHANDLER NV   GAL 54 02
  PILGRIMAGE TO EARTH (LOVE, INCORPORATED)
                              SHECKLEY, ROBERT   SS   PBY 56 09
  BY HIS BOOTSTRAPS (ALSO AS THE TIME GATE)
                              HEINLEIN, ROBERT A.   NV   ASF 41 10

SPECTRUM 2   AMIS & CONQUEST   AN H HBW 63
  INTRODUCTION   AMIS, KINGSLEY
                              AND CONQUEST, ROBERT IN C
  BEYOND BEDLAM   GUIN, WYMAN   NA   GAL 51 08
  BRIDGE   BLISH, JAMES   NV   ASF 52 02
  THERE IS A TIDE   ALDISS, BRIAN W.   SS   NWS 56 02
  SECOND VARIETY   DICK, PHILIP K.   NV   SSF 53 05
  FEELING OF POWER, THE   ASIMOV, ISAAC   SS   IFS 58 02
  SENSE FROM THOUGHT DIVIDE   CLIFTON, MARK   NV   ASF 55 03
  RESURRECTION (THE MONSTER) VAN VOGT, A. E.   SS   ASF 48 08
  VINTAGE SEASON   KUTTNER, HENRY   NV   ASF 46 09

SPECTRUM 3   AMIS & CONQUEST   AN H HBW 64
  INTRODUCTION   AMIS, KINGSLEY
                              AND CONQUEST, ROBERT IN C
  KILLDOZER   STURGEON, THEODORE   SN   ASF 44 11
  VOICES OF TIME, THE   BALLARD, J. G.   SS   NWS 60 10
  CALL ME JOE   ANDERSON, POUL   NV   ASF 57 04
  WE WOULD SEE A SIGN   ROSE, MARK   SS   NEW 64 AN
  DREAMS ARE SACRED   PHILLIPS, PETER   SS   ASF 48 09
  EXPLORATION TEAM (ALSO AS COMBAT TEAM)
                              LEINSTER, MURRAY   NV   ASF 56 03
  FONDLY FAHRENHEIT   BESTER, ALFRED   SS   FSF 54 08
  SENTINEL, THE (SENTINEL OF ETERNITY)
                              CLARKE, ARTHUR C.   SS   TSF 51 SP

SPECTRUM 4   AMIS & CONQUEST   AN H HBW 65
  PREFACE   AMIS, KINGSLEY
                              AND CONQUEST, ROBERT IN C
  UNREAL ESTATES   LEWIS, C. S.
                              ALDISS, BRIAN W.
                              AND AMIS, KINGSLEY   MS C SFH 64 01
  MARCHING MORONS, THE   KORNBLUTH, C. M.   NV   GAL 51 04
  GADGET VS. TREND   ANVIL, CHRISTOPHER   SS   ASF 62 10
  SUCH STUFF   BRUNNER, JOHN   SS   FSF 62 06
  SELLERS OF THE DREAM, THE   JAKES, JOHN W.   NA   GAL 63 06
  LARGE ANT, THE (THE BIG ANT) FAST, HOWARD   SS   FUN 60 02
  BARRIER   BOUCHER, ANTHONY   NV   ASF 42 09
  GREAT NEBRASKA SEA, THE   DANZIG, ALLAN   FA   GAL 63 08
  COMPASSION CIRCUIT   WYNDHAM, JOHN   SS   FUN 54 12
  PLANET NAMED SHAYOL, A   SMITH, CORDWAINER   NA   GAL 61 10
  INTO THE SHOP   GOULART, RON   SS   FSF 64 04
  SECRET SONGS, THE   LEIBER, FRITZ   SS   FSF 62 08
  STRANGER STATION   KNIGHT, DAMON   NV   FSF 56 12
  HOT PLANET   CLEMENT, HAL   NV   GAL 63 08
  CHOICE, THE   HILTON-YOUNG,WAYLAND SS   PUN 52 03

SPECTRUM 5   AMIS & CONQUEST   AN H HBW 67
  INTRODUCTION   AMIS, KINGSLEY

SPECTRUM 5

	AND CONQUEST, ROBERT	IN	C	
STUDENT BODY	WALLACE, F. L.	NV	GAL 53 03
CRUCIFIXUS ETIAM	MILLER, WALTER M. JR	SS	ASF 53 02
NOISE LEVEL	JONES, RAYMOND F.	NV	ASF 52 12
GRANDPA	SCHMITZ, JAMES H.	SS	ASF 55 02
MOTHER OF INVENTION	GODWIN, TOM	SN	ASF 53 12
FAR LOOK, THE	THOMAS, THEODORE L.	NV	ASF 56 08
BIG SWORD	ASH, PAUL	NV	ASF 58 10
COMMENCEMENT NIGHT	ASHBY, RICHARD	SS	ASF 53 08

SPECTRUM OF WORLDS, A   CLARESON, THOMAS D.   AN H DBL 72
INTRODUCTION: A SPECTRUM OF WORLDS

	CLARESON, THOMAS D.	IN	
DAMNED THING, THE (1893)	BIERCE, AMBROSE	SS	WRT 23 09
SEA-RAIDERS, THE	WELLS, H. G.	SS	WSL 96 12
RED ONE, THE	LONDON, JACK	NV	CMP 18 10
METAL MAN, THE	WILLIAMSON, JACK	SS	AMZ 28 12
BY THE WATERS OF BABYLON (THE PLACE OF THE GODS)	BENET, STEPHEN V.	SS	SEP 37 07
TRENDS	ASIMOV, ISAAC	SS	ASF 39 07
FAR CENTAURUS	VAN VOGT, A. E.	SS	ASF 44 01
IF I FORGET THEE, OH EARTH...	CLARKE, ARTHUR C.	SS	FUT 51 09
DESERTION	SIMAK, CLIFFORD D.	SS	ASF 44 11
THIRTEEN TO CENTAURUS	BALLARD, J. G.	NV	AMZ 62 04
CAPTAIN HONARIO HARPPLAYER, R.N.	HARRISON, HARRY	SS	FSF 63 03
DRIFTGLASS	DELANY, SAMUEL R.	NV	IFS 67 06
STILL TRAJECTORIES	ALDISS, BRIAN W.	SS	NWS 67 09
SUNDANCE	SILVERBERG, ROBERT	SS	FSF 69 06

SPECULATIONS   SANDERS, THOMAS E.   AN L GLN 73

THEMATIC CONTENTS	MISC. MATERIAL	MS	
PREFACE	SANDERS, THOMAS E.	IN	
INTRODUCTION	SANDERS, THOMAS E.	IN	
POETRY	SANDERS, THOMAS E.	SI	
SCIENCE FICTION	AMIS, KINGSLEY	PM	ENC 60 05
MISFIT, THE	AMMONS, A. R.	PM	65
SIX HAIKU	ANDERSON, KAREN	PM	FSF 62 07
MOON LANDING	AUDEN, W. H.	PM	NYM 69
UNKNOWN CITIZEN, THE	AUDEN, W. H.	PM	40
NIGHTMARE NUMBER THREE	BENET, STEPHEN V.	PM	35
E=MC2	BISHOP, MORRIS	PM	NYM 46
LET THE TREES	BOOTH, PHILIP	PM	PNW 69 FL
OUTER BECOMING INNER, THE	BRONK, WILLIAM	PM	SAR 49
COMPASS, THE	CORMAN, CID	PM	67
MAN SAID TO THE UNIVERSE, A	CRANE, STEPHEN	PM	
PITY THIS BUSY MONSTER, MANUNKIND	CUMMINGS, E. E.	PM	44
RHYMES FOR A MODERN NURSERY (FROM "QUAKE, QUAKE, QUAKE")	DEHN, PAUL	PM	61
TO THE MOON, 1969	DEUTSCH, BABETTE	PM	
APOLLO	DICKEY, JAMES	PM	LIF 69
POEM ROCKET	GINSBERG, ALLEN	PM	61
GREAT BEAR, THE	HOLLANDER, JOHN	PM	58
SCIENCE	JEFFERS, ROBINSON	PM	25
PLANETARY EXCHANGE	JONES, LEROI	PM	69
SPACE: FOR MARTIN GREEN	KENNEDY, X. J.	PM	
FLIGHT OF APOLLO, THE	KUNITZ, STANLEY	PM	69
STAR-GAZE POEM	LYNE, STANDFORD	PM	69
SONNET: TO SCIENCE (1829)	POE, EDGAR ALLEN	PM	29
COMING, THE	POULIN, A. JR.	PM	63
EARTH WILL NOT LET GO	SWENSON, MAY	PM	70
WHEN I HEARD THE LEARN'D ASTRONOMER	WHITMAN, WALT	PM	
HEEL & TOE TO THE END	WILLIAMS, WILLIAM C.	PM	62
FICTION	SANDERS, THOMAS E.	SI	
MISBEGOTTEN MISSIONARY (ALSO AS GREEN PATCHES)	ASIMOV, ISAAC	SS	GAL 50 11
GARDEN OF TIME, THE	BALLARD, J. G.	SS	FSF 62 02
BY THE WATERS OF BABYLON (THE PLACE OF THE GODS)	BENET, STEPHEN V.	SS	SEP 37 07
IT'S A GOOD LIFE	BIXBY, JEROME	SS	STR 53 02
FOG HORN, THE (THE BEAST FROM 20,000 FATHOMS)	BRADBURY, RAY	SS	SEP 51 06
WAVERIES, THE	BROWN, FREDRIC	SS	ASF 45 01
PORTABLE PHONOGRAPH, THE	CLARK, WALTER VAN T.	SS	41
STAR, THE	CLARKE, ARTHUR C.	SS	INF 55 11
STAR, BRIGHT	CLIFTON, MARK	NV	GAL 52 07
HILIFTER	DICKSON, GORDON R.	SS	ASF 63 02
"REPENT, HARLEQUIN!" SAID THE TICKTOCKMAN	ELLISON, HARLAN	SS	GAL 65 12
CATO THE MARTIAN	FAST, HOWARD	SS	FSF 60 06
FRANCES HARKINS	GOGGIN, RICHARD	SS	FSF 52 12
DISCOVERY IN THE WOODS, A	GREENE, GRAHAM	NV	63
EARTH'S HOLOCAUST	HAWTHORNE, NATHANIEL	SS	GLG 44 05
GREEN HILLS OF EARTH, THE	HEINLEIN, ROBERT A.	SS	SEP 47 02
AS EASY AS A. B. C.	KIPLING, RUDYARD	NV	LOM 12 04
INVASION FROM MARS	KOCH, HOWARD	PL	CBS 38 10
ALTAR AT MIDNIGHT, THE	KORNBLUTH, C. M.	SS	GAL 52 11
CONTINUED ON NEXT ROCK	LAFFERTY, R. A.	NV	ORB 70 07
EEL BY THE TAIL, AN	LANG, ALLEN KIM	SS	IMG 51 04
THIS STAR SHALL BE FREE	LEINSTER, MURRAY	NV	SSS 49 11
PAIL OF AIR, A	LEIBER, FRITZ	SS	GAL 51 12
OUTSIDER, THE	LOVECRAFT, H. P.	SS	WRT 26 04
PICTURES DON'T LIE	MACLEAN, KATHERINE	SS	GAL 51 08
TARTARUS OF MAIDS, THE	MELVILLE, HERMAN	SS	
THAT ONLY A MOTHER	MERRIL, JUDITH	SS	ASF 48 06
NEUTRON STAR	NIVEN, LARRY	NV	IFS 66 10
MELLONTA TAUTA	POE, EDGAR ALLEN	SS	GDY 49 02
WHAT TO DO TILL THE ANALYST COMES (EVERYBODY'S HAPPY BUT ME!)	POHL, FREDERIK	SS	IMG 56 02
SREDNI VASHTAR	SAKI	SS	
STREET OF DREAMS, FEET OF CLAY	SHECKLEY, ROBERT	NV	GAL 68 02
LAST MAN, THE (1826)	SHELLEY, MARY W.	EX	

BLACK IS BEAUTIFUL	SILVERBERG, ROBERT	SS	YRT 70
SUNDANCE	SILVERBERG, ROBERT	SS	FSF 69 0.
SLOW SCULPTURE	STURGEON, THEODORE	NV	GAL 70 0.
DATE TO REMEMBER, A	TEMPLE, WILLIAM F.	SS	TWS 49 0.
FRESH GUY	TUBB, E. C.	SS	SCF 58 0.
AUTOMATON	VAN VOGT, A. E.	SS	OWS 50 0.
REPORT ON THE BARNHOUSE EFFECT	VONNEGUT, KURT JR.	SS	COL 50 02
CHRONIC ARGONAUTS, THE	WELLS, H. G.	NV	SSJ 88 0.
ESSAY, AN EXPLANATION, AND AN EXCERPT, AN	SANDERS, THOMAS E.	SI	
WHEN ARISTOTLE FAILS, TRY SCIENCE FICTION	ASIMOV, ISAAC	AR	ITL 71
GHOST OF AN APPREHENSION, THE	CLARK, WALTER VAN T.	AR	PSP 49 S.
AGE OF CLIMAX, THE (FROM "THE GHOST IN THE MACHINE")	KOESTLER, ARTHUR	EX	MAC 67

SPELL OF SEVEN, THE   DE CAMP, L. SPRAGUE   AN   PYR 65 06

WIZARDS AND WARRIORS	DE CAMP, L. SPRAGUE	IN	
BAZAAR OF THE BIZARRE	LEIBER, FRITZ	NV	SOI 63 08
DARK EIDOLON, THE	SMITH, CLARK ASHTON	NV	WRT 35 0
HOARD OF THE GIBBELINS, THE	DUNSANY, LORD	SS	AFR 47 0.
HUNGRY HERCYNIAN, THE	DE CAMP, L. SPRAGUE	NV	USF 53 1.
KINGS IN DARKNESS	MOORCOCK, MICHAEL	NV	SCF 62 08
MAZIRIAN THE MAGICIAN	VANCE, JACK	SS	50
SHADOWS IN ZAMBOULA	HOWARD, ROBERT E.	NV	WRT 35 11

SPRAGUE DE CAMP'S NEW ANTHOLOGY   DE CAMP, L. SPRAGUE   AC H HML 53

CALORIES	DE CAMP, L. SPRAGUE	SS	TST 51 S.
COLORFUL CHARACTER, THE	DE CAMP, L. SPRAGUE	SS	TWS 49 12
JUICE	DE CAMP, L. SPRAGUE	SS	SSS 40 05
PROPOSAL	DE CAMP, L. SPRAGUE	SS	STS 52 1.
SAXON PRETENDER, THE	DE CAMP, L. SPRAGUE	SS	
SPACE CLAUSE, THE	DE CAMP, L. SPRAGUE	SS	IFS 52 0.

SQUARE ROOT OF MAN, THE   TENN, WILLIAM   AC   BAL 68 06

AUTHOR'S NOTE	TENN, WILLIAM	IN	
ALEXANDER THE BAIT	TENN, WILLIAM	SS	ASF 46 05
LAST BOUNCE, THE	TENN, WILLIAM	NV	FAD 50 09
SHE ONLY GOES OUT AT NIGHT	TENN, WILLIAM	SS	FUN 56 10
MY MOTHER WAS A WITCH	TENN, WILLIAM	SS	66
JESTER, THE	TENN, WILLIAM	SS	TWS 51 08
CONFUSION CARGO	TENN, WILLIAM	SS	PLS 48 S.
VENUS IS A MAN'S WORLD	TENN, WILLIAM	NV	GAL 51 07
CONSULATE	TENN, WILLIAM	SS	TWS 48 06
LEMON-GREEN SPAGHETTI-LOUD DYNAMITE-DRIBBLE DAY (DID YOUR COFFE. TASTE FUNNY THIS MORNING?)	TENN, WILLIAM	SS	CAV 67 0.

STAR FOURTEEN   POHL, FREDERIK   AN H WHW 66
SEE "STAR OF STARS"

STAR FOX, THE   ANDERSON, POUL   AC H DBL 65

MARQUE AND REPRISAL	ANDERSON, POUL	SN	FSF 65 02
ARSENAL PORT	ANDERSON, POUL	SN	FSF 65 04
ADMIRALTY	ANDERSON, POUL	SN	FSF 65 06

STAR LIGHT, STAR BRIGHT   BESTER, ALFRED   AC H BKP 76
ALSO IN "STARLIGHT"

ADAM AND NO EVE	BESTER, ALFRED	SS	ASF 41 09
TIME IS THE TRAITOR	BESTER, ALFRED	NV	FSF 53 09
ODDY AND ID (THE DEVIL'S INVENTION)	BESTER, ALFRED	SS	ASF 50 08
HOBSON'S CHOICE	BESTER, ALFRED	SS	FSF 52 08
STAR LIGHT, STAR BRIGHT	BESTER, ALFRED	SS	FSF 53 07
THEY DON'T MAKE LIFE LIKE THEY USED TO	BESTER, ALFRED	NV	FSF 63 10
OF TIME AND THIRD AVENUE	BESTER, ALFRED	SS	FSF 51 10
ISAAC ASIMOV	BESTER, ALFRED	AR	PBW 73
PI MAN, THE	BESTER, ALFRED	SS	FSF 59 10
SOMETHING UP THERE LIKES ME	BESTER, ALFRED	NV	AMA 73
MY AFFAIR WITH SCIENCE FICTION	BESTER, ALFRED	AR	NOV 74 0.

STAR OF STARS   POHL, FREDERIK   AN   BAL 60
IN ENGLAND AS "STAR FOURTEEN"

INTRODUCTION	POHL, FREDERIK	IN	
WHATEVER HAPPENED TO CORPORAL CUCKOO? (1953)	KERSH, GERALD	NV	STR 54 03
ADVENT ON CHANNEL TWELVE, THE	KORNBLUTH, C. M.	SS	STR 58 04
DISAPPEARING ACT	BESTER, ALFRED	SS	STR 53 02
TWIN'S WAIL	BORGESE, ELISABETH M	NV	STR 59 06
COUNTRY DOCTOR	MORRISON, WILLIAM	NV	STR 53 0.
DAYBROKE	BLOCH, ROBERT	SS	SMG 58 01
DEEP RANGE, THE (ARB 54 04)	CLARKE, ARTHUR C.	NV	STR 54 03
CROSS OF CENTURIES, A	KUTTNER, HENRY	SS	STR 58 04
MAN WITH ENGLISH, THE	GOLD, H. L.	SS	STR 53 0.
SPARKIE'S FALL	HYDE, GAVIN	SS	STR 59 05
SPACE-TIME FOR SPRINGERS	LEIBER, FRITZ	SS	STR 58 04
DANCE OF THE DEAD	MATHESON, RICHARD	SS	STR 54 03
HAPPIEST CREATURE, THE	WILLIAMSON, JACK	SS	STR 53 02
IT'S A GOOD LIFE	BIXBY, JEROME	SS	STR 53 02

STAR ROAD, THE   DICKSON, GORDON R.   AC H DBL 73

WHATEVER GODS THERE BE	DICKSON, GORDON R.	SS	AMZ 61 07
HILIFTER	DICKSON, GORDON R.	SS	ASF 63 02
BUILDING ON THE LINE	DICKSON, GORDON R.	NV	GAL 68 11
CHRISTMAS PRESENT, THE	DICKSON, GORDON R.	SS	FSF 58 10
THREE-PART PUZZLE	DICKSON, GORDON R.	SS	ASF 62 06
ON MESSENGER MOUNTAIN	DICKSON, GORDON R.	NV	WOT 64 06
CATCH, THE	DICKSON, GORDON R.	SS	ASF 59 04
JACKAL'S MEAL	DICKSON, GORDON R.	SS	ASF 69 06
MOUSETRAP, THE	DICKSON, GORDON R.	SS	GAL 52 09

STAR SCIENCE FICTION STORIES   STAR TREK 7

STAR SCIENCE FICTION STORIES POHL, FREDERIK   OA H BAL 53
  EDITOR'S NOTE   POHL, FREDERIK   IN
  COUNTRY DOCTOR   MORRISON, WILLIAM   NV   STR 53 01
  DOMINOES   KORNBLUTH, C. M.   SS   STR 53 01
  IDEALIST   DEL REY, LESTER   SS   STR 53 01
  NIGHT HE CRIED, THE   LEIBER, FRITZ   SS   STR 53 01
  CONTRAPTION   SIMAK, CLIFFORD D.   SS   STR 53 01
  CHRONOCLASM, THE   WYNDHAM, JOHN   NV   STR 53 01
  DESERTER, THE   TENN, WILLIAM   SS   STR 53 01
  MAN WITH ENGLISH, THE   GOLD, H. L.   SS   STR 53 01
  SO PROUDLY WE HAIL   MERRIL, JUDITH   SS   STR 53 01
  SCENT OF SARSAPARILLA, A   BRADBURY, RAY   SS   STR 53 01
  NOBODY HERE BUT-   ASIMOV, ISAAC   SS   STR 53 01
  LAST WEAPON, THE   SHECKLEY, ROBERT   SS   STR 53 01
  WILD SURMISE, A   KUTTNER, HENRY
                               AND MOORE, C. L.   SS C STR 53 01
  JOURNEY, THE   LEINSTER, MURRAY   SS   STR 53 01
  NINE BILLION NAMES OF GOD, THE
                               CLARKE, ARTHUR C.   SS   STR 53 01

STAR SCIENCE FICTION STORIES NO. 2
                               POHL, FREDERIK   OA H BAL 53
  EDITOR'S NOTE   POHL, FREDERIK   IN
  DISAPPEARING ACT   BESTER, ALFRED   SS   STR 53 02
  CLINIC, THE   STURGEON, THEODORE   SS   STR 53 02
  CONGRUENT PEOPLE, THE   BUDRYS, ALGIS   SS   STR 53 02
  CRITICAL FACTOR   CLEMENT, HAL   SS   STR 53 02
  IT'S A GOOD LIFE   BIXBY, JEROME   SS   STR 53 02
  POUND OF CURE, A   DEL REY, LESTER   SS   STR 53 02
  PURPLE FIELDS, THE   CRANE, ROBERT   SS   STR 53 02
  F Y I   BLISH, JAMES   SS   STR 53 02
  CONQUEST   BOUCHER, ANTHONY   SS   STR 53 02
  HORMONES   PRATT, FLETCHER   SS   STR 53 02
  ODOR OF THOUGHT, THE   SHECKLEY, ROBERT   SS   STR 53 02
  HAPPIEST CREATURE, THE   WILLIAMSON, JACK   SS   STR 53 02
  REMORSEFUL, THE   KORNBLUTH, C. M.   SS   STR 53 02
  FRIEND OF THE FAMILY   WILSON, RICHARD   SS   STR 53 02

STAR SCIENCE FICTION STORIES NO. 3
                               POHL, FREDERIK   OA H BAL 54
  EDITOR'S NOTE   POHL, FREDERIK   IN
  IT'S SUCH A BEAUTIFUL DAY   ASIMOV, ISAAC   NV   STR 54 03
  STRAWBERRY WINDOW, THE   BRADBURY, RAY   NV   STR 54 03
  DEEP RANGE, THE (ARB 54 04) CLARKE, ARTHUR C.   NV   STR 54 03
  ALIEN   DEL REY, LESTER   SS   STR 54 03
  FOSTER, YOU'RE DEAD   DICK, PHILIP K.   NV   STR 54 03
  WHATEVER HAPPENED TO CORPORAL CUCKOO? (1953)
                               KERSH, GERALD   NV   STR 54 03
  DANCE OF THE DEAD   MATHESON, RICHARD   SS   STR 54 03
  ANY MORE AT HOME LIKE YOU?   OLIVER, CHAD   SS   STR 54 03
  DEVIL ON SALVATION BLUFF, THE
                               VANCE, JACK   NV   STR 54 03
  GUINEVERE FOR EVERYBODY   WILLIAMSON, JACK   SS   STR 54 03

STAR SCIENCE FICTION STORIES NO. 4
                               POHL, FREDERIK   OA   BAL 58
  PINCH OF STARDUST, A   POHL, FREDERIK   IN
  CROSS OF CENTURIES, A   KUTTNER, HENRY   SS   STR 58 04
  ADVENT ON CHANNEL TWELVE, THE
                               KORNBLUTH, C. M.   SS   STR 58 04
  SPACE-TIME FOR SPRINGERS   LEIBER, FRITZ   SS   STR 58 04
  MAN WORKING   WILSON, RICHARD   SS   STR 58 04
  HELPING HAND   DEL REY, LESTER   NV   STR 58 04
  LONG ECHO, THE   DEFORD, MIRIAM ALLEN   SS   STR 58 04
  TOMORROW'S GIFT   COOPER, EDMUND   SS   STR 58 04
  IDIOT STICK   KNIGHT, DAMON   SS   STR 58 04
  IMMORTALS, THE (ALSO AS IMMORTAL)
                               GUNN, JAMES E.   NV   STR 58 04

STAR SCIENCE FICTION STORIES NO. 5
                               POHL, FREDERIK   OA   BAL 59
  TROUBLE WITH TREATIES   MACLEAN, KATHERINE
                               AND CONDIT, TOM   NV C STR 59 05
  TOUCH OF GRAPEFRUIT, A (ALSO AS THE CREEPING TERROR)
                               MATHESON, RICHARD   SS   STR 59 05
  COMPANY STORE   SILVERBERG, ROBERT   SS   STR 59 05
  ADRIFT ON THE POLICY LEVEL   DAVIS, CHAN   SS   STR 59 05
  SPARKIE'S FALL   HYDE, GAVIN   SS   STR 59 05
  STAR DESCENDING   BUDRYS, ALGIS   SS   STR 59 05
  DIPLOMATIC COOP   GALOUYE, DANIEL F.   SS   STR 59 05
  SCENE SHIFTER, THE   SELLINGS, ARTHUR   SS   STR 59 05
  HAIR-RAISING ADVENTURE   BROWN, ROSEL GEORGE   SS   STR 59 05

STAR SCIENCE FICTION STORIES NO. 6
                               POHL, FREDERIK   OA   BAL 59
  DANGER! CHILD AT LARGE   COTTRELL, C. L.   NV   STR 59 06
  TWIN'S WAIL   BORGESE, ELISABETH M   NV   STR 59 06
  HOLY GRAIL, THE   PURDOM, TOM   SS   STR 59 06
  ANGERHELM   SMITH, CORDWAINER   NV   STR 59 06
  DREAMSMAN, THE   DICKSON, GORDON R.   SS   STR 59 06
  TO CATCH AN ALIEN   MCGUIRE, JOHN J.   SS   STR 59 06
  PRESS CONFERENCE   DEFORD, MIRIAM ALLEN   SS   STR 59 06
  INVASION FROM INNER SPACE   KOCH, HOWARD   NV   STR 59 06

STAR SHINE   BROWN, FREDRIC   AC   BAN 56 02
  SEE "ANGELS AND SPACESHIPS"

STAR SHORT NOVELS   POHL, FREDERIK   OA   BAL 54 10
  INTRODUCTION   POHL, FREDERIK   IN
  LITTLE MEN   WEST, JESSAMYN   SN   SSN 54
  FOR I AM A JEALOUS PEOPLE!   DEL REY, LESTER   SN   SSN 54
  TO HERE AND THE EASEL   STURGEON, THEODORE   SN   SSN 54
  ABOUT THE AUTHORS   MISC. MATERIAL   MS

STAR TREK   BLISH, JAMES   OC   BAN 67
  ALSO IN "THE STAR TREK READER II"

  CHARLIE'S LAW (CHARLIE X, FONTANA & RODDENBERRY)
                               BLISH, JAMES   SA   STK 67 01
  DAGGER OF THE MIND (S. BAR-DAVID)
                               BLISH, JAMES   SA   STK 67 01
  UNREAL MCCOY, THE (THE MAN TRAP, GEORGE C. JOHNSON)
                               BLISH, JAMES   SA   STK 67 01
  BALANCE OF TERROR (PAUL SCHNEIDER)
                               BLISH, JAMES   SA   STK 67 01
  NAKED TIME, THE (JOHN D. F. BLACK)
                               BLISH, JAMES   SA   STK 67 01
  MIRI (ADRIAN SPIES)   BLISH, JAMES   SA   STK 67 01
  CONSCIENCE OF THE KING, THE (BARRY TRIVERS)
                               BLISH, JAMES   SA   STK 67 01

STAR TREK   2   BLISH, JAMES   OC   BAN 68
  ALSO IN "THE STAR TREK READER"
  ARENA (GENE L. COON)   BLISH, JAMES   SA   STK 68 02
  TASTE OF ARMAGEDDON, A (R. HAMNER & G. L. COON)
                               BLISH, JAMES   SA   STK 68 02
  TOMORROW IS YESTERDAY (D. C. FONTANA)
                               BLISH, JAMES   SA   STK 68 02
  ERRAND OF MERCY (GENE L. COON)
                               BLISH, JAMES   SA   STK 68 02
  COURT MARTIAL (D. M. MANKIEWICZ & S. CARABATSOS)
                               BLISH, JAMES   SA   STK 68 02
  OPERATION- ANNIHILATE! (S. W. CARABATSOS)
                               BLISH, JAMES   SA   STK 68 02
  CITY ON THE EDGE OF FOREVER, THE (HARLAN ELLISON)
                               BLISH, JAMES   SA   STK 68 02
  SPACE SEED (C. WILBER & GENE L. COON)
                               BLISH, JAMES   SA   STK 68 02

STAR TREK   3   BLISH, JAMES   OC   BAN 69 04
  ALSO IN "THE STAR TREK READER"
  PREFACE: SOME AWARDS FOR STAR TREK- AND AN OPEN LETTER
                               BLISH, JAMES   IN
  TROUBLE WITH TRIBBLES, THE (DAVID GERROLD)
                               BLISH, JAMES   SA   STK 69 03
  LAST GUNFIGHT, THE (LEE CRONIN)
                               BLISH, JAMES   SA   STK 69 03
  DOOMSDAY MACHINE, THE (NORMAN SPINRAD)
                               BLISH, JAMES   SA   STK 69 03
  ASSIGNMENT: EARTH (GENE RODDENBERRY & ART WALLACE)
                               BLISH, JAMES   SA   STK 69 03
  MIRROR, MIRROR (JEROME BIXBY)
                               BLISH, JAMES   SA   STK 69 03
  FRIDAY'S CHILD (D. C. FONTANA)
                               BLISH, JAMES   SA   STK 69 03
  AMOK TIME (THEODORE STURGEON)
                               BLISH, JAMES   SA   STK 69 03

STAR TREK   4   BLISH, JAMES   OC   BAN 71 07
  ALSO IN "THE STAR TREK READER II"
  PREFACE   BLISH, JAMES   IN
  ALL OUR YESTERDAYS (JEAN LISETTE AROESTE)
                               BLISH, JAMES   SA   STK 71 04
  DEVIL IN THE DARK, THE (GENE L. COON)
                               BLISH, JAMES   SA   STK 71 04
  JOURNEY TO BABEL (D. C. FONTANA)
                               BLISH, JAMES   SA   STK 71 04
  MENAGERIE (GENE RODDENBERRY) BLISH, JAMES   SA   STK 71 04
  ENTERPRISE INCIDENT, THE (D. C. FONTANA)
                               BLISH, JAMES   SA   STK 71 04
  PIECE OF THE ACTION, A (D. P. HARMON & G. L. COON)
                               BLISH, JAMES   SA   STK 71 04

STAR TREK   5   BLISH, JAMES   OC   BAN 72 02
  PREFACE   BLISH, JAMES   IN
  WHOM GODS DESTROY (LEE ERWIN & JERRY SOHL)
                               BLISH, JAMES   SA   STK 72 05
  THOLIAN WEB, THE (JUDY BURNS & CHET RICHARDS)
                               BLISH, JAMES   SA   STK 72 05
  LET THAT BE YOUR LAST BATTLEFIELD (CRAWFORD & CRONIN)
                               BLISH, JAMES   SA   STK 72 05
  THIS SIDE OF PARADISE (N. BUTLER & D. C. FONTANA)
                               BLISH, JAMES   SA   STK 72 05
  TURNABOUT INTRUDER (G. RODDENBERRY & A. H. SINGER)
                               BLISH, JAMES   SA   STK 72 05
  REQUIEM FOR METHUSELAH (JEROME BIXBY)
                               BLISH, JAMES   SA   STK 72 05
  WAY TO EDEN, THE (A. HEINEMANN & M. RICHARDS)
                               BLISH, JAMES   SA   STK 72 05

STAR TREK   6   BLISH, JAMES   OC   BAN 72 04
  PREFACE   BLISH, JAMES   IN
  SAVAGE CURTAIN, THE (G. RODDENBERRY & A. HEINEMANN)
                               BLISH, JAMES   SA   STK 72 06
  LIGHTS OF ZETAR, THE (JEREMY TARCHER & SHARI LEWIS)
                               BLISH, JAMES   SA   STK 72 06
  APPLE, THE (MAX EHRLICH & GENE L. COON)
                               BLISH, JAMES   SA   STK 72 06
  BY ANY OTHER NAME (D. C. FONTANA & JEROME BIXBY)
                               BLISH, JAMES   SA   STK 72 06
  CLOUD MINERS, THE (ARMEN, GERROLD & CRAWFORD)
                               BLISH, JAMES   SA   STK 72 06
  MARK OF GIDEON, THE (G. F. SLAVIN & S. ADAMS)
                               BLISH, JAMES   SA   STK 72 06

STAR TREK   7   BLISH, JAMES   OC   BAN 72 07
  WHO MOURNS FOR ADONAIS? (G. RALSTON & G. COON)
                               BLISH, JAMES   SA   STK 72 07
  CHANGELING, THE (JOHN MEREDYTH LUCAS)
                               BLISH, JAMES   SA   STK 72 07
  PARADISE SYNDROME, THE (MARGARET ARMEN)
                               BLISH, JAMES   SA   STK 72 07
  METAMORPHOSIS (GENE L. COON) BLISH, JAMES   SA   STK 72 07

DEADLY YEARS, THE (DAVID P. HARMON)
                              BLISH, JAMES   SA   STK 72 07
ELAAN OF TROYIUS (JOHN MEREDYTH LUCAS)
                              BLISH, JAMES   SA   STK 72 07

STAR TREK   8   BLISH, JAMES   OC   BAN 72 11
   ALSO IN "THE STAR TREK READER"
SPOCK'S BRAIN (LEE CRONIN)   BLISH, JAMES   SA   STK 72 08
ENEMY WITHIN, THE (RICHARD MATHESON)
                              BLISH, JAMES   SA   STK 72 08
CATSPAW (ROBERT BLOCH)   BLISH, JAMES   SA   STK 72 08
WHERE NO MAN HAS GONE BEFORE (SAMUEL A. PEEPLES)
                              BLISH, JAMES   SA   STK 72 08
WOLF IN THE FOLD (ROBERT BLOCH)
                              BLISH, JAMES   SA   STK 72 08
FOR THE WORLD IS HOLLOW AND I HAVE TOUCHED THE SKY
   (RIK VOLLAERTS) BLISH, JAMES   SA   STK 72 08

STAR TREK   9   BLISH, JAMES   OC   BAN 73 08
   ALSO IN "THE STAR TREK READER II"
PREFACE   BLISH, JAMES   IN
RETURN TO TOMORROW (G. RODDENBERRY & J. T. DOUGAN)
                              BLISH, JAMES   SA   STK 73 09
ULTIMATE COMPUTER, THE (D. C. FONTANA & L. WOLFE)
                              BLISH, JAMES   SA   STK 73 09
THAT WHICH SURVIVES (J. M. LUCAS & D. C. FONTANA)
                              BLISH, JAMES   SA   STK 73 09
OBSESSION (ART WALLACE)   BLISH, JAMES   SA   STK 73 09
RETURN OF THE ARCHONS, THE (BORIS SOBELMAN)
                              BLISH, JAMES   SA   STK 73 09
IMMUNITY SYNDROME, THE (ROBERT SABAROFF)
                              BLISH, JAMES   SA   STK 73 09

STAR TREK   10   BLISH, JAMES   OC   BAN 74 02
PREFACE   BLISH, JAMES   IN
ALTERNATIVE FACTOR, THE (DON INGALLS)
                              BLISH, JAMES   SA   STK 74 10
EMPATH, THE (JOYCE MUSKAT)   BLISH, JAMES   SA   STK 74 10
GALILEO SEVEN, THE (S. WINCELBERG & O. CRAWFORD)
                              BLISH, JAMES   SA   STK 74 10
IS THERE NO TRUTH IN BEAUTY? (JEAN LISETTE AROESTE)
                              BLISH, JAMES   SA   STK 74 10
PRIVATE LITTLE WAR, A (D. INGALLS & G. RODDENBERRY)
                              BLISH, JAMES   SA   STK 74 10
OMEGA GLORY, THE (GENE RODDENBERRY)
                              BLISH, JAMES   SA   STK 74 10

STAR TREK   11   BLISH, JAMES   OC   BAN 75 04
PREFACE   BLISH, JAMES   IN
WHAT ARE LITTLE GIRLS MADE OF? (ROBERT BLOCH)
                              BLISH, JAMES   SA   STK 75 11
SQUIRE OF GOTHOS, THE (PAUL SCHNEIDER)
                              BLISH, JAMES   SA   STK 75 11
WINK OF AN EYE (ARTHUR HEINEMANN & LEE CRONIN)
                              BLISH, JAMES   SA   STK 75 11
BREAD AND CIRCUSES (GENE RODDENBERRY & G. L. COON)
                              BLISH, JAMES   SA   STK 75 11
DAY OF THE DOVE (JEROME BIXBY)
                              BLISH, JAMES   SA   STK 75 11
PLATO'S STEPCHILDREN (MEYER DOLINSKY)
                              BLISH, JAMES   SA   STK 75 11

STAR TREK LOG FIVE   FOSTER, ALAN DEAN   OC   BAL 75 08
AMBERGRIS ELEMENT, THE (MARGARET ARMEN)
                              FOSTER, ALAN DEAN   SA   SLG 75 05
PIRATES OF ORION, THE (HOWARD WEINSTEIN)
                              FOSTER, ALAN DEAN   SA   SLG 75 05
JIHAD (STEPHEN KANDEL)   FOSTER, ALAN DEAN   SA   SLG 75 05

STAR TREK LOG FOUR   FOSTER, ALAN DEAN   OC   BAL 75 03
TERRATIN INCIDENT, THE (PAUL SCHNEIDER)
                              FOSTER, ALAN DEAN   SA   SLG 75 04
TIME TRAP (JOYCE PERRY)   FOSTER, ALAN DEAN   SA   SLG 75 04
MORE TRIBBLES, MORE TROUBLES (DAVID GERROLD)
                              FOSTER, ALAN DEAN   SA   SLG 75 04

STAR TREK LOG ONE   FOSTER, ALAN DEAN   OC   BAL 74 06
BEYOND THE FARTHEST STAR (SAMUEL A. PEEPLES)
                              FOSTER, ALAN DEAN   SA   SLG 74 01
YESTERYEAR (D. C. FONTANA)   FOSTER, ALAN DEAN   SA   SLG 74 01
ONE OF OUR PLANETS IS MISSING (MARC DANIELS)
                              FOSTER, ALAN DEAN   SA   SLG 74 01

STAR TREK LOG SIX   FOSTER, ALAN DEAN   OC   BAL 76 03
ALBATROSS (DARIO FINELLI)   FOSTER, ALAN DEAN   SA   SLG 76 06
PRACTICAL JOKER, THE (CHUCK MENVILLE)
                              FOSTER, ALAN DEAN   SA   SLG 76 06
HOW SHARPER THAN A SERPENT'S TOOTH (RUSSELL BATES &DAVID WISE)
                              FOSTER, ALAN DEAN   SA   SLG 76 06

STAR TREK LOG THREE FOSTER, ALAN DEAN   OC   BAL 75 01
ONCE UPON A PLANET (LEN JANSON & CHUCK MENVILLE)
                              FOSTER, ALAN DEAN   SA   SLG 75 03
MUDD'S PASSION (STEPHEN KANDEL)
                              FOSTER, ALAN DEAN   SA   SLG 75 03
MAGICKS OF MEGAS-TU, THE (LARRY BRODY)
                              FOSTER, ALAN DEAN   SA   SLG 75 03

STAR TREK LOG TWO   FOSTER, ALAN DEAN   OC   BAL 74 09
SURVIVOR, THE (JAMES SCHERMER)
                              FOSTER, ALAN DEAN   SA   SLG 74 02
LORELEI SIGNAL, THE (MARGARET ARMEN)
                              FOSTER, ALAN DEAN   SA   SLG 74 02
INFINITE VULCAN, THE (WALTER KOENIG)
                              FOSTER, ALAN DEAN   SA   SLG 74 02

STAR TREK READER II, THE   BLISH, JAMES   AC H DUT 77
   STAR TREK   BLISH, JAMES   OC   BAN 67
   STAR TREK   4   BLISH, JAMES   OC   BAN 71 07
   STAR TREK   9   BLISH, JAMES   OC   BAN 73 08

STAR TREK READER, THE   BLISH, JAMES   AC H DUT 76
   STAR TREK   2   BLISH, JAMES   OC   BAN 68
   STAR TREK   3   BLISH, JAMES   OC   BAN 69 04
   STAR TREK   8   BLISH, JAMES   OC   BAN 72 11

STAR TREK: THE NEW VOYAGES MARSHAK, S&CULBREATH OA BAN 76 03
FOREWORD   RODDENBERRY, GENE   IN
INTRODUCTION: THE ONCE AND FUTURE VOYAGES
                              MARSHAK, SONDRA
                           AND CULBREATH, MYRNA   IN C
INTRODUCTION TO NI VAR   NIMOY, LEONARD   IN
NI VAR   GABRIEL, CLAIRE   NV
INTRODUCTION TO INTERSECTION POINT
                              DOOHAN, JAMES   IN
INTERSECTION POINT   COULSON, JUANITA   NV
INTRODUCTION TO THE ENCHANTED POOL
                              NICHOLS, NICHELLE   IN
ENCHANTED POOL, THE   ERICSON, MARCIA   NV
INTRODUCTION TO VISIT TO A WEIRD PLANET REVISITED
                              RODDENBERRY, MAJEL B IN
VISIT TO A WEIRD PLANET REVISITED
                              BERMAN, RUTH   SS
INTRODUCTION TO THE FACE ON THE BARROOM FLOOR
                              TAKEI, GEORGE   IN
FACE ON THE BARROOM FLOOR, THE
                              ARNASON, ELEANOR
                           AND BERMAN, RUTH   NV C
INTRODUCTION TO THE HUNTING   MARSHAK, SONDRA
                           AND CULBREATH, MYRNA   IN C
HUNTING, THE   BEETEM, DORIS   SS
INTRODUCTION TO THE WINGED DREAMERS
                              KELLEY, DEFOREST   IN
WINGED DREAMERS, THE   GUTTRIDGE, JENNIFER NV
INTRODUCTION TO MIND-SIFTER   SHATNER, WILLIAM   IN
MIND-SIFTER   MAIEWSKI, SHIRLEY S. NA
SONNET FROM THE VULCAN: OMICRON CETI THREE
                              MEECH, SHIRLEY   PM

STARBURST   BESTER, ALFRED   AC   SIG 58
DISAPPEARING ACT   BESTER, ALFRED   SS   STR 53 02
ADAM AND NO EVE   BESTER, ALFRED   SS   ASF 41 09
STAR LIGHT, STAR BRIGHT   BESTER, ALFRED   SS   FSF 53 07
ROLLER COASTER, THE   BESTER, ALFRED   SS   FAN 53 06
ODDY AND ID (THE DEVIL'S INVENTION)
                              BESTER, ALFRED   SS   ASF 50 08
STARCOMBER, THE (5,271,009)   BESTER, ALFRED   NV   FSF 54 03
TRAVEL DIARY   BESTER, ALFRED   SS   NEW 54 AC
FONDLY FAHRENHEIT   BESTER, ALFRED   SS   FSF 54 08
HOBSON'S CHOICE   BESTER, ALFRED   SS   FSF 52 08
DIE-HARD, THE   BESTER, ALFRED   SS   NEW 58 AC
OF TIME AND THIRD AVENUE   BESTER, ALFRED   SS   FSF 51 10

STARDREAMER   SMITH, CORDWAINER   AC   BEA 71 08
THINK BLUE, COUNT TWO   SMITH, CORDWAINER   NA   GAL 63 02
UNDER OLD EARTH   SMITH, CORDWAINER   NV   GAL 66 02
CRIME AND THE GLORY OF COMMANDER SUZDAL, THE
                              SMITH, CORDWAINER   SS   AMZ 64 05
GOOD FRIENDS, THE   SMITH, CORDWAINER   SS   WOT 63 10
FIFE OF BODIDHARMA, THE   SMITH, CORDWAINER   SS   FAN 59 06
WHEN THE PEOPLE FELL   SMITH, CORDWAINER   SS   GAL 59 04
ANGERHELM   SMITH, CORDWAINER   NV   STR 59 06
WESTERN SCIENCE IS SO WONDERFUL
                              SMITH, CORDWAINER   SS   IFS 58 12

STARDRIFT AND OTHER FANTASTIC FLOTSAM
                              PETAJA, EMIL   AC H FPB 71
INTRODUCTION   ACKERMAN, FORREST J. IN
STARDRIFT (SKYDRIFT)   PETAJA, EMIL   SS   WRT 49 11
MOON FEVER (MILLION-MILE HUNT)
                              PETAJA, EMIL   SS   IFS 65 03
WHERE IS THY STING   PETAJA, EMIL   SS   FSF 67 05
DOG'S BEST FRIEND, A   PETAJA, EMIL   SS
PEACEMONGER (THE MAN WHO HATED WAR)
                              PETAJA, EMIL   SS   AMZ 44 12
DARK BALCONY, THE   PETAJA, EMIL   SS   FAD 51 02
HUNGER (THE HUNGRY GHOST)   PETAJA, EMIL   SS   WRT 50 03
DARK HOLLOW   PETAJA, EMIL   SS   MOH 66 WI
DODECAGON GARDEN (CUBE IN A DODECAGON GARDEN)
                              PETAJA, EMIL   SS   SWY 70 06
ONLY GONE BEFORE   PETAJA, EMIL   SS   MOH 68 03
ANSWER, THE   PETAJA, EMIL   SS   IMG 51 09
BE A WINGDINGER, EARN BIG MONEY
                              PETAJA, EMIL   SS
PATTERN FOR PLUNDER   PETAJA, EMIL   NV
FOUND OBJECTS   PETAJA, EMIL   SS

STARDUST VOYAGES, THE   TALL, STEPHEN   AC   BKM 75 10
FOREWORD   TALL, STEPHEN   IN
STAR CALLED CYRENE, A (70 LIGHT-YEARS FROM SOL)
                              TALL, STEPHEN   NV   WOT 66 11
BEAR WITH THE KNOT ON HIS TAIL, THE
                              TALL, STEPHEN   NV   FSF 71 05
BIRDS FLY SOUTH IN WINTER   TALL, STEPHEN   NV   GAL 71 11
GODS ON OLYMPUS, THE   TALL, STEPHEN   NA   IFS 72 10
INVADERS, THE   TALL, STEPHEN   NV   IFS 73 08
MUSHROOM WORLD   TALL, STEPHEN   NA   FSF 74 11

STARLIGHT   BESTER, ALFRED   AC H NDB 76
LIGHT FANTASTIC, THE   BESTER, ALFRED   AC   BKP 76
STAR LIGHT, STAR BRIGHT   BESTER, ALFRED   AC   BKP 76

```
STARLIT CORRIDOR, THE          MANSFIELD, ROGER        AN H PGM 67
  INTRODUCTION                 MANSFIELD, ROGER        IN
  SPACE: THE THIRD MILLENNIUM  PETHEBRIDGE, DENIS      PM
  BEFORE EDEN                  CLARKE, ARTHUR C.       SS   AMZ 61 06
  RETURN OF THE MOON MAN (ALSO AS WHEN GRANDFATHER FLEW
    TO THE MOON)               MALPASS, E. L.          SS   LOB 55 01
  SPACE PILOT, THE             BLACKIE, J.             PM
  SPACE PROBE TO VENUS         FITZGIBBON, C.          PM
  DISAPPEARING ACT             BESTER, ALFRED          SS   STR 53 02
  TO SEE THE RABBIT            BROWNJOHN, ALAN         PM
  PAWLEY'S PEEPHOLES (OPERATION PEEP)
                               WYNDHAM, JOHN           SS   SCF 51 WI
  TEA IN A SPACE-SHIP          KIRKUP, JAMES           PM
  MONSTERS, THE                SHECKLEY, ROBERT        SS   FSF 53 03
  HARRISON BERGERON            VONNEGUT, KURT JR.      SS   FSF 61 10
  HAPPY MAN, THE               PAGE, GERALD W.         NV   ASF 63 03
  BEDTIME STORY                MACBETH, GEORGE         PM        63
  LIBERATION OF EARTH, THE     TENN, WILLIAM           SS   FUT 53 05
  SCIENCE FICTION              AMIS, KINGSLEY          PM   ENC 60 05

STARS AND UNDER, THE           CRISPIN, EDMUND         AN H FAB 68
  WHAT SCIENCE FICTION IS      CRISPIN, EDMUND         IN
  SOUND OF THUNDER, A          BRADBURY, RAY           SS   COL 52 06
  FOOD TO ALL FLESH            HENDERSON, ZENNA        SS   FSF 53 12
  RUUM, THE                    PORGES, ARTHUR          SS   FSF 53 10
  LITTLE LOST ROBOT            ASIMOV, ISAAC           SS   ASF 47 03
  ANSWER                       BROWN, FREDRIC          SS   NEW 54 AC
  STAR DUCKS, THE              BROWN, BILL             SS   FSF 50 FL
  NULL-P                       TENN, WILLIAM           SS   WBY 51 01
  BILLENIUM                    BALLARD, J. G.          SS   NWS 61 11
  FORGOTTEN ENEMY, THE         CLARKE, ARTHUR C.       SS   NWS 49 05

STARS AROUND US, THE           HOSKINS, ROBERT         AN   SIG 70 03
  INTRODUCTION                 HOSKINS, ROBERT         IN
  PEDDLER'S NOSE, THE          WILLIAMSON, JACK        SS   ASF 51 04
  LISTENERS, THE (ALSO AS ROBERT MACDONALD- 2025)
                               GUNN, JAMES E.          NV   GAL 68 09
  GHOST FLEET                  ANVIL, CHRISTOPHER      SS   ASF 61 02
  FONDLY FAHRENHEIT            BESTER, ALFRED          SS   FSF 54 08
  WITH REDFERN ON CAPELLA XII (AS CHAS. SATTERFIELD)
                               POHL, FREDERIK          NV   GAL 55 11
  UNDERFOLLOW                  JAKES, JOHN W.          SS   FSF 63 05
  FEELING OF POWER, THE        ASIMOV, ISAAC           SS   IFS 58 02
  HELPING HAND, THE            ANDERSON, POUL          NV   ASF 50 05
  WORK OF ART, A (ART-WORK)    BLISH, JAMES            SS   SFS 56 07
  GREAT SLOW KINGS, THE        ZELAZNY, ROGER          SS   WOT 63 12

STARSHADOWS                    SARGENT, PAMELA         AC   ACE 77 06
  INTRODUCTION                 CARR, TERRY             IN
  SHADOWS                      SARGENT, PAMELA         NV   POS 74
  GATHER BLUE ROSES            SARGENT, PAMELA         SS   FSF 72 02
  JULIO 204                    SARGENT, PAMELA         SS   NWQ 72 03
  IMT                          SARGENT, PAMELA         SS   TVW 73
  DESERT PLACES                SARGENT, PAMELA         SS   UNI 74 04
  OTHER PERCEIVER, THE         SARGENT, PAMELA         SS   UNI 72 02
  BOND AND FREE                SARGENT, PAMELA         NV   FSF 74 06
  IF EVER I SHOULD LEAVE YOU (REVISED)
                               SARGENT, PAMELA         SS   IFS 74 02
  CLONE SISTER                 SARGENT, PAMELA         NV   EIO 73

STARSHINE                      STURGEON, THEODORE      AC   PYR 66 12
  DERM FOOL                    STURGEON, THEODORE      SS   UNK 40 03
  HAUNT, THE                   STURGEON, THEODORE      SS   UNK 41 04
  ARTNAN PROCESS               STURGEON, THEODORE      NV   ASF 41 06
  WORLD WELL LOST, THE         STURGEON, THEODORE      SS   USF 53 06
  POD AND THE BARRIER, THE     STURGEON, THEODORE      NA   GAL 57 09
  HOW TO KILL AUNTY            STURGEON, THEODORE      NV   MSM 61 03

STARSWARM                      ALDISS, BRIAN W.        AC   SIG 64 01
  KIND OF ARTISTRY, A          ALDISS, BRIAN W.        SS   FSF 62 10
  HEARTS AND ENGINES (SOLDIERS RUNNING)
                               ALDISS, BRIAN W.        SS   NWS 60 06
  UNDERPRIVILEGED, THE         ALDISS, BRIAN W.        SS   NWS 63 05
  GAME OF GOD, THE (SEGREGATION)
                               ALDISS, BRIAN W.        NV   NWS 58 07
  SHARDS                       ALDISS, BRIAN W.        SS   FSF 62 04
  LEGENDS OF SMITH'S BURST     ALDISS, BRIAN W.        SS   NEB 59 06
  O MOON OF MY DELIGHT! (MOON OF DELIGHT)
                               ALDISS, BRIAN W.        NV   NWS 61 03
  OLD HUNDREDTH                ALDISS, BRIAN W.        SS   NWS 60 11

STARTLING STORIES              MINES, SAMUEL           AN H CAS 54
  SEE "THE BEST FROM STARTLING STORIES"

STATION IN SPACE               GUNN, JAMES E.          AC   BAN 58
  CAVE OF NIGHT, THE           GUNN, JAMES E.          SS   GAL 55 02
  HOAX                         GUNN, JAMES E.          NV   IFS 55 12
  BIG WHEEL, THE               GUNN, JAMES E.          SS   FUN 56 09
  POWDER KEG                   GUNN, JAMES E.          NV   IFS 58 04
  SPACE IS A LONELY PLACE      GUNN, JAMES E.          NV   VSF 57 05

STELLAR MISSILES, THE          REPP, ED EARL           AC H FPB 49
  STELLAR MISSILE, THE         REPP, ED EARL           SS   SWS 29 11
  SECOND MISSILE, THE          REPP, ED EARL           NV   AMZ 30 12
  QUEST OF THE IMMORTAL, THE (BUCCANEER OF THE STAR SEAS)
                               REPP, ED EARL           SS   PLS 40 FL

STELLAR SHORT NOVELS           DEL REY, JUDY-LYNN      OA   BAL 76 10
  INTRODUCTION: AN ENDANGERED SPECIES
                               DEL REY, JUDY-LYNN      IN
  MORTAL AND THE MONSTER, THE  DICKSON, GORDON R.      NA
  GREENHOUSE DEFECT, THE       OFFUTT, ANDREW J.       NA
  OCEANS AWAY                  WEINSTEIN, RICHARD S    NA

STELLAR 1                      DEL REY, JUDY-LYNN      OA   BAL 74 09
  WHY ANTHOLOGIZE?             DEL REY, JUDY-LYNN      IN

  BIRCH CLUMP CYLINDER, THE    SIMAK, CLIFFORD D.      NV   STL 74 01
  FUSION                       ROTHMAN, MILTON A.      NV   STL 74 01
  MIRACLE OF SMALL FISHES, A   FOSTER, ALAN DEAN       NV   STL 74 01
  WHIRLIGIG OF TIME, THE       VINGE, VERNOR           SS   STL 74 01
  SCHWARTZ BETWEEN THE GALAXIES
                               SILVERBERG, ROBERT      SS   STL 74 01
  MR. HAMADRYAD                LAFFERTY, R. A.         NV   STL 74 01
  SINGULARITIES MAKE ME NERVOUS
                               NIVEN, LARRY            SS   STL 74 01
  LOGICAL LIFE, THE            CLEMENT, HAL            SS   STL 74 01
  TWIG                         DICKSON, GORDON R.      NV   STL 74 01

STELLAR 2                      DEL REY, JUDY-LYNN      OA   BAL 76 02
  CUSTOM FITTING               WHITE, JAMES            NV   STL 76 02
  STUCK WITH IT                CLEMENT, HAL            NV   STL 76 02
  SONGS OF DYING SWANS         HALDEMAN, JACK C. II    SS   STL 76 02
  MISTAKE                      NIVEN, LARRY            SS   STL 76 02
  BICENTENNIAL MAN, THE        ASIMOV, ISAAC           NV   STL 76 02
  TINDAR-B                     CONNER, PATRICK G.      NV   STL 76 02
  SIC TRANSIT...?, A SHAGGY HAIRLESS-DOG STORY
                               UTLEY, STEVEN
                               AND WALDROP, HOWARD     SS C STL 76 02
  UNSILENT SPRING              SIMAK, RICHARD S.
                               AND SIMAK, CLIFFORD D.  NV C STL 76 02

STEP OUTSIDE YOUR MIND         CARR, TERRY             AC H DOB 69
  SEE "NEW WORLDS OF FANTASY"

STOLEN BACILLUS AND OTHER INCIDENTS, THE
                               WELLS, H. G.            AC H MTH 95
  STOLEN BACILLUS, THE         WELLS, H. G.            SS   PMB 94 06
  FLOWERING OF THE STRANGE ORCHID, THE (ALSO AS THE STRANGE
    ORCHID)                    WELLS, H. G.            SS   PMB 94 08
  IN THE AVU OBSERVATORY       WELLS, H. G.            SS   PMB 94 08
  TRIUMPHS OF A TAXIDERMIST, THE
                               WELLS, H. G.            SS   PGZ 94
  DEAL IN OSTRICHES, A         WELLS, H. G.            SS   PMB 94
  THROUGH A WINDOW (AT A WINDOW)
                               WELLS, H. G.            SS   BAW 94 08
  TEMPTATION OF HARRINGAY, THE WELLS, H. G.            SS   SJG 95 02
  FLYING MAN, THE (THE ADVENT OF THE FLYING MAN)
                               WELLS, H. G.            SS   PGZ 93 12
  DIAMOND MAKER, THE           WELLS, H. G.            SS   PMB 94
  AEPYORNIS ISLAND             WELLS, H. G.            SS   PMB 94 12
  REMARKABLE CASE OF DAVIDSON'S EYES, THE
                               WELLS, H. G.            SS   PMB 95 03
  LORD OF THE DYNAMOS, THE     WELLS, H. G.            SS   PMB 94 09
  HAMMERPOUND PARK BURGLARY, THE
                               WELLS, H. G.            SS   PMB 94
  MOTH, THE (A MOTH- GENUS NOVO)
                               WELLS, H. G.            SS   PGZ 95 03
  TREASURE IN THE FOREST, THE  WELLS, H. G.            SS   PMB 94

STOPWATCH                      HAY, GEORGE             OA H NEL 74 10
  INTRODUCTION                 HAY, GEORGE             IN
  PROTOCOLS OF THE ELDERS OF BRITAIN, THE
                               BRUNNER, JOHN           SS
  ARE YOUR HOME GROWN VEGETABLES RADIOACTIVE?
                               BRENNAN, KATHLEEN       SS
  ASH, ASH                     HOLDSTOCK, ROBERT P.    SS
  ALL WE HAVE ON THIS PLANET   VAN VOGT, A. E.         SS
  EA 5000: REPORT ON THE EFFECTS OF RIOT GAS
                               WATSON, IAN             SS
  INTRACOM                     LE GUIN, URSULA K.      PL
  BEDTIME STORY, A             LETTS, D.               SS
  INVISIBLE MEN, THE           PRIEST, CHRISTOPHER     SS
  NOW IS FOREVER               ALLEN, EDWARD           SS
  CHARLEY                      CHAPDELAINE, PERRY A    SS
  WHEN THE MUSIC'S OVER        DARLINGTON, ANDREW      SS
  IN MEMORIAM, JEANNIE         SAXTON, JOSEPHINE       SS
  DOCTOR FAUSTA                MASSON, DAVID I.        NV

STORE OF INFINITY              SHECKLEY, ROBERT        AC   BAN 60 11
  PRIZE OF PERIL, THE          SHECKLEY, ROBERT        SS   FSF 58 05
  HUMORS, THE (JOIN NOW)       SHECKLEY, ROBERT        NA   GAL 58 12
  TRIPLICATION                 SHECKLEY, ROBERT        SS   PBY 59 05
  MINIMUM MAN, THE             SHECKLEY, ROBERT        NV   GAL 58 06
  IF THE RED SLAYER            SHECKLEY, ROBERT        SS   AMZ 59 07
  STORE OF THE WORLDS, THE (THE WORLD OF HEART'S DESIRE)
                               SHECKLEY, ROBERT        SS   PBY 59 09
  GUN WITHOUT A BANG, THE      SHECKLEY, ROBERT        NV   GAL 58 06
  DEATHS OF BEN BAXTER, THE    SHECKLEY, ROBERT        NV   GAL 57 07

STORIES                        YEFREMOV, IVAN          AC H FLP 54
  FOREWORD                     YEFREMOV, IVAN          IN
  SHADOWS OF THE PAST          YEFREMOV, IVAN          SS
  NUR-I-DESHT OBSERVATORY, THE YEFREMOV, IVAN          SS
  MEETING OVER THE TUSCARORA   YEFREMOV, IVAN          SS
  MOON MOUNTAIN                YEFREMOV, IVAN          SS
  LAKE OF THE MOUNTAIN SPIRITS, THE
                               YEFREMOV, IVAN          SS
  OLGOI-KHORKHOI               YEFREMOV, IVAN          SS
  WHITE HORN                   YEFREMOV, IVAN          SS
  STELLAR SHIPS                YEFREMOV, IVAN          SS

STORIES FOR TOMORROW           SLOANE, WILLIAM         AN H FKW 54 06
  ABOUT THIS BOOK              SLOANE, WILLIAM         IN
  WILDERNESS, THE              BRADBURY, RAY           SS   FSF 52 11
  STAR BRIDE                   BOUCHER, ANTHONY        SS   TWS 51 12
  SECOND CHILDHOOD             SIMAK, CLIFFORD D.      SS   GAL 51 02
  HOMELAND (THE STATUE)        WOLFE, MARI             NV   IFS 53 03
  LET NOTHING YOU DISMAY       SLOANE, WILLIAM         SS   NEW 55 AN
  SCENT OF SARSAPARILLA, A     BRADBURY, RAY           SS   STR 53 01
  EXILE, THE                   COPPEL, ALFRED          SS   ASF 52 10
  FARTHEST HORIZON, THE        JONES, RAYMOND F.       SS   ASF 52 04
  NOISE LEVEL                  JONES, RAYMOND F.       NV   ASF 52 12
```

STORIES FOR TOMORROW

FIRST CONTACT	LEINSTER, MURRAY	NV	ASF 45 05
FRANCHISE	NEVILLE, KRIS	SS	ASF 51 02
IN VALUE DECEIVED	FYFE, H. B.	SS	ASF 50 11
OKIE	BLISH, JAMES	NV	ASF 50 04
BLACK EYES AND THE DAILY GRIND			
	LESSER, MILTON	SS	IFS 52 03
SOCRATES	CHRISTOPHER, JOHN	SS	GAL 51 03
IN HIDING	SHIRAS, WILMAR H.	NV	ASF 48 11
BETTYANN	NEVILLE, KRIS	NV	NTS 51
ANT AND THE EYE, THE	OLIVER, CHAD	NV	ASF 53 04
BEEP	BLISH, JAMES	NV	GAL 54 02
AND THEN THERE WERE NONE	RUSSELL, ERIC FRANK	NV	ASF 51 06
GIRLS FROM EARTH, THE	ROBINSON, FRANK M.	NV	GAL 52 01
MINISTER WITHOUT PORTFOLIO	CLINGERMAN, MILDRED	SS	FSF 52 02
HEAD HUNTERS, THE	WILLIAMS, RALPH	SS	ASF 51 10
DUNE ROLLER	MAY, JULIAN C.	NV	ASF 51 12
DISGUISE	WOLLHEIM, DONALD A.	SS	OWS 53 02
SHED, THE	EVANS, E. EVERETT	SS	ASR 53 01
NINE BILLION NAMES OF GOD, THE			
	CLARKE, ARTHUR C.	SS	STR 53 01
FORGOTTEN ENEMY, THE	CLARKE, ARTHUR C.	SS	NWS 49 05
ANSWERS, THE (AND THE TRUTH SHALL MAKE YOU FREE)			
	SIMAK, CLIFFORD D.	SS	FUT 53 03

STORIES FOR TOMORROW (BRITISH)

	SLOANE, WILLIAM	AN H	EYR 55
ABOUT THIS BOOK	SLOANE, WILLIAM	IN	
WILDERNESS, THE	BRADBURY, RAY	SS	FSF 52 11
STAR BRIDE	BOUCHER, ANTHONY	SS	TWS 51 12
HOMELAND (THE STATUE)	WOLFE, MARI	NV	IFS 53 01
LET NOTHING YOU DISMAY	SLOANE, WILLIAM	SS	NEW 55 AN
SCENT OF SARSAPARILLA, A	BRADBURY, RAY	SS	STR 53 01
NOISE LEVEL	JONES, RAYMOND F.	NV	ASF 52 12
FIRST CONTACT	LEINSTER, MURRAY	NV	ASF 45 05
FRANCHISE	NEVILLE, KRIS	SS	ASF 51 02
IN VALUE DECEIVED	FYFE, H. B.	SS	ASF 50 11
BLACK EYES AND THE DAILY GRIND			
	LESSER, MILTON	SS	IFS 52 03
SOCRATES	CHRISTOPHER, JOHN	SS	GAL 51 03
IN HIDING	SHIRAS, WILMAR H.	NV	ASF 48 11
BETTYANN	NEVILLE, KRIS	NV	NTS 51
ANT AND THE EYE, THE	OLIVER, CHAD	NV	ASF 53 04
BEEP	BLISH, JAMES	NV	GAL 54 02
AND THEN THERE WERE NONE	RUSSELL, ERIC FRANK	NV	ASF 51 06
GIRLS FROM EARTH, THE	ROBINSON, FRANK M.	NV	GAL 52 01
MINISTER WITHOUT PORTFOLIO	CLINGERMAN, MILDRED	SS	FSF 52 02
HEAD HUNTERS, THE	WILLIAMS, RALPH	SS	ASF 51 10
NINE BILLION NAMES OF GOD, THE			
	CLARKE, ARTHUR C.	SS	STR 53 01
FORGOTTEN ENEMY, THE	CLARKE, ARTHUR C.	SS	NWS 49 05
ANSWERS, THE (AND THE TRUTH SHALL MAKE YOU FREE)			
	SIMAK, CLIFFORD D.	SS	FUT 53 03

STORIES FROM SCIENCE FICTION DOHERTY, G. D.   AN H NLS 66

INTRODUCTION	DOHERTY, G. D.	IN	
WHO CAN REPLACE A MAN? (BUT WHO CAN REPLACE A MAN)			
	ALDISS, BRIAN W.	SS	INF 58 06
GOLDEN APPLES OF THE SUN, THE			
	BRADBURY, RAY	SS	PLS 53 11
ETAOIN SHRDLU	BROWN, FREDRIC	SS	UNK 42 02
HUNTING PROBLEM	SHECKLEY, ROBERT	SS	GAL 55 09
SUNJAMMER (ALSO AS THE WIND FROM THE SUN)			
	CLARKE, ARTHUR C.	SS	BLF 64
RESCUE OPERATION	HARRISON, HARRY	SS	ASF 64 12
LORD OF THE DYNAMOS, THE	WELLS, H. G.	SS	PMB 94 09
ASTEROIDS, 2194, THE (THE EMPTYNESS OF SPACE, NWS 60 11)			
	WYNDHAM, JOHN	SS	AMZ 61 01
FLOWERS FOR ALGERNON	KEYES, DANIEL	SS	FSF 59 04
MAN WHO TASTED ASHES, THE	BUDRYS, ALGIS	SS	IFS 59 02
SUBLIMINAL MAN, THE	BALLARD, J. G.	SS	NWS 63 01

STORIES FROM THE HUGO WINNERS VOLUME 2
ASIMOV, ISAAC   AN FCR 73 08

FIRST 6 STORIES

STORIES FROM THE TWILIGHT ZONE

	SERLING, ROD	OC	BAN 60 04
MIGHTY CASEY, THE	SERLING, ROD	SA	
ESCAPE CLAUSE	SERLING, ROD	SA	
WALKING DISTANCE	SERLING, ROD	SA	
FEVER, THE	SERLING, ROD	SA	
WHERE IS EVERYBODY?	SERLING, ROD	SA	
MONSTERS ARE DUE ON MAPLE STREET, THE			
	SERLING, ROD	SA	

STORIES OF SCIENTIFIC IMAGINATION

	GALLANT, JOSEPH	AN	OXF 54
PREFACE	GALLANT, JOSEPH	IN	
BLACK PITS OF LUNA, THE	HEINLEIN, ROBERT A.	SS	SEP 48 01
PLANET PASSAGE	WOLLHEIM, DONALD A.	SS	FUT 42 10
IN VALUE DECEIVED	FYFE, H. B.	SS	ASF 50 11
PERIL OF THE BLUE WORLD	ABERNATHY, ROBERT	SS	PLS 42 WI
PROPAGANDIST	LEINSTER, MURRAY	SS	ASF 47 08
SYMBIOSIS	JENKINS, WILL F.	SS	COL 47 06
CONQUEROR'S ISLE	BOND, NELSON S.	SS	BBM 46 06
WHITE ARMY, THE	DRESSLER, DR. DANIEL	SS	AMZ 29 09
CONNECTICUT YANKEE IN KING ARTHUR'S COURT, A			
	TWAIN, MARK	EX	HRP 89

STRANGE ADVENTURES IN SCIENCE FICTION
CONKLIN, GROFF   AN H GRY 54

STORIES FROM "OMNIBUS OF SCIENCE FICTION"

INTRODUCTION	CONKLIN, GROFF	IN	
NEVER UNDERESTIMATE...	STURGEON, THEODORE	SS	IFS 52 03
DOORBELL, THE	KELLER, DAVID H. MD.	SS	WOS 34 06
BOX, THE	BLISH, JAMES	SS	TWS 49 04

CATCH THAT MARTIAN	KNIGHT, DAMON	SS	GAL 52 03
PLAGUE	LEINSTER, MURRAY	NV	ASF 44 02
ENVIRONMENT	GEIER, CHESTER S.	SS	ASF 44 05
SPECTATOR SPORT	MACDONALD, JOHN D.	SS	TWS 50 02
RECRUITING STATION (ALSO AS MASTERS OF TIME)			
	VAN VOGT, A. E.	NV	ASF 42 03
CHOICE, THE	HILTON-YOUNG, WAYLAND	SS	PUN 52 03

STRANGE BEASTS AND UNNATURAL MONSTERS
STERN, PHILIP VAN D. AN   FCR 68 08

INTRODUCTION	STERN, PHILIP VAN D.	IN	
NATURE OF THE EVIDENCE, THE	SINCLAIR, MAY	SS	FOR 23 08
SLIME	BRENNAN, JOSEPH P.	NV	WRT 53 03
GARDEN OF PARIS, THE	WILLIAMS, ERIC C.	SS	NEW 65 AN
DOOMSDAY DEFERRED	JENKINS, WILL F.	SS	SEP 49 09
COCOON, THE	GOODWIN, JOHN B. L.	SS	STO 46 10
AEPYORNIS ISLAND	WELLS, H. G.	SS	PMB 94 12
TERROR OF BLUE JOHN GAP, THE	DOYLE, ARTHUR CONAN	SS	10
BIRDS, THE	DU MAURIER, DAPHNE	NV	GHK 52 10
JUDGE'S HOUSE, THE	STOKER, BRAM	SS	
KILL, THE	FLEMING, PETER	SS	42
MRS. AMWORTH (1922)	BENSON, E. F.	SS	FFM 50 06
SKELETON	BRADBURY, RAY	SS	WRT 45 09
ELEPHANT MAN, THE	TREVES, FREDERICK	SS	23

STRANGE BED FELLOWS   SCORTIA, THOMAS N.   AN H RDM 72
"WHERE HAVE ALL THE DEFLOWERERS GONE?"

	SCORTIA, THOMAS N.	IN	
PUSH NO MORE	SILVERBERG, ROBERT	NV	NEW 72 AN
GENETIC FAUX PAS	BILKER, HARVEY L.	SS	RLS 65 03
FIRST LOVE, FIRST FEAR	ZEBROWSKI, GEORGE	SS	NEW 72 AN
WORLD WELL LOST, THE	STURGEON, THEODORE	SS	USF 53 06
DO ANDROIDS DREAM OF ELECTRIC LOVE?			
	LEIBSCHER, WALT	SS	NEW 72 AN
DINNER AT HELEN'S	CARLSON, WILLIAM	SS	NEW 72 AN
CRIMINAL, THE	GORES, JOE	SS	ADM 70 12
MECHANICAL SWEETHEART, THE	ALPER, GERALD ARTHUR	SS	NEW 72 AN
FALSE DAWN	YARBRO, CHELSEA Q.	SS	NEW 72 AN
I'M WITH YOU IN ROCKLAND	DANN, JACK M.	SS	NEW 72 AN
DR. BIRDMOUSE	BRETNOR, REGINALD	SS	FAN 62 04
LOOKING-GLASS SEA	YEP, LAURENCE	SS	NEW 72 AN
WHAT ABOUT US GRILS?	GILDEN, MEL	SS	CLR 71 01
LAMBETH BLOSSOM	ALDISS, BRIAN W.	SS	KNT 66 09
WIDENING CIRCLE, THE	MCCLOUD, RICHARD	SS	NEW 72 AN
ICEBOX BLONDE, THE	SCORTIA, THOMAS N.	SS	ROG 59 06
KHARTOUM: A PROSE LIMERICK	BOUCHER, ANTHONY	SS	STF 55 08
MOTHER	FARMER, PHILIP JOSE	NV	TWS 53 04
DAUGHTER OF THE TREE, THE	DEFORD, MIRIAM ALLEN	SS	FSF 51 08

STRANGE DOINGS   LAFFERTY, R. A.   AC H SCB 72

RAINBIRD	LAFFERTY, R. A.	SS	GAL 61 12
CAMELS AND DROMEDARIES, CLEM	LAFFERTY, R. A.	SS	FSF 67 10
CONTINUED ON NEXT ROCK	LAFFERTY, R. A.	NV	ORB 70 07
ONCE ON ARANEA	LAFFERTY, R. A.	SS	NEW 72 AC
SODOM AND GOMORRAH, TEXAS	LAFFERTY, R. A.	SS	GAL 62 12
MAN WITH THE SPECKLED EYES, THE			
	LAFFERTY, R. A.	SS	FSF 64 12
ALL BUT THE WORDS	LAFFERTY, R. A.	SS	GAL 71 07
TRANSCENDENT TIGERS, THE	LAFFERTY, R. A.	SS	WOT 64 02
WORLD ABOUNDING	LAFFERTY, R. A.	NV	FSF 71 12
DREAM (DREAMWORLD)	LAFFERTY, R. A.	SS	GAL 62 06
RIDE A TIN CAN	LAFFERTY, R. A.	SS	IFS 70 04
ALOYS	LAFFERTY, R. A.	SS	GAL 61 08
ENTIRE AND PERFECT CHRYSOLITE			
	LAFFERTY, R. A.	SS	ORB 70 06
INCASED IN ANCIENT RIND	LAFFERTY, R. A.	NV	QRK 71 03
UGLY SEA, THE	LAFFERTY, R. A.	SS	LRV 60 FL
CLIFFS THAT LAUGHED	LAFFERTY, R. A.	SS	MOH 69 03

STRANGE ECSTASIES   PARRY, MICHEL   AN   PIN 74 10

INTRODUCTION	PARRY, MICHEL	IN	
PLUTONIAN DRUG, THE	SMITH, CLARK ASHTON	SS	AMZ 34 09
DREAM PILLS, THE	DAVIS, F. H.	SS	20
WHITE POWDER, THE	MACHEN, ARTHUR	NV	FFM 44 09
NEW ACCELERATOR, THE	WELLS, H. G.	SS	SND 01 12
BIG PIX, THE	WILSON, RICHARD	NV	INF 56 08
SECRET SONGS, THE	LEIBER, FRITZ	SS	FSF 62 08
HOUNDS OF TINDALOS, THE	LONG, FRANK BELKNAP	SS	WRT 29 03
SUBJECTIVITY	SPINRAD, NORMAN	SS	ASF 64 01
WHAT TO DO TILL THE ANALYST COMES (EVERYBODY'S HAPPY BUT ME!)			
	POHL, FREDERIK	SS	IMG 56 02
PIPE DREAM	MILLER, CHRIS	SS	NLP 72 06

STRANGE ENCOUNTERS   BISCHOFF, DAVID   OA H RTR 77

DEMON MACHINE, THE	LITTKE, LAEL J.	SS	
SPACESHIP, THE	DE WEESE, GENE	SS	
NIGHT SEARCH	FRANKLIN, DONALD	SS	
CAPTURED!	TOFTE, ARTHUR	SS	
WEALTH OF THE SUN, THE	LAMPTON, CHRIS	SS	

STRANGE GIFTS   SILVERBERG, ROBERT   AN H NEL 75

INTRODUCTION	SILVERBERG, ROBERT	IN	
GOLDEN MAN, THE	DICK, PHILIP K.	NV	IFS 54 04
DANGER- HUMAN!	DICKSON, GORDON R.	SS	ASF 57 12
ALL THE PEOPLE	LAFFERTY, R. A.	SS	GAL 61 04
ODDY AND ID (THE DEVIL'S INVENTION)			
	BESTER, ALFRED	SS	ASF 50 08
MAN WITH ENGLISH, THE	GOLD, H. L.	SS	STR 53 01
TO BE CONTINUED	SILVERBERG, ROBERT	SS	ASF 56 05
HUMPTY DUMPTY HAD A GREAT FALL			
	LONG, FRANK BELKNAP	SS	STS 48 11
BETTYANN	NEVILLE, KRIS	NV	NTS 51

STRANGE GODS   ELWOOD, ROGER   OA   PKT 74 09
WHATEVER GODS THERE BE: SPACE-TIME AND DEITY IN SF
ZEBROWSKI, GEORGE   IN   STG 74

STRANGE GODS

HIGH PRIEST	BONE, J. F.	SS	STG 74
OVERSIGHT	O'DONNELL, K. M.	SS	STG 74
ONE AFTERNOON IN BUSTERVILLE	GRASTY, WILLIAM K.	SS	STG 74
PROPHET OF ZORAYNE, THE	DIXON, TERRY	SS	STG 74
IN HIS OWN IMAGE	PAYES, RACHEL C.	SS	STG 74
TRY AGAIN	MALZBERG, BARRY N.	SS	STG 74
CHOLOM	KIDD, VIRGINIA	PM	STG 74
WHAT HATH GOD WROUGHT!	BIGGLE, LLOYD JR.	NV	STG 74
THROWBACK	ELWOOD, ROGER	SS	STG 74
DIRECTOR, THE	HOWARD, JAMES	NV	STG 74
RETURN TO A HOSTILE PLANET	THOMAS, JOHN B.	SS	STG 74
MUSSPELSHEIM	LUPOFF, RICHARD A.	NV	STG 74

STRANGE HARVEST WANDREI, DONALD AC H ARK 65

ATOM SMASHER, THE	WANDREI, DONALD	SS	ASF 34 04
CHUCKLER, THE	WANDREI, DONALD	SS	
DESTROYING HORDE, THE	WANDREI, DONALD	SS	WRT 33 02
FIRE VAMPIRES, THE	WANDREI, DONALD	SS	WRT 39 02
GIANT-PLASM	WANDREI, DONALD	SS	WRT 30 07
GREEN FLAME, THE	WANDREI, DONALD	SS	ASF 36 10
INFINITY ZERO	WANDREI, DONALD	SS	ASF 35 04
LIFE CURRENT	WANDREI, DONALD	SS	ASF 34 03
MAN WHO NEVER LIVED, THE	WANDREI, DONALD	SS	ASF 35 06
MURRAY'S LIGHT	WANDREI, DONALD	SS	
NIGHTMARE	WANDREI, DONALD	NV	WRT 30 12
SOMETHING FROM ABOVE	WANDREI, DONALD	NV	WRT 33 05
SPAWN OF THE SEA	WANDREI, DONALD	NV	WRT 53 05
STRANGE HARVEST	WANDREI, DONALD	NV	
TRIP TO INFINITY, A	WANDREI, DONALD	NV	
UNEASY LIE THE DROWNED	WANDREI, DONALD	NV	WRT 37 12

STRANGE LOVE STORIES ANONYMOUS AN UTP 46

DESERT ROMANCE (SHADOW GUIDE)			
	PRICE, E. HOFFMANN	SS	
REIGN OF THE ROBOTS, THE	HAMILTON, EDMOND	SS	WOS 31 12
EVE WAS A SNAKE (SNAKE GODDESS)			
	PRICE, E. HOFFMANN	SS	STE 39 08
STAR BRIGHT	WILLIAMSON, JACK	NV	ARG 39 11

STRANGE PORTS OF CALL DERLETH, AUGUST AN H PEL 48

INTRODUCTION	DERLETH, AUGUST	IN	
CUNNING OF THE BEAST, THE (ANOTHER WORLD BEGINS)			
	BOND, NELSON S.	SS	BBM 42 11
WORM, THE	KELLER, DAVID H. MD.	SS	AMZ 29 03
CRYSTAL BULLET, THE	WANDREI, DONALD	SS	WRT 41 03
THING FROM OUTSIDE, THE (AMZ 26 04)			
	ENGLAND, GEORGE A.	SS	SAI 23 04
AT THE MOUNTAINS OF MADNESS	LOVECRAFT, H. P.	NO	ASF 36 02
MARS ON THE ETHER	DUNSANY, LORD	SS	CRT 37 09
GOD-BOX, THE	WANDREI, HOWARD E.	SS	ASF 34 04
MR. BAUER AND THE ATOMS	LEIBER, FRITZ	SS	WRT 46 01
CRYSTAL EGG, THE	WELLS, H. G.	SS	NRV 97 05
JOHN JONES' DOLLAR	KELLER, HARRY S.	SS	BLC 15 08
CALL HIM DEMON	KUTTNER, HENRY	SS	TWS 46 FL
MASTER OF THE ASTEROID	SMITH, CLARK ASHTON	SS	WOS 32 10
GUEST IN THE HOUSE	LONG, FRANK BELKNAP	SS	ASF 46 03
LOST STREET, THE (THE STREET THAT WASN'T THERE)			
	JACOBI, CARL		
AND	SIMAK, CLIFFORD D.	SS C	CMT 41 07
FORGOTTEN (THE FORGOTTEN MAN OF SPACE)			
	MILLER, P. SCHUYLER	SS	WOS 33 04
FAR CENTAURUS	VAN VOGT, A. E.	SS	ASF 44 01
GREEN HILLS OF EARTH, THE	HEINLEIN, ROBERT A.	SS	SEP 47 02
THUNDER AND ROSES	STURGEON, THEODORE	SS	ASF 47 11
BLUNDER	WYLIE, PHILIP	SS	COL 46 01
MILLION-YEAR PICNIC, THE	BRADBURY, RAY	SS	PLS 46 SU

STRANGE PORTS OF CALL (10 OF 20)
DERLETH, AUGUST AN BRK 58

CUNNING OF THE BEAST, THE (ANOTHER WORLD BEGINS)			
	BOND, NELSON S.	SS	BBM 42 11
CRYSTAL BULLET, THE	WANDREI, DONALD	SS	WRT 41 03
MR. BAUER AND THE ATOMS	LEIBER, FRITZ	SS	WRT 46 01
CALL HIM DEMON	KUTTNER, HENRY	SS	TWS 46 FL
MASTER OF THE ASTEROID	SMITH, CLARK ASHTON	SS	WOS 32 10
GUEST IN THE HOUSE	LONG, FRANK BELKNAP	SS	ASF 46 03
FORGOTTEN (THE FORGOTTEN MAN OF SPACE)			
	MILLER, P. SCHUYLER	SS	WOS 33 04
FAR CENTAURUS	VAN VOGT, A. E.	SS	ASF 44 01
BLUNDER	WYLIE, PHILIP	SS	COL 46 01
MILLION-YEAR PICNIC, THE	BRADBURY, RAY	SS	PLS 46 SU

STRANGE RELATIONS FARMER, PHILIP JOSE AC BAL 60

MOTHER	FARMER, PHILIP JOSE	NV	TWS 53 04
DAUGHTER	FARMER, PHILIP JOSE	SS	TWS 54 WI
FATHER	FARMER, PHILIP JOSE	NV	FSF 55 07
SON (QUEEN OF THE DEEP)	FARMER, PHILIP JOSE	SS	ARG 54 03
MY SISTER'S BROTHER (OPEN TO ME, MY SISTER)			
	FARMER, PHILIP JOSE	NV	FSF 60 05

STRANGE SEAS AND SHORES DAVIDSON, AVRAM AC H DBL 71

PREFACE	DAVIDSON, AVRAM	IN	
INTRODUCTION	DAVIDSON, AVRAM	IN	
SACHEVERELL	DAVIDSON, AVRAM	SS	FSF 64 03
TAKE WOODEN INDIANS	DAVIDSON, AVRAM	NV	GAL 59 06
VAT, THE	DAVIDSON, AVRAM	SS	FSF 61 10
TAIL-TIED KINGS, THE	DAVIDSON, AVRAM	SS	GAL 62 04
PARAMOUNT ULJ	DAVIDSON, AVRAM	SS	GAL 58 10
BOTTLE FULL OF KISMET, A	DAVIDSON, AVRAM	SS	
GOOBERS, THE	DAVIDSON, AVRAM	SS	SWK 65 11
DR. MORRIS GOLDPEPPER RETURNS			
	DAVIDSON, AVRAM	SS	GAL 62 12
CERTIFICATE, THE	DAVIDSON, AVRAM	SS	FSF 59 03
OGRE IN THE VLY	DAVIDSON, AVRAM	SS	IFS 59 07
APRES NOUS	DAVIDSON, AVRAM	SS	FSF 60 03
CLIMACTERIC	DAVIDSON, AVRAM	SS	FSF 60 08

YO-HO, AND UP	DAVIDSON, AVRAM	SS	FSF 60 12
SIXTY-THIRD STREET STATION, THE			
	DAVIDSON, AVRAM	SS	FSF 62 03
HOUSE THE BLAKENEYS BUILT, THE			
	DAVIDSON, AVRAM	SS	FSF 65 01
POWER OF EVERY ROOT, THE	DAVIDSON, AVRAM	NV	FSF 67 10
SOURCES OF THE NILE, THE	DAVIDSON, AVRAM	NV	FSF 61 01

STRANGE SIGNPOSTS ELWOOD & MOSKOWITZ AN H HRW 66

OTHER SIDE OF THE CURTAIN- A REFLECTION OF THE FUTURE, THE			
	ELWOOD, ROGER		
AND	MOSKOWITZ, SAM	IN C	
LAST MAN, THE (1826)	SHELLEY, MARY W.	EX	
MELLONTA TAUTA	POE, EDGAR ALLEN	SS	GDY 49 02
RAPPACCINI'S DAUGHTER (1844)	HAWTHORNE, NATHANIEL	NV	DMR 44 12
HANS SCHNAP'S SPY-GLASS	ERCKMANN-CHATRIAN	SS	
CHRONIC ARGONAUTS, THE	WELLS, H. G.	NV	SSJ 88 04
BEGUM'S FORTUNE, THE (1879)	VERNE, JULES	EX	
FRANK READE JUNIOR'S AIR WONDER (1876)			
	SENARENS, LOUIS P.	SS	BNY 76
WHISPERER IN DARKNESS, THE	LOVECRAFT, H. P.	NV	WRT 31 08
MAN WHO SAW THE FUTURE, THE	HAMILTON, EDMOND	SS	AMZ 30 10
PROWLER OF THE WASTELANDS	VINCENT, HARL	SS	ASF 35 04
SKELETON MEN OF JUPITER	BURROUGHS, EDGAR R.	NV	AMZ 43 02
DOODAD	BRADBURY, RAY	SS	ASF 43 09
COSMIC EXPRESS, THE	WILLIAMSON, JACK	SS	AMZ 30 11
CASTAWAY	CLARKE, ARTHUR C.	SS	FSB 47 04
ONE WAY TO MARS	BLOCH, ROBERT	SS	WRT 45 07

STRANGE TOMORROWS HOSKINS, ROBERT AN LAN 72

INTRODUCTION	HOSKINS, ROBERT	IN	
SHADOW ON THE SAND	MACDONALD, JOHN D.	SN	TWS 50 10
COMEDIAN'S CHILDREN, THE	STURGEON, THEODORE	NV	VSF 58 05
FIREWATER	TENN, WILLIAM	SN	ASF 52 02
GREATEST INVENTION, THE	WILLIAMSON, JACK	NV	ASF 51 07
PLANETFALL (PLANET FOR PLUNDER)			
	CLEMENT, HAL	SN	SAT 57 02

STRANGE TRAVELS IN SCIENCE FICTION
CONKLIN, GROFF AN H GRY 53

STORIES FROM "OMNIBUS OF SCIENCE FICTION"			
INTRODUCTION	CONKLIN, GROFF	IN	
JOHN THOMAS'S CUBE	LEIMERT, JOHN	SS	ATL 45 08
SUBWAY NAMED MOBIUS, A	DEUTSCH, A. J.	SS	ASF 50 12
COLOUR OUT OF SPACE, THE (ALSO AS MONSTER OF TERROR)			
	LOVECRAFT, H. P.	SS	AMZ 27 09
STAR DUMMY, THE	BOUCHER, ANTHONY	SS	FAN 52 FL
SHIPSHAPE HOME	MATHESON, RICHARD	SS	GAL 52 07
KALEIDOSCOPE	BRADBURY, RAY	SS	TWS 49 10
NOTHING HAPPENS ON THE MOON	ERNST, PAUL	SS	ASF 39 02
HIGH THRESHOLD	NOURSE, ALAN E.	SS	ASF 51 03
STONE AND A SPEAR, A	JONES, RAYMOND F.	NV	GAL 50 12
PLEASANT DREAMS	ROBIN, RALPH	SS	GAL 51 10
MANNERS OF THE AGE	FYFE, H. B.	SS	GAL 52 03
WEAPON, THE	BROWN, FREDRIC	SS	ASF 51 04
SCARLET PLAGUE, THE	LONDON, JACK	NA	LOM 12 06

STRANGE WORLD OF SCIENCE FICTION
ANONYMOUS OA NLB 75 10

SPECIMEN, THE	ANONYMOUS	SS	
HARRY AMONG THE ALIENS	ANONYMOUS	SS	
MAN FROM OCCAM, THE	ANONYMOUS	SS	
SPACE PEDLAR, THE	MARSH, JOYCE	SS	
VOYAGE OF THE MORNING STAR, THE			
	SMYTH, ROBIN	SS	
PARALLEL DEVELOPMENT, THE	WEINER, GUY	SS	
MYSTERIOUS FOOTPRINTS, THE	ANONYMOUS	SS	
ZARGON MENACE, THE	ANONYMOUS	SS	

STRANGE WORLDS FARLEY, RALPH MILNE AC H FPB 52

RADIO MAN, THE	FARLEY, RALPH MILNE	NO	AAS 24 06
HIDDEN UNIVERSE, THE	FARLEY, RALPH MILNE	NO	AMZ 39 11
WE, THE MIST (THE LIVING MIST)			
	FARLEY, RALPH MILNE	NV	AMZ 40 08

STRANGER THAN YOU THINK EDMONDSON, G. C. DC ACE 65

MISFIT, THE	EDMONDSON, G. C.	SS	FSF 59 02
"FROM CARIBOU TO CARRY NATION"			
	EDMONDSON, G. C.	SS	FSF 59 11
GALACTIC CALABASH, THE	EDMONDSON, G. C.	SS	FSF 60 01
SIGN OF THE GOOSE, THE	EDMONDSON, G. C.	SS	FSF 60 08
COUNTRY BOY, THE	EDMONDSON, G. C.	SS	FSF 61 05
WORLD MUST NEVER KNOW, THE	EDMONDSON, G. C.	SS	FSF 63 04
THIRD BUBBLE, THE	EDMONDSON, G. C.	SS	FSF 64 06

STRANGERS FROM EARTH ANDERSON, POUL AC BAL 61 05

EARTHMAN, BEWARE!	ANDERSON, POUL	NV	SSS 51 06
QUIXOTE AND THE WINDMILL	ANDERSON, POUL	SS	ASF 50 11
GYPSY	ANDERSON, POUL	SS	ASF 50 01
FOR THE DURATION	ANDERSON, POUL	SS	VSF 57 09
DUEL ON SYRTIS	ANDERSON, POUL	SS	PLS 51 03
STAR BEAST, THE	ANDERSON, POUL	NV	SSS 50 09
DISINTEGRATING SKY, THE	ANDERSON, POUL	NV	FUN 53 08
AMONG THIEVES	ANDERSON, POUL	NV	ASF 57 06

STRANGERS IN THE UNIVERSE SIMAK, CLIFFORD D. AC H SAS 56

SHADOW SHOW	SIMAK, CLIFFORD D.	NV	FSF 53 11
CONTRAPTION	SIMAK, CLIFFORD D.	SS	STR 53 01
ANSWERS, THE (AND THE TRUTH SHALL MAKE YOU FREE)			
	SIMAK, CLIFFORD D.	SS	FUT 53 03
FENCE, THE	SIMAK, CLIFFORD D.	SS	SSF 52 09
TARGET GENERATION	SIMAK, CLIFFORD D.	NV	
BEACHHEAD (YOU'LL NEVER GO HOME AGAIN)			
	SIMAK, CLIFFORD D.	SS	FAD 51 07
KINDERGARTEN	SIMAK, CLIFFORD D.	NV	GAL 53 07
MIRAGE	SIMAK, CLIFFORD D.	NV	

```
STRANGERS IN THE UNIVERSE

  SKIRMISH (BATHE YOUR BEARINGS IN BLOOD)
                        SIMAK, CLIFFORD D.    SS    AMZ 50 12
  RETROGRADE EVOLUTION  SIMAK, CLIFFORD D.    NV    SFP 53 04
  IMMIGRANT             SIMAK, CLIFFORD D.    SN    ASP 54 03

STRANGERS IN THE UNIVERSE (BRITISH)
                        SIMAK, CLIFFORD D.    AC H FAB 58
  FENCE, THE            SIMAK, CLIFFORD D.    SS    SSP 52 09
  TARGET GENERATION     SIMAK, CLIFFORD D.    NV
  BEACHHEAD (YOU'LL NEVER GO HOME AGAIN)
                        SIMAK, CLIFFORD D.    SS    FAD 51 07
  KINDERGARTEN          SIMAK, CLIFFORD D.    NV    GAL 53 07
  MIRAGE                SIMAK, CLIFFORD D.    NV
  SKIRMISH (BATHE YOUR BEARINGS IN BLOOD)
                        SIMAK, CLIFFORD D.    SS    AMZ 50 12
  IMMIGRANT             SIMAK, CLIFFORD D.    SN    ASP 54 03

STRANGERS IN THE UNIVERSE (7 OF 11)
                        SIMAK, CLIFFORD D.    AC    BKM 57 09
  TARGET GENERATION     SIMAK, CLIFFORD D.    NV
  MIRAGE                SIMAK, CLIFFORD D.    NV
  BEACHHEAD (YOU'LL NEVER GO HOME AGAIN)
                        SIMAK, CLIFFORD D.    SS    FAD 51 07
  ANSWERS, THE (AND THE TRUTH SHALL MAKE YOU FREE)
                        SIMAK, CLIFFORD D.    SS    FUT 53 03
  RETROGRADE EVOLUTION  SIMAK, CLIFFORD D.    NV    SFP 53 04
  FENCE, THE            SIMAK, CLIFFORD D.    SS    SSP 52 09
  SHADOW SHOW           SIMAK, CLIFFORD D.    NV    FSF 53 11

STURGEON IN ORBIT       STURGEON, THEODORE    AC    PYR 64 02
  INTRODUCTION          STURGEON, THEODORE    IN
  EXTRAPOLATION (BEWARE THE FURY)
                        STURGEON, THEODORE    SS    FAN 54 04
  WAGES OF SYNERGY, THE STURGEON, THEODORE    NV    STS 53 08
  MAKE ROOM FOR ME      STURGEON, THEODORE    NV    FAD 51 05
  HEART, THE            STURGEON, THEODORE    SS    OWS 55 05
  INCUBI OF PARALLEL X, THE  STURGEON, THEODORE  NA  PLS 51 09

STURGEON IS ALIVE AND WELL...
                        STURGEON, THEODORE    AC H PUT 71
  FOREWORD              STURGEON, THEODORE    IN
  TO HERE AND THE EASEL STURGEON, THEODORE    SN    SSN 54
  SLOW SCULPTURE        STURGEON, THEODORE    NV    GAL 70 02
  IT'S YOU!             STURGEON, THEODORE    SS    KNT 70
  TAKE CARE OF JOEY     STURGEON, THEODORE    SS    70
  CRATE                 STURGEON, THEODORE    SS    70
  GIRL WHO KNEW WHAT THEY MENT, THE
                        STURGEON, THEODORE    SS    70
  JORRY'S GAP           STURGEON, THEODORE    SS    KNT 69
  IT WAS NOTHING- REALLY!  STURGEON, THEODORE SS    69
  BROWNSHOES            STURGEON, THEODORE    SS    KNT 69
  UNCLE FREMMIS         STURGEON, THEODORE    SS    KNT 70
  PATTERNS OF DORNE, THE  STURGEON, THEODORE  SS    70
  SUICIDE               STURGEON, THEODORE    SS    KNT 70

SUN DESTROYERS, THE     ROCKLYNNE, ROSS       DC    ACE 73 03
  INTO THE DARKNESS     ROCKLYNNE, ROSS       NV    AST 40 06
  DAUGHTER OF DARKNESS  ROCKLYNNE, ROSS       NA    AST 41 11
  ABYSS OF DARKNESS     ROCKLYNNE, ROSS       NV    AST 42 12
  REBEL OF THE DARKNESS (REVOLT OF THE DEVIL STAR)
                        ROCKLYNNE, ROSS       NV    IMG 51 02

SUNDANCE AND OTHER SCIENCE FICTION STORIES
                        SILVERBERG, ROBERT    AC H NEL 74
  SUNDANCE              SILVERBERG, ROBERT    SS    FSF 69 06
  NEIGHBOR              SILVERBERG, ROBERT    SS    GAL 64 08
  PASSPORT TO SIRIUS    SILVERBERG, ROBERT    SS    IFS 58 04
  CAUGHT IN THE ORGAN DRAFT  SILVERBERG, ROBERT  SS  WLK 73
  NEUTRAL PLANET        SILVERBERG, ROBERT    SS    SFS 57 07
  PAIN PEDDLERS, THE    SILVERBERG, ROBERT    SS    GAL 63 08
  OVERLORD'S THUMB, THE SILVERBERG, ROBERT    NV    INF 58 03
  OUTBREEDERS, THE      SILVERBERG, ROBERT    SS    FUN 59 09
  SOMETHING WILD IS LOOSE  SILVERBERG, ROBERT  NV   MWS 71

SUNLESS WORLD, THE      JONES, NEIL R.        AC    ACE 67
  INTO THE HYDROSPHERE  JONES, NEIL R.        SS    AMZ 33 10
  TIME'S MAUSOLEUM      JONES, NEIL R.        SS    AMZ 33 12
  SUNLESS WORLD, THE    JONES, NEIL R.        NV    AMZ 34 12

SUNRISE ON MERCURY AND OTHER SCIENCE FICTION STORIES
                        SILVERBERG, ROBERT    OA L NDB 75
  SUNRISE ON MERCURY    SILVERBERG, ROBERT    SS    SFS 57 05
  HI DIDDLE DIDDLE!     SILVERBERG, ROBERT    NV    ASF 59 02
  BIRDS OF A FEATHER    SILVERBERG, ROBERT    NV    GAL 58 11
  THERE WAS AN OLD WOMAN-  SILVERBERG, ROBERT SS    INF 58 11
  ALAREE               SILVERBERG, ROBERT     SS    STN 58 03
  MACAULEY CIRCUIT, THE SILVERBERG, ROBERT    SS    FUN 56 10
  COMPANY STORE         SILVERBERG, ROBERT    SS    STR 59 05
  AFTER THE MYTHS WENT HOME  SILVERBERG, ROBERT  SS FSF 69 11

SUPER SCIENCE STORIES   ELAM, RICHARD M. JR. AC    LPB 67 02
  SEE "TEEN-AGE SUPER SCIENCE STORIES"

SUPERNATURAL READER, THE  CONKLIN, G&L.       AN H LIP 53
  INTRODUCTION          CONKLIN, GROFF        IN
  ANGEL WITH PURPLE HAIR, THE  PAUL, HERB      SS    FSF 50 12
  FOR THE BLOOD IS THE LIFE  CRAWFORD, F. MARION  SS  11
  STRANGER, THE         HUGHES, RICHARD       SS    31
  MRS. MANIFOLD         GRENDON, STEPHEN      SS    49
  PIFFINGCAP            COPPARD, A. E.        SS    21
  SHOTTLE BOP           STURGEON, THEODORE    SS    UNK 41 02
  GABRIEL-ERNEST        MUNRO, H. H.          SS    30
  LOST ROOM, THE        O'BRIEN, FITZ-JAMES   SS    WRT 29 10
  TRAITOR, THE          HART, JAMES S.        SS    FSF 50 FL
  ANGUS MACAULIFFE AND THE GOWDEN TOOCH
                        TANNER, CHARLES R.    SS    OWS 51 03

  ARE YOU RUN-DOWN, TIRED-  ROSMOND, BABETTE
                    AND LAKE, LEONARD M.      SS C UNK 42 10
  NATURE OF THE EVIDENCE, THE  SINCLAIR, MAY   SS    WRT 23 10
  TREE'S WIFE, THE      COUNSELMAN, MARY E.   SS    WRT 50 03
  PAVILION, THE         NESBIT, EDITH         SS    23
  PICKUP FOR OLYMPUS    PANGBORN, EDGAR       SS    NEW 53 AN
  SWAP, THE             HEARD, H. F.          SS    44
  TOMBLING DAY, THE     BRADBURY, RAY         SS    SHN 52 FL
  MINUKE                KNEALE, NIGEL         SS    HRP 50 09
  BIRD OF PREY          COLLIER, JOHN         SS    41
  THING IN THE CELLAR, THE  KELLER, DAVID H. MD. SS  WRT 32 13
  DEVIL'S HENCHMAN      JENKINS, WILL F.      SS    ARG 52 05
  LOST HEARTS           JAMES, M. R.          SS    31
  THIRTEEN AT TABLE     DUNSANY, LORD         SS    16
  LIGHTS                FISHER, PHILIP M. JR  SS    AAS 22 07
  SILVER HIGHWAY, THE   LAWLOR, HAROLD        SS    WRT 46 05
  MOONLIT ROAD, THE     BIERCE, AMBROSE       SS    93
  CURATE'S FRIEND, THE  FORSTER, E. M.        SS    47

SURVIVAL FROM INFINITY  ELWOOD, ROGER         OA H WAT 74
  EDITOR'S NOTE         ELWOOD, ROGER         IN
  SURVIVAL ON A PRIMATIVE PLANET
                        TOFTE, ARTHUR         NV
  INSTITUTIONS          MALZBERG, BARRY N.    SS
  I HAVE HEARD THE MERMAIDS  TUTTLE, LISA      SS
  SURVIVAL, A.D. 2000   REYNOLDS, MACK        SS
  SERPENTINE            SCHAUB, MARY H.        NV
  MEETING THE ALIENS ON ALGOL IV
                        SCHAEFFER, ROBIN      SS
  WALLS                 KINSOLVING, MAY R.    NV
  REFLECTIONS FROM A STAR  JONES, RAYMOND F.   SS

SURVIVAL PRINTOUT       TOTAL EFFECT          AN    VNT 73
  PRINTOUT              TOTAL EFFECT          IN
  STAR THROWER, THE     EISELEY, SIMON        AR    69
  TERMINAL BEACH, THE   BALLARD, J. G.        SS    NWS 64 03
  FONDLY FAHRENHEIT     BESTER, ALFRED        SS    FSF 54 08
  FOR A BREATH I TARRY  ZELAZNY, ROGER        NV    NWS 66 03
  SOCIAL CONSEQUENCES OF COMMUNICATIONS SATELLITES, THE
                        CLARKE, ARTHUR C.     AR    65
  HAPPY DAY IN 2381, A  SILVERBERG, ROBERT    SS    NOV 70 01
  INTERURBAN QUEEN      LAFFERTY, R. A.       SS    ORB 70 08
  I HAVE NO MOUTH, AND I MUST SCREAM
                        ELLISON, HARLAN       SS    IFS 67 03
  EXPLODING STARS       CALDER, NIGEL         AR    69
  SECRET SONGS, THE     LEIBER, FRITZ         SS    FSF 62 08
  DRIFTGLASS            DELANY, SAMUEL R.     NV    IFS 67 06
  DESERTION             SIMAK, CLIFFORD D.    SS    ASF 44 11
  DIRECT CONTACT AMONG GALACTIC CIVILIZATIONS
                        SHKLOVSKII, I. S.
                    AND SAGAN, CARL           AR C  66
  SCANNERS LIVE IN VAIN SMITH, CORDWAINER     NA    FBK 50 06
  ALL YOU ZOMBIES-      HEINLEIN, ROBERT A.   SS    FSF 59 03
  COMMON TIME           BLISH, JAMES          SS    SFQ 53 08
  EDITORS, THE          MISC. MATERIAL        MS
  AUTHORS, THE          MISC. MATERIAL        MS

SURVIVAL SHIP AND OTHER STORIES
                        MERRIL, JUDITH        AC    KAK 74
  INTRODUCTION          THEALL, DONALD F.     IN
  PROLOGUE              MERRIL, JUDITH        IN
  SURVIVAL SHIP         MERRIL, JUDITH        SS    WBY 51 01
  WISH UPON A STAR      MERRIL, JUDITH        SS    FSF 58 12
  EXILE FROM SPACE      MERRIL, JUDITH        NV    FUN 56 11
  CONNECTION COMPLETED  MERRIL, JUDITH        SS    USF 54 SU
  SHRINE OF TEMPTATION, THE  MERRIL, JUDITH    SS    FAN 62 04
  PEEPING TOM           MERRIL, JUDITH        NV    STS 54 SP
  LADY WAS A TRAMP, THE MERRIL, JUDITH        SS    VSF 57 03
  AUCTION PIT           MERRIL, JUDITH        PM    46
  SO PROUDLY WE HAIL    MERRIL, JUDITH        SS    STR 53 01
  DEEP DOWN DRAGON, THE MERRIL, JUDITH        SS    GAL 61 08
  WHOEVER YOU ARE       MERRIL, JUDITH        NV    STS 52 12
  DEATH IS THE PENALTY  MERRIL, JUDITH        SS    ASF 49 01
  LONELY, THE           MERRIL, JUDITH        SS    WOT 63 10

SURVIVOR AND OTHER STORIES, THE
                        LOVECRAFT & DERLETH   AC H ARK 57
  SURVIVOR, THE         LOVECRAFT, H. P.
                    AND DERLETH, AUGUST       NV C WRT 54 07
  WENTWORTH'S DAY       LOVECRAFT, H. P.
                    AND DERLETH, AUGUST       SS C
  PEABODY HERITAGE, THE LOVECRAFT, H. P.
                    AND DERLETH, AUGUST       NV C
  GABEL WINDOW, THE (THE MURKY GLASS)
                        LOVECRAFT, H. P.
                    AND DERLETH, AUGUST       SS C STN 57 05
  ANCESTOR, THE         LOVECRAFT, H. P.
                    AND DERLETH, AUGUST       SS C
  SHADOW OUT OF SPACE, THE  LOVECRAFT, H. P.
                    AND DERLETH, AUGUST       NV C
  LAMP OF ALHAZRED, THE LOVECRAFT, H. P.
                    AND DERLETH, AUGUST       SS C

SWORD OF CONAN, THE     HOWARD, ROBERT E.     AC H GNM 55
  PEOPLE OF THE BLACK CIRCLE, THE
                        HOWARD, ROBERT E.     NA    WRT 34 09
  SLITHERING SHADOW, THE  HOWARD, ROBERT E.    SS    WRT 33 09
  POOL OF THE BLACK ONE, THE  HOWARD, ROBERT E. SS   WRT 33 10
  RED NAILS             HOWARD, ROBERT E.     NA    WRT 36 07

SWORDSMEN IN THE SKY    WOLLHEIM, DONALD A.   AN    ACE 64
  SWORDSMAN OF LOST TERRA  ANDERSON, POUL      NA    PLS 51 11
  PEOPLE OF THE CRATER  NORTON, ANDRE         NV    FBK 47 01
  MOON THAT VANISHED, THE  BRACKETT, LEIGH     NV    TWS 48 10
  VISION OF VENUS, A    KLINE, OTIS ADELBERT  SS    AMZ 33 12
  KALDAR, WORLD OF ANTARES  HAMILTON, EDMOND   NV    MGC 33 04
```

TALES AND STORIES

```
TALES AND STORIES          SHELLEY, MARY W.      AC H GRG 75
   REPRINT OF 1891 EDITION PUBLISHED BY WM. PATERSON & CO, LONDON
   INTRODUCTION            RUSS, JOANNA          IN
   INTRODUCTION            GARNETT, RICHARD,LLD  IN
   FERDINANDO EBOLI        SHELLEY, MARY W.      NV    KPS 29
   EVIL EYE, THE           SHELLEY, MARY W.      NV    KPS 30
   DREAM, THE              SHELLEY, MARY W.      SS    KPS 32
   MOURNER, THE            SHELLEY, MARY W.      NV    KPS 30
   FALSE RHYME, THE        SHELLEY, MARY W.      SS    KPS 30
   TALE OF THE PASSIONS: OR, THE DEATH OF DESPINA, A
                          SHELLEY, MARY W.       NV    LIB 22 01
   MORTAL IMMORTAL, THE (1834) SHELLEY, MARY W.  SS    KPS 34
   TRANSFORMATION          SHELLEY, MARY W.      NV    KPS 31
   SWISS PEASANT, THE      SHELLEY, MARY W.      NV    KPS 31
   INVISIBLE GIRL, THE     SHELLEY, MARY W.      SS    KPS 33
   BROTHER AND SISTER, THE SHELLEY, MARY W.      NV    KPS 33
   PARVENUE, THE           SHELLEY, MARY W.      SS    KPS 37
   POLE, THE               SHELLEY, MARY W.      NV    CMG 32 08
   EUPHRASIA               SHELLEY, MARY W.      SS    KPS 39
   ELDER SON, THE          SHELLEY, MARY W.      NV        35
   PILGRIMS, THE           SHELLEY, MARY W.      NV    KPS 38

TALES BEYOND TIME          DE CAMP, L. S.&C.     AN H LOT 73
   INTRODUCTION: YESTERDAY, TOMORROW, AND MAYBY
                          DE CAMP, L. SPRAGUE
                       AND DE CAMP, CATHERINE C  IN C
   ICARUS                 DE CAMP, CATHERINE C   SS    NEW 73 AN
   BOY WHO FOUND FEAR, THE KUNOS, IGNAZ          SS        07
   MARVELOUS POWDER OF LIFE, THE (FROM THE LAND OF OZ)
                          BAUM, L. FRANK         EX    REL 04
   SACRED CITY OF CATS, THE (FROM TIME CAT)
                          ALEXANDER, LLOYD       EX    HRW 63
   SHED, THE              EVANS, E. EVERETT      SS    ASR 53 01
   SOMETHING BRIGHT       HENDERSON, ZENNA       SS    GAL 60 02
   ROCKET MAN, THE        LUDWIG, EDWARD W.      SS    OWS 51 05
   NATIVE SON             HAMM, THELMA D.        SS    IMG 53 07
   PLAYMATE               CROUTCH, LESLIE A.     SS    IMG 51 11
   ROBBIE (STRANGE PLAYFELLOW) ASIMOV, ISAAC     SS    SSS 40 09
   LONGER STORIES TOO GOOD TO BE MISSED
                          MISC. MATERIAL         MS

TALES FROM GAVAGAN'S BAR   DE CAMP, L. S.&PRATT  AC H TWN 53
   GIFT OF GOD, THE        DE CAMP, L. SPRAGUE
                       AND PRATT, FLETCHER       SS C FSF 50 WS
   CORPUS DELECTABLE       DE CAMP, L. SPRAGUE
                       AND PRATT, FLETCHER       SS C NEW 53 AC
   BETTER MOUSETRAP, THE   DE CAMP, L. SPRAGUE
                       AND PRATT, FLETCHER       SS C FSF 50 12
   ELEPHAS FRUMENTI        DE CAMP, L. SPRAGUE
                       AND PRATT, FLETCHER       SS C FSF 50 WS
   BEASTS OF BOURBON       DE CAMP, L. SPRAGUE
                       AND PRATT, FLETCHER       SS C FSF 51 10
   LOVE-NEST, THE          DE CAMP, L. SPRAGUE
                       AND PRATT, FLETCHER       SS C NEW 53 AC
   STONE OF THE SAGES, THE DE CAMP, L. SPRAGUE
                       AND PRATT, FLETCHER       SS C NEW 53 AC
   WHERE TO, PLEASE?       DE CAMP, L. SPRAGUE
                       AND PRATT, FLETCHER       SS C WRT 52 09
   PALIMPSEST OF ST. AUGUSTINE, THE
                          DE CAMP, L. SPRAGUE
                       AND PRATT, FLETCHER       SS C NEW 53 AC
   MORE THAN SKIN DEEP     DE CAMP, L. SPRAGUE
                       AND PRATT, FLETCHER       SS C FSF 51 04
   NO FORWARDING ADDRESS   DE CAMP, L. SPRAGUE
                       AND PRATT, FLETCHER       SS C NEW 53 AC
   WHEN THE NIGHT WIND HOWLS DE CAMP, L. SPRAGUE
                       AND PRATT, FLETCHER       SS C WRT 51 11
   MY BROTHER'S KEEPER     DE CAMP, L. SPRAGUE
                       AND PRATT, FLETCHER       SS C NEW 53 AC
   DIME BRINGS YOU SUCCESS, A DE CAMP, L. SPRAGUE
                       AND PRATT, FLETCHER       SS C NEW 53 AC
   RAPE OF THE LOCK, THE   DE CAMP, L. SPRAGUE
                       AND PRATT, FLETCHER       SS C FSF 52 02
   ALL THAT GLITTERS       DE CAMP, L. SPRAGUE
                       AND PRATT, FLETCHER       SS C NEW 53 AC
   HERE, PUTZI¡            DE CAMP, L. SPRAGUE
                       AND PRATT, FLETCHER       SS C NEW 53 AC
   GIN COMES IN BOTTLES    DE CAMP, L. SPRAGUE
                       AND PRATT, FLETCHER       SS C NEW 53 AC
   BLACK BALL, THE         DE CAMP, L. SPRAGUE
                       AND PRATT, FLETCHER       SS C FSF 52 10
   GREEN THUMB, THE        DE CAMP, L. SPRAGUE
                       AND PRATT, FLETCHER       SS C FSF 53 02
   CAVEAT EMPTOR           DE CAMP, L. SPRAGUE
                       AND PRATT, FLETCHER       SS C WRT 53 03
   EVE OF ST. JOHN, THE    DE CAMP, L. SPRAGUE
                       AND PRATT, FLETCHER       SS C NEW 53 AC
   ANCESTRAL AMETHYST, THE DE CAMP, L. SPRAGUE
                       AND PRATT, FLETCHER       SS C FSF 52 08

TALES FROM THE GALAXIES    WILLIAMS-ELLIS& P.    AN    PPL 73
   PREFACE                PEARSON, MICHAEL
                       AND WILLIAMS-ELLIS, A.    IN C
   RED STUFF, THE         WYNDHAM, JOHN          NV    MSS 51 02
   MISS INMAN AND THE KLOOTS WILLIAMS-ELLIS, A.  NV    NEW 73 AN
   HERITAGE, THE          STOKES, MALCOM         CT
   ODOR OF THOUGHT, THE   SHECKLEY, ROBERT       SS    STR 53 02
   EXPLORATION TEAM (ALSO AS COMBAT TEAM)
                          LEINSTER, MURRAY       NV    ASF 56 03

TALES FROM THE WHITE HART  CLARKE, ARTHUR C.     AC    BAL 57
   PREFACE                CLARKE, ARTHUR C.      IN
   SILENCE, PLEASE        CLARKE, ARTHUR C.      SS    SCF 50 WI
   BIG GAME HUNT          CLARKE, ARTHUR C.      SS        54
   PATENT PENDING         CLARKE, ARTHUR C.      SS        54
   ARMAMENTS RACE         CLARKE, ARTHUR C.      SS    ADV 54 04
```

TALES OF KNOWN SPACE: THE UNIVERSE OF LARRY NIVEN

```
   CRITICAL MASS (ORIGINAL VERSION IN LILLIPUT MARCH 1949)
                          CLARKE, ARTHUR C.      SS    SPM 57 08
   ULTIMATE MELODY, THE    CLARKE, ARTHUR C.      SS    IFS 57 02
   PACIFIST, THE           CLARKE, ARTHUR C.      SS    FUN 56 10
   NEXT TENANTS, THE       CLARKE, ARTHUR C.      SS    SAT 57 02
   MOVING SPIRIT           CLARKE, ARTHUR C.      SS
   MAN WHO PLOUGHED THE SEA, THE
                          CLARKE, ARTHUR C.      SS    SAT 57 06
   RELUCTANT ORCHID, THE   CLARKE, ARTHUR C.      SS    SAT 56 12
   COLD WAR                CLARKE, ARTHUR C.      SS    SAT 57 04
   WHAT GOES UP            CLARKE, ARTHUR C.      SS    FSF 56 01
   SLEEPING BEAUTY (THE CASE OF THE SNORING HEIR)
                          CLARKE, ARTHUR C.      SS    INF 57 04
   DEFENESTRATION OF ERMINTRUDE INCH, THE
                          CLARKE, ARTHUR C.      SS

TALES FROM UNDERWOOD       KELLER, DAVID H. MD. AC H PEL 52
   WORM, THE               KELLER, DAVID H. MD. SS    AMZ 29 03
   REVOLT OF THE PEDESTRIANS, THE
                          KELLER, DAVID H. MD. SS    AMZ 28 02
   YEAST MEN, THE          KELLER, DAVID H. MD. SS    AMZ 28 04
   IVY WAR, THE            KELLER, DAVID H. MD. SS    AMZ 30 05
   DOORBELL, THE           KELLER, DAVID H. MD. SS    WOS 34 06
   FLYING FOOL, THE        KELLER, DAVID H. MD. SS    AMZ 29 07
   PSYCHOPHONIC NURSE, THE KELLER, DAVID H. MD. NV    AMZ 28 11
   BIOLOGICAL EXPERIMENT, A KELLER, DAVID H. MD. SS   AMZ 28 06
   FREE AS AIR             KELLER, DAVID H. MD. SS    AMZ 31 06
   BRIDLE, THE             KELLER, DAVID H. MD. SS    WRT 42 09
   TIGER CAT               KELLER, DAVID H. MD. SS    WRT 37 10
   GOD WHEEL, THE          KELLER, DAVID H. MD. SS
   GOLDEN BOUGH, THE       KELLER, DAVID H. MD. SS    MVT 34 WI
   JELLY FISH, THE         KELLER, DAVID H. MD. SS    WRT 29 01
   OPIUM EATER, THE        KELLER, DAVID H. MD. SS
   THING IN THE CELLAR, THE KELLER, DAVID H. MD. SS   WRT 32 03
   CREATION UNFORGIVABLE   KELLER, DAVID H. MD. SS    WRT 30 04
   MOON ARTIST, THE        KELLER, DAVID H. MD. SS    STI 41 06
   DEAD WOMAN, THE (STE 39 04) KELLER, DAVID H. MD. SS FMG 34 04
   DOOR, THE               KELLER, DAVID H. MD. SS    ARS 49 SU
   PERFUMED GARDEN, THE    KELLER, DAVID H. MD. SS
   LITERARY CORKSCREW, THE KELLER, DAVID H. MD. SS    WOS 34 03
   PIECE OF LINOLEUM, A (AS AMY WORTH)
                          KELLER, DAVID H. MD. SS    TST 33 12

TALES IN A JUGULAR VEIN    BLOCH, ROBERT         AC    PYR 65 02
   SABBATICAL             BLOCH, ROBERT          SS    GAL 59 12
   DOUBLE-CROSS (DOUBLE TRAGEDY)
                          BLOCH, ROBERT          SS    MSM 59 10
   PAST MASTER, THE        BLOCH, ROBERT          NV    BBM 55 01
   TERROR OVER HOLLYWOOD   BLOCH, ROBERT          SS    FUN 57 06
   HOME AWAY FROM HOME, A  BLOCH, ROBERT          SS    AHM 61 06
   RHYME NEVER PAYS (CRIME IN RHYME)
                          BLOCH, ROBERT          SS    EQM 57 09
   NIGHT SCHOOL            BLOCH, ROBERT          SS    ROG 59 08
   PIN-UP GIRL             BLOCH, ROBERT          SS    SHK 60 07
   FOUNDING FATHERS        BLOCH, ROBERT          SS    FUN 56 07
   DEADLIEST ART, THE      BLOCH, ROBERT          SS    BMM 58 11

TALES OF CONAN             HOWARD, R. & DE CAMP AC H GNM 55
   INTRODUCTION           MILLER, P. SCHUYLER    IN
   BLOOD-STAINED GOD, THE  HOWARD, ROBERT E.     NV    FUN 56 04
   HAWKS OVER SHEM (FROM "HAWKS OVER EGYPT" BY REH.)
                          HOWARD, ROBERT E.
                       AND DE CAMP, L. SPRAGUE  NV C FUN 55 10
   ROAD OF THE EAGLES, THE (CONAN, MAN OF DESTINY)
                          HOWARD, ROBERT E.
                       AND DE CAMP, L. SPRAGUE  NV C FUN 55 12
   FLAME KNIFE, THE        HOWARD, ROBERT E.     SS

TALES OF GOOSEFLESH AND LAUGHTER
                          WYNDHAM, JOHN          AC    BAL 56 12
   CHINESE PUZZLE (A STRAY FROM CATHAY)
                          WYNDHAM, JOHN          NV    FNF 53 08
   UNA (THE PERFECT CREATURE, TOW 37 01)
                          WYNDHAM, JOHN          NV    FSF 53 01
   WHEEL, THE              WYNDHAM, JOHN          SS    STS 52 01
   JIZZLE (REVISED FROM COL 49 01)
                          WYNDHAM, JOHN          SS    FSF 52 02
   HEAVEN SCENT            WYNDHAM, JOHN          SS
   COMPASSION CIRCUIT      WYNDHAM, JOHN          SS    FUN 54 12
   MORE SPINNED AGAINST    WYNDHAM, JOHN          SS    FNF 53 06
   PRESENT FROM BRUNSWICK, A (BARGAIN FROM BRUNSWICK)
                          WYNDHAM, JOHN          SS    FSF 51 06
   CONFIDENCE TRICK        WYNDHAM, JOHN          SS    FAN 53 08
   OPPOSITE NUMBERS        WYNDHAM, JOHN          SS    NWS 54 04
   WILD FLOWER             WYNDHAM, JOHN          SS    FUN 55 11

TALES OF KNOWN SPACE: THE UNIVERSE OF LARRY NIVEN
                          NIVEN, LARRY           AC    BAL 75 08
   TIMELINE FOR KNOWN SPACE NIVEN, LARRY          MS
   INTRODUCTION: MY UNIVERSE AND WELCOME TO IT¡
                          NIVEN, LARRY           IN
   COLDEST PLACE, THE      NIVEN, LARRY           SS    IFS 64 12
   BECALMED IN HELL        NIVEN, LARRY           SS    FSF 65 07
   WAIT IT OUT             NIVEN, LARRY           SS    FUP 68
   EYE OF AN OCTOPUS       NIVEN, LARRY           SS    GAL 66 02
   HOW THE HEROES DIE      NIVEN, LARRY           NV    GAL 66 10
   JIGSAW MAN, THE         NIVEN, LARRY           SS    DVS 67 01
   AT THE BOTTOM OF A HOLE NIVEN, LARRY           NV    GAL 66 12
   INTENT TO DECEIVE (THE DECEIVERS)
                          NIVEN, LARRY           SS    GAL 68 04
   CLOAK OF ANARCHY        NIVEN, LARRY           NV    ASF 72 03
   WARRIORS, THE           NIVEN, LARRY           SS    IFS 66 02
   BORDERLAND OF SOL, THE  NIVEN, LARRY           NV    ASF 75 01
   THERE IS A TIDE         NIVEN, LARRY           NV    GAL 68 07
   SAFE AT ANY SPEED       NIVEN, LARRY           SS    FSF 67 05
   AFTERTHOUGHTS           NIVEN, LARRY           MS
```

TALES OF KNOWN SPACE: THE UNIVERSE OF LARRY NIVEN

BIBLIOGRAPHY: THE WORLDS OF LARRY NIVEN
                                      MISC. MATERIAL   MS
ABOUT THE COVER   STERNBACH, RICK   MS

TALES OF OUTER SPACE   WOLLHEIM, DONALD A.   DA   ACE 54
DOORWAY IN THE SKY (BERTHA) WILLIAMS, RALPH   NV   ASF 54 01
HERE LIE WE   HOLDEN, FOX B.   NV   STS 53 06
OPERATION MERCURY (MASQUERADE)
                         SIMAK, CLIFFORD D.   NV   ASF 41 03
LORD OF A THOUSAND SUNS ANDERSON, POUL   NV   PLS 51 09
BEHIND THE BLACK NEBULA (THE INVADERS)
                         HUBBARD, L. RON   NV   ASF 42 01

TALES OF SCIENCE AND SORCERY SMITH, CLARK ASHTON AC H ARK 64
GREAT GOD AWTO, THE   SMITH, CLARK ASHTON   SS   TWS 40 02
IMMORTALS OF MERCURY, THE SMITH, CLARK ASHTON   NV   32
MAKER OF GARGOYLES, THE SMITH, CLARK ASHTON   SS   WRT 32 08
MASTER OF THE ASTEROID   SMITH, CLARK ASHTON   SS   WOS 32 10
MORTHYLLA   SMITH, CLARK ASHTON   SS   WRT 53 05
MOTHER OF TOADS   SMITH, CLARK ASHTON   SS   WRT 38 07
MURDER IN THE FOURTH DIMENSION
                         SMITH, CLARK ASHTON   SS   AMD 30 10
ROOT OF AMPOI, THE   SMITH, CLARK ASHTON   SS   ARS 49 SP
SCHIZOID CREATOR   SMITH, CLARK ASHTON   SS   FNF 53 11
SEED FROM THE SEPULCHRE, THE SMITH, CLARK ASHTON SS   WRT 33 10
SEEDLING OF MARS (THE PLANET ENTITY)
                         SMITH, CLARK ASHTON   NV   WSQ 31 FL
SYMPOSIUM OF THE GORGON SMITH, CLARK ASHTON   SS   FUN 58 10
THEFT OF THE THIRTY-NINE GIRDLES, THE (THE POWER OF THE
  HYPERBOREA)   SMITH, CLARK ASHTON   SS   STN 58 03
TOMB-SPAWN, THE   SMITH, CLARK ASHTON   SS   WRT 34 05

TALES OF SCIENCE FICTION BALL, BRIAN N.   AN H HML 64
HIDE AND SEEK   CLARKE, ARTHUR C.   SS   ASF 49 09
RETURN OF THE MOON MAN (ALSO AS WHEN GRANDFATHER FLEW
  TO THE MOON)   MALPASS, E. L.   SS   LOB 55 01
LIFE-LINE   HEINLEIN, ROBERT A.   SS   ASF 39 08
ESCAPE VELOCITY   BALL, BRIAN N.   SS
NOTHING HAPPENS ON THE MOON ERNST, PAUL   SS   ASF 39 02
MR. KOWTSHOOK   CHRISTOPHER, JOHN   SS   ASR 53 01
METEOR (PHONEY METEOR)   WYNDHAM, JOHN   SS   AMZ 41 03
ALLAMAGOOSA   RUSSELL, ERIC FRANK   SS   ASF 55 05
BUT WHO CAN REPLACE A MAN? ALDISS, BRIAN W.   SS   INF 58 06

TALES OF SPACE AND TIME WELLS, H. G.   AC H HPR 99
CRYSTAL EGG, THE   WELLS, H. G.   SS   NRV 97 05
STAR, THE   WELLS, H. G.   SS   GRP 97 12
STORY OF THE STONE AGE, A WELLS, H. G.   NA   IDL 97 05
STORY OF THE DAYS TO COME, A WELLS, H. G.   NA   PGZ 97
MAN WHO COULD WORK MIRACLES, THE
                         WELLS, H. G.   SS   ILN 98 07

TALES OF TEN WORLDS   CLARKE, ARTHUR C.   AC H HBW 62
I REMEMBER BABYLON   CLARKE, ARTHUR C.   SS   PBY 60 05
SUMMERTIME ON ICARUS (THE HOTTEST PIECE OF REAL ESTATE IN THE
  SOLAR SYSTEM)   CLARKE, ARTHUR C.   SS   VOG 60 06
OUT OF THE CRADLE, ENDLESSLY ORBITING
                         CLARKE, ARTHUR C.   SS   DUD 59 03
WHO'S THERE? (ALSO AS THE HAUNTED SPACESUIT)
                         CLARKE, ARTHUR C.   SS   NWS 58 11
HATE (AT THE END OF THE ORBIT)
                         CLARKE, ARTHUR C.   NV   IFS 61 11
INTO THE COMET (INSIDE THE COMET)
                         CLARKE, ARTHUR C.   SS   FSF 60 10
APE ABOUT THE HOUSE, AN CLARKE, ARTHUR C.   SS   DUD 62
SATURN RISING   CLARKE, ARTHUR C.   SS   FSF 61 03
LET THERE BE LIGHT   CLARKE, ARTHUR C.   SS   PBY 58 02
DEATH AND THE SENATOR   CLARKE, ARTHUR C.   NV   ASF 61 05
TROUBLE WITH TIME (CRIME ON MARS, EQM 60 07)
                         CLARKE, ARTHUR C.   SS   FSF 61 06
BEFORE EDEN   CLARKE, ARTHUR C.   SS   AMZ 61 06
SLIGHT CASE OF SUNSTROKE, A (STROKE OF THE SUN)
                         CLARKE, ARTHUR C.   SS   GAL 58 09
DOG STAR (MOONDOG)   CLARKE, ARTHUR C.   SS   GAL 62 04
ROAD TO THE SEA, THE (SEEKER OF THE SPHINX)
                         CLARKE, ARTHUR C.   NV   TCS 51 SP

TALES OF TERROR FROM OUTER SPACE
                         CHETWYND-HAYES, R.   AN   FON 75 05
INTRODUCTION   CHETWYND-HAYES, R.   IN
I, MARS   BRADBURY, RAY   SS   SSS 49 04
EIGHT O'CLOCK IN THE MORNING NELSON, RAY   SS   FSF 63 11
GIRL FROM MARS, THE   BLOCH, ROBERT   SS   FAD 50 03
HERESIES OF THE HUGE GOD ALDISS, BRIAN W.   FA   GAL 66 08
HEAD HUNTERS, THE   WILLIAMS, RALPH   SS   ASF 51 10
ANIMATORS, THE   BOUNDS, SYDNEY J.   SS   NEW 75 AN
NIGHT OF THE SEVENTH FINGER, THE
                         PRESSLIE, ROBERT   SS   NWR 66 07
NO MORE FOR MARY   BIRKIN, CHARLES   SS   66
INVASION OF PRIVACY   SHAW, BOB   NV   AMZ 70 07
RUUM, THE   PORGES, ARTHUR   SS   FSF 53 10
FIRST DAYS OF MAY, THE (FCT 60 05)
                         VEILLOT, CLAUDE   SS   FSF 61 12
SPECIALIST   SHECKLEY, ROBERT   SS   GAL 53 05
NO MORNING AFTER   CLARKE, ARTHUR C.   SS   FSF 56 07
SHIPWRECK   CHETWYND-HAYES, R.   SS   NEW 75 AN

TALES OF THE FLYING MOUNTAINS
                         ANDERSON, POUL   AC H MAC 70
PROLOGUE   ANDERSON, POUL   IN
NOTHING SUCCEEDS LIKE FAILURE
                         ANDERSON, POUL   SS   NEW 70 AC
ROGUE, THE (INDUSTRIAL REVOLUTION)
                         ANDERSON, POUL   SN   ASF 63 09
SAY IT WITH FLOWERS   ANDERSON, POUL   SS   ASF 65 09
RAMBLE WITH A GAMBLIN' MAN ANDERSON, POUL   NV   NEW 70 AC

TEN THOUSAND LIGHT-YEARS FROM HOME

QUE DONN'REZ VOUS? (WHAT'LL YOU GIVE?)
                         ANDERSON, POUL   NV   ASF 63 04
SUNJAMMER   ANDERSON, POUL   NV   ASF 64 04
RECRUITING NATION   ANDERSON, POUL   NV   NEW 70 AC
EPILOGUE   ANDERSON, POUL   MS

TALES OF THREE PLANETS   BURROUGHS, EDGAR R. AC H CAN 64
ILLUSTRATIONS   KRENKEL, R.   IL
BEYOND THE FARTHEST STAR (INCLUDES UNPUBLISHED SEQUEL,
  TANGOR RETURNS)   BURROUGHS, EDGAR R.   NV   BBM 42 01
RESURRECTION OF JIMBER-JAW, THE
                         BURROUGHS, EDGAR R.   NV   ARG 37 02
WIZARD OF VENUS, THE   BURROUGHS, EDGAR R.   NV   NEW 64 AC

TALES OF TIME AND SPACE OLNEY, ROSS R.   AN H WPC 69
YESTERDAY'S FANTASY, TODAY'S FACT- AN INTRODUCTION
                         OLNEY, ROSS R.   IN
ALL THE TIME IN THE WORLD CLARKE, ARTHUR C.   SS   STS 52 07
PUPPET SHOW   BROWN, FREDRIC   SS   PBY 62 11
BIRDS OF A FEATHER   SILVERBERG, ROBERT   NV   GAL 58 11
CLUTCH OF MORPHEUS   STERNIG, LARRY   NV   TWS 46 WI
LAST COMMAND, THE   LAUMER, KEITH   SS   ASF 67 01
FOG   GAULT, WILLIAM C.   SS   TWS 51 06
MARTIAN CROWN JEWELS, THE ANDERSON, POUL   SS   EQM 58 02
OF MISSING PERSONS   FINNEY, JACK   SS   GHK 55 03

TEEN-AGE OUTER SPACE STORIES FURMAN, A. L.   AN H LPB 62
ALSO AS "OUTER SPACE STORIES"
SIGN AMONG THE STARS   PRIESTLEY, LEE   SS   58
CRASH ALERT   PEARL, CLINTON   SS   59
NEW GAME, A   LIGHTNER, A. M.   SS   BLF 59
FLYING TEACUP   GOHMAN, FRED   SS   53
ROCKET RIDER   COOMBS, CHARLES   SS   BLF 59
SHAKE HANDS WITH THE MAN IN THE MOON
                         LEYSON, CAPT. BURR W   SS   BLF 59
MOON GOLD   HARMON, SETH   SS   58
SPACE SECRET   PEARL, CLINTON   SS   58

TEEN-AGE SCIENCE FICTION STORIES
                         ELAM, RICHARD M. JR. AC H LPB 52
ALSO AS "YOUNG READERS SCIENCE FICTION STORIES" AND
  "SCIENCE FICTION STORIES"
WHAT TIME IS IT?   ELAM, RICHARD M. JR. NV
STRANGE MEN, THE   ELAM, RICHARD M. JR. SS
PROJECT OCEAN FLOOR   ELAM, RICHARD M. JR. SS
LUNAR TRAP   ELAM, RICHARD M. JR. NV   BLF 49
RED SANDS   ELAM, RICHARD M. JR. SS
IRON MOON, THE   ELAM, RICHARD M. JR. NV   BLF 51
VENUSWAY   ELAM, RICHARD M. JR. SS   BLF 51
BY JUPITER   ELAM, RICHARD M. JR. SS
SOL'S LITTLE BROTHER   ELAM, RICHARD M. JR. SS
DAY THE FLAG FELL, THE   ELAM, RICHARD M. JR. SS
HANDS ACROSS THE DEEP   ELAM, RICHARD M. JR. SS

TEEN-AGE SPACE ADVENTURES FURMAN, A. L.   AN   LPB 72
ALSO AS "SPACE ADVENTURES"
TOTAL RECALL   STERNIG, LARRY   SS   PLS 46 FL
GREAT DAY FOR THE IRISH, A LIGHTNER, A. M.   SS   IFS 60 05
MASTER RACE   ASHBY, RICHARD   SS   IMG 51 09
FATEFUL FIRST DAY ON XENE TOFTE, ARTHUR   NV   NEW 72 AN
BEST FRIEND   LIGHTNER, A. M.   SS   BLF 61
VENUSIAN INVADER   STERNIG, LARRY   SS   PLS 45 WI
MARS-STATION   KEVLES, BETTYANN   SS
MARS JAR, THE   LIGHTNER, A. M.   SS   66

TEEN-AGE SUPER SCIENCE STORIES
                         ELAM, RICHARD M. JR. AC H LPB 58
ALSO AS "SUPER SCIENCE STORIES"
FIRST MAN INTO SPACE, THE ELAM, RICHARD M. JR. NV
MYSTERY EYES OVER EARTH ELAM, RICHARD M. JR. SS
RACE AROUND THE SUN   ELAM, RICHARD M. JR. SS
FLIGHT OF THE CENTAURUS ELAM, RICHARD M. JR. SS
EXPEDITION PLUTO   ELAM, RICHARD M. JR. NV
MERCY FLIGHT TO LUNA   ELAM, RICHARD M. JR. SS
PERIL FROM OUTER SPACE, THE ELAM, RICHARD M. JR. NV
GHOST SHIP OF SPACE, THE ELAM, RICHARD M. JR. NV
SPACE STEWARD   ELAM, RICHARD M. JR. NV

TELZEY TOY, THE   SCHMITZ, JAMES H.   NO   DAW 73 12
TELZEY TOY, THE   SCHMITZ, JAMES H.   NV   ASF 71 01
RESIDENT WITCH   SCHMITZ, JAMES H.   NV   ASF 70 05
COMPULSION   SCHMITZ, JAMES H.   NV   ASF 70 06
COMPANY PLANET   SCHMITZ, JAMES H.   NV   ASF 71 05

TEN FROM TOMORROW   TUBB, E. C.   AC H HDV 66
MING VASE, THE   TUBB, E. C.   SS   ASF 63 05
TELL THE TRUTH   TUBB, E. C.   SS   ASF 59 12
LAST DAY OF SUMMER, THE TUBB, E. C.   SS   SCF 55 02
FRESH GUY   TUBB, E. C.   SS   SCF 58 06
VIGIL   TUBB, E. C.   SS   GAL 56 11
PIEBALD HORSE   TUBB, E. C.   SS   ASF 60 11
SENSE OF PROPORTION   TUBB, E. C.   NV   NEB 58 07
GREATER THAN INFINITY   TUBB, E. C.   SS   NWS 60 11
LAST OF THE MORTICIANS   TUBB, E. C.   SS   GAL 59 10
WORM IN THE WOODWORK   TUBB, E. C.   NV   ASF 62 01

TEN THOUSAND LIGHT-YEARS FROM HOME
                         TIPTREE, JAMES JR.   AC   ACE 73 07
INTRODUCTION   HARRISON, HARRY   IN
AND I AWOKE AND FOUND ME HERE ON THE COLD HILL'S SIDE
                         TIPTREE, JAMES JR.   SS   FSF 72 03
SNOWS ARE MELTED, THE SNOWS ARE GONE, THE
                         TIPTREE, JAMES JR.   SS   VSF 69 11
PEACEFULNESS OF VIVYAN, THE TIPTREE, JAMES JR.   SS   AMZ 71 07
MAMMA COME HOME (THE MOTHER SHIP)
                         TIPTREE, JAMES JR.   NV   IFS 68 06

Title	Author	Type	Mag	Yr	Mo
HELP (PUPA KNOWS BEST)	TIPTREE, JAMES JR.	NV	IFS	68	10
PAINWISE	TIPTREE, JAMES JR.	SS	FSF	72	02
FAITHFUL TO THEE, TERRA, IN OUR FASHION (PARAMUTUEL PLANET)	TIPTREE, JAMES JR.	NV	GAL	69	01
MAN DOORS SAID HELLO TO, THE	TIPTREE, JAMES JR.	SS	WOF	70	WI
MAN WHO WALKED HOME, THE	TIPTREE, JAMES JR.	NV	AMZ	72	05
FOREVER TO A HUDSON BAY BLANKET	TIPTREE, JAMES JR.	SS	FAN	72	08
I'LL BE WAITING FOR YOU WHEN THE SWIMMING POOL IS EMPTY	TIPTREE, JAMES JR.	SS	PRT	71	
I'M TOO BIG BUT I LOVE TO PLAY	TIPTREE, JAMES JR.	NV	AMZ	70	03
BIRTH OF A SALESMAN	TIPTREE, JAMES JR.	SS	ASF	68	03
MOTHER IN THE SKY WITH DIAMONDS	TIPTREE, JAMES JR.	NV	GAL	71	03
BEAM US HOME	TIPTREE, JAMES JR.	SS	GAL	69	04

Title	Author	Type	Mag	Yr	Mo
TEN TOMORROWS	ELWOOD, ROGER	OA	FGM	73	09
MS. FOUND IN AN ABANDONED TIME MACHINE	SILVERBERG, ROBERT	SS	TTM	73	
YAHRZEIT	MALZBERG, BARRY N.	SS	TTM	73	
FEW MINUTES, A	JANIFER, LAURENCE M.	SS	TTM	73	
FRESHMAN ANGLE, THE	PANGBORN, EDGAR	NV	TTM	73	
RESCUED GIRLS OF REFUGEE, THE	MCCAFFREY, ANNE	SS	TTM	73	
MATTHEW	SARGENT, PAMELA	SS	TTM	73	
DEFENSELESS DEAD, THE	NIVEN, LARRY	NV	TTM	73	
INFINITY OF LOVING, AN	GERROLD, DAVID	SS	TTM	73	
TRUE BILL, A	BLISH, JAMES	NV	TTM	73	
IN A CROOKED YEAR	DOZOIS, GARDNER R.	NV	TTM	73	

Title	Author	Type	Mag	Yr	Mo
TENTH GALAXY READER, THE	POHL, FREDERIK	AN H	DBL	67	

ALSO AS "DOOR TO ANYWHERE"

Title	Author	Type	Mag	Yr	Mo
WALL OF CRYSTAL, EYE OF NIGHT	BUDRYS, ALGIS	NV	GAL	61	12
ELEPHANT FOR THE PRINKIP, AN	STECHER, L. J. JR.	SS	GAL	60	08
PLACE WHERE CHICAGO WAS, THE	HARMON, JIM	NV	GAL	62	02
HERESIES OF THE HUGE GOD	ALDISS, BRIAN W.	FA	GAL	66	08
DEVIL CAR	ZELAZNY, ROGER	SS	GAL	65	06
TUNNEL UNDER THE WORLD, THE	POHL, FREDERIK	NV	GAL	55	01
AUTO-DA-FE	KNIGHT, DAMON	SS	GAL	61	02
DOOR TO ANYWHERE	ANDERSON, POUL	NV	GAL	66	12
PRIMATIVES, THE	HERBERT, FRANK	NV	GAL	66	04
IF YOU WERE THE ONLY-	WILSON, RICHARD	SS	GAL	53	06
"REPENT, HARLEQUIN!" SAID THE TICKTOCKMAN	ELLISON, HARLAN	SS	GAL	65	12

Title	Author	Type	Mag	Yr	Mo
TERMINAL BEACH (AMERICAN VERSION)	BALLARD, J. G.	AC	BKM	64	06
END-GAME	BALLARD, J. G.	SS	NWS	63	06
SUBLIMINAL MAN, THE	BALLARD, J. G.	SS	NWS	63	01
LAST WORLD OF MR. GODDARD, THE	BALLARD, J. G.	SS	SCF	60	10
TIME-TOMBS, THE	BALLARD, J. G.	NV	IFS	63	03
NOW WAKES THE SEA	BALLARD, J. G.	SS	FSF	63	05
VENUS HUNTERS, THE (THE ENCOUNTER)	BALLARD, J. G.	NV	AMZ	63	06
MINUS ONE	BALLARD, J. G.	SS	SCF	63	06
SUDDEN AFTERNOON, THE	BALLARD, J. G.	SS	FAN	63	09
TERMINAL BEACH, THE	BALLARD, J. G.	SS	NWS	64	03

Title	Author	Type	Mag	Yr	Mo
TERMINAL BEACH (BRITISH VERSION)	BALLARD, J. G.	AC H	GOL	64	06
TERMINAL BEACH, THE	BALLARD, J. G.	SS	NWS	64	03
QUESTION OF RE-ENTRY, A	BALLARD, J. G.	NV	FAN	63	03
DROWNED GIANT, THE (SOUVENIR)	BALLARD, J. G.	SS	PBY	65	05
END-GAME	BALLARD, J. G.	SS	NWS	63	06
ILLUMINATED MAN, THE	BALLARD, J. G.	NV	FSF	64	05
REPTILE ENCLOSURE, THE (THE SHERRINGTON THEORY)	BALLARD, J. G.	SS	AMZ	63	03
DELTA AT SUNSET, THE	BALLARD, J. G.	SS	NEW	64	AC
DEEP END	BALLARD, J. G.	SS	NWS	61	05
VOLCANO DANCES, THE	BALLARD, J. G.	SS	NEW	64	AC
BILLENIUM	BALLARD, J. G.	SS	NWS	61	11
GIOCONDA OF THE TWILIGHT NOON, THE	BALLARD, J. G.	SS	NEW	64	AC
LOST LEONARDO, THE	BALLARD, J. G.	SS	FSF	64	03

Title	Author	Type	Mag	Yr	Mo
TERROR IN THE MODERN VEIN	WOLLHEIM, DONALD A.	AN H	HAN	55	04

ENGLISH DERIVATIVE ANTHOLOGY "MORE TERROR IN THE MODERN VEIN"

Title	Author	Type	Mag	Yr	Mo
CROQUET PLAYER, THE	WELLS, H. G.	EX		36	
THEY	HEINLEIN, ROBERT A.	SS	UNK	41	04
FRITZCHEN	BEAUMONT, CHARLES	SS	OSF	53	01
GIRL WITH THE HUNGRY EYES, THE	LEIBER, FRITZ	SS		49	
FISHING SEASON	SHECKLEY, ROBERT	SS	TWS	53	08
CROWD, THE	BRADBURY, RAY	SS	WRT	43	05
HE	LOVECRAFT, H. P.	SS	WRT	26	09
STRANGE CASE OF LEMUEL JENKINS, THE	FISHER, PHILIP M. JR	SS	ASW	19	07
RAG THING, THE	GRINNELL, DAVID	SS	FSF	51	10
BURROW, THE	KAFKA, FRANZ	SS		46	
GONE AWAY	COPPARD, A. E.	SS		46	
SILENCE, THE	MCLAUGHLIN, BERNARD	SS	STI	41	06
MIMIC	WOLLHEIM, DONALD A.	SS	AST	42	12
SHIPSHAPE HOME	MATHESON, RICHARD	SS	GAL	52	07
DREAM MAKERS, THE	BLOCH, ROBERT	NV	BEY	53	09
REPUBLIC OF THE SOUTHERN CROSS, THE	BRUSSOV, VALERY	SS		19	
INHERITORS, THE	LOWNDES, ROBERT W. AND MICHAEL, JOHN	SS C	FFS	42	10

Title	Author	Type	Mag	Yr	Mo
TERROR IN THE MODERN VEIN (BRITISH PB)	WOLLHEIM, DONALD A.	AN	DIG	61	
THEY	HEINLEIN, ROBERT A.	SS	UNK	41	04

Title	Author	Type	Mag	Yr	Mo
FRITZCHEN	BEAUMONT, CHARLES	SS	OSF	53	01
GIRL WITH THE HUNGRY EYES, THE	LEIBER, FRITZ	SS		49	
FISHING SEASON	SHECKLEY, ROBERT	SS	TWS	53	08
CROWD, THE	BRADBURY, RAY	SS	WRT	43	05
HE	LOVECRAFT, H. P.	SS	WRT	26	09
STRANGE CASE OF LEMUEL JENKINS, THE	FISHER, PHILIP M. JR	SS	ASW	19	07
RAG THING, THE	GRINNELL, DAVID	SS	FSF	51	10

Title	Author	Type	Mag	Yr	Mo
THEMES IN SCIENCE FICTION	KELLEY, LEO P.	AN L	MGH	72	

A JOURNEY INTO WONDER

Title	Author	Type	Mag	Yr	Mo
LAST OF THE ROMANY, THE	SPINRAD, NORMAN	SS	ASF	63	05
TOTAL EXPERIENCE KICK, THE	PLATT, CHARLES	SS	NWS	66	12
SHORTSTACK	RICHMOND, WALT AND RICHMOND, LEIGH	SS C	ASF	64	12
FAR FROM THIS EARTH	OLIVER, CHAD	SS	YRT	70	
MAELSTROM II	CLARKE, ARTHUR C.	SS	PBY	65	04
FOUNDING FATHER	ASIMOV, ISAAC	SS	GAL	65	10
HOLDOUT	SHECKLEY, ROBERT	SS	FSF	57	12
COLD EQUATIONS, THE	GODWIN, TOM	NV	ASF	54	08
FATHER-THING, THE	DICK, PHILIP K.	SS	FSF	54	12
SILK AND THE SONG, THE	FONTENAY, CHARLES L.	NV	FSF	56	07
EYEBEM	WOLFE, GENE	SS	ORB	70	07
PUPPET SHOW	BROWN, FREDRIC	SS	PBY	62	11
LOOK, YOU THINK YOU'VE GOT TROUBLES	CARR, CAROL	SS	ORB	69	05
YOUNG GIRL AT AN OPEN HALF-DOOR	SABERHAGEN, FRED	SS	FSF	68	11
MAN WHO CAME EARLY, THE	ANDERSON, POUL	NV	FSF	56	06
SOLDIER (SOLDIER FROM TOMORROW)	ELLISON, HARLAN	SS	FUN	57	10
GOOD PROVIDER, THE	GROSS, MARION	SS	FSF	52	09
MESSAGE FROM CHARITY, A	LEE, WILLIAM M.	SS	FSF	67	11
WITCH WAR	MATHESON, RICHARD	SS	STS	51	07
GOMEZ	KORNBLUTH, C. M.	NV	NEW	54	AC
MUSE	KOONTZ, DEAN R.	SS	FSF	69	09
WORLD OF MYRION FLOWERS, THE	POHL, FREDERIK AND KORNBLUTH, C. M.	SS C	FSF	61	10
X MARKS THE PEDWALK	LEIBER, FRITZ	SS	WOT	63	04
EPICAC	VONNEGUT, KURT JR.	SS	COL	50	11
LAST COMMAND, THE	LAUMER, KEITH	SS	ASF	67	01
LOST MEMORY	PHILLIPS, PETER	SS	GAL	52	05
SURVIVOR, THE	MOUDY, WALTER F.	NV	AMZ	65	05
POST-MORTEM PEOPLE, THE (ALSO AS BEYOND THE WEEDS)	TATE, PETER	SS	NWS	66	03
TRAVELIN' MAN, THE	KELLEY, LEO P.	SS	FSF	70	09
ONE LOVE HAVE I	YOUNG, ROBERT F.	SS	IFS	55	04
WHO SHALL DWELL...	NEAL, H. C.	SS	PBY	62	07

Title	Author	Type	Mag	Yr	Mo
THING AND OTHER STORIES, THE	CAMPBELL, JOHN W. JR	AC	KEM	52	

SEE "WHO GOES THERE?"

Title	Author	Type	Mag	Yr	Mo
THING FROM OUTER SPACE, THE	CAMPBELL, JOHN W. JR	AC	TDM	66	

SEE "WHO GOES THERE?"

Title	Author	Type	Mag	Yr	Mo
WHO GOES THERE?	CAMPBELL, JOHN W. JR	NV	ASF	38	08
BLINDNESS	CAMPBELL, JOHN W. JR	SS	ASF	35	03
FRICTIONAL LOSSES	CAMPBELL, JOHN W. JR	NV	ASF	36	07
DEAD KNOWLEDGE	CAMPBELL, JOHN W. JR	NV	ASF	38	01
ELIMINATION	CAMPBELL, JOHN W. JR	SS	ASF	36	05
TWILIGHT	CAMPBELL, JOHN W. JR	SS	ASF	34	11
NIGHT	CAMPBELL, JOHN W. JR	NV	ASF	35	10

Title	Author	Type	Mag	Yr	Mo
THINGS	HOWARD, IVAN	AN	BEL	64	02
GIFT OF THE GODS, THE	JONES, RAYMOND F.	NV	SFS	55	01
TURN OF A CENTURY	BLISH, JAMES	SS	DSF	53	03
COURIER OF CHAOS	ANDERSON, POUL	NV	FUT	53	03
MIND OF TOMORROW (ALSO AS CONDITIONED REFLEX)	DEL REY, LESTER	SS	FUT	51	05
IN THE BEGINNING	KNIGHT, DAMON	NV	FUT	53	01
LITTLE GREEN MAN	LOOMIS, NOEL	SS	DSF	53	03

Title	Author	Type	Mag	Yr	Mo
THIRD EYE, THE	COGSWELL, THEODORE R	AC	BEL	68	09
NO GUN TO THE VICTOR (ALSO AS CONSUMER'S REPORT)	COGSWELL, THEODORE R	SS	IMG	55	10
MR. HOSKIN'S HEEL	COGSWELL, THEODORE R	SS	FUN	54	11
CABBAGE PATCH, THE	COGSWELL, THEODORE R	SS	FSF	57	12
LIMITING FACTOR	COGSWELL, THEODORE R	SS	GAL	54	04
DISASSEMBLY LINE	COGSWELL, THEODORE R	SS	BEY	54	07
SPUDGET FOR THWILBERT, A	COGSWELL, THEODORE R	SS	FUN	58	04
TRAINING DEVICE	COGSWELL, THEODORE R	SS	IMG	55	03
IMPACT WITH THE DEVIL	COGSWELL, THEODORE R	SS	FSF	56	11
MACHINE RECORD	COGSWELL, THEODORE R	SS	SFA	61	05
ONE TO A CUSTOMER	COGSWELL, THEODORE R	SS	SUP	58	06
MAN WHO KNEW GRODNIK, THE	COGSWELL, THEODORE R	SS	SCF	62	06
LOVER BOY	COGSWELL, THEODORE R	SS	BEY	54	03
OTHER CHEEK, THE	COGSWELL, THEODORE R	NA	SFA	53	05
MINIMUM SENTENCE	COGSWELL, THEODORE R	SS	GAL	53	08
SHORT COUNT	COGSWELL, THEODORE R	SS	AVS	53	01
CONVENTIONAL ENDING	COGSWELL, THEODORE R	SS	FUT	54	10

Title	Author	Type	Mag	Yr	Mo
THIRD FROM THE SUN	MATHESON, RICHARD	AC	BAN	55	02

SELECTIONS FROM "BORN OF MAN AND WOMAN"

Title	Author	Type	Mag	Yr	Mo
BORN OF MAN AND WOMAN	MATHESON, RICHARD	SS	FSF	50	SU
THIRD FROM THE SUN	MATHESON, RICHARD	SS	GAL	50	10
LOVER, WHEN YOU'RE NEAR ME	MATHESON, RICHARD	NV	GAL	52	05
SRL AD	MATHESON, RICHARD	AD			
MAD HOUSE	MATHESON, RICHARD	NV	FAN	53	02
F--- (THE FOODLEGGER)	MATHESON, RICHARD	SS	TWS	52	04
DEAR DIARY	MATHESON, RICHARD	SS	NEW	54	AN
TO FIT THE CRIME	MATHESON, RICHARD	SS	FAN	52	12
DRESS OF WHITE SILK	MATHESON, RICHARD	SS	FSF	51	10
DISAPPEARING ACT	MATHESON, RICHARD	SS	FSF	53	03
WEDDING, THE	MATHESON, RICHARD	SS	BEY	53	07
SHIPSHAPE HOME	MATHESON, RICHARD	SS	GAL	52	07
TRAVELER, THE	MATHESON, RICHARD	SS	FSF	62	02

```
THIRD GALAXY READER, THE                                            THREE TIMES INFINITY

THIRD GALAXY READER, THE   GOLD, H. L.          AN H DBL 58    LONELY ROAD              WILSON, RICHARD      SS  FSF 56 09
  PROGRAM NOTES            GOLD, H. L.          IN             LOVE                     WILSON, RICHARD      SS  FSF 52 06
  LIMITING FACTOR          COGSWELL, THEODORE R SS  GAL 54 04  HONOR                    WILSON, RICHARD      SS  SFQ 52 02
  PROTECTION               SHECKLEY, ROBERT     SS  GAL 56 04  88 BEATS 266 (SUCCESS STORY) WILSON, RICHARD  SS  FUN 57 02
  VILBAR PARTY, THE        SMITH, EVELYN E.     SS  GAL 55 01  DON'T FENCE ME IN        WILSON, RICHARD      SS  FSF 56 04
  END AS A WORLD           WALLACE, F. L.       SS  GAL 55 09  PRESS CONFERENCE (VISITOR FROM THE VOID)
  TIME IN THE ROUND        LEIBER, FRITZ        NV  GAL 57 05                           WILSON, RICHARD      SS  AMZ 53 11
  HELP! I AM DR. MORRIS GOLDPEPPER                             IT'S COLD OUTSIDE        WILSON, RICHARD      NV  IFS 56 12
                           DAVIDSON, AVRAM      NV  GAL 57 07
  WIND IS RISING, A        O'DONNEVAN, FINN     SS  GAL 57 07  THOSE WHO CAN: A SCIENCE FICTION READER
  IDEAS DIE HARD           ASIMOV, ISAAC        NV  GAL 57 10                           WILSON, ROBIN SCOTT  AN    MNT 73 09
  DEAD RINGER (ALSO AS AND THE TRUTH)                            INTRODUCTION: TO THE READER WILSON, ROBIN SCOTT IN
                           DEL REY, LESTER      SS  GAL 56 11    PLOT: THE TANGELED WEB WILSON, ROBIN SCOTT  SI
  HAUNTED CORPSE, THE      POHL, FREDERIK       SS  GAL 57 01    JAMBOREE               WILLIAMSON, JACK     SS  GAL 69 12
  MODEL OF A JUDGE, THE    MORRISON, WILLIAM    SS  GAL 53 10    PLOTTING "JAMBOREE"    WILLIAMSON, JACK     AR
  MAN IN THE JAR           KNIGHT, DAMON        SS  GAL 54 07    WE, IN SOME STRANGE POWER'S EMPLOY, MOVE ON A RIGOROUS LINE
  VOLPLA                   GUIN, WYMAN          NV  GAL 56 05                           DELANY, SAMUEL R.    NV  FSF 68 05
  HONORABLE OPPONENT       SIMAK, CLIFFORD D.   SS  GAL 56 08    THICKENING THE PLOT    DELANY, SAMUEL R.    AR
  GAME OF RAT AND DRAGON, THE  SMITH, CORDWAINER NV GAL 55 10    CHARACTER: THE DETERMINANT OF INCIDENT
                                                                                        WILSON, ROBIN SCOTT  SI
THIRD LEVEL, THE           FINNEY, JACK         AC H RIN 57      CRAZY MARO             KEYES, DANIEL        NV  FSF 60 04
  IN ENGLAND AS "THE CLOCK OF TIME"                              HOW MUCH DOES A CHARACTER COST?
                                                                                        KEYES, DANIEL        AR
THIRST QUENCHERS, THE      RAPHAEL, RICK        AC H GOL 65      PRETTY MAGGIE MONEYEYES ELLISON, HARLAN     NV  KNT 67 05
  THIRST QUENCHERS, THE    RAPHAEL, RICK        NV  ASF 63 09    WHORE WITH A HEART OF IRON PYRITES: OR, WHERE DOES A WRITER GO
  GUTTERSNIPE              RAPHAEL, RICK        NV  ASF 64 11       TO FIND A MAGGIE?   ELLISON, HARLAN      AR
  MAILMAN COMETH, THE      RAPHAEL, RICK        NV  ASF 65 02    SETTING: A LOCAL HABITATION AND A NAME
  ODD MAN IN               RAPHAEL, RICK        NV                                      WILSON, ROBIN SCOTT  SI
                                                               MAN WHO COULD NOT SEE DEVILS, THE
THIRTEEN O'CLOCK AND OTHER ZERO HOURS                                                   RUSS, JOANNA         SS  ANA 70
                           KORNBLUTH, C. M.     AC  DEL 70      ON SETTING               RUSS, JOANNA         AR
  CECIL CORWIN STORIES, EDITED BY JAMES BLISH                   SUNDANCE                 SILVERBERG, ROBERT   SS  FSF 69 06
  PREFACE                  BLISH, JAMES         IN              INTRODUCTION TO "SUNDANCE"  SILVERBERG, ROBERT AR
  THIRTEEN O'CLOCK & MR. PACKER GOES TO HELL                    THEME: TO MEAN INTENSELY WILSON, ROBIN SCOTT  SI
                           KORNBLUTH, C. M.     NV  STI 41 02    NINE LIVES             LE GUIN, URSULA K.   NV  PBY 69 11
  ROCKET OF 1955, THE      KORNBLUTH, C. M.     SS  STI 41 04    ON THEME               LE GUIN, URSULA K.   AR
  WHAT SORGHUM SAYS        KORNBLUTH, C. M.     SS  COS 41 05    ANNOTATED "MASKS", A   KNIGHT, DAMON        SS  PBY 68 07
  CRISIS!                  KORNBLUTH, C. M.     SS  SFQ 42 SP    POINT OF VIEW: WHO'S MINDING THE STORE
  REVERSIBLE REVOLUTIONS, THE  KORNBLUTH, C. M. SS  COS 41 03                            WILSON, ROBIN SCOTT  SI
  CITY IN THE SOFA, THE    KORNBLUTH, C. M.     SS  COS 41 07    PLANNERS, THE          WILHELM, KATE        SS  ORB 68 03
  GOLDEN ROAD, THE         KORNBLUTH, C. M.     NV  STI 42 03    ON POINT OF VIEW       WILHELM, KATE        AR
  MS. FOUND IN A CHINESE FORTUNE COOKIE                         FOR A WHILE THERE, HERBERT MARCUSE, I THOUGHT YOU WERE MAYBE
                           KORNBLUTH, C. M.     SS  FSF 57 07      RIGHT ABOUT ALIENATION AND  WILSON, ROBIN SCOTT  SS  FSF 72 07
                                                               POINT OF VIEW: THE QUICK-CHANGE ARTIST IN THE TYPE
THIRTY STRANGE STORIES     WELLS, H. G.         AC H ANL 97                              WILSON, ROBIN SCOTT  AR
  STRANGE ORCHID, THE (THE FLOWERING OF THE STRANGE ORCHID)     STYLE: THE DRESS OF THOUGHT  WILSON, ROBIN SCOTT  SI
                           WELLS, H. G.         SS  PMB 94 08  LISTENERS, THE (ALSO AS ROBERT MACDONALD- 2025)
  AEPYORNIS ISLAND         WELLS, H. G.         SS  PMB 94 12                            GUNN, JAMES E.       NV  GAL 68 09
  PLATTNER STORY, THE      WELLS, H. G.         SS  NRV 96 04    ON STYLE               GUNN, JAMES E.       AR
  ARGONAUTS OF THE AIR, THE  WELLS, H. G.       SS  PMY 95       GRANDY DEVIL           POHL, FREDERIK       SS  GAL 55 06
  STORY OF THE LATE MR. ELVESHAM, THE                           DAY MILLION            POHL, FREDERIK       SS  ROG 66 02
                           WELLS, H. G.         SS  IDL 96 05    ON VELOCITY EXERCISES  POHL, FREDERIK       AR
  STOLEN BACILLUS, THE     WELLS, H. G.         SS  PMB 94 06
  RED ROOM, THE            WELLS, H. G.         SS  IDL 96 03  THREADS OF TIME          SILVERBERG, ROBERT   OA H NDB 74
  MOTH, THE (A MOTH- GENUS NOVO)                                 INTRODUCTION           SILVERBERG, ROBERT   IN
                           WELLS, H. G.         SS  PGZ 95 03    THREADS OF TIME        BENFORD, GREGORY     NA  TOT 74
  IN THE ABYSS             WELLS, H. G.         SS  PRS 96 08    MARATHON PHOTOGRAPH, THE  SIMAK, CLIFFORD D. NA  TOT 74
  SLIP UNDER THE KNIFE (ALSO AS UNDER THE KNIFE)                 RIDING THE TORCH       SPINRAD, NORMAN      NA  TOT 74
                           WELLS, H. G.         SS  NRV 96 01
  RECONCILIATION, THE (THE BULLA)                             THREE BY HEINLEIN          HEINLEIN, ROBERT A.  AC H DBL 51
                           WELLS, H. G.         SS  WSL 95 12    IN ENGLAND AS "A HEINLEIN TRIAD"
  SLIP UNDER THE MICROSCOPE, A WELLS, H. G.     SS  YBK 96 01    PUPPET MASTERS, THE    HEINLEIN, ROBERT A.  NO  GAL 51 09
  IN THE AVU OBSERVATORY   WELLS, H. G.         SS  PMB 94 08    WALDO                  HEINLEIN, ROBERT A.  SN  ASF 42 08
  TRIUMPHS OF A TAXIDERMIST, THE                                MAGIC, INC. (THE DEVIL MAKES THE LAW)
                           WELLS, H. G.         SS  PGZ 94                               HEINLEIN, ROBERT A.  SN  UNK 40 09
  DEAL IN OSTRICHES, A     WELLS, H. G.         SS  PMB 94
  RAJAH'S TREASURE, THE    WELLS, H. G.         SS  PRS 96 07  THREE FOR TOMORROW        SILVERBERG, ROBERT   OA H MDT 69
  STORY OF DAVIDSON'S EYES, THE                                 EDITOR'S INTRODUCTION   SILVERBERG, ROBERT   IN
                           WELLS, H. G.         SS  PMB 95 03    FOREWORD               CLARKE, ARTHUR C.    IN
  CONE, THE                WELLS, H. G.         SS  UCN 95 09    HOW IT WAS WHEN THE PAST WENT AWAY
  PURPLE PILEUS, THE       WELLS, H. G.         SS  BAW 96 12                            SILVERBERG, ROBERT   NA  TFT 69
  CATASTROPHE, A           WELLS, H. G.         SS  NBG 95 08    EVE OF RUMOKO, THE     ZELAZNY, ROGER       NA  TFT 69
  MARI TERRIBLE            WELLS, H. G.         SS  97           WE ALL DIE NAKED       BLISH, JAMES         NA  TFT 69
  APPLE, THE               WELLS, H. G.         SS  IDL 96 10
  SAD STORY OF A DRAMATIC CRITIC, THE                         THREE MARTIAN NOVELS      BURROUGHS, EDGAR R.  AC L DOV 62
                           WELLS, H. G.         SS  BON 15       ILLUSTRATIONS          ST. JOHN, J. ALLEN   IL
  JILTING OF JANE, THE     WELLS, H. G.         SS  97           THUVIA, MAID OF MARS   BURROUGHS, EDGAR R.  NO  ASW 16 04
  LOST INHERITANCE, THE    WELLS, H. G.         SS  97           CHESSMEN OF MARS, THE  BURROUGHS, EDGAR R.  NO  AAS 22 02
  POLLOCK AND THE PORROH MAN  WELLS, H. G.      SS  NBG 95 05    MASTER MINDS OF MARS, THE  BURROUGHS, EDGAR R. NO  ASA 27
  SEA-RAIDERS, THE         WELLS, H. G.         SS  WSL 96 12
  IN THE MODERN VEIN: AN UNSYMPATHETIC LOVE STORY (A BARDLET'S  THREE NOVELS            KNIGHT, DAMON        AC H DBL 67
     ROMANCE)              WELLS, H. G.         SS  TTH 94 03    RULE GOLDEN            KNIGHT, DAMON        NV  SFA 54 06
  LORD OF THE DYNAMOS, THE WELLS, H. G.         SS  PMB 94 09    NATURAL STATE          KNIGHT, DAMON        NA  GAL 54 01
  TREASURE IN THE FOREST, THE  WELLS, H. G.     SS  PMB 94       DYING MAN, THE (DIO)   KNIGHT, DAMON        SN  INF 57 09

THIS ISLAND EARTH          JONES, RAYMOND F.    NO H SHS 52   THREE SCIENCE FICTION NOVELS  BURROUGHS, EDGAR R. AC L DOV 63
  ALIEN MACHINE, THE       JONES, RAYMOND F.    NV  TWS 49 06    ILLUSTRATIONS          ST. JOHN, J. ALLEN   IL
  SHROUD OF SECRECY, THE   JONES, RAYMOND F.    NV  TWS 49 12    AT THE EARTH'S CORE    BURROUGHS, EDGAR R.  NO  ASW 14 04
  GREATER CONFLICT, THE    JONES, RAYMOND F.    NV  TWS 50 02    PELLUCIDAR             BURROUGHS, EDGAR R.  NO  ASC 15 05
                                                                TANAR OF PELLUCIDAR    BURROUGHS, EDGAR R.  NO  BBM 29 03
THIS SIDE OF INFINITY      CARR, TERRY          AN  ACE 72 09
  INTRODUCTION             CARR, TERRY          IN            THREE SCIENCE FICTION NOVELS  TAINE, JOHN       AC L DOV 64
  REALITY TRIP, THE        SILVERBERG, ROBERT   NV  IFS 70 05    TIME STREAM, THE       TAINE, JOHN          NO  WOS 31 12
  THIS MORTAL MOUNTAIN     ZELAZNY, ROGER       NV  IFS 67 03    PURPLE SAPPHIRE, THE   TAINE, JOHN          NO  DUT 24
  SUNDOWN                  REDD, DAVID          NV  FSF 67 12
  TOYS                     PURDOM, TOM          SS  ASF 67 10  THREE STORIES            MOSKOWITZ, SAM       AN H DBL 67
  RIDE A TIN CAN           LAFFERTY, R. A.      SS  IFS 70 04    ALSO AS "THE MOON ERA" AND "A SENSE OF WONDER"
  LAST CRUSADE, THE        SMITH, GEORGE HUDSON SS  IFS 55 02    SENSE OF WONDER, THE   MOSKOWITZ, SAM       IN
  RESIDENT WITCH           SCHMITZ, JAMES H.    NV  ASF 70 05    MOLE PIRATE, THE       LEINSTER, MURRAY     SN  ASF 34 11
  AND THE STAGNATION OF THE HEART                               MOON ERA, THE          WILLIAMSON, JACK     NV  WOS 32 02
                           ALDISS, BRIAN W.     SS  NWS 68 12    EXILES ON ASPERUS      WYNDHAM, JOHN        NV  WSQ 33 WI

THOSE IDIOTS FROM EARTH    WILSON, RICHARD      AC  BAL 57    THREE TIMES INFINITY      MARGULIES, LEO       AN  GMB 58
  THOSE IDIOTS FROM EARTH  WILSON, RICHARD      SS  NEW 57 AC   LORELEI OF THE RED MIST  BRADBURY, RAY
  INHABITED, THE           WILSON, RICHARD      NV  GAL 53 01                           AND BRACKETT, LEIGH  NV C PLS 46 SU
  HOAXTERS, THE            WILSON, RICHARD      NV  GAL 52 06    GOLDEN HELIX, THE      STURGEON, THEODORE   NA  TWS 54 SU
```

DESTINATION MOON	HEINLEIN, ROBERT A.	NV	SSM	50	09
THREE TO DORSAI!	DICKSON, GORDON R.	AC H	NDB	75	
INTRODUCTION	DICKSON, GORDON R.	IN			
PROLOGUE	DICKSON, GORDON R.	MS			
NECROMANCER	DICKSON, GORDON R.	NO	DBL	62	
INTERLUDE	DICKSON, GORDON R.	MS			
TACTICS OF MISTAKE	DICKSON, GORDON R.	NO	ASF	70	10
INTERLUDE	DICKSON, GORDON R.	MS			
DORSAI!	DICKSON, GORDON R.	NO	ASF	59	05
EPILIGUE	DICKSON, GORDON R.	MS			
THREE TRIPS IN TIME AND SPACE	SILVERBERG, ROBERT	OA H	HAW	73	
FOREWORD	SILVERBERG, ROBERT	IN			
INTRODUCTION	SILVERBERG, ROBERT	IN			
FLASH CROWD	NIVEN, LARRY	NA	TTT	73	
YOU'LL TAKE THE HIGH ROAD	BRUNNER, JOHN	NA	TTT	73	
RUMFUDDLE	VANCE, JACK	NA	TTT	73	
THREE WORLDS OF FUTURITY	ST. CLAIR, MARGARET	DC	ACE	64	
EVERLASTING FOOD, THE	ST. CLAIR, MARGARET	NV	TWS	50	12
IDRIS' PIG (THE SACRED MARTIAN PIG)					
	ST. CLAIR, MARGARET	NV	STS	49	07
RAGES, THE (RATIONS OF TANTALUS)					
	ST. CLAIR, MARGARET	NV	FUN	54	07
ROBERTA	ST. CLAIR, MARGARET	SS	GAL	62	10
ISLAND OF THE HANDS, THE	ST. CLAIR, MARGARET	SS	WRT	52	09
THRONE OF SATURN, THE	WRIGHT, S. FOWLER	AC H	ARK	49	
NEW GODS LEAD, THE	WRIGHT, S. FOWLER	AC	JAR	32	
TEMPERATURE OF GEHENNA SUE, THE					
	WRIGHT, S. FOWLER	SS			
ORIGINAL SIN	WRIGHT, S. FOWLER	SS	AFR	50	13
THROUGH A GLASS, CLEARLY	ASIMOV, ISAAC	AC	FSP	67	
IT'S SUCH A BEAUTIFUL DAY	ASIMOV, ISAAC	NV	STR	54	03
BELIEF	ASIMOV, ISAAC	NV	ASF	53	10
BREEDS THERE A MAN...?	ASIMOV, ISAAC	NV	ASF	51	06
C-CHUTE, THE	ASIMOV, ISAAC	NV	GAL	51	10
THROUGH TIME AND SPACE WITH FERDINAND FEGHOOT					
	BRIARTON, GRENDEL	AC H	PDX	62	
IN "THE COMPLETE FEGHOOT"					
ILLUSTRATIONS	ARISS, BRUCE	IL			
50 FEGHOOT PUNS, 45 FROM F&SF AND 5 ORIGINAL					
	BRIARTON, GRENDEL	MS			
THUNDER AND ROSES	STURGEON, THEODORE	AC H	JOS	57	
8 STORIES FROM "A WAY HOME"					
INTRODUCTION	CONKLIN, GROFF	IN			
MEWHU'S JET	STURGEON, THEODORE	NV	ASF	46	11
AND MY FEAR IS GREAT	STURGEON, THEODORE	NA	BEY	53	07
MINORITY REPORT	STURGEON, THEODORE	SS	FSF	49	FL
HURKLE IS A HAPPY BEAST, THE	STURGEON, THEODORE	SS	FSF	49	FL
THUNDER AND ROSES	STURGEON, THEODORE	SS	ASF	47	11
BULKHEAD (WHO?)	STURGEON, THEODORE	NV	GAL	55	03
TINY AND THE MONSTER	STURGEON, THEODORE	NV	ASF	47	05
WAY HOME, A	STURGEON, THEODORE	SS	AMZ	53	05
TIGER BY THE TAIL	NOURSE, ALAN E.	AC H	MCK	61	
AND OTHER SCIENCE FICTION STORIES					
IN ENGLAND AS "BEYOND INFINITY"					
TIGER BY THE TAIL	NOURSE, ALAN E.	SS	GAL	51	11
NIGHTMARE BROTHER	NOURSE, ALAN E.	NV	ASF	53	02
PROBLEM	NOURSE, ALAN E.	SS	GAL	56	10
COFFIN CURE, THE	NOURSE, ALAN E.	SS	GAL	57	04
BRIGHTSIDE CROSSING	NOURSE, ALAN E.	NV	GAL	56	01
NATIVE SOIL, THE	NOURSE, ALAN E.	SS	FUN	57	07
LOVE THY VIMP	NOURSE, ALAN E.	SS	FSF	52	04
LETTER OF THE LAW	NOURSE, ALAN E.	SS	IFS	54	01
FAMILY RESEMBLANCE	NOURSE, ALAN E.	SS	ASF	53	12
TIME AND STARS	ANDERSON, POUL	AC H	DBL	64	
BRITISH EDITION OMITS "EVE TIMES FOUR"					
NO TRUCE WITH KINGS	ANDERSON, POUL	NV	FSF	63	06
TURNING POINT	ANDERSON, POUL	NV	IFS	63	05
ESCAPE FROM ORBIT	ANDERSON, POUL	NV	AMZ	62	10
EPILOGUE	ANDERSON, POUL	SN	ASF	62	03
CRITIQUE OF IMPURE REASON, THE					
	ANDERSON, POUL	NV	IFS	62	11
EVE TIMES FOUR	ANDERSON, POUL	NV	FAN	60	04
TIME AND THE RIDDLE	FAST, HOWARD	AC H	WRP	75	
FOREWORD	FAST, HOWARD	IN			
INTRODUCTION	FAST, HOWARD	IN			
EDGE OF TOMORROW, THE (OMITS STORY "THE FIRST MEN")					
	FAST, HOWARD	AC	BAN	61	06
GENERAL ZAPPED AN ANGEL, THE	FAST, HOWARD	OC	MOR	70	
TOUCH OF INFINITY, A	FAST, HOWARD	OC	MOR	73	
ECHINOMASTUS CONTENTII	FAST, HOWARD	SS			
TRAP, THE	FAST, HOWARD	NA			
HUNTER, THE	FAST, HOWARD	NV			
AFTERWORD	FAST, HOWARD	MS			
TIME CURVE, THE	MOSKOWITZ & ELWOOD	AN	TWR	68	
UNTO HIM THAT HATH	DEL REY, LESTER	NV	SSF	52	11
NICE GIRL WITH FIVE HUSBANDS	LEIBER, FRITZ	SS	GAL	51	04
DEATH OF A DINOSAUR	MOSKOWITZ, SAM	SS	AMZ	56	08
TERROR OUT OF TIME	WILLIAMSON, JACK	SS	ASF	33	12
TIME WOUNDS ALL HEELS	BLOCH, ROBERT	SS	FAD	42	04
OVER THE RIVER AND THROUGH THE WOODS					
	SIMAK, CLIFFORD D.	SS	AMZ	65	05
GUN FOR DINOSAUR, A	DE CAMP, L. SPRAGUE	NV	GAL	56	03
OPERATION PEEP (ALSO AS PAWLEY'S PEEPHOLES)					
	WYNDHAM, JOHN	SS	SUS	51	SU

GREAT JUDGE, THE	VAN VOGT, A. E.	SS	FBK	48	03
GIFTS OF ASTI, THE	NORTON, ANDRE	SS	FBK	48	03
TIME DWELLER, THE	MOORCOCK, MICHAEL	AC H	HDV	69	
TIME DWELLER, THE	MOORCOCK, MICHAEL	SS	NWS	64	02
ESCAPE FROM EVENING	MOORCOCK, MICHAEL	NV	NWS	65	03
DEEP FIX, THE (AS JAMES COLVIN)					
	MOORCOCK, MICHAEL	NV	SCF	64	04
GOLDEN BARGE, THE (AS WILLIAM BARCLAY)					
	MOORCOCK, MICHAEL	SS	NWS	65	10
WOLF	MOORCOCK, MICHAEL	SS		66	
CONSUMING PASSION	MOORCOCK, MICHAEL	SS	NWS	66	04
RUINS, THE (AS JAMES COLVIN)	MOORCOCK, MICHAEL	SS	NWS	66	04
PLEASURE GARDEN OF FELIPE SAGITTARIUS, THE					
	MOORCOCK, MICHAEL	SS	NWS	65	09
MOUNTAIN, THE	MOORCOCK, MICHAEL	SS	NWS	65	02
TIME IN ADVANCE	TENN, WILLIAM	AC	BAN	58	06
FIREWATER	TENN, WILLIAM	SN	ASF	52	02
TIME IN ADVANCE	TENN, WILLIAM	NV	GAL	56	08
SICKNESS, THE	TENN, WILLIAM	NV	INF	55	11
WINTHROP WAS STUBBORN (TIME WAITS FOR WINTHROP)					
	TENN, WILLIAM	NA	GAL	57	08
TIME MACHINE AND OTHER STORIES, THE					
	WELLS, H. G.	AC H	HLT	95	
TIME MACHINE, THE	WELLS, H. G.	NA	NRV	95	01
EMPIRE OF THE ANTS, THE	WELLS, H. G.	SS	SND	05	12
VISION OF JUDGEMENT, A	WELLS, H. G.	SS	BUT	99	09
LAND IRONCLADS, THE	WELLS, H. G.	NV	SND	03	12
BEAUTIFUL SUIT, THE (A MOONLIGHT FABLE)					
	WELLS, H. G.	SS	COL	09	04
DOOR IN THE WALL, THE	WELLS, H. G.	SS	DCH	06	07
PEARL OF LOVE, THE	WELLS, H. G.	SS		24	
COUNTRY OF THE BLIND, THE	WELLS, H. G.	SS	SND	04	04
TIME MACHINE AND OTHER STORIES, THE (PB)					
	WELLS, H. G.	AC	SBS	63	
WORD TO THE READER, A	HURLEY, RICHARD J.	IN			
TIME MACHINE, THE	WELLS, H. G.	NA	NRV	95	01
EMPIRE OF THE ANTS, THE	WELLS, H. G.	SS	SND	05	12
COUNTRY OF THE BLIND, THE	WELLS, H. G.	SS	SND	04	04
MAN WHO COULD WORK MIRACLES, THE					
	WELLS, H. G.	SS	ILN	98	07
TIME OF INFINITY, THE	DERLETH, AUGUST	AN	CNL	63	
LAST 9 STORIES FROM "THE OUTER REACHES"					
TIME OF THE EYE, THE	ELLISON, HARLAN	AC	PTH	74	
LAST 12 STORIES FROM "ALONE AGAINST TOMORROW"					
TIME OUT FOR TOMORROW	WILSON, RICHARD	AC	BAL	62	
KIN (SHOW YOUR MIGHT)	WILSON, RICHARD	SS	FUN	56	05
BIG FIX, THE	WILSON, RICHARD	NV	INF	56	08
WASP (THE WASP)	WILSON, RICHARD	SS	FAN	54	06
ABUNDANCE OF GOOD THINGS, AN (HAVE IT YOUR OWN WAY)					
	WILSON, RICHARD	SS	AMZ	54	05
TIME OUT FOR TOMORROW	WILSON, RICHARD	SS	SCF	57	12
TUNNEL UNDER THE WORLD, THE (TRAVELING COMPANION WANTED)					
	WILSON, RICHARD	SS	GAL	59	06
BEST POSSIBLE WORLD, THE	WILSON, RICHARD	SS	NWS	60	09
VOICE OF THE DIAPHRAGM, THE	WILSON, RICHARD	SS	GAL	58	05
QRM	WILSON, RICHARD	SS	FSF	57	04
UBIQUITOUS YOU, THE (THE IN-BETWEENS)					
	WILSON, RICHARD	SS	FUT	57	SP
JUST CALL ME IRISH	WILSON, RICHARD	SS	FUT	58	06
LOCUS FOCUS, THE	WILSON, RICHARD	SS	SFQ	57	08
TIME OUT OF MIND	BOULLE, PIERRE	OC H	VAN	66	
TIME OUT OF MIND	BOULLE, PIERRE	NV			
MAN WHO PICKED UP PINS, THE	BOULLE, PIERRE	SS			
MIRACLE, THE	BOULLE, PIERRE	SS			
PERFECT ROBOT, THE	BOULLE, PIERRE	SS			
ENIGMATIC SAINT, THE	BOULLE, PIERRE	NV			
LUNIANS, THE	BOULLE, PIERRE	NV			
DIABOLICAL WEAPON, THE	BOULLE, PIERRE	SS			
AGE OF WISDOM, THE	BOULLE, PIERRE	NV			
MAN WHO HATED MACHINES, THE	BOULLE, PIERRE	NV			
LOVE AND GRAVITY	BOULLE, PIERRE	SS			
HALLUCINATION, THE	BOULLE, PIERRE	SS			
E=MC2	BOULLE, PIERRE	NV			
TIME PROBE: THE SCIENCES IN SF.					
	CLARKE, ARTHUR C.	AN H	DCT	66	
SCIENCE AND SCIENCE FICTION	CLARKE, ARTHUR C.	IN			
AND HE BUILT A CROOKED HOUSE	HEINLEIN, ROBERT A.	SS	ASF	41	02
WABBLER, THE	LEINSTER, MURRAY	SS	ASF	42	10
WEATHER MAN, THE	THOMAS, THEODORE L.	SN	ASF	62	06
ARTIFACT BUSINESS, THE	SILVERBERG, ROBERT	SS	FUN	57	04
GRANDPA	SCHMITZ, JAMES H.	SS	ASF	55	02
NOT FINAL!	ASIMOV, ISAAC	SS	ASF	41	10
LITTLE BLACK BAG, THE	KORNBLUTH, C. M.	NV	ASF	50	07
BLINDNESS, THE	LATHAM, PHILIP	NV	ASF	46	07
TAKE A DEEP BREATH (THE OTHER SIDE OF THE SKY)					
	CLARKE, ARTHUR C.	SS	INF	57	09
POTTERS OF FIRSK, THE	VANCE, JACK	SS	ASF	50	05
TISSUE-CULTURE KING, THE	HUXLEY, JULIAN	SS	AMZ	27	08
TIME TO COME	DERLETH, AUGUST	OA H	FSY	54	
FOREWORD	DERLETH, AUGUST	IN			
BUTCH	ANDERSON, POUL	NV	NWS	55	07
PAUSE, THE	ASIMOV, ISAAC	SS			
KEEPER OF THE DREAM	BEAUMONT, CHARLES	SS		54	
NO MORNING AFTER	CLARKE, ARTHUR C.	SS	FSF	56	07
BLIGHT, THE	COX, ARTHUR JEAN	NV			
HOLE IN THE SKY	COX, IRVING E. JR.	NV			

```
TIME TO COME
  JON'S WORLD              DICK, PHILIP K.         NV
  WHITE PINNACLE, THE      JACOBI, CARL           SS
  WINNER TAKE ALL          ROCKLYNNE, ROSS        NV
  PARADISE II              SHECKLEY, ROBERT       SS   NWS 55 07
  PHOENIX                  SMITH, CLARK ASHTON    SS
  BAXBR DAXBR              SMITH, EVELYN E.       SS   FSF 56 09

TIME TO COME (10 OF 12, BRK 58)
                          DERLETH, AUGUST        OA   BRK 58 12
  PARADISE II              SHECKLEY, ROBERT       SS   NWS 55 07
  PHOENIX                  SMITH, CLARK ASHTON    SS
  BUTCH                    ANDERSON, POUL         NV   NWS 55 07
  PAUSE, THE               ASIMOV, ISAAC         SS
  KEEPER OF THE DREAM      BEAUMONT, CHARLES      SS        54
  NO MORNING AFTER         CLARKE, ARTHUR C.      SS   FSF 56 07
  HOLE IN THE SKY          COX, IRVING E. JR.     NV
  JON'S WORLD              DICK, PHILIP K.        NV
  WHITE PINNACLE, THE      JACOBI, CARL           SS
  WINNER TAKE ALL          ROCKLYNNE, ROSS        NV

TIME TO COME (10 OF 12, TWR 65)
                          DERLETH, AUGUST        OA   TWR 65
  BUTCH                    ANDERSON, POUL         NV   NWS 55 07
  PAUSE, THE               ASIMOV, ISAAC         SS
  KEEPER OF THE DREAM      BEAUMONT, CHARLES      SS        54
  NO MORNING AFTER         CLARKE, ARTHUR C.      SS   FSF 56 07
  BLIGHT, THE              COX, ARTHUR JEAN       NV
  HOLE IN THE SKY          COX, IRVING E. JR.     NV
  JON'S WORLD              DICK, PHILIP K.        NV
  WINNER TAKE ALL          ROCKLYNNE, ROSS        NV
  PARADISE II              SHECKLEY, ROBERT       SS   NWS 55 07
  PHOENIX                  SMITH, CLARK ASHTON    SS

TIME TRANSFER             SELLINGS, ARTHUR       AC H JOS 56
  WORDLESS ONES, THE       SELLINGS, ARTHUR       SS
  AWAKENING, THE           SELLINGS, ARTHUR       SS
  SOLILOQUY                SELLINGS, ARTHUR       SS
  ESCAPE MECHANISM         SELLINGS, ARTHUR       SS   FUN 55 08
  JUKEBOX                  SELLINGS, ARTHUR       SS   FUN 55 12
  CATEGORICAL IMPERATIVE (THE CATEGORY INVENTORS)
                          SELLINGS, ARTHUR       NV   GAL 56 02
  PENTAGRAM                SELLINGS, ARTHUR       SS   SAT 58 10
  PROXIES, THE             SELLINGS, ARTHUR       SS   IFS 55 10
  FROM UP THERE            SELLINGS, ARTHUR       SS
  START IN LIFE, A         SELLINGS, ARTHUR       SS   GAL 54 09
  TIME TRANSFER            SELLINGS, ARTHUR       SS
  HAUNTING, THE            SELLINGS, ARTHUR       SS   AUT 53 10
  CONTROL ROOM             SELLINGS, ARTHUR       SS
  AGE OF KINDNESS, THE     SELLINGS, ARTHUR       SS   GAL 54 11
  FIGMENT, THE             SELLINGS, ARTHUR       SS   FUN 55 02
  TRANSFER, THE            SELLINGS, ARTHUR       SS

TIME TRANSFER (11 OF 16)  SELLINGS, ARTHUR       AC   CPT 66
  WORDLESS ONES, THE       SELLINGS, ARTHUR       SS
  ESCAPE MECHANISM         SELLINGS, ARTHUR       SS   FUN 55 08
  JUKEBOX                  SELLINGS, ARTHUR       SS   FUN 55 12
  CATEGORICAL IMPERATIVE (THE CATEGORY INVENTORS)
                          SELLINGS, ARTHUR       NV   GAL 56 02
  PROXIES, THE             SELLINGS, ARTHUR       SS   IFS 55 10
  FROM UP THERE            SELLINGS, ARTHUR       SS
  START IN LIFE, A         SELLINGS, ARTHUR       SS   GAL 54 09
  TIME TRANSFER            SELLINGS, ARTHUR       SS
  CONTROL ROOM             SELLINGS, ARTHUR       SS
  AGE OF KINDNESS, THE     SELLINGS, ARTHUR       SS   GAL 54 11
  FIGMENT, THE             SELLINGS, ARTHUR       SS   FUN 55 02

TIME UNTAMED              HOWARD, IVAN           AN   BEL 67
  SALLY                    ASIMOV, ISAAC         SS   FAN 53 05
  YOU'LL NEVER GO HOME AGAIN (ALSO AS BEACHHEAD)
                          SIMAK, CLIFFORD D.     SS   FAD 51 07
  EYE OF TANDYLA, THE      DE CAMP, L. SPRAGUE    NV   FAD 51 05
  TOMORROW AND TOMORROW    BRADBURY, RAY         SS   FAN 51 11
  HUNGRY EYE, THE          BLOCH, ROBERT         NV   FAN 59 05
  DARK ROOM, THE           STURGEON, THEODORE    NV   FAN 53 08
  ETERNAL EVE, THE         WYNDHAM, JOHN         NV   AMZ 50 09
  I'M LOOKING FOR "JEFF"   LEIBER, FRITZ         SS   FAN 52 FL

TIME WAITS FOR WINTHROP, AND FOUR OTHER SHORT NOVELS
                          POHL, FREDERIK        AN H DBL 62
  TIME WAITS FOR WINTHROP (ALSO AS WINTHROP WAS STUBBORN)
                          TENN, WILLIAM         NA   GAL 57 08
  ACCIDENTAL FLIGHT        WALLACE, F. L.        NA   GAL 52 04
  TO MARRY MEDUSA          STURGEON, THEODORE    NA   GAL 58 08
  NATURAL STATE            KNIGHT, DAMON         NA   GAL 54 01
  GALLEY SLAVE             ASIMOV, ISAAC         NV   GAL 57 12

TIME: X                   TUCKER, WILSON        AC   BAN 55 12
  SEE "THE SCIENCE FICTION SUBTREASURY"

TIME-JUMP                 BRUNNER, JOHN         AC   DEL 73 12
  INTRODUCTION             BRUNNER, JOHN         IN
  GALACTIC CONSUMER REPORT NO. 1: INEXPENSIVE TIME MACHINES
                          BRUNNER, JOHN         FA   GAL 65 12
  SPEECH IS SILVER         BRUNNER, JOHN         SS   AMZ 65 04
  WARP AND THE WOOF-WOOF, THE  BRUNNER, JOHN     SS   SCF 66 02
  PRODUCT OF THE MASSES, THE   BRUNNER, JOHN     NV   IFS 68 04
  GALACTIC CONSUMER REPORT NO. 2: AUTOMATIC TWIN-TUBE WISHING
    MACHINES               BRUNNER, JOHN         FA   GAL 66 06
  DEATH DO US PART         BRUNNER, JOHN         SS   SCF 55 11
  COINCIDENCE DAY          BRUNNER, JOHN         SS   ASF 65 02
  WHIRLIGIG|               BRUNNER, JOHN         SS   BYI 67 11
  GALACTIC CONSUMER REPORT NO. 3: A SURVEY OF THE MEMBERSHIP
                          BRUNNER, JOHN         FA   GAL 67 12
  NOBODY AXED YOU          BRUNNER, JOHN         NV   NWS 65 05

TIMELESS STORIES FOR TODAY AND TOMORROW
                          BRADBURY, RAY         AN   BAN 52 09
  INTRODUCTION             BRADBURY, RAY         IN
  HOUR AFTER WESTERLY, THE COATES, ROBERT M.     SS   NYM 47 11
  HOUSING PROBLEM          KUTTNER, HENRY        SS   CHM 44 10
  PORTABLE PHONOGRAPH, THE CLARK, WALTER VAN T.  SS        41
  NONE BEFORE ME           CARROLL, SIDNEY       SS   CMP 49 07
  PUTZI                    BEMLEMANS, LUDWIG     SS        39
  DAEMON LOVER, THE        JACKSON, SHIRLEY      NV        48
  MISS WINTERS AND THE WIND  GOVAN, CHRISTINE N. SS   TOM 46 05
  MR. DEATH AND THE REDHEADED WOMAN
                          EUSTIS, HELEN         SS   SEP 50 02
  JEREMY IN THE WIND       KNEALE, NIGEL         SS        50
  GLASS EYE, THE           CROSS, JOHN KEIR      SS        46
  SAINT KATY THE VIRGIN    STEINBECK, JOHN       SS        38
  NIGHT FLIGHT             JOHNSON, JOSEPHINE    SS   HRP 44 02
  COCOON, THE              GOODWIN, JOHN B. L.   SS   STO 46 10
  HAND, THE                SMITTER, WESSEL H.    SS   STO 47 02
  SOUND MACHINE, THE       DAHL, ROALD           SS   NYM 49 09
  LAOCOON COMPLEX, THE     FURNAS, J. C.         SS   ESQ 37 04
  I AM WAITING             ISHERWOOD, C.         SS   NYM 39 10
  WITNESSES, THE           SANSOM, WILLIAM       SS        44
  ENORMOUS RADIO, THE      CHEEVER, JOHN         SS   NYM 47 05
  HEARTBURN                CALISHER, HORTENSE    SS   AMM 51 01
  SUPREMACY OF URUGUAY, THE  WHITE, E. B.        SS   NYM 33 11
  PEDESTRIAN, THE (REP 51 08)  BRADBURY, RAY     SS   FSF 52 02
  NOTE FOR THE MILKMAN, A   CARROLL, SIDNEY       SS   TDW 50 04
  EIGHT MISTRESSES, THE     HROLDA, JEAN          SS   ESQ 37 08
  IN THE PENAL COLONY       KAFKA, FRANZ          SS        48
  INFLEXIBLE LOGIC          MALONEY, RUSSELL      SS   NYM 40 02

TIMES WITHOUT NUMBER      BRUNNER, JOHN         NO   ACE 62
  SPOIL OF YESTERDAY       BRUNNER, JOHN         NV   SFA 62 03
  WORD NOT WRITTEN, THE    BRUNNER, JOHN         NV   SFA 62 06
  FULLNESS OF TIME, THE    BRUNNER, JOHN         NV   SFA 62 07

TIMES 4 (ABRIDGED STORIES)  ALLEN, VIRGINIA F.   AN   FAL
  TIME MACHINE, THE        WELLS, H. G.          NA   NRV 95 01
  THIEF IN TIME, A         SHECKLEY, ROBERT      NV   GAL 54 07
  FACE IN THE PHOTO, THE (TIME HAS NO BOUNDARIES)
                          FINNEY, JACK          SS   SEP 62 10
  BUSINESS, AS USUAL, THE  REYNOLDS, MACK        SS   FSF 52 06

TIMETRACKS               LAUMER, KEITH         AC   BAL 72 04
  TIMESWEEPERS, THE        LAUMER, KEITH         NV   ASF 69 08
  DEVIL YOU DON'T, THE     LAUMER, KEITH         NV   ANA 70
  TIME THIEVES, THE (THE STAR-SENT KNAVES)
                          LAUMER, KEITH         NV   WOT 63 06
  OTHER SKY, THE (THE FURTHER SKY)
                          LAUMER, KEITH         SN   AMZ 64 12
  MIND OUT OF TIME, THE    LAUMER, KEITH         SS   FRS 68

TITAN, THE               MILLER, P. SCHUYLER   AC H FPS 52
  BRITISH EDITION OMITS "THE ARRHENIUS HORROR"
  TITAN, THE               MILLER, P. SCHUYLER   NV   MVT 34 WI
  AS NEVER WAS             MILLER, P. SCHUYLER   SS   ASF 44 01
  OLD MAN MULLIGAN         MILLER, P. SCHUYLER   NV   ASF 40 12
  SPAWN                    MILLER, P. SCHUYLER   SS   WRT 39 08
  IN THE GOOD OLD SUMMERTIME  MILLER, P. SCHUYLER  SS  ASF 40 03
  GLEEPS                   MILLER, P. SCHUYLER   SS   ASF 43 07
  ARRHENIUS HORROR, THE    MILLER, P. SCHUYLER   SS   AMZ 31 09
  FORGOTTEN (THE FORGOTTEN MAN OF SPACE)
                          MILLER, P. SCHUYLER   SS   WOS 33 04

TO HERE AND THE EASEL     STURGEON, THEODORE    AC H GOL 73
  TO HERE AND THE EASEL    STURGEON, THEODORE    SN   SSN 54
  SKILLS OF XANADU, THE    STURGEON, THEODORE    NV   GAL 56 07
  THERE IS NO DEFENSE      STURGEON, THEODORE    NV   ASF 48 02
  PERFECT HOST, THE        STURGEON, THEODORE    NV   WRT 48 11
  GRAVEYARD READER, THE    STURGEON, THEODORE    NV   SCF 58 10
  SHOTTLE BOP              STURGEON, THEODORE    SS   UNK 41 02

TO OPEN THE SKY           SILVERBERG, ROBERT    NO   BAL 67 05
  BLUE FIRE                SILVERBERG, ROBERT    NV   GAL 65 06
  WARRIORS OF LIGHT, THE   SILVERBERG, ROBERT    NV   GAL 65 12
  WHERE THE CHANGED ONES GO  SILVERBERG, ROBERT  NV   GAL 66 02
  LAZARUS COME FORTH|      SILVERBERG, ROBERT    NV   GAL 66 04
  TO OPEN THE SKY (OPEN THE SKY)
                          SILVERBERG, ROBERT    NV   GAL 66 06

TO RIDE PEGASUS           MCCAFFREY, ANNE       AC   BAL 73 08
  TO RIDE PEGASUS          MCCAFFREY, ANNE       NV   NEW 73 AC
  WOMANLY TALENT, A        MCCAFFREY, ANNE       SN   ASF 69 02
  APPLE                    MCCAFFREY, ANNE       NV   NEW 69 AN
  BRIDLE FOR PEGASUS, A    MCCAFFREY, ANNE       NV   ASF 73 07

TO THE END OF TIME        STAPLEDON, OLAF       AC H FKW 53
  THE BEST OF OLAF STAPLEDON, EDITED BY BASIL DAVENPORT
  VISION OF OLAF STAPLEDON, THE
                          DAVENPORT, BASIL      AR
  LAST AND FIRST MEN       STAPLEDON, OLAF       NO   MTH 30
  STAR MAKER, THE          STAPLEDON, OLAF       NO   MTH 37
  ODD JOHN                 STAPLEDON, OLAF       NO   MTH 35
  SIRIUS                   STAPLEDON, OLAF       NO   SKW 44
  FLAMES, THE              STAPLEDON, OLAF       NO   SKW 47

TO THE END OF TIME AND OTHER STORIES
                          WILLIAMS, ROBERT M.   DC   ACE 60
  TO THE END OF TIME       WILLIAMS, ROBERT M.   SS   SSS 50 04
  WHERE TALL TOWERS GLEAM  WILLIAMS, ROBERT M.   SS   FAD 50 08
  HOMEWARD BOUND           WILLIAMS, ROBERT M.   SS   STS 49 11
  WHEN THE SPOILERS CAME   WILLIAMS, ROBERT M.   NV   PLS 52 05
  LIKE ALARM BELLS RINGING WILLIAMS, ROBERT M.   SS   AMZ 47 01

TO THE STARS             SILVERBERG, ROBERT    AN H HAW 71
  INTRODUCTION             SILVERBERG, ROBERT    IN
```

TO THE STARS

COMMON TIME	BLISH, JAMES	SS	SFQ	53	08
FOUR IN ONE	KNIGHT, DAMON	NV	GAL	53	02
OZYMANDIAS	SILVERBERG, ROBERT	SS	INF	58	11
END OF THE LINE, THE	SCHMITZ, JAMES H.	NV	ASF	51	07
WALK IN THE DARK, A	CLARKE, ARTHUR C.	SS	TWS	50	08
PLANETOID IDIOT	GOTLEIB, PHYLLIS	NV	FSF	67	05
KEYS TO DECEMBER, THE	ZELAZNY, ROGER	SS	NWS	66	08
GYPSY	ANDERSON, POUL	SS	ASF	50	01

TO WORLDS BEYOND — SILVERBERG, ROBERT — AC H CHL 65

OLD MAN, THE	SILVERBERG, ROBERT	SS	IMG	57	04
NEW MEN FOR MARS	SILVERBERG, ROBERT	NV	SUP	57	06
COLLECTING TEAM	SILVERBERG, ROBERT	SS	AUT	57	06
DOUBLE DARE	SILVERBERG, ROBERT	SS	GAL	56	11
OVERLORD'S THUMB, THE	SILVERBERG, ROBERT	NV	INF	58	03
OZYMANDIAS	SILVERBERG, ROBERT	SS	INF	58	11
CERTAINTY	SILVERBERG, ROBERT	SS	ASF	59	11
MIND FOR BUSINESS	SILVERBERG, ROBERT	SS	ASF	56	09
MISFIT	SILVERBERG, ROBERT	SS	SUP	57	12

TOMORROW AND TOMORROW — KNIGHT, DAMON — AN H SAS 73

SOUND-SWEEP, THE	BALLARD, J. G.	NV	SCF	60	02
HOBSON'S CHOICE	BESTER, ALFRED	SS	FSF	52	08
MAN WHO ALWAYS KNEW, THE	BUDRYS, ALGIS	SS	ASF	56	04
SIGN IN SPACE, A	CALVINO, ITALO	SS		68	
PORTABLE PHONOGRAPH, THE	CLARK, WALTER VAN T.	SS		41	
GOMEZ	KORNBLUTH, C. M.	NV	NEW	54	AC
AND NOW THE NEWS...	STURGEON, THEODORE	SS	FSF	56	12
LIBERATION OF EARTH, THE	TENN, WILLIAM	SS	FUT	53	05
ROGUE SHIP (ALSO AS THE TWISTED MEN)					
	VAN VOGT, A. E.	NV	SSS	50	03
SELF PORTRAIT	WOLFE, BERNARD	NV	GAL	51	11

TOMORROW AND TOMORROW AND THE FAIRY CHESSMEN
— PADGETT, LEWIS — AC H GNM 51

TOMORROW AND TOMORROW	PADGETT, LEWIS	SN	ASF	47	01
FAIRY CHESSMEN, THE	PADGETT, LEWIS	SN	ASF	46	01

TOMORROW CAME — COOPER, EDMUND — AC PTH 63

WELCOME HOME	COOPER, EDMUND	SS			
DEATH WATCH	COOPER, EDMUND	SS			
PICCADILLY INTERVAL	COOPER, EDMUND	SS			
MOUSE THAT ROARED, THE	COOPER, EDMUND	SS			
NINETEEN NINETY-FOUR	COOPER, EDMUND	SS			
WHEN THE SAUCERS CAME	COOPER, EDMUND	SS			
FIRST MARTIAN, THE	COOPER, EDMUND	SS			
LIZARD OF WOZ, THE	COOPER, EDMUND	SS	FUN	58	08
LIFE AND DEATH OF PLUNKY GOO, THE					
	COOPER, EDMUND	SS			
JUDGEMENT DAY	COOPER, EDMUND	SS			
VERTICAL HOLD	COOPER, EDMUND	SS			
DOOMSDAY STORY, THE	COOPER, EDMUND	SS			

TOMORROW LIES IN AMBUSH — SHAW, BOB — AC ACE 73 02
ENGLISH EDITION (GOL 73) OMITS STORIES "STORMSEEKER"
AND "ELEMENT OF CHANCE"

CALL ME DUMBO	SHAW, BOB	NV	IFS	66	12
STORMSEEKER	SHAW, BOB	SS	GAL	72	01
REPEAT PERFORMANCE	SHAW, BOB	SS	FSF	71	02
AND ISLES WHERE GOOD MEN LIE	SHAW, BOB	SS	NWS	65	10
WHAT TIME DO YOU CALL THIS?	SHAW, BOB	SS	AMZ	71	09
COMMUNICATION	SHAW, BOB	NV	FAN	70	06
COSMIC COCKTAIL PARTY, THE (HAROLD WILSON AT THE COSMIC					
COCKTAIL PARTY)	SHAW, BOB	SS	SAG	70	
HAPPIEST DAY OF YOUR LIFE, THE					
	SHAW, BOB	SS	ASF	70	10
ELEMENT OF CHANCE	SHAW, BOB	SS	GAL	69	10
WEAPONS OF ISHER II, THE	SHAW, BOB	SS	AMZ	71	05
PILOT PLANT	SHAW, BOB	NV	NWS	66	05
TELEMART THREE	SHAW, BOB	SS	IFS	70	03
INVASION OF PRIVACY	SHAW, BOB	NV	AMZ	70	07

TOMORROW MIDNIGHT — BRADBURY, RAY — AC BAL 66
STORIES IN CARTOON FORM

ADAPTATION	FELDSTEIN, ALBERT B.	MS			
FOREWORD	BRADBURY, RAY	IN			
PUNISHMENT WITHOUT CRIME	BRADBURY, RAY	SS	OWS	50	03
I, ROCKET	BRADBURY, RAY	SS	AMZ	44	05
KING OF THE GRAY SPACES (ALSO AS R IS FOR ROCKET)					
	BRADBURY, RAY	SS	FFM	43	12
ONE WHO WAITS, THE	BRADBURY, RAY	SS	FSF	51	02
LONG YEARS, THE (ALSO AS DWELLERS IN SILENCE)					
	BRADBURY, RAY	SS	MCL	48	09
THERE WILL COME SOFT RAINS	BRADBURY, RAY	SS	COL	50	05
MARS IS HEAVEN!	BRADBURY, RAY	SS	PLS	48	PL
OUTCASTS OF THE STARS (ALSO AS THE ROCKET)					
	BRADBURY, RAY	SS	SSS	50	03

TOMORROW TIMES SEVEN — POHL, FREDERIK — AC BAL 59 07

HAUNTED CORPSE, THE	POHL, FREDERIK	SS	GAL	57	01
MIDDLE OF NOWHERE, THE	POHL, FREDERIK	SS	GAL	55	05
GENTLE VENUSIAN, THE (THE GENTLEST UNPEOPLE)					
	POHL, FREDERIK	NV	GAL	58	06
DAY OF THE BOOMER DUKES, THE	POHL, FREDERIK	SS	FUT	56	30
SURVIVAL KIT	POHL, FREDERIK	NV	GAL	57	05
KNIGHTS OF ARTHUR, THE	POHL, FREDERIK	NA	GAL	58	01
TO SEE ANOTHER MOUNTAIN	POHL, FREDERIK	SS	FSF	59	04

TOMORROW TODAY — ZEBROWSKI, GEORGE — OA L UPR 75
INTRODUCTION: TODAY'S TOMORROWS

	MCHALE, JOHN	IN			
INTO MY OWN	YARBRO, CHELSEA Q.	SS			
JOHN OF THE APOCALYPSE	BENFORD, JAMES				
	AND BENFORD, GREGORY	SS	C		
VISITOR	REYNOLDS, MACK	NV			
IN THE WIND	COOK, GLEN	NV			

TOMORROW, AND TOMORROW, AND TOMORROW...

HARPER CONAN & SINGER DAVID	PANGBORN, EDGAR	NV			
SYN	STEVENS, JAMES	SS			
COUNTER ECOLOGY	KAGAN, NORMAN	SS			
ABOUT THE AUTHORS	MISC. MATERIAL	MS			

TOMORROW X 4 — KNIGHT, DAMON — AN GMB 64

INTRODUCTION	KNIGHT, DAMON	IN			
NIGHT OF HOGGY DARN, THE	MCKENNA, RICHARD M.	NV	IFS	58	12
SOURCES OF THE NILE, THE	DAVIDSON, AVRAM	NV	FSF	61	01
NO WOMAN BORN	MOORE, C. L.	NV	ASF	44	12
ROADS MUST ROLL, THE	HEINLEIN, ROBERT A.	NV	ASF	40	06

TOMORROW 1 — HOSKINS, ROBERT — AN SIG 71 06

INTRODUCTION	HOSKINS, ROBERT	IN			
CIVILIZATION GAME, THE	SIMAK, CLIFFORD D.	NV	GAL	58	11
TROJAN HORSE LAUGH	MACDONALD, JOHN D.	NV	ASF	49	08
END OF THE LINE, THE	SCHMITZ, JAMES H.	NV	ASF	51	07
TERRITORY	ANDERSON, POUL	SN	ASF	63	06
SICKNESS, THE	TENN, WILLIAM	NV	INF	55	11

TOMORROW: NEW WORLDS OF SCIENCE FICTION
— ELWOOD, ROGER — OA H EVN 76

PREFACE	ELWOOD, ROGER	IN	
COME SEE THE LAST MAN CRY	HOLLY, J. HUNTER	NA	
NIZE KITTY	NOURSE, ALAN E.	SS	
KELLEY'S EYE, THE	HOSKINS, ROBERT	SS	
ARCTIC RESCUE	MASON, JOHN KEITH	SS	
ALWAYS SOMEBODY THERE	ALDISS, BRIAN W.	SS	
DEATH OR CONSEQUENCES	DORMAN, SONYA	SS	
CASTLE IN THE STARS	CARR, TERRY	SS	
JOURNEY OF THE SOUL	SHAPIRO, NEIL	NV	
ENCHANTE	OFFUTT, ANDREW J.	SS	
PERIHESPERON	BEAR, GREG	SS	

TOMORROW'S ALTERNATIVES — ELWOOD, ROGER — OA H MAC 73
SEE "FRONTIERS 1; TOMORROW'S ALTERNATIVES"

TOMORROW'S CHILDREN — ASIMOV, ISAAC — AN H DBL 66

INTRODUCTION	ASIMOV, ISAAC	IN			
NO LIFE OF THEIR OWN	SIMAK, CLIFFORD D.	NA	GAL	59	08
ACCOUNTANT, THE	SHECKLEY, ROBERT	SS	FSF	54	07
NOVICE	SCHMITZ, JAMES H.	NV	ASF	62	06
CHILD OF VOID	ST. CLAIR, MARGARET	SS	SSS	49	11
WHEN THE BOUGH BREAKS	PADGETT, LEWIS	NV	ASF	44	11
PAIL OF AIR, A	LEIBER, FRITZ	SS	GAL	51	12
JUNIOR ACHIEVEMENT	LEE, WILLIAM M.	SS	ASF	62	07
CABIN BOY	KNIGHT, DAMON	NV	GAL	51	09
LITTLE TERROR, THE	JENKINS, WILL F.	SS	SEP	53	08
GILEAD	HENDERSON, ZENNA	SS	FSF	54	08
MENACE FROM EARTH, THE	HEINLEIN, ROBERT A.	SS	FSF	57	08
WAYWARD CRAVAT, THE	FRIEDBERG, GERTRUDE	SS		58	
FATHER-THING, THE	DICK, PHILIP K.	SS	FSF	54	12
STAR, BRIGHT	CLIFTON, MARK	NV	GAL	52	07
ALL SUMMER IN A DAY	BRADBURY, RAY	SS	FSF	54	03
IT'S A GOOD LIFE	BIXBY, JEROME	SS	STR	53	02
PLACE OF THE GODS, THE	BENET, STEPHEN V.	SS	SEP	37	07
UGLY LITTLE BOY, THE (LASTBORN)					
	ASIMOV, ISAAC	NA	GAL	58	09

TOMORROW'S GIFT — COOPER, EDMUND — AC BAL 58

TOMORROW'S GIFT	COOPER, EDMUND	SS	STR	58	04
QUESTION OF TIME, A	COOPER, EDMUND	NV	FUN	56	05
BUTTERFLIES, THE	COOPER, EDMUND	SS			
REPEAT PERFORMANCE	COOPER, EDMUND	SS			
BRAIN CHILD (INVISIBLE BOY)	COOPER, EDMUND	SS	SEP	56	06
FALCON CHASE	COOPER, EDMUND	SS			
JAR OF LATAKIA, THE	COOPER, EDMUND	SS	AUT	54	09
M81: URSA MAJOR (THE END OF THE JOURNEY)					
	COOPER, EDMUND	SS	FUN	56	02
ENLIGHTENED ONES, THE	COOPER, EDMUND	NV	FUN	59	01
INTRUDERS (INTRUDERS ON THE MOON)					
	COOPER, EDMUND	NV	FUN	57	04

TOMORROW'S UNIVERSE — CAMPBELL, H. J. — AN H HML 54 05

HERITAGE	HARNESS, CHARLES L.	SS	FSF	50	FL
IT PAYS TO ADVERTISE	NEVILLE, KRIS	SS	FSF	53	06
TICKING HIS LIFE AWAY	HAMM, THELMA D.	SS	NEW	54	AN
M 33 IN ANDROMEDA	VAN VOGT, A. E.	SS	ASF	43	08
IMMORTAL, THE	ROCKLYNNE, ROSS	SS	CMT	41	03
SHORE OF TOMORROW, THE	OLIVER, CHAD	NV	STS	53	03
SOARING STATUE, THE	DE CAMP, L. SPRAGUE	SS	NEW	54	AN
EXTERRAN	LESSER, MILTON	SS	NEW	54	AN

TOMORROW'S WORLDS — SILVERBERG, ROBERT — AN H MDT 69

INTRODUCTION	SILVERBERG, ROBERT	IN			
SUNRISE ON MERCURY	SILVERBERG, ROBERT	SS	SFS	57	05
BEFORE EDEN	CLARKE, ARTHUR C.	SS	AMZ	61	06
SEEDS OF THE DUSK	GALLUN, RAYMOND Z.	NV	ASF	38	06
BLACK PITS OF LUNA, THE	HEINLEIN, ROBERT A.	SS	SEP	48	01
CRUCIFIXUS ETIAM	MILLER, WALTER M. JR	SS	ASF	53	02
DESERTION	SIMAK, CLIFFORD D.	SS	ASF	44	11
PRESSURE	HARRISON, HARRY	SS	ASF	69	08
PLANET OF DOUBT, THE	WEINBAUM, STANLEY G.	NV	ASF	35	10
ONE SUNDAY IN NEPTUNE	PANSHIN, ALEXEI	SS	NEW	69	AN
WAIT IT OUT	NIVEN, LARRY	SS	FUP	68	

TOMORROW, AND TOMORROW, AND TOMORROW...

	HEINTZ/HERBERT/JOOS/	AN L HRW 74			
PREFACE	HEINTZ, BONNIE L.				
	HERBERT, FRANK				
	JOOS, DONALD A.				
	AND MCGEE, JANE AGORN	IN C			
SCIENCE FICTION AND YOU	HERBERT, FRANK	IN			
STAR, THE	WELLS, H. G.	SS	GRP	97	12
SUBLIMINAL MAN, THE	BALLARD, J. G.	SS	NWS	63	01
WAVERIES, THE	BROWN, FREDRIC	SS	ASF	45	01

TOMORROW, AND TOMORROW, AND TOMORROW...   TRAPS OF TIME, THE

NIGHTFALL	ASIMOV, ISAAC	NV	ASF 41 09	
NOTHING, THE	HERBERT, FRANK	SS	FUN 56 01	
BITTER END	RUSSELL, ERIC FRANK	SS	SFP 53 12	
WINNER, THE	WESTLAKE, DONALD E.	SS	NOV 70 01	
LAWGIVER, THE	LAUMER, KEITH	SS	YRT 70	
UTOPIAN	REYNOLDS, MACK	SS	YRT 70	
RESCUE PARTY	CLARKE, ARTHUR C.	NV	ASF 46 05	
FOR THE SAKE OF GRACE	ELGIN, SUZETTE HADEN	NV	FSF 69 05	
OTHER FOOT, THE	BRADBURY, RAY	SS	NST 51 03	
CRATE	STURGEON, THEODORE	SS	70	
CLOUDBUILDERS, THE	KAPP, COLIN	NV	NWR 68 12	
SHORTEST SCIENCE FICTION STORY EVER TOLD, THE				
	ACKERMAN, FORREST J.	SS	VTX 73 06	
STREET OF DREAMS, FEET OF CLAY				
	SHECKLEY, ROBERT	NV	GAL 68 02	
VELDT, THE (THE WORLD THE CHILDREN MADE)				
	BRADBURY, RAY	SS	SEP 50 09	
AFTER THE MYTHS WENT HOME	SILVERBERG, ROBERT	SS	FSF 69 11	
ARENA	BROWN, FREDRIC	NV	ASF 44 06	
"REPENT, HARLEQUIN!" SAID THE TICKTOCKMAN				
	ELLISON, HARLAN	SS	GAL 65 12	
HOLE ON THE CORNER, THE	LAFFERTY, R. A.	SS	ORB 67 02	
TEXAS WEEK	HERNHUNTER, ALBERT	SS	FUN 54 01	
HEMEAC	VON WALD, E. G.	SS	GAL 68 03	
THIS GRAND CARCASS	LAFFERTY, R. A.	SS	AMZ 68 11	
PERFECT WOMAN, THE	SHECKLEY, ROBERT	SS	AMZ 54 01	
DESERTION	SIMAK, CLIFFORD D.	SS	ASF 44 11	
HERE THERE BE TYGERS	BRADBURY, RAY	SS	NTS 51	
CRUCIFIXUS ETIAM	MILLER, WALTER M. JR	SS	ASF 53 02	
SUNRISE ON MERCURY	SILVERBERG, ROBERT	SS	SFS 57 05	
OMNILINGUAL	PIPER, H. BEAM	NV	ASF 57 02	
SENTINEL, THE (SENTINEL OF ETERNITY)				
	CLARKE, ARTHUR C.	SS	TSF 51 SP	
SEEDS OF THE DUSK	GALLUN, RAYMOND Z.	NV	ASF 38 06	
SPECIALIST	SHECKLEY, ROBERT	SS	GAL 53 05	
HALF-BREED	ASIMOV, ISAAC	SS	AST 40 02	
BOMB SCARE	VINGE, VERNOR	SS	ASF 70 11	
KEYHOLE	LEINSTER, MURRAY	SS	TWS 51 12	
SUNDANCE	SILVERBERG, ROBERT	SS	FSF 69 06	
GOLDFISH BOWL	HEINLEIN, ROBERT A.	NV	ASF 42 03	
SWORD GAME	HOLLIS, H. H.	SS	GAL 68 04	
SINGING BELL, THE	ASIMOV, ISAAC	SS	FSF 55 01	
PRIVATE EYE	PADGETT, LEWIS	NV	ASF 49 01	

TOMORROW, INC.   GREENBERG& OLANDER   AN L TAP 76
INTRODUCTION	GREENBERG, MARTIN H.	IN C		
	AND OLANDER, JOSEPH D.			
AGE OF INVENTION, THE	SPINRAD, NORMAN	SS	FSF 66 07	
BRAVE NEW WORD	MCCOMAS, J. FRANCIS	SS	FSF 54 09	
TUNNEL UNDER THE WORLD, THE	POHL, FREDERIK	NV	GAL 55 01	
CAPTIVE AUDIENCE	GRIFFITH, ANN WARREN	SS	FSF 53 08	
SELLERS OF THE DREAM, THE	JAKES, JOHN W.	NA	GAL 63 06	
SUBLIMINAL MAN, THE	BALLARD, J. G.	SS	NWS 63 01	
DREAMING IS A PRIVATE THING	ASIMOV, ISAAC	SS	FSF 55 12	
COMPANY STORE	SILVERBERG, ROBERT	SS	STR 59 05	
BUSINESS AS USUAL, DURING ALTERATIONS				
	WILLIAMS, RALPH	NV	ASF 58 07	
CRIMINAL IN UTOPIA	REYNOLDS, MACK	NV	GAL 68 10	
OWE ME	PHILLIFENT, JOHN T.	SS	ASF 74 05	
PATENT PENDING	CLARKE, ARTHUR C.	SS	54	
CAPTIVE MARKET	DICK, PHILIP K.	SS	IFS 55 04	
SOMETHING FOR NOTHING	SHECKLEY, ROBERT	SS	GAL 54 06	

TOMORROW, THE STARS   HEINLEIN, ROBERT A.   AN H DBL 51
INTRODUCTION	HEINLEIN, ROBERT A.	IN		
I'M SCARED	FINNEY, JACK	SS	COL 51 09	
SILLY SEASON, THE	KORNBLUTH, C. M.	SS	FSF 50 FL	
REPORT ON THE BARNHOUSE EFFECT				
	VONNEGUT, KURT JR.	SS	COL 50 02	
TOURIST TRADE, THE	TUCKER, BOB	SS	WBY 51 01	
RAINMAKER	REESE, JOHN	SS	SEP 49 02	
ABSALOM	KUTTNER, HENRY	SS	STS 46 FL	
MONSTER, THE	DEL REY, LESTER	SS	ARG 51 06	
JAY SCORE	RUSSELL, ERIC FRANK	SS	ASF 41 05	
BETELGEUSE BRIDGE	TENN, WILLIAM	SS	GAL 51 04	
SURVIVAL SHIP	MERRIL, JUDITH	SS	WBY 51 01	
KEYHOLE	LEINSTER, MURRAY	SS	TWS 51 12	
MISBEGOTTEN MISSIONARY (ALSO AS GREEN PATCHES)				
	ASIMOV, ISAAC	SS	GAL 50 11	
SACK, THE	MORRISON, WILLIAM	SS	ASF 50 09	
POOR SUPERMAN (APPOINTMENT IN TOMORROW)				
	LEIBER, FRITZ	NV	GAL 51 07	

TORRENT OF FACES, A   BLISH & KNIGHT, N.   NO H DBL 67
SHIPWRECKED HOTEL, THE	BLISH, JAMES			
	AND KNIGHT, NORMAN L.	NV C	GAL 65 08	
PIPER OF DIS, THE	BLISH, JAMES			
	AND KNIGHT, NORMAN L.	NV C	GAL 66 08	
TO LOVE ANOTHER	BLISH, JAMES			
	AND KNIGHT, NORMAN L.	NV C	ASF 67 04	

TOUCH OF INFINITY, A   ELLISON, HARLAN   DC   ACE 59
INTRODUCTION	ELLISON, HARLAN	IN		
RUN FOR THE STARS	ELLISON, HARLAN	NV	SFA 57 06	
BACK TO THE DRAWING BOARDS	ELLISON, HARLAN	SS	FUN 58 08	
LIFE HUTCH	ELLISON, HARLAN	SS	IFS 56 04	
SKY IS BURNING, THE	ELLISON, HARLAN	SS	IFS 58 08	
FINAL TROPHY	ELLISON, HARLAN	NV	SUP 57 06	
BLIND LIGHTNING	ELLISON, HARLAN	SS	FUN 56 06	

TOUCH OF INFINITY, A   FAST, HOWARD   OC H MOR 73
ALSO IN "TIME AND THE RIDDLE"
HOOP, THE	FAST, HOWARD	SS	FSF 72 10	
PRICE, THE	FAST, HOWARD	SS		
MATTER OF SIZE, A	FAST, HOWARD	SS		
HOLE IN THE FLOOR, THE	FAST, HOWARD	SS		

GENERAL HARDY'S PROFESSION	FAST, HOWARD	SS		
SHOW CAUSE	FAST, HOWARD	SS		
NOT WITH A BANG	FAST, HOWARD	SS		
TALENT OF HARVEY, THE	FAST, HOWARD	NV		
MIND OF GOD, THE	FAST, HOWARD	SS		
UFO	FAST, HOWARD	SS		
CEPHES 5	FAST, HOWARD	SS		
PRAGMATIC SEED, THE	FAST, HOWARD	SS		
EGG, THE	FAST, HOWARD	SS		

TOUCH OF STRANGE, A   STURGEON, THEODORE   AC H DBL 58
POD AND THE BARRIER, THE	STURGEON, THEODORE	NA	GAL 57 09	
MR. COSTELLO, HERO	STURGEON, THEODORE	NV	GAL 53 12	
TOUCH OF YOUR HAND, THE	STURGEON, THEODORE	NA	GAL 53 09	
AFFAIR WITH A GREEN MONKEY	STURGEON, THEODORE	SS	VSF 57 05	
CRIME FOR LLEWELLYN, A	STURGEON, THEODORE	NV	NEW 58 AC	
GIRL HAD GUTS, THE	STURGEON, THEODORE	SS	VSF 57 01	
IT OPENS THE SKY	STURGEON, THEODORE	NV	VSF 57 11	
TOUCH OF STRANGE, A	STURGEON, THEODORE	SS	FSF 58 01	
OTHER CELIA, THE	STURGEON, THEODORE	NV	GAL 57 03	

TOUCH OF STRANGE, A (7 OF 9)   STURGEON, THEODORE   AC   BRK 59
MR. COSTELLO, HERO	STURGEON, THEODORE	NV	GAL 53 12	
TOUCH OF YOUR HAND, THE	STURGEON, THEODORE	NA	GAL 53 09	
AFFAIR WITH A GREEN MONKEY	STURGEON, THEODORE	SS	VSF 57 05	
CRIME FOR LLEWELLYN, A	STURGEON, THEODORE	NV	NEW 58 AC	
IT OPENS THE SKY	STURGEON, THEODORE	NV	VSF 57 11	
TOUCH OF STRANGE, A	STURGEON, THEODORE	SS	FSF 58 01	
OTHER CELIA, THE	STURGEON, THEODORE	NV	GAL 57 03	

TOWARD INFINITY   KNIGHT, DAMON   AN H SAS 68
INTRODUCTION	KNIGHT, DAMON	IN		
MAN WHO LOST THE SEA, THE	STURGEON, THEODORE	SS	FSF 59 10	
MARCH HARE MISSION	MCCORMACK, FORD	NV	WBY 51 01	
EARTH MEN, THE	BRADBURY, RAY	SS	TWS 48 08	
WHO GOES THERE?	STUART, DON A.	NV	ASF 38 08	
IN HIDING	SHIRAS, WILMAR H.	NV	ASF 48 11	
NOT FINAL!	ASIMOV, ISAAC	SS	ASF 41 10	
AND BE MERRY... (ALSO AS THE PYRAMID IN THE DESERT)				
	MACLEAN, KATHERINE	SS	ASF 50 02	
WITCHES OF KARRES, THE	SCHMITZ, JAMES H.	NV	ASF 49 12	
RESURRECTION (THE MONSTER)	VAN VOGT, A. E.	SS	ASF 48 08	

TOYMAKER, THE   JONES, RAYMOND F.   AC H FPB 51
MODEL SHOP, THE	JONES, RAYMOND F.	SS	ASF 47 06	
DEADLY HOST	JONES, RAYMOND F.	SS	ASF 45 09	
UTILITY	JONES, RAYMOND F.	SS	ASF 44 07	
FORECAST	JONES, RAYMOND F.	NV	ASF 46 06	
TOYMAKER, THE	JONES, RAYMOND F.	NV	ASF 46 09	
CHILDREN'S HOUR, THE	JONES, RAYMOND F.	NV	FAD 47 09	

TRADER TO THE STARS   ANDERSON, POUL   AC H DBL 64
HIDING PLACE	ANDERSON, POUL	NV	ASF 61 03	
TERRITORY	ANDERSON, POUL	SN	ASF 63 06	
MASTER KEY, THE	ANDERSON, POUL	NV	ASF 64 07	

TRANSFORMATIONS   ROSELLE, DANIEL   AN   FPR 73 12
UNDERSTANDING WORLD HISTORY THROUGH SCIENCE FICTION
SOUND OF THUNDER, A	BRADBURY, RAY	SS	COL 52 06	
GORGON'S HEAD, THE	BACON, GERTRUDE	SS		
THUS WE FRUSTRATE CHARLEMAGNE				
	LAFFERTY, R. A.	SS	GAL 67 02	
SMILE, THE	BRADBURY, RAY	SS	FAN 52 SU	
MAN ON TOP, THE (SCH 51 10)	BRETNOR, REGINALD	SS	FSF 60 09	
IT'S SUCH A BEAUTIFUL DAY	ASIMOV, ISAAC	NV	STR 54 03	
I KILL MYSELF	KAWALEC, JULIAN	SS	62	
THAT ONLY A MOTHER	MERRIL, JUDITH	SS	ASF 48 06	
SURVIVAL SHIP	MERRIL, JUDITH	SS	WBY 51 01	
ABSALOM	KUTTNER, HENRY	SS	STS 46 FL	
"REPENT, HARLEQUIN!" SAID THE TICKTOCKMAN				
	ELLISON, HARLAN	SS	GAL 65 12	

TRANSFORMATIONS II   ROSELLE, DANIEL   AN   FAW 74 11
UNDERSTANDING AMERICAN HISTORY THROUGH SCIENCE FICTION
INTRODUCTION	ROSELLE, DANIEL	IN		
HISTORY LESSON	CLARKE, ARTHUR C.	SS	STS 49 05	
CONQUEST OF THE MOON, THE	IRVING, WASHINGTON	SS		
I DO NOT HEAR YOU, SIR	DAVIDSON, AVRAM	SS	FSF 58 02	
REMEMBER THE ALAMO!	FEHRENBACH, T. R.	SS	ASF 61 12	
DRUMMER BOY OF SHILOH, THE	BRADBURY, RAY	SS	SEP 60 04	
SCENT OF SARSAPARILLA, A	BRADBURY, RAY	SS	STR 53 01	
TRANSLATION ERROR	SILVERBERG, ROBERT	SS	ASF 59 03	
BEYOND THE GAME	AANDAHL, VANCE	SS	FSF 68 05	
COMPUTERS DON'T ARGUE	DICKSON, GORDON R.	SS	ASF 65 09	
PORTABLE PHONOGRAPH, THE	CLARK, WALTER VAN T.	SS	41	

TRANSIT OF EARTH   PLAYBOY, EDITORS OF AN   PBP 71
TRANSIT OF EARTH	CLARKE, ARTHUR C.	SS	PBY 71 01	
BUTTON, BUTTON	MATHESON, RICHARD	SS	PBY 70 06	
MACHINERIES OF JOY, THE	BRADBURY, RAY	SS	PBY 62 12	
INVASION, THE	DAVIDSON, AVRAM	SS	PBY 65 07	
BERNIE THE FAUST	TENN, WILLIAM	NV	PBY 63 11	
CEPHALOTRON (ALSO AS FUN WITH YOUR NEW HEAD)				
	DISCH, THOMAS M.	SS	PBY 66 12	
IT DIDN'T HAPPEN	BROWN, FREDRIC	SS	PBY 63 10	
MAN IN THE RORSCHACH SHIRT, THE				
	BRADBURY, RAY	SS	PBY 66 10	
WASTE NOT, WANT NOT	ATHERTON, JOHN	SS	PBY 59 06	
CONTROL SOMNAMBULE	SAMBROT, WILLIAM	SS	PBY 62 05	
LET THERE BE LIGHT	CLARKE, ARTHUR C.	SS	PBY 58 02	
SPEED TRAP	POHL, FREDERIK	SS	PBY 67 11	
SOUVENIR (ALSO AS THE DROWNED GIANT)				
	BALLARD, J. G.	SS	PBY 65 05	

TRAPS OF TIME, THE   MOORCOCK, MICHAEL   AN H RPW 68
INTRODUCTION	MOORCOCK, MICHAEL	IN		

TRAPS OF TIME, THE

Title	Author				
MAN IN HIS TIME	ALDISS, BRIAN W.	SS	SCF	65	04
TIME TRAP	HARNESS, CHARLES L.	NV	ASF	48	08
GREAT CLOCK, THE	JONES, LANGDON	SS	NWS	66	03
MR. F IS MR. F	BALLARD, J. G.	SS	SCF	61	08
TRAVELER'S REST	MASSON, DAVID I.	SS	NWS	65	09
GARDEN OF FORKING PATHS, THE	BORGES, JORGE LUIS	SS		62	
UNIFICATION DAY	COLLYN, GEORGE	SS	NWS	66	05
NOW IS FOREVER	DISCH, THOMAS M.	SS	AMZ	64	03
DIVINE MADNESS	ZELAZNY, ROGER	SS	MOH	66	SU
HOW TO CONSTRUCT A TIME MACHINE	JARRY, ALFRED	SS			

TRAVELER IN BLACK, THE — BRUNNER, JOHN — AC — ACE 71

Title	Author				
IMPRINT OF CHAOS	BRUNNER, JOHN	NV	SCF	60	08
BREAK THE DOOR OF HELL	BRUNNER, JOHN	NV	IMP	66	04
WAGER LOST BY WINNING, THE	BRUNNER, JOHN	NV	FAN	70	04
DREAD EMPIRE	BRUNNER, JOHN	SN	FAN	71	04

TRAVELERS IN TIME — STERN, PHILIP VAN D. — AN H DBL 47 07

Title	Author				
TIME MACHINE, THE	WELLS, H. G.	NA	NRV	95	01
ELSEWHERE AND OTHERWISE	BLACKWOOD, ALGERNON	SS		36	
ENOCH SOAMES	BEERBOHM, MAX	NV	CNY	16	05
BETWEEN THE MINUTE AND THE HOUR	BURRAGE, A. M.	SS		27	
ROCKING-HORSE WINNER, THE	LAWRENCE, D. H.	SS		33	
ON THE STAIRCASE	GEROULD, KATHERINE F	SS	SCR	13	12
AUGUST HEAT	HARVEY, WILLIAM F.	SS		28	
ANTICIPATOR, THE (1898)	ROBERTS, MORLEY	SS		98	
OLD MAN, THE	HORN, HOLLOWAY	SS		32	
TAIPAN, THE	MAUGHAM, W. SOMERSET	SS	PRS	22	10
ROUSING OF MR. BRADEGAR, THE	HEARD, H. F.	SS		44	
FINEST STORY IN THE WORLD, THE	KIPLING, RUDYARD	NV	CRV	91	07
ETCHED IN MOONLIGHT	STEPHENS, JAMES	SS		28	
VIEW FROM A HILL, A	JAMES, M. R.	SS		26	
FRIEND TO ALEXANDER, A	THURBER, JAMES	SS	NYM	42	01
SILVER MIRROR, THE	DOYLE, ARTHUR CONAN	SS			
NO SHIPS PASS	SMITH, LADY ELEANOR	NV	CSL	32	04
CLOCK, THE	MASON, A. E. W.	SS		17	
OPENING THE DOOR	MACHEN, ARTHUR	SS		31	
CURIOUS CASE OF BENJAMIN BUTTON, THE	FITZGERALD, F. SCOTT	SS	COL	22	05
ALTERNATIVE, THE	BARING, MAURICE	SS		25	
MR. STRENBERRY'S TALE	PRIESTLEY, J. B.	SS		34	
PHANTAS	ONIONS, OLIVER	SS		11	
HOMELESS ONE, THE	COPPARD, A. E.	SS		46	

TRAVELLERS BY NIGHT — DERLETH, AUGUST — OA H ARK 67

Title	Author				
CICERONES, THE	AICKMAN, ROBERT	SS			
EPISODE ON CAIN STREET	BRENNAN, JOSEPH P.	SS			
CELLARS, THE	CAMPBELL, J. RAMSEY	SS			
MAN WHO RODE THE TRAINS, THE	CARTER, PAUL A.	SS			
HANDFUL OF SILVER, A	COUNSELMAN, MARY E.	SS			
DENKIRK	DRAKE, DAVID	SS			
WILD MAN OF THE SEA, THE	HODGSON, WILLIAM H.	SS			
UNPLEASANTNESS AT CARVER HOUSE, THE	JACOBI, CARL	SS			
TERROR OF ANERLY HOUSE SCHOOL, THE	LAWRENCE, MARGERY	SS			
HORROR FROM THE MIDDLE SPAN, THE	LOVECRAFT, H. P.	SS			
NOT THERE	METCALF, JOHN	SS			
FAMILY TREE	THAYER, FRANK D.	SS			
DEATH OF A BUMBLEBEE	WAKEFIELD, H.RUSSELL	SS			
CRATER, THE	WANDREI, DONALD	SS			

TRAVELLERS OF SPACE — GREENBERG , MARTIN — AN H GNM 51

Title	Author				
FOREWORD	GREENBERG , MARTIN	IN			
INTRODUCTION	LEY, WILLY	IN			
ROCKETEERS HAVE SHAGGY EARS, THE	BENNETT, KEITH	NV	PLS	50	SP
CHRISTMAS TREE (ALSO AS CHRISTMAS ROSES)	YOUD, CHRISTOPHER	SS	ASF	49	02
FORGIVENESS OF TENCHU TAEN, THE	KUMMER, FREDERICK A.	SS	ASF	38	11
EPISODE ON DHEE MINOR	WALTON, HARRY	SS	ASF	39	10
SHAPE OF THINGS, THE	BRADBURY, RAY	SS	TWS	48	02
COLUMBUS WAS A DOPE	MONROE, LYLE	SS	STS	47	05
ATTITUDE	CLEMENT, HAL	NV	ASF	43	09
IONIAN CIRCLE, THE	TENN, WILLIAM	SS	TWS	49	08
TROUBLE ON TANTALUS	MILLER, P. SCHUYLER	NV	ASF	41	02
PLACET IS A CRAZY PLACE	BROWN, FREDRIC	SS	ASF	46	05
ACTION ON AZURA (ALSO AS CONTACT, INCORPORATED)	OSBORNE, ROBERTSON	NV	PLS	49	FL
RULL, THE	VAN VOGT, A. E.	NV	ASF	48	05
DOUBLE DYED VILLAINS, THE	ANDERSON, POUL	NV	ASF	49	09
BUREAU OF SLICK TRICKS	FYFE, H. B.	SS	ASF	48	12
LIFE ON OTHER WORLDS	CARTIER, EDD	IL			
INTERSTELLAR ZOO, THE	KYLE, DAVID A.	AR			
SCIENCE FICTION DICTIONARY	MISC. MATERIAL	MS			

TREASURY OF GREAT SCIENCE FICTION, A VOL.1 — BOUCHER, ANTHONY — AN H DBL 59

Title	Author				
BEFORE THE CURTAIN...	BOUCHER, ANTHONY	IN			
RE-BIRTH (ALSO AS THE CHRYSALIDS)	WYNDHAM, JOHN	NO	BAL	55	
SHAPE OF THINGS THAT CAME, THE	DEMING, RICHARD	SS	FSF	51	10
PILLAR OF FIRE	BRADBURY, RAY	NV	PLS	48	SU
WALDO	HEINLEIN, ROBERT A.	SN	ASF	42	08
FATHER-THING, THE	DICK, PHILIP K.	SS	FSF	54	12
CHILDREN'S HOUR, THE	KUTTNER, HENRY AND MOORE, C. L.	NV C	ASF	44	03
GOMEZ	KORNBLUTH, C. M.	NV	NEW	54	AC
(WIDGET), THE (WADGET), AND BOFF, THE	STURGEON, THEODORE	SN	FSF	55	11

SANDRA	ELLIOTT, GEORGE P.	SS	FSF	57	10
BEYOND SPACE AND TIME	ROGERS, JOEL T.	SS	SSS	50	09
MARTIAN CROWN JEWELS, THE	ANDERSON, POUL	SS	EQM	58	02
WEAPON SHOPS OF ISHER, THE	VAN VOGT, A. E.	NO	GBG	51	

TREASURY OF GREAT SCIENCE FICTION, A VOL.2 — BOUCHER, ANTHONY — AN H DBL 59

Title	Author				
BRAIN WAVE	ANDERSON, POUL	NO	BAL	54	
BULLARD REFLECTS	JAMESON, MALCOLM	SS	ASF	41	12
LOST YEARS, THE	LEWIS, OSCAR	EX	KNP	51	
DEAD CENTER	MERRIL, JUDITH	NV	FSF	54	11
LOST ART	SMITH, GEORGE O.	NV	ASF	43	12
OTHER SIDE OF THE SKY, THE	CLARKE, ARTHUR C.	GR	INF	57	09
MAN WHO SOLD THE MOON, THE	HEINLEIN, ROBERT A.	NV	NEW	50	AC
MAGIC CITY	BOND, NELSON S.	NV	ASF	41	02
MORNING OF THE DAY THEY DID IT, THE	WHITE, E. B.	SS	NYM	50	02
PIGGY BANK	KUTTNER, HENRY	NV	ASF	42	12
LETTERS FROM LAURA	CLINGERMAN, MILDRED	SS	FSF	54	10
STARS MY DESTINATION, THE (ALSO AS TIGER! TIGER!)	BESTER, ALFRED	NO	GAL	56	10

TREASURY OF SCIENCE FICTION CLASSICS, THE — KUEBLER, HAROLD W. — AN H HAN 54

Title	Author				
INTRODUCTION	KUEBLER, HAROLD W.	IN			
CONVERSATION OF EIROS AND CHARMION, THE	POE, EDGAR ALLEN	SS	BGM	39	12
STAR, THE	WELLS, H. G.	SS	GRP	97	12
FROM "WHEN WORLDS COLLIDE"	BALMER, EDWIN AND WYLIE, PHILIP	EX C	LIP	32	
MARACOT DEEP, THE	DOYLE, ARTHUR CONAN	NO	SEP	27	10
ROUND THE MOON (1870)	VERNE, JULES	NO			
LAST TERRESTRIALS, THE (FROM "LAST AND FIRST MEN")	STAPLEDON, OLAF	EX	MTH	30	
MACHINE STOPS, THE	FORSTER, E. M.	NV		28	
R.U.R.	CAPEK, KAREL	PL		21	
FROM "BRAVE NEW WORLD"	HUXLEY, ALDOUS	EX	WND	32	
INVASION FROM MARS	KOCH, HOWARD	PL	CBS	38	10
EDISON'S CONQUEST OF MARS (ABRIDGED)	SERVISS, GARRETT P.	SS	NYE	98	01
MARTIANS, THE (FROM "LAST AND FIRST MEN")	STAPLEDON, OLAF	EX	MTH	30	
TIME MACHINE, THE	WELLS, H. G.	NA	NRV	95	01
CURIOUS CASE OF BENJAMIN BUTTON, THE	FITZGERALD, F. SCOTT	SS	COL	22	05
RAT, THE	WRIGHT, S. FOWLER	SS	WRT	29	03
DAMNED THING, THE (1893)	BIERCE, AMBROSE	SS	WRT	23	09
MR. STRENBERRY'S TALE	PRIESTLEY, J. B.	SS		34	

TREASURY OF SCIENCE FICTION, A — CONKLIN, GROFF — AN H CRN 48 11

Title	Author				
INTRODUCTION	CONKLIN, GROFF	IN			
NIGHTMARE, THE	DAVIS, CHAN	NV	ASF	46	05
TOMORROW'S CHILDREN	ANDERSON, POUL AND WALDROP, F. N.	NV C	ASF	47	03
LAST OBJECTIVE, THE	CARTER, PAUL A.	NV	ASF	46	08
LOOPHOLE	CLARKE, ARTHUR C.	SS	ASF	46	04
FIGURE, THE	GRENDON, EDWARD	SS	ASF	47	07
GREAT FOG, THE	HEARD, H. F.	SS		44	
CHRYSALIS, THE	MILLER, P. SCHUYLER	SS	ASF	36	04
LIVING FOSSIL	DE CAMP, L. SPRAGUE	SS	ASF	39	02
N DAY	LATHAM, PHILIP	SS	ASF	46	01
WITH FOLDED HANDS...	WILLIAMSON, JACK	NV	ASF	47	07
NO WOMAN BORN	MOORE, C. L.	NV	ASF	44	12
WITH FLAMING SWORDS	CARTMILL, CLEVE	NV	ASF	42	09
CHILDREN OF THE "BETSY B"	JAMESON, MALCOLM	SS	ASF	39	03
CHILD'S PLAY	TENN, WILLIAM	NV	ASF	47	03
PERSON FROM PORLOCK, THE	JONES, RAYMOND F.	NV	ASF	47	08
JUGGERNAUT	VAN VOGT, A. E.	SS	ASF	48	08
ETERNAL MAN, THE	SHARP, D. D.	SS	SWS	29	08
MIMSY WERE THE BOROGOVES	PADGETT, LEWIS	NV	ASF	43	02
TIME AND TIME AGAIN	PIPER, H. BEAM	SS	ASF	47	04
HOUSING SHORTAGE	WALTON, HARRY	SS	ASF	47	01
FLIGHT OF THE DAWN STAR	WILLIAMS, ROBERT M.	SS	ASF	38	03
VINTAGE SEASON	O'DONNELL, LAWRENCE	NV	ASF	46	09
OF JOVIAN BUILD	FRIEND, OSCAR J.	SS	TWS	38	10
WINGS ACROSS THE COSMOS	CROSS, POLTON	SS	TWS	38	06
EMBASSY, THE	PEARSON, MARTIN	SS	ASF	42	03
DARK MISSION	DEL REY, LESTER	SS	ASF	40	07
ETHICAL EQUATIONS, THE	LEINSTER, MURRAY	SS	ASF	45	06
IT'S GREAT TO BE BACK!	HEINLEIN, ROBERT A.	SS	SEP	47	07
TOOLS	SIMAK, CLIFFORD D.	NV	ASF	42	07
RESCUE PARTY	CLARKE, ARTHUR C.	NV	ASF	46	05

TREASURY OF SCIENCE FICTION, A (8 OF 30) — CONKLIN, GROFF — AN — BRK 57 07

Title	Author				
RESCUE PARTY	CLARKE, ARTHUR C.	NV	ASF	46	05
JUGGERNAUT	VAN VOGT, A. E.	SS	ASF	48	08
WITH FOLDED HANDS...	WILLIAMSON, JACK	NV	ASF	47	07
GREAT FOG, THE	HEARD, H. F.	SS		44	
MIMSY WERE THE BOROGOVES	PADGETT, LEWIS	NV	ASF	43	02
ETHICAL EQUATIONS, THE	LEINSTER, MURRAY	SS	ASF	45	06
IT'S GREAT TO BE BACK!	HEINLEIN, ROBERT A.	SS	SEP	47	07
LOOPHOLE	CLARKE, ARTHUR C.	SS	ASF	46	04

TRIAD — VAN VOGT, A. E. — AC H SAS 51

Title	Author				
WORLD OF NULL A, THE	VAN VOGT, A. E.	NO	ASF	45	08
VOYAGE OF THE SPACE BEAGLE, THE	VAN VOGT, A. E.	NO	SAS	50	
SLAN	VAN VOGT, A. E.	NO	ASF	40	09

TRIAL OF TERRA, THE — WILLIAMSON, JACK — NO — ACE 62

Title	Author				
MAN FROM OUTSIDE, THE	WILLIAMSON, JACK	SS	ASF	51	03
MAN DOWN	WILLIAMSON, JACK	NV	ASF	52	03
HAPPIEST CREATURE, THE	WILLIAMSON, JACK	SS	STR	53	02
PLANET FOR PLUNDERING, A	WILLIAMSON, JACK	NA	GAL	62	04

```
TRIANGLE                       ASIMOV, ISAAC        AC H DBL 61
    IN ENGLAND AS "AN ISAAC ASIMOV SECOND OMNIBUS"
    CURRENTS OF SPACE, THE      ASIMOV, ISAAC        NO    ASF 52 10
    PEBBLE IN THE SKY           ASIMOV, ISAAC        NO    DBL 50
    STARS LIKE DUST, THE        ASIMOV, ISAAC        NO    GAL 51 01
TRILOGY OF THE FUTURE           WOLLHEIM, DONALD A.  AN H  SID 62
    SEE "ACE SCIENCE FICTION READER"
TRITONIAN RING, THE             DE CAMP, L. SPRAGUE  AC H TWN 53
    TRITONIAN RING, THE         DE CAMP, L. SPRAGUE  NO    TCS 51 WI
    STRONGER SPELL, THE         DE CAMP, L. SPRAGUE  SS    FNF 53 11
    OWL AND THE APE, THE        DE CAMP, L. SPRAGUE  SS    IMG 51 11
    EYE OF TANDYLA, THE         DE CAMP, L. SPRAGUE  NV    FAD 51 05
TROUBLE TWISTERS, THE           ANDERSON, POUL       AC H DBL 66
    THREE-CORNERED WHEEL, THE   ANDERSON, POUL       NV    ASF 63 10
    SUN INVISIBLE, A            ANDERSON, POUL       NV    ASF 66 04
    TROUBLE TWISTERS, THE (TRADER TEAM)
                                ANDERSON, POUL       NA    ASF 65 07
TUNNEL AND OTHER STORIES, THE
                                ELWOOD, ROGER        OA H LER 74
    FOREWORD                    ASIMOV, ISAAC        IN
    TUNNEL, THE                 LYTLE, B. J.         SS
    SMALLEST STARSHIP, THE      ORGILL, MICHAEL      SS
    TO THE WORLD OF ZZZD        STREET, CLAIRE EDWIN SS
TURN LEFT AT THURSDAY           POHL, FREDERIK       AC    BAL 61 03
    MARS BY MOONLIGHT           POHL, FREDERIK       NA    GAL 58 06
    RICHEST MAN IN LEVITTOWN, THE (THE BITTEREST PILL)
                                POHL, FREDERIK       SS    GAL 59 04
    SEVEN DEADLY VIRTUES, THE   POHL, FREDERIK       NV    GAL 58 08
    MARTIAN IN THE ATTIC, THE   POHL, FREDERIK       SS    IFS 60 07
    THIRD OFFENSE (AS CHARLES SATTERFIELD)
                                POHL, FREDERIK       SS    GAL 58 08
    HATED, THE                  POHL, FREDERIK       SS    GAL 58 01
    I PLINGLOT, WHO YOU?        POHL, FREDERIK       NV    GAL 59 02
TURNING ON                      KNIGHT, DAMON        AC H DBL 66
    ACE 67 EDITION OMITS STORY "THE HANDLER"
    SEMPER FI (SATISFACTION)    KNIGHT, DAMON        SS    ASF 64 08
    BIG PAT BOOM, THE           KNIGHT, DAMON        SS    GAL 63 12
    MAN IN THE JAR              KNIGHT, DAMON        SS    GAL 57 04
    HANDLER, THE                KNIGHT, DAMON        SS    ROG 60 08
    MARY (AN ANCIENT MADNESS)   KNIGHT, DAMON        NV    GAL 64 06
    AUTO-DA-FE                  KNIGHT, DAMON        SS    GAL 61 02
    TO THE PURE                 KNIGHT, DAMON        SS    NWS 66 10
    ERIPMAV                     KNIGHT, DAMON        SS    FSF 58 06
    BACKWARD, O TIME (THIS WAY TO THE REGRESS)
                                KNIGHT, DAMON        SS    GAL 56 08
    NIGHT OF LIES, THE          KNIGHT, DAMON        SS    FSF 58 10
    MAID TO MEASURE             KNIGHT, DAMON        SS    FSF 64 10
    COLLECTOR'S ITEM (THE END OF THE SEARCH)
                                KNIGHT, DAMON        SS    WOT 63 06
    LIKELY STORY, A             KNIGHT, DAMON        SS    INF 56 02
    DON'T LIVE IN THE PAST      KNIGHT, DAMON        NV    GAL 51 06
TURNING PLACE, THE              KARL, JEAN E.        OC H DUT 76
    STORIES OF A FUTURE PAST
    TURNING PLACE, THE          KARL, JEAN E.        NV
    OVER THE HILL               KARL, JEAN E.        SS
    ENOUGH                      KARL, JEAN E.        SS
    ACCORD                      KARL, JEAN E.        NV
    CATABILID CONQUEST          KARL, JEAN E.        NV
    QUIET AND A WHITE BUSH      KARL, JEAN E.        SS
    TALKAROUND, THE             KARL, JEAN E.        SS
    CENTRAL QUESTION, A         KARL, JEAN E.        NV
    OUT OF THE FLICKER PATH     KARL, JEAN E.        SS
    SOME NOTES ON SOURCES       KARL, JEAN E.        MS
TWELVE STORIES AND A DREAM      WELLS, H. G.         AC H MCM 03
    FILMER                      WELLS, H. G.         SS    GRP 01
    MAGIC SHOP, THE             WELLS, H. G.         SS    SND 03 06
    VALLEY OF SPIDERS, THE      WELLS, H. G.         SS    PRS 03 03
    TRUTH ABOUT PYECRAFT, THE   WELLS, H. G.         SS    SND 03 04
    MR. SKELMERSDALE IN FAIRYLAND
                                WELLS, H. G.         SS    SND 01
    INEXPERIENCED GHOST, THE (THE STORY OF THE INEXPERIENCED GHOST)
                                WELLS, H. G.         SS    SND 02 03
    JIMMY GOGGLES THE GOD       WELLS, H. G.         SS    GRP 98 12
    NEW ACCELERATOR, THE        WELLS, H. G.         SS    SND 01 12
    MR. LEDBETTER'S VACATION    WELLS, H. G.         SS    SND 98 10
    STOLEN BODY, THE            WELLS, H. G.         SS    SND 98 11
    MR. BRISHER'S TREASURE      WELLS, H. G.         SS    SND 99 04
    MISS WINCHELSEA'S HEART     WELLS, H. G.         SS    QUN 98 10
    DREAM OF ARMAGEDDON, A      WELLS, H. G.         NV    BAW 01
TWENTY YEARS OF FANTASY & SCIENCE FICTION
                                FERMAN & MILLS       AN H PUT 70
    F & SF AND I                ASIMOV, ISAAC        IN
    5,271,009 (ALSO AS THE STARCOMBER)
                                BESTER, ALFRED       NV    FSF 54 03
    FREE DIRT                   BEAUMONT, CHARLES    SS    FSF 55 05
    BECALMED IN HELL            NIVEN, LARRY         SS    FSF 65 07
    PRIVATE- KEEP OUT!          MACDONALD, PHILIP    SS    FSF 49 FL
    GLADYS'S GREGORY            WEST, JOHN ANTHONY   SS    FSF 63 02
    FEMININE INTUITION          ASIMOV, ISAAC        NV    FSF 69 10
    THAT HELL-BOUND TRAIN       BLOCH, ROBERT        SS    FSF 58 09
    TOUCH OF STRANGE, A         STURGEON, THEODORE   SS    FSF 58 01
    GRATITUDE GUARANTEED        BRETNOR, REGINALD
                                AND NEVILLE, KRIS    SS C FSF 53 08
    PRIME-TIME TEASER           MCALLISTER, BRUCE    SS    FSF 68 12
    AS LONG AS YOU'RE HERE      STANTON, WILL        SS    FSF 63 07
    SWEET HELEN                 RUNYON, CHARLES W.   SS    FSF 69 09
```

```
    FINAL SCEPTRE, A LASTING CROWN, A (ALSO AS HENRY THE NINTH)
                                BRADBURY, RAY        SS    FSF 69 10
    YES, WE HAVE NO RITCHARD    FRIEDMAN, BRUCE JAY  SS    FSF 60 11
    WE CAN REMEMBER IT FOR YOU WHOLESALE
                                DICK, PHILIP K.      NV    FSF 66 04
    237 TALKING STATUES, ETC.   LEIBER, FRITZ        SS    FSF 63 09
    M-1                         WILSON, GAHAN        SS    FSF 70 02
    SILLY SEASON, THE           KORNBLUTH, C. M.     SS    FSF 50 FL
    HOLIDAY MAN, THE            MATHESON, RICHARD    SS    FSF 57 07
    SOMETHING ELSE              TILLEY, ROBERT J.    SS    FSF 65 10
TWENTY-EIGHT SCIENCE FICTION STORIES
                                WELLS, H. G.         AC H DOV 52
    AEPYORNIS ISLAND            WELLS, H. G.         SS    PMB 94 12
    ARGONAUTS OF THE AIR, THE   WELLS, H. G.         SS    PMY 95
    COUNTRY OF THE BLIND, THE   WELLS, H. G.         SS    SND 04 04
    CRYSTAL EGG, THE            WELLS, H. G.         SS    NRV 97 05
    DREAM OF ARMAGEDDON, A      WELLS, H. G.         NV    BAW 01
    EMPIRE OF THE ANTS, THE     WELLS, H. G.         SS    SND 05 12
    FILMER                      WELLS, H. G.         SS    GRP 01
    FLOWERING OF THE STRANGE ORCHID, THE (ALSO AS THE STRANGE
        ORCHID)                 WELLS, H. G.         SS    PMB 94 08
    IN THE ABYSS                WELLS, H. G.         SS    PRS 96 08
    IN THE AVU OBSERVATORY      WELLS, H. G.         SS    PMB 94 08
    LAND IRONCLADS, THE         WELLS, H. G.         NV    SND 03 12
    MAGIC SHOP, THE             WELLS, H. G.         SS    SND 03 06
    MAN WHO COULD WORK MIRACLES, THE
                                WELLS, H. G.         SS    ILN 98 07
    MEN LIKE GODS               WELLS, H. G.         NO    HRS 22 11
    NEW ACCELERATOR, THE        WELLS, H. G.         SS    SND 01 12
    PLATTNER STORY, THE         WELLS, H. G.         SS    NRV 96 04
    REMARKABLE CASE OF DAVIDSON'S EYES, THE
                                WELLS, H. G.         SS    PMB 95 03
    SEA-RAIDERS, THE            WELLS, H. G.         SS    WSL 96 12
    STAR, THE                   WELLS, H. G.         SS    GRP 97 12
    STAR BEGOTTEN               WELLS, H. G.         NO    VIK 37
    STOLEN BACILLUS, THE        WELLS, H. G.         SS    PMB 94 06
    STOLEN BODY, THE            WELLS, H. G.         SS    SND 98 11
    STORY OF THE DAYS TO COME, A WELLS, H. G.        NA    PGZ 97
    STORY OF THE LATE MR. ELVESHAM, THE
                                WELLS, H. G.         SS    IDL 96 05
    STORY OF THE STONE AGE, A   WELLS, H. G.         NA    IDL 97 05
    TRUTH ABOUT PYECRAFT, THE   WELLS, H. G.         SS    SND 03 04
    UNDER THE KNIFE (SLIP UNDER THE KNIFE)
                                WELLS, H. G.         SS    NRV 96 01
    VALLEY OF SPIDERS, THE      WELLS, H. G.         SS    PRS 03 03
TWENTY-SECOND CENTURY, THE      CHRISTOPHER, JOHN    AC H GRY 54
    COLONIAL                    CHRISTOPHER, JOHN    NV    ASF 49 04
    PROPHET, THE                CHRISTOPHER, JOHN    SS    NWS 53 03
    BREAKING POINT              CHRISTOPHER, JOHN    SS    NWS 53 04
    DECOY                       CHRISTOPHER, JOHN    SS    SFS 55 07
    TREE, THE                   CHRISTOPHER, JOHN    SS    NWS 51 FL
    CHRISTMAS ROSES (CHRISTMAS TREE)
                                CHRISTOPHER, JOHN    SS    ASF 49 02
    OCCUPATIONAL RISK           CHRISTOPHER, JOHN    SS    SFS 57 01
    MR. KOWTSHOOK               CHRISTOPHER, JOHN    SS    ASR 53 01
    NEW WINE, THE               CHRISTOPHER, JOHN    SS    FSM 54 SU
    SENTENCE OF DEATH (DEATH SENTENCE)
                                CHRISTOPHER, JOHN    SS    IMG 53 06
    MUSEUM PIECE                CHRISTOPHER, JOHN    SS    NWS 54 04
    RICH AND STRANGE            CHRISTOPHER, JOHN    SS
    RATHER IMPROBABLE HISTORY OF HILIARY KIFFER, THE
                                CHRISTOPHER, JOHN    SS    AVS 53 04
    MONSTER                     CHRISTOPHER, JOHN    SS    SCF 50 SU
    WEAPON                      CHRISTOPHER, JOHN    SS    NEW 54 AC
    TIME OF PEACE, A            CHRISTOPHER, JOHN    SS    STN 57 10
    $64 QUESTION, THE           CHRISTOPHER, JOHN    SS    NEW 54 AC
    BLEMISH                     CHRISTOPHER, JOHN    SS    AUT 53 11
    ROCK-A-BYE                  CHRISTOPHER, JOHN    SS
    BEGIN AGAIN                 CHRISTOPHER, JOHN    SS    ESQ
TWICE 22                        BRADBURY, RAY        AC H DBL 66
    GOLDEN APPLES OF THE SUN    BRADBURY, RAY        AC    DBL 53
    MEDICINE FOR MELANCHOLY, A  BRADBURY, RAY        AC    DBL 58
TWILIGHT WORLD                  ANDERSON, POUL       NO H TOR 61
    TOMORROW'S CHILDREN         ANDERSON, POUL       NV    ASF 47 03
    CHAIN OF LOGIC (LOGIC)      ANDERSON, POUL       NV    ASF 47 07
    CHILDREN OF FORTUNE         ANDERSON, POUL       NV    NEW 61 NO
TWIN WORLDS                     JONES, NEIL R.       AC    ACE 67
    TWIN WORLDS                 JONES, NEIL R.       NV    AMZ 37 04
    ON THE PLANET FRAGMENT      JONES, NEIL R.       NV    AMZ 37 10
    MUSIC MONSTERS, THE         JONES, NEIL R.       NV    AMZ 38 04
TWISTED                         CONKLIN, GROFF       AN    BEL 62
    INTRODUCTION                CONKLIN, GROFF       IN
    PLAYGROUND, THE             BRADBURY, RAY        SS    ESQ 53 10
    OTHER HAND, THE             LANGELAAN, GEORGE    SS    FSF 61 10
    THING IN THE CELLAR, THE    KELLER, DAVID H. MD. SS    WRT 32 03
    DIARY OF A MADMAN, THE      DE MAUPASSANT, GUY   SS
    UPTURNED FACE, THE          CRANE, STEPHEN       SS
    LITTLE MAN WHO WASN'T QUITE, THE
                                STUART, WILLIAM W.   NV    GAL 61 12
    NIGHT DRIVE                 JENKINS, WILL F.     SS    TDW 60
    SONG OF MARYA, THE (VENGEANCE FOR NIKOLAI)
                                MILLER, WALTER M. JR NV    VSF 57 03
    MRS. MANIFOLD               GRENDON, STEPHEN     SS          49
    HOLY TERROR, A              BIERCE, AMBROSE      SS          91
    IMPULSE                     RUSSELL, ERIC FRANK  SS    ASF 38 09
    BRENDA                      ST. CLAIR, MARGARET  SS    WRT 54 03
    TELL-TALE HEART, THE        POE, EDGAR ALLEN     SS    POI 43 01
    SHUNNED HOUSE, THE          LOVECRAFT, H. P.     NV    WRT 37 10
    WORLD WELL LOST, THE        STURGEON, THEODORE   SS    USF 53 06
```

TWISTED (BRITISH)   CONKLIN, GROFF   AN   HWZ 63
  INTRODUCTION   CONKLIN, GROFF   IN
  PLAYGROUND, THE   BRADBURY, RAY   SS   ESQ 53 10
  OTHER HAND, THE   LANGELAAN, GEORGE   SS   FSF 61 10
  THING IN THE CELLAR, THE   KELLER, DAVID H. MD. SS   WRT 32 03
  DIARY OF A MADMAN, THE   DE MAUPASSANT, GUY   SS
  UPTURNED FACE, THE   CRANE, STEPHEN   SS
  LITTLE MAN WHO WASN'T QUITE, THE
                               STUART, WILLIAM W.   NV   GAL 61 12
  NIGHT DRIVE   JENKINS, WILL F.   SS   TDW 60
  SONG OF MARYA, THE (VENGEANCE FOR NIKOLAI)
                               MILLER, WALTER M. JR SS   VSF 57 03
  MRS. MANIFOLD   GRENDON, STEPHEN   SS   49
  IMPULSE   RUSSELL, ERIC FRANK   SS   ASF 38 09

TWISTED MEN, THE   VAN VOGT, A. E.   DC   ACE 64
  TWISTED MEN, THE (ROGUE SHIP)
                               VAN VOGT, A. E.   NV   SSS 50 03
  STAR-SAINT, THE   VAN VOGT, A. E.   NV   PLS 51 03
  EARTH KILLERS, THE   VAN VOGT, A. E.   NV   SSS 49 04

TWISTS IN TIME   LEINSTER, MURRAY   AC   AVN 60
  ROGUE STAR   LEINSTER, MURRAY   NV   NEW 60 AC
  DEAR CHARLES   LEINSTER, MURRAY   SS   FSM 53 05
  DEAD CITY (ALSO AS MALIGNANT MARAUDER)
                               LEINSTER, MURRAY   NV   TWS 46 SU
  SAM, THIS IS YOU   LEINSTER, MURRAY   NV   GAL 55 05
  OTHER NOW, THE   LEINSTER, MURRAY   SS   GAL 51 03
  FOURTH-DIMENSIONAL DEMONSTRATOR, THE
                               LEINSTER, MURRAY   SS   ASF 35 12
  END, THE   LEINSTER, MURRAY   NV   TWS 46 12

TWO DOZEN DRAGON EGGS   WOLLHEIM, DONALD A.   AC   POW 69 09
  EGGS AND I, THE   ACKERMAN, FORREST J. IN
  INTRODUCTION   WOLLHEIM, DONALD A.   IN
  MIMIC   WOLLHEIM, DONALD A.   SS   AST 42 12
  EXTENDING THE HOLDINGS   WOLLHEIM, DONALD A.   SS   FSF 51 04
  STORM WARNING   WOLLHEIM, DONALD A.   SS   FUT 42 10
  POETESS AND THE 21 GRAY-HAIRED CADAVERS, THE
                               WOLLHEIM, DONALD A.   SS
  MALICE AFORETHOUGHT   WOLLHEIM, DONALD A.   SS   FSF 52 11
  SANTA RIDES A SAUCER   WOLLHEIM, DONALD A.   SS
  GANYMEDE HOUSE   WOLLHEIM, DONALD A.   SS   OSF 53 01
  ROAD TO ROME   WOLLHEIM, DONALD A.   SS   FUT 53 07
  RAG THING, THE   WOLLHEIM, DONALD A.   SS   FSF 51 10
  FEMININE FRACTION, THE   WOLLHEIM, DONALD A.   SS   MOH 64 11
  EIN BLICK IN DIE ZUKUNFT   WOLLHEIM, DONALD A.   SS
  TOP SECRET   WOLLHEIM, DONALD A.   SS   FSF 50 FL
  HOW MANY MILES TO BABYLON? (BABYLON: 70 M.)
                               WOLLHEIM, DONALD A.   SS   MOH 63 08
  SHOO, FLY!   WOLLHEIM, DONALD A.   SS
  LYSENKO MAZE, THE   WOLLHEIM, DONALD A.   SS   FSF 54 07
  LANDRAGON   WOLLHEIM, DONALD A.   SS
  GIVE HER HELL   WOLLHEIM, DONALD A.   SS
  DISGUISE   WOLLHEIM, DONALD A.   SS   OWS 53 02
  GARRISON, THE   WOLLHEIM, DONALD A.   SS   MOH 65 04
  DOORSLAMMER   WOLLHEIM, DONALD A.   SS   MOH 63 11
  EGG FROM ALPHA CENTAURI, THE WOLLHEIM, DONALD A.   SS
  LAST STAND OF A SPACE GRENADIER
                               WOLLHEIM, DONALD A.   SS   SFQ 54 02
  ADVANCE POST IN THE WAR BETWEEN THE SEXES, AN
                               WOLLHEIM, DONALD A.   SS
  WEB SIXTY-FOUR   WOLLHEIM, DONALD A.   SS

TWO TALES AND EIGHT TOMORROWS
                               HARRISON, HARRY   AC   BAN 68 05
  INTRODUCTION   ALDISS, BRIAN W.   IN
  STREETS OF ASHKELON, THE (ALSO AS AN ALIEN AGONY)
                               HARRISON, HARRY   SS   NWS 62 09
  PORTRAIT OF THE ARTIST   HARRISON, HARRY   SS   FSF 64 11
  RESCUE OPERATION   HARRISON, HARRY   SS   ASF 64 12
  CAPTAIN BEDLAM   HARRISON, HARRY   SS   SPA 57 12
  FINAL ENCOUNTER   HARRISON, HARRY   NV   GAL 64 04
  UNTO MY MANIFOLD DOOMS (THE MANY DOOMS)
                               HARRISON, HARRY   SS   GAL 64 06
  PLIABLE ANIMAL, THE   HARRISON, HARRY   NV   SDM 62 09
  CAPTAIN HONARIO HARPPLAYER, R.N.
                               HARRISON, HARRY   SS   FSF 63 03
  ACCORDING TO HIS ABILITIES   HARRISON, HARRY   SS   AMZ 64 05
  I ALWAYS DO WHAT TEDDY SAYS HARRISON, HARRY   SS   EQM 65 06

TWO VIEWS OF WONDER   SCORTIA & YARBRO   OA   BAL 73 12
  "VIVE LAQUELLE DIFFERENCE?" SCORTIA, THOMAS N.
                               AND YARBRO, CHELSEA Q. IN C
  FAULTY REGISTER   GORES, JOE   SS   TVW 73
  LONE WARRIOR   DEFORD, MIRIAM ALLEN SS   TVW 73
  IMT   SARGENT, PAMELA   SS   TVW 73
  SMALL WORLD   KURLAND, MICHAEL J.   NV   TVW 73
  WHEN PETALS FALL   VAN SCYOC, SYDNEY J. NV   TVW 73
  PAPA SCHIMMELHORN AND THE S.O.D.O.M. SERUM
                               BRETNOR, REGINALD   NV   TVW 73
  ROPE OF GLASS   ZEBROWSKI, GEORGE   SS   TVW 73
  QUALITY OF MERCY, THE   ASHE, TAMSIN   SS   TVW 73
  UN BEL DI   YARBRO, CHELSEA Q.   NV   TVW 73
  KISS OF FIRE   ELLISON, HARLAN   SS   TVW 73
  PERSONAGE OF ROYAL BLOOD, A ROBERTS, WILLO DAVIS SS   TVW 73
  THOU GOOD AND FAITHFUL   SCORTIA, THOMAS N.   SS   TVW 73
  APPENDIX OF THEMES   MISC. MATERIAL   MS

TYRANT OF TIME, THE   ESHBACH, LLOYD A.   AC H FPS 55
  TYRANT OF TIME, THE (THE TIME CONQUEROR)
                               ESHBACH, LLOYD A.   SS   WOS 32 07
  METEOR MINERS, THE   ESHBACH, LLOYD A.   SS   AMZ 35 12
  SPACEWAYS INCIDENT   ESHBACH, LLOYD A.   SS
  LIGHT FROM BEYOND, THE (GOD OF LIGHT)
                               ESHBACH, LLOYD A.   SS   TWS 44 SU

  PLACE OF ORCHIDS, THE (THE GOD THAT SCIENCE MADE)
                               ESHBACH, LLOYD A.   SS   SFS 39 08
  CITY OF DREAD, THE   ESHBACH, LLOYD A.   SS
  SINGING BLADES   ESHBACH, LLOYD A.   SS   SRS 40 02
  CAULDRON OF LIFE, THE (THE CAULDRON)
                               ESHBACH, LLOYD A.   SS   SRS 40 04

UBERWINDUNG VON RAUM UND ZEIT
                               GUNTHER, GOTTHARD   AN H KRP 52
  CONQUEST OF SPACE AND TIME, STORIES IN GERMAN
  DESERTION   SIMAK, CLIFFORD D.   SS   ASF 44 11
  NIGHTFALL   ASIMOV, ISAAC   NV   ASF 41 09
  WHO GOES THERE?   CAMPBELL, JOHN W. JR NV   ASF 38 08
  LOTUS EATERS, THE   WEINBAUM, STANLEY G. NV   ASF 35 04
  TIME AND TIME AGAIN   PIPER, H. BEAM   SS   ASF 47 04
  RESURRECTION (THE MONSTER)   VAN VOGT, A. E.   SS   ASF 48 08
  MIMSY WERE THE BOROGOVES   PADGETT, LEWIS   NV   ASF 43 02

ULTIMATE INVADER, AND OTHER SCIENCE FICTION, THE
                               WOLLHEIM, DONALD A.   DA   ACE 54
  ULTIMATE INVADER, THE (DESIGN FOR GREAT-DAY)
                               RUSSELL, ERIC FRANK   NO   PLS 53 01
  ALIEN ENVOY   JAMESON, MALCOLM   SS   ASF 44 11
  MALIGNANT MARAUDER (DEAD CITY)
                               LEINSTER, MURRAY   NV   TWS 46 SU
  TEMPORAL TRANSGRESSOR, THE (BRIDGEHEAD)
                               LONG, FRANK BELKNAP   NV   ASF 44 08

ULTIMATE THRESHOLD, THE   GINSBURG, MIRRA   AN H HRW 70
  PREFACE   GINSBURG, MIRRA   IN
  ICARUS AND DAEDALUS   ALTOV, HENRIK   SS   68
  EREM   ANFILOV, GLEB   SS   63
  FORMULA FOR IMMORTALITY   DNIEPROV, ANATOLY   NV   63
  WHEN QUESTIONS ARE ASKED   DNIEPROV, ANATOLY   SS   63
  HORN OF PLENTY, THE   GRIGORIEV, VLADIMIR   SS   GAL 69 12
  USELESS PLANET, THE   LARIONOVA, OLGA   NV   67
  ULTIMATE THRESHOLD, THE   MAXIMOV, HERMAN   SS   65
  INVASION   PODOLNY, ROMAN   SS   66
  WHEN YOU RETURN   ROSOKHOVATSKY, IGOR   NV   67
  ONE LESS   ROSOKHOVATSKY, IGOR   SS   66
  WE PLAYED UNDER YOUR WINDOW SHCHERBAKOV, VLADIMIR SS   66
  PRELIMINARY RESEARCH   VARSHAVSKY, ILYA   SS   65
  HE WHO LEAVES NO TRACE   YEMTSEV, MIKHAIL
                               AND PARNOV, YEREMEY   NV C   63

UN-MAN AND OTHER NOVELLAS   ANDERSON, POUL   DC   ACE 62
  UN-MAN   ANDERSON, POUL   SN   ASF 53 01
  MARGIN OF PROFIT   ANDERSON, POUL   SS   ASF 56 09
  LIVE COWARD, THE   ANDERSON, POUL   SS   ASF 56 06

UNBORN TOMORROW   COOPER, EDMUND   AC H HAL 71
  INTRODUCTION   COOPER, EDMUND   IN
  INTRUDERS (INTRUDERS ON THE MOON)
                               COOPER, EDMUND   NV   FUN 57 04
  SECOND CHANCE   COOPER, EDMUND   SS
  M81: URSA MAJOR (THE END OF THE JOURNEY)
                               COOPER, EDMUND   SS   FUN 56 02
  LIZARD OF WOZ, THE   COOPER, EDMUND   SS   FUN 58 08
  BUTTERFLIES, THE   COOPER, EDMUND   SS
  WHEN THE SAUCERS CAME   COOPER, EDMUND   SS
  ENLIGHTENED ONES, THE   COOPER, EDMUND   NV   FUN 59 01
  LIFE AND DEATH OF PLUNKY GOO, THE
                               COOPER, EDMUND   SS

UNDEFEATED, THE   LAUMER, KEITH   AC   DEL 74 06
  WORLDMASTER   LAUMER, KEITH   NV   WOT 65 11
  NIGHT OF THE TROLLS, THE   LAUMER, KEITH   SN   WOT 63 10
  THUNDERHEAD   LAUMER, KEITH   NV   GAL 67 04
  END AS A HERO   LAUMER, KEITH   NA   GAL 63 06

UNDER COMPULSION   DISCH, THOMAS M.   AC H HDV 68
  SEE "FUN WITH YOUR NEW HEAD"

UNDER THE MOONS OF MARS   MOSKOWITZ, SAM   AN H HRW 70
  PREFACE   MOSKOWITZ, SAM   IN
  UNDER THE MOONS OF MARS (ALSO AS A PRINCESS OF MARS)
                               BURROUGHS, EDGAR R.   NV   ASM 12 02
  DARKNESS AND DAWN   ENGLAND, GEORGE A.   NO   CSB 12 01
  POLARIS OF THE SNOWS   STILSON, CHARLES B.   NV   ASW 15 12
  PALOS OF THE DOG STAR PACK   GIESY, J. U.   NV   ASW 18 07
  FRIEND ISLAND   STEVENS, FRANCIS   SS   ASW 18 09
  MOON POOL, THE   MERRITT, A.   NA   ASW 18 06
  GIRL IN THE GOLDEN ATOM, THE CUMMINGS, RAY   NA   ASW 19 03
  MAD PLANET, THE   LEINSTER, MURRAY   NA   ARG 20 06
  BLIND SPOT, THE   HALL, AUSTIN
                               AND FLINT, HOMER EON NV.C AAS 21 05
  HISTORY OF "THE SCIENTIFIC ROMANCE" IN THE MUNSEY MAGAZINES,
  1912-1920, A   MOSKOWITZ, SAM   AR

UNEXPECTED DIMENSION, THE   BUDRYS, ALGIS   AC   BAL 60
  END OF SUMMER, THE   BUDRYS, ALGIS   NV   ASF 54 11
  DISTANT SOUND OF ENGINES, THE
                               BUDRYS, ALGIS   SS   FSF 59 03
  NEVER MEET AGAIN   BUDRYS, ALGIS   SS   INF 58 03
  BURNING WORLD, THE   BUDRYS, ALGIS   NV   INF 57 07
  FIRST TO SERVE   BUDRYS, ALGIS   SS   ASF 54 05
  GO AND BEHOLD THEM (THE END OF WINTER, AS WILLIAM SCARFF)
                               BUDRYS, ALGIS   NV   VSF 58 01
  EXECUTIONER, THE   BUDRYS, ALGIS   NV   ASF 56 01

UNEXPECTED, THE   MARGULIES, LEO   AN   PYR 61 02
  INTRODUCTION   MARGULIES, LEO   IN
  PROFESSOR'S TEDDY-BEAR, THE STURGEON, THEODORE   SS   WRT 48 03
  LEGAL RITES   ASIMOV, ISAAC
                               AND POHL, FREDERIK   NV C WRT 50 09
  STRANGE ISLAND OF DR. NORK, THE

```
                        BLOCH, ROBERT         SS  WRT 49 03      WORLD IS A SPHERE, THE    PANGBORN, EDGAR      NV  UNI 73 03
MRS. HAWK               ST. CLAIR, MARGARET   SS  WRT 50 07      LEGEND OF COUGAR LOU LANDIS, THE
HANDLER, THE            BRADBURY, RAY         SS  WRT 47 01                                BRYANT, EDWARD       SS  UNI 73 03
AUTOMATIC PISTOL, THE   LEIBER, FRITZ         SS  WRT 40 05      FREE CITY BLUES           EKLUND, GORDON       NV  UNI 73 03
UNWANTED, THE           COUNSELMAN, MARY E.   SS  WRT 51 01
VALLEY WAS STILL, THE   WELLMAN, MANLY WADE   SS  WRT 39 08      UNIVERSE 4                CARR, TERRY          OA H RDM 74
SCRAWNY ONE, THE        BOUCHER, ANTHONY      SS  WRT 49 05      ASSAULT ON A CITY         VANCE, JACK          NV  UNI 74 04
COME AND GO MAD         BROWN, FREDRIC        NV  WRT 49 07      SEA OF FACES, A           SILVERBERG, ROBERT   SS  UNI 74 04
BIG SHOT, THE           RUSSELL, ERIC FRANK   SS  WRT 49 01      AND READ THE FLESH BETWEEN THE LINES
                                                                                          LAFFERTY, R. A.      SS  UNI 74 04
UNFAMILIAR TERRITORY    SILVERBERG, ROBERT    AC H SCB 73        MY SWEET LADY JO          WALDROP, HOWARD      SS  UNI 74 04
CAUGHT IN THE ORGAN DRAFT  SILVERBERG, ROBERT SS  WLK 73         STUNGUN SLIM              GOULART, RON         SS  UNI 74 04
(NOW+N), (NOW-N)        SILVERBERG, ROBERT    NV  NOV 72 02      DESERT PLACES             SARGENT, PAMELA      SS  UNI 74 04
SOME NOTES ON THE PREDYNASTIC EPOCH                             IF THE STARS ARE GODS     EKLUND, GORDON
                        SILVERBERG, ROBERT    SS  BMR 73                                  AND BENFORD, GREGORY NV C UNI 74 04
IN THE GROUP            SILVERBERG, ROBERT    SS  EIO 73         WHEN THE VERTICAL WORLD BECOMES HORIZONTAL
CALIBAN                 SILVERBERG, ROBERT    SS  INY 72 03                                PANSHIN, ALEXEI      SS  UNI 74 04
MANY MANSIONS           SILVERBERG, ROBERT    NV  UNI 73 03
GOOD NEWS FROM THE VATICAN  SILVERBERG, ROBERT SS  UNI 71 01     UNIVERSE 5                CARR, TERRY          OA H RDM 74
PUSH NO MORE            SILVERBERG, ROBERT    NV  NEW 72 AN      IF THIS IS WINNETKA, YOU MUST BE JUDY
MUTANT WEAPON, THE      SILVERBERG, ROBERT    SS  NEW 73 AN                                BUSBY, F. M.         NV  UNI 74 05
WHEN WE WENT TO SEE THE END OF THE WORLD                        SCHRODINGER'S CAT         LE GUIN, URSULA K.   SS  UNI 74 05
                        SILVERBERG, ROBERT    SS  UNI 72 02      HOW IT FELT               EFFINGER, GEO. ALEC  SS  UNI 74 05
WHAT WE LEARNED FROM THIS MORNING'S NEWSPAPER                   NIGHT IS COLD, THE STARS ARE FAR AWAY, THE
                        SILVERBERG, ROBERT    SS  INY 72 04                                BROXON, MILDRED D.   SS  UNI 74 05
IN ENTROPY'S JAWS       SILVERBERG, ROBERT    NV  INY 72 02      MYSTERIOUS DOINGS IN THE METROPOLITAN MUSEUM
WIND AND THE RAIN, THE  SILVERBERG, ROBERT    SS  SVW 73                                   LEIBER, FRITZ        SS  UNI 74 05
                                                                M IS FOR THE MANY         RUSS, J. J.          SS  UNI 74 05
UNFRIENDLY FUTURE, THE  BOARDMAN, TOM JR.     AN  FSP 65         NIGHT WIND, THE           PANGBORN, EDGAR      SS  UNI 74 05
INTRODUCTION            BOARDMAN, TOM JR.     IN                 SURVIVAL PROBLEMS         NEVILLE, KRIS        SS  UNI 74 05
RUSSKIES GO HOME!       REYNOLDS, MACK        SS  FSF 60 11      PASSION PLAY              REAVES, J. MICHAEL   SS  UNI 74 05
FOOD GOES IN THE TOP, THE  WORTHINGTON, WILL  SS  SCF 61 08      RUBBER BEND, THE          WOLFE, GENE          NV  UNI 74 05
DANGER: RELIGION! (MATRIX)  ALDISS, BRIAN W.  TC  SCF 62 10      BUT, AS A SOLDIER, FOR HIS COUNTRY
RESCUE OPERATION        HARRISON, HARRY       SS  ASF 64 12                                GOLDIN, STEPHEN      SS  UNI 74 05
HADES BUSINESS, THE     PRATCHETT, TERRY      SS  SCF 63 08      RAMPARTS, THE             BAILEY, HILARY       NV  UNI 74 05
SEED OF VIOLENCE, THE   WILLIAMS, JAY         SN  FUN 58 11
                                                                UNIVERSE 6                CARR, TERRY          OA H DBL 76
UNIVERSE AHEAD          ENGDAHL & ROBERSON    AN H ATH 76        JOURNEY TO THE HEARTLAND  ALDISS, BRIAN W.     NV  UNI 76 06
PREFACE                 ENGDAHL, SYLVIA       IN                 WHAT DID YOU DO LAST YEAR?  EKLUND, GORDON
INTRODUCTION            ROBERSON, RICK        IN                                          AND BENFORD, GREGORY SS C UNI 76 06
ANIMAL, THE             STEPHENS, ROSEMARY    SS                 CUSTER'S LAST JUMP        UTLEY, STEVEN
IT'S SUCH A BEAUTIFUL DAY  ASIMOV, ISAAC      NV  STR 54 03                                AND WALDROP, HOWARD  NV C UNI 76 06
ARARAT                  HENDERSON, ZENNA      SS  FSF 52 10      WINE HAS BEEN LEFT OPEN TOO LONG AND THE MEMORY HAS
WILDERNESS, THE         BRADBURY, RAY         SS  FSF 52 11        GONE FLAT, THE          ELLISON, HARLAN      SS  UNI 76 06
CLOUDLAB, THE           ROBERSON, RICK        NV  NEW 76 AN       UNDER THE GENERATOR       SHIRLEY, JOHN        NV  UNI 76 06
OLD MAN HENDERSON       NEVILLE, KRIS         SS  FSF 51 06      STARS AND DARKNESS        CHANG, GLENN         NV  UNI 76 06
NIGHTMARE BROTHER       NOURSE, ALAN E.       NV  ASF 53 02      SHIFTING PARAMETERS IN DISAPPEARANCE AND MEMORY
SAMARITAN, THE          HARPER, RICHARD       SS  BLF                                      HAAS, CHARLIE        NV  UNI 76 06
LOWER THAN ANGELS       BUDRYS, ALGIS         SN  INF 56 10
KYRIE                   ANDERSON, POUL        SS  FRS 68         UNIVERSE 7                CARR, TERRY          OA H DBL 77 01
CHRISTMAS PRESENT, THE  DICKSON, GORDON R.    SS  FSF 58 01      RITE OF SPRING, A         LEIBER, FRITZ        NV  UNI 77 07
RANGING                 JAKES, JOHN W.        SS  FRS 68         MY LADY OF PSYCHIATRIC SORROWS
BECKONING TRAIL, THE    ENGDAHL, SYLVIA                                                    ALDISS, BRIAN W.     SS  UNI 77 07
                        AND ROBERSON, RICK    NV C NEW 76 AN     PROBABILITY STORM         REID, JULIA          NV  UNI 77 07
                                                                PEOPLE REVIEWS            CHILSON, ROBERT      SS  UNI 77 07
UNIVERSE DAY            O'DONNELL, K. M.      NO  AVN 71 04      IBID                      EFFINGER, GEO. ALEC  SS  UNI 77 07
MAKING TITAN            O'DONNELL, K. M.      SS  FSF 70 07      MARVELOUS BRASS CHESSPLAYING AUTOMATON, THE
TRIPTYCH, A             O'DONNELL, K. M.      SS  FSF 69 07                                WOLFE, GENE          NV  UNI 77 07
TERMINUS EST            O'DONNELL, K. M.      SS  NOV 70 11      BRAIN FEVER SEASON        LAFFERTY, R. A.      SS  UNI 77 07
TWO ODYSSEYS INTO THE CENTER  O'DONNELL, K. M. SS NOV 72 02      NINTH SYMPHONY OF LUDWIG VAN BEETHOVEN AND OTHER LOST SONGS
PACEM EST               O'DONNELL, K. M.      SS  INY 70 01                                SCHOLZ, CARTER       NV  UNI 77 07
ELEPHANTS               O'DONNELL, K. M.      SS  INY 71 02
                                                                UNKNOWN 5, THE            BENSEN, D. R.        AN  PYR 64 01
UNIVERSE 1              CARR, TERRY           OA  ACE 71         INTRODUCTION              BENSEN, D. R.        IN
INTRODUCTION            CARR, TERRY           IN                 AUTHOR! AUTHOR!           ASIMOV, ISAAC        NV  NEW 64 AN
WEST WIND, FALLING      BENFORD, GREGORY                        BARGAIN, THE              CARTMILL, CLEVE      SS  UNK 42 08
                        AND EKLUND, GORDON    NV C UNI 71 01     HAG SELEEN, THE           STURGEON, THEODORE   SS  UNK 42 12
GOOD NEWS FROM THE VATICAN  SILVERBERG, ROBERT SS  UNI 71 01     HELL IS FOREVER           BESTER, ALFRED       SS  UNK 42 08
JADE BLUE               BRYANT, EDWARD        SS  UNI 71 01      CREST OF THE WAVE, THE    RICE, JANE           SS  UNK 41 06
NOR LIMESTONE ISLANDS   LAFFERTY, R. A.       SS  UNI 71 01
TIME EXPOSURES          TUCKER, WILSON        NV  UNI 71 01      UNKNOWN, THE              BENSEN, D. R.        AN  PYR 63 04
MINDSHIP                CONWAY, GERARD F.     SS  UNI 71 01      INTRODUCTION              BENSEN, D. R.        IN
NOTES FOR A NOVEL ABOUT THE FIRST SHIP EVER TO VENUS            FOREWORD                  ASIMOV, ISAAC        IN
                        MALZBERG, BARRY N.    SS  UNI 71 01      MISGUIDED HALO, THE       KUTTNER, HENRY       SS  UNK 39 08
POOR MAN, BEGGER MAN    RUSS, JOANNA          NV  UNI 71 01      PRESCIENCE                BOND, NELSON S.      SS  UNK 41 10
HUMAN SIDE OF THE VILLAGE MONSTER, THE                          YESTERDAY WAS MONDAY      STURGEON, THEODORE   SS  UNK 41 06
                        BRYANT, EDWARD        SS  UNI 71 01      GNARLY MAN, THE           DE CAMP, L. SPRAGUE  NV  UNK 39 06
ROMANCE OF DR. TANNER, THE  GOULART, RON      SS  UNI 71 01      BLEAK SHORE, THE          LEIBER, FRITZ        SS  UNK 40 11
MOUNT CHARITY           PANGBORN, EDGAR       NV  UNI 71 01      TROUBLE WITH WATER        GOLD, H. L.          SS  UNK 39 03
ALL THE LAST WARS AT ONCE  EFFINGER, GEO. ALEC SS  UNI 71 01     DOUBLED AND REDOUBLED     JAMESON, MALCOLM     SS  UNK 41 02
                                                                WHEN IT WAS MOONLIGHT     WELLMAN, MANLY WADE  SS  UNK 40 02
UNIVERSE 2              CARR, TERRY           OA  ACE 72         MR. JINX                  ARTHUR, ROBERT       SS  UNK 41 08
RETROACTIVE             SHAW, BOB             NV  UNI 72 02      SNULBUG (FIRST IN UNKNOWN, DEC. 1941)
WHEN WE WENT TO SEE THE END OF THE WORLD                                                  BOUCHER, ANTHONY     SS  FSF 53 05
                        SILVERBERG, ROBERT    SS  UNI 72 02      ARMAGEDDON                BROWN, FREDRIC       SS  UNK 41 08
FUNERAL SERVICE         CONWAY, GERARD F.     SS  UNI 72 02
SPECIAL CONDITION IN SUMMIT CITY, A                             UNPLEASANT PROFESSION OF JONATHAN HOAG, THE
                        LAFFERTY, R. A.       SS  UNI 72 02                                HEINLEIN, ROBERT A.  AC H GNM 59
PATRON OF THE ARTS      ROTSLER, WILLIAM      NV  UNI 72 02          ALSO AS "6 X H"
USEFUL PHRASES FOR THE TOURIST                                 UNPLEASANT PROFESSION OF JONATHAN HOAG, THE
                        RUSS, JOANNA          SS  UNI 72 02                                HEINLEIN, ROBERT A.  SN  UNK 42 10
ON THE DOWNHILL SIDE    ELLISON, HARLAN       SS  UNI 72 02      MAN WHO TRAVELED IN ELEPHANTS, THE (THE ELEPHANT CIRCUIT)
OTHER PERCEIVER, THE    SARGENT, PAMELA       SS  UNI 72 02                                HEINLEIN, ROBERT A.  SS  STN 57 10
MY HEAD'S IN A DIFFERENT PLACE, NOW                            ALL YOU ZOMBIES-          HEINLEIN, ROBERT A.  SS  FSF 59 03
                        DAVIS, GRANIA         NV  UNI 72 02      THEY                      HEINLEIN, ROBERT A.  SS  UNK 41 04
STALKING THE SUN        EKLUND, GORDON        NV  UNI 72 02      OUR FAIR CITY             HEINLEIN, ROBERT A.  SS  WRT 49 01
MAN WHO WAVED HELLO, THE  DOZOIS, GARDNER R.  SS  UNI 72 02      AND HE BUILT A CROOKED HOUSE  HEINLEIN, ROBERT A. SS  ASF 41 02
HEADLESS MAN, THE       WOLFE, GENE           SS  UNI 72 02
TIGER BOY               PANGBORN, EDGAR       NV  UNI 72 02      UNTOUCHED BY HUMAN HANDS  SHECKLEY, ROBERT     AC H BAL 54 03
                                                                MONSTERS, THE             SHECKLEY, ROBERT     SS  FSF 53 03
UNIVERSE 3              CARR, TERRY           OA H RDM 73        COST OF LIVING            SHECKLEY, ROBERT     SS  GAL 52 12
INTRODUCTION            CARR, TERRY           IN                 ALTAR, THE                SHECKLEY, ROBERT     SS  FAN 53 08
DEATH OF DOCTOR ISLAND, THE  WOLFE, GENE      NV  UNI 73 03      SHAPE (KEEP YOUR SHAPE)   SHECKLEY, ROBERT     NV  GAL 53 11
GHOST WRITER, THE       EFFINGER, GEO. ALEC   SS  UNI 73 03      IMPACTED MAN, THE         SHECKLEY, ROBERT     SS  ASF 52 12
MANY MANSIONS           SILVERBERG, ROBERT    NV  UNI 73 03      UNTOUCHED BY HUMAN HANDS (ONE MAN'S POISON)
RANDY-TANDY MAN         ROCKLYNNE, ROSS       SS  UNI 73 03                                SHECKLEY, ROBERT     SS  GAL 53 12
```

UNTOUCHED BY HUMAN HANDS

KING'S WISHES, THE	SHECKLEY, ROBERT	SS	FSF 53 07
WARM	SHECKLEY, ROBERT	SS	GAL 53 06
DEMONS, THE	SHECKLEY, ROBERT	SS	FNF 53 02
SPECIALIST	SHECKLEY, ROBERT	SS	GAL 53 05
SEVENTH VICTIM	SHECKLEY, ROBERT	SS	GAL 53 04
RITUAL (STRANGE RITUAL)	SHECKLEY, ROBERT	SS	CLM 53
BESIDE STILL WATERS	SHECKLEY, ROBERT	SS	AMZ 53 11

UNTOUCHED BY HUMAN HANDS (BRITISH)

	SHECKLEY, ROBERT	AC	FSP 67
MONSTERS, THE	SHECKLEY, ROBERT	SS	FSF 53 03
COST OF LIVING	SHECKLEY, ROBERT	SS	GAL 52 12
ALTAR, THE	SHECKLEY, ROBERT	SS	FAN 53 08
SHAPE (KEEP YOUR SHAPE)	SHECKLEY, ROBERT	NV	GAL 53 11
IMPACTED MAN, THE	SHECKLEY, ROBERT	SS	ASF 52 12

UNTOUCHED BY HUMAN HANDS (ONE MAN'S POISON)

	SHECKLEY, ROBERT	SS	GAL 53 12
WARM	SHECKLEY, ROBERT	SS	GAL 53 06
SPECIALIST	SHECKLEY, ROBERT	SS	GAL 53 05
SEVENTH VICTIM	SHECKLEY, ROBERT	SS	GAL 53 04
WATCHBIRD	SHECKLEY, ROBERT	NV	GAL 53 02

UNTRAVELLED WORLDS

	BARTER & WILSON	AN	MCM 66
FOREWORD	BARTER, ALAN FRANK		
	AND WILSON, R.	IN C	
IMPOSTOR	DICK, PHILIP K.	SS	ASF 53 06
METEOR (PHONEY METEOR)	WYNDHAM, JOHN	SS	AMZ 41 03
WINDOWS OF HEAVEN, THE	ANONYMOUS	SS	
VELDT, THE (THE WORLD THE CHILDREN MADE)			
	BRADBURY, RAY	SS	SEP 50 09
CREATURE OF THE SNOWS	SAMBROT, WILLIAM	SS	SEP 60 10
GRENVILLE'S PLANET	SHAARA, MICHAEL	SS	FSF 52 10
GENTLEMAN IS AN EPWA, THE	JACOBI, CARL	NV	NEW 53 AN
SUMMERTIME ON ICARUS (THE HOTTEST PIECE OF REAL ESTATE IN THE			
SOLAR SYSTEM)	CLARKE, ARTHUR C.	SS	VOG 60 06
ONE FOR THE BOOKS	MATHESON, RICHARD	NV	GAL 55 09
BITTER END	RUSSELL, ERIC FRANK	SS	SFP 53 12
CRICKET BALL, THE	MANHATTAN, AVRO	SS	FSF 55 10
FUN THEY HAD, THE (NEA 51 12)			
	ASIMOV, ISAAC	SS	FSF 54 02

VALLEY BEYOND TIME

	SILVERBERG, ROBERT	AC	DEL 73 01
INTRODUCTION	SILVERBERG, ROBERT	IN	
VALLEY BEYOND TIME	SILVERBERG, ROBERT	SN	SFA 57 12
SPACEROGUE (AS WEBBER MARTIN)			
	SILVERBERG, ROBERT	SN	INF 58 11
FLAME AND THE HAMMER, THE	SILVERBERG, ROBERT	NO	SFA 57 09
WAGES OF DEATH, THE	SILVERBERG, ROBERT	NV	IFS 58 08

VAMPIRES, LTD. | NESVADBA, JOSEF | AC | VNS 64
SEE "THE LOST FACE"

VAN VOGT OMNIBUS, A

	VAN VOGT, A. E.	AC H	SID 67
PLANETS FOR SALE	HULL, E. MAYNE		
	AND VAN VOGT, A. E.	AC C	FEL 54
BEAST, THE	VAN VOGT, A. E.	NO	DBL 63
BOOK OF PTATH, THE	VAN VOGT, A. E.	NO	UNK 43 10

VARIABLE MAN, THE

	DICK, PHILIP K.	AC	ACE 57
VARIABLE MAN, THE	DICK, PHILIP K.	NA	SSF 53 09
SECOND VARIETY	DICK, PHILIP K.	NV	SSF 53 05
MINORITY REPORT, THE	DICK, PHILIP K.	SS	FUN 56 01
AUTOFAC	DICK, PHILIP K.	NV	GAL 55 11
WORLD OF TALENT, A	DICK, PHILIP K.	NV	GAL 54 10

VENUS EQUILATERAL

	SMITH, GEORGE O.	AC H	PRM 47
INTRODUCTION	CAMPBELL, JOHN W. JR	IN	
ILLUSTRATIONS	LEVIN, SOL	IL	
QRM-INTERPLANETARY	SMITH, GEORGE O.	NV	ASF 42 10
CALLING THE EMPRESS	SMITH, GEORGE O.	NV	ASF 43 06
RECOIL	SMITH, GEORGE O.	NV	ASF 43 11
OFF THE BEAM	SMITH, GEORGE O.	NV	ASF 44 02
LONG WAY, THE	SMITH, GEORGE O.	NV	ASF 44 04
BEAM PIRATE	SMITH, GEORGE O.	NV	ASF 44 10
FIRING LINE	SMITH, GEORGE O.	NV	ASF 44 12
SPECIAL DELIVERY	SMITH, GEORGE O.	NV	ASF 45 03
PANDORA'S MILLIONS	SMITH, GEORGE O.	NV	ASF 45 06
MAD HOLIDAY	SMITH, GEORGE O.	NV	NEW 47 AC

VENUS FACTOR, THE | GHIDALIA, V.& ELWOOD | AN | MBB 72
GOD GRANTE THAT SHE LYE STILLE

	ASQUITH, CYNTHIA	NV	31
FOGHORN, THE	ATHERTON, GERTRUDE	SS	
LAST SEANCE, THE (1926)	CHRISTIE, AGATHA	SS	EQM 71 11
AGAINST AUTHORITY	DEFORD, MIRIAM ALLEN	NV	FSF 66 02
J-LINE TO NOWHERE	HENDERSON, ZENNA	NV	FSF 69 09
SHIP WHO DISAPPEARED, THE (ALSO AS THE SHIP WHO DISSEMBLED)			
	MCCAFFREY, ANNE	NV	IFS 69 03
LADY WAS A TRAMP, THE	MERRIL, JUDITH	SS	VSF 57 03
DARK LAND, THE	MOORE, C. L.	NV	WRT 36 01

VERMILLION SANDS

	BALLARD, J. G.	AC	BKM 71 04
PRIMA BELLADONNA	BALLARD, J. G.	SS	SCF 56 12
THOUSAND DREAMS OF STELLAVISTA, THE			
	BALLARD, J. G.	SS	AMZ 62 03
CRY HOPE, CRY FURY¡	BALLARD, J. G.	SS	FSF 67 10
VENUS SMILES (MOBILE)	BALLARD, J. G.	NV	IFS 67 09
STUDIO 5, THE STARS	BALLARD, J. G.	NV	SCF 61 02
CLOUD-SCULPTORS OF CORAL D, THE			
	BALLARD, J. G.	SS	FSF 67 12
SAY GOODBYE TO THE WIND	BALLARD, J. G.	SS	FAN 70 08
SCREEN GAME, THE	BALLARD, J. G.	NV	FAN 63 10

VERMILLION SANDS (BRITISH) | BALLARD, J. G. | AC H | CAP 73
CLOUD-SCULPTORS OF CORAL D, THE

	BALLARD, J. G.	SS	FSF 67 12

PRIMA BELLADONNA	BALLARD, J. G.	SS	SCF 56 12
SCREEN GAME, THE	BALLARD, J. G.	NV	FAN 63 10
SINGING STATUES, THE	BALLARD, J. G.	SS	FAN 62 07
CRY HOPE, CRY FURY¡	BALLARD, J. G.	SS	FSF 67 10
VENUS SMILES (MOBILE)	BALLARD, J. G.	NV	IFS 67 09
SAY GOODBYE TO THE WIND	BALLARD, J. G.	SS	FAN 70 08
STUDIO 5, THE STARS	BALLARD, J. G.	NV	SCF 61 02
THOUSAND DREAMS OF STELLAVISTA, THE			
	BALLARD, J. G.	SS	AMZ 62 03

VIEW FROM ANOTHER SHORE | ROTTENSTEINER, FRANZ | AN H | SEA 73

INTRODUCTION	ROTTENSTEINER, FRANZ	IN	
IN HOT PURSUIT OF HAPPINESS	LEM, STANISLAW	NV	
VALLEY OF ECHOES, THE	KLEIN, GERARD	SS	
OBSERVATION OF QUADRAGNES	ANDREVON, JEAN-PIERRE	SS	
GOOD RING, THE	MADSEN, SVEND AGE	SS	
SLUM	FRANKE, HERBERT W.	SS	
CAPTAIN NEMO'S LAST ADVENTURE			
	NESVADBA, JOSEF	NV	73
ALTAR OF THE RANDOM GODS, THE			
	ROGOZ, ADRIAN	SS	
GOOD NIGHT, SOPHIE	ALDANI, LINO	NV	
PROVING GROUND, THE	GANSOVSKY, SEVER	SS	
SISYPHUS, THE SON OF AEOLUS	IVANOV, VSEVOLOD	SS	
MODEST GENIUS, A	SHEFNER, VADIM	SS	
NOTES ON THE AUTHORS	MISC. MATERIAL	MS	

VIEW FROM THE STARS, THE | MILLER, WALTER M. JR | AC | BAL 65 01
YOU TRIFLIN' SKUNK¡ (TRIFLIN' MAN)

	MILLER, WALTER M. JR	SS	FUN 55 01
WILL, THE	MILLER, WALTER M. JR	SS	FAN 54 02
ANYBODY ELSE LIKE ME? (COMMAND PERFORMANCE)			
	MILLER, WALTER M. JR	NV	GAL 52 11
CRUCIFIXUS ETIAM	MILLER, WALTER M. JR	SS	ASF 53 02
I, DREAMER	MILLER, WALTER M. JR	SS	AMZ 53 07
DUMB WAITER	MILLER, WALTER M. JR	NV	ASF 52 04
BLOOD BANK	MILLER, WALTER M. JR	NV	ASF 52 06
BIG JOE AND THE NTH GENERATION (IT TAKES A THIEF)			
	MILLER, WALTER M. JR	SS	IFS 52 05
BIG HUNGER, THE	MILLER, WALTER M. JR	SS	ASF 52 10

VINTAGE ANTHOLOGY OF SCIENCE FANTASY, THE

	CERF, CHRISTOPHER	AN	VNT 66 02
INTRODUCTION	CERF, CHRISTOPHER	IN	
GREAT AUTOMATIC GRAMMATISATOR, THE			
	DAHL, ROALD	SS	53
EGG A MONTH FROM ALL OVER, AN			
	SEABRIGHT, IDRIS	SS	FSF 52 10
THERE WILL COME SOFT RAINS	BRADBURY, RAY	SS	COL 50 05
AND NOW THE NEWS...	STURGEON, THEODORE	SS	FSF 56 12
NO-SIDED PROFESSOR (ESQ 47 01)			
	GARDNER, MARTIN	SS	FSF 51 02
RANDOM QUEST	WYNDHAM, JOHN	NV	NEW 61 AC
ROCKET OF 1955, THE	KORNBLUTH, C. M.	SS	STI 41 04
SOMETHING FOR NOTHING	SHECKLEY, ROBERT	SS	GAL 54 06
DEATH OF THE SEA, THE	GIRONELLA,JOSE MARIA	SS	64
RED WHITE AND BLUE RUM COLLINS, THE			
	BRUST, JOHN C. M.	SS	HLP
PIE IN THE SKY	STYRON, WILLIAM	SS	NEW 66 AN
ANALOGUES, THE	KNIGHT, DAMON	SS	ASF 52 01
IMMORTALITY (GREAT LOST DISCOVERIES III)			
	BROWN, FREDRIC	SS	NEW 61 AC
SHADOW SHOW	SIMAK, CLIFFORD D.	NV	FSF 53 11
CHRONOPOLIS	BALLARD, J. G.	NV	NWS 60 06
OR ALL THE SEAS WITH OYSTERS	DAVIDSON, AVRAM	SS	GAL 58 05
PATENT PENDING	CLARKE, ARTHUR C.	SS	54
I KILL MYSELF	KAWALEC, JULIAN	SS	62
MEN WHO MURDERED MOHAMMED, THE			
	BESTER, ALFRED	SS	FSF 58 10
CANTICLE FOR LEIBOWITZ, A	MILLER, WALTER M. JR	NV	FSF 55 04

VINTAGE BRADBURY, THE | BRADBURY, RAY | AC | VNT 65

INTRODUCTION	HIGHET, GILBERT	IN	
WATCHFUL POKER CHIP OF H. MATISSE, THE			
	BRADBURY, RAY	SS	BEY 54 03
VELDT, THE (THE WORLD THE CHILDREN MADE)			
	BRADBURY, RAY	SS	SEP 50 09
HAIL AND FAREWELL	BRADBURY, RAY	SS	TDY 53 03
MEDICINE FOR MELANCHOLY, A	BRADBURY, RAY	SS	NEW 59 AC
FRUIT AT THE BOTTOM OF THE BOWL, THE (TOUCH AND GO)			
	BRADBURY, RAY	SS	DBM 48 11
YLLA (I'LL NOT LOOK FOR WINE)			
	BRADBURY, RAY	SS	MCL 50 01
LITTLE MICE, THE (THE MICE)	BRADBURY, RAY	SS	ESC 55 10
SMALL ASSASSIN, THE	BRADBURY, RAY	SS	DMN 46 11
ANTHEM SPRINTERS, THE (THE QUEEN'S OWN EVADERS)			
	BRADBURY, RAY	SS	PBY 63 06
AND THE ROCK CRIED OUT (THE MILLIONTH MURDER)			
	BRADBURY, RAY	SS	MHT 53 09
INVISIBLE BOY	BRADBURY, RAY	SS	MAD 45 11
NIGHT MEETING	BRADBURY, RAY	SS	NEW 51 AC
FOX AND THE FOREST, THE (TO THE FUTURE)			
	BRADBURY, RAY	SS	COL 50 05
SKELETON	BRADBURY, RAY	SS	WRT 45 09
KALEIDOSCOPE	BRADBURY, RAY	SS	TWS 49 10
SUN AND SHADOW	BRADBURY, RAY	SS	REP 53 03
ILLUSTRATED MAN, THE	BRADBURY, RAY	SS	NEW 51 AC
FOG HORN, THE (THE BEAST FROM 20,000 FATHOMS)			
	BRADBURY, RAY	SS	SEP 51 06
DWARF, THE	BRADBURY, RAY	SS	FAN 54 01
FEVER DREAM	BRADBURY, RAY	SS	WRT 48 09
WONDERFUL ICE CREAM SUIT, THE (THE MAGIC WHITE SUIT)			
	BRADBURY, RAY	SS	SEP 58 10
THERE WILL COME SOFT RAINS	BRADBURY, RAY	SS	COL 50 05
ILLUMINATION	BRADBURY, RAY	SS	REP 57 05
DANDELION WINE	BRADBURY, RAY	SS	GOR 53 06

VINTAGE BRADBURY, THE

```
STATUES                          BRADBURY, RAY            SS   NEW 57 NO
GREEN WINE FOR DREAMING          BRADBURY, RAY            SS   NEW 57 NO
VISIONS OF TOMORROW              ELWOOD, ROGER            AN   PKT 76 11
CHRONIC ARGONAUTS, THE           WELLS, H. G.             NV   SSJ 88 04
SUNJAMMER (ALSO AS THE WIND FROM THE SUN)
                                 CLARKE, ARTHUR C.        SS   BLF 64
MS. FOUND IN AN ABANDONED TIME MACHINE
                                 SILVERBERG, ROBERT       SS   TTM 73
STORM, THE                       DOZOIS, GARDNER R.       NV   FCR 75
LAST MAN, THE (1826)             SHELLEY, MARY W.         EX
BEGUM'S FORTUNE, THE (1879)      VERNE, JULES             EX
WITH THE NIGHT MAIL              KIPLING, RUDYARD         NV   MCS 05 11
LAND IRONCLADS, THE              WELLS, H. G.             NV   SND 03 12
LENNY                            ASIMOV, ISAAC            SS   INF 58 01
RUNNING, THE                     POSNER, RICHARD          SS   NEW 73 AN
CRYSTAL EGG, THE                 WELLS, H. G.             SS   NRV 97 05
ARIEL                            ELWOOD, ROGER            SS   NDM 74 04
SERPENT IN EDEN, THE             ANDERSON, POUL           NV   OMG 73
WEARIEST RIVER, THE              SCORTIA, THOMAS N.       NV   FUC 73
RESCUED GIRLS OF REFUGEE, THE
                                 MCCAFFREY, ANNE          SS   TTM 73
SHINING ONE, THE                 SCHACHNER, NAT           SS   ASF 37 05
MY FRIEND KLATU                  YEP, LAURENCE            NV   SAW 72
GENTLE CAPTIVE, THE              GODWIN, TOM              SS   SAW 72
LAST CONGREGATION, THE           GOLDSMITH, HOWARD        SS   FCR 75
TOWARDS THE BELOVED CITY         FARMER, PHILIP JOSE      NV   SAW 72
HIGH PRIEST                      BONE, J. F.              SS   STG 74

VISITOR FROM OUTER SPACE, A  ANONYMOUS                    AN H FLP 61
    SEE "SOVIET SCIENCE FICTION"

VOICE OF THE DOLPHINS, AND OTHER STORIES, THE
                                 SZILARD, LEO             AC H SAS 61
NIGHTMARE FOR FUTURE REFERENCE
                                 BENET, STEPHEN V.        PM   SCH 38 09
VOICE OF THE DOLPHINS, THE       SZILARD, LEO             SS
MY TRIAL AS A WAR CRIMINAL       SZILARD, LEO             SS   UCL 49 FL
MARK GABLE FOUNDATION, THE       SZILARD, LEO             SS       61
CALLING ALL STARS                SZILARD, LEO             SS       61
REPORT ON "GRAND CENTRAL TERMINAL"
                                 SZILARD, LEO             SS   UCM 52 06

VOICES IN THE DARK                COOPER, EDMUND          AC   DIG 60
UNICORN, THE                     COOPER, EDMUND           SS
SIX EGGS FOR MAFEKING            COOPER, EDMUND           SS
BOY DAVID, THE                   COOPER, EDMUND           SS
MOUSE THAT ROARED, THE           COOPER, EDMUND           SS
I AM A GHOST                     COOPER, EDMUND           SS
NINETEEN NINETY-FOUR             COOPER, EDMUND           SS
SENTIMENTAL JOURNEY              COOPER, EDMUND           SS
BURNT UMBER                      COOPER, EDMUND           SS
MILLER'S DAUGHTER                COOPER, EDMUND           SS
WHEN THE SAUCERS CAME            COOPER, EDMUND           SS
LIONS AND THE HARP, THE          COOPER, EDMUND           SS
FIRST MARTIAN, THE               COOPER, EDMUND           SS
DUET FOR ONE FINGER              COOPER, EDMUND           SS
SO I NEVER LEFT HOME             COOPER, EDMUND           SS
LAST ACT, THE                    COOPER, EDMUND           SS

VOICES OF TIME AND OTHER STORIES, THE
                                 BALLARD, J. G.           AC   BKM 62 02
VOICES OF TIME, THE              BALLARD, J. G.           SS   NWS 60 10
SOUND-SWEEP, THE                 BALLARD, J. G.           NV   SCF 60 02
OVERLOADED MAN, THE              BALLARD, J. G.           SS   NWS 61 07
ZONE OF TERROR                   BALLARD, J. G.           SS   NWS 60 03
MANHOLE 69                       BALLARD, J. G.           SS   NWS 57 11
WAITING GROUNDS, THE             BALLARD, J. G.           NV   NWS 59 11
DEEP END                         BALLARD, J. G.           SS   NWS 61 05

VOID BEYOND, AND OTHER STORIES, THE
                                 WILLIAMS, ROBERT M.      DC   ACE 58
VOID BEYOND, THE                 WILLIAMS, ROBERT M.      NV   TWS 51 04
REFUGE FOR TONIGHT               WILLIAMS, ROBERT M.      NV   BBM 49 03
CHALLENGE, THE                   WILLIAMS, ROBERT M.      SS   TWS 50 10
WEAPON, THE                      WILLIAMS, ROBERT M.      SS   AMZ 47 07
STUBBORN MEN, THE                WILLIAMS, ROBERT M.      SS   SSS 48 11
FINAL FRONTIER, THE              WILLIAMS, ROBERT M.      SS   SSS 50 01

VORTEX BLASTERS, THE             MOSKOWITZ, SAM           AN   MBB 65
    AND OTHER STORIES FROM MODERN MASTERPIECES OF SCIENCE FICTION
VORTEX BLASTER, THE              SMITH, EDWARD E. PHD     SS   CMT 41 07
REQUIEM                          HAMILTON, EDMOND         SS   AMZ 62 04
WITNESS, THE                     RUSSELL, ERIC FRANK      SS   OWS 51 09
KINDNESS                         DEL REY, LESTER          SS   ASF 44 10
WE ALSO WALK DOGS                HEINLEIN, ROBERT A.      SS   ASF 41 07
COMING ATTRACTION                LEIBER, FRITZ            SS   GAL 50 11
WE GUARD THE BLACK PLANET!       KUTTNER, HENRY           NV   SSS 42 11

VOYAGE OF THE SPACE BEAGLE, THE
                                 VAN VOGT, A. E.          NO H SAS 50
    IN "TRIAD"
    ALSO AS "MISSION: INTERPLANETARY"
BLACK DESTROYER                  VAN VOGT, A. E.          NV   ASF 39 07
DISCORD IN SCARLET               VAN VOGT, A. E.          NV   ASF 39 12
WAR OF NERVES                    VAN VOGT, A. E.          SS   OWS 50 05

VOYAGERS IN TIME                 SILVERBERG, ROBERT       AN H MDT 67
INTRODUCTION                     SILVERBERG, ROBERT       IN
SANDS OF TIME, THE               MILLER, P. SCHUYLER      SN   ASF 37 04
AND IT COMES OUT HERE            DEL REY, LESTER          SS   GAL 51 02
BROOKLYN PROJECT                 TENN, WILLIAM            SS   PLS 48 FL
MEN WHO MURDERED MOHAMMED, THE
                                 BESTER, ALFRED           SS   FSF 58 10
TIME HEALS                       ANDERSON, POUL           SS   ASF 49 10
WRONG-WAY STREET                 NIVEN, LARRY             SS   GAL 65 04
```

WANDERING STARS

```
FLUX                             MOORCOCK, MICHAEL        NV   NWS 63 07
DOMINOES                         KORNBLUTH, C. M.         SS   STR 53 01
BULLETIN FROM THE TRUSTEES, A
                                 SHORE, WILMA             SS   FSF 64 08
TRAVELER'S REST                  MASSON, DAVID I.         SS   NWS 65 09
ABSOLUTELY INFLEXIBLE            SILVERBERG, ROBERT       SS   FUN 56 07
TIME MACHINE, THE (CHAPTER XI, XII-PART)
                                 WELLS, H. G.             EX   NRV 95 01

VOYAGES: SCENARIOS FOR A SHIP CALLED EARTH
                                 SAUER, ROB               AN   BAL 71 04
FOREWORD                         EHRLICH, DR. PAUL R.
                                 AND EHRLICH, ANNE H.     IN C
ZERO POPULATION GROWTH: A STATEMENT
                                 MISC. MATERIAL           MS
NIGGER OF THE NARCISSUS          CONRAD, JOSEPH           EX
BILLENIUM                        BALLARD, J. G.           SS   NWS 61 11
OTHER, THE                       MACLEAN, KATHERINE       SS   NWS 66 07
PATTERN                          BROWN, FREDRIC           SS   NEW 54 AC
PURPLE CHILD, THE                BELAVAL, EMILIO S.       SS       66
ALL SUMMER IN A DAY              BRADBURY, RAY            SS   FSF 54 03
AUTO-DA-FE                       ZELAZNY, ROGER           SS   DVS 67 01
HEAT DEATH OF THE UNIVERSE, THE
                                 ZOLINE, PAMELA A.        SS   NWS 67 07
FOOD FARM, THE                   REED, KIT                SS   ORB 67 02
STUDENT BODY                     WALLACE, F. L.           NV   GAL 53 03
MILD ATTACK OF LOCUSTS, A        LESSING, DORIS           SS       51
DOCTOR SCHMIDT                   SHAMIR, MOSHE            SS       52
GOLDEN ACRES                     REED, KIT                NV       68
CHOICE, THE                      HILTON-YOUNG, WAYLAND    SS   FUN 52 03
BIG FLASH, THE                   SPINRAD, NORMAN          NV   ORB 69 05
POPULATION CONTROL, 1986         PAREDES, HORACIO V.      SS   ATS 70 04
TUNNEL AHEAD, THE                GLASER, ALICE            SS   FSF 61 11
CONSUMER'S REPORT (NO GUN TO THE VICTOR)
                                 COGSWELL, THEODORE R     SS   IMG 55 10
SHARK SHIP (REAP THE DARK TIDE)
                                 KORNBLUTH, C. M.         NV   VAN 58 06
LETTER TO THOSE WHO SEE NO THREAT, A
                                 POPE, CARL               AR
GENERALIZED NONFICTION BIBLIOGRAPHY
                                 MISC. MATERIAL           MS
CHARTING A BETTER VOYAGE- ZPG
                                 ROGERS, NORMAN L.        AR

WALKER THROUGH WALLS, THE        AYME, MARCEL             AC   BRK 62
    IN ENGLAND AS "ACROSS PARIS AND OTHER STORIES"
WALKER-THROUGH-WALLS, THE        AYME, MARCEL             SS   FSF 59 08
RUE D'EVANGILE                   AYME, MARCEL             SS
WINE OF PARIS, THE               AYME, MARCEL             SS
MARTIN THE NOVELIST              AYME, MARCEL             SS
DWARF, THE                       AYME, MARCEL             SS
STATE OF GRACE, THE              AYME, MARCEL             SS   FSF 59 12
SEVEN-LEAGUE BOOTS, THE          AYME, MARCEL             SS
DERMUCHE                         AYME, MARCEL             SS
ROLL OF DAUGHTERS, A             AYME, MARCEL             SS
PICTURE-WELL, THE                AYME, MARCEL             SS
LEGEND OF POLDEVIA               AYME, MARCEL             SS
ACROSS PARIS                     AYME, MARCEL             SS

WALL AROUND THE WORLD, THE   COGSWELL, THEODORE R  AC   PYR 62 02
FANTASY AND/OR SCIENCE FICTION
                                 BOUCHER, ANTHONY         IN
FANTASY IN SCIENCE FICTION- NO
                                 POHL, FREDERIK           IN
MASTERS, THE                     COGSWELL, THEODORE R     SS   TWS 54 SU
SPECTER GENERAL, THE             COGSWELL, THEODORE R     NV   ASF 52 06
WOLFIE                           COGSWELL, THEODORE R     SS   BEY 54 SU
EMERGENCY RATIONS                COGSWELL, THEODORE R     SS   IMG 53 09
BURNING, THE                     COGSWELL, THEODORE R     SS   FSF 60 07
THINGS                           COGSWELL, THEODORE R     SS   FSF 58 05
TEST AREA                        COGSWELL, THEODORE R     SS   FUN 55 02
PRISONER OF LOVE                 COGSWELL, THEODORE R     SS   NEW 62 AC
INVASION REPORT                  COGSWELL, THEODORE R     SS   GAL 54 08
WALL AROUND THE WORLD, THE       COGSWELL, THEODORE R     NV   BEY 53 09

WANDERERS OF TIME                WYNDHAM, JOHN            AC   CNT 73
BEFORE THE TRIFFIDS...           GILLINGS, WALTER         IN
WANDERERS OF TIME                WYNDHAM, JOHN            NV   TOW 41 WI
DERELICT OF SPACE                WYNDHAM, JOHN            NV   FSB 39 03
CHILD OF POWER                   WYNDHAM, JOHN            NV   FSB 39 03
LAST LUNARIANS, THE              WYNDHAM, JOHN            SS   TOW 38 SU
PUFF-BALL MENACE, THE            WYNDHAM, JOHN            NV   TOW 38 SU

WANDERING STARS                  DANN, JACK M.            AN H HPR 74
WHY ME?                          ASIMOV, ISAAC            IN
ON VENUS, HAVE WE GOT A RABBI
                                 TENN, WILLIAM            NV   NEW 74 AN
GOLEM, THE                       DAVIDSON, AVRAM          SS   FSF 55 03
UNTO THE FOURTH GENERATION       ASIMOV, ISAAC            SS   FSF 59 04
LOOK, YOU THINK YOU'VE GOT TROUBLES
                                 CARR, CAROL              SS   ORB 69 05
GOSLIN DAY                       DAVIDSON, AVRAM          SS   ORB 70 06
DYBBUK OF MAZEL TOV IV, THE      SILVERBERG, ROBERT       SS   NEW 74 AN
TROUBLE WITH WATER               GOLD, H. L.              SS   UNK 39 03
GATHER BLUE ROSES                SARGENT, PAMELA          SS   FSF 72 02
JEWBIRD, THE                     MALAMUD, BERNARD         SS   REP 63 04
PARADISE LAST                    EFFINGER, GEO. ALEC      NV   NEW 74 AN
STREET OF DREAMS, FEET OF CLAY
                                 SHECKLEY, ROBERT         NV   GAL 68 02
JACHID AND JECHIDAH              SINGER, ISAAC B.         SS       64
I'M LOOKING FOR KADAK            ELLISON, HARLAN          NV   NEW 74 AN
ELLISON'S GRAMMATICAL GUIDE AND GLOSSARY FOR GOYIM
                                 ELLISON, HARLAN          MS
EVISE, THE ZSOUCHMOID            KIRK, TIM                IL
```

WAR AGAINST THE RULL, THE   WHAT STRANGE STARS AND SKIES

WAR AGAINST THE RULL, THE   VAN VOGT, A. E.   NO H SAS 59 09
    REPETITION (ALSO AS THE GRYB)
                             VAN VOGT, A. E.   NV   ASF 40 04
    CO-OPERATE- OR ELSE| VAN VOGT, A. E.   NV   ASF 42 04
    SECOND SOLUTION, THE   VAN VOGT, A. E.   SS   ASF 42 10
    RULL, THE   VAN VOGT, A. E.   NV   ASF 48 05
    GREEN FOREST, THE   VAN VOGT, A. E.   NV   ASF 49 06
    SOUND, THE   VAN VOGT, A. E.   NV   ASF 50 02

WAR OF THE WORLDS, THE TIME MACHINE AND SELECTED SHORT STORIES
                             WELLS, H. G.   AC H PLM 63
    H. G. WELLS   AMIS, KINGSLEY   IN
    WAR OF THE WORLDS, THE   WELLS, H. G.   NA   PRS 97 04
    TIME MACHINE, THE   WELLS, H. G.   NA   NRV 95 01
    CRYSTAL EGG, THE   WELLS, H. G.   SS   NRV 97 05
    STORY OF THE LATE MR. ELVESHAM, THE
                             WELLS, H. G.   SS   IDL 96 05
    RED ROOM, THE   WELLS, H. G.   SS   IDL 96 03
    VALLEY OF SPIDERS, THE   WELLS, H. G.   SS   PRS 03 03
    IN THE ABYSS   WELLS, H. G.   SS   PRS 96 08
    IN THE AVU OBSERVATORY   WELLS, H. G.   SS   PMB 94 08
    TRUTH ABOUT PYECRAFT, THE WELLS, H. G.   SS   SND 03 04
    ABOUT H. G. WELLS: BIOGRAPHICAL NOTES
                             MISC. MATERIAL   MS

WAR WITH THE ROBOTS   HARRISON, HARRY   AC   PYR 62 09
    WORD FROM THE (HUMAN) EDITOR..., A
                             HARRISON, HARRY   IN
    SIMULATED TRAINER (TRAINEE FOR MARS)
                             HARRISON, HARRY   SS   FUN 58 06
    VELVET GLOVE, THE   HARRISON, HARRY   NV   FUN 56 11
    ARM OF THE LAW   HARRISON, HARRY   SS   FUN 58 08
    ROBOT WHO WANTED TO KNOW, THE
                             HARRISON, HARRY   SS   FUN 58 03
    I SEE YOU (ROBOT JUSTICE, FUN 59 07)
                             HARRISON, HARRY   SS   NWS 59 05
    REPAIRMAN, THE   HARRISON, HARRY   SS   GAL 58 02
    SURVIVAL PLANET   HARRISON, HARRY   SS   FSF 61 08
    WAR WITH THE ROBOTS   HARRISON, HARRY   SS   SFE 62 07

WARM WORLDS AND OTHERWISE   TIPTREE, JAMES JR.   AC   BAL 75 02
    WHO IS TIPTREE, WHAT IS HE? SILVERBERG, ROBERT IN
    ALL THE KINDS OF YES (FILOMENA & GREG & RIKKI-TIKKI & BARLOW &
        THE ALIEN)   TIPTREE, JAMES JR.   NV   NDM 72 02
    MILK OF PARADISE, THE   TIPTREE, JAMES JR.   SS   DVS 72 02
    AND I HAVE COME UPON THIS PLACE BY LOST WAYS
                             TIPTREE, JAMES JR.   NV   NOV 72 02
    LAST FLIGHT OF DR. AIN, THE TIPTREE, JAMES JR. SS GAL 69 03
    AMBERJACK   TIPTREE, JAMES JR.   SS   GEN 72
    THROUGH A LASS DARKLY   TIPTREE, JAMES JR.   SS   GEN 72
    GIRL WHO WAS PLUGGED IN, THE TIPTREE, JAMES JR. NV NDM 73 03
    NIGHTBLOOMING SAURIAN, THE TIPTREE, JAMES JR. SS IFS 70 05
    WOMEN MEN DON'T SEE, THE TIPTREE, JAMES JR. NV   FSF 73 12
    FAULT   TIPTREE, JAMES JR.   SS   FAN 68 08
    LOVE IS THE PLAN THE PLAN IS DEATH
                             TIPTREE, JAMES JR.   SS   ALC 73
    ON THE LAST AFTERNOON   TIPTREE, JAMES JR.   NA   AMZ 72 11

WAY HOME, A   STURGEON, THEODORE   AC H FKW 55
    EDITED BY GROFF CONKLIN
    ENGLISH DERIVATIVE COLLECTION "THUNDER AND ROSES"
    INTRODUCTION   CONKLIN, GROFF   IN
    UNITE AND CONQUER   STURGEON, THEODORE   NV   ASF 48 10
    SPECIAL APTITUDE (LAST LAUGH)
                             STURGEON, THEODORE   SS   OWS 51 03
    MEWHU'S JET   STURGEON, THEODORE   NV   ASF 46 11
    HURRICANE TRIO   STURGEON, THEODORE   NV   GAL 55 04
    AND MY FEAR IS GREAT   STURGEON, THEODORE   NA   BEY 53 07
    MINORITY REPORT   STURGEON, THEODORE   SS   ASF 49 06
    HURKLE IS A HAPPY BEAST, THE STURGEON, THEODORE SS FSF 49 FL
    THUNDER AND ROSES   STURGEON, THEODORE   SS   ASF 47 11
    BULKHEAD (WHO?)   STURGEON, THEODORE   NV   GAL 55 03
    TINY AND THE MONSTER   STURGEON, THEODORE   NV   ASF 47 05
    WAY HOME, A   STURGEON, THEODORE   SS   AMZ 53 05

WAY HOME, A (9 OF 11)   STURGEON, THEODORE   AC   PYR 56
    EDITED BY GROFF CONKLIN
    INTRODUCTION   CONKLIN, GROFF   IN
    UNITE AND CONQUER   STURGEON, THEODORE   NV   ASF 48 10
    SPECIAL APTITUDE (LAST LAUGH)
                             STURGEON, THEODORE   SS   OWS 51 03
    MEWHU'S JET   STURGEON, THEODORE   NV   ASF 46 11
    HURRICANE TRIO   STURGEON, THEODORE   NV   GAL 55 04
    HURKLE IS A HAPPY BEAST, THE STURGEON, THEODORE SS FSF 49 FL
    THUNDER AND ROSES   STURGEON, THEODORE   SS   ASF 47 11
    BULKHEAD (WHO?)   STURGEON, THEODORE   NV   GAL 55 03
    TINY AND THE MONSTER   STURGEON, THEODORE   NV   ASF 47 05
    WAY HOME, A   STURGEON, THEODORE   SS   AMZ 53 05

WAY OUT   HOWARD, IVAN   AN   BEL 63 12
    ENNUI   LESSER, MILTON   SS   DSF 52 12
    KNOWLEDGE IS POWER   FYFE, H. B.   NV   DSF 52 12
    SNAIL'S PACE   BUDRYS, ALGIS   SS   DSF 53 10
    "X" FOR "EXPENDABLE"   BAILEY, WILLIAM C.   SS   DSF 52 12
    BLOOD LANDS   COPPEL, ALFRED   NV   DSF 52 12
    BLUNDER ENLIGHTENING   DRYFOOS, DAVE   NV   DSF 52 12
    HONORABLE ENEMIES   ANDERSON, POUL   NV   FUT 51 05

WEAPON SHOPS OF ISHER, THE   VAN VOGT, A. E.   NO H GBG 51
    ALSO IN "A TREASURY OF GREAT SCIENCE FICTION VOL. 1"
    SEESAW, THE   VAN VOGT, A. E.   SS   ASF 41 07
    WEAPON SHOP, THE   VAN VOGT, A. E.   NV   ASF 42 12
    WEAPON SHOPS OF ISHER, THE VAN VOGT, A. E.   NA   TWS 49 02

WEIGHER OF SOULS AND THE EARTH DWELLERS, THE
                             MAUROIS, ANDRE   AC H MAC 63

INTRODUCTION   MAUROIS, ANDRE   IN
TRANSLATION   MILES, HAMIS   MS
ILLUSTRATIONS   FISHER, LEONARD E.   IL
WEIGHER OF SOULS, THE   MAUROIS, ANDRE   NV   PFM 50 10
EARTH DWELLERS, THE   MAUROIS, ANDRE   NV   63
EPILOGUE   CHORON, JACQUES   MS

WEIRD ONES, THE   HOWARD, IVAN   AN   BEL 62 07
    MY WORD   GOLD, H. L.   IN
    SMALL LORDS   POHL, FREDERIK   NV   SFQ 57 02
    SENTIMENT, INC.   ANDERSON, POUL   NV   SFS 53 01
    NAME YOUR TIGER   LESSER, MILTON   NV   SFQ 57 05
    IRON MAN   BINDER, EANDO   SS   FUT 55 28
    HUNTED ONES, THE   REYNOLDS, MACK   NV   SFS 59 11
    HAIL TO THE CHIEF   SACKETT, SAM   SN   FUT 54 06
    IMPRACTICAL JOKE   DE CAMP, L. SPRAGUE SS   FUT 56 29

WEIRD SHADOWS FROM BEYOND CARNELL, JOHN   AN   AVN 69 04
    INTRODUCTION   CARNELL, JOHN   IN
    DANSE MACABRE   PEAKE, MERVYN   SS   SCF 63 10
    BLOOD OFFERING   KIPPAX, JOHN   SS   SCF 61 06
    SAME TIME, SAME PLACE PEAKE, MERVYN   SS   SCF 63 08
    MASTER OF CHAOS   MOORCOCK, MICHAEL   SS   FAN 64 05
    WEDNESDAY'S CHILD   TENN, WILLIAM   SS   FUN 56 01
    DIAL "O" FOR OPERATOR PRESSLIE, ROBERT   SS   SCF 58 02
    FLOWERS OF THE FOREST, THE ALDISS, BRIAN W. SS SCF 57 08
    FRESH GUY   TUBB, E. C.   SS   SCF 58 06
    GARDEN OF PARIS, THE WILLIAMS, ERIC C.   SS   NEW 65 AN
    GRAVEYARD READER, THE STURGEON, THEODORE SS SCF 58 10

WEIRD SHOW   PLAYBOY, EDITORS OF AN   PBP 71
    PREFACE   PLAYBOY, EDITORS OF IN
    WEIRD SHOW   GOLD, HERBERT   SS   PBY 58 04
    RECLUSE AND HIS GUEST, A WILLIAMS, TENNESSEE SS PBY 70 01
    I DO NOT LIKE THEE, DR. FELDMAN
                         SLESAR, HENRY   SS   PBY 59 06
    ACCIDENTS OF A COUNTRY ROAD DIONNE, ROGER SS PBY 70 11
    BY APPOINTMENT ONLY MATHESON, RICHARD   SS   PBY 70 04
    LIFE IN THE DAY OF, A ROBINSON, FRANK M. SS PBY 69 06
    SOFTLY WALKS THE BEETLE COLLIER, JOHN   SS   PBY 60 01
    CONVERT, THE   PURDY, KEN W.   SS   PBY 70 03
    DOUBLE EXPOSURE   REESE, JOHN   SS   PBY 65 02
    MACHINE IN WARD ELEVEN, THE WILLEFORD, CHARLES NV PBY 61 03
    ACADEMY, THE   ELY, DAVID   SS   PBY 65 06
    PARTY, THE   NOLAN, WILLIAM F.   SS   PBY 67 04
    NASTY   BROWN, FREDRIC   SS   PBY 59 04
    I'M YOURS   SCHAFHAUSER, CHARLES SS   PBY 54 12
    TASTE OF FEAR, THE   FOSTER, HUGH G.   SS   PBY 59 09
    KONG OF KUXAN   RUSSELL, RAY   SS   PBY 70 10

WEIRD TALES   MARGULIES, LEO   AN   PYR 64 05
    INTRODUCTION   MARGULIES, LEO   IN
    MAN WHO RETURNED, THE HAMILTON, EDMOND   SS   WRT 34 02
    SPIDER MANSION   LEIBER, FRITZ   SS   WRT 42 09
    QUESTION OF ETIQUETTE, A BLOCH, ROBERT   SS   WRT 42 09
    SEA WITCH, THE   DYALHIS, NICTZIN   NV   WRT 37 12
    STRANGE HIGH HOUSE IN THE MIST, THE
                         LOVECRAFT, H. P.   SS   WRT 31 10
    DRIFTING SNOW, THE   DERLETH, AUGUST   SS   WRT 39 02
    BODY-MASTERS, THE   LONG, FRANK BELKNAP SS   WRT 35 02
    PIGEONS FROM HELL   HOWARD, ROBERT E.   NV   WRT 38 05

WELCOME TO THE MONKEY HOUSE VONNEGUT, KURT JR. AC H DCT 68
    PREFACE   VONNEGUT, KURT JR.   IN
    WHERE I LIVE (YOU'VE NEVER BEEN TO BARNSTABLE?)
                         VONNEGUT, KURT JR.   AR   VTR 64 10
    HARRISON BERGERON   VONNEGUT, KURT JR.   SS   FSF 61 10
    WHO AM I THIS TIME? (MY NAME IS EVERYONE)
                         VONNEGUT, KURT JR.   SS   SEP 61 12
    WELCOME TO THE MONKEY HOUSE VONNEGUT, KURT JR. SS PBY 68 01
    LONG WALK TO FOREVER VONNEGUT, KURT JR. SS   LHJ 60 08
    FOSTER PORTFOLIO, THE VONNEGUT, KURT JR. SS   COL 51 09
    MISS TEMPTATION   VONNEGUT, KURT JR.   SS   SEP 56 04
    ALL THE KING'S HORSES VONNEGUT, KURT JR. SS   COL 51 02
    TOM EDISON'S SHAGGY DOG VONNEGUT, KURT JR. SS COL 53 03
    NEW DICTIONARY (THE RANDOM HOUSE DICTIONARY)
                         VONNEGUT, KURT JR.   BR   NYT 66 10
    NEXT DOOR   VONNEGUT, KURT JR.   SS   CMP 55 04
    MORE STATELY MANSIONS VONNEGUT, KURT JR. SS   COL 51 12
    HYANNIS PORT STORY, THE VONNEGUT, KURT JR. SS NEW 68 AC
    D.P.   VONNEGUT, KURT JR.   SS   LHJ 53 08
    REPORT ON THE BARNHOUSE EFFECT
                         VONNEGUT, KURT JR.   SS   COL 50 02
    EUPHIO QUESTION, THE VONNEGUT, KURT JR. SS   COL 51 05
    GO BACK TO YOUR PRECIOUS WIFE AND SON
                         VONNEGUT, KURT JR.   SS   LHJ 62 07
    DEER IN THE WORKS   VONNEGUT, KURT JR.   SS   ESQ 55 04
    LIE, THE   VONNEGUT, KURT JR.   SS   SEP 62 02
    UNREADY TO WEAR   VONNEGUT, KURT JR.   SS   GAL 53 04
    KID NOBODY COULD HANDLE, THE VONNEGUT, KURT JR. SS SEP 55 09
    MANNED MISSILES, THE VONNEGUT, KURT JR. SS   CMP 58 07
    EPICAC   VONNEGUT, KURT JR.   SS   COL 50 11
    ADAM   VONNEGUT, KURT JR.   SS   CMP 54 04
    TOMORROW AND TOMORROW AND TOMORROW (THE BIG TRIP UP YONDER)
                         VONNEGUT, KURT JR.   SS   GAL 54 01

WHAT STRANGE STARS AND SKIES DAVIDSON, AVRAM   AC   ACE 65
    INTRODUCTION   DAVIDSON, AVRAM   IN
    WHAT STRANGE STARS AND SKIES DAVIDSON, AVRAM SS FSF 63 12
    BOUNTY HUNTER, THE   DAVIDSON, AVRAM   SS   FUN 58 03
    OGRE, THE   DAVIDSON, AVRAM   SS   IFS 59 07
    FAIR TRADE   DAVIDSON, AVRAM   SS   FSF 60 07
    LOVE CALLED THIS THING DAVIDSON, AVRAM
                         AND GOFORTH, LAURA   SS C GAL 59 04
    FAED-OUT   DAVIDSON, AVRAM   SS   FSF 63 10

WHAT STRANGE STARS AND SKIES   WINDOW ON THE FUTURE

LINEAMENTS OF GRATIFIED DESIRE, THE
                                   DAVIDSON, AVRAM   SS
TEETH OF DESPAIR, THE   DAVIDSON, AVRAM
                                   AND KLEIN, SIDNEY   SS C FSF 61 05
JURY-RIG   DAVIDSON, AVRAM   SS   VSF 57 11
MISS BUTTERMOUTH   DAVIDSON, AVRAM   SS   FSF 62 05
WHERE DO YOU LIVE, QUEEN ESTHER?
                                   DAVIDSON, AVRAM   SS   FSF 64 11
MR. STILWELL'S STAGE   DAVIDSON, AVRAM   SS   FSF 57 09
UNKNOWN LAW, THE   DAVIDSON, AVRAM   NV   FSF 64 06
SINGULAR EVENTS WHICH OCCURRED IN THE HOVEL ON THE ALLEY OFF
  OF EYE STREET, THE   DAVIDSON, AVRAM   SS   FSF 62 02

WHAT'S BECOME OF SCREWLOOSE? AND OTHER INQUIRIES
                                   GOULART, RON   AC H SCB 71
WHAT'S BECOME OF SCREWLOOSE?   GOULART, RON   SS   IFS 70 07
JUNIOR PARTNER   GOULART, RON   SS   FAN 62 09
HARDCASTLE   GOULART, RON   SS   NEW 71 AC
INTO THE SHOP   GOULART, RON   SS   FSF 64 04
PREZ   GOULART, RON   SS   IFS 70 02
CONFESSIONS   GOULART, RON   NV   FSF 70 08
MONTE CRISTO COMPLEX   GOULART, RON   SS
YES-MEN OF VENUS, THE   GOULART, RON   SS   AMZ 63 07
KEEPING AN EYE ON JANEY   GOULART, RON   SS   INY 70 01
HOBO JUNGLE   GOULART, RON   NV   FSF 70 06

WHAT'S IT LIKE OUT THERE? AND OTHER STORIES
                                   HAMILTON, EDMOND   AC ACE 74
WHAT'S IT LIKE OUT THERE?   HAMILTON, EDMOND   NV   TWS 52 12
KING OF SHADOWS, THE   HAMILTON, EDMOND   NV   WRT 47 01
CASTAWAY   HAMILTON, EDMOND   SS   68
SERPENT PRINCESS   HAMILTON, EDMOND   NV   WRT 48 01
STARS, MY BROTHERS, THE   HAMILTON, EDMOND   NV   AMZ 62 05
DREAMER'S WORLD   HAMILTON, EDMOND   NV   WRT 41 11
TWILIGHT OF THE GODS   HAMILTON, EDMOND   NV   WRT 48 07
SUNFIRE!   HAMILTON, EDMOND   SS   AMZ 62 09
INN OUTSIDE THE WORLD, THE   HAMILTON, EDMOND   SS   WRT 45 07
WATCHER OF THE AGES, THE   HAMILTON, EDMOND   SS   WRT 48 09
TRANSURANIC   HAMILTON, EDMOND   SS   TWS 48 02
ISLE OF THE SLEEPER, THE   HAMILTON, EDMOND   SS   WRT 51 05

WHEELS OF IF, THE   DE CAMP, L. SPRAGUE   AC H SHS 48
FOREWORD   DE CAMP, L. SPRAGUE   IN
WHEELS OF IF, THE   DE CAMP, L. SPRAGUE   SN   UNK 40 10
BEST-LAID SCHEME, THE   DE CAMP, L. SPRAGUE   SS   ASF 41 02
WARRIOR RACE, THE   DE CAMP, L. SPRAGUE   SS   ASF 40 10
HYPERPELOSITY   DE CAMP, L. SPRAGUE   SS   ASF 38 04
MERMAN, THE   DE CAMP, L. SPRAGUE   SS   ASF 38 12
CONTRABAND COW, THE   DE CAMP, L. SPRAGUE   SS   ASF 42 07
GNARLY MAN, THE   DE CAMP, L. SPRAGUE   NV   UNK 39 06

WHEN HARLIE WAS ONE   GERROLD, DAVID   NO H NDB 72
ORACLE FOR A WHITE RABBIT   GERROLD, DAVID   NV   GAL 69 12
GOD MACHINE, THE   GERROLD, DAVID   NV   GAL 70 05
TROUBLE WITH G.O.D., THE   GERROLD, DAVID   NV   GAL 72 05
FOR G.O.D.'S SAKE   GERROLD, DAVID   NV   GAL 72 07

WHEN TWO WORLDS MEET   WILLIAMS, ROBERT M.   AC CUR 70
  STORIES OF MEN ON MARS
WHEN TWO WORLDS MEET   WILLIAMS, ROBERT M.   NV   AMZ 50 04
AUROCHS CAME WALKING   WILLIAMS, ROBERT M.   SS   FSF 53 12
ON PAIN OF DEATH   WILLIAMS, ROBERT M.   NV   ASF 42 06
SOUND OF BUGLES, THE   WILLIAMS, ROBERT M.   SS   STS 49 03
FINAL FRONTIER, THE   WILLIAMS, ROBERT M.   SS   SSS 50 01
WHEN THE SPOILERS CAME   WILLIAMS, ROBERT M.   NV   PLS 52 05

WHEN WOMEN RULE   MOSKOWITZ, SAM   AN H WKR 72
WHEN WOMEN RULE   MOSKOWITZ, SAM   AR   IFS 67 08
AMAZONS, THE (500 B.C.)   HERODOTUS   AR
QUEEN OF CALIFORNIA, THE (1510, TRANSLATION AND NOTES BY
  EDWARD EVERETT HALE)   MONTALVO, GARCIA O.   NV
REVOLT OF THE..., THE   BARR, ROBERT   SS   IDL 94 05
JUNE 6, 2016   ENGLAND, GEORGE A.   NV   COL 16 04
VEILED FEMINISTS OF ATLANTIS, THE
                                   TARKINGTON, BOOTH   SS   FRM 26 03
LAST MAN, THE   WEST, WALLACE   NV   AMZ 29 02
LAST WOMAN, THE   GARDNER, THOMAS S.   SS   WOS 32 04
FEMININE METAMORPHOSIS, THE   KELLER, DAVID H. MD.   NA   SWS 29 08
PRIESTESS WHO REBELLED, THE (ALSO AS PILGRIMAGE)
                                   BOND, NELSON S.   SS   AMZ 39 10

WHERE DO WE GO FROM HERE?   ASIMOV, ISAAC   AN H DBL 71
INTRODUCTION   ASIMOV, ISAAC   IN
MARTIAN ODYSSEY, A   WEINBAUM, STANLEY G.   NV   WOS 34 07
NIGHT   CAMPBELL, JOHN W. JR   NV   ASF 35 10
DAY IS DONE, THE   DEL REY, LESTER   SS   ASF 39 05
HEAVY PLANET   ROTHMAN, MILTON A.   SS   ASF 39 08
AND HE BUILT A CROOKED HOUSE   HEINLEIN, ROBERT A.   SS   ASF 41 02
PROOF   CLEMENT, HAL   SS   ASF 42 06
SUBWAY NAMED MOBIUS, A   DEUTSCH, A. J.   SS   ASF 50 12
SURFACE TENSION   BLISH, JAMES   NA   GAL 52 08
COUNTRY DOCTOR   MORRISON, WILLIAM   NV   STR 53 01
HOLES AROUND MARS, THE   BIXBY, JEROME   SS   GAL 54 01
DEEP RANGE, THE (ARB 54 04)   CLARKE, ARTHUR C.   NV   STR 54 03
CAVE OF NIGHT, THE   GUNN, JAMES E.   SS   GAL 55 02
DUST RAG   CLEMENT, HAL   SS   ASF 56 09
PATE DE FOIE GRAS   ASIMOV, ISAAC   SF   ASF 56 09
OMNILINGUAL   PIPER, H. BEAM   NV   ASF 57 02
BIG BOUNCE, THE   TEVIS, WALTER S. JR.   SS   GAL 58 02
NEUTRON STAR   NIVEN, LARRY   NV   IFS 66 10

WHITE FANG GOES DINGO AND OTHER FUNNY S.F. STORIES
                                   DISCH, THOMAS M.   AC ARW 71
102 H-BOMBS   DISCH, THOMAS M.   NV   FAN 65 03
BONE OF CONTENTION   DISCH, THOMAS M.   SS   AHM 66
DANGEROUS FLAGS   DISCH, THOMAS M.   SS   FAN 64 08

DEMI-URGE, THE   DISCH, THOMAS M.   SS   AMZ 63 06
FINAL AUDIT   DISCH, THOMAS M.   SS   FAN 63 07
UTOPIA? NEVER!   DISCH, THOMAS M.   SS   AMZ 63 08
PRINCESS' CARILLON, THE (THE ENCHANTED PRINCE)
                                   DISCH, THOMAS M.   SS   FAN 63 08
GENETIC CODA   DISCH, THOMAS M.   SS   FAN 64 06
INVADED BY LOVE   DISCH, THOMAS M.   SS   NWS 66 09
VAMP, THE   DISCH, THOMAS M.   SS   FAN 65 02
RETURN OF THE MEDUSAE, THE   DISCH, THOMAS M.   SS   FAN 63 08
INVASION OF THE GIANT STUPID DINOSAURS, THE
                                   DISCH, THOMAS M.   SS   AMZ 69 03
DESCENT OF THE WEST END, THE   DISCH, THOMAS M.   SS   NWS 67 03
HAPPY STORY, THE   DISCH, THOMAS M.   SS
WONDERFUL WORLD OF GRISWALD TRACTORS, THE
                                   DISCH, THOMAS M.   SS   NWQ 72 03
DISCOVERY OF THE NULLITRON, THE
                                   DISCH, THOMAS M.
                                   AND SLADEK, JOHN T.   PA C GAL 67 02
DANNY'S NEW FRIENDS FROM DENEB
                                   DISCH, THOMAS M.
                                   AND SLADEK, JOHN T.   SS C
AFFLUENCE OF EDWIN LOLLARD, THE
                                   DISCH, THOMAS M.   SS   NWR 67 10
WHITE FANG GOES DINGO   DISCH, THOMAS M.   NV   IFS 65 04

WHO CAN REPLACE A MAN?   ALDISS, BRIAN W.   AC H HBW 66
    SEE "BEST SCIENCE FICTION STORIES OF BRIAN W. ALDISS"

WHO FEARS THE DEVIL?   WELLMAN, MANLY WADE   AC H ARK 63
WONDER AS I WANDER   WELLMAN, MANLY WADE   SS   FSF 62 03
O UGLY BIRD!   WELLMAN, MANLY WADE   SS   FSF 51 12
ONE OTHER   WELLMAN, MANLY WADE   SS   FSF 53 08
SHIVER IN THE PINES   WELLMAN, MANLY WADE   SS   FSF 55 02
OLD DEVILNS WAS A-WAITING   WELLMAN, MANLY WADE   SS   FSF 57 02
DESRICK ON YANDRO, THE   WELLMAN, MANLY WADE   SS   FSF 52 06
VANDY, VANDY   WELLMAN, MANLY WADE   SS   FSF 53 03
DUMB SUPPER (CALL ME FROM THE VALLEY)
                                   WELLMAN, MANLY WADE   SS   FSF 54 03
LITTLE BLACK TRAIN, THE   WELLMAN, MANLY WADE   SS   FSF 54 08
WALK LIKE A MOUNTAIN   WELLMAN, MANLY WADE   SS   FSF 55 06
ON THE HILLS AND EVERYWHERE   WELLMAN, MANLY WADE   SS   FSF 56 01
NINE YARDS OF OTHER CLOTH   WELLMAN, MANLY WADE   SS   FSF 58 07

WHO GOES THERE?   CAMPBELL, JOHN W. JR AC H SHS 48
    IN ENGLAND AS "THE THING AND OTHER STORIES" AND
    "THE THING FROM OUTER SPACE"

WHO GOES THERE? AND OTHER STORIES
                                   CAMPBELL, JOHN W. JR AC DEL 55
ABOUT JOHN CAMPBELL   STURGEON, THEODORE   MS
WHO GOES THERE?   CAMPBELL, JOHN W. JR NV   ASF 38 08
TWILIGHT   CAMPBELL, JOHN W. JR SS   ASF 34 11
NIGHT   CAMPBELL, JOHN W. JR NV   ASF 35 10
BLINDNESS   CAMPBELL, JOHN W. JR SS   ASF 35 03
OUT OF NIGHT   CAMPBELL, JOHN W. JR NV   ASF 37 10
CLOAK OF AESIR   CAMPBELL, JOHN W. JR NV   ASF 39 03

WHOLE MAN, THE   BRUNNER, JOHN   NO   BAL 64 08
CITY OF THE TIGER   BRUNNER, JOHN   SN   SCF 58 12
WHOLE MAN, THE   BRUNNER, JOHN   SN   SCF 59 04
CURATIVE TELEPATH   BRUNNER, JOHN   NV   FUN 59 12

WILDERNESS OF STARS, A   NOLAN, WILLIAM F.   AN H SHB 69
INTRODUCTION   LOWENKOPF, SHELLY   IN
LINEMAN, THE   MILLER, WALTER M. JR SN   FSF 57 07
I, MARS   BRADBURY, RAY   SS   SSS 49 04
SUNJAMMER (ALSO AS THE WIND FROM THE SUN)
                                   CLARKE, ARTHUR C.   SS   BLF 64
BETTER MAN, THE   RUSSELL, RAY   SS   PBY 66 07
CARRIER   SHECKLEY, ROBERT   NV   IFS 54 04
CASTAWAY, THE   FRITCH, CHARLES E.   SS   GAM 63 02
GHETTO   ANDERSON, POUL   NV   FSF 54 05
HAPPILY EVER AFTER   NOLAN, WILLIAM F.   SS   GAM 65 04
NORTH WIND   OLIVER, CHAD   SS   FSF 56 03
DEATH OF A SPACEMAN (ALSO AS MOMENTO HOMO)
                                   MILLER, WALTER M. JR SS   AMZ 54 03
EDITOR'S POSTSCRIPT   NOLAN, WILLIAM F.   MS

WIND FROM THE SUN, THE   CLARKE, ARTHUR C.   AC H HBJ 72
PREFACE   CLARKE, ARTHUR C.   IN
FOOD OF THE GODS, THE   CLARKE, ARTHUR C.   SS   PBY 64 05
MAELSTROM II   CLARKE, ARTHUR C.   SS   PBY 65 04
SHINING ONES, THE   CLARKE, ARTHUR C.   SS   PBY 64 08
WIND FROM THE SUN, THE (SUNJAMMER)
                                   CLARKE, ARTHUR C.   SS   BLF 64
SECRET, THE   CLARKE, ARTHUR C.   SS
LAST COMMAND, THE   CLARKE, ARTHUR C.   SS   BIZ 65 11
DIAL "F" FOR FRANKENSTEIN   CLARKE, ARTHUR C.   SS   PBY 65 01
REUNION   CLARKE, ARTHUR C.   SS   INY 71 02
PLAYBACK   CLARKE, ARTHUR C.   SS   PBY 66 12
LIGHT OF DARKNESS, THE   CLARKE, ARTHUR C.   SS
LONGEST SCIENCE-FICTION STORY EVER TOLD, THE
                                   CLARKE, ARTHUR C.   SS
HERBERT GEORGE MORLEY ROBERTS WELLS, ESQ.
                                   CLARKE, ARTHUR C.   ED   IFS 67 12
LOVE THAT UNIVERSE   CLARKE, ARTHUR C.   SS
CRUSADE   CLARKE, ARTHUR C.   SS   FRS 68
CRUEL SKY, THE   CLARKE, ARTHUR C.   SS
NEUTRON TIDE, THE   CLARKE, ARTHUR C.   SS   GAL 70 05
TRANSIT OF EARTH   CLARKE, ARTHUR C.   SS   PBY 71 01
MEETING WITH MEDUSA, A   CLARKE, ARTHUR C.   NA   PBY 71 12

WINDOW ON THE FUTURE   HILL, DOUGLAS   AN H HDV 66
SUBLIMINAL MAN, THE   BALLARD, J. G.   SS   NWS 63 01
DISPOSAL UNIT MAN, THE   ALEXANDER, DAVID   SS   NWS 63 08
WASTED ON THE YOUNG   BRUNNER, JOHN   SS   GAL 65 04

WINDOW ON THE FUTURE

CATEGORICAL IMPERATIVE (THE CATEGORY INVENTORS)
    SELLINGS, ARTHUR   NV   GAL 56 02
FACTS OF LIFE, THE   HILLMAN, MARTIN   SS
SENSE OF PROPORTION   TUBB, E. C.   NV   NEB 58 07
CIRCULATION OF THE BLOOD, THE
    ALDISS, BRIAN W.   NV   IMP 66 03

WINDOWS INTO TOMORROW   SILVERBERG, ROBERT   AN H HAW 74
INTRODUCTION   SILVERBERG, ROBERT   IN
YEAR OF THE JACKPOT, THE   HEINLEIN, ROBERT A.   NV   GAL 52 03
BILLENIUM   BALLARD, J. G.   SS   NWS 61 11
PAIL OF AIR, A   LEIBER, FRITZ   SS   GAL 51 12
ELECTRIC ANT, THE   DICK, PHILIP K.   NV   FSF 69 10
LAST OF THE ROMANY, THE   SPINRAD, NORMAN   SS   ASF 63 05
BATTLEFIELD (HIS FIRST DAY AT WAR)
    ELLISON, HARLAN   SS   STM 58 11
ALL THE LAST WARS AT ONCE   EFFINGER, GEO. ALEC   SS   UNI 71 01
PAIN PEDDLERS, THE   SILVERBERG, ROBERT   SS   GAL 63 08
DODKIN'S JOB   VANCE, JACK   NV   ASF 59 10

WINDS TWELVE QUARTERS, THE   LE GUIN, URSULA .K.   AC H HPR 75
FOREWORD   LE GUIN, URSULA K.   IN
SEMLEY'S NECKLACE (DOWRY OF THE ANGYAR)
    LE GUIN, URSULA K.   SS   AMZ 64 09
APRIL IN PARIS   LE GUIN, URSULA K.   SS   FAN 62 09
MASTERS, THE   LE GUIN, URSULA K.   SS   FAN 63 02
DARKNESS BOX   LE GUIN, URSULA K.   SS   FAN 63 11
WORD OF UNBINDING, THE   LE GUIN, URSULA K.   SS   FAN 64 01
RULE OF NAMES, THE   LE GUIN, URSULA K.   SS   FAN 64 04
WINTER'S KING   LE GUIN, URSULA K.   NV   ORB 69 05
GOOD TRIP, THE   LE GUIN, URSULA K.   SS   FAN 70 08
NINE LIVES   LE GUIN, URSULA K.   NV   PBY 69 11
THINGS (THE END)   LE GUIN, URSULA K.   SS   ORB 70 06
TRIP TO THE HEAD, A   LE GUIN, URSULA K.   SS   QRK 70 01
VASTER THAN EMPIRES AND MORE SLOW
    LE GUIN, URSULA K.   NV   NDM 71 01
STARS BELOW, THE   LE GUIN, URSULA K.   SS   ORB 74 14
FIELD OF VISION, THE   LE GUIN, URSULA K.   SS   GAL 73 10
DIRECTION OF THE ROAD   LE GUIN, URSULA K.   SS   ORB 73 12
ONES WHO WALK AWAY FROM OMELAS, THE
    LE GUIN, URSULA K.   SS   NDM 73 03
DAY BEFORE THE REVOLUTION, THE   LE GUIN, URSULA K.   SS   GAL 74 08

WINGS ACROSS TIME   ARNOLD, FRANK EDWARD AC   PND 46
WINGS ACROSS TIME   ARNOLD, FRANK EDWARD NV   SFQ 42 WI
MAD MACHINES, THE (CITY OF MACHINES)
    ARNOLD, FRANK EDWARD NV   TOW 39 SU
ENDLESS DIMENSIONS   ARNOLD, FRANK EDWARD NV
TWILIGHT PEOPLE, THE   ARNOLD, FRANK EDWARD NV   CMT 41 01

WITCHES THREE   PRATT, FLETCHER   AN H TWN 52
BLUE STAR, THE   PRATT, FLETCHER   NA   NEW 52 AN
CONJURE WIFE   LEIBER, FRITZ   SN   UNK 43 04
THERE SHALL BE NO DARKNESS   BLISH, JAMES   SS   TWS 50 04

WITCHFINDER, THE   WRIGHT, S. FOWLER   AC H BFT 46
WITCHFINDER, THE   WRIGHT, S. FOWLER   SS
STATUS   WRIGHT, S. FOWLER   SS
WHO ELSE BUT SHE?   WRIGHT, S. FOWLER   SS
BURGLAR'S AID   WRIGHT, S. FOWLER   SS
CARROTS   WRIGHT, S. FOWLER   SS
TEMPERATURE OF GEHENNA SUE, THE
    WRIGHT, S. FOWLER   SS
CONGO CAT, THE   WRIGHT, S. FOWLER   SS
ORIGINAL SIN   WRIGHT, S. FOWLER   SS   AFR 50 13
QUESTION OF E.D.D., A   WRIGHT, S. FOWLER   SS
TERROR OF WILLIAM STICKERS, THE
    WRIGHT, S. FOWLER   SS

WITCHING HOUR, THE   GUNN, JAMES E.   AC   DEL 70 06
RELUCTANT WITCH, THE (WHEREVER YOU MAY BE)
    GUNN, JAMES E.   NA   GAL 53 05
BEAUTIFUL BREW, THE   GUNN, JAMES E.   NV   BEY 54 09
MAGICIANS, THE (SINE OF THE MAGUS)
    GUNN, JAMES E.   NA   BEY 54 05

WITH A FINGER IN MY I   GERROLD, DAVID   AC   BAL 72 06
ALL OF THEM WERE EMPTY   GERROLD, DAVID   SS   NEW 72 AC
ORACLE FOR A WHITE RABBIT   GERROLD, DAVID   NV   GAL 69 12
LOVE STORY IN THREE ACTS   GERROLD, DAVID   SS   NOV 70 01
YARST!   GERROLD, DAVID   SS   NEW 72 AC
BATTLE HUM AND THE BOJE   GERROLD, DAVID   NV   NEW 72 AC
WITH A FINGER IN MY I   GERROLD, DAVID   SS   DVS 72 02
HOW WE SAVED THE HUMAN RACE   GERROLD, DAVID   NV   NEW 72 AC
CRYSTAL CASTLE, THE   GERROLD, DAVID   SS   NEW 72 AC
IN THE DEADLANDS   GERROLD, DAVID   NV   NEW 72 AC

WITHOUT SORCERY   STURGEON, THEODORE   AC H PRM 48
    DERIVATIVE COLLECTION "NOT WITHOUT SORCERY"
INTRODUCTION   BRADBURY, RAY   IN
ULTIMATE EGOIST, THE   STURGEON, THEODORE   NV   UNK 41 02
IT   STURGEON, THEODORE   NV   UNK 40 08
POKER FACE   STURGEON, THEODORE   SS   ASF 41 03
SHOTTLE BOP   STURGEON, THEODORE   SS   UNK 41 02
ARTNAN PROCESS   STURGEON, THEODORE   NV   ASF 41 06
MEMORIAL (SEE ALSO ATOMIC MEMORIAL)
    STURGEON, THEODORE   SS   ASF 46 04
ETHER BREATHER   STURGEON, THEODORE   SS   ASF 39 09
BUTYL AND THE BREATHER   STURGEON, THEODORE   NV   ASF 40 10
BRAT   STURGEON, THEODORE   SS   UNK 41 12
TWO PERCENT INSPIRATION   STURGEON, THEODORE   SS   ASF 41 10
CARGO   STURGEON, THEODORE   NV   UNK 40 11
MATURITY   STURGEON, THEODORE   NV   ASF 47 02
MICROCOSMIC GOD   STURGEON, THEODORE   NV   ASF 41 04

WIZARDS AND WARLOCKS   GHIDALIA, VIC   AN   MAN 72
SECRET OF SEBEK, THE   BLOCH, ROBERT   SS   WRT 37 11
IN THE LEFT WING   SCHORER, MARK
    AND DERLETH, AUGUST   SS C WRT 32 06
NECROMANTIC TALE, THE   SMITH, CLARK ASHTON   SS   WRT 31 01
BATTLE OF WIZARDS   HUBBARD, L. RON   SS   FBK 49 05
YOUNG GOODMAN BROWN (1835)   HAWTHORNE, NATHANIEL SS   NEM 35 04
CASTING THE RUNES   JAMES, M. R.   NV
DISAPPEARANCE OF MRS. MACRECHAM, THE
    MARSH, RICHARD   NV
SO SWEET AS MAGIC...   ELLIOTT, BRUCE   NV   FNF 53 08
APPRENTICE MAGICIAN   PRICE, E. HOFFMANN   SS   WRT 39 08

WOLFSHEAD   HOWARD, ROBERT E.   AC   LAN 68
BLACK STONE, THE   HOWARD, ROBERT E.   SS   WRT 31 11
VALLEY OF THE WORM, THE   HOWARD, ROBERT E.   SS   WRT 34 02
WOLFSHEAD   HOWARD, ROBERT E.   SS   WRT 26 04
FIRE OF ASSHURBANIPAL, THE   HOWARD, ROBERT E.   SS   WRT 36 12
HOUSE OF ARABU, THE   HOWARD, ROBERT E.   SS
HORROR FROM THE MOUND, THE   HOWARD, ROBERT E.   SS   WRT 32 05
CAIRN ON THE HEADLAND, THE   HOWARD, ROBERT E.   SS   STT 33 01

WOMEN OF WONDER   SARGENT, PAMELA   AN   VNT 75 01
WOMEN IN SCIENCE FICTION   SARGENT, PAMELA   IN
CHILD DREAMS, THE   DORMAN, SONYA   PM
THAT ONLY A MOTHER   MERRIL, JUDITH   SS   ASF 48 06
CONTAGION   MACLEAN, KATHERINE   NV   GAL 50 10
WIND PEOPLE, THE   BRADLEY, MARION Z.   SS   IFS 59 02
SHIP WHO SANG, THE   MCCAFFREY, ANNE   SS   FSF 61 04
WHEN I WAS MISS DOW   DORMAN, SONYA   SS   GAL 66 06
FOOD FARM, THE   REED, KIT   SS   ORB 67 02
BABY, YOU WERE GREAT   WILHELM, KATE   SS   ORB 67 02
SEX AND/OR MR. MORRISON   EMSHWILLER, CAROL   SS   DVS 67 01
VASTER THAN EMPIRES AND MORE SLOW
    LE GUIN, URSULA K.   NV   NDM 71 01
FALSE DAWN   YARBRO, CHELSEA Q.   SS   NEW 72 AN
NOBODY'S HOME   RUSS, JOANNA   SS   NDM 72 02
OF MIST, AND GRASS, AND SAND MCINTYRE, VONDA N.   SS   ASF 73 10

WONDER EFFECT, THE   POHL, F. & KORNBLUTH AC   BAL 62
INTRODUCTION   POHL, FREDERIK   IN
CRITICAL MASS   POHL, FREDERIK
    AND KORNBLUTH, C. M.   NA C GAL 62 02
GENTLE DYING, A   POHL, FREDERIK
    AND KORNBLUTH, C. M.   SS C GAL 61 06
NIGHTMARE WITH ZEPPELINS   POHL, FREDERIK
    AND KORNBLUTH, C. M.   NV C GAL 58 12
BEST FRIEND   POHL, FREDERIK
    AND KORNBLUTH, C. M.   SS C SSS 41 05
WORLD OF MYRION FLOWERS, THE   POHL, FREDERIK
    AND KORNBLUTH, C. M.   SS C FSF 61 10
TROUBLE IN TIME   POHL, FREDERIK
    AND KORNBLUTH, C. M.   SS C AST 40 12
ENGINEER, THE   POHL, FREDERIK
    AND KORNBLUTH, C. M.   SS C INF 56 02
MARS-TUBE   POHL, FREDERIK
    AND KORNBLUTH, C. M.   SS C AST 41 09
QUAKER CANNON, THE   POHL, FREDERIK
    AND KORNBLUTH, C. M.   NV C ASF 61 08

WONDERFUL ICE CREAM SUIT AND OTHER PLAYS, THE
    BRADBURY, RAY   AC   BAN 72 04
INTRODUCTION, WITH NOTES ON STAGING
    BRADBURY, RAY   IN
WONDERFUL ICE CREAM SUIT, THE
    BRADBURY, RAY   PL   SEP 58 10
VELDT, THE   BRADBURY, RAY   PL   SEP 50 09
TO THE CHICAGO ABYSS   BRADBURY, RAY   PL   FSF 63 05

WONDERMAKERS   HOSKINS, ROBERT   AN   FAW 72 05
SOMETHING NEW UNDER THE SUN   WILSON, ROBIN SCOTT   IN
PRIZE OF WONDER, THE   HOSKINS, ROBERT   IN
BALLOON-HOAX, THE   POE, EDGAR ALLEN   SS   SUN 44 04
FLATLAND: TWO EXCERPTS   ABBOTT, EDWIN A.   EX   SEE 84
MOXON'S MASTER   BIERCE, AMBROSE   SS   93
LAND IRONCLADS, THE   WELLS, H. G.   NV   SND 03 12
WITH THE NIGHT MAIL   KIPLING, RUDYARD   NV   MCS 05 11
MACHINE STOPS, THE   FORSTER, E. M.   NV   28
UNPARALLELED INVASION, THE   LONDON, JACK   SS   MCS 10 07
DISINTEGRATION MACHINE, THE   DOYLE, ARTHUR CONAN   SS   CMP 28
METROPOLITAN NIGHTMARE   BENET, STEPHEN V.   PM   27
NIGHTMARE NUMBER THREE   BENET, STEPHEN V.   PM   35
KILLDOZER!   STURGEON, THEODORE   SN   ASF 44 11
SURFACE TENSION   BLISH, JAMES   NA   GAL 52 08

WONDERMAKERS 2   HOSKINS, ROBERT   AN   FPR 74 02
REACHING OUT OF TOMORROW   HOSKINS, ROBERT   IN
DOMINIONS BEYOND (THE SECOND TRIP TO MARS)
    MOORE, WARD   SS   SEP 54 08
LIVING SPACE   ASIMOV, ISAAC   SS   SFS 56 05
GUN WITHOUT A BANG, THE   SHECKLEY, ROBERT   NV   GAL 58 06
WE NEVER MENTION AUNT NORA (AS PAUL FLEHR)
    POHL, FREDERIK   SS   GAL 58 07
AND MILES TO GO BEFORE I SLEEP
    NOLAN, WILLIAM F.   SS   INF 58 08
EASTWARD HO!   TENN, WILLIAM   SS   FSF 58 10
REPORT ON THE NATURE OF THE LUNAR SURFACE
    BRUNNER, JOHN   SS   ASF 60 08
HORN OF TIME THE HUNTER, THE (HOMO AQUATICUS)
    ANDERSON, POUL   SS   AMZ 63 09
MONSTER AND THE MAIDEN, THE   ZELAZNY, ROGER   SS   GAL 64 12
COMPUTERS DON'T ARGUE   DICKSON, GORDON R.   SS   ASF 65 09
I HAVE MY VIGIL   HARRISON, HARRY   SS   FSF 68 02
TWELFTH BED, THE   KOONTZ, DEAN R.   SS   FSF 68 08
HIGH WEIR   DELANY, SAMUEL R.   NV   IFS 68 10

WONDERMAKERS 2

ADVENTURE OF THE MARTIAN CLIENT, THE
    WELLMAN, MANLY WADE
    AND WELLMAN, WADE   SS C FSF 69 12
FALCON AND THE FALCONEER, THE
    MALZBERG, BARRY N.   SS   FSF 69 12
EVERGREEN LIBRARY, THE   PRONZINI, BILL
    AND WALLMANN, JEFFREY SS C VSF 70 05
XONG OF XUXAN   RUSSELL, RAY   SS   PBY 70 10
VASTER THAN EMPIRES AND MORE SLOW
    LE GUIN, URSULA K.   NV   NDM 71 01
CAUGHT IN THE ORGAN DRAFT   SILVERBERG, ROBERT SS   WLK 73

WOODEN STAR, THE   TENN, WILLIAM   AC BAL 68 06
  AUTHOR'S NOTE   TENN, WILLIAM   IN
  GENERATION OF NOAH   TENN, WILLIAM   SS   SUS 51 SP
  BROOKLYN PROJECT   TENN, WILLIAM   SS   PLS 48 FL
  DARK STAR, THE   TENN, WILLIAM   SS   GAL 57 09
  NULL-P   TENN, WILLIAM   SS   WBY 51 01
  EASTWARD HO!   TENN, WILLIAM   SS   FSF 58 10
  DESERTER, THE   TENN, WILLIAM   SS   STR 53 01
  BETELGEUSE BRIDGE   TENN, WILLIAM   SS   GAL 51 04
  WILL YOU WALK A LITTLE FASTER?
    TENN, WILLIAM   SS   MAR 51 11
  IT ENDS WITH A FLICKER (OF ALL POSSIBLE WORLDS)
    TENN, WILLIAM   SS   GAL 56 12
  LISBON CUBED   TENN, WILLIAM   NV   GAL 58 10
  MASCULINIST REVOLT, THE   TENN, WILLIAM   NV   FSF 65 08

WORLD BETWEEN AND OTHER STORIES, THE
    VANCE, JACK   DC ACE 65
  IN ENGLAND AS "THE MOON MOTH AND OTHER STORIES"

WORLD BY THE TALE, A   CAMPBELL, JOHN W. JR AN CUR 65
  SEE "ANALOG 3"

WORLD INSIDE, THE   SILVERBERG, ROBERT NO H DBL 71
  THROWBACKS, THE   SILVERBERG, ROBERT NV GAL 70 07
  WORLD OUTSIDE, THE   SILVERBERG, ROBERT NA GAL 70 10
  WE ARE WELL ORGANIZED   SILVERBERG, ROBERT NV GAL 70 12
  ALL THE WAY UP, ALL THE WAY DOWN
    SILVERBERG, ROBERT NV GAL 71 07

WORLD NAMED CLEOPATRA, A ANDERSON, POUL   OA PYR 77 03
  PRODUCED BY ROGER ELWOOD
WORLD NAMED CLEOPATRA, A ANDERSON, POUL   FA NEW 74 AC
SERPENT IN EDEN, THE   ANDERSON, POUL   NV OMG 73
FABER-MASTER   ORGILL, MICHAEL   NV
AMONG THE MOUNTAINS   DANN, JACK M.   NV
WAYSIDE WORLD   ZEBROWSKI, GEORGE   NV
ABOUT THE AUTHORS   MISC. MATERIAL   MS

WORLD OF WONDER   PRATT, FLETCHER   AN H TWN 51
  FOREWORD   MIRRIELEES, EDITH   IN
  NATURE OF IMAGINATIVE LITERATURE, THE
    PRATT, FLETCHER   IN
  HE WALKED AROUND THE HORSES PIPER, H. BEAM   NV ASF 48 04
  ROADS OF DESTINY   HENRY, O.   NV   09
  RED QUEEN'S RACE, THE   ASIMOV, ISAAC   NV ASF 49 01
  CHILD'S PLAY   TENN, WILLIAM   NV ASF 47 03
  FINEST STORY IN THE WORLD, THE
    KIPLING, RUDYARD   NV CRV 91 07
  ETAOIN SHRDLU   BROWN, FREDRIC   SS UNK 42 02
  MISTAKE INSIDE   BLISH, JAMES   NV STS 48 03
  PRIVATE- KEEP OUT!   MACDONALD, PHILIP SS FSF 49 FL
  THEY   HEINLEIN, ROBERT A. SS UNK 41 04
  METAMORPHOSIS   KAFKA, FRANZ   NV   37
  BACK THERE IN THE GRASS   MORRIS, GOUVERNEUR SS   22
  MARK OF THE BEAST, THE   KIPLING, RUDYARD SS PIO 90 07
  MUSEUM PIECE   CARLSON, ESTHER   SS   47
  BLUE GIRAFFE, THE   DE CAMP, L. SPRAGUE NV ASF 39 08
  THAT ONLY A MOTHER   MERRIL, JUDITH   SS ASF 48 06
  OPERATION RSVP   PIPER, H. BEAM   SS AMZ 51 01
  CONQUEROR'S ISLE   BOND, NELSON S.   SS BBM 46 06
  GIANT KILLER   CHANDLER, A. BERTRAM NV ASF 45 10
  MILLION-YEAR PICNIC, THE   BRADBURY, RAY   SS PLS 46 SU

WORLD OUT OF TIME, A   NIVEN, LARRY   NO H HRW 76
  RAMMER   NIVEN, LARRY   NV GAL 71 11
  DOWN AND OUT   NIVEN, LARRY   NV GAL 76 02
  CHILDREN OF THE STATE   NIVEN, LARRY   NO GAL 76 09

WORLD THAT COULDN'T BE AND 8 OTHER SF NOVELETS
    GOLD, H. L.   AN H DBL 59
  HOW DO YOU KNOW YOU CAN'T WRITE SCIENCE FICTION?
    GOLD, H. L.   IN
  WORLD THAT COULDN'T BE, THE SIMAK, CLIFFORD D. NV GAL 58 01
  BRIGHTSIDE CROSSING   NOURSE, ALAN E.   NV GAL 56 01
  MEZZEROW LOVES COMPANY WALLACE, F. L.   NV GAL 56 06
  EYE FOR A WHAT?, AN   KNIGHT, DAMON   NV GAL 57 03
  WOMAN'S PLACE, A   CLIFTON, MARK   NV GAL 55 05
  GUN FOR DINOSAUR, A   DE CAMP, L. SPRAGUE NV GAL 56 03
  ONE FOR THE BOOKS   MATHESON, RICHARD NV GAL 55 09
  MUSIC MASTER OF BABYLON, THE PANGBORN, EDGAR   NV GAL 54 11
  ONCE A GREECH   SMITH, EVELYN E.   NV GAL 57 04

WORLD'S BEST SCIENCE FICTION: 1965
    WOLLHEIM & CARR   AN ACE 65
  INTRODUCTION   WOLLHEIM, DONALD A.
    AND CARR, TERRY   IN C
  GREENPLACE   PURDOM, TOM   SS FSF 64 11
  MEN OF GOOD WILL   BOVA, BEN
    AND LEWIS, MYRON R. SS C GAL 64 06
  BILL FOR DELIVERY   ANVIL, CHRISTOPHER SS ASF 64 11
  FOUR BRANDS OF IMPOSSIBLE KAGAN, NORMAN   NV FSF 64 09
  NICHE IN TIME, A   TEMPLE, WILLIAM F. SS ASF 64 05
  SEA WRACK   JESBY, EDWARD   NV FSF 64 05

FOR EVERY ACTION   MACAPP, C. C.   SS AMZ 64 05
VAMPIRES LTD.   NESVADBA, JOSEF   SS   64
LAST LONELY MAN, THE   BRUNNER, JOHN   SS NWS 64 06
STAR PARTY, THE   LORY, ROBERT   SS FSF 64 09
WEATHER IN THE UNDERWORLD, THE
    FREE, COLIN   SS SQU 65 06
OH, TO BE A BLOBEL!   DICK, PHILIP K.   SS GAL 64 02
UNREMEMBERED, THE   MACKIN, EDWARD   SS NWS 64 03
WHAT HAPPENED TO SERGEANT MASURO?
    NULISCH, HARRY   NV   64
NOW IS FOREVER   DISCH, THOMAS M.   SS AMZ 64 03
COMPETITORS, THE   LAWSON, JACK B.   NV IFS 64 01
WHEN THE CHANGE-WINDS BLOW LEIBER, FRITZ   SS FSF 64 08

WORLD'S BEST SCIENCE FICTION: 1966
    WOLLHEIM & CARR   AN ACE 66
  INTRODUCTION   WOLLHEIM, DONALD A.
    AND CARR, TERRY   IN C
  SUNJAMMER (ALSO AS THE WIND FROM THE SUN)
    CLARKE, ARTHUR C.   SS BLP 64
  CALLING DR. CLOCKWORK   GOULART, RON   SS AMZ 65 03
  BECALMED IN HELL   NIVEN, LARRY   SS FSF 65 07
  APARTNESS   VINGE, VERNOR   SS NWS 65 06
  OVER THE RIVER AND THROUGH THE WOODS
    SIMAK, CLIFFORD D.   SS AMZ 65 05
  PLANET OF FORGETTING   SCHMITZ, JAMES H. NV GAL 65 02
  "REPENT, HARLEQUIN!" SAID THE TICKTOCKMAN
    ELLISON, HARLAN   SS GAL 65 12
  DECISION MAKERS, THE   GREEN, JOSEPH   NV GAL 65 04
  TRAVELER'S REST   MASSON, DAVID I.   SS NWS 65 09
  UNCOLLECTED WORKS   CARTER, LIN   SS FSF 65 03
  VANISHING POINT   BRAND, JONATHAN   NV IFS 65 01
  IN OUR BLOCK   LAFFERTY, R. A.   SS IFS 65 07
  MASQUE OF THE RED SHIFT SABERHAGEN, FRED   NV IFS 65 11
  CAPTIVE DJINN, THE   ANVIL, CHRISTOPHER SS ASF 65 05
  GOOD NEW DAYS, THE   LEIBER, FRITZ   SS GAL 65 10

WORLD'S BEST SCIENCE FICTION: 1967
    WOLLHEIM & CARR   AN ACE 67
  INTRODUCTION   WOLLHEIM, DONALD A.
    AND CARR, TERRY   IN C
  WE CAN REMEMBER IT FOR YOU WHOLESALE
    DICK, PHILIP K.   NV FSF 66 04
  LIGHT OF OTHER DAYS   SHAW, BOB   SS ASF 66 08
  KEYS TO DECEMBER, THE   ZELAZNY, ROGER   SS NWS 66 08
  NINE HUNDRED GRANDMOTHERS LAFFERTY, R. A.   SS IFS 66 02
  BIRCHER   WALDE, A. A.   NV IFS 66 07
  BEHOLD THE MAN   MOORCOCK, MICHAEL NV NWS 66 09
  BUMBERBOOM   DAVIDSON, AVRAM   NV FSF 66 12
  DAY MILLION   POHL, FREDERIK   SS ROG 66 02
  WINGS OF A BAT, THE   ASH, PAUL   NV ASF 66 05
  MAN FROM WHEN, THE   PLACHTA, DANNIE   SS IFS 66 07
  AMEN AND OUT   ALDISS, BRIAN W.   SS NWS 66 08
  FOR A BREATH I TARRY   ZELAZNY, ROGER   NV NWS 66 03

WORLD'S BEST SCIENCE FICTION: 1968
    WOLLHEIM & CARR   AN ACE 68
  INTRODUCTION   WOLLHEIM, DONALD A.
    AND CARR, TERRY   IN C
  SEE ME NOT   WILSON, RICHARD   NV IMP 67 02
  DRIFTGLASS   DELANY, SAMUEL R.   NV IFS 67 06
  AMBASSADOR TO VERDAMMT KAPP, COLIN   SS ASF 67 04
  MAN WHO NEVER WAS, THE LAFFERTY, R. A.   SS MOH 67 SU
  BILLIARD BALL, THE   ASIMOV, ISAAC   NV IFS 67 03
  HAWKSBILL STATION   SILVERBERG, ROBERT NV GAL 67 08
  NUMBER YOU HAVE REACHED, THE DISCH, THOMAS M.   SS IMP 67 07
  MAN WHO LOVED THE FAIOLI, THE
    ZELAZNY, ROGER   SS GAL 67 06
  POPULATION IMPLOSION   OFFUTT, ANDREW J. NV IFS 67 07
  I HAVE NO MOUTH, AND I MUST SCREAM
    ELLISON, HARLAN   SS IFS 67 03
  SWORD SWALLOWER, THE   GOULART, RON   NV FSF 67 11
  CORANDA   ROBERTS, KEITH   SS NWS 67 01
  THUS WE FRUSTRATE CHARLEMAGNE
    LAFFERTY, R. A.   SS GAL 67 02
  HANDICAP (ALSO AS THE HANDICAPPED)
    NIVEN, LARRY   NV GAL 67 12
  FULL SUN   ALDISS, BRIAN W.   SS ORB 67 02
  IT'S SMART TO HAVE AN ENGLISH ADDRESS
    COMPTON, D. G.   SS IMP 67 02

WORLD'S BEST SCIENCE FICTION: 1969
    WOLLHEIM & CARR   AN ACE 69
  INTRODUCTION   WOLLHEIM, DONALD A.
    AND CARR, TERRY   IN C
  STREET OF DREAMS, FEET OF CLAY
    SHECKLEY, ROBERT   NV GAL 68 02
  BACKTRACKED   FILER, BURT K.   SS FSF 68 06
  KYRIE   ANDERSON, POUL   SS FRS 68
  GOING DOWN SMOOTH   SILVERBERG, ROBERT SS GAL 68 08
  WORM THAT FLIES, THE   ALDISS, BRIAN W.   SS FRS 68
  MASKS   KNIGHT, DAMON   SS PBY 68 07
  TIME CONSIDERED AS A HELIX OF SEMI-PRECIOUS STONES
    DELANY, SAMUEL R.   SS NWS 68 12
  HEMEAC   VON WALD, E. G.   SS GAL 68 08
  CLOUDBUILDERS, THE   KAPP, COLIN   NV NWR 68 12
  THIS GRAND CARCASS   LAFFERTY, R. A.   SS AMZ 68 11
  VISIT TO CLEVELAND GENERAL, A
    VAN SCYOC, SYDNEY J. SS GAL 68 10
  SELCHEY KIDS, THE   YEP, LAURENCE   NV IFS 68 04
  WELCOME TO THE MONKEY HOUSE VONNEGUT, KURT JR. SS PBY 68 01
  DANCE OF THE CHANGER AND THE THREE, THE
    CARR, TERRY   SS FRS 68
  SWORD GAME   HOLLIS, H. H.   SS GAL 68 04
  TOTAL ENVIRONMENT   ALDISS, BRIAN W.   NV GAL 68 02
  SQUARE ROOT OF BRAIN, THE LEIBER, FRITZ   SS NWS 68 02

WORLD'S BEST SCIENCE FICTION: 1969

STARSONG	SABERHAGEN, FRED	SS	IFS 68 01	
FEAR HOUND	MACLEAN, KATHERINE	NV	ASF 68 05	

WORLD'S BEST SCIENCE FICTION: 1970

	WOLLHEIM & CARR	AN	ACE 70	
INTRODUCTION	WOLLHEIM, DONALD A.			
	AND CARR, TERRY	IN C		
MAN SPEKITH, A	WILSON, RICHARD	NV	GAL 69 05	
AFTER THE MYTHS WENT HOME	SILVERBERG, ROBERT	SS	FSF 69 11	
DEATH BY ECSTASY (THE ORGANLEGGERS)				
	NIVEN, LARRY	NV	GAL 69 01	
ONE SUNDAY IN NEPTUNE	PANSHIN, ALEXEI	SS	NEW 69 AN	
FOR THE SAKE OF GRACE	ELGIN, SUZETTE HADEN	NV	FSF 69 05	
YOUR HAPLOID HEART	TIPTREE, JAMES JR.	NV	ASF 69 09	
THERAPY 2000	ROBERTS, KEITH	SS	NWR 69 15	
SIXTH SENSE	CONEY, MICHAEL G.	SS	VOT 69 08	
BOY AND HIS DOG, A	ELLISON, HARLAN	NV	NWS 69 04	
AND SO SAY ALL OF US	MCALLISTER, BRUCE	SS	IFS 69 09	
SHIP OF SHADOWS	LEIBER, FRITZ	SN	FSF 69 07	
NINE LIVES	LE GUIN, URSULA K.	NV	PBY 69 11	
BIG FLASH, THE	SPINRAD, NORMAN	NV	ORB 69 05	

WORLD'S BEST SCIENCE FICTION: 1971

	WOLLHEIM & CARR	AN	ACE 71	
INTRODUCTION	WOLLHEIM, DONALD A.			
	AND CARR, TERRY	IN C		
SLOW SCULPTURE	STURGEON, THEODORE	NV	GAL 70 02	
BIRD IN THE HAND	NIVEN, LARRY	SS	FSF 70 10	
ISHMAEL IN LOVE	SILVERBERG, ROBERT	SS	FSF 70 07	
INVASION OF PRIVACY	SHAW, BOB	NV	AMZ 70 07	
WATERCLAP	ASIMOV, ISAAC	NV	IFS 70 04	
CONTINUED ON NEXT ROCK	LAFFERTY, R. A.	NV	ORB 70 07	
THING IN THE STONE, THE	SIMAK, CLIFFORD D.	NV	IFS 70 03	
NOBODY LIVES ON BURTON STREET				
	BENFORD, GREGORY	SS	AMZ 70 05	
WHATEVER BECAME OF THE MCGOWANS?				
	CONEY, MICHAEL G.	NV	GAL 70 05	
LAST TIME AROUND, THE	SELLINGS, ARTHUR	NV	NWR 68 12	
GREYSPUN'S GIFT	BARRETT, NEAL JR.	SS	WOT 70 WI	
SHAKER REVIVAL, THE	JONAS, GERALD	NV	GAL 70 02	
DEAR AUNT ANNIE	EKLUND, GORDON	NV	FAN 70 04	
CONFESSIONS	GOULART, RON	NV	FSF 70 08	
GONE ARE THE LUPO	HICKEY, H. B.	SS	QRK 70 01	

WORLD'S BEST SF SHORT STORIES NO. 1, THE
WOLLHEIM, DONALD A. AN H ELM 75
SEE "THE 1974 ANNUAL WORLD'S BEST SF"

WORLD'S BEST SF SHORT STORIES NO. 2, THE
WOLLHEIM, DONALD A. AN H ELM 76
SEE "THE 1975 ANNUAL WORLD'S BEST SF"

WORLDS APART   LOCKE, GEORGE   AN H CMK
AN ANTHOLOGY OF INTERPLANETARY FICTION

INTRODUCTION	LOCKE, GEORGE	IN		
LETTERS FROM THE PLANETS	LACH-SZYRMA, D. S.	GR		
RUINED CITY IN THE MOON, A	LACH-SZYRMA, D. S.	SS	CSL 87 01	
IN THE ANTARCTIC REGIONS OF MARS				
	LACH-SZYRMA, D. S.	SS	CSL 87 04	
QUEEN OF BEAUTY, OR THE PLANET OF LOVE, THE				
	LACH-SZYRMA, D. S.	SS	CSL 87 08	
MERCURY	LACH-SZYRMA, D. S.	SS	CSL 87 10	
PORTALS OF THE KING OF DAY, THE				
	LACH-SZYRMA, D. S.	SS	CSL 88 01	
OUR SECOND VOYAGE TO MARS	LACH-SZYRMA, D. S.	SS	CSL 89 02	
CANAL LIFE ON MARS	LACH-SZYRMA, D. S.	SS	CSL 90 04	
TRIP TO JUPITER'S MOONLET, A	LACH-SZYRMA, D. S.	SS	CSL 91 12	
CORRESPONDING WITH THE PLANETS				
	LACH-SZYRMA, D. S.	SS	CSL 93 06	
REJECTED PLANET, THE	WILSON, JOHN FLEMING	SS	PRS 12 06	
GREAT SACRIFICE, THE	WALLIS, GEORGE C.	SS	LOM 03 06	
IN THE DEEP OF TIME	LATHROP, GEORGE P.	NV	EIM 97 03	
STRANGE CASE OF ALAN MORAINE, THE				
	ATKEY, BERTRAM	SS	GND 12 09	
WHEELS OF DR. GINOCHIO GYVES, THE				
	DOUGLASS, ELLSWORTH			
	AND PALLANDER, EDWIN	SS C	CSL 99 09	
MESSAGE FROM THE MOON, A	ENGLAND, GEORGE A.	SS	PRS 07 04	
BLACK SHADOW, THE	OLIVER, OWEN	SS	CSL 03 02	
STORIES OF OTHER WORLDS	GRIFFITH, GEORGE	GR		
VISIT TO THE MOON, A	GRIFFITH, GEORGE	SS	PRS 00 01	
WORLD OF THE WAR GOD, THE	GRIFFITH, GEORGE	SS	PRS 00 02	
GLIMPSE OF THE SINLESS STAR, A				
	GRIFFITH, GEORGE	SS	PRS 00 03	
WORLD OF CRYSTAL CITIES, THE	GRIFFITH, GEORGE	SS	PRS 00 04	
IN SATURN'S REALM	GRIFFITH, GEORGE	SS	PRS 00 05	
HOMEWARD BOUND	GRIFFITH, GEORGE	SS	PRS 00 06	

WORLDS APART   WILLIAMS-ELLIS & OWEN AN H BLK 66

DOCTOR	LEINSTER, MURRAY	NV	GAL 61 02	
CONSIDER HER WAYS	WYNDHAM, JOHN	NV	56	
EYE FOR A WHAT?, AN	KNIGHT, DAMON	NV	GAL 57 03	
CAPTIVITY	HENDERSON, ZENNA	SS	FSF 58 06	
O'MARA'S ORPHAN (ALSO AS MEDIC)				
	WHITE, JAMES	NV	NWS 60 01	
NUMBER TEN Q STREET	MCCLOY, HELEN	SS	EQM 63 09	
ENORMOUS ROOM, THE	KREPPS, ROBERT W.			
	AND GOLD, H. L.	SN C	AMZ 53 11	
LAST AND FIRST MEN	STAPLEDON, OLAF	EX	MTH 30	
ANARCHIST; OR, THE DOOM OF THE GREAT CITY, THE				
	FAWCETT, DOUGLAS	SS		
INFRA DRACONIS	GUREVICH, G.	NV		

WORLDS AT WAR   RAYER, FRANCIS G. AN TPS

FEARFUL BANNER	RAYER, FRANCIS G.	SS		
MASQUE	DRACO, S.	SS		

WORLDS OF FRITZ LEIBER, THE

DODIE SLAMMED THE DOOR	JAMES, E. R.	SS		
SCAPEGOAT	HANNAH, E.	SS		
CLEVERJACKS AND THE MOONSTALKS, THE				
	JAMES, E. R.	SS		

WORLDS FAR AND NEAR   CARR, TERRY   AN H NEL 74

INTRODUCTION	CARR, TERRY	IN		
FOUR GHOSTS IN HAMLET	LEIBER, FRITZ	NV	FSF 65 01	
DYBBUK OF MAZEL TOV IV, THE	SILVERBERG, ROBERT	SS	NEW 74 AN	
ONE AT A TIME	LAFFERTY, R. A.	SS	ORB 68 04	
DISPLACED PERSON	RUSSELL, ERIC FRANK	SS	WRT 48 09	
IF SOMETHING BEGINS	MOORE, RAYLYN	SS		
THEY LIVE ON LEVELS	CARR, TERRY	SS	NDM 73 03	
HORSE WITH ONE LEG, THE	EFFINGER, GEO. ALEC	SS	NEW 74 AN	
KAZAM COLLECTS	KORNBLUTH, C. M.	SS	STI 41 06	
FEATHER TIGERS	WOLFE, GENE	SS		

WORLDS OF A. E. VAN VOGT, THE

	VAN VOGT, A. E.	AC	ACE 74 01	
ABOUT THE AUTHOR	ACKERMAN, FORREST J.	IN		
REPLICATORS, THE	VAN VOGT, A. E.	NV	IFS 65 02	
FIRST MARTIAN, THE (THIS JOE)				
	VAN VOGT, A. E.	SS	39	
PURPOSE, THE	VAN VOGT, A. E.	NV	ASF 45 05	
EARTH KILLERS, THE	VAN VOGT, A. E.	NV	SSS 49 04	
CATAAAAA, THE	VAN VOGT, A. E.	SS	FBK 47 01	
AUTOMATON	VAN VOGT, A. E.	SS	OWS 50 09	
ITSELF!	VAN VOGT, A. E.	SS	GAM 63 01	
PROCESS	VAN VOGT, A. E.	SS	FSF 50 12	
NOT THE FIRST	VAN VOGT, A. E.	SS	ASF 41 04	
FULFILLMENT	VAN VOGT, A. E.	NV	NTS 51	
SHIP OF DARKNESS	VAN VOGT, A. E.	SS	FBK 47 02	
ULTRA MAN, THE	VAN VOGT, A. E.	NV	WOT 66 05	
STORM, THE	VAN VOGT, A. E.	NV	ASF 43 10	
EXPENDABLES, THE	VAN VOGT, A. E.	NV	IFS 63 09	
REFLECTED MEN, THE	VAN VOGT, A. E.	NV	GAL 71 02	

WORLDS OF CLIFFORD SIMAK, THE

	SIMAK, CLIFFORD D.	AC H SAS 60		
DERIVATIVE COLLECTION "OTHER WORLDS OF CLIFFORD SIMAK"				
IN ENGLAND AS "ALIENS FOR NEIGHBOURS"				
DUSTY ZEBRA	SIMAK, CLIFFORD D.	NV	GAL 54 09	
HONORABLE OPPONENT	SIMAK, CLIFFORD D.	SS	GAL 56 08	
CARBON COPY	SIMAK, CLIFFORD D.	NA	GAL 57 12	
FOUNDING FATHER	SIMAK, CLIFFORD D.	SS	GAL 57 05	
IDIOT'S CRUSADE	SIMAK, CLIFFORD D.	SS	GAL 54 10	
BIG FRONT YARD, THE	SIMAK, CLIFFORD D.	NV	ASF 58 10	
OPERATION STINKY	SIMAK, CLIFFORD D.	NV	GAL 57 04	
JACKPOT	SIMAK, CLIFFORD D.	NV	GAL 56 10	
DEATH SCENE	SIMAK, CLIFFORD D.	SS	INF 57 10	
GREEN THUMB	SIMAK, CLIFFORD D.	NV	GAL 54 07	
LULU	SIMAK, CLIFFORD D.	NV	GAL 57 06	
NEIGHBOR	SIMAK, CLIFFORD D.	NV	ASF 54 06	

WORLDS OF CLIFFORD SIMAK, THE (BRITISH PB)

	SIMAK, CLIFFORD D.	AC	FSP 63	
DUSTY ZEBRA	SIMAK, CLIFFORD D.	NV	GAL 54 09	
HONORABLE OPPONENT	SIMAK, CLIFFORD D.	SS	GAL 56 08	
IDIOT'S CRUSADE	SIMAK, CLIFFORD D.	SS	GAL 54 10	
OPERATION STINKY	SIMAK, CLIFFORD D.	NV	GAL 57 04	
JACKPOT	SIMAK, CLIFFORD D.	NV	GAL 56 10	
NEIGHBOR	SIMAK, CLIFFORD D.	NV	ASF 54 06	

WORLDS OF CLIFFORD SIMAK, THE (6 OF 12)

	SIMAK, CLIFFORD D.	AC	AVN 61	
HONORABLE OPPONENT	SIMAK, CLIFFORD D.	SS	GAL 56 08	
BIG FRONT YARD, THE	SIMAK, CLIFFORD D.	NV	ASF 58 10	
OPERATION STINKY	SIMAK, CLIFFORD D.	NV	GAL 57 04	
JACKPOT	SIMAK, CLIFFORD D.	NV	GAL 56 10	
LULU	SIMAK, CLIFFORD D.	NV	GAL 57 06	
NEIGHBOR	SIMAK, CLIFFORD D.	NV	ASF 54 06	

WORLDS OF FRANK HERBERT, THE HERBERT, FRANK   AC ACE 71

TACTFUL SABOTEUR, THE	HERBERT, FRANK	NV	GAL 64 10	
BY THE BOOK	HERBERT, FRANK	NV	ASF 66 08	
COMMITTEE OF THE WHOLE	HERBERT, FRANK	NV	GAL 65 04	
MATING CALL	HERBERT, FRANK	SS	GAL 61 10	
ESCAPE FELICITY	HERBERT, FRANK	SS	ASF 66 06	
GM EFFECT, THE	HERBERT, FRANK	SS	ASF 65 06	
FEATHERBEDDERS, THE	HERBERT, FRANK	NV	ASF 67 08	
OLD RAMBLING HOUSE	HERBERT, FRANK	SS	GAL 58 04	
A-W-F, UNLIMITED	HERBERT, FRANK	NV	GAL 61 06	

WORLDS OF FRITZ LEIBER, THE LEIBER, FRITZ   AC ACE 76 11

INTRODUCTION	LEIBER, FRITZ	IN		
HATCHERY OF DREAMS	LEIBER, FRITZ	SS	FAN 61 11	
GOGGLES OF DR. DRAGONET, THE	LEIBER, FRITZ	SS	FAN 61 07	
FAR REACH TO CYGNUS	LEIBER, FRITZ	SS	AMZ 65 02	
NIGHT PASSAGE	LEIBER, FRITZ	NV	75	
NICE GIRL WITH FIVE HUSBANDS	LEIBER, FRITZ	SS	GAL 51 04	
WHEN THE CHANGE-WINDS BLOW	LEIBER, FRITZ	SS	FSF 64 08	
237 TALKING STATUES, ETC.	LEIBER, FRITZ	SS	FSF 63 09	
IMPROPER AUTHORITIES, THE	LEIBER, FRITZ	SS	FAN 59 11	
OUR SAUCER VACATION	LEIBER, FRITZ	AR	FUN 59 12	
PIPE DREAM	LEIBER, FRITZ	SS	IFS 59 02	
WHAT'S HE DOING IN THERE?	LEIBER, FRITZ	SS	GAL 57 12	
FRIENDS AND ENEMIES	LEIBER, FRITZ	SS	INF 57 04	
LAST LETTER, THE	LEIBER, FRITZ	SS	GAL 58 06	
ENDFRAY OF THE OFAY	LEIBER, FRITZ	SS	IFS 69 03	
CYCLOPS	LEIBER, FRITZ	NV	WOT 65 09	
MYSTERIOUS DOINGS IN THE METROPOLITAN MUSEUM				
	LEIBER, FRITZ	SS	UNI 74 05	
BAIT, THE	LEIBER, FRITZ	SS	73	
LOTUS EATERS, THE	LEIBER, FRITZ	SS	FSF 72 10	
WAIF	LEIBER, FRITZ	NV	74	

```
WORLDS OF FRITZ LEIBER, THE

  MYTHS MY GREAT-GRANDDAUGHTER TAUGHT ME
                            LEIBER, FRITZ        SS   FSF 63 01
  CATCH THAT ZEPPELIN|      LEIBER, FRITZ        SS   FSF 75 03
  LAST                      LEIBER, FRITZ        SS   FSF 57 03

WORLDS OF JACK VANCE, THE   VANCE, JACK          AC   ACE 73 12
  WORLD BETWEEN, THE        VANCE, JACK          NV
  MOON MOTH, THE            VANCE, JACK          NA   GAL 61 08
  BRAIN OF THE GALAXY       VANCE, JACK          NV   WBY 51 02
  DEVIL ON SALVATION BLUFF, THE
                            VANCE, JACK          NV   STR 54 03
  MEN RETURN, THE           VANCE, JACK          SS   INF 57 07
  KOKOD WARRIORS, THE       VANCE, JACK          NV   TWS 52 10
  KING OF THIEVES, THE      VANCE, JACK          NV   STS 49 11
  COUPE DE GRACE            VANCE, JACK          NV
  BRAINS OF EARTH, THE      VANCE, JACK          NA       66

WORLDS OF MAYBE            SILVERBERG, ROBERT  AN H  NEL 70
  INTRODUCTION             SILVERBERG, ROBERT   IN
  SIDEWISE IN TIME         LEINSTER, MURRAY     SN   ASF 34 06
  SAIL ON! SAIL ON!        FARMER, PHILIP JOSE  SS   STS 52 12
  SLIPS TAKE OVER          DEFORD, MIRIAM ALLEN SS   FSF 64 09
  ALL THE MYRIAD WAYS      NIVEN, LARRY         SS   GAL 68 10
  LIVING SPACE             ASIMOV, ISAAC        SS   SFS 56 05
  TRANSLATION ERROR        SILVERBERG, ROBERT   SS   ASF 59 03
  DELENDA EST              ANDERSON, POUL       NV   FSF 55 12

WORLDS OF POUL ANDERSON, THE  ANDERSON, POUL   AC   ACE 74
  PLANET OF NO RETURN (QUESTION AND ANSWER)
                            ANDERSON, POUL      NO   ASF 54 06
  WAR OF TWO WORLDS, THE (SILENT VICTORY)
                            ANDERSON, POUL      NO   TCS 53 WI
  WORLD WITHOUT STARS (THE ANCIENT GODS)
                            ANDERSON, POUL      NO   ASF 66 06

WORLDS OF ROBERT A. HEINLEIN, THE
                  HEINLEIN, ROBERT A.  AC   ACE 66
  PANDORA'S BOX (WHERE TO?) HEINLEIN, ROBERT A. IN   GAL 52 02
  FREE MEN                 HEINLEIN, ROBERT A.  NV   NEW 66 AC
  BLOWUPS HAPPEN           HEINLEIN, ROBERT A.  NV   ASF 40 09
  SEARCHLIGHT              HEINLEIN, ROBERT A.  SS   SAM 62 08
  LIFE-LINE                HEINLEIN, ROBERT A.  SS   ASF 39 08
  SOLUTION UNSATISFACTORY  HEINLEIN, ROBERT A.  NV   ASF 41 05

WORLDS OF ROBERT F. YOUNG, THE
                  YOUNG, ROBERT F.   AC H  SAS 65
  GIRL WHO MADE TIME STOP, THE YOUNG, ROBERT F. SS   SEP 61 04
  ADDED INDUCEMENT         YOUNG, ROBERT F.     SS   FSF 57 03
  HOPSOIL                  YOUNG, ROBERT F.     SS   FSF 61 01
  FLYING PAN               YOUNG, ROBERT F.     SS   FSF 56 11
  EMILY AND THE BARDS SUBLIME YOUNG, ROBERT F.  SS   FSF 56 07
  DANDELION GIRL, THE      YOUNG, ROBERT F.     SS   SEP 61 04
  STARS ARE CALLING, MR. KEATS, THE
                            YOUNG, ROBERT F.    SS   AMZ 59 06
  GODDESS IN GRANITE       YOUNG, ROBERT F.     NV   FSF 57 09
  PROMISED PLANET          YOUNG, ROBERT F.     SS   IFS 55 12
  ROMANCE IN A 21ST CENTURY USED CAR LOT
                            YOUNG, ROBERT F.    SS   FSF 60 11
  COURTS OF JAMSHYD, THE   YOUNG, ROBERT F.     SS   INF 57 09
  PRODUCTION PROBLEM       YOUNG, ROBERT F.     SS   FSF 59 06
  LITTLE RED SCHOOLHOUSE   YOUNG, ROBERT F.     SS   GAL 56 03
  WRITTEN IN THE STARS     YOUNG, ROBERT F.     SS   VSF 57 09
  DRINK OF DARKNESS, A     YOUNG, ROBERT F.     SS   FAN 62 07
  INTRODUCTION             DAVIDSON, AVRAM      IN
  YOUR GHOST WILL WALK...  YOUNG, ROBERT F.     SS   FSF 57 07

WORLDS OF SCIENCE FICTION, THE
                  MILLS, ROBERT P.   AN   PBK 63
  INTRODUCTION             MILLS, ROBERT P.     IN
  FIRST MEN, THE           FAST, HOWARD         NV   FSF 60 02
  WORK OF ART, A (ART-WORK) BLISH, JAMES        SS   SFS 56 07
  EVENING PRIMROSE (1941)  COLLIER, JOHN        SS   APR 47 03
  MOMENTO HOMO (DEATH OF A SPACEMAN)
                            MILLER, WALTER M. JR SS  AMZ 54 03
  MIRACLE OF RARE DEVICE, A BRADBURY, RAY       SS   PBY 62 01
  ALL YOU ZOMBIES-         HEINLEIN, ROBERT A.  SS   FSF 59 03
  FAQ!                     ELLIOTT, GEORGE P.   SS   FSF 61 11
  BABEL II                 KNIGHT, DAMON        NV   BEY 53 07
  SAUCER OF LONELINESS     STURGEON, THEODORE   SS   GAL 53 02
  NIGHT PIECE              ANDERSON, POUL       SS   FSF 61 07
  NOW LET US SLEEP         DAVIDSON, AVRAM      SS   VSF 57 09
  STRANGE GIRL, THE        VAN DOREN, MARK      SS       62
  QUEST FOR SAINT AQUIN, THE BOUCHER, ANTHONY   SS   NTS 51
  WAR IN THE AIR, THE      CASSILL, R. V.       SS   FSF 56 09
  UGLY LITTLE BOY, THE (LASTBORN)
                            ASIMOV, ISAAC       NA   GAL 58 09
  MY PRIVATE WORLD OF SCIENCE FICTION
                            BESTER, ALFRED      MS

WORLDS OF THEODORE STURGEON, THE
                  STURGEON, THEODORE  AC   ACE 72
  FROM PLYNCK TO PLANCK    STURGEON, THEODORE   SF   IFS 62 01
  SKILLS OF XANADU, THE    STURGEON, THEODORE   NV   GAL 56 07
  THERE IS NO DEFENSE      STURGEON, THEODORE   NV   ASF 48 02
  PERFECT HOST, THE        STURGEON, THEODORE   NV   WRT 48 11
  GRAVEYARD READER, THE    STURGEON, THEODORE   SS   SCF 58 10
  OTHER MAN, THE           STURGEON, THEODORE   NA   GAL 56 09
  SKY WAS FULL OF SHIPS, THE STURGEON, THEODORE SS   TWS 47 06
  SHOTTLE BOP              STURGEON, THEODORE   SS   UNK 41 02
  MATURITY                 STURGEON, THEODORE   NV   ASF 47 02
  MEMORIAL (SEE ALSO ATOMIC MEMORIAL)
                            STURGEON, THEODORE  SS   ASF 46 04

WORLDS OF TOMORROW         DERLETH, AUGUST   AN H PEL 53
  ENGLISH DERIVATIVE ANTHOLOGY "NEW WORLDS FOR OLD"
  INTRODUCTION             DERLETH, AUGUST      IN

  TINKLER, THE             ANDERSON, POUL       SS   WBY 51 02
  SMILE, THE               BRADBURY, RAY        SS   FAN 52 SU
  FIRES WITHIN, THE        CLARKE, ARTHUR C.    SS   FSB 47 08
  SUPERIORITY              CLARKE, ARTHUR C.    SS   FSF 51 08
  MCILVAINE'S STAR         DERLETH, AUGUST      SS   IFS 52 07
  BROTHERS BEYOND THE VOID FAIRMAN, PAUL W.     SS   FAD 52 03
  BEAUTIFUL, BEAUTIFUL, BEAUTIFUL|
                            FRIEDMAN, STUART    SS   FUT 52 03
  DEAD PLANET, THE         HAMILTON, EDMOND     SS   STS 46 SP
  LIKE A BIRD, LIKE A FISH HICKEY, H. B.        SS   WBY 51 02
  GENTLEMAN IS AN EPWA, THE JACOBI, CARL        NV   NEW 53 AN
  ENCHANTED FOREST, THE    LEIBER, FRITZ        SS   ASF 50 10
  GREAT COLD, THE          LONG, FRANK BELKNAP  SS   ASF 35 02
  FROM BEYOND              LOVECRAFT, H. P.     SS   WRT 38 02
  LINE TO TOMORROW         PADGETT, LEWIS       SS   ASF 45 11
  BUSINESS, AS USUAL, THE  REYNOLDS, MACK       SS   FSF 52 06
  GARDENER, THE            ST. CLAIR, MARGARET  SS   TWS 49 10
  MARTIAN AND THE MORON, THE STURGEON, THEODORE NV   WRT 49 03
  NULL-P                   TENN, WILLIAM        SS   WBY 51 01
  STRANGE HARVEST          WANDREI, DONALD      NV   WRT 53 05

WORLDS OF TOMORROW (BRITISH PB)
                            DERLETH, AUGUST     AN   FSP 63
  10 STORIES FROM AMERICAN EDITION,
     REMAINING 9 IN "NEW WORLDS FOR OLD"
  INTRODUCTION             DERLETH, AUGUST      IN
  TINKLER, THE             ANDERSON, POUL       SS   WBY 51 02
  SUPERIORITY              CLARKE, ARTHUR C.    SS   FSF 51 08
  MCILVAINE'S STAR         DERLETH, AUGUST      SS   IFS 52 07
  BROTHERS BEYOND THE VOID FAIRMAN, PAUL W.     SS   FAD 52 03
  BEAUTIFUL, BEAUTIFUL, BEAUTIFUL|
                            FRIEDMAN, STUART    SS   FUT 52 03
  DEAD PLANET, THE         HAMILTON, EDMOND     SS   STS 46 SP
  LIKE A BIRD, LIKE A FISH HICKEY, H. B.        SS   WBY 51 02
  GARDENER, THE            ST. CLAIR, MARGARET  SS   TWS 49 10
  NULL-P                   TENN, WILLIAM        SS   WBY 51 01
  STRANGE HARVEST          WANDREI, DONALD      NV   WRT 53 05

WORLDS OF TOMORROW (BRITISH) DERLETH, AUGUST   AN H WEI 55
  INTRODUCTION             DERLETH, AUGUST      IN
  SMILE, THE               BRADBURY, RAY        SS   FAN 52 SU
  FIRES WITHIN, THE        CLARKE, ARTHUR C.    SS   FSB 47 08
  SUPERIORITY              CLARKE, ARTHUR C.    SS   FSF 51 08
  MCILVAINE'S STAR         DERLETH, AUGUST      SS   IFS 52 07
  BROTHERS BEYOND THE VOID FAIRMAN, PAUL W.     SS   FAD 52 03
  DEAD PLANET, THE         HAMILTON, EDMOND     SS   STS 46 SP
  LIKE A BIRD, LIKE A FISH HICKEY, H. B.        SS   WBY 51 02
  ENCHANTED FOREST, THE    LEIBER, FRITZ        SS   ASF 50 10
  GREAT COLD, THE          LONG, FRANK BELKNAP  SS   ASF 35 02
  FROM BEYOND              LOVECRAFT, H. P.     SS   WRT 38 02
  LINE TO TOMORROW         PADGETT, LEWIS       SS   ASF 45 11
  GARDENER, THE            ST. CLAIR, MARGARET  SS   TWS 49 10
  MARTIAN AND THE MORON, THE STURGEON, THEODORE NV   WRT 49 03
  NULL-P                   TENN, WILLIAM        SS   WBY 51 01
  STRANGE HARVEST          WANDREI, DONALD      NV   WRT 53 05

WORLDS OF TOMORROW (10 OF 19)
                            DERLETH, AUGUST     AN   BRK 58 10
  DEAD PLANET, THE         HAMILTON, EDMOND     SS   STS 46 SP
  MCILVAINE'S STAR         DERLETH, AUGUST      SS   IFS 52 07
  GREAT COLD, THE          LONG, FRANK BELKNAP  SS   ASF 35 02
  FIRES WITHIN, THE        CLARKE, ARTHUR C.    SS   FSB 47 08
  BROTHERS BEYOND THE VOID FAIRMAN, PAUL W.     SS   FAD 52 03
  GENTLEMAN IS AN EPWA, THE JACOBI, CARL        NV   NEW 53 AN
  ENCHANTED FOREST, THE    LEIBER, FRITZ        SS   ASF 50 10
  BUSINESS, AS USUAL, THE  REYNOLDS, MACK       SS   FSF 52 06
  MARTIAN AND THE MORON, THE STURGEON, THEODORE NV   WRT 49 03
  NULL-P                   TENN, WILLIAM        SS   WBY 51 01

WORLDS OF WEIRD            MARGULIES, LEO     AN   PYR 65
  FORGOTTEN CREATOR OF WEIRD TALES, THE
                            MOSKOWITZ, SAM      IN
  ROADS                    QUINN, SEABURY       SS   WRT 38 01
  VALLEY OF THE WORM, THE  HOWARD, ROBERT E.    SS   WRT 34 02
  SAPPHIRE GODDESS, THE    DYALHIS, NICTZIN     NV   WRT 34 02
  HE THAT HATH WINGS       HAMILTON, EDMOND     SS   WRT 38 07
  MOTHER OF TOADS          SMITH, CLARK ASHTON  SS   WRT 38 07
  THING IN THE CELLAR, THE KELLER, DAVID H. MD. SS   WRT 32 03
  GIANTS IN THE SKY        LONG, FRANK BELKNAP  SS   WRT 39 08

WORLDS OF WHEN            CONKLIN, GROFF     AN   PYR 62 05
  INTRODUCTORY NOTE        CONKLIN, GROFF       IN
  TRANSFUSION              OLIVER, CHAD         NV   ASF 59 06
  BULLET WITH HIS NAME     LEIBER, FRITZ        NV   GAL 58 07
  DEATH AND THE SENATOR    CLARKE, ARTHUR C.    NV   ASF 61 05
  FARMER                   REYNOLDS, MACK       NV   GAL 61 06
  RATIONS OF TANTALUS (ALSO AS THE RAGES)
                            ST. CLAIR, MARGARET NV   FUN 54 07

WORLDS OF WONDER          HARRISON, HARRY    AN H DBL 69
  INTRODUCTION             HARRISON, HARRY      IN
  SUNJAMMER (ALSO AS THE WIND FROM THE SUN)
                            CLARKE, ARTHUR C.   SS   BLF 64
  WE DIDN'T DO ANYTHING WRONG, HARDLY
                            KUYKENDALL, ROGER   SS   ASF 59 05
  WHO CAN REPLACE A MAN? (BUT WHO CAN REPLACE A MAN)
                            ALDISS, BRIAN W.    SS   INF 58 06
  TRICKY TONNAGE           JAMESON, MALCOLM     SS   ASF 44 12
  APPOINTMENT ON PRILA     SHAW, BOB            SS   ASF 68 08
  HI DIDDLE DIDDLE|        SILVERBERG, ROBERT   NV   ASF 59 02
  IF (PRAISEWORTHY SAUR)   HARRISON, HARRY      SS   IFS 69 02
  PAIL OF AIR, A           LEIBER, FRITZ        SS   GAL 51 12
  HOWLING BOUNDERS, THE    VANCE, JACK          NV   STS 49 03
  MIRROR OF ICE            WRIGHT, GARY         SS   GAL 67 06
  HEAVY PLANET             ROTHMAN, MILTON A.   SS   ASF 39 08
  KEYHOLE                  LEINSTER, MURRAY     SS   TWS 51 12
```

WORLDS OF WONDER

WALL AROUND THE WORLD, THE	COGSWELL, THEODORE R	NV	BEY 53 09
PRONE	REYNOLDS, MACK	SS	FSF 54 09
ESCAPE THE MORNING	ANDERSON, POUL	SS	BLF 66 11
SOMEDAY	ASIMOV, ISAAC	SS	INF 56 08

WORLDS OF WONDER STAPLEDON, OLAF AC H FPB 49

DEATH INTO LIFE	STAPLEDON, OLAF	NO	MTH 46
FLAMES, THE	STAPLEDON, OLAF	NO	SKW 47
OLD MAN IN A NEW WORLD	STAPLEDON, OLAF	NO	ALN 44

WORLDS TO COME KNIGHT, DAMON AN H HPR 67

INTRODUCTION	KNIGHT, DAMON	IN	
SENTINEL, THE (SENTINEL OF ETERNITY)	CLARKE, ARTHUR C.	SS	TSF 51 SP
MOONWALK	FYFE, H. B.	NA	SSF 52 11
MARS IS HEAVEN!	BRADBURY, RAY	SS	PLS 48 FL
EDGE OF THE SEA, THE	BUDRYS, ALGIS	SS	VSF 58 03
MARTIAN WAY, THE	ASIMOV, ISAAC	NA	GAL 52 11
BIG CONTEST, THE	MACDONALD, JOHN D.	SS	WBY 50 12
ORDEAL IN SPACE	HEINLEIN, ROBERT A.	SS	TAC 48 05
THAT SHARE OF GLORY	KORNBLUTH, C. M.	NV	ASF 52 01
SUNKEN UNIVERSE (AS ARTHUR MERLYN, SEE ALSO SURFACE TENSION)	BLISH, JAMES	NV	SSS 42 05
MORE GOOD READING IN SCIENCE FICTION	KNIGHT, DAMON	MS	

WORLDS WITHOUT END SIMAK, CLIFFORD D. AC BEL 64 04

WORLDS WITHOUT END	SIMAK, CLIFFORD D.	NA	FUT 56 WI
SPACEMAN'S VAN GOGH, THE	SIMAK, CLIFFORD D.	NA	SFS 56 03
FULL CYCLE	SIMAK, CLIFFORD D.	NA	SFS 55 11

WOUNDED PLANET, THE ELWOOD, ROGER AN BAN 74 08
SEE "SAVING WORLDS"

XENOGENESIS DEFORD, MIRIAM ALLEN AC BAL 69 03

DAUGHTER OF THE TREE, THE	DEFORD, MIRIAM ALLEN	SS	FSF 51 08
SUPERIOR SEX, THE	DEFORD, MIRIAM ALLEN	SS	FSF 68 04
AJERI DIARY, THE	DEFORD, MIRIAM ALLEN	SS	FSF 68 03
QUICK TO HASTE	DEFORD, MIRIAM ALLEN	SS	NEW 69 AC
SMILING FUTURE, THE	DEFORD, MIRIAM ALLEN	SS	IFS 65 10
GATHI	DEFORD, MIRIAM ALLEN	SS	FSF 58 06
CHILDREN, THE	DEFORD, MIRIAM ALLEN	NV	STS 52 12
THROWBACK	DEFORD, MIRIAM ALLEN	SS	STS 52 10
ONE-WAY JOURNEY (ONE WAY)	DEFORD, MIRIAM ALLEN	SS	GAL 55 03
SEASON OF THE BABIES, THE	DEFORD, MIRIAM ALLEN	SS	FUN 59 12
FEATHERBED ON CHLYNTHA	DEFORD, MIRIAM ALLEN	SS	VSF 57 11
TRANSIT OF VENUS, THE	DEFORD, MIRIAM ALLEN	SS	FSF 62 06
ALL IN GOOD TIME	DEFORD, MIRIAM ALLEN	SS	FSF 60 07
ABSOLUTELY PERFECT MURDER, THE	DEFORD, MIRIAM ALLEN	SS	FSF 65 02
OPERATION CASSANDRA	DEFORD, MIRIAM ALLEN	NV	FUN 58 11
LAST GENERATION, THE	DEFORD, MIRIAM ALLEN	SS	FSF 50 12

YEAR AFTER TOMORROW, THE DEL REY, L/MATSCHAT/ AN H JCW 51

FOREWORD	DEL REY, LESTER	IN	
LUCK OF IGNATZ, THE	DEL REY, LESTER	NV	ASF 39 08
MIND MASTERS OF MARS, THE	CLAUDY, CARL H.	NV	AMB 31 09
BY VIRTUE OF CIRCUMFERENCE	VAN DRESSER, PETER	SS	AMB 37 11
RED DEATH OF MARS, THE	WILLIAMS, ROBERT M.	NV	ASF 40 07
LAND OF NO SHADOW, THE	CLAUDY, CARL H.	NV	AMB 31 02
PLUM DUFF	VAN DRESSER, PETER	SS	AMB 35 12
KINDNESS	DEL REY, LESTER	SS	ASF 44 10
TONGUE OF BEAST	CLAUDY, CARL H.	SS	AMB 39 05
ROCKET TO THE SUN	VAN DRESSER, PETER	SS	AMB 39 07

YEAR 2000, THE HARRISON, HARRY OA H DBL 70

AMERICA THE BEAUTIFUL	LEIBER, FRITZ	SS	YRT 70
PROMETHEUS REBOUND	GALOUYE, DANIEL F.	NV	YRT 70
FAR FROM THIS EARTH	OLIVER, CHAD	SS	YRT 70
AFTER THE ACCIDENT	MITCHISON, NAOMI	SS	YRT 70
UTOPIAN	REYNOLDS, MACK	SS	YRT 70
ORGY OF THE LIVING AND THE DYING	ALDISS, BRIAN W.	NV	YRT 70
SEA CHANGE	CHANDLER, A. BERTRAM	NV	YRT 70
BLACK IS BEAUTIFUL	SILVERBERG, ROBERT	SS	YRT 70
TAKE IT OR LEAVE IT	MASSON, DAVID I.	SS	YRT 70
LAWGIVER, THE	LAUMER, KEITH	SS	YRT 70
TO BE A MAN	COUPLING, J. J.	SS	YRT 70
JUDAS FISH	SCORTIA, THOMAS N.	SS	YRT 70
AMERICAN DEAD	HARRISON, HARRY	SS	YRT 70

YEAR 2018! BLISH, JAMES NO AVN 57
IN ENGLAND AS "THEY SHALL HAVE STARS"

BRIDGE	BLISH, JAMES	NV	ASF 52 02
AT DEATH'S END	BLISH, JAMES	NV	ASF 54 05
CHRONOLOGY OF CITIES IN FLIGHT	BLISH, JAMES	MS	

YEAR'S BEST HORROR STORIES: SERIES II, THE DAVIS, RICHARD AN DAW 74 07

FOREWORD	LEE, CHRISTOPHER	IN	
DAVID'S WORM	LUMLEY, BRIAN	SS	71
PRICE OF A DEMON, THE	BRANDNER, GARY	SS	WTS 72 07
KNOCKER AT THE PORTICO, THE	COPPER, BASIL	SS	
ANIMAL FAIR, THE	BLOCH, ROBERT	SS	PBY 71 05
NAPIER COURT	CAMPBELL, J. RAMSEY	SS	
HAUNTS OF THE VERY RICH	BROWN, T. K. III	NV	PBY 71 05
LONG-TERM RESIDENTS, THE	PEDLER, KIT	SS	
LIKE TWO WHITE SPIDERS	BERTIN, EDDY C.	SS	
OLD HORNS, THE	CAMPBELL, J. RAMSEY	SS	
HAGGOPIAN	LUMLEY, BRIAN	NV	FSF 73 06
EVENTS AT POROTH FARM, THE	KLEIN, T. E. D.	NV	

YEAR'S BEST HORROR STORIES: SERIES III, THE DAVIS, RICHARD AN DAW 75 06

INTRODUCTION	DAVIS, RICHARD	IN	

YEAR'S BEST SCIENCE FICTION NOVELS: 1952

WHIMPER OF WHIPPED DOGS, THE	ELLISON, HARLAN	NV	BMR 73
MAN IN THE UNDERPASS, THE	CAMPBELL, J. RAMSEY	SS	NEW 75 AN
S.F.	KLEIN, T. E. D.	SS	NEW 75 AN
UNCLE VLAD	SINCLAIR, CLIVE	SS	TRV 73
JUDAS STORY	STABLEFORD, BRIAN M.	SS	NEW 75 AN
HOUSE OF CTHULHU, THE	LUMLEY, BRIAN	SS	WHS 73
SATANESQUE	WEISS, ALAN	SS	LMF 74
BURGER CREATURE	CHAPMAN, STEVE	SS	ORB 73 12
WAKE UP DEAD	STOUT, TIM	SS	NEW 75 AN
FORGET-ME-NOT	TAYLOR, BERNARD	SS	NEW 75 AN
HALLOWEEN STORY	FITZ GERALD, GREGORY	SS	BTH 73
BIG, WIDE, WONDERFUL WORLD	PRITCH, CHARLES E.	SS	FSF 58 03
TASTE OF YOUR LOVE, THE	BERTIN, EDDY C.	SS	71

YEAR'S BEST HORROR STORIES: SERIES IV, THE PAGE, GERALD W. AN DAW 76 11

INTRODUCTION	PAGE, GERALD W.	IN	
FOREVER STAND THE STONES	PUMILIA, JOSEPH F.	SS	75
AND DON'T FORGET THE ONE RED ROSE	DAVIDSON, AVRAM	SS	PBY 75 09
CHRISTMAS PRESENT	CAMPBELL, J. RAMSEY	SS	BBC 69 12
QUESTION OF GUILT, A	CLEMENT, HAL	NV	NEW 76 AN
HOUSE ON STILLCROFT STREET, THE	BRENNAN, JOSEPH P.	SS	AHM 75 06
RECRUDESCENCE OF GEOFFREY MARVELL, THE	GABBARD, G. N.	SS	NEW 76 AN
SOMETHING HAD TO BE DONE	DRAKE, DAVID	SS	FSF 75 02
COTTAGE TENANT	LONG, FRANK BELKNAP	NV	FAN 75 04
MAN WITH THE AURA, THE	LAFFERTY, R. A.	SS	FSF 75 04
WHITE WOLF CALLING	GRANT, C. L.	SS	FSF 75 04
LIFEGUARD	COVER, ARTHUR BYRON	SS	75
BLACK CAPTAIN, THE	MUNN, H. WARNER	SS	75
GLOVE, THE	LEIBER, FRITZ	SS	WHS 75 03
NO WAY HOME	LUMLEY, BRIAN	SS	FSF 75 09
LOVECRAFT CONTROVERSY- WHY?, THE	PRICE, E. HOFFMANN	AR	NEW 76 AN

YEAR'S BEST HORROR STORIES, THE DAVIS, RICHARD AN DAW 71

DOUBLE WHAMMY	BLOCH, ROBERT	SS	FAN 70 02
SISTER CITY, THE	LUMLEY, BRIAN	SS	70
WHEN MORNING COMES	FANCETT, ELIZABETH	SS	69
PREY	MATHESON, RICHARD	SS	PBY 69 04
WINTER	REED, KIT	SS	ARG 70
LUCIFER!	TUBB, E. C.	SS	VOT 69 11
I WONDER WHAT HE WANTED	BERTIN, EDDY C.	SS	70
PROBLEM CHILD	OLDALE, PETER	SS	VOT 70 06
SCAR, THE	CAMPBELL, J. RAMSEY	SS	SMS 69 SU
WARP	NORTON, RALPH	SS	MAY 68
HATE, THE	PINCKARD, TERRI E.	SS	WTS 71 01
QUIET GAME, A	FREMLIN, CELIA	SS	ARG 70
AFTER NIGHTFALL	RILEY, DAVE	SS	70
DEATH'S DOOR	MCNEAR, ROBERT	SS	PBY 69 03

YEAR'S BEST SCIENCE FICTION NO. 1, THE HARRISON & ALDISS AN SPH 68
SEE "BEST SF: 1967"

YEAR'S BEST SCIENCE FICTION NO. 2, THE HARRISON & ALDISS AN SPH 69
SEE "BEST SF: 1968"

YEAR'S BEST SCIENCE FICTION NO. 3, THE HARRISON & ALDISS AN SPH 70
SEE "BEST SF: 1969"

YEAR'S BEST SCIENCE FICTION NO. 4, THE HARRISON & ALDISS AN SPH 71
SEE "BEST SF: 1970"

YEAR'S BEST SCIENCE FICTION NO. 5, THE HARRISON & ALDISS AN SPH 72
SEE "BEST SF: 1971"

YEAR'S BEST SCIENCE FICTION NO. 6, THE HARRISON & ALDISS AN SPH 73
SEE "BEST SF: 1972"

YEAR'S BEST SCIENCE FICTION NO. 7, THE HARRISON & ALDISS AN SPH 74
SEE "BEST SF: 1973"

YEAR'S BEST SCIENCE FICTION NO. 8, THE HARRISON & ALDISS AN SPH 75
SEE "BEST SF: 1974"

YEAR'S BEST SCIENCE FICTION NO. 9, THE HARRISON & ALDISS AN H WEI 76
SEE "BEST SF: 75, THE NINTH ANNUAL"

YEAR'S BEST SCIENCE FICTION NOVELS: SECOND SERIES, THE BLEILER & DIKTY AN H GRY 55
SEE "YEAR'S BEST SCIENCE FICTION NOVELS: 1954"
OMITS "SECOND VARIETY"

YEAR'S BEST SCIENCE FICTION NOVELS: 1952 BLEILER & DIKTY AN H FEL 52
IN ENGLAND AS "THE YEAR'S BEST SCIENCE FICTION NOVELS"

IZZARD AND THE MEMBRANE	MILLER, WALTER M. JR	NV	ASF 51 05
AND THEN THERE WERE NONE	RUSSELL, ERIC FRANK	NV	ASF 51 06
FLIGHT TO FOREVER	ANDERSON, POUL	NV	SSS 50 11
HUNTING SEASON, THE	ROBINSON, FRANK M.	SN	ASF 51 11
SEEKER OF THE SPHINX (ALSO AS THE ROAD TO THE SEA)	CLARKE, ARTHUR C.	NV	TCS 51 SP

YEAR'S BEST SCIENCE FICTION NOVELS: 1953

YEAR'S BEST SCIENCE FICTION NOVELS: 1953
                              BLEILER & DIKTY   AN H FEL 53 03
   IN ENGLAND AS "CATEGORY PHOENIX"
   INTRODUCTION   BLEILER, EVERETT F.
                            AND DIKTY, T. E.   IN C
   FIREWATER   TENN, WILLIAM   SN   ASF 52 02
   CATEGORY PHOENIX   ELLANBY, BOYD   NA   GAL 52 05
   SURFACE TENSION   BLISH, JAMES   NA   GAL 52 08
   GADGET HAD A GHOST, THE   LEINSTER, MURRAY   NV   TWS 52 06
   CONDITIONALLY HUMAN   MILLER, WALTER M. JR NV   GAL 52 02

YEAR'S BEST SCIENCE FICTION NOVELS: 1954
                              BLEILER & DIKTY   AN H FEL 54 03
   IN ENGLAND AS
   "THE YEAR'S BEST SCIENCE FICTION NOVELS: SECOND SERIES
   INTRODUCTION   BLEILER, EVERETT F.
                            AND DIKTY, T. E.   IN C
   ENORMOUS ROOM, THE   GOLD, H. L.
                            AND KREPPS, ROBERT W.   SN C AMZ 53 11
   ASSIGNMENT IN ALDEBARAN   CROSSEN, KENDELL F.   NV   TWS 53 02
   OCEANS ARE WIDE, THE   ROBINSON, FRANK M.   SN   SST 54 04
   SENTIMENTALISTS, THE   LEINSTER, MURRAY   NV   GAL 53 04
   SECOND VARIETY   DICK, PHILIP K.   NV   SSF 53 05

YEAR'S BEST SCIENCE FICTION NOVELS, THE
                              BLEILER & DIKTY   AN H GRY 54
   SEE "YEAR'S BEST SCIENCE FICTION NOVELS: 1952"
   OMITS "SEEKER OF THE SPHINX"

YESTERDAY AND TOMORROW   VERNE, JULES   AC H ARC 64
   EDITED BY I. O. EVANS
   INTRODUCTION   EVANS, I. O.   IN
   ETERNAL ADAM, THE (1905) VERNE, JULES   NV   STN 57 03
   FATE OF JEAN MORENAS, THE VERNE, JULES   SS
   IDEAL CITY, AN   VERNE, JULES   SS
   TEN HOURS HUNTING   VERNE, JULES   SS
   FRRITT-FLACC (1884)   VERNE, JULES   SS   FSF 59 11
   GIL BRALTAR (1857)   VERNE, JULES   SS   FSF 58 07
   IN THE TWENTY NINTH CENTURY (ARS 49 SU)
                            VERNE, JULES   SS   FRM 89 02
   MR. RAY SHARP AND MISS ME FLAT (1893)
                            VERNE, JULES   SS

YET MORE PENGUIN SCIENCE FICTION
                              ALDISS, BRIAN W.   AN   PEN 64
   ALSO IN "THE PENGUIN SCIENCE FICTION OMNIBUS"
   INTRODUCTION   ALDISS, BRIAN W.   IN
   WALL AROUND THE WORLD, THE COGSWELL, THEODORE R NV   BEY 53 09
   PROTECTED SPECIES   FYFE, H. B.   SS   ASF 51 03
   BEFORE EDEN   CLARKE, ARTHUR C.   SS   AMZ 61 06
   RESCUER, THE   PORGES, ARTHUR   SS   ASF 62 07
   I MADE YOU   MILLER, WALTER M. JR SS   ASF 54 03
   COUNTRY OF THE KIND, THE KNIGHT, DAMON   SS   FSF 56 02
   MS. FOUND IN A CHINESE FORTUNE COOKIE
                            KORNBLUTH, C. M.   SS   FSF 57 07
   CAGE, THE   CHANDLER, A. BERTRAM   SS   FSF 57 06
   EASTWARD HO!   TENN, WILLIAM   SS   FSF 58 10
   WINDOWS OF HEAVEN, THE (TWO BY TWO)
                            BRUNNER, JOHN   SS   NWS 56 05
   COMMON TIME   BLISH, JAMES   SS   SFQ 53 08
   FULFILLMENT   VAN VOGT, A. E.   NV   NTS 51

YONDER   BEAUMONT, CHARLES   AC   BAN 58 04
   YOU CAN'T HAVE THEM ALL   BEAUMONT, CHARLES   SS   PBY 56 08
   FRITZCHEN   BEAUMONT, CHARLES   SS   OSF 53 01
   LAST RITES   BEAUMONT, CHARLES   SS   IFS 55 10
   PLACE OF MEETING   BEAUMONT, CHARLES   SS   OSF 54 02
   WORLD OF DIFFERENTS, A   BEAUMONT, CHARLES   SS   NEW 58 AC
   ANTHEM   BEAUMONT, CHARLES   SS   NEW 58 AC
   IN HIS IMAGE (THE MAN WHO MADE HIMSELF)
                            BEAUMONT, CHARLES   NV   IMG 57 02
   JUNGLE, THE   BEAUMONT, CHARLES   NV   IFS 54 12
   QUADRIOPTICON, THE   BEAUMONT, CHARLES   SS   FSF 54 08
   HAIR OF THE DOG   BEAUMONT, CHARLES   SS   OSF 54 03
   BEAUTIFUL PEOPLE, THE (ALSO AS THE BEAUTIFUL WOMAN)
                            BEAUMONT, CHARLES   SS   IFS 52 09
   LAST CAPER, THE   BEAUMONT, CHARLES   SS   FSF 54 03
   MOTHER'S DAY   BEAUMONT, CHARLES   SS   NEW 58 AC
   TRAUMEREI   BEAUMONT, CHARLES   SS   INF 56 02
   MONSTER SHOW, THE   BEAUMONT, CHARLES   SS   PBY 56 05
   NEW SOUND, THE   BEAUMONT, CHARLES   SS   FSF 55 06

YOU AND SCIENCE FICTION   HOLLISTER, BERNARD C AN L NTC 76
   A HUMANISTIC APPROACH TO SCIENCE FICTION
   INTRODUCTION   HOLLISTER, BERNARD C IN
   WHO AM I THIS TIME? (MY NAME IS EVERYONE)
                            VONNEGUT, KURT JR.   SS   SEP 61 12
   PROFESSION (EDITED)   ASIMOV, ISAAC   SS   ASF 57 07
   RAT RACE   JONES, RAYMOND F.   SS   ASF 66 04
   SURVIVAL SHIP   MERRIL, JUDITH   SS   WBY 51 01
   SMILE, THE   BRADBURY, RAY   SS   FAN 52 SU
   GILEAD   HENDERSON, ZENNA   SS   FSF 54 08
   ALL SUMMER IN A DAY   BRADBURY, RAY   SS   FSF 54 03
   DAY OF TRUCE   SIMAK, CLIFFORD D.   NV   GAL 63 02
   SUBLIMINAL MAN, THE   BALLARD, J. G.   NV   NWS 63 01
   IT'S SUCH A BEAUTIFUL DAY ASIMOV, ISAAC   NV   STR 54 03
   NOW LET US SLEEP   DAVIDSON, AVRAM   SS   VSF 57 09
   WHAT TO DO TILL THE ANALYST COMES (EVERYBODY'S HAPPY BUT ME!)
                            POHL, FREDERIK   SS   IMG 56 02
   CONSUMER'S REPORT (NO GUN TO THE VICTOR)
                            COGSWELL, THEODORE R SS   IMG 55 10
   COMPUTERS DON'T ARGUE   DICKSON, GORDON R.   SS   ASF 65 09
   INTO THE SHOP   GOULART, RON   SS   FSF 64 04
   CAUGHT IN THE ORGAN DRAFT SILVERBERG, ROBERT   SS   WLK 73
   PILL, THE   NADLER, MAGGIE   SS   FAN 72 04
   BIRDS, THE   DU MAURIER, DAPHNE   NV   GHK 52 10

FROG POND   YARBRO, CHELSEA Q.   SS   GAL 71 03
BILLENIUM   BALLARD, J. G.   SS   NWS 61 11
CENSUS TAKERS, THE   POHL, FREDERIK   SS   FSF 56 02
CRAWLERS, THE   DICK, PHILIP K.   SS   IMG 54 07
EPILOG   HOLLISTER, BERNARD C MS

YOU WILL NEVER BE THE SAME SMITH, CORDWAINER   AC   BKM 63
   NO, NO, NOT ROGOV!   SMITH, CORDWAINER   SS   IFS 59 02
   LADY WHO SAILED THE SOUL, THE
                            SMITH, CORDWAINER   NV   GAL 60 04
   SCANNERS LIVE IN VAIN   SMITH, CORDWAINER   NA   FBK 50 06
   GAME OF RAT AND DRAGON, THE SMITH, CORDWAINER   NV   GAL 55 10
   BURNING OF THE BRAIN, THE SMITH, CORDWAINER   SS   IFS 58 10
   GOLDEN THE SHIP WAS- OH! OH! OH!
                            SMITH, CORDWAINER   SS   AMZ 59 04
   ALPHA RALPHA BOULEVARD   SMITH, CORDWAINER   NV   FSF 61 06
   MARK ELF   SMITH, CORDWAINER   SS   STN 57 05

YOU'RE ALL ALONE   LEIBER, FRITZ   AC   ACE 72
   YOU'RE ALL ALONE   LEIBER, FRITZ   NO   FAD 50 07
   FOUR GHOSTS IN HAMLET   LEIBER, FRITZ   NV   FSF 65 01
   CREATURE FROM CLEVELAND DEPTHS, THE (ALSO AS THE LONE WOLF)
                            LEIBER, FRITZ   NA   GAL 62 12

YOUNG DEMONS   ELWOOD & GHIDALIA   AN   AVN 72 04
   INTRODUCTION   STURGEON, THEODORE   IN
   SREDNI VASHTAR   SAKI   SS
   BETTYANN   NEVILLE, KRIS   NV   NTS 51
   TRANSCENDENT TIGERS, THE LAFFERTY, R. A.   SS   WOT 64 02
   APPLE   MCCAFFREY, ANNE   NV   NEW 69 AN
   SMALL ASSASSIN, THE   BRADBURY, RAY   SS   DMN 46 11
   SHUT THE LAST DOOR   HENSLEY, JOE L.   SS   ANA 70
   GAMES   MACLEAN, KATHERINE   SS   GAL 53 03
   JAMBOREE   WILLIAMSON, JACK   SS   GAL 69 12

YOUNG READERS SCIENCE FICTION STORIES
                              ELAM, RICHARD M. JR. AC H LPB 57
   SEE "TEEN-AGE SCIENCE FICTION STORIES"

YOURS TRULY, JACK THE RIPPER BLOCH, ROBERT   AC   BEL 62
   IN ENGLAND AS "THE HOUSE OF THE HATCHET AND OTHER TALES OF
   HORROR"
   INTRODUCTION   BLOCH, ROBERT   IN
   SWEETS TO THE SWEET   BLOCH, ROBERT   SS   WRT 47 03
   DREAM MAKERS, THE   BLOCH, ROBERT   NV   BEY 53 09
   YOURS TRULY, JACK THE RIPPER BLOCH, ROBERT   SS   WRT 43 07
   EYES OF THE MUMMY, THE   BLOCH, ROBERT   SS   WRT 38 04
   MANNIKIN, THE (ALSO AS MANNIKINS OF HORROR)
                            BLOCH, ROBERT   SS   WRT 37 04
   HOUSE OF THE HATCHET, THE BLOCH, ROBERT   SS   WRT 41 01
   CLOAK, THE   BLOCH, ROBERT   SS   UNK 39 05
   BEETLES   BLOCH, ROBERT   SS   WRT 38 12
   FACELESS GOD, THE   BLOCH, ROBERT   SS   WRT 36 05

ZACHERLEY'S MIDNIGHT SNACKS ZACHERLEY   AN   BAL 60
   SORRY, RIGHT NUMBER (ALSO AS LONG DISTANCE CALL)
                            MATHESON, RICHARD   SS   BEY 53 11
   SHARE ALIKE   BIXBY, JEROME
                            AND DEAN, JOE E.   SS C BEY 53 07
   TALENT   STURGEON, THEODORE   SS   BEY 53 09
   LISTEN, CHILDREN, LISTEN WEST, WALLACE   SS   FUN 53 10
   WHISPERING GALLERY, THE   TEMPLE, WILLIAM F.   SS   FUN 53 10
   PIPING DEATH, THE   WILLIAMS, ROBERT M.   SS   UNK 39 05
   GHOST, THE   VAN VOGT, A. E.   NV   UNK 42 08
   CARILLON OF SKULLS   JAMES, PHILIP   SS   UNK 41 02
   PILE OF TROUBLE   KUTTNER, HENRY   SS   TWS 48 04

ZACHERLEY'S VULTURE STEW ZACHERLEY   AN   BAL 60
   HE DIDN'T LIKE CATS   HUBBARD, L. RON   SS   UNK 42 02
   DR. JACOBUS MELIFLORE'S LAST PATIENT
                            LORD, MINDRET   SS   FSF 53 11
   DEVIL IS NOT MOCKED, THE WELLMAN, MANLY WADE   SS   UNK 43 06
   BONES   WOLLHEIM, DONALD A.   SS   STI 41 02
   OUT OF THE JAR   TANNER, CHARLES R.   SS   STI 41 02
   WITCH, THE   VAN VOGT, A. E.   SS   UNK 43 02
   THEY BITE   BOUCHER, ANTHONY   SS   UNK 43 08
   SHED, THE   EVANS, E. EVERETT   SS   ASR 53 01
   THERE SHALL BE NO DARKNESS BLISH, JAMES   SS   TWS 50 04

ZOO 2000   YOLEN, JANE   AN H SEA 73
   INTRODUCTION   YOLEN, JANE   IN
   ZOO 2000   CURTIS, RICHARD   SS   NEW 72 AN
   HURKLE IS A HAPPY BEAST, THE STURGEON, THEODORE   SS   FSF 49 FL
   DEEP RANGE, THE (A&B 54 04) CLARKE, ARTHUR C.   NV   STR 54 03
   THERE'S A WOLF IN MY TIME MACHINE
                            NIVEN, LARRY   SS   FSF 71 06
   APPLE   BAXTER, JOHN   SS   NWR 67 10
   INTERVIEW WITH A LEMMING THURBER, JAMES   SS   43
   ALL CATS ARE GRAY (AS ANDREW NORTH)
                            NORTON, ANDRE   SS   FUN 53 08
   MOUSE, THE   FAST, HOWARD   SS   FSF 69 11
   ISLAND OF THE ENDANGERED, THE
                            FERGUSON, DALE   SS   NEW 72 AN
   COUNTRY DOCTOR   MORRISON, WILLIAM   NV   STR 53 01
   DAY OF THE DRAGON, THE   ENDORE, GUY   NV   APR 47 02
   KING OF THE BEASTS, THE   FARMER, PHILIP JOSE   SS   GAL 64 06

1,000 YEAR PLAN, THE   ASIMOV, ISAAC   DN   ACE 55
   ABRIDGED VERSION OF "FOUNDATION"

10TH ANNUAL OF THE YEAR'S BEST S-F, THE
                              MERRIL, JUDITH   AN H DCT 65
   AUTOMATIC TIGER   REED, KIT   SS   FSF 64 03
   CARSON EFFECT, THE   WILSON, RICHARD   SS   WOT 64 11
   SHINING ONES, THE   CLARKE, ARTHUR C.   SS   PBY 64 08
   PACIFIST   REYNOLDS, MACK   SS   FSF 64 01

10TH ANNUAL OF THE YEAR'S BEST S-F, THE

NEW ENCYCLOPAEDIST, THE	BECKER, STEPHEN	SS	FSF 64 05	
LEGEND OF JOE LEE, THE	MACDONALD, JOHN D.	SS	CMP 64	
GAS MASK	HOUSTON, JAMES D.	SS	NUG 64	
SINISTER METAMORPHOSIS, A	BAKER, RUSSELL	SS	NYT 65	
SONNY	RAPHAEL, RICK	SS	ASF 63 04	
LAST SECRET WEAPON OF THE THIRD REICH, THE				
	NESVADBA, JOSEF	SS	64	
DESCENDING	DISCH, THOMAS M.	SS	FAN 64 07	
DECADENCE (TRANSLATED BY RICHARD HOWARD)				
	GARY, ROMAIN	SS	SGA 64	
BE OF GOOD CHEER	LEIBER, FRITZ	SS	GAL 64 10	
IT COULD BE YOU	ROBERTS, FRANK	SS	SSI 64	
BENEFACTOR OF HUMANITY, A	FARRELL, JAMES T.	SS	SSI 58	
SYNCHROMOCRACY	CAWOOD, HAP	SS	MOT 64	
SEARCH, THE	SIMONDS, BRUCE	PM	FSF 64 06	
PIROKIN EFFECT, THE	EISENBERG, LARRY	SS	AMZ 64 06	
TWERLIK, THE	SHARKEY, JACK	SS	WOT 64 06	
ROSE FOR ECCLESIASTES, A	ZELAZNY, ROGER	NV	FSF 63 11	
TERMINAL BEACH, THE	BALLARD, J. G.	SS	NWS 64 03	
PROBLEM CHILD	PORGES, ARTHUR	SS	ASF 64 04	
WONDERFUL DOG SUIT, THE	HALL, DONALD	SS		
MATHENAUTS, THE	KAGAN, NORMAN	NV	IFS 64 07	
FAMILY PORTRAIT	KENT, MORGAN	SS	FAN 64 08	
RED EGG, A (TRANSLATED BY TERRY BROCH FONTSERE)				
	GIRONELLA, JOSE MARIA	SS	64	
POWER OF POSITIVE THINKING, THE				
	WHITE, M. E.	SS	NDR 64 18	
LIVING DOLL, A	WALLACE, ROBERT	SS	HRP 64 01	
TRAINING TALK	BUNCH, DAVID R.	SS	FAN 64 03	
MIRACLE TOO MANY, A	SMITH, PHILIP H.			
	AND NOURSE, ALAN E.	SS C	FSF 64 09	
LAST LONELY MAN, THE	BRUNNER, JOHN	SS	NWS 64 06	
MAN WHO FOUND PROTEUS, THE	ROHRER, ROBERT	SS	FAN 64 11	
YACHID AND YECHIDA	SINGER, ISAAC B.	SS	64	
SUMMATION	MERRIL, JUDITH	MS		
HONORABLE MENTIONS	MISC. MATERIAL	MS		

11TH ANNUAL OF THE YEAR'S BEST S-F, THE

	MERRIL, JUDITH	AN H	DCT 66	
INTRODUCTION	MERRIL, JUDITH	IN		
SOMETHING ELSE	TILLEY, ROBERT J.	SS	FSF 65 10	
VOLCANO DANCES, THE	BALLARD, J. G.	SS	NEW 64 AC	
SLOW TUESDAY NIGHT	LAFFERTY, R. A.	SS	GAL 65 04	
BETTER THAN EVER	KIRS, ALEX	SS	FSF 65 03	
COMING-OF-AGE DAY	JORGENSSON, A. K.	SS	SCF 65 09	
WALL, THE	SAXTON, JOSEPHINE	SS	SCF 65 11	
SURVIVOR, THE	MOUDY, WALTER F.	NV	AMZ 65 05	
MOON DUEL	LEIBER, FRITZ	SS	IFS 65 09	
PROJECT INHUMANE	MALEC, ALEXANDER B.	SS	COQ 64 SP	
THOSE WHO CAN, DO	KUROSAKA, BOB	SS	FSF 65 01	
SUSAN	BEVAN, ALISTAIR	SS	SCF 65 04	
YESTERDAYS' GARDENS	BYRNE, JOHNNY	SS	SCF 65 11	
ROACHES, THE	DISCH, THOMAS M.	SS	ESC 65 10	
GAME	BARTHELME, DONALD	SS	NYM 65 07	
J IS FOR JEANNE	TUBB, E. C.	SS	NWS 65 12	
TERMINAL	GOULART, RON	SE	FAN 65 05	
PLOT, THE	HERZOG, TOM	SS	ROG 65	
INVESTIGATING THE BIDWELL ENDEAVORS				
	BUNCH, DAVID R.	SS	65	
CASE, THE	REDGROVE, PETER	PM	NWS 66 01	
THERE'S A STARMAN IN WARD 7	ROME, DAVID	SS	NWS 65 01	
EYES DO MORE THAN SEE	ASIMOV, ISAAC	SS	FSF 65 04	
MAELSTROM II	CLARKE, ARTHUR C.	SS	PBY 65 04	
TWO TELEPATHIC LETTERS TO LORD KELVIN				
	JARRY, ALFRED	SS	65	
WARRIOR	DICKSON, GORDON R.	SS	ASF 65 12	
MARS IS OURS!	BUCHWALD, ART	SS	65	
SCARFE'S WORLD	ALDISS, BRIAN W.	NV	WOT 65 03	
SINGULAR CASE OF EXTREME ELECTROLYTE BALANCE ASSOCIATED WITH				
FOLIE A DEUX	TSCHIRGI, ROBERT D.	FA	65	
MAGUS, A	CIARDI, JOHN	PM	SRV 65 12	
CIRCULAR RUINS, THE (TRANSLATED BY JAMES E. IRBY)				
	BORGES, JORGE LUIS	SS	62	
GIRL WHO DREW THE GODS, THE	JACOBS, HARVEY	NV	MAD 65 05	
DROWNED GIANT, THE (SOUVENIR)				
	BALLARD, J. G.	SS	PBY 65 05	
CIRCE UNDERSEA	MACBETH, GEORGE	PM	65	
SOMEWHERE NOT FAR FROM HERE	KERSH, GERALD	SS	PBY 65 03	
IN THE RUINS	DAHL, ROALD	SS	64	
TRAVELER'S REST	MASSON, DAVID I.	SS	NWS 65 09	
ADO ABOUT NOTHING	OTTUM, BOB JR.	SS	FSF 65 03	
SUMMATION	MERRIL, JUDITH	MS		

12 GREAT CLASSICS OF SCIENCE FICTION

	CONKLIN, GROFF	AN	FGM 63	
INTRODUCTION	CONKLIN, GROFF	IN		
DUE PROCESS	BUDRYS, ALGIS	SS	ASF 60 02	
EARTHMEN BEARING GIFTS	BROWN, FREDRIC	SS	GAL 60 06	
THINGS	HENDERSON, ZENNA	SS	FSF 60 07	
TOP, THE	ALBEE, GEORGE SUMNER	SS	FSF 62 08	
MY OBJECT ALL SUBLIME	ANDERSON, POUL	SS	GAL 61 06	
HUMAN MAN'S BURDEN	SHECKLEY, ROBERT	SS	GAL 56 09	
ON THE FOURTH PLANET	BONE, J. F.	SS	GAL 63 04	
BALLAD OF LOST C'MELL, THE	SMITH, CORDWAINER	NV	GAL 62 10	
THIRTY DAYS HAD SEPTEMBER	YOUNG, ROBERT F.	SS	FSF 57 10	
CAGE, THE	CHANDLER, A. BERTRAM	SS	FSF 57 06	
STAR-CROSSED LOVER	STUART, WILLIAM W.	NV	GAL 60 04	
IMMORTALITY...FOR SOME	MCINTOSH, J. T.	NV	ASF 60 03	

13 ABOVE THE NIGHT

	CONKLIN, GROFF	AN	DEL 65	
INTRODUCTION	CONKLIN, GROFF	IN		
FOUNDING FATHER	BONE, J. F.	NA	GAL 62 04	
MATING CALL	HERBERT, FRANK	SS	GAL 61 10	
NICE GIRL WITH FIVE HUSBANDS	LEIBER, FRITZ	SS	GAL 51 04	
PRONE	REYNOLDS, MACK	SS	FSF 54 09	

EDUCATION OF TIGRESS MACARDLE, THE

	KORNBLUTH, C. M.	SS	VSF 57 07	
NOW INHALE	RUSSELL, ERIC FRANK	SS	ASF 59 04	
BACK OF OUR HEADS, THE	BARR, STEPHEN	NV	GAL 58 07	
BUTTON, BUTTON	ASIMOV, ISAAC	SS	STS 53 01	
DEEP DOWN DRAGON, THE	MERRIL, JUDITH	SS	GAL 61 08	
KAPPA NU NEXUS, THE	DAVIDSON, AVRAM			
	AND KLASS, MORTON	SS C	FSF 61 08	
IDIOT SOLVANT	DICKSON, GORDON R.	SS	ASF 62 01	
COUNTER SECURITY	WHITE, JAMES	NV	FSF 63 02	
DREISTEIN CASE, THE	PAINE, J. LINCOLN	SS	FSF 58 06	

13 FRENCH SCIENCE-FICTION STORIES

	KNIGHT, DAMON	AN	BAN 65	
INTRODUCTION	KNIGHT, DAMON	IN		
JULIETTE	CHEINISSE, CLAUDE F.	SS	59	
BLIND PILOT, THE (TRANSLATED BY DAMON KNIGHT)				
	HENNEBERG, CHARLES	SS	FSF 60 01	
OLIVIA	DAMONTI, HENRI	SS	60	
NOTARY AND THE CONSPIRACY, THE				
	DAMONTI, HENRI	SS	62	
VANA, THE	DOREMIEUX, ALAIN	SS	59	
DEVIL'S GODDAUGHTER	MALAVAL, SUZANNE	SS	60	
MOON-FISHERS	HENNEBERG, CHARLES	NV	59	
NON-HUMANS, THE	HENNEBERG, CHARLES	SS	58	
AFTER THREE HUNDRED YEARS	MILLE, PIERRE	SS	22	
MONSTEE, THE	KLEIN, GERARD	SS	58	
LITTLE MORE CAVIAR?, A	VEILLOT, CLAUDE	SS	63	
CHAIN OF LOVE, THE	CLIFF, CATHERINE	SS	55	
DEAD FISH, THE	VIAN, BORIS	SS	55	
ABOUT THE AUTHORS	KNIGHT, DAMON	MS		

13 GREAT STORIES OF SCIENCE FICTION

	CONKLIN, GROFF	AN	FGM 60	
INTRODUCTION	CONKLIN, GROFF	IN		
WAR IS OVER, THE	BUDRYS, ALGIS	SS	ASF 57 02	
LIGHT, THE	ANDERSON, POUL	NV	GAL 57 03	
COMPASSION CIRCUIT	WYNDHAM, JOHN	SS	FUN 54 12	
VOLPLA	GUIN, WYMAN	NV	GAL 56 05	
SILENCE, PLEASE	CLARKE, ARTHUR C.	SS	SCF 50 WI	
ALLEGORY	POWERS, WILLIAM T.	SS	ASF 53 04	
SOAP OPERA	NELSON, ALAN	SS	FSF 53 04	
SHIPPING CLERK	MORRISON, WILLIAM	SS	GAL 52 06	
TECHNOLOGICAL RETREAT	EDMONDSON, G. C.	SS	FSF 56 05	
ANALOGUES, THE	KNIGHT, DAMON	SS	ASF 52 01	
AVAILABLE DATA ON THE WORP REACTION, THE				
	MILLER, LION	SS	FSF 53 09	
SKILLS OF XANADU, THE	STURGEON, THEODORE	NV	GAL 56 07	
MACHINE, THE	GEHMAN, RICHARD	SS	COL 46 12	

14 GREAT TALES OF ESP

	STONE, IDELLA P.	AN	FGM 69 11	
INTRODUCTION	CAMPBELL, JOHN W. JR	IN		
FOREIGN HAND TIE, THE	GARRETT, RANDALL	NV	ASF 61 12	
LEADER, THE	LEINSTER, MURRAY	SS	ASF 60 02	
WHAT THIN PARTITIONS	CLIFTON, MARK			
	AND APOSTOLIDES, ALEX	NV C	ASF 53 09	
PROJECT NIGHTMARE	HEINLEIN, ROBERT A.	NV	AMZ 53 05	
PREPOSTEROUS	BROWN, FREDRIC	SS	NEW 54 AC	
MODUS VIVENDI	BUPP, WALTER	NV	ASF 61 09	
BELIEF	ASIMOV, ISAAC	NV	ASF 53 10	
I'M A STRANGER HERE MYSELF	REYNOLDS, MACK	SS	AMZ 60 12	
MAN ON TOP, THE (SCH 51 10)	BRETNOR, REGINALD	SS	FSF 60 09	
FALSE IMAGE	WILLIAMS, JAY	SS	ASF 58 10	
ARARAT	HENDERSON, ZENNA	SS	FSF 52 10	
THESE ARE THE ARTS	SCHMITZ, JAMES H.	SS	FSF 62 09	
GARDEN IN THE FOREST, THE	YOUNG, ROBERT F.	SS	ASF 53 09	
AND STILL IT MOVES	RUSSELL, ERIC FRANK	AR	ASF 57 06	

17 X INFINITY

	CONKLIN, GROFF	AN	DEL 63 08	
INTRODUCTION	CONKLIN, GROFF	IN		
SIMIAN PROBLEM, THE	ALPERT, HOLLIS	SS	FSF 60 07	
STRIKEBREAKER (MALE STRIKEBREAKER)				
	ASIMOV, ISAAC	SS	SFS 57 01	
COME INTO MY CELLAR (ALSO AS BOYS, RAISE GIANT MUSHROOMS				
IN YOUR CELLAR)	BRADBURY, RAY	SS	GAL 62 10	
MS FND IN A LBRY	DRAPER, HAL	SS	FSF 61 12	
MS FOUND IN A LBRY	DRAPER, HAL	SS	FSF 61 12	
CATO THE MARTIAN	FAST, HOWARD	SS	FSF 60 06	
SPACEMAN COMETH, THE	FELSEN, HENRY GREGOR	SS	FSF 56 04	
MACHINE STOPS, THE	FORSTER, E. M.	NV	28	
FRANCES HARKINS	GOGGIN, RICHARD	SS	FSF 52 12	
DAY THEY GOT BOSTON, THE	GOLD, HERBERT	SS	FSF 61 09	
A-W-F, UNLIMITED	HERBERT, FRANK	NV	GAL 61 06	
AS EASY AS A. B. C.	KIPLING, RUDYARD	NV	LOM 12 04	
MACDONOUGH'S SONG	KIPLING, RUDYARD	PM	MPM 12 03	
SILENZIA	NELSON, ALAN	SS	FSF 53 09	
WHAT TO DO TILL THE ANALYST COMES (EVERYBODY'S HAPPY BUT ME!)				
	POHL, FREDERIK	SS	IMG 56 02	
SHORT IN THE CHEST	SEABRIGHT, IDRIS	SS	FUN 54 07	
LAST OF THE SPODE, THE	SMITH, EVELYN E.	SS	FSF 53 06	
NEVER UNDERESTIMATE...	STURGEON, THEODORE	SS	IFS 52 03	
BROOKLYN PROJECT	TENN, WILLIAM	SS	PLS 48 FL	

18 GREAT SCIENCE FICTION STORIES

	JANIFER, LAURENCE M.	AN	TMP 71 01	

SEE "MASTERS' CHOICE"

1972 ANNUAL WORLD'S BEST SF, THE

	WOLLHEIM, DONALD A.	AN H	DAW 72	
INTRODUCTION	WOLLHEIM, DONALD A.	IN		
FOURTH PROFESSION, THE	NIVEN, LARRY	NV	QRK 71 04	
GLEEPSITE	RUSS, JOANNA	SS	ORB 71 09	
BEAR WITH THE KNOT ON HIS TAIL, THE				
	TALL, STEPHEN	NV	FSF 71 05	
SHARKS OF PENTREATH, THE	CONEY, MICHAEL G.	SS	GAL 71 02	
LITTLE KNOWLEDGE, A	ANDERSON, POUL	NV	ASF 71 08	

1972 ANNUAL WORLD'S BEST SF, THE   593

REAL-TIME WORLD   PRIEST, CHRISTOPHER   NV   NWR 71 19
ALL PIECES OF A RIVER SHORE LAFFERTY, R. A.   SS   ORB 70 08
WITH FRIENDS LIKE THESE... FOSTER, ALAN DEAN   SS   ASF 71 06
AUNT JENNIE'S TONIC   TUSHNET, LEONARD   SS   FSF 71 12
TIMESTORM   BERTIN, EDDY C.   SS   71
TRANSIT OF EARTH   CLARKE, ARTHUR C.   SS   PBY 71 01
GEHENNA   MALZBERG, BARRY N.   SS   GAL 71 03
ONE LIFE, FURNISHED IN EARLY POVERTY
                           ELLISON, HARLAN   SS   ORB 70 08
OCCAM'S SCALPEL   STURGEON, THEODORE   NV   IFS 71 08

1973 ANNUAL WORLD'S BEST SF, THE
                           WOLLHEIM, DONALD A. AN H DAW 73
INTRODUCTION   WOLLHEIM, DONALD A. IN
GOAT SONG   ANDERSON, POUL   NV   FSF 72 02
MAN WHO WALKED HOME, THE   TIPTREE, JAMES JR.   NV   AMZ 72 05
OH, VALINDA!   CONEY, MICHAEL G.   NV   NWR 72 20
GOLD AT THE STARBOW'S END, THE
                           POHL, FREDERIK   NV   ASF 72 03
TO WALK A CITY'S STREET   SIMAK, CLIFFORD D.   SS   INY 72 03
RORQUAL MARU   BASS, T. J.   NV   GAL 72 01
CHANGING WOMAN   MACFARLANE, WALLACE   SS   GAL 72 09
"WILLIE'S BLUES"   TILLEY, ROBERT J.   NV   FSF 72 05
LONG SHOT   VINGE, VERNOR   SS   ASF 72 08
THUS LOVE BETRAYS US   MACLENNAN, PHYLLIS   SS   FSF 72 09

1974 ANNUAL WORLD'S BEST SF, THE
                           WOLLHEIM, DONALD A. AN H DAW 74
  IN ENGLAND AS "THE WORLD'S BEST SF SHORT STORIES NO. 1"
INTRODUCTION   WOLLHEIM, DONALD A. IN
SUPPLIANT IN SPACE, A   SHECKLEY, ROBERT   NV   GAL 73 11
PARTHEN   LAFFERTY, R. A.   SS   GAL 73 05
DOOMSHIP   POHL, FREDERIK
                           AND WILLIAMSON, JACK NA C IFS 73 04
WEED OF TIME, THE   SPINRAD, NORMAN   SS   ANA 70
MODEST GENIUS, A   SHEFNER, VADIM   SS
DEATHBIRD, THE   ELLISON, HARLAN   NV   FSF 73 03
EVANE   TUBB, E. C.   SS   NWR 73 22
MOBY, TOO   EKLUND, GORDON   SS   AMZ 73 12
DEATH AND DESIGNATION AMONG THE ASADI
                           BISHOP, MICHAEL   NA   IFS 73 02
CONSTRUCTION SHACK   SIMAK, CLIFFORD D.   SS   IFS 73 02

1975 ANNUAL WORLD'S BEST SF, THE
                           WOLLHEIM, DONALD A. AN   DAW 75
  IN ENGLAND AS "THE WORLD'S BEST SF SHORT STORIES NO. 2"
INTRODUCTION   WOLLHEIM, DONALD A. IN
SONG FOR LYA, A   MARTIN, GEORGE R. R. NV   ASF 74 06
DEATHSONG   VAN SCYOC, SYDNEY J. NA   GAL 74 02
FULL MEMBER OF THE CLUB, A SHAW, BOB   NV   GAL 74 07
SUN'S TEARS, THE   STABLEFORD, BRIAN M. SS   AMZ 74 10
GIFT OF GARIGOLLI, THE   POHL, FREDERIK
                           AND KORNBLUTH, C. M. NV C GAL 74 08
FOUR-HOUR FUGUE, THE   BESTER, ALFRED   SS   ASF 74 06
TWIG   DICKSON, GORDON R.   NV   STL 74 01
CATHADONIAN ODYSSEY   BISHOP, MICHAEL   SS   FSF 74 09
BLEEDING MAN, THE   STRETE, CRAIG   NV   GAL 74 12
STRANGER IN PARADISE   ASIMOV, ISAAC   NV   IFS 74 06

1976 ANNUAL WORLD'S BEST SF, THE
                           WOLLHEIM, DONALD A. AN   DAW 76 05
INTRODUCTION   WOLLHEIM, DONALD A. IN
CATCH THAT ZEPPELIN!   LEIBER, FRITZ   SS   FSF 75 03
PEDDLER'S APPRENTICE, THE VINGE, JOAN D.
                           AND VINGE, VERNOR   NV C ASF 75 08
BEES OF KNOWLEDGE, THE   BAYLEY, BARRINGTON J NV   NWB 75 08
STORMS OF WINDHAVEN, THE   TUTTLE, LISA
                           AND MARTIN, GEORGE R. R. NV C ASF 75 05
ENGINEER AND THE EXECUTIONER, THE
                           STABLEFORD, BRIAN M. NV   AMZ 75 05
ALLEGIANCES   BISHOP, MICHAEL   NA   GAL 75 02
CHILD OF ALL AGES   PLAUGER, P. J.   SS   ASF 75 03
HELBENT 4   ROBINETT, STEPHEN   NV   GAL 75 10
PROTOCOLS OF THE ELDERS OF BRITAIN, THE
                           BRUNNER, JOHN   SS
CUSTODIANS, THE   COWPER, RICHARD   NV   FSF 75 10

1977 ANNUAL WORLD'S BEST SF, THE
                           WOLLHEIM, DONALD A. AN   DAW 77 05
  WITH ARTHUR W. SAHA
INTRODUCTION   WOLLHEIM, DONALD A. IN
APPEARANCE OF LIFE   ALDISS, BRIAN W.   SS   76
OVERDRAWN AT THE MEMORY BANK VARLEY, JOHN   NV   GAL 76 05
THOSE GOOD OLD DAYS OF LIQUID FUEL
                           CONEY, MICHAEL G.   SS   FSF 76 01
HERTFORD MANUSCRIPT, THE   COWPER, RICHARD   NV   FSF 76 10
NATURAL ADVANTAGE   DEL REY, LESTER   SS   AMZ 76 06
BICENTENNIAL MAN, THE   ASIMOV, ISAAC   NV   STL 76 02
CABINET OF OLIVER NAYLOR, THE
                           BAYLEY, BARRINGTON J SS   NWB 76 10
MY BOAT   RUSS, JOANNA   SS   FSF 76 01
HOUSTON, HOUSTON, DO YOU READ?
                           TIPTREE, JAMES JR.   NA
I SEE YOU   KNIGHT, DAMON   SS   FSF 76 11

2020 VISION   POURNELLE, JERRY   AN   AVN 74 02
PREFACE   POURNELLE, JERRY   IN
DO WE LIVE IN A GOLDEN AGE? POURNELLE, JERRY   IN
BUILD ME A MOUNTAIN   BOVA, BEN   SS   NEW 74 AN
CLOAK OF ANARCHY   NIVEN, LARRY   NV   ASF 72 03
SILENT IN GEHENNA   ELLISON, HARLAN   SS   MWS 71
PUGILIST, THE   ANDERSON, POUL   NV   FSF 73 11
EAT, DRINK, AND BE MERRY   GIRAD, DIAN   SS   NEW 74 AN
PROGNOSIS: TERMINAL   MCDANIEL, DAVE   NV   NEW 74 AN
FUTURE PERFECT   VAN VOGT, A. E.   SS   VTX 73 08
THING OF BEAUTY, A   SPINRAD, NORMAN   SS   ASF 73 01

2076: THE AMERICAN TRICENTENNIAL
                           BRYANT, EDWARD   OA   PYR 77
INTRODUCTION: FLASHFORWARD TO 2076
                           ALTERMAN, PETER S.   AR
RED, WHITE AND BLUE FOURTH OF JULY, A
                           HANSEN, KARL   NV
ESCAPE IS NO ACCIDENT   EMSHWILLER, CAROL   SS
FEMININE DEMYSTIFICATION   HARPER, JO ANN   PM
DUST OF EVENING, THE   CRAIS, ROBERT   SS
DEATH OF SAPPHO, THE   PIERCY, MARGE   NV
LIKE SNOW-HUMPED FIELDS AFRAID OF RAIN
                           WATKINS, WILLIAM JON PM
AND I FOR AN EYE   STEVENS, JAMES   SS
EMISSARY FROM HAMELIN   ELLISON, HARLAN   SS
CORRUPTION OF METALS   DORMAN, SONYA   PM
AZTECS   MCINTYRE, VONDA N.   NA
X-2076   DILLINGHAM, PETER   PM
BIOLOGICAL REVOLUTION, THE VARDEMAN, ROBERT E.
                           AND SLATEN, JEFF   SS C
ONE ROAD TO DAMASCUS   SALLIS, JAMES
                           AND LUNDE, DAVID   SS C
WELCOME TO THE TRICENTENNIAL PRENTICE, PATRICK H. NV

25 MODERN STORIES OF MYSTERY AND IMAGINATION
                           STONG, PHILIP D.   AN H GCB 42
     SEE "THE OTHER WORLDS"

3 FROM OUT THERE   MARGULIES, LEO   AN   CRS 59 03
MOTHER EARTH   ASIMOV, ISAAC   NV   ASF 49 05
DOUBLE MEANING   KNIGHT, DAMON   NA   STS 53 01
SON OF TWO WORLDS   HAMILTON, EDMOND   NA   TWS 41 08

3 IN 1   MARGULIES, LEO   AN   PYR 63 08
INTRODUCTION   MARGULIES, LEO   IN
THERE IS NO DEFENSE   STURGEON, THEODORE   NV   ASF 48 02
GALACTIC CHEST   SIMAK, CLIFFORD D.   NV   SFS 56 09
WEST WIND   LEINSTER, MURRAY   NV   ASF 48 03

3 PROPHETIC SCIENCE FICTION NOVELS OF H. G. WELLS
                           WELLS, H. G.   AC L DOV 60
INTRODUCTION TO THE DOVER EDITION
                           BLEILER, EVERETT F. IN
WHEN THE SLEEPER WAKES   WELLS, H. G.   NO   HPR 99
STORY OF THE DAYS TO COME, A WELLS, H. G.   NA   PGZ 97
TIME MACHINE, THE   WELLS, H. G.   NA   NRV 95 01

3 TO THE HIGHEST POWER   NOLAN, WILLIAM F.   AN   AVN 68 02
RAY BRADBURY   NOLAN, WILLIAM F.   AR
LOST CITY OF MARS, THE   BRADBURY, RAY   NV   PBY 67 01
RAY BRADBURY SF/FANTASY INDEX, A
                           MISC. MATERIAL   MS
THEODORE STURGEON   NOLAN, WILLIAM F.   AR
ONE FOOT AND THE GRAVE   STURGEON, THEODORE   NV   WRT 49 09
THEODORE STURGEON SF/FANTASY INDEX, A
                           MISC. MATERIAL   MS
CHAD OLIVER   NOLAN, WILLIAM F.   AR
MARGINAL MAN, THE (GUARDIAN SPIRIT)
                           OLIVER, CHAD   NV   FSF 58 04
CHAD OLIVER SF/FANTASY INDEX, A
                           MISC. MATERIAL   MS
CHAD OLIVER SF|FANTASY INDEX, A
                           MISC. MATERIAL   MS

3000 YEARS OF FANTASY AND SCIENCE FICTION
                           DE CAMP, L. S.&C.   AN H LOT 72
FOREWORD- WHY READ SCIENCE FICTION?
                           ASIMOV, ISAAC   IN
INTRODUCTION- BEYOND THE WORLD WE KNOW
                           DE CAMP, L. SPRAGUE
                           AND DE CAMP, CATHERINE C IN C
ODYSSEY, THE (EXCERPT)   HOMER   EX
TIMAIOS (EXCERPT)   PLATO   EX
JOURNEY TO THE MOON, A (ABRIDGED)
                           DE BERGERAC, CYRANO   NV
NEW ACCELERATOR, THE   WELLS, H. G.   SS   SND 01 12
CATS OF ULTHAR, THE   LOVECRAFT, H. P.   SS   TRY 20 11
MARTIAN ODYSSEY, A   WEINBAUM, STANLEY G. NV   WOS 34 07
HELEN O'LOY   DEL REY, LESTER   SS   ASF 38 12
COLD EQUATIONS, THE   GODWIN, TOM   NV   ASF 54 08
GUN FOR DINOSAUR, A   DE CAMP, L. SPRAGUE   NV   GAL 56 03
BEFORE EDEN   CLARKE, ARTHUR C.   SS   AMZ 61 06
LAST QUESTION, THE   ASIMOV, ISAAC   SS   SFQ 56 11
MILESTONES . NOVELS WORTH READING
                           MISC. MATERIAL   MS

31ST OF FEBRUARY, THE   BOND, NELSON S.   AC H GNM 49
SPORTSMAN, THE   BOND, NELSON S.   SS
MASK OF MEDUSA, THE   BOND, NELSON S.   SS
MY NEPHEW NORVELL   BOND, NELSON S.   SS
RING, THE   BOND, NELSON S.   SS
GRIPES OF WRAITH, THE   BOND, NELSON S.   SS
CUNNING OF THE BEAST, THE (ANOTHER WORLD BEGINS)
                           BOND, NELSON S.   SS   BBM 42 11
FIVE LIVES OF ROBERT JORDAN, THE
                           BOND, NELSON S.   SS
TAKE MY DRUM TO ENGLAND-   BOND, NELSON S.   SS   UNK 41 08
SAINT MULLIGAN   BOND, NELSON S.   SS   FAD 43 05
MONSTER FROM NOWHERE, THE BOND, NELSON S.   SS   FAD 39 07
MAN WHO WALKED THROUGH GLASS, THE
                           BOND, NELSON S.   SS   ESQ 38 11
ENCHANTED PENCIL, THE   BOND, NELSON S.   SS
PILGRIMAGE (THE PRIESTESS WHO REBELLED)
                           BOND, NELSON S.   SS   AMZ 39 10

334   DISCH, THOMAS M.   NO   AVN 74 02
DEATH OF SOCRATES, THE   DISCH, THOMAS M.   NV

Title	Author	Type	Source
BODIES	DISCH, THOMAS M.	NV	QRK 71 04
EVERYDAY LIFE IN THE LATER ROMAN EMPIRE	DISCH, THOMAS M.	NV	BMR 73
EMANCIPATION: A ROMANCE OF THE TIMES TO COME	DISCH, THOMAS M.	NV	NDM 71 01
ANGOULEME	DISCH, THOMAS M.	SS	NWQ 71 01
334	DISCH, THOMAS M.	NA	NWQ 72 04

Title	Author	Type	Source
5 GALAXY SHORT NOVELS	GOLD, H. L.	AN H	DBL 58
TODAY'S TOMORROWS	GOLD, H. L.	IN	
TANGLE HOLD	WALLACE, F. L.	NA	GAL 53 06
WORLD WITHOUT CHILDREN	KNIGHT, DAMON	NA	GAL 51 12
WHEREVER YOU MAY BE (ALSO AS THE RELUCTANT WITCH)	GUNN, JAMES E.	NA	GAL 53 05
MIND ALONE	MCINTOSH, J. T.	NA	GAL 53 08
GRANNY WON'T KNIT	STURGEON, THEODORE	NA	GAL 54 05

Title	Author	Type	Source
5 TALES FROM TOMORROW	DIKTY, T. E.	AN	CRS 57 12
5 STORIES FROM "BEST SCIENCE FICTION STORIES AND NOVELS: 1955"			
PUSH-BUTTON PASSION (CARELESS LOVE)	FRIBORG, ALBERT C.	SS	FSF 54 07
COLD EQUATIONS, THE	GODWIN, TOM	SS	ASF 54 08
HOW-2	SIMAK, CLIFFORD D.	NV	GAL 54 11
DEEP SPACE (AXOLOTL)	ABERNATHY, ROBERT	SS	FSF 54 01
EXILE	COLE, EVERETT B.	SN	ASF 54 01

Title	Author	Type	Source
5 UNEARTHLY VISIONS	CONKLIN, GROFF	AN	FGM 65
LEGWORK	RUSSELL, ERIC FRANK	NV	ASF 56 04
CONDITIONALLY HUMAN	MILLER, WALTER M. JR	NV	GAL 52 02
STAMPED CAUTION	GALLUN, RAYMOND Z.	NV	GAL 53 08
DIO (ALSO AS THE DYING MAN)	KNIGHT, DAMON	SN	INF 57 09
SHADOW WORLD	SIMAK, CLIFFORD D.	NV	GAL 57 09

Title	Author	Type	Source
5TH ANNUAL OF THE YEAR'S BEST S-F, THE	MERRIL, JUDITH	AN H	SAS 60
IN ENGLAND AS "THE BEST OF SCIENCE FICTION 5"			
INTRODUCTION	MERRIL, JUDITH	IN	
HANDLER, THE	KNIGHT, DAMON	SS	ROG 60 08
OTHER WIFE, THE (ALSO AS THE COIN COLLECTOR)	FINNEY, JACK	SS	SEP 60 01
NO FIRE BURNS	DAVIDSON, AVRAM	SS	PBY 60 02
NO, NO, NOT ROGOV!	SMITH, CORDWAINER	SS	IFS 59 02
SHORELINE AT SUNSET, THE (ALSO AS THE SUNSET HARP)	BRADBURY, RAY	SS	FSF 59 03
DREAMSMAN, THE	DICKSON, GORDON R.	SS	STR 59 06
MULTUM IN PARVO	SHARKEY, JACK	SS	GNT 59 12
FLOWERS FOR ALGERNON	KEYES, DANIEL	SS	FSF 59 04
"WHAT DO YOU MEAN...HUMAN?"	CAMPBELL, JOHN W. JR	ED	ASF 59 09
SIERRA SAM	DIGHTON, RALPH	AR	NYT 60 01
DEATH IN THE HOUSE, A	SIMAK, CLIFFORD D.	NV	GAL 59 10
MARIANA	LEIBER, FRITZ	SS	FAN 60 02
INQUIRY CONCERNING THE CURVATURE OF THE EARTH'S SURFACE	PRICE, ROGER	SS	MON 59 WI
DAY AT THE BEACH	EMSHWILLER, CAROL	SS	FSF 59 08
HOT ARGUMENT	GARRETT, RANDALL	PM	FSF 60 02
WHAT THE LEFT HAND WAS DOING	LANGART, DARREL T.	NV	ASF 60 02
SOUND-SWEEP, THE	BALLARD, J. G.	NV	SCF 60 02
PLENITUDE	WORTHINGTON, WILL	SS	FSF 59 11
MAN WHO LOST THE SEA, THE	STURGEON, THEODORE	SS	FSF 59 10
MAKE A PRISON	BLOCK, LAWRENCE	SS	SFS 59 01
WHAT NOW, LITTLE MAN?	CLIFTON, MARK	NV	FSF 59 12
ME	SCHENCK, HILBERT JR.	PM	FSF 59 08
YEAR'S S-F, THE, SUMMATION AND HONORABLE MENTIONS	MERRIL, JUDITH	MS	

Title	Author	Type	Source
6 AND THE SILENT SCREAM	HOWARD, IVAN	AN	BEL 63 05
VULCAN'S HAMMER	DICK, PHILIP K.	NV	FUT 56 29
RIDDLE OF THE DEADLY PARADISE	LONG, FRANK BELKNAP	NV	SFS 58 11
EAR-FRIEND, THE	BANKS, RAYMOND E.	NV	SFS 55 03
PEACE ON EARTH	COX, IRVING E. JR.	NV	FUT 54 06
ASK A FOOLISH QUESTION	SHECKLEY, ROBERT	SS	SFS 53 01
CHILDREN OF FORTUNE	JOURDAN, D. A.	NV	SFQ 57 02

Title	Author	Type	Source
6 FINGERS OF TIME AND 5 OTHER SCIENCE FICTION NOVELETS, THE	ANONYMOUS	AN	MBB 65
SIX FINGERS OF TIME, THE	LAFFERTY, R. A.	NV	IFS 60 09
PRIDE OF ISLANDS, A	MACAPP, C. C.	NV	IFS 60 05
SITTING DUCK	GALOUYE, DANIEL F.	SS	IFS 59 07
I.O.U.	WELLEN, EDWARD	NV	IFS 61 03
TO EACH HIS OWN	SHARKEY, JACK	SS	IFS 60 01
JUNKMAKERS, THE	TEICHNER, ALBERT	NV	IFS 61 07

Title	Author	Type	Source
6 FROM WORLDS BEYOND	DIKTY, T. E.	AN	CRS 58 12
6 STORIES FROM "BEST SCIENCE FICTION STORIES AND NOVELS: 1956"			
JUNGLE DOCTOR	YOUNG, ROBERT F.	NV	STS 55 FL
GAME OF RAT AND DRAGON, THE	SMITH, CORDWAINER	NV	GAL 55 10
DREAM STREET	ROBINSON, FRANK M.	SS	IMT 55 03
YOU CREATED US	GODWIN, TOM	SS	FUN 55 10
I DO NOT LOVE THEE, DOCTOR FELL	BLOCH, ROBERT	SS	FSF 55 03
SHORES OF NIGHT, THE (EXPANDED FROM "SEA CHANGE")	SCORTIA, THOMAS N.	SS	ASF 56 06

Title	Author	Type	Source
6 GREAT SHORT NOVELS OF SCIENCE FICTION	CONKLIN, GROFF	AN	DEL 54
INTRODUCTION	CONKLIN, GROFF	IN	
BLAST, THE	CLOETE, STUART	NV	COL 47 04
COVENTRY	HEINLEIN, ROBERT A.	NV	ASF 40 07
OTHER WORLD, THE	LEINSTER, MURRAY	NA	STS 49 11
OTHER WORLD, THE	LEINSTER, MURRAY	NV	STS 49 11
BARRIER	BOUCHER, ANTHONY	NV	ASF 42 09
SURFACE TENSION	BLISH, JAMES	NA	GAL 52 08
MATURITY	STURGEON, THEODORE	NV	ASF 47 02

Title	Author	Type	Source
6 X H	HEINLEIN, ROBERT A.	AC	PYR 61 08
SEE "THE UNPLEASANT PROFESSION OF JONATHAN HOAG"			

Title	Author	Type	Source
6TH ANNUAL OF THE YEAR'S BEST S-F, THE	MERRIL, JUDITH	AN H	SAS 61
IN ENGLAND AS "THE BEST OF SCIENCE FICTION"			
INTRODUCTION	MERRIL, JUDITH	IN	
DOUBLE, DOUBLE, TOIL AND TROUBLE	CANTINE, HOLLEY	SS	FSF 60 01
NEVER ENDING PENNY, THE	WOLFE, BERNARD	SS	PBY 60 09
FELLOW WHO MARRIED THE MAXILL GIRL, THE	MOORE, WARD	NV	FSF 60 02
SOMETHING INVENTED ME	PHELAN, R. C.	SS	REP 60 10
SIGH FOR CYBERNETICS, A	LAMPORT, FELICIA	PM	HRP 61 01
OBVIOUS!	FFOLKES, MICHAEL	CT	PUN 56 10
I REMEMBER BABYLON	CLARKE, ARTHUR C.	SS	PBY 60 05
LAGGING PROFESSION, THE	LOCKHARD, LEONARD	SF	ASF 61 01
DISTORTION, THE	SILVERSTEIN, SHEL	CT	PBY 60 05
REPORT ON THE NATURE OF THE LUNAR SURFACE	BRUNNER, JOHN	SS	ASF 60 08
J.G. (FROM "J.G. THE UPRIGHT APE")	PRICE, ROGER	EX	60
CHIEF	SLESAR, HENRY	SS	PBY 60 06
PSALM	DEL REY, LESTER	PM	FUN 60 02
LARGE ANT, THE (THE BIG ANT)	FAST, HOWARD	SS	FUN 60 02
ROSE BY OTHER NAME, A	ANVIL, CHRISTOPHER	SS	ASF 60 01
ENCHANTMENT	EMMETT, ELIZABETH	SS	SEP 60 10
THIOTIMOLINE AND THE SPACE AGE	ASIMOV, ISAAC	SF	ASF 60 10
BEACH SCENE	KING, MARSHALL	SS	GAL 60 10
CREATURE OF THE SNOWS	SAMBROT, WILLIAM	SS	SEP 60 10
ABOMINABLE	BROWN, FREDRIC	SS	DUD 60 03
MAN ON TOP, THE (SCH 51 10)	BRETNOR, REGINALD	SS	FSF 60 09
DAVID'S DADDY	BROWN, ROSEL GEORGE	SS	FAN 60 06
THINKERS, THE	KELLY, WALT	CT	HAS 61 01
SOMETHING BRIGHT	HENDERSON, ZENNA	SS	GAL 60 02
IN THE HOUSE, ANOTHER	WHITEHILL, JOSEPH	SS	FSF 60 04
SERIOUS SEARCH FOR WEIRD WORLDS, A	BRADBURY, RAY	AR	LIF 60 10
ED LEAR WASN'T SO CRAZY!	SCHENCK, HILBERT JR.	PM	FSF 60 06
INSTRUCTOR	THELWELL	CT	PUN 61 01
BROTHERHOOD OF KEEPERS, THE	MCLAUGHLIN, DEAN	NV	ASF 60 07
HEMINGWAY IN SPACE	AMIS, KINGSLEY	SS	PUN 60 12
MINE OWN WAYS	MCKENNA, RICHARD M.	SS	FSF 60 02
OLD HUNDREDTH	ALDISS, BRIAN W.	SS	NWS 60 11
RADIATION BLUES	COGSWELL, THEODORE R	SG	60
BLOWUP BLUES	COGSWELL, THEODORE R	SG	60
BALLAD OF THE SHOSHONU	DICKSON, GORDON R.	SG	NEW 61 AN
HOW TO THINK A SCIENCE FICTION STORY (EXCERPT)	STINE, G. HARRY	AR	ASF 61 05
YEAR IN S-F, THE	MERRIL, JUDITH	MS	
S-F BOOKS- 1960	BOUCHER, ANTHONY	MS	
HONORABLE MENTIONS	MISC. MATERIAL	MS	

Title	Author	Type	Source
7 CONQUESTS	ANDERSON, POUL	AC H	MAC 69
FOREWORD	ANDERSON, POUL	IN	
KINGS WHO DIE	ANDERSON, POUL	NV	IFS 62 03
WILDCAT	ANDERSON, POUL	NV	FSF 58 11
COLD VICTORY	ANDERSON, POUL	SS	FSF 57 05
INSIDE STRAIGHT	ANDERSON, POUL	SS	FSF 55 08
DETAILS	ANDERSON, POUL	SS	IFS 56 10
LICENSE	ANDERSON, POUL	NV	FSF 57 04
STRANGE BEDFELLOWS (TO BUILD A WORLD)	ANDERSON, POUL	SN	GAL 64 06

Title	Author	Type	Source
7TH ANNUAL OF THE YEAR'S BEST S-F, THE	MERRIL, JUDITH	AN H	SAS 62
IN ENGLAND AS "THE BEST OF SCIENCE FICTION 2"			
ONEIROMACHIA	AIKEN, CONRAD	PM	ATL 61 10
PASSAGE FROM THE STARS, A	HURLBUT, KAATJE	SS	SEP 61 05
AMONG THE DANGS (EXCERPT)	ELLIOTT, GEORGE P.	EX	ESQ 58 06
IMMEDIATELY YOURS	HALE, ROBERT BEVERLY	SS	MAD 61 11
PARKY	ROME, DAVID	SS	SCF 61 08
FASTEST GUN DEAD, THE	GROW, JULIAN F.	SS	IFS 61 03
ALL THE TEA IN CHINA	BRETNOR, REGINALD	SS	FSF 61 05
PORTOBELLO ROAD, THE	SPARK, MURIEL	NV	CMP 58
OTTMAR BALLEAU X 2	BAMBER, GEORGE	SS	ROG 61 03
DANDELION GIRL, THE	YOUNG, ROBERT F.	SS	SEP 61 04
NIGHTMARE IN TIME	BROWN, FREDRIC	SS	DUD 61
LOOKING BACKWARD	FEIFFER, JULES	CT	HAS 61 12
THREE PROLOGUES AND AN EPILOGUE	DOS PASSOS, JOHN	PM	ADT 61 SP
IT BECOMES NECESSARY (THE COLD PEACE)	MOORE, WARD	SS	GNT 61
MY TRIAL AS A WAR CRIMINAL	SZILARD, LEO	SS	UCL 49 FL
PRIZE FOR EDIE, A	BONE, J. F.	SS	ASF 61 04
FREEDOM	REYNOLDS, MACK	NV	ASF 61 02
HIGH BARBARY	DURRELL, LAWRENCE	SS	MAD 61 09
QUAKER CANNON, THE	POHL, FREDERIK AND KORNBLUTH, C. M.	NV C	ASF 61 08
QUAKE, QUAKE, QUAKE (EXCERPT)	DEHN, PAUL	PM	61
QUAKE, QUAKE, QUAKE (EXCERPT)	GOREY, EDWARD	IL	61
JUDAS BOMB	REED, KIT	SS	FSF 61 04
SMALL MIRACLE OF FISHHOOKS AND STRAIGHT PINS, A	BUNCH, DAVID R.	NV	FAN 61 06
TUNNEL AHEAD, THE	GLASER, ALICE	SS	FSF 61 11
EXTRATERRESTRIAL TRILOGY ON TERRAN SELF-DESTRUCTION	EBERHART, SHERI	PM	GAL 61 08
COUNTDOWN, THE	HAASE, JOHN	SS	NYM 61 10
BEAT CLUSTER, THE	LEIBER, FRITZ	SS	GAL 61 10
IN TOMORROW'S LITTLE BLACK BAG	BLISH, JAMES	AR	
SHIP WHO SANG, THE	MCCAFFREY, ANNE	SS	FSF 61 04
PLANET NAMED SHAYOL, A	SMITH, CORDWAINER	NA	GAL 61 10

7TH ANNUAL OF THE YEAR'S BEST S-F, THE

ASTEROIDS, 2194, THE (THE EMPTYNESS OF SPACE, NWS 60 11)
    WYNDHAM, JOHN   SS   AMZ 61 01
LONG NIGHT, THE (THE EXPLOITS OF ARGO)
    RUSSELL, RAY   SS   ROG 61 04
TO AN ASTRONAUT DYING YOUNG KUMIN, MAXINE W. PM   ATL 61 12
SUMMATION: S-F, 1961 MERRIL, JUDITH MS
BOOKS BOUCHER, ANTHONY MS
HONORABLE MENTIONS MISC. MATERIAL MS

8TH ANNUAL OF THE YEAR'S BEST S-F, THE
    MERRIL, JUDITH AN H SAS 63
    IN ENGLAND AS "THE BEST OF SCIENCE FICTION 4"
UNSAFE DEPOSIT BOX, THE KERSH, GERALD SS SEP 62 04
SEVEN-DAY TERROR LAFFERTY, R. A. SS IFS 62 03
TOY SHOP HARRISON, HARRY SS ASF 62 04
FACE IN THE PHOTO, THE (TIME HAS NO BOUNDARIES)
    FINNEY, JACK SS SEP 62 10
CIRCUIT RIDERS, THE FITZPATRICK, R. C. SS ASF 62 04
SUCH STUFF BRUNNER, JOHN SS FSF 62 06
MAN WHO MADE FRIENDS WITH ELECTRICITY, THE
    LEIBER, FRITZ SS FSF 62 03
KINGS WHO DIE ANDERSON, POUL NV IFS 62 03
UNFORTUNATE MR. MORKY, THE AANDAHL, VANCE SS FSF 62 10
CHRISTMAS TREASON WHITE, JAMES NV FSF 62 01
MIRACLE OF RARE DEVICE, A BRADBURY, RAY SS PBY 62 01
ALL THE SOUNDS OF FEAR ELLISON, HARLAN SS SDM 62 07
ONE OF THOSE DAYS NOLAN, WILLIAM F. SS FSF 62 05
DAY REMBRANDT WENT PUBLIC, THE
    AUERBACH, ARNOLD M. SS HRP 62 07
MS. FOUND IN A BUS BAKER, RUSSELL SS NYT 62
INSANE ONES, THE BALLARD, J. G. SS AMZ 62 01
LEPRECHAUN SAMBROT, WILLIAM SS ESC 62
CHANGE OF HEART WHITLEY, GEORGE SS NWS 61 09
ANGELA'S SATYR CLEEVE, BRIAN SS SEP 62 11
PUPPET SHOW BROWN, FREDRIC SS PBY 62 11
HANG HEAD, VANDAL! CLIFTON, MARK SS AMZ 62 04
EARTHLINGS GO HOME! REYNOLDS, MACK SS ROG 62 08
MARTIAN STAR-GAZERS, THE POHL, FREDERIK FA GAL 62 02
PLANETARY EFFULGENCE RUSSELL, BERTRAND SS 61
DEADLY GAME, THE WELLEN, EDWARD SS IFS 62 05
SUBCOMMITTEE HENDERSON, ZENNA NV FSF 62 07
PIEBALD HIPPOGRIFF, THE ANDERSON, KAREN SS FAN 62 05
HOME FROM THE SHORE DICKSON, GORDON R. NA GAL 63 02
SUMMATION: S-F, 1962 MERRIL, JUDITH MS
BOOKS BOUCHER, ANTHONY MS
HONORABLE MENTIONS MISC. MATERIAL MS

9TH ANNUAL OF THE YEAR'S BEST S-F, THE

9 TALES OF SPACE AND TIME HEALY, RAYMOND J. OA H HLT 54
IDEALIST, THE CAMPBELL, JOHN W. JR NV NTL 54
SHOCK TREATMENT MCCOMAS, J. FRANCIS NV FSF 56 04
GENIUS OF THE SPECIES BRETNOR, REGINALD SS FSF 56 06
OVERTURE NEVILLE, KRIS SS NTL 54
COMPOUND B FINK, DAVID H. MD. NV NTL 54
CHICKEN OR THE EGG-HEAD, THE FENTON, FRANK SS NTL 54
GREAT DEVON MYSTERY, THE HEALY, RAYMOND J. SS NTL 54
BALAAM BOUCHER, ANTHONY SS NTL 54
MAN OF PARTS GOLD, H. L. SS NTL 54

9TH ANNUAL OF THE YEAR'S BEST S-F, THE
    MERRIL, JUDITH AN H SAS 64
BERNIE THE FAUST TENN, WILLIAM NV PBY 63 10
FORTRESS SHIP (ALSO AS WITHOUT A THOUGHT)
    SABERHAGEN, FRED SS IFS 63 01
MR. WATERMAN REDGROVE, PETER SS PRV 63 29
MRS. PIGAFETTA SWIMS WELL BRETNOR, REGINALD SS FSF 63 05
TREE TRUNKS GALLAGHER, JOHN CT SEP 63
THEY DON'T MAKE LIFE LIKE THEY USED TO
    BESTER, ALFRED NV FSF 63 10
GREAT NEBRASKA SEA, THE DANZIG, ALLAN FA GAL 63 08
FACES OUTSIDE, THE MCALLISTER, BRUCE SS IFS 63 07
SLIGHT CASE OF LIMBO, A BIGGLE, LLOYD JR. SS ASF 63 04
237 TALKING STATUES, ETC. LEIBER, FRITZ SS FSF 63 09
JAZZ MACHINE, THE MATHESON, RICHARD PM FSF 63 02
MOURNING SONG BEAUMONT, CHARLES SS GAM 63 01
DOG EAT DOG PEIFFER, JULES CT 63
JEWBIRD, THE MALAMUD, BERNARD SS REP 63 04
ON THE FOURTH PLANET BONE, J. F. SS GAL 63 04
POPPA NEEDS SHORTS RICHMOND, WALT
    AND RICHMOND, LEIGH SS C ASF 64 01
DOUBLE STANDARD BROWN, FREDRIC SS PBY 63
INTERVIEW JAVOR, FRANK A. SS ASF 63 11
EIGHT O'CLOCK IN THE MORNING NELSON, RAY SS FSF 63 11
WHERE IS EVERYBODY? BOVA, BEN AR AMZ 63 05
EARTH DWELLERS, THE MAUROIS, ANDRE NV 63
NOBEL PRIZE WINNERS GORDON, W. J. J. SS ATL 63 11
HOT PLANET CLEMENT, HAL NV GAL 63 08
IBM GERNBERG, MORT CT DUD 63
CONFESSIONS OF THE FIRST NUMBER
    OWSLEY, CLIFF SS SRV 63
MING VASE, THE TUBB, E. C. SS ASF 63 05
BARGAIN WITH CASHEL, A KERSH, GERALD SS SEP 63 04
DRUNKBOAT SMITH, CORDWAINER NV AMZ 63 10
SUMMATION: S-F, 1963 MERRIL, JUDITH MS
BOOKS BOUCHER, ANTHONY MS
HONORABLE MENTIONS MISC. MATERIAL MS